Demsi Barton

George Knightley, Esquire

A Novel in Two Parts

Book 1
Charity Envieth Not

by

Barbara Cornthwaite

Cover art: Guy's Cliffe, Wiltshire, unknown artist, from *Picturesque Views of Seats of the Noblemen and Gentlemen of Great Britain and Ireland*, ed. F.O. Morris (1870)

To my husband

Thanks are due to many, many people:

The ladies of the Crownhill Writers' Guild – for inviting me to join your ranks and offering encouragement along the way

Jeena — for being absolutely the most enthusiastic draft-reader and cheerleader a writer could have

Chautona — for giving valuable feedback and *lots* of help

Joan and Brenna — for being proofreaders extraordinaire

And, lastly, my family — for always asking me how "the book about Mr. Knightley" was coming, and for loving me the same no matter what the answer was.

1

The moon had just risen as Knightley left the grounds of Donwell Abbey and walked the familiar road to Hartfield. He had left his brother's house in London only that afternoon, later than he had intended. Even apart from his own reluctance to leave the homely atmosphere of Brunswick-square, it had been difficult to extricate himself from the family. The children had hung about him and begged him not to leave, and Isabella had delayed him further by entrusting him with long, affectionate messages for her father and sister. Even John, though not demonstrative, had not wanted to see him go. But at length he had made his final farewells, and only John had followed him out of the house to see him off.

"You might have stayed a few more days, George," John had said as the groom brought the horses around to where they were standing and checked to see that the luggage was securely loaded onto one of them. "The children would have liked you to see the Royal Menagerie with them."

"Had I only my own inclination to consult, I would stay until Christmas. But the quarter sessions are approaching and William Larkins is anxious that I come and approve his plan for moving that fence on the north side of the sheep pasture before he dismisses the workmen that have been building the new barn. And I must see how Hartfield is sustaining the loss of Miss Taylor."

"Yes." John smiled wryly. "I do not envy you the task of cheering my father-in-law. Though you and Emma together might just do it—temporarily, at least. I fear you will be entirely surrounded by morose and irritable people: Hartfield will be sober for several weeks at least, and William Larkins and Mrs. Hodges are never cheerful."

"Not exactly *never*, John. There was a day last spring..."

John snorted. "I suppose all the sheep had twin lambs, pleasing Larkins with the thought of profit and Mrs. Hodges with the thought of lamb cutlets?"

"Not quite. It was the cows that had twin calves, and even then Mrs. Hodges only smiled because the asparagus was early."

John groaned even as he smiled. "I do not know how you can bear with them with such good humour. It seems to me that you spend a good deal of your time smoothing over fractious tempers or putting up with difficult and tedious people."

"No more than is good for me."

"And you are sadly in want of rational conversation."

"Not at all. I have told you that Cole is on the parish committee for Poor Relief, and he is a good fellow. And I have Gilbert and Dr. Hughes. Dr. Hughes, particularly, is well-read and intelligent. And then I am often surprised by good conversation when I am not looking for it. Young Martin came the other week to discuss the new rams he had bought and found me reading the road surveyor's report of that bridge near Highbury. We had a most interesting talk on the subject of roads, bridges, and improvements."

"And Weston is settled there now, as well."

"Yes, though I'm not sure any newly-married man is good for *rational* conversation. I recall you, for example, seven years ago—"

"No, no, that is enough of that. You had better be off now, or you will be too late to give Isabella's greetings to Hartfield."

And so he had travelled home and eaten his dinner and was now going to raise the spirits of Mr. Woodhouse and Emma. He might have deferred his visit to the morrow, but he felt that a visit to Hartfield was as necessary to his mood as it was to theirs. After the noisy cheerfulness of his brother's house, Donwell Abbey seemed lonely and silent—even more so than usual. A little bit of conversation at Hartfield was just the thing he needed.

The road was well lit by the nearly-full moon, and the weather was just right for an evening in late September. The weather would certainly not hinder the final days of work on the new barn, in spite of William Larkins' gloomy predictions. His brother's words came back to him and made him smile: *I fear you will be entirely surrounded by morose and irritable people.* John pitied him, he knew, for living alone at Donwell with no connections nearby—unless one could count the Woodhouse family as connections. But even so, he was usually content. His brother's home was not too distant for frequent visits, and Hartfield was so familiar to him as to be almost a second home. Mr. Woodhouse could not take the place of a father with him, but he was the sort of man that one must respect, and it felt good and right to Knightley that there was such a man in the neighbourhood for him to pay deference to. Even his brother, who at times allowed Mr. Woodhouse's weak understanding and nervous temperament to vex him, knew the real generosity and goodness of the old man's heart. Knightley's father had been Mr. Woodhouse's friend and advisor, and the son had taken up the mantle when he became the master of Donwell. It was a satisfaction to him to be of use to the fussy, kind-hearted old gentleman.

This usefulness extended to the daughter; it lifted Emma's burden a little when he was there to calm Mr. Woodhouse's fears and make him cheerful with small, happy items of news. *You and Emma together might just do it...* Yes, he feared that the loss of Miss Taylor would be such a blow to Mr. Woodhouse that Emma alone would not be able to do much to prevent his lamentations. And Emma herself would be feeling melancholy after the loss of such a friend. Not for the first time did Knightley wish that there was another companion in Highbury for Emma. Her loss was the heavier of the two.

He was nearly to Hartfield now; the knowledge that Emma was labouring alone to bring her father to contentment while feeling rather dismal on her own account had hastened his steps. A few moments later, the hall porter, a dignified elderly servant, answered the door to his knock and greeted him with his usual quiet, "Good evening, Mr. Knightley." As he took Knightley's coat, he added, "I thought you might come tonight, sir."

The footman announced him as he walked into the drawing room. The faces of the two occupants of the room brightened with unfeigned pleasure at the sight of him. Mr. Woodhouse was seated, as usual, near the blazing fire, and Emma was evidently arranging the playing pieces on the backgammon table in preparation for a game with her father. She came forward to meet him with a smile and a lively greeting, and he fancied there was even a little bit of relief in her expression as she led him to the empty chair near her father and bid him be seated.

"All well here, I trust?" he asked, as Emma put the backgammon aside. "I left Isabella and John in excellent health and spirits not three hours ago."

"How good of you to come and tell us so, Mr. Knightley!" said Mr. Woodhouse. "But the children? How are the dear children?"

"They are all in excellent health, sir."

"Poor Isabella, my poor dear Isabella," murmured Mr. Woodhouse. To a stranger this remark would have been puzzling enough, following as it did on the heels of a good report, but to Knightley, who understood it, it gave gentle amusement. Emma's eyes rested lovingly on her father, but there was humour in them, too.

"And had poor Isabella a headache while you were there? She often has a headache, you know, Mr. Knightley, though she never complains."

"I do not believe she had any. She said that she has had very few since they returned from South End. And that little Bella's throat was much better as well."

"Oh! That miserable South End and that sea-bathing! They had much better not have gone. Sea-bathing with a weak throat! Perry said that he had never heard of such folly. And the baby, too—so young, and so liable to infection! Are you sure, Mr. Knightley, that the baby caught no infection at South End?"

"Perfectly sure. All the children are in remarkably good health. The boys are strong and healthy fellows. I took them to the park one day, and Henry rolled his hoop the length of it with no assistance from anyone."

"Did he, indeed? Well, he is a clever boy, to be sure."

"And little Bella," said Emma, "is it true that she knows her alphabet already?"

"In truth, she does know it, and can recite it whenever she is called upon. She's a precocious little thing. She reminds me of Emma, sir, when Emma was a child."

"Yes, Emma was always very quick, was she not, Mr. Knightley? You were like your dear mother, Emma. It is no wonder that Isabella's children take after her."

After Mr. Woodhouse was satisfied that the Knightleys in London were in no worse health than they were when he had last seen them, he was at leisure to express his concern for Mr. Knightley's comfort, as he had walked all the way from Donwell Abbey on such a dark and damp night. Mr. Knightley made his usual protests against such solicitude, as it was perfectly unnecessary, and then gently broached the topic of Miss Taylor's marriage.

"Ah! Poor Miss Taylor!" said Mr. Woodhouse immediately, his countenance clouding over again. "'tis a sad business."

Knightley looked at Emma to see how she took the mention of this change in her life. Her elegant posture did droop a little at this reminder, though her face retained the smile it had been wearing. *Poor Miss Taylor, indeed!* thought Knightly. *No one in this room needs sympathy less than she!* He would do what he could to comfort Emma, at least. An appeal to her love for Miss Taylor and her desire for Miss Taylor's happiness would do more than anything else to reconcile her.

"Poor Mr. and Miss Woodhouse, if you please," he said, "But I cannot possibly say 'poor Miss Taylor.' I have a great regard for you and Emma; but when it comes to the question of dependence or independence! At any rate, it must be better to have only one to please, than two."

Emma's left eyebrow lifted, as it always did when she was about to tease him. "Especially when *one* of those two is such a fanciful, troublesome creature! That is what you have in your head, I know—and what you would certainly say if my father were not by."

He grinned and opened his mouth to respond to this, but was checked by Mr. Woodhouse's breaking in with, "I believe it is very true, my dear, indeed. I am afraid I am sometimes very fanciful and troublesome."

Emma quickly reassured her father that she had herself in view, certainly not him, and that it was all a joke, anyway—Mr. Knightley liked to *pretend* to find fault with her, and that was what the joke was about. Knightley watched this familial interplay with quiet amusement. He knew she wished his reminders and reprimands were all mere teasing, though she knew very well they were not. However, these few well-chosen words from Emma quieted Mr. Woodhouse's fears and brought him back to complacency. Even so, Knightley judged that his nerves were not in a state that made it possible to tell Emma now—again—that he had only her own good in view when he brought her faults to her attention. Instead, he merely clarified his own statement, saying that anyone who had only one person to please instead of two must find it a gain.

"Well," said Emma, starting a new subject, "You want to hear about the wedding, and I shall be happy to tell you, for we all behaved charmingly. Everybody was punctual, everybody in their best looks. Not a tear and hardly a long face to be seen." Emma glanced at her father—she could not honestly say that there had been *no* long faces. "Oh no! We all felt that we were going to be only half a mile apart, and were sure of meeting every day."

Perhaps Mr. Woodhouse thought Emma sounded rather heartless, for he shook his head and said, "Dear Emma bears everything so well. But, Mr. Knightley, she is really very sorry to lose poor Miss Taylor, and I am sure she *will* miss her more than she thinks for."

Emma's determined cheerfulness wavered at this—the truth of her father's words could not be denied. She turned away, but not before Knightley saw tears forming in her eyes.

"It is impossible that Emma should not miss such a companion," he said. "We should not like her so well as we do, sir, if we could suppose it." He meant to show her that he understood her feelings, and could never think her wanting in affection for her friend. It was, in fact, that affection which would be the most material help in soothing the pangs of separation; the more Emma thought of Miss Taylor's happiness, the less she would regret her own loss. So he said all he could on the subject of Miss Taylor's comforts and advantages, and was rewarded by the return of a smile to Emma's face and the good omen of a raised left eyebrow.

Knightley walked home to Donwell less content than he had been on the walk to Hartfield. The marriage of the Westons was undoubtedly a good thing for *them,* but he foresaw that it would be a bad thing for Emma. Though not as firm in her authority as she might have been, Miss Taylor had been a good companion and teacher for her charge; she had instructed her commendably in the art of being a gentlewoman, had nourished her love of her father and her compassion for the poor, and had given her right principles to live by. Those principles had taken root in Emma; when once convinced that something was her duty, she would do it, regardless of cost to herself. Emma really was, in many ways, an admirable young woman. But she might be still more admirable than she was. She could be a very knowledgeable and accomplished woman indeed, but she had not disciplined herself to read, practice, or study when she did not feel like it, and Miss Taylor had not forced her. He felt that her intellect was often wasted on trivial matters. She was clever, but there was no one around her but himself who would oppose any scheme she had. He had no doubt that the scheme she had spoken of tonight would be diligently pursued. Probably nothing he could have said would have deterred her, but had he goaded her into it by any misspoken word?

How had it started? Ah, yes. She had taken credit for the Westons' marriage, saying that she had planned it four years ago and that as it was the greatest amusement in the world, she would continue to make matches for other people. *Amusement!* He bit his lip in frustration. Meddling in the lives of good, honest men and women all for the sake of her own *amusement*! And then when he had protested that the Westons' marriage was really not due to her own endeavours but that she had merely made a lucky guess, she asserted that she had at least smoothed the progress of the courtship and assured its successful conclusion.

"A straight-forward, open-hearted man like Weston and a rational, unaffected woman like Miss Taylor may be safely left to manage their own concerns," he had told her. "You are more likely to have done harm to yourself than good to them, by interference."

Mr. Woodhouse had also urged Emma not to make any more matches, though it was more on his own account than anyone else's. But Emma would not be dissuaded by either her father or himself, and there was no one else to check her. She had declared that she meant to make a match for Mr. Elton, the vicar, and Knightley was sure that however weak her determination proved to be when she planned a course of improving study for herself, it would be firm in this enterprise.

Mr. Woodhouse had suggested that an invitation to dinner would be far more helpful to Mr. Elton, and Knightley could not help laughing as he concurred. But the more he thought about it, the less humorous he found it. Deprived of Miss Taylor's steadying influence, she would be more headstrong than ever; deprived of Miss Taylor's society, she would amuse herself with employments unworthy of her intelligence and abilities. For years—since Emma was about twelve—he had thought that if he had a wife she might be a help to Emma. The right sort of woman...virtuous but also lively, domestic but intelligent, able to appreciate and meet Emma's wit...such a woman would be an ideal companion for Emma no less than for himself. But no such woman had crossed his path, and he was not prepared to let a lesser woman take the title of mistress of Donwell Abbey.

He sighed as he walked through Donwell's sweep-gate. He had some little hope that he had been able to raise the spirits of those at Hartfield, but *his* feelings were rather more depressed than they had been two hours ago.

2

"So then, gentlemen, we are all agreed? Good. Charles Burton is hereby appointed constable for this parish," said Knightley. "I will call on him this evening and inform him of our decision."

"Very good," said Weston. "He's an excellent man for the job. Full of energy and good spirits—just the sort of man that position needs. That concludes our business today, Knightley, does it not? I need to be getting home."

"Ah," said Cole with a wink. "It's no wonder you're so keen to get back to Randalls—you've only been married three weeks. Give it three years and you won't be in such a hurry."

Weston laughed good-naturedly and rose from his seat. "For such a remark as that I ought to deny you any wedding cake."

"Too late," said Cole, rising also. "My wife and daughters were to call on Mrs. Weston this very day while we have been meeting, and I am certain your good wife will have given them each a piece as well as one to carry home for myself."

"No doubt. Well, the sooner it is all gone the sooner poor Mr. Woodhouse will be relieved from his anxiety on the score of everyone's health. Elton, you ought to call again and help us to eat it up."

"I should be very happy to," said Elton, and stood up, stretching surreptitiously as he did so. He took up his hat and gloves and moved toward the door, glancing out the window as he passed it. Something he saw arrested his attention, causing him to stop suddenly and forcing Knightley, who was coming behind him, to stop as well. Knightley looked out the window and saw instantly what had stayed the vicar's steps: Emma was across the road, looking into the shop window of Ford's, and with her was a young woman. Knightley could not remember the last time he had seen Emma out together with another young lady, and he gazed at the pair for several moments trying to determine who it might be.

By this time Weston had gathered that there was something of interest outside the window. "What is it, Elton? Something amiss?"

"Ah—no, no," said Elton. "I see John Abdy walking along—looking very frail, I must say. I was wondering whether—ah—he was looking more feeble than he used to look."

Weston joined them at the window. "Yes, he does look bad, poor thing. No doubt he's failing a bit. And there's Miss Woodhouse and her new little friend, Miss Smith. Do you know Miss Smith, Knightley? No? Such a pleasant young girl—only seventeen, I believe—and Emma will do her a great deal of good. Bring her out in society more, you know, and that sort of thing. She was a pupil of Mrs. Goddard's. Still lives there as parlour-border. Mrs. Weston is so pleased that she can be a companion for Emma. And there they go into Ford's. I tell Mrs. Weston that Ford's is like a magnet that draws in all the young ladies. No lady can come into Highbury without stopping there, what?"

"Mrs. Cole cannot, at any rate," said that lady's husband, who declined to add himself to the party at the window, "And if she cannot shop there herself, she gives me commissions to attend to on her behalf. I have one today, as it happens, and I'm afraid I must part company with you, gentlemen. I'll see you tomorrow, Weston, Elton. Good afternoon, Mr. Knightley."

"Well, now, Knightley," said Weston after they had all quitted the Crown, "Can you come to Randalls now and eat up more of the wedding cake? Mrs. Weston would be very pleased to see you."

"No, I thank you. I promised William Larkins that I would go and inspect some cottages this afternoon."

"Very well, very well. I mustn't interfere with promises made to William Larkins, I know. I suppose I will see you Thursday evening at Hartfield?"

"Yes, indeed. Hartfield's first dinner in honour of the Westons cannot be missed. Give my regards to Mrs. Weston."

"Of course. And mine to William Larkins," said Weston with a twinkle in his eye. "Until Thursday, then."

William Larkins received the regards of Mr. Weston from Knightley with a very modified rapture. He was a short man of about fifty-five with greying hair and a rather severe expression. He nodded his acknowledgement of the courtesy, but quickly got to the business at hand.

"I sent a message to the cottagers this morning to say that we would be along this afternoon, sir, so as not to embarrass them with an unexpected visit."

"And which cottages are these, exactly?" asked Knightley as the two men set forth.

"The ones along the mill road. The assistant game-keeper Green's cottage is among them. They are the oldest on the estate, and they are in such a condition now that they ought to be replaced."

Knightley nodded. Larkins was nearly always right about these things.

"There have been no new cottages built here in the last ten years, have there, Larkins?"

"No, sir. The last cottages to be built were the four near the stables, twelve years ago."

"The year '01. Yes, I remember now. That was the last thing my father built, wasn't it?"

"Yes, sir," said Larkins.

"You had better look out some new pattern books of designs for cottages. Green needs to have a good place to live. I should hate to lose him as assistant game-keeper on account of an unimproved cottage."

As usual, Larkins received Knightley's humour with all seriousness.

"I do not think such a consideration would ever tempt Green to leave your service, Mr. Knightley. He is as loyal to Donwell Abbey as anyone could well be. But I must tell you, sir, that *Mrs.* Green is not as happy as she might be with her present cottage. I have heard her holding forth on the subject to the lodge-keeper's wife."

Knightley hid a smile. Larkins always played the role of an unwilling bearer of disagreeable news to someone who ought to know it. It was in this way that he spread more gossip than anyone else in the parish of Donwell. His communications usually began with the words, "I fear I must tell you…"

The three old cottages came into view. They looked well enough on the outside, but they were rather small: one room on the ground floor and one on the floor above. Each room was fairly spacious, but they were definitely built to an old design.

Larkins knocked on the first door and Mrs. Green opened it. She was a plump woman, just past middle age, but she made a graceful curtsey to the men and ushered them into the house. To their surprise, the women who occupied the other cottages were also there.

"I beg your pardon, Mr. Knightley," said Mrs. Green as the other ladies rose and curtseyed. "I wasn't expecting you for another hour or so."

"Not at all, Mrs. Green. You can answer our questions just as easily all together as you could separately. Mrs. Shaw, Mrs. Bull, do be seated again. Tea? Yes, thank you, Mrs. Green. And now you must all tell me every single thing that is wrong with these cottages."

The list was long, although the women made as light of it as they could. The ceilings were low; the floors were rather damp; windows were scarce and small which made the cottages dark; they would like to have more rooms—at least two upstairs; the stairs were awkward. Larkins drank his tea in silence and let his master do the talking. Knightley asked questions, listened to the women, and gratified Mrs. Green by taking another cup of tea. He made no promises except that something would be done for them very shortly.

At the end of half an hour, the men rose and took their leave. Larkins departed in quest of the head gardener to find out how many bushels of apples the orchard had yielded, and Knightley walked back to the house alone, thinking about designs for cottages. It seemed to him that Weston had built a cottage on his small estate a year or so ago; he might know if there were any new books to be got on the topic. He might even have one that Knightley could borrow.

He would ask him at the dinner at Hartfield on Thursday. Emma would laugh at him, of course, for asking to borrow a book instead of buying it for himself. She thought he was altogether too frugal. Of course she must know that he would buy a book if it merited purchase, but he preferred to glance through a book first if he could before laying out money to make it part of his library.

Emma....yes, what about this new friendship of Emma's? A girl of seventeen, was she? That did not bode well. What Emma needed was to be influenced by a woman she respected, one who was superior to Emma in just those points where Emma was lacking, and equal enough to her accomplishments to provide a basis for a friendship. A girl of seventeen would hardly fit that description. Perhaps there was something in the girl's situation that merited Emma's interest or compassion. But what sort of situation would that be? Emma, who was usually so scrupulous as to distinctions in rank, would seem to be the last young lady to choose a girl with low connections as a companion. There must be more to it than met the eye. There was no time today to call at Hartfield, but tomorrow he would pay a visit to the Woodhouses and see what he could discover.

"Ah! Mr. Knightley," said Mr. Woodhouse from his usual chair by the fire. "It is so good of you to come, particularly on a cold day such as this. Does it rain? I looked out of the window not long ago and there seemed to be some very threatening clouds."

"Not at all," said Knightley. "I saw nothing that looked like rain. And it is not so very cold, sir, as it looks. It is rather warmer than one expects a day in October to be." He took a chair near Mr. Woodhouse, but a little further from the fire.

"Well, you relieve my mind, Mr. Knightley, very much. Emma and her little friend Miss Smith are out walking to Randalls and I was quite afraid that they might be caught in the rain. But if you say there is no chance of it, then I am content. I fear there is a great deal to trouble my mind just now—I have had a letter from my banker in London, and I cannot understand what it is he wants me to do. It is all about the funds and interest and things of that nature. Between my anxiety over the letter and my worry for dear Emma and her little friend I have been exceedingly distracted all the afternoon."

"Would you wish me to see the letter, sir? I might be able to understand what is wanted."

"Ah! That is very good of you. I do not wish to trouble you, but then you are so very clever at understanding these difficult things. The letter is in my library—perhaps you would be good enough to come with me and read it there?"

Knightley assented and followed Mr. Woodhouse into the library. It was a beautiful room, housing an impressive collection of books, though very few of them were new in the last fifty years. Mr. Woodhouse was no sort of scholar and had neither disturbed his collection nor added to it in several decades. Emma was not a great reader, either, and it always made Knightley a little wistful to see the wealth of knowledge on the library shelves and know that it was not being used.

Mr. Woodhouse found his letter and gave it to Knightley. Three minutes were sufficient for him to master its contents, and he was able to give such a clear explanation of the matter that even Mr. Woodhouse could hardly fail to comprehend it. The only thing remaining was to write a letter in response, and, as usual, Knightley obliged by doing the task himself.

"I am a very troublesome neighbour to you, Mr. Knightley," said Mr. Woodhouse as he signed his name at the bottom of the letter. "And I am very sorry to inconvenience you so often with my business affairs."

"It is my pleasure to serve you, sir," said Knightley sincerely. "I am indebted to you for your constant hospitality and friendship; you have no need to thank me."

"It is very handsome of you to say so, Mr. Knightley. And now, perhaps we ought to return to the drawing room; I wonder if Emma and Miss Smith have come back?"

As the gentlemen entered the drawing room they saw that the ladies had indeed returned and were sitting cosily together, talking. Emma had a book in her hand, though it was closed, and whatever the conversation was about it did not seem to include the book. Emma rose and went to greet her father with affection and escort him to his chair. Miss Smith rose also and she and Knightley were introduced. She certainly was a pretty girl, a little awed by her introduction to Mr. Knightley, but not awkwardly shy.

"And how did you find poor Miss Taylor?" asked Mr. Woodhouse when all were seated again.

"Mrs. Weston is very well, Papa, and she sent her best regards to you. She says that she is quite impatient for Thursday to come, to be dining at Hartfield again with us."

"Ah! It is very sad indeed that she should have to dine anywhere else. I am sure she is always very welcome here. I hope, Miss Smith, that you enjoyed your visit to Randalls?"

"Oh yes, indeed, sir. Mrs. Weston is so very kind."

"I hope you did not eat any wedding cake, Miss Smith; it is most unwise to eat wedding cake."

"Oh, Papa," said Emma, breaking in, "Mrs. Weston showed Harriet her letter from Mr. Frank Churchill. Harriet agreed that it was a very handsome letter, didn't you, Harriet?"

"Yes, very handsome, Miss Woodhouse."

"Ah! I think anyone who has seen the letter must agree, do not you, Mr. Knightley?" said Mr. Woodhouse. "You have seen the young man's letter, I believe?"

"Yes, I have. I thought it very proper of him to write to Mrs. Weston on the occasion of her marriage. What is that book you were reading, Emma, when I came in?"

"It is Dr. Watts' *On The Improvement of the Mind.* Harriet and I have been reading it together." She spoke with some smugness; she knew he believed that she did not do enough serious reading. "And when we have finished with it we will begin on Rollin's *Ancient History.*"

Knightley looked at the bookmark, reposing in what appeared to be the first chapter of the book.

"Are you fond of reading, Miss Smith?" was his next question.

"Oh, yes, sir. I have read all of Miss Edgeworth's novels as well as *The Vicar of Wakefield* and several more besides. I have not read many books of the sort that Miss Woodhouse has chosen for us to read—I had not heard of Dr. Watts' book before we began to read it together last week—but I do think reading is a delightful occupation."

"As do I, Miss Smith. I hope you will enjoy the book you have started—'some books are to be tasted, others to be swallowed, and some few to be chewed and digested'—and I believe Dr. Watts' work is in the last category."

Harriet looked rather puzzled than edified by Bacon's dictum.

"Mr. Knightley is only quoting Pope, Harriet," said Emma. "He is comparing reading to eating—not a particularly elegant metaphor, I must say."

"Oh! Of course, it is a quote, and a metaphor," said Harriet. "I ought to have known. But you are so clever, Miss Woodhouse, to know so quickly which author said anything! I do not think that I will ever be able to learn such things."

"Well, Harriet, I think that you will improve a good deal as we study together." Emma's tone was authoritative and confident.

"Be careful, Emma," said Knightley, smiling. "'A little learning is a dangerous thing'—Pope did say *that,* before you hazard another guess."

"Yes," said Mr. Woodhouse, whose attention had been caught by the mention of tasting and swallowing. "One must always be careful what one eats. Digestion is so apt to be impaired by the wrong foods. I think it is very wise to be cautious about what you eat. But you need not fear while you are at Hartfield, Miss Smith. We have no unwholesome food here. Emma, my dear, will you ring for tea?"

An involuntary smile passed between Knightley and Emma as she rose to ring the bell.

3

Knightley closed the account book and put down his pen. Another good harvest this year – better than last year, in fact. Next year there would be enough money to drain the land around the Fisher farm and create another smallholding. He finished the remains of the spruce beer in his glass and looked into the cheerful fire of the library. It had always given him a feeling of plenitude and satisfaction when the work of the autumn was completed and winter was free to do its worst. The home farm, at any rate, was ready for the coming season. The larders were full, the animals were well provided for, the winter crops of vegetables were sown, and the roofs of the outbuildings had been examined and found free of leaks. He had every reason to feel the contentment that ought to come with the completion of a fruitful harvest season.

This year, however, he was conscious of a lack. Instead of feeling that he was free now to enjoy the social engagements of the winter months, he felt as if he wanted to be doing something more in the way of work to fill his time. Donwell Abbey, which had always seemed to him to be a sheltered refuge, was beginning to seem just a bit *too* sheltered – too far away from friendly society. He shook his head at the notion. Donwell was what it always had been. It was no more isolated than it ever was, and he had never had cause to be lonely. Perhaps the colder weather today and the shortening of the daylight hours had given him a fit of melancholy. Well, he ought to shake off this unfounded discontent before the Hartfield dinner. A book – an amusing book – would clear his mind. He had only begun to consider which volume might answer the purpose when the butler, a short, slight, middle-aged man, came in.

"Yes, Baxter?"

"I thought you would like to know, sir, that Dr. Hughes has broken his leg."

"Broken his leg!" Knightley stared at the butler in surprise.

"Yes, Mr. Knightley. William Larkins heard it from the Hughes' maid only this morning."

"When did it happen? And how?"

"I believe the accident occurred yesterday, sir. William Larkins said something about a tumble down stairs, but I am not certain of exactly what transpired."

"I must see him at once, of course," said Knightley, rising. "Do you know what has been done for him?"

"William Larkins says that Mr. Perry was sent for immediately, and then a surgeon was brought from Kingston late last evening. Thomas has your things by the door, sir."

"Thank you, Baxter."

Knightley collected his hat, gloves, coat, and walking stick from the footman and took the path to the rectory of Donwell. This was a blow not only to Dr. Hughes but to all of the parish of Donwell. For a man who had reached his five-and-sixtieth year, the vicar was very busy: not only did he prepare sermons that were thoughtful and scholarly, yet not out of the mental reach of the largely unlettered congregation, but he regularly visited his parishioners and he had a place on the Donwell parish council. How long did broken legs take to mend? It probably took longer in an older man than a younger one. Perhaps the news was all wrong and it was merely a bad sprain instead of a break.

The Hughes' housemaid answered the door and curtseyed when she saw Mr. Knightley.

"May I see Dr. Hughes?" said Knightley. "Or failing that, Mrs. Hughes?"

"Oh, yes, sir. Come this way, if you please, sir. If you'll wait in the drawing room, sir, I'll fetch Mrs. Hughes." The maid ushered him into the room, curtseyed again, and disappeared.

Knightley wandered over to the window and looked out over the tidy garden that Mrs. Hughes tended so well. There were only grass and shrubs to be seen now; the bulbs of next year's flowers were buried under the earth, waiting for March. *'Daffodils,'* he quoted to himself, *'that come before the swallow dares, and take the winds of March with beauty.'* They would all have to wait until spring to come out of their graves, like Lazarus.

He heard footsteps coming down the stairs and turned to meet Mrs. Hughes as she came in.

"Mr. Knightley! How very good of you to come."

"And how is Dr. Hughes?"

"He is in a good deal of pain, I fear. But he is in bed, resting."

"And how long did the surgeon say he would be housebound?"

"Months, I'm afraid."

Knightley sighed, although this was exactly what he had expected.

"Is there anything I can do for him?"

"Yes, you can go and talk to him."

"I would not wish to disturb him if he is in pain."

"It would be an act of charity on your part to give him some amusement for this last half-hour before I can give him the draught that Mr. Perry left for him to take three times a day. Believe me when I say that he will be most disappointed if you go away without speaking to him. Come with me now."

Knightley could not do otherwise but follow Mrs. Hughes up the stairs and into the bedroom. Dr. Hughes was sitting in bed, his face rather ashen, but the serenity that usually marked his countenance was still there, and the shadows lifted from his eyes for a moment when he saw the younger man.

"My dear sir," said Knightley. "I am extremely sorry to see you in this condition."

"For my part I am thankful that I am still here for you to see, Mr. Knightley. The fall was not so sinister as it might have been."

"You fell, then?"

"Yes. It was all rather foolish, really. I was coming down the stairs, reading a book, I confess, instead of looking at my feet. I missed a step and tumbled the rest of the way down. I might have been much more grievously injured, but Heaven was merciful and I suffered only a broken leg."

"It is serious enough, I think. How will you manage?"

"I will have to lay aside my duties for a time. My dear wife has written to the bishop for me already to see about getting a curate for several months to carry on the work of the parish. I expect that in a week or two you will have a youthful and energetic man filling my place."

"No one could fill your place, sir."

Dr. Hughes smiled – a thin, slight smile, but a smile. "You over-estimate me, Mr. Knightley, but I thank you for your kind words. I return the compliment by telling you that your old valet, Richards, was singing your praises to me only last week. According to him, he is supported by you in a style which no other retired valet in the history of England has laid claim to."

Knightley chuckled. "He was a loyal, faithful, and devoted servant to my father and to me, and he thoroughly deserves what little pension he gets."

"He worries about you, Mr. Knightley. He thinks that since you no longer keep a valet you must be entirely neglected. I wanted to tell him that your appearance is as well as ever, but of course that would have hurt his pride terribly to think that a mere butler could do as well as he. I could only murmur that I believed Baxter was as anxious to serve you in your dress and toilet as anyone could be."

"He is that."

A spasm of pain crossed the rector's face.

"Are you all right, sir? May I get you anything?"

"No, nothing, thank you, Mr. Knightley. I will not deny that I am in some pain, but your conversation is directing my thoughts to other things. Pray, continue."

"Very well, then. I will enquire of you how young Richard getting on."

"Quite well, thank you. He is extremely grateful for Mr. John Knightley's patronage and help. He hopes to be called to the bar next term."

"I'm certain he will be. John says he will be an excellent barrister, and he is quite taken with him personally as well."

"It is such a comfort to me to have Mr. John Knightley watching over him, as it were. London is full of temptations, as you know, and Richard is a charming young man. I had some fears that he might be led astray, but your brother has him well in hand."

Mrs. Hughes entered the room with a glass of water, a spoon, and a paper packet full of powdered medicine. Knightley rose.

"I must be going away now, I'm afraid. There is a dinner tonight at Hartfield for Mr. and Mrs. Weston which I cannot miss."

"To be sure. Give them my greetings, if you will, Mr. Knightley. I am thoroughly happy for every man who finds a good wife, and Mr. Weston has found an excellent one. Please do take care down the steps, Mr. Knightley—if *you* break your leg I will be deprived of your company all winter, and my poor wife will be forced to endure all my conversation by herself!"

Knightley arrived at Hartfield at the same time as the Westons, and they were shown in together. To Knightley's surprise, Miss Smith was also included in the party. Elton was already there, of course—he always arrived at the earliest possible moment in order (as Knightley assumed) to gaze upon Miss Woodhouse's beauty for as long as he could. Emma had never seemed to notice this; there was so little worldliness in her and so little vanity about her appearance that she never guessed that she had made a conquest. She took it for granted that his excessive deference was only his way of showing due respect. It was just as well, of course. Elton would never presume to make her an offer – his position being so very inferior to hers – and it was best for her to continue to think of Elton as merely the vicar of Highbury who had access to Hartfield simply because of his office. Knightley supposed he could hardly blame the man for admiring Emma; even beside Miss Smith, whom everyone must call pretty, Emma's beauty shone out. And her thirty thousand pounds surely did not make her less attractive to a man like Elton.

Elton's attention was certainly fixed on the young ladies this evening. He made the slightest possible greetings to the Westons and to Knightley, and then resumed his conversation with Emma and Miss Smith. Emma said something, apparently of a humorous nature, at which Elton laughed heartily and Miss Smith giggled like the young girl she was.

Why was she included in this party? Emma would not even condescend to invite the Coles, good people that they were, and yet here was this girl of no birth or class at all evidently become Emma's favourite companion!

"Well, Knightley!" Weston's voice boomed in his ear. "I hear that Dr. Hughes is ailing. Cracked his skull, did he?"

Knightley could not stifle a smile. Gossip was, as usual, swift and inaccurate. "No, there's nothing whatever the matter with his head; it's his leg that's broken."

"Poor fellow! I suppose he'll be laid up for some time?"

"Yes, I expect it will be a few months at least."

"What a pity! That will be difficult for so active a man. I do hope he'll have a curate to preach and so on?"

"Oh, yes. I know he has written to the bishop about it."

"Good, good. I suppose if one cannot be got very soon, Elton could preach at both churches. You could change the time of the service at Donwell, you know, and then he could preach in both places."

Knightley tried very hard not to shudder. Elton made a passable sort of vicar for Highbury, he supposed, but that was as much as he could say for him.

"Well," Weston went on, "I must go and visit him one of these days. Cheer his weary hours of recovery and that sort of thing. At least he's a bookish man. It must be a comfort to him that he's got a library to keep him occupied while he heals."

"I daresay it will be some consolation. Descartes says that the reading of all good books is like a conversation with the finest men of past centuries—and Dr. Hughes is the sort of man who enjoys that. Speaking of books, Weston, I was wondering if you had any pattern books for cottages that I might borrow. I recall you building one on your estate last year some time."

"Why, yes, I believe I do have one. It wasn't much use to me—I didn't like any of the plans – but it may be to you. Come to Randalls tomorrow and get it, if you like."

At this moment the bell rang to signal that dinner was ready. Mr. Woodhouse, with delighted alacrity, asked Mrs. Weston if he would be allowed to take her in to the dining room.

Behind him, Knightley heard Elton say, "Miss Woodhouse, may—"

"Oh!" exclaimed Emma, "I must get a cushion for my father. He is so much easier at table with a cushion at his back. Mr. Elton, would you have the goodness to take Miss Smith in while I see what has become of the blue cushion?"

Knightley's eyebrows lifted. He had never seen Mr. Woodhouse with a cushion in his dining-room chair. And yet Emma had said it so naturally that it was just possible…

"By all means," said Elton with an ingratiating smile. "Anything to be of service!" And he offered his arm ceremoniously to Miss Smith.

Knightley watched Emma as she bustled around, looking for a blue cushion in very unlikely places. On her face was a self-satisfied little smile—the one she always wore when she was successful at something. But what had she accomplished now? Emma paused in her search behind a curtain to glance at the figures passing out of the room.

Aha! Knightley nearly laughed aloud. So that was it! Emma was following through on her resolution to find a wife for Elton. Miss Smith was evidently the bride-elect.

"Come, Emma, come, Knightley," said Weston. "We mustn't keep Mr. Woodhouse waiting."

"Ah, there it is," said Emma, retrieving a blue cushion from a window seat. She smiled up at Weston as she took his arm. Knightley followed the two of them into the dining room, trying to feel the impatience with her that he ought to feel and succeeding only in suppressing a chuckle

The dinner was over and the ladies were gone back to the drawing room, leaving the men to their port and whatever masculine topics of conversation they chose.

"So, the workmen are to begin on that bridge on Monday next, I understand," said Elton. "How long do you think it will take them to replace it?"

"Not long, I hope," said Weston. "Everyone will be forced to go around by Aston until it is completed."

"I was assured that it would not be above three weeks," said Knightley, "but I expect it will be longer if we have bad weather."

"I sincerely hope we will have fine weather, then," said Elton. "I will get a steady stream of complaints from parishioners about it until it is completed, just as if the whole thing was my responsibility."

"Bear up, Elton," said Weston. "It's only natural for people to think that if they complain to you, you might put a word in with the Almighty and get some change in their circumstances, isn't it?

Elton rolled his eyes. "I'm sure they think so. I have a cousin who perpetually writes to me of all his difficulties 'so that I may mention them in prayer', he says. I'm sure he blames me if none of his burdens are lifted."

The mention of a cousin evidently suggested a new topic of conversation to Mr. Woodhouse.

"Mr. Weston, are all of your cousins quite well? Miss Bates said something a week or two ago about some illness in that house. And knowing how you visit them, and Mrs. Weston, too, I was quite anxious about you."

"All very well again, now, thank you, sir," said Weston. "I think it was nothing but a cold that was passed from one to the other."

"Ah, but a cold, Mr. Weston, may be very serious indeed if it is not properly attended to. Perry has often told me of very serious complaints resulting from a lack of care taken with a cold. However, I am relieved to hear they are well now. And your son – is he in health?"

"Never better, sir, never better. He is at Weymouth just now, but I expect we will see him here in Highbury very soon. That will be something for the young people here, eh?" Weston smiled at the other men at the table, sure of their concurrence. "Emma, I am sure, would welcome a new face here among us all. We will be a much livelier set when Frank comes."

Knightley was amused to see consternation instead of assent on the faces of the other men. To Mr. Woodhouse, of course, the idea of a *new* person could do nothing but disturb his peace, and Mr. Elton did not look as if he wanted anyone else's help in entertaining Emma. Knightley managed a polite smile, but did not think that Mr. Weston's son would be any great addition to their company. Frank had the reputation of being very good-looking and a great favourite wherever he went, but then that was the reputation of half the idle, rich, and foolish young men in the kingdom. If he were a truly commendable young man, he would have visited his father and his father's new wife by now.

When the men had finished their wine, they joined the ladies in the drawing room. The three ladies were seated together, and Elton moved a chair close to them and attached himself to their group. Mr. Woodhouse took his seat by the fire, and Weston and Knightley sat down near him. Mr. Woodhouse enquired after Hannah, the daughter of his coachman, now a servant at Randalls, and while Weston answered his minute enquiries, Knightley found his gaze wandering over to the cluster around Emma. Elton was relating a story about a friend of his who had either bought or sold a horse not worth his price, and Knightley watched the faces of all three listeners. Mrs. Weston listened with good-hearted politeness, Miss Smith listened with wide-eyed interest, and Emma listened with one eye on Miss Smith to see her reaction to Elton. That was a mistake, thought Knightley. She ought to be keeping her eye on Elton, to see his reaction to Miss Smith. Knightley could easily see that Emma's matchmaking efforts were in vain; a man like Elton would never be drawn to a girl like Miss Smith. Emma would soon find that out.

"I must be in London in a fortnight," Weston was saying. "Business. I shall probably have to stay a week. I used to find Town very exciting, but I suspect it will seem dull now. I don't suppose there's any chance of you visiting your brother, Knightley, in the next three weeks or so?"

"None whatever, I'm sorry to say. The Kingston fair is on the thirteenth and I must be there."

"I dare say you will get better prices for your cattle than anyone. William Larkins says you have a bull nearly the size of the Durham Ox."

"I think that was Larkins' idea of a joke. The home farm does have a large bull, but nothing like so large as the Durham Ox."

"I saw it once — in '03, it was, at the agricultural fair. I paid a shilling for the privilege, too. Extremely impressive! How large do you reckon it was?"

"Two hundred and seventy stone, I believe, and it stood five feet, five inches at the shoulder. Magnificent creature."

"Yes, I remember the man standing near it was at a level with its head. And it was all done by feeding the beast turnips, I hear."

"And a few other things besides, I fancy."

His eye caught Emma's; she had a curious expression on her face and he wondered what it was about. Next moment she had turned to say something to Mrs. Weston, and Knightley gave his attention back to Mr. Woodhouse, who was extolling the merits of mashed turnips.

The hour was still somewhat early when the guests departed, Mr. Woodhouse being unable to tolerate late evening parties. Knightley lingered when the others had gone; he was not quite ready yet to go back to Donwell and give up the family atmosphere of Hartfield. He sat by the fire with Mr. Woodhouse and Emma and gave himself another fifteen minutes to enjoy their company before he would leave.

"I hope Miss Smith enjoyed herself tonight, Emma," he said.

"Yes, she did, Mr. Knightley, thank you. She is full of sweetness and gratitude, and I do not feel that I could ever do enough for her."

"A fine sentiment, Emma. I believe you do mean to do her good."

She looked surprised. "Do you doubt it, Mr. Knightley? I certainly did not befriend her to do her harm!"

"No, I am sure you did not. I do not recall you ever purposing to do another person harm. Intention, however, is not everything."

Emma's left eyebrow lifted. "Take care, Mr. Knightley. If you begin to lecture me I shall begin to tease *you* about the beautiful Unknown Lady you were praising this evening."

"Unknown Lady! I was not aware that I had praised any lady, known or unknown."

"You were telling Mr. Weston about her. Five feet, five inches tall, I believe you said, and also that she was magnificent. Who is she, pray?"

Knightley laughed. "My dear Emma, that was no lady I was speaking of! Mr. Weston and I were discussion the dimensions of the Durham bull, a famous ox that is known all over England!"

Emma joined in his laughter. "I did think it odd that Mr. Weston should mention her love of turnips!"

He laughed even harder at that, and it was some moments before they could compose themselves again.

"Well, Emma," he said when he had breath again for speaking, "I must say you have a very suspicious mind. And, I may say, a decided taste for matchmaking. I do not think you have any great skill at it, however."

Emma's chin lifted. "We shall see, Mr. Knightley. My *hearing* might be a little faulty, but my judgement, I think, may be safely trusted."

Knightley sighed. He wondered what it would take to dislodge these inflated ideas she had about her own powers. It was certainly beyond *his* abilities to do anything. Rather frustrated with himself and with her, he took his leave and went back to Donwell Abbey; if it was lacking in family atmosphere, at least there were no headstrong young ladies.

4

"And isn't it shocking, Mr. Knightley, about poor Dr. Hughes?" said Miss Bates. "He was a friend of my father's, you know, quite a friend, although my father must have been twenty years his senior, at least. Dr. Hughes is such a good man, such a *very* good man that it is doubly sad that he should have this miserable accident. But we may safely say, mayn't we, that no one could meet suffering with a greater fortitude than he? And dear Mrs. Hughes as well, of course. Indeed, I think she may have the heavier burden of the two—it is very taxing to see a loved one in pain, is it not?"

"Yes, indeed," Knightley managed to say before Miss Bates continued.

"But then she is so very patient herself! I called on her yesterday—no, it could not have been yesterday, because I was at Hartfield yesterday—but the day before yesterday I called at the Donwell vicarage and saw Mrs. Hughes, and I must say that she looked as peaceful as ever she did. My mother said the same."

"Was Mrs. Bates—"

"Oh! yes, my mother was able to go with me, as Mr. Woodhouse kindly sent us his carriage so that we could both visit Mrs. Hughes. My mother was so pleased to see Mrs. Hughes again, as she would tell you if she were not resting. She is very well for her age, Mr. Knightley, but she will sometimes rest in her bedroom in the afternoon as she did today. She is as well as she can be, however, and Mrs. Hughes remarked on it. My mother has always been a good friend to her, and to Dr. Hughes, of course, as well, and also the dear children, Mr. Richard and Miss Phoebe—oh! Mrs. Elson, I should say—it seems impossible that little Miss Phoebe is old enough to be married! But so she is. It ought not surprise me, as Miss Phoebe—Mrs. Elson, that is—is two years older than Jane. She was always so kind to dear Jane, and still is, whenever Jane visits. Mr. Knightley, do have another piece of this cake which Mrs. Weston sent to us. Oh, you must! After all your liberality to us, Mr. Knightley, you must allow us to share with you as much cake as we can when you call! Ah, I knew you would have another piece. I never can persuade Mr. Elton to take more than one piece of cake. His calls here are never very long, but then he is such a busy man! And he has so many people to call on, you know, in the way of parish business and so forth. He makes a great many calls at Hartfield, I know —calling on dear Mr. Woodhouse. He is quite devoted to Mr. Woodhouse, Mr. Knightley, else he would not give so much of his time to Hartfield. He was there yesterday, in fact, when I was there, and with Miss Woodhouse and Miss Smith we were quite a merry party."

"I would imagine so." And Knightley *could* imagine it...Elton eager to please and in the best of spirits, Harriet delighting in the attentions of a superior social set, Emma trying to give many little encouragements and smooth many little matters, as she had done—or thought she had done—for the Westons, and Miss Bates, probably rather ignored by the younger people, but sure of Mr. Woodhouse's regard, and finding her joy in merely being in company with them all.

"Mrs. Goddard says that Miss Smith has spent some nights at Hartfield, as well as many of her days. So obliging of Miss Woodhouse to take such an interest in Miss Smith! Mrs. Goddard believes that it will greatly improve Miss Smith's prospects."

"Yes, well," said Knightley, and looked at his watch. "I fear I must leave you, Miss Bates. William Larkins will be waiting for me at Donwell if I do not hurry. No, thank you, Miss Bates, I *cannot* have another piece of cake. Give my best regards to your mother, and to your niece when next you write to her. Not at all. Good day, Miss Bates."

Regaining the street, he put on his hat and began the walk to Donwell—rather reluctantly, as he had rather have been going to Hartfield. Mischief was being done there, and he wished to have a better knowledge of the facts. It was clear that Emma was making much of Harriet Smith, no doubt with a view to matching her with Elton. It was a mistake on Emma's part, showing a lack of judgement and several false ideas. It would be rather good for Emma to make a mistake—even a large mistake—and have to acknowledge it. But it did not follow that such a mistake would be good for Harriet Smith. Knightley knew little of her, but it was probable that Emma would tell Harriet that she deserved a man such as Elton, and Harriet, trusting implicitly in everything Emma said, would raise her expectations to just such a level. Disappointed hopes, at least, would follow.

And then Elton was being misled as well. It was just possible that he was vain enough to believe that Miss Woodhouse was beginning to prefer him to all other men. And if he really believed that, there was every reason to suppose that he would make her an offer. It might be good for Elton to make a mistake as well, if only he would profit by the lesson it taught him. Knightley had not much faith in *that*; Elton seemed the sort of man who would respond to embarrassment over a blunder with anger instead of contrition. All in all it would be better for him to be undeceived soon.

And even apart from the injury Emma was doing Elton and Harriet, there was mischief working the other way, too. To have someone like Harriet who relied so totally on one's judgement, who believed so completely in all one said, and who admired everything one did without any hesitation or reservation—that was a dangerous thing to anyone's ego. And when it came to Emma...that was absolutely the last thing she needed.

Of course, if there had still been a Miss Taylor living at Hartfield, she would have seen how Elton was interpreting Emma's behaviour and given her a quiet hint. Uneasily, Knightley wondered if *he* ought to say something to Emma. Perhaps it was a brother's place, and he was as close to holding that position as anyone. But something within him shrank at addressing such a topic with her. He could not quite reason out why, but the thought of discussing with Emma Elton's attraction to her made him unreasonably embarrassed and uncomfortable. No, he could not do it. Perhaps if this went on much longer he could talk to Mrs. Weston about it.

They had often talked about Emma before, and now and then she had taken his advice. It could be tried, at any rate.

Knightley arrived home just before Larkins, who came into the library with his brows knit ominously.

"I believe we will have more trouble with that Adam Mefford, Mr. Knightley."

"His rent is still in arrears, isn't it?"

"Yes, in spite of your very lenient terms. And he still has not cultivated that field, though you drained it for him. And he has been very insolent to me."

"Has he?"

"Yes, Mr. Knightley. I was passing the widow Hunt's cottage this afternoon as she was driving her geese back into her little enclosure. They had all got out, it seems, and she told me that one was still missing and asked me to look out for it. Of course I said I would do so, Mr. Knightley, and I asked those I passed on the road if they had seen it. When I came to the Mefford farm I saw Adam sitting on the low wall, just sitting there in the middle of the day, and I said, 'Have you seen a goose come down this road?" and he said, 'Just the one I'm talking to.' That was very impertinent, was it not, Mr. Knightley? And so I thought I would just take it out of him. I said, 'Mr. Knightley's been talking to me. He wants to give you a job up at the Abbey.' 'Oh? What job's that?' says he. 'He wants you to go up there and play the fool,' I said. And he said, 'Is he giving you the sack or is he going to keep two of us?'"

Knightley's mouth twitched into a smile before he could stop himself. Mefford, though something of a rascal, was a witty rascal, and Knightley had been more lenient with him than he ought to have been partly because he was so amusing. He could understand how a man like Mefford would be tempted to taunt an over-serious fellow like Larkins, who did have a tendency to stand upon his dignity. Nevertheless, it was inexcusable and Larkins was correct in saying that there would likely be more trouble coming from that quarter. It had been a long time since a tenant was evicted from Donwell, but it might come to that.

Knightley sighed. "Well, his manner certainly is impertinent, and he is not a model tenant. I will have to consider his case very shortly. I would have acted before now if it were not for his family."

Larkins' indignant face softened. "Indeed, Mr. Knightley. I feel for them most sincerely. His wife is a good creature, and the son, Harry, has the makings of a good young man, if only he got the chance. Well, sir, have you looked over the pattern book of Mr. Weston's?"

"I have, but I did not see any that I thought appropriate. Some of these designs are impressive to the eye, but hopelessly inconvenient for an occupant. Look here at this one —a gate-keeper's cottage. It consists of two rooms—a living room and a bedroom—but one on either side of the gate! To be sure, it looks symmetrical and neat, but who would want to walk twenty feet across the road to get to their bed?"

"Yes. It seemed to me that these cottages were designed more for their contribution to the appearance of the estate's grandeur than for the comfort of the resident."

"Exactly. Are there any more pattern books we might consult?"

"Yes, Mr. Knightley. I have ordered two that sounded promising; they should be delivered next week."

"Very good."

"And the head stockman tells me that he wishes he could use the home meadow next year for grazing the cattle."

"It would be rather inconvenient for the Highbury people making their way to Langham to take their chances with the bull every time they crossed the meadow."

"Yes," said Larkins gravely, "I do not think they would wish to hazard their safety on so regular a basis. However, it occurred to me that the path might be moved a little to the right, and so avoid the meadow altogether."

"Hmm. It might be possible. We shall see about it."

"And you ought to know, Mr. Knightley, that the widow Hunt thinks it was most unwise for Mr. Elton to preach in Donwell church on Sunday."

"It was not— "

"Oh, be assured, sir, I told her it was not due to *your* influence that Mr. Elton filled the pulpit, and she said she was quite aware of that. But she said that all the young girls were in a flutter over such a handsome young man...those were *her* words, Mr. Knightley, not mine."

"Well, Larkins, the bishop has acted promptly on Dr. Hughes' letter, and the new curate will be arriving Monday next. So there will be only one more Sunday for Mr. Elton to preach in Donwell."

"Yes, sir. But then the new curate might be just such a young man as Mr. Elton, and then what will be the consequence to the parish?"

"Let us hope, then, for the sake of the peace of the young ladies of the parish, that the new curate is old and ugly."

"That would answer, Mr. Knightley, indeed it would. But there is no assurance that he will be anything near so desirable. And now, sir, I have the accounts ready for your examination, if you would care to look at them."

Knightley nodded, and the two men submerged themselves in the welcome world of verifiable facts—a logical, reliable, and manageable realm.

5

Knightley climbed over the stile and cocked an eye skyward. It was going to rain. He had known it would rain before he set out to look at the Langham path that cut through the home meadow, but he had convinced himself it would hold off for another hour. He wanted to be out of the house. Whatever he had tried to do that afternoon—reading, writing letters, drawing up a new lease—he had found his mind constantly wandering back to the problem of Emma, Elton, and Harriet Smith. Ought he to say something? Was there any way to discourage Emma or Elton without speaking? Should he talk to Mrs. Weston about Emma's inappropriate friendship with Harriet? Or would it be best to let the matter go and allow the consequences to follow?

At last he had decided that what he needed was to clear his mind by going to look at that path and see if it could be moved. Without even pausing to take his umbrella or great-coat, he had walked out into the blustery day.

Now that he was here, he regretted that he had been so impetuous. Before he could even begin to survey the land adjoining the home meadow, the first sprinkles of rain were felt. The clouds were dark and it was evident that this would not be a passing shower. There was nothing to do but turn around and go back.

Very quickly the light drizzle turned into a heavy pelting rain, and long before Donwell Abbey was in sight the rain was pouring down. Just ahead was a large oak, and he hastened toward it for the partial shelter it could give. As he neared the tree he could see that someone else was taking refuge under its branches. The driving rain became large irregular drips under the tree's broad leaves, and he took out his handkerchief and dried his face before turning to greet his fellow shelter-seeker.

He was a stranger, young and well-dressed, with fair hair and a rather plain face. He returned Knightley's "How do you do" with a quiet "Very well, I thank you, sir." The young man looked embarrassed and nervous, and Knightley hoped to put him at ease by asking if he was visiting in the country.

"No," said the young man uncomfortably. "I fear I am now a resident of this parish."

Knightley smiled. "Is it a very fearsome thing?"

The man blushed. "Not at all, sir. It seems a pleasant place. I only meant that it is rather mortifying as a resident to have lost my way. All the more as it is now *my* parish. Mr. Knightley will not think much of the new curate if he learns that I could not even find my own house after a walk."

Knightley hesitated, reluctant to make the poor young man more unhappy than he already was. But of course, he really had no choice. He summoned a light-hearted smile and said, "As it happens, I am Mr. Knightley."

The young man gasped and grew rather pale.

"And," Knightley went on, "I fear you will not think much of *me* when you realize that I was so imprudent as to set off on a threatening day without so much as an umbrella. So you see, we have already shown our worst faces to each other and there is nothing more to dread."

The young man bowed, with his eyes on the ground. "Peter Spencer, at your service," he said.

"I met the new curate yesterday afternoon, quite accidentally," Knightley said to Dr. Hughes the next day. "We were both taking shelter under the same tree."

Dr. Hughes leaned back against the pillows in his bed and nodded.

"Yes, so he informed me when he came to see me last evening. And what did you think of him?"

"Well..." said Knightley slowly, and paused.

"Yes?"

"He seems rather timid."

Dr. Hughes chuckled but made no reply.

"I have met many clergymen who were quiet or reserved, but none who were so very bashful. He did answer my questions, and I managed to learn that he was born in Norfolk, was up at Oxford, and was ordained three months ago. Beyond that, however, I know nothing but his name—not even the colour of his eyes, as I do not believe that he looked me full in the face even once."

"And you have misgivings about his ability to 'feed the flock of God,' haven't you?" Dr. Hughes usually knew what Knightley was thinking.

"I confess I have."

"I think he will surprise you, Mr. Knightley. His manner may be hesitating, but you will find him to be a sound man. Very sound."

"Very well. I trust your judgement, sir, and will reserve my own until I know Spencer better."

"A wise policy, Mr. Knightley. Hasty appraisals are rarely accurate."

"He will please William Larkins, at any rate; his greatest fear was that the new curate would be a handsome, pleasing young man who would discompose the feelings of all the single young women of his parish."

"Well then, he pleases me and William Larkins. That means there are two in his favour already. Oh! And there is a third: Mrs. Martin told me yesterday that she highly approves of him as well. She discovered that he was born in the parish of Diss, in Norfolk, which is where her grandfather was born. Evidently being born in Diss is a guarantee of good character."

Knightley smiled. "The Martins are all well, I trust?"

"Oh, yes. Mrs. Martin brought some Madeira wine which she said was remarkably healing. Robert was with her. He has done very well with his sheep, has he not? He has high hopes for the selling of his wool at the Kingston fair on Saturday next."

"Indeed, I only wish my own flock were prospering as well. But then his whole farm is very well-managed. His father was an excellent farmer, of course, but it is to young Martin's credit that the farm has not declined at all—if anything, it has improved since he has taken the lease."

"I don't suppose you know if he means to marry soon?"

"Marry? No, I do not. Has he said something?"

"Not directly. I would not be astonished, however, to know that he has something of the kind in contemplation. A man in love usually has an aspect of great abstractedness, and there is further evidence of it when he stops talking about sheep and cattle and begins talking about improvements to the furnishing of his house."

"I confess I have never noticed such a thing."

"Ah, well, you see, Mr. Knightley, you're not married. Never even thought of it, I think." He looked rather steadily at Knightley.

Knightley was a little taken aback, not at the words, but at the searching look, and did not know how to respond. But in a moment Dr. Hughes went on, more naturally.

"I have been the repository of the lovelorn confessions of countless young men over the years. I suppose it is only natural that I should develop a consciousness of these things."

"I only remember my brother suffering the agonies of uncertainty over Isabella," said Knightley. "Perhaps subtler signs were present as well, but the thing I remember most is his real anguish as he said one day, 'What if she should not love me after all?' I suppose all young men seem insufferably cocksure to their older brothers, but those weeks of apprehension took away all John's conceit. He grew exceedingly humble. Unfortunately, once he was in no doubt of his love's being returned, his usual demeanour was restored."

Dr. Hughes laughed. "Lovesickness is a good remedy for arrogance. If only we could prescribe it as Mr. Perry does his medicines! I can think of half a dozen people who would benefit from such a treatment."

At this moment the housemaid entered and dropped a deferential curtsey to Knightley.

"If you please, sir, there's a servant downstairs with a message for you," she said.

Knightley rose and followed her downstairs to where his footman was waiting in the hall.

"Yes, Thomas?"

"Mr. Baxter wishes to inform you, sir, that Constable Burton is waiting to see you at Donwell Abbey. He has two men with him, sir. Mr. Baxter thought you would wish to be informed."

"Yes, thank you, Thomas. I will come directly." Knightley dismissed the servant with a courteous nod and climbed back up the stairs to Dr. Hughes' room.

"I must go, sir. The duties of a magistrate await me in my own drawing room. It must be somewhat important—whoever it is did not care to wait until my usual day at the Crown."

"Goodbye, then, Mr. Knightley. Come again soon." It was not spoken out of mere politeness, and Knightley knew it.

It was only a short walk back to the Abbey—hardly long enough to wonder who might want him so urgently. It was someone from Highbury, obviously, as Burton was the constable for that parish, and if there were two men with him it was probably the victim of a crime and its suspected perpetrator. He hoped it would not be something very serious.

Baxter met him at the door. "I have shown them into the drawing room, sir."

"Thank you, Baxter."

The three men rose as Knightley entered the room. There was Burton, of course, a farmer called Mitchell, and a young man whom Knightley recognized by sight but could not immediately put a name to. He greeted them as they bowed and then asked how he might be of service.

"Well, now, Mr. Knightley," said Mitchell. "I want William here committed and tried at the petty sessions. He's committed a felony, he has, and he must pay for it."

Knightley looked at the young man. Ah yes, William Plover, that was his name. A character rather notorious for petty pilfering and small damages to property. William looked back at Knightley with impudent eyes.

"What exactly was the felony?" said Knightley.

"Stealing eggs," said Mitchell. "It mayn't sound like much, but it's an indictable offence, and I want him taken for it. He's stolen a quantity of small things from all the farms hereabouts, and this time I caught him red-handed. He was in my poultry house—and that's trespass, too—and he was filling this here sack that Mr. Burton is holding with my eggs. And I said, 'Now then, you thief, you're caught *this* time, anyway," and I had my lad run for the constable and he came and took him in hand and we've come straight to you for justice." Mitchell paused here, out of breath with the speed of his narrative and with the energy of his indignation.

"Is this so?" Knightley questioned William.

William shrugged.

"I take it that you admit your guilt," Knightley said sternly. "All right. Mr. Burton, would you be so good as to take William into the hall and wait with him there until I ask you to return? Thank you."

The men were silent until the door was shut again.

"Will you commit him?" asked Mitchell. "You know he is a troublemaker and must be stopped. No amount of warnings and threats have had any effect on his behaviour thus far. He doesn't believe he will ever be prosecuted."

"I know," said Knightley. "Does he work at all?"

"A little," Mitchell sniffed. "Odd jobs for a few farmers."

"He has a mother, hasn't he?"

"Yes. A poor woman with a bad foot who deserves a better son."

"You realize, of course, that if he is committed the support of his mother will fall upon the parish? And the rates will have to be raised if any more people are given parish help."

Mitchell paused. "I had not thought of that," he said. "Nevertheless, there ought to be some kind of justice done."

"Indeed there ought. I could commit him to the petty sessions, but I must tell you that I think it unlikely that he would be imprisoned for such a crime. I could fine him, but then there will be even less money in his mother's house. And I have no doubt she would suffer more from it than he would."

"True enough," said Mitchell, whose zeal had noticeably flagged.

"However, there is one thing which may be sufficient to check his criminal activities. I think it is the best solution for now."

He walked to the door, opened it, and asked the men to return to the room.

"William Plover," said Knightley, "I am inclined to have the judges at the petty sessions hear this case."

William looked unconcernedly at the magistrate, not believing that Mr. Knightley was really inclined to do any such thing. He knew he was unlikely to be imprisoned for stealing eggs. It was only another empty threat, and threats did not bother him.

"There is a particular need just now for more men in His Majesty's Navy. Napoleon is not yet defeated. The penalty given for your sort of theft is often conscription into the army or navy. You could send home a little money to your mother, you know, that way, and the experience may teach you a few things you are lacking."

William's eyes lost their contemptuous look as the meaning of Knightley's words sank in. This was not an empty threat, it was rather a real and sinister one. He would have no one to witness to his character if he were brought to court, and as he would not be able to pay a large fine, the justices might very well think he ought to be entered in the lists of soldiers or sailors as his punishment. He began to look actually worried.

"Please, sir," he said, speaking for the first time, "don't send me on. I'll make satisfaction, truly I will."

"Will you pay Mr. Mitchell the worth of the eggs you stole?"

"That would be sixpence," put in Mitchell.

"I will, sir."

"I think there ought to be something more," mused Knightley. "Have you a job, Mitchell, that young William might labour at for a day or so?"

"I do, Mr. Knightley. I have a wall that wants repairing, and I know he can do it."

"Very well. William Plover, I find you guilty of theft. Your punishment is to pay Mr. Mitchell sixpence and to mend his fence in a manner that satisfies him."

"Yes, sir," said William.

"Thank you, Mr. Knightley," said Mitchell.

The men bowed and left. Knightley could see them walking away through the drawing room window. He hoped he had done enough. William's widowed mother ought not to suffer any more for her son's sake. He hoped she was doing well enough now. He would ask Emma about her; Emma would know.

6

11th November
Wellyn House
Brunswick-square

Dear George,

Thank you for yours of the 2nd. We are all well here; that is to say, Isabella is as usual and the children are very healthy. Little Bella's fourth birthday was last week, and she was presented – rather against my inclination – with a white French cat. It is made much of by everyone but myself, and though it is confined to the nursery most of the time, Bella brings it down every evening after dinner so that it may pay its respects to the rest of the family. Bella asked me what name the cat should have and I suggested "Madam Duval" – out of Evelina, *you know. I fear the joke is lost on everyone here.*

I hauled myself over to the Club last night for the annual dinner – thank God only one dinner is required all year. Good food is a weak substitute for poor company. I ought not to speak so harshly, I suppose; the fellows are not so bad. But the talk is everlastingly the same: the War, politics, Prinny, the theatre and all the other sort of gossip that sends me to sleep over the port.

I met up with Graham and he asked to be remembered to you. He has suddenly inherited an estate in Northamptonshire – cousin died unexpectedly, apparently, and the whole lot was entailed to Graham. He's in a quandary, though, as to how to make the estate pay. He says it's in a poor state, the previous owners having lived in London and relied on a worthless bailiff to manage the place. He wants your advice. I told him there was nothing you liked so much as arranging everyone else's business. I think he believed me.

Thank you for the kind invitation to stay with you at Christmas. You know as well as I that it would be too difficult for Mr. Woodhouse to have Isabella anywhere else but Hartfield at Christmas, but I value your offer of hospitality. It makes little difference, really, as we will see you every day. The boys continually ask how many days must pass before they can see Uncle Knightley again.

Isabella sends all her kind wishes, as usual, and I remain,

Your favourite brother,
John

"Ah, my dear Mr. Knightley!" said Mr. Woodhouse. "It is indeed a delight to have you dining here once again. How weary you must be after that dreadful fair in Kingston! And here is Mr. Weston returned from Town as well, as you see. I am sure you must both be extremely thankful to be home." Mr. Woodhouse would have been wrung to the depths of his soul if he had been required to leave his home and travel elsewhere, and he had the utmost pity for anyone else obliged to do so.

"I am very glad to be dining here again, sir," said Knightley. "I regret that I have been engaged for so many days together which prevented me from calling at Hartfield."

"It is always so dismal when you cannot come, Mr. Knightley," said Mr. Woodhouse, faintly reproachful. "Emma and I miss you so."

Knightley looked around for Emma. There she was, dressed in a new green print gown that brought out the rich hazel of her eyes.

"And here is Mr. Elton come," said Mr. Woodhouse. "If you will excuse me, Mr. Knightley..." He gave a courtly little bow and moved off to welcome the vicar as he entered the room.

Knightley went over to Emma. For once she was standing alone; Harriet was talking to the Westons.

"You look very well," he said. "That is a new gown, is it not?"

"It is," Emma smiled—her natural smile, with all its openness and sincerity, "but I am surprised that you perceived such a thing. You never noticed whether a gown of mine was new or not before, I am sure."

"I have never needed to. Miss Bates has always informed me when you had a new gown."

Emma laughed. "I see. How did you fail to hear about this one, then?"

"I have not been near the Bates' for several days; in fact, I have not had leisure to call on anyone."

"Ah! Well then, I must give you all the news that Miss Bates would otherwise have informed you of. Mrs. Weston has a new silver teapot which Mr. Weston brought her from Town, the bridge is finally completed, and"—lowering her voice—"Mrs. Bates has a cold. My father has not heard of it yet. Pray don't mention it to him; it would disturb his comfort so."

"No, of course I will not."

"There must be other news as well...Oh! Mrs. Saunders was delivered of a baby girl yesterday, and Mrs. Plover's son was...but then you would know about him already."

"Yes. Have you visited Mrs. Plover? Is she well?"

Emma's brow wrinkled thoughtfully. "Well enough, I suppose. I wish she had a better son. She manages to keep from relying on the parish, but only just. I do not believe she would be able to do it without the help of her neighbours."

"And the help of Hartfield," added Knightley, "for I know what you do. Well, will you let me know if I may be of service to her?"

Emma smiled and nodded. She did indeed look very well this evening, Knightley thought, and he was on the verge of telling her so when he remembered that he had already said it once.

"Well now, Elton!" Weston hailed the vicar from across the room. "What took you so long to get here? I've never known you to be the last to arrive at a Hartfield gathering."

"I was detained at the Bates'," said Elton with a polite smile on his face but a note of frustration in his voice. "Mrs. Bates has caught a bad cold and Miss Bates was very worried about it."

Blast the man! thought Knightley, as Mr. Woodhouse's face revealed his dismay. *Cannot he learn when to keep silent? Mr. Woodhouse's peace will be cut up for the entire evening now.*

"Emma, my dear," said Mr. Woodhouse in consternation, "Should not Perry be sent for? Should we not send a message for Perry to see Mrs. Bates? And we ought to send her some beef-tea. Oh dear, oh dear. Poor Mrs. Bates!"

"I'm sure Mr. Perry has been to see her already," said Emma soothingly, "Has he not, Mr. Elton?"

"Oh, yes. He came twice today, I believe."

"There, Papa! You know that Mr. Perry is very attentive to Mrs. Bates. I was sure he would not neglect her. And when Mr. Perry calls here tomorrow we may ask him what we may do for her. We will suggest beef-tea and he will tell us if that is what we ought to send."

"And I will call on the Bates' tomorrow, Mr. Woodhouse," said Mrs. Weston, coming over to him. "I shall bring you a report of her health. A cold, you know, if carefully watched, is seldom *very* serious. She has a strong constitution, as well, sir. I think we need not be uneasy for her."

"No indeed!" said Emma. "Miss Bates loves her mother so much that it is natural she should be nervous at the slightest symptoms of ill-health, but we who have seen her come through many a cold may safely trust to Mr. Perry, I think."

"You must be right, of course, my dear Emma," sighed Mr. Woodhouse, endeavouring to be comforted by her logic. "My dear Mrs. Weston, I am sure you are right; you always are. But it is a dangerous season."

A new topic of conversation was needed now, and Mrs. Weston took the responsibility of finding it.

"Mr. Knightley, how does the new curate at Donwell get on?"

There was a pause as Knightley felt the eyes of the entire company on him. In his opinion, Spencer was not getting on very well. Knightley had now sat through two of Spencer's sermons and the experience had been rather painful. The poor young man had read his sermons with a quiet voice and faltering manner, never once lifting his eyes to the congregation. For a parish used to the masterful and eloquent sermons of Dr. Hughes, Spencer was an enormous disappointment. Furthermore, the first Sunday he had actually left out a whole set of responses through sheer nervousness.

Out of the corner of his eye, Knightley saw Elton smirk. No doubt he had heard reports of the curate's sermons. He determined to represent Spencer as well as he could.

"Not so badly," he said. "Dr. Hughes tells me that he has visited half the families in the parish already—he began visiting the day after he arrived! And his sermons are very…thoughtful." Now that he had said it, it struck him that it was entirely true. The content of the sermon *had* been thoughtful, however feeble the delivery had been. "He is young yet," Knightley went on, "But he is very sincere. I think the parish may consider itself fortunate to have him." Elton's eyebrows went up at that, and even Knightley knew he was overreaching what he really felt. It was best to leave the subject altogether.

"Mrs. Weston, I have heard rumours that you have a handsome new silver teapot. I do hope Weston brought you a matching sugar bowl."

Knightley sat at the breakfast table the next morning with his eyes on his bread but his mind recalling the previous evening. He was thoroughly impatient with Elton. His sneering attitude toward poor Spencer was disgraceful, and the way he fawned over and flattered Emma was scarcely less so. Knightley would not interfere. Let him offer for Miss Woodhouse and be refused. It would do him good.

It would also do Emma good. She would find that her manner was *not* always flawless, and she would be disappointed in her scheme to marry Harriet to Elton. She must be disabused of the notion that she could arrange the lives of everyone in Highbury as if she were a master chess player, moving and positioning the pieces at will.

Then again, it was no wonder she had the idea that she could do so with poor Harriet admiring and supporting everything she said or did. Last night had been specimen enough of that. "Yes, Miss Woodhouse…You are so clever, Miss Woodhouse!...Of course, Miss Woodhouse…Do you think so, Miss Woodhouse?" The silly girl could not even make up her mind whether or not to eat peaches, even though she owned that she disliked them! Miss Woodhouse must advise her first.

Knightley pushed his plate away and looked out the breakfast room window at the trees which were now completely bare. It was impossible to be annoyed with Harriet. The girl was transparently free of design in all she did. Emma might have seen through a girl who meant to flatter her for her own advantage, but Harriet's artless veneration pleased her. Harriet was only too grateful to be directed and Emma thought herself a philanthropist for directing her. And, unfortunately, Emma's direction would not make Harriet a better woman. Harriet would most likely become the wife of an artisan or shopkeeper, and she needed to learn how to be a capable manager and a resourceful housewife. But all she would learn from Emma would be how to sit in polite society without reproach, how to dress with taste and elegance, and how to play backgammon. Much good that would do her!

Knightley rose from the table and walked over to the window to look at the sky. It was grey, but not threatening. A solitary robin perched in the tree just outside. Knightley watched as it hopped along the branch and then flew away.

Emma and Harriet...It was a sorry business for both of them. The only thing to be done was to enlist help. If those Emma respected most—the Westons or the London Knightleys—united with him in discouraging the friendship, Emma might gradually let the acquaintance drop. He ought to return that book of plans for cottages to Weston; he would bring it back that afternoon and speak to the Westons about Harriet at the same time.

He had almost reached Randalls when he met Weston on the road.

"Coming to see me?"

"I was returning your book to the library at Randalls, and thought I might spend a congenial hour in the drawing room with you and your lady. But I see you are off somewhere."

"I have some business with William Cox. I ought to have been there a half hour ago, otherwise I would go back to Randalls with you and help to enliven that congenial hour."

"Perhaps I ought to call tomorrow instead."

"Not at all, not at all. Do go and call on Mrs. Weston; she will be glad to see you."

So Knightley went on and fifteen minutes later he was seated in the drawing room, embarking on the subject of Emma and Harriet.

"I do not know what your opinion may be, Mrs. Weston," he began, "of this great intimacy between Emma and Harriet Smith, but I think it a bad thing."

"A bad thing!" Mrs. Weston was truly surprised. "Do you really think it a bad thing? Why so?"

Knightley's heart sank. She had not seen anything amiss, then. Bother! He would have to convince her. "I think they will neither of them do the other any good."

"You surprise me! Emma must do Harriet good; and by supplying her with a new object of interest, Harriet may be said to do Emma good. I have been seeing their intimacy with the greatest pleasure. How very differently we feel! Not think they will do each other any good! This will certainly be the beginning of one of our quarrels about Emma, Mr. Knightley."

Knightley grinned at that. They had "quarrelled" over Emma several times in the past—always good-naturedly—but Knightley, at least, had been serious about trying to correct the faults in Emma's education.

"Perhaps you think I am come on purpose to quarrel with you, knowing Weston to be out, and that you must still fight your own battle."

Mrs. Weston protested that it made not the slightest difference, for she knew Mr. Weston to be entirely on her side of the question. They both agreed that it was fortunate for Emma to have secured a female companion after she had been used to it all her life.

"Mr. Knightley," she continued, "I shall not allow you to be a fair judge in this case. You are so much used to live alone that you do not know the value of a companion; and perhaps no man can be a good judge of the comfort a woman feels in the society of one of her own sex after being used to it all her life."

I do not know the value of a companion? thought Knightley. But Mrs. Weston was still speaking.

"I can imagine your objection to Harriet Smith. She is not the superior young woman which Emma's friend ought to be. But on the other hand as Emma wants to see her better informed, it will be an inducement to her to read more herself. They will read together. She means it, I know."

Well, at least Mrs. Weston saw something less than ideal in the friendship. Perhaps he could build on this. He reminded her that Emma had always had great plans for improving reading, but had never actually read the books, in spite of Miss Taylor's urging. He knew he was on firm ground by saying that anything requiring industry and patience would never be mastered by Emma. Mrs. Weston, however, seemed to be reluctant to grant him that point, and so he elaborated.

"Emma is spoiled," said he, "by being the cleverest of her family. At ten years old she had the misfortune of being able to answer questions which puzzled her sister at seventeen. She was always quick and assured, Isabella slow and diffident. And ever since she was twelve, Emma has been mistress of the house and of you all. In her mother she lost the only person able to cope with her. She inherits her mother's talents, and must have been under subjection to her."

"I should have been sorry, Mr. Knightley," laughed Mrs. Weston, "to be dependent on *your* recommendation, had I quitted Mr. Woodhouse's family and wanted another situation; I do not think you would have spoken a good word for me to anybody. I am sure you always thought me unfit for the office I held."

"Yes," said he, smiling. "You are better placed *here*; very fit for a wife, but not at all for a governess. But you were preparing yourself to be an excellent wife all the time you were at Hartfield. You might not give Emma such a complete education as your powers would seem to promise; but you were receiving a very good education from *her*, on the very material matrimonial point of submitting your own will, and doing as you were bid; and if Weston had asked me to recommend him a wife, I should certainly have named Miss Taylor."

"Thank you," said Mrs. Weston, acknowledging his humour with a graceful incline of her head. "There will be very little merit in making a good wife to such a man as Mr. Weston."

"Why, to own the truth, I am afraid you are rather thrown away, and that with every disposition to bear, there will be nothing to be borne. We will not despair, however. Weston may grow cross from the wantonness of comfort, or his son may plague him."

"I hope not *that*. It is not likely. No, Mr. Knightley, do not foretell vexation from that quarter."

"Not I, indeed. I only name possibilities. I do not pretend to Emma's genius for foretelling and guessing. I hope, with all my heart, the young man may be a Weston in merit, and a Churchill in fortune." *However unlikely that appears to be at the moment,* he added silently.

"But Harriet Smith," he continued, "I have not half done about Harriet Smith. I think her the very worst sort of companion that Emma could possibly have. She knows nothing herself, and looks upon Emma as knowing everything. She is a flatterer in all her ways; and so much the worse, because undesigned. Her ignorance is hourly flattery. How can Emma imagine she has any thing to learn herself while Harriet is presenting such a delightful inferiority? And as for Harriet, I will venture to say that *she* cannot gain by the acquaintance. Hartfield will only put her out of conceit with all the other places she belongs to. She will grow just refined enough to be uncomfortable with those among whom birth and circumstances have placed her home. I am much mistaken if Emma's doctrines give any strength of mind, or tend at all to make a girl adapt herself rationally to the varieties of her situation in life. They only give a little polish."

"I either depend more upon Emma's good sense than you do, or am more anxious for her present comfort; for I cannot lament the acquaintance. How well she looked last night!"

"Oh! You would rather talk of her person than her mind, would you? Very well; I shall not attempt to deny Emma's being pretty."

"Pretty! Say beautiful rather. Can you imagine any thing nearer perfect beauty than Emma altogether—face and figure?"

A sudden vision of how Emma had looked the night before came into his mind. Yes, she was beautiful. She was very beautiful.

"I do not know what I could imagine," he said after trying for a moment to improve on the vision and failing, "but I confess that I have seldom seen a face or figure more pleasing to me than hers. But I am a partial old friend."

"Such an eye! The true hazel eye—and so brilliant! Regular features, open countenance, with a complexion! Oh! What a bloom of full health, and such a pretty height and size; such a firm and upright figure. There is health, not merely in her bloom, but in her air, her head, her glance. One hears sometimes of a child being 'the picture of health'; now Emma always gives me the idea of being the complete picture of grown-up health. She is loveliness itself, Mr. Knightley, is not she?"

"I have not a fault to find with her person," he replied. "I think her all you describe. I love to look at her" (even now he was strangely reluctant to put the picture of her out of his mind) "and I will add this praise, that I do not think her personally vain. Considering how very handsome she is, she appears to be little occupied with it; her vanity lies another way. Mrs. Weston, I am not to be talked out of my dislike of her intimacy with Harriet Smith, or my dread of its doing them both harm."

"And I, Mr. Knightley, am equally stout in my confidence of its not doing them any harm. With all dear Emma's little faults, she is an excellent creature. Where shall we see a better daughter, or a kinder sister, or a truer friend? No, no. She has qualities which may be trusted; she will never lead any one really wrong; she will make no lasting blunder; where Emma errs once, she is in the right a hundred times."

It was useless; he could see that. The Westons would not aid him in separating the two young ladies. He gave way amiably, therefore, and said that he would not plague her about it any more, but would instead wait for the Christmas visit of John and Isabella, who would be sure to think as he did.

Mrs. Weston, however, dissuaded him from even that plan of action, saying that she did not think that Emma would listen to John and Isabella even were they to disapprove of her friendship with Harriet, as Mr. Woodhouse completely endorsed it. Furthermore, Isabella was easily worried and might fret over her sister.

This was all very true, and Knightley realized that there was nothing for it but to sit silently by and let Emma do as she pleased. He promised to keep quiet. It vexed him very much to leave her to her fate; his impulse was to protect her even from her own folly.

"I have a very sincere interest in Emma," he said, explaining his wish to intervene as much to himself as to Mrs. Weston. "Isabella does not seem more my sister—has never excited a greater interest—perhaps hardly so great. There is an anxiety, a curiosity in what one feels for Emma. I wonder what will become of her."

"So do I, very much," said Mrs. Weston.

"She always declares she will never marry, which, of course, means just nothing at all. But I have no idea that she has yet ever seen a man she cared for." That was a thought; what would Emma be like if she *had* seen such a man? Perhaps she would alter as John had when he had fallen in love with Isabella: apprehension and uncertainty would make her humble. "It would not be a bad thing for her to be very much in love with a proper object," he said, thinking aloud. "I should like to see Emma in love, and in some doubt of a return; it would do her good. But there is nobody hereabouts to attach her, and she goes so seldom from home."

"There does, indeed, seem as little to tempt her to break her resolution, at present," said Mrs. Weston, "as can well be; and while she is so happy at Hartfield, I cannot wish her to be forming any attachment which would be creating such difficulties on poor Mr. Woodhouse's account. I do not recommend matrimony at present to Emma, though I mean no slight to the state I assure you."

Mrs. Weston managed to say it very naturally, but Knightley knew from the way that she looked at her hands as she said it that she had other thoughts she was not expressing. He had been too closely acquainted with Hartfield for too many years not to be able to read the expressions and mannerisms of its inmates. It did not take him many moments to surmise what she was not saying; she likely had some young man in mind that would tempt Emma to break her resolution of remaining single, and he would be very much surprised if the young man was not Frank Churchill.

However, there was nothing he could say about that if Mrs. Weston said nothing, and although he himself had started the topic of Emma being in love, for some reason the thought of Emma *marrying* was one he was disinclined to dwell on. For the second time in two days he felt he ought to change the course of the conversation.

"What does Weston think of the weather?" was the first thing that came into his head. "Shall we have rain?"

Knightley stayed another quarter of an hour before excusing himself. He had plenty of time on the walk home to review the frustrating conversation. Oddly enough, the words that most needled him were "You are so much used to live alone that you do not know the value of a companion." *But I do,* he argued with the ghost of Mrs. Weston. *I do know the value of a companion. I may live alone but I have not yet retreated entirely from the world and become a hermit! Not know the value of a companion, indeed! One would think that to live alone condemns a man to be insensible to all human feeling and friendship! Ridiculous! There is nothing wrong with living alone.*

"It is not good that the man should be alone." The words darted into his mind, startling him and halting his steps for an instant. He was not prepared to do battle with *that* quotation. Very deliberately he pushed the whole subject out of his mind and strode on toward Donwell.

7

The day dawned sullenly, rain dribbling down the windows of the dressing room.

"I dine with the Gilberts this evening, Baxter," said Knightley as the butler helped him on with his waistcoat.

"Yes, sir. Mrs. Hodges informed me this morning of the circumstance."

Knightley's lips quirked in amusement. He had received an invitation only the day before and had not spoken of it to anyone, but somehow he was not surprised that Baxter knew. Where his staff got their information was anyone's guess, although he suspected that William Larkins was usually responsible. It was a wonder that Larkins had time to do any work at all, so much of his time being spent spreading intelligence of one kind or another.

"Well, Baxter, are you also knowledgeable about the guest list for this gathering?"

"Yes, Mr. Knightley."

"And?" prompted Knightley.

"Young Mr. Gilbert, of course, the elder Mr. Gilbert's sister Miss Gilbert, Miss Gilbert's companion, Mr. Spencer, Mrs. Hughes, and yourself."

"Thank you. I presume that the companion to Miss Gilbert was an unexpected addition to their party, thus necessitating my invitation in order to make an equal number of ladies and gentlemen."

"I believe you are correct, sir," said Baxter. "She is evidently a widow who has begun to accompany Miss Gilbert when she goes visiting. Would you prefer the grey coat? It is a trifle warmer than the black for such a day as this."

"Yes, the grey. The rain is very heavy, and even if it lets up the roads will be muddy. Better send Thomas to get horses from the Crown for this evening. I will use the carriage and take Mr. Spencer and Mrs. Hughes with me. Would you send a message to Mrs. Hughes, saying that the carriage will be at her door at seven o'clock? I have a meeting at the Crown this morning, and will visit Spencer myself when I return."

"Very good, sir. Your coat, sir."

Baxter assisted Knightley in putting on the coat and gave it a final brush as expertly as Richards had ever done. Emma had been horrified when he had told her, at his old valet Richards' retirement, that he did not intend to hire another valet but instead have Baxter perform those services.

"My dear Emma," he had said, "I do not need a distinct servant to look after my attire. Baxter can manage it easily with his other duties. I can save…"

Her left eyebrow arched as she interrupted with "Oh, if it has to do with *saving money* on servants' wages *and* the servant tax, then I can see there will be no dissuading you. Your living up to your position as landowner, magistrate, and head of the ancient Knightley family is nothing in comparison to the opportunity of economising."

"No," he said solemnly, "There is no hope of persuading me otherwise when I have occasion to save a guinea. And when Mrs. Hodges retires I shall have William Larkins take on her tasks as well as his own. He will scold the kitchen maids just as well as she, I dare say, and will learn to bake an apple tart that will rival even hers."

Emma laughed in spite of herself to think of grim William Larkins fussing about the kitchen. "He could do the scolding bit very well, at least. And perhaps *then* you will have saved enough to purchase horses to ride and drive instead of always hiring them."

"What?" he cried in mock horror. "Pay the tax for pleasure horses *and* hire another groom *and* lay out money to feed the beasts all so that I can put them to use once a fortnight? Emma, Emma, you know that putting the money into the estate yields better profits—"

"There! I knew you would not listen to the voice of reason, though I believe you protest loudly because you know I am right. You remind me of Shakespeare's description of someone: 'e'en though vanquished he could argue still.'"

"I believe the author of that remark was *Goldsmith,* Emma. Though I can recall something Shakespeare did write that could be properly aimed at you."

"And what might that be?"

"'Get thee to a nunnery.'"

Knightley smiled at the memory of that conversation. Emma was to this day unconvinced that he did right by not keeping his own riding horses. And, he owned, she did have a point. The rain was still coming down and the wind felt icy as he left the house. It would be easy to use one of the home farm horses for saddle, as less scrupulous men did—the tax for farm horses being less than those kept for pleasure. But his conscience was rather finely-tuned in matters of honesty, and he never seriously entertained the notion.

He was thoroughly chilled by the time he reached the Crown. He scraped the mud off his boots and went to the little parlour where the vestry council held their meetings. Thankfully, Mrs. Stokes had built a prosperous fire and he warmed himself by it. Elton arrived shortly thereafter with a sheaf of papers, and Mrs. Stokes appeared with brandy. Knightley poured out two glasses and offered one to Elton, saying, "Terrible weather."

"Yes, horrible. The mud just past the Mitchell farm was dreadful. I had to use the path that comes around by Mr. Cole's stable."

So Elton had come from Hartfield, had he? It was very early for a social call. Well, he *might* have been visiting the Mitchells. To put the matter beyond doubt, Knightley asked, "And how is Mr. Woodhouse this morning?"

"Pretty well, although storms make him nervous. It is a pity that poor Miss Woodhouse must always stay so near to him when he is anxious. He is fretful so much of the time! It will be much better for her when..." He let his sentence trail off and busied himself arranging the papers he had brought.

When...what? thought Knightley. *When Mr. Woodhouse dies? When Miss Woodhouse marries? When she marries* you? He took another sip of his brandy before replying as evenly as he could,

"Miss Woodhouse would not wish to be anywhere else but with her father."

"Yes, yes, of course, and very noble of her, I'm sure."

Knightley was tempted out of sheer perversity to ask after the health of the Misses Carson, of Bath, who had been the aspiration of Elton before Miss Woodhouse had attained the ascendancy. He wavered, but then Cole and Weston bustled in and the moment was gone. Drinks were poured, hands were warmed at the fire, small talk was bantered about, and then Knightley cleared his throat. "Gentlemen, shall we begin?"

He was thankful that the rain held off as he walked to Spencer's cottage. Dr. Hughes had arranged a cottage for the curate to reside in and had installed an ancient, nearly deaf, but very competent maiden lady whom everyone called Old Maggie as housekeeper. Gratefully he stepped beneath the little ledge that projected over the door just as the heavens opened again. The door was opened by Maggie, of course, who gave a deep curtsey when she saw who it was and said in that loud voice peculiar to those who cannot hear much, "How d'ye do, Mr. Knightley, sir?"

Knightley raised his voice to match her volume. "Very well, Maggie, I thank you. And you?"

"'E's in the parlour, sir. This way, if you please."

Knightley followed her in and gave her his hat, coat, walking stick and umbrella before she opened the parlour door and bawled, "'Ere's Mr. Knightly, sir."

Spencer could be in no way surprised by Knightley's entrance, having heard the shouted exchange at the door. He laid aside his book and rose to shake Knightley's hand. Knightley was glad to see that though his manner could not be called easy, still he was not so timid and withdrawn as he had been at their first meeting. He motioned Knightley to a seat near the respectable fire.

"Would you like some refreshment, Mr. Knightley?"

"No, I thank you. My visit will be brief. May I enquire how you are settling in?"

"Well enough, I think."

"You have a comfortable home here."

"Yes, Dr. Hughes has been very kind to arrange it all for me, even to fitting out the cottage with furniture."

Knightley looked with admiration at the sturdy, serviceable chairs and occasional tables and the bookcase crammed with books. Stacks of books were placed on the wooden crate next to the shelves; the crate, presumably, held more books.

"It seems you will need another bookcase or two. You're something of a scholar, are you?"

"I do not think I consider myself a scholar, sir, but I do like to read."

"A very good thing in a clergyman. Which are your favourites?"

"Well, when you came in I was reading the poetry of Mr. George Herbert."

"Ah, that is one of Dr. Hughes' treasured volumes. I can see why he approves of you so highly."

"That is no good reason, sir. But Dr. Hughes has been most liberal and thoughtful. Not only did he organize the cottage and its furnishings, but he arranged for Maggie to be housekeeper."

"I've heard she is an excellent cook."

"Oh, indeed; and a wonder for scrubbing and polishing. And then her deafness makes for amusing conversations, as she always answers what she *thinks* I said rather than making any effort to really understand. Of course it makes it rather a loud household—passers-by must think we are perpetually quarrelling." He smiled for the first time at Mr. Knightley.

Knightley laughed. "No, everyone hereabouts knows Old Maggie. And if I may say so, you seem like you would be the least inclined to heated exchanges of any man I ever met."

"True, I am not really given to shouting or even loud bursts of feeling." He gave a self-deprecating smile. "I believe Mr. Whitefield would think my sermons very lacking in fervour."

"You seemed more at ease in the pulpit last Sunday than you were in previous weeks."

Spencer blushed, but answered readily enough. "I fear that I have an inordinate dread of strangers, Mr. Knightley, which was the reason for the inferior way I conducted the first services. But now I have called on most of the parishioners, they seem a little more like friends."

"I am surprised that someone with a horror of strangers would so immediately and so thoroughly visit every house in Donwell."

"Ah, well, sometimes I cannot help being afraid. But I have determined that it will not stop me from doing my duty."

"I see. *That* is a worthy reason for Dr. Hughes to approve of you, and you have won my approval as well. But I did not come to embarrass you with flattery"—for another blush was creeping over Spencer's face—"I came to see if you would like to share my carriage on the way to the Gilberts' this evening.

"Oh, are you of the party?"

"I am. I thought that as the roads are muddy and Langham is two miles distant, you and Mrs. Hughes might consent to ride with me."

"Yes, thank you. I am glad you will be one of the company. I have not met the Gilberts yet; I knew no one but Mrs. Hughes."

"Oh, they are good people—not unreasonably fine or awe-inspiring."

"I did hear a mention of a Miss Gilbert and her companion—and I dread elegant young ladies."

"There is nothing to fear on that score. Miss Gilbert is the sister of the elder Mr. Gilbert, not his daughter. She must be over forty. She travels with an old widowed companion, who will, I'm sure, be a nice, motherly soul."

"That relieves my mind somewhat. I never know what to say to ladies."

"You might talk of books. If the lady has read the same books you have, then your way is clear. You may compare opinions for the rest of the evening."

"And if the lady has not read anything?"

"Then you may expound at length on whatever book you have lately read."

Spencer smiled. "Do you not think that a summary of Mr. Herbert's poems will be construed as more of a sermon than a lecture on literature?"

"Well, if you frighten the lady away with a sermon, at least you will not be plagued with her for the rest of the evening."

"That is so. Very well, I shall attack her with 'The Window' then."

"Is that what you were reading when I came in?"

"Yes. 'Lord, how can man preach thy eternal word? He is brittle, crazy glass', and so on. I found it very fortifying."

"Fortifying? That is a new commendation for a poet."

Spencer smiled again. "I suppose it is. I was a bit of a fool this morning and I felt very like 'brittle, crazy glass'."

"A fool? How so?" Knightley had a feeling that Spencer often felt foolish over things he had no reason to be ashamed of.

"I was visiting one of the farms, and I said something silly. I mentioned that my mother died several years ago and the farmer's wife asked what she had died of. I was still rather nervous, I suppose, and without thinking I said, "It wasn't anything serious." And the farmer laughed said "Wussock" under his breath."

"*Wussock*? What on earth is that?"

"It's an old word from the Midlands—it means idiot. I learned it from one of the college servants. It was rather a funny thing for me to say, but his calling me *wussock* stung a bit."

"It must have been Mefford—I can guess the name even though you will not gossip about him. He came from Cambridgeshire, and he's rather a bad lot. Even so, I am surprised that he would insult you to your face."

"Well, I daresay he didn't know I would understand him."

"That is no excuse for him. So instead of 'rendering railing for railing' you came back and read poetry?"

Spencer gave a wry smile. "I sound very virtuous, don't I? But my first impulse was to say that he was wet as tripe and a tatchy barley-bump—he'd know what that meant if he knew the other."

Knightley chuckled. "I wish you had said it. I've never seen him get back as good as he gave."

"It would have been a satisfaction. But you remember what Chaucer said about the Parson: 'If gold rust, what shall iron do?'"

"Hmmm, yes. I suppose it would be difficult to expect forbearance in your flock if *you* show none." He stood up and offered Spencer his hand. "I must be off now, but I will see you this evening. The coach will be here at a little past seven."

"Do please come again, Mr. Knightley," Spencer said, just as Dr. Hughes always did. And with him they were not idle words, either.

8

The carriage containing the three guests from Donwell sloshed its way to Langham through heavy rain. It was a miserable night to be going anywhere, and no doubt the weather had contributed to the agitation of Spencer, who had reverted to his former manner, twisting at his glove buttons and playing with the brim of the hat on his lap. Mrs. Hughes spent the short journey talking brightly to Knightley about the annual distribution of Christmas boxes among the tenants of Donwell, either not seeing Spencer's unease or kindly leaving him alone to gather his courage. When the carriage discharged its occupants and they were ushered into the drawing room of the Hall, determination was warring with panic on Spencer's face. So busy was he watching the young man that Knightley only vaguely attended to Gilbert as he performed the introductions. The only person not previously known to him was an overdressed woman aged about thirty, who was introduced as "Mrs. Whitney." Knightley made his bow, and then turned his eyes to the curate. Spencer's comportment was the same as it had been on the day Knightley had met him; his eyes were on the floor and his face was flushed a dark red.

Mrs. Hughes was carried off immediately by Mrs. Gilbert to stand near the fire and talk. Young Mr. Edmund Gilbert, aged only eighteen, retired to a sofa to continue a conversation with his aunt, Miss Gilbert, which had evidently begun before the guests from

Donwell had arrived. Knightley looked around for the elderly widow he had been expecting; she would be the one to bring Spencer back to equanimity. This other woman, Mrs. Whitney, was too close to being a fine young lady to do anything but increase the curate's alarm. And where on earth was *Mr.* Whitney?

He realized his error in a moment. Mrs. Whitney *was* the widowed companion of Miss Gilbert. *Blast,* he thought. And here was Gilbert coming over to them with Mrs. Whitney on his arm. She was fluttering a painted fan, which was odd on such a cold and stormy night. Good fires were a matter of course at the Gilberts', but the room was not so warm as made a fan necessary.

"Mr. Knightley," began Gilbert, "I have discovered that Mrs. Whitney knows the John Knightleys."

"Indeed?" said Knightley, trying to smile pleasantly at her. It was hardly her fault that she was the wrong age.

"Yes," said Mrs. Whitney, simpering and fanning herself energetically. "I dined at their house two days ago. When I informed them that I was to come to the Gilberts', Mr. John Knightley told me to be sure to give you his kind regards and a message…what was it?...something about hoping you are pleased with the first in his string. I am not certain I have remembered it correctly, but it was something very near that."

Oh mercy, thought Knightley and very nearly rolled his eyes. On his last visit to London, John had railed him about still being a bachelor and threatened to send a string of impossible old maids his way until he chose someone—anyone—as his wife. Evidently a widow was close enough to an old maid to begin the parade.

"Mr. John Knightley is such a droll man," Mrs. Whitney continued with a giggle. "There is no understanding half of what he says. I was seated beside him at dinner, and he talked very seriously about a houseguest of his for a long time, a Madam Duval, who he said slept most of the day away, was fond of mice, and caused the baby to sneeze whenever she came near. I was quite amazed at his description of the old lady, only to discover that it was a *cat* he was talking about! It was so very diverting!" She giggled again as the fan waved rhythmically in front of her face. Knightley could not be certain, but the scene painted on it appeared to depict Marius among the ruins of Carthage. He had never been more inclined to feel sympathy with poor Marius than at that moment.

Knightley was not really surprised to find Mrs. Whitney seated next to him at dinner. He was grateful that at least Spencer was placed beside Mrs. Hughes, and was recovering his spirits enough to converse quietly with her. It was, alas, his only comfort during that meal.

"Your brother tells me that you are an improver," said Mrs. Whitney as the fish course was being cleared. Her fan slid off her lap to the floor. "Oh, how provoking! I believe it is under my chair. Thank you, Mr. Knightley. As I was saying, your brother told me all about Donwell Abbey, and what an improver you are. You must have had Repton in, or that other man who is all the rage—Loudon, that is the name."

"Not at all. I believe my brother meant that I work to improve the buildings on the estate and the land for farming. The gardens are laid out very much as they have been for centuries."

"Oh." Her face registered such disappointment that he felt he ought to soften the blow.

"Donwell Abbey is the sort of house that is best complemented by the old styles. The main part of the house is nearly unchanged from the days, centuries ago, when it really was an abbey."

"But surely you must wish to see it brought into modern times. Have you any groves of trees? Yes, I thought you would. Those old groves are so unhealthy—they preserve dampness, you know—and they obstruct the views."

"Well, I suppose I am old-fashioned enough to prefer that kind of obstruction."

"I see that you—oh! I declare, my fan is gone again—under the table this time—I am so sorry to trouble you again—Can you see it? Thank you, Mr. Knightley, you are very good. Well, I see that as a bachelor you are loathe to change a familiar landscape. But the day may come, Mr. Knightley, when you cease to be single." She dropped her eyes and allowed a faint blush to colour her cheeks. "There may someday be a mistress at Donwell Abbey who prefers the modern style and who persuades you at the last to pull down that grove."

Never, thought Knightley. The lime walk was one of his favourite retreats when he had something to think over. He had been known to pace it for hours when an important decision had to be made. And Emma liked it.

"The French have it that an ordered garden reflects an ordered mind," he said. "They have not yet given up their formal flower beds and shrubberies."

"Ah, the French," said Mrs. Whitney, nodding her head meditatively. "You have seen their gardens, I suppose, when you had a Tour on the Continent?"

"No, we were at war with France from the time I was seventeen until I was twenty-five, and by then my father's health was failing. I regret that I have never travelled further than Scotland. Still, I have seen engravings and heard descriptions of French gardens by those who have travelled there."

"Oh, if only you had been able to go abroad, as I have! Mr. Whitney took me to the Isle of Wight, and I assure you it was a revelation to me! I was never the same afterwards."

A revelation of what? thought Knightley, but his curiosity did not remain unsatisfied for long.

"I learned," said Mrs. Whitney, putting down her fork and bringing her fan into play again, "that travelling on one's own does not give one the true sense of a place. The romance of a scene can only be appreciated when..." here she paused, looked away, and seemed to expect to be prompted. Knightley could not bring himself to do it.

"...When," she said at last, "one is with one's beloved."

"I see," was all the response she got.

"Of course, I have no heart for travel now," she continued sorrowfully. "With Mr. Whitney gone, all the wellsprings of passion in me have dried up. I feel old before my time. I don't suppose I will ever meet anyone who can call them forth again." Her head drooped sadly, and Knightley wondered with some panic if she was about to cry. He saw her glance at him as if to judge his reaction, and he had a premonition that he was about to be asked if she could borrow his handkerchief. The sight of Spencer at the other end of the table gave him a sudden inspiration.

"Do you read at all, Mrs. Whitney?"

Her head came up again, her expression all eagerness for any subject he should introduce.

"Oh, my, yes. Widows have all too much time for reading. As do bachelors, I daresay."

"Not as much as I would wish, I'm afraid. I was only thinking of a book in my library that I thought my be a help to you."

"Really? And what book is that? I should adore to hear all about it! Please, do tell me!"

"It is a most edifying volume by that excellent divine, Jeremiah Burroughs, entitled *The Rare Jewel of Christian Contentment*. As you have so kindly expressed such an interest in the book, allow me to share with you the principle arguments of his thesis…"

He was saved.

The ladies withdrew before he had exhausted the subject, and he assured Mrs. Whitney that he could finish his recital of Burroughs' salient points for her when the whole company reassembled. She nodded, but he thought that he would be very surprised if she came anywhere near him for the rest of the evening. His advice to Spencer had been sound after all. Who would have guessed, when his clergyman tutor all those years ago had insisted he read the book very thoroughly and make a précis of its contents, that it would be so very useful at such a time!

"Well, Knightley," said Gilbert who was seated near him, "On Saturday next there will be a small shooting party here to reduce the population of pheasants on the estate. You would be most welcome to join us. I think you bagged more birds than anyone last year. And that dog of yours put all of our dogs to shame. You lost him, though, didn't you?"

Knightley nodded.

"Have you got another dog yet? I mean, another one like that?"

"No, not yet."

Homer, the best pointer in the world, had died the year before. Of course there were other dogs at Donwell, but none that had access to the house. It seemed even to himself a foolish thing that he could not bring himself to get another dog, but the empty spot on the library hearth seemed to belong only to Homer.

"If it is only a matter of finding a dog to suit, my spaniel had a litter of puppies last week. You're welcome to any of them."

"I thank you…but not yet."

Gilbert nodded. "I had a dog like that once, too," he said with a sympathetic smile. "Went with me everywhere, slept by my bed…my wife complained that I talked more to the hound than I did to her."

Knightley smiled slightly. "I'm afraid I talked poor Homer's ear off as well. The library is a much more silent place than it used to be."

"Yes," said Gilbert. "Funny how an animal can take the place of a confidant." He picked up the decanter and offered it to Knightley, who shook his head.

"Well," said Gilbert, pouring himself a little more, "if the silence becomes too oppressive, let me know. I'll save a pup for you."

That night the rumble of thunder awakened Knightley from his nightmare. Without lighting a candle he could not be sure of the time, but it seemed to him to be the very darkest part of the night. It had been an extraordinary dream, and had seemed so very real!

He had dreamed that it was morning, and that Baxter was waking him by telling him that the parish council had been persuaded by Elton to pull down the lime walk at Donwell. The workmen were already there, ready to begin felling the trees. All Knightley needed to do was to go quickly to the walk and tell them to stop. But everything conspired to prevent him. He could not get dressed because Baxter could find no shirt for him, and when Knightley impatiently looked for one himself, he could not find one, either. He pulled on an old coat instead of a shirt and left the bedroom. But Larkins was just outside the door, pleading with him to go over the accounts at just that moment, "for you know, Mr. Knightley, 'business is the salt of life', as the old saying goes. Mrs. Hodges says that she has very little salt left." For some reason, Knightley felt he had to take the time to explain that the salt in the old proverb was not literal salt. It took a little while to convince

Larkins of that, and even longer to convince him that he would have to go over the accounts some other time. Finally Larkins left and Knightley got as far as the top of the stairs.

There was Dr. Hughes, with his leg still broken, proposing to descend the stairs by hopping gently down on his good leg. Of course, Knightley could only offer to help him, but their progress was agonizingly slow. As they reached the bottom, he was accosted by Mrs. Whitney who needed help finding her fan. She looked so distressed that Knightley made a cursory search around the ground floor rooms to see if it was anywhere about. She followed him as he hunted for it, talking all the time about her sad life as a widow and how she really ought to be mistress of an estate like Donwell. He felt acutely his lack of a shirt and pulled the coat as tightly around him as he could, but knew that she could tell that he was not fully dressed. At last Knightley managed to excuse himself and escaped out of the house. He tried to run to the lime walk, but kept tripping over stones and bushes that seemed to spring up out of the ground. At last he could see the trees and the workmen already hacking at a tree with their axes. Elton was there, looking on, fanning himself with Mrs. Whitney's painted fan. Knightley tried to shout at the men to stop, but his voice made no sound. Before he could reach them, the trunk was severed and the tree crashed to the ground.

He woke up then, sweating and panting, and lay there for a moment wondering if any of it had really happened. A second rumble of thunder made him realize that the sound of the tree falling had been made by thunder. The lime walk must be safe, then, and Mrs. Whitney was not really waiting for him downstairs. The relief he felt was overwhelming. Still, it was over an hour before he fell back into an uneasy slumber.

By morning the rain had mellowed into a light drizzle, but the ground was still so muddy that Knightley rode one of the Crown horses over to Hartfield to give them the greetings Isabella had included in the letter he had received from John the day before. Knightley was amply repaid for his kindness by the heartfelt gratitude of Mr. Woodhouse, and by the refreshing sight of two beautiful and wholesome young women, Emma and Harriet, sitting together with their embroidery. The spectre of Mrs. Whitney with all her affected nonsense had been haunting him all morning—the share she had in his nightmare had been perhaps the most horrifying part of it.

When all the little items of news in John's letter had been talked over, Mr. Woodhouse said, "And now, Emma, we must ask Mr. Knightley if he knows where the book is."

Knightley turned an enquiring face to Emma.

"Papa is speaking of the book John and Isabella gave him last year, *The Antiquities of England and Wales.* Harriet is interested in seeing the engravings of Reading Abbey. The book ought to be in the library, but we could not find it."

"Yes," said Mr. Woodhouse. "I fear my memory is not what it was—and then my eyes are not as good as they once were. But as you kindly arranged some of my books for me a month or two ago, I thought perhaps you might remember where we might find that particular book."

"I believe I do, sir. If you will excuse me one moment, I will go to the library and look."

It did not take Knightley long to find the book, though he could scarcely blame Emma or her father for not knowing where it was. He ought to have remembered that it was one of the few books that Mr. Woodhouse did peruse on occasion and put it in a more prominent place.

"Ah, you have found it," said Mr. Woodhouse when Knightley reappeared with the book. "I am very grateful, Mr. Knightley. I do not know what I should do without you. And now, Miss Smith, if you will sit in the chair beside mine, I will show you the engravings we were speaking of."

"You look very tired," said Emma to Knightley as her father opened the book eagerly and read to Harriet the titles under each picture. "I've seen you twice stifle a yawn. Are you quite well?"

"Oh, yes. I am rather tired, I suppose—the storm woke me last night." He did not want to tell her about the nightmare. She would appreciate the humour in it, but then she would tease him about Mrs. Whitney. John was bad enough about matchmaking; to have Emma harassing him about finding a wife was somehow even more dreadful.

"You ought to have rested this morning, then, instead of coming here. To ride out in the rain in order to get chilled and wet when you are already tired must make you ill."

He smiled and shook his head at her. "Emma, Emma, I have people enough fussing over my health." He glanced at Mr. Woodhouse. "Have the goodness to let me take care of myself."

"Ah, but *do* you take care of yourself? You are always busy about parish business or the home farm or visiting tenants or helping Papa. If you fall prey to nervous exhaustion from too many parish meetings, who will scold you for taking too much upon yourself? William Larkins, I am sure, never thinks of such a thing. As long as you can go over the accounts with him he will think you are fit enough."

Knightley remembered Larkins' behaviour in his dream and laughed. "Never mind, Emma. If I ever do suffer from nervous exhaustion, I promise to come to Hartfield to be coddled by you and your father. Will that satisfy you?"

"I suppose it must," she smiled back, though the concern in her face was not entirely gone. "But prevention is better than cure, and as Papa said, we could not do without you."

He inclined his head in thanks, and was about to tell her that she, at least, looked very well, when Harriet broke in.

"Miss Woodhouse, was it St. George's Chapel that Mr. Weston was telling us he had seen? Or was it another chapel of the same name?"

She turned to answer Harriet, and Knightley watched her as she conversed with her friend. Emma did indeed look very well. She was all that was graceful and poised, and another woman with such elegance might have been haughty and cold. But Emma's affectionate nature for those she loved prevented this. Indeed, she seemed to be even improving in her solicitude for others. She had always been attentive to her father, of course, but now she was even careful for his own health. And he could see in the way that she looked at and spoke to Harriet that she was sincerely fond of the girl. It may have been a sort of maternal interest—he had seen that same look on Isabella's face often enough as she spoke to her children—but there was plenty of benevolence in her attentions. However misguided Emma's notions were, there was no doubt, as she had once protested, that she meant to do Harriet good.

The words *she is loveliness itself* came into his mind. Someone had said that about Emma recently...who was it? Mr. Woodhouse? No, not him. He frowned in concentration. It was the sort of thing that Elton would say, but Elton was not quite rash enough to say such a thing to Knightley—yet. Where had he been when he had heard those words? They were quite true. Her hazel eyes sparkled when she was being mischievous and shone when she looked at her father. And her voice was lovely: sweet without being affected and clear without being shrill. If it wasn't Elton, then who…

"Mr. Knightley, if you *will* look so sternly you must at least tell us what it is about Mrs. Weston's plan that you disapprove."

Knightley came out of his reverie with a start. "I beg your pardon?"

"Oh, come now, Mr. Knightley," said Emma with a raised eyebrow, "What is it that offends you? Ought the pupils to have no celebration at all? Or is it only the particulars of the entertainment that you distain? I perceive the latter is the true reason for your censure."

Knightley was completely at a loss. He had no idea what they had been talking about. Something about a celebration, evidently, but what on earth was he to say? He shrugged his shoulders and tried to smile as complacently as possible.

"Very well then," Emma continued when he said nothing, "We shall apply to you to draw up a list of Christmas entertainments suitable for Mrs. Goddard's pupils."

"But pray, Mr. Knightley," interjected Mr. Woodhouse, "do not recommend snap-dragon as one of the diversions. I tremble to think of the consequence if one of the young ladies were to burn herself! Whoever can have invented such an amusement? Plucking raisins from burning brandy! Such folly!"

"Have no fear, Mr. Woodhouse," said Knightley. "I have no inclination to do any such thing—no inclination at all. Miss Smith would be a far better judge of what Mrs. Goddard's pupils would enjoy, and I suggest that Emma should take the advice of her friend in such matters. She will not propose anything untoward." He inclined his head with a smile to Harriet.

"Thank you, sir," said Harriet, flushing with pleasure but without the usual giggle, as Knightley noted with approval. Emma's lessons in manner were evidently having some effect.

"My dear Emma," said Mr. Woodhouse, "perhaps Mr. Knightley would take tea and a little something to eat… perhaps a dish of gruel?"

"No, thank you, sir," said Knightley, rising. "I would greatly enjoy a longer visit here, but I must get back to Donwell. I have a letter to write."

6th December
Donwell Abbey

Dear John,

Where on earth did you scrape up an acquaintance with Mrs. Whitney? I cannot believe that you, who cherish sensible conversation, invited that woman to dine at Wellyn House. And if she is the first in a string of similar potential brides, I beg to inform you that I will quit Donwell Abbey immediately and retire to Northamptonshire where I will handle Graham's estate business for him.

Speaking of Graham, tell him that Lord Carrick's bailiff in Scotland wants a new situation in a warmer climate. As you know, many of the Scots have done wonders with their estates, and Lord Carrick in particular has a model system in place. Of course his bailiff will want a large salary, but I shouldn't think Graham would mind that.

Mr. Woodhouse and Emma are very well, and both send all the usual wishes to you and yours. I was going to say more about this business of a "string of old maids" but must close this epistle now – someone needing my counsel as a magistrate has just been announced. If you dare to send another woman in this direction I will never write to you again.

Yours in brotherly friendship – for now,
George

8th December
Wellyn House
Brunswick-square

Dear George,

So Mrs. Whitney is not to your taste? I am very sorry to hear it. I thought that you would at least admire her fan. It will do you no good to run to Northamptonshire – Graham has a spinster sister who lives with him and is every bit as charming as Mrs. Whitney. I don't suppose you know if Lord Carrick's bailiff is a single man? If he is, Graham will probably hire him sight unseen, grasping at the opportunity to get his sister married. I suppose I ought not to have told you this – I ought to have let you go to Graham's and discover his sister for yourself. I shall do better another time…

Yours in the eternal friendship of brotherhood,
John

9

"Mr. Woodhouse is taking the air in the garden, Mr. Knightley," said the hall porter at Hartfield. "Will you join him there or wait for him indoors? Miss Woodhouse, Miss Smith and Mr. Elton are in the morning room."

"I shall go and find him in the garden, thank you," said Knightley. Perhaps Elton would leave before Mr. Woodhouse finished his exercise, although that seemed rather unlikely. Elton was now nearly part of the furniture at Hartfield. He wished that Elton would hurry up and offer for Emma so that he could be refused and spend his days elsewhere. There were rumours enough already about. Even Spencer had asked him if it was true that the vicar of Highbury was going to marry Miss Woodhouse of Hartfield—evidently William Larkins had paid Spencer a visit and unburdened himself of that speculation. It was a bad thing for a vicar to be the main subject of local gossip, and he hated Emma's name being coupled with that...*wussock.*

No, no, he chided himself with a sigh. *Show respect for the office, if not for the man.* He opened the garden door and stepped out onto the terrace. Mr. Woodhouse was slowly pacing the rose walk that led from the terrace to the shrubbery.

"Ah, Mr. Knightley!" said Mr. Woodhouse, as the younger man joined him. "You find me taking my winter walk. You ought to have waited for me indoors, by the fire. You have no doubt walked all the way from Donwell, and must be chilled."

"Not at all, sir. The sky is wonderfully clear and there is no wind to speak of. I would rather walk with you, if you can tolerate my company."

"That would give me great pleasure, Mr. Knightley, if only my slow pace of walking will not inconvenience you."

"Not at all." The slower, the better, as far as Knightley was concerned.

"I suppose you have come about the portrait?" said Mr. Woodhouse.

"What portrait is that?"

"Oh, have you not heard, then? Emma is drawing a portrait of Miss Smith. That is, she has nearly completed the drawing in pencil, and then she is to finish it in watercolours. Everyone who has seen it has admired it extremely. I was sure Mrs. Weston had mentioned it to you."

"I'm certain she would have if I had seen her in these last few days, but I have not."

"Dear Emma is so clever with her drawings and paintings! She has a natural talent, does she not, Mr. Knightley?"

"Indeed, yes," said Knightley, and it was quite true. Emma had a great deal of natural talent, and a little teaching and practice would have made her an excellent artist. Her drawings showed promise, and he never saw them without being struck by the simplicity of line and form that yet conveyed so much. If only she had taken the time to really work at her drawing! She had not drawn much recently, and he would have been eager to go inside to see the latest endeavour if only he could be sure Elton had gone.

It was not long before Mr. Woodhouse was finished with his walk and ready to return to the house to see what had been done to Harriet's portrait. The morning room had large windows that made the most of the winter sun, and Emma was seated at her low easel near one of them. A bright shaft of sunlight came through the window and illuminated her. Her cream-coloured gown glowed almost golden, and her hair was touched with radiance. *That* is a picture, thought Knightley. Harriet was sitting a few feet away in an obviously posed attitude, and Elton was, regrettably, seated near Emma. He had been reading aloud, but put the book aside and rose to his feet when Mr. Woodhouse and Knightley entered.

"Emma, my dear," said Mr. Woodhouse, "Mr. Knightley would like to see the portrait. There it is, Mr. Knightley. What do you think?"

It was a beautiful picture. Emma had caught the sweetness and guileless-ness of Harriet's countenance, though she had taken liberties with the details of her appearance, altering Harriet's height and something about the face. It was an idealized picture of Harriet: Harriet as Emma would have made her. The real Harriet was very pretty; the Harriet of the portrait was perfection. A little *too* perfect, in Knightley's opinion. A human creature, even with faults, was better than an ethereal ideal. A familiar sense of impatience welled up in him. Emma evidently intended to "improve" her friend in every possible way—manner, mind, connections must all be enhanced. And what could not be changed in reality must be attempted at least in art.

"Well?" said Emma. "Is it a good likeness?"

"You have made her too tall, Emma," said Knightley.

"No, indeed I have not! It represents her height completely."

"Oh, no! certainly not too tall," put in Elton warmly, "Not in the least too tall. Consider, she is sitting down—which naturally presents a different—" He paused, searching for words. "Which in short," he went on, "gives exactly the idea—and the proportions must be preserved, you know. Proportions, fore-shortening." He stopped again, somewhat confused, but returned to the material point with vigour. "Oh, no! it gives one exactly the idea of such a height as Miss Smith's. Exactly so indeed!"

Knightley mastered the laughter that threatened to burst out at the comical expression on Emma's face. Though gratified to have her side of the debate championed, Emma obviously felt that Elton's indignant defence of her drawing was less able than might be wished. The drawing *should* have an able defence; it should have the praise it deserved. Very well, then.

"You have caught Miss Smith's air and expression admirably," Knightley said. "And the composition is perfect. It really is very well done."

Emma smiled her gratitude for this bit of commendation.

"Thank you, Mr. Knightley," she said. "I think it will look better when I have finished it. It is to be a watercolour, you know."

"Oh, yes, indeed," put in Elton. "It looks very well now; it will be truly magnificent when it is completed! And watercolour is the perfect choice—much better than crayon for such a portrait!"

"What do you think of it, Miss Smith?" said Knightley, more to put a stop to Elton's panegyric than because he had any real uncertainty as to how Harriet would view Miss Woodhouse's work.

"I think it is very beautiful," said Harriet. "I do not know anyone who can draw so well!"

"Quite right," said Elton, "There is no one who draws as well as Miss Woodhouse!"

Knightley decided that a complete change of topic would be needed to stem the flow of Elton's compliments.

"I'm sorry to intrude with business into such a scene of artistic inspiration, but Isabella included a note with John's last letter, saying that she was sending a parcel of used baby linen for Christmas boxes, to be distributed evenly between Donwell and Highbury. Will you let me know when the parcel arrives?"

"Of course. That is just like Isabella: she never forgets those in need, even when she is so far away."

"But it is the less surprising," said Elton, "when one considers how renowned Hartfield is for generosity. The voices of all the poor in Highbury resound with the praises of Miss Woodhouse. And Mr. Woodhouse," he added as an afterthought.

Knightley could bear it no longer. He wished them all good day and took his leave.

"You wished to see me, sir?" said Mrs. Hodges, dropping a perfunctory curtsey as she entered the breakfast room where Knightley was just finishing his morning meal. Mrs. Hodges had been housekeeper at Donwell Abbey for twenty-five years, and Knightley always thought of her as "the great and grim Mrs. Hodges"—his boyhood appellation for her. She was a little more grey and her figure was considerably fuller than it had been when she had first arrived, but her face seemed changeless. Her countenance now showed a mixture of emotions: the deference she owed to an employer, the proud loyalty she felt to the master of Donwell, and the irritation she suffered in being summoned out of the kitchen when she ought to be supervising the kitchen maid's first attempt at pickling walnuts.

"Yes, I did," said Knightley. "I wondered how the spruce beer is holding out. You know John and Mrs. Knightley come for Christmas, and it is a particular favourite of theirs. And I wanted some sent to Hartfield as well."

"Well, sir, I wouldn't say there is a great deal left. Christmas is near two weeks off…we'll just have time to make more. Is there anything else, sir?"

"Nothing. Oh, I presume the Bates' have received a bushel of apples?"

"Yes, sir," said Mrs. Hodges in a melancholy tone. She did not like Donwell produce being given away as freely as it was, but it was not her place to say so.

"Thank you, Mrs. Hodges. That will be all."

Mrs. Hodges curtseyed and left, nearly bumping into Baxter as he entered the room with a note on a small silver tray.

"This came just now from Hartfield, sir," he said, "And William Larkins desires to see you as soon as may be. I have put him in the library."

"Thank you, Baxter," said Knightley. He took the note and opened it; it was from Emma, to say that Isabella's baby linen had arrived. He put the note into his waistcoat pocket and got up from the table. The library was at the other end of the house, and as he walked the long hallway he could hear only the sound of his own footsteps. It was a lonely sound. For years, the click-click-click of Homer's toenails on the polished floors had followed him as he walked around the house. Perhaps he ought to get a puppy from Gilbert after all.

Larkins was standing by the fire warming himself as Knightley entered the library.

"Good morning, Larkins. I did not expect to see you this morning."

"Good morning, Mr. Knightley. I had not anticipated seeing you this morning, either, sir. However, it has come to my attention that the farmer Mefford has been very insulting indeed to the widow Hunt. I thought it only right that you should know."

"In what way was he insulting?"

"She passed him on the road, and, being the kindly soul she is, she asked after his health. 'Never better,' said he, 'And you?'

"'Well,' she said, 'I'm not as young as I once was, and this earthen vessel is beginning to crack here and there. Still, I forget how old I really am until I look in a mirror and see that I have a wrinkle for every year of my age.'

"She said it half in jest, Mr. Knightley, but Mefford said, 'Ah, well, at least we know there's nothing wrong with your eyes!'

"It really was most unkind, Mr. Knightley, for as you know, the widow Hunt is not very wrinkled at all. She went away crying bitterly."

"You were there, then?" said Knightley.

"No, but the Shaw boy was. He heard it all. Something must be done, Mr. Knightley."

"Yes. But I cannot evict him merely because he insulted Mrs. Hunt—or any number of other people, for that matter."

"No, sir. But you know that he has not paid his rent in full for the last three quarters—in fact, he paid less than half last quarter. And I have it on good authority that he means to pay very little on Christmas Day when this quarter's rent is due."

"Good authority?"

"Mr. Sloan heard it from John Farnsworth at the 'Dog and Duck'. His wife told me. I know there have been no evictions at Donwell for decades, but I truly think it is called for in this case."

Knightley looked into the fire and sighed. He agreed with Larkins in theory, but the thought of putting Mrs. Mefford and young Harry Mefford out of their home right before Christmas made him reluctant. Could nothing else be done? And then he remembered something Gilbert had done with one of his tenants.

"There is one thing left to try," said Knightley. "We shall draw up a document for Mefford to sign, saying that he intends to give up his lease at the next quarter day—that is, in two weeks—as he is unable to meet the rent. If he signs it, Donwell will be free of a bad tenant without having to evict him; even if he does not it may show that we are serious about collecting the rent due. He may give up the rest of what he owes. If he neither signs the document nor pays the rent, then I will have to evict him."

"Mr. Knightley! So good of you to come!"

"I was just passing, Miss Bates, and thought I would enquire after your mother's health. Is she completely recovered from—?"

"Oh yes, Mr. Knightley, I believe the cough has gone at last. I will just tell her what you said, for she is a little deaf, you know. Mother, Mr. Knightley has come to enquire after you, to see if your health has improved. To ask after your *health*. Isn't it kind of him? Not but what you are always kind, Mr. Knightley, and Mr. Elton, too. Mr. Elton was here not a half-hour ago. Such kind friends! I am sorry you missed him—you must enjoy each other's company so! Clever men always do enjoy talking with each other, I think. I am exceedingly sorry you missed him. However, you both call so frequently—you are so very good to us!—that I would not be surprised if you happened to meet each other here quite accidentally some day."

Knightley coughed and asked if Miss Woodhouse had called recently. Miss Bates hesitated for a moment before answering.

"Miss Woodhouse called on us—not long ago. She calls whenever she is able—she has much to occupy her time, you know, Mr. Knightley. She is so careful for dear Mr. Woodhouse, and of course she cannot leave him often. And then she has been painting a portrait of Miss Smith—did you know? Mr. Elton says it is the finest thing he ever saw, which is not surprising at all, is it? Miss Woodhouse is so very skilled at taking portraits! I do quite long to see this one. Mr. Elton says that it is complete now—he saw the finished picture last evening. Mr. Knightley, I declare, you are still standing! You must come and sit down and take a little something."

"No, Miss Bates. You are very kind, and there is nothing I should like better than to sit with you for a few moments, but I really must be getting on. I allowed myself to come and enquire after your mother because I have been anxious about her, and I am very glad to know she is well."

Miss Bates had too much to say to allow him to leave that very instant, but it was not long before he was descending the stairs and able to think. If Elton was in Highbury this morning, Knightley could put off his business with Cox and visit Hartfield without fear of having to listen to Elton flatter Emma. He would go now and see the finished portrait and bring back the baby linen to Donwell, assuming it was not too large and awkward a bundle. He felt ridiculously pleased with the idea of being alone with the occupants of Hartfield. Ah, no, Harriet would probably be there. Still, it would be rather comfortable than otherwise.

He had not gone far when a voice came from behind him: "Going to Hartfield?"

Knightley turned to see Elton catching him up.

"Yes, I am. And you?"

"Oh, I am bound for Hartfield as well," said Elton cheerfully.

It was impossible for Knightley not to sigh, but he managed to do it quietly.

Miss Bates would have been a little surprised to see how silently the two clever men walked along together. Knightley was loathe to say anything at all, lest Elton turn it into yet another compliment to Miss Woodhouse. Elton was lost in his own thoughts—happy thoughts, if the look on his face signified anything. Knightley felt a sudden pang of pity for the man.

When the men were shown into the drawing room, Mr. Woodhouse was slumbering peacefully in his chair by the fire and Emma and Harriet were seated near him, talking. The finished portrait was on its easel, and after the first greetings—which woke Mr. Woodhouse—the men were invited to come and admire it. Elton, though he had seen it the night before, was just as fulsome in his admiration as if he were looking at it for the first time, but Knightley felt Emma's eyes on him and knew that she was waiting for his verdict.

"Beautiful," said Knightley, and was rewarded with her smile of relief. "It ought to be given pride of place. How will you frame it?"

"That is the difficulty," said Emma. "Of course the frame must be got in London, but who is to get it for us is less certain."

"Could not Isabella—" began Knightley, but Emma shook her head, and Mr. Woodhouse added,

"My dear Mr. Knightley, you forget that Isabella has a delicate constitution, very delicate indeed. To ask her to stir outside her own home in the fogs of December would be most reckless. It must not be thought of."

"I will be in London in January," said Knightley, "though that is several weeks away and you may not think much of my taste in choosing a frame."

"No sir," said Emma with a smile and a lifted eyebrow, "I have no faith in your taste. Ever since the day you told me I ought to have one of those bonnets that were decorated with stuffed birds I have been certain that I can not trust your judgement on matters of that sort."

"If I had known that my incautious remark would be thrown up in my face regularly for the next five years, I would certainly have kept my opinion to myself," said Knightley, grinning back at her. "And in order that I might not make another blunder that I will be reminded of monthly—if not weekly—for years to come, I gladly withdraw my offer of assistance in getting the picture framed."

"Might I be trusted with the commission?" said Elton. "What infinite pleasure I should have in executing it! I could ride to London at any time, you know. It is impossible to say how much I should be gratified by being employed on such an errand."

"Oh, Mr. Elton, you are too good! That is really very kind of you, but of course you have many duties and responsibilities that keep you here. I could not endure the thought of you giving up so much of your time for such a thing. And I well know that it is a tedious sort of task for a man; I would not give you such a troublesome office for the world!"

"Upon my honour, Miss Woodhouse, it is no trouble to me! I greatly enjoy a ride to London, and shopping is my delight!"

Knightley rose and moved off toward the window. He was afraid that the others would hear his teeth grinding if he stayed next to them any longer. In a few moments all was settled: Elton would take the drawing to London, choose the frame, and give the directions. Emma had offered to pack it up that evening, and it would be ready for him the next morning. She assured Elton that the picture could be rolled and encased in such a way that it could be safely fixed to his saddle, and that he would hardly know he was carrying it. Elton was energetic in *his* assurances that it would not matter whether he had to carry it fixed to his saddle or held in his arms or clenched in his teeth—this last being a jest at which Emma and Harriet laughed appreciatively—it was enough that he should be allowed be of service in this small way.

Knightley turned away from the window and looked at Emma. Surely she must see this as it was meant: open flattery to herself. But no, Emma was looking at Harriet with a delighted, knowing expression that showed exactly who she thought the compliment was intended for. Harriet flushed with pleasure; she obviously shared Emma's view. How easy it would be to set them all straight! A few plain words would do all that was needed: "Emma, Elton wants to marry you, not Harriet. Elton, Emma is planning for you to marry Harriet. Harriet, I'm afraid your hopes with regard to Elton have no foundation." But of course he could not say such things. He would never be forgiven by any of them.

Rather abruptly he walked back to the group around the fire and said, "I received your note about the baby linen, Emma. Is it the sort of bundle I can bring back with me or will I need a horse and cart?"

"No, it is not so very large. You may carry it very well under your arm."

"Or clenched in my teeth?"

Emma laughed. *She* could see Elton's absurdity.

"Even that, I suppose, if you were very determined. Isabella would, however, be somewhat startled to learn that her charitable gifts were transported in such a manner."

"Have you much preparation to make for John and Isabella's visit?"

"Not really. They will occupy the rooms they always do. It is fortunate they stay here instead of at Donwell. I cannot think Mrs. Hodges would enjoy the addition of five children to the usually empty Abbey."

"Empty?"

"Well, nearly empty. I suppose the children will visit you every day as they did before, but Mrs. Hodges will think that a lesser evil than having them resident. As it is she will have very little preparation to do."

"Well, I did ask her to brew more spruce beer; it should be just ready when they arrive. I shall have some sent on here, too—I know how you like it."

"Oh, thank you, Mr. Knightley. That will be delightful. Do you like spruce beer, Harriet?" asked Emma, suddenly aware that she and Mr. Knightley had excluded the others from their conversation.

"Oh, yes, very much. That is, I have not drunk it often. But I believe I like it."

"And you, Mr. Elton?" prompted Emma.

"I regret to say that I have not tasted it above once. It did not seem to agree with me then, but I daresay I would like it if I tried it again. I drank it at a coaching inn; perhaps the quality was inferior to what is generally drunk."

"Very likely," put in Knightley. "I have never had tolerable spruce beer at an inn."

"Perhaps I might have my housekeeper make me some. I should very much like to drink it again. Is it very difficult to brew?"

"Not at all. It is very like brewing ginger beer. It can be made with sugar or treacle—I much prefer it made with treacle. But be sure to tell your housekeeper to cut off the resinous part of the spruce before boiling it; that will prevent it being bitter."

"I must put that down so that I remember it," said Elton, taking out his pocket-book and drawing the pencil from its holder. "Let me see…oh, I must sharpen this."

"There is a knife on the table there," said Emma, and Elton went over to the table to sharpen his pencil. "No good," he said after a few moments. "There is not enough lead left in it."

"Never mind, Mr. Elton," said Emma. "Here is another in my pocket that you may use."

Elton left the old bit of pencil on the table and beamed as he took Emma's, looking for all the world like a knight receiving a token from his lady just before a jousting match. The image of Elton seated on a charger in full armour—still with that silly smile on his face—was enough to keep Knightley in a good humour while he slowly repeated his brewing advice and Elton wrote down every word.

"Thank you," said Elton when he had finished. "I am sure I will enjoy spruce beer that has been properly brewed. I will set my housekeeper to making some as soon as possible. I am afraid I must be going now, but I will return tomorrow immediately after breakfast for the portrait. Miss Woodhouse, how may I thank you for the privilege of getting a frame for it?"

"That is very gallant of you, Mr. Elton, to turn your kind service to us into an occasion requiring your thanks! Miss Smith and I are both very sensible of the honour you show to my little portrait of her."

Knightley watched Harriet as Elton took his leave. Her face was still glowing with happiness; she was sure of Elton's regard for her. *Oh Emma,* he thought. *You are doing your friend no favours at all. She will be badly hurt before all this is finished.*

He was rather glad that the noise of Elton's going woke Mr. Woodhouse from the doze into which he had fallen, for he felt that he could not talk to Emma or Harriet just then without betraying some of his thoughts. Therefore he talked to Mr. Woodhouse exclusively and determinedly until he could use the approaching dinner hour as his excuse and go away.

10

It was the following evening that Knightley, trying to amuse himself with *Tristram Shandy,* was surprised by Baxter entering the library and announcing Mr. Martin. Knightley put down his book with very little regret and greeted his tenant with something of relief in his manner. An intelligent, friendly conversation was a much better prospect than another evening alone.

"I am not disturbing you, Mr. Knightley?"

"No, Martin, not at all. I had thought to occupy myself with a favourite book this evening—I was trying to counter the dull winter weather with something humorous, but it is not as entertaining as I remembered it. You have saved me from several hours of tedious solitude. Do please be seated."

"Thank you, Mr. Knightley. I have often thought that bachelors are the least comfortable people in the country during long winter evenings."

"*You* cannot be too miserable," said Knightley. "You have a kind mother and charming sisters to keep you company. I'll not forget the very pleasant evening I spent at your house last winter; nothing could have been cosier."

"It is kind of you to say so, Mr. Knightley. But there are times when even such an agreeable domestic circle cannot answer all a man's hopes."

"Oh?"

"To speak plainly, Mr. Knightley, I had some thought of getting married."

And then Knightley remembered what Dr. Hughes had said about Robert Martin; he had been right, as usual.

"And who is the lady?"

"A Miss Smith—Miss Harriet Smith."

"The same Miss Smith who has been so much at Hartfield lately?"

"Yes, the very same. She knew my sisters at Mrs. Goddard's school, and she made a visit of some weeks to us last summer. I confess, Mr. Knightley,"—he flushed a little but went on in his straightforward way—"I have not been the same man since. I had not meant to settle quite so early in life, but as I cannot seem to do any of my work properly for thinking of her, I thought perhaps I ought to end my own misery and get married."

"And have you spoken to Miss Smith?"

"No, Mr. Knightley. I wanted your advice first. Still, I think she would have me if I asked her. She appeared to enjoy my company very much...and there was a look in her eyes sometimes...I don't know how to explain it. But, what is more to the purpose, my sisters and my mother believe she would not refuse my suit."

Knightley smiled. So here was the end of all Emma's matchmaking!

"It seems an agreeable thing for all concerned," he said. "Miss Smith is a beautiful and sweet-tempered young lady and you are a fine, prosperous young man; that is enough for most people. But you said you wanted my advice about it."

"Yes, I had some matters that I wanted your opinion on. If you tell me I am unwise to take this step, then I will try to reconsider my plans...though I do not know if I really could bring myself to let her go." He paused a moment and looked into the fire with a more sober expression than Knightley had ever seen on his face.

"What are your concerns?" prompted Knightley after a few moments of silence.

"First, whether I ought to be thinking of marriage at all—is it prudent? Am I too young? Can I afford it?"

"I think your age has very little to do with your maturity. You are a good farmer and have a fine head for business as well. And you have an uncanny knack for getting good farm help—your shepherd is worth his weight in...well, silver, at least. Yours is easily the most prosperous farm of all the tenants in Donwell. To be truthful, I often forget what your age is. When people speak of a man marrying too young, they usually mean that he has the vices of youth—irresponsibility, impulsiveness, and general foolishness—and you are free of these. Or they may mean that he has not yet the ability to provide for a wife with no dowry—I am assuming Miss Smith will have none—but that does not apply to you, either. You make a clear profit every year, do you not?"

"I do. Last year there was a profit of four hundred pounds, and this year is likely to be a bit more than that."

"No worries on that score, then. I suppose the only other matter that might merit consideration would be the arrangement of your household—would you and Miss Smith live in the house with your mother and sisters? All the ladies who bear the name of Martin are, to my knowledge, most amiable and kind, and Miss Smith is affability itself. However, I have heard that women who must suddenly share a house sometimes find it difficult to maintain perfect harmony."

"I have heard the same thing, Mr. Knightley, and what is more, so has my mother. We have all talked about it, and decided that if Miss Smith and I should marry, she and I would live in the empty cottage a stone's throw from the main house. My mother and sisters proposed their moving there, but I thought they should not have to leave the home they have known for so long. I suggested that Harthat Miss Smith and I should live there until we have children. By then, one of my sisters may have married and Miss Smith might be more accustomed to household duties and would not find being mistress of the main house so daunting."

"You are proposing not to have any housemaids at the cottage?"

"One of the maids will come at times during the day to help."

"That sounds very reasonable. I see you have thought it over very carefully. Had you any other worries?"

"Yes, Mr. Knightley. I know that you have seen Miss Smith at Hartfield, and I wondered—do you think she is too young to marry? Ought I to wait until she is older?"

"For what purpose?"

"I don't know, really. I overheard someone the other day talking about a bride who was seventeen, and their companion said, 'She is so very young to be getting married!' I suppose it *is* rather a young age for matrimony. Miss Smith has not much experience of the wide world, Mr. Knightley, but I must say that I prefer her just as she is. There is something...sweet... about her innocence, and she is nothing like the artificial young ladies whose affected airs drive me to distraction."

Knightley knew just what Martin meant. Hadn't he felt exactly the same about Emma after his evening of conversation with Mrs. Whitney? Although there was something in Martin's concern that *was* valid: Harriet was not an intelligent girl, and there would be no companionship of the mind in that marriage. There was always a tendency to dissatisfaction when one partner was much more intelligent than the other; he saw something of that kind almost daily with Emma and her father.

"Do you think," said Knightley cautiously, "that you might tire of Miss Smith's company after a time if she did not fully share your interests in reading and commerce and so on?"

"Tire of her company?" said Martin. Clearly such a thing was inconceivable to him. "I think she does share my interests, sir. She was very happy to listen when I read aloud, and was always interested in what I had to tell her about the farm and so on."

Knightley could not argue the point with him without being rather insulting to Harriet, and he felt sure that a good relationship with his best tenant would be destroyed if he called the girl dim-witted to his face. She was not the sort of girl he would have picked for Robert Martin. She would bring nothing to the marriage—no money, no connections worth having, no skills, no cleverness. On the other hand, there was no harm in her, either. She was not vicious, shrewish, selfish, or deceitful. She had a simple goodness, and would likely make an adoring wife and doting mother. And she was very pretty, too. A man might do far worse.

"I do not think waiting for Miss Smith to be older will materially change anything," said Knightley. "In my opinion you have no reason to wait."

Martin grinned—he could not help it—and said, "It is a very great relief, sir, to hear you say that. That was my own opinion, but of course I am biased by my own wishes. Miss Smith seems perfectly suited to me...that is,"—his face darkened a bit with doubt again—"she was last summer when she stayed with us. She moves in rather different circles now than she did then. I have begun to wonder if perhaps I am not worthy of her—in regard to her place in society, I mean. I *am* only a farmer, when all is said and done, while she receives invitations to dine with the first families of the neighbourhood. I would not wish to bring her down to a level beneath her deserts by marrying me."

Knightley chuckled. "Put away your fears, Martin. You will be *raising* her to your level by marrying her. She may dine at Hartfield, but that does not essentially elevate her station. You are not beneath her in any way. I predict a very happy union between you. As I said before, she is the very soul of amiability, and she is very beautiful. Furthermore, she is the sort of girl who will have eyes for no one but her husband. I think you a very lucky man."

There might have been something a little wistful in Knightley's tone, for Martin smiled and said, "Perhaps you ought to think of matrimony for yourself, Mr. Knightley."

Knightley groaned. "Not you matchmaking as well! If you tell me that you know a lovely young widow for me, I will—"

"Oh no, Mr. Knightley," protested Martin. "I would never presume such a thing."

"I am glad to hear it. I only wish everyone had your delicacy. At least I am safe in your company. Let us hope your felicity in marriage will occupy your mind so entirely that you have no leisure for arranging the happiness of anyone else."

"If I knew Miss Smith would accept me, I think I would be so happy that I could not think of anything else. But I have such fears sometimes. When I think of the way we talked and laughed together, nothing seems more certain than our marriage. And yet—what if she should refuse? How could I bear to meet her on the road and merely lift my hat to her and say, 'Good day, Miss Smith' and keep walking?"

"Nonsense, Martin. Miss Smith will be very pleased to give you her hand in marriage, I am sure. I look forward to calling on you both at your new cottage in about two months' time."

Knightley went to bed that evening feeling that a heavy burden had been lifted. Robert Martin's proposal to Harriet would solve all the problems he had been fretting about for the last two months. He was quite sure that Harriet, with her pliable will and her fond regard for Martin, would be very happy to become Mrs. Martin. Emma, of course, would miss her friend, but would not mind letting her companion go when she realized what a good match Harriet was going to make. The friendship would gradually drop and its bad effects on both of them would cease. Possibly Emma might find another companion that would be more suitable. And with Harriet gone, Emma would stop unconsciously encouraging Elton. It might embarrass both Emma and Elton to find how far they had misunderstood each other, but it was better than an outright proposal and rejection. Perhaps the salutary humiliation they both needed might not have to be so explicit. All in all, he could not have asked for a neater solution to the entire problem.

The next day brought more good news: Larkins announced that Mefford had signed the document, giving up his lease.

"At first Mefford refused to sign it, Mr. Knightley, which I had rather expected. So I said, 'Very wise of you, I'm sure. You'll never be able to get another lease if you give up this one.'

"'What do you mean?' he said.

"And I said, 'Landlords have a way of enquiring how prospective tenants managed their last farms. And I must say that as you have done so poorly with the farm here, no landlord would be likely to offer you another lease.'

"Then he said a rude word, Mr. Knightley, and told me that it was a rotten farm to begin with and that no one could have done anything with it, that the rent was unreasonable for such a place, and that any landlord with half a mind would understand that. So I told him that if he could believe such a thing, then it was well for him that he was not going to give up the lease and test his assumption. I believe that stung his pride, Mr. Knightley, for he snatched the document out of my hand and signed it and said, 'We'll see about that.' So you are free of a bad tenant, Mr. Knightley, and without any real unpleasantness."

"You look uncommonly pleased, Mr. Knightley," said Baxter the next morning.

Knightley smiled. "I suppose I do, Baxter." He had been thinking of Robert Martin's face, illuminated with joy, as he had said goodnight the other evening. He could pardon Emma for feeling that she had a hand in the Westons' match, for he felt the same now about Martin and Harriet. He wondered how long it would take him to propose. Not long, he guessed. Perhaps in a day or two Emma would be confiding to him that Harriet would not be single much longer.

Suddenly, he wanted to be the one confiding the secret to *her*. He had to share the news with someone, and as it concerned Emma's protégé, it would surely do no harm for her to know what was coming. If he left now, he could probably be there when Mr. Woodhouse took his morning walk and he could have a word with Emma alone. Ah, no, Harriet would probably be there. He hesitated, but the chance that he would find a way to talk to Emma anyway proved irresistible and he yielded to his first impulse.

He called at Hartfield, and by some miracle stroke, Harriet was not there. He sat down with Mr. Woodhouse and Emma and helped to talk away Mr. Woodhouse's fears on the subject of Miss Smith's health—"she ate pickled onions when she was here for dinner yesterday. I tried to dissuade her from it, and I am sure she was very quiet all the evening. And now she is gone to Mrs. Goddard's again, and I fear it is due to ill-health, though she would not own it."

"But Papa, Harriet is only gone to fetch a few of her things, and she is coming back directly to spend several days with us. And she has eaten pickled onions all her life, and it has never disagreed with her before."

"If she had a good breakfast this morning," said Knightley, "then I think her health must be well enough. Do you not agree, sir?"

"I suppose so, Mr. Knightley. And she did eat a good breakfast, I think, did she not, Emma?"

"Yes, indeed, Papa."

"Well, it must be as you say, Mr. Knightley. But all the same, I do not think she ought to have eaten the onions."

Having restored Miss Smith's health, they talked over other small items of news until Knightley was sure that Mr. Woodhouse had given up the idea of having a walk at all that day. But at last Emma mentioned that perhaps he ought to take his walk now, and after making his usual lengthy apologies and explanations, Mr. Woodhouse agreed and allowed Knightley to get him his great coat and open the garden door for him.

At last Knightley was alone with Emma, and he opened the subject immediately by praising Harriet's beauty and good nature, and then giving Emma the compliment she wanted: "You have improved her. You have cured her of her school-girl's giggle," he said. "She really does you credit."

"Thank you," said Emma. "I should be mortified indeed if I did not believe I had been of some use; but it is not everybody who will bestow praise where they may. *You* do not often overpower me with it."

No, thought Knightley. *I know better than to give you even more flattery than you are currently receiving!* However, he said merely, "You are expecting her again, you say, this morning?"

"Almost every moment. She has been gone longer already than she intended."

Aha! thought Knightley.

"Something has happened to delay her," he said. "Some visitors perhaps." *One visitor in particular...*

"Highbury gossips! Tiresome wretches!"

"Harriet may not consider everybody tiresome that you would," said Knightley, and Emma conceded the point by looking away.

"I do not pretend to fix on times or places," Knightley went on, "but I must tell you that I have good reason to believe your little friend will soon hear of something to her advantage."

"Indeed! How so? Of what sort?"

"A very serious sort, I assure you," said Knightley, smiling.

"Very serious! I can think of but one thing—who is in love with her? Who makes you their confidant?"

"I have reason to think," he replied, "that Harriet Smith will soon have an offer of marriage, and from a most unexceptionable quarter: Robert Martin is the man. Her visit to Abbey Mill this summer seems to have done his business. He is desperately in love and means to marry her."

"He is very obliging," said Emma, "but is he sure that Harriet means to marry him?"

"Well, well, means to make her an offer then. Will that do?" said Knightley, and went on to tell of Robert Martin's visit two days before, giving Martin all the praise he was due. It was a good sign, he thought, that Emma smiled through this explanation. In spite of the fact that she would lose her companion, she could already see that this marriage was a good thing.

"Now," he concluded, "as we may fairly suppose he would not allow much time to pass before he spoke to the lady, and as he does not appear to have spoken yesterday, it is not unlikely that he should be at Mrs. Goddard's today... and she may be detained by a visitor without thinking him at all a tiresome wretch."

"Pray, Mr. Knightley," said Emma, "how do you know that Mr. Martin did not speak yesterday?"

"Certainly I do not absolutely know it, but it may be inferred. Was not she the whole day with you?" His heart sank a little; was he not going to be the bearer of news after all?

"Come, I will tell you something, in return for what you have told me. He did speak yesterday—that is, he wrote, and was refused."

"What?"

"He wrote, and she refused him."

Refused him? Impossible! He could see Robert Martin's earnest face in his mind's eye and he began to feel a knot growing inside him. Could the girl not see what she was rejecting?

"Then she is a greater simpleton than I ever believed her," he said, standing up and feeling his face grow red with indignation. "What is the foolish girl about?" He took a couple strides away from her.

"Oh, to be sure," said Emma, "it is always incomprehensible to a man that a woman should ever refuse an offer of marriage. A man always imagines a woman to be ready for anybody who asks her."

Knightley did not know which was more absurd: her ridiculous assertion or the fact that she thought *she* knew anything at all about men!

"Nonsense!" he said, beginning to pace the floor, "A man does not imagine any such thing. But what is the meaning of this? Harriet Smith refuse Robert Martin? Madness, if it is so, but I hope you are mistaken." He could imagine Martin's despair if it was really true. It must be a mistake. It *must* be! Martin had left the Abbey so expectant and happy...

"I saw her answer; nothing could be clearer."

"You saw her answer!" What strange creatures women were. To write a refusal letter and then show it to a friend...*Rubbish!* Harriet would have done no such thing! The thought of Harriet Smith composing her own letter was preposterous. He turned and faced Emma.

"You *wrote* her answer, too."

The quick downward cast of her eyes confirmed it.

"Emma, this is your doing. You persuaded her to refuse him."

"And if I did," retorted Emma, "which, however, I am far from allowing—I should not feel that I had done wrong. Mr. Martin is a very respectable young man, but I cannot admit him to be Harriet's equal; and am rather surprised indeed that he should have ventured to address her. By your account, he does seem to have had some scruples. It is a pity that they were ever got over."

"Not Harriet's equal!" The words came out louder than he had meant them to, but he could hardly believe what he was hearing. He had hardly thought Emma could be so deluded about Harriet as that! Perhaps if he reasoned with her she might reconsider—she did respect his judgement. He could tell Martin to try again, and Emma could encourage Harriet to accept him this time. He took a deep breath, sat down, and then said in what he hoped was a reasonable tone, "No, he is not her equal indeed, for he is as much her superior in sense as in situation."

He explained as clearly as he could that Harriet had no claims to any high connection, and that she was unlikely to receive a better offer than Robert Martin's; indeed, she would probably never get another one anywhere near as good. He even appealed to Emma's good sense, saying that he had been quite sure that she would see the match favourably.

But it was all in vain. Emma was certain that Harriet was the natural daughter of a gentleman, and that this made her eligible for a match with a man of what Emma called "good society."

"Whoever might be her parents," said Knightley patiently, "whoever may have had the charge of her, it does not appear to have been any part of their plan to introduce her into what you would call good society. After receiving a very indifferent education she is left in Mrs. Goddard's hands to shift as she can—to move, in short, in Mrs. Goddard's line, to have Mrs. Goddard's acquaintance. Her friends evidently thought this good enough for her; and it *was* good enough. She desired nothing better herself. Till you chose to turn her into a friend, her mind had no distaste for her own set, nor any ambition beyond it. She was as happy as possible with the Martins in the summer. She had no sense of superiority then. If she has it now, you have given it. You have been no friend to Harriet Smith, Emma. Robert Martin would never have proceeded so far, if he had not felt persuaded of her not being disinclined to him. I know him well. He has too much real feeling to address any woman on the haphazard of selfish passion. And as to conceit, he is the farthest from it of any man I know. Depend upon it he had encouragement."

There. Perhaps the thought of breaking the heart of an honest man would change Emma's mind.

She paused before she spoke again, and he began to hope. But when she did speak, it was only to reiterate the commendations of Harriet that Knightley had given—that she was pretty and good-tempered—and argue that these alone were enough to make Harriet admired and sought after by many men of the sort Emma approved of.

"I am very much mistaken," she said, "if your sex in general would not think such beauty, and such temper, the highest claims a woman could possess."

"Upon my word, Emma," he said quietly, "to hear you abusing the reason you have is almost enough to make me think so too. Better be without sense, than misapply it as you do."

It cost him something to say those words; he was more disappointed in her than he could express, and he was more earnest in this reproof than he had ever been before.

It grated on him all the more, then, when she said in a teasing tone, "To be sure! I know *that* is the feeling of you all. I know that such a girl as Harriet is exactly what every man delights in—what at once bewitches his senses and satisfies his judgment. Oh! Harriet may pick and choose. Were you, yourself, ever to marry, she is the very woman for you."

This ludicrous statement almost made him laugh—almost.

"And is she, at seventeen, just entering into life, just beginning to be known, to be wondered at because she does not accept the first offer she receives? No—pray let her have time to look about her."

She would have plenty of time, Knightley knew. She would likely have an entire lifetime to wait for an offer of marriage from a gentleman. He told Emma this. Why would she not listen to him? She knew nothing about men! He tried to explain to her that it was very unlikely that a gentleman would wish to ally himself with a girl in Harriet's position, no matter how beautiful she was; that a man of sense would not choose a silly wife; and that Harriet was being puffed up by Emma to expect something that had no likelihood of coming to pass.

"Let her marry Robert Martin," he concluded, "and she is safe, respectable, and happy for ever; but if you encourage her to expect to marry greatly, and teach her to be satisfied with nothing less than a man of consequence and large fortune, she may be a parlour-boarder at Mrs. Goddard's all the rest of her life; or, at least—for Harriet Smith is a girl who will marry somebody or other—till she grow desperate, and is glad to catch at the old writing master's son."

Emma refused to reply directly to this, saying that there was no use arguing over something about which they thought so differently. There was a note of triumph in her voice as she declared that Robert Martin had been repulsed so definitely that there was no chance of him renewing his suit, and though she might have influenced Harriet a *little* in her decision, his manner, appearance, and education were so bad that Harriet would not be disposed to think much of him now that she knew what real gentlemen were.

"Nonsense, errant nonsense, as ever was talked!" said Knightley, getting angry again. Emma knew nothing of Martin, nothing at all, and it exasperated him to hear her abusing him. "Robert Martin's manners have sense, sincerity, and good-humour to recommend them; and his mind has more true gentility than Harriet Smith could understand."

Emma looked away again; she had nothing to say to that, of course.

Knightley sat for a few moments in silence, confounded, irritated, despondent, and feeling wretchedly guilty for having encouraged Martin to expect a positive answer to his proposal. What on earth could he say to the man? He had no doubt that Martin could find a better wife in time, but he would suffer much in the meantime.

Emma fidgeted uncomfortably. "The weather is certainly good for December, is it not?" she said.

He ignored her. Only an hour ago he had been so thankful for the way Harriet's marriage was going to do away with the problem of Elton, Emma, and Harriet, and now that infuriating circumstance was going to go on and on.

Stay, why should he not say something about that? Things had gone so far now, at least he might induce her to give up the attempt to match Harriet with Elton.

"Robert Martin has no great loss," he began, "if he can but think so, and I hope it will not be long before he does. Your views for Harriet are best known to yourself, but as you make no secret of your love of match-making, it is fair to suppose that views, and plans, and projects you have—and as a friend I shall just hint to you that if Elton is the man, I think it will be all labour in vain."

Emma laughed—a rather brittle laugh—and said, "Oh, no, Mr. Knightley, I have no plans in that direction."

He ignored this blatant falsehood and went on. "Depend upon it, Elton will not do. Elton is a very good sort of man, and a very respectable vicar of Highbury, but not at all likely to make an imprudent match. He knows the value of a good income as well as anybody. Elton may talk sentimentally, but he will act rationally. He is as well acquainted with his own claims as you can be with Harriet's. He knows that he is a very handsome young man, and a great favourite wherever he goes. And from his general way of talking in unreserved moments, when there are only men present, I am convinced that he does not mean to throw himself away."

He paused here; was this the time to tell Emma that Elton was hoping to marry her? Somehow, he could not—the great awkwardness of telling her and the uncomfortable conversation that would follow were beyond him just now. No, the Misses Carson would illustrate his point just as well.

"I have heard him speak with great animation of a large family of young ladies that his sisters are intimate with, who have all twenty thousand apiece." There, if that would not convince her, nothing would.

Emma gave another false laugh and said, "I am very much obliged to you. If I had set my heart on Mr. Elton's marrying Harriet, it would have been very kind to open my eyes; but at present I only want to keep Harriet to myself. I have done with match-making, indeed. I could never hope to equal my own doings at Randalls. I shall leave off while I am well."

Enough! He could no longer torture himself by listening to such obvious lies and observing such a perfect example of self-delusion.

He rose abruptly and said, "Good morning to you." Without waiting for an answer, he left the room, resisting with great difficulty the temptation to slam the door shut behind him.

11

The parish committee met at The Crown as usual the next Wednesday. After an hour in conference they had nearly got through all the items slated for deliberation. They had discussed the distressing fact that the newly repaired bridge already showed a crack in its north side and debated whether the fault lay with the workmen, the architect, or Random Mischance. Knightley said he would undertake to speak to the Surveyor of Highways about it and see what ought to be done. Parish rates had been analysed: was the help given sufficient? Could any more poor be added to the rolls without rates being raised again? Elton referred often to the papers he had brought to support his opinions, which were, on the whole, reasonable, though he did seem to rely overmuch on the generosity of Hartfield for the support of the poor. And finally they embarked on the topic of the farmer Freeman's draining a boggy field.

"Of course there's no quarrel with Freeman reclaiming that land," said Cole, "but it's the harm it's doing the river that's the trouble."

"The river?" said Elton, stifling a yawn.

"Yes," said Knightley. "The field had three or four feet of peat on top of good soil. Freeman is taking the peat off so that he may use that field for crops. There's no harm in that, but he is getting rid of the peat by throwing it into the river, which runs through his property."

"Yes," put in Weston, "And the river's getting blocked up a little downstream and fish are dying and so on."

Elton nodded a little absently and let the men argue the matter without any contribution from him. Weston thought that no lasting harm would be done, and Cole thought there might be. Weston said that as the river flowed through Freeman's land, there wasn't much that could be done about it. He had already spoken to Freeman and found him unwilling to stop putting the peat in the river. Cole thought that there must be some remedy for the situation and appealed to Knightley. As Knightley began speaking, Elton took out his pencil and, uncharacteristically, began making notes on a blank sheet of paper. Surprised but pleased at Elton's diligence, Knightley gave his opinion that William Cox ought to be applied to. He might know of a law that would strengthen their hand.

"Is there not a law about disrupting the course of a river?" said Cole, "Or one about fouling a water supply?"

Weston's view was that the mere threat of the law might be enough to deter Freeman, and the talk drifted into stories about miscreants who were warned off bad behaviour by well-worded threats. Elton appeared to find these fascinating, for he jotted down more notes as the talk went on.

"Well then," said Knightley finally. "Cole will speak to William Cox about this matter and we can decide what to do on this subject next week. I think that closes our business today. And our timing is perfect—it appears the rain has stopped."

"Has it?" said Cole. "But only for a moment, I'll wager. Dash it all, I meant to talk to Mrs. Stokes when I came in about changing the whist-club night to Thursdays. I'll do it now before I forget." He went out, leaving the door open.

Weston went to the window, and as was his habit, threw up the sash and stuck his head out. The draught caused by the open door and window caught Elton's papers which were stacked on the table in front of him. They flew up in confusion and then fluttered gracefully to the floor.

Unheeding, Weston gave his report. "Yes, no rain at present, though there are more dark clouds coming and the wind is still howling. Brrrrr..." He brought his head back inside and shut the window. Elton glowered but said nothing as he bent down to pick up the scattered pages. Knightley handed him the two which had come to rest nearest his foot, and Elton grunted his thanks.

The men left the room together, Knightley pausing before going outside to ask John Ostler, whom he met in the passageway, about his father's health.

"Not so bad, Mr. Knightley, I thank you, but then not so good, either," said John.

"You'll let me know how he gets on, will you?" said Knightley.

"I will, sir, and thank you."

Knightley turned to go, but was stopped by Mrs. Stokes' saying, "Mr. Knightley, I think you've left one of your papers behind. It was in the little parlour, on the floor."

Knightley took the page from her outstretched hand. It looked like one of Elton's sheets of paper, but the words on it had nothing to do with parish business.

> *My first must show ~~the treasures~~ the wealth and display of ~~rulers~~ kings*
> *Lords of the ~~land~~ earth, their riches and ease*
>
> > *cheese*
> > *trees*
> > *~~fleas~~*
> > *please*

It was Elton's writing. Well, that explained why Elton had looked so studious during the meeting; he must fancy himself a poet whose first duty was to the Muse that inspired him at inopportune moments. Looking at it again, he saw that it appeared to be a charade. *My first must show…*

Then Knightley became aware that Mrs. Stokes was still waiting for him to speak.

"Thank you, Mrs. Stokes. I'll see that this is returned to its owner."

He had no wish to give the charade back to its owner personally and see Elton's embarrassment (at least he *ought* to be embarrassed to be caught writing riddles during parish meetings) and hear his excuses. Instead, he went to the vicarage and gave it to the housemaid that opened the door. Then, reluctantly, he walked to Hartfield. It had been nearly a week since he had been there, and he must go and call on Mr. Woodhouse. He hoped that Emma might be out during his visit; he did not want to see her yet. He had met Robert Martin on the road that morning on his way to the meeting at the Crown, and though nothing was said about Martin's disappointment, the grief on his face was almost enough to make Knightley fall to his knees and beg forgiveness for having given him so much encouragement.

He had often been annoyed by Emma's faults, but this time he was really angry. *How dare she!* was the refrain that had been playing itself over in his mind during the last week. And his resentment was not toward Emma alone: Mrs. Weston, for example—why could she not have used a firmer hand with Emma when she was governess? That would have warded off this trouble. And Harriet—why must Harriet flatter Emma so much? It was the excess of Harriet's adoration that had given Emma such an exalted view of her own powers. And then there was Elton. Elton's admiration for Emma was supposed by her to be disinterested, as she thought he was pursuing Harriet. Emma no doubt took all his gallantries as literal truth, which only puffed her up more. He was also angry with himself. He ought to have said something sooner, or talked more seriously to her when she was younger and more impressionable ...

He had not finished reproaching himself when he arrived at Hartfield.

To his chagrin, both Emma and Harriet were there. Emma gave him a tentative smile of greeting, which faded when he gave her a civil, formal salutation and sat down near Mr. Woodhouse. He had intended to talk exclusively with Mr. Woodhouse, but that elderly gentleman drew Emma into the conversation almost at once.

"My dear Emma, we must ask Mr. Knightley if he has anything for Miss Smith's book. Mr. Knightley is so very clever, I am sure he knows a score of riddles."

"This is the book of riddles and charades that Harriet is collecting, Mr. Knightley," Emma said, taking a thin book from a side table. "Perhaps you may like to see it."

"Yes, indeed," said Knightley politely. This must have some connection with the charade that Elton had written. Presumably Mr. Woodhouse had also importuned him for a contribution, and Elton was obliging by writing one himself. The first few pages of Harriet's book had several riddles and charades already copied neatly onto them, and they were ornamented very tastefully with little ciphers and trophies—Emma's work, Knightley could tell. Most of the conundrums were well known to him, but one he had never heard before caught his eye:

When my first is a task to a young girl of spirit,
And my second confines her to finish the piece,
How hard is her fate! But how great is her merit
If by taking my whole she effects her release!

He contemplated the hints for a moment, and then smiled briefly as understanding came. *Hemlock,* of course.

"I have tried to remember the riddles I knew when I was young," said Mr. Woodhouse, "but my memory is not what it was. It is very strange that I cannot remember any of them except 'Kitty, a fair but frozen maid,' and then only a part of it. But Mr. Knightley, I dare say, knows several."

"I have no doubt that Mr. Knightley does know a number of charades," said Emma. "They are all very likely highly instructive and exceptionally moral, and will improve everyone who reads them." She spoke as if she were teasing him, but she was not really teasing. There was no humour in her eyes. "The collection would not be complete without a contribution from Mr. Knightley."

Very well, then, he would contribute something that ought to instruct Emma—and Elton, who was sure to read the book as well—if only they had ears to hear.

"If you insist," said Knightley, "I do happen to know a charade which is very much to the purpose. Quite *instructive,* as you have said. It is not too difficult. I will write it out for you, if you will give me a moment." He crossed to the little table in the corner, where a pencil and paper were to be found, and quickly wrote:

My first denotes a muted song
With which the jaw can never tire
The next is a beast with horns quite long
And proves to be the new calf's sire.

The whole's a virtue some despise
But makes one exalted in Heaven's eyes.

"There," he said, coming over to Emma and giving her the paper. "Can you tell the answer?"

Emma read the whole aloud, and then applied herself to deciphering its meaning.

"Hmmm…" she said. "'A muted song with which the jaw can never tire.' Well, I suppose a jaw would never tire if it didn't move, but then how could you have a song if you didn't move your jaw? Well, leave that for the present. A beast with long horns…the calf's sire…that would be a bull. Something-bull. 'The whole's a virtue…makes one exalted…' A virtue? You were quite serious about this being an edifying riddle!"

Knightley's grave eyes met hers, and she looked back at the paper.

"I'm sure I must be mistaken," said Harriet timidly, "but the part about being exalted in heaven's eyes reminds me of the text Mr. Elton read out on Sunday, from St. Luke: 'He that humbleth himself shall be exalted.' But of course 'humbleth' is too many syllables."

"Humble…muted song…hum…bull…yes, of course! Harriet, you have found it out!" Emma's face beamed at Harriet with delight; *Like a proud mother,* thought Knightley.

"Have I?" said Harriet. "I do not believe I have ever found out the answer to a riddle before."

"Well, Miss Smith, it is to your credit that it was your familiarity with Holy Writ that gave you the clue," said Knightley civilly.

"As to that, sir, it was only that Mr. Elton had read it out recently, else I might not have remembered it so quickly."

"Never mind, Harriet," said Emma. "It is a worthy addition to your collection, and one that particularly belongs to you—not only because you discovered the answer but because it is a virtue that you display to perfection. There are few who would tax *you* with arrogance, whoever else might be accused of it"—this said with a slight glance in his direction.

"I am glad the charade has your approval," said Knightley drily. "I hope it may prove *useful* to those who read Miss Smith's collection."

"Excuse me, sir, but here's Mr. Knightley for you."

Dr. Hughes looked up from his book at the housemaid's announcement and his eyes brightened.

"And how are you, Mr. Knightley?"

"Well in body, though rather agitated in mind. I was hoping that conversation with you might give me a more tranquil spirit."

"Then I am afraid you will be disappointed, I am not in the best of tempers myself."

"I am very sorry—and greatly surprised—to hear that, sir. I do not think I have ever seen you otherwise than uncomplaining and patient. What has troubled you?"

"Oh, everything. The pain in my leg has subsided a great deal, but it still hurts and I am tired of lying in this bed, tired of reading, and tired of every visitor beginning the conversation by asking if my leg is improving."

Knightley grinned sheepishly; he had entered the room ready to enquire after that very thing.

"Of course," Dr. Hughes went on, "it is very reasonable for them to ask; it is what I should ask if I were visiting an invalid. But you have no idea how annoying it is to answer the same question time and time again."

"I shall go away and come another time if you prefer," said Knightley.

"Not at all; you have improved my ill-humour by coming. Sit down. And I had something I wanted to say to you."

"What is that?"

"You know, of course, that Mefford has given up his lease and will be moving."

"Yes."

"Mrs. Mefford came to see me yesterday, asking if there was something that could be done for her son, Harry. He is nearly twenty, you know, and has never really taken to farming. And she fears that her husband will not be able to lease another farm elsewhere. She wondered if he might go into service somewhere, and if I knew of an open position hereabouts."

"Were you hoping there was a place at Donwell?"

"I know there is a place at Donwell. Betty, our housemaid, told Mrs. Hughes this morning that one of your footmen has given notice. His older brother has died and he is needed at home—I think his father is a corset-maker."

"William Larkins called at the vicarage this morning, did he?" smiled Knightley.

"Yes, I've no doubt the information came through him. You did not know it?"

"No. Baxter had not yet mentioned it to me."

"Well, will you ask Baxter if young Harry could take Thomas's place?

"He's certainly tall enough for a footman, but—forgive me—my impression of him is that he is better fitted for feeding poultry than serving it at table."

Dr. Hughes chuckled. "No doubt. But he may learn." Seeing that Knightley still hesitated, he added, "I can well believe that he is not an ideal choice for the position from your point of view, but from *his* point of view, nothing could be better."

"I am not likely to suffer as much from his inexperience as Baxter is," said Knightley. "I will ask Baxter if he is willing to train him. Heretofore I have had nothing to do with the hiring of under-servants."

"No, I imagine not. If you give it good consideration, I will be content."

"Very well, I will think on it."

"Thank you. That is one burden less. Now, if you could only find a balm for broken hearts you would remove another cause of my troubled state."

"If you mean Robert Martin, I heartily wish I had a cure. Healing his heart would remove my aggravation as well."

"How so?"

Knightley hesitated. As angry as he was with Emma, it pained him to think of others censuring her too. She was quite mistaken, but there was still a great deal of goodness in her. People would be apt to forget that. Of course, the rector was the very last person who would spread tales about others; telling him about Emma's folly would not be making it public. But then he didn't really want to discuss Emma's misdeeds even with Dr. Hughes.

"I don't think I can explain it fully to you, sir. But I do feel most sincerely for Robert Martin."

"Anyone must. I confess I had rather it happened to almost anyone else."

"Will he confide in Spencer, do you think? He is about his own age."

"Oh, I don't know," said Dr. Hughes with a touch of impatience. "He very well might." He looked away from Knightley and out the window with a rather cross expression, which was such a contrast to his usually cheerful countenance that Knightley wondered if perhaps he really ought to go. But before he could move, Dr. Hughes sighed and said, "Forgive me. You see now another reason for my peevishness. When Spencer first came, I was distressed that he was not more generally liked by the parish. I knew his worth and was unhappy that his merit was unseen by most. Now, however, his kindness and humility have earned him the respect he is worthy of. I should be pleased, and yet…and yet I fear now that the parish will come to prefer him to me. Is that not a disgraceful confession? That I should be envious of my curate! I may say that I had no idea of the state of my heart until I realized that my vanity was wounded at the thought of 'my flock' preferring another."

"An entirely reasonable and natural feeling, I should think," said Knightley. "I am sure I would feel the same. But you have nothing at all to fear, sir; your flock will never favour another over you. They have loved you too well and too long to give your curate the preference."

"That may be true. And also true, as you have said, that it is *natural* for me to feel as I do. But there is a higher Law, which I have violated. 'Charity envieth not', you know, and therefore I know that I am lacking in charity. It is a frightful admission."

"'O! beware, my lord, of jealousy'," murmured Knightley.

"Indeed. The Bard knew what he was about when he wrote that." Dr. Hughes looked out the window again, but now he looked contemplative instead of annoyed. After a moment he sighed again and then looked at Knightley once again. "Your brother and sister arrive soon, do they not?"

"On Saturday. I will be very glad to see them again."

"You will ask them to visit me, will you not? Tell Mrs. Knightley that I want to see *all* the children."

"My dear sir," said Knightley, rising to go, "You could not evade seeing them if you wanted to. Nothing would induce my sister to leave her children behind when she calls on old friends. And they will be at the Abbey frequently—you know they always visit Donwell every day. They can be so much noisier there than at Hartfield where their Grandpapa likes tranquillity."

"Good. I am glad the Abbey will have children's voices echoing down its halls, however briefly. It needs a little life in it; you are too much alone there."

Knightley opened his mouth to protest, and then closed it. It was not worth arguing over. He bowed and bid the rector good day.

12

Knightley was glad there was nothing to take him to Hartfield in the days leading up to Saturday. Almost against his will, his anger at Emma was beginning to ebb away. She had been wrong—very, very wrong—and she would not admit it; he hoped that his steady disapproval might in a sober moment make her reconsider her actions. But he was tired of being at odds with her. He kept thinking of things he wanted to tell her or ask her, only to remember that he was supposed to be preserving a dignified reserve toward her. He was afraid that the more he was in her company, the more impossible it would be to maintain an adequate show of displeasure.

For this reason he did not come to Hartfield until Saturday evening, to ensure that his brother's family arrived first. In a room full of people—Mr. Woodhouse, Emma, John, Isabella, the five children and, with any luck, two nursery maids—he hoped there would be no reason to talk much to Emma. He could be grave and civil from a distance.

He was unlucky. When he arrived at Hartfield, he found the drawing room much emptier than he wished it. Mr. Woodhouse was sitting by the fire with Isabella, and Emma was standing near them, holding the baby. Of John and the other children there was no sign.

"My dear sir," said Mr. Woodhouse, rising with Isabella to greet him, "how are you on this dreadfully cold night? I hope you have not caught a chill."

"I am very well indeed. And Isabella, it is good to see you again in Surrey."

"Thank you, George. We are very pleased to be here again. John is upstairs, but I expect he will join us very shortly. And the children, too."

"They tolerated the journey well, I hope?"

"Oh yes. They enjoyed the ride in the carriage immensely, and have been resting since we arrived."

"My dear," said Mr. Woodhouse, seating himself again, "you ought to have rested, too. It is a frightfully long journey."

"I could not rest, Papa, when I was longing so to talk to you and Emma," said Isabella, taking her seat as well.

"Well, that may be so, but I fear you will suffer for it. But you said something about Mr. Wingfield a moment ago. Do tell me what it was he was saying to you."

Knightley's eyes drifted over to Emma. He thought she had never looked so lovely. *"If to her share some female errors fall, look on her face and you'll forget 'em all,"* he quoted to himself, the aptness of the couplet making him want to chuckle. But no, he must remain steady to his resolution of formality with Emma. He had not greeted her at all yet, and he must do so. And, of course, he did want to see the baby. Mr. Woodhouse and Isabella were deep in conversation and did not mark him as he came over to Emma.

"Good evening," he said. He hoped there was not too much warmth in his tone.

"Good evening, Mr. Knightley." She said it without either archness or apprehension; there was only sincerity in her manner.

"Do you think her looking well?" he said, shifting his gaze from Emma's hazel eyes to those of the baby.

"Oh yes. Does it seem to you that she is eight months old? I remember her birth as being only a few weeks ago. But then, you have seen her more recently than I have. Has she grown much?"

"Yes, very much."

"I was surprised to see how the other children have changed and grown since I saw them last, though I know that children do grow rapidly and the only astonishing thing is that I *was* surprised . They are acutely anxious to see you, Mr. Knightley. Bella has whispered to me that she has a very particular gift for you. You must remember to be all enthusiasm for whatever it is, or you will crush her tender feelings."

"Of course." He was tempted to add a teasing remark about knowing the consideration due a niece, having been an uncle *nearly* as long she had had been an aunt, but he remembered in time and restrained himself.

The baby had been looking at him with wide eyes all this time, but now she turned back to her aunt and gently patted her face. Emma smiled and kissed her, which prompted a laugh from the baby and another little caress for her aunt.

"She's an affectionate little thing, rather like Bella, isn't she?" said Knightley without thinking. "Little George was always more interested in observing things than playing with his relatives."

"Yes, I remember. You thought it was unpardonable in a namesake not to show more interest in you."

He smiled at the memory and said, "It was disgraceful. He sat on my lap for a whole half-hour with his attention fixed on my watch fob."

Baby Emma turned to him and smiled, and without even making a conscious decision to do so, he took the baby into his arms.

"You remember Uncle Knightley, don't you?" said Emma to the baby. "I am certain you do."

And then Knightley remembered that he wasn't supposed to be smiling and talking in this friendly way with Emma. For half a moment he contemplated reverting back to his former demeanour and perhaps making some excuse and walking away with the baby. No, it was impossible. He could hardly go back now without open rudeness, and anyway, the longing to be friends again was irresistible. He gave up the struggle.

"You are a clever child, aren't you?" he said to the infant. "Of course you remember me. I was the one who kept telling you how beautiful you are."

"I thought you despised flattery, Mr. Knightley," said Emma with a raised left eyebrow.

"So I do. It was not flattery to tell the baby she is beautiful—I meant every word."

"What a comfort it is," said Emma, "that we think alike about our nephews and nieces. As to men and women, our opinions are sometimes very different; but with regard to these children, I observe we never disagree."

"If you were as much guided by nature in your estimate of men and women, and as little under the power of fancy and whim in your dealings with them as you are where these children are concerned, we might always think alike."

"To be sure—our discordancies must always arise from my being in the wrong." She said it a little petulantly, but her eyes held a smile.

"Yes, and reason good. I was sixteen years old when you were born."

"A material difference then," she replied, "and no doubt you were much my superior in judgment at that period of our lives. But does not the lapse of one-and-twenty years bring our understandings a good deal nearer?"

"Yes—a good deal *nearer.*"

"But still, not near enough to give me a chance of being right if we think differently." There was just a hint of a challenge in her tone.

"I have still the advantage of you by sixteen years' experience, and by not being a pretty young woman and a spoiled child," he began, and then stopped. He was not ready for another verbal battle with her. "Come, my dear Emma," he said, "let us be friends and say no more about it. Tell your aunt, little Emma, that she ought to set you a better example than to be renewing old grievances, and that if she were not wrong before, she is now."

"That's true," said Emma heartily, "very true. Little Emma, grow up a better woman than your aunt. Be infinitely cleverer and not half so conceited."

Her words lifted his spirits. Was it possible that she had she taken some of his rebuke to heart?

"Now, Mr. Knightley," continued Emma, "a word or two more, and I have done. As far as good intentions went, we were *both* right, and I must say that no effects on my side of the argument have yet proved wrong. I only want to know that Mr. Martin is not very, very bitterly disappointed."

The image of Robert Martin's dejected face came immediately before his eyes.

"A man cannot be more so," was all he could say.

"Ah! Indeed I am very sorry. Come, shake hands with me."

She looked as if she meant it, and he could not refuse her. It was a relief, after the strain of the last two weeks, to be done with the discord between the two of them, not to mention the discord between his resolution and his inclination. He was almost disappointed when John chose that moment to come into the room; now that harmony was restored he might have had a satisfying talk with Emma.

"The children's supper has already been sent to the nursery," said John after greeting his brother. "It took all the force of my authority to make them stay there and eat instead of rushing down to the drawing room to see you. But they will be down the moment we finish our dinner and send for them, you can be sure. And here is the nurse come for baby Emma."

Knightley reluctantly gave the baby to her nurse, and, dinner being announced, took Emma in to the dining room.

"And how is the new vicar, Mr. Elton, getting on?" asked Isabella over the dessert.

"He is not so new, Isabella," said Emma, with a smile. "He has been here well over a year."

"Yes, I suppose that must be so," said Isabella. "I have only seen him once, last Christmas. He seemed a very good sort of man."

Knightley kept his face perfectly serious.

"He is attentive," said Mr. Woodhouse. "Most attentive. He calls nearly every day, whatever the weather. He is always welcome, of course, and he greatly enjoys the society at Hartfield."

John's eyebrows rose in surprise at this statement, and he looked at Knightley. Knightley shook his head slightly at his brother. Explanations would have to wait.

"He met with a sad accident today," said Mr. Woodhouse. "He cut himself—actually cut himself—with Emma's new penknife. I advised him to go home and rest, but he would not do it."

"But Papa, he was able to use the court plaister to bind it up and it did not pain him at all, he said."

"Ah, yes, I remember now. You will see him Sunday, my dear Isabella."

The gentlemen lingered only a very little while behind the ladies, but the children were in the drawing room waiting for them when they entered.

"Uncle Knightley!" said the three older children in unison, rushing upon him like so many bedlamites. Little George, who had just reached the age of two, followed his siblings at a slower pace. Knightley glanced at Emma; her face beamed as she watched the scene.

"Mama," said Henry, after the tumult of the initial greetings was over, "May we show Uncle Knightley how well we can drive our hoops?"

"Of course, my dear."

"Now?"

"No, not now. It is not a game you may play indoors and it is dark outside."

"Yes, Mama," said the boy sadly.

"You will come and visit the Abbey tomorrow," said Knightley to Henry. "You may show me then how well you can roll your hoop down the length of the lime walk."

The little boy's face brightened and he nodded vigorously.

Young Bella now claimed his attention. "Uncle Knightley, I have brought you a gift for Christmas."

"Have you? I can hardly wait to see what it is."

"It is Madam Duval."

"Madam Duval?" He could not immediately work out what she meant.

"Yes, Madam Duval, my cat."

"Your cat!" He looked at her blankly for a moment. "But, Bella, that is *your* cat. I know you love her very much. Why do you want to give her to me?" The very last thing he wanted was a French cat!

"She makes little George ill. If she comes near him he sneezes and becomes all over red with bumps and Nurse says there's no keeping her away from him. And Papa said that Madam Duval had better come to you."

He shot a glare at John, who grinned and walked to the other side of the room.

"But should you not like to give her to Aunt Emma instead? I am sure Aunt Emma would like another lady about the house."

"But you have no lady at all in your house." Bella's eyes were very serious, and she spoke softly. "Papa says every house should have a lady in it."

"Does he, indeed?" said Knightley. He looked over at his brother, whose back was turned to him but whose shoulders were shaking with suppressed laughter.

"Madam Duval wishes to come to you, too," said Bella solemnly. "I asked her if she would rather go to Aunt Emma or to Uncle Knightley, and she said she wanted to go to the Abbey." Her trusting little face looked up at Knightley; she was perfectly confident that he saw the necessity as well as she did.

Knightley hesitated, but he knew very well that there was nothing to do but acknowledge defeat. He summoned a smile.

"Thank you, Bella. I am honoured that your cat has chosen to live with me."

"You will be kind to her, Uncle? And write in every letter to Papa how she is doing?"

"Yes, I will. I promise."

Satisfied, Bella wrapped her arms around him and then ran off to play with her brothers, who were busy about the box of letters that Aunt Emma had purchased for them.

Little George remained, having stared at his uncle through the greater part of the conversation, and he now raised his arms and said, "Up, peese."

Knightley lifted up the little boy and went to talk to John.

"Shall I call you Captain Mirvan?" said John with a smirk.

"You cannot. You heard me promise to be kind to the creature. Though I may occasionally call her 'Madam Frog' as the worthy captain did when the lady annoyed him. I do wonder at you, John. Do you lie awake at night thinking of ways to provoke me?"

"Yes," said John. "It takes a great deal of contemplation."

Knightley chuckled. Little George squirmed and Knightley put him down and watched him run to his mother.

"You know I am right."

"Right?"

"Yes. Every house needs a lady in it."

"John— "

"I know, I know. Never mind. Let us be seated. What is this about Mefford giving up his lease?"

"Perfectly true." He told John how William Larkins had effected this miracle.

"So! Mefford will be gone this day week, and new tenants will come. Have you any ready to take over the place?"

"Larkins has had an application from a man who he says seems to be a good prospect. He is making enquiries now."

"Larkins is a treasure. To have a bailiff whose judgement one can trust so completely in these matters is a blessing. Graham hopes his new bailiff will be as reliable as I tell him Larkins is. He is indebted to you, by the way, for mentioning Lord Carrick's man. He has hired him—his name is MacIntyre, I think—sight unseen for that estate he inherited. He wanted to meet him before hiring him, but of course, Scotland is a bit far for such an errand and Graham is very busy."

In the slight pause that followed this statement, both brothers heard Mr. Woodhouse mention "Mr. John Knightley."

"What is the matter, sir? Did you speak to me?" said John, turning to Mr. Woodhouse.

"I am sorry to find, my love, that my father does not think you looking well," said Isabella. "But I hope it is only from being a little fatigued. I could have wished, however, as you know, that you had seen Mr. Wingfield before you left home."

"My dear Isabella," said John quickly and with a shade of annoyance, "pray do not concern yourself about my looks. Be satisfied with doctoring and coddling yourself and the children, and let me look as I choose."

Knightley stifled a sigh. John *would* let little things perturb him, especially if he was already slightly irritated. John would never have owned it, but he was as fond of his own fireside as Mr. Woodhouse was of his, and travelling never improved his temper. Emma knew this as well as he, and she came to the rescue this time.

"I do not thoroughly understand what you were telling your brother," she interjected, "about your friend Mr. Graham's intending to have a bailiff from Scotland, to look after his new estate. But will it answer? Will not the old prejudice be too strong?"

"No, I think he will be all right," said John. "He is a lowland Scot, and has spent some time in England. Apart from his name, there is not much that is Scottish about him at all."

Knightley smiled at Emma to thank her, and her eyes sparkled back at him. It was very, very good to be at peace with her again.

The rest of the evening passed off well enough, save for the incident brought about by Mr. Woodhouse, who injudiciously represented Mr. Perry as being highly critical of the Knightleys' sojourn in South End. Thus attacked (so it seemed) by Mr. Perry, John burst out in a spirited censure of the medical gentleman. The eruption did not last long, however. As soon as he had finished speaking, Knightley turned the conversation back to the Langham path which they had been discussing a moment before, and Emma was able to soothe her father back to equanimity.

Knightley took his leave as the children were shepherded off to bed. There would have been tears from Bella as she said goodbye to her cat had not Knightley reminded her that she could come to the Abbey the next day and see her. The cat was put into a cunning little basket that had a lid that could be fastened, and Knightley held it as carefully as Bella desired him to as he said his farewells.

Madam Duval meowed piteously throughout the walk to Donwell. After five minutes, Knightley was thoroughly exasperated with the animal and would have willingly opened the basket and let her run free if it had not been for his promise to Bella. What on earth was he to do with a cat? And *such* a cat. Long, pure white fur that needed to be combed daily, Bella said. One could hardly imagine she would be any good at catching mice—she would probably sit on a cushion all day, growing fat. And who would be given the task of combing her daily? Mrs. Hodges? The thought of what Mrs. Hodges' expression would be if she were required to comb a cat made him laugh aloud. Well then, Baxter? Or the new footman, Harry? Perhaps one of the housemaids would like the chore.

Baxter greeted his master as usual and helped him to remove his greatcoat. He nodded at the basket.

"A gift, sir?"

"Yes."

At that moment, Madam Duval meowed again. Baxter's busy hands paused at the sound and he stared at the basket.

Knightley cleared his throat. "My niece, Bella, has given me her cat."

Baxter recovered himself. "Very good, Mr. Knightley."

"It was an unexpected gift, and not entirely welcome, but it seems duty requires me to keep the cat. It has been a long walk home, Baxter, and I find that I require a glass of your excellent punch. I will be in the library—with the cat."

"Pardon me, Mr. Knightley, but have you made any arrangements for the cat's...er...calls of nature?"

"Ah, yes. My brother tells me that a shallow box filled with fresh earth will be satisfactory."

"In the library, sir?"

"Well, no. In the scullery, perhaps."

"Very good, sir."

Knightley carried the basket into the library and set it on the floor in front of his favourite chair. He sat down and then reached down and unfastened the lid of the basket, opened it, and picked up the cat.

"Meeeow," said Madam Duval.

"Hmph," said Knightley, resting the creature on his lap. "I daresay you would rather be with Bella, and I wish with all my heart that you were. However, here we are together and we must make the best of it, I suppose."

To his great surprise, the cat curled up on his lap and began to purr. Absently, Knightley began to stroke the soft fur as he mused on the evening. He had gone to Hartfield with only one goal, that of remaining aloof from Emma. In that he had been completely unsuccessful. And yet it was one of the best evenings he'd had all winter. It was always good to see John—and Isabella and the children, of course, too. He was glad to have John in Surrey to talk to about plans for the home farm, and about moving that path...and about Emma and Elton. John might know what to do. And though he hadn't been able to talk much to Emma after amity had been restored, it had been *almost* enough to be able to smile at her again and know that there would be plenty of time for talking later.

The library door opened and Baxter entered with the punch. Madam Duval jumped off Knightley's lap and disappeared under his chair. Knightley took the drink and sipped it, rather wishing that the cat had stayed on his lap—it had kept his legs warm. He looked down at his breeches and then sighed; they were covered with long, white cat hairs.

13

"Watch me, Uncle Knightley! Watch me!"

It was the third day of John and Isabella's stay in Surrey, and therefore the third time that Henry and John had rolled their hoops down the lime walk at Donwell Abbey. Uncle Knightley had been present each time, but the thrill of having him as an audience had not yet faded.

"Yes, I see you, Henry. Well done!" said Knightley. He and John were pacing sedately down the walk as the little boys raced ahead of them.

"And how is Hartfield today?" said Knightley.

"Much as usual. Mr. Woodhouse wanted us to give up the walk to Donwell, as it appeared to him to be very likely to rain. Emma talked away his fears, of course. Oh, and Elton appeared again this morning." John gave his brother a sidelong glance. "Very good of him to give up so much of his time to visiting Mr. Woodhouse."

"Yes."

"And how very agreeable Emma can be to the vicar."

"Indeed."

John waited for an explanation, but none came. He gave an exasperated sigh.

"George, what is all this? Elton behaves as if he is about to offer for Emma, and Emma responds as if he could not do so fast enough. I cannot understand it—she has too much sense to be in love with him, and I can think of no other reason for her to conduct herself in such a manner."

"Emma," said Knightley, "thinks that Elton is in love with her friend Harriet—Miss Smith."

"What? The Miss Smith I met at Hartfield yesterday, who thought *prima facie* was a city in Italy?"

"The very same."

"Humph! I do not know Elton well, but anyone with half an eye could see that he would set his sights a good deal higher."

"Quite. But Emma's eyesight in regard to matchmaking is very poor."

"Could you not have said something?"

"I did. That is, I told her that Elton was not likely to marry a girl like Harriet Smith."

"And she did not believe you?"

"No."

"Well, perhaps if you told her that Elton obviously sees *her* as the future mistress of the parsonage—preposterous as that would be—she would give more weight to your opinion."

Knightley's conscience pricked him; he had thought the same. Still, he had no inclination for discussing suitors with Emma.

"I don't know," he hedged.

"It is rather a brother's place to do so. Although," John continued thoughtfully, "perhaps you are more like an uncle to her."

Knightley bristled. "An uncle! Certainly not!"

"You are eighteen years her senior."

"Only sixteen!"

"Well, sixteen then, but still nearly a generation older. I can imagine she might see you in that light, and therefore consider your assistance in such a matter as elderly interference."

"Nonsense!" said Knightley warmly. "She may not always listen to me, but my age has nothing to do with it. You know there is very little that she allows to influence her opinions, and there is no one whose judgement she relies upon so much as her own."

"True enough. -Henry! John! The hoops must stay on the path! I must say, it's a pity Elton is not more eligible. It would be good for Emma to be married—to the right man, of course. Can you not think of anyone who might be suitable?"

"No," said Knightley shortly.

"Ah," said John. "I've put you into a bad humour. No doubt your approaching the years of senility has made you sensitive to remarks about your age."

"And I suppose you lay awake all last night thinking up a new subject to provoke me with?"

"No need. Bella made me promise to ask how Madam Duval is faring at the Abbey. I knew that would be aggravation enough."

Knightley groaned. "That cat has thrown my well-ordered house into complete confusion. I told you about the first night, did I not?"

"You did. As I recall, you gave her freedom of the house as you had always done with Homer, and she ignored the box of earth in the scullery and left a surprise for Mrs. Hodges in the dining room."

"Yes. She also scratched and screeched at my bedroom door for an hour until I got out of bed and let her in. Then she leapt onto the bed and insisted on lying next to me. I woke with her wrapped around my head."

John chuckled. "Who has the task of combing her? One of the housemaids?"

Knightley shook his head and remained silent.

John looked at his brother for a long moment before giving a shout of laughter. "You're doing it *yourself*?"

Knightley scowled. "I had no choice. It isn't just the door and the furniture that cat scratches—it's all the servants, too. I didn't dare ask Mrs. Hodges to do it after the incident in the dining room, but Baxter tried and the housemaid tried and even the new footman made an attempt. It was no good; she scratched every last one of them."

"But not you."

Knightley gave a despairing little shrug. "I don't know why. She follows me around. If I sit down, she tries to jump into my lap. She is giving Baxter fits as he tries to keep my clothes free of cat hairs. And contrary to my expectations, she has managed to catch a mouse."

"Is that not some consolation? At least she is being useful."

"She left it on my bed."

John chortled again, but the laughter died away when his brother did not join in. The two men walked together in silence for a few moments, and then John shook his head and said, "I'm sorry, George. If I had known it would be this much bother, I would have told Bella to give the cat to someone else. Even now, I suppose I might..."

"No, no. Tempting as it is, I made a promise to Bella. It is a point of honour now."

"Ever the soul of honour, George. I hope you will be rewarded, and that Madam Duval will be a prop and comfort to you in your old age."

"Well, she *has* been the impetus for something rather remarkable already."

"And that is...?"

"You apologized to me. It must be fully ten years since you last did that."

"Yes, it must be. I am so rarely in the wrong, you see."

On the twenty-third of December, Knightley sat in his library going over his accounts and waiting for William Larkins. On his foot, fast asleep, was Madam Duval. John had advised him that cats adored warmth, and that the surest way to keep the cat from following him around was to put a soft cushion near a warm fire. Accordingly, a tremendous fire had been built in the library, and an array of cushions and blankets had been placed around the hearth, but the cat ignored these arrangements and, as usual, jumped into Knightley's lap as soon as he sat down. He put her down on the floor three times in quick succession, and finally she conceded the point and curled up on his shoe, purring loudly. Knightley could not imagine her position being very comfortable, but he really had not the heart to kick her off.

"William Larkins, sir," announced Baxter.

Knightley stood to greet his bailiff, and the cat, offended, retreated beneath his chair in high dudgeon.

"Good afternoon, Larkins. You are in very good time."

"Good afternoon, Mr. Knightley. Yes, I walked quickly—the weather is very brisk, very brisk indeed, sir. I did not realize just how chilly it was until I came into this room. It feels much warmer than usual—the contrast with the cold outside, I suppose. Now, I have here the information about the possible new tenant—Foote is his name—if you would care to see it before I prepare the lease."

Knightley took the paper Larkins held out to him and glanced over it. "And you think he will not disappoint?"

"I think we may have reasonable expectations of him. He grew up on a farm near Ewell; a fine, prosperous place. His elder brother is the leaseholder there now, and evidently Foote has always wanted a farm of his own. He came into some little money and started looking for a small place that would suit his means."

"Will he improve the place, do you think?"

"I do. His brother's farm is considerably improved these last twenty years and he is eager to do the same. He will buy Mefford's stock from him and add to it."

"And has he a family?"

"A wife, but no children. His widowed sister lives with them, and I think he said she had a young child."

"Well, if you are satisfied, Larkins, I see no reason he should not have it."

"Very good, Mr. Knightley; I will draw up the lease. I should think he will take possession next week."

"Thank you, Larkins. I hope this business with the lease will not delay your travels—I think I heard you say that you will be spending Christmas with your sister's family?"

Larkins heaved a deep sigh. "Yes, Mr. Knightley."

"It does not seem a matter of joy to you."

"To be completely candid, Mr. Knightley, my sister has seven children and a small home, and there is nothing of quiet or solitude to be had there. I confess I much prefer the order and silence of my own little house, and of the Abbey."

"You have my sincere sympathy, Larkins. At any rate, I need not worry about you returning to your duties at the proper time."

"No, indeed, Mr. Knightley. And now, if we could look at the accounts—there was an item I particularly wanted to draw to your attention."

For the next half-hour the two men devoted themselves to the examination of the account-books, and they had only just finished when Baxter entered and said, "Mr. Elton for you, sir. Shall I ask him to wait?"

"No, send him in, Baxter."

Elton was sent in accordingly.

"Good afternoon, Knightley. And how do you do, Mr. Larkins?" said Elton, bowing slightly. "I trust I do not interrupt your business."

"Not at all, sir," said Larkins with a stiff bow in return. "Our conference is at an end, and I must be off now."

"Well then, permit me to wish you a happy Christmas."

"Thank you, Mr. Elton. I will endeavour to endure it with patience. Good afternoon, Mr. Elton. Good afternoon, Mr. Knightley."

"Now then, Elton," said Knightley when Larkins had quitted the room, "How may I be of service?"

"I came to ask what the Surveyor of Highways said about that bridge. You were to meet with him yesterday, were you not?"

"I was, but he sent a note saying he was ill. I'm afraid I will not be able to speak with him until the new year now."

Elton frowned. "That is very unfortunate. Several people in Highbury have said that the crack in the bridge is worse and they wanted my opinion as to its safety. I know nothing about these things and was hoping the surveyor might have an opinion."

"Well, I do not know that my judgement on such matters is worth very much, but I will go tomorrow and look at it and give you my opinion. You will be at the Westons' dinner tomorrow evening, I think?"

"Yes, indeed!" Elton's face brightened immediately. "It is sure to be a delightful evening!"

"I only hope the weather will hold; Mr. Woodhouse will be extremely uneasy if it is very stormy."

"Ah, yes. Poor man. One almost wishes he might stay at home. Miss Woodhouse is always so busy ensuring his comfort—it must be a relief to her to leave him at Hartfield when she goes out."

Knightley could scarcely conceal the irritation in his voice as he said, "I assure you that Miss Woodhouse is never tired of her father's company, or happy to leave him behind."

"Well, perhaps. Certainly she never complains. But it must be a burden nonetheless. And there will come a day—not too long hence, I trust—when she will leave Hartfield for her own home, and I think she will discover then that she has been relieved of a great encumbrance."

Knightley did not trust himself to speak. He turned and walked to the hearth, picked up the poker, and made several vicious little stabs at the burning logs. The fire blazed up fiercely. *Arrogant, selfish, ignorant...wussock!* The thought that Elton was a clergyman was no check on his thoughts this time; it only increased his outrage.

"I suppose a substantial fire is an excellent thing in a library," said Elton conversationally. "Keeps the books from getting damp, I presume. I must remember that. One never knows when one might acquire a house with a library."

Knightley still had the poker in his hand, and the urge to use it on the vicar was almost overpowering. Reason mastered emotion, however, and he dropped the poker with a clatter, making Elton start and Madam Duval slink out from under the chair.

"Oh, you have a cat!" said Elton, coming close to her. "And a very fine specimen, too. I have heard that many aristocratic ladies keep them, and are very fond of them. Perhaps I ought to see if I can acquire one…Here puss, puss…"

Madam Duval looked with utter distain at the hand stretched out toward her.

"Does it have a name?" said Elton.

"Madam Duval," said Knightley.

"Indeed!" said Elton. He looked at the cat with respect. "Of a noble lineage, then, is she? Here, puss. Here, Madam."

The cat made no movement at all.

"Come here, puss." Elton moved to pick her up. Instantly the cat batted her paw and left Elton with four long, deep scratches on the back of his hand.

"Aaahh!" he cried, jumping back and flapping his hand as if he could shake off the smart.

Knightley had a great desire to laugh, but kept his face sober as he held out a handkerchief and Elton wrapped it around the injury.

"Rather wicked, isn't she?" said Elton.

"Oh yes," Knightley said. "These aristocratic cats are all very temperamental, you know. Ah, blood seeping through there, I see. Yes, very nasty scratch. Quite unfortunate. You ought to go home and get a proper dressing on it. If it has good treatment now there will be no need for you to wear a bandage tomorrow night to the Westons' dinner."

"Yes, very true. I ought to go and see to it—nothing worse than eating with a bandage on one's hand. I will see you tomorrow evening, then, Knightley. Good day."

The door shut behind him and Knightley dropped into his chair, his feelings divided between amusement and indignation. How presumptuous, how conceited the man was! He did not deserve to be in the same room with Emma, let alone marry her! Who could possibly think that Emma enjoyed getting away from her father, or that Mr. Woodhouse was a burden to be discarded? Absolutely insufferable! And, it appeared, Elton was determined to ask Emma for her hand—and soon, by the sound of it. Well, good. He could hardly wait for Elton to realize his own folly.

A meow at his feet told him that the cat was about to jump onto his lap, and he let her. "I must say, Madam, that you are an excellent judge of character," he told her. "I beg your pardon for underestimating your usefulness. And I forgive you the mouse on my bed."

The weather was so threatening on Christmas Eve that Knightley ordered horses from the Crown so that he could go to the Westons' dinner in his carriage. He was the first to arrive, and so was the sole auditor to the effusions of Weston, who, with all the enthusiasm of a newlywed, drew his attention to the greenery and ribbons his wife had so skilfully arranged around the drawing room for the festive season. It was not long, however, before Mr. Woodhouse and Isabella came and offered a diversion. Knightley helped Mr. Woodhouse to the seat nearest the fire.

"Thank you, my dear Mr. Knightley. Oh yes, my dear Miss Tay—Mrs. Weston, I am very well. But have you heard about Miss Smith? Such a melancholy thing! A bad cold and a sore throat. She became ill yesterday, in the evening, and I wanted her to stay the night at Hartfield. But she did so want to have Mrs. Goddard nurse her that she *would* go back to the school. And now she is miserably feverish and unwell. So Isabella and I came in the carriage without her (for she was to have gone in our carriage), and Mr. John Knightley and Emma are to follow—and I believe they are to bring Mr. Elton with them. If he had not come we would have needed but one carriage, for we would be only four together. You may be sure,

Mr. Knightley, I would not like to have put James and the horses to so much trouble on such a night as this if it could be avoided. But as it is, James can see his daughter, as he does whenever he comes here, you know, as his daughter is housemaid."

There was a little bustle at the door and Mrs. Weston turned from Mr. Woodhouse to greet the newcomers. Knightley was surprised to reflect that he had never noticed before how Emma could brighten a room simply by entering it. He watched as she greeted Mrs. Weston with genuine affection, and the sheer happiness on her face was a lovely sight. There was a kind of radiance about her that had nothing to do with mere beauty or fine clothes—Isabella was a handsome woman and her gown was more elaborate than Emma's, but she had not the same quality of brilliance as her younger sister. Elton plainly had eyes for no one else. He paid his respects to his host and hostess, and then attached himself to Emma. Knightley presumed that he was hovering near her until they should all be seated so that he could claim the chair nearest hers. Knightley noticed that his cuffs were as long as they could be, and one could hardly perceive that the back of his hand was faintly yellow—tinted with the salve he must be using instead of a court plaister.

John finished greeting the Westons and came over to his brother.

"Of all the exuberant companions I have ever known, Elton is unsurpassed."

"He does seem to be in rather lively spirits this evening."

"Oh, he has great hopes of us all being snowed up here at Randalls—for a week, I think he said. How Emma listens to him with any degree of composure is beyond my understanding. By the bye, I gave Emma a hint today about Elton's designs."

"And what did she say?"

"She assured me that I was quite mistaken, and that she and Elton were only very good friends."

"Naturally."

"I even told her that I thought her manner toward him was encouraging."

"And she did not welcome your advice?"

"No. Truth be told, she looked rather annoyed."

"Well, don't be cast down. Better men than you have tried and failed to persuade Emma that her judgement is fallible."

John chuckled. "I will not take it too much to heart. Elton will speak for himself before long, I wager, and then she will be undeceived."

"And humbled."

"That too." John looked at Emma and the expression on his face softened. "Poor girl," he murmured.

Weston's voice could be heard now, urging everyone to be seated, and the company obeyed. Elton attained his object: he sat down at Emma's side and talked to her continuously, effectively dividing her from the rest of the party.

"I do hope you have been enjoying your time in Surrey, Mrs. Knightley," said Weston.

"Oh, indeed I have," said Isabella. "It is delightful to be at Hartfield with Papa and Emma, of course, and such a pleasure to see all my old friends and acquaintances and hear all their news."

"Ah," said Mr. Weston. "What would meeting old friends be if they had no news? As it happens, *I* have a fresh piece of news for you about my son, Frank."

"I do hope he is well," said Isabella.

"He is exceedingly well, I thank you. I received a letter from him this very morning, announcing that he is coming at last. He proposes to be here about the second week of January—less than a fortnight from now. My son has never been able to come to Highbury, you know, though he has often wished to."

"What a wonderful occasion that will be!" said Isabella. "What a pity he could not come for Christmas."

"Yes, that would have been a great thing. However, it will not be long now until he is here."

John murmured an appropriate sentiment, and Knightley managed a polite nod, but could not feel any real eagerness. His suspicion that the Westons thought of Frank Churchill as a match for Emma had never been challenged by contradictory evidence, and he was tired of thinking about suitors for Emma. He looked over at Elton; he was talking to Emma with great energy and without any intermission. She was listening to him with every appearance of courtesy, but Knightley could see that her patience was being tested.

He was relieved for her sake when dinner was announced, and glad to see that Elton was seated near Mrs. Weston, at the other end of the table from Emma, who sat beside Mr. Weston. Knightley was across the table from Emma—not directly in front of her, but near enough to see and hear her. On one side of him was Mr. Woodhouse and on the other was Isabella, and between answering the questions of the one, reassuring all the anxieties of the other, and trying to follow the conversation of the pair across the table, he hardly had leisure to eat his excellent roast mutton.

"I am entirely of your opinion," Emma was saying. "If only Miss Smith and Mr. Frank Churchill were here, our party would be quite complete."

"He has been wanting to come to us ever since September," said Weston. "Every letter has been full of it; but he cannot command his own time. He has those to please who must be pleased, and who—between ourselves—are sometimes to be pleased only by a good many sacrifices. But now I have no doubt of seeing him here about the second week in January."

Weston was an eternal optimist, thought Knightley. He had been in no doubt of seeing his son "very shortly" ever since the end of September. Knightley wanted to catch Emma's eye and share his amusement with her, but she was too interested in the subject to notice him.

"What a very great pleasure it will be to you!" said Emma, her eyes sparkling. "And Mrs. Weston is so anxious to be acquainted with him that she must be almost as happy as yourself."

"George," said Isabella at his elbow, "How does William Larkins do? Is his health as good as ever?"

Knightley answered briefly, but was immediately importuned with another question, this time about Mrs. Hodges. When he could again listen to the conversation across the table, Emma was saying, "I am sorry there should be any thing like doubt in the case, but am disposed to side with you, Mr. Weston. If you think he will come, I shall think so too, for you know Enscombe."

Knightley was a little puzzled. Was Emma sincere in her declaration or was she merely being polite? She ought to know better than to depend on Weston's predictions of anything! The expression on her face showed nothing but genuine interest as she listened to Weston's explanation of the whims of Mrs. Churchill which kept dear Frank away from Highbury. But that expression must be due to good manners. She could not really be delighted over the visit of a dissipated young man who could not be bothered to visit his father—could she?

"Mr. Knightley," said Mr. Woodhouse, "What is your opinion of the caper sauce on the mutton? Do you not think it indigestible?" And by the time that issue had been settled, Emma and Weston had begun talking about the improvements planned for the gardens at Randalls.

When the ladies had withdrawn after dinner, John and Elton moved from the further end of the table to join the other men.

"I looked at that bridge today, Elton," said Knightley when the port had been distributed. "And I concur with the good people of Highbury: the crack in the bridge *is* worse."

Elton sighed. "Is it unsafe, then?"

"Not yet. But if will be soon if the crack continues to grow."

Elton made a wry face. "Then I shall have to prepare myself for another onslaught of complaints from everyone in the parish about the incompetence of workmen and the inconvenience of having to take the other road through Aston. As if I didn't hear enough grumbling about the river that Freeman is blocking up with his peat."

"Has William Cox been able to find out anything about laws preventing the fouling of rivers?" asked Knightley.

"I don't believe he has," said Weston, "But perhaps Mr. John Knightley could give us his opinion."

"My dear Mr. Weston," interjected Mr. Woodhouse, "You will not take it amiss, I hope, if I excuse myself to join the ladies?"

"By no means," said Mr. Weston. "The fire in the drawing room is much warmer, and the chairs are without doubt more comfortable."

"Thank you, Mr. Weston. I believe I had better have my cup of tea now—late hours do not agree with me. No, I thank you, Mr. Knightley, you need not accompany me—I would not take you away from your friends."

Mr. Woodhouse bowed and made his way out of the dining room, leaving the men to talk about parish business for another quarter of an hour, until Weston observed that this was not a meeting at the Crown, but a dinner party—and moreover it was Christmas Eve. "We ought to be able to put aside these matters for a few hours, at least," he said. "And Mr. John Knightley must find it all extremely dull."

"Not at all, sir," said John. "I have a keen interest in everything that relates to Donwell and Highbury. But as we have changed the topic, I may observe that wedlock seems to suit you very well. I don't know when I've seen you look so flourishing."

"Yes indeed, matrimony is splendid physic! Never felt better in my life."

"I am surprised," John went on, "that with such an example before them our two bachelors here have not been convinced to change their state as well."

Knightley scowled at John, who grinned impudently back at him.

"Oh, everyone knows that Knightley will be a bachelor to the end of time," said Elton dismissively. "On the other hand, I would like nothing better than to try marriage for myself."

"Ha!" said Weston. "Got a lady in mind already, I'll warrant. Well, what I say is, don't hesitate if your mind is made up. A fine, well-set-up young man like yourself need have no reason for delay. You'll amaze us all next week, I daresay, with an announcement. That would be a surprise for Highbury, now, wouldn't it?"

John nudged Knightley and murmured, "Nothing would surprise me more."

"What's that you say?" said Weston, turning his gaze from Elton's flushed and happy face to query John.

"I was merely agreeing with you, sir, that it *would* be a surprise," said John. "A great and lasting one, if I am any judge."

"Well, what do you say to rejoining the ladies?" said Weston, downing the last of his wine.

The men moved out of the dining room into the hall, and were about to enter the drawing room when John paused outside the door.

"I believe I will step outside for a moment and look at the weather," said John.

"By all means," said Weston, and followed Elton into the drawing room.

"How very droll Weston is," said John to Knightley, who had stayed behind in the hall with him. "He wants Elton to marry Emma, then?"

"No, I am quite sure he does not. His perception in the matter of other people's tender feelings is about the same as Emma's."

"Oh, that acute, is he? So he has no idea that Elton…Hmph. He merely wants everyone to be married—on principle, as it were. Well, he ought to have held his tongue."

"You introduced the subject."

"I don't think *everyone* ought to get married. Only you."

Knightley's patience gave out. The topic of matrimony had become intolerable, and he refused to banter with John about it any more.

"Enough," he said coldly and walked into the drawing room. The scene that met his eyes there was hardly likely to improve his temper: Elton was sitting on a sofa between Emma and Mrs. Weston, talking earnestly to Emma again. This time, however, there was no look of affable politeness—actual or assumed—on Emma's face. She looked nothing but astonished. Knightley turned away; once he would have been amused by the scene, but now it was merely painful. He moved to the table in the corner where coffee was being served, and accepted a steaming cup from the servant. His eyes wandered back to the group on the sofa; he could only see the back of Emma from where he was, but her posture was rigid and tense. Perhaps he ought to intervene. But would it really do any good to forestall the inevitable?

All at once, Emma got up from the sofa and walked over to the empty chair beside Isabella. It could mean only one thing: Emma meant to give Elton a set-down. But Elton looked perplexed, not dejected; Emma's reproof was quite lost on him. She was talking to Isabella now with an intensity that matched Elton's—a sign that she meant to ignore him for the rest of the evening. Knightley had little hope that such a hint would be understood by Elton, but at least now Emma's eyes were opened.

John came in then and said in a voice that all could hear, "Well! The ground is covered in snow, there is more snow falling fast, and the wind is blowing hard. This will prove a spirited beginning of your winter engagements, sir," he said, turning to Mr. Woodhouse, "—something new for your coachman and horses to be making their way through a storm of snow."

There was a moment of silence and then a volley of exclamations. Mr. Woodhouse's face showed his complete alarm, and Knightley muttered an imprecation against John for being so unfeeling. There was only one thing for it—check the weather himself. Otherwise there would be no hope of calming Mr. Woodhouse or anyone else.

He walked out, relieved to be alone and feeling that the cold air would clear his head. It took only a moment to discover that John had been exaggerating. The snow was not in the least deep, barely covering the ground in most places. He walked all the way out to the Highbury road and a little distance along it, and it was the same all the way along. There were a few flakes of snow drifting down from the sky, but he could see some stars between the clouds, and it was evident that there would be no more snow falling that night. The wind was blowing, but not strongly, and there was certainly nothing to fear in travelling home.

John could be the most exasperating man! It was one thing to needle his brother about marriage, but quite another to intentionally stir up the fears of his father-in-law, and Isabella, too. He suspected that his own bad humour had contributed to John's, but that did not excuse him. Altogether it had been a most aggravating evening and he would be very pleased to get home again.

To further allay any fears on the score of safety, he found the coachmen and asked them if they thought there was any cause for worry about the journey home. None at all, they said. He walked back into the drawing room—how very hot the room was!—and gave his report to the company. The relief on Isabella's face repaid him for his exertions, and the agitation of Mr. Woodhouse was greatly reduced. It did not vanish, however, and he asked Knightley several times if he was quite sure that there was not more snow piling up on the roads at that very moment. Knightley assured him that there was not, and Emma did her best to pacify her father, but Knightley knew that nothing would make him really tranquil as long as he remained at Randalls. He took a few steps behind Mr. Woodhouse's chair and beckoned Emma with a small movement of his head.

She came over to him, and he said quietly, "Your father will not be easy; why do not you go?"

She nodded and matched his quiet tone as she said, "I am ready, if the others are."

"Shall I ring the bell?"

"Yes, do."

It was the shortest conversation he had had all evening, but it soothed his irritated feelings remarkably. For a moment it was as if he and Emma were the only adults present—the only ones with sense and compassion, who knew what ought to be done and were able to do it without hesitation. The others were like children, who lacked either the wit or the confidence to do what they ought.

It was only a few minutes until the carriages came, and Knightley and Weston escorted Mr. Woodhouse to his.

"Oh, there is indeed snow!" exclaimed Mr. Woodhouse. "And the night is fearfully dark! I am afraid we shall have a very bad drive. Poor Isabella will not like it. And poor Emma will be in the carriage behind. I do not know what we had best do—we must keep as much together as we can. Where is the coachman? James! Ah, James, you must go very slow and wait for the other carriage. Very slow. And wait for the other carriage. Yes. Thank you, Mr. Weston. Yes, the blanket is here; thank you, Mr. Knightley."

John had conducted Isabella to the carriage, and when she was safely inside, he got in after her and the door was shut. Knightley and Weston were going back into the house when they passed Elton escorting Emma to her carriage. It took a few seconds for Knightley to realize what had happened. John ought not to be with Isabella and Mr. Woodhouse; he ought to be with Emma and Elton.

Oh mercy, thought Knightley. *Emma and Elton shut up together all the way back to the vicarage. Elton will probably think this is the perfect opportunity…*He sighed. *Poor Emma.*

14

Knightley awoke to the same thoughts he had closed his eyes against the night before. He lay in bed, staring at the canopy above him, while his thoughts wandered. How had Emma fared on the carriage ride home? Presumably, Elton had offered and she had refused, and therefore he ought to feel relief that this affair was over. Most probably, also, Emma now realized her own error—Elton was *not* attracted to Harriet, as Knightley had told her, and she *was* Elton's object, as John had warned her. She must also now be aware of her own conceit. And he knew Emma: where she knew she was in the wrong, she would endeavour to change. Elton's unsuccessful proposal would bring many good things to Emma—and to Elton as well, if he would condescend to profit by it. Really, he should be full of relief and thanks.

Instead, he was uneasy. Whatever the scene had been, it must have been supremely uncomfortable for Emma. Humility was not a virtue that sat easily with her. Good for her it might be to be caught out in her error, but the pain and embarrassment that must be hers awakened all his compassion. And then a new doubt assailed him: what if Elton had seen Emma's displeasure and bided his time in making his proposals? *Had* he taken Emma's hint? Or had he declared himself?

He threw off the bedclothes and went over to the window, looking out at a landscape that had its own snowy blanket. For the moment, the world was fresh and peaceful; nothing could be more appropriate for Christmas morning. Peace… He felt greatly in need of some peace of mind. The evening before had been full of turmoil, though now that he came to consider it, he was not entirely sure why. Of course Elton was an idiot and a nuisance, but that was nothing new. Neither were John's hints about marriage. He hadn't been vexed when he had arrived at Randalls, so what was it that had turned the evening sour?

The sound of the door being opened ended his musing, and he turned to greet his butler.

"Good morning, sir," said Baxter. "Permit me to wish you a happy Christmas."

"Thank you, Baxter, and you have my wishes for the same."

"I thank you, sir. May I propose the grey coat for this morning? I fear the inclement weather will render the church extremely frigid."

"Yes, I will have the grey. However, I will return here after church to change it for a lighter one before I go to Hartfield—there will be no need to be dressed warmly there."

The church *was* very cold; poor Spencer could be seen shivering as he read out the lesson. Knightley suspected that his was not the only mind not fixed on the text, but he was distracted by more than just the temperature. His thoughts were at Hartfield, and he spent most of the service wondering what Emma's state of mind might be, and whether John's temper was restored. If Emma had been troubled by the events of last evening, John being out of humour would distress her still more. He must be ready to assist in keeping harmony between John and the rest of them, and to show Emma by quiet friendliness that, in spite of unpleasant scenes, all was well.

"O God, who art the author of peace and lover of concord," he found himself saying with the rest of the congregation, and started at the relevance of the words. *Author of peace and lover of concord*...peace and concord...the very things he hoped to restore at Hartfield. It might well take divine assistance to accomplish that.

His fears were a little relieved by Emma's greeting him with a smile, and although she was rather more quiet than usual, she did not look anxious or unduly shaken. She busied herself with the children, reading to them and keeping them occupied with quiet play while they were in the same room as their grandfather. John, too, was remarkably good-humoured and talked to Mr. Woodhouse for a full half-hour without once betraying any emotion but kindly sympathy, and what is more, without manoeuvring to get Knightley to take his place. Knightley settled himself near Emma and entertained his toddler namesake with a spinning top. At length Isabella joined her father, and John excused himself from the fireside to talk to his brother.

"Well, George, you seem to have recovered from your ill humour last evening."

"I was going to say the same to you."

"Quite true. The wind must have carried away my bad temper during the night; I was a perfect lamb when I woke this morning."

Knightley laughed. "I take it you bleated your apologies to all and sundry this morning?"

John grimaced. "Not exactly. Really, I ought not to have gone at all—I so dislike that sort of evening. I would have done better to feign a headache. But I never thought you had an aversion to such gatherings. I don't know when I've seen you so out of sorts."

"It must have been the company we were forced to keep."

"Ah. Elton, you mean."

"I suppose. And how did Emma—that is, did Elton—"

"I have no idea. She seemed…preoccupied when she first arrived home, but I only saw her for a few moments. And she would have said nothing, of course, even if—"

"Of course."

"John," said Isabella, coming over to them, "John and Henry are asking when they may play the bullet pudding game."

"I think we may as well do it now."

"Bullet pudding?" said Knightley. "At Hartfield?"

John smiled. "In the nursery, dear brother. I would not subject Mr. Woodhouse to such a boisterous amusement."

"Good. For a moment I thought the wind in the night must have carried away your good sense as well as your ill temper."

So John, Knightley and Emma brought the three older children up to the nursery and watched them play. A bullet was balanced on a cone of flour, and each child took turns cutting away slices of the flour. The object was to keep the bullet in place, but when it fell, the one whose cut had dislodged it had to pick up the bullet with their teeth, thus getting well powdered. When the children had played long enough that each was dusted with white, they clamoured for their elders to have a game.

John rolled his eyes and looked at Knightley, who shrugged. Emma laughed.

"And who do you think will lose?" she asked the children.

"Papa! Papa!" shouted Henry and John, and Bella giggled.

"You have so little confidence in me?" said John, taking off his coat and rolling up his sleeves. "You think Aunt Emma and Uncle Knightley will get the better of me? Well, we shall see about that!"

One of the nursemaids gathered up the flour and put it back into the cone mould.

"Do you not think you should wear an apron of some sort to protect your dress?" said John to Emma as the mould was inverted on the table and lifted away to reveal a perfectly smooth cone of flour.

"I do not intend to let the bullet fall," said Emma. "But I can get *you* an apron."

"I won't need it. George might."

Emma turned mischievous eyes to Knightley. "Shall I fetch one for you? I have a very pretty one..."

The children laughed.

"Thank you, no. I prefer to keep whatever dignity I have."

"Very well, then," said John. "Bullet ready? There, all arranged. Ladies first, Emma."

Emma took up the knife and cut away some of the flour without hesitation, and handed it to John who did the same. Knightley did pause when it was his turn—the others had changes of clothes at Hartfield, but he did not.

"Worried, Mr. Knightley?" said Emma. He looked up and saw the challenge in her eye.

"Never," he answered. "'Courage mounteth with occasion.'" He took the knife and with a show of bravado, made a cut in the flour. The bullet stayed at the top of the cone.

"Pope is singularly inspiring," said Emma.

"Not at all," said Knightley dryly.

"Shakespeare, dear sister, Shakespeare," murmured John.

"Oh! I do beg his pardon," said Emma, cutting away another portion and smiling when the bullet did not move.

"Oh Emma," said John, "That was 'the most unkindest cut of all.' How is anyone to carve any more without the whole thing toppling? Have no fear, however; I see the place which may be attacked without consequence." He scrutinized the cone and put the knife to the flour as if he were a great surgeon. "No one but such a master as I am could possibly—"

But at that moment the cone collapsed, and the bullet was buried in a mound of flour. The children shrieked and clapped their hands with delight and the adults in the room laughed.

Emma grinned and said "Pride goeth before—"

"I know, I know," interrupted John and sighed. "I had better get this over with. I shall 'go down to the vile dust' and get myself powdered white with it."

"'Unwept, unhonoured and unsung?'" suggested Knightley.

"No doubt," said John, and proceeded to gratify the very ungenteel desires of his children (and of his near relations) by getting himself thoroughly covered with flour.

The next day, a Sunday, followed the exact pattern of the day before it: another morning with snow on the ground, another frozen hour in church, another afternoon at Hartfield. He spent the time there observing Emma closely to see if by manner or by word she would betray what had happened between herself and Elton on Christmas Eve, but she continued to be subdued yet not unhappy and made him no wiser than he was before. John continued to be agreeable, which was fortunate as the inclement weather would force the Knightleys to stay on at Hartfield for another day or two.

Knightley had formed the habit of calling on Dr. Hughes every Monday, and as he set off for the rectory the next day, he wondered if the invalid would be interested in a game of chess. He wanted something to take his mind off that infernal question of how things stood between Emma and Elton. Was the whole business at an end? Or would it die a yet more lingering death?

He was surprised to see Elton himself coming away from the rectory as he approached it.

"Good afternoon, Knightley," said Elton as he came within speaking distance. "I was just coming to tell you that I won't be at the parish meeting this week—I am away to Bath on Thursday."

"Bath? On Thursday? I hope you have not had any distressing news which requires your leaving Surrey with such haste."

"No, nothing like that. I have friends who have been urging me to visit them for some time, and I mustn't keep them waiting any longer." He did not look particularly happy *or* despondent; in fact, he rather had an air of studied carelessness. Certainly there was something artificial in his bearing. And what a peculiar time of year to suddenly hare off with such an unconvincing excuse!

"I'm afraid you will find Bath very quiet at this time of year," said Knightley.

"Oh," said Elton, moving his foot restlessly, "I won't mind the quiet. A change of scene…that is, I am extremely anxious to see my friends, and *they* remain the same, no matter what the weather."

So it appeared that he *had* spoken and been refused and was now going away to nurse his injured dignity.

"How long will you be staying?"

"That is not yet decided. Several weeks, I daresay. I've just been to Dr. Hughes, asking if he can loan Spencer to the church in Highbury while I am away. He has agreed, and therefore I am free to go."

"That was very generous of him."

"Oh!" said Elton, with a hint of surprise in his tone, "Yes, I suppose it was. Well, I will excuse myself if I may. I have several letters of farewell to write."

"Will you be calling at Hartfield this afternoon? I may see you there."

"No, I will not." The sharpness of Elton's tone cleared away any remaining doubts about what had happened on that carriage ride.

"Very well, then," said Knightley, feeling a burden lifted. "I wish you a safe and happy journey."

"Thank you," said Elton briefly, and the men bowed and parted.

On Tuesday Knightley went to visit the Bates', bringing a mince pie. He was forced to stay and eat some of it, of course, and was given a full treatise by Miss Bates on the minutiae of the Christmas festivities at Mrs. Goddard's school. He stayed above an hour and was returning to Donwell when he passed Old Maggie, Spencer's housekeeper, shuffling along the road with a basket on her arm. She curtseyed as she drew near, and he said loudly, "How are you this afternoon, Maggie?"

"Quite cold, sir," she said in strident tones, "And rather windy."

He was a little taken aback by this personal disclosure, but then realized that she was talking of the weather.

"Yes, it is," he said, raising his voice. "I think it may even be colder than yesterday...the snow from last night is not yet completely gone."

"Yes, Mr. Knightley, 'e would be most 'appy to see you. If you go on to the house now, sir, I'll be back to fix the tea afore long."

"I was just going home *to the Abbey,*" he said at full volume. "I was not intending to call on Mr. Spencer today."

Maggie beamed and nodded. ""E'll be ever so pleased you called, sir. Tell 'im I'll be there very shortly."

Knightley sighed and yielded. "Thank you," he said, smiling faintly. "I believe there is nothing I would like better than a short visit with Mr. Spencer."

It was a curious thing, he thought as he continued down the road to the cottage, that everyone continued to talk in their loudest voices to Old Maggie when clearly it made not the slightest difference whether one whispered or shouted.

Spencer opened the door to his knock, and looked relieved when he saw who it was.

"Good afternoon, Mr. Knightley. Please, do come in. May I get you some refreshment? Maggie is out at the moment, but I can make tea..."

"No, I thank you, not just now. I spoke to Maggie a moment ago on the road. We were a little at cross purposes, I fancy, and she was convinced that I intended to call here."

Spencer smiled. "And so you came to call rather than disappoint her. Dear Maggie. I cannot tell you how often I have done something I had not anticipated doing because it was too much trouble to explain that she was mistaken."

"At least I am in good company, then. At any rate, she said to tell you she would be here soon to make some tea."

"I hope you were not completely disinclined to see me."

"Not at all. I ought to have been here sooner, but lately my time has been taken up with my brother's visit."

"Oh, yes. Pray be seated. Is your brother's family still at Hartfield?"

"They are. They had planned to leave yesterday, but the snow hindered them. If the weather is fair tomorrow, they will leave in the afternoon."

"I trust the visit has been a pleasant one."

"Yes, quite like old times. No one else understands Donwell like John does, of course, and I like to have his opinion on things there. He still teases me mercilessly, but I suppose all younger brothers do that. And I know that Miss Woodhouse and her father greatly enjoy having all the family there. They would not think Christmas a time of much cheer unless the Knightleys were there to share it—nor I. I have spent a good part of nearly every day with the family at either Donwell or Hartfield. I will miss them when they go."

"You are fortunate in having them so near—you must see them several times every year."

"Yes, London is a great deal closer than Norfolk. Have you any plans to return there for a visit?"

"Not for several months, at least."

"No, I suppose you will be too busy for that—especially in light of your new extra duties in Highbury."

"Dr. Hughes has told you?"

"I heard it first from Elton."

"I see. Yes, I will be busier than usual for the next few weeks."

"You look as if you do not relish the added work, and I'm sure no one could blame you. I fear Elton thought little of the inconvenience it would be to you."

"Oh, I am not so much inconvenienced. I will conduct both services on Sundays, of course, but there will not be many extra duties above that. If I seem unhappy it is probably because ... do you remember my telling you that I have a dread of meeting new people?"

"I do."

"Highbury is full of people that I do not know," Spencer said, looking into the fire. "The thought of standing at the pulpit in

Highbury church with that sea of strange faces looking back at me ... And there is to be a new tenant, you know, in the old Mefford farm, and William Larkins thought the family might move in today, in spite of the bad weather. In fact, when I heard your knock at the door I thought you were William Larkins coming to tell me they had arrived. I was gathering up my courage to greet them and ask if I might be of service." He looked up at Knightley with a wry smile. "I must appear very foolish to you—such irrational fears."

"Not at all, I assure you. I am prey to unreasonable fears myself."

"I suppose you must have some fears—everyone does—though I must say you appear as imperturbable as a piece of granite. But I can't believe that there is any time when you are afraid of people."

"You are mistaken in thinking so. Perhaps there are not many scenes which make me nervous—my position has accustomed me to public life—however I do have a particular dislike of any sort of performance. Fortunately, I am not a young lady that would be expected to entertain the assembled company of an evening, and I daresay hardly anyone knows how much I should dislike a group of people watching me exhibit."

"You don't go in much for display, do you?" said Spencer thoughtfully.

"No. Our family has never been ostentatious. I do not know whether it has been due to modesty or to laziness in following the fashions of the hour, but however it has come about, the Knightleys of Donwell Abby are a bit too ordinary for society's elite."

"And I am exceedingly grateful that neither you nor your estate have grand pretensions. I could never feel at home in a place that flaunted its affluence. But have you ever displayed a talent in public? If it is merely your *family's* habit to refrain from performing in front of others and you have never done it yourself, perhaps you would not find it nearly as disagreeable as you think."

It was Knightley's turn to look into the fire. "I have done it," he said slowly, "though it was a long time ago." He took a deep breath and glanced at Spencer, whose face was alight with interest. "When I was ten years old, a dancing master came to Highbury—it was a more populous place in my youth than it is now—and my father elected to have me attend his school rather than have private lessons at home. At first I had no aversion whatever to learning alongside the twenty-odd other children, but soon I began to hate it. The dancing master was a bit of a sycophant and he wanted to be on the good side of any rich and important people, which meant that he was particularly attentive to me. He told everyone to 'watch Master George' every time there was a new pattern to learn, and I was always chosen to demonstrate the correct steps to children who were not doing them properly. I knew perfectly well why I was made much of, and such praise was hardly gratifying. There was no telling if I was really any good or not, and the thought that perhaps they all knew me to be a poor dancer even as they politely applauded my performance vexed me. I loathe flattery. All the crowd was watching me—judging me—and there was no way for me to ever determine what their true judgement was. The whole business made me detest dancing."

Spencer nodded. "I'm certain I should feel the same. And how did you overcome your dislike?"

"I never did. I still do not like to dance. The thought of standing up at a ball, for example, with the eyes of all the company on me as the music begins to play twists my stomach into knots."

"But surely not everyone would have their eyes on you," said Spencer reasonably. "The young flirting couples, for example, might be more inclined to look at each other."

"I know it. And the chances that anyone would take such an opportunity to flatter me on my dancing abilities are very remote. I told you that it was an unreasonable fear. It is so unreasonable that I am sure no one has guessed it. When I do not take the very few opportunities for dancing presented to me everyone simply assumes I do not like the music or the motion of the dance."

"Well, they will not learn the truth from me unless I find myself in need of a secret with which to blackmail you," said Spencer with a smile. "But what will you do if there is ever a young lady that you are anxious to please and who wants you to dance?"

"Faint, most likely," said Knightley.

Spencer laughed. "The very last thing anyone would expect you to do! But I do not think you would fall prey to such an extremity. Holy Writ tells us that 'perfect love casteth out fear,' you know. Under the influence of a great love you may find the courage to dance after all."

"Well," said Knightley, chuckling, "You have given me the perfect test by which to judge any future infatuations; if I am willing to dance in public for her sake, it must be true love."

15

For a week Knightley basked in the restoration of comfortable circumstances: Elton undeceived and gone, Emma undeceived and chastened, and John back in London where he could not tease except by letter. The daily visits to Hartfield were once again pleasant and comfortable, even if Harriet was very much there. Indeed, her presence at Hartfield was evidence that Emma was endeavouring to make amends with her friend by showing her great attention. The long-neglected *On the Improvement of the Mind* was taken out again, and the bookmark moved a little forward as a result.

"I do not think, Mr. Knightley, that Mr. Elton was very wise in going to Bath at this time of year, or so suddenly," said Mr. Woodhouse one day when Harriet was not at Hartfield and Knightley had been persuaded to take tea with them in her absence. "He may very well catch a chill during this cold weather. And going about among strangers he may be exposed to infection. The whole excursion is most imprudent."

Knightley agreed politely, just as he had on each of the other seventeen occasions that Mr. Woodhouse had expressed these thoughts in the last few days. He looked over at Emma, who was quietly smiling over her embroidery. She radiated the natural grace that was indicative of the poise she seemed to have in any situation. Indeed, considering the ordeal she had recently experienced, her behaviour was the model of dignity when contrasted with Elton's. Emma had responded very well to the humiliating affair. She had swallowed her dose of mortification, learnt from her mistake, and begun to atone for her misguided actions. Elton, on the other hand, had merely become embarrassed and angry and then run away.

"Oh! Mrs. Weston was here this morning, Mr. Knightley," said Emma, turning the subject firmly away from Elton. "She left her compliments for you."

"Thank you. And how do the Westons do?"

"As well as might be expected, considering their disappointment."

"Disappointment?"

"Oh, have you not heard? Mr. Frank Churchill will not be coming next week after all; his aunt and uncle cannot spare him."

"Indeed?" said Knightley, with a dim sense that he ought to feel sorry on behalf of the Westons but not really feeling unhappy at all.

"Yes, and it is too provoking!" said Emma warmly. "Here we have for all these months been anticipating an addition to our confined society—someone new to look at instead of the same dull procession of faces—and now we must wait some more. It would have been as good as a holiday to Highbury to have a new young man about. I am quite out of patience with the Churchills—they could let him come if they would, I am sure."

Emma's outburst gave Knightley pause. She had appeared fascinated by this subject once before, at the Westons' dinner, though at the time he had put it down to simple politeness. Whatever the Westons might imagine with regard to Frank Churchill and Emma, he had been sure that Emma was in no danger of being captivated by such a trivial, frivolous young man. For all that she had been mistaken in Elton's nature, she generally recognized an honourable character; and she, more than most people, took a firm view of what was due to a father. She could not possibly be captivated by the mere thought of a man like Frank Churchill. But this enthusiasm for the topic when there was no one else to hear her (for even Mr. Woodhouse had begun to nod) denoted some genuine interest. Perhaps in her desire for something new she had forgotten this imperfection of Mr. Churchill's. As her plans for Elton to wed Harriet had come to nothing, she must feel that life was very dull and be eager for any novelty. It was but a temporary lapse, of course.

When reminded of what she knew already, her interest in Frank Churchill would disappear.

"The Churchills are very likely in fault, but I dare say he might come if he would," said Knightley.

"I do not know why you should say so. He wishes exceedingly to come; but his uncle and aunt will not spare him."

"I cannot believe that he has not the power of coming, if he made a point of it. It is too unlikely for me to believe it without proof."

"How odd you are! What has Mr. Frank Churchill done to make you suppose him such an unnatural creature?"

And so Knightley explained why Mr. Frank Churchill could not possibly be blameless in staying away from Randalls, and why he gave every indication of being proud, luxurious and selfish. It was not long before the conversation began to have a familiar feel to it; once again he was asserting things that were clear as day, and Emma was wilfully closing her eyes to those facts. Back and forth they went, Knightley giving sound reasons for his opinions, and Emma stubbornly arguing with every one of them. She made excuse after excuse for Churchill's negligence, and it was the more aggravating because he would have thought she was the last person to make light of such errors.

"We shall never agree about him," said Emma after ten minutes of combat, "but that is nothing extraordinary."

Nothing extraordinary at all, thought Knightley. *I have only to open my mouth to be sure that you will contradict whatever I say.*

"I have not the least idea of his being a weak young man," she went on. "I feel sure that he is not. Mr. Weston would not be blind to folly, though in his own son. But he is very likely to have a more yielding, complying, mild disposition than would suit your notions of man's perfection. I dare say he has; and though it may cut him off from some advantages, it will secure him many others."

The image Emma's words conjured up—that of a simpering, weak-minded fop—was so very much at odds with his notion of man's perfection that he responded with more acerbity than he was wont.

"Yes, all the advantages of sitting still when he ought to move, and of leading a life of mere idle pleasure, and fancying himself extremely expert in finding excuses for it. He can sit down and write a fine flourishing letter, full of professions and falsehoods, and persuade himself that he has hit upon the very best method in the world of preserving peace at home and preventing his father's having any right to complain. His letters disgust me."

He could see from Emma's face that she was a little taken aback by his harsh words. He did not repent them, however. She had been wrong before and suffered humiliation; if he could keep her from doing the same again, he would.

"Your feelings are singular," said Emma, recovering. "They seem to satisfy everybody else."

"I suspect they do not satisfy Mrs. Weston," said Knightley, hoping that the mention of her dear friend would aid him in bringing Emma to reason. "They hardly can satisfy a woman of her good sense and quick feelings, standing in a mother's place, but without a mother's affection to blind her. It is on her account that attention to Randalls is doubly due, and she must doubly feel the omission. Had she been a person of consequence herself, he would have come, I dare say, and it would not have signified whether he did or no. Can you think your friend behindhand in these sort of considerations? Do you suppose she does not often say all this to herself? No, Emma, your amiable young man can be amiable only in French, not in English. He may be very 'amiable', have very good manners and be very agreeable, but he can have no English delicacy towards the feelings of other people—nothing really amiable about him."

"You seem determined to think ill of him," said Emma, reverting, as usual, to a change of subject when she could not refute his point.

"Me! Not at all. I do not want to think ill of him. I should be as ready to acknowledge his merits as any other man; but I hear of none, except what are merely personal—that he is well grown and good-looking, with smooth, plausible manners."

"Well, if he have nothing else to recommend him," said Emma, smiling, "he will be a treasure at Highbury. We do not often look upon fine young men, well-bred and agreeable. We must not be nice and ask for all the virtues into the bargain. Cannot you imagine, Mr. Knightley, what a *sensation* his coming will produce? There will be but one subject throughout the parishes of Donwell and Highbury; but one interest—one object of curiosity; it will be all Mr. Frank Churchill. We shall think and speak of nobody else."

The idea of, say, Mrs. Hodges thinking and speaking of nothing but Frank Churchill as she went about her duties made him smile in spite of his vexation. Such an exaggeration tempted him to retort in kind, but he stopped himself. It was better to be the voice of reason in this dispute.

"You will excuse my being so much overpowered," he said. "If I find him conversable, I shall be glad of his acquaintance; but if he is only a chattering coxcomb, he will not occupy much of my time or thoughts."

"My idea of him," said Emma, ignoring this bit of good sense, "is that he can adapt his conversation to the taste of everybody, and has the power as well as the wish of being universally agreeable. To you, he will talk of farming; to me, of drawing or music; and so on to everybody, having that general information on all subjects which will enable him to follow the lead, or take the lead, just as propriety may require, and to speak extremely well on each. That is my idea of him."

Good heavens! thought Knightley. She was absolutely *determined* to admire this fellow. Without ever having laid eyes on him she had decided his personality, his talents and his manners! *Her* idea of him, indeed!

"And mine," he said in a tone that sounded less reasonable than he liked, "is that if he turn out any thing like it, he will be the most insufferable fellow breathing! What! At three-and-twenty to be the king of his company—the great man—the practised politician—who is to read everybody's character, and make everybody's talents conduce to the display of his own superiority! To be dispensing his flatteries around, that he may make all appear like fools compared with himself! My dear Emma, your own good sense could not endure such a puppy when it came to the point."

"I will say no more about him. You turn everything to evil," said Emma, picking up the embroidery that she had laid aside when the argument began. "We are both prejudiced: you against, I for him. And we have no chance of agreeing till he is really here."

"Prejudiced!" *Of all the ridiculous accusations!* "I am not prejudiced."

"But I am very much, and without being at all ashamed of it. My love for Mr. and Mrs. Weston gives me a decided prejudice in his favour."

Prejudiced! thought Knightley, still fuming at the word. *She imagines that I spend all my time thinking up malicious slanders against the man!*

"He is a person I never think of from one month's end to another," he said, irritated beyond caring what his tone conveyed.

Emma looked at him for a moment in surprise and then turned her attention to her needle. "Well then, let us talk of something else. Has William Larkins returned to Donwell since his Christmas visit?"

Knightley took a deep breath and willed himself to put aside his annoyance and answer calmly.

"Yes, he has. He came back from his sister's house with such evident relief that he was almost cheerful. I am to meet with him this afternoon—in an hour, to be exact—to discuss the winter planting of vegetables in the hot-beds at the Abbey."

"And your new tenants have come?"

"Yes. The farmer presented himself at the Abbey yesterday. He seems a decent fellow—earnest and dedicated. Not much of a sense of humour, though, from what I could see."

"Rather like William Larkins himself, then."

"I suppose so, except that he is twenty years younger, and I doubt that he is quite as full of amusing information."

William Larkins came to the Abbey and left again an hour later, having received his instructions about what should be sown in the hot-beds and having imparted the news ("I think you should know, Mr. Knightley…") that Robert Martin's best ram was injured and not likely to live, that the maid at Starling Farm was engaged to a labourer from Langham, and that the little boy living with his widowed mother at the Foote farm was blind.

It was this last bit of information that Knightley sat musing on as he was once again alone in his library with Madam Duval purring contentedly on his lap. He remembered once, years ago, that there had been a child in Highbury that was subject to fits, and the family had been almost shunned by the parish in consequence. But the child had died and the family moved away and no one seemed to remember it anymore. He hoped Donwell would not be too disturbed by the presence of this sightless child in their midst. It took so little to unsettle people. Look what the thought of Frank Churchill's advent was doing to even such a generally steady female as Emma. She was more than steady; she was clever—the cleverest woman he knew, in fact—and she had firm principles and a good heart. And with those characteristics, her view of the young man was completely unaccountable. No one could doubt Emma's devotion to her own father; she showed him unceasing kindness and consideration, even though he could be a very tedious companion. How then could she treat so lightly Churchill's indifference to Weston, a man who was by no means a tedious companion, and who, if not due a visit before now, was certainly owed one on the occasion of his marriage? Knightley could not understand it.

She could not possibly share the unspoken sentiments of the Westons and wish to marry the man. Could she? His brow furrowed as he considered the idea. Suppose Churchill was both good looking and a smooth talker? With her scant knowledge of the world she just might be taken in. In his mind's eye he could see a dandified fop (ludicrously dressed in the fashion of twenty years ago) prancing up to Emma and uttering flattering nonsense, and Emma (no doubt taken in by the show of worldly sophistication) smiling graciously and allowing his attentions. No, no, that would never be. The prancing alone would make her laugh. Ah, but what if he walked *without* prancing—say he had an ordinary, manly gait. The apparition in his mind changed accordingly to one which strode purposefully up to Emma and said his piece with insinuating cleverness (still, however, dressed like a macaroni). Emma might be in some danger from a fellow like that.

The cat suddenly leapt off his lap and huddled under the chair as Baxter came into the library and said, "Mr. Spencer to see you, sir. Are you at leisure?"

"By all means, Baxter, send him in. How do you do, Spencer? Come and sit near the fire. The snow is gone, but the wind is still biting; I know, for I was out in it today."

"Thank you, Mr. Knightley. Yes, perhaps I will take a little something to drive away the chill. Thank you."

Spencer took the glass that was offered him and sat down in the chair that Knightley indicated. "I suppose you haven't heard the latest gossip around Donwell."

"If it concerns anyone connected with Randalls then I am already well-informed."

"The Westons? No, it has nothing to do with them. No, it is concerning Mrs. Catherwood."

"Mrs. Catherwood," repeated Knightley, searching his memory for anyone by that name.

"She is the widowed sister of Edward Foote, your new tenant," supplied Spencer.

"Ah, yes. I had not heard her name before."

"I passed Mrs. Catherwood and her son on the road today and stopped to say a few words of greeting to them. I went down on one knee to talk to the little boy, as one does with children, you know, and I put out my hand for him to shake, and he ignored it. I noticed then that he was looking *toward* me, but not *at* me."

"He is blind," said Knightley.

"You know, then?"

"William Larkins told me a half-hour ago."

"Yes, of course," said Spencer with a half-smile. "I saw him coming away from the Abbey—I ought to have guessed that he would have told you."

"I am quite sure the whole parish is aware of the fact by this time. I hope there will not be any trouble about it."

"Trouble?"

"You know the superstitious ideas that fester in the country. Some people think that any malady is a visitation of judgement on the sufferer. I only hope that Mrs. Catherwood may not suffer any harassment from pious simpletons. "

Spencer looked startled. "I confess I had not thought of that. I was only struck by the difficulty of Mrs. Catherwood's situation—to bring up a fatherless boy is a difficult thing for any woman, but when the boy is blind as well! His prospects must be very bleak."

"Yes, they must. You shame me, Spencer. I was so mindful of my own affairs that I gave the situation no more thought than to hope it would not cause uneasiness in the parish."

"Could it really upset the populace to any extent?"

"I think it could. If folk really think that the boy or his mother have done something so wicked that they merit divine retribution..."

"But that is absurd! Of all the mystical nonsense— Pious simpletons, you called them? Simpletons, yes, but *pious*... Humph! If they were truly devout they would remember 'neither hath this man sinned, nor his parents'—that was about the man born blind, remember. I wish someone might broach the subject with me. I'd give them a lecture they'd not soon forget!"

Knightley had never seen Spencer speak so forcefully. He'd not imagined that the curate could ever be angry; it seemed too far outside his nature. But there were depths in him, evidently, that had been hidden heretofore.

"Well," said Knightley, "A sermon or two on the topic may go a long way in influencing the general opinion. If you preached with *that* look on your face, you may be sure the parish would take notice!"

"Whether they take notice or not, they shall certainly hear the truth on this matter. And surely if you undertook to speak to any disruptive troublemakers, your arguments on the subject would convince them of their error. No one would consider disputing *your* judgement."

Knightley gave a short laugh. "My judgement is not so universally esteemed as you think. I was told very lately, after a debate that lasted twenty minutes, that I am quite prejudiced and no judge of anyone else's situation. So you see, I have little faith in my persuasive powers."

Spencer sat up straight in his chair. "Who on earth had the effrontery to say such a thing to you?"

"Oh, a lady of my acquaintance—a connection of my family's."

"What an extraordinary thing to say to a gentleman."

"Well, she was provoked, and, I think, rather attached to the subject of our debate."

"I see. Something to do with tender feelings?"

"I hope it has not gone quite as far as that. But I fear she is in some danger of being captivated by a silly, worthless young man."

"Oh, that sort. Good looking, too, I suppose."

"Well, he has that reputation, but as our description of him rests solely on the authority of his relatives, we cannot be certain."

"Have you not met the young man in question, then?"

"Well, no. But one can make a fair estimation of his character from the fragments of news that one hears of him—forever at some watering place or dancing attendance on rich relatives—and from his lack of attention to his real duties."

"Perhaps he is not so bad as you think him. Charity 'hopeth all things', you know. One may get hold of quite a false notion about a person, and then everything one hears about him only serves to make the impression stronger. But with a further knowledge of his circumstances some of his behaviour may be defended."

"You take the young lady's side, I see."

"I did not mean to. But I have suffered before now under the preconceived ideas of others, and it pains me to see the same injustice being done to another. Perhaps the lady can distinguish in him something good that you cannot perceive, but which will become clear if you meet him yourself."

Knightley snorted. "She has not met him, either! Which is why her seeming attachment to him is so strange."

"Well, women *have* been known to fall in love with men by reputation alone. Izaak Walton, you know, wrote that George Herbert's wife fell in love with him before she had even seen him; her father's description of the man was enough for her. And by all accounts they had a happy marriage."

Knightley found very little comfort in this anecdote.

"At any rate," Spencer went on, "I do think you ought to reserve judgement until the man actually appears. You may be surprised to find him, if not perfect, at least estimable. Then you could be easy whether the lady was in love with him or not."

"That would be worse," said Knightley, frowning. "Then there would be nothing to stop her marrying him."

Spencer had been on the point of taking a sip of his drink, but at Knightley's words he lowered the glass and stared at him in surprise. "Then—" He stopped abruptly.

"Yes?"

Spencer shook his head. "Never mind. I had almost forgotten what I came to see you about, and I ought to ask you now before it slips my mind again. Can anything be done for the little Catherwood boy?"

"About his eyesight? I doubt it, but you might ask a medical man what his opinion is."

"No, I meant is there anything we might do for the boy's prospects? Some sort of trade or craft that he might be taught so that he can support himself when he is grown?"

"Oh! Well, he might do something in the literary way, I suppose, following in the footsteps of Homer and Milton."

"That is possible, of course, if he is gifted with words. But if he is not?"

"A musician? That has been the traditional trade of many blind people."

"That is a good thought. Perhaps when he is a little older I will see what can be done about finding a master to teach him." He put the glass on the small table beside him and stood up.

"Thank you, Mr. Knightley, for your counsel and your hospitality."

"Not at all. I enjoy our discussions; they always reveal some new aspect of your character."

"I might say the same thing to you," said Spencer with a smile that seemed too knowing for such an unworldly curate. "Good day." He bowed and quit the room, leaving Knightley to puzzle out what he meant.

16

14th January
Wellyn House
Brunswick-square

Dear George,

I wonder if you might spare us a short visit when the quarter sessions have finished with you. We are not far from Newington, after all, and there is a matter on which I should like your advice.

Bella would like to know who is going to comb Madam Duval while you are away at the quarter sessions. Isabella would like to know if William Larkins' sister and all her children are well. John and Henry would like to know if you ever found the painted horse that they brought to Donwell to show you one day and left behind. I, however, don't want to know anything except whether we may expect you next week.

Your uninquisitive brother,
John

You will come, won't you?

"You seem a little troubled," said John, pouring his brother a drink and handing it to him. Dinner was ended, the children were in bed, and Isabella had left the two brothers alone in the library to talk.

"Do I?" Knightley took the brandy and settled into his chair. "In what way?"

"You didn't have much to say this evening."

"Perhaps that is because we parted company a mere two weeks ago. Very little has changed since then."

"Yes, I was afraid our dinner was likely to be a dull affair. I invited Mrs. Whitney to dine with us this evening in order to enliven the family party, but she was engaged elsewhere. However, we are secure of her company for tomorrow's dinner, at least."

Knightley stared at his younger brother, aghast, until John broke down and laughed.

"No, no, I was only joking. As dearly as I would love to see you married, I am not willing to put *myself* through such torture for the cause."

"No; you never do put yourself to any inconvenience if you can help it," said Knightley severely; he was not in the least amused by John's little joke.

"And such an unwarranted personal attack only strengthens my suspicion," said John coolly. "You have something weighing on your mind. Come now, you didn't really think I wouldn't notice, did you?"

Knightley sighed. "I was not thinking about you at all—only pondering that line from *Timon of Athens:* 'Nothing emboldens sin so much as mercy.'"

"I see. And is it often that a sentence from an obscure play—Shakespeare though it may be—dominates your thoughts to such an extent? Out with it; no more demurs. I conjecture something happened at the quarter sessions."

Knightley nodded slowly. "There was a fellow brought up on a game-stealing charge. I recognized him—he was up before me last year, too—a poor man with a large family. I let him off rather lightly last time—he didn't seem a practiced hand. I thought it was only his great poverty that drove him to it. But there he was again today on the same charge. Mind you, he may have been in dire need both times. How can I know?"

"You can't," said John promptly. "Not without personal knowledge of the man."

"No. But all the same, I wonder…did my leniency persuade him to try his luck again? Would he have tried some honest way to feed his family first if I had dealt more harshly with him the first time? Sibbes—of Blanchard Hall, you know—chided me for showing too much clemency. He said as a landowner I must be especially careful to enforce the game laws. Of course, Sibbes has always been ruthless on the bench, especially about game offences. He loves to hunt."

"Yes. And since *you* are always afraid that you will act out of self-interest, you show more mercy than you would if the victim of the crime was not a landowner."

"Do I?"

John smiled. "You do. A crime against a poor widow gets a harsher penalty from you than an offence against a squire would. Ever the soul of honour, George."

"Yes, well…the difficulty remains: how does one know whether to 'temper justice with mercy' or to exact the harshest penalty? Which best serves the accused? And their families? And the general population?"

John sighed. "You will hardly believe me, George, but it was just such a dilemma that I wanted your advice on. I had no idea it would be a philosophical bone that you were already worrying."

"You might as well tell me about it."

"It's about Richard."

"Richard?"

"Dr. Hughes' son."

"Oh yes. I thought he was doing well; Dr. Hughes told me he thought Richard would be called to the bar this term."

"It's likely he will be. However, he has begun to associate with unfortunate companions."

"Undesirable, you mean?"

"Exactly. He has a friend—he told me the name but I've forgotten it—who is a member at the Union Club. I understand that Richard was invited along to a dinner with some of the fellows who frequent the place and they were all taken with him. He's the sort of young man those dandies admire: intelligent, well-looking, and able to make a memorable *bon mot.* I think Lord Byron's friends

Hobhouse and Davies were among them. At any rate, he was invited to more dinners and more outings—they took him to Newmarket with them, too, once—and before long he was a member at the club."

"The Union Club. Not very illustrious, is it?"

"No. Respectable enough, but really it is little more than a gaming-house."

"I see. He's begun to gamble."

John nodded his head and traced the rim of his glass with his finger. "Sometimes on horses, but usually on games of chance—chiefly 'hazard', I fancy."

"Does his father know?"

"No."

"And have you said nothing to dissuade him?"

"You know I have."

"Then what do you want my advice about?"

John sighed and ran his fingers through his hair. "It's beginning to be a tangled mess. I knew nothing about any of this until just before Christmas. Richard came to me the week before I left for Surrey and told me that he had just lost five hundred pounds at hazard."

Knightley's eyebrows went up. "He had that much cash available?"

"No, he did not. He had exactly twenty pounds and was therefore in debt for four hundred and eighty pounds, with no way to raise the money. I suppose Dr. Hughes *might* have been able to cover it, but he was frantic that his father not find out."

"That explains why he did not come home to Donwell for Christmas. Dr. Hughes said he had accepted an invitation from friends in Somerset for a holiday visit. I thought it rather odd at the time, but now everything becomes clear. Well, what did you tell him?"

John looked a little sheepish. "I lent him the money myself. Better I than the money-lenders. *That* is a slavery I could not countenance."

Knightley nodded in agreement. "I probably would have done the same. And do you think he will repay you? I imagine he will."

"That is not the worst of it. Last week—the day I wrote to you—Richard came to see me again. He was very distraught, and yet I could hardly get a word out of him. At last he confessed that he had taken the money I lent him and gambled it, hoping to get enough to pay me back rapidly."

"Good God!"

"Of course he lost it all, and another three hundred besides."

"Do you mean to say that he is now in debt for—" Knightley paused to add the amounts together—*"one thousand two hundred and sixty pounds?"*

"Precisely."

Knightley shook his head, finding no words.

"And so you see my difficulty. I had some doubts about giving him the money in the first place; and now to find out that he only used the money to dig himself deeper into debt...."

"And it seems madness to lend him any more." Knightley finished. "Does Dr. Hughes know anything now?"

"I don't think so."

"He will have to be told."

"Of course he will."

"It will be a terrible blow for him."

"I know," said John, leaning his head back against the chair and staring at the ceiling. "The thought of it made *me* feel ill for three days."

Knightley smiled sympathetically. John's usual demeanour was that of a dispassionate, rather nonchalant man, and those who knew him little never guessed at the warm heart beneath the façade. Emma saw it, of course, and had remarked on it only two or three weeks before. "John *tries* to be a cynic," she had said as she watched him play with baby Emma, "but his affection overpowers his inclination too often for him to make the attempt successful." Emma was always quick to appreciate devotion to family. Which made her attitude toward Frank Churchill all the more confusing. She ought to see that his behaviour was completely at odds with his professions of filial affection, and that he was nothing but a—

"So what do you advise?"

John's words recalled Knightley's thoughts to the problem at hand.

"I don't know without thinking it over," he said. "Give me a night. At least."

"Every evening I have hoped that the answer would be easier to see in the morning," said John forlornly, "but the problem is just as ugly when the sun comes up as when it went down."

John was already at breakfast when Knightley came down for it the next morning.

"Sleep well?" John asked.

"Not particularly."

"Nor did I." John moodily stirred sugar into his tea. "It will do Richard no good if I discover that he has been sleeping soundly for the last several weeks. Well, did your musings at midnight enlighten you as to a solution?"

"I only wish they had. If it were just Richard to consider, it would be a different thing."

"Yes. But there is Dr. Hughes—and Mrs. Hughes, for that matter. We cannot leave them out of the reckoning."

Knightley buttered a hot roll. "Has Richard been to see you since last week?"

"No. I told him he would be sent for when I had something to tell him. Though I made him promise he wouldn't see Smith in the meantime."

"Smith?"

"Money-lender."

"Ah." Knightley took a sip of his chocolate. "Did you tell him about what happened….?"

"No, of course not. That's for you to tell—if you choose."

"I suppose so." Knightley put down his cup and looked at his brother. "Do you think this was the momentary lapse in judgement of a good fellow who is rather easily led? Or is it the beginning manifestations of a character going bad?"

John considered the question for a moment. "I hope my fondness for the boy is not distorting my view, but I think he is a good fellow at the core. I believe he was genuinely distressed at the disaster he brought about by losing the five hundred pounds, and was so eager to pay me back and get it all put right that he took the risk of gambling with what I had given him."

"It is hard to believe he is as stupid as all that—what chance did he think he had of suddenly winning so much?"

"He said something about it when he came to tell me of the great calamity, but he was so incoherent I could hardly understand him. Something about comprehending the odds and thinking it would make a difference."

"Oh, I know what he meant, especially if he was playing hazard. I think I would like to speak to him. Perhaps you ought to ask him to come this evening."

The door of the breakfast-room opened to admit Isabella, who bestowed a friendly smile on her brother and a tender one on her husband. Isabella's smile was so like Emma's that it gave him a start, and it struck him that this was what Emma would look like when *she* smiled tenderly at someone. Against his will, his mind called up the vision of the dandified young man that did duty for Frank Churchill in his imagination, and the Emma in his mind smiled tenderly at the vision. Something about the look in her eyes made him catch his breath. Then the young man smiled back at Emma—the sardonic, superficial smile that such a man would have—and Knightley found himself gripping the butter knife with unaccustomed intensity. That fellow was no good for Emma; no good at all.

This unsettling image was dispelled by a servant bringing in the letters: three for John and one for Isabella. Isabella's was addressed in a hand he knew very well.

"Dear Emma is always so faithful to write," said Isabella, opening her letter and beginning to read. "I see Mr. Elton is still away in Bath... Emma says that young Mr. Spencer has been preaching in Highbury church...he is very shy, but seems to be quite sincere...Mrs. Weston is very well...Oh! Jane Fairfax will soon be in Highbury. Miss Bates has had a letter from Jane saying that she will be there within a week."

"That seems a very sudden visit," said John. "How long has it been since she was last in Highbury?"

"It must be nearly two years," said Isabella. "What a lovely thing for dear Emma!"

"How do you mean?" asked her husband.

"It must be very agreeable for her to have another companion, since she has lost Mrs. Weston. Miss Smith is a charming girl, but Jane Fairfax is such an excellent young woman that it must be to Emma's great advantage to keep company with her."

"Yes," said Knightley, "No doubt it would be a great advantage, if only it could be contrived." But as he finished his breakfast, he wondered if Emma might not, after all, begin to appreciate the worth of Jane Fairfax. She had lately not only tried to improve Harriet, but to make amends for her own mistakes. She might now even be of a mind to improve herself. If so, the companionship of such a genteel and accomplished young lady could only assist the endeavour. Perhaps during Jane's stay in Highbury, Emma might see the benefits of friendship with an intellectual equal. And Jane, too, might learn to be more open and less reserved if Emma befriended her. If Emma could overcome the young lady's reticence—which was about the only fault her disposition had—a closer acquaintance would be very satisfactory for both of them. And a new friendship might very well drive away all thoughts of Frank Churchill from Emma's mind. Yes, Jane Fairfax's visiting Highbury at this time was a very good thing.

Knightley had not seen Richard for several months, and that evening he thought that he had never seen a man's demeanour so completely changed in so short a time. Richard was used to be open, confident, and cheerful; now he stood in front of the library fire twisting the ring on his finger and looking humbled, restless, and altogether wretched.

"Do, please, sit down, Richard," said John.

"Thank you, Mr. Knightley," said Richard and gingerly lowered himself into the nearest chair.

"You're not looking very well," said Knightley.

"No, I suppose not. I haven't slept well for…a long time."

The Knightley brothers exchanged faint smiles.

"I am glad to see you take a serious view of the matter," said Knightley.

"How could I not?" said Richard. "Believe me, Mr. Knightley, I know too well that I have disgraced my own name and my family's name, and I am surprised that Mr. John Knightley has even allowed me to enter his house this evening."

"And yet I know many a young man who would merely curse his luck and shrug his shoulders and find a willing lender in order to try again," said Knightley. "You are not quite the disgrace that you could be. At least, not yet."

Richard's eyes were on the floor. "I know you have no reason to believe me, but I will never gamble again. *Nothing* would induce me to play for money, even once."

"That is very good to hear," said John, "though you are right in saying that we have no reason to trust you in this matter. You seem very sincere, and I am inclined to believe you. But then you seemed very sincere when I lent you that four hundred and eighty pounds, too."

"I was sincere, sir. When I took that money I had no notion—none at all—of spending it on more gaming. I took it around to the Club, you know, but before I could pay the debt I ran into Davies." He paused and looked at Knightley. "Do you know him?"

"I know *of* him. Lord Byron's great friend."

"That's right. He told me not to be a fool and pay all that money when I could double it very easily in a few hours."

"And you believed him?" said John.

"He made it sound so very simple," said Richard. "He has lived by gaming for upwards of eight or ten years, and lived very well. He told me that it is quite easy to win at hazard, if you know the laws of chance."

"It sounds like double-talk," said John.

"Not at all," said Knightley. "You have not been exposed to enough gaming, dear brother. Winning at hazard is chiefly a matter of mastering the odds. You cannot manipulate the dice, but the reality is that it is easier to throw some numbers than others. There are, for example, only three chances in thirty-six of throwing a four, but six chances in thirty-six of throwing a seven. Once you are able to determine the probabilities, your chances of winning are greatly improved."

"Yes, that was what he told me," said Richard. "And he said he would advise me at play." He lifted his eyes to Knightley's face. "It seemed a sure thing, and I was so desperate to be in the clear, and to spare my father—my parents—the knowledge of my folly, that it seemed the best course."

"Why did you not stop when you began losing?"

"Davies told me that he often loses at the beginning of an evening and then his luck turns. And I have seen it myself, watching others play."

"And," said Knightley, "the more you lost the less likely you were to be able to pay back the money by any other method. How else could you ever get hold of more than a thousand pounds?"

Richard winced at this reminder of the enormity of his debt but nodded in agreement. "By the time I had lost several hundred pounds I felt the only course open to me was to keep on and hope my luck would change."

"But you did stop eventually," said John.

"Yes. It was Davies that called a halt. 'Not a lucky night,' he said. 'Best to try again another day.' He had the grace to apologize for interfering, and said he would introduce me to Smith and get me a good rate of interest, but I told him I had to see someone first." He looked at John. "I knew nothing would ever be really right again, but I meant to do what I could. I came to confess, at least, what I had done. I did not know what you would say, but I comforted myself that there's a big, dark river runs through London, and at the worst I could..."

"That would hardly make things easier for Dr. and Mrs. Hughes," said Knightley.

"Nor for me, by my father's reckoning. At any rate, I made my confession and have been waiting ever since to be led away to the Marshalsea, to rot along with all the other insolvent debtors."

"Oh, I think the Club will give you a little time before calling in your debt," said John. "I'm sure they expect you to find a bill-broker or money-lender, as most of the members do."

"*That* is something I shall not do," said Richard firmly. "I have contemplated the idea in the last week—though of course I did nothing about it, as I had promised you I would not—but I soon realized that such a step would do nothing but keep me out of gaol...for a time. Most of the fellows who begin borrowing never seem to get clear, and they often end by flying to France or the Low Countries. And even if I were, by some miracle, able to raise the money to pay the original debt, it would have grown enormously if a bill-broker had put his fingerprints on it."

"Exactly," said John.

"I am determined to earn the money needed honestly," said Richard. "It may take a lifetime, but I know I may earn something as a schoolmaster or a clerk. I hardly think I will be called to the bar now; such a weakness in my character might well make good men shrink from adding me to their number. All these months I knew I was doing what I ought not, but had not the strength of mind to resist as long as I was able to remain solvent."

"Your excursion into the world of gaming has ended very fortunately," said Knightley.

"Fortunately, you say?" said Richard. "I can scarcely imagine how it could be worse!"

"It could be far worse," said Knightley. "You might have kept winning."

Richard stared at the older man with his mouth slightly agape.

"When I was up at Cambridge," went on Knightley, "I became friends with a man whose passion was gambling. He was a good fellow in many ways—generous, amusing, and quite a scholar—but he did love gaming. I had never bet on anything in my life, my father's notions on the subject being quite strict. But I was persuaded by him and his other friends to play with them. His specialty was hazard, and he taught me well. I won frequently. One night I won six hundred pounds. About a week later I received an urgent summons to Donwell. I hurried home, fearing for my father's life, and was relieved to be told, on my arrival, that my father was waiting for me in the library, not in bed. But my relief was short-lived. My father had heard about my gaming and was more angry than I had ever seen him. I excused myself as well as I could and added that I had at least won more than I had lost. 'That is what frightens me,' he said. 'If you had lost I would have scolded you and then trusted to your good sense to prevent you indulging in such folly again. But since you won frequently I will tell you that if I hear of you gaming again, or going to Newmarket or any other races, I will have no qualms in leaving the entire estate to your brother John.' Donwell is not entailed, you know, Richard; it was my father's, to dispose of as he saw fit. 'I'll not have the estate gambled away,' he said."

"Did you not resent that threat?" said Richard. "Most of my acquaintance would."

"No. I knew he was right. And I knew also that he *would* give the lot to John if I gambled another farthing."

"So you gave it all up. And your friends?"

"I gave them up, too. They were a little resentful at first—they gave me a nickname with which I will not defile your chaste ears—but I don't think they bore me any lasting grudge."

"What happened to the friend who loved hazard?"

"He died last year. Abroad."

"I see why you say I've been fortunate. Though it *has* cost me dearly." Richard sighed. "I suppose I ought to start searching out vacant schoolmaster posts. God knows who will give me a reference after this…"

"Stop a minute," said John and glanced at Knightley, who gave him the briefest of nods. "I think we may be able to help you."

"Help me?"

"Yes," said Knightley. "You must understand that we do this as much for your parents as for you, and I do not think I can express what our outrage will be if we find that you have misused our generosity."

"Indeed, sir, I'll not abuse your kindness, whatever it is!" said Richard earnestly. "I deserve nothing, I know, but I am exceedingly grateful for any help you could give!"

"Very well. John and I will advance you the entire sum you owe, on several conditions…pray be seated again, Richard"—for the young man had sprung out of his chair at Knightley's words. "As I said, there are several conditions. First, you must resign your membership at the Union Club immediately."

"Already done," said Richard. "Several days ago."

"And are you a member anywhere else?"

"No, sir."

"Very well. The second condition is that you must go home and give a full account of this business to your parents."

Richard licked his lips, but nodded.

"The third condition is that when you are called to the bar, which my brother assures me you soon will be, you will live the life of a very frugal monk. You will repay us as quickly as you are able, and you will by no means live up to your income. And I hardly need add that there must be no more gambling of any sort. Can you meet all those conditions?"

"I can, sir. I only wish there were something else I could do to show my gratitude…my penitence…my earnest desire…"

"All right," said John. "No speeches. Save them for the courtroom. Your conduct will show your sincerity. Don't forget: 'Some often repent, yet never reform.'"

"You will see me reform, I swear it," said Richard. "And perhaps you might take the money to the Club yourself? I would rather not appear there again, for any reason."

"By all means," said John.

"I hope we did right," said Knightley an hour later when Richard was gone.

"So do I," said John. "But I believe we did."

"I almost think he has punishment enough in confessing his idiocy to his parents."

"Quite. It's no wonder he stayed away at Christmas. It would have been torture for him to visit his father, knowing what misery his father would suffer if the truth were all told."

"Yes. Avoiding the parental home is of great consequence to those in the throes of dissipation," said Knightley, wondering suddenly if *this* was the reason for Frank Churchill's non-appearance at Randalls. Could he be gambling away his expected inheritance, and feeling guilty enough to avoid his upright, honest father? *Just the sort of thing he would do,* thought Knightley. *Expensive, useless, idle fellow. Nothing to occupy his time but following the racing calendar and gaming at some club whenever he is in town. I hope Weston is on his guard; Churchill may come to him for a loan under some pretence. And if he were ever to come to me for money…*

"What is it?" said John.

"Hmm?"

"You look as if you regret helping Richard after all."

"No, no. Richard is all right. But I tell you truly, John, if *any other* dissolute young man crosses my path and threatens the happiness of my friends, I will show no mercy—none at all."

"Then heaven help the poor fellow."

"Heaven won't want to help him, either," said Knightley.

17

Two days later Knightley stood on a little rise overlooking the home meadow, watching the workmen cut the new path toward Langham. The air was as cold as one might expect on a day in mid-January, but the sky was clear and the breeze carried the welcome song of throstles to his ears. There was really no reason for him to be standing there idly in the middle of the day; the men knew their work well enough and did not need an overseer. He stood there anyway, however, basking in the diminished strength of the winter sun and the feeling of satisfaction borne of agreeable circumstances.

Only the day before on the journey from London he had pondered whether there was any way to promote a friendship between Jane Fairfax and Emma—a friendship which he thought would be the most desirable thing in the world for both of them. Of course, Emma would have to initiate anything of that nature: Miss Fairfax was too reserved and unassuming to make any overtures herself. He had been unsure if speaking to Emma would help or hinder his object—in days gone by she had been unreceptive to any of his hints in that direction. He suspected that Emma thought of Jane Fairfax as a rival for the admiration of those of consequence in Highbury. Though Emma was, to his eye, much more beautiful, there was no denying that Jane's accomplishments deserved all the praise they were generally given. Envy might well be lying hidden in the dark corners of Emma's heart, and if it were so, open praise of the lady might only feed that monster. He had gone to Hartfield that morning still undecided as to the best course.

But to his surprise, Emma seemed to be making a beginning without any contribution from him. She had voluntarily started the subject of Miss Bates' niece, and answered him pleasantly when he had enquired after Miss Fairfax's health.

"She looks a little pale, I think. But she is quite as elegant as ever, and I hope she will have a very pleasant stay with her aunt and grandmother."

There was no hint of jealousy in that speech. Cautiously he said, "I have always thought she was a very well-looking young woman."

"Well-looking? You are very sparing in your praise! She is certainly handsome; she is better than handsome!"

Yes, the state of affairs in Highbury was entirely agreeable: Emma was showing signs of admiration of the one young woman who would make an excellent companion for her, Elton was still away, and there was no sign at all of that Churchill fellow.

"Mr. Knightley!"

Knightley turned to see who had hailed him; it was Robert Martin coming over the stile toward him.

"Good day, Martin," said Knightley, advancing to meet him. "How do you do?"

"Pretty well, Mr. Knightley, I thank you."

There was no smile in Martin's eyes to match the one on his face, but then there never was anymore. A certain sort of settled resignation marked his manner, as if he had done battle and come to a tenuous peace, but he had not so far recovered as to become cheerful.

"I meant to ask you—did you lose that ram after all?" said Knightley.

"No, Mr. Knightley. I thought we would, but he pulled through."

"I am glad to hear it."

"I see you're moving that path."

"Yes, the home meadow was wanted as pasture this spring. I wouldn't have moved the path if it would inconvenience anyone, but you see it is only a few steps further around to the right."

Both men watched as the workmen paused in their labour to help a woman with a small child find her way around the piles of earth and vegetation where the new path was being cut.

"I suppose that is Mrs. Catherwood," said Knightley. "I think I should recognize anyone else."

"Yes. She takes her son for a walk almost every day. Poor little fellow."

"And how is she—how are *they*—settling in, do you think?"

Martin hesitated, and Knightley's heart sank.

"I presume there is some ill-feeling in the parish toward the boy?"

"Oh, no, sir, nothing like that," said Martin. "And if there had been any such thing, the sermon Mr. Spencer preached two weeks ago would have snuffed it out. I've never seen him so severe about anything."

"People took it to heart, did they?"

"They did. It's a bit of an honour now to do something for the boy."

"Good. But there is still something, isn't there, that is difficult for the Catherwoods?"

Martin's brow furrowed. "I'm not one to tell tales, Mr. Knightley."

"No, you are not. But I may be able to help, if I know what it is."

Martin gave a short laugh. "I don't think you could be of any assistance with this problem, sir."

"You've not been sworn to secrecy, have you?"

"No, nothing like that. My sisters have befriended Mrs. Catherwood, and I hear things through them." Martin deliberated with himself for a moment, and then shrugged. "I suppose I could tell you. It seems that her brother's wife—Mrs. Foote, you know—is not the easiest of women to live with."

"I see."

"She seems to be unhappy about having to host her husband's sister as well as a blind child."

"How did Mrs. Catherwood lose her husband?" said Knightley.

"A sudden illness, I believe, about two years ago. She lived with her mother until recently, but her mother died—in September, if memory serves."

"Poor woman," said Knightley with feeling. "Her circumstances would be difficult enough even without uncomfortable domestic arrangements."

"Very true, Mr. Knightley."

Knightley watched the retreating figures

"She ought to marry again," said Knightley.

Immediately the look of compassion on Martin's face vanished and was replaced with a stoic, even defiant, expression.

"Have I said something amiss?" said Knightley.

Martin's eyes looked determinedly across the meadow but his voice wavered a little as he said, "Mr. Knightley, you once asked me to refrain from matchmaking where you were concerned. With respect, sir, I would ask you to do the same."

Knightley was stricken. "Truly, Martin," he said, "I had no intention of matchmaking! It was but an idle comment. I had no notion of hinting such a thing to *you.*"

Martin nodded, but his eyes still did not meet Knightley's. "I beg your pardon, sir. I ought not to have assumed you meant anything of the sort. It is only that my mother said something to me the other day about it, and it cut me to the heart—to think that she thought I could so easily set aside—" He swallowed and fell silent.

Not for the first time did Knightley wish he could beg forgiveness for the part he had played in Martin's blighted hopes. He had been right when he had told Emma that a man could not be more disappointed than Robert Martin.

"I ought to have waited," said Martin, low. "I ought to have been more certain of her regard before I asked."

Guilt threatened to engulf Knightley. "Martin, I—"

"Please, sir," interrupted Martin, "do not blame yourself for the advice you gave me—I am certain I would have spoken to her before long, regardless of what you said. The fault was mine...and impatience has brought about its own penalty."

Dr. Hughes was sitting in a chair by the fire in his own drawing room when Knightley was shown in, and he smiled at the surprise on Knightley's face.

"Downstairs!" exclaimed Knightley. "My dear sir, I had no idea you were so far mended! I would have thought it would be several weeks yet before you could use the stairs."

"It will be," said Dr. Hughes. "Richard fairly carried me down the stairs this morning and will have to tote me up again later, like a sack of meal. But he was determined that I should see the first snowdrops, and I may say that I was entirely ready for a change of scene. I was able to walk a little in the garden today—he brought me this rosewood cane, you see."

"Very handsome," said Knightley. "I wish it were a warmer season, for your sake, so that you might sit in the garden and recover your strength."

"That would be delightful. I have often found that a garden can be very healing, to the spirit if not to the body."

"Indeed," said Knightley, remembering that only the night before he had dreamt that he was walking around the gardens, talking with Emma, and had woken with a remarkable sense of peace and well-being. He had been surprised that merely dreaming about a garden could effect such tranquillity of spirits.

"I met Richard in the lane and he told me you were asking for me."

"I was," said Dr. Hughes. "I had wondered at your keeping away from me—only that one brief call since you came back from the quarter sessions—but when Richard arrived yesterday it all became clear."

"He spoke to you, then?"

"He did." Dr. Hughes paused to clear his throat, and then said, "My dear Mr. Knightley, the debt we owe to you and to Mr. John Knightley is beyond anything—"

"Oh, never mind that, sir," interrupted Knightley. "I understand your feelings—truly, I do—but we did no more than you would have done for us had we ever been in Richard's position."

"Oh, but—"

"Tell me faithfully, now," said Knightley earnestly. "You *would* have done the same, would you not?"

"Well..." Dr. Hughes hesitated, looked at Knightley, and gave a rueful smile. "I suppose I would."

"Exactly. You would also have some gracious and subtle way of avoiding thanks, whereas I can only, in my unpolished way, forbid the expression of gratitude. Therefore, to spare my feelings, you will be good enough to let the matter rest."

"You are denying me the opportunity of delivering the speech I have been preparing since yesterday, you know."

"Good. You ought not to have spent your time on such a thing. A sermon would have been the better thing to prepare; your leg is evidently mending so well that you will be back in the pulpit before long."

"Will you join us for dinner this evening? I will eat in my own dining room tonight, and would be very pleased to have you with us to mark such a great event. And I might be able to slip in bits of my speech between the courses."

"I do thank you, sir, but I regret that Hartfield has the prior claim on me tonight."

"Tomorrow evening, then?"

"With very great pleasure."

The one advantage of being seated next to Miss Bates at dinner was that absolutely no thought was needed to keep a conversation going—a nod or murmur now and then was all the contribution one needed to make.

"And as I was telling Jane, Mr. Knightley—at breakfast, I believe—yes, it was, for she was eating her bread—generally she has only the one piece of bread with butter for her breakfast—just the one, if you can imagine such a thing—even my mother has two—But as I was saying, I told her that she ought to have eaten more of the mutton the night before, as she had the smallest piece—at least, I think it was the smallest—there were two that were very like, and perhaps the other one was a little thinner—but however, it was not enough for her, I am sure. She has not the appetite of a sparrow, and has not eaten a full meal since—oh, it must have been Thursday last, when we had some pork, but that was the last of it, and now there is nothing in the larder but mutton. But mutton is so very wholesome for an invalid—Mr. Perry says so—and she is not *absolutely* an invalid—and we are so very fortunate that there is a good bit of mutton in the larder, and we do not lack for anything, Mr. Knightley."

He let Miss Bates talk on while he watched Emma. It was a good sign, he thought, that Emma was showing an interest in Miss Fairfax. He could see her asking questions of her and listening intently to the answers. What they were speaking of he had no idea—Miss Bates' chatter effectively drowned out the low voices of the well-bred young ladies—but he caught the word "Weymouth" and presumed the topic must be Jane's recent travels. He was pleased: Emma was cultivating Jane Fairfax for her own sake and on her own initiative. He could have wished Miss Fairfax a little more energetic in her responses, but perhaps in time she would be more open with Emma.

Mr. Woodhouse and Knightley lingered only a very few minutes in the dining room after the ladies had retired; neither wanted any more to drink, and Mr. Woodhouse much preferred his comfortable seat by the drawing-room fire. He had no sooner settled into this seat than he drew Miss Bates and her niece into conversation; he had overheard enough at dinner to make him extremely anxious on the score of Miss Fairfax's appetite.

As much as he respected both Miss Bates and Mr. Woodhouse, Knightley was happy to have a little respite from conversing with them, and he sat down next to Emma with a small sigh of relief. The gleam in Emma's eye meant she knew exactly what he was feeling, and found it amusing.

"I was remiss, Mr. Knightley," she said. "I ought to have invited another gentleman so that you might have had more masculine discussion this evening."

"Masculine discussion? Come now, Emma, tell me: what is it that you think gentlemen talk about?"

"Oh, politics, most likely, or perhaps hunting. But then you are not like most men, are you? You would rather discuss farming methods, I think."

"Certainly. You must know that I spent the entire dinner wishing that William Larkins was seated beside me so that we could discuss my new Romney Marsh ram and the chances of an early rhubarb harvest."

Emma laughed. "I regret to say that I have no other acquaintance who can converse intelligently with you about rams.

But if you like, you may slip out now and spend the rest of the evening with Tadgett, the gardener. He is quite as cheerful a person as William Larkins, you know, and he will be sure to tell you that the frost is likely to kill all the early vegetables."

"All the early vegetables killed!" said Knightley. "And the early flowers, too, no doubt. How very disturbing! Thank goodness I have already had my dinner.

O how I am troubled!
Bamboozled, and bit!
My distresses are doubled."

"That song always reminds me of Tadgett," said Emma. "It would do for William Larkins as well—it might have been written for either of them. It sums up their view completely."

"So it does. Some songs seem meant for certain people."

"Oh, yes. There's another song from *The Beggar's Opera* that always makes me think of John," said Emma. "You know the one:

The gamesters and lawyers are jugglers alike,
If they meddle, your all is in danger.
Like gypsies, if once they can finger a souse
Your pockets they pick, and they pilfer your house
And give your estate to a stranger."

Knightley laughed. "I must tell that to John—he would find it amusing. Of course, he would take great pleasure in finding a song to fit *you*."

"That should be a very easy task. He must know several songs that mention angels. But I must ask Miss Fairfax to favour us with some music now; she has answered enough of my father's questions about her health for the present, I think."

Miss Fairfax very properly obliged the company. It could not be denied that she was a superior performer; both by natural talent and by training her music was excellent. She sang "I Attempt From Love's Sickness to Fly," which to Knightley's mind seemed the perfect song for Robert Martin. Poor Martin! If anyone could be said to be sick from love, it would be he. His pain was still raw and recovery any time soon seemed doubtful, as he was evidently blaming himself for Harriet's rejection. Was it possible that he could ever forget Harriet enough to look at another woman; say, Mrs. Catherwood?

The song came to an end, and Knightley was pleased to see Emma urging Miss Fairfax to stay at the piano-forte and indulge them with more music, even requesting a particular concerto. The old Emma would have been too anxious for her own musical reputation to be pressing Miss Fairfax for another performance.

Knightley closed his eyes and leaned back in his chair and let the music of Mozart wash over him. It was not a song, but still it seemed to him to represent Emma perfectly. After all, it was beautiful and lively and …complicated. He had used to think he understood her, but lately he had been surprised by the complexity of her character. On the one hand, she had been wilfully blind in the matter of Harriet Smith and Robert Martin, but then she had unselfishly tried to make amends with Harriet when she realized her error. It must be unselfish, for Harriet Smith could be a tedious companion for a young lady such as Emma; she could not be spending so much time with Harriet merely for her own pleasure. Again, Emma was all consideration and tenderness for those she loved—her father and Mrs. Weston, for example, but Frank Churchill's iniquities seemed of no account to her, even when his actions slighted the Westons. And though she still stayed aloof from the Coles and the Perrys, she was at last making an effort to befriend Jane Fairfax. It was all very puzzling.

The intricate melody ceased, and the fair performer received her just praise.

"You will play for us now, I hope," said Knightley to Emma.

"Very well, but you may be sorry you asked."

"How so?" Surely she could not think her own performance would be so inferior that those assembled would rather not hear her at all!

"I have determined to sing the song that most reminds me of *you.*"

"'Pastime With Good Company', is it?"

"For you?" she said, raising an eyebrow. "I think not."

She seated herself at the piano-forte, and played the introductory flourish with a smirk on her face.

He could not help but chuckle when she began to sing.

"As I was going to Darby, Sir,
All on a market day,
I met the finest Ram, Sir,
That ever was fed on hay.
Daddle-i-day, daddle-i-day,
Fal-de-ral, fal-de-ral, daddle-i-day.

This Ram was fat behind, Sir,
This Ram was fat before,
This Ram was ten yards high, Sir,
Indeed he was no more.
Daddle-i-day, daddle-i-day,
Fal-de-ral, fal-de-ral, daddle-i-day.

The Wool upon his back, Sir,
Reached up unto the sky,
The Eagles made their nests there, Sir,
For I heard the young ones cry.
Daddle-i-day, daddle-i-day,
Fal-de-ral, fal-de-ral, daddle-i-day."

She sang her way though all fifteen verses of the old song, which expounded the enormous size of the mythical ram, and played the final notes with a triumphant grin at Knightley.

"Well, now," she said when she had regained her seat and Miss Fairfax was turning over music to see what she might play next, "Was that not an apt choice for you?"

"I would have preferred something more like 'Genteel is My Damon, Engaging is His Air'."

"Oh, nonsense! Your farm looms far larger in your thoughts than does your air. I have no doubt that your dreams are full of large farm animals—England's biggest ox, for example, or a horse strong enough to drag a house."

"I have never once dreamt of a large farm animal."

"Then what do you dream of?"

You. The thought came unexpectedly, inexplicably. He would never have remembered her part in his dream of the night before if her face had not worn the same expression then as now. He opened his mouth to answer her question, and then realized he had no idea what to say. For a long moment he hesitated, and then the sound of the piano-forte came to his relief. He turned his attention to Miss Fairfax and gladly put aside the whole confusing muddle.

18

Knightley liked the Coles. While not genteel enough for Emma's taste, they were nonetheless hospitable, amiable, and full of genuine friendship. In spite of their recently increased means they had neither snubbed former acquaintance nor assumed superior airs. It was characteristic that Cole was the only man on the parish council who called him "Mr. Knightley", instead of plain "Knightley". Knightley could not decide whether it was mere habit left over from the days when the difference in rank had been more marked, or whether Cole still saw himself as much the inferior. Knightley was slightly the elder of the two men; perhaps that had something to do with it.

The Coles had lately enlarged their home to include a grander dining room and a library, and it was into the latter that Knightley was shown the morning after the dinner at Hartfield. Cole was seated behind his handsome new desk, reading a letter, but he smiled as he rose to greet his visitor.

"Good morning, Mr. Knightley. You've come about that bridge, haven't you? I thought so. But here is a piece of news you won't have expected." He waved the letter at Knightley, who took it and read it silently.

Dear Cole,

I write to inform you that I am the happiest of men, having been so fortunate as to win the heart and the hand of the beautiful and accomplished Miss Hawkins of Bath. I intend to be in Highbury next week, on or about the 2nd, and stay long enough to prepare the vicarage for its new mistress.

Yours in haste,
P. Elton

"Quick work, eh?" said Cole.

"Very quick," said Knightley. Hardly a month had passed since Elton had offered for Emma, and here he was engaged to someone else! He had never supposed that Elton had any real devotion to Emma, but it seemed unbelievable that even a man of shallow feelings could recover from an attachment to Emma with such unseemly haste.

"I confess myself rather surprised," said Cole. "I had thought that Elton's interests had been more local in nature."

Of course, Cole knew. Everyone knew.

"Well," said Knightley lightly, "perhaps it's a case of '*repente amor victum mihi*', and he has been caught unawares and swept away."

"Perhaps," said Cole, without much conviction.

"At any rate," said Knightley, returning the letter, "the tea-parties of Highbury will be much enlivened by this news. I suppose there is no reason for secrecy, is there?"

"No. He would have said something it if he didn't want the engagement known. And he must have assumed that I would tell Mrs. Cole, and that she would tell Miss Bates…"

"Indeed," said Knightley. Elton would know that once Mrs. Cole told Miss Bates, every soul in Highbury and Donwell would be in possession of that knowledge by sundown. And no doubt he would be only too pleased to have his conquest published.

"I suppose we shan't know any more about the fair young lady until Elton comes next week," said Cole. "He'll be too busy holding her hand to write more letters."

"Let us hope that when he arrives, his state of bliss will be such that the difficulties with the bridge will be as nothing to him."

"Ah, the bridge. You've talked with the surveyor, then?"

"Yes. The bridge will have to be repaired again."

"As we suspected. Can it be done quickly?"

"Two weeks, the surveyor said—if we had able workmen."

"Well, it could be worse, I suppose."

"It could. I had been afraid he would say that the whole thing would have to be demolished and built again. The thing we must be sure of this time is that the workmen are really skilled."

"That was the trouble, then?"

"So the surveyor said. Do you know anyone that might have enough knowledge to undertake the job—hire the stonemasons, oversee the work, and so on?"

"I think Carson might do it well. I'll speak to him."

"Good. Let me know how you get on, will you? I must be going—I have some business at Hartfield."

"Hartfield," repeated Cole. "I say, Mr. Knightley, do you mind if I ask your advice about a rather delicate matter?"

"Not at all."

"Now that the dining room is complete, Mrs. Cole is anxious to have a dinner party. She has set her heart on returning the hospitality of the Westons and gaining a better acquaintance with the Gilberts...and of course, we are depending on your company, and that of the Coxes as well. But she wonders if she should venture to invite the Woodhouses—we have never dined at Hartfield, you know, and greatly as we would enjoy the company of Mr. and Miss Woodhouse at our dinner, we would not wish to offend them by presuming intimacy with them. Then again, *not* to extend an invitation to them may be interpreted as a slight, particularly when all their friends will be invited. It is difficult to know which would be most agreeable to them."

"I see your difficulty," said Knightley.

"I hoped you might. I thought that perhaps with your knowledge of Hartfield you could advise us as to the best course."

Knightley thought rapidly. Emma ought to come to the dinner; it would do her good to have a better acquaintance with the Coles and see that they were not so far beneath her as she thought they were. And the dinner would be a good deal more interesting if she were there, contributing beauty and wit to the party.

"I think you ought to invite Hartfield," said Knightley. "If you particularly solicit the presence of Mr. Woodhouse and show great sensibility for his comfort, I think there will be no suspicion of presumption."

"You think so? Mrs. Cole thought of ordering a screen for the benefit of Mr. Woodhouse—so that he would be protected from any draughts of air, you know."

"That is precisely the sort of thing that would put—Hartfield—in charity with you, and with the invitation."

"I will tell Mrs. Cole, then. I thank you, Mr. Knightley. You said you had business at Hartfield...I ought not to keep you."

It was pleasant walking to Hartfield with the knowledge that Elton would never again be found loitering there, flattering Emma and deceiving himself. He had not thought the vicar likely to renew his addresses to Emma, and there was clearly no danger of that now. And what would Emma make of Elton's approaching nuptials? Knightley did not know whether or not she reproached herself for being the instrument of disappointed hopes, but this news would certainly do away with any guilt she might feel. It was not often that Emma was completely surprised at anything, but this announcement was sure to astonish her. He anticipated seeing the expression on her face.

Of course she would ask him all about the lady, and there was not much he could say. He had the same questions himself. What sort of woman would engage herself to Elton after such a short acquaintance? Was she a desperate young lady, not fastidious enough to insist on solid worth in a suitor? Or perhaps she was of a romantic turn of mind: Elton's person and manners were good enough that a young lady might be swept away by them. He shook his head. Neither a reckless woman nor an overly romantic one would be good companions for Emma. But then it probably did not matter so much anymore, now that Jane Fairfax was in favour. What a relief it was to see Emma on friendly terms with her!

The pleasure of that thought sustained him through the rather trying ordeal of attempting to explain financial matters to Mr. Woodhouse. The simple old gentleman could not understand his banker's queries any more than he could answer them. But Knightley was accustomed to helping Mr. Woodhouse in his business dealings, and knew what course to take. After going through the formality of an explanation, he persuaded Mr. Woodhouse that the changes he was authorizing were not only inevitable but would also make his daughters' inheritance more secure. Nothing appealed to Mr. Woodhouse so much as an increase of security, and he was willing, even eager, to sign his name to the documents put before him.

"Well, Mr. Knightley," said Emma when the business was finished, "have you recovered from the dissipations of yesterday's gathering? I hope you enjoyed yourself."

"A very pleasant evening," he said. "Particularly pleasant. You and Miss Fairfax gave us some very good music. I do not know a more luxurious state, sir, than sitting at one's ease to be entertained a whole evening by two such young women, sometimes with music and sometimes with conversation. I am sure Miss Fairfax must have found the evening pleasant, Emma. You left nothing undone. I was glad you made her play so much, for having no instrument at her grandmother's, it must have been a real indulgence."

Emma smiled at these words of praise and said, "I am happy you approved, but I hope I am not often deficient in what is due to guests at Hartfield."

Mr. Woodhouse was quick to assure his daughter that, if anything, she was too attentive, but Knightley was not to be put off. She had shown special attention to Miss Fairfax after years of neglect, and he wanted her to know that he marked *that* and approved it highly.

"No," he said, "you are not often deficient; not often deficient either in manner or comprehension. I think you understand me, therefore."

She did understand him; he could tell from the sly look on her face. She could not pretend that she had always taken care to make Miss Fairfax's visits pleasant.

"Miss Fairfax is reserved," she said, defending past conduct by implication.

"I always told you she was—a little," said Knightley. "But you will soon overcome all that part of her reserve which ought to be overcome, all that has its foundation in diffidence. What arises from discretion must be honoured."

"You think her diffident," said Emma coolly. "I do not see it."

What was this? Was Emma saying that she was not disposed to approve of Miss Fairfax after all? He moved to a chair closer to her.

"My dear Emma, you are not going to tell me, I hope, that you had not a pleasant evening." Had all her friendliness been a mere pretence?

"Oh, no," said Emma. "I was pleased with my own perseverance in asking questions, and amused to think how little information I obtained."

His heart sank. She was not beginning to admire Miss Fairfax, then.

"I am disappointed," he said, and fell silent. He did not want to say too much.

"I hope everybody had a pleasant evening," said Mr. Woodhouse, who was, as usual, lagging behind the course of their conversation. "I had. Once, I felt the fire rather too much; but then I moved back my chair a little, a very little, and it did not disturb me. Miss Bates was very chatty and good-humoured, as she always is, though she speaks rather too quick. However, she is very agreeable, and Mrs. Bates too, in a different way. I like old friends. And Miss Jane Fairfax is a very pretty sort of young lady, a very pretty and a very well-behaved young lady indeed. She must have found the evening agreeable, Mr. Knightley, because she had Emma."

"True, sir," said Knightley in spite of his melancholy. How could spending an evening in company with Emma be anything but agreeable? He glanced at Emma, and added, "And Emma, because she had Miss Fairfax." Now, what would she say to that?

She understood the glance, and replied to his unspoken query.

"She is a sort of elegant creature that one cannot keep one's eyes from. I am always watching her to admire, and I do pity her from my heart."

There was no pretence in *that* statement, at least. His spirits rose a little.

"It is a great pity that their circumstances should be so confined!" said Mr. Woodhouse. "A great pity indeed! and I have often wished—but it is so little one can venture to do—small, trifling presents of anything uncommon. Now we have killed a porker, and Emma thinks of sending them a loin or a leg."

So Emma had heard Miss Bates' comment that they had no pork left, and was quietly making them a gift of some. That was just like Emma. He was not even surprised to hear, a moment later, that she had sent them the whole hind-quarter. Some parts of Emma's character were unexceptionable, and both Harriet and Miss Fairfax might be influenced for good by a friendship with her. So might Elton's new wife, for that matter. But Emma did not know about her yet.

"Emma, I have a piece of news for you," he said. "You like news—and I heard an article in my way hither that I think will interest you."

"News! Oh yes, I always like news." Her face was alight with curiosity, and he smiled at her eagerness.

"What is it?" she said. "Why do you smile so? Where did you hear it? At Randalls?"

Randalls? What sort of news would come from—and then he knew. *Churchill.*

"No, not at Randalls," he said, pushing back the foolish irritation that her question had begotten. "I have not been near Randalls..."

The sound of the drawing room door opening interrupted him, and one look at those entering told him that he would not be able to resume his discourse any time soon—Miss Bates and Miss Fairfax had come to call.

"Oh! My dear sir, how are you this morning? My dear Miss Woodhouse—I come quite overpowered. Such a beautiful hind-quarter of pork! You are too bountiful! Have you heard the news? Mr. Elton is going to be married."

If Knightley could not tell Emma himself, at least he was not denied the amusement of seeing Emma so surprised that she forgot to be composed. He saw her start and blush, and then after a moment of gaping slightly at Miss Bates, she recovered her poise and glanced to see if he had noticed. He smiled and said quietly,

"There is my news. I thought it would interest you."

For an instant their eyes held, and he could see she understood that he knew what had happened between her and Elton.

"But where could *you* hear it?" exclaimed Miss Bates. "Where could you possibly hear it, Mr. Knightley? For it is not five minutes since I received Mrs. Cole's note—no, it cannot be more than five—or at least ten—for I had got my bonnet and spencer on, just ready to come out—I was only gone down to speak to Patty again about the pork—Jane was standing in the passage—were not you, Jane? For my mother was so afraid that we had not any salting-pan large enough. So I said I would go down and see, and Jane said, 'Shall I go down instead? For I think you have a little cold, and Patty has been washing the kitchen.' 'Oh! my dear,' said I—well, and just then came the note. A Miss Hawkins—that's all I know. A Miss Hawkins of Bath. But, Mr. Knightley, how could you possibly have heard it? For the very moment Mr. Cole told Mrs. Cole of it, she sat down and wrote to me. A Miss Hawkins—"

"I was with Mr. Cole on business an hour and a half ago," said Knightley. "He had just read Elton's letter as I was shown in, and handed it to me directly."

"Well! That is quite—I suppose there never was a piece of news more generally interesting. My dear sir, you really are too bountiful. My mother desires her very best compliments and regards, and a thousand thanks, and says you really quite oppress her."

Mr. Woodhouse smiled beatifically and said, "We consider our Hartfield pork—indeed it certainly is—so very superior to all other pork, that Emma and I cannot have a greater pleasure than—"

But Miss Bates could not wait to hear the rest of her benefactor's speech.

"Oh! my dear sir, as my mother says, our friends are only too good to us. If ever there were people who, without having great wealth themselves, had everything they could wish for, I am sure it is us. We may well say that 'our lot is cast in a goodly heritage.' Well, Mr. Knightley," she said, turning to him, "and so you actually saw the letter. Well—"

"It was short, merely to announce—but cheerful, exulting, of course." He glanced mischievously at Emma. He knew she could well imagine the style Elton would use on such an occasion. "He had been so fortunate as to—I forget the precise words—one has no business to remember them. The information was, as you state, that he was going to be married to a Miss Hawkins. By his style, I should imagine it just settled."

Finally, Emma found her voice. "Mr. Elton going to be married! He will have everybody's wishes for his happiness." A very correct and irreproachable sentiment, even if she would not have been able to say it while meeting his eye.

He quitted Hartfield at the same time as Miss Bates and her niece and escorted them back to their home. He was fortunate to spy Spencer coming out of Ford's, and was able to excuse himself from Miss Bates' pressing invitation to join them for some small refreshment by representing his need to talk to the curate. The rain that had long been threatening began to fall as the two men met.

"What brings you to Highbury, Spencer?"

"I was visiting someone who is ill, and I wanted to speak to Mr. Ford. I meant to speak to him yesterday, but hadn't time."

"I see you're as busy as ever. Well, at least Elton's return is in sight."

"Elton is returning soon?"

"Oh—you won't have heard yet. I say, the rain is getting heavy. Ford's looks a little crowded—shall we step into the Crown to wait it out?"

"Yes, let's."

The Crown was comfortable in its faded glory, as was Mrs. Stokes who bustled up to greet them.

"Good afternoon, Mr. Knightley, Mr. Spencer. Heavens! Look at that rain come down. Was you wanting to hire a horse, Mr. Knightley? I'm sorry to say that Columbus was hired for the day by William Cox, but Paris is still in the stable..."

"No, thank you, Mrs. Stokes, I haven't come for a horse," said Knightley. "I'm afraid we have no business here except to keep dry."

"By all means, sir. Go into the great room, if you please. Would you like I should build a fire there?"

"No, no, the shower will be soon over, I'm sure. If you will allow us to linger here until the rain stops we would be most grateful."

"Of course, Mr. Knightley."

The two men went into the great room and stood near the window, watching the rain form puddles on the ground outside.

"So Elton is returning, you say?"

"Yes, next week, in fact, but he will not stay long. According to the note he sent to Cole, he comes only to prepare the vicarage for his new bride."

"*New bride*?" said Spencer, looking, if anything, slightly more shocked than Emma had.

"Yes. A woman he met in Bath, apparently."

"But I thought...well, I suppose not," said Spencer.

Knightley sighed. Everyone said the same thing. Though Miss Bates, to do her justice, had merely alluded to *Mrs. Cole's* suspicions, and hinted that she herself did not think Mr. Elton was really a worthy match for Emma. Miss Bates had uncommonly good sense; Knightley liked her very much indeed.

"Well, I wish them joy, I am sure," said Spencer.

"It will be a relief for you to confine your activities to Donwell once again, I think."

"In some ways it will. But I have grown very fond of many in Highbury, and shall miss seeing them often. Do you think Elton would mind if I continued to call on some of them—Mrs. Plover, for example?"

"I can't imagine he would object. How is Mrs. Plover faring?"

"Not very well."

"Her foot again, is it?

"Yes, the ulcer is worse. And of course, her son is a great worry to her."

"Has he got into more trouble?"

"Not really, but she is afraid it is only for lack of opportunity. She calls him a 'bad boy', and I could not contradict her. She is inclined to blame herself, I think, but she has no reason to. From all I hear, she has been a good mother; it is only that he has been a difficult child from the beginning."

"I believe he has. And, of course, she was widowed when he was very young. It might have made a difference if there had been a father in the home."

"Yes, I was thinking about that," said Spencer slowly. "It must be difficult for widows with any children, but especially for those with sons. I wonder how they manage?"

"You could ask Mrs. Hunt. She was widowed when her sons were young."

"Did they turn out well?"

"They did. One died a few years ago, but the other is a captain in the Navy."

"That is good to hear. Is that usual? I mean, do most boys who lose their fathers early still do well in life?"

Knightley searched his memory for a moment. "I can't say, really. I think most of the widows I know re-married before long, and so have not raised their boys alone."

"True. And of course, that is what St. Paul advised young widows to do—marry again. But it occurred to me that the widows of our day do not have it in their power to remarry if no one offers for them."

"A considerable difficulty."

"And I wonder," said Spencer more earnestly, "if our Christian duty to care for widows and orphans might not extend to more than our contribution to the Poor Relief and giving baskets of food now and then. It might mean that single men ought to consider marrying widows with children."

"Spencer," said Knightley, "I agree with you in principle, but I really do not think I have it in me to marry Mrs. Plover."

"Mrs. Plover!" exclaimed Spencer, looking thoroughly bewildered.

"Were you not speaking of Mrs. Plover?"

"Oh! I suppose it was her situation that started me thinking, but I had no thought of her remarrying."

"Then it was merely a philosophical abstraction that you were grappling with?"

"Not really, no. I was thinking of Mrs. Catherwood."

"Ah, yes. Widowed, and with a blind son."

"And her life at home rather difficult."

"She told you so?'

"No, no, but I hear things." He gave a faint grin. "I suppose I ought to ask you to keep that information to yourself, but I have no doubt that you have heard it already. Donwell far outstrips Diss in gossip."

"I can well believe it. What with—well, never mind. So, you are trying to find a bachelor to marry Mrs. Catherwood?"

"Not you, Mr. Knightley," said Spencer, blushing.

"Thank you—you relieve my mind. And I wouldn't speak to Martin about it, either…the idea was not well-received when it was suggested to him."

"Martin? No, I never thought of him."

"You have someone else in mind?"

Spencer looked at the floor and then out the window. "Yes," he said, "someone else."

"I think he meant himself," said Knightley to Madam Duval that evening in the library. She was curled up on his foot, as usual, but he knew she was not asleep because he could hear her purring. "A noble fellow. I wonder what the lady would say if he asked her? One would think she would be happy to have him, if only to secure a better life for herself and her son. But one never knows...look at Martin and Harriet Smith. I saw them today, you know. It was while we were at the Crown—we saw them through the window. Miss Smith was leaving Ford's, and Martin came out after her. We couldn't hear what he said, of course, but I think Spencer and I both held our breath, hoping that his speaking to her meant some kind of rapprochement between them. It couldn't have been, though, because she seemed to thank him in a flurried kind of a way and then she hurried off, and he turned back with a face as grey as ash. I would like to forget the sight of his face, Madam."

He wanted another splash of brandy, but he would have had to walk across the room to get it, and he didn't like to disturb the cat.

"I did have one moment of complete satisfaction today, though," he continued, reaching down to stroke the soft fur for a moment. "I found William Larkins when I came home from Highbury and said to him, 'Have you heard the news, Larkins?' He looked slightly panicked; no doubt he was worried that I might know something he didn't. 'And what news is that, Mr. Knightley?' he said. I think he actually trembled a bit. 'Why, that Mr. Elton is getting married to a Miss Hawkins of Bath.' He was so affected by the news that he dropped the papers he was holding. I had a sudden fright that he would die of apoplexy on the spot. However, by the time I had helped him gather the papers together he was breathing all right, and I am hopeful that I have not shortened his life significantly."

The cat looked up at him and gave a soft meow.

"Oh, his spirits might have drooped for an hour or so, but the opportunity to enlighten everyone else in Donwell must have restored his confidence by now. It was a very brief triumph, Madam—but it was gratifying all the same."

19

Knightley saw a little too much of Elton during the week of his stay in Highbury. He reminded Knightley of a little boy who, put into breeches for the first time, forces himself on the notice of everyone he sees so that he might hear over and over what a big boy he is to leave dresses and pantalons behind him. Elton seemed to spend most of his time wandering around Highbury and even Donwell, hoping to be teased and congratulated by everyone he met. The triumph in his manner was regrettable, but Knightley could make allowances for him. After being rejected by a woman like Emma, it was no wonder that Elton would grasp at anything to soothe his pain. Finding another woman might numb a broken heart, even if she could not immediately heal it. And furthermore—No, no, no, that wasn't right at all. What was he thinking? Elton didn't *have* a broken heart, only an offended one. He had never loved Emma; it was only that his vanity had been flattered and he had been delighted at the prospect of such a sizable dowry. True, it was hard to imagine that any man could be confronted with such an enchanting portrait of womanhood as Emma and not be in love with her, but then he never had understood Elton.

The vicar's brief stay in Highbury was nearing its end when Weston came to Donwell one afternoon and found Knightley in the kitchen garden, watching the under-gardeners prepare the hot-beds for planting.

"I must say, Knightley, you take more interest in your kitchen gardens than anyone else I know. Are you always in attendance at the sowing of spring vegetables?"

"Not usually, no," said Knightley. "But I'm growing a new variety of strawberry this year—*fragraria chiloensis*—and I wanted to see that they were planted correctly. Apparently they produce bigger fruit than hautboys, but are more difficult to grow. And I don't know that they will be any sweeter. Still, I thought it was worth trying. But I don't suppose you came all the way to the Abbey to hear about my strawberries."

"No, though if they turn out well, I hope you'll let us have some of them—in the name of scientific enquiry, of course." Weston winked. "No, what I really came about was the Crow's Nest over at Langham. Do you know it?"

"Of course. More a tavern than an inn, though I think they have a room or two."

"That's the one. My housekeeper's niece married the fellow that owns the place, and Mrs. Brown is worried about her—thinks there might be something amiss there. I thought you might know if she has any cause to worry. You are the magistrate for Langham, are you not?"

"Yes, but I don't remember any trouble with the Crow's Nest—not recently, at any rate. I can't think of the proprietor's name…Carson? Culver?"

"Cooper, I think."

"That's it. No, I don't know anything against him, but I can ask a few questions. It wouldn't surprise me greatly to discover something unlawful going on in the place—it's not the haunt of the more respectable citizens of Langham."

"Thank you, Knightley. I'd like to set Mrs. Brown's mind at rest. She doesn't usually worry about things, you know—level-headed woman. I hope there's nothing in it, but there might be." Weston stared absently at the espalier trees growing along the garden wall for a moment, murmuring, "She's a good girl. Hope there's nothing in it."

He sighed and shook his head and then said, "So, Elton leaves for Bath again tomorrow, does he?"

"Yes. I heard him tell William Cox so. He said something about expecting to be gone for three weeks."

"The population of Highbury is growing rapidly. Miss Fairfax is come, and Elton's new wife will be here, and—I may as well tell you, Knightley—Randalls will be making its own contribution to the expansion."

A feeling very like dread began to seep into Knightley's soul. *Churchill.* He cleared his throat. "So your son's visit is imminent, is it?"

"Frank? No, no. I expect a letter from him any day, but that is not the person I meant. I was speaking of a *much younger* person."

It was the gleam in Weston's eye rather than his words that brought enlightenment.

"A *very* young person, I see," said Knightley, with all gloom of spirits vanished. "Excellent news! And the newcomer will arrive at the end of summer, I suppose?"

"We expect so."

"Well, you have my very heartiest congratulations."

8 February
Donwell Abbey

Dear John,

Tell Bella that Madam Duval is very well. She has caught another mouse, which event produced half a smile from Mrs. Hodges—the first one in over a year. Madam left the mouse on the sideboard, which event produced a gasp from Baxter—also the first one in over a year. You can see what a lively domestic life I have; all your fears on that score can be laid to rest.

Speaking of domestic life, Elton left for Bath today to claim his bride. We have therefore three weeks to speculate about her before she arrives in the flesh to put an end to the conjectures of the gossips. The most outlandish I have heard came from Mrs. Green (through Larkins, of course), whose theory is that the new Mrs. Elton is the daughter of a highwayman who made his fortune in Essex—evidently there was a highwayman called Hawkins in those parts thirty years ago. She is divided between horror at the misalliance of a clergyman and a felon's daughter and delight at the dubious distinction that such a notorious personage will give to Highbury.

You asked about the Mefford farm – or as we should now call it, the Foote farm. Foote has done very well with it, even in winter and after such a short time. Larkins tells me that Mefford has not been able to lease another farm, and that they are living with his wife's family. Is it very uncharitable of me to be pleased? I am *sorry when I remember Mrs. Mefford. For her sake I am glad I was able to do something for Harry, though I fear he will not make a superior footman. He is the sort that breaks dishes and stumbles over rugs, whose livery never fits quite correctly and whose wig is always slightly askew. However, Baxter says he is a willing worker, and he hasn't broken anything for a week, so I suppose I'll keep him on.*

Since you ask, Miss Fairfax is in tolerable health, I think. A great deal of nourishing, wholesome food, such as she is used to, would be the most useful method of restoring her health completely, but she will not get it at the Bates'. I intend to call tomorrow and see if there is anything I might contribute without giving offence. Emma seemed to show Miss Fairfax marked attention when she first came, and I had hopes that Emma was beginning to appreciate her as a companion. Unfortunately, the warm feeling seems to have cooled and I don't know that it can be revived. A pity.

Give my love to Isabella and the children, and be assured that I will not *attend any such dinner at your house unless I receive assurance in writing that there will be no single women and no widows under the age of forty among the guests. I have no faith at all that your invitations to dine are given in the name of disinterested brotherhood.*

I am, as ever, your older (but not yet decrepit) brother,
George

Knightley called on the Bates' the next morning, and discovered, quite fortuitously, that Miss Fairfax was very fond of baked apples. He made them admit that their supply of apples was nearly gone, and happily promised them more. Innate politeness kept them from refusing his gift, and he felt satisfied that he had done some small thing for Miss Fairfax's recovery. There was, of course, no escaping the profuse thanks of Miss Bates, but after the first gush of gratitude, he changed the subject by asking after the servant, Patty.

"Oh! Patty is very well, thank you, Mr. Knightley. Although to say truly, she is very well *today*, although yesterday—she has her half-day on Tuesdays, you know, and she goes to see her brother in Langham. And Patty went to see James and we were here at home—Jane had been telling us about Miss Campbell's new gowns—and Patty came in so angry—not at us, I don't mean—I do not believe she has ever been angry with *us*—but with someone who cheated her brother—the one who lives at Langham, you know, Mr. Knightley. He was playing cards of an evening at an ale-house, and he said he was cheated. A terrible thing, is it not? And Patty says that there is often crooked play there, and the proprietor does nothing about it, and so she was very distressed. But I told her—and Jane said the same, did you not, Jane?—that one can hardly believe such a thing would be allowed to go on, and very likely there is some confusion. James is a very good fellow, you know, but rather young, and it may be—one can easily be mistaken, you know."

It was on the tip of Knightley's tongue to ask the name of the ale-house where James had been cheated, but he checked himself. Anything he said that showed his attention to the story was sure to be repeated by Miss Bates and very possibly Patty. If there *was* anything wrong, it would be best for his interest to be completely unheralded. He would go to Langham himself and find James and talk to him—no, that would be sure to be remarked on. No, he would go and speak to Gilbert, who was the principal landowner around Langham. He might be aware of something. When his visit at the Bates' was finished, he went to the Crown, hired a horse, and rode the three miles to Langham. He found Gilbert in the stables, looking over a litter of spaniels.

"So, you've come for a pup after all, have you, Knightley?"

"No, not yet."

"Want to wait a bit longer, eh? Have a look at them anyway."

Knightley crouched down and picked up one of the pups. She was a lovely brown, and his hands stroked the silky fur on her ears.

"About two months old, are they?"

"Yes, very nearly weaned."

Knightley was tempted; he could probably bring this little one home that very day. In his mind's eye he could see her flopped down on the library hearth, next to—oh yes, next to the cat. Bother.

He had a feeling Madam Duval would not take kindly to a puppy. There was enough upheaval with a domestic animal already. He put the puppy down and straightened up.

"Very tempting, Gilbert, but I will resist a while longer. I came to ask if you have heard anything unpleasant recently concerning the Crows' Nest."

"Aside from their beer? No, nothing of any note. Why?"

"I have heard rumours of crooked play left unchecked, and there was a hint of something more sinister, though no particulars were offered."

"Hmm. Well, the fact that nothing has been brought to my attention doesn't mean there isn't something in it. Frankly, I don't like that fellow Cooper, and—Say, I've just remembered something. My wife was visiting one of the cottagers a week or two ago and heard that Cooper was a cousin of Finchley—you know, that man everyone suspected of robbing those houses."

"He was never caught, was he?"

"No, he disappeared. Probably well-hidden in London now. My wife asked if we ought to do something—let someone know about the cousinship, I mean—but I told her that the gossip of an old woman didn't amount to much, and even if it was true, it didn't mean that Cooper was guilty of anything."

"But you say no one knew they were related?"

"I never heard it, at any rate. Finchley was from some other place and never mentioned a connection. And the old woman appeared to think she was divulging a great secret."

"Hmm. Well, nothing to be done now, of course, but perhaps you might let me know if you hear anything more about Cooper or the ale-house. Cooper's wife is the niece of a very respectable woman who is worried about her, and I'm growing uneasy myself."

"Certainly; and I'll see what I can learn in a discreet kind of way around the village."

Knightley thanked him and rode slowly back to the Crown. It did seem that there was something in Mrs. Brown's suspicions, though it could be that the mention Miss Bates had made of an ale-house in Langham had disposed him to give too much weight to rumours. He could not even be sure that Patty's brother was talking about the Crow's Nest. At any rate, he could ask Weston if he might speak with Mrs. Brown. And he ought to talk to Spencer, too—people talked to clergymen sometimes, especially Spencer's sort. He stopped at Spencer's cottage on his way to the Abbey, and put his question to him.

"The Crow's Nest?" said Spencer, watching Old Maggie pour his guest a cup of tea. "Do you mean the one Patty Lovett's brother was cheated at?"

"How did you—"

"I called on the Bates' yesterday."

"In the evening?"

"Well, I was passing the house, and Miss Bates called out to me to come and sit with them..."

"Oh, yes. Many an unwary passer-by has been caught in the same way."

Spencer smiled and took his own cup from Old Maggie. "I didn't mind being caught this time. I had nowhere else I needed to be, and Miss Bates is the least fearsome woman in England. Miss Fairfax was there, too, and it was quite a homely little family circle."

"And Miss Bates told you what Patty said when she came in from her half-day?"

"Only that Patty's brother said he had been cheated at cards at the Crow's Nest, and that he thinks the owner has some hand in it—allowing it to continue, at least."

"Anything more?"

Spencer frowned as he tried to remember. "No, I can't think of anything else that was said about it. The subject turned to Miss Fairfax's health, and Patty's brother was not mentioned again."

"I see. Well, if you hear anything else from that quarter or anywhere else, would you let me know?"

"Of course, Mr. Knightley. Am I right to assume I shouldn't mention your interest in the matter to anyone?"

"Please do not. It may be nothing, but if it is, I would rather make discoveries without any fanfare. There are enough people talking, I fancy."

"Miss Bates," nodded Spencer. "But Miss Fairfax seems well able to hold her tongue when required—or even when not required. She's very quiet, isn't she?"

"Rather reserved, yes, but very intelligent and refined. And quite handsome."

Spencer eyed him speculatively over the rim of his teacup. "May I ask, Mr. Knightley—has Miss Fairfax some connection with your family?"

"With my family?" repeated Knightley. "No, not at all. Why do you ask?"

"Something you said once—a lady taking you to task about something. A lady who had some connection with your family."

"And you thought Miss Fairfax was the sort to criticize me?"

"Not at all—that is why I asked. Never mind. I will keep my mouth closed and my ears open and anything I learn I will pass on to you."

Knightly wondered at the curate's strange question as he walked back to the Abbey. He remembered now what he had said to Spencer that day—that a lady had told him that he was no fit judge of anyone else's situation. So why had his words of praise for Jane Fairfax today made Spencer curious if she was the lady? It was very strange. In any case, at least he knew without doubt that the cheating had been done at the Crow's Nest. He could affirm that much to Weston.

"Thank you, Baxter," he said as the butler helped him out of his coat. "I was gone longer than I intended. Any callers?"

"Mr. Weston is in the drawing room, sir, and—"

"Weston? Good. I needed to speak to him."

Without waiting to hear anything more, he went into the drawing room and was met with the sight of Weston...and someone else, too: a tall young man, well-dressed and handsome, with eyes that exactly matched Weston's.

Frank Churchill.

Damn.

They stayed no longer than a quarter of an hour, parting with an invitation to come and drink tea at Randalls that evening. Knightley felt he could not do other than accept; and although he saw them off with his usual calm civility, a complete riot of thoughts and emotions held sway in his inner man. He stood perfectly still as he watched them mount their horses and ride away. When they had gone, he took a deep breath and willed himself to put aside the outrageous desire to throw something or hit someone. Tending to his responsibilities would settle his mind, he thought, and he sought solace in his library. He sat down at his desk and attempted to look over the final plans and estimated costs for the new cottages, but before long the papers were thrust aside. He was much too confused to give his attention to any business just now, and there was only one remedy. He gave the bell pull a sharp tug and fought to keep himself from pacing while he waited for Baxter.

"I need my greatcoat," he said when the butler appeared. "I will be in the lime walk."

"Very good, Mr. Knightley," said Baxter. He knew what that meant: Mr. Knightley was not to be disturbed for anything less than the overthrow of the monarchy.

The overcast sky did nothing to cheer the rather gloomy aspect of the lime walk in winter. The leafless trees lifted their black branches to the heavens in a gesture of mute resignation, or so it seemed to him. At least he was alone; the only sound he heard was the crunch of gravel beneath his feet as he stalked severely between the rows of trees.

Frank Churchill. He looked nothing like the simpering fop that Knightley had imagined. The real Churchill looked intelligent and well-bred, and he was altogether more *manly* than Knightley had envisioned. Weston had long styled his son a charming young man, and Knightley must admit that there was some justice in that description. He had asked Knightley about Donwell parish, about the history of the house, and about the problems of enclosure in rural Surrey, all with a lively interest that seemed perfectly sincere. Knightley could not suppose that Churchill had any real thirst for knowledge about these things, but undoubtedly he had excellent powers of conversation. *Smooth,* Knightley thought, *very smooth. Slippery, in fact.*

He remembered his argument with Emma all those weeks ago when she had informed him of the sort of young man she thought Churchill would be. He would be able to adapt his conversation to the taste of everybody, she had said, and able to follow the lead or take the lead on almost any subject. From what Knightley had seen today, she had been very near the mark. And by now she knew it: Weston had been quick to inform him that they had already been to Hartfield that day—had been there, in fact, as early as propriety would allow. Weston was eager, much too eager, to promote a match between his son and Emma. There was a real possibility that she would be annoyed at having a young man thrown at her head; she might, out of pure stubbornness, refuse to have any more than a distant acquaintance with him. But then again, she might not.

He reached the end of the lime walk and looked out over the low wall to where Abbey Mill farm could be seen in the distance, the thin ribbon of river winding lazily around it. Sheep with their new lambs were in the meadow before him, the bank full of timber was beyond it. It was his world—his peaceful world—and now this conceited, selfish fellow had come into it and upset everything. It was exceedingly aggravating. He turned abruptly and started back up the walk toward the house.

"He has no right," Knightley said aloud, "to come here and display his charms to an unsuspecting population." There was no one to agree with him; his words hung in the air, as hollow as the reasoning that had provoked them. No right to come? Ridiculous. Churchill had every right to come. Was not the biggest blot on his character that he had not visited Randalls sooner? It was nonsensical to fault him for coming.

Then what was it, Knightley wondered, that made him feel justified in his anger? No, it was not anger, not altogether. There was something else—some other emotion that he could not immediately put a name to. Anger would make his jaw tense and his fingers clench, as they were doing now. But it would not twist something inside him and produce the sensation of dread which seemed to appear every time he thought of Churchill. It was almost as if he were afraid of…

Afraid. Yes, that was it: the other emotion was fear. Fear of what, exactly? Well, he had been afraid that Churchill would dupe his father into giving him money that he might squander in gambling or some other unwholesome thing, but he knew it was not only that. It was Emma. He was afraid of Churchill's effect on Emma. It was clear as anything, now that he thought about it. He had always been afraid that she might be taken in by this plausible gentleman and not notice, or not care, about the machinations of the Westons. It was probably a groundless fear; in spite of her defence of Churchill, Emma was too clever to be fooled by such a glib, shallow puppy. She must be aware of his deficiencies. He knew she was. *She must be.* He was not worried about that.

No, his concern was centred on Emma's naiveté about men. She had unwittingly led Elton to believe that she was in love with him;

might she not accidentally do the same with Churchill? She might, for example, look at Churchill with nothing more than friendly interest on her face, but a man could get lost in those beautiful hazel eyes of hers, and then what would be the result? If she happened to smile at him, he might regard it as a sign of particular favour. Emma's smile was one that lingered in the memory and warmed the heart at each recollection. Of course, aware of Churchill's faults as she was, she would never entangle herself permanently with him, but it would be another embarrassment, another regret. He must see what he could do to prevent such a misunderstanding.

Taking tea at Randalls that evening was not quite as tedious as Knightley had feared. The Coles had been invited as well, and it was not Weston's fault if the assembled party was not still larger.

"I would have liked to invite Mr. and Miss Woodhouse to come, too," said Weston to his son. "But Mr. Woodhouse seldom stirs from home, and is nervous about Miss Woodhouse going anywhere by herself in the evening."

"What a pity," said Churchill. "I would have liked to see more of them."

"So you will, so you will," said his father, cheerfully. "But only during daylight hours."

"Or perhaps at our dinner," said Cole, "if the folding screen we ordered arrives in time for us to issue the invitation to Hartfield. It ought to have come by now. I hope, Mr. Churchill, your father has told you how disappointed we will be if you do not favour us with your company at that dinner."

"He has," said Churchill, "and I would not fail you on any account. I am very eager to make the acquaintance of all my father's friends."

"I heard you had some acquaintance in Highbury even before you came," said Mrs. Cole. "Do I understand correctly that you have previously been in company with Miss Fairfax?"

"Yes, indeed," said Churchill. "We met at Weymouth." He smiled politely.

"She has not been well, you know," said Mrs. Cole. "When you see her again her appearance may surprise you."

Churchill bowed his head briefly in acknowledgement, but whether he would have replied or not was a mystery, for Weston said immediately, "Oh, he saw her this morning. Yes, he paid a call on the Bates' and she was there, of course."

"And how did she appear to you?" persisted Mrs. Cole. "Is there a great alteration in her?"

"She did not look as well as she did at Weymouth," said Churchill, "although I have no doubt that the air of Highbury and the care of her relatives will restore her completely."

"That is just what I think," said Mrs. Cole. "And Miss Woodhouse thinks the same. At least, that is what Miss Bates told me."

"Miss Woodhouse is generally correct," said Weston. "Is that not right, my dear?"

"Oh yes," said Mrs. Weston. "She visits the sick in Highbury very often, you know," she added, turning to Churchill, "and she is usually right when she thinks Mr. Perry ought to be called in or when she perceives some improvement in the ill person."

"Yes, Miss Woodhouse is very good about visiting," said Weston. "She is not one of those fine young ladies that give themselves airs and think they are above visiting the poor and sick of Highbury. I dare say she gives the poor as much relief as the parish does."

What Weston said was perfectly true, but it irritated Knightley nonetheless. It seemed to him that Weston was trying to advertise Emma to his son, as if she were Atkinson's Original Curling Fluid. *Miss Emma Woodhouse,* he thought sardonically, *is eminently calculated to be far superior to any other Woman ever invented. This Female is reputed to be in demand in the Highest Circles, and will never fail in beauty, vigour, and gloss.* Well, perhaps "gloss" was out of place. In any case, Emma needed no panegyrics to recommend her to anyone, especially to Churchill.

It occurred to Knightley that he was not contributing much to the talk this evening; he hoped the Westons would not be offended at his taking so little effort to converse with Churchill. He thought it was better if he did not affect comradeship with the young man: he could observe his behaviour much more effectually from a distance.

"I am anxious to see your new pianoforté," Mrs. Weston was saying to Mrs. Cole.

"And I am anxious to hear you play it," replied Mrs. Cole. "It has not yet been done justice to and I am hoping that at our dinner we may persuade several of the ladies to try it."

"Excellent!" said Weston. "I do hope that Miss Woodhouse will be there—I believe she has a very good style of playing."

"And Miss Fairfax, too," said Mrs. Cole, "It has been a long time since I have heard her play."

Knightley seized on this—it would keep Weston from going on about Emma.

"I greatly look forward to hearing Miss Fairfax play again," he said. "She is a very superior musician. And I hope she may be persuaded to sing a little as well."

"Oh, yes," agreed Mrs. Weston. "I do hope she may sing."

"It will be a pleasure for her also, I think," pursued Knightley, "as she has no instrument to play at the Bates'. It is quite a pity that she does not; it would be a delightful occupation for her and give great enjoyment to her family."

"Oh, indeed," said Weston. "It is a shame that she doesn't have a pianoforté of her own. However, I know she plays whenever she comes to Hartfield—Miss Woodhouse insists on it, you know—such a kind-hearted woman."

"The young ladies are two of a kind," said Knightley hastily. "Miss Fairfax is extremely benevolent and thoughtful—something not often seen in women as elegant as she." He had no definite examples of Jane Fairfax's compassionate nature to offer, and he hoped no one would press him about it; he was only hoping to keep Weston quiet.

"She's a handsome young lady, as well," said Cole. "It's rather surprising that she hasn't caught the eye of any worthy young man while living with the Campbells."

"Certainly," said Knightley, "And—"

But Weston was too quick for him.

"Quite right—a very handsome young lady, indeed. Though I think perhaps Miss Woodhouse is considered the greater beauty. They are both very fair and agreeable, however, and it will be very pleasant to be in company with them again. We are full of anticipation for your dinner, Mrs. Cole. Aren't we, Frank?"

20

"May I venture to hope, sir, that you will be at Donwell on St. Valentine's Day as usual?" said Knightley to Dr. Hughes. He had called on the rector and found Spencer there, and the three men were sitting comfortably in the rectory drawing room.

"I fear not," said the elder gentleman. "Mr. Perry says that I ought not to go anywhere for two more weeks at the least—I asked him particularly. But perhaps Mr. Spencer will come in my place."

"Oh yes," said Knightley, turning to Spencer, "I hope you will. It has always been the custom at Donwell—at least since my grandfather's time—to give small gifts of money to the children of the parish on St. Valentine's Day."

"A very commendable tradition," said Spencer.

"Dr. Hughes has always come up to the Abbey on the day because he says he ought to help with the arduous task of giving out the money—a very thin excuse, I must say."

Dr. Hughes chuckled. "You don't expect me to tell everyone that I only come because I dote on the children of the parish and like to see the joy on their faces when given a gift, do you? Whatever would become of my reputation as a curmudgeon of the first order?"

"I'm afraid that reputation is in tatters, and has been ever since you started slipping your own pennies into the hands of the children as they leave the Abby—I've seen you do it every fourteenth of

February for the past five years."

Dr. Hughes glanced at the curate with a guilty smile. "Found out! And I thought I was being so clever. I hope you do not mind, Mr. Knightley?"

"Not in the least. 'In charity there is no excess.'"

"That has always been my own view," agreed Dr. Hughes. "Well, Spencer, if you will kindly take my place at the Abbey, I will give you a small sack of pennies to distribute on my behalf."

"Certainly. And perhaps I could even—"

"No, no. You must not think of it. I know what your income is, remember." There was a twinkle in the rector's eye as he added, "'Obey them that have the rule over you', you know."

"I fear there is no argument against that," said Spencer. "But you will not stop me giving them what I can—a smile, a friendly word, and a place in my prayers."

"This fellow," said Dr. Hughes to Knightley, "is far more pert than he seems on first acquaintance, isn't he? You must keep a watch over your lips, Spencer—your obstinacy may get you something you don't expect. Like a bishopric. Very well, you go and hand out my pennies and give them what is far more valuable from yourself. Now then, you might take it upon yourself to inform any new people in the parish of this little benefaction. That is, if there *are* any recent arrivals with children..."

The rector looked unnaturally blank for a moment, but Spencer said immediately, "Mrs. Catherwood and her son are at the Foote farm."

"Ah, yes, quite right," said the rector. "You must be sure they know." His amusement was thinly veiled, and Knightley wondered at Spencer's not noticing it, but the curate looked as earnest as usual when he assured Dr. Hughes that he would take care to do so.

"I would tell them immediately, but I must meet with the verger in Highbury soon—in fact, I must be going or I will be late. However, I will visit the Foote farm on my return."

"Perhaps I might walk with you," said Knightley. "I have business with William Cox."

"Certainly, sir."

"Mr. Elton's absence has given me the opportunity for plenty of exercise," said Spencer as they walked companionably toward Highbury. "I think it has been good for my health."

"I suppose that is some compensation for the demanding nature of the last few weeks."

"Yes. To be truthful, after the first week or two I didn't mind so much. But my duties being reduced now will enable me to pursue…other things."

Knightley was tempted to ask Spencer if marriage with Mrs. Catherwood was one of those things, but he forbore. It seemed unlikely that Spencer had spoken of it to anyone—if he had, Dr. Hughes' gentle teasing would surely have been met with a blush. Dr. Hughes had no doubt deduced the state of things for himself from Spencer's chance comments, the same way Knightley had. Poor Spencer! To be so transparent and evidently unconscious of it! Knightley would hate to think that someone else could read his heart without his being aware of it. It seemed a weakness, somehow.

The men parted at the church, and Knightley went to see William Cox with a question about the leases for the new cottages. He left Cox's office a half hour later with his mind full of terms and percentages, and rather anxious that he get back to Donwell in time to talk to Larkins about the leases before he drew them up. He wondered if Emma was right after all: perhaps he ought to keep a saddle horse for occasions like this.

And then, with a start, he recognized just who was walking ahead of him: it was Churchill, with Emma on one side and Mrs. Weston on the other. They were perhaps ten yards away—too far for him to hear what they were saying, but close enough that he heard Emma laugh. What were they speaking of? He was tempted to creep up behind them and listen, but knew it would be less than honourable. More than that, it would be nearly impossible to do without someone noticing.

Their progress down the street was slow, and in spite of the haste he had been in only moments before, Knightley kept well behind. Emma seemed very much interested in what Churchill was saying. One could only hope he was not making up stories for her benefit. Knightley wondered who had proposed the walk through Highbury. Would Emma have suggested it? No, no, of course not, and nor would Mrs. Weston have done so. It must have been Churchill. He was the sort to want to parade himself around the village and give the appearance of intimacy with Emma.

The trio turned in to the church, and Knightley, after wavering for a moment, went on to Donwell. There was nothing to be gained by following the little group through the town, and he did not feel equal to making himself a fourth to their party. After he had finished with William Larkins there would be time to reflect on this state of affairs and determine what could be done about it.

Perhaps he was putting too much weight on this little incident. After all, Churchill's faults were heavy and numerous, were they not? He had neglected his father and failed to show Mrs. Weston the honour due her, for one thing. And for another, he...he had...well, he must have done something else worthy of censure. Oh yes, he had frivoled his time away at Weymouth. And Emma knew that; she would not let herself fall in love with such a fellow. He was not worth worrying over.

He assured himself of that fact often throughout the long evening and more than once as he lay in his bed. But when he found himself picking at his breakfast, wondering again if Churchill would visit Hartfield that morning, he decided that action was necessary. He would go and prove to himself that Churchill was not at Hartfield—or that even if he was, there was nothing to worry about. But he would not go immediately. To hasten to Hartfield so early in the morning merely to reassure himself of something that was not really a threat would be ridiculous. No, he would look over those leases again first; he had been distracted the day before when he drew them up, and he ought to examine them again before they were signed.

He dealt with the leases, and then, just to show that he could, waited an extra half-hour before setting off for Hartfield. He even kept his pace moderate and stopped to talk to John Page for a few minutes when he met him on the road.

In spite of his laborious nonchalance, it was a relief to find that Churchill was not at Hartfield after all. Mr. Woodhouse and Emma were sitting together just as they usually did in the mornings, Emma working at her embroidery and Mr. Woodhouse seated by the fire, ready to chat or to doze as the desire took him. All was comfortable and familiar. Knightley dropped into a chair and picked up a newspaper to look over during the companionable silence that would follow Mr. Woodhouse's enquiries as to his health and well-being. But after these questions were answered, Mr. Woodhouse had another communication to make.

"I suppose you know, Mr. Knightley, that Emma is going to dine at the Coles'."

Knightley could not help the smile that flickered over his face.

"No, I did not know it, sir," he said, "but I am glad to hear it."

"I wish the Coles had rather chosen to take their tea with us here some afternoon instead of requiring people go out in the evening to dine. I consider it a very ill-advised scheme. But they are so anxious to have dear Emma come, and of course the Westons will be there, and yourself—Emma will be well taken care of, you know—and I suppose it is as well that she goes."

"I own that I am delighted that she will be one of the party."

"It seems a very large party," said Mr. Woodhouse. "The Gilberts and some of the Coxes are to be there with the Westons and you and Emma."

"And Mr. Churchill," put in Emma.

It meant nothing, of course. She was merely supplying a name that her father had forgotten. Knightley forced himself to be unconcerned. He opened the newspaper and began to scan its contents.

"My dear, you forget," said Mr. Woodhouse. "He cannot be there. He has gone to London."

"It is only for the day, Papa," said Emma. "You remember, he wanted to get his hair cut."

"Ah, yes, I had forgotten," said Mr. Woodhouse. "Mrs. Weston said that as he was eating his breakfast this morning he said he must have his hair cut and that no place would answer for it but London. It was a long way to go for such an errand, I think."

Gone to London to have his hair cut? "Hmph! Just the trifling, silly fellow I took him for." The words were out of his mouth before he realized he was saying them aloud. The triumph he felt at having his opinion of Churchill vindicated was tempered by anxiety that Emma would take issue with his words. What an idiot he was to have voiced them! He did not want to be drawn into another argument with her about Frank Churchill. She said nothing to him, however, and gradually his fear subsided.

14 February
Donwell Abbey

Dear John,

Yes, the annual distribution of coins to the children of Donwell is going forward in a few hours in spite of the fact that Dr. Hughes is not well enough to come to the Abbey this year. Spencer is coming in his place, much to the apprehension of Larkins. He is afraid that Spencer will be unwary enough to give money to someone who is ineligible for it – a tragedy without equal in Larkins' mind. To be sure, Peter Ross has been 'fourteen' for the last two years and will certainly try his luck again, but I think Spencer will be equal to the challenge. Of course, Larkins is also worried about damage to the gardens – the day is fine and we will hold the great event out of doors, as we did several years ago. As the children arrive, they will be brought to me and Spencer and then allowed to roam the gardens until three o'clock. Larkins has taken it upon himself to see that all gardeners and under-gardeners will be posted in various places around the gardens to help keep watch. I cannot think what his anxiety would be if anything was actually flowering or producing fruit! The garden is a poor place in February. But the children will no doubt enjoy the fountain and the fish-ponds.

If it were All Fool's Day instead of the Feast of St. Valentine, I would tell you that I am about to be wed to either the Martins' dairymaid or a beautiful heiress – I don't know which you would find harder to believe. As it is, I will answer your most impertinent inquiry by saying that I believe there are *romantic attachments forming in Donwell, but none of them have anything to do with*

your long-suffering brother,
George

"Oh, Mr. Knightley, how very kind of you to call!" said Miss Bates, beaming. "We were only this moment talking of you, and saying that we would be sure to see you this evening, when I spied you coming across the street. 'Oh, look!' said I, 'Here is Mr. Knightley come to see us—or perhaps not'—because you know, Mr. Knightley, you may have been going somewhere else—but indeed you came straight to us. How do you do?"

Miss Bates bustled about, taking care of his hat and coat and ushering him toward the preferred seat in their little parlour. They advanced only a little way, however, before Knightley spied a small but very handsome piano-forte against the wall where there had been empty space before.

"What a very fine-looking instrument!" he exclaimed.

"I quite agree, Mr. Knightley, and you are no more astonished than we were yesterday when it arrived—only yesterday—and such a magnificent thing! You can imagine how surprised we all were, and Jane especially, for she says she had not the least notion—and indeed, how could she have guessed anything of the sort? But it was directed to "Miss Fairfax", so we know there was no mistake—only whoever sent it did not include their own name, and we are quite in the dark about the giver."

"How very mysterious! I am extremely gratified that Miss Fairfax should have such an instrument; it is exactly what all her friends must have wished for. A Broadwood, too! Most satisfactory. The manner of giving is very strange, though, isn't it? Perhaps Col. Campbell might—"

"Yes, Mr. Knightley, that is just what we think—it could only be from the Campbells—so generous and thoughtful as they are! And they think so highly of Jane—excuse my saying so to you, Mr. Knightley—I hope you do not think it unbecoming in an aunt to boast a little about her niece—but they *are* very fond of dear Jane and nothing could be more natural than their sending a gift—although indeed they have never done so before, but—however, we are quite sure that it must have come from the Campbells."

"A very generous gift."

"Ah, you may say so, Mr. Knightley, you who are so generous yourself—the most liberal benefactor in three parishes, I am sure. Mrs. Hughes came this morning—such an old friend! So delightful!—and she told us how sorry Dr. Hughes was to miss the St. Valentine's tradition—so very sad that he is not yet mended enough to have come! But Mrs. Hughes said that Mr. Spencer came in his place—such a fine young man—so kind—I do hope he got on well?"

Knightley smiled. It had been most amusing to watch Spencer the previous day as he was exceedingly distracted from his task of distributing Dr. Hughes' pennies. His eyes constantly scanned the gardens for Mrs. Catherwood and her little son as he absently doled out a penny to each child that approached him. Even more amusing was the sudden "Oh!" that he had uttered when he saw the Catherwoods, and the way he had hurried to greet them and then wandered the garden paths with them until he remembered the little purse of coins in his hand and reluctantly went back to his post.

"Yes," said Knightley, "I believe Mr. Spencer did get on very well."

"I am *so* happy to hear it—though of course he is such a favourite with all the children, and with their parents, too, I am sure. Mrs. Hughes speaks so very highly of him! Working so hard—at both parishes, too—missing dear Mr. Elton—such a pity he has been gone so long! But then, of course, when he returns, he will bring a mistress for the vicarage! So many new people in the parish—with Mr. Churchill, of course. Such a congenial young man! And so very handsome! I'm sure I've never seen a finer—excepting yourself, of course, Mr. Knightley—but then he is such a *young* man that there ought to be no comparison—"

Knightley cleared his throat.

"I understand from Mr. Cole that you and Miss Fairfax will come to the Coles' this evening to take tea with the assembled party."

"Oh, yes, Mr. Knightley! So thoughtful—so kind of Mrs. Cole to invite us! Able to see so many friends at once! "

"May I entreat you to let my carriage convey you there and home again?"

"Oh, Mr. Knightley, there is no need for any such attention, I assure you! We are well able to walk."

"Indeed you are, but we must be careful for the health of Miss Fairfax, you know. She is looking stronger, I think, and we ought to take care that nothing hinders her full recovery."

"That is very true, Mr. Knightley, and I don't know but that I ought to let you take Jane, at least."

"Oh, I do think you ought to share the carriage with her, Miss Bates—otherwise she may be unwilling to let you walk alone and refuse the carriage altogether."

"Quite true, Mr. Knightley, I had not thought of it. Perhaps we had better both ride in your carriage then—we would be most grateful."

21

Knightley dressed with particular care for the dinner party. Baxter was surprised to hear his master express a preference for the striped waistcoat rather than the green, and at his unwonted interest in the way his neckcloth was tied. Miss Bates' words about the congenial and handsome Frank Churchill had rankled a bit, and Knightley was determined not to look drab and middle-aged in his company. When Baxter had done his best and gone out, Knightley looked at himself in the mirror. Nothing remarkable there; he looked, as always, like a conventional country gentleman of the dependable sort. No one could ever have mistaken him for a man of fashion and intrigue, and for an instant he rather regretted it. He turned from the mirror impatiently.

Until last week, he had been looking forward to this evening. To see Emma enjoying herself *at the Coles'* would be very satisfying—a triumph of good sense over silly prejudice. Now, with the addition of Churchill to the party, all was changed. Uppermost in his mind was the worry that Emma would unconsciously encourage Churchill. An image from yesterday's encounter in Highbury was imprinted on his mind: that of Emma smiling up at Churchill and laughing at his nonsense. That was the sort of thing that might very well make Churchill think there was more to her amiability than mere politeness. And consider what *that* might lead to! Churchill might have enough encouragement that he would actually offer for her, as any man would if he had the smallest hope of succeeding.

And Emma just might take pity on him—she was that compassionate—and accept him in spite of everything. That would be a disaster. He felt sick at the thought of it.

"Well," he said to Madam Duval, who had watched him dress with a gravity that rivalled his own, "I fear it will be a very disagreeable evening, but there is really nothing for it but to go on and hope for the best. No, you may *not* brush up against my leg; I want no cat hairs on my clothing tonight!" He sidestepped the cat and went downstairs to the waiting carriage.

When he arrived at the Coles', Emma's carriage was found to be just behind his own, and he was glad for the opportunity—all too rare—of handing her out himself.

She smiled when she saw him, and said, "This is coming as you should do—like a gentleman. I am quite glad to see you."

"Thank you," he said, and bowed with mock formality. "How lucky that we should arrive at the same moment! For if we had met first in the drawing-room, I doubt whether you would have discerned me to be more of a gentleman than usual. You might not have distinguished how I came, by my look or manner."

It was reassuring to see her left eyebrow lift quite in the old way as she said "Yes, I should, I am sure I should. There is always a look of consciousness or bustle when people come in a way which they know to be beneath them. You think you carry it off very well, I dare say, but with you it is a sort of bravado, an air of affected unconcern; I always observe it whenever I meet you under those circumstances. *Now* you have nothing to try for. You are not afraid of being supposed ashamed. You are not striving to look taller than anybody else. *Now* I shall really be very happy to walk into the same room with you."

No one but Emma would have said such a thing to him, and he revelled in it as proof that she had not changed. The attention of one conceited young man was not enough to alter his Emma. He smiled and told her that she was nonsensical—as she was, of course—and took her into the house.

Knightley and Emma were the first to arrive, and he could see that she was gratified by the deference paid to her by the Coles. More than that, Mrs. Cole asked after Mr. Woodhouse almost before the first greetings were over. Emma's smile at this was most genuine, and Knightley reflected that Mrs. Cole might now make quite a number of ungenteel blunders before Emma would feel any disdain for her.

Mr. and Mrs. Gilbert and their son Edmund were the next to arrive, and while the Coles greeted them, Emma said, "I suppose the children of Donwell are very happy today—they always are on the fifteenth of February."

"I hope so. We opened the gardens to them this year."

"And William Larkins approved?"

"Well, I don't say that. But they were all very quiet and well-behaved, and no accidents beyond little James Wenham's falling into a fish-pond."

"Not seriously injured, I hope?"

"Not at all—unless you take a serious view of the fact that he was still dripping while being thoroughly scolded by his mother; he was trying to touch a fish despite having been forbidden to do so a moment before."

Emma laughed. "He sounds rather like our nephew John. I wish I had been there to see him."

"I wish you had, too." He wondered suddenly why he had never before invited Emma to be present. It was exactly the sort of thing she enjoyed—the giving of charity, the antics of children—she ought to have been a part of it.

"Come next year," he said impulsively. "You can be the one to distribute the coins."

She looked at him, surprised at his earnest tone; but before she could answer, a new group of guests claimed her attention.

"Oh look! The Westons and Mr. Churchill have come," she said, and walked off precipitately to greet them, leaving him standing alone. He watched her meet the Westons with all the warmth and affection that she ought to have for such friends. Nothing could be more proper or more endearing. But she ought not to look so delighted with the very obvious admiration of Churchill, who not only approached her the instant propriety would allow, but also stayed at her side without seeming to notice anyone else in the room. Even when the Mr. Coxes arrived, he merely bowed to them from his place near Emma and continued his conversation with her. Knightley could not insert himself into their discussion, but he wished he knew what they were saying. He did not feel himself in a humour to talk to anyone, really, and found himself skulking around the edges of the party.

He was glad to see, when dinner was announced, that Weston was the one escorting Emma to the dining room. But as they were all seating themselves around the table, Churchill murmured a few words in the ear of his father, who nodded at him and then said, smiling, "Here, Frank—this is your seat, next to Miss Woodhouse." Knightley was not surprised to see that Emma looked pleased.

It was a most aggravating dinner. Knightley was seated far enough away from Churchill and Emma that he could not hear anything they were saying. The only clues he might have had about their subject matter would have come from watching their lips, and he could not very well do that and still be civil to Mrs. Gilbert, who was seated beside him. She was new to the story of Mr. Elton's sudden engagement, and pressed him for details about the length of their courtship and the antecedents of Miss Hawkins. From time to time he stole glances at Emma and Churchill; they seemed wholly absorbed in their conversation. To be sure, they did listen to Mrs. Cole when she spoke of Miss Fairfax's new pianoforte—Emma must not have heard of it yet—but when Mrs. Cole had finished her tale, they resumed their conversation and talked only to each other.

After dessert, the Coles' children were ushered by their caregivers into the dining room, and Knightley hoped that the presence of the little ones would awaken Emma's interest in something besides her neighbour. It seemed to. She smiled at the cherubs and even engaged the oldest daughter in a few minutes' conversation, which gratified Mrs. Cole immensely. For nearly fifteen minutes Churchill and Emma behaved in such a way that an impartial observer might think there was no particular interest between them. But when at length the ladies excused themselves, Knightley saw Emma look back at Churchill as she left the room.

"Well, I suppose we ought to join the others," said Cole.

"Indeed," said Knightley with feeling. The annoyance he had felt during dinner was nothing to what he had suffered while the gentlemen lingered over the port. Churchill had left the dining room for the company of the ladies before much time had passed, and Knightley would have followed him if he could. But Cole and Weston had got on to the topic of poor rates, and the issue was such that Knightley could not leave in the middle of the discussion. He tried to keep his mind on the plight of the young widow Rigsby, but the thought that Churchill had very likely been seated next to Emma for the last twenty minutes kept recurring. Why had she looked back at Churchill when she left the room? Did she not *know* that it could only give him encouragement? If they were tête-à-tête again now—well, he could not answer for the consequences.

And in point of fact, when Knightley drifted with the remaining gentlemen into the drawing room, the two of them *were* seated next to each other, and evidently having a lively conversation. They were interrupted by Cole, who engaged Emma in some banter, leaving Churchill to contemplate something on the far side of the room. Knightley wondered briefly if he ought to go and talk to Churchill himself and distract his attention away from Emma, but the thought of trying to keep all Frank Churchill's conversation to himself for an entire evening was more than he could endure.

It came to him that he ought not to stand here alone, staring, like this—he ought to find someone to talk to. He looked around to see who was disengaged. Miss Bates and her niece had arrived for the tea and music, along with a few other females, but none of them looked neglected. Edmund Gilbert caught his eye; the youth was sitting alone and looked as if he found the evening very tedious. He was only eighteen, and Knightley had never before seen him at a dinner party given by any but his parents. He was to have begun university this year, but a serious illness just before the term began had delayed his education. He had always seemed like a pleasant enough fellow, though Knightley had the feeling that he had a tendency to strain at the parental leading-strings.

"Well, Edmund," he began, taking the empty seat next to the young man, "I fear this not so amusing an evening as you would wish."

Edmund grinned. "Is my boredom that apparent, sir?"

"I'm afraid it is."

"I ought to hide it better, then. I believe I was invited on the assumption that the other younger guests would extend the hand of friendship to one so callow as I." His eyes drifted toward Emma and Churchill, who were, Knightley noticed, talking again. Edmund was right: Churchill ought to be the one talking to him. Emma would have done so, he was sure, if only Churchill had not distracted her so entirely. There was no end to the mischief that fellow was doing!

"I suppose the evening has not been even half as long as it has seemed," said Edmund. "I have only been here for…" Edmund paused and seemed to feel for a watch; finding nothing, he glanced down and then looked sheepishly at Knightley. "I keep forgetting that my watch is gone."

"Broken, is it?"

"N-no…I…lost it."

"Bad luck," said Knightley.

"It is, rather. I'll get another, of course, but this one was a gift from my grandfather. I don't think I fully appreciated it until it was gone."

"That seems to be usual with lost things. Someone once stole a walking stick of mine, and though I never thought much of it while I had it, I have regretted its loss a hundred times since."

"Yes. Mother says, 'The most precious jewel is always the one that was lost.'"

"It must be a celebrated maternal aphorism…I recall my own mother saying the same."

Knightley's eyes turned toward Emma again. She was now talking to Mrs. Weston and Churchill was across the room, conversing with Miss Fairfax.

"I hope your evening may improve," said Knightley, feeling that *his* evening had just improved a great deal. "I have it on good authority that there will be music before long."

"Yes, I have heard that Miss Fairfax is expected to play and sing. It was said with great anticipation, so I presume she performs very well."

"She does. And she rarely has opportunity to display her skills in Highbury—though I suppose she will have more occasion now that she has been given a pianoforte."

"Yes, I heard Mrs. Cole mention it at dinner. It was a generous gift, but rather an odd method of giving it. But perhaps it is the Colonel's usual way."

"I don't think it is," said Knightley, "At least I never heard of him doing such a thing before. He has always seemed to me to be a very sensible man—too sensible for such a scheme. Elaborate surprises have a tendency to turn awkward."

"Oh yes," said Edmund, smiling. "I know of a fellow who wanted to give a gift to his sweetheart—a necklace, I think. He thought he would surprise her with it and tried to get it into her room during her evening out. But he got into the wrong room by mistake and surprised the—well, someone else. He was taken up as a housebreaker, and only just managed to get off by getting a dozen testimonials as to his character."

Knightley stared at Edmund. He knew the story well; he had, in fact, been the presiding magistrate in the case several years past. The farm labourer (a young man with no foresight at all) had thought he was climbing through a window into a housemaid's room, but found himself instead in one of the family bedrooms. But how did Edmund come to know of it? Could Larkins possibly...? No, he was quite sure Larkins would not carry tales about such things. Local quarrels and romances were fair game for Larkins' tongue, but he was too loyal to Donwell to gossip about legal proceedings. Who, then?

"Most amusing," said Knightley, pleasantly. "I fancy I have heard the story before somewhere. Where did *you* hear it?"

Edmund paused and then said quietly, "Oh, playing at cards with some of the lads."

"The lads?"

"In the village." He looked up at Knightley. "Don't tell my father, if you please. He wouldn't approve."

"You have nothing to fear from me; I have no wish to interfere. All the same, I do hope that in keeping that sort of company you will not get into a scrape."

"Oh, no. It's only—there's nothing to do at home. A fellow must have some amusement."

Knightley was fairly certain that it was this particular amusement that had lost Edmund his watch. "A very natural sentiment," was all he said, however.

Ah, there was Cole coming up to Emma again; likely he would be asking her to play for them. And Churchill was not far behind him, ready to flatter away any unwillingness on her part. In a very few moments, it was apparent that the men had been successful.

Emma stood and moved toward the pianoforte, while Cole and Churchill brought several chairs closer to the instrument. Knightley noticed that Churchill seemed to be deliberately placing one chair in a spot where the performer would clearly see the face of its occupant. No doubt Churchill meant to sit there so that Emma would see his eager face whenever she lifted her eyes from the keys or the music. That would be a very bad thing. Without any compunction at all, Knightley crossed the room and sat in the chair himself.

Emma seated herself at the instrument, and the other guests arranged themselves to listen, some near to the pianoforte and some further away, where they could converse in low tones without disturbing the musician. Knightley was glad that Churchill was not sitting in his chair; it afforded him a perfect view of Emma. She was wearing the green print gown, and he thought she had never looked more beautiful. Everything in her appearance and demeanour—her eyes, her smile, her delicate colouring, the graceful way she fingered the keys—could only bewitch a man. Her voice, though not as polished as Jane Fairfax's, was delightful, and perfectly suited to the song, which was one of his favourites.

I prithee send me back my heart
Since I cannot have thine
For if from yours you will not part
Why then shouldst thou have mine?

Yet now I think on't, let it lie
To find it were in vain;
For th' hast a thief in either eye
Would steal it back again.

Why should two hearts in one breast lie
And yet not lodge together?
O love, where is thy sympathy
If thus our breasts thou sever?

It was at this point that Knightley heard another voice—a male voice—Churchill's voice—take up the song and softly sing in harmony with Emma.

But love is such a mystery

I cannot find it out;
For when I think I'm best resolved
I then am most in doubt

Then farewell care and farewell woe
I will no longer pine
For I'll believe I have her heart
As much as she hath mine.

Knightley fought to keep a frown from his face as the song ended. How impudent of the fellow to make Emma share her applause with him! Of course he made a show of begging pardon for his intrusion, and of course Emma expressed warm admiration of his singing. He was all that was charming as he deprecated his own voice (and he did so at length), but all his denials did not keep him from getting up from his chair and standing beside Emma to sing another song with her. Knightley could have wished his voice much worse than it was, and his singing without so much expression.

Why should thy cheek be pale,
Shaded with sorrow's veil?
Why should'st thou grieve me?
I will never, never leave thee.
'Mid my deepest sadness,
'Mid my gayest gladness,
I am thine, believe me;
I will never, never leave thee.

Emma looked up at Churchill and smiled. Knightley felt his jaw tense.

Life's storms may rudely blow,
Laying hope and pleasure low:
I'd ne'er deceive thee;
I could never, never leave thee.
Ne'er till my cheek grow pale,
And my heart pulses fail,
And my last breath grieve thee.
Can I ever, ever leave thee!

The last lines were sung by Churchill with his eyes on Emma's face. *Never, ever leave thee, indeed!* thought Knightley. *The sort of thing a libertine always says! Don't you trust him, Emma. He is exactly the sort that* would *leave you, in spite of fine words and soulful looks!*

Emma resigned her place at the pianoforte to Jane Fairfax and went to sit in one of the chairs further back in the room. Knightley was prepared to see Churchill follow her and claim the seat next to hers, but he did not; he stayed at the pianoforte, ready to sing with Miss Fairfax. It appeared that the prospect of exhibiting his fine voice was more appealing to him even than remaining at Emma's side.

In spite of Churchill's contribution to the music, it was a delight to hear Miss Fairfax. For several minutes he listened to "Soave sia il vento" with no other thoughts intruding. Knightley's Italian was imperfect, but he knew enough to appreciate the sentiments of the song: a tender adieu that wishes the winds to be gentle and the waves to be calm for the departing lovers. He imagined Frank Churchill to be departing forever from England's shores, and found that under those conditions he would have no difficulty wishing him as well as the words of the song did other young men.

If only he could be kept away from Emma! Knightley had not spoken a word to her since Churchill had arrived this evening. It looked as if those few words they had exchanged at the start of the evening were all he was going to have. Stay, Churchill was occupied; why should he not talk to her now? He glanced back to see that she was sitting alone; she was. He rose quietly and moved to the empty seat, glad to see her smile as he approached.

"Miss Fairfax sounds extremely well tonight; do you not think so?" he said softly.

"Yes, indeed. I have not heard her perform this piece before, but it is very beautiful."

"It is written for a trio, but as there are only two singers, she has arranged the piece a little to compensate for the missing soprano. It is not an easy thing to do."

"Her abilities are certainly very high."

"And her voice, too. Even the highest notes are perfectly clear and strong."

"Yes," said Emma.

They listened for a few more moments before Emma said, "You showed great kindness in sending your carriage for her and Miss

Bates. I know how much they are obliged to you."

"It was a mere nothing, and you know it. How can the offer of my carriage be supposed to demand any sacrifice on my part?"

She smiled at that—too reasonable to give him more credit than he deserved.

"I often feel concerned," she said, "that I dare not make *our* carriage more useful on such occasions. It is not that I am without the wish; but you know how impossible my father would deem it that James should put-to for such a purpose."

"Quite out of the question," he said, smiling, "Quite out of the question. But you must often wish it, I am sure." Of course she could not act on her inclination, but the generous impulse should be applauded. And here was proof that she *had* increased in sympathy toward the Bates'.

Emma smiled at him in return and listened silently to the music for a moment. Then she said, "This present from the Campbells—this pianoforte—is very kindly given."

"Yes, but they would have done better had they given her notice of it. Surprises are foolish things. The pleasure is not enhanced, and the inconvenience is often considerable. I should have expected better judgment in Colonel Campbell."

She seemed extraordinarily pleased with his reply, but said no more. They listened together in silence to a second offering by Jane Fairfax and Churchill. It was another beautiful piece in Italian that tested the range of its vocalists. Miss Fairfax acquitted herself well in that regard, but Knightley could tell that her voice was suffering near the end of the song, and he saw the relief on her face when it was finished.

"That will do," he muttered. "You have sung quite enough for one evening; now, be quiet."

But the auditors around the instrument had not noticed the strain on her voice, or else were less considerate than they ought to be. Several clamoured for another song, and Churchill promoted the notion by hunting through the stack of music on the pianoforte to find a song which might be supposed to be less taxing. He seized one and said, "I think you could manage this without effort; the first part is so trifling. The strength of the song falls on the second."

"That fellow thinks of nothing but showing off his own voice," said Knightley to Emma. "This must not be."

Miss Bates was passing by just at that moment, and he reached out his hand and touched her arm to attract her notice.

"Miss Bates," he said quietly, "Are you mad, to let your niece sing herself hoarse in this manner? Go and interfere. They have no mercy on her."

Miss Bates had evidently been worried about Jane already, for she said only briefly, "Yes, thank you, Mr. Knightley!" before she hastened to Jane's side and begged her to come away from the instrument and rest herself. There could be no resisting Miss Bates, and the audience gave up their entreaties and began to talk again among themselves.

Knightley felt rather smug in having captured the seat next to Emma. For a little while he would have her all to himself. He wanted to talk to her about the Coles, to see if her idea of them had changed at all by being a guest in their home. He wanted to talk to her about Jane Fairfax, to hear again some evidence that she was beginning to appreciate her true worth. He wanted to talk to her about—oh, anything. Anything at all. As long as she would smile at him and look at him with her hazel eyes and raise her left eyebrow now and then when she teased him.

"Well now, what do you think of the furnishings in the room?" he said. He knew they were elegant and wanted to hear her say so.

"Very fine. Much finer than I would have—"

She stopped to listen to the voices that had begun to murmur around them; Knightley caught the word "dancing" among the babble.

"A dance!" Emma exclaimed, eyes sparkling. "I had hoped there would be one!"

All around the room the word 'dancing' was heard as the idea was taken up, and when once Cole began moving chairs to the outer edge of the room, Knightley knew it was inevitable. For a moment he was conscious of a pang of disappointment—there would be no long talk with Emma, then. But the delight on her face made it impossible to regret it completely. It was rare enough that Emma had the opportunity to dance, and she ought to have that pleasure now and then. Knightley stood reluctantly and moved his chair to the outer edge of the room; as he returned he was arrested by the sight of Churchill making a slight bow to Emma and asking her to dance.

His heart stopped. He ought to have known—ought to have guessed—that it would happen, and done something to prevent it.

He ought not to have left her side, or perhaps got someone else to ask her. He stood there cursing himself as she took Churchill's arm and walked with him to the top of the set that was forming. He suddenly felt as if Churchill was taking away the loveliest creature on the face of the earth, and he wanted nothing more than to walk up to him with a drawn sword and say, "Unhand that young woman!" *He ought to have asked her himself.* That would have prevented this catastrophe. He frowned. The idea of his asking a lady to dance seemed to suggest a train of thought, but he couldn't quite remember…he couldn't *think* with all the bustle around him…it was something about…that if he ever brought himself to dance with someone, it would mean…something…

He became conscious that once again he was standing alone, staring at Churchill and Emma, and willed himself to look away. Mrs. Cole was standing nearby, alone. Resolutely he composed his features into an expression of polite interest and approached her with a handsome compliment about the new pianoforte on his lips. She received it graciously, and for a few moments they talked of the performers and the music. His attention was divided, however. Again and again he caught himself looking toward the dancers, until Mrs. Cole said, "Do you not dance, Mr. Knightley? Shall we find you a partner? I think Miss Fairfax is—ah, no, young Mr. Gilbert has asked her." She smiled archly as the music began. "I fear you are cut out, Mr. Knightley."

"Yes," he said slowly, watching Churchill and Emma lead off the dancing. "I believe I am."

The eyes of all in the room were on the couple as they met and retreated, turned and crossed—the other dancers waiting patiently for their turn to begin the figures, the observers at the edges of the room looking on with admiration, and Knightley, who, seeing suddenly what he had never seen before, could hardly hear the music for the clamour in his own mind condemning him as the blindest fool in England. How could he have been so unconscious of what was in his own heart?

He was in love with Emma. She was the most beautiful woman he had ever seen; the most lively, the most entrancing creature in the world. He cared more for her happiness than anyone else's—even his own. He remembered his mother's proverb and smiled bitterly. *The most precious jewel is always the one that was lost.* The cherished jewel was now slipping through his fingers...or, more accurately, dancing off with Frank Churchill. And it was all his own fault. What had he ever done to make her love him? He should have been trying to woo her for the last year, to slowly move her from her present regard for him to love. It might not have been very difficult. He knew that she treasured their friendship; she always looked to him to advise her, and his opinion did have weight with her. He was the only one of their circle that she could not get the upper hand over, and though she chafed at it, he knew she liked the challenge he presented. And her teasing was almost always for him alone. He had been so close to having all he could have hoped for in a life's companion, but like an imbecile he had been unaware of his real feelings and wasted the opportunity.

The dance seemed to go on and on and on. Mrs. Cole moved away to talk to someone else, and Knightley was left standing alone to watch his dearest Emma whirl and bound and weave in and out of the other dancers and smile at her partner. He was thankful no one else came to talk to him; he could not have said anything intelligible. All he wanted was to get home and to think.

After two dances, the lateness of the hour prompted Miss Bates to express her wish of getting home. This ended the dancing and gave Knightley something to do: he ordered his carriage for Miss Bates and her niece and escorted them out to it. He saw them off and then started back to the house, passing Churchill with Emma on his arm as they went out to her carriage. They said goodnight to him and he returned it with as much heartiness as he could summon up.

At least the dreaded evening was over. No more bustle and noise, no more agitation and turmoil. The guests were melting away into the night to take their repose in their own peaceful homes with those they loved the most. He would be back at the Abbey soon, too, with his…cat. Well, he had no one to blame but himself.

"Wussock," he muttered.

22

"Good evening, sir," said Baxter as he took Knightley's greatcoat. "I trust you had a pleasant evening."

"Very pleasant," returned Knightley, out of habit; it was not until the words left his mouth that he realized they were untrue. It seemed too much effort to correct them.

"Will you be retiring immediately, sir?"

"No, I believe I will sit in the library for a little while first."

"Certainly, sir. I will send Harry to tend to the fire. Would you wish any refreshment, sir?"

"None, thank you. And I will see to the fire myself. You need not wait up for me."

There was a slight pause before Baxter said, "Very good, sir."

The library was dark and cold; Knightley stirred up the fire which had almost expired and lighted a candle from the one he had carried in with him. He sank into the chair nearest the fire and began his mortifying reflections.

The fact that he was in love with Emma had been confronting him for some time, but he had pushed it away and given other names to the emotions that ought to have enlightened him. He had blundered on, deaf to the pleadings of his heart until the revelation of them burst on him in a surprising and, it must be said, inconvenient way. No doubt he had appeared as a complete imbecile tonight, standing there in a trance and unable to do anything but watch Emma as he acknowledged to himself for the first time that it was not because he was a partial old friend that he admired her dancing and her figure and her liveliness—it was because he wanted her for himself.

What on earth could have kept him from realizing that Emma was exactly the sort of woman he had always wanted in a wife? Intelligent, good-hearted, witty, loving...and so very, very beautiful. Incomparable. Why could he not have seen it and secured her love before Churchill came?

True, she had not always been a woman. His memories of her as a child were a little dim, although he could clearly recall being sorry when told that the Woodhouse girls had lost their mother. Isabella was twelve then, the same age he had been when his own mother had died. His mother would have liked Emma. She had been a pretty child, a clever child. She had also been wilful enough to make him anxious about her as she grew. He smiled as his memory brought forward the scene ten years earlier when John had come to him begging for his aid with his courtship of Isabella.

"You have no idea," he had said, "of the difficulty of conversing with Isabella while her father and sister are in the room. That little Emma—she seems to know exactly what I'm about and contrives to embarrass me in any way she can by her questions and her knowing looks. And Mr. Woodhouse—you know how he goes on, asking question after question about the most trivial, commonplace—"

"John—"

"I know, I know. I do respect him, George. A more benevolent man never lived. But as he doesn't seem to know what I am doing there, and Emma *does*—I am perpetually parrying the queries of both and can say precious little to Isabella."

"And where is Miss Taylor all this time?"

"Oh, she is sometimes there, too, of course, but naturally she can only command the attention of one or the other of them, leaving one free to torment me."

"You could ask Isabella to walk with you in the garden."

"I did, last week. Emma immediately asked if she could join us, and Isabella was too soft-hearted to deny her. She made a very intrusive third. George, you *must* come with me when I go to Hartfield and distract the attention of Emma and Mr. Woodhouse."

So he had done it, and been diverted beyond his expectation by little Emma's precocious banter and delightful sense of humour. As time went on, he was never quite satisfied to leave Hartfield unless he had seen Emma and talked with her a little. It was not only that she amused him; he was sincerely interested in her welfare. She had great promise, but he could see the wilfulness that was not checked, either by her father or by Miss Taylor. She was never disobedient or impudent to them; she was clever enough to get what she wanted without that. She was also clever enough to surmise that Knightley seemed to want a hand in her upbringing, even though he had no authority to enforce any of his ideas, and she took great delight in letting him know that she was allowed to do something that his judgement would have denied her.

Somehow, as time went on, his concern grew into a feeling of responsibility for her; he became a sort of self-appointed guardian. Did guardians ever fall in love with their charges when they grew up? For she *had* grown up. He wondered when he had first realized it. He seemed to remember one particular occasion ....yes, it was two or three years ago—the day he had overheard a stable-boy at the Crown Inn talking about Miss Woodhouse as "monstrous pretty and ripe for plucking". Knightley had not made his presence known at the time—the temptation to commit some physical violence against the fellow was so powerful that he had not trusted himself to make any sort of confrontation. He had, however, warned Mrs. Stokes that the lad had an insolent mouth and ought to be watched, and was very gratified to learn, a week or two later, that the stable-boy had been dismissed. Knightley could recall dining at Hartfield that evening and seeing Emma's lovely face and pleasing figure with new eyes, privately acknowledging for the first time that a grown man could be attracted to Emma. He remembered the thought making him uncomfortable.

Well, what was to be done now? Could Emma ever really fancy herself—no, no, better face up to the thing honestly; he had deluded himself long enough. Could Emma ever really *be* in love with Churchill? The thought was like the stab of a knife, but he had to own that it was possible that, in time, she could. Indeed, he was very much afraid that even now she seemed to prefer Churchill's society to his, though no doubt she had a certain amount of affection for him—rather like a favourite uncle, as John had once said. And who could blame her for desiring the company of a fascinating young man over that of an uncle? *Uncle,* indeed! Yet it would be very natural for her to think of him in just that way: his behaviour to her would suggest nothing else. She must see him as a well-intentioned, lecturing old busybody who was always interfering in her affairs and meddling in all her concerns.

The library clock chimed twelve o'clock. The fire was dying again and the coal scuttle was empty. Perhaps he ought to go to bed and try to sleep. With an effort he rose from his chair, blew out one candle and took up the other one. He paused at the window and looked out. The lawn was bathed in moonlight, which painted the cyprus trees silver and threw their long shadows across the gravel walk. Down the road a mile hence was Hartfield, where Emma was sleeping.

"Goodnight, sweet Emma," he whispered. "May your slumber be restful and your dreams—" He stopped and smiled ruefully. Her dreams were likely to be of Frank Churchill. No matter. "Goodnight nonetheless, Emma. Goodnight...my love."

It spite of a shortened night, Knightley opened his eyes before Baxter came to wake him. His first thought was to see Emma. He would dress and go to Hartfield and—and what? Sit with Emma and Mr. Woodhouse and talk over small items of news in the usual way, wondering all the while if Emma was thinking of Churchill? It would be maddening. No, he ought to stay away from Hartfield until he had pondered the situation a little more. He would go to the lime walk directly after breakfast and do his thinking there.

He found, however, that it was impossible to keep his mind from the subject while he dressed and ate. Questions crowded into his mind; difficult, unpleasant questions that had no intention of letting him perform his morning rituals in peace. Was it too late to try to win Emma? Was Churchill seriously pursuing her? If he was, would it be dishonourable to enter the lists and compete for her affection?

Just as he was finishing his breakfast, the footman came in with a note.

"Thank you, Harry," he said as he put down his cup and took the note. It was written in a clear, feminine hand, and asked him if he would have the kindness to visit the cottage of John Page in the course of the morning, on urgent business.

He frowned. John Page was one of the under-gardeners; a hard worker and one on whom the head gardener depended greatly. Well, he should go immediately, of course; the lime walk must wait.

The day was bright and clear with little wind: good weather for the transplanting of the melons and cucumbers into new hot-beds. He saw the work going forward as he walked past the kitchen gardens. Seeing Rooker, the head gardener, he asked him if he knew what was wrong with John Page.

"I hear he's quite ill, Mr. Knightley, but I don't know that they'll be ringing the bells for him yet."

Page's cottage was not far from the Abbey; it was one of the newer sort with two rooms on the ground floor. Knightley's knock was answered by Page's wife, Sarah, who said, "Oh, good morning, sir! Thank you ever so much for comin'!" and curtsied deeply before opening the door wide to let him in. The room seemed full of people, but a moment's survey revealed the occupants to be Mrs. Catherwood, Granny Page, and three or four older children. There was also a little boy sitting in a chair against the wall; Knightley recognized him as Mrs. Catherwood's son.

"Come, children!" said Sarah, "Show manners to Mr. Knightley." The children bobbed or bowed and murmured, "Good morning, sir." Mrs. Catherwood whispered to her son and held his hand while he stood up and made his bow.

"Now then, you children—Mags, Peter, Johnny—you go outside." Sarah turned from her children to Mrs. Catherwood and said, "Will James be goin' out with 'em or will he stay here?"

"I think he would like to be near the other children. Perhaps I should go out with them and settle him someplace near the door. Granny—" She turned to the old woman. "I will return in a moment to help with the poultice."

"May I bring the whistle, Mama?" said James, holding up a roughly-carved instrument. Mrs. Catherwood looked to Sarah.

"Of course he may, bless 'im," said Sarah.

"Poor thing," she added to Knightley when the others were gone. "He's a lovely little chap—sweet as a nut and never complains when he has to sit and wait for 'is mother—which happens regular, as she's such a good soul, always nursing the sick or helping those with troubles. And he always comes with 'er, as the missus at the farm can't be bothered with the boy. Now then, sir, I'll take you in to see John."

She opened the door to the other room and ushered Knightley in before her. The sick man was lying in bed, very pale but still alert.

"Mr. Knightley, sir," he wheezed. "I thank you for coming."

"Of course." Knightley waved the thanks aside. "I'm sorry to see you poorly, John."

"Eh, I'm not so bad," said the man, but broke off with a cough.

"It's only talking makes it worse," said his wife. "Shall I tell Mr. Knightley then, John?"

John nodded.

"Well then, sir, it's this way. John's brother lives in Kingston—he's ostler at The Black Lion. He was here a fortnight since to visit us."

"Yes. He came to church with you, didn't he? I remember seeing you both with someone new in the churchyard."

"That's it, sir. Well, he sent us this letter here—it come yesterday while John was sleeping. I can't read, so I set it aside, and it weren't until this morning that we knew what it said." She held out the letter to Knightley, who unfolded and read it.

Deer John, Mister Gibbens thinks he saw me steele two Bags o oates and a Gold Watch on the frist day o Febr. but as you know I was with you then. The Justis is holdin me over but ses he will not send me on if I can bring a Witness to my being out of Kinston on that day. You must come and tell him John.

Yr. brother Sam

"I see," said Knightley. "But it ought to be easy enough to prove his innocence."

"Aye, it would, sir," said John faintly, "if I could get out of bed and go." Once more his body was wracked by coughs.

"Here, John," said his wife kindly. "Take a little water. There. I don't think 'e ought to go off, Mr. Knightley, sir, even if he could get around a little. Mrs. Catherwood says it's like to be pleurisy. He might have got away with only a cold, only he *would* go and dig the asparagus beds in the rain last week, though Mr. Rooker said he might rest at home until his throat was better." She looked at her husband with concern and reproach mingled on her face.

John exerted himself again to say, "But I can't let Sam—"

"I know you can't, John," said Sarah. "Mrs. Catherwood thought of sending for you, Mr. Knightley, in case you could do something."

"Of course. I will send a letter to the magistrate—it must be Carver—and tell him—stay, I could ride there and back this afternoon and tell Carver myself that I know the man to be innocent as I saw him in my parish. I suppose I did not see him personally on the day in question, but I trust you, John, and I daresay your neighbours saw him here on the first of February?"

"Oh, yes, sir!" put in Sarah. "Ask any of 'em that you like—they'll all say the same. We ought not to put you to so much trouble, sir—"

"It is far less trouble than you think. I would welcome a long ride today, and I do believe this will be the quickest way of getting Sam free. I'll take the letter, if I may, and talk to a few of your neighbours—must be able to tell Carver I interviewed witnesses personally, you know. Farewell, John. If I don't see you this evening I'll send a message to say that all is well. No, Mrs. Page, you needn't bother to see me out; I can find my way."

When he passed through the main room again, Mrs. Catherwood was alone, sitting at the table cutting squares of muslin. He paused for a moment, watching her. She was no more than twenty-four or so, and rather pretty. She would be an admirable wife for Spencer, and he wished he could say something to help the curate's suit along; nothing occurred to him, however.

She looked up. "Did you wish to see Granny, sir? I can fetch her for you..."

"No, no. I only wanted to offer my thanks for the help you are giving here."

Mrs. Catherwood smiled. "It is not much, sir."

"I think they would not agree with you. It means a great deal to them."

"I hope I can do a little. I was greatly helped by kind friends in my own times of difficulty; I am only too glad to do the same for others."

Perfect, thought Knightley. *Spencer could find no better wife in all of Surrey.* He bid her good day and went to talk to those in the neighbouring cottages. In less than an hour he had got assurances from half a dozen people that John Page's brother Sam had been in Donwell on the first of February. That was all right, then. He would go and get a horse from the Crown and ride to Kingston.

He passed Page's cottage once again on the way to Highbury.

Little James Catherwood was sitting in the sunshine outside the door on the stump of a tree, apparently contented. He was still turning the whistle over and over in his hands, feeling every hole and bump and running his fingers down its length. Perhaps the little chap would have an interest in music, as Spencer had suggested. Knightley smiled, and then frowned as he heard John Page cough inside the cottage. Poor fellow. Perhaps he would rest better with his mind at ease over his brother.

Rest was so often the best cure, Knightley mused as he walked on. It was because he had continued to work—and in the rain—when he already had a cold that Page's illness had become serious. It was a shame he had not listened to the voice of his wife and stayed home that day. Those who were ill needed plenty of rest. Jane Fairfax, for example, needed to take care; perhaps she ought not to have gone to the Coles'. Her health was still fragile, and too much exertion was sure to lay her low. Of course, Churchill had been no help at all, pressing her to sing in spite of her discomfort. It was just like him, really. No thought for anyone but himself. At least Miss Fairfax had been able to travel in a carriage. When he returned from Kingston he would call on the Bates' and enquire after her health.

The Crown obligingly supplied him with a light meal and a horse. His favourite mount was not available, and the one he was given was not very fast. He was glad for it, however; it meant that he would have nearly a whole hour alone to think before he reached Kingston. He had just left the stable when he heard Miss Bates' voice.

"Mr. Knightley! How d'ye do? how d'ye do?" She had opened the window and was calling down to him as he passed her house.

"Quite, well, Miss Bates, thank you, and how are—"

"Very well, I thank you. So obliged to you for the carriage last night! We were just in time—my mother just ready for us. Pray come in—do come in. You will find some friends here."

"How is your niece, Miss Bates? I want to inquire after you all, but particularly your niece. How is Miss Fairfax? I hope she caught no cold last night."

"Last night! Indeed, it was such a lovely—"

"How is she today? Tell me how Miss Fairfax is."

"Oh! She is very well, Mr. Knightley. She caught no cold at all. So obliged to you! So very much obliged to you for the carriage," said Miss Bates.

"I am going to Kingston. Can I do any thing for you?"

"Oh! dear, Kingston—are you? Mrs. Cole was saying the other day she wanted something from Kingston."

"Mrs. Cole has servants to send. Can I do any thing for *you*?"

"No, I thank you. But do come in. Who do you think is here? Miss Woodhouse and Miss Smith—"

Emma... He hardly heard what was said after that. He ought not to stop, of course, but the desire to see Emma was powerful enough to make him say, "Well, for five minutes, perhaps."

"And here is Mrs. Weston and Mr. Frank Churchill too!" went on Miss Bates. "Quite delightful; so many friends!"

The desire vanished.

"No, not now, I thank you. I could not stay two minutes. I must get on to Kingston as fast as I can."

"Oh! Do come in. They will be so very happy to see you."

Knightley thought that unlikely.

"No, no," he said, "your room is full enough. I will call another day, and hear the pianoforté."

"Well, I am so sorry! Oh! Mr. Knightley, what a delightful party last night; how extremely pleasant. Did you ever see such dancing? Was not it delightful? Miss Woodhouse and Mr. Frank Churchill—I never saw any thing equal to it."

Knightley could imagine the smirks on the faces of those inside the house as they overheard this description of themselves.

"Oh! Very delightful indeed. I can say nothing less, for I suppose Miss Woodhouse and Mr. Frank Churchill are hearing everything that passes." Emma would be amused at his saying that. "And I do not see why Miss Fairfax should not be mentioned too," he went on. "I think Miss Fairfax dances very well, and Mrs. Weston is the very best country-dance player, without exception, in England. Now, if your friends have any gratitude, they will say something pretty loud about you and me in return, but I cannot stay to hear it."

"Oh! Mr. Knightley, one moment more—something of consequence—so shocked! Jane and I are both so shocked about the apples!"

Apples?

"What is the matter now?" he asked.

"To think of your sending us all your store apples! You said you had a great many, and now you have not one left."

Oh, that was all. She had thanked him three times already, but every time she was reminded of a past kindness she thanked the giver again. He waved his hand in farewell and gave the horse a nudge. Her chatter followed him as he moved away.

"We really are so shocked! Mrs. Hodges may well be angry. William Larkins mentioned it here. You should not have done it, indeed you should not..."

No sooner had Miss Bates voice' faded than he heard the sound of a horse behind him; he turned to see Cole riding up and grinning at him.

"How do you do, Cole?"

"Very well, thank you, Mr. Knightley. I would ask you the same, but I have already heard you announce your good health to Miss Bates."

"Ah. Well then, I shall be spared answering questions about where I am going and what I thought of the dancing last evening and whatever other information I inadvertently bellowed to the residents of Highbury. I only wanted to know that Miss Fairfax was none the worse for being out last night."

"Very good of you to be so concerned for her health."

"Not at all. But where are you going? Out of Highbury, at least."

"Yes, I am bearing you company to Kingston, if you have no objection."

It seemed he was destined to have no time alone to think at all today.

"Of course not," said Knightley courteously. "You have business there?"

"Well, I am acting as envoy for Mrs. Cole: she is commissioning another fire screen to match the one we lately acquired. I have no notion why fire screens in different rooms must look alike, but there you have it. Having rooms new-furnished is an expensive business, I can tell you, Mr. Knightley. I give you fair warning."

"Warning?"

"Well, you may be buying new furnishings at no distant period. When the new mistress comes to Donwell she may very likely wish to change a few things—if she is like most other women, that is."

Knightley looked at him in bewilderment.

"Are you not thinking of bringing home a wife to Donwell?" said Cole.

Knightley felt the blood drain from his face. Was his love for Emma so very obvious? Had everyone known it except himself?

And what could he possibly say to Cole? But Cole did not wait for an answer.

"As I said a day or two ago, I am surprised that Miss Fairfax has not caught the eye of any worthy young man these last few years. Perhaps it is because she was destined for you."

"Oh!" Relief flowed through him; he had not been so obvious after all. "I am sorry to disappoint you, Cole, but I have never thought of Miss Fairfax in that way."

"Indeed? Then I beg your pardon, Mr. Knightley; I should not have spoken."

"No need to be sorry, Cole; a mistake anyone might make." Knightley supposed he *had* shown a good deal of attention to Miss Fairfax's health lately, and of course he had just advertised his concern to all of Highbury a few moments ago. And Cole had heard him praise her at that little gathering at Weston's, too, in an effort to stop Weston's going on about Emma. It was no wonder he had assumed a partiality for Miss Fairfax. Did everyone else think the same? Could Emma possibly…? No. She, at least, knew him too well to think any such thing. Didn't she?

Knightley knew Carver from the quarter sessions and had even dined once at his house. He found him at home and at leisure, and from the comfort of a deep chair in the library told him Page's story. He listened sympathetically to Knightley's tale, and accepted without any difficulty the evidence that Sam Page was in Donwell on the day he had supposedly committed a crime in Kingston.

"Well, Knightley, there doesn't seem to be any question that this man Gibbons mistook the matter, and it couldn't have been Page who stole those things. Here, I'll write a note to my man to have Page released. You can go and tell his brother that he'll be free tonight. I'm glad, to say the truth. He seemed a decent fellow."

"Yes, I believe he is. Thank you."

"You are quite welcome to dine here this evening, you know. Garrett will be here—you know Garrett? Yes—well, he will be here at seven."

"I had better not, but I thank you for the offer. Another time, perhaps."

"As you say. I'll see you at the Easter quarter sessions, then."

Knightley took his leave and started back to Donwell with a mind free to give to his own thoughts for the first time all day.

The important question before him was this: was Emma's heart already lost to Churchill? If at this moment she were asked to choose between them, whom would she prefer? Knightley had the advantage of established intimacy with her family. She regarded him highly, appreciated his friendship, and was pleased with his company: these were his assets. Then again, perhaps his familiarity with Emma was also a liability. After all, Churchill's great charm was probably that he was new and young and handsome.

Well, suppose her heart was not yet given to either of them? Ought he to declare himself openly now in order to forestall Churchill? What would happen if he rode straight to Hartfield immediately, told her of his love, and asked her to marry him? It was a heady thought. By the time he went to bed tonight he would have his heart's desire. He could look into her eyes and call her "my darling Emma." He could walk with her in the garden—in his mind's eye it would be a summer's eve—and they could talk and laugh and tease without restraint, and then in some secluded spot...

No! He could not let himself imagine it; if there was any hope of his thinking rationally he must keep his mind from wandering down that path. For, of course, Emma was not likely to consent to marry him now. She would be both startled and bewildered by his proposal, and there was little doubt that she would regretfully—but definitely—refuse him. That would be the end of everything, for he could never ask her again: a lady must not be pestered by an unwanted suit. He ought to wait.

But then, what if Churchill spoke first? He was not worthy of her, and there was no one to caution her except himself. Perhaps he ought to speak—hazard everything on the chance that friendly affection would be enough to secure her. He could teach her to love him afterwards. Perhaps it was cowardly to hesitate. *'None but the brave deserves the fair,'* he thought. But this was immediately countered with *'The better part of valour is discretion.'*

Well, he would not act today, at least. He would give himself another night to think it over. Perhaps by morning he would have some certainty about which course to take.

23

"Sir?"

Baxter's light touch woke him. He groaned and struggled to open his eyes.

"Sir? Are you unwell?" There was a note of anxiety in Baxter's voice.

Knightley could not remember the last time he had needed to be prodded awake. How long had he slept? Long enough, it seemed; the sunlight coming through the windows was bright and the fire in his room well established.

"I am well enough, Baxter; only a little over-tired." In truth, he had lain awake much of the night, trying without success to determine what Emma's reaction might be to any one of the possible actions he might take. The only thing he was certain of this morning was that he needed to see Emma again. He had not laid eyes on her since his revelation, and he wondered if observation alone could tell him how deep her affection for him might be. Perhaps it was foolish to be in her presence—he might betray himself by some word or action or even incautiously speak to her of his love before he was fully decided on such a course. It could not be helped, however. He was aching for the sight of her.

He was careful to pay no particular attention to his appearance as he dressed; Emma should not detect any change in him, no matter how trivial, until he was sure of her feelings. He was a little afraid of being summoned away on some urgent business while he was eating his breakfast, but Harry brought in nothing but the ordinary post. There was a letter from John, but Knightley deferred the reading of it until another time.

He set off for Hartfield almost immediately after breakfast. He was not much past the sweep-gate when the thought crossed his mind that he should have enquired after Page's welfare. He had sent a message to the cottage last evening to say that Sam was free, but he knew he ought to call in person. *Later,* he told himself. *After I see Emma.* The possibility of there being some need that would require more of his time was a real threat, and he did not want to postpone seeing her. Still, it was not his habit to put off a visit to a sick tenant for his own selfish pleasure—and did he not want to be as unchanged in behaviour as in appearance?

He stood still, hesitating, conscience warring with desire. His eye fell on the curate's cottage. Of course! He could ask Spencer—very briefly—if there was any news; he was sure to know if John had taken a turn for the worse. Most likely there had been no such change, and he could then visit Hartfield with a clear conscience.

Old Maggie answered his rap on the door.

"How d'ye do, Mr. Knightley, sir?"

"I was hoping to speak to Mr. Spencer for just a moment," said Knightley in his loudest voice.

"Yes, indeed, a very fine day, sir. Do come in, sir."

She took his hat and walking stick and motioned him past the parlour.

"He's in the study, sir—been writin' his sermon all morning, he has. You'll be wantin' a bit of a chat with him, sir—I'll bring the tea directly."

"No, I thank you, Maggie, I cannot stay!" he shouted desperately. "I will go and come again when he is more at leisure!"

"No, not to worry sir; no trouble to me at all, sir." She opened the door of the study and announced Knightley. Spencer was sitting at his desk, but rose to greet Knightley with a faint smile and gestured toward a chair.

"I heard you tell Maggie you could not stay long, sir," he said when the servant withdrew. "I am sorry about the tea. You may escape whenever you wish and I will explain to Maggie that you were obliged to go." He spoke quietly, and Knightley noticed that there was only one book open on the desk beside a virgin sheaf of writing paper, and the quill was still in its stand. Something was amiss.

"Oh, I think I may stay long enough for a cup of tea," said Knightley, sitting down. "I came to ask if there was any news about John Page this morning."

"I don't know. I have not heard anything."

"Did you know he was ill?"

"Oh, yes—I beg your pardon—I ought to have explained more fully. I *did* know he was ill, but have heard nothing of his condition since late last evening. Had you any reason to suppose he was worse?"

"No, no…It was only that I was passing and thought I might enquire…"

"Of course. I *am* usually informed of such things, so I think we may be easy about him for the present."

"Good. I am sorry to have interrupted your work."

Spencer looked at him blankly for a moment and then gave a light laugh. "Oh, yes, my sermon. I was not getting on very well—a distraction is quite welcome. I…slept poorly last night."

So that was it. Yes, Spencer did look tired; it was no wonder his manner was so subdued.

"I slept poorly myself," offered Knightley, "and I would be hard pressed to do any work at my desk this morning. I feel unequal even to making an attempt. At least you are endeavouring to do what you ought."

He expected his words to call forth a slight blush and a self-deprecating remark, but Spencer only nodded.

"You do appear to be exhausted," said Knightley. "Perhaps you ought to have risen later in the morning."

The sound of Old Maggie's clumping footsteps could be heard in the passageway, along with the rattle of china.

"I would have liked to do that," said Spencer, "but as Maggie is not aware of how loud she is…" His eyes twinkled briefly.

"I can imagine," said Knightley as the door opened and the tea was brought in.

They were silent as Maggie poured the tea. Knightley glanced at the curate who was watching the proceedings with an expression that could almost be called morose. His spirits were definitely dejected, and it seemed to Knightley that something more than lack of sleep was to blame. Likely there was some difficulty about a parishioner, or perhaps he had received bad news from Norfolk. Things must be very bad for Spencer to keep staring mutely into his teacup, even after Maggie had left them alone again.

"I saw Mrs. Catherwood and her son yesterday at Page's cottage," said Knightley, hoping to see a spark of interest in his eyes.

Spencer nodded but made no answer. Knightley began to feel dread. If that did not bring a smile to his face, there must be something terribly wrong. Well, there was nothing to be lost by asking a forthright question.

"Are you ill?"

Spencer looked up and gave a short laugh. "In a manner of speaking, I suppose I am."

"In a manner of speaking?"

"'Hope deferred maketh the heart sick.'"

"You've had a hope deferred, I take it."

Spencer nodded again and looked out of the window. Knightley studied the pattern on his teacup. The only hope he knew of in Spencer's case had to do with Mrs. Catherwood. Probably he had encountered some impediment to his marriage plans. Perhaps he had an overbearing father or grandfather who threatened to cut him out of his inheritance if he married a widow with a blind child.

"Is there any possibility of a change in circumstances?" Knightley said after several moments. "Is it the sort of trouble that my influence can do anything to lighten?"

Spencer stirred and said, "No, nothing, I thank you." He was silent for another moment, but then took a deep breath and said, "I suppose I ought to have told you, Mr. Knightley—I had thought of taking a wife."

"There was no need."

"Do you mean that I was not obliged to tell you, or that you already knew?"

"Both."

Spencer digested this news with only a blink of his eyes. "And did you also know that the lady was Mrs. Catherwood?" At a nod from Knightley, he sighed and said, "I did not know my interest was so apparent. I hope I have not acted unbecomingly..."

"Not at all, not in the least. But am I correct in surmising that there is some impediment to the marriage?

"Yes, a very great one: I made her an offer, and she declined it."

"No!" The word broke from Knightley with such force that Spencer stared at him. "Forgive me—I did not mean to startle you. I confess I am *greatly* surprised." Was there some sort of curse on the men of Donwell? First Martin, now Spencer…

"You do not think I was a fool for offering, then?"

"Good heavens, no!"

"She told me I did her great honour—*very great* honour, she said—by asking, and that I was all that was generous, but that she was certain I would regret my choice before long, and she could not allow me to forfeit my happiness for the sake of my noble ideals."

"*Noble ideals*? She thinks love nothing but a noble ideal?"

Spencer gave a wry smile and looked into his teacup again. "I fear she thinks I offered for her out of pity. It is my own doing—I went about the business in a very clumsy way. I knew I had very little to recommend myself…small income, unpolished manners, dull conversation…"

Knightley opened his mouth to protest this description, but Spencer put up his hand and said, "I know—and I am thankful for your good opinion, Mr. Knightley; but even you must admit that I am not the sort of man likely to quicken the pulse of any young lady. I, at least, am well aware of it."

Knightley admitted this with a reluctant nod.

"However," Spencer went on, "I thought that perhaps her situation—her love for her son—she would be willing enough to be my wife. I spoke too much about the practical advantages of the match, and she must have assumed I offered only out of a sense of duty. It is true that her situation was what first excited my compassion, and I suppose I went on thinking that my primary motive for offering was dispassionate benevolence."

"But it was not?"

"No. Not in the end. I do not think I understood my own heart until she refused me. Then I knew that I loved her."

"Do you think that if you told her—it is not usual, I know, but perhaps if you spoke to her once more—"

"I think not, sir. It is very likely she would not have me even if she thought I offered only out of the very deepest love. After all, whatever I was, I am still. She may have been very glad of the excuse that she did not want to accept the charity of a conscience-stricken benefactor. More than that, she might feel that I was trying to compel her against her will, or even that I was inventing this new information about the state of my heart; after all, what man in love would have said nothing about it when he proposed marriage?"

"Surely she would not think you were telling a falsehood, Spencer. It is so far outside your character that it would not even occur to her; I am certain of that."

"Perhaps; but who can guess what a woman will think?"

This remark found its way straight to the heart.

"No one," said Knightley glumly. "No one ever knows."

Spencer looked at him for a long moment, and then heaved a deep sigh. "I will do what I ought to have done all along: pray for another man to marry her. It is a husband she needs, not....*me*."

The helpless feeling that swelled within him whenever he thought of Martin had appeared again for Spencer.

"I wish there was *anything* I could do," Knightley said.

A slight smile hovered around Spencer's mouth. "I suppose I ought to ask you to look out a husband for Mrs. Catherwood, but I cannot yet bring myself to take even so feeble a step to bring it to pass. And when someone finally *does* win her hand, I do not know how I will be able to conduct the ceremony."

"'Jealousy is cruel as the grave.'"

"It is. It is cruel even when the object of one's envy does not yet exist. And yet...Well, 'charity envieth not.' True charity will guard my heart from such a state, I trust. Only—" Spencer smiled again. "I believe there will be some difficulty in cultivating enough love for a non-existent person to make this cruel jealousy disappear."

"You have my full sympathy, Spencer." *More full than you know.*

"I am sorry to have taken so much of your time, Mr. Knightley; I did not mean to burden you with my troubles."

"Not at all—'bear ye one another's burdens', and so on. And who knows?" Knightley added lightly. "You may yet have opportunity to bear some of mine."

"I do hope you will allow me the privilege," said Spencer, rising as Knightley did. "You would be assured of my understanding."

There was so much significance in his tone and such a knowing look on his face that Knightley could almost believe that Spencer knew his secret, and he faltered for a moment. If he really knew—But it was impossible, of course. He thanked the curate and went off to Hartfield to indulge in the sight and presence of his lady-love. He did not, however, walk quite so quickly as he had before.

"And so," said Knightley to Madam Duval, "I spent an hour in Emma's drawing room without making a fool of myself. I had been afraid that knowing my own heart would make me uncomfortable and ill-at-ease in her company, but in fact, everything seemed to go on as comfortably as it did before. Mr. Woodhouse had another letter from his banker for me to interpret, and Emma and Harriet talked to each other much of the time; no doubt those things aided in the appearance of normalcy. Still, I was thankful it went off so well."

Knightley was sitting in the library with the cat curled up at his feet. The fire danced in its grate in front of them, the glow making a cheerful spot in the otherwise dark room. It was a setting that seemed to invite the sharing of confidences, even if it was only with a cat.

"I have come to a decision, Madam," he went on. "I will not venture an immediate proposal of marriage. When I saw her today—I have told you, haven't I, that she is the most beautiful, most entrancing, most adorable creature in all the world?—I knew to a certainty that she is the complete mistress of my heart; I am not, however, the master of hers. I watched her carefully today, and there was nothing at all in her words or demeanor to show that she felt any more for me than she would for a brother. A much older brother."

He reached for the glass of spruce beer on the table beside him and took a sip before continuing: "John reminded me in his letter today that I will be thirty-eight next week. Emma is twenty-one. When I was twenty-one, men who were thirty-eight seemed to be very nearly grandfathers. I don't say she is anticipating my descent into senility in the coming months, but I can well understand her not conceiving of me as an ideal husband. And as it happens, Churchill is leaving in exactly five days; it is my earnest hope that when he is gone, she will see him for what he is: an egotistical, inconsiderate blockhead who is utterly unworthy of her notice."

The cat looked up at him; his voice had become harsh. "You think me uncharitable, Madam? Well, perhaps I am. Spencer, poor fellow, is already trying to tolerate—nay, *love*—the possible future bridegroom of Mrs. Catherwood. And that is another reason for restraint; I have no wish to become the third rejected bachelor in Donwell. Surely Emma has even less reason to marry me than those women had to marry their suitors; there is no reason to think she would accept my offer. And what is more, presenting her with such a decision to make could only distress her. I am persuaded that she would reject me, but she would feel badly over it—and our future relations would be most awkward. It is best that I say nothing."

There was only a little spruce beer left in the glass; Knightley finished it and put the glass down.

"I met Weston on the road today; he taxed me—as a joke—with avoiding Randalls, and told me to come to tea on Saturday. I really think I must go, Madam. I *have* been avoiding Randalls, and I ought not to. I fear that more time spent in the presence of Churchill will not help me to be any more forbearing toward him, but I suppose there is some satisfaction in doing one's duty."

He reached down and stroked the cat for a moment. "I cannot say you are as good a listener as Homer was; and if anyone had told me six months ago that I would be telling my troubles to a *cat*—no offense intended, of course, Madam—I would not have believed them. But I may say that you are not quite as intolerable as I had thought you would be. I wish you a good night."

He stood then and walked over to the window. It was cloudy and the moon gave very little light, but he gazed toward Hartfield just as he had done before. The thought of Emma there, deep in untroubled sleep, made him glad.

"Good night, my dear Emma. If I had asked you to marry me today, you would have had a sleepless night; it is better as it is. Sleep well, my love."

He went to Hartfield late in the afternoon of the next day, bringing the greetings and news John's letter had contained. As accustomed as he was to the sight of Emma, it was an effort of the will to keep himself from staring at her. She seemed almost to glow with health and good spirits—or could he hope that perhaps some of her joy came at seeing him? He tried to remember if she had always looked this happy when he was announced; perhaps she had and he had been blind to that as well.

"I suppose you have heard about this ball of the Weston's," said Mr. Woodhouse. "Emma has been very busy about it today."

"No, sir, I had not." His hopes faded; this explained her unusually cheerful looks.

"Yes, Mr. Knightley, the Westons are giving a ball!" Emma said. "And there will be musicians and a supper and enough guests to fill the room—all at the Crown. That is, we *hope* there is to be a ball. It is impossible to arrange such a thing in a day or two, you know, and so the ball cannot be held until next week. Mr. Churchill has written to Enscombe to ask that he may extend his stay by a day or two. Until we have Mrs. Churchill's answer we may not depend on it absolutely."

He ought to have expected something of the kind. Naturally, Churchill would have been the one to start this scheme; he must want another opportunity to display his talents to all of Highbury, and especially to Emma. And now he would be staying longer in Highbury because of it!

"But Mr. Churchill says he believes she will give consent," Emma went on. "Is it not wonderful, Mr. Knightley? There has not been a ball in Highbury since—well, I cannot remember one. It will give such pleasure to all the neighbourhood!"

He wished she would not be so exuberant about it, as if she *wanted* to see Churchill showing off again. Some belligerent impulse to quell her enthusiasm made him say dismissively, "Very well. If the Westons think it worthwhile to be at all this trouble for a few hours of noisy entertainment, I have nothing to say against it—but that they shall not choose pleasures for me."

His tone stopped Emma short. She looked at him, surprised.

"You will come—you would not refuse to come!"

"Oh! yes, I must be there; I could not refuse. And I will keep as much awake as I can, but I would rather be at home, looking over William Larkins's week's account. Much rather, I confess."

"But you will see your friends; and if you will not dance yourself, at least you will have pleasure in seeing other people dance."

"Pleasure in seeing dancing!" As if he could be amused by watching Frank Churchill dance! "Not I, indeed—I never look at it—

I do not know who does. Fine dancing, I believe, like virtue, must be its own reward. Those who are standing by are usually thinking of something very different."

A flash of some emotion passed across Emma's face; Knightley thought it was anger, but he could not see why she should be angry. If he had no desire to dress in his finest clothes and stand about all evening, watching that—well, watching Churchill do his best to electrify the room with his skilful dancing, what should it matter to anyone but himself? He wanted to talk of something else, something they could not argue about. He remembered the letter.

"John says that the boys may be coming to Hartfield for a fortnight or so in May; if the visit comes to pass, I hope that you will share them with me. I enjoy their company quite as much as you do, you know."

Her face softened at the mention of their nephews, and in the shared admiration of their little relations the rest of the visit passed in perfect amity.

18 February
Donwell Abbey

Dear John,

Yes, Weston's son is still in Highbury. He was to leave in a very few days, but somehow he has contrived that the Westons will be giving a ball next week at the Crown, and therefore his going is deferred until after the Grand Occasion. I shall attend, of course, unless I am fortunate enough to be called away by some urgent necessity. You would not happen to desire my presence for any reason, I suppose?

Tell Bella that Madam Duval has found a source of amusement: my pencils. She discovered one on the floor the other day and batted it around for ten minutes before the noise of it rolling around the library was more than my nerves could bear. The next day she saw one on my desk (she was in my lap—yes, laugh at that if you will) and swatted it to the floor where it occupied her for quite some time. I have found three pencils in various corners of the library since then; I shall have to start hiding them.

How splendid that Isabella has found such a sweet friend in Miss Hartley! From your description she seems a perfectly delightful lady – and if you do anything to effect our introduction I shall make Bella the gift of a monkey to animate the nursery, and indeed the entire house.

Faithfully yours,
George

Knightley went to Randalls on Saturday with a mind resolute to do his duty to the Westons, and to be as affable to Frank Churchill as he could bear to be. He was surprised, therefore, to be greeted with the news that Churchill was not there.

"Frank asked me to make his apologies for not joining us," said Weston. "He hopes you will not be offended by his absence."

"Not at all." Knightley was tempted to ask if Frank's hair had needed cutting again, but restrained himself.

"He has gone to Hartfield," explained Weston, "to give Emma the good news—he has just received word from Enscombe that he may stay a little longer, and the ball can proceed as planned."

Weston said it with such certainty of giving delight that Knightley felt obliged to say, "Good news, indeed! It will be greatly enjoyed by all of Highbury, I am sure."

"So we hope," said Mrs. Weston. "Emma is very much looking forward to it."

"As well she might," said Knightley. "She loves to dance and rarely has opportunity." He felt a slight pang at this admission; he ought to have shown more sympathy at Emma's pleasure in the prospect of dancing.

"Yes, a ball is just the thing for a young lady," said Weston. "And for a young man, too, eh? Nothing like a ball to promote affection. Music is the food of love, they say; isn't that right? It is just as well there was no ball here five years ago, my dear—had I danced with you I certainly would have thrown over all my carefully-laid plans and married you within the month." Weston winked at his wife and she smiled and blushed; Knightley looked away. The sheer happiness on their faces awakened the very longing in his heart that he was trying to lull to sleep.

He left Randalls an hour later, more troubled even than he had been before. Weston was right: a dance could very likely fuel whatever affection was between Emma and Churchill. The thought flitted across his mind that perhaps *he* could ask Emma to dance, and his heart had just time to leap at the thought before he pushed it down again. Everyone would mark such a completely unprecedented thing as Mr. Knightley dancing, and his object was to keep his behaviour unchanged. Moreover, if he danced with Emma after Churchill did, she would compare her two partners, and no doubt his dancing would be much inferior to Churchill's. No, he could not dance with her. He would have to stand aside and watch, just as he had before.

Spencer conducted the service as usual on Sunday; Knightley fancied he could see a little depression of spirits in the curate, but otherwise he carried out his duties admirably for one who had lately experienced such a blow. He felt a kinship with Spencer, and indeed with Robert Martin, who was still suffering. Martin had in the last week rejected the opportunity to rent out the little cottage where he had planned to live with Harriet, because (Knightley guessed) although it must be heartbreaking to see the cottage standing empty when he had hoped to fill it, it would be more painful still to see it occupied by others. He ought to invite Spencer and Martin to Donwell some evening: the first meeting of The Society for Lovelorn Bachelors in Donwell. Then again, perhaps that would be unwise. It could scarcely be a lively party; none of them were the sort that would try to mask their sorrows with an evening of drinking and cards. And hours of polite talk might make them all more melancholy than they were before.

Knightley spent Monday and Tuesday going about his business as well as he could, putting aside the thought of the ball whenever it intruded into his consciousness. Thinking of it would do no good and only put him into a bad humour. He avoided Hartfield for the same reason; Emma would talk about the ball, and he would respond in some way he ought not, he was sure. It was better to keep away from the subject entirely until the ball itself; he would suffer through that evening somehow and then be done with it.

21 February
Wellyn House
Brunswick Square

Dear George,

Of course I have no need of you here; you must go to the ball and dance. Miss Gilbert has gone to visit her brother again; perhaps Mrs. Whitney will accompany her? I hear she quite enjoys dancing.

Bella says she is very glad Madam Duval has found a plaything and she hopes you will not really hide all your pencils. She also bids me tell you that she can sing "The Lass of Killashee" quite as well as her mama does and she will sing it for you when next you come. Perhaps she thinks you will take it to heart and find a winsome lass to woo. We live in hope…but I do not depend upon it.

I am, as always, your most cherished brother,
John

Larkins came to the Abbey for his usual meeting on Tuesday afternoon bristling with news.

"I suppose you have heard, Mr. Knightley, that Mr. Churchill has left Highbury?"

The quill fell from Knightley's fingers as he stared at Larkins.

"Left Highbury? To go where?"

"To Yorkshire, I understand. It appears he was recalled by his relatives there only this morning, and set off without delay. There is great regret in Highbury over the cancellation of the ball."

Churchill gone! His relief was so great he nearly clapped Larkins on the back and thanked him for bringing the information.

"Miss Bates fears her niece is very dejected by the news," Larkins went on, "And Mr. Weston says Miss Woodhouse will be exceedingly disappointed."

Very true, it was a misfortune for Emma. Though Knightley could not be sorry the ball was no more, he wished Emma might have had the pleasure of dancing. If he had not taken to heart (as he ought to have) the injunction to "rejoice with them that do rejoice", at least he might now try to "weep with them that weep".

Never had his business with Larkins been so swiftly dealt with, and the speed with which various matters were considered and dispatched left the poor bailiff almost gasping. He left for Hartfield as soon as Larkins was gone, and it struck him as he hurried along that he had used to walk this road with no other feelings than the mild anticipation of a pleasant visit with agreeable companions. How long had it been since he had walked past these same trees and cottages to Hartfield without any disquiet at all? It seemed a long, long time. The worry had begun when Emma befriended Harriet, and had only increased during those tedious weeks when Elton thought he was wooing Emma. Lately, of course, anxiety had been his constant companion on these walks as he dreaded the possibility of an attachment between Emma and Churchill. What a fool he was for not seeing that so much concern over Emma was cause for suspecting his own heart! But it had taken the genuine threat of Churchill's attentions to Emma to wake him from his stupor. Grudgingly he acknowledged that he owed Churchill a small debt of gratitude for his awakening. He could even wish him well, so long as he stayed in Yorkshire.

And now he was walking the same road again with a mind...well, he could not say that his mind was free of apprehension, but he did feel a good measure of relief. The immediate threat was lifted: Churchill was gone, perhaps never to return. Knightley could not be so foolish as to offer for Emma now, but in time, perhaps, she might see him as something other than an interfering older relative.

Knightley arrived at Hartfield in time for tea, happy to see that although Emma was undoubtedly disappointed, she had a smile for him when he came in.

"I heard about the ball—that it must be abandoned," said Knightley. "I am sorry for the thwarted expectations of so many."

"Not for yourself, of course."

"Well, no, I cannot say that. But you, Emma, who have so few opportunities of dancing—you are really out of luck; you are very much out of luck!" He spoke as kindly as he could and she seemed grateful for his sympathy.

"I think it is very well that they gave it up," said Mr. Woodhouse. "It would have been a perilous thing to be dancing in a ball-room in February! In a house it is not so draughty, of course, and one knows the people who own the house. But at the Crown! It was a very imprudent idea."

"Well, it is a comfort to know that there are two people, at least, who are not in mourning," said Emma, smiling at her father.

"My dear, you must tell Mr. Knightley about Isabella's letter. He will be very pleased to hear about little Bella—such a clever child!"

"Papa means that Isabella says Bella has learnt a song, and sings it very well."

"Ah, yes, John told me of that; it is "The Lass of Kilashee", I think:

For tho' she scorned to give her hand
His patience constant won the day
He woo'd by stealth with sighs and smiles
And gently stole her heart away."

"Yes, that is the song Isabella mentioned, is it not?" said Mr. Woodhouse. "My dear, you ought to write and remind Isabella not to let Bella sing too constantly. Remember that she had that little weakness in the throat a month or two ago; excessive singing will bring it back. Perry says…"

Mr. Woodhouse went on talking, but Knightley forgot to listen, arrested by the train of thought the song had suggested. *He woo'd by stealth…*

Indeed. Perhaps, though he could not pursue Emma openly, he might still begin to plan an assault on the stronghold of Emma's heart. There was no need now for feverish haste in trying to secure

Emma's affections; he could rather, by kindness and smiles, win her gradually; there would be nothing hurried or pressing about his courtship. Love could ripen in its own time. *And gently steal her heart away.*

"Perhaps Mr. Knightley knows when Mr. Elton will return with his bride," said Mr. Woodhouse, drawing Knightley's attention back to the conversation.

"He is planning to return in a little more than a week, I believe," said Knightley.

"He could not have married at a better time," said Emma. "The new Mrs. Elton will usurp the ball as an item of interest to be talked over amongst the gossips."

"And have the gossips determined what her leading qualities are yet? For of course they must establish such points before she appears in person. Tell me what they have decided; I am certain you have heard something of it."

Emma laughed. "Miss Bates reports it all faithfully to me, you may be sure. Miss Hawkins evidently excels at everything—a great authority on dress, a better musician than Miss Fairfax, and so skilful a card-player that no one will play with her for stakes higher than tuppence."

"Poor woman, to have to endeavour to match such a reputation! Let us hope that she is not easily intimidated by the judgement of others."

"Oh, they are all disposed to like her, you know; Mr. Elton is still a favourite, and whatever his wife is, she must be acceptable to the general populace."

"True enough. She may count herself fortunate that she is coming to a society that is so easily pleased. I trust she will be just as eager to be impressed with us."

"*You* need not worry, I am sure," said Emma with a smile and a raised left eyebrow. "Only show her the Abbey, giving special attention to the things you are most proud of—your favourite milk-cow and fine new ram, for example—and she will give you all the admiration you could wish for."

Knightley chuckled. "No doubt she will weep bitter tears that she married Mr. Elton before she had seen my poultry-yard."

"Any woman would," said Emma.

Any woman...like you, Emma?

"I am uneasy, Mr. Knightley," said Mr. Woodhouse, "that you are contemplating showing the new Mrs. Elton about the Abbey in these depths of winter. It is a dangerous season, you know, and she may become chilled."

"Oh, Papa, Mr. Knightley would never keep anyone out of doors so long that they became chilled! Mr. Knightley is very careful for the health of all our friends."

"Very true, my dear, very true. Mr. Knightley is always watchful for the safety of others. But he is often out of doors himself; my dear sir," he said, turning to Knightley, "you know you are often out of doors."

"I am indeed, sir, and I thank you for your concern; but I am always careful to dress warmly when it is cold."

"Well, I suppose you do, Mr. Knightley. You are always very prudent."

Knightley nearly laughed. Prudent, yes; too prudent to declare his affection at this moment when his heart would have dictated nothing less. What man could behold Emma's beauty, watch her tenderly soothe the fears of her father, and be the recipient of her impish teasing without feeling an overpowering urge to confess his love? And yet he was resisting the temptation. Oh, yes, he was very prudent. He was also, however, scheming. *His patience constant won the day…*He would be silent now and wait. But he would not wait helplessly, hoping the mere passage of time would incline her to him; no, he would be planning and working all the time. *He woo'd by stealth with sighs and smiles…*

"Of course, Papa," said Emma was saying, "We will all be careful; Mr. Knightley will take care as well. Isn't that so, Mr. Knightley?"

"Yes," he said. "You may be sure that I will." *Oh yes, my dearest Emma, I will take care. I will take very great care…to steal your heart away.*

FINIS

Note: The first charade on page 104 was written by Jane Austen

12855972R00148

Made in the USA
Lexington, KY
06 January 2012

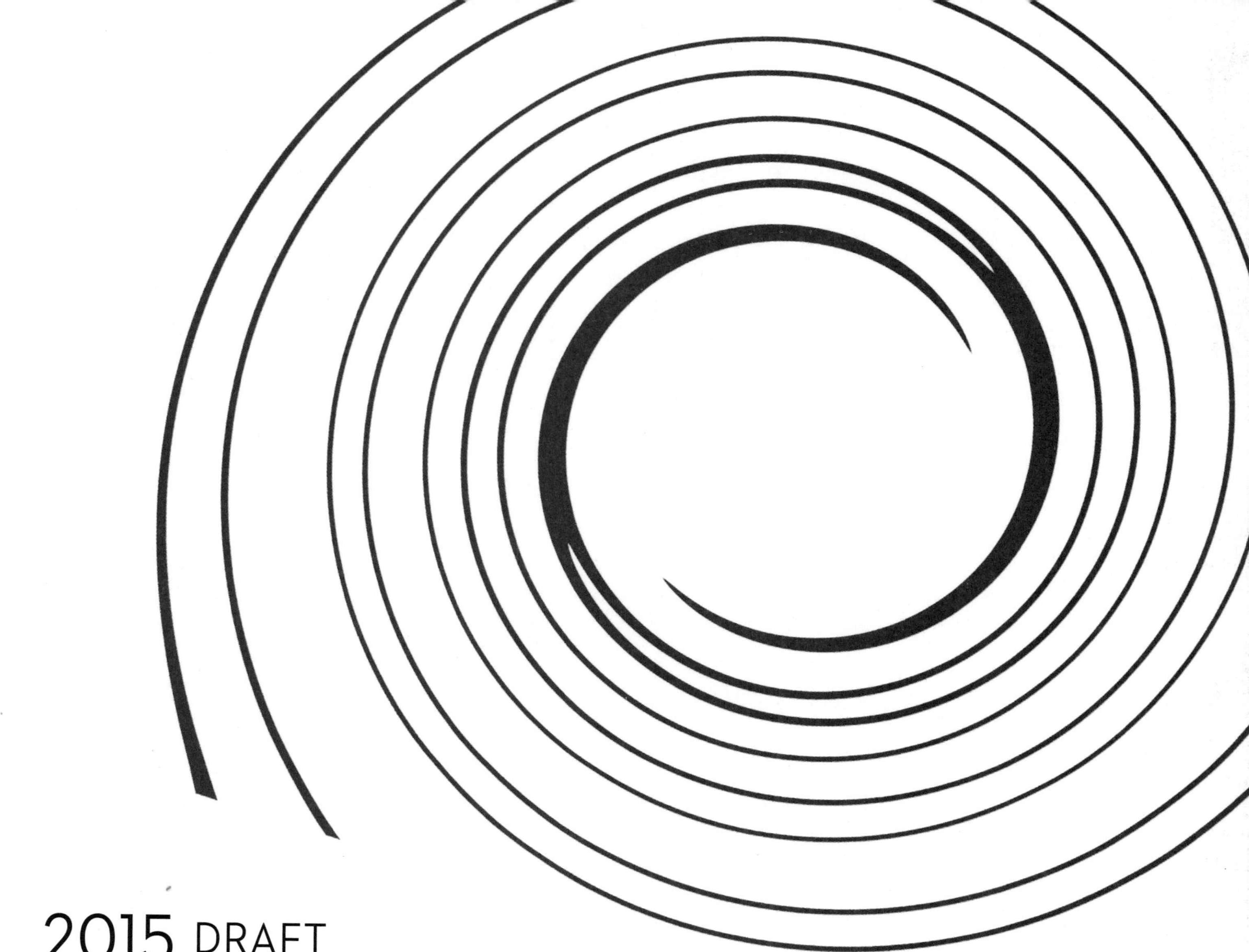

2015 DRAFT

ICD-10-CM Code Book

Anne B. Casto, RHIA, CCS
Consulting Editor

AHIMA
American Health Information Management Association®

ISBN: 978-1-58426-440-8
AHIMA Product No.: AC221014

AHIMA Staff:
Patricia E. Buttner, RHIA, CDIP, CCS, Technical Review
Angie Comfort, RHIA, CDIP, CCS, Technical Review
Melanie Endicott, MBA/HCM, RHIA, CDIP, CCS, CCS-P, FAHIMA, Technical Review
Katherine M. Greenock, MS, Production Development Editor
Megan Grennan, Production Development Editor
Jason O. Malley, Vice President, Business Innovation
Caitlin Wilson, Assistant Editor
Pamela Woolf, Director of Publications

For more information about AHIMA Press publications, including updates, visit http://www.ahima.org/publications/updates.aspx

American Health Information Management Association
233 North Michigan Avenue, 21st Floor
Chicago, Illinois 60601-5809
ahima.org

Contents

About the Consulting Editor

Anne B. Casto, RHIA, CCS, is the president of Casto Consulting, LLC. Casto Consulting, LLC is a consulting firm that provides services to hospitals and other healthcare stakeholders primarily in the areas of reimbursement and coding. Casto Consulting, LLC specializes in linking coding and billing practices to positive revenue cycle outcomes. Additionally, the firm provides guidance to consulting firms, healthcare organizations and healthcare insurers regarding reimbursement methodologies and Medicare regulations.

Prior to founding the firm Anne was the program manager of the HIMS Division at The Ohio State University School of Allied Medical Professions. Ms. Casto taught healthcare reimbursement, ICD-9-CM coding and CPT coding courses for several years. Additionally, Ms. Casto was responsible for curriculum revisions in the areas of chargemaster management, clinical data management and healthcare reimbursement.

Additionally, Ms. Casto was the vice president of clinical information for Cleverley & Associates where she worked very closely with APC regulations and guidelines, preparing hospitals for the implementation of the Medicare OPPS. Ms. Casto was also the clinical information product manager for CHIPS/Ingenix. She joined CHIPS/Ingenix in 1998 and spent the majority of her time developing coding compliance products for the inpatient and outpatient settings.

Ms. Casto has been responsible for inpatient and outpatient coding activities in several large hospitals including Mt. Sinai Medical Center (NYC), Beth Israel Medical Center (NYC), and The Ohio State University. She has worked extensively with CMI, quality measures, physician documentation, and coding accuracy efforts at these facilities.

Ms. Casto received her degree in Health Information Management at The Ohio State University in 1995. She received her Certified Coding Specialist credential in 1998 from the American Health Information Management Association. Ms. Casto is the co-author of an AHIMA published text book entitled *Principles of Healthcare Reimbursement*. Additionally, Ms. Casto was a contributing author to the published AHIMA books: *Severity DRGs and Reimbursement; A MS-DRG Primer* and *Effective Management of Coding Services.* Most recently Ms. Casto authored the AHIMA published text entitled *The CDM Handbook.*

Ms. Casto received the AHIMA Legacy Award, part of the FORE Triumph Awards, in 2007 which honors a significant contribution to the knowledge base of the HIM field through an insightful publication. Additionally, Ms. Casto was honored with the Ohio Health Information Management Association's Distinguished Member Award in 2008 and the Ohio Health Information Management Association's Professional Achievement Award in 2011.

Acknowledgments

Many thanks to my family for their support during this project. Thanks to Dr. Susan White, The Ohio State University; your data manipulation skills are second to none. Thanks to Drew Beverick for providing valuable insight from the students perspective. Many thanks to Linda Hyde for her very thorough technical review of the book. I thank the reviewers for their thoughtful comments and suggestions.

History of ICD-10-CM

The International Classification of Diseases, Tenth Revision, Clinical Modification (ICD-10-CM) is the United Stated modification to the World Health Organization's (WHO) International Classification of Diseases, Tenth Revision (ICD-10). The WHO adopted the tenth revision in 1990. Since that time, several countries, including Australia and Canada, have developed their own modification to ICD-10 and have implemented it for use.

In 1994, the National Center for Health Statistics (NCHS) began the process of determining the viability of ICD-10 and the applicability of a clinical modification of the code set for the United States. The NCHS has made draft versions of ICD-10-CM available since 2002. NCHS continued to refine and update the code set for use in the United States while the healthcare community waited for adoption of the code set by Congress. On August 22, 2008, the long-awaited official Notice of Proposed Rule Making (NPRM) regarding the adopting of the ICD-10-CM and ICD-10-PCS classifications was published in the *Federal Register*. On January 16, 2009, the Centers for Medicare and Medicaid Services (CMS) published the Final Rule for adoption of the ICD-10-CM and ICD-10-PCS code sets udders rules, 45 CFR Parts 160 and 162 of the Health Insurance Portability and Accountability Act of 1996 (HIPAA). Within this rule, a compliance (implementation) date of October 1, 2013 was released. The compliance date has been revised to October 1, 2015. Since the compliance date was released, the healthcare community has been developing implementation plans for a successful adoption of the new code sets.

Organizational and Structural Changes in ICD-10-CM

ICD-10-CM represents a significant improvement over ICD-9-CM. Although the hierarchical structure of the code set is the same, there are differences seen in the organization of the code set including:

- Increase from 17 to 21 chapters
- Inclusion of External Cases of Morbidity and Factors Influencing Health Status and Contact with Health Services incorporated into the main classification
- New separate chapters for Diseases of Eye and Adnexa and Diseases of Ear and Mastoid Process
- Certain diseases have been reclassified to new chapters based on current medical knowledge
- Injuries are now grouped by specific site and then by type of injury
- Movement of postoperative complications to procedure-specific body system chapters
- ICD-10-CM codes are alphanumeric and up to seven characters in length
- ICD-10-CM Tabular includes full code titles for all codes

New Features in ICD-10-CM

There are several new features in ICD-10-CM will allow for a greater level of specificity and clinical detail. The new features include:

- Combination codes for conditions and common symptoms or manifestations
- Combination codes for poisonings and external causes
- Added laterality
- Added seventh characters for episode of care
- Expanded code categories
- Inclusion of trimesters in obstetrics codes
- Changes in time frames specified in certain codes
- Added standard definitions for two types of "excludes" notes

With the adoption of the revised classification system comes the need for coders and other users to familiarize themselves with the large number of changes in ICD-10-CM. Although this draft of ICD-10-CM is available, the codes in ICD-10-CM are not currently valid for any purpose or use. Updates to this draft are anticipated to continue until the implementation of ICD-10-CM, which is expected to take place October 1, 2015. In the meantime, this draft of ICD-10-CM can be used as an educational tool to prepare the healthcare community for the adoption of ICD-10-CM.

Official Conventions

ICD-10-CM Official Guidelines for Coding and Reporting 2015

Narrative changes appear in bold text Items <u>underlined</u> have been moved within the guidelines since the 2014 version *Italics* are used to indicate revisions to heading changes

The Centers for Medicare and Medicaid Services (CMS) and the National Center for Health Statistics (NCHS), two departments within the US Federal Government's Department of Health and Human Services (HHS) provide the following guidelines for coding and reporting using the International Classification of Diseases, Tenth Revision, Clinical Modification (ICD-10-CM). These guidelines should be used as a companion document to the official version of the ICD-10-CM as published on the NCHS website. The ICD-10-CM is a morbidity classification published by the United States for classifying diagnoses and reason for visits in all healthcare settings. The ICD-10-CM is based on the ICD-10, the statistical classification of disease published by the World Health Organization (WHO).

These guidelines have been approved by the four organizations that make up the Cooperating Parties for the ICD-10-CM: the American Hospital Association (AHA), the American Health Information Management Association (AHIMA), CMS, and NCHS.

These guidelines are a set of rules that have been developed to accompany and complement the official conventions and instructions provided within the ICD-10-CM itself. The instructions and conventions of the classification take precedence over guidelines. These guidelines are based on the coding and sequencing instructions in the Tabular List and Alphabetic Index of ICD-10-CM, but provide additional instruction. Adherence to these guidelines when assigning ICD-10-CM diagnosis codes is required under the Health Insurance Portability and Accountability Act (HIPAA). The diagnosis codes (Tabular List and Alphabetic Index) have been adopted under HIPAA for all healthcare settings. A joint effort between the healthcare provider and the coder is essential to achieve complete and accurate documentation, code assignment, and reporting of diagnoses and procedures. These guidelines have been developed to assist both the healthcare provider and the coder in identifying those diagnoses that are to be reported. The importance of consistent, complete documentation in the medical record cannot be overemphasized. Without such documentation accurate coding cannot be achieved. The entire record should be reviewed to determine the specific reason for the encounter and the conditions treated.

The term encounter is used for all settings, including hospital admissions. In the context of these guidelines, the term provider is used throughout the guidelines to mean physician or any qualified healthcare practitioner who is legally accountable for establishing the patient's diagnosis. Only this set of guidelines, approved by the Cooperating Parties, is official.

The guidelines are organized into sections. Section I includes the structure and conventions of the classification and general guidelines that apply to the entire classification, and chapter-specific guidelines that correspond to the chapters as they are arranged in the classification. Section II includes guidelines for selection of principal diagnosis for non-outpatient settings. Section III includes guidelines for reporting additional diagnoses in non-outpatient settings. Section IV is for outpatient coding and reporting. It is necessary to review all sections of the guidelines to fully understand all of the rules and instructions needed to code properly.

Section I. Conventions, General Coding Guidelines and Chapter Specific Guidelines

The conventions, general guidelines and chapter-specific guidelines are applicable to all healthcare settings unless otherwise indicated. The conventions and instructions of the classification take precedence over guidelines.

A. Conventions for the ICD-10-CM

The conventions for the ICD-10-CM are the general rules for use of the classification independent of the guidelines. These conventions are incorporated within the Alphabetic Index and Tabular List of the ICD-10-CM as instructional notes.

1. The Alphabetic Index and Tabular List

The ICD-10-CM is divided into the Alphabetic Index, an alphabetical list of terms and their corresponding code, and the Tabular List, a structured list of codes divided into chapters based on body system or condition. The Alphabetic Index consists of the following parts: the Index of Diseases and Injury, the Index of External Causes of Injury, the Table of Neoplasms, and the Table of Drugs and Chemicals.

See Section I.C2. General guidelines

See Section I.C.19. Adverse effects, poisoning, underdosing and toxic effects

2. Format and Structure

The ICD-10-CM Tabular List contains categories, subcategories and codes. Characters for categories, subcategories and codes may be either a letter or a number. All categories are 3 characters. A three-character category that has no further subdivision is equivalent to a code. Subcategories are either 4 or 5 characters. Codes may be 3, 4, 5, 6, or 7 characters. That is, each level of subdivision after a category is a subcategory. The final level of subdivision is a code. Codes that have applicable 7th characters are still referred to as codes, not subcategories. A code that has an applicable 7th character is considered invalid without the 7th character.

The ICD-10-CM uses an indented format for ease in reference.

3. Use of Codes for Reporting Purposes

For reporting purposes only codes are permissible, not categories or subcategories, and any applicable 7th character is required.

4. Placeholder Character

The ICD-10-CM utilizes a placeholder character X. The X is used as a placeholder at certain codes to allow for future expansion. An example of this is at the poisoning, adverse effect and underdosing codes, categories T36–T50.

Where a placeholder exists, the X must be used in order for the code to be considered a valid code.

5. 7th Characters

Certain ICD-10-CM categories have applicable 7th characters. The applicable 7th character is required for all codes within the category, or as the notes in the Tabular List instruct. The 7th character must always be the 7th character in the data field. If a code that requires a 7th character is not 6 characters, a placeholder X must be used to fill in the empty characters.

6. Abbreviations

a. Alphabetic Index Abbreviations

NEC "Not elsewhere classifiable"

This abbreviation in the Alphabetic Index represents "other specified". When a specific code is not available for a condition, the Alphabetic Index directs the coder to the "other specified" code in the Tabular List.

NOS "Not otherwise specified"
This abbreviation is the equivalent of unspecified.

b. Tabular List Abbreviations

NEC "Not elsewhere classifiable"
This abbreviation in the Tabular List represents "other specified". When a specific code is not available for a condition the Tabular List includes an NEC entry under a code to identify the code as the "other specified" code.

NOS "Not otherwise specified"
This abbreviation is the equivalent of unspecified.

7. Punctuation

[ ] Brackets are used in the Tabular List to enclose synonyms, alternative wording or explanatory phrases. Brackets are used in the Alphabetic Index to identify manifestation codes.

( ) Parentheses are used in both the Alphabetic Index and Tabular List to enclose supplementary words that may be present or absent in the statement of a disease or procedure without affecting the code number to which it is assigned. The terms within the parentheses are referred to as nonessential modifiers. The nonessential modifiers in the Alphabetic Index to Diseases apply to subterms following a main term except when a nonessential modifier and a subentry are mutually exclusive, the subentry takes precedence. For example, in the ICD-10-CM Alphabetic Index under the main term Enteritis, "acute" is a nonessential modifier and "chronic" is a subentry. In this case, the nonessential modifier "acute" does not apply to the subentry "chronic".

: Colons are used in the Tabular List after an incomplete term which needs one or more of the modifiers following the colon to make it assignable to a given category.

8. Use of "and"

See Section I.A.14. Use of the term "And"

9. Other and Unspecified Codes

a. "Other" Codes

Codes titled "other" or "other specified" are for use when the information in the medical record provides detail for which a specific code does not exist. Alphabetic Index entries with NEC in the line designate "other" codes in the Tabular List. These Alphabetic Index entries represent specific disease entities for which no specific code exists so the term is included within an "other" code.

b. "Unspecified" Codes

Codes titled "unspecified" are for use when the information in the medical record is insufficient to assign a more specific code. For those categories for which an unspecified code is not provided, the "other specified" code may represent both other and unspecified.

See Section I.B.18 Use of Signs/Symptom/Unspecified Codes

10. Includes Notes

This note appears immediately under a three character code title to further define, or give examples of, the content of the category.

11. Inclusion Terms

List of terms is included under some codes. These terms are the conditions for which that code is to be used. The terms may be synonyms of the code title, or, in the case of "other specified" codes, the terms are a list of the various conditions assigned to that code. The inclusion terms are not necessarily exhaustive. Additional terms found only in the Alphabetic Index may also be assigned to a code.

12. Excludes Notes

The ICD-10-CM has two types of excludes notes. Each type of note has a different definition for use but they are all similar in that they indicate that codes excluded from each other are independent of each other.

a. Excludesl

A type 1 Excludes note is a pure excludes note. It means "NOT CODED HERE!" An Excludes1 note indicates that the code excluded should never be used at the same time as the code above the Excludes1 note. An Excludes1 is used when two conditions cannot occur together, such as a congenital form versus an acquired form of the same condition.

b. Excludes2

A type 2 Excludes note represents "Not included here". An Excludes2 note indicates that the condition excluded is not part of the condition represented by the code, but a patient may have both conditions at the same time. When an Excludes2 note appears under a code, it is acceptable to use both the code and the excluded code together, when appropriate.

13. Etiology/Manifestation Convention ("Code first", "Use additional code" and "In Diseases Classified Elsewhere" Notes)

Certain conditions have both an underlying etiology and multiple body system manifestations due to the underlying etiology. For such conditions, the ICD-10-CM has a coding convention that requires the underlying condition be sequenced first followed by the manifestation. Wherever such a combination exists, there is a "use additional code" note at the etiology code, and a "code first" note at the manifestation code. These instructional notes indicate the proper sequencing order of the codes, etiology followed by manifestation.

In most cases the manifestation codes will have in the code title, "in diseases classified elsewhere." Codes with this title are a component of the etiology/manifestation convention. The code title indicates that it is a manifestation code. "In diseases classified elsewhere" codes are never permitted to be used as first-listed or principal diagnosis codes. They must be used in conjunction with an underlying condition code and they must be listed following the underlying condition. See category F02, Dementia in other diseases classified elsewhere, for an example of this convention.

There are manifestation codes that do not have "in diseases classified elsewhere" in the title. For such codes, there is a "use additional code" note at the etiology code and a "code first" note at the manifestation code and the rules for sequencing apply.

In addition to the notes in the Tabular List, these conditions also have a specific Alphabetic Index entry structure. In the Alphabetic Index both conditions are listed together with the etiology code first followed by the manifestation codes in brackets. The code in brackets is always to be sequenced second.

An example of the etiology/manifestation convention is dementia in Parkinson's disease. In the Alphabetic Index, code G20 is listed first, followed by code F02.80 or F02.81 in brackets. Code G20 represents the underlying etiology, Parkinson's disease, and must be sequenced first, whereas codes F02.80 and F02.81 represent the manifestation of dementia in diseases classified elsewhere, with or without behavioral disturbance.

"Code first" and "Use additional code" notes are also used as sequencing rules in the classification for certain codes that are not part of an etiology/ manifestation combination.

See Section I.B. 7. Multiple coding for a single condition.

14. "And"
The word "and" should be interpreted to mean either "and" or "or" when it appears in a title.

For example, cases of "tuberculosis of bones", "tuberculosis of joints" and "tuberculosis of bones and joints" are classified to subcategory A18.0, Tuberculosis of bones and joints.

15. "With"
The word "with" should be interpreted to mean "associated with" or "due to" when it appears in a code title, the Alphabetic Index, or an instructional note in the Tabular List.

The word "with" in the Alphabetic Index is sequenced immediately following the main term, not in alphabetical order.

16. "See" and "See Also"
The "see" instruction following a main term in the Alphabetic Index indicates that another term should be referenced. It is necessary to go to the main term referenced with the "see" note to locate the correct code.

A "see also" instruction following a main term in the Alphabetic Index instructs that there is another main term that may also be referenced that may provide additional Alphabetic Index entries that may be useful. It is not necessary to follow the "see also" note when the original main term provides the necessary code.

17. "Code Also Note"
A "code also" note instructs that two codes may be required to fully describe a condition, but this note does not provide sequencing direction.

18. Default Codes
A code listed next to a main term in the ICD-10-CM Alphabetic Index is referred to as a default code. The default code represents that condition that is most commonly associated with the main term, or is the unspecified code for the condition. If a condition is documented in a medical record (for example, appendicitis) without any additional information, such as acute or chronic, the default code should be assigned.

B. General Coding Guidelines

1. Locating a Code in the ICD-10-CM
To select a code in the classification that corresponds to a diagnosis or reason for visit documented in a medical record, first locate the term in the Alphabetic Index, and then verify the code in the Tabular List. Read and be guided by instructional notations that appear in both the Alphabetic Index and the Tabular List.

It is essential to use both the Alphabetic Index and Tabular List when locating and assigning a code. The Alphabetic Index does not always provide the full code. Selection of the full code, including laterality and any applicable 7th character can only be done in the Tabular List. A dash (-) at the end of an Alphabetic Index entry indicates that additional characters are required. Even if a dash is not included at the Alphabetic Index entry, it is necessary to refer to the Tabular List to verify that no 7th character is required.

2. Level of Detail in Coding
Diagnosis codes are to be used and reported at their highest number of characters available.

ICD-10-CM diagnosis codes are composed of codes with 3, 4, 5, 6, or 7 characters. Codes with three characters are included in ICD-10-CM as the heading of a category of codes that may be further subdivided by the use of fourth and/or fifth characters and/or sixth characters, which provide greater detail.

A three-character code is to be used only if it is not further subdivided. A code is invalid if it has not been coded to the full number of characters required for that code, including the 7th character, if applicable.

3. Code or Codes from A00.0–T88.9, Z00–Z99.8
The appropriate code or codes from A00.0–T88.9, Z00–Z99.8 must be used to identify diagnoses, symptoms, conditions, problems, complaints or other reason(s) for the encounter/visit.

4. Signs and Symptoms

Codes that describe symptoms and signs, as opposed to diagnoses, are acceptable for reporting purposes when a related definitive diagnosis has not been established (confirmed) by the provider. Chapter 18 of ICD-10-CM, Symptoms, Signs, and Abnormal Clinical and Laboratory Findings, Not Elsewhere Classified (codes R00.0–R99) contains many, but not all codes for symptoms.

See Section I.B.18 Use of Signs/Symptom/Unspecified Codes

5. Conditions that are an Integral Part of a Disease Process

Signs and symptoms that are associated routinely with a disease process should not be assigned as additional codes, unless otherwise instructed by the classification.

6. Conditions that are not an Integral Part of a Disease Process

Additional signs and symptoms that may not be associated routinely with a disease process should be coded when present.

7. Multiple Coding for a Single Condition

In addition to the etiology/manifestation convention that requires two codes to fully describe a single condition that affects multiple body systems, there are other single conditions that also require more than one code. "Use additional code" notes are found in the Tabular List at codes that are not part of an etiology/manifestation pair where a secondary code is useful to fully describe a condition. The sequencing rule is the same as the etiology/manifestation pair, "use additional code" indicates that a secondary code should be added.

For example, for bacterial infections that are not included in chapter 1, a secondary code from category B95, Streptococcus, Staphylococcus, and Enterococcus, as the cause of diseases classified elsewhere, or B96, Other bacterial agents as the cause of diseases classified elsewhere, may be required to identify the bacterial organism causing the infection. A "use additional code" note will normally be found at the infectious disease code, indicating a need for the organism code to be added as a secondary code.

"Code first" notes are also under certain codes that are not specifically manifestation codes but may be due to an underlying cause. When there is a "code first" note and an underlying condition is present, the underlying condition should be sequenced first.

"Code, if applicable, any causal condition first", notes indicate that this code may be assigned as a principal diagnosis when the causal condition is unknown or not applicable. If a causal condition is known, the code for that condition should be sequenced as the principal or first-listed diagnosis.

Multiple codes may be needed for sequela, complication codes and obstetric codes to more fully describe a condition. See the specific guidelines for these conditions for further instruction.

8. Acute and Chronic Conditions

If the same condition is described as both acute (subacute) and chronic, and separate subentries exist in the Alphabetic Index at the same indentation level, code both and sequence the acute (subacute) code first.

9. Combination Code

A combination code is a single code used to classify:

- Two diagnoses, or
- A diagnosis with an associated secondary process (manifestation)
- A diagnosis with an associated complication

Combination codes are identified by referring to subterm entries in the Alphabetic Index and by reading the inclusion and exclusion notes in the Tabular List.

Assign only the combination code when that code fully identifies the diagnostic conditions involved or when the Alphabetic Index so directs. Multiple coding should not be used when the classification provides a combination code that clearly identifies all of the elements documented in the diagnosis. When the combination code lacks necessary specificity in describing the manifestation or complication, an additional code should be used as a secondary code.

10. Sequela (Late Effects)

A sequela is the residual effect (condition produced) after the acute phase of an illness or injury has terminated. There is no time limit on when a sequela code can be used. The residual may be apparent early, such as in cerebral infarction, or it may occur months or years later, such as that due to a previous injury. **Examples of sequela include: scar formation resulting from a burn, deviated septum due to a nasal fracture, and infertility due to tubal occlusion from old tuberculosis.** Coding of sequela generally requires two codes sequenced in the following order: The condition or nature of the sequela is sequenced first.

The sequela code is sequenced second.

An exception to the above guidelines are those instances where the code for the sequela is followed by a manifestation code identified in the Tabular List and title, or the sequela code has been expanded (at the fourth, fifth or sixth, character levels) to include the manifestation(s). The code for the acute phase of an illness or injury that led to the sequela is never used with a code for the late effect.

- *See Section I.C.9. Sequelae of cerebrovascular disease*
- *See Section I.C.15. Sequelae of complication of pregnancy, childbirth and the puerperium*
- *See Section I.C.19. Application of 7th characters for Chapter 19*

11. Impending or Threatened Condition

Code any condition described at the time of discharge as "impending" or "threatened" as follows:

- If it did occur, code as confirmed diagnosis.
- If it did not occur, reference the Alphabetic Index to determine if the condition has a subentry term for "impending" or "threatened" and also reference main term entries for "Impending" and for "Threatened."
- If the subterms are listed, assign the given code.
- If the subterms are not listed, code the existing underlying condition(s) and not the condition described as impending or threatened.

12. Reporting Same Diagnosis Code More than Once

Each unique ICD-10-CM diagnosis code may be reported only once for an encounter. This applies to bilateral conditions when there are no distinct codes identifying laterality or two different conditions classified to the same ICD-10-CM diagnosis code.

13. Laterality

Some ICD-10-CM codes indicate laterality, specifying whether the condition occurs on the left, right or is bilateral. If no bilateral code is provided and the condition is bilateral, assign separate codes for both the left and right side. If the side is not identified in the medical record, assign the code for the unspecified side.

14. Documentation for BMI, Non-Pressure Ulcers and Pressure Ulcer Stages

For the body mass index (BMI), depth of non-pressure chronic ulcers and pressure ulcer stage codes, code assignment may be based on medical record documentation from clinicians who are not the patient's provider (i.e., physician or other qualified healthcare practitioner legally accountable for establishing the patient's diagnosis), since this information is typically documented by other clinicians involved in the care of the patient (e.g., a dietitian often documents the BMI and nurses often documents the pressure ulcer stages). However, the associated diagnosis (such as overweight, obesity, or pressure ulcer) must be documented by the patient's provider. If there is conflicting medical record documentation, either from the same clinician or different clinicians, the patient's attending provider should be queried for clarification.

The BMI codes should only be reported as secondary diagnoses. As with all other secondary diagnosis codes, the BMI codes should only be assigned when they meet the definition of a reportable additional diagnosis (see Section III, Reporting Additional Diagnoses).

15. Syndromes

Follow the Alphabetic Index guidance when coding syndromes. In the absence of Alphabetic Index guidance, assign codes for the documented manifestations of the syndrome. Additional codes for manifestations that are not an integral part of the disease process may also be assigned when the condition does not have a unique code.

16. Documentation of Complications of Care

Code assignment is based on the provider's documentation of the relationship between the condition and the care or procedure. The guideline extends to any complications of care, regardless of the chapter the code is located in. It is important to note that not all conditions that occur during or following medical care or surgery are classified as complications. There must be a cause-and-effect relationship between the care provided and the condition, and an indication in the documentation that it is a complication. Query the provider for clarification, if the complication is not clearly documented.

17. Borderline Diagnosis

If the provider documents a "borderline" diagnosis at the time of discharge, the diagnosis is coded as confirmed, unless the classification provides a specific entry (e.g., borderline diabetes). If a borderline condition has a specific index entry in ICD-10-CM, it should be coded as such. Since borderline conditions are not uncertain diagnoses, no distinction is made between the care setting (inpatient versus outpatient). Whenever the documentation is unclear regarding a borderline condition, coders are encouraged to query for clarification.

18. Use of Sign/Symptom/Unspecified Codes

Sign/symptom and "unspecified" codes have acceptable, even necessary, uses. While specific diagnosis codes should be reported when they are supported by the available medical record documentation and clinical knowledge of the patient's health condition, there are instances when signs/symptoms or unspecified codes are the best choices for accurately reflecting the healthcare encounter. Each healthcare encounter should be coded to the level of certainty known for that encounter.

If a definitive diagnosis has not been established by the end of the encounter, it is appropriate to report codes for sign(s) and/or symptom(s) in lieu of a definitive diagnosis. When sufficient clinical information isn't known or available about a particular health condition to assign a more specific code, it is acceptable to report the appropriate "unspecified" code (e.g., a diagnosis of pneumonia has been determined, but not the specific type). Unspecified codes should be reported when they are the codes that most accurately reflects what is known about the patient's condition at the time of that particular encounter. It would be inappropriate to select a specific code that is not supported by the medical record documentation or conduct medically unnecessary diagnostic testing in order to determine a more specific code.

C. Chapter-Specific Coding Guidelines

Consulting Editor Note

In this book the Chapter-Specific Coding Guidelines are included in the Tabular List of Diseases and Injuries at the beginning of the chapter for which they are applicable.

Additionally, notes have been added throughout the Diagnosis and Procedure Tabular to alert the coder when the code under review is included in a chapter specific coding guideline. The user can then reference the coding guideline prior to making their final code selection. For example:

A41 Other sepsis

Review coding guideline C.1.d

This note alerts the coder to reference the chapter specific coding guidelines (C), chapter 1, guideline d, before making the final code selection. The guidelines for chapter 1, Certain Infectious and Parasitic Diseases, is located at the beginning of Chapter 1 in the Diagnosis Tabular. Please note that the coding guideline notes may be provided at the category, sub-category, or sub-classification level, whichever is applicable to the coding guidance.

II. Selection of Principal Diagnosis

The circumstances of inpatient admission always govern the selection of principal diagnosis. The principal diagnosis is defined in the Uniform Hospital Discharge Data Set (UHDDS) as "that condition established after study to be chiefly responsible for occasioning the admission of the patient to the hospital for care."

The UHDDS definitions are used by hospitals to report inpatient data elements in a standardized manner. These data elements and their definitions can be found in the July 31, 1985, Federal Register (Vol. 50, No, 147), pp. 31038–40.

Since that time the application of the UHDDS definitions has been expanded to include all non-outpatient settings (acute care, short term, long term care and psychiatric hospitals; home health agencies; rehab facilities; nursing homes, etc).

In determining principal diagnosis, coding conventions in the ICD-10-CM, the Tabular List and Alphabetic Index take precedence over these official coding guidelines.

(See Section I.A., Conventions for the ICD-10-CM)

The importance of consistent, complete documentation in the medical record cannot be overemphasized. Without such documentation the application of all coding guidelines is a difficult, if not impossible, task.

A. Codes for Symptoms, Signs, and Ill-Defined Conditions

Codes for symptoms, signs, and ill-defined conditions from Chapter 18 are not to be used as principal diagnosis when a related definitive diagnosis has been established.

B. Two or More Interrelated Conditions, Each Potentially Meeting the Definition for Principal Diagnosis

When there are two or more interrelated conditions (such as diseases in the same ICD-10-CM chapter or manifestations characteristically associated with a certain disease) potentially meeting the definition of principal diagnosis, either condition may be sequenced first, unless the circumstances of the admission, the therapy provided, the Tabular List, or the Alphabetic Index indicate otherwise.

C. Two or More Diagnoses that Equally Meet the Definition for Principal Diagnosis

In the unusual instance when two or more diagnoses equally meet the criteria for principal diagnosis as determined by the circumstances of admission, diagnostic workup and/or therapy provided, and the Alphabetic Index, Tabular List, or another coding guidelines does not provide sequencing direction, any one of the diagnoses may be sequenced first.

D. Two or More Comparative or Contrasting Conditions

In those rare instances when two or more contrasting or comparative diagnoses are documented as "either/or" (or similar terminology), they are coded as if the diagnoses were confirmed and the diagnoses are sequenced according to the circumstances of the admission. If no further determination can be made as to which diagnosis should be principal, either diagnosis may be sequenced first.

E. A Symptom(s) Followed by Contrasting/Comparative Diagnoses

GUIDELINE HAS BEEN DELETED EFFECTIVE OCTOBER 1, 2014.

F. Original Treatment Plan not Carried out

Sequence as the principal diagnosis the condition, which after study occasioned the admission to the hospital, even though treatment may not have been carried out due to unforeseen circumstances.

G. Complications of Surgery and Other Medical Care

When the admission is for treatment of a complication resulting from surgery or other medical care, the complication code is sequenced as the principal diagnosis. If the complication is classified to the T80–T88 series and the code lacks the necessary specificity in describing the complication, an additional code for the specific complication should be assigned.

H. Uncertain Diagnosis

If the diagnosis documented at the time of discharge is qualified as "probable", "suspected", "likely", "questionable", "possible", or "still to be ruled out", or other similar terms indicating uncertainty, code the condition as if it existed or was established. The bases for these guidelines are the diagnostic workup, arrangements for further workup or observation, and initial therapeutic approach that correspond most closely with the established diagnosis.

Note: This guideline is applicable only to inpatient admissions to short-term, acute, long-term care and psychiatric hospitals.

I. Admission from Observation Unit

1. Admission Following Medical Observation

When a patient is admitted to an observation unit for a medical condition, which either worsens or does not improve, and is subsequently admitted as an inpatient of the same hospital for this same medical condition, the principal diagnosis would be the medical condition which led to the hospital admission.

2. Admission Following Post-Operative Observation

When a patient is admitted to an observation unit to monitor a condition (or complication) that develops following outpatient surgery, and then is subsequently admitted as an inpatient of the same hospital, hospitals should apply the Uniform Hospital Discharge Data Set (UHDDS) definition of principal diagnosis as "that condition established after study to be chiefly responsible for occasioning the admission of the patient to the hospital for care."

J. Admission from Outpatient Surgery

When a patient receives surgery in the hospital's outpatient surgery department and is subsequently admitted for continuing inpatient care at the same hospital, the following guidelines should be followed in selecting the principal diagnosis for the inpatient admission:

- If the reason for the inpatient admission is a complication, assign the complication as the principal diagnosis.
- If no complication, or other condition, is documented as the reason for the inpatient admission, assign the reason for the outpatient surgery as the principal diagnosis.
- If the reason for the inpatient admission is another condition unrelated to the surgery, assign the unrelated condition as the principal diagnosis.

K. Admissions/Encounters for Rehabilitation

When the purpose for the admission/encounter is rehabilitation, sequence first the code for the condition for which the service is being performed. For example, for an admission/encounter for rehabilitation for rightsided dominant hemiplegia following a cerebrovascular infarction, report code I69.351, Hemiplegia and hemiparesis following cerebral infarction affecting right dominant side, as the first-listed or principal diagnosis.

If the condition for which the rehabilitation service is no longer present, report the appropriate aftercare code as the first-listed or principal diagnosis. For example, if a patient with severe degenerative osteoarthritis of the hip, underwent hip replacement and the current encounter/admission is for rehabilitation, report code Z47.1, Aftercare following joint replacement surgery, as the first-listed or principal diagnosis.

See Section I.C.21.c.7, Factors influencing health states and contact with health services, Aftercare.

III. Reporting Additional Diagnoses

GENERAL RULES FOR OTHER (ADDITIONAL) DIAGNOSES

For reporting purposes the definition for "other diagnoses" is interpreted as additional conditions that affect patient care in terms of requiring:

- clinical evaluation; or
- therapeutic treatment; or
- diagnostic procedures; or
- extended length of hospital stay; or
- increased nursing care and/or
- monitoring

The UHDDS item #11-b defines Other Diagnoses as "all conditions that coexist at the time of admission, that develop subsequently, or that affect the treatment received and/or the length of stay. Diagnoses that relate to an earlier episode which have no bearing on the current hospital stay are to be excluded." UHDDS definitions apply to inpatients in acute-care, short-term, long term care and psychiatric hospital setting. The UHDDS definitions are used by acute-care shortterm hospitals to report inpatient data elements in a standardized manner. These data elements and their definitions can be found in the July 31, 1985, *Federal Register* (Vol. 50, No, 147), pp. 31038–40.

Since that time the application of the UHDDS definitions has been expanded to include all nonoutpatient settings (acute-care, short-term, long-term care and psychiatric hospitals; home health agencies; rehab facilities; nursing homes, etc.).

The following guidelines are to be applied in designating "other diagnoses" when neither the Alphabetic Index nor the Tabular List in ICD-10-CM provide direction. The listing of the diagnoses in the patient record is the responsibility of the attending provider.

A. Previous Conditions

If the provider has included a diagnosis in the final diagnostic statement, such as the discharge summary or the face sheet, it should ordinarily be coded. Some providers include in the diagnostic statement resolved conditions or diagnoses and status-post procedures from previous admission that have no bearing on the current stay. Such conditions are not to be reported and are coded only if required by hospital policy.

However, history codes (categories Z80–Z87) may be used as secondary codes if the historical condition or family history has an impact on current care or influences treatment.

B. Abnormal Findings

Abnormal findings (laboratory, x-ray, pathologic, and other diagnostic results) are not coded and reported unless the provider indicates their clinical significance. If the findings are outside the normal range and the attending provider has ordered other tests to evaluate the condition or prescribed treatment, it is appropriate to ask the provider whether the abnormal finding should be added.

Note: This differs from the coding practices in the outpatient setting for coding encounters for diagnostic tests that have been interpreted by a provider.

C. Uncertain Diagnosis

If the diagnosis documented at the time of discharge is qualified as "probable", "suspected", "likely", "questionable", "possible", or "still to be ruled out" or other similar terms indicating uncertainty, code the condition as if it existed or was established. The bases for these guidelines are the diagnostic workup, arrangements for further workup or observation, and initial therapeutic approach that correspond most closely with the established diagnosis.

Note: This guideline is applicable only to inpatient admissions to short-term, acute-care, long-term care and psychiatric hospitals.

IV. Diagnostic Coding and Reporting Guidelines for Outpatient Services

These coding guidelines for outpatient diagnoses have been approved for use by hospitals/ providers in coding and reporting hospital-based outpatient services and provider-based office visits.

Information about the use of certain abbreviations, punctuation, symbols, and other conventions used in the ICD-10-CM Tabular List (code numbers and titles), can be found in Section IA of these guidelines, under "Conventions Used in the Tabular List." Section I.B. contains general guidelines that apply to the entire classification. Section I.C. contains chapter-specific guidelines that correspond to the chapters as they are arranged in the classification. Information about the correct sequence to use in finding a code is also described in Section I.

The terms encounter and visit are often used interchangeably in describing outpatient service contacts and, therefore, appear together in these guidelines without distinguishing one from the other.

Though the conventions and general guidelines apply to all settings, coding guidelines for outpatient and provider reporting of diagnoses will vary in a number of instances from those for inpatient diagnoses, recognizing that:

The Uniform Hospital Discharge Data Set (UHDDS) definition of principal diagnosis applies only to inpatients in acute, short-term, long-term care and psychiatric hospitals.

Coding guidelines for inconclusive diagnoses (probable, suspected, rule out, etc.) were developed for inpatient reporting and do not apply to outpatients.

A. Selection of First-Listed Condition

In the outpatient setting, the term first-listed diagnosis is used in lieu of principal diagnosis.

In determining the first-listed diagnosis the coding conventions of ICD-10-CM, as well as the general and disease specific guidelines take precedence over the outpatient guidelines.

Diagnoses often are not established at the time of the initial encounter/visit. It may take two or more visits before the diagnosis is confirmed.

The most critical rule involves beginning the search for the correct code assignment through the Alphabetic Index. Never begin searching initially in the Tabular List as this will lead to coding errors.

1. Outpatient Surgery

When a patient presents for outpatient surgery (same day surgery), code the reason for the surgery as the first-listed diagnosis (reason for the encounter), even if the surgery is not performed due to a contraindication.

2. Observation Stay

When a patient is admitted for observation for a medical condition, assign a code for the medical condition as the first-listed diagnosis.

When a patient presents for outpatient surgery and develops complications requiring admission to observation, code the reason for the surgery as the first reported diagnosis (reason for the encounter), followed by codes for the complications as secondary diagnoses.

B. Codes from A00.0–T88.9, Z00–Z99

The appropriate code(s) from A00.0–T88.9, Z00–Z99 must be used to identify diagnoses, symptoms, conditions, problems, complaints, or other reason(s) for the encounter/visit.

C. Accurate Reporting of ICD-10-CM Diagnosis Codes

For accurate reporting of ICD-10-CM diagnosis codes, the documentation should describe the patient's condition, using terminology which includes specific diagnoses as well as symptoms, problems, or reasons for the encounter. There are ICD-10-CM codes to describe all of these.

D. Codes that Describe Symptoms and Signs

Codes that describe symptoms and signs, as opposed to diagnoses, are acceptable for reporting purposes when a diagnosis has not been established (confirmed) by the provider. Chapter 18 of ICD-10-CM, Symptoms, Signs, and Abnormal Clinical, and Laboratory Findings Not Elsewhere Classified (codes R00–R99) contain many, but not all codes for symptoms.

E. Encounters for Circumstances Other than a Disease or Injury

ICD-10-CM provides codes to deal with encounters for circumstances other than a disease or injury. The Factors Influencing Health Status and Contact with Health Services codes (Z00–Z99) are provided to deal with occasions when circumstances other than a disease or injury are recorded as diagnosis or problems.

See Section I.C.21. Factors influencing health status and contact with health services.

F. Level of Detail in Coding

1. ICD-10-CM Codes with 3, 4, 5, 6, Or 7 Characters

ICD-10-CM is composed of codes with 3, 4, 5, 6, or 7 characters. Codes with three characters are included in ICD-10-CM as the heading of a category of codes that may be further subdivided by the use of fourth, fifth, sixth, or seventh characters to provide greater specificity.

2. Use of Full Number of *Characters* Required for a Code

A three-character code is to be used only if it is not further subdivided. A code is invalid if it has not been coded to the full number of characters required for that code, including the 7th character, if applicable.

G. ICD-10-CM Code for the Diagnosis, Condition, Problem, or Other Reason for Encounter/Visit

List first the ICD-10-CM code for the diagnosis, condition, problem, or other reason for encounter/visit shown in the medical record to be chiefly responsible for the services provided. List additional codes that describe any coexisting conditions. In some cases the first-listed diagnosis may be a symptom when a diagnosis has not been established (confirmed) by the physician.

H. Uncertain Diagnosis

Do not code diagnoses documented as "probable", "suspected," "questionable," "rule out," or "working diagnosis" or other similar terms indicating uncertainty. Rather, code the condition(s) to the highest degree of certainty for that encounter/visit, such as symptoms, signs, abnormal test results, or other reason for the visit.

Note: This differs from the coding practices used by short-term, acute-care, long-term care and psychiatric hospitals.

I. Chronic Diseases

Chronic diseases treated on an ongoing basis may be coded and reported as many times as the patient receives treatment and care for the condition(s).

J. Code All Documented Conditions that Coexist

Code all documented conditions that coexist at the time of the encounter/visit, and require or affect patient care treatment or management. Do not code conditions that were previously treated and no longer exist. However, history codes (categories Z80–Z87) may be used as secondary codes if the historical condition or family history has an impact on current care or influences treatment.

K. Patients Receiving Diagnostic Services Only

For patients receiving diagnostic services only during an encounter/visit, sequence first the diagnosis, condition, problem, or other reason for encounter/visit shown in the medical record to be chiefly responsible for the outpatient services provided during the encounter/visit. Codes for other diagnoses (e.g., chronic conditions) may be sequenced as additional diagnoses.

For encounters for routine laboratory/radiology testing in the absence of any signs, symptoms, or associated diagnosis, assign Z01.89, Encounter for other specified special examinations. If routine testing is performed during the same encounter as a test to evaluate a sign, symptom, or diagnosis, it is appropriate to assign both the Z code and the code describing the reason for the non-routine test.

For outpatient encounters for diagnostic tests that have been interpreted by a physician, and the final report is available at the time of coding, code any confirmed or definitive diagnosis(es) documented in the interpretation. Do not code related signs and symptoms as additional diagnoses.

Note: This differs from the coding practice in the hospital inpatient setting regarding abnormal findings on test results.

L. Patients Receiving Therapeutic Services Only

For patients receiving therapeutic services only during an encounter/visit, sequence first the diagnosis, condition, problem, or other reason for encounter/visit shown in the medical record to be chiefly responsible for the outpatient services provided during the encounter/visit. Codes for other diagnoses (e.g., chronic conditions) may be sequenced as additional diagnoses.

The only exception to this rule is that when the primary reason for the admission/encounter is chemotherapy or radiation therapy, the appropriate Z code for the service is listed first, and the diagnosis or problem for which the service is being performed listed second.

M. Patients Receiving Preoperative Evaluations Only

For patients receiving preoperative evaluations only, sequence first a code from subcategory Z01.81, Encounter for pre-procedural examinations, to describe the pre-op consultations. Assign a code for the condition to describe the reason for the surgery as an additional diagnosis. Code also any findings related to the pre-op evaluation.

N. Ambulatory Surgery

For ambulatory surgery, code the diagnosis for which the surgery was performed. If the postoperative diagnosis is known to be different from the preoperative diagnosis at the time the diagnosis is confirmed, select the postoperative diagnosis for coding, since it is the most definitive.

O. Routine Outpatient Prenatal Visits

See Section I.C.15. Routine outpatient prenatal visits.

P. Encounters for General Medical Examinations with Abnormal Findings

The subcategories for encounters for general medical examinations, Z00.0-, provide codes for with and without abnormal findings. Should a general medical examination result in an abnormal finding, the code for general medical examination with abnormal finding should be assigned as the first-listed diagnosis. A secondary code for the abnormal finding should also be coded.

Q. Encounters for Routine Health Screenings

See Section I.C.21. Factors influencing health status and contact with health services, Screening

Appendix I Present on Admission Reporting Guidelines

Introduction

These guidelines are to be used as a supplement to the *ICD-10-CM Official Guidelines for Coding and Reporting* to facilitate the assignment of the Present on Admission (POA) indicator for each diagnosis and external cause of injury code reported on claim forms (UB-04 and 837 Institutional).

These guidelines are not intended to replace any guidelines in the main body of the *ICD-10-CM Official Guidelines for Coding and Reporting.* The POA guidelines are not intended to provide guidance on when a condition should be coded, but rather, how to apply the POA indicator to the final set of diagnosis codes that have been assigned in accordance with Sections I, II, and III of the official coding guidelines. Subsequent to the assignment of the ICD-10-CM codes, the POA indicator should then be assigned to those conditions that have been coded.

As stated in the Introduction to the ICD-10-CM Official Guidelines for Coding and Reporting, a joint effort between the healthcare provider and the coder is essential to achieve complete and accurate documentation, code assignment, and reporting of diagnoses and procedures. The importance of consistent, complete documentation in the medical record cannot be overemphasized. Medical record documentation from any provider involved in the care and treatment of the patient may be used to support the determination of whether a condition was present on admission or not. In the context of the official coding guidelines, the term "provider" means a physician or any qualified healthcare practitioner who is legally accountable for establishing the patient's diagnosis.

These guidelines are not a substitute for the provider's clinical judgment as to the determination of whether a condition was or was not present on admission. The provider should be queried regarding issues related to the linking of signs/symptoms, timing of test results, and the timing of findings.

General Reporting Requirements

All claims involving inpatient admissions to general acute-care hospitals or other facilities that are subject to a law or regulation mandating collection of present on admission information.

Present on admission is defined as present at the time the order for inpatient admission occurs—conditions that develop during an outpatient encounter, including emergency department, observation, or outpatient surgery, are considered as present on admission.

POA indicator is assigned to principal and secondary diagnoses (as defined in Section II of the Official Guidelines for Coding and Reporting) and the external cause of injury codes.

Issues related to inconsistent, missing, conflicting or unclear documentation must still be resolved by the provider.

If a condition would not be coded and reported based on UHDDS definitions and current official coding guidelines, then the POA indicator would not be reported.

Reporting Options

Y—Yes
N—No
U—Unknown
W—Clinically undetermined
Unreported/Not used—(Exempt from POA reporting)

Reporting Definitions

Y = present at the time of inpatient admission
N = not present at the time of inpatient admission

U = documentation is insufficient to determine if condition is present on admission
W = provider is unable to clinically determine whether condition was present on admission or not

Timeframe for POA Identification and Documentation

There is no required timeframe as to when a provider (per the definition of "provider" used in these guidelines) must identify or document a condition to be present on admission. In some clinical situations, it may not be possible for a provider to make a definitive diagnosis (or a condition may not be recognized or reported by the patient) for a period of time after admission. In some cases it may be several days before the provider arrives at a definitive diagnosis. This does not mean that the condition was not present on admission. Determination of whether the condition was present on admission or not will be based on the applicable POA guideline as identified in this document, or on the provider's best clinical judgment.

If at the time of code assignment the documentation is unclear as to whether a condition was present on admission or not, it is appropriate to query the provider for clarification.

Assigning the POA Indicator

Condition is on the "Exempt from Reporting" list

Leave the "present on admission" field blank if the condition is on the list of ICD-10-CM codes for which this field is not applicable. This is the only circumstance in which the field may be left blank.

POA Explicitly Documented

Assign "Y" for any condition the provider explicitly documents as being present on admission.

Assign "N" for any condition the provider explicitly documents as not present at the time of admission.

Conditions diagnosed prior to inpatient admission

Assign "Y" for conditions that were diagnosed prior to admission (example: hypertension, diabetes mellitus, asthma)

Conditions diagnosed during the admission but clearly present before admission

Assign "Y" for conditions diagnosed during the admission that were clearly present but not diagnosed until after admission occurred.

Diagnoses subsequently confirmed after admission are considered present on admission if at the time of admission they are documented as suspected, possible, rule out, differential diagnosis, or constitute an underlying cause of a symptom that is present at the time of admission.

Condition develops during outpatient encounter prior to inpatient admission

Assign "Y" for any condition that develops during an outpatient encounter prior to a written order for inpatient admission.

Documentation does not indicate whether condition was present on admission

Assign "U" when the medical record documentation is unclear as to whether the condition was present on admission. "U" should not be routinely assigned and used only in very limited circumstances. Coders are encouraged to query the providers when the documentation is unclear.

Documentation states that it cannot be determined whether the condition was or was not present on admission

Assign "W" when the medical record documentation indicates that it cannot be clinically determined whether or not the condition was present on admission.

Chronic condition with acute exacerbation during the admission

If a single code identifies both the chronic condition and the acute exacerbation, see POA guidelines pertaining to combination codes.

If a single code only identifies the chronic condition and not the acute exacerbation (e.g., acute exacerbation of chronic leukemia), assign "Y."

Conditions documented as possible, probable, suspected, or rule out at the time of discharge

If the final diagnosis contains a possible, probable, suspected, or rule out diagnosis, and this diagnosis was based on signs, symptoms or clinical findings suspected at the time of inpatient admission, assign "Y."

If the final diagnosis contains a possible, probable, suspected, or rule out diagnosis, and this diagnosis was based on signs, symptoms or clinical findings that were not present on admission, assign "N".

Conditions documented as impending or threatened at the time of discharge

If the final diagnosis contains an impending or threatened diagnosis, and this diagnosis is based on symptoms or clinical findings that were present on admission, assign "Y".

If the final diagnosis contains an impending or threatened diagnosis, and this diagnosis is based on symptoms or clinical findings that were not present on admission, assign "N".

Acute and Chronic Conditions

Assign "Y" for acute conditions that are present at time of admission and N for acute conditions that are not present at time of admission.

Assign "Y" for chronic conditions, even though the condition may not be diagnosed until after admission.

If a single code identifies both an acute and chronic condition, see the POA guidelines for combination codes.

Combination Codes

Assign "N" if any part of the combination code was not present on admission (e.g., COPD with acute exacerbation and the exacerbation was not present on admission; gastric ulcer that does not start bleeding until after admission; asthma patient develops status asthmaticus after admission)

Assign "Y" if all parts of the combination code were present on admission (e.g., patient with acute prostatitis admitted with hematuria)

If the final diagnosis includes comparative or contrasting diagnoses, and both were present, or suspected, at the time of admission, assign "Y".

For infection codes that include the causal organism, assign "Y" if the infection (or signs of the infection) was present on admission, even though the culture results may not be known until after admission (e.g., patient is admitted with pneumonia and the provider documents pseudomonas as the causal organism a few days later).

Same Diagnosis Code for Two or More Conditions

When the same ICD-10-CM diagnosis code applies to two or more conditions during the same encounter (e.g. two separate conditions classified to the same ICD-10-CM diagnosis code):

Assign "Y" if all conditions represented by the single ICD-10-CM code were present on admission (e.g. bilateral unspecified age-related cataracts).

Assign "N" if any of the conditions represented by the single ICD-10-CM code was not present on admission (e.g. traumatic secondary and recurrent hemorrhage and seroma is assigned to a single code T79.2, but only one of the conditions was present on admission).

Obstetrical Conditions

Whether or not the patient delivers during the current hospitalization does not affect assignment of the POA indicator.
The determining factor for POA assignment is whether the pregnancy complication or obstetrical condition described by the code was present at the time of admission or not.

If the pregnancy complication or obstetrical condition was present on admission (e.g., patient admitted in preterm labor), assign "Y".

If the pregnancy complication or obstetrical condition was not present on admission (e.g., 2nd degree laceration during delivery, postpartum hemorrhage that occurred during current hospitalization, fetal distress develops after admission), assign "N".

If the obstetrical code includes more than one diagnosis and any of the diagnoses identified by the code were not present on admission assign "N". (e.g., Category O11, Pre-existing hypertension with pre-eclampsia)

Perinatal Conditions

Newborns are not considered to be admitted until after birth. Therefore, any condition present at birth or that developed in utero is considered present at admission and should be assigned "Y". This includes conditions that occur during delivery (e.g., injury during delivery, meconium aspiration, exposure to streptococcus B in the vaginal canal).

Congenital Conditions and Anomalies

Assign "Y" for congenital conditions and anomalies except for categories Q00–Q99, Congenital anomalies, which are on the exempt list. Congenital conditions are always considered present on admission.

External Cause of Injury Codes

Assign "Y" for any external cause code representing an external cause of morbidity that occurred prior to inpatient admission (e.g., patient fell out of bed at home, patient fell out of bed in emergency room prior to admission)

Assign "N" for any external cause code representing an external cause of morbidity that occurred during inpatient hospitalization (e.g., patient fell out of hospital bed during hospital stay, patient experienced an adverse reaction to a medication administered after inpatient admission)

Categories and Codes Exempt from Diagnosis Present on Admission Requirement

Note: "Diagnosis present on admission" for these code categories are exempt because they represent circumstances regarding the healthcare encounter or factors influencing health status that do not represent a current disease or injury or are always present on admission

B90–B94	Sequelae of infectious and parasitic diseases
E64	Sequelae of malnutrition and other nutritional deficiencies
I25.2	Old myocardial infarction
I69	Sequelae of cerebrovascular disease
O09	Supervision of high risk pregnancy
O66.5	Attempted application of vacuum extractor and forceps
O80	Encounter for full-term uncomplicated delivery
O94	Sequelae of complication of pregnancy, childbirth, and the puerperium
P00	Newborn (suspected to be) affected by maternal conditions that may be unrelated to present pregnancy
Q00–Q99	Congenital malformations, deformations and chromosomal abnormalities
S00–T88.9	Injury, poisoning and certain other consequences of external causes with 7th character representing subsequent encounter or sequela
V00–V09	Pedestrian injured in transport accident
	Except V00.81-, Accident with wheelchair (powered)
	V00.83-, Accident with motorized mobility scooter
V10–V19	Pedal cycle rider injured in transport accident
V20–V29	Motorcycle rider injured in transport accident
V30–V39	Occupant of three-wheeled motor vehicle injured in transport accident
V40–V49	Car occupant injured in transport accident
V50–V59	Occupant of pick-up truck or van injured in transport accident
V60–V69	Occupant of heavy transport vehicle injured in transport accident
V70–V79	Bus occupant injured in transport accident
V80–V89	Other land transport accidents
V90–V94	Water transport accidents
V95–V97	Air and space transport accidents

V98–V99	Other and unspecified transport accidents
W09	Fall on and from playground equipment
W14	Fall from tree
W15	Fall from cliff
W17.0	Fall into well
W17.1	Fall into storm drain or manhole
W18.01	Striking against sports equipment with subsequent fall
W21	Striking against or struck by sports equipment
W30	Contact with agricultural machinery
W31	Contact with other and unspecified machinery
W32–W34	Accidental handgun discharge and malfunction
W35–W40	Exposure to inanimate mechanical forces
W52	Crushed, pushed or stepped on by crowd or human stampede
W56	Contact with nonvenomous marine animal
W58	Contact with crocodile or alligator
W61	Contact with birds (domestic) (wild)
W62	Contact with nonvenomous amphibians
W89	Exposure to man-made visible and ultraviolet light
X02	Exposure to controlled fire in building or structure
X03	Exposure to controlled fire, not in building or structure
X04	Exposure to ignition of highly flammable material
X52	Prolonged stay in weightless environment
X71	Intentional self-harm by drowning and submersion
	Except X71.0-, Intentional self-harm by drowning and submersion while in bath tub
X72	Intentional self-harm by handgun discharge
X73	Intentional self-harm by rifle, shotgun and larger firearm discharge
X74	Intentional self-harm by other and unspecified firearm and gun discharge
X75	Intentional self-harm by explosive material
X76	Intentional self-harm by smoke, fire and flames
X77	Intentional self-harm by steam, hot vapors and hot objects
X81	Intentional self-harm by jumping or lying in front of moving object
X82	Intentional self-harm by crashing of motor vehicle
X83	Intentional self-harm by other specified means
Y03	Assault by crashing of motor vehicle
Y07	Perpetrator of assault, maltreatment and neglect
Y08.8	Assault by strike by sports equipment
Y21	Drowning and submersion, undetermined intent
Y22	Handgun discharge, undetermined intent
Y23	Rifle, shotgun and larger firearm discharge, undetermined intent
Y24	Other and unspecified firearm discharge, undetermined intent
Y30	Falling, jumping or pushed from a high place, undetermined intent
Y32	Assault by crashing of motor vehicle, undetermined intent
Y37	Military operations
Y36	Operations of war
Y92	Place of occurrence of the external cause
Y93	Activity code
Y99	External cause status
Z00	Encounter for general examination without complaint, suspected or reported diagnosis
Z01	Encounter for other special examination without complaint, suspected or reported diagnosis
Z02	Encounter for administrative examination
Z03	Encounter for medical observation for suspected diseases and conditions ruled out
Z08	Encounter for follow-up examination following completed treatment for malignant neoplasm
Z09	Encounter for follow-up examination after completed treatment for conditions other than malignant neoplasm

Z11	Encounter for screening for infectious and parasitic diseases
Z11.8	Encounter for screening for other infectious and parasitic diseases
Z12	Encounter for screening for malignant neoplasms
Z13	Encounter for screening for other diseases and disorders
Z13.4	Encounter for screening for certain developmental disorders in childhood
Z13.5	Encounter for screening for eye and ear disorders
Z13.6	Encounter for screening for cardiovascular disorders
Z13.83	Encounter for screening for respiratory disorder NEC
Z13.89	Encounter for screening for other disorder
Z13.89	Encounter for screening for other disorder
Z14	Genetic carrier
Z15	Genetic susceptibility to disease
Z17	Estrogen receptor status
Z18	Retained foreign body fragments
Z22	Carrier of infectious disease
Z23	Encounter for immunization
Z28	Immunization not carried out and underimmunization status
Z28.3	Underimmunization status
Z30	Encounter for contraceptive management
Z31	Encounter for procreative management
Z34	Encounter for supervision of normal pregnancy
Z36	Encounter for antenatal screening of mother
Z37	Outcome of delivery
Z38	Liveborn infants according to place of birth and type of delivery
Z39	Encounter for maternal postpartum care and examination
Z41	Encounter for procedures for purposes other than remedying health state
Z42	Encounter for plastic and reconstructive surgery following medical procedure or healed injury
Z43	Encounter for attention to artificial openings
Z44	Encounter for fitting and adjustment of external prosthetic device
Z45	Encounter for adjustment and management of implanted device
Z46	Encounter for fitting and adjustment of other devices
Z47.8	Encounter for other orthopedic aftercare
Z49	Encounter for care involving renal dialysis
Z51	Encounter for other aftercare
Z51.5	Encounter for palliative care
Z51.8	Encounter for other specified aftercare
Z52	Donors of organs and tissues
Z59	Problems related to housing and economic circumstances
Z63	Other problems related to primary support group, including family circumstances
Z65	Problems related to other psychosocial circumstances
Z65.8	Other specified problems related to psychosocial circumstances
Z67.1–Z67.9	Blood type
Z68	Body mass index (BMI)
Z72	Problems related to lifestyle
Z74.01	Bed confinement status
Z76	Persons encountering health services in other circumstances
Z77.110–Z77.128	Environmental pollution and hazards in the physical environment
Z78	Other specified health status
Z79	Long-term (current) drug therapy
Z80	Family history of primary malignant neoplasm
Z81	Family history of mental and behavioral disorders
Z82	Family history of certain disabilities and chronic diseases (leading to disablement)

Z83	Family history of other specific disorders
Z84	Family history of other conditions
Z85	Personal history of primary malignant neoplasm
Z86	Personal history of certain other diseases
Z87	Personal history of other diseases and conditions
Z87.828	Personal history of other (healed) physical injury and trauma
Z87.891	Personal history of nicotine dependence
Z88	Allergy status to drugs, medicaments and biological substances
Z89	Acquired absence of limb
Z90.710	Acquired absence of both cervix and uterus
Z91.0	Allergy status, other than to drugs and biological substances
Z91.4	Personal history of psychological trauma, not elsewhere classified
Z91.5	Personal history of self-harm
Z91.8	Other specified risk factors, not elsewhere classified
Z92	Personal history of medical treatment
Z93	Artificial opening status
Z94	Transplanted organ and tissue status
Z95	Presence of cardiac and vascular implants and grafts
Z97	Presence of other devices
Z98	Other postprocedural states
Z99	Dependence on enabling machines and devices, not elsewhere classified

Additional Conventions

The use of symbols and color-coding has been added to this code book to alert the user to Medicare reimbursement logic and edits that are impacted by diagnosis coding. Although some third-party payers have adopted Medicare's reimbursement methodology, others have not. Therefore, it is important to review your facilities payer reporting requirements for non-Medicare payers prior to diagnosis coding.

Some codes may be included in multiple reimbursement issues and, therefore, may have more than one symbol or color-coding feature. For a quick reference review, the legend at the bottom of each page of the Tabular as well as the inside cover of the code book. The symbols and color-coding features are described in detail here.

Tabular Enhancements

In an effort to make the Tabular more user-friendly, the following symbols and color-coding features have been added. These features are indented to help the user in selecting a complete and accurate diagnosis code.

Final Character Indicator

ICD-10-CM codes range in length from 3 to 7 characters. In order for a code to be "valid" it must be listed to the fullest character length available. For example, if a fourth character is available, a three-character code is considered invalid.

To help users comply with this convention, a red plus sign (+) is listed to the left of any subcategory or subclassification code that requires an additional character. For example:

+ J45.2 Mild intermittent asthma

The assignment of the seventh character can, at times, be tricky. There are designated categories of codes that require a seventh character even though the code may not already have six characters present. For these codes, the user must insert the placeholder character of X after the code to fill any open characters prior to the seventh character.

To help users comply with this convention, in this book, the phrase **X+7th** is in red and is located to the left of the code that requires the placeholder of X and/or the seventh character. For example:

X+7th M80.00 Age-related osteoporosis with current pathological fracture

Additionally, there are six character codes that require the application of a seventh character. For these codes a placeholder X is not required. To help users differentiate these codes, in this book, the phrase **+7th** is in red and is located to the left of the code that requires the seventh character. For example:

+7th S72.021 Displaced fracture of epiphysis (separation) (upper) of right femur

Lastly, there are some codes that have only three characters. They require no further specification with additional characters and are therefore valid codes. The following note: Valid 3-character code, no further characters required is located below the code description in this book. This note alerts the coder that the three-character code is valid and can be used for reporting.

Color Identification

The Tabular section of this code book contains many instructional notes for the user. In order to help navigate the various types of instructional notes, a color-coding system has been applied:

- Category block headers are presented in dark green font.
- Category codes (three characters) are presented in blue font.
- Includes notes have a gray color bar over the **Includes**
- Excludes1 notes have a yellow color bar over the ***Excludes1***
- Excludes2 notes have a bright green color bar over the ***Excludes2***
- Notes have a maroon color bar over the **NOTE**
- *Use additional code* notes are presented in red font
- *Code also* notes are presented in red font
- *Code first* notes are presented in red font
- Seventh character options are presented in a box and are highlighted in gray

The following excerpt from the Tabular illustrates the color-coding applied in this code book.

Disorders of bone density and structure (M80–M85)

M80 Osteoporosis with current pathological fracture

Includes: osteoporosis with current fragility fracture

Use additional code to identify major osseous defect, if applicable (M89.7-)

Excludes1: *collapsed vertebra NOS (M48.5)*
pathological fracture NOS (M84.4)
wedging of vertebra NOS (M48.5)

Excludes2: *personal history of (healed) osteoporosis fracture (Z87.310)*

The appropriate 7th character is to be added to each code from category M80:
A initial encounter for fracture
D subsequent encounter for fracture with routine healing
G subsequent encounter for fracture with delayed healing
K subsequent encounter for fracture with nonunion
P subsequent encounter for fracture with malunion
S sequela

Medicare Code Edits

Hospital inpatient Medicare claims paid under the Inpatient Prospective payment System (IPPS) are processed through the MCE prior to payment by the Medicare administrative contractor (MAC). The code edits are intended to ensure that all claims processed by the MAC are accurate and complete. Medicare has released an ICD-10 version of the MCE v31R and is provided to the general public as a tool to assist in the implementation of ICD-10-CM/PCS. The information in this manual is based on the MCE v31R.

Several of the MCE edits pertain to diagnoses. We have identified the codes included in these edits throughout the Tabular section this manual to assist users with preparing accurate and complete claims. The MCE edits included in this manual:

- Age conflict
- Sex Conflict Edit
- Manifestation codes not allowed as principal diagnosis
- Unacceptable principal diagnoses

Note: It is important to remember these edits are Medicare edits and may not apply to other third-party payers claim processing.

Age Conflict

The age conflict edit is activated when the age of the patient and the type diagnosis code reported does not match. The following symbols are used to identify the four age conflict categories.

- Newborn diagnosis age 0: This symbol appears to the left of the applicable code in the Tabular.
- Pediatric diagnosis age 0–17: This symbol appears to the left of the applicable code in the Tabular.
- Maternity diagnosis age 12–55: This symbol appears to the left of the applicable code in the Tabular.
- Adult diagnosis age 15–124: This symbol appears to the left of the applicable code in the Tabular.

Sex Conflict Edit

The sex conflict edit is activated when the sex of the patient and the diagnosis reported does not match. The following symbols are used to identify female-only and male-only diagnoses.

♀ Female-only diagnosis: This symbol appears to the left of the applicable code in the Tabular.

♂ Male-only diagnosis: This symbol appears to the left of the applicable code in the Tabular.

Manifestation Code Not Allowed as Principal Diagnosis

Manifestation codes are used to report the manifestation of an underlying disease, not to report the disease itself. Therefore, within ICD-10-CM the manifestation should not be reported as the principal diagnosis; rather it should always be reported as a secondary diagnosis.

Manifestation codes are identified with a light green color bar over the code in the Tabular. For example:

D63.0 Anemia in neoplastic disease

Unacceptable Principal Diagnosis

There are specified codes that describe a circumstance which influences an individual's health status but not a current illness or injury, or codes that are not specific manifestations but may be due to an underlying cause. These codes are considered unacceptable as a principal diagnosis.

Unacceptable principal diagnosis codes are identified with a light blue color bar over the code in the Tabular:

B60.13 Keratoconjunctivitis due to Acanthamoeba

MS-DRG Diagnosis Designations

The MS-DRG system is utilized within the IPPS to determine the unadjusted reimbursement amount for Medicare hospital inpatient claims. The MS-DRG Definitions Manual includes the logic for MS-DRG refinement and selection as well as logic based on the IPPS final rules released each August. CMS has released an ICD-10-CM/PCS version of the MS-DRG v31R. The information in this book is based on the MS-DRG v31R. *Note:* It is important to remember that these edits are Medicare edits and may not apply to other third-party payers claim processing.

CC and MCC Codes

Within the MS-DRG system, one of the refinement pathways is whether there is a complication/comorbidity (CC) or major complication/comorbidity (MCC) code reported as a secondary diagnosis. For some of the MS-DRG families, the presence of a CC or MCC allows for an MS-DRG assignment that has a higher relative weight and, therefore, a higher reimbursement amount. There are exceptions to the application of the CC or MCC codes and the exceptions are referred to as *CC Exclusions* or *MCC Exclusions*. If exclusions apply, the CC/MCC code is assigned a principal diagnosis collection. Within this collection are the codes that, when reported as principal diagnosis, excludes the CC/MCC status from the secondary diagnosis code under review. Essentially, it takes away the CC/MCC code's ability to influence the MS-DRG assignment.

Codes that are considered CC codes have a purple **CC** to the left of the code in the Tabular. Below the code description, the phrase ***CC Exclusion see Appendix A PDX collection xxxx*** appears, alerting the coder to review the principal diagnosis collection identified if required for the task at hand. If the code requires a seventh character, the characters that are eligible for CC status are included within the CC Exclusion note.

Codes that are considered MCC codes have a purple **MCC** to the left of the code in the Tabular. Below the code description, the phrase ***MCC Exclusion see Appendix A PDX collection xxxx*** appears, alerting the coder to review the principal diagnosis collection identified if required for the task at hand. If the code requires a seventh character, the characters that are eligible for MCC status are included within the MCC Exclusion note.

Hospital-Acquired Conditions Related Diagnoses

As part of the Medicare Value-Based Purchasing program, CMS has implemented a Paying for Value program entitled Hospital-Acquired Conditions (HACs). This program is designed to reduce reimbursements to facilities where value of the medical or surgical has been comprised due to preventable conditions. The HAC program identifies diagnosis and procedure codes that when reported as "not present on admission" activate the HAC reduced reimbursement logic. In this manual, the HAC-associated procedures are identified with an orange rectangle HAC with HAC. The orange rectangle is located below the code description in the code listing. If there is conditional logic for the diagnosis code, it is included in Appendix B.

Basic Steps in ICD-10-CM Coding

To code each disease or condition completely and accurately, the coder should:

1. Identify all main terms included in the diagnostic statement.
2. Locate each main term in the Alphabetic Index.
3. Refer to any sub terns indented under the main term. The subterms form individual line entries and describe essential differences by site, etiology, or clinical type.
4. Follow cross-reference instructions if the needed code is not located under the first main entry consulted.
5. Verify the code selected in the Tabular List.
6. Read and be guided by any instructional terms in the Tabular List.
7. Assign codes to their highest level of specificity.
   - Assign three-character codes only when no four-character codes appear within the category.
   - Assign a seventh character for any subcategory where a seventh-character subclassification is provided.
8. Continue coding the diagnostic statement until all the component elements are fully identified.

(*Source:* Schraffenberger, L.A. *Basic ICD-10-CM/PCS Coding*, 2013 Edition, pg 27. AHIMA.)

Index to Diseases and Injuries

A

Abnormal, abnormality, abnormalities *(continued)*
gait —*see* Gait
hysterical F44.4
gastrin secretion E16.4
globulin R77.1
cortisol-binding E27.8
thyroid-binding E07.89
glomerular, minor —*see also* N00-N07 with fourth character .0 N05.0
glucagon secretion E16.3
glucose tolerance (test) (non-fasting) R73.09
gravitational (G) forces or states (effect of) T75.81
hair (color) (shaft) L67.9
specified NEC L67.8
hard tissue formation in pulp (dental) K04.3
head movement R25.0
heart
rate R00.9
specified NEC R00.8
shadow R93.1
sounds NEC R01.2
hemoglobin (disease) —*see also* Disease, hemoglobin D58.2
trait —*see* Trait, hemoglobin, abnormal
histology NEC R89.7
immunological findings R89.4
in serum R76.9
specified NEC R76.8
increase in appetite R63.2
involuntary movement —*see* Abnormal, movement, involuntary
jaw closure M26.51
karyotype R89.8
kidney function test R94.4
knee jerk R29.2
leukocyte (cell) (differential) NEC D72.9
liver
loss of
height R29.890
weight R63.4
mammogram NEC R92.8
calcification (calculus) R92.1
microcalcification R92.0
Mantoux test R76.11
movement (disorder) —*see also* Disorder, movement
head R25.0
involuntary R25.9
fasciculation R25.3
of head R25.0
spasm R25.2
specified type NEC R25.8
tremor R25.1
myoglobin (Aberdeen) (Annapolis) R89.7
neonatal screening P09
oculomotor study R94.113
palmar creases Q82.8
Papanicolaou (smear)
anus R85.619
atypical squamous cells cannot exclude high grade squamous intraepithelial lesion(ASC-H) R85.611
atypical squamous cells of undetermined significance(ASC-US) R85.610
cytologic evidence of malignancy R85.614
high grade squamous intraepithelial lesion (HGSIL) R85.613

Abnormal, abnormality, abnormalities *(continued)*
Papanicolaou *(continued)*
anus *(continued)*
human papillomavirus (HPV) DNA test
high risk positive R85.81
low risk postive R85.82
inadequate smear R85.615
low grade squamous intraepithelial lesion (LGSIL) R85.612
satisfactory anal smear but lacking transformation zone R85.616
specified NEC R85.618
unsatisfactory smear R85.615
bronchial washings R84.6
cerebrospinal fluid R83.6
cervix R87.619
atypical squamous cells cannot exclude high grade squamous intraepithelial lesion(ASC-H) R87.611
atypical squamous cells of undetermined significance(ASC-US) R87.610
cytologic evidence of malignancy R87.614
high grade squamous intraepithelial lesion (HGSIL) R87.613
inadequate smear R87.615
low grade squamous intraepithelial lesion (LGSIL) R87.612
non-atypical endometrial cells R87.618
satisfactory cervical smear but lacking transformation zone R87.616
specified NEC R87.618
thin preparaton R87.619
unsatisfactory smear R87.615
nasal secretions R84.6
nipple discharge R89.6
peritoneal fluid R85.69
pleural fluid R84.6
prostatic secretions R86.6
saliva R85.69
seminal fluid R86.6
sites NEC R89.6
sputum R84.6
synovial fluid R89.6
throat scrapings R84.6
vagina R87.629
atypical squamous cells cannot exclude high grade squamous intraepithelial lesion(ASC-H) R87.621
atypical squamous cells of undetermined significance(ASC-US) R87.620
cytologic evidence of malignancy R87.624
high grade squamous intraepithelial lesion (HGSIL) R87.623
inadequate smear R87.625
low grade squamous intraepithelial lesion (LGSIL) R87.622
specified NEC R87.628
thin preparation R87.629
unsatisfactory smear R87.625
vulva R87.69
wound secretions R89.6
partial thromboplastin time (PTT) R79.1
pelvis (bony) —*see* Deformity, pelvis

Abnormal, abnormality, abnormalities *(continued)*
percussion, chest (tympany) R09.89
periods (grossly) —*see* Menstruation
phonocardiogram R94.39
plantar reflex R29.2
plasma
protein R77.9
specified NEC R77.8
viscosity R70.1
pleural (folds) Q34.0
posture R29.3
product of conception O02.9
specified type NEC O02.89
prothrombin time (PT) R79.1
pulmonary
artery, congenital Q25.79
function, newborn P28.89
test results R94.2
pulsations in neck R00.2
pupillary H21.56-
function (reaction) (reflex) —*see* Anomaly, pupil, function
radiological examination —*see* Abnormal, diagnostic imaging
red blood cell (s) (morphology) (volume) R71.8
reflex —*see* Reflex
renal function test R94.4
response to nerve stimulation R94.130
retinal correspondence H53.31
retinal function study R94.111
rhythm, heart —*see also* Arrhythmia
saliva —*see* Abnormal, specimen, digestive organs
scan
kidney R94.4
liver R93.2
thyroid R94.6
secretion
gastrin E16.4
glucagon E16.3
semen, seminal fluid —*see* Abnormal, specimen, male genital organs
serum level (of)
acid phosphatase R74.8
alkaline phosphatase R74.8
amylase R74.8
enzymes R74.9
specified NEC R74.8
lipase R74.8
triacylglycerol lipase R74.8
shape
gravid uterus —*see* Anomaly, uterus
sinus venosus Q21.1
size, tooth, teeth K00.2
spacing, tooth, teeth, fully erupted M26.30
specimen
digestive organs(peritoneal fluid) (saliva) R85.9
cytology R85.69
drug level R85.2
enzyme level R85.0
histology R85.7
hormones R85.1
immunology R85.4
microbiology R85.5
nonmedicinal level R85.3
specified type NEC R85.89
female genital organs (secretions) (smears) R87.9
cytology R87.69
cervix R87.619
human papillomavirus (HPV) DNA test
high risk positive R87.810
low risk positive R87.820

Abnormal, abnormality, abnormalities *(continued)*
specimen *(continued)*
female genital organs *(continued)*
cytology *(continued)*
cervix *(continued)*
inadequate (unsatisfactory) smear R87.615
non-atypical endometrial cells R87.618
specified NEC R87.618
vagina R87.629
human papillomavirus (HPV) DNA test
high risk positive R87.811
low risk positive R87.821
inadequate (unsatisfactory) smear R87.625
vulva R87.69
drug level R87.2
enzyme level R87.0
histological R87.7
hormones R87.1
immunology R87.4
microbiology R87.5
nonmedicinal level R87.3
specified type NEC R87.89
male genital organs(prostatic secretions) (semen) R86.9
cytology R86.6
drug level R86.2
enzyme level R86.0
histological R86.7
hormones R86.1
immunology R86.4
microbiology R86.5
nonmedicinal level R86.3
specified type NEC R86.8
nipple discharge —*see* Abnormal, specimen, specified
respiratory organs(bronchial washings) (nasal secretions) (pleural fluid) (sputum) R84.9
cytology R84.6
drug level R84.2
enzyme level R84.0
histology R84.7
hormones R84.1
immunology R84.4
microbiology R84.5
nonmedicinal level R84.3
specified type NEC R84.8
specified organ, system and tissue NOS R89.9
cytology R89.6
drug level R89.2
enzyme level R89.0
histology R89.7
hormones R89.1
immunology R89.4
microbiology R89.5
nonmedicinal level R89.3
specified type NEC R89.8
synovial fluid —*see* Abnormal, specimen, specified
thorax(bronchial washings) (pleural fluids) —*see* Abnormal, specimen, respiratory organs
vagina (secretion) (smear) R87.629
vulva (secretion) (smear) R87.69
wound secretion —*see* Abnormal, specimen, specified
spermatozoa —*see* Abnormal, specimen, male genital organs
sputum (amount) (color) (odor) R09.3
stool (color) (contents) (mucus) R19.5
bloody K92.1
guaiac positive R19.5
synchondrosis Q78.8

Abnormal, abnormality, abnormalities *(continued)*
thermography —*see also* Abnormal, diagnostic imaging R93.8
thyroid-binding globulin E07.89
tooth, teeth (form) (size) K00.2
toxicology (findings) R78.9
transport protein E88.09
tumor marker NEC R97.8
ultrasound results —*see* Abnormal, diagnostic imaging
umbilical cord complicating delivery O69.9
urination NEC R39.19
urine (constituents) R82.90
bile R82.2
cytological examination R82.8
drugs R82.5
fat R82.0
glucose R81
heavy metals R82.6
hemoglobin R82.3
histological examination R82.8
ketones R82.4
microbiological examination (culture) R82.7
myoglobin R82.1
positive culture R82.7
protein —*see* Proteinuria
specified substance NEC R82.99
chromoabnormality NEC R82.91
substances nonmedical R82.6
uterine hemorrhage —*see* Hemorrhage, uterus
vectorcardiogram R94.39
visually evoked potential (VEP) R94.112
white blood cells D72.9
specified NEC D72.89
X-ray examination —*see* Abnormal, diagnostic imaging

Abnormity(any organ or part) —*see* Anomaly

Abocclusion M26.29
hemolytic disease (newborn) P55.1
incompatibility reaction ABO —*see* Complication (s), transfusion, incompatibility reaction, ABO

Abolition, language R48.8

Aborter, habitual or recurrent —*see* Loss (of), pregnancy, recurrent

Abortion (complete) (spontaneous) O03.9
with
retained products of conception —*see* Abortion, incomplete
attempted (elective) (failed) O07.4
complicated by O07.30
afibrinogenemia O07.1
cardiac arrest O07.36
chemical damage of pelvic organ (s) O07.34
circulatory collapse O07.31
cystitis O07.38
defibrination syndrome O07.1
electrolyte imbalance O07.33
embolism (air) (amniotic fluid) (blood clot) (fat) (pulmonary) (septic) (soap) O07.2
endometritis O07.0
genital tract and pelvic infection O07.0
hemolysis O07.1
hemorrhage (delayed) (excessive) O07.1
infection
genital tract or pelvic O07.0
urinary tract tract O07.38
intravascular coagulation O07.1

Abortion *(continued)*
attempted (elective) (failed) *(continued)*
complicated by *(continued)*
laceration of pelvic organ (s) O07.34
metabolic disorder O07.33
oliguria O07.32
oophoritis O07.0
parametritis O07.0
pelvic peritonitis O07.0
perforation of pelvic organ (s) O07.34
renal failure or shutdown O07.32
salpingitis or salpingo-oophoritis O07.0
sepsis O07.37
shock O07.31
specified condition NEC O07.39
tubular necrosis (renal) O07.32
uremia O07.32
urinary tract infection O07.38
venous complication NEC O07.35
embolism (air) (amniotic fluid) (blood clot) (fat) (pulmonary) (septic) (soap) O07.2
complicated (by) (following) O03.80
afibrinogenemia O03.6
cardiac arrest O03.86
chemical damage of pelvic organ (s) O03.84
circulatory collapse O03.81
cystitis O03.88
defibrination syndrome O03.6
electrolyte imbalance O03.83
embolism (air) (amniotic fluid) (blood clot) (fat) (pulmonary) (septic) (soap) O03.7
endometritis O03.5
genital tract and pelvic infection O03.5
hemolysis O03.6
hemorrhage (delayed) (excessive) O03.6
infection
genital tract or pelvic O03.5
urinary tract O03.88
intravascular coagulation O03.6
laceration of pelvic organ (s) O03.84
metabolic disorder O03.83
oliguria O03.82
oophoritis O03.5
parametritis O03.5
pelvic peritonitis O03.5
perforation of pelvic organ (s) O03.84
renal failure or shutdown O03.82
salpingitis or salpingo-oophoritis O03.5
sepsis O03.87
shock O03.81
specified condition NEC O03.89
tubular necrosis (renal) O03.82
uremia O03.82
urinary tract infection O03.88
venous complication NEC O03.85
embolism (air) (amniotic fluid) (blood clot) (fat) (pulmonary) (septic) (soap) O03.7
failed —*see* Abortion, attempted
habitual or recurrent N96
with current abortion —*see* categories O03-O06
without current pregnancy N96
care in current pregnancy O26.2-
incomplete (spontaneous) O03.4
complicated (by) (following) O03.30

Abortion *(continued)*
incomplete (spontaneous) *(continued)*
complicated (by) (following) *(continued)*
afibrinogenemia O03.1
cardiac arrest O03.36
chemical damage of pelvic organ (s) O03.34
circulatory collapse O03.31
cystitis O03.38
defibrination syndrome O03.1
electrolyte imbalance O03.33
embolism (air) (amniotic fluid) (blood clot) (fat) (pulmonary) (septic) (soap) O03.2
endometritis O03.0
genital tract and pelvic infection O03.0
hemolysis O03.1
hemorrhage (delayed) (excessive) O03.1
infection
genital tract or pelvic O03.0
urinary tract O03.38
intravascular coagulation O03.1
laceration of pelvic organ (s) O03.34
metabolic disorder O03.33
oliguria O03.32
oophoritis O03.0
parametritis O03.0
pelvic peritonitis O03.0
perforation of pelvic organ (s) O03.34
renal failure or shutdown O03.32
salpingitis or salpingo-oophoritis O03.0
sepsis O03.37
shock O03.31
specified condition NEC O03.39
tubular necrosis (renal) O03.32
uremia O03.32
urinary infection O03.38
venous complication NEC O03.35
embolism (air) (amniotic fluid) (blood clot) (fat) (pulmonary) (septic) (soap) O03.2
induced(encounter for) Z33.2
complicated by O04.80
afibrinogenemia O04.6
cardiac arrest O04.86
chemical damage of pelvic organ (s) O04.84
circulatory collapse O04.81
cystitis O04.88
defibrination syndrome O04.6
electrolyte imbalance O04.83
embolism (air) (amniotic fluid) (blood clot) (fat) (pulmonary) (septic) (soap) O04.7
endometritis O04.5
genital tract and pelvic infection O04.5
hemolysis O04.6
hemorrhage (delayed) (excessive) O04.6
infection
genital tract or pelvic O04.5
urinary tract O04.88
intravascular coagulation O04.6
laceration of pelvic organ (s) O04.84
metabolic disorder O04.83
oliguria O04.82
oophoritis O04.5
parametritis O04.5
pelvic peritonitis O04.5

Abortion *(continued)*
induced(encounter for) *(continued)*
complicated by *(continued)*
perforation of pelvic organ (s) O04.84
renal failure or shutdown O04.82
salpingitis or salpingo-oophoritis O04.5
sepsis O04.87
shock O04.81
specified condition NEC O04.89
tubular necrosis (renal) O04.82
uremia O04.82
urinary tract infection O04.88
venous complication NEC O04.85
embolism (air) (amniotic fluid) (blood clot) (fat) (pulmonary) (septic) (soap) O04.7
missed O02.1
spontaneous —*see* Abortion (complete) (spontaneous)
threatened O20.0
threatened (spontaneous) O20.0
tubal O00.1

Abortus fever A23.1

Aboulomania F60.7

Abrami's disease D59.8

Abramov-Fiedler myocarditis(acute isolated myocarditis) I40.1

Abrasion T14.8
abdomen, abdominal (wall) S30.811
alveolar process S00.512
ankle S90.51-
antecubital space —*see* Abrasion, elbow
anus S30.817
arm (upper) S40.81-
auditory canal —*see* Abrasion, ear
auricle —*see* Abrasion, ear
axilla —*see* Abrasion, arm
back, lower S30.810
breast S20.11-
brow S00.81
buttock S30.810
calf —*see* Abrasion, leg
canthus —*see* Abrasion, eyelid
cheek S00.81
internal S00.512
chest wall —*see* Abrasion, thorax
chin S00.81
clitoris S30.814
cornea S05.0-
costal region —*see* Abrasion, thorax
dental K03.1
digit (s)
foot —*see* Abrasion, toe
hand —*see* Abrasion, finger
ear S00.41-
elbow S50.31-
epididymis S30.813
epigastric region S30.811
epiglottis S10.11
esophagus (thoracic) S27.818
cervical S10.11
eyebrow —*see* Abrasion, eyelid
eyelid S00.21-
face S00.81
finger (s) S60.41-
index S60.41-
little S60.41-
middle S60.41-
ring S60.41-
flank S30.811
foot (except toe (s) alone) S90.81-
toe —*see* Abrasion, toe

Abrasion *(continued)*
- forearm S50.81-
  - elbow only —*see* Abrasion, elbow
- forehead S00.81
- genital organs, external
  - female S30.816
  - male S30.815
- groin S30.811
- gum S00.512
- hand S60.51-
- head S00.91
  - ear —*see* Abrasion, ear
  - eyelid —*see* Abrasion, eyelid
  - lip S00.511
  - nose S00.31
  - oral cavity S00.512
  - scalp S00.01
  - specified site NEC S00.81
- heel —*see* Abrasion, foot
- hip S70.21-
- inguinal region S30.811
- interscapular region S20.419
- jaw S00.81
- knee S80.21-
- labium (majus) (minus) S30.814
- larynx S10.11
- leg (lower) S80.81-
  - knee —*see* Abrasion, knee
  - upper —*see* Abrasion, thigh
- lip S00.511
- lower back S30.810
- lumbar region S30.810
- malar region S00.81
- mammary —*see* Abrasion, breast
- mastoid region S00.81
- mouth S00.512
- nail
  - finger —*see* Abrasion, finger
  - toe —*see* Abrasion, toe
- nape S10.81
- nasal S00.31
- neck S10.91
  - specified site NEC S10.81
  - throat S10.11
- nose S00.31
- occipital region S00.01
- oral cavity S00.512
- orbital region —*see* Abrasion, eyelid
- palate S00.512
- palm —*see* Abrasion, hand
- parietal region S00.01
- pelvis S30.810
- penis S30.812
- perineum
  - female S30.814
  - male S30.810
- periocular area —*see* Abrasion, eyelid
- phalanges
  - finger —*see* Abrasion, finger
  - toe —*see* Abrasion, toe
- pharynx S10.11
- pinna —*see* Abrasion, ear
- popliteal space —*see* Abrasion, knee
- prepuce S30.812
- pubic region S30.810
- pudendum
  - female S30.816
  - male S30.815
- sacral region S30.810
- scalp S00.01
- scapular region —*see* Abrasion, shoulder
- scrotum S30.813
- shin —*see* Abrasion, leg
- shoulder S40.21-
- skin NEC T14.8
- sternal region S20.319
- submaxillary region S00.81
- submental region S00.81
- subungual
  - finger (s) —*see* Abrasion, finger
  - toe (s) —*see* Abrasion, toe

Abrasion *(continued)*
- supraclavicular fossa S10.81
- supraorbital S00.81
- temple S00.81
- temporal region S00.81
- testis S30.813
- thigh S70.31-
- thorax, thoracic (wall) S20.91
  - back S20.41-
  - front S20.31-
- throat S10.11
- thumb S60.31-
- toe (s) (lesser) S90.416
  - great S90.41-
- tongue S00.512
- tooth, teeth (dentifrice) (habitual) (hard tissues) (occupational) (ritual) (traditional) K03.1
- trachea S10.11
- tunica vaginalis S30.813
- tympanum, tympanic membrane —*see* Abrasion, ear
- uvula S00.512
- vagina S30.814
- vocal cords S10.11
- vulva S30.814
- wrist S60.81-

Abrism —*see* Poisoning, food, noxious, plant

Abruptio placentae O45.9-
- with
  - afibrinogenemia O45.01-
  - coagulation defect O45.00-
    - specified NEC O45.09-
  - disseminated intravascular coagulation O45.02-
  - hypofibrinogenemia O45.01-
- specified NEC O45.8-

Abruption, placenta —*see* Abruptio placentae

Abscess (connective tissue) (embolic) (fistulous) (infective) (metastatic) (multiple) (pernicious) (pyogenic) (septic) L02.91
- with
  - diverticular disease (intestine) K57.80
    - with bleeding K57.81
    - large intestine K57.20
      - with
        - bleeding K57.21
        - small intestine K57.40
          - with bleeding K57.41
    - small intestine K57.00
      - with
        - bleeding K57.01
        - large intestine K57.40
          - with bleeding K57.41
  - lymphangitis - code by site under Abscess
- abdomen, abdominal
  - cavity K65.1
  - wall L02.211
- abdominopelvic K65.1
- accessory sinus —*see* Sinusitis
- adrenal (capsule) (gland) E27.8
- alveolar K04.7
  - with sinus K04.6
- amebic A06.4
  - brain(and liver or lung abscess) A06.6
  - genitourinary tract A06.82
  - liver(without mention of brain or lung abscess) A06.4
  - lung(and liver) (without mention of brain abscess) A06.5
  - specified site NEC A06.89
  - spleen A06.89
- anerobic A48.0
- ankle —*see* Abscess, lower limb

Abscess *(continued)*
- anorectal K61.2
- antecubital space —*see* Abscess, upper limb
- antrum (chronic) (Highmore) —*see* Sinusitis, maxillary
- anus K61.0
- apical (tooth) K04.7
  - with sinus (alveolar) K04.6
- appendix K35.3
- areola (acute) (chronic) (nonpuerperal) N61
  - puerperal, postpartum or gestational —*see* Infection, nipple
- arm(any part) —*see* Abscess, upper limb
- artery (wall) I77.89
- atheromatous I77.2
- auricle, ear —*see* Abscess, ear, external
- axilla (region) L02.41-
  - lymph gland or node L04.2
- back(any part, except buttock) L02.212
- Bartholin's gland N75.1
  - with
    - abortion —*see* Abortion, by type complicated by, sepsis
    - ectopic or molar pregnancy O08.0
  - following ectopic or molar pregnancy O08.0
- Bezold's —*see* Mastoiditis, acute
- bilharziasis B65.1
- bladder (wall) —*see* Cystitis, specified type NEC
- bone (subperiosteal) —*see also* Osteomyelitis, specified type NEC
  - accessory sinus (chronic) —*see* Sinusitis
  - chronic or old —*see* Osteomyelitis, chronic
  - jaw (lower) (upper) M27.2
  - mastoid —*see* Mastoiditis, acute, subperiosteal
  - petrous —*see* Petrositis
  - spinal (tuberculous) A18.01
    - nontuberculous —*see* Osteomyelitis, vertebra
- bowel K63.0
- brain(any part) (cystic) (otogenic) G06.0
  - amebic(with abscess of any other site) A06.6
  - gonococcal A54.82
  - pheomycotic (chromomycotic) B43.1
  - tuberculous A17.81
- breast (acute) (chronic) (nonpuerperal) N61
  - newborn P39.0
  - puerperal, postpartum, gestational —*see* Mastitis, obstetric, purulent
- broad ligament N73.2
  - acute N73.0
  - chronic N73.1
- Brodie's (localized) (chronic) M86.8X-
- bronchi J98.09
- buccal cavity K12.2
- bulbourethral gland N34.0
- bursa M71.00
  - ankle M71.07-
  - elbow M71.02-
  - foot M71.07-
  - hand M71.04-
  - hip M71.05-

Abscess *(continued)*
- bursa *(continued)*
  - knee M71.06-
  - multiple sites M71.09
  - pharyngeal J39.1
  - shoulder M71.01-
  - specified site NEC M71.08
  - wrist M71.03-
- buttock L02.31
- canthus —*see* Blepharoconjunctivitis
- cartilage —*see* Disorder, cartilage, specified type NEC
- cecum K35.3
- cerebellum, cerebellar G06.0
  - sequelae G09
- cerebral (embolic) G06.0
  - sequelae G09
- cervical(meaning neck) L02.11
  - lymph gland or node L04.0
- cervix (stump) (uteri) —*see* Cervicitis
- cheek (external) L02.01
  - inner K12.2
- chest J86.9
  - with fistula J86.0
  - wall L02.213
- chin L02.01
- choroid —*see* Inflammation, chorioretinal
- circumtonsillar J36
- cold (lung) (tuberculous) —*see also* Tuberculosis, abscess, lung
  - articular —*see* Tuberculosis, joint
- colon (wall) K63.0
- colostomy K94.02
- conjunctiva —*see* Conjunctivitis, acute
- cornea H16.31-
- corpus
  - cavernosum N48.21
  - luteum —*see* Oophoritis
- Cowper's gland N34.0
- cranium G06.0
- cul-de-sac(Douglas') (posterior) —*see* Peritonitis, pelvic, female
- cutaneous —*see* Abscess, by site
- dental K04.7
  - with sinus (alveolar) K04.6
- dentoalveolar K04.7
  - with sinus K04.6
- diaphragm, diaphragmatic K65.1
- Douglas' cul-de-sac or pouch —*see* Peritonitis, pelvic, female
- Dubois A50.59
- ear (middle) —*see also* Otitis, media, suppurative
  - acute —*see* Otitis, media, suppurative, acute
  - external H60.0-
- entamebic —*see* Abscess, amebic
- enterostomy K94.12
- epididymis N45.4
- epidural G06.2
  - brain G06.0
  - spinal cord G06.1
- epiglottis J38.7
- epiploon, epiploic K65.1
- erysipelatous —*see* Erysipelas
- esophagus K20.8
- ethmoid (bone) (chronic) (sinus) J32.2
- external auditory canal —*see* Abscess, ear, external
- extradural G06.2
  - brain G06.0
    - sequelae G09
  - spinal cord G06.1
- extraperitoneal K68.19
- eye —*see* Endophthalmitis, purulent
- eyelid H00.03-

Abscess *(continued)*
- face (any part, except ear, eye and nose) L02.01
- fallopian tube —*see* Salpingitis
- fascia M72.8
- fauces J39.1
- fecal K63.0
- femoral (region) —*see* Abscess, lower limb
- filaria, filarial —*see* Infestation, filarial
- finger (any) —*see also* Abscess, hand
  - nail —*see* Cellulitis, finger
- foot L02.61-
- forehead L02.01
- frontal sinus (chronic) J32.1
- gallbladder K81.0
- genital organ or tract
  - female (external) N76.4
  - male N49.9
    - multiple sites N49.8
    - specified NEC N49.8
- gestational mammary O91.11-
- gestational subareolar O91.11-
- gingival K05.21
- gland, glandular (lymph) (acute) —*see* Lymphadenitis, acute
- gluteal (region) L02.31
- gonorrheal —*see* Gonococcus
- groin L02.214
- gum K05.21
- hand L02.51-
- head NEC L02.811
  - face(any part, except ear, eye and nose) L02.01
- heart —*see* Carditis
- heel —*see* Abscess, foot
- helminthic —*see* Infestation, helminth
- hepatic (cholangitic) (hematogenic) (lymphogenic) (pylephlebitic) K75.0
  - amebic A06.4
- hip (region) —*see* Abscess, lower limb
- ileocecal K35.3
- ileostomy (bud) K94.12
- iliac (region) L02.214
  - fossa K35.3
- infraclavicular (fossa) —*see* Abscess, upper limb
- inguinal (region) L02.214
  - lymph gland or node L04.1
- intestine, intestinal NEC K63.0
  - rectal K61.1
- intra-abdominal —*see also* Abscess, peritoneum K65.1
  - postoperative T81.4
    - retroperitoneal K68.11
- intracranial G06.0
- intramammary —*see* Abscess, breast
- intraorbital —*see* Abscess, orbit
- intraperitoneal K65.1
- intrasphincteric (anus) K61.4
- intraspinal G06.1
- intratonsillar J36
- ischiorectal (fossa) K61.3
- jaw (bone) (lower) (upper) M27.2
- joint —*see* Arthritis, pyogenic or pyemic
  - spine (tuberculous) A18.01
    - nontuberculous —*see* Spondylopathy, infective
- kidney N15.1
  - with calculus N20.0
    - with hydronephrosis N13.6
  - puerperal (postpartum) O86.21
- knee —*see also* Abscess, lower limb
  - joint M00.9

Abscess *(continued)*
- labium (majus) (minus) N76.4
- lacrimal
  - caruncle —*see* Inflammation, lacrimal, passages, acute
  - gland —*see* Dacryoadenitis
  - passages (duct) (sac) —*see* Inflammation, lacrimal, passages, acute
- lacunar N34.0
- larynx J38.7
- lateral (alveolar) K04.7
  - with sinus K04.6
- leg(any part) —*see* Abscess, lower limb
- lens H27.8
- lingual K14.0
  - tonsil J36
- lip K13.0
- Littre's gland N34.0
- liver (cholangitic) (hematogenic) (lymphogenic) (pylephlebitic) (pyogenic) K75.0
  - amebic(due to Entamoeba histolytica) (dysenteric) (tropical) A06.4
    - with
      - brain abscess(and liver or lung abscess) A06.6
      - lung abscess A06.5
- loin (region) L02.211
- lower limb L02.41-
- lumbar (tuberculous) A18.01
  - nontuberculous L02.212
- lung (miliary) (putrid) J85.2
  - with pneumonia J85.1
    - due to specified organism(*see* Pneumonia, in (due to))
  - amebic (with liver abscess) A06.5
    - with
      - brain abscess A06.6
      - pneumonia A06.5
- lymph, lymphatic, gland or node (acute) —*see also* Lymphadenitis, acute
  - mesentery I88.0
- malar M27.2
- mammary gland —*see* Abscess, breast
- marginal, anus K61.0
- mastoid —*see* Mastoiditis, acute
- maxilla, maxillary M27.2
  - molar (tooth) K04.7
    - with sinus K04.6
  - premolar K04.7
  - sinus (chronic) J32.0
- mediastinum J85.3
- meibomian gland —*see* Hordeolum
- meninges G06.2
- mesentery, mesenteric K65.1
- mesosalpinx —*see* Salpingitis
- mons pubis L02.215
- mouth (floor) K12.2
- muscle —*see* Myositis, infective
- myocardium I40.0
- nabothian (follicle) —*see* Cervicitis
- nasal J32.9
- nasopharyngeal J39.1
- navel L02.216
  - newborn P38.9
    - with mild hemorrhage P38.1
    - without hemorrhage P38.9
- neck (region) L02.11
  - lymph gland or node L04.0
- nephritic —*see* Abscess, kidney
- nipple N61
  - associated with
    - lactation —*see* Pregnancy, complicated by,

Abscess *(continued)*
- nipple *(continued)*
  - associated with *(continued)*
    - pregnancy —*see* Pregnancy, complicated by
- nose (external) (fossa) (septum) J34.0
  - sinus (chronic) —*see* Sinusitis
- omentum K65.1
- operative wound T81.4
- orbit, orbital —*see* Cellulitis, orbit
- otogenic G06.0
- ovary, ovarian(corpus luteum) —*see* Oophoritis
- oviduct —*see* Oophoritis
- palate (soft) K12.2
  - hard M27.2
- palmar (space) —*see* Abscess, hand
- pancreas (duct) —*see* Pancreatitis, acute
- parafrenal N48.21
- parametric, parametrium N73.2
  - acute N73.0
  - chronic N73.1
- paranephric N15.1
- parapancreatic —*see* Pancreatitis, acute
- parapharyngeal J39.0
- pararectal K61.1
- parasinus —*see* Sinusitis
- parauterine —*see also* Disease, pelvis, inflammatory N73.2
- paravaginal —*see* Vaginitis
- parietal region (scalp) L02.811
- parodontal K05.21
- parotid (duct) (gland) K11.3
  - region K12.2
- pectoral (region) L02.213
- pelvis, pelvic
  - female —*see* Disease, pelvis, inflammatory
  - male, peritoneal K65.1
- penis N48.21
  - gonococcal(accessory gland) (periurethral) A54.1
- perianal K61.0
- periapical K04.7
  - with sinus (alveolar) K04.6
- periappendicular K35.3
- pericardial I30.1
- pericecal K35.3
- pericemental K05.21
- pericholecystic —*see* Cholecystitis, acute
- pericoronal K05.21
- peridental K05.21
- perimetric —*see also* Disease, pelvis, inflammatory N73.2
- perinephric, perinephritic —*see* Abscess, kidney
- perineum, perineal (superficial) L02.215
  - urethra N34.0
- periodontal (parietal) K05.21
  - apical K04.7
- periosteum, periosteal —*see also* Osteomyelitis, specified type NEC
  - with osteomyelitis —*see also* Osteomyelitis, specified type NEC
    - acute —*see* Osteomyelitis, acute
    - chronic —*see* Osteomyelitis, chronic
- peripharyngeal J39.0
- peripleuritic J86.9
  - with fistula J86.0
- periprostatic N41.2
- perirectal K61.1
- perirenal (tissue) —*see* Abscess, kidney

Abscess *(continued)*
- perisinuous (nose) —*see* Sinusitis
- peritoneum, peritoneal (perforated) (ruptured) K65.1
  - with appendicitis K35.3
  - pelvic
    - female —*see* Peritonitis, pelvic, female
    - male K65.1
  - postoperative T81.4
  - puerperal, postpartum, childbirth O85
  - tuberculous A18.31
- peritonsillar J36
- perityphlic K35.3
- periureteral N28.89
- periurethral N34.0
  - gonococcal(accessory gland) (periurethral) A54.1
- periuterine —*see also* Disease, pelvis, inflammatory N73.2
- perivesical —*see* Cystitis, specified type NEC
- petrous bone —*see* Petrositis
- phagedenic NOS L02.91
  - chancroid A57
- pharynx, pharyngeal (lateral) J39.1
- pilonidal L05.01
- pituitary (gland) E23.6
- pleura J86.9
  - with fistula J86.0
- popliteal —*see* Abscess, lower limb
- postcecal K35.3
- postlaryngeal J38.7
- postnasal J34.0
- postoperative(any site) T81.4
  - retroperitoneal K68.11
- postpharyngeal J39.0
- posttonsillar J36
- post-typhoid A01.09
- pouch of Douglas —*see* Peritonitis, pelvic, female
- premammary —*see* Abscess, breast
- prepatellar —*see* Abscess, lower limb
- prostate N41.2
  - gonococcal (acute) (chronic) A54.22
- psoas muscle K68.12
- puerperal - code by site under Puerperal, abscess
- pulmonary —*see* Abscess, lung
- pulp, pulpal (dental) K04.0
- rectovaginal septum K63.0
- rectovesical —*see* Cystitis, specified type NEC
- rectum K61.1
- renal —*see* Abscess, kidney
- retina —*see* Inflammation, chorioretinal
- retrobulbar —*see* Abscess, orbit
- retrocecal K65.1
- retrolaryngeal J38.7
- retromammary —*see* Abscess, breast
- retroperitoneal NEC K68.19
  - postprocedural K68.11
- retropharyngeal J39.0
- retrouterine —*see* Peritonitis, pelvic, female
- retrovesical —*see* Cystitis, specified type NEC
- root, tooth K04.7
  - with sinus (alveolar) K04.6
- round ligament —*see also* Disease, pelvis, inflammatory N73.2
- rupture (spontaneous) NOS L02.91
- sacrum (tuberculous) A18.01
  - nontuberculous M46.28
- salivary (duct) (gland) K11.3
- scalp (any part) L02.811

Abscess *(continued)*
- scapular —*see* Osteomyelitis, specified type NEC
- sclera —*see* Scleritis
- scrofulous (tuberculous) A18.2
- scrotum N49.2
- seminal vesicle N49.0
- septal, dental K04.7
  - with sinus (alveolar) K04.6
- serous —*see* Periostitis
- shoulder (region) —*see* Abscess, upper limb
- sigmoid K63.0
- sinus (accessory) (chronic) (nasal) —*see also* Sinusitis
  - intracranial venous (any) G06.0
- Skene's duct or gland N34.0
- skin —*see* Abscess, by site
- specified site NEC L02.818
- spermatic cord N49.1
- sphenoidal (sinus) (chronic) J32.3
- spinal cord(any part) (staphylococcal) G06.1
  - tuberculous A17.81
- spine (column) (tuberculous) A18.01
  - epidural G06.1
  - nontuberculous —*see*
    - Osteomyelitis, vertebra
- spleen D73.3
  - amebic A06.89
- stitch T81.4
- subarachnoid G06.2
  - brain G06.0
  - spinal cord G06.1
- subareolar —*see* Abscess, breast
- subcecal K35.3
- subcutaneous —*see also* Abscess, by site
  - pheomycotic (chromomycotic) B43.2
- subdiaphragmatic K65.1
- subdural G06.2
  - brain G06.0
    - sequelae G09
  - spinal cord G06.1
- subgaleal L02.811
- subhepatic K65.1
- sublingual K12.2
  - gland K11.3
- submammary —*see* Abscess, breast
- submandibular (region) (space) (triangle) K12.2
  - gland K11.3
- submaxillary (region) L02.01
  - gland K11.3
- submental L02.01
  - gland K11.3
- subperiosteal —*see* Osteomyelitis, specified type NEC
- subphrenic K65.1
  - postoperative T81.4
- suburethral N34.0
- sudoriparous L75.8
- supraclavicular (fossa) —*see* Abscess, upper limb
- suprapelvic, acute N73.0
- suprarenal (capsule) (gland) E27.8
- sweat gland L74.8
- tear duct —*see* Inflammation, lacrimal, passages, acute
- temple L02.01
- temporal region L02.01
- temporosphenoidal G06.0
- tendon (sheath) M65.00
  - ankle M65.07-
  - foot M65.07-
  - forearm M65.03-
  - hand M65.04-
  - lower leg M65.06-
  - pelvic region M65.05-
  - shoulder region M65.01-
  - specified site NEC M65.08

Abscess *(continued)*
- tendon (sheath) *(continued)*
  - thigh M65.05-
  - upper arm M65.02-
- testis N45.4
- thigh —*see* Abscess, lower limb
- thorax J86.9
  - with fistula J86.0
- throat J39.1
- thumb —*see also* Abscess, hand
  - nail —*see* Cellulitis, finger
- thymus (gland) E32.1
- thyroid (gland) E06.0
- toe (any) —*see also* Abscess, foot
  - nail —*see* Cellulitis, toe
- tongue (staphylococcal) K14.0
- tonsil (s) (lingual) J36
- tonsillopharyngeal J36
- tooth, teeth (root) K04.7
  - with sinus (alveolar) K04.6
  - supporting structures NEC K05.21
- trachea J39.8
- trunk L02.219
  - abdominal wall L02.211
  - back L02.212
  - chest wall L02.213
  - groin L02.214
  - perineum L02.215
  - umbilicus L02.216
- tubal —*see* Salpingitis
- tuberculous —*see* Tuberculosis, abscess
- tubo-ovarian —*see* Salpingo-oophoritis
- tunica vaginalis N49.1
- umbilicus L02.216
- upper
  - limb L02.41-
  - respiratory J39.8
- urethral (gland) N34.0
- urinary N34.0
- uterus, uterine (wall) —*see also* Endometritis
  - ligament —*see also* Disease, pelvis, inflammatory N73.2
  - neck —*see* Cervicitis
- uvula K12.2
- vagina (wall) —*see* Vaginitis
- vaginorectal —*see* Vaginitis
- vas deferens N49.1
- vermiform appendix K35.3
- vertebra (column) (tuberculous) A18.01
  - nontuberculous —*see*
    - Osteomyelitis, vertebra
- vesical —*see* Cystitis, specified type NEC
- vesico-uterine pouch —*see* Peritonitis, pelvic, female
- vitreous (humor) —*see* Endophthalmitis, purulent
- vocal cord J38.3
- von Bezold's —*see* Mastoiditis, acute
- vulva N76.4
- vulvovaginal gland N75.1
- web space —*see* Abscess, hand
- wound T81.4
- wrist —*see* Abscess, upper limb

Absence (of) (organ or part) (complete or partial)
- adrenal (gland) (congenital) Q89.1
  - acquired E89.6
- albumin in blood E88.09
- alimentary tract (congenital) Q45.8
  - upper Q40.8
- alveolar process (acquired) —*see* Anomaly, alveolar
- ankle (acquired) Z89.44-
- anus (congenital) Q42.3
  - with fistula Q42.2
- aorta (congenital) Q25.4

Absence *(continued)*
- appendix, congenital Q42.8
- arm (acquired) Z89.20-
  - above elbow Z89.22-
    - congenital(with hand present) —*see* Agenesis, arm, with hand present
      - and hand —*see* Agenesis, forearm, and hand
  - below elbow Z89.21-
    - congenital(with hand present) —*see* Agenesis, arm, with hand present
      - and hand —*see* Agenesis, forearm, and hand
  - congenital —*see* Defect, reduction, upper limb
  - shoulder(following explantation of shoulder joint prosthesis) (joint) (with or without presence of antibiotic-impregnated cement spacer) Z89.23-
    - congenital(with hand present) —*see* Agenesis, arm, with hand present
- artery (congenital) (peripheral) Q27.8
  - brain Q28.3
  - coronary Q24.5
  - pulmonary Q25.79
  - specified NEC Q27.8
  - umbilical Q27.0
- atrial septum (congenital) Q21.1
- auditory canal (congenital) (external) Q16.1
- auricle (ear), congenital Q16.0
- bile, biliary duct, congenital Q44.5
- bladder (acquired) Z90.6
  - congenital Q64.5
- bowel sounds R19.11
- brain Q00.0
  - part of Q04.3
- breast (s) (and nipple (s)) (acquired) Z90.1-
  - congenital Q83.8
- broad ligament Q50.6
- bronchus (congenital) Q32.4
- canaliculus lacrimalis, congenital Q10.4
- cerebellum (vermis) Q04.3
- cervix (acquired) (with uterus) Z90.710
  - with remaining uterus Z90.712
  - congenital Q51.5
- chin, congenital Q18.8
- cilia (congenital) Q10.3
  - acquired —*see* Madarosis
- clitoris (congenital) Q52.6
- coccyx, congenital Q76.49
- cold sense R20.8
- congenital
  - lumen —*see* Atresia
  - organ or site NEC —*see* Agenesis
  - septum —*see* Imperfect, closure
- corpus callosum Q04.0
- cricoid cartilage, congenital Q31.8
- diaphragm(with hernia), congenital Q79.1
- digestive organ (s) or tract, congenital Q45.8
  - acquired NEC Z90.49
  - upper Q40.8
- ductus arteriosus Q28.8
- duodenum (acquired) Z90.49
  - congenital Q41.0
- ear, congenital Q16.9
  - acquired H93.8-
  - auricle Q16.0
  - external Q16.0
  - inner Q16.5
  - lobe, lobule Q17.8
  - middle, except ossicles Q16.4

Absence *(continued)*
- ear *(continued)*
  - middle *(continued)*
    - ossicles Q16.3
  - ossicles Q16.3
- ejaculatory duct (congenital) Q55.4
- endocrine gland (congenital) NEC Q89.2
  - acquired E89.89
- epididymis (congenital) Q55.4
  - acquired Z90.79
- epiglottis, congenital Q31.8
- esophagus (congenital) Q39.8
  - acquired (partial) Z90.49
- eustachian tube (congenital) Q16.2
- extremity (acquired) Z89.9
  - congenital Q73.0
  - knee(following explantation of knee joint prosthesis) (joint) (with or without presence of antibiotic-impregnated cement spacer) Z89.52-
  - lower(above knee) Z89.619
    - below knee Z89.51-
  - upper —*see* Absence, arm
- eye (acquired) Z90.01
  - congenital Q11.1
  - muscle (congenital) Q10.3
- eyeball (acquired) Z90.01
- eyelid (fold) (congenital) Q10.3
  - acquired Z90.01
- face, specified part NEC Q18.8
- fallopian tube (s) (acquired) Z90.79
  - congenital Q50.6
- family member(causing problem in home) NEC —*see also* Disruption, family Z63.32
- femur, congenital —*see* Defect, reduction, lower limb, longitudinal, femur
- fibrinogen (congenital) D68.2
  - acquired D65
- finger (s) (acquired) Z89.02-
  - congenital —*see* Agenesis, hand
- foot (acquired) Z89.43-
  - congenital —*see* Agenesis, foot
- forearm (acquired) —*see* Absence, arm, below elbow
- gallbladder (acquired) Z90.49
  - congenital Q44.0
- gamma globulin in blood D80.1
  - hereditary D80.0
- genital organs
  - acquired (female) (male) Z90.79
  - female, congenital Q52.8
    - external Q52.71
    - internal NEC Q52.8
  - male, congenital Q55.8
- genitourinary organs, congenital NEC
  - female Q52.8
  - male Q55.8
- globe (acquired) Z90.01
  - congenital Q11.1
- glottis, congenital Q31.8
- hand and wrist (acquired) Z89.11-
  - congenital —*see* Agenesis, hand
- head, part (acquired) NEC Z90.09
- heat sense R20.8
- hip (following explantation of hip joint prosthesis) (joint) (with or without presence of antibiotic-impregnated cement spacer) Z89.62-
- hymen (congenital) Q52.4
- ileum (acquired) Z90.49
  - congenital Q41.2
- immunoglobulin, isolated NEC D80.3
  - IgA D80.2
  - IgG D80.3
  - IgM D80.4
- incus (acquired) —*see* Loss, ossicles, ear
  - congenital Q16.3

Absence *(continued)*
- inner ear, congenital Q16.5
- intestine (acquired) (small) Z90.49
  - congenital Q41.9
    - specified NEC Q41.8
  - large Z90.49
    - congenital Q42.9
      - specified NEC Q42.8
- iris, congenital Q13.1
- jejunum (acquired) Z90.49
  - congenital Q41.1
- joint
  - acquired
    - hip(following explantation of hip joint prosthesis) (with or without presence of antibiotic-impregnated cement spacer) Z89.62-
    - knee(following explantation of knee joint prosthesis) (with or without presence of antibiotic-impregnated cement spacer) Z89.52-
    - shoulder (following explantation of shoulder joint prosthesis) (with or without presence of antibiotic-impregnated cement spacer) Z89.23-
  - congenital NEC Q74.8
- kidney (s) (acquired) Z90.5
  - congenital Q60.2
    - bilateral Q60.1
    - unilateral Q60.0
- knee(following explantation of knee joint prosthesis) (joint) (with or without presence of antibiotic-impregnated cement spacer) Z89.52-
- labyrinth, membranous Q16.5
- larynx (congenital) Q31.8
  - acquired Z90.02
- leg (acquired) (above knee) Z89.61-
  - below knee (acquired) Z89.51-
  - congenital —*see* Defect, reduction, lower limb
- lens (acquired) —*see also* Aphakia
  - congenital Q12.3
  - post cataract extraction Z98.4-
- limb (acquired) —*see* Absence, extremity
- lip Q38.6
- liver (congenital) Q44.7
- lung (fissure) (lobe) (bilateral) (unilateral) (congenital) Q33.3
  - acquired(any part) Z90.2
- menstruation —*see* Amenorrhea
- muscle (congenital) (pectoral) Q79.8
  - ocular Q10.3
- neck, part Q18.8
- neutrophil —*see* Agranulocytosis
- nipple (s) (with breast (s)) (acquired) Z90.1-
  - congenital Q83.2
- nose (congenital) Q30.1
  - acquired Z90.09
- organ
  - of Corti, congenital Q16.5
  - or site, congenital NEC Q89.8
    - acquired NEC Z90.89
- osseous meatus (ear) Q16.4
- ovary (acquired)
  - bilateral Z90.722
  - congenital
    - bilateral Q50.02
    - unilateral Q50.01
  - unilateral Z90.721
- oviduct (acquired)
  - bilateral Z90.722
  - congenital Q50.6
  - unilateral Z90.721

Absence *(continued)*
- pancreas (congenital) Q45.0
  - acquired Z90.410
    - complete Z90.410
    - partial Z90.411
    - total Z90.410
- parathyroid gland (acquired) E89.2
  - congenital Q89.2
- patella, congenital Q74.1
- penis (congenital) Q55.5
  - acquired Z90.79
- pericardium (congenital) Q24.8
- pituitary gland (congenital) Q89.2
  - acquired E89.3
- prostate (acquired) Z90.79
  - congenital Q55.4
- pulmonary valve Q22.0
- punctum lacrimale (congenital) Q10.4
- radius, congenital —*see* Defect, reduction, upper limb, longitudinal, radius
- rectum (congenital) Q42.1
  - with fistula Q42.0
  - acquired Z90.49
- respiratory organ NOS Q34.9
- rib (acquired) Z90.89
  - congenital Q76.6
- sacrum, congenital Q76.49
- salivary gland (s), congenital Q38.4
- scrotum, congenital Q55.29
- seminal vesicles (congenital) Q55.4
  - acquired Z90.79
- septum
  - atrial (congenital) Q21.1
  - between aorta and pulmonary artery Q21.4
  - ventricular (congenital) Q20.4
- sex chromosome
  - female phenotype Q97.8
  - male phenotype Q98.8
- skull bone (congenital) Q75.8
  - with
    - anencephaly Q00.0
    - encephalocele —*see* Encephalocele
    - hydrocephalus Q03.9
      - with spina bifida —*see* Spina bifida, by site, with hydrocephalus
    - microcephaly Q02
- spermatic cord, congenital Q55.4
- spine, congenital Q76.49
- spleen (congenital) Q89.01
  - acquired Z90.81
- sternum, congenital Q76.7
- stomach (acquired) (partial) Z90.3
  - congenital Q40.2
- superior vena cava, congenital Q26.8
- teeth, tooth (congenital) K00.0
  - acquired (complete) K08.109
    - class I K08.101
    - class II K08.102
    - class III K08.103
    - class IV K08.104
    - due to
      - caries K08.139
        - class I K08.131
        - class II K08.132
        - class III K08.133
        - class IV K08.134
      - periodontal disease K08.129
        - class I K08.121
        - class II K08.122
        - class III K08.123
        - class IV K08.124
      - specified NEC K08.199
        - class I K08.191
        - class II K08.192
        - class III K08.193
        - class IV K08.194
      - trauma K08.119
        - class I K08.111

Absence *(continued)*
- teeth, tooth *(continued)*
  - acquired *(continued)*
    - due to *(continued)*
      - trauma *(continued)*
        - class II K08.112
        - class III K08.113
        - class IV K08.114
  - partial K08.409
    - class I K08.401
    - class II K08.402
    - class III K08.403
    - class IV K08.404
    - due to
      - caries K08.439
        - class I K08.431
        - class II K08.432
        - class III K08.433
        - class IV K08.434
      - periodontal disease K08.429
        - class I K08.421
        - class II K08.422
        - class III K08.423
        - class IV K08.424
      - specified NEC K08.499
        - class I K08.491
        - class II K08.492
        - class III K08.493
        - class IV K08.494
      - trauma K08.419
        - class I K08.411
        - class II K08.412
        - class III K08.413
        - class IV K08.414
- tendon (congenital) Q79.8
- testis (congenital) Q55.0
  - acquired Z90.79
- thumb (acquired) Z89.01-
  - congenital —*see* Agenesis, hand
- thymus gland Q89.2
- thyroid (gland) (acquired) E89.0
  - cartilage, congenital Q31.8
  - congenital E03.1
- toe (s) (acquired) Z89.42-
  - with foot —*see* Absence, foot and ankle
  - congenital —*see* Agenesis, foot
  - great Z89.41-
- tongue, congenital Q38.3
- trachea (cartilage), congenital Q32.1
- transverse aortic arch, congenital Q25.4
- tricuspid valve Q22.4
- umbilical artery, congenital Q27.0
- upper arm and forearm with hand present, congenital —*see* Agenesis, arm, with hand present
- ureter (congenital) Q62.4
  - acquired Z90.6
- urethra, congenital Q64.5
- uterus (acquired) Z90.710
  - with cervix Z90.710
  - with remaining cervical stump Z90.711
  - congenital Q51.0
- uvula, congenital Q38.5
- vagina, congenital Q52.0
- vas deferens (congenital) Q55.4
  - acquired Z90.79
- vein (peripheral) congenital NEC Q27.8
  - cerebral Q28.3
  - digestive system Q27.8
  - great Q26.8
  - lower limb Q27.8
  - portal Q26.5
  - precerebral Q28.1
  - specified site NEC Q27.8
  - upper limb Q27.8
- vena cava (inferior) (superior), congenital Q26.8

Absence *(continued)*
- ventricular septum Q20.4
- vertebra, congenital Q76.49
- vulva, congenital Q52.71
- wrist (acquired) Z89.12-

Absorbent system disease I87.8

Absorption
- carbohydrate, disturbance K90.4
- chemical —*see* Table of Drugs and Chemicals
  - through placenta (newborn) P04.9
    - environmental substance P04.6
    - nutritional substance P04.5
    - obstetric anesthetic or analgesic drug P04.0
- drug NEC —*see* Table of Drugs and Chemicals
  - addictive
    - through placenta (newborn) P04.49
      - cocaine P04.41
  - medicinal
    - through placenta (newborn) P04.1
  - through placenta (newborn) P04.1
    - obstetric anesthetic or analgesic drug P04.0
- fat, disturbance K90.4
  - pancreatic K90.3
- noxious substance —*see* Table of Drugs and Chemicals
- protein, disturbance K90.4
- starch, disturbance K90.4
- toxic substance —*see* Table of Drugs and Chemicals
- uremic —*see* Uremia

Abstinence symptoms, syndrome
- alcohol F10.239
  - with delirium F10.231
- cocaine F14.23
- neonatal P96.1
- nicotine —*see* Dependence, drug, nicotine, with, withdrawal
- opioid F11.93
  - with dependence F11.23
- psychoactive NEC F19.939
  - with
    - delirium F19.931
    - dependence F19.239
      - with
        - delirium F19.231
        - perceptual disturbance F19.232
      - uncomplicated F19.230
    - perceptual disturbance F19.932
  - uncomplicated F19.930
- sedative F13.939
  - with
    - delirium F13.931
    - dependence F13.239
      - with
        - delirium F13.231
        - perceptual disturbance F13.232
      - uncomplicated F13.230
    - perceptual disturbance F13.932
  - uncomplicated F13.930
- stimulant NEC F15.93
  - with dependence F15.23

Abulia R68.89

Abulomania F60.7

Abuse
- adult —*see* Maltreatment, adult
  - as reason for
    - couple *see*king advice(including offender) Z63.0
- alcohol (non-dependent) F10.10
  - with
    - anxiety disorder F10.180

Abuse *(continued)*
alcohol *(continued)*
with *(continued)*
intoxication F10.129
with delirium F10.121
uncomplicated F10.120
mood disorder F10.14
other specified disorder F10.188
psychosis F10.159
delusions F10.150
hallucinations F10.151
sexual dysfunction F10.181
sleep disorder F10.182
unspecified disorder F10.19
counseling and surveillance Z71.41
amphetamine(or related substance) —*see* Abuse, drug, stimulant NEC
analgesics(non-prescribed) (over the counter) F55.8
antacids F55.0
antidepressants —*see* Abuse, drug, psychoactive NEC
anxiolytic —*see* Abuse, drug, sedative
barbiturates —*see* Abuse, drug, sedative
caffeine —*see* Abuse, drug, stimulant NEC
cannabis, cannabinoids —*see* Abuse, drug, cannabis
child —*see* Maltreatment, child
cocaine —*see* Abuse, drug, cocaine
drug NEC (non-dependent) F19.10
with sleep disorder F19.182
amphetamine type —*see* Abuse, drug, stimulant NEC
analgesics(non-prescribed) (over the counter) F55.8
antacids F55.0
antidepressants —*see* Abuse, drug, psychoactive NEC
anxiolytics —*see* Abuse, drug, sedative
barbiturates —*see* Abuse, drug, sedative
caffeine —*see* Abuse, drug, stimulant NEC
cannabis F12.10
with
anxiety disorder F12.180
intoxication F12.129
with
delirium F12.121
perceptual disturbance F12.122
uncomplicated F12.120
other specified disorder F12.188
psychosis F12.159
delusions F12.150
hallucinations F12.151
unspecified disorder F12.19
cocaine F14.10
with
anxiety disorder F14.180
intoxication F14.129
with
delirium F14.121
perceptual disturbance F14.122
uncomplicated F14.120
mood disorder F14.14
other specified disorder F14.188
psychosis F14.159
delusions F14.150
hallucinations F14.151
sexual dysfunction F14.181
sleep disorder F14.182
unspecified disorder F14.19

Abuse *(continued)*
drug NEC *(continued)*
counseling and surveillance Z71.51
hallucinogen F16.10
with
anxiety disorder F16.180
flashbacks F16.183
intoxication F16.129
with
delirium F16.121
perceptual disturbance F16.122
uncomplicated F16.120
mood disorder F16.14
other specified disorder F16.188
perception disorder, persisting F16.183
psychosis F16.159
delusions F16.150
hallucinations F16.151
unspecified disorder F16.19
hashish —*see* Abuse, drug, cannabis
herbal or folk remedies F55.1
hormones F55.3
hypnotics —*see* Abuse, drug, sedative
inhalant F18.10
with
anxiety disorder F18.180
dementia, persisting F18.17
intoxication F18.129
with delirium F18.121
uncomplicated F18.120
mood disorder F18.14
other specified disorder F18.188
psychosis F18.159
delusions F18.150
hallucinations F18.151
unspecified disorder F18.19
laxatives F55.2
LSD —*see* Abuse, drug, hallucinogen
marihuana —*see* Abuse, drug, cannabis
morphine type (opioids) —*see* Abuse, drug, opioid
opioid F11.10
with
intoxication F11.129
with
delirium F11.121
perceptual disturbance F11.122
uncomplicated F11.120
mood disorder F11.14
other specified disorder F11.188
psychosis F11.159
delusions F11.150
hallucinations F11.151
sexual dysfunction F11.181
sleep disorder F11.182
unspecified disorder F11.19
PCP (phencyclidine) (or related substance) —*see* Abuse, drug, hallucinogen
psychoactive NEC F19.10
with
amnestic disorder F19.16
anxiety disorder F19.180
dementia F19.17
intoxication F19.129
with
delirium F19.121
perceptual disturbance F19.122
uncomplicated F19.120
mood disorder F19.14

Abuse *(continued)*
drug NEC *(continued)*
psychoactive *(continued)*
with *(continued)*
other specified disorder F19.188
psychosis F19.159
delusions F19.150
hallucinations F19.151
sexual dysfunction F19.181
sleep disorder F19.182
unspecified disorder F19.19
sedative, hypnotic or anxiolytic F13.10
with
anxiety disorder F13.180
intoxication F13.129
with delirium F13.121
uncomplicated F13.120
mood disorder F13.14
other specified disorder F13.188
psychosis F13.159
delusions F13.150
hallucinations F13.151
sexual dysfunction F13.181
sleep disorder F13.182
unspecified disorder F13.19
solvent —*see* Abuse, drug, inhalant
steroids F55.3
stimulant NEC F15.10
with
anxiety disorder F15.180
intoxication F15.129
with
delirium F15.121
perceptual disturbance F15.122
uncomplicated F15.120
mood disorder F15.14
other specified disorder F15.188
psychosis F15.159
delusions F15.150
hallucinations F15.151
sexual dysfunction F15.181
sleep disorder F15.182
unspecified disorder F15.19
tranquilizers —*see* Abuse, drug, sedative
vitamins F55.4
hallucinogens —*see* Abuse, drug, hallucinogen
hashish —*see* Abuse, drug, cannabis
herbal or folk remedies F55.1
hormones F55.3
hypnotic —*see* Abuse, drug, sedative
inhalant —*see* Abuse, drug, inhalant
laxatives F55.2
LSD —*see* Abuse, drug, hallucinogen
marihuana —*see* Abuse, drug, cannabis
morphine type (opioids) —*see* Abuse, drug, opioid
non-psychoactive substance NEC F55.8
antacids F55.0
folk remedies F55.1
herbal remedies F55.1
hormones F55.3
laxatives F55.2
steroids F55.3
vitamins F55.4
opioids —*see* Abuse, drug, opioid
PCP (phencyclidine) (or related substance) —*see* Abuse, drug, hallucinogen
physical (adult) (child) —*see* Maltreatment
psychoactive substance —*see* Abuse, drug, psychoactive NEC

Abuse *(continued)*
psychological (adult) (child) —*see* Maltreatment
sedative —*see* Abuse, drug, sedative
sexual —*see* Maltreatment
solvent —*see* Abuse, drug, inhalant
steroids F55.3
vitamins F55.4
Acalculia R48.8
developmental F81.2
Acanthamebiasis (with) B60.10
conjunctiva B60.12
keratoconjunctivitis B60.13
meningoencephalitis B60.11
other specified B60.19
Acanthocephaliasis B83.8
Acanthocheilonemiasis B74.4
Acanthocytosis E78.6
Acantholysis L11.9
Acanthosis (acquired) (nigricans) L83
benign Q82.8
congenital Q82.8
seborrheic L82.1
inflamed L82.0
tongue K14.3
Acapnia E87.3
Acarbia E87.2
Acardia, acardius Q89.8
Acardiacus amorphus Q89.8
Acardiotrophia I51.4
Acariasis B88.0
scabies B86
Acarodermatitis (urticarioides) B88.0
Acarophobia F40.218
Acatalasemia, acatalasia E80.3
Acathisia (drug induced) G25.71
Accelerated atrioventricular conduction I45.6
Accentuation of personality traits (type A) Z73.1
Accessory (congenital)
adrenal gland Q89.1
anus Q43.4
appendix Q43.4
atrioventricular conduction I45.6
auditory ossicles Q16.3
auricle (ear) Q17.0
biliary duct or passage Q44.5
bladder Q64.79
blood vessels NEC Q27.9
coronary Q24.5
bone NEC Q79.8
breast tissue, axilla Q83.1
carpal bones Q74.0
cecum Q43.4
chromosome (s) NEC (nonsex) Q92.9
with complex rearrangements NEC Q92.5
*see*n only at prometaphase Q92.8
partial Q92.9
sex
female phenotype Q97.8
13 —*see* Trisomy, 13
18 —*see* Trisomy, 18
21 —*see* Trisomy, 21
coronary artery Q24.5
cusp (s), heart valve NEC Q24.8
pulmonary Q22.3
cystic duct Q44.5
digit (s) Q69.9
ear (auricle) (lobe) Q17.0
endocrine gland NEC Q89.2
eye muscle Q10.3
eyelid Q10.3
face bone (s) Q75.8
fallopian tube (fimbria) (ostium) Q50.6

- **Accessory** *(continued)*
  - finger (s) Q69.0
  - foreskin N47.8
  - frontonasal process Q75.8
  - gallbladder Q44.1
  - genital organ (s)
    - female Q52.8
      - external Q52.79
      - internal NEC Q52.8
    - male Q55.8
  - genitourinary organs NEC Q89.8
    - female Q52.8
    - male Q55.8
  - hallux Q69.2
  - heart Q24.8
    - valve NEC Q24.8
      - pulmonary Q22.3
  - hepatic ducts Q44.5
  - hymen Q52.4
  - intestine (large) (small) Q43.4
  - kidney Q63.0
  - lacrimal canal Q10.6
  - leaflet, heart valve NEC Q24.8
  - ligament, broad Q50.6
  - liver Q44.7
    - duct Q44.5
  - lobule (ear) Q17.0
  - lung (lobe) Q33.1
  - muscle Q79.8
  - navicular of carpus Q74.0
  - nervous system, part NEC Q07.8
  - nipple Q83.3
  - nose Q30.8
  - organ or site not listed —*see* Anomaly, by site
  - ovary Q50.31
  - oviduct Q50.6
  - pancreas Q45.3
  - parathyroid gland Q89.2
  - parotid gland(and duct) Q38.4
  - pituitary gland Q89.2
  - preauricular appendage Q17.0
  - prepuce N47.8
  - renal arteries (multiple) Q27.2
  - rib Q76.6
    - cervical Q76.5
  - roots (teeth) K00.2
  - salivary gland Q38.4
  - sesamoid bones Q74.8
    - foot Q74.2
    - hand Q74.0
  - skin tags Q82.8
  - spleen Q89.09
  - sternum Q76.7
  - submaxillary gland Q38.4
  - tarsal bones Q74.2
  - teeth, tooth K00.1
  - tendon Q79.8
  - thumb Q69.1
  - thymus gland Q89.2
  - thyroid gland Q89.2
  - toes Q69.2
  - tongue Q38.3
  - tooth, teeth K00.1
  - tragus Q17.0
  - ureter Q62.5
  - urethra Q64.79
  - urinary organ or tract NEC Q64.8
  - uterus Q51.2
  - vagina Q52.10
  - valve, heart NEC Q24.8
    - pulmonary Q22.3
  - vertebra Q76.49
  - vocal cords Q31.8
  - vulva Q52.79
- **Accident**
  - birth —*see* Birth, injury
  - cardiac —*see* Infarct, myocardium
  - cerebral I63.9
  - cerebrovascular (embolic) (ischemic) (thrombotic) I63.9
    - aborted I63.9
    - hemorrhagic —*see* Hemorrhage, intracranial, intracerebral
    - old(without sequelae) Z86.73
      - with sequelae (of) —*see* Sequelae, infarction, cerebral
  - coronary —*see* Infarct, myocardium
  - craniovascular I63.9
  - vascular, brain I63.9
- **Accidental** —*see* condition
- **Accommodation** (disorder) —*see also* condition
  - hysterical paralysis of F44.89
  - insufficiency of H52.4
  - paresis —*see* Paresis, of accommodation
  - spasm —*see* Spasm, of accommodation
- **Accouchement** —*see* Delivery
- **Accreta placenta** O43.21-
- **Accretio cordis** (nonrheumatic) I31.0
- **Accretions, tooth, teeth** K03.6
- **Acculturation difficulty** Z60.3
- **Accumulation secretion, prostate** N42.89
- **Acephalia, acephalism, acephalus, acephaly** Q00.0
- **Acephalobrachia monster** Q89.8
- **Acephalochirus monster** Q89.8
- **Acephalogaster** Q89.8
- **Acephalostomus monster** Q89.8
- **Acephalothorax** Q89.8
- **Acerophobia** F40.298
- **Acetonemia** R79.89
  - in Type 1 diabetes E10.10
    - with coma E10.11
- **Acetonuria** R82.4
- **Achalasia** (cardia) (esophagus) K22.0
  - congenital Q39.5
  - pylorus Q40.0
  - sphincteral NEC K59.8
- **Ache** (s) —*see* Pain
- **Acheilia** Q38.6
- **Achillobursitis** —*see* Tendinitis, Achilles
- **Achillodynia** —*see* Tendinitis, Achilles
- **Achlorhydria, achlorhydric** (neurogenic) K31.83
  - anemia D50.8
  - diarrhea K31.83
  - psychogenic F45.8
  - secondary to vagotomy K91.1
- **Achluophobia** F40.228
- **Acholia** K82.8
- **Acholuric jaundice** (familial) (splenomegalic) —*see also* Spherocytosis
  - acquired D59.8
- **Achondrogenesis** Q77.0
- **Achondroplasia** (osteosclerosis congenita) Q77.4
- **Achroma, cutis** L80
- **Achromat** (ism), achromatopsia (acquired) (congenital) H53.51
- **Achromia, congenital** —*see* Albinism
- **Achromia parasitica** B36.0
- **Achylia gastrica** K31.89
  - psychogenic F45.8
- **Acid**
  - burn —*see* Corrosion
  - deficiency
    - amide nicotinic E52
    - ascorbic E54
    - folic E53.8
    - nicotinic E52
    - pantothenic E53.8
  - intoxication E87.2
  - peptic disease K30
  - phosphatase deficiency E83.39
  - stomach K30
    - psychogenic F45.8
- **Acidemia** E87.2
  - argininosuccinic E72.22
  - isovaleric E71.110
  - metabolic (newborn) P19.9
    - first noted before onset of labor P19.0
    - first noted during labor P19.1
    - noted at birth P19.2
  - methylmalonic E71.120
  - pipecolic E72.3
  - propionic E71.121
- **Acidity, gastric** (high) K30
  - psychogenic F45.8
- **Acidocytopenia** —*see* Agranulocytosis
- **Acidocytosis** D72.1
- **Acidopenia** —*see* Agranulocytosis
- **Acidosis** (lactic) (respiratory) E87.2
  - in Type 1 diabetes E10.10
    - with coma E10.11
  - kidney, tubular N25.89
  - lactic E87.2
  - metabolic NEC E87.2
    - with respiratory acidosis E87.4
    - late, of newborn P74.0
  - mixed metabolic and respiratory, newborn P84
  - newborn P84
  - renal (hyperchloremic) (tubular) N25.89
  - respiratory E87.2
    - complicated by
      - metabolic
        - acidosis E87.4
        - alkalosis E87.4
- **Aciduria**
  - argininosuccinic E72.22
  - glutaric(type I) E72.3
    - type II E71.313
    - type III E71.5-
  - orotic (congenital) (hereditary) (pyrimidine deficiency) E79.8
    - anemia D53.0
- **Acladiosis** (skin) B36.0
- **Aclasis, diaphyseal** Q78.6
- **Acleistocardia** Q21.1
- **Aclusion** —*see* Anomaly, dentofacial, malocclusion
- **Acne** L70.9
  - artificialis L70.8
  - atrophica L70.2
  - cachecticorum (Hebra) L70.8
  - conglobata L70.1
  - cystic L70.0
  - decalvans L66.2
  - excoriée des jeunes filles L70.5
  - frontalis L70.2
  - indurata L70.0
  - infantile L70.4
  - keloid L73.0
  - lupoid L70.2
  - necrotic, necrotica (miliaris) L70.2
  - neonatal L70.4
  - nodular L70.0
  - occupational L70.8
  - picker's L70.5
  - pustular L70.0
  - rodens L70.2
  - rosacea L71.9
  - specified NEC L70.8
  - tropica L70.3
  - varioliformis L70.2
  - vulgaris L70.0
- **Acnitis** (primary) A18.4
- **Acosta's disease** T70.29
- **Acoustic** —*see* condition
- **Acousticophobia** F40.298
- **Acquired** —*see also* condition
  - immunodeficiency syndrome (AIDS) B20
- **Acrania** Q00.0
- **Acroangiodermatitis** I78.9
- **Acroasphyxia, chronic** I73.89
- **Acrobystitis** N47.7
- **Acrocephalopolysyndactyly** Q87.0
- **Acrocephalosyndactyly** Q87.0
- **Acrocephaly** Q75.0
- **Acrochondrohyperplasia** —*see* Syndrome, Marfan's
- **Acrocyanosis** I73.8
  - newborn P28.2
    - meaning transient blue hands and feet - omit code
- **Acrodermatitis** L30.8
  - atrophicans (chronica) L90.4
  - continua (Hallopeau) L40.2
  - enteropathica (hereditary) E83.2
  - Hallopeau's L40.2
  - infantile papular L44.4
  - perstans L40.2
  - pustulosa continua L40.2
  - recalcitrant pustular L40.2
- **Acrodynia** —*see* Poisoning, mercury
- **Acromegaly, acromegalia** E22.0
- **Acromelalgia** I73.81
- **Acromicria, acromikria** Q79.8
- **Acronyx** L60.0
- **Acropachy, thyroid** —*see* Thyrotoxicosis
- **Acroparesthesia** (simple) (vasomotor) I73.89
- **Acropathy, thyroid** —*see* Thyrotoxicosis
- **Acrophobia** F40.241
- **Acroposthitis** N47.7
- **Acroscleriasis, acroscleroderma, acrosclerosis** —*see* Sclerosis, systemic
- **Acrosphacelus** I96
- **Acrospiroma, eccrine** —*see* Neoplasm, skin, benign
- **Acrostealgia** —*see* Osteochondropathy
- **Acrotrophodynia** —*see* Immersion
- **ACTH ectopic syndrome** E24.3
- **Actinic** —*see* condition
- **Actinobacillosis, actinobacillus** A28.8
  - mallei A24.0
  - muris A25.1
- **Actinomyces israelii** (infection) —*see* Actinomycosis
- **Actinomycetoma** (foot) B47.1
- **Actinomycosis, actinomycotic** A42.9
  - with pneumonia A42.0
  - abdominal A42.1
  - cervicofacial A42.2
  - cutaneous A42.89

Actinomycosis, actinomycotic *(continued)*
  gastrointestinal A42.1
  pulmonary A42.0
  sepsis A42.7
  specified site NEC A42.89
Actinoneuritis G62.82
Action, heart
  disorder I49.9
  irregular I49.9
    psychogenic F45.8
Activated protein C resistance D68.51
Active —*see* condition
Acute —*see also* condition
  abdomen R10.0
  gallbladder —*see* Cholecystitis, acute
Acyanotic heart disease (congenital) Q24.9
Acystia Q64.5
Adair-Dighton syndrome (brittle bones and blue sclera, deafness) Q78.0
Adamantinoblastoma —*see* Ameloblastoma
Adamantinoma —*see also* Cyst, calcifying odontogenic
  long bones C40.90
    lower limb C40.2-
    upper limb C40.0-
  malignant C41.1
    jaw (bone) (lower) C41.1
      upper C41.0
  tibial C40.2-
Adamantoblastoma —*see* Ameloblastoma
Adams-Stokes (-Morgagni) **disease or syndrome** I45.9
Adaption reaction —*see* Disorder, adjustment
Addiction —*see also* Dependence F19.20
  alcohol, alcoholic (ethyl) (methyl) (wood) (without remission) F10.20
    with remission F10.21
  drug —*see* Dependence, drug
  ethyl alcohol(without remission) F10.20
    with remission F10.21
  heroin —*see* Dependence, drug, opioid
  methyl alcohol(without remission) F10.20
    with remission F10.21
  methylated spirit(without remission) F10.20
    with remission F10.21
  morphine(-like substances) —*see* Dependence, drug, opioid
  nicotine —*see* Dependence, drug, nicotine
  opium and opioids —*see* Dependence, drug, opioid
  tobacco —*see* Dependence, drug, nicotine
Addisonian crisis E27.2
Addison's
  anemia (pernicious) D51.0
  disease (bronze) or syndrome E27.1
    tuberculous A18.7
  keloid L94.0
Addison-Biermer anemia (pernicious) D51.0
Addison-Schilder complex E71.528
Additional —*see also* Accessory
  chromosome (s) Q99.8
    sex —*see* Abnormal, chromosome, sex
    21 —*see* Trisomy, 21
Adduction contracture, hip or other joint —*see* Contraction, joint
Adenitis —*see also* Lymphadenitis
  acute, unspecified site L04.9
  axillary I88.9
    acute L04.2
    chronic or subacute I88.1
  Bartholin's gland N75.8
  bulbourethral gland —*see* Urethritis
  cervical I88.9
    acute L04.0
    chronic or subacute I88.1
  chancroid(Hemophilus ducreyi) A57
  chronic, unspecified site I88.1
  Cowper's gland —*see* Urethritis
  due to Pasteurella multocida(p. septica) A28.0
  epidemic, acute B27.09
  gangrenous L04.9
  gonorrheal NEC A54.89
  groin I88.9
    acute L04.1
    chronic or subacute I88.1
  infectious (acute) (epidemic) B27.09
  inguinal I88.9
    acute L04.1
    chronic or subacute I88.1
  lymph gland or node, except mesenteric I88.9
    acute —*see* Lymphadenitis, acute
    chronic or subacute I88.1
  mesenteric (acute) (chronic) (nonspecific) (subacute) I88.0
  parotid gland (suppurative) —*see* Sialoadenitis
  salivary gland (any) (suppurative) —*see* Sialoadenitis
  scrofulous (tuberculous) A18.2
  Skene's duct or gland —*see* Urethritis
  strumous, tuberculous A18.2
  subacute, unspecified site I88.1
  sublingual gland (suppurative) —*see* Sialoadenitis
  submandibular gland (suppurative) —*see* Sialoadenitis
  submaxillary gland (suppurative) —*see* Sialoadenitis
  tuberculous —*see* Tuberculosis, lymph gland
  urethral gland —*see* Urethritis
  Wharton's duct (suppurative) —*see* Sialoadenitis
Adenoacanthoma —*see* Neoplasm, malignant, by site
Adenoameloblastoma —*see* Cyst, calcifying odontogenic
Adenocarcinoid (tumor) —*see* Neoplasm, malignant, by site
Adenocarcinoma —*see also* Neoplasm, malignant, by site
  acidophil
    specified site —*see* Neoplasm, malignant, by site
    unspecified site C75.1
  adrenal cortical C74.0-
  alveolar —*see* Neoplasm, lung, malignant
  apocrine
    breast —*see* Neoplasm, breast, malignant
    in situ
      breast D05.8-
      specified site NEC —*see* Neoplasm, skin, in situ
      unspecified site D04.9
Adenocarcinoma *(continued)*
  apocrine *(continued)*
    specified site NEC —*see* Neoplasm, skin, malignant
    unspecified site C44.99
  basal cell
    specified site —*see* Neoplasm, skin, malignant
    unspecified site C08.9
  basophil
    specified site —*see* Neoplasm, malignant, by site
    unspecified site C75.1
  bile duct type C22.1
    liver C22.1
    specified site NEC —*see* Neoplasm, malignant, by site
    unspecified site C22.1
  bronchiolar —*see* Neoplasm, lung, malignant
  bronchioloalveolar —*see* Neoplasm, lung, malignant
  ceruminous C44.29-
  cervix, in situ —*see also* Carcinoma, cervix uteri, in situ D06.9
  chromophobe
    specified site —*see* Neoplasm, malignant, by site
    unspecified site C75.1
  diffuse type
    specified site —*see* Neoplasm, malignant, by site
    unspecified site C16.9
  duct
    infiltrating
      with Paget's disease —*see* Neoplasm, breast, malignant
      specified site —*see* Neoplasm, malignant, by site
      unspecified site (female) C50.91-
        male C50.92-
    specified site —*see* Neoplasm, malignant, by site
    unspecified site
      female C56.9
      male C61
  eosinophil
    specified site —*see* Neoplasm, malignant, by site
    unspecified site C75.1
  follicular
    with papillary C73
    moderately differentiated C73
    specified site —*see* Neoplasm, malignant, by site
    trabecular C73
    unspecified site C73
    well differentiated C73
  Hurthle cell C73
  in
    adenomatous
      polyposis coli C18.9
  infiltrating duct
    with Paget's disease —*see* Neoplasm, breast, malignant
    specified site —*see* Neoplasm, by site, malignant
    unspecified site (female) C50.91-
      male C50.92-
  inflammatory
    specified site —*see* Neoplasm, by site, malignant
    unspecified site (female) C50.91-
      male C50.92-
  intestinal type
    specified site —*see* Neoplasm, by site, malignant
    unspecified site C16.9
  intracystic papillary
  intraductal
    breast D05.1-
Adenocarcinoma *(continued)*
  intraductal *(continued)*
    noninfiltrating
      breast D05.1-
      papillary
        with invasion
          specified site —*see* Neoplasm, by site, malignant
          unspecified site (female) C50.91-
            male C50.92-
        breast D05.1-
        specified site NEC —*see* Neoplasm, in situ, by site
        unspecified site D05.1-
      specified site NEC —*see* Neoplasm, in situ, by site
      unspecified site D05.1-
    papillary
      with invasion
        specified site —*see* Neoplasm, malignant, by site
        unspecified site (female) C50.91-
          male C50.92-
      breast D05.1-
      specified site —*see* Neoplasm, in situ, by site
      unspecified site D05.1-
    specified site NEC —*see* Neoplasm, in situ, by site
    unspecified site D05.1-
  islet cell
    with exocrine, mixed
      specified site —*see* Neoplasm, malignant, by site
      unspecified site C25.9
    pancreas C25.4
    specified site NEC —*see* Neoplasm, malignant, by site
    unspecified site C25.4
  lobular
    in situ
      breast D05.0-
      specified site NEC —*see* Neoplasm, in situ, by site
      unspecified site D05.0-
    specified site —*see* Neoplasm, malignant, by site
    unspecified site (female) C50.91-
      male C50.92-
  mucoid —*see also* Neoplasm, malignant, by site
    cell
      specified site —*see* Neoplasm, malignant, by site
      unspecified site C75.1
  nonencapsulated sclerosing C73
  papillary
    with follicular C73
    follicular variant C73
    intraductal (noninfiltrating)
      with invasion
        specified site —*see* Neoplasm, malignant, by site
        unspecified site (female) C50.91-
          male C50.92-
      breast D05.1-
      specified site NEC —*see* Neoplasm, in situ, by site
      unspecified site D05.1-
    serous
      specified site —*see* Neoplasm, malignant, by site
      unspecified site C56.9
  papillocystic
    specified site —*see* Neoplasm, malignant, by site
    unspecified site C56.9

Adenocarcinoma *(continued)*
  pseudomucinous
    specified site —*see* Neoplasm, malignant, by site
    unspecified site C56.9
  renal cell C64-
  sebaceous —*see* Neoplasm, skin, malignant
  serous —*see also* Neoplasm, malignant, by site
    papillary
      specified site —*see* Neoplasm, malignant, by site
      unspecified site C56.9
  sweat gland —*see* Neoplasm, skin, malignant
  water-clear cell C75.0

Adenocarcinoma-in-situ —*see also* Neoplasm, in situ, by site
  breast D05.9-

Adenofibroma
  clear cell —*see* Neoplasm, benign, by site
  endometrioid D27.9
    borderline malignancy D39.10
    malignant C56-
  mucinous
    specified site —*see* Neoplasm, benign, by site
    unspecified site D27.9
  papillary
    specified site —*see* Neoplasm, benign, by site
    unspecified site D27.9
  prostate —*see* Enlargement, enlarged, prostate
  serous
    specified site —*see* Neoplasm, benign, by site
    unspecified site D27.9
  specified site —*see* Neoplasm, benign, by site
  unspecified site D27.9

Adenofibrosis
  breast —*see* Fibroadenosis, breast
  endometrioid N80.0

Adenoiditis (chronic) J35.02
  with tonsillitis J35.03
  acute J03.90
    recurrent J03.91
    specified organism NEC J03.80
      recurrent J03.81
    staphylococcal J03.80
      recurrent J03.81
    streptococcal J03.00
      recurrent J03.01

Adenoids —*see* condition

Adenolipoma —*see* Neoplasm, benign, by site

Adenolipomatosis, Launois-Bensaude E88.89

Adenolymphoma
  specified site —*see* Neoplasm, benign, by site
  unspecified site D11.9

Adenoma —*see also* Neoplasm, benign, by site
  acidophil
    specified site —*see* Neoplasm, benign, by site
    unspecified site D35.2
  acidophil-basophil, mixed
    specified site —*see* Neoplasm, benign, by site
    unspecified site D35.2
  adrenal (cortical) D35.00
    clear cell D35.00
    compact cell D35.00
    glomerulosa cell D35.00

Adenoma *(continued)*
  adrenal *(continued)*
    heavily pigmented variant D35.00
    mixed cell D35.00
  alpha-cell
    pancreas D13.7
    specified site NEC —*see* Neoplasm, benign, by site
    unspecified site D13.7
  alveolar D14.30
  apocrine
    breast D24-
    specified site NEC —*see* Neoplasm, skin, benign, by site
    unspecified site D23.9
  basal cell D11.9
  basophil
    specified site —*see* Neoplasm, benign, by site
    unspecified site D35.2
  basophil-acidophil, mixed
    specified site —*see* Neoplasm, benign, by site
    unspecified site D35.2
  beta-cell
    pancreas D13.7
    specified site NEC —*see* Neoplasm, benign, by site
    unspecified site D13.7
  bile duct D13.4
    common D13.5
    extrahepatic D13.5
    intrahepatic D13.4
    specified site NEC —*see* Neoplasm, benign, by site
    unspecified site D13.4
  black D35.00
  bronchial D38.1
    cylindroid type —*see* Neoplasm, lung, malignant
  ceruminous D23.2-
  chief cell D35.1
  chromophobe
    specified site —*see* Neoplasm, benign, by site
    unspecified site D35.2
  colloid
    specified site —*see* Neoplasm, benign, by site
    unspecified site D34
  duct
  eccrine, papillary —*see* Neoplasm, skin, benign
  endocrine, multiple
    single specified site —*see* Neoplasm, uncertain behavior, by site
    two or more specified sites D44-
    unspecified site D44.9
  endometrioid —*see also* Neoplasm, benign
    borderline malignancy —*see* Neoplasm, uncertain behavior, by site
  eosinophil
    specified site —*see* Neoplasm, benign, by site
    unspecified site D35.2
  fetal
    specified site —*see* Neoplasm, benign, by site
    unspecified site D34
  follicular
    specified site —*see* Neoplasm, benign, by site
    unspecified site D34
  hepatocellular D13.4
  Hurthle cell D34
  islet cell
    pancreas D13.7
    specified site NEC —*see* Neoplasm, benign, by site

Adenoma *(continued)*
  islet cell *(continued)*
    unspecified site D13.7
  liver cell D13.4
  macrofollicular
    specified site —*see* Neoplasm, benign, by site
    unspecified site D34
  malignant, malignum —*see* Neoplasm, malignant, by site
  microcystic
    pancreas D13.7
    specified site NEC —*see* Neoplasm, benign, by site
    unspecified site D13.7
  microfollicular
    specified site —*see* Neoplasm, benign, by site
    unspecified site D34
  mucoid cell
    specified site —*see* Neoplasm, benign, by site
    unspecified site D35.2
  multiple endocrine
    single specified site —*see* Neoplasm, uncertain behavior, by site
    two or more specified sites D44-
    unspecified site D44.9
  nipple D24-
  papillary —*see also* Neoplasm, benign, by site
    eccrine —*see* Neoplasm, skin, benign, by site
  Pick's tubular
    specified site —*see* Neoplasm, benign, by site
    unspecified site
      female D27.9
      male D29.20
  pleomorphic
    carcinoma in —*see* Neoplasm, salivary gland, malignant
      specified site —*see* Neoplasm, malignant, by site
      unspecified site C08.9
  polypoid —*see also* Neoplasm, benign
    adenocarcinoma in —*see* Neoplasm, malignant, by site
    adenocarcinoma in situ —*see* Neoplasm, in situ, by site
  prostate —*see* Neoplasm, benign, prostate
  rete cell D29.20
  sebaceous —*see* Neoplasm, skin, benign
  Sertoli cell
    specified site —*see* Neoplasm, benign, by site
    unspecified site
      female D27.9
      male D29.20
  skin appendage —*see* Neoplasm, skin, benign
  sudoriferous gland —*see* Neoplasm, skin, benign
  sweat gland —*see* Neoplasm, skin, benign
  testicular
    specified site —*see* Neoplasm, benign, by site
    unspecified site
      female D27.9
      male D29.20
  tubular —*see also* Neoplasm, benign, by site
    adenocarcinoma in —*see* Neoplasm, malignant, by site
    adenocarcinoma in situ —*see* Neoplasm, in situ, by site

Adenoma *(continued)*
  tubular *(continued)*
    Pick's
      specified site —*see* Neoplasm, benign, by site
      unspecified site
        female D27.9
        male D29.20
  tubulovillous —*see also* Neoplasm, benign, by site
    adenocarcinoma in —*see* Neoplasm, malignant, by site
    adenocarcinoma in situ —*see* Neoplasm, in situ, by site
  villous —*see* Neoplasm, uncertain behavior, by site
    adenocarcinoma in —*see* Neoplasm, malignant, by site
    adenocarcinoma in situ —*see* Neoplasm, in situ, by site
  water-clear cell D35.1

Adenomatosis
  endocrine (multiple) E31.20
    single specified site —*see* Neoplasm, uncertain behavior, by site
  erosive of nipple D24-
  pluriendocrine —*see* Adenomatosis, endocrine
  pulmonary D38.1
    malignant —*see* Neoplasm, lung, malignant
  specified site —*see* Neoplasm, benign, by site
  unspecified site D12.6

Adenomatous
  goiter (nontoxic) E04.9
    with hyperthyroidism —*see* Hyperthyroidism, with, goiter, nodular
    toxic —*see* Hyperthyroidism, with, goiter, nodular

Adenomyoma —*see also* Neoplasm, benign, by site
  prostate —*see* Enlarged, prostate

Adenomyometritis N80.0

Adenomyosis N80.0

Adenopathy (lymph gland) R59.9
  generalized R59.1
  inguinal R59.0
  localized R59.0
  mediastinal R59.0
  mesentery R59.0
  syphilitic (secondary) A51.49
  tracheobronchial R59.0
    tuberculous A15.4
      primary (progressive) A15.7
  tuberculous —*see also* Tuberculosis, lymph gland
    tracheobronchial A15.4
      primary (progressive) A15.7

Adenosalpingitis —*see* Salpingitis

Adenosarcoma —*see* Neoplasm, malignant, by site

Adenosclerosis I88.8

Adenosis (sclerosing) breast —*see* Fibroadenosis, breast

Adenovirus, as cause of disease classified elsewhere B97.0

Adentia (complete) (partial) —*see* Absence, teeth

Adherent —*see also* Adhesions
  labia (minora) N90.89
  pericardium (nonrheumatic) I31.0
    rheumatic I09.2
  placenta(with hemorrhage) O72.0
    without hemorrhage O73.0

Adherent *(continued)*
  prepuce, newborn N47.0
  scar (skin) L90.5
  tendon in scar L90.5

Adhesions, adhesive (postinfective) K66.0
  with intestinal obstruction K56.5
  abdominal (wall) —*see* Adhesions, peritoneum
  appendix K38.8
  bile duct (common) (hepatic) K83.8
  bladder (sphincter) N32.89
  bowel —*see* Adhesions, peritoneum
  cardiac I31.0
    rheumatic I09.2
  cecum —*see* Adhesions, peritoneum
  cervicovaginal N88.1
    congenital Q52.8
    postpartal O90.89
      old N88.1
  cervix N88.1
  ciliary body NEC —*see* Adhesions, iris
  clitoris N90.89
  colon —*see* Adhesions, peritoneum
  common duct K83.8
  congenital —*see also* Anomaly, by site
    fingers —*see* Syndactylism, complex, fingers
    omental, anomalous Q43.3
    peritoneal Q43.3
    tongue (to gum or roof of mouth) Q38.3
  conjunctiva (acquired) H11.21-
    congenital Q15.8
  cystic duct K82.8
  diaphragm —*see* Adhesions, peritoneum
  due to foreign body —*see* Foreign body
  duodenum —*see* Adhesions, peritoneum
  ear
    middle H74.1-
  epididymis N50.8
  epidural —*see* Adhesions, meninges
  epiglottis J38.7
  eyelid H02.59
  female pelvis N73.6
  gallbladder K82.8
  globe H44.89
  heart I31.0
    rheumatic I09.2
  ileocecal (coil) —*see* Adhesions, peritoneum
  ileum —*see* Adhesions, peritoneum
  intestine —*see also* Adhesions, peritoneum
    with obstruction K56.5
  intra-abdominal —*see* Adhesions, peritoneum
  iris H21.50-
    anterior H21.51-
    goniosynechiae H21.52-
    posterior H21.54-
    to corneal graft T85.89
  joint —*see* Ankylosis
    knee M23.8X
    temporomandibular M26.61
  labium (majus) (minus), congenital Q52.5
  liver —*see* Adhesions, peritoneum
  lung J98.4
  mediastinum J98.5
  meninges (cerebral) (spinal) G96.12
    congenital Q07.8
    tuberculous (cerebral) (spinal) A17.0
  mesenteric —*see* Adhesions, peritoneum
  nasal (septum) (to turbinates) J34.89
  ocular muscle —*see* Strabismus, mechanical
  omentum —*see* Adhesions, peritoneum
  ovary N73.6
    congenital(to cecum, kidney or omentum) Q50.39
  paraovarian N73.6
  pelvic (peritoneal)
    female N73.6
      postprocedural N99.4
    male —*see* Adhesions, peritoneum
    postpartal (old) N73.6
    tuberculous A18.17
  penis to scrotum (congenital) Q55.8
  periappendiceal —*see also* Adhesions, peritoneum
  pericardium (nonrheumatic) I31.0
    focal I31.8
    rheumatic I09.2
    tuberculous A18.84
  pericholecystic K82.8
  perigastric —*see* Adhesions, peritoneum
  periovarian N73.6
  periprostatic N42.89
  perirectal —*see* Adhesions, peritoneum
  perirenal N28.89
  peritoneum, peritoneal (postinfective) (postprocedural) K66.0
    with obstruction (intestinal) K56.5
    congenital Q43.3
    pelvic, female N73.6
      postprocedural N99.4
    postpartal, pelvic N73.6
    to uterus N73.6
  peritubal N73.6
  periureteral N28.89
  periuterine N73.6
  perivesical N32.89
  perivesicular(seminal vesicle) N50.8
  pleura, pleuritic J94.8
    tuberculous NEC A15.6
  pleuropericardial J94.8
  postoperative(gastrointestinal tract) K66.0
    with obstruction K91.3
    due to foreign body accidentally left in wound —*see* Foreign body, accidentally left during a procedure
    pelvic peritoneal N99.4
    urethra —*see* Stricture, urethra, postprocedural
    vagina N99.2
  postpartal, old (vulva or perineum) N90.89
  preputial, prepuce N47.5
  pulmonary J98.4
  pylorus —*see* Adhesions, peritoneum
  sciatic nerve —*see* Lesion, nerve, sciatic
  seminal vesicle N50.8
  shoulder (joint) —*see* Capsulitis, adhesive
  sigmoid flexure —*see* Adhesions, peritoneum
  spermatic cord (acquired) N50.8
    congenital Q55.4
  spinal canal G96.12
  stomach —*see* Adhesions, peritoneum
  subscapular —*see* Capsulitis, adhesive
  temporomandibular M26.61
  tendinitis —*see also* Tenosynovitis, specified type NEC
    shoulder —*see* Capsulitis, adhesive
  testis N44.8
  tongue, congenital(to gum or roof of mouth) Q38.3
    acquired K14.8
  trachea J39.8
  tubo-ovarian N73.6
  tunica vaginalis N44.8
  uterus N73.6
    internal N85.6
    to abdominal wall N73.6
  vagina (chronic) N89.5
    postoperative N99.2
  vitreomacular H43.82-
  vitreous H43.89
  vulva N90.89

Adiaspiromycosis B48.8

Adie (-Holmes) **pupil or syndrome** —*see* Anomaly, pupil, function, tonic pupil

Adiponecrosis neonatorum P83.8

Adiposis —*see also* Obesity
  cerebralis E23.6
  dolorosa E88.2

Adiposity —*see also* Obesity
  heart —*see* Degeneration, myocardial
  localized E65

Adiposogenital dystrophy E23.6

Adjustment
  disorder —*see* Disorder, adjustment
  implanted device —*see* Encounter (for), adjustment (of)
  prosthesis, external —*see* Fitting
  reaction —*see* Disorder, adjustment

Administration of tPA (rtPA) **in a different facility within the last 24 hours prior to admission to current facility** Z92.82

Admission (for) —*see also* Encounter (for)
  adjustment (of)
    artificial
      arm Z44.00-
        complete Z44.01-
        partial Z44.02-
      eye Z44.2
      leg Z44.10-
        complete Z44.11-
        partial Z44.12-
    brain neuropacemaker Z46.2
      implanted Z45.42
    breast
      implant Z45.81
      prosthesis (external) Z44.3
    colostomy belt Z46.89
    contact lenses Z46.0
    cystostomy device Z46.6
    dental prosthesis Z46.3
    device NEC
      abdominal Z46.89
      implanted Z45.89
        cardiac Z45.09
          defibrillator(with synchronous cardiace pacemaker) Z45.02
          pacemaker Z45.018
            pulse generator Z45.010
        hearing device Z45.328
          bone conduction Z45.320
          cochlear Z45.321
        infusion pump Z45.1
        nervous system Z45.49
          CSF drainage Z45.41
          hearing device —*see* Admission, adjustment, device, implanted, hearing device
          neuropacemaker Z45.42
          visual substitution Z45.31
        specified NEC Z45.89

Admission *(continued)*
  adjustment *(continued)*
    device NEC *(continued)*
      implanted *(continued)*
        vascular access Z45.2
        visual substitution Z45.31
      nervous system Z46.2
        implanted —*see* Admission, adjustment, device, implanted, nervous system
      orthodontic Z46.4
      prosthetic Z44.9
        arm —*see* Admission, adjustment, artificial, arm
        breast Z44.3
        dental Z46.3
        eye Z44.2
        leg —*see* Admission, adjustment, artificial, leg
        specified type NEC Z44.8
      substitution
        auditory Z46.2
          implanted —*see* Admission, adjustment, device, implanted, hearing device
        nervous system Z46.2
          implanted —*see* Admission, adjustment, device, implanted, nervous system
        visual Z46.2
          implanted Z45.31
      urinary Z46.6
    hearing aid Z46.1
      implanted —*see* Admission, adjustment, device, implanted, hearing device
    ileostomy device Z46.89
    intestinal appliance or device NEC Z46.89
    neuropacemaker (brain) (peripheral nerve) (spinal cord) Z46.2
      implanted Z45.42
    orthodontic device Z46.4
    orthopedic (brace) (cast) (device) (shoes) Z46.89
    pacemaker
      cardiac Z45.018
        pulse generator Z45.010
      nervous system Z46.2
        implanted Z45.42
    portacath(port-a-cath) Z45.2
    prosthesis Z44.9
      arm —*see* Admission, adjustment, artificial, arm
      breast Z44.3
      dental Z46.3
      eye Z44.2
      leg —*see* Admission, adjustment, artificial, leg
      specified NEC Z44.8
    spectacles Z46.0
  aftercare —*see also* Aftercare Z51.89
    postpartum
      immediately after delivery Z39.0
      routine follow-up Z39.2
    radiation therapy (antineoplastic) Z51.0
  attention to artificial opening (of) Z43.9
    artificial vagina Z43.7
    colostomy Z43.3
    cystostomy Z43.5
    enterostomy Z43.4
    gastrostomy Z43.1
    ileostomy Z43.2
    jejunostomy Z43.4
    nephrostomy Z43.6
    specified site NEC Z43.8
      intestinal tract Z43.4
      urinary tract Z43.6

- **Admission** *(continued)*
  - attention to artificial opening *(continued)*
    - tracheostomy Z43.0
    - ureterostomy Z43.6
    - urethrostomy Z43.6
  - breast augmentation or reduction Z41.1
  - breast reconstruction following mastectomy Z42.1
  - change of
    - dressing (nonsurgical) Z48.00
    - neuropacemaker device (brain) (peripheral nerve) (spinal cord) Z46.2
      - implanted Z45.42
    - surgical dressing Z48.01
  - circumcision, ritual or routine(in absence of diagnosis) Z41.2
  - clinical research investigation (control) (normal comparison) (participant) Z00.6
  - contraceptive management Z30.9
  - cosmetic surgery NEC Z41.1
  - counseling —*see also* Counseling
    - dietary Z71.3
    - HIV Z71.7
    - human immunodeficiency virus Z71.7
    - nonattending third party Z71.0
    - procreative management NEC Z31.69
  - delivery, full-term, uncomplicated O80
    - cesarean, without indication O82
  - dietary surveillance and counseling Z71.3
  - ear piercing Z41.3
  - examination at health care facility (adult) —*see also* Examination Z00.00
    - with abnormal findings Z00.01
    - clinical research investigation (control) (normal comparison) (participant) Z00.6
    - dental Z01.20
      - with abnormal findings Z01.21
    - donor (potential) Z00.5
    - ear Z01.10
      - with abnormal findings NEC Z01.118
    - eye Z01.00
      - with abnormal findings Z01.01
    - general, specified reason NEC Z00.8
    - hearing Z01.10
      - with abnormal findings NEC Z01.118
    - postpartum checkup Z39.2
    - psychiatric (general) Z00.8
      - requested by authority Z04.6
    - vision Z01.00
      - with abnormal findings Z01.01
  - fitting (of)
    - artificial
      - arm —*see* Admission, adjustment, artificial, arm
      - eye Z44.2
      - leg —*see* Admission, adjustment, artificial, leg
    - brain neuropacemaker Z46.2
      - implanted Z45.42
    - breast prosthesis (external) Z44.3
    - colostomy belt Z46.89
    - contact lenses Z46.0
    - cystostomy device Z46.6
    - dental prosthesis Z46.3
    - dentures Z46.3
    - device NEC
      - abdominal Z46.89

- **Admission** *(continued)*
  - fitting (of) *(continued)*
    - device NEC *(continued)*
      - nervous system Z46.2
        - implanted —*see* Admission, adjustment, device, implanted, nervous system
      - orthodontic Z46.4
      - prosthetic Z44.9
        - breast Z44.3
        - dental Z46.3
        - eye Z44.2
      - substitution
        - auditory Z46.2
          - implanted —*see* Admission, adjustment, device, implanted, hearing device
        - nervous system Z46.2
          - implanted —*see* Admission, adjustment, device, implanted, nervous system
        - visual Z46.2
          - implanted Z45.31
    - hearing aid Z46.1
    - ileostomy device Z46.89
    - intestinal appliance or device NEC Z46.89
    - neuropacemaker (brain) (peripheral nerve) (spinal cord) Z46.2
      - implanted Z45.42
    - orthodontic device Z46.4
    - orthopedic device (brace) (cast) (shoes) Z46.89
    - prosthesis Z44.9
      - arm —*see* Admission, adjustment, artificial, arm
      - breast Z44.3
      - dental Z46.3
      - eye Z44.2
      - leg —*see* Admission, adjustment, artificial, leg
      - specified type NEC Z44.8
    - spectacles Z46.0
  - follow-up examination Z09
  - intrauterine device management Z30.431
    - initial prescription Z30.014
  - mental health evaluation Z00.8
    - requested by authority Z04.6
  - observation —*see* Observation
  - Papanicolaou smear, cervix Z12.4
    - for suspected malignant neoplasm Z12.4
  - plastic and reconstructive surgery following medical procedure or healed injury NEC Z42.8
  - plastic surgery, cosmetic NEC Z41.1
  - postpartum observation
    - immediately after delivery Z39.0
    - routine follow-up Z39.2
  - poststerilization(for restoration) Z31.0
    - aftercare Z31.42
  - procreative management Z31.9
  - prophylactic (measure)
    - organ removal Z40.00
      - breast Z40.01
      - ovary Z40.02
      - specified organ NEC Z40.09
      - testes Z40.09
    - vaccination Z23
  - psychiatric examination (general) Z00.8
    - requested by authority Z04.6
  - radiation therapy (antineoplastic) Z51.0
  - reconstructive surgery following medical procedure or healed injury NEC Z42.8

- **Admission** *(continued)*
  - removal of
    - cystostomy catheter Z43.5
    - drains Z48.03
    - dressing (nonsurgical) Z48.00
    - intrauterine contraceptive device Z30.432
    - neuropacemaker (brain) (peripheral nerve) (spinal cord) Z46.2
      - implanted Z45.42
    - staples Z48.02
    - surgical dressing Z48.01
    - sutures Z48.02
    - ureteral stent Z46.6
  - respirator [ventilator] use during power failure Z99.12
  - restoration of organ continuity (poststerilization) Z31.0
    - aftercare Z31.42
  - sensitivity test —*see also* Test, skin
    - allergy NEC Z01.82
    - Mantoux Z11.1
  - tuboplasty following previous sterilization Z31.0
    - aftercare Z31.42
  - vasoplasty following previous sterilization Z31.0
    - aftercare Z31.42
  - vision examination Z01.00
    - with abnormal findings Z01.01
  - waiting period for admission to other facility Z75.1
- **Adnexitis** (suppurative) —*see* Salpingo-oophoritis
- **Adolescent X-linked adrenoleukodystrophy** E71.521
- **Adrenal** (gland) —*see* condition
- **Adrenalism, tuberculous** A18.7
- **Adrenalitis, adrenitis** E27.8
  - autoimmune E27.1
  - meningococcal, hemorrhagic A39.1
- **Adrenarche, premature** E27.0
- **Adrenocortical syndrome** —*see* Cushing's, syndrome
- **Adrenogenital syndrome** E25.9
  - acquired E25.8
  - congenital E25.0
  - salt loss E25.0
- **Adrenogenitalism, congenital** E25.0
- **Adrenoleukodystrophy** E71.529
  - neonatal E71.511
  - X-linked E71.529
    - Addison only phenotype E71.528
    - Addison-Schilder E71.528
    - adolescent E71.521
    - adrenomyeloneuropathy E71.522
    - childhood cerebral E71.520
    - other specified E71.528
- **Adrenomyeloneuropathy** E71.522
- **Adventitious bursa** —*see* Bursopathy, specified type NEC
- **Adverse effect** —*see* Table of Drugs and Chemicals, categories T36-T50, with 6th character 5
- **Advice** —*see* Counseling
- **Adynamia** (episodica) (hereditary) (periodic) G72.3
- **Aeration lung imperfect, newborn** —*see* Atelectasis
- **Aerobullosis** T70.3
- **Aerocele** —*see* Embolism, air
- **Aerodermectasia**
  - subcutaneous (traumatic) T79.7
- **Aerodontalgia** T70.29
- **Aeroembolism** T70.3

- **Aerogenes capsulatus infection** A48.0
- **Aero-otitis media** T70.0
- **Aerophagy, aerophagia** (psychogenic) F45.8
- **Aerophobia** F40.228
- **Aerosinusitis** T70.1
- **Aerotitis** T70.0
- **Affection** —*see* Disease
- **Afibrinogenemia** —*see also* Defect, coagulation D68.8
  - acquired D65
  - congenital D68.2
  - following ectopic or molar pregnancy O08.1
  - in abortion —*see* Abortion, by type, complicated by, afibrinogenemia
  - puerperal O72.3
- **African**
  - sleeping sickness B56.9
  - tick fever A68.1
  - trypanosomiasis B56.9
    - gambian B56.0
    - rhodesian B56.1
- **Aftercare** —*see also* Care Z51.89
  - following surgery (for) (on)
    - amputation Z47.81
    - attention to
      - drains Z48.03
      - dressings (nonsurgical) Z48.00
        - surgical Z48.01
      - sutures Z48.02
    - circulatory system Z48.812
    - delayed (planned) wound closure Z48.1
    - digestive system Z48.815
    - explantation of joint prosthesis(staged procedure)
      - hip Z47.32
      - knee Z47.33
      - shoulder Z47.31
    - genitourinary system Z48.816
    - joint replacement Z47.1
    - neoplasm Z48.3
    - nervous system Z48.811
    - oral cavity Z48.814
    - organ transplant
      - bone marrow Z48.290
      - heart Z48.21
      - heart-lung Z48.280
      - kidney Z48.22
      - liver Z48.23
      - lung Z48.24
      - multiple organs NEC Z48.288
      - specified NEC Z48.298
    - orthopedic NEC Z47.89
    - planned wound closure Z48.1
    - removal of internal fixation device Z47.2
    - respiratory system Z48.813
    - scoliosis Z47.82
    - sense organs Z48.810
    - skin and subcutaneous tissue Z48.817
    - specified body system
      - circulatory Z48.812
      - digestive Z48.815
      - genitourinary Z48.816
      - nervous Z48.811
      - oral cavity Z48.814
      - respiratory Z48.813
      - sense organs Z48.810
      - skin and subcutaneous tissue Z48.817
      - teeth Z48.814
    - specified NEC Z48.89
    - spinal Z48.89
    - teeth Z48.814
  - fracture - code to fracture with seventh character D

Aftercare *(continued)*
- involving
  - removal of
    - drains Z48.03
    - dressings (nonsurgical) Z48.00
    - staples Z48.02
    - surgical dressings Z48.01
    - sutures Z48.02
  - neuropacemaker (brain) (peripheral nerve) (spinal cord) Z46.2
    - implanted Z45.42
  - orthopedic NEC Z47.89
  - postprocedural —*see* Aftercare, following surgery

After-cataract —*see* Cataract, secondary

Agalactia (primary) O92.3
- elective, secondary or therapeutic O92.5

Agammaglobulinemia (acquired (secondary)) (nonfamilial) D80.1
- with
  - immunoglobulin-bearing B-lymphocytes D80.1
  - lymphopenia D81.9
- autosomal recessive (Swiss type) D80.0
- Bruton's X-linked D80.0
- common variable (CVAgamma) D80.1
- congenital sex-linked D80.0
- hereditary D80.0
- lymphopenic D81.9
- Swiss type(autosomal recessive) D80.0
- X-linked(with growth hormone deficiency) (Bruton) D80.0

Aganglionosis (bowel) (colon) Q43.1

Age (old) —*see* Senility

Agenesis
- adrenal (gland) Q89.1
- alimentary tract (complete) (partial) NEC Q45.8
  - upper Q40.8
- anus, anal (canal) Q42.3
  - with fistula Q42.2
- aorta Q25.4
- appendix Q42.8
- arm (complete) Q71.0-
  - with hand present Q71.1-
- artery (peripheral) Q27.9
  - brain Q28.3
  - coronary Q24.5
  - pulmonary Q25.79
  - specified NEC Q27.8
  - umbilical Q27.0
- auditory (canal) (external) Q16.1
- auricle (ear) Q16.0
- bile duct or passage Q44.5
- bladder Q64.5
- bone Q79.9
- brain Q00.0
  - part of Q04.3
- breast(with nipple present) Q83.8
  - with absent nipple Q83.0
- bronchus Q32.4
- canaliculus lacrimalis Q10.4
- carpus —*see* Agenesis, hand
- cartilage Q79.9
- cecum Q42.8
- cerebellum Q04.3
- cervix Q51.5
- chin Q18.8
- cilia Q10.3
- circulatory system, part NOS Q28.9
- clavicle Q74.0
- clitoris Q52.6
- coccyx Q76.49
- colon Q42.9
  - specified NEC Q42.8
- corpus callosum Q04.0

Agenesis *(continued)*
- cricoid cartilage Q31.8
- diaphragm(with hernia) Q79.1
- digestive organ (s) or tract (complete) (partial) NEC Q45.8
  - upper Q40.8
- ductus arteriosus Q28.8
- duodenum Q41.0
- ear Q16.9
  - auricle Q16.0
  - lobe Q17.8
- ejaculatory duct Q55.4
- endocrine (gland) NEC Q89.2
- epiglottis Q31.8
- esophagus Q39.8
- eustachian tube Q16.2
- eye Q11.1
  - adnexa Q15.8
- eyelid (fold) Q10.3
- face
  - bones NEC Q75.8
  - specified part NEC Q18.8
- fallopian tube Q50.6
- femur —*see* Defect, reduction, lower limb, longitudinal, femur
- fibula —*see* Defect, reduction, lower limb, longitudinal, fibula
- finger (complete) (partial) —*see* Agenesis, hand
- foot(and toes) (complete) (partial) Q72.3-
- forearm(with hand present) —*see* Agenesis, arm, with hand present
  - and hand Q71.2-
- gallbladder Q44.0
- gastric Q40.2
- genitalia, genital(organ (s))
  - female Q52.8
    - external Q52.71
    - internal NEC Q52.8
  - male Q55.8
- glottis Q31.8
- hair Q84.0
- hand(and fingers) (complete) (partial) Q71.3-
- heart Q24.8
  - valve NEC Q24.8
    - pulmonary Q22.0
- hepatic Q44.7
- humerus —*see* Defect, reduction, upper limb
- hymen Q52.4
- ileum Q41.2
- incus Q16.3
- intestine (small) Q41.9
  - large Q42.9
    - specified NEC Q42.8
- iris(dilator fibers) Q13.1
- jaw M26.09
- jejunum Q41.1
- kidney (s) (partial) Q60.2
  - bilateral Q60.1
  - unilateral Q60.0
- labium (majus) (minus) Q52.71
- labyrinth, membranous Q16.5
- lacrimal apparatus Q10.4
- larynx Q31.8
- leg (complete) Q72.0-
  - with foot present Q72.1-
  - lower leg(with foot present) —*see* Agenesis, leg, with foot present
    - and foot Q72.2-
- lens Q12.3
- limb (complete) Q73.0
  - lower —*see* Agenesis, leg
  - upper —*see* Agenesis, arm
- lip Q38.0
- liver Q44.7
- lung (fissure) (lobe) (bilateral) (unilateral) Q33.3
- mandible, maxilla M26.09
- metacarpus —*see* Agenesis, hand

Agenesis *(continued)*
- metatarsus —*see* Agenesis, foot
- muscle Q79.8
  - eyelid Q10.3
  - ocular Q15.8
- musculoskeletal system NEC Q79.8
- nail (s) Q84.3
- neck, part Q18.8
- nerve Q07.8
- nervous system, part NEC Q07.8
- nipple Q83.2
- nose Q30.1
- nuclear Q07.8
- organ
  - of Corti Q16.5
  - or site not listed —*see* Anomaly, by site
- osseous meatus (ear) Q16.1
- ovary
  - bilateral Q50.02
  - unilateral Q50.01
- oviduct Q50.6
- pancreas Q45.0
- parathyroid (gland) Q89.2
- parotid gland (s) Q38.4
- patella Q74.1
- pelvic girdle (complete) (partial) Q74.2
- penis Q55.5
- pericardium Q24.8
- pituitary (gland) Q89.2
- prostate Q55.4
- punctum lacrimale Q10.4
- radioulnar —*see* Defect, reduction, upper limb
- radius —*see* Defect, reduction, upper limb, longitudinal, radius
- rectum Q42.1
  - with fistula Q42.0
- renal Q60.2
  - bilateral Q60.1
  - unilateral Q60.0
- respiratory organ NEC Q34.8
- rib Q76.6
- roof of orbit Q75.8
- round ligament Q52.8
- sacrum Q76.49
- salivary gland Q38.4
- scapula Q74.0
- scrotum Q55.29
- seminal vesicles Q55.4
- septum
  - atrial Q21.1
  - between aorta and pulmonary artery Q21.4
  - ventricular Q20.4
- shoulder girdle (complete) (partial) Q74.0
- skull (bone) Q75.8
  - with
    - anencephaly Q00.0
    - encephalocele —*see* Encephalocele
    - hydrocephalus Q03.9
      - with spina bifida —*see* Spina bifida, by site, with hydrocephalus
    - microcephaly Q02
- spermatic cord Q55.4
- spinal cord Q06.0
- spine Q76.49
- spleen Q89.01
- sternum Q76.7
- stomach Q40.2
- submaxillary gland (s) (congenital) Q38.4
- tarsus —*see* Agenesis, foot
- tendon Q79.8
- testicle Q55.0
- thymus (gland) Q89.2
- thyroid (gland) E03.1
  - cartilage Q31.8

Agenesis *(continued)*
- tibia —*see* Defect, reduction, lower limb, longitudinal, tibia
- tibiofibular —*see* Defect, reduction, lower limb, specified type NEC
- toe(and foot) (complete) (partial) —*see* Agenesis, foot
- tongue Q38.3
- trachea (cartilage) Q32.1
- ulna —*see* Defect, reduction, upper limb, longitudinal, ulna
- upper limb —*see* Agenesis, arm
- ureter Q62.4
- urethra Q64.5
- urinary tract NEC Q64.8
- uterus Q51.0
- uvula Q38.5
- vagina Q52.0
- vas deferens Q55.4
- vein (s) (peripheral) Q27.9
  - brain Q28.3
  - great NEC Q26.8
  - portal Q26.5
- vena cava (inferior) (superior) Q26.8
- vermis of cerebellum Q04.3
- vertebra Q76.49
- vulva Q52.71

Ageusia R43.2

Agitated —*see* condition

Agitation R45.1

Aglossia (congenital) Q38.3

Aglossia-adactylia syndrome Q87.0

Aglycogenosis E74.00

Agnosia (body image) (other senses) (tactile) R48.1
- developmental F88
- verbal R48.1
  - auditory R48.1
    - developmental F80.2
  - developmental F80.2
- visual (object) R48.3

Agoraphobia F40.00
- with panic disorder F40.01
- without panic disorder F40.02

Agrammatism R48.8

Agranulocytopenia —*see* Agranulocytosis

Agranulocytosis (chronic) (cyclical) (genetic) (infantile) (periodic) (pernicious) —*see also* Neutropenia D70.9
- congenital D70.0
- cytoreductive cancer chemotherapy sequela D70.1
- drug-induced D70.2
  - due to cytoreductive cancer chemotherapy D70.1
- due to infection D70.3
- secondary D70.4
  - drug-induced D70.2
    - due to cytoreductive cancer chemotherapy D70.1

Agraphia (absolute) R48.8
- with alexia R48.0
- developmental F81.81

Ague (dumb) —*see* Malaria

Agyria Q04.3

Ahumada-del Castillo syndrome E23.0

Aichomophobia F40.298

AIDS (related complex) B20

Ailment heart —*see* Disease, heart

Ailurophobia F40.218

Ainhum (disease) L94.6

AIPHI (acute idiopathic pulmonary hemorrhage in infants (over 28 days old)) R04.81

Air
- anterior mediastinum J98.2
- compressed, disease T70.3
- conditioner lung or pneumonitis J67.7
- embolism (artery) (cerebral) (any site) T79.0
  - with ectopic or molar pregnancy O08.2
  - due to implanted device NEC —*see* Complications, by site and type, specified NEC
  - following
    - abortion —*see* Abortion by type, complicated by, embolism
    - ectopic or molar pregnancy O08.2
    - infusion, therapeutic injection or transfusion T80.0
  - in pregnancy, childbirth or puerperium —*see* Embolism, obstetric
  - traumatic T79.0
- hunger, psychogenic F45.8
- rarefied, effects of —*see* Effect, adverse, high altitude
- sickness T75.3

Airplane sickness T75.3

Akathisia(drug-induced) (treatment-induced) G25.71
- neuroleptic induced (acute) G25.71

Akinesia R29.898

Akinetic mutism R41.89

Akureyri's disease G93.3

Alactasia, congenital E73.0

Alagille's syndrome Q44.7

Alastrim B03

Albers-Schönberg syndrome Q78.2

Albert's syndrome —*see* Tendinitis, Achilles

Albinism, albino E70.30
- with hematologic abnormality E70.339
  - Chédiak-Higashi syndrome E70.330
  - Hermansky-Pudlak syndrome E70.331
  - other specified E70.338
- I E70.320
- II E70.321
- ocular E70.319
  - autosomal recessive E70.311
  - other specified E70.318
  - X-linked E70.310
- oculocutaneous E70.329
  - other specified E70.328
  - tyrosinase (ty) negative E70.320
  - tyrosinase (ty) positive E70.321
- other specified E70.39

Albinismus E70.30

Albright (-McCune)(-Sternberg) syndrome Q78.1

Albuminous —*see* condition

Albuminuria, albuminuric (acute) (chronic) (subacute) —*see also* Proteinuria R80.9
- complicating pregnancy —*see* Proteinuria, gestational
  - with
    - gestational hypertension —*see* Pre-eclampsia
    - pre-existing hypertension —*see* Hypertension, complicating pregnancy, pre-existing, with, pre-eclampsia

Albuminuria, albuminuric *(continued)*
- gestational —*see* Proteinuria, gestational
  - with
    - gestational hypertension —*see* Pre-eclampsia
    - pre-existing hypertension —*see* Hypertension, complicating pregnancy, pre-existing, with, pre-eclampsia
- orthostatic R80.2
- postural R80.2
- pre-eclamptic —*see* Pre-eclampsia
- scarlatinal A38.8

Albuminurophobia F40.298

Alcaptonuria E70.29

Alcohol, alcoholic, alcohol-induced
- addiction(without remission) F10.20
  - with remission F10.21
- amnestic disorder, persisting F10.96
  - with dependence F10.26
- brain syndrome, chronic F10.97
  - with dependence F10.27
- cardiopathy I42.6
- counseling and surveillance Z71.41
  - family member Z71.42
- delirium (acute) (tremens) (withdrawal) F10.231
  - with intoxication F10.921
    - in
      - abuse F10.121
      - dependence F10.221
- dementia F10.97
  - with dependence F10.27
- deterioration F10.97
  - with dependence F10.27
- hallucinosis (acute) F10.951
  - in
    - abuse F10.151
    - dependence F10.251
- insanity F10.959
- intoxication (acute) (without dependence) F10.129
  - with
    - delirium F10.121
    - dependence F10.229
      - with delirium F10.221
      - uncomplicated F10.220
  - uncomplicated F10.120
- jealousy F10.988
- Korsakoff's, Korsakov's, Korsakow's F10.26
- liver K70.9
  - acute —*see* Disease, liver, alcoholic, hepatitis
- mania (acute) (chronic) F10.959
- paranoia, paranoid (type) psychosis F10.950
- pellagra E52
- poisoning, accidental (acute) NEC —*see* Table of Drugs and Chemicals, alcohol, poisoning
- psychosis —*see* Psychosis, alcoholic
- withdrawal(without convulsions) F10.239
  - with delirium F10.231

Alcoholism (chronic) (without remission) F10.20
- with
  - psychosis —*see* Psychosis, alcoholic
  - remission F10.21
- Korsakov's F10.96
  - with dependence F10.26

Alder (-Reilly) anomaly or syndrome (leukocyte granulation) D72.0

Aldosteronism E26.9
- familial(type I) E26.02
- glucocorticoid-remediable E26.02

Aldosteronism *(continued)*
- primary(due to (bilateral) adrenal hyperplasia) E26.09
- primary NEC E26.09
- secondary E26.1
- specified NEC E26.89

Aldosteronoma D44.10

Aldrich (-Wiskott) syndrome (eczema-thrombocytopenia) D82.0

Alektorophobia F40.218

Aleppo boil B55.1

Aleukemic —*see* condition

Aleukia
- congenital D70.0
- hemorrhagica D61.9
  - congenital D61.09
- splenica D73.1

Alexia R48.0
- developmental F81.0
- secondary to organic lesion R48.0

Algoneurodystrophy M89.00
- ankle M89.07-
- foot M89.07-
- forearm M89.03-
- hand M89.04-
- lower leg M89.06-
- multiple sites M89.0-
- shoulder M89.01-
- specified site NEC M89.08
- thigh M89.05-
- upper arm M89.02-

Algophobia F40.298

Alienation, mental —*see* Psychosis

Alkalemia E87.3

Alkalosis E87.3
- metabolic E87.3
  - with respiratory acidosis E87.4
- respiratory E87.3

Alkaptonuria E70.29

Allen-Masters syndrome N83.8

Allergy, allergic (reaction) (to) T78.40
- air-borne substance NEC (rhinitis) J30.89
- alveolitis (extrinsic) J67.9
  - due to
    - Aspergillus clavatus J67.4
    - Cryptostroma corticale J67.6
    - organisms(fungal, thermophilic actinomycete) growing in ventilation (air conditioning) systems J67.7
  - specified type NEC J67.8
- anaphylactic reaction or shock T78.2
- angioneurotic edema T78.3
- animal (dander) (epidermal) (hair) (rhinitis) J30.81
- bee sting(anaphylactic shock) —*see* Toxicity, venom, arthropod, bee
- biological —*see* Allergy, drug
- colitis K52.2
- dander (animal) (rhinitis) J30.81
- dandruff (rhinitis) J30.81
- dental restorative material (existing) K08.55
- dermatitis —*see* Dermatitis, contact, allergic
- diathesis —*see* History, allergy
- drug, medicament & biological (any) (external) (internal) T78.40
  - correct substance properly administered —*see* Table of Drugs and Chemicals, by drug, adverse effect
  - wrong substance given or taken NEC (by accident) —*see* Table of Drugs and Chemicals, by drug, poisoning

Allergy, allergic *(continued)*
- due to pollen J30.1
- dust (house) (stock) (rhinitis) J30.89
  - with asthma —*see* Asthma, allergic extrinsic
- eczema —*see* Dermatitis, contact, allergic
- epidermal (animal) (rhinitis) J30.81
- feathers (rhinitis) J30.89
- food (any) (ingested) NEC T78.1
  - anaphylactic shock —*see* Shock, anaphylactic, due to food
  - dermatitis —*see* Dermatitis, due to, food
  - dietary counseling and surveillance Z71.3
  - in contact with skin L23.6
  - rhinitis J30.5
  - status(without reaction) Z91.018
    - eggs Z91.012
    - milk products Z91.011
    - peanuts Z91.010
    - seafood Z91.013
    - specified NEC Z91.018
- gastrointestinal K52.2
- grain J30.1
- grass(hay fever) (pollen) J30.1
  - asthma —*see* Asthma, allergic extrinsic
- hair (animal) (rhinitis) J30.81
- history (of) —*see* History, allergy
- horse serum —*see* Allergy, serum
- inhalant (rhinitis) J30.89
  - pollen J30.1
- kapok (rhinitis) J30.89
- medicine —*see* Allergy, drug
- milk protein K52.2
- nasal, seasonal due to pollen J30.1
- pneumonia J82
- pollen (any) (hay fever) J30.1
  - asthma —*see* Asthma, allergic extrinsic
- primrose J30.1
- primula J30.1
- purpura D69.0
- ragweed(hay fever) (pollen) J30.1
  - asthma —*see* Asthma, allergic extrinsic
- rose (pollen) J30.1
- seasonal NEC J30.2
- Senecio jacobae (pollen) J30.1
- serum —*see also* Reaction, serum T80.69
  - anaphylactic shock T80.59
- shock (anaphylactic) T78.2
  - due to
    - administration of blood and blood products T80.51
    - adverse effect of correct medicinal substance properly administered T88.6
    - immunization T80.52
    - serum NEC T80.59
    - vaccination T80.52
- specific NEC T78.49
- tree (any) (hay fever) (pollen) J30.1
  - asthma —*see* Asthma, allergic extrinsic
- upper respiratory J30.9
- urticaria L50.0
- vaccine —*see* Allergy, serum
- wheat —*see* Allergy, food

Allescheriasis B48.2

Alligator skin disease Q80.9

Allocheiria, allochiria R20.8

Almeida's disease —*see* Paracoccidioidomycosis

Alopecia (hereditaria) (seborrheica) L65.9

Alopecia *(continued)*
  androgenic L64.9
    drug-induced L64.0
    specified NEC L64.8
  areata L63.9
    ophiasis L63.2
    specified NEC L63.8
    totalis L63.0
    universalis L63.1
  cicatricial L66.9
    specified NEC L66.8
  circumscripta L63.9
  congenital, congenitalis Q84.0
  due to cytotoxic drugs NEC L65.8
  mucinosa L65.2
  postinfective NEC L65.8
  postpartum L65.0
  premature L64.8
  specific (syphilitic) A51.32
  specified NEC L65.8
  syphilitic (secondary) A51.32
  totalis (capitis) L63.0
  universalis(entire body) L63.1
  X-ray L58.1
Alpers' disease G31.81
Alpine sickness T70.29
Alport syndrome Q87.81
ALTE (apparent life threatening event) in newborn and infant R68.13
Alteration (of), **Altered**
  awareness, transient R40.4
  mental status R41.82
  pattern of family relationships affecting child Z62.898
  sensation
    following
      cerebrovascular disease I69.998
        cerebral infarction I69.398
        intracerebral hemorrhage I69.198
        nontraumatic intracranial hemorrhage NEC I69.298
        specified disease NEC I69.898
        subarachnoid hemorrhage I69.098
Alternating —*see* condition
Altitude, high (effects) —*see* Effect, adverse, high altitude
Aluminosis (of lung) J63.0
Alveolitis
  allergic (extrinsic) —*see* Pneumonitis, hypersensitivity
  due to
    Aspergillus clavatus J67.4
    Cryptostroma corticale J67.6
  fibrosing (cryptogenic) (idiopathic) J84.112
  jaw M27.3
  sicca dolorosa M27.3
Alveolus, alveolar —*see* condition
Alymphocytosis D72.810
  thymic(with immunodeficiency) D82.1
Alymphoplasia, thymic D82.1
Alzheimer's disease or sclerosis —*see* Disease, Alzheimer's
Amastia (with nipple present) Q83.8
  with absent nipple Q83.0
Amathophobia F40.228
Amaurosis (acquired) (congenital) —*see also* Blindness
  fugax G45.3
  hysterical F44.6
  Leber's congenital H35.50
  uremic —*see* Uremia
Amaurotic idiocy (infantile) (juvenile) (late) E75.4
Amaxophobia F40.248
Ambiguous genitalia Q56.4
Amblyopia (congenital) (ex anopsia) (partial) (suppression) H53.00-
  anisometropic —*see* Amblyopia, refractive
  deprivation H53.01-
  hysterical F44.6
  nocturnal —*see also* Blindness, night
    vitamin A deficiency E50.5
  refractive H53.02-
  strabismic H53.03-
  tobacco H53.8
  toxic NEC H53.8
  uremic —*see* Uremia
Ameba, amebic (histolytica) —*see also* Amebiasis
  abscess (liver) A06.4
Amebiasis A06.9
  with abscess —*see* Abscess, amebic
  acute A06.0
  chronic (intestine) A06.1
    with abscess —*see* Abscess, amebic
  cutaneous A06.7
  cutis A06.7
  cystitis A06.81
  genitourinary tract NEC A06.82
  hepatic —*see* Abscess, liver, amebic
  intestine A06.0
  nondysenteric colitis A06.2
  skin A06.7
  specified site NEC A06.89
Ameboma (of intestine) A06.3
Amelia Q73.0
  lower limb —*see* Agenesis, leg
  upper limb —*see* Agenesis, arm
Ameloblastoma —*see also* Cyst, calcifying odontogenic
  long bones C40.9-
    lower limb C40.2-
    upper limb C40.0-
  malignant C41.1
    jaw (bone) (lower) C41.1
      upper C41.0
  tibial C40.2-
Amelogenesis imperfecta K00.5
  nonhereditaria (segmentalis) K00.4
Amenorrhea N91.2
  hyperhormonal E28.8
  primary N91.0
  secondary N91.1
Amentia —*see* Disability, intellectual
  Meynert's (nonalcoholic) F04
American
  leishmaniasis B55.2
  mountain tick fever A93.2
Ametropia —*see* Disorder, refraction
Amianthosis J61
Amimia R48.8
Amino-acid disorder E72.9
  anemia D53.0
Aminoacidopathy E72.9
Aminoaciduria E72.9
Amnes(t)**ic syndrome** (post-traumatic) F04
  induced by
    alcohol F10.96
      with dependence F10.26
    psychoactive NEC F19.96
      with
        abuse F19.16
        dependence F19.26
    sedative F13.96
      with dependence F13.26
Amnesia R41.3
  anterograde R41.1
  auditory R48.8
  dissociative F44.0
  hysterical F44.0
  postictal in epilepsy —*see* Epilepsy
  psychogenic F44.0
  retrograde R41.2
  transient global G45.4
Amnion, amniotic —*see* condition
Amnionitis —*see* Pregnancy, complicated by
Amok F68.8
Amoral traits F60.89
Ampulla
  lower esophagus K22.8
  phrenic K22.8
Amputation —*see also* Absence, by site, acquired
  neuroma (postoperative) (traumatic) —*see* Complications, amputation stump, neuroma
  stump (surgical)
    abnormal, painful, or with complication (late) —*see* Complications, amputation stump
    healed or old NOS Z89.9
  traumatic (complete) (partial)
    arm (upper) (complete) S48.91-
      at
        elbow S58.01-
          partial S58.02-
        shoulder joint (complete) S48.01-
          partial S48.02-
      between
        elbow and wrist (complete) S58.11-
          partial S58.12-
        shoulder and elbow (complete) S48.11-
          partial S48.12-
      partial S48.92-
    breast (complete) S28.21-
      partial S28.22-
    clitoris (complete) S38.211
      partial S38.212
    ear (complete) S08.11-
      partial S08.12-
    finger (complete) (metacarpophalangeal) S68.11-
      index S68.11-
      little S68.11-
      middle S68.11-
      partial S68.12-
        index S68.12-
        little S68.12-
        middle S68.12-
        ring S68.12-
      ring S68.11-
      thumb —*see* Amputation, traumatic, thumb
      transphalangeal (complete) S68.61-
        index S68.61-
        little S68.61-
        middle S68.61-
        partial S68.62-
          index S68.62-
          little S68.62-
          middle S68.62-
          ring S68.62-
        ring S68.61-
    foot (complete) S98.91-
      at ankle level S98.01-
        partial S98.02-
      midfoot S98.31-
        partial S98.32-
      partial S98.92-
Amputation *(continued)*
  traumatic *(continued)*
    forearm (complete) S58.91-
      at elbow level (complete) S58.01-
        partial S58.02-
      between elbow and wrist (complete) S58.11-
        partial S58.12-
      partial S58.92-
    genital organ (s) (external)
      female (complete) S38.211
        partial S38.212
      male
        penis (complete) S38.221
          partial S38.222
        scrotum (complete) S38.231
          partial S38.232
        testes (complete) S38.231
          partial S38.232
    hand (complete) (wrist level) S68.41-
      finger (s) alone —*see* Amputation, traumatic, finger
      partial S68.42-
      thumb alone —*see* Amputation, traumatic, thumb
      transmetacarpal (complete) S68.71-
        partial S68.72-
    head
      ear —*see* Amputation, traumatic, ear
      nose (partial) S08.812
        complete S08.811
      part S08.89
        scalp S08.0
    hip(and thigh) (complete) S78.91-
      at hip joint (complete) S78.01-
        partial S78.02-
      between hip and knee (complete) S78.11-
        partial S78.12-
      partial S78.92-
    labium (majus) (minus) (complete) S38.21-
      partial S38.21-
    leg (lower) S88.91-
      at knee level S88.01-
        partial S88.02-
      between knee and ankle S88.11-
        partial S88.12-
      partial S88.92-
    nose (partial) S08.812
      complete S08.811
    penis (complete) S38.221
      partial S38.222
    scrotum (complete) S38.231
      partial S38.232
    shoulder —*see* Amputation, traumatic, arm
      at shoulder joint —*see* Amputation, traumatic, arm, at shoulder joint
    testes (complete) S38.231
      partial S38.232
    thigh —*see* Amputation, traumatic, hip
    thorax, part of S28.1
      breast —*see* Amputation, traumatic, breast
    thumb (complete) (metacarpophalangeal) S68.01-
      partial S68.02-
      transphalangeal (complete) S68.51-
        partial S68.52-
    toe (lesser) S98.13-
      great S98.11-
        partial S98.12-
      more than one S98.21-
        partial S98.22-
      partial S98.14-

Amputation *(continued)*
  traumatic *(continued)*
    vulva (complete) S38.211
      partial S38.212
Amputee (bilateral) (old) Z89.9
Amsterdam dwarfism Q87.1
Amusia R48.8
  developmental F80.89
Amyelencephalus, amyelencephaly Q00.0
Amyelia Q06.0
Amygdalitis —*see* Tonsillitis
Amygdalolith J35.8
Amyloid heart (disease) E85.4 *[I43]*
Amyloidosis (generalized) (primary) E85.9
  with lung involvement E85.4 *[J99]*
  familial E85.2
  genetic E85.2
  heart E85.4 *[I43]*
  hemodialysis-associated E85.3
  liver E85.4 *[K77]*
  localized E85.4
  neuropathic heredofamilial E85.1
  non-neuropathic heredofamilial E85.0
  organ limited E85.4
  Portuguese E85.1
  pulmonary E85.4 *[J99]*
  secondary systemic E85.3
  skin (lichen) (macular) E85.4 *[L99]*
  specified NEC E85.8
  subglottic E85.4 *[J99]*
Amylopectinosis(brancher enzyme deficiency) E74.03
Amylophagia —*see* Pica
Amyoplasia congenita Q79.8
Amyotonia M62.89
  congenita G70.2
Amyotrophia, amyotrophy, amyotrophic G71.8
  congenita Q79.8
  diabetic —*see* Diabetes, amyotrophy
  lateral sclerosis G12.21
  neuralgic G54.5
  spinal progressive G12.21
Anacidity, gastric K31.83
  psychogenic F45.8
Anaerosis of newborn P28.89
Analbuminemia E88.09
Analgesia —*see* Anesthesia
Analphalipoproteinemia E78.6
Anaphylactic
  purpura D69.0
  shock or reaction —*see* Shock, anaphylactic
Anaphylactoid shock or reaction —*see* Shock, anaphylactic
Anaphylactoid syndrome of pregnancy O88.01-
Anaphylaxis —*see* Shock, anaphylactic
Anaplasia cervix —*see also* Dysplasia, cervix N87.9
Anaplasmosis, human A77.49
Anarthria R47.1
Anasarca R60.1
  cardiac —*see* Failure, heart, congestive
  lung J18.2
  newborn P83.2
  nutritional E43
  pulmonary J18.2
  renal N04.9

Anastomosis
  aneurysmal —*see* Aneurysm
  arteriovenous ruptured brain I60.8
  intestinal K63.89
    complicated NEC K91.89
      involving urinary tract N99.89
  retinal and choroidal vessels (congenital) Q14.8
Anatomical narrow angle H40.03-
Ancylostoma, ancylostomiasis (braziliense) (caninum) (ceylanicum) (duodenale) B76.0
  Necator americanus B76.1
Andersen's disease (glycogen storage) E74.09
Anderson-Fabry disease E75.21
Andes disease T70.29
Andrews' disease (bacterid) L08.89
Androblastoma
  benign
    specified site —*see* Neoplasm, benign, by site
    unspecified site
      female D27.9
      male D29.20
  malignant
    specified site —*see* Neoplasm, malignant, by site
    unspecified site
      female C56.9
      male C62.90
  specified site —*see* Neoplasm, uncertain behavior, by site
  tubular
    with lipid storage
      specified site —*see* Neoplasm, benign, by site
      unspecified site
        female D27.9
        male D29.20
    specified site —*see* Neoplasm, benign, by site
    unspecified site
      female D27.9
      male D29.20
  unspecified site
    female D39.10
    male D40.10
Androgen insensitivity syndrome —*see also* Syndrome, androgen insensitivity E34.50
Androgen resistance syndrome —*see also* Syndrome, androgen insensitivity E34.50
Android pelvis Q74.2
  with disproportion (fetopelvic) O33.3
    causing obstructed labor O65.3
Androphobia F40.290
Anectasis, pulmonary (newborn) —*see* Atelectasis
Anemia (essential) (general) (hemoglobin deficiency) (infantile) (primary) (profound) D64.9
  with(due to) (in)
    disorder of
      anaerobic glycolysis D55.2
      pentose phosphate pathway D55.1
    koilonychia D50.9
  achlorhydric D50.8
  achrestic D53.1
  Addison (-Biermer) (pernicious) D51.0
  agranulocytic —*see* Agranulocytosis
  amino-acid-deficiency D53.0

Anemia *(continued)*
  aplastic D61.9
    congenital D61.09
    drug-induced D61.1
    due to
      drugs D61.1
      external agents NEC D61.2
      infection D61.2
      radiation D61.2
    idiopathic D61.3
    red cell (pure) D60.9
      chronic D60.0
      congenital D61.01
      specified type NEC D60.8
      transient D60.1
    specified type NEC D61.89
    toxic D61.2
  aregenerative
    congenital D61.09
  asiderotic D50.9
  atypical (primary) D64.9
  Baghdad spring D55.0
  Balantidium coli A07.0
  Biermer's (pernicious) D51.0
  blood loss (chronic) D50.0
    acute D62
  bothriocephalus B70.0 *[D63.8]*
  brickmaker's B76.9 *[D63.8]*
  cerebral I67.89
  childhood D58.9
  chlorotic D50.8
  chronic
    blood loss D50.0
    hemolytic D58.9
      idiopathic D59.9
    simple D53.9
  chronica congenita aregenerativa D61.09
  combined system disease NEC D51.0 *[G32.0]*
    due to dietary vitamin B12 deficiency D51.3 *[G32.0]*
  complicating pregnancy, childbirth or puerperium —*see* Pregnancy, complicated by (management affected by), anemia
  congenital P61.4
    aplastic D61.09
    due to isoimmunization NOS P55.9
    dyserythropoietic, dyshematopoietic D64.4
    following fetal blood loss P61.3
    Heinz body D58.2
    hereditary hemolytic NOS D58.9
    pernicious D51.0
    spherocytic D58.0
  Cooley's (erythroblastic) D56.1
  cytogenic D51.0
  deficiency D53.9
    2, 3 diphosphoglycurate mutase D55.2
    2, 3 PG D55.2
    6 phosphogluconate dehydrogenase D55.1
    6-PGD D55.1
    amino-acid D53.0
    combined B12 and folate D53.1
    enzyme D55.9
      drug-induced (hemolytic) D59.2
      glucose-6-phosphate dehydrogenase(G6PD) D55.0
      glycolytic D55.2
      nucleotide metabolism D55.3
      related to hexose monophosphate (HMP) shunt pathway NEC D55.1
      specified type NEC D55.8
    erythrocytic glutathione D55.1
    folate D52.9
      dietary D52.0
      drug-induced D52.1

Anemia *(continued)*
  deficiency *(continued)*
    folic acid D52.9
      dietary D52.0
      drug-induced D52.1
    G SH D55.1
    GGS-R D55.1
    glucose-6-phosphate dehydrogenase D55.0
    glutathione reductase D55.1
    glyceraldehyde phosphate dehydrogenase D55.2
    G6PD D55.0
    hexokinase D55.2
    iron D50.9
      secondary to blood loss (chronic) D50.0
    nutritional D53.9
      with
        poor iron absorption D50.8
        specified deficiency NEC D53.8
    phosphofructo-aldolase D55.2
    phosphoglycerate kinase D55.2
    PK D55.2
    protein D53.0
    pyruvate kinase D55.2
    transcobalamin II D51.2
    triose-phosphate isomerase D55.2
    vitamin B12 NOS D51.9
      dietary D51.3
      due to
        intrinsic factor deficiency D51.0
        selective vitamin B12 malabsorption with proteinuria D51.1
      pernicious D51.0
      specified type NEC D51.8
  Diamond-Blackfan(congenital hypoplastic) D61.01
  dibothriocephalus B70.0 *[D63.8]*
  dimorphic D53.1
  diphasic D53.1
  Diphyllobothrium (Dibothriocephalus) B70.0 *[D63.8]*
  due to (in) (with)
    antineoplastic chemotherapy D64.81
    blood loss (chronic) D50.0
      acute D62
    chemotherapy, antineoplastic D64.81
    chronic disease classified elsewhere NEC D63.8
    chronic kidney disease D63.1
    deficiency
      amino-acid D53.0
      copper D53.8
      folate(folic acid) D52.9
        dietary D52.0
        drug-induced D52.1
      molybdenum D53.8
      protein D53.0
      zinc D53.8
    dietary vitamin B12 deficiency D51.3
    disorder of
      glutathione metabolism D55.1
      nucleotide metabolism D55.3
    drug —*see* Anemia, by type —*see also* Table of Drugs and Chemicals
    end stage renal disease D63.1
    enzyme disorder D55.9
    fetal blood loss P61.3
    fish tapeworm(D.latum) infestation B70.0 *[D63.8]*
    hemorrhage (chronic) D50.0
      acute D62
    impaired absorption D50.9

Anemia *(continued)*
- due to *(continued)*
  - loss of blood (chronic) D50.0
    - acute D62
  - myxedema E03.9 *[D63.8]*
  - Necator americanus B76.1 *[D63.8]*
  - prematurity P61.2
  - selective vitamin B12
    - malabsorption with proteinuria D51.1
  - transcobalamin II deficiency D51.2
- Dyke-Young type (secondary) (symptomatic) D59.1
- dyserythropoietic (congenital) D64.4
- dyshematopoietic (congenital) D64.4
- Egyptian B76.9 *[D63.8]*
- elliptocytosis —*see* Elliptocytosis
- enzyme-deficiency, drug-induced D59.2
- epidemic —*see also* Ancylostomiasis B76.9 *[D63.8]*
- erythroblastic
  - familial D56.1
  - newborn —*see also* Disease, hemolytic P55.9
  - of childhood D56.1
- erythrocytic glutathione deficiency D55.1
- erythropoietin-resistant anemia(EPO resistant anemia) D63.1
- Faber's(achlorhydric anemia) D50.9
- factitious(self-induced blood letting) D50.0
- familial erythroblastic D56.1
- Fanconi's(congenital pancytopenia) D61.09
- favism D55.0
- fish tapeworm(D. latum) infestation B70.0 *[D63.8]*
- folate(folic acid) deficiency D52.9
- glucose-6-phosphate dehydrogenase(G6PD) deficiency D55.0
- glutathione-reductase deficiency D55.1
- goat's milk D52.0
- granulocytic —*see* Agranulocytosis
- Heinz body, congenital D58.2
- hemolytic D58.9
  - acquired D59.9
    - with hemoglobinuria NEC D59.6
    - autoimmune NEC D59.1
    - infectious D59.4
    - specified type NEC D59.8
    - toxic D59.4
  - acute D59.9
    - due to enzyme deficiency
      - specified type NEC D55.8
    - Lederer's D59.1
  - autoimmune D59.1
    - drug-induced D59.0
  - chronic D58.9
    - idiopathic D59.9
  - cold type (secondary) (symptomatic) D59.1
  - congenital (spherocytic) —*see* Spherocytosis
  - due to
    - cardiac conditions D59.4
    - drugs (nonautoimmune) D59.2
      - autoimmune D59.0
    - enzyme disorder D55.9
      - drug-induced D59.2
    - presence of shunt or other internal prosthetic device D59.4
  - familial D58.9
  - hereditary D58.9
    - due to enzyme disorder D55.9
      - specified type NEC D55.8
    - specified type NEC D58.8

Anemia *(continued)*
- hemolytic *(continued)*
  - idiopathic (chronic) D59.9
  - mechanical D59.4
  - microangiopathic D59.4
  - nonautoimmune D59.4
    - drug-induced D59.2
  - nonspherocytic
    - congenital or hereditary NEC D55.8
      - glucose-6-phosphate dehydrogenase deficiency D55.0
      - pyruvate kinase deficiency D55.2
      - type
        - I D55.1
        - II D55.2
    - type
      - I D55.1
      - II D55.2
  - secondary D59.4
    - autoimmune D59.1
  - specified (hereditary) type NEC D58.8
  - Stransky-Regala type —*see also* Hemoglobinopathy D58.8
  - symptomatic D59.4
    - autoimmune D59.1
  - toxic D59.4
  - warm type (secondary) (symptomatic) D59.1
- hemorrhagic (chronic) D50.0
  - acute D62
- Herrick's D57.1
- hexokinase deficiency D55.2
- hookworm B76.9 *[D63.8]*
- hypochromic (idiopathic) (microcytic) (normoblastic) D50.9
  - due to blood loss (chronic) D50.0
    - acute D62
  - familial sex-linked D64.0
  - pyridoxine-responsive D64.3
  - sideroblastic, sex-linked D64.0
- hypoplasia, red blood cells D61.9
  - congenital or familial D61.01
- hypoplastic (idiopathic) D61.9
  - congenital or familial(of childhood) D61.01
- hypoproliferative (refractive) D61.9
- idiopathic D64.9
  - aplastic D61.3
  - hemolytic, chronic D59.9
- in(due to) (with)
  - chronic kidney disease D63.1
  - end stage renal disease D63.1
  - failure, kidney (renal) D63.1
  - neoplastic disease —*see also* Neoplasm D63.0
- intertropical —*see also* Ancylostomiasis D63.8
- iron deficiency D50.9
  - secondary to blood loss (chronic) D50.0
    - acute D62
  - specified type NEC D50.8
- Joseph-Diamond-Blackfan (congenital hypoplastic) D61.01
- Lederer's (hemolytic) D59.1
- leukoerythroblastic D61.82
- macrocytic D53.9
  - nutritional D52.0
  - tropical D52.8
- malarial —*see also* Malaria B54 *[D63.8]*
- malignant (progressive) D51.0
- malnutrition D53.9
- marsh —*see also* Malaria B54 D63.8
- Mediterranean(with other hemoglobinopathy) D56.9

Anemia *(continued)*
- megaloblastic D53.1
  - combined B12 and folate deficiency D53.1
  - hereditary D51.1
  - nutritional D52.0
  - orotic aciduria D53.0
  - refractory D53.1
  - specified type NEC D53.1
- megalocytic D53.1
- microcytic (hypochromic) D50.9
  - due to blood loss (chronic) D50.0
    - acute D62
  - familial D56.8
- microdrepanocytosis D57.40
- microelliptopoikilocytic (Rietti-Greppi- Micheli) D56.9
- miner's B76.9 *[D63.8]*
- myelodysplastic D46.9
- myelofibrosis D75.81
- myelogenous D64.89
- myelopathic D64.89
- myelophthisic D61.82
- myeloproliferative D47.Z9
- newborn P61.4
  - due to
    - ABO (antibodies, isoimmunization, maternal/fetal incompatibility) P55.1
    - Rh(antibodies, isoimmunization, maternal/fetal incompatibility) P55.0
  - following fetal blood loss P61.3
  - posthemorrhagic (fetal) P61.3
- nonspherocytic hemolytic —*see* Anemia, hemolytic, nonspherocytic
- normocytic (infectional) D64.9
  - due to blood loss (chronic) D50.0
    - acute D62
  - myelophthisic D61.82
- nutritional (deficiency) D53.9
  - with
    - poor iron absorption D50.8
    - specified deficiency NEC D53.8
  - megaloblastic D52.0
- of prematurity P61.2
- orotaciduric (congenital) (hereditary) D53.0
- osteosclerotic D64.89
- ovalocytosis (hereditary) —*see* Elliptocytosis
- paludal —*see also* Malaria B54 *[D63.8]*
- pernicious (congenital) (malignant) (progressive) D51.0
- pleochromic D64.89
  - of sprue D52.8
- posthemorrhagic (chronic) D50.0
  - acute D62
  - newborn P61.3
- postoperative (postprocedural)
  - due to (acute) blood loss D62
    - chronic blood loss D50.0
  - specified NEC D64.9
- postpartum O90.81
- pressure D64.89
- progressive D64.9
  - malignant D51.0
  - pernicious D51.0
- protein-deficiency D53.0
- pseudoleukemica infantum D64.89
- pure red cell D60.9
  - congenital D61.01
- pyridoxine-responsive D64.3
- pyruvate kinase deficiency D55.2
- refractory D46.4
  - with
    - excess of blasts D46.20
      - 1(RAEB 1) D46.21
      - 2(RAEB 2) D46.22
      - in transformation(RAEB T) —*see* Leukemia, acute myeloblastic

Anemia *(continued)*
- refractory *(continued)*
  - with *(continued)*
    - hemochromatosis D46.1
    - sideroblasts (ring) (RARS) D46.1
  - megaloblastic D53.1
  - sideroblastic D46.1
  - sideropenic D50.9
  - without ring sideroblasts, so stated D46.0
  - without sideroblasts without excess of blasts D46.0
- Rietti-Greppi-Micheli D56.9
- scorbutic D53.2
- secondary to
  - blood loss (chronic) D50.0
    - acute D62
  - hemorrhage (chronic) D50.0
    - acute D62
- semiplastic D61.89
- sickle-cell —*see* Disease, sickle-cell
- sideroblastic D64.3
  - hereditary D64.0
  - hypochromic, sex-linked D64.0
  - pyridoxine-responsive NEC D64.3
  - refractory D46.1
  - secondary(due to)
    - disease D64.1
    - drugs and toxins D64.2
  - specified type NEC D64.3
- sideropenic (refractory) D50.9
  - due to blood loss (chronic) D50.0
    - acute D62
- simple chronic D53.9
- specified type NEC D64.89
- spherocytic (hereditary) —*see* Spherocytosis
- splenic D64.89
- splenomegalic D64.89
- stomatocytosis D58.8
- syphilitic (acquired) (late) A52.79 *[D63.8]*
- target cell D64.89
- thalassemia D56.9
- thrombocytopenic —*see* Thrombocytopenia
- toxic D61.2
- tropical B76.9 *[D63.8]*
  - macrocytic D52.8
- tuberculous A18.89 *[D63.8]*
- vegan D51.3
- vitamin
  - B6-responsive D64.3
  - B12 deficiency (dietary) pernicious D51.0
- von Jaksch's D64.89
- Witts'(achlorhydric anemia) D50.8

Anemophobia F40.228

Anencephalus, anencephaly Q00.0

Anergasia —*see* Psychosis, organic

Anesthesia, anesthetic R20.0
- complication or reaction NEC —*see also* Complications, anesthesia T88.59
  - due to
    - correct substance properly administered —*see* Table of Drugs and Chemicals, by drug, adverse effect
    - overdose or wrong substance given —*see* Table of Drugs and Chemicals, by drug, poisoning
- cornea H18.81-
- dissociative F44.6
- functional (hysterical) F44.6
- hyperesthetic, thalamic G89.0
- hysterical F44.6
- local skin lesion R20.0
- sexual (psychogenic) F52.1
- shock (due to) T88.2

- **Anesthesia, anesthetic** *(continued)*
  - skin R20.0
  - testicular N50.9
- **Anetoderma** (maculosum) (of) L90.8
  - Jadassohn-Pellizzari L90.2
  - Schweniger-Buzzi L90.1
- **Aneurin deficiency** E51.9
- **Aneurysm** (anastomotic) (artery) (cirsoid) (diffuse) (false) (fusiform) (multiple) (saccular) I72.9
  - abdominal (aorta) I71.4
    - ruptured I71.3
    - syphilitic A52.01
  - aorta, aortic (nonsyphilitic) I71.9
    - abdominal I71.4
      - ruptured I71.3
    - arch I71.2
      - ruptured I71.1
    - arteriosclerotic I71.9
      - ruptured I71.8
    - ascending I71.2
      - ruptured I71.1
    - congenital Q25.4
    - descending I71.9
      - abdominal I71.4
        - ruptured I71.3
      - ruptured I71.8
      - thoracic I71.2
        - ruptured I71.1
    - ruptured I71.8
    - sinus, congenital Q25.4
    - syphilitic A52.01
    - thoracic I71.2
      - ruptured I71.1
    - thoracoabdominal I71.6
      - ruptured I71.5
    - thorax, thoracic (arch) I71.2
      - ruptured I71.1
    - transverse I71.2
      - ruptured I71.1
    - valve (heart) —*see also* Endocarditis, aortic I35.8
  - arteriosclerotic I72.9
    - cerebral I67.1
      - ruptured —*see* Hemorrhage, intracranial, subarachnoid
  - arteriovenous (congenital) —*see also* Malformation, arteriovenous
    - acquired I77.0
      - brain I67.1
      - coronary I25.41
      - pulmonary I28.0
    - brain Q28.2
      - ruptured I60.8
    - peripheral —*see* Malformation, arteriovenous, peripheral
    - precerebral vessels Q28.0
    - specified site NEC —*see also* Malformation, arteriovenous
      - acquired I77.0
  - basal —*see* Aneurysm, brain
  - berry (congenital) (nonruptured) I67.1
    - ruptured I60.7
  - brain I67.1
    - arteriosclerotic I67.1
      - ruptured —*see* Hemorrhage, intracranial, subarachnoid
    - arteriovenous (congenital) (nonruptured) Q28.2
      - acquired I67.1
        - ruptured I60.8
      - ruptured I60.8
    - berry (congenital) (nonruptured) I67.1
      - ruptured —*see also* Hemorrhage, intracranial, subarachnoid I60.7
    - congenital Q28.3
      - ruptured I60.7
    - meninges I67.1
      - ruptured I60.8
- **Aneurysm** *(continued)*
  - brain *(continued)*
    - miliary (congenital) (nonruptured) I67.1
      - ruptured —*see also* Hemorrhage, intracranial, subarachnoid I60.7
    - mycotic I33.0
    - ruptured —*see* Hemorrhage, intracranial, subarachnoid
    - syphilitic (hemorrhage) A52.05
  - cardiac (false) —*see also* Aneurysm, heart I25.3
  - carotid artery (common) (external) I72.0
    - internal (intracranial) I67.1
      - extracranial portion I72.0
    - ruptured into brain I60.0-
    - syphilitic A52.09
      - intracranial A52.05
  - cavernous sinus I67.1
    - arteriovenous (congenital) (nonruptured) Q28.3
      - ruptured I60.8
  - celiac I72.8
  - central nervous system, syphilitic A52.05
  - cerebral —*see* Aneurysm, brain
  - chest —*see* Aneurysm, thorax
  - circle of Willis I67.1
    - congenital Q28.3
      - ruptured I60.6
    - ruptured I60.6
  - common iliac artery I72.3
  - congenital (peripheral) Q27.8
    - brain Q28.3
      - ruptured I60.7
    - coronary Q24.5
    - digestive system Q27.8
    - lower limb Q27.8
    - pulmonary Q25.79
    - retina Q14.1
    - specified site NEC Q27.8
    - upper limb Q27.8
  - conjunctiva —*see* Abnormality, conjunctiva, vascular
  - conus arteriosus —*see* Aneurysm, heart
  - coronary (arteriosclerotic) (artery) I25.41
    - arteriovenous, congenital Q24.5
    - congenital Q24.5
    - ruptured —*see* Infarct, myocardium
    - syphilitic A52.06
    - vein I25.89
  - cylindroid (aorta) I71.9
    - ruptured I71.8
    - syphilitic A52.01
  - ductus arteriosus Q25.0
  - endocardial, infective(any valve) I33.0
  - femoral (artery) (ruptured) I72.4
  - gastroduodenal I72.8
  - gastroepiploic I72.8
  - heart (wall) (chronic or with a stated duration of over 4 weeks) I25.3
    - valve —*see* Endocarditis
  - hepatic I72.8
  - iliac (common) (artery) (ruptured) I72.3
  - infective I72.9
    - endocardial(any valve) I33.0
  - innominate (nonsyphilitic) I72.8
    - syphilitic A52.09
  - interauricular septum —*see* Aneurysm, heart
  - interventricular septum —*see* Aneurysm, heart
  - intrathoracic (nonsyphilitic) I71.2
    - ruptured I71.1
    - syphilitic A52.01
- **Aneurysm** *(continued)*
  - lower limb I72.4
  - lung(pulmonary artery) I28.1
  - mediastinal (nonsyphilitic) I72.8
    - syphilitic A52.09
  - miliary (congenital) I67.1
    - ruptured —*see* Hemorrhage, intracerebral, subarachnoid, intracranial
  - mitral (heart) (valve) I34.8
  - mural —*see* Aneurysm, heart
  - mycotic I72.9
    - endocardial(any valve) I33.0
    - ruptured, brain —*see* Hemorrhage, intracerebral, subarachnoid
  - myocardium —*see* Aneurysm, heart
  - neck I72.0
  - pancreaticoduodenal I72.8
  - patent ductus arteriosus Q25.0
  - peripheral NEC I72.8
    - congenital Q27.8
      - digestive system Q27.8
      - lower limb Q27.8
      - specified site NEC Q27.8
      - upper limb Q27.8
  - popliteal (artery) (ruptured) I72.4
  - precerebral, congenital (nonruptured) Q28.1
  - pulmonary I28.1
    - arteriovenous Q25.72
      - acquired I28.0
    - syphilitic A52.09
    - valve (heart) —*see* Endocarditis, pulmonary
  - racemose (peripheral) I72.9
    - congenital —*see* Aneurysm, congenital
  - radial I72.1
  - Rasmussen NEC A15.0
  - renal (artery) I72.2
  - retina —*see also* Disorder, retina, microaneurysms
    - congenital Q14.1
    - diabetic —*see* Diabetes, microaneurysms, retinal
  - sinus of Valsalva Q25.4
  - specified NEC I72.8
  - spinal (cord) I72.8
    - syphilitic (hemorrhage) A52.09
  - splenic I72.8
  - subclavian (artery) (ruptured) I72.8
    - syphilitic A52.09
  - superior mesenteric I72.8
  - syphilitic (aorta) A52.01
    - central nervous system A52.05
    - congenital (late) A50.54 *[I79.0]*
    - spine, spinal A52.09
  - thoracoabdominal (aorta) I71.6
    - ruptured I71.5
    - syphilitic A52.01
  - thorax, thoracic (aorta) (arch) (nonsyphilitic) I71.2
    - ruptured I71.1
    - syphilitic A52.01
  - traumatic (complication) (early), specified site —*see* Injury, blood vessel
  - tricuspid (heart) (valve) I07.8
  - ulnar I72.1
  - upper limb (ruptured) I72.1
  - valve, valvular —*see* Endocarditis
  - venous —*see also* Varix I86.8
    - congenital Q27.8
      - digestive system Q27.8
      - lower limb Q27.8
      - specified site NEC Q27.8
      - upper limb Q27.8
  - ventricle —*see* Aneurysm, heart
  - visceral NEC I72.8
- **Angelman syndrome** Q93.5
- **Anger** R45.4
- **Angiectasis, angiectopia** I99.8
- **Angiitis** I77.6
  - allergic granulomatous M30.1
  - hypersensitivity M31.0
  - necrotizing M31.9
    - specified NEC M31.8
  - nervous system, granulomatous I67.7
- **Angina** (attack) (cardiac) (chest) (heart) (pectoris) (syndrome) (vasomotor) I20.9
  - with
    - atherosclerotic heart disease — *see* Arteriosclerosis, coronary (artery),
    - documented spasm I20.1
  - abdominal K55.1
  - accelerated —*see* Angina, unstable
  - agranulocytic —*see* Agranulocytosis
  - angiospastic —*see* Angina, with documented spasm
  - aphthous B08.5
  - crescendo —*see* Angina, unstable
  - croupous J05.0
  - cruris I73.9
  - de novo effort —*see* Angina, unstable
  - diphtheritic, membranous A36.0
  - equivalent I20.8
  - exudative, chronic J37.0
  - following acute myocardial infarction I23.7
  - gangrenous diphtheritic A36.0
  - intestinal K55.1
  - Ludovici K12.2
  - Ludwig's K12.2
  - malignant diphtheritic A36.0
  - membranous J05.0
    - diphtheritic A36.0
    - Vincent's A69.1
  - mesenteric K55.1
  - monocytic —*see* Mononucleosis, infectious
  - of effort —*see* Angina, specified NEC
  - phlegmonous J36
    - diphtheritic A36.0
  - post-infarctional I23.7
  - pre-infarctional —*see* Angina, unstable
  - Prinzmetal —*see* Angina, with documented spasm
  - progressive —*see* Angina, unstable
  - pseudomembranous A69.1
  - pultaceous, diphtheritic A36.0
  - spasm-induced —*see* Angina, with documented spasm
  - specified NEC I20.8
  - stable I20.9
  - stenocardia —*see* Angina, specified NEC
  - stridulous, diphtheritic A36.2
  - tonsil J36
  - trachealis J05.0
  - unstable I20.0
  - variant —*see* Angina, with documented spasm
  - Vincent's A69.1
  - worsening effort —*see* Angina, unstable
- **Angioblastoma** —*see* Neoplasm, connective tissue, uncertain behavior
- **Angiocholecystitis** —*see* Cholecystitis, acute
- **Angiocholitis** —*see also* Cholecystitis, acute K83.0
- **Angiodysgenesis spinalis** G95.19
- **Angiodysplasia** (cecum) (colon) K55.20
  - with bleeding K55.21
  - duodenum(and stomach) K31.819
    - with bleeding K31.811
  - stomach(and duodenum) K31.819
    - with bleeding K31.811

Angioedema (allergic) (any site) (with urticaria) T78.3
- hereditary D84.1

Angioendothelioma —*see* Neoplasm, uncertain behavior, by site
- benign D18.00
  - intra-abdominal D18.03
  - intracranial D18.02
  - skin D18.01
  - specified site NEC D18.09
- bone —*see* Neoplasm, bone, malignant
- Ewing's —*see* Neoplasm, bone, malignant

Angioendotheliomatosis C85.8-

Angiofibroma —*see also* Neoplasm, benign, by site
- juvenile
  - specified site —*see* Neoplasm, benign, by site
  - unspecified site D10.6

Angiohemophilia (A) (B) D68.0

Angioid streaks (choroid) (macula) (retina) H35.33

Angiokeratoma —*see* Neoplasm, skin, benign
- corporis diffusum E75.21

Angioleiomyoma —*see* Neoplasm, connective tissue, benign

Angiolipoma —*see also* Lipoma
- infiltrating —*see* Lipoma

Angioma —*see also* Hemangioma, by site
- capillary I78.1
- hemorrhagicum hereditaria I78.0
- intra-abdominal D18.03
- intracranial D18.02
- malignant —*see* Neoplasm, connective tissue, malignant
- plexiform D18.00
  - intra-abdominal D18.03
  - intracranial D18.02
  - skin D18.01
  - specified site NEC D18.09
- senile I78.1
- serpiginosum L81.7
- skin D18.01
- specified site NEC D18.09
- spider I78.1
- stellate I78.1
- venous Q28.3

Angiomatosis Q82.8
- bacillary A79.89
- encephalotrigeminal Q85.8
- hemorrhagic familial I78.0
- hereditary familial I78.0
- liver K76.4

Angiomyolipoma —*see* Lipoma

Angiomyoliposarcoma —*see* Neoplasm, connective tissue, malignant

Angiomyoma —*see* Neoplasm, connective tissue, benign

Angiomyosarcoma —*see* Neoplasm, connective tissue, malignant

Angiomyxoma —*see* Neoplasm, connective tissue, uncertain behavior

Angioneurosis F45.8

Angioneurotic edema (allergic) (any site) (with urticaria) T78.3
- hereditary D84.1

Angiopathia, angiopathy I99.9
- cerebral I67.9
  - amyloid E85.4 *[I68.0]*
- diabetic (peripheral) —*see* Diabetes, angiopathy

Angiopathia, angiopathy *(continued)*
- peripheral I73.9
  - diabetic —*see* Diabetes, angiopathy
  - specified type NEC I73.89
- retinae syphilitica A52.05
- retinalis (juvenilis)
  - diabetic —*see* Diabetes, retinopathy
  - proliferative —*see* Retinopathy, proliferative

Angiosarcoma —*see also* Neoplasm, connective tissue, malignant
- liver C22.3

Angiosclerosis —*see* Arteriosclerosis

Angiospasm (peripheral) (traumatic) (vessel) I73.9
- brachial plexus G54.0
- cerebral G45.9
- cervical plexus G54.2
- nerve
  - arm —*see* Mononeuropathy, upper limb
    - axillary G54.0
    - median —*see* Lesion, nerve, median
    - ulnar —*see* Lesion, nerve, ulnar
  - axillary G54.0
  - leg —*see* Mononeuropathy, lower limb
  - median —*see* Lesion, nerve, median
  - plantar —*see* Lesion, nerve, plantar
  - ulnar —*see* Lesion, nerve, ulnar

Angiospastic disease or edema I73.9

Angiostrongyliasis
- due to
  - Parastrongylus
    - cantonensis B83.2
    - costaricensis B81.3
- intestinal B81.3

Anguillulosis —*see* Strongyloidiasis

Angulation
- cecum —*see* Obstruction, intestine
- coccyx (acquired) —*see also* subcategory M43.8
  - congenital NEC Q76.49
- femur (acquired) —*see also* Deformity, limb, specified type NEC, thigh
  - congenital Q74.2
- intestine (large) (small) —*see* Obstruction, intestine
- sacrum (acquired) —*see also* subcategory M43.8
  - congenital NEC Q76.49
- sigmoid (flexure) —*see* Obstruction, intestine
- spine —*see* Dorsopathy, deforming, specified NEC
- tibia (acquired) —*see also* Deformity, limb, specified type NEC, lower leg
  - congenital Q74.2
- ureter N13.5
  - with infection N13.6
- wrist (acquired) —*see also* Deformity, limb, specified type NEC, forearm
  - congenital Q74.0

Angulus infectiosus (lips) K13.0

Anhedonia R45.84

Anhidrosis L74.4

Anhydration, anhydremia E86.0
- with
  - hypernatremia E87.0
  - hyponatremia E87.1

Anhydremia E86.0
- with
  - hypernatremia E87.0
  - hyponatremia E87.1

Anidrosis L74.4

Aniridia (congenital) Q13.1

Anisakiasis (infection) (infestation) B81.0

Anisakis larvae infestation B81.0

Aniseikonia H52.32

Anisocoria (pupil) H57.02
- congenital Q13.2

Anisocytosis R71.8

Anisometropia (congenital) H52.31

Ankle —*see* condition

Ankyloblepharon (eyelid) (acquired) —*see also* Blepharophimosis
- filiforme (adnatum) (congenital) Q10.3
- total Q10.3

Ankyloglossia Q38.1

Ankylosis (fibrous) (osseous) (joint) M24.60
- ankle M24.67-
- arthrodesis status Z98.1
- cricoarytenoid (cartilage) (joint) (larynx) J38.7
- dental K03.5
- ear ossicles H74.31-
- elbow M24.62-
- foot M24.67-
- hand M24.64-
- hip M24.65-
- incostapedial joint (infectional) —*see* Ankylosis, ear ossicles
- jaw (temporomandibular) M26.61
- knee M24.66-
- lumbosacral (joint) M43.27
- postoperative (status) Z98.1
- produced by surgical fusion, status Z98.1
- sacro-iliac (joint) M43.28
- shoulder M24.61-
- spine (joint) —*see also* Fusion, spine
  - spondylitic —*see* Spondylitis, ankylosing
- surgical Z98.1
- temporomandibular M26.61
- tooth, teeth(hard tissues) K03.5
- wrist M24.63-

Ankylostoma —*see* Ancylostoma

Ankylostomiasis —*see* Ancylostomiasis

Ankylurethria —*see* Stricture, urethra

Annular —*see also* condition
- detachment, cervix N88.8
- organ or site, congenital NEC —*see* Distortion
- pancreas (congenital) Q45.1

Anodontia (complete) (partial) (vera) K00.0
- acquired K08.10

Anomaly, anomalous (congenital) (unspecified type) Q89.9
- abdominal wall NEC Q79.59
- acoustic nerve Q07.8
- adrenal (gland) Q89.1
- Alder(-Reilly) (leukocyte granulation) D72.0
- alimentary tract Q45.9
  - upper Q40.9
- alveolar M26.70
  - hyperplasia M26.79
    - mandibular M26.72
    - maxillary M26.71

Anomaly, anomalous *(continued)*
- alveolar *(continued)*
  - hypoplasia M26.79
    - mandibular M26.74
    - maxillary M26.73
  - ridge (process) M26.79
  - specified NEC M26.79
- ankle (joint) Q74.2
- anus Q43.9
- aorta (arch) NEC Q25.4
  - coarctation (preductal) (postductal) Q25.1
- aortic cusp or valve Q23.9
- appendix Q43.8
- apple peel syndrome Q41.1
- aqueduct of Sylvius Q03.0
  - with spina bifida —*see* Spina bifida, with hydrocephalus
- arm Q74.0
- arteriovenous NEC
  - coronary Q24.5
  - gastrointestinal Q27.33
    - acquired —*see* Angiodysplasia
- artery (peripheral) Q27.9
  - basilar NEC Q28.1
  - cerebral Q28.3
  - coronary Q24.5
  - digestive system Q27.8
  - eye Q15.8
  - great Q25.9
    - specified NEC Q25.8
  - lower limb Q27.8
  - peripheral Q27.9
    - specified NEC Q27.8
  - pulmonary NEC Q25.79
  - renal Q27.2
  - retina Q14.1
  - specified site NEC Q27.8
  - subclavian Q27.8
  - umbilical Q27.0
  - upper limb Q27.8
  - vertebral NEC Q28.1
- aryteno-epiglottic folds Q31.8
- atrial
  - bands or folds Q20.8
  - septa Q21.1
- atrioventricular
  - excitation I45.6
  - septum Q21.0
- auditory canal Q17.8
- auricle
  - ear Q17.8
    - causing impairment of hearing Q16.9
  - heart Q20.8
- Axenfeld's Q15.0
- back Q89.9
- band
  - atrial Q20.8
  - heart Q24.8
  - ventricular Q24.8
- Bartholin's duct Q38.4
- biliary duct or passage Q44.5
- bladder Q64.70
  - absence Q64.5
  - diverticulum Q64.6
  - exstrophy Q64.10
    - cloacal Q64.12
    - extroversion Q64.19
    - specified type NEC Q64.19
    - supravesical fissure Q64.11
  - neck obstruction Q64.31
  - specified type NEC Q64.79
- bone Q79.9
  - arm Q74.0
  - face Q75.9
  - leg Q74.2
  - pelvic girdle Q74.2
  - shoulder girdle Q74.0

Anomaly, anomalous *(continued)*
- lumbosacral (joint) (region) Q76.49
  - kyphosis —*see* Kyphosis, congenital
  - lordosis —*see* Lordosis, congenital
- lung (fissure) (lobe) Q33.9
- mandible —*see* Anomaly, dentofacial
- maxilla —*see* Anomaly, dentofacial
- May(-Hegglin) D72.0
- meatus urinarius NEC Q64.79
- meningeal bands or folds Q07.9
  - constriction of Q07.8
  - spinal Q06.9
- meninges Q07.9
  - cerebral Q04.8
  - spinal Q06.9
- meningocele Q05.9
- mesentery Q45.9
- metacarpus Q74.0
- metatarsus NEC Q74.2
- middle ear Q16.4
  - ossicles Q16.3
- mitral (leaflets) (valve) Q23.9
  - insufficiency Q23.3
  - specified NEC Q23.8
  - stenosis Q23.2
- mouth Q38.6
- Müllerian —*see also* Anomaly, by site
  - uterus NEC Q51.818
- multiple NEC Q89.7
- muscle Q79.9
  - eyelid Q10.3
- musculoskeletal system, except limbs Q79.9
- myocardium Q24.8
- nail Q84.6
- narrowness, eyelid Q10.3
- nasal sinus (wall) Q30.8
- neck(any part) Q18.9
- nerve Q07.9
  - acoustic Q07.8
  - optic Q07.8
- nervous system (central) Q07.9
- nipple Q83.9
- nose, nasal (bones) (cartilage) (septum) (sinus) Q30.9
  - specified NEC Q30.8
- ocular muscle Q15.8
- omphalomesenteric duct Q43.0
- opening, pulmonary veins Q26.4
- optic
  - disc Q14.2
  - nerve Q07.8
- opticociliary vessels Q13.2
- orbit (eye) Q10.7
- organ Q89.9
  - of Corti Q16.5
- origin
  - artery
    - innominate Q25.8
    - pulmonary Q25.79
    - renal Q27.2
    - subclavian Q25.8
- osseous meatus (ear) Q16.1
- ovary Q50.39
- oviduct Q50.6
- palate (hard) (soft) NEC Q38.5
- pancreas or pancreatic duct Q45.3
- papillary muscles Q24.8
- parathyroid gland Q89.2
- paraurethral ducts Q64.79
- parotid (gland) Q38.4
- patella Q74.1
- Pelger-Huët(hereditary hyposegmentation) D72.0
- pelvic girdle NEC Q74.2
- pelvis (bony) NEC Q74.2
  - rachitic E64.3
- penis (glans) Q55.69
- pericardium Q24.8
- peripheral vascular system Q27.9

Anomaly, anomalous *(continued)*
- Peter's Q13.4
- pharynx Q38.8
- pigmentation L81.9
  - congenital Q82.8
- pituitary (gland) Q89.2
- pleural (folds) Q34.0
- portal vein Q26.5
  - connection Q26.5
- position, tooth, teeth, fully erupted M26.30
  - specified NEC M26.39
- precerebral vessel Q28.1
- prepuce Q55.69
- prostate Q55.4
- pulmonary Q33.9
  - artery NEC Q25.79
  - valve Q22.3
    - atresia Q22.0
    - insufficiency Q22.2
    - specified type NEC Q22.3
    - stenosis Q22.1
      - infundibular Q24.3
      - subvalvular Q24.3
  - venous connection Q26.4
    - partial Q26.3
    - total Q26.2
- pupil Q13.2
  - function H57.00
    - anisocoria H57.02
    - Argyll Robertson pupil H57.01
    - miosis H57.03
    - mydriasis H57.04
    - specified type NEC H57.09
    - tonic pupil H57.05-
- pylorus Q40.3
- radius Q74.0
- rectum Q43.9
- reduction (extremity) (limb)
  - femur (longitudinal) —*see* Defect, reduction, lower limb, longitudinal, femur
  - fibula (longitudinal) —*see* Defect, reduction, lower limb, longitudinal, fibula
  - lower limb —*see* Defect, reduction, lower limb
  - radius (longitudinal) —*see* Defect, reduction, upper limb, longitudinal, radius
  - tibia (longitudinal) —*see* Defect, reduction, lower limb, longitudinal, tibia
  - ulna (longitudinal) —*see* Defect, reduction, upper limb, longitudinal, ulna
  - upper limb —*see* Defect, reduction, upper limb
- refraction —*see* Disorder, refraction
- renal Q63.9
  - artery Q27.2
  - pelvis Q63.9
    - specified NEC Q63.8
- respiratory system Q34.9
  - specified NEC Q34.8
- retina Q14.1
- rib Q76.6
  - cervical Q76.5
- Rieger's Q13.81
- rotation —*see* Malrotation
  - hip or thigh Q65.89
- round ligament Q52.8
- sacroiliac (joint) NEC Q74.2
- sacrum NEC Q76.49
  - kyphosis —*see* Kyphosis, congenital
  - lordosis —*see* Lordosis, congenital
- saddle nose, syphilitic A50.57
- salivary duct or gland Q38.4
- scapula Q74.0
- scrotum —*see* Malformation, testis and scrotum

Anomaly, anomalous *(continued)*
- sebaceous gland Q82.9
- seminal vesicles Q55.4
- sense organs NEC Q07.8
- sex chromosomes NEC —*see also* Anomaly, chromosomes
  - female phenotype Q97.8
  - male phenotype Q98.9
- shoulder (girdle) (joint) Q74.0
- sigmoid (flexure) Q43.9
- simian crease Q82.8
- sinus of Valsalva Q25.4
- skeleton generalized Q78.9
- skin (appendage) Q82.9
- skull Q75.9
  - with
    - anencephaly Q00.0
    - encephalocele —*see* Encephalocele
    - hydrocephalus Q03.9
      - with spina bifida —*see* Spina bifida, by site, with hydrocephalus
    - microcephaly Q02
- specified organ or site NEC Q89.8
- spermatic cord Q55.4
- spine, spinal NEC Q76.49
  - column NEC Q76.49
    - kyphosis —*see* Kyphosis, congenital
    - lordosis —*see* Lordosis, congenital
  - cord Q06.9
    - nerve root Q07.8
- spleen Q89.09
  - agenesis Q89.01
- stenonian duct Q38.4
- sternum NEC Q76.7
- stomach Q40.3
- submaxillary gland Q38.4
- tarsus NEC Q74.2
- tendon Q79.9
- testis —*see* Malformation, testis and scrotum
- thigh NEC Q74.2
- thorax (wall) Q67.8
  - bony Q76.9
- throat Q38.8
- thumb Q74.0
- thymus gland Q89.2
- thyroid (gland) Q89.2
  - cartilage Q31.8
- tibia NEC Q74.2
  - saber A50.56
- toe Q74.2
- tongue Q38.3
- tooth, teeth K00.9
  - eruption K00.6
  - position, fully erupted M26.30
  - spacing, fully erupted M26.30
- trachea (cartilage) Q32.1
- tragus Q17.9
- tricuspid (leaflet) (valve) Q22.9
  - atresia or stenosis Q22.4
  - Ebstein's Q22.5
- Uhl's(hypoplasia of myocardium, right ventricle) Q24.8
- ulna Q74.0
- umbilical artery Q27.0
- union
  - cricoid cartilage and thyroid cartilage Q31.8
  - thyroid cartilage and hyoid bone Q31.8
  - trachea with larynx Q31.8
- upper limb Q74.0
- urachus Q64.4
- ureter Q62.8
  - obstructive NEC Q62.39
    - cecoureterocele Q62.32
    - orthotopic ureterocele Q62.31

Anomaly, anomalous *(continued)*
- urethra Q64.70
  - absence Q64.5
  - double Q64.74
  - fistula to rectum Q64.73
  - obstructive Q64.39
    - stricture Q64.32
  - prolapse Q64.71
  - specified type NEC Q64.79
- urinary tract Q64.9
- uterus Q51.9
  - with only one functioning horn Q51.4
- uvula Q38.5
- vagina Q52.4
- valleculae Q31.8
- valve (heart) NEC Q24.8
  - coronary sinus Q24.5
  - inferior vena cava Q24.8
  - pulmonary Q22.3
  - sinus coronario Q24.5
  - venae cavae inferioris Q24.8
- vas deferens Q55.4
- vascular Q27.9
  - brain Q28.3
  - ring Q25.4
- vein (s) (peripheral) Q27.9
  - brain Q28.3
  - cerebral Q28.3
  - coronary Q24.5
  - developmental Q28.3
  - great Q26.9
    - specified NEC Q26.8
- vena cava (inferior) (superior) Q26.9
- venous —*see* Anomaly, vein (s)
- venous return Q26.8
- ventricular
  - bands or folds Q24.8
  - septa Q21.0
- vertebra Q76.49
  - kyphosis —*see* Kyphosis, congenital
  - lordosis —*see* Lordosis, congenital
- vesicourethral orifice Q64.79
- vessel (s) Q27.9
  - optic papilla Q14.2
  - precerebral Q28.1
- vitelline duct Q43.0
- vitreous body or humor Q14.0
- vulva Q52.70
- wrist (joint) Q74.0

Anomia R48.8

Anonychia (congenital) Q84.3
- acquired L60.8

Anophthalmos, anophthalmus (congenital) (globe) Q11.1
- acquired Z90.01

Anopia, anopsia H53.46-
- quadrant H53.46-

Anorchia, anorchism, anorchidism Q55.0

Anorexia R63.0
- hysterical F44.89
- nervosa F50.00
  - atypical F50.9
  - binge-eating type F50.2
    - with purging F50.02
  - restricting type F50.01

Anorgasmy, psychogenic (female) F52.31
- male F52.32

Anosmia R43.0
- hysterical F44.6
- postinfectional J39.8

Anosognosia R41.89

Anosteoplasia Q78.9

Anovulatory cycle N97.0

Anoxemia R09.02
- newborn P84

Anoxia (pathological) R09.02
- altitude T70.29
- cerebral G93.1
  - complicating
    - anesthesia (general) (local) or other sedation T88.59
      - in labor and delivery O74.3
      - in pregnancy O29.21-
      - postpartum, puerperal O89.2
    - delivery (cesarean) (instrumental) O75.4
  - during a procedure G97.81
  - newborn P84
  - resulting from a procedure G97.82
- due to
  - drowning T75.1
  - high altitude T70.29
- heart —*see* Insufficiency, coronary
- intrauterine P84
- myocardial —*see* Insufficiency, coronary
- newborn P84
- spinal cord G95.11
- systemic(by suffocation) (low content in atmosphere) —*see* Asphyxia, traumatic

Anteflexion —*see* Anteversion

Antenatal
- care(normal pregnancy) Z34.90
- screening(encounter for) of mother Z36

Antepartum —*see* condition

Anterior —*see* condition

Antero-occlusion M26.220

Anteversion
- cervix —*see* Anteversion, uterus
- femur (neck), congenital Q65.89
- uterus, uterine (cervix) (postinfectional) (postpartal, old) N85.4
  - congenital Q51.818
  - in pregnancy or childbirth —*see* Pregnancy, complicated by

Anthophobia F40.228

Anthracosilicosis J60

Anthracosis (lung) (occupational) J60
- lingua K14.3

Anthrax A22.9
- with pneumonia A22.1
- cerebral A22.8
- colitis A22.2
- cutaneous A22.0
- gastrointestinal A22.2
- inhalation A22.1
- intestinal A22.2
- meningitis A22.8
- pulmonary A22.1
- respiratory A22.1
- sepsis A22.7
- specified manifestation NEC A22.8

Anthropoid pelvis Q74.2
- with disproportion (fetopelvic) O33.0

Anthropophobia F40.10
- generalized F40.11

Antibodies, maternal (blood group) —*see* Isoimmunization, affecting management of pregnancy
- anti-D —*see* Isoimmunization, affecting management of pregnancy, Rh
  - newborn P55.0

Antibody
- anticardiolipin R76.0
  - with
    - hemorrhagic disorder D68.312
    - hypercoagulable state D68.61

Antibody *(continued)*
- antiphosphatidylglycerol R76.0
  - with
    - hemorrhagic disorder D68.312
    - hypercoagulable state D68.61
- antiphosphatidylinositol R76.0
  - with
    - hemorrhagic disorder D68.312
    - hypercoagulable state D68.61
- antiphosphatidylserine R76.0
  - with
    - hemorrhagic disorder D68.312
    - hypercoagulable state D68.61
- antiphospholipid R76.0
  - with
    - hemorrhagic disorder D68.312
    - hypercoagulable state D68.61

Anticardiolipin syndrome D68.61

Anticoagulant, circulating (intrinsic) —*see also* - Disorder, hemorrhagic D68.318
- drug-induced (extrinsic) —*see also* - Disorder, hemorrhagic D68.32

Antidiuretic hormone syndrome E22.2

Antimonial cholera —*see* Poisoning, antimony

Antiphospholipid
- antibody
  - with hemorrhagic disorder D68.312
  - syndrome D68.61

Antisocial personality F60.2

Antithrombinemia —*see* Circulating anticoagulants

Antithromboplastinemia D68.318

Antithromboplastinogenemia D68.318

Antitoxin complication or reaction — *see* Complications, vaccination

Antlophobia F40.228

Antritis J32.0
- maxilla J32.0
  - acute J01.00
    - recurrent J01.01
- stomach K29.60
  - with bleeding K29.61

Antrum, antral —*see* condition

Anuria R34
- calculous (impacted) (recurrent) —*see also* Calculus, urinary N20.9
- following
  - abortion —*see* Abortion by type complicated by, renal failure
  - ectopic or molar pregnancy O08.4
- newborn P96.0
- postprocedural N99.0
- postrenal N13.8
- traumatic(following crushing) T79.5

Anus, anal —*see* condition

Anusitis K62.89

Anxiety F41.9
- depression F41.8
- episodic paroxysmal F41.0
- generalized F41.1
- hysteria F41.8
- neurosis F41.1
- panic type F41.0
- reaction F41.1
- separation, abnormal(of childhood) F93.0
- specified NEC F41.8
- state F41.1

Aorta, aortic —*see* condition

Aortectasia —*see* Ectasia, aorta
- with aneurysm —*see* Aneurysm, aorta

Aortitis (nonsyphilitic) (calcific) I77.6
- arteriosclerotic I70.0
- Doehle-Heller A52.02
- luetic A52.02
- rheumatic —*see* Endocarditis, acute, rheumatic
- specific (syphilitic) A52.02
- syphilitic A52.02
  - congenital A50.54 *[I79.1]*

Apathetic thyroid storm —*see* Thyrotoxicosis

Apathy R45.3

Apeirophobia F40.228

Apepsia K30
- psychogenic F45.8

Aperistalsis, esophagus K22.0

Apertognathia M26.29

Apert's syndrome Q87.0

Aphagia R13.0
- psychogenic F50.9

Aphakia (acquired) (postoperative) H27.0-
- congenital Q12.3

Aphasia (amnestic) (global) (nominal) (semantic) (syntactic) R47.01
- acquired, with epilepsy(Landau-Kleffner syndrome) —*see* Epilepsy, specified NEC
- auditory (developmental) F80.2
- developmental(receptive type) F80.2
  - expressive type F80.1
  - Wernicke's F80.2
- following
  - cerebrovascular disease I69.920
    - cerebral infarction I69.320
    - intracerebral hemorrhage I69.120
    - nontraumatic intracranial hemorrhage NEC I69.220
    - specified disease NEC I69.820
    - subarachnoid hemorrhage I69.020
- primary progressive G31.01 *[F02.80]*
  - with behavioral disturbance G31.01 *[F02.81]*
- progressive isolated G31.01 *[F02.80]*
  - with behavioral disturbance G31.01 *[F02.81]*
- sensory F80.2
- syphilis, tertiary A52.19
- Wernicke's (developmental) F80.2

Aphonia (organic) R49.1
- hysterical F44.4
- psychogenic F44.4

Aphthae, aphthous —*see also* condition
- Bednar's K12.0
- cachectic K14.0
- epizootic B08.8
- fever B08.8
- oral (recurrent) K12.0
- stomatitis (major) (minor) K12.0
- thrush B37.0
- ulcer (oral) (recurrent) K12.0
  - genital organ (s) NEC
    - female N76.6
    - male N50.8
  - larynx J38.7

Apical —*see* condition

Apiphobia F40.218

Aplasia —*see also* Agenesis
- abdominal muscle syndrome Q79.4
- alveolar process (acquired) —*see* Anomaly, alveolar
  - congenital Q38.6
- aorta (congenital) Q25.4

Aplasia *(continued)*
- axialis extracorticalis (congenita) E75.29
- bone marrow (myeloid) D61.9
  - congenital D61.01
- brain Q00.0
  - part of Q04.3
- bronchus Q32.4
- cementum K00.4
- cerebellum Q04.3
- cervix (congenital) Q51.5
- congenital pure red cell D61.01
- corpus callosum Q04.0
- cutis congenita Q84.8
- erythrocyte congenital D61.01
- extracortical axial E75.29
- eye Q11.1
- fovea centralis (congenital) Q14.1
- gallbladder, congenital Q44.0
- iris Q13.1
- labyrinth, membranous Q16.5
- limb (congenital) Q73.8
  - lower —*see* Defect, reduction, lower limb
  - upper —*see* Agenesis, arm
- lung, congenital (bilateral) (unilateral) Q33.3
- pancreas Q45.0
- parathyroid-thymic D82.1
- Pelizaeus-Merzbacher E75.29
- penis Q55.5
- prostate Q55.4
- red cell(with thymoma) D60.9
  - acquired D60.9
    - due to drugs D60.9
  - adult D60.9
  - chronic D60.0
  - congenital D61.01
  - constitutional D61.01
  - due to drugs D60.9
  - hereditary D61.01
  - of infants D61.01
  - primary D61.01
  - pure D61.01
    - due to drugs D60.9
  - specified type NEC D60.8
  - transient D60.1
- round ligament Q52.8
- skin Q84.8
- spermatic cord Q55.4
- spleen Q89.01
- testicle Q55.0
- thymic, with immunodeficiency D82.1
- thyroid (congenital) (with myxedema) E03.1
- uterus Q51.0
- ventral horn cell Q06.1

Apnea, apneic (of) (spells) R06.81
- newborn NEC P28.4
  - obstructive P28.4
  - sleep (central) (obstructive) (primary) P28.3
- prematurity P28.4
- sleep G47.30
  - central (primary) G47.31
    - in conditions classified elsewhere G47.37
  - obstructive (adult) (pediatric) G47.33
  - primary central G47.31
  - specified NEC G47.39

Apneumatosis, newborn P28.0

Apocrine metaplasia (breast) —*see* Dysplasia, mammary, specified type NEC

Apophysitis (bone) —*see also* Osteochondropathy
- calcaneus M92.8
- juvenile M92.9

Apoplectiform convulsions (cerebral ischemia) I67.82

Apoplexia, apoplexy, apoplectic
- adrenal A39.1
- heart (auricle) (ventricle) —*see* Infarct, myocardium
- heat T67.0
- hemorrhagic (stroke) —*see* Hemorrhage, intracranial
- meninges, hemorrhagic —*see* Hemorrhage, intracranial, subarachnoid
- uremic N18.9 *[I68.8]*

Appearance
- bizarre R46.1
- specified NEC R46.89
- very low level of personal hygiene R46.0

Appendage
- epididymal(organ of Morgagni) Q55.4
- intestine (epiploic) Q43.8
- preauricular Q17.0
- testicular(organ of Morgagni) Q55.29

Appendicitis (pneumococcal) (retrocecal) K37
- with
  - perforation or rupture K35.2
  - peritoneal abscess K35.3
  - peritonitis NEC K35.3
    - generalized(with perforation or rupture) K35.2
    - localized(with perforation or rupture) K35.3
- acute (catarrhal) (fulminating) (gangrenous) (obstructive) (retrocecal) (suppurative) K35.80
  - with
    - peritoneal abscess K35.3
    - peritonitis NEC K35.3
      - generalized(with perforation or rupture) K35.2
      - localized(with perforation or rupture) K35.3
  - specified NEC K35.89
- amebic A06.89
- chronic (recurrent) K36
- exacerbation —*see* Appendicitis, acute
- gangrenous —*see* Appendicitis, acute
- healed (obliterative) K36
- interval K36
- neurogenic K36
- obstructive K36
- recurrent K36
- relapsing K36
- subacute (adhesive) K36
- subsiding K36
- suppurative —*see* Appendicitis, acute
- tuberculous A18.32

Appendicopathia oxyurica B80

Appendix, appendicular —*see also* condition
- epididymis Q55.4
- Morgagni
  - female Q50.5
  - male (epididymal) Q55.4
    - testicular Q55.29
- testis Q55.29

Appetite
- depraved —*see* Pica
- excessive R63.2
- lack or loss —*see also* Anorexia R63.0
  - nonorganic origin F50.8
  - psychogenic F50.8
- perverted (hysterical) —*see* Pica

Apple peel syndrome Q41.1

Apprehension state F41.1

Apprehensiveness, abnormal F41.9

Approximal wear K03.0

Apraxia (classic) (ideational) (ideokinetic) (ideomotor) (motor) (verbal) R48.2
- following
  - cerebrovascular disease I69.990
    - cerebral infarction I69.390
    - intracerebral hemorrhage I69.190
    - nontraumatic intracranial hemorrhage NEC I69.290
    - specified disease NEC I69.890
    - subarachnoid hemorrhage I69.090
- oculomotor, congenital H51.8

Aptyalism K11.7

Apudoma —*see* Neoplasm, uncertain behavior, by site

Aqueous misdirection H40.83-

Arabicum elephantiasis —*see* Infestation, filarial

Arachnitis —*see* Meningitis

Arachnodactyly —*see* Syndrome, Marfan's

Arachnoiditis (acute) (adhesive) (basal) (brain) (cerebrospinal) —*see* Meningitis

Arachnophobia F40.210

Arboencephalitis, Australian A83.4

Arborization block (heart) I45.5

ARC (AIDS-related complex) B20

Arches —*see* condition

Arcuate uterus Q51.810

Arcuatus uterus Q51.810

Arcus (cornea) **senilis** —*see* Degeneration, cornea, senile

Arc-welder's lung J63.4

Areflexia R29.2

Areola —*see* condition

Argentaffinoma —*see also* Neoplasm, uncertain behavior, by site
- malignant —*see* Neoplasm, malignant, by site
- syndrome E34.0

Argininemia E72.21

Arginosuccinic aciduria E72.22

Argyll Robertson phenomenon, pupil or syndrome (syphilitic) A52.19
- atypical H57.09
- nonsyphilitic H57.09

Argyria, argyriasis
- conjunctival H11.13-
- from drug or medicament —*see* Table of Drugs and Chemicals, by substance

Argyrosis, conjunctival H11.13-

Arhinencephaly Q04.1

Ariboflavinosis E53.0

Arm —*see* condition

Arnold-Chiari disease, obstruction or syndrome (type II) Q07.00
- with
  - hydrocephalus Q07.02
    - with spina bifida Q07.03
  - spina bifida Q07.01
    - with hydrocephalus Q07.03
- type III —*see* Encephalocele
- type IV Q04.8

Aromatic amino-acid metabolism disorder E70.9
- specified NEC E70.8

Arousals, confusional G47.51

Arrest, arrested
- cardiac I46.9
  - complicating
    - abortion —*see* Abortion, by type, complicated by, cardiac arrest
    - anesthesia (general) (local) or other sedation —*see* Table of Drugs and Chemicals, by drug,
      - in labor and delivery O74.2
      - in pregnancy O29.11-
      - postpartum, puerperal O89.1
    - delivery (cesarean) (instrumental) O75.4
  - due to
    - cardiac condition I46.2
    - specified condition NEC I46.8
  - intraoperative I97.71-
  - newborn P29.81
  - postprocedural I97.12-
    - obstetric procedure O75.4
- cardiorespiratory —*see* Arrest, cardiac
- circulatory —*see* Arrest, cardiac
- deep transverse O64.0
- development or growth
  - bone —*see* Disorder, bone, development or growth
  - child R62.50
  - tracheal rings Q32.1
- epiphyseal
  - complete
    - femur M89.15-
    - humerus M89.12-
    - tibia M89.16-
    - ulna M89.13-
  - forearm M89.13-
    - specified NEC M89.13-
    - ulna —*see* Arrest, epiphyseal, by type, ulna
  - lower leg M89.16-
    - specified NEC M89.168
    - tibia —*see* Arrest, epiphyseal, by type, tibia
  - partial
    - femur M89.15-
    - humerus M89.12-
    - tibia M89.16-
    - ulna M89.13-
  - specified NEC M89.18
- granulopoiesis —*see* Agranulocytosis
- growth plate —*see* Arrest, epiphyseal
- heart —*see* Arrest, cardiac
- legal, anxiety concerning Z65.3
- physeal —*see* Arrest, epiphyseal
- respiratory R09.2
  - newborn P28.81
- sinus I45.5
- spermatogenesis (complete) —*see* Azoospermia
  - incomplete —*see* Oligospermia
- transverse (deep) O64.0

Arrhenoblastoma
- benign
  - specified site —*see* Neoplasm, benign, by site
  - unspecified site
    - female D27.9
    - male D29.20
- malignant
  - specified site —*see* Neoplasm, malignant, by site
  - unspecified site
    - female C56.9
    - male C62.90
- specified site —*see* Neoplasm, uncertain behavior, by site
- unspecified site
  - female D39.10
  - male D40.10

Arrhythmia (auricle)(cardiac) (juvenile)(nodal) (reflex)(sinus) (supraventricular)(transitory) (ventricle) I49.9
- block I45.9
- extrasystolic I49.49
- newborn
  - bradycardia P29.12
  - occurring before birth P03.819
    - before onset of labor P03.810
    - during labor P03.811
  - tachycardia P29.11
- psychogenic F45.8
- specified NEC I49.8
- vagal R55
- ventricular re-entry I47.0

Arrillaga-Ayerza syndrome (pulmonary sclerosis with pulmonary hypertension) I27.0

Arsenical pigmentation L81.8
- from drug or medicament —*see* Table of Drugs and Chemicals

Arsenism —*see* Poisoning, arsenic

Arterial —*see* condition

Arteriofibrosis —*see* Arteriosclerosis

Arteriolar sclerosis —*see* Arteriosclerosis

Arteriolith —*see* Arteriosclerosis

Arteriolitis I77.6
- necrotizing, kidney I77.5
- renal —*see* Hypertension, kidney

Arteriolosclerosis —*see* Arteriosclerosis

Arterionephrosclerosis —*see* Hypertension, kidney

Arteriopathy I77.9

Arteriosclerosis, arteriosclerotic (diffuse) (obliterans) (of) (senile) (with calcification) I70.90
- aorta I70.0
- arteries of extremities —*see* Arteriosclerosis, extremities
- brain I67.2
- bypass graft
  - coronary —*see* Arteriosclerosis, coronary, bypass graft
  - extremities —*see* Arteriosclerosis, extremities, bypass graft
- cardiac —*see* Disease, heart, ischemic, atherosclerotic
- cardiopathy —*see* Disease, heart, ischemic, atherosclerotic
- cardiorenal —*see* Hypertension, cardiorenal
- cardiovascular —*see* Disease, heart, ischemic, atherosclerotic
- carotid —*see also* Occlusion, artery, carotid I65.2-
- central nervous system I67.2
- cerebral I67.2
- cerebrovascular I67.2
- coronary (artery) I25.10
  - due to
    - calcified coronary lesion (severely) I25.84
    - lipid rich plaque I25.83
  - bypass graft I25.810
    - with
      - angina pectoris I25.709
        - with documented spasm I25.701
        - specified type NEC I25.708
        - unstable I25.700
      - ischemic chest pain I25.709

Arteriosclerosis, arteriosclerotic *(continued)*

- autologous artery I25.810
  - with
    - angina pectoris I25.729
      - with documented spasm I25.721
      - specified type I25.728
      - unstable I25.720
    - ischemic chest pain I25.729
- autologous vein I25.810
  - with
    - angina pectoris I25.719
      - with documented spasm I25.711
      - specified type I25.718
      - unstable I25.710
    - ischemic chest pain I25.719
- nonautologous biological I25.810
  - with
    - angina pectoris I25.739
      - with documented spasm I25.731
      - specified type I25.738
      - unstable I25.730
    - ischemic chest pain I25.739
- specified type NEC I25.810
  - with
    - angina pectoris I25.799
      - with documented spasm I25.791
      - specified type I25.798
      - unstable I25.790
    - ischemic chest pain I25.799

native vessel
- with
  - angina pectoris I25.119
    - with documented spasm I25.111
    - specified type NEC I25.118
    - unstable I25.110
  - ischemic chest pain I25.119

transplanted heart I25.811
- bypass graft I25.812
  - with
    - angina pectoris I25.769
      - with documented spasm I25.761
      - specified type I25.768
      - unstable I25.760
    - ischemic chest pain I25.769
- native coronary artery I25.811
  - with
    - angina pectoris I25.759
      - with documented spasm I25.751
      - specified type I25.758
      - unstable I25.750
    - ischemic chest pain I25.759

extremities (native arteries) I70.209
- bypass graft I70.309
  - autologous vein graft I70.409
    - leg I70.409
      - with
        - gangrene(and intermittent claudication, rest pain and ulcer) I70.469
        - intermittent claudication I70.419
        - rest pain(and intermittent claudication) I70.429
      - bilateral I70.403
        - with
          - gangrene(and intermittent claudication, rest pain and ulcer) I70.463
          - intermittent claudication I70.413

Arteriosclerosis, arteriosclerotic *(continued)*

extremities *(continued)*
- bypass graft *(continued)*
  - autologous vein graft *(continued)*
    - leg *(continued)*
      - bilateral *(continued)*
        - with *(continued)*
          - rest pain (and intermittent claudication) I70.423
        - specified type NEC I70.493
      - left I70.402
        - with
          - gangrene(and intermittent claudication, rest pain and ulcer) I70.462
          - intermittent claudication I70.412
          - rest pain(and intermittent claudication) I70.422
          - ulceration(and intermittent claudication and rest pain) I70.449
            - ankle I70.443
            - calf I70.442
            - foot site NEC I70.445
            - heel I70.444
            - lower leg NEC I70.448
            - midfoot I70.444
            - thigh I70.441
        - specified type NEC I70.492
      - right I70.401
        - with
          - gangrene(and intermittent claudication, rest pain and ulcer) I70.461
          - intermittent claudication I70.411
          - rest pain(and intermittent claudication) I70.421
          - ulceration(and intermittent claudication and rest pain) I70.439
            - ankle I70.433
            - calf I70.432
            - foot site NEC I70.435
            - heel I70.434
            - lower leg NEC I70.438
            - midfoot I70.434
            - thigh I70.431
        - specified type NEC I70.491
      - specified type NEC I70.499
    - specified NEC I70.408
      - with
        - gangrene(and intermittent claudication, rest pain and ulcer) I70.468
        - intermittent claudication I70.418
        - rest pain(and intermittent claudication) I70.428

Arteriosclerosis, arteriosclerotic *(continued)*

extremities *(continued)*
- bypass graft *(continued)*
  - autologous vein graft *(continued)*
    - specified NEC *(continued)*
      - with *(continued)*
        - ulceration (and intermittent claudication and rest pain) I70.45
      - specified type NEC I70.498
  - leg I70.309
    - with
      - gangrene(and intermittent claudication, rest pain and ulcer) I70.369
      - intermittent claudication I70.319
      - rest pain(and intermittent claudication) I70.329
    - bilateral I70.303
      - with
        - gangrene(and intermittent claudication, rest pain and ulcer) I70.363
        - intermittent claudication I70.313
        - rest pain (and intermittent claudication) I70.323
      - specified type NEC I70.393
    - left I70.302
      - with
        - gangrene(and intermittent claudication, rest pain and ulcer) I70.362
        - intermittent claudication I70.312
        - rest pain(and intermittent claudication) I70.322
        - ulceration(and intermittent claudication and rest pain) I70.349
          - ankle I70.343
          - calf I70.342
          - foot site NEC I70.345
          - heel I70.344
          - lower leg NEC I70.348
          - midfoot I70.344
          - thigh I70.341
      - specified type NEC I70.392
    - right I70.301
      - with
        - gangrene(and intermittent claudication, rest pain and ulcer) I70.361
        - intermittent claudication I70.311
        - rest pain(and intermittent claudication) I70.321
        - ulceration(and intermittent claudication and rest pain) I70.339
          - ankle I70.333
          - calf I70.332
          - foot site NEC I70.335
          - heel I70.334
          - lower leg NEC I70.338
          - midfoot I70.334
          - thigh I70.331
      - specified type NEC I70.391
    - specified type NEC I70.399

Arteriosclerosis, arteriosclerotic *(continued)*

extremities *(continued)*
- bypass graft *(continued)*
  - nonautologous biological graft I70.509
    - leg I70.509
      - with
        - gangrene(and intermittent claudication, rest pain and ulcer) I70.569
        - intermittent claudication I70.519
        - rest pain(and intermittent claudication) I70.529
      - bilateral I70.503
        - with
          - gangrene(and intermittent claudication, rest pain and ulcer) I70.563
          - intermittent claudication I70.513
          - rest pain(and intermittent claudication) I70.523
        - specified type NEC I70.593
      - left I70.502
        - with
          - gangrene(and intermittent claudication, rest pain and ulcer) I70.562
          - intermittent claudication I70.512
          - rest pain(and intermittent claudication) I70.522
          - ulceration(and intermittent claudication and rest pain) I70.549
            - ankle I70.543
            - calf I70.542
            - foot site NEC I70.545
            - heel I70.544
            - lower leg NEC I70.548
            - midfoot I70.544
            - thigh I70.541
        - specified type NEC I70.592
      - right I70.501
        - with
          - gangrene(and intermittent claudication, rest pain and ulcer) I70.561
          - intermittent claudication I70.511
          - rest pain(and intermittent claudication) I70.521
          - ulceration (and intermittent claudication and rest pain) I70.539
            - ankle I70.533
            - calf I70.532
            - foot site NEC I70.535
            - heel I70.534

Arteriosclerosis, arteriosclerotic *(continued)*
extremities *(continued)*
bypass graft *(continued)*
nonautologous biological graft *(continued)*
leg *(continued)*
right *(continued)*
with *(continued)*
ulceration *(continued)*
lower leg NEC I70.538
midfoot I70.534
thigh I70.531
specified type NEC I70.591
specified type NEC I70.599
specified NEC I70.508
with
gangrene(and intermittent claudication, rest pain and ulcer) I70.568
intermittent claudication I70.518
rest pain(and intermittent claudication) I70.528
ulceration(and intermittent claudication and rest pain) I70.55
specified type NEC I70.598
nonbiological graft I70.609
leg I70.609
with
gangrene(and intermittent claudication, rest pain and ulcer) I70.669
intermittent claudication I70.619
rest pain(and intermittent claudication) I70.629
bilateral I70.603
with
gangrene(and intermittent claudication, rest pain and ulcer) I70.663
intermittent claudication I70.613
rest pain(and intermittent claudication) I70.623
specified type NEC I70.693
left I70.602
with
gangrene(and intermittent claudication, rest pain and ulcer) I70.662
intermittent claudication I70.612
rest pain(and intermittent claudication) I70.622
ulceration (and intermittent claudication and rest pain) I70.649
ankle I70.643
calf I70.642
foot site NEC I70.645
heel I70.644
lower leg NEC I70.648

Arteriosclerosis, arteriosclerotic *(continued)*
extremities *(continued)*
bypass graft *(continued)*
nonbiological graft *(continued)*
leg *(continued)*
left *(continued)*
with *(continued)*
ulceration *(continued)*
midfoot I70.644
thigh I70.641
specified type NEC I70.692
right I70.601
with
gangrene(and intermittent claudication, rest pain and ulcer) I70.661
intermittent claudication I70.611
rest pain (and intermittent claudication) I70.621
ulceration(and intermittent claudication and rest pain) I70.639
ankle I70.633
calf I70.632
foot site NEC I70.635
heel I70.634
lower leg NEC I70.638
midfoot I70.634
thigh I70.631
specified type NEC I70.691
specified type NEC I70.699
specified NEC I70.608
with
gangrene(and intermittent claudication, rest pain and ulcer) I70.668
intermittent claudication I70.618
rest pain(and intermittent claudication) I70.628
ulceration (and intermittent claudication and rest pain) I70.65
specified type NEC I70.698
specified graft NEC I70.709
leg I70.709
with
gangrene (and intermittent claudication, rest pain and ulcer) I70.769
intermittent claudication I70.719
rest pain(and intermittent claudication) I70.729
bilateral I70.703
with
gangrene (and intermittent claudication, rest pain and ulcer) I70.763
intermittent claudication I70.713
rest pain (and intermittent claudication) I70.723

Arteriosclerosis, arteriosclerotic *(continued)*
extremities *(continued)*
bypass graft *(continued)*
specified graft NEC *(continued)*
leg *(continued)*
bilateral *(continued)*
specified type NEC I70.793
left I70.702
with
gangrene (and intermittent claudication, rest pain and ulcer) I70.762
intermittent claudication I70.712
rest pain(and intermittent claudication) I70.722
ulceration(and intermittent claudication and rest pain) I70.749
ankle I70.743
calf I70.742
foot site NEC I70.745
heel I70.744
lower leg NEC I70.748
midfoot I70.744
thigh I70.741
specified type NEC I70.792
right I70.701
with
gangrene (and intermittent claudication, rest pain and ulcer) I70.761
intermittent claudication I70.711
rest pain(and intermittent claudication) I70.721
ulceration(and intermittent claudication and rest pain) I70.739
ankle I70.733
calf I70.732
foot site NEC I70.735
heel I70.734
lower leg NEC I70.738
midfoot I70.734
thigh I70.731
specified type NEC I70.791
specified type NEC I70.799
specified NEC I70.708
with
gangrene(and intermittent claudication, rest pain and ulcer) I70.768
intermittent claudication I70.718
rest pain (and intermittent claudication) I70.728
ulceration(and intermittent claudication and rest pain) I70.75
specified type NEC I70.798

Arteriosclerosis, arteriosclerotic *(continued)*
extremities *(continued)*
bypass graft *(continued)*
specified NEC I70.308
with
gangrene(and intermittent claudication, rest pain and ulcer) I70.368
intermittent claudication I70.318
rest pain(and intermittent claudication) I70.328
ulceration(and intermittent claudication and rest pain) I70.35
specified type NEC I70.398
leg I70.209
with
gangrene(and intermittent claudication, rest pain and ulcer) I70.269
intermittent claudication I70.219
rest pain(and intermittent claudication) I70.229
bilateral I70.203
with
gangrene(and intermittent claudication, rest pain and ulcer) I70.263
intermittent claudication I70.213
rest pain(and intermittent claudication) I70.223
specified type NEC I70.293
left I70.202
with
gangrene(and intermittent claudication, rest pain and ulcer) I70.262
intermittent claudication I70.212
rest pain(and intermittent claudication) I70.222
ulceration(and intermittent claudication and rest pain) I70.249
ankle I70.243
calf I70.242
foot site NEC I70.245
heel I70.244
lower leg NEC I70.248
midfoot I70.244
thigh I70.241
specified type NEC I70.292
right I70.201
with
gangrene(and intermittent claudication, rest pain and ulcer) I70.261
intermittent claudication I70.211
rest pain(and intermittent claudication) I70.221
ulceration(and intermittent claudication and rest pain) I70.239
ankle I70.233
calf I70.232
foot site NEC I70.235
heel I70.234
lower leg NEC I70.238
midfoot I70.234
thigh I70.231
specified type NEC I70.291
specified type NEC I70.299
specified site NEC I70.208
with
gangrene (and intermittent claudication, rest pain and ulcer) I70.268

Arteriosclerosis, arteriosclerotic *(continued)*
extremities *(continued)*
specified site NEC *(continued)*
with *(continued)*
intermittent claudication I70.218
rest pain (and intermittent claudication) I70.228
ulceration (and intermittent claudication and rest pain) I70.25
specified type NEC I70.298
generalized I70.91
heart (disease) *—see* Arteriosclerosis, coronary (artery),
kidney *—see* Hypertension, kidney
medial *—see* Arteriosclerosis, extremities
mesenteric (artery) K55.1
Mönckeberg's *—see* Arteriosclerosis, extremities
myocarditis I51.4
peripheral(of extremities) *—see* Arteriosclerosis, extremities
pulmonary (idiopathic) I27.0
renal (arterioles) *—see also* Hypertension, kidney
artery I70.1
retina (vascular) I70.8 *[H35.0]-*
specified artery NEC I70.8
spinal (cord) G95.19
vertebral (artery) I67.2

Arteriospasm I73.9

Arteriovenous *—see* condition

Arteritis I77.6
allergic M31.0
aorta (nonsyphilitic) I77.6
syphilitic A52.02
aortic arch M31.4
brachiocephalic M31.4
brain I67.7
syphilitic A52.04
cerebral I67.7
in
diseases classified elsewhere I68.2
systemic lupus erythematosus M32.19
listerial A32.89
syphilitic A52.04
tuberculous A18.89
coronary (artery) I25.89
rheumatic I01.8
chronic I09.89
syphilitic A52.06
cranial (left) (right), giant cell M31.6
deformans *—see* Arteriosclerosis
giant cell NEC M31.6
with polymyalgia rheumatica M31.5
necrosing or necrotizing M31.9
specified NEC M31.8
nodosa M30.0
obliterans *—see* Arteriosclerosis
pulmonary I28.8
rheumatic *—see* Fever, rheumatic
senile *—see* Arteriosclerosis
suppurative I77.2
syphilitic (general) A52.09
brain A52.04
coronary A52.06
spinal A52.09
temporal, giant cell M31.6
young female aortic arch syndrome M31.4

Artery, arterial *—see also* condition
abscess I77.89
single umbilical Q27.0

Arthralgia (allergic) *—see also* Pain, joint
in caisson disease T70.3
temporomandibular M26.62

Arthritis, arthritic (acute) (chronic) (nonpyogenic) (subacute) M19.90
allergic *—see* Arthritis, specified form NEC
ankylosing (crippling) (spine) *—see also* Spondylitis, ankylosing
sites other than spine *—see* Arthritis, specified form NEC
atrophic *—see* Osteoarthritis
spine *—see* Spondylitis, ankylosing
back *—see* Spondylopathy, inflammatory
blennorrhagic (gonococcal) A54.42
Charcot's *—see* Arthropathy, neuropathic
diabetic *—see* Diabetes, arthropathy, neuropathic
syringomyelic G95.0
chylous (filarial) *—see also* category M01 *[B74.9]*
climacteric(any site) NEC *—see* Arthritis, specified form NEC
crystal(-induced) *—see* Arthritis, in, crystals
deformans *—see* Osteoarthritis
degenerative *—see* Osteoarthritis
due to or associated with
acromegaly E22.0
brucellosis *—see* Brucellosis
caisson disease T70.3
diabetes *—see* Diabetes, arthropathy
dracontiasis *—see also* category M01 *[B72]*
enteritis NEC
regional *—see* Enteritis, regional
erysipelas *—see also* category M01 *[A46]*
erythema
epidemic A25.1
nodosum L52
filariasis NOS B74.9
glanders A24.0
helminthiasis *—see also* category M01 *[B83.9]*
hemophilia D66 *[M36.2]*
Henoch-(Schönlein) purpura D69.0 *[M36.4]*
human parvovirus *—see also* category M01 *[B97.6]*
infectious disease NEC M01
leprosy(*see* also category M01) *—see also* Leprosy A30.9
Lyme disease A69.23
mycobacteria *—see also* category M01 *[A31.8]*
parasitic disease NEC *—see also* category M01 *[B89]*
paratyphoid fever(*see* also category M01) *—see also* Fever, paratyphoid A01.4
rat bite fever *—see also* category M01 *[A25.1]*
regional enteritis *—see* Enteritis, regional
respiratory disorder NOS J98.9
serum sickness *—see also* Reaction, serum T80.69
syringomyelia G95.0
typhoid fever A01.04
epidemic erythema A25.1
febrile *—see* Fever, rheumatic
gonococcal A54.42
gouty (acute) *—see* Gout, idiopathic

Arthritis, arthritic *(continued)*
in (due to)
acromegaly *—see also* subcategory M14.8- E22.0
amyloidosis *—see also* subcategory M14.8- E85.4
bacterial disease *—see also* subcategory M01 *[A49.9]*
Behçet's syndrome M35.2
caisson disease *—see also* subcategory M14.8- T70.3
coliform bacilli(Escherichia coli) *—see* Arthritis, in, pyogenic organism NEC
crystals M11.9
dicalcium phosphate *—see* Arthritis, in, crystals, specified type NEC
hydroxyapatite M11.0-
pyrophosphate *—see* Arthritis, in, crystals, specified type NEC
specified type NEC M11.80
ankle M11.87-
elbow M11.82-
foot joint M11.87-
hand joint M11.84-
hip M11.85-
knee M11.86-
multiple sites M11.8-
shoulder M11.81-
vertebrae M11.88
wrist M11.83-
dermatoarthritis, lipoid E78.81
dracontiasis (dracunculiasis) *—see also* category M01 *[B72]*
endocrine disorder NEC *—see also* subcategory M14.8- E34.9
enteritis, infectious NEC *—see also* category M01 *[A09]*
specified organism NEC *—see also* category M01 *[A08.8]*
erythema
multiforme *—see also* subcategory M14.8- L51.9
nodosum *—see also* subcategory M14.8- L52
gout *—see* Gout, idiopathic
helminthiasis NEC *—see also* category M01 *[B83.9]*
hemochromatosis *—see also* subcategory M14.8- E83.118
hemoglobinopathy NEC D58.2 *[M36.3]*
hemophilia NEC D66 *[M36.2]*
Hemophilus influenzae M00.8- B96.3
Henoch(-Schönlein) purpura D69.0 *[M36.4]*
hyperparathyroidism NEC *—see also* subcategory M14.8- E21.3
hypersensitivity reaction NEC T78.49 *[M36.4]*
hypogammaglobulinemia *—see also* subcategory M14.8- D80.1
hypothyroidism NEC *—see also* subcategory M14.8- E03.9
infection *—see* Arthritis, pyogenic or pyemic
spine *—see* Spondylopathy, infective
infectious disease NEC M01
leprosy *—see also* category M01 *[A30.9]*
leukemia NEC C95.9- M36.1
lipoid dermatoarthritis E78.81
Lyme disease A69.23
Mediterranean fever, familial *—see also* subcategory M14.8- E85.0
Meningococcus A39.83
metabolic disorder NEC *—see also* subcategory M14.8- E88.9

Arthritis, arthritic *(continued)*
in *(continued)*
multiple myelomatosis C90.0-M36.1
mumps B26.85
mycosis NEC *—see also* category M01 *[B49]*
myelomatosis (multiple) C90.0-M36.1
neurological disorder NEC G98.0
ochronosis *—see also* subcategory M14.8- E70.29
O'nyong-nyong *—see also* category M01 *[A92.1]*
parasitic disease NEC *—see also* category M01 *[B89]*
paratyphoid fever *—see also* category M01 *[A01.4]*
Pseudomonas *—see* Arthritis, pyogenic, bacterial NEC
psoriasis L40.50
pyogenic organism NEC *—see* Arthritis, pyogenic, bacterial NEC
Reiter's disease *—see* Reiter's disease
respiratory disorder NEC *—see also* subcategory M14.8- J98.9
reticulosis, malignant *—see also* subcategory M14.8- C86.0
rubella B06.82
Salmonella (arizonae) (cholerae-suis) (enteritidis) (typhimurium) A02.23
sarcoidosis D86.86
specified bacteria NEC *—see* Arthritis, pyogenic, bacterial NEC
sporotrichosis B42.82
syringomyelia G95.0
thalassemia NEC D56.9 *[M36.3]*
tuberculosis *—see* Tuberculosis, arthritis
typhoid fever A01.04
urethritis, Reiter's *—see* Reiter's disease
viral disease NEC *—see also* category M01 *[B34.9]*
infectious or infective *—see also* Arthritis, pyogenic or pyemic
spine *—see* Spondylopathy, infective
juvenile M08.90
with systemic onset *—see* Still's disease
ankle M08.97-
elbow M08.92-
foot joint M08.97-
hand joint M08.94-
hip M08.95-
knee M08.96-
multiple site M08.99
pauciarticular M08.40
ankle M08.47-
elbow M08.42-
foot joint M08.47-
hand joint M08.44-
hip M08.45-
knee M08.46-
shoulder M08.41-
vertebrae M08.48
wrist M08.43-
psoriatic L40.54
rheumatoid *—see* Arthritis, rheumatoid, juvenile
shoulder M08.91-
vertebra M08.98
specified type NEC M08.80
ankle M08.87-
elbow M08.82-
foot joint M08.87-
hand joint M08.84-

Arthritis, arthritic *(continued)*
- juvenile *(continued)*
  - specified type NEC *(continued)*
    - hip M08.85-
    - knee M08.86-
    - multiple site M08.89
    - shoulder M08.81-
    - specified joint NEC M08.88
    - vertebrae M08.88
    - wrist M08.83-
  - wrist M08.93-
- meaning osteoarthritis —*see* Osteoarthritis
- meningococcal A39.83
- menopausal(any site) NEC —*see* Arthritis, specified form NEC
- mutilans (psoriatic) L40.52
- mycotic NEC —*see also* category M01 *[B49]*
- neuropathic (Charcot) —*see* Arthropathy, neuropathic
  - diabetic —*see* Diabetes, arthropathy, neuropathic
  - nonsyphilitic NEC G98.0
  - syringomyelic G95.0
- ochronotic —*see also* subcategory M14.8- E70.29
- palindromic(any site) —*see* Rheumatism, palindromic
- pneumococcal M00.10
  - ankle M00.17-
  - elbow M00.12-
  - foot joint —*see* Arthritis, pneumococcal, ankle
  - hand joint M00.14-
  - hip M00.15-
  - knee M00.16-
  - multiple site M00.19
  - shoulder M00.11-
  - vertebra M00.18
  - wrist M00.13-
- postdysenteric —*see* Arthropathy, postdysenteric
- postmeningococcal A39.84
- postrheumatic, chronic —*see* Arthropathy, postrheumatic, chronic
- primary progressive —*see also* Arthritis, specified form NEC
  - spine —*see* Spondylitis, ankylosing
- psoriatic L40.50
- purulent(any site except spine) —*see* Arthritis, pyogenic or pyemic
  - spine —*see* Spondylopathy, infective
- pyogenic or pyemic(any site except spine) M00.9
  - bacterial NEC M00.80
    - ankle M00.87-
    - elbow M00.82-
    - foot joint —*see* Arthritis, pyogenic, bacterial NEC, ankle
    - hand joint M00.84-
    - hip M00.85-
    - knee M00.86-
    - multiple site M00.89
    - shoulder M00.81-
    - vertebra M00.88
    - wrist M00.83-
  - pneumococcal —*see* Arthritis, pneumococcal
  - spine —*see* Spondylopathy, infective
  - staphylococcal —*see* Arthritis, staphylococcal
  - streptococcal —*see* Arthritis, streptococcal NEC
    - pneumococcal —*see* Arthritis, pneumococcal
- reactive —*see* Reiter's disease

Arthritis, arthritic *(continued)*
- rheumatic —*see also* Arthritis, rheumatoid
  - acute or subacute —*see* Fever, rheumatic
- rheumatoid M06.9
  - with
    - carditis —*see* Rheumatoid, carditis
    - endocarditis —*see* Rheumatoid, carditis
    - heart involvement NEC —*see* Rheumatoid, carditis
    - lung involvement —*see* Rheumatoid, lung
    - myocarditis —*see* Rheumatoid, carditis
    - myopathy —*see* Rheumatoid, myopathy
    - pericarditis —*see* Rheumatoid, carditis
    - polyneuropathy —*see* Rheumatoid, polyneuropathy
    - rheumatoid factor —*see* Arthritis, rheumatoid, seropositive
    - splenoadenomegaly and leukopenia —*see* Felty's syndrome
    - vasculitis —*see* Rheumatoid, vasculitis
    - visceral involvement NEC —*see* Rheumatoid, arthritis, with involvement of organs NEC
  - juvenile (with or without rheumatoid factor) M08.00
    - ankle M08.07-
    - elbow M08.02-
    - foot joint M08.07-
    - hand joint M08.04-
    - hip M08.05-
    - knee M08.06-
    - multiple site M08.09
    - shoulder M08.01-
    - vertebra M08.08
    - wrist M08.03-
  - seronegative M06.00
    - ankle M06.07-
    - elbow M06.02-
    - foot joint M06.07-
    - hand joint M06.04-
    - hip M06.05-
    - knee M06.06-
    - multiple site M06.09
    - shoulder M06.01-
    - vertebra M06.08
    - wrist M06.03-
  - seropositive M05.9
    - specified NEC M05.80
      - ankle M05.87-
      - elbow M05.82-
      - foot joint M05.87-
      - hand joint M05.84-
      - hip M05.85-
      - knee M05.86-
      - multiple sites M05.89
      - shoulder M05.81-
      - vertebra —*see* Spondylitis, ankylosing
      - wrist M05.83-
    - without organ involvement M05.70
      - ankle M05.77-
      - elbow M05.72-
      - foot joint M05.77-
      - hand joint M05.74-
      - hip M05.75-
      - knee M05.76-
      - multiple sites M05.79
      - shoulder M05.71-
      - vertebra —*see* Spondylitis, ankylosing
      - wrist M05.73-

Arthritis, arthritic *(continued)*
- rheumatoid *(continued)*
  - specified type NEC M06.80
    - ankle M06.87-
    - elbow M06.82-
    - foot joint M06.87-
    - hand joint M06.84-
    - hip M06.85-
    - knee M06.86-
    - multiple site M06.89
    - shoulder M06.81-
    - vertebra M06.88
    - wrist M06.83-
  - spine —*see* Spondylitis, ankylosing
- rubella B06.82
- scorbutic —*see also* subcategory M14.8- E54
- senile or senescent —*see* Osteoarthritis
- septic(any site except spine) —*see* Arthritis, pyogenic or pyemic
  - spine —*see* Spondylopathy, infective
- serum (nontherapeutic) (therapeutic) —*see* Arthropathy, postimmunization
- specified form NEC M13.80
  - ankle M13.87-
  - elbow M13.82-
  - foot joint M13.87-
  - hand joint M13.84-
  - hip M13.85-
  - knee M13.86-
  - multiple site M13.89
  - shoulder M13.81-
  - specified joint NEC M13.88
  - wrist M13.83-
- spine —*see also* Spondylopathy, inflammatory
  - infectious or infective NEC —*see* Spondylopathy, infective
  - Marie-Strümpell —*see* Spondylitis, ankylosing
  - pyogenic —*see* Spondylopathy, infective
  - rheumatoid —*see* Spondylitis, ankylosing
  - traumatic (old) —*see* Spondylopathy, traumatic
  - tuberculous A18.01
- staphylococcal M00.00
  - ankle M00.07-
  - elbow M00.02-
  - foot joint —*see* Arthritis, staphylococcal, ankle
  - hand joint M00.04-
  - hip M00.05-
  - knee M00.06-
  - multiple site M00.09
  - shoulder M00.01-
  - vertebra M00.08
  - wrist M00.03-
- streptococcal NEC M00.20
  - ankle M00.27-
  - elbow M00.22-
  - foot joint —*see* Arthritis, streptococcal, ankle
  - hand joint M00.24-
  - hip M00.25-
  - knee M00.26-
  - multiple site M00.29
  - shoulder M00.21-
  - vertebra M00.28
  - wrist M00.23-
- suppurative —*see* Arthritis, pyogenic or pyemic
- syphilitic (late) A52.16
  - congenital A50.55 *[M12.80]*
- syphilitica deformans (Charcot) A52.16
- temporomandibular M26.69

Arthritis, arthritic *(continued)*
- toxic of menopause(any site) —*see* Arthritis, specified form NEC
- transient —*see* Arthropathy, specified form NEC
- traumatic (chronic) —*see* Arthropathy, traumatic
- tuberculous A18.02
  - spine A18.01
- uratic —*see* Gout, idiopathic
- urethritica(Reiter's) —*see* Reiter's disease
- vertebral —*see* Spondylopathy, inflammatory
- villous(any site) —*see* Arthropathy, specified form NEC

Arthrocele —*see* Effusion, joint

Arthrodesis status Z98.1

Arthrodynia —*see also* Pain, joint

Arthrodysplasia Q74.9

Arthrofibrosis, joint —*see* Ankylosis

Arthrogryposis (congenital) Q68.8
- multiplex congenita Q74.3

Arthrokatadysis M24.7

Arthropathy —*see also* Arthritis M12.9
- Charcot's —*see* Arthropathy, neuropathic
  - diabetic —*see* Diabetes, arthropathy, neuropathic
  - syringomyelic G95.0
- cricoarytenoid J38.7
- crystal (-induced) —*see* Arthritis, in, crystals
- diabetic NEC —*see* Diabetes, arthropathy
- distal interphalangeal, psoriatic L40.51
- enteropathic M07.60
  - ankle M07.67-
  - elbow M07.62-
  - foot joint M07.67-
  - hand joint M07.64-
  - hip M07.65-
  - knee M07.66-
  - multiple site M07.69
  - shoulder M07.61-
  - vertebra M07.68
  - wrist M07.63-
- following intestinal bypass M02.00
  - ankle M02.07-
  - elbow M02.02-
  - foot joint M02.07-
  - hand joint M02.04-
  - hip M02.05-
  - knee M02.06-
  - multiple site M02.09
  - shoulder M02.01-
  - vertebra M02.08
  - wrist M02.03-
- gouty —*see also* Gout, idiopathic
  - in (due to)
    - Lesch-Nyhan syndrome E79.1 *[M14.8]-*
    - sickle-cell disorders D57- M14.8-
- hemophilic NEC D66 *[M36.2]*
  - in (due to)
    - hyperparathyroidism NEC E21.3 *[M14.8]-*
    - metabolic disease NOS E88.9 *[M14.8]-*
- in (due to)
  - acromegaly E22.0 *[M14.8]-*
  - amyloidosis E85.4 *[M14.8]-*
  - blood disorder NOS D75.9 *[M36.3]*
  - diabetes —*see* Diabetes, arthropathy
  - endocrine disease NOS E34.9 *[M14.8]-*

- **Arthropathy** *(continued)*
  - in *(continued)*
    - erythema
      - multiforme L51.9 *[M14.8]*-
      - nodosum L52 *[M14.8]*-
    - hemochromatosis E83.118 M14.8-
    - hemoglobinopathy NEC D58.2 *[M36.3]*
    - hemophilia NEC D66 *[M36.2]*
    - Henoch-Schönlein purpura D69.0 *[M36.4]*
    - hyperthyroidism E05.90 *[M14.8]*-
    - hypothyroidism E03.9 *[M14.8]*-
    - infective endocarditis I33.0 M12.80
    - leukemia NEC C95.9- M36.1
    - malignant histiocytosis C96.A M36.1
    - metabolic disease NOS E88.9 *[M14.8]*-
    - multiple myeloma C90.0- M36.1
    - neoplastic disease NOS (*see* also Neoplasm) D49.9 *[M36.1]*
    - nutritional deficiency —*see also* subcategory M14.8- E63.9
    - psoriasis NOS L40.50
    - sarcoidosis D86.86
    - syphilis (late) A52.77
      - congenital A50.55 *[M12.80]*
    - thyrotoxicosis —*see also* subcategory M14.8- E05.90
    - ulcerative colitis K51.90 *[M07.60]*
    - viral hepatitis (postinfectious) NEC B19.9 *[M12.80]*
    - Whipple's disease —*see also* subcategory M14.8- K90.81
  - Jaccoud —*see* Arthropathy, postrheumatic, chronic
  - juvenile —*see* Arthritis, juvenile
    - psoriatic L40.54
  - mutilans (psoriatic) L40.52
  - neuropathic (Charcot) M14.60
    - ankle M14.67-
    - diabetic —*see* Diabetes, arthropathy, neuropathic
    - elbow M14.62-
    - foot joint M14.67-
    - hand joint M14.64-
    - hip M14.65-
    - knee M14.66-
    - multiple site M14.69
    - nonsyphilitic NEC G98.0
    - shoulder M14.61-
    - syringomyelic G95.0
    - vertebra M14.68
    - wrist M14.63-
  - osteopulmonary —*see* Osteoarthropathy, hypertrophic, specified NEC
  - postdysenteric M02.10
    - ankle M02.17-
    - elbow M02.12-
    - foot joint M02.17-
    - hand joint M02.14-
    - hip M02.15-
    - knee M02.16-
    - multiple site M02.19
    - shoulder M02.11-
    - vertebra M02.18
    - wrist M02.13-
  - postimmunization M02.20
    - ankle M02.27-
    - elbow M02.22-
    - foot joint M02.27-
    - hand joint M02.24-
    - hip M02.25-
    - knee M02.26-
    - multiple site M02.29
    - shoulder M02.21-
    - vertebra M02.28
    - wrist M02.23-

- **Arthropathy** *(continued)*
  - postinfectious NEC B99 *[M12.80]*
    - in (due to)
      - enteritis due to Yersinia enterocolitica A04.6 *[M12.80]*
      - syphilis A52.77
      - viral hepatitis NEC B19.9 *[M12.80]*
  - postrheumatic, chronic (Jaccoud) M12.00
    - ankle M12.07-
    - elbow M12.02-
    - foot joint M12.07-
    - hand joint M12.04-
    - hip M12.05-
    - knee M12.06-
    - multiple site M12.09
    - shoulder M12.01-
    - specified joint NEC M12.08
    - vertebrae M12.08
    - wrist M12.03-
  - psoriatic NEC L40.59
    - interphalangeal, distal L40.51
  - reactive M02.9
    - in(due to)
      - infective endocarditis I33.0 *[M02.9]*
    - specified type NEC M02.80
      - ankle M02.87-
      - elbow M02.82-
      - foot joint M02.87-
      - hand joint M02.84-
      - hip M02.85-
      - knee M02.86-
      - multiple site M02.89
      - shoulder M02.81-
      - vertebra M02.88
      - wrist M02.83-
  - specified form NEC M12.80
    - ankle M12.87-
    - elbow M12.82-
    - foot joint M12.87-
    - hand joint M12.84-
    - hip M12.85-
    - knee M12.86-
    - multiple site M12.89
    - shoulder M12.81-
    - specified joint NEC M12.88
    - vertebrae M12.88
    - wrist M12.83-
  - syringomyelic G95.0
  - tabes dorsalis A52.16
  - tabetic A52.16
  - transient —*see* Arthropathy, specified form NEC
  - traumatic M12.50
    - ankle M12.57-
    - elbow M12.52-
    - foot joint M12.57-
    - hand joint M12.54-
    - hip M12.55-
    - knee M12.56-
    - multiple site M12.59
    - shoulder M12.51-
    - specified joint NEC M12.58
    - vertebrae M12.58
    - wrist M12.53-
- **Arthropyosis** —*see* Arthritis, pyogenic or pyemic
- **Arthrosis** (deformans) (degenerative) (localized) —*see also* Osteoarthritis M19.90
  - spine —*see* Spondylosis
- **Arthus' phenomenon or reaction** T78.41
  - due to
    - drug —*see* Table of Drugs and Chemicals, by drug
- **Articular** —*see* condition
- **Articulation, reverse** (teeth) M26.24

- **Artificial**
  - insemination complication —*see* Complications, artificial, fertilization
  - opening status (functioning) (without complication) Z93.9
    - anus (colostomy) Z93.3
    - colostomy Z93.3
    - cystostomy Z93.50
      - appendico-vesicostomy Z93.52
      - cutaneous Z93.51
      - specified NEC Z93.59
    - enterostomy Z93.4
    - gastrostomy Z93.1
    - ileostomy Z93.2
    - intestinal tract NEC Z93.4
    - jejunostomy Z93.4
    - nephrostomy Z93.6
    - specified site NEC Z93.8
    - tracheostomy Z93.0
    - ureterostomy Z93.6
    - urethrostomy Z93.6
    - urinary tract NEC Z93.6
    - vagina Z93.8
  - vagina status Z93.8
- **Arytenoid** —*see* condition
- **Asbestosis** (occupational) J61
- **ASC-H** (atypical squamous cells cannot exclude high grade squamous intraepithelial lesion on cytologic smear)
  - anus R85.611
  - cervix R87.611
  - vagina R87.621
- **ASC-US** (atypical squamous cells of undetermined significance on cytologic smear)
  - anus R85.610
  - cervix R87.610
  - vagina R87.620
- **Ascariasis** B77.9
  - with
    - complications NEC B77.89
    - intestinal complications B77.0
    - pneumonia, pneumonitis B77.81
- **Ascaridosis, ascaridiasis** —*see* Ascariasis
- **Ascaris** (infection) (infestation) (lumbricoides) —*see* Ascariasis
- **Ascending** —*see* condition
- **Aschoff's bodies** —*see* Myocarditis, rheumatic
- **Ascites** (abdominal) R18.8
  - cardiac I50.9
  - chylous (nonfilarial) I89.8
    - filarial —*see* Infestation, filarial
  - due to
    - cirrhosis, alcoholic K70.31
    - hepatitis
      - alcoholic K70.11
      - chronic active K71.51
    - S. japonicum B65.2
  - heart I50.9
  - malignant R18.0
  - pseudochylous R18.8
  - syphilitic A52.74
  - tuberculous A18.31
- **Aseptic** —*see* condition
- **Asherman's syndrome** N85.6
- **Asialia** K11.7
- **Asiatic cholera** —*see* Cholera
- **Asimultagnosia** (simultanagnosia) R48.3
- **Askin's tumor** —*see* Neoplasm, connective tissue, malignant
- **Asocial personality** F60.2

- **Asomatognosia** R41.4
- **Aspartylglucosaminuria** E77.1
- **Asperger's disease or syndrome** F84.5
- **Aspergilloma** —*see* Aspergillosis
- **Aspergillosis** (with pneumonia) B44.9
  - bronchopulmonary, allergic B44.81
  - disseminated B44.7
  - generalized B44.7
  - pulmonary NEC B44.1
    - allergic B44.81
    - invasive B44.0
  - specified NEC B44.89
  - tonsillar B44.2
- **Aspergillus** (flavus) (fumigatus) (infection) (terreus) —*see* Aspergillosis
- **Aspermatogenesis** —*see* Azoospermia
- **Aspermia** (testis) —*see* Azoospermia
- **Asphyxia, asphyxiation** (by) R09.01
  - antenatal P84
  - birth P84
  - bunny bag —*see* Asphyxia, due to, mechanical threat to breathing, trapped in bed clothes
  - crushing S28.0
  - drowning T75.1
  - gas, fumes, or vapor —*see* Table of Drugs and Chemicals
  - inhalation —*see* Inhalation
  - intrauterine P84
  - local I73.00
    - with gangrene I73.01
  - mucus —*see also* Foreign body, respiratory tract, causing asphyxia
  - newborn P84
  - pathological R09.01
  - postnatal P84
    - mechanical —*see* Asphyxia, due to, mechanical threat to breathing
  - prenatal P84
  - reticularis R23.1
  - strangulation —*see* Asphyxia, due to, mechanical threat to breathing
  - submersion T75.1
  - traumatic T71.9
    - due to
      - crushed chest S28.0
      - foreign body (in) —*see* Foreign body, respiratory tract, causing asphyxia
      - low oxygen content of ambient air T71.20
        - due to
          - being trapped in
            - low oxygen environment T71.29
              - in car trunk T71.221
                - circumstances undetermined T71.224
                - done with intent to harm by
                  - another person T71.223
                  - self T71.222
              - in refrigerator T71.231
                - circumstances undetermined T71.234
                - done with intent to harm by
                  - another person T71.233
                  - self T71.232
          - cave-in T71.21

Asphyxia, asphyxiation *(continued)*
- traumatic *(continued)*
  - due to *(continued)*
    - mechanical threat to breathing (accidental) T71.191
      - circumstances undetermined T71.194
      - done with intent to harm by
        - another person T71.193
        - self T71.192
    - hanging T71.161
      - circumstances
        - undetermined T71.164
      - done with intent to harm by
        - another person T71.163
        - self T71.162
    - plastic bag T71.121
      - circumstances
        - undetermined T71.124
      - done with intent to harm by
        - another person T71.123
        - self T71.122
    - smothering
      - in furniture T71.151
        - circumstances
          - undetermined T71.154
        - done with intent to harm by
          - another person T71.153
          - self T71.152
      - under
        - another person's body T71.141
          - circumstances
            - undetermined T71.144
          - done with intent to harm T71.143
        - pillow T71.111
          - circumstances
            - undetermined T71.114
          - done with intent to harm by
            - another person T71.113
            - self T71.112
    - trapped in bed clothes T71.131
      - circumstances
        - undetermined T71.134
      - done with intent to harm by
        - another person T71.133
        - self T71.132
- vomiting, vomitus —*see* Foreign body, respiratory tract, causing asphyxia

Aspiration
- amniotic (clear) fluid (newborn) P24.10
  - with
    - pneumonia (pneumonitis) P24.11
    - respiratory symptoms P24.11
- blood
  - newborn(without respiratory symptoms) P24.20
    - with
      - pneumonia (pneumonitis) P24.21
      - respiratory symptoms P24.21
  - specified age NEC —*see* Foreign body, respiratory tract
- bronchitis J69.0
- food or foreign body(with asphyxiation) —*see* Asphyxia, food
- liquor (amnii) (newborn) P24.10
  - with
    - pneumonia (pneumonitis) P24.11
    - respiratory symptoms P24.11

Aspiration *(continued)*
- meconium (newborn) (without respiratory symptoms) P24.00
  - with
    - pneumonitis (pneumonitis) P24.01
    - respiratory symptoms P24.01
- milk (newborn) (without respiratory symptoms) P24.30
  - with
    - pneumonia (pneumonitis) P24.31
    - respiratory symptoms P24.31
  - specified age NEC —*see* Foreign body, respiratory tract
- mucus —*see also* Foreign body, by site, causing asphyxia
  - newborn P24.10
    - with
      - pneumonia (pneumonitis) P24.11
      - respiratory symptoms P24.11
- neonatal P24.9
  - specific NEC (without respiratory symptoms) P24.80
    - with
      - pneumonia (pneumonitis) P24.81
      - respiratory symptoms P24.81
- newborn P24.9
  - specific NEC (without respiratory symptoms) P24.80
    - with
      - pneumonia (pneumonitis) P24.81
      - respiratory symptoms P24.81
- pneumonia J69.0
- pneumonitis J69.0
- syndrome of newborn —*see* Aspiration, by substance, with pneumonia
- vernix caseosa (newborn) P24.80
  - with
    - pneumonia (pneumonitis) P24.81
    - respiratory symptoms P24.81
- vomitus —*see also* Foreign body, respiratory tract
  - newborn(without respiratory symptoms) P24.30
    - with
      - pneumonia (pneumonitis) P24.31
      - respiratory symptoms P24.31

Asplenia (congenital) Q89.01
- postsurgical Z90.81

Assam fever B55.0

Assault, sexual —*see* Maltreatment

Assmann's focus NEC A15.0

Astasia(-abasia) (hysterical) F44.4

Asteatosis cutis L85.3

Astereognosia, astereognosis R48.1

Asterixis R27.8
- in liver disease K71.3

Asteroid hyalitis —*see* Deposit, crystalline

Asthenia, asthenic R53.1
- cardiac —*see also* Failure, heart I50.9
  - psychogenic F45.8
- cardiovascular —*see also* Failure, heart I50.9
  - psychogenic F45.8
- heart —*see also* Failure, heart I50.9
  - psychogenic F45.8
- hysterical F44.4
- myocardial —*see also* Failure, heart I50.9
  - psychogenic F45.8
- nervous F48.8
- neurocirculatory F45.8

Asthenia, asthenic *(continued)*
- neurotic F48.8
- psychogenic F48.8
- psychoneurotic F48.8
- psychophysiologic F48.8
- reaction (psychophysiologic) F48.8
- senile R54

Asthenopia —*see also* Discomfort, visual
- hysterical F44.6
- psychogenic F44.6

Asthenospermia —*see* Abnormal, specimen, male genital organs

Asthma, asthmatic (bronchial) (catarrh) (spasmodic) J45.909
- with
  - chronic obstructive bronchitis J44.9
    - with
      - acute lower respiratory infection J44.0
      - exacerbation (acute) J44.1
  - chronic obstructive pulmonary disease J44.9
    - with
      - acute lower respiratory infection J44.0
      - exacerbation (acute) J44.1
  - exacerbation (acute) J45.901
  - hay fever —*see* Asthma, allergic extrinsic
  - rhinitis, allergic —*see* Asthma, allergic extrinsic
  - status asthmaticus J45.902
- allergic extrinsic J45.909
  - with
    - exacerbation (acute) J45.901
    - status asthmaticus J45.902
- atopic —*see* Asthma, allergic extrinsic
- cardiac —*see* Failure, ventricular, left
- cardiobronchial I50.1
- childhood J45.909
  - with
    - exacerbation (acute) J45.901
    - status asthmaticus J45.902
- chronic obstructive J44.9
  - with
    - acute lower respiratory infection J44.0
    - exacerbation (acute) J44.1
- collier's J60
- cough variant J45.991
- detergent J69.8
- due to
  - detergent J69.8
  - inhalation of fumes J68.3
- eosinophilic J82
- extrinsic, allergic —*see* Asthma, allergic extrinsic
- grinder's J62.8
- hay —*see* Asthma, allergic extrinsic
- heart I50.1
- idiosyncratic —*see* Asthma, nonallergic
- intermittent (mild) J45.20
  - with
    - exacerbation (acute) J45.21
    - status asthmaticus J45.22
- intrinsic, nonallergic —*see* Asthma, nonallergic
- Kopp's E32.8
- late-onset J45.909
  - with
    - exacerbation (acute) J45.901
    - status asthmaticus J45.902
- mild intermittent J45.20
  - with
    - exacerbation (acute) J45.21
    - status asthmaticus J45.22

Asthma, asthmatic *(continued)*
- mild persistent J45.30
  - with
    - exacerbation (acute) J45.31
    - status asthmaticus J45.32
- Millar's(laryngismus stridulus) J38.5
- miner's J60
- mixed J45.909
  - with
    - exacerbation (acute) J45.901
    - status asthmaticus J45.902
- moderate persistent J45.40
  - with
    - exacerbation (acute) J45.41
    - status asthmaticus J45.42
- nervous —*see* Asthma, nonallergic
- nonallergic (intrinsic) J45.909
  - with
    - exacerbation (acute) J45.901
    - status asthmaticus J45.902
- persistent
  - mild J45.30
    - with
      - exacerbation (acute) J45.31
      - status asthmaticus J45.32
  - moderate J45.40
    - with
      - exacerbation (acute) J45.41
      - status asthmaticus J45.42
  - severe J45.50
    - with
      - exacerbation (acute) J45.51
      - status asthmaticus J45.52
- platinum J45.998
- pneumoconiotic NEC J64
- potter's J62.8
- predominantly allergic J45.909
- psychogenic F54
- pulmonary eosinophilic J82
- red cedar J67.8
- Rostan's I50.1
- sandblaster's J62.8
- sequoiosis J67.8
- severe persistent J45.50
  - with
    - exacerbation (acute) J45.51
    - status asthmaticus J45.52
- specified NEC J45.998
- stonemason's J62.8
- thymic E32.8
- tuberculous —*see* Tuberculosis, pulmonary
- Wichmann's(laryngismus stridulus) J38.5
- wood J67.8

Astigmatism (compound) (congenital) H52.20-
- irregular H52.21-
- regular H52.22-

Astraphobia F40.220

Astroblastoma
- specified site —*see* Neoplasm, malignant, by site
- unspecified site C71.9

Astrocytoma (cystic)
- anaplastic
  - specified site —*see* Neoplasm, malignant, by site
  - unspecified site C71.9
- fibrillary
  - specified site —*see* Neoplasm, malignant, by site
  - unspecified site C71.9
- fibrous
  - specified site —*see* Neoplasm, malignant, by site
  - unspecified site C71.9
- gemistocytic
  - specified site —*see* Neoplasm, malignant, by site
  - unspecified site C71.9

Astrocytoma *(continued)*
- juvenile
  - specified site *—see* Neoplasm, malignant, by site
  - unspecified site C71.9
- pilocytic
  - specified site *—see* Neoplasm, malignant, by site
  - unspecified site C71.9
- piloid
  - specified site *—see* Neoplasm, malignant, by site
  - unspecified site C71.9
- protoplasmic
  - specified site *—see* Neoplasm, malignant, by site
  - unspecified site C71.9
- specified site NEC *—see* Neoplasm, malignant, by site
- subependymal D43.2
  - giant cell
    - specified site *—see* Neoplasm, uncertain behavior, by site
    - unspecified site D43.2
  - specified site *—see* Neoplasm, uncertain behavior, by site
  - unspecified site D43.2
- unspecified site C71.9

Astroglioma
- specified site *—see* Neoplasm, malignant, by site
- unspecified site C71.9

Asymbolia R48.8

Asymmetry *—see also* Distortion
- between native and reconstructed breast N65.1
- face Q67.0
- jaw (lower) *—see* Anomaly, dentofacial, jaw-cranial base relationship, asymmetry

Asynergia, asynergy R27.8
- ventricular I51.89

Asystole (heart) *—see* Arrest, cardiac

At risk
- for falling Z91.81

Ataxia, ataxy, ataxic R27.0
- acute R27.8
- brain (hereditary) G11.9
- cerebellar (hereditary) G11.9
  - with defective DNA repair G11.3
  - alcoholic G31.2
  - early-onset G11.1
  - in
    - alcoholism G31.2
    - myxedema E03.9 *[G13.2]*
    - neoplastic disease *—see also* Neoplasm D49.9 *[G13.1]*
    - specified disease NEC G32.81
  - late-onset(Marie's) G11.2
- cerebral (hereditary) G11.9
- congenital nonprogressive G11.0
- family, familial *—see* Ataxia, hereditary
- following
  - cerebrovascular disease I69.993
    - cerebral infarction I69.393
    - intracerebral hemorrhage I69.193
    - nontraumatic intracranial hemorrhage NEC I69.293
    - specified disease NEC I69.893
    - subarachnoid hemorrhage I69.093
- Friedreich's (heredofamilial) (cerebellar) (spinal) G11.1
- gait R26.0
  - hysterical F44.4
- general R27.8
- gluten M35.9 *[G32.81]*
  - with celiac disease K90.0 *[G32.81]*

Ataxia, ataxy, ataxic *(continued)*
- hereditary G11.9
  - with neuropathy G60.2
  - cerebellar *—see* Ataxia, cerebellar
  - spastic G11.4
  - specified NEC G11.8
  - spinal(Friedreich's) G11.1
- heredofamilial *—see* Ataxia, hereditary
- Hunt's G11.1
- hysterical F44.4
- locomotor (progressive) (syphilitic) (partial) (spastic) A52.11
  - diabetic *—see* Diabetes, ataxia
- Marie's (cerebellar) (heredofamilial) (late- onset) G11.2
- nonorganic origin F44.4
- nonprogressive, congenital G11.0
- psychogenic F44.4
- Roussy-Lévy G60.0
- Sanger-Brown's (hereditary) G11.2
- spastic hereditary G11.4
- spinal
  - hereditary(Friedreich's) G11.1
  - progressive (syphilitic) A52.11
- spinocerebellar, X-linked recessive G11.1
- telangiectasia(Louis-Bar) G11.3

Ataxia-telangiectasia (Louis-Bar) G11.3

Atelectasis (massive) (partial) (pressure) (pulmonary) J98.11
- newborn P28.10
  - due to resorption P28.11
  - partial P28.19
  - primary P28.0
  - secondary P28.19
- primary (newborn) P28.0
- tuberculous *—see* Tuberculosis, pulmonary

Atelocardia Q24.9

Atelomyelia Q06.1

Atheroembolism
- of
  - extremities
    - lower I75.02-
    - upper I75.01-
  - kidney I75.81
  - specified NEC I75.89

Atheroma, atheromatous *—see also* Arteriosclerosis I70.90
- aorta, aortic I70.0
  - valve *—see also* Endocarditis, aortic I35.8
- aorto-iliac I70.0
- artery *—see* Arteriosclerosis
- basilar (artery) I67.2
- carotid (artery) (common) (internal) I67.2
- cerebral (arteries) I67.2
- coronary (artery) I25.10
  - with angina pectoris *—see* Arteriosclerosis, coronary (artery),
- degeneration *—see* Arteriosclerosis
- heart, cardiac *—see* Disease, heart, ischemic, atherosclerotic
- mitral (valve) I34.8
- myocardium, myocardial *—see* Disease, heart, ischemic, atherosclerotic
- pulmonary valve (heart) *—see also* Endocarditis, pulmonary I37.8
- tricuspid (heart) (valve) I36.8
- valve, valvular *—see* Endocarditis
- vertebral (artery) I67.2

Atheromatosis *—see* Arteriosclerosis

Atherosclerosis *—see also* Arteriosclerosis
- coronary
  - artery I25.10
    - with angina pectoris *—see* Arteriosclerosis, coronary (artery),
    - due to
      - calcified coronary lesion (severely) I25.84
      - lipid rich plaque I25.83
  - transplanted heart I25.811
    - bypass graft I25.812
      - with angina pectoris *—see* Arteriosclerosis, coronary (artery),
    - native coronary artery I25.811
      - with angina pectoris *—see* Arteriosclerosis, coronary (artery),

Athetosis (acquired) R25.8
- bilateral (congenital) G80.3
- congenital (bilateral) (double) G80.3
- double (congenital) G80.3
- unilateral R25.8

Athlete's
- foot B35.3
- heart I51.7

Athrepsia E41

Athyrea (acquired) *—see also* Hypothyroidism
- congenital E03.1

Atonia, atony, atonic
- bladder (sphincter) (neurogenic) N31.2
- capillary I78.8
- cecum K59.8
  - psychogenic F45.8
- colon *—see* Atony, intestine
- congenital P94.2
- esophagus K22.8
- intestine K59.8
  - psychogenic F45.8
- stomach K31.89
  - neurotic or psychogenic F45.8
- uterus(during labor) O62.2
  - with hemorrhage (postpartum) O72.1
  - postpartum(with hemorrhage) O72.1
    - without hemorrhage O75.89

Atopy *—see* History, allergy

Atransferrinemia, congenital E88.09

Atresia, atretic
- alimentary organ or tract NEC Q45.8
  - upper Q40.8
- ani, anus, anal (canal) Q42.3
  - with fistula Q42.2
- aorta (arch) (ring) Q25.2
- aortic (orifice) (valve) Q23.0
  - arch Q25.2
  - congenital with hypoplasia of ascending aorta and defective development of left ventricle (with mitral stenosis) Q23.4
  - in hypoplastic left heart syndrome Q23.4
- aqueduct of Sylvius Q03.0
  - with spina bifida *—see* Spina bifida, with hydrocephalus
- artery NEC Q27.8
  - cerebral Q28.3
  - coronary Q24.5
  - digestive system Q27.8
  - eye Q15.8
  - lower limb Q27.8
  - pulmonary Q25.5
  - specified site NEC Q27.8
  - umbilical Q27.0
  - upper limb Q27.8

Atresia, atretic *(continued)*
- auditory canal (external) Q16.1
- bile duct (common) (congenital) (hepatic) Q44.2
  - acquired *—see* Obstruction, bile duct
- bladder (neck) Q64.39
  - obstruction Q64.31
- bronchus Q32.4
- cecum Q42.8
- cervix (acquired) N88.2
  - congenital Q51.828
  - in pregnancy or childbirth *—see* Anomaly, cervix, in pregnancy or childbirth
    - causing obstructed labor O65.5
- choana Q30.0
- colon Q42.9
  - specified NEC Q42.8
- common duct Q44.2
- cricoid cartilage Q31.8
- cystic duct Q44.2
  - acquired K82.8
    - with obstruction K82.0
- digestive organs NEC Q45.8
- duodenum Q41.0
- ear canal Q16.1
- ejaculatory duct Q55.4
- epiglottis Q31.8
- esophagus Q39.0
  - with tracheoesophageal fistula Q39.1
- eustachian tube Q17.8
- fallopian tube (congenital) Q50.6
  - acquired N97.1
- follicular cyst N83.0
- foramen of
  - Luschka Q03.1
    - with spina bifida *—see* Spina bifida, with hydrocephalus
  - Magendie Q03.1
    - with spina bifida *—see* Spina bifida, with hydrocephalus
- gallbladder Q44.1
- genital organ
  - external
    - female Q52.79
    - male Q55.8
  - internal
    - female Q52.8
    - male Q55.8
- glottis Q31.8
- gullet Q39.0
  - with tracheoesophageal fistula Q39.1
- heart valve NEC Q24.8
  - pulmonary Q22.0
  - tricuspid Q22.4
- hymen Q52.3
  - acquired (postinfective) N89.6
- ileum Q41.2
- intestine (small) Q41.9
  - large Q42.9
    - specified NEC Q42.8
- iris, filtration angle Q15.0
- jejunum Q41.1
- lacrimal apparatus Q10.4
- larynx Q31.8
- meatus urinarius Q64.33
- mitral valve Q23.2
  - in hypoplastic left heart syndrome Q23.4
- nares (anterior) (posterior) Q30.0
- nasopharynx Q34.8
- nose, nostril Q30.0
  - acquired J34.89
- organ or site NEC Q89.8
- osseous meatus (ear) Q16.1
- oviduct (congenital) Q50.6
  - acquired N97.1
- parotid duct Q38.4
  - acquired K11.8

Atresia, atretic *(continued)*
  pulmonary (artery) Q25.5
    valve Q22.0
  pulmonic Q22.0
  pupil Q13.2
  rectum Q42.1
    with fistula Q42.0
  salivary duct Q38.4
    acquired K11.8
  sublingual duct Q38.4
    acquired K11.8
  submandibular duct Q38.4
    acquired K11.8
  submaxillary duct Q38.4
    acquired K11.8
  thyroid cartilage Q31.8
  trachea Q32.1
  tricuspid valve Q22.4
  ureter Q62.10
    pelvic junction Q62.11
    vesical orifice Q62.12
  ureteropelvic junction Q62.11
  ureterovesical orifice Q62.12
  urethra (valvular) Q64.39
    stricture Q64.32
  urinary tract NEC Q64.8
  uterus Q51.818
    acquired N85.8
  vagina (congenital) Q52.4
    acquired (postinfectional) (senile) N89.5
  vas deferens Q55.3
  vascular NEC Q27.8
    cerebral Q28.3
    digestive system Q27.8
    lower limb Q27.8
    specified site NEC Q27.8
    upper limb Q27.8
  vein NEC Q27.8
    digestive system Q27.8
    great Q26.8
    lower limb Q27.8
    portal Q26.5
    pulmonary Q26.3
    specified site NEC Q27.8
    upper limb Q27.8
  vena cava (inferior) (superior) Q26.8
  vesicourethral orifice Q64.31
  vulva Q52.79
    acquired N90.5

Atrichia, atrichosis *—see* Alopecia

Atrophia *—see also* Atrophy
  cutis senilis L90.8
    due to radiation L57.8
  gyrata of choroid and retina H31.23
  senilis R54
    dermatological L90.8
      due to radiation (nonionizing) (solar) L57.8
  unguium L60.3
    congenita Q84.6

Atrophie blanche (en plaque) (de Milian) L95.0

Atrophoderma, atrophodermia (of) L90.9
  diffusum (idiopathic) L90.4
  maculatum L90.8
    et striatum L90.8
      due to syphilis A52.79
    syphilitic A51.39
  neuriticum L90.8
  Pasini and Pierini L90.3
  pigmentosum Q82.1
  reticulatum symmetricum faciei L66.4
  senile L90.8
    due to radiation (nonionizing) (solar) L57.8
  vermiculata (cheeks) L66.4

Atrophy, atrophic (of)
  adrenal (capsule) (gland) E27.49
    primary (autoimmune) E27.1
  alveolar process or ridge (edentulous) K08.20
  anal sphincter (disuse) N81.84
  appendix K38.8
  arteriosclerotic *—see* Arteriosclerosis
  bile duct (common) (hepatic) K83.8
  bladder N32.89
    neurogenic N31.8
  blanche(en plaque) (of Milian) L95.0
  bone (senile) NEC *—see also* Disorder, bone, specified type NEC
    due to
      tabes dorsalis (neurogenic) A52.11
  brain (cortex) (progressive) G31.9
    frontotemporal circumscribed G31.01 *[F02.80]*
      with behavioral disturbance G31.01 *[F02.81]*
    senile NEC G31.1
  breast N64.2
    obstetric *—see* Disorder, breast, specified type NEC
  buccal cavity K13.79
  cardiac *—see* Degeneration, myocardial
  cartilage (infectional) (joint) *—see* Disorder, cartilage, specified NEC
  cerebellar *—see* Atrophy, brain
  cerebral *—see* Atrophy, brain
  cervix (mucosa) (senile) (uteri) N88.8
    menopausal N95.8
  Charcot-Marie-Tooth G60.0
  choroid (central) (macular) (myopic) (retina) H31.10-
    diffuse secondary H31.12-
    gyrate H31.23
    senile H31.11-
  ciliary body *—see* Atrophy, iris
  conjunctiva (senile) H11.89
  corpus cavernosum N48.89
  cortical *—see* Atrophy, brain
  cystic duct K82.8
  Déjérine-Thomas G23.8
  disuse NEC *—see* Atrophy, muscle
  Duchenne-Aran G12.21
  ear H93.8-
  edentulous alveolar ridge K08.20
  endometrium (senile) N85.8
    cervix N88.8
  enteric K63.89
  epididymis N50.8
  eyeball *—see* Disorder, globe, degenerated condition, atrophy
  eyelid (senile) *—see* Disorder, eyelid, degenerative
  facial (skin) L90.9
  fallopian tube (senile) N83.32
    with ovary N83.33
  fascioscapulohumeral(Landouzy-Déjérine) G71.0
  fatty, thymus (gland) E32.8
  gallbladder K82.8
  gastric K29.40
    with bleeding K29.41
  gastrointestinal K63.89
  glandular I89.8
  globe H44.52-
  gum K06.0
  hair L67.8
  heart (brown) *—see* Degeneration, myocardial
  hemifacial Q67.4
    Romberg G51.8
  infantile E41
    paralysis, acute *—see* Poliomyelitis, paralytic
  intestine K63.89

Atrophy, atrophic *(continued)*
  iris (essential) (progressive) H21.26-
    specified NEC H21.29
  kidney (senile) (terminal) *—see also* Sclerosis, renal N26.1
    congenital or infantile Q60.5
      bilateral Q60.4
      unilateral Q60.3
    hydronephrotic *—see* Hydronephrosis
  lacrimal gland (primary) H04.14-
    secondary H04.15-
  Landouzy-Déjérine G71.0
  laryngitis, infective J37.0
  larynx J38.7
  Leber's optic (hereditary) H47.22
  lip K13.0
  liver (yellow) K72.90
    with coma K72.91
    acute, subacute K72.00
      with coma K72.01
    chronic K72.10
      with coma K72.11
  lung (senile) J98.4
  macular (dermatological) L90.8
    syphilitic, skin A51.39
      striated A52.79
  mandible (edentulous) K08.20
    minimal K08.21
    moderate K08.22
    severe K08.23
  maxilla K08.20
    minimal K08.24
    moderate K08.25
    severe K08.26
  muscle, muscular (diffuse) (general) (idiopathic) (primary) M62.50
    ankle M62.57-
    Duchenne-Aran G12.21
    foot M62.57-
    forearm M62.53-
    hand M62.54-
    infantile spinal G12.0
    lower leg M62.56-
    multiple sites M62.59
    myelopathic *—see* Atrophy, muscle, spinal
    myotonic G71.11
    neuritic G58.9
    neuropathic (peroneal) (progressive) G60.0
    pelvic (disuse) N81.84
    peroneal G60.0
    progressive (bulbar) G12.21
      adult G12.1
      infantile (spinal) G12.0
      spinal G12.9
        adult G12.1
        infantile G12.0
    pseudohypertrophic G71.0
    shoulder region M62.51-
    specified site NEC M62.58
    spinal G12.9
      adult form G12.1
      Aran-Duchenne G12.21
      childhood form, type II G12.1
      distal G12.1
      hereditary NEC G12.1
      infantile, type I (Werdnig-Hoffmann) G12.0
      juvenile form, type III (Kugelberg- Welander) G12.1
      progressive G12.21
      scapuloperoneal form G12.1
      specified NEC G12.8
    syphilitic A52.78
    thigh M62.55-
    upper arm M62.52-
  myocardium *—see* Degeneration, myocardial
  myometrium (senile) N85.8
    cervix N88.8

Atrophy, atrophic *(continued)*
  myopathic NEC *—see* Atrophy, muscle
  myotonia G71.11
  nail L60.3
  nasopharynx J31.1
  nerve *—see also* Disorder, nerve
    abducens *—see* Strabismus, paralytic, sixth nerve
    accessory G52.8
    acoustic or auditory H93.3
    cranial G52.9
      eighth (auditory) H93.3
      eleventh (accessory) G52.8
      fifth (trigeminal) G50.8
      first (olfactory) G52.0
      fourth (trochlear) *—see* Strabismus, paralytic, fourth nerve
      second (optic) H47.20
      sixth (abducens) *—see* Strabismus, paralytic, sixth nerve
      tenth (pneumogastric) (vagus) G52.2
      third (oculomotor) *—see* Strabismus, paralytic, third nerve
      twelfth (hypoglossal) G52.3
    hypoglossal G52.3
    oculomotor *—see* Strabismus, paralytic, third nerve
    olfactory G52.0
    optic(papillomacular bundle)
      syphilitic (late) A52.15
        congenital A50.44
    pneumogastric G52.2
    trigeminal G50.8
    trochlear *—see* Strabismus, paralytic, fourth nerve
    vagus (pneumogastric) G52.2
  neurogenic, bone, tabetic A52.11
  nutritional E41
  old age R54
  olivopontocerebellar G23.8
  optic (nerve) H47.20
    glaucomatous H47.23-
    hereditary H47.22
    primary H47.21-
    specified type NEC H47.29-
    syphilitic (late) A52.15
      congenital A50.44
  orbit H05.31-
  ovary (senile) N83.31
    with fallopian tube N83.33
  oviduct (senile) *—see* Atrophy, fallopian tube
  palsy, diffuse (progressive) G12.22
  pancreas (duct) (senile) K86.8
  parotid gland K11.0
  pelvic muscle N81.84
  penis N48.89
  pharynx J39.2
  pluriglandular E31.8
    autoimmune E31.0
  polyarthritis M15.9
  prostate N42.89
  pseudohypertrophic (muscle) G71.0
  renal *—see also* Sclerosis, renal N26.1
  retina, retinal (postinfectional) H35.89
  rhinitis J31.0
  salivary gland K11.0
  scar L90.5
  sclerosis, lobar(of brain) G31.09 *[F02.80]*
    with behavioral disturbance G31.09 *[F02.81]*
  scrotum N50.8
  seminal vesicle N50.8

- **Atrophy, atrophic** *(continued)*
  - senile R54
    - due to radiation (nonionizing) (solar) L57.8
  - skin (patches) (spots) L90.9
    - degenerative (senile) L90.8
    - due to radiation (nonionizing) (solar) L57.8
    - senile L90.8
  - spermatic cord N50.8
  - spinal (acute) (cord) G95.89
    - muscular —*see* Atrophy, muscle, spinal
    - paralysis G12.20
      - acute —*see* Poliomyelitis, paralytic
      - meaning progressive muscular atrophy G12.21
  - spine (column) —*see* Spondylopathy, specified NEC
  - spleen (senile) D73.0
  - stomach K29.40
    - with bleeding K29.41
  - striate (skin) L90.6
    - syphilitic A52.79
  - subcutaneous L90.9
  - sublingual gland K11.0
  - submandibular gland K11.0
  - submaxillary gland K11.0
  - Sudeck's —*see* Algoneurodystrophy
  - suprarenal (capsule) (gland) E27.49
    - primary E27.1
  - systemic affecting central nervous system
    - in
      - myxedema E03.9 *[G13.2]*
      - neoplastic disease —*see also* Neoplasm D49.9 *[G13.1]*
    - specified disease NEC G13.8
  - tarso-orbital fascia, congenital Q10.3
  - testis N50.0
  - thenar, partial —*see* Syndrome, carpal tunnel
  - thymus (fatty) E32.8
  - thyroid (gland) (acquired) E03.4
    - with cretinism E03.1
    - congenital(with myxedema) E03.1
  - tongue (senile) K14.8
    - papillae K14.4
  - trachea J39.8
  - tunica vaginalis N50.8
  - turbinate J34.89
  - tympanic membrane (nonflaccid) H73.82-
    - flaccid H73.81-
  - upper respiratory tract J39.8
  - uterus, uterine (senile) N85.8
    - cervix N88.8
    - due to radiation(intended effect) N85.8
      - adverse effect or misadventure N99.89
  - vagina (senile) N95.2
  - vas deferens N50.8
  - vascular I99.8
  - vertebra (senile) —*see* Spondylopathy, specified NEC
  - vulva (senile) N90.5
  - Werdnig-Hoffmann G12.0
  - yellow —*see* Failure, hepatic
- **Attack, attacks**
  - with alteration of consciousness (with automatisms) —*see* Epilepsy, localization-related, symptomatic, with complex partial seizures
  - Adams-Stokes I45.9
  - akinetic —*see* Epilepsy, generalized, specified NEC
  - angina —*see* Angina
  - atonic —*see* Epilepsy, generalized, specified NEC
- **Attack, attacks** *(continued)*
  - benign shuddering G25.83
  - cataleptic —*see* Catalepsy
  - coronary —*see* Infarct, myocardium
  - cyanotic, newborn P28.2
  - drop NEC R55
  - epileptic —*see* Epilepsy
  - heart —*see* infarct, myocardium
  - hysterical F44.9
  - jacksonian —*see* Epilepsy, localization-related, symptomatic, with simple partial seizures
  - myocardium, myocardial —*see* Infarct, myocardium
  - myoclonic —*see* Epilepsy, generalized, specified NEC
  - panic F41.0
  - psychomotor —*see* Epilepsy, localization-related, symptomatic, with complex partial seizures
  - salaam —*see* Epilepsy, spasms
  - schizophreniform, brief F23
  - shuddering, benign G25.83
  - Stokes-Adams I45.9
  - syncope R55
  - transient ischemic (TIA) G45.9
    - specified NEC G45.8
  - unconsciousness R55
    - hysterical F44.89
  - vasomotor R55
  - vasovagal (paroxysmal) (idiopathic) R55
  - without alteration of consciousness —*see* Epilepsy, localization-related, symptomatic, with simple partial seizures
- **Attention** (to)
  - artificial
    - opening (of) Z43.9
      - digestive tract NEC Z43.4
        - colon Z43.3
        - ilium Z43.2
        - stomach Z43.1
      - specified NEC Z43.8
      - trachea Z43.0
      - urinary tract NEC Z43.6
        - cystostomy Z43.5
        - nephrostomy Z43.6
        - ureterostomy Z43.6
        - urethrostomy Z43.6
      - vagina Z43.7
  - colostomy Z43.3
  - cystostomy Z43.5
  - deficit disorder or syndrome F98.8
    - with hyperactivity —*see* Disorder, attention-deficit hyperactivity
  - gastrostomy Z43.1
  - ileostomy Z43.2
  - jejunostomy Z43.4
  - nephrostomy Z43.6
  - surgical dressings Z48.01
  - sutures Z48.02
  - tracheostomy Z43.0
  - ureterostomy Z43.6
  - urethrostomy Z43.6
- **Attrition**
  - gum K06.0
  - tooth, teeth (excessive) (hard tissues) K03.0
- **Atypical, atypism** —*see also* condition
  - cells(on cytolgocial smear) (endocervical) (endometrial) (glandular)
    - cervix R87.619
    - vagina R87.629
  - cervical N87.9
  - endometrium N85.9
    - hyperplasia N85.00
  - parenting situation Z62.9
- **Auditory** —*see* condition
- **Aujeszky's disease** B33.8
- **Aurantiasis, cutis** E67.1
- **Auricle, auricular** —*see also* condition
  - cervical Q18.2
- **Auriculotemporal syndrome** G50.8
- **Austin Flint murmur** (aortic insufficiency) I35.1
- **Australian**
  - Q fever A78
  - X disease A83.4
- **Autism, autistic** (childhood) (infantile) F84.0
  - atypical F84.9
- **Autodigestion** R68.89
- **Autoerythrocyte sensitization** (syndrome) D69.2
- **Autographism** L50.3
- **Autoimmune**
  - disease (systemic) M35.9
  - inhibitors to clotting factors D68.311
  - lymphoproliferative syndrome [ALPS] D89.82
  - thyroiditis E06.3
- **Autointoxication** R68.89
- **Automatism** G93.89
  - with temporal sclerosis G93.81
  - epileptic —*see* Epilepsy, localization-related, symptomatic, with complex partial seizures
  - paroxysmal, idiopathic —*see* Epilepsy, localization-related, symptomatic, with complex partial seizures
- **Autonomic, autonomous**
  - bladder (neurogenic) N31.2
  - hysteria seizure F44.5
- **Autosensitivity, erythrocyte** D69.2
- **Autosensitization, cutaneous** L30.2
- **Autosome** —*see* condition by chromosome involved
- **Autotopagnosia** R48.1
- **Autotoxemia** R68.89
- **Autumn** —*see* condition
- **Avellis' syndrome** G46.8
- **Aversion**
  - oral R63.3
    - newborn P92.-
    - nonorganic origin F98.2
  - sexual F52.1
- **Aviator's**
  - disease or sickness —*see* Effect, adverse, high altitude
  - ear T70.0
- **Avitaminosis** (multiple) —*see also* Deficiency, vitamin E56.9
  - B E53.9
    - with
      - beriberi E51.11
      - pellagra E52
  - B2 *[E53.0]*
  - B6 *[E53.1]*
  - B12 *[E53.8]*
  - D E55.9
    - with rickets E55.0
  - G E53.0
  - K E56.1
  - nicotinic acid E52
- **AVNRT** (atrioventricular nodal re-entrant tachycardia) I47.1
- **AVRT** (atrioventricular nodal re-entrant tachycardia) I47.1
- **Avulsion** (traumatic)
  - blood vessel —*see* Injury, blood vessel
  - bone —*see* Fracture, by site
  - cartilage —*see also* Dislocation, by site
    - symphyseal (inner), complicating delivery O71.6
  - external site other than limb —*see* Wound, open, by site
  - eye S05.7-
  - head (intracranial)
    - external site NEC S08.89
    - scalp S08.0
  - internal organ or site —*see* Injury, by site
  - joint —*see also* Dislocation, by site
    - capsule —*see* Sprain, by site
  - kidney S37.06-
  - ligament —*see* Sprain, by site
  - limb —*see also* Amputation, traumatic, by site
    - skin and subcutaneous tissue —*see* Wound, open, by site
  - muscle —*see* Injury, muscle
  - nerve (root) —*see* Injury, nerve
  - scalp S08.0
  - skin and subcutaneous tissue —*see* Wound, open, by site
  - spleen S36.032
  - symphyseal cartilage (inner), complicating delivery O71.6
  - tendon —*see* Injury, muscle
  - tooth S03.2
- **Awareness of heart beat** R00.2
- **Axenfeld's**
  - anomaly or syndrome Q15.0
  - degeneration (calcareous) Q13.4
- **Axilla, axillary** —*see also* condition
  - breast Q83.1
- **Axonotmesis** —*see* Injury, nerve
- **Ayerza's disease or syndrome**(pulmonary artery sclerosis with pulmonary hypertension) I27.0
- **Azoospermia** (organic) N46.01
  - due to
    - drug therapy N46.021
    - efferent duct obstruction N46.023
    - infection N46.022
    - radiation N46.024
    - specified cause NEC N46.029
    - systemic disease N46.025
- **Azotemia** R79.89
  - meaning uremia N19
- **Aztec ear** Q17.3
- **Azygos**
  - continuation inferior vena cava Q26.8
  - lobe (lung) Q33.1

B

- **Baastrup's disease** —*see* Kissing spine
- **Babesiosis** B60.0
- **Babington's disease** (familial hemorrhagic telangiectasia) I78.0
- **Babinski's syndrome** A52.79
- **Baby**
  - crying constantly R68.11
  - floppy (syndrome) P94.2
- **Bacillary** —*see* condition
- **Bacilluria** N39.0
- **Bacillus** —*see also* Infection, bacillus
  - abortus infection A23.1
  - anthracis infection A22.9

Bacillus *(continued)*
  coli infection *—see also* Escherichia coli B96.20
  Flexner's A03.1
  mallei infection A24.0
  Shiga's A03.0
  suipestifer infection *—see* Infection, salmonella

Back *—see* condition

Backache (postural) M54.9
  sacroiliac M53.3
  specified NEC M54.89

Backflow *—see* Reflux

Backward reading (dyslexia) F81.0

Bacteremia R78.81
  with sepsis *—see* Sepsis

Bactericholia *—see* Cholecystitis, acute

Bacterid, bacteride (pustular) L40.3

Bacterium, bacteria, bacterial
  agent NEC, as cause of disease classified elsewhere B96.89
  in blood *—see* Bacteremia
  in urine *—see* Bacteriuria

Bacteriuria, bacteruria N39.0
  asymptomatic N39.0

Bacteroides
  fragilis, as cause of disease classified elsewhere B96.6

Bad
  heart *—see* Disease, heart
  trip
    due to drug abuse *—see* Abuse, drug, hallucinogen
    due to drug dependence *—see* Dependence, drug, hallucinogen

Baelz's disease (cheilitis glandularis apostematosa) K13.0

Baerensprung's disease (eczema marginatum) B35.6

Bagasse disease or pneumonitis J67.1

Bagassosis J67.1

Baker's cyst *—see* Cyst, Baker's

Bakwin-Krida syndrome (craniometaphyseal dysplasia) Q78.5

Balancing side interference M26.56

Balanitis (circinata) (erosiva) (gangrenosa) (phagedenic) (vulgaris) N48.1
  amebic A06.82
  candidal B37.42
  due to Haemophilus ducreyi A57
  gonococcal (acute) (chronic) A54.09
  xerotica obliterans N48.0

Balanoposthitis N47.6
  gonococcal (acute) (chronic) A54.09
  ulcerative (specific) A63.8

Balanorrhagia *—see* Balanitis

Balantidiasis, balantidiosis A07.0

Bald tongue K14.4

Baldness *—see also* Alopecia
  male-pattern *—see* Alopecia, androgenic

Balkan grippe A78

Balloon disease *—see* Effect, adverse, high altitude

Balo's disease (concentric sclerosis) G37.5

Bamberger-Marie disease *—see* Osteoarthropathy, hypertrophic, specified type NEC

Bancroft's filariasis B74.0

Band (s)
  adhesive *—see* Adhesions, peritoneum
  anomalous or congenital *—see also* Anomaly, by site
    heart (atrial) (ventricular) Q24.8
    intestine Q43.3
    omentum Q43.3
  cervix N88.1
  constricting, congenital Q79.8
  gallbladder (congenital) Q44.1
  intestinal (adhesive) *—see* Adhesions, peritoneum
  obstructive
    intestine K56.5
    peritoneum K56.5
  periappendiceal, congenital Q43.3
  peritoneal (adhesive) *—see* Adhesions, peritoneum
  uterus N73.6
    internal N85.6
  vagina N89.5

Bandemia D72.825

Bandl's ring (contraction), **complicating delivery** O62.4

Bangkok hemorrhagic fever A91

Bang's disease (brucella abortus) A23.1

Bankruptcy, anxiety concerning Z59.8

Bannister's disease T78.3
  hereditary D84.1

Banti's disease or syndrome (with cirrhosis) (with portal hypertension) K76.6

Bar, median, prostate *—see* Enlargement, enlarged, prostate

Barcoo disease or rot *—see* Ulcer, skin

Barlow's disease E54

Barodontalgia T70.29

Baron Münchausen syndrome *—see* Disorder, factitious

Barosinusitis T70.1

Barotitis T70.0

Barotrauma T70.29
  odontalgia T70.29
  otitic T70.0
  sinus T70.1

Barraquer (-Simons) **disease or syndrome** (progressive lipodystrophy) E88.1

Barré-Guillain disease or syndrome G61.0

Barré-Liéou syndrome (posterior cervical sympathetic) M53.0

Barrel chest M95.4

Barrett's
  disease *—see* Barrett's, esophagus
  esophagus K22.70
    with dysplasia K22.719
      high grade K22.711
      low grade K22.710
    without dysplasia K22.70
  syndrome *—see* Barrett's, esophagus
  ulcer K22.10
    with bleeding K22.11
    without bleeding K22.10

Bársony (-Polgár) (-Teschendorf) syndrome (corkscrew esophagus) K22.4

Bartholinitis (suppurating) N75.8
  gonococcal (acute) (chronic) (with abscess) A54.1

Barth syndrome E78.71

Bartonellosis A44.9
  cutaneous A44.1
  mucocutaneous A44.1
  specified NEC A44.8
  systemic A44.0

Barton's fracture S52.56-

Bartter's syndrome E26.81

Basal *—see* condition

Basan's (hidrotic) **ectodermal dysplasia** Q82.4

Baseball finger *—see* Dislocation, finger

Basedow's disease (exophthalmic goiter) *—see* Hyperthyroidism, with, goiter

Basic *—see* condition

Basilar *—see* condition

Bason's (hidrotic) **ectodermal dysplasia** Q82.4

Basopenia *—see* Agranulocytosis

Basophilia D72.824

Basophilism (cortico-adrenal) (Cushing's) (pituitary) E24.0

Bassen-Kornzweig disease or syndrome E78.6

Bat ear Q17.5

Bateman's
  disease B08.1
  purpura (senile) D69.2

Bathing cramp T75.1

Bathophobia F40.248

Batten (-Mayou) **disease** E75.4
  retina E75.4 *[H36]*

Batten-Steinert syndrome G71.11

Battered *—see* Maltreatment

Battey Mycobacterium infection A31.0

Battle exhaustion F43.0

Battledore placenta O43.19-

Baumgarten-Cruveilhier cirrhosis, disease or syndrome K74.69

Bauxite fibrosis(of lung) J63.1

Bayle's disease (general paresis) A52.17

Bazin's disease (primary) (tuberculous) A18.4

Beach ear *—see* Swimmer's, ear

Beaded hair (congenital) Q84.1

Béal conjunctivitis or syndrome B30.2

Beard's disease (neurasthenia) F48.8

Beat (s)
  atrial, premature I49.1
  ectopic I49.49
  elbow *—see* Bursitis, elbow
  escaped, heart I49.49
  hand *—see* Bursitis, hand
  knee *—see* Bursitis, knee
  premature I49.40
    atrial I49.1
    auricular I49.1
    supraventricular I49.1

Beau's
  disease or syndrome *—see* Degeneration, myocardial
  lines(transverse furrows on fingernails) L60.4

Bechterev's syndrome *—see* Spondylitis, ankylosing

Beck's syndrome (anterior spinal artery occlusion) I65.8

Becker's
  cardiomyopathy I42.8
  disease
    idiopathic mural endomyocardial disease I42.3
    myotonia congenita, recessive form G71.12
  dystrophy G71.0
  pigmented hairy nevus D22.5

Beckwith-Wiedemann syndrome Q87.3

Bed confinement status Z74.01

Bed sore *—see* Ulcer, pressure, by site

Bedbug bite (s) *—see* Bite (s), by site, superficial, insect

Bedclothes, asphyxiation or suffocation by *—see* Asphyxia, traumatic, due to, mechanical, trapped

Bednar's
  aphthae K12.0
  tumor *—see* Neoplasm, malignant, by site

Bedridden Z74.01

Bedsore *—see* Ulcer, pressure, by site

Bedwetting *—see* Enuresis

Bee sting (with allergic or anaphylactic shock) *—see* Toxicity, venom, arthropod, bee

Beer drinker's heart (disease) I42.6

Begbie's disease (exophthalmic goiter) *—see* Hyperthyroidism, with, goiter

Behavior
  antisocial
    adult Z72.811
    child or adolescent Z72.810
  disorder, disturbance *—see* Disorder, conduct
  disruptive *—see* Disorder, conduct
  drug *see*king Z72.89
  inexplicable R46.2
  marked evasiveness R46.5
  obsessive-compulsive R46.81
  overactivity R46.3
  poor responsiveness R46.4
  self-damaging(life-style) Z72.89
  sleep-incompatible Z72.821
  slowness R46.4
  specified NEC R46.89
  strange(and inexplicable) R46.2
  suspiciousness R46.5
  type A pattern Z73.1
  undue concern or preoccupation with stressful events R46.6
  verbosity and circumstantial detail obscuring reason for contact R46.7

Behçet's disease or syndrome M35.2

Behr's disease *—see* Degeneration, macula

Beigel's disease or morbus (white piedra) B36.2

Bejel A65

Bekhterev's syndrome *—see* Spondylitis, ankylosing

Belching *—see* Eructation

Bell's
  mania F30.8
  palsy, paralysis G51.0
    infant or newborn P11.3
  spasm G51.3

Bence Jones albuminuria or proteinuria NEC R80.3

Bends T70.3

Benedikt's paralysis or syndrome G46.3

Bite *(continued)*
- digit (s)
  - hand —*see* Bite, finger
  - toe —*see* Bite, toe
- ear (canal) (external) S01.35-
  - superficial NEC S00.47-
    - insect S00.46-
- elbow S51.05-
  - superficial NEC S50.37-
    - insect S50.36-
- epididymis —*see* Bite, testis
- epigastric region —*see* Bite, abdomen
- epiglottis —*see* Bite, neck, specified site NEC
- esophagus, cervical S11.25
  - superficial NEC S10.17
    - insect S10.16
- eyebrow —*see* Bite, eyelid
- eyelid S01.15-
  - superficial NEC S00.27-
    - insect S00.26-
- face NEC —*see* Bite, head, specified site NEC
- finger (s) S61.259
  - with
    - damage to nail S61.359
  - index S61.258
    - with
      - damage to nail S61.358
    - left S61.251
      - with
        - damage to nail S61.351
    - right S61.250
      - with
        - damage to nail S61.350
    - superficial NEC S60.478
      - insect S60.46-
  - little S61.25-
    - with
      - damage to nail S61.35-
    - superficial NEC S60.47-
      - insect S60.46-
  - middle S61.25-
    - with
      - damage to nail S61.35-
    - superficial NEC S60.47-
      - insect S60.46-
  - ring S61.25-
    - with
      - damage to nail S61.35-
    - superficial NEC S60.47-
      - insect S60.46-
  - superficial NEC S60.479
    - insect S60.469
  - thumb —*see* Bite, thumb
- flank —*see* Bite, abdomen, wall
- flea —*see* Bite, by site, superficial, insect
- foot(except toe (s) alone) S91.35-
  - superficial NEC S90.87-
    - insect S90.86-
  - toe —*see* Bite, toe
- forearm S51.85-
  - elbow only —*see* Bite, elbow
  - superficial NEC S50.87-
    - insect S50.86-
- forehead —*see* Bite, head, specified site NEC
- genital organs, external
  - female S31.552
    - superficial NEC S30.876
      - insect S30.866
    - vagina and vulva —*see* Bite, vulva
  - male S31.551
    - penis —*see* Bite, penis
    - scrotum —*see* Bite, scrotum
    - superficial NEC S30.875
      - insect S30.865
    - testes —*see* Bite, testis
- groin —*see* Bite, abdomen, wall
- gum —*see* Bite, oral cavity

Bite *(continued)*
- hand S61.45-
  - finger —*see* Bite, finger
  - superficial NEC S60.57-
    - insect S60.56-
  - thumb —*see* Bite, thumb
- head S01.95
  - cheek —*see* Bite, cheek
  - ear —*see* Bite, ear
  - eyelid —*see* Bite, eyelid
  - lip —*see* Bite, lip
  - nose —*see* Bite, nose
  - oral cavity —*see* Bite, oral cavity
  - scalp —*see* Bite, scalp
  - specified site NEC S01.85
    - superficial NEC S00.87
      - insect S00.86
  - superficial NEC S00.97
    - insect S00.96
  - temporomandibular area —*see* Bite, cheek
- heel —*see* Bite, foot
- hip S71.05-
  - superficial NEC S70.27-
    - insect S70.26-
- hymen S31.45
- hypochondrium —*see* Bite, abdomen, wall
- hypogastric region —*see* Bite, abdomen, wall
- inguinal region —*see* Bite, abdomen, wall
- insect —*see* Bite, by site, superficial, insect
- instep —*see* Bite, foot
- interscapular region —*see* Bite, thorax, back
- jaw —*see* Bite, head, specified site NEC
- knee S81.05-
  - superficial NEC S80.27-
    - insect S80.26-
- labium (majus) (minus) —*see* Bite, vulva
- lacrimal duct —*see* Bite, eyelid
- larynx S11.015
  - superficial NEC S10.17
    - insect S10.16
- leg (lower) S81.85-
  - ankle —*see* Bite, ankle
  - foot —*see* Bite, foot
  - knee —*see* Bite, knee
  - superficial NEC S80.87-
    - insect S80.86-
  - toe —*see* Bite, toe
  - upper —*see* Bite, thigh
- lip S01.551
  - superficial NEC S00.571
    - insect S00.561
- lizard (venomous) —*see* Venom, bite, reptile
- loin —*see* Bite, abdomen, wall
- lower back —*see* Bite, back, lower
- lumbar region —*see* Bite, back, lower
- malar region —*see* Bite, head, specified site NEC
- mammary —*see* Bite, breast
- marine animals (venomous) —*see* Toxicity, venom, marine animal
- mastoid region —*see* Bite, head, specified site NEC
- mouth —*see* Bite, oral cavity
- nail
  - finger —*see* Bite, finger
  - toe —*see* Bite, toe
- nape —*see* Bite, neck, specified site NEC
- nasal (septum) (sinus) —*see* Bite, nose
- nasopharynx —*see* Bite, head, specified site NEC

Bite *(continued)*
- neck S11.95
  - involving
    - cervical esophagus —*see* Bite, esophagus, cervical
    - larynx —*see* Bite, larynx
    - pharynx —*see* Bite, pharynx
    - thyroid gland S11.15
    - trachea —*see* Bite, trachea
  - specified site NEC S11.85
    - superficial NEC S10.87
      - insect S10.86
  - superficial NEC S10.97
    - insect S10.96
  - throat S11.85
    - superficial NEC S10.17
      - insect S10.16
- nose (septum) (sinus) S01.25
  - superficial NEC S00.37
    - insect S00.36
- occipital region —*see* Bite, scalp
- oral cavity S01.552
  - superficial NEC S00.572
    - insect S00.562
- orbital region —*see* Bite, eyelid
- palate —*see* Bite, oral cavity
- palm —*see* Bite, hand
- parietal region —*see* Bite, scalp
- pelvis S31.050
  - with penetration into retroperitoneal space S31.051
  - superficial NEC S30.870
    - insect S30.860
- penis S31.25
  - superficial NEC S30.872
    - insect S30.862
- perineum
  - female —*see* Bite, vulva
  - male —*see* Bite, pelvis
- periocular area(with or without lacrimal passages) —*see* Bite, eyelid
- phalanges
  - finger —*see* Bite, finger
  - toe —*see* Bite, toe
- pharynx S11.25
  - superficial NEC S10.17
    - insect S10.16
- pinna —*see* Bite, ear
- poisonous —*see* Venom
- popliteal space —*see* Bite, knee
- prepuce —*see* Bite, penis
- pubic region —*see* Bite, abdomen, wall
- rectovaginal septum —*see* Bite, vulva
- red bug B88.0
- reptile NEC —*see also* Venom, bite, reptile
  - nonvenomous —*see* Bite, by site
  - snake —*see* Venom, bite, snake
- sacral region —*see* Bite, back, lower
- sacroiliac region —*see* Bite, back, lower
- salivary gland —*see* Bite, oral cavity
- scalp S01.05
  - superficial NEC S00.07
    - insect S00.06
- scapular region —*see* Bite, shoulder
- scrotum S31.35
  - superficial NEC S30.873
    - insect S30.863
- sea-snake (venomous) —*see* Toxicity, venom, snake, sea snake
- shin —*see* Bite, leg
- shoulder S41.05-
  - superficial NEC S40.27-
    - insect S40.26-
- snake —*see also* Venom, bite, snake
  - nonvenomous —*see* Bite, by site
- spermatic cord —*see* Bite, testis
- spider (venomous) —*see* Toxicity, venom, spider
  - nonvenomous —*see* Bite, by site, superficial, insect

Bite *(continued)*
- sternal region —*see* Bite, thorax, front
- submaxillary region —*see* Bite, head, specified site NEC
- submental region —*see* Bite, head, specified site NEC
- subungual
  - finger (s) —*see* Bite, finger
  - toe —*see* Bite, toe
- superficial —*see* Bite, by site, superficial
- supraclavicular fossa S11.85
- supraorbital —*see* Bite, head, specified site NEC
- temple, temporal region —*see* Bite, head, specified site NEC
- temporomandibular area —*see* Bite, cheek
- testis S31.35
  - superficial NEC S30.873
    - insect S30.863
- thigh S71.15-
  - superficial NEC S70.37-
    - insect S70.36-
- thorax, thoracic (wall) S21.95
  - back S21.25-
    - with penetration into thoracic cavity S21.45-
  - breast —*see* Bite, breast
  - front S21.15-
    - with penetration into thoracic cavity S21.35-
  - superficial NEC S20.97
    - back S20.47-
    - front S20.37-
    - insect S20.96
      - back S20.46-
      - front S20.36-
- throat —*see* Bite, neck, throat
- thumb S61.05-
  - with
    - damage to nail S61.15-
  - superficial NEC S60.37-
    - insect S60.36-
- thyroid S11.15
  - superficial NEC S10.87
    - insect S10.86
- toe (s) S91.15-
  - with
    - damage to nail S91.25-
  - great S91.15-
    - with
      - damage to nail S91.25-
  - lesser S91.15-
    - with
      - damage to nail S91.25-
  - superficial NEC S90.47-
    - great S90.47-
    - insect S90.46-
      - great S90.46-
- tongue S01.552
- trachea S11.025
  - superficial NEC S10.17
    - insect S10.16
- tunica vaginalis —*see* Bite, testis
- tympanum, tympanic membrane —*see* Bite, ear
- umbilical region S31.155
- uvula —*see* Bite, oral cavity
- vagina —*see* Bite, vulva
- venomous —*see* Venom
- vocal cords S11.035
  - superficial NEC S10.17
    - insect S10.16
- vulva S31.45
  - superficial NEC S30.874
    - insect S30.864
- wrist S61.55-
  - superficial NEC S60.87-
    - insect S60.86-

- **Biting, cheek or lip** K13.1
- **Biventricular failure** (heart) I50.9
- **Björck**(-Thorson) **syndrome** (malignant carcinoid) E34.0
- **Black**
  - death A20.9
  - eye S00.1-
  - hairy tongue K14.3
  - heel (foot) S90.3-
  - lung (disease) J60
  - palm (hand) S60.22-
- **Blackfan-Diamond anemia or syndrome** (congenital hypoplastic anemia) D61.01
- **Blackhead** L70.0
- **Blackout** R55
- **Bladder** *—see* condition
- **Blast** (air) (hydraulic) (immersion) (underwater)
  - blindness S05.8X-
  - injury
    - abdomen or thorax *—see* Injury, by site
    - ear (acoustic nerve trauma) *—see* Injury, nerve, acoustic, specified type NEC
    - syndrome NEC T70.8
- **Blastoma** *—see* Neoplasm, malignant, by site
  - pulmonary *—see* Neoplasm, lung, malignant
- **Blastomycosis, blastomycotic** B40.9
  - Brazilian *—see* Paracoccidioidomycosis
  - cutaneous B40.3
  - disseminated B40.7
  - European *—see* Cryptococcosis
  - generalized B40.7
  - keloidal B48.0
  - North American B40.9
  - primary pulmonary B40.0
  - pulmonary B40.2
    - acute B40.0
    - chronic B40.1
  - skin B40.3
  - South American *—see* Paracoccidioidomycosis
  - specified NEC B40.89
- **Bleb** (s) R23.8
  - emphysematous (lung) (solitary) J43.9
  - endophthalmitis H59.43
  - filtering (vitreous), after glaucoma surgery Z98.83
  - inflammed (infected), postprocedural H59.40
    - stage 1 H59.41
    - stage 2 H59.42
    - stage 3 H59.43
  - lung (ruptured) J43.9
    - congenital *—see* Atelectasis
    - newborn P25.8
  - subpleural (emphysematous) J43.9
- **Blebitis, postprocedural** H59.40
  - stage 1 H59.41
  - stage 2 H59.42
  - stage 3 H59.43
- **Bleeder** (familial) (hereditary) *—see* Hemophilia
- **Bleeding** *—see also* Hemorrhage
  - anal K62.5
  - anovulatory N97.0
  - atonic, following delivery O72.1
  - capillary I78.8
    - puerperal O72.2
  - contact (postcoital) N93.0
  - due to uterine subinvolution N85.3
  - ear *—see* Otorrhagia

- **Bleeding** *(continued)*
  - excessive, associated with menopausal onset N92.4
  - familial *—see* Defect, coagulation
  - following intercourse N93.0
  - gastrointestinal K92.2
  - hemorrhoids *—see* Hemorrhoids
  - intermenstrual (regular) N92.3
    - irregular N92.1
  - intraoperative *—see* Complication, intraoperative, hemorrhage
  - irregular N92.6
  - menopausal N92.4
  - newborn, intraventricular *—see* Newborn, affected by, hemorrhage, intraventricular
  - nipple N64.59
  - nose R04.0
  - ovulation N92.3
  - postclimacteric N95.0
  - postcoital N93.0
  - postmenopausal N95.0
  - postoperative *—see* Complication, postprocedural, hemorrhage
  - preclimacteric N92.4
  - puberty (excessive, with onset of menstrual periods) N92.2
  - rectum, rectal K62.5
    - newborn P54.2
  - tendencies *—see* Defect, coagulation
  - throat R04.1
  - tooth socket (post-extraction) K91.840
  - umbilical stump P51.9
  - uterus, uterine NEC N93.9
    - climacteric N92.4
    - dysfunctional of functional N93.8
    - menopausal N92.4
    - preclimacteric or premenopausal N92.4
    - unrelated to menstrual cycle N93.9
  - vagina, vaginal (abnormal) N93.9
    - dysfunctional or functional N93.8
    - newborn P54.6
  - vicarious N94.89
- **Blennorrhagia, blennorrhagic** *—see* Gonorrhea
- **Blennorrhea** (acute) (chronic) *—see also* Gonorrhea
  - inclusion (neonatal) (newborn) P39.1
  - lower genitourinary tract (gonococcal) A54.00
  - neonatorum(gonococcal ophthalmia) A54.31
- **Blepharelosis** *—see* Entropion
- **Blepharitis** (angularis) (ciliaris) (eyelid) (marginal) (nonulcerative) H01.009
  - herpes zoster B02.39
  - left H01.006
    - lower H01.005
    - upper H01.004
  - right H01.003
    - lower H01.002
    - upper H01.001
  - squamous H01.029
    - left H01.026
      - lower H01.025
      - upper H01.024
    - right H01.023
      - lower H01.022
      - upper H01.021
  - ulcerative H01.019
    - left H01.016
      - lower H01.015
      - upper H01.014
    - right H01.013
      - lower H01.012
      - upper H01.011

- **Blepharochalasis** H02.30
  - congenital Q10.0
  - left H02.36
    - lower H02.35
    - upper H02.34
  - right H02.33
    - lower H02.32
    - upper H02.31
- **Blepharoclonus** H02.59
- **Blepharoconjunctivitis** H10.50-
  - angular H10.52-
  - contact H10.53-
  - ligneous H10.51-
- **Blepharophimosis** (eyelid) H02.529
  - congenital Q10.3
  - left H02.526
    - lower H02.525
    - upper H02.524
  - right H02.523
    - lower H02.522
    - upper H02.521
- **Blepharoptosis** H02.40-
  - congenital Q10.0
  - mechanical H02.41-
  - myogenic H02.42-
  - neurogenic H02.43-
  - paralytic H02.43-
- **Blepharopyorrhea, gonococcal** A54.39
- **Blepharospasm** G24.5
  - drug induced G24.01
- **Blighted ovum** O02.0
- **Blind** *—see also* Blindness
  - bronchus (congenital) Q32.4
  - loop syndrome K90.2
    - congenital Q43.8
  - sac, fallopian tube (congenital) Q50.6
  - spot, enlarged *—see* Defect, visual field, localized, scotoma, blind spot area
  - tract or tube, congenital NEC *—see* Atresia, by site
- **Blindness** (acquired) (congenital) (both eyes) H54.0
  - blast S05.8X-
  - color *—see* Deficiency, color vision
  - concussion S05.8X-
  - cortical H47.619
    - left brain H47.612
    - right brain H47.611
  - day H53.11
  - due to injury (current episode) S05.9-
    - sequelae -- code to injury with seventh character S
  - eclipse (total) *—see* Retinopathy, solar
  - emotional (hysterical) F44.6
  - face H53.16
  - hysterical F44.6
  - legal (both eyes) (USA definition) H54.8
  - mind R48.8
  - night H53.60
    - abnormal dark adaptation curve H53.61
    - acquired H53.62
    - congenital H53.63
    - specified type NEC H53.69
    - vitamin A deficiency E50.5
  - one eye(other eye normal) H54.40
    - left(normal vision on right) H54.42
      - low vision on right H54.12
    - low vision, other eye H54.10
    - right(normal vision on left) H54.41
      - low vision on left H54.11
  - psychic R48.8
  - river B73.01
  - snow *—see* Photokeratitis
  - sun, solar *—see* Retinopathy, solar
  - transient *—see* Disturbance, vision, subjective, loss, transient

- **Blindness** *(continued)*
  - traumatic (current episode) S05.9-
  - word (developmental) F81.0
    - acquired R48.0
    - secondary to organic lesion R48.0
- **Blister** (nonthermal)
  - abdominal wall S30.821
  - alveolar process S00.522
  - ankle S90.52-
  - antecubital space *—see* Blister, elbow
  - anus S30.827
  - arm (upper) S40.82-
  - auditory canal *—see* Blister, ear
  - auricle *—see* Blister, ear
  - axilla *—see* Blister, arm
  - back, lower S30.820
  - beetle dermatitis L24.89
  - breast S20.12-
  - brow S00.82
  - calf *—see* Blister, leg
  - canthus *—see* Blister, eyelid
  - cheek S00.82
    - internal S00.522
  - chest wall *—see* Blister, thorax
  - chin S00.82
  - costal region *—see* Blister, thorax
  - digit (s)
    - foot *—see* Blister, toe
    - hand *—see* Blister, finger
  - due to burn *—see* Burn, by site, second degree
  - ear S00.42-
  - elbow S50.32-
  - epiglottis S10.12
  - esophagus, cervical S10.12
  - eyebrow *—see* Blister, eyelid
  - eyelid S00.22-
  - face S00.82
  - fever B00.1
  - finger (s) S60.429
    - index S60.42-
    - little S60.42-
    - middle S60.42-
    - ring S60.42-
  - foot (except toe (s) alone) S90.82-
    - toe *—see* Blister, toe
  - forearm S50.82-
    - elbow only *—see* Blister, elbow
  - forehead S00.82
  - fracture - omit code
  - genital organ
    - female S30.826
    - male S30.825
  - gum S00.522
  - hand S60.52-
  - head S00.92
    - ear *—see* Blister, ear
    - eyelid *—see* Blister, eyelid
    - lip S00.521
    - nose S00.32
    - oral cavity S00.522
    - scalp S00.02
    - specified site NEC S00.82
  - heel *—see* Blister, foot
  - hip S70.22-
  - interscapular region S20.429
  - jaw S00.82
  - knee S80.22-
  - larynx S10.12
  - leg (lower) S80.82-
    - knee *—see* Blister, knee
    - upper *—see* Blister, thigh
  - lip S00.521
  - malar region S00.82
  - mammary *—see* Blister, breast
  - mastoid region S00.82
  - mouth S00.522
  - multiple, skin, nontraumatic R23.8
  - nail
    - finger *—see* Blister, finger
    - toe *—see* Blister, toe
  - nasal S00.32

- **Blister** *(continued)*
  - neck S10.92
    - specified site NEC S10.82
    - throat S10.12
  - nose S00.32
  - occipital region S00.02
  - oral cavity S00.522
  - orbital region —*see* Blister, eyelid
  - palate S00.522
  - palm —*see* Blister, hand
  - parietal region S00.02
  - pelvis S30.820
  - penis S30.822
  - periocular area —*see* Blister, eyelid
  - phalanges
    - finger —*see* Blister, finger
    - toe —*see* Blister, toe
  - pharynx S10.12
  - pinna —*see* Blister, ear
  - popliteal space —*see* Blister, knee
  - scalp S00.02
  - scapular region —*see* Blister, shoulder
  - scrotum S30.823
  - shin —*see* Blister, leg
  - shoulder S40.22-
  - sternal region S20.329
  - submaxillary region S00.82
  - submental region S00.82
  - subungual
    - finger (s) —*see* Blister, finger
    - toe (s) —*see* Blister, toe
  - supraclavicular fossa S10.82
  - supraorbital S00.82
  - temple S00.82
  - temporal region S00.82
  - testis S30.823
  - thermal —*see* Burn, second degree, by site
  - thigh S70.32-
  - thorax, thoracic (wall) S20.92
    - back S20.42-
    - front S20.32-
  - throat S10.12
  - thumb S60.32-
  - toe (s) S90.42-
    - great S90.42-
  - tongue S00.522
  - trachea S10.12
  - tympanum, tympanic membrane —*see* Blister, ear
  - upper arm —*see* Blister, arm (upper)
  - uvula S00.522
  - vagina S30.824
  - vocal cords S10.12
  - vulva S30.824
  - wrist S60.82-
- **Bloating** R14.0
- **Bloch-Sulzberger disease or syndrome** Q82.3
- **Block, blocked**
  - alveolocapillary J84.10
  - arborization (heart) I45.5
  - arrhythmic I45.9
  - atrioventricular (incomplete) (partial) I44.30
    - with atrioventricular dissociation I44.2
    - complete I44.2
      - congenital Q24.6
    - congenital Q24.6
    - first degree I44.0
    - second degree(types I and II) I44.1
    - specified NEC I44.39
    - third degree I44.2
    - types I and II I44.1
  - auriculoventricular —*see* Block, atrioventricular
  - bifascicular (cardiac) I45.2
- **Block, blocked** *(continued)*
  - bundle-branch (complete) (false) (incomplete) I45.4
    - bilateral I45.2
    - left I44.7
      - with right bundle branch block I45.2
      - hemiblock I44.60
        - anterior I44.4
        - posterior I44.5
      - incomplete I44.7
        - with right bundle branch block I45.2
    - right I45.10
      - with
        - left bundle branch block I45.2
        - left fascicular block I45.2
      - specified NEC I45.19
    - Wilson's type I45.19
  - cardiac I45.9
  - conduction I45.9
    - complete I44.2
  - fascicular (left) I44.60
    - anterior I44.4
    - posterior I44.5
    - right I45.0
    - specified NEC I44.69
  - foramen Magendie (acquired) G91.1
    - congenital Q03.1
      - with spina bifida —*see* Spina bifida, by site, with hydrocephalus
  - heart I45.9
    - bundle branch I45.4
      - bilateral I45.2
    - complete (atrioventricular) I44.2
    - congenital Q24.6
    - first degree (atrioventricular) I44.0
    - second degree (atrioventricular) I44.1
    - specified type NEC I45.5
    - third degree (atrioventricular) I44.2
  - hepatic vein I82.0
  - intraventricular (nonspecific) I45.4
    - bundle branch
      - bilateral I45.2
  - kidney N28.9
    - postcystoscopic or postprocedural N99.0
  - Mobitz (types I and II) I44.1
  - myocardial —*see* Block, heart
  - nodal I45.5
  - organ or site, congenital NEC —*see* Atresia, by site
  - portal (vein) I81
  - second degree(types I and II) I44.1
  - sinoatrial I45.5
  - sinoauricular I45.5
  - third degree I44.2
  - trifascicular I45.3
  - tubal N97.1
  - vein NOS I82.90
  - Wenckebach (types I and II) I44.1
- **Blockage** —*see* Obstruction
- **Blocq's disease** F44.4
- **Blood**
  - constituents, abnormal R78.9
  - disease D75.9
  - donor —*see* Donor, blood
  - dyscrasia D75.9
    - with
      - abortion —*see* Abortion, by type, complicated by, hemorrhage
      - ectopic pregnancy O08.1
      - molar pregnancy O08.1
    - following ectopic or molar pregnancy O08.1
    - newborn P61.9
    - puerperal, postpartum O72.3
  - flukes NEC —*see* Schistosomiasis
- **Blood** *(continued)*
  - in
    - feces K92.1
      - occult R19.5
    - urine —*see* Hematuria
  - mole O02.0
  - occult in feces R19.5
  - pressure
    - decreased, due to shock following injury T79.4
    - examination only Z01.30
    - fluctuating I99.8
    - high —*see* Hypertension
      - borderline R03.0
      - incidental reading, without diagnosis of hypertension R03.0
    - low —*see also* Hypotension
      - incidental reading, without diagnosis of hypotension R03.1
  - spitting —*see* Hemoptysis
  - staining cornea —*see* Pigmentation, cornea, stromal
  - transfusion
    - reaction or complication —*see* Complications, transfusion
  - type
    - A (Rh positive) Z67.10
      - Rh negative Z67.11
    - AB (Rh positive) Z67.30
      - Rh negative Z67.31
    - B (Rh positive) Z67.20
      - Rh negative Z67.21
    - O (Rh positive) Z67.40
      - Rh negative Z67.41
    - Rh (positive) Z67.90
      - negative Z67.91
  - vessel rupture —*see* Hemorrhage
  - vomiting —*see* Hematemesis
- **Blood-forming organs, disease** D75.9
- **Bloodgood's disease** —*see* Mastopathy, cystic
- **Bloom** (-Machacek)(-Torre) syndrome Q82.8
- **Blount's disease or osteochondrosis** —*see* Osteochondrosis, juvenile, tibia
- **Blue**
  - baby Q24.9
  - diaper syndrome E72.09
  - dome cyst (breast) —*see* Cyst, breast
  - dot cataract Q12.0
  - nevus D22.9
  - sclera Q13.5
    - with fragility of bone and deafness Q78.0
  - toe syndrome I75.02-
- **Blueness** —*see* Cyanosis
- **Blues, postpartal** O90.6
  - baby O90.6
- **Blurring, visual** H53.8
- **Blushing** (abnormal) (excessive) R23.2
- **BMI** —*see* Body, mass index
- **Boarder, hospital NEC** Z76.4
  - accompanying sick person Z76.3
  - healthy infant or child Z76.2
    - foundling Z76.1
- **Bockhart's impetigo** L01.02
- **Bodechtel-Guttman disease** (subacute sclerosing panencephalitis) A81.1
- **Boder-Sedgwick syndrome** (ataxia-telangiectasia) G11.3
- **Body, bodies**
  - Aschoff's —*see* Myocarditis, rheumatic
  - asteroid, vitreous —*see* Deposit, crystalline
- **Body, bodies** *(continued)*
  - cytoid (retina) —*see* Occlusion, artery, retina
  - drusen (degenerative) (macula) (retinal) —*see also* Degeneration, macula, drusen
    - optic disc —*see* Drusen, optic disc
  - foreign —*see* Foreign body
  - loose
    - joint, except knee —*see* Loose, body, joint
      - knee M23.4-
    - sheath, tendon —*see* Disorder, tendon, specified type NEC
  - mass index (BMI)
    - adult
      - 19 or less Z68.1
      - 20.0-20.9 Z68.20
      - 21.0-21.9 Z68.21
      - 22.0-22.9 Z68.22
      - 23.0-23.9 Z68.23
      - 24.0-24.9 Z68.24
      - 25.0-25.9 Z68.25
      - 26.0-26.9 Z68.26
      - 27.0-27.9 Z68.27
      - 28.0-28.9 Z68.28
      - 29.0-29.9 Z68.29
      - 30.0-30.9 Z68.30
      - 31.0-31.9 Z68.31
      - 32.0-32.9 Z68.32
      - 33.0-33.9 Z68.33
      - 34.0-34.9 Z68.34
      - 35.0-35.9 Z68.35
      - 36.0-36.9 Z68.36
      - 37.0-37.9 Z68.37
      - 38.0-38.9 Z68.38
      - 39.0-39.9 Z68.39
      - 40.0-44.9 Z68.41
      - 45.0-49.9 Z68.42
      - 50.0-59.9 Z68.43
      - 60.0-69.9 Z68.44
      - 70 and over Z68.45
    - pediatric
      - 5th percentile to less than 85th percentile for age Z68.52
      - 85th percentile to less than 95th percentile for age Z68.53
      - greater than or equal to ninety-fifth percentile for age Z68.54
      - less than fifth percentile for age Z68.51
  - Mooser's A75.2
  - rice —*see also* Loose, body, joint
    - knee M23.4-
  - rocking F98.4
- **Boeck's**
  - disease or sarcoid —*see* Sarcoidosis
  - lupoid (miliary) D86.3
- **Boerhaave's syndrome** (spontaneous esophageal rupture) K22.3
- **Boggy**
  - cervix N88.8
  - uterus N85.8
- **Boil** —*see also* Furuncle, by site
  - Aleppo B55.1
  - Baghdad B55.1
  - Delhi B55.1
  - lacrimal
    - gland —*see* Dacryoadenitis
    - passages (duct) (sac) —*see* Inflammation, lacrimal, passages, acute
  - Natal B55.1
  - orbit, orbital —*see* Abscess, orbit
  - tropical B55.1
- **Bold hives** —*see* Urticaria
- **Bombé, iris** —*see* Membrane, pupillary
- **Bone** —*see* condition
- **Bonnevie-Ullrich syndrome** Q87.1

Bonnier's syndrome —*see* subcategory H81.8
Bonvale dam fever T73.3
Bony block of joint —*see* Ankylosis
BOOP (bronchiolitis obliterans organized pneumonia) J84.89
Borderline
- diabetes mellitus R73.09
- hypertension R03.0
- osteopenia M85.8-
- pelvis, with obstruction during labor O65.1
- personality F60.3

Borna disease A83.9
Bornholm disease B33.0
Boston exanthem A88.0
Botalli, ductus (patent) (persistent) Q25.0
Bothriocephalus latus infestation B70.0
Botulism (foodborne intoxication) A05.1
- infant A48.51
- non-foodborne A48.52
- wound A48.52

Bouba —*see* Yaws
Bouchard's nodes (with arthropathy) M15.2
Bouffée délirante F23
Bouillaud's disease or syndrome (rheumatic heart disease) I01.9
Bourneville's disease Q85.1
Boutonniere deformity (finger) —*see* Deformity, finger, boutonniere
Bouveret (-Hoffmann) syndrome (paroxysmal tachycardia) I47.9
Bovine heart —*see* Hypertrophy, cardiac
Bowel —*see* condition
Bowen's
- dermatosis (precancerous) —*see* Neoplasm, skin, in situ
- disease —*see* Neoplasm, skin, in situ
- epithelioma —*see* Neoplasm, skin, in situ
- type
  - epidermoid carcinoma-in-situ — *see* Neoplasm, skin, in situ
  - intraepidermal squamous cell carcinoma —*see* Neoplasm, skin, in situ

Bowing
- femur —*see also* Deformity, limb, specified type NEC, thigh
  - congenital Q68.3
- fibula —*see also* Deformity, limb, specified type NEC, lower leg
  - congenital Q68.4
- forearm —*see* Deformity, limb, specified type NEC, forearm
- leg (s), long bones, congenital Q68.5
- radius —*see* Deformity, limb, specified type NEC, forearm
- tibia —*see also* Deformity, limb, specified type NEC, lower leg
  - congenital Q68.4

Bowleg (s) (acquired) M21.16-
- congenital Q68.5
- rachitic E64.3

Boyd's dysentery A03.2
Brachial —*see* condition
Brachycardia R00.1
Brachycephaly Q75.0
Bradley's disease A08.19
Bradyarrhythmia, cardiac I49.8
Bradycardia (sinoatrial) (sinus) (vagal) R00.1
- neonatal P29.12
- reflex G90.09
- tachycardia syndrome I49.5

Bradykinesia R25.8
Bradypnea R06.89
Bradytachycardia I49.5
Brailsford's disease or osteochondrosis —*see* Osteochondrosis, juvenile, radius
Brain —*see also* condition
- death G93.82
- syndrome —*see* Syndrome, brain

Branched-chain amino-acid disorder E71.2
Branchial —*see* condition
- cartilage, congenital Q18.2

Branchiogenic remnant (in neck) Q18.0
Brandt's syndrome (acrodermatitis enteropathica) E83.2
Brash (water) R12
Bravais-jacksonian epilepsy —*see* Epilepsy, localization-related, symptomatic, with simple partial seizures
Braxton Hicks contractions —*see* False, labor
Brazilian leishmaniasis B55.2
BRBPR K62.5
Break, retina (without detachment) H33.30-
- with retinal detachment —*see* Detachment, retina
- horseshoe tear H33.31-
- multiple H33.33-
- round hole H33.32-

Breakdown
- device, graft or implant —*see also* Complications, by site and type, mechanical T85.618
  - arterial graft NEC —*see* Complication, cardiovascular device, mechanical, vascular
  - breast (implant) T85.41
  - catheter NEC T85.618
    - cystostomy T83.010
    - dialysis (renal) T82.41
      - intraperitoneal T85.611
    - infusion NEC T82.514
      - spinal (epidural) (subdural) T85.610
    - urinary (indwelling) T83.018
  - electronic (electrode) (pulse generator) (stimulator)
    - bone T84.310
    - cardiac T82.119
      - electrode T82.110
      - pulse generator T82.111
      - specified type NEC T82.118
    - nervous system —*see* Complication, prosthetic device, mechanical, electronic nervous system stimulator
    - urinary —*see* Complication, genitourinary, device, urinary, mechanical
  - fixation, internal (orthopedic) NEC —*see* Complication, fixation device, mechanical
  - gastrointestinal —*see* Complications, prosthetic device, mechanical, gastrointestinal device

Breakdown *(continued)*
- device, graft or implant —*see also* Complications, by site and type, mechanical *(continued)*
  - genital NEC T83.418
    - intrauterine contraceptive device T83.31
    - penile prosthesis T83.410
  - heart NEC —*see* Complication, cardiovascular device, mechanical
  - joint prosthesis —*see* Complications..., joint prosthesis,internal, mechanical, by site
  - ocular NEC —*see* Complications, prosthetic device, mechanical, ocular device
  - orthopedic NEC —*see* Complication, orthopedic, device, mechanical
  - specified NEC T85.618
  - sutures, permanent T85.612
    - used in bone repair —*see* Complications, fixation device, internal (orthopedic), mechanical
  - urinary NEC —*see also* Complication, genitourinary, device, urinary, mechanical
    - graft T83.21
  - vascular NEC —*see* Complication, cardiovascular device, mechanical
  - ventricular intracranial shunt T85.01
- nervous F48.8
- perineum O90.1
- respirator J95.850
  - specified NEC J95.859
- ventilator J95.850
  - specified NEC J95.859

Breast —*see also* condition
- buds E30.1
  - in newborn P96.89
- dense R92.2
- nodule N63

Breath
- foul R19.6
- holder, child R06.89
- holding spell R06.89
- shortness R06.02

Breathing
- labored —*see* Hyperventilation
- mouth R06.5
  - causing malocclusion M26.5
- periodic R06.3
  - high altitude G47.32

Breathlessness R06.81
Breda's disease —*see* Yaws
Breech presentation (mother) O32.1
- causing obstructed labor O64.1
- footling O32.8
  - causing obstructed labor O64.8
- incomplete O32.8
  - causing obstructed labor O64.8

Breisky's disease N90.4
Brennemann's syndrome I88.0
Brenner
- tumor (benign) D27.9
  - borderline malignancy D39.1-
  - malignant C56
  - proliferating D39.1-

Bretonneau's disease or angina A36.0
Breus' mole O02.0
Brevicollis Q76.49
Brickmakers' anemia B76.9 *[D63.8]*
Bridge, myocardial Q24.5
Bright red blood per rectum (BRBPR) K62.5
Bright's disease —*see also* Nephritis
- arteriosclerotic —*see* Hypertension, kidney

Brill (-Zinsser) disease (recrudescent typhus) A75.1
- flea-borne A75.2
- louse-borne A75.1

Brill-Symmers' disease C82.90
Brion-Kayser disease —*see* Fever, parathyroid
Briquet's disorder or syndrome F45.0
Brissaud's
- infantilism or dwarfism E23.0
- motor-verbal tic F95.2

Brittle
- bones disease Q78.0
- nails L60.3
  - congenital Q84.6

Broad —*see also* condition
- beta disease E78.2
- ligament laceration syndrome N83.8

Broad- or floating-betalipoproteinemia E78.2
Brock's syndrome (atelectasis due to enlarged lymph nodes) J98.19
Brocq-Duhring disease (dermatitis herpetiformis) L13.0
Brodie's abscess or disease M86.8X-
Broken
- arches —*see also* Deformity, limb, flat foot
- arm (meaning upper limb) —*see* Fracture, arm
- back —*see* Fracture, vertebra
- bone —*see* Fracture
- implant or internal device —*see* Complications, by site and type, mechanical
- leg (meaning lower limb) —*see* Fracture, leg
- nose S02.2
- tooth, teeth —*see* Fracture, tooth

Bromhidrosis, bromidrosis L75.0
Bromidism, bromism G92
- due to
  - correct substance properly administered —*see* Table of Drugs and Chemicals, by drug, adverse effect
  - overdose or wrong substance given or taken —*see* Table of Drugs and Chemicals, by drug, poisoning
- chronic (dependence) F13.20

Bromidrosiphobia F40.298
Bronchi, bronchial —*see* condition
Bronchiectasis (cylindrical) (diffuse) (fusiform) (localized) (saccular) J47.9
- with
  - acute
    - bronchitis J47.0
    - lower respiratory infection J47.0
  - exacerbation (acute) J47.1
- congenital Q33.4
- tuberculous NEC —*see* Tuberculosis, pulmonary

Bronchiolectasis —*see* Bronchiectasis
Bronchiolitis (acute) (infective) (subacute) J21.9
- with
  - bronchospasm or obstruction J21.9
  - influenza, flu or grippe —*see* Influenza, with, respiratory manifestations NEC

- **Bronchiolitis** *(continued)*
  - chemical (chronic) J68.4
    - acute J68.0
  - chronic (fibrosing) (obliterative) J44.9
  - due to
    - external agent —*see* Bronchitis, acute, due to
    - human metapneumovirus J21.1
    - respiratory syncytial virus J21.0
    - specified organism NEC J21.8
  - fibrosa obliterans J44.9
  - influenzal —*see* Influenza, with, respiratory manifestations NEC
  - obliterans J42
    - with organizing pneumonia (BOOP) J84.89
  - obliterative (chronic) (subacute) J44.9
    - due to fumes or vapors J68.4
    - due to chemicals, gases, fumes or vapors (inhalation) J68.4
  - respiratory, interstitial lung disease J84.115
- **Bronchitis** (diffuse) (fibrinous) (hypostatic) (infective) (membranous) J40
  - with
    - influenza, flu or grippe —*see* Influenza, with, respiratory manifestations NEC
    - obstruction (airway) (lung) J44.9
    - tracheitis (15 years of age and above) J40
      - acute or subacute J20.9
      - chronic J42
      - under 15 years of age J20.9
  - acute or subacute (with bronchospasm or obstruction) J20.9
    - with
      - bronchiectasis J47.0
      - chronic obstructive pulmonary disease J44.0
    - chemical (due to gases, fumes or vapors) J68.0
    - due to
      - fumes or vapors J68.0
      - Haemophilus influenzae J20.1
      - Mycoplasma pneumoniae J20.0
      - radiation J70.0
      - specified organism NEC J20.8
      - Streptococcus J20.2
      - virus
        - coxsackie J20.3
        - echovirus J20.7
        - parainfluenzae J20.4
        - respiratory syncytial J20.5
        - rhinovirus J20.6
    - viral NEC J20.8
  - allergic (acute) J45.909
    - with
      - exacerbation (acute) J45.901
      - status asthmaticus J45.902
  - arachidic T17.528
  - aspiration (due to fumes or vapors) J68.0
  - asthmatic J45.9
    - chronic J44.9
      - with
        - acute lower respiratory infection J44.0
        - exacerbation (acute) J44.1
  - capillary —*see* Pneumonia, broncho
  - caseous (tuberculous) A15.5
  - Castellani's A69.8
  - catarrhal (15 years of age and above) J40
    - acute —*see* Bronchitis, acute
    - chronic J41.0
    - under 15 years of age J20.9
- **Bronchitis** *(continued)*
  - chemical (acute) (subacute) J68.0
    - chronic J68.4
    - due to fumes or vapors J68.0
      - chronic J68.4
  - chronic J42
    - with
      - airways obstruction J44.9
      - tracheitis (chronic) J42
    - asthmatic (obstructive) J44.9
    - catarrhal J41.0
    - chemical (due to fumes or vapors) J68.4
    - due to
      - chemicals, gases, fumes or vapors (inhalation) J68.4
      - radiation J70.1
      - tobacco smoking J41.0
    - emphysematous J44.9
    - mucopurulent J41.1
    - non-obstructive J41.0
    - obliterans J44.9
    - obstructive J44.9
    - purulent J41.1
    - simple J41.0
  - croupous —*see* Bronchitis, acute
  - due to gases, fumes or vapors (chemical) J68.0
  - emphysematous (obstructive) J44.9
  - exudative —*see* Bronchitis, acute
  - fetid J41.1
  - grippal —*see* Influenza, with, respiratory manifestations NEC
  - in those under 15 years age —*see* Bronchitis, acute
    - chronic —*see* Bronchitis, chronic
  - influenzal —*see* Influenza, with, respiratory manifestations NEC
  - mixed simple and mucopurulent J41.8
  - moulder's J62.8
  - mucopurulent (chronic) (recurrent) J41.1
    - acute or subacute J20.9
    - simple (mixed) J41.8
  - obliterans (chronic) J44.9
  - obstructive (chronic) (diffuse) J44.9
  - pituitous J41.1
  - pneumococcal, acute or subacute J20.2
  - pseudomembranous, acute or subacute —*see* Bronchitis, acute
  - purulent (chronic) (recurrent) J41.1
    - acute or subacute —*see* Bronchitis, acute
  - putrid J41.1
  - senile (chronic) J42
  - simple and mucopurulent (mixed) J41.8
  - smokers' J41.0
  - spirochetal NEC A69.8
  - subacute —*see* Bronchitis, acute
  - suppurative (chronic) J41.1
    - acute or subacute —*see* Bronchitis, acute
  - tuberculous A15.5
  - under 15 years of age —*see* Bronchitis, acute
    - chronic —*see* Bronchitis, chronic
  - viral NEC, acute or subacute —*see also* Bronchitis, acute J20.8
- **Bronchoalveolitis** J18.0
- **Bronchoaspergillosis** B44.1
- **Bronchocele meaning goiter** E04.0
- **Broncholithiasis** J98.09
  - tuberculous NEC A15.5
- **Bronchomalacia** J98.09
  - congenital Q32.2
- **Bronchomycosis NOS** B49 *[J99]*
  - candidal B37.1
- **Bronchopleuropneumonia** —*see* Pneumonia, broncho
- **Bronchopneumonia** —*see* Pneumonia, broncho
- **Bronchopneumonitis** —*see* Pneumonia, broncho
- **Bronchopulmonary** —*see* condition
- **Bronchopulmonitis** —*see* Pneumonia, broncho
- **Bronchorrhagia** (*see* Hemoptysis)
- **Bronchorrhea** J98.09
  - acute J20.9
  - chronic (infective) (purulent) J42
- **Bronchospasm** (acute) J98.01
  - with
    - bronchiolitis, acute J21.9
    - bronchitis, acute (conditions in J20) —*see* Bronchitis, acute
  - due to external agent —*see* condition, respiratory, acute, due to
  - exercise induced J45.990
- **Bronchospirochetosis** A69.8
  - Castellani A69.8
- **Bronchostenosis** J98.09
- **Bronchus** —*see* condition
- **Brontophobia** F40.220
- **Bronze baby syndrome** P83.8
- **Brooke's tumor** —*see* Neoplasm, skin, benign
- **Brown enamel of teeth** (hereditary) K00.5
- **Brown's sheath syndrome** H50.61-
- **Brown-Séquard disease, paralysis or syndrome** G83.81
- **Bruce sepsis** A23.0
- **Brucellosis** (infection) A23.9
  - abortus A23.1
  - canis A23.3
  - dermatitis A23.9
  - melitensis A23.0
  - mixed A23.8
  - sepsis A23.9
    - melitensis A23.0
    - specified NEC A23.8
  - suis A23.2
- **Bruck-de Lange disease** Q87.1
- **Bruck's disease** —*see* Deformity, limb
- **Brugsch's syndrome** Q82.8
- **Bruise** (skin surface intact) —*see also* Contusion
  - with
    - open wound —*see* Wound, open
  - internal organ —*see* Injury, by site
  - newborn P54.5
  - scalp, due to birth injury, newborn P12.3
  - umbilical cord O69.5
- **Bruit** (arterial) R09.89
  - cardiac R01.1
- **Brush burn** —*see* Abrasion, by site
- **Bruton's X-linked agammaglobulinemia** D80.0
- **Bruxism**
  - psychogenic F45.8
  - sleep related G47.63
- **Bubbly lung syndrome** P27.0
- **Bubo** I88.8
  - blennorrhagic (gonococcal) A54.89
  - chancroidal A57
  - climatic A55
  - due to Haemophilus ducreyi A57
  - gonococcal A54.89
  - indolent (nonspecific) I88.8
- **Bubo** *(continued)*
  - inguinal (nonspecific) I88.8
    - chancroidal A57
    - climatic A55
    - due to H. ducreyi A57
    - infective I88.8
  - scrofulous (tuberculous) A18.2
  - soft chancre A57
  - suppurating —*see* Lymphadenitis, acute
  - syphilitic (primary) A51.0
    - congenital A50.07
  - tropical A55
  - virulent (chancroidal) A57
- **Bubonic plague** A20.0
- **Bubonocele** —*see* Hernia, inguinal
- **Buccal** —*see* condition
- **Buchanan's disease or osteochondrosis** M91.0
- **Buchem's syndrome** (hyperostosis corticalis) M85.2
- **Bucket-handle fracture or tear** (semilunar cartilage) —*see* Tear, meniscus
- **Budd-Chiari syndrome** (hepatic vein thrombosis) I82.0
- **Budgerigar fancier's disease or lung** J67.2
- **Buds**
  - breast E30.1
    - in newborn P96.89
- **Buerger's disease** (thromboangiitis obliterans) I73.1
- **Bulbar** —*see* condition
- **Bulbus cordis** (left ventricle) (persistent) Q21.8
- **Bulimia** (nervosa) F50.2
  - atypical F50.9
  - normal weight F50.9
- **Bulky**
  - stools R19.5
  - uterus N85.2
- **Bulla** (e) R23.8
  - lung (emphysematous) (solitary) J43.9
    - newborn P25.8
- **Bullet wound** —*see also* Wound, open
  - fracture - code as Fracture, by site
  - internal organ —*see* Injury, by site
- **Bundle**
  - branch block (complete) (false) (incomplete) —*see* Block, bundle-branch
  - of His —*see* condition
- **Bunion** —*see* Deformity, toe, hallux valgus
- **Buphthalmia, buphthalmos** (congenital) Q15.0
- **Burdwan fever** B55.0
- **Bürger-Grütz disease or syndrome** E78.3
- **Buried**
  - penis (congenital) Q55.64
    - acquired N48.83
  - roots K08.3
- **Burke's syndrome** K86.8
- **Burkitt**
  - cell leukemia C91.0-
  - lymphoma (malignant) C83.7-
    - small noncleaved, diffuse C83.7-
    - spleen C83.77
    - undifferentiated C83.7-

Burn *(continued)*
- finger *(continued)*
  - right T23.021
    - first degree T23.121
    - second degree T23.221
    - third degree T23.321
  - second degree T23.229
  - third degree T23.329
- flank —*see* Burn, abdominal wall
- foot T25.029
  - first degree T25.129
  - left T25.022
    - first degree T25.122
    - second degree T25.222
    - third degree T25.322
  - multiple with ankle —*see* Burn, lower, limb, multiple, ankle and foot
  - right T25.021
    - first degree T25.121
    - second degree T25.221
    - third degree T25.321
  - second degree T25.229
  - third degree T25.329
- forearm T22.019
  - first degree T22.119
  - left T22.012
    - first degree T22.112
    - second degree T22.212
    - third degree T22.312
  - right T22.011
    - first degree T22.111
    - second degree T22.211
    - third degree T22.311
  - second degree T22.219
  - third degree T22.319
- forehead T20.06
  - first degree T20.16
  - second degree T20.26
  - third degree T20.36
- fourth degree - code as Burn, third degree, by site
- friction —*see* Burn, by site
- from swallowing caustic or corrosive substance NEC —*see* Corrosion, by site
- full thickness skin loss - code as Burn, third degree, by site
- gastrointestinal tract NEC T28.2
  - from swallowing caustic or corrosive substance T28.7
- genital organs
  - external
    - female T21.07
      - first degree T21.17
      - second degree T21.27
      - third degree T21.37
    - male T21.06
      - first degree T21.16
      - second degree T21.26
      - third degree T21.36
  - internal T28.3
    - from caustic or corrosive substance T28.8
- groin —*see* Burn, abdominal wall
- hand (s) T23.009
  - back —*see* Burn, dorsum of hand
  - finger —*see* Burn, finger
  - first degree T23.109
  - left T23.002
    - first degree T23.102
    - second degree T23.202
    - third degree T23.302
  - multiple sites with wrist T23.099
    - first degree T23.199
    - left T23.092
      - first degree T23.192
      - second degree T23.292
      - third degree T23.392
    - right T23.091
      - first degree T23.191
      - second degree T23.291

Burn *(continued)*
- hand *(continued)*
  - multiple sites with wrist *(continued)*
    - right *(continued)*
      - third degree T23.391
    - second degree T23.299
    - third degree T23.399
  - palm —*see* Burn, palm
  - right T23.001
    - first degree T23.101
    - second degree T23.201
    - third degree T23.301
  - second degree T23.209
  - third degree T23.309
  - thumb —*see* Burn, thumb
- head (and face) (and neck) T20.00
  - cheek —*see* Burn, cheek
  - chin —*see* Burn, chin
  - ear —*see* Burn, ear
  - eye (s) only —*see* Burn, eye
  - first degree T20.10
  - forehead —*see* Burn, forehead
  - lip —*see* Burn, lip
  - multiple sites T20.09
    - first degree T20.19
    - second degree T20.29
    - third degree T20.39
  - neck —*see* Burn, neck
  - nose —*see* Burn, nose
  - scalp —*see* Burn, scalp
  - second degree T20.20
  - third degree T20.30
- hip (s) —*see* Burn, lower, limb
- inhalation —*see* Burn, respiratory tract
  - caustic or corrosive substance (fumes) —*see* Corrosion, respiratory tract
- internal organ (s) T28.40
  - alimentary tract T28.2
    - esophagus T28.1
  - eardrum T28.41
  - esophagus T28.1
  - from caustic or corrosive substance (swallowing) NEC —*see* Corrosion, by site
  - genitourinary T28.3
  - mouth T28.0
  - pharynx T28.0
  - respiratory tract —*see* Burn, respiratory tract
  - specified organ NEC T28.49
- interscapular region —*see* Burn, back, upper
- intestine (large) (small) T28.2
- knee T24.029
  - first degree T24.129
  - left T24.022
    - first degree T24.122
    - second degree T24.222
    - third degree T24.322
  - right T24.021
    - first degree T24.121
    - second degree T24.221
    - third degree T24.321
  - second degree T24.229
  - third degree T24.329
- labium (majus) (minus) —*see* Burn, genital organs, external, female
- lacrimal apparatus, duct, gland or sac —*see* Burn, eye, specified site NEC
- larynx T27.0
  - with lung T27.1
- leg (s) (lower) (upper) —*see* Burn, lower, limb
- lightning —*see* Burn, by site
- limb (s)
  - lower (except ankle or foot alone) —*see* Burn, lower, limb
  - upper —*see* Burn, upper limb

Burn *(continued)*
- lip (s) T20.02
  - first degree T20.12
  - second degree T20.22
  - third degree T20.32
- lower
  - back —*see* Burn, back
  - limb T24.009
    - ankle —*see* Burn, ankle
    - calf —*see* Burn, calf
    - first degree T24.109
    - foot —*see* Burn, foot
    - hip —*see* Burn, thigh
    - knee —*see* Burn, knee
    - left T24.002
      - first degree T24.102
      - second degree T24.202
      - third degree T24.302
    - multiple sites, except ankle and foot T24.099
      - ankle and foot T25.099
        - first degree T25.199
        - left T25.092
          - first degree T25.192
          - second degree T25.292
          - third degree T25.392
        - right T25.091
          - first degree T25.191
          - second degree T25.291
          - third degree T25.391
        - second degree T25.299
        - third degree T25.399
      - first degree T24.199
      - left T24.092
        - first degree T24.192
        - second degree T24.292
        - third degree T24.392
      - right T24.091
        - first degree T24.191
        - second degree T24.291
        - third degree T24.391
      - second degree T24.299
      - third degree T24.399
    - right T24.001
      - first degree T24.101
      - second degree T24.201
      - third degree T24.301
    - second degree T24.209
    - thigh —*see* Burn, thigh
    - third degree T24.309
    - toe —*see* Burn, toe
- lung (with larynx and trachea) T27.1
- mouth T28.0
- neck T20.07
  - first degree T20.17
  - second degree T20.27
  - third degree T20.37
- nose (septum) T20.04
  - first degree T20.14
  - second degree T20.24
  - third degree T20.34
- ocular adnexa —*see* Burn, eye
- orbit region —*see* Burn, eyelid
- palm T23.059
  - first degree T23.159
  - left T23.052
    - first degree T23.152
    - second degree T23.252
    - third degree T23.352
  - right T23.051
    - first degree T23.151
    - second degree T23.251
    - third degree T23.351
  - second degree T23.259
  - third degree T23.359
- partial thickness - code as Burn, unspecified degree, by site
- pelvis —*see* Burn, trunk
- penis —*see* Burn, genital organs, external, male

Burn *(continued)*
- perineum
  - female —*see* Burn, genital organs, external, female
  - male —*see* Burn, genital organs, external, male
- periocular area —*see* Burn, eyelid
- pharynx T28.0
- rectum T28.2
- respiratory tract T27.3
  - larynx —*see* Burn, larynx
  - specified part NEC T27.2
  - trachea —*see* Burn, trachea
- sac, lacrimal —*see* Burn, eye, specified site NEC
- scalp T20.05
  - first degree T20.15
  - second degree T20.25
  - third degree T20.35
- scapular region T22.069
  - first degree T22.169
  - left T22.062
    - first degree T22.162
    - second degree T22.262
    - third degree T22.362
  - right T22.061
    - first degree T22.161
    - second degree T22.261
    - third degree T22.361
  - second degree T22.269
  - third degree T22.369
- sclera —*see* Burn, eye, specified site NEC
- scrotum —*see* Burn, genital organs, external, male
- shoulder T22.059
  - first degree T22.159
  - left T22.052
    - first degree T22.152
    - second degree T22.252
    - third degree T22.352
  - right T22.051
    - first degree T22.151
    - second degree T22.251
    - third degree T22.351
  - second degree T22.259
  - third degree T22.359
- stomach T28.2
- temple —*see* Burn, head
- testis —*see* Burn, genital organs, external, male
- thigh T24.019
  - first degree T24.119
  - left T24.012
    - first degree T24.112
    - second degree T24.212
    - third degree T24.312
  - right T24.011
    - first degree T24.111
    - second degree T24.211
    - third degree T24.311
  - second degree T24.219
  - third degree T24.319
- thorax (external) —*see* Burn, trunk
- throat (meaning pharynx) T28.0
- thumb (s) T23.019
  - first degree T23.119
  - left T23.012
    - first degree T23.112
    - second degree T23.212
    - third degree T23.312
  - multiple sites with fingers T23.049
    - first degree T23.149
    - left T23.042
      - first degree T23.142
      - second degree T23.242
      - third degree T23.342
    - right T23.041
      - first degree T23.141
      - second degree T23.241
      - third degree T23.341

Burn *(continued)*
thumb *(continued)*
multiple sites with fingers *(continued)*
second degree T23.249
third degree T23.349
right T23.011
first degree T23.111
second degree T23.211
third degree T23.311
second degree T23.219
third degree T23.319
toe T25.039
first degree T25.139
left T25.032
first degree T25.132
second degree T25.232
third degree T25.332
right T25.031
first degree T25.131
second degree T25.231
third degree T25.331
second degree T25.239
third degree T25.339
tongue T28.0
tonsil (s) T28.0
trachea T27.0
with lung T27.1
trunk T21.00
abdominal wall —*see* Burn, abdominal wall
anus —*see* Burn, buttock
axilla —*see* Burn, upper limb
back —*see* Burn, back
breast —*see* Burn, chest wall
buttock —*see* Burn, buttock
chest wall —*see* Burn, chest wall
first degree T21.10
flank —*see* Burn, abdominal wall
genital
female —*see* Burn, genital organs, external, female
male —*see* Burn, genital organs, external, male
groin —*see* Burn, abdominal wall
interscapular region —*see* Burn, back, upper
labia —*see* Burn, genital organs, external, female
lower back —*see* Burn, back
penis —*see* Burn, genital organs, external, male
perineum
female —*see* Burn, genital organs, external, female
male —*see* Burn, genital organs, external, male
scapula region —*see* Burn, scapular region
scrotum —*see* Burn, genital organs, external, male
second degree T21.20
specified site NEC T21.09
first degree T21.19
second degree T21.29
third degree T21.39
testes —*see* Burn, genital organs, external, male
third degree T21.30
upper back —*see* Burn, back, upper
vulva —*see* Burn, genital organs, external, female
unspecified site with extent of body surface involved specified
less than 10 per cent T31.0
10-19 per cent (0-9 percent third degree) T31.10
with 10-19 percent third degree T31.11

Burn *(continued)*
unspecified site with extent of body surface involved specified *(continued)*
20-29 per cent (0-9 percent third degree) T31.20
with
10-19 percent third degree T31.21
20-29 percent third degree T31.22
30-39 per cent (0-9 percent third degree) T31.30
with
10-19 percent third degree T31.31
20-29 percent third degree T31.32
30-39 percent third degree T31.33
40-49 per cent (0-9 percent third degree) T31.40
with
10-19 percent third degree T31.41
20-29 percent third degree T31.42
30-39 percent third degree T31.43
40-49 percent third degree T31.44
50-59 per cent (0-9 percent third degree) T31.50
with
10-19 percent third degree T31.51
20-29 percent third degree T31.52
30-39 percent third degree T31.53
40-49 percent third degree T31.54
50-59 percent third degree T31.55
60-69 per cent (0-9 percent third degree) T31.60
with
10-19 percent third degree T31.61
20-29 percent third degree T31.62
30-39 percent third degree T31.63
40-49 percent third degree T31.64
50-59 percent third degree T31.65
60-69 percent third degree T31.66
70-79 per cent (0-9 percent third degree) T31.70
with
10-19 percent third degree T31.71
20-29 percent third degree T31.72
30-39 percent third degree T31.73
40-49 percent third degree T31.74
50-59 percent third degree T31.75
60-69 percent third degree T31.76
70-79 percent third degree T31.77
80-89 per cent (0-9 percent third degree) T31.80
with
10-19 percent third degree T31.81

Burn *(continued)*
unspecified site with extent of body surface involved specified *(continued)*
80-89 per cent (0-9 percent third degree) *(continued)*
with *(continued)*
20-29 percent third degree T31.82
30-39 percent third degree T31.83
40-49 percent third degree T31.84
50-59 percent third degree T31.85
60-69 percent third degree T31.86
70-79 percent third degree T31.87
80-89 percent third degree T31.88
90 per cent or more (0-9 percent third degree) T31.90
with
10-19 percent third degree T31.91
20-29 percent third degree T31.92
30-39 percent third degree T31.93
40-49 percent third degree T31.94
50-59 percent third degree T31.95
60-69 percent third degree T31.96
70-79 percent third degree T31.97
80-89 percent third degree T31.98
90-99 percent third degree T31.99
upper limb T22.00
above elbow —*see* Burn, above elbow
axilla —*see* Burn, axilla
elbow —*see* Burn, elbow
first degree T22.10
forearm —*see* Burn, forearm
hand —*see* Burn, hand
interscapular region —*see* Burn, back, upper
multiple sites T22.099
first degree T22.199
left T22.092
first degree T22.192
second degree T22.292
third degree T22.392
right T22.091
first degree T22.191
second degree T22.291
third degree T22.391
second degree T22.299
third degree T22.399
scapular region —*see* Burn, scapular region
second degree T22.20
shoulder —*see* Burn, shoulder
third degree T22.30
wrist —*see* Burn, wrist
uterus T28.3
vagina T28.3
vulva —*see* Burn, genital organs, external, female
wrist T23.079
first degree T23.179
left T23.072
first degree T23.172
second degree T23.272
third degree T23.372
multiple sites with hand T23.099
first degree T23.199

Burn *(continued)*
wrist *(continued)*
multiple sites with hand *(continued)*
left T23.092
first degree T23.192
second degree T23.292
third degree T23.392
right T23.091
first degree T23.191
second degree T23.291
third degree T23.391
second degree T23.299
third degree T23.399
right T23.071
first degree T23.171
second degree T23.271
third degree T23.371
second degree T23.279
third degree T23.379

Burnett's syndrome E83.52

Burning
feet syndrome E53.9
sensation R20.8
tongue K14.6

Burn-out (state) Z73.0

Burns' disease or osteochondrosis — *see* Osteochondrosis, juvenile, ulna

Bursa —*see* condition

Bursitis M71.9
Achilles —*see* Tendinitis, Achilles
adhesive —*see* Bursitis, specified NEC
ankle —*see* Enthesopathy, lower limb, ankle, specified type NEC
calcaneal —*see* Enthesopathy, foot, specified type NEC
collateral ligament, tibial —*see* Bursitis, tibial collateral
due to use, overuse, pressure —*see also* Disorder, soft tissue, due to use, specified type NEC
specified NEC —*see* Disorder, soft tissue, due to use, specified NEC
Duplay's M75.0
elbow NEC M70.3-
olecranon M70.2-
finger —*see* Disorder, soft tissue, due to use, specified type NEC, hand
foot —*see* Enthesopathy, foot, specified type NEC
gonococcal A54.49
gouty —*see* Gout, idiopathic
hand M70.1-
hip NEC M70.7-
trochanteric M70.6-
infective NEC M71.10
abscess —*see* Abscess, bursa
ankle M71.17-
elbow M71.12-
foot M71.17-
hand M71.14-
hip M71.15-
knee M71.16-
multiple sites M71.19
shoulder M71.11-
specified site NEC M71.18
wrist M71.13-
ischial —*see* Bursitis, hip
knee NEC M70.5-
prepatellar M70.4-
occupational NEC —*see also* Disorder, soft tissue, due to, use
olecranon —*see* Bursitis, elbow, olecranon
pharyngeal J39.1
popliteal —*see* Bursitis, knee
prepatellar M70.4-
radiohumeral M77.8

Bursitis *(continued)*
  rheumatoid M06.20
    ankle M06.27-
    elbow M06.22-
    foot joint M06.27-
    hand joint M06.24-
    hip M06.25-
    knee M06.26-
    multiple site M06.29
    shoulder M06.21-
    vertebra M06.28
    wrist M06.23-
  scapulohumeral —*see* Bursitis, shoulder
  semimembranous muscle (knee) —*see* Bursitis, knee
  shoulder M75.5-
    adhesive —*see* Capsulitis, adhesive
  specified NEC M71.50
    ankle M71.57-
    due to use, overuse or pressure —*see* Disorder, soft tissue, due to, use
    elbow M71.52-
    foot M71.57-
    hand M71.54-
    hip M71.55-
    knee M71.56-
    shoulder —*see* Bursitis, shoulder
    specified site NEC M71.58
    tibial collateral M76.4-
    wrist M71.53-
  subacromial —*see* Bursitis, shoulder
  subcoracoid —*see* Bursitis, shoulder
  subdeltoid —*see* Bursitis, shoulder
  syphilitic A52.78
  Thornwaldt, Tornwaldt J39.2
  tibial collateral —*see* Bursitis, tibial collateral
  toe —*see* Enthesopathy, foot, specified type NEC
  trochanteric (area) —*see* Bursitis, hip, trochanteric
  wrist —*see* Bursitis, hand

Bursopathy M71.9
  specified type NEC M71.80
    ankle M71.87-
    elbow M71.82-
    foot M71.87-
    hand M71.84-
    hip M71.85-
    knee M71.86-
    multiple sites M71.89
    shoulder M71.81-
    specified site NEC M71.88
    wrist M71.83-

Burst stitches or sutures (complication of surgery) T81.31
  external operation wound T81.31
  internal operation wound T81.32

Buruli ulcer A31.1

Bury's disease L95.1

Buschke's
  disease B45.3
  scleredema —*see* Sclerosis, systemic

Busse-Buschke disease B45.3

Buttock —*see* condition

Button
  Biskra B55.1
  Delhi B55.1
  oriental B55.1

Buttonhole deformity (finger) —*see* Deformity, finger, boutonniere

Bwamba fever A92.8

Byssinosis J66.0

Bywaters' syndrome T79.5

C

Cachexia R64
  cancerous R64
  cardiac —*see* Disease, heart
  dehydration E86.0
    with
      hypernatremia E87.0
      hyponatremia E87.1
  due to malnutrition R64
  exophthalmic —*see* Hyperthyroidism
  heart —*see* Disease, heart
  hypophyseal E23.0
  hypopituitary E23.0
  lead —*see* Poisoning, lead
  malignant R64
  marsh —*see* Malaria
  nervous F48.8
  old age R54
  paludal —*see* Malaria
  pituitary E23.0
  renal N28.9
  saturnine —*see* Poisoning, lead
  senile R54
  Simmonds' E23.0
  splenica D73.0
  strumipriva E03.4
  tuberculous NEC —*see* Tuberculosis

Café, au lait spots L81.3

Caffey's syndrome Q78.8

Caisson disease T70.3

Cake kidney Q63.1

Caked breast (puerperal, postpartum) O92.79

Calabar swelling B74.3

Calcaneal spur —*see* Spur, bone, calcaneal

Calcaneo-apophysitis M92.8

Calcareous —*see* condition

Calcicosis J62.8

Calciferol (vitamin D) **deficiency** E55.9
  with rickets E55.0

Calcification
  adrenal (capsule) (gland) E27.49
    tuberculous E35 *[B90.8]*
  aorta I70.0
  artery (annular) —*see* Arteriosclerosis
  auricle (ear) —*see* Disorder, pinna, specified type NEC
  basal ganglia G23.8
  bladder N32.89
    due to Schistosoma hematobium B65.0
  brain (cortex) —*see* Calcification, cerebral
  bronchus J98.09
  bursa M71.40
    ankle M71.47-
    elbow M71.42-
    foot M71.47-
    hand M71.44-
    hip M71.45-
    knee M71.46-
    multiple sites M71.49
    shoulder M75.3-
    specified site NEC M71.48
    wrist M71.43-
  cardiac —*see* Degeneration, myocardial
  cerebral (cortex) G93.89
    artery I67.2
  cervix (uteri) N88.8
  choroid plexus G93.89
  conjunctiva —*see* Concretion, conjunctiva
  corpora cavernosa (penis) N48.89
  cortex (brain) —*see* Calcification, cerebral

Calcification *(continued)*
  dental pulp (nodular) K04.2
  dentinal papilla K00.4
  fallopian tube N83.8
  falx cerebri G96.19
  gallbladder K82.8
  general E83.59
  heart —*see also* Degeneration, myocardial
    valve —*see* Endocarditis
  idiopathic infantile arterial (IIAC) Q28.8
  intervertebral cartilage or disc (postinfective) —*see* Disorder, disc, specified NEC
  intracranial —*see* Calcification, cerebral
  joint —*see* Disorder, joint, specified type NEC
  kidney N28.89
    tuberculous N29 *[B90.1]*
  larynx (senile) J38.7
  lens —*see* Cataract, specified NEC
  lung (active) (postinfectional) J98.4
    tuberculous B90.9
  lymph gland or node (postinfectional) I89.8
    tuberculous —*see also* Tuberculosis, lymph gland B90.8
  mammographic R92.1
  massive (paraplegic) —*see* Myositis, ossificans, in, quadriplegia
  medial —*see* Arteriosclerosis, extremities
  meninges (cerebral) (spinal) G96.19
  metastatic E83.59
  Mönckeberg's —*see* Arteriosclerosis, extremities
  muscle M61.9
    due to burns —*see* Myositis, ossificans, in, burns
    paralytic —*see* Myositis, ossificans, in, quadriplegia
    specified type NEC M61.40
      ankle M61.47-
      foot M61.47-
      forearm M61.43-
      hand M61.44-
      lower leg M61.46-
      multiple sites M61.49
      pelvic region M61.45-
      shoulder region M61.41-
      specified site NEC M61.48
      thigh M61.45-
      upper arm M61.42-
  myocardium, myocardial —*see* Degeneration, myocardial
  ovary N83.8
  pancreas K86.8
  penis N48.89
  periarticular —*see* Disorder, joint, specified type NEC
  pericardium —*see also* Pericarditis I31.1
  pineal gland E34.8
  pleura J94.8
    postinfectional J94.8
    tuberculous NEC B90.9
  pulpal (dental) (nodular) K04.2
  sclera H15.89
  spleen D73.89
  subcutaneous L94.2
  suprarenal (capsule) (gland) E27.49
  tendon (sheath) —*see also* Tenosynovitis, specified type NEC
    with bursitis, synovitis or tenosynovitis —*see* Tendinitis, calcific
  trachea J39.8
  ureter N28.89
  uterus N85.8
  vitreous —*see* Deposit, crystalline

Calcified —*see* Calcification

Calcinosis (interstitial) (tumoral) (universalis) E83.59
  with Raynaud's phenomenon, esophageal dysfunction, sclerodactyly, telangiectasia (CREST syndrome) M34.1
  circumscripta (skin) L94.2
  cutis L94.2

Calciphylaxis —*see also* Calcification, by site E83.59

Calcium
  deposits —*see* Calcification, by site
  metabolism disorder E83.50
  salts or soaps in vitreous —*see* Deposit, crystalline

Calciuria R82.99

Calculi —*see* Calculus

Calculosis, intrahepatic —*see* Calculus, bile duct

Calculus, calculi, calculous
  ampulla of Vater —*see* Calculus, bile duct
  anuria (impacted) (recurrent) —*see also* Calculus, urinary N20.9
  appendix K38.1
  bile duct (common) (hepatic) K80.50
    with
      calculus of gallbladder —*see* Calculus, gallbladder and bile duct
      cholangitis K80.30
        with
          cholecystitis —*see* Calculus, bile duct, with cholecystitis
          obstruction K80.31
        acute K80.32
          with
            chronic cholangitis K80.36
              with obstruction K80.37
            obstruction K80.33
        chronic K80.34
          with
            acute cholangitis K80.36
              with obstruction K80.37
            obstruction K80.35
      cholecystitis (with cholangitis) K80.40
        with obstruction K80.41
        acute K80.42
          with
            chronic cholecystitis K80.46
              with obstruction K80.47
            obstruction K80.43
        chronic K80.44
          with
            acute cholecystitis K80.46
              with obstruction K80.47
            obstruction K80.45
      obstruction K80.51
  biliary —*see also* Calculus, gallbladder
    specified NEC K80.80
      with obstruction K80.81
  bilirubin, multiple —*see* Calculus, gallbladder
  bladder (encysted) (impacted) (urinary) (diverticulum) N21.0
  bronchus J98.09
  calyx (kidney) (renal) —*see* Calculus, kidney

Calculus, calculi, calculous *(continued)*
cholesterol (pure) (solitary) —*see* Calculus, gallbladder
common duct (bile) —*see* Calculus, bile duct
conjunctiva —*see* Concretion, conjunctiva
cystic N21.0
duct —*see* Calculus, gallbladder
dental (subgingival) (supragingival) K03.6
diverticulum
bladder N21.0
kidney N20.0
epididymis N50.8
gallbladder K80.20
with
bile duct calculus —*see* Calculus, gallbladder and bile duct
cholecystitis K80.10
with obstruction K80.11
acute K80.00
with
chronic cholecystitis K80.12
with obstruction K80.13
obstruction K80.01
chronic K80.10
with
acute cholecystitis K80.12
with obstruction K80.13
obstruction K80.11
specified NEC K80.18
with obstruction K80.19
obstruction K80.21
gallbladder and bile duct K80.70
with
cholecystitis K80.60
with obstruction K80.61
acute K80.62
with
chronic cholecystitis K80.66
with obstruction K80.67
obstruction K80.63
chronic K80.64
with
acute cholecystitis K80.66
with obstruction K80.67
obstruction K80.65
obstruction K80.71
hepatic (duct) —*see* Calculus, bile duct
hepatobiliary K80.80
with obstruction K80.81
ileal conduit N21.8
intestinal (impaction) (obstruction) K56.49
kidney (impacted) (multiple) (pelvis) (recurrent) (staghorn) N20.0
with calculus, ureter N20.2
congenital Q63.8
lacrimal passages —*see* Dacryolith
liver (impacted) —*see* Calculus, bile duct
lung J98.4
mammographic R92.1
nephritic (impacted) (recurrent) —*see* Calculus, kidney
nose J34.89
pancreas (duct) K86.8
parotid duct or gland K11.5
pelvis, encysted —*see* Calculus, kidney
prostate N42.0
pulmonary J98.4
pyelitis (impacted) (recurrent) N20.0
with hydronephrosis N13.2
pyelonephritis (impacted) (recurrent) N20
with hydronephrosis N13.2
renal (impacted) (recurrent) —*see* Calculus, kidney
salivary (duct) (gland) K11.5
seminal vesicle N50.8
staghorn —*see* Calculus, kidney
Stensen's duct K11.5
stomach K31.89
sublingual duct or gland K11.5
congenital Q38.4
submandibular duct, gland or region K11.5
submaxillary duct, gland or region K11.5
suburethral N21.8
tonsil J35.8
tooth, teeth (subgingival) (supragingival) K03.6
tunica vaginalis N50.8
ureter (impacted) (recurrent) N20.1
with calculus, kidney N20.2
with hydronephrosis N13.2
with infection N13.6
urethra (impacted) N21.1
urinary (duct) (impacted) (passage) (tract) N20.9
with hydronephrosis N13.2
with infection N13.6
in (due to)
lower N21.9
specified NEC N21.8
vagina N89.8
vesical (impacted) N21.0
Wharton's duct K11.5
xanthine E79.8 *[N22]*

Calicectasis N28.89

Caliectasis N28.89

California
disease B38.9
encephalitis A83.5

Caligo cornea —*see* Opacity, cornea, central

Callositas, callosity (infected) L84

Callus (infected) L84
bone —*see* Osteophyte
excessive, following fracture - code as Sequelae of fracture

Calorie deficiency or malnutrition —*see also* Malnutrition E46

Calvé-Perthes disease —*see* Legg-Calvé-Perthes disease

Calvé's disease —*see* Osteochondrosis, juvenile, spine

Calvities —*see* Alopecia, androgenic

Cameroon fever —*see* Malaria

Camptocormia (hysterical) F44.4

Camurati-Engelmann syndrome Q78.3

Canal —*see also* condition
atrioventricular common Q21.2

Canaliculitis (lacrimal) (acute) (subacute) H04.33-
Actinomyces A42.89
chronic H04.42-

Canavan's disease E75.29

Canceled procedure (surgical) Z53.9
because of
contraindication Z53.09
smoking Z53.01

Canceled procedure *(continued)*
because of *(continued)*
left against medical advice (AMA) Z53.21
patient's decision Z53.20
for reasons of belief or group pressure Z53.1
specified reason NEC Z53.29
specified reason NEC Z53.8

Cancer —*see also* Neoplasm, by site, malignant
bile duct type liver C22.1
blood —*see* Leukemia
breast —*see also* Neoplasm, breast, malignant C50.91-
hepatocellular C22.0
lung —*see also* Neoplasm, lung, malignant C34.90-
ovarian —*see also* Neoplasm ovary, malignant C56.9-
unspecified site (primary) C80.1

Cancer (o)**phobia** F45.29

Cancerous —*see* Neoplasm, malignant, by site

Cancrum oris A69.0

Candidiasis, candidal B37.9
balanitis B37.42
bronchitis B37.1
cheilitis B37.83
congenital P37.5
cystitis B37.41
disseminated B37.7
endocarditis B37.6
enteritis B37.82
esophagitis B37.81
intertrigo B37.2
lung B37.1
meningitis B37.5
mouth B37.0
nails B37.2
neonatal P37.5
onychia B37.2
oral B37.0
osteomyelitis B37.89
otitis externa B37.84
paronychia B37.2
perionyxis B37.2
pneumonia B37.1
proctitis B37.82
pulmonary B37.1
pyelonephritis B37.49
sepsis B37.7
skin B37.2
specified site NEC B37.89
stomatitis B37.0
systemic B37.7
urethritis B37.41
urogenital site NEC B37.49
vagina B37.3
vulva B37.3
vulvovaginitis B37.3

Candidid L30.2

Candidosis —*see* Candidiasis

Candiru infection or infestation B88.8

Canities (premature) L67.1
congenital Q84.2

Canker (mouth) (sore) K12.0
rash A38.9

Cannabinosis J66.2

Canton fever A75.9

Cantrell's syndrome Q87.89

Capillariasis (intestinal) B81.1
hepatic B83.8

Capillary —*see* condition

Caplan's syndrome —*see* Rheumatoid, lung

Capsule —*see* condition

Capsulitis (joint) —*see also* Enthesopathy
adhesive (shoulder) M75.0-
hepatic K65.8
labyrinthine —*see* Otosclerosis, specified NEC
thyroid E06.9

Caput
crepitus Q75.8
medusae I86.8
succedaneum P12.81

Car sickness T75.3

Carapata (disease) A68.0

Carate —*see* Pinta

Carbon lung J60

Carbuncle L02.93
abdominal wall L02.231
anus K61.0
auditory canal, external —*see* Abscess, ear, external
auricle ear —*see* Abscess, ear, external
axilla L02.43-
back (any part) L02.232
breast N61
buttock L02.33
cheek (external) L02.03
chest wall L02.233
chin L02.03
corpus cavernosum N48.21
ear (any part) (external) (middle) —*see* Abscess, ear, external
external auditory canal —*see* Abscess, ear, external
eyelid —*see* Abscess, eyelid
face NEC L02.03
femoral (region) —*see* Carbuncle, lower limb
finger —*see* Carbuncle, hand
flank L02.231
foot L02.63-
forehead L02.03
genital —*see* Abscess, genital
gluteal (region) L02.33
groin L02.234
hand L02.53-
head NEC L02.831
heel —*see* Carbuncle, foot
hip —*see* Carbuncle, lower limb
kidney —*see* Abscess, kidney
knee —*see* Carbuncle, lower limb
labium (majus) (minus) N76.4
lacrimal
gland —*see* Dacryoadenitis
passages (duct) (sac) —*see* Inflammation, lacrimal, passages, acute
leg —*see* Carbuncle, lower limb
lower limb L02.43-
malignant A22.0
navel L02.236
neck L02.13
nose (external) (septum) J34.0
orbit, orbital —*see* Abscess, orbit
palmar (space) —*see* Carbuncle, hand
partes posteriores L02.33
pectoral region L02.233
penis N48.21
perineum L02.235
pinna —*see* Abscess, ear, external
popliteal —*see* Carbuncle, lower limb
scalp L02.831
seminal vesicle N49.0
shoulder —*see* Carbuncle, upper limb
specified site NEC L02.838
temple (region) L02.03
thumb —*see* Carbuncle, hand
toe —*see* Carbuncle, foot

Carbuncle *(continued)*
- trunk L02.239
  - abdominal wall L02.231
  - back L02.232
  - chest wall L02.233
  - groin L02.234
  - perineum L02.235
  - umbilicus L02.236
- umbilicus L02.236
- upper limb L02.43-
- urethra N34.0
- vulva N76.4

Carbunculus *—see* Carbuncle

Carcinoid (tumor) *—see* Tumor, carcinoid

Carcinoidosis E34.0

Carcinoma (malignant) *—see also* Neoplasm, by site, malignant
- acidophil
  - specified site *—see* Neoplasm, malignant, by site
  - unspecified site C75.1
- acidophil-basophil, mixed
  - specified site *—see* Neoplasm, malignant, by site
  - unspecified site C75.1
- adnexal (skin) *—see* Neoplasm, skin, malignant
- adrenal cortical C74.0-
- alveolar *—see* Neoplasm, lung, malignant
  - cell *—see* Neoplasm, lung, malignant
- ameloblastic C41.1
  - upper jaw (bone) C41.0
- apocrine
  - breast *—see* Neoplasm, breast, malignant
  - specified site NEC *—see* Neoplasm, skin, malignant
  - unspecified site C44.99
- basal cell (pigmented) (*see also* Neoplasm, skin, malignant) C44.91
  - fibro-epithelial *—see* Neoplasm, skin, malignant
  - morphea *—see* Neoplasm, skin, malignant
  - multicentric *—see* Neoplasm, skin, malignant
- basaloid
- basal-squamous cell, mixed *—see* Neoplasm, skin, malignant
- basophil
  - specified site *—see* Neoplasm, malignant, by site
  - unspecified site C75.1
- basophil-acidophil, mixed
  - specified site *—see* Neoplasm, malignant, by site
  - unspecified site C75.1
- basosquamous *—see* Neoplasm, skin, malignant
- bile duct
  - with hepatocellular, mixed C22.0
  - liver C22.1
  - specified site NEC *—see* Neoplasm, malignant, by site
  - unspecified site C22.1
- branchial or branchiogenic C10.4
- bronchial or bronchogenic *—see* Neoplasm, lung, malignant
- bronchiolar *—see* Neoplasm, lung, malignant
- bronchioloalveolar *—see* Neoplasm, lung, malignant
- C cell
  - specified site *—see* Neoplasm, malignant, by site
  - unspecified site C73
- ceruminous C44.29-

Carcinoma *(continued)*
- cervix uteri
  - in situ D06.9
    - endocervix D06.0
    - exocervix D06.1
    - specified site NEC D06.7
- chorionic
  - specified site *—see* Neoplasm, malignant, by site
  - unspecified site
    - female C58
    - male C62.90
- chromophobe
  - specified site *—see* Neoplasm, malignant, by site
  - unspecified site C75.1
- cloacogenic
  - specified site *—see* Neoplasm, malignant, by site
  - unspecified site C21.2
- diffuse type
  - specified site *—see* Neoplasm, malignant, by site
  - unspecified site C16.9
- duct (cell)
  - with Paget's disease *—see* Neoplasm, breast, malignant
  - infiltrating
    - with lobular carcinoma (in situ)
      - specified site *—see* Neoplasm, malignant, by site
      - unspecified site (female) C50.91-
        - male C50.92-
    - specified site *—see* Neoplasm, malignant, by site
    - unspecified site (female) C50.91-
      - male C50.92-
- ductal
  - with lobular
    - specified site *—see* Neoplasm, malignant, by site
    - unspecified site (female) C50.91-
      - male C50.92-
- ductular, infiltrating
  - specified site *—see* Neoplasm, malignant, by site
  - unspecified site (female) C50.91-
    - male C50.92-
- embryonal
  - liver C22.7
- endometrioid
  - specified site *—see* Neoplasm, malignant, by site
  - unspecified site
    - female C56.9
    - male C61
- eosinophil
  - specified site *—see* Neoplasm, malignant, by site
  - unspecified site C75.1
- epidermoid *—see also* Neoplasm, skin malignant
  - in situ, Bowen's type *—see* Neoplasm, skin, in situ
- fibroepithelial, basal cell *—see* Neoplasm, skin, malignant
- follicular
  - with papillary (mixed) C73
  - moderately differentiated C73
  - pure follicle C73
  - specified site *—see* Neoplasm, malignant, by site
  - trabecular C73
  - unspecified site C73
  - well differentiated C73
- generalized, with unspecified primary site C80.0
- glycogen-rich *—see* Neoplasm, breast, malignant

Carcinoma *(continued)*
- granulosa cell C56-
- hepatic cell C22.0
- hepatocellular C22.0
  - with bile duct, mixed C22.0
  - fibrolamellar C22.0
- hepatocholangiolitic C22.0
- Hurthle cell C73
- in
  - adenomatous
    - polyposis coli C18.9
  - pleomorphic adenoma *—see* Neoplasm, salivary glands, malignant
  - situ *—see* Carcinoma-in-situ
- infiltrating
  - duct
    - with lobular
      - specified site *—see* Neoplasm, malignant, by site
      - unspecified site (female) C50.91-
        - male C50.92-
    - with Paget's disease *—see* Neoplasm, breast, malignant
    - specified site *—see* Neoplasm, malignant
    - unspecified site (female) C50.91-
      - male C50.92-
  - ductular
    - specified site *—see* Neoplasm, malignant
    - unspecified site (female) C50.91-
      - male C50.92-
  - lobular
    - specified site *—see* Neoplasm, malignant
    - unspecified site (female) C50.91-
      - male C50.92-
- inflammatory
  - specified site *—see* Neoplasm, malignant
  - unspecified site (female) C50.91-
    - male C50.92-
- intestinal type
  - specified site *—see* Neoplasm, malignant, by site
  - unspecified site C16.9
- intracystic
  - noninfiltrating *—see* Neoplasm, in situ, by site
- intraductal (noninfiltrating)
  - with Paget's disease *—see* Neoplasm, breast, malignant
  - breast D05.1-
  - papillary
    - with invasion
      - specified site *—see* Neoplasm, malignant, by site
      - unspecified site (female) C50.91-
        - male C50.92-
    - breast D05.1-
    - specified site NEC *—see* Neoplasm, in situ, by site
    - unspecified site (female) D05.1-
  - specified site NEC *—see* Neoplasm, in situ, by site
  - unspecified site (female) D05.1-
- intraepidermal *—see* Neoplasm, in situ
  - squamous cell, Bowen's type *—see* Neoplasm, skin, in situ
- intraepithelial *—see* Neoplasm, in situ, by site
  - squamous cell *—see* Neoplasm, in situ, by site
- intraosseous C41.1
  - upper jaw (bone) C41.0

Carcinoma *(continued)*
- islet cell
  - with exocrine, mixed
    - specified site *—see* Neoplasm, malignant, by site
    - unspecified site C25.9
  - pancreas C25.4
  - specified site NEC *—see* Neoplasm, malignant, by site
  - unspecified site C25.4
- juvenile, breast *—see* Neoplasm, breast, malignant
- large cell
  - small cell
    - specified site *—see* Neoplasm, malignant, by site
    - unspecified site C34.90
- Leydig cell (testis)
  - specified site *—see* Neoplasm, malignant, by site
  - unspecified site
    - female C56.9
    - male C62.90
- lipid-rich (female) C50.91-
  - male C50.92-
- liver cell C22.0
- liver NEC C22.7
- lobular (infiltrating)
  - with intraductal
    - specified site *—see* Neoplasm, malignant, by site
    - unspecified site (female) C50.91-
      - male C50.92-
  - noninfiltrating
    - breast D05.0-
    - specified site NEC *—see* Neoplasm, in situ, by site
    - unspecified site D05.0-
  - specified site *—see* Neoplasm, malignant, by site
  - unspecified site (female) C50.91-
    - male C50.92-
- medullary
  - with
    - amyloid stroma
      - specified site *—see* Neoplasm, malignant, by site
      - unspecified site C73
    - lymphoid stroma
      - specified site *—see* Neoplasm, malignant, by site
      - unspecified site (female) C50.91-
        - male C50.92-
- Merkel cell C4A.9
  - anal margin C4A.51
  - anal skin C4A.51
  - canthus C4A.1-
  - ear and external auricular canal C4A.2-
  - external auricular canal C4A.2-
  - eyelid, including canthus C4A.1-
  - face C4A.30
    - specified NEC C4A.39
  - hip C4A.7-
  - lip C4A.0
  - lower limb, including hip C4A.7-
  - neck C4A.4
  - nodal presentation C7B.1
  - nose C4A.31
  - overlapping sites C4A.8
  - perianal skin C4A.51
  - scalp C4A.4
  - secondary C7B.1
  - shoulder C4A.6-
  - skin of breast C4A.52
  - trunk NEC C4A.59
  - upper limb, including shoulder C4A.6-
  - visceral metastatic C7B.1

Carcinoma *(continued)*
metastatic —*see* Neoplasm, secondary, by site
metatypical —*see* Neoplasm, skin, malignant
morphea, basal cell —*see* Neoplasm, skin, malignant
mucoid
cell
specified site —*see* Neoplasm, malignant, by site
unspecified site C75.1
neuroendocrine —*see also* Tumor, neuroendocrine
high grade, any site C7A.1
poorly differentiated, any site C7A.1
nonencapsulated sclerosing C73
noninfiltrating
intracystic —*see* Neoplasm, in situ, by site
intraductal
breast D05.1-
papillary
breast D05.1-
specified site NEC —*see* Neoplasm, in situ, by site
unspecified site D05.1-
specified site —*see* Neoplasm, in situ, by site
unspecified site D05.1-
lobular
breast D05.0-
specified site NEC —*see* Neoplasm, in situ, by site
unspecified site (female) D05.0-
oat cell
specified site —*see* Neoplasm, malignant, by site
unspecified site C34.90
odontogenic C41.1
upper jaw (bone) C41.0
papillary
with follicular (mixed) C73
follicular variant C73
intraductal (noninfiltrating)
with invasion
specified site —*see* Neoplasm, malignant, by site
unspecified site (female) C50.91-
male C50.92-
breast D05.1-
specified site NEC —*see* Neoplasm, in situ, by site
unspecified site D05.1-
serous
specified site —*see* Neoplasm, malignant, by site
surface
specified site —*see* Neoplasm, malignant, by site
unspecified site C56.9
unspecified site C56.9
papillocystic
specified site —*see* Neoplasm, malignant, by site
unspecified site C56.9
parafollicular cell
specified site —*see* Neoplasm, malignant, by site
unspecified site C73
pilomatrix —*see* Neoplasm, skin, malignant
pseudomucinous
specified site —*see* Neoplasm, malignant, by site
unspecified site C56.9
renal cell C64-
Schmincke —*see* Neoplasm, nasopharynx, malignant

Carcinoma *(continued)*
Schneiderian
specified site —*see* Neoplasm, malignant, by site
unspecified site C30.0
sebaceous —*see* Neoplasm, skin, malignant
secondary —*see also* Neoplasm, secondary, by site
Merkel cell C7B.1
secretory, breast —*see* Neoplasm, breast, malignant
serous
papillary
specified site —*see* Neoplasm, malignant, by site
unspecified site C56.9
surface, papillary
specified site —*see* Neoplasm, malignant, by site
unspecified site C56.9
Sertoli cell
specified site —*see* Neoplasm, malignant, by site
unspecified site C62.90
female C56.9
male C62.90
skin appendage —*see* Neoplasm, skin, malignant
small cell
fusiform cell
specified site —*see* Neoplasm, malignant, by site
unspecified site C34.90
intermediate cell
specified site —*see* Neoplasm, malignant, by site
unspecified site C34.90
large cell
specified site —*see* Neoplasm, malignant, by site
unspecified site C34.90
solid
with amyloid stroma
specified site —*see* Neoplasm, malignant, by site
unspecified site C73
microinvasive
specified site —*see* Neoplasm, malignant, by site
unspecified site C53.9
sweat gland —*see* Neoplasm, skin, malignant
theca cell C56.-
thymic C37
unspecified site (primary) C80.1
water-clear cell C75.0

Carcinoma-in-situ —*see also* Neoplasm, in situ, by site
breast NOS D05.9-
specified type NEC D05.8-
epidermoid —*see also* Neoplasm, in situ, by site
with questionable stromal invasion
cervix D06.9
specified site NEC —*see* Neoplasm, in situ, by site
unspecified site D06.9
Bowen's type —*see* Neoplasm, skin, in situ
intraductal
breast D05.1-
specified site NEC —*see* Neoplasm, in situ, by site
unspecified site D05.1-
lobular
with
infiltrating duct
breast (female) C50.91-
male C50.92-
specified site NEC —*see* Neoplasm, malignant

Carcinoma-in-situ *(continued)*
lobular *(continued)*
with *(continued)*
infiltrating duct *(continued)*
unspecified site (female) C50.91-
male C50.92-
intraductal
breast D05.8-
specified site NEC —*see* Neoplasm, in situ, by site
unspecified site (female) D05.8-
breast D05.0-
specified site NEC —*see* Neoplasm, in situ, by site
unspecified site D05.0-
squamous cell —*see also* Neoplasm, in situ, by site
with questionable stromal invasion
cervix D06.9
specified site NEC —*see* Neoplasm, in situ, by site
unspecified site D06.9

Carcinomaphobia F45.29

Carcinomatosis C80.0
peritonei C78.6
unspecified site (primary) (secondary) C80.0

Carcinosarcoma —*see* Neoplasm, malignant, by site
embryonal —*see* Neoplasm, malignant, by site

Cardia, cardial —*see* condition

Cardiac —*see also* condition
death, sudden —*see* Arrest, cardiac
pacemaker
in situ Z95.0
management or adjustment Z45.018
tamponade I31.4

Cardialgia —*see* Pain, precordial

Cardiectasis —*see* Hypertrophy, cardiac

Cardiochalasia K21.9

Cardiomalacia I51.5

Cardiomegalia glycogenica diffusa E74.02 *[I43]*

Cardiomegaly —*see also* Hypertrophy, cardiac
congenital Q24.8
glycogen E74.02 *[I43]*
idiopathic I51.7

Cardiomyoliposis I51.5

Cardiomyopathy (familial) (idiopathic) I42.9
alcoholic I42.6
amyloid E85.4 *[I43]*
arteriosclerotic —*see* Disease, heart, ischemic, atherosclerotic
beriberi E51.12
cobalt-beer I42.6
congenital I42.4
congestive I42.0
constrictive NOS I42.5
dilated I42.0
due to
alcohol I42.6
beriberi E51.12
cardiac glycogenosis E74.02 *[I43]*
drugs I42.7
external agents NEC I42.7
Friedreich's ataxia G11.1
myotonia atrophica G71.11 *[I43]*
progressive muscular dystrophy G71.0
glycogen storage E74.02 *[I43]*

Cardiomyopathy *(continued)*
hypertensive —*see* Hypertension, heart
hypertrophic (nonobstructive) I42.2
obstructive I42.1
congenital Q24.8
in
Chagas' disease (chronic) B57.2
acute B57.0
sarcoidosis D86.85
ischemic I25.5
metabolic E88.9 *[I43]*
thyrotoxic E05.90 *[I43]*
with thyroid storm E05.91 *[I43]*
newborn I42.8
congenital I42.4
nutritional E63.9 *[I43]*
beriberi E51.12
obscure of Africa I42.8
peripartum O90.3
postpartum O90.3
restrictive NEC I42.5
rheumatic I09.0
secondary I42.9
stress induced I51.81
takotsubo I51.81
thyrotoxic E05.90 *[I43]*
with thyroid storm E05.91 *[I43]*
toxic NEC I42.7
tuberculous A18.84
viral B33.24

Cardionephritis —*see* Hypertension, cardiorenal

Cardionephropathy —*see* Hypertension, cardiorenal

Cardionephrosis —*see* Hypertension, cardiorenal

Cardiopathia nigra I27.0

Cardiopathy —*see also* Disease, heart I51.9
idiopathic I42.9
mucopolysaccharidosis E76.3 *[I52]*

Cardiopericarditis —*see* Pericarditis

Cardiophobia F45.29

Cardiorenal —*see* condition

Cardiorrhexis —*see* Infarct, myocardium

Cardiosclerosis —*see* Disease, heart, ischemic, atherosclerotic

Cardiosis —*see* Disease, heart

Cardiospasm (esophagus) (reflex) (stomach) K22.0
congenital Q39.5
with megaesophagus Q39.5

Cardiostenosis —*see* Disease, heart

Cardiosymphysis I31.0

Cardiovascular —*see* condition

Carditis (acute) (bacterial) (chronic) (subacute) I51.89
meningococcal A39.50
rheumatic —*see* Disease, heart, rheumatic
rheumatoid —*see* Rheumatoid, carditis
viral B33.20

Care (of) (for) (following)
child (routine) Z76.2
family member (handicapped) (sick)
creating problem for family Z63.6
provided away from home for holiday relief Z75.5
unavailable, due to
absence (person rendering care) (sufferer) Z74.2
inability (any reason) of person rendering care Z74.2

Care *(continued)*
- foundling Z76.1
- holiday relief Z75.5
- improper —*see* Maltreatment
- lack of (at or after birth) (infant) —*see* Maltreatment, child, neglect
- lactating mother Z39.1
- palliative Z51.5
- postpartum
  - immediately after delivery Z39.0
  - routine follow-up Z39.2
- respite Z75.5
- unavailable, due to
  - absence of person rendering care Z74.2
  - inability (any reason) of person rendering care Z74.2
- well-baby Z76.2

Caries
- bone NEC A18.03
- dental K02.9
  - arrested (coronal) (root) K02.3
  - chewing surface
    - limited to enamel K02.51
    - penetrating into dentin K02.52
    - penetrating into pulp K02.53
  - coronal surface
    - chewing surface
      - limited to enamel K02.51
      - penetrating into dentin K02.52
      - penetrating into pulp K02.53
    - pit and fissure surface
      - limited to enamel K02.51
      - penetrating into dentin K02.52
      - penetrating into pulp K02.53
    - smooth surface
      - limited to enamel K02.61
      - penetrating into dentin K02.62
      - penetrating into pulp K02.63
  - pit and fissure surface
    - limited to enamel K02.51
    - penetrating into dentin K02.52
    - penetrating into pulp K02.53
  - root K02.7
  - smooth surface
    - limited to enamel K02.61
    - penetrating into dentin K02.62
    - penetrating into pulp K02.63
- external meatus —*see* Disorder, ear, external, specified type NEC
- hip (tuberculous) A18.02
- initial (tooth)
  - chewing surface K02.51
  - pit and fissure surface K02.51
  - smooth surface K02.61
- knee (tuberculous) A18.02
- labyrinth —*see* subcategory H83.8
- limb NEC (tuberculous) A18.03
- mastoid process (chronic) —*see* Mastoiditis, chronic
  - tuberculous A18.03
- middle ear —*see* subcategory H74.8
- nose (tuberculous) A18.03
- orbit (tuberculous) A18.03
- ossicles, ear —*see* Abnormal, ear ossicles
- petrous bone —*see* Petrositis
- root (dental) (tooth) K02.7
- sacrum (tuberculous) A18.01
- spine, spinal (column) (tuberculous) A18.01
- syphilitic A52.77
  - congenital (early) A50.02 *[M90.80]*
- tooth, teeth —*see* Caries, dental
- tuberculous A18.03
- vertebra (column) (tuberculous) A18.01

Carious teeth —*see* Caries, dental

Carneous mole O02.0

Carnitine insufficiency E71.40

Carotid body or sinus syndrome G90.01

Carotidynia G90.01

Carotinemia (dietary) E67.1

Carotinosis (cutis) (skin) E67.1

Carpal tunnel syndrome —*see* Syndrome, carpal tunnel

Carpenter's syndrome Q87.0

Carpopedal spasm —*see* Tetany

Carr-Barr-Plunkett syndrome Q97.1

Carrier (suspected) **of**
- amebiasis Z22.1
- bacterial disease NEC Z22.39
  - diphtheria Z22.2
  - intestinal infectious NEC Z22.1
    - typhoid Z22.0
  - meningococcal Z22.31
  - sexually transmitted Z22.4
  - specified NEC Z22.39
  - staphylococcal (Methicillin susceptible) Z22.321
    - Methicillin resistant Z22.322
  - streptococcal Z22.338
    - group B Z22.330
  - typhoid Z22.0
- cholera Z22.1
- diphtheria Z22.2
- gastrointestinal pathogens NEC Z22.1
- genetic Z14.8
  - cystic fibrosis Z14.1
  - hemophilia A (asymptomatic) Z14.01
    - symptomatic Z14.02
- gonorrhea Z22.4
- HAA (hepatitis Australian-antigen) Z22.59
- HB (c)(s)-AG Z22.51
- hepatitis (viral) Z22.50
  - Australia-antigen (HAA) Z22.59
  - B surface antigen (HBsAg) Z22.51
    - with acute delta-(super) infection B17.0
  - C Z22.52
  - specified NEC Z22.59
- human T-cell lymphotropic virus type-1(HTLV-1) infection Z22.6
- infectious organism Z22.9
  - specified NEC Z22.8
- meningococci Z22.31
- Salmonella typhosa Z22.0
- serum hepatitis —*see* Carrier, hepatitis
- staphylococci (Methicillin susceptible) Z22.321
  - Methicillin resistant Z22.322
- streptococci Z22.338
  - group B Z22.330
- syphilis Z22.4
- typhoid Z22.0
- venereal disease NEC Z22.4

Carrion's disease A44.0

Carter's relapsing fever (Asiatic) A68.1

Cartilage —*see* condition

Caruncle (inflamed)
- conjunctiva (acute) —*see* Conjunctivitis, acute
- labium (majus) (minus) N90.89
- lacrimal —*see* Inflammation, lacrimal, passages
- myrtiform N89.8
- urethral (benign) N36.2

Cascade stomach K31.2

Caseation lymphatic gland (tuberculous) A18.2

Cassidy (-Scholte) **syndrome** (malignant carcinoid) E34.0

Castellani's disease A69.8

Castration, traumatic, male S38.231

Casts in urine R82.99

Cat
- cry syndrome Q93.4
- ear Q17.3
- eye syndrome Q92.8

Catabolism, senile R54

Catalepsy (hysterical) F44.2
- schizophrenic F20.2

Cataplexy (idiopathic) —*see* -Narcolepsy

Cataract (cortical) (immature) (incipient) H26.9
- with
  - neovascularization —*see* Cataract, complicated
- age-related —*see* Cataract, senile
- anterior
  - and posterior axial embryonal Q12.0
  - pyramidal Q12.0
- associated with
  - galactosemia E74.21 *[H28]*
  - myotonic disorders G71.19 *[H28]*
- blue Q12.0
- central Q12.0
- cerulean Q12.0
- complicated H26.20
  - with
    - neovascularization H26.21-
    - ocular disorder H26.22-
  - glaucomatous flecks H26.23-
- congenital Q12.0
- coraliform Q12.0
- coronary Q12.0
- crystalline Q12.0
- diabetic —*see* Diabetes, cataract
- drug-induced H26.3-
- due to
  - ocular disorder —*see* Cataract, complicated
  - radiation H26.8
- electric H26.8
- extraction status Z98.4-
- glass-blower's H26.8
- heat ray H26.8
- heterochromic —*see* Cataract, complicated
- hypermature —*see* Cataract, senile, morgagnian type
- in (due to)
  - chronic iridocyclitis —*see* Cataract, complicated
  - diabetes —*see* Diabetes, cataract
  - endocrine disease E34.9 *[H28]*
  - eye disease —*see* Cataract, complicated
  - hypoparathyroidism E20.9 *[H28]*
  - malnutrition-dehydration E46 *[H28]*
  - metabolic disease E88.9 *[H28]*
  - myotonic disorders G71.19 *[H28]*
  - nutritional disease E63.9 *[H28]*
- infantile —*see* Cataract, presenile
- irradiational —*see* Cataract, specified NEC
- juvenile —*see* Cataract, presenile
- malnutrition-dehydration E46 *[H28]*
- morgagnian —*see* Cataract, senile, morgagnian type
- myotonic G71.19 *[H28]*
- myxedema E03.9 *[H28]*
- nuclear
  - embryonal Q12.0
  - sclerosis —*see* Cataract, senile, nuclear

Cataract *(continued)*
- presenile H26.00-
  - combined forms H26.06-
  - cortical H26.01-
  - lamellar —*see* Cataract, presenile, cortical
  - nuclear H26.03-
  - specified NEC H26.09
  - subcapsular polar (anterior) H26.04-
    - posterior H26.05-
  - zonular —*see* Cataract, presenile, cortical
- secondary H26.40
  - Soemmering's ring H26.41-
  - specified NEC H26.49-
  - to eye disease —*see* Cataract, complicated
- senile H25.9
  - brunescens —*see* Cataract, senile, nuclear
  - combined forms H25.81-
  - coronary —*see* Cataract, senile, incipient
  - cortical H25.01-
  - hypermature —*see* Cataract, senile, morgagnian type
  - incipient (mature) (total) H25.09-
    - cortical —*see* Cataract, senile, cortical
    - subcapsular —*see* Cataract, senile, subcapsular
  - morgagnian type (hypermature) H25.2-
  - nuclear (sclerosis) H25.1-
  - polar subcapsular (anterior) (posterior) —*see* Cataract, senile, incipient
  - punctate —*see* Cataract, senile, incipient
  - specified NEC H25.89
  - subcapsular polar (anterior) H25.03-
    - posterior H25.04-
- snowflake —*see* Diabetes, cataract
- specified NEC H26.8
- toxic —*see* Cataract, drug-induced
- traumatic H26.10-
  - localized H26.11-
  - partially resolved H26.12-
  - total H26.13-
- zonular (perinuclear) Q12.0

Cataracta —*see also* Cataract
- brunescens —*see* Cataract, senile, nuclear
- centralis pulverulenta Q12.0
- cerulea Q12.0
- complicata —*see* Cataract, complicated
- congenita Q12.0
- coralliformis Q12.0
- coronaria Q12.0
- diabetic —*see* Diabetes, cataract
- membranacea
  - accreta —*see* Cataract, secondary
  - congenita Q12.0
- nigra —*see* Cataract, senile, nuclear
- sunflower —*see* Cataract, complicated

Catarrh, catarrhal (acute) (febrile) (infectious) (inflammation) —*see also* condition J00
- bronchial —*see* Bronchitis
- chest —*see* Bronchitis
- chronic J31.0
- due to congenital syphilis A50.03
- enteric —*see* Enteritis
- eustachian H68.009
- fauces —*see* Pharyngitis
- gastrointestinal —*see* Enteritis

Catarrh, catarrhal *(continued)*
- gingivitis K05.00
  - nonplaque induced K05.01
  - plaque induced K05.00
- hay —*see* Fever, hay
- intestinal —*see* Enteritis
- larynx, chronic J37.0
- liver B15.9
  - with hepatic coma B15.0
- lung —*see* Bronchitis
- middle ear, chronic —*see* Otitis, media, nonsuppurative, chronic, serous
- mouth K12.1
- nasal (chronic) —*see* Rhinitis
- nasobronchial J31.1
- nasopharyngeal (chronic) J31.1
  - acute J00
- pulmonary —*see* Bronchitis
- spring (eye) (vernal) —*see* Conjunctivitis, acute, atopic
- summer (hay) —*see* Fever, hay
- throat J31.2
- tubotympanal —*see also* Otitis, media, nonsuppurative
  - chronic —*see* Otitis, media, nonsuppurative, chronic, serous

Catatonia (schizophrenic) F20.2

Catatonic
- disorder due to known physiologic condition F06.1
- schizophrenia F20.2
- stupor R40.1

Cat-scratch —*see also* Abrasion
- disease or fever A28.1

Cauda equina —*see* condition

Cauliflower ear M95.1-

Causalgia (upper limb) G56.4-
- lower limb G57.7-

Cause
- external, general effects T75.89

Caustic burn —*see* Corrosion, by site

Cavare's disease (familial periodic paralysis) G72.3

Cave-in, injury
- crushing (severe) —*see* Crush
- suffocation —*see* Asphyxia, traumatic, due to low oxygen, due to cave-in

Cavernitis (penis) N48.29

Cavernositis N48.29

Cavernous —*see* condition

Cavitation of lung —*see also* Tuberculosis, pulmonary
- nontuberculous J98.4

Cavities, dental —*see* Caries, dental

Cavity
- lung —*see* Cavitation of lung
- optic papilla Q14.2
- pulmonary —*see* Cavitation of lung

Cavovarus foot, congenital Q66.1

Cavus foot (congenital) Q66.7
- acquired —*see* Deformity, limb, foot, specified NEC

Cazenave's disease L10.2

Cecitis K52.9
- with perforation, peritonitis, or rupture K65.8

Cecum —*see* condition

Celiac
- artery compression syndrome I77.4
- disease K90.0
- infantilism K90.0

Cell (s), **cellular** —*see also* condition
- in urine R82.99

Cellulitis (diffuse) (phlegmonous) (septic) (suppurative) L03.90
- abdominal wall L03.311
- anaerobic A48.0
- ankle —*see* Cellulitis, lower limb
- anus K61.0
- arm —*see* Cellulitis, upper limb
- auricle (ear) —*see* Cellulitis, ear
- axilla L03.11-
- back (any part) L03.312
- broad ligament
  - acute N73.0
- buttock L03.317
- cervical (meaning neck) L03.221
- cervix (uteri) —*see* Cervicitis
- cheek (external) L03.211
  - internal K12.2
- chest wall L03.313
- chronic L03.90
- clostridial A48.0
- corpus cavernosum N48.22
- digit
  - finger —*see* Cellulitis, finger
  - toe —*see* Cellulitis, toe
- Douglas' cul-de-sac or pouch
  - acute N73.0
- drainage site (following operation) T81.4
- ear (external) H60.1-
- eosinophilic (granulomatous) L98.3
- erysipelatous —*see* Erysipelas
- external auditory canal —*see* Cellulitis, ear
- eyelid —*see* Abscess, eyelid
- face NEC L03.211
- finger (intrathecal) (periosteal) (subcutaneous) (subcuticular) L03.01-
- foot —*see* Cellulitis, lower limb
- gangrenous —*see* Gangrene
- genital organ NEC
  - female (external) N76.4
  - male N49.9
    - multiple sites N49.8
    - specified NEC N49.8
- gluteal (region) L03.317
- gonococcal A54.89
- groin L03.314
- hand —*see* Cellulitis, upper limb
- head NEC L03.811
  - face (any part, except ear, eye and nose) L03.211
- heel —*see* Cellulitis, lower limb
- hip —*see* Cellulitis, lower limb
- jaw (region) L03.211
- knee —*see* Cellulitis, lower limb
- labium (majus) (minus) —*see* Vulvitis
- lacrimal passages —*see* Inflammation, lacrimal, passages
- larynx J38.7
- leg —*see* Cellulitis, lower limb
- lip K13.0
- lower limb L03.11-
  - toe —*see* Cellulitis, toe
- mouth (floor) K12.2
- multiple sites, so stated L03.90
- nasopharynx J39.1
- navel L03.316
  - newborn P38.9
    - with mild hemorrhage P38.1
    - without hemorrhage P38.9
- neck (region) L03.221
- nose (septum) (external) J34.0
- orbit, orbital H05.01-
- palate (soft) K12.2
- pectoral (region) L03.313

Cellulitis *(continued)*
- pelvis, pelvic (chronic)
  - female —*see also* Disease, pelvis, inflammatory N73.2
    - acute N73.0
  - following ectopic or molar pregnancy O08.0
  - male K65.0
- penis N48.22
- perineal, perineum L03.315
- perirectal K61.1
- peritonsillar J36
- periurethral N34.0
- periuterine —*see also* Disease, pelvis, inflammatory N73.2
  - acute N73.0
- pharynx J39.1
- rectum K61.1
- retroperitoneal K68.9
- round ligament
  - acute N73.0
- scalp (any part) L03.811
- scrotum N49.2
- seminal vesicle N49.0
- shoulder —*see* Cellulitis, upper limb
- specified site NEC L03.818
- submandibular (region) (space) (triangle) K12.2
  - gland K11.3
- submaxillary (region) K12.2
  - gland K11.3
- thigh —*see* Cellulitis, lower limb
- thumb (intrathecal) (periosteal) (subcutaneous) (subcuticular) —*see* Cellulitis, finger
- toe (intrathecal) (periosteal) (subcutaneous) (subcuticular) L03.03-
- tonsil J36
- trunk L03.319
  - abdominal wall L03.311
  - back (any part) L03.312
  - buttock L03.317
  - chest wall L03.313
  - groin L03.314
  - perineal, perineum L03.315
  - umbilicus L03.316
- tuberculous (primary) A18.4
- umbilicus L03.316
- upper limb L03.11-
  - axilla —*see* Cellulitis, axilla
  - finger —*see* Cellulitis, finger
  - thumb —*see* Cellulitis, finger
- vaccinal T88.0
- vocal cord J38.3
- vulva —*see* Vulvitis
- wrist —*see* Cellulitis, upper limb

Cementoblastoma, benign —*see* Cyst, calcifying odontogenic

Cementoma —*see* Cyst, calcifying odontogenic

Cementoperiostitis —*see* Periodontitis

Cementosis K03.4

Central auditory processing disorder H93.25

Central pain syndrome G89.0

Cephalematocele, cephal (o)**hematocele**
- newborn P52.8
  - birth injury P10.8
- traumatic —*see* Hematoma, brain

Cephalematoma, cephalhematoma (calcified)
- newborn (birth injury) P12.0
- traumatic —*see* Hematoma, brain

Cephalgia, cephalalgia —*see also* Headache
- histamine G44.009
  - intractable G44.001
  - not intractable G44.009

Cephalgia, cephalalgia *(continued)*
- trigeminal autonomic (TAC) NEC G44.099
  - intractable G44.091
  - not intractable G44.099

Cephalic —*see* condition

Cephalitis —*see* Encephalitis

Cephalocele —*see* Encephalocele

Cephalomenia N94.89

Cephalopelvic —*see* condition

Cerclage (with cervical incompetence) **in pregnancy** —*see* Incompetence, cervix, in pregnancy

Cerebellitis —*see* Encephalitis

Cerebellum, cerebellar —*see* condition

Cerebral —*see* condition

Cerebritis —*see* Encephalitis

Cerebro-hepato-renal syndrome Q87.89

Cerebromalacia —*see* Softening, brain
- sequelae of cerebrovascular disease I69.398

Cerebroside lipidosis E75.22

Cerebrospasticity (congenital) G80.1

Cerebrospinal —*see* condition

Cerebrum —*see* condition

Ceroid-lipofuscinosis, neuronal E75.4

Cerumen (accumulation) (impacted) H61.2-

Cervical —*see also* condition
- auricle Q18.2
- dysplasia in pregnancy —*see* Abnormal, cervix, in pregnancy or childbirth
- erosion in pregnancy —*see* Abnormal, cervix, in pregnancy or childbirth
- fibrosis in pregnancy —*see* Abnormal, cervix, in pregnancy or childbirth
- fusion syndrome Q76.1
- rib Q76.5
- shortening (complicating pregnancy) O26.87-

Cervicalgia M54.2

Cervicitis (acute) (chronic) (nonvenereal) (senile (atrophic)) (subacute) (with ulceration) N72
- with
  - abortion —*see* Abortion, by type complicated by genital tract and pelvic infection
  - ectopic pregnancy O08.0
  - molar pregnancy O08.0
- chlamydial A56.09
- gonococcal A54.03
- herpesviral A60.03
- puerperal (postpartum) O86.11
- syphilitic A52.76
- trichomonal A59.09
- tuberculous A18.16

Cervicocolpitis (emphysematosa) (*see also* Cervicitis) N72

Cervix —*see* condition

Cesarean delivery, previous, affecting management of pregnancy O34.21

Céstan (-Chenais) **paralysis or syndrome** G46.3

Céstan-Raymond syndrome I65.8

Cestode infestation B71.9
- specified type NEC B71.8

Cestodiasis B71.9

- **Chabert's disease** A22.9
- **Chacaleh** E53.8
- **Chafing** L30.4
- **Chagas'** (-Mazza) **disease** (chronic) B57.2
  - with
    - cardiovascular involvement NEC B57.2
    - digestive system involvement B57.30
      - megacolon B57.32
      - megaesophagus B57.31
      - other specified B57.39
    - megacolon B57.32
    - megaesophagus B57.31
    - myocarditis B57.2
    - nervous system involvement B57.40
      - meningitis B57.41
      - meningoencephalitis B57.42
      - other specified B57.49
    - specified organ involvement NEC B57.5
  - acute (with) B57.1
    - cardiovascular NEC B57.0
    - myocarditis B57.0
- **Chagres fever** B50.9
- **Chairridden** Z74.09
- **Chalasia** (cardiac sphincter) K21.9
- **Chalazion** H00.19
  - left H00.16
    - lower H00.15
    - upper H00.14
  - right H00.13
    - lower H00.12
    - upper H00.11
- **Chalcosis** —*see also* Disorder, globe, degenerative, chalcosis
  - cornea —*see* Deposit, cornea
  - crystalline lens —*see* Cataract, complicated
  - retina H35.89
- **Chalicosis** (pulmonum) J62.8
- **Chancre** (any genital site) (hard) (hunterian) (mixed) (primary) (seronegative) (seropositive) (syphilitic) A51.0
  - congenital A50.07
  - conjunctiva NEC A51.2
  - Ducrey's A57
  - extragenital A51.2
  - eyelid A51.2
  - lip A51.2
  - nipple A51.2
  - Nisbet's A57
  - of
    - carate A67.0
    - pinta A67.0
    - yaws A66.0
  - palate, soft A51.2
  - phagedenic A57
  - simple A57
  - soft A57
    - bubo A57
    - palate A51.2
  - urethra A51.0
  - yaws A66.0
- **Chancroid** (anus) (genital) (penis) (perineum) (rectum) (urethra) (vulva) A57
- **Chandler's disease** (osteochondritis dissecans, hip) —*see* Osteochondritis, dissecans, hip
- **Change** (s) (in) (of) —*see also* Removal
  - arteriosclerotic —*see* Arteriosclerosis
  - bone —*see also* Disorder, bone
    - diabetic —*see* Diabetes, bone change

Change *(continued)*
  - bowel habit R19.4
  - cardiorenal (vascular) —*see* Hypertension, cardiorenal
  - cardiovascular —*see* Disease, cardiovascular
  - circulatory I99.9
  - cognitive (mild) (organic) R41.89
  - color, tooth, teeth
    - during formation K00.8
    - posteruptive K03.7
  - contraceptive device Z30.433
  - corneal membrane H18.30
    - Bowman's membrane fold or rupture H18.31-
    - Descemet's membrane
      - fold H18.32-
      - rupture H18.33-
  - coronary —*see* Disease, heart, ischemic
  - degenerative, spine or vertebra —*see* Spondylosis
  - dental pulp, regressive K04.2
  - dressing (nonsurgical) Z48.00
    - surgical Z48.01
  - heart —*see* Disease, heart
  - hip joint —*see* Derangement, joint, hip
  - hyperplastic larynx J38.7
  - hypertrophic
    - nasal sinus J34.89
    - turbinate, nasal J34.3
    - upper respiratory tract J39.8
  - indwelling catheter Z46.6
  - inflammatory —*see also* Inflammation
    - sacroiliac M46.1
  - job, anxiety concerning Z56.1
  - joint —*see* Derangement, joint
  - life —*see* Menopause
  - mental status R41.82
  - minimal (glomerular) —*see also* N00-N07 with fourth character .0
    - N05.0
  - myocardium, myocardial —*see* Degeneration, myocardial
  - of life —*see* Menopause
  - pacemaker Z45.018
    - pulse generator Z45.010
  - personality (enduring) F68.8
    - due to (secondary to)
      - general medical condition F07.0
    - secondary (nonspecific) F60.89
  - regressive, dental pulp K04.2
  - renal —*see* Disease, renal
  - retina H35.9
    - myopic H44.2-
  - sacroiliac joint M53.3
  - senile —*see also* condition R54
  - sensory R20.8
  - skin R23.9
    - acute, due to ultraviolet radiation L56.9
      - specified NEC L56.8
    - chronic, due to nonionizing radiation L57.9
      - specified NEC L57.8
    - cyanosis R23.0
    - flushing R23.2
    - pallor R23.1
    - petechiae R23.3
    - specified change NEC R23.8
    - swelling —*see* Mass, localized
    - texture R23.4
  - trophic
    - arm —*see* Mononeuropathy, upper limb
    - leg —*see* Mononeuropathy, lower limb
  - vascular I99.9
  - vasomotor I73.9

Change *(continued)*
  - voice R49.9
    - psychogenic F44.4
    - specified NEC R49.8
- **Changing sleep-work schedule, affecting sleep** G47.26
- **Changuinola fever** A93.1
- **Chapping skin** T69.8
- **Charcot-Marie-Tooth disease, paralysis or syndrome** G60.0
- **Charcot's**
  - arthropathy —*see* Arthropathy, neuropathic
  - cirrhosis K74.3
  - disease (tabetic arthropathy) A52.16
  - joint (disease) (tabetic) A52.16
    - diabetic —*see* Diabetes, with, arthropathy
    - syringomyelic G95.0
  - syndrome (intermittent claudication) I73.9
- **CHARGE association** Q89.8
- **Charley-horse** (quadriceps) M62.831
  - traumatic (quadriceps) S76.11-
- **Charlouis' disease** —*see* Yaws
- **Cheadle's disease** E54
- **Checking** (of)
  - cardiac pacemaker (battery) (electrode (s)) Z45.018
    - pulse generator Z45.010
  - intrauterine contraceptive device Z30.431
- **Check-up** —*see* Examination
- **Chédiak-Higashi** (-Steinbrinck) **syndrome** (congenital gigantism of peroxidase granules) E70.330
- **Cheek** —*see* condition
- **Cheese itch** B88.0
- **Cheese-washer's lung** J67.8
- **Cheese-worker's lung** J67.8
- **Cheilitis** (acute) (angular) (catarrhal) (chronic) (exfoliative) (gangrenous) (glandular) (infectional) (suppurative) (ulcerative) (vesicular) K13.0
  - actinic (due to sun) L56.8
    - other than from sun L59.8
  - candidal B37.83
- **Cheilodynia** K13.0
- **Cheiloschisis** —*see* Cleft, lip
- **Cheilosis** (angular) K13.0
  - with pellagra E52
  - due to
    - vitamin B2(riboflavin) deficiency E53.0
- **Cheiromegaly** M79.89
- **Cheiropompholyx** L30.1
- **Cheloid** —*see* Keloid
- **Chemical burn** —*see* Corrosion, by site
- **Chemodectoma** —*see* Paraganglioma, nonchromaffin
- **Chemosis, conjunctiva** —*see* Edema, conjunctiva
- **Chemotherapy** (session) (for)
  - cancer Z51.11
  - neoplasm Z51.11
- **Cherubism** M27.8
- **Chest** —*see* condition
- **Cheyne-Stokes breathing** (respiration) R06.3
- **Chiari's**
  - disease or syndrome (hepatic vein thrombosis) I82.0

Chiari's *(continued)*
  - malformation
    - type I G93.5
    - type II —*see* Spina bifida
  - net Q24.8
- **Chicago disease** B40.9
- **Chickenpox** —*see* Varicella
- **Chiclero ulcer or sore** B55.1
- **Chigger** (infestation) B88.0
- **Chignon** (disease) B36.8
  - newborn (from vacuum extraction) (birth injury) P12.1
- **Chilaiditi's syndrome** (subphrenic displacement, colon) Q43.3
- **Chilblain** (s) (lupus) T69.1
- **Child**
  - custody dispute Z65.3
- **Childbirth** —*see* Delivery
- **Childhood**
  - cerebral X-linked
    - adrenoleukodystrophy E71.520
  - period of rapid growth Z00.2
- **Chill** (s) R68.83
  - with fever R50.9
  - congestive in malarial regions B54
  - without fever R68.83
- **Chilomastigiasis** A07.8
- **Chimera 46,XX/46,XY** Q99.0
- **Chin** —*see* condition
- **Chinese dysentery** A03.9
- **Chionophobia** F40.228
- **Chitral fever** A93.1
- **Chlamydia, chlamydial** A74.9
  - cervicitis A56.09
  - conjunctivitis A74.0
  - cystitis A56.01
  - endometritis A56.11
  - epididymitis A56.19
  - female
    - pelvic inflammatory disease A56.11
    - pelviperitonitis A56.11
  - orchitis A56.19
  - peritonitis A74.81
  - pharyngitis A56.4
  - proctitis A56.3
  - psittaci (infection) A70
  - salpingitis A56.11
  - sexually-transmitted infection NEC A56.8
  - specified NEC A74.89
  - urethritis A56.01
  - vulvovaginitis A56.02
- **Chlamydiosis** —*see* Chlamydia
- **Chloasma** (skin) (idiopathic) (symptomatic) L81.1
  - eyelid H02.719
    - hyperthyroid E05.90 *[H02.719]*
      - with thyroid storm E05.91 *[H02.719]*
    - left H02.716
      - lower H02.715
      - upper H02.714
    - right H02.713
      - lower H02.712
      - upper H02.711
- **Chloroma** C92.3-
- **Chlorosis** D50.9
  - Egyptian B76.9 *[D63.8]*
  - miner's B76.9 *[D63.8]*
- **Chlorotic anemia** D50.8
- **Chocolate cyst** (ovary) N80.1

Choked
- disc or disk —*see* Papilledema
- on food, phlegm, or vomitus NOS —*see* Foreign body, by site
- while vomiting NOS —*see* Foreign body, by site

Chokes (resulting from bends) T70.3

Choking sensation R09.89

Cholangiectasis K83.8

Cholangiocarcinoma
- with hepatocellular carcinoma, combined C22.0
- liver C22.1
- specified site NEC —*see* Neoplasm, malignant, by site
- unspecified site C22.1

Cholangiohepatitis K83.8
- due to fluke infestation B66.1

Cholangiohepatoma C22.0

Cholangiolitis (acute) (chronic) (extrahepatic) (gangrenous) (intrahepatic) K83.0
- paratyphoidal —*see* Fever, paratyphoid
- typhoidal A01.09

Cholangioma D13.4
- malignant —*see* Cholangiocarcinoma

Cholangitis (ascending) (primary) (recurrent) (sclerosing) (secondary) (stenosing) (suppurative) K83.0
- with calculus, bile duct —*see* Calculus, bile duct, with cholangitis
- chronic nonsuppurative destructive K74.3

Cholecystectasia K82.8

Cholecystitis K81.9
- with
  - calculus, stones in
    - bile duct (common) (hepatic) —*see* Calculus, bile duct, with cholecystitis
    - cystic duct —*see* Calculus, gallbladder, with cholecystitis
    - gallbladder —*see* Calculus, gallbladder, with cholecystitis
  - choledocholithiasis —*see* Calculus, bile duct, with cholecystitis
  - cholelithiasis —*see* Calculus, gallbladder, with cholecystitis
- acute (emphysematous) (gangrenous) (suppurative) K81.0
  - with
    - calculus, stones in
      - cystic duct —*see* Calculus, gallbladder, with cholecystitis, acute
      - gallbladder —*see* Calculus, gallbladder, with cholecystitis, acute
    - choledocholithiasis —*see* Calculus, bile duct, with cholecystitis, acute
    - cholelithiasis —*see* Calculus, gallbladder, with cholecystitis, acute
    - chronic cholecystitis K81.2
      - with gallbladder calculus K80.12
        - with obstruction K80.13
- chronic K81.1
  - with acute cholecystitis K81.2
    - with gallbladder calculus K80.12
      - with obstruction K80.13
- emphysematous (acute) —*see* Cholecystitis, acute
- gangrenous —*see* Cholecystitis, acute
- paratyphoidal, current A01.4

Cholecystitis *(continued)*
- suppurative —*see* Cholecystitis, acute
- typhoidal A01.09

Cholecystolithiasis —*see* Calculus, gallbladder

Choledochitis (suppurative) K83.0

Choledocholith —*see* Calculus, bile duct

Choledocholithiasis (common duct) (hepatic duct) —*see* Calculus, bile duct
- cystic —*see* Calculus, gallbladder
- typhoidal A01.09

Cholelithiasis (cystic duct) (gallbladder) (impacted) (multiple) —*see* Calculus, gallbladder
- bile duct (common) (hepatic) —*see* Calculus, bile duct
- hepatic duct —*see* Calculus, bile duct
- specified NEC K80.80
  - with obstruction K80.81

Cholemia —*see also* Jaundice
- familial (simple) (congenital) E80.4
- Gilbert's E80.4

Choleperitoneum, choleperitonitis K65.3

Cholera (Asiatic) (epidemic) (malignant) A00.9
- antimonial —*see* Poisoning, antimony
- classical A00.0
- due to Vibrio cholerae 01 A00.9
  - biovar cholerae A00.0
  - biovar eltor A00.1
  - el tor A00.1
- el tor A00.1

Cholerine —*see* Cholera

Cholestasis NEC K83.1
- with hepatocyte injury K71.0
- due to total parenteral nutrition (TPN) K76.89
- pure K71.0

Cholesteatoma (ear) (middle) (with reaction) H71.9-
- attic H71.0-
- external ear (canal) H60.4-
- mastoid H71.2-
- postmastoidectomy cavity (recurrent) —*see* Complications, postmastoidectomy, recurrent cholesteatoma
- recurrent (postmastoidectomy) —*see* Complications, postmastoidectomy, recurrent cholesteatoma
- tympanum H71.1-

Cholesteatosis, diffuse H71.3-

Cholesteremia E78.0

Cholesterin in vitreous —*see* Deposit, crystalline

Cholesterol
- deposit
  - retina H35.89
  - vitreous —*see* Deposit, crystalline
- elevated (high) E78.0
  - with elevated (high) triglycerides E78.2
  - screening for Z13.220
- imbibition of gallbladder K82.4

Cholesterolemia (essential) (familial) (hereditary) (pure) E78.0

Cholesterolosis, cholesterosis (gallbladder) K82.4
- cerebrotendinous E75.5

Cholocolic fistula K82.3

Choluria R82.2

Chondritis M94.8X9
- aurical H61.03-
- costal (Tietze's) M94.0
- external ear H61.03-
- patella, posttraumatic —*see* Chondromalacia, patella
- pinna H61.03-
- purulent M94.8X-
- tuberculous NEC A18.02
  - intervertebral A18.01

Chondroblastoma —*see also* Neoplasm, bone, benign
- malignant —*see* Neoplasm, bone, malignant

Chondrocalcinosis M11.20
- ankle M11.27-
- elbow M11.22-
- familial M11.10
  - ankle M11.17-
  - elbow M11.12-
  - foot joint M11.17-
  - hand joint M11.14-
  - hip M11.15-
  - knee M11.16-
  - multiple site M11.19
  - shoulder M11.11-
  - vertebrae M11.18
  - wrist M11.13-
- foot joint M11.27-
- hand joint M11.24-
- hip M11.25-
- knee M11.26-
- multiple site M11.29
- shoulder M11.21-
- vertebrae M11.28
- specified type NEC M11.20
  - ankle M11.27-
  - elbow M11.22-
  - foot joint M11.27-
  - hand joint M11.24-
  - hip M11.25-
  - knee M11.26-
  - multiple site M11.29
  - shoulder M11.21-
  - vertebrae M11.28
  - wrist M11.23-
- wrist M11.23-

Chondrodermatitis nodularis helicis or anthelicis —*see* Perichondritis, ear

Chondrodysplasia Q78.9
- with hemangioma Q78.4
- calcificans congenita Q77.3
- fetalis Q77.4
- metaphyseal (Jansen's) (McKusick's) (Schmid's) Q78.5
- punctata Q77.3

Chondrodystrophy, chondrodystrophia (familial) (fetalis) (hypoplastic) Q78.9
- calcificans congenita Q77.3
- myotonic (congenital) G71.13
- punctata Q77.3

Chondroectodermal dysplasia Q77.6

Chondrogenesis imperfecta Q77.4

Chondrolysis M94.35-

Chondroma —*see also* Neoplasm, cartilage, benign
- juxtacortical —*see* Neoplasm, bone, benign
- periosteal —*see* Neoplasm, bone, benign

Chondromalacia (systemic) M94.20
- acromioclavicular joint M94.21-
- ankle M94.27-
- elbow M94.22-
- foot joint M94.27-
- glenohumeral joint M94.21-

Chondromalacia *(continued)*
- hand joint M94.24-
- hip M94.25-
- knee M94.26-
  - patella M22.4-
- multiple sites M94.29
- patella M22.4-
- rib M94.28
- sacroiliac joint M94.259
- shoulder M94.21-
- sternoclavicular joint M94.21-
- vertebral joint M94.28
- wrist M94.23-

Chondromatosis —*see also* Neoplasm, cartilage, uncertain behavior
- internal Q78.4

Chondromyxosarcoma —*see* Neoplasm, cartilage, malignant

Chondro-osteodysplasia (Morquio-Brailsford type) E76.219

Chondro-osteodystrophy E76.29

Chondro-osteoma —*see* Neoplasm, bone, benign

Chondropathia tuberosa M94.0

Chondrosarcoma —*see* Neoplasm, cartilage, malignant
- juxtacortical —*see* Neoplasm, bone, malignant
- mesenchymal —*see* Neoplasm, connective tissue, malignant
- myxoid —*see* Neoplasm, cartilage, malignant

Chordee (nonvenereal) N48.89
- congenital Q54.4
- gonococcal A54.09

Chorditis (fibrinous) (nodosa) (tuberosa) J38.2

Chordoma —*see* Neoplasm, vertebral (column), malignant

Chorea (chronic) (gravis) (posthemiplegic) (senile) (spasmodic) G25.5
- with
  - heart involvement I02.0
    - active or acute (conditions in I01-) I02.0
    - rheumatic I02.9
      - with valvular disorder I02.0
  - rheumatic heart disease (chronic) (inactive)(quiescent) - code to rheumatic heart condition involved
- drug-induced G25.4
- habit F95.8
- hereditary G10
- Huntington's G10
- hysterical F44.4
- minor I02.9
  - with heart involvement I02.0
- progressive G25.5
  - hereditary G10
- rheumatic (chronic) I02.9
  - with heart involvement I02.0
- Sydenham's I02.9
  - with heart involvement —*see* Chorea, with rheumatic heart disease
  - nonrheumatic G25.5

Choreoathetosis (paroxysmal) G25.5

Chorioadenoma (destruens) D39.2

Chorioamnionitis O41.12-

Chorioangioma D26.7

Choriocarcinoma *—see* Neoplasm, malignant, by site
- combined with
  - embryonal carcinoma *—see* Neoplasm, malignant, by site
  - other germ cell elements *—see* Neoplasm, malignant, by site
  - teratoma *—see* Neoplasm, malignant, by site
- specified site *—see* Neoplasm, malignant, by site
- unspecified site
  - female C58
  - male C62.90

Chorioencephalitis (acute) (lymphocytic) (serous) A87.2

Chorioepithelioma *—see* Choriocarcinoma

Choriomeningitis (acute) (lymphocytic) (serous) A87.2

Chorionepithelioma *—see* Choriocarcinoma

Chorioretinitis *—see also* Inflammation, chorioretinal
- disseminated *—see also* Inflammation, chorioretinal, disseminated
  - in neurosyphilis A52.19
- Egyptian B76.9 *[D63.8]*
- focal *—see also* Inflammation, chorioretinal, focal
- histoplasmic B39.9 *[H32]*
- in (due to)
  - histoplasmosis B39.9 *[H32]*
  - syphilis (secondary) A51.43
    - late A52.71
  - toxoplasmosis (acquired) B58.01
    - congenital (active) P37.1 *[H32]*
  - tuberculosis A18.53
- juxtapapillary, juxtapapillaris *—see* Inflammation, chorioretinal, focal, juxtapapillary
- leprous A30.9 *[H32]*
- miner's B76.9 *[D63.8]*
- progressive myopia (degeneration) H44.2-
- syphilitic (secondary) A51.43
  - congenital (early) A50.01 *[H32]*
    - late A50.32
  - late A52.71
- tuberculous A18.53

Chorioretinopathy, central serous H35.71-

Choroid *—see* condition

Choroideremia H31.21

Choroiditis *—see* Chorioretinitis

Choroidopathy *—see* Disorder, choroid

Choroidoretinitis *—see* Chorioretinitis

Choroidoretinopathy, central serous *—see* Chorioretinopathy, central serous

Christian-Weber disease M35.6

Christmas disease D67

Chromaffinoma *—see also* Neoplasm, benign, by site
- malignant *—see* Neoplasm, malignant, by site

Chromatopsia *—see* Deficiency, color vision

Chromhidrosis, chromidrosis L75.1

Chromoblastomycosis *—see* Chromomycosis

Chromoconversion R82.91

Chromomycosis B43.9
- brain abscess B43.1
- cerebral B43.1
- cutaneous B43.0
- skin B43.0
- specified NEC B43.8
- subcutaneous abscess or cyst B43.2

Chromophytosis B36.0

Chromosome *—see* condition by chromosome involved
- D (1) *—see* condition, chromosome 13
- E (3) *—see* condition, chromosome 18
- G *—see* condition, chromosome 21

Chromotrichomycosis B36.8

Chronic *—see* condition
- fracture *—see* Fracture, pathological

Churg-Strauss syndrome M30.1

Chyle cyst, mesentery I89.8

Chylocele (nonfilarial) I89.8
- filarial *—see also* Infestation, filarial B74.9 *[N51]*
- tunica vaginalis N50.8
  - filarial *—see also* Infestation, filarial B74.9 *[N51]*

Chylomicronemia (fasting) (with hyperprebetalipoproteinemia) E78.3

Chylopericardium I31.3
- acute I30.9

Chylothorax (nonfilarial) I89.8
- filarial *—see also* Infestation, filarial B74.9 *[J91.8]*

Chylous *—see* condition

Chyluria (nonfilarial) R82.0
- due to
  - bilharziasis B65.0
  - Brugia (malayi) B74.1
    - timori B74.2
  - schistosomiasis (bilharziasis) B65.0
  - Wuchereria (bancrofti) B74.0
- filarial *—see* Infestation, filarial

Cicatricial (deformity) *—see* Cicatrix

Cicatrix (adherent) (contracted) (painful) (vicious) *—see also* Scar L90.5
- adenoid (and tonsil) J35.8
- alveolar process M26.79
- anus K62.89
- auricle *—see* Disorder, pinna, specified type NEC
- bile duct (common) (hepatic) K83.8
- bladder N32.89
- bone *—see* Disorder, bone, specified type NEC
- brain G93.89
- cervix (postoperative) (postpartal) N88.1
- common duct K83.8
- cornea H17.9
  - tuberculous A18.59
- duodenum (bulb), obstructive K31.5
- esophagus K22.2
- eyelid *—see* Disorder, eyelid function
- hypopharynx J39.2
- lacrimal passages *—see* Obstruction, lacrimal
- larynx J38.7
- lung J98.4
- middle ear H74.8
- mouth K13.79
- muscle M62.89
  - with contracture *—see* Contraction, muscle NEC
- nasopharynx J39.2
- palate (soft) K13.79
- penis N48.89

Cicatrix *(continued)*
- pharynx J39.2
- prostate N42.89
- rectum K62.89
- retina *—see* Scar, chorioretinal
- semilunar cartilage *—see* Derangement, meniscus
- seminal vesicle N50.8
- skin L90.5
  - infected L08.89
  - postinfective L90.5
  - tuberculous B90.8
- specified site NEC L90.5
- throat J39.2
- tongue K14.8
- tonsil (and adenoid) J35.8
- trachea J39.8
- tuberculous NEC B90.9
- urethra N36.8
- uterus N85.8
- vagina N89.8
  - postoperative N99.2
- vocal cord J38.3
- wrist, constricting (annular) L90.5

CIDP(chronic inflammatory demyelinating polyneuropathy) G61.81

CIN *—see* Neoplasia, intraepithelial, cervix

Cinchonism *—see* Deafness, ototoxic
- correct substance properly administered *—see* Table of Drugs and Chemicals, by drug, adverse effect
- overdose or wrong substance given or taken *—see* Table of Drugs and Chemicals, by drug, poisoning

Circle of Willis *—see* condition

Circular *—see* condition

Circulating anticoagulants *—see also* - Disorder, hemorrhagic D68.318
- due to drugs *—see also* - Disorder, hemorrhagic D68.32
- following childbirth O72.3

Circulation
- collateral, any site I99.8
- defective (lower extremity) I99.8
  - congenital Q28.9
- embryonic Q28.9
- failure (peripheral) R57.9
  - newborn P29.89
- fetal, persistent P29.3
- heart, incomplete Q28.9

Circulatory system *—see* condition

Circulus senilis (cornea) *—see* Degeneration, cornea, senile

Circumcision (in absence of medical indication) (ritual) (routine) Z41.2

Circumscribed *—see* condition

Circumvallate placenta O43.11-

Cirrhosis, cirrhotic (hepatic) (liver) K74.60
- alcoholic K70.30
  - with ascites K70.31
- atrophic *—see* Cirrhosis, liver
- Baumgarten-Cruveilhier K74.69
- biliary (cholangiolitic) (cholangitic) (hypertrophic) (obstructive) (pericholangiolitic) K74.5
  - due to
    - Clonorchiasis B66.1
    - flukes B66.3
  - primary K74.3
  - secondary K74.4
- cardiac (of liver) K76.1
- Charcot's K74.3
- cholangiolitic, cholangitic, cholostatic (primary) K74.3

Cirrhosis, cirrhotic *(continued)*
- congestive K76.1
- Cruveilhier-Baumgarten K74.69
- cryptogenic (liver) K74.69
- due to
  - hepatolenticular degeneration E83.01
  - Wilson's disease E83.01
  - xanthomatosis E78.2
- fatty K76.0
  - alcoholic K70.0
- Hanot's (hypertrophic) K74.3
- hepatic *—see* Cirrhosis, liver
- hypertrophic K74.3
- Indian childhood K74.69
- kidney *—see* Sclerosis, renal
- Laennec's K70.30
  - with ascites K70.31
  - alcoholic K70.30
    - with ascites K70.31
  - nonalcoholic K74.69
- liver K74.60
  - alcoholic K70.30
    - with ascites K70.31
    - fatty K70.0
  - congenital P78.81
  - syphilitic A52.74
- lung (chronic) J84.10
- macronodular K74.69
  - alcoholic K70.30
    - with ascites K70.31
- micronodular K74.69
  - alcoholic K70.30
    - with ascites K70.31
- mixed type K74.69
- monolobular K74.3
- nephritis *—see* Sclerosis, renal
- nutritional K74.69
  - alcoholic K70.30
    - with ascites K70.31
- obstructive *—see* Cirrhosis, biliary
- ovarian N83.8
- pancreas (duct) K86.8
- pigmentary E83.110
- portal K74.69
  - alcoholic K70.30
    - with ascites K70.31
- postnecrotic K74.69
  - alcoholic K70.30
    - with ascites K70.31
- pulmonary J84.10
- renal *—see* Sclerosis, renal
- spleen D73.2
- stasis K76.1
- Todd's K74.3
- unilobar K74.3
- xanthomatous (biliary) K74.5
  - due to xanthomatosis (familial) (metabolic) (primary) E78.2

Cistern, subarachnoid R93.0

Citrullinemia E72.23

Citrullinuria E72.23

Civatte's disease or poikiloderma L57.3

Clam digger's itch B65.3

Clammy skin R23.1

Clap *—see* Gonorrhea

Clarke-Hadfield syndrome (pancreatic infantilism) K86.8

Clark's paralysis G80.9

Clastothrix L67.8

Claude Bernard-Horner syndrome G90.2
- traumatic *—see* Injury, nerve, cervical sympathetic

Claude's disease or syndrome G46.3

Claudication, intermittent I73.9
- cerebral (artery) G45.9
- spinal cord (arteriosclerotic) G95.19
  - syphilitic A52.09
- venous (axillary) I87.8

Claudicatio venosa intermittens I87.8

Claustrophobia F40.240

Clavus (infected) L84

Clawfoot (congenital) Q66.89
- acquired —*see* Deformity, limb, clawfoot

Clawhand (acquired) —*see also* Deformity, limb, clawhand
- congenital Q68.1

Clawtoe (congenital) Q66.89
- acquired —*see* Deformity, toe, specified NEC

Clay eating —*see* Pica

Cleansing of artificial opening —*see* Attention to, artificial, opening

Cleft (congenital) —*see also* Imperfect, closure
- alveolar process M26.79
- branchial (cyst) (persistent) Q18.2
- cricoid cartilage, posterior Q31.8
- lip (unilateral) Q36.9
  - with cleft palate Q37.9
    - hard Q37.1
      - with soft Q37.5
    - soft Q37.3
      - with hard Q37.5
  - bilateral Q36.0
    - with cleft palate Q37.8
      - hard Q37.0
        - with soft Q37.4
      - soft Q37.2
        - with hard Q37.4
  - median Q36.1
- nose Q30.2
- palate Q35.9
  - with cleft lip (unilateral) Q37.9
    - bilateral Q37.8
  - hard Q35.1
    - with
      - cleft lip (unilateral) Q37.1
        - bilateral Q37.0
  - soft Q35.5
    - with cleft lip (unilateral) Q37.5
      - bilateral Q37.4
  - medial Q35.5
  - soft Q35.3
    - with
      - cleft lip (unilateral) Q37.3
        - bilateral Q37.2
      - hard Q35.5
        - with cleft lip (unilateral) Q37.5
          - bilateral Q37.4
- penis Q55.69
- scrotum Q55.29
- thyroid cartilage Q31.8
- uvula Q35.7

Cleidocranial dysostosis Q74.0

Cleptomania F63.2

Clicking hip (newborn) R29.4

Climacteric (female) —*see also* Menopause
- arthritis (any site) NEC —*see* Arthritis, specified form NEC
- depression (single episode) F32.8
- male (symptoms) (syndrome) NEC N50.8
- paranoid state F22
- polyarthritis NEC —*see* Arthritis, specified form NEC
- symptoms (female) N95.1

Clinical research investigation (clinical trial) (control subject) (normal comparison) (participant) Z00.6

Clitoris —*see* condition

Cloaca (persistent) Q43.7

Clonorchiasis, clonorchis infection (liver) B66.1

Clonus R25.8

Closed bite M26.29

Clostridium (C.) **perfringens, as cause of disease classified elsewhere** B96.7

Closure
- congenital, nose Q30.0
- cranial sutures, premature Q75.0
- defective or imperfect NEC —*see* Imperfect, closure
- fistula, delayed —*see* Fistula
- foramen ovale, imperfect Q21.1
- hymen N89.6
- interauricular septum, defective Q21.1
- interventricular septum, defective Q21.0
- lacrimal duct —*see also* Stenosis, lacrimal, duct
  - congenital Q10.5
- nose (congenital) Q30.0
  - acquired M95.0
- of artificial opening —*see* Attention to, artificial, opening
- primary angle, without glaucoma damage H40.06-
- vagina N89.5
- valve —*see* Endocarditis
- vulva N90.5

Clot (blood) —*see also* Embolism
- artery (obstruction) (occlusion) —*see* Embolism
- bladder N32.89
- brain (intradural or extradural) —*see* Occlusion, artery, cerebral
- circulation I74.9
- heart —*see also* Infarct, myocardium
  - not resulting in infarction I24.0
- vein —*see* Thrombosis

Clouded state R40.1
- epileptic —*see* Epilepsy, specified NEC
- paroxysmal —*see* Epilepsy, specified NEC

Cloudy antrum, antra J32.0

Clouston's (hidrotic) **ectodermal dysplasia** Q82.4

Clubbed nail pachydermoperiostosis M89.40 *[L62]*

Clubbing of finger (s) (nails) R68.3

Clubfinger R68.3
- congenital Q68.1

Clubfoot (congenital) Q66.89
- acquired —*see* Deformity, limb, clubfoot
- equinovarus Q66.0
- paralytic —*see* Deformity, limb, clubfoot

Clubhand (congenital) (radial) Q71.4-
- acquired —*see* Deformity, limb, clubhand

Clubnail R68.3
- congenital Q84.6

Clump, kidney Q63.1

Clumsiness, clumsy child syndrome F82

Cluttering F80.81

Clutton's joints A50.51 *[M12.80]*

Coagulation, intravascular (diffuse) (disseminated) —*see also* Defibrination syndrome
- complicating abortion —*see* Abortion, by type, complicated by, intravascular coagulation
- following ectopic or molar pregnancy O08.1

Coagulopathy —*see also* Defect, coagulation
- consumption D65
- intravascular D65
  - newborn P60

Coalition
- calcaneo-scaphoid Q66.89
- tarsal Q66.89

Coalminer's
- elbow —*see* Bursitis, elbow, olecranon
- lung or pneumoconiosis J60

Coalworker's lung or pneumoconiosis J60

Coarctation
- aorta (preductal) (postductal) Q25.1
- pulmonary artery Q25.71

Coated tongue K14.3

Coats' disease (exudative retinopathy) —*see* Retinopathy, exudative

Cocainism —*see* Dependence, drug, cocaine

Coccidioidomycosis B38.9
- cutaneous B38.3
- disseminated B38.7
- generalized B38.7
- meninges B38.4
- prostate B38.81
- pulmonary B38.2
  - acute B38.0
  - chronic B38.1
- skin B38.3
- specified NEC B38.89

Coccidioidosis —*see* Coccidioidomycosis

Coccidiosis (intestinal) A07.3

Coccydynia, coccygodynia M53.3

Coccyx —*see* condition

Cochin-China diarrhea K90.1

Cockayne's syndrome Q87.1

Cocked up toe —*see* Deformity, toe, specified NEC

Cock's peculiar tumor L72.3

Codman's tumor —*see* Neoplasm, bone, benign

Coenurosis B71.8

Coffee-worker's lung J67.8

Cogan's syndrome H16.32-
- oculomotor apraxia H51.8

Coitus, painful (female) N94.1
- male N53.12
- psychogenic F52.6

Cold J00
- with influenza, flu, or grippe —*see* Influenza, with, respiratory manifestations NEC
- agglutinin disease or hemoglobinuria (chronic) D59.1
- bronchial —*see* Bronchitis
- chest —*see* Bronchitis
- common (head) J00
- effects of T69.9
  - specified effect NEC T69.8
- excessive, effects of T69.9
  - specified effect NEC T69.8
- exhaustion from T69.8

Cold *(continued)*
- exposure to T69.9
  - specified effect NEC T69.8
- head J00
- injury syndrome (newborn) P80.0
- on lung —*see* Bronchitis
- rose J30.1
- sensitivity, auto-immune D59.1
- virus J00

Coldsore B00.1

Colibacillosis A49.8
- as the cause of other disease —*see also* Escherichia coli B96.20
- generalized A41.50

Colic (bilious) (infantile) (intestinal) (recurrent) (spasmodic) R10.83
- abdomen R10.83
  - psychogenic F45.8
- appendix, appendicular K38.8
- bile duct —*see* Calculus, bile duct
- biliary —*see* Calculus, bile duct
- common duct —*see* Calculus, bile duct
- cystic duct —*see* Calculus, gallbladder
- Devonshire NEC —*see* Poisoning, lead
- gallbladder —*see* Calculus, gallbladder
- gallstone —*see* Calculus, gallbladder
  - gallbladder or cystic duct —*see* Calculus, gallbladder
- hepatic (duct) —*see* Calculus, bile duct
- hysterical F45.8
- kidney N23
- lead NEC —*see* Poisoning, lead
- mucous K58.9
  - with diarrhea K58.0
  - psychogenic F54
- nephritic N23
- painter's NEC —*see* Poisoning, lead
- pancreas K86.8
- psychogenic F45.8
- renal N23
- saturnine NEC —*see* Poisoning, lead
- ureter N23
- urethral N36.8
  - due to calculus N21.1
- uterus NEC N94.89
  - menstrual —*see* Dysmenorrhea
- worm NOS B83.9

Colicystitis —*see* Cystitis

Colitis (acute) (catarrhal) (chronic) (noninfective) (hemorrhagic) —*see also* Enteritis K52.9
- allergic K52.2
- amebic (acute) —*see also* Amebiasis A06.0
  - nondysenteric A06.2
- anthrax A22.2
- bacillary —*see* Infection, Shigella
- balantidial A07.0
- Clostridium difficile A04.7
- coccidial A07.3
- collagenous K52.89
- cystica superficialis K52.89
- dietary counseling and surveillance (for) Z71.3
- dietetic K52.2
- drug-induced K52.1
- due to radiation K52.0
- eosinophilic K52.82
- food hypersensitivity K52.2
- giardial A07.1
- granulomatous —*see* Enteritis, regional, large intestine
- infectious —*see* Enteritis, infectious

- **Colitis** *(continued)*
  - ischemic K55.9
    - acute (fulminant) (subacute) K55.0
    - chronic K55.1
    - due to mesenteric artery insufficiency K55.1
    - fulminant (acute) K55.0
  - left sided K51.50
    - with
      - abscess K51.514
      - complication K51.519
        - specified NEC K51.518
      - fistula K51.513
      - obstruction K51.512
      - rectal bleeding K51.511
  - lymphocytic K52.89
  - membranous
    - psychogenic F54
  - microscopic (collagenous) (lymphocytic) K52.89
  - mucous —*see* Syndrome, irritable, bowel
    - psychogenic F54
  - noninfective K52.9
    - specified NEC K52.89
  - polyposa —*see* Polyp, colon, inflammatory
  - protozoal A07.9
  - pseudomembranous A04.7
  - pseudomucinous —*see* Syndrome, irritable, bowel
  - regional —*see* Enteritis, regional, large intestine
  - segmental —*see* Enteritis, regional, large intestine
  - septic —*see* Enteritis, infectious
  - spastic K58.9
    - with diarrhea K58.0
    - psychogenic F54
  - staphylococcal A04.8
    - foodborne A05.0
  - subacute ischemic K55.0
  - thromboulcerative K55.0
  - toxic NEC K52.1
    - due to Clostridium difficile A04.7
  - transmural —*see* Enteritis, regional, large intestine
  - trichomonal A07.8
  - tuberculous (ulcerative) A18.32
  - ulcerative (chronic) K51.90
    - with
      - complication K51.919
        - abscess K51.914
        - fistula K51.913
        - obstruction K51.912
        - rectal bleeding K51.911
        - specified complication NEC K51.918
    - enterocolitis —*see* Enterocolitis, ulcerative
    - ileocolitis —*see* Ileocolitis, ulcerative
    - mucosal proctocolitis —*see* Proctocolitis, mucosal
    - proctitis —*see* Proctitis, ulcerative
    - pseudopolyposis —*see* Polyp, colon, inflammatory
    - psychogenic F54
    - rectosigmoiditis —*see* Rectosigmoiditis, ulcerative
    - specified type NEC K51.80
      - with
        - complication K51.819
          - abscess K51.814
          - fistula K51.813
          - obstruction K51.812
          - rectal bleeding K51.811
          - specified complication NEC K51.818

- **Collagenosis, collagen disease** (nonvascular) (vascular) M35.9
  - cardiovascular I42.8
  - reactive perforating L87.1
  - specified NEC M35.8

- **Collapse** R55
  - adrenal E27.2
  - cardiorespiratory R57.0
  - cardiovascular R57.0
    - newborn P29.89
  - circulatory (peripheral) R57.9
    - during or after labor and delivery O75.1
    - following ectopic or molar pregnancy O08.3
    - newborn P29.89
  - during or
    - after labor and delivery O75.1
    - resulting from a procedure, not elsewhere classified T81.10
  - external ear canal —*see* Stenosis, external ear canal
  - general R55
  - heart —*see* Disease, heart
  - heat T67.1
  - hysterical F44.89
  - labyrinth, membranous (congenital) Q16.5
  - lung (massive) —*see also* Atelectasis J98.19
    - pressure due to anesthesia (general) (local) or other sedation T88.2
      - during labor and delivery O74.1
      - in pregnancy O29.02-
      - postpartum, puerperal O89.09
  - myocardial —*see* Disease, heart
  - nervous F48.8
  - neurocirculatory F45.8
  - nose M95.0
  - postoperative T81.10
  - pulmonary —*see also* Atelectasis J98.19
    - newborn —*see* Atelectasis
  - trachea J39.8
  - tracheobronchial J98.09
  - valvular —*see* Endocarditis
  - vascular (peripheral) R57.9
    - during or after labor and delivery O75.1
    - following ectopic or molar pregnancy O08.3
    - newborn P29.89
  - vertebra M48.50-
    - cervical region M48.52-
    - cervicothoracic region M48.53-
    - in (due to)
      - metastasis —*see* Collapse, vertebra, in, specified disease NEC
      - osteoporosis —*see also* Osteoporosis M80.88
        - cervical region M80.88
        - cervicothoracic region M80.88
        - lumbar region M80.88
        - lumbosacral region M80.88
        - multiple sites M80.88
        - occipito-atlanto-axial region M80.88
        - sacrococcygeal region M80.88
        - thoracic region M80.88
        - thoracolumbar region M80.88
      - specified disease NEC M48.50-
        - cervical region M48.52-
        - cervicothoracic region M48.53-
        - lumbar region M48.56-
        - lumbosacral region M48.57-
        - occipito-atlanto-axial region M48.51-

- **Collapse** *(continued)*
  - vertebra *(continued)*
    - in *(continued)*
      - specified disease NEC *(continued)*
        - sacrococcygeal region M48.58-
        - thoracic region M48.54-
        - thoracolumbar region M48.55-
    - lumbar region M48.56-
    - lumbosacral region M48.57-
    - occipito-atlanto-axial region M48.51-
    - sacrococcygeal region M48.58-
    - thoracic region M48.54-
    - thoracolumbar region M48.55-
- **Collateral** —*see also* condition
  - circulation (venous) I87.8
  - dilation, veins I87.8
- **Colles' fracture** S52.53-
- **Collet** (-Sicard) **syndrome** G52.7
- **Collier's asthma or lung** J60
- **Collodion baby** Q80.2
- **Colloid nodule** (of thyroid) (cystic) E04.1
- **Coloboma** (iris) Q13.0
  - eyelid Q10.3
  - fundus Q14.8
  - lens Q12.2
  - optic disc (congenital) Q14.2
    - acquired H47.31-
- **Coloenteritis** —*see* Enteritis
- **Colon** —*see* condition
- **Colonization**
  - MRSA(Methicillin resistant Staphylococcus aureus) Z22.322
  - MSSA(Methicillin susceptible Staphylococcus aureus) Z22.321
  - status —*see* Carrier (suspected) of
- **Coloptosis** K63.4
- **Color blindness** —*see* Deficiency, color vision
- **Colostomy**
  - attention to Z43.3
  - fitting or adjustment Z46.89
  - malfunctioning K94.03
  - status Z93.3
- **Colpitis** (acute) —*see* Vaginitis
- **Colpocele** N81.5
- **Colpocystitis** —*see* Vaginitis
- **Colpospasm** N94.2
- **Column, spinal, vertebral** —*see* condition
- **Coma** R40.20
  - with
    - motor response (none) R40.231
      - abnormal R40.233
      - extension R40.232
      - flexion withdrawal R40.234
      - localizes pain R40.235
      - obeys commands R40.236
    - opening of eyes (never) R40.211
      - in response to
        - pain R40.212
        - sound R40.213
      - spontaneous R40.214
    - verbal response (none) R40.221
      - confused conversation R40.224
      - inappropriate words R40.223
      - incomprehensible words R40.222
      - oriented R40.225
  - eclamptic —*see* Eclampsia
  - epileptic —*see* Epilepsy

- **Coma** *(continued)*
  - Glasgow, scale score —*see* Glasgow coma scale
  - hepatic —*see* Failure, hepatic, by type, with coma
  - hyperglycemic (diabetic) —*see* Diabetes, coma
  - hyperosmolar (diabetic) —*see* Diabetes, coma
  - hypoglycemic (diabetic) —*see* Diabetes, coma, hypoglycemic
    - nondiabetic E15
  - in diabetes —*see* Diabetes, coma
  - insulin-induced —*see* Coma, hypoglycemic
  - myxedematous E03.5
  - newborn P91.5
  - persistent vegetative state R40.3
  - specified NEC, without documented Glasgow coma scale score, or with partial Glasgow coma scale score reported R40.244
- **Comatose** —*see* Coma
- **Combat fatigue** F43.0
- **Combined** —*see* condition
- **Comedo, comedones** (giant) L70.0
- **Comedocarcinoma** —*see also* Neoplasm, breast, malignant
  - noninfiltrating
    - breast D05.8-
    - specified site —*see* Neoplasm, in situ, by site
    - unspecified site D05.8-
- **Comedomastitis** —*see* Ectasia, mammary duct
- **Comminuted fracture - code as Fracture, closed**
- **Common**
  - arterial trunk Q20.0
  - atrioventricular canal Q21.2
  - atrium Q21.1
  - cold (head) J00
  - truncus (arteriosus) Q20.0
  - variable immunodeficiency —*see* Immunodeficiency, common variable
  - ventricle Q20.4
- **Commotio, commotion** (current)
  - brain —*see* Injury, intracranial, concussion
  - cerebri —*see* Injury, intracranial, concussion
  - retinae S05.8X-
  - spinal cord —*see* Injury, spinal cord, by region
  - spinalis —*see* Injury, spinal cord, by region
- **Communication**
  - between
    - base of aorta and pulmonary artery Q21.4
    - left ventricle and right atrium Q20.5
    - pericardial sac and pleural sac Q34.8
    - pulmonary artery and pulmonary vein, congenital Q25.72
  - congenital between uterus and digestive or urinary tract Q51.7
- **Compartment syndrome** (deep) (posterior) (traumatic) T79.A0
  - abdomen T79.A3
  - lower extremity (hip, buttock, thigh, leg, foot, toes) T79.A2
  - nontraumatic
    - abdomen M79.A3
    - lower extremity (hip, buttock, thigh, leg, foot, toes) M79.A2-

Compartment syndrome *(continued)*
- nontraumatic *(continued)*
  - specified site NEC M79.A9
  - upper extremity (shoulder, arm, forearm, wrist, hand, fingers) M79.A1-
- specified site NEC T79.A9
- upper extremity (shoulder, arm, forearm, wrist, hand, fingers) T79.A1

Compensation
- failure *—see* Disease, heart
- neurosis, psychoneurosis *—see* Disorder, factitious

Complaint *—see also* Disease
- bowel, functional K59.9
  - psychogenic F45.8
- intestine, functional K59.9
  - psychogenic F45.8
- kidney *—see* Disease, renal
- miners' J60

Complete *—see* condition

Complex
- Addison-Schilder E71.528
- cardiorenal *—see* Hypertension, cardiorenal
- Costen's M26.69
- disseminated mycobacterium avium-intracellulare (DMAC) A31.2
- Eisenmenger's (ventricular septal defect) I27.89
- hypersexual F52.8
- jumped process, spine *—see* Dislocation, vertebra
- primary, tuberculous A15.7
- Schilder-Addison E71.528
- subluxation (vertebral) M99.19
  - abdomen M99.19
  - acromioclavicular M99.17
  - cervical region M99.11
  - cervicothoracic M99.11
  - costochondral M99.18
  - costovertebral M99.18
  - head region M99.10
  - hip M99.15
  - lower extremity M99.16
  - lumbar region M99.13
  - lumbosacral M99.13
  - occipitocervical M99.10
  - pelvic region M99.15
  - pubic M99.15
  - rib cage M99.18
  - sacral region M99.14
  - sacrococcygeal M99.14
  - sacroiliac M99.14
  - specified NEC M99.19
  - sternochondral M99.18
  - sternoclavicular M99.17
  - thoracic region M99.12
  - thoracolumbar M99.12
  - upper extremity M99.17
- Taussig-Bing (transposition, aorta and overriding pulmonary artery) Q20.1

Complication (s) (from) (of)
- accidental puncture or laceration during a procedure (of) *—see* Complications, intraoperative (intraprocedural), puncture or laceration
- amputation stump (surgical) (late) NEC T87.9
  - dehiscence T87.81
  - infection or inflammation T87.40
    - lower limb T87.4-
    - upper limb T87.4-
  - necrosis T87.50
    - lower limb T87.5-
    - upper limb T87.5-
  - neuroma T87.30
    - lower limb T87.3-
    - upper limb T87.3-
  - specified type NEC T87.89
- anastomosis (and bypass) *—see also* Complications, prosthetic device or implant
  - intestinal (internal) NEC K91.89
    - involving urinary tract N99.89
  - urinary tract (involving intestinal tract) N99.89
  - vascular *—see* Complications, cardiovascular device or implant
- anesthesia, anesthetic *—see also* Anesthesia, complication T88.59
  - brain, postpartum, puerperal O89.2
  - cardiac
    - in
      - labor and delivery O74.2
      - pregnancy O29.19-
    - postpartum, puerperal O89.1
  - central nervous system
    - in
      - labor and delivery O74.3
      - pregnancy O29.29-
    - postpartum, puerperal O89.2
  - difficult or failed intubation T88.4
    - in pregnancy O29.6-
  - failed sedation (conscious) (moderate) during procedure T88.52
  - hyperthermia, malignant T88.3
  - hypothermia T88.51
  - intubation failure T88.4
  - malignant hyperthermia T88.3
  - pulmonary
    - in
      - labor and delivery O74.1
      - pregnancy NEC O29.09-
    - postpartum, puerperal O89.09
  - shock T88.2
  - spinal and epidural
    - in
      - labor and delivery NEC O74.6
        - headache O74.5
      - pregnancy NEC O29.5X-
    - postpartum, puerperal NEC O89.5
      - headache O89.4
- anti-reflux device *—see* Complications, esophageal anti-reflux device
- aortic (bifurcation) graft *—see* Complications, graft, vascular
- aortocoronary (bypass) graft *—see* Complications, coronary artery (bypass) graft
- aortofemoral (bypass) graft *—see* Complications, extremity artery (bypass) graft
- arteriovenous
  - fistula, surgically created T82.9
    - embolism T82.818
    - fibrosis T82.828
    - hemorrhage T82.838
    - infection or inflammation T82.7
    - mechanical
      - breakdown T82.510
      - displacement T82.520
      - leakage T82.530
      - malposition T82.520
      - obstruction T82.590
      - perforation T82.590
      - protrusion T82.590
    - pain T82.848
    - specified type NEC T82.898
    - stenosis T82.858
    - thrombosis T82.868

Complication *(continued)*
- arteriovenous *(continued)*
  - shunt, surgically created T82.9
    - embolism T82.818
    - fibrosis T82.828
    - hemorrhage T82.838
    - infection or inflammation T82.7
    - mechanical
      - breakdown T82.511
      - displacement T82.521
      - leakage T82.531
      - malposition T82.521
      - obstruction T82.591
      - perforation T82.591
      - protrusion T82.591
    - pain T82.848
    - specified type NEC T82.898
    - stenosis T82.858
    - thrombosis T82.868
- arthroplasty *—see* Complications, joint prosthesis
- artificial
  - fertilization or insemination N98.9
    - attempted introduction (of)
      - embryo in embryo transfer N98.3
      - ovum following in vitro fertilization N98.2
    - hyperstimulation of ovaries N98.1
    - infection N98.0
    - specified NEC N98.8
  - heart T82.9
    - embolism T82.817
    - fibrosis T82.827
    - hemorrhage T82.837
    - infection or inflammation T82.7
    - mechanical
      - breakdown T82.512
      - displacement T82.522
      - leakage T82.532
      - malposition T82.522
      - obstruction T82.592
      - perforation T82.592
      - protrusion T82.592
    - pain T82.847
    - specified type NEC T82.897
    - stenosis T82.857
    - thrombosis T82.867
  - opening
    - cecostomy *—see* Complications, colostomy
    - colostomy *—see* Complications, colostomy
    - cystostomy *—see* Complications, cystostomy
    - enterostomy *—see* Complications, enterostomy
    - gastrostomy *—see* Complications, gastrostomy
    - ileostomy *—see* Complications, enterostomy
    - jejunostomy *—see* Complications, enterostomy
    - nephrostomy *—see* Complications, stoma, urinary tract
    - tracheostomy *—see* Complications, tracheostomy
    - ureterostomy *—see* Complications, stoma, urinary tract
    - urethrostomy *—see* Complications, stoma, urinary tract
- balloon implant or device
  - gastrointestinal T85.9
    - embolism T85.81
    - fibrosis T85.82
    - hemorrhage T85.83
    - infection and inflammation T85.79

Complication *(continued)*
- balloon implant or device *(continued)*
  - gastrointestinal *(continued)*
    - pain T85.84
    - specified type NEC T85.89
    - stenosis T85.85
    - thrombosis T85.86
  - vascular (counterpulsation) T82.9
    - embolism T82.818
    - fibrosis T82.828
    - hemorrhage T82.838
    - infection or inflammation T82.7
    - mechanical
      - breakdown T82.513
      - displacement T82.523
      - leakage T82.533
      - malposition T82.523
      - obstruction T82.593
      - perforation T82.593
      - protrusion T82.593
    - pain T82.848
    - specified type NEC T82.898
    - stenosis T82.858
    - thrombosis T82.868
- bariatric procedure
  - gastric band procedure K95.09
    - infection K95.01
  - specified procedure NEC K95.89
    - infection K95.81
- bile duct implant (prosthetic) T85.9
  - embolism T85.81
  - fibrosis T85.82
  - hemorrhage T85.83
  - infection and inflammation T85.79
  - mechanical
    - breakdown T85.510
    - displacement T85.520
    - malfunction T85.510
    - malposition T85.520
    - obstruction T85.590
    - perforation T85.590
    - protrusion T85.590
    - specified NEC T85.590
  - pain T85.84
  - specified type NEC T85.89
  - stenosis T85.85
  - thrombosis T85.86
- bladder device (auxiliary) *—see* Complications, genitourinary, device or implant, urinary system
- bleeding (postoperative) *—see* Complication, postoperative, hemorrhage
  - intraoperative *—see* Complication, intraoperative, hemorrhage
- blood vessel graft *—see* Complications, graft, vascular
- bone
  - device NEC T84.9
    - embolism T84.81
    - fibrosis T84.82
    - hemorrhage T84.83
    - infection or inflammation T84.7
    - mechanical
      - breakdown T84.318
      - displacement T84.328
      - malposition T84.328
      - obstruction T84.398
      - perforation T84.398
      - protrusion T84.398
    - pain T84.84
    - specified type NEC T84.89
    - stenosis T84.85
    - thrombosis T84.86
  - graft *—see* Complications, graft, bone
  - growth stimulator (electrode) *— see* Complications, electronic stimulator device, bone

Complication *(continued)*
- bone *(continued)*
  - marrow transplant —*see* Complications, transplant, bone, marrow
- brain neurostimulator (electrode) —*see* Complications, electronic stimulator device, brain
- breast implant (prosthetic) T85.9
  - capsular contracture T85.44
  - embolism T85.81
  - fibrosis T85.82
  - hemorrhage T85.83
  - infection and inflammation T85.79
  - mechanical
    - breakdown T85.41
    - displacement T85.42
    - leakage T85.43
    - malposition T85.42
    - obstruction T85.49
    - perforation T85.49
    - protrusion T85.49
    - specified NEC T85.49
  - pain T85.84
  - specified type NEC T85.89
  - stenosis T85.85
  - thrombosis T85.86
- bypass —*see also* Complications, prosthetic device or implant
  - aortocoronary —*see* Complications, coronary artery (bypass) graft
  - arterial —*see also* Complications, graft, vascular
    - extremity —*see* Complications, extremity artery (bypass) graft
- cardiac —*see also* Disease, heart
  - device, implant or graft T82.9
    - embolism T82.817
    - fibrosis T82.827
    - hemorrhage T82.837
    - infection or inflammation T82.7
      - valve prosthesis T82.6
    - mechanical
      - breakdown T82.519
        - specified device NEC T82.518
      - displacement T82.529
        - specified device NEC T82.528
      - leakage T82.539
        - specified device NEC T82.538
      - malposition T82.529
        - specified device NEC T82.528
      - obstruction T82.599
        - specified device NEC T82.598
      - perforation T82.599
        - specified device NEC T82.598
      - protrusion T82.599
        - specified device NEC T82.598
    - pain T82.847
    - specified type NEC T82.897
    - stenosis T82.857
    - thrombosis T82.867
- cardiovascular device, graft or implant T82.9
  - aortic graft —*see* Complications, graft, vascular
  - arteriovenous
    - fistula, artificial —*see* Complication, arteriovenous, fistula, surgically created
    - shunt —*see* Complication, arteriovenous, shunt, surgically created
  - artificial heart —*see* Complication, artificial, heart

Complication *(continued)*
- cardiovascular device, graft or implant *(continued)*
  - balloon (counterpulsation) device —*see* Complication, balloon implant, vascular
  - carotid artery graft —*see* Complications, graft, vascular
  - coronary bypass graft —*see* Complication, coronary artery (bypass) graft
  - dialysis catheter (vascular) —*see* Complication, catheter, dialysis
  - electronic T82.9
    - electrode T82.9
      - embolism T82.817
      - fibrosis T82.827
      - hemorrhage T82.837
      - infection T82.7
      - mechanical
        - breakdown T82.110
        - displacement T82.120
        - leakage T82.190
        - obstruction T82.190
        - perforation T82.190
        - protrusion T82.190
        - specified type NEC T82.190
      - pain T82.847
      - specified NEC T82.897
      - stenosis T82.857
      - thrombosis T82.867
    - embolism T82.817
    - fibrosis T82.827
    - hemorrhage T82.837
    - infection T82.7
    - mechanical
      - breakdown T82.119
      - displacement T82.129
      - leakage T82.199
      - obstruction T82.199
      - perforation T82.199
      - protrusion T82.199
      - specified type NEC T82.199
    - pain T82.847
    - pulse generator T82.9
      - embolism T82.817
      - fibrosis T82.827
      - hemorrhage T82.837
      - infection T82.7
      - mechanical
        - breakdown T82.111
        - displacement T82.121
        - leakage T82.191
        - obstruction T82.191
        - perforation T82.191
        - protrusion T82.191
        - specified type NEC T82.191
      - pain T82.847
      - specified NEC T82.897
      - stenosis T82.857
      - thrombosis T82.867
    - specified condition NEC T82.897
    - specified device NEC T82.9
      - embolism T82.817
      - fibrosis T82.827
      - hemorrhage T82.837
      - infection T82.7
      - mechanical
        - breakdown T82.118
        - displacement T82.128
        - leakage T82.198
        - obstruction T82.198
        - perforation T82.198
        - protrusion T82.198
        - specified type NEC T82.198
      - pain T82.847
      - specified NEC T82.897
      - stenosis T82.857
      - thrombosis T82.867
    - stenosis T82.857
    - thrombosis T82.867

Complication *(continued)*
- cardiovascular device, graft or implant *(continued)*
  - extremity artery graft —*see* Complication, extremity artery (bypass) graft
  - femoral artery graft —*see* Complication, extremity artery (bypass) graft
  - heart-lung transplant —*see* Complication, transplant, heart, with lung
  - heart
    - transplant —*see* Complication, transplant, heart
    - valve —*see* Complication, prosthetic device, heart valve
      - graft —*see* Complication, heart, valve, graft
  - infection or inflammation T82.7
  - umbrella device —*see* Complication, umbrella device, vascular
  - vascular graft (or anastomosis) —*see* Complication, graft, vascular
- carotid artery (bypass) graft —*see* Complications, graft, vascular
- catheter (device) NEC —*see also* Complications, prosthetic device or implant
  - cystostomy T83.9
    - embolism T83.81
    - fibrosis T83.82
    - hemorrhage T83.83
    - infection and inflammation T83.59
    - mechanical
      - breakdown T83.010
      - displacement T83.020
      - leakage T83.030
      - malposition T83.020
      - obstruction T83.090
      - perforation T83.090
      - protrusion T83.090
      - specified NEC T83.090
    - pain T83.84
    - specified type NEC T83.89
    - stenosis T83.85
    - thrombosis T83.86
  - dialysis (vascular) T82.9
    - embolism T82.818
    - fibrosis T82.828
    - hemorrhage T82.838
    - infection and inflammation T82.7
    - intraperitoneal —*see* Complications, catheter, intraperitoneal
    - mechanical
      - breakdown T82.41
      - displacement T82.42
      - leakage T82.43
      - malposition T82.42
      - obstruction T82.49
      - perforation T82.49
      - protrusion T82.49
    - pain T82.848
    - specified type NEC T82.898
    - stenosis T82.858
    - thrombosis T82.868
  - epidural infusion T85.9
    - embolism T85.81
    - fibrosis T85.82
    - hemorrhage T85.83
    - infection and inflammation T85.79
    - mechanical
      - breakdown T85.610
      - displacement T85.620
      - leakage T85.630
      - malfunction T85.610
      - malposition T85.620
      - obstruction T85.690
      - perforation T85.690
      - protrusion T85.690
      - specified NEC T85.690

Complication *(continued)*
- catheter *(continued)*
    - pain T85.84
    - specified type NEC T85.89
    - stenosis T85.85
    - thrombosis T85.86
  - intraperitoneal dialysis T85.9
    - embolism T85.81
    - fibrosis T85.82
    - hemorrhage T85.83
    - infection and inflammation T85.71
    - mechanical
      - breakdown T85.611
      - displacement T85.621
      - leakage T85.631
      - malfunction T85.611
      - malposition T85.621
      - obstruction T85.691
      - perforation T85.691
      - protrusion T85.691
      - specified NEC T85.691
    - pain T85.84
    - specified type NEC T85.89
    - stenosis T85.85
    - thrombosis T85.86
  - intravenous infusion T82.9
    - embolism T82.818
    - fibrosis T82.828
    - hemorrhage T82.838
    - infection or inflammation T82.7
    - mechanical
      - breakdown T82.514
      - displacement T82.524
      - leakage T82.534
      - malposition T82.524
      - obstruction T82.594
      - perforation T82.594
      - protrusion T82.594
    - pain T82.848
    - specified type NEC T82.898
    - stenosis T82.858
    - thrombosis T82.868
  - subdural infusion T85.9
    - embolism T85.81
    - fibrosis T85.82
    - hemorrhage T85.83
    - infection and inflammation T85.79
    - mechanical
      - breakdown T85.610
      - displacement T85.620
      - leakage T85.630
      - malfunction T85.610
      - malposition T85.620
      - obstruction T85.690
      - perforation T85.690
      - protrusion T85.690
      - specified NEC T85.690
    - pain T85.84
    - specified type NEC T85.89
    - stenosis T85.85
    - thrombosis T85.86
  - urethral, indwelling T83.9
    - displacement T83.028
    - embolism T83.81
    - fibrosis T83.82
    - hemorrhage T83.83
    - infection and inflammation T83.51
    - leakage T83.038
    - malposition T83.028
    - mechanical
      - breakdown T83.018
    - obstruction (mechanical) T83.098
    - pain T83.84
    - perforation T83.098
    - protrusion T83.098
    - specified type NEC T83.098
    - stenosis T83.85
    - thrombosis T83.86
  - urinary (indwelling) —*see* Complications, catheter, urethral, indwelling

Complication *(continued)*
- cecostomy (stoma) —*see* Complications, colostomy
- cesarean delivery wound NEC O90.89
  - disruption O90.0
  - hematoma O90.2
  - infection (following delivery) O86.0
- chemotherapy (antineoplastic) NEC T88.7
- chin implant (prosthetic) —*see* Complication, prosthetic device or implant, specified NEC
- circulatory system I99.8
  - intraoperative I97.88
  - postprocedural I97.89
    - following cardiac surgery I97.19-
      - postcardiotomy syndrome I97.0
    - hypertension I97.3
    - lymphedema after mastectomy I97.2
    - postcardiotomy syndrome I97.0
    - specified NEC I97.89
- colostomy (stoma) K94.00
  - hemorrhage K94.01
  - infection K94.02
  - malfunction K94.03
  - mechanical K94.03
  - specified complication NEC K94.09
- contraceptive device, intrauterine —*see* Complications, intrauterine, contraceptive device
- cord (umbilical) —*see* Complications, umbilical cord
- corneal graft —*see* Complications, graft, cornea
- coronary artery (bypass) graft T82.9
  - atherosclerosis —*see* Arteriosclerosis, coronary (artery),
  - embolism T82.818
  - fibrosis T82.828
  - hemorrhage T82.838
  - infection and inflammation T82.7
  - mechanical
    - breakdown T82.211
    - displacement T82.212
    - leakage T82.213
    - malposition T82.212
    - obstruction T82.218
    - perforation T82.218
    - protrusion T82.218
    - specified NEC T82.218
  - pain T82.848
  - specified type NEC T82.897
  - stenosis T82.858
  - thrombosis T82.868
- counterpulsation device (balloon), intra- aortic —*see* Complications, balloon implant, vascular
- cystostomy (stoma) N99.518
  - catheter —*see* Complications, catheter, cystostomy
  - hemorrhage N99.510
  - infection N99.511
  - malfunction N99.512
  - specified type NEC N99.518
- delivery —*see also* Complications, obstetric O75.9
  - procedure (instrumental) (manual) (surgical) O75.4
  - specified NEC O75.89
- dialysis (peritoneal) (renal) —*see also* Complications, infusion
  - catheter (vascular) —*see* Complication, catheter, dialysis
  - peritoneal, intraperitoneal —*see* Complications, catheter, intraperitoneal

Complication *(continued)*
- dorsal column (spinal) neurostimulator —*see* Complications, electronic stimulator device, spinal cord
- drug NEC T88.7
- ear procedure —*see also* Disorder, ear
  - intraoperative H95.88
    - hematoma —*see* Complications, intraoperative, hemorrhage (hematoma) (of), ear
    - hemorrhage —*see* Complications, intraoperative, hemorrhage (hematoma) (of), ear
    - laceration —*see* Complications, intraoperative, puncture or laceration..., ear
    - specified NEC H95.88
  - postoperative H95.89
    - external ear canal stenosis H95.81-
    - hematoma —*see* Complications, postprocedural, hemorrhage (hematoma) (of), ear
    - hemorrhage —*see* Complications, postprocedural, hemorrhage (hematoma) (of), ear
    - postmastoidectomy —*see* Complications, postmastoidectomy
    - specified NEC H95.89
- ectopic pregnancy O08.9
  - damage to pelvic organs O08.6
  - embolism O08.2
  - genital infection O08.0
  - hemorrhage (delayed) (excessive) O08.1
  - metabolic disorder O08.5
  - renal failure O08.4
  - shock O08.3
  - specified type NEC O08.0
  - venous complication NEC O08.7
- electronic stimulator device
  - bladder (urinary) —*see* Complications, electronic stimulator device, urinary
  - bone T84.9
    - breakdown T84.310
    - displacement T84.320
    - embolism T84.81
    - fibrosis T84.82
    - hemorrhage T84.83
    - infection or inflammation T84.7
    - malfunction T84.310
    - malposition T84.320
    - mechanical NEC T84.390
    - obstruction T84.390
    - pain T84.84
    - perforation T84.390
    - protrusion T84.390
    - specified type NEC T84.89
    - stenosis T84.85
    - thrombosis T84.86
  - brain T85.9
    - embolism T85.81
    - fibrosis T85.82
    - hemorrhage T85.83
    - infection and inflammation T85.79
    - mechanical
      - breakdown T85.110
      - displacement T85.120
      - leakage T85.190
      - malposition T85.120
      - obstruction T85.190
      - perforation T85.190
      - protrusion T85.190
      - specified NEC T85.190
    - pain T85.84
    - specified type NEC T85.89
    - stenosis T85.85
    - thrombosis T85.86

Complication *(continued)*
- electronic stimulator device *(continued)*
  - cardiac (defibrillator) (pacemaker) —*see* Complications, cardiovascular device or implant, electronic
  - muscle T84.9
    - breakdown T84.418
    - displacement T84.428
    - embolism T84.81
    - fibrosis T84.82
    - hemorrhage T84.83
    - infection or inflammation T84.7
    - mechanical NEC T84.498
    - pain T84.84
    - specified type NEC T84.89
    - stenosis T84.85
    - thrombosis T84.86
  - nervous system T85.9
    - brain —*see* Complications, electronic stimulator device, brain
    - embolism T85.81
    - fibrosis T85.82
    - hemorrhage T85.83
    - infection and inflammation T85.79
    - mechanical
      - breakdown T85.118
      - displacement T85.128
      - leakage T85.199
      - malposition T85.128
      - obstruction T85.199
      - perforation T85.199
      - protrusion T85.199
      - specified NEC T85.199
    - pain T85.84
    - peripheral nerve —*see* Complications, electronic stimulator device, peripheral nerve
    - specified type NEC T85.89
    - spinal cord —*see* Complications, electronic stimulator device, spinal cord
    - stenosis T85.85
    - thrombosis T85.86
  - peripheral nerve T85.9
    - embolism T85.81
    - fibrosis T85.82
    - hemorrhage T85.83
    - infection and inflammation T85.79
    - mechanical
      - breakdown T85.111
      - displacement T85.121
      - leakage T85.191
      - malposition T85.121
      - obstruction T85.191
      - perforation T85.191
      - protrusion T85.191
      - specified NEC T85.191
    - pain T85.84
    - specified type NEC T85.89
    - stenosis T85.85
    - thrombosis T85.86
  - spinal cord T85.9
    - embolism T85.81
    - fibrosis T85.82
    - hemorrhage T85.83
    - infection and inflammation T85.79
    - mechanical
      - breakdown T85.112
      - displacement T85.122
      - leakage T85.192
      - malposition T85.122
      - obstruction T85.192
      - perforation T85.192
      - protrusion T85.192
      - specified NEC T85.192

Complication *(continued)*
- electronic stimulator device *(continued)*
  - spinal cord *(continued)*
    - pain T85.84
    - specified type NEC T85.89
    - stenosis T85.85
    - thrombosis T85.86
  - urinary T83.9
    - embolism T83.81
    - fibrosis T83.82
    - hemorrhage T83.83
    - infection and inflammation T83.59
    - mechanical
      - breakdown T83.110
      - displacement T83.120
      - malposition T83.120
      - perforation T83.190
      - protrusion T83.190
      - specified NEC T83.190
    - pain T83.84
    - specified type NEC T83.89
    - stenosis T83.85
    - thrombosis T83.86
- electroshock therapy T88.9
  - specified NEC T88.8
- endocrine E34.9
  - postprocedural
    - adrenal hypofunction E89.6
    - hypoinsulinemia E89.1
    - hypoparathyroidism E89.2
    - hypopituitarism E89.3
    - hypothyroidism E89.0
    - ovarian failure E89.40
      - asymptomatic E89.40
      - symptomatic E89.41
    - specified NEC E89.89
    - testicular hypofunction E89.5
- endodontic treatment NEC M27.59
- enterostomy (stoma) K94.10
  - hemorrhage K94.11
  - infection K94.12
  - malfunction K94.13
  - mechanical K94.13
  - specified complication NEC K94.19
- episiotomy, disruption O90.1
- esophageal anti-reflux device T85.9
  - embolism T85.81
  - fibrosis T85.82
  - hemorrhage T85.83
  - infection and inflammation T85.79
  - mechanical
    - breakdown T85.511
    - displacement T85.521
    - malfunction T85.511
    - malposition T85.521
    - obstruction T85.591
    - perforation T85.591
    - protrusion T85.591
    - specified NEC T85.591
  - pain T85.84
  - specified type NEC T85.89
  - stenosis T85.85
  - thrombosis T85.86
- esophagostomy K94.30
  - hemorrhage K94.31
  - infection K94.32
  - malfunction K94.33
  - mechanical K94.33
  - specified complication NEC K94.39
- extracorporeal circulation T80.90
- extremity artery (bypass) graft T82.9
  - arteriosclerosis —*see* Arteriosclerosis, extremities, bypass graft
  - embolism T82.818
  - fibrosis T82.828
  - hemorrhage T82.838
  - infection and inflammation T82.7

- **Complication** *(continued)*
  - extremity artery (bypass) graft *(continued)*
    - mechanical
      - breakdown T82.318
        - femoral artery T82.312
      - displacement T82.328
        - femoral artery T82.322
      - leakage T82.338
        - femoral artery T82.332
      - malposition T82.328
        - femoral artery T82.322
      - obstruction T82.398
        - femoral artery T82.392
      - perforation T82.398
        - femoral artery T82.392
      - protrusion T82.398
        - femoral artery T82.392
    - pain T82.848
    - specified type NEC T82.898
    - stenosis T82.858
    - thrombosis T82.868
  - eye H57.9
    - corneal graft —*see* Complications, graft, cornea
    - implant (prosthetic) T85.9
      - embolism T85.81
      - fibrosis T85.82
      - hemorrhage T85.83
      - infection and inflammation T85.79
      - mechanical
        - breakdown T85.318
        - displacement T85.328
        - leakage T85.398
        - malposition T85.328
        - obstruction T85.398
        - perforation T85.398
        - protrusion T85.398
        - specified NEC T85.398
      - pain T85.84
      - specified type NEC T85.89
      - stenosis T85.85
      - thrombosis T85.86
    - intraocular lens —*see* Complications, intraocular lens
    - orbital prosthesis —*see* Complications, orbital prosthesis
  - female genital N94.9
    - device, implant or graft NEC —*see* Complications, genitourinary, device or implant, genital tract
  - femoral artery (bypass) graft —*see* Complication, extremity artery (bypass) graft
  - fixation device, internal (orthopedic) T84.9
    - infection and inflammation T84.60
      - arm T84.61-
        - humerus T84.61-
        - radius T84.61-
        - ulna T84.61-
      - leg T84.629
        - femur T84.62-
        - fibula T84.62-
        - tibia T84.62-
      - specified site NEC T84.69
      - spine T84.63
    - mechanical
      - breakdown
        - limb T84.119
          - carpal T84.210
          - femur T84.11-
          - fibula T84.11-
          - humerus T84.11-
          - metacarpal T84.210
          - metatarsal T84.213
          - phalanx
            - foot T84.213
            - hand T84.210
          - radius T84.11-
          - tarsal T84.213

- **Complication** *(continued)*
  - fixation device, internal (orthopedic) *(continued)*
    - mechanical *(continued)*
      - breakdown *(continued)*
        - limb *(continued)*
          - tibia T84.11-
          - ulna T84.11-
        - specified bone NEC T84.218
        - spine T84.216
      - displacement
        - limb T84.129
          - carpal T84.220
          - femur T84.12-
          - fibula T84.12-
          - humerus T84.12-
          - metacarpal T84.220
          - metatarsal T84.223
          - phalanx
            - foot T84.223
            - hand T84.220
          - radius T84.12-
          - tarsal T84.223
          - tibia T84.12-
          - ulna T84.12-
        - specified bone NEC T84.228
        - spine T84.226
      - malposition —*see* Complications, fixation device, internal, mechanical, displacement
      - obstruction —*see* Complications, fixation device, internal, mechanical, specified type NEC
      - perforation —*see* Complications, fixation device, internal, mechanical, specified type NEC
      - protrusion —*see* Complications, fixation device, internal, mechanical, specified type NEC
      - specified type NEC
        - limb T84.199
          - carpal T84.290
          - femur T84.19-
          - fibula T84.19-
          - humerus T84.19-
          - metacarpal T84.290
          - metatarsal T84.293
          - phalanx
            - foot T84.293
            - hand T84.290
          - radius T84.19-
          - tarsal T84.293
          - tibia T84.19-
          - ulna T84.19-
        - specified bone NEC T84.298
        - vertebra T84.296
    - specified type NEC T84.89
      - embolism T84.81
      - fibrosis T84.82
      - hemorrhage T84.83
      - pain T84.84
      - specified complication NEC T84.89
      - stenosis T84.85
      - thrombosis T84.86
  - following
    - acute myocardial infarction NEC I23.8
      - aneurysm (false) (of cardiac wall) (of heart wall) (ruptured) I23.3
      - angina I23.7
      - atrial
        - septal defect I23.1
        - thrombosis I23.6
      - cardiac wall rupture I23.3
      - chordae tendinae rupture I23.4

- **Complication** *(continued)*
  - following *(continued)*
    - acute myocardial infarction NEC *(continued)*
      - defect
        - septal
          - atrial (heart) I23.1
          - ventricular (heart) I23.2
      - hemopericardium I23.0
      - papillary muscle rupture I23.5
      - rupture
        - cardiac wall I23.3
          - with hemopericardium I23.0
        - chordae tendineae I23.4
        - papillary muscle I23.5
      - specified NEC I23.8
      - thrombosis
        - atrium I23.6
        - auricular appendage I23.6
        - ventricle (heart) I23.6
      - ventricular
        - septal defect I23.2
        - thrombosis I23.6
    - ectopic or molar pregnancy O08.9
      - cardiac arrest O08.81
      - sepsis O08.82
      - specified type NEC O08.89
      - urinary tract infection O08.83
    - termination of pregnancy —*see* Abortion
  - gastrointestinal K92.9
    - bile duct prosthesis —*see* Complications, bile duct implant
    - esophageal anti-reflux device —*see* Complications, esophageal anti-reflux device
    - postoperative
      - colostomy —*see* Complications, colostomy
      - dumping syndrome K91.1
      - enterostomy —*see* Complications, enterostomy
      - gastrostomy —*see* Complications, gastrostomy
      - malabsorption NEC K91.2
      - obstruction K91.3
      - postcholecystectomy syndrome K91.5
      - specified NEC K91.89
      - vomiting after GI surgery K91.0
    - prosthetic device or implant
      - bile duct prosthesis —*see* Complications, bile duct implant
      - esophageal anti-reflux device —*see* Complications, esophageal anti-reflux device
      - specified type NEC
        - embolism T85.81
        - fibrosis T85.82
        - hemorrhage T85.83
        - mechanical
          - breakdown T85.518
          - displacement T85.528
          - malfunction T85.518
          - malposition T85.528
          - obstruction T85.598
          - perforation T85.598
          - protrusion T85.598
          - specified NEC T85.598
        - pain T85.84
        - specified complication NEC T85.89
        - stenosis T85.85
        - thrombosis T85.86
  - gastrostomy (stoma) K94.20
    - hemorrhage K94.21
    - infection K94.22
    - malfunction K94.23
    - mechanical K94.23
    - specified complication NEC K94.29

- **Complication** *(continued)*
  - genitourinary
    - device or implant T83.9
      - genital tract T83.9
        - infection or inflammation T83.6
        - intrauterine contraceptive device —*see* Complications, intrauterine, contraceptive device
        - mechanical —*see* Complications, by device, mechanical
        - mesh —*see* Complications, mesh
        - penile prosthesis —*see* Complications, prosthetic device, penile
        - specified type NEC T83.89
          - embolism T83.81
          - fibrosis T83.82
          - hemorrhage T83.83
          - pain T83.84
          - specified complication NEC T83.89
          - stenosis T83.85
          - thrombosis T83.86
        - vaginal mesh —*see* Complications, mesh
      - urinary system T83.9
        - cystostomy catheter —*see* Complication, catheter, cystostomy
        - electronic stimulator —*see* Complications, electronic stimulator device, urinary
        - indwelling urethral catheter —*see* Complications, catheter, urethral, indwelling
        - infection or inflammation T83.59
          - indwelling urinary catheter T83.51
        - kidney transplant —*see* Complication, transplant, kidney
        - organ graft —*see* Complication, graft, urinary organ
        - specified type NEC T83.89
          - embolism T83.81
          - fibrosis T83.82
          - hemorrhage T83.83
          - mechanical T83.198
            - breakdown T83.118
            - displacement T83.128
            - malfunction T83.118
            - malposition T83.128
            - obstruction T83.198
            - perforation T83.198
            - protrusion T83.198
            - specified NEC T83.198
          - pain T83.84
          - specified complication NEC T83.89
          - stenosis T83.85
          - thrombosis T83.86
        - sphincter implant —*see* Complications, implant, urinary sphincter
    - postprocedural
      - pelvic peritoneal adhesions N99.4
      - renal failure N99.0
      - specified NEC N99.89
      - stoma —*see* Complications, stoma, urinary tract
      - urethral stricture —*see* Stricture, urethra, postprocedural
      - vaginal
        - adhesions N99.2
        - vault prolapse N99.3

Complication *(continued)*
- graft (bypass) (patch) *—see also* Complications, prosthetic device or implant
  - aorta *—see* Complications, graft, vascular
  - arterial *—see* Complication, graft, vascular
  - bone T86.839
    - failure T86.831
    - infection T86.832
    - mechanical T84.318
      - breakdown T84.318
      - displacement T84.328
      - protrusion T84.398
      - specified type NEC T84.398
    - rejection T86.830
    - specified type NEC T86.838
  - carotid artery *—see* Complications, graft, vascular
  - cornea T86.849
    - failure T86.841
    - infection T86.842
    - mechanical T85.398
      - breakdown T85.318
      - displacement T85.328
      - protrusion T85.398
      - specified type NEC T85.398
    - rejection T86.840
    - retroprosthetic membrane T85.398
    - specified type NEC T86.848
  - femoral artery (bypass) *—see* Complication, extremity artery (bypass) graft
  - genital organ or tract *—see* Complications, genitourinary, device or implant, genital tract
  - muscle T84.9
    - breakdown T84.410
    - displacement T84.420
    - embolism T84.81
    - fibrosis T84.82
    - hemorrhage T84.83
    - infection and inflammation T84.7
    - mechanical NEC T84.490
    - pain T84.84
    - specified type NEC T84.89
    - stenosis T84.85
    - thrombosis T84.86
  - nerve *—see* Complication, prosthetic device or implant, specified NEC
  - skin *—see* Complications, prosthetic device or implant, skin graft
  - tendon T84.9
    - breakdown T84.410
    - displacement T84.420
    - embolism T84.81
    - fibrosis T84.82
    - hemorrhage T84.83
    - infection and inflammation T84.7
    - mechanical NEC T84.490
    - pain T84.84
    - specified type NEC T84.89
    - stenosis T84.85
    - thrombosis T84.86
  - urinary organ T83.9
    - embolism T83.81
    - fibrosis T83.82
    - hemorrhage T83.83
    - infection and inflammation T83.59
      - indwelling urinary catheter T83.51
    - mechanical
      - breakdown T83.21
      - displacement T83.22
      - leakage T83.23
      - malposition T83.22
      - obstruction T83.29
      - perforation T83.29
      - protrusion T83.29
      - specified NEC T83.29

Complication *(continued)*
- graft *(continued)*
  - urinary organ *(continued)*
    - pain T83.84
    - specified type NEC T83.89
    - stenosis T83.85
    - thrombosis T83.86
  - vascular T82.9
    - embolism T82.818
    - femoral artery *—see* Complication, extremity artery (bypass) graft
    - fibrosis T82.828
    - hemorrhage T82.838
    - mechanical
      - breakdown T82.319
        - aorta (bifurcation) T82.310
        - carotid artery T82.311
        - specified vessel NEC T82.318
      - displacement T82.329
        - aorta (bifurcation) T82.320
        - carotid artery T82.321
        - specified vessel NEC T82.328
      - leakage T82.339
        - aorta (bifurcation) T82.330
        - carotid artery T82.331
        - specified vessel NEC T82.338
      - malposition T82.329
        - aorta (bifurcation) T82.320
        - carotid artery T82.321
        - specified vessel NEC T82.328
      - obstruction T82.399
        - aorta (bifurcation) T82.390
        - carotid artery T82.391
        - specified vessel NEC T82.398
      - perforation T82.399
        - aorta (bifurcation) T82.390
        - carotid artery T82.391
        - specified vessel NEC T82.398
      - protrusion T82.399
        - aorta (bifurcation) T82.390
        - carotid artery T82.391
        - specified vessel NEC T82.398
    - pain T82.848
    - specified complication NEC T82.898
    - stenosis T82.858
    - thrombosis T82.868
- heart I51.9
  - assist device
    - infection and inflammation T82.7
  - following acute myocardial infarction *—see* Complications, following, acute myocardial infarction
  - postoperative *—see* Complications, circulatory system
  - transplant *—see* Complication, transplant, heart
    - and lung (s) *—see* Complications, transplant, heart, with lung
  - valve
    - graft (biological) T82.9
      - embolism T82.817
      - fibrosis T82.827
      - hemorrhage T82.837
      - infection and inflammation T82.7
      - mechanical T82.228
        - breakdown T82.221
        - displacement T82.222
        - leakage T82.223
        - malposition T82.222

Complication *(continued)*
- heart *(continued)*
  - valve *(continued)*
    - graft *(continued)*
      - mechanical *(continued)*
        - obstruction T82.228
        - perforation T82.228
        - protrusion T82.228
      - pain T82.847
      - specified type NEC T82.897
      - stenosis T82.857
      - thrombosis T82.867
    - prosthesis T82.9
      - embolism T82.817
      - fibrosis T82.827
      - hemorrhage T82.837
      - infection or inflammation T82.6
      - mechanical T82.09
        - breakdown T82.01
        - displacement T82.02
        - leakage T82.03
        - malposition T82.02
        - obstruction T82.09
        - perforation T82.09
        - protrusion T82.09
      - pain T82.847
      - specified type NEC T82.897
        - mechanical T82.09
      - stenosis T82.857
      - thrombosis T82.867
- hematoma
  - intraoperative *—see* Complication, intraoperative, hemorrhage
  - postprocedural *—see* Complication, postprocedural, hemorrhage
- hemodialysis *—see* Complications, dialysis
- hemorrhage
  - intraoperative *—see* Complication, intraoperative, hemorrhage
  - postprocedural *—see* Complication, postprocedural, hemorrhage
- ileostomy (stoma) *—see* Complications, enterostomy
- immunization (procedure) *—see* Complications, vaccination
- implant *—see also* Complications, by site and type
  - urinary sphincter T83.9
    - embolism T83.81
    - fibrosis T83.82
    - hemorrhage T83.83
    - infection and inflammation T83.59
    - mechanical
      - breakdown T83.111
      - displacement T83.121
      - leakage T83.191
      - malposition T83.121
      - obstruction T83.191
      - perforation T83.191
      - protrusion T83.191
      - specified NEC T83.191
    - pain T83.84
    - specified type NEC T83.89
    - stenosis T83.85
    - thrombosis T83.86
- infusion (procedure) T80.90
  - air embolism T80.0
  - blood *—see* Complications, transfusion
  - catheter *—see* Complications, catheter
  - infection T80.29
  - pump *—see* Complications, cardiovascular, device or implant
  - sepsis T80.29
  - serum reaction *—see also* Reaction, serum T80.69
    - anaphylactic shock *—see also* Shock, anaphylactic T80.59
  - specified type NEC T80.89

Complication *(continued)*
- inhalation therapy NEC T81.81
- injection (procedure) T80.90
  - drug reaction *—see* Reaction, drug
  - infection T80.29
  - sepsis T80.29
  - serum (prophylactic) (therapeutic) *—see* Complications, vaccination
  - specified type NEC T80.89
  - vaccine (any) *—see* Complications, vaccination
- inoculation (any) *—see* Complications, vaccination
- insulin pump
  - infection and inflammation T85.72
  - mechanical
    - breakdown T85.614
    - displacement T85.624
    - leakage T85.633
    - malposition T85.624
    - obstruction T85.694
    - perforation T85.694
    - protrusion T85.694
    - specified NEC T85.694
- intestinal pouch NEC K91.858
- intraocular lens (prosthetic) T85.9
  - embolism T85.81
  - fibrosis T85.82
  - hemorrhage T85.83
  - infection and inflammation T85.79
  - mechanical
    - breakdown T85.21
    - displacement T85.22
    - malposition T85.22
    - obstruction T85.29
    - perforation T85.29
    - protrusion T85.29
    - specified NEC T85.29
  - pain T85.84
  - specified type NEC T85.89
  - stenosis T85.85
  - thrombosis T85.86
- intraoperative (intraprocedural)
  - cardiac arrest
    - during cardiac surgery I97.710
    - during other surgery I97.711
  - cardiac functional disturbance NEC
    - during cardiac surgery I97.790
    - during other surgery I97.791
  - hemorrhage (hematoma) (of)
    - circulatory system organ or structure
      - during cardiac bypass I97.411
      - during cardiac catheterization I97.410
      - during other circulatory system procedure I97.418
      - during other procedure I97.42
    - digestive system organ
      - during procedure on digestive system K91.61
      - during procedure on other organ K91.62
    - ear
      - during procedure on ear and mastoid process H95.21
      - during procedure on other organ H95.22
    - endocrine system organ or structure
      - during procedure on endocrine system organ or structure E36.01
      - during procedure on other organ E36.02
    - eye and adnexa
      - during ophthalmic procedure H59.11-
      - during other procedure H59.12-

Complication *(continued)*
- prosthetic device or implant *(continued)*
  - intraperitoneal (dialysis) catheter —*see* Complications, catheter, intraperitoneal
  - joint —*see* Complications, joint prosthesis, internal
  - mechanical NEC T85.698
    - dialysis catheter (vascular) —*see also* Complication, catheter, dialysis, mechanical
      - peritoneal —*see* Complication, catheter, intraperitoneal, mechanical
    - gastrointestinal device T85.598
    - ocular device T85.398
    - subdural (infusion) catheter T85.690
    - suture, permanent T85.692
      - that for bone repair —*see* Complications, fixation device, internal (orthopedic), mechanical
    - ventricular shunt
      - breakdown T85.01
      - displacement T85.02
      - leakage T85.03
      - malposition T85.02
      - obstruction T85.09
      - perforation T85.09
      - protrusion T85.09
      - specified NEC T85.09
  - mesh
    - erosion (to surrounding organ or tissue) T83.718
      - vaginal (into pelvic floor muscles) T83.711
    - exposure (into surrounding organ or tissue) T83.728
      - vaginal (into vagina) (through vaginal wall) T83.721
  - orbital —*see* Complications, orbital prosthesis
  - penile T83.9
    - embolism T83.81
    - fibrosis T83.82
    - hemorrhage T83.83
    - infection and inflammation T83.6
    - mechanical
      - breakdown T83.410
      - displacement T83.420
      - leakage T83.490
      - malposition T83.420
      - obstruction T83.490
      - perforation T83.490
      - protrusion T83.490
      - specified NEC T83.490
    - pain T83.84
    - specified type NEC T83.89
    - stenosis T83.85
    - thrombosis T83.86
  - prosthetic materials NEC
    - erosion (to surrounding organ or tissue) T83.718
      - vaginal (into pelvic floor muscles) T83.711
    - exposure (into surrounding organ or tissue) T83.728
      - vaginal (into vagina) (through vaginal wall) T83.721
  - skin graft T86.829
    - artificial skin or decellularized allodermis
      - embolism T85.81
      - fibrosis T85.82
      - hemorrhage T85.83
      - infection and inflammation T85.79

Complication *(continued)*
- prosthetic device or implant *(continued)*
  - skin graft *(continued)*
    - artificial skin or decellularized allodermis *(continued)*
      - mechanical
        - breakdown T85.613
        - displacement T85.623
        - malfunction T85.613
        - malposition T85.623
        - obstruction T85.693
        - perforation T85.693
        - protrusion T85.693
        - specified NEC T85.693
      - pain T85.84
      - specified type NEC T85.89
      - stenosis T85.85
      - thrombosis T85.86
    - failure T86.821
    - infection T86.822
    - rejection T86.820
    - specified NEC T86.828
  - specified NEC T85.9
    - embolism T85.81
    - fibrosis T85.82
    - hemorrhage T85.83
    - infection and inflammation T85.79
    - mechanical
      - breakdown T85.618
      - displacement T85.628
      - leakage T85.638
      - malfunction T85.618
      - malposition T85.628
      - obstruction T85.698
      - perforation T85.698
      - protrusion T85.698
      - specified NEC T85.698
    - pain T85.84
    - specified type NEC T85.89
    - stenosis T85.85
    - thrombosis T85.86
  - subdural infusion catheter —*see* Complications, catheter, subdural
  - sutures —*see* Complications, sutures
  - urinary organ or tract NEC —*see* Complications, genitourinary, device or implant, urinary system
  - vascular —*see* Complications, cardiovascular device or implant
  - ventricular shunt —*see* Complications, ventricular shunt (device)
- puerperium —*see* Puerperal
- puncture, spinal G97.1
  - cerebrospinal fluid leak G97.0
  - headache or reaction G97.1
- pyelogram N99.89
- radiation
  - kyphosis M96.2
  - scoliosis M96.5
- reattached
  - extremity (infection) (rejection)
    - lower T87.1X-
    - upper T87.0X-
  - specified body part NEC T87.2
- reconstructed breast
  - asymmetry between native and reconstructed breast N65.1
  - deformity N65.0
  - disproportion between native and reconstructed breast N65.1
  - excess tissue N65.0
  - misshappen N65.0

Complication *(continued)*
- reimplant NEC —*see also* Complications, prosthetic device or implant
  - limb (infection) (rejection) —*see* Complications, reattached, extremity
  - organ (partial) (total) —*see* Complications, transplant
  - prosthetic device NEC —*see* Complications, prosthetic device
- renal N28.9
  - allograft —*see* Complications, transplant, kidney
  - dialysis —*see* Complications, dialysis
- respirator
  - mechancial J95.850
    - specified NEC J95.859
- respiratory system J98.9
  - device, implant or graft —*see* Complication, prosthetic device or implant, specified NEC
  - lung transplant —*see* Complications, prosthetic device or implant, lung transplant
  - postoperative J95.89
    - air leak J95.812
    - Mendelson's syndrome (chemical pneumonitis) J95.4
    - pneumothorax J95.811
    - pulmonary insufficiency (acute) (after nonthoracic surgery) J95.2
      - chronic J95.3
      - following thoracic surgery J95.1
    - respiratory failure (acute) J95.821
      - acute and chronic J95.822
    - specified NEC J95.89
    - subglottic stenosis J95.5
    - tracheostomy complication —*see* Complications, tracheostomy
  - therapy T81.89
- sedation during labor and delivery O74.9
  - cardiac O74.2
  - central nervous system O74.3
  - pulmonary NEC O74.1
- shunt —*see also* Complications, prosthetic device or implant
  - arteriovenous —*see* Complications, arteriovenous, shunt
  - ventricular (communicating) —*see* Complications, ventricular shunt
- skin
  - graft T86.829
    - failure T86.821
    - infection T86.822
    - rejection T86.820
    - specified type NEC T86.828
- spinal
  - anesthesia —*see* Complications, anesthesia, spinal
  - catheter (epidural) (subdural) —*see* Complications, catheter
  - puncture or tap G97.1
    - cerebrospinal fluid leak G97.0
    - headache or reaction G97.1
- stent
  - bile duct —*see* Complications, bile duct prosthesis
  - urinary T83.9
    - embolism T83.81
    - fibrosis T83.82
    - hemorrhage T83.83
    - infection and inflammation T83.59

Complication *(continued)*
- stent *(continued)*
  - urinary *(continued)*
    - mechanical
      - breakdown T83.112
      - displacement T83.122
      - leakage T83.192
      - malposition T83.122
      - obstruction T83.192
      - perforation T83.192
      - protrusion T83.192
      - specified NEC T83.192
    - pain T83.84
    - specified type NEC T83.89
    - stenosis T83.85
    - thrombosis T83.86
- stoma
  - digestive tract
    - colostomy —*see* Complications, colostomy
    - enterostomy —*see* Complications, enterostomy
    - esophagostomy —*see* Complications, esophagostomy
    - gastrostomy —*see* Complications, gastrostomy
  - urinary tract N99.538
    - cystostomy —*see* Complications, cystostomy
    - external NOS N99.528
      - hemorrhage N99.520
      - infection N99.521
      - malfunction N99.522
      - specified type NEC N99.528
    - hemorrhage N99.530
    - infection N99.531
    - malfunction N99.532
    - specified type NEC N99.538
- stomach banding —*see* Complication(s), bariatric procedure
- stomach stapling —*see* Complication(s), bariatric procedure
- surgical material, nonabsorbable —*see* Complication, suture, permanent
- surgical procedure (on) T81.9
  - amputation stump (late) —*see* Complications, amputation stump
  - cardiac —*see* Complications, circulatory system
  - cholesteatoma, recurrent —*see* Complications, postmastoidectomy, recurrent cholesteatoma
  - circulatory (early) —*see* Complications, circulatory system
  - digestive system —*see* Complications, gastrointestinal
  - dumping syndrome (postgastrectomy) K91.1
  - ear —*see* Complications, ear
  - elephantiasis or lymphedema I97.89
    - postmastectomy I97.2
  - emphysema (surgical) T81.82
  - endocrine —*see* Complications, endocrine
  - eye —*see* Complications, eye
  - fistula (persistent postoperative) T81.83
  - foreign body inadvertently left in wound (sponge) (suture) (swab) —*see* Foreign body, accidentally left during a procedure
  - gastrointestinal —*see* Complications, gastrointestinal
  - genitourinary NEC N99.89

- **Complication** *(continued)*
  - surgical procedure *(continued)*
    - hematoma
      - intraoperative —*see* Complication, intraoperative, hemorrhage
      - postprocedural —*see* Complication, postprocedural, hemorrhage
    - hemorrhage
      - intraoperative —*see* Complication, intraoperative, hemorrhage
      - postprocedural —*see* Complication, postprocedural, hemorrhage
    - hepatic failure K91.82
    - hyperglycemia (postpancreatectomy) E89.1
    - hypoinsulinemia (postpancreatectomy) E89.1
    - hypoparathyroidism (postparathyroidectomy) E89.2
    - hypopituitarism (posthypophysectomy) E89.3
    - hypothyroidism (post-thyroidectomy) E89.0
    - intestinal obstruction K91.3
    - intracranial hypotension following ventricular shunting (ventriculostomy) G97.2
    - lymphedema I97.89
      - postmastectomy I97.2
    - malabsorption (postsurgical) NEC K91.2
      - osteoporosis —*see* Osteoporosis, postsurgical malabsorption
    - mastoidectomy cavity NEC —*see* Complications, postmastoidectomy
    - metabolic E89.89
      - specified NEC E89.89
    - musculoskeletal —*see* Complications, musculoskeletal system
    - nervous system (central) (peripheral) —*see* Complications, nervous system
    - ovarian failure E89.40
      - asymptomatic E89.40
      - symptomatic E89.41
    - peripheral vascular —*see* Complications, surgical procedure, vascular
    - postcardiotomy syndrome I97.0
    - postcholecystectomy syndrome K91.5
    - postcommissurotomy syndrome I97.0
    - postgastrectomy dumping syndrome K91.1
    - postlaminectomy syndrome NEC M96.1
      - kyphosis M96.3
    - postmastectomy lymphedema syndrome I97.2
    - postmastoidectomy cholesteatoma —*see* Complications, postmastoidectomy, recurrent cholesteatoma
    - postvagotomy syndrome K91.1
    - postvalvulotomy syndrome I97.0
    - pulmonary insufficiency (acute) J95.2
      - chronic J95.3
      - following thoracic surgery J95.1
    - reattached body part —*see* Complications, reattached
    - respiratory —*see* Complications, respiratory system
    - shock (hypovolemic) T81.19

- **Complication** *(continued)*
  - surgical procedure *(continued)*
    - spleen (postoperative) D78.89
      - intraoperative D78.81
    - stitch abscess T81.4
    - subglottic stenosis (postsurgical) J95.5
    - testicular hypofunction E89.5
    - transplant —*see* Complications, organ or tissue transplant
    - urinary NEC N99.89
    - vaginal vault prolapse (posthysterectomy) N99.3
    - vascular (peripheral)
      - artery T81.719
        - mesenteric T81.710
        - renal T81.711
        - specified NEC T81.718
      - vein T81.72
    - wound infection T81.4
  - suture, permanent (wire) NEC T85.9
    - with repair of bone —*see* Complications, fixation device, internal
    - embolism T85.81
    - fibrosis T85.82
    - hemorrhage T85.83
    - infection and inflammation T85.79
    - mechanical
      - breakdown T85.612
      - displacement T85.622
      - malfunction T85.612
      - malposition T85.622
      - obstruction T85.692
      - perforation T85.692
      - protrusion T85.692
      - specified NEC T85.692
    - pain T85.84
    - specified type NEC T85.89
    - stenosis T85.85
    - thrombosis T85.86
  - tracheostomy J95.00
    - granuloma J95.09
    - hemorrhage J95.01
    - infection J95.02
    - malfunction J95.03
    - mechanical J95.03
    - obstruction J95.03
    - specified type NEC J95.09
    - tracheo-esophageal fistula J95.04
  - transfusion (blood) (lymphocytes) (plasma) T80.92
    - air emblism T80.0
    - circulatory overload E87.71
    - febrile nonhemolytic transfusion reaction R50.84
    - hemolysis T80.89
    - hemochromatosis E83.111
    - hemolytic reaction (antigen unspecified) T80.919
    - incompatibility reaction (antigen unspecified) T80.919
      - ABO T80.30
        - delayed serologic (DSTR) T80.39
        - hemolytic transfusion reaction (HTR) (unspecified time after transfusion) T80.319
          - acute (AHTR) (less than 24 hours after transfusion) T80.310
          - delayed (DHTR) (24 hours or more after transfusion) T80.311
        - specified NEC T80.39
      - acute (antigen unspecified) T80.910
      - delayed (antigen unspecified) T80.911
      - delayed serologic (DSTR) T80.89

- **Complication** *(continued)*
  - transfusion *(continued)*
    - incompatibility reaction *(continued)*
      - Non-ABO(minor antigens (Duffy) (Kell) (Kidd) (Lewis) (M) (N) (P) (S)) T80.A0
        - delayed serologic (DSTR) T80.A9
        - hemolytic transfusion reaction (HTR) (unspecified time after transfusion) T80.A19
          - acute (AHTR) (less than 24 hours after transfusion) T80.A10
          - delayed (DHTR) (24 hours or more after transfusion) T80.A11
        - specified NEC T80.A9
      - Rh (antigens (C) (c) (D) (E) (e)) (factor) T80.40
        - delayed serologic (DSTR) T80.49
        - hemolytic transfusion reaction (HTR) (unspecified time after transfusion) T80.419
          - acute (AHTR) (less than 24 hours after transfusion) T80.410
          - delayed (DHTR) (24 hours or more after transfusion) T80.411
        - specified NEC T80.49
    - infection T80.29
      - acute T80.22
    - reaction NEC T80.89
    - sepsis T80.29
    - shock T80.89
  - transplant T86.90
    - bone T86.839
      - failure T86.831
      - infection T86.832
      - rejection T86.830
      - specified type NEC T86.838
    - bone marrow T86.00
      - failure T86.02
      - infection T86.03
      - rejection T86.01
      - specified type NEC T86.09
    - cornea T86.849
      - failure T86.841
      - infection T86.842
      - rejection T86.840
      - specified type NEC T86.848
    - failure T86.92
    - heart T86.20
      - with lung T86.30
      - cardiac allograft vasculopathy T86.290
        - failure T86.32
        - infection T86.33
        - rejection T86.31
        - specified type NEC T86.39
      - failure T86.22
      - infection T86.23
      - rejection T86.21
      - specified type NEC T86.298
    - infection T86.93
    - intestine T86.859
      - failure T86.851
      - infection T86.852
      - rejection T86.850
      - specified type NEC T86.858
    - kidney T86.10
      - failure T86.12
      - infection T86.13
      - rejection T86.11
      - specified type NEC T86.19
    - liver T86.40
      - failure T86.42
      - infection T86.43

- **Complication** *(continued)*
  - transplant *(continued)*
    - liver *(continued)*
      - rejection T86.41
      - specified type NEC T86.49
    - lung T86.819
      - with heart T86.30
        - failure T86.32
        - infection T86.33
        - rejection T86.31
        - specified type NEC T86.39
      - failure T86.811
      - infection T86.812
      - rejection T86.810
      - specified type NEC T86.818
    - malignant neoplasm C80.2
    - pancreas T86.899
      - failure T86.891
      - infection T86.892
      - rejection T86.890
      - specified type NEC T86.898
    - peripheral blood stem cells T86.5
    - post-transplant lymphoproliferative disorder (PTLD) D47.Z1
    - rejection T86.91
    - skin T86.829
      - failure T86.821
      - infection T86.822
      - rejection T86.820
      - specified type NEC T86.828
    - specified
      - tissue T86.899
        - failure T86.891
        - infection T86.892
        - rejection T86.890
        - specified type NEC T86.898
      - type NEC T86.99
    - stem cell (from peripheral blood) (from umbilical cord) T86.5
    - umbilical cord stem cells T86.5
  - trauma (early) T79.9
    - specified NEC T79.8
  - ultrasound therapy NEC T88.9
  - umbilical cord NEC
    - complicating delivery O69.9
      - specified NEC O69.89
  - umbrella device, vascular T82.9
    - embolism T82.818
    - fibrosis T82.828
    - hemorrhage T82.838
    - infection or inflammation T82.7
    - mechanical
      - breakdown T82.515
      - displacement T82.525
      - leakage T82.535
      - malposition T82.525
      - obstruction T82.595
      - perforation T82.595
      - protrusion T82.595
    - pain T82.848
    - specified type NEC T82.898
    - stenosis T82.858
    - thrombosis T82.868
  - urethral catheter —*see* Complications, catheter, urethral, indwelling
  - vaccination T88.1
    - anaphylaxis NEC T80.52
    - arthropathy —*see* Arthropathy, postimmunization
    - cellulitis T88.0
    - encephalitis or encephalomyelitis G04.02
    - infection (general) (local) NEC T88.0
    - meningitis G03.8
    - myelitis G04.89
    - protein sickness T80.62
    - rash T88.1
    - reaction (allergic) T88.1
      - serum T80.62
    - sepsis T88.0

- **Complication** *(continued)*
  - vaccination *(continued)*
    - serum intoxication, sickness, rash, or other serum reaction NEC T80.62
      - anaphylactic shock T80.52
    - shock (allergic) (anaphylactic) T80.52
    - vaccinia (generalized) (localized) T88.1
  - vas deferens device or implant *—see* Complications, genitourinary, device or implant, genital tract
  - vascular I99.9
    - device or implant T82.9
      - embolism T82.818
      - fibrosis T82.828
      - hemorrhage T82.838
      - infection or inflammation T82.7
      - mechanical
        - breakdown T82.519
          - specified device NEC T82.518
        - displacement T82.529
          - specified device NEC T82.528
        - leakage T82.539
          - specified device NEC T82.538
        - malposition T82.529
          - specified device NEC T82.528
        - obstruction T82.599
          - specified device NEC T82.598
        - perforation T82.599
          - specified device NEC T82.598
        - protrusion T82.599
          - specified device NEC T82.598
      - pain T82.848
      - specified type NEC T82.898
      - stenosis T82.858
      - thrombosis T82.868
    - dialysis catheter *—see* Complication, catheter, dialysis
    - following infusion, therapeutic injection or transfusion T80.1
    - graft T82.9
      - embolism T82.818
      - fibrosis T82.828
      - hemorrhage T82.838
      - mechanical
        - breakdown T82.319
          - aorta (bifurcation) T82.310
          - carotid artery T82.311
          - specified vessel NEC T82.318
        - displacement T82.329
          - aorta (bifurcation) T82.320
          - carotid artery T82.321
          - specified vessel NEC T82.328
        - leakage T82.339
          - aorta (bifurcation) T82.330
          - carotid artery T82.331
          - specified vessel NEC T82.338
        - malposition T82.329
          - aorta (bifurcation) T82.320
          - carotid artery T82.321
          - specified vessel NEC T82.328
        - obstruction T82.399
          - aorta (bifurcation) T82.390
          - carotid artery T82.391
          - specified vessel NEC T82.398
        - perforation T82.399
          - aorta (bifurcation) T82.390
          - carotid artery T82.391

- **Complication** *(continued)*
  - vascular *(continued)*
    - graft *(continued)*
      - mechanical *(continued)*
        - obstruction *(continued)*
          - specified vessel NEC T82.398
        - protrusion T82.399
          - aorta (bifurcation) T82.390
          - carotid artery T82.391
          - specified vessel NEC T82.398
      - pain T82.848
      - specified complication NEC T82.898
      - stenosis T82.858
      - thrombosis T82.868
    - postoperative *—see* Complications, postoperative, circulatory
  - vena cava device (filter) (sieve) (umbrella) *—see* Complications, umbrella device, vascular
  - ventilation therapy NEC T81.81
  - ventilator
    - mechanical J95.850
      - specified NEC J95.859
  - ventricular (communicating) shunt (device) T85.9
    - embolism T85.81
    - fibrosis T85.82
    - hemorrhage T85.83
    - infection and inflammation T85.79
    - mechanical
      - breakdown T85.01
      - displacement T85.02
      - leakage T85.03
      - malposition T85.02
      - obstruction T85.09
      - perforation T85.09
      - protrusion T85.09
      - specified NEC T85.09
    - pain T85.84
    - specified type NEC T85.89
    - stenosis T85.85
    - thrombosis T85.86
  - wire suture, permanent (implanted) *—see* Complications, suture, permanent

- **Compressed air disease** T70.3

- **Compression**
  - with injury - code by Nature of injury
  - artery I77.1
    - celiac, syndrome I77.4
  - brachial plexus G54.0
  - brain (stem) G93.5
    - due to
      - contusion (diffuse) *—see* Injury, intracranial, diffuse
        - focal *—see* Injury, intracranial, focal
      - injury NEC *—see* Injury, intracranial, diffuse
    - traumatic *—see* Injury, intracranial, diffuse
  - bronchus J98.09
  - cauda equina G83.4
  - celiac (artery) (axis) I77.4
  - cerebral *—see* Compression, brain
  - cervical plexus G54.2
  - cord
    - spinal *—see* Compression, spinal
    - umbilical *—see* Compression, umbilical cord
  - cranial nerve G52.9
    - eighth H93.3
    - eleventh G52.8
    - fifth G50.8
    - first G52.0
    - fourth *—see* Strabismus, paralytic, fourth nerve
    - ninth G52.1

- **Compression** *(continued)*
  - cranial nerve *(continued)*
    - second *—see* Disorder, nerve, optic
    - seventh G52.8
    - sixth *—see* Strabismus, paralytic, sixth nerve
    - tenth G52.2
    - third *—see* Strabismus, paralytic, third nerve
    - twelfth G52.3
  - diver's squeeze T70.3
  - during birth (newborn) P15.9
  - esophagus K22.2
  - eustachian tube *—see* Obstruction, eustachian tube, cartilaginous
  - facies Q67.1
  - fracture *—see* Fracture
  - heart *—see* Disease, heart
  - intestine *—see* Obstruction, intestine
  - laryngeal nerve, recurrent G52.2
    - with paralysis of vocal cords and larynx J38.00
      - bilateral J38.02
      - unilateral J38.01
  - lumbosacral plexus G54.1
  - lung J98.4
  - lymphatic vessel I89.0
  - medulla *—see* Compression, brain
  - nerve *—see also* Disorder, nerve G58.9
    - arm NEC *—see* Mononeuropathy, upper limb
    - axillary G54.0
    - cranial *—see* Compression, cranial nerve
    - leg NEC *—see* Mononeuropathy, lower limb
    - median (in carpal tunnel) *—see* Syndrome, carpal tunnel
    - optic *—see* Disorder, nerve, optic
    - plantar *—see* Lesion, nerve, plantar
    - posterior tibial (in tarsal tunnel) *—see* Syndrome, tarsal tunnel
    - root or plexus NOS (in) G54.9
      - intervertebral disc disorder NEC *—see* Disorder, disc, with, radiculopathy
        - with myelopathy *—see* Disorder, disc, with, myelopathy
      - neoplastic disease *—see also* Neoplasm D49.9 *[G55]*
      - spondylosis *—see* Spondylosis, with radiculopathy
    - sciatic (acute) *—see* Lesion, nerve, sciatic
    - sympathetic G90.8
    - traumatic *—see* Injury, nerve
    - ulnar *—see* Lesion, nerve, ulnar
    - upper extremity NEC *—see* Mononeuropathy, upper limb
  - spinal (cord) G95.20
    - by displacement of intervertebral disc NEC *—see also* Disorder, disc, with, myelopathy
    - nerve root NOS G54.9
      - due to displacement of intervertebral disc NEC *—see* Disorder, disc, with, radiculopathy
        - with myelopathy *—see* Disorder, disc, with, myelopathy
    - specified NEC G95.29
    - spondylogenic (cervical) (lumbar, lumbosacral) (thoracic) *—see* Spondylosis, with myelopathy NEC
      - anterior *—see* Syndrome, anterior, spinal artery, compression
    - traumatic *—see* Injury, spinal cord, by region

- **Compression** *(continued)*
  - subcostal nerve (syndrome) *—see* Mononeuropathy, upper limb, specified NEC
  - sympathetic nerve NEC G90.8
  - syndrome T79.5
  - trachea J39.8
  - ulnar nerve (by scar tissue) *—see* Lesion, nerve, ulnar
  - umbilical cord
    - complicating delivery O69.2
      - cord around neck O69.1
      - prolapse O69.0
      - specified NEC O69.2
  - ureter N13.5
  - vein I87.1
  - vena cava (inferior) (superior) I87.1

- **Compulsion, compulsive**
  - gambling F63.0
  - neurosis F42
  - personality F60.5
  - states F42
  - swearing F42
    - in Gilles de la Tourette's syndrome F95.2
  - tics and spasms F95.9

- **Concato's disease** (pericardial polyserositis) A19.9
  - nontubercular I31.1
  - pleural *—see* Pleurisy, with effusion

- **Concavity chest wall** M95.4

- **Concealed penis** Q55.69

- **Concern** (normal) about sick person in family Z63.6

- **Concrescence** (teeth) K00.2

- **Concretio cordis** I31.1
  - rheumatic I09.2

- **Concretion** *—see also* Calculus
  - appendicular K38.1
  - canaliculus *—see* Dacryolith
  - clitoris N90.89
  - conjunctiva H11.12-
  - eyelid *—see* Disorder, eyelid, specified type NEC
  - lacrimal passages *—see* Dacryolith
  - prepuce (male) N47.8
  - salivary gland (any) K11.5
  - seminal vesicle N50.8
  - tonsil J35.8

- **Concussion** (brain) (cerebral) (current) S06.0X-
  - blast (air) (hydraulic) (immersion) (underwater)
    - abdomen or thorax *—see* Injury, blast, by site
    - ear with acoustic nerve injury *—see* Injury, nerve, acoustic, specified type NEC
  - cauda equina S34.3
  - conus medullaris S34.02
  - ocular S05.8X-
  - spinal (cord)
    - cervical S14.0
    - lumbar S34.01
    - sacral S34.02
    - thoracic S24.0
  - syndrome F07.81

- **Condition** *—see* Disease

- **Conditions arising in the perinatal period** *—see* Newborn, affected by

- **Conduct disorder** *—see* Disorder, conduct

- **Condyloma** A63.0
  - acuminatum A63.0
  - gonorrheal A54.09
  - latum A51.31

Condyloma *(continued)*
- syphilitic A51.31
  - congenital A50.07
- venereal, syphilitic A51.31

Conflagration —*see also* Burn
- asphyxia (by inhalation of gases, fumes or vapors) —*see also* Table of Drugs and Chemicals T59.9-

Conflict (with) —*see also* Discord
- family Z73.9
- marital Z63.0
  - involving divorce or estrangement Z63.5
- parent-child Z62.820
  - parent-adopted child Z62.821
  - parent-biological child Z62.820
  - parent-foster child Z62.822
- social role NEC Z73.5

Confluent —*see* condition

Confusion, confused R41.0
- epileptic F05
- mental state (psychogenic) F44.89
- psychogenic F44.89
- reactive (from emotional stress, psychological trauma) F44.89

Confusional arousals G47.51

Congelation T69.9

Congenital —*see also* condition
- aortic septum Q25.4
- intrinsic factor deficiency D51.0
- malformation —*see* Anomaly

Congestion, congestive
- bladder N32.89
- bowel K63.89
- brain G93.89
- breast N64.59
- bronchial J98.09
- catarrhal J31.0
- chest R09.89
- chill, malarial —*see* Malaria
- circulatory NEC I99.8
- duodenum K31.89
- eye —*see* Hyperemia, conjunctiva
- facial, due to birth injury P15.4
- general R68.89
- glottis J37.0
- heart —*see* Failure, heart, congestive
- hepatic K76.1
- hypostatic (lung) —*see* Edema, lung
- intestine K63.89
- kidney N28.89
- labyrinth —*see* subcategory H83.8
- larynx J37.0
- liver K76.1
- lung R09.89
  - active or acute —*see* Pneumonia
- malaria, malarial —*see* Malaria
- nasal R09.81
- nose R09.81
- orbit, orbital —*see also* Exophthalmos
  - inflammatory (chronic) —*see* Inflammation, orbit
- ovary N83.8
- pancreas K86.8
- pelvic, female N94.89
- pleural J94.8
- prostate (active) N42.1
- pulmonary —*see* Congestion, lung
- renal N28.89
- retina H35.81
- seminal vesicle N50.1
- spinal cord G95.19
- spleen (chronic) D73.2
- stomach K31.89
- trachea —*see* Tracheitis
- urethra N36.8
- uterus N85.8
  - with subinvolution N85.3

Congestion, congestive *(continued)*
- venous (passive) I87.8
- viscera R68.89

Congestive —*see* Congestion

Conical
- cervix (hypertrophic elongation) N88.4
- cornea —*see* Keratoconus
- teeth K00.2

Conjoined twins Q89.4

Conjugal maladjustment Z63.0
- involving divorce or estrangement Z63.5

Conjunctiva —*see* condition

Conjunctivitis (staphylococcal) (streptococcal) **NOS** H10.9
- Acanthamoeba B60.12
- acute H10.3-
  - atopic H10.1-
  - mucopurulent H10.02-
    - follicular H10.01-
  - chemical —*see also* Corrosion, cornea H10.21-
  - pseudomembranous H10.22-
  - serous except viral H10.23-
    - viral —*see* Conjunctivitis, viral
  - toxic H10.21-
- adenoviral (acute) (follicular) B30.1
- allergic (acute) —*see* Conjunctivitis, acute, atopic
  - chronic H10.45
    - vernal H10.44
- anaphylactic —*see* Conjunctivitis, acute, atopic
- Apollo B30.3
- atopic (acute) —*see* Conjunctivitis, acute, atopic
- Béal's B30.2
- blennorrhagic (gonococcal) (neonatorum) A54.31
- chemical (acute) —*see also* Corrosion, cornea H10.21-
- chlamydial A74.0
  - due to trachoma A71.1
  - neonatal P39.1
- chronic (nodosa) (petrificans) (phlyctenular) H10.40-
  - allergic H10.45
    - vernal H10.44
  - follicular H10.43-
  - giant papillary H10.41-
  - simple H10.42-
  - vernal H10.44
- coxsackievirus 24 B30.3
- diphtheritic A36.86
- due to
  - dust —*see* Conjunctivitis, acute, atopic
  - filariasis B74.9
  - mucocutaneous leishmaniasis B55.2
- enterovirus type 70 (hemorrhagic) B30.3
- epidemic (viral) B30.9
  - hemorrhagic B30.3
- gonococcal (neonatorum) A54.31
- granular (trachomatous) A71.1
  - sequelae (late effect) B94.0
- hemorrhagic (acute) (epidemic) B30.3
- herpes zoster B02.31
- in (due to)
  - Acanthamoeba B60.12
  - adenovirus (acute) (follicular) B30.1
  - Chlamydia A74.0
  - coxsackievirus 24 B30.3
  - diphtheria A36.86
  - enterovirus type 70 (hemorrhagic) B30.3

Conjunctivitis *(continued)*
- in *(continued)*
  - filariasis B74.9
  - gonococci A54.31
  - herpes (simplex) virus B00.53
    - zoster B02.31
  - infectious disease NEC B99
  - meningococci A39.89
  - mucocutaneous leishmaniasis B55.2
  - rosacea L71.9
  - syphilis (late) A52.71
  - zoster B02.31
- inclusion A74.0
- infantile P39.1
  - gonococcal A54.31
- Koch-Weeks' —*see* Conjunctivitis, acute, mucopurulent
- light —*see* Conjunctivitis, acute, atopic
- ligneous —*see* Blepharoconjunctivitis, ligneous
- meningococcal A39.89
- mucopurulent —*see* Conjunctivitis, acute, mucopurulent
- neonatal P39.1
  - gonococcal A54.31
- Newcastle B30.8
- of Béal B30.2
- parasitic
  - filariasis B74.9
  - mucocutaneous leishmaniasis B55.2
- Parinaud's H10.89
- petrificans H10.89
- rosacea L71.9
- specified NEC H10.89
- swimming-pool B30.1
- trachomatous A71.1
  - acute A71.0
  - sequelae (late effect) B94.0
- traumatic NEC H10.89
- tuberculous A18.59
- tularemic A21.1
- tularensis A21.1
- viral B30.9
  - due to
    - adenovirus B30.1
    - enterovirus B30.3
  - specified NEC B30.8

Conjunctivochalasis H11.82-

Connective tissue —*see* condition

Conn's syndrome E26.01

Conradi (-Hunermann) **disease** Q77.3

Consanguinity Z84.3
- counseling Z71.89

Conscious simulation (of illness) Z76.5

Consecutive —*see* condition

Consolidation lung (base) —*see* Pneumonia, lobar

Constipation (atonic) (neurogenic) (simple) (spastic) K59.00
- drug-induced —*see* Table of Drugs and Chemicals
- outlet dysfunction K59.02
- psychogenic F45.8
- slow transit K59.01
- specified NEC K59.09

Constitutional —*see also* condition
- substandard F60.7

Constitutionally substandard F60.7

Constriction —*see also* Stricture
- auditory canal —*see* Stenosis, external ear canal
- bronchial J98.09
- duodenum K31.5
- esophagus K22.2

Constriction *(continued)*
- external
  - abdomen, abdominal (wall) S30.841
  - alveolar process S00.542
  - ankle S90.54-
  - antecubital space —*see* Constriction, external, forearm
  - arm (upper) S40.84-
  - auricle —*see* Constriction, external, ear
  - axilla —*see* Constriction, external, arm
  - back, lower S30.840
  - breast S20.14-
  - brow S00.84
  - buttock S30.840
  - calf —*see* Constriction, external, leg
  - canthus —*see* Constriction, external, eyelid
  - cheek S00.84
    - internal S00.542
  - chest wall —*see* Constriction, external, thorax
  - chin S00.84
  - clitoris S30.844
  - costal region —*see* Constriction, external, thorax
  - digit (s)
    - foot —*see* Constriction, external, toe
    - hand —*see* Constriction, external, finger
  - ear S00.44-
  - elbow S50.34-
  - epididymis S30.843
  - epigastric region S30.841
  - esophagus, cervical S10.14
  - eyebrow —*see* Constriction, external, eyelid
  - eyelid S00.24-
  - face S00.84
  - finger (s) S60.44-
    - index S60.44-
    - little S60.44-
    - middle S60.44-
    - ring S60.44-
  - flank S30.841
  - foot (except toe(s) alone) S90.84-
    - toe —*see* Constriction, external, toe
  - forearm S50.84-
    - elbow only —*see* Constriction, external, elbow
  - forehead S00.84
  - genital organs, external
    - female S30.846
    - male S30.845
  - groin S30.841
  - gum S00.542
  - hand S60.54-
  - head S00.94
    - ear —*see* Constriction, external, ear
    - eyelid —*see* Constriction, external, eyelid
    - lip S00.541
    - nose S00.34
    - oral cavity S00.542
    - scalp S00.04
    - specified site NEC S00.84
  - heel —*see* Constriction, external, foot
  - hip S70.24-
  - inguinal region S30.841
  - interscapular region S20.449
  - jaw S00.84
  - knee S80.24-
  - labium (majus) (minus) S30.844

- **Constriction** *(continued)*
  - external *(continued)*
    - larynx S10.14
    - leg (lower) S80.84-
      - knee —*see* Constriction, external, knee
      - upper —*see* Constriction, external, thigh
    - lip S00.541
    - lower back S30.840
    - lumbar region S30.840
    - malar region S00.84
    - mammary —*see* Constriction, external, breast
    - mastoid region S00.84
    - mouth S00.542
    - nail
      - finger —*see* Constriction, external, finger
      - toe —*see* Constriction, external, toe
    - nasal S00.34
    - neck S10.94
      - specified site NEC S10.84
      - throat S10.14
    - nose S00.34
    - occipital region S00.04
    - oral cavity S00.542
    - orbital region —*see* Constriction, external, eyelid
    - palate S00.542
    - palm —*see* Constriction, external, hand
    - parietal region S00.04
    - pelvis S30.840
    - penis S30.842
    - perineum
      - female S30.844
      - male S30.840
    - periocular area —*see* Constriction, external, eyelid
    - phalanges
      - finger —*see* Constriction, external, finger
      - toe —*see* Constriction, external, toe
    - pharynx S10.14
    - pinna —*see* Constriction, external, ear
    - popliteal space —*see* Constriction, external, knee
    - prepuce S30.842
    - pubic region S30.840
    - pudendum
      - female S30.846
      - male S30.845
    - sacral region S30.840
    - scalp S00.04
    - scapular region —*see* Constriction, external, shoulder
    - scrotum S30.843
    - shin —*see* Constriction, external, leg
    - shoulder S40.24-
    - sternal region S20.349
    - submaxillary region S00.84
    - submental region S00.84
    - subungual
      - finger (s) —*see* Constriction, external, finger
      - toe (s) —*see* Constriction, external, toe
    - supraclavicular fossa S10.84
    - supraorbital S00.84
    - temple S00.84
    - temporal region S00.84
    - testis S30.843
    - thigh S70.34-
    - thorax, thoracic (wall) S20.94
      - back S20.44-
      - front S20.34-
    - throat S10.14

- **Constriction** *(continued)*
  - external *(continued)*
    - thumb S60.34-
    - toe (s) (lesser) S90.44-
      - great S90.44-
    - tongue S00.542
    - trachea S10.14
    - tunica vaginalis S30.843
    - uvula S00.542
    - vagina S30.844
    - vulva S30.844
    - wrist S60.84-
  - gallbladder —*see* Obstruction, gallbladder
  - intestine —*see* Obstruction, intestine
  - larynx J38.6
    - congenital Q31.8
      - specified NEC Q31.8
      - subglottic Q31.1
  - organ or site, congenital NEC —*see* Atresia, by site
  - prepuce (acquired) (congenital) N47.1
  - pylorus (adult hypertrophic) K31.1
    - congenital or infantile Q40.0
    - newborn Q40.0
  - ring dystocia (uterus) O62.4
  - spastic —*see also* Spasm
    - ureter N13.5
  - ureter N13.5
    - with infection N13.6
  - urethra —*see* Stricture, urethra
  - visual field (peripheral) (functional) —*see* Defect, visual field
- **Constrictive** —*see* condition
- **Consultation**
  - medical —*see* Counseling, medical
  - religious Z71.81
  - specified reason NEC Z71.89
  - spiritual Z71.81
  - without complaint or sickness Z71.9
    - feared complaint unfounded Z71.1
    - specified reason NEC Z71.89
- **Consumption** —*see* Tuberculosis
- **Contact** (with) —*see also* Exposure (to)
  - acariasis Z20.7
  - AIDS virus Z20.6
  - air pollution Z77.110
  - algae and algae toxins Z77.121
  - algae bloom Z77.121
  - anthrax Z20.810
  - aromatic amines Z77.020
  - aromatic (hazardous) compounds NEC Z77.028
  - aromatic dyes NOS Z77.028
  - arsenic Z77.010
  - asbestos Z77.090
  - bacterial disease NEC Z20.818
  - benzene Z77.021
  - blue-green algae bloom Z77.121
  - body fluids (potentially hazardous) Z77.21
  - brown tide Z77.121
  - chemicals (chiefly nonmedicinal) (hazardous) NEC Z77.098
  - cholera Z20.09
  - chromium compounds Z77.018
  - communicable disease Z20.9
    - bacterial NEC Z20.818
    - specified NEC Z20.89
    - viral NEC Z20.828
  - cyanobacteria bloom Z77.121
  - dyes Z77.098
  - Escherichia coli (E. coli) Z20.01
  - fiberglass —*see* Table of Drugs and Chemicals, fiberglass
  - German measles Z20.4
  - gonorrhea Z20.2
  - hazardous metals NEC Z77.018
  - hazardous substances NEC Z77.29

- **Contact** *(continued)*
  - hazards in the physical environment NEC Z77.128
  - hazards to health NEC Z77.9
  - HIV Z20.6
  - HTLV-III/LAV Z20.6
  - human immunodeficiency virus (HIV) Z20.6
  - infection Z20.9
    - specified NEC Z20.89
  - infestation (parasitic) NEC Z20.7
  - intestinal infectious disease NEC Z20.09
    - Escherichia coli (E. coli) Z20.01
  - lead Z77.011
  - meningococcus Z20.811
  - mold (toxic) Z77.120
  - nickel dust Z77.018
  - noise Z77.122
  - parasitic disease Z20.7
  - pediculosis Z20.7
  - pfiesteria piscicida Z77.121
  - poliomyelitis Z20.89
  - pollution
    - air Z77.110
    - environmental NEC Z77.118
    - soil Z77.112
    - water Z77.111
  - polycyclic aromatic hydrocarbons Z77.028
  - rabies Z20.3
  - radiation, naturally occurring NEC Z77.123
  - radon Z77.123
  - red tide (Florida) Z77.121
  - rubella Z20.4
  - sexually-transmitted disease Z20.2
  - smallpox (laboratory) Z20.89
  - syphilis Z20.2
  - tuberculosis Z20.1
  - uranium Z77.012
  - varicella Z20.820
  - venereal disease Z20.2
  - viral disease NEC Z20.828
  - viral hepatitis Z20.5
  - water pollution Z77.111
- **Contamination, food** —*see* Intoxication, foodborne
- **Contraception, contraceptive**
  - advice Z30.09
  - counseling Z30.09
  - device (intrauterine) (in situ) Z97.5
    - causing menorrhagia T83.83
    - checking Z30.431
    - complications —*see* Complications, intrauterine, contraceptive device
    - in place Z97.5
    - initial prescription Z30.014
    - reinsertion Z30.433
    - removal Z30.432
    - replacement Z30.433
  - emergency (postcoital) Z30.012
  - initial prescription Z30.019
    - injectable Z30.013
    - intrauterine device Z30.014
    - pills Z30.011
    - postcoital (emergency) Z30.012
    - specified type NEC Z30.018
    - subdermal implantable Z30.019
  - maintenance Z30.40
    - examination Z30.8
    - injectable Z30.42
    - intrauterine device Z30.431
    - pills Z30.41
    - specified type NEC Z30.49
    - subdermal implantable Z30.49
  - management Z30.9
    - specified NEC Z30.8
  - postcoital (emergency) Z30.012

- **Contraception, contraceptive** *(continued)*
  - prescription Z30.019
    - repeat Z30.40
  - sterilization Z30.2
  - surveillance (drug) —*see* Contraception, maintenance
- **Contraction(s), contracture, contracted**
  - Achilles tendon —*see also* Short, tendon, Achilles
    - congenital Q66.89
  - amputation stump (surgical) (flexion) (late) (next proximal joint) T87.89
  - anus K59.8
  - bile duct (common) (hepatic) K83.8
  - bladder N32.89
    - neck or sphincter N32.0
  - bowel, cecum, colon or intestine, any part —*see* Obstruction, intestine
  - Braxton Hicks —*see* False, labor
  - breast implant, capsular T85.44
  - bronchial J98.09
  - burn (old) —*see* Cicatrix
  - cervix —*see* Stricture, cervix
  - cicatricial —*see* Cicatrix
  - conjunctiva, trachomatous, active A71.1
    - sequelae (late effect) B94.0
  - Dupuytren's M72.0
  - eyelid —*see* Disorder, eyelid function
  - fascia (lata) (postural) M72.8
    - Dupuytren's M72.0
    - palmar M72.0
    - plantar M72.2
  - finger NEC —*see also* Deformity, finger
    - congenital Q68.1
    - joint —*see* Contraction, joint, hand
  - flaccid —*see* Contraction, paralytic
  - gallbladder K82.0
  - heart valve —*see* Endocarditis
  - hip —*see* Contraction, joint, hip
  - hourglass
    - bladder N32.89
      - congenital Q64.79
    - gallbladder K82.0
      - congenital Q44.1
    - stomach K31.89
      - congenital Q40.2
      - psychogenic F45.8
    - uterus (complicating delivery) O62.4
  - hysterical F44.4
  - internal os —*see* Stricture, cervix
  - joint (abduction) (acquired) (adduction) (flexion) (rotation) M24.50
    - ankle M24.57-
    - congenital NEC Q68.8
      - hip Q65.89
    - elbow M24.52-
    - foot joint M24.57-
    - hand joint M24.54-
    - hip M24.55-
      - congenital Q65.89
    - hysterical F44.4
    - knee M24.56-
    - shoulder M24.51-
    - wrist M24.53-
  - kidney (granular) (secondary) N26.9
    - congenital Q63.8
    - hydronephritic —*see* Hydronephrosis
    - Page N26.2
    - pyelonephritic —*see* Pyelitis, chronic
    - tuberculous A18.11
  - ligament —*see also* Disorder, ligament
    - congenital Q79.8

Contraception, contraceptive *(continued)*
- muscle (postinfective) (postural) NEC M62.40
  - with contracture of joint —*see* Contraction, joint
  - ankle M62.47-
  - congenital Q79.8
    - sternocleidomastoid Q68.0
  - extraocular —*see* Strabismus
  - eye (extrinsic) —*see* Strabismus
  - foot M62.47-
  - forearm M62.43-
  - hand M62.44-
  - hysterical F44.4
  - ischemic (Volkmann's) T79.6
  - lower leg M62.46-
  - multiple sites M62.49
  - pelvic region M62.45-
  - posttraumatic —*see* Strabismus, paralytic
  - psychogenic F45.8
    - conversion reaction F44.4
  - shoulder region M62.41-
  - specified site NEC M62.48
  - thigh M62.45-
  - upper arm M62.42-
- neck —*see* Torticollis
- ocular muscle —*see* Strabismus
- organ or site, congenital NEC —*see* Atresia, by site
- outlet (pelvis) —*see* Contraction, pelvis
- palmar fascia M72.0
- paralytic
  - joint —*see* Contraction, joint
  - muscle —*see also* Contraction, muscle NEC
    - ocular —*see* Strabismus, paralytic
- pelvis (acquired) (general) M95.5
  - with disproportion (fetopelvic) O33.1
    - causing obstructed labor O65.1
    - inlet O33.2
    - mid-cavity O33.3
    - outlet O33.3
- plantar fascia M72.2
- premature
  - atrium I49.1
  - auriculoventricular I49.49
  - heart I49.49
  - junctional I49.2
  - supraventricular I49.1
  - ventricular I49.3
- prostate N42.89
- pylorus NEC —*see also* Pylorospasm
  - psychogenic F45.8
- rectum, rectal (sphincter) K59.8
- ring (Bandl's) (complicating delivery) O62.4
- scar —*see* Cicatrix
- spine —*see* Dorsopathy, deforming
- sternocleidomastoid (muscle), congenital Q68.0
- stomach K31.89
  - hourglass K31.89
    - congenital Q40.2
    - psychogenic F45.8
  - psychogenic F45.8
- tendon (sheath) M62.40
  - with contracture of joint —*see* Contraction, joint
  - Achilles —*see* Short, tendon, Achilles
  - ankle M62.47-
    - Achilles —*see* Short, tendon, Achilles
  - foot M62.47-
  - forearm M62.43-
  - hand M62.44-
  - lower leg M62.46-

Contraception, contraceptive *(continued)*
  - multiple sites M62.49
  - neck M62.48
  - pelvic region M62.45-
  - shoulder region M62.41-
  - specified site NEC M62.48
  - thigh M62.45-
  - thorax M62.48
  - trunk M62.48
  - upper arm M62.42-
- toe —*see* Deformity, toe, specified NEC
- ureterovesical orifice (postinfectional) N13.5
  - with infection N13.6
- urethra —*see also* Stricture, urethra
  - orifice N32.0
- uterus N85.8
  - abnormal NEC O62.9
  - clonic (complicating delivery) O62.4
  - dyscoordinate (complicating delivery) O62.4
  - hourglass (complicating delivery) O62.4
  - hypertonic O62.4
  - hypotonic NEC O62.2
  - inadequate
    - primary O62.0
    - secondary O62.1
  - incoordinate (complicating delivery) O62.4
  - poor O62.2
  - tetanic (complicating delivery) O62.4
- vagina (outlet) N89.5
- vesical N32.89
  - neck or urethral orifice N32.0
- visual field —*see* Defect, visual field, generalized
- Volkmann's (ischemic) T79.6

Contusion (skin surface intact) T14.8
- abdomen, abdominal (muscle) (wall) S30.1
- adnexa, eye NEC S05.8X-
- adrenal gland S37.812
- alveolar process S00.532
- ankle S90.0-
- antecubital space —*see* Contusion, forearm
- anus S30.3
- arm (upper) S40.02-
  - lower (with elbow) —*see* Contusion, forearm
- auditory canal —*see* Contusion, ear
- auricle —*see* Contusion, ear
- axilla —*see* Contusion, arm, upper
- back —*see also* Contusion, thorax, back
  - lower S30.0
- bile duct S36.13
- bladder S37.22
- bone NEC T14.8
- brain (diffuse) —*see* Injury, intracranial, diffuse
  - focal —*see* Injury, intracranial, focal
- brainstem S06.38-
- breast S20.0-
- broad ligament S37.892
- brow S00.83
- buttock S30.0
- canthus, eye S00.1-
- cauda equina S34.3
- cerebellar, traumatic S06.37-
- cerebral S06.33-
  - left side S06.32-
  - right side S06.31-
- cheek S00.83
  - internal S00.532

Contusion *(continued)*
- chest (wall) —*see* Contusion, thorax
- chin S00.83
- clitoris S30.23
- colon —*see* Injury, intestine, large, contusion
- common bile duct S36.13
- conjunctiva S05.1-
  - with foreign body (in conjunctival sac) —*see* Foreign body, conjunctival sac
- conus medullaris (spine) S34.139
- cornea —*see* Contusion, eyeball
  - with foreign body —*see* Foreign body, cornea
- corpus cavernosum S30.21
- cortex (brain) (cerebral) —*see* Injury, intracranial, diffuse
  - focal —*see* Injury, intracranial, focal
- costal region —*see* Contusion, thorax
- cystic duct S36.13
- diaphragm S27.802
- duodenum S36.420
- ear S00.43-
- elbow S50.0-
  - with forearm —*see* Contusion, forearm
- epididymis S30.22
- epigastric region S30.1
- epiglottis S10.0
- esophagus (thoracic) S27.812
  - cervical S10.0
- eyeball S05.1-
- eyebrow S00.1-
- eyelid (and periocular area) S00.1-
- face NEC S00.83
- fallopian tube S37.529
  - bilateral S37.522
  - unilateral S37.521
- femoral triangle S30.1
- finger (s) S60.00
  - with damage to nail (matrix) S60.10
  - index S60.02-
    - with damage to nail S60.12-
  - little S60.05-
    - with damage to nail S60.15-
  - middle S60.03-
    - with damage to nail S60.13-
  - ring S60.04-
    - with damage to nail S60.14-
  - thumb —*see* Contusion, thumb
- flank S30.1
- foot (except toe(s) alone) S90.3-
  - toe —*see* Contusion, toe
- forearm S50.1-
  - elbow only —*see* Contusion, elbow
- forehead S00.83
- gallbladder S36.122
- genital organs, external
  - female S30.202
  - male S30.201
- globe (eye) —*see* Contusion, eyeball
- groin S30.1
- gum S00.532
- hand S60.22-
  - finger (s) —*see* Contusion, finger
  - wrist —*see* Contusion, wrist
- head S00.93
  - ear —*see* Contusion, ear
  - eyelid —*see* Contusion, eyelid
  - lip S00.531
  - nose S00.33
  - oral cavity S00.532
  - scalp S00.03
  - specified part NEC S00.83
- heel —*see* Contusion, foot
- hepatic duct S36.13
- hip S70.0-
- ileum S36.428
- iliac region S30.1

Contusion *(continued)*
- inguinal region S30.1
- interscapular region S20.229
- intra-abdominal organ S36.92
  - colon —*see* Injury, intestine, large, contusion
  - liver S36.112
  - pancreas —*see* Contusion, pancreas
  - rectum S36.62
  - small intestine —*see* Injury, intestine, small, contusion
  - specified organ NEC S36.892
  - spleen —*see* Contusion, spleen
  - stomach S36.32
- iris (eye) —*see* Contusion, eyeball
- jaw S00.83
- jejunum S36.428
- kidney S37.01-
  - major (greater than 2 cm) S37.02-
  - minor (less than 2 cm) S37.01-
- knee S80.0-
- labium (majus) (minus) S30.23
- lacrimal apparatus, gland or sac S05.8X-
- larynx S10.0
- leg (lower) S80.1-
  - knee —*see* Contusion, knee
- lens —*see* Contusion, eyeball
- lip S00.531
- liver S36.112
- lower back S30.0
- lumbar region S30.0
- lung S27.329
  - bilateral S27.322
  - unilateral S27.321
- malar region S00.83
- mastoid region S00.83
- membrane, brain —*see* Injury, intracranial, diffuse
  - focal —*see* Injury, intracranial, focal
- mesentery S36.892
- mesosalpinx S37.892
- mouth S00.532
- muscle —*see* Contusion, by site
- nail
  - finger —*see* Contusion, finger, with damage to nail
  - toe —*see* Contusion, toe, with damage to nail
- nasal S00.33
- neck S10.93
  - specified site NEC S10.83
  - throat S10.0
- nerve —*see* Injury, nerve
- newborn P54.5
- nose S00.33
- occipital
  - lobe (brain) —*see* Injury, intracranial, diffuse
    - focal —*see* Injury, intracranial, focal
  - region (scalp) S00.03
- orbit (region) (tissues) S05.1-
- ovary S37.429
  - bilateral S37.422
  - unilateral S37.421
- palate S00.532
- pancreas S36.229
  - body S36.221
  - head S36.220
  - tail S36.222
- parietal
  - lobe (brain) —*see* Injury, intracranial, diffuse
    - focal —*see* Injury, intracranial, focal
  - region (scalp) S00.03
- pelvic organ S37.92
  - adrenal gland S37.812
  - bladder S37.22

Contusion *(continued)*
pelvic organ *(continued)*
fallopian tube —*see* Contusion, fallopian tube
kidney —*see* Contusion, kidney
ovary —*see* Contusion, ovary
prostate S37.822
specified organ NEC S37.892
ureter S37.12
urethra S37.32
uterus S37.62
pelvis S30.0
penis S30.21
perineum
female S30.23
male S30.0
periocular area S00.1-
peritoneum S36.81
periurethral tissue —*see* Contusion, urethra
pharynx S10.0
pinna —*see* Contusion, ear
popliteal space —*see* Contusion, knee
prepuce S30.21
prostate S37.822
pubic region S30.1
pudendum
female S30.202
male S30.201
quadriceps femoris —*see* Contusion, thigh
rectum S36.62
retroperitoneum S36.892
round ligament S37.892
sacral region S30.0
scalp S00.03
due to birth injury P12.3
scapular region —*see* Contusion, shoulder
sclera —*see* Contusion, eyeball
scrotum S30.22
seminal vesicle S37.892
shoulder S40.01-
skin NEC T14.8
small intestine —*see* Injury, intestine, small, contusion
spermatic cord S30.22
spinal cord —*see* Injury, spinal cord, by region
cauda equina S34.3
conus medullaris S34.139
spleen S36.029
major S36.021
minor S36.020
sternal region S20.219
stomach S36.32
subconjunctival S05.1-
subcutaneous NEC T14.8
submaxillary region S00.83
submental region S00.83
subperiosteal NEC T14.8
subungual
finger —*see* Contusion, finger, with damage to nail
toe —*see* Contusion, toe, with damage to nail
supraclavicular fossa S10.83
supraorbital S00.83
suprarenal gland S37.812
temple (region) S00.83
temporal
lobe (brain) —*see* Injury, intracranial, diffuse
focal —*see* Injury, intracranial, focal
region S00.83
testis S30.22
thigh S70.1-
thorax (wall) S20.20
back S20.22-
front S20.21-
throat S10.0

Contusion *(continued)*
thumb S60.01-
with damage to nail S60.11-
toe (s) (lesser) S90.12-
with damage to nail S90.22-
great S90.11-
with damage to nail S90.21-
specified type NEC S90.221
tongue S00.532
trachea (cervical) S10.0
thoracic S27.52
tunica vaginalis S30.22
tympanum, tympanic membrane —*see* Contusion, ear
ureter S37.12
urethra S37.32
urinary organ NEC S37.892
uterus S37.62
uvula S00.532
vagina S30.23
vas deferens S37.892
vesical S37.22
vocal cord (s) S10.0
vulva S30.23
wrist S60.21-

Conus (congenital) (any type) Q14.8
cornea —*see* Keratoconus
medullaris syndrome G95.81

Conversion hysteria, neurosis or reaction F44.9

Converter, tuberculosis (test reaction) R76.11

Conviction (legal)**, anxiety concerning** Z65.0
with imprisonment Z65.1

Convulsions (idiopathic) —*see also* Seizure (s) R56.9
apoplectiform (cerebral ischemia) I67.82
benign neonatal (familial) —*see* Epilepsy, generalized, idiopathic
dissociative F44.5
epileptic —*see* Epilepsy
epileptiform, epileptoid —*see* Seizure, epileptiform
ether (anesthetic) —*see* Table of Drugs and Chemicals, by drug
febrile R56.00
with status epilepticus G40.901
complex R56.01
with status epilepticus G40.901
simple R56.00
hysterical F44.5
infantile P90
epilepsy —*see* Epilepsy
jacksonian —*see* Epilepsy, localization-related, symptomatic, with simple partial seizures
myoclonic G25.3
neonatal, benign (familial) —*see* Epilepsy, generalized, idiopathic
newborn P90
obstetrical (nephritic) (uremic) —*see* Eclampsia
paretic A52.17
post traumatic R56.1
psychomotor —*see* Epilepsy, localization-related, symptomatic, with complex partial seizures
recurrent R56.9
reflex R25.8
scarlatinal A38.8
tetanus, tetanic —*see* Tetanus
thymic E32.8

Convulsive —*see also* Convulsions

Cooley's anemia D56.1

Coolie itch B76.9

Cooper's
disease —*see* Mastopathy, cystic
hernia —*see* Hernia, abdomen, specified site NEC

Copra itch B88.0

Coprophagy F50.8

Coprophobia F40.298

Coproporphyria, hereditary E80.29

Cor
biloculare Q20.8
bovis, bovinum —*see* Hypertrophy, cardiac
pulmonale (chronic) I27.81
acute I26.09
triatriatum, triatrium Q24.2
triloculare Q20.8
biatrium Q20.4
biventriculare Q21.1

Corbus' disease (gangrenous balanitis) N48.1

Cord —*see also* condition
around neck (tightly) (with compression)
complicating delivery O69.1
bladder G95.89
tabetic A52.19

Cordis ectopia Q24.8

Corditis (spermatic) N49.1

Corectopia Q13.2

Cori's disease (glycogen storage) E74.03

Corkhandler's disease or lung J67.3

Corkscrew esophagus K22.4

Corkworker's disease or lung J67.3

Corn (infected) L84

Cornea —*see also* condition
donor Z52.5
plana Q13.4

Cornelia de Lange syndrome Q87.1

Cornu cutaneum L85.8

Cornual gestation or pregnancy O00.8

Coronary (artery) —*see* condition

Coronavirus, as cause of disease classified elsewhere B97.29
SARS-associated B97.21

Corpora —*see also* condition
amylacea, prostate N42.89
cavernosa —*see* condition

Corpulence —*see* Obesity

Corpus —*see* condition

Corrected transposition Q20.5

Corrosion (injury) (acid) (caustic) (chemical) (lime) (external) (internal) T30.4
abdomen, abdominal (muscle) (wall) T21.42
first degree T21.52
second degree T21.62
third degree T21.72
above elbow T22.439
first degree T22.539
left T22.432
first degree T22.532
second degree T22.632
third degree T22.732
right T22.431
first degree T22.531
second degree T22.631
third degree T22.731
second degree T22.639
third degree T22.739
alimentary tract NEC T28.7

Corrosion *(continued)*
ankle T25.419
first degree T25.519
left T25.412
first degree T25.512
second degree T25.612
third degree T25.712
multiple with foot —*see* Corrosion, lower, limb, multiple, ankle and foot
right T25.411
first degree T25.511
second degree T25.611
third degree T25.711
second degree T25.619
third degree T25.719
anus —*see* Corrosion, buttock
arm (s) (meaning upper limb (s)) —*see* Corrosion, upper limb
axilla T22.449
first degree T22.549
left T22.442
first degree T22.542
second degree T22.642
third degree T22.742
right T22.441
first degree T22.541
second degree T22.641
third degree T22.741
second degree T22.649
third degree T22.749
back (lower) T21.44
first degree T21.54
second degree T21.64
third degree T21.74
upper T21.43
first degree T21.53
second degree T21.63
third degree T21.73
blisters - code as Corrosion, second degree, by site
breast (s) —*see* Corrosion, chest wall
buttock (s) T21.45
first degree T21.55
second degree T21.65
third degree T21.75
calf T24.439
first degree T24.539
left T24.432
first degree T24.532
second degree T24.632
third degree T24.732
right T24.431
first degree T24.531
second degree T24.631
third degree T24.731
second degree T24.639
third degree T24.739
canthus (eye) —*see* Corrosion, eyelid
cervix T28.8
cheek T20.46
first degree T20.56
second degree T20.66
third degree T20.76
chest wall T21.41
first degree T21.51
second degree T21.61
third degree T21.71
chin T20.43
first degree T20.53
second degree T20.63
third degree T20.73
colon T28.7
conjunctiva (and cornea) —*see* Corrosion, cornea
cornea (and conjunctiva) T26.6-
deep necrosis of underlying tissue - code as Corrosion, third degree, by site

- **Corrosion** *(continued)*
  - unspecified site with extent of body surface involved specified *(continued)*
    - 60-69 per cent *(continued)*
      - with *(continued)*
        - 40-49 percent third degree T32.64
        - 50-59 percent third degree T32.65
        - 60-69 percent third degree T32.66
    - 70-79 per cent (0-9 percent third degree) T32.70
      - with
        - 10-19 percent third degree T32.71
        - 20-29 percent third degree T32.72
        - 30-39 percent third degree T32.73
        - 40-49 percent third degree T32.74
        - 50-59 percent third degree T32.75
        - 60-69 percent third degree T32.76
        - 70-79 percent third degree T32.77
    - 80-89 per cent (0-9 percent third degree) T32.80
      - with
        - 10-19 percent third degree T32.81
        - 20-29 percent third degree T32.82
        - 30-39 percent third degree T32.83
        - 40-49 percent third degree T32.84
        - 50-59 percent third degree T32.85
        - 60-69 percent third degree T32.86
        - 70-79 percent third degree T32.87
        - 80-89 percent third degree T32.88
    - 90 per cent or more (0-9 percent third degree) T32.90
      - with
        - 10-19 percent third degree T32.91
        - 20-29 percent third degree T32.92
        - 30-39 percent third degree T32.93
        - 40-49 percent third degree T32.94
        - 50-59 percent third degree T32.95
        - 60-69 percent third degree T32.96
        - 70-79 percent third degree T32.97
        - 80-89 percent third degree T32.98
        - 90-99 percent third degree T32.99
  - upper limb (axilla) (scapular region) T22.40
    - above elbow —*see* Corrosion, above elbow
    - axilla —*see* Corrosion, axilla
    - elbow —*see* Corrosion, elbow
    - first degree T22.50
    - forearm —*see* Corrosion, forearm
    - hand —*see* Corrosion, hand
    - interscapular region —*see* Corrosion, back, upper

- **Corrosion** *(continued)*
  - upper limb *(continued)*
    - multiple sites T22.499
      - first degree T22.599
      - left T22.492
        - first degree T22.592
        - second degree T22.692
        - third degree T22.792
      - right T22.491
        - first degree T22.591
        - second degree T22.691
        - third degree T22.791
      - second degree T22.699
      - third degree T22.799
    - scapular region —*see* Corrosion, scapular region
    - second degree T22.60
    - shoulder —*see* Corrosion, shoulder
    - third degree T22.70
    - wrist —*see* Corrosion, hand
  - uterus T28.8
  - vagina T28.8
  - vulva —*see* Corrosion, genital organs, external, female
  - wrist T23.479
    - first degree T23.579
    - left T23.472
      - first degree T23.572
      - second degree T23.672
      - third degree T23.772
    - multiple sites with hand T23.499
      - first degree T23.599
      - left T23.492
        - first degree T23.592
        - second degree T23.692
        - third degree T23.792
      - right T23.491
        - first degree T23.591
        - second degree T23.691
        - third degree T23.791
      - second degree T23.699
      - third degree T23.799
    - right T23.471
      - first degree T23.571
      - second degree T23.671
      - third degree T23.771
    - second degree T23.679
    - third degree T23.779
- **Corrosive burn** —*see* Corrosion
- **Corsican fever** —*see* Malaria
- **Cortical** —*see* condition
- **Cortico-adrenal** —*see* condition
- **Coryza** (acute) J00
  - with grippe or influenza —*see* Influenza, with, respiratory manifestations NEC
  - syphilitic
    - congenital (chronic) A50.05
- **Costen's syndrome or complex** M26.69
- **Costiveness** —*see* Constipation
- **Costochondritis** M94.0
- **Cotard's syndrome** F22
- **Cot death** R99
- **Cotia virus** B08.8
- **Cotton wool spots** (retinal) H35.81
- **Cotungo's disease** —*see* Sciatica
- **Cough** (affected) (chronic) (epidemic) (nervous) R05
  - with hemorrhage —*see* Hemoptysis
  - bronchial R05
    - with grippe or influenza —*see* Influenza, with, respiratory manifestations NEC
  - functional F45.8
  - hysterical F45.8
  - laryngeal, spasmodic R05

- **Cough** *(continued)*
  - psychogenic F45.8
  - smokers' J41.0
  - tea taster's B49
- **Counseling** (for) Z71.9
  - abuse NEC
    - perpetrator Z69.82
    - victim Z69.81
  - alcohol abuser Z71.41
    - family Z71.42
  - child abuse
    - nonparental
      - perpetrator Z69.021
      - victim Z69.020
    - parental
      - perpetrator Z69.011
      - victim Z69.010
  - consanguinity Z71.89
  - contraceptive Z30.09
  - dietary Z71.3
  - drug abuser Z71.51
    - family member Z71.52
  - family Z71.89
  - fertility preservation (prior to cancer therapy) (prior to removal of gonads) Z31.62
  - for non-attending third party Z71.0
    - related to sexual behavior or orientation Z70.2
  - genetic NEC Z31.5
  - health (advice) (education) (instruction) —*see* Counseling, medical
  - human immunodeficiency virus (HIV) Z71.7
  - impotence Z70.1
  - insulin pump use Z46.81
  - medical (for) Z71.9
    - boarding school resident Z59.3
    - consanguinity Z71.89
    - feared complaint and no disease found Z71.1
    - human immunodeficiency virus (HIV) Z71.7
    - institutional resident Z59.3
    - on behalf of another Z71.0
      - related to sexual behavior or orientation Z70.2
    - person living alone Z60.2
    - specified reason NEC Z71.89
  - natural family planning
    - procreative Z31.61
    - to avoid pregnancy Z30.02
  - perpetrator (of)
    - abuse NEC Z69.82
    - child abuse
      - non-parental Z69.021
      - parental Z69.011
    - rape NEC Z69.82
    - spousal abuse Z69.12
  - procreative NEC Z31.69
    - fertility preservation (prior to cancer therapy) (prior to removal of gonads) Z31.62
    - using natural family planning Z31.61
  - promiscuity Z70.1
  - rape victim Z69.81
  - religious Z71.81
  - sex, sexual (related to) Z70.9
    - attitude (s) Z70.0
    - behavior or orientation Z70.1
    - combined concerns Z70.3
    - non-responsiveness Z70.1
    - on behalf of third party Z70.2
    - specified reason NEC Z70.8
  - specified reason NEC Z71.89
  - spiritual Z71.81
  - spousal abuse (perpetrator) Z69.12
    - victim Z69.11
  - substance abuse Z71.89
    - alcohol Z71.41
    - drug Z71.51
    - tobacco Z71.6

- **Counseling** *(continued)*
  - tobacco use Z71.6
  - use (of)
    - insulin pump Z46.81
  - victim (of)
    - abuse Z69.81
    - child abuse
      - by parent Z69.010
      - non-parental Z69.020
    - rape NEC Z69.81
- **Coupled rhythm** R00.8
- **Couvelaire syndrome or uterus** (complicating delivery) O45.8X-
- **Cowperitis** —*see* Urethritis
- **Cowper's gland** —*see* condition
- **Cowpox** B08.010
  - due to vaccination T88.1
- **Coxa**
  - magna M91.4-
  - plana M91.2-
  - valga (acquired) —*see also* Deformity, limb, specified type NEC, thigh
    - congenital Q65.81
    - sequelae (late effect) of rickets E64.3
  - vara (acquired) —*see also* Deformity, limb, specified type NEC, thigh
    - congenital Q65.82
    - sequelae (late effect) of rickets E64.3
- **Coxalgia, coxalgic** (nontuberculous) —*see also* Pain, joint, hip
  - tuberculous A18.02
- **Coxitis** —*see* Monoarthritis, hip
- **Coxsackie** (virus) (infection) B34.1
  - as cause of disease classified elsewhere B97.11
  - carditis B33.20
  - central nervous system NEC A88.8
  - endocarditis B33.21
  - enteritis A08.39
  - meningitis (aseptic) A87.0
  - myocarditis B33.22
  - pericarditis B33.23
  - pharyngitis B08.5
  - pleurodynia B33.0
  - specific disease NEC B33.8
- **Crabs, meaning pubic lice** B85.3
- **Crack baby** P04.41
- **Cracked nipple** N64.0
  - associated with
    - lactation O92.13
    - pregnancy O92.11-
    - puerperium O92.12
- **Cracked tooth** K03.81
- **Cradle cap** L21.0
- **Craft neurosis** F48.8
- **Cramp** (s) R25.2
  - abdominal —*see* Pain, abdominal
  - bathing T75.1
  - colic R10.83
    - psychogenic F45.8
  - due to immersion T75.1
  - fireman T67.2
  - heat T67.2
  - immersion T75.1
  - intestinal —*see* Pain, abdominal
    - psychogenic F45.8
  - leg, sleep related G47.62
  - limb (lower) (upper) NEC R25.2
    - sleep related G47.62
  - linotypist's F48.8
    - organic G25.89
  - muscle (limb) (general) R25.2
    - due to immersion T75.1
    - psychogenic F45.8

Cramp *(continued)*
  occupational (hand) F48.8
    organic G25.89
  salt-depletion E87.1
  sleep related, leg G47.62
  stoker's T67.2
  swimmer's T75.1
  telegrapher's F48.8
    organic G25.89
  typist's F48.8
    organic G25.89
  uterus N94.89
    menstrual —*see* Dysmenorrhea
  writer's F48.8
    organic G25.89

Cranial —*see* condition

Craniocleidodysostosis Q74.0

Craniofenestria (skull) Q75.8

Craniolacunia (skull) Q75.8

Craniopagus Q89.4

Craniopathy, metabolic M85.2

Craniopharyngeal —*see* condition

Craniopharyngioma D44.4

Craniorachischisis (totalis) Q00.1

Cranioschisis Q75.8

Craniostenosis Q75.0

Craniosynostosis Q75.0

Craniotabes (cause unknown) M83.8
  neonatal P96.3
  rachitic E64.3
  syphilitic A50.56

Cranium —*see* condition

Craw-craw —*see* Onchocerciasis

Creaking joint —*see* Derangement, joint, specified type NEC

Creeping
  eruption B76.9
  palsy or paralysis G12.22

Crenated tongue K14.8

Creotoxism A05.9

Crepitus
  caput Q75.8
  joint —*see* Derangement, joint, specified type NEC

Crescent or conus choroid, congenital Q14.3

CREST syndrome M34.1

Cretin, cretinism (congenital) (endemic) (nongoitrous) (sporadic) E00.9
  pelvis
    with disproportion (fetopelvic) O33.0
      causing obstructed labor O65.0
  type
    hypothyroid E00.1
    mixed E00.2
    myxedematous E00.1
    neurological E00.0

Creutzfeldt-Jakob disease or syndrome (with dementia) A81.00
  familial A81.09
  iatrogenic A81.09
  specified NEC A81.09
  sporadic A81.09
  variant (vCJD) A81.01

Crib death R99

Cribriform hymen Q52.3

Cri-du-chat syndrome Q93.4

Crigler-Najjar disease or syndrome E80.5

Crime, victim of Z65.4

Crimean hemorrhagic fever A98.0

Criminalism F60.2

Crisis
  abdomen R10.0
  acute reaction F43.0
  addisonian E27.2
  adrenal (cortical) E27.2
  celiac K90.0
  Dietl's N13.8
  emotional —*see also* Disorder, adjustment
    acute reaction to stress F43.0
    specific to childhood and adolescence F93.8
  glaucomatocyclitic —*see* Glaucoma, secondary, inflammation
  heart —*see* Failure, heart
  nitritoid I95.2
    correct substance properly administered —*see* Table of Drugs and Chemicals, by drug, adverse effect
    overdose or wrong substance given or taken —*see* Table of Drugs and Chemicals, by drug, poisoning
  oculogyric H51.8
    psychogenic F45.8
  Pel's (tabetic) A52.11
  psychosexual identity F64.2
  renal N28.0
  sickle-cell D57.00
    with
      acute chest syndrome D57.01
      splenic sequestration D57.02
  state (acute reaction) F43.0
  tabetic A52.11
  thyroid —*see* Thyrotoxicosis with thyroid storm
  thyrotoxic —*see* Thyrotoxicosis with thyroid storm

Crocq's disease (acrocyanosis) I73.89

Crohn's disease —*see* Enteritis, regional

Crooked septum, nasal J34.2

Cross syndrome E70.328

Crossbite (anterior) (posterior) M26.24

Cross-eye —*see* Strabismus, convergent concomitant

Croup, croupous (catarrhal) (infectious) (inflammatory) (nondiphtheritic) J05.0
  bronchial J20.9
  diphtheritic A36.2
  false J38.5
  spasmodic J38.5
    diphtheritic A36.2
  stridulous J38.5
    diphtheritic A36.2

Crouzon's disease Q75.1

Crowding, tooth, teeth, fully erupted M26.31

CRST syndrome M34.1

Cruchet's disease A85.8

Cruelty in children —*see also* Disorder, conduct

Crural ulcer —*see* Ulcer, lower limb

Crush, crushed, crushing T14.8
  abdomen S38.1
  ankle S97.0-
  arm (upper) (and shoulder) S47.-
  axilla —*see* Crush, arm
  back, lower S38.1
  buttock S38.1
  cheek S07.0
  chest S28.0

Crush, crushed, crushing *(continued)*
  cranium S07.1
  ear S07.0
  elbow S57.0-
  extremity
    lower
      ankle —*see* Crush, ankle
      below knee —*see* Crush, leg
      foot —*see* Crush, foot
      hip —*see* Crush, hip
      knee —*see* Crush, knee
      thigh —*see* Crush, thigh
      toe —*see* Crush, toe
    upper
      below elbow S67.9-
      elbow —*see* Crush, elbow
      finger —*see* Crush, finger
      forearm —*see* Crush, forearm
      hand —*see* Crush, hand
      thumb —*see* Crush, thumb
      upper arm —*see* Crush, arm
      wrist —*see* Crush, wrist
  face S07.0
  finger (s) S67.1-
    with hand (and wrist) —*see* Crush, hand, specified site NEC
    index S67.19-
    little S67.19-
    middle S67.19-
    ring S67.19-
    thumb —*see* Crush, thumb
  foot S97.8-
    toe —*see* Crush, toe
  forearm S57.8-
  genitalia, external
    female S38.002
      vagina S38.03
      vulva S38.03
    male S38.001
      penis S38.01
      scrotum S38.02
      testis S38.02
  hand (except fingers alone) S67.2-
    with wrist S67.4-
  head S07.9
    specified NEC S07.8
  heel —*see* Crush, foot
  hip S77.0-
    with thigh S77.2-
  internal organ (abdomen, chest, or pelvis) NEC T14.8
  knee S87.0-
  labium (majus) (minus) S38.03
  larynx S17.0
  leg (lower) S87.8-
    knee —*see* Crush, knee
  lip S07.0
  lower
    back S38.1
    leg —*see* Crush, leg
  neck S17.9
  nerve —*see* Injury, nerve
  nose S07.0
  pelvis S38.1
  penis S38.01
  scalp S07.8
  scapular region —*see* Crush, arm
  scrotum S38.02
  severe, unspecified site T14.8
  shoulder (and upper arm) —*see* Crush, arm
  skull S07.1
  syndrome (complication of trauma) T79.5
  testis S38.02
  thigh S77.1-
    with hip S77.2-
  throat S17.8
  thumb S67.0-
    with hand (and wrist) —*see* Crush, hand, specified site NEC

Crush, crushed, crushing *(continued)*
  toe (s) S97.10-
    great S97.11-
    lesser S97.12-
  trachea S17.0
  vagina S38.03
  vulva S38.03
  wrist S67.3-
    with hand S67.4-

Crusta lactea L21.0

Crusts R23.4

Crutch paralysis —*see* Injury, brachial plexus

Cruveilhier-Baumgarten cirrhosis, disease or syndrome K74.69

Cruveilhier's atrophy or disease G12.8

Crying (constant) (continuous) (excessive)
  child, adolescent, or adult R45.83
  infant (baby) (newborn) R68.11

Cryofibrinogenemia D89.2

Cryoglobulinemia (essential) (idiopathic) (mixed) (primary) (purpura) (secondary) (vasculitis) D89.1
  with lung involvement D89.1 *[J99]*

Cryptitis (anal) (rectal) K62.89

Cryptococcosis, cryptococcus (infection) (neoformans) B45.9
  bone B45.3
  cerebral B45.1
  cutaneous B45.2
  disseminated B45.7
  generalized B45.7
  meningitis B45.1
  meningocerebralis B45.1
  osseous B45.3
  pulmonary B45.0
  skin B45.2
  specified NEC B45.8

Cryptopapillitis (anus) K62.89

Cryptophthalmos Q11.2
  syndrome Q87.0

Cryptorchid, cryptorchism, cryptorchidism Q53.9
  bilateral Q53.20
    abdominal Q53.21
    perineal Q53.22
  unilateral Q53.10
    abdominal Q53.11
    perineal Q53.12

Cryptosporidiosis A07.2
  hepatobiliary B88.8
  respiratory B88.8

Cryptostromosis J67.6

Crystalluria R82.99

Cubitus
  congenital Q68.8
  valgus (acquired) M21.0-
    congenital Q68.8
    sequelae (late effect) of rickets E64.3
  varus (acquired) M21.1-
    congenital Q68.8
    sequelae (late effect) of rickets E64.3

Cultural deprivation or shock Z60.3

Curling esophagus K22.4

Curling's ulcer —*see* Ulcer, peptic, acute

Curschmann (-Batten) (-Steinert) **disease or syndrome** G71.11

Curse, Ondine's —*see* Apnea, sleep

Curvature
- organ or site, congenital NEC —*see* Distortion
- penis (lateral) Q55.61
- Pott's (spinal) A18.01
- radius, idiopathic, progressive (congenital) Q74.0
- spine (acquired) (angular) (idiopathic) (incorrect) (postural) —*see* Dorsopathy, deforming
  - congenital Q67.5
  - due to or associated with
    - Charcot-Marie-Tooth disease —*see also* subcategory M49.8 *[G60.0]*
    - osteitis
      - deformans M88.88
      - fibrosa cystica —*see also* subcategory M49.8 *[E21.0]*
    - tuberculosis (Pott's curvature) A18.01
  - sequelae (late effect) of rickets E64.3
  - tuberculous A18.01

Cushingoid due to steroid therapy E24.2
- correct substance properly administered —*see* Table of Drugs and Chemicals, by drug, adverse effect
- overdose or wrong substance given or taken —*see* Table of Drugs and Chemicals, by drug, poisoning

Cushing's
- syndrome or disease E24.9
  - drug-induced E24.2
  - iatrogenic E24.2
  - pituitary-dependent E24.0
  - specified NEC E24.8
- ulcer —*see* Ulcer, peptic, acute

Cusp, Carabelli - omit code

Cut (external) —*see also* Laceration
- muscle —*see* Injury, muscle

Cutaneous —*see also* condition
- hemorrhage R23.3
- larva migrans B76.9

Cutis —*see also* condition
- hyperelastica Q82.8
  - acquired L57.4
- laxa (hyperelastica) —*see* Dermatolysis
- marmorata R23.8
- osteosis L94.2
- pendula —*see* Dermatolysis
- rhomboidalis nuchae L57.2
- verticis gyrata Q82.8
  - acquired L91.8

Cyanosis R23.0
- due to
  - patent foramen botalli Q21.1
  - persistent foramen ovale Q21.1
- enterogenous D74.8
- paroxysmal digital —*see* Raynaud's disease
  - with gangrene I73.01
- retina, retinal H35.89

Cyanotic heart disease I24.9
- congenital Q24.9

Cycle
- anovulatory N97.0
- menstrual, irregular N92.6

Cyclencephaly Q04.9

Cyclical vomiting —*see also* Vomiting, cyclical G43.A0
- psychogenic F50.8

Cyclitis —*see also* Iridocyclitis H20.9
- chronic —*see* Iridocyclitis, chronic
- Fuchs' heterochromic H20.81-
- granulomatous —*see* Iridocyclitis, chronic
- lens-induced —*see* Iridocyclitis, lens-induced
- posterior H30.2-

Cycloid personality F34.0

Cyclophoria H50.54

Cyclopia, cyclops Q87.0

Cyclopism Q87.0

Cyclosporiasis A07.4

Cyclothymia F34.0

Cyclothymic personality F34.0

Cyclotropia H50.41-

Cylindroma —*see also* Neoplasm, malignant, by site
- eccrine dermal —*see* Neoplasm, skin, benign
- skin —*see* Neoplasm, skin, benign

Cylindruria R82.99

Cynanche
- diphtheritic A36.2
- tonsillaris J36

Cynophobia F40.218

Cynorexia R63.2

Cyphosis —*see* Kyphosis

Cyprus fever —*see* Brucellosis

Cyst (colloid) (mucous) (simple) (retention)
- adenoid (infected) J35.8
- adrenal gland E27.8
  - congenital Q89.1
- air, lung J98.4
- allantoic Q64.4
- alveolar process (jaw bone) M27.40
- amnion, amniotic O41.8X-
- anterior
  - chamber (eye) —*see* Cyst, iris
  - nasopalatine K09.1
- antrum J34.1
- anus K62.89
- apical (tooth) (periodontal) K04.8
- appendix K38.8
- arachnoid, brain (acquired) G93.0
  - congenital Q04.6
- arytenoid J38.7
- Baker's M71.2-
  - ruptured M66.0
  - tuberculous A18.02
- Bartholin's gland N75.0
- bile duct (common) (hepatic) K83.5
- bladder (multiple) (trigone) N32.89
- blue dome (breast) —*see* Cyst, breast
- bone (local) NEC M85.60
  - aneurysmal M85.50
    - ankle M85.57-
    - foot M85.57-
    - forearm M85.53-
    - hand M85.54-
    - jaw M27.49
    - lower leg M85.56-
    - multiple site M85.59
    - neck M85.58
    - rib M85.58
    - shoulder M85.51-
    - skull M85.58
    - specified site NEC M85.58
    - thigh M85.55-
    - toe M85.57-
    - upper arm M85.52-
    - vertebra M85.58

Cyst *(continued)*
- bone *(continued)*
  - solitary M85.40
    - ankle M85.47-
    - fibula M85.46-
    - foot M85.47-
    - hand M85.44-
    - humerus M85.42-
    - jaw M27.49
    - neck M85.48
    - pelvis M85.45-
    - radius M85.43-
    - rib M85.48
    - shoulder M85.41-
    - skull M85.48
    - specified site NEC M85.48
    - tibia M85.46-
    - toe M85.47-
    - ulna M85.43-
    - vertebra M85.48
  - specified type NEC M85.60
    - ankle M85.67-
    - foot M85.67-
    - forearm M85.63-
    - hand M85.64-
    - jaw M27.40
      - developmental (nonodontogenic) K09.1
        - odontogenic K09.0
      - latent M27.0
    - lower leg M85.66-
    - multiple site M85.69
    - neck M85.68
    - rib M85.68
    - shoulder M85.61-
    - skull M85.68
    - specified site NEC M85.68
    - thigh M85.65-
    - toe M85.67-
    - upper arm M85.62-
    - vertebra M85.68
- brain (acquired) G93.0
  - congenital Q04.6
  - hydatid B67.99 *[G94]*
  - third ventricle (colloid), congenital Q04.6
- branchial (cleft) Q18.0
- branchiogenic Q18.0
- breast (benign) (blue dome) (pedunculated) (solitary) N60.0-
  - involution —*see* Dysplasia, mammary, specified type NEC
  - sebaceous —*see* Dysplasia, mammary, specified type NEC
- broad ligament (benign) N83.8
- bronchogenic (mediastinal) (sequestration) J98.4
  - congenital Q33.0
- buccal K09.8
- bulbourethral gland N36.8
- bursa, bursal NEC M71.30
  - with rupture —*see* Rupture, synovium
  - ankle M71.37-
  - elbow M71.32-
  - foot M71.37-
  - hand M71.34-
  - hip M71.35-
  - multiple sites M71.39
  - pharyngeal J39.2
  - popliteal space —*see* Cyst, Baker's
  - shoulder M71.31-
  - specified site NEC M71.38
  - wrist M71.33-
- calcifying odontogenic D16.5
  - upper jaw (bone) (maxilla) D16.4
- canal of Nuck (female) N94.89
  - congenital Q52.4
- canthus —*see* Cyst, conjunctiva
- carcinomatous —*see* Neoplasm, malignant, by site
- cauda equina G95.89

Cyst *(continued)*
- cavum septi pellucidi —*see* Cyst, brain
- celomic (pericardium) Q24.8
- cerebellopontine (angle) —*see* Cyst, brain
- cerebellum —*see* Cyst, brain
- cerebral —*see* Cyst, brain
- cervical lateral Q18.1
- cervix NEC N88.8
  - embryonic Q51.6
  - nabothian N88.8
- chiasmal optic NEC —*see* Disorder, optic, chiasm
- chocolate (ovary) N80.1
- choledochus, congenital Q44.4
- chorion O41.8X-
- choroid plexus G93.0
- ciliary body —*see* Cyst, iris
- clitoris N90.7
- colon K63.89
- common (bile) duct K83.5
- congenital NEC Q89.8
  - adrenal gland Q89.1
  - epiglottis Q31.8
  - esophagus Q39.8
  - fallopian tube Q50.4
  - kidney Q61.00
    - more than one (multiple) Q61.02
      - specified as polycystic Q61.3
        - adult type Q61.2
        - infantile type NEC Q61.19
          - collecting duct dilation Q61.11
    - solitary Q61.01
  - larynx Q31.8
  - liver Q44.6
  - lung Q33.0
  - mediastinum Q34.1
  - ovary Q50.1
  - oviduct Q50.4
  - periurethral (tissue) Q64.79
  - prepuce Q55.69
  - salivary gland (any) Q38.4
  - sublingual Q38.6
  - submaxillary gland Q38.6
  - thymus (gland) Q89.2
  - tongue Q38.3
  - ureterovesical orifice Q62.8
  - vulva Q52.79
- conjunctiva H11.44-
- cornea H18.89-
- corpora quadrigemina G93.0
- corpus
  - albicans N83.29
  - luteum (hemorrhagic) (ruptured) N83.1
- Cowper's gland (benign) (infected) N36.8
- cranial meninges G93.0
- craniobuccal pouch E23.6
- craniopharyngeal pouch E23.6
- cystic duct K82.8
- Cysticercus —*see* Cysticercosis
- Dandy-Walker Q03.1
  - with spina bifida —*see* Spina bifida
- dental (root) K04.8
  - developmental K09.0
  - eruption K09.0
  - primordial K09.0
- dentigerous (mandible) (maxilla) K09.0
- dermoid —*see* Neoplasm, benign, by site
  - with malignant transformation C56.-
  - implantation
    - external area or site (skin) NEC L72.0
    - iris —*see* Cyst, iris, implantation
    - vagina N89.8
    - vulva N90.7

Cyst *(continued)*
- dermoid —*see* Neoplasm, benign, by site *(continued)*
  - mouth K09.8
  - oral soft tissue K09.8
  - sacrococcygeal —*see* Cyst, pilonidal
- developmental K09.1
  - odontogenic K09.0
  - oral region (nonodontogenic) K09.1
  - ovary, ovarian Q50.1
- dura (cerebral) G93.0
  - spinal G96.19
- ear (external) Q18.1
- echinococcal —*see* Echinococcus
- embryonic
  - cervix uteri Q51.6
  - fallopian tube Q50.4
  - vagina Q51.6
- endometrium, endometrial (uterus) N85.8
  - ectopic —*see* Endometriosis
- enterogenous Q43.8
- epidermal, epidermoid (inclusion) (*see also* Cyst, skin) L72.0
  - mouth K09.8
  - oral soft tissue K09.8
- epididymis N50.3
- epiglottis J38.7
- epiphysis cerebri E34.8
- epithelial (inclusion) L72.0
- epoophoron Q50.5
- eruption K09.0
- esophagus K22.8
- ethmoid sinus J34.1
- external female genital organs NEC N90.7
- eye NEC H57.8
  - congenital Q15.8
- eyelid (sebaceous) H02.829
  - infected —*see* Hordeolum
  - left H02.826
    - lower H02.825
    - upper H02.824
  - right H02.823
    - lower H02.822
    - upper H02.821
- fallopian tube N83.8
  - congenital Q50.4
- fimbrial (twisted) Q50.4
- fissural (oral region) K09.1
- follicle (graafian) (hemorrhagic) N83.0
  - nabothian N88.8
- follicular (atretic) (hemorrhagic) (ovarian) N83.0
  - dentigerous K09.0
  - odontogenic K09.0
  - skin L72.9
    - specified NEC L72.8
- frontal sinus J34.1
- gallbladder K82.8
- ganglion —*see* Ganglion
- Gartner's duct Q52.4
- gingiva K09.0
- gland of Moll —*see* Cyst, eyelid
- globulomaxillary K09.1
- graafian follicle (hemorrhagic) N83.0
- granulosal lutein (hemorrhagic) N83.1
- hemangiomatous D18.00
  - intra-abdominal D18.03
  - intracranial D18.02
  - skin D18.01
  - specified site NEC D18.09
- hydatid —*see also* Echinococcus B67.90
  - brain B67.99 *[G94]*
  - liver —*see also* Cyst, liver, hydatid B67.8
  - lung NEC B67.99 *[J99]*

Cyst *(continued)*
- hydatid —*see also* Echinococcus *(continued)*
  - Morgagni
    - female Q50.5
    - male (epididymal) Q55.4
      - testicular Q55.29
  - specified site NEC B67.99
- hymen N89.8
  - embryonic Q52.4
- hypopharynx J39.2
- hypophysis, hypophyseal (duct) (recurrent) E23.6
  - cerebri E23.6
- implantation (dermoid)
  - external area or site (skin) NEC L72.0
  - iris —*see* Cyst, iris, implantation
  - vagina N89.8
  - vulva N90.7
- incisive canal K09.1
- inclusion (epidermal) (epithelial) (epidermoid) (squamous) L72.0
  - not of skin - code under Cyst, by site
- intestine (large) (small) K63.89
- intracranial —*see* Cyst, brain
- intraligamentous —*see also* Disorder, ligament
  - knee —*see* Derangement, knee
- intrasellar E23.6
- iris H21.309
  - exudative H21.31-
  - idiopathic H21.30-
  - implantation H21.32-
  - parasitic H21.33-
  - pars plana (primary) H21.34-
    - exudative H21.35-
- jaw (bone) M27.40
  - aneurysmal M27.49
  - developmental (odontogenic) K09.0
  - fissural K09.1
  - hemorrhagic M27.49
  - traumatic M27.49
- joint NEC —*see* Disorder, joint, specified type NEC
- kidney (acquired) N28.1
  - calyceal —*see* Hydronephrosis
  - congenital Q61.00
  - more than one (multiple) Q61.02
    - specified as polycystic Q61.3
      - adult type (autosomal dominant) Q61.2
      - infantile type (autosomal recessive) NEC Q61.19
        - collecting duct dilation Q61.11
  - pyelogenic —*see* Hydronephrosis
  - simple N28.1
  - solitary (single) Q61.01
    - acquired N28.1
- labium (majus) (minus) N90.7
  - sebaceous N90.7
- lacrimal —*see also* Disorder, lacrimal system, specified NEC
  - gland H04.13-
  - passages or sac —*see* Disorder, lacrimal system, specified NEC
- larynx J38.7
- lateral periodontal K09.0
- lens H27.8
  - congenital Q12.8
- lip (gland) K13.0
- liver (idiopathic) (simple) K76.89
  - congenital Q44.6
  - hydatid B67.8
    - granulosus B67.0
    - multilocularis B67.5
- lung J98.4
  - congenital Q33.0
  - giant bullous J43.9

Cyst *(continued)*
- lutein N83.1
- lymphangiomatous D18.1
- lymphoepithelial, oral soft tissue K09.8
- macula —*see* Degeneration, macula, hole
- malignant —*see* Neoplasm, malignant, by site
- mammary gland —*see* Cyst, breast
- mandible M27.40
  - dentigerous K09.0
  - radicular K04.8
- maxilla M27.40
  - dentigerous K09.0
  - radicular K04.8
- medial, face and neck Q18.8
- median
  - anterior maxillary K09.1
  - palatal K09.1
- mediastinum, congenital Q34.1
- meibomian (gland) —*see* Chalazion
  - infected —*see* Hordeolum
- membrane, brain G93.0
- meninges (cerebral) G93.0
  - spinal G96.19
- meniscus, knee —*see* Derangement, knee, meniscus, cystic
- mesentery, mesenteric K66.8
  - chyle I89.8
- mesonephric duct
  - female Q50.5
  - male Q55.4
- milk N64.89
- Morgagni (hydatid)
  - female Q50.5
  - male (epididymal) Q55.4
    - testicular Q55.29
- mouth K09.8
- Müllerian duct Q50.4
  - appendix testis Q55.29
  - cervix Q51.6
  - fallopian tube Q50.4
  - female Q50.4
  - male Q55.29
  - prostatic utricle Q55.4
  - vagina (embryonal) Q52.4
- multilocular (ovary) D39.10
  - benign —*see* Neoplasm, benign, by site
- myometrium N85.8
- nabothian (follicle) (ruptured) N88.8
- nasoalveolar K09.1
- nasolabial K09.1
- nasopalatine (anterior) (duct) K09.1
- nasopharynx J39.2
- neoplastic —*see* Neoplasm, uncertain behavior, by site
  - benign —*see* Neoplasm, benign, by site
- nervous system NEC G96.8
- neuroenteric (congenital) Q06.8
- nipple —*see* Cyst, breast
- nose (turbinates) J34.1
  - sinus J34.1
- odontogenic, developmental K09.0
- omentum (lesser) K66.8
  - congenital Q45.8
- ora serrata —*see* Cyst, retina, ora serrata
- oral
  - region K09.9
    - developmental (nonodontogenic) K09.1
    - specified NEC K09.8
  - soft tissue K09.9
    - specified NEC K09.8
- orbit H05.81-
- ovary, ovarian (twisted) N83.20
  - adherent N83.20
  - chocolate N80.1

Cyst *(continued)*
- ovary, ovarian *(continued)*
  - corpus
    - albicans N83.29
    - luteum (hemorrhagic) N83.1
  - dermoid D27.9
  - developmental Q50.1
  - due to failure of involution NEC N83.20
  - endometrial N80.1
  - follicular (graafian) (hemorrhagic) N83.0
  - hemorrhagic N83.20
  - in pregnancy or childbirth O34.8-
    - with obstructed labor O65.5
  - multilocular D39.10
  - pseudomucinous D27.9
  - retention N83.29
  - serous N83.20
  - specified NEC N83.29
  - theca lutein (hemorrhagic) N83.1
  - tuberculous A18.18
- oviduct N83.8
- palate (median) (fissural) K09.1
- palatine papilla (jaw) K09.1
- pancreas, pancreatic (hemorrhagic) (true) K86.2
  - congenital Q45.2
  - false K86.3
- paralabral
  - hip M24.85-
  - shoulder S43.43-
- paramesonephric duct Q50.4
  - female Q50.4
  - male Q55.29
- paranephric N28.1
- paraphysis, cerebri, congenital Q04.6
- parasitic B89
- parathyroid (gland) E21.4
- paratubal N83.8
- paraurethral duct N36.8
- paroophoron Q50.5
- parotid gland K11.6
- parovarian Q50.5
- pelvis, female N94.89
  - in pregnancy or childbirth O34.8-
    - causing obstructed labor O65.5
- penis (sebaceous) N48.89
- periapical K04.8
- pericardial (congenital) Q24.8
  - acquired (secondary) I31.8
- pericoronal K09.0
- periodontal K04.8
  - lateral K09.0
- peripelvic (lymphatic) N28.1
- peritoneum K66.8
  - chylous I89.8
- periventricular, acquired, newborn P91.1
- pharynx (wall) J39.2
- pilar L72.11
- pilonidal (infected) (rectum) L05.91
  - with abscess L05.01
  - malignant C44.59-
- pituitary (duct) (gland) E23.6
- placenta O43.19-
- pleura J94.8
- popliteal —*see* Cyst, Baker's
- porencephalic Q04.6
  - acquired G93.0
- postanal (infected) —*see* Cyst, pilonidal
- postmastoidectomy cavity (mucosal) —*see* Complications, postmastoidectomy, cyst
- preauricular Q18.1
- prepuce N47.4
  - congenital Q55.69
- primordial (jaw) K09.0
- prostate N42.83
- pseudomucinous (ovary) D27.9
- pupillary, miotic H21.27-

Cyst *(continued)*
radicular (residual) K04.8
radiculodental K04.8
ranular K11.8
Rathke's pouch E23.6
rectum (epithelium) (mucous) K62.89
renal —*see* Cyst, kidney
residual (radicular) K04.8
retention (ovary) N83.29
salivary gland K11.6
retina H33.19-
ora serrata H33.11-
parasitic H33.12-
retroperitoneal K68.9
sacrococcygeal (dermoid) —*see* Cyst, pilonidal
salivary gland or duct (mucous extravasation or retention) K11.6
Sampson's N80.1
sclera H15.89
scrotum L72.9
sebaceous L72.3
sebaceous (duct) (gland) L72.3
breast —*see* Dysplasia, mammary, specified type NEC
eyelid —*see* Cyst, eyelid
genital organ NEC
female N94.89
male N50.8
scrotum L72.3
semilunar cartilage (knee) (multiple) —*see* Derangement, knee, meniscus, cystic
seminal vesicle N50.8
serous (ovary) N83.20
sinus (accessory) (nasal) J34.1
Skene's gland N36.8
skin L72.9
breast —*see* Dysplasia, mammary, specified type NEC
epidermal, epidermoid L72.0
epithelial L72.0
eyelid —*see* Cyst, eyelid
genital organ NEC
female N90.7
male N50.8
inclusion L72.0
scrotum L72.9
sebaceous L72.3
sweat gland or duct L74.8
solitary
bone —*see* Cyst, bone, solitary
jaw M27.40
kidney N28.1
spermatic cord N50.8
sphenoid sinus J34.1
spinal meninges G96.19
spleen NEC D73.4
congenital Q89.09
hydatid —*see also* Echinococcus B67.99 *[D77]*
Stafne's M27.0
subarachnoid intrasellar R93.0
subcutaneous, pheomycotic (chromomycotic) B43.2
subdural (cerebral) G93.0
spinal cord G96.19
sublingual gland K11.6
submandibular gland K11.6
submaxillary gland K11.6
suburethral N36.8
suprarenal gland E27.8
suprasellar —*see* Cyst, brain
sweat gland or duct L74.8
synovial —*see also* Cyst, bursa
ruptured —*see* Rupture, synovium
tarsal —*see* Chalazion
tendon (sheath) —*see* Disorder, tendon, specified type NEC
testis N44.2
tunica albuginea N44.1
theca lutein (ovary) N83.1

Cyst *(continued)*
Thornwaldt's J39.2
thymus (gland) E32.8
thyroglossal duct (infected) (persistent) Q89.2
thyrolingual duct (infected) (persistent) Q89.2
thyroid (gland) E04.1
tongue K14.8
tonsil J35.8
tooth —*see* Cyst, dental
Tornwaldt's J39.2
trichilemmal (proliferating) L72.12
trichodermal L72.12
tubal (fallopian) N83.8
inflammatory —*see* Salpingitis, chronic
tubo-ovarian N83.8
inflammatory N70.13
tunica
albuginea testis N44.1
vaginalis N50.8
turbinate (nose) J34.1
Tyson's gland N48.89
urachus, congenital Q64.4
ureter N28.89
ureterovesical orifice N28.89
urethra, urethral (gland) N36.8
uterine ligament N83.8
uterus (body) (corpus) (recurrent) N85.8
embryonic Q51.818
cervix Q51.6
vagina, vaginal (implantation) (inclusion) (squamous cell) (wall) N89.8
embryonic Q52.4
vallecula, vallecular (epiglottis) J38.7
vesical (orifice) N32.89
vitreous body H43.89
vulva (implantation) (inclusion) N90.7
congenital Q52.79
sebaceous gland N90.7
vulvovaginal gland N90.7
wolffian
female Q50.5
male Q55.4

Cystadenocarcinoma —*see* Neoplasm, malignant, by site
bile duct C22.1
endometrioid —*see* Neoplasm, malignant, by site
specified site —*see* Neoplasm, malignant, by site
unspecified site
female C56.9
male C61
mucinous
papillary
specified site —*see* Neoplasm, malignant, by site
unspecified site C56.9
specified site —*see* Neoplasm, malignant, by site
unspecified site C56.9
papillary
mucinous
specified site —*see* Neoplasm, malignant, by site
unspecified site C56.9
pseudomucinous
specified site —*see* Neoplasm, malignant, by site
unspecified site C56.9
serous
specified site —*see* Neoplasm, malignant, by site
unspecified site C56.9
specified site —*see* Neoplasm, malignant, by site
unspecified site C56.9

Cyst *(continued)*
pseudomucinous
papillary
specified site —*see* Neoplasm, malignant, by site
unspecified site C56.9
specified site —*see* Neoplasm, malignant, by site
unspecified site C56.9
serous
papillary
specified site —*see* Neoplasm, malignant, by site
unspecified site C56.9
specified site —*see* Neoplasm, malignant, by site
unspecified site C56.9

Cystadenofibroma
clear cell —*see* Neoplasm, benign, by site
endometrioid D27.9
borderline malignancy D39.1-
malignant C56.-
mucinous
specified site —*see* Neoplasm, benign, by site
unspecified site D27.9
serous
specified site —*see* Neoplasm, benign, by site
unspecified site D27.9
specified site —*see* Neoplasm, benign, by site
unspecified site D27.9

Cystadenoma —*see also* Neoplasm, benign, by site
bile duct D13.4
endometrioid —*see* Neoplasm, benign, by site
borderline malignancy —*see* Neoplasm, uncertain behavior, by site
malignant —*see* Neoplasm, malignant, by site
mucinous
borderline malignancy
ovary C56.-
specified site NEC —*see* Neoplasm, uncertain behavior, by site
unspecified site C56.9
papillary
borderline malignancy
ovary C56.-
specified site NEC —*see* Neoplasm, uncertain behavior, by site
unspecified site C56.9
specified site —*see* Neoplasm, benign, by site
unspecified site D27.9
specified site —*see* Neoplasm, benign, by site
unspecified site D27.9
papillary
borderline malignancy
ovary C56.-
specified site NEC —*see* Neoplasm, uncertain behavior, by site
unspecified site C56.9
lymphomatosum
specified site —*see* Neoplasm, benign, by site
unspecified site D11.9
mucinous
borderline malignancy
ovary C56.-
specified site NEC —*see* Neoplasm, uncertain behavior, by site

Cystadenoma *(continued)*
papillary *(continued)*
mucinous *(continued)*
borderline malignancy *(continued)*
unspecified site C56.9
specified site —*see* Neoplasm, benign, by site
unspecified site D27.9
pseudomucinous
borderline malignancy
ovary C56.-
specified site NEC —*see* Neoplasm, uncertain behavior, by site
unspecified site C56.9
specified site —*see* Neoplasm, benign, by site
unspecified site D27.9
serous
borderline malignancy
ovary C56.-
specified site NEC —*see* Neoplasm, uncertain behavior, by site
unspecified site C56.9
specified site —*see* Neoplasm, benign, by site
unspecified site D27.9
specified site —*see* Neoplasm, benign, by site
unspecified site D27.9
pseudomucinous
borderline malignancy
ovary C56.-
specified site NEC —*see* Neoplasm, uncertain behavior, by site
unspecified site C56.9
papillary
borderline malignancy
ovary C56.-
specified site NEC —*see* Neoplasm, uncertain behavior, by site
unspecified site C56.9
specified site —*see* Neoplasm, benign, by site
unspecified site D27.9
specified site —*see* Neoplasm, benign, by site
unspecified site D27.9
serous
borderline malignancy
ovary C56.-
specified site NEC —*see* Neoplasm, uncertain behavior, by site
unspecified site C56.9
papillary
borderline malignancy
ovary C56.-
specified site NEC —*see* Neoplasm, uncertain behavior, by site
unspecified site C56.9
specified site —*see* Neoplasm, benign, by site
unspecified site D27.9
specified site —*see* Neoplasm, benign, by site
unspecified site D27.9

Cystathionine synthase deficiency E72.11

Cystathioninemia E72.19

Cystathioninuria E72.19

Cystic —*see also* condition
breast (chronic) —*see* Mastopathy, cystic
corpora lutea (hemorrhagic) N83.1
duct —*see* condition

Cystic *(continued)*
- eyeball (congenital) Q11.0
- fibrosis *—see* Fibrosis, cystic
- kidney (congenital) Q61.9
  - adult type Q61.2
  - infantile type NEC Q61.19
    - collecting duct dilatation Q61.11
  - medullary Q61.5
- liver, congenital Q44.6
- lung disease J98.4
  - congenital Q33.0
- mastitis, chronic *—see* Mastopathy, cystic
- medullary, kidney Q61.5
- meniscus *—see* Derangement, knee, meniscus, cystic
- ovary N83.20

Cysticercosis, cysticerciasis B69.9
- with
  - epileptiform fits B69.0
  - myositis B69.81
- brain B69.0
- central nervous system B69.0
- cerebral B69.0
- ocular B69.1
- specified NEC B69.89

Cysticercus cellulose infestation *—see* Cysticercosis

Cystinosis (malignant) E72.04

Cystinuria E72.01

Cystitis (exudative) (hemorrhagic) (septic) (suppurative) N30.90
- with
  - fibrosis *—see* Cystitis, chronic, interstitial
  - hematuria N30.91
  - leukoplakia *—see* Cystitis, chronic, interstitial
  - malakoplakia *—see* Cystitis, chronic, interstitial
  - metaplasia *—see* Cystitis, chronic, interstitial
  - prostatitis N41.3
- acute N30.00
  - with hematuria N30.01
  - of trigone N30.30
    - with hematuria N30.31
- allergic *—see* Cystitis, specified type NEC
- amebic A06.81
- bilharzial B65.9 *[N33]*
- blennorrhagic (gonococcal) A54.01
- bullous *—see* Cystitis, specified type NEC
- calculous N21.0
- chlamydial A56.01
- chronic N30.20
  - with hematuria N30.21
  - interstitial N30.10
    - with hematuria N30.11
  - of trigone N30.30
    - with hematuria N30.31
  - specified NEC N30.20
    - with hematuria N30.21
- cystic (a) *—see* Cystitis, specified type NEC
- diphtheritic A36.85
- echinococcal
  - granulosus B67.39
  - multilocularis B67.69
- emphysematous *—see* Cystitis, specified type NEC
- encysted *—see* Cystitis, specified type NEC
- eosinophilic *—see* Cystitis, specified type NEC
- follicular *—see* Cystitis, of trigone
- gangrenous *—see* Cystitis, specified type NEC

Cystitis *(continued)*
- glandularis *—see* Cystitis, specified type NEC
- gonococcal A54.01
- incrusted *—see* Cystitis, specified type NEC
- interstitial (chronic) *—see* Cystitis, chronic, interstitial
- irradiation N30.40
  - with hematuria N30.41
- irritation *—see* Cystitis, specified type NEC
- malignant *—see* Cystitis, specified type NEC
- of trigone N30.30
  - with hematuria N30.31
- panmural *—see* Cystitis, chronic, interstitial
- polyposa *—see* Cystitis, specified type NEC
- prostatic N41.3
- puerperal (postpartum) O86.22
- radiation *—see* Cystitis, irradiation
- specified type NEC N30.80
  - with hematuria N30.81
- subacute *—see* Cystitis, chronic
- submucous *—see* Cystitis, chronic, interstitial
- syphilitic (late) A52.76
- trichomonal A59.03
- tuberculous A18.12
- ulcerative *—see* Cystitis, chronic, interstitial

Cystocele (-urethrocele)
- female N81.10
  - with prolapse of uterus *—see* Prolapse, uterus
  - lateral N81.12
  - midline N81.11
  - paravaginal N81.12
- in pregnancy or childbirth O34.8-
  - causing obstructed labor O65.5
- male N32.89

Cystolithiasis N21.0

Cystoma *—see also* Neoplasm, benign, by site
- endometrial, ovary N80.1
- mucinous
  - specified site *—see* Neoplasm, benign, by site
  - unspecified site D27.9
- serous
  - specified site *—see* Neoplasm, benign, by site
  - unspecified site D27.9
- simple (ovary) N83.29

Cystoplegia N31.2

Cystoptosis N32.89

Cystopyelitis *—see* Pyelonephritis

Cystorrhagia N32.89

Cystosarcoma phyllodes D48.6-
- benign D24-
- malignant *—see* Neoplasm, breast, malignant

Cystostomy
- attention to Z43.5
- complication *—see* Complications, cystostomy
- status Z93.50
  - appendico-vesicostomy Z93.52
  - cutaneous Z93.51
  - specified NEC Z93.59

Cystourethritis *—see* Urethritis

Cystourethrocele *—see also* Cystocele
- female N81.10
  - with uterine prolapse *—see* Prolapse, uterus
  - lateral N81.12

Cystourethrocele *(continued)*
- female *(continued)*
  - midline N81.11
  - paravaginal N81.12
- male N32.89

Cytomegalic inclusion disease
- congenital P35.1

Cytomegalovirus infection B25.9

Cytomycosis (reticuloendothelial) B39.4

Cytopenia D75.9
- refractory
  - with multilineage dysplasia D46.A
    - and ring sideroblasts (RCMD RS) D46.B

Czerny's disease (periodic hydrarthrosis of the knee) *—see* Effusion, joint, knee

D

Daae (-Finsen) **disease** (epidemic pleurodynia) B33.0

Da Costa's syndrome F45.8

Dabney's grip B33.0

Dacryoadenitis, dacryadenitis H04.00-
- acute H04.01-
- chronic H04.02-

Dacryocystitis H04.30-
- acute H04.32-
- chronic H04.41-
- neonatal P39.1
- phlegmonous H04.31-
- syphilitic A52.71
  - congenital (early) A50.01
- trachomatous, active A71.1
  - sequelae (late effect) B94.0

Dacryocystoblenorrhea *—see* Inflammation, lacrimal, passages, chronic

Dacryocystocele *—see* Disorder, lacrimal system, changes

Dacryolith, dacryolithiasis H04.51-

Dacryoma *—see* Disorder, lacrimal system, changes

Dacryopericystitis *—see* Dacryocystitis

Dacryops H04.11-

Dacryostenosis *—see also* Stenosis, lacrimal
- congenital Q10.5

Dactylitis
- bone *—see* Osteomyelitis
- sickle-cell D57.00
  - Hb C D57.219
  - Hb SS D57.00
  - specified NEC D57.819
- skin L08.9
- syphilitic A52.77
- tuberculous A18.03

Dactylolysis spontanea (ainhum) L94.6

Dactylosymphysis Q70.9
- fingers *—see* Syndactylism, complex, fingers
- toes *—see* Syndactylism, complex, toes

Damage
- arteriosclerotic *—see* Arteriosclerosis
- brain (nontraumatic) G93.9
  - anoxic, hypoxic G93.1
    - resulting from a procedure G97.82
  - child NEC G80.9
  - due to birth injury P11.2
- cardiorenal (vascular) *—see* Hypertension, cardiorenal

Damage *(continued)*
- cerebral NEC *—see* Damage, brain
- coccyx, complicating delivery O71.6
- coronary *—see* Disease, heart, ischemic
- eye, birth injury P15.3
- liver (nontraumatic) K76.9
  - alcoholic K70.9
  - due to drugs *—see* Disease, liver, toxic
  - toxic *—see* Disease, liver, toxic
- medication T88.7
- pelvic
  - joint or ligament, during delivery O71.6
  - organ NEC
    - during delivery O71.5
    - following ectopic or molar pregnancy O08.6
- renal *—see* Disease, renal
- subendocardium, subendocardial *—see* Degeneration, myocardial
- vascular I99.9

Dana-Putnam syndrome (subacute combined sclerosis with pernicious anemia) *—see* Degeneration, combined

Danbolt (-Cross) **syndrome** (acrodermatitis enteropathica) E83.2

Dandruff L21.0

Dandy-Walker syndrome Q03.1
- with spina bifida *—see* Spina bifida

Danlos' syndrome Q79.6

Darier (-White) disease (congenital) Q82.8
- meaning erythema annulare centrifugum L53.1

Darier-Roussy sarcoid D86.3

Darling's disease or histoplasmosis B39.4

Darwin's tubercle Q17.8

Dawson's (inclusion body) **encephalitis** A81.1

De Beurmann (-Gougerot) **disease** B42.1

De la Tourette's syndrome F95.2

De Lange's syndrome Q87.1

De Morgan's spots (senile angiomas) I78.1

De Quervain's
- disease (tendon sheath) M65.4
- syndrome E34.51
- thyroiditis (subacute granulomatous thyroiditis) E06.1

De Toni-Fanconi (-Debré) **syndrome** E72.09
- with cystinosis E72.04

Dead
- fetus, retained (mother) O36.4
  - early pregnancy O02.1
- labyrinth H83.2
- ovum, retained O02.0

Deaf nonspeaking NEC H91.3

Deafmutism (acquired) (congenital) **NEC** H91.3
- hysterical F44.6
- syphilitic, congenital *—see also* subcategory H94.8 *[A50.09]*

Deafness (acquired) (complete) (hereditary) (partial) H91.9-
- with blue sclera and fragility of bone Q78.0
- auditory fatigue *—see* Deafness, specified type NEC

Defect, defective *(continued)*
reduction
limb Q73.8
lower Q72.9-
absence —*see* Agenesis, leg
foot —*see* Agenesis, foot
longitudinal
femur Q72.4-
fibula Q72.6-
tibia Q72.5-
specified type NEC Q72.89-
split foot Q72.7-
specified type NEC Q73.8
upper Q71.9-
absence —*see* Agenesis, arm
forearm —*see* Agenesis, forearm
hand —*see* Agenesis, hand
lobster-claw hand Q71.6-
longitudinal
radius Q71.4-
ulna Q71.5-
specified type NEC Q71.89-
renal pelvis Q63.8
obstructive Q62.39
respiratory system, congenital Q34.9
restoration, dental K08.50
specified NEC K08.59
retinal nerve bundle fibers H35.89
septal (heart) NOS Q21.9
acquired (atrial) (auricular) (ventricular) (old) I51.0
atrial Q21.1
concurrent with acute myocardial infarction —*see* Infarct, myocardium
following acute myocardial infarction (current complication) I23.1
ventricular —*see also* Defect, ventricular septal Q21.0
sinus venosus Q21.1
speech R47.9
developmental F80.9
specified NEC R47.89
Taussig-Bing (aortic transposition and overriding pulmonary artery) Q20.1
teeth, wedge K03.1
vascular (local) I99.9
congenital Q27.9
ventricular septal Q21.0
concurrent with acute myocardial infarction —*see* Infarct, myocardium
following acute myocardial infarction (current complication) I23.2
in tetralogy of Fallot Q21.3
vision NEC H54.7
visual field H53.40
bilateral
heteronymous H53.47
homonymous H53.46-
generalized contraction H53.48-
localized
arcuate H53.43-
scotoma (central area) H53.41-
blind spot area H53.42-
sector H53.43-
specified type NEC H53.45-
voice R49.9
specified NEC R49.8
wedge, tooth, teeth (abrasion) K03.1

Deferentitis N49.1
gonorrheal (acute) (chronic) A54.23

Defibrination (syndrome) D65
antepartum —*see* Hemorrhage, antepartum, with coagulation defect, disseminated intravascular coagulation

Defibrination *(continued)*
following ectopic or molar pregnancy O08.1
intrapartum O67.0
newborn P60
postpartum O72.3

Deficiency, deficient
3-beta hydroxysteroid dehydrogenase E25.0
5-alpha reductase (with male pseudohermaphroditism) E29.1
11-hydroxylase E25.0
21-hydroxylase E25.0
abdominal muscle syndrome Q79.4
accelerator globulin (Ac G) (blood) D68.2
AC globulin (congenital) (hereditary) D68.2
acquired D68.4
acid phosphatase E83.39
activating factor (blood) D68.2
adenosine deaminase (ADA) D81.3
aldolase (hereditary) E74.19
alpha-1-antitrypsin E88.01
amino-acids E72.9
anemia —*see* Anemia
aneurin E51.9
antibody with
hyperimmunoglobulinemia D80.6
near-normal immunoglobins D80.6
antidiuretic hormone E23.2
anti-hemophilic
factor (A) D66
B D67
C D68.1
globulin (AHG) NEC D66
antithrombin (antithrombin III) D68.59
ascorbic acid E54
attention (disorder) (syndrome) F98.8
with hyperactivity —*see* Disorder, attention-deficit hyperactivity
autoprothrombin
I D68.2
II D67
C D68.2
beta-glucuronidase E76.29
biotin E53.8
biotin-dependent carboxylase D81.819
biotinidase D81.810
brancher enzyme (amylopectinosis) E74.03
calciferol E55.9
with
adult osteomalacia M83.8
rickets —*see* Rickets
calcium (dietary) E58
calorie, severe E43
with marasmus E41
and kwashiorkor E42
cardiac —*see* Insufficiency, myocardial
carnitine E71.40
due to
hemodialysis E71.43
inborn errors of metabolism E71.42
Valproic acid therapy E71.43
iatrogenic E71.43
muscle palmityltransferase E71.314
primary E71.41
secondary E71.448
carotene E50.9
central nervous system G96.8
ceruloplasmin (Wilson) E83.01
choline E53.8
Christmas factor D67
chromium E61.4

Deficiency, deficient *(continued)*
clotting (blood) —*see also* Deficiency, coagulation factor D68.9
clotting factor NEC (hereditary) —*see also* Deficiency, factor D68.2
coagulation NOS D68.9
with
ectopic pregnancy O08.1
molar pregnancy O08.1
acquired (any) D68.4
antepartum hemorrhage —*see* Hemorrhage, antepartum, with coagulation defect
clotting factor NEC —*see also* Deficiency, factor D68.2
due to
hyperprothrombinemia D68.4
liver disease D68.4
vitamin K deficiency D68.4
newborn, transient P61.6
postpartum O72.3
specified NEC D68.8
cognitive F09
color vision H53.50
achromatopsia H53.51
acquired H53.52
deuteranomaly H53.53
protanomaly H53.54
specified type NEC H53.59
tritanomaly H53.55
combined glucocorticoid and mineralocorticoid E27.49
contact factor D68.2
copper (nutritional) E61.0
corticoadrenal E27.40
primary E27.1
craniofacial axis Q75.0
cyanocobalamin E53.8
C1 esterase inhibitor (C1-INH) D84.1
debrancher enzyme (limit dextrinosis) E74.03
dehydrogenase
long chain/very long chain acyl CoA E71.310
medium chain acyl CoA E71.311
short chain acyl CoA E71.312
diet E63.9
dihydropyrimidine dehydrogenase (DPD) E88.89
disaccharidase E73.9
edema —*see* Malnutrition, severe
endocrine E34.9
energy-supply —*see* Malnutrition
enzymes, circulating NEC E88.09
ergosterol E55.9
with
adult osteomalacia M83.8
rickets —*see* Rickets
essential fatty acid (EFA) E63.0
factor —*see also* Deficiency, coagulation
Hageman D68.2
I (congenital) (hereditary) D68.2
II (congenital) (hereditary) D68.2
IX (congenital) (functional) (hereditary) (with functional defect) D67
multiple (congenital) D68.8
acquired D68.4
V (congenital) (hereditary) D68.2
VII (congenital) (hereditary) D68.2
VIII (congenital) (functional) (hereditary) (with functional defect) D66
with vascular defect D68.0
X (congenital) (hereditary) D68.2
XI (congenital) (hereditary) D68.1
XII (congenital) (hereditary) D68.2
XIII (congenital) (hereditary) D68.2

Deficiency, deficient *(continued)*
femoral, proximal focal (congenital) —*see* Defect, reduction, lower limb, longitudinal, femur
fibrin-stabilizing factor (congenital) (hereditary) D68.2
acquired D68.4
fibrinase D68.2
fibrinogen (congenital) (hereditary) D68.2
acquired D65
folate E53.8
folic acid E53.8
foreskin N47.3
fructokinase E74.11
fructose 1,6-diphosphatase E74.19
fructose-1-phosphate aldolase E74.19
galactokinase E74.29
galactose-1-phosphate uridyl transferase E74.29
gammaglobulin in blood D80.1
hereditary D80.0
glass factor D68.2
glucocorticoid E27.49
mineralocorticoid E27.49
glucose-6-phosphatase E74.01
glucose-6-phosphate dehydrogenase anemia D55.0
glucuronyl transferase E80.5
glycogen synthetase E74.09
gonadotropin (isolated) E23.0
growth hormone (idiopathic) (isolated) E23.0
Hageman factor D68.2
hemoglobin D64.9
hepatophosphorylase E74.09
homogentisate 1,2-dioxygenase E70.29
hormone
anterior pituitary (partial) NEC E23.0
growth E23.0
growth (isolated) E23.0
pituitary E23.0
testicular E29.1
hypoxanthine-(guanine)-phosphoribosyltransferase (HG-PRT) (total H-PRT) E79.1
immunity D84.9
cell-mediated D84.8
with thrombocytopenia and eczema D82.0
combined D81.9
humoral D80.9
IgA (secretory) D80.2
IgG D80.3
IgM D80.4
immuno —*see* Immunodeficiency
immunoglobulin, selective
A (IgA) D80.2
G (IgG) (subclasses) D80.3
M (IgM) D80.4
inositol (B complex) E53.8
intrinsic
factor (congenital) D51.0
sphincter N36.42
with urethral hypermobility N36.43
iodine E61.8
congenital syndrome —*see* Syndrome, iodine-deficiency, congenital
iron E61.1
anemia D50.9
kalium E87.6
kappa-light chain D80.8
labile factor (congenital) (hereditary) D68.2
acquired D68.4
lacrimal fluid (acquired) —*see also* Syndrome, dry eye
congenital Q10.6

Deficiency, deficient *(continued)*
lactase
congenital E73.0
secondary E73.1
Laki-Lorand factor D68.2
lecithin cholesterol acyltransferase E78.6
lipocaic K86.8
lipoprotein (familial) (high density) E78.6
liver phosphorylase E74.09
lysosomal alpha-1, 4 glucosidase E74.02
magnesium E61.2
major histocompatibility complex
class I D81.6
class II D81.7
manganese E61.3
menadione (vitamin K) E56.1
newborn P53
mental (familial) (hereditary) —*see* Disability, intellectual
methylenetetrahydrofolate reductase (MTHFR) E72.12
mineral NEC E61.8
mineralocorticoid E27.49
with glucocorticoid E27.49
molybdenum (nutritional) E61.5
moral F60.2
multiple nutrient elements E61.7
muscle
carnitine (palmityltransferase) E71.314
phosphofructokinase E74.09
myoadenylate deaminase E79.2
myocardial —*see* Insufficiency, myocardial
myophosphorylase E74.04
NADH diaphorase or reductase (congenital) D74.0
NADH-methemoglobin reductase (congenital) D74.0
natrium E87.1
niacin (amide) (-tryptophan) E52
nicotinamide E52
nicotinic acid E52
number of teeth —*see* Anodontia
nutrient element E61.9
multiple E61.7
specified NEC E61.8
nutrition, nutritional E63.9
sequelae —*see* Sequelae, nutritional deficiency
specified NEC E63.8
ornithine transcarbamylase E72.4
ovarian E28.39
oxygen —*see* Anoxia
pantothenic acid E53.8
parathyroid (gland) E20.9
perineum (female) N81.89
phenylalanine hydroxylase E70.1
phosphoenolpyruvate carboxykinase E74.4
phosphofructokinase E74.19
phosphomannomutuse E74.8
phosphomannose isomerase E74.8
phosphomannosyl mutase E74.8
phosphorylase kinase, liver E74.09
pituitary hormone (isolated) E23.0
plasma thromboplastin
antecedent (PTA) D68.1
component (PTC) D67
platelet NEC D69.1
constitutional D68.0
polyglandular E31.8
autoimmune E31.0
potassium (K) E87.6
prepuce N47.3
proaccelerin (congenital) (hereditary) D68.2
acquired D68.4

Deficiency, deficient *(continued)*
proconvertin factor (congenital) (hereditary) D68.2
acquired D68.4
protein —*see also* Malnutrition E46
anemia D53.0
C D68.59
S D68.59
prothrombin (congenital) (heredItary) D68.2
acquired D68.4
Prower factor D68.2
pseudocholinesterase E88.09
PTA(plasma thromboplastin antecedent) D68.1
PTC(plasma thromboplastin component) D67
purine nucleoside phosphorylase (PNP) D81.5
pyracin (alpha) (beta) E53.1
pyridoxal E53.1
pyridoxamine E53.1
pyridoxine (derivatives) E53.1
pyruvate
carboxylase E74.4
dehydrogenase E74.4
riboflavin (vitamin B2) E53.0
salt E87.1
secretion
ovary E28.39
salivary gland (any) K11.7
urine R34
selenium (dietary) E59
serum antitrypsin, familial E88.01
short stature homeobox gene (SHOX)
with
dyschondrosteosis Q78.8
short stature (idiopathic) E34.3
Turner's syndrome Q96.9
sodium (Na) E87.1
SPCA(factor VII) D68.2
sphincter, intrinsic N36.42
with urethral hypermobility N36.43
stable factor (congenital) (hereditary) D68.2
acquired D68.4
Stuart-Prower (factor X) D68.2
sucrase E74.39
sulfatase E75.29
sulfite oxidase E72.19
thiamin, thiaminic (chloride) E51.9
beriberi (dry) E51.11
wet E51.12
thrombokinase D68.2
newborn P53
thyroid (gland) —*see* Hypothyroidism
tocopherol E56.0
tooth bud K00.0
transcobalamine II (anemia) D51.2
vanadium E61.6
vascular I99.9
vasopressin E23.2
viosterol —*see* Deficiency, calciferol
vitamin (multiple) NOS E56.9
A E50.9
with
Bitot's spot (corneal) E50.1
follicular keratosis E50.8
keratomalacia E50.4
manifestations NEC E50.8
night blindness E50.5
scar of cornea, xerophthalmic E50.6
xeroderma E50.8
xerophthalmia E50.7
xerosis
conjunctival E50.0
and Bitot's spot E50.1
cornea E50.2
and ulceration E50.3
sequelae E64.1

Deficiency, deficient *(continued)*
vitamin *(continued)*
B (complex) NOS E53.9
with
beriberi (dry) E51.11
wet E51.12
pellagra E52
B1 NOS E51.9
beriberi (dry) E51.11
with circulatory system manifestations E51.11
wet E51.12
B12 *[E53.8]*
B2 (riboflavin) E53.0
B6 *[E53.1]*
C E54
sequelae E64.2
D E55.9
with
adult osteomalacia M83.8
rickets —*see* Rickets
25-hydroxylase E83.32
E E56.0
folic acid E53.8
G E53.0
group B E53.9
specified NEC E53.8
H (biotin) E53.8
K E56.1
of newborn P53
nicotinic E52
P E56.8
PP(pellagra-preventing) E52
specified NEC E56.8
thiamin E51.9
beriberi —*see* Beriberi
zinc, dietary E60

Deficit —*see also* Deficiency
attention and concentration R41.840
disorder —*see* Attention, deficit
cognitive communication R41.841
cognitive NEC R41.89
following
cerebral infarction I69.31
cerebrovascular disease I69.91
specified disease NEC I69.81
intracerebral hemorrhage I69.11
nontraumatic intracranial hemorrhage NEC I69.21
subarachnoid hemorrhage I69.01
concentration R41.840
executive function R41.844
frontal lobe R41.844
neurologic NEC R29.818
ischemic
reversible (RIND) I63.9
prolonged (PRIND) I63.9
oxygen R09.02
prolonged reversible ischemic neurologic (PRIND) I63.9
psychomotor R41.843
visuospatial R41.842

Deflection
radius —*see* Deformity, limb, specified type NEC, forearm
septum (acquired) (nasal) (nose) J34.2
spine —*see* Curvature, spine
turbinate (nose) J34.2

Defluvium
capillorum —*see* Alopecia
ciliorum —*see* Madarosis
unguium L60.8

Deformity Q89.9
abdomen, congenital Q89.9
abdominal wall
acquired M95.8
congenital Q79.59
acquired (unspecified site) M95.9
adrenal gland Q89.1

Deformity *(continued)*
alimentary tract, congenital Q45.9
upper Q40.9
ankle (joint) (acquired) —*see also* Deformity, limb, lower leg
abduction —*see* Contraction, joint, ankle
congenital Q68.8
contraction —*see* Contraction, joint, ankle
specified type NEC —*see* Deformity, limb, foot, specified NEC
anus (acquired) K62.89
congenital Q43.9
aorta (arch) (congenital) Q25.4
acquired I77.89
aortic
arch, acquired I77.89
cusp or valve (congenital) Q23.8
acquired —*see also* Endocarditis, aortic I35.8
arm (acquired) (upper) —*see also* Deformity, limb, upper arm
congenital Q68.8
forearm —*see* Deformity, limb, forearm
artery (congenital) (peripheral) NOS Q27.9
acquired I77.89
coronary (acquired) I25.9
congenital Q24.5
umbilical Q27.0
atrial septal Q21.1
auditory canal (external) (congenital) —*see also* Malformation, ear, external
acquired —*see* Disorder, ear, external, specified type NEC
auricle
ear (congenital) —*see also* Malformation, ear, external
acquired —*see* Disorder, pinna, deformity
back —*see* Dorsopathy, deforming
bile duct (common) (congenital) (hepatic) Q44.5
acquired K83.8
biliary duct or passage (congenital) Q44.5
acquired K83.8
bladder (neck) (trigone) (sphincter) (acquired) N32.89
congenital Q64.79
bone (acquired) NOS M95.9
congenital Q79.9
turbinate M95.0
brain (congenital) Q04.9
acquired G93.89
reduction Q04.3
breast (acquired) N64.89
congenital Q83.9
reconstructed N65.0
bronchus (congenital) Q32.4
acquired NEC J98.09
bursa, congenital Q79.9
canaliculi (lacrimalis) (acquired) —*see also* Disorder, lacrimal system, changes
congenital Q10.6
canthus, acquired —*see* Disorder, eyelid, specified type NEC
capillary (acquired) I78.8
cardiovascular system, congenital Q28.9
caruncle, lacrimal (acquired) —*see also* Disorder, lacrimal system, changes
congenital Q10.6
cascade, stomach K31.2
cecum (congenital) Q43.9
acquired K63.89

Deformity *(continued)*
- cerebral, acquired G93.89
  - congenital Q04.9
- cervix (uterus) (acquired) NEC N88.8
  - congenital Q51.9
- cheek (acquired) M95.2
  - congenital Q18.9
- chest (acquired) (wall) M95.4
  - congenital Q67.8
  - sequelae (late effect) of rickets E64.3
- chin (acquired) M95.2
  - congenital Q18.9
- choroid (congenital) Q14.3
  - acquired H31.8
  - plexus Q07.8
    - acquired G96.19
- cicatricial —*see* Cicatrix
- cilia, acquired —*see* Disorder, eyelid, specified type NEC
- clavicle (acquired) M95.8
  - congenital Q68.8
- clitoris (congenital) Q52.6
  - acquired N90.89
- clubfoot —*see* Clubfoot
- coccyx (acquired) M43.8
- colon (congenital) Q43.9
  - acquired K63.89
- concha (ear), congenital —*see also* Malformation, ear, external
  - acquired —*see* Disorder, pinna, deformity
- cornea (acquired) H18.70
  - congenital Q13.4
  - descemetocele —*see* Descemetocele
  - ectasia —*see* Ectasia, cornea
  - specified NEC H18.79-
  - staphyloma —*see* Staphyloma, cornea
- coronary artery (acquired) I25.9
  - congenital Q24.5
- cranium (acquired) —*see* Deformity, skull
- cricoid cartilage (congenital) Q31.8
  - acquired J38.7
- cystic duct (congenital) Q44.5
  - acquired K82.8
- Dandy-Walker Q03.1
  - with spina bifida —*see* Spina bifida
- diaphragm (congenital) Q79.1
  - acquired J98.6
- digestive organ NOS Q45.9
- ductus arteriosus Q25.0
- duodenal bulb K31.89
- duodenum (congenital) Q43.9
  - acquired K31.89
- dura —*see* Deformity, meninges
- ear (acquired) —*see also* Disorder, pinna, deformity
  - congenital (external) Q17.9
    - internal Q16.5
    - middle Q16.4
      - ossicles Q16.3
    - ossicles Q16.3
- ectodermal (congenital) NEC Q84.9
- ejaculatory duct (congenital) Q55.4
  - acquired N50.8
- elbow (joint) (acquired) —*see also* Deformity, limb, upper arm
  - congenital Q68.8
  - contraction —*see* Contraction, joint, elbow
- endocrine gland NEC Q89.2
- epididymis (congenital) Q55.4
  - acquired N50.8
- epiglottis (congenital) Q31.8
  - acquired J38.7
- esophagus (congenital) Q39.9
  - acquired K22.8
- eustachian tube (congenital) NEC Q17.8

Deformity *(continued)*
- eye, congenital Q15.9
- eyebrow (congenital) Q18.8
- eyelid (acquired) —*see also* Disorder, eyelid, specified type NEC
  - congenital Q10.3
- face (acquired) M95.2
  - congenital Q18.9
- fallopian tube, acquired N83.8
- femur (acquired) —*see* Deformity, limb, specified type NEC, thigh
- fetal
  - with fetopelvic disproportion O33.7
  - causing obstructed labor O66.3
- finger (acquired) M20.00-
  - boutonniere M20.02-
  - congenital Q68.1
  - flexion contracture —*see* Contraction, joint, hand
  - mallet finger M20.01-
  - specified NEC M20.09-
  - swan-neck M20.03-
- flexion (joint) (acquired) —*see also* Deformity, limb, flexion M21.20
  - congenital NOS Q74.9
    - hip Q65.89
- foot (acquired) —*see also* Deformity, limb, lower leg
  - cavovarus (congenital) Q66.1
  - congenital NOS Q66.9
    - specified type NEC Q66.89
  - specified type NEC —*see* Deformity, limb, foot, specified NEC
  - valgus (congenital) Q66.6
    - acquired —*see* Deformity, valgus, ankle
  - varus (congenital) NEC Q66.3
    - acquired —*see* Deformity, varus, ankle
- forearm (acquired) —*see also* Deformity, limb, forearm
  - congenital Q68.8
- forehead (acquired) M95.2
  - congenital Q75.8
- frontal bone (acquired) M95.2
  - congenital Q75.8
- gallbladder (congenital) Q44.1
  - acquired K82.8
- gastrointestinal tract (congenital) NOS Q45.9
  - acquired K63.89
- genitalia, genital organ (s) or system NEC
  - female (congenital) Q52.9
    - acquired N94.89
    - external Q52.70
  - male (congenital) Q55.9
    - acquired N50.8
- globe (eye) (congenital) Q15.8
  - acquired H44.89
- gum, acquired NEC K06.8
- hand (acquired) —*see* Deformity, limb, hand
  - congenital Q68.1
- head (acquired) M95.2
  - congenital Q75.8
- heart (congenital) Q24.9
  - septum Q21.9
    - auricular Q21.1
    - ventricular Q21.0
  - valve (congenital) NEC Q24.8
    - acquired —*see* Endocarditis
- heel (acquired) —*see* Deformity, foot
- hepatic duct (congenital) Q44.5
  - acquired K83.8
- hip (joint) (acquired) —*see also* Deformity, limb, thigh
  - congenital Q65.9
  - due to (previous) juvenile osteochondrosis —*see* Coxa, plana
  - flexion —*see* Contraction, joint, hip

Deformity *(continued)*
- hourglass —*see* Contraction, hourglass
- humerus (acquired) M21.82-
  - congenital Q74.0
- hypophyseal (congenital) Q89.2
- ileocecal (coil) (valve) (acquired) K63.89
  - congenital Q43.9
- ileum (congenital) Q43.9
  - acquired K63.89
- ilium (acquired) M95.5
  - congenital Q74.2
- integument (congenital) Q84.9
- intervertebral cartilage or disc (acquired) —*see* Disorder, disc, specified NEC
- intestine (large) (small) (congenital) NOS Q43.9
  - acquired K63.89
- intrinsic minus or plus (hand) —*see* Deformity, limb, specified type NEC, forearm
- iris (acquired) H21.89
  - congenital Q13.2
- ischium (acquired) M95.5
  - congenital Q74.2
- jaw (acquired) (congenital) M26.9
- joint (acquired) NEC M21.90
  - congenital Q68.8
  - elbow M21.92-
  - hand M21.94-
  - hip M21.95-
  - knee M21.96-
  - shoulder M21.92-
  - wrist M21.93-
- kidney (s) (calyx) (pelvis) (congenital) Q63.9
  - acquired N28.89
  - artery (congenital) Q27.2
    - acquired I77.89
- Klippel-Feil (brevicollis) Q76.1
- knee (acquired) NEC —*see also* Deformity, limb, lower leg
  - congenital Q68.2
- labium (majus) (minus) (congenital) Q52.79
  - acquired N90.89
- lacrimal passages or duct (congenital) NEC Q10.6
  - acquired —*see* Disorder, lacrimal system, changes
- larynx (muscle) (congenital) Q31.8
  - acquired J38.7
  - web (glottic) Q31.0
- leg (upper) (acquired) NEC —*see also* Deformity, limb, thigh
  - congenital Q68.8
  - lower leg —*see* Deformity, limb, lower leg
- lens (acquired) H27.8
  - congenital Q12.9
- lid (fold) (acquired) —*see also* Disorder, eyelid, specified type NEC
  - congenital Q10.3
- ligament (acquired) —*see* Disorder, ligament
  - congenital Q79.9
- limb (acquired) M21.90
  - clawfoot M21.53-
  - clawhand M21.51-
  - clubfoot M21.54-
  - clubhand M21.52-
  - congenital, except reduction deformity Q74.9
  - flat foot M21.4-
  - flexion M21.20
    - ankle M21.27-
    - elbow M21.22-
    - finger M21.24-
    - hip M21.25-

Deformity *(continued)*
- limb *(continued)*
  - flexion *(continued)*
    - knee M21.26-
    - shoulder M21.21-
    - toe M21.27-
    - wrist M21.23-
  - foot
    - claw —*see* Deformity, limb, clawfoot
    - club —*see* Deformity, limb, clubfoot
    - drop M21.37-
    - flat —*see* Deformity, limb, flat foot
    - specified NEC M21.6X-
  - forearm M21.93-
  - hand M21.94-
  - lower leg M21.96-
  - specified type NEC M21.80
    - forearm M21.83-
    - lower leg M21.86-
    - thigh M21.85-
    - upper arm M21.82-
  - thigh M21.95-
  - unequal length M21.70
    - short site is
      - femur M21.75-
      - fibula M21.76-
      - humerus M21.72-
      - radius M21.73-
      - tibia M21.76-
      - ulna M21.73-
  - upper arm M21.92-
  - valgus —*see* Deformity, valgus
  - varus —*see* Deformity, varus
  - wrist drop M21.33-
- lip (acquired) NEC K13.0
  - congenital Q38.0
- liver (congenital) Q44.7
  - acquired K76.89
- lumbosacral (congenital) (joint) (region) Q76.49
  - acquired M43.8
  - kyphosis —*see* Kyphosis, congenital
  - lordosis —*see* Lordosis, congenital
- lung (congenital) Q33.9
  - acquired J98.4
- lymphatic system, congenital Q89.9
- Madelung's (radius) Q74.0
- mandible (acquired) (congenital) M26.9
- maxilla (acquired) (congenital) M26.9
- meninges or membrane (congenital) Q07.9
  - cerebral Q04.8
    - acquired G96.19
  - spinal cord (congenital) G96.19
    - acquired G96.19
- metacarpus (acquired) —*see* Deformity, limb, forearm
  - congenital Q74.0
- metatarsus (acquired) —*see* Deformity, foot
  - congenital Q66.9
- middle ear (congenital) Q16.4
  - ossicles Q16.3
- mitral (leaflets) (valve) I05.8
  - parachute Q23.2
  - stenosis, congenital Q23.2
- mouth (acquired) K13.79
  - congenital Q38.6
- multiple, congenital NEC Q89.7
- muscle (acquired) M62.89
  - congenital Q79.9
    - sternocleidomastoid Q68.0
- musculoskeletal system (acquired) M95.9
  - congenital Q79.9
  - specified NEC M95.8

Deformity *(continued)*
- nail (acquired) L60.8
  - congenital Q84.6
- nasal —*see* Deformity, nose
- neck (acquired) M95.3
  - congenital Q18.9
    - sternocleidomastoid Q68.0
- nervous system (congenital) Q07.9
- nipple (congenital) Q83.9
  - acquired N64.89
- nose (acquired) (cartilage) M95.0
  - bone (turbinate) M95.0
  - congenital Q30.9
    - bent or squashed Q67.4
  - saddle M95.0
    - syphilitic A50.57
  - septum (acquired) J34.2
    - congenital Q30.8
  - sinus (wall) (congenital) Q30.8
    - acquired M95.0
  - syphilitic (congenital) A50.57
    - late A52.73
- ocular muscle (congenital) Q10.3
  - acquired —*see* Strabismus, mechanical
- opticociliary vessels (congenital) Q13.2
- orbit (eye) (acquired) H05.30
  - atrophy —*see* Atrophy, orbit
  - congenital Q10.7
  - due to
    - bone disease NEC H05.32-
    - trauma or surgery H05.33-
  - enlargement —*see* Enlargement, orbit
  - exostosis —*see* Exostosis, orbit
- organ of Corti (congenital) Q16.5
- ovary (congenital) Q50.39
  - acquired N83.8
- oviduct, acquired N83.8
- palate (congenital) Q38.5
  - acquired M27.8
  - cleft (congenital) —*see* Cleft, palate
- pancreas (congenital) Q45.3
  - acquired K86.8
- parathyroid (gland) Q89.2
- parotid (gland) (congenital) Q38.4
  - acquired K11.8
- patella (acquired) —*see* Disorder, patella, specified NEC
- pelvis, pelvic (acquired) (bony) M95.5
  - with disproportion (fetopelvic) O33.0
    - causing obstructed labor O65.0
  - congenital Q74.2
  - rachitic sequelae (late effect) E64.3
- penis (glans) (congenital) Q55.69
  - acquired N48.89
- pericardium (congenital) Q24.8
  - acquired —*see* Pericarditis
- pharynx (congenital) Q38.8
  - acquired J39.2
- pinna, acquired —*see also* Disorder, pinna, deformity
  - congenital Q17.9
- pituitary (congenital) Q89.2
- posture —*see* Dorsopathy, deforming
- prepuce (congenital) Q55.69
  - acquired N47.8
- prostate (congenital) Q55.4
  - acquired N42.89
- pupil (congenital) Q13.2
  - acquired —*see* Abnormality, pupillary
- pylorus (congenital) Q40.3
  - acquired K31.89
- rachitic (acquired), old or healed E64.3

Deformity *(continued)*
- radius (acquired) —*see also* Deformity, limb, forearm
  - congenital Q68.8
- rectum (congenital) Q43.9
  - acquired K62.89
- reduction (extremity) (limb), congenital —*see also* condition and site Q73.8
  - brain Q04.3
  - lower —*see* Defect, reduction, lower limb
  - upper —*see* Defect, reduction, upper limb
- renal —*see* Deformity, kidney
- respiratory system (congenital) Q34.9
- rib (acquired) M95.4
  - congenital Q76.6
    - cervical Q76.5
- rotation (joint) (acquired) —*see* Deformity, limb, specified site NEC
  - congenital Q74.9
  - hip —*see* Deformity, limb, specified type NEC, thigh
    - congenital Q65.89
- sacroiliac joint (congenital) Q74.2
  - acquired —*see* subcategory M43.8
- sacrum (acquired) —*see* subcategory M43.8
- saddle
  - back —*see* Lordosis
  - nose M95.0
    - syphilitic A50.57
- salivary gland or duct (congenital) Q38.4
  - acquired K11.8
- scapula (acquired) M95.8
  - congenital Q68.8
- scrotum (congenital) —*see also* Malformation, testis and scrotum
  - acquired N50.8
- seminal vesicles (congenital) Q55.4
  - acquired N50.8
- septum, nasal (acquired) J34.2
- shoulder (joint) (acquired) —*see* Deformity, limb, upper arm
  - congenital Q74.0
  - contraction —*see* Contraction, joint, shoulder
- sigmoid (flexure) (congenital) Q43.9
  - acquired K63.89
- skin (congenital) Q82.9
- skull (acquired) M95.2
  - congenital Q75.8
    - with
      - anencephaly Q00.0
      - encephalocele —*see* Encephalocele
      - hydrocephalus Q03.9
        - with spina bifida —*see* Spina bifida, by site, with hydrocephalus
      - microcephaly Q02
- soft parts, organs or tissues (of pelvis)
  - in pregnancy or childbirth NEC O34.8-
    - causing obstructed labor O65.5
- spermatic cord (congenital) Q55.4
  - acquired N50.8
    - torsion —*see* Torsion, spermatic cord
- spinal —*see* Dorsopathy, deforming
  - column (acquired) —*see* Dorsopathy, deforming
    - congenital Q67.5
  - cord (congenital) Q06.9
    - acquired G95.89
  - nerve root (congenital) Q07.9
- spine (acquired) —*see also* Dorsopathy, deforming
  - congenital Q67.5
  - rachitic E64.3

Deformity *(continued)*
- spine *(continued)*
  - specified NEC —*see* Dorsopathy, deforming, specified NEC
- spleen
  - acquired D73.89
  - congenital Q89.09
- Sprengel's (congenital) Q74.0
- sternocleidomastoid (muscle), congenital Q68.0
- sternum (acquired) M95.4
  - congenital NEC Q76.7
- stomach (congenital) Q40.3
  - acquired K31.89
- submandibular gland (congenital) Q38.4
- submaxillary gland (congenital) Q38.4
  - acquired K11.8
- talipes —*see* Talipes
- testis (congenital) —*see also* Malformation, testis and scrotum
  - acquired N44.8
    - torsion —*see* Torsion, testis
- thigh (acquired) —*see also* Deformity, limb, thigh
  - congenital NEC Q68.8
- thorax (acquired) (wall) M95.4
  - congenital Q67.8
  - sequelae of rickets E64.3
- thumb (acquired) —*see also* Deformity, finger
  - congenital NEC Q68.1
- thymus (tissue) (congenital) Q89.2
- thyroid (gland) (congenital) Q89.2
  - cartilage Q31.8
    - acquired J38.7
- tibia (acquired) —*see also* Deformity, limb, specified type NEC, lower leg
  - congenital NEC Q68.8
  - saber (syphilitic) A50.56
- toe (acquired) M20.6-
  - congenital Q66.9
  - hallux rigidus M20.2-
  - hallux valgus M20.1-
  - hallux varus M20.3-
  - hammer toe M20.4-
  - specified NEC M20.5X-
- tongue (congenital) Q38.3
  - acquired K14.8
- tooth, teeth K00.2
- trachea (rings) (congenital) Q32.1
  - acquired J39.8
- transverse aortic arch (congenital) Q25.4
- tricuspid (leaflets) (valve) I07.8
  - atresia or stenosis Q22.4
  - Ebstein's Q22.5
- trunk (acquired) M95.8
  - congenital Q89.9
- ulna (acquired) —*see also* Deformity, limb, forearm
  - congenital NEC Q68.8
- urachus, congenital Q64.4
- ureter (opening) (congenital) Q62.8
  - acquired N28.89
- urethra (congenital) Q64.79
  - acquired N36.8
- urinary tract (congenital) Q64.9
  - urachus Q64.4
- uterus (congenital) Q51.9
  - acquired N85.8
- uvula (congenital) Q38.5
- vagina (acquired) N89.8
  - congenital Q52.4
- valgus NEC M21.00
  - ankle M21.07-
  - elbow M21.02-
  - hip M21.05-
  - knee M21.06-

Deformity *(continued)*
- valve, valvular (congenital) (heart) Q24.8
  - acquired —*see* Endocarditis
- varus NEC M21.10
  - ankle M21.17-
  - elbow M21.12-
  - hip M21.15
  - knee M21.16-
  - tibia —*see* Osteochondrosis, juvenile, tibia
- vas deferens (congenital) Q55.4
  - acquired N50.8
- vein (congenital) Q27.9
  - great Q26.9
- vertebra —*see* Dorsopathy, deforming
- vertical talus (congenital) Q66.80
  - left foot Q66.82
  - right foot Q66.81
- vesicourethral orifice (acquired) N32.89
  - congenital NEC Q64.79
- vessels of optic papilla (congenital) Q14.2
- visual field (contraction) —*see* Defect, visual field
- vitreous body, acquired H43.89
- vulva (congenital) Q52.79
  - acquired N90.89
- wrist (joint) (acquired) —*see also* Deformity, limb, forearm
  - congenital Q68.8
  - contraction —*see* Contraction, joint, wrist

Degeneration, degenerative
- adrenal (capsule) (fatty) (gland) (hyaline) (infectional) E27.8
- amyloid —*see also* Amyloidosis E85.9
- anterior cornua, spinal cord G12.29
- anterior labral S43.49-
- aorta, aortic I70.0
  - fatty I77.89
- aortic valve (heart) —*see* Endocarditis, aortic
- arteriovascular —*see* Arteriosclerosis
- artery, arterial (atheromatous) (calcareous) —*see also* Arteriosclerosis
  - cerebral, amyloid E85.4 *[I68.0]*
  - medial —*see* Arteriosclerosis, extremities
- articular cartilage NEC —*see* Derangement, joint, articular cartilage, by site
- atheromatous —*see* Arteriosclerosis
- basal nuclei or ganglia G23.9
  - specified NEC G23.8
- bone NEC —*see* Disorder, bone, specified type NEC
- brachial plexus G54.0
- brain (cortical) (progressive) G31.9
  - alcoholic G31.2
  - arteriosclerotic I67.2
  - childhood G31.9
    - specified NEC G31.89
  - cystic G31.89
    - congenital Q04.6
  - in
    - alcoholism G31.2
    - beriberi E51.2
    - cerebrovascular disease I67.9
    - congenital hydrocephalus Q03.9
      - with spina bifida —*see also* Spina bifida
    - Fabry-Anderson disease E75.21
    - Gaucher's disease E75.22
    - Hunter's syndrome E76.1

Degeneration, degenerative *(continued)*
- brain *(continued)*
  - in *(continued)*
    - lipidosis
      - cerebral E75.4
      - generalized E75.6
    - mucopolysaccharidosis —*see* Mucopolysaccharidosis
    - myxedema E03.9 *[G32.89]*
    - neoplastic disease —*see also* Neoplasm D49.6 *[G32.89]*
    - Niemann-Pick disease E75.249 *[G32.89]*
    - sphingolipidosis E75.3 *[G32.89]*
    - vitamin B12 deficiency E53.8 *[G32.89]*
  - senile NEC G31.1
- breast N64.89
- Bruch's membrane —*see* Degeneration, choroid
- capillaries (fatty) I78.8
  - amyloid E85.8 *[I79.8]*
- cardiac —*see also* Degeneration, myocardial
  - valve, valvular —*see* Endocarditis
- cardiorenal —*see* Hypertension, cardiorenal
- cardiovascular —*see also* Disease, cardiovascular
  - renal —*see* Hypertension, cardiorenal
- cerebellar NOS G31.9
  - alcoholic G31.2
  - primary (hereditary) (sporadic) G11.9
- cerebral —*see* Degeneration, brain
- cerebrovascular I67.9
  - due to hypertension I67.4
- cervical plexus G54.2
- cervix N88.8
  - due to radiation (intended effect) N88.8
    - adverse effect or misadventure N99.89
- chamber angle H21.21-
- changes, spine or vertebra —*see* Spondylosis
- chorioretinal —*see also* Degeneration, choroid
  - hereditary H31.20
- choroid (colloid) (drusen) H31.10-
  - atrophy —*see* Atrophy, choroidal
  - hereditary —*see* Dystrophy, choroidal, hereditary
- ciliary body H21.22-
- cochlear H83.8
- combined (spinal cord) (subacute) E53.8 *[G32.0]*
  - with anemia (pernicious) D51.0 *[G32.0]*
    - due to dietary vitamin B12 deficiency D51.3 *[G32.0]*
  - in (due to)
    - vitamin B12 deficiency E53.8 *[G32.0]*
      - anemia D51.9 *[G32.0]*
- conjunctiva H11.10
  - concretions —*see* Concretion, conjunctiva
  - deposits —*see* Deposit, conjunctiva
  - pigmentations —*see* Pigmentation, conjunctiva
  - pinguecula —*see* Pinguecula
  - xerosis —*see* Xerosis, conjunctiva
- cornea H18.40
  - calcerous H18.43
    - band keratopathy H18.42-
  - familial, hereditary —*see* Dystrophy, cornea
  - hyaline (of old scars) H18.49
  - keratomalacia —*see* Keratomalacia

Degeneration, degenerative *(continued)*
- cornea *(continued)*
  - nodular H18.45-
  - peripheral H18.46-
  - senile H18.41-
  - specified type NEC H18.49
- cortical (cerebellar) (parenchymatous) G31.89
  - alcoholic G31.2
  - diffuse, due to arteriopathy I67.2
- corticobasal G31.85
- cutis L98.8
  - amyloid E85.4 *[L99]*
- dental pulp K04.2
- disc disease —*see* Degeneration, intervertebral disc NEC
- dorsolateral (spinal cord) —*see* Degeneration, combined
- extrapyramidal G25.9
- eye, macular —*see also* Degeneration, macula
  - congenital or hereditary —*see* Dystrophy, retina
- facet joints —*see* Spondylosis
- fatty
  - liver NEC K76.0
    - alcoholic K70.0
- grey matter (brain) (Alpers') G31.81
- heart —*see also* Degeneration, myocardial
  - amyloid E85.4 *[I43]*
  - atheromatous —*see* Disease, heart, ischemic, atherosclerotic
  - ischemic —*see* Disease, heart, ischemic
- hepatolenticular (Wilson's) E83.01
- hepatorenal K76.7
- hyaline (diffuse) (generalized)
  - localized —*see* Degeneration, by site
- infrapatellar fat pad M79.4
- intervertebral disc NOS
  - with
    - myelopathy —*see* Disorder, disc, with, myelopathy
    - radiculitis or radiculopathy —*see* Disorder, disc, with, radiculopathy
  - cervical, cervicothoracic —*see* Disorder, disc, cervical, degeneration
    - with
      - myelopathy —*see* Disorder, disc, cervical, with myelopathy
      - neuritis, radiculitis or radiculopathy —*see* Disorder, disc, cervical, with neuritis
  - lumbar region M51.36
    - with
      - myelopathy M51.06
      - neuritis, radiculitis, radiculopathy or sciatica M51.16
  - lumbosacral region M51.37
    - with
      - neuritis, radiculitis, radiculopathy or sciatica M51.17
  - sacrococcygeal region M53.3
  - thoracic region M51.34
    - with
      - myelopathy M51.04
      - neuritis, radiculitis, radiculopathy M51.14
  - thoracolumbar region M51.35
    - with
      - myelopathy M51.05
      - neuritis, radiculitis, radiculopathy M51.15

Degeneration, degenerative *(continued)*
- intestine, amyloid E85.4
- iris (pigmentary) H21.23-
- ischemic —*see* Ischemia
- joint disease —*see* Osteoarthritis
- kidney N28.89
  - amyloid E85.4 *[N29]*
  - cystic, congenital Q61.9
  - fatty N28.89
  - polycystic Q61.3
    - adult type (autosomal dominant) Q61.2
    - infantile type (autosomal recessive) NEC Q61.19
      - collecting duct dilatation Q61.11
- Kuhnt-Junius —*see also* Degeneration, macula H35.32
- lens —*see* Cataract
- lenticular (familial) (progressive) (Wilson's) (with cirrhosis of liver) E83.01
- liver (diffuse) NEC K76.89
  - amyloid E85.4 *[K77]*
  - cystic K76.89
    - congenital Q44.6
  - fatty NEC K76.0
    - alcoholic K70.0
  - hypertrophic K76.89
  - parenchymatous, acute or subacute K72.00
    - with coma K72.01
  - pigmentary K76.89
  - toxic (acute) K71.9
- lung J98.4
- lymph gland I89.8
  - hyaline I89.8
- macula, macular (acquired) (age-related) (senile) H35.30
  - angioid streaks H35.33
  - atrophic age-related H35.31
  - congenital or hereditary —*see* Dystrophy, retina
  - cystoid H35.35-
  - drusen H35.36-
  - exudative H35.32
  - hole H35.34-
  - nonexudative H35.31
  - puckering H35.37-
  - toxic H35.38-
- membranous labyrinth, congenital (causing impairment of hearing) Q16.5
- meniscus —*see* Derangement, meniscus
- mitral —*see* Insufficiency, mitral
- Mönckeberg's —*see* Arteriosclerosis, extremities
- motor centers, senile G31.1
- multi-system G90.3
- mural —*see* Degeneration, myocardial
- muscle (fatty) (fibrous) (hyaline) (progressive) M62.89
  - heart —*see* Degeneration, myocardial
- myelin, central nervous system G37.9
- myocardial, myocardium (fatty) (hyaline) (senile) I51.5
  - with rheumatic fever (conditions in I00) I09.0
    - active, acute or subacute I01.2
      - with chorea I02.0
    - inactive or quiescent (with chorea) I09.0
  - hypertensive —*see* Hypertension, heart
  - rheumatic —*see* Degeneration, myocardial, with rheumatic fever
  - syphilitic A52.06

Degeneration, degenerative *(continued)*
- nasal sinus (mucosa) J32.9
  - frontal J32.1
  - maxillary J32.0
- nerve —*see* Disorder, nerve
- nervous system G31.9
  - alcoholic G31.2
  - amyloid E85.4 *[G99.8]*
  - autonomic G90.9
  - fatty G31.89
  - specified NEC G31.89
- nipple N64.89
- olivopontocerebellar (hereditary) (familial) G23.8
- osseous labyrinth —*see* subcategory H83.8
- ovary N83.8
  - cystic N83.20
  - microcystic N83.20
- pallidal pigmentary (progressive) G23.0
- pancreas K86.8
  - tuberculous A18.83
- penis N48.89
- pigmentary (diffuse) (general)
  - localized —*see* Degeneration, by site
  - pallidal (progressive) G23.0
- pineal gland E34.8
- pituitary (gland) E23.6
- popliteal fat pad M79.4
- posterolateral (spinal cord) —*see* Degeneration, combined
- pulmonary valve (heart) I37.8
- pulp (tooth) K04.2
- pupillary margin H21.24-
- renal —*see* Degeneration, kidney
- retina H35.9
  - hereditary (cerebroretinal) (congenital) (juvenile) (macula) (peripheral) (pigmentary) —*see* Dystrophy, retina
  - Kuhnt-Junius —*see also* Degeneration, macula H35.32
  - macula (cystic) (exudative) (hole) (nonexudative) (pseudohole) (senile) (toxic) —*see* Degeneration, macula
  - peripheral H35.40
    - lattice H35.41-
    - microcystoid H35.42-
    - paving stone H35.43-
    - secondary
      - pigmentary H35.45-
      - vitreoretinal H35.46-
    - senile reticular H35.44-
  - pigmentary (primary) —*see also* Dystrophy, retina
    - secondary —*see* Degeneration, retina, peripheral, secondary
  - posterior pole —*see* Degeneration, macula
- saccule, congenital (causing impairment of hearing) Q16.5
- senile R54
  - brain G31.1
  - cardiac, heart or myocardium —*see* Degeneration, myocardial
  - motor centers G31.1
  - vascular —*see* Arteriosclerosis
- sinus (cystic) —*see also* Sinusitis
  - polypoid J33.1
- skin L98.8
  - amyloid E85.4 *[L99]*
  - colloid L98.8
- spinal (cord) G31.89
  - amyloid E85.4 *[G32.89]*
  - combined (subacute) —*see* Degeneration, combined
  - dorsolateral —*see* Degeneration, combined
  - familial NEC G31.89

- **Delivery** *(continued)*
  - cesarean *(continued)*
    - previous
      - cesarean delivery O34.21
      - surgery (to)
        - cervix O34.4-
        - gynecological NEC O34.8-
        - rectum O34.7-
        - uterus O34.29
        - vagina O34.6-
    - prolapse
      - arm or hand O32.2
      - uterus O34.52-
    - prolonged labor NOS O63.9
    - rectocele O34.8-
    - retroversion
      - uterus O34.53-
    - rigid
      - cervix O34.4-
      - pelvic floor O34.8-
      - perineum O34.7-
      - vagina O34.6-
      - vulva O34.7-
    - sacculation, pregnant uterus O34.59-
    - scar (s)
      - cervix O34.4-
      - cesarean delivery O34.21
      - uterus O34.29
    - Shirodkar suture in situ O34.3-
    - shoulder presentation O32.2
    - stenosis or stricture, cervix O34.4-
    - streptococcus B carrier state O99.824
    - transverse presentation or lie O32.2
    - tumor, pelvic organs or tissues NEC O34.8-
      - cervix O34.4-
    - umbilical cord presentation or prolapse O69.0
    - without indication O82
  - completely normal case O80
  - complicated O75.9
    - by
      - abnormal, abnormality (of)
        - forces of labor O62.9
          - specified type NEC O62.8
        - glucose O99.814
        - uterine contractions NOS O62.9
      - abruptio placentae —*see also* Abruptio placentae O45.9-
      - abuse
        - physical O9A.32
        - psychological O9A.52
        - sexual O9A.42
      - adherent placenta O72.0
        - without hemorrhage O73.0
      - alcohol use O99.314
      - anemia (pre-existing) O99.02
      - anesthetic death O74.8
      - annular detachment of cervix O71.3
      - atony, uterus O62.2
      - attempted vacuum extraction and forceps O66.5
      - Bandl's ring O62.4
      - bariatric surgery status O99.844
      - biliary tract disorder O26.62
      - bleeding —*see* Delivery, complicated by, hemorrhage
      - blood disorder NEC O99.12
      - cervical dystocia (hypotonic) O62.2
        - primary O62.0
        - secondary O62.1
      - circulatory system disorder O99.42
      - compression of cord (umbilical) NEC O69.2
      - condition NEC O99.89

- **Delivery** *(continued)*
  - complicated *(continued)*
    - by *(continued)*
      - contraction, contracted ring O62.4
      - cord (umbilical)
        - around neck
          - with compression O69.1
          - without compression O69.81
        - bruising O69.5
        - complication O69.9
          - specified NEC O69.89
        - compression NEC O69.2
        - entanglement O69.2
          - without compression O69.82
        - hematoma O69.5
        - presentation O69.0
        - prolapse O69.0
        - short O69.3
        - thrombosis (vessels) O69.5
        - vascular lesion O69.5
      - Couvelaire uterus O45.8X-
      - damage to (injury to) NEC
        - perineum O71.82
        - periurethral tissue O71.82
        - vulva O71.82
      - delay following rupture of membranes (spontaneous) —*see* Pregnancy, complicated by, premature rupture of membranes
      - depressed fetal heart tones O76
      - diabetes O24.92
        - gestational O24.429
          - diet controlled O24.420
          - insulin controlled O24.424
        - pre-existing O24.32
          - specified NEC O24.82
          - type 1 O24.02
          - type 2 O24.12
      - diastasis recti (abdominis) O71.89
      - dilatation
        - bladder O66.8
        - cervix incomplete, poor or slow O62.0
      - disease NEC O99.89
      - disruptio uteri —*see* Delivery, complicated by, rupture, uterus
      - drug use O99.324
      - dysfunction, uterus NOS O62.9
        - hypertonic O62.4
        - hypotonic O62.2
          - primary O62.0
          - secondary O62.1
        - incoordinate O62.4
      - eclampsia O15.1
      - embolism (pulmonary) —*see* Embolism, obstetric
      - endocrine, nutritional or metabolic disease NEC O99.284
      - failed
        - attempted vaginal birth after previous cesarean delivery O66.41
        - induction of labor O61.9
          - instrumental O61.1
          - mechanical O61.1
          - medical O61.0
          - specified NEC O61.8
          - surgical O61.1
        - trial of labor O66.40
      - female genital mutilation O65.5
      - fetal
        - abnormal acid-base balance O68
        - acidemia O68
        - acidosis O68

- **Delivery** *(continued)*
  - complicated *(continued)*
    - by *(continued)*
      - fetal *(continued)*
        - alkalosis O68
        - death, early O02.1
        - deformity O66.3
        - heart rate or rhythm (abnormal) (non-reassuring) O76
        - hypoxia O77.8
        - stress O77.9
          - due to drug administration O77.1
          - electrocardiographic evidence of O77.8
          - specified NEC O77.8
          - ultrasound evidence of O77.8
      - fever during labor O75.2
      - gastric banding status O99.844
      - gastric bypass status O99.844
      - gastrointestinal disease NEC O99.62
      - gestational diabetes O24.429
        - diet controlled O24.420
        - insulin (and diet) controlled O24.424
      - gonorrhea O98.22
      - hematoma O71.7
        - ischial spine O71.7
        - pelvic O71.7
        - vagina O71.7
        - vulva or perineum O71.7
      - hemorrhage (uterine) O67.9
        - associated with
          - afibrinogenemia O67.0
          - coagulation defect O67.0
          - hyperfibrinolysis O67.0
          - hypofibrinogenemia O67.0
        - due to
          - low-lying placenta O44.1-
          - placenta previa O44.1-
          - premature separation of placenta (normally implanted) —*see also* Abruptio placentae O45.9-
          - retained placenta O72.0
          - uterine leiomyoma O67.8
        - placenta NEC O67.8
        - postpartum NEC (atonic) (immediate) O72.1
          - with retained or trapped placenta O72.0
          - delayed O72.2
          - secondary O72.2
          - third stage O72.0
      - hourglass contraction, uterus O62.4
      - hypertension, hypertensive (pre-existing) —*see* Hypertension, complicated by, childbirth (labor)
      - hypotension O26.5-
      - incomplete dilatation (cervix) O62.0
      - incoordinate uterus contractions O62.4
      - inertia, uterus O62.2
        - during latent phase of labor O62.0
        - primary O62.0
        - secondary O62.1
      - infection (maternal) O98.92
        - carrier state NEC O99.834
        - gonorrhea O98.22
        - human immunodeficiency virus (HIV) O98.72
        - sexually transmitted NEC O98.32
        - specified NEC O98.82

- **Delivery** *(continued)*
  - complicated *(continued)*
    - by *(continued)*
      - infection *(continued)*
        - syphilis O98.12
        - tuberculosis O98.02
        - viral hepatitis O98.42
        - viral NEC O98.52
      - injury (to mother) —*see also* Delivery, complicated, by, damage to O71.9
        - nonobstetric O9A.22
          - caused by abuse —*see* Delivery, complicated by, abuse
      - intrauterine fetal death, early O02.1
      - inversion, uterus O71.2
      - laceration (perineal) O70.9
        - anus (sphincter) O70.4
          - with third degree laceration O70.2
            - with mucosa O70.3
          - without third degree laceration O70.4
        - bladder (urinary) O71.5
        - bowel O71.5
        - cervix (uteri) O71.3
        - fourchette O70.0
        - hymen O70.0
        - labia O70.0
        - pelvic
          - floor O70.1
          - organ NEC O71.5
        - perineum, perineal O70.9
          - first degree O70.0
          - fourth degree O70.3
          - muscles O70.1
          - second degree O70.1
          - skin O70.0
          - slight O70.0
          - third degree O70.2
        - peritoneum (pelvic) O71.5
        - rectovaginal (septum) (without perineal laceration) O71.4
          - with perineum O70.2
            - with anal or rectal mucosa O70.3
        - specified NEC O71.89
        - sphincter ani —*see* Delivery, complicated, by, laceration, anus (sphincter)
        - urethra O71.5
        - uterus O71.81
          - before labor O71.81
        - vagina, vaginal (deep) (high) (without perineal laceration) O71.4
          - with perineum O70.0
          - muscles, with perineum O70.1
        - vulva O70.0
      - liver disorder O26.62
      - malignancy O9A.12
      - malnutrition O25.2
      - malposition, malpresentation
        - placenta (with hemorrhage) O44.1-
          - without hemorrhage O44.0-
        - uterus or cervix O65.5
        - without obstruction —*see also* Delivery, complicated by, obstruction O32.9
          - breech O32.1
          - compound O32.6
          - face (brow) (chin) O32.3
          - footling O32.8
          - high head O32.4
          - oblique O32.2
          - specified NEC O32.8
          - transverse O32.2
          - unstable lie O32.0

Delivery *(continued)*
complicated *(continued)*
by *(continued)*
meconium in amniotic fluid O77.0
mental disorder NEC O99.344
metrorrhexis *—see* Delivery, complicated by, rupture, uterus
nervous system disorder O99.354
obesity (pre-existing) O99.214
obesity surgery status O99.844
obstetric trauma O71.9
specified NEC O71.89
obstructed labor
due to
breech (complete) (frank)
presentation O64.1
incomplete O64.8
brow presenation O64.3
buttock presentation O64.1
chin presentation O64.2
compound presentation O64.5
contracted pelvis O65.1
deep transverse arrest O64.0
deformed pelvis O65.0
dystocia (fetal) O66.9
due to
conjoined twins O66.3
fetal
abnormality NEC O66.3
ascites O66.3
hydrops O66.3
meningomyelocele O66.3
sacral teratoma O66.3
tumor O66.3
hydrocephalic fetus O66.3
shoulder O66.0
face presentation O64.2
fetopelvic disproportion O65.4
footling presentation O64.8
impacted shoulders O66.0
incomplete rotation of fetal head O64.0
large fetus O66.2
locked twins O66.1
malposition O64.9
specified NEC O64.8
malpresentation O64.9
specified NEC O64.8
multiple fetuses NEC O66.6
pelvic
abnormality (maternal) O65.9
organ O65.5
specified NEC O65.8
contraction
inlet O65.2
mid-cavity O65.3
outlet O65.3
persistent (position)
occipitoiliac O64.0
occipitoposterior O64.0
occipitosacral O64.0
occipitotransverse O64.0
prolapsed arm O64.4
shoulder presentation O64.4
specified NEC O66.8
pathological retraction ring, uterus O62.4
penetration, pregnant uterus by instrument O71.1

Delivery *(continued)*
complicated *(continued)*
by *(continued)*
perforation *—see* Delivery, complicated by, laceration
placenta, placental
ablatio *—see also* Abruptio placentae O45.9-
abnormality O43.9-
specified NEC O43.89-
abruptio *—see also* Abruptio placentae O45.9-
accreta O43.21-
adherent (with hemorrhage) O72.0
without hemorrhage O73.0
detachment (premature) *—see also* Abruptio placentae O45.9-
disorder O43.9-
specified NEC O43.89-
hemorrhage NEC O67.8
increta O43.22-
low (implantation) O44.1-
without hemorrhage O44.0-
malformation O43.10-
malposition O44.1-
without hemorrhage O44.0-
percreta O43.23-
previa (central) (lateral) (low) (marginal) (partial) (total) O44.1-
without hemorrhage O44.0-
retained (with hemorrhage) O72.0
without hemorrhage O73.0
separation (premature) O45.9-
specified NEC O45.8X-
vicious insertion O44.1-
precipitate labor O62.3
premature rupture, membranes *—see also* Pregnancy, complicated by, premature rupture of membranes O42.90
prolapse
arm or hand O32.2
cord (umbilical) O69.0
foot or leg O32.8
uterus O34.52-
prolonged labor O63.9
first stage O63.0
second stage O63.1
protozoal disease (maternal) O98.62
respiratory disease NEC O99.52
retained membranes or portions of placenta O72.2
without hemorrhage O73.1
retarded birth O63.9
retention of secundines (with hemorrhage) O72.0
without hemorrhage O73.0
partial O72.2
without hemorrhage O73.1
rupture
bladder (urinary) O71.5
cervix O71.3
pelvic organ NEC O71.5
urethra O71.5
uterus (during or after labor) O71.1
before labor O71.0-
separation, pubic bone (symphysis pubis) O71.6
shock O75.1
shoulder presentation O64.4
skin disorder NEC O99.72
spasm, cervix O62.4
stenosis or stricture, cervix O65.5
streptococcus B carrier state O99.824

Delivery *(continued)*
complicated *(continued)*
by *(continued)*
subluxation of symphysis (pubis) O26.72
syphilis (maternal) O98.12
tear *—see* Delivery, complicated by, laceration
tetanic uterus O62.4
trauma (obstetrical) *—see also* Delivery, complicated, by, damage to O71.9
non-obstetric O9A.22
periurethral O71.82
specified NEC O71.89
tuberculosis (maternal) O98.02
tumor, pelvic organs or tissues NEC O65.5
umbilical cord around neck
with compression O69.1
without compression O69.81
uterine inertia O62.2
during latent phase of labor O62.0
primary O62.0
secondary O62.1
vasa previa O69.4
velamentous insertion of cord O43.12-
specified complication NEC O75.89
delayed NOS O63.9
following rupture of membranes
artificial O75.5
second twin, triplet, etc. O63.2
forceps, low following failed vacuum extraction O66.5
missed (at or near term) O36.4
normal O80
obstructed *—see* Delivery, complicated by, obstruction
precipitate O62.3
preterm *—see also* Pregnancy, complicated by, preterm labor O60.10
spontaneous O80
term pregnancy NOS O80
uncomplicated O80
vaginal, following previous cesarean delivery O34.21

Delusions (paranoid) *—see* Disorder, delusional

Dementia (degenerative (primary)) (old age) (persisting) F03.90
with
aggressive behavior F03.91
behavioral disturbance F03.91
combative behavior F03.91
Lewy bodies G31.83 *[F02.80]*
with behavioral disturbance G31.83 *[F02.81]*
Parkinsonism G31.83 *[F02.80]*
with behavioral disturbance G31.83 *[F02.81]*
Parkinson's disease G20 *[F02.80]*
with behavioral disturbance G20 *[F02.81]*
violent behavior F03.91
alcoholic F10.97
with dependence F10.27
Alzheimer's type *—see* Disease, Alzheimer's
arteriosclerotic *—see* Dementia, vascular
atypical, Alzheimer's type *—see* Disease, Alzheimer's, specified NEC
congenital *—see* Disability, intellectual
frontal (lobe) G31.09 *[F02.80]*
with behavioral disturbance G31.09 *[F02.81]*

Dementia *(continued)*
frontotemporal G31.09 *[F02.80]*
with behavioral disturbance G31.09 *[F02.81]*
specified NEC G31.09 *[F02.80]*
with behavioral disturbance G31.09 *[F02.81]*
in (due to)
alcohol F10.97
with dependence F10.27
Alzheimer's disease *—see* Disease, Alzheimer's
arteriosclerotic brain disease *—see* Dementia, vascular
cerebral lipidoses E75.- *[F02.80]*
with behavioral disturbance E75.- *[F02.81]*
Creutzfeldt-Jakob disease *—see also* Creutzfeldt-Jakob disease or syndrome (with dementia) A81.00
epilepsy G40.- *[F02.80]*
with behavioral disturbance G40.- *[F02.81]*
hepatolenticular degeneration E83.01 *[F02.80]*
with behavioral disturbance E83.01 *[F02.81]*
human immunodeficiency virus (HIV) disease B20 *[F02.80]*
with behavioral disturbance B20 *[F02.81]*
Huntington's disease or chorea G10
hypercalcemia E83.52 *[F02.80]*
with behavioral disturbance E83.52 *[F02.81]*
hypothyroidism, acquired E03.9 *[F02.80]*
with behavioral disturbance E03.9 *[F02.81]*
due to iodine deficiency E01.8 *[F02.80]*
with behavioral disturbance E01.8 *[F02.81]*
inhalants F18.97
with dependence F18.27
multiple
etiologies F03
sclerosis G35 *[F02.80]*
with behavioral disturbance G35 *[F02.81]*
neurosyphilis A52.17 *[F02.80]*
with behavioral disturbance A52.17 *[F02.81]*
juvenile A50.49 *[F02.80]*
with behavioral disturbance A50.49 *[F02.81]*
niacin deficiency E52 *[F02.80]*
with behavioral disturbance E52 *[F02.81]*
paralysis agitans G20 *[F02.80]*
with behavioral disturbance G20 *[F02.81]*
Parkinson's disease G20 *[F02.80]*
pellagra E52 *[F02.80]*
with behavioral disturbance E52 *[F02.81]*
Pick's G31.01 *[F02.80]*
with behavioral disturbance G31.01 *[F02.81]*
polyarteritis nodosa M30.0 *[F02.80]*
with behavioral disturbance M30.0 *[F02.81]*
psychoactive drug F19.97
with dependence F19.27
inhalants F18.97
with dependence F18.27
sedatives, hypnotics or anxiolytics F13.97
with dependence F13.27

Dementia *(continued)*
  in *(continued)*
    sedatives, hypnotics or anxiolytics F13.97
      with dependence F13.27
    systemic lupus erythematosus M32.- F02.80
      with behavioral disturbance M32.- F02.81
    trypanosomiasis
      African B56.9 *[F02.80]*
        with behavioral disturbance B56.9 *[F02.81]*
    unknown etiology F03
    vitamin B12 deficiency E53.8 *[F02.80]*
      with behavioral disturbance E53.8 *[F02.81]*
    volatile solvents F18.97
      with dependence F18.27
    with behavioral disturbance G31.83 *[F02.81]*
  infantile, infantilis F84.3
  Lewy body G31.83 *[F02.80]*
    with behavioral disturbance G31.83 *[F02.81]*
  multi-infarct —*see* Dementia, vascular
  paralytica, paralytic (syphilitic) A52.17 *[F02.80]*
    with behavioral disturbance A52.17 *[F02.81]*
    juvenilis A50.45
  paretic A52.17
  praecox —*see* Schizophrenia
  presenile F03
    Alzheimer's type —*see* Disease, Alzheimer's, early onset
  primary degenerative F03
  progressive, syphilitic A52.17
  senile F03
    with acute confusional state F05
    Alzheimer's type —*see* Disease, Alzheimer's, late onset
    depressed or paranoid type F03
  vascular (acute onset) (mixed) (multi-infarct) (subcortical) F01.50
    with behavioral disturbance F01.51

Demineralization, bone —*see* Osteoporosis

Demodex folliculorum (infestation) B88.0

Demophobia F40.248

Demoralization R45.3

Demyelination, demyelinization
  central nervous system G37.9
    specified NEC G37.8
  corpus callosum (central) G37.1
  disseminated, acute G36.9
    specified NEC G36.8
  global G35
  in optic neuritis G36.0

Dengue (classical) (fever) A90
  hemorrhagic A91
  sandfly A93.1

Dennie-Marfan syphilitic syndrome A50.45

Dens evaginatus, in dente or invaginatus K00.2

Dense breasts R92.2

Density
  increased, bone (disseminated) (generalized) (spotted) —*see* Disorder, bone, density and structure, specified type NEC
  lung (nodular) J98.4

Dental —*see also* condition
  examination Z01.20
    with abnormal findings Z01.21
  restoration
    aesthetically inadequate or displeasing K08.56
    defective K08.50
      specified NEC K08.59
    failure of marginal integrity K08.51
    failure of periodontal anatomical integrity K08.54

Dentia praecox K00.6

Denticles (pulp) K04.2

Dentigerous cyst K09.0

Dentin
  irregular (in pulp) K04.3
  opalescent K00.5
  secondary (in pulp) K04.3
  sensitive K03.89

Dentinogenesis imperfecta K00.5

Dentinoma —*see* Cyst, calcifying odontogenic

Dentition (syndrome) K00.7
  delayed K00.6
  difficult K00.7
  precocious K00.6
  premature K00.6
  retarded K00.6

Dependence (on) (syndrome) F19.20
  with remission F19.21
  alcohol (ethyl) (methyl) (without remission) F10.20
    with
      amnestic disorder, persisting F10.26
      anxiety disorder F10.280
      dementia, persisting F10.27
      intoxication F10.229
        with delirium F10.221
        uncomplicated F10.220
      mood disorder F10.24
      psychotic disorder F10.259
        with
          delusions F10.250
          hallucinations F10.251
      remission F10.21
      sexual dysfunction F10.281
      sleep disorder F10.282
      specified disorder NEC F10.288
      withdrawal F10.239
        with
          delirium F10.231
          perceptual disturbance F10.232
        uncomplicated F10.230
    counseling and surveillance Z71.41
  amobarbital —*see* Dependence, drug, sedative
  amphetamine (s) (type) —*see* Dependence, drug, stimulant NEC
  amytal (sodium) —*see* Dependence, drug, sedative
  analgesic NEC F55.8
  anesthetic (agent) (gas) (general) (local) NEC —*see* Dependence, drug, psychoactive NEC
  anxiolytic NEC —*see* Dependence, drug, sedative
  barbital (s) —*see* Dependence, drug, sedative
  barbiturate (s) (compounds) (drugs classifiable to T42) —*see* Dependence, drug, sedative
  benzedrine —*see* Dependence, drug, stimulant NEC
  bhang —*see* Dependence, drug, cannabis
  bromide (s) NEC —*see* Dependence, drug, sedative

Dependence *(continued)*
  caffeine —*see* Dependence, drug, stimulant NEC
  cannabis (sativa) (indica) (resin) (derivatives) (type) —*see* Dependence, drug, cannabis
  chloral (betaine) (hydrate) —*see* Dependence, drug, sedative
  chlordiazepoxide —*see* Dependence, drug, sedative
  coca (leaf) (derivatives) —*see* Dependence, drug, cocaine
  cocaine —*see* Dependence, drug, cocaine
  codeine —*see* Dependence, drug, opioid
  combinations of drugs F19.20
  dagga —*see* Dependence, drug, cannabis
  demerol —*see* Dependence, drug, opioid
  dexamphetamine —*see* Dependence, drug, stimulant NEC
  dexedrine —*see* Dependence, drug, stimulant NEC
  dextromethorphan —*see* Dependence, drug, opioid
  dextromoramide —*see* Dependence, drug, opioid
  dextro-nor-pseudo-ephedrine —*see* Dependence, drug, stimulant NEC
  dextrorphan —*see* Dependence, drug, opioid
  diazepam —*see* Dependence, drug, sedative
  dilaudid —*see* Dependence, drug, opioid
  D-lysergic acid diethylamide —*see* Dependence, drug, hallucinogen
  drug NEC F19.20
    with sleep disorder F19.282
    cannabis F12.20
      with
        anxiety disorder F12.280
        intoxication F12.229
          with
            delirium F12.221
            perceptual disturbance F12.222
          uncomplicated F12.220
        other specified disorder F12.288
        psychosis F12.259
          delusions F12.250
          hallucinations F12.251
        unspecified disorder F12.29
      in remission F12.21
    cocaine F14.20
      with
        anxiety disorder F14.280
        intoxication F14.229
          with
            delirium F14.221
            perceptual disturbance F14.222
          uncomplicated F14.220
        mood disorder F14.24
        other specified disorder F14.288
        psychosis F14.259
          delusions F14.250
          hallucinations F14.251
        sexual dysfunction F14.281
        sleep disorder F14.282
        unspecified disorder F14.29
        withdrawal F14.23
      in remission F14.21
      withdrawal symptoms in newborn P96.1
    counseling and surveillance Z71.51

Dependence *(continued)*
  drug NEC *(continued)*
    hallucinogen F16.20
      with
        anxiety disorder F16.280
        flashbacks F16.283
        intoxication F16.229
          with delirium F16.221
          uncomplicated F16.220
        mood disorder F16.24
        other specified disorder F16.288
        perception disorder, persisting F16.283
        psychosis F16.259
          delusions F16.250
          hallucinations F16.251
        unspecified disorder F16.29
      in remission F16.21
    in remission F19.21
    inhalant F18.20
      with
        anxiety disorder F18.280
        dementia, persisting F18.27
        intoxication F18.229
          with delirium F18.221
          uncomplicated F18.220
        mood disorder F18.24
        other specified disorder F18.288
        psychosis F18.259
          delusions F18.250
          hallucinations F18.251
        unspecified disorder F18.29
      in remission F18.21
    nicotine F17.200
      with disorder F17.209
        remission F17.201
        specified disorder NEC F17.208
        withdrawal F17.203
      chewing tobacco F17.220
        with disorder F17.229
          remission F17.221
          specified disorder NEC F17.228
          withdrawal F17.223
      cigarettes F17.210
        with disorder F17.219
          remission F17.211
          specified disorder NEC F17.218
          withdrawal F17.213
      specified product NEC F17.290
        with disorder F17.299
          remission F17.291
          specified disorder NEC F17.298
          withdrawal F17.293
    opioid F11.20
      with
        intoxication F11.229
          with
            delirium F11.221
            perceptual disturbance F11.222
          uncomplicated F11.220
        mood disorder F11.24
        other specified disorder F11.288
        psychosis F11.259
          delusions F11.250
          hallucinations F11.251
        sexual dysfunction F11.281
        sleep disorder F11.282
        unspecified disorder F11.29
        withdrawal F11.23
      in remission F11.21

Dependence *(continued)*
  drug NEC *(continued)*
    psychoactive NEC F19.20
      with
        amnestic disorder F19.26
        anxiety disorder F19.280
        dementia F19.27
        intoxication F19.229
          with
            delirium F19.221
            perceptual disturbance F19.222
          uncomplicated F19.220
        mood disorder F19.24
        other specified disorder F19.288
        psychosis F19.259
          delusions F19.250
          hallucinations F19.251
        sexual dysfunction F19.281
        sleep disorder F19.282
        unspecified disorder F19.29
        withdrawal F19.239
          with
            delirium F19.231
            perceptual disturbance F19.232
          uncomplicated F19.230
    sedative, hypnotic or anxiolytic F13.20
      with
        amnestic disorder F13.26
        anxiety disorder F13.280
        dementia, persisting F13.27
        intoxication F13.229
          with delirium F13.221
          uncomplicated F13.220
        mood disorder F13.24
        other specified disorder F13.288
        psychosis F13.259
          delusions F13.250
          hallucinations F13.251
        sexual dysfunction F13.281
        sleep disorder F13.282
        unspecified disorder F13.29
        withdrawal F13.239
          with
            delirium F13.231
            perceptual disturbance F13.232
          uncomplicated F13.230
      in remission F13.21
    stimulant NEC F15.20
      with
        anxiety disorder F15.280
        intoxication F15.229
          with
            delirium F15.221
            perceptual disturbance F15.222
          uncomplicated F15.220
        mood disorder F15.24
        other specified disorder F15.288
        psychosis F15.259
          delusions F15.250
          hallucinations F15.251
        sexual dysfunction F15.281
        sleep disorder F15.282
        unspecified disorder F15.29
        withdrawal F15.23
      in remission F15.21
  ethyl
    alcohol (without remission) F10.20
      with remission F10.21
    bromide —*see* Dependence, drug, sedative
    carbamate F19.20
    chloride F19.20
    morphine —*see* Dependence, drug, opioid

Dependence *(continued)*
  ganja —*see* Dependence, drug, cannabis
  glue (airplane) (sniffing) —*see* Dependence, drug, inhalant
  glutethimide —*see* Dependence, drug, sedative
  hallucinogenics —*see* Dependence, drug, hallucinogen
  hashish —*see* Dependence, drug, cannabis
  hemp —*see* Dependence, drug, cannabis
  heroin (salt) (any) —*see* Dependence, drug, opioid
  hypnotic NEC —*see* Dependence, drug, sedative
  Indian hemp —*see* Dependence, drug, cannabis
  inhalants —*see* Dependence, drug, inhalant
  khat —*see* Dependence, drug, stimulant NEC
  laudanum —*see* Dependence, drug, opioid
  LSD(-25) (derivatives) —*see* Dependence, drug, hallucinogen
  luminal —*see* Dependence, drug, sedative
  lysergic acid —*see* Dependence, drug, hallucinogen
  maconha —*see* Dependence, drug, cannabis
  marihuana —*see* Dependence, drug, cannabis
  meprobamate —*see* Dependence, drug, sedative
  mescaline —*see* Dependence, drug, hallucinogen
  methadone —*see* Dependence, drug, opioid
  methamphetamine (s) —*see* Dependence, drug, stimulant NEC
  methaqualone —*see* Dependence, drug, sedative
  methyl
    alcohol (without remission) F10.20
      with remission F10.21
    bromide —*see* Dependence, drug, sedative
    morphine —*see* Dependence, drug, opioid
    phenidate —*see* Dependence, drug, stimulant NEC
    sulfonal —*see* Dependence, drug, sedative
  morphine (sulfate) (sulfite) (type) —*see* Dependence, drug, opioid
  narcotic (drug) NEC —*see* Dependence, drug, opioid
  nembutal —*see* Dependence, drug, sedative
  neraval —*see* Dependence, drug, sedative
  neravan —*see* Dependence, drug, sedative
  neurobarb —*see* Dependence, drug, sedative
  nicotine —*see* Dependence, drug, nicotine
  nitrous oxide F19.20
  nonbarbiturate sedatives and tranquilizers with similar effect —*see* Dependence, drug, sedative
  on
    artificial heart (fully implantable) (mechanical) Z95.812
    aspirator Z99.0
    care provider (because of) Z74.9
      impaired mobility Z74.09

Dependence *(continued)*
  on *(continued)*
    care provider *(continued)*
      need for
        assistance with personal care Z74.1
        continuous supervision Z74.3
      no other household member able to render care Z74.2
      specified reason NEC Z74.8
    machine Z99.89
      enabling NEC Z99.89
      specified type NEC Z99.89
    renal dialysis (hemodialysis) (peritoneal) Z99.2
    respirator Z99.11
    ventilator Z99.11
    wheelchair Z99.3
  opiate —*see* Dependence, drug, opioid
  opioids —*see* Dependence, drug, opioid
  opium (alkaloids) (derivatives) (tincture) —*see* Dependence, drug, opioid
  oxygen (long-term) (supplemental) Z99.81
  paraldehyde —*see* Dependence, drug, sedative
  paregoric —*see* Dependence, drug, opioid
  PCP (phencyclidine) —*see also* Abuse, drug, hallucinogen F16.20
  pentobarbital —*see* Dependence, drug, sedative
  pentobarbitone (sodium) —*see* Dependence, drug, sedative
  pentothal —*see* Dependence, drug, sedative
  peyote —*see* Dependence, drug, hallucinogen
  phencyclidine (PCP) (and related substances) —*see also* Abuse, drug, hallucinogen F16.20
  phenmetrazine —*see* Dependence, drug, stimulant NEC
  phenobarbital —*see* Dependence, drug, sedative
  polysubstance F19.20
  psilocibin, psilocin, psilocyn, psilocyline —*see* Dependence, drug, hallucinogen
  psychostimulant NEC —*see* Dependence, drug, stimulant NEC
  secobarbital —*see* Dependence, drug, sedative
  seconal —*see* Dependence, drug, sedative
  sedative NEC —*see* Dependence, drug, sedative
  specified drug NEC —*see* Dependence, drug
  stimulant NEC —*see* Dependence, drug, stimulant NEC
  substance NEC —*see* Dependence, drug
  supplemental oxygen Z99.81
  tobacco —*see* Dependence, drug, nicotine
    counseling and surveillance Z71.6
  tranquilizer NEC —*see* Dependence, drug, sedative
  vitamin B6 *[E53.1]*
  volatile solvents —*see* Dependence, drug, inhalant

Dependency
  care-provider Z74.9
  passive F60.7
  reactions (persistent) F60.7

Depersonalization (in neurotic state) (neurotic) (syndrome) F48.1

Depletion
  extracellular fluid E86.9
  plasma E86.1
  potassium E87.6
    nephropathy N25.89
  salt or sodium E87.1
    causing heat exhaustion or prostration T67.4
    nephropathy N28.9
  volume NOS E86.9

Deployment (current) (military) **status** Z56.82
  in theater or in support of military war, peacekeeping and humanitarian operations Z56.82
  personal history of Z91.82
    military war, peacekeeping and humanitarian deployment (current or past conflict) Z91.82
  returned from Z91.82

Depolarization, premature I49.40
  atrial I49.1
  junctional I49.2
  specified NEC I49.49
  ventricular I49.3

Deposit
  bone in Boeck's sarcoid D86.89
  calcareous, calcium —*see* Calcification
  cholesterol
    retina H35.89
    vitreous (body) (humor) —*see* Deposit, crystalline
  conjunctiva H11.11-
  cornea H18.00-
    argentous H18.02-
    due to metabolic disorder H18.03-
    Kayser-Fleischer ring H18.04-
    pigmentation —*see* Pigmentation, cornea
  crystalline, vitreous (body) (humor) H43.2-
  hemosiderin in old scars of cornea —*see* Pigmentation, cornea, stromal
  metallic in lens —*see* Cataract, specified NEC
  skin R23.8
  tooth, teeth (betel) (black) (green) (materia alba) (orange) (tobacco) K03.6
  urate, kidney —*see* Calculus, kidney

Depraved appetite —*see* Pica

Depressed
  HDL cholesterol E78.6

Depression (acute) (mental) F32.9
  agitated (single episode) F32.2
  anaclitic —*see* Disorder, adjustment
  anxiety F41.8
    persistent F34.1
  arches —*see also* Deformity, limb, flat foot
  atypical (single episode) F32.8
  basal metabolic rate R94.8
  bone marrow D75.89
  central nervous system R09.2
  cerebral R29.818
    newborn P91.4
  cerebrovascular I67.9
  chest wall M95.4
  climacteric (single episode) F32.8
  endogenous (without psychotic symptoms) F33.2
    with psychotic symptoms F33.3
  functional activity R68.89
  hysterical F44.89
  involutional (single episode) F32.8
  major F32.9
    with psychotic symptoms F32.3
    recurrent —*see* Disorder, depressive, recurrent

- **Depression** *(continued)*
  - manic-depressive —*see* Disorder, depressive, recurrent
  - masked (single episode) F32.8
  - medullary G93.89
  - menopausal (single episode) F32.8
  - metatarsus —*see* Depression, arches
  - monopolar F33.9
  - nervous F34.1
  - neurotic F34.1
  - nose M95.0
  - postnatal F53
  - postpartum F53
  - post-psychotic of schizophrenia F32.8
  - post-schizophrenic F32.8
  - psychogenic (reactive) (single episode) F32.9
  - psychoneurotic F34.1
  - psychotic (single episode) F32.3
    - recurrent F33.3
  - reactive (psychogenic) (single episode) F32.9
    - psychotic (single episode) F32.3
  - recurrent —*see* Disorder, depressive, recurrent
  - respiratory center G93.89
  - seasonal —*see* Disorder, depressive, recurrent
  - senile F03
  - severe, single episode F32.2
  - situational F43.21
  - skull Q67.4
  - specified NEC(single episode) F32.8
  - sternum M95.4
  - visual field —*see* Defect, visual field
  - vital (recurrent) (without psychotic symptoms) F33.2
    - with psychotic symptoms F33.3
    - single episode F32.2
- **Deprivation**
  - cultural Z60.3
  - effects NOS T73.9
    - specified NEC T73.8
  - emotional NEC Z65.8
    - affecting infant or child —*see* Maltreatment, child, psychological
  - food T73.0
  - protein —*see* Malnutrition
  - sleep Z72.820
  - social Z60.4
    - affecting infant or child —*see* Maltreatment, child, psychological
  - specified NEC T73.8
  - vitamins —*see* Deficiency, vitamin
  - water T73.1
- **Derangement**
  - ankle (internal) —*see* Derangement, joint, ankle
  - cartilage (articular) NEC —*see* Derangement, joint, articular cartilage, by site
    - recurrent —*see* Dislocation, recurrent
  - cruciate ligament, anterior, current injury —*see* Sprain, knee, cruciate, anterior
  - elbow (internal) —*see* Derangement, joint, elbow
  - hip (joint) (internal) (old) —*see* Derangement, joint, hip
  - joint (internal) M24.9
    - ankylosis —*see* Ankylosis
    - articular cartilage M24.10
      - ankle M24.17-
      - elbow M24.12-
      - foot M24.17-
      - hand M24.14-
      - hip M24.15-
      - knee NEC M23.9-

- **Derangement** *(continued)*
  - joint *(continued)*
    - articular cartilage *(continued)*
      - loose body —*see* Loose, body
      - shoulder M24.11-
      - wrist M24.13-
    - contracture —*see* Contraction, joint
    - current injury —*see also* Dislocation
      - knee, meniscus or cartilage —*see* Tear, meniscus
    - dislocation
      - pathological —*see* Dislocation, pathological
      - recurrent —*see* Dislocation, recurrent
    - knee —*see* Derangement, knee
    - ligament —*see* Disorder, ligament
    - loose body —*see* Loose, body
    - recurrent —*see* Dislocation, recurrent
    - specified type NEC M24.80
      - ankle M24.87-
      - elbow M24.82-
      - foot joint M24.87-
      - hand joint M24.84-
      - hip M24.85-
      - shoulder M24.81-
      - wrist M24.83-
    - temporomandibular M26.69
  - knee (recurrent) M23.9-
    - ligament disruption, spontaneous M23.60-
      - anterior cruciate M23.61-
      - capsular M23.67-
      - instability, chronic M23.5-
      - lateral collateral M23.64-
      - medial collateral M23.63-
      - posterior cruciate M23.62-
    - loose body M23.4-
    - meniscus M23.30-
      - cystic M23.00-
        - lateral M23.002
          - anterior horn M23.04-
          - posterior horn M23.05-
          - specified NEC M23.06-
        - medial M23.005
          - anterior horn M23.01-
          - posterior horn M23.02-
          - specified NEC M23.03-
      - degenerate —*see* Derangement, knee, meniscus, specified NEC
      - detached —*see* Derangement, knee, meniscus, specified NEC
      - due to old tear or injury M23.20-
        - lateral M23.20-
          - anterior horn M23.24-
          - posterior horn M23.25-
          - specified NEC M23.26-
        - medial M23.20-
          - anterior horn M23.21-
          - posterior horn M23.22-
          - specified NEC M23.23-
      - retained —*see* Derangement, knee, meniscus, specified NEC
      - specified NEC M23.30-
        - lateral M23.30-
          - anterior horn M23.34-
          - posterior horn M23.35-
          - specified NEC M23.36-
        - medial M23.30-
          - anterior horn M23.31-
          - posterior horn M23.32-
          - specified NEC M23.33-
    - old M23.8X-
    - specified NEC —*see* subcategory M23.8
  - low back NEC —*see* Dorsopathy, specified NEC

- **Derangement** *(continued)*
  - meniscus —*see* Derangement, knee, meniscus
  - mental —*see* Psychosis
  - patella, specified NEC —*see* Disorder, patella, derangement NEC
  - semilunar cartilage (knee) —*see* Derangement, knee, meniscus, specified NEC
  - shoulder (internal) —*see* Derangement, joint, shoulder
- **Dercum's disease** E88.2
- **Derealization** (neurotic) F48.1
- **Dermal** —*see* condition
- **Dermaphytid** —*see* Dermatophytosis
- **Dermatitis** (eczematous) L30.9
  - ab igne L59.0
  - acarine B88.0
  - actinic (due to sun) L57.8
    - other than from sun L59.8
  - allergic —*see* Dermatitis, contact, allergic
  - ambustionis, due to burn or scald —*see* Burn
  - amebic A06.7
  - ammonia L22
  - arsenical (ingested) L27.8
  - artefacta L98.1
    - psychogenic F54
  - atopic L20.9
    - psychogenic F54
    - specified NEC L20.89
  - autoimmune progesterone L30.8
  - berlock, berloque L56.2
  - blastomycotic B40.3
  - blister beetle L24.89
  - bullous, bullosa L13.9
    - mucosynechial, atrophic L12.1
    - seasonal L30.8
    - specified NEC L13.8
  - calorica L59.0
    - due to burn or scald —*see* Burn
  - caterpillar L24.89
  - cercarial B65.3
  - combustionis L59.0
    - due to burn or scald —*see* Burn
  - congelationis T69.1
  - contact (occupational) L25.9
    - allergic L23.9
      - due to
        - adhesives L23.1
        - cement L23.5
        - chemical products NEC L23.5
        - chromium L23.0
        - cosmetics L23.2
        - dander (cat) (dog) L23.81
        - drugs in contact with skin L23.3
        - dyes L23.4
        - food in contact with skin L23.6
        - hair (cat) (dog) L23.81
        - insecticide L23.5
        - metals L23.0
        - nickel L23.0
        - plants, non-food L23.7
        - plastic L23.5
        - rubber L23.5
        - specified agent NEC L23.89
    - due to
      - cement L25.3
      - chemical products NEC L25.3
      - cosmetics L25.0
      - dander (cat) (dog) L23.81
      - drugs in contact with skin L25.1
      - dyes L25.2
      - food in contact with skin L25.4
      - hair (cat) (dog) L23.81
      - plants, non-food L25.5
      - specified agent NEC L25.8

- **Dermatitis** *(continued)*
  - contact *(continued)*
    - irritant L24.9
      - due to
        - cement L25.3
        - chemical products NEC L24.5
        - cosmetics L24.3
        - detergents L24.0
        - drugs in contact with skin L24.4
        - food in contact with skin L24.6
        - oils and greases L24.1
        - plants, non-food L24.7
        - solvents L24.2
        - specified agent NEC L24.89
  - contusiformis L52
  - diabetic —*see* E08-E13 with .620
  - diaper L22
  - diphtheritica A36.3
  - dry skin L85.3
  - due to
    - acetone (contact) (irritant) L24.2
    - acids (contact) (irritant) L24.5
    - adhesive (s) (allergic) (contact) (plaster) L23.1
      - irritant L24.5
    - alcohol (irritant) (skin contact) (substances in category T51) L24.2
      - taken internally L27.8
    - alkalis (contact) (irritant) L24.5
    - arsenic (ingested) L27.8
    - carbon disulfide (contact) (irritant) L24.2
    - caustics (contact) (irritant) L24.5
    - cement (contact) L25.3
    - cereal (ingested) L27.2
    - chemical (s) NEC L25.3
      - taken internally L27.8
    - chlorocompounds L24.2
    - chromium (contact) (irritant) L24.81
    - coffee (ingested) L27.2
    - cold weather L30.8
    - cosmetics (contact) L25.0
      - allergic L23.2
      - irritant L24.3
    - cyclohexanes L24.2
    - dander (cat) (dog) L23.81
    - Demodex species B88.0
    - Dermanyssus gallinae B88.0
    - detergents (contact) (irritant) L24.0
    - dichromate L24.81
    - drugs and medicaments (generalized) (internal use) L27.0
      - external —*see* Dermatitis, due to, drugs, in contact with skin
      - in contact with skin L25.1
        - allergic L23.3
        - irritant L24.4
      - localized skin eruption L27.1
      - specified substance —*see* Table of Drugs and Chemicals
    - dyes (contact) L25.2
      - allergic L23.4
      - irritant L24.89
    - epidermophytosis —*see* Dermatophytosis
    - esters L24.2
    - external irritant NEC L24.9
    - fish (ingested) L27.2
    - flour (ingested) L27.2
    - food (ingested) L27.2
      - in contact with skin L25.4
    - fruit (ingested) L27.2
    - furs (allergic) (contact) L23.81
    - glues —*see* Dermatitis, due to, adhesives
    - glycols L24.2

- **Dermographia, dermographism** L50.3
- **Dermoid** (cyst) —*see also* Neoplasm, benign, by site
  - with malignant transformation C56-
  - due to radiation (nonionizing) L57.8
- **Dermopathy**
  - infiltrative with thyrotoxicosis —*see* Thyrotoxicosis
  - nephrogenic fibrosing L90.8
- **Dermophytosis** —*see* Dermatophytosis
- **Descemetocele** H18.73-
- **Descemet's membrane** —*see* condition
- **Descending** —*see* condition
- **Descensus uteri** —*see* Prolapse, uterus
- **Desert**
  - rheumatism B38.0
  - sore —*see* Ulcer, skin
- **Desertion** (newborn) —*see* Maltreatment
- **Desmoid** (extra-abdominal) (tumor) —*see* Neoplasm, connective tissue, uncertain behavior
  - abdominal D48.1
- **Despondency** F32.9
- **Desquamation, skin** R23.4
- **Destruction, destructive** —*see also* Damage
  - articular facet —*see also* Derangement, joint, specified type NEC
    - knee M23.8X-
    - vertebra —*see* Spondylosis
  - bone —*see also* Disorder, bone, specified type NEC
    - syphilitic A52.77
  - joint —*see also* Derangement, joint, specified type NEC
    - sacroiliac M53.3
  - rectal sphincter K62.89
  - septum (nasal) J34.89
  - tuberculous NEC —*see* Tuberculosis
  - tympanum, tympanic membrane (nontraumatic) —*see* Disorder, tympanic membrane, specified NEC
  - vertebral disc —*see* Degeneration, intervertebral disc
- **Destructiveness** —*see also* Disorder, conduct
  - adjustment reaction —*see* Disorder, adjustment
- **Desultory labor** O62.2
- **Detachment**
  - cartilage —*see* Sprain
  - cervix, annular N88.8
    - complicating delivery O71.3
  - choroid (old) (postinfectional) (simple) (spontaneous) H31.40-
    - hemorrhagic H31.41-
    - serous H31.42-
  - ligament —*see* Sprain
  - meniscus (knee) —*see also* Derangement, knee, meniscus, specified NEC
    - current injury —*see* Tear, meniscus
    - due to old tear or injury —*see* Derangement, knee, meniscus, due to old tear
  - retina (without retinal break) (serous) H33.2-
    - with retinal:
      - break H33.00-
        - giant H33.03-
        - multiple H33.02-
        - single H33.01-
      - dialysis H33.04-

- **Detachment** *(continued)*
    - pigment epithelium —*see* Degeneration, retina, separation of layers, pigment epithelium detachment
    - rhegmatogenous —*see* Detachment, retina, with retinal, break
    - specified NEC H33.8
    - total H33.05-
    - traction H33.4-
  - vitreous (body) H43.81
- **Detergent asthma** J69.8
- **Deterioration**
  - epileptic F06.8
  - general physical R53.81
  - heart, cardiac —*see* Degeneration, myocardial
  - mental —*see* Psychosis
  - myocardial, myocardium —*see* Degeneration, myocardial
  - senile (simple) R54
- **Deuteranomaly** (anomalous trichromat) H53.53
- **Deuteranopia** (complete) (incomplete) H53.53
- **Development**
  - abnormal, bone Q79.9
  - arrested R62.50
    - bone —*see* Arrest, development or growth, bone
    - child R62.50
    - due to malnutrition E45
  - defective, congenital —*see also* Anomaly, by site
    - cauda equina Q06.3
    - left ventricle Q24.8
      - in hypoplastic left heart syndrome Q23.4
    - valve Q24.8
      - pulmonary Q22.3
  - delayed —*see also* Delay, development R62.50
    - arithmetical skills F81.2
    - language (skills) (expressive) F80.1
    - learning skill F81.9
    - mixed skills F88
    - motor coordination F82
    - reading F81.0
    - specified learning skill NEC F81.89
    - speech F80.9
    - spelling F81.81
    - written expression F81.81
  - imperfect, congenital —*see also* Anomaly, by site
    - heart Q24.9
    - lungs Q33.6
  - incomplete
    - bronchial tree Q32.4
    - organ or site not listed —*see* Hypoplasia, by site
    - respiratory system Q34.9
  - sexual, precocious NEC E30.1
  - tardy, mental —*see also* Disability, intellectual F79
- **Developmental** —*see* condition
  - testing, child —*see* Examination, child
- **Devergie's disease** (pityriasis rubra pilaris) L44.0
- **Deviation** (in)
  - conjugate palsy (eye) (spastic) H51.0
  - esophagus (acquired) K22.8
  - eye, skew H51.8
  - midline (jaw) (teeth) (dental arch) M26.29
    - specified site NEC —*see* Malposition

- **Deviation** *(continued)*
  - nasal septum J34.2
    - congenital Q67.4
  - opening and closing of the mandible M26.53
  - organ or site, congenital NEC —*see* Malposition, congenital
  - septum (nasal) (acquired) J34.2
    - congenital Q67.4
  - sexual F65.9
    - bestiality F65.89
    - erotomania F52.8
    - exhibitionism F65.2
    - fetishism, fetishistic F65.0
      - transvestism F65.1
    - frotteurism F65.81
    - masochism F65.51
    - multiple F65.89
    - necrophilia F65.89
    - nymphomania F52.8
    - pederosis F65.4
    - pedophilia F65.4
    - sadism, sadomasochism F65.52
    - satyriasis F52.8
    - specified type NEC F65.89
    - transvestism F64.1
    - voyeurism F65.3
  - teeth, midline M26.29
  - trachea J39.8
  - ureter, congenital Q62.61
- **Device**
  - cerebral ventricle (communicating) in situ Z98.2
  - contraceptive —*see* Contraceptive, device
  - drainage, cerebrospinal fluid, in situ Z98.2
- **Devic's disease** G36.0
- **Devil's**
  - grip B33.0
  - pinches (purpura simplex) D69.2
- **Devitalized tooth** K04.99
- **Devonshire colic** —*see* Poisoning, lead
- **Dextraposition, aorta** Q20.3
  - in tetralogy of Fallot Q21.3
- **Dextrinosis, limit** (debrancher enzyme deficiency) E74.03
- **Dextrocardia** (true) Q24.0
  - with
    - complete transposition of viscera Q89.3
    - situs inversus Q89.3
- **Dextrotransposition, aorta** Q20.3
- **d-glycericacidemia** E72.59
- **Dhat syndrome** F48.8
- **Dhobi itch** B35.6
- **Di George's syndrome** D82.1
- **Di Guglielmo's disease** C94.0-
- **Diabetes, diabetic** (mellitus) (sugar) E11.9
  - with
    - amyotrophy E11.44
    - arthropathy NEC E11.618
    - autonomic (poly)neuropathy E11.43
    - cataract E11.36
    - Charcot's joints E11.610
    - chronic kidney disease E11.22
    - circulatory complication NEC E11.59
    - complication E11.8
      - specified NEC E11.69
    - dermatitis E11.620
    - foot ulcer E11.621
    - gangrene E11.52
    - gastroparesis E11.43

- **Diabetes, diabetic** *(continued)*
  - with *(continued)*
    - glomerulonephrosis, intracapillary E11.21
    - glomerulosclerosis, intercapillary E11.21
    - hyperglycemia E11.65
    - hyperosmolarity E11.00
      - with coma E11.01
    - hypoglycemia E11.649
      - with coma E11.641
    - kidney complications NEC E11.29
    - Kimmelsteil-Wilson disease E11.21
    - loss of protective sensation (LOPS) —*see* Diabetes, by type, with neuropathy
    - mononeuropathy E11.41
    - myasthenia E11.44
    - necrobiosis lipoidica E11.620
    - nephropathy E11.21
    - neuralgia E11.42
    - neurologic complication NEC E11.49
    - neuropathic arthropathy E11.610
    - neuropathy E11.40
    - ophthalmic complication NEC E11.39
    - oral complication NEC E11.638
    - periodontal disease E11.630
    - peripheral angiopathy E11.51
      - with gangrene E11.52
    - polyneuropathy E11.42
    - renal complication NEC E11.29
    - renal tubular degeneration E11.29
    - retinopathy E11.319
      - with macular edema E11.311
      - nonproliferative E11.329
        - with macular edema E11.321
        - mild E11.329
          - with macular edema E11.321
        - moderate E11.339
          - with macular edema E11.331
        - severe E11.349
          - with macular edema E11.341
      - proliferative E11.359
        - with macular edema E11.351
    - skin complication NEC E11.628
    - skin ulcer NEC E11.622
  - bronzed E83.110
  - complicating pregnancy —*see* Pregnancy, complicated by, diabetes
  - dietary counseling and surveillance Z71.3
  - due to drug or chemical E09.9
    - with
      - amyotrophy E09.44
      - arthropathy NEC E09.618
      - autonomic (poly)neuropathy E09.43
      - cataract E09.36
      - Charcot's joints E09.610
      - chronic kidney disease E09.22
      - circulatory complication NEC E09.59
      - complication E09.8
        - specified NEC E09.69
      - dermatitis E09.620
      - foot ulcer E09.621
      - gangrene E09.52
      - gastroparesis E09.43
      - glomerulonephrosis, intracapillary E09.21
      - glomerulosclerosis, intercapillary E09.21
      - hyperglycemia E09.65

Diabetes, diabetic *(continued)*
type 2 *(continued)*
with *(continued)*
glomerulonephrosis, intracapillary E11.21
glomerulosclerosis, intercapillary E11.21
hyperglycemia E11.65
hyperosmolarity E11.00
with coma E11.01
hypoglycemia E11.649
with coma E11.641
kidney complications NEC E11.29
Kimmelsteil-Wilson disease E11.21
mononeuropathy E11.41
myasthenia E11.44
necrobiosis lipoidica E11.620
nephropathy E11.21
neuralgia E11.42
neurologic complication NEC E11.49
neuropathic arthropathy E11.610
neuropathy E11.40
ophthalmic complication NEC E11.39
oral complication NEC E11.638
periodontal disease E11.630
peripheral angiopathy E11.51
with gangrene E11.52
polyneuropathy E11.42
renal complication NEC E11.29
renal tubular degeneration E11.29
retinopathy E11.319
with macular edema E11.311
nonproliferative E11.329
with macular edema E11.321
mild E11.329
with macular edema E11.321
moderate E11.339
with macular edema E11.331
severe E11.349
with macular edema E11.341
proliferative E11.359
with macular edema E11.351
skin complication NEC E11.628
skin ulcer NEC E11.622

Diacyclothrombopathia D69.1

Diagnosis deferred R69

Dialysis (intermittent) (treatment)
noncompliance (with) Z91.15
renal (hemodialysis) (peritoneal), status Z99.2
retina, retinal —*see* Detachment, retina, with retinal, dialysis

Diamond-Blackfan anemia (congenital hypoplastic) D61.01

Diamond-Gardener syndrome (autoerythrocyte sensitization) D69.2

Diaper rash L22

Diaphoresis (excessive) R61

Diaphragm —*see* condition

Diaphragmalgia R07.1

Diaphragmatitis, diaphragmitis J98.6

Diaphysial aclasis Q78.6

Diaphysitis —*see* Osteomyelitis, specified type NEC

Diarrhea, diarrheal (disease) (infantile) (inflammatory) R19.7
achlorhydric K31.83

Diarrhea, diarrheal *(continued)*
allergic K52.2
amebic —*see also* Amebiasis A06.0
with abscess —*see* Abscess, amebic
acute A06.0
chronic A06.1
nondysenteric A06.2
bacillary —*see* Dysentery, bacillary
balantidial A07.0
cachectic NEC K52.89
Chilomastix A07.8
choleriformis A00.1
chronic (noninfectious) K52.9
coccidial A07.3
Cochin-China K90.1
strongyloidiasis B78.0
Dientamoeba A07.8
dietetic K52.2
drug-induced K52.1
due to
bacteria A04.9
specified NEC A04.8
Campylobacter A04.5
Capillaria philippinensis B81.1
Clostridium difficile A04.7
Clostridium perfringens (C) (F) A04.8
Cryptosporidium A07.2
drugs K52.1
Escherichia coli A04.4
enteroaggregative A04.4
enterohemorrhagic A04.3
enteroinvasive A04.2
enteropathogenic A04.0
enterotoxigenic A04.1
specified NEC A04.4
food hypersensitivity K52.2
Necator americanus B76.1
S. japonicum B65.2
specified organism NEC A08.8
bacterial A04.8
viral A08.39
Staphylococcus A04.8
Trichuris trichiuria B79
virus —*see* Enteritis, viral
Yersinia enterocolitica A04.6
dysenteric A09
endemic A09
epidemic A09
flagellate A07.9
Flexner's (ulcerative) A03.1
functional K59.1
following gastrointestinal surgery K91.89
psychogenic F45.8
Giardia lamblia A07.1
giardial A07.1
hill K90.1
infectious A09
malarial —*see* Malaria
mite B88.0
mycotic NEC B49
neonatal (noninfectious) P78.3
nervous F45.8
neurogenic K59.1
noninfectious K52.9
postgastrectomy K91.1
postvagotomy K91.1
protozoal A07.9
specified NEC A07.8
psychogenic F45.8
specified
bacterium NEC A04.8
virus NEC A08.39
strongyloidiasis B78.0
toxic K52.1
trichomonal A07.8
tropical K90.1
tuberculous A18.32
viral —*see* Enteritis, viral

Diastasis
cranial bones M84.88
congenital NEC Q75.8
joint (traumatic) —*see* Dislocation
muscle M62.00
ankle M62.07-
congenital Q79.8
foot M62.07-
forearm M62.03-
hand M62.04-
lower leg M62.06-
pelvic region M62.05-
shoulder region M62.01-
specified site NEC M62.08
thigh M62.05-
upper arm M62.02-
recti (abdomen)
complicating delivery O71.89
congenital Q79.59

Diastema, tooth, teeth, fully erupted M26.32

Diastematomyelia Q06.2

Diataxia, cerebral G80.4

Diathesis
allergic —*see* History, allergy
bleeding (familial) D69.9
cystine (familial) E72.00
gouty —*see* Gout
hemorrhagic (familial) D69.9
newborn NEC P53
spasmophilic R29.0

Diaz's disease or osteochondrosis (juvenile) (talus) —*see* Osteochondrosis, juvenile, tarsus

Dibothriocephalus, dibothriocephaliasis (latus) (infection) (infestation) B70.0
larval B70.1

Dicephalus, dicephaly Q89.4

Dichotomy, teeth K00.2

Dichromat, dichromatopsia (congenital) —*see* Deficiency, color vision

Dichuchwa A65

Dicroceliasis B66.2

Didelphia, didelphys —*see* Double uterus

Didymytis N45.1
with orchitis N45.3

Dietary
inadequacy or deficiency E63.9
surveillance and counseling Z71.3

Dietl's crisis N13.8

Dieulafoy lesion (hemorrhagic)
duodenum K31.82
esophagus K22.8
intestine (colon) K63.81
stomach K31.82

Difficult, difficulty (in)
acculturation Z60.3
feeding R63.3
newborn P92.9
breast P92.5
specified NEC P92.8
nonorganic (infant or child) F98.29
intubation, in anesthesia T88.4
mechanical, gastroduodenal stoma K91.89
causing obstruction K91.3
reading (developmental) F81.0
secondary to emotional disorders F93.9
spelling (specific) F81.81
with reading disorder F81.89
due to inadequate teaching Z55.8
swallowing —*see* Dysphagia

Difficult, difficulty *(continued)*
walking R26.2
work
conditions NEC Z56.5
schedule Z56.3

Diffuse —*see* condition

DiGeorge's syndrome (thymic hypoplasia) D82.1

Digestive —*see* condition

Dihydropyrimidine dehydrogenase disease (DPD) E88.89

Diktyoma —*see* Neoplasm, malignant, by site

Dilaceration, tooth K00.4

Dilatation
anus K59.8
venule —*see* Hemorrhoids
aorta (focal) (general) —*see* Ectasia, aorta
with aneuysm —*see* Aneurysm, aorta
artery —*see* Aneurysm
bladder (sphincter) N32.89
congenital Q64.79
blood vessel I99.8
bronchial J47.9
with
exacerbation (acute) J47.1
lower respiratory infection J47.0
calyx (due to obstruction) —*see* Hydronephrosis
capillaries I78.8
cardiac (acute) (chronic) —*see also* Hypertrophy, cardiac
congenital Q24.8
valve NEC Q24.8
pulmonary Q22.3
valve —*see* Endocarditis
cavum septi pellucidi Q06.8
cervix (uteri) —*see also* Incompetency, cervix
incomplete, poor, slow
complicating delivery O62.0
colon K59.3
congenital Q43.1
psychogenic F45.8
common duct (acquired) K83.8
congenital Q44.5
cystic duct (acquired) K82.8
congenital Q44.5
duct, mammary —*see* Ectasia, mammary duct
duodenum K59.8
esophagus K22.8
congenital Q39.5
due to achalasia K22.0
eustachian tube, congenital Q17.8
gallbladder K82.8
gastric —*see* Dilatation, stomach
heart (acute) (chronic) —*see also* Hypertrophy, cardiac
congenital Q24.8
valve —*see* Endocarditis
ileum K59.8
psychogenic F45.8
jejunum K59.8
psychogenic F45.8
kidney (calyx) (collecting structures) (cystic) (parenchyma) (pelvis) (idiopathic) N28.89
lacrimal passages or duct —*see* Disorder, lacrimal system, changes
lymphatic vessel I89.0
mammary duct —*see* Ectasia, mammary duct
Meckel's diverticulum (congenital) Q43.0
malignant —*see* Table of Neoplasms, small intestine, malignant

Dilatation *(continued)*
myocardium (acute) (chronic) —*see* Hypertrophy, cardiac
organ or site, congenital NEC —*see* Distortion
pancreatic duct K86.8
pericardium —*see* Pericarditis
pharynx J39.2
prostate N42.89
pulmonary
artery (idiopathic) I28.8
valve, congenital Q22.3
pupil H57.04
rectum K59.3
saccule, congenital Q16.5
salivary gland (duct) K11.8
sphincter ani K62.89
stomach K31.89
acute K31.0
psychogenic F45.8
submaxillary duct K11.8
trachea, congenital Q32.1
ureter (idiopathic) N28.82
congenital Q62.2
due to obstruction N13.4
urethra (acquired) N36.8
vasomotor I73.9
vein I86.8
ventricular, ventricle (acute) (chronic) —*see also* Hypertrophy, cardiac
cerebral, congenital Q04.8
venule NEC I86.8
vesical orifice N32.89

Dilated, dilation —*see* Dilatation

Diminished, diminution
hearing (acuity) —*see* Deafness
sense or sensation (cold) (heat) (tactile) (vibratory) R20.8
vision NEC H54.7
vital capacity R94.2

Diminuta taenia B71.0

Dimitri-Sturge-Weber disease Q85.8

Dimple
parasacral, pilonidal or postanal —*see* Cyst, pilonidal

Dioctophyme renalis (infection) (infestation) B83.8

Dipetalonemiasis B74.4

Diphallus Q55.69

Diphtheria, diphtheritic (gangrenous) (hemorrhagic) A36.9
carrier (suspected) Z22.2
cutaneous A36.3
faucial A36.0
infection of wound A36.3
laryngeal A36.2
myocarditis A36.81
nasal, anterior A36.89
nasopharyngeal A36.1
neurological complication A36.89
pharyngeal A36.0
specified site NEC A36.89
tonsillar A36.0

Diphyllobothriasis (intestine) B70.0
larval B70.1

Diplacusis H93.22-

Diplegia (upper limbs) G83.0
congenital (cerebral) G80.8
facial G51.0
lower limbs G82.20
spastic G80.1

Diplococcus, diplococcal —*see* condition

Diplopia H53.2

Dipsomania F10.20
with
psychosis —*see* Psychosis, alcoholic
remission F10.21

Dipylidiasis B71.1

Direction, teeth, abnormal, fully erupted M26.30

Dirofilariasis B74.8

Dirt-eating child F98.3

Disability, disabilities
heart —*see* Disease, heart
intellectual F79
with
autistic features F84.9
mild (I.Q.50-69) F70
moderate (I.Q.35-49) F71
profound (I.Q. under 20) F73
severe (I.Q.20-34) F72
specified level NEC F78
knowledge acquisition F81.9
learning F81.9
limiting activities Z73.6
spelling, specific F81.81

Disappearance of family member Z63.4

Disarticulation —*see* Amputation
meaning traumatic amputation —*see* Amputation, traumatic

Discharge (from)
abnormal finding in —*see* Abnormal, specimen
breast (female) (male) N64.52
diencephalic autonomic idiopathic —*see* Epilepsy, specified NEC
ear —*see also* Otorrhea
blood —*see* Otorrhagia
excessive urine R35.8
nipple N64.52
penile R36.9
postnasal R09.82
prison, anxiety concerning Z65.2
urethral R36.9
without blood R36.0
hematospermia R36.1
vaginal N89.8

Discitis, diskitis M46.40
cervical region M46.42
cervicothoracic region M46.43
lumbar region M46.46
lumbosacral region M46.47
multiple sites M46.49
occipito-atlanto-axial region M46.41
pyogenic —*see* Infection, intervertebral disc, pyogenic
sacrococcygeal region M46.48
thoracic region M46.44
thoracolumbar region M46.45

Discoid
meniscus (congenital) Q68.6
semilunar cartilage (congenital) —*see* Derangement, knee, meniscus, specified NEC

Discoloration
nails L60.8
teeth (posteruptive) K03.7
during formation K00.8

Discomfort
chest R07.89
visual H53.14-

Discontinuity, ossicles, ear H74.2-

Discord (with)
boss Z56.4
classmates Z55.4
counselor Z64.4
employer Z56.4
family Z63.8
fellow employees Z56.4
in-laws Z63.1
landlord Z59.2
lodgers Z59.2
neighbors Z59.2

Discord *(continued)*
probation officer Z64.4
social worker Z64.4
teachers Z55.4
workmates Z56.4

Discordant connection
atrioventricular (congenital) Q20.5
ventriculoarterial Q20.3

Discrepancy
centric occlusion maximum intercuspation M26.55
leg length (acquired) —*see* Deformity, limb, unequal length
congenital —*see* Defect, reduction, lower limb
uterine size date O26.84-

Discrimination
ethnic Z60.5
political Z60.5
racial Z60.5
religious Z60.5
sex Z60.5

Disease, diseased —*see also* Syndrome
absorbent system I87.8
acid-peptic K30
Acosta's T70.29
Adams-Stokes (-Morgagni) (syncope with heart block) I45.9
Addison's anemia (pernicious) D51.0
adenoids (and tonsils) J35.9
adrenal (capsule) (cortex) (gland) (medullary) E27.9
hyperfunction E27.0
specified NEC E27.8
ainhum L94.6
airway
obstructive, chronic J44.9
due to
cotton dust J66.0
specific organic dusts NEC J66.8
reactive —*see* Asthma
akamushi (scrub typhus) A75.3
Albers-Schönberg (marble bones) Q78.2
Albert's —*see* Tendinitis, Achilles
alimentary canal K63.9
alligator-skin Q80.9
acquired L85.0
alpha heavy chain C88.3
alpine T70.29
altitude T70.20
alveolar ridge
edentulous K06.9
specified NEC K06.8
alveoli, teeth K08.9
Alzheimer's G30.9 *[F02.80]*
with behavioral disturbance G30.9 *[F02.81]*
early onset G30.0 *[F02.80]*
with behavioral disturbance G30.0 *[F02.81]*
late onset G30.1 *[F02.80]*
with behavioral disturbance G30.1 *[F02.81]*
specified NEC G30.8 *[F02.80]*
with behavioral disturbance G30.8 *[F02.81]*
amyloid —*see* Amyloidosis
Andersen's (glycogenosis IV) E74.09
Andes T70.29
Andrews'(bacterid) L08.89
angiospastic I73.9
cerebral G45.9
vein I87.8
anterior
chamber H21.9
horn cell G12.29
antiglomerular basement membrane (anti- GBM) antibody M31.0
tubulo-interstitial nephritis N12

Disease, diseased *(continued)*
antral —*see* Sinusitis, maxillary
anus K62.9
specified NEC K62.89
aorta (nonsyphilitic) I77.9
syphilitic NEC A52.02
aortic (heart) (valve) I35.9
rheumatic I06.9
Apollo B30.3
aponeuroses —*see* Enthesopathy
appendix K38.9
specified NEC K38.8
aqueous (chamber) H21.9
Arnold-Chiari —*see* Arnold-Chiari disease
arterial I77.9
occlusive —*see* Occlusion, by site
due to stricture or stenosis I77.1
arteriocardiorenal —*see* Hypertension, cardiorenal
arteriolar (generalized) (obliterative) I77.9
arteriorenal —*see* Hypertension, kidney
arteriosclerotic —*see also* Arteriosclerosis
cardiovascular —*see* Disease, heart, ischemic, atherosclerotic
coronary (artery) —*see* Disease, heart, ischemic, atherosclerotic
heart —*see* Disease, heart, ischemic, atherosclerotic
artery I77.9
cerebral I67.9
coronary I25.10
with angina pectoris —*see* Arteriosclerosis, coronary (artery),
arthropod-borne NOS (viral) A94
specified type NEC A93.8
atticoantral, chronic H66.20
left H66.22
with right H66.23
right H66.21
with left H66.23
auditory canal —*see* Disorder, ear, external
auricle, ear NEC —*see* Disorder, pinna
Australian X A83.4
autoimmune (systemic) NOS M35.9
hemolytic (cold type) (warm type) D59.1
drug-induced D59.0
thyroid E06.3
aviator's —*see* Effect, adverse, high altitude
Ayala's Q78.5
Ayerza's (pulmonary artery sclerosis with pulmonary hypertension) I27.0
Babington's (familial hemorrhagic telangiectasia) I78.0
bacterial A49.9
specified NEC A48.8
zoonotic A28.9
specified type NEC A28.8
Baelz's (cheilitis glandularis apostematosa) K13.0
bagasse J67.1
balloon —*see* Effect, adverse, high altitude
Bang's (brucella abortus) A23.1
Bannister's T78.3
barometer makers' —*see* Poisoning, mercury
Barraquer (-Simons') (progressive lipodystrophy) E88.1
Barrett's —*see* Barrett's, esophagus
Bartholin's gland N75.9
basal ganglia G25.9
degenerative G23.9
specified NEC G23.8

Disease, diseased *(continued)*
- basal ganglia *(continued)*
  - specified NEC G25.89
- Basedow's (exophthalmic goiter) —*see* Hyperthyroidism, with, goiter (diffuse)
- Bateman's B08.1
- Batten-Steinert G71.11
- Battey A31.0
- Beard's (neurasthenia) F48.8
- Becker
  - idiopathic mural endomyocardial I42.3
  - myotonia congenita G71.12
- Begbie's (exophthalmic goiter) —*see* Hyperthyroidism, with, goiter (diffuse)
- behavioral, organic F07.9
- Beigel's (white piedra) B36.2
- Benson's —*see* Deposit, crystalline
- Bernard-Soulier (thrombopathy) D69.1
- Bernhardt (-Roth) —*see* Mononeuropathy, lower limb, meralgia paresthetica
- Biermer's (pernicious anemia) D51.0
- bile duct (common) (hepatic) K83.9
  - with calculus, stones —*see* Calculus, bile duct
  - specified NEC K83.8
- biliary (tract) K83.9
  - specified NEC K83.8
- Billroth's —*see* Spina bifida
- bird fancier's J67.2
- black lung J60
- bladder N32.9
  - in (due to)
    - schistosomiasis (bilharziasis) B65.0 *[N33]*
  - specified NEC N32.89
- bleeder's D66
- blood D75.9
  - forming organs D75.9
  - vessel I99.9
- Bloodgood's —*see* Mastopathy, cystic
- Bodechtel-Guttmann (subacute sclerosing panencephalitis) A81.1
- bone —*see also* Disorder, bone
  - aluminum M83.4
  - fibrocystic NEC
    - jaw M27.49
- bone-marrow D75.9
- Borna A83.9
- Bornholm (epidemic pleurodynia) B33.0
- Bouchard's (myopathic dilatation of the stomach) K31.0
- Bouillaud's (rheumatic heart disease) I01.9
- Bourneville (-Brissaud) (tuberous sclerosis) Q85.1
- Bouveret (-Hoffmann) (paroxysmal tachycardia) I47.9
- bowel K63.9
  - functional K59.9
    - psychogenic F45.8
- brain G93.9
  - arterial, artery I67.9
  - arteriosclerotic I67.2
  - congenital Q04.9
  - degenerative —*see* Degeneration, brain
  - inflammatory —*see* Encephalitis
  - organic G93.9
    - arteriosclerotic I67.2
  - parasitic NEC B71.9 *[G94]*
  - senile NEC G31.1
  - specified NEC G93.89
- breast —*see also* Disorder, breast N64.9

Disease, diseased *(continued)*
- breast —*see also* Disorder, breast *(continued)*
  - cystic (chronic) —*see* Mastopathy, cystic
  - fibrocystic —*see* Mastopathy, cystic
  - Paget's
    - female, unspecified side C50.91-
    - male, unspecified side C50.92-
  - specified NEC N64.89
- Breda's —*see* Yaws
- Bretonneau's (diphtheritic malignant angina) A36.0
- Bright's —*see* Nephritis
  - arteriosclerotic —*see* Hypertension, kidney
- Brill's (recrudescent typhus) A75.1
- Brill-Zinsser (recrudescent typhus) A75.1
- Brion-Kayser —*see* Fever, paratyphoid
- broad
  - beta E78.2
  - ligament (noninflammatory) N83.9
    - inflammatory —*see* Disease, pelvis, inflammatory
    - specified NEC N83.8
- Brocq-Duhring (dermatitis herpetiformis) L13.0
- Brocq's
  - meaning
    - dermatitis herpetiformis L13.0
    - prurigo L28.2
- bronchopulmonary J98.4
- bronchus NEC J98.09
- bronze Addison's E27.1
  - tuberculous A18.7
- budgerigar fancier's J67.2
- bullous L13.9
  - chronic of childhood L12.2
  - specified NEC L13.8
- Buerger's (thromboangiitis obliterans) I73.1
- Bürger-Grütz (essential familial hyperlipemia) E78.3
- bursa —*see* Bursopathy
- caisson T70.3
- California —*see* Coccidioidomycosis
- capillaries I78.9
  - specified NEC I78.8
- Carapata A68.0
- cardiac —*see* Disease, heart
- cardiopulmonary, chronic I27.9
- cardiorenal (hepatic) (hypertensive) (vascular) —*see* Hypertension, cardiorenal
- cardiovascular (atherosclerotic) I25.10
  - with angina pectoris —*see* Arteriosclerosis, coronary (artery),
  - congenital Q28.9
  - newborn P29.9
    - specified NEC P29.89
  - hypertensive —*see* Hypertension, heart
  - renal (hypertensive) —*see* Hypertension, cardiorenal
  - syphilitic (asymptomatic) A52.00
- cartilage —*see* Disorder, cartilage
- Castellani's A69.8
- cat-scratch A28.1
- Cavare's (familial periodic paralysis) G72.3
- cecum K63.9
- celiac (adult) (infantile) K90.0
- cellular tissue L98.9
- central core G71.2
- cerebellar, cerebellum —*see* Disease, brain
- cerebral —*see also* Disease, brain
  - degenerative —*see* Degeneration, brain

Disease, diseased *(continued)*
- cerebrospinal G96.9
- cerebrovascular I67.9
  - acute I67.89
    - embolic I63.4-
    - thrombotic I63.3-
  - arteriosclerotic I67.2
  - specified NEC I67.89
- cervix (uteri) (noninflammatory) N88.9
  - inflammatory —*see* Cervicitis
  - specified NEC N88.8
- Chabert's A22.9
- Chandler's (osteochondritis dissecans, hip) —*see* Osteochondritis, dissecans, hip
- Charlouis —*see* Yaws
- Chédiak-Steinbrinck (-Higashi) (congenital gigantism of peroxidase granules) E70.330
- chest J98.9
- Chiari's (hepatic vein thrombosis) I82.0
- Chicago B40.9
- Chignon B36.8
- chigo, chigoe B88.1
- childhood granulomatous D71
- Chinese liver fluke B66.1
- chlamydial A74.9
  - specified NEC A74.89
- cholecystic K82.9
- choroid H31.9
  - specified NEC H31.8
- Christmas D67
- chronic bullous of childhood L12.2
- chylomicron retention E78.3
- ciliary body H21.9
  - specified NEC H21.89
- circulatory (system) NEC I99.8
  - newborn P29.9
  - syphilitic A52.00
    - congenital A50.54
- coagulation factor deficiency (congenital) —*see* Defect, coagulation
- coccidioidal —*see* Coccidioidomycosis
- cold
  - agglutinin or hemoglobinuria D59.1
    - paroxysmal D59.6
  - hemagglutinin (chronic) D59.1
- collagen NOS (nonvascular) (vascular) M35.9
  - specified NEC M35.8
- colon K63.9
  - functional K59.9
    - congenital Q43.2
  - ischemic K55.0
- combined system —*see* Degeneration, combined
- compressed air T70.3
- Concato's (pericardial polyserositis) A19.9
  - nontubercular I31.1
  - pleural —*see* Pleurisy, with effusion
- conjunctiva H11.9
  - chlamydial A74.0
  - specified NEC H11.89
  - viral B30.9
    - specified NEC B30.8
- connective tissue, systemic (diffuse) M35.9
  - in (due to)
    - hypogammaglobulinemia D80.1 *[M36.8]*
    - ochronosis E70.29 *[M36.8]*
  - specified NEC M35.8
- Conor and Bruch's (boutonneuse fever) A77.1
- Cooper's —*see* Mastopathy, cystic

Disease, diseased *(continued)*
- Cori's (glycogenosis III) E74.03
- corkhandler's or corkworker's J67.3
- cornea H18.9
  - specified NEC H18.89-
- coronary (artery) —*see* Disease, heart, ischemic, atherosclerotic
  - congenital Q24.5
  - ostial, syphilitic (aortic) (mitral) (pulmonary) A52.03
- corpus cavernosum N48.9
  - specified NEC N48.89
- Cotugno's —*see* Sciatica
- coxsackie (virus) NEC B34.1
- cranial nerve NOS G52.9
- Creutzfeldt-Jakob —*see* Creutzfeldt-Jakob disease or syndrome
- Crocq's (acrocyanosis) I73.89
- Crohn's —*see* Enteritis, regional
- Curschmann G71.11
- cystic
  - breast (chronic) —*see* Mastopathy, cystic
  - kidney, congenital Q61.9
  - liver, congenital Q44.6
  - lung J98.4
    - congenital Q33.0
- cytomegalic inclusion (generalized) B25.9
  - with pneumonia B25.0
  - congenital P35.1
- cytomegaloviral B25.9
  - specified NEC B25.8
- Czerny's (periodic hydrarthrosis of the knee) —*see* Effusion, joint, knee
- Daae (-Finsen) (epidemic pleurodynia) B33.0
- Darling's —*see* Histoplasmosis capsulati
- Débove's (splenomegaly) R16.1
- deer fly —*see* Tularemia
- Degos' I77.89
- demyelinating, demyelinizating (nervous system) G37.9
  - multiple sclerosis G35
  - specified NEC G37.8
- dense deposit —*see also* N00-N07
  - with fourth character .6 N05.6
- deposition, hydroxyapatite —*see* Disease, hydroxyapatite deposition
- de Quervain's (tendon sheath) M65.4
  - thyroid (subacute granulomatous thyroiditis) E06.1
- Devergie's (pityriasis rubra pilaris) L44.0
- Devic's G36.0
- diaphorase deficiency D74.0
- diaphragm J98.6
- diarrheal, infectious NEC A09
- digestive system K92.9
  - specified NEC K92.89
- disc, degenerative —*see* Degeneration, intervertebral disc
- discogenic —*see also* Displacement, intervertebral disc NEC
  - with myelopathy —*see* Disorder, disc, with, myelopathy
- diverticular —*see* Diverticula
- Dubois (thymus) A50.59 *[E35]*
- Duchenne-Griesinger G71.0
- Duchenne's
  - muscular dystrophy G71.0
  - pseudohypertrophy, muscles G71.0
- ductless glands E34.9
- Duhring's (dermatitis herpetiformis) L13.0
- duodenum K31.9
  - specified NEC K31.89
- Dupré's (meningism) R29.1
- Dupuytren's (muscle contracture) M72.0

Disease, diseased *(continued)*
  Durand-Nicholas-Favre (climatic bubo) A55
  Duroziez's (congenital mitral stenosis) Q23.2
  ear —*see* Disorder, ear
  Eberth's —*see* Fever, typhoid
  Ebola (virus) A98.4
  Ebstein's heart Q22.5
  Echinococcus —*see* Echinococcus
  echovirus NEC B34.1
  Eddowes'(brittle bones and blue sclera) Q78.0
  edentulous (alveolar) ridge K06.9
    specified NEC K06.8
  Edsall's T67.2
  Eichstedt's (pityriasis versicolor) B36.0
  Ellis-van Creveld (chondroectodermal dysplasia) Q77.6
  end stage renal (ESRD) N18.6
    due to hypertension I12.0
  endocrine glands or system NEC E34.9
  endomyocardial (eosinophilic) I42.3
  English (rickets) E55.0
  enteroviral, enterovirus NEC B34.1
    central nervous system NEC A88.8
  epidemic B99.9
    specified NEC B99.8
  epididymis N50.9
  Erb (-Landouzy) G71.0
  Erdheim-Chester (ECD) E88.89
  esophagus K22.9
    functional K22.4
    psychogenic F45.8
    specified NEC K22.8
  Eulenburg's (congenital paramyotonia) G71.19
  eustachian tube —*see* Disorder, eustachian tube
  external
    auditory canal —*see* Disorder, ear, external
    ear —*see* Disorder, ear, external
  extrapyramidal G25.9
    specified NEC G25.89
  eye H57.9
    anterior chamber H21.9
    inflammatory NEC H57.8
    muscle (external) —*see* Strabismus
    specified NEC H57.8
    syphilitic —*see* Oculopathy, syphilitic
  eyeball H44.9
    specified NEC H44.89
  eyelid —*see* Disorder, eyelid
    specified NEC —*see* Disorder, eyelid, specified type NEC
  eyeworm of Africa B74.3
  facial nerve (seventh) G51.9
    newborn (birth injury) P11.3
  Fahr (of brain) G23.8
  Fahr Volhard (of kidney) I12.-
  fallopian tube (noninflammatory) N83.9
    inflammatory —*see* Salpingo-oophoritis
    specified NEC N83.8
  familial periodic paralysis G72.3
  Fanconi's (congenital pancytopenia) D61.09
  fascia NEC —*see also* Disorder, muscle
    inflammatory —*see* Myositis
    specified NEC M62.89
  Fauchard's (periodontitis) —*see* Periodontitis
  Favre-Durand-Nicolas (climatic bubo) A55
  Fede's K14.0
  Feer's —*see* Poisoning, mercury

Disease, diseased *(continued)*
  female pelvic inflammatory —*see also* Disease, pelvis, inflammatory N73.9
    syphilitic (secondary) A51.42
    tuberculous A18.17
  Fernels'(aortic aneurysm) I71.9
  fibrocaseous of lung —*see* Tuberculosis, pulmonary
  fibrocystic —*see* Fibrocystic disease
  Fiedler's (leptospiral jaundice) A27.0
  fifth B08.3
  file-cutter's —*see* Poisoning, lead
  fish-skin Q80.9
    acquired L85.0
  Flajani (-Basedow) (exophthalmic goiter) —*see* Hyperthyroidism, with, goiter (diffuse)
  flax-dresser's J66.1
  fluke —*see* Infestation, fluke
  foot and mouth B08.8
  foot process N04.9
  Forbes'(glycogenosis III) E74.03
  Fordyce-Fox (apocrine miliaria) L75.2
  Fordyce's (ectopic sebaceous glands) (mouth) Q38.6
  Forestier's (rhizomelic pseudopolyarthritis) M35.3
    meaning ankylosing hyperostosis —*see* Hyperostosis, ankylosing
  Fothergill's
    neuralgia —*see* Neuralgia, trigeminal
    scarlatina anginosa A38.9
  Fournier (gangrene) N49.3
    female N76.89
  fourth B08.8
  Fox (-Fordyce) (apocrine miliaria) L75.2
  Francis' —*see* Tularemia
  Franklin C88.2
  Frei's (climatic bubo) A55
  Friedreich's
    combined systemic or ataxia G11.1
    myoclonia G25.3
  frontal sinus —*see* Sinusitis, frontal
  fungus NEC B49
  Gaisböck's (polycythemia hypertonica) D75.1
  gallbladder K82.9
    calculus —*see* Calculus, gallbladder
    cholecystitis —*see* Cholecystitis
    cholesterolosis K82.4
    fistula —*see* Fistula, gallbladder
    hydrops K82.1
    obstruction —*see* Obstruction, gallbladder
    perforation K82.2
    specified NEC K82.8
  gamma heavy chain C88.2
  Gamna's (siderotic splenomegaly) D73.2
  Gamstorp's (adynamia episodica hereditaria) G72.3
  Gandy-Nanta (siderotic splenomegaly) D73.2
  ganister J62.8
  gastric —*see* Disease, stomach
  gastroesophageal reflux (GERD) K21.9
    with esophagitis K21.0
  gastrointestinal (tract) K92.9
    amyloid E85.4
    functional K59.9
      psychogenic F45.8
    specified NEC K92.89
  Gee (-Herter) (-Heubner) (-Thaysen) (nontropical sprue) K90.0
  genital organs
    female N94.9
    male N50.9

Disease, diseased *(continued)*
  Gerhardt's (erythromelalgia) I73.81
  Gibert's (pityriasis rosea) L42
  Gierke's (glycogenosis I) E74.01
  Gilles de la Tourette's (motor-verbal tic) F95.2
  gingiva K06.9
    specified NEC K06.8
  gland (lymph) I89.9
  Glanzmann's (hereditary hemorrhagic thrombasthenia) D69.1
  glass-blower's (cataract) —*see* Cataract, specified NEC
    salivary gland hypertrophy K11.1
  Glisson's —*see* Rickets
  globe H44.9
    specified NEC H44.89
  glomerular —*see also* Glomerulonephritis
    with edema —*see* Nephrosis
    acute —*see* Nephritis, acute
    chronic —*see* Nephritis, chronic
    minimal change N05.0
    rapidly progressive N01.9
  glycogen storage E74.00
    Andersen's E74.09
    Cori's E74.03
    Forbes' E74.03
    generalized E74.00
    glucose-6-phosphatase deficiency E74.01
    heart E74.02 *[I43]*
    hepatorenal E74.09
    Hers' E74.09
    liver and kidney E74.09
    McArdle's E74.04
    muscle phosphofructokinase E74.09
    myocardium E74.02 *[I43]*
    Pompe's E74.02
    Tauri's E74.09
    type 0 E74.09
    type I E74.01
    type II E74.02
    type III E74.03
    type IV E74.09
    type V E74.04
    type VI-XI E74.09
    Von Gierke's E74.01
  Goldstein's (familial hemorrhagic telangiectasia) I78.0
  gonococcal NOS A54.9
  graft-versus-host (GVH) D89.813
    acute D89.810
    acute on chronic D89.812
    chronic D89.811
  grainhandler's J67.8
  granulomatous (childhood) (chronic) D71
  Graves'(exophthalmic goiter) —*see* Hyperthyroidism, with, goiter (diffuse)
  Griesinger's —*see* Ancylostomiasis
  Grisel's M43.6
  Gruby's (tinea tonsurans) B35.0
  Guillain-Barré G61.0
  Guinon's (motor-verbal tic) F95.2
  gum K06.9
  gynecological N94.9
  H(Hartnup's) E72.02
  Haff —*see* Poisoning, mercury
  Hageman (congenital factor XII deficiency) D68.2
  hair (color) (shaft) L67.9
    follicles L73.9
      specified NEC L73.8
  Hamman's (spontaneous mediastinal emphysema) J98.2
  hand, foot and mouth B08.4
  Hansen's —*see* Leprosy
  Hantavirus, with pulmonary manifestations B33.4
    with renal manifestations A98.5

Disease, diseased *(continued)*
  Harada's H30.81-
  Hartnup (pellagra-cerebellar ataxia-renal aminoaciduria) E72.02
  Hart's (pellagra-cerebellar ataxia-renal aminoaciduria) E72.02
  Hashimoto's (struma lymphomatosa) E06.3
  Hb —*see* Disease, hemoglobin
  heart (organic) I51.9
    with
      pulmonary edema (acute) —*see also* Failure, ventricular, left I50.1
      rheumatic fever (conditions in I00)
        active I01.9
          with chorea I02.0
          specified NEC I01.8
        inactive or quiescent (with chorea) I09.9
          specified NEC I09.89
    amyloid E85.4 *[I43]*
    aortic (valve) I35.9
    arteriosclerotic or sclerotic (senile) —*see* Disease, heart, ischemic, atherosclerotic
    artery, arterial —*see* Disease, heart, ischemic, atherosclerotic
    beer drinkers' I42.6
    beriberi (wet) E51.12
    black I27.0
    congenital Q24.9
      cyanotic Q24.9
      specified NEC Q24.8
    coronary —*see* Disease, heart, ischemic
    cryptogenic I51.9
    fibroid —*see* Myocarditis
    functional I51.89
      psychogenic F45.8
    glycogen storage E74.02 *[I43]*
    gonococcal A54.83
    hypertensive —*see* Hypertension, heart
    hyperthyroid —*see also* Hyperthyroidism E05.90 *[I43]*
      with thyroid storm E05.91 *[I43]*
    ischemic (chronic or with a stated duration of over 4 weeks) I25.9
      atherosclerotic (of) I25.10
        with angina pectoris —*see* Arteriosclerosis, coronary (artery)
        coronary artery bypass graft —*see* Arteriosclerosis, coronary (artery),
      cardiomyopathy I25.5
      diagnosed on ECG or other special investigation, but currently presenting no symptoms I25.6
      silent I25.6
      specified form NEC I25.89
    kyphoscoliotic I27.1
    meningococcal A39.50
      endocarditis A39.51
      myocarditis A39.52
      pericarditis A39.53
    mitral I05.9
      specified NEC I05.8
    muscular —*see* Degeneration, myocardial
    psychogenic (functional) F45.8
    pulmonary (chronic) I27.9
      in schistosomiasis B65.9 *[I52]*
      specified NEC I27.89
    rheumatic (chronic) (inactive) (old) (quiescent) (with chorea) I09.9
      active or acute I01.9
        with chorea (acute) (rheumatic) (Sydenham's) I02.0
      specified NEC I09.89

Disease, diseased *(continued)*
- heart *(continued)*
  - senile *—see* Myocarditis
  - syphilitic A52.06
    - aortic A52.03
      - aneurysm A52.01
    - congenital A50.54 *[I52]*
  - thyrotoxic *—see also* Thyrotoxicosis E05.90 *[I43]*
    - with thyroid storm E05.91 *[I43]*
  - valve, valvular (obstructive) (regurgitant) *—see also* Endocarditis
    - congenital NEC Q24.8
      - pulmonary Q22.3
  - vascular *—see* Disease, cardiovascular
- heavy chain NEC C88.2
  - alpha C88.3
  - gamma C88.2
  - mu C88.2
- Hebra's
  - pityriasis
    - maculata et circinata L42
    - rubra pilaris L44.0
  - prurigo L28.2
- hematopoietic organs D75.9
- hemoglobin or Hb
  - abnormal (mixed) NEC D58.2
    - with thalassemia D56.9
  - AS genotype D57.3
  - Bart's D56.0
  - C(Hb-C) D58.2
    - with other abnormal hemoglobin NEC D58.2
    - elliptocytosis D58.1
    - Hb-S D57.2-
    - sickle-cell D57.2-
    - thalassemia D56.8
  - Constant Spring D58.2
  - D(Hb-D) D58.2
  - E(Hb-E) D58.2
  - E-beta thalassemia D56.5
  - elliptocytosis D58.1
  - H(Hb-H) (thalassemia) D56.0
    - with other abnormal hemoglobin NEC D56.9
    - Constant Spring D56.0
  - I thalassemia D56.9
  - M D74.0
  - S or SS D57.1
  - SC D57.2-
  - SD D57.8-
  - SE D57.8-
  - spherocytosis D58.0
  - unstable, hemolytic D58.2
- hemolytic (newborn) P55.9
  - autoimmune (cold type) (warm type) D59.1
  - drug-induced D59.0
  - due to or with
    - incompatibility
      - ABO(blood group) P55.1
      - blood (group) (Duffy) (K (ell)) (Kidd) (Lewis) (M) (S) NEC P55.8
      - Rh (blood group) (factor) P55.0
    - Rh negative mother P55.0
  - specified type NEC P55.8
  - unstable hemoglobin D58.2
- hemorrhagic D69.9
  - newborn P53
- Henoch (-Schönlein) (purpura nervosa) D69.0
- hepatic *—see* Disease, liver
- hepatobiliary K83.9
  - toxic K71.9
- hepatolenticular E83.01
- heredodegenerative NEC
  - spinal cord G95.89
- herpesviral, disseminated B00.7

Disease, diseased *(continued)*
- Hers'(glycogenosis VI) E74.09
- Herter (-Gee) (-Heubner) (nontropical sprue) K90.0
- Heubner-Herter (nontropical sprue) K90.0
- high fetal gene or hemoglobin thalassemia D56.9
- Hildenbrand's *—see* Typhus
- hip (joint) M25.9
  - congenital Q65.89
  - suppurative M00.9
  - tuberculous A18.02
- His (-Werner) (trench fever) A79.0
- Hodgson's I71.2
  - ruptured I71.1
- Holla *—see* Spherocytosis
- hookworm B76.9
  - specified NEC B76.8
- host-versus-graft D89.813
  - acute D89.810
  - acute on chronic D89.812
  - chronic D89.811
- human immunodeficiency virus (HIV) B20
- Huntington's G10
- Hutchinson's (cheiropompholyx) — *see* Hutchinson's disease
- hyaline (diffuse) (generalized)
  - membrane (lung) (newborn) P22.0
    - adult J80
- hydatid *—see* Echinococcus
- hydroxyapatite deposition M11.00
  - ankle M11.07-
  - elbow M11.02-
  - foot joint M11.07-
  - hand joint M11.04-
  - hip M11.05-
  - knee M11.06-
  - multiple site M11.09
  - shoulder M11.01-
  - vertebra M11.08
  - wrist M11.03-
- hyperkinetic *—see* Hyperkinesia
- hypertensive *—see* Hypertension
- hypophysis E23.7
- Iceland G93.3
- I-cell E77.0
- immune D89.9
- immunoproliferative (malignant) C88.9
  - small intestinal C88.3
  - specified NEC C88.8
- inclusion B25.9
  - salivary gland B25.9
- infectious, infective B99.9
  - congenital P37.9
    - specified NEC P37.8
    - viral P35.9
      - specified type NEC P35.8
  - specified NEC B99.8
- inflammatory
  - penis N48.29
    - abscess N48.21
    - cellulitis N48.22
  - prepuce N47.7
    - balanoposthitis N47.6
  - tubo-ovarian *—see* Salpingo-oophoritis
- intervertebral disc *—see also* Disorder, disc
  - with myelopathy *—see* Disorder, disc, with, myelopathy
  - cervical, cervicothoracic *—see* Disorder, disc, cervical
    - with
      - myelopathy *—see* Disorder, disc, cervical, with myelopathy
      - neuritis, radiculitis or radiculopathy *—see* Disorder, disc, cervical, with neuritis

Disease, diseased *(continued)*
- intervertebral disc *—see also* Disorder, disc *(continued)*
  - cervical, cervicothoracic — *see* Disorder, disc, cervical *(continued)*
    - with *(continued)*
      - specified NEC *—see* Disorder, disc, cervical, specified type NEC
  - lumbar (with)
    - myelopathy M51.06
    - neuritis, radiculitis, radiculopathy or sciatica M51.16
    - specified NEC M51.86
  - lumbosacral (with)
    - neuritis, radiculitis, radiculopathy or sciatica M51.17
    - specified NEC M51.87
  - specified NEC *—see* Disorder, disc, specified NEC
  - thoracic (with)
    - myelopathy M51.04
    - neuritis, radiculitis or radiculopathy M51.14
    - specified NEC M51.84
  - thoracolumbar (with)
    - myelopathy M51.05
    - neuritis, radiculitis or radiculopathy M51.15
    - specified NEC M51.85
- intestine K63.9
  - functional K59.9
    - psychogenic F45.8
    - specified NEC K59.8
  - organic K63.9
  - protozoal A07.9
  - specified NEC K63.89
- iris H21.9
  - specified NEC H21.89
- iron metabolism or storage E83.10
- island (scrub typhus) A75.3
- itai-itai *—see* Poisoning, cadmium
- Jakob-Creutzfeldt *—see* Creutzfeldt-Jakob disease or syndrome
- jaw M27.9
  - fibrocystic M27.49
  - specified NEC M27.8
- jigger B88.1
- joint *—see also* Disorder, joint
  - Charcot's *—see* Arthropathy, neuropathic (Charcot)
  - degenerative *—see* Osteoarthritis
    - multiple M15.9
    - spine *—see* Spondylosis
  - hypertrophic *—see* Osteoarthritis
  - sacroiliac M53.3
  - specified NEC *—see* Disorder, joint, specified type NEC
  - spine NEC *—see* Dorsopathy
  - suppurative *—see* Arthritis, pyogenic or pyemic
- Jourdain's (acute gingivitis) K05.00
  - nonplaque induced K05.01
  - plaque induced K05.00
- Kaschin-Beck (endemic polyarthritis) M12.10
  - ankle M12.17-
  - elbow M12.12-
  - foot joint M12.17-
  - hand joint M12.14-
  - hip M12.15-
  - knee M12.16-
  - multiple site M12.19
  - shoulder M12.11-
  - vertebra M12.18
  - wrist M12.13-
- Katayama B65.2
- Kedani (scrub typhus) A75.3
- Keshan E59

Disease, diseased *(continued)*
- kidney (functional) (pelvis) N28.9
  - chronic N18.9
    - hypertensive *—see* Hypertension, kidney
    - stage 1 N18.1
    - stage 2(mild) N18.2
    - stage 3(moderate) N18.3
    - stage 4(severe) N18.4
    - stage 5 N18.5
  - complicating pregnancy *—see* Pregnancy, complicated by, renal disease
  - cystic (congenital) Q61.9
  - diabetic *—see* E08-E13 with .22
  - fibrocystic (congenital) Q61.8
  - hypertensive *—see* Hypertension, kidney
  - in (due to)
    - schistosomiasis (bilharziasis) B65.9 *[N29]*
  - multicystic Q61.4
  - polycystic Q61.3
    - adult type Q61.2
    - childhood type NEC Q61.19
      - collecting duct dilatation Q61.11
- Kimmelstiel (-Wilson) (intercapillary polycystic (congenital) glomerulosclerosis) *—see* E08-E13 with .21
- Kimura D21.9
  - specified site (*see* Neoplasm, connective tissue benign)
- Kinnier Wilson's (hepatolenticular degeneration) E83.01
- kissing *—see* Mononucleosis, infectious
- Klebs' *—see also* Glomerulonephritis N05.-
- Klippel-Feil (brevicollis) Q76.1
- Köhler-Pellegrini-Stieda (calcification, knee joint) *—see* Bursitis, tibial collateral
- Kok Q89.8
- König's (osteochondritis dissecans) *—see* Osteochondritis, dissecans
- Korsakoff's (nonalcoholic) F04
  - alcoholic F10.96
    - with dependence F10.26
- Kostmann's (infantile genetic agranulocytosis) D70.0
- kuru A81.81
- Kyasanur Forest A98.2
- labyrinth, ear *—see* Disorder, ear, inner
- lacrimal system *—see* Disorder, lacrimal system
- Lafora's *—see* Epilepsy, generalized, idiopathic
- Lancereaux-Mathieu (leptospiral jaundice) A27.0
- Landry's G61.0
- Larrey-Weil (leptospiral jaundice) A27.0
- larynx J38.7
- legionnaires' A48.1
  - nonpneumonic A48.2
- Lenegre's I44.2
- lens H27.9
  - specified NEC H27.8
- Lev's (acquired complete heart block) I44.2
- Lewy body (dementia) G31.83 *[F02.80]*
  - with behavioral disturbance G31.83 *[F02.81]*
- Lichtheim's (subacute combined sclerosis with pernicious anemia) D51.0
- Lightwood's (renal tubular acidosis) N25.89

Disease, diseased *(continued)*
Lignac's (cystinosis) E72.04
lip K13.0
lipid-storage E75.6
specified NEC E75.5
Lipschütz's N76.6
liver (chronic) (organic) K76.9
alcoholic (chronic) K70.9
acute —*see* Disease, liver, alcoholic, hepatitis
cirrhosis K70.30
with ascites K70.31
failure K70.40
with coma K70.41
fatty liver K70.0
fibrosis K70.2
hepatitis K70.10
with ascites K70.11
sclerosis K70.2
cystic, congenital Q44.6
drug-induced (idiosyncratic) (toxic) (predictable) (unpredictable) — *see* Disease, liver, toxic
end stage K72.90
due to hepatitis —*see* Hepatitis
fatty, nonalcoholic (NAFLD) K76.0
alcoholic K70.0
fibrocystic (congenital) Q44.6
fluke
Chinese B66.1
oriental B66.1
sheep B66.3
glycogen storage E74.09 *[K77]*
in (due to)
schistosomiasis (bilharziasis) B65.9 *[K77]*
inflammatory K75.9
alcoholic K70.1
specified NEC K75.89
polycystic (congenital) Q44.6
toxic K71.9
with
cholestasis K71.0
cirrhosis (liver) K71.7
fibrosis (liver) K71.7
focal nodular hyperplasia K71.8
hepatic granuloma K71.8
hepatic necrosis K71.10
with coma K71.11
hepatitis NEC K71.6
acute K71.2
chronic
active K71.50
with ascites K71.51
lobular K71.4
persistent K71.3
lupoid K71.50
with ascites K71.51
peliosis hepatis K71.8
veno-occlusive disease (VOD) of liver K71.8
veno-occlusive K76.5
Lobo's (keloid blastomycosis) B48.0
Lobstein's (brittle bones and blue sclera) Q78.0
Ludwig's (submaxillary cellulitis) K12.2
lumbosacral region M53.87
lung J98.4
black J60
congenital Q33.9
cystic J98.4
congenital Q33.0
fibroid (chronic) —*see* Fibrosis, lung
fluke B66.4
oriental B66.4
in
amyloidosis E85.4 *[J99]*
sarcoidosis D86.0

Disease, diseased *(continued)*
lung *(continued)*
in *(continued)*
Sjögren's syndrome M35.02
systemic
lupus erythematosus M32.13
sclerosis M34.81
interstitial J84.9
of childhood, specified NEC J84.848
respiratory bronchiolitis J84.115
specified NEC J84.89
obstructive (chronic) J44.9
with
acute
bronchitis J44.0
exacerbation NEC J44.1
lower respiratory infection J44.0
alveolitis, allergic J67.9
asthma J44.9
bronchiectasis J47.9
with
exacerbation (acute) J47.1
lower respiratory infection J47.0
bronchitis J44.9
with
exacerbation (acute) J44.1
lower respiratory infection J44.0
emphysema J44.9
hypersensitivity pneumonitis J67.9
decompensated J44.1
with
exacerbation (acute) J44.1
polycystic J98.4
congenital Q33.0
rheumatoid (diffuse) (interstitial) —*see* Rheumatoid, lung
Lutembacher's (atrial septal defect with mitral stenosis) Q21.1
Lyme A69.20
lymphatic (gland) (system) (channel) (vessel) I89.9
lymphoproliferative D47.9
specified NEC D47.Z9
T-gamma D47.Z9
X-linked D82.3
Magitot's M27.2
malarial —*see* Malaria
malignant —*see also* Neoplasm, malignant, by site
Manson's B65.1
maple bark J67.6
maple-syrup-urine E71.0
Marburg (virus) A98.3
Marion's (bladder neck obstruction) N32.0
Marsh's (exophthalmic goiter) —*see* Hyperthyroidism, with, goiter (diffuse)
mastoid (process) —*see* Disorder, ear, middle
Mathieu's (leptospiral jaundice) A27.0
Maxcy's A75.2
McArdle (-Schmid-Pearson) (glycogenosis V) E74.04
mediastinum J98.5
medullary center (idiopathic) (respiratory) G93.89
Meige's (chronic hereditary edema) Q82.0
meningococcal —*see* Infection, meningococcal
mental F99
organic F09
mesenchymal M35.9

Disease, diseased *(continued)*
mesenteric embolic K55.0
metabolic, metabolism E88.9
bilirubin E80.7
metal-polisher's J62.8
metastatic —*see also* Neoplasm, secondary, by site C79.9
microvascular - code to condition
microvillus
atrophy Q43.8
inclusion (MVD) Q43.8
middle ear —*see* Disorder, ear, middle
Mikulicz'(dryness of mouth, absent or decreased lacrimation) K11.8
Milroy's (chronic hereditary edema) Q82.0
Minamata —*see* Poisoning, mercury
minicore G71.2
Minor's G95.19
Minot's (hemorrhagic disease, newborn) P53
Minot-von Willebrand-Jürgens (angiohemophilia) D68.0
Mitchell's (erythromelalgia) I73.81
mitral (valve) I05.9
nonrheumatic I34.9
mixed connective tissue M35.1
moldy hay J67.0
Monge's T70.29
Morgagni-Adams-Stokes (syncope with heart block) I45.9
Morgagni's (syndrome) (hyperostosis frontalis interna) M85.2
Morton's (with metatarsalgia) —*see* Lesion, nerve, plantar
Morvan's G60.8
motor neuron (bulbar) (familial) (mixed type) (spinal) G12.20
amyotrophic lateral sclerosis G12.21
progressive bulbar palsy G12.22
specified NEC G12.29
moyamoya I67.5
mu heavy chain disease C88.2
multicore G71.2
muscle —*see also* Disorder, muscle
inflammatory —*see* Myositis
ocular (external) —*see* Strabismus
musculoskeletal system, soft tissue — *see also* Disorder, soft tissue
specified NEC —*see* Disorder, soft tissue, specified type NEC
mushroom workers' J67.5
mycotic B49
myelodysplastic, not classified C94.6
myeloproliferative, not classified C94.6
chronic D47.1
myocardium, myocardial —*see also* Degeneration, myocardial I51.5
primary (idiopathic) I42.9
myoneural G70.9
Naegeli's D69.1
nails L60.9
specified NEC L60.8
Nairobi (sheep virus) A93.8
nasal J34.9
nemaline body G71.2
nerve —*see* Disorder, nerve
nervous system G98.8
autonomic G90.9
central G96.9
specified NEC G96.8
congenital Q07.9
parasympathetic G90.9
specified NEC G98.8
sympathetic G90.9
vegetative G90.9
neuromuscular system G70.9
Newcastle B30.8

Disease, diseased *(continued)*
Nicolas (-Durand)-Favre (climatic bubo) A55
nipple N64.9
Paget's C50.01-
female C50.01-
male C50.02-
Nishimoto (-Takeuchi) I67.5
nonarthropod-borne NOS (viral) B34.9
enterovirus NEC B34.1
nonautoimmune hemolytic D59.4
drug-induced D59.2
Nonne-Milroy-Meige (chronic hereditary edema) Q82.0
nose J34.9
nucleus pulposus —*see* Disorder, disc
nutritional E63.9
oast-house-urine E72.19
ocular
herpesviral B00.50
zoster B02.30
obliterative vascular I77.1
Ohara's —*see* Tularemia
Opitz's (congestive splenomegaly) D73.2
Oppenheim-Urbach (necrobiosis lipoidica diabeticorum) —*see* E08-E13 with .620
optic nerve NEC —*see* Disorder, nerve, optic
orbit —*see* Disorder, orbit
Oriental liver fluke B66.1
Oriental lung fluke B66.4
Ormond's N13.5
Oropouche virus A93.0
Osler-Rendu (familial hemorrhagic telangiectasia) I78.0
osteofibrocystic E21.0
Otto's M24.7
outer ear —*see* Disorder, ear, external
ovary (noninflammatory) N83.9
cystic N83.20
inflammatory —*see* Salpingo-oophoritis
polycystic E28.2
specified NEC N83.8
Owren's (congenital) —*see* Defect, coagulation
pancreas K86.9
cystic K86.2
fibrocystic E84.9
specified NEC K86.8
panvalvular I08.9
specified NEC I08.8
parametrium (noninflammatory) N83.9
parasitic B89
cerebral NEC B71.9 *[G94]*
intestinal NOS B82.9
mouth B37.0
skin NOS B88.9
specified type —*see* Infestation
tongue B37.0
parathyroid (gland) E21.5
specified NEC E21.4
Parkinson's G20
parodontal K05.6
Parrot's (syphilitic osteochondritis) A50.02
Parry's (exophthalmic goiter) —*see* Hyperthyroidism, with, goiter (diffuse)
Parson's (exophthalmic goiter) —*see* Hyperthyroidism, with, goiter (diffuse)
Paxton's (white piedra) B36.2
pearl-worker's —*see* Osteomyelitis, specified type NEC
Pellegrini-Stieda (calcification, knee joint) —*see* Bursitis, tibial collateral

Disease, diseased *(continued)*
pelvis, pelvic
female NOS N94.9
specified NEC N94.89
gonococcal (acute) (chronic) A54.24
inflammatory (female) N73.9
acute N73.0
chronic N73.1
specified NEC N73.8
syphilitic (secondary) A51.42
late A52.76
tuberculous A18.17
organ, female N94.9
peritoneum, female NEC N94.89
penis N48.9
inflammatory N48.29
abscess N48.21
cellulitis N48.22
specified NEC N48.89
periapical tissues NOS K04.90
periodontal K05.6
specified NEC K05.5
periosteum —*see* Disorder, bone, specified type NEC
peripheral
arterial I73.9
autonomic nervous system G90.9
nerves —*see* Polyneuropathy
vascular NOS I73.9
peritoneum K66.9
pelvic, female NEC N94.89
specified NEC K66.8
persistent mucosal (middle ear) H66.20
left H66.22
with right H66.23
right H66.21
with left H66.23
Petit's —*see* Hernia, abdomen, specified site NEC
pharynx J39.2
specified NEC J39.2
Phocas' —*see* Mastopathy, cystic
photochromogenic (acid-fast bacilli) (pulmonary) A31.0
nonpulmonary A31.9
Pick's G31.01 *[F02.80]*
with behavioral disturbance G31.01 *[F02.81]*
pigeon fancier's J67.2
pineal gland E34.8
pink —*see* Poisoning, mercury
Pinkus'(lichen nitidus) L44.1
pinworm B80
Piry virus A93.8
pituitary (gland) E23.7
pituitary-snuff-taker's J67.8
pleura (cavity) J94.9
specified NEC J94.8
pneumatic drill (hammer) T75.21
Pollitzer's (hidradenitis suppurativa) L73.2
polycystic
kidney or renal Q61.3
adult type Q61.2
childhood type NEC Q61.19
collecting duct dilatation Q61.11
liver or hepatic Q44.6
lung or pulmonary J98.4
congenital Q33.0
ovary, ovaries E28.2
spleen Q89.09
polyethylene T84.05-
Pompe's (glycogenosis II) E74.02
Posadas-Wernicke B38.9
Potain's (pulmonary edema) —*see* Edema, lung
prepuce N47.8
inflammatory N47.7
balanoposthitis N47.6

Disease, diseased *(continued)*
Pringle's (tuberous sclerosis) Q85.1
prion, central nervous system A81.9
specified NEC A81.89
prostate N42.9
specified NEC N42.89
protozoal B64
acanthamebiasis —*see* Acanthamebiasis
African trypanosomiasis —*see* African trypanosomiasis
babesiosis B60.0
Chagas disease —*see* Chagas disease
intestine, intestinal A07.9
leishmaniasis —*see* Leishmaniasis
malaria —*see* Malaria
naegleriasis B60.2
pneumocystosis B59
specified organism NEC B60.8
toxoplasmosis —*see* Toxoplasmosis
pseudo-Hurler's E77.0
psychiatric F99
psychotic —*see* Psychosis
Puente's (simple glandular cheilitis) K13.0
puerperal —*see also* Puerperal O90.89
pulmonary —*see also* Disease, lung
artery I28.9
chronic obstructive J44.9
with
acute bronchitis J44.0
exacerbation (acute) J44.1
lower respiratory infection (acute) J44.0
decompensated J44.1
with
exacerbation (acute) J44.1
heart I27.9
specified NEC I27.89
hypertensive (vascular) I27.0
valve I37.9
rheumatic I09.89
pulp (dental) NOS K04.90
pulseless M31.4
Putnam's (subacute combined sclerosis with pernicious anemia) D51.0
Pyle (-Cohn) (craniometaphyseal dysplasia) Q78.5
ragpicker's or ragsorter's A22.1
Raynaud's —*see* Raynaud's disease
reactive airway —*see* Asthma
Reclus'(cystic) —*see* Mastopathy, cystic
rectum K62.9
specified NEC K62.89
Refsum's (heredopathia atactica polyneuritiformis) G60.1
renal (functional) (pelvis) —*see also* Disease, kidney N28.9
with
edema —*see* Nephrosis
glomerular lesion —*see* Glomerulonephritis
with edema —*see* Nephrosis
interstitial nephritis N12
acute N28.9
chronic —*see also* Disease, kidney, chronic N18.9
cystic, congenital Q61.9
diabetic —*see* E08-E13 with .22
end-stage (failure) N18.6
due to hypertension I12.0
fibrocystic (congenital) Q61.8
hypertensive —*see* Hypertension, kidney
lupus M32.14
phosphate-losing (tubular) N25.0

Disease, diseased *(continued)*
renal *(continued)*
polycystic (congenital) Q61.3
adult type Q61.2
childhood type NEC Q61.19
collecting duct dilatation Q61.11
rapidly progressive N01.9
subacute N01.9
Rendu-Osler-Weber (familial hemorrhagic telangiectasia) I78.0
renovascular (arteriosclerotic) —*see* Hypertension, kidney
respiratory (tract) J98.9
acute or subacute NOS J06.9
due to
chemicals, gases, fumes or vapors (inhalation) J68.3
external agent J70.9
specified NEC J70.8
radiation J70.0
smoke inhalation J70.5
noninfectious J39.8
chronic NOS J98.9
due to
chemicals, gases, fumes or vapors J68.4
external agent J70.9
specified NEC J70.8
radiation J70.1
newborn P27.9
specified NEC P27.8
due to
chemicals, gases, fumes or vapors J68.9
acute or subacute NEC J68.3
chronic J68.4
external agent J70.9
specified NEC J70.8
newborn P28.9
specified type NEC P28.89
upper J39.9
acute or subacute J06.9
noninfectious NEC J39.8
specified NEC J39.8
streptococcal J06.9
retina, retinal H35.9
Batten's or Batten-Mayou E75.4 *[H36]*
specified NEC H35.89
rheumatoid —*see* Arthritis, rheumatoid
rickettsial NOS A79.9
specified type NEC A79.89
Riga (-Fede) (cachectic aphthae) K14.0
Riggs'(compound periodontitis) —*see* Periodontitis
Ritter's L00
Rivalta's (cervicofacial actinomycosis) A42.2
Robles'(onchocerciasis) B73.01
Roger's (congenital interventricular septal defect) Q21.0
Rosenthal's (factor XI deficiency) D68.1
Rossbach's (hyperchlorhydria) K30
Ross River B33.1
Rotes Quérol —*see* Hyperostosis, ankylosing
Roth (-Bernhardt) —*see* Mononeuropathy, lower limb, meralgia paresthetica
Runeberg's (progressive pernicious anemia) D51.0
sacroiliac NEC M53.3
salivary gland or duct K11.9
inclusion B25.9
specified NEC K11.8
virus B25.9
sandworm B76.9

Disease, diseased *(continued)*
Schimmelbusch's —*see* Mastopathy, cystic
Schmorl's —*see* Schmorl's disease or nodes
Schönlein (-Henoch) (purpura rheumatica) D69.0
Schottmüller's —*see* Fever, paratyphoid
Schultz's (agranulocytosis) —*see* Agranulocytosis
Schwalbe-Ziehen-Oppenheim G24.1
Schwartz-Jampel G71.13
sclera H15.9
specified NEC H15.89
scrofulous (tuberculous) A18.2
scrotum N50.9
sebaceous glands L73.9
semilunar cartilage, cystic —*see also* Derangement, knee, meniscus, cystic
seminal vesicle N50.9
serum NEC —*see also* Reaction, serum T80.69
sexually transmitted A64
anogenital
herpesviral infection —*see* Herpes, anogenital
warts A63.0
chancroid A57
chlamydial infection —*see* Chlamydia
gonorrhea —*see* Gonorrhea
granuloma inguinale A58
specified organism NEC A63.8
syphilis —*see* Syphilis
trichomoniasis —*see* Trichomoniasis
Sézary C84.1-
shimamushi (scrub typhus) A75.3
shipyard B30.0
sickle-cell D57.1
with crisis (vasoocclusive pain) D57.00
with
acute chest syndrome D57.01
splenic sequestration D57.02
elliptocytosis D57.8-
Hb-C D57.20
with crisis (vasoocclusive pain) D57.219
with
acute chest syndrome D57.211
splenic sequestration D57.212
without crisis D57.20
Hb-SD D57.80
with crisis D57.819
with
acute chest syndrome D57.811
splenic sequestration D57.812
Hb-SE D57.80
with crisis D57.819
with
acute chest syndrome D57.811
splenic sequestration D57.812
specified NEC D57.80
with crisis D57.819
with
acute chest syndrome D57.811
splenic sequestration D57.812

Dislocation (articular)
- with fracture —*see* Fracture
- acromioclavicular (joint) S43.10-
  - with displacement
    - 100%-200% S43.12-
    - more than 200% S43.13-
  - inferior S43.14-
  - posterior S43.15-
- ankle S93.0-
- astragalus —*see* Dislocation, ankle
- atlantoaxial S13.121
- atlantooccipital S13.111
- atloidooccipital S13.111
- breast bone S23.29
- capsule, joint - code by site under Dislocation
- carpal (bone) —*see* Dislocation, wrist
- carpometacarpal (joint) NEC S63.05-
  - thumb S63.04-
- cartilage (joint) - code by site under Dislocation
- cervical spine (vertebra) —*see* Dislocation, vertebra, cervical
- chronic —*see* Dislocation, recurrent
- clavicle —*see* Dislocation, acromioclavicular joint
- coccyx S33.2
- congenital NEC Q68.8
- coracoid —*see* Dislocation, shoulder
- costal cartilage S23.29
- costochondral S23.29
- cricoarytenoid articulation S13.29
- cricothyroid articulation S13.29
- dorsal vertebra —*see* Dislocation, vertebra, thoracic
- ear ossicle —*see* Discontinuity, ossicles, ear
- elbow S53.10-
  - congenital Q68.8
  - pathological —*see* Dislocation, pathological NEC, elbow
  - radial head alone —*see* Dislocation, radial head
  - recurrent —*see* Dislocation, recurrent, elbow
  - traumatic S53.10-
    - anterior S53.11-
    - lateral S53.14-
    - medial S53.13-
    - posterior S53.12-
    - specified type NEC S53.19-
- eye, nontraumatic —*see* Luxation, globe
- eyeball, nontraumatic —*see* Luxation, globe
- femur
  - distal end —*see* Dislocation, knee
  - proximal end —*see* Dislocation, hip
- fibula
  - distal end —*see* Dislocation, ankle
  - proximal end —*see* Dislocation, knee
- finger S63.25-
  - index S63.25-
  - interphalangeal S63.27-
    - distal S63.29-
      - index S63.29-
      - little S63.29-
      - middle S63.29-
      - ring S63.29-
    - index S63.27-
    - little S63.27-
    - middle S63.27-
    - proximal S63.28-
      - index S63.28-
      - little S63.28-
      - middle S63.28-
      - ring S63.28-
    - ring S63.27-

Dislocation *(continued)*
- finger *(continued)*
  - little S63.25-
  - metacarpophalangeal S63.26-
    - index S63.26-
    - little S63.26-
    - middle S63.26-
    - ring S63.26-
  - middle S63.25-
  - recurrent —*see* Dislocation, recurrent, finger
  - ring S63.25-
  - thumb —*see* Dislocation, thumb
- foot S93.30-
  - recurrent —*see* Dislocation, recurrent, foot
  - specified site NEC S93.33-
  - tarsal joint S93.31-
  - tarsometatarsal joint S93.32-
  - toe —*see* Dislocation, toe
- fracture —*see* Fracture
- glenohumeral (joint) —*see* Dislocation, shoulder
- glenoid —*see* Dislocation, shoulder
- habitual —*see* Dislocation, recurrent
- hip S73.00-
  - anterior S73.03-
    - obturator S73.02-
  - central S73.04-
  - congenital (total) Q65.2
    - bilateral Q65.1
    - partial Q65.5
      - bilateral Q65.4
      - unilateral Q65.3-
    - unilateral Q65.0-
  - developmental M24.85-
  - pathological —*see* Dislocation, pathological NEC, hip
  - posterior S73.01-
  - recurrent —*see* Dislocation, recurrent, hip
- humerus, proximal end —*see* Dislocation, shoulder
- incomplete —*see* Subluxation, by site
- incus —*see* Discontinuity, ossicles, ear
- infracoracoid —*see* Dislocation, shoulder
- innominate (pubic junction) (sacral junction) S33.39
  - acetabulum —*see* Dislocation, hip
- interphalangeal (joint(s))
  - finger S63.279
    - distal S63.29-
      - index S63.29-
      - little S63.29-
      - middle S63.29-
      - ring S63.29-
    - index S63.27-
    - little S63.27-
    - middle S63.27-
    - proximal S63.28-
      - index S63.28-
      - little S63.28-
      - middle S63.28-
      - ring S63.28-
    - ring S63.27-
  - foot or toe —*see* Dislocation, toe
  - thumb S63.12-
    - distal joint S63.14-
    - proximal joint S63.13-
- jaw (cartilage) (meniscus) S03.0
- joint prosthesis —*see* Complications, joint prosthesis, mechanical, displacement, by site
- knee S83.106
  - cap —*see* Dislocation, patella
  - congenital Q68.2
  - old M23.8X-
  - patella —*see* Dislocation, patella
  - pathological —*see* Dislocation, pathological NEC, knee

Dislocation *(continued)*
- knee *(continued)*
  - proximal tibia
    - anteriorly S83.11-
    - laterally S83.14-
    - medially S83.13-
    - posteriorly S83.12-
  - recurrent —*see also* Derangement, knee, specified NEC
  - specified type NEC S83.19-
- lacrimal gland H04.16-
- lens (complete) H27.10
  - anterior H27.12-
  - congenital Q12.1
  - ocular implant —*see* Complications, intraocular lens
  - partial H27.11-
  - posterior H27.13-
  - traumatic S05.8X-
- ligament - code by site under Dislocation
- lumbar (vertebra) —*see* Dislocation, vertebra, lumbar
- lumbosacral (vertebra) —*see also* Dislocation, vertebra, lumbar
  - congenital Q76.49
- mandible S03.0
- meniscus (knee) —*see* Tear, meniscus
  - other sites - code by site under Dislocation
- metacarpal (bone)
  - distal end —*see* Dislocation, finger
  - proximal end S63.06-
- metacarpophalangeal (joint)
  - finger S63.26-
    - index S63.26-
    - little S63.26-
    - middle S63.26-
    - ring S63.26-
  - thumb S63.11-
- metatarsal (bone) —*see* Dislocation, foot
- metatarsophalangeal (joint(s)) —*see* Dislocation, toe
- midcarpal (joint) S63.03-
- midtarsal (joint) —*see* Dislocation, foot
- neck S13.20
  - specified site NEC S13.29
  - vertebra —*see* Dislocation, vertebra, cervical
- nose (septal cartilage) S03.1
- occipitoatloid S13.111
- old —*see* Derangement, joint, specified type NEC
- ossicles, ear —*see* Discontinuity, ossicles, ear
- partial —*see* Subluxation, by site
- patella S83.006
  - congenital Q74.1
  - lateral S83.01-
  - recurrent (nontraumatic) M22.0-
    - incomplete M22.1-
  - specified type NEC S83.09-
- pathological NEC M24.30
  - ankle M24.37-
  - elbow M24.32-
  - foot joint M24.37-
  - hand joint M24.34-
  - hip M24.35-
  - knee M24.36-
  - lumbosacral joint —*see* subcategory M53.2
  - pelvic region —*see* Dislocation, pathological, hip
  - sacroiliac —*see* subcategory M53.2
  - shoulder M24.31-
  - wrist M24.33-
- pelvis NEC S33.30
  - specified NEC S33.39
- phalanx
  - finger or hand —*see* Dislocation, finger

Dislocation *(continued)*
- phalanx *(continued)*
  - foot or toe —*see* Dislocation, toe
- prosthesis, internal —*see* Complications, prosthetic device, by site, mechanical
- radial head S53.006
  - anterior S53.01-
  - posterior S53.02-
  - specified type NEC S53.09-
- radiocarpal (joint) S63.02-
- radiohumeral (joint) —*see* Dislocation, radial head
- radioulnar (joint)
  - distal S63.01-
  - proximal —*see* Dislocation, elbow
- radius
  - distal end —*see* Dislocation, wrist
  - proximal end —*see* Dislocation, radial head
- recurrent M24.40
  - ankle M24.47-
  - elbow M24.42-
  - finger M24.44-
  - foot joint M24.47-
  - hand joint M24.44-
  - hip M24.45-
  - knee M24.46-
    - patella —*see* Dislocation, patella, recurrent
  - patella —*see* Dislocation, patella, recurrent
  - sacroiliac —*see* subcategory M53.
  - shoulder M24.41-
  - toe M24.47-
  - vertebra —*see also* subcategory M43.
    - atlantoaxial M43.4
      - with myelopathy M43.3
  - wrist M24.43-
- rib (cartilage) S23.29
- sacrococcygeal S33.2
- sacroiliac (joint) (ligament) S33.2
  - congenital Q74.2
  - recurrent M53.2
- sacrum S33.2
- scaphoid (bone) (hand) (wrist) —*see* Dislocation, wrist
  - foot —*see* Dislocation, foot
- scapula —*see* Dislocation, shoulder, girdle, scapula
- semilunar cartilage, knee —*see* Tear, meniscus
- septal cartilage (nose) S03.1
- septum (nasal) (old) J34.2
- sesamoid bone - code by site under Dislocation
- shoulder (blade) (ligament) (joint) (traumatic) S43.006
  - acromioclavicular —*see* Dislocation, acromioclavicular
  - chronic —*see* Dislocation, recurrent, shoulder
  - congenital Q68.8
  - girdle S43.30-
    - scapula S43.31-
    - specified site NEC S43.39-
  - humerus S43.00-
    - anterior S43.01-
    - inferior S43.03-
    - posterior S43.02-
  - pathological —*see* Dislocation, pathological NEC, shoulder
  - recurrent —*see* Dislocation, recurrent, shoulder
  - specified type NEC S43.08-
- spine
  - cervical —*see* Dislocation, vertebra, cervical
  - congenital Q76.49
  - due to birth trauma P11.5
  - lumbar —*see* Dislocation, vertebra lumbar

Dislocation *(continued)*
- spine *(continued)*
  - thoracic *—see* Dislocation, vertebra, thoracic
- spontaneous *—see* Dislocation, pathological
- sternoclavicular (joint) S43.206
  - anterior S43.21-
  - posterior S43.22-
- sternum S23.29
- subglenoid *—see* Dislocation, shoulder
- symphysis pubis S33.4
- talus *—see* Dislocation, ankle
- tarsal (bone(s)) (joint (s)) *—see* Dislocation, foot
- tarsometatarsal (joint(s)) *—see* Dislocation, foot
- temporomandibular (joint) S03.0
- thigh, proximal end *—see* Dislocation, hip
- thorax S23.20
  - specified site NEC S23.29
  - vertebra *—see* Dislocation, vertebra
- thumb S63.10-
  - interphalangeal joint *—see* Dislocation, interphalangeal (joint), thumb
  - metacarpophalangeal joint *—see* Dislocation, metacarpophalangeal (joint), thumb
- thyroid cartilage S13.29
- tibia
  - distal end *—see* Dislocation, ankle
  - proximal end *—see* Dislocation, knee
- tibiofibular (joint)
  - distal *—see* Dislocation, ankle
  - superior *—see* Dislocation, knee
- toe (s) S93.106
  - great S93.10-
    - interphalangeal joint S93.11-
    - metatarsophalangeal joint S93.12-
  - interphalangeal joint S93.119
  - lesser S93.106
    - interphalangeal joint S93.11-
    - metatarsophalangeal joint S93.12-
  - metatarsophalangeal joint S93.12-
- tooth S03.2
- trachea S23.29
- ulna
  - distal end S63.07-
  - proximal end *—see* Dislocation, elbow
- ulnohumeral (joint) *—see* Dislocation, elbow
- vertebra (articular process) (body) (traumatic)
  - cervical S13.101
    - atlantoaxial joint S13.121
    - atlantooccipital joint S13.111
    - atloidooccipital joint S13.111
    - joint between
      - C0 and C1 S13.111
      - C1 and C2 S13.121
      - C2 and C3 S13.131
      - C3 and C4 S13.141
      - C4 and C5 S13.151
      - C5and C6 S13.161
      - C6and C7 S13.171
      - C7and T1 S13.181
    - occipitoatloid joint S13.111
  - congenital Q76.49
  - lumbar S33.101
    - joint between
      - L1and L2 S33.111
      - L2and L3 S33.121
      - L3 and L4 S33.131
      - L4and L5 S33.141

Dislocation *(continued)*
- vertebra *(continued)*
  - nontraumatic *—see* Displacement, intervertebral disc
  - partial *—see* Subluxation, by site
  - recurrent NEC *—see* subcategory M43.5
  - thoracic S23.101
    - joint between
      - T1 and T2 S23.111
      - T2 and T3 S23.121
      - T3 and T4 S23.123
      - T4 and T5 S23.131
      - T5 and T6 S23.133
      - T6 and T7 S23.141
      - T7 and T8 S23.143
      - T8 and T9 S23.151
      - T9 and T10 S23.153
      - T10 and T11 S23.161
      - T11 and T12 S23.163
      - T12 and L1 S23.171
- wrist (carpal bone) S63.006
  - carpometacarpal joint *—see* Dislocation, carpometacarpal (joint)
  - distal radioulnar joint *—see* Dislocation, radioulnar (joint), distal
  - metacarpal bone, proximal *—see* Dislocation, metacarpal (bone), proximal end
  - midcarpal *—see* Dislocation, midcarpal (joint)
  - radiocarpal joint *—see* Dislocation, radiocarpal (joint)
  - recurrent *—see* Dislocation, recurrent, wrist
  - specified site NEC S63.09-
  - ulna *—see* Dislocation, ulna, distal end
- xiphoid cartilage S23.29

Disorder (of) *—see also* Disease
- acantholytic L11.9
  - specified NEC L11.8
- acute
  - psychotic *—see* Psychosis, acute
  - stress F43.0
- adjustment (grief) F43.20
  - with
    - anxiety F43.22
      - with depressed mood F43.23
    - conduct disturbance F43.24
      - with emotional disturbance F43.25
    - depressed mood F43.21
      - with anxiety F43.23
    - other specified symptom F43.29
- adrenal (capsule) (gland) (medullary) E27.9
  - specified NEC E27.8
- adrenogenital E25.9
  - drug-induced E25.8
  - iatrogenic E25.8
  - idiopathic E25.8
- adult personality (and behavior) F69
  - specified NEC F68.8
- affective (mood) *—see* Disorder, mood
- aggressive, unsocialized F91.1
- alcohol-related F10.99
  - with
    - amnestic disorder, persisting F10.96
    - anxiety disorder F10.980
    - dementia, persisting F10.97
    - intoxication F10.929
      - with delirium F10.921
      - uncomplicated F10.920
    - mood disorder F10.94
    - other specified F10.988

Disorder *(continued)*
- alcohol-related *(continued)*
  - with *(continued)*
    - psychotic disorder F10.959
      - with
        - delusions F10.950
        - hallucinations F10.951
    - sexual dysfunction F10.981
    - sleep disorder F10.982
- allergic *—see* Allergy
- alveolar NEC J84.09
- amino-acid
  - cystathioninuria E72.19
  - cystinosis E72.04
  - cystinuria E72.01
  - glycinuria E72.09
  - homocystinuria E72.11
  - metabolism *—see* Disturbance, metabolism, amino-acid
    - specified NEC E72.8
  - neonatal, transitory P74.8
  - renal transport NEC E72.09
  - transport NEC E72.09
- amnesic, amnestic
  - alcohol-induced F10.96
    - with dependence F10.26
  - due to (secondary to) general medical condition F04
  - psychoactive NEC-induced F19.96
    - with
      - abuse F19.16
      - dependence F19.26
  - sedative, hypnotic or anxiolytic-induced F13.96
    - with dependence F13.26
- anaerobic glycolysis with anemia D55.2
- anxiety F41.9
  - due to (secondary to)
    - alcohol F10.980
    - amphetamine F15.980
      - in
        - abuse F15.180
        - dependence F15.280
    - anxiolytic F13.980
      - in
        - abuse F13.180
        - dependence F13.280
    - caffeine F15.980
      - in
        - abuse F15.180
        - dependence F15.280
    - cannabis F12.980
      - in
        - abuse F12.180
        - dependence F12.280
    - cocaine F14.980
      - in
        - abuse F14.180
        - dependence F14.180
    - general medical condition F06.4
    - hallucinogen F16.980
      - in
        - abuse F16.180
        - dependence F16.280
    - hypnotic F13.980
      - in
        - abuse F13.180
        - dependence F13.280
    - inhalant F18.980
      - in
        - abuse F18.180
        - dependence F18.280
    - phencyclidine F16.980
      - in
        - abuse F16.180
        - dependence F16.280
    - psychoactive substance NEC F19.980
      - in
        - abuse F19.180
        - dependence F19.280

Disorder *(continued)*
- anxiety *(continued)*
  - due to *(continued)*
    - sedative F13.980
      - in
        - abuse F13.180
        - dependence F13.280
    - volatile solvents F18.980
      - in
        - abuse F18.180
        - dependence F18.280
  - generalized F41.1
  - mixed
    - with depression (mild) F41.8
    - specified NEC F41.3
  - organic F06.4
  - phobic F40.9
    - of childhood F40.8
  - specified NEC F41.8
- aortic valve *—see* Endocarditis, aortic
- aromatic amino-acid metabolism E70.9
  - specified NEC E70.8
- arteriole NEC I77.89
- artery NEC I77.89
- articulation *—see* Disorder, joint
- attachment (childhood)
  - disinhibited F94.2
  - reactive F94.1
- attention-deficit hyperactivity (adolescent) (adult) (child) F90.9
  - combined type F90.2
  - hyperactive type F90.1
  - inattentive type F90.0
  - specified type NEC F90.8
- attention-deficit without hyperactivity (adolescent) (adult) (child) F90.0
- auditory processing (central) H93.25
- autistic F84.0
- autonomic nervous system G90.9
  - specified NEC G90.8
- avoidant, child or adolescent F40.10
- balance
  - acid-base E87.8
    - mixed E87.4
  - electrolyte E87.8
  - fluid NEC E87.8
- behavioral (disruptive) *—see* Disorder, conduct
- beta-amino-acid metabolism E72.8
- bile acid and cholesterol metabolism E78.70
  - Barth syndrome E78.71
  - other specified E78.79
  - Smith-Lemli-Opitz syndrome E78.72
- bilirubin excretion E80.6
- binocular
  - movement H51.9
    - convergence
      - excess H51.12
      - insufficiency H51.11
    - internuclear ophthalmoplegia *—see* Ophthalmoplegia, internuclear
    - palsy of conjugate gaze H51.0
    - specified type NEC H51.8
  - vision NEC *—see* Disorder, vision, binocular
- bipolar (I) F31.9
  - current episode
    - depressed F31.9
      - with psychotic features F31.5
      - without psychotic features F31.30
        - mild F31.31
        - moderate F31.32
        - severe (without psychotic features) F31.4
          - with psychotic features F31.5

Disorder *(continued)*
developmental *(continued)*
expressive writing F81.81
language F80.9
expressive F80.1
mixed receptive and expressive F80.2
receptive type F80.2
specified NEC F80.89
learning F81.9
arithmetical F81.2
reading F81.0
mixed F88
motor coordination or function F82
pervasive F84.9
specified NEC F84.8
phonological F80.0
reading F81.0
scholastic skills *—see also* Disorder, learning
mixed F81.89
specified NEC F88
speech F80.9
articulation F80.0
specified NEC F80.89
written expression F81.81
diaphragm J98.6
digestive (system) K92.9
newborn P78.9
specified NEC P78.89
postprocedural *—see* Complication, gastrointestinal
psychogenic F45.8
disc (intervertebral) M51.9
with
myelopathy
cervical region M50.00
cervicothoracic region M50.03
high cervical region M50.01
lumbar region M51.06
mid-cervical region M50.02
sacrococcygeal region M53.3
thoracic region M51.04
thoracolumbar region M51.05
radiculopathy
cervical region M50.10
cervicothoracic region M50.13
high cervical region M50.11
lumbar region M51.16
lumbosacral region M51.17
mid-cervical region M50.12
sacrococcygeal region M53.3
thoracic region M51.14
thoracolumbar region M51.15
cervical M50.90
with
myelopathy M50.00
C2-C3 M50.01
C3-C4 M50.01
C4-C5 M50.02
C5-C6 M50.02
C6-C7 M50.02
C7-T1 M50.03
cervicothoracic region M50.03
high cervical region M50.01
mid-cervical region M50.02
neuritis, radiculitis or radiculopathy M50.10
C2-C3 M50.11
C3-C4 M50.11
C4-C5 M50.12
C5-C6 M50.12
C6-C7 M50.12
C7-T1 M50.13
cervicothoracic region M50.13
high cervical region M50.11
mid-cervical region M50.12

Disorder *(continued)*
disc *(continued)*
cervical *(continued)*
C2-C3 M50.91
C3-C4 M50.91
C4-C5 M50.92
C5-C6 M50.92
C6-C7 M50.92
C7-T1 M50.93
cervicothoracic region M50.93
degeneration M50.30
C2-C3 M50.31
C3-C4 M50.31
C4-C5 M50.32
C5-C6 M50.32
C6-C7 M50.32
C7-T1 M50.33
cervicothoracic region M50.33
high cervical region M50.31
mid-cervical region M50.32
displacement M50.20
C2-C3 M50.21
C3-C4 M50.21
C4-C5 M50.22
C5-C6 M50.22
C6-C7 M50.22
C7-T1 M50.23
cervicothoracic region M50.23
high cervical region M50.21
mid-cervical region M50.22
high cervical region M50.91
mid-cervical region M50.92
specified type NEC M50.80
C2-C3 M50.81
C3-C4 M50.81
C4-C5 M50.82
C5-C6 M50.82
C6-C7 M50.82
C7-T1 M50.83
cervicothoracic region M50.83
high cervical region M50.81
mid-cervical region M50.82
specified NEC
lumbar region M51.86
lumbosacral region M51.87
sacrococcygeal region M53.3
thoracic region M51.84
thoracolumbar region M51.85
disinhibited attachment (childhood) F94.2
disintegrative, childhood NEC F84.3
disruptive behavior F98.9
dissocial personality F60.2
dissociative F44.9
affecting
motor function F44.4
and sensation F44.7
sensation F44.6
and motor function F44.7
brief reactive F43.0
due to (secondary to) general medical condition F06.8
mixed F44.7
organic F06.8
other specified NEC F44.89
double heterozygous sickling *—see* Disease, sickle-cell
dream anxiety F51.5
drug induced hemorrhagic D68.32
drug related F19.99
abuse *—see* Abuse, drug
dependence *—see* Dependence, drug
dysmorphic body F45.1
dysthymic F34.1
ear H93.9-
bleeding *—see* Otorrhagia
deafness *—see* Deafness
degenerative H93.09-

Disorder *(continued)*
ear *(continued)*
discharge *—see* Otorrhea
external H61.9-
auditory canal stenosis *—see* Stenosis, external ear canal
exostosis *—see* Exostosis, external ear canal
impacted cerumen *—see* Impaction, cerumen
otitis *—see* Otitis, externa
perichondritis *—see* Perichondritis, ear
pinna *—see* Disorder, pinna
specified type NEC H61.89-
in diseases classified elsewhere H62.8X-
inner H83.9-
vestibular dysfunction *—see* Disorder, vestibular function
middle H74.9-
adhesive H74.1-
ossicle *—see* Abnormal, ear ossicles
polyp *—see* Polyp, ear (middle)
specified NEC, in diseases classified elsewhere H75.8-
postprocedural *—see* Complications, ear, procedure
specified NEC, in diseases classified elsewhere H94.8-
eating (adult) (psychogenic) F50.9
anorexia *—see* Anorexia
bulimia F50.2
child F98.29
pica F98.3
rumination disorder F98.21
pica F50.8
childhood F98.3
electrolyte (balance) NEC E87.8
with
abortion *—see* Abortion by type complicated by specified condition NEC
ectopic pregnancy O08.5
molar pregnancy O08.5
acidosis (metabolic) (respiratory) E87.2
alkalosis (metabolic) (respiratory) E87.3
elimination, transepidermal L87.9
specified NEC L87.8
emotional (persistent) F34.9
of childhood F93.9
specified NEC F93.8
endocrine E34.9
postprocedural E89.89
specified NEC E89.89
erectile (male) (organic) *—see also* Dysfunction, sexual, male, erectile N52.9
nonorganic F52.21
erythematous *—see* Erythema
esophagus K22.9
functional K22.4
psychogenic F45.8
eustachian tube H69.9-
infection *—see* Salpingitis, eustachian
obstruction *—see* Obstruction, eustachian tube
patulous *—see* Patulous, eustachian tube
specified NEC H69.8-
extrapyramidal G25.9
in diseases classified elsewhere *—see* category G26
specified type NEC G25.89
eye H57.9
postprocedural *—see* Complication, postprocedural, eye

Disorder *(continued)*
eyelid H02.9
cyst *—see* Cyst, eyelid
degenerative H02.70
chloasma *—see* Chloasma, eyelid
madarosis *—see* Madarosis
specified type NEC H02.79
vitiligo *—see* Vitiligo, eyelid
xanthelasma *—see* Xanthelasma
dermatochalasis *—see* Dermatochalasis
edema *—see* Edema, eyelid
elephantiasis *—see* Elephantiasis, eyelid
foreign body, retained *—see* Foreign body, retained, eyelid
function H02.59
abnormal innervation syndrome *—see* Syndrome, abnormal innervation
blepharochalasis *—see* Blepharochalasis
blepharoclonus *—see* Blepharoclonus
blepharophimosis *—see* Blepharophimosis
blepharoptosis *—see* Blepharoptosis
lagophthalmos *—see* Lagophthalmos
lid retraction *—see* Retraction, lid
hypertrichosis *—see* Hypertrichosis, eyelid
specified type NEC H02.89
vascular H02.879
left H02.876
lower H02.875
upper H02.874
right H02.873
lower H02.872
upper H02.871
factitious F68.10
with predominantly
psychological symptoms F68.11
with physical symptoms F68.13
physical symptoms F68.12
with psychological symptoms F68.13
factor, coagulation *—see* Defect, coagulation
fatty acid
metabolism E71.30
specified NEC E71.39
oxidation
LCAD E71.310
MCAD E71.311
SCAD E71.312
specified deficiency NEC E71.318
feeding (infant or child) *—see also* Disorder, eating R63.3
feigned (with obvious motivation) Z76.5
without obvious motivation *—see* Disorder, factitious
female
hypoactive sexual desire F52.0
orgasmic F52.31
sexual arousal F52.22
fibroblastic M72.9
specified NEC M72.8
fluency
adult onset F98.5
childhood onset F80.81
following
cerebral infarction I69.323

Disorder *(continued)*
  fluency *(continued)*
    following *(continued)*
      cerebrovascular disease I69.923
        specified disease NEC I69.823
      intracerebral hemorrhage I69.123
      nontraumatic intracranial hemorrhage NEC I69.223
      subarachnoid hemorrhage I69.023
    in conditions classified elsewhere R47.82
  fluid balance E87.8
  follicular (skin) L73.9
    specified NEC L73.8
  fructose metabolism E74.10
    essential fructosuria E74.11
    fructokinase deficiency E74.11
    fructose-1, 6-diphosphatase deficiency E74.19
    hereditary fructose intolerance E74.12
    other specified E74.19
  functional polymorphonuclear neutrophils D71
  gallbladder, biliary tract and pancreas in diseases classified elsewhere K87
  gamma-glutamyl cycle E72.8
  gastric (functional) K31.9
    motility K30
    psychogenic F45.8
    secretion K30
  gastrointestinal (functional) NOS K92.9
    newborn P78.9
    psychogenic F45.8
  gender-identity or -role F64.9
    childhood F64.2
    effect on relationship F66
    of adolescence or adulthood (nontranssexual) F64.1
    specified NEC F64.8
    uncertainty F66
  genitourinary system
    female N94.9
    male N50.9
    psychogenic F45.8
  globe H44.9
    degenerated condition H44.50
      absolute glaucoma H44.51-
      atrophy H44.52-
      leucocoria H44.53-
    degenerative H44.30
      chalcosis H44.31-
      myopia H44.2-
      siderosis H44.32-
      specified type NEC H44.39-
    endophthalmitis *—see* Endophthalmitis
    foreign body, retained *—see* Foreign body, intraocular, old, retained
    hemophthalmos *—see* Hemophthalmos
    hypotony H44.40
      due to
        ocular fistula H44.42-
        specified disorder NEC H44.43-
      flat anterior chamber H44.41-
      primary H44.44-
    luxation *—see* Luxation, globe
    specified type NEC H44.89
  glomerular (in) N05.9
    amyloidosis E85.4 *[N08]*
    cryoglobulinemia D89.1 *[N08]*
    disseminated intravascular coagulation D65 *[N08]*
    Fabry's disease E75.21 *[N08]*

Disorder *(continued)*
  glomerular *(continued)*
    familial lecithin cholesterol acyltransferase deficiency E78.6 *[N08]*
    Goodpasture's syndrome M31.0
    hemolytic-uremic syndrome D59.3
    Henoch (-Schönlein) purpura D69.0 *[N08]*
    malariae malaria B52.0
    microscopic polyangiitis M31.7 *[N08]*
    multiple myeloma C90.0- *[N08]*
    mumps B26.83
    schistosomiasis B65.9 *[N08]*
    sepsis NEC A41.- N08
      streptococcal A40.- [N08]
    sickle-cell disorders D57.- *[N08]*
    strongyloidiasis B78.9 *[N08]*
    subacute bacterial endocarditis I33.0 *[N08]*
    syphilis A52.75
    systemic lupus erythematosus M32.14
    thrombotic thrombocytopenic purpura M31.1 *[N08]*
    Waldenström macroglobulinemia C88.0 *[N08]*
    Wegener's granulomatosis M31.31
  gluconeogenesis E74.4
  glucosaminoglycan metabolism *—see* Disorder, metabolism, glucosaminoglycan
  glycine metabolism E72.50
    d-glycericacidemia E72.59
    hyperhydroxyprolinemia E72.59
    hyperoxaluria E72.53
    hyperprolinemia E72.59
    non-ketotic hyperglycinemia E72.51
    oxalosis E72.53
    oxaluria E72.53
    sarcosinemia E72.59
    trimethylaminuria E72.52
  glycoprotein metabolism E77.9
    specified NEC E77.8
  habit (and impulse) F63.9
    involving sexual behavior NEC F65.9
    specified NEC F63.89
  heart action I49.9
  hematological D75.9
    newborn (transient) P61.9
      specified NEC P61.8
  hematopoietic organs D75.9
  hemorrhagic NEC D69.9
    drug-induced D68.32
    due to
      extrinsic circulating anticoagulants D68.32
      increase in
        anti-IIa D68.32
        anti-Xa D68.32
      intrinsic
        circulating anticoagulants D68.318
        increase in
          antithrombin D68.318
          anti-VIIIa D68.318
          anti-IXa D68.318
          anti-XIa D68.318
    following childbirth O72.3
  hemostasis *—see* Defect, coagulation
  histidine metabolism E70.40
    histidinemia E70.41
    other specified E70.49
  hyperkinetic *—see* Disorder, attention-deficit hyperactivity
  hyperleucine-isoleucinemia E71.19
  hypervalinemia E71.19
  hypoactive sexual desire F52.0

Disorder *(continued)*
  hypochondriacal F45.20
    body dysmorphic F45.22
    neurosis F45.21
    other specified F45.29
  identity
    dissociative F44.81
    of childhood F93.8
  immune mechanism (immunity) D89.9
    specified type NEC D89.89
  impaired renal tubular function N25.9
    specified NEC N25.89
  impulse (control) F63.9
  inflammatory
    pelvic, in diseases classified elsewhere *—see* category N74
    penis N48.29
      abscess N48.21
      cellulitis N48.22
  integument, newborn P83.9
    specified NEC P83.8
  intermittent explosive F63.81
  internal secretion pancreas *—see* Increased, secretion, pancreas, endocrine
  intestine, intestinal
    carbohydrate absorption NEC E74.39
      postoperative K91.2
    functional NEC K59.9
      postoperative K91.89
    psychogenic F45.8
    vascular K55.9
      chronic K55.1
      specified NEC K55.8
  intraoperative (intraprocedural) *—see* Complications, intraoperative
  involuntary emotional expression (IEED) F48.2
  iris H21.9
    adhesions *—see* Adhesions, iris
    atrophy *—see* Atrophy, iris
    chamber angle recession *—see* Recession, chamber angle
    cyst *—see* Cyst, iris
    degeneration *—see* Degeneration, iris
    in diseases classified elsewhere H22
    iridodialysis *—see* Iridodialysis
    iridoschisis *—see* Iridoschisis
    miotic pupillary cyst *—see* Cyst, pupillary
    pupillary
      abnormality *—see* Abnormality, pupillary
      membrane *—see* Membrane, pupillary
    specified type NEC H21.89
    vascular NEC H21.1X-
  iron metabolism E83.10
    specified NEC E83.19
  isovaleric acidemia E71.110
  jaw, developmental M27.0
    temporomandibular *—see* Anomaly, dentofacial, temporomandibular joint
  joint M25.9
    derangement *—see* Derangement, joint
    effusion *—see* Effusion, joint
    fistula *—see* Fistula, joint
    hemarthrosis *—see* Hemarthrosis
    instability *—see* Instability, joint
    osteophyte *—see* Osteophyte
    pain *—see* Pain, joint
    psychogenic F45.8
    specified type NEC M25.80
      ankle M25.87-
      elbow M25.82-
      foot joint M25.87-

Disorder *(continued)*
  joint *(continued)*
    specified type NEC *(continued)*
      hand joint M25.84-
      hip M25.85-
      knee M25.86-
      shoulder M25.81-
      wrist M25.83-
    stiffness *—see* Stiffness, joint
  ketone metabolism E71.32
  kidney N28.9
    functional (tubular) N25.9
    in
      schistosomiasis B65.9 *[N29]*
    tubular function N25.9
      specified NEC N25.89
  lacrimal system H04.9
    changes H04.69
      fistula *—see* Fistula, lacrimal
    gland H04.19
      atrophy *—see* Atrophy, lacrimal gland
      cyst *—see* Cyst, lacrimal, gland
      dacryops *—see* Dacryops
      dislocation *—see* Dislocation, lacrimal gland
      dry eye syndrome *—see* Syndrome, dry eye
      infection *—see* Dacryoadenitis
    granuloma *—see* Granuloma, lacrimal
    inflammation *—see* Inflammation, lacrimal
    obstruction *—see* Obstruction, lacrimal
    specified NEC H04.89
  lactation NEC O92.79
  language (developmental) F80.9
    expressive F80.1
    mixed receptive and expressive F80.2
    receptive F80.2
  late luteal phase dysphoric N94.89
  learning (specific) F81.9
    acalculia R48.8
    alexia R48.0
    mathematics F81.2
    reading F81.0
    specified NEC F81.89
    spelling F81.81
    written expression F81.81
  lens H27.9
    aphakia *—see* Aphakia
    cataract *—see* Cataract
    dislocation *—see* Dislocation, lens
    specified type NEC H27.8
  ligament M24.20
    ankle M24.27-
    attachment, spine *—see* Enthesopathy, spinal
    elbow M24.22-
    foot joint M24.27-
    hand joint M24.24-
    hip M24.25-
    knee *—see* Derangement, knee, specified NEC
    shoulder M24.21-
    vertebra M24.28
    wrist M24.23-
  ligamentous attachments *—see also* Enthesopathy
    spine *—see* Enthesopathy, spinal
  lipid
    metabolism, congenital E78.9
    storage E75.6
      specified NEC E75.5
  lipoprotein
    deficiency (familial) E78.6
    metabolism E78.9
      specified NEC E78.89
  liver K76.9
    malarial B54 *[K77]*

Disorder *(continued)*
- low back —*see also* Dorsopathy, specified NEC
- lumbosacral
  - plexus G54.1
  - root (nerve) NEC G54.4
- lung, interstitial, drug-induced J70.4
  - acute J70.2
  - chronic J70.3
- lymphoproliferative, post-transplant (PTLD) D47.Z1
- lysine and hydroxylysine metabolism E72.3
- male
  - erectile (organic) —*see also* Dysfunction, sexual, male, erectile N52.9
    - nonorganic F52.21
  - hypoactive sexual desire F52.0
  - orgasmic F52.32
- manic F30.9
  - organic F06.33
- mastoid —*see also* Disorder, ear, middle
  - postprocedural —*see* Complications, ear, procedure
- meniscus —*see* Derangement, knee, meniscus
- menopausal N95.9
  - specified NEC N95.8
- menstrual N92.6
  - psychogenic F45.8
  - specified NEC N92.5
- mental (or behavioral) (nonpsychotic) F99
  - due to (secondary to)
    - amphetamine
      - due to drug abuse —*see* Abuse, drug, stimulant
      - due to drug dependence —*see* Dependence, drug, stimulant
    - brain disease, damage and dysfunction F09
    - caffeine use
      - due to drug abuse —*see* Abuse, drug, stimulant
      - due to drug dependence —*see* Dependence, drug, stimulant
    - cannabis use
      - due to drug abuse —*see* Abuse, drug, cannabis
      - due to drug dependence —*see* Dependence, drug, cannabis
    - general medical condition F09
    - sedative or hypnotic use
      - due to drug abuse —*see* Abuse, drug, sedative
      - due to drug dependence —*see* Dependence, drug, sedative
    - tobacco (nicotine) use —*see* Dependence, drug, nicotine
  - following organic brain damage F07.9
    - frontal lobe syndrome F07.0
    - personality change F07.0
    - postconcussional syndrome F07.81
    - specified NEC F07.89
  - infancy, childhood or adolescence F98.9
  - neurotic —*see* Neurosis
  - organic or symptomatic F09
  - presenile, psychotic F03
  - problem NEC
  - psychoneurotic —*see* Neurosis
  - psychotic —*see* Psychosis
  - puerperal F53
  - senile, psychotic NEC F03
- metabolic, amino acid, transitory, newborn P74.8

Disorder *(continued)*
- metabolism NOS E88.9
  - amino-acid E72.9
    - aromatic E70.9
      - albinism —*see* Albinism
      - histidine E70.40
        - histidinemia E70.41
        - other specified E70.49
      - hyperphenylalaninemia E70.1
        - classical phenylketonuria E70.0
      - other specified E70.8
      - tryptophan E70.5
      - tyrosine E70.20
        - hypertyrosinemia E70.21
        - other specified E70.29
    - branched chain E71.2
      - 3-methylglutaconic aciduria E71.111
      - hyperleucine-isoleucinemia E71.19
      - hypervalinemia E71.19
      - isovaleric acidemia E71.110
      - maple syrup urine disease E71.0
      - methylmalonic acidemia E71.120
      - organic aciduria NEC E71.118
      - other specified E71.19
      - proprionate NEC E71.128
      - proprionic acidemia E71.121
    - glycine E72.50
      - d-glycericacidemia E72.59
      - hyperhydroxyprolinemia E72.59
      - hyperoxaluria E72.53
      - hyperprolinemia E72.59
      - non-ketotic hyperglycinemia E72.51
      - other specified E72.59
      - sarcosinemia E72.59
      - trimethylaminuria E72.52
    - hydroxylysine E72.3
    - lysine E72.3
    - ornithine E72.4
    - other specified E72.8
      - beta-amino acid E72.8
      - gamma-glutamyl cycle E72.8
    - straight-chain E72.8
    - sulfur-bearing E72.10
      - homocystinuria E72.11
      - methylenetetrahydrofolate reductase deficiency E72.12
      - other specified E72.19
  - bile acid and cholesterol metabolism E78.70
  - bilirubin E80.7
    - specified NEC E80.6
  - calcium E83.50
    - hypercalcemia E83.52
    - hypocalcemia E83.51
    - other specified E83.59
  - carbohydrate E74.9
    - specified NEC E74.8
  - cholesterol and bile acid metabolism E78.70
  - congenital E88.9
  - copper E83.00
    - Wilson's disease E83.01
    - specified type NEC E83.09
  - cystinuria E72.01
  - fructose E74.10
  - galactose E74.20
  - glucosaminoglycan E76.9
    - mucopolysaccharidosis —*see* Mucopolysaccharidosis
    - specified NEC E76.8
  - glutamine E72.8
  - glycine E72.50
  - glycogen storage (hepatorenal) E74.09
  - glycoprotein E77.9
    - specified NEC E77.8

Disorder *(continued)*
- metabolism NOS *(continued)*
  - glycosaminoglycan E76.9
    - specified NEC E76.8
  - in labor and delivery O75.89
  - iron E83.10
  - isoleucine E71.19
  - leucine E71.19
  - lipoid E78.9
  - lipoprotein E78.9
    - specified NEC E78.89
  - magnesium E83.40
    - hypermagnesemia E83.41
    - hypomagnesemia E83.42
    - other specified E83.49
  - mineral E83.9
    - specified NEC E83.89
  - mitochondrial E88.40
    - MELAS syndrome E88.41
    - MERRF syndrome (myoclonic epilepsy associated with ragged-red fibers) E88.42
    - other specified E88.49
  - ornithine E72.4
  - phosphatases E83.30
  - phosphorus E83.30
    - acid phosphatase deficiency E83.39
    - hypophosphatasia E83.39
    - hypophosphatemia E83.39
      - familial E83.31
    - other specified E83.39
    - pseudovitamin D deficiency E83.32
  - plasma protein NEC E88.09
  - porphyrin —*see* Porphyria
  - postprocedural E89.89
    - specified NEC E89.89
  - purine E79.9
    - specified NEC E79.8
  - pyrimidine E79.9
    - specified NEC E79.8
  - pyruvate E74.4
  - serine E72.8
  - sodium E87.8
  - specified NEC E88.89
  - threonine E72.8
  - valine E71.19
  - zinc E83.2
- methylmalonic acidemia E71.120
- micturition NEC R39.19
  - feeling of incomplete emptying R39.14
  - hesitancy R39.11
  - poor stream R39.12
  - psychogenic F45.8
  - split stream R39.13
  - straining R39.16
  - urgency R39.15
- mitochondrial metabolism E88.40
- mitral (valve) —*see* Endocarditis, mitral
- mixed
  - anxiety and depressive F41.8
  - of scholastic skills (developmental) F81.89
  - receptive expressive language F80.2
- mood F39
  - bipolar —*see* Disorder, bipolar
  - depressive —*see* Disorder, depressive
  - due to (secondary to)
    - alcohol F10.94
    - amphetamine F15.94
      - in
        - abuse F15.14
        - dependence F15.24
    - anxiolytic F13.94
      - in
        - abuse F13.14
        - dependence F13.24

Disorder *(continued)*
- mood *(continued)*
  - due to *(continued)*
    - cocaine F14.94
      - in
        - abuse F14.14
        - dependence F14.24
    - general medical condition F06.30
    - hallucinogen F16.94
      - in
        - abuse F16.14
        - dependence F16.24
    - hypnotic F13.94
      - in
        - abuse F13.14
        - dependence F13.24
    - inhalant F18.94
      - in
        - abuse F18.14
        - dependence F18.24
    - opioid F11.94
      - in
        - abuse F11.14
        - dependence F11.24
    - phencyclidine (PCP) F16.94
      - in
        - abuse F16.14
        - dependence F16.24
    - physiological condition F06.30
      - with
        - depressive features F06.31
        - major depressive-like episode F06.32
        - manic features F06.33
        - mixed features F06.34
    - psychoactive substance NEC F19.94
      - in
        - abuse F19.14
        - dependence F19.24
    - sedative F13.94
      - in
        - abuse F13.14
        - dependence F13.24
    - volatile solvents F18.94
      - in
        - abuse F18.14
        - dependence F18.24
  - manic episode F30.9
    - with psychotic symptoms F30.2
    - in remission (full) F30.4
      - partial F30.3
    - specified type NEC F30.8
    - without psychotic symptoms F30.10
      - mild F30.11
      - moderate F30.12
      - severe F30.13
  - organic F06.30
    - right hemisphere F07.89
  - persistent F34.9
    - cyclothymia F34.0
    - dysthymia F34.1
    - specified type NEC F34.8
  - recurrent F39
  - right hemisphere organic F07.89
- movement G25.9
  - drug-induced G25.70
    - akathisia G25.71
    - specified NEC G25.79
  - hysterical F44.4
  - in diseases classified elsewhere —*see* category G26
  - periodic limb G47.61
    - sleep related G47.61
  - specified NEC G25.89
  - sleep related NEC G47.69
  - stereotyped F98.4
  - treatment-induced G25.9
- multiple personality F44.81

Disorder *(continued)*
muscle M62.9
attachment, spine —*see* Enthesopathy, spinal
in trichinellosis —*see* Trichinellosis, with muscle disorder
psychogenic F45.8
specified type NEC M62.89
tone, newborn P94.9
specified NEC P94.8
muscular
attachments —*see also* Enthesopathy
spine —*see* Enthesopathy, spinal
urethra N36.44
musculoskeletal system, soft tissue —*see* Disorder, soft tissue
postprocedural M96.89
psychogenic F45.8
myoneural G70.9
due to lead G70.1
specified NEC G70.89
toxic G70.1
myotonic NEC G71.19
nail, in diseases classified elsewhere L62
neck region NEC —*see* Dorsopathy, specified NEC
nerve G58.9
abducent NEC —*see* Strabismus, paralytic, sixth nerve
accessory G52.8
acoustic —*see* subcategory H93.3
auditory —*see* subcategory H93.3
auriculotemporal G50.8
axillary G54.0
cerebral —*see* Disorder, nerve, cranial
cranial G52.9
eighth —*see* subcategory H93.3
eleventh G52.8
fifth G50.9
first G52.0
fourth NEC —*see* Strabismus, paralytic, fourth nerve
multiple G52.7
ninth G52.1
second NEC —*see* Disorder, nerve, optic
seventh NEC G51.8
sixth NEC —*see* Strabismus, paralytic, sixth nerve
specified NEC G52.8
tenth G52.2
third NEC —*see* Strabismus, paralytic, third nerve
twelfth G52.3
entrapment —*see* Neuropathy, entrapment
facial G51.9
specified NEC G51.8
femoral —*see* Lesion, nerve, femoral
glossopharyngeal NEC G52.1
hypoglossal G52.3
intercostal G58.0
lateral
cutaneous of thigh —*see* Mononeuropathy, lower limb, meralgia paresthetica
popliteal —*see* Lesion, nerve, popliteal
lower limb —*see* Mononeuropathy, lower limb
medial popliteal —*see* Lesion, nerve, popliteal, medial
median NEC —*see* Lesion, nerve, median
multiple G58.7
oculomotor NEC —*see* Strabismus, paralytic, third nerve

Disorder *(continued)*
nerve *(continued)*
olfactory G52.0
optic NEC H47.09-
hemorrhage into sheath —*see* Hemorrhage, optic nerve
ischemic H47.01-
peroneal —*see* Lesion, nerve, popliteal
phrenic G58.8
plantar —*see* Lesion, nerve, plantar
pneumogastric G52.2
posterior tibial —*see* Syndrome, tarsal tunnel
radial —*see* Lesion, nerve, radial
recurrent laryngeal G52.2
root G54.9
cervical G54.2
lumbosacral G54.1
specified NEC G54.8
thoracic G54.3
sciatic NEC —*see* Lesion, nerve, sciatic
specified NEC G58.8
lower limb —*see* Mononeuropathy, lower limb, specified NEC
upper limb —*see* Mononeuropathy, upper limb, specified NEC
sympathetic G90.9
tibial —*see* Lesion, nerve, popliteal, medial
trigeminal G50.9
specified NEC G50.8
trochlear NEC —*see* Strabismus, paralytic, fourth nerve
ulnar —*see* Lesion, nerve, ulnar
upper limb —*see* Mononeuropathy, upper limb
vagus G52.2
nervous system G98.8
autonomic (peripheral) G90.9
specified NEC G90.8
central G96.9
specified NEC G96.8
parasympathetic G90.9
specified NEC G98.8
sympathetic G90.9
vegetative G90.9
neurohypophysis NEC E23.3
neurological NEC R29.818
neuromuscular G70.9
hereditary NEC G71.9
specified NEC G70.89
toxic G70.1
neurotic F48.9
specified NEC F48.8
neutrophil, polymorphonuclear D71
nicotine use —*see* Dependence, drug, nicotine
nightmare F51.5
nose J34.9
specified NEC J34.89
obsessive-compulsive F42
odontogenesis NOS K00.9
opioid use
with
opioid-induced psychotic disorder F11.959
with
delusions F11.950
hallucinations F11.951
due to drug abuse —*see* Abuse, drug, opioid
due to drug dependence —*see* Dependence, drug, opioid
oppositional defiant F91.3
optic
chiasm H47.49
due to
inflammatory disorder H47.41

Disorder *(continued)*
optic *(continued)*
chiasm *(continued)*
due to *(continued)*
neoplasm H47.42
vascular disorder H47.43
disc H47.39-
coloboma —*see* Coloboma, optic disc
drusen —*see* Drusen, optic disc
pseudopapilledema —*see* Pseudopapilledema
radiations —*see* Disorder, visual, pathway
tracts —*see* Disorder, visual, pathway
orbit H05.9
cyst —*see* Cyst, orbit
deformity —*see* Deformity, orbit
edema —*see* Edema, orbit
enophthalmos —*see* Enophthalmos
exophthalmos —*see* Exophthalmos
hemorrhage —*see* Hemorrhage, orbit
inflammation —*see* Inflammation, orbit
myopathy —*see* Myopathy, extraocular muscles
retained foreign body —*see* Foreign body, orbit, old
specified type NEC H05.89
organic
anxiety F06.4
catatonic F06.1
delusional F06.2
dissociative F06.8
emotionally labile (asthenic) F06.8
mood (affective) F06.30
schizophrenia-like F06.2
orgasmic (female) F52.31
male F52.32
ornithine metabolism E72.4
overanxious F41.1
of childhood F93.8
pain
with related psychological factors F45.42
exclusively related to psychological factors F45.41
pancreatic internal secretion E16.9
specified NEC E16.8
panic F41.0
with agoraphobia F40.01
papulosquamous L44.9
in diseases classified elsewhere L45
specified NEC L44.8
paranoid F22
induced F24
shared F24
parathyroid (gland) E21.5
specified NEC E21.4
parietoalveolar NEC J84.09
paroxysmal, mixed R56.9
patella M22.9-
chondromalacia —*see* Chondromalacia, patella
derangement NEC M22.3X-
recurrent
dislocation —*see* Dislocation, patella, recurrent
subluxation —*see* Dislocation, patella, recurrent, incomplete
specified NEC M22.8X-
patellofemoral M22.2X-
pentose phosphate pathway with anemia D55.1
perception, due to hallucinogens F16.983
in
abuse F16.183
dependence F16.283

Disorder *(continued)*
peripheral nervous system NEC G64
peroxisomal E71.50
biogenesis
neonatal adrenoleukodystrophy E71.511
specified disorder NEC E71.518
Zellweger syndrome E71.510
rhizomelic chondrodysplasia punctata E71.540
specified form NEC E71.548
group 1 E71.518
group 2 E71.53
group 3 E71.542
X-linked adrenoleukodystrophy E71.529
adolescent E71.521
adrenomyeloneuropathy E71.522
childhood E71.520
specified form NEC E71.528
Zellweger-like syndrome E71.541
persistent
(somatoform) pain F45.41
affective (mood) F34.9
personality —*see also* Personality F60.9
affective F34.0
aggressive F60.3
amoral F60.2
anankastic F60.5
antisocial F60.2
anxious F60.6
asocial F60.2
asthenic F60.7
avoidant F60.6
borderline F60.3
change (secondary) due to general medical condition F07.0
compulsive F60.5
cyclothymic F34.0
dependent (passive) F60.7
depressive F34.1
dissocial F60.2
emotional instability F60.3
expansive paranoid F60.0
explosive F60.3
following organic brain damage F07.9
histrionic F60.4
hyperthymic F34.0
hypothymic F34.1
hysterical F60.4
immature F60.89
inadequate F60.7
labile F60.3
mixed (nonspecific) F60.89
moral deficiency F60.2
narcissistic F60.81
negativistic F60.89
obsessional F60.5
obsessive (-compulsive) F60.5
organic F07.9
overconscientious F60.5
paranoid F60.0
passive (-dependent) F60.7
passive-aggressive F60.89
pathological NEC F60.9
pseudosocial F60.2
psychopathic F60.2
schizoid F60.1
schizotypal F21
self-defeating F60.7
specified NEC F60.89
type A F60.5
unstable (emotional) F60.3
pervasive, developmental F84.9
phobic anxiety, childhood F40.8
phosphate-losing tubular N25.0

Disorder *(continued)*
- pigmentation L81.9
  - choroid, congenital Q14.3
  - diminished melanin formation L81.6
  - iron L81.8
  - specified NEC L81.8
- pinna (noninfective) H61.10-
  - deformity, acquired H61.11-
  - hematoma H61.12-
  - perichondritis —*see* Perichondritis, ear
  - specified type NEC H61.19-
- pituitary gland E23.7
  - iatrogenic (postprocedural) E89.3
  - specified NEC E23.6
- platelets D69.1
- plexus G54.9
  - specified NEC G54.8
- polymorphonuclear neutrophils D71
- porphyrin metabolism —*see* Porphyria
- postconcussional F07.81
- posthallucinogen perception F16.983
  - in
    - abuse F16.183
    - dependence F16.283
- postmenopausal N95.9
  - specified NEC N95.8
- postprocedural (postoperative) —*see* Complications, postprocedural
- post-transplant lymphoproliferative D47.Z1
- post-traumatic stress (PTSD) F43.10
  - acute F43.11
  - chronic F43.12
- premenstrual dysphoric (PMDD) N94.3
- prepuce N47.8
- propionic acidemia E71.121
- prostate N42.9
  - specified NEC N42.89
- psychogenic NOS —*see also* condition F45.9
  - anxiety F41.8
  - appetite F50.9
  - asthenic F48.8
  - cardiovascular (system) F45.8
  - compulsive F42
  - cutaneous F54
  - depressive F32.9
  - digestive (system) F45.8
  - dysmenorrheic F45.8
  - dyspneic F45.8
  - endocrine (system) F54
  - eye NEC F45.8
  - feeding —*see* Disorder, eating
  - functional NEC F45.8
  - gastric F45.8
  - gastrointestinal (system) F45.8
  - genitourinary (system) F45.8
  - heart (function) (rhythm) F45.8
  - hyperventilatory F45.8
  - hypochondriacal —*see* Disorder, hypochondriacal
  - intestinal F45.8
  - joint F45.8
  - learning F81.9
  - limb F45.8
  - lymphatic (system) F45.8
  - menstrual F45.8
  - micturition F45.8
  - monoplegic NEC F44.4
  - motor F44.4
  - muscle F45.8
  - musculoskeletal F45.8
  - neurocirculatory F45.8
  - obsessive F42
  - occupational F48.8
  - organ or part of body NEC F45.8
  - paralytic NEC F44.4
  - phobic F40.9

Disorder *(continued)*
- psychogenic NOS —*see also* condition *(continued)*
  - physical NEC F45.8
  - rectal F45.8
  - respiratory (system) F45.8
  - rheumatic F45.8
  - sexual (function) F52.9
  - skin (allergic) (eczematous) F54
  - sleep F51.9
  - specified part of body NEC F45.8
  - stomach F45.8
- psychological F99
  - associated with
    - disease classified elsewhere F54
    - sexual
      - development F66
      - relationship F66
    - uncertainty about gender identity F66
- psychomotor NEC F44.4
  - hysterical F44.4
- psychoneurotic —*see also* Neurosis
  - mixed NEC F48.8
- psychophysiologic —*see* Disorder, somatoform
- psychosexual F65.9
  - development F66
  - identity of childhood F64.2
- psychosomatic NOS —*see* Disorder, somatoform
  - multiple F45.0
  - undifferentiated F45.1
- psychotic —*see* Psychosis
  - transient (acute) F23
- puberty E30.9
  - specified NEC E30.8
- pulmonary (valve) —*see* Endocarditis, pulmonary
- purine metabolism E79.9
- pyrimidine metabolism E79.9
- pyruvate metabolism E74.4
- reactive attachment (childhood) F94.1
- reading R48.0
  - developmental (specific) F81.0
- receptive language F80.2
- receptor, hormonal, peripheral —*see also* Syndrome, androgen insensitivity E34.50
- recurrent brief depressive F33.8
- reflex R29.2
- refraction H52.7
  - aniseikonia H52.32
  - anisometropia H52.31
  - astigmatism —*see* Astigmatism
  - hypermetropia —*see* Hypermetropia
  - myopia —*see* Myopia
  - presbyopia H52.4
  - specified NEC H52.6
- relationship F68.8
  - due to sexual orientation F66
- REM sleep behavior G47.52
- renal function, impaired (tubular) N25.9
- resonance R49.9
  - specified NEC R49.8
- respiratory function, impaired —*see also* Failure, respiration
  - postprocedural —*see* Complication, postoperative, respiratory system
  - psychogenic F45.8
- retina H35.9
  - angioid streaks H35.33
  - changes in vascular appearance H35.01-
  - degeneration —*see* Degeneration, retina
  - dystrophy (hereditary) —*see* Dystrophy, retina
  - edema H35.81

Disorder *(continued)*
- retina H35.9 *(continued)*
  - hemorrhage —*see* Hemorrhage, retina
  - ischemia H35.82
  - macular degeneration —*see* Degeneration, macula
  - microaneurysms H35.04-
  - microvascular abnormality NEC H35.09
  - neovascularization —*see* Neovascularization, retina
  - retinopathy —*see* Retinopathy
  - separation of layers H35.70
    - central serous chorioretinopathy H35.71-
    - pigment epithelium detachment (serous) H35.72-
      - hemorrhagic H35.73-
  - specified type NEC H35.89
  - telangiectasis —*see* Telangiectasis, retina
  - vasculitis —*see* Vasculitis, retina
- retroperitoneal K68.9
- right hemisphere organic affective F07.89
- rumination (infant or child) F98.21
- sacrum, sacrococcygeal NEC M53.3
- schizoaffective F25.9
  - bipolar type F25.0
  - depressive type F25.1
  - manic type F25.0
  - mixed type F25.0
  - specified NEC F25.8
- schizoid of childhood F84.5
- schizophreniform F20.81
  - brief F23
- schizotypal (personality) F21
- secretion, thyrocalcitonin E07.0
- seizure —*see also* Epilepsy G40.909
  - intractable G40.919
    - with status epilepticus G40.911
- semantic pragmatic F80.89
  - with autism F84.0
- sense of smell R43.1
  - psychogenic F45.8
- separation anxiety, of childhood F93.0
- sexual
  - arousal, female F52.22
  - aversion F52.1
  - function, psychogenic F52.9
  - maturation F66
  - nonorganic F52.9
  - preference —*see also* Deviation, sexual F65.9
    - fetishistic transvestism F65.1
  - relationship F66
- shyness, of childhood and adolescence F40.10
- sibling rivalry F93.8
- sickle-cell (sickling) (homozygous) —*see* Disease, sickle-cell
  - heterozygous D57.3
  - specified type NEC D57.8-
  - trait D57.3
- sinus (nasal) J34.9
  - specified NEC J34.89
- skin L98.9
  - atrophic L90.9
    - specified NEC L90.8
  - granulomatous L92.9
    - specified NEC L92.8
  - hypertrophic L91.9
    - specified NEC L91.8
  - infiltrative NEC L98.6
  - newborn P83.9
    - specified NEC P83.8
  - psychogenic (allergic) (eczematous) F54
- sleep G47.9
  - breathing-related —*see* Apnea, sleep

Disorder *(continued)*
- sleep *(continued)*
  - circadian rhythm G47.20
    - advance sleep phase type G47.22
    - delayed sleep phase type G47.21
    - due to
      - alcohol
        - abuse F10.182
        - dependence F10.282
        - use F10.982
      - amphetamines
        - abuse F15.182
        - dependence F15.282
        - use F15.982
      - caffeine
        - abuse F15.182
        - dependence F15.282
        - use F15.982
      - cocaine
        - abuse F14.182
        - dependence F14.282
        - use F14.982
      - drug NEC
        - abuse F19.182
        - dependence F19.282
        - use F19.982
      - opioid
        - abuse F11.182
        - dependence F11.282
        - use F11.982
      - psychoactive substance NEC
        - abuse F19.182
        - dependence F19.282
        - use F19.982
      - sedative, hypnotic, or anxiolytic
        - abuse F13.182
        - dependence F13.282
        - use F13.982
      - stimulant NEC
        - abuse F15.182
        - dependence F15.282
        - use F15.982
    - free running type G47.24
    - in conditions classified elsewhere G47.27
    - irregular sleep wake type G47.23
    - jet lag type G47.25
    - shift work type G47.26
    - specified NEC G47.29
  - due to
    - alcohol
      - abuse F10.182
      - dependence F10.282
      - use F10.982
    - amphetamine
      - abuse F15.182
      - dependence F15.282
      - use F15.982
    - anxiolytic
      - abuse F13.182
      - dependence F13.282
      - use F13.982
    - caffeine
      - abuse F15.182
      - dependence F15.282
      - use F15.982
    - cocaine
      - abuse F14.182
      - dependence F14.282
      - use F14.982
    - drug NEC
      - abuse F19.182
      - dependence F19.282
      - use F19.982
    - hypnotic
      - abuse F13.182
      - dependence F13.282
      - use F13.982
    - opioid
      - abuse F11.182
      - dependence F11.282

- **Disorder** *(continued)*
  - sleep *(continued)*
    - due to *(continued)*
      - opioid *(continued)*
        - use F11.982
      - psychoactive substance NEC
        - abuse F19.182
        - dependence F19.282
        - use F19.982
      - sedative
        - abuse F13.182
        - dependence F13.282
        - use F13.982
      - stimulant NEC
        - abuse F15.182
        - dependence F15.282
        - use F15.982
    - emotional F51.9
    - excessive somnolence *—see* Hypersomnia
    - hypersomnia type *—see* Hypersomnia
    - initiating or maintaining *—see* Insomnia
    - nightmares F51.5
    - nonorganic F51.9
      - specified NEC F51.8
    - parasomnia type G47.50
    - specified NEC G47.8
    - terrors F51.4
    - walking F51.3
  - sleep-wake pattern or schedule *—see* Disorder, sleep, circadian rhythm
  - social
    - anxiety of childhood F40.10
    - functioning in childhood F94.9
      - specified NEC F94.8
  - soft tissue M79.9
    - ankle M79.9
    - due to use, overuse and pressure M70.90
      - ankle M70.97-
      - bursitis *—see* Bursitis
      - foot M70.97-
      - forearm M70.93-
      - hand M70.94-
      - lower leg M70.96-
      - multiple sites M70.99
      - pelvic region M70.95-
      - shoulder region M70.91-
      - specified site NEC M70.98
      - specified type NEC M70.80
        - ankle M70.87-
        - foot M70.87-
        - forearm M70.83-
        - hand M70.84-
        - lower leg M70.86-
        - multiple sites M70.89
        - pelvic region M70.85-
        - shoulder region M70.81-
        - specified site NEC M70.88
        - thigh M70.85-
        - upper arm M70.82-
      - thigh M70.95-
      - upper arm M70.92-
    - foot M79.9
    - forearm M79.9
    - hand M79.9
    - lower leg M79.9
    - multiple sites M79.9
    - occupational *—see* Disorder, soft tissue, due to use, overuse and pressure
    - pelvic region M79.9
    - shoulder region M79.9
    - specified type NEC M79.89
    - thigh M79.9
    - upper arm M79.9
  - somatization F45.0
  - somatoform F45.9
    - pain (persistent) F45.41

- **Disorder** *(continued)*
  - somatoform *(continued)*
    - somatization (multiple) (long-lasting) F45.0
    - specified NEC F45.8
    - undifferentiated F45.1
  - somnolence, excessive *—see* Hypersomnia
  - specific
    - arithmetical F81.2
    - developmental, of motor F82
    - reading F81.0
    - speech and language F80.9
    - spelling F81.81
    - written expression F81.81
  - speech R47.9
    - articulation (functional) (specific) F80.0
    - developmental F80.9
    - specified NEC R47.89
  - spelling (specific) F81.81
  - spine *—see also* Dorsopathy
    - ligamentous or muscular attachments, peripheral *—see* Enthesopathy, spinal
    - specified NEC *—see* Dorsopathy, specified NEC
  - stereotyped, habit or movement F98.4
  - stomach (functional) *—see* Disorder, gastric
  - stress F43.9
    - post-traumatic F43.10
      - acute F43.11
      - chronic F43.12
  - sulfur-bearing amino-acid metabolism E72.10
  - sweat gland (eccrine) L74.9
    - apocrine L75.9
      - specified NEC L75.8
    - specified NEC L74.8
  - synovium M67.90
    - acromioclavicular M67.91-
    - ankle M67.97-
    - elbow M67.92-
    - foot M67.97-
    - forearm M67.93-
    - hand M67.94-
    - hip M67.95-
    - knee M67.96-
    - multiple sites M67.99
    - rupture *—see* Rupture, synovium
    - shoulder M67.91-
    - specified type NEC M67.80
      - acromioclavicular M67.81-
      - ankle M67.87-
      - elbow M67.82-
      - foot M67.87-
      - hand M67.84-
      - hip M67.85-
      - knee M67.86-
      - multiple sites M67.89
      - wrist M67.83-
    - synovitis *—see* Synovitis
    - upper arm M67.92-
    - wrist M67.93-
  - temperature regulation, newborn P81.9
    - specified NEC P81.8
  - temporomandibular joint *—see* Anomaly, dentofacial, temporomandibular joint
  - tendon M67.90
    - acromioclavicular M67.91-
    - ankle M67.97-
    - contracture *—see* Contracture, tendon
    - elbow M67.92-
    - foot M67.97-
    - forearm M67.93-
    - hand M67.94-
    - hip M67.95-
    - knee M67.96-

- **Disorder** *(continued)*
  - tendon *(continued)*
    - multiple sites M67.99
    - rupture *—see* Rupture, tendon
    - shoulder M67.91-
    - specified type NEC M67.80
      - acromioclavicular M67.81-
      - ankle M67.87-
      - elbow M67.82-
      - foot M67.87-
      - hand M67.84-
      - hip M67.85-
      - knee M67.86-
      - multiple sites M67.89
      - trunk M67.88
      - wrist M67.83-
    - synovitis *—see* Synovitis
    - tendinitis *—see* Tendinitis
    - tenosynovitis *—see* Tenosynovitis
    - trunk M67.98
    - upper arm M67.92-
    - wrist M67.93-
  - thoracic root (nerve) NEC G54.3
  - thyrocalcitonin hypersecretion E07.0
  - thyroid (gland) E07.9
    - function NEC, neonatal, transitory P72.2
    - iodine-deficiency related E01.8
    - specified NEC E07.89
  - tic *—see* Tic
  - tooth K08.9
    - development K00.9
      - specified NEC K00.8
    - eruption K00.6
  - Tourette's F95.2
  - trance and possession F44.89
  - tricuspid (valve) *—see* Endocarditis, tricuspid
  - tryptophan metabolism E70.5
  - tubular, phosphate-losing N25.0
  - tubulo-interstitial (in)
    - brucellosis A23.9 *[N16]*
    - cystinosis E72.04
    - diphtheria A36.84
    - glycogen storage disease E74.00 *[N16]*
    - leukemia NEC C95.9- *[N16]*
    - lymphoma NEC C85.9- *[N16]*
    - mixed cryoglobulinemia D89.1 *[N16]*
    - multiple myeloma C90.0- *[N16]*
    - Salmonella infection A02.25
    - sarcoidosis D86.84
    - sepsis A41.9 *[N16]*
      - streptococcal A40.9 *[N16]*
    - systemic lupus erythematosus M32.15
    - toxoplasmosis B58.83
    - transplant rejection T86.91 *[N16]*
    - Wilson's disease E83.01 *[N16]*
  - tubulo-renal function, impaired N25.9
    - specified NEC N25.89
  - tympanic membrane H73.9-
    - atrophy *—see* Atrophy, tympanic membrane
    - infection *—see* Myringitis
    - perforation *—see* Perforation, tympanum
    - specified NEC H73.89-
  - unsocialized aggressive F91.1
  - urea cycle metabolism E72.20
    - argininemia E72.21
    - arginosuccinic aciduria E72.22
    - citrullinemia E72.23
    - ornithine transcarbamylase deficiency E72.4
    - other specified E72.29
  - ureter (in) N28.9
    - schistosomiasis B65.0 *[N29]*
    - tuberculosis A18.11
  - urethra N36.9
    - specified NEC N36.8

- **Disorder** *(continued)*
  - urinary system N39.9
    - specified NEC N39.8
  - valve, heart
    - aortic *—see* Endocarditis, aortic
    - mitral *—see* Endocarditis, mitral
    - pulmonary *—see* Endocarditis, pulmonary
    - rheumatic
      - aortic *—see* Endocarditis, aortic, rheumatic
      - mitral *—see* Endocarditis, mitral
      - pulmonary *—see* Endocarditis, pulmonary, rheumatic
      - tricuspid *—see* Endocarditis, tricuspid
    - tricuspid *—see* Endocarditis, tricuspid
  - vestibular function H81.9-
    - specified NEC *—see* subcategory H81.8
      - in diseases classified elsewhere H82.-
    - vertigo *—see* Vertigo
  - vision, binocular H53.30
    - abnormal retinal correspondence H53.31
    - diplopia H53.2
    - fusion with defective stereopsis H53.32
    - simultaneous perception H53.33
    - suppression H53.34
  - visual
    - cortex
      - blindness H47.619
        - left brain H47.612
        - right brain H47.611
      - due to
        - inflammatory disorder H47.62
          - left brain H47.622
          - right brain H47.621
        - neoplasm H47.639
          - left brain H47.632
          - right brain H47.631
        - vascular disorder H47.649
          - left brain H47.642
          - right brain H47.641
    - pathway H47.9
      - due to
        - inflammatory disorder H47.51-
        - neoplasm H47.52-
        - vascular disorder H47.53-
      - optic chiasm *—see* Disorder, optic, chiasm
  - vitreous body H43.9
    - crystalline deposits *—see* Deposit, crystalline
    - degeneration *—see* Degeneration, vitreous
    - hemorrhage *—see* Hemorrhage, vitreous
    - opacities *—see* Opacity, vitreous
    - prolapse *—see* Prolapse, vitreous
    - specified type NEC H43.89
  - voice R49.9
    - specified type NEC R49.8
  - volatile solvent use
    - due to drug abuse *—see* Abuse, drug, inhalant
    - due to drug dependence *—see* Dependence, drug, inhalant
  - white blood cells D72.9
    - specified NEC D72.89
  - withdrawing, child or adolescent F40.10

- **Disorientation** R41.0

- **Displacement, displaced**
  - acquired traumatic of bone, cartilage, joint, tendon NEC *—see* Dislocation

Displacement, displaced *(continued)*
adrenal gland (congenital) Q89.1
appendix, retrocecal (congenital) Q43.8
auricle (congenital) Q17.4
bladder (acquired) N32.89
congenital Q64.19
brachial plexus (congenital) Q07.8
brain stem, caudal (congenital) Q04.8
canaliculus (lacrimalis), congenital Q10.6
cardia through esophageal hiatus (congenital) Q40.1
cerebellum, caudal (congenital) Q04.8
cervix —*see* Malposition, uterus
colon (congenital) Q43.3
device, implant or graft —*see also* Complications, by site and type, mechanical T85.628
arterial graft NEC —*see* Complication, cardiovascular device, mechanical, vascular
breast (implant) T85.42
catheter NEC T85.628
dialysis (renal) T82.42
intraperitoneal T85.621
infusion NEC T82.524
spinal (epidural) (subdural) T85.620
urinary (indwelling) T83.028
cystostomy T83.020
electronic (electrode) (pulse generator) (stimulator) —*see* Complication, electronic stimulator
fixation, internal (orthopedic) NEC —*see* Complication, fixation device, mechanical
gastrointestinal —*see* Complications, prosthetic device, mechanical, gastrointestinal device
genital NEC T83.428
intrauterine contraceptive device T83.32
penile prosthesis T83.420
heart NEC —*see* Complication, cardiovascular device, mechanical
joint prosthesis —*see* Complications, joint prosthesis, mechanical
ocular —*see* Complications, prosthetic device, mechanical, ocular device
orthopedic NEC —*see* Complication, orthopedic, device or graft, mechanical
specified NEC T85.628
urinary NEC —*see also* Complication, genitourinary, device, urinary, mechanical
graft T83.22
vascular NEC —*see* Complication, cardiovascular device, mechanical
ventricular intracranial shunt T85.02
electronic stimulator
bone T84.320
cardiac —*see* Complications, cardiac device, electronic
nervous system —*see* Complication, prosthetic device, mechanical, electronic nervous system stimulator
urinary —*see* Complications, electronic stimulator, urinary
esophageal mucosa into cardia of stomach, congenital Q39.8

Displacement, displaced *(continued)*
esophagus (acquired) K22.8
congenital Q39.8
eyeball (acquired) (lateral) (old) —*see* Displacement, globe
congenital Q15.8
current —*see* Avulsion, eye
fallopian tube (acquired) N83.4
congenital Q50.6
opening (congenital) Q50.6
gallbladder (congenital) Q44.1
gastric mucosa (congenital) Q40.2
globe (acquired) (old) (lateral) H05.21-
current —*see* Avulsion, eye
heart (congenital) Q24.8
acquired I51.89
hymen (upward) (congenital) Q52.4
intervertebral disc NEC
with myelopathy —*see* Disorder, disc, with, myelopathy
cervical, cervicothoracic (with) M50.20
myelopathy —*see* Disorder, disc, cervical, with myelopathy
neuritis, radiculitis or radiculopathy —*see* Disorder, disc, cervical, with neuritis
due to trauma —*see* Dislocation, vertebra
lumbar region M51.26
with
myelopathy M51.06
neuritis, radiculitis, radiculopathy or sciatica M51.16
lumbosacral region M51.27
with
neuritis, radiculitis, radiculopathy or sciatica M51.17
sacrococcygeal region M53.3
thoracic region M51.24
with
myelopathy M51.04
neuritis, radiculitis, radiculopathy M51.14
thoracolumbar region M51.25
with
myelopathy M51.05
neuritis, radiculitis, radiculopathy M51.15
intrauterine device T83.32
kidney (acquired) N28.83
congenital Q63.2
lachrymal, lacrimal apparatus or duct (congenital) Q10.6
lens, congenital Q12.1
macula (congenital) Q14.1
Meckel's diverticulum Q43.0
malignant —*see* Table of Neoplasms, small intestine, malignant
nail (congenital) Q84.6
acquired L60.8
opening of Wharton's duct in mouth Q38.4
organ or site, congenital NEC —*see* Malposition, congenital
ovary (acquired) N83.4
congenital Q50.39
free in peritoneal cavity (congenital) Q50.39
into hernial sac N83.4
oviduct (acquired) N83.4
congenital Q50.6
parathyroid (gland) E21.4
parotid gland (congenital) Q38.4
punctum lacrimale (congenital) Q10.6
sacro-iliac (joint) (congenital) Q74.2
current injury S33.2
old —*see* subcategory M53.2

Displacement, displaced *(continued)*
salivary gland (any) (congenital) Q38.4
spleen (congenital) Q89.09
stomach, congenital Q40.2
sublingual duct Q38.4
tongue (downward) (congenital) Q38.3
tooth, teeth, fully erupted M26.30
horizontal M26.33
vertical M26.34
trachea (congenital) Q32.1
ureter or ureteric opening or orifice (congenital) Q62.62
uterine opening of oviducts or fallopian tubes Q50.6
uterus, uterine —*see* Malposition, uterus
ventricular septum Q21.0
with rudimentary ventricle Q20.4

Disproportion
between native and reconstructed breast N65.1
fiber-type G71.2

Disruptio uteri —*see* Rupture, uterus

Disruption (of)
ciliary body NEC H21.89
closure of
cornea T81.31
craniotomy T81.32
fascia (muscular) (superficial) T81.32
internal organ or tissue T81.32
laceration (external) (internal) T81.33
ligament T81.32
mucosa T81.31
muscle or muscle flap T81.32
ribs or rib cage T81.32
skin and subcutaneous tissue (full-thickness) (superficial) T81.31
skull T81.32
sternum (sternotomy) T81.32
tendon T81.32
traumatic laceration (external) (internal) T81.33
family Z63.8
due to
absence of family member due to military deployment Z63.31
absence of family member NEC Z63.32
alcoholism and drug addiction in family Z63.72
bereavement Z63.4
death (assumed) or disappearance of family member Z63.4
divorce or separation Z63.5
drug addiction in family Z63.72
return of family member from military deployment (current or past conflict) Z63.71
stressful life events NEC Z63.79
iris NEC H21.89
ligament (s) —*see also* Sprain
knee
current injury —*see* Dislocation, knee
old (chronic) —*see* Derangement, knee, ligament, instability, chronic
spontaneous NEC —*see* Derangement, knee, disruption ligament
ossicular chain —*see* Discontinuity, ossicles, ear
pelvic ring (stable) S32.810
unstable S32.811
wound T81.30
episiotomy O90.1

Disruption *(continued)*
wound *(continued)*
operation T81.31
cesarean O90.0
external operation wound (superficial) T81.31
internal operation wound (deep) T81.32
perineal (obstetric) O90.1
traumatic injury repair T81.33
traumatic injury wound repair T81.33

Dissatisfaction with
employment Z56.9
school environment Z55.4

Dissecting —*see* condition

Dissection
aorta I71.00
abdominal I71.02
thoracic I71.01
thoracoabdominal I71.03
artery
carotid I77.71
cerebral (nonruptured) I67.0
ruptured —*see* Hemorrhage, intracranial, subarachnoid
coronary I25.42
iliac I77.72
renal I77.73
specified NEC I77.79
vertebral I77.74
traumatic —*see* Wound, open, by site
vascular I99.8
wound —*see* Wound, open

Disseminated —*see* condition

Dissociation
auriculoventricular or atrioventricular (AV) (any degree) (isorhythmic) I45.89
with heart block I44.2
interference I45.89

Dissociative reaction, state F44.9

Dissolution, vertebra —*see* Osteoporosis

Distension, distention
abdomen R14.0
bladder N32.89
cecum K63.89
colon K63.89
gallbladder K82.8
intestine K63.89
kidney N28.89
liver K76.89
seminal vesicle N50.8
stomach K31.89
acute K31.0
psychogenic F45.8
ureter —*see* Dilatation, ureter
uterus N85.8

Distoma hepaticum infestation B66.3

Distomiasis B66.9
bile passages B66.3
hemic B65.9
hepatic B66.3
due to Clonorchis sinensis B66.1
intestinal B66.5
liver B66.3
due to Clonorchis sinensis B66.1
lung B66.4
pulmonary B66.4

Distomolar (fourth molar) K00.1

Disto-occlusion (Division I) (Division II) M26.212

Distortion (s) (congenital)
adrenal (gland) Q89.1
arm NEC Q68.8
bile duct or passage Q44.5
bladder Q64.79
brain Q04.9

Disturbance *(continued)*
polyglandular E31.9
specified NEC E31.8
potassium balance, newborn P74.3
psychogenic F45.9
psychomotor F44.4
psychophysical visual H53.16
pupillary *—see* Anomaly, pupil, function
reflex R29.2
rhythm, heart I49.9
salivary secretion K11.7
sensation (cold) (heat) (localization) (tactile discrimination) (texture) (vibratory) NEC R20.9
hysterical F44.6
skin R20.9
anesthesia R20.0
hyperesthesia R20.3
hypoesthesia R20.1
paresthesia R20.2
specified type NEC R20.8
smell R43.9
and taste (mixed) R43.8
anosmia R43.0
parosmia R43.1
specified NEC R43.8
taste R43.9
and smell (mixed) R43.8
parageusia R43.2
specified NEC R43.8
sensory *—see* Disturbance, sensation
situational (transient) *—see also* Disorder, adjustment
acute F43.0
sleep G47.9
nonorganic origin F51.9
smell *—see* Disturbance, sensation, smell
sociopathic F60.2
sodium balance, newborn P74.2
speech R47.9
developmental F80.9
specified NEC R47.89
stomach (functional) K31.9
sympathetic (nerve) G90.9
taste *—see* Disturbance, sensation, taste
temperature
regulation, newborn P81.9
specified NEC P81.8
sense R20.8
hysterical F44.6
tooth
eruption K00.6
formation K00.4
structure, hereditary NEC K00.5
touch *—see* Disturbance, sensation
vascular I99.9
arteriosclerotic *—see* Arteriosclerosis
vasomotor I73.9
vasospastic I73.9
vision, visual H53.9
following
cerebral infarction I69.398
cerebrovascular disease I69.998
specified NEC I69.898
intracerebral hemorrhage I69.198
nontraumatic intracranial hemorrhage NEC I69.298
specified disease NEC I69.898
subarachnoid hemorrhage I69.098
psychophysical H53.16
specified NEC H53.8

Disturbance *(continued)*
vision, visual *(continued)*
subjective H53.10
day blindness H53.11
discomfort H53.14-
distortions of shape and size H53.15
loss
sudden H53.13-
transient H53.12-
specified type NEC H53.19
voice R49.9
psychogenic F44.4
specified NEC R49.8

Diuresis R35.8

Diver's palsy, paralysis or squeeze T70.3

Diverticulitis (acute) K57.92
bladder *—see* Cystitis
ileum *—see* Diverticulitis, intestine, small
intestine K57.92
with
abscess, perforation or peritonitis K57.80
with bleeding K57.81
bleeding K57.93
congenital Q43.8
large K57.32
with
abscess, perforation or peritonitis K57.20
with bleeding K57.21
bleeding K57.33
small intestine K57.52
with
abscess, perforation or peritonitis K57.40
with bleeding K57.41
bleeding K57.53
small K57.12
with
abscess, perforation or peritonitis K57.00
with bleeding K57.01
bleeding K57.13
large intestine K57.52
with
abscess, perforation or peritonitis K57.40
with bleeding K57.41
bleeding K57.53

Diverticulosis K57.90
with bleeding K57.91
large intestine K57.30
with
bleeding K57.31
small intestine K57.50
with bleeding K57.51
small intestine K57.10
with
bleeding K57.11
large intestine K57.50
with bleeding K57.51

Diverticulum, diverticula (multiple) K57.90
appendix (noninflammatory) K38.2
bladder (sphincter) N32.3
congenital Q64.6
bronchus (congenital) Q32.4
acquired J98.09
calyx, calyceal (kidney) N28.89
cardia (stomach) K31.4
cecum *—see* Diverticulosis, intestine, large
congenital Q43.8
colon *—see* Diverticulosis, intestine, large
congenital Q43.8

Diverticulum, diverticula *(continued)*
duodenum *—see* Diverticulosis, intestine, small
congenital Q43.8
epiphrenic (esophagus) K22.5
esophagus (congenital) Q39.6
acquired (epiphrenic) (pulsion) (traction) K22.5
eustachian tube *—see* Disorder, eustachian tube, specified NEC
fallopian tube N83.8
gastric K31.4
heart (congenital) Q24.8
ileum *—see* Diverticulosis, intestine, small
jejunum *—see* Diverticulosis, intestine, small
kidney (pelvis) (calyces) N28.89
with calculus *—see* Calculus, kidney
Meckel's (displaced) (hypertrophic) Q43.0
malignant *—see* Table of Neoplasms, small intestine, malignant
midthoracic K22.5
organ or site, congenital NEC *—see* Distortion
pericardium (congenital) (cyst) Q24.8
acquired I31.8
pharyngoesophageal (congenital) Q39.6
acquired K22.5
pharynx (congenital) Q38.7
rectosigmoid *—see* Diverticulosis, intestine, large
congenital Q43.8
rectum *—see* Diverticulosis, intestine, large
Rokitansky's K22.5
seminal vesicle N50.8
sigmoid *—see* Diverticulosis, intestine, large
congenital Q43.8
stomach (acquired) K31.4
congenital Q40.2
trachea (acquired) J39.8
ureter (acquired) N28.89
congenital Q62.8
ureterovesical orifice N28.89
urethra (acquired) N36.1
congenital Q64.79
ventricle, left (congenital) Q24.8
vesical N32.3
congenital Q64.6
Zenker's (esophagus) K22.5

Division
cervix uteri (acquired) N88.8
glans penis Q55.69
labia minora (congenital) Q52.79
ligament (partial or complete) (current) *—see also* Sprain
with open wound *—see* Wound, open
muscle (partial or complete) (current) *—see also* Injury, muscle
with open wound *—see* Wound, open
nerve (traumatic) *—see* Injury, nerve
spinal cord *—see* Injury, spinal cord, by region
vein I87.8

Divorce, causing family disruption Z63.5

Dix-Hallpike neurolabyrinthitis *—see* Neuronitis, vestibular

Dizziness R42
hysterical F44.89
psychogenic F45.8

DMAC (disseminated mycobacterium avium- intracellulare complex) A31.2

DNR (do not resuscitate) Z66

Doan-Wiseman syndrome (primary splenic neutropenia) *—see* Agranulocytosis

Doehle-Heller aortitis A52.02

Dog bite *—see* Bite

Dohle body panmyelopathic syndrome D72.0

Dolichocephaly Q67.2

Dolichocolon Q43.8

Dolichostenomelia *—see* Syndrome, Marfan's

Donohue's syndrome E34.8

Donor (organ or tissue) Z52.9
blood (whole) Z52.000
autologous Z52.010
specified component (lymphocytes) (platelets) NEC Z52.008
autologous Z52.018
specified donor NEC Z52.098
specified donor NEC Z52.090
stem cells Z52.001
autologous Z52.011
specified donor NEC Z52.091
bone Z52.20
autologous Z52.21
marrow Z52.3
specified type NEC Z52.29
cornea Z52.5
egg (Oocyte) Z52.819
age 35 and over Z52.812
anonymous recipient Z52.812
designated recipient Z52.813
under age 35 Z52.810
anonymous recipient Z52.810
designated recipient Z52.811
kidney Z52.4
liver Z52.6
lung Z52.89
lymphocyte *—see* Donor, blood, specified components NEC
Oocyte *—see* Donor, egg
platelets Z52.008
potential, examination of Z00.5
semen Z52.89
skin Z52.10
autologous Z52.11
specified type NEC Z52.19
specified organ or tissue NEC Z52.89
sperm Z52.89

Donovanosis A58

Dorsalgia M54.9
psychogenic F45.41
specified NEC M54.89

Dorsopathy M53.9
deforming M43.9
specified NEC *—see* subcategory M43.8
specified NEC M53.80
cervical region M53.82
cervicothoracic region M53.83
lumbar region M53.86
lumbosacral region M53.87
occipito-atlanto-axial region M53.81
sacrococcygeal region M53.88
thoracic region M53.84
thoracolumbar region M53.85

Double
albumin E88.09
aortic arch Q25.4
auditory canal Q17.8
auricle (heart) Q20.8
bladder Q64.79

Double *(continued)*
- cervix Q51.820
  - with doubling of uterus (and vagina) Q51.10
    - with obstruction Q51.11
- inlet ventricle Q20.4
- kidney with double pelvis (renal) Q63.0
- meatus urinarius Q64.75
- monster Q89.4
- outlet
  - left ventricle Q20.2
  - right ventricle Q20.1
- pelvis (renal) with double ureter Q62.5
- tongue Q38.3
- ureter (one or both sides) Q62.5
  - with double pelvis (renal) Q62.5
- urethra Q64.74
- urinary meatus Q64.75
- uterus Q51.2
  - with
    - doubling of cervix (and vagina) Q51.10
      - with obstruction Q51.11
  - in pregnancy or childbirth O34.59-
    - causing obstructed labor O65.5
- vagina Q52.10
  - with doubling of uterus (and cervix) Q51.10
    - with obstruction Q51.11
- vision H53.2
- vulva Q52.79

Douglas' pouch, cul-de-sac *—see* condition

Down syndrome Q90.9
- meiotic nondisjunction Q90.0
- mitotic nondisjunction Q90.1
- mosaicism Q90.1
- translocation Q90.2

DPD(dihydropyrimidine dehydrogenase deficiency) E88.89

Dracontiasis B72

Dracunculiasis, dracunculosis B72

Dream state, hysterical F44.89

Dreschlera (hawaiiensis) (infection) B43.8

Drepanocytic anemia *—see* Disease, sickle-cell

Dresbach's syndrome (elliptocytosis) D58.1

Dressler's syndrome I24.1

Drift, ulnar *—see* Deformity, limb, specified type NEC, forearm

Drinking (alcohol)
- excessive, to excess NEC(without dependence) F10.10
  - habitual (continual) (without remission) F10.20
    - with remission F10.21

Drip, postnasal (chronic) R09.82
- due to
  - allergic rhinitis *—see* Rhinitis, allergic
  - common cold J00
  - gastroesophageal reflux *—see* Reflux, gastroesophageal
  - nasopharyngitis *—see* Nasopharyngitis
  - other know condition - code to condition
  - sinusitis *—see* Sinusitis

Droop
- facial R29.810
  - cerebrovascular disease I69.992
    - cerebral infarction I69.392

Droop *(continued)*
- facial *(continued)*
  - cerebrovascular disease *(continued)*
    - intracerebral hemorrhage I69.192
    - nontraumatic intracranial hemorrhage NEC I69.292
    - specified disease NEC I69.892
    - subarachnoid hemorrhage I69.092

Drop (in)
- attack NEC R55
- finger *—see* Deformity, finger
- foot *—see* Deformity, limb, foot, drop
- hematocrit (precipitous) R71.0
- hemoglobin R71.0
- toe *—see* Deformity, toe, specified NEC
- wrist *—see* Deformity, limb, wrist drop

Dropped heart beats I45.9

Dropsy, dropsical *—see also* Hydrops
- abdomen R18.8
- brain *—see* Hydrocephalus
- cardiac, heart *—see* Failure, heart, congestive
- gangrenous *—see* Gangrene
- heart *—see* Failure, heart, congestive
- kidney *—see* Nephrosis
- lung *—see* Edema, lung
- newborn due to isoimmunization P56.0
- pericardium *—see* Pericarditis

Drowned, drowning (near) T75.1

Drowsiness R40.0

Drug
- abuse counseling and surveillance Z71.51
- addiction *—see* Dependence
- dependence *—see* Dependence
- habit *—see* Dependence
- harmful use *—see* Abuse, drug
- induced fever R50.2
- overdose *—see* Table of Drugs and Chemicals, by drug, poisoning
- poisoning *—see* Table of Drugs and Chemicals, by drug, poisoning
- resistant organism infection *—see also* Resistant, organism, to, drug Z16.30
- therapy
  - long term (current) (prophylactic) *—see* Therapy, drug long-term (current) (prophylactic)
  - short term - omit code
- wrong substance given or taken in error *—see* Table of Drugs and Chemicals, by drug, poisoning

Drunkenness (without dependence) F10.129
- acute in alcoholism F10.229
- chronic (without remission) F10.20
  - with remission F10.21
- pathological (without dependence) F10.129
  - with dependence F10.229
- sleep F51.9

Drusen
- macula (degenerative) (retina) *—see* Degeneration, macula, drusen
- optic disc H47.32-

Dry, dryness *—see also* condition
- larynx J38.7
- mouth R68.2
  - due to dehydration E86.0
- nose J34.89
- socket (teeth) M27.3
- throat J39.2

DSAP L56.5

Duane's syndrome H50.81-

Dubin-Johnson disease or syndrome E80.6

Dubois' disease (thymus gland) A50.59 *[E35]*

Dubowitz' syndrome Q87.1

Duchenne-Aran muscular atrophy G12.21

Duchenne-Griesinger disease G71.0

Duchenne's
- disease or syndrome
  - motor neuron disease G12.22
  - muscular dystrophy G71.0
- locomotor ataxia (syphilitic) A52.11
- paralysis
  - birth injury P14.0
  - due to or associated with
    - motor neuron disease G12.22
    - muscular dystrophy G71.0

Ducrey's chancre A57

Duct, ductus *—see* condition

Duhring's disease (dermatitis herpetiformis) L13.0

Dullness, cardiac (decreased) (increased) R01.2

Dumb ague *—see* Malaria

Dumbness *—see* Aphasia

Dumdum fever B55.0

Dumping syndrome (postgastrectomy) K91.1

Duodenitis (nonspecific) (peptic) K29.80
- with bleeding K29.81

Duodenocholangitis *—see* Cholangitis

Duodenum, duodenal *—see* condition

Duplay's bursitis or periarthritis *— see* Tendinitis, calcific, shoulder

Duplication, duplex *—see also* Accessory
- alimentary tract Q45.8
- anus Q43.4
- appendix (and cecum) Q43.4
- biliary duct (any) Q44.5
- bladder Q64.79
- cecum (and appendix) Q43.4
- cervix Q51.820
- chromosome NEC
  - with complex rearrangements NEC Q92.5
  - seen only at prometaphase Q92.8
- cystic duct Q44.5
- digestive organs Q45.8
- esophagus Q39.8
- frontonasal process Q75.8
- intestine (large) (small) Q43.4
- kidney Q63.0
- liver Q44.7
- pancreas Q45.3
- penis Q55.69
- respiratory organs NEC Q34.8
- salivary duct Q38.4
- spinal cord (incomplete) Q06.2
- stomach Q40.2

Dupré's disease (meningism) R29.1

Dupuytren's contraction or disease M72.0

Durand-Nicolas-Favre disease A55

Durotomy (inadvertent) (incidental) G97.41

Duroziez's disease (congenital mitral stenosis) Q23.2

Dutton's relapsing fever (West African) A68.1

Dwarfism E34.3
- achondroplastic Q77.4
- congenital E34.3
- constitutional E34.3
- hypochondroplastic Q77.4
- hypophyseal E23.0
- infantile E34.3
- Laron-type E34.3
- Lorain (-Levi) type E23.0
- metatropic Q77.8
- nephrotic-glycosuric (with hypophosphatemic rickets) E72.09
- nutritional E45
- pancreatic K86.8
- pituitary E23.0
- renal N25.0
- thanatophoric Q77.1

Dyke-Young anemia (secondary) (symptomatic) D59.1

Dysacusis *—see* Abnormal, auditory perception

Dysadrenocortism E27.9
- hyperfunction E27.0

Dysarthria R47.1
- following
  - cerebral infarction I69.322
  - cerebrovascular disease I69.922
    - specified disease NEC I69.822
  - intracerebral hemorrhage I69.122
  - nontraumatic intracranial hemorrhage NEC I69.222
  - subarachnoid hemorrhage I69.022

Dysautonomia (familial) G90.1

Dysbarism T70.3

Dysbasia R26.2
- angiosclerotica intermittens I73.9
- hysterical F44.4
- lordotica (progressiva) G24.1
- nonorganic origin F44.4
- psychogenic F44.4

Dysbetalipoproteinemia (familial) E78.2

Dyscalculia R48.8
- developmental F81.2

Dyschezia K59.00

Dyschondroplasia (with hemangiomata) Q78.4

Dyschromia (skin) L81.9

Dyscollagenosis M35.9

Dyscranio-pygo-phalangy Q87.0

Dyscrasia
- blood (with) D75.9
  - antepartum hemorrhage *—see* Hemorrhage, antepartum, with coagulation defect
  - newborn P61.9
    - specified type NEC P61.8
  - intrapartum hemorrhage O67.0
  - puerperal, postpartum O72.3
- polyglandular, pluriglandular E31.9

Dysendocrinism E34.9

Dysentery, dysenteric (catarrhal) (diarrhea) (epidemic) (hemorrhagic) (infectious) (sporadic) (tropical) A09
- abscess, liver A06.4
- amebic *—see also* Amebiasis A06.0
  - with abscess *—see* Abscess, amebic
  - acute A06.0
  - chronic A06.1
- arthritis *—see also* category M01 *[A09]*
  - bacillary *—see also* category M01 *[A03.9]*

- **Dysentery, dysenteric** *(continued)*
  - bacillary A03.9
    - arthritis —*see also* category M01 *[A03.9]*
    - Boyd A03.2
    - Flexner A03.1
    - Schmitz (-Stutzer) A03.0
    - Shiga (-Kruse) A03.0
    - Shigella A03.9
      - boydii A03.2
      - dysenteriae A03.0
      - flexneri A03.1
      - group A A03.0
      - group B A03.1
      - group C A03.2
      - group D A03.3
      - sonnei A03.3
      - specified type NEC A03.8
    - Sonne A03.3
    - specified type NEC A03.8
  - balantidial A07.0
  - Balantidium coli A07.0
  - Boyd's A03.2
  - candidal B37.82
  - Chilomastix A07.8
  - Chinese A03.9
  - coccidial A07.3
  - Dientamoeba (fragilis) A07.8
  - Embadomonas A07.8
  - Entamoeba, entamebic —*see* Dysentery, amebic
  - Flexner-Boyd A03.2
  - Flexner's A03.1
  - Giardia lamblia A07.1
  - Hiss-Russell A03.1
  - Lamblia A07.1
  - leishmanial B55.0
  - malarial —*see* Malaria
  - metazoal B82.0
  - monilial B37.82
  - protozoal A07.9
  - Salmonella A02.0
  - schistosomal B65.1
  - Schmitz (-Stutzer) A03.0
  - Shiga (-Kruse) A03.0
  - Shigella NOS —*see* Dysentery, bacillary
  - Sonne A03.3
  - strongyloidiasis B78.0
  - trichomonal A07.8
  - viral —*see also* Enteritis, viral A08.4

- **Dysequilibrium** R42

- **Dysesthesia** R20.8
  - hysterical F44.6

- **Dysfibrinogenemia** (congenital) D68.2

- **Dysfunction**
  - adrenal E27.9
    - hyperfunction E27.0
  - autonomic
    - due to alcohol G31.2
    - somatoform F45.8
  - bladder N31.9
    - neurogenic NOS —*see* Dysfunction, bladder, neuromuscular
    - neuromuscular NOS N31.9
      - atonic (motor) (sensory) N31.2
      - autonomous N31.2
      - flaccid N31.2
      - nonreflex N31.2
      - reflex N31.1
      - specified NEC N31.8
      - uninhibited N31.0
  - bleeding, uterus N93.8
  - cerebral G93.89
  - colon K59.9
    - psychogenic F45.8
  - colostomy K94.03
  - cystic duct K82.8

- **Dysfunction** *(continued)*
  - cystostomy (stoma) —*see* Complications, cystostomy
  - ejaculatory N53.19
    - anejaculatory orgasm N53.13
    - painful N53.12
    - premature F52.4
    - retarded N53.11
  - endocrine NOS E34.9
  - endometrium N85.8
  - enterostomy K94.13
  - gallbladder K82.8
  - gastrostomy (stoma) K94.23
  - gland, glandular NOS E34.9
  - heart I51.89
  - hemoglobin D75.89
  - hepatic K76.89
  - hypophysis E23.7
  - hypothalamic NEC E23.3
  - ileostomy (stoma) K94.13
  - jejunostomy (stoma) K94.13
  - kidney —*see* Disease, renal
  - labyrinthine —*see* subcategory H83.2
  - left ventricular, following sudden emotional stress I51.81
  - liver K76.89
  - male —*see* Dysfunction, sexual, male
  - orgasmic (female) F52.31
    - male F52.32
  - ovary E28.9
    - specified NEC E28.8
  - papillary muscle I51.89
  - parathyroid E21.4
  - physiological NEC R68.89
    - psychogenic F59
  - pineal gland E34.8
  - pituitary (gland) E23.3
  - platelets D69.1
  - polyglandular E31.9
    - specified NEC E31.8
  - psychophysiologic F59
  - psychosexual F52.9
    - with
      - dyspareunia F52.6
      - premature ejaculation F52.4
      - vaginismus F52.5
  - pylorus K31.9
  - rectum K59.9
    - psychogenic F45.8
  - reflex (sympathetic) —*see* Syndrome, pain, complex regional I
  - segmental —*see* Dysfunction, somatic
  - senile R54
  - sexual (due to) R37
    - alcohol F10.981
    - amphetamine F15.981
      - in
        - abuse F15.181
        - dependence F15.281
    - anxiolytic F13.981
      - in
        - abuse F13.181
        - dependence F13.281
    - cocaine F14.981
      - in
        - abuse F14.181
        - dependence F14.281
    - excessive sexual drive F52.8
    - failure of genital response (male) F52.21
      - female F52.22
    - female N94.9
      - aversion F52.1
      - dyspareunia N94.1
        - psychogenic F52.6
      - frigidity F52.22
      - nymphomania F52.8
      - orgasmic F52.31
      - psychogenic F52.9
        - aversion F52.1
        - dyspareunia F52.6

- **Dysfunction** *(continued)*
  - sexual *(continued)*
    - female *(continued)*
      - psychogenic *(continued)*
        - frigidity F52.22
        - nymphomania F52.8
        - orgasmic F52.31
        - vaginismus F52.5
      - vaginismus N94.2
        - psychogenic F52.5
    - hypnotic F13.981
      - in
        - abuse F13.181
        - dependence F13.281
    - inhibited orgasm (female) F52.31
      - male F52.32
    - lack
      - of sexual enjoyment F52.1
      - or loss of sexual desire F52.0
    - male N53.9
      - anejaculatory orgasm N53.13
      - ejaculatory N53.19
        - painful N53.12
        - premature F52.4
        - retarded N53.11
      - erectile N52.9
        - drug induced N52.2
        - due to
          - disease classified elsewhere N52.1
          - drug N52.2
        - postoperative (postprocedural) N52.39
          - following
            - prostatectomy N52.34
              - radical N52.31
            - radical cystectomy N52.32
            - urethral surgery N52.33
        - psychogenic F52.21
        - specified cause NEC N52.8
        - vasculogenic
          - arterial insufficiency N52.01
            - with corporo-venous occlusive N52.03
          - corporo-venous occlusive N52.02
            - with arterial insufficiency N52.03
      - impotence —*see* Dysfunction, sexual, male, erectile
      - psychogenic F52.9
        - aversion F52.1
        - erectile F52.21
        - orgasmic F52.32
        - premature ejaculation F52.4
        - satyriasis F52.8
        - specified type NEC F52.8
      - specified type NEC N53.8
    - nonorganic F52.9
      - specified NEC F52.8
    - opioid F11.981
      - in
        - abuse F11.181
        - dependence F11.281
    - orgasmic dysfunction (female) F52.31
      - male F52.32
    - premature ejaculation F52.4
    - psychoactive substances NEC F19.981
      - in
        - abuse F19.181
        - dependence F19.281
    - psychogenic F52.9
    - sedative F13.981
      - in
        - abuse F13.181
        - dependence F13.281
    - sexual aversion F52.1
    - vaginismus (nonorganic) (psychogenic) F52.5

- **Dysfunction** *(continued)*
  - sinoatrial node I49.5
  - somatic M99.09
    - abdomen M99.09
    - acromioclavicular M99.07
    - cervical region M99.01
    - cervicothoracic M99.01
    - costochondral M99.08
    - costovertebral M99.08
    - head region M99.00
    - hip M99.05
    - lower extremity M99.06
    - lumbar region M99.03
    - lumbosacral M99.03
    - occipitocervical M99.00
    - pelvic region M99.05
    - pubic M99.05
    - rib cage M99.08
    - sacral region M99.04
    - sacrococcygeal M99.04
    - sacroiliac M99.04
    - specified NEC M99.09
    - sternochondral M99.08
    - sternoclavicular M99.07
    - thoracic region M99.02
    - thoracolumbar M99.02
    - upper extremity M99.07
  - somatoform autonomic F45.8
  - stomach K31.89
    - psychogenic F45.8
  - suprarenal E27.9
    - hyperfunction E27.0
  - symbolic R48.9
    - specified type NEC R48.8
  - temporomandibular (joint) M26.69
    - joint-pain syndrome M26.62
  - testicular (endocrine) E29.9
    - specified NEC E29.8
  - thymus E32.9
  - thyroid E07.9
  - ureterostomy (stoma) —*see* Complications, stoma, urinary tract
  - urethrostomy (stoma) —*see* Complications, stoma, urinary tract
  - uterus, complicating delivery O62.9
    - hypertonic O62.4
    - hypotonic O62.2
      - primary O62.0
      - secondary O62.1
  - ventricular I51.9
    - with congestive heart failure I50.9-
      - left, reversible, following sudden emotional stress I51.81

- **Dysgenesis**
  - gonadal (due to chromosomal anomaly) Q96.9
    - pure Q99.1
  - renal Q60.5
    - bilateral Q60.4
    - unilateral Q60.3
  - reticular D72.0
  - tidal platelet D69.3

- **Dysgerminoma**
  - specified site —*see* Neoplasm, malignant, by site
  - unspecified site
    - female C56.9
    - male C62.90

- **Dysgeusia** R43.2

- **Dysgraphia** R27.8

- **Dyshidrosis, dysidrosis** L30.1

- **Dyskaryotic cervical smear** R87.619

- **Dyskeratosis** L85.8
  - cervix —*see* Dysplasia, cervix
  - congenital Q82.8
  - uterus NEC N85.8

- **Dyskinesia** G24.9
  - biliary (cystic duct or gallbladder) K82.8

- **Dyskinesia** *(continued)*
  - drug induced
    - orofacial G24.01
  - esophagus K22.4
  - hysterical F44.4
  - intestinal K59.8
  - nonorganic origin F44.4
  - orofacial (idiopathic) G24.4
    - drug induced G24.01
  - psychogenic F44.4
  - subacute, drug induced G24.01
  - tardive G24.01
    - neuroleptic induced G24.01
  - trachea J39.8
  - tracheobronchial J98.09
- **Dyslalia** (developmental) F80.0
- **Dyslexia** R48.0
  - developmental F81.0
- **Dyslipidemia** E78.5
  - depressed HDL cholesterol E78.6
  - elevated fasting triglycerides E78.1
- **Dysmaturity** *—see also* Light for dates
  - pulmonary (newborn) (Wilson-Mikity) P27.0
- **Dysmenorrhea** (essential) (exfoliative) N94.6
  - congestive (syndrome) N94.6
  - primary N94.4
  - psychogenic F45.8
  - secondary N94.5
- **Dysmetabolic syndrome X** E88.81
- **Dysmetria** R27.8
- **Dysmorphism** (due to)
  - alcohol Q86.0
  - exogenous cause NEC Q86.8
  - hydantoin Q86.1
  - warfarin Q86.2
- **Dysmorphophobia** (nondelusional) F45.22
  - delusional F22
- **Dysnomia** R47.01
- **Dysorexia** R63.0
  - psychogenic F50.8
- **Dysostosis**
  - cleidocranial, cleidocranialis Q74.0
  - craniofacial Q75.1
  - Fairbank's (idiopathic familial generalized osteophytosis) Q78.9
  - mandibulofacial (incomplete) Q75.4
  - multiplex E76.01
  - oculomandibular Q75.5
- **Dyspareunia** (female) N94.1
  - male N53.12
  - nonorganic F52.6
  - psychogenic F52.6
  - secondary N94.1
- **Dyspepsia** R10.13
  - atonic K30
  - functional (allergic) (congenital) (gastrointestinal) (occupational) (reflex) K30
  - intestinal K59.8
  - nervous F45.8
  - neurotic F45.8
  - psychogenic F45.8
- **Dysphagia** R13.10
  - cervical R13.19
  - following
    - cerebral infarction I69.391
    - cerebrovascular disease I69.991
      - specified NEC I69.891
    - intracerebral hemorrhage I69.191
    - nontraumatic intracranial hemorrhage NEC I69.291
    - specified disease NEC I69.891
    - subarachnoid hemorrhage I69.091
  - functional (hysterical) F45.8
- **Dysphagia** *(continued)*
  - hysterical F45.8
  - nervous (hysterical) F45.8
  - neurogenic R13.19
  - oral phase R13.11
  - oropharyngeal phase R13.12
  - pharyneal phase R13.13
  - pharyngoesophageal phase R13.14
  - psychogenic F45.8
  - sideropenic D50.1
  - spastica K22.4
  - specified NEC R13.19
- **Dysphagocytosis, congenital** D71
- **Dysphasia** R47.02
  - developmental
    - expressive type F80.1
    - receptive type F80.2
  - following
    - cerebrovascular disease I69.921
      - cerebral infarction I69.321
      - intracerebral hemorrhage I69.121
      - nontraumatic intracranial hemorrhage NEC I69.221
      - specified disease NEC I69.821
      - subarachnoid hemorrhage I69.021
- **Dysphonia** R49.0
  - functional F44.4
  - hysterical F44.4
  - psychogenic F44.4
  - spastica J38.3
- **Dysphoria, postpartal** O90.6
- **Dyspituitarism** E23.3
- **Dysplasia** *—see also* Anomaly
  - acetabular, congenital Q65.89
  - alveolar capillary, with vein misalignment J84.843
  - anus (histologically confirmed) (mild) (moderate) K62.82
    - severe D01.3
  - arrhythmogenic right ventricular I42.8
  - arterial, fibromuscular I77.3
  - asphyxiating thoracic (congenital) Q77.2
  - brain Q07.9
  - bronchopulmonary, perinatal P27.1
  - cervix (uteri) N87.9
    - mild N87.0
    - moderate N87.1
    - severe D06.9
  - chondroectodermal Q77.6
  - colon D12.6
  - craniometaphyseal Q78.5
  - dentinal K00.5
  - diaphyseal, progressive Q78.3
  - dystrophic Q77.5
  - ectodermal (anhidrotic) (congenital) (hereditary) Q82.4
    - hydrotic Q82.8
  - epithelial, uterine cervix *—see* Dysplasia, cervix
  - eye (congenital) Q11.2
  - fibrous
    - bone NEC (monostotic) M85.00
      - ankle M85.07-
      - foot M85.07-
      - forearm M85.03-
      - hand M85.04-
      - lower leg M85.06-
      - multiple site M85.09
      - neck M85.08
      - rib M85.08
      - shoulder M85.01-
      - skull M85.08
      - specified site NEC M85.08
      - thigh M85.05-
      - toe M85.07-
      - upper arm M85.02-
      - vertebra M85.08
- **Dysplasia** *(continued)*
  - fibrous *(continued)*
    - diaphyseal, progressive Q78.3
    - jaw M27.8
    - polyostotic Q78.1
  - florid osseous *—see also* Cyst, calcifying odontogenic
  - high grade, focal D12.6
  - hip, congenital Q65.89
  - joint, congenital Q74.8
  - kidney Q61.4
    - multicystic Q61.4
  - leg Q74.2
  - lung, congenital (not associated with short gestation) Q33.6
  - mammary (gland) (benign) N60.9-
    - cyst (solitary) *—see* Cyst, breast
    - cystic *—see* Mastopathy, cystic
    - duct ectasia *—see* Ectasia, mammary duct
    - fibroadenosis *—see* Fibroadenosis, breast
    - fibrosclerosis *—see* Fibrosclerosis, breast
    - specified type NEC N60.8-
  - metaphyseal (Jansen's) (McKusick's) (Schmid's) Q78.5
  - muscle Q79.8
  - oculodentodigital Q87.0
  - periapical (cemental) (cemento-osseous) *—see* Cyst, calcifying odontogenic
  - periosteum *—see* Disorder, bone, specified type NEC
  - polyostotic fibrous Q78.1
  - prostate *—see also* Neoplasia, intraepithelial, prostate N42.3
    - severe D07.5
  - renal Q61.4
    - multicystic Q61.4
  - retinal, congenital Q14.1
  - right ventricular, arrhythmogenic I42.8
  - septo-optic Q04.4
  - skin L98.8
  - spinal cord Q06.1
  - spondyloepiphyseal Q77.7
  - thymic, with immunodeficiency D82.1
  - vagina N89.3
    - mild N89.0
    - moderate N89.1
    - severe NEC D07.2
  - vulva N90.3
    - mild N90.0
    - moderate N90.1
    - severe NEC D07.1
- **Dyspnea** (nocturnal) (paroxysmal) R06.00
  - asthmatic (bronchial) J45.909
    - with
      - exacerbation (acute) J45.901
      - bronchitis J45.909
        - with
          - exacerbation (acute) J45.901
          - status asthmaticus J45.902
        - chronic J44.9
      - status asthmaticus J45.902
    - cardiac *—see* Failure, ventricular, left
  - cardiac *—see* Failure, ventricular, left
  - functional F45.8
  - hyperventilation R06.4
  - hysterical F45.8
  - newborn P28.89
  - orthopnea R06.01
  - psychogenic F45.8
  - shortness of breath R06.02
  - specified type NEC R06.09
- **Dyspraxia** R27.8
  - developmental (syndrome) F82
- **Dysproteinemia** E88.09
- **Dysreflexia, autonomic** G90.4
- **Dysrhythmia**
  - cardiac I49.9
    - newborn
      - bradycardia P29.12
      - occurring before birth P03.819
        - before onset of labor P03.810
        - during labor P03.811
      - tachycardia P29.11
    - postoperative I97.89
  - cerebral or cortical *—see* Epilepsy
- **Dyssomnia** *—see* Disorder, sleep
- **Dyssynergia**
  - biliary K83.8
  - bladder sphincter N36.44
  - cerebellaris myoclonica (Hunt's ataxia) G11.1
- **Dysthymia** F34.1
- **Dysthyroidism** E07.9
- **Dystocia** O66.9
  - affecting newborn P03.1
  - cervical (hypotonic) O62.2
    - affecting newborn P03.6
    - primary O62.0
    - secondary O62.1
  - contraction ring O62.4
  - fetal O66.9
    - abnormality NEC O66.3
    - conjoined twins O66.3
    - oversize O66.2
  - maternal O66.9
  - positional O64.9
  - shoulder (girdle) O66.0
    - causing obstructed labor O66.0
  - uterine NEC O62.4
- **Dystonia** G24.9
  - deformans progressiva G24.1
  - drug induced NEC G24.09
    - acute G24.02
    - specified NEC G24.09
  - familial G24.1
  - idiopathic G24.1
    - familial G24.1
    - nonfamilial G24.2
    - orofacial G24.4
  - lenticularis G24.8
  - musculorum deformans G24.1
  - neuroleptic induced (acute) G24.02
  - orofacial (idiopathic) G24.4
  - oromandibular G24.4
    - due to drug G24.01
  - specified NEC G24.8
  - torsion (familial) (idiopathic) G24.1
    - acquired G24.8
    - genetic G24.1
    - symptomatic (nonfamilial) G24.2
- **Dystonic movements** R25.8
- **Dystrophy, dystrophia**
  - adiposogenital E23.6
  - Becker's type G71.0
  - cervical sympathetic G90.2
  - choroid (hereditary) H31.20
    - central areolar H31.22
    - choroideremia H31.21
    - gyrate atrophy H31.23
    - specified type NEC H31.29
  - cornea (hereditary) H18.50
    - endothelial H18.51
    - epithelial H18.52
    - granular H18.53
    - lattice H18.54
    - macular H18.55
    - specified type NEC H18.59
  - Duchenne's type G71.0
  - due to malnutrition E45
  - Erb's G71.0

- **Dystrophy, dystrophia** *(continued)*
  - Fuchs' H18.51
  - Gower's muscular G71.0
  - hair L67.8
  - infantile neuraxonal G31.89
  - Landouzy-Déjérine G71.0
  - Leyden-Möbius G71.0
  - muscular G71.0
    - benign (Becker type) G71.0
    - congenital (hereditary) (progressive) (with specific morphological abnormalities of the muscle fiber) G71.0
      - myotonic G71.11
    - distal G71.0
    - Duchenne type G71.0
    - Emery-Dreifuss G71.0
    - Erb type G71.0
    - facioscapulohumeral G71.0
    - Gower's G71.0
    - hereditary (progressive) G71.0
    - Landouzy-Déjérine type G71.0
    - limb-girdle G71.0
    - myotonic G71.11
    - progressive (hereditary) G71.0
      - Charcot-Marie (-Tooth) type G60.0
    - pseudohypertrophic (infantile) G71.0
    - severe (Duchenne type) G71.0
  - myocardium, myocardial —*see* Degeneration, myocardial
  - nail L60.3
    - congenital Q84.6
  - nutritional E45
  - ocular G71.0
  - oculocerebrorenal E72.03
  - oculopharyngeal G71.0
  - ovarian N83.8
  - polyglandular E31.8
  - reflex (neuromuscular) (sympathetic) —*see* Syndrome, pain, complex regional I
  - retinal (hereditary) H35.50
    - in
      - lipid storage disorders E75.6 *[H36]*
      - systemic lipidoses E75.6 *[H36]*
    - involving
      - pigment epithelium H35.54
      - sensory area H35.53
    - pigmentary H35.52
    - vitreoretinal H35.51
  - Salzmann's nodular —*see* Degeneration, cornea, nodular
  - scapuloperoneal G71.0
  - skin NEC L98.8
  - sympathetic (reflex) —*see* Syndrome, pain, complex regional I
    - cervical G90.2
  - tapetoretinal H35.54
  - thoracic, asphyxiating Q77.2
  - unguium L60.3
    - congenital Q84.6
  - vitreoretinal H35.51
  - vulva N90.4
  - yellow (liver) —*see* Failure, hepatic
- **Dysuria** R30.0
  - psychogenic F45.8

E

- **Eales' disease** H35.06-
- **Ear** —*see also* condition
  - piercing Z41.3
  - tropical B36.8
  - wax (impacted) H61.20
    - left H61.22
      - with right H61.23
    - right H61.21
      - with left H61.23
- **Earache** —*see* subcategory H92.0
- **Early satiety** R68.81
- **Eaton-Lambert syndrome** —*see* Syndrome, Lambert-Eaton
- **Eberth's disease** (typhoid fever) A01.00
- **Ebola virus disease** A98.4
- **Ebstein's anomaly or syndrome** (heart) Q22.5
- **Eccentro-osteochondrodysplasia** E76.29
- **Ecchondroma** —*see* Neoplasm, bone, benign
- **Ecchondrosis** D48.0
- **Ecchymosis** R58
  - conjunctiva —*see* Hemorrhage, conjunctiva
  - eye (traumatic) —*see* Contusion, eyeball
  - eyelid (traumatic) —*see* Contusion, eyelid
  - newborn P54.5
  - spontaneous R23.3
  - traumatic —*see* Contusion
- **Echinococciasis** —*see* Echinococcus
- **Echinococcosis** —*see* Echinococcus
- **Echinococcus** (infection) B67.90
  - granulosus B67.4
    - bone B67.2
    - liver B67.0
    - lung B67.1
    - multiple sites B67.32
    - specified site NEC B67.39
    - thyroid B67.31 *[E35]*
  - liver NOS B67.8
    - granulosus B67.0
    - multilocularis B67.5
  - lung NEC B67.99
    - granulosus B67.1
    - multilocularis B67.69
  - multilocularis B67.7
    - liver B67.5
    - multiple sites B67.61
    - specified site NEC B67.69
  - specified site NEC B67.99
    - granulosus B67.39
    - multilocularis B67.69
  - thyroid NEC B67.99
    - granulosus B67.31 *[E35]*
    - multilocularis B67.69 *[E35]*
- **Echinorhynchiasis** B83.8
- **Echinostomiasis** B66.8
- **Echolalia** R48.8
- **Echovirus, as cause of disease classified elsewhere** B97.12
- **Eclampsia, eclamptic** (coma) (convulsions) (delirium) (with hypertension) **NEC** O15.9
  - during labor and delivery O15.1
  - postpartum O15.2
  - pregnancy O15.0-
  - puerperal O15.2
- **Economic circumstances affecting care** Z59.9
- **Economo's disease** A85.8
- **Ectasia, ectasis**
  - annuloaortic I35.8
  - aorta I77.819
    - with aneurysm —*see* Aneurysm, aorta
    - abdominal I77.811
    - thoracic I77.810
    - thoracoabdominal I77.812
  - breast —*see* Ectasia, mammary duct
  - capillary I78.8
- **Ectasia, ectasis** *(continued)*
  - cornea H18.71-
  - gastric antral vascular (GAVE) K31.819
    - with hemorrhage K31.811
    - without hemorrhage K31.819
  - mammary duct N60.4-
  - salivary gland (duct) K11.8
  - sclera —*see* Sclerectasia
- **Ecthyma** L08.0
  - contagiosum B08.02
  - gangrenosum L08.0
  - infectiosum B08.02
- **Ectocardia** Q24.8
- **Ectodermal dysplasia** (anhidrotic) Q82.4
- **Ectodermosis erosiva pluriorificialis** L51.1
- **Ectopic, ectopia** (congenital)
  - abdominal viscera Q45.8
    - due to defect in anterior abdominal wall Q79.59
  - ACTH syndrome E24.3
  - adrenal gland Q89.1
  - anus Q43.5
  - atrial beats I49.1
  - beats I49.49
    - atrial I49.1
    - ventricular I49.3
  - bladder Q64.10
  - bone and cartilage in lung Q33.5
  - brain Q04.8
  - breast tissue Q83.8
  - cardiac Q24.8
  - cerebral Q04.8
  - cordis Q24.8
  - endometrium —*see* Endometriosis
  - gastric mucosa Q40.2
  - gestation —*see* Pregnancy, by site
  - heart Q24.8
  - hormone secretion NEC E34.2
  - kidney (crossed) (pelvis) Q63.2
  - lens, lentis Q12.1
  - mole —*see* Pregnancy, by site
  - organ or site NEC —*see* Malposition, congenital
  - pancreas Q45.3
  - pregnancy —*see* Pregnancy, ectopic
  - pupil —*see* Abnormality, pupillary
  - renal Q63.2
  - sebaceous glands of mouth Q38.6
  - spleen Q89.09
  - testis Q53.00
    - bilateral Q53.02
    - unilateral Q53.01
  - thyroid Q89.2
  - tissue in lung Q33.5
  - ureter Q62.63
  - ventricular beats I49.3
  - vesicae Q64.10
- **Ectromelia** Q73.8
  - lower limb —*see* Defect, reduction, limb, lower, specified type NEC
  - upper limb —*see* Defect, reduction, limb, upper, specified type NEC
- **Ectropion** H02.109
  - cervix N86
    - with cervicitis N72
  - congenital Q10.1
  - eyelid (paralytic) H02.109
    - cicatricial H02.119
      - left H02.116
        - lower H02.115
        - upper H02.114
      - right H02.113
        - lower H02.112
        - upper H02.111
    - congenital Q10.1
- **Ectropion** *(continued)*
  - eyelid *(continued)*
    - left H02.106
      - lower H02.105
      - upper H02.104
    - mechanical H02.129
      - left H02.126
        - lower H02.125
        - upper H02.124
      - right H02.123
        - lower H02.122
        - upper H02.121
    - right H02.103
      - lower H02.102
      - upper H02.101
    - senile H02.139
      - left H02.136
        - lower H02.135
        - upper H02.134
      - right H02.133
        - lower H02.132
        - upper H02.131
    - spastic H02.149
      - left H02.146
        - lower H02.145
        - upper H02.144
      - right H02.143
        - lower H02.142
        - upper H02.141
  - iris H21.89
  - lip (acquired) K13.0
    - congenital Q38.0
  - urethra N36.8
  - uvea H21.89
- **Eczema** (acute) (chronic) (erythematous) (fissum) (rubrum) (squamous) —*see also* Dermatitis L30.9
  - contact —*see* Dermatitis, contact
  - dyshydrotic L30.1
  - external ear —*see* Otitis, externa, acute, eczematoid
  - flexural L20.82
  - herpeticum B00.0
  - hypertrophicum L28.0
  - hypostatic —*see* Varix, leg, with, inflammation
  - impetiginous L01.1
  - infantile (due to any substance) L20.83
    - intertriginous L21.1
    - seborrheic L21.1
  - intertriginous NEC L30.4
    - infantile L21.1
  - intrinsic (allergic) L20.84
  - lichenified NEC L28.0
  - marginatum (hebrae) B35.6
  - pustular L30.3
  - stasis —*see* Varix, leg, with, inflammation
  - vaccination, vaccinatum T88.1
  - varicose —*see* Varix, leg, with, inflammation
- **Eczematid** L30.2
- **Eddowes** (-Spurway) **syndrome** Q78.0
- **Edema, edematous** (infectious) (pitting) (toxic) R60.9
  - with nephritis —*see* Nephrosis
  - allergic T78.3
  - amputation stump (surgical) (sequelae (late effect)) T87.89
  - angioneurotic (allergic) (any site) (with urticaria) T78.3
    - hereditary D84.1
  - angiospastic I73.9
  - Berlin's (traumatic) S05.8X-
  - brain (cytotoxic) (vasogenic) G93.6
    - due to birth injury P11.0
    - newborn (anoxia or hypoxia) P52.4
      - birth injury P11.0
    - traumatic —*see* Injury, intracranial, cerebral edema

Edema, edematous *(continued)*
- cardiac —*see* Failure, heart, congestive
- cardiovascular —*see* Failure, heart, congestive
- cerebral —*see* Edema, brain
- cerebrospinal —*see* Edema, brain
- cervix (uteri) (acute) N88.8
  - puerperal, postpartum O90.89
- chronic hereditary Q82.0
- circumscribed, acute T78.3
  - hereditary D84.1
- conjunctiva H11.42-
- cornea H18.2-
  - idiopathic H18.22-
  - secondary H18.23-
    - due to contact lens H18.21-
- due to
  - lymphatic obstruction I89.0
  - salt retention E87.0
- epiglottis —*see* Edema, glottis
- essential, acute T78.3
  - hereditary D84.1
- extremities, lower —*see* Edema, legs
- eyelid NEC H02.849
  - left H02.846
    - lower H02.845
    - upper H02.844
  - right H02.843
    - lower H02.842
    - upper H02.841
- familial, hereditary Q82.0
- famine —*see* Malnutrition, severe
- generalized R60.1
- glottis, glottic, glottidis (obstructive) (passive) J38.4
  - allergic T78.3
    - hereditary D84.1
- heart —*see* Failure, heart, congestive
- heat T67.7
- hereditary Q82.0
- inanition —*see* Malnutrition, severe
- intracranial G93.6
- iris H21.89
- joint —*see* Effusion, joint
- larynx —*see* Edema, glottis
- legs R60.0
  - due to venous obstruction I87.1
  - hereditary Q82.0
- localized R60.0
  - due to venous obstruction I87.1
- lower limbs —*see* Edema, legs
- lung J81.1
  - with heart condition or failure —*see* Failure, ventricular, left
  - acute J81.0
  - chemical (acute) J68.1
    - chronic J68.1
  - chronic J81.1
    - due to
      - chemicals, gases, fumes or vapors (inhalation) J68.1
      - external agent J70.9
        - specified NEC J70.8
      - radiation J70.1
  - due to
    - chemicals, fumes or vapors (inhalation) J68.1
    - external agent J70.9
      - specified NEC J70.8
    - high altitude T70.29
    - near drowning T75.1
    - radiation J70.0
  - meaning failure, left ventricle I50.1
- lymphatic I89.0
  - due to mastectomy I97.2
- macula H35.81
  - cystoid, following cataract surgery —*see* Complications, postprocedural, following cataract surgery
  - diabetic —*see* Diabetes, by type, with, retinopathy, with macular edema
- malignant —*see* Gangrene, gas
- Milroy's Q82.0
- nasopharynx J39.2
- newborn P83.30
  - hydrops fetalis —*see* Hydrops, fetalis
  - specified NEC P83.39
- nutritional —*see also* Malnutrition, severe
  - with dyspigmentation, skin and hair E40
- optic disc or nerve —*see* Papilledema
- orbit H05.22-
- pancreas K86.8
- papilla, optic —*see* Papilledema
- penis N48.89
- periodic T78.3
  - hereditary D84.1
- pharynx J39.2
- pulmonary —*see* Edema, lung
- Quincke's T78.3
  - hereditary D84.1
- renal —*see* Nephrosis
- retina H35.81
  - diabetic —*see* Diabetes, by type, with, retinopathy, with macular edema
- salt E87.0
- scrotum N50.8
- seminal vesicle N50.8
- spermatic cord N50.8
- spinal (cord) (vascular) (nontraumatic) G95.19
- starvation —*see* Malnutrition, severe
- stasis —*see* Hypertension, venous, (chronic)
- subglottic —*see* Edema, glottis
- supraglottic —*see* Edema, glottis
- testis N44.8
- tunica vaginalis N50.8
- vas deferens N50.8
- vulva (acute) N90.89

Edentulism —*see* Absence, teeth, acquired

Edsall's disease T67.2

Educational handicap Z55.9
- specified NEC Z55.8

Edward's syndrome —*see* Trisomy, 18

Effect, adverse
- abnormal gravitational (G) forces or states T75.81
- abuse —*see* Maltreatment
- air pressure T70.9
  - specified NEC T70.8
- altitude (high) —*see* Effect, adverse, high altitude
- anesthesia —*see also* Anesthesia T88.59
  - in labor and delivery O74.9
  - in pregnancy NEC O29.3-
  - local, toxic
    - in labor and delivery O74.4
    - postpartum, puerperal O89.3
  - postpartum, puerperal O89.9
  - specified NEC T88.59
    - in labor and delivery O74.8
    - postpartum, puerperal O89.8
  - spinal and epidural T88.59
    - headache T88.59
      - in labor and delivery O74.5
      - postpartum, puerperal O89.4
    - specified NEC
      - in labor and delivery O74.6
      - postpartum, puerperal O89.5
- antitoxin —*see* Complications, vaccination
- atmospheric pressure T70.9
  - due to explosion T70.8
  - high T70.3
  - low —*see* Effect, adverse, high altitude
  - specified effect NEC T70.8
- biological, correct substance properly administered —*see* Effect, adverse, drug
- blood (derivatives) (serum) (transfusion) —*see* Complications, transfusion
- chemical substance —*see* Table of Drugs and Chemicals
- cold (temperature) (weather) T69.9
  - chilblains T69.1
  - frostbite —*see* Frostbite
  - specified effect NEC T69.8
- drugs and medicaments T88.7
  - specified drug —*see* Table of Drugs and Chemicals, by drug, adverse effect
  - specified effect - code to condition
- electric current, electricity (shock) T75.4
  - burn —*see* Burn
- exertion (excessive) T73.3
- exposure —*see* Exposure
- external cause NEC T75.89
- foodstuffs T78.1
  - allergic reaction —*see* Allergy, food
    - causing anaphylaxis —*see* Shock, anaphylactic, due to food
  - noxious —*see* Poisoning, food, noxious
- gases, fumes, or vapors T59.9-
  - specified agent —*see* Table of Drugs and Chemicals
- glue (airplane) sniffing
  - due to drug abuse —*see* Abuse, drug, inhalant
  - due to drug dependence —*see* Dependence, drug, inhalant
- heat —*see* Heat
- high altitude NEC T70.29
  - anoxia T70.29
  - on
    - ears T70.0
    - sinuses T70.1
  - polycythemia D75.1
- high pressure fluids T70.4
- hot weather —*see* Heat
- hunger T73.0
- immersion, foot —*see* Immersion
- immunization —*see* Complications, vaccination
- immunological agents —*see* Complications, vaccination
- infrared (radiation) (rays) NOS T66
  - dermatitis or eczema L59.8
- infusion —*see* Complications, infusion
- lack of care of infants —*see* Maltreatment, child
- lightning —*see* Lightning
- medical care T88.9
  - specified NEC T88.8
- medicinal substance, correct, properly administered —*see* Effect, adverse, drug
- motion T75.3
- noise, on inner ear —*see* subcategory H83.3
- overheated places —*see* Heat
- psychosocial, of work environment Z56.5
- radiation (diagnostic) (infrared) (natural source) (therapeutic) (ultraviolet) (X-ray) NOS T66
  - dermatitis or eczema —*see* Dermatitis, due to, radiation
  - fibrosis of lung J70.1
  - pneumonitis J70.0
  - pulmonary manifestations
    - acute J70.0
    - chronic J70.1
  - skin L59.9
- radioactive substance NOS
  - dermatitis or eczema —*see* Radiodermatitis
- reduced temperature T69.9
  - immersion foot or hand —*see* Immersion
  - specified effect NEC T69.8
- serum NEC —*see also* Reaction, serum T80.69
- specified NEC T78.8
  - external cause NEC T75.89
- strangulation —*see* Asphyxia, traumatic
- submersion T75.1
- thirst T73.1
- toxic —*see* Toxicity
- transfusion —*see* Complications, transfusion
- ultraviolet (radiation) (rays) NOS T66
  - burn —*see* Burn
  - dermatitis or eczema —*see* Dermatitis, due to, ultraviolet rays
    - acute L56.8
- vaccine (any) —*see* Complications, vaccination
- vibration —*see* Vibration, adverse effects
- water pressure NEC T70.9
  - specified NEC T70.8
- weightlessness T75.82
- whole blood —*see* Complications, transfusion
- work environment Z56.5

Effect (s) (of) (from) —*see* Effect, adverse NEC

Effects, late —*see* Sequelae

Effluvium
- anagen L65.1
- telogen L65.0

Effort syndrome (psychogenic) F45.8

Effusion
- amniotic fluid —*see* Pregnancy, complicated by, prematue rupture of membranes
- brain (serous) G93.6
- bronchial —*see* Bronchitis
- cerebral G93.6
- cerebrospinal —*see also* Meningitis
  - vessel G93.6
- chest —*see* Effusion, pleura
- chylous, chyliform (pleura) J94.0
- intracranial G93.6
- joint M25.40
  - ankle M25.47-
  - elbow M25.42-
  - foot joint M25.47-
  - hand joint M25.44-
  - hip M25.45-
  - knee M25.46-
  - shoulder M25.41-
  - specified joint NEC M25.48
  - wrist M25.43-
- malignant pleural J91.0
- meninges —*see* Meningitis
- pericardium, pericardial (noninflammatory) I31.3
  - acute —*see* Pericarditis, acute

ffusion *(continued)*
peritoneal (chronic) R18.8
pleura, pleurisy, pleuritic, pleuropericardial J90
chylous, chyliform J94.0
due to systemic lupus erythematosis M32.13
influenzal —*see* Influenza, with, respiratory manifestations NEC
malignant J91.0
newborn P28.89
tuberculous NEC A15.6
primary (progressive) A15.7
spinal —*see* Meningitis
thorax, thoracic —*see* Effusion, pleura

gg shell nails L60.3
congenital Q84.6

gyptian splenomegaly B65.1

hrlichiosis A77.40
due to
E. chafeensis A77.41
E. sennetsu A79.81
specified organism NEC A77.49

hlers-Danlos syndrome Q79.6

ichstedt's disease B36.0

isenmenger's
complex or syndrome I27.89
defect Q21.8

jaculation
painful N53.12
premature F52.4
retarded N53.11
retrograde N53.14
semen, painful N53.12
psychogenic F52.6

kbom's syndrome (restless legs) G25.81

kman's syndrome (brittle bones and blue sclera) Q78.0

lastic skin Q82.8
acquired L57.4

lastofibroma —*see* Neoplasm, connective tissue, benign

lastoma (juvenile) Q82.8
Miescher's L87.2

lastomyofibrosis I42.4

lastosis
actinic, solar L57.8
atrophicans (senile) L57.4
perforans serpiginosa L87.2
senilis L57.4

lbow —*see* condition

lectric current, electricity, effects (concussion) (fatal) (nonfatal) (shock) T75.4
burn —*see* Burn

lectric feet syndrome E53.8

lectrocution T75.4
from electroshock gun (taser) T75.4

lectrolyte imbalance E87.8
with
abortion —*see* Abortion by type, complicated by, electrolyte imbalance
ectopic pregnancy O08.5
molar pregnancy O08.5

lephantiasis (nonfilarial) I89.0
arabicum —*see* Infestation, filarial
bancroftian B74.0
congenital (any site) (hereditary) Q82.0
due to
Brugia (malayi) B74.1
timori B74.2

Elephantiasis *(continued)*
due to *(continued)*
mastectomy I97.2
Wuchereria (bancrofti) B74.0
eyelid H02.859
left H02.856
lower H02.855
upper H02.854
right H02.853
lower H02.852
upper H02.851
filarial, filariensis —*see* Infestation, filarial
glandular I89.0
graecorum A30.9
lymphangiectatic I89.0
lymphatic vessel I89.0
due to mastectomy I97.2
scrotum (nonfilarial) I89.0
streptococcal I89.0
surgical I97.89
postmastectomy I97.2
telangiectodes I89.0
vulva (nonfilarial) N90.89

Elevated, elevation
antibody titer R76.0
basal metabolic rate R94.8
blood pressure —*see also* Hypertension
reading (incidental) (isolated) (nonspecific), no diagnosis of hypertension R03.0
blood sugar R73.9
body temperature (of unknown origin) R50.9
C-reactive protein (CRP) R79.82
cancer antigen 125 [CA 125] R97.1
carcinoembryonic antigen [CEA] R97.0
cholesterol E78.0
with high triglycerides E78.2
conjugate, eye H51.0
diaphragm, congenital Q79.1
erythrocyte sedimentation rate R70.0
fasting glucose R73.01
fasting triglycerides E78.1
finding on laboratory examination —*see* Findings, abnormal, inconclusive, without diagnosis, by type of exam
GFR(glomerular filtration rate) —*see* Findings, abnormal, inconclusive, without diagnosis, by type of exam
glucose tolerance (oral) R73.02
immunoglobulin level R76.8
indoleacetic acid R82.5
lactic acid dehydrogenase (LDH) level R74.0
leukocytes D72.829
lipoprotein a level E78.8
liver function
study R94.5
test R79.89
alkaline phosphatase R74.8
aminotransferase R74.0
bilirubin R17
hepatic enzyme R74.8
lactate dehydrogenase R74.0
lymphocytes D72.820
prostate specific antigen [PSA] R97.2
Rh titer —*see* Complication (s), transfusion, incompatibility reaction, Rh (factor)
scapula, congenital Q74.0
sedimentation rate R70.0
SGOT R74.0
SGPT R74.0
transaminase level R74.0
triglycerides E78.1
with high cholesterol E78.2

Elevated, elevation *(continued)*
tumor associated antigens [TAA] NEC R97.8
tumor specific antigens [TSA] NEC R97.8
urine level of
catecholamine R82.5
indoleacetic acid R82.5
17-ketosteroids R82.5
steroids R82.5
vanillylmandelic acid (VMA) R82.5
venous pressure I87.8
white blood cell count D72.829
specified NEC D72.828

Elliptocytosis (congenital) (hereditary) D58.1
Hb C (disease) D58.1
hemoglobin disease D58.1
sickle-cell (disease) D57.8-
trait D57.3

Ellison-Zollinger syndrome E16.4

Ellis-van Creveld syndrome (chondroectodermal dysplasia) Q77.6

Elongated, elongation (congenital) —*see also* Distortion
bone Q79.9
cervix (uteri) Q51.828
acquired N88.4
hypertrophic N88.4
colon Q43.8
common bile duct Q44.5
cystic duct Q44.5
frenulum, penis Q55.69
labia minora (acquired) N90.6
ligamentum patellae Q74.1
petiolus (epiglottidis) Q31.8
tooth, teeth K00.2
uvula Q38.6

Eltor cholera A00.1

Emaciation (due to malnutrition) E41

Embadomoniasis A07.8

Embedded tooth, teeth K01.0
root only K08.3

Embolic —*see* condition

Embolism (multiple) (paradoxical) I74.9
air (any site) (traumatic) T79.0
following
abortion —*see* Abortion by type complicated by embolism
ectopic pregnancy O08.2
infusion, therapeutic injection or transfusion T80.0
molar pregnancy O08.2
procedure NEC
artery T81.719
mesenteric T81.710
renal T81.711
specified NEC T81.718
vein T81.72
in pregnancy, childbirth or puerperium —*see* Embolism, obstetric
amniotic fluid (pulmonary) —*see also* Embolism, obstetric
following
abortion —*see* Abortion by type complicated by embolism
ectopic pregnancy O08.2
molar pregnancy O08.2
aorta, aortic I74.10
abdominal I74.09
saddle I74.01
bifurcation I74.09
saddle I74.01
thoracic I74.11

Embolism *(continued)*
artery I74.9
auditory, internal I65.8
basilar —*see* Occlusion, artery, basilar
carotid (common) (internal) —*see* Occlusion, artery, carotid
cerebellar (anterior inferior) (posterior inferior) (superior) I66.3
cerebral —*see* Occlusion, artery, cerebral
choroidal (anterior) I66.8
communicating posterior I66.8
coronary —*see also* Infarct, myocardium
not resulting in infarction I24.0
extremity I74.4
lower I74.3
upper I74.2
hypophyseal I66.8
iliac I74.5
limb I74.4
lower I74.3
upper I74.2
mesenteric (with gangrene) K55.0
ophthalmic —*see* Occlusion, artery, retina
peripheral I74.4
pontine I66.8
precerebral —*see* Occlusion, artery, precerebral
pulmonary —*see* Embolism, pulmonary
renal N28.0
retinal —*see* Occlusion, artery, retina
septic I76
specified NEC I74.8
vertebral —*see* Occlusion, artery, vertebral
basilar (artery) I65.1
blood clot
following
abortion —*see* Abortion by type complicated by embolism
ectopic or molar pregnancy O08.2
in pregnancy, childbirth or puerperium —*see* Embolism, obstetric
brain —*see also* Occlusion, artery, cerebral
following
abortion —*see* Abortion by type complicated by embolism
ectopic or molar pregnancy O08.2
puerperal, postpartum, childbirth —*see* Embolism, obstetric
capillary I78.8
cardiac —*see also* Infarct, myocardium
not resulting in infarction I24.0
carotid (artery) (common) (internal) —*see* Occlusion, artery, carotid
cavernous sinus (venous) —*see* Embolism, intracranial venous sinus
cerebral —*see* Occlusion, artery, cerebral
cholesterol —*see* Atheroembolism
coronary (artery or vein) (systemic) —*see* Occlusion, coronary
due to device, implant or graft —*see also* Complications, by site and type, specified NEC
arterial graft NEC T82.818
breast (implant) T85.81
catheter NEC T85.81
dialysis (renal) T82.818
intraperitoneal T85.81

Embolism *(continued)*
due to device, implant or graft —*see also* Complications, by site and type, specified NEC *(continued)*
catheter NEC *(continued)*
infusion NEC T82.818
spinal (epidural) (subdural) T85.81
urinary (indwelling) T83.81
electronic (electrode) (pulse generator) (stimulator)
bone T84.81
cardiac T82.817
nervous system (brain) (peripheral nerve) (spinal) T85.81
urinary T83.81
fixation, internal (orthopedic) NEC T84.81
gastrointestinal (bile duct) (esophagus) T85.81
genital NEC T83.81
heart (graft) (valve) T82.817
joint prosthesis T84.81
ocular (corneal graft) (orbital implant) T85.81
orthopedic (bone graft) NEC T86.838
specified NEC T85.81
urinary (graft) NEC T83.81
vascular NEC T82.818
ventricular intracranial shunt T85.81
extremities
lower —*see* Embolism, vein, lower extremity
arterial I74.3
upper I74.2
eye H34.9
fat (cerebral) (pulmonary) (systemic) T79.1
following
abortion —*see* Abortion by type complicated by embolism
ectopic or molar pregnancy O08.2
complicating delivery —*see* Embolism, obstetric
following
abortion —*see* Abortion by type complicated by embolism
ectopic or molar pregnancy O08.2
infusion, therapeutic injection or transfusion
air T80.0
heart (fatty) —*see also* Infarct, myocardium
not resulting in infarction I24.0
hepatic (vein) I82.0
in pregnancy, childbirth or puerperium —*see* Embolism, obstetric
intestine (artery) (vein) (with gangrene) K55.0
intracranial —*see also* Occlusion, artery, cerebral
venous sinus (any) G08
nonpyogenic I67.6
intraspinal venous sinuses or veins G08
nonpyogenic G95.19
kidney (artery) N28.0
lateral sinus (venous) —*see* Embolism, intracranial, venous sinus
leg —*see* Embolism, vein, lower extremity
arterial I74.3
longitudinal sinus (venous) —*see* Embolism, intracranial, venous sinus

Embolism *(continued)*
lung (massive) —*see* Embolism, pulmonary
meninges I66.8
mesenteric (artery) (vein) (with gangrene) K55.0
obstetric (in) (pulmonary)
childbirth O88.82
air O88.02
amniotic fluid O88.12
blood clot O88.22
fat O88.82
pyemic O88.32
septic O88.32
specified type NEC O88.82
pregnancy O88.81-
air O88.01-
amniotic fluid O88.11-
blood clot O88.21-
fat O88.81-
pyemic O88.31-
septic O88.31-
specified type NEC O88.81-
puerperal O88.83
air O88.03
amniotic fluid O88.13
blood clot O88.23
fat O88.83
pyemic O88.33
septic O88.33
specified type NEC O88.83
ophthalmic —*see* Occlusion, artery, retina
penis N48.81
peripheral artery NOS I74.4
pituitary E23.6
popliteal (artery) I74.3
portal (vein) I81
postoperative, postrpocedural
artery T81.719
mesenteric T81.710
renal T81.711
specified NEC T81.718
vein T81.72
precerebral artery —*see* Occlusion, artery, precerebral
puerperal —*see* Embolism, obstetric
pulmonary (acute) (artery) (vein) I26.99
with acute cor pulmonale I26.09
chronic I27.82
following
abortion —*see* Abortion by type complicated by embolism
ectopic or molar pregnancy O08.2
healed or old Z86.711
in pregnancy, childbirth or puerperium —*see* Embolism, obstetric
personal history of Z86.711
saddle I26.92
with acute cor pulmonale I26.02
septic I26.90
with acute cor pulmonale I26.01
pyemic (multiple) I76
following
abortion —*see* Abortion by type complicated by embolism
ectopic or molar pregnancy O08.2
Hemophilus influenzae A41.3
pneumococcal A40.3
with pneumonia J13
puerperal, postpartum, childbirth (any organism) —*see* Embolism, obstetric
specified organism NEC A41.89
staphylococcal A41.2
streptococcal A40.9
renal (artery) N28.0
vein I82.3

Embolism *(continued)*
retina, retinal —*see* Occlusion, artery, retina
saddle
abdominal aorta I74.01
pulmonary artery I26.92
with acute cor pulmonale I26.02
septic (arterial) I76
complicating abortion —*see* Abortion, by type, complicated by, embolism
sinus —*see* Embolism, intracranial, venous sinus
soap complicating abortion —*see* Abortion, by type, complicated by, embolism
spinal cord G95.19
pyogenic origin G06.1
spleen, splenic (artery) I74.8
upper extremity I74.2
vein (acute) I82.90
antecubital I82.61-
chronic I82.71-
axillary I82.A1-
chronic I82.A2-
basilic I82.61-
chronic I82.71-
brachial I82.62-
chronic I82.72-
brachiocephalic (innominate) I82.290
chronic I82.291
cephalic I82.61-
chronic I82.71-
chronic I82.91
deep (DVT) I82.40-
calf I82.4Z-
chronic I82.5Z-
lower leg I82.4Z-
chronic I82.5Z-
thigh I82.4Y-
chronic I82.5Y-
upper leg I82.4Y
chronic I82.5y-
femoral I82.41-
chronic I82.51-
iliac (iliofemoral) I82.42-
chronic I82.52-
innominate I82.290
chronic I82.291
internal jugular I82.C1-
chronic I82.C2-
lower extremity
deep I82.40-
chronic I82.50-
specified NEC I82.49-
chronic NEC I82.59-
distal
deep I82.4Z-
proximal
deep I82.4Y-
chronic I82.5Y-
superficial I82.81-
popliteal I82.43-
chronic I82.53-
radial I82.62-
chronic I82.72-
renal I82.3
saphenous (greater) (lesser) I82.81-
specified NEC I82.890
chronic NEC I82.891
subclavian I82.B1-
chronic I82.B2-
thoracic NEC I82.290
chronic I82.291
tibial I82.44-
chronic I82.54-
ulnar I82.62-
chronic I82.72-

Embolism *(continued)*
vein *(continued)*
upper extremity I82.60-
chronic I82.70-
deep I82.62-
chronic I82.72-
superficial I82.61-
chronic I82.71-
vena cava
inferior (acute) I82.220
chronic I82.221
superior (acute) I82.210
chronic I82.211
venous sinus G08
vessels of brain —*see* Occlusion, artery, cerebral

Embolus —*see* Embolism

Embryoma —*see also* Neoplasm, uncertain behavior, by site
benign —*see* Neoplasm, benign, by site
kidney C64.-
liver C22.0
malignant —*see also* Neoplasm, malignant, by site
kidney C64.-
liver C22.0
testis C62.9-
descended (scrotal) C62.1-
undescended C62.0-
testis C62.9-
descended (scrotal) C62.1-
undescended C62.0-

Embryonic
circulation Q28.9
heart Q28.9
vas deferens Q55.4

Embryopathia NOS Q89.9

Embryotoxon Q13.4

Emesis —*see* Vomiting

Emotional lability R45.86

Emotionality, pathological F60.3

Emotogenic disease —*see* Disorder, psychogenic

Emphysema (atrophic) (bullous) (chronic) (interlobular) (lung) (obstructive) (pulmonary) (senile) (vesicular) J43.9
cellular tissue (traumatic) T79.7
surgical T81.82
centrilobular J43.2
compensatory J98.3
congenital (interstitial) P25.0
conjunctiva H11.89
connective tissue (traumatic) T79.7
surgical T81.82
due to chemicals, gases, fumes or vapors J68.4
eyelid (s) —*see* Disorder, eyelid, specified type NEC
surgical T81.82
traumatic T79.7
interstitial J98.2
congenital P25.0
perinatal period P25.0
laminated tissue T79.7
surgical T81.82
mediastinal J98.2
newborn P25.2
orbit, orbital —*see* Disorder, orbit, specified type NEC
panacinar J43.1
panlobular J43.1
specified NEC J43.8
subcutaneous (traumatic) T79.7
nontraumatic J98.2
postprocedural T81.82
surgical T81.82

- **Encephalopathy** *(continued)*
  - posthypoglycemic (coma) E16.1 *[G94]*
  - postradiation G93.89
  - saturnine *—see* Poisoning, lead
  - septic G93.41
  - specified NEC G93.49
  - spongioform, subacute (viral) A81.09
  - toxic G92
    - metabolic G92
  - traumatic (postconcussional) F07.81
    - current injury *—see* Injury, intracranial
  - vitamin B deficiency NEC E53.9 *[G32.89]*
    - vitamin B1 *[E51.2]*
  - Wernicke's E51.2
- **Encephalorrhagia** *—see* Hemorrhage, intracranial, intracerebral
- **Encephalosis, posttraumatic** F07.81
- **Enchondroma** *—see also* Neoplasm, bone, benign
- **Enchondromatosis** (cartilaginous) (multiple) Q78.4
- **Encopresis** R15.9
  - functional F98.1
  - nonorganic origin F98.1
  - psychogenic F98.1
- **Encounter** (with health service) (for) Z76.89
  - adjustment and management (of)
    - breast implant Z45.81
    - implanted device NEC Z45.89
    - myringotomy device (stent) (tube) Z45.82
  - administrative purpose only Z02.9
    - examination for
      - adoption Z02.82
      - armed forces Z02.3
      - disability determination Z02.71
      - driving license Z02.4
      - employment Z02.1
      - insurance Z02.6
      - medical certificate NEC Z02.79
      - paternity testing Z02.81
      - residential institution admission Z02.2
      - school admission Z02.0
      - sports Z02.5
    - specified reason NEC Z02.89
  - aftercare *—see* Aftercare
  - antenatal screening Z36
  - assisted reproductive fertility procedure cycle Z31.83
  - blood typing Z01.83
    - Rh typing Z01.83
  - breast augmentation or reduction Z41.1
  - breast implant exchange (different material) (different size) Z45.81
  - breast reconstruction following mastectomy Z42.1
  - check-up *—see* Examination
  - chemotherapy for neoplasm Z51.11
  - colonoscopy, screening Z12.11
  - counseling *—see* Counseling
  - delivery, full-term, uncomplicated O80
    - cesarean, without indication O82
  - ear piercing Z41.3
  - examination *—see* Examination
  - expectant parent (s) (adoptive) pre-birth pediatrician visit Z76.81
  - fertility preservation procedure (prior to cancer therapy) (prior to removal of gonads) Z31.84
  - fitting (of) *—see* Fitting (and adjustment) (of)

- **Encounter** *(continued)*
  - genetic
    - counseling Z31.5
    - testing *—see* Test, genetic
  - hearing conservation and treatment Z01.12
  - immunotherapy for neoplasm Z51.12
  - in vitro fertilization cycle Z31.83
  - instruction (in)
    - childbirth Z32.2
    - child care (postpartal) (prenatal) Z32.3
    - natural family planning
      - procreative Z31.61
      - to avoid pregnancy Z30.02
  - insulin pump titration Z46.81
  - joint prosthesis insertion following prior explantation of joint prosthesis (staged procedure)
    - hip Z47.32
    - knee Z47.33
    - shoulder Z47.31
  - laboratory (as part of a general medical examination) Z00.00
    - with abnormal findings Z00.01
  - mental health services (for)
    - abuse NEC
      - perpetrator Z69.82
      - victim Z69.81
    - child abuse
      - nonparental
        - perpetrator Z69.021
        - victim Z69.020
      - parental
        - perpetrator Z69.011
        - victim Z69.010
    - spousal or partner abuse
      - perpetrator Z69.12
      - victim Z69.11
  - observation (for) (ruled out)
    - exposure to (suspected)
      - anthrax Z03.810
      - biological agent NEC Z03.818
  - pediatrician visit, by expectant parent (s) (adoptive) Z76.81
  - plastic and reconstructive surgery following medical procedure or healed injury NEC Z42.8
  - pregnancy
    - supervision of *—see* Pregnancy, supervision of
    - test Z32.00
      - result negative Z32.02
      - result positive Z32.01
  - radiation therapy (antineoplastic) Z51.0
  - radiological (as part of a general medical examination) Z00.00
    - with abnormal findings Z00.01
  - reconstructive surgery following medical procedure or healed injury NEC Z42.8
  - removal (of) *—see also* Removal
    - artificial
      - arm Z44.00-
        - complete Z44.01-
        - partial Z44.02-
      - eye Z44.2-
      - leg Z44.10-
        - complete Z44.11-
        - partial Z44.12-
    - breast implant Z45.81
      - tissue expander (without synchronous insertion of permanent implant) Z45.81
    - device Z46.9
      - specified NEC Z46.89
    - external
      - fixation device - code to fracture with seventh character D
      - prosthesis, prosthetic device Z44.9
        - breast Z44.3-
        - specified NEC Z44.8

- **Encounter** *(continued)*
  - removal *(continued)*
    - implanted device NEC Z45.89
    - insulin pump Z46.81
    - internal fixation device Z47.2
    - myringotomy device (stent) (tube) Z45.82
    - nervous system device NEC Z46.2
      - brain neuropacemaker Z46.2
      - visual substitution device Z46.2
        - implanted Z45.31
    - non-vascular catheter Z46.82
    - orthodontic device Z46.4
    - stent
      - ureteral Z46.6
    - urinary device Z46.6
  - repeat cervical smear to confirm findings of recent normal smear following initial abnormal smear Z01.42
  - respirator [ventilator] use during power failure Z99.12
  - Rh typing Z01.83
  - screening *—see* Screening
  - specified NEC Z76.89
  - sterilization Z30.2
  - suspected condition, ruled out
    - amniotic cavity and membrane Z03.71
    - cervical shortening Z03.75
    - fetal anomaly Z03.73
    - fetal growth Z03.74
    - maternal and fetal conditions NEC Z03.79
    - oligohydramnios Z03.71
    - placental problem Z03.72
    - polyhydramnios Z03.71
  - suspected exposure (to), ruled out
    - anthrax Z03.810
    - biological agents NEC Z03.818
  - termination of pregnancy, elective Z33.2
  - testing *—see* Test
  - therapeutic drug level monitoring Z51.81
  - titration, insulin pump Z46.81
  - to determine fetal viability of pregnancy O36.80
  - training
    - insulin pump Z46.81
  - X-ray of chest (as part of a general medical examination) Z00.00
    - with abnormal findings Z00.01
- **Encystment** *—see* Cyst
- **Endarteritis** (bacterial, subacute) (infective) I77.6
  - brain I67.7
  - cerebral or cerebrospinal I67.7
  - deformans *—see* Arteriosclerosis
  - embolic *—see* Embolism
  - obliterans *—see also* Arteriosclerosis
    - pulmonary I28.8
  - pulmonary I28.8
  - retina *—see* Vasculitis, retina
  - senile *—see* Arteriosclerosis
  - syphilitic A52.09
    - brain or cerebral A52.04
    - congenital A50.54 *[I79.8]*
  - tuberculous A18.89
- **Endemic** *—see* condition
- **Endocarditis** (chronic) (marantic) (nonbacterial) (thrombotic) (valvular) I38
  - with rheumatic fever (conditions in I00)
    - active *—see* Endocarditis, acute, rheumatic
    - inactive or quiescent (with chorea) I09.1

- **Endocarditis** *(continued)*
  - acute or subacute I33.9
    - infective I33.0
    - rheumatic (aortic) (mitral) (pulmonary) (tricuspid) I01.1
      - with chorea (acute) (rheumatic) (Sydenham's) I02.0
  - aortic (heart) (nonrheumatic) (valve) I35.8
    - with
      - mitral disease I08.0
        - with tricuspid (valve) disease I08.3
        - active or acute I01.1
          - with chorea (acute) (rheumatic) (Sydenham's) I02.0
      - rheumatic fever (conditions in I00)
        - active *—see* Endocarditis, acute, rheumatic
        - inactive or quiescent (with chorea) I06.9
      - tricuspid (valve) disease I08.2
        - with mitral (valve) disease I08.3
    - acute or subacute I33.9
    - arteriosclerotic I35.8
    - rheumatic I06.9
      - with mitral disease I08.0
        - with tricuspid (valve) diseas[e] I08.3
        - active or acute I01.1
          - with chorea (acute) (rheumatic) (Sydenham's) I02.0
      - active or acute I01.1
        - with chorea (acute) (rheumatic) (Sydenham's) I02.0
      - specified NEC I06.8
    - specified cause NEC I35.8
    - syphilitic A52.03
  - arteriosclerotic I38
  - atypical verrucous (Libman-Sacks) M32.11
  - bacterial (acute) (any valve) (subacute) I33.0
  - candidal B37.6
  - congenital Q24.8
  - constrictive I33.0
  - Coxiella burnetii A78 *[I39]*
  - Coxsackie B33.21
  - due to
    - prosthetic cardiac valve T82.6
    - Q fever A78 *[I39]*
    - Serratia marcescens I33.0
    - typhoid (fever) A01.02
  - gonococcal A54.83
  - infectious or infective (acute) (any valve) (subacute) I33.0
  - lenta (acute) (any valve) (subacute) I33.0
  - Libman-Sacks M32.11
  - listerial A32.82
  - Löffler's I42.3
  - malignant (acute) (any valve) (subacute) I33.0
  - meningococcal A39.51
  - mitral (chronic) (double) (fibroid) (heart) (inactive) (valve) (with chorea) I05.9
    - with
      - aortic (valve) disease I08.0
        - with tricuspid (valve) dise[ase] I08.3
        - active or acute I01.1
          - with chorea (acute) (rheumatic) (Sydenham's) I02.0
      - rheumatic fever (conditions [in] I00)

Endocarditis *(continued)*
- mitral *(continued)*
  - with *(continued)*
    - rheumatic fever *(continued)*
      - active —*see* Endocarditis, acute, rheumatic
      - inactive or quiescent (with chorea) I05.9
    - tricuspid (valve) disease I08.1
      - with aortic (valve) disease I08.3
  - active or acute I01.1
    - with chorea (acute) (rheumatic) (Sydenham's) I02.0
    - bacterial I33.0
  - arteriosclerotic I34.8
  - nonrheumatic I34.8
    - acute or subacute I33.9
  - specified NEC I05.8
- monilial B37.6
- multiple valves I08.9
  - specified disorders I08.8
- mycotic (acute) (any valve) (subacute) I33.0
- pneumococcal (acute) (any valve) (subacute) I33.0
- pulmonary (chronic) (heart) (valve) I37.8
  - with rheumatic fever (conditions in I00)
    - active —*see* Endocarditis, acute, rheumatic
    - inactive or quiescent (with chorea) I09.89
      - with aortic, mitral or tricuspid disease I08.8
  - acute or subacute I33.9
    - rheumatic I01.1
      - with chorea (acute) (rheumatic) (Sydenham's) I02.0
  - arteriosclerotic I37.8
  - congenital Q22.2
  - rheumatic (chronic) (inactive) (with chorea) I09.89
    - active or acute I01.1
      - with chorea (acute) (rheumatic) (Sydenham's) I02.0
  - syphilitic A52.03
- purulent (acute) (any valve) (subacute) I33.0
- Q fever A78 *[I39]*
- rheumatic (chronic) (inactive) (with chorea) I09.1
  - active or acute (aortic) (mitral) (pulmonary) (tricuspid) I01.1
    - with chorea (acute) (rheumatic) (Sydenham's) I02.0
- rheumatoid —*see* Rheumatoid, carditis
- septic (acute) (any valve) (subacute) I33.0
- streptococcal (acute) (any valve) (subacute) I33.0
- subacute —*see* Endocarditis, acute
- suppurative (acute) (any valve) (subacute) I33.0
- syphilitic A52.03
- toxic I33.9
- tricuspid (chronic) (heart) (inactive) (rheumatic) (valve) (with chorea) I07.9
  - with
    - aortic (valve) disease I08.2
      - mitral (valve) disease I08.3
    - mitral (valve) disease I08.1
      - aortic (valve) disease I08.3
    - rheumatic fever (conditions in I00)
      - active —*see* Endocarditis, acute, rheumatic
      - inactive or quiescent (with chorea) I07.8

Endocarditis *(continued)*
- tricuspid *(continued)*
  - active or acute I01.1
    - with chorea (acute) (rheumatic) (Sydenham's) I02.0
  - arteriosclerotic I36.8
  - nonrheumatic I36.8
    - acute or subacute I33.9
  - specified cause, except rheumatic I36.8
- tuberculous —*see* Tuberculosis, endocarditis
- typhoid A01.02
- ulcerative (acute) (any valve) (subacute) I33.0
- vegetative (acute) (any valve) (subacute) I33.0
- verrucous (atypical) (nonbacterial) (nonrheumatic) M32.11

Endocardium, endocardial —*see also* condition
- cushion defect Q21.2

Endocervicitis —*see also* Cervicitis
- due to intrauterine (contraceptive) device T83.6
- hyperplastic N72

Endocrine —*see* condition

Endocrinopathy, pluriglandular E31.9

Endodontic
- overfill M27.52
- underfill M27.53

Endodontitis K04.0

Endomastoiditis —*see* Mastoiditis

Endometrioma N80.9

Endometriosis N80.9
- appendix N80.5
- bladder N80.8
- bowel N80.5
- broad ligament N80.3
- cervix N80.0
- colon N80.5
- cul-de-sac (Douglas') N80.3
- exocervix N80.0
- fallopian tube N80.2
- female genital organ NEC N80.8
- gallbladder N80.8
- in scar of skin N80.6
- internal N80.0
- intestine N80.5
- lung N80.8
- myometrium N80.0
- ovary N80.1
- parametrium N80.3
- pelvic peritoneum N80.3
- peritoneal (pelvic) N80.3
- rectovaginal septum N80.4
- rectum N80.5
- round ligament N80.3
- skin (scar) N80.6
- specified site NEC N80.8
- stromal D39.0
- umbilicus N80.8
- uterus (internal) N80.0
- vagina N80.4
- vulva N80.8

Endometritis (decidual) (nonspecific) (purulent) (senile) (atrophic) (suppurative) N71.9
- with ectopic pregnancy O08.0
- acute N71.0
- blenorrhagic (gonococcal) (acute) (chronic) A54.24
- cervix, cervical (with erosion or ectropion) —*see also* Cervicitis
  - hyperplastic N72
- chlamydial A56.11
- chronic N71.1

Endometritis *(continued)*
- following
  - abortion —*see* Abortion by type complicated by genital infection
  - ectopic or molar pregnancy O08.0
- gonococcal, gonorrheal (acute) (chronic) A54.24
- hyperplastic —*see also* Hyperplasia, endometrial N85.00-
  - cervix N72
- puerperal, postpartum, childbirth O86.12
- subacute N71.0
- tuberculous A18.17

Endometrium —*see* condition

Endomyocardiopathy, South African I42.3

Endomyocarditis —*see* Endocarditis

Endomyofibrosis I42.3

Endomyometritis —*see* Endometritis

Endopericarditis —*see* Endocarditis

Endoperineuritis —*see* Disorder, nerve

Endophlebitis —*see* Phlebitis

Endophthalmia —*see* Endophthalmitis, purulent

Endophthalmitis (acute) (infective) (metastatic) (subacute) H44.009
- bleb associated H59.4 —*see also* Bleb, inflammed (infected), postprocedural
- gonorrheal A54.39
- in (due to)
  - cysticercosis B69.1
  - onchocerciasis B73.01
  - toxocariasis B83.0
- panuveitis —*see* Panuveitis
- parasitic H44.12-
- purulent H44.00-
  - panophthalmitis —*see* Panophthalmitis
  - vitreous abscess H44.02-
- specified NEC H44.19
- sympathetic —*see* Uveitis, sympathetic

Endosalpingioma D28.2

Endosalpingiosis N94.89

Endosteitis —*see* Osteomyelitis

Endothelioma, bone —*see* Neoplasm, bone, malignant

Endotheliosis (hemorrhagic infectional) D69.8

Endotoxemia - code to condition

Endotrachelitis —*see* Cervicitis

Engelmann (-Camurati) **syndrome** Q78.3

English disease —*see* Rickets

Engman's disease L30.3

Engorgement
- breast N64.59
  - newborn P83.4
  - puerperal, postpartum O92.79
- lung (passive) —*see* Edema, lung
- pulmonary (passive) —*see* Edema, lung
- stomach K31.89
- venous, retina —*see* Occlusion, retina, vein, engorgement

Enlargement, enlarged —*see also* Hypertrophy
- adenoids J35.2
  - with tonsils J35.3
- alveolar ridge K08.8
  - congenital —*see* Anomaly, alveolar
- apertures of diaphragm (congenital) Q79.1

Enlargement, enlarged *(continued)*
- gingival K06.1
- heart, cardiac —*see* Hypertrophy, cardiac
- lacrimal gland, chronic H04.03-
- liver —*see* Hypertrophy, liver
- lymph gland or node R59.9
  - generalized R59.1
  - localized R59.0
- orbit H05.34-
- organ or site, congenital NEC —*see* Anomaly, by site
- parathyroid (gland) E21.0
- pituitary fossa R93.0
- prostate N40.0
  - with lower urinary tract symptoms (LUTS) N40.1
  - without lower urinary tract symtpoms (LUTS) N40.0
- sella turcica R93.0
- spleen —*see* Splenomegaly
- thymus (gland) (congenital) E32.0
- thyroid (gland) —*see* Goiter
- tongue K14.8
- tonsils J35.1
  - with adenoids J35.3
- uterus N85.2

Enophthalmos H05.40-
- due to
  - orbital tissue atrophy H05.41-
  - trauma or surgery H05.42-

Enostosis M27.8

Entamebic, entamebiasis —*see* Amebiasis

Entanglement
- umbilical cord (s) O69.2
  - with compression O69.2
    - without compression O69.82
  - around neck (with compression) O69.1
    - without compression O69.81
  - of twins in monoamniotic sac O69.2

Enteralgia —*see* Pain, abdominal

Enteric —*see* condition

Enteritis (acute) (diarrheal) (hemorrhagic) (noninfective) (septic) K52.9
- adenovirus A08.2
- aertrycke infection A02.0
- allergic K52.2
- amebic (acute) A06.0
  - with abscess —*see* Abscess, amebic
  - chronic A06.1
    - with abscess —*see* Abscess, amebic
    - nondysenteric A06.2
  - nondysenteric A06.2
- astrovirus A08.32
- bacillary NOS A03.9
- bacterial A04.9
  - specified NEC A04.8
- calicivirus A08.31
- candidal B37.82
- Chilomastix A07.8
- choleriformis A00.1
- chronic (noninfectious) K52.9
  - ulcerative —*see* Colitis, ulcerative
- cicatrizing (chronic) —*see* Enteritis, regional, small intestine
- Clostridium
  - botulinum (food poisoning) A05.1
  - difficile A04.7
- coccidial A07.3
- coxsackie virus A08.39
- dietetic K52.2
- drug-induced K52.1

Enteritis *(continued)*
- due to
  - astrovirus A08.32
  - calicivirus A08.31
  - coxsackie virus A08.39
  - drugs K52.1
  - echovirus A08.39
  - enterovirus NEC A08.39
  - food hypersensitivity K52.2
  - infectious organism (bacterial) (viral) —*see* Enteritis, infectious
  - torovirus A08.39
  - Yersinia enterocolitica A04.6
- echovirus A08.39
- eltor A00.1
- enterovirus NEC A08.39
- eosinophilic K52.81
- epidemic (infectious) A09
- fulminant K55.0
- gangrenous —*see* Enteritis, infectious
- giardial A07.1
- infectious NOS A09
  - due to
    - adenovirus A08.2
    - Aerobacter aerogenes A04.8
    - Arizona (bacillus) A02.0
    - bacteria NOS A04.9
      - specified NEC A04.8
    - Campylobacter A04.5
    - Clostridium difficile A04.7
    - Clostridium perfringens A04.8
    - Enterobacter aerogenes A04.8
    - enterovirus A08.39
    - Escherichia coli A04.4
      - enteroaggregative A04.4
      - enterohemorrhagic A04.3
      - enteroinvasive A04.2
      - enteropathogenic A04.0
      - enterotoxigenic A04.1
      - specified NEC A04.4
    - specified
      - bacteria NEC A04.8
      - virus NEC A08.39
    - Staphylococcus A04.8
    - virus NEC A08.4
      - specified type NEC A08.39
    - Yersinia enterocolitica A04.6
  - specified organism NEC A08.8
- influenzal —*see* Influenza, with, digestive manifestations
- ischemic K55.9
  - acute K55.0
  - chronic K55.1
- microsporidial A07.8
- mucomembranous, myxomembranous —*see* Syndrome, irritable bowel
- mucous —*see* Syndrome, irritable bowel
- necroticans A05.2
- necrotizing of newborn —*see* Enterocolitis, necrotizing, in newborn
- neurogenic —*see* Syndrome, irritable bowel
- newborn necrotizing —*see* Enterocolitis, necrotizing, in newborn
- noninfectious K52.9
- norovirus A08.11
- parasitic NEC B82.9
- paratyphoid (fever) —*see* Fever, paratyphoid
- protozoal A07.9
  - specified NEC A07.8
- radiation K52.0
- regional (of) K50.90
  - with
    - complication K50.919
      - abscess K50.914
      - fistula K50.913
      - intestinal obstruction K50.912
      - rectal bleeding K50.911
      - specified complication NEC K50.918
  - colon —*see* Enteritis, regional, large intestine
  - duodenum —*see* Enteritis, regional, small intestine
  - ileum —*see* Enteritis, regional, small intestine
  - jejunum —*see* Enteritis, regional, small intestine
  - large bowel —*see* Enteritis, regional, large intestine
  - large intestine (colon) (rectum) K50.10
    - with
      - complication K50.119
        - abscess K50.114
        - fistula K50.113
        - intestinal obstruction K50.112
        - rectal bleeding K50.111
        - small intestine (duodenum) (ileum) (jejunum) involvement K50.80
          - with
            - complication K50.819
              - abscess K50.814
              - fistula K50.813
              - intestinal obstruction K50.812
              - rectal bleeding K50.811
              - specified complication NEC K50.818
        - specified complication NEC K50.118
  - rectum —*see* Enteritis, regional, large intestine
  - small intestine (duodenum) (ileum) (jejunum) K50.00
    - with
      - complication K50.019
        - abscess K50.014
        - fistula K50.013
        - intestinal obstruction K50.012
        - large intestine (colon) (rectum) involvement K50.80
          - with
            - complication K50.819
              - abscess K50.814
              - fistula K50.813
              - intestinal obstruction K50.812
              - rectal bleeding K50.811
              - specified complication NEC K50.818
        - rectal bleeding K50.011
        - specified complication NEC K50.018
- rotaviral A08.0
- Salmonella, salmonellosis (arizonae) (cholerae-suis) (enteritidis) (typhimurium) A02.0
- segmental —*see* Enteritis, regional
- septic A09
- Shigella —*see* Infection, Shigella
- small round structured NEC A08.19
- spasmodic, spastic —*see* Syndrome, irritable bowel
- staphylococcal A04.8
  - due to food A05.0
- torovirus A08.39
- toxic NEC K52.1
  - due to Clostridium difficile A04.7
- trichomonal A07.8
- tuberculous A18.32
- typhosa A01.00
- ulcerative (chronic) —*see* Colitis, ulcerative
- viral A08.4
  - adenovirus A08.2
  - enterovirus A08.39
  - Rotavirus A08.0
  - small round structured NEC A08.19
  - specified NEC A08.39
  - virus specified NEC A08.39

Enterobiasis B80

Enterobius vermicularis (infection) (infestation) B80

Enterocele —*see also* Hernia, abdomen
- pelvic, pelvis (acquired) (congenital) N81.5
- vagina, vaginal (acquired) (congenital) NEC N81.5

Enterocolitis —*see also* Enteritis K52.9
- due to Clostridium difficile A04.7
- fulminant ischemic K55.0
- granulomatous —*see* Enteritis, regional
- hemorrhagic (acute) K55.0
  - chronic K55.1
- infectious NEC A09
- ischemic K55.9
- necrotizing
  - due to Clostridium difficile A04.7
  - in newborn P77.9
    - stage 1 (without pneumatosis, without perforation) P77.1
    - stage 2 (with pneumatosis, without perforation) P77.2
    - stage 3 (with pneumatosis, with perforation) P77.3
- noninfectious K52.9
  - newborn —*see* Enterocolitis, necrotizing, in newborn
- pseudomembranous (newborn) A04.7
- radiation K52.0
  - newborn —*see* Enterocolitis, necrotizing, in newborn
- ulcerative (chronic) —*see* Pancolitis, ulcerative (chronic)

Enterogastritis —*see* Enteritis

Enteropathy K63.9
- gluten-sensitive K90.0
- hemorrhagic, terminal K55.0
- protein-losing K90.4

Enteroperitonitis —*see* Peritonitis

Enteroptosis K63.4

Enterorrhagia K92.2

Enterospasm —*see also* Syndrome, irritable, bowel
- psychogenic F45.8

Enterostenosis —*see also* Obstruction, intestine K56.69

Enterostomy
- complication —*see* Complication, enterostomy
- status Z93.4

Enterovirus, as cause of disease classified elsewhere B97.10
- coxsackievirus B97.11
- echovirus B97.12
- other specified B97.19

Enthesopathy (peripheral) M77.9
- Achilles tendinitis —*see* Tendinitis, Achilles
- ankle and tarsus M77.9
  - specified type NEC —*see* Enthesopathy, foot, specified type NEC
- anterior tibial syndrome M76.81-
- calcaneal spur —*see* Spur, bone, calcaneal
- elbow region M77.8
  - lateral epicondylitis —*see* Epicondylitis, lateral
  - medial epicondylitis —*see* Epicondylitis, medial
- foot NEC M77.9
  - metatarsalgia —*see* Metatarsalgia
  - specified type NEC M77.5-
- forearm M77.9
- gluteal tendinitis —*see* Tendinitis, gluteal
- hand M77.9
- hip —*see* Enthesopathy, lower limb, specified type NEC
- iliac crest spur —*see* Spur, bone, iliac crest
- iliotibial band syndrome —*see* Syndrome, iliotibial band
- knee —*see* Enthesopathy, lower limb, lower leg, specified type NEC
- lateral epicondylitis —*see* Epicondylitis, lateral
- lower limb (excluding foot) M76.9
  - Achilles tendinitis —*see* Tendinitis, Achilles
  - anterior tibial syndrome M76.81-
  - gluteal tendinitis —*see* Tendinitis, gluteal
  - iliac crest spur —*see* Spur, bone, iliac crest
  - iliotibial band syndrome —*see* Syndrome, iliotibial band
  - patellar tendinitis —*see* Tendinitis, patellar
  - pelvic region —*see* Enthesopathy, lower limb, specified type NEC
  - peroneal tendinitis —*see* Tendinitis, peroneal
  - posterior tibial syndrome M76.82-
  - psoas tendinitis —*see* Tendinitis, psoas
  - shoulder M77.9
  - specified type NEC M76.89-
  - tibial collateral bursitis —*see* Bursitis, tibial collateral
- medial epicondylitis —*see* Epicondylitis, medial
- metatarsalgia —*see* Metatarsalgia
- multiple sites M77.9
- patellar tendinitis —*see* Tendinitis, patellar
- pelvis M77.9
- periarthritis of wrist —*see* Periarthritis, wrist
- peroneal tendinitis —*see* Tendinitis, peroneal
- posterior tibial syndrome M76.82-
- psoas tendinitis —*see* Tendinitis, psoas
- shoulder region —*see* Lesion, shoulder
- specified site NEC M77.9
- specified type NEC M77.8
- spinal M46.00
  - cervical region M46.02
  - cervicothoracic region M46.03
  - lumbar region M46.06
  - lumbosacral region M46.07
  - multiple sites M46.09
  - occipito-atlanto-axial region M46.01
  - sacrococcygeal region M46.08
  - thoracic region M46.04
  - thoracolumbar region M46.05
- tibial collateral bursitis —*see* Bursitis, tibial collateral
- upper arm M77.9

Epilepsy, epileptic, epilepsia *(continued)*
  progressive (familial) myoclonic —*see* Epilepsy, generalized, idiopathic
  reflex —*see* Epilepsy, specified NEC
  related to
    alcohol G40.509
      not intractable G40.509
        with status epilepticus G40.501
        without status eplilepticus G40.509
    drugs G40.509
      not intractable G40.509
        with status epilepticus G40.501
        without status eplilepticus G40.509
    external causes G40.509
      not intractable G40.509
        with status epilepticus G40.501
        without status eplilepticus G40.509
    hormonal changes G40.509
      not intractable G40.509
        with status epilepticus G40.501
        without status eplilepticus G40.509
    sleep deprivation G40.509
      not intractable G40.509
        with status epilepticus G40.501
        without status eplilepticus G40.509
    stress G40.509
      not intractable G40.509
        with status epilepticus G40.501
        without status eplilepticus G40.509
  somatomotor —*see* Epilepsy, localization-related, symptomatic, with simple partial seizures
  somatosensory —*see* Epilepsy, localization-related, symptomatic, with simple partial seizures
  spasms G40.822
    intractable G40.824
      with status epilepticus G40.823
      without status epilepticus G40.824
    not intractable G40.822
      with status epilepticus G40.821
      without status epilepticus G40.822
  specified NEC G40.802
    intractable G40.804
      with status epilepticus G40.803
      without status epilepticus G40.804
    not intractable G40.802
      with status epilepticus G40.801
      without status epilepticus G40.802
  syndromes
    generalized
      idiopathic G40.309
        intractable G40.319
          with status epilepticus G40.311
          without status epilepticus G40.319
        not intractable G40.309
          with status epilepticus G40.301
          without status epilepticus G40.309

Epilepsy, epileptic, epilepsia *(continued)*
  syndromes *(continued)*
    generalized *(continued)*
      specified NEC G40.409
        intractable G40.419
          with status epilepticus G40.411
          without status epilepticus G40.419
        not intractable G40.409
          with status epilepticus G40.401
          without status epilepticus G40.409
    localization-related (focal) (partial)
      idiopathic G40.009
        with seizures of localized onset G40.009
          intractable G40.019
            with status epilepticus G40.011
            without status epilepticus G40.019
          not intractable G40.009
            with status epilepticus G40.001
            without status epilepticus G40.009
      symptomatic
        with complex partial seizures G40.209
          intractable G40.219
            with status epilepticus G40.211
            without status epilepticus G40.219
          not intractable G40.209
            with status epilepticus G40.201
            without status epilepticus G40.209
        with simple partial seizures G40.109
          intractable G40.119
            with status epilepticus G40.111
            without status epilepticus G40.119
          not intractable G40.109
            with status epilepticus G40.101
            without status epilepticus G40.109
    specified NEC G40.802
      intractable G40.804
        with status epilepticus G40.803
        without status epilepticus G40.804
      not intractable G40.802
        with status epilepticus G40.801
        without status epilepticus G40.802
  tonic (-clonic) —*see* Epilepsy, generalized, specified NEC
  twilight F05
  uncinate (gyrus) —*see* Epilepsy, localization-related, symptomatic, with complex partial seizures
  Unverricht (-Lundborg) (familial myoclonic) —*see* Epilepsy, generalized, idiopathic
  visceral —*see* Epilepsy, specified NEC
  visual —*see* Epilepsy, specified NEC

Epiloia Q85.1

Epimenorrhea N92.0

Epipharyngitis —*see* Nasopharyngitis

Epiphora H04.20-
  due to
    excess lacrimation H04.21-
    insufficient drainage H04.22-

Epiphyseal arrest —*see* Arrest, epiphyseal

Epiphyseolysis, epiphysiolysis —*see* Osteochondropathy

Epiphysitis —*see also* Osteochondropathy
  juvenile M92.9
  syphilitic (congenital) A50.02

Epiplocele —*see* Hernia, abdomen

Epiploitis —*see* Peritonitis

Epiplosarcomphalocele —*see* Hernia, umbilicus

Episcleritis (suppurative) H15.10-
  in (due to)
    syphilis A52.71
    tuberculosis A18.51
  nodular H15.12-
  periodica fugax H15.11-
    angioneurotic —*see* Edema, angioneurotic
  syphilitic (late) A52.71
  tuberculous A18.51

Episode
  affective, mixed F39
  depersonalization (in neurotic state) F48.1
  depressive F32.9
    major F32.9
      mild F32.0
      moderate F32.1
      severe (without psychotic symptoms) F32.2
        with psychotic symptoms F32.3
    recurrent F33.9
      brief F33.8
    specified NEC F32.8
  hypomanic F30.8
  manic F30.9
    with
      psychotic symptoms F30.2
      remission (full) F30.4
        partial F30.3
    other specified F30.8
    recurrent F31.89
    without psychotic symptoms F30.10
      mild F30.11
      moderate F30.12
      severe (without psychotic symptoms) F30.13
        with psychotic symptoms F30.2
  psychotic F23
    organic F06.8
  schizophrenic (acute) NEC, brief F23

Epispadias (female) (male) Q64.0

Episplenitis D73.89

Epistaxis (multiple) R04.0
  hereditary I78.0
  vicarious menstruation N94.89

Epithelioma (malignant) —*see* also Neoplasm, malignant, by site
  adenoides cysticum —*see* Neoplasm, skin, benign
  basal cell —*see* Neoplasm, skin, malignant
  benign —*see* Neoplasm, benign, by site
  Bowen's —*see* Neoplasm, skin, in situ
  calcifying, of Malherbe —*see* Neoplasm, skin, benign

Epithelioma *(continued)*
  external site —*see* Neoplasm, skin, malignant
  intraepidermal, Jadassohn —*see* Neoplasm, skin, benign
  squamous cell —*see* Neoplasm, malignant, by site

Epitheliomatosis pigmented Q82.1

Epitheliopathy, multifocal placoid pigment H30.14-

Epithelium, epithelial —*see* condition

Epituberculosis (with atelectasis) (allergic) A15.7

Eponychia Q84.6

Epstein's
  nephrosis or syndrome —*see* Nephrosis
  pearl K09.8

Epulis (gingiva) (fibrous) (giant cell) K06.8

Equinia A24.0

Equinovarus (congenital) (talipes) Q66.0
  acquired —*see* Deformity, limb, clubfoot

Equivalent
  convulsive (abdominal) —*see* Epilepsy, specified NEC
  epileptic (psychic) —*see* Epilepsy, localization-related, symptomatic, with complex partial seizures

Erb (-Duchenne) **paralysis** (birth injury) (newborn) P14.0

Erb-Goldflam disease or syndrome G70.00
  with exacerbation (acute) G70.01
  in crisis G70.01

Erb's
  disease G71.0
  palsy, paralysis (brachial) (birth) (newborn) P14.0
    spinal (spastic) syphilitic A52.17
  pseudohypertrophic muscular dystrophy G71.0

Erdheim's syndrome (acromegalic macrospondylitis) E22.0

Erection, painful (persistent) —*see* Priapism

Ergosterol deficiency (vitamin D) E55.9
  with
    adult osteomalacia M83.8
    rickets —*see* Rickets

Ergotism —*see also* Poisoning, food, noxious, plant
  from ergot used as drug (migraine therapy) —*see* Table of Drugs and Chemicals

Erosio interdigitalis blastomycetica B37.2

Erosion
  artery I77.2
    without rupture I77.89
  bone —*see* Disorder, bone, density and structure, specified NEC
  bronchus J98.09
  cartilage (joint) —*see* Disorder, cartilage, specified type NEC
  cervix (uteri) (acquired) (chronic) (congenital) N86
    with cervicitis N72
  cornea (nontraumatic) —*see* Ulcer, cornea
    recurrent H18.83-
    traumatic —*see* Abrasion, cornea

Erosion *(continued)*
- dental (idiopathic) (occupational) (due to diet, drugs or vomiting) K03.2
- duodenum, postpyloric —*see* Ulcer, duodenum
- esophagus K22.10
  - with bleeding K22.11
- gastric —*see* Ulcer, stomach
- gastrojejunal —*see* Ulcer, gastrojejunal
- implanted mesh —*see* Complications, mesh
- intestine K63.3
- lymphatic vessel I89.8
- pylorus, pyloric (ulcer) —*see* Ulcer, stomach
- spine, aneurysmal A52.09
- stomach —*see* Ulcer, stomach
- teeth (idiopathic) (occupational) (due to diet, drugs or vomiting) K03.2
- urethra N36.8
- uterus N85.8

Erotomania F52.8

Error
- metabolism, inborn -- se Disorder, metabolism
- refractive —*see* Disorder, refraction

Eructation R14.2
- nervous or psychogenic F45.8

Eruption
- creeping B76.9
- drug (generalized) (taken internally) L27.0
  - fixed L27.1
  - in contact with skin —*see* Dermatitis, due to drugs
  - localized L27.1
- Hutchinson, summer L56.4
- Kaposi's varicelliform B00.0
- napkin L22
- polymorphous light (sun) L56.4
- recalcitrant pustular L13.8
- ringed R23.8
- skin (nonspecific) R21
  - creeping (meaning hookworm) B76.9
  - due to inoculation/vaccination (generalized) —*see also* Dermatitis, due to, vaccine L27.0
    - localized L27.1
  - erysipeloid A26.0
  - feigned L98.1
  - Kaposi's varicelliform B00.0
  - lichenoid L28.0
  - meaning dermatitis —*see* Dermatitis
  - toxic NEC L53.0
- tooth, teeth, abnormal (incomplete) (late) (premature) (sequence) K00.6
- vesicular R23.8

Erysipelas (gangrenous) (infantile) (newborn) (phlegmonous) (suppurative) A46
- external ear A46 *[H62.40]*
- puerperal, postpartum O86.89

Erysipeloid A26.9
- cutaneous (Rosenbach's) A26.0
- disseminated A26.8
- sepsis A26.7
- specified NEC A26.8

Erythema, erythematous (infectional) (inflammation) L53.9
- ab igne L59.0
- annulare (centrifugum) (rheumaticum) L53.1
- arthriticum epidemicum A25.1
- brucellum —*see* Brucellosis

Erythema, erythematous *(continued)*
- chronic figurate NEC L53.3
- chronicum migrans (Borrelia burgdorferi) A69.20
- diaper L22
- due to
  - chemical NEC L53.0
    - in contact with skin L24.5
  - drug (internal use) —*see* Dermatitis, due to, drugs
- elevatum diutinum L95.1
- endemic E52
- epidemic, arthritic A25.1
- figuratum perstans L53.3
- gluteal L22
- heat - code by site under Burn, first degree
- ichthyosiforme congenitum bullous Q80.3
- in diseases classified elsewhere L54
- induratum (nontuberculous) L52
  - tuberculous A18.4
- infectiosum B08.3
- intertrigo L30.4
- iris L51.9
- marginatum L53.2
  - in (due to) acute rheumatic fever I00
- medicamentosum —*see* Dermatitis, due to, drugs
- migrans A26.0
  - chronicum A69.20
  - tongue K14.1
- multiforme (major) (minor) L51.9
  - bullous, bullosum L51.1
  - conjunctiva L51.1
  - nonbullous L51.0
  - pemphigoides L12.0
  - specified NEC L51.8
- napkin L22
- neonatorum P83.8
  - toxic P83.1
- nodosum L52
  - tuberculous A18.4
- palmar L53.8
- pernio T69.1
- rash, newborn P83.8
- scarlatiniform (recurrent) (exfoliative) L53.8
- solare L55.0
- specified NEC L53.8
- toxic, toxicum NEC L53.0
  - newborn P83.1
- tuberculous (primary) A18.4

Erythematous, erythematosus —*see* condition

Erythermalgia (primary) I73.81

Erythralgia I73.81

Erythrasma L08.1

Erythredema (polyneuropathy) —*see* Poisoning, mercury

Erythremia (acute) C94.0-
- chronic D45
- secondary D75.1

Erythroblastopenia —*see also* Aplasia, red cell D60.9
- congenital D61.01

Erythroblastophthisis D61.09

Erythroblastosis (fetalis) (newborn) P55.9
- due to
  - ABO (antibodies) (incompatibility) (isoimmunization) P55.1
  - Rh (antibodies) (incompatibility) (isoimmunization) P55.0

Erythrocyanosis (crurum) I73.89

Erythrocythemia —*see* Erythremia

Erythrocytosis (megalosplenic) (secondary) D75.1
- familial D75.0
- oval, hereditary —*see* Elliptocytosis
- secondary D75.1
- stress D75.1

Erythroderma (secondary) —*see also* Erythema L53.9
- bullous ichthyosiform, congenital Q80.3
- desquamativum L21.1
- ichthyosiform, congenital (bullous) Q80.3
- neonatorum P83.8
- psoriaticum L40.8

Erythrodysesthesia, palmar plantar (PPE) L27.1

Erythrogenesis imperfecta D61.09

Erythroleukemia C94.0-

Erythromelalgia I73.81

Erythrophagocytosis D75.89

Erythrophobia F40.298

Erythroplakia, oral epithelium, and tongue K13.29

Erythroplasia (Queyrat) D07.4
- specified site —*see* Neoplasm, skin, in situ
- unspecified site D07.4

Escherichia coli (E. coli)**, as cause of disease classified elsewhere** B96.20
- non-O157 Shiga toxin-producing (with known O group) B96.22
- non-Shiga toxin-producing B96.29
- O157 with confirmation of Shiga toxin when H antigen is unknown, or is not H7 B96.21
- O157:H-(nonmotile) with confirmation of Shiga toxin B96.21
- O157:H7 with or without confirmation of Shiga toxin-production B96.21
- Shiga toxin-producing (with unspecified O group) (STEC) B96.23
  - O157 B96.21
  - O157:H7 with or without confirmation of Shiga toxin-production B96.21
  - specified NEC B96.22
- specified NEC B96.29

Esophagismus K22.4

Esophagitis (acute) (alkaline) (chemical) (chronic) (infectional) (necrotic) (peptic) (postoperative) K20.9
- candidal B37.81
- due to gastrointestinal reflux disease K21.0
- eosinophilic K20.0
- reflux K21.0
- specified NEC K20.8
- tuberculous A18.83
- ulcerative K22.10
  - with bleeding K22.11

Esophagocele K22.5

Esophagomalacia K22.8

Esophagospasm K22.4

Esophagostenosis K22.2

Esophagostomiasis B81.8

Esophagotracheal —*see* condition

Esophagus —*see* condition

Esophoria H50.51
- convergence, excess H51.12
- divergence, insufficiency H51.8

Esotropia —*see* Strabismus, convergent concomitant

Espundia B55.2

Essential —*see* condition

Esthesioneuroblastoma C30.0

Esthesioneurocytoma C30.0

Esthesioneuroepithelioma C30.0

Esthiomene A55

Estivo-autumnal malaria (fever) B50.9

Estrangement (marital) Z63.5
- parent-child NEC Z62.890

Estriasis —*see* Myiasis

Ethanolism —*see* Alcoholism

Etherism —*see* Dependence, drug, inhalant

Ethmoid, ethmoidal —*see* condition

Ethmoiditis (chronic) (nonpurulent) (purulent) —*see also* Sinusitis, ethmoidal
- influenzal —*see* Influenza, with, respiratory manifestations NEC
- Woakes' J33.1

Ethylism —*see* Alcoholism

Eulenburg's disease (congenital paramyotonia) G71.19

Eumycetoma B47.0

Eunuchoidism E29.1
- hypogonadotropic E23.0

European blastomycosis —*see* Cryptococcosis

Eustachian —*see* condition

Evaluation (for) (of)
- development state
  - adolescent Z00.3
  - period of
    - delayed growth in childhood Z00.70
      - with abnormal findings Z00.71
    - rapid growth in childhood Z00.2
  - puberty Z00.3
- growth and developmental state (period of rapid growth) Z00.2
  - delayed growth Z00.70
    - with abnormal findings Z00.71
- mental health (status) Z00.8
  - requested by authority Z04.6
- period of
  - delayed growth in childhood Z00.70
    - with abnormal findings Z00.71
  - rapid growth in childhood Z00.2
- suspected condition —*see* Observation

Evans syndrome D69.41

Event, apparent life threatening in newborn and infant (ALTE) R68.13

Eventration —*see also* Hernia, ventral
- colon into chest —*see* Hernia, diaphragm
- diaphragm (congenital) Q79.1

Eversion
- bladder N32.89
- cervix (uteri) N86
  - with cervicitis N72
- foot NEC —*see also* Deformity, valgus, ankle
  - congenital Q66.6
- punctum lacrimale (postinfectional) (senile) H04.52-
- ureter (meatus) N28.89
- urethra (meatus) N36.8
- uterus N81.4

Evidence
cytologic
of malignancy on anal smear R85.614
of malignancy on cervical smear R87.614
of malignancy on vaginal smear R87.624

Evisceration
birth injury P15.8
traumatic NEC
eye —*see* Enucleated eye

Evulsion —*see* Avulsion

Ewing's sarcoma or tumor - —*see* Neoplasm, bone, malignant

Examination (for) (following) (general) (of) (routine) Z00.00
with abnormal findings Z00.01
abuse, physical (alleged), ruled out
adult Z04.71
child Z04.72
adolescent (development state) Z00.3
alleged rape or sexual assault (victim), ruled out
adult Z04.41
child Z04.42
allergy Z01.82
annual (adult) (periodic) (physical) Z00.00
with abnormal findings Z00.01
gynecological Z01.419
with abnormal findings Z01.411
antibody response Z01.84
blood —*see* Examination, laboratory
blood pressure Z01.30
with abnormal findings Z01.31
cancer staging —*see* Neoplasm, malignant, by site
cervical Papanicolaou smear Z12.4
as part of routine gynecological examination Z01.419
with abnormal findings Z01.411
child (over 28 days old) Z00.129
with abnormal findings Z00.121
under 28 days old —*see* Newborn, examination
clinical research control or normal comparison (control) (participant) Z00.6
contraceptive (drug) maintenance (routine) Z30.8
device (intrauterine) Z30.431
dental Z01.20
with abnormal findings Z01.21
developmental —*see* Examination, child
donor (potential) Z00.5
ear Z01.10
with abnormal findings NEC Z01.118
eye Z01.00
with abnormal findings Z01.01
following
accident NEC Z04.3
transport Z04.1
work Z04.2
assault, alleged, ruled out
adult Z04.71
child Z04.72
motor vehicle accident Z04.1
treatment (for) Z09
combined NEC Z09
fracture Z09
malignant neoplasm Z08
malignant neoplasm Z08
mental disorder Z09
specified condition NEC Z09
follow-up (routine) (following) Z09
chemotherapy NEC Z09
malignant neoplasm Z08

Examination *(continued)*
follow-up *(continued)*
fracture Z09
malignant neoplasm Z08
postpartum Z39.2
psychotherapy Z09
radiotherapy NEC Z09
malignant neoplasm Z08
surgery NEC Z09
malignant neoplasm Z08
gynecological Z01.419
with abnormal findings Z01.411
for contraceptive maintenance Z30.8
health —*see* Examination, medical
hearing Z01.10
with abnormal findings NEC Z01.118
following failed hearing screening Z01.110
immunity status testing Z01.84
laboratory (as part of a general medical examination) Z00.00
with abnormal findings Z00.01
preprocedural Z01.812
lactating mother Z39.1
medical (adult) (for) (of) Z00.00
with abnormal findings Z00.01
administrative purpose only Z02.9
specified NEC Z02.89
admission to
armed forces Z02.3
old age home Z02.2
prison Z02.89
residential institution Z02.2
school Z02.0
following illness or medical treatment Z02.0
summer camp Z02.89
adoption Z02.82
blood alcohol or drug level Z02.83
camp (summer) Z02.89
clinical research, normal subject (control) (participant) Z00.6
control subject in clinical research (normal comparison) (participant) Z00.6
donor (potential) Z00.5
driving license Z02.4
general (adult) Z00.00
with abnormal findings Z00.01
immigration Z02.89
insurance purposes Z02.6
marriage Z02.89
medicolegal reasons NEC Z04.8
naturalization Z02.89
participation in sport Z02.5
paternity testing Z02.81
population survey Z00.8
pre-employment Z02.1
pre-operative —*see* Examination, pre-procedural
pre-procedural
cardiovascular Z01.810
respiratory Z01.811
specified NEC Z01.818
preschool children
for admission to school Z02.0
prisoners
for entrance into prison Z02.89
recruitment for armed forces Z02.3
specified NEC Z00.8
sport competition Z02.5
medicolegal reason NEC Z04.8
newborn —*see* Newborn, examination
pelvic (annual) (periodic) Z01.419
with abnormal findings Z01.411
period of rapid growth in childhood Z00.2

Examination *(continued)*
periodic (adult) (annual) (routine) Z00.00
with abnormal findings Z00.01
physical (adult) —*see also* Examination, medical Z00.00
sports Z02.5
postpartum
immediately after delivery Z39.0
routine follow-up Z39.2
prenatal (normal pregnancy) —*see also* Pregnancy, normal Z34.9-
pre-chemotherapy (antineoplastic) Z01.818
pre-procedural (pre-operative)
cardiovascular Z01.810
laboratory Z01.812
respiratory Z01.811
specified NEC Z01.818
prior to chemotherapy (antineoplastic) Z01.818
psychiatric NEC Z00.8
follow-up not needing further care Z09
requested by authority Z04.6
radiological (as part of a general medical examination) Z00.00
with abnormal findings Z00.01
repeat cervical smear to confirm findings of recent normal smear following initial abnormal smear Z01.42
skin (hypersensitivity) Z01.82
special —*see also* Examination, by type Z01.89
specified type NEC Z01.89
specified type or reason NEC Z04.8
teeth Z01.20
with abnormal findings Z01.21
urine —*see* Examination, laboratory
vision Z01.00
with abnormal findings Z01.01

Exanthem, exanthema —*see also* Rash
with enteroviral vesicular stomatitis B08.4
Boston A88.0
epidemic with meningitis A88.0 *[G02]*
subitum B08.20
due to human herpesvirus 6 B08.21
due to human herpesvirus 7 B08.22
viral, virus B09
specified type NEC B08.8

Excess, excessive, excessively
alcohol level in blood R78.0
androgen (ovarian) E28.1
attrition, tooth, teeth K03.0
carotene, carotin (dietary) E67.1
cold, effects of T69.9
specified effect NEC T69.8
convergence H51.12
crying
in child, adolescent, or adult R45.83
in infant R68.11
development, breast N62
divergence H51.8
drinking (alcohol) NEC (without dependence) F10.10
habitual (continual) (without remission) F10.20
eating R63.2
estrogen E28.0
fat —*see also* Obesity
in heart —*see* Degeneration, myocardial
localized E65
foreskin N47.8
gas R14.0
glucagon E16.3
heat —*see* Heat

Excess, excessive, excessively *(continued)*
intermaxillary vertical dimension of fully erupted teeth M26.37
interocclusal distance of fully erupted teeth M26.37
kalium E87.5
large
colon K59.3
congenital Q43.8
infant P08.0
organ or site, congenital NEC —*see* Anomaly, by site
long
organ or site, congenital NEC —*see* Anomaly, by site
menstruation (with regular cycle) N92.0
with irregular cycle N92.1
napping Z72.821
natrium E87.0
number of teeth K00.1
nutrient (dietary) NEC R63.2
potassium (K) E87.5
salivation K11.7
secretion —*see also* Hypersecretion
milk O92.6
sputum R09.3
sweat R61
sexual drive F52.8
short
organ or site, congenital NEC —*see* Anomaly, by site
umbilical cord in labor or delivery O69.3
skin, eyelid (acquired) —*see* Blepharochalasis
congenital Q10.3
sodium (Na) E87.0
spacing of fully erupted teeth M26.32
sputum R09.3
sweating R61
thirst R63.1
due to deprivation of water T73.1
tuberosity of jaw M26.07
vitamin
A (dietary) E67.0
administered as drug (prolonged intake) —*see* Table of Drugs and Chemicals, vitamins, adverse effect
overdose or wrong substance given or taken —*see* Table of Drugs and Chemicals, vitamins, poisoning
D (dietary) E67.3
administered as drug (prolonged intake) —*see* Table of Drugs and Chemicals, vitamins, adverse effect
overdose or wrong substance given or taken —*see* Table of Drugs and Chemicals, vitamins, poisoning
weight
gain R63.5
loss R63.4

Excitability, abnormal, under minor stress (personality disorder) F60.3

Excitation
anomalous atrioventricular I45.6
psychogenic F30.8
reactive (from emotional stress, psychological trauma) F30.8

Excitement
hypomanic F30.8
manic F30.9
mental, reactive (from emotional stress, psychological trauma) F30.8
state, reactive (from emotional stress, psychological trauma) F30.8

F

Failure, failed *(continued)*
- cardiorenal (chronic) I50.9
  - hypertensive I13.2
- cardiorespiratory —*see also* Failure, heart R09.2
- cardiovascular (chronic) —*see* Failure, heart
- cerebrovascular I67.9
- cervical dilatation in labor O62.0
- circulation, circulatory (peripheral) R57.9
  - newborn P29.89
- compensation —*see* Disease, heart
- compliance with medical treatment or regimen —*see* Noncompliance
- congestive —*see* Failure, heart, congestive
- dental implant (endosseous) M27.69
  - due to
    - failure of dental prosthesis M27.63
    - lack of attached gingiva M27.62
    - occlusal trauma (poor prosthetic design) M27.62
    - parafunctional habits M27.62
    - periodontal infection (peri-implantitis) M27.62
    - poor oral hygiene M27.62
  - osseointegration M27.61
    - due to
      - complications of systemic disease M27.61
      - poor bone quality M27.61
    - iatrogenic M27.61
  - post-osseointegration
    - biological M27.62
    - due to complications of systemic disease M27.62
    - iatrogenic M27.62
    - mechanical M27.63
  - pre-integration M27.61
  - pre-osseointegration M27.61
  - specified NEC M27.69
- descent of head (at term) of pregnancy (mother) O32.4
- endosseous dental implant —*see* Failure, dental implant
- engagement of head (term of pregnancy) (mother) O32.4
- erection (penile) —*see also* Dysfunction, sexual, male, erectile N52.9
  - nonorgqanic F52.21
- examination (s), anxiety concerning Z55.2
- expansion terminal respiratory units (newborn) (primary) P28.0
- forceps NOS (with subsequent cesarean delivery) O66.5
- gain weight (child over 28 days old) R62.51
  - adult R62.7
  - newborn P92.6
- genital response (male) F52.21
  - female F52.22
- heart (acute) (senile) (sudden) I50.9
  - with
    - acute pulmonary edema —*see* Failure, ventricular, left
    - decompensation —*see* Failure, heart, congestive
    - dilatation —*see* Disease, heart
  - arteriosclerotic I70.90
  - biventricular I50.9
  - combined left-right sided I50.9
  - compensated I50.9
  - complicating
    - anesthesia (general) (local) or other sedation
      - in labor and delivery O74.2
      - in pregnancy O29.12-
      - postpartum, puerperal O89.1
    - delivery (cesarean) (instrumental) O75.4
  - congestive (compensated) (decompensated) I50.9
    - with rheumatic fever (conditions in I00)
      - active I01.8
      - inactive or quiescent (with chorea) I09.81
    - newborn P29.0
    - rheumatic (chronic) (inactive) (with chorea) I09.81
      - active or acute I01.8
        - with chorea I02.0
  - decompensated I50.9
  - degenerative —*see* Degeneration, myocardial
  - diastolic (congestive) I50.30
    - acute (congestive) I50.31
      - and (on) chronic (congestive) I50.33
    - chronic (congestive) I50.32
      - and (on) acute (congestive) I50.33
    - combined with systolic (congestive) I50.40
      - acute (congestive) I50.41
        - and (on) chronic (congestive) I50.43
      - chronic (congestive) I50.42
        - and (on) acute (congestive) I50.43
  - due to presence of cardiac prosthesis I97.13-
  - following cardiac surgery I97.13-
  - high output NOS I50.9
  - hypertensive —*see* Hypertension, heart
  - left (ventricular) —*see* Failure, ventricular, left
  - low output (syndrome) NOS I50.9
  - newborn P29.0
  - organic —*see* Disease, heart
  - peripartum O90.3
  - postprocedural I97.13-
  - rheumatic (chronic) (inactive) I09.9
  - right (ventricular) (secondary to left heart failure) —*see* Failure, heart, congestive
  - systolic (congestive) I50.20
    - acute (congestive) I50.21
      - and (on) chronic (congestive) I50.23
    - chronic (congestive) I50.22
      - and (on) acute (congestive) I50.23
    - combined with diastolic (congestive) I50.40
      - acute (congestive) I50.41
        - and (on) chronic (congestive) I50.43
      - chronic (congestive) I50.42
        - and (on) acute (congestive) I50.43
  - thyrotoxic —*see also* Thyrotoxicosis E05.90 *[I43]*
    - with thyroid storm E05.91 *[I43]*
  - valvular —*see* Endocarditis
- hepatic K72.90
  - with coma K72.91
  - acute or subacute K72.00
    - with coma K72.01
    - due to drugs K71.10
      - with coma K71.11
  - alcoholic (acute) (chronic) (subacute) K70.40
    - with coma K70.41
  - chronic K72.10
    - with coma K72.11
    - due to drugs (acute) (subacute) (chronic) K71.10
      - with coma K71.11
  - due to drugs (acute) (subacute) (chronic) K71.10
    - with coma K71.11
  - postprocedural K91.82
- hepatorenal K76.7
- induction (of labor) O61.9
  - abortion —*see* Abortion, attempted by
    - oxytocic drugs O61.0
    - prostaglandins O61.0
  - instrumental O61.1
  - mechanical O61.1
  - medical O61.0
  - specified NEC O61.8
  - surgical O61.1
- intubation during anesthesia T88.4
  - in pregnancy O29.6-
  - labor and delivery O74.7
  - postpartum, puerperal O89.6
- involution, thymus (gland) E32.0
- kidney —*see also* Disease, kidney, chronic N19
  - acute —*see also* Failure, renal, acute N17.9-
  - diabetic —*see* E08-E13 with .22
- lactation (complete) O92.3
  - partial O92.4
- Leydig's cell, adult E29.1
- liver —*see* Failure, hepatic
- menstruation at puberty N91.0
- mitral I05.8
- myocardial, myocardium —*see also* Failure, heart I50.9
  - chronic —*see also* Failure, heart, congestive I50.9
  - congestive —*see also* Failure, heart, congestive I50.9
- orgasm (female) (psychogenic) F52.31
  - male F52.32
- ovarian (primary) E28.39
  - iatrogenic E89.40
    - asymptomatic E89.40
    - symptomatic E89.41
  - postprocedural (postablative) (postirradiation) (postsurgical) E89.40
    - asymptomatic E89.40
    - symptomatic E89.41
- ovulation causing infertility N97.0
- polyglandular, autoimmune E31.0
- prosthetic joint implant —*see* Complications, joint prosthesis, mechanical, breakdown, by site
- renal N19
  - with
    - tubular necrosis (acute) N17.0
  - acute N17.9
    - with
      - cortical necrosis N17.1
      - medullary necrosis N17.2
      - tubular necrosis N17.0
    - specified NEC N17.8
  - chronic N18.9
    - hypertensive —*see* Hypertension, kidney
  - congenital P96.0
  - end stage (chronic) N18.6
    - due to hypertension I12.0
  - following
    - abortion —*see* Abortion by type complicated by specified condition NEC
    - crushing T79.5
    - ectopic or molar pregnancy O08.4
    - labor and delivery (acute) O90.4
  - hypertensive —*see* Hypertension, kidney
  - postprocedural N99.0
- respiration, respiratory J96.90
  - with
    - hypercapnia J96.92
    - hypoxia J96.91
  - acute J96.00
    - with
      - hypercapnia J96.02
      - hypoxia J96.01
  - center G93.89
  - acute and (on) chronic J96.20
    - with
      - hypercapnia J96.22
      - hypoxia J96.21
  - chronic J96.10
    - with
      - hypercapnia J96.12
      - hypoxia J96.11
  - newborn P28.5
  - postprocedural (acute) J95.821
    - acute and chronic J95.822
- rotation
  - cecum Q43.3
  - colon Q43.3
  - intestine Q43.3
  - kidney Q63.2
- sedation (conscious) (moderate)
  - during procedure T88.52
  - history of Z92.83
- segmentation —*see also* Fusion
  - fingers —*see* Syndactylism, complex, fingers
  - vertebra Q76.49
    - with scoliosis Q76.3
- seminiferous tubule, adult E29.1
- senile (general) R54
- sexual arousal (male) F52.21
  - female F52.22
- testicular endocrine function E29.1
- to thrive (child over 28 days old) R62.51
  - adult R62.7
  - newborn P92.6
- transplant T86.92
  - bone T86.831
    - marrow T86.02
  - cornea T86.841
  - heart T86.22
    - with lung (s) T86.32
  - intestine T86.851
  - kidney T86.12
  - liver T86.42
  - lung (s) T86.811
    - with heart T86.32
  - pancreas T86.891
  - skin (allograft) (autograft) T86.821
  - specified organ or tissue NEC T86.891
  - stem cell (peripheral blood) (umbilical cord) T86.5
- trial of labor (with subsequent cesarean delivery) O66.40
  - following previous cesarean delivery O66.41
- tubal ligation N99.89
- urinary —*see* Disease, kidney, chronic
- vacuum extraction NOS (with subsequent cesarean delivery) O66.5
- vasectomy N99.89
- ventouse NOS (with subsequent cesarean delivery) O66.5
- ventricular —*see also* Failure, heart I50.9

- **Failure, failed** *(continued)*
  - ventricular —*see also* Failure, heart *(continued)*
    - left I50.1
      - with rheumatic fever (conditions in I00)
        - active I01.8
          - with chorea I02.0
        - inactive or quiescent (with chorea) I09.81
      - rheumatic (chronic) (inactive) (with chorea) I09.81
        - active or acute I01.8
          - with chorea I02.0
    - right —*see also* Failure, heart, congestive I50.9
  - vital centers, newborn P91.8
- **Fainting** (fit) R55
- **Fallen arches** —*see* Deformity, limb, flat foot
- **Falling, falls** (repeated) R29.6
  - any organ or part —*see* Prolapse
- **Fallopian**
  - insufflation Z31.41
  - tube —*see* condition
- **Fallot's**
  - pentalogy Q21.8
  - tetrad or tetralogy Q21.3
  - triad or trilogy Q22.3
- **False** —*see also* condition
  - croup J38.5
  - joint —*see* Nonunion, fracture
  - labor (pains) O47.9
    - at or after 37 completed weeks of gestation O47.1
    - before 37 completed weeks of gestation O47.0-
  - passage, urethra (prostatic) N36.5
  - pregnancy F45.8
- **Family, familial** —*see also* condition
  - disruption Z63.8
    - involving divorce or separation Z63.5
  - Li-Fraumeni (syndrome) Z15.01
  - planning advice Z30.09
  - problem Z63.9
    - specified NEC Z63.8
  - retinoblastoma C69.2-
- **Famine** (effects of) T73.0
  - edema —*see* Malnutrition, severe
- **Fanconi** (-de Toni)(-Debré) **syndrome** E72.09
  - with cystinosis E72.04
- **Fanconi's anemia** (congenital pancytopenia) D61.09
- **Farber's disease or syndrome** E75.29
- **Farcy** A24.0
- **Farmer's**
  - lung J67.0
  - skin L57.8
- **Farsightedness** —*see* Hypermetropia
- **Fascia** —*see* condition
- **Fasciculation** R25.3
- **Fasciitis** M72.9
  - diffuse (eosinophilic) M35.4
  - infective M72.8
    - necrotizing M72.6
  - necrotizing M72.6
  - nodular M72.4
  - perirenal (with ureteral obstruction) N13.5
    - with infection N13.6
  - plantar M72.2
  - specified NEC M72.8
  - traumatic (old) M72.8
    - current - code by site under Sprain
- **Fascioliasis** B66.3
- **Fasciolopsis, fasciolopsiasis** (intestinal) B66.5
- **Fascioscapulohumeral myopathy** G71.0
- **Fast pulse** R00.0
- **Fat**
  - embolism —*see* Embolism, fat
  - excessive —*see also* Obesity
    - in heart —*see* Degeneration, myocardial
  - in stool R19.5
  - localized (pad) E65
    - heart —*see* Degeneration, myocardial
    - knee M79.4
    - retropatellar M79.4
  - necrosis
    - breast N64.1
    - mesentery K65.4
    - omentum K65.4
  - pad E65
    - knee M79.4
- **Fatigue** R53.83
  - auditory deafness —*see* Deafness
  - chronic R53.82
  - combat F43.0
  - general R53.83
    - psychogenic F48.8
  - heat (transient) T67.6
  - muscle M62.89
  - myocardium —*see* Failure, heart
  - neoplasm-related R53.0
  - nervous, neurosis F48.8
  - operational F48.8
  - psychogenic (general) F48.8
  - senile R54
  - voice R49.8
- **Fatness** —*see* Obesity
- **Fatty** —*see also* condition
  - apron E65
  - degeneration —*see* Degeneration, fatty
  - heart (enlarged) —*see* Degeneration, myocardial
  - liver NEC K76.0
    - alcoholic K70.0
    - nonalcoholic K76.0
  - necrosis —*see* Degeneration, fatty
- **Fauces** —*see* condition
- **Fauchard's disease** (periodontitis) —*see* Periodontitis
- **Faucitis** J02.9
- **Favism** (anemia) D55.0
- **Favus** —*see* Dermatophytosis
- **Fazio-Londe disease or syndrome** G12.1
- **Fear complex or reaction** F40.9
- **Fear of** —*see* Phobia
- **Feared complaint unfounded** Z71.1
- **Febris, febrile** —*see also* Fever
  - flava —*see also* Fever, yellow A95.9
  - melitensis A23.0
  - pestis —*see* Plague
  - recurrens —*see* Fever, relapsing
  - rubra A38.9
- **Fecal**
  - incontinence R15.9
  - smearing R15.1
  - soiling R15.1
  - urgency R15.2
- **Fecalith** (impaction) K56.41
  - appendix K38.1
  - congenital P76.8
- **Fede's disease** K14.0
- **Feeble rapid pulse due to shock following injury** T79.4
- **Feeble-minded** F70
- **Feeding**
  - difficulties R63.3
  - problem R63.3
    - newborn P92.9
      - specified NEC P92.8
    - nonorganic (adult) —*see* Disorder, eating
- **Feeling** (of)
  - foreign body in throat R09.89
- **Feer's disease** —*see* Poisoning, mercury
- **Feet** —*see* condition
- **Feigned illness** Z76.5
- **Feil-Klippel syndrome** (brevicollis) Q76.1
- **Feinmesser's** (hidrotic) **ectodermal dysplasia** Q82.4
- **Felinophobia** F40.218
- **Felon** —*see also* Cellulitis, digit
  - with lymphangitis —*see* Lymphangitis, acute, digit
- **Felty's syndrome** M05.00
  - ankle M05.07-
  - elbow M05.02-
  - foot joint M05.07-
  - hand joint M05.04-
  - hip M05.05-
  - knee M05.06-
  - multiple site M05.09
  - shoulder M05.01-
  - vertebra —*see* Spondylitis, ankylosing
  - wrist M05.03-
- **Female genital cutting status** —*see* Female genital mutilation status (FGM)
- **Female genital mutilation status** (FGM) N90.810
  - specified NEC N90.818
  - type I (clitorectomy status) N90.811
  - type II (clitorectomy with excision of labia minora status) N90.812
  - type III (infibulation status) N90.813
  - type IV N90.818
- **Femur, femoral** —*see* condition
- **Fenestration, fenestrated** —*see also* Imperfect, closure
  - aortico-pulmonary Q21.4
  - cusps, heart valve NEC Q24.8
    - pulmonary Q22.3
  - pulmonic cusps Q22.3
- **Fernell's disease** (aortic aneurysm) I71.9
- **Fertile eunuch syndrome** E23.0
- **Fetid**
  - breath R19.6
  - sweat L75.0
- **Fetishism** F65.0
  - transvestic F65.1
- **Fetus, fetal** —*see also* condition
  - alcohol syndrome (dysmorphic) Q86.0
  - compressus O31.0-
  - hydantoin syndrome Q86.1
  - lung tissue P28.0
  - papyraceous O31.0-
- **Fever** (inanition) (of unknown origin) (persistent) (with chills) (with rigor) R50.9
  - abortus A23.1
  - Aden (dengue) A90
  - African tick-borne A68.1
- **Fever** *(continued)*
  - American
    - mountain (tick) A93.2
    - spotted A77.0
  - aphthous B08.8
  - arbovirus, arboviral A94
    - hemorrhagic A94
    - specified NEC A93.8
  - Argentinian hemorrhagic A96.0
  - Assam B55.0
  - Australian Q A78
  - Bangkok hemorrhagic A91
  - Barmah forest A92.8
  - Bartonella A44.0
  - bilious, hemoglobinuric B50.8
  - blackwater B50.8
  - blister B00.1
  - Bolivian hemorrhagic A96.1
  - Bonvale dam T73.3
  - boutonneuse A77.1
  - brain —*see* Encephalitis
  - Brazilian purpuric A48.4
  - breakbone A90
  - Bullis A77.0
  - Bunyamwera A92.8
  - Burdwan B55.0
  - Bwamba A92.8
  - Cameroon —*see* Malaria
  - Canton A75.9
  - catarrhal (acute) J00
    - chronic J31.0
  - cat-scratch A28.1
  - Central Asian hemorrhagic A98.0
  - cerebral —*see* Encephalitis
  - cerebrospinal meningococcal A39.0
  - Chagres B50.9
  - Chandipura A92.8
  - Changuinola A93.1
  - Charcot's (biliary) (hepatic) (intermittent) - —*see* Calculus, bile duct
  - Chikungunya (viral) (hemorrhagic) A92.0
  - Chitral A93.1
  - Colombo —*see* Fever, paratyphoid
  - Colorado tick (virus) A93.2
  - congestive (remittent) —*see* Malaria
  - Congo virus A98.0
  - continued malarial B50.9
  - Corsican —*see* Malaria
  - Crimean-Congo hemorrhagic A98.0
  - Cyprus —*see* Brucellosis
  - dandy A90
  - deer fly —*see* Tularemia
  - dengue (virus) A90
    - hemorrhagic A91
    - sandfly A93.1
  - desert B38.0
  - drug induced R50.2
  - due to
    - conditions classified elsewhere R50.81
    - heat T67.0
  - enteric A01.00
  - enteroviral exanthematous (Boston exanthem) A88.0
  - ephemeral (of unknown origin) R50.9
  - epidemic hemorrhagic A98.5
  - erysipelatous —*see* Erysipelas
  - estivo-autumnal (malarial) B50.9
  - famine A75.0
  - five day A79.0
  - following delivery O86.4
  - Fort Bragg A27.89
  - gastroenteric A01.00
  - gastromalarial —*see* Malaria
  - Gibraltar —*see* Brucellosis
  - glandular —*see* Mononucleosis, infectious
  - Guama (viral) A92.8
  - Haverhill A25.1

Fibrinopurulent —*see* condition

Fibrinous —*see* condition

Fibroadenoma
- cellular intracanalicular D24-
- giant D24-
- intracanalicular
  - cellular D24-
  - giant D24-
  - specified site —*see* Neoplasm, benign, by site
  - unspecified site D24-
- juvenile D24-
- pericanalicular
  - specified site —*see* Neoplasm, benign, by site
  - unspecified site D24-
- phyllodes D24-
- prostate D29.1
- specified site NEC —*see* Neoplasm, benign, by site
- unspecified site D24-

Fibroadenosis, breast (chronic) (cystic) (diffuse) (periodic) (segmental) N60.2-

Fibroangioma —*see also* Neoplasm, benign, by site
- juvenile
  - specified site —*see* Neoplasm, benign, by site
  - unspecified site D10.6

Fibrochondrosarcoma —*see* Neoplasm, cartilage, malignant

Fibrocystic
- disease —*see also* Fibrosis, cystic
  - breast —*see* Mastopathy, cystic
  - jaw M27.49
  - kidney (congenital) Q61.8
  - liver Q44.6
  - pancreas E84.9
- kidney (congenital) Q61.8

Fibrodysplasia ossificans progressiva
- —*see* Myositis, ossificans, progressiva

Fibroelastosis (cordis) (endocardial) (endomyocardial) I42.4

Fibroid (tumor) —*see also* Neoplasm, connective tissue, benign
- disease, lung (chronic) —*see* Fibrosis, lung
- heart (disease) —*see* Myocarditis
- in pregnancy or childbirth O34.1-
  - causing obstructed labor O65.5
- induration, lung (chronic) —*see* Fibrosis, lung
- lung —*see* Fibrosis, lung
- pneumonia (chronic) —*see* Fibrosis, lung
- uterus D25.9

Fibrolipoma —*see* Lipoma

Fibroliposarcoma —*see* Neoplasm, connective tissue, malignant

Fibroma —*see also* Neoplasm, connective tissue, benign
- ameloblastic —*see* Cyst, calcifying odontogenic
- bone (nonossifying) —*see* Disorder, bone, specified type NEC
  - ossifying —*see* Neoplasm, bone, benign
- cementifying —*see* Neoplasm, bone, benign
- chondromyxoid —*see* Neoplasm, bone, benign
- desmoplastic —*see* Neoplasm, connective tissue, uncertain behavior
- durum —*see* Neoplasm, connective tissue, benign

Fibroma *(continued)*
- fascial —*see* Neoplasm, connective tissue, benign
- invasive —*see* Neoplasm, connective tissue, uncertain behavior
- molle —*see* Lipoma
- myxoid —*see* Neoplasm, connective tissue, benign
- nasopharynx, nasopharyngeal (juvenile) D10.6
- nonosteogenic (nonossifying) —*see* Dysplasia, fibrous
- odontogenic (central) —*see* Cyst, calcifying odontogenic
- ossifying —*see* Neoplasm, bone, benign
- periosteal —*see* Neoplasm, bone, benign
- soft —*see* Lipoma

Fibromatosis M72.9
- abdominal —*see* Neoplasm, connective tissue, uncertain behavior
- aggressive —*see* Neoplasm, connective tissue, uncertain behavior
- congenital generalized —*see* Neoplasm, connective tissue, uncertain behavior
- Dupuytren's M72.0
- gingival K06.1
- palmar (fascial) M72.0
- plantar (fascial) M72.2
- pseudosarcomatous (proliferative) (subcutaneous) M72.4
- retroperitoneal D48.3
- specified NEC M72.8

Fibromyalgia M79.7

Fibromyoma —*see also* Neoplasm, connective tissue, benign
- uterus (corpus) —*see also* Leiomyoma, uterus
  - in pregnancy or childbirth —*see* Fibroid, in pregnancy or childbirth
    - causing obstructed labor O65.5

Fibromyositis M79.7

Fibromyxolipoma D17.9

Fibromyxoma —*see* Neoplasm, connective tissue, benign

Fibromyxosarcoma —*see* Neoplasm, connective tissue, malignant

Fibro-odontoma, ameloblastic —*see* Cyst, calcifying odontogenic

Fibro-osteoma —*see* Neoplasm, bone, benign

Fibroplasia, retrolental H35.17-

Fibropurulent —*see* condition

Fibrosarcoma —*see also* Neoplasm, connective tissue, malignant
- ameloblastic C41.1
  - upper jaw (bone) C41.0
- congenital —*see* Neoplasm, connective tissue, malignant
- fascial —*see* Neoplasm, connective tissue, malignant
- infantile —*see* Neoplasm, connective tissue, malignant
- odontogenic C41.1
  - upper jaw (bone) C41.0
- periosteal —*see* Neoplasm, bone, malignant

Fibrosclerosis
- breast N60.3-
- multifocal M35.5
- penis (corpora cavernosa) N48.6

Fibrosis, fibrotic
- adrenal (gland) E27.8
- amnion O41.8X-
- anal papillae K62.89
- arteriocapillary —*see* Arteriosclerosis
- bladder N32.89
  - interstitial —*see* Cystitis, chronic, interstitial
  - localized submucosal —*see* Cystitis, chronic, interstitial
  - panmural —*see* Cystitis, chronic, interstitial
- breast —*see* Fibrosclerosis, breast
- capillary —*see also* Arteriosclerosis I70.90
  - lung (chronic) —*see* Fibrosis, lung
- cardiac —*see* Myocarditis
- cervix N88.8
- chorion O41.8X-
- corpus cavernosum (sclerosing) N48.6
- cystic (of pancreas) E84.9
  - with
    - distal intestinal obstruction syndrome E84.19
    - fecal impaction E84.19
    - intestinal manifestations NEC E84.19
    - pulmonary manifestations E84.0
    - specified manifestations NEC E84.8
- due to device, implant or graft —*see also* Complications, by site and type, specified NEC T85.82
  - arterial graft NEC T82.828
  - breast (implant) T85.82
  - catheter NEC T85.82
    - dialysis (renal) T82.828
      - intraperitoneal T85.82
    - infusion NEC T82.828
      - spinal (epidural) (subdural) T85.82
    - urinary (indwelling) T83.82
  - electronic (electrode) (pulse generator) (stimulator)
    - bone T84.82
    - cardiac T82.827
    - nervous system (brain) (peripheral nerve) (spinal) T85.82
    - urinary T83.82
  - fixation, internal (orthopedic) NEC T84.82
  - gastrointestinal (bile duct) (esophagus) T85.82
  - genital NEC T83.82
  - heart NEC T82.827
  - joint prosthesis T84.82
  - ocular (corneal graft) (orbital implant) NEC T85.82
  - orthopedic NEC T84.82
  - specified NEC T85.82
  - urinary NEC T83.82
  - vascular NEC T82.828
  - ventricular intracranial shunt T85.82
- ejaculatory duct N50.8
- endocardium —*see* Endocarditis
- endomyocardial (tropical) I42.3
- epididymis N50.8
- eye muscle —*see* Strabismus, mechanical
- heart —*see* Myocarditis
- hepatic —*see* Fibrosis, liver
- hepatolienal (portal hypertension) K76.6
- hepatosplenic (portal hypertension) K76.6
- infrapatellar fat pad M79.4
- intrascrotal N50.8
- kidney N26.9

Fibrosis, fibrotic *(continued)*
- liver K74.0
  - with sclerosis K74.2
  - alcoholic K70.2
- lung (atrophic) (chronic) (confluent) (massive) (perialveolar) (peribronchial) J84.10
  - with
    - anthracosilicosis J60
    - anthracosis J60
    - asbestosis J61
    - bagassosis J67.1
    - bauxite J63.1
    - berylliosis J63.2
    - byssinosis J66.0
    - calcicosis J62.8
    - chalicosis J62.8
    - dust reticulation J64
    - farmer's lung J67.0
    - ganister disease J62.8
    - graphite J63.3
    - pneumoconiosis NOS J64
    - siderosis J63.4
    - silicosis J62.8
  - capillary J84.10
  - congenital P27.8
  - diffuse (idiopathic) J84.10
    - chemicals, gases, fumes or vapors (inhalation) J68.4
    - interstitial J84.10
      - acute J84.114
    - talc J62.0
  - following radiation J70.1
  - idiopathic J84.112
  - postinflammatory J84.10
  - silicotic J62.8
  - tuberculous —*see* Tuberculosis, pulmonary
- lymphatic gland I89.8
- median bar —*see* Hyperplasia, prostate
- mediastinum (idiopathic) J98.5
- meninges G96.19
- myocardium, myocardial —*see* Myocarditis
- ovary N83.8
- oviduct N83.8
- pancreas K86.8
- penis NEC N48.6
- pericardium I31.0
- perineum, in pregnancy or childbirth O34.7-
  - causing obstructed labor O65.5
- pleura J94.1
- popliteal fat pad M79.4
- prostate (chronic) —*see* Hyperplasia, prostate
- pulmonary —*see also* Fibrosis, lung J84.10
  - congenital P27.8
  - idiopathic J84.112
- rectal sphincter K62.89
- retroperitoneal, idiopathic (with ureteral obstruction) N13.5
  - with infection N13.6
- sclerosing mesenteric (idiopathic) K65.4
- scrotum N50.8
- seminal vesicle N50.8
- senile R54
- skin L90.5
- spermatic cord N50.8
- spleen D73.89
  - in schistosomiasis (bilharziasis) B65.9 *[D77]*
- subepidermal nodular —*see* Neoplasm, skin, benign
- submucous (oral) (tongue) K13.5
- testis N44.8
  - chronic, due to syphilis A52.76
- thymus (gland) E32.8
- tongue, submucous K13.5

Fibrosis, fibrotic *(continued)*
- tunica vaginalis N50.8
- uterus (non-neoplastic) N85.8
- vagina N89.8
- valve, heart —*see* Endocarditis
- vas deferens N50.8
- vein I87.8

Fibrositis (periarticular) M79.7
- nodular, chronic (Jaccoud's) (rheumatoid) —*see* Arthropathy, postrheumatic, chronic

Fibrothorax J94.1

Fibrotic —*see* Fibrosis

Fibrous —*see* condition

Fibroxanthoma —*see also* Neoplasm, connective tissue, benign
- atypical —*see* Neoplasm, connective tissue, uncertain behavior
- malignant —*see* Neoplasm, connective tissue, malignant

Fibroxanthosarcoma —*see* Neoplasm, connective tissue, malignant

Fiedler's
- disease (icterohemorrhagic leptospirosis) A27.0
- myocarditis (acute) I40.1

Fifth disease B08.3
- venereal A55

Filaria, filarial, filariasis —*see* Infestation, filarial

Filatov's disease —*see* Mononucleosis, infectious

File-cutter's disease —*see* Poisoning, lead

Filling defect
- biliary tract R93.2
- bladder R93.4
- duodenum R93.3
- gallbladder R93.2
- gastrointestinal tract R93.3
- intestine R93.3
- kidney R93.4
- stomach R93.3
- ureter R93.4

Fimbrial cyst Q50.4

Financial problem affecting care NOS Z59.9
- bankruptcy Z59.8
- foreclosure on loan Z59.8

Findings, abnormal, inconclusive, without diagnosis —*see also* Abnormal
- 17-ketosteroids, elevated R82.5
- acetonuria R82.4
- alcohol in blood R78.0
- anisocytosis R71.8
- antenatal screening of mother O28.9
  - biochemical O28.1
  - chromosomal O28.5
  - cytological O28.2
  - genetic O28.5
  - hematological O28.0
  - radiological O28.4
  - specified NEC O28.8
  - ultrasonic O28.3
- antibody titer, elevated R76.0
- anticardiolipin antibody R76.0
- antiphosphatidylglycerol antibody R76.0
- antiphosphatidylinositol antibody R76.0
- antiphosphatidylserine antibody R76.0
- antiphospholipid antibody R76.0
- bacteriuria N39.0
- bicarbonate E87.8
- bile in urine R82.2

Findings, abnormal, inconclusive, without diagnosis *(continued)*
- blood sugar R73.09
  - high R73.9
  - low (transient) E16.2
- body fluid or substance, specified NEC R88.8
- casts, urine R82.99
- catecholamines R82.5
- cells, urine R82.99
- chloride E87.8
- cholesterol E78.9
  - high E78.0
    - with high triglycerides E78.2
- chyluria R82.0
- cloudy
  - dialysis effluent R88.0
  - urine R82.90
- creatinine clearance R94.4
- crystals, urine R82.99
- culture
  - blood R78.81
  - positive —*see* Positive, culture
- echocardiogram R93.1
- electrolyte level, urinary R82.99
- function study NEC R94.8
  - bladder R94.8
  - endocrine NEC R94.7
    - thyroid R94.6
  - kidney R94.4
  - liver R94.5
  - pancreas R94.8
  - placenta R94.8
  - pulmonary R94.2
  - spleen R94.8
- gallbladder, nonvisualization R93.2
- glucose (tolerance test) (non-fasting) R73.09
- glycosuria R81
- heart
  - shadow R93.1
  - sounds R01.2
- hematinuria R82.3
- hematocrit drop (precipitous) R71.0
- hemoglobinuria R82.3
- human papillomavirus (HPV) DNA test positive
  - cervix
    - high risk R87.810
    - low risk R87.820
  - vagina
    - high risk R87.811
    - low risk R87.821
- in blood (of substance not normally found in blood) R78.9
  - addictive drug NEC R78.4
  - alcohol (excessive level) R78.0
  - cocaine R78.2
  - hallucinogen R78.3
  - heavy metals (abnormal level) R78.79
  - lead R78.71
  - lithium (abnormal level) R78.89
  - opiate drug R78.1
  - psychotropic drug R78.5
  - specified substance NEC R78.89
  - steroid agent R78.6
- indoleacetic acid, elevated R82.5
- ketonuria R82.4
- lactic acid dehydrogenase (LDH) R74.0
- liver function test R79.89
- mammogram NEC R92.8
  - calcification (calculus) R92.1
  - inconclusive result (due to dense breasts) R92.2
  - microcalcification R92.0
- mediastinal shift R93.8
- melanin, urine R82.99
- myoglobinuria R82.1
- neonatal screening P09
- nonvisualization of gallbladder R93.2

Findings, abnormal, inconclusive, without diagnosis *(continued)*
- odor of urine NOS R82.90
- Papanicolaou cervix R87.619
  - non-atypical endometrial cells R87.618
- pneumoencephalogram R93.0
- poikilocytosis R71.8
- potassium (deficiency) E87.6
  - excess E87.5
- PPD R76.11
- radiologic (X-ray) R93.8
  - abdomen R93.5
  - biliary tract R93.2
  - breast R92.8
  - gastrointestinal tract R93.3
  - genitourinary organs R93.8
  - head R93.0
  - inconclusive due to excess body fat of patient R93.9
  - intrathoracic organs NEC R93.1
  - placenta R93.8
  - retroperitoneum R93.5
  - skin R93.8
  - skull R93.0
  - subcutaneous tissue R93.8
- red blood cell (count) (morphology) (sickling) (volume) R71.8
- scan NEC R94.8
  - bladder R94.8
  - bone R94.8
  - kidney R94.4
  - liver R93.2
  - lung R94.2
  - pancreas R94.8
  - placental R94.8
  - spleen R94.8
  - thyroid R94.6
- sedimentation rate, elevated R70.0
- SGOT R74.0
- SGPT R74.0
- sodium (deficiency) E87.1
  - excess E87.0
- specified body fluid NEC R88.8
- stress test R94.39
- thyroid (function) (metabolic rate) (scan) (uptake) R94.6
- transaminase (level) R74.0
- triglycerides E78.9
  - high E78.1
    - with high cholesterol E78.2
- tuberculin skin test (without active tuberculosis) R76.11
- urine R82.90
  - acetone R82.4
  - bacteria N39.0
  - bile R82.2
  - casts or cells R82.99
  - chyle R82.0
  - culture positive R82.7
  - glucose R81
  - hemoglobin R82.3
  - ketone R82.4
  - sugar R81
- vanillylmandelic acid (VMA), elevated R82.5
- vectorcardiogram (VCG) R94.39
- ventriculogram R93.0
- white blood cell (count) (differential) (morphology) D72.9
- xerography R92.8

Finger —*see* condition

Fire, Saint Anthony's —*see* Erysipelas

Fire-setting
- pathological (compulsive) F63.1

Fish hook stomach K31.89

Fishmeal-worker's lung J67.8

Fissure, fissured
- anus, anal K60.2
  - acute K60.0
  - chronic K60.1
  - congenital Q43.8
- ear, lobule, congenital Q17.8
- epiglottis (congenital) Q31.8
- larynx J38.7
  - congenital Q31.8
- lip K13.0
  - congenital —*see* Cleft, lip
- nipple N64.0
  - associated with
    - lactation O92.13
    - pregnancy O92.11-
    - puerperium O92.12
- nose Q30.2
- palate (congenital) —*see* Cleft, palate
- skin R23.4
- spine (congenital) —*see also* Spina bifida
  - with hydrocephalus —*see* Spina bifida, by site, with hydrocephalus
- tongue (acquired) K14.5
  - congenital Q38.3

Fistula (cutaneous) L98.8
- abdomen (wall) K63.2
  - bladder N32.2
  - intestine NEC K63.2
  - ureter N28.89
  - uterus N82.5
- abdominorectal K63.2
- abdominosigmoidal K63.2
- abdominothoracic J86.0
- abdominouterine N82.5
  - congenital Q51.7
- abdominovesical N32.2
- accessory sinuses —*see* Sinusitis
- actinomycotic —*see* Actinomycosis
- alveolar antrum —*see* Sinusitis, maxillary
- alveolar process K04.6
- anorectal K60.5
- antrobuccal —*see* Sinusitis, maxillary
- antrum —*see* Sinusitis, maxillary
- anus, anal (recurrent) (infectional) K60.3
  - congenital Q43.6
    - with absence, atresia and stenosis Q42.2
  - tuberculous A18.32
- aorta-duodenal I77.2
- appendix, appendicular K38.3
- arteriovenous (acquired) (nonruptured) I77.0
  - brain I67.1
    - congenital Q28.2
      - ruptured I60.8
    - ruptured I60.8
  - cerebral —*see* Fistula, arteriovenous, brain
  - congenital (peripheral) —*see also* Malformation, arteriovenous
    - brain Q28.2
      - ruptured I60.8
    - coronary Q24.5
    - pulmonary Q25.72
  - coronary I25.41
    - congenital Q24.5
  - pulmonary I28.0
    - congenital Q25.72
  - surgically created (for dialysis) Z99.2
    - complication —*see* Complication, arteriovenous, fistula, surgically created
  - traumatic —*see* Injury, blood vessel
- artery I77.2

Fistula *(continued)*
- aural (mastoid) —*see* Mastoiditis, chronic
- auricle —*see also* Disorder, pinna, specified type NEC
  - congenital Q18.1
- Bartholin's gland N82.8
- bile duct (common) (hepatic) K83.3
  - with calculus, stones —*see* Calculus, bile duct
- biliary (tract) —*see* Fistula, bile duct
- bladder (sphincter) NEC —*see also* Fistula, vesico- N32.2
  - into seminal vesicle N32.2
- bone —*see also* Disorder, bone, specified type NEC
  - with osteomyelitis, chronic —*see* Osteomyelitis, chronic, with draining sinus
- brain G93.89
  - arteriovenous (acquired) I67.1
    - congenital Q28.2
- branchial (cleft) Q18.0
- branchiogenous Q18.0
- breast N61
  - puerperal, postpartum or gestational, due to mastitis (purulent) —*see* Mastitis, obstetric, purulent
- bronchial J86.0
- bronchocutaneous, bronchomediastinal, bronchopleural, bronchopleuromediastinal (infective) J86.0
  - tuberculous NEC A15.5
- bronchoesophageal J86.0
  - congenital Q39.2
    - with atresia of esophagus Q39.1
- bronchovisceral J86.0
- buccal cavity (infective) K12.2
- cecosigmoidal K63.2
- cecum K63.2
- cerebrospinal (fluid) G96.0
- cervical, lateral Q18.1
- cervicoaural Q18.1
- cervicosigmoidal N82.4
- cervicovesical N82.1
- cervix N82.8
- chest (wall) J86.0
- cholecystenteric —*see* Fistula, gallbladder
- cholecystocolic —*see* Fistula, gallbladder
- cholecystocolonic —*see* Fistula, gallbladder
- cholecystoduodenal —*see* Fistula, gallbladder
- cholecystogastric —*see* Fistula, gallbladder
- cholecystointestinal —*see* Fistula, gallbladder
- choledochoduodenal —*see* Fistula, bile duct
- cholocolic K82.3
- coccyx —*see* Sinus, pilonidal
- colon K63.2
- colostomy K94.09
- common duct —*see* Fistula, bile duct
- congenital, site not listed —*see* Anomaly, by site
- coronary, arteriovenous I25.41
  - congenital Q24.5
- costal region J86.0
- cul-de-sac, Douglas' N82.8
- cystic duct —*see also* Fistula, gallbladder
  - congenital Q44.5
- dental K04.6
- diaphragm J86.0
- duodenum K31.6

Fistula *(continued)*
- ear (external) (canal) —*see* Disorder, ear, external, specified type NEC
- enterocolic K63.2
- enterocutaneous K63.2
- enterouterine N82.4
  - congenital Q51.7
- enterovaginal N82.4
  - congenital Q52.2
  - large intestine N82.3
  - small intestine N82.2
- enterovesical N32.1
- epididymis N50.8
  - tuberculous A18.15
- esophagobronchial J86.0
  - congenital Q39.2
    - with atresia of esophagus Q39.1
- esophagocutaneous K22.8
- esophagopleural-cutaneous J86.0
- esophagotracheal J86.0
  - congenital Q39.2
    - with atresia of esophagus Q39.1
- esophagus K22.8
  - congenital Q39.2
    - with atresia of esophagus Q39.1
- ethmoid —*see* Sinusitis, ethmoidal
- eyeball (cornea) (sclera) —*see* Disorder, globe, hypotony
- eyelid H01.8
- fallopian tube, external N82.5
- fecal K63.2
  - congenital Q43.6
- from periapical abscess K04.6
- frontal sinus —*see* Sinusitis, frontal
- gallbladder K82.3
  - with calculus, cholelithiasis, stones —*see* Calculus, gallbladder
- gastric K31.6
- gastrocolic K31.6
  - congenital Q40.2
  - tuberculous A18.32
- gastroenterocolic K31.6
- gastroesophageal K31.6
- gastrojejunal K31.6
- gastrojejunocolic K31.6
- genital tract (female) N82.9
  - specified NEC N82.8
  - to intestine NEC N82.4
  - to skin N82.5
- hepatic artery-portal vein, congenital Q26.6
- hepatopleural J86.0
- hepatopulmonary J86.0
- ileorectal or ileosigmoidal K63.2
- ileovaginal N82.2
- ileovesical N32.1
- ileum K63.2
- in ano K60.3
  - tuberculous A18.32
- inner ear (labyrinth) H83.1
- intestine NEC K63.2
- intestinocolonic (abdominal) K63.2
- intestinoureteral N28.89
- intestinouterine N82.4
- intestinovaginal N82.4
  - large intestine N82.3
  - small intestine N82.2
- intestinovesical N32.1
- ischiorectal (fossa) K61.3
- jejunum K63.2
- joint M25.10
  - ankle M25.17-
  - elbow M25.12-
  - foot joint M25.17-
  - hand joint M25.14-
  - hip M25.15-
  - knee M25.16-
  - shoulder M25.11-
  - specified joint NEC M25.18
  - tuberculous —*see* Tuberculosis, joint
  - vertebrae M25.18
  - wrist M25.13-

Fistula *(continued)*
- kidney N28.89
- labium (majus) (minus) N82.8
- labyrinth H83.1
- lacrimal (gland) (sac) H04.61-
- lacrimonasal duct —*see* Fistula, lacrimal
- laryngotracheal, congenital Q34.8
- larynx J38.7
- lip K13.0
  - congenital Q38.0
- lumbar, tuberculous A18.01
- lung J86.0
- lymphatic I89.8
- mammary (gland) N61
- mastoid (process) (region) —*see* Mastoiditis, chronic
- maxillary J32.0
- medial, face and neck Q18.8
- mediastinal J86.0
- mediastinobronchial J86.0
- mediastinocutaneous J86.0
- middle ear H74.8
- mouth K12.2
- nasal J34.89
  - sinus —*see* Sinusitis
- nasopharynx J39.2
- nipple N64.0
- nose J34.89
- oral (cutaneous) K12.2
  - maxillary J32.0
  - nasal (with cleft palate) —*see* Cleft, palate
- orbit, orbital —*see* Disorder, orbit, specified type NEC
- oroantral J32.0
- oviduct, external N82.5
- palate (hard) M27.8
- pancreatic K86.8
- pancreaticoduodenal K86.8
- parotid (gland) K11.4
  - region K12.2
- penis N48.89
- perianal K60.3
- pericardium (pleura) (sac) —*see* Pericarditis
- pericecal K63.2
- perineorectal K60.4
- perineosigmoidal K63.2
- perineum, perineal (with urethral involvement) NEC N36.0
  - tuberculous A18.13
  - ureter N28.89
- perirectal K60.4
  - tuberculous A18.32
- peritoneum K65.9
- pharyngoesophageal J39.2
- pharynx J39.2
  - branchial cleft (congenital) Q18.0
- pilonidal (infected) (rectum) —*see* Sinus, pilonidal
- pleura, pleural, pleurocutaneous, pleuroperitoneal J86.0
  - tuberculous NEC A15.6
- pleuropericardial I31.8
- portal vein-hepatic artery, congenital Q26.6
- postauricular H70.81-
- postoperative, persistent T81.83
  - specified site —*see* Fistula, by site
- preauricular (congenital) Q18.1
- prostate N42.89
- pulmonary J86.0
  - arteriovenous I28.0
    - congenital Q25.72
  - tuberculous —*see* Tuberculosis, pulmonary
- pulmonoperitoneal J86.0
- rectolabial N82.4
- rectosigmoid (intercommunicating) K63.2
- rectoureteral N28.89

Fistula *(continued)*
- rectourethral N36.0
  - congenital Q64.73
- rectouterine N82.4
  - congenital Q51.7
- rectovaginal N82.3
  - congenital Q52.2
  - tuberculous A18.18
- rectovesical N32.1
  - congenital Q64.79
- rectovesicovaginal N82.3
- rectovulval N82.4
  - congenital Q52.79
- rectum (to skin) K60.4
  - congenital Q43.6
    - with absence, atresia and stenosis Q42.0
  - tuberculous A18.32
- renal N28.89
- retroauricular —*see* Fistula, postauricular
- salivary duct or gland (any) K11.4
  - congenital Q38.4
- scrotum (urinary) N50.8
  - tuberculous A18.15
- semicircular canals H83.1
- sigmoid K63.2
  - to bladder N32.1
- sinus —*see* Sinusitis
- skin L98.8
  - to genital tract (female) N82.5
- splenocolic D73.89
- stercoral K63.2
- stomach K31.6
- sublingual gland K11.4
- submandibular gland K11.4
- submaxillary (gland) K11.4
  - region K12.2
- thoracic J86.0
  - duct I89.8
- thoracoabdominal J86.0
- thoracogastric J86.0
- thoracointestinal J86.0
- thorax J86.0
- thyroglossal duct Q89.2
- thyroid E07.89
- trachea, congenital (external) (internal) Q32.1
- tracheoesophageal J86.0
  - congenital Q39.2
    - with atresia of esophagus Q39.1
  - following tracheostomy J95.04
- traumatic arteriovenous —*see* Injury, blood vessel, by site
- tuberculous - code by site under Tuberculosis
- typhoid A01.09
- umbilicourinary Q64.8
- urachus, congenital Q64.4
- ureter (persistent) N28.89
- ureteroabdominal N28.89
- ureterorectal N28.89
- ureterosigmoido-abdominal N28.89
- ureterovaginal N82.1
- ureterovesical N32.2
- urethra N36.0
  - congenital Q64.79
  - tuberculous A18.13
- urethroperineal N36.0
- urethroperineovesical N32.2
- urethrorectal N36.0
  - congenital Q64.73
- urethroscrotal N50.8
- urethrovaginal N82.1
- urethrovesical N32.2
- urinary (tract) (persistent) (recurrent) N36.0
- uteroabdominal N82.5
  - congenital Q51.7
- uteroenteric, uterointestinal N82.4
  - congenital Q51.7

Foreign body *(continued)*
superficial, without open wound *(continued)*
jaw S00.85
knee S80.25-
labium (majus) (minus) S30.854
larynx S10.15
leg (lower) S80.85-
knee —*see* Foreign body, superficial, knee
upper —*see* Foreign body, superficial, thigh
lip S00.551
lower back S30.850
lumbar region S30.850
malar region S00.85
mammary —*see* Foreign body, superficial, breast
mastoid region S00.85
mouth S00.552
nail
finger —*see* Foreign body, superficial, finger
toe —*see* Foreign body, superficial, toe
nape S10.85
nasal S00.35
neck S10.95
specified site NEC S10.85
throat S10.15
nose S00.35
occipital region S00.05
oral cavity S00.552
orbital region —*see* Foreign body, superficial, eyelid
palate S00.552
palm —*see* Foreign body, superficial, hand
parietal region S00.05
pelvis S30.850
penis S30.852
perineum
female S30.854
male S30.850
periocular area —*see* Foreign body, superficial, eyelid
phalanges
finger —*see* Foreign body, superficial, finger
toe —*see* Foreign body, superficial, toe
pharynx S10.15
pinna —*see* Foreign body, superficial, ear
popliteal space —*see* Foreign body, superficial, knee
prepuce S30.852
pubic region S30.850
pudendum
female S30.856
male S30.855
sacral region S30.850
scalp S00.05
scapular region —*see* Foreign body, superficial, shoulder
scrotum S30.853
shin —*see* Foreign body, superficial, leg
shoulder S40.25-
sternal region S20.359
submaxillary region S00.85
submental region S00.85
subungual
finger (s) —*see* Foreign body, superficial, finger
toe (s) —*see* Foreign body, superficial, toe
supraclavicular fossa S10.85
supraorbital S00.85
temple S00.85
temporal region S00.85
testis S30.853

Foreign body *(continued)*
superficial, without open wound *(continued)*
thigh S70.35-
thorax, thoracic (wall) S20.95
back S20.45-
front S20.35-
throat S10.15
thumb S60.35-
toe (s) (lesser) S90.456
great S90.45-
tongue S00.552
trachea S10.15
tunica vaginalis S30.853
tympanum, tympanic
membrane —*see* Foreign body, superficial, ear
uvula S00.552
vagina S30.854
vocal cords S10.15
vulva S30.854
wrist S60.85-
swallowed T18.9
trachea T17.408
causing
asphyxiation T17.400
food (bone) (seed) T17.420
gastric contents (vomitus) T17.410
specified type NEC T17.490
injury NEC T17.408
food (bone) (seed) T17.428
gastric contents (vomitus) T17.418
specified type NEC T17.498
type of fragment —*see* Retained, foreign body fragments (type of)
vitreous (humor) S05.5-

Forestier's disease (rhizomelic pseudopolyarthritis) M35.3
meaning ankylosing hyperostosis —*see* Hyperostosis, ankylosing

Formation
hyalin in cornea —*see* Degeneration, cornea
sequestrum in bone (due to infection) —*see* Osteomyelitis, chronic
valve
colon, congenital Q43.8
ureter (congenital) Q62.39

Formication R20.2

Fort Bragg fever A27.89

Fossa —*see also* condition
pyriform —*see* condition

Foster-Kennedy syndrome H47.14-

Fothergill's
disease (trigeminal neuralgia) —*see also* Neuralgia, trigeminal
scarlatina anginosa A38.9

Foul breath R19.6

Foundling Z76.1

Fournier disease or gangrene N49.3
female N76.89

Fourth
cranial nerve —*see* condition
molar K00.1

Foville's (peduncular) **disease or syndrome** G46.3

Fox (-Fordyce) disease (apocrine miliaria) L75.2

Fracture, burst —*see* Fracture, traumatic, by site

Fracture, chronic —*see* Fracture, pathological

Fracture, insufficiency —*see* Fracture, pathologic, by site

Fracture, pathological (pathologic) —*see also* Fracture, traumatic M84.40
ankle M84.47-
carpus M84.44-
clavicle M84.41-
dental implant M27.63
dental restorative material K08.539
with loss of material K08.531
without loss of material K08.530
due to
neoplastic disease NEC —*see also* Neoplasm M84.50
ankle M84.57-
carpus M84.54-
clavicle M84.51-
femur M84.55-
fibula M84.56-
finger M84.54-
hip M84.559
humerus M84.52-
ilium M84.550
ischium M84.550
metacarpus M84.54-
metatarsus M84.57-
neck M84.58
pelvis M84.550
radius M84.53-
rib M84.58
scapula M84.51-
skull M84.58
specified site NEC M84.58
tarsus M84.57-
tibia M84.56-
toe M84.57-
ulna M84.53-
vertebra M84.58
osteoporosis M80.80
disuse —*see* Osteoporosis, specified type NEC, with pathological fracture
drug-induced —*see* Osteoporosis, drug induced, with pathological fracture
idiopathic —*see* Osteoporosis, specified type NEC, with pathological fracture
postmenopausal —*see* Osteoporosis, postmenopausal, with pathological fracture
postoophorectomy —*see* Osteoporosis, postoophorectomy, with pathological fracture
postsurgical malabsorption —*see* Osteoporosis, specified type NEC, with pathological fracture
specified cause NEC —*see* Osteoporosis, specified type NEC, with pathological fracture
specified disease NEC M84.60
ankle M84.67-
carpus M84.64-
clavicle M84.61-
femur M84.65-
fibula M84.66-
finger M84.64-
hip M84.65-
humerus M84.62-
ilium M84.650
ischium M84.650
metacarpus M84.64-
metatarsus M84.67-
neck M84.68
radius M84.63-
rib M84.68
scapula M84.61-
skull M84.68
tarsus M84.67-
tibia M84.66-

Fracture, pathological *(continued)*
due to *(continued)*
specified disease NEC *(continued)*
toe M84.67-
ulna M84.63-
vertebra M84.68
femur M84.45-
fibula M84.46-
finger M84.44-
hip M84.459
humerus M84.42-
ilium M84.454
ischium M84.454
joint prosthesis —*see* Complications, joint prosthesis, mechanical, breakdown, by site
periprosthetic —*see* Complications, joint prosthesis, mechanical, periprosthesis, fracture, by site
metacarpus M84.44-
metatarsus M84.47-
neck M84.48
pelvis M84.454
radius M84.43-
restorative material (dental) K08.539
with loss of material K08.531
without loss of material K08.530
rib M84.48
scapula M84.41-
skull M84.48
tarsus M84.47-
tibia M84.46-
toe M84.47-
ulna M84.43-
vertebra M84.48

Fracture, traumatic (abduction) (adduction) (separation) —*see also* Fracture, pathological T14.8
acetabulum S32.40-
column
anterior (displaced) (iliopubic) S32.43-
nondisplaced S32.436
posterior (displaced) (ilioischial) S32.443
nondisplaced S32.44-
dome (displaced) S32.48-
nondisplaced S32.48
specified NEC S32.49-
transverse (displaced) S32.45-
with associated posterior wall fracture (displaced) S32.46-
nondisplaced S32.46-
nondisplaced S32.45-
wall
anterior (displaced) S32.41-
nondisplaced S32.41-
medial (displaced) S32.47-
nondisplaced S32.47-
posterior (displaced) S32.42-
with associated transverse fracture (displaced) S32.46-
nondisplaced S32.46-
nondisplaced S32.42-
acromion —*see* Fracture, scapula, acromial process
ankle S82.899
bimalleolar (displaced) S82.84-
nondisplaced S82.84-
lateral malleolus only (displaced) S82.6-
nondisplaced S82.6-
medial malleolus (displaced) S82.5-
associated with Maisonneuve's fracture —*see* Fracture, Maisonneuve's
nondisplaced S82.5-
talus —*see* Fracture, tarsal, talus
trimalleolar (displaced) S82.85-
nondisplaced S82.85-

Fracture, traumatic *(continued)*
- arm (upper) —*see also* Fracture, humerus, shaft
  - humerus —*see* Fracture, humerus
  - radius —*see* Fracture, radius
  - ulna —*see* Fracture, ulna
- astragalus —*see* Fracture, tarsal, talus
- atlas —*see* Fracture, neck, cervical vertebra, first
- axis —*see* Fracture, neck, cervical vertebra, second
- back —*see* Fracture, vertebra
- Barton's —*see* Barton's fracture
- base of skull —*see* Fracture, skull, base
- basicervical (basal) (femoral) S72.0
- Bennett's —*see* Bennett's fracture
- bimalleolar —*see* Fracture, ankle, bimalleolar
- blow-out S02.3
- bone NEC T14.8
  - birth injury P13.9
  - following insertion of orthopedic implant, joint prosthesis or bone plate —*see* Fracture, following insertion of orthopedic implant, joint prosthesis or bone plate
  - in (due to) neoplastic disease NEC —*see* Fracture, pathological, due to, neoplastic disease
  - pathological (cause unknown) —*see* Fracture, pathological
- breast bone —*see* Fracture, sternum
- bucket handle (semilunar cartilage) —*see* Tear, meniscus
- burst —*see* Fracture, traumatic, by site
- calcaneus —*see* Fracture, tarsal, calcaneus
- carpal bone (s) S62.10-
  - capitate (displaced) S62.13-
    - nondisplaced S62.13-
  - cuneiform —*see* Fracture, carpal bone, triquetrum
  - hamate (body) (displaced) S62.143
    - hook process (displaced) S62.15-
      - nondisplaced S62.15-
    - nondisplaced S62.14-
  - larger multangular —*see* Fracture, carpal bones, trapezium
  - lunate (displaced) S62.12-
    - nondisplaced S62.12-
  - navicular S62.00-
    - distal pole (displaced) S62.01-
      - nondisplaced S62.01-
    - middle third (displaced) S62.02-
      - nondisplaced S62.02-
    - proximal third (displaced) S62.03-
      - nondisplaced S62.03-
    - volar tuberosity —*see* Fracture, carpal bones, navicular, distal pole
  - os magnum —*see* Fracture, carpal bones, capitate
  - pisiform (displaced) S62.16-
    - nondisplaced S62.16-
  - semilunar —*see* Fracture, carpal bones, lunate
  - smaller multangular —*see* Fracture, carpal bones, trapezoid
  - trapezium (displaced) S62.17-
    - nondisplaced S62.17-
  - trapezoid (displaced) S62.18-
    - nondisplaced S62.18-
  - triquetrum (displaced) S62.11-
    - nondisplaced S62.11-
  - unciform —*see* Fracture, carpal bones, hamate
- cervical —*see* Fracture, vertebra, cervical

Fracture, traumatic *(continued)*
- clavicle S42.00-
  - acromial end (displaced) S42.03-
    - nondisplaced S42.03-
  - birth injury P13.4
  - lateral end —*see* Fracture, clavicle, acromial end
  - shaft (displaced) S42.02-
    - nondisplaced S42.02-
  - sternal end (anterior) (displaced) S42.01-
    - nondisplaced S42.01-
    - posterior S42.01-
- coccyx S32.2
- collapsed —*see* Collapse, vertebra
- collar bone —*see* Fracture, clavicle
- Colles' —*see* Colles' fracture
- compression, not due to trauma —*see* Collapse, vertebra
- coronoid process —*see* Fracture, ulna, upper end, coronoid process
- corpus cavernosum penis S39.840
- costochondral cartilage S23.41
- costochondral, costosternal junction —*see* Fracture, rib
- cranium —*see* Fracture, skull
- cricoid cartilage S12.8
- cuboid (ankle) —*see* Fracture, tarsal, cuboid
- cuneiform
  - foot —*see* Fracture, tarsal, cuneiform
  - wrist —*see* Fracture, carpal, triquetrum
- delayed union —*see* Delay, union, fracture
- dental restorative material K08.539
  - with loss of material K08.531
  - without loss of material K08.530
- due to
  - birth injury —*see* Birth, injury, fracture
  - osteoporosis —*see* Osteoporosis, with fracture
- Dupuytren's —*see* Fracture, ankle, lateral malleolus
- elbow S42.40-
- ethmoid (bone) (sinus) —*see* Fracture, skull, base
- face bone S02.92
- fatigue —*see also* Fracture, stress
  - vertebra M48.40
    - cervical region M48.42
    - cervicothoracic region M48.43
    - lumbar region M48.46
    - lumbosacral region M48.47
    - occipito-atlanto-axial region M48.41
    - sacrococcygeal region M48.48
    - thoracic region M48.44
    - thoracolumbar region M48.45
- femur, femoral S72.9-
  - basicervical (basal) S72.0
  - birth injury P13.2
  - capital epiphyseal S79.01-
  - condyles, epicondyles —*see* Fracture, femur, lower end
  - distal end —*see* Fracture, femur, lower end
  - epiphysis
    - head —*see* Fracture, femur, upper end, epiphysis
    - lower —*see* Fracture, femur, lower end, epiphysis
    - upper —*see* Fracture, femur, upper end, epiphysis
  - following insertion of implant, prosthesis or plate M96.66-
  - head —*see* Fracture, femur, upper end, head
  - intertrochanteric —*see* Fracture, femur, trochanteric

Fracture, traumatic *(continued)*
- femur, femoral *(continued)*
  - intratrochanteric —*see* Fracture, femur, trochanteric
  - lower end S72.40-
    - condyle (displaced) S72.41-
      - lateral (displaced) S72.42-
        - nondisplaced S72.42-
      - medial (displaced) S72.43-
        - nondisplaced S72.43-
      - nondisplaced S72.41-
    - epiphysis (displaced) S72.44-
      - nondisplaced S72.44-
    - physeal S79.10-
      - Salter-Harris
        - Type I S79.11-
        - Type II S79.12-
        - Type III S79.13-
        - Type IV S79.14-
      - specified NEC S79.19-
    - specified NEC S72.49-
    - supracondylar (displaced) S72.45-
      - with intracondylar extension (displaced) S72.46-
        - nondisplaced S72.46-
      - nondisplaced S72.45-
    - torus S72.47-
  - neck —*see* Fracture, femur, upper end, neck
  - pertrochanteric —*see* Fracture, femur, trochanteric
  - shaft (lower third) (middle third) (upper third) S72.30-
    - comminuted (displaced) S72.35-
      - nondisplaced S72.35-
    - oblique (displaced) S72.33-
      - nondisplaced S72.33-
    - segmental (displaced) S72.36-
      - nondisplaced S72.36-
    - specified NEC S72.39-
    - spiral (displaced) S72.34-
      - nondisplaced S72.34-
    - transverse (displaced) S72.32-
      - nondisplaced S72.32-
  - specified site NEC S72.8
  - subcapital (displaced) S72.01-
  - subtrochanteric (region) (section) (displaced) S72.2-
    - nondisplaced S72.2-
  - transcervical —*see* Fracture, femur, upper end, neck
  - transtrochanteric —*see* Fracture, femur, trochanteric
  - trochanteric S72.10-
    - apophyseal (displaced) S72.13-
      - nondisplaced S72.13-
    - greater trochanter (displaced) S72.11-
      - nondisplaced S72.11-
    - intertrochanteric (displaced) S72.14-
      - nondisplaced S72.14-
    - lesser trochanter (displaced) S72.12-
      - nondisplaced S72.12-
  - upper end S72.00-
    - apophyseal (displaced) S72.13-
      - nondisplaced S72.13-
    - cervicotrochanteric —*see* Fracture, femur, upper end, neck, base
    - epiphysis (displaced) S72.02-
      - nondisplaced S72.02-
    - head S72.05-
      - articular (displaced) S72.06-
        - nondisplaced S72.06-
      - specified NEC S72.09-
    - intertrochanteric (displaced) S72.14-
      - nondisplaced S72.14-
    - intracapsular S72.01-

Fracture, traumatic *(continued)*
- femur, femoral *(continued)*
  - upper end *(continued)*
    - midcervical (displaced) S72.03-
      - nondisplaced S72.03-
    - neck S72.00-
      - base (displaced) S72.04-
        - nondisplaced S72.04-
      - specified NEC S72.09-
    - pertrochanteric —*see* Fracture, femur, upper end, trochanteric
    - physeal S79.00-
      - Salter-Harris type I S79.01-
      - specified NEC S79.09-
    - subcapital (displaced) S72.01-
    - subtrochanteric (displaced) S72.2-
      - nondisplaced S72.2-
    - transcervical —*see* Fracture, femur, upper end, midcervical
    - trochanteric S72.10-
      - greater (displaced) S72.11-
        - nondisplaced S72.11-
      - lesser (displaced) S72.12-
        - nondisplaced S72.12-
- fibula (shaft) (styloid) S82.40-
  - comminuted (displaced) S82.45-
    - nondisplaced S82.45-
  - following insertion of implant, prosthesis or plate M96.67-
  - involving ankle or malleolus —*see* Fracture, fibula, lateral malleolus
  - lateral malleolus (displaced) S82.6-
    - nondisplaced S82.6-
  - lower end
    - physeal S89.30-
      - Salter-Harris
        - Type I S89.31-
        - Type II S89.32-
      - specified NEC S89.39-
    - specified NEC S82.83-
    - torus S82.82-
  - oblique (displaced) S82.43-
    - nondisplaced S82.43-
  - segmental (displaced) S82.46-
    - nondisplaced S82.46-
  - specified NEC S82.49-
  - spiral (displaced) S82.44-
    - nondisplaced S82.44-
  - transverse (displaced) S82.42-
    - nondisplaced S82.42-
  - upper end
    - physeal S89.20-
      - Salter-Harris
        - Type I S89.21-
        - Type II S89.22-
      - specified NEC S89.29-
    - specified NEC S82.83-
    - torus S82.81-
- finger (except thumb) S62.60-
  - distal phalanx (displaced) S62.63-
    - nondisplaced S62.66-
  - index S62.60-
    - distal phalanx (displaced) S62.63-
      - nondisplaced S62.66-
    - medial phalanx (displaced) S62.62-
      - nondisplaced S62.65-
    - proximal phalanx (displaced) S62.61-
      - nondisplaced S62.64-
  - little S62.60-
    - distal phalanx (displaced) S62.63-
      - nondisplaced S62.66-
    - medial phalanx (displaced) S62.62-
      - nondisplaced S62.65-
    - proximal phalanx (displaced) S62.61-
      - nondisplaced S62.64-

Fracture, traumatic *(continued)*

- metastatic —*see* Fracture, pathological, due to, neoplastic disease —*see also* Neoplasm
- metatarsal bone S92.30-
  - fifth (displaced) S92.35-
    - nondisplaced S92.35-
  - first (displaced) S92.31-
    - nondisplaced S92.31-
  - fourth (displaced) S92.34-
    - nondisplaced S92.34-
  - second (displaced) S92.32-
    - nondisplaced S92.32-
  - third (displaced) S92.33-
    - nondisplaced S92.33-
- Monteggia's —*see* Monteggia's fracture
- multiple
  - hand (and wrist) NEC —*see* Fracture, by site
  - ribs —*see* Fracture, rib, multiple
- nasal (bone(s)) S02.2
- navicular (scaphoid) (foot) —*see also* Fracture, tarsal, navicular
  - hand —*see* Fracture, carpal, navicular
- neck S12.9
  - cervical vertebra S12.9
    - fifth (displaced) S12.400
      - nondisplaced S12.401
      - specified type NEC (displaced) S12.490
        - nondisplaced S12.491
    - first (displaced) S12.000
      - burst (stable) S12.01
        - unstable S12.02
      - lateral mass (displaced) S12.040
        - nondisplaced S12.041
      - nondisplaced S12.001
      - posterior arch (displaced) S12.030
        - nondisplaced S12.031
      - specified type NEC (displaced) S12.090
        - nondisplaced S12.091
    - fourth (displaced) S12.300
      - nondisplaced S12.301
      - specified type NEC (displaced) S12.390
        - nondisplaced S12.391
    - second (displaced) S12.100
      - nondisplaced S12.101
      - dens (anterior) (displaced) (type II) S12.110
        - nondisplaced S12.112
        - posterior S12.111
        - specified type NEC (displaced) S12.120
          - nondisplaced S12.121
      - specified type NEC (displaced) S12.190
        - nondisplaced S12.191
    - seventh (displaced) S12.600
      - nondisplaced S12.601
      - specified type NEC (displaced) S12.690
        - displaced S12.691
    - sixth (displaced) S12.500
      - nondisplaced S12.501
      - specified type NEC (displaced) S12.590
        - displaced S12.591
    - third (displaced) S12.200
      - nondisplaced S12.201
      - specified type NEC (displaced) S12.290
        - displaced S12.291
  - hyoid bone S12.8
  - larynx S12.8
  - specified site NEC S12.8
  - thyroid cartilage S12.8

Fracture, traumatic *(continued)*

- neck *(continued)*
  - trachea S12.8
- neoplastic NEC —*see* Fracture, pathological, due to, neoplastic disease
- neural arch —*see* Fracture, vertebra
- newborn —*see* Birth, injury, fracture
- nontraumatic —*see* Fracture, pathological
- nonunion —*see* Nonunion, fracture
- nose, nasal (bone) (septum) S02.2
- occiput —*see* Fracture, skull, base, occiput
- odontoid process —*see* Fracture, neck, cervical vertebra, second
- olecranon (process) (ulna) —*see* Fracture, ulna, upper end, olecranon process
- orbit, orbital (bone) (region) S02.8
  - floor (blow-out) S02.3
  - roof S02.19
- os
  - calcis —*see* Fracture, tarsal, calcaneus
  - magnum —*see* Fracture, carpal, capitate
  - pubis —*see* Fracture, pubis
- palate S02.8
- parietal bone (skull) S02.0
- patella S82.00-
  - comminuted (displaced) S82.04-
    - nondisplaced S82.04-
  - longitudinal (displaced) S82.02-
    - nondisplaced S82.02-
  - osteochondral (displaced) S82.01-
    - nondisplaced S82.01-
  - specified NEC S82.09-
  - transverse (displaced) S82.03-
    - nondisplaced S82.03-
- pedicle (of vertebral arch) —*see* Fracture, vertebra
- pelvis, pelvic (bone) S32.9
  - acetabulum —*see* Fracture, acetabulum
  - circle —*see* Disruption, pelvic ring
  - following insertion of implant, prosthesis or plate M96.65
  - ilium —*see* Fracture, ilium
  - ischium —*see* Fracture, ischium
  - multiple
    - with disruption of pelvic ring (circle) —*see* Disruption, pelvic ring
    - without disruption of pelvic ring (circle) S32.82
  - pubis —*see* Fracture, pubis
  - specified site NEC S32.89
  - sacrum —*see* Fracture, sacrum
- phalanx
  - foot —*see* Fracture, toe
  - hand —*see* Fracture, finger
- pisiform —*see* Fracture, carpal, pisiform
- pond —*see* Fracture, skull
- prosthetic device, internal —*see* Complications, prosthetic device, by site, mechanical
- pubis S32.50-
  - with disruption of pelvic ring —*see* Disruption, pelvic ring
  - specified site NEC S32.59-
  - superior rim S32.51-
- radius S52.9-
  - distal end —*see* Fracture, radius, lower end
  - following insertion of implant, prosthesis or plate M96.63-
  - head —*see* Fracture, radius, upper end, head
  - lower end S52.50-
    - Barton's —*see* Barton's fracture

Fracture, traumatic *(continued)*

- radius *(continued)*
  - lower end *(continued)*
    - Colles' —*see* Colles' fracture
    - extraarticular NEC S52.55-
    - intraarticular NEC S52.57-
    - physeal S59.20-
      - Salter-Harris
        - Type I S59.21-
        - Type II S59.22-
        - Type III S59.23-
        - Type IV S59.24-
      - specified NEC S59.29-
    - Smith's —*see* Smith's fracture
    - specified NEC S52.59-
    - styloid process (displaced) S52.51-
      - nondisplaced S52.51-
    - torus S52.52-
  - neck —*see* Fracture, radius, upper end
  - proximal end —*see* Fracture, radius, upper end
  - shaft S52.30-
    - bent bone S52.38-
    - comminuted (displaced) S52.35-
      - nondisplaced S52.35-
    - Galeazzi's —*see* Galeazzi's fracture
    - greenstick S52.31-
    - oblique (displaced) S52.33-
      - nondisplaced S52.33-
    - segmental (displaced) S52.36-
      - nondisplaced S52.36-
    - specified NEC S52.39-
    - spiral (displaced) S52.34-
      - nondisplaced S52.34-
    - transverse (displaced) S52.32-
      - nondisplaced S52.32-
  - upper end S52.10-
    - head (displaced) S52.12-
      - nondisplaced S52.12-
    - neck (displaced) S52.13-
      - nondisplaced S52.13-
    - specified NEC S52.18-
    - physeal S59.10-
      - Salter-Harris
        - Type I S59.11-
        - Type II S59.12-
        - Type III S59.13-
        - Type IV S59.14-
      - specified NEC S59.19-
    - torus S52.11-
- ramus
  - inferior or superior, pubis —*see* Fracture, pubis
  - mandible —*see* Fracture, mandible
- restorative material (dental) K08.539
  - with loss of material K08.531
  - without loss of material K08.530
- rib S22.3-
  - with flail chest —*see* Flail, chest
  - multiple S22.4-
    - with flail chest —*see* Flail, chest
- root, tooth —*see* Fracture, tooth
- sacrum S32.10
  - specified NEC S32.19
  - Type
    - 1 S32.14
    - 2 S32.15
    - 3 S32.16
    - 4 S32.17
  - Zone
    - I S32.119
      - displaced (minimally) S32.111
        - severely S32.112
      - nondisplaced S32.110
    - II S32.129
      - displaced (minimally) S32.121
        - severely S32.122
      - nondisplaced S32.120

Fracture, traumatic *(continued)*

- sacrum *(continued)*
  - Zone *(continued)*
    - III S32.139
      - displaced (minimally) S32.131
        - severely S32.132
      - nondisplaced S32.130
- scaphoid (hand) —*see also* Fracture, carpal, navicular
  - foot —*see* Fracture, tarsal, navicular
- scapula S42.10-
  - acromial process (displaced) S42.12-
    - nondisplaced S42.12-
  - body (displaced) S42.11-
    - nondisplaced S42.11-
  - coracoid process (displaced) S42.13-
    - nondisplaced S42.13-
  - glenoid cavity (displaced) S42.14-
    - nondisplaced S42.14-
  - neck (displaced) S42.15-
    - nondisplaced S42.15-
  - specified NEC S42.19-
- semilunar bone, wrist —*see* Fracture, carpal, lunate
- sequelae —*see* Sequelae, fracture
- sesamoid bone
  - hand —*see* Fracture, carpal
  - other - code by site under Fracture
- shepherd's —*see* Fracture, tarsal, talus
- shoulder (girdle) S42.9-
  - blade —*see* Fracture, scapula
- sinus (ethmoid) (frontal) S02.19
- skull S02.91
  - base S02.10
    - occiput S02.119
      - condyle S02.113
        - type I S02.110
        - type II S02.111
        - type III S02.112
      - specified NEC S02.118
    - specified NEC S02.19
  - birth injury P13.0
  - frontal bone S02.0
  - parietal bone S02.0
  - specified site NEC S02.8
  - temporal bone S02.19
  - vault S02.0
- Smith's —*see* Smith's fracture
- sphenoid (bone) (sinus) S02.19
- spine —*see* Fracture, vertebra
- spinous process —*see* Fracture, vertebra
- spontaneous (cause unknown) —*see* Fracture, pathological
- stave (of thumb) —*see* Fracture, metacarpal, first
- sternum S22.20
  - with flail chest —*see* Flail, chest
  - body S22.22
  - manubrium S22.21
  - xiphoid (process) S22.24
- stress M84.30
  - ankle M84.37-
  - carpus M84.34-
  - clavicle M84.31-
  - femoral neck M84.359
  - femur M84.35-
  - fibula M84.36-
  - finger M84.34-
  - hip M84.359
  - humerus M84.32-
  - ilium M84.350
  - ischium M84.350
  - metacarpus M84.34-
  - metatarsus M84.37-
  - neck —*see* Fracture, fatigue, vertebra

- **Fracture, traumatic** *(continued)*
  - uniform —*see* Fracture, carpal, hamate
  - vault of skull S02.0
  - vertebra, vertebral (arch) (body) (column) (neural arch) (pedicle) (spinous process) (transverse process)
    - atlas —*see* Fracture, neck, cervical vertebra, first
    - axis —*see* Fracture, neck, cervical vertebra, second
    - cervical (teardrop) S12.9
      - axis —*see* Fracture, neck, cervical vertebra, second
      - first (atlas) —*see* Fracture, neck, cervical vertebra, first
      - second (axis) —*see* Fracture, neck, cervical vertebra, second
    - chronic M84.48
    - coccyx S32.2
    - dorsal —*see* Fracture, thorax, vertebra
    - lumbar S32.009
      - burst (stable) S32.001
        - unstable S32.002
      - fifth S32.059
        - burst (stable) S32.051
          - unstable S32.052
        - specified type NEC S32.058
        - wedge compression S32.050
      - first S32.019
        - burst (stable) S32.011
          - unstable S32.012
        - specified type NEC S32.018
        - wedge compression S32.010
      - fourth S32.049
        - burst (stable) S32.041
          - unstable S32.042
        - specified type NEC S32.048
        - wedge compression S32.040
      - second S32.029
        - burst (stable) S32.021
          - unstable S32.022
        - specified type NEC S32.028
        - wedge compression S32.020
      - specified type NEC S32.008
      - third S32.039
        - burst (stable) S32.031
          - unstable S32.032
        - specified type NEC S32.038
        - wedge compression S32.030
      - wedge compression S32.000
    - metastatic —*see* Collapse, vertebra, in, specified disease NEC —*see also* Neoplasm
    - newborn (birth injury) P11.5
    - sacrum S32.10
      - specified NEC S32.19
      - Type
        - 1 S32.14
        - 2 S32.15
        - 3 S32.16
        - 4 S32.17
      - Zone
        - I S32.119
          - displaced (minimally) S32.111
            - severely S32.112
          - nondisplaced S32.110
        - II S32.129
          - displaced (minimally) S32.121
            - severely S32.122
          - nondisplaced S32.120
        - III S32.139
          - displaced (minimally) S32.131
            - severely S32.132
          - nondisplaced S32.130
    - thoracic —*see* Fracture, thorax, vertebra

- **Fracture, traumatic** *(continued)*
  - vertex S02.0
  - vomer (bone) S02.2
  - wrist S62.10-
    - carpal —*see* Fracture, carpal bone
    - navicular (scaphoid) (hand) —*see* Fracture, carpal, navicular
  - xiphisternum, xiphoid (process) S22.24
  - zygoma S02.402
- **Fragile, fragility**
  - autosomal site Q95.5
  - bone, congenital (with blue sclera) Q78.0
  - capillary (hereditary) D69.8
  - hair L67.8
  - nails L60.3
  - non-sex chromosome site Q95.5
  - X chromosome Q99.2
- **Fragilitas**
  - crinium L67.8
  - ossium (with blue sclerae) (hereditary) Q78.0
  - unguium L60.3
    - congenital Q84.6
- **Fragments, cataract** (lens)**, following cataract surgery** H59.02-
  - retained foreign body —*see* Retained, foreign body fragments (type of)
- **Frailty** (frail) R54
  - mental R41.81
- **Frambesia, frambesial** (tropica) —*see also* Yaws
  - initial lesion or ulcer A66.0
  - primary A66.0
- **Frambeside**
  - gummatous A66.4
  - of early yaws A66.2
- **Frambesioma** A66.1
- **Franceschetti-Klein** (-Wildervanck) **disease or syndrome** Q75.4
- **Francis' disease** —*see* Tularemia
- **Franklin disease** C88.2
- **Frank's essential thrombocytopenia** D69.3
- **Fraser's syndrome** Q87.0
- **Freckle** (s) L81.2
  - malignant melanoma in —*see* Melanoma
  - melanotic (Hutchinson's) —*see* Melanoma, in situ
  - retinal D49.81
- **Frederickson's hyperlipoproteinemia, type**
  - I and V E78.3
  - IIA E78.0
  - IIB and III E78.2
  - IV E78.1
- **Freeman Sheldon syndrome** Q87.0
- **Freezing** —*see also* Effect, adverse, cold T69.9
- **Freiberg's disease** (infraction of metatarsal head or osteochondrosis) —*see* Osteochondrosis, juvenile, metatarsus
- **Frei's disease** A55
- **Fremitus, friction, cardiac** R01.2
- **Frenum, frenulum**
  - external os Q51.828
  - tongue (shortening) (congenital) Q38.1
- **Frequency micturition** (nocturnal) R35.0
  - psychogenic F45.8

- **Frey's syndrome**
  - auriculotemporal G50.8
  - hyperhidrosis L74.52
- **Friction**
  - burn —*see* Burn, by site
  - fremitus, cardiac R01.2
  - precordial R01.2
  - sounds, chest R09.89
- **Friderichsen-Waterhouse syndrome or disease** A39.1
- **Friedländer's B** (bacillus) **NEC** —*see also* condition A49.8
- **Friedreich's**
  - ataxia G11.1
  - combined systemic disease G11.1
  - facial hemihypertrophy Q67.4
  - sclerosis (cerebellum) (spinal cord) G11.1
- **Frigidity** F52.22
- **Fröhlich's syndrome** E23.6
- **Frontal** —*see also* condition
  - lobe syndrome F07.0
- **Frostbite** (superficial) T33.90
  - with
    - partial thickness skin loss —*see* Frostbite (superficial), by site
    - tissue necrosis T34.90
  - abdominal wall T33.3
    - with tissue necrosis T34.3
  - ankle T33.81-
    - with tissue necrosis T34.81-
  - arm T33.4-
    - with tissue necrosis T34.4-
    - finger (s) —*see* Frostbite, finger
    - hand —*see* Frostbite, hand
    - wrist —*see* Frostbite, wrist
  - ear T33.01-
    - with tissue necrosis T34.01-
  - face T33.09
    - with tissue necrosis T34.09
  - finger T33.53-
    - with tissue necrosis T34.53-
  - foot T33.82-
    - with tissue necrosis T34.82-
  - hand T33.52-
    - with tissue necrosis T34.52-
  - head T33.09
    - with tissue necrosis T34.09
    - ear —*see* Frostbite, ear
    - nose —*see* Frostbite, nose
  - hip (and thigh) T33.6-
    - with tissue necrosis T34.6-
  - knee T33.7-
    - with tissue necrosis T34.7-
  - leg T33.9-
    - with tissue necrosis T34.9-
    - ankle —*see* Frostbite, ankle
    - foot —*see* Frostbite, foot
    - knee —*see* Frostbite, knee
    - lower T33.7-
      - with tissue necrosis T34.7-
    - thigh —*see* Frostbite, hip
    - toe —*see* Frostbite, toe
  - limb
    - lower T33.99
      - with tissue necrosis T34.99
    - upper —*see* Frostbite, arm
  - neck T33.1
    - with tissue necrosis T34.1
  - nose T33.02
    - with tissue necrosis T34.02
  - pelvis T33.3
    - with tissue necrosis T34.3
  - specified site NEC T33.99
    - with tissue necrosis T34.99
  - thigh —*see* Frostbite, hip
  - thorax T33.2
    - with tissue necrosis T34.2
  - toes T33.83-
    - with tissue necrosis T34.83-

- **Frostbite** *(continued)*
  - trunk T33.99
    - with tissue necrosis T34.99
  - wrist T33.51-
    - with tissue necrosis T34.51-
- **Frotteurism** F65.81
- **Frozen** —*see also* Effect, adverse, cold T69.9
  - pelvis (female) N94.89
    - male K66.8
  - shoulder —*see* Capsulitis, adhesive
- **Fructokinase deficiency** E74.11
- **Fructose 1,6 diphosphatase deficiency** E74.19
- **Fructosemia** (benign) (essential) E74.12
- **Fructosuria** (benign) (essential) E74.11
- **Fuchs'**
  - black spot (myopic) H44.2-
  - dystrophy (corneal endothelium) H18.51
  - heterochromic cyclitis —*see* Cyclitis, Fuchs' heterochromic
- **Fucosidosis** E77.1
- **Fugue** R68.89
  - dissociative F44.1
  - hysterical (dissociative) F44.1
  - postictal in epilepsy —*see* Epilepsy
  - reaction to exceptional stress (transient) F43.0
- **Fulminant, fulminating** —*see* condition
- **Functional** —*see also* condition
  - bleeding (uterus) N93.8
- **Functioning, intellectual, borderline** R41.83
- **Fundus** —*see* condition
- **Fungemia NOS** B49
- **Fungus, fungous**
  - cerebral G93.89
  - disease NOS B49
  - infection —*see* Infection, fungus
- **Funiculitis** (acute) (chronic) (endemic) N49.1
  - gonococcal (acute) (chronic) A54.23
  - tuberculous A18.15
- **Funnel**
  - breast (acquired) M95.4
    - congenital Q67.6
    - sequelae (late effect) of rickets E64.3
  - chest (acquired) M95.4
    - congenital Q67.6
    - sequelae (late effect) of rickets E64.3
  - pelvis (acquired) M95.5
    - with disproportion (fetopelvic) O33.3
      - causing obstructed labor O65.3
    - congenital Q74.2
- **FUO** (fever of unknown origin) R50.9
- **Furfur** L21.0
  - microsporon B36.0
- **Furrier's lung** J67.8
- **Furrowed** K14.5
  - nail (s) (transverse) L60.4
    - congenital Q84.6
  - tongue K14.5
    - congenital Q38.3
- **Furuncle** L02.92
  - abdominal wall L02.221
  - ankle —*see* Furuncle, lower limb
  - anus K61.0
  - antecubital space —*see* Furuncle, upper limb

Gangrene, gangrenous *(continued)*
- intestine, intestinal (hemorrhagic) (massive) K55.0
  - with
    - mesenteric embolism K55.0
    - obstruction —*see* Obstruction, intestine
- laryngitis J04.0
- limb (lower) (upper) I96
- lung J85.0
  - spirochetal A69.8
- lymphangitis I89.1
- Meleney's (synergistic) —*see* Ulcer, skin
- mesentery K55.0
  - with
    - embolism K55.0
    - intestinal obstruction —*see* Obstruction, intestine
- mouth A69.0
- ovary —*see* Oophoritis
- pancreas K85.9
- penis N48.29
  - noninfective N48.89
- perineum I96
- pharynx —*see also* Pharyngitis
  - Vincent's A69.1
- presenile I73.1
- progressive synergistic —*see* Ulcer, skin
- pulmonary J85.0
- pulpal (dental) K04.1
- quinsy J36
- Raynaud's (symmetric gangrene) I73.01
- retropharyngeal J39.2
- scrotum N49.3
  - noninfective N50.8
- senile (atherosclerotic) —*see* Arteriosclerosis, extremities, with, gangrene
- spermatic cord N49.1
  - noninfective N50.8
- spine I96
- spirochetal NEC A69.8
- spreading cutaneous I96
- stomatitis A69.0
- symmetrical I73.01
- testis (infectional) N45.2
  - noninfective N44.8
- throat —*see also* Pharyngitis
  - diphtheritic A36.0
  - Vincent's A69.1
- thyroid (gland) E07.89
- tooth (pulp) K04.1
- tuberculous NEC —*see* Tuberculosis
- tunica vaginalis N49.1
  - noninfective N50.8
- umbilicus I96
- uterus —*see* Endometritis
- uvulitis K12.2
- vas deferens N49.1
  - noninfective N50.8
- vulva N76.89

Ganister disease J62.8

Ganser's syndrome (hysterical) F44.89

Gardner-Diamond syndrome (autoerythrocyte sensitization) D69.2

Gargoylism E76.01

Garré's disease, osteitis (sclerosing), **osteomyelitis** —*see* Osteomyelitis, specified type NEC

Garrod's pad, knuckle M72.1

Gartner's duct
- cyst Q52.4
- persistent Q50.6

Gas R14.3
- asphyxiation, inhalation, poisoning, suffocation NEC —*see* Table of Drugs and Chemicals

Gas *(continued)*
- excessive R14.0
- gangrene A48.0
  - following
    - abortion —*see* Abortion by type complicated by infection
    - ectopic or molar pregnancy O08.0
- on stomach R14.0
- pains R14.1

Gastralgia —*see also* Pain, abdominal

Gastrectasis K31.0
- psychogenic F45.8

Gastric —*see* condition

Gastrinoma
- malignant
  - pancreas C25.4
  - specified site NEC —*see* Neoplasm, malignant, by site
  - unspecified site C25.4
- specified site —*see* Neoplasm, uncertain behavior
- unspecified site D37.9

Gastritis (simple) K29.70
- with bleeding K29.71
- acute (erosive) K29.00
  - with bleeding K29.01
- alcoholic K29.20
  - with bleeding K29.21
- allergic K29.60
  - with bleeding K29.61
- atrophic (chronic) K29.40
  - with bleeding K29.41
- chronic (antral) (fundal) K29.50
  - with bleeding K29.51
  - atrophic K29.40
    - with bleeding K29.41
  - superficial K29.30
    - with bleeding K29.31
- dietary counseling and surveillance Z71.3
- due to diet deficiency E63.9
- eosinophilic K52.81
- giant hypertrophic K29.60
  - with bleeding K29.61
- granulomatous K29.60
  - with bleeding K29.61
- hypertrophic (mucosa) K29.60
  - with bleeding K29.61
- nervous F54
- spastic K29.60
  - with bleeding K29.61
- specified NEC K29.60
  - with bleeding K29.61
- superficial chronic K29.30
  - with bleeding K29.31
- tuberculous A18.83
- viral NEC A08.4

Gastrocarcinoma —*see* Neoplasm, malignant, stomach

Gastrocolic —*see* condition

Gastrodisciasis, gastrodiscoidiasis B66.8

Gastroduodenitis K29.90
- with bleeding K29.91
- virus, viral A08.4
  - specified type NEC A08.39

Gastrodynia —*see* Pain, abdominal

Gastroenteritis (acute) (chronic) (noninfectious) —*see also* Enteritis K52.9
- allergic K52.2
- dietetic K52.2
- drug-induced K52.1
- due to
  - Cryptosporidium A07.2
  - drugs K52.1
  - food poisoning —*see* Intoxication, foodborne
  - radiation K52.0

Gastroenteritis *(continued)*
- eosinophilic K52.81
- epidemic (infectious) A09
- food hypersensitivity K52.2
- infectious —*see* Enteritis, infectious
- influenzal —*see* Influenza, with gastroenteritis
- noninfectious K52.9
  - specified NEC K52.89
- rotaviral A08.0
- Salmonella A02.0
- toxic K52.1
- viral NEC A08.4
  - acute infectious A08.39
    - type Norwalk A08.11
  - infantile (acute) A08.39
  - Norwalk agent A08.11
  - rotaviral A08.0
  - severe of infants A08.39
  - specified type NEC A08.39

Gastroenteropathy —*see also* Gastroenteritis K52.9
- acute, due to Norwalk agent A08.11
- acute, due to Norovirus A08.11
- infectious A09

Gastroenteroptosis K63.4

Gastroesophageal laceration-hemorrhage syndrome K22.6

Gastrointestinal —*see* condition

Gastrojejunal —*see* condition

Gastrojejunitis —*see also* Enteritis K52.9

Gastrojejunocolic —*see* condition

Gastroliths K31.89

Gastromalacia K31.89

Gastroparalysis K31.84
- diabetic —*see* Diabetes, gastroparalysis

Gastroparesis K31.84
- diabetic —*see* Diabetes, by type, with gastroparesis

Gastropathy K31.9
- congestive portal K31.89
- erythematous K29.70
- exudative K90.89
- portal hypertensive K31.89

Gastroptosis K31.89

Gastrorrhagia K92.2
- psychogenic F45.8

Gastroschisis (congenital) Q79.3

Gastrospasm (neurogenic) (reflex) K31.89
- neurotic F45.8
- psychogenic F45.8

Gastrostaxis —*see* Gastritis, with bleeding

Gastrostenosis K31.89

Gastrostomy
- attention to Z43.1
- status Z93.1

Gastrosuccorrhea (continuous) (intermittent) K31.89
- neurotic F45.8
- psychogenic F45.8

Gatophobia F40.218

Gaucher's disease or splenomegaly (adult) (infantile) E75.22

Gee (-Herter)(-Thaysen) **disease** (nontropical sprue) K90.0

Gélineau's syndrome G47.419
- with cataplexy G47.411

Gemination, tooth, teeth K00.2

Gemistocytoma
- specified site —*see* Neoplasm, malignant, by site
- unspecified site C71.9

General, generalized —*see* condition

Genetic
- carrier (status)
  - cystic fibrosis Z14.1
  - hemophilia A (asymptomatic) Z14.01
    - symptomatic Z14.02
  - specified NEC Z14.8
- susceptibility to disease NEC Z15.89
  - malignant neoplasm Z15.09
    - breast Z15.01
    - endometrium Z15.04
    - ovary Z15.02
    - prostate Z15.03
    - specified NEC Z15.09
  - multiple endocrine neoplasia Z15.81

Genital —*see* condition

Genito-anorectal syndrome A55

Genitourinary system —*see* condition

Genu
- congenital Q74.1
- extrorsum (acquired) —*see also* Deformity, varus, knee
  - congenital Q74.1
  - sequelae (late effect) of rickets E64.3
- introrsum (acquired) —*see also* Deformity, valgus, knee
  - congenital Q74.1
  - sequelae (late effect) of rickets E64.3
- rachitic (old) E64.3
- recurvatum (acquired) —*see also* Deformity, limb, specified type NEC, lower leg
  - congenital Q68.2
  - sequelae (late effect) of rickets E64.3
- valgum (acquired) (knock-knee) M21.06-
  - congenital Q74.1
  - sequelae (late effect) of rickets E64.3
- varum (acquired) (bowleg) M21.16-
  - congenital Q74.1
  - sequelae (late effect) of rickets E64.3

Geographic tongue K14.1

Geophagia —*see* Pica

Geotrichosis B48.3
- stomatitis B48.3

Gephyrophobia F40.242

Gerbode defect Q21.0

GERD (gastroesophageal reflux disease) K21.9

Gerhardt's
- disease (erythromelalgia) I73.81
- syndrome (vocal cord paralysis) J38.00
  - bilateral J38.02
  - unilateral J38.01

German measles —*see also* Rubella
- exposure to Z20.4

Germinoblastoma (diffuse) C85.9-
- follicular C82.9-

Germinoma —*see* Neoplasm, malignant, by site

Gerontoxon —*see* Degeneration, cornea, senile

Gerstmann-Sträussler-Scheinker syndrome (GSS) A81.82

erstmann's syndrome R48.8
- developmental F81.2

estation (period) *—see also* Pregnancy
- ectopic *—see* Pregnancy, by site
- multiple O30.9-
  - greater than quadruplets *—see* Pregnancy, multiple (gestation), specified NEC
  - specified NEC *—see* Pregnancy, multiple (gestation), specified NEC

estational
- mammary abscess O91.11-
- purulent mastitis O91.11-
- subareolar abscess O91.11-

hon tubercle, primary infection A15.7

host
- teeth K00.4
- vessels (cornea) H16.41-

houl hand A66.3

ianotti-Crosti disease L44.4

iant
- cell
  - epulis K06.8
  - peripheral granuloma K06.8
- esophagus, congenital Q39.5
- kidney, congenital Q63.3
- urticaria T78.3
  - hereditary D84.1

iardiasis A07.1

ibert's disease or pityriasis L42

iddiness R42
- hysterical F44.89
- psychogenic F45.8

ierke's disease (glycogenosis I) E74.01

igantism (cerebral) (hypophyseal) (pituitary) E22.0
- constitutional E34.4

ilbert's disease or syndrome E80.4

ilchrist's disease B40.9

ilford-Hutchinson disease E34.8

illes de la Tourette's disease or syndrome (motor-verbal tic) F95.2

ingivitis K05.10
- acute (catarrhal) K05.00
  - necrotizing A69.1
  - nonplaque induced K05.01
  - plaque induced K05.00
- chronic (desquamative) (hyperplastic) (simple marginal) (ulcerative) K05.10
  - nonplaque induced K05.11
  - plaque induced K05.10
- expulsiva *—see* Periodontitis
- necrotizing ulcerative (acute) A69.1
- pellagrous E52
  - acute necrotizing A69.1
- Vincent's A69.1

Gingivoglossitis K14.0

Gingivopericementitis *—see* Periodontitis

Gingivosis *—see* Gingivitis, chronic

Gingivostomatitis K05.10
- herpesviral B00.2
- necrotizing ulcerative (acute) A69.1

Gland, glandular *—see* condition

Glanders A24.0

Glanzmann (-Naegeli) **disease or thrombasthenia** D69.1

Glasgow coma scale
- total score
  - 3-8 R40.243
  - 9-12 R40.242
  - 13-15 R40.241

Glass-blower's disease (cataract) *—see* Cataract, specified NEC

Glaucoma H40.9
- with
  - increased episcleral venous pressure H40.81-
  - pseudoexfoliation of lens *—see* Glaucoma, open angle, primary, capsular
- absolute H44.51-
- angle-closure (primary) H40.20-
  - acute (attack) (crisis) H40.21-
  - chronic H40.22-
  - intermittent H40.23-
  - residual stage H40.24-
- borderline H40.00-
- capsular (with pseudoexfoliation of lens) *—see* Glaucoma, open angle, primary, capsular
- childhood Q15.0
- closed angle *—see* Glaucoma, angle-closure
- congenital Q15.0
- corticosteroid-induced *—see* Glaucoma, secondary, drugs
- hypersecretion H40.82-
- in (due to)
  - amyloidosis E85.4 *[H42]*
  - aniridia Q13.1 *[H42]*
  - concussion of globe *—see* Glaucoma, secondary, trauma
  - dislocation of lens *—see* Glaucoma, secondary
  - disorder of lens NEC *—see* Glaucoma, secondary
  - drugs *—see* Glaucoma, secondary, drugs
  - endocrine disease NOS E34.9 *[H42]*
  - eye
    - inflammation *—see* Glaucoma, secondary, inflammation
    - trauma *—see* Glaucoma, secondary, trauma
  - hypermature cataract *—see* Glaucoma, secondary
  - iridocyclitis *—see* Glaucoma, secondary, inflammation
  - lens disorder *—see* Glaucoma, secondary,
  - Lowe's syndrome E72.03 *[H42]*
  - metabolic disease NOS E88.9 *[H42]*
  - ocular disorders NEC *—see* Glaucoma, secondary
  - onchocerciasis B73.02
  - pupillary block *—see* Glaucoma, secondary
  - retinal vein occlusion *—see* Glaucoma, secondary
  - Rieger's anomaly Q13.81 *[H42]*
  - rubeosis of iris *—see* Glaucoma, secondary
  - tumor of globe *—see* Glaucoma, secondary
- infantile Q15.0
- low tension *—see* Glaucoma, open angle, primary, low-tension
- malignant H40.83-
- narrow angle *—see* Glaucoma, angle-closure
- newborn Q15.0
- noncongestive (chronic) *—see* Glaucoma, open angle
- nonobstructive *—see* Glaucoma, open angle
- obstructive *—see also* Glaucoma, angle-closure
  - due to lens changes *—see* Glaucoma, secondary
- open angle H40.10-
  - primary H40.11-
    - capsular (with pseudoexfoliation of lens) H40.14-
    - low-tension H40.12-
    - pigmentary H40.13-
    - residual stage H40.15-
- phacolytic *—see* Glaucoma, secondary
- pigmentary *—see* Glaucoma, open angle, primary, pigmentary
- postinfectious *—see* Glaucoma, secondary, inflammation
- secondary (to) H40.5-
  - drugs H40.6-
  - inflammation H40.4-
  - trauma H40.3-
- simple (chronic) H40.11
- simplex H40.11
- specified type NEC H40.89
- suspect H40.00-
- syphilitic A52.71
- traumatic *—see also* Glaucoma, secondary, trauma
  - newborn (birth injury) P15.3
- tuberculous A18.59

Glaucomatous flecks (subcapsular) *—see* Cataract, complicated

Glazed tongue K14.4

Gleet (gonococcal) A54.01

Glénard's disease K63.4

Glioblastoma (multiforme)
- with sarcomatous component
  - specified site *—see* Neoplasm, malignant, by site
  - unspecified site C71.9
- giant cell
  - specified site *—see* Neoplasm, malignant, by site
  - unspecified site C71.9
- specified site *—see* Neoplasm, malignant, by site
- unspecified site C71.9

Glioma (malignant)
- astrocytic
  - specified site *—see* Neoplasm, malignant, by site
  - unspecified site C71.9
- mixed
  - specified site *—see* Neoplasm, malignant, by site
  - unspecified site C71.9
- nose Q30.8
- specified site NEC *—see* Neoplasm, malignant, by site
- subependymal D43.2
  - specified site *—see* Neoplasm, uncertain behavior, by site
  - unspecified site D43.2
- unspecified site C71.9

Gliomatosis cerebri C71.0

Glioneuroma *—see* Neoplasm, uncertain behavior, by site

Gliosarcoma
- specified site *—see* Neoplasm, malignant, by site
- unspecified site C71.9

Gliosis (cerebral) G93.89
- spinal G95.89

Glisson's disease *—see* Rickets

Globinuria R82.3

Globus (hystericus) F45.8

Glomangioma D18.00
- intra-abdominal D18.03
- intracranial D18.02
- skin D18.01
- specified site NEC D18.09

Glomangiomyoma D18.00
- intra-abdominal D18.03
- intracranial D18.02
- skin D18.01
- specified site NEC D18.09

Glomangiosarcoma *—see* Neoplasm, connective tissue, malignant

Glomerular
- disease in syphilis A52.75
- nephritis *—see* Glomerulonephritis

Glomerulitis *—see* Glomerulonephritis

Glomerulonephritis *—see also* Nephritis N05.9
- with
  - edema *—see* Nephrosis
  - minimal change N05.0
  - minor glomerular abnormality N05.0
- acute N00.9
- chronic N03.9
- crescentic (diffuse) NEC *—see also* N00-N07 with fourth character .7 N05.7
- dense deposit *—see also* N00-N07 with fourth character .6 N05.6
- diffuse
  - crescentic *—see also* N00-N07 with fourth character .7 N05.7
  - endocapillary proliferative *—see also* N00-N07 with fourth character .4 N05.4
  - membranous *—see also* N00-N07 with fourth character .2 N05.2
  - mesangial proliferative *—see also* N00-N07 with fourth character .3 N05.3
  - mesangiocapillary *—see also* N00-N07 with fourth character .5 N05.5
  - sclerosing N05.8
- endocapillary proliferative (diffuse) NEC *—see also* N00-N07 with fourth character .4 N05.4
- extracapillary NEC *—see also* N00-N07 with fourth character .7 N05.7
- focal (and segmental) *—see also* N00-N07 with fourth character .1 N05.1
- hypocomplementemic *—see* Glomerulonephritis, membranoproliferative
- IgA *—see* Nephropathy, IgA
- immune complex (circulating) NEC N05.8
- in (due to)
  - amyloidosis E85.4 *[N08]*
  - bilharziasis B65.9 *[N08]*
  - cryoglobulinemia D89.1 *[N08]*
  - defibrination syndrome D65 *[N08]*
  - diabetes mellitus *—see* Diabetes, glomerulosclerosis
  - disseminated intravascular coagulation D65 *[N08]*
  - Fabry (-Anderson) disease E75.21 *[N08]*
  - Goodpasture's syndrome M31.0
  - hemolytic-uremic syndrome D59.3
  - Henoch (-Schönlein) purpura D69.0 *[N08]*
  - lecithin cholesterol acyltransferase deficiency E78.6 *[N08]*
  - microscopic polyangiitis M31.7 *[N08]*
  - multiple myeloma C90.0- *[N08]*

- **Glomerulonephritis** *(continued)*
    - Plasmodium malariae B52.0
    - schistosomiasis B65.9 *[N08]*
    - sepsis A41.9 *[N08]*
        - streptococcal A40- *[N08]*
    - sickle-cell disorders D57.- *[N08]*
    - strongyloidiasis B78.9 *[N08]*
    - subacute bacterial endocarditis I33.0 *[N08]*
    - syphilis (late) congenital A50.59 *[N08]*
    - systemic lupus erythematosus M32.14
    - thrombotic thrombocytopenic purpura M31.1 *[N08]*
    - typhoid fever A01.09
    - Waldenström macroglobulinemia C88.0 *[N08]*
    - Wegener's granulomatosis M31.31
  - latent or quiescent N03.9
  - lobular, lobulonodular — *see* Glomerulonephritis, membranoproliferative
  - membranoproliferative (diffuse) (type 1 or 3) —*see also* N00-N07 with fourth character .5 N05.5
    - dense deposit (type 2) NEC —*see also* N00-N07 with fourth character .6 N05.6
  - membranous (diffuse) NEC —*see also* N00-N07 with fourth character .2 N05.2
  - mesangial
    - IgA/IgG —*see* Nephropathy, IgA
    - proliferative (diffuse) NEC —*see also* N00-N07 with fourth character .3 N05.3
  - mesangiocapillary (diffuse) NEC —*see also* N00-N07 with fourth character .5 N05.5
  - necrotic, necrotizing NEC —*see also* N00-N07 with fourth character .8 N05.8
  - nodular —*see* Glomerulonephritis, membranoproliferative
  - poststreptococcal NEC N05.9
    - acute N00.9
    - chronic N03.9
    - rapidly progressive N01.9
  - proliferative NEC —*see also* N00-N07 with fourth character .8 N05.8
    - diffuse (lupus) M32.14
  - rapidly progressive N01.9
  - sclerosing, diffuse N05.8
  - specified pathology NEC —*see also* N00-N07 with fourth character .8 N05.8
  - subacute N01.9
- **Glomerulopathy** —*see* Glomerulonephritis
- **Glomerulosclerosis** —*see also* Sclerosis, renal
  - intercapillary (nodular) (with diabetes) —*see* Diabetes, glomerulosclerosis
  - intracapillary —*see* Diabetes, glomerulosclerosis
- **Glossagra** K14.6
- **Glossalgia** K14.6
- **Glossitis** (chronic superficial) (gangrenous) (Moeller's) K14.0
  - areata exfoliativa K14.1
  - atrophic K14.4
  - benign migratory K14.1
  - cortical superficial, sclerotic K14.0
  - Hunter's D51.0
  - interstitial, sclerous K14.0
  - median rhomboid K14.2
  - pellagrous E52
  - superficial, chronic K14.0
- **Glossocele** K14.8
- **Glossodynia** K14.6
  - exfoliativa K14.4
- **Glossoncus** K14.8
- **Glossopathy** K14.9
- **Glossophytia** K14.3
- **Glossoplegia** K14.8
- **Glossoptosis** K14.8
- **Glossopyrosis** K14.6
- **Glossotrichia** K14.3
- **Glossy skin** L90.8
- **Glottis** —*see* condition
- **Glottitis** —*see also* Laryngitis J04.0
- **Glucagonoma**
  - pancreas
    - benign D13.7
    - malignant C25.4
    - uncertain behavior D37.8
  - specified site NEC
    - benign —*see* Neoplasm, benign, by site
    - malignant —*see* Neoplasm, malignant, by site
    - uncertain behavior —*see* Neoplasm, uncertain behavior, by site
  - unspecified site
    - benign D13.7
    - malignant C25.4
    - uncertain behavior D37.8
- **Glucoglycinuria** E72.51
- **Glucose-galactose malabsorption** E74.39
- **Glue**
  - ear —*see* Otitis, media, nonsuppurative, chronic, mucoid
  - sniffing (airplane) —*see* Abuse, drug, inhalant
    - dependence —*see* Dependence, drug, inhalant
- **Glutaric aciduria** E72.3
- **Glycinemia** E72.51
- **Glycinuria** (renal) (with ketosis) E72.09
- **Glycogen**
  - infiltration —*see* Disease, glycogen storage
  - storage disease —*see* Disease, glycogen storage
- **Glycogenosis** (diffuse) (generalized) —*see also* Disease, glycogen storage
  - cardiac E74.02 *[I43]*
  - diabetic, secondary —*see* Diabetes, glycogenosis, secondary
  - pulmonary interstitial J84.842
- **Glycopenia** E16.2
- **Glycosuria** R81
  - renal E74.8
- **Gnathostoma spinigerum** (infection) (infestation), **gnathostomiasis** (wandering swelling) B83.1
- **Goiter** (plunging) (substernal) E04.9
  - with
    - hyperthyroidism (recurrent) —*see* Hyperthyroidism, with, goiter
    - thyrotoxicosis —*see* Hyperthyroidism, with, goiter
  - adenomatous —*see* Goiter, nodular
  - cancerous C73
  - congenital (nontoxic) E03.0
    - diffuse E03.0
    - parenchymatous E03.0
    - transitory, with normal functioning P72.0
- **Goiter** *(continued)*
  - cystic E04.2
    - due to iodine-deficiency E01.1
  - due to
    - enzyme defect in synthesis of thyroid hormone E07.1
    - iodine-deficiency (endemic) E01.2
  - dyshormonogenetic (familial) E07.1
  - endemic (iodine-deficiency) E01.2
    - diffuse E01.0
    - multinodular E01.1
  - exophthalmic —*see* Hyperthyroidism, with, goiter
  - iodine-deficiency (endemic) E01.2
    - diffuse E01.0
    - multinodular E01.1
    - nodular E01.1
  - lingual Q89.2
  - lymphadenoid E06.3
  - malignant C73
  - multinodular (cystic) (nontoxic) E04.2
    - toxic or with hyperthyroidism E05.20
      - with thyroid storm E05.21
  - neonatal NEC P72.0
  - nodular (nontoxic) (due to) E04.9
    - with
      - hyperthyroidism E05.20
        - with thyroid storm E05.21
      - thyrotoxicosis E05.20
        - with thyroid storm E05.21
    - endemic E01.1
    - iodine-deficiency E01.1
    - sporadic E04.9
    - toxic E05.20
      - with thyroid storm E05.21
  - nontoxic E04.9
    - diffuse (colloid) E04.0
    - multinodular E04.2
    - simple E04.0
    - specified NEC E04.8
    - uninodular E04.1
  - simple E04.0
  - toxic —*see* Hyperthyroidism, with, goiter
  - uninodular (nontoxic) E04.1
    - toxic or with hyperthyroidism E05.10
      - with thyroid storm E05.11
- **Goiter-deafness syndrome** E07.1
- **Goldberg syndrome** Q89.8
- **Goldberg-Maxwell syndrome** E34.51
- **Goldblatt's hypertension or kidney** I70.1
- **Goldenhar** (-Gorlin) **syndrome** Q87.0
- **Goldflam-Erb disease or syndrome** G70.00
  - with exacerbation (acute) G70.01
  - in crisis G70.01
- **Goldscheider's disease** Q81.8
- **Goldstein's disease** (familial hemorrhagic telangiectasia) I78.0
- **Golfer's elbow** —*see* Epicondylitis, medial
- **Gonadoblastoma**
  - specified site —*see* Neoplasm, uncertain behavior, by site
  - unspecified site
    - female D39.10
    - male D40.10
- **Gonecystitis** —*see* Vesiculitis
- **Gongylonemiasis** B83.8
- **Goniosynechiae** —*see* Adhesions, iris, goniosynechiae
- **Gonococcemia** A54.86
- **Gonococcus, gonococcal** (disease) (infection) —*see also* condition A54.9
  - anus A54.6
  - bursa, bursitis A54.49
  - conjunctiva, conjunctivitis (neonatorum) A54.31
  - endocardium A54.83
  - eye A54.30
    - conjunctivitis A54.31
    - iridocyclitis A54.32
    - keratitis A54.33
    - newborn A54.31
    - other specified A54.39
  - fallopian tubes (acute) (chronic) A54.24
  - genitourinary (organ) (system) (tract (acute)
    - lower A54.00
      - with abscess (accessory gland) (periurethral) A54.1
    - upper —*see also* condition A54.29
  - heart A54.83
  - iridocyclitis A54.32
  - joint A54.42
  - lymphatic (gland) (node) A54.89
  - meninges, meningitis A54.81
  - musculoskeletal A54.40
    - arthritis A54.42
    - osteomyelitis A54.43
    - other specified A54.49
    - spondylopathy A54.41
  - pelviperitonitis A54.24
  - pelvis (acute) (chronic) A54.24
  - pharynx A54.5
  - proctitis A54.6
  - pyosalpinx (acute) (chronic) A54.24
  - rectum A54.6
  - skin A54.89
  - specified site NEC A54.89
  - tendon sheath A54.49
  - throat A54.5
  - urethra (acute) (chronic) A54.01
    - with abscess (accessory gland) (periurethral) A54.1
  - vulva (acute) (chronic) A54.02
- **Gonocytoma**
  - specified site —*see* Neoplasm, uncertain behavior, by site
  - unspecified site
    - female D39.10
    - male D40.10
- **Gonorrhea** (acute) (chronic) A54.9
  - Bartholin's gland (acute) (chronic) (purulent) A54.02
    - with abscess (accessory gland) (periurethral) A54.1
  - bladder A54.01
  - cervix A54.03
  - conjunctiva, conjunctivitis (neonatorum) A54.31
  - contact Z20.2
  - Cowper's gland (with abscess) A54.1
  - exposure to Z20.2
  - fallopian tube (acute) (chronic) A54.24
  - kidney (acute) (chronic) A54.21
  - lower genitourinary tract A54.00
    - with abscess (accessory gland) (periurethral) A54.1
  - ovary (acute) (chronic) A54.24
  - pelvis (acute) (chronic) A54.24
    - female pelvic inflammatory disease A54.24
  - penis A54.09
  - prostate (acute) (chronic) A54.22
  - seminal vesicle (acute) (chronic) A54.23
  - specified site not listed —*see also* Gonococcus A54.89

Granuloma *(continued)*
- spine
  - syphilitic (epidural) A52.19
  - tuberculous A18.01
- stitch (postoperative) T81.89
- suppurative (skin) L98.0
- swimming pool A31.1
- talc —*see also* Granuloma, foreign body
  - in operation wound —*see* Foreign body, accidentally left during a procedure
- telangiectaticum (skin) L98.0
- tracheostomy J95.09
- trichophyticum B35.8
- tropicum A66.4
- umbilicus L92.9
- urethra N36.8
- uveitis —*see* Iridocyclitis, chronic
- vagina A58
- venereum A58
- vocal cord J38.3

Granulomatosis L92.9
- lymphoid C83.8-
- miliary (listerial) A32.89
- necrotizing, respiratory M31.30
- progressive septic D71
- specified NEC L92.8
- Wegener's M31.30
  - with renal involvement M31.31

Granulomatous tissue (abnormal) (excessive) L92.9

Granulosis rubra nasi L74.8

Graphite fibrosis (of lung) J63.3

Graphospasm F48.8
- organic G25.89

Grating scapula M89.8X1

Gravel (urinary) —*see* Calculus, urinary

Graves' disease —*see* Hyperthyroidism, with, goiter

Gravis —*see* condition

Grawitz tumor C64.-

Gray syndrome (newborn) P93.0

Grayness, hair (premature) L67.1
- congenital Q84.2

Green sickness D50.8

Greenfield's disease
- meaning
  - concentric sclerosis (encephalitis periaxialis concentrica) G37.5
  - metachromatic leukodystrophy E75.25

Greenstick fracture - code as Fracture, by site

Grey syndrome (newborn) P93.0

Grief F43.21
- prolonged F43.29
- reaction —*see also* Disorder, adjustment F43.20

Griesinger's disease B76.9

Grinder's lung or pneumoconiosis J62.8

Grinding, teeth
- psychogenic F45.8
- sleep related G47.63

Grip
- Dabney's B33.0
- devil's B33.0

Grippe, grippal —*see also* Influenza
- Balkan A78
- summer, of Italy A93.1

Grisel's disease M43.6

Groin —*see* condition

Grooved tongue K14.5

Ground itch B76.9

Grover's disease or syndrome L11.1

Growing pains, children R29.898

Growth (fungoid) (neoplastic) (new) —*see also* Neoplasm
- adenoid (vegetative) J35.8
- benign —*see* Neoplasm, benign, by site
- malignant —*see* Neoplasm, malignant, by site
- rapid, childhood Z00.2
- secondary —*see* Neoplasm, secondary, by site

Gruby's disease B35.0

Gubler-Millard paralysis or syndrome G46.3

Guerin-Stern syndrome Q74.3

Guidance, insufficient anterior (occlusal) M26.54

Guillain-Barré disease or syndrome G61.0
- sequelae G65.0

Guinea worms (infection) (infestation) B72

Guinon's disease (motor-verbal tic) F95.2

Gull's disease E03.4

Gum —*see* condition

Gumboil K04.7
- with sinus K04.6

Gumma (syphilitic) A52.79
- artery A52.09
  - cerebral A52.04
- bone A52.77
  - of yaws (late) A66.6
- brain A52.19
- cauda equina A52.19
- central nervous system A52.3
- ciliary body A52.71
- congenital A50.59
- eyelid A52.71
- heart A52.06
- intracranial A52.19
- iris A52.71
- kidney A52.75
- larynx A52.73
- leptomeninges A52.19
- liver A52.74
- meninges A52.19
- myocardium A52.06
- nasopharynx A52.73
- neurosyphilitic A52.3
- nose A52.73
- orbit A52.71
- palate (soft) A52.79
- penis A52.76
- pericardium A52.06
- pharynx A52.73
- pituitary A52.79
- scrofulous (tuberculous) A18.4
- skin A52.79
- specified site NEC A52.79
- spinal cord A52.19
- tongue A52.79
- tonsil A52.73
- trachea A52.73
- tuberculous A18.4
- ulcerative due to yaws A66.4
- ureter A52.75
- yaws A66.4
  - bone A66.6

Gunn's syndrome Q07.8

Gunshot wound —*see also* Wound, open
- fracture - code as Fracture, by site
- internal organs —*see* Injury, by site

Gynandrism Q56.0

Gynandroblastoma
- specified site —*see* Neoplasm, uncertain behavior, by site
- unspecified site
  - female D39.10
  - male D40.10

Gynecological examination (periodic) (routine) Z01.419
- with abnormal findings Z01.411

Gynecomastia N62

Gynephobia F40.291

Gyrate scalp Q82.8

H

H(Hartnup's) **disease** E72.02

Haas' disease or osteochondrosis (juvenile) (head of humerus) —*see* Osteochondrosis, juvenile, humerus

Habit, habituation
- bad sleep Z72.821
- chorea F95.8
- disturbance, child F98.9
- drug —*see* Dependence, drug
- irregular sleep Z72.821
- laxative F55.2
- spasm —*see* Tic
- tic —*see* Tic

Haemophilus (H.) **influenzae, as cause of disease classified elsewhere** B96.3

Haff disease —*see* Poisoning, mercury

Hageman's factor defect, deficiency or disease D68.2

Haglund's disease or osteochondrosis (juvenile) (os tibiale externum) —*see* Osteochondrosis, juvenile, tarsus

Hailey-Hailey disease Q82.8

Hair —*see also* condition
- plucking F63.3
  - in stereotyped movement disorder F98.4
- tourniquet syndrome —*see also* Constriction, external, by site
  - finger S60.44-
  - penis S30.842
  - thumb S60.34-
  - toe S90.44-

Hairball in stomach T18.2

Hair-pulling, pathological (compulsive) F63.3

Hairy black tongue K14.3

Half vertebra Q76.49

Halitosis R19.6

Hallerman-Streiff syndrome Q87.0

Hallervorden-Spatz disease G23.0

Hallopeau's acrodermatitis or disease L40.2

Hallucination R44.3
- auditory R44.0
- gustatory R44.2
- olfactory R44.2
- specified NEC R44.2
- tactile R44.2
- visual R44.1

Hallucinosis (chronic) F28
- alcoholic (acute) F10.951
  - in
    - abuse F10.151
    - dependence F10.251
- drug-induced F19.951
  - cannabis F12.951
  - cocaine F14.951
  - hallucinogen F16.151

Hallucinosis *(continued)*
- drug-induced *(continued)*
  - in
    - abuse F19.151
      - cannabis F12.151
      - cocaine F14.151
      - hallucinogen F16.151
      - inhalant F18.151
      - opioid F11.151
      - sedative, anxiolytic or hypnotic F13.151
      - stimulant NEC F15.151
    - dependence F19.251
      - cannabis F12.251
      - cocaine F14.251
      - hallucinogen F16.251
      - inhalant F18.251
      - opioid F11.251
      - sedative, anxiolytic or hypnotic F13.251
      - stimulant NEC F15.251
  - inhalant F18.951
  - opioid F11.951
  - sedative, anxiolytic or hypnotic F13.951
  - stimulant NEC F15.951
- organic F06.0

Hallux
- deformity (acquired) NEC M20.5X-
- limitus M20.5X-
- malleus (acquired) NEC M20.3-
- rigidus (acquired) M20.2-
  - congenital Q74.2
  - sequelae (late effect) of rickets E64.3
- valgus (acquired) M20.1-
  - congenital Q66.6
- varus (acquired) M20.3-
  - congenital Q66.3

Halo, visual H53.19

Hamartoma, hamartoblastoma Q85.9
- epithelial (gingival), odontogenic, central or peripheral —*see* Cyst, calcifying odontogenic

Hamartosis Q85.9

Hamman-Rich syndrome J84.114

Hammer toe (acquired) **NEC** —*see also* Deformity, toe, hammer toe
- congenital Q66.89
- sequelae (late effect) of rickets E64.3

Hand —*see* condition

Hand-foot syndrome L27.1

Handicap, handicapped
- educational Z55.9
  - specified NEC Z55.8

Hand-Schüller-Christian disease or syndrome C96.5

Hanging (asphyxia) (strangulation) (suffocation) —*see* Asphyxia, traumatic, due to mechanical threat

Hangnail —*see also* Cellulitis, digit
- with lymphangitis —*see* Lymphangitis, acute, digit

Hangover (alcohol) F10.129

Hanhart's syndrome Q87.0

Hanot-Chauffard (-Troisier) **syndrome** E83.19

Hanot's cirrhosis or disease K74.3

Hansen's disease —*see* Leprosy

Hantaan virus disease (Korean hemorrhagic fever) A98.5

Hantavirus disease (with renal manifestations) (Dobrava) (Puumala) (Seoul) A98.5
- with pulmonary manifestations (Andes) (Bayou) (Bermejo) (Black Creek Canal) (Choclo) (Juquitiba) (Laguna negra) (Lechiguanas) (New York) (Oran) (Sin nombre) B33.4

Happy puppet syndrome Q93.5

Harada's disease or syndrome H30.81-

Hardening
- artery —*see* Arteriosclerosis
- brain G93.89

Harelip (complete) (incomplete) —*see* Cleft, lip

Harlequin (newborn) Q80.4

Harley's disease D59.6

Harmful use (of)
- alcohol F10.10
- anxiolytics —*see* Abuse, drug, sedative
- cannabinoids —*see* Abuse, drug, cannabis
- cocaine —*see* Abuse, drug, cocaine
- drug —*see* Abuse, drug
- hallucinogens —*see* Abuse, drug, hallucinogen
- hypnotics —*see* Abuse, drug, sedative
- opioids —*see* Abuse, drug, opioid
- PCP (phencyclidine) —*see* Abuse, drug, hallucinogen
- sedatives —*see* Abuse, drug, sedative
- stimulants NEC —*see* Abuse, drug, stimulant

Harris' lines —*see* Arrest, epiphyseal

Hartnup's disease E72.02

Harvester's lung J67.0

Harvesting ovum for in vitro fertilization Z31.83

Hashimoto's disease or thyroiditis E06.3

Hashitoxicosis (transient) E06.3

Hassal-Henle bodies or warts (cornea) H18.49

Haut mal —*see* Epilepsy, generalized, specified NEC

Haverhill fever A25.1

Hay fever —*see also* Fever, hay J30.1

Hayem-Widal syndrome D59.8

Haygarth's nodes M15.8

Haymaker's lung J67.0

Hb (abnormal)
- Bart's disease D56.0
- disease —*see* Disease, hemoglobin
- trait —*see* Trait

Head —*see* condition

Headache R51
- allergic NEC G44.89
- associated with sexual activity G44.82
- chronic daily R51
- cluster G44.009
  - chronic G44.029
    - intractable G44.021
    - not intractable G44.029
  - episodic G44.019
    - intractable G44.011
    - not intractable G44.019
  - intractable G44.001
  - not intractable G44.009
- cough (primary) G44.83
- daily chronic R51

Headache *(continued)*
- drug-induced NEC G44.40
  - intractable G44.41
  - not intractable G44.40
- exertional (primary) G44.84
- histamine G44.009
  - intractable G44.001
  - not intractable G44.009
- hypnic G44.81
- lumbar puncture G97.1
- medication overuse G44.40
  - intractable G44.41
  - not intractable G44.40
- menstrual —*see* Migraine, menstrual
- migraine (type) —*see also* Migraine G43.909
- nasal septum R51
- neuralgiform, short lasting unilateral, with conjunctival injection and tearing (SUNCT) G44.059
  - intractable G44.051
  - not intractable G44.059
- new daily persistent (NDPH) G44.52
- orgasmic G44.82
- periodic syndromes in adults and children G43.C0
  - with refractory migraine G43.C1
  - intractable G43.C1
  - not intractable G43.C0
  - without refractory migraine G43.C0
- postspinal puncture G97.1
- post-traumatic G44.309
  - acute G44.319
    - intractable G44.311
    - not intractable G44.319
  - chronic G44.329
    - intractable G44.321
    - not intractable G44.329
  - intractable G44.301
  - not intractable G44.309
- pre-menstrual —*see* Migraine, menstrual
- preorgasmic G44.82
- primary
  - cough G44.83
  - exertional G44.84
  - stabbing G44.85
  - thunderclap G44.53
- rebound G44.40
  - intractable G44.41
  - not intractable G44.40
- short lasting unilateral neuralgiform, with conjunctival injection and tearing (SUNCT) G44.059
  - intractable G44.051
  - not intractable G44.059
- specified syndrome NEC G44.89
- spinal and epidural anesthesia - induced T88.59
  - in labor and delivery O74.5
  - in pregnancy O29.4-
  - postpartum, puerperal O89.4
- spinal fluid loss (from puncture) G97.1
- stabbing (primary) G44.85
- tension (-type) G44.209
  - chronic G44.229
    - intractable G44.221
    - not intractable G44.229
  - episodic G44.219
    - intractable G44.211
    - not intractable G44.219
  - intractable G44.201
  - not intractable G44.209
- thunderclap (primary) G44.53
- vascular NEC G44.1

Healthy
- infant
  - accompanying sick mother Z76.3
  - receiving care Z76.2
- person accompanying sick person Z76.3

Hearing examination Z01.10
- with abnormal findings NEC Z01.118
- following failed hearing screening Z01.110
- for hearing conservation and treatment Z01.12

Heart —*see* condition

Heart beat
- abnormality R00.9
  - specified NEC R00.8
- awareness R00.2
- rapid R00.0
- slow R00.1

Heartburn R12
- psychogenic F45.8

Heat (effects) T67.9
- apoplexy T67.0
- burn —*see also* Burn L55.9
- collapse T67.1
- cramps T67.2
- dermatitis or eczema L59.0
- edema T67.7
- erythema - code by site under Burn, first degree
- excessive T67.9
  - specified effect NEC T67.8
- exhaustion T67.5
  - anhydrotic T67.3
  - due to
    - salt (and water) depletion T67.4
    - water depletion T67.3
      - with salt depletion T67.4
- fatigue (transient) T67.6
- fever T67.0
- hyperpyrexia T67.0
- prickly L74.0
- prostration —*see* Heat, exhaustion
- pyrexia T67.0
- rash L74.0
- specified effect NEC T67.8
- stroke T67.0
- sunburn —*see* Sunburn
- syncope T67.1

Heavy-for-dates NEC (infant) (4000g to 4499g) P08.1
- exceptionally (4500g or more) P08.0

Hebephrenia, hebephrenic (schizophrenia) F20.1

Heberden's disease or nodes (with arthropathy) M15.1

Hebra's
- pityriasis L26
- prurigo L28.2

Heel —*see* condition

Heerfordt's disease D86.89

Hegglin's anomaly or syndrome D72.0

Heilmeyer-Schoner disease D45

Heine-Medin disease A80.9

Heinz body anemia, congenital D58.2

Heliophobia F40.228

Heller's disease or syndrome F84.3

HELLP syndrome (hemolysis, elevated liver enzymes and low platelet count) O14.2-

Helminthiasis —*see also* Infestation, helminth
- Ancylostoma B76.0
- intestinal B82.0
  - mixed types (types classifiable to more than one of the titles B65.0-B81.3 and B81.8) B81.4
  - specified type NEC B81.8
- mixed types (intestinal) (types classifiable to more than one of the titles B65.0-B81.3 and B81.8) B81.4

Helminthiasis *(continued)*
- Necator (americanus) B76.1
- specified type NEC B83.8

Heloma L84

Hemangioblastoma —*see* Neoplasm, connective tissue, uncertain behavior
- malignant —*see* Neoplasm, connective tissue, malignant

Hemangioendothelioma —*see also* Neoplasm, uncertain behavior, by site
- benign D18.00
  - intra-abdominal D18.03
  - intracranial D18.02
  - skin D18.01
  - specified site NEC D18.09
- bone (diffuse) —*see* Neoplasm, bone, malignant
- epithelioid —*see also* Neoplasm, uncertain behavior, by site
  - malignant —*see* Neoplasm, malignant, by site
- malignant —*see* Neoplasm, connective tissue, malignant

Hemangiofibroma —*see* Neoplasm, benign, by site

Hemangiolipoma —*see* Lipoma

Hemangioma D18.00
- arteriovenous D18.00
  - intra-abdominal D18.03
  - intracranial D18.02
  - skin D18.01
  - specified site NEC D18.09
- capillary D18.00
  - intra-abdominal D18.03
  - intracranial D18.02
  - skin D18.01
  - specified site NEC D18.09
- cavernous D18.00
  - intra-abdominal D18.03
  - intracranial D18.02
  - skin D18.01
  - specified site NEC D18.09
- epithelioid D18.00
  - intra-abdominal D18.03
  - intracranial D18.02
  - skin D18.01
  - specified site NEC D18.09
- histiocytoid D18.00
  - intra-abdominal D18.03
  - intracranial D18.02
  - skin D18.01
  - specified site NEC D18.09
- infantile D18.00
  - intra-abdominal D18.03
  - intracranial D18.02
  - skin D18.01
  - specified site NEC D18.09
- intra-abdominal D18.03
- intracranial D18.02
- intramuscular D18.00
  - intra-abdominal D18.03
  - intracranial D18.02
  - skin D18.01
  - specified site NEC D18.09
- juvenile D18.00
- malignant —*see* Neoplasm,connective tissue, malignant
- plexiform D18.00
  - intra-abdominal D18.03
  - intracranial D18.02
  - skin D18.01
  - specified site NEC D18.09
- racemose D18.00
  - intra-abdominal D18.03
  - intracranial D18.02
  - skin D18.01
  - specified site NEC D18.09
- sclerosing —*see* Neoplasm,skin, benign

Hemangioma *(continued)*
  simplex D18.00
    intra-abdominal D18.03
    intracranial D18.02
    skin D18.01
    specified site NEC D18.09
  skin D18.01
  specified site NEC D18.09
  venous D18.00
    intra-abdominal D18.03
    intracranial D18.02
    skin D18.01
    specified site NEC D18.09
  verrucous keratotic D18.00
    intra-abdominal D18.03
    intracranial D18.02
    skin D18.01
    specified site NEC D18.09

Hemangiomatosis (systemic) I78.8
  involving single site —*see* Hemangioma

Hemangiopericytoma —*see also* Neoplasm, connective tissue, uncertain behavior
  benign —*see* Neoplasm, connective tissue, benign
  malignant —*see* Neoplasm, connective tissue, malignant

Hemangiosarcoma —*see* Neoplasm, connective tissue, malignant

Hemarthrosis (nontraumatic) M25.00
  ankle M25.07-
  elbow M25.02-
  foot joint M25.07-
  hand joint M25.04-
  hip M25.05-
  in hemophilic arthropathy —*see* Arthropathy, hemophilic
  knee M25.06-
  shoulder M25.01-
  specified joint NEC M25.08
  traumatic —*see* Sprain, by site
  vertebrae M25.08
  wrist M25.03-

Hematemesis K92.0
  with ulcer - code by site under Ulcer, with hemorrhage K27.4
  newborn, neonatal P54.0
    due to swallowed maternal blood P78.2

Hematidrosis L74.8

Hematinuria —*see also* Hemoglobinuria
  malarial B50.8

Hematobilia K83.8

Hematocele
  female NEC N94.89
    with ectopic pregnancy O00.9
    ovary N83.8
  male N50.1

Hematochezia —*see also* Melena K92.1

Hematochyluria —*see also* Infestation, filarial
  schistosomiasis (bilharziasis) B65.0

Hematocolpos (with hematometra or hematosalpinx) N89.7

Hematocornea —*see* Pigmentation, cornea, stromal

Hematogenous —*see* condition

Hematoma (traumatic) (skin surface intact) —*see also* Contusion
  with
    injury of internal organs —*see* Injury, by site
    open wound —*see* Wound, open

Hematoma *(continued)*
  amputation stump (surgical) (late) T87.89
  aorta, dissecting I71.00
    abdominal I71.02
    thoracic I71.01
    thoracoabdominal I71.03
  aortic intramural —*see* Dissection, aorta
  arterial (complicating trauma) —*see* Injury, blood vessel, by site
  auricle —*see* Contusion, ear
    nontraumatic —*see* Disorder, pinna, hematoma
  birth injury NEC P15.8
  brain (traumatic)
    with
      cerebral laceration or contusion (diffuse) —*see* Injury, intracranial, diffuse
        focal —*see* Injury, intracranial, focal
    cerebellar, traumatic S06.37-
    newborn NEC P52.4
      birth injury P10.1
    intracerebral, traumatic —*see* Injury, intracranial, intracerebral hemorrhage
    nontraumatic —*see* Hemorrhage, intracranial
    subarachnoid, arachnoid, traumatic —*see* Injury, intracranial, subarachnoid hemorrhage
    subdural, traumatic —*see* Injury, intracranial, subdural hemorrhage
  breast (nontraumatic) N64.89
  broad ligament (nontraumatic) N83.7
    traumatic S37.892
  cerebellar, traumatic S06.37-
  cerebral —*see* Hematoma, brain
  cerebrum S06.36-
    left S06.35-
    right S06.34-
  cesarean delivery wound O90.2
  complicating delivery (perineal) (pelvic) (vagina) (vulva) O71.7
  corpus cavernosum (nontraumatic) N48.89
  epididymis (nontraumatic) N50.1
  epidural (traumatic) —*see* Injury, intracranial, epidural hemorrhage
    spinal —*see* Injury, spinal cord, by region
  episiotomy O90.2
  face, birth injury P15.4
  genital organ NEC (nontraumatic)
    female (nonobstetric) N94.89
      traumatic S30.202
    male N50.1
      traumatic S30.201
  internal organs —*see* Injury, by site
  intracerebral, traumatic —*see* Injury, intracranial, intracerebral hemorrhage
  intraoperative —*see* Complications, intraoperative, hemorrhage
  labia (nontraumatic) (nonobstetric) N90.89
  liver (subcapsular) (nontraumatic) K76.89
    birth injury P15.0
  mediastinum —*see* Injury, intrathoracic
  mesosalpinx (nontraumatic) N83.7
    traumatic S37.898
  muscle - code by site under Contusion
  nontraumatic
    muscle M79.81
    soft tissue M79.81
  obstetrical surgical wound O90.2

  orbit, orbital (nontraumatic) —*see also* Hemorrhage, orbit
    traumatic —*see* Contusion, orbit
  pelvis (female) (nontraumatic) (nonobstetric) N94.89
    obstetric O71.7
    traumatic —*see* Injury, by site
  penis (nontraumatic) N48.89
    birth injury P15.5
  perianal (nontraumatic) K64.5
  perineal S30.23
    complicating delivery O71.7
  perirenal —*see* Injury, kidney
  pinna —*see* Contusion, ear
    nontraumatic —*see* Disorder, pinna, hematoma
  placenta O43.89-
  postoperative (postprocedural) —*see* Complication, postprocedural, hemorrhage
  retroperitoneal (nontraumatic) K66.1
    traumatic S36.892
  scrotum, superficial S30.22
    birth injury P15.5
  seminal vesicle (nontraumatic) N50.1
    traumatic S37.892
  spermatic cord (traumatic) S37.892
    nontraumatic N50.1
  spinal (cord) (meninges) —*see also* Injury, spinal cord, by region
    newborn (birth injury) P11.5
  spleen D73.5
    intraoperative —*see* Complications, intraoperative, hemorrhage, spleen
    postprocedural (postoperative) —*see* Complications, postprocedural, hemorrhage, spleen
  sternocleidomastoid, birth injury P15.2
  sternomastoid, birth injury P15.2
  subarachnoid (traumatic) —*see* Injury, intracranial, subarachnoid hemorrhage
    newborn (nontraumatic) P52.5
      due to birth injury P10.3
    nontraumatic —*see* Hemorrhage, intracranial, subarachnoid
  subdural (traumatic) —*see* Injury, intracranial, subdural hemorrhage
    newborn (localized) P52.8
      birth injury P10.0
    nontraumatic —*see* Hemorrhage, intracranial, subdural
  superficial, newborn P54.5
  testis (nontraumatic) N50.1
    birth injury P15.5
  tunica vaginalis (nontraumatic) N50.1
  umbilical cord, complicating delivery O69.5
  uterine ligament (broad) (nontraumatic) N83.7
    traumatic S37.892
  vagina (ruptured) (nontraumatic) N89.8
    complicating delivery O71.7
  vas deferens (nontraumatic) N50.1
    traumatic S37.892
  vitreous —*see* Hemorrhage, vitreous
  vulva (nontraumatic) (nonobstetric) N90.89
    complicating delivery O71.7
    newborn (birth injury) P15.5

Hematometra N85.7
  with hematocolpos N89.7

Hematomyelia (central) G95.19
  newborn (birth injury) P11.5
  traumatic T14.8

Hematomyelitis G04.90

  Hemoperitoneum

Hematophobia F40.230

Hematopneumothorax (*see* Hemothorax)

Hematopoiesis, cyclic D70.4

Hematoporphyria —*see* Porphyria

Hematorachis, hematorrhachis G95.
  newborn (birth injury) P11.5

Hematosalpinx N83.6
  with
    hematocolpos N89.7
    hematometra N85.7
      with hematocolpos N89.7
  infectional —*see* Salpingitis

Hematospermia R36.1

Hematothorax (see Hemothorax)

Hematuria R31.9
  due to sulphonamide, sulfonamide *see* Table of Drugs and Chemica by drug
  benign (familial) (of childhood) — *also* Hematuria, idiopathic
    essential microscopic R31.1
  endemic —*see also* Schistosomias B65.0
  gross R31.0
  idiopathic N02.9
    with glomerular lesion
      crescentic (diffuse) glomerulonephritis N02.7
      dense deposit disease N02.6
      endocapillary proliferative glomerulonephritis N02.4
      focal and segmental hyalinos or sclerosis N02.1
      membranoproliferative (diffu N02.5
      membranous (diffuse) N02.2
      mesangial proliferative (diffu N02.3
      mesangiocapillary (diffuse) N02.5
      minor abnormality N02.0
      proliferative NEC N02.8
      specified pathology NEC NC
  intermittent —*see* Hematuria, idiopathic
  malarial B50.8
  microscopic NEC R31.2
    benign essential R31.1
  paroxysmal —*see also* Hematuri idiopathic
    nocturnal D59.5
  persistent —*see* Hematuria, idiopathic
  recurrent —*see* Hematuria, idiop
  tropical —*see also* Schistosomia B65.0
  tuberculous A18.13

Hemeralopia (day blindness) H53
  vitamin A deficiency E50.5

Hemi-akinesia R41.4

Hemianalgesia R20.0

Hemianencephaly Q00.0

Hemianesthesia R20.0

Hemianopia, hemianopsia (heteronymous) H53.47
  homonymous H53.46-
  syphilitic A52.71

Hemiathetosis R25.8

Hemiatrophy R68.89
  cerebellar G31.9
  face, facial, progressive (Rombe G51.8
  tongue K14.8

Hemiballism (us) G25.5

Hemicardia Q24.8

Hemicephalus, hemicephaly Q00.0

Hemichorea G25.5

Hemicolitis, left —*see* Colitis, left sided

Hemicrania
- congenital malformation Q00.0
- continua G44.51
- meaning migraine —*see also* Migraine G43.909
- paroxysmal G44.039
  - chronic G44.049
    - intractable G44.041
    - not intractable G44.049
  - episodic G44.039
    - intractable G44.031
    - not intractable G44.039
  - intractable G44.031
  - not intractable G44.039

Hemidystrophy —*see* Hemiatrophy

Hemiectromelia Q73.8

Hemihypalgesia R20.8

Hemihypesthesia R20.1

Hemi-inattention R41.4

Hemimelia Q73.8
- lower limb —*see* Defect, reduction, lower limb, specified type NEC
- upper limb —*see* Defect, reduction, upper limb, specified type NEC

Hemiparalysis —*see* Hemiplegia

Hemiparesis —*see* Hemiplegia

Hemiparesthesia R20.2

Hemiparkinsonism G20

Hemiplegia G81.9-
- alternans facialis G83.89
- ascending NEC G81.90
  - spinal G95.89
- congenital (cerebral) G80.8
  - spastic G80.2
- embolic (current episode) I63.4-
- flaccid G81.0-
- following
  - cerebrovascular disease I69.959
    - cerebral infarction I69.35-
    - intracerebral hemorrhage I69.15-
    - nontraumatic intracranial hemorrhage NEC I69.25-
    - specified disease NEC I69.85-
    - stroke NOS I69.35-
    - subarachnoid hemorrhage I69.05-
- hysterical F44.4
- newborn NEC P91.8
  - birth injury P11.9
- spastic G81.1-
  - congenital G80.2
- thrombotic (current episode) I63.3

Hemisection, spinal cord —*see* Injury, spinal cord, by region

Hemispasm (facial) R25.2

Hemisporosis B48.8

Hemitremor R25.1

Hemivertebra Q76.49
- failure of segmentation with scoliosis Q76.3
- fusion with scoliosis Q76.3

Hemochromatosis E83.119
- with refractory anemia D46.1
- due to repeated red blood cell transfusion E83.111
- hereditary (primary) E83.110
- primary E83.110
- specified NEC E83.118

Hemoglobin —*see also* condition
- abnormal (disease) —*see* Disease, hemoglobin
- AS genotype D57.3
- Constant Spring D58.2
- E-beta thalassemia D56.5
- fetal, hereditary persistence (HPFH) D56.4
- H Constant Spring D56.0
- low NOS D64.9
- S(Hb S), heterozygous D57.3

Hemoglobinemia D59.9
- due to blood transfusion T80.89
- paroxysmal D59.6
  - nocturnal D59.5

Hemoglobinopathy (mixed) D58.2
- with thalassemia D56.8
- sickle-cell D57.1
  - with thalassemia D57.40
    - with crisis (vasoocclusive pain) D57.419
      - with
        - acute chest syndrome D57.411
        - splenic sequestration D57.412
    - without crisis D57.40

Hemoglobinuria R82.3
- with anemia, hemolytic, acquired (chronic) NEC D59.6
- cold (agglutinin) (paroxysmal) (with Raynaud's syndrome) D59.6
- due to exertion or hemolysis NEC D59.6
- intermittent D59.6
- malarial B50.8
- march D59.6
- nocturnal (paroxysmal) D59.5
- paroxysmal (cold) D59.6
  - nocturnal D59.5

Hemolymphangioma D18.1

Hemolysis
- intravascular
  - with
    - abortion —*see* Abortion, by type, complicated by, hemorrhage
    - ectopic or molar pregnancy O08.1
    - hemorrhage
      - antepartum —*see* Hemorrhage, antepartum, with coagulation defect
      - intrapartum —*see also* Hemorrhage, complicating, delivery O67.0
  - postpartum O72.3
- neonatal (excessive) P58.9
  - specified NEC P58.8

Hemolytic —*see* condition

Hemopericardium I31.2
- following acute myocardial infarction (current complication) I23.0
- newborn P54.8
- traumatic —*see* Injury, heart, with hemopericardium

Hemoperitoneum K66.1
- infectional K65.9
- traumatic S36.899
  - with open wound —*see* Wound, open, with penetration into peritoneal cavity

Hemophilia (classical) (familial) (hereditary) D66
- A D66
- B D67
- C D68.1
- acquired D68.311
- autoimmune D68.311

Hemophilia
- calcipriva —*see also* Defect, coagulation D68.4
- nonfamilial —*see also* Defect, coagulation D68.4
- secondary D68.311
- vascular D68.0

Hemophthalmos H44.81-

Hemopneumothorax —*see also* Hemothorax
- traumatic S27.2

Hemoptysis R04.2
- newborn P26.9
- tuberculous —*see* Tuberculosis, pulmonary

Hemorrhage, hemorrhagic
- (concealed) R58
- abdomen R58
- accidental antepartum —*see* Hemorrhage, antepartum
- acute idiopathic pulmonary, in infants R04.81
- adenoid J35.8
- adrenal (capsule) (gland) E27.49
  - medulla E27.8
  - newborn P54.4
- after delivery —*see* Hemorrhage, postpartum
- alveolar
  - lung, newborn P26.8
  - process K08.8
- alveolus K08.8
- amputation stump (surgical) T87.89
- anemia (chronic) D50.0
  - acute D62
- antepartum (with) O46.90
  - with coagulation defect O46.00-
    - afibrinogenemia O46.01-
    - disseminated intravascular coagulation O46.02-
    - hypofibrinogenemia O46.01-
    - specified defect NEC O46.09-
  - before 20 weeks gestation O20.9
    - specified type NEC O20.8
    - threatened abortion O20.0
  - due to
    - abruptio placenta —*see also* Abruptio placentae O45.9-
    - leiomyoma, uterus —*see* Hemorrhage, antepartum, specified cause NEC
    - placenta previa O44.1-
  - specified cause NEC O46.8X-
- anus (sphincter) K62.5
- apoplexy (stroke) —*see* Hemorrhage, intracranial, intracerebral
- arachnoid —*see* Hemorrhage, intracranial, subarachnoid
- artery R58
  - brain —*see* Hemorrhage, intracranial, intracerebral
- basilar (ganglion) I61.0
- bladder N32.89
- bowel K92.2
  - newborn P54.3
- brain (miliary) (nontraumatic) —*see* Hemorrhage, intracranial, intracerebral
  - due to
    - birth injury P10.1
    - syphilis A52.05
  - epidural or extradural (traumatic) —*see* Injury, intracranial, epidural hemorrhage
  - newborn P52.4
    - birth injury P10.1
  - subarachnoid —*see* Hemorrhage, intracranial, subarachnoid
  - subdural —*see* Hemorrhage, intracranial, subdural

Hemorrhage, hemorrhagic *(continued)*
- brainstem (nontraumatic) I61.3
  - traumatic S06.38-
- breast N64.59
- bronchial tube —*see* Hemorrhage, lung
- bronchopulmonary —*see* Hemorrhage, lung
- bronchus —*see* Hemorrhage, lung
- bulbar I61.5
- capillary I78.8
  - primary D69.8
- cecum K92.2
- cerebellar, cerebellum (nontraumatic) I61.4
  - newborn P52.6
  - traumatic S06.37-
- cerebral, cerebrum —*see also* Hemorrhage, intracranial, intracerebral
  - newborn (anoxic) P52.4
    - birth injury P10.1
  - lobe I61.1
- cerebromeningeal I61.8
- cerebrospinal —*see* Hemorrhage, intracranial, intracerebral
- cervix (uteri) (stump) NEC N88.8
- chamber, anterior (eye) —*see* Hyphema
- childbirth —*see* Hemorrhage, complicating, delivery
- choroid H31.30-
  - expulsive H31.31-
- ciliary body —*see* Hyphema
- cochlea —*see* subcategory H83.8
- colon K92.2
- complicating
  - abortion —*see* Abortion, by type, complicated by, hemorrhage
  - delivery O67.9
    - associated with coagulation defect (afibrinogenemia) (DIC) (hyperfibrinolysis) O67.0
    - specified cause NEC O67.8
  - surgical procedure —*see* Hemorrhage, intraoperative
- conjunctiva H11.3-
  - newborn P54.8
- cord, newborn (stump) P51.9
- corpus luteum (ruptured) cyst N83.1
- cortical (brain) I61.1
- cranial —*see* Hemorrhage, intracranial
- cutaneous R23.3
  - due to autosensitivity, erythrocyte D69.2
  - newborn P54.5
- delayed
  - following ectopic or molar pregnancy O08.1
  - postpartum O72.2
- diathesis (familial) D69.9
- disease D69.9
  - newborn P53
  - specified type NEC D69.8
- due to or associated with
  - afibrinogenemia or other coagulation defect (conditions in categories D65-D69)
    - antepartum —*see* Hemorrhage, antepartum, with coagulation defect
    - intrapartum O67.0
  - dental implant M27.61
  - device, implant or graft —*see also* Complications, by site and type, specified NEC T85.83
    - arterial graft NEC T82.838
    - breast T85.83

Hemorrhage, hemorrhagic *(continued)*
- due to or associated with *(continued)*
  - device, implant or graft —*see also* Complications, by site and type, specified NEC *(continued)*
    - catheter NEC T85.83
      - dialysis (renal) T82.838
        - intraperitoneal T85.83
      - infusion NEC T82.838
        - spinal (epidural) (subdural) T85.83
      - urinary (indwelling) T83.83
    - electronic (electrode) (pulse generator) (stimulator)
      - bone T84.83
      - cardiac T82.837
      - nervous system (brain) (peripheral nerve) (spinal) T85.83
      - urinary T83.83
    - fixation, internal (orthopedic) NEC T84.83
    - gastrointestinal (bile duct) (esophagus) T85.83
    - genital NEC T83.83
    - heart NEC T82.837
    - joint prosthesis T84.83
    - ocular (corneal graft) (orbital implant) NEC T85.83
    - orthopedic NEC T84.83
      - bone graft T86.838
    - specified NEC T85.83
    - urinary NEC T83.83
    - vascular NEC T82.838
    - ventricular intracranial shunt T85.83
- duodenum, duodenal K92.2
  - ulcer —*see* Ulcer, duodenum, with hemorrhage
- dura mater —*see* Hemorrhage, intracranial, subdural
- endotracheal —*see* Hemorrhage, lung
- epicranial subaponeurotic (massive), birth injury P12.2
- epidural (traumatic) —*see also* Injury, intracranial, epidural hemorrhage
  - nontraumatic I62.1
- esophagus K22.8
  - varix I85.01
    - secondary I85.11
- excessive, following ectopic gestation (subsequent episode) O08.1
- extradural (traumatic) —*see* Injury, intracranial, epidural hemorrhage
  - birth injury P10.8
  - newborn (anoxic) (nontraumatic) P52.8
  - nontraumatic I62.1
- eye NEC H57.8
  - fundus —*see* Hemorrhage, retina
  - lid —*see* Disorder, eyelid, specified type NEC
- fallopian tube N83.6
- fibrinogenolysis —*see* Fibrinolysis
- fibrinolytic (acquired) —*see* Fibrinolysis
- from
  - ear (nontraumatic) —*see* Otorrhagia
  - tracheostomy stoma J95.01
- fundus, eye —*see* Hemorrhage, retina
- funis —*see* Hemorrhage, umbilicus, cord
- gastric —*see* Hemorrhage, stomach
- gastroenteric K92.2
  - newborn P54.3
- gastrointestinal (tract) K92.2
  - newborn P54.3
- genital organ, male N50.1
- genitourinary (tract) NOS R31.9
- gingiva K06.8
- globe (eye) —*see* Hemophthalmos

Hemorrhage, hemorrhagic *(continued)*
- graafian follicle cyst (ruptured) N83.0
- gum K06.8
- heart I51.89
- hypopharyngeal (throat) R04.1
- intermenstrual (regular) N92.3
  - irregular N92.1
- internal (organs) NEC R58
  - capsule I61.0
  - ear H83.8
  - newborn P54.8
- intestine K92.2
  - newborn P54.3
- intra-abdominal R58
- intra-alveolar (lung), newborn P26.8
- intracerebral (nontraumatic) —*see* Hemorrhage, intracranial, intracerebral
- intracranial (nontraumatic) I62.9
  - birth injury P10.9
  - epidural, nontraumatic I62.1
  - extradural, nontraumatic I62.1
  - newborn P52.9
    - specified NEC P52.8
  - intracerebral (nontraumatic) (in) I61.9
    - brain stem I61.3
    - cerebellum I61.4
    - newborn P52.4
      - birth injury P10.1
    - hemisphere I61.2
      - cortical (superficial) I61.1
      - subcortical (deep) I61.0
    - intraoperative
      - during a nervous system procedure G97.31
      - during other procedure G97.32
    - intraventricular I61.5
    - multiple localized I61.6
    - postprocedural
      - following a nervous system procedure G97.51
      - following other procedure G97.52
    - specified NEC I61.8
    - superficial I61.1
    - traumatic (diffuse) —*see* Injury, intracranial, diffuse
      - focal —*see* Injury, intracranial, focal
  - subarachnoid (nontraumatic) (from) I60.9
    - newborn P52.5
      - birth injury P10.3
    - intracranial (cerebral) artery I60.7
      - anterior communicating I60.2-
      - basilar I60.4
      - carotid siphon and bifurcation I60.0-
      - communicating I60.7
        - anterior I60.2-
        - posterior I60.3-
      - middle cerebral I60.1-
      - posterior communicating I60.3-
      - specified artery NEC I60.6
      - vertebral I60.5-
    - specified NEC I60.8
    - traumatic S06.6X-
  - subdural (nontraumatic) I62.00
    - acute I62.01
    - birth injury P10.0
    - chronic I62.03
    - newborn (anoxic) (hypoxic) P52.8
      - birth injury P10.0
    - spinal G95.19
    - subacute I62.02
    - traumatic —*see* Injury, intracranial, subdural hemorrhage
  - traumatic —*see* Injury, intracranial, focal brain injury

Hemorrhage, hemorrhagic *(continued)*
- intramedullary NEC G95.19
- intraocular —*see* Hemophthalmos
- intraoperative, intraprocedural —*see* Complication, hemorrhage (hematoma), intraoperative (intraprocedural), by site
- intrapartum —*see* Hemorrhage, complicating, delivery
- intrapelvic
  - female N94.89
  - male K66.1
- intraperitoneal K66.1
- intrapontine I61.3
- intraprocedural —*see* Complication, hemorrhage (hematoma), intraoperative (intraprocedural), by site
- intrauterine N85.7
  - complicating delivery —*see also* Hemorrhage, complicating, delivery O67.9
  - postpartum —*see* Hemorrhage, postpartum
- intraventricular I61.5
  - newborn (nontraumatic) —*see also* Newborn, affected by, hemorrhage P52.3
    - due to birth injury P10.2
    - grade
      - 1 P52.0
      - 2 P52.1
      - 3 P52.21
      - 4 P52.22
- intravesical N32.89
- iris (postinfectional) (postinflammatory) (toxic) —*see* Hyphema
- joint (nontraumatic) —*see* Hemarthrosis
- kidney N28.89
- knee (joint) (nontraumatic) —*see* Hemarthrosis, knee
- labyrinth —*see* subcategory H83.8
- lenticular striate artery I61.0
- ligature, vessel —*see* Hemorrhage, postoperative
- liver K76.89
- lung R04.89
  - newborn P26.9
    - massive P26.1
    - specified NEC P26.8
  - tuberculous —*see* Tuberculosis, pulmonary
- massive umbilical, newborn P51.0
- mediastinum —*see* Hemorrhage, lung
- medulla I61.3
- membrane (brain) I60.8
  - spinal cord —*see* Hemorrhage, spinal cord
- meninges, meningeal (brain) (middle) I60.8
  - spinal cord —*see* Hemorrhage, spinal cord
- mesentery K66.1
- metritis —*see* Endometritis
- mouth K13.79
- mucous membrane NEC R58
  - newborn P54.8
- muscle M62.89
- nail (subungual) L60.8
- nasal turbinate R04.0
  - newborn P54.8
- navel, newborn P51.9
- newborn P54.9
  - specified NEC P54.8
- nipple N64.59
- nose R04.0
  - newborn P54.8
- omentum K66.1
- optic nerve (sheath) H47.02-
- orbit, orbital H05.23-

Hemorrhage, hemorrhagic *(continued)*
- ovary NEC N83.8
- oviduct N83.6
- pancreas K86.8
- parathyroid (gland) (spontaneous) E21.4
- parturition —*see* Hemorrhage, complicating, delivery
- penis N48.89
- pericardium, pericarditis I31.2
- peritoneum, peritoneal K66.1
- peritonsillar tissue J35.8
  - due to infection J36
- petechial R23.3
  - due to autosensitivity, erythrocyte D69.2
- pituitary (gland) E23.6
- pleura —*see* Hemorrhage, lung
- polioencephalitis, superior E51.2
- polymyositis —*see* Polymyositis
- pons, pontine I61.3
- posterior fossa (nontraumatic) I61.8
  - newborn P52.6
- postmenopausal N95.0
- postnasal R04.0
- postoperative —*see* Complications, postprocedural, hemorrhage, by site
- postpartum NEC(following delivery of placenta) O72.1
  - delayed or secondary O72.2
  - retained placenta O72.0
  - third stage O72.0
- pregnancy —*see* Hemorrhage, antepartum
- preretinal —*see* Hemorrhage, retina
- prostate N42.1
- puerperal —*see* Hemorrhage, postpartum
  - delayed or secondary O72.2
- pulmonary R04.89
  - newborn P26.9
    - massive P26.1
    - specified NEC P26.8
  - tuberculous —*see* Tuberculosis, pulmonary
- purpura (primary) D69.3
- rectum (sphincter) K62.5
  - newborn P54.2
- recurring, following initial hemorrhage at time of injury T79.2
- renal N28.89
- respiratory passage or tract R04.9
  - specified NEC R04.89
- retina, retinal (vessels) H35.6-
  - diabetic —*see* Diabetes, retinal, hemorrhage
- retroperitoneal R58
- scalp R58
- scrotum N50.1
- secondary (nontraumatic) R58
  - following initial hemorrhage at time of injury T79.2
- seminal vesicle N50.1
- skin R23.3
  - newborn P54.5
- slipped umbilical ligature P51.8
- spermatic cord N50.1
- spinal (cord) G95.19
  - newborn (birth injury) P11.5
- spleen D73.5
  - intraoperative —*see* Complications, intraoperative, hemorrhage, spleen
  - postprocedural —*see* Complications, postprocedural, hemorrhage, spleen
- stomach K92.2
  - newborn P54.3
  - ulcer —*see* Ulcer, stomach, with hemorrhage

Hemorrhage, hemorrhagic *(continued)*
  subarachnoid (nontraumatic) — *see* Hemorrhage, intracranial, subarachnoid
  subconjunctival —*see also* Hemorrhage, conjunctiva
    birth injury P15.3
  subcortical (brain) I61.0
  subcutaneous R23.3
  subdiaphragmatic R58
  subdural (acute) (nontraumatic) —*see* Hemorrhage, intracranial, subdural
  subependymal
    newborn P52.0
      with intraventricular extension P52.1
        and intracerebral extension P52.22
  subgaleal P12.1
  subhyaloid —*see* Hemorrhage, retina
  subperiosteal —*see* Disorder, bone, specified type NEC
  subretinal —*see* Hemorrhage, retina
  subtentorial —*see* Hemorrhage, intracranial, subdural
  subungual L60.8
  suprarenal (capsule) (gland) E27.49
    newborn P54.4
  tentorium (traumatic) NEC —*see* Hemorrhage, brain
    newborn (birth injury) P10.4
  testis N50.1
  third stage (postpartum) O72.0
  thorax —*see* Hemorrhage, lung
  throat R04.1
  thymus (gland) E32.8
  thyroid (cyst) (gland) E07.89
  tongue K14.8
  tonsil J35.8
  trachea —*see* Hemorrhage, lung
  tracheobronchial R04.89
    newborn P26.0
  traumatic - code to specific injury
    cerebellar —*see* Hemorrhage, brain
    intracranial —*see* Hemorrhage, brain
    recurring or secondary (following initial hemorrhage at time of injury) T79.2
  tuberculous NEC —*see also* Tuberculosis, pulmonary A15.0
  tunica vaginalis N50.1
  ulcer - code by site under Ulcer, with hemorrhage K27.4
  umbilicus, umbilical
    cord
      after birth, newborn P51.9
      complicating delivery O69.5
    newborn P51.9
      massive P51.0
      slipped ligature P51.8
    stump P51.9
  urethra (idiopathic) N36.8
  uterus, uterine (abnormal) N93.9
    climacteric N92.4
    complicating delivery —*see* Hemorrhage, complicating, delivery
    dysfunctional or functional N93.8
    intermenstrual (regular) N92.3
      irregular N92.1
    postmenopausal N95.0
    postpartum —*see* Hemorrhage, postpartum
    preclimacteric or premenopausal N92.4
    prepubertal N93.8
    pubertal N92.2
  vagina (abnormal) N93.9
    newborn P54.6
  vas deferens N50.1
  vasa previa O69.4

Hemorrhage, hemorrhagic *(continued)*
  ventricular I61.5
  vesical N32.89
  viscera NEC R58
    newborn P54.8
  vitreous (humor) (intraocular) H43.1-
  vulva N90.89

Hemorrhoids (bleeding) (without mention of degree) K64.9
  1st degree (grade/stage I) (without prolapse outside of anal canal) K64.0
  2nd degree (grade/stage II) (that prolapse with straining but retract spontaneously) K64.1
  3rd degree (grade/stage III) (that prolapse with straining and require manual replacement back inside anal canal) K64.2
  4th degree (grade/stage IV) (with prolapsed tissue that cannot be manually replaced) K64.3
  complicating
    pregnancy O22.4
    puerperium O87.2
  external K64.4
    with
      thrombosis K64.5
  internal (without mention of degree) K64.8
  prolapsed K64.8
  skin tags
    anus K64.4
    residual K64.4
  specified NEC K64.8
  strangulated —*see also* Hemorrhoids, by degree K64.8
  thrombosed —*see also* Hemorrhoids, by degree K64.5
  ulcerated —*see also* Hemorrhoids, by degree K64.8

Hemosalpinx N83.6
  with
    hematocolpos N89.7
    hematometra N85.7
      with hematocolpos N89.7

Hemosiderosis (dietary) E83.19
  pulmonary, idiopathic E83.1- *[J84.03]*
  transfusion T80.89

Hemothorax (bacterial) (nontuberculous) J94.2
  newborn P54.8
  traumatic S27.1
    with pneumothorax S27.2
  tuberculous NEC A15.6

Henoch (-Schönlein) **disease or syndrome** (purpura) D69.0

Henpue, henpuye A66.6

Hepar lobatum (syphilitic) A52.74

Hepatalgia K76.89

Hepatitis K75.9
  acute B17.9
    with coma K72.01
    with hepatic failure —*see* Failure, hepatic
    alcoholic —*see* Hepatitis, alcoholic
    infectious B15.9
      with hepatic coma B15.0
    viral B17.9
  alcoholic (acute) (chronic) K70.10
    with ascites K70.11
  amebic —*see* Abscess, liver, amebic
  anicteric,(viral) —*see* Hepatitis, viral
  antigen-associated (HAA) —*see* Hepatitis, B
  Australia-antigen (positive) —*see* Hepatitis, B
  autoimmune K75.4

Hepatitis *(continued)*
  B B19.10
    with hepatic coma B19.11
    acute B16.9
      with
        delta-agent (coinfection) (without hepatic coma) B16.1
          with hepatic coma B16.0
        hepatic coma (without delta-agent coinfection) B16.2
    chronic B18.1
      with delta-agent B18.0
  bacterial NEC K75.89
  C (viral) B19.20
    with hepatic coma B19.21
    acute B17.10
      with hepatic coma B17.11
    chronic B18.2
  catarrhal (acute) B15.9
    with hepatic coma B15.0
  cholangiolitic K75.89
  cholestatic K75.89
  chronic K73.9
    active NEC K73.2
    lobular NEC K73.1
    persistent NEC K73.0
    specified NEC K73.8
  cytomegaloviral B25.1
  due to ethanol (acute) (chronic) —*see* Hepatitis, alcoholic
  epidemic B15.9
    with hepatic coma B15.0
  fulminant NEC (viral) —*see* Hepatitis, viral
  neonatal giant cell P59.29
  granulomatous NEC K75.3
  herpesviral B00.81
  history of
    B Z86.19
    C Z86.19
  homologous serum —*see* Hepatitis, viral, type B
  in (due to)
    mumps B26.81
    toxoplasmosis (acquired) B58.1
      congenital (active) P37.1 *[K77]*
  infectious, infective (acute) (chronic) (subacute) B15.9
    with hepatic coma B15.0
  inoculation —*see* Hepatitis, viral, type B
  interstitial (chronic) K74.69
  lupoid NEC K75.4
  malignant NEC(with hepatic failure) K72.90
    with coma K72.91
  neonatal (idiopathic) (toxic) P59.29
  newborn P59.29
  postimmunization —*see* Hepatitis, viral, type B
  post-transfusion —*see* Hepatitis, viral, type B
  reactive, nonspecific K75.2
  serum —*see* Hepatitis, viral, type B
  specified type NEC
    with hepatic failure —*see* Failure, hepatic
  syphilitic (late) A52.74
    congenital (early) A50.08 *[K77]*
      late A50.59 *[K77]*
    secondary A51.45
  toxic —*see also* Disease, liver, toxic K71.6
  tuberculous A18.83
  viral, virus B19.9
    with hepatic coma B19.0
    acute B17.9

Hepatitis *(continued)*
  viral, virus *(continued)*
    chronic B18.9
      specified NEC B18.8
      type
        B B18.1
          with delta-agent B18.0
        C B18.2
    congenital P35.3
    coxsackie B33.8 *[K77]*
    cytomegalic inclusion B25.1
    in remission, any type - code to Hepatitis, chronic, by type
    non-A, non-B B17.8
    specified type NEC (with or without coma) B17.8
    type
      A B15.9
        with hepatic coma B15.0
      B B19.10
        with hepatic coma B19.11
        acute B16.9
          with
            delta-agent (coinfection) (without hepatic coma) B16.1
              with hepatic coma B16.0
            hepatic coma (without delta-agent coinfection) B16.2
        chronic B18.1
          with delta-agent B18.0
      C B19.20
        with hepatic coma B19.21
        acute B17.10
          with hepatic coma B17.11
        chronic B18.2
      E B17.2
      non-A, non-B B17.8

Hepatization lung (acute) —*see* Pneumonia, lobar

Hepatoblastoma C22.2

Hepatocarcinoma C22.0

Hepatocholangiocarcinoma C22.0

Hepatocholangioma, benign D13.4

Hepatocholangitis K75.89

Hepatolenticular degeneration E83.01

Hepatoma (malignant) C22.0
  benign D13.4
  embryonal C22.0

Hepatomegaly —*see also* Hypertrophy, liver
  with splenomegaly R16.2
  congenital Q44.7
  in mononucleosis
    gammaherpesviral B27.09
    infectious specified NEC B27.89

Hepatoptosis K76.89

Hepatorenal syndrome following labor and delivery O90.4

Hepatosis K76.89

Hepatosplenomegaly R16.2
  hyperlipemic (Bürger-Grütz type) E78.3 *[K77]*

Hereditary —*see* condition

Heredodegeneration, macular —*see* Dystrophy, retina

Heredopathia atactica polyneuritiformis G60.1

Heredosyphilis —*see* Syphilis, congenital

Herlitz' syndrome Q81.1

Hermansky-Pudlak syndrome E70.331

Hermaphrodite, hermaphroditism
- (true) Q56.0
- 46,XX with streak gonads Q99.1
- 46,XX/46,XY Q99.0
- 46,XY with streak gonads Q99.1
- chimera 46,XX/46,XY Q99.0

Hernia, hernial (acquired) (recurrent) K46.9
- with
  - gangrene —*see* Hernia, by site, with, gangrene
  - incarceration —*see* Hernia, by site, with, obstruction
  - irreducible —*see* Hernia, by site, with, obstruction
  - obstruction —*see* Hernia, by site, with, obstruction
  - strangulation —*see* Hernia, by site, with, obstruction
- abdomen, abdominal K46.9
  - with
    - gangrene (and obstruction) K46.1
    - obstruction K46.0
  - femoral —*see* Hernia, femoral
  - incisional —*see* Hernia, incisional
  - inguinal —*see* Hernia, inguinal
  - specified site NEC K45.8
    - with
      - gangrene (and obstruction) K45.1
      - obstruction K45.0
  - umbilical —*see* Hernia, umbilical
  - wall —*see* Hernia, ventral
- appendix —*see* Hernia, abdomen
- bladder (mucosa) (sphincter)
  - congenital (female) (male) Q79.51
  - female —*see* Cystocele
  - male N32.89
- brain, congenital —*see* Encephalocele
- cartilage, vertebra —*see* Displacement, intervertebral disc
- cerebral, congenital —*see also* Encephalocele
  - endaural Q01.8
- ciliary body (traumatic) S05.2-
- colon —*see* Hernia, abdomen
- Cooper's —*see* Hernia, abdomen, specified site NEC
- crural —*see* Hernia, femoral
- diaphragm, diaphragmatic K44.9
  - with
    - gangrene (and obstruction) K44.1
    - obstruction K44.0
  - congenital Q79.0
- direct (inguinal) —*see* Hernia, inguinal
- diverticulum, intestine —*see* Hernia, abdomen
- double (inguinal) —*see* Hernia, inguinal, bilateral
- due to adhesions (with obstruction) K56.5
- epigastric —*see also* Hernia, ventral K43.9
- esophageal hiatus —*see* Hernia, hiatal
- external (inguinal) —*see* Hernia, inguinal
- fallopian tube N83.4
- fascia M62.89
- femoral K41.90
  - with
    - gangrene (and obstruction) K41.40
      - not specified as recurrent K41.40
      - recurrent K41.41
    - obstruction K41.30
      - not specified as recurrent K41.30
      - recurrent K41.31

Hernia, hernial *(continued)*
- femoral *(continued)*
  - bilateral K41.20
    - with
      - gangrene (and obstruction) K41.10
        - not specified as recurrent K41.10
        - recurrent K41.11
      - obstruction K41.00
        - not specified as recurrent K41.00
        - recurrent K41.01
    - not specified as recurrent K41.20
    - recurrent K41.21
  - unilateral K41.90
    - with
      - gangrene (and obstruction) K41.40
        - not specified as recurrent K41.40
        - recurrent K41.41
      - obstruction K41.30
        - not specified as recurrent K41.30
        - recurrent K41.31
    - not specified as recurrent K41.90
    - recurrent K41.91
  - not specified as recurrent K41.90
  - recurrent K41.91
- foramen magnum G93.5
  - congenital Q01.8
- funicular (umbilical) —*see also* Hernia, umbilicus
  - spermatic (cord) —*see* Hernia, inguinal
- gastrointestinal tract —*see* Hernia, abdomen
- Hesselbach's —*see* Hernia, femoral, specified site NEC
- hiatal (esophageal) (sliding) K44.9
  - with
    - gangrene (and obstruction) K44.1
    - obstruction K44.0
  - congenital Q40.1
- hypogastric —*see* Hernia, ventral
- incarcerated —*see also* Hernia, by site, with obstruction
  - with gangrene —*see* Hernia, by site, with gangrene
- incisional K43.2
  - with
    - gangrene (and obstruction) K43.1
    - obstruction K43.0
- indirect (inguinal) —*see* Hernia, inguinal
- inguinal (direct) (external) (funicular) (indirect) (internal) (oblique) (scrotal) (sliding) K40.90
  - with
    - gangrene (and obstruction) K40.40
      - not specified as recurrent K40.40
      - recurrent K40.41
    - obstruction K40.30
      - not specified as recurrent K40.30
      - recurrent K40.31
  - not specified as recurrent K40.90
  - recurrent K40.91
  - bilateral K40.20
    - with
      - gangrene (and obstruction) K40.10
        - not specified as recurrent K40.10
        - recurrent K40.11

Hernia, hernial *(continued)*
- inguinal *(continued)*
  - bilateral *(continued)*
    - with *(continued)*
      - obstruction K40.00
        - not specified as recurrent K40.00
        - recurrent K40.01
    - not specified as recurrent K40.20
    - recurrent K40.21
  - unilateral K40.90
    - with
      - gangrene (and obstruction) K40.40
        - not specified as recurrent K40.40
        - recurrent K40.41
      - obstruction K40.30
        - not specified as recurrent K40.30
        - recurrent K40.31
    - not specified as recurrent K40.90
    - recurrent K40.91
- internal —*see also* Hernia, abdomen
  - inguinal —*see* Hernia, inguinal
- interstitial —*see* Hernia, abdomen
- intervertebral cartilage or disc —*see* Displacement, intervertebral disc
- intestine, intestinal —*see* Hernia, by site
- intra-abdominal —*see* Hernia, abdomen
- iris (traumatic) S05.2-
- irreducible —*see also* Hernia, by site, with obstruction
  - with gangrene —*see* Hernia, by site, with gangrene
- ischiatic —*see* Hernia, abdomen, specified site NEC
- ischiorectal —*see* Hernia, abdomen, specified site NEC
- lens (traumatic) S05.2-
- linea (alba) (semilunaris) —*see* Hernia, ventral
- Littre's —*see* Hernia, abdomen
- lumbar —*see* Hernia, abdomen, specified site NEC
- lung (subcutaneous) J98.4
- mediastinum J98.5
- mesenteric (internal) —*see* Hernia, abdomen
- midline —*see* Hernia, ventral
- muscle (sheath) M62.89
- nucleus pulposus —*see* Displacement, intervertebral disc
- oblique (inguinal) —*see* Hernia, inguinal
- obstructive —*see also* Hernia, by site, with obstruction
  - with gangrene —*see* Hernia, by site, with gangrene
- obturator —*see* Hernia, abdomen, specified site NEC
- omental —*see* Hernia, abdomen
- ovary N83.4
- oviduct N83.4
- paraesophageal —*see also* Hernia, diaphragm
  - congenital Q40.1
- parastomal K43.5
  - with
    - gangrene (and obstruction) K43.4
    - obstruction K43.3
- paraumbilical —*see* Hernia, umbilicus
- perineal —*see* Hernia, abdomen, specified site NEC
- Petit's —*see* Hernia, abdomen, specified site NEC
- postoperative —*see* Hernia, incisional

Hernia, hernial *(continued)*
- pregnant uterus —*see* Abnormal, uterus in pregnancy or childbirth
- prevesical N32.89
- properitoneal —*see* Hernia, abdomen, specified site NEC
- pudendal —*see* Hernia, abdomen, specified site NEC
- rectovaginal N81.6
- retroperitoneal —*see* Hernia, abdomen, specified site NEC
- Richter's —*see* Hernia, abdomen, with obstruction
- Rieux's, Riex's —*see* Hernia, abdomen, specified site NEC
- sac condition (adhesion) (dropsy) (inflammation) (laceration) (suppuration) - code by site under Hernia
- sciatic —*see* Hernia, abdomen, specified site NEC
- scrotum, scrotal —*see* Hernia, inguinal
- sliding (inguinal) —*see also* Hernia, inguinal
  - hiatus —*see* Hernia, hiatal
- spigelian —*see* Hernia, ventral
- spinal —*see* Spina bifida
- strangulated —*see also* Hernia, by site, with obstruction
  - with gangrene —*see* Hernia, by site, with gangrene
- subxiphoid —*see* Hernia, ventral
- supra-umbilicus —*see* Hernia, ventral
- tendon —*see* Disorder, tendon, specified type NEC
- Treitz's (fossa) —*see* Hernia, abdomen, specified site NEC
- tunica vaginalis Q55.29
- umbilicus, umbilical K42.9
  - with
    - gangrene (and obstruction) K42.1
    - obstruction K42.0
- ureter N28.89
- urethra, congenital Q64.79
- urinary meatus, congenital Q64.79
- uterus N81.4
  - pregnant —*see* Abnormal, uterus in pregnancy or childbirth
- vaginal (anterior) (wall) —*see* Cystocele
- Velpeau's —*see* Hernia, femoral
- ventral K43.9
  - with
    - gangrene (and obstruction) K43.7
    - obstruction K43.6
  - recurrent —*see* Hernia, incisional
  - incisional K43.2
    - with
      - gangrene (and obstruction) K43.1
      - obstruction K43.0
  - specified NEC K43.9
    - with
      - gangrene (and obstruction) K43.7
      - obstruction K43.6
- vesical
  - congenital (female) (male) Q79.51
  - female —*see* Cystocele
  - male N32.89
- vitreous (into wound) S05.2-
  - into anterior chamber —*see* Prolapse, vitreous

Herniation —*see also* Hernia
- brain (stem) G93.5
- cerebral G93.5
- mediastinum J98.5

- **erniation** *(continued)*
  - nucleus pulposus *—see* Displacement, intervertebral disc
- **erpangina** B08.5
- **erpes, herpesvirus, herpetic** B00.9
  - anogenital A60.9
    - perianal skin A60.1
    - rectum A60.1
    - urogenital tract A60.00
      - cervix A60.03
      - male genital organ NEC A60.02
      - penis A60.01
      - specified site NEC A60.09
      - vagina A60.04
      - vulva A60.04
  - blepharitis (zoster) B02.39
    - simplex B00.59
  - circinatus B35.4
    - bullosus L12.0
  - conjunctivitis (simplex) B00.53
    - zoster B02.31
  - cornea B02.33
  - encephalitis B00.4
    - due to herpesvirus 6 B10.01
    - due to herpesvirus 7 B10.09
    - specified NEC B10.09
  - eye (zoster) B02.30
    - simplex B00.50
  - eyelid (zoster) B02.39
    - simplex B00.59
  - facialis B00.1
  - febrilis B00.1
  - geniculate ganglionitis B02.21
  - genital, genitalis A60.00
    - female A60.09
    - male A60.02
  - gestational, gestationis O26.4-
  - gingivostomatitis B00.2
  - human B00.9
    - 1 *—see* Herpes, simplex
    - 2 *—see* Herpes, simplex
    - 3 *—see* Varicella
    - 4 *—see* Mononucleosis, Epstein-Barr (virus)
    - 5 *—see* Disease, cytomegalic inclusion (generalized)
    - 6
      - encephalitis B10.01
      - specified NEC B10.81
    - 7
      - encephalitis B10.09
      - specified NEC B10.82
    - 8 B10.89
  - infection NEC B10.89
    - Kaposi's sarcoma associated B10.89
  - iridocyclitis (simplex) B00.51
    - zoster B02.32
  - iris (vesicular erythema multiforme) L51.9
  - iritis (simplex) B00.51
  - Kaposi's sarcoma associated B10.89
  - keratitis (simplex) (dendritic) (disciform) (interstitial) B00.52
    - zoster (interstitial) B02.33
  - keratoconjunctivitis (simplex) B00.52
    - zoster B02.33
  - labialis B00.1
  - lip B00.1
  - meningitis (simplex) B00.3
    - zoster B02.1
  - ophthalmicus (zoster) NEC B02.30
    - simplex B00.50
  - penis A60.01
  - perianal skin A60.1
  - pharyngitis, pharyngotonsillitis B00.2

- **Herpes, herpesvirus, herpetic** *(continued)*
  - rectum A60.1
  - scrotum A60.02
  - sepsis B00.7
  - simplex B00.9
    - complicated NEC B00.89
    - congenital P35.2
    - conjunctivitis B00.53
    - external ear B00.1
    - eyelid B00.59
    - hepatitis B00.81
    - keratitis (interstitial) B00.52
    - myleitis B00.82
    - specified complication NEC B00.89
    - visceral B00.89
  - stomatitis B00.2
  - tonsurans B35.0
  - visceral B00.89
  - vulva A60.04
  - whitlow B00.89
  - zoster *—see also* condition B02.9
    - auricularis B02.21
    - complicated NEC B02.8
    - conjunctivitis B02.31
    - disseminated B02.7
    - encephalitis B02.0
    - eye (lid) B02.39
    - geniculate ganglionitis B02.21
    - keratitis (interstitial) B02.33
    - meningitis B02.1
    - myelitis B02.24
    - neuritis, neuralgia B02.29
    - ophthalmicus NEC B02.30
    - oticus B02.21
    - polyneuropathy B02.23
    - specified complication NEC B02.8
    - trigeminal neuralgia B02.22
- **Herpesvirus** (human) *—see* Herpes
- **Herpetophobia** F40.218
- **Herrick's anemia** *—see* Disease, sickle-cell
- **Hers' disease** E74.09
- **Herter-Gee syndrome** K90.0
- **Herxheimer's reaction** R68.89
- **Hesitancy**
  - of micturition R39.11
  - urinary R39.11
- **Hesselbach's hernia** *—see* Hernia, femoral, specified site NEC
- **Heterochromia** (congenital) Q13.2
  - cataract *—see* Cataract, complicated
  - cyclitis (Fuchs) *—see* Cyclitis, Fuchs' heterochromic
  - hair L67.1
  - iritis *—see* Cyclitis, Fuchs' heterochromic
  - retained metallic foreign body (nonmagnetic) *—see* Foreign body, intraocular, old, retained
    - magnetic *—see* Foreign body, intraocular, old, retained, magnetic
  - uveitis *—see* Cyclitis, Fuchs' heterochromic
- **Heterophoria** *—see* Strabismus, heterophoria
- **Heterophyes, heterophyiasis** (small intestine) B66.8
- **Heterotopia, heterotopic** *—see also* Malposition, congenital
  - cerebralis Q04.8
- **Heterotropia** *—see* Strabismus
- **Heubner-Herter disease** K90.0
- **Hexadactylism** Q69.9

- **HGSIL** (cytology finding) (high grade squamous intraepithelial lesion on cytologic smear) (Pap smear finding)
  - anus R85.613
  - cervix R87.613
    - biopsy (histology) finding - code to CIN II or CIN III
  - vagina R87.623
    - biopsy (histology) finding - code to VAIN II or VAIN III
- **Hibernoma** *—see* Lipoma
- **Hiccup, hiccough** R06.6
  - epidemic B33.0
  - psychogenic F45.8
- **Hidden penis** (congenital) Q55.64
  - acquired N48.83
- **Hidradenitis** (axillaris) (suppurative) L73.2
- **Hidradenoma** (nodular) *—see also* Neoplasm, skin, benign
  - clear cell *—see* Neoplasm, skin, benign
  - papillary *—see* Neoplasm, skin, benign
- **Hidrocystoma** *—see* Neoplasm, skin, benign
- **High**
  - altitude effects T70.20
    - anoxia T70.29
    - on
      - ears T70.0
      - sinuses T70.1
    - polycythemia D75.1
  - arch
    - foot Q66.7
    - palate, congenital Q38.5
  - arterial tension *—see* Hypertension
  - basal metabolic rate R94.8
  - blood pressure *—see also* Hypertension
    - borderline R03.0
    - reading (incidental) (isolated) (nonspecific), without diagnosis of hypertension R03.0
  - cholesterol E78.0
    - with high triglycerides E78.2
  - diaphragm (congenital) Q79.1
  - expressed emotional level within family Z63.8
  - head at term O32.4
  - palate, congenital Q38.5
  - risk
    - infant NEC Z76.2
    - sexual behavior (heterosexual) Z72.51
      - bisexual Z72.53
      - homosexual Z72.52
  - temperature (of unknown origin) R50.9
  - thoracic rib Q76.6
  - triglycerides E78.1
    - with high cholesterol E78.2
- **Hildenbrand's disease** A75.0
- **Hilum** *—see* condition
- **Hip** *—see* condition
- **Hippel's disease** Q85.8
- **Hippophobia** F40.218
- **Hippus** H57.09
- **Hirschsprung's disease or megacolon** Q43.1
- **Hirsutism, hirsuties** L68.0
- **Hirudiniasis**
  - external B88.3
  - internal B83.4
- **Hiss-Russell dysentery** A03.1
- **Histidinemia, histidinuria** E70.41

- **Histiocytoma** *—see also* Neoplasm, skin, benign
  - fibrous *—see also* Neoplasm, skin, benign
    - atypical *—see* Neoplasm, connective tissue, uncertain behavior
    - malignant *—see* Neoplasm, connective tissue, malignant
- **Histiocytosis** D76.3
  - acute differentiated progressive C96.0
  - Langerhans' cell NEC C96.6
    - multifocal X
      - multisystemic (disseminated) C96.0
      - unisystemic C96.5
    - pulmonary, adult (adult PLCH) J84.82
    - unifocal (X) C96.6
  - lipid, lipoid D76.3
    - essential E75.29
  - malignant C96.A
  - mononuclear phagocytes NEC D76.1
    - Langerhans' cells C96.6
  - non-Langerhans cell D76.3
  - polyostotic sclerosing D76.3
  - sinus, with massive lymphadenopathy D76.3
  - syndrome NEC D76.3
  - X NEC C96.6
    - acute (progressive) C96.0
    - chronic C96.6
    - multifocal C96.5
    - multisystemic C96.0
    - unifocal C96.6
- **Histoplasmosis** B39.9
  - with pneumonia NEC B39.2
  - African B39.5
  - American *—see* Histoplasmosis, capsulati
  - capsulati B39.4
    - disseminated B39.3
    - generalized B39.3
    - pulmonary B39.2
      - acute B39.0
      - chronic B39.1
  - Darling's B39.4
  - duboisii B39.5
  - lung NEC B39.2
- **History**
  - family (of) *—see also* History, personal (of)
    - alcohol abuse Z81.1
    - allergy NEC Z84.89
    - anemia Z83.2
    - arthritis Z82.61
    - asthma Z82.5
    - blindness Z82.1
    - cardiac death (sudden) Z82.41
    - carrier of genetic disease Z84.81
    - chromosomal anomaly Z82.79
    - chronic
      - disabling disease NEC Z82.8
      - lower respiratory disease Z82.5
    - colonic polyps Z83.71
    - congenital malformations and deformations Z82.79
      - polycystic kidney Z82.71
    - consanguinity Z84.3
    - deafness Z82.2
    - diabetes mellitus Z83.3
    - disability NEC Z82.8
    - disease or disorder (of)
      - allergic NEC Z84.89
      - behavioral NEC Z81.8
      - blood and blood-forming organs Z83.2
      - cardiovascular NEC Z82.49
      - chronic disabling NEC Z82.8
      - digestive Z83.79
      - ear NEC Z83.52

History *(continued)*
  family *(continued)*
    disease or disorder *(continued)*
      endocrine NEC Z83.49
      eye NEC Z83.518
        glaucoma Z83.511
      genitourinary NEC Z84.2
      glaucoma Z83.511
      hematological Z83.2
      immune mechanism Z83.2
      infectious NEC Z83.1
      ischemic heart Z82.49
      kidney Z84.1
      mental NEC Z81.8
      metabolic Z83.49
      musculoskeletal NEC Z82.69
      neurological NEC Z82.0
      nutritional Z83.49
      parasitic NEC Z83.1
      psychiatric NEC Z81.8
      respiratory NEC Z83.6
      skin and subcutaneous tissue NEC Z84.0
      specified NEC Z84.89
    drug abuse NEC Z81.3
    epilepsy Z82.0
    genetic disease carrier Z84.81
    glaucoma Z83.511
    hearing loss Z82.2
    human immunodeficiency virus (HIV) infection Z83.0
    Huntington's chorea Z82.0
    intellectual disability Z81.0
    leukemia Z80.6
    malignant neoplasm (of) NOS Z80.9
      bladder Z80.52
      breast Z80.3
      bronchus Z80.1
      digestive organ Z80.0
      gastrointestinal tract Z80.0
      genital organ Z80.49
        ovary Z80.41
        prostate Z80.42
        specified organ NEC Z80.49
        testis Z80.43
      hematopoietic NEC Z80.7
      intrathoracic organ NEC Z80.2
      kidney Z80.51
      lung Z80.1
      lymphatic NEC Z80.7
      ovary Z80.41
      prostate Z80.42
      respiratory organ NEC Z80.2
      specified site NEC Z80.8
      testis Z80.43
      trachea Z80.1
      urinary organ or tract Z80.59
        bladder Z80.52
        kidney Z80.51
    mental
      disorder NEC Z81.8
    multiple endocrine neoplasia (MEN) syndrome Z83.41
    osteoporosis Z82.62
    polycystic kidney Z82.71
    polyps (colon) Z83.71
    psychiatric disorder Z81.8
    psychoactive substance abuse NEC Z81.3
    respiratory condition NEC Z83.6
      asthma and other lower respiratory conditions Z82.5
    self-harmful behavior Z81.8
    skin condition Z84.0
    specified condition NEC Z84.89
    stroke (cerebrovascular) Z82.3
    substance abuse NEC Z81.4
      alcohol Z81.1
      drug NEC Z81.3
      psychoactive NEC Z81.3
      tobacco Z81.2

History *(continued)*
  family *(continued)*
    sudden cardiac death Z82.41
    tobacco abuse Z81.2
    violence, violent behavior Z81.8
    visual loss Z82.1
  personal (of) —*see also* History, family (of)
    abuse
      childhood Z62.819
        physical Z62.810
        psychological Z62.811
        sexual Z62.810
      adult Z91.419
        physical and sexual Z91.410
        psychological Z91.411
    alcohol dependence F10.21
    allergy (to) Z88.9
      analgesic agent NEC Z88.6
      anesthetic Z88.4
      antibiotic agent NEC Z88.1
      anti-infective agent NEC Z88.3
      contrast media Z91.041
      drugs, medicaments and biological substances Z88.9
        specified NEC Z88.8
      food Z91.018
        additives Z91.02
        eggs Z91.012
        milk products Z91.011
        peanuts Z91.010
        seafood Z91.013
        specified food NEC Z91.018
      insect Z91.038
        bee Z91.030
      latex Z91.040
      medicinal agents Z88.9
        specified NEC Z88.8
      narcotic agent NEC Z88.5
      nonmedicinal agents Z91.048
      penicillin Z88.0
      serum Z88.7
      specified NEC Z91.09
      sulfonamides Z88.2
      vaccine Z88.7
    anaphylactic shock Z87.892
    anaphylaxis Z87.892
    behavioral disorders Z86.59
    benign carcinoid tumor Z86.012
    benign neoplasm Z86.018
      carcinoid Z86.012
      brain Z86.011
      colonic polyps Z86.010
    brain injury (traumatic) Z87.820
    breast implant removal Z98.86
    calculi, renal Z87.442
    cancer —*see* History, personal (of), malignant neoplasm (of)
    cardiac arrest (death), successfully resuscitated Z86.74
    cerebral infarction without residual deficit Z86.73
    cervical dysplasia Z87.410
    chemotherapy for neoplastic condition Z92.21
    childhood abuse —*see* History, personal (of), abuse
    cleft lip (corrected) Z87.730
    cleft palate (corrected) Z87.730
    collapsed vertebra (healed) Z87.311
      due to osteoporosis Z87.310
    combat and operational stress reaction Z86.51
    congenital malformation (corrected) Z87.798
      circulatory system (corrected) Z87.74
      digestive system (corrected) NEC Z87.738
      ear (corrected) Z87.720
      eye (corrected) Z87.721

History *(continued)*
  personal *(continued)*
    congenital malformation *(continued)*
      face and neck (corrected) Z87.790
      genitourinary system (corrected) NEC Z87.718
      heart (corrected) Z87.74
      integument (corrected) Z87.76
      limb (s) (corrected) Z87.76
      musculoskeletal system (corrected) Z87.76
      neck (corrected) Z87.790
      nervous system (corrected) NEC Z87.728
      respiratory system (corrected) Z87.75
      sense organs (corrected) NEC Z87.728
      specified NEC Z87.798
    contraception Z92.0
    deployment (military) Z91.82
    diabetic foot ulcer Z86.31
    disease or disorder (of) Z87.898
      blood and blood-forming organs Z86.2
      circulatory system Z86.79
        specified condition NEC Z86.79
      connective tissue NEC Z87.39
      digestive system Z87.19
        colonic polyp Z86.010
        peptic ulcer disease Z87.11
        specified condition NEC Z87.19
      ear Z86.69
      endocrine Z86.39
        diabetic foot ulcer Z86.31
        gestational diabetes Z86.32
        specified type NEC Z86.39
      eye Z86.69
      genital (track) system NEC
        female Z87.42
        male Z87.438
      hematological Z86.2
      Hodgkin Z85.71
      immune mechanism Z86.2
      infectious Z86.19
        malaria Z86.13
        Methicillin resistant Staphylococcus aureus (MRSA) Z86.14
        poliomyelitis Z86.12
        specified NEC Z86.19
        tuberculosis Z86.11
      mental NEC Z86.59
      metabolic Z86.39
        diabetic foot ulcer Z86.31
        gestational diabetes Z86.32
        specified type NEC Z86.39
      musculoskeletal NEC Z87.39
      nervous system Z86.69
      nutritional Z86.39
      parasitic Z86.19
      respiratory system NEC Z87.09
      sense organs Z86.69
      skin Z87.2
      specified site or type NEC Z87.898
      subcutaneous tissue Z87.2
      trophoblastic Z87.59
      urinary system NEC Z87.448
    drug dependence —*see* Dependence, drug, by type, in remission
    drug therapy
      antineoplastic chemotherapy Z92.21
      estrogen Z92.23
      immunosupression Z92.25
      inhaled steroids Z92.240

History *(continued)*
  personal *(continued)*
    drug therapy *(continued)*
      monoclonal drug Z92.22
      specified NEC Z92.29
      steroid Z92.241
      systemic steroids Z92.241
    dysplasia
      cervical Z87.410
      prostatic Z87.430
      vaginal Z87.411
      vulvar Z87.412
    embolism (venous) Z86.718
      pulmonary Z86.711
    encephalitis Z86.61
    estrogen therapy Z92.23
    extracorporeal membrane oxygenation (ECMO) Z92.81
    failed moderate sedation Z92.83
    failed conscious sedation Z92.83
    fall, falling Z91.81
    fracture (healed)
      fatigue Z87.312
      fragility Z87.310
      osteoporosis Z87.310
      pathological NEC Z87.311
      stress Z87.312
      traumatic Z87.81
    gestational diabetes Z86.32
    hepatitis
      B Z86.19
      C Z86.19
    Hodgkin disease Z85.71
    hyperthermia, malignant Z88.4
    hypospadias (corrected) Z87.710
    hysterectomy Z90.710
    immunosupression therapy Z92.25
    in situ neoplasm
      breast Z86.000
      cervix uteri Z86.001
      specified NEC Z86.008
    infection NEC Z86.19
      central nervous system Z86.61
      Methicillin resistant Staphylococcus aureus (MRSA) Z86.14
      urinary (recurrent) (tract) Z87.440
    injury NEC Z87.828
    in utero procedure during pregnancy Z98.870
    in utero procedure while a fetus Z98.871
    irradiation Z92.3
    kidney stones Z87.442
    leukemia Z85.6
    lymphoma (non-Hodgkin) Z85.72
    malignant melanoma (skin) Z85.820
    malignant neoplasm (of) Z85.9
      accessory sinuses Z85.22
      anus NEC Z85.048
        carcinoid Z85.040
      bladder Z85.51
      bone Z85.830
      brain Z85.841
      breast Z85.3
      bronchus NEC Z85.118
        carcinoid Z85.110
      carcinoid —*see* History, personal (of), malignant neoplasm, by site, carcinioid
      cervix Z85.41
      colon NEC Z85.038
        carcinoid Z85.030
      digestive organ Z85.00
        specified NEC Z85.09
      endocrine gland NEC Z85.858
      epididymis Z85.48
      esophagus Z85.01
      eye Z85.840

- **History** *(continued)*
  - personal *(continued)*
    - malignant neoplasm *(continued)*
      - gastrointestinal tract *—see* History, malignant neoplasm, digestive organ
      - genital organ
        - female Z85.40
          - specified NEC Z85.44
        - male Z85.45
          - specified NEC Z85.49
      - hematopoietic NEC Z85.79
      - intrathoracic organ Z85.20
      - kidney NEC Z85.528
        - carcinoid Z85.520
      - large intestine NEC Z85.038
        - carcinoid Z85.030
      - larynx Z85.21
      - liver Z85.05
      - lung NEC Z85.118
        - carcinoid Z85.110
      - mediastinum Z85.29
      - Merkel cell Z85.821
      - middle ear Z85.22
      - nasal cavities Z85.22
      - nervous system NEC Z85.848
      - oral cavity Z85.819
        - specified site NEC Z85.818
      - ovary Z85.43
      - pancreas Z85.07
      - pharynx Z85.819
        - specified site NEC Z85.818
      - pelvis Z85.53
      - pleura Z85.29
      - prostate Z85.46
      - rectosigmoid junction NEC Z85.048
        - carcinoid Z85.040
      - rectum NEC Z85.048
        - carcinoid Z85.040
      - respiratory organ Z85.20
      - sinuses, accessory Z85.22
      - skin NEC Z85.828
        - melanoma Z85.820
        - Merkel cell Z85.821
      - small intestine NEC Z85.068
        - carcinoid Z85.060
      - soft tissue Z85.831
      - specified site NEC Z85.89
      - stomach NEC Z85.028
        - carcinoid Z85.020
      - testis Z85.47
      - thymus NEC Z85.238
        - carcinoid Z85.230
      - thyroid Z85.850
      - tongue Z85.810
      - trachea Z85.12
      - ureter Z85.54
      - urinary organ or tract Z85.50
        - specified NEC Z85.59
      - uterus Z85.42
    - maltreatment Z91.89
    - medical treatment NEC Z92.89
    - melanoma (malignant) (skin) Z85.820
    - meningitis Z86.61
    - mental disorder Z86.59
    - Merkel cell carcinoma (skin) Z85.821
    - Methicillin resistant Staphylococcus aureus (MRSA) Z86.14
    - military deployment Z91.82
    - military war, peacekeeping and humanitarian deployment (current or past conflict) Z91.82
    - myocardial infarction (old) I25.2
    - neglect (in)
      - adult Z91.412
      - childhood Z62.812
    - neoplasm

- **History** *(continued)*
  - personal *(continued)*
    - neoplasm *(continued)*
      - benign Z86.018
        - brain Z86.011
        - colon polyp Z86.010
      - in situ
        - breast Z86.000
        - cervix uteri Z86.001
        - specified NEC Z86.008
      - malignant *—see* History of, malignant neoplasm
      - uncertain behavior Z86.03
    - nephrotic syndrome Z87.441
    - nicotine dependence Z87.891
    - noncompliance with medical treatment or regimen *—see* Noncompliance
    - nutritional deficiency Z86.39
    - obstetric complications Z87.59
      - childbirth Z87.59
      - pregnancy Z87.59
      - pre-term labor Z87.51
      - puerperium Z87.59
    - osteoporosis fractures Z87.31
    - parasuicide (attempt) Z91.5
    - physical trauma NEC Z87.828
      - self-harm or suicide attempt Z91.5
    - poisoning NEC Z91.89
      - self-harm or suicide attempt Z91.5
    - poor personal hygiene Z91.89
    - pneumonia (recurrent) Z87.01
    - preterm labor Z87.51
    - prolonged reversible ischemic neurologic deficit (PRIND) Z86.73
    - procedure during pregnancy Z98.870
    - procedure while a fetus Z98.871
    - prostatic dysplasia Z87.430
    - psychological
      - abuse
        - adult Z91.411
        - child Z62.811
      - trauma, specified NEC Z91.49
    - radiation therapy Z92.3
    - removal
      - implant
        - breast Z98.86
    - renal calculi Z87.442
    - respiratory condition NEC Z87.09
    - retained foreign body fully removed Z87.821
    - risk factors NEC Z91.89
    - self-harm Z91.5
    - self-poisoning attempt Z91.5
    - sex reassignment Z87.890
    - sleep-wake cycle problem Z72.821
    - specified NEC Z87.898
    - steroid therapy (systemic) Z92.241
      - inhaled Z92.240
    - stroke without residual deficits Z86.73
    - substance abuse NEC F10-F19 with fifth character 1
    - sudden cardiac arrest Z86.74
    - sudden cardiac death successfully resuscitated Z86.74
    - suicide attempt Z91.5
    - surgery NEC Z98.89
      - sex reassignment Z87.890
      - transplant *—see* Transplant
    - thrombophlebitis Z86.72
    - thrombosis (venous) Z86.718
      - pulmonary Z86.711
    - tobacco dependence Z87.891
    - transient ischemic attack (TIA) without residual deficits Z86.73
    - trauma (physical) NEC Z87.828
      - psychological NEC Z91.49
      - self-harm Z91.5

- **History** *(continued)*
  - personal *(continued)*
    - traumatic brain injury Z87.820
    - unhealthy sleep-wake cycle Z72.821
    - urinary calculi Z87.442
    - urinary (recurrent) (tract) infection (s) Z87.440
    - vaginal dysplasia Z87.411
    - venous thrombosis or embolism Z86.718
      - pulmonary Z86.711
    - vulvar dysplasia Z87.412
- **His-Werner disease** A79.0
- **HIV** *—see also* Human, immunodeficiency virus B20
  - laboratory evidence (nonconclusive) R75
  - positive, seropositive Z21
  - nonconclusive test (in infants) R75
- **Hives** (bold) *—see* Urticaria
- **Hoarseness** R49.0
- **Hobo** Z59.0
- **Hodgkin disease** *—see* Lymphoma, Hodgkin
- **Hodgson's disease** I71.2
  - ruptured I71.1
- **Hoffa-Kastert disease** E88.89
- **Hoffa's disease** E88.89
- **Hoffmann-Bouveret syndrome** I47.9
- **Hoffmann's syndrome** E03.9 *[G73.7]*
- **Hole** (round)
  - macula H35.34-
  - retina (without detachment) *—see* Break, retina, round hole
    - with detachment *—see* Detachment, retina, with retinal, break
- **Holiday relief care** Z75.5
- **Hollenhorst's plaque** *—see* Occlusion, artery, retina
- **Hollow foot** (congenital) Q66.7
  - acquired *—see* Deformity, limb, foot, specified NEC
- **Holoprosencephaly** Q04.2
- **Holt-Oram syndrome** Q87.2
- **Homelessness** Z59.0
- **Homesickness** *—see* Disorder, adjustment
- **Homocystinemia, homocystinuria** E72.11
- **Homogentisate 1,2-dioxygenase deficiency** E70.29
- **Homologous serum hepatitis** (prophylactic) (therapeutic) *—see* Hepatitis, viral, type B
- **Honeycomb lung** J98.4
  - congenital Q33.0
- **Hooded**
  - clitoris Q52.6
  - penis Q55.69
- **Hookworm** (anemia) (disease) (infection) (infestation) B76.9
  - specified NEC B76.8
- **Hordeolum** (eyelid) (externum) (recurrent) H00.019
  - internum H00.029
    - left H00.026
      - lower H00.025
      - upper H00.024
    - right H00.023
      - lower H00.022
      - upper H00.021

- **Hordeolum** *(continued)*
  - left H00.016
    - lower H00.015
    - upper H00.014
  - right H00.013
    - lower H00.012
    - upper H00.011
- **Horn**
  - cutaneous L85.8
  - nail L60.2
    - congenital Q84.6
- **Horner** (-Claude Bernard) **syndrome** G90.2
  - traumatic *—see* Injury, nerve, cervical sympathetic
- **Horseshoe kidney** (congenital) Q63.1
- **Horton's headache or neuralgia** G44.099
  - intractable G44.091
  - not intractable G44.099
- **Hospital hopper syndrome** *—see* Disorder, factitious
- **Hospitalism in children** *—see* Disorder, adjustment
- **Hostility** R45.5
  - towards child Z62.3
- **Hot flashes**
  - menopausal N95.1
- **Hourglass** (contracture) *—see also* Contraction, hourglass
  - stomach K31.89
    - congenital Q40.2
    - stricture K31.2
- **Household, housing circumstance affecting care** Z59.9
  - specified NEC Z59.8
- **Housemaid's knee** *—see* Bursitis, prepatellar
- **Hudson** (-Stähli) **line** (cornea) *—see* Pigmentation, cornea, anterior
- **Human**
  - bite (open wound) *—see also* Bite
    - intact skin surface *—see* Bite, superficial
  - herpesvirus *—see* Herpes
  - immunodeficiency virus (HIV)
    - disease (infection) B20
    - asymptomatic status Z21
    - contact Z20.6
    - counseling Z71.7
    - dementia B20 *[F02.80]*
      - with behavioral disturbance B20 *[F02.81]*
    - exposure to Z20.6
    - laboratory evidence R75
    - type-2(HIV 2) as cause of disease classified elsewhere B97.35
  - papillomavirus (HPV)
    - DNA test positive
      - high risk
        - cervix R87.810
        - vagina R87.811
      - low risk
        - cervix R87.820
        - vagina R87.821
    - screening for Z11.51
  - T-cell lymphotropic virus
    - type-1(HTLV-I) infection B33.3
      - as cause of disease classified elsewhere B97.33
      - carrier Z22.6
    - type-2(HTLV-II) as cause of disease classified elsewhere B97.34
- **Humidifier lung or pneumonitis** J67.7
- **Humiliation** (experience) **in childhood** Z62.898

- **Humpback** (acquired) —*see* Kyphosis
- **Hunchback** (acquired) —*see* Kyphosis
- **Hunger** T73.0
  - air, psychogenic F45.8
- **Hungry bone syndrome** E83.81
- **Hunner's ulcer** —*see* Cystitis, chronic, interstitial
- **Hunter's**
  - glossitis D51.0
  - syndrome E76.1
- **Huntington's disease or chorea** G10
  - with dementia G10 *[F02.80]*
    - with behavioral disturbance G10 *[F02.81]*
- **Hunt's**
  - disease or syndrome (herpetic geniculate ganglionitis) B02.21
    - dyssynergia cerebellaris myoclonica G11.1
  - neuralgia B02.21
- **Hurler** (-Scheie) **disease or syndrome** E76.02
- **Hurst's disease** G36.1
- **Hurthle cell**
  - adenocarcinoma C73
  - adenoma D34
  - carcinoma C73
  - tumor D34
- **Hutchinson-Boeck disease or syndrome** —*see* Sarcoidosis
- **Hutchinson-Gilford disease or syndrome** E34.8
- **Hutchinson's**
  - disease, meaning
    - angioma serpiginosum L81.7
    - pompholyx (cheiropompholyx) L30.1
    - prurigo estivalis L56.4
    - summer eruption or summer prurigo L56.4
  - melanotic freckle —*see* Melanoma, in situ
    - malignant melanoma in —*see* Melanoma
  - teeth or incisors (congenital syphilis) A50.52
  - triad (congenital syphilis) A50.53
- **Hyalin plaque, sclera, senile** H15.89
- **Hyaline membrane** (disease) (lung) (pulmonary) (newborn) P22.0
- **Hyalinosis**
  - cutis (et mucosae) E78.89
  - focal and segmental (glomerular) —*see also* N00-N07 with fourth character .1 N05.1
- **Hyalitis, hyalosis, asteroid** —*see also* Deposit, crystalline
  - syphilitic (late) A52.71
- **Hydatid**
  - cyst or tumor —*see* Echinococcus
  - mole —*see* Hydatidiform mole
  - Morgagni
    - female Q50.5
    - male (epididymal) Q55.4
      - testicular Q55.29
- **Hydatidiform mole** (benign) (complicating pregnancy) (delivered) (undelivered) O01.9
  - classical O01.0
  - complete O01.0
  - incomplete O01.1
  - invasive D39.2
  - malignant D39.2
  - partial O01.1
- **Hydatidosis** —*see* Echinococcus
- **Hydradenitis** (axillaris) (suppurative) L73.2
- **Hydradenoma** —*see* Hidradenoma
- **Hydramnios** O40.-
- **Hydrancephaly, hydranencephaly** Q04.3
  - with spina bifida —*see* Spina bifida, with hydrocephalus
- **Hydrargyrism NEC** —*see* Poisoning, mercury
- **Hydrarthrosis** —*see also* Effusion, joint
  - gonococcal A54.42
  - intermittent M12.40
    - ankle M12.47-
    - elbow M12.42-
    - foot joint M12.47-
    - hand joint M12.44-
    - hip M12.45-
    - knee M12.46-
    - multiple site M12.49
    - shoulder M12.41-
    - specified joint NEC M12.48
    - wrist M12.43-
  - of yaws (early) (late) —*see also* subcategory M14.8- A66.6
  - syphilitic (late) A52.77
    - congenital A50.55 *[M12.80]*
- **Hydremia** D64.89
- **Hydrencephalocele** (congenital) —*see* Encephalocele
- **Hydrencephalomeningocele** (congenital) —*see* Encephalocele
- **Hydroa** R23.8
  - aestivale L56.4
  - vacciniforme L56.4
- **Hydroadenitis** (axillaris) (suppurative) L73.2
- **Hydrocalycosis** —*see* Hydronephrosis
- **Hydrocele** (spermatic cord) (testis) (tunica vaginalis) N43.3
  - canal of Nuck N94.89
  - communicating N43.2
    - congenital P83.5
  - congenital P83.5
  - encysted N43.0
  - female NEC N94.89
  - infected N43.1
  - newborn P83.5
  - round ligament N94.89
  - specified NEC N43.2
  - spinalis —*see* Spina bifida
  - vulva N90.89
- **Hydrocephalus** (acquired) (external) (internal) (malignant) (recurrent) G91.9
  - aqueduct Sylvius stricture Q03.0
  - causing disproportion O33.6
    - with obstructed labor O66.3
  - communicating G91.0
  - congenital (external) (internal) Q03.9
    - with spina bifida Q05.4
      - cervical Q05.0
      - dorsal Q05.1
      - lumbar Q05.2
      - lumbosacral Q05.2
      - sacral Q05.3
      - thoracic Q05.1
      - thoracolumbar Q05.1
    - specified NEC Q03.8
  - due to toxoplasmosis (congenital) P37.1
  - foramen Magendie block (acquired) G91.1
    - congenital —*see also* Hydrocephalus, congenital Q03.1

Hydrocephalus *(continued)*

  - in (due to)
    - infectious disease NEC B89 *[G91.4]*
    - neoplastic disease NEC(*see* also Neoplasm) G91.4
    - parasitic disease B89 *[G91.4]*
  - newborn Q03.9
    - with spina bifida —*see* Spina bifida, with hydrocephalus
  - noncommunicating G91.1
  - normal pressure G91.2
    - secondary G91.0
  - obstructive G91.1
  - otitic G93.2
  - post-traumatic NEC G91.3
  - secondary G91.4
    - post-traumatic G91.3
  - specified NEC G91.8
  - syphilitic, congenital A50.49
- **Hydrocolpos** (congenital) N89.8
- **Hydrocystoma** —*see* Neoplasm, skin, benign
- **Hydroencephalocele** (congenital) —*see* Encephalocele
- **Hydroencephalomeningocele** (congenital) —*see* Encephalocele
- **Hydrohematopneumothorax** —*see* Hemothorax
- **Hydromeningitis** —*see* Meningitis
- **Hydromeningocele** (spinal) —*see also* Spina bifida
  - cranial —*see* Encephalocele
- **Hydrometra** N85.8
- **Hydrometrocolpos** N89.8
- **Hydromicrocephaly** Q02
- **Hydromphalos** (since birth) Q45.8
- **Hydromyelia** Q06.4
- **Hydromyelocele** —*see* Spina bifida
- **Hydronephrosis** (atrophic) (early) (functionless) (intermittent) (primary) (secondary) **NEC** N13.30
  - with
    - infection N13.6
    - obstruction (by) (of)
      - renal calculus N13.2
        - with infection N13.6
      - ureteral NEC N13.1
        - with infection N13.6
        - calculus N13.2
          - with infection N13.6
      - ureteropelvic junction (congenital) Q62.0
        - with infection N13.6
    - ureteral stricture NEC N13.1
      - with infection N13.6
  - congenital Q62.0
  - specified type NEC N13.39
  - tuberculous A18.11
- **Hydropericarditis** —*see* Pericarditis
- **Hydropericardium** —*see* Pericarditis
- **Hydroperitoneum** R18.8
- **Hydrophobia** —*see* Rabies
- **Hydrophthalmos** Q15.0
- **Hydropneumohemothorax** —*see* Hemothorax
- **Hydropneumopericarditis** —*see* Pericarditis
- **Hydropneumopericardium** —*see* Pericarditis
- **Hydropneumothorax** J94.8
  - traumatic —*see* Injury, intrathoracic, lung
  - tuberculous NEC A15.6
- **Hydrops** R60.9
  - abdominis R18.8
  - articulorum intermittens —*see* Hydrarthrosis, intermittent
  - cardiac —*see* Failure, heart, congestive
  - causing obstructed labor (mother) O66.3
  - endolymphatic H81.0-
  - fetal —*see* Pregnancy, complicated by, hydrops, fetalis
  - fetalis P83.2
    - due to
      - ABO isoimmunization P56.0
      - alpha thalassemia D56.0
      - hemolytic disease P56.90
        - specified NEC P56.99
      - isoimmunization (ABO) (Rh) P56.0
      - other specified nonhemolytic disease NEC P83.2
      - Rh incompatibility P56.0
    - during pregnancy —*see* Pregnancy, complicated by, hydrops, fetalis
  - gallbladder K82.1
  - joint —*see* Effusion, joint
  - labyrinth H81.0-
  - newborn (idiopathic) P83.2
    - due to
      - ABO isoimmunization P56.0
      - alpha thalassemia D56.0
      - hemolytic disease P56.90
        - specified NEC P56.99
      - isoimmunization (ABO) (Rh) P56.0
      - Rh incompatibility P56.0
  - nutritional —*see* Malnutrition, severe
  - pericardium —*see* Pericarditis
  - pleura —*see* Hydrothorax
  - spermatic cord —*see* Hydrocele
- **Hydropyonephrosis** N13.6
- **Hydrorachis** Q06.4
- **Hydrorrhea** (nasal) J34.89
  - pregnancy —*see* Rupture, membranes, premature
- **Hydrosadenitis** (axillaris) (suppurative) L73.2
- **Hydrosalpinx** (fallopian tube) (follicularis) N70.11
- **Hydrothorax** (double) (pleura) J94.8
  - chylous (nonfilarial) I89.8
    - filarial —*see also* Infestation, filarial B74.9 *[J91.8]*
  - traumatic —*see* Injury, intrathoracic
  - tuberculous NEC(non primary) A15.6
- **Hydroureter** —*see also* Hydronephrosis N13.4
  - with infection N13.6
  - congenital Q62.39
- **Hydroureteronephrosis** —*see* Hydronephrosis
- **Hydrourethra** N36.8
- **Hydroxykynureninuria** E70.8
- **Hydroxylysinemia** E72.3
- **Hydroxyprolinemia** E72.59
- **Hygiene, sleep**
  - abuse Z72.821
  - inadequate Z72.821
  - poor Z72.821
- **Hygroma** (congenital) (cystic) D18.1
  - praepatellare, prepatellar —*see* Bursitis, prepatellar
- **Hymen** —*see* condition
- **Hymenolepis, hymenolepiasis** (diminuta) (infection) (infestation) (nana) B71.0

ypalgesia R20.8
yperacidity (gastric) K31.89
psychogenic F45.8
yperactive, hyperactivity F90.9
basal cell, uterine cervix *—see* Dysplasia, cervix
bowel sounds R19.12
cervix epithelial (basal) *—see* Dysplasia, cervix
child F90.9
attention deficit *—see* Disorder, attention-deficit hyperactivity
detrusor muscle N32.81
gastrointestinal K31.89
psychogenic F45.8
nasal mucous membrane J34.3
stomach K31.89
thyroid (gland) *—see* Hyperthyroidism
yperacusis H93.23-
yperadrenalism E27.5
yperadrenocorticism E24.9
congenital E25.0
iatrogenic E24.2
correct substance properly administered *—see* Table of Drugs and Chemicals, by drug, adverse effect
overdose or wrong substance given or taken *—see* Table of Drugs and Chemicals, by drug, poisoning
not associated with Cushing's syndrome E27.0
pituitary-dependent E24.0
yperaldosteronism E26.9
familial (type I) E26.02
glucocorticoid-remediable E26.02
primary (due to (bilateral) adrenal hyperplasia) E26.09
primary NEC E26.09
secondary E26.1
specified NEC E26.89
yperalgesia R20.8
yperalimentation R63.2
carotene, carotin E67.1
specified NEC E67.8
vitamin
A E67.0
D E67.3
yperaminoaciduria
arginine E72.21
cystine E72.01
lysine E72.3
ornithine E72.4
yperammonemia (congenital) E72.20
yperazotemia *—see* Uremia
yperbetalipoproteinemia (familial) E78.0
with prebetalipoproteinemia E78.2
yperbilirubinemia
constitutional E80.6
familial conjugated E80.6
neonatal (transient) *—see* Jaundice, newborn
Hypercalcemia, hypocalciuric, familial E83.52
Hypercalciuria, idiopathic E83.52
Hypercapnia R06.89
newborn P84
Hypercarotenemia, hypercarotinemia (dietary) E67.1
Hypercementosis K03.4
Hyperchloremia E87.8
Hyperchlorhydria K31.89
neurotic F45.8
psychogenic F45.8
Hypercholesterinemia *—see* Hypercholesterolemia
Hypercholesterolemia (essential) (familial) (hereditary) (primary) (pure) E78.0
with hyperglyceridemia, endogenous E78.2
dietary counseling and surveillance Z71.3
Hyperchylia gastrica, psychogenic F45.8
Hyperchylomicronemia (familial) (primary) E78.3
with hyperbetalipoproteinemia E78.3
Hypercoagulable (state) D68.59
activated protein C resistance D68.51
antithrombin (III) deficiency D68.59
factor V Leiden mutation D68.51
primary NEC D68.59
protein C deficiency D68.59
protein S deficiency D68.59
prothrombin gene mutation D68.52
secondary D68.69
specified NEC D68.69
Hypercoagulation (state) D68.59
Hypercorticalism, pituitary-dependent E24.0
Hypercorticosolism *—see* Cushing's, syndrome
Hypercorticosteronism E24.2
correct substance properly administered *—see* Table of Drugs and Chemicals, by drug, adverse effect
overdose or wrong substance given or taken *—see* Table of Drugs and Chemicals, by drug, poisoning
Hypercortisonism E24.2
correct substance properly administered *—see* Table of Drugs and Chemicals, by drug, adverse effect
overdose or wrong substance given or taken *—see* Table of Drugs and Chemicals, by drug, poisoning
Hyperekplexia Q89.8
Hyperelectrolytemia E87.8
Hyperemesis R11.10
with nausea R11.2
gravidarum (mild) O21.0
with
carbohydrate depletion O21.1
dehydration O21.1
electrolyte imbalance O21.1
metabolic disturbance O21.1
severe (with metabolic disturbance) O21.1
projectile R11.12
psychogenic F45.8
Hyperemia (acute) (passive) R68.89
anal mucosa K62.89
bladder N32.89
cerebral I67.89
conjunctiva H11.43-
ear internal, acute H83.0
enteric K59.8
eye *—see* Hyperemia, conjunctiva
eyelid (active) (passive) *—see* Disorder, eyelid, specified type NEC
intestine K59.8
iris *—see* Disorder, iris, vascular
kidney N28.89
labyrinth H83.0
Hyperemia *(continued)*
liver (active) K76.89
lung (passive) *—see* Edema, lung
pulmonary (passive) *—see* Edema, lung
renal N28.89
retina H35.89
stomach K31.89
Hyperesthesia (body surface) R20.3
larynx (reflex) J38.7
hysterical F44.89
pharynx (reflex) J39.2
hysterical F44.89
Hyperestrogenism (drug-induced) (iatrogenic) E28.0
Hyperexplexia Q89.8
Hyperfibrinolysis *—see* Fibrinolysis
Hyperfructosemia E74.19
Hyperfunction
adrenal cortex, not associated with Cushing's syndrome E27.0
medulla E27.5
adrenomedullary E27.5
virilism E25.9
congenital E25.0
ovarian E28.8
pancreas K86.8
parathyroid (gland) E21.3
pituitary (gland) (anterior) E22.9
specified NEC E22.8
polyglandular E31.1
testicular E29.0
Hypergammaglobulinemia D89.2
polyclonal D89.0
Waldenström D89.0
Hypergastrinemia E16.4
Hyperglobulinemia R77.1
Hyperglycemia, hyperglycemic (transient) R73.9
coma *—see* Diabetes, by type, with coma
postpancreatectomy E89.1
Hyperglyceridemia (endogenous) (essential) (familial) (hereditary) (pure) E78.1
mixed E78.3
Hyperglycinemia (non-ketotic) E72.51
Hypergonadism
ovarian E28.8
testicular (primary) (infantile) E29.0
Hyperheparinemia D68.32
Hyperhidrosis, hyperidrosis R61
focal
primary L74.519
axilla L74.510
face L74.511
palms L74.512
soles L74.513
secondary L74.52
generalized R61
localized
primary L74.519
axilla L74.510
face L74.511
palms L74.512
soles L74.513
secondary L74.52
psychogenic F45.8
secondary R61
focal L74.52
Hyperhistidinemia E70.41
Hyperhomocysteinemia E72.11
Hyperhydroxyprolinemia E72.59
Hyperinsulinism (functional) E16.1
with
coma (hypoglycemic) E15
encephalopathy E16.1 *[G94]*
ectopic E16.1
therapeutic misadventure (from administration of insulin) T38.3
Hyperkalemia E87.5
Hyperkeratosis *—see also* Keratosis L85.9
cervix N88.0
due to yaws (early) (late) (palmar or plantar) A66.3
follicularis Q82.8
penetrans (in cutem) L87.0
palmoplantaris climacterica L85.1
pinta A67.1
senile (with pruritus) L57.0
universalis congenita Q80.8
vocal cord J38.3
vulva N90.4
Hyperkinesia, hyperkinetic (disease) (reaction) (syndrome) (childhood) (adolescence) *—see also* Disorder, attention-deficit hyperactivity
heart I51.89
Hyperleucine-isoleucinemia E71.19
Hyperlipemia, hyperlipidemia E78.5
combined E78.2
familial E78.4
group
A E78.0
B E78.1
C E78.2
D E78.3
mixed E78.2
specified NEC E78.4
Hyperlipidosis E75.6
hereditary NEC E75.5
Hyperlipoproteinemia E78.5
Fredrickson's type
I E78.3
IIa E78.0
IIb E78.2
III E78.2
IV E78.1
V E78.3
low-density-lipoprotein-type (LDL) E78.0
very-low-density-lipoprotein-type (VLDL) E78.1
Hyperlucent lung, unilateral J43.0
Hyperlysinemia E72.3
Hypermagnesemia E83.41
neonatal P71.8
Hypermenorrhea N92.0
Hypermethioninemia E72.19
Hypermetropia (congenital) H52.0-
Hypermobility, hypermotility
cecum *—see* Syndrome, irritable bowel
coccyx *—see* subcategory M53.2
colon *—see* Syndrome, irritable bowel
psychogenic F45.8
ileum K58.9
intestine *—see also* Syndrome, irritable bowel K58.9
psychogenic F45.8
meniscus (knee) *—see* Derangement, knee, meniscus
scapula *—see* Instability, joint, shoulder
stomach K31.89
psychogenic F45.8

- **Hypermobility, hypermotility** *(continued)*
  - syndrome M35.7
  - urethra N36.41
    - with intrinsic sphincter deficiency N36.43
- **Hypernasality** R49.21
- **Hypernatremia** E87.0
- **Hypernephroma** C64.-
- **Hyperopia** —*see* Hypermetropia
- **Hyperorexia nervosa** F50.2
- **Hyperornithinemia** E72.4
- **Hyperosmia** R43.1
- **Hyperosmolality** E87.0
- **Hyperostosis** (monomelic) —*see also* Disorder, bone, density and structure, specified NEC
  - ankylosing (spine) M48.10
    - cervical region M48.12
    - cervicothoracic region M48.13
    - lumbar region M48.16
    - lumbosacral region M48.17
    - multiple sites M48.19
    - occipito-atlanto-axial region M48.11
    - sacrococcygeal region M48.18
    - thoracic region M48.14
    - thoracolumbar region M48.15
  - cortical (skull) M85.2
    - infantile M89.8X-
  - frontal, internal of skull M85.2
  - interna frontalis M85.2
  - skeletal, diffuse idiopathic —*see* Hyperostosis, ankylosing
  - skull M85.2
    - congenital Q75.8
  - vertebral, ankylosing —*see* Hyperostosis, ankylosing
- **Hyperovarism** E28.8
- **Hyperoxaluria** (primary) E72.53
- **Hyperparathyroidism** E21.3
  - primary E21.0
  - secondary (renal) N25.81
    - non-renal E21.1
  - specified NEC E21.2
  - tertiary E21.2
- **Hyperpathia** R20.8
- **Hyperperistalsis** R19.2
  - psychogenic F45.8
- **Hyperpermeability, capillary** I78.8
- **Hyperphagia** R63.2
- **Hyperphenylalaninemia NEC** E70.1
- **Hyperphoria** (alternating) H50.53
- **Hyperphosphatemia** E83.39
- **Hyperpiesis, hyperpiesia** —*see* Hypertension
- **Hyperpigmentation** —*see also* Pigmentation
  - melanin NEC L81.4
  - postinflammatory L81.0
- **Hyperpinealism** E34.8
- **Hyperpituitarism** E22.9
- **Hyperplasia, hyperplastic**
  - adenoids J35.2
  - adrenal (capsule) (cortex) (gland) E27.8
    - with
      - sexual precocity (male) E25.9
        - congenital E25.0
      - virilism, adrenal E25.9
        - congenital E25.0
      - virilization (female) E25.9
        - congenital E25.0
    - congenital E25.0
      - salt-losing E25.0

- **Hyperplasia, hyperplastic** *(continued)*
  - adrenomedullary E27.5
  - angiolymphoid, eosinophilia (ALHE) D18.01
  - appendix (lymphoid) K38.0
  - artery, fibromuscular I77.3
  - bone —*see also* Hypertrophy, bone
    - marrow D75.89
  - breast —*see also* Hypertrophy, breast
    - ductal (atypical) N60.9-
  - C-cell, thyroid E07.0
  - cementation (tooth) (teeth) K03.4
  - cervical gland R59.0
  - cervix (uteri) (basal cell) (endometrium) (polypoid) —*see also* Dysplasia, cervix
    - congenital Q51.828
  - clitoris, congenital Q52.6
  - denture K06.2
  - endocervicitis N72
  - endometrium, endometrial (adenomatous) (benign) (cystic) (glandular) (glandular-cystic) (polypoid) N85.00
    - with atypia N85.02
    - cervix —*see* Dysplasia, cervix
    - complex (without atypia) N85.01
    - simple (without atypia) N85.01
  - epithelial L85.9
    - focal, oral, including tongue K13.29
    - nipple N62
    - skin L85.9
    - tongue K13.29
    - vaginal wall N89.3
  - erythroid D75.89
  - fibromuscular of artery (carotid) (renal) I77.3
  - genital
    - female NEC N94.89
    - male N50.8
  - gingiva K06.1
  - glandularis cystica uteri (interstitialis) —*see also* Hyperplasia, endometrial N85.00-
  - gum K06.1
  - hymen, congenital Q52.4
  - irritative, edentulous (alveolar) K06.2
  - jaw M26.09
    - alveolar M26.79
    - lower M26.03
      - alveolar M26.72
    - upper M26.01
      - alveolar M26.71
  - kidney (congenital) Q63.3
  - labia N90.6
    - epithelial N90.3
  - liver (congenital) Q44.7
    - nodular, focal K76.89
  - lymph gland or node R59.9
  - mandible, mandibular M26.03
    - alveolar M26.72
    - unilateral condylar M27.8
  - maxilla, maxillary M26.01
    - alveolar M26.71
  - myometrium, myometrial N85.2
  - neuroendocrine cell, of infancy J84.841
  - nose
    - lymphoid J34.89
    - polypoid J33.9
  - oral mucosa (irritative) K13.6
  - organ or site, congenital NEC —*see* Anomaly, by site
  - ovary N83.8
  - palate, papillary (irritative) K13.6
  - pancreatic islet cells E16.9
    - alpha E16.8
      - with excess
        - gastrin E16.4
        - glucagon E16.3
    - beta E16.1

- **Hyperplasia, hyperplastic** *(continued)*
  - parathyroid (gland) E21.0
  - pharynx (lymphoid) J39.2
  - prostate (adenofibromatous) (nodular) N40.0
    - with lower urinary tract symptoms (LUTS) N40.1
    - without lower urinary tract symtpoms (LUTS) N40.0
  - renal artery I77.89
  - reticulo-endothelial (cell) D75.89
  - salivary gland (any) K11.1
  - Schimmelbusch's —*see* Mastopathy, cystic
  - suprarenal capsule (gland) E27.8
  - thymus (gland) (persistent) E32.0
  - thyroid (gland) —*see* Goiter
  - tonsils (faucial) (infective) (lingual) (lymphoid) J35.1
    - with adenoids J35.3
  - unilateral condylar M27.8
  - uterus, uterine N85.2
    - endometrium (glandular) —*see also* Hyperplasia, endometrial N85.00-
  - vulva N90.6
    - epithelial N90.3
- **Hyperpnea** —*see* Hyperventilation
- **Hyperpotassemia** E87.5
- **Hyperprebetalipoproteinemia** (familial) E78.1
- **Hyperprolactinemia** E22.1
- **Hyperprolinemia** (type I) (type II) E72.59
- **Hyperproteinemia** E88.09
- **Hyperprothrombinemia, causing coagulation factor deficiency** D68.4
- **Hyperpyrexia** R50.9
  - heat (effects) T67.0
  - malignant, due to anesthetic T88.3
  - rheumatic —*see* Fever, rheumatic
  - unknown origin R50.9
- **Hyper-reflexia** R29.2
- **Hypersalivation** K11.7
- **Hypersecretion**
  - ACTH (not associated with Cushing's syndrome) E27.0
    - pituitary E24.0
  - adrenaline E27.5
  - adrenomedullary E27.5
  - androgen (testicular) E29.0
    - ovarian (drug-induced) (iatrogenic) E28.1
  - calcitonin E07.0
  - catecholamine E27.5
  - corticoadrenal E24.9
  - cortisol E24.9
  - epinephrine E27.5
  - estrogen E28.0
  - gastric K31.89
    - psychogenic F45.8
  - gastrin E16.4
  - glucagon E16.3
  - hormone (s)
    - ACTH(not associated with Cushing's syndrome) E27.0
      - pituitary E24.0
    - antidiuretic E22.2
    - growth E22.0
    - intestinal NEC E34.1
    - ovarian androgen E28.1
    - pituitary E22.9
    - testicular E29.0
    - thyroid stimulating E05.80
      - with thyroid storm E05.81
  - insulin —*see* Hyperinsulinism
  - lacrimal glands —*see* Epiphora
  - medulloadrenal E27.5

- **Hypersecretion** *(continued)*
  - milk O92.6
  - ovarian androgens E28.1
  - salivary gland (any) K11.7
  - thyrocalcitonin E07.0
  - upper respiratory J39.8
- **Hypersegmentation, leukocytic, hereditary** D72.0
- **Hypersensitive, hypersensitiveness, hypersensitivity** —*see also* Allergy
  - carotid sinus G90.01
  - colon —*see* Irritable, colon
  - drug T88.7
  - gastrointestinal K52.2
    - psychogenic F45.8
  - labyrinth H83.2
  - pain R20.8
  - pneumonitis —*see* Pneumonitis, allergic
  - reaction T78.40
    - upper respiratory tract NEC J39.3
- **Hypersomnia** (organic) G47.10
  - due to
    - alcohol
      - abuse F10.182
      - dependence F10.282
      - use F10.982
    - amphetamines
      - abuse F15.182
      - dependence F15.282
      - use F15.982
    - caffeine
      - abuse F15.182
      - dependence F15.282
      - use F15.982
    - cocaine
      - abuse F14.182
      - dependence F14.282
      - use F14.982
    - drug NEC
      - abuse F19.182
      - dependence F19.282
      - use F19.982
    - medical condition G47.14
    - mental disorder F51.13
    - opioid
      - abuse F11.182
      - dependence F11.282
      - use F11.982
    - psychoactive substance NEC
      - abuse F19.182
      - dependence F19.282
      - use F19.982
    - sedative, hypnotic, or anxiolytic
      - abuse F13.182
      - dependence F13.282
      - use F13.982
    - stimulant NEC
      - abuse F15.182
      - dependence F15.282
      - use F15.982
  - idiopathic G47.11
    - with long sleep time G47.11
    - without long sleep time G47.12
  - menstrual related G47.13
  - nonorganic origin F51.11
    - specified NEC F51.19
  - not due to a substance or known physiological condition F51.11
    - specified NEC F51.19
  - primary F51.11
  - recurrent G47.13
  - specified NEC G47.19
- **Hypersplenia, hypersplenism** D73.1
- **Hyperstimulation, ovaries** (associated with induced ovulation) N98.1
- **Hypersusceptibility** —*see* Allergy
- **Hypertelorism** (ocular) (orbital) Q75.2

Hypertrophy, hypertrophic *(continued)*
- liver *(continued)*
  - cirrhotic —*see* Cirrhosis, liver
  - fatty —*see* Fatty, liver
- lymph, lymphatic gland R59.9
  - generalized R59.1
  - localized R59.0
  - tuberculous —*see* Tuberculosis, lymph gland
- mammary gland —*see* Hypertrophy, breast
- Meckel's diverticulum (congenital) Q43.0
  - malignant —*see* Table of Neoplasms, small intestine, malignant
- median bar —*see* Hyperplasia, prostate
- meibomian gland —*see* Chalazion
- meniscus, knee, congenital Q74.1
- metatarsal head —*see* Hypertrophy, bone, metatarsus
- metatarsus —*see* Hypertrophy, bone, metatarsus
- mucous membrane
  - alveolar ridge K06.2
  - gum K06.1
  - nose (turbinate) J34.3
- muscle M62.89
- muscular coat, artery I77.89
- myocardium —*see also* Hypertrophy, cardiac
  - idiopathic I42.2
- myometrium N85.2
- nail L60.2
  - congenital Q84.5
- nasal J34.89
  - alae J34.89
  - bone J34.89
  - cartilage J34.89
  - mucous membrane (septum) J34.3
  - sinus J34.89
  - turbinate J34.3
- nasopharynx, lymphoid (infectional) (tissue) (wall) J35.2
- nipple N62
- organ or site, congenital NEC —*see* Anomaly, by site
- ovary N83.8
- palate (hard) M27.8
  - soft K13.79
- pancreas, congenital Q45.3
- parathyroid (gland) E21.0
- parotid gland K11.1
- penis N48.89
- pharyngeal tonsil J35.2
- pharynx J39.2
  - lymphoid (infectional) (tissue) (wall) J35.2
- pituitary (anterior) (fossa) (gland) E23.6
- prepuce (congenital) N47.8
  - female N90.89
- prostate —*see* Enlargement, enlarged, prostate
  - congenital Q55.4
- pseudomuscular G71.0
- pylorus (adult) (muscle) (sphincter) K31.1
  - congenital or infantile Q40.0
- rectal, rectum (sphincter) K62.89
- rhinitis (turbinate) J31.0
- salivary gland (any) K11.1
  - congenital Q38.4
- scaphoid (tarsal) —*see* Hypertrophy, bone, tarsus
- scar L91.0
- scrotum N50.8
- seminal vesicle N50.8
- sigmoid —*see* Megacolon
- skin L91.9
  - specified NEC L91.8

Hypertrophy, hypertrophic *(continued)*
- spermatic cord N50.8
- spleen —*see* Splenomegaly
- spondylitis —*see* Spondylosis
- stomach K31.89
- sublingual gland K11.1
- submandibular gland K11.1
- suprarenal cortex (gland) E27.8
- synovial NEC M67.20
  - acromioclavicular M67.21-
  - ankle M67.27-
  - elbow M67.22-
  - foot M67.27-
  - hand M67.24-
  - hip M67.25-
  - knee M67.26-
  - multiple sites M67.29
  - specified site NEC M67.28
  - wrist M67.23-
- tendon —*see* Disorder, tendon, specified type NEC
- testis N44.8
  - congenital Q55.29
- thymic, thymus (gland) (congenital) E32.0
- thyroid (gland) —*see* Goiter
- toe (congenital) Q74.2
  - acquired —*see also* Deformity, toe, specified NEC
- tongue K14.8
  - congenital Q38.2
  - papillae (foliate) K14.3
- tonsils (faucial) (infective) (lingual) (lymphoid) J35.1
  - with adenoids J35.3
- tunica vaginalis N50.8
- ureter N28.89
- urethra N36.8
- uterus N85.2
  - neck (with elongation) N88.4
  - puerperal O90.89
- uvula K13.79
- vagina N89.8
- vas deferens N50.8
- vein I87.8
- ventricle, ventricular (heart) —*see also* Hypertrophy, cardiac
  - congenital Q24.8
  - in tetralogy of Fallot Q21.3
- verumontanum N36.8
- vocal cord J38.3
- vulva N90.6
  - stasis (nonfilarial) N90.6

Hypertropia H50.2-

Hypertyrosinemia E70.21

Hyperuricemia (asymptomatic) E79.0

Hypervalinemia E71.19

Hyperventilation (tetany) R06.4
- hysterical F45.8
- psychogenic F45.8
- syndrome F45.8

Hypervitaminosis (dietary) **NEC** E67.8
- A E67.0
  - administered as drug (prolonged intake) —*see* Table of Drugs and Chemicals, vitamins, adverse effect
  - overdose or wrong substance given or taken —*see* Table of Drugs and Chemicals, vitamins, poisoning
- B6 *[E67.2]*
- D E67.3
  - administered as drug (prolonged intake) —*see* Table of Drugs and Chemicals, vitamins, adverse effect
  - overdose or wrong substance given or taken —*see* Table of Drugs and Chemicals, vitamins, poisoning

Hypervitaminosis *(continued)*
- K E67.8
  - administered as drug (prolonged intake) —*see* Table of Drugs and Chemicals, vitamins, adverse effect
  - overdose or wrong substance given or taken —*see* Table of Drugs and Chemicals, vitamins, poisoning

Hypervolemia E87.70
- specified NEC E87.79

Hypesthesia R20.1
- cornea —*see* Anesthesia, cornea

Hyphema H21.0-
- traumatic S05.1-

Hypoacidity, gastric K31.89
- psychogenic F45.8

Hypoadrenalism, hypoadrenia E27.40
- primary E27.1
- tuberculous A18.7

Hypoadrenocorticism E27.40
- pituitary E23.0
- primary E27.1

Hypoalbuminemia E88.09

Hypoaldosteronism E27.40

Hypoalphalipoproteinemia E78.6

Hypobarism T70.29

Hypobaropathy T70.29

Hypobetalipoproteinemia (familial) E78.6

Hypocalcemia E83.51
- dietary E58
- neonatal P71.1
  - due to cow's milk P71.0
- phosphate-loading (newborn) P71.1

Hypochloremia E87.8

Hypochlorhydria K31.89
- neurotic F45.8
- psychogenic F45.8

Hypochondria, hypochondriac, hypochondriasis (reaction) F45.21
- sleep F51.03

Hypochondrogenesis Q77.0

Hypochondroplasia Q77.4

Hypochromasia, blood cells D50.8

Hypodontia —*see* Anodontia

Hypoeosinophilia D72.89

Hypoesthesia R20.1

Hypofibrinogenemia D68.8
- acquired D65
- congenital (hereditary) D68.2

Hypofunction
- adrenocortical E27.40
  - drug-induced E27.3
  - postprocedural E89.6
  - primary E27.1
- adrenomedullary, postprocedural E89.6
- cerebral R29.818
- corticoadrenal NEC E27.40
- intestinal K59.8
- labyrinth H83.2
- ovary E28.39
- pituitary (gland) (anterior) E23.0
- testicular E29.1
  - postprocedural (postsurgical) (postirradiation) (iatrogenic) E89.5

Hypogalactia O92.4

Hypogammaglobulinemia —*see also* Agammaglobulinemia D80.1
- hereditary D80.0

Hypogammaglobulinemia *(continued)*
- nonfamilial D80.1
- transient, of infancy D80.7

Hypogenitalism (congenital) —*see* Hypogonadism

Hypoglossia Q38.3

Hypoglycemia (spontaneous) E16.2
- coma E15
  - diabetic —*see* Diabetes, coma
- diabetic —*see* Diabetes, hypoglycemia
- dietary counseling and surveillance Z71.3
- drug-induced E16.0
  - with coma (nondiabetic) E15
- due to insulin E16.0
  - with coma (nondiabetic) E15
  - therapeutic misadventure —*see* subcategory T38.3
- functional, nonhyperinsulinemic E16.1
- iatrogenic E16.0
  - with coma (nondiabetic) E15
- in infant of diabetic mother P70.1
  - gestational diabetes P70.0
- infantile E16.1
- leucine-induced E71.19
- neonatal (transitory) P70.4
  - iatrogenic P70.3
- reactive (not drug-induced) E16.1
- transitory neonatal P70.4

Hypogonadism
- female E28.39
- hypogonadotropic E23.0
- male E29.1
- ovarian (primary) E28.39
- pituitary E23.0
- testicular (primary) E29.1

Hypohidrosis, hypoidrosis L74.4

Hypoinsulinemia, postprocedural E89.1

Hypokalemia E87.6

Hypoleukocytosis —*see* Agranulocytosis

Hypolipoproteinemia (alpha) (beta) E78.6

Hypomagnesemia E83.42
- neonatal P71.2

Hypomania, hypomanic reaction F30

Hypomenorrhea —*see* Oligomenorrhea

Hypometabolism R63.8

Hypomotility
- gastrointestinal (tract) K31.89
  - psychogenic F45.8
- intestine K59.8
  - psychogenic F45.8
- stomach K31.89
  - psychogenic F45.8

Hyponasality R49.22

Hyponatremia E87.1

Hypo-osmolality E87.1

Hypo-ovarianism, hypo-ovarism E28.39

Hypoparathyroidism E20.9
- familial E20.8
- idiopathic E20.0
- neonatal, transitory P71.4
- postprocedural E89.2
- specified NEC E20.8

Hypoperfusion (in)
- newborn P96.89

Hypopharyngitis —*see* Laryngopharyngitis

- **ypophoria** H50.53
- **ypophosphatemia, hypophosphatasia** (acquired) (congenital) (renal) E83.39
  - familial E83.31
- **ypophyseal, hypophysis** —*see also* condition
  - dwarfism E23.0
  - gigantism E22.0
- **ypopiesis** —*see* Hypotension
- **ypopinealism** E34.8
- **ypopituitarism** (juvenile) E23.0
  - drug-induced E23.1
  - due to
    - hypophysectomy E89.3
    - radiotherapy E89.3
  - iatrogenic NEC E23.1
  - postirradiation E89.3
  - postpartum E23.0
  - postprocedural E89.3
- **ypoplasia, hypoplastic**
  - adrenal (gland), congenital Q89.1
  - alimentary tract, congenital Q45.8
    - upper Q40.8
  - anus, anal (canal) Q42.3
    - with fistula Q42.2
  - aorta, aortic Q25.4
    - ascending, in hypoplastic left heart syndrome Q23.4
    - valve Q23.1
      - in hypoplastic left heart syndrome Q23.4
  - areola, congenital Q83.8
  - arm (congenital) —*see* Defect, reduction, upper limb
  - artery (peripheral) Q27.8
    - brain (congenital) Q28.3
    - coronary Q24.5
    - digestive system Q27.8
    - lower limb Q27.8
    - pulmonary Q25.79
      - functional, unilateral J43.0
    - retinal (congenital) Q14.1
    - specified site NEC Q27.8
    - umbilical Q27.0
    - upper limb Q27.8
  - auditory canal Q17.8
    - causing impairment of hearing Q16.9
  - biliary duct or passage Q44.5
  - bone NOS Q79.9
    - face Q75.8
    - marrow D61.9
      - megakaryocytic D69.49
    - skull —*see* Hypoplasia, skull
  - brain Q02
    - gyri Q04.3
    - part of Q04.3
  - breast (areola) N64.82
  - bronchus Q32.4
  - cardiac Q24.8
  - carpus —*see* Defect, reduction, upper limb, specified type NEC
  - cartilage hair Q78.5
  - cecum Q42.8
  - cementum K00.4
  - cephalic Q02
  - cerebellum Q04.3
  - cervix (uteri), congenital Q51.821
  - clavicle (congenital) Q74.0
  - coccyx Q76.49
  - colon Q42.9
    - specified NEC Q42.8
  - corpus callosum Q04.0
  - cricoid cartilage Q31.2
  - digestive organ (s) or tract NEC Q45.8
    - upper (congenital) Q40.8
  - ear (auricle) (lobe) Q17.2
    - middle Q16.4

Hypoplasia, hypoplastic *(continued)*

  - enamel of teeth (neonatal) (postnatal) (prenatal) K00.4
  - endocrine (gland) NEC Q89.2
  - endometrium N85.8
  - epididymis (congenital) Q55.4
  - epiglottis Q31.2
  - erythroid, congenital D61.01
  - esophagus (congenital) Q39.8
  - eustachian tube Q17.8
  - eye Q11.2
  - eyelid (congenital) Q10.3
  - face Q18.8
    - bone (s) Q75.8
  - femur (congenital) —*see* Defect, reduction, lower limb, specified type NEC
  - fibula (congenital) —*see* Defect, reduction, lower limb, specified type NEC
  - finger (congenital) —*see* Defect, reduction, upper limb, specified type NEC
  - focal dermal Q82.8
  - foot —*see* Defect, reduction, lower limb, specified type NEC
  - gallbladder Q44.0
  - genitalia, genital organ (s)
    - female, congenital Q52.8
      - external Q52.79
      - internal NEC Q52.8
    - in adiposogenital dystrophy E23.6
  - glottis Q31.2
  - hair Q84.2
  - hand (congenital) —*see* Defect, reduction, upper limb, specified type NEC
  - heart Q24.8
  - humerus (congenital) —*see* Defect, reduction, upper limb, specified type NEC
  - intestine (small) Q41.9
    - large Q42.9
      - specified NEC Q42.8
  - jaw M26.09
    - alveolar M26.79
    - lower M26.04
      - alveolar M26.74
    - upper M26.02
      - alveolar M26.73
  - kidney (s) Q60.5
    - bilateral Q60.4
    - unilateral Q60.3
  - labium (majus) (minus), congenital Q52.79
  - larynx Q31.2
  - left heart syndrome Q23.4
  - leg (congenital) —*see* Defect, reduction, lower limb
  - limb Q73.8
    - lower (congenital) —*see* Defect, reduction, lower limb
    - upper (congenital) —*see* Defect, reduction, upper limb
  - liver Q44.7
  - lung (lobe) (not associated with short gestation) Q33.6
    - associated with immaturity, low birth weight, prematurity, or short gestation P28.0
  - mammary (areola), congenital Q83.8
  - mandible, mandibular M26.04
    - alveolar M26.74
    - unilateral condylar M27.8
  - maxillary M26.02
    - alveolar M26.73
  - medullary D61.9
  - megakaryocytic D69.49
  - metacarpus —*see* Defect, reduction, upper limb, specified type NEC
  - metatarsus —*see* Defect, reduction, lower limb, specified type NEC

Hypoplasia, hypoplastic *(continued)*

  - muscle Q79.8
  - nail (s) Q84.6
  - nose, nasal Q30.1
  - optic nerve H47.03-
  - osseous meatus (ear) Q17.8
  - ovary, congenital Q50.39
  - pancreas Q45.0
  - parathyroid (gland) Q89.2
  - parotid gland Q38.4
  - patella Q74.1
  - pelvis, pelvic girdle Q74.2
  - penis (congenital) Q55.62
  - peripheral vascular system Q27.8
    - digestive system Q27.8
    - lower limb Q27.8
    - specified site NEC Q27.8
    - upper limb Q27.8
  - pituitary (gland) (congenital) Q89.2
  - pulmonary (not associated with short gestation) Q33.6
    - artery, functional J43.0
    - associated with short gestation P28.0
  - radioulnar —*see* Defect, reduction, upper limb, specified type NEC
  - radius —*see* Defect, reduction, upper limb
  - rectum Q42.1
    - with fistula Q42.0
  - respiratory system NEC Q34.8
  - rib Q76.6
  - right heart syndrome Q22.6
  - sacrum Q76.49
  - scapula Q74.0
  - scrotum Q55.1
  - shoulder girdle Q74.0
  - skin Q82.8
  - skull (bone) Q75.8
    - with
      - anencephaly Q00.0
      - encephalocele —*see* Encephalocele
      - hydrocephalus Q03.9
        - with spina bifida —*see* Spina bifida, by site, with hydrocephalus
      - microcephaly Q02
  - spinal (cord) (ventral horn cell) Q06.1
  - spine Q76.49
  - sternum Q76.7
  - tarsus —*see* Defect, reduction, lower limb, specified type NEC
  - testis Q55.1
  - thymic, with immunodeficiency D82.1
  - thymus (gland) Q89.2
    - with immunodeficiency D82.1
  - thyroid (gland) E03.1
    - cartilage Q31.2
  - tibiofibular (congenital) —*see* Defect, reduction, lower limb, specified type NEC
  - toe —*see* Defect, reduction, lower limb, specified type NEC
  - tongue Q38.3
  - Turner's K00.4
  - ulna (congenital) —*see* Defect, reduction, upper limb
  - umbilical artery Q27.0
  - unilateral condylar M27.8
  - ureter Q62.8
  - uterus, congenital Q51.811
  - vagina Q52.4
  - vascular NEC peripheral Q27.8
    - brain Q28.3
    - digestive system Q27.8
    - lower limb Q27.8
    - specified site NEC Q27.8
    - upper limb Q27.8

Hypoplasia, hypoplastic *(continued)*

  - vein (s) (peripheral) Q27.8
    - brain Q28.3
    - digestive system Q27.8
    - great Q26.8
    - lower limb Q27.8
    - specified site NEC Q27.8
    - upper limb Q27.8
  - vena cava (inferior) (superior) Q26.8
  - vertebra Q76.49
  - vulva, congenital Q52.79
  - zonule (ciliary) Q12.8
- **Hypopotassemia** E87.6
- **Hypoproconvertinemia, congenital** (hereditary) D68.2
- **Hypoproteinemia** E77.8
- **Hypoprothrombinemia** (congenital) (hereditary) (idiopathic) D68.2
  - acquired D68.4
  - newborn, transient P61.6
- **Hypoptyalism** K11.7
- **Hypopyon** (eye) (anterior chamber) —*see* Iridocyclitis, acute, hypopyon
- **Hypopyrexia** R68.0
- **Hyporeflexia** R29.2
- **Hyposecretion**
  - ACTH E23.0
  - antidiuretic hormone E23.2
  - ovary E28.39
  - salivary gland (any) K11.7
  - vasopressin E23.2
- **Hyposegmentation, leukocytic, hereditary** D72.0
- **Hyposiderinemia** D50.9
- **Hypospadias** Q54.9
  - balanic Q54.0
  - coronal Q54.0
  - glandular Q54.0
  - penile Q54.1
  - penoscrotal Q54.2
  - perineal Q54.3
  - specified NEC Q54.8
- **Hypospermatogenesis** —*see* Oligospermia
- **Hyposplenism** D73.0
- **Hypostasis pulmonary, passive** —*see* Edema, lung
- **Hypostatic** —*see* condition
- **Hyposthenuria** N28.89
- **Hypotension** (arterial) (constitutional) I95.9
  - chronic I95.89
  - due to (of) hemodialysis I95.3
  - drug-induced I95.2
  - iatrogenic I95.89
  - idiopathic (permanent) I95.0
  - intracranial, following ventricular shunting (ventriculostomy) G97.2
  - intra-dialytic I95.3
  - maternal, syndrome (following labor and delivery) O26.5-
  - neurogenic, orthostatic G90.3
  - orthostatic (chronic) I95.1
    - due to drugs I95.2
    - neurogenic G90.3
  - postoperative I95.81
  - postural I95.1
  - specified NEC I95.89
- **Hypothermia** (accidental) T68
  - due to anesthesia, anesthetic T88.51
  - low environmental temperature T68
  - neonatal P80.9
    - environmental (mild) NEC P80.8
    - mild P80.8

Hypothermia *(continued)*
- neonatal *(continued)*
  - severe (chronic) (cold injury syndrome) P80.0
  - specified NEC P80.8
- not associated with low environmental temperature R68.0

Hypothyroidism (acquired) E03.9
- congenital (without goiter) E03.1
  - with goiter (diffuse) E03.0
- due to
  - exogenous substance NEC E03.2
  - iodine-deficiency, acquired E01.8
    - subclinical E02
  - irradiation therapy E89.0
  - medicament NEC E03.2
  - P-aminosalicylic acid (PAS) E03.2
  - phenylbutazone E03.2
  - resorcinol E03.2
  - sulfonamide E03.2
  - surgery E89.0
  - thiourea group drugs E03.2
- iatrogenic NEC E03.2
- iodine-deficiency (acquired) E01.8
  - congenital —*see* Syndrome, iodine- deficiency, congenital
  - subclinical E02
- neonatal, transitory P72.2
- postinfectious E03.3
- postirradiation E89.0
- postprocedural E89.0
- postsurgical E89.0
- specified NEC E03.8
- subclinical, iodine-deficiency related E02

Hypotonia, hypotonicity, hypotony
- bladder N31.2
- congenital (benign) P94.2
- eye —*see* Disorder, globe, hypotony

Hypotrichosis —*see* Alopecia

Hypotropia H50.2-

Hypoventilation R06.89
- congenital central alveolar G47.35
- sleep related
  - idiopathic nonobstructive alveolar G47.34
  - in conditions classified elsewhere G47.36

Hypovitaminosis —*see* Deficiency, vitamin

Hypovolemia E86.1
- surgical shock T81.19
- traumatic (shock) T79.4

Hypoxemia R09.02
- newborn P84
- sleep related, in conditions classified elsewhere G47.36

Hypoxia —*see also* Anoxia R09.02
- cerebral, during a procedure NEC G97.81
  - postprocedural NEC G97.82
- intrauterine P84
- myocardial —*see* Insufficiency, coronary
- newborn P84
- sleep-related G47.34

Hypsarhythmia —*see* Epilepsy, generalized, specified NEC

Hysteralgia, pregnant uterus O26.89-

Hysteria, hysterical (conversion) (dissociative state) F44.9
- anxiety F41.8
- convulsions F44.5
- psychosis, acute F44.9

Hysteroepilepsy F44.5

I

Ichthyoparasitism due to Vandellia cirrhosa B88.8

Ichthyosis (congenital) Q80.9
- acquired L85.0
- fetalis Q80.4
- hystrix Q80.8
- lamellar Q80.2
- lingual K13.29
- palmaris and plantaris Q82.8
- simplex Q80.0
- vera Q80.8
- vulgaris Q80.0
- X-linked Q80.1

Ichthyotoxism —*see* Poisoning, fish
- bacterial —*see* Intoxication, foodborne

Icteroanemia, hemolytic (acquired) D59.9
- congenital —*see* Spherocytosis

Icterus —*see also* Jaundice
- conjunctiva R17
- newborn P59.9
- gravis, newborn P55.0
- hematogenous (acquired) D59.9
- hemolytic (acquired) D59.9
  - congenital —*see* Spherocytosis
- hemorrhagic (acute) (leptospiral) (spirochetal) A27.0
  - newborn P53
- infectious B15.9
  - with hepatic coma B15.0
  - leptospiral A27.0
  - spirochetal A27.0
- neonatorum —*see* Jaundice, newborn
- spirochetal A27.0

Ictus solaris, solis T67.0

Ideation
- homicidal R45.850
- suicidal R45.851

Identity disorder (child) F64.9
- gender role F64.2
- psychosexual F64.2

Id reaction (due to bacteria) L30.2

Idioglossia F80.0

Idiopathic —*see* condition

Idiot, idiocy (congenital) F73
- amaurotic (Bielschowsky(-Jansky)) (family) (infantile (late)) (juvenile (late)) (Vogt-Spielmeyer) E75.4
- microcephalic Q02

IgE asthma J45.909

IIAC (idiopathic infantile arterial calcification) Q28.8

Ileitis (chronic) (noninfectious) —*see also* Enteritis K52.9
- backwash —*see* Pancolitis, ulcerative (chronic)
- infectious A09
- regional (ulcerative) —*see* Enteritis, regional, small intestine
- segmental —*see* Enteritis, regional
- terminal (ulcerative) —*see* Enteritis, regional, small intestine

Ileocolitis —*see also* Enteritis K52.9
- regional —*see* Enteritis, regional
- infectious A09

Ileostomy
- attention to Z43.2
- malfunctioning K94.13
- status Z93.2
  - with complication —*see* Complications, enterostomy

Ileotyphus —*see* Typhoid

Ileum —*see* condition

Ileus (bowel) (colon) (inhibitory) (intestine) K56.7
- adynamic K56.0
- due to gallstone (in intestine) K56.3
- duodenal (chronic) K31.5
- gallstone K56.3
- mechanical NEC K56.69
- meconium P76.0
  - in cystic fibrosis E84.11
  - meaning meconium plug (without cystic fibrosis) P76.0
- myxedema K59.8
- neurogenic K56.0
  - Hirschsprung's disease or megacolon Q43.1
- newborn
  - due to meconium P76.0
    - in cystic fibrosis E84.11
    - meaning meconium plug (without cystic fibrosis) P76.0
  - transitory P76.1
- obstructive K56.69
- paralytic K56.0

Iliac —*see* condition

Iliotibial band syndrome M76.3-

Illiteracy Z55.0

Illness —*see also* Disease R69
- manic-depressive —*see* Disorder, bipolar

Imbalance R26.89
- autonomic G90.8
- constituents of food intake E63.1
- electrolyte E87.8
  - with
    - abortion —*see* Abortion by type, complicated by, electrolyte imbalance
    - molar pregnancy O08.5
  - due to hyperemesis gravidarum O21.1
  - following ectopic or molar pregnancy O08.5
  - neonatal, transitory NEC P74.4
    - potassium P74.3
    - sodium P74.2
- endocrine E34.9
- eye muscle NOS H50.9
- hormone E34.9
- hysterical F44.4
- labyrinth H83.2
- posture R29.3
- protein-energy —*see* Malnutrition
- sympathetic G90.8

Imbecile, imbecility (I.Q.35-49) F71

Imbedding, intrauterine device T83.39

Imbibition, cholesterol (gallbladder) K82.4

Imbrication, teeth,, fully erupted M26.30

Imerslund (-Gräsbeck) **syndrome** D51.1

Immature —*see also* Immaturity
- birth (less than 37 completed weeks) —*see* Preterm, newborn
  - extremely (less than 28 completed weeks) —*see* Immaturity, extreme
- personality F60.89

Immaturity (less than 37 completed weeks) —*see also* Preterm, newborn
- extreme of newborn (less than 28 completed weeks of gestation) (less than 196 completed days of gestation) (unspecified weeks of gestation) P07.20
  - gestational age
    - 23 completed weeks (23 weeks 0 days through 23 weeks, 6 days) P07.22
    - 24 completed weeks (24 weeks 0 days through 24 weeks, 6 days) P07.23
    - 25 completed weeks (25 weeks 0 days through 25 weeks, 6 days) P07.24
    - 26 completed weeks (26 weeks 0 days through 26 weeks, 6 days) P07.25
    - 27 completed weeks (27 weeks 0 days through 27 weeks, 6 days) P07.26
    - less than 23 completed weeks P07.21
- fetus or infant light-for-dates —*see* Light-for-dates
- lung, newborn P28.0
- organ or site NEC —*see* Hypoplasia
- pulmonary, newborn P28.0
- reaction F60.89
- sexual (female) (male), after puberty E30.0

Immersion T75.1
- hand T69.01-
- foot T69.02-

Immobile, immobility
- complete, due to severe physical disability or frailty R53.2
- intestine K59.8
- syndrome (paraplegic) M62.3

Immune reconstitution (inflammatory) **syndrome [IRIS]** D89.3

Immunization —*see also* Vaccination
- ABO —*see* Incompatibility, ABO
  - in newborn P55.1
- complication —*see* Complications, vaccination
- encounter for Z23
- not done (not carried out) Z28.9
  - because (of)
    - acute illness of patient Z28.01
    - allergy to vaccine (or component) Z28.04
    - caregiver refusal Z28.82
    - chronic illness of patient Z28.02
    - contraindication NEC Z28.09
    - group pressure Z28.1
    - guardian refusal Z28.82
    - immune compromised state of patient Z28.03
    - parent refusal Z28.82
    - patient's belief Z28.1
    - patient had disease being vaccinated against Z28.81
    - patient refusal Z28.21
    - religious beliefs of patient Z28.1
    - specified reason NEC Z28.89
      - of patient Z28.29
    - unspecified patient reason Z28.20
- Rh factor
  - affecting management of pregnancy NEC O36.09-
    - anti-D antibody O36.01-
  - from transfusion —*see* Complication(s), transfusion, incompatibility reaction, Rh (factor)

Immunocytoma C83.0-

munodeficiency D84.9
with
adenosine-deaminase deficiency D81.3
antibody defects D80.9
specified type NEC D80.8
hyperimmunoglobulinemia D80.6
increased immunoglobulin M (IgM) D80.5
major defect D82.9
specified type NEC D82.8
partial albinism D82.8
short-limbed stature D82.2
thrombocytopenia and eczema D82.0
antibody with
hyperimmunoglobulinemia D80.6
near-normal immunoglobulins D80.6
autosomal recessive, Swiss type D80.0
combined D81.9
biotin-dependent carboxylase D81.819
biotinidase D81.810
holocarboxylase synthetase D81.818
specified type NEC D81.818
severe (SCID) D81.9
with
low or normal B-cell numbers D81.2
low T- and B-cell numbers D81.1
reticular dysgenesis D81.0
specified type NEC D81.89
common variable D83.9
with
abnormalities of B-cell numbers and function D83.0
autoantibodies to B- or T-cells D83.2
immunoregulatory T-cell disorders D83.1
specified type NEC D83.8
following hereditary defective response to Epstein-Barr virus (EBV) D82.3
selective, immunoglobulin
A (IgA) D80.2
G (IgG) (subclasses) D80.3
M (IgM) D80.4
severe combined (SCID) D81.9
specified type NEC D84.8
X-linked, with increased IgM D80.5

munotherapy (encounter for)
antineoplastic Z51.12

paction, impacted
bowel, colon, rectum —*see also* Impaction, fecal K56.49
by gallstone K56.3
calculus —*see* Calculus
cerumen (ear) (external) H61.2-
cuspid —*see* Impaction, tooth
dental (same or adjacent tooth) K01.1
fecal, feces K56.41
fracture —*see* Fracture, by site
gallbladder —*see* Calculus, gallbladder
gallstone (s) —*see* Calculus, gallbladder
bile duct (common) (hepatic) —*see* Calculus, bile duct
cystic duct —*see* Calculus, gallbladder
in intestine, with obstruction (any part) K56.3

Impaction, impacted *(continued)*
intestine (calculous) NEC —*see also* Impaction, fecal K56.49
gallstone, with ileus K56.3
intrauterine device (IUD) T83.39
molar —*see* Impaction, tooth
shoulder, causing obstructed labor O66.0
tooth, teeth K01.1
turbinate J34.89

Impaired, impairment (function)
auditory discrimination —*see* Abnormal, auditory perception
cognitive, mild, so stated G31.84
dual sensory Z73.82
fasting glucose R73.01
glucose tolerance (oral) R73.02
hearing —*see* Deafness
heart —*see* Disease, heart
kidney N28.9
disorder resulting from N25.9
specified NEC N25.89
liver K72.90
with coma K72.91
mastication K08.8
mild cognitive, so stated G31.84
mobility
ear ossicles —*see* Ankylosis, ear ossicles
requiring care provider Z74.09
myocardium, myocardial —*see* Insufficiency, myocardial
rectal sphincter R19.8
renal (acute) (chronic) N28.9
disorder resulting from N25.9
specified NEC N25.89
vision NEC H54.7
both eyes H54.3

Impediment, speech R47.9
psychogenic (childhood) F98.8
slurring R47.81
specified NEC R47.89

Impending
coronary syndrome I20.0
delirium tremens F10.239
myocardial infarction I20.0

Imperception auditory (acquired) —*see also* Deafness
congenital H93.25

Imperfect
aeration, lung (newborn) NEC —*see* Atelectasis
closure (congenital)
alimentary tract NEC Q45.8
lower Q43.8
upper Q40.8
atrioventricular ostium Q21.2
atrium (secundum) Q21.1
branchial cleft or sinus Q18.0
choroid Q14.3
cricoid cartilage Q31.8
cusps, heart valve NEC Q24.8
pulmonary Q22.3
ductus
arteriosus Q25.0
Botalli Q25.0
ear drum (causing impairment of hearing) Q16.4
esophagus with communication to bronchus or trachea Q39.1
eyelid Q10.3
foramen
botalli Q21.1
ovale Q21.1
genitalia, genital organ (s) or system
female Q52.8
external Q52.79
internal NEC Q52.8
male Q55.8

Imperfect *(continued)*
closure *(continued)*
glottis Q31.8
interatrial ostium or septum Q21.1
interauricular ostium or septum Q21.1
interventricular ostium or septum Q21.0
larynx Q31.8
lip —*see* Cleft, lip
nasal septum Q30.3
nose Q30.2
omphalomesenteric duct Q43.0
optic nerve entry Q14.2
organ or site not listed —*see* Anomaly, by site
ostium
interatrial Q21.1
interauricular Q21.1
interventricular Q21.0
palate —*see* Cleft, palate
preauricular sinus Q18.1
retina Q14.1
roof of orbit Q75.8
sclera Q13.5
septum
aorticopulmonary Q21.4
atrial (secundum) Q21.1
between aorta and pulmonary artery Q21.4
heart Q21.9
interatrial (secundum) Q21.1
interauricular (secundum) Q21.1
interventricular Q21.0
in tetralogy of Fallot Q21.3
nasal Q30.3
ventricular Q21.0
with pulmonary stenosis or atresia, dextraposition of aorta, and hypertrophy of right ventricle Q21.3
in tetralogy of Fallot Q21.3
skull Q75.0
with
anencephaly Q00.0
encephalocele —*see* Encephalocele
hydrocephalus Q03.9
with spina bifida —*see* Spina bifida, by site, with hydrocephalus
microcephaly Q02
spine (with meningocele) —*see* Spina bifida
trachea Q32.1
tympanic membrane (causing impairment of hearing) Q16.4
uterus Q51.818
vitelline duct Q43.0
erection —*see* Dysfunction, sexual, male, erectile
fusion —*see* Imperfect, closure
inflation, lung (newborn) —*see* Atelectasis
posture R29.3
rotation, intestine Q43.3
septum, ventricular Q21.0

Imperfectly descended testis —*see* Cryptorchid

Imperforate (congenital) —*see also* Atresia
anus Q42.3
with fistula Q42.2
cervix (uteri) Q51.828
esophagus Q39.0
with tracheoesophageal fistula Q39.1
hymen Q52.3
jejunum Q41.1
pharynx Q38.8

Imperforate *(continued)*
rectum Q42.1
with fistula Q42.0
urethra Q64.39
vagina Q52.4

Impervious (congenital) —*see also* Atresia
anus Q42.3
with fistula Q42.2
bile duct Q44.2
esophagus Q39.0
with tracheoesophageal fistula Q39.1
intestine (small) Q41.9
large Q42.9
specified NEC Q42.8
rectum Q42.1
with fistula Q42.0
ureter —*see* Atresia, ureter
urethra Q64.39

Impetiginization of dermatoses L01.1

Impetigo (any organism) (any site) (circinate) (contagiosa) (simplex) (vulgaris) L01.00
Bockhart's L01.02
bullous, bullosa L01.03
external ear L01.00 *[H62.40]*
follicularis L01.02
furfuracea L30.5
herpetiformis L40.1
nonobstetrical L40.1
neonatorum L01.03
nonbullous L01.01
specified type NEC L01.09
ulcerative L01.09

Impingement (on teeth)
soft tissue
anterior M26.81
posterior M26.82

Implant, endometrial N80.9

Implantation
anomalous —*see* Anomaly, by site
ureter Q62.63
cyst
external area or site (skin) NEC L72.0
iris —*see* Cyst, iris, implantation
vagina N89.8
vulva N90.7
dermoid (cyst) —*see* Implantation, cyst

Impotence (sexual) N52.9
counseling Z70.1
organic origin —*see also* Dysfunction, sexual, male, erectile N52.9
psychogenic F52.21

Impression, basilar Q75.8

Imprisonment, anxiety concerning Z65.1

Improper care (child) (newborn) —*see* Maltreatment

Improperly tied umbilical cord (causing hemorrhage) P51.8

Impulsiveness (impulsive) R45.87

Inability to swallow —*see* Aphagia

Inaccessible, inaccessibility
health care NEC Z75.3
due to
waiting period Z75.2
for admission to facility elsewhere Z75.1
other helping agencies Z75.4

Inactive —*see* condition

Inadequate, inadequacy
- aesthetics of dental restoration K08.56
- biologic, constitutional, functional, or social F60.7
- development
  - child R62.50
  - genitalia
    - after puberty NEC E30.0
    - congenital
      - female Q52.8
        - external Q52.79
        - internal Q52.8
      - male Q55.8
  - lungs Q33.6
    - associated with short gestation P28.0
  - organ or site not listed —*see* Anomaly, by site
- diet (causing nutritional deficiency) E63.9
- eating habits Z72.4
- environment, household Z59.1
- family support Z63.8
- food (supply) NEC Z59.4
  - hunger effects T73.0
- functional F60.7
- household care, due to
  - family member
    - handicapped or ill Z74.2
    - on vacation Z75.5
    - temporarily away from home Z74.2
  - technical defects in home Z59.1
  - temporary absence from home of person rendering care Z74.2
- housing (heating) (space) Z59.1
- income (financial) Z59.6
- intrafamilial communication Z63.8
- material resources Z59.9
- mental —*see* Disability, intellectual
- parental supervision or control of child Z62.0
- personality F60.7
- pulmonary
  - function R06.89
    - newborn P28.5
  - ventilation, newborn P28.5
- sample of cytologic smear
  - anus R85.615
  - cervix R87.615
  - vagina R87.625
- social F60.7
  - insurance Z59.7
  - skills NEC Z73.4
- supervision of child by parent Z62.0
- teaching affecting education Z55.8
- welfare support Z59.7

Inanition R64
- with edema —*see* Malnutrition, severe
- due to
  - deprivation of food T73.0
  - malnutrition —*see* Malnutrition
- fever R50.9

Inappropriate
- change in quantitative human chorionic gonadotropin (hCG) in early pregnancy O02.81
- diet or eating habits Z72.4
- level of quantitative human chorionic gonadotropin (hCG) for gestational age in early pregnancy O02.81
- secretion
  - antidiuretic hormone (ADH) (excessive) E22.2
    - deficiency E23.2
  - pituitary (posterior) E22.2

Inattention at or after birth —*see* Neglect

Incarceration, incarcerated
- enterocele K46.0
  - gangrenous K46.1
- epiplocele K46.0
  - gangrenous K46.1
- exophthalmos K42.0
  - gangrenous K42.1
- hernia —*see also* Hernia, by site, with obstruction
  - with gangrene —*see* Hernia, by site, with gangrene
- iris, in wound —*see* Injury, eye, laceration, with prolapse
- lens, in wound —*see* Injury, eye, laceration, with prolapse
- omphalocele K42.0
- prison, anxiety concerning Z65.1
- rupture —*see* Hernia, by site
- sarcoepiplocele K46.0
  - gangrenous K46.1
- sarcoepiplomphalocele K42.0
  - with gangrene K42.1
- uterus N85.8
  - gravid O34.51-
    - causing obstructed labor O65.5

Incised wound
- external —*see* Laceration
- internal organs —*see* Injury, by site

Incision, incisional
- hernia K43.2
  - with
    - gangrene (and obstruction) K43.1
    - obstruction K43.0
- surgical, complication —*see* Complications, surgical procedure
- traumatic
  - external —*see* Laceration
  - internal organs —*see* Injury, by site

Inclusion
- azurophilic leukocytic D72.0
- blennorrhea (neonatal) (newborn) P39.1
- gallbladder in liver (congenital) Q44.1

Incompatibility
- ABO
  - affecting management of pregnancy O36.11-
    - anti-A sensitization O36.11-
    - anti-B sensitization O36.19-
    - specified NEC O36.19-
  - infusion or transfusion reaction —*see* Complication(s), transfusion, incompatibility reaction, ABO
  - newborn P55.1
- blood (group) (Duffy) (K(ell)) (Kidd) (Lewis) (M) (S) NEC
  - affecting management of pregnancy O36.11-
    - anti-A sensitization O36.11-
    - anti-B sensitization O36.19-
  - infusion or transfusion reaction T80.89
  - newborn P55.8
- divorce or estrangement Z63.5
- Rh (blood group) (factor) Z31.82
  - affecting management of pregnancy NEC O36.09-
    - anti-D antibody O36.01-
  - infusion or transfusion reaction —*see* Complication (s), transfusion, incompatibility reaction, Rh (factor)
  - newborn P55.0
- rhesus —*see* Incompatibility, Rh

Incompetency, incompetent, incompetence
- annular
  - aortic (valve) —*see* Insufficiency, aortic
  - mitral (valve) I34.0
  - pulmonary valve (heart) I37.1
- aortic (valve) —*see* Insufficiency, aortic
- cardiac valve —*see* Endocarditis
- cervix, cervical (os) N88.3
  - in pregnancy O34.3-
- chronotropic I45.89
  - with
    - autonomic dysfunction G90.8
    - ischemic heart disease I25.89
    - left ventricular dysfunction I51.89
    - sinus node dysfunction I49.8
- esophagogastric (junction) (sphincter) K22.0
- mitral (valve) —*see* Insufficiency, mitral
- pelvic fundus N81.89
- pubocervical tissue N81.82
- pulmonary valve (heart) I37.1
  - congenital Q22.3
- rectovaginal tissue N81.83
- tricuspid (annular) (valve) —*see* Insufficiency, tricuspid
- valvular —*see* Endocarditis
  - congenital Q24.8
- vein, venous (saphenous) (varicose) —*see* Varix, leg

Incomplete —*see also* condition
- bladder, emptying R33.9
- defecation R15.0
- expansion lungs (newborn) NEC —*see* Atelectasis
- rotation, intestine Q43.3

Inconclusive
- diagnostic imaging due to excess body fat of patient R93.9
- findings on diagnostic imaging of breast NEC R92.8
- mammogram (due to dense breasts) R92.2

Incontinence R32
- anal sphincter R15.9
- feces R15.9
  - nonorganic origin F98.1
- overflow N39.490
- psychogenic F45.8
- rectal R15.9
- reflex N39.498
- stress (female) (male) N39.3
  - and urge N39.46
- urethral sphincter R32
- urge N39.41
  - and stress (female) (male) N39.46
- urine (urinary) R32
  - continuous N39.45
  - due to cognitive impairment, or severe physical disability or immobility R39.81
  - functional R39.81
  - mixed (stress and urge) N39.46
  - nocturnal N39.44
  - nonorganic origin F98.0
  - overflow N39.490
  - post dribbling N39.43
  - reflex N39.498
  - specified NEC N39.498
  - stress (female) (male) N39.3
    - and urge N39.46
  - total N39.498
  - unaware N39.42
  - urge N39.41
    - and stress (female) (male) N39.46

Incontinentia pigmenti Q82.3

Incoordinate, incoordination
- esophageal-pharyngeal (newborn) —*see* Dysphagia
- muscular R27.8
- uterus (action) (contractions) (complicating delivery) O62.4

Increase, increased
- abnormal, in development R63.8
- androgens (ovarian) E28.1
- anticoagulants (antithrombin) (anti-VIIIa) (anti-IXa) (anti-Xa) (anti-XIa) —*see* Circulating anticoagulants
- cold sense R20.8
- estrogen E28.0
- function
  - adrenal
    - cortex —*see* Cushing's, syndrome
    - medulla E27.5
  - pituitary (gland) (anterior) (lobe) E22.9
    - posterior E22.2
- heat sense R20.8
- intracranial pressure (benign) G93.2
- permeability, capillaries I78.8
- pressure, intracranial G93.2
- secretion
  - gastrin E16.4
  - glucagon E16.3
  - pancreas, endocrine E16.9
    - growth hormone-releasing hormone E16.8
    - pancreatic polypeptide E16.8
    - somatostatin E16.8
    - vasoactive-intestinal polypeptide E16.8
- sphericity, lens Q12.4
- splenic activity D73.1
- venous pressure I87.8
  - portal K76.6

Increta placenta O43.22-

Incrustation, cornea, foreign body (lead)(zinc) —*see* Foreign body, cornea

Incyclophoria H50.54

Incyclotropia —*see* Cyclotropia

Indeterminate sex Q56.4

India rubber skin Q82.8

Indigestion (acid) (bilious) (functional) K30
- catarrhal K31.89
- due to decomposed food NOS A05.9
- nervous F45.8
- psychogenic F45.8

Indirect —*see* condition

Induratio penis plastica N48.6

Induration, indurated
- brain G93.89
- breast (fibrous) N64.51
  - puerperal, postpartum O92.29
- broad ligament N83.8
- chancre
  - anus A51.1
  - congenital A50.07
  - extragenital NEC A51.2
- corpora cavernosa (penis) (plastic) N48.6
- liver (chronic) K76.89
- lung (black) (chronic) (fibroid) —*see also* Fibrosis, lung J84.10
  - essential brown J84.03
- penile (plastic) N48.6
- phlebitic —*see* Phlebitis
- skin R23.4

Inebriety (without dependence) —*see* Alcohol, intoxication

- **fficiency, kidney** N28.9
- **lasticity, skin** R23.4
- **quality, leg** (length) (acquired) —*ee also* Deformity, limb, unequal ength
  - ongenital —*see* Defect, reduction, lower limb
  - ɔwer leg —*see* Deformity, limb, unequal length
- **rtia**
  - ladder (neurogenic) N31.2
  - tomach K31.89
    - psychogenic F45.8
  - terus, uterine during labor O62.2
    - during latent phase of labor O62.0
    - primary O62.0
    - secondary O62.1
  - esical (neurogenic) N31.2
- **ancy, infantile, infantilism** —*see lso* condition
  - eliac K90.0
  - enitalia, genitals (after puberty) E30.0
  - Ierter's (nontropical sprue) K90.0
  - ntestinal K90.0
  - orain E23.0
  - ancreatic K86.8
  - elvis M95.5
    - with disproportion (fetopelvic) O33.1
      - causing obstructed labor O65.1
  - ituitary E23.0
  - enal N25.0
  - terus —*see* Infantile, genitalia
- **ant** (s) —*see also* Infancy
  - xcessive crying R68.11
  - rritable child R68.12
  - ack of care —*see* Neglect
  - veborn (singleton) Z38.2
    - born in hospital Z38.00
      - by cesarean Z38.01
    - born outside hospital Z38.1
    - multiple NEC Z38.8
      - born in hospital Z38.68
        - by cesarean Z38.69
      - born outside hospital Z38.7
    - quadruplet Z38.8
      - born in hospital Z38.63
        - by cesarean Z38.64
      - born outside hospital Z38.7
    - quintuplet Z38.8
      - born in hospital Z38.65
        - by cesarean Z38.66
      - born outside hospital Z38.7
    - triplet Z38.8
      - born in hospital Z38.61
        - by cesarean Z38.62
      - born outside hospital Z38.7
    - twin Z38.5
      - born in hospital Z38.30
        - by cesarean Z38.31
      - born outside hospital Z38.4
  - of diabetic mother (syndrome of) P70.1
    - gestational diabetes P70.0
- **antile** —*see also* condition
  - genitalia, genitals E30.0
  - ɔs, uterine E30.0
  - enis E30.0
  - estis E29.1
  - terus E30.0
- **antilism** —*see* Infancy
- **arct, infarction**
  - adrenal (capsule) (gland) E27.49
  - appendices epiploicae K55.0
  - bowel K55.0
  - brain (stem) —*see* Infarct, cerebral
  - breast N64.89
  - brewer's (kidney) N28.0

Infarct, infarction *(continued)*

- cardiac —*see* Infarct, myocardium
- cerebellar —*see* Infarct, cerebral
- cerebral —*see also* Occlusion, artery cerebral or precerebral, with infarction I63.9-
  - aborted I63.9
  - cortical I63.9
  - due to
    - cerebral venous thrombosis, nonpyogenic I63.6
    - embolism
      - cerebral arteries I63.4-
      - precerebral arteries I63.1-
    - occlusion NEC
      - cerebral arteries I63.5-
      - precerebral arteries I63.2-
    - stenosis NEC
      - cerebral arteries I63.5-
      - precerebral arteries I63.2-
    - thrombosis
      - cerebral artery I63.3-
      - precerebral artery I63.0-
  - intraoperative
    - during cardiac surgery I97.810
    - during other surgery I97.811
  - postprocedural
    - following cardiac surgery I97.820
    - following other surgery I97.821
  - specified NEC I63.8
- colon (acute) (agnogenic) (embolic) (hemorrhagic) (nonocclusive) (nonthrombotic) (occlusive) (segmental) (thrombotic) (with gangrene) K55.0
- coronary artery —*see* Infarct, myocardium
- embolic —*see* Embolism
- fallopian tube N83.8
- gallbladder K82.8
- heart —*see* Infarct, myocardium
- hepatic K76.3
- hypophysis (anterior lobe) E23.6
- impending (myocardium) I20.0
- intestine (acute) (agnogenic) (embolic) (hemorrhagic) (nonocclusive) (nonthrombotic) (occlusive) (thrombotic) (with gangrene) K55.0
- kidney N28.0
- liver K76.3
- lung (embolic) (thrombotic) —*see* Embolism, pulmonary
- lymph node I89.8
- mesentery, mesenteric (embolic) (thrombotic) (with gangrene) K55.0
- muscle (ischemic) M62.20
  - ankle M62.27-
  - foot M62.27-
  - forearm M62.23-
  - hand M62.24-
  - lower leg M62.26-
  - pelvic region M62.25-
  - shoulder region M62.21-
  - specified site NEC M62.28
  - thigh M62.25-
  - upper arm M62.22-
- myocardium, myocardial (acute) (with stated duration of 4 weeks or less) I21.3
  - diagnosed on ECG, but presenting no symptoms I25.2
  - healed or old I25.2
  - intraoperative
    - during cardiac surgery I97.790
    - during other surgery I97.791
  - non-Q wave I21.4
  - non-ST elevation (NSTEMI) I21.4
    - subsequent I22.2
  - nontransmural I21.4

Infarct, infarction *(continued)*

- myocardium, myocardial *(continued)*
  - past (diagnosed on ECG or other investigation, but currently presenting no symptoms) I25.2
  - postprocedural
    - following cardiac surgery I97.190
    - following other surgery I97.191
  - Q wave (*see* also, Infarct, myocardium, by site) I21.3
  - ST elevation (STEMI) I21.3
    - anterior (anteroapical) (anterolateral) (anteroseptal) (Q wave) (wall) I21.09
      - subsequent I22.0
    - inferior (diaphragmatic) (inferolateral) (inferoposterior) (wall) NEC I21.19
      - subsequent I22.1
    - inferoposterior transmural (Q wave) I21.11
    - involving
      - coronary artery of anterior wall NEC I21.09
      - coronary artery of inferior wall NEC I21.19
      - diagonal coronary artery I21.02
      - left anterior descending coronary artery I21.02
      - left circumflex coronary artery I21.21
      - left main coronary artery I21.01
      - oblique marginal coronary artery I21.21
      - right coronary artery I21.11
    - lateral (apical-lateral) (basal-lateral) (high) I21.29
      - subsequent I22.8
    - posterior (posterobasal) (posterolateral) (posteroseptal) (true) I21.29
      - subsequent I22.8
    - septal I21.29
      - subsequent I22.8
    - specified NEC I21.29
      - subsequent I22.8
    - subsequent I22.9
  - subsequent (recurrent) (reinfarction) I22.9
    - anterior (anteroapical) (anterolateral) (anteroseptal) (wall) I22.0
    - diaphragmatic (wall) I22.1
    - inferior (diaphragmatic) (inferolateral) (inferoposterior) (wall) I22.1
    - lateral (apical-lateral) (basal-lateral) (high) I22.8
    - non-ST elevation (NSTEMI) I22.2
    - posterior (posterobasal) (posterolateral) (posteroseptal) (true) I22.8
    - septal I22.8
    - specified NEC I22.8
    - ST elevation I22.9
      - anterior (anteroapical) (anterolateral) (anteroseptal) (wall) I22.0
      - inferior (diaphragmatic) (inferolateral) (inferoposterior) (wall) I22.1
      - specified NEC I22.8
    - subendocardial I22.2
    - transmural I22.9
      - anterior (anteroapical) (anterolateral) (anteroseptal) (wall) I22.0

Infarct, infarction *(continued)*

- myocardium, myocardial *(continued)*
  - subsequent *(continued)*
    - transmural
      - diaphragmatic (wall) I22.1
      - inferior (diaphragmatic) (inferolateral) (inferoposterior) (wall) I22.1
      - lateral (apical-lateral) (basal-lateral) (high) I22.8
      - posterior (posterobasal) (posterolateral) (posteroseptal) (true) I22.8
      - specified NEC I22.8
  - syphilitic A52.06
  - transmural I21.3
    - anterior (anteroapical) (anterolateral) (anteroseptal) (Q wave) (wall) NEC I21.09
    - inferior (diaphragmatic) (inferolateral) (inferoposterior) (Q wave) (wall) NEC I21.19
    - inferoposterior (Q wave) I21.11
    - lateral (apical-lateral) (basal-lateral) (high) NEC I21.29
    - posterior (posterobasal) (posterolateral) (posteroseptal) (true) NEC I21.29
    - septal NEC I21.29
    - specified NEC I21.29
- nontransmural I21.4
- omentum K55.0
- ovary N83.8
- pancreas K86.8
- papillary muscle —*see* Infarct, myocardium
- parathyroid gland E21.4
- pituitary (gland) E23.6
- placenta O43.81-
- prostate N42.89
- pulmonary (artery) (vein) (hemorrhagic) —*see* Embolism, pulmonary
- renal (embolic) (thrombotic) N28.0
- retina, retinal (artery) —*see* Occlusion, artery, retina
- spinal (cord) (acute) (embolic) (nonembolic) G95.11
- spleen D73.5
  - embolic or thrombotic I74.8
- subendocardial (acute) (nontransmural) I21.4
- suprarenal (capsule) (gland) E27.49
- testis N50.1
- thrombotic —*see also* Thrombosis
  - artery, arterial —*see* Embolism
- thyroid (gland) E07.89
- ventricle (heart) —*see* Infarct, myocardium

Infecting —*see* condition

Infection, infected, infective (opportunistic) B99.9

- with
  - drug resistant organism —*see* Resistance (to), drug —*see also* specific organism
  - lymphangitis —*see* Lymphangitis
  - organ dysfunction (acute) R65.20
    - with septic shock R65.21
- abscess (skin)- code by site under Abscess
- Absidia —*see* Mucormycosis
- Acanthamoeba —*see* Acanthamebiasis
- Acanthocheilonema (perstans) (streptocerca) B74.4
- accessory sinus (chronic) —*see* Sinusitis
- achorion —*see* Dermatophytosis

Infection, infected, infective *(continued)*
- Acremonium falciforme B47.0
- acromioclavicular M00.9
- Actinobacillus (actinomycetem-comitans) A28.8
  - mallei A24.0
  - muris A25.1
- Actinomadura B47.1
- Actinomyces (israelii) —*see also* Actinomycosis A42.9
- Actinomycetales —*see* Actinomycosis
- actinomycotic NOS —*see* Actinomycosis
- adenoid (and tonsil) J03.90
  - chronic J35.02
- adenovirus NEC
  - as cause of disease classified elsewhere B97.0
  - unspecified nature or site B34.0
- aerogenes capsulatus A48.0
- aertrycke —*see* Infection, salmonella
- alimentary canal NOS —*see* Enteritis, infectious
- Allescheria boydii B48.2
- Alternaria B48.8
- alveolus, alveolar (process) K04.7
- Ameba, amebic (histolytica) —*see* Amebiasis
- amniotic fluid, sac or cavity O41.10-
  - chorioamnionitis O41.12-
  - placentitis O41.14-
- amputation stump (surgical) —*see* Complication, amputation stump, infection
- Ancylostoma (duodenalis) B76.0
- Anisakiasis, Anisakis larvae B81.0
- anthrax —*see* Anthrax
- antrum (chronic) —*see* Sinusitis, maxillary
- anus, anal (papillae) (sphincter) K62.89
- arbovirus (arbor virus) A94
  - specified type NEC A93.8
- artificial insemination N98.0
- Ascaris lumbricoides —*see* Ascariasis
- Ascomycetes B47.0
- Aspergillus (flavus) (fumigatus) (terreus) —*see* Aspergillosis
- atypical
  - acid-fast (bacilli) —*see* Mycobacterium, atypical
  - mycobacteria —*see* Mycobacterium, atypical
  - virus A81.9
    - specified type NEC A81.89
- auditory meatus (external) —*see* Otitis, externa, infective
- auricle (ear) —*see* Otitis, externa, infective
- axillary gland (lymph) L04.2
- Bacillus A49.9
  - abortus A23.1
  - anthracis —*see* Anthrax
  - Ducrey's (any location) A57
  - Flexner's A03.1
  - Friedländer's NEC A49.8
  - gas (gangrene) A48.0
  - mallei A24.0
  - melitensis A23.0
  - paratyphoid, paratyphosus A01.4
    - A A01.1
    - B A01.2
    - C A01.3
  - Shiga (-Kruse) A03.0
  - suipestifer —*see* Infection, salmonella
  - swimming pool A31.1
  - typhosa A01.00
  - welchii —*see* Gangrene, gas
- bacterial NOS A49.9
  - as cause of disease classified elsewhere B96.89
    - Clostridium perfringens [C. perfringens] B96.7
    - Bacteroides fragilis [B. fragilis] B96.6
    - Enterobacter sakazakii B96.89
    - Enterococcus B95.2
    - Escherichia coli [E. coli] —*see also* Escherichia coli B96.20
    - Helicobacter pylori [H.pylori] B96.81
    - Hemophilus influenzae [H. influenzae] B96.3
    - Klebsiella pneumoniae [K. pneumoniae] B96.1
    - Mycoplasma pneumoniae [M. pneumoniae] B96.0
    - Proteus (mirabilis) (morganii) B96.4
    - Pseudomonas (aeruginosa) (mallei) (pseudomallei) B96.5
    - Staphylococcus B95.8
      - aureus (methicillin susceptible) (MSSA) B95.61
        - methicillin resistant (MRSA) B95.62
      - specified NEC B95.7
    - Streptococcus B95.5
      - group A B95.0
      - group B B95.1
      - pneumoniae B95.3
      - specified NEC B95.4
    - Vibrio vulnificus B96.82
  - specified NEC A48.8
- Bacterium
  - paratyphosum A01.4
    - A A01.1
    - B A01.2
    - C A01.3
  - typhosum A01.00
- Bacteroides NEC A49.8
  - fragilis, as cause of disease classified elsewhere B96.6
- Balantidium coli A07.0
- Bartholin's gland N75.8
- Basidiobolus B46.8
- bile duct (common) (hepatic) —*see* Cholangitis
- bladder —*see* Cystitis
- Blastomyces, blastomycotic —*see also* Blastomycosis
  - brasiliensis —*see* Paracoccidioidomycosis
  - dermatitidis —*see* Blastomycosis
  - European —*see* Cryptococcosis
  - Loboi B48.0
  - North American B40.9
  - South American —*see* Paracoccidioidomycosis
- bleb, postprocedure —*see* Blebitis
- bone —*see* Osteomyelitis
- Bordetella —*see* Whooping cough
- Borrelia bergdorfi A69.20
- brain —*see also* Encephalitis G04.90
  - membranes —*see* Meningitis
  - septic G06.0
    - meninges —*see* Meningitis, bacterial
- branchial cyst Q18.0
- breast —*see* Mastitis
- bronchus —*see* Bronchitis
- Brucella A23.9
  - abortus A23.1
  - canis A23.3
  - melitensis A23.0
  - mixed A23.8
  - specified NEC A23.8
  - suis A23.2

Infection, infected, infective *(continued)*
- Brugia (malayi) B74.1
  - timori B74.2
- bursa —*see* Bursitis, infective
- buttocks (skin) L08.9
- Campylobacter, intestinal A04.5
  - as cause of disease classified elsewhere B96.81
- Candida (albicans) (tropicalis) —*see* Candidiasis
- candiru B88.8
- Capillaria (intestinal) B81.1
  - hepatica B83.8
  - philippinensis B81.1
- cartilage —*see* Disorder, cartilage, specified type NEC
- catheter-related bloodstream (CRBSI) T80.211
- cat liver fluke B66.0
- cellulitis - code by site under Cellulitis
- central line-associated T80.219
  - bloodstream (CLABSI) T80.211
  - specified NEC T80.218
- Cephalosporium falciforme B47.0
- cerebrospinal —*see* Meningitis
- cervical gland (lymph) L04.0
- cervix —*see* Cervicitis
- cesarean delivery wound (puerperal) O86.0
- cestodes —*see* Infestation, cestodes
- chest J22
- Chilomastix (intestinal) A07.8
- Chlamydia, chlamydial A74.9
  - anus A56.3
  - genitourinary tract A56.2
    - lower A56.00
    - specified NEC A56.19
  - lymphogranuloma A55
  - pharynx A56.4
  - psittaci A70
  - rectum A56.3
  - sexually transmitted NEC A56.8
- cholera —*see* Cholera
- Cladosporium
  - bantianum (brain abscess) B43.1
  - carrionii B43.0
  - castellanii B36.1
  - trichoides (brain abscess) B43.1
  - werneckii B36.1
- Clonorchis (sinensis) (liver) B66.1
- Clostridium NEC
  - bifermentans A48.0
  - botulinum (food poisoning) A05.1
    - infant A48.51
    - wound A48.52
  - difficile
    - as cause of disease classified elsewhere B96.89
    - foodborne (disease) A04.7
    - gas gangrene A48.0
    - necrotizing enterocolitis A04.7
    - sepsis A41.4
  - gas-forming NEC A48.0
  - histolyticum A48.0
  - novyi, causing gas gangrene A48.0
  - oedematiens A48.0
  - perfringens
    - as cause of disease classified elsewhere B96.7
    - due to food A05.2
    - foodborne (disease) A05.2
    - gas gangrene A48.0
    - sepsis A41.4
  - septicum, causing gas gangrene A48.0
  - sordellii, causing gas gangrene A48.0
  - welchii
    - as cause of disease classified elsewhere B96.7

Infection, infected, infective *(continued)*
- Clostridium *(continued)*
  - welchii *(continued)*
    - foodborne (disease) A05.2
    - gas gangrene A48.0
    - necrotizing enteritis A05.2
    - sepsis A41.4
- Coccidioides (immitis) —*see* Coccidioidomycosis
- colon —*see* Enteritis, infectious
- colostomy K94.02
- common duct —*see* Cholangitis
- congenital P39.9
  - Candida (albicans) P37.5
  - cytomegalovirus P35.1
  - hepatitis, viral P35.3
  - herpes simplex P35.2
  - infectious or parasitic disease P37.9
    - specified NEC P37.8
  - listeriosis (disseminated) P37.2
  - malaria NEC P37.4
    - falciparum P37.3
  - Plasmodium falciparum P37.3
  - poliomyelitis P35.8
  - rubella P35.0
  - skin P39.4
  - toxoplasmosis (acute) (subacute) (chronic) P37.1
  - tuberculosis P37.0
  - urinary (tract) P39.3
  - vaccinia P35.8
  - virus P35.9
    - specified type NEC P35.8
- Conidiobolus B46.8
- coronavirus NEC B34.2
  - as cause of disease classified elsewhere B97.29
  - severe acute respiratory syndrom (SARS associated) B97.21
- corpus luteum —*see* Salpingo-oophoritis
- Corynebacterium diphtheriae —*see* Diphtheria
- cotia virus B08.8
- Coxiella burnetii A78
- coxsackie —*see* Coxsackie
- Cryptococcus neoformans —*see* Cryptococcosis
- Cryptosporidium A07.2
- Cunninghamella —*see* Mucormyco
- cyst —*see* Cyst
- cystic duct —*see also* Cholecystitis K81.9
- Cysticercus cellulosae —*see* Cysticercosis
- cytomegalovirus, cytomegaloviral B25.9
  - congenital P35.1
  - maternal, maternal care for (suspected) damage to fetus O35.3
  - mononucleosis B27.10
    - with
      - complication NEC B27.19
      - meningitis B27.12
      - polyneuropathy B27.11
- delta-agent (acute), in hepatitis B carrier B17.0
- dental (pulpal origin) K04.7
- Deuteromycetes B47.0
- Dicrocoelium dendriticum B66.2
- Dipetalonema (perstans) (streptocerca) B74.4
- diphtherial —*see* Diphtheria
- Diphyllobothrium (adult) (latum) (pacificum) B70.0
  - larval B70.1
- Diplogonoporus (grandis) B71.8
- Dipylidium caninum B67.4
- Dirofilaria B74.8

Infection, infected, infective
(continued)
- leptospirochetal NEC —*see* Leptospirosis
- Listeria monocytogenes —*see also* Listeriosis
  - congenital P37.2
- Loa loa B74.3
  - with conjunctival infestation B74.3
  - eyelid B74.3
- Loboa loboi B48.0
- local, skin (staphylococcal) (streptococcal) L08.9
  - abscess - code by site under Abscess
  - cellulitis - code by site under Cellulitis
  - specified NEC L08.89
  - ulcer —*see* Ulcer, skin
- Loefflerella mallei A24.0
- lung —*see also* Pneumonia J18.9
  - atypical Mycobacterium A31.0
  - spirochetal A69.8
  - tuberculous —*see* Tuberculosis, pulmonary
  - virus —*see* Pneumonia, viral
- lymph gland —*see also* Lymphadenitis, acute
  - mesenteric I88.0
- lymphoid tissue, base of tongue or posterior pharynx, NEC (chronic) J35.03
- Madurella (grisea) (mycetomii) B47.0
- major
  - following ectopic or molar pregnancy O08.0
  - puerperal, postpartum, childbirth O85
- Malassezia furfur B36.0
- Malleomyces
  - mallei A24.0
  - pseudomallei (whitmori) —*see* Melioidosis
- mammary gland N61
- Mansonella (ozzardi) (perstans) (streptocerca) B74.4
- mastoid —*see* Mastoiditis
- maxilla, maxillary M27.2
  - sinus (chronic) —*see* Sinusitis, maxillary
- mediastinum J98.5
- Medina (worm) B72
- meibomian cyst or gland —*see* Hordeolum
- meninges —*see* Meningitis, bacterial
- meningococcal —*see also* condition A39.9
  - adrenals A39.1
  - brain A39.81
  - cerebrospinal A39.0
  - conjunctiva A39.89
  - endocardium A39.51
  - heart A39.50
    - endocardium A39.51
    - myocardium A39.52
    - pericardium A39.53
  - joint A39.83
  - meninges A39.0
  - meningococcemia A39.4
    - acute A39.2
    - chronic A39.3
  - myocardium A39.52
  - pericardium A39.53
  - retrobulbar neuritis A39.82
  - specified site NEC A39.89
- mesenteric lymph nodes or glands NEC I88.0
- Metagonimus B66.8
- metatarsophalangeal M00.9

Infection, infected, infective
(continued)
- methicillin
  - resistant Staphylococcus aureus (MRSA) A49.02
  - susceptible Staphylococcus aureus (MSSA) A49.01
- Microsporum, microsporic —*see* Dermatophytosis
- mixed flora (bacterial) NEC A49.8
- Monilia —*see* Candidiasis
- Monosporium apiospermum B48.2
- mouth, parasitic B37.0
- Mucor —*see* Mucormycosis
- muscle NEC —*see* Myositis, infective
- mycelium NOS B49
- mycetoma B47.9
  - actinomycotic NEC B47.1
  - mycotic NEC B47.0
- Mycobacterium, mycobacterial —*see* Mycobacterium
- Mycoplasma NEC A49.3
  - pneumoniae, as cause of disease classified elsewhere B96.0
- mycotic NOS B49
  - pathogenic to compromised host only B48.8
  - skin NOS B36.9
- myocardium NEC I40.0
- nail (chronic)
  - with lymphangitis —*see* Lymphangitis, acute, digit
  - finger L03.01-
    - fungus B35.1
  - ingrowing L60.0
  - toe L03.03-
    - fungus B35.1
- nasal sinus (chronic) —*see* Sinusitis
- nasopharynx —*see* Nasopharyngitis
- navel L08.82
- Necator americanus B76.1
- Neisseria —*see* Gonococcus
- Neotestudina rosatii B47.0
- newborn P39.9
  - intra-amniotic NEC P39.2
  - skin P39.4
  - specified type NEC P39.8
- nipple N61
  - associated with
    - lactation O91.03
    - pregnancy O91.01-
    - puerperium O91.02
- Nocardia —*see* Nocardiosis
- obstetrical surgical wound (puerperal) O86.0
- Oesophagostomum (apiostomum) B81.8
- Oestrus ovis —*see* Myiasis
- Oidium albicans B37.9
- Onchocerca (volvulus) —*see* Onchocerciasis
- oncovirus, as cause of disease classified elsewhere B97.32
- operation wound T81.4
- Opisthorchis (felineus) (viverrini) B66.0
- orbit, orbital —*see* Inflammation, orbit
- orthopoxvirus NEC B08.09
- ovary —*see* Salpingo-oophoritis
- Oxyuris vermicularis B80
- pancreas (acute) K85.9
  - abscess —*see* Pancreatitis, acute
  - specified NEC K85.8
- papillomavirus, as cause of disease classified elsewhere B97.7
- papovavirus NEC B34.4
- Paracoccidioides brasiliensis —*see* Paracoccidioidomycosis
- Paragonimus (westermani) B66.4
- parainfluenza virus B34.8
- parameningococcus NOS A39.9

Infection, infected, infective
(continued)
- parapoxvirus B08.60
  - specified NEC B08.69
- parasitic B89
- Parastrongylus
  - cantonensis B83.2
  - costaricensis B81.3
  - paratyphoid A01.4
    - Type A A01.1
    - Type B A01.2
    - Type C A01.3
- paraurethral ducts N34.2
- parotid gland —*see* Sialoadenitis
- parvovirus NEC B34.3
  - as cause of disease classified elsewhere B97.6
- Pasteurella NEC A28.0
  - multocida A28.0
  - pestis —*see* Plague
  - pseudotuberculosis A28.0
  - septica (cat bite) (dog bite) A28.0
  - tularensis —*see* Tularemia
- pelvic, female —*see* Disease, pelvis, inflammatory
- Penicillium (marneffei) B48.4
- penis (glans) (retention) NEC N48.29
- periapical K04.5
- peridental, periodontal K05.20
  - generalized K05.22
  - localized K05.21
- perinatal period P39.9
  - specified type NEC P39.8
- perineal repair (puerperal) O86.0
- periorbital —*see* Inflammation, orbit
- perirectal K62.89
- perirenal —*see* Infection, kidney
- peritoneal —*see* Peritonitis
- periureteral N28.89
- Petriellidium boydii B48.2
- pharynx —*see also* Pharyngitis
  - coxsackievirus B08.5
  - posterior, lymphoid (chronic) J35.03
- Phialophora
  - gougerotii (subcutaneous abscess or cyst) B43.2
  - jeanselmei (subcutaneous abscess or cyst) B43.2
  - verrucosa (skin) B43.0
- Piedraia hortae B36.3
- pinta A67.9
  - intermediate A67.1
  - late A67.2
  - mixed A67.3
  - primary A67.0
- pinworm B80
- pityrosporum furfur B36.0
- pleuro-pneumonia-like organism (PPLO) NEC A49.3
  - as cause of disease classified elsewhere B96.0
- pneumococcus, pneumococcal NEC A49.1
  - as cause of disease classified elsewhere B95.3
  - generalized (purulent) A40.3
    - with pneumonia J13
- Pneumocystis carinii (pneumonia) B59
- Pneumocystis jiroveci (pneumonia) B59
- port or reservoir T80.212
- postoperative T81.4
- postoperative wound T81.4
- postprocedural T81.4
- postvaccinal T88.0
- prepuce NEC N47.7
  - with penile inflammation N47.6
- prion —*see* Disease, prion, central nervous system
- prostate (capsule) —*see* Prostatitis

Infection, infected, infective
(continued)
- Proteus (mirabilis) (morganii) (vulgaris) NEC A49.8
  - as cause of disease classified elsewhere B96.4
- protozoal NEC B64
  - intestinal A07.9
    - specified NEC A07.8
  - specified NEC B60.8
- Pseudoallescheria boydii B48.2
- Pseudomonas NEC A49.8
  - as cause of disease classified elsewhere B96.5
  - mallei A24.0
  - pneumonia J15.1
  - pseudomallei —*see* Melioidosis
- puerperal O86.4
  - genitourinary tract NEC O86.89
  - major or generalized O85
  - minor O86.4
  - specified NEC O86.89
- pulmonary —*see* Infection, lung
- purulent —*see* Abscess
- Pyrenochaeta romeroi B47.0
- Q fever A78
- rectum (sphincter) K62.89
- renal —*see also* Infection, kidney
  - pelvis and ureter (cystic) N28.85
- reovirus, as cause of disease classifi elsewhere B97.5
- respiratory (tract) NEC J98.8
  - acute J22
  - chronic J98.8
  - influenzal (upper) (acute) —*see* Influenza, with, respiratory manifestations NEC
  - lower (acute) J22
    - chronic —*see* Bronchitis, chronic
  - rhinovirus J00
  - syncytial virus, as cause of diseas classified elsewhere B97.4
  - upper (acute) NOS J06.9
    - chronic J39.8
    - streptococcal J06.9
    - viral NOS J06.9
- resulting from
  - presence of internal prosthesis, implant, graft —*see* Complications, by site and type infection
- retortamoniasis A07.8
- retroperitoneal NEC K68.9
- retrovirus B33.3
  - as cause of disease classified elsewhere B97.30
    - human
      - immunodeficiency, type 2(HIV 2) B97.35
      - T-cell lymphotropic
        - type I(HTLV-I) B97.33
        - type II(HTLV-II) B97.34
    - lentivirus B97.31
    - oncovirus B97.32
    - specified NEC B97.39
- Rhinosporidium (*see*beri) B48.1
- rhinovirus
  - as cause of disease classified elsewhere B97.89
  - unspecified nature or site B34.8
- Rhizopus —*see* Mucormycosis
- rickettsial NOS A79.9
- roundworm (large) NEC B82.0
  - Ascariasis —*see also* Ascariasis B77.9
- rubella —*see* Rubella
- Saccharomyces —*see* Candidiasis
- salivary duct or gland (any) —*see* Sialoadenitis

Infestation *(continued)*
Pediculus *(continued)*
head B85.0
mixed (classifiable to more than one of the titles B85.0-B85.3) B85.4
pubis (any site) B85.3
Pentastoma B88.8
Phthirus (pubis) (any site) B85.3
with any infestation classifiable to B85.0-B85.2 B85.4
pinworm B80
pork tapeworm (adult) B68.0
protozoal NEC B64
intestinal A07.9
specified NEC A07.8
specified NEC B60.8
pubic, louse B85.3
rat tapeworm B71.0
red bug B88.0
roundworm (large) NEC B82.0
Ascariasis —*see also* Ascariasis B77.9
sandflea B88.1
Sarcoptes scabiei B86
scabies B86
Schistosoma B65.9
bovis B65.8
cercariae B65.3
haematobium B65.0
intercalatum B65.8
japonicum B65.2
mansoni B65.1
mattheei B65.8
mekongi B65.8
specified type NEC B65.8
spindale B65.8
screw worms —*see* Myiasis
skin NOS B88.9
Sparganum (mansoni) (proliferum) (baxteri) B70.1
larval B70.1
specified type NEC B88.8
Spirometra larvae B70.1
Stellantchasmus falcatus B66.8
Strongyloides stercoralis —*see* Strongyloidiasis
Taenia B68.9
diminuta B71.0
echinococcus —*see* Echinococcus
mediocanellata B68.1
nana B71.0
saginata B68.1
solium (intestinal form) B68.0
larval form —*see* Cysticercosis
Taeniarhynchus saginatus B68.1
tapeworm B71.9
beef B68.1
broad B70.0
larval B70.1
dog B67.4
dwarf B71.0
fish B70.0
larval B70.1
pork B68.0
rat B71.0
Ternidens diminutus B81.8
Tetranychus molestissimus B88.0
threadworm B80
tongue B37.0
Toxocara (canis) (cati) (felis) B83.0
trematode (s) NEC —*see* Infestation, fluke
Trichinella (spiralis) B75
Trichocephalus B79
Trichomonas —*see* Trichomoniasis
Trichostrongylus B81.2
Trichuris (trichiura) B79
Trombicula (irritans) B88.0
Tunga penetrans B88.1
Uncinaria americana B76.1
Vandellia cirrhosa B88.8

Infestation *(continued)*
whipworm B79
worms B83.9
intestinal B82.0
Wuchereria (bancrofti) B74.0

Infiltrate, infiltration
amyloid (generalized) (localized) —*see* Amyloidosis
calcareous NEC R89.7
localized —*see* Degeneration, by site
calcium salt R89.7
cardiac
fatty —*see* Degeneration, myocardial
glycogenic E74.02 *[I43]*
corneal —*see* Edema, cornea
eyelid —*see* Inflammation, eyelid
glycogen, glycogenic —*see* Disease, glycogen storage
heart, cardiac
fatty —*see* Degeneration, myocardial
glycogenic E74.02 *[I43]*
inflammatory in vitreous H43.89
kidney N28.89
leukemic —*see* Leukemia
liver K76.89
fatty —*see* Fatty, liver NEC
glycogen —*see also* Disease, glycogen storage E74.03 *[K77]*
lung R91.8
eosinophilic J82
lymphatic —*see also* Leukemia, lymphatic C91.9-
gland I88.9
muscle, fatty M62.89
myocardium, myocardial
fatty —*see* Degeneration, myocardial
glycogenic E74.02 *[I43]*
on chest x-ray R91.8
pulmonary R91.8
with eosinophilia J82
skin (lymphocytic) L98.6
thymus (gland) (fatty) E32.8
urine R39.0
vesicant agent
antineoplastic chemotherapy T80.810
other agent NEC T80.818
vitreous body H43.89

Infirmity R68.89
senile R54

Inflammation, inflamed, inflammatory (with exudation)
abducent (nerve) —*see* Strabismus, paralytic, sixth nerve
accessory sinus (chronic) —*see* Sinusitis
adrenal (gland) E27.8
alveoli, teeth M27.3
scorbutic E54
anal canal, anus K62.89
antrum (chronic) —*see* Sinusitis, maxillary
appendix —*see* Appendicitis
arachnoid —*see* Meningitis
areola N61
puerperal, postpartum or gestational —*see* Infection, nipple
areolar tissue NOS L08.9
artery —*see* Arteritis
auditory meatus (external) —*see* Otitis, externa
Bartholin's gland N75.8
bile duct (common) (hepatic) or passage —*see* Cholangitis
bladder —*see* Cystitis
bone —*see* Osteomyelitis

Inflammation, inflamed, inflammatory *(continued)*
brain —*see also* Encephalitis
membrane —*see* Meningitis
breast N61
puerperal, postpartum, gestational —*see* Mastitis, obstetric
broad ligament —*see* Disease, pelvis, inflammatory
bronchi —*see* Bronchitis
catarrhal J00
cecum —*see* Appendicitis
cerebral —*see also* Encephalitis
membrane —*see* Meningitis
cerebrospinal
meningococcal A39.0
cervix (uteri) —*see* Cervicitis
chest J98.8
chorioretinal H30.9-
cyclitis —*see* Cyclitis
disseminated H30.10-
generalized H30.13-
peripheral H30.12-
posterior pole H30.11-
epitheliopathy —*see* Epitheliopathy
focal H30.00-
juxtapapillary H30.01-
macular H30.04-
paramacular —*see* Inflammation, chorioretinal, focal, macular
peripheral H30.03-
posterior pole H30.02-
specified type NEC H30.89-
choroid —*see* Inflammation, chorioretinal
chronic, postmastoidectomy cavity —*see* Complications, postmastoidectomy, inflammation
colon —*see* Enteritis
connective tissue (diffuse) NEC —*see* Disorder, soft tissue, specified type NEC
cornea —*see* Keratitis
corpora cavernosa N48.29
cranial nerve —*see* Disorder, nerve, cranial
Douglas' cul-de-sac or pouch (chronic) N73.0
due to device, implant or graft —*see also* Complications, by site and type, infection or inflammation
arterial graft T82.7
breast (implant) T85.79
catheter T85.79
dialysis (renal) T82.7
intraperitoneal T85.71
infusion T82.7
spinal (epidural) (subdural) T85.79
urinary (indwelling) T83.51
electronic (electrode) (pulse generator) (stimulator)
bone T84.7
cardiac T82.7
nervous system (brain) (peripheral nerve) (spinal) T85.79
urinary T83.59
fixation, internal (orthopedic) NEC —*see* Complication, fixation device, infection
gastrointestinal (bile duct) (esophagus) T85.79
genital NEC T83.6
heart NEC T82.7
valve (prosthesis) T82.6
graft T82.7
joint prosthesis —*see* Complication, joint prosthesis, infection

Inflammation, inflamed, inflammatory *(continued)*
due to device, implant or graft —*see also* Complications, by site and type, infection or inflammation *(continued)*
ocular (corneal graft) (orbital implant) NEC T85.79
orthopedic NEC T84.7
specified NEC T85.79
urinary NEC T83.59
vascular NEC T82.7
ventricular intracranial shunt T85.79
duodenum K29.80
with bleeding K29.81
dura mater —*see* Meningitis
ear (middle) —*see also* Otitis, media
external —*see* Otitis, externa
inner —*see* subcategory H83.0
epididymis —*see* Epididymitis
esophagus K20.9
ethmoidal (sinus) (chronic) —*see* Sinusitis, ethmoidal
eustachian tube (catarrhal) —*see* Salpingitis, eustachian
eyelid H01.9
abscess —*see* Abscess, eyelid
blepharitis —*see* Blepharitis
chalazion —*see* Chalazion
dermatosis (noninfectious) —*see* Dermatosis, eyelid
hordeolum —*see* Hordeolum
specified NEC H01.8
fallopian tube —*see* Salpingo-oophoritis
fascia —*see* Myositis
follicular, pharynx J31.2
frontal (sinus) (chronic) —*see* Sinusitis, frontal
gallbladder —*see* Cholecystitis
gastric —*see* Gastritis
gastrointestinal —*see* Enteritis
genital organ (internal) (diffuse)
female —*see* Disease, pelvis, inflammatory
male N49.9
multiple sites N49.8
specified NEC N49.8
gland (lymph) —*see* Lymphadenitis
glottis —*see* Laryngitis
granular, pharynx J31.2
gum K05.10
nonplaque induced K05.11
plaque induced K05.10
heart —*see* Carditis
hepatic duct —*see* Cholangitis
ileoanal (internal) pouch K91.850
ileum —*see also* Enteritis
regional or terminal —*see* Enteritis, regional
intestine (any part) —*see* Enteritis
intestinal pouch K91.850
jaw (acute) (bone) (chronic) (lower) (suppurative) (upper) M27.2
joint NEC —*see* Arthritis
sacroiliac M46.1
kidney —*see* Nephritis
knee (joint) M13.169
tuberculous A18.02
labium (majus) (minus) —*see* Vulvitis
lacrimal
gland —*see* Dacryoadenitis
passages (duct) (sac) —*see also* Dacryocystitis
canaliculitis —*see* Canaliculitis, lacrimal
larynx —*see* Laryngitis
leg NOS L08.9
lip K13.0

Inflammation, inflamed, inflammatory *(continued)*
- liver (capsule) —*see also* Hepatitis
  - chronic K73.9
  - suppurative K75.0
- lung (acute) —*see also* Pneumonia
  - chronic J98.4
- lymph gland or node —*see* Lymphadenitis
- lymphatic vessel —*see* Lymphangitis
- maxilla, maxillary M27.2
  - sinus (chronic) —*see* Sinusitis, maxillary
- membranes of brain or spinal cord —*see* Meningitis
- meninges —*see* Meningitis
- mouth K12.1
- muscle —*see* Myositis
- myocardium —*see* Myocarditis
- nasal sinus (chronic) —*see* Sinusitis
- nasopharynx —*see* Nasopharyngitis
- navel L08.82
- nerve NEC —*see* Neuralgia
- nipple N61
  - puerperal, postpartum or gestational —*see* Infection, nipple
- nose —*see* Rhinitis
- oculomotor (nerve) —*see* Strabismus, paralytic, third nerve
- optic nerve —*see* Neuritis, optic
- orbit (chronic) H05.10
  - acute H05.00
    - abscess —*see* Abscess, orbit
    - cellulitis —*see* Cellulitis, orbit
    - osteomyelitis —*see* Osteomyelitis, orbit
    - periostitis —*see* Periostitis, orbital
    - tenonitis —*see* Tenonitis, eye
  - granuloma —*see* Granuloma, orbit
  - myositis —*see* Myositis, orbital
- ovary —*see* Salpingo-oophoritis
- oviduct —*see* Salpingo-oophoritis
- pancreas (acute) —*see* Pancreatitis
- parametrium N73.0
- parotid region L08.9
- pelvis, female —*see* Disease, pelvis, inflammatory
- penis (corpora cavernosa) N48.29
- perianal K62.89
- pericardium —*see* Pericarditis
- perineum (female) (male) L08.9
- perirectal K62.89
- peritoneum —*see* Peritonitis
- periuterine —*see* Disease, pelvis, inflammatory
- perivesical —*see* Cystitis
- petrous bone (acute) (chronic) —*see* Petrositis
- pharynx (acute) —*see* Pharyngitis
- pia mater —*see* Meningitis
- pleura —*see* Pleurisy
- polyp, colon —*see also* Polyp, colon, inflammatory K51.40
- prostate —*see also* Prostatitis
  - specified type NEC N41.8
- rectosigmoid —*see* Rectosigmoiditis
- rectum —*see also* Proctitis K62.89
- respiratory, upper —*see also* Infection, respiratory, upper J06.9
  - acute, due to radiation J70.0
  - chronic, due to external agent —*see* condition, respiratory, chronic, due to
  - due to
    - chemicals, gases, fumes or vapors (inhalation) J68.2
    - radiation J70.1
- retina —*see* Chorioretinitis
- retrocecal —*see* Appendicitis
- retroperitoneal —*see* Peritonitis

Inflammation, inflamed, inflammatory *(continued)*
- salivary duct or gland (any) (suppurative) —*see* Sialoadenitis
- scorbutic, alveoli, teeth E54
- scrotum N49.2
- seminal vesicle —*see* Vesiculitis
- sigmoid —*see* Enteritis
- sinus —*see* Sinusitis
- Skene's duct or gland —*see* Urethritis
- skin L08.9
- spermatic cord N49.1
- sphenoidal (sinus) —*see* Sinusitis, sphenoidal
- spinal
  - cord —*see* Encephalitis
  - membrane —*see* Meningitis
  - nerve —*see* Disorder, nerve
- spine —*see* Spondylopathy, inflammatory
- spleen (capsule) D73.89
- stomach —*see* Gastritis
- subcutaneous tissue L08.9
- suprarenal (gland) E27.8
- synovial —*see* Tenosynovitis
- tendon (sheath) NEC —*see* Tenosynovitis
- testis —*see* Orchitis
- throat (acute) —*see* Pharyngitis
- thymus (gland) E32.8
- thyroid (gland) —*see* Thyroiditis
- tongue K14.0
- tonsil —*see* Tonsillitis
- trachea —*see* Tracheitis
- trochlear (nerve) —*see* Strabismus, paralytic, fourth nerve
- tubal —*see* Salpingo-oophoritis
- tuberculous NEC —*see* Tuberculosis
- tubo-ovarian —*see* Salpingo-oophoritis
- tunica vaginalis N49.1
- tympanic membrane —*see* Tympanitis
- umbilicus, umbilical L08.82
- uterine ligament —*see* Disease, pelvis, inflammatory
- uterus (catarrhal) —*see* Endometritis
- uveal tract (anterior) NOS —*see also* Iridocyclitis
  - posterior —*see* Chorioretinitis
- vagina —*see* Vaginitis
- vas deferens N49.1
- vein —*see also* Phlebitis
  - intracranial or intraspinal (septic) G08
  - thrombotic I80.9
    - leg —*see* Phlebitis, leg
    - lower extremity —*see* Phlebitis, leg
- vocal cord J38.3
- vulva —*see* Vulvitis
- Wharton's duct (suppurative) —*see* Sialoadenitis

Inflation, lung, imperfect (newborn) —*see* Atelectasis

Influenza (bronchial) (epidemic) (respiratory (upper)) (unidentified influenza virus) J11.1
- with
  - digestive manifestations J11.2
  - encephalopathy J11.81
  - enteritis J11.2
  - gastroenteritis J11.2
  - gastrointestinal manifestations J11.2
  - laryngitis J11.1
  - myocarditis J11.82
  - otitis media J11.83
  - pharyngitis J11.1
  - pneumonia J11.00
    - specified type J11.08

Influenza *(continued)*
- with *(continued)*
  - respiratory manifestations NEC J11.1
  - specified manifestation NEC J11.89
- A/H5N1 —*see also* Influenza, due to, identified novel influenza A virus J09.X2
- avian —*see also* Influenza, due to, identified novel influenza A virus J09.X2
- bird —*see also* Influenza, due to, identified novel influenza A virus J09.X2
- novel (2009) H1N1 influenza —*see also* Influenza, due to, identified influenza virus NEC J10.1
- novel influenza A/H1N1 —*see also* Influenza, due to, identified influenza virus NEC J10.1
- due to
  - avian —*see also* Influenza, due to, identified novel influenza A virus J09.X2
  - identified influenza virus NEC J10.1
    - with
      - digestive manifestations J10.2
      - encephalopathy J10.81
      - enteritis J10.2
      - gastroenteritis J10.2
      - gastrointestinal manifestations J10.2
      - laryngitis J10.1
      - myocarditis J10.82
      - otitis media J10.83
      - pharyngitis J10.1
      - pneumonia (unspecified type) J10.00
        - with same identified influenza virus J10.01
        - specified type NEC J10.08
      - respiratory manifestations NEC J10.1
      - specified manifestation NEC J10.89
  - identified novel influenza A virus J09.X2
    - with
      - digestive manifestations J09.X3
      - encephalopathy J09.X9
      - enteritis J09.X3
      - gastroenteritis J09.X3
      - gastrointestinal manifestations J09.X3
      - laryngitis J09.X2
      - myocarditis J09.X9
      - otitis media J09.X9
      - pharyngitis J09.X2
      - pneumonia J09.X1
      - respiratory manifestations NEC J09.X2
      - specified manifestation NEC J09.X9
      - upper respiratory symptoms J09.X2
- of other animal origin, not bird or swine —*see also* Influenza, due to, identified novel influenza A virus J09.X2
- swine (viruses that normally cause infections in pigs) —*see also* Influenza, due to, identified novel influenza A virus J09.X2

Influenza-like disease —*see* Influenza

Influenzal —*see* Influenza

Infraction, Freiberg's (metatarsal head) —*see* Osteochondrosis, juvenile, metatarsus

Infraeruption of tooth (teeth) M26.3

Infusion complication, misadventur or reaction —*see* Complications, infusion

Ingestion
- chemical —*see* Table of Drugs and Chemicals, by substance, poisoni
- drug or medicament
  - correct substance properly administered —*see* Table of Drugs and Chemicals, by drug adverse effect
  - overdose or wrong substance given or taken —*see* Table of Drugs and Chemicals, by drug poisoning
- foreign body —*see* Foreign body, alimentary tract
- tularemia A21.3

Ingrowing
- hair (beard) L73.1
- nail (finger) (toe) L60.0

Inguinal —*see also* condition
- testicle Q53.9
  - bilateral Q53.21
  - unilateral Q53.11

Inhalation
- anthrax A22.1
- flame T27.3
- food or foreign body —*see* Foreign body, by site
- gases, fumes, or vapors NEC T59.9
  - specified agent —*see* Table of Drugs and Chemicals, by substance
- liquid or vomitus —*see* Asphyxia
- meconium (newborn) P24.00
  - with
    - pneumonia (pneumonitis) P24.01
    - with respiratory symptoms P24.01
- mucus —*see* Asphyxia, mucus
- oil or gasoline (causing suffocation) —*see* Foreign body, by site
- smoke J70.5
  - due to chemicals, gases, fumes an vapors J68.9
- steam —*see* Toxicity, vapors
- stomach contents or secretions —*se* Foreign body, by site
  - due to anesthesia (general) (local) or other sedation T88.59
    - in labor and delivery O74.0
    - in pregnancy O29.01-
    - postpartum, puerperal O89.01

Inhibition, orgasm
- female F52.31
- male F52.32

Inhibitor, systemic lupus erythematosus (presence of) D68.6

Iniencephalus, iniencephaly Q00.2

Injection, traumatic jet (air) (industrial) (water) (paint or dye) T70.4

Injury —*see also* specified injury type T14.90
- abdomen, abdominal S39.91
  - blood vessel —*see* Injury, blood vessel, abdomen
  - cavity —*see* Injury, intra-abdominal
  - contusion S30.1
  - internal —*see* Injury, intra-abdominal
  - intra-abdominal organ —*see* Injur intra-abdominal
  - nerve —*see* Injury, nerve, abdome

Injury *(continued)*
- eye *(continued)*
  - conjunctiva S05.0-
  - cornea
    - abrasion S05.0-
  - laceration S05.3-
    - with prolapse S05.2-
  - lacrimal apparatus S05.8X-
  - orbit penetration S05.4-
  - specified site NEC S05.8X-
- eyeball S05.8X-
  - contusion S05.1-
  - penetrating S05.6-
    - with
      - foreign body S05.5-
      - prolapse or loss of intraocular tissue S05.2-
    - without prolapse or loss of intraocular tissue S05.3-
  - specified type NEC S05.8-
- eyebrow S09.93
- eyelid S09.93
  - abrasion —*see* Abrasion, eyelid
  - contusion —*see* Contusion, eyelid
  - open —*see* Wound, open, eyelid
- face S09.93
- fallopian tube S37.509
  - bilateral S37.502
    - blast injury S37.512
    - contusion S37.522
    - laceration S37.532
    - specified type NEC S37.592
  - blast injury (primary) S37.519
    - bilateral S37.512
    - secondary —*see* Injury, fallopian tube, specified type NEC
    - unilateral S37.511
  - contusion S37.529
    - bilateral S37.522
    - unilateral S37.521
  - laceration S37.539
    - bilateral S37.532
    - unilateral S37.531
  - specified type NEC S37.599
    - bilateral S37.592
    - unilateral S37.591
  - unilateral S37.501
    - blast injury S37.511
    - contusion S37.521
    - laceration S37.531
    - specified type NEC S37.591
- fascia —*see* Injury, muscle
- fifth cranial nerve (trigeminal) —*see* Injury, nerve, trigeminal
- finger (nail) S69.9-
  - blood vessel —*see* Injury, blood vessel, finger
  - contusion —*see* Contusion, finger
  - dislocation —*see* Dislocation, finger
  - fracture —*see* Fracture, finger
  - muscle —*see* Injury, muscle, finger
  - nerve —*see* Injury, nerve, digital, finger
  - open —*see* Wound, open, finger
  - specified NEC S69.8-
  - sprain —*see* Sprain, finger
  - superficial —*see* Injury, superficial, finger
- first cranial nerve (olfactory) —*see* Injury, nerve, olfactory
- flank —*see* Injury, abdomen
- foot S99.92-
  - blood vessel —*see* Injury, blood vessel, foot
  - contusion —*see* Contusion, foot
  - dislocation —*see* Dislocation, foot
  - fracture —*see* Fracture, foot
  - muscle —*see* Injury, muscle, foot
  - open —*see* Wound, open, foot
  - specified type NEC S99.82-
  - sprain —*see* Sprain, foot

Injury *(continued)*
- foot *(continued)*
  - superficial —*see* Injury, superficial, foot
- forceps NOS P15.9
- forearm S59.91-
  - blood vessel —*see* Injury, blood vessel, forearm
  - contusion —*see* Contusion, forearm
  - fracture —*see* Fracture, forearm
  - muscle —*see* Injury, muscle, forearm
  - nerve —*see* Injury, nerve, forearm
  - open —*see* Wound, open, forearm
  - specified NEC S59.81-
  - superficial —*see* Injury, superficial, forearm
- forehead S09.90
- fourth cranial nerve (trochlear) —*see* Injury, nerve, trochlear
- gallbladder S36.129
  - contusion S36.122
  - laceration S36.123
  - specified NEC S36.128
- ganglion
  - celiac, coeliac —*see* Injury, nerve, lumbosacral, sympathetic
  - gasserian —*see* Injury, nerve, trigeminal
  - stellate —*see* Injury, nerve, thorax, sympathetic
  - thoracic sympathetic —*see* Injury, nerve, thorax, sympathetic
- gasserian ganglion —*see* Injury, nerve, trigeminal
- gastric artery —*see* Injury, blood vessel, celiac artery, branch
- gastroduodenal artery —*see* Injury, blood vessel, celiac artery, branch
- gastrointestinal tract —*see* Injury, intra-abdominal
  - with open wound into abdominal cavity —*see* Wound, open, with penetration into peritoneal cavity
  - colon —*see* Injury, intestine, large
  - rectum —*see* Injury, intestine, large, rectum
    - with open wound into abdominal cavity S36.61
  - specified site NEC —*see* Injury, intra-abdominal, specified, site NEC
  - stomach —*see* Injury, stomach
  - small intestine —*see* Injury, intestine, small
- genital organ (s)
  - external S39.94
    - specified NEC S39.848
  - internal S37.90
    - fallopian tube —*see* Injury, fallopian tube
    - ovary —*see* Injury, ovary
    - prostate —*see* Injury, prostate
    - seminal vesicle —*see* Injury, pelvis, organ, specified site NEC
    - uterus —*see* Injury, uterus
    - vas deferens —*see* Injury, pelvis, organ, specified site NEC
  - obstetrical trauma O71.9
- gland
  - lacrimal laceration —*see* Injury, eye, specified site NEC
  - salivary S09.90
  - thyroid NEC S19.84
- globe (eye) S05.90
  - specified NEC S05.8X-
- groin —*see* Injury, abdomen
- gum S09.90

Injury *(continued)*
- hand S69.9-
  - blood vessel —*see* Injury, blood vessel, hand
  - contusion —*see* Contusion, hand
  - fracture —*see* Fracture, hand
  - muscle —*see* Injury, muscle, hand
  - nerve —*see* Injury, nerve, hand
  - open —*see* Wound, open, hand
  - specified NEC S69.8-
  - sprain —*see* Sprain, hand
  - superficial —*see* Injury, superficial, hand
- head S09.90
  - with loss of consciousness S06.9-
  - specified NEC S09.8
- heart S26.90
  - with hemopericardium S26.00
    - contusion S26.01
    - laceration (mild) S26.020
      - moderate S26.021
      - major S26.022
    - specified type NEC S26.09
  - contusion S26.91
  - laceration S26.92
  - specified type NEC S26.99
  - without hemopericardium S26.10
    - contusion S26.11
    - laceration S26.12
    - specified type NEC S26.19
- heel —*see* Injury, foot
- hepatic
  - artery —*see* Injury, blood vessel, celiac artery, branch
  - duct —*see* Injury, liver
  - vein —*see* Injury, vena cava, inferior
- hip S79.91-
  - blood vessel —*see* Injury, blood vessel, hip
  - contusion —*see* Contusion, hip
  - dislocation —*see* Dislocation, hip
  - fracture —*see* Fracture, femur, neck
  - muscle —*see* Injury, muscle, hip
  - nerve —*see* Injury, nerve, hip
  - open —*see* Wound, open, hip
  - sprain —*see* Sprain, hip
  - superficial —*see* Injury, superficial, hip
  - specified NEC S79.81-
- hymen S39.94
- hypogastric
  - blood vessel —*see* Injury, blood vessel, iliac
  - plexus —*see* Injury, nerve, lumbosacral, sympathetic
- ileum —*see* Injury, intestine, small
- iliac region S39.91
- instrumental (during surgery) —*see* Laceration, accidental complicating surgery
  - birth injury —*see* Birth, injury
  - nonsurgical —*see* Injury, by site
  - obstetrical O71.9
    - bladder O71.5
    - cervix O71.3
    - high vaginal O71.4
    - perineal NOS O70.9
    - urethra O71.5
    - uterus O71.5
      - with rupture or perforation O71.1
- internal T14.8
  - aorta —*see* Injury, aorta
  - bladder (sphincter) —*see* Injury, bladder
    - with
      - ectopic or molar pregnancy O08.6
    - following ectopic or molar pregnancy O08.6
    - obstetrical trauma O71.5

Injury *(continued)*
- internal *(continued)*
  - bronchus, bronchi —*see* Injury, intrathoracic, bronchus
  - cecum —*see* Injury, intestine, large
  - cervix (uteri) —*see also* Injury, uterus
    - with ectopic or molar pregnancy O08.6
    - following ectopic or molar pregnancy O08.6
    - obstetrical trauma O71.3
  - chest —*see* Injury, intrathoracic
  - gastrointestinal tract —*see* Injury, intra-abdominal
  - heart —*see* Injury, heart
  - intestine NEC —*see* Injury, intestine
  - intrauterine —*see* Injury, uterus
  - mesentery —*see* Injury, intra-abdominal, specified, site NEC
  - pelvis, pelvic (organ) S37.90
    - following ectopic or molar pregnancy (subsequent episode) O08.6
    - obstetrical trauma NEC O71.5
      - rupture or perforation O71.1
    - specified NEC S39.83
  - rectum —*see* Injury, intestine, large, rectum
  - stomach —*see* Injury, stomach
  - ureter —*see* Injury, ureter
  - urethra (sphincter) following ectopic or molar pregnancy O08.6
  - uterus —*see* Injury, uterus
- interscapular area —*see* Injury, thorax
- intestine
  - large S36.509
    - ascending (right) S36.500
      - blast injury (primary) S36.510
        - secondary S36.590
      - contusion S36.520
      - laceration S36.530
      - specified type NEC S36.590
    - blast injury (primary) S36.519
      - ascending (right) S36.510
      - descending (left) S36.512
      - rectum S36.61
      - sigmoid S36.513
      - specified site NEC S36.518
      - transverse S36.511
    - contusion S36.529
      - ascending (right) S36.520
      - descending (left) S36.522
      - rectum S36.62
      - sigmoid S36.523
      - specified site NEC S36.528
      - transverse S36.521
    - descending (left) S36.502
      - blast injury (primary) S36.512
        - secondary S36.592
      - contusion S36.522
      - laceration S36.532
      - specified type NEC S36.592
    - laceration S36.539
      - ascending (right) S36.530
      - descending (left) S36.532
      - rectum S36.63
      - sigmoid S36.533
      - specified site NEC S36.538
      - transverse S36.531
    - rectum S36.60
      - blast injury (primary) S36.61
        - secondary S36.69
      - contusion S36.62
      - laceration S36.63
      - specified type NEC S36.69
    - sigmoid S36.503
      - blast injury (primary) S36.513
        - secondary S36.593
      - contusion S36.523

Injury *(continued)*
intestine *(continued)*
large *(continued)*
sigmoid *(continued)*
laceration S36.533
specified type NEC S36.593
specified
site NEC S36.508
blast injury (primary) S36.518
secondary S36.598
contusion S36.528
laceration S36.538
specified type NEC S36.598
type NEC S36.599
ascending (right) S36.590
descending (left) S36.592
rectum S36.69
sigmoid S36.593
specified site NEC S36.598
transverse S36.591
transverse S36.501
blast injury (primary) S36.511
secondary S36.591
contusion S36.521
laceration S36.531
specified type NEC S36.591
small S36.409
blast injury (primary) S36.419
duodenum S36.410
secondary S36.499
duodenum S36.490
specified site NEC S36.498
specified site NEC S36.418
contusion S36.429
duodenum S36.420
specified site NEC S36.428
duodenum S36.400
blast injury (primary) S36.410
secondary S36.490
contusion S36.420
laceration S36.430
specified NEC S36.490
laceration S36.439
duodenum S36.430
specified site NEC S36.438
specified
type NEC S36.499
duodenum S36.490
specified site NEC S36.498
site NEC S36.408
intra-abdominal S36.90
adrenal gland —*see* Injury, adrenal gland
bladder —*see* Injury, bladder
colon —*see* Injury, intestine, large
contusion S36.92
fallopian tube —*see* Injury, fallopian tube
gallbladder —*see* Injury, gallbladder
intestine —*see* Injury, intestine
laceration S36.93
liver —*see* Injury, liver
kidney —*see* Injury, kidney
ovary —*see* Injury, ovary
pancreas —*see* Injury, pancreas
pelvic NOS S37.90
peritoneum —*see* Injury, intra-abdominal, specified, site NEC
prostate —*see* Injury, prostate
rectum —*see* Injury, intestine, large, rectum
retroperitoneum —*see* Injury, intra-abdominal, specified, site NEC
seminal vesicle —*see* Injury, pelvis, organ, specified site NEC
small intestine —*see* Injury, intestine, small

Injury *(continued)*
intra-abdominal *(continued)*
specified
site NEC S36.899
contusion S36.892
laceration S36.893
specified type NEC S36.898
type NEC S36.99
pelvic S37.90
specified
site NEC S37.899
specified type NEC S37.898
type NEC S37.99
spleen —*see* Injury, spleen
stomach —*see* Injury, stomach
ureter —*see* Injury, ureter
urethra —*see* Injury, urethra
uterus —*see* Injury, uterus
vas deferens —*see* Injury, pelvis, organ, specified site NEC
intracranial (traumatic) S06.9-
cerebellar hemorrhage, traumatic —*see* Injury, intracranial, focal
cerebral edema, traumatic S06.1X-
diffuse S06.1X-
focal S06.1X-
diffuse (axonal) S06.2X-
epidural hemorrhage (traumatic) S06.4X-
focal brain injury S06.30-
contusion —*see* Contusion, cerebral
laceration —*see* Laceration, cerebral
intracerebral hemorrhage, traumatic S06.36-
left side S06.35-
right side S06.34-
subarachnoid hemorrhage, traumatic S06.6X-
subdural hemorrhage, traumatic S06.5X-
intraocular —*see* Injury, eyeball, penetrating
intrathoracic S27.9
bronchus S27.409
bilateral S27.402
blast injury (primary) S27.419
bilateral S27.412
secondary —*see* Injury, intrathoracic, bronchus, specified type NEC
unilateral S27.411
contusion S27.429
bilateral S27.422
unilateral S27.421
laceration S27.439
bilateral S27.432
unilateral S27.431
specified type NEC S27.499
bilateral S27.492
unilateral S27.491
unilateral S27.401
diaphragm S27.809
contusion S27.802
laceration S27.803
specified type NEC S27.808
esophagus (thoracic) S27.819
contusion S27.812
laceration S27.813
specified type NEC S27.818
heart —*see* Injury, heart
hemopneumothorax S27.2
hemothorax S27.1
lung S27.309
aspiration J69.0
bilateral S27.302
blast injury (primary) S27.319
bilateral S27.312

Injury *(continued)*
intrathoracic *(continued)*
lung *(continued)*
blast injury *(continued)*
secondary —*see* Injury, intrathoracic, lung, specified type NEC
unilateral S27.311
contusion S27.329
bilateral S27.322
unilateral S27.321
laceration S27.339
bilateral S27.332
unilateral S27.331
specified type NEC S27.399
bilateral S27.392
unilateral S27.391
unilateral S27.301
pleura S27.60
laceration S27.63
specified type NEC S27.69
pneumothorax S27.0
specified organ NEC S27.899
contusion S27.892
laceration S27.893
specified type NEC S27.898
thoracic duct —*see* Injury, intrathoracic, specified organ NEC
thymus gland —*see* Injury, intrathoracic, specified organ NEC
trachea, thoracic S27.50
blast (primary) S27.51
contusion S27.52
laceration S27.53
specified type NEC S27.59
iris —*see* Injury, eye, specified site NEC
penetrating —*see* Injury, eyeball, penetrating
jaw S09.93
jejunum —*see* Injury, intestine, small
joint NOS T14.8
old or residual —*see* Disorder, joint, specified type NEC
kidney S37.00-
acute (nontraumatic) N17.9
contusion —*see* Contusion, kidney
laceration —*see* Laceration, kidney
specified NEC S37.09-
knee S89.9-
contusion —*see* Contusion, knee
dislocation —*see* Dislocation, knee
meniscus (lateral) (medial) —*see* Sprain, knee, specified site NEC
old injury or tear —*see* Derangement, knee, meniscus, due to old injury
open —*see* Wound, open, knee
specified NEC S89.8-
sprain —*see* Sprain, knee
superficial —*see* Injury, superficial, knee
labium (majus) (minus) S39.94
labyrinth, ear S09.30-
lacrimal apparatus, duct, gland, or sac —*see* Injury, eye, specified site NEC
larynx NEC S19.81
leg (lower) S89.9-
blood vessel —*see* Injury, blood vessel, leg
contusion —*see* Contusion, leg
fracture —*see* Fracture, leg
muscle —*see* Injury, muscle, leg
nerve —*see* Injury, nerve, leg
open —*see* Wound, open, leg
specified NEC S89.8-
superficial —*see* Injury, superficial, leg

Injury *(continued)*
lens, eye —*see* Injury, eye, specified site NEC
penetrating —*see* Injury, eyeball, penetrating
limb NEC T14.8
lip S09.93
liver S36.119
contusion S36.112
laceration S36.113
major (stellate) S36.116
minor S36.114
moderate S36.115
specified NEC S36.118
lower back S39.92
specified NEC S39.82
lumbar, lumbosacral (region) S39.92
plexus —*see* Injury, lumbosacral plexus
lumbosacral plexus S34.4
lung —*see also* Injury, intrathoracic, lung
aspiration J69.0
transfusion-related (TRALI) J95.8
lymphatic thoracic duct —*see* Injury, intrathoracic, specified organ NEC
malar region S09.93
mastoid region S09.90
maxilla S09.93
mediastinum —*see* Injury, intrathoracic, specified organ NEC
membrane, brain —*see* Injury, intracranial
meningeal artery —*see* Injury, intracranial, subdural hemorrhage
meninges (cerebral) —*see* Injury, intracranial
mesenteric
artery
branch S35.299
laceration (minor) (superficial) S35.291
major S35.292
specified NEC S35.298
inferior S35.239
laceration (minor) (superficial) S35.231
major S35.232
specified NEC S35.238
superior S35.229
laceration (minor) (superficial) S35.221
major S35.222
specified NEC S35.228
plexus (inferior) (superior) —*see* Injury, nerve, lumbosacral, sympathetic
vein
inferior S35.349
laceration S35.341
specified NEC S35.348
superior S35.339
laceration S35.331
specified NEC S35.338
mesentery —*see* Injury, intra-abdominal, specified site NEC
mesosalpinx —*see* Injury, pelvic organ, specified site NEC
middle ear S09.30-
midthoracic region NOS S29.9
mouth S09.93
multiple NOS T07
muscle (and fascia) (and tendon)
abdomen S39.001
laceration S39.021
specified type NEC S39.091
strain S39.011
abductor
thumb, forearm level —*see* Injury, muscle, thumb, abductor

Injury *(continued)*
- nerve NEC *(continued)*
  - sixth cranial (abducent) —*see* Injury, nerve, abducens
  - spinal
    - plexus —*see* Injury, nerve, plexus, spinal
    - root
      - cervical S14.2
      - dorsal S24.2
      - lumbar S34.21
      - sacral S34.22
      - thoracic —*see* Injury, nerve, spinal, root, dorsal
  - splanchnic —*see* Injury, nerve, lumbosacral, sympathetic
  - sympathetic NEC —*see* Injury, nerve, lumbosacral, sympathetic
    - cervical —*see* Injury, nerve, cervical sympathetic
  - tenth cranial (pneumogastric or vagus) —*see* Injury, nerve, vagus
  - thigh (level) —*see* Injury, nerve, hip
    - cutaneous sensory —*see* Injury, nerve, cutaneous sensory, hip
    - femoral —*see* Injury, nerve, femoral
    - sciatic —*see* Injury, nerve, sciatic
    - specified NEC —*see* Injury, nerve, hip
  - third cranial (oculomotor) —*see* Injury, nerve, oculomotor
  - thorax S24.9
    - peripheral S24.3
    - specified site NEC S24.8
    - sympathetic S24.4
  - thumb, digital —*see* Injury, nerve, digital, thumb
  - tibial (lower leg level) (posterior) S84.0-
  - toe —*see* Injury, nerve, ankle
  - trigeminal S04.3-
    - contusion S04.3-
    - laceration S04.3-
    - specified type NEC S04.3-
  - trochlear S04.2-
    - contusion S04.2-
    - laceration S04.2-
    - specified type NEC S04.2-
  - twelfth cranial (hypoglossal) —*see* Injury, nerve, hypoglossal
  - ulnar (forearm level) S54.0-
    - arm (upper) (level) S44.0-
    - hand (level) S64.0-
    - wrist (level) —*see* Injury, nerve, ulnar, hand
  - vagus S04.89-
    - specified type NEC S04.89-
  - wrist (level) —*see* Injury, nerve, hand
- ninth cranial nerve (glossopharyngeal) —*see* Injury, nerve, glossopharyngeal
- nose (septum) S09.92
- obstetrical O71.9
  - specified NEC O71.89
- occipital (region) (scalp) S09.90
  - lobe —*see* Injury, intracranial
- optic chiasm S04.02
- optic radiation S04.03-
- optic tract and pathways S04.03-
- orbit, orbital (region) —*see* Injury, eye
  - penetrating (with foreign body) —*see* Injury, eye, orbit, penetrating
  - specified NEC —*see* Injury, eye, specified site NEC
- ovary, ovarian S37.409
  - bilateral S37.402
    - contusion S37.422
    - laceration S37.432
    - specified type NEC S37.492
  - blood vessel —*see* Injury, blood vessel, ovarian
  - contusion S37.429
    - bilateral S37.422
    - unilateral S37.421
  - laceration S37.439
    - bilateral S37.432
    - unilateral S37.431
  - specified type NEC S37.499
    - bilateral S37.492
    - unilateral S37.491
  - unilateral S37.401
    - contusion S37.421
    - laceration S37.431
    - specified type NEC S37.491
- palate (hard) (soft) S09.93
- pancreas S36.209
  - body S36.201
    - contusion S36.221
    - laceration S36.231
      - major S36.261
      - minor S36.241
      - moderate S36.251
    - specified type NEC S36.291
  - contusion S36.229
  - head S36.200
    - contusion S36.220
    - laceration S36.230
      - major S36.260
      - minor S36.240
      - moderate S36.250
    - specified type NEC S36.290
  - laceration S36.239
    - major S36.269
    - minor S36.249
    - moderate S36.259
  - specified type NEC S36.299
  - tail S36.202
    - contusion S36.222
    - laceration S36.232
      - major S36.262
      - minor S36.242
      - moderate S36.252
    - specified type NEC S36.292
- parietal (region) (scalp) S09.90
  - lobe —*see* Injury, intracranial
- patellar ligament (tendon) S76.10-
  - laceration S76.12-
  - specified NEC S76.19-
  - strain S76.11-
- pelvis, pelvic (floor) S39.93
  - complicating delivery O70.1
  - joint or ligament, complicating delivery O71.6
  - organ S37.90
    - with ectopic or molar pregnancy O08.6
    - complication of abortion —*see* Abortion
    - contusion S37.92
    - following ectopic or molar pregnancy O08.6
    - laceration S37.93
    - obstetrical trauma NEC O71.5
    - specified
      - site NEC S37.899
        - contusion S37.892
        - laceration S37.893
        - specified type NEC S37.898
      - type NEC S37.99
  - specified NEC S39.83
- penis S39.94
- perineum S39.94
- peritoneum S36.81
  - laceration S36.893

Injury *(continued)*
- periurethral tissue —*see* Injury, urethra
  - complicating delivery O71.82
- phalanges
  - foot —*see* Injury, foot
  - hand —*see* Injury, hand
- pharynx NEC S19.85
- pleura —*see* Injury, intrathoracic, pleura
- plexus
  - brachial —*see* Injury, brachial plexus
  - cardiac —*see* Injury, nerve, thorax, sympathetic
  - celiac, coeliac —*see* Injury, nerve, lumbosacral, sympathetic
  - esophageal —*see* Injury, nerve, thorax, sympathetic
  - hypogastric —*see* Injury, nerve, lumbosacral, sympathetic
  - lumbar, lumbosacral —*see* Injury, lumbosacral plexus
  - mesenteric —*see* Injury, nerve, lumbosacral, sympathetic
  - pulmonary —*see* Injury, nerve, thorax, sympathetic
- postcardiac surgery (syndrome) I97.0
- prepuce S39.94
- prostate S37.829
  - contusion S37.822
  - laceration S37.823
  - specified type NEC S37.828
- pubic region S39.94
- pudendum S39.94
- pulmonary plexus —*see* Injury, nerve, thorax, sympathetic
- rectovaginal septum NEC S39.83
- rectum —*see* Injury, intestine, large, rectum
- retina —*see* Injury, eye, specified site NEC
  - penetrating —*see* Injury, eyeball, penetrating
- retroperitoneal —*see* Injury, intra-abdominal, specified site NEC
- rotator cuff (muscle(s)) (tendon(s)) S46.00-
  - laceration S46.02-
  - specified type NEC S46.09-
  - strain S46.01-
- round ligament —*see* Injury, pelvic organ, specified site NEC
- sacral plexus —*see* Injury, lumbosacral plexus
- salivary duct or gland S09.93
- scalp S09.90
  - newborn (birth injury) P12.9
    - due to monitoring (electrode) (sampling incision) P12.4
    - specified NEC P12.89
      - caput succedaneum P12.81
- scapular region —*see* Injury, shoulder
- sclera —*see* Injury, eye, specified site NEC
  - penetrating —*see* Injury, eyeball, penetrating
- scrotum S39.94
- second cranial nerve (optic) —*see* Injury, nerve, optic
- seminal vesicle —*see* Injury, pelvic organ, specified site NEC
- seventh cranial nerve (facial) —*see* Injury, nerve, facial
- shoulder S49.9-
  - blood vessel —*see* Injury, blood vessel, arm
  - contusion —*see* Contusion, shoulder
  - dislocation —*see* Dislocation, shoulder
  - fracture —*see* Fracture, shoulder

Injury *(continued)*
- shoulder S49.9-
  - muscle —*see* Injury, muscle, shoulder
  - nerve —*see* Injury, nerve, shoulder
  - open —*see* Wound, open, shoulder
  - specified type NEC S49.8-
  - sprain —*see* Sprain, shoulder girdle
  - superficial —*see* Injury, superficial, shoulder
- sinus
  - cavernous —*see* Injury, intracranial
  - nasal S09.92
- sixth cranial nerve (abducent) —*see* Injury, nerve, abducens
- skeleton, birth injury P13.9
  - specified part NEC P13.8
- skin NEC T14.8
  - surface intact —*see* Injury, superficial
- skull NEC S09.90
- specified NEC T14.8
- spermatic cord (pelvic region) S37.898
  - scrotal region S39.848
- spinal (cord)
  - cervical (neck) S14.109
    - anterior cord syndrome S14.139
      - C1 level S14.131
      - C2 level S14.132
      - C3 level S14.133
      - C4 level S14.134
      - C5 level S14.135
      - C6 level S14.136
      - C7 level S14.137
      - C8 level S14.138
    - Brown-Séquard syndrome S14.149
      - C1 level S14.141
      - C2 level S14.142
      - C3 level S14.143
      - C4 level S14.144
      - C5 level S14.145
      - C6 level S14.146
      - C7 level S14.147
      - C8 level S14.148
    - C1 level S14.101
    - C2 level S14.102
    - C3 level S14.103
    - C4 level S14.104
    - C5 level S14.105
    - C6 level S14.106
    - C7 level S14.107
    - C8 level S14.108
    - central cord syndrome S14.129
      - C1 level S14.121
      - C2 level S14.122
      - C3 level S14.123
      - C4 level S14.124
      - C5 level S14.125
      - C6 level S14.126
      - C7 level S14.127
      - C8 level S14.128
    - complete lesion S14.119
      - C1 level S14.111
      - C2 level S14.112
      - C3 level S14.113
      - C4 level S14.114
      - C5 level S14.115
      - C6 level S14.116
      - C7 level S14.117
      - C8 level S14.118
    - concussion S14.0
    - edema S14.0
    - incomplete lesion specified NEC S14.159
      - C1 level S14.151
      - C2 level S14.152
      - C3 level S14.153
      - C4 level S14.154
      - C5 level S14.155

Insufficiency, insufficient *(continued)*
- gastroesophageal K22.8
- gonadal
  - ovary E28.39
  - testis E29.1
- heart *—see also* Insufficiency, myocardial
  - newborn P29.0
  - valve *—see* Endocarditis
- hepatic *—see* Failure, hepatic
- idiopathic autonomic G90.09
- interocclusal distance of fully erupted teeth (ridge) M26.36
- kidney N28.9
  - acute N28.9
  - chronic N18.9
- lacrimal (secretion) H04.12-
  - passages *—see* Stenosis, lacrimal
- liver *—see* Failure, hepatic
- lung *—see* Insufficiency, pulmonary
- mental (congenital) *—see* Disability, intellectual
- mesenteric K55.1
- mitral (valve) I34.0
  - with
    - aortic valve disease I08.0
      - with tricuspid (valve) disease I08.3
    - obstruction or stenosis I05.2
      - with aortic valve disease I08.0
    - tricuspid (valve) disease I08.1
      - with aortic (valve) disease I08.3
  - congenital Q23.3
  - rheumatic I05.1
    - with
      - aortic valve disease I08.0
        - with tricuspid (valve) disease I08.3
      - obstruction or stenosis I05.2
        - with aortic valve disease I08.0
          - with tricuspid (valve) disease I08.3
      - tricuspid (valve) disease I08.1
        - with aortic (valve) disease I08.3
    - active or acute I01.1
      - with chorea, rheumatic (Sydenham's) I02.0
  - specified cause, except rheumatic I34.0
- muscle *—see also* Disease, muscle
  - heart *—see* Insufficiency, myocardial
  - ocular NEC H50.9
- myocardial, myocardium (with arteriosclerosis) I50.9
  - with
    - rheumatic fever (conditions in I00) I09.0
      - active, acute or subacute I01.2
        - with chorea I02.0
      - inactive or quiescent (with chorea) I09.0
  - congenital Q24.8
  - hypertensive *—see* Hypertension, heart
  - newborn P29.0
  - rheumatic I09.0
    - active, acute, or subacute I01.2
  - syphilitic A52.06
- nourishment T73.0
- pancreatic K86.8
- parathyroid (gland) E20.9
- peripheral vascular (arterial) I73.9
- pituitary E23.0
- placental (mother) O36.51-
- platelets D69.6
- prenatal care affecting management of pregnancy O09.3-
- progressive pluriglandular E31.0

Insufficiency, insufficient *(continued)*
- pulmonary J98.4
  - acute, following surgery (nonthoracic) J95.2
    - thoracic J95.1
  - chronic, following surgery J95.3
  - following
    - shock J98.4
    - trauma J98.4
  - newborn P28.5
  - valve I37.1
    - with stenosis I37.2
    - congenital Q22.2
    - rheumatic I09.89
      - with aortic, mitral or tricuspid (valve) disease I08.8
- pyloric K31.89
- renal (acute) N28.9
  - chronic N18.9
- respiratory R06.89
  - newborn P28.5
- rotation *—see* Malrotation
- sleep syndrome F51.12
- social insurance Z59.7
- suprarenal E27.40
  - primary E27.1
- tarso-orbital fascia, congenital Q10.3
- testis E29.1
- thyroid (gland) (acquired) E03.9
  - congenital E03.1
- tricuspid (valve) (rheumatic) I07.1
  - with
    - aortic (valve) disease I08.2
      - with mitral (valve) disease I08.3
    - mitral (valve) disease I08.1
      - with aortic (valve) disease I08.3
    - obstruction or stenosis I07.2
      - with aortic (valve) disease I08.2
        - with mitral (valve) disease I08.3
  - congenital Q22.8
  - nonrheumatic I36.1
    - with stenosis I36.2
- urethral sphincter R32
- valve, valvular (heart) *—see* Endocarditis
  - congenital Q24.8
- vascular I99.8
  - intestine K55.9
    - acute K55.0
  - mesenteric K55.1
  - peripheral I73.9
  - renal *—see* Hypertension, kidney
- velopharyngeal
  - acquired K13.79
  - congenital Q38.8
- venous (chronic) (peripheral) I87.2
- ventricular *—see* Insufficiency, myocardial
- welfare support Z59.7

Insufflation, fallopian Z31.41

Insular *—see* condition

Insulinoma
- pancreas
  - benign D13.7
  - malignant C25.4
  - uncertain behavior D37.8
- specified site
  - benign *—see* Neoplasm, by site, benign
  - malignant *—see* Neoplasm, by site, malignant
  - uncertain behavior *—see* Neoplasm, by site, uncertain behavior
- unspecified site
  - benign D13.7
  - malignant C25.4
  - uncertain behavior D37.8

Insuloma *—see* Insulinoma

Interference
- balancing side M26.56
- non-working side M26.56

Intermenstrual *—see* condition

Intermittent *—see* condition

Internal *—see* condition

Interrogation
- cardiac defibrillator (automatic) (implantable) Z45.02
- cardiac pacemaker Z45.018
- cardiac (event) (loop) recorder Z45.09
- infusion pump (implanted) (intrathecal) Z45.1
- neurostimulator Z46.2

Interruption
- bundle of His I44.30
- phase-shift, sleep cycle *—see* Disorder, sleep, circadian rhythm
- sleep phase-shift, or 24 hour sleep-wake cycle *—see* Disorder, sleep, circadian rhythm

Interstitial *—see* condition

Intertrigo L30.4
- labialis K13.0

Intervertebral disc *—see* condition

Intestine, intestinal *—see* condition

Intolerance
- carbohydrate K90.4
- disaccharide, hereditary E73.0
- fat NEC K90.4
  - pancreatic K90.3
- food K90.4
  - dietary counseling and surveillance Z71.3
- fructose E74.10
  - hereditary E74.12
- glucose (-galactose) E74.39
- gluten K90.0
- lactose E73.9
  - specified NEC E73.8
- lysine E72.3
- milk NEC K90.4
  - lactose E73.9
- protein K90.4
- starch NEC K90.4
- sucrose (-isomaltose) E74.31

Intoxicated NEC (without dependence) *—see* Alcohol, intoxication

Intoxication
- acid E87.2
- alcoholic (acute) (without dependence) *—see* Alcohol, intoxication
- alimentary canal K52.1
- amphetamine (without dependence) *—see* Abuse, drug, stimulant, with intoxication
  - with dependence *—see* Dependence, drug, stimulant, with intoxication
- anxiolytic (acute) (without dependence) *—see* Abuse, drug, sedative, with intoxication
  - with dependence *—see* Dependence, drug, sedative, with intoxication
- caffeine (acute) (without dependence) *—see* Abuse, drug, stimulant, with intoxication
  - with dependence *—see* Dependence, drug, stimulant, with intoxication
- cannabinoids (acute) (without dependence) *—see* Abuse, drug, cannabis, with intoxication
  - with dependence *—see* Dependence, drug, cannabis, with intoxication

Intoxication *(continued)*
- chemical *—see* Table of Drugs and Chemicals
  - via placenta or breast milk *—see* - Absorption, chemical, through placenta
- cocaine (acute) (without dependence) *—see* Abuse, drug, cocaine, with intoxication
  - with dependence *—see* Dependence, drug, cocaine, with intoxication
- drug
  - acute (without dependence) *—see* Abuse, drug, by type with intoxication
    - with dependence *—see* Dependence, drug, by type with intoxication
  - addictive
    - via placenta or breast milk *—see* Absorption, drug, addictive, through placenta
  - newborn P93.8
    - gray baby syndrome P93.0
  - overdose or wrong substance given or taken *—see* Table of Drugs and Chemicals, by drug, poisoning
- enteric K52.1
- foodborne A05.9
  - bacterial A05.9
  - classical (Clostridium botulinum) A05.1
  - due to
    - Bacillus cereus A05.4
    - bacterium A05.9
      - specified NEC A05.8
    - Clostridium
      - botulinum A05.1
      - perfringens A05.2
      - welchii A05.2
    - Salmonella A02.9
      - with
        - (gastro)enteritis A02.0
        - localized infection (s) A02.20
          - arthritis A02.23
          - meningitis A02.21
          - osteomyelitis A02.24
          - pneumonia A02.22
          - pyelonephritis A02.25
          - specified NEC A02.29
        - sepsis A02.1
        - specified manifestation NEC A02.8
    - Staphylococcus A05.0
    - Vibrio
      - parahaemolyticus A05.3
      - vulnificus A05.5
  - enterotoxin, staphylococcal A05.0
  - noxious *—see* Poisoning, food, noxious
- gastrointestinal K52.1
- hallucinogenic (without dependence) *—see* Abuse, drug, hallucinogen, with intoxication
  - with dependence *—see* Dependence, drug, hallucinogen, with intoxication
- hypnotic (acute) (without dependence) *—see* Abuse, drug, sedative, with intoxication
  - with dependence *—see* Dependence, drug, sedative, with intoxication
- inhalant (acute) (without dependence) *—see* Abuse, drug, inhalant, with intoxication
  - with dependence *—see* Dependence, drug, inhalant, with intoxication

Intoxication *(continued)*
meaning
inebriation F10
poisoning —*see* Table of Drugs and Chemicals
methyl alcohol (acute) (without dependence) —*see* Alcohol, intoxication
opioid (acute) (without dependence) —*see* Abuse, drug, opioid, with intoxication
with dependence —*see* Dependence, drug, opioid, with intoxication
pathologic NEC(without dependence) —*see* Alcohol, intoxication
phencyclidine (without dependence) —*see* Abuse, drug, psychoactive NEC, with intoxication
with dependence —*see* Dependence, drug, psychoactive NEC, with intoxication
potassium (K) E87.5
psychoactive substance NEC(without dependence) —*see* Abuse, drug, psychoactive NEC, with intoxication
with dependence —*see* Dependence, drug, psychoactive NEC, with intoxication
sedative (acute) (without dependence) —*see* Abuse, drug, sedative, with intoxication
with dependence —*see* Dependence, drug, sedative, with intoxication
serum —*see also* Reaction, serum T80.69
uremic —*see* Uremia
volatile solvents (acute) (without dependence) —*see* Abuse, drug, inhalant, with intoxication
with dependence —*see* Dependence, drug, inhalant, with intoxication
water E87.79

Intracranial —*see* condition

Intrahepatic gallbladder Q44.1

Intraligamentous —*see* condition

Intrathoracic —*see also* condition
kidney Q63.2

Intrauterine contraceptive device
checking Z30.431
insertion Z30.430
immediately following removal Z30.433
in situ Z97.5
management Z30.431
reinsertion Z30.433
removal Z30.432
replacement Z30.433
retention in pregnancy O26.3-

Intraventricular —*see* condition

Intrinsic deformity —*see* Deformity

Intubation, difficult or failed T88.4

Intumescence, lens (eye) (cataract) —*see* Cataract

Intussusception (bowel) (colon) (enteric) (ileocecal) (ileocolic) (intestine) (rectum) K56.1
appendix K38.8
congenital Q43.8
ureter (with obstruction) N13.5

Invagination (bowel, colon, intestine or rectum) K56.1

Inversion
albumin-globulin (A-G) ratio E88.09
bladder N32.89

Inversion *(continued)*
cecum —*see* Intussusception
cervix N88.8
chromosome in normal individual Q95.1
circadian rhythm —*see* Disorder, sleep, circadian rhythm
nipple N64.59
congenital Q83.8
gestational —*see* Retraction, nipple
puerperal, postpartum —*see* Retraction, nipple
nyctohemeral rhythm —*see* Disorder, sleep, circadian rhythm
optic papilla Q14.2
organ or site, congenital NEC —*see* Anomaly, by site
sleep rhythm —*see* Disorder, sleep, circadian rhythm
testis (congenital) Q55.29
uterus (chronic) (postinfectional) (postpartal, old) N85.5
postpartum O71.2
vagina (posthysterectomy) N99.3
ventricular Q20.5

Investigation —*see also* Examination Z04.9
clinical research subject (control) (normal comparison) (participant) Z00.6

Involuntary movement, abnormal R25.9

Involution, involutional —*see also* condition
breast, cystic —*see* Dysplasia, mammary, specified type NEC
depression (single episode) F32.8
recurrent episode F33.9
melancholia (recurrent episode) (single episode) F32.8
ovary, senile —*see* Atrophy, ovary
thymus failure E32.8

I.Q.
under 20 F73
20-34 F72
35-49 F71
50-69 F70

IRDS (type I) P22.0
type II P22.1

Irideremia Q13.1

Iridis rubeosis —*see* Disorder, iris, vascular

Iridochoroiditis (panuveitis) —*see* Panuveitis

Iridocyclitis H20.9
acute H20.0-
hypopyon H20.05-
primary H20.01-
recurrent H20.02-
secondary (noninfectious) H20.04-
infectious H20.03-
chronic H20.1-
due to allergy —*see* Iridocyclitis, acute, secondary
endogenous —*see* Iridocyclitis, acute, primary
Fuchs' —*see* Cyclitis, Fuchs' heterochromic
gonococcal A54.32
granulomatous —*see* Iridocyclitis, chronic
herpes, herpetic (simplex) B00.51
zoster B02.32
hypopyon —*see* Iridocyclitis, acute, hypopyon
in (due to)
ankylosing spondylitis M45.9
gonococcal infection A54.32

Iridocyclitis *(continued)*
in *(continued)*
herpes (simplex) virus B00.51
zoster B02.32
infectious disease NOS B99
parasitic disease NOS B89 *[H22]*
sarcoidosis D86.83
syphilis A51.43
tuberculosis A18.54
zoster B02.32
lens-induced H20.2-
nongranulomatous —*see* Iridocyclitis, acute
recurrent —*see* Iridocyclitis, acute, recurrent
rheumatic —*see* Iridocyclitis, chronic
subacute —*see* Iridocyclitis, acute
sympathetic —*see* Uveitis, sympathetic
syphilitic (secondary) A51.43
tuberculous (chronic) A18.54
Vogt-Koyanagi H20.82-

Iridocyclochoroiditis (panuveitis) —*see* Panuveitis

Iridodialysis H21.53-

Iridodonesis H21.89

Iridoplegia (complete) (partial) (reflex) H57.09

Iridoschisis H21.25-

Iris —*see also* condition
bombé —*see* Membrane, pupillary

Iritis —*see also* Iridocyclitis
chronic —*see* Iridocyclitis, chronic
diabetic —*see* E08-E13 with .39
due to
herpes simplex B00.51
leprosy A30.9 *[H22]*
gonococcal A54.32
gouty M10.9
granulomatous —*see* Iridocyclitis, chronic
lens induced —*see* Iridocyclitis, lens-induced
papulosa (syphilitic) A52.71
rheumatic —*see* Iridocyclitis, chronic
syphilitic (secondary) A51.43
congenital (early) A50.01
late A52.71
tuberculous A18.54

Iron —*see* condition

Iron-miner's lung J63.4

Irradiated enamel (tooth, teeth) K03.89

Irradiation effects, adverse T66

Irreducible, irreducibility —*see* condition

Irregular, irregularity
action, heart I49.9
alveolar process K08.8
bleeding N92.6
breathing R06.89
contour of cornea (acquired) —*see* Deformity, cornea
congenital Q13.4
contour, reconstructed breast N65.0
dentin (in pulp) K04.3
eye movements H55.89
nystagmus —*see* Nystagmus
saccadic H55.81
labor O62.2
menstruation (cause unknown) N92.6
periods N92.6
prostate N42.9
pupil —*see* Abnormality, pupillary
reconstructed breast N65.0
respiratory R06.89
septum (nasal) J34.2

Irregular, irregularity *(continued)*
shape, organ or site, congenital NEC —*see* Distortion
sleep-wake pattern (rhythm) G47.23

Irritable, irritability R45.4
bladder N32.89
bowel (syndrome) K58.9
with diarrhea K58.0
psychogenic F45.8
bronchial —*see* Bronchitis
cerebral, in newborn P91.3
colon K58.9
with diarrhea K58.0
psychogenic F45.8
duodenum K59.8
heart (psychogenic) F45.8
hip —*see* Derangement, joint, specified type NEC, hip
ileum K59.8
infant R68.12
jejunum K59.8
rectum K59.8
stomach K31.89
psychogenic F45.8
sympathetic G90.8
urethra N36.8

Irritation
anus K62.89
axillary nerve G54.0
bladder N32.89
brachial plexus G54.0
bronchial —*see* Bronchitis
cervical plexus G54.2
cervix —*see* Cervicitis
choroid, sympathetic —*see* Endophthalmitis
cranial nerve —*see* Disorder, nerve, cranial
gastric K31.89
psychogenic F45.8
globe, sympathetic —*see* Uveitis, sympathetic
labyrinth —*see* subcategory H83.2
lumbosacral plexus G54.1
meninges (traumatic) —*see* Injury, intracranial
nontraumatic —*see* Meningismus
nerve —*see* Disorder, nerve
nervous R45.0
penis N48.89
perineum NEC L29.3
peripheral autonomic nervous system G90.8
peritoneum —*see* Peritonitis
pharynx J39.2
plantar nerve —*see* Lesion, nerve, plantar
spinal (cord) (traumatic) —*see also* Injury, spinal cord, by region
nerve G58.9
root NEC —*see* Radiculopathy
nontraumatic —*see* Myelopathy
stomach K31.89
psychogenic F45.8
sympathetic nerve NEC G90.8
ulnar nerve —*see* Lesion, nerve, ulnar
vagina N89.8

Ischemia, ischemic I99.8
brain —*see* Ischemia, cerebral
bowel (transient)
acute K55.0
chronic K55.1
due to mesenteric artery insufficiency K55.1
cardiac (*see* Disease, heart, ischemic)
cardiomyopathy I25.5
cerebral (chronic) (generalized) I67.82
arteriosclerotic I67.2
intermittent G45.9
newborn P91.0
recurrent focal G45.8

chemia, ischemic *(continued)*
  cerebral *(continued)*
    transient G45.9
  colon chronic (due to mesenteric artery insufficiency) K55.1
  coronary —*see* Disease, heart, ischemic
  demand (coronary) —*see also* Angina I24.8
  heart (chronic or with a stated duration of over 4 weeks) I25.9
    acute or with a stated duration of 4 weeks or less I24.9
    subacute I24.9
  infarction, muscle —*see* Infarct, muscle
  intestine (large) (small) (transient) K55.9
    acute K55.0
    chronic K55.1
    due to mesenteric artery insufficiency K55.1
  kidney N28.0
  mesenteric, acute K55.0
  muscle, traumatic T79.6
  myocardium, myocardial (chronic or with a stated duration of over 4 weeks) I25.9
    acute, without myocardial infarction I24.0
    silent (asymptomatic) I25.6
    transient of newborn P29.4
  renal N28.0
  retina, retinal —*see* Occlusion, artery, retina
  small bowel
    acute K55.0
    chronic K55.1
    due to mesenteric artery insufficiency K55.1
  spinal cord G95.11
  subendocardial —*see* Insufficiency, coronary
  supply (coronary) —*see also* Angina I25.9
    due to vasospasm I20.1

schial spine —*see* condition

schialgia —*see* Sciatica

schiopagus Q89.4

schium, ischial —*see* condition

schuria R34

selin's disease or osteochondrosis —*see* Osteochondrosis, juvenile, metatarsus

slands of
  parotid tissue in
    lymph nodes Q38.6
    neck structures Q38.6
  submaxillary glands in
    fascia Q38.6
    lymph nodes Q38.6
    neck muscles Q38.6

slet cell tumor, pancreas D13.7

Isoimmunization NEC —*see also* Incompatibility
  affecting management of pregnancy (ABO) (with hydrops fetalis) O36.11-
    anti-A sensitization O36.11-
    anti-B sensitization O36.19-
    anti-c sensitization O36.09-
    anti-C sensitization O36.09-
    anti-e sensitization O36.09-
    anti-E sensitization O36.09-
    Rh NEC O36.09-
      anti-D antibody O36.01-
    specified NEC O36.19-

Isoimmunization NEC *(continued)*
  newborn P55.9
    with
      hydrops fetalis P56.0
      kernicterus P57.0
    ABO(blood groups) P55.1
    Rhesus (Rh) factor P55.0
    specified type NEC P55.8

Isolation, isolated
  dwelling Z59.8
  family Z63.79
  social Z60.4

Isoleucinosis E71.19

Isomerism atrial appendages (with asplenia or polysplenia) Q20.6

Isosporiasis, isosporosis A07.3

Isovaleric acidemia E71.110

Issue of
  medical certificate Z02.79
    for disability determination Z02.71
  repeat prescription (appliance) (glasses) (medicinal substance, medicament, medicine) Z76.0
    contraception —*see* Contraception

Itch, itching —*see also* Pruritus
  baker's L23.6
  barber's B35.0
  bricklayer's L24.5
  cheese B88.0
  clam digger's B65.3
  coolie B76.9
  copra B88.0
  dew B76.9
  dhobi B35.6
  filarial —*see* Infestation, filarial
  grain B88.0
  grocer's B88.0
  ground B76.9
  harvest B88.0
  jock B35.6
  Malabar B35.5
    beard B35.0
    foot B35.3
    scalp B35.0
  meaning scabies B86
  Norwegian B86
  perianal L29.0
  poultrymen's B88.0
  sarcoptic B86
  scabies B86
  scrub B88.0
  straw B88.0
  swimmer's B65.3
  water B76.9
  winter L29.8

Ivemark's syndrome (asplenia with congenital heart disease) Q89.01

Ivory bones Q78.2

Ixodiasis NEC B88.8

J

Jaccoud's syndrome —*see* Arthropathy, postrheumatic, chronic

Jackson's
  membrane Q43.3
  paralysis or syndrome G83.89
  veil Q43.3

Jacquet's dermatitis (diaper dermatitis) L22

Jadassohn-Pellizari's disease or anetoderma L90.2

Jadassohn's
  blue nevus —*see* Nevus
  intraepidermal epithelioma —*see* Neoplasm, skin, benign

Jaffe-Lichtenstein (-Uehlinger) **syndrome** —*see* Dysplasia, fibrous, bone NEC

Jakob-Creutzfeldt disease or syndrome —*see* Creutzfeldt-Jakob disease or syndrome

Jaksch-Luzet disease D64.89

Jamaican
  neuropathy G92
  paraplegic tropical ataxic-spastic syndrome G92

Janet's disease F48.8

Janiceps Q89.4

Jansky-Bielschowsky amaurotic idiocy E75.4

Japanese
  B-type encephalitis A83.0
  river fever A75.3

Jaundice (yellow) R17
  acholuric (familial) (splenomegalic) —*see also* Spherocytosis
    acquired D59.8
  breast-milk (inhibitor) P59.3
  catarrhal (acute) B15.9
    with hepatic coma B15.0
  cholestatic (benign) R17
  due to or associated with
    delayed conjugation P59.8
      associated with (due to) preterm delivery P59.0
    preterm delivery P59.0
  epidemic (catarrhal) B15.9
    with hepatic coma B15.0
    leptospiral A27.0
    spirochetal A27.0
  familial nonhemolytic (congenital) (Gilbert) E80.4
    Crigler-Najjar E80.5
  febrile (acute) B15.9
    with hepatic coma B15.0
    leptospiral A27.0
    spirochetal A27.0
  hematogenous D59.9
  hemolytic (acquired) D59.9
    congenital —*see* Spherocytosis
  hemorrhagic (acute) (leptospiral) (spirochetal) A27.0
  infectious (acute) (subacute) B15.9
    with hepatic coma B15.0
    leptospiral A27.0
    spirochetal A27.0
  leptospiral (hemorrhagic) A27.0
  malignant (without coma) K72.90
    with coma K72.91
  newborn P59.9
    due to or associated with
      ABO
        antibodies P55.1
        incompatibility, maternal/fetal P55.1
        isoimmunization P55.1
      absence or deficiency of enzyme system for bilirubin conjugation (congenital) P59.8
      bleeding P58.1
      breast milk inhibitors to conjugation P59.3
        associated with preterm delivery P59.0
      bruising P58.0
      Crigler-Najjar syndrome E80.5
      delayed conjugation P59.8
        associated with preterm delivery P59.0
      drugs or toxins
        given to newborn P58.42
        transmitted from mother P58.41

Jaundice *(continued)*
  newborn *(continued)*
    due to or associated with *(continued)*
      excessive hemolysis P58.9
        due to
          bleeding P58.1
          bruising P58.0
          drugs or toxins
            given to newborn P58.42
            transmitted from mother P58.41
          infection P58.2
          polycythemia P58.3
          swallowed maternal blood P58.5
        specified type NEC P58.8
      galactosemia E74.21
      Gilbert syndrome E80.4
      hemolytic disease P55.9
        ABO isoimmunization P55.1
        Rh isoimmunization P55.0
        specified NEC P55.8
      hepatocellular damage P59.20
        specified NEC P59.29
      hereditary hemolytic anemia P58.8
      hypothyroidism, congenital E03.1
      incompatibility, maternal/fetal NOS P55.9
      infection P58.2
      inspissated bile syndrome P59.1
      isoimmunization NOS P55.9
      mucoviscidosis E84.9
      polycythemia P58.3
      preterm delivery P59.0
      Rh
        antibodies P55.0
        incompatibility, maternal/fetal P55.0
        isoimmunization P55.0
      specified cause NEC P59.8
      swallowed maternal blood P58.5
    spherocytosis (congenital) D58.0
  neonatal —*see* Jaundice, newborn
  nonhemolytic congenital familial (Gilbert) E80.4
  nuclear, newborn —*see also* Kernicterus of newborn P57.9
  obstructive —*see also* Obstruction, bile duct K83.1
  post-immunization —*see* Hepatitis, viral, type, B
  post-transfusion —*see* Hepatitis, viral, type, B
  regurgitation —*see also* Obstruction, bile duct K83.1
  serum (homologous) (prophylactic) (therapeutic) —*see* Hepatitis, viral, type, B
  spirochetal (hemorrhagic) A27.0
  symptomatic R17
    newborn P59.9

Jaw —*see* condition

Jaw-winking phenomenon or syndrome Q07.8

Jealousy
  alcoholic F10.988
  childhood F93.8
  sibling F93.8

Jejunitis —*see* Enteritis

Jejunostomy status Z93.4

Jejunum, jejunal —*see* condition

Jensen's disease —*see* Inflammation, chorioretinal, focal, juxtapapillary

Jerks, myoclonic G25.3

Jervell-Lange-Nielsen syndrome I45.81

- **Jeune's disease** Q77.2
- **Jigger disease** B88.1
- **Job's syndrome** (chronic granulomatous disease) D71
- **Joint** *—see also* condition
  - mice *—see* Loose, body, joint
    - knee M23.4-
- **Jordan's anomaly or syndrome** D72.0
- **Joseph-Diamond-Blackfan anemia** (congenital hypoplastic) D61.01
- **Jungle yellow fever** A95.0
- **Jüngling's disease** *—see* Sarcoidosis
- **Juvenile** *—see* condition

K

- **Kahler's disease** C90.0-
- **Kakke** E51.11
- **Kala-azar** B55.0
- **Kallmann's syndrome** E23.0
- **Kanner's syndrome** (autism) *—see* Psychosis, childhood
- **Kaposi's**
  - dermatosis (xeroderma pigmentosum) Q82.1
  - lichen ruber L44.0
    - acuminatus L44.0
  - sarcoma
    - colon C46.4
    - connective tissue C46.1
    - gastrointestinal organ C46.4
    - lung C46.5-
    - lymph node (multiple) C46.3
    - palate (hard) (soft) C46.2
    - rectum C46.4
    - skin (multiple sites) C46.0
    - specified site NEC C46.7
    - stomach C46.4
    - unspecified site C46.9
  - varicelliform eruption B00.0
    - vaccinia T88.1
- **Kartagener's syndrome or triad** (sinusitis, bronchiectasis, situs inversus) Q89.3
- **Karyotype**
  - with abnormality except iso (Xq) Q96.2
  - 45,X Q96.0
  - 46,X
    - iso (Xq) Q96.1
  - 46,XX Q98.3
    - with streak gonads Q50.32
    - hermaphrodite (true) Q99.1
    - male Q98.3
  - 46,XY
    - with streak gonads Q56.1
    - female Q97.3
    - hermaphrodite (true) Q99.1
  - 47,XXX Q97.0
  - 47,XXY Q98.0
  - 47,XYY Q98.5
- **Kaschin-Beck disease** *—see* Disease, Kaschin-Beck
- **Katayama's disease or fever** B65.2
- **Kawasaki's syndrome** M30.3
- **Kayser-Fleischer ring** (cornea) (pseudosclerosis) H18.04-
- **Kaznelson's syndrome** (congenital hypoplastic anemia) D61.01
- **Kearns-Sayre syndrome** H49.81-
- **Kedani fever** A75.3
- **Kelis** L91.0
- **Kelly** (-Patterson) **syndrome** (sideropenic dysphagia) D50.1
- **Keloid, cheloid** L91.0
  - acne L73.0
  - Addison's L94.0
  - cornea *—see* Opacity, cornea
  - Hawkin's L91.0
  - scar L91.0
- **Keloma** L91.0
- **Kenya fever** A77.1
- **Keratectasia** *—see also* Ectasia, cornea
  - congenital Q13.4
- **Keratinization of alveolar ridge mucosa**
  - excessive K13.23
  - minimal K13.22
- **Keratinized residual ridge mucosa**
  - excessive K13.23
  - minimal K13.22
- **Keratitis** (nodular) (nonulcerative) (simple) (zonular) H16.9
  - with ulceration (central) (marginal) (perforated) (ring) *—see* Ulcer, cornea
  - actinic *—see* Photokeratitis
  - arborescens (herpes simplex) B00.52
  - areolar H16.11-
  - bullosa H16.8
  - deep H16.309
    - specified type NEC H16.399
  - dendritic (a) (herpes simplex) B00.52
  - disciform (is) (herpes simplex) B00.52
    - varicella B01.81
  - filamentary H16.12-
  - gonococcal (congenital or prenatal) A54.33
  - herpes, herpetic (simplex) B00.52
    - zoster B02.33
  - in (due to)
    - acanthamebiasis B60.13
    - adenovirus B30.0
    - exanthema *—see also* Exanthem B09
    - herpes (simplex) virus B00.52
    - measles B05.81
    - syphilis A50.31
    - tuberculosis A18.52
    - zoster B02.33
  - interstitial (nonsyphilitic) H16.30-
    - diffuse H16.32-
    - herpes, herpetic (simplex) B00.52
      - zoster B02.33
    - sclerosing H16.33-
    - specified type NEC H16.39-
    - syphilitic (congenital) (late) A50.31
    - tuberculous A18.52
  - macular H16.11-
  - nummular H16.11-
  - oyster shuckers' H16.8
  - parenchymatous *—see* Keratitis, interstitial
  - petrificans H16.8
  - postmeasles B05.81
  - punctata
    - leprosa A30.9 *[H16.14]*-
    - syphilitic (profunda) A50.31
  - punctate H16.14-
  - purulent H16.8
  - rosacea L71.8
  - sclerosing H16.33-
  - specified type NEC H16.8
  - stellate H16.11-
  - striate H16.11-
  - superficial H16.10-
    - with conjunctivitis *—see* Keratoconjunctivitis
    - due to light *—see* Photokeratitis
  - suppurative H16.8
  - syphilitic (congenital) (prenatal) A50.31

- **Keratitis** *(continued)*
  - trachomatous A71.1
    - sequelae B94.0
  - tuberculous A18.52
  - vesicular H16.8
  - xerotic *—see also* Keratomalacia H16.8
    - vitamin A deficiency E50.4
- **Keratoacanthoma** L85.8
- **Keratocele** *—see* Descemetocele
- **Keratoconjunctivitis** H16.20-
  - Acanthamoeba B60.13
  - adenoviral B30.0
  - epidemic B30.0
  - exposure H16.21-
  - herpes, herpetic (simplex) B00.52
    - zoster B02.33
  - in exanthema *—see also* Exanthem B09
  - infectious B30.0
  - lagophthalmic *—see* Keratoconjunctivitis, specified type NEC
  - neurotrophic H16.23-
  - phlyctenular H16.25-
  - postmeasles B05.81
  - shipyard B30.0
  - sicca (Sjogren's) M35.0-
    - not Sjogren's H16.22-
  - specified type NEC H16.29-
  - tuberculous (phlyctenular) A18.52
  - vernal H16.26-
- **Keratoconus** H18.60-
  - congenital Q13.4
  - stable H18.61-
  - unstable H18.62-
- **Keratocyst** (dental) (odontogenic) *—see* Cyst, calcifying odontogenic
- **Keratoderma, keratodermia** (congenital) (palmaris et plantaris) (symmetrical) Q82.8
  - acquired L85.1
    - in diseases classified elsewhere L86
  - climactericum L85.1
  - gonococcal A54.89
  - gonorrheal A54.89
  - punctata L85.2
  - Reiter's *—see* Reiter's disease
- **Keratodermatocele** *—see* Descemetocele
- **Keratoglobus** H18.79
  - congenital Q15.8
    - with glaucoma Q15.0
- **Keratohemia** *—see* Pigmentation, cornea, stromal
- **Keratoiritis** *—see also* Iridocyclitis
  - syphilitic A50.39
  - tuberculous A18.54
- **Keratoma** L57.0
  - palmaris and plantaris hereditarium Q82.8
  - senile L57.0
- **Keratomalacia** H18.44-
  - vitamin A deficiency E50.4
- **Keratomegaly** Q13.4
- **Keratomycosis** B49
  - nigrans, nigricans (palmaris) B36.1
- **Keratopathy** H18.9
  - band H18.42-
  - bullous H18.1-
  - bullous (aphakic), following cataract surgery H59.01-
- **Keratoscleritis, tuberculous** A18.52
- **Keratosis** L57.0
  - actinic L57.0

- **Keratosis** *(continued)*
  - arsenical L85.8
  - congenital, specified NEC Q80.8
  - female genital NEC N94.89
  - follicularis Q82.8
    - acquired L11.0
    - congenita Q82.8
    - et parafollicularis in cutem penetrans L87.0
    - spinulosa (decalvans) Q82.8
    - vitamin A deficiency E50.8
  - gonococcal A54.89
  - male genital (external) N50.8
  - nigricans L83
  - obturans, external ear (canal) *—see* Cholesteatoma, external ear
  - palmaris et plantaris (inherited) (symmetrical) Q82.8
    - acquired L85.1
  - penile N48.89
  - pharynx J39.2
  - pilaris, acquired L85.8
  - punctata (palmaris et plantaris) L85.2
  - scrotal N50.8
  - seborrheic L82.1
    - inflamed L82.0
  - senile L57.0
  - solar L57.0
  - tonsillaris J35.8
  - vagina N89.4
  - vegetans Q82.8
  - vitamin A deficiency E50.8
  - vocal cord J38.3
- **Kerato-uveitis** *—see* Iridocyclitis
- **Kerunoparalysis** T75.09
- **Kerion** (celsi) B35.0
- **Kernicterus of newborn** (not due to isoimmunization) P57.9
  - due to isoimmunization (conditions in P55.0-P55.9) P57.0
  - specified type NEC P57.8
- **Keshan disease** E59
- **Ketoacidosis** E87.2
  - diabetic *—see* Diabetes, by type, wit ketoacidosis
- **Ketonuria** R82.4
- **Ketosis NEC** E88.89
  - diabetic *—see* Diabetes, by type, with with ketoacidosis
- **Kew Garden fever** A79.1
- **Kidney** *—see* condition
- **Kienböck's disease** *—see also* Osteochondrosis, juvenile, hand, carpal lunate
  - adult M93.1
- **Kimmelstiel** (-Wilson) **disease** *—see* Diabetes, Kimmelstiel (-Wilson) disease
- **Kimura disease** D21.9
  - specified site *—see* Neoplasm, connective tissue benign
- **Kink, kinking**
  - artery I77.1
  - hair (acquired) L67.8
  - ileum or intestine *—see* Obstruction, intestine
  - Lane's *—see* Obstruction, intestine
  - organ or site, congenital NEC *—see* Anomaly, by site
  - ureter (pelvic junction) N13.5
    - with
      - hydronephrosis N13.1
        - with infection N13.6
      - pyelonephritis (chronic) N11.1
    - congenital Q62.39

ink, kinking *(continued)*
vein (s) I87.8
caval I87.1
peripheral I87.1
innier Wilson's disease (hepatolenticular degeneration) E83.01
issing spine M48.20
cervical region M48.22
cervicothoracic region M48.23
lumbar region M48.26
lumbosacral region M48.27
occipito-atlanto-axial region M48.21
thoracic region M48.24
thoracolumbar region M48.25
latskin's tumor C24.0
lauder's disease A26.8
lebs' disease —*see also* Glomerulonephritis N05.-
lebsiella (K.) **pneumoniae, as cause of disease classified elsewhere** B96.1
lein (e)**-Levin syndrome** G47.13
leptomania F63.2
linefelter's syndrome Q98.4
karyotype 47,XXY Q98.0
male with more than two X chromosomes Q98.1
lippel-Feil deficiency, disease, or syndrome (brevicollis) Q76.1
lippel's disease I67.2
lippel-Trenaunay (-Weber) **syndrome** Q87.2
lumpke (-Déjerine) palsy, paralysis (birth) (newborn) P14.1
nee —*see* condition
nock knee (acquired) M21.06-
congenital Q74.1
not (s)
intestinal, syndrome (volvulus) K56.2
surfer S89.8-
umbilical cord (true) O69.2
Knotting (of)
hair L67.8
intestine K56.2
Knuckle pad (Garrod's) M72.1
Koch's
infection —*see* Tuberculosis
relapsing fever A68.9
Koch-Weeks' conjunctivitis —*see* Conjunctivitis, acute, mucopurulent
Köebner's syndrome Q81.8
Köenig's disease (osteochondritis dissecans) —*see* Osteochondritis, dissecans
Köhler-Pellegrini-Steida disease or syndrome (calcification, knee joint) —*see* Bursitis, tibial collateral
Köhler's disease
patellar —*see* Osteochondrosis, juvenile, patella
tarsal navicular —*see* Osteochondrosis, juvenile, tarsus
Koilonychia L60.3
congenital Q84.6
Kojevnikov's, epilepsy —*see* Kozhevnikof's epilepsy
Koplik's spots B05.9
Kopp's asthma E32.8
Korsakoff's (Wernicke) disease, psychosis or syndrome (alcoholic) F10.96
with dependence F10.26

Korsakoff's *(continued)*
drug-induced
due to drug abuse —*see* Abuse, drug, by type, with amnestic disorder
due to drug dependence —*see* Dependence, drug, by type, with amnestic disorder
nonalcoholic F04
Korsakov's disease, psychosis or syndrome —*see* Korsakoff's disease
Korsakow's disease, psychosis or syndrome —*see* Korsakoff's disease
Kostmann's disease or syndrome (infantile genetic agranulocytosis) —*see* Agranulocytosis
Kozhevnikof's epilepsy G40.109
intractable G40.119
with status epilepticus G40.111
without status epilepticus G40.119
not intractable G40.109
with status epilepticus G40.101
without status epilepticus G40.109
Krabbe's
disease E75.23
syndrome, congenital muscle hypoplasia Q79.8
Kraepelin-Morel disease —*see* Schizophrenia
Kraft-Weber-Dimitri disease Q85.8
Kraurosis
ani K62.89
penis N48.0
vagina N89.8
vulva N90.4
Kreotoxism A05.9
Krukenberg's
spindle —*see* Pigmentation, cornea, posterior
tumor C79.6-
Kufs' disease E75.4
Kugelberg-Welander disease G12.1
Kuhnt-Junius degeneration —*see also* Degeneration, macula H35.32
Kümmell's disease or spondylitis —*see* Spondylopathy, traumatic
Kupffer cell sarcoma C22.3
Kuru A81.81
Kussmaul's
disease M30.0
respiration E87.2
in diabetic acidosis —*see* Diabetes, by type, with ketoacidosis
Kwashiorkor E40
marasmic, marasmus type E42
Kyasanur Forest disease A98.2
Kyphoscoliosis, kyphoscoliotic (acquired) —*see also* Scoliosis M41.9
congenital Q67.5
heart (disease) I27.1
sequelae of rickets E64.3
tuberculous A18.01
Kyphosis, kyphotic (acquired) M40.209
cervical region M40.202
cervicothoracic region M40.203
congenital Q76.419
cervical region Q76.412
cervicothoracic region Q76.413
occipito-atlanto-axial region Q76.411
thoracic region Q76.414
thoracolumbar region Q76.415

Kyphosis, kyphotic *(continued)*
Morquio-Brailsford type (spinal) —*see also* subcategory M49.8 *[E76.219]*
postlaminectomy M96.3
postradiation therapy M96.2
postural (adolescent) M40.00
cervicothoracic region M40.03
thoracic region M40.04
thoracolumbar region M40.05
secondary NEC M40.10
cervical region M40.12
cervicothoracic region M40.13
thoracic region M40.14
thoracolumbar region M40.15
sequelae of rickets E64.3
specified type NEC M40.299
cervical region M40.292
cervicothoracic region M40.293
thoracic region M40.294
thoracolumbar region M40.295
syphilitic, congenital A50.56
thoracic region M40.204
thoracolumbar region M40.205
tuberculous A18.01
Kyrle disease L87.0

L

Labia, labium —*see* condition
Labile
blood pressure R09.89
vasomotor system I73.9
Labioglossal paralysis G12.29
Labium leporinum —*see* Cleft, lip
Labor —*see* Delivery
Labored breathing —*see* Hyperventilation
Labyrinthitis (circumscribed) (destructive) (diffuse) (inner ear) (latent) (purulent) (suppurative) —*see also* subcategory H83.0
syphilitic A52.79
Laceration
with abortion —*see* Abortion, by type, complicated by laceration of pelvic organs
abdomen, abdominal
wall S31.119
with
foreign body S31.129
penetration into peritoneal cavity S31.619
with foreign body S31.629
epigastric region S31.112
with
foreign body S31.122
penetration into peritoneal cavity S31.612
with foreign body S31.622
left
lower quadrant S31.114
with
foreign body S31.124
penetration into peritoneal cavity S31.614
with foreign body S31.624
upper quadrant S31.111
with
foreign body S31.121
penetration into peritoneal cavity S31.611
with foreign body S31.621

Laceration *(continued)*
abdomen, abdominal *(continued)*
wall *(continued)*
periumbilic region S31.115
with
foreign body S31.125
penetration into peritoneal cavity S31.615
with foreign body S31.625
right
lower quadrant S31.113
with
foreign body S31.123
penetration into peritoneal cavity S31.613
with foreign body S31.623
upper quadrant S31.110
with
foreign body S31.120
penetration into peritoneal cavity S31.610
with foreign body S31.620
accidental, complicating surgery —*see* Complications, surgical, accidental puncture or laceration
Achilles tendon S86.02-
adrenal gland S37.813
alveolar (process) —*see* Laceration, oral cavity
ankle S91.01-
with
foreign body S91.02-
antecubital space —*see* Laceration, elbow
anus (sphincter) S31.831
with
ectopic or molar pregnancy O08.6
foreign body S31.832
complicating delivery —*see* Delivery, complicated, by, laceration, anus (sphincter)
following ectopic or molar pregnancy O08.6
nontraumatic, nonpuerperal —*see* Fissure, anus
arm (upper) S41.11-
with foreign body S41.12-
lower —*see* Laceration, forearm
auditory canal (external) (meatus) —*see* Laceration, ear
auricle, ear —*see* Laceration, ear
axilla —*see* Laceration, arm
back —*see also* Laceration, thorax, back
lower S31.010
with
foreign body S31.020
with penetration into retroperitoneal space S31.021
penetration into retroperitoneal space S31.011
bile duct S36.13
bladder S37.23
with ectopic or molar pregnancy O08.6
following ectopic or molar pregnancy O08.6
obstetrical trauma O71.5
blood vessel —*see* Injury, blood vessel
bowel —*see also* Laceration, intestine
with ectopic or molar pregnancy O08.6

Laceration *(continued)*
- leg (lower) S81.819
  - with foreign body S81.829
  - foot —*see* Laceration, foot
  - knee —*see* Laceration, knee
  - left S81.812
    - with foreign body S81.822
  - right S81.811
    - with foreign body S81.821
  - upper —*see* Laceration, thigh
- ligament —*see* Sprain
- lip S01.511
  - with foreign body S01.521
- liver S36.113
  - major (stellate) S36.116
  - minor S36.114
  - moderate S36.115
- loin —*see* Laceration, abdomen, wall
- lower back —*see* Laceration, back, lower
- lumbar region —*see* Laceration, back, lower
- lung S27.339
  - bilateral S27.332
  - unilateral S27.331
- malar region —*see* Laceration, head, specified site NEC
- mammary —*see* Laceration, breast
- mastoid region —*see* Laceration, head, specified site NEC
- meninges —*see* Injury, intracranial, diffuse
- meniscus —*see* Tear, meniscus
- mesentery S36.893
- mesosalpinx S37.893
- mouth —*see* Laceration, oral cavity
- muscle —*see* Injury, muscle, by site, laceration
- nail
  - finger —*see* Laceration, finger, with damage to nail
  - toe —*see* Laceration, toe, with damage to nail
- nasal (septum) (sinus) —*see* Laceration, nose
- nasopharynx —*see* Laceration, head, specified site NEC
- neck S11.91
  - with foreign body S11.92
  - involving
    - cervical esophagus S11.21
      - with foreign body S11.22
    - larynx —*see* Laceration, larynx
    - pharynx —*see* Laceration, pharynx
    - thyroid gland —*see* Laceration, thyroid gland
    - trachea —*see* Laceration, trachea
  - specified site NEC S11.81
    - with foreign body S11.82
- nerve —*see* Injury, nerve
- nose (septum) (sinus) S01.21
  - with foreign body S01.22
- ocular NOS S05.3-
  - adnexa NOS S01.11-
- oral cavity S01.512
  - with foreign body S01.522
- orbit (eye) —*see* Wound, open, ocular, orbit
- ovary S37.439
  - bilateral S37.432
  - unilateral S37.431
- palate —*see* Laceration, oral cavity
- palm —*see* Laceration, hand
- pancreas S36.239
  - body S36.231
    - major S36.261
    - minor S36.241
    - moderate S36.251

Laceration *(continued)*
- pancreas *(continued)*
  - head S36.230
    - major S36.260
    - minor S36.240
    - moderate S36.250
  - major S36.269
  - minor S36.249
  - moderate S36.259
  - tail S36.232
    - major S36.262
    - minor S36.242
    - moderate S36.252
- pelvic S31.010
  - with
    - foreign body S31.020
      - penetration into retroperitoneal cavity S31.021
    - penetration into retroperitoneal cavity S31.011
  - floor —*see also* Laceration, back, lower
    - with ectopic or molar pregnancy O08.6
    - complicating delivery O70.1
    - following ectopic or molar pregnancy O08.6
    - old (postpartal) N81.89
  - organ S37.93
    - with ectopic or molar pregnancy O08.6
    - adrenal gland S37.813
    - bladder S37.23
    - fallopian tube —*see* Laceration, fallopian tube
    - following ectopic or molar pregnancy O08.6
    - kidney —*see* Laceration, kidney
    - obstetrical trauma O71.5
    - ovary —*see* Laceration, ovary
    - prostate S37.823
    - specified site NEC S37.893
    - ureter S37.13
    - urethra S37.33
    - uterus S37.63
- penis S31.21
  - with foreign body S31.22
- perineum
  - female S31.41
    - with
      - ectopic or molar pregnancy O08.6
      - foreign body S31.42
    - during delivery O70.9
      - first degree O70.0
      - fourth degree O70.3
      - second degree O70.1
      - third degree O70.2
    - old (postpartal) N81.89
    - postpartal N81.89
    - secondary (postpartal) O90.1
  - male S31.119
    - with foreign body S31.129
- periocular area (with or without lacrimal passages) —*see* Laceration, eyelid
- peritoneum S36.893
- periumbilic region —*see* Laceration, abdomen, wall, periumbilic
- periurethral tissue —*see* Laceration, urethra
- phalanges
  - finger —*see* Laceration, finger
  - toe —*see* Laceration, toe
- pharynx S11.21
  - with foreign body S11.22
- pinna —*see* Laceration, ear
- popliteal space —*see* Laceration, knee
- prepuce —*see* Laceration, penis
- prostate S37.823

Laceration *(continued)*
- pubic region S31.119
  - with foreign body S31.129
- pudendum —*see* Laceration, genital organs, external
- rectovaginal septum —*see* Laceration, vagina
- rectum S36.63
- retroperitoneum S36.893
- round ligament S37.893
- sacral region —*see* Laceration, back, lower
- sacroiliac region —*see* Laceration, back, lower
- salivary gland —*see* Laceration, oral cavity
- scalp S01.01
  - with foreign body S01.02
- scapular region —*see* Laceration, shoulder
- scrotum S31.31
  - with foreign body S31.32
- seminal vesicle S37.893
- shin —*see* Laceration, leg
- shoulder S41.019
  - with foreign body S41.029
  - left S41.012
    - with foreign body S41.022
  - right S41.011
    - with foreign body S41.021
- small intestine —*see* Laceration, intestine, small
- spermatic cord —*see* Laceration, testis
- spinal cord (meninges) —*see also* Injury, spinal cord, by region
  - due to injury at birth P11.5
  - newborn (birth injury) P11.5
- spleen S36.039
  - major (massive) (stellate) S36.032
  - moderate S36.031
  - superficial (minor) S36.030
- sternal region —*see* Laceration, thorax, front
- stomach S36.33
- submaxillary region —*see* Laceration, head, specified site NEC
- submental region —*see* Laceration, head, specified site NEC
- subungual
  - finger (s) —*see* Laceration, finger, with damage to nail
  - toe (s) —*see* Laceration, toe, with damage to nail
- suprarenal gland —*see* Laceration, adrenal gland
- temple, temporal region —*see* Laceration, head, specified site NEC
- temporomandibular area —*see* Laceration, cheek
- tendon —*see* Injury, muscle, by site, laceration
  - Achilles S86.02-
- tentorium cerebelli —*see* Injury, intracranial, diffuse
- testis S31.31
  - with foreign body S31.32
- thigh S71.11-
  - with foreign body S71.12-
- thorax, thoracic (wall) S21.91
  - with foreign body S21.92
    - back S21.22-
      - with penetration into thoracic cavity S21.42-
    - front S21.12-
      - with penetration into thoracic cavity S21.32-
  - back S21.21-
    - with
      - foreign body S21.22-
        - with penetration into thoracic cavity S21.42-

Laceration *(continued)*
- thorax, thoracic *(continued)*
  - back *(continued)*
    - with *(continued)*
      - penetration into thoracic cavity S21.41-
  - breast —*see* Laceration, breast
  - front S21.11-
    - with
      - foreign body S21.12-
        - with penetration into thoracic cavity S21.32-
      - penetration into thoracic cavity S21.31-
- thumb S61.019
  - with
    - damage to nail S61.119
      - with
        - foreign body S61.129
    - foreign body S61.029
  - left S61.012
    - with
      - damage to nail S61.112
        - with
          - foreign body S61.122
      - foreign body S61.022
  - right S61.011
    - with
      - damage to nail S61.111
        - with
          - foreign body S61.121
      - foreign body S61.021
- thyroid gland S11.11
  - with foreign body S11.12
- toe (s) S91.119
  - with
    - damage to nail S91.219
      - with
        - foreign body S91.229
    - foreign body S91.129
  - great S91.113
    - with
      - damage to nail S91.213
        - with
          - foreign body S91.223
      - foreign body S91.123
    - left S91.112
      - with
        - damage to nail S91.212
          - with
            - foreign body S91.222
        - foreign body S91.122
    - right S91.111
      - with
        - damage to nail S91.211
          - with
            - foreign body S91.221
        - foreign body S91.121
  - lesser S91.116
    - with
      - damage to nail S91.216
        - with
          - foreign body S91.226
      - foreign body S91.126
    - left S91.115
      - with
        - damage to nail S91.215
          - with
            - foreign body S91.225
        - foreign body S91.125
    - right S91.114
      - with
        - damage to nail S91.214
          - with
            - foreign body S91.224
        - foreign body S91.124
- tongue —*see* Laceration, oral cavity
- trachea S11.021
  - with foreign body S11.022
- tunica vaginalis —*see* Laceration, testis

Laceration *(continued)*
tympanum, tympanic membrane — *see* Laceration, ear, drum
umbilical region S31.115
with foreign body S31.125
ureter S37.13
urethra S37.33
with or following ectopic or molar pregnancy O08.6
obstetrical trauma O71.5
urinary organ NEC S37.893
uterus S37.63
with ectopic or molar pregnancy O08.6
following ectopic or molar pregnancy O08.6
nonpuerperal, nontraumatic N85.8
obstetrical trauma NEC O71.81
old (postpartal) N85.8
uvula —*see* Laceration, oral cavity
vagina S31.41
with
ectopic or molar pregnancy O08.6
foreign body S31.42
during delivery O71.4
with perineal laceration —*see* Laceration, perineum, female, during delivery
following ectopic or molar pregnancy O08.6
nonpuerperal, nontraumatic N89.8
old (postpartal) N89.8
vas deferens S37.893
vesical —*see* Laceration, bladder
vocal cords S11.031
with foreign body S11.032
vulva S31.41
with
ectopic or molar pregnancy O08.6
foreign body S31.42
complicating delivery O70.0
following ectopic or molar pregnancy O08.6
nonpuerperal, nontraumatic N90.89
old (postpartal) N90.89
wrist S61.519
with
foreign body S61.529
left S61.512
with
foreign body S61.522
right S61.511
with
foreign body S61.521

Lack of
achievement in school Z55.3
adequate
food Z59.4
intermaxillary vertical dimension of fully erupted teeth M26.36
sleep Z72.820
appetite (*see* Anorexia) R63.0
awareness R41.9
care
in home Z74.2
of infant (at or after birth) T76.02
confirmed T74.02
cognitive functions R41.9
coordination R27.9
ataxia R27.0
specified type NEC R27.8
development (physiological) R62.50
failure to thrive (child over 28 days old) R62.51
adult R62.7
newborn P92.6
short stature R62.52
specified type NEC R62.59
energy R53.83

Lack of *(continued)*
financial resources Z59.6
food T73.0
growth R62.52
heating Z59.1
housing (permanent) (temporary) Z59.0
adequate Z59.1
learning experiences in childhood Z62.898
leisure time (affecting life-style) Z73.2
material resources Z59.9
memory —*see also* Amnesia
mild, following organic brain damage F06.8
ovulation N97.0
parental supervision or control of child Z62.0
person able to render necessary care Z74.2
physical exercise Z72.3
play experience in childhood Z62.898
posterior occlusal support M26.57
relaxation (affecting life-style) Z73.2
sexual
desire F52.0
enjoyment F52.1
shelter Z59.0
sleep (adequate) Z72.820
supervision of child by parent Z62.0
support, posterior occlusal M26.57
water T73.1

Lacrimal —*see* condition

Lacrimation, abnormal —*see* Epiphora

Lacrimonasal duct —*see* condition

Lactation, lactating (breast) (puerperal, postpartum)
associated
cracked nipple O92.13
retracted nipple O92.03
defective O92.4
disorder NEC O92.79
excessive O92.6
failed (complete) O92.3
partial O92.4
mastitis NEC —*see* Mastitis, obstetric
mother (care and/or examination) Z39.1
nonpuerperal N64.3

Lacticemia, excessive E87.2

Lacunar skull Q75.8

Laennec's cirrhosis K74.69
alcoholic K70.30
with ascites K70.31

Lafora's disease —*see* Epilepsy, generalized, idiopathic

Lag, lid (nervous) —*see* Retraction, lid

Lagophthalmos (eyelid) (nervous) H02.209
cicatricial H02.219
left H02.216
lower H02.215
upper H02.214
right H02.213
lower H02.212
upper H02.211
keratoconjunctivitis —*see* Keratoconjunctivitis
left H02.206
lower H02.205
upper H02.204
mechanical H02.229
left H02.226
lower H02.225
upper H02.224

Lagophthalmos *(continued)*
mechanical *(continued)*
right H02.223
lower H02.222
upper H02.221
paralytic H02.239
left H02.236
lower H02.235
upper H02.234
right H02.233
lower H02.232
upper H02.231
right H02.203
lower H02.202
upper H02.201

Laki-Lorand factor deficiency —*see* Defect, coagulation, specified type NEC

Lalling F80.0

Lambert-Eaton syndrome —*see* Syndrome, Lambert-Eaton

Lambliasis, lambliosis A07.1

Landau-Kleffner syndrome —*see* Epilepsy, specified NEC

Landouzy-Déjérine dystrophy or facioscapulohumeral atrophy G71.0

Landouzy's disease (icterohemorrhagic leptospirosis) A27.0

Landry-Guillain-Barré, syndrome or paralysis G61.0

Landry's disease or paralysis G61.0

Lane's
band Q43.3
kink —*see* Obstruction, intestine
syndrome K90.2

Langdon Down syndrome —*see* Trisomy, 21

Lapsed immunization schedule status Z28.3

Large
baby (regardless of gestational age) (4000g to 4499g) P08.1
ear, congenital Q17.1
physiological cup Q14.2
stature R68.89

Large-for-dates NEC (infant) (4000g to 4499g) P08.1
affecting management of pregnancy O36.6-
exceptionally (4500g or more) P08.0

Larsen-Johansson disease orosteochondrosis —*see* Osteochondrosis, juvenile, patella

Larsen's syndrome (flattened facies and multiple congenital dislocations) Q74.8

Larva migrans
cutaneous B76.9
Ancylostoma B76.0
visceral B83.0

Laryngeal —*see* condition

Laryngismus (stridulus) J38.5
congenital P28.89
diphtheritic A36.2

Laryngitis (acute) (edematous) (fibrinous) (infective) (infiltrative) (malignant) (membranous) (phlegmonous) (pneumococcal) (pseudomembranous) (septic) (subglottic) (suppurative) (ulcerative) J04.0
with
influenza, flu, or grippe —*see* Influenza, with, laryngitis
tracheitis (acute) —*see* Laryngotracheitis

Laryngitis *(continued)*
atrophic J37.0
catarrhal J37.0
chronic J37.0
with tracheitis (chronic) J37.1
diphtheritic A36.2
due to external agent —*see* Inflammation, respiratory, upper, due to
Hemophilus influenzae J04.0
H. influenzae J04.0
hypertrophic J37.0
influenzal —*see* Influenza, with, respiratory manifestations NEC
obstructive J05.0
sicca J37.0
spasmodic J05.0
acute J04.0
streptococcal J04.0
stridulous J05.0
syphilitic (late) A52.73
congenital A50.59 *[J99]*
early A50.03 *[J99]*
tuberculous A15.5
Vincent's A69.1

Laryngocele (congenital) (ventricular Q31.3

Laryngofissure J38.7
congenital Q31.8

Laryngomalacia (congenital) Q31.5

Laryngopharyngitis (acute) J06.0
chronic J37.0
due to external agent —*see* Inflammation, respiratory, upper, due to

Laryngoplegia J38.00
bilateral J38.02
unilateral J38.01

Laryngoptosis J38.7

Laryngospasm J38.5

Laryngostenosis J38.6

Laryngotracheitis (acute) (Infectiona (infective) (viral) J04.2
atrophic J37.1
catarrhal J37.1
chronic J37.1
diphtheritic A36.2
due to external agent —*see* Inflammation, respiratory, upper, due to
Hemophilus influenzae J04.2
hypertrophic J37.1
influenzal —*see* Influenza, with, respiratory manifestations NEC
pachydermic J38.7
sicca J37.1
spasmodic J38.5
acute J05.0
streptococcal J04.2
stridulous J38.5
syphilitic (late) A52.73
congenital A50.59 *[J99]*
early A50.03 *[J99]*
tuberculous A15.5
Vincent's A69.1

Laryngotracheobronchitis —*see* Bronchitis

Larynx, laryngeal —*see* condition

Lassa fever A96.2

Lassitude —*see* Weakness

Late
talker R62.0
walker R62.0

Late effect (s) —*see* Sequelae

Latent —*see* condition

Laterocession —*see* Lateroversion

- **ateroflexion** —*see* Lateroversion
- **ateroversion**
  - cervix —*see* Lateroversion, uterus
  - uterus, uterine (cervix) (postinfectional) (postpartal, old) N85.4
    - congenital Q51.818
    - in pregnancy or childbirth O34.59-
- **athyrism** —*see* Poisoning, food, noxious, plant
- **aunois' syndrome** (pituitary gigantism) E22.0
- **aunois-Bensaude adenolipomatosis** E88.89
- **aurence-Moon** (-Bardet)-**Biedl syndrome** Q87.89
- **ax, laxity** —*see also* Relaxation
  - ligament (ous) —*see also* Disorder, ligament
    - familial M35.7
    - knee —*see* Derangement, knee
  - skin (acquired) L57.4
    - congenital Q82.8
- **axative habit** F55.2
- **azy leukocyte syndrome** D70.8
- **ead miner's lung** J63.6
- **eak, leakage**
  - air NEC J93.82
    - postprocedural J95.812
  - amniotic fluid —*see* Rupture, membranes, premature
  - blood (microscopic), fetal, into maternal circulation affecting management of pregnancy —*see* Pregnancy, complicated by
  - cerebrospinal fluid G96.0
    - from spinal (lumbar) puncture G97.0
  - device, implant or graft —*see also* Complications, by site and type, mechanical
    - arterial graft NEC —*see* Complication, cardiovascular device, mechanical, vascular
    - breast (implant) T85.43
    - catheter NEC T85.638
      - urinary, indwelling T83.038
        - cystostomy T83.030
      - dialysis (renal) T82.43
        - intraperitoneal T85.631
      - infusion NEC T82.534
        - spinal (epidural) (subdural) T85.630
    - gastrointestinal —*see* Complications, prosthetic device, mechanical, gastrointestinal device
    - genital NEC T83.498
      - penile prosthesis T83.490
    - heart NEC —*see* Complication, cardiovascular device, mechanical
    - joint prosthesis —*see* Complications, joint prosthesis, mechanical, specified NEC, by site
    - ocular NEC —*see* Complications, prosthetic device, mechanical, ocular device
    - orthopedic NEC —*see* Complication, orthopedic, device, mechanical
    - persistent air J93.82
    - specified NEC T85.638
    - urinary NEC —*see also* Complication, genitourinary, device, urinary, mechanical
      - graft T83.23

Leak, leakage *(continued)*
- device, implant or graft —*see also* Complications, by site and type, mechanical *(continued)*
  - vascular NEC —*see* Complication, cardiovascular device, mechanical
  - ventricular intracranial shunt T85.03
- urine —*see* Incontinence

- **Leaky heart** —*see* Endocarditis
- **Learning defect** (specific) F81.9
- **Leather bottle stomach** C16.9
- **Leber's**
  - congenital amaurosis H35.50
  - optic atrophy (hereditary) H47.22
- **Lederer's anemia** D59.1
- **Leeches** (external) —*see* Hirudiniasis
- **Leg** —*see* condition
- **Legg** (-Calvé)-**Perthes disease, syndrome or osteochondrosis** M91.1-
- **Legionellosis** A48.1
  - nonpneumonic A48.2
- **Legionnaires'**
  - disease A48.1
    - nonpneumonic A48.2
  - pneumonia A48.1
- **Leigh's disease** G31.82
- **Leiner's disease** L21.1
- **Leiofibromyoma** —*see* Leiomyoma
- **Leiomyoblastoma** —*see* Neoplasm, connective tissue, benign
- **Leiomyofibroma** —*see also* Neoplasm, connective tissue, benign
  - uterus (cervix) (corpus) D25.9
- **Leiomyoma** —*see also* Neoplasm, connective tissue, benign
  - bizarre —*see* Neoplasm, connective tissue, benign
  - cellular —*see* Neoplasm, connective tissue, benign
  - epithelioid —*see* Neoplasm, connective tissue, benign
  - uterus (cervix) (corpus) D25.9
    - intramural D25.1
    - submucous D25.0
    - subserosal D25.2
  - vascular —*see* Neoplasm, connective tissue, benign
- **Leiomyoma, leiomyomatosis** (intravascular) —*see* Neoplasm, connective tissue, uncertain behavior
- **Leiomyosarcoma** —*see also* Neoplasm, connective tissue, malignant
  - epithelioid —*see* Neoplasm, connective tissue, malignant
  - myxoid —*see* Neoplasm, connective tissue, malignant
- **Leishmaniasis** B55.9
  - American (mucocutaneous) B55.2
    - cutaneous B55.1
  - Asian Desert B55.1
  - Brazilian B55.2
  - cutaneous (any type) B55.1
  - dermal —*see also* Leishmaniasis, cutaneous
    - post-kala-azar B55.0
  - eyelid B55.1
  - infantile B55.0
  - Mediterranean B55.0
  - mucocutaneous (American) (New World) B55.2
  - naso-oral B55.2
  - nasopharyngeal B55.2

Leishmaniasis *(continued)*
- old world B55.1
- tegumentaria diffusa B55.1
- visceral B55.0

- **Leishmanoid, dermal** —*see also* Leishmaniasis, cutaneous
  - post-kala-azar B55.0
- **Lenegre's disease** I44.2
- **Lengthening, leg** —*see* Deformity, limb, unequal length
- **Lennert's lymphoma** —*see* Lymphoma, Lennert's
- **Lennox-Gastaut syndrome** G40.812
  - intractable G40.814
    - with status epilepticus G40.813
    - without status epilepticus G40.814
  - not intractable G40.812
    - with status epilepticus G40.811
    - without status epilepticus G40.812
- **Lens** —*see* condition
- **Lenticonus** (anterior) (posterior) (congenital) Q12.8
- **Lenticular degeneration, progressive** E83.01
- **Lentiglobus** (posterior) (congenital) Q12.8
- **Lentigo** (congenital) L81.4
  - maligna —*see also* Melanoma, in situ
    - melanoma —*see* Melanoma
- **Lentivirus, as cause of disease classified elsewhere** B97.31
- **Leontiasis**
  - ossium M85.2
  - syphilitic (late) A52.78
    - congenital A50.59
- **Lepothrix** A48.8
- **Lepra** —*see* Leprosy
- **Leprechaunism** E34.8
- **Leprosy** A30.-
  - with muscle disorder A30.9 *[M63.80]*
    - ankle A30.9 *[M63.87]-*
    - foot A30.9 *[M63.87]-*
    - forearm A30.9 *[M63.83]-*
    - hand A30.9 *[M63.84]-*
    - lower leg A30.9 *[M63.86]-*
    - multiple sites A30.9 *[M63.89]*
    - pelvic region A30.9 *[M63.85]-*
    - shoulder region A30.9 *[M63.81]-*
    - specified site NEC A30.9 *[M63.88]*
    - thigh A30.9 *[M63.85]-*
    - upper arm A30.9 *[M63.82]-*
  - anesthetic A30.9
  - BB A30.3
  - BL A30.4
  - borderline (infiltrated) (neuritic) A30.3
    - lepromatous A30.4
    - tuberculoid A30.2
  - BT A30.2
  - dimorphous (infiltrated) (neuritic) A30.3
  - I A30.0
  - indeterminate (macular) (neuritic) A30.0
  - lepromatous (diffuse) (infiltrated) (macular) (neuritic) (nodular) A30.5
  - LL A30.5
  - macular (early) (neuritic) (simple) A30.9
  - maculoanesthetic A30.9
  - mixed A30.3
  - neural A30.9
  - nodular A30.5
  - primary neuritic A30.3
  - specified type NEC A30.8
  - TT A30.1
  - tuberculoid (major) (minor) A30.1

- **Leptocytosis, hereditary** D56.9
- **Leptomeningitis** (chronic) (circumscribed) (hemorrhagic) (nonsuppurative) —*see* Meningitis
- **Leptomeningopathy** G96.19
- **Leptospiral** —*see* condition
- **Leptospirochetal** —*see* condition
- **Leptospirosis** A27.9
  - canicola A27.89
  - due to Leptospira interrogans serovar icterohaemorrhagiae A27.0
  - icterohemorrhagica A27.0
  - pomona A27.89
  - Weil's disease A27.0
- **Leptus dermatitis** B88.0
- **Leriche's syndrome** (aortic bifurcation occlusion) I74.09
- **Leri's pleonosteosis** Q78.8
- **Leri-Weill syndrome** Q77.8
- **Lermoyez' syndrome** —*see* Vertigo, peripheral NEC
- **Lesch-Nyhan syndrome** E79.1
- **Leser-Trélat disease** L82.1
  - inflamed L82.0
- **Lesion**(s) (nontraumatic)
  - abducens nerve —*see* Strabismus, paralytic, sixth nerve
  - alveolar process K08.9
  - angiocentric immunoproliferative D47.Z9
  - anorectal K62.9
  - aortic (valve) I35.9
  - auditory nerve —*see* subcategory H93.3
  - basal ganglion G25.9
  - bile duct —*see* Disease, bile duct
  - biomechanical M99.9
    - specified type NEC M99.89
      - abdomen M99.89
      - acromioclavicular M99.87
      - cervical region M99.81
      - cervicothoracic M99.81
      - costochondral M99.88
      - costovertebral M99.88
      - head region M99.80
      - hip M99.85
      - lower extremity M99.86
      - lumbar region M99.83
      - lumbosacral M99.83
      - occipitocervical M99.80
      - pelvic region M99.85
      - pubic M99.85
      - rib cage M99.88
      - sacral region M99.84
      - sacrococcygeal M99.84
      - sacroiliac M99.84
      - specified NEC M99.89
      - sternochondral M99.88
      - sternoclavicular M99.87
      - thoracic region M99.82
      - thoracolumbar M99.82
      - upper extremity M99.87
  - bladder N32.9
  - bone —*see* Disorder, bone
  - brachial plexus G54.0
  - brain G93.9
    - congenital Q04.9
    - vascular I67.9
      - degenerative I67.9
      - hypertensive I67.4
  - buccal cavity K13.79
  - calcified —*see* Calcification
  - canthus —*see* Disorder, eyelid
  - carate —*see* Pinta, lesions
  - cardia K22.9
  - cardiac —*see also* Disease, heart I51.9
    - congenital Q24.9
    - valvular —*see* Endocarditis

eukomelanopathy, hereditary D72.0
eukonychia (punctata) (striata)
L60.8
congenital Q84.4
eukopathia unguium L60.8
congenital Q84.4
eukopenia D72.819
basophilic D72.818
chemotherapy (cancer) induced D70.1
congenital D70.0
cyclic D70.0
drug induced NEC D70.2
due to cytoreductive cancer
chemotherapy D70.1
eosinophilic D72.818
familial D70.0
infantile genetic D70.0
malignant D70.9
periodic D70.0
transitory neonatal P61.5
eukopenic —*see* condition
eukoplakia
anus K62.89
bladder (postinfectional) N32.89
buccal K13.21
cervix (uteri) N88.0
esophagus K22.8
gingiva K13.21
hairy (oral mucosa) (tongue)
K13.3
kidney (pelvis) N28.89
larynx J38.7
lip K13.21
mouth K13.21
oral epithelium, including tongue
(mucosa) K13.21
palate K13.21
pelvis (kidney) N28.89
penis (infectional) N48.0
rectum K62.89
syphilitic (late) A52.79
tongue K13.21
ureter (postinfectional) N28.89
urethra (postinfectional) N36.8
uterus N85.8
vagina N89.4
vocal cord J38.3
vulva N90.4
Leukorrhea N89.8
due to Trichomonas (vaginalis)
A59.00
trichomonal A59.00
Leukosarcoma C85.9-
Levocardia (isolated) Q24.1
with situs inversus Q89.3
Levotransposition Q20.5
Lev's disease or syndrome (acquired
complete heart block) I44.2
Levulosuria —*see* Fructosuria
Levurid L30.2
Lewy body (ies) (dementia) (disease)
G31.83
Leyden-Moebius dystrophy G71.0
Leydig cell
carcinoma
specified site —*see* Neoplasm,
malignant, by site
unspecified site
female C56.9
male C62.9-
tumor
benign
specified site —*see* Neoplasm,
benign, by site
unspecified site
female D27.-
male D29.2-

Leydig cell *(continued)*
tumor *(continued)*
malignant
specified site —*see* Neoplasm,
malignant, by site
unspecified site
female C56.-
male C62.9-
specified site —*see* Neoplasm,
uncertain behavior, by site
unspecified site
female D39.1-
male D40.1-
Leydig-Sertoli cell tumor
specified site —*see* Neoplasm,
benign, by site
unspecified site
female D27.-
male D29.2-
LGSIL(Low grade squamous
intraepithelial lesion on cytologic
smear of)
anus R85.612
cervix R87.612
vagina R87.622
Liar, pathologic F60.2
Libido
decreased R68.82
Libman-Sacks disease M32.11
Lice (infestation) B85.2
body (Pediculus corporis) B85.1
crab B85.3
head (Pediculus capitis) B85.0
mixed (classifiable to more than one
of the titles B85.0-B85.3) B85.4
pubic (Phthirus pubis) B85.3
Lichen L28.0
albus L90.0
penis N48.0
vulva N90.4
amyloidosis E85.4 *[L99]*
atrophicus L90.0
penis N48.0
vulva N90.4
congenital Q82.8
myxedematosus L98.5
nitidus L44.1
pilaris Q82.8
acquired L85.8
planopilaris L66.1
planus (chronicus) L43.9
annularis L43.8
bullous L43.1
follicular L66.1
hypertrophic L43.0
moniliformis L44.3
of Wilson L43.9
specified NEC L43.8
subacute (active) L43.3
tropicus L43.3
ruber
acuminatus L44.0
moniliformis L44.3
planus L43.9
sclerosus (et atrophicus) L90.0
penis N48.0
vulva N90.4
scrofulosus (primary) (tuberculous)
A18.4
simplex (chronicus) (circumscriptus)
L28.0
striatus L44.2
urticatus L28.2
Lichenification L28.0
Lichenoides tuberculosis (primary)
A18.4
Lichtheim's disease or syndrome —
see Degeneration, combined

Lien migrans D73.89
Ligament —*see* condition
Light
for gestational age —*see* Light for
dates
headedness R42
Light-for-dates (infant) P05.00
with weight of
499 grams or less P05.01
500-749 grams P05.02
750-999 grams P05.03
1000-1249 grams P05.04
1250-1499 grams P05.05
1500-1749 grams P05.06
1750-1999 grams P05.07
2000-2499 grams P05.08
and small-for-dates —*see* Small for
dates
affecting management of pregnancy
O36.59-
Lightning (effects) (stroke) (struck by)
T75.00
burn —*see* Burn
foot E53.8
shock T75.01
specified effect NEC T75.09
Lightwood-Albright syndrome N25.89
Lightwood's disease or syndrome
(renal tubular acidosis) N25.89
Lignac (-de Toni) (-Fanconi) (-Debré)
disease or syndrome E72.09
with cystinosis E72.04
Ligneous thyroiditis E06.5
Likoff's syndrome I20.8
Limb —*see* condition
Limbic epilepsy personality syndrome
F07.0
Limitation, limited
activities due to disability Z73.6
cardiac reserve —*see* Disease, heart
eye muscle duction, traumatic —*see*
Strabismus, mechanical
mandibular range of motion M26.52
Lindau (-von Hippel) **disease** Q85.8
Line (s)
Beau's L60.4
Harris' —*see* Arrest, epiphyseal
Hudson's (cornea) —*see*
Pigmentation, cornea, anterior
Stähli's (cornea) —*see* Pigmentation,
cornea, anterior
Linea corneae senilis —*see* Change,
cornea, senile
Lingua
geographica K14.1
nigra (villosa) K14.3
plicata K14.5
tylosis K13.29
Lingual —*see* condition
Linguatulosis B88.8
Linitis (gastric) **plastica C16.9**
Lip —*see* condition
Lipedema —*see* Edema
Lipemia —*see also* Hyperlipidemia
retina, retinalis E78.3
Lipidosis E75.6
cerebral (infantile) (juvenile) (late)
E75.4
cerebroretinal E75.4
cerebroside E75.22
cholesterol (cerebral) E75.5
glycolipid E75.21
hepatosplenomegalic E78.3

Lipidosis *(continued)*
sphingomyelin —*see* Niemann-Pick
disease or syndrome
sulfatide E75.29
Lipoadenoma —*see* Neoplasm, benign,
by site
Lipoblastoma —*see* Lipoma
Lipoblastomatosis —*see* Lipoma
Lipochondrodystrophy E76.01
Lipodermatosclerosis —*see* Varix, leg,
with, inflammation
ulcerated —*see* Varix, leg, with, ulcer,
with inflammation by site
Lipochrome histiocytosis (familial)
D71
Lipodystrophia progressiva E88.1
Lipodystrophy (progressive) E88.1
insulin E88.1
intestinal K90.81
mesenteric K65.4
Lipofibroma —*see* Lipoma
Lipofuscinosis, neuronal (with
ceroidosis) E75.4
Lipogranuloma, sclerosing L92.8
Lipogranulomatosis E78.89
Lipoid —*see also* condition
histiocytosis D76.3
essential E75.29
nephrosis N04.9
proteinosis of Urbach E78.89
Lipoidemia —*see* Hyperlipidemia
Lipoidosis —*see* Lipidosis
Lipoma D17.9
fetal D17.9
fat cell D17.9
infiltrating D17.9
intramuscular D17.9
pleomorphic D17.9
site classification
arms (skin) (subcutaneous)
D17.2-
connective tissue D17.30
intra-abdominal D17.5
intrathoracic D17.4
peritoneum D17.79
retroperitoneum D17.79
specified site NEC D17.39
spermatic cord D17.6
face (skin) (subcutaneous) D17.0
genitourinary organ NEC D17.72
head (skin) (subcutaneous) D17.0
intra-abdominal D17.5
intrathoracic D17.4
kidney D17.71
legs (skin) (subcutaneous) D17.2-
neck (skin) (subcutaneous) D17.0
peritoneum D17.79
retroperitoneum D17.79
skin D17.30
specified site NEC D17.39
specified site NEC D17.79
spermatic cord D17.6
subcutaneous D17.30
specified site NEC D17.39
trunk (skin) (subcutaneous) D17.1
unspecified D17.9
spindle cell D17.9
Lipomatosis E88.2
dolorosa (Dercum) E88.2
fetal —*see* Lipoma
Launois-Bensaude E88.89
Lipomyoma —*see* Lipoma
Lipomyxoma —*see* Lipoma
Lipomyxosarcoma —*see* Neoplasm,
connective tissue, malignant

Lipoprotein metabolism disorder E78.9

Lipoproteinemia E78.5
- broad-beta E78.2
- floating-beta E78.2
- hyper-pre-beta E78.1

Liposarcoma —*see also* Neoplasm, connective tissue, malignant
- dedifferentiated —*see* Neoplasm, connective tissue, malignant
- differentiated type —*see* Neoplasm, connective tissue, malignant
- embryonal —*see* Neoplasm, connective tissue, malignant
- mixed type —*see* Neoplasm, connective tissue, malignant
- myxoid —*see* Neoplasm, connective tissue, malignant
- pleomorphic —*see* Neoplasm, connective tissue, malignant
- round cell —*see* Neoplasm, connective tissue, malignant
- well differentiated type —*see* Neoplasm, connective tissue, malignant

Liposynovitis prepatellaris E88.89

Lipping, cervix N86

Lipschütz disease or ulcer N76.6

Lipuria R82.0
- schistosomiasis (bilharziasis) B65.0

Lisping F80.0

Lissauer's paralysis A52.17

Lissencephalia, lissencephaly Q04.3

Listeriosis, listerellosis A32.9
- congenital (disseminated) P37.2
- cutaneous A32.0
- neonatal, newborn (disseminated) P37.2
- oculoglandular A32.81
- specified NEC A32.89

Lithemia E79.0

Lithiasis —*see* Calculus

Lithosis J62.8

Lithuria R82.99

Litigation, anxiety concerning Z65.3

Little leaguer's elbow —*see* Epicondylitis, medial

Little's disease G80.9

Littre's
- gland —*see* condition
- hernia —*see* Hernia, abdomen

Littritis —*see* Urethritis

Livedo (annularis) (racemosa) (reticularis) R23.1

Liver —*see* condition

Living alone (problems with) Z60.2
- with handicapped person Z74.2

Lloyd's syndrome —*see* Adenomatosis, endocrine

Loa loa, loaiasis, loasis B74.3

Lobar —*see* condition

Lobomycosis B48.0

Lobo's disease B48.0

Lobotomy syndrome F07.0

Lobstein (-Ekman) **disease or syndrome** Q78.0

Lobster-claw hand Q71.6-

Lobulation (congenital) —*see also* Anomaly, by site
- kidney, Q63.1
- liver, abnormal Q44.7
- spleen Q89.09

Lobule, lobular —*see* condition

Local, localized —*see* condition

Locked-in state G83.5

Locked twins causing obstructed labor O66.1

Locking
- joint —*see* Derangement, joint, specified type NEC
  - knee —*see* Derangement, knee

Lockjaw —*see* Tetanus

Löffler's
- endocarditis I42.3
- eosinophilia J82
- pneumonia J82
- syndrome (eosinophilic pneumonitis) J82

Loiasis (with conjunctival infestation) (eyelid) B74.3

Lone Star fever A77.0

Long
- labor O63.9
  - first stage O63.0
  - second stage O63.1
- QT syndrome I45.81

Long-term (current) (prophylactic)
- drug therapy (use of)
- agents affecting estrogen receptors and estrogen levels NEC Z79.818
- anastrozole (Arimidex) Z79.811
- antibiotics Z79.2
  - short-term use - omit code
- anticoagulants Z79.01
- anti-inflammatory, non-steroidal (NSAID) Z79.1
- antiplatelet Z79.02
- antithrombotics Z79.02
- aromatase inhibitors Z79.811
- aspirin Z79.82
- birth control pill or patch Z79.3
- bisphosphonates Z79.83
- contraceptive, oral Z79.3
- drug, specified NEC Z79.899
- estrogen receptor downregulators Z79.818
- Evista Z79.810
- exemestane (Aromasin) Z79.811
- Fareston Z79.810
- fulvestrant (Faslodex) Z79.818
- gonadotropin-releasing hormone (GnRH) agonist Z79.818
- goserelin acetate (Zoladex) Z79.818
- hormone replacement (postmenopausal) Z79.890
- insulin Z79.4
- letrozole (Femara) Z79.811
- leuprolide acetate (leuprorelin) (Lupron) Z79.818
- megestrol acetate (Megace) Z79.818
- methadone for pain management Z79.891
- Nolvadex Z79.810
- non-steroidal anti-inflammatories (NSAID) Z79.1
- opiate analgesic Z79.891
- oral contraceptive Z79.3
- raloxifene (Evista) Z79.810
- selective estrogen receptor modulators (SERMs) Z79.810
- steroids
  - inhaled Z79.51
  - systemic Z79.52
- tamoxifen (Nolvadex) Z79.810
- toremifene (Fareston) Z79.810

Longitudinal stripes or grooves, nails L60.8
- congenital Q84.6

Loop
- intestine —*see* Volvulus
- vascular on papilla (optic) Q14.2

Loose —*see also* condition
- body
  - joint M24.00
    - ankle M24.07-
    - elbow M24.02-
    - hand M24.04-
    - hip M24.05-
    - knee M23.4-
    - shoulder (region) M24.01-
    - specified site NEC M24.08
    - vertebra M24.08
    - toe M24.07-
    - wrist M24.03-
  - knee M23.4-
  - sheath, tendon —*see* Disorder, tendon, specified type NEC
- cartilage —*see* Loose, body, joint
- tooth, teeth K08.8

Loosening
- aseptic
  - joint prosthesis —*see* Complications, joint prosthesis, mechanical, loosening, by site
- epiphysis —*see* Osteochondropathy
- mechanical
  - joint prosthesis —*see* Complications, joint prosthesis, mechanical, loosening, by site

Looser-Milkman (-Debray) **syndrome** M83.8

Lop ear (deformity) Q17.3

Lorain (-Levi) **short stature syndrome** E23.0

Lordosis M40.50
- acquired —*see* Lordosis, specified type NEC
- congenital Q76.429
  - lumbar region Q76.426
  - lumbosacral region Q76.427
  - sacral region Q76.428
  - sacrococcygeal region Q76.428
  - thoracolumbar region Q76.425
- lumbar region M40.56
- lumbosacral region M40.57
- postsurgical M96.4
- postural —*see* Lordosis, specified type NEC
- rachitic (late effect) (sequelae) E64.3
- sequelae of rickets E64.3
- specified type NEC M40.40
  - lumbar region M40.46
  - lumbosacral region M40.47
  - thoracolumbar region M40.45
- thoracolumbar region M40.55
- tuberculous A18.01

Loss (of)
- appetite (*see* Anorexia) R63.0
  - hysterical F50.8
  - nonorganic origin F50.8
  - psychogenic F50.8
- blood —*see* Hemorrhage
- control, sphincter, rectum R15.9
  - nonorganic origin F98.1
- consciousness, transient R55
  - traumatic —*see* Injury, intracranial
- elasticity, skin R23.4
- family (member) in childhood Z62.898
- fluid (acute) E86.9
  - with
    - hypernatremia E87.0
    - hyponatremia —*see* subcategory E87.1
- function of labyrinth H83.2
- hair, nonscarring —*see* Alopecia

Loss *(continued)*
- hearing —*see also* Deafness
  - central NOS H90.5
  - neural NOS H90.5
  - perceptive NOS H90.5
  - sensorineural NOS H90.5
  - sensory NOS H90.5
- height R29.890
- limb or member, traumatic, current —*see* Amputation, traumatic
- love relationship in childhood Z62.898
- memory —*see also* Amnesia
  - mild, following organic brain damage F06.8
- mind —*see* Psychosis
- occlusal vertical dimension of fully erupted teeth M26.37
- organ or part —*see* Absence, by site, acquired
- ossicles, ear (partial) H74.32-
- parent in childhood Z63.4
- pregnancy, recurrent N96
  - care in current pregnancy O26.2-
  - without current pregnancy N96
- recurrent pregnancy —*see* Loss, pregnancy, recurrent
- self-esteem, in childhood Z62.898
- sense of
  - smell —*see* Disturbance, sensation, smell
  - taste —*see* Disturbance, sensation, taste
  - touch R20.8
- sensory R44.9
  - dissociative F44.6
- sexual desire F52.0
- sight (acquired) (complete) (congenital) —*see* Blindness
- substance of
  - bone —*see* Disorder, bone, density and structure, specified NEC
  - cartilage —*see* Disorder, cartilage, specified type NEC
    - auricle (ear) —*see* Disorder, pinna, specified type NEC
  - vitreous (humor) H15.89
- tooth, teeth —*see* Absence, teeth, acquired
- vision, visual H54.7
  - both eyes H54.3
  - one eye H54.60
    - left (normal vision on right) H54.62
    - right (normal vision on left) H54.61
  - specified as blindness —*see* Blindness
  - subjective
    - sudden H53.13-
    - transient H53.12-
- vitreous —*see* Prolapse, vitreous
- voice —*see* Aphonia
- weight (abnormal) (cause unknown) R63.4

Louis-Bar syndrome (ataxia-telangiectasia) G11.3

Louping ill (encephalitis) A84.8

Louse, lousiness —*see* Lice

Low
- achiever, school Z55.3
- back syndrome M54.5
- basal metabolic rate R94.8
- birthweight (2499 grams or less) P07.10
  - with weight of
    - 1000-1249 grams P07.14
    - 1250-1499 grams P07.15
    - 1500-1749 grams P07.16
    - 1750-1999 grams P07.17
    - 2000-2499 grams P07.18

Lymphangitis *(continued)*
acute *(continued)*
toe (intrathecal) (periosteal) (subcutaneous) (subcuticular) L03.04-
trunk L03.329
abdominal wall L03.321
back (any part) L03.322
buttock L03.327
chest wall L03.323
groin L03.324
perineal, perineum L03.325
umbilicus L03.326
umbilicus L03.326
upper limb L03.12-
axilla *—see* Lymphangitis, acute, axilla
finger *—see* Lymphangitis, acute, finger
thumb *—see* Lymphangitis, acute, finger
wrist *—see* Lymphangitis, acute, upper limb
breast
gestational *—see* Mastitis, obstetric
chancroidal A57
chronic (any site) I89.1
due to
Brugia (malayi) B74.1
timori B74.2
Wuchereria bancrofti B74.0
following ectopic or molar pregnancy O08.89
penis
acute N48.29
gonococcal (acute) (chronic) A54.09
puerperal, postpartum, childbirth O86.89
strumous, tuberculous A18.2
subacute (any site) I89.1
tuberculous *—see* Tuberculosis, lymph gland

Lymphatic (vessel) *—see* condition

Lymphatism E32.8

Lymphectasia I89.0

Lymphedema (acquired) *—see also* Elephantiasis
congenital Q82.0
hereditary (chronic) (idiopathic) Q82.0
postmastectomy I97.2
praecox I89.0
secondary I89.0
surgical NEC I97.89
postmastectomy (syndrome) I97.2

Lymphoblastic *—see* condition

Lymphoblastoma (diffuse) *—see* Lymphoma, lymphoblastic (diffuse)
giant follicular *—see* Lymphoma, lymphoblastic (diffuse)
macrofollicular *—see* Lymphoma, lymphoblastic (diffuse)

Lymphocele I89.8

Lymphocytic
chorioencephalitis (acute) (serous) A87.2
choriomeningitis (acute) (serous) A87.2
meningoencephalitis A87.2

Lymphocytoma, benign cutis L98.8

Lymphocytopenia D72.810

Lymphocytosis (symptomatic) D72.820
infectious (acute) B33.8

Lymphoepithelioma *—see* Neoplasm, malignant, by site

Lymphogranuloma (malignant) *—see also* Lymphoma, Hodgkin
chlamydial A55
inguinale A55
venereum (any site) (chlamydial) (with stricture of rectum) A55

Lymphogranulomatosis (malignant) *— see also* Lymphoma, Hodgkin
benign (Boeck's sarcoid) (Schaumann's) D86.1

Lymphohistiocytosis, hemophagocytic (familial) D76.1

Lymphoid *—see* condition

Lymphoma (of) (malignant) C85.90
adult T-cell (HTLV-1-associated) (acute variant) (chronic variant) (lymphomatoid variant) (smouldering variant) C91.5-
anaplastic large cell
ALK-negative C84.7-
ALK-positive C84.6-
CD30-positive C84.6-
primary cutaneous C86.6
angioimmunoblastic T-cell C86.5
BALT C88.4
B-cell C85.1-
B-precursor C83.5-
blastic NK-cell C86.4
bronchial-associated lymphoid tissue [BALT-lymphoma] C88.4
Burkitt (atypical) C83.7-
Burkitt-like C83.7-
centrocytic C83.1-
cutaneous follicle center C82.6-
cutaneous T-cell C84.A-
diffuse follicle center C82.5-
diffuse large cell C83.3-
anaplastic C83.3-
B-cell C83.3-
CD30-positive C83.3-
centroblastic C83.3-
immunoblastic C83.3-
plasmablastic C83.3-
subtype not specified C83.3-
T-cell rich C83.3-
enteropathy-type (associated) (intestinal) T-cell C86.2
extranodal NK/T-cell, nasal type C86.0
extranodal marginal zone B-cell lymphoma of mucosa-associated lymphoid tissue [MALT-lymphoma] C88.4
follicular C82.9-
grade
I C82.0-
II C82.1-
III C82.2-
IIIa C82.3-
IIIb C82.4-
specified NEC C82.8-
hepatosplenic T-cell (alpha-beta) (gamma-delta) C86.1
histiocytic C85.9-
true C96.A
Hodgkin C81.9
classical C81.7-
lymphocyte-rich C81.4-
lymphocyte depleted C81.3-
mixed cellularity C81.2-
nodular sclerosis C81.1-
specified NEC C81.7-
lymphocyte-rich classical C81.4-
lymphocyte depleted classical C81.3-
mixed cellularity classical C81.2-
nodular
lymphocyte predominant C81.0-
sclerosis classical C81.1-
intravascular large B-cell C83.8-

Lymphoma *(continued)*
Lennert's C84.4-
lymphoblastic B-cell C83.5-
lymphoblastic (diffuse) C83.5-
lymphoblastic T-cell C83.5-
lymphoepithelioid C84.4-
lymphoplasmacytic C83.0-
with IgM-production C88.0
MALT C88.4
mantle cell C83.1-
mature T-cell NEC C84.4-
mature T/NK-cell C84.9-
specified NEC C84.Z-
mediastinal (thymic) large B-cell C85.2-
Mediterranean C88.3
mucosa-associated lymphoid tissue [MALT-lymphoma] C88.4
NK/T cell C84.9-
nodal marginal zone C83.0-
non-follicular (diffuse) C83.9-
specified NEC C83.8-
non-Hodgkin *—see also* Lymphoma, by type C85.9-
specified NEC C85.8-
non-leukemic variant of B-CLL C83.0-
peripheral T-cell, not classified C84.4-
primary cutaneous
anaplastic large cell C86.6
CD30-positive large T-cell C86.6
primary effusion B-cell C83.8-
SALT C88.4
skin-associated lymphoid tissue [SALT-lymphoma] C88.4
small cell B-cell C83.0-
splenic marginal zone C83.0-
subcutaneous panniculitis-like T-cell C86.3
T-precursor C83.5-
true histiocytic C96.A

Lymphomatosis *—see* Lymphoma

Lymphopathia venereum, veneris A55

Lymphopenia D72.810

Lymphoplasmacytic leukemia *—see* Leukemia, chronic lymphocytic, B-cell type

Lymphoproliferation, X-linked disease D82.3

Lymphoreticulosis, benign (of inoculation) A28.1

Lymphorrhea I89.8

Lymphosarcoma (diffuse) *—see also* Lymphoma C85.9-

Lymphostasis I89.8

Lypemania *—see* Melancholia

Lysine and hydroxylysine metabolism disorder E72.3

Lyssa *—see* Rabies

M

Macacus ear Q17.3

Maceration, wet feet, tropical (syndrome) T69.02-

MacLeod's syndrome J43.0

Macrocephalia, macrocephaly Q75.3

Macrocheilia, macrochilia (congenital) Q18.6

Macrocolon *—see also* Megacolon Q43.1

Macrocornea Q15.8
with glaucoma Q15.0

Macrocytic *—see* condition

Macrocytosis D75.89

Macrodactylia, macrodactylism (fingers) (thumbs) Q74.0
toes Q74.2

Macrodontia K00.2

Macrogenia M26.05

Macrogenitosomia (adrenal) (male) (praecox) E25.9
congenital E25.0

Macroglobulinemia (idiopathic) (primary) C88.0
monoclonal (essential) D47.2
Waldenström C88.0

Macroglossia (congenital) Q38.2
acquired K14.8

Macrognathia, macrognathism (congenital) (mandibular) (maxillary) M26.09

Macrogyria (congenital) Q04.8

Macrohydrocephalus *—see* Hydrocephalus

Macromastia *—see* Hypertrophy, breast

Macrophthalmos Q11.3
in congenital glaucoma Q15.0

Macropsia H53.15

Macrosigmoid K59.3
congenital Q43.2

Macrospondylitis, acromegalic E22.0

Macrostomia (congenital) Q18.4

Macrotia (external ear) (congenital) Q17.1

Macula
cornea, corneal *—see* Opacity, cornea
degeneration (atrophic) (exudative) (senile) *—see also* Degeneration, macula
hereditary *—see* Dystrophy, retina

Maculae ceruleae -- B85.1

Maculopathy, toxic *—see* Degeneration, macula, toxic

Madarosis (eyelid) H02.729
left H02.726
lower H02.725
upper H02.724
right H02.723
lower H02.722
upper H02.721

Madelung's
deformity (radius) Q74.0
disease
radial deformity Q74.0
symmetrical lipomas, neck E88.89

Madness *—see* Psychosis

Madura
foot B47.9
actinomycotic B47.1
mycotic B47.0

Maduromycosis B47.0

Maffucci's syndrome Q78.4

Magnesium metabolism disorder *— see* Disorder, metabolism, magnesium

Main en griffe (acquired) *—see also* Deformity, limb, clawhand
congenital Q74.0

Maintenance (encounter for)
antineoplastic chemotherapy Z51.11
antineoplastic radiation therapy Z51.0
methadone F11.20

Majocchi's
disease L81.7
granuloma B35.8

Malposition *(continued)*
congenital *(continued)*
peripheral vascular system Q27.8
pituitary (gland) Q89.2
respiratory organ or system NEC Q34.8
rib (cage) Q76.6
supernumerary in cervical region Q76.5
scapula Q74.0
shoulder Q74.0
spinal cord Q06.8
spleen Q89.09
sternum NEC Q76.7
stomach Q40.2
symphysis pubis Q74.2
thymus (gland) Q89.2
thyroid (gland) (tissue) Q89.2
cartilage Q31.8
toe (s) Q66.9
supernumerary Q69.2
tongue Q38.3
trachea Q32.1
ureter Q62.60
deviation Q62.61
displacement Q62.62
ectopia Q62.63
specified type NEC Q62.69
uterus Q51.818
vein (s) (peripheral) Q27.8
great Q26.8
vena cava (inferior) (superior) Q26.8
device, implant or graft —*see also* Complications, by site and type, mechanical T85.628
arterial graft NEC —*see* Complication, cardiovascular device, mechanical, vascular
breast (implant) T85.42
catheter NEC T85.628
cystostomy T83.020
dialysis (renal) T82.42
intraperitoneal T85.621
infusion NEC T82.524
spinal (epidural) (subdural) T85.620
urinary, indwelling T83.028
electronic (electrode) (pulse generator) (stimulator)
bone T84.320
cardiac T82.129
electrode T82.120
pulse generator T82.121
specified type NEC T82.128
nervous system —*see* Complication, prosthetic device, mechanical, electronic nervous system stimulator
urinary —*see* Complication, genitourinary, device, urinary, mechanical
fixation, internal (orthopedic) NEC —*see* Complication, fixation device, mechanical
gastrointestinal —*see* Complications, prosthetic device, mechanical, gastrointestinal device
genital NEC T83.428
intrauterine contraceptive device T83.32
penile prosthesis T83.420
heart NEC —*see* Complication, cardiovascular device, mechanical
joint prosthesis —*see* Complication, joint prosthesis, mechanical
ocular NEC —*see* Complications, prosthetic device, mechanical, ocular device

Malposition *(continued)*
device, implant or graft —*see also* Complications, by site and type, mechanical *(continued)*
orthopedic NEC —*see* Complication, orthopedic, device, mechanical
specified NEC T85.628
urinary NEC —*see also* Complication, genitourinary, device, urinary, mechanical
graft T83.22
vascular NEC —*see* Complication, cardiovascular device, mechanical
ventricular intracranial shunt T85.02
fetus —*see* Pregnancy, complicated by (management affected by), presentation, fetal
gallbladder K82.8
gastrointestinal tract, congenital Q45.8
heart, congenital NEC Q24.8
joint prosthesis —*see* Complications, joint prosthesis, mechanical, displacement, by site
stomach K31.89
congenital Q40.2
tooth, teeth, fully erupted M26.30
uterus (acute) (acquired) (adherent) (asymptomatic) (postinfectional) (postpartal, old) N85.4
anteflexion or anteversion N85.4
congenital Q51.818
flexion N85.4
lateral —*see* Lateroversion, uterus
inversion N85.5
lateral (flexion) (version) —*see* Lateroversion, uterus
in pregnancy or childbirth —*see* subcategory O34.5
retroflexion or retroversion —*see* Retroversion, uterus

Malposture R29.3

Malrotation
cecum Q43.3
colon Q43.3
intestine Q43.3
kidney Q63.2

Maltreatment
adult
abandonment
confirmed T74.01
suspected T76.01
confirmed T74.91
history of Z91.419
neglect
confirmed T74.01
suspected T76.01
physical abuse
confirmed T74.11
suspected T76.11
psychological abuse
confirmed T74.31
suspected T76.31
history of Z91.411
sexual abuse
confirmed T74.21
suspected T76.21
suspected T76.91
child
abandonment
confirmed T74.02
suspected T76.02
confirmed T74.92
history of —*see* History, personal (of), abuse
neglect
confirmed T74.02
history of —*see* History, personal (of), abuse
suspected T76.02

Maltreatment *(continued)*
child *(continued)*
physical abuse
confirmed T74.12
history of —*see* History, personal (of), abuse
suspected T76.12
psychological abuse
confirmed T74.32
history of —*see* History, personal (of), abuse
suspected T76.32
sexual abuse
confirmed T74.22
history of —*see* History, personal (of), abuse
suspected T76.22
suspected T76.92
personal history of Z91.89

Malta fever —*see* Brucellosis

Maltworker's lung J67.4

Malunion, fracture —*see* Fracture, by site

Mammillitis N61
puerperal, postpartum O91.02

Mammitis —*see* Mastitis

Mammogram (examination) Z12.39
routine Z12.31

Mammoplasia N62

Management (of)
bone conduction hearing device (implanted) Z45.320
cardiac pacemaker NEC Z45.018
cerebrospinal fluid drainage device Z45.41
cochlear device (implanted) Z45.321
contraceptive Z30.9
specified NEC Z30.8
implanted device Z45.9
specified NEC Z45.89
infusion pump Z45.1
procreative Z31.9
male factor infertility in female Z31.81
specified NEC Z31.89
prosthesis (external) —*see also* Fitting Z44.9
implanted Z45.9
specified NEC Z45.89
renal dialysis catheter Z49.01
vascular access device Z45.2

Mangled —*see* specified injury by site

Mania (monopolar) —*see also* Disorder, mood, manic episode
with psychotic symptoms F30.2
without psychotic symptoms F30.10
mild F30.11
moderate F30.12
severe F30.13
Bell's F30.8
chronic (recurrent) F31.89
hysterical F44.89
puerperal F30.8
recurrent F31.89

Manic-depressive insanity, psychosis, or syndrome —*see* Disorder, bipolar

Mannosidosis E77.1

Mansonelliasis, mansonellosis B74.4

Manson's
disease B65.1
schistosomiasis B65.1

Manual —*see* condition

Maple-bark-stripper's lung (disease) J67.6

Maple-syrup-urine disease E71.0

Marable's syndrome (celiac artery compression) I77.4

Marasmus E41
due to malnutrition E41
intestinal E41
nutritional E41
senile R54
tuberculous NEC —*see* Tuberculosis

Marble
bones Q78.2
skin R23.8

Marburg virus disease A98.3

March
fracture —*see* Fracture, traumatic, stress, by site
hemoglobinuria D59.6

Marchesani (-Weill) **syndrome** Q87.0

Marchiafava (-Bignami) **syndrome or disease** G37.1

Marchiafava-Micheli syndrome D59.5

Marcus Gunn's syndrome Q07.8

Marfan's syndrome —*see* Syndrome, Marfan's

Marie-Bamberger disease —*see* Osteoarthropathy, hypertrophic, specified NEC

Marie-Charcot-Tooth neuropathic muscular atrophy G60.0

Marie's
cerebellar ataxia (late-onset) G11.2
disease or syndrome (acromegaly) E22.0

Marie-Strümpell arthritis, disease or spondylitis —*see* Spondylitis, ankylosing

Marion's disease (bladder neck obstruction) N32.0

Marital conflict Z63.0

Mark
port wine Q82.5
raspberry Q82.5
strawberry Q82.5
stretch L90.6
tattoo L81.8

Marker heterochromatin —*see* Extra, marker chromosomes

Maroteaux-Lamy syndrome (mild) (severe) E76.29

Marrow (bone)
arrest D61.9
poor function D75.89

Marseilles fever A77.1

Marsh fever —*see* Malaria

Marshall's (hidrotic) **ectodermal dysplasia** Q82.4

Marsh's disease (exophthalmic goiter) E05.00
with storm E05.01

Masculinization (female) **with adrenal hyperplasia** E25.9
congenital E25.0

Masculinovoblastoma D27.-

Masochism (sexual) F65.51

Mason's lung J62.8

Mass
abdominal R19.00
epigastric R19.06
generalized R19.07
left lower quadrant R19.04
left upper quadrant R19.02
periumbilic R19.05
right lower quadrant R19.03

Mass *(continued)*
- abdominal *(continued)*
  - right upper quadrant R19.01
  - specified site NEC R19.09
- breast N63
- chest R22.2
- cystic —*see* Cyst
- ear H93.8-
- head R22.0
- intra-abdominal (diffuse) (generalized) —*see* Mass, abdominal
- kidney N28.89
- liver R16.0
- localized (skin) R22.9
  - chest R22.2
  - head R22.0
  - limb
    - lower R22.4-
    - upper R22.3-
  - neck R22.1
  - trunk R22.2
- lung R91.8
- malignant —*see* Neoplasm, malignant, by site
- neck R22.1
- pelvic (diffuse) (generalized) —*see* Mass, abdominal
- specified organ NEC —*see* Disease, by site
- splenic R16.1
- substernal thyroid —*see* Goiter
- superficial (localized) R22.9
- umbilical (diffuse) (generalized) R19.09

Massive —*see* condition

Mast cell
- disease, systemic tissue D47.0
- leukemia C94.3-
- sarcoma C96.2
- tumor D47.0
  - malignant C96.2

Mastalgia N64.4

Masters-Allen syndrome N83.8

Mastitis (acute) (diffuse) (nonpuerperal) (subacute) N61
- chronic (cystic) —*see* Mastopathy, cystic
- cystic (Schimmelbusch's type) —*see* Mastopathy, cystic
- fibrocystic —*see* Mastopathy, cystic
- infective N61
  - newborn P39.0
- interstitial, gestational or puerperal —*see* Mastitis, obstetric
- neonatal (noninfective) P83.4
  - infective P39.0
- obstetric (interstitial) (nonpurulent)
  - associated with
    - lactation O91.23
    - pregnancy O91.21-
    - puerperium O91.22
  - purulent
    - associated with
      - lactation O91.13
      - pregnancy O91.11-
      - puerperium O91.12
- periductal —*see* Ectasia, mammary duct
- phlegmonous —*see* Mastopathy, cystic
- plasma cell —*see* Ectasia, mammary duct

Mastocytoma D47.0
- malignant C96.2

Mastocytosis Q82.2
- aggressive systemic C96.2
- indolent systemic D47.0
- malignant C96.2

Mastocytosis *(continued)*
- systemic, associated with clonal hematopoetic non-mast-cell disease (SM-AHNMD) D47.0

Mastodynia N64.4

Mastoid —*see* condition

Mastoidalgia —*see* subcategory H92.0

Mastoiditis (coalescent) (hemorrhagic) (suppurative) H70.9-
- acute, subacute H70.00-
  - complicated NEC H70.09-
  - subperiosteal H70.01-
- chronic (necrotic) (recurrent) H70.1-
- in (due to)
  - infectious disease NEC B99 *[H75.0]-*
  - parasitic disease NEC B89 *[H75.0]-*
  - tuberculosis A18.03
- petrositis —*see* Petrositis
- postauricular fistula —*see* Fistula, postauricular
- specified NEC H70.89-
- tuberculous A18.03

Mastopathy, mastopathia N64.9
- chronica cystica —*see* Mastopathy, cystic
- cystic (chronic) (diffuse) N60.1-
  - with epithelial proliferation N60.3-
- diffuse cystic —*see* Mastopathy, cystic
- estrogenic, oestrogenica N64.89
- ovarian origin N64.89

Mastoplasia, mastoplastia N62

Masturbation (excessive) F98.8

Maternal care (for) —*see* Pregnancy (complicated by) (management affected by)

Matheiu's disease (leptospiral jaundice) A27.0

Mauclaire's disease or osteochondrosis —*see* Osteochondrosis, juvenile, hand, metacarpal

Maxcy's disease A75.2

Maxilla, maxillary —*see* condition

May (-Hegglin) **anomaly or syndrome** D72.0

McArdle (-Schmid)(-Pearson) **disease** (glycogen storage) E74.04

McCune-Albright syndrome Q78.1

McQuarrie's syndrome (idiopathic familial hypoglycemia) E16.2

Meadow's syndrome Q86.1

Measles (black) (hemorrhagic) (suppressed) B05.9
- with
  - complications NEC B05.89
  - encephalitis B05.0
  - intestinal complications B05.4
  - keratitis (keratoconjunctivitis) B05.81
  - meningitis B05.1
  - otitis media B05.3
  - pneumonia B05.2
- French —*see* Rubella
- German —*see* Rubella
- Liberty —*see* Rubella

Meatitis, urethral —*see* Urethritis

Meatus, meatal —*see* condition

Meat-wrappers' asthma J68.9

Meckel-Gruber syndrome Q61.9

Meckel's diverticulitis, diverticulum (displaced) (hypertrophic) Q43.0
- malignant —*see* Table of Neoplasms, small intestine, malignant

Meconium
- ileus, newborn P76.0
  - in cystic fibrosis E84.11
  - meaning meconium plug (without cystic fibrosis) P76.0
- obstruction, newborn P76.0
  - due to fecaliths P76.0
  - in mucoviscidosis E84.11
- peritonitis P78.0
- plug syndrome (newborn) NEC P76.0

Median —*see also* condition
- arcuate ligament syndrome I77.4
- bar (prostate) (vesical orifice) —*see* Hyperplasia, prostate
- rhomboid glossitis K14.2

Mediastinal shift R93.8

Mediastinitis (acute) (chronic) J98.5
- syphilitic A52.73
- tuberculous A15.8

Mediastinopericarditis —*see also* Pericarditis
- acute I30.9
- adhesive I31.0
- chronic I31.8
  - rheumatic I09.2

Mediastinum, mediastinal —*see* condition

Medicine poisoning —*see* Table of Drugs and Chemicals, by drug, poisoning

Mediterranean
- fever —*see* Brucellosis
  - familial E85.0
  - tick A77.1
- kala-azar B55.0
- leishmaniasis B55.0
- tick fever A77.1

Medulla —*see* condition

Medullary cystic kidney Q61.5

Medullated fibers
- optic (nerve) Q14.8
- retina Q14.1

Medulloblastoma
- desmoplastic C71.6
- specified site —*see* Neoplasm, malignant, by site
- unspecified site C71.6

Medulloepithelioma —*see also* Neoplasm, malignant, by site
- teratoid —*see* Neoplasm, malignant, by site

Medullomyoblastoma
- specified site —*see* Neoplasm, malignant, by site
- unspecified site C71.6

Meekeren-Ehlers-Danlos syndrome Q79.6

Megacolon (acquired) (functional) (not Hirschsprung's disease) (in) K59.3
- Chagas' disease B57.32
- congenital, congenitum (aganglionic) Q43.1
- Hirschsprung's (disease) Q43.1
- toxic NEC K59.3
  - due to Clostridium difficile A04.7

Megaesophagus (functional) K22.0
- congenital Q39.5
- in (due to) Chagas' disease B57.31

Megalencephaly Q04.5

Megalerythema (epidemic) B08.3

Megaloappendix Q43.8

Megalocephalus, megalocephaly NE Q75.3

Megalocornea Q15.8
- with glaucoma Q15.0

Megalocytic anemia D53.1

Megalodactylia (fingers) (thumbs) (congenital) Q74.0
- toes Q74.2

Megaloduodenum Q43.8

Megaloesophagus (functional) K22.0
- congenital Q39.5

Megalogastria (acquired) K31.89
- congenital Q40.2

Megalophthalmos Q11.3

Megalopsia H53.15

Megalosplenia —*see* Splenomegaly

Megaloureter N28.82
- congenital Q62.2

Megarectum K62.89

Megasigmoid K59.3
- congenital Q43.2

Megaureter N28.82
- congenital Q62.2

Megavitamin-B6 syndrome E67.2

Megrim —*see* Migraine

Meibomian
- cyst, infected —*see* Hordeolum
- gland —*see* condition
- sty, stye —*see* Hordeolum

Meibomitis —*see* Hordeolum

Meige-Milroy disease (chronic hereditary edema) Q82.0

Meige's syndrome Q82.0

Melalgia, nutritional E53.8

Melancholia F32.9
- climacteric (single episode) F32.8
  - recurrent episode F33.9
- hypochondriac F45.29
- intermittent (single episode) F32.8
  - recurrent episode F33.9
- involutional (single episode) F32.8
  - recurrent episode F33.9
- menopausal (single episode) F32.8
  - recurrent episode F33.9
- puerperal F32.8
- reactive (emotional stress or trauma) F32.3
- recurrent F33.9
- senile F03
- stuporous (single episode) F32.8
  - recurrent episode F33.9

Melanemia R79.89

Melanoameloblastoma —*see* Neoplasm, bone, benign

Melanoblastoma —*see* Melanoma

Melanocarcinoma —*see* Melanoma

Melanocytoma, eyeball D31.4-

Melanocytosis, neurocutaneous Q82.8

Melanoderma, melanodermia L81.4

Melanodontia, infantile K03.89

Melanodontoclasia K03.89

Melanoepithelioma —*see* Melanoma

Melanoma (malignant) C43.9
- acral lentiginous, malignant —*see* Melanoma, skin, by site
- amelanotic —*see* Melanoma, skin, by site
- balloon cell —*see* Melanoma, skin, by site
- benign —*see* Nevus

elanoma *(continued)*
desmoplastic, malignant —*see* Melanoma, skin, by site
epithelioid cell —*see* Melanoma, skin, by site
  with spindle cell, mixed —*see* Melanoma, skin, by site
in
  giant pigmented nevus —*see* Melanoma, skin, by site
  Hutchinson's melanotic freckle — *see* Melanoma, skin, by site
  junctional nevus —*see* Melanoma, skin, by site
  precancerous melanosis —*see* Melanoma, skin, by site
in situ D03.9
  abdominal wall D03.59
  ala nasi D03.39
  ankle D03.7-
  anus, anal (margin) (skin) D03.51
  arm D03.6-
  auditory canal D03.2-
  auricle (ear) D03.2-
  auricular canal (external) D03.2-
  axilla, axillary fold D03.59
  back D03.59
  breast D03.52
  brow D03.39
  buttock D03.59
  canthus (eye) D03.1-
  cheek (external) D03.39
  chest wall D03.59
  chin D03.39
  choroid D03.8
  conjunctiva D03.8
  ear (external) D03.2-
  external meatus (ear) D03.2-
  eye D03.8
  eyebrow D03.39
  eyelid (lower) (upper) D03.1-
  face D03.30
    specified NEC D03.39
  female genital organ (external) NEC D03.8
  finger D03.6-
  flank D03.59
  foot D03.7-
  forearm D03.6-
  forehead D03.39
  foreskin D03.8
  gluteal region D03.59
  groin D03.59
  hand D03.6-
  heel D03.7-
  helix D03.2-
  hip D03.7-
  interscapular region D03.59
  iris D03.8
  jaw D03.39
  knee D03.7-
  labium (majus) (minus) D03.8
  lacrimal gland D03.8
  leg D03.7-
  lip (lower) (upper) D03.0
  lower limb NEC D03.7-
  male genital organ (external) NEC D03.8
  nail D03.9
    finger D03.6-
    toe D03.7-
  neck D03.4
  nose (external) D03.39
  orbit D03.8
  penis D03.8
  perianal skin D03.51
  perineum D03.51
  pinna D03.2-
  popliteal fossa or space D03.7-
  prepuce D03.8
  pudendum D03.8
  retina D03.8

Melanoma *(continued)*
in situ *(continued)*
  retrobulbar D03.8
  scalp D03.4
  scrotum D03.8
  shoulder D03.6-
  specified site NEC D03.8
  submammary fold D03.52
  temple D03.39
  thigh D03.7-
  toe D03.7-
  trunk NEC D03.59
  umbilicus D03.59
  upper limb NEC D03.6-
  vulva D03.8
juvenile —*see* Nevus
malignant, of soft parts except skin —*see* Neoplasm, connective tissue, malignant
metastatic
  breast C79.81
  genital organ C79.82
  specified site NEC C79.89
neurotropic, malignant —*see* Melanoma, skin, by site
nodular —*see* Melanoma, skin, by site
regressing, malignant —*see* Melanoma, skin, by site
skin C43.9
  abdominal wall C43.59
  ala nasi C43.31
  ankle C43.7-
  anus, anal (skin) C43.51
  arm C43.6-
  auditory canal (external) C43.2-
  auricle (ear) C43.2-
  auricular canal (external) C43.2-
  axilla, axillary fold C43.59
  back C43.59
  breast (female) (male) C43.52
  brow C43.39
  buttock C43.59
  canthus (eye) C43.1-
  cheek (external) C43.39
  chest wall C43.59
  chin C43.39
  ear (external) C43.2-
  elbow C43.6-
  external meatus (ear) C43.2-
  eyebrow C43.39
  eyelid (lower) (upper) C43.1-
  face C43.30
    specified NEC C43.39
  female genital organ (external) NEC C51.9
  finger C43.6-
  flank C43.59
  foot C43.7-
  forearm C43.6-
  forehead C43.39
  foreskin C60.0
  glabella C43.39
  gluteal region C43.59
  groin C43.59
  hand C43.6-
  heel C43.7-
  helix C43.2-
  hip C43.7-
  interscapular region C43.59
  jaw (external) C43.39
  knee C43.7-
  labium C51.9
    majus C51.0
    minus C51.1
  leg C43.7-
  lip (lower) (upper) C43.0
  lower limb NEC C43.7-
  male genital organ (external) NEC C63.9
  nail
    finger C43.6-
    toe C43.7-

Melanoma *(continued)*
skin *(continued)*
  nasolabial groove C43.39
  nates C43.59
  neck C43.4
  nose (external) C43.31
  overlapping site C43.8
  palpebra C43.1-
  penis C60.9
  perianal skin C43.51
  perineum C43.51
  pinna C43.2-
  popliteal fossa or space C43.7-
  prepuce C60.0
  pudendum C51.9
  scalp C43.4
  scrotum C63.2
  shoulder C43.6-
  skin NEC C43.9
  submammary fold C43.52
  temple C43.39
  thigh C43.7-
  toe C43.7-
  trunk NEC C43.59
  umbilicus C43.59
  upper limb NEC C43.6-
  vulva C51.9
    overlapping sites C51.8
spindle cell
  with epithelioid, mixed —*see* Melanoma, skin, by site
  type A C69.4-
  type B C69.4-
superficial spreading —*see* Melanoma, skin, by site

Melanosarcoma —*see also* Melanoma
epithelioid cell —*see* Melanoma

Melanosis L81.4
addisonian E27.1
  tuberculous A18.7
adrenal E27.1
colon K63.89
conjunctiva —*see* Pigmentation, conjunctiva
  congenital Q13.89
cornea (presenile) (senile) —*see also* Pigmentation, cornea
  congenital Q13.4
eye NEC H57.8
  congenital Q15.8
lenticularis progressiva Q82.1
liver K76.89
precancerous —*see also* Melanoma, in situ
  malignant melanoma in —*see* Melanoma
Riehl's L81.4
sclera H15.89
  congenital Q13.89
suprarenal E27.1
tar L81.4
toxic L81.4

Melanuria R82.99

MELAS syndrome E88.41

Melasma L81.1
adrenal (gland) E27.1
suprarenal (gland) E27.1

Melena K92.1
with ulcer - code by site under Ulcer, with hemorrhage K27.4
due to swallowed maternal blood P78.2
newborn, neonatal P54.1
  due to swallowed maternal blood P78.2

Meleney's
gangrene (cutaneous) —*see* Ulcer, skin
ulcer (chronic undermining) —*see* Ulcer, skin

Melioidosis A24.9
acute A24.1
chronic A24.2
fulminating A24.1
pneumonia A24.1
pulmonary (chronic) A24.2
  acute A24.1
  subacute A24.2
sepsis A24.1
specified NEC A24.3
subacute A24.2

Melitensis, febris A23.0

Melkersson (-Rosenthal) **syndrome** G51.2

Mellitus, diabetes —*see* Diabetes

Melorheostosis (bone) —*see* Disorder, bone, density and structure, specified NEC

Meloschisis Q18.4

Melotia Q17.4

Membrana
capsularis lentis posterior Q13.89
epipapillaris Q14.2

Membranacea placenta O43.19-

Membranaceous uterus N85.8

Membrane (s), **membranous** —*see also* condition
cyclitic —*see* Membrane, pupillary
folds, congenital —*see* Web
Jackson's Q43.3
over face of newborn P28.9
premature rupture —*see* Rupture, membranes, premature
pupillary H21.4-
  persistent Q13.89
retained (with hemorrhage) (complicating delivery) O72.2
  without hemorrhage O73.1
secondary cataract —*see* Cataract, secondary
unruptured (causing asphyxia) —*see* Asphyxia, newborn
vitreous —*see* Opacity, vitreous, membranes and strands

Membranitis —*see* Chorioamnionitis

Memory disturbance, lack or loss —*see also* Amnesia
mild, following organic brain damage F06.8

Menadione deficiency E56.1

Menarche
delayed E30.0
precocious E30.1

Mendacity, pathologic F60.2

Mendelson's syndrome (due to anesthesia) J95.4
in labor and delivery O74.0
in pregnancy O29.01-
obstetric O74.0
postpartum, puerperal O89.01

Ménétrier's disease or syndrome K29.60
with bleeding K29.61

Ménière's disease, syndrome or vertigo H81.0-

Meninges, meningeal —*see* condition

Meningioma —*see also* Neoplasm, meninges, benign
angioblastic —*see* Neoplasm, meninges, benign
angiomatous —*see* Neoplasm, meninges, benign
endotheliomatous —*see* Neoplasm, meninges, benign

Meningioma *(continued)*
fibroblastic —*see* Neoplasm, meninges, benign
fibrous —*see* Neoplasm, meninges, benign
hemangioblastic —*see* Neoplasm, meninges, benign
hemangiopericytic —*see* Neoplasm, meninges, benign
malignant —*see* Neoplasm, meninges, malignant
meningiothelial —*see* Neoplasm, meninges, benign
meningotheliomatous —*see* Neoplasm, meninges, benign
mixed —*see* Neoplasm, meninges, benign
multiple —*see* Neoplasm, meninges, uncertain behavior
papillary —*see* Neoplasm, meninges, uncertain behavior
psammomatous —*see* Neoplasm, meninges, benign
syncytial —*see* Neoplasm, meninges, benign
transitional —*see* Neoplasm, meninges, benign

Meningiomatosis (diffuse) —*see* Neoplasm, meninges, uncertain behavior

Meningism —*see* Meningismus

Meningismus (infectional) (pneumococcal) R29.1
due to serum or vaccine R29.1
influenzal —*see* Influenza, with, manifestations NEC

Meningitis (basal) (basic) (brain) (cerebral) (cervical) (congestive) (diffuse) (hemorrhagic) (infantile) (membranous) (metastatic) (nonspecific) (pontine) (progressive) (simple) (spinal) (subacute) (sympathetic) (toxic) G03.9
abacterial G03.0
actinomycotic A42.81
adenoviral A87.1
arbovirus A87.8
aseptic (acute) G03.0
bacterial G00.9
Escherichia coli (E. coli) G00.8
Friedländer (bacillus) G00.8
gram-negative G00.9
H. influenzae G00.0
Klebsiella G00.8
pneumococcal G00.1
specified organism NEC G00.8
staphylococcal G00.3
streptococcal (acute) G00.2
benign recurrent (Mollaret) G03.2
candidal B37.5
caseous (tuberculous) A17.0
cerebrospinal A39.0
chronic NEC G03.1
clear cerebrospinal fluid NEC G03.0
coxsackievirus A87.0
cryptococcal B45.1
diplococcal (gram positive) A39.0
echovirus A87.0
enteroviral A87.0
eosinophilic B83.2
epidemic NEC A39.0
Escherichia coli (E. coli) G00.8
fibrinopurulent G00.9
specified organism NEC G00.8
Friedländer (bacillus) G00.8
gonococcal A54.81
gram-negative cocci G00.9
gram-positive cocci G00.9
Haemophilus (influenzae) G00.0
H. influenzae G00.0

Meningitis *(continued)*
in (due to)
adenovirus A87.1
African trypanosomiasis B56.9 *[G02]*
anthrax A22.8
bacterial disease NEC A48.8 *[G01]*
Chagas' disease (chronic) B57.41
chickenpox B01.0
coccidioidomycosis B38.4
Diplococcus pneumoniae G00.1
enterovirus A87.0
herpes (simplex) virus B00.3
zoster B02.1
infectious mononucleosis B27.92
leptospirosis A27.81
Listeria monocytogenes A32.11
Lyme disease A69.21
measles B05.1
mumps (virus) B26.1
neurosyphilis (late) A52.13
parasitic disease NEC B89 *[G02]*
poliovirus A80.9 *[G02]*
preventive immunization, inoculation or vaccination G03.8
rubella B06.02
Salmonella infection A02.21
specified cause NEC G03.8
typhoid fever A01.01
varicella B01.0
viral disease NEC A87.8
whooping cough A37.90
zoster B02.1
infectious G00.9
influenzal (H. influenzae) G00.0
Klebsiella G00.8
leptospiral (aseptic) A27.81
lymphocytic (acute) (benign) (serous) A87.2
meningococcal A39.0
Mima polymorpha G00.8
Mollaret (benign recurrent) G03.2
monilial B37.5
mycotic NEC B49 *[G02]*
Neisseria A39.0
nonbacterial G03.0
nonpyogenic NEC G03.0
ossificans G96.19
pneumococcal G00.1
poliovirus A80.9 *[G02]*
postmeasles B05.1
purulent G00.9
specified organism NEC G00.8
pyogenic G00.9
specified organism NEC G00.8
Salmonella (arizonae) (Cholerae-Suis) (enteritidis) (typhimurium) A02.21
septic G00.9
specified organism NEC G00.8
serosa circumscripta NEC G03.0
serous NEC G93.2
specified organism NEC G00.8
sporotrichosis B42.81
staphylococcal G00.3
sterile G03.0
streptococcal (acute) G00.2
suppurative G00.9
specified organism NEC G00.8
syphilitic (late) (tertiary) A52.13
acute A51.41
congenital A50.41
secondary A51.41
Torula histolytica (cryptococcal) B45.1
traumatic (complication of injury) T79.8
tuberculous A17.0
typhoid A01.01
viral NEC A87.9
Yersinia pestis A20.3

Meningocele (spinal) —*see also* Spina bifida
with hydrocephalus —*see* Spina bifida, by site, with hydrocephalus
acquired (traumatic) G96.19
cerebral —*see* Encephalocele

Meningocerebritis —*see* Meningoencephalitis

Meningococcemia A39.4
acute A39.2
chronic A39.3

Meningococcus, meningococcal —*see also* condition A39.9
adrenalitis, hemorrhagic A39.1
carrier (suspected) of Z22.31
meningitis (cerebrospinal) A39.0

Meningoencephalitis —*see also* Encephalitis G04.90
acute NEC —*see also* Encephalitis, viral A86
bacterial NEC G04.2
California A83.5
diphasic A84.1
eosinophilic B83.2
epidemic A39.81
herpesviral, herpetic B00.4
due to herpesvirus 6 B10.01
due to herpesvirus 7 B10.09
specified NEC B10.09
in (due to)
blastomycosis NEC B40.81
diseases classified elsewhere G05.3
free-living amebae B60.2
Hemophilus influenzae (H .influenzae) G04.2
herpes B00.4
due to herpesvirus 6 B10.01
due to herpesvirus 7 B10.09
specified NEC B10.09
H. influenzae G00.0
Lyme disease A69.22
mercury —*see* subcategory T56.1
mumps B26.2
Naegleria (amebae) (organisms) (fowleri) B60.2
Parastrongylus cantonensis B83.2
toxoplasmosis (acquired) B58.2
congenital P37.1
infectious (acute) (viral) A86
influenzal (H. influenzae) G04.2
Listeria monocytogenes A32.12
lymphocytic (serous) A87.2
mumps B26.2
parasitic NEC B89 *[G05.3]*
pneumococcal G00.1
primary amebic B60.2
specific (syphilitic) A52.14
specified organism NEC G04.81
staphylococcal G04.2
streptococcal G04.2
syphilitic A52.14
toxic NEC G92
due to mercury —*see* subcategory T56.1
tuberculous A17.82
virus NEC A86

Meningoencephalocele —*see also* Encephalocele
syphilitic A52.19
congenital A50.49

Meningoencephalomyelitis —*see also* Meningoencephalitis
acute NEC (viral) A86
disseminated G04.00
postimmunization or postvaccination G04.02
postinfectious G04.01
due to
actinomycosis A42.82
Torula B45.1

Meningoencephalomyelitis *(continue*
due to *(continued)*
Toxoplasma or toxoplasmosis (acquired) B58.2
congenital P37.1
postimmunization or postvaccinatio
G04.02

Meningoencephalomyelopathy G96.

Meningoencephalopathy G96.9

Meningomyelitis —*see also* Meningoencephalitis
bacterial NEC G04.2
blastomycotic NEC B40.81
cryptococcal B45.1
in diseases classified elsewhere G05
meningococcal A39.81
syphilitic A52.14
tuberculous A17.82

Meningomyelocele —*see also* Spina bifida
syphilitic A52.19

Meningomyeloneuritis —*see* Meningoencephalitis

Meningoradiculitis —*see* Meningitis

Meningovascular —*see* condition

Menkes' disease or syndrome E83.09
meaning maple-syrup-urine disease E71.0

Menometrorrhagia N92.1

Menopause, menopausal (asymptomatic) (state) Z78.0
arthritis (any site) NEC —*see* Arthritis, specified form NEC
bleeding N92.4
depression (single episode) F32.8
agitated (single episode) F32.2
recurrent episode F33.9
psychotic (single episode) F32.8
recurrent episode F33.9
recurrent episode F33.9
melancholia (single episode) F32.8
recurrent episode F33.9
paranoid state F22
premature E28.319
asymptomatic E28.319
postirradiation E89.40
postsurgical E89.40
symptomatic E28.310
postirradiation E89.41
postsurgical E89.41
psychosis NEC F28
symptomatic N95.1
toxic polyarthritis NEC —*see* Arthritis, specified form NEC

Menorrhagia (primary) N92.0
climacteric N92.4
menopausal N92.4
menopausal N92.4
postclimacteric N95.0
postmenopausal N95.0
preclimacteric or premenopausal N92.4
pubertal (menses retained) N92.2

Menostaxis N92.0

Menses, retention N94.89

Menstrual —*see* Menstruation

Menstruation
absent —*see* Amenorrhea
anovulatory N97.0
cycle, irregular N92.6
delayed N91.0
disorder N93.9
psychogenic F45.8
during pregnancy O20.8
excessive (with regular cycle) N92.0
with irregular cycle N92.1
at puberty N92.2

Menstruation *(continued)*
- frequent N92.0
- infrequent *—see* Oligomenorrhea
- irregular N92.6
  - specified NEC N92.5
- latent N92.5
- membranous N92.5
- painful *—see also* Dysmenorrhea N94.6
  - primary N94.4
  - psychogenic F45.8
  - secondary N94.5
- passage of clots N92.0
- precocious E30.1
- protracted N92.5
- rare *—see* Oligomenorrhea
- retained N94.89
- retrograde N92.5
- scanty *—see* Oligomenorrhea
- suppression N94.89
- vicarious (nasal) N94.89

Mental *—see also* condition
- deficiency *—see* Disability, intellectual
- deterioration *—see* Psychosis
- disorder *—see* Disorder, mental
- exhaustion F48.8
- insufficiency (congenital) *—see* Disability, intellectual
- observation without need for further medical care Z03.89
- retardation *—see* Disability, intellectual
- subnormality *—see* Disability, intellectuall
- upset *—see* Disorder, mental

Meralgia paresthetica G57.1-

Mercurial *—see* condition

Mercurialism *—see* subcategory T56.1

MERRF syndrome (myoclonic epilepsy associated with ragged-red fiber) E88.42

Merkel cell tumor *—see* Carcinoma, Merkel cell

Merocele *—see* Hernia, femoral

Meromelia
- lower limb *—see* Defect, reduction, lower limb
  - intercalary
    - femur *—see* Defect, reduction, lower limb, specified type NEC
    - tibiofibular (complete) (incomplete) *—see* Defect, reduction, lower limb
- upper limb *—see* Defect, reduction, upper limb
  - intercalary, humeral, radioulnar *—see* Agenesis, arm, with hand present

Merzbacher-Pelizaeus disease E75.29

Mesaortitis *—see* Aortitis

Mesarteritis *—see* Arteritis

Mesencephalitis *—see* Encephalitis

Mesenchymoma *—see also* Neoplasm, connective tissue, uncertain behavior
- benign *—see* Neoplasm, connective tissue, benign
- malignant *—see* Neoplasm, connective tissue, malignant

Mesenteritis
- retractile K65.4
- sclerosing K65.4

Mesentery, mesenteric *—see* condition

Mesiodens, mesiodentes K00.1

Mesio-occlusion M26.213

Mesocolon *—see* condition

Mesonephroma (malignant) *—see* Neoplasm, malignant, by site
- benign *—see* Neoplasm, benign, by site

Mesophlebitis *—see* Phlebitis

Mesostromal dysgenesia Q13.89

Mesothelioma (malignant) C45.9
- benign
  - mesentery D19.1
  - mesocolon D19.1
  - omentum D19.1
  - peritoneum D19.1
  - pleura D19.0
  - specified site NEC D19.7
  - unspecified site D19.9
- biphasic C45.9
  - benign
    - mesentery D19.1
    - mesocolon D19.1
    - omentum D19.1
    - peritoneum D19.1
    - pleura D19.0
    - specified site NEC D19.7
    - unspecified site D19.9
- cystic D48.4
- epithelioid C45.9
  - benign
    - mesentery D19.1
    - mesocolon D19.1
    - omentum D19.1
    - peritoneum D19.1
    - pleura D19.0
    - specified site NEC D19.7
    - unspecified site D19.9
- fibrous C45.9
  - benign
    - mesentery D19.1
    - mesocolon D19.1
    - omentum D19.1
    - peritoneum D19.1
    - pleura D19.0
    - specified site NEC D19.7
    - unspecified site D19.9
- site classification
  - liver C45.7
  - lung C45.7
  - mediastinum C45.7
  - mesentery C45.1
  - mesocolon C45.1
  - omentum C45.1
  - pericardium C45.2
  - peritoneum C45.1
  - pleura C45.0
    - parietal C45.0
  - retroperitoneum C45.7
  - specified site NEC C45.7
  - unspecified C45.9

Metabolic syndrome E88.81

Metagonimiasis B66.8

Metagonimus infestation (intestine) B66.8

Metal
- pigmentation L81.8
- polisher's disease J62.8

Metamorphopsia H53.15

Metaplasia
- apocrine (breast) *—see* Dysplasia, mammary, specified type NEC
- cervix (squamous) *—see* Dysplasia, cervix
- endometrium (squamous) (uterus) N85.8
- esophagus
- kidney (pelvis) (squamous) N28.89
- myelogenous D73.1
- myeloid (agnogenic) (megakaryocytic) D73.1

Metaplasia *(continued)*
- spleen D73.1
- squamous cell, bladder N32.89

Metastasis, metastatic
- abscess *—see* Abscess
- calcification E83.59
- cancer
  - from specified site *—see* Neoplasm, malignant, by site
  - to specified site *—see* Neoplasm, secondary, by site
- deposits (in) *—see* Neoplasm, secondary, by site
- disease *—see also* Neoplasm, secondary, by site C79.9
- spread (to) *—see* Neoplasm, secondary, by site

Metastrongyliasis B83.8

Metatarsalgia M77.4-
- anterior G57.6-
- Morton's G57.6-

Metatarsus, metatarsal *—see also* condition
- valgus (abductus), congenital Q66.6
- varus (adductus) (congenital) Q66.2

Methadone use F11.20

Methemoglobinemia D74.9
- acquired (with sulfhemoglobinemia) D74.8
- congenital D74.0
- enzymatic (congenital) D74.0
- Hb M disease D74.0
- hereditary D74.0
- toxic D74.8

Methemoglobinuria *—see* Hemoglobinuria

Methioninemia E72.19

Methylmalonic acidemia E71.120

Metritis (catarrhal) (hemorrhagic) (septic) (suppurative) *—see also* Endometritis
- cervical *—see* Cervicitis

Metropathia hemorrhagica N93.8

Metroperitonitis *—see* Peritonitis, pelvic, female

Metrorrhagia N92.1
- climacteric N92.4
- menopausal N92.4
- postpartum NEC (atonic) (following delivery of placenta) O72.1
  - delayed or secondary O72.2
- preclimacteric or premenopausal N92.4
- psychogenic F45.8

Metrorrhexis *—see* Rupture, uterus

Metrosalpingitis N70.91

Metrostaxis N93.8

Metrovaginitis *—see* Endometritis

Meyer-Schwickerath and Weyers syndrome Q87.0

Meynert's amentia (nonalcoholic) F04
- alcoholic F10.96
  - with dependence F10.26

Mibelli's disease (porokeratosis) Q82.8

Mice, joint *—see* Loose, body, joint
- knee M23.4-

Micrencephalon, micrencephaly Q02

Microalbuminuria R80.9

Microaneurysm, retinal *—see also* Disorder, retina, microaneurysms
- diabetic *—see* E08-E13 with .31

Microangiopathy (peripheral) I73.9
- thrombotic M31.1

Microcalcifications, breast R92.0

Microcephalus, microcephalic, microcephaly Q02
- due to toxoplasmosis (congenital) P37.1

Microcheilia Q18.7

Microcolon (congenital) Q43.8

Microcornea (congenital) Q13.4

Microcytic *—see* condition

Microdeletions NEC Q93.88

Microdontia K00.2

Microdrepanocytosis D57.40
- with crisis (vasoocclusive pain) D57.419
  - with
    - acute chest syndrome D57.411
    - splenic sequestration D57.412

Microembolism
- atherothrombotic *—see* Atheroembolism
- retinal *—see* Occlusion, artery, retina

Microencephalon Q02

Microfilaria streptocerca infestation *—see* Onchocerciasis

Microgastria (congenital) Q40.2

Microgenia M26.06

Microgenitalia, congenital
- female Q52.8
- male Q55.8

Microglioma *—see* Lymphoma, non-Hodgkin, specified NEC

Microglossia (congenital) Q38.3

Micrognathia, micrognathism (congenital) (mandibular) (maxillary) M26.09

Microgyria (congenital) Q04.3

Microinfarct of heart *—see* Insufficiency, coronary

Microlentia (congenital) Q12.8

Microlithiasis, alveolar, pulmonary J84.02

Micromastia N64.82

Micromyelia (congenital) Q06.8

Micropenis Q55.62

Microphakia (congenital) Q12.8

Microphthalmos, microphthalmia (congenital) Q11.2
- due to toxoplasmosis P37.1

Micropsia H53.15

Microscopic polyangiitis (polyarteritis) M31.7

Microsporidiosis B60.8
- intestinal A07.8

Microsporon furfur infestation B36.0

Microsporosis *—see also* Dermatophytosis
- nigra B36.1

Microstomia (congenital) Q18.5

Microtia (congenital) (external ear) Q17.2

Microtropia H50.40

Microvillus inclusion disease (MVD) (MVID) Q43.8

Micturition
- disorder NEC R39.19
  - psychogenic F45.8
- frequency R35.0
  - psychogenic F45.8
- hesitancy R39.11
- incomplete emptying R39.14

Micturition *(continued)*
- nocturnal R35.1
- painful R30.9
  - dysuria R30.0
  - psychogenic F45.8
  - tenesmus R30.1
- poor stream R39.12
- split stream R39.13
- straining R39.16
- urgency R39.15

Mid plane *—see* condition

Middle
- ear *—see* condition
- lobe (right) syndrome J98.19

Miescher's elastoma L87.2

Mietens' syndrome Q87.2

Migraine (idiopathic) G43.909
- with refractory migraine G43.919
  - with status migrainosus G43.911
  - without status migrainosus G43.919
- with aura (acute-onset) (prolonged) (typical) (without headache) G43.109
  - with refractory migraine G43.119
    - with status migrainosus G43.111
    - without status migrainosus G43.119
  - intractable G43.119
    - with status migrainosus G43.111
    - without status migrainosus G43.119
  - not intractable G43.109
    - with status migrainosus G43.101
    - without status migrainosus G43.109
  - persistent G43.509
    - with cerebral infarction G43.609
      - with refractory migraine G43.619
        - with status migrainosus G43.611
        - without status migrainosus G43.619
      - intractable G43.619
        - with status migrainosus G43.611
        - without status migrainosus G43.619
      - not intractable G43.609
        - with status migrainosus G43.601
        - without status migrainosus G43.609
      - without refractory migraine G43.609
        - with status migrainosus G43.601
        - without status migrainosus G43.609
    - without cerebral infarction G43.509
      - with refractory migraine G43.519
        - with status migrainosus G43.511
        - without status migrainosus G43.519
      - intractable G43.519
        - with status migrainosus G43.511
        - without status migrainosus G43.519
      - not intractable G43.509
        - with status migrainosus G43.501
        - without status migrainosus G43.509

Migraine *(continued)*
- with aura *(continued)*
  - persistent *(continued)*
    - without cerebral infarction *(continued)*
      - without refractory migraine G43.509
        - with status migrainosus G43.501
        - without status migrainosus G43.509
  - without mention of refractory migraine G43.109
    - with status migrainosus G43.101
    - without status migrainosus G43.109
- abdominal G43.D0
  - with refractory migraine G43.D1
  - intractable G43.D1
  - not intractable G43.D0
  - without refractory migraine G43.D0
- basilar *—see* Migraine, with aura
- classical *—see* Migraine, with aura
- common *—see* Migraine, without aura
- complicated G43.109
- equivalents *—see* Migraine, with aura
- familiar *—see* Migraine, hemiplegic
- hemiplegic G43.409
  - with refractory migraine G43.419
    - with status migrainosus G43.411
    - without status migrainosus G43.419
  - intractable G43.419
    - with status migrainosus G43.411
    - without status migrainosus G43.419
  - not intractable G43.409
    - with status migrainosus G43.401
    - without status migrainosus G43.409
  - without refractory migraine G43.409
    - with status migrainosus G43.401
    - without status migrainosus G43.409
- intractable G43.919
  - with status migrainosus G43.911
  - without status migrainosus G43.919
- menstrual G43.829
  - with refractory migraine G43.839
    - with status migrainosus G43.831
    - without status migrainosus G43.839
  - intractable G43.839
    - with status migrainosus G43.831
    - without status migrainosus G43.839
  - not intractable 4G43.829
    - with status migrainosus G43.821
    - without status migrainosus G43.829
  - without refractory migraine G43.829
    - with status migrainosus G43.821
    - without status migrainosus G43.829
- menstrually related *—see* Migraine, menstrual
- not intractable G43.909
  - with status migrainosus G43.901
  - without status migrainosus G43.919
- ophthalmoplegic G43.B0
  - with refractory migraine G43.B1
  - intractable G43.B1
  - not intractable G43.B0
  - without refractory migraine G43.B0

Migraine *(continued)*
- persistent aura (with, without)
  - cerebral infarction *—see* Migraine, with aura, persistent
- preceded or accompanied by transient focal neurological phenomena *—see* Migraine, with aura
- pre-menstrual *—see* Migraine, menstrual
- pure menstrual *—see* Migraine, menstrual
- retinal *—see* Migraine, with aura
- specified NEC G43.809
  - intractable G43.819
    - with status migrainosus G43.811
    - without status migrainosus G43.819
  - not intractable G43.809
    - with status migrainosus G43.801
    - without status migrainosus G43.809
- sporadic *—see* Migraine, hemiplegic
- transformed *—see* Migraine, without aura, chronic
- triggered seizures *—see* Migraine, with aura
- without aura G43.009
  - with refractory migraine G43.019
    - with status migrainosus G43.011
    - without status migrainosus G43.019
  - chronic G43.709
    - with refractory migraine G43.719
      - with status migrainosus G43.711
      - without status migrainosus G43.719
    - intractable
      - with status migrainosus G43.711
      - without status migrainosus G43.719
    - not intractable
      - with status migrainosus G43.701
      - without status migrainosus G43.709
    - without refractory migraine G43.709
      - with status migrainosus G43.701
      - without status migrainosus G43.709
  - intractable
    - with status migrainosus G43.011
    - without status migrainosus G43.019
  - not intractable
    - with status migrainosus G43.001
    - without status migrainosus G43.009
  - without mention of refractory migraine G43.009
    - with status migrainosus G43.001
    - without status migrainosus G43.009
- without refractory migraineG43.909
  - with status migrainosus G43.901
  - without status migrainosus G43.919

Migrant, social Z59.0

Migration, anxiety concerning Z60.3

Migratory, migrating *—see also* condition
- person Z59.0
- testis Q55.29

Mikity-Wilson disease or syndrome P27.0

Mikulicz' disease or syndrome K11.8

Miliaria L74.3
- alba L74.1
- apocrine L75.2
- crystallina L74.1
- profunda L74.2
- rubra L74.0
- tropicalis L74.2

Miliary *—see* condition

Milium L72.0
- colloid L57.8

Milk
- crust L21.0
- excessive secretion O92.6
- poisoning *—see* Poisoning, food, noxious
- retention O92.79
- sickness *—see* Poisoning, food, noxious
- spots I31.0

Milk-alkali disease or syndrome E83.52

Milk-leg (deep vessels) (nonpuerperal) *—see* Embolism, vein, lower extremity
- complicating pregnancy O22.3-
- puerperal, postpartum, childbirth O87.1

Milkman's disease or syndrome M83.8

Milky urine *—see* Chyluria

Millard-Gubler (-Foville) **paralysis or syndrome** G46.3

Millar's asthma J38.5

Miller Fisher syndrome G61.0

Mills' disease *—see* Hemiplegia

Millstone maker's pneumoconiosis J62.8

Milroy's disease (chronic hereditary edema) Q82.0

Minamata disease T26.1-

Miners' asthma or lung J60

Minkowski-Chauffard syndrome *— see* Spherocytosis

Minor *—see* condition

Minor's disease (hematomyelia) G95.19

Minot's disease (hemorrhagic disease), **newborn** P53

Minot-von Willebrand-Jurgens disease or syndrome (angiohemophilia) D68.0

Minus (and plus) hand (intrinsic) *—see* Deformity, limb, specified type NEC, forearm

Miosis (pupil) H57.03

Mirizzi's syndrome (hepatic duct stenosis) K83.1

Mirror writing F81.0

Misadventure (of) (prophylactic) (therapeutic) *—see also* Complications T88.9
- administration of insulin (by accident) T38.3
- infusion *—see* Complications, infusion
- local applications (of fomentations, plasters, etc.) T88.9
  - burn or scald *—see* Burn
  - specified NEC T88.8
- medical care (early) (late) T88.9
  - adverse effect of drugs or chemicals *—see* Table of Drugs and Chemicals

Morgagni-Stokes-Adams syndrome I45.9

Morgagni-Stewart-Morel syndrome M85.2

Morgagni-Turner (-Albright) **syndrome** Q96.9

Moria F07.0

Moron (I.Q.50-69) F70

Morphea L94.0

Morphinism (without remission) F11.20
- with remission F11.21

Morphinomania (without remission) F11.20
- with remission F11.21

Morquio (-Ullrich) (-Brailsford) **disease or syndrome** *—see* Mucopolysaccharidosis

Mortification (dry) (moist) *—see* Gangrene

Morton's metatarsalgia (neuralgia) (neuroma) (syndrome) G57.6-

Morvan's disease or syndrome G60.8

Mosaicism, mosaic (autosomal) (chromosomal)
- 45,X/other cell lines NEC with abnormal sex chromosome Q96.4
- 45,X/46,XX Q96.3
- sex chromosome
  - female Q97.8
  - lines with various numbers of X chromosomes Q97.2
  - male Q98.7
- XY Q96.3

Moschowitz' disease M31.1

Mother yaw A66.0

Motion sickness (from travel, any vehicle) (from roundabouts or swings) T75.3

Mottled, mottling, teeth (enamel) (endemic) (nonendemic) K00.3

Mounier-Kuhn syndrome Q32.4
- with bronchiectasis J47.9
  - exacerbation (acute) J47.1
  - lower respiratory infection J47.0
- acquired J98.09
  - with bronchiectasis J47.9
    - with
      - exacerbation (acute) J47.1
      - lower respiratory infection J47.0

Mountain
- sickness T70.29
  - with polycythemia, acquired (acute) D75.1
- tick fever A93.2

Mouse, joint *—see* Loose, body, joint knee M23.4-

Mouth *—see* condition

Movable
- coccyx *—see* subcategory M53.2
- kidney N28.89
  - congenital Q63.8
- spleen D73.89

Movements, dystonic R25.8

Moyamoya disease I67.5

MRSA (Methicillin resistant Staphylococcus aureus)
- infection A49.02
  - as the cause of diseases classified elsewhere B95.62
- sepsis A41.02

MSSA (Methicillin susceptible Staphylococcus aureus)
- infection A49.01
  - as the cause of diseases classified elsewhere B95.61
- sepsis A41.01

Mucha-Habermann disease L41.0

Mucinosis (cutaneous) (focal) (papular) (reticular erythematous) (skin) L98.5
- oral K13.79

Mucocele
- appendix K38.8
- buccal cavity K13.79
- gallbladder K82.1
- lacrimal sac, chronic H04.43-
- nasal sinus J34.1
- nose J34.1
- salivary gland (any) K11.6
- sinus (accessory) (nasal) J34.1
- turbinate (bone) (middle) (nasal) J34.1
- uterus N85.8

Mucolipidosis
- I E77.1
- II, III E77.0
- IV E75.11

Mucopolysaccharidosis E76.3
- beta-gluduronidase deficiency E76.29
- cardiopathy E76.3 *[I52]*
- Hunter's syndrome E76.1
- Hurler's syndrome E76.01
- Hurler-Scheie syndrome E76.02
- Maroteaux-Lamy syndrome E76.29
- Morquio syndrome E76.219
  - A E76.210
  - B E76.211
  - classic E76.210
- Sanfilippo syndrome E76.22
- Scheie's syndrome E76.03
- specified NEC E76.29
- type
  - I
    - Hurler's syndrome E76.01
    - Hurler-Scheie syndrome E76.02
    - Scheie's syndrome E76.03
  - II E76.1
  - III E76.22
  - IV E76.219
  - IVA E76.210
  - IVB E76.211
  - VI E76.29
  - VII E76.29

Mucormycosis B46.5
- cutaneous B46.3
- disseminated B46.4
- gastrointestinal B46.2
- generalized B46.4
- pulmonary B46.0
- rhinocerebral B46.1
- skin B46.3
- subcutaneous B46.3

Mucositis (ulcerative) K12.30
- due to drugs NEC K12.32
- gastrointestinal K92.81
- mouth (oral) (oropharyngeal) K12.30
  - due to antineoplastic therapy K12.31
  - due to drugs NEC K12.32
  - due to radiation K12.33
  - specified NEC K12.39
  - viral K12.39
- nasal J34.81
- oral cavity *—see* Mucositis, mouth
- oral soft tissues *—see* Mucositis, mouth
- vagina and vulva N76.81

Mucositis necroticans agranulocytica *—see* Agranulocytosis

Mucous *—see also* condition
- patches (syphilitic) A51.39
  - congenital A50.07

Mucoviscidosis E84.9
- with meconium obstruction E84.11

Mucus
- asphyxia or suffocation *—see* Asphyxia, mucus
- in stool R19.5
- plug *—see* Asphyxia, mucus

Muguet B37.0

Mulberry molars (congenital syphilis) A50.52

Müllerian mixed tumor
- specified site *—see* Neoplasm, malignant, by site
- unspecified site C54.9

Multicystic kidney (development) Q61.4

Multiparity (grand) Z64.1
- affecting management of pregnancy, labor and delivery (supervision only) O09.4-
- requiring contraceptive management *—see* Contraception

Multipartita placenta O43.19-

Multiple, multiplex *—see also* condition
- digits (congenital) Q69.9
- endocrine neoplasia *—see* Neoplasia, endocrine, multiple (MEN)
- personality F44.81

Mumps B26.9
- arthritis B26.85
- complication NEC B26.89
- encephalitis B26.2
- hepatitis B26.81
- meningitis (aseptic) B26.1
- meningoencephalitis B26.2
- myocarditis B26.82
- oophoritis B26.89
- orchitis B26.0
- pancreatitis B26.3
- polyneuropathy B26.84

Mumu *—see also* Infestation, filarial B74.9 *[N51]*

Münchhausen's syndrome *—see* Disorder, factitious

Münchmeyer's syndrome *—see* Myositis, ossificans, progressiva

Mural *—see* condition

Murmur (cardiac) (heart) (organic) R01.1
- abdominal R19.15
- aortic (valve) *—see* Endocarditis, aortic
- benign R01.0
- diastolic *—see* Endocarditis
- Flint I35.1
- functional R01.0
- Graham Steell I37.1
- innocent R01.0
- mitral (valve) *—see* Insufficiency, mitral
- nonorganic R01.0
- presystolic, mitral *—see* Insufficiency, mitral
- pulmonic (valve) I37.8
- systolic (valvular) *—see* Endocarditis
- tricuspid (valve) I07.9
- valvular *—see* Endocarditis

Murri's disease (intermittent hemoglobinuria) D59.6

Muscle, muscular *—see also* condition
- carnitine (palmityltransferase) deficiency E71.314

Musculoneuralgia *—see* Neuralgia

Mushroom-workers'(pickers') **disease or lung** J67.5

Mushrooming hip *—see* Derangement, joint, specified NEC, hip

Mutation (s)
- factor V Leiden D68.51
- surfactant, of lung J84.83
- prothrombin gene D68.52

Mutism *—see also* Aphasia
- deaf (acquired) (congenital) NEC H91.3
- elective (adjustment reaction) (childhood) F94.0
- hysterical F44.4
- selective (childhood) F94.0

MVD (microvillus inclusion disease) Q43.8

MVID (microvillus inclusion disease) Q43.8

Myalgia M79.1
- epidemic (cervical) B33.0
- traumatic NEC T14.8

Myasthenia G70.9
- congenital G70.2
- cordis *—see* Failure, heart
- developmental G70.2
- gravis G70.00
  - with exacerbation (acute) G70.01
  - in crisis G70.01
  - neonatal, transient P94.0
  - pseudoparalytica G70.00
    - with exacerbation (acute) G70.01
    - in crisis G70.01
- stomach, psychogenic F45.8
- syndrome
  - in
    - diabetes mellitus *—see* E08-E13 with .44
    - neoplastic disease *—see also* Neoplasm D49.9 *[G73.3]*
    - pernicious anemia D51.0 *[G73.3]*
    - thyrotoxicosis E05.90 *[G73.3]*
      - with thyroid storm E05.91 *[G73.3]*

Myasthenic M62.81

Mycelium infection B49

Mycetismus *—see* Poisoning, food, noxious, mushroom

Mycetoma B47.9
- actinomycotic B47.1
- bone (mycotic) B47.9 *[M90.80]*
- eumycotic B47.0
- foot B47.9
  - actinomycotic B47.1
  - mycotic B47.0
- madurae NEC B47.9
  - mycotic B47.0
- maduromycotic B47.0
- mycotic B47.0
- nocardial B47.1

Mycobacteriosis *—see* Mycobacterium

Mycobacterium, mycobacterial (infection) A31.9
- anonymous A31.9
- atypical A31.9
  - cutaneous A31.1
  - pulmonary A31.0
    - tuberculous *—see* Tuberculosis, pulmonary
  - specified site NEC A31.8
- avium (intracellulare complex) A31.0
- balnei A31.1
- Battey A31.0
- chelonei A31.8

ycobacterium, mycobacterial *(continued)*
cutaneous A31.1
extrapulmonary systemic A31.8
fortuitum A31.8
intracellulare (Battey bacillus) A31.0
kansasii (yellow bacillus) A31.0
kakaferifu A31.8
kasongo A31.8
leprae —*see also* Leprosy A30.9
luciflavum A31.1
marinum (M. balnei) A31.1
nonspecific —*see* Mycobacterium, atypical
pulmonary (atypical) A31.0
tuberculous —*see* Tuberculosis, pulmonary
scrofulaceum A31.8
simiae A31.8
systemic, extrapulmonary A31.8
szulgai A31.8
terrae A31.8
triviale A31.8
tuberculosis (human, bovine) - see Tuberculosis
ulcerans A31.1
xenopi A31.8

lycoplasma (M.) **pneumoniae, as cause of disease classified elsewhere** B96.0

lycosis, mycotic B49
cutaneous NEC B36.9
ear B36.8
fungoides (extranodal) (solid organ) C84.0-
mouth B37.0
nails B35.1
opportunistic B48.8
skin NEC B36.9
specified NEC B48.8
stomatitis B37.0
vagina, vaginitis (candidal) B37.3

lydriasis (pupil) H57.04

lyelatelia Q06.1

lyelinolysis, pontine, central G37.2

lyelitis (acute) (ascending) (childhood) (chronic) (descending) (diffuse) (disseminated) (idiopathic) (pressure) (progressive) (spinal cord) (subacute) —*see also* Encephalitis G04.91
herpes simplex B00.82
herpes zoster B02.24
in diseases classified elsewhere G05.4
necrotizing, subacute G37.4
optic neuritis in G36.0
postchickenpox B01.12
postherpetic B02.24
postimmunization G04.02
postinfectious NEC G04.89
postvaccinal G04.02
specified NEC G04.89
syphilitic (transverse) A52.14
toxic G92
transverse (in demyelinating diseases of central nervous system) G37.3
tuberculous A17.82
varicella B01.12

Myeloblastic —*see* condition

Myeloblastoma
granular cell —*see also* Neoplasm, connective tissue
malignant —*see* Neoplasm, connective tissue, malignant
tongue D10.1

Myelocele —*see* Spina bifida

Myelocystocele —*see* Spina bifida

Myelocytic —*see* condition

Myelodysplasia D46.9
specified NEC D46.Z
spinal cord (congenital) Q06.1

Myelodysplastic syndrome D46.9
with
5q deletion D46.C
isolated del (5q) chromosomal abnormality D46.C
specified NEC D46.Z

Myeloencephalitis —*see* Encephalitis

Myelofibrosis D75.81
with myeloid metaplasia D47.4
acute C94.4-
idiopathic (chronic) D47.4
primary D47.1
secondary D75.81
in myeloproliferative disease D47.4

Myelogenous —*see* condition

Myeloid —*see* condition

Myelokathexis D70.9

Myeloleukodystrophy E75.29

Myelolipoma —*see* Lipoma

Myeloma (multiple) C90.0-
monostotic C90.3
plasma cell C90.0-
plasma cell C90.0-
solitary —*see also* Plasmacytoma, solitary C90.3-

Myelomalacia G95.89

Myelomatosis C90.0-

Myelomeningitis —*see* Meningoencephalitis

Myelomeningocele (spinal cord) —*see* Spina bifida

Myelo-osteo-musculodysplasia hereditaria Q79.8

Myelopathic
anemia D64.89
muscle atrophy —*see* Atrophy, muscle, spinal
pain syndrome G89.0

Myelopathy (spinal cord) G95.9
drug-induced G95.89
in (due to)
degeneration or displacement, intervertebral disc NEC —*see* Disorder, disc, with, myelopathy
infection —*see* Encephalitis
intervertebral disc disorder —*see also* Disorder, disc, with, myelopathy
mercury —*see* subcategory T56.1
neoplastic disease —*see also* Neoplasm D49.9 *[G99.2]*
pernicious anemia D51.0 *[G99.2]*
spondylosis —*see* Spondylosis, with myelopathy NEC
necrotic (subacute) (vascular) G95.19
radiation-induced G95.89
spondylogenic NEC —*see* Spondylosis, with myelopathy NEC
toxic G95.89
transverse, acute G37.3
vascular G95.19
vitamin B12 E53.8 *[G32.0]*

Myelophthisis D61.82

Myeloradiculitis G04.91

Myeloradiculodysplasia (spinal) Q06.1

Myelosarcoma C92.3-

Myelosclerosis D75.89
with myeloid metaplasia D47.4
disseminated, of nervous system G35
megakaryocytic D47.4
with myeloid metaplasia D47.4

Myelosis
acute C92.0-
aleukemic C92.9-
chronic D47.1
erythremic (acute) C94.0-
megakaryocytic C94.2-
nonleukemic D72.828
subacute C92.9-

Myiasis (cavernous) B87.9
aural B87.4
creeping B87.0
cutaneous B87.0
dermal B87.0
ear (external) (middle) B87.4
eye B87.2
genitourinary B87.81
intestinal B87.82
laryngeal B87.3
nasopharyngeal B87.3
ocular B87.2
orbit B87.2
skin B87.0
specified site NEC B87.89
traumatic B87.1
wound B87.1

Myoadenoma, prostate —*see* Hyperplasia, prostate

Myoblastoma
granular cell —*see also* Neoplasm, connective tissue, benign
malignant —*see* Neoplasm, connective tissue, malignant
tongue D10.1

Myocardial —*see* condition

Myocardiopathy (congestive) (constrictive) (familial) (hypertrophic nonobstructive) (idiopathic) (infiltrative) (obstructive) (primary) (restrictive) (sporadic) —*see also* Cardiomyopathy I42.9
alcoholic I42.6
cobalt-beer I42.6
glycogen storage E74.02 *[I43]*
hypertrophic obstructive I42.1
in (due to)
beriberi E51.12
cardiac glycogenosis E74.02 *[I43]*
Friedreich's ataxia G11.1 *[I43]*
myotonia atrophica G71.11 *[I43]*
progressive muscular dystrophy G71.0 *[I43]*
obscure (African) I42.8
secondary I42.9
thyrotoxic E05.90 *[I43]*
with storm E05.91 *[I43]*
toxic NEC I42.7

Myocarditis (with arteriosclerosis) (chronic) (fibroid) (interstitial) (old) (progressive) (senile) I51.4
with
rheumatic fever (conditions in I00) I09.0
active —*see* Myocarditis, acute, rheumatic
inactive or quiescent (with chorea) I09.0
active I40.9
rheumatic I01.2
with chorea (acute) (rheumatic) (Sydenham's) I02.0
acute or subacute (interstitial) I40.9
due to
streptococcus (beta-hemolytic) I01.2
idiopathic I40.1
rheumatic I01.2
with chorea (acute) (rheumatic) (Sydenham's) I02.0
specified NEC I40.8

Myocarditis *(continued)*
aseptic of newborn B33.22
bacterial (acute) I40.0
Coxsackie (virus) B33.22
diphtheritic A36.81
eosinophilic I40.1
epidemic of newborn (Coxsackie) B33.22
Fiedler's (acute) (isolated) I40.1
giant cell (acute) (subacute) I40.1
gonococcal A54.83
granulomatous (idiopathic) (isolated) (nonspecific) I40.1
hypertensive —*see* Hypertension, heart
idiopathic (granulomatous) I40.1
in (due to)
diphtheria A36.81
epidemic louse-borne typhus A75.0 *[I41]*
Lyme disease A69.29
sarcoidosis D86.85
scarlet fever A38.1
toxoplasmosis (acquired) B58.81
typhoid A01.02
typhus NEC A75.9 *[I41]*
infective I40.0
influenzal —*see* Influenza, with, myocarditis
isolated (acute) I40.1
meningococcal A39.52
mumps B26.82
nonrheumatic, active I40.9
parenchymatous I40.9
pneumococcal I40.0
rheumatic (chronic) (inactive) (with chorea) I09.0
active or acute I01.2
with chorea (acute) (rheumatic) (Sydenham's) I02.0
rheumatoid —*see* Rheumatoid, carditis
septic I40.0
staphylococcal I40.0
suppurative I40.0
syphilitic (chronic) A52.06
toxic I40.8
rheumatic —*see* Myocarditis, acute, rheumatic
tuberculous A18.84
typhoid A01.02
valvular —*see* Endocarditis
virus, viral I40.0
of newborn (Coxsackie) B33.22

Myocardium, myocardial —*see* condition

Myocardosis —*see* Cardiomyopathy

Myoclonus, myoclonic, myoclonia (familial) (essential) (multifocal) (simplex) G25.3
drug-induced G25.3
epilepsy —*see also* Epilepsy, generalized, specified NEC G40.4-
familial (progressive) G25.3
epileptica G40.409
with status epilepticus G40.401
facial G51.3
familial progressive G25.3
Friedreich's G25.3
jerks G25.3
massive G25.3
palatal G25.3
pharyngeal G25.3

Myocytolysis I51.5

Myodiastasis —*see* Diastasis, muscle

Myoendocarditis —*see* Endocarditis

Myoepithelioma —*see* Neoplasm, benign, by site

Myofasciitis (acute) —*see* Myositis

- **Myofibroma** —*see also* Neoplasm, connective tissue, benign
  - uterus (cervix) (corpus) —*see* Leiomyoma
- **Myofibromatosis** D48.1
  - infantile Q89.8
- **Myofibrosis** M62.89
  - heart —*see* Myocarditis
  - scapulohumeral —*see* Lesion, shoulder, specified NEC
- **Myofibrositis** M79.7
  - scapulohumeral —*see* Lesion, shoulder, specified NEC
- **Myoglobulinuria, myoglobinuria** (primary) R82.1
- **Myokymia, facial** G51.4
- **Myolipoma** —*see* Lipoma
- **Myoma** —*see also* Neoplasm, connective tissue, benign
  - malignant —*see* Neoplasm, connective tissue, malignant
  - prostate D29.1
  - uterus (cervix) (corpus) —*see* Leiomyoma
- **Myomalacia** M62.89
- **Myometritis** —*see* Endometritis
- **Myometrium** —*see* condition
- **Myonecrosis, clostridial** A48.0
- **Myopathy** G72.9
  - acute
    - necrotizing G72.81
    - quadriplegic G72.81
  - alcoholic G72.1
  - benign congenital G71.2
  - central core G71.2
  - centronuclear G71.2
  - congenital (benign) G71.2
  - critical illness G72.81
  - distal G71.0
  - drug-induced G72.0
  - endocrine NEC E34.9 *[G73.7]*
  - extraocular muscles H05.82-
  - facioscapulohumeral G71.0
  - hereditary G71.9
    - specified NEC G71.8
  - immune NEC G72.49
  - in (due to)
    - Addison's disease E27.1 *[G73.7]*
    - alcohol G72.1
    - amyloidosis E85.0 *[G73.7]*
    - cretinism E00.9 *[G73.7]*
    - Cushing's syndrome E24.9 *[G73.7]*
    - drugs G72.0
    - endocrine disease NEC E34.9 *[G73.7]*
    - giant cell arteritis M31.6 *[G73.7]*
    - glycogen storage disease E74.00 *[G73.7]*
    - hyperadrenocorticism E24.9 *[G73.7]*
    - hyperparathyroidism NEC E21.3 *[G73.7]*
    - hypoparathyroidism E20.9 *[G73.7]*
    - hypopituitarism E23.0 *[G73.7]*
    - hypothyroidism E03.9 *[G73.7]*
    - infectious disease NEC B99 *[G73.7]*
    - lipid storage disease E75.6 *[G73.7]*
    - metabolic disease NEC E88.9 *[G73.7]*
    - myxedema E03.9 *[G73.7]*
    - parasitic disease NEC B89 *[G73.7]*
    - polyarteritis nodosa M30.0 *[G73.7]*
    - rheumatoid arthritis —*see* Rheumatoid, myopathy
    - sarcoidosis D86.87
    - scleroderma M34.82
    - sicca syndrome M35.03

- **Myopathy** *(continued)*
  - in *(continued)*
    - Sjögren's syndrome M35.03
    - systemic lupus erythematosus M32.19
    - thyrotoxicosis (hyperthyroidism) E05.90 *[G73.7]*
      - with thyroid storm E05.91 *[G73.7]*
    - toxic agent NEC G72.2
  - inflammatory NEC G72.49
  - intensive care (ICU) G72.81
  - limb-girdle G71.0
  - mitochondrial NEC G71.3
  - mytonic, proximal (PROMM) G71.11
  - myotubular G71.2
  - nemaline G71.2
  - ocular G71.0
  - oculopharyngeal G71.0
  - of critical illness G72.81
  - primary G71.9
    - specified NEC G71.8
  - progressive NEC G72.89
  - proximal myotonic (PROMM) G71.11
  - rod G71.2
  - scapulohumeral G71.0
  - specified NEC G72.89
  - toxic G72.2
- **Myopericarditis** —*see also* Pericarditis
  - chronic rheumatic I09.2
- **Myopia** (axial) (congenital) H52.1-
  - degenerative (malignant) H44.2-
  - malignant H44.2-
  - pernicious H44.2-
  - progressive high (degenerative) H44.2-
- **Myosarcoma** —*see* Neoplasm, connective tissue, malignant
- **Myosis** (pupil) H57.03
  - stromal (endolymphatic) D39.0
- **Myositis** M60.9
  - clostridial A48.0
  - due to posture —*see* Myositis, specified type NEC
  - epidemic B33.0
  - fibrosa or fibrous (chronic), Volkmann's T79.6
  - foreign body granuloma —*see* Granuloma, foreign body
  - in (due to)
    - bilharziasis B65.9 *[M63.8]-*
    - cysticercosis B69.81
    - leprosy A30.9 *[M63.8]-*
    - mycosis B49 *[M63.8]-*
    - sarcoidosis D86.87
    - schistosomiasis B65.9 *[M63.8]-*
    - syphilis
      - late A52.78
      - secondary A51.49
    - toxoplasmosis (acquired) B58.82
    - trichinellosis B75 *[M63.8]-*
    - tuberculosis A18.09
  - inclusion body [IBM] G72.41
  - infective M60.009
    - arm M60.002
      - left M60.001
      - right M60.000
    - leg M60.005
      - left M60.004
      - right M60.003
    - lower limb M60.005
      - ankle M60.07-
      - foot M60.07-
      - lower leg M60.06-
      - thigh M60.05-
      - toe M60.07-
    - multiple sites M60.09
    - specified site NEC M60.08

- **Myositis** *(continued)*
  - infective *(continued)*
    - upper limb M60.002
      - finger M60.04-
      - forearm M60.03-
      - hand M60.04-
      - shoulder region M60.01-
      - upper arm M60.02-
  - interstitial M60.10
    - ankle M60.17-
    - foot M60.17-
    - forearm M60.13-
    - hand M60.14-
    - lower leg M60.16-
    - multiple sites M60.19
    - shoulder region M60.11-
    - specified site NEC M60.18
    - thigh M60.15-
    - upper arm M60.12-
  - mycotic B49 *[M63.8]-*
  - orbital, chronic H05.12-
  - ossificans or ossifying (circumscripta) —*see also* Ossification, muscle, specified NEC
    - in (due to)
      - burns M61.30
        - ankle M61.37-
        - foot M61.37-
        - forearm M61.33-
        - hand M61.34-
        - lower leg M61.36-
        - multiple sites M61.39
        - pelvic region M61.35-
        - shoulder region M61.31-
        - specified site NEC M61.38
        - thigh M61.35-
        - upper arm M61.32-
      - quadriplegia or paraplegia M61.20
        - ankle M61.27-
        - foot M61.27-
        - forearm M61.23-
        - hand M61.24-
        - lower leg M61.26-
        - multiple sites M61.29
        - pelvic region M61.25-
        - shoulder region M61.21-
        - specified site NEC M61.28
        - thigh M61.25-
        - upper arm M61.22-
    - progressiva M61.10
      - ankle M61.17-
      - finger M61.14-
      - foot M61.17-
      - forearm M61.13-
      - hand M61.14-
      - lower leg M61.16-
      - multiple sites M61.19
      - pelvic region M61.15-
      - shoulder region M61.11-
      - specified site NEC M61.18
      - thigh M61.15-
      - toe M61.17-
      - upper arm M61.12-
    - traumatica M61.00
      - ankle M61.07-
      - foot M61.07-
      - forearm M61.03-
      - hand M61.04-
      - lower leg M61.06-
      - multiple sites M61.09
      - pelvic region M61.05-
      - shoulder region M61.01-
      - specified site NEC M61.08
      - thigh M61.05-
      - upper arm M61.02-
  - purulent —*see* Myositis, infective
  - specified type NEC M60.80
    - ankle M60.87-
    - foot M60.87-
    - forearm M60.83-
    - hand M60.84-

- **Myositis** *(continued)*
  - specified type NEC *(continued)*
    - lower leg M60.86-
    - multiple sites M60.89
    - pelvic region M60.85-
    - shoulder region M60.81-
    - specified site NEC M60.88
    - thigh M60.85-
    - upper arm M60.82-
  - suppurative —*see* Myositis, infective
  - traumatic (old) —*see* Myositis, specified type NEC
- **Myospasia impulsiva** F95.2
- **Myotonia** (acquisita) (intermittens) M62.89
  - atrophica G71.11
  - chondrodystrophic G71.13
  - congenita (acetazolamide responsive (dominant) (recessive) G71.12
  - drug-induced G71.14
  - dystrophica G71.11
  - fluctuans G71.19
  - levior G71.12
  - permanens G71.19
  - symptomatic G71.19
- **Myotonic pupil** —*see* Anomaly, pupil, function, tonic pupil
- **Myriapodiasis** B88.2
- **Myringitis** H73.2-
  - with otitis media —*see* Otitis, media
  - acute H73.00-
    - bullous H73.01-
    - specified NEC H73.09-
  - bullous —*see* Myringitis, acute, bullous
  - chronic H73.1-
- **Mysophobia** F40.228
- **Mytilotoxism** —*see* Poisoning, fish
- **Myxadenitis labialis** K13.0
- **Myxedema** (adult) (idiocy) (infantile) (juvenile) —*see also* Hypothyroidism E03.9
  - circumscribed E05.90
    - with storm E05.91
  - coma E03.5
  - congenital E00.1
  - cutis L98.5
  - localized (pretibial) E05.90
    - with storm E05.91
  - papular L98.5
- **Myxochondrosarcoma** —*see* Neoplasm, cartilage, malignant
- **Myxofibroma** —*see* Neoplasm, connective tissue, benign
  - odontogenic —*see* Cyst, calcifying odontogenic
- **Myxofibrosarcoma** —*see* Neoplasm, connective tissue, malignant
- **Myxolipoma** D17.9
- **Myxoliposarcoma** —*see* Neoplasm, connective tissue, malignant
- **Myxoma** —*see also* Neoplasm, connective tissue, benign
  - nerve sheath —*see* Neoplasm, nerve, benign
  - odontogenic —*see* Cyst, calcifying odontogenic
- **Myxosarcoma** —*see* Neoplasm, connective tissue, malignant

N

- **Naegeli's**
  - disease Q82.8
  - leukemia, monocytic C93.1-

Neonatal *(continued)*
- tachycardia P29.11
- screening, abnormal findings on P09
- tooth, teeth K00.6

Neonatorum —*see* condition

Neoplasia
- endocrine, multiple (MEN) E31.20
  - type I E31.21
  - type IIA E31.22
  - type IIB E31.23
- intraepithelial (histologically confirmed)
  - anal (AIN) (histologically confirmed) K62.82
    - grade I K62.82
    - grade II K62.82
    - severe D01.3
  - cervical glandular (histologically confirmed) D06.9
  - cervix (uteri) (CIN) (histologically confirmed) N87.9
    - glandular D06.9
    - grade I N87.0
    - grade II N87.1
    - grade III (severe dysplasia) —*see also* Carcinoma, cervix uteri, in situ D06.9
  - prostate (histologically confirmed) (PIN I) (PIN II) N42.3
    - grade I N42.3
    - grade II N42.3
    - severe D07.5
  - vagina (histologically confirmed) (VAIN) N89.3
    - grade I N89.0
    - grade II N89.1
    - grade III (severe dysplasia) D07.2
  - vulva (histologically confirmed) (VIN) N90.3
    - grade I N90.0
    - grade II N90.1
    - grade III (severe dysplasia) D07.1

Neoplasm, neoplastic —*see also* Table of Neoplasms
- lipomatous, benign —*see* Lipoma

Neovascularization
- ciliary body —*see* Disorder, iris, vascular
- cornea H16.40-
  - deep H16.44-
  - ghost vessels —*see* Ghost, vessels
  - localized H16.43-
  - pannus —*see* Pannus
- iris —*see* Disorder, iris, vascular
- retina H35.05-

Nephralgia N23

Nephritis, nephritic (albuminuric) (azotemic) (congenital) (disseminated) (epithelial) (familial) (focal) (granulomatous) (hemorrhagic) (infantile) (nonsuppurative, excretory) (uremic) N05.9
- with
  - dense deposit disease N05.6
  - diffuse
    - crescentic glomerulonephritis N05.7
    - endocapillary proliferative glomerulonephritis N05.4
    - membranous glomerulonephritis N05.2
    - mesangial proliferative glomerulonephritis N05.3
    - mesangiocapillary glomerulonephritis N05.5
  - edema —*see* Nephrosis

Nephritis, nephritic *(continued)*
- with *(continued)*
  - focal and segmental glomerular lesions N05.1
  - foot process disease N04.9
  - glomerular lesion
    - diffuse sclerosing N05.8
    - hypocomplementemic —*see* Nephritis, membranoproliferative
    - IgA —*see* Nephropathy, IgA
    - lobular, lobulonodular —*see* Nephritis, membranoproliferative
    - nodular —*see* Nephritis, membranoproliferative
  - lesion of
    - glomerulonephritis, proliferative N05.8
    - renal necrosis N05.9
  - minor glomerular abnormality N05.0
  - specified morphological changes NEC N05.8
- acute N00.9
  - with
    - dense deposit disease N00.6
    - diffuse
      - crescentic glomerulonephritis N00.7
      - endocapillary proliferative glomerulonephritis N00.4
      - membranous glomerulonephritis N00.2
      - mesangial proliferative glomerulonephritis N00.3
      - mesangiocapillary glomerulonephritis N00.5
    - focal and segmental glomerular lesions N00.1
    - minor glomerular abnormality N00.0
    - specified morphological changes NEC N00.8
- amyloid E85.4 *[N08]*
- antiglomerular basement membrane (anti-GBM) antibody NEC
  - in Goodpasture's syndrome M31.0
- antitubular basement membrane (tubulo-interstitial) NEC N12
  - toxic —*see* Nephropathy, toxic
- arteriolar —*see* Hypertension, kidney
- arteriosclerotic —*see* Hypertension, kidney
- ascending —*see* Nephritis, tubulo-interstitial
- atrophic N03.9
- Balkan (endemic) N15.0
- calculous, calculus —*see* Calculus, kidney
- cardiac —*see* Hypertension, kidney
- cardiovascular —*see* Hypertension, kidney
- chronic N03.9
  - with
    - dense deposit disease N03.6
    - diffuse
      - crescentic glomerulonephritis N03.7
      - endocapillary proliferative glomerulonephritis N03.4
      - membranous glomerulonephritis N03.2
      - mesangial proliferative glomerulonephritis N03.3
      - mesangiocapillary glomerulonephritis N03.5
    - focal and segmental glomerular lesions N03.1
    - minor glomerular abnormality N03.0

Nephritis, nephritic *(continued)*
- chronic *(continued)*
  - with *(continued)*
    - specified morphological changes NEC N03.8
  - arteriosclerotic —*see* Hypertension, kidney
- cirrhotic N26.9
- complicating pregnancy O26.83-
- croupous N00.9
- degenerative —*see* Nephrosis
- diffuse sclerosing N05.8
- due to
  - diabetes mellitus —*see* E08-E13 with .21
  - subacute bacterial endocarditis I33.0
  - systemic lupus erythematosus (chronic) M32.14
  - typhoid fever A01.09
- gonococcal (acute) (chronic) A54.21
- hypocomplementemic —*see* Nephritis, membranoproliferative
- IgA —*see* Nephropathy, IgA
- immune complex (circulating) NEC N05.8
- infective —*see* Nephritis, tubulo-interstitial
- interstitial —*see* Nephritis, tubulo-interstitial
- lead N14.3
- membranoproliferative (diffuse) (type 1 or 3) —*see also* N00-N07 with fourth character .5 N05.5
  - type 2 —*see also* N00-N07 with fourth character .6 N05.6
- minimal change N05.0
- necrotic, necrotizing NEC —*see also* N00-N07 with fourth character .8 N05.8
- nephrotic —*see* Nephrosis
- nodular —*see* Nephritis, membranoproliferative
- polycystic Q61.3
  - adult type Q61.2
  - autosomal
    - dominant Q61.2
    - recessive NEC Q61.19
  - childhood type NEC Q61.19
  - infantile type NEC Q61.19
- poststreptococcal N05.9
  - acute N00.9
  - chronic N03.9
  - rapidly progressive N01.9
- proliferative NEC —*see also* N00-N07 with fourth character .8 N05.8
- purulent —*see* Nephritis, tubulo-interstitial
- rapidly progressive N01.9
  - with
    - dense deposit disease N01.6
    - diffuse
      - crescentic glomerulonephritis N01.7
      - endocapillary proliferative glomerulonephritis N01.4
      - membranous glomerulonephritis N01.2
      - mesangial proliferative glomerulonephritis N01.3
      - mesangiocapillary glomerulonephritis N01.5
    - focal and segmental glomerular lesions N01.1
    - minor glomerular abnormality N01.0
    - specified morphological changes NEC N01.8
- salt losing or wasting NEC N28.89
- saturnine N14.3
- sclerosing, diffuse N05.8

Nephritis, nephritic *(continued)*
- septic —*see* Nephritis, tubulo-interstitial
- specified pathology NEC —*see als*
  - N00-N07 with fourth character .
  - N05.8
- subacute N01.9
- suppurative —*see* Nephritis, tubulo interstitial
- syphilitic (late) A52.75
  - congenital A50.59 *[N08]*
  - early (secondary) A51.44
- toxic —*see* Nephropathy, toxic
- tubal, tubular —*see* Nephritis, tubu interstitial
- tuberculous A18.11
- tubulo-interstitial (in) N12
  - acute (infectious) N10
  - chronic (infectious) N11.9
    - nonobstructive N11.8
      - reflux-associated N11.0
    - obstructive N11.1
    - specified NEC N11.8
  - due to
    - brucellosis A23.9 *[N16]*
    - cryoglobulinemia D89.1 *[N16*
    - glycogen storage disease E74. *[N16]*
  - Sjögren's syndrome M35.04
- vascular —*see* Hypertension, kidne
- war N00.9

Nephroblastoma (epithelial) (mesenchymal) C64-

Nephrocalcinosis E83.59 *[N29]*

Nephrocystitis, pustular —*see* Nephritis, tubulo-interstitial

Nephrolithiasis (congenital) (pelvis) (recurrent) —*see also* Calculus, kidn

Nephroma C64-
- mesoblastic D41.0-

Nephronephritis —*see* Nephrosis

Nephronophthisis Q61.5

Nephropathia epidemica A98.5

Nephropathy —*see also* Nephritis N28
- with
  - edema —*see* Nephrosis
  - glomerular lesion —*see* Glomerulonephritis
- amyloid, hereditary E85.0
- analgesic N14.0
  - with medullary necrosis, acute N17
- Balkan (endemic) N15.0
- chemical —*see* Nephropathy, toxic
- diabetic —*see* E08-E13 with .21
- drug-induced N14.2
  - specified NEC N14.1
- focal and segmental hyalinosis or sclerosis N02.1
- heavy metal-induced N14.3
- hereditary NEC N07.9
  - with
    - dense deposit disease N07.6
    - diffuse
      - crescentic glomerulonephritis N07.7
      - endocapillary proliferative glomerulonephritis N07.4
      - membranous glomerulonephritis N07.2
      - mesangial proliferative glomerulonephritis N07.3
      - mesangiocapillary glomerulonephritis N07.5
    - focal and segmental glomerular lesions N07.1
    - minor glomerular abnormality N07.0
    - specified morphological changes NEC N07.8

phropathy *(continued)*
ıypercalcemic N25.89
ıypertensive *—see* Hypertension, kidney
ıypokalemic (vacuolar) N25.89
gA N02.8
with glomerular lesion N02.9
focal and segmental hyalinosis or sclerosis N02.1
membranoproliferative (diffuse) N02.5
membranous (diffuse) N02.2
mesangial proliferative (diffuse) N02.3
mesangiocapillary (diffuse) N02.5
proliferative NEC N02.8
specified pathology NEC N02.8
lead N14.3
membranoproliferative (diffuse) N02.5
membranous (diffuse) N02.2
mesangial (IgA/IgG) *—see* Nephropathy, IgA
proliferative (diffuse) N02.3
mesangiocapillary (diffuse) N02.5
obstructive N13.8
phenacetin N17.2
phosphate-losing N25.0
potassium depletion N25.89
pregnancy-related O26.83-
proliferative NEC *—see also* N00-N07 with fourth character .8
N05.8
protein-losing N25.89
saturnine N14.3
sickle-cell D57.- *[N08]*
toxic NEC N14.4
due to
drugs N14.2
analgesic N14.0
specified NEC N14.1
heavy metals N14.3
vasomotor N17.0
water-losing N25.89

ephroptosis N28.83

ephropyosis *—see* Abscess, kidney

ephrorrhagia N28.89

ephrosclerosis (arteriolar) (arteriosclerotic) (chronic) (hyaline) *—see also* Hypertension, kidney
hyperplastic *—see* Hypertension, kidney
senile N26.9

ephrosis, nephrotic (Epstein's) (syndrome) (congenital) N04.9
with
foot process disease N04.9
glomerular lesion N04.1
hypocomplementemic N04.5
acute N04.9
anoxic *—see* Nephrosis, tubular
chemical *—see* Nephrosis, tubular
cholemic K76.7
diabetic *—see* E08-E13 with .21
Finnish type (congenital) Q89.8
hemoglobin N10
hemoglobinuric *—see* Nephrosis, tubular
in
amyloidosis E85.4 *[N08]*
diabetes mellitus *—see* E08-E13 with .21
epidemic hemorrhagic fever A98.5
malaria (malariae) B52.0
ischemic *—see* Nephrosis, tubular
lipoid N04.9
lower nephron *—see* Nephrosis, tubular
malarial (malariae) B52.0

Nephrosis, nephrotic *(continued)*
minimal change N04.0
myoglobin N10
necrotizing *—see* Nephrosis, tubular
osmotic (sucrose) N25.89
radiation N04.9
syphilitic (late) A52.75
toxic *—see* Nephrosis, tubular
tubular (acute) N17.0
postprocedural N99.0
radiation N04.9

Nephrosonephritis, hemorrhagic (endemic) A98.5

Nephrostomy
attention to Z43.6
status Z93.6

Nerve *—see also* condition
injury *—see* Injury, nerve, by body site

Nerves R45.0

Nervous *—see also* condition R45.0
heart F45.8
stomach F45.8
tension R45.0

Nervousness R45.0

Nesidioblastoma
pancreas D13.7
specified site NEC *—see* Neoplasm, benign, by site
unspecified site D13.7

Nettleship's syndrome Q82.2

Neumann's disease or syndrome L10.1

Neuralgia, neuralgic (acute) M79.2
accessory (nerve) G52.8
acoustic (nerve) H93.3
auditory (nerve) H93.3
ciliary G44.009
intractable G44.001
not intractable G44.009
cranial
nerve *—see also* Disorder, nerve, cranial
fifth or trigeminal *—see* Neuralgia, trigeminal
postherpetic, postzoster B02.29
ear *—see* subcategory H92.0
facialis vera G51.1
Fothergill's *—see* Neuralgia, trigeminal
glossopharyngeal (nerve) G52.1
Horton's G44.099
intractable G44.091
not intractable G44.099
Hunt's B02.21
hypoglossal (nerve) G52.3
infraorbital *—see* Neuralgia, trigeminal
malarial *—see* Malaria
migrainous G44.009
intractable G44.001
not intractable G44.009
Morton's G57.6-
nerve, cranial *—see* Disorder, nerve, cranial
nose G52.0
occipital M54.81
olfactory G52.0
penis N48.9
perineum R10.2
postherpetic NEC B02.29
trigeminal B02.22
pubic region R10.2
scrotum R10.2
Sluder's G44.89
specified nerve NEC G58.8
spermatic cord R10.2
sphenopalatine (ganglion) G90.09

Neuralgia, neuralgic *(continued)*
trifacial *—see* Neuralgia, trigeminal
trigeminal G50.0
postherpetic, postzoster B02.22
vagus (nerve) G52.2
writer's F48.8
organic G25.89

Neurapraxia *—see* Injury, nerve

Neurasthenia F48.8
cardiac F45.8
gastric F45.8
heart F45.8

Neurilemmoma *—see also* Neoplasm, nerve, benign
acoustic (nerve) D33.3
malignant *—see also* Neoplasm, nerve, malignant
acoustic (nerve) C72.4-

Neurilemmosarcoma *—see* Neoplasm, nerve, malignant

Neurinoma *—see* Neoplasm, nerve, benign

Neurinomatosis *—see* Neoplasm, nerve, uncertain behavior

Neuritis (rheumatoid) M79.2
abducens (nerve) *—see* Strabismus, paralytic, sixth nerve
accessory (nerve) G52.8
acoustic (nerve) *—see also* subcategory H93.3
in (due to)
infectious disease NEC B99 *[H94.0]-*
parasitic disease NEC B89 *[H94.0]-*
syphilitic A52.15
alcoholic G62.1
with psychosis *—see* Psychosis, alcoholic
amyloid, any site E85.4 *[G63]*
auditory (nerve) *—see* subcategory H93.3
brachial *—see* Radiculopathy
due to displacement, intervertebral disc *—see* Disorder, disc, cervical, with neuritis
cranial nerve
due to Lyme disease A69.22
eighth or acoustic or auditory H93.3
eleventh or accessory G52.8
fifth or trigeminal G51.0
first or olfactory G52.0
fourth or trochlear *—see* Strabismus, paralytic, fourth nerve
second or optic *—see* Neuritis, optic
seventh or facial G51.8
newborn (birth injury) P11.3
sixth or abducent *—see* Strabismus, paralytic, sixth nerve
tenth or vagus G52.2
third or oculomotor *—see* Strabismus, paralytic, third nerve
twelfth or hypoglossal G52.3
Déjérine-Sottas G60.0
diabetic (mononeuropathy) *—see* E08-E13 with .41
polyneuropathy *—see* E08-E13 with .42
due to
beriberi E51.11
displacement, prolapse or rupture, intervertebral disc *—see* Disorder, disc, with, radiculopathy
herniation, nucleus pulposus M51.9 *[G55]*

Neuritis *(continued)*
endemic E51.11
facial G51.8
newborn (birth injury) P11.3
general *—see* Polyneuropathy
geniculate ganglion G51.1
due to herpes (zoster) B02.21
gouty M10.00 *[G63]*
hypoglossal (nerve) G52.3
ilioinguinal (nerve) G57.9-
infectious (multiple) NEC G61.0
interstitial hypertrophic progressive G60.0
lumbar M54.16
lumbosacral M54.17
multiple *—see also* Polyneuropathy
endemic E51.11
infective, acute G61.0
multiplex endemica E51.11
nerve root *—see* Radiculopathy
oculomotor (nerve) *—see* Strabismus, paralytic, third nerve
olfactory nerve G52.0
optic (nerve) (hereditary) (sympathetic) H46.9
with demyelination G36.0
in myelitis G36.0
nutritional H46.2
papillitis *—see* Papillitis, optic
retrobulbar H46.1-
specified type NEC H46.8
toxic H46.3
peripheral (nerve) G62.9
multiple *—see* Polyneuropathy
single *—see* Mononeuritis
pneumogastric (nerve) G52.2
postherpetic, postzoster B02.29
progressive hypertrophic interstitial G60.0
retrobulbar *—see also* Neuritis, optic, retrobulbar
in (due to)
late syphilis A52.15
meningococcal infection A39.82
meningococcal A39.82
syphilitic A52.15
sciatic (nerve) *—see also* Sciatica
due to displacement of intervertebral disc *—see* Disorder, disc, with, radiculopathy
serum *—see also* Reaction, serum T80.69
shoulder-girdle G54.5
specified nerve NEC G58.8
spinal (nerve) root *—see* Radiculopathy
syphilitic A52.15
thenar (median) G56.1-
thoracic M54.14
toxic NEC G62.2
trochlear (nerve) *—see* Strabismus, paralytic, fourth nerve
vagus (nerve) G52.2

Neuroastrocytoma *—see* Neoplasm, uncertain behavior, by site

Neuroavitaminosis E56.9 *[G99.8]*

Neuroblastoma
olfactory C30.0
specified site *—see* Neoplasm, malignant, by site
unspecified site C74.90

Neurochorioretinitis *—see* Chorioretinitis

Neurocirculatory asthenia F45.8

Neurocysticercosis B69.0

Neurocytoma *—see* Neoplasm, benign, by site

- **Neurodermatitis** (circumscribed) (circumscripta) (local) L28.0
  - atopic L20.81
  - diffuse (Brocq) L20.81
  - disseminated L20.81
- **Neuroencephalomyelopathy, optic** G36.0
- **Neuroepithelioma** *—see also* Neoplasm, malignant, by site
  - olfactory C30.0
- **Neurofibroma** *—see also* Neoplasm, nerve, benign
  - melanotic *—see* Neoplasm, nerve, benign
  - multiple *—see* Neurofibromatosis
  - plexiform *—see* Neoplasm, nerve, benign
- **Neurofibromatosis** (multiple) (nonmalignant) Q85.00
  - acoustic Q85.02
  - malignant *—see* Neoplasm, nerve, malignant
  - specified NEC Q85.09
  - type 1 (von Recklinghausen) Q85.01
  - type 2 Q85.02
- **Neurofibrosarcoma** *—see* Neoplasm, nerve, malignant
- **Neurogenic** *—see also* condition
  - bladder *—see also* Dysfunction, bladder, neuromuscular N31.9
    - cauda equina syndrome G83.4
  - bowel NEC K59.2
  - heart F45.8
- **Neuroglioma** *—see* Neoplasm, uncertain behavior, by site
- **Neurolabyrinthitis** (of Dix and Hallpike) *—see* Neuronitis, vestibular
- **Neurolathyrism** *—see* Poisoning, food, noxious, plant
- **Neuroleprosy** A30.9
- **Neuroma** *—see also* Neoplasm, nerve, benign
  - acoustic (nerve) D33.3
  - amputation (stump) (traumatic) (surgical complication) (late) T87.3-
    - arm T87.3-
    - leg T87.3-
  - digital (toe) G57.6-
  - interdigital (toe) G58.8
    - lower limb G57.8-
    - upper limb G56.8-
  - intermetatarsal G57.8-
  - Morton's G57.6-
  - nonneoplastic
    - arm G56.9-
    - leg G57.9-
    - lower extremity G57.9-
    - upper extremity G56.9-
  - optic (nerve) D33.3
  - plantar G57.6-
  - plexiform *—see* Neoplasm, nerve, benign
  - surgical (nonneoplastic)
    - arm G56.9-
    - leg G57.9-
    - lower extremity G57.9-
    - upper extremity G56.9-
- **Neuromyalgia** *—see* Neuralgia
- **Neuromyasthenia** (epidemic) (postinfectious) G93.3
- **Neuromyelitis** G36.9
  - ascending G61.0
  - optica G36.0
- **Neuromyopathy** G70.9
  - paraneoplastic D49.9 *[G13.0]*
- **Neuromyotonia** (Isaacs) G71.19
- **Neuronevus** *—see* Nevus
- **Neuronitis** G58.9
  - ascending (acute) G57.2-
  - vestibular H81.2-
- **Neuroparalytic** *—see* condition
- **Neuropathy, neuropathic** G62.9
  - acute motor G62.81
  - alcoholic G62.1
    - with psychosis *—see* Psychosis, alcoholic
  - arm G56.9-
  - autonomic, peripheral *—see* Neuropathy, peripheral, autonomic
  - axillary G56.9-
  - bladder N31.9
    - atonic (motor) (sensory) N31.2
    - autonomous N31.2
    - flaccid N31.2
    - nonreflex N31.2
    - reflex N31.1
    - uninhibited N31.0
  - brachial plexus G54.0
  - cervical plexus G54.2
  - chronic
    - progressive segmentally demyelinating G62.89
    - relapsing demyelinating G62.89
  - Déjérine-Sottas G60.0
  - diabetic *—see* E08-E13 with .40
    - mononeuropathy *—see* E08-E13 with .41
    - polyneuropathy *—see* E08-E13 with .42
  - entrapment G58.9
    - iliohypogastric nerve G57.8-
    - ilioinguinal nerve G57.8-
    - lateral cutaneous nerve of thigh G57.1-
    - median nerve G56.0-
    - obturator nerve G57.8-
    - peroneal nerve G57.3-
    - posterior tibial nerve G57.5-
    - saphenous nerve G57.8-
    - ulnar nerve G56.2-
  - facial nerve G51.9
  - hereditary G60.9
    - motor and sensory (types I-IV) G60.0
    - sensory G60.8
    - specified NEC G60.8
  - hypertrophic G60.0
    - Charcot-Marie-Tooth G60.0
    - Déjérine-Sottas G60.0
    - interstitial progressive G60.0
    - of infancy G60.0
    - Refsum G60.1
  - idiopathic G60.9
    - progressive G60.3
    - specified NEC G60.8
  - in association with hereditary ataxia G60.2
  - intercostal G58.0
  - ischemic *—see* Disorder, nerve
  - Jamaica (ginger) G62.2
  - leg NEC G57.9-
  - lower extremity G57.9-
  - lumbar plexus G54.1
  - median nerve G56.1-
  - motor and sensory *—see also* Polyneuropathy
    - hereditary (types I-IV) G60.0
  - multiple (acute) (chronic) *—see* Polyneuropathy
  - optic (nerve) *—see also* Neuritis, optic
    - ischemic H47.01-
  - paraneoplastic (sensorial) (Denny Brown) D49.9 *[G13.0]*

Neuropathy, neuropathic *(continued)*

  - peripheral (nerve) *—see also* Polyneuropathy G62.9
    - autonomic G90.9
      - idiopathic G90.09
      - in (due to)
        - amyloidosis E85.4 *[G99.0]*
        - diabetes mellitus *—see* E08-E13 with .43
        - endocrine disease NEC E34.9 *[G99.0]*
        - gout M10.00 *[G99.0]*
        - hyperthyroidism E05.90 *[G99.0]*
          - with thyroid storm E05.91 *[G99.0]*
        - metabolic disease NEC E88.9 *[G99.0]*
    - idiopathic G60.9
      - progressive G60.3
    - in (due to)
      - antitetanus serum G62.0
      - arsenic G62.2
      - drugs NEC G62.0
      - lead G62.2
      - organophosphate compounds G62.2
      - toxic agent NEC G62.2
  - plantar nerves G57.6-
  - progressive
    - hypertrophic interstitial G60.0
    - inflammatory G62.81
  - radicular NEC *—see* Radiculopathy
  - sacral plexus G54.1
  - sciatic G57.0-
  - serum G61.1
  - toxic NEC G62.2
  - trigeminal sensory G50.8
  - ulnar nerve G56.2-
  - uremic N18.9 *[G63]*
  - vitamin B12 *[E53.8]* G63
    - with anemia (pernicious) D51.0 *[G63]*
      - due to dietary deficiency D51.3 *[G63]*
- **Neurophthisis** *—see also* Disorder, nerve
  - peripheral, diabetic *—see* E08-E13 with .42
- **Neuroretinitis** *—see* Chorioretinitis
- **Neuroretinopathy, hereditary optic** H47.22
- **Neurosarcoma** *—see* Neoplasm, nerve, malignant
- **Neurosclerosis** *—see* Disorder, nerve
- **Neurosis, neurotic** F48.9
  - anankastic F42
  - anxiety (state) F41.1
    - panic type F41.0
  - asthenic F48.8
  - bladder F45.8
  - cardiac (reflex) F45.8
  - cardiovascular F45.8
  - character F60.9
  - colon F45.8
  - compensation F68.1
  - compulsive, compulsion F42
  - conversion F44.9
  - craft F48.8
  - cutaneous F45.8
  - depersonalization F48.1
  - depressive (reaction) (type) F34.1
  - environmental F48.8
  - excoriation L98.1
  - fatigue F48.8
  - functional *—see* Disorder, somatoform
  - gastric F45.8
  - gastrointestinal F45.8
  - heart F45.8

Neurosis, neurotic *(continued)*

  - hypochondriacal F45.21
  - hysterical F44.9
  - incoordination F45.8
    - larynx F45.8
    - vocal cord F45.8
  - intestine F45.8
  - larynx (sensory) F45.8
    - hysterical F44.4
  - mixed NEC F48.8
  - musculoskeletal F45.8
  - obsessional F42
  - obsessive-compulsive F42
  - occupational F48.8
  - ocular NEC F45.8
  - organ *—see* Disorder, somatoform
  - pharynx F45.8
  - phobic F40.9
  - posttraumatic (situational) F43.10
    - acute F43.11
    - chronic F43.12
  - psychasthenic (type) F48.8
  - railroad F48.8
  - rectum F45.8
  - respiratory F45.8
  - rumination F45.8
  - sexual F65.9
  - situational F48.8
  - social F40.10
    - generalized F40.11
  - specified type NEC F48.8
  - state F48.9
    - with depersonalization episode F48.1
  - stomach F45.8
  - traumatic F43.10
    - acute F43.11
    - chronic F43.12
  - vasomotor F45.8
  - visceral F45.8
  - war F48.8
- **Neurospongioblastosis diffusa** Q85.1
- **Neurosyphilis** (arrested) (early) (gumma) (late) (latent) (recurrent) (relapse) A52.3
  - with ataxia (cerebellar) (locomotor) (spastic) (spinal) A52.19
  - aneurysm (cerebral) A52.05
  - arachnoid (adhesive) A52.13
  - arteritis (any artery) (cerebral) A52.0
  - asymptomatic A52.2
  - congenital A50.40
  - dura (mater) A52.13
  - general paresis A52.17
  - hemorrhagic A52.05
  - juvenile (asymptomatic) (meningeal) A50.40
  - leptomeninges (aseptic) A52.13
  - meningeal, meninges (adhesive) A52.13
  - meningitis A52.13
  - meningovascular (diffuse) A52.13
  - optic atrophy A52.15
  - parenchymatous (degenerative) A52.19
  - paresis, paretic A52.17
    - juvenile A50.45
  - remission in (sustained) A52.3
  - serological (without symptoms) A52.2
  - specified nature or site NEC A52.19
  - tabes, tabetic (dorsalis) A52.11
    - juvenile A50.45
  - taboparesis A52.17
    - juvenile A50.45
  - thrombosis (cerebral) A52.05
  - vascular (cerebral) NEC A52.05
- **Neurothekeoma** *—see* Neoplasm, nerve, benign
- **Neurotic** *—see* Neurosis

- **urotoxemia** —*see* Toxemia
- **utroclusion** M26.211
- **utropenia, neutropenic** (chronic) (genetic) (idiopathic) (immune) (infantile) (malignant) (pernicious) (splenic) D70.9
  - congenital (primary) D70.0
  - cyclic D70.4
  - cytoreductive cancer chemotherapy sequela D70.1
  - drug-induced D70.2
    - due to cytoreductive cancer chemotherapy D70.1
  - due to infection D70.3
  - fever D70.9
  - neonatal, transitory (isoimmune) (maternal transfer) P61.5
  - periodic D70.4
  - secondary (cyclic) (periodic) (splenic) D70.4
    - drug-induced D70.2
      - due to cytoreductive cancer chemotherapy D70.1
  - toxic D70.8
- **eutrophilia, hereditary giant** D72.0
- **evocarcinoma** —*see* Melanoma
- **evus** D22.9
  - achromic —*see* Neoplasm, skin, benign
  - amelanotic —*see* Neoplasm, skin, benign
  - angiomatousD18.00
    - intra-abdominal D18.03
    - intracranial D18.02
    - skin D18.01
    - specified site NEC D18.09
  - araneus I78.1
  - balloon cell —*see* Neoplasm, skin, benign
  - bathing trunk D48.5
  - blue —*see* Neoplasm, skin, benign
    - cellular —*see* Neoplasm, skin, benign
    - giant —*see* Neoplasm, skin, benign
    - Jadassohn's —*see* Neoplasm, skin, benign
    - malignant —*see* Melanoma
  - capillary D18.00
    - intra-abdominal D18.03
    - intracranial D18.02
    - skin D18.01
    - specified site NEC D18.09
  - cavernous D18.00
    - intra-abdominal D18.03
    - intracranial D18.02
    - skin D18.01
    - specified site NEC D18.09
  - cellular —*see* Neoplasm, skin, benign
    - blue —*see* Neoplasm, skin, benign
  - choroid D31.3-
  - comedonicus Q82.5
  - conjunctiva D31.0-
  - dermal —*see* Neoplasm, skin, benign
    - with epidermal nevus —*see* Neoplasm, skin, benign
  - dysplastic —*see* Neoplasm, skin, benign
  - eye D31.9-
  - flammeus Q82.5
  - hemangiomatous D18.00
    - intra-abdominal D18.03
    - intracranial D18.02
    - skin D18.01
    - specified site NEC D18.09
  - iris D31.4-
  - lacrimal gland D31.5-
  - lymphatic D18.1
  - magnocellular
    - specified site —*see* Neoplasm, benign, by site
    - unspecified site D31.40

Nevus *(continued)*

  - malignant —*see* Melanoma
  - meaning hemangioma D18.00
    - intra-abdominal D18.03
    - intracranial D18.02
    - skin D18.01
    - specified site NEC D18.09
  - mouth (mucosa) D10.30
    - specified site NEC D10.39
    - white sponge Q38.6
  - multiplex Q85.1
  - non-neoplastic I78.1
  - oral mucosa D10.30
    - specified site NEC D10.39
    - white sponge Q38.6
  - orbit D31.6-
  - pigmented
    - giant —*see also* Neoplasm, skin, uncertain behavior D48.5
      - malignant melanoma in —*see* Melanoma
  - portwine Q82.5
  - retina D31.2-
  - retrobulbar D31.6-
  - sanguineous Q82.5
  - senile I78.1
  - skin D22.9
    - abdominal wall D22.5
    - ala nasi D22.39
    - ankle D22.7-
    - anus, anal D22.5
    - arm D22.6-
    - auditory canal (external) D22.2-
    - auricle (ear) D22.2-
    - auricular canal (external) D22.2-
    - axilla, axillary fold D22.5
    - back D22.5
    - breast D22.5
    - brow D22.39
    - buttock D22.5
    - canthus (eye) D22.1-
    - cheek (external) D22.39
    - chest wall D22.5
    - chin D22.39
    - ear (external) D22.2-
    - external meatus (ear) D22.2-
    - eyebrow D22.39
    - eyelid (lower) (upper) D22.1-
    - face D22.30
      - specified NEC D22.39
    - female genital organ (external) NEC D28.0
    - finger D22.6-
    - flank D22.5
    - foot D22.7-
    - forearm D22.6-
    - forehead D22.39
    - foreskin D29.0
    - genital organ (external) NEC
      - female D28.0
      - male D29.9
    - gluteal region D22.5
    - groin D22.5
    - hand D22.6-
    - heel D22.7-
    - helix D22.2-
    - hip D22.7-
    - interscapular region D22.5
    - jaw D22.39
    - knee D22.7-
    - labium (majus) (minus) D28.0
    - leg D22.7-
    - lip (lower) (upper) D22.0
    - lower limb D22.7-
    - male genital organ (external) D29.9
    - nail D22.9
      - finger D22.6-
      - toe D22.7-
    - nasolabial groove D22.39
    - nates D22.5
    - neck D22.4
    - nose (external) D22.39

Nevus *(continued)*

  - skin *(continued)*
    - palpebra D22.1-
    - penis D29.0
    - perianal skin D22.5
    - perineum D22.5
    - pinna D22.2-
    - popliteal fossa or space D22.7-
    - prepuce D29.0
    - pudendum D28.0
    - scalp D22.4
    - scrotum D29.4
    - shoulder D22.6-
    - submammary fold D22.5
    - temple D22.39
    - thigh D22.7-
    - toe D22.7-
    - trunk NEC D22.5
    - umbilicus D22.5
    - upper limb D22.6-
    - vulva D28.0
  - specified site NEC —*see* Neoplasm, by site, benign
  - spider I78.1
  - stellar I78.1
  - strawberry Q82.5
  - Sutton's —*see* Neoplasm, skin, benign
  - unius lateris Q82.5
  - Unna's Q82.5
  - vascular Q82.5
  - verrucous Q82.5
- **Newborn** (infant) (liveborn) (singleton) Z38.2
  - acne L70.4
  - abstinence syndrome P96.1
  - affected by (suspected to be)
    - abnormalities of membranes P02.9
      - specified NEC P02.8
    - abruptio placenta P02.1
    - amino-acid metabolic disorder, transitory P74.8
    - amniocentesis (while in utero) P00.6
    - amnionitis P02.7
    - apparent life threatening event (ALTE) R68.13
    - bleeding (into)
      - cerebral cortex P52.22
      - germinal matrix P52.0
      - ventricles P52.1
    - breech delivery P03.0
    - cardiac arrest P29.81
    - cardiomyopathy I42.8
      - congenital I42.4
    - cerebral ischemia P91.0
    - Cesarean delivery P03.4
    - chemotherapy agents P04.1
    - chorioamnionitis P02.7
    - cocaine (crack) P04.41
    - complications of labor and delivery P03.9
      - specified NEC P03.89
    - compression of umbilical cord NEC P02.5
    - contracted pelvis P03.1
    - delivery P03.9
      - Cesarean P03.4
      - forceps P03.2
      - vacuum extractor P03.3
    - environmental chemicals P04.6
    - entanglement (knot) in umbilical cord P02.5
    - fetal (intrauterine)
      - growth retardation P05.9
      - malnutrition not light or small for gestational age P05.2
    - forceps delivery P03.2
    - heart rate abnormalities
      - bradycardia P29.12

Newborn *(continued)*

  - affected by *(continued)*
    - heart rate abnormalities *(continued)*
      - intrauterine P03.819
        - before onset of labor P03.810
        - during labor P03.811
      - tachycardia P29.11
    - hemorrhage (antepartum) P02.1
      - cerebellar (nontraumatic) P52.6
      - intracerebral (nontraumatic) P52.4
      - intracranial (nontraumatic) P52.9
        - specified NEC P52.8
      - intraventricular (nontraumatic) P52.3
        - grade 1 P52.0
        - grade 2 P52.1
        - grade 3 P52.21
        - grade 4 P52.22
      - posterior fossa (nontraumatic) P52.6
      - subarachnoid (nontraumatic) P52.5
      - subependymal P52.0
        - with intracerebral extension P52.22
        - with intraventricular extension P52.1
          - with enlargment of ventricles P52.21
        - without intraventricular extension P52.0
    - hypoxic ischemic encephalopathy [HIE] P91.60
      - mild P91.61
      - moderate P91.62
      - severe P91.63
    - induction of labor P03.89
    - intestinal perforation P78.0
    - intrauterine (fetal) blood loss P50.9
      - due to (from)
        - cut end of co-twin cord P50.5
        - hemorrhage into
          - co-twin P50.3
          - maternal circulation P50.4
        - placenta P50.2
        - ruptured cord blood P50.1
        - vasa previa P50.0
      - specified NEC P50.8
    - intrauterine (fetal) hemorrhage P50.9
    - intrauterine (in utero) procedure P96.5
    - malpresentation (malposition) NEC P03.1
    - maternal (complication of) (use of)
      - alcohol P04.3
      - analgesia (maternal) P04.0
      - anesthesia (maternal) P04.0
      - blood loss P02.1
      - circulatory disease P00.3
      - condition P00.9
        - specified NEC P00.89
      - delivery P03.9
        - Cesarean P03.4
        - forceps P03.2
        - vacuum extractor P03.3
      - diabetes mellitus (pre-existing) P70.1
      - disorder P00.9
        - specified NEC P00.89
      - drugs (addictive) (illegal) NEC P04.49
      - ectopic pregnancy P01.4
      - gestational diabetes P70.0
      - hemorrhage P02.1
      - hypertensive disorder P00.0
      - incompetent cervix P01.0
      - infectious disease P00.2
      - injury P00.5
      - labor and delivery P03.9

Obstruction, obstructed, obstructive *(continued)*
- device, implant or graft —*see also* Complications, by site and type, mechanical T85.698
  - arterial graft NEC —*see* Complication, cardiovascular device, mechanical, vascular
  - catheter NEC T85.628
    - cystostomy T83.090
    - dialysis (renal) T82.49
      - intraperitoneal T85.691
    - infusion NEC T82.594
      - spinal (epidural) (subdural) T85.690
    - urinary, indwelling T83.098
  - due to infection T85.79
  - gastrointestinal —*see* Complications, prosthetic device, mechanical, gastrointestinal device
  - genital NEC T83.498
    - intrauterine contraceptive device T83.39
    - penile prosthesis T83.490
  - heart NEC —*see* Complication, cardiovascular device, mechanical
  - joint prosthesis —*see* Complications, joint prosthesis, mechanical, specified NEC, by site
  - orthopedic NEC —*see* Complication, orthopedic, device, mechanical
  - specified NEC T85.628
  - urinary NEC —*see also* Complication, genitourinary, device, urinary, mechanical
    - graft T83.29
  - vascular NEC —*see* Complication, cardiovascular device, mechanical
  - ventricular intracranial shunt T85.09
- due to foreign body accidentally left in operative wound T81.529
- duodenum K31.5
- ejaculatory duct N50.8
- esophagus K22.2
- eustachian tube (complete) (partial) H68.10-
  - cartilagenous (extrinsic) H68.13-
    - intrinsic H68.12-
  - osseous H68.11-
- fallopian tube (bilateral) N97.1
- fecal K56.41
  - with hernia —*see* Hernia, by site, with obstruction
- foramen of Monro (congenital) Q03.8
  - with spina bifida —*see* Spina bifida, by site, with hydrocephalus
- foreign body —*see* Foreign body
- gallbladder K82.0
  - with calculus, stones K80.21
  - congenital Q44.1
- gastric outlet K31.1
- gastrointestinal —*see* Obstruction, intestine
- hepatic K76.89
  - duct (noncalculous) K83.1
- hepatobiliary K83.1
- ileum —*see* Obstruction, intestine
- iliofemoral (artery) I74.5
- intestine K56.60
  - with
    - adhesions (intestinal) (peritoneal) K56.5
  - adynamic K56.0
  - by gallstone K56.3

Obstruction, obstructed, obstructive *(continued)*
- intestine *(continued)*
  - congenital (small) Q41.9
    - large Q42.9
      - specified part NEC Q42.8
  - neurogenic K56.0
    - Hirschsprung's disease or megacolon Q43.1
  - newborn P76.9
    - due to
      - fecaliths P76.8
      - inspissated milk P76.2
      - meconium (plug) P76.0
        - in mucoviscidosis E84.11
    - specified NEC P76.8
  - postoperative K91.3
  - reflex K56.0
  - specified NEC K56.69
  - volvulus K56.2
- intracardiac ball valve prosthesis T82.09
- jejunum —*see* Obstruction, intestine
- joint prosthesis —*see* Complications, joint prosthesis, mechanical, specified NEC, by site
- kidney (calices) N28.89
- labor —*see* Delivery
- lacrimal (passages) (duct)
  - by
    - dacryolith —*see* Dacryolith
    - stenosis —*see* Stenosis, lacrimal
  - congenital Q10.5
  - neonatal H04.53-
- lacrimonasal duct —*see* Obstruction, lacrimal
- lacteal, with steatorrhea K90.2
- laryngitis —*see* Laryngitis
- larynx NEC J38.6
  - congenital Q31.8
- lung J98.4
  - disease, chronic J44.9
- lymphatic I89.0
- meconium (plug)
  - newborn P76.0
    - due to fecaliths P76.0
    - in mucoviscidosis E84.11
- mitral —*see* Stenosis, mitral
- nasal J34.89
- nasolacrimal duct —*see also* Obstruction, lacrimal
  - congenital Q10.5
- nasopharynx J39.2
- nose J34.89
- organ or site, congenital NEC —*see* Atresia, by site
- pancreatic duct K86.8
- parotid duct or gland K11.8
- pelviureteral junction N13.5
  - congenital Q62.39
- pharynx J39.2
- portal (circulation) (vein) I81
- prostate —*see also* Hyperplasia, prostate
  - valve (urinary) N32.0
- pulmonary valve (heart) I37.0
- pyelonephritis (chronic) N11.1
- pylorus
  - adult K31.1
  - congenital or infantile Q40.0
- rectosigmoid —*see* Obstruction, intestine
- rectum K62.4
- renal N28.89
  - outflow N13.8
  - pelvis, congenital Q62.39
- respiratory J98.8
  - chronic J44.9
- retinal (vessels) H34.9
- salivary duct (any) K11.8
  - with calculus K11.5
- sigmoid —*see* Obstruction, intestine

Obstruction, obstructed, obstructive *(continued)*
- sinus (accessory) (nasal) J34.89
- Stensen's duct K11.8
- stomach NEC K31.89
  - acute K31.0
  - congenital Q40.2
  - due to pylorospasm K31.3
- submandibular duct K11.8
- submaxillary gland K11.8
  - with calculus K11.5
- thoracic duct I89.0
- thrombotic —*see* Thrombosis
- trachea J39.8
- tracheostomy airway J95.03
- tricuspid (valve) —*see* Stenosis, tricuspid
- upper respiratory, congenital Q34.8
- ureter (functional) (pelvic junction) NEC N13.5
  - with
    - hydronephrosis N13.1
      - with infection N13.6
    - pyelonephritis (chronic) N11.1
  - congenital Q62.39
  - due to calculus —*see* Calculus, ureter
- urethra NEC N36.8
  - congenital Q64.39
- urinary (moderate) N13.9
  - due to hyperplasia (hypertrophy) of prostate —*see* Hyperplasia, prostate
  - organ or tract (lower) N13.9
  - prostatic valve N32.0
  - specified NEC N13.8
- uropathy N13.9
- uterus N85.8
- vagina N89.5
- valvular —*see* Endocarditis
- vein, venous I87.1
  - caval (inferior) (superior) I87.1
  - thrombotic —*see* Thrombosis
- vena cava (inferior) (superior) I87.1
- vesical NEC N32.0
- vesicourethral orifice N32.0
  - congenital Q64.31
- vessel NEC I99.8

Obturator —*see* condition

Occlusal wear, teeth K03.0

Occlusio pupillae —*see* Membrane, pupillary

Occlusion, occluded
- anus K62.4
  - congenital Q42.3
    - with fistula Q42.2
- aortoiliac (chronic) I74.09
- aqueduct of Sylvius G91.1
  - congenital Q03.0
    - with spina bifida —*see* Spina bifida, by site, with hydrocephalus
- artery —*see also* Embolism, artery I74.9
  - auditory, internal I65.8
  - basilar I65.1
    - with
      - infarction I63.22
        - due to
          - embolism I63.12
          - thrombosis I63.02
  - brain or cerebral I66.9
    - with infarction (due to) I63.5
      - embolism I63.4
      - thrombosis I63.3
  - carotid I65.2-
    - with
      - infarction I63.23-
        - due to
          - embolism I63.13-
          - thrombosis I63.03-

Occlusion, occluded *(continued)*
- artery —*see also* Embolism, artery *(continued)*
  - cerebellar (anterior inferior) (posterior inferior) (superior) I66.3
    - with infarction I63.54-
      - due to
        - embolism I63.44-
        - thrombosis I63.34-
  - cerebral I66.9
    - with infarction I63.50
      - due to
        - embolism I63.40
          - specified NEC I63.49
        - thrombosis I63.30
          - specified NEC I63.39
    - anterior I66.1-
      - with infarction I63.52-
        - due to
          - embolism I63.42-
          - thrombosis I63.32-
    - middle I66.0-
      - with infarction I63.51-
        - due to
          - embolism I63.41-
          - thrombosis I63.31-
    - posterior I66.2-
      - with infarction I63.53-
        - due to
          - embolism I63.43-
          - thrombosis I63.33-
    - specified NEC I66.8
      - with infarction I63.59
        - due to
          - embolism I63.4
          - thrombosis I63.3
  - choroidal (anterior) —*see* Occlusion, artery, precerebral, specified NEC
  - communicating posterior —*see* Occlusion, artery, cerebral, specified NEC
  - complete
    - coronary I25.82
    - extremities I70.92
  - coronary (acute) (thrombotic) (without myocardial infarction) I24.0
    - with myocardial infarction —*see* Infarction, myocardium
    - chronic total I25.82
    - complete I25.82
    - healed or old I25.2
    - total (chronic) I25.82
  - hypophyseal —*see* Occlusion, artery, precerebral, specified NEC
  - iliac I74.5
  - lower extremities due to stenosis o stricture I77.1
  - mesenteric (embolic) (thrombotic) K55.0
  - perforating —*see* Occlusion, arter cerebral, specified NEC
  - peripheral I77.9
    - thrombotic or embolic I74.4
  - pontine —*see* Occlusion, artery, cerebral, specified NEC
  - precerebral I65.9
    - with infarction I63.20
      - specified NEC I63.29
      - due to
        - embolism I63.10
          - specified NEC I63.19
        - thrombosis I63.00
          - specified NEC I63.09
    - basilar —*see* Occlusion, artery, basilar
    - carotid —*see* Occlusion, artery, carotid

teoarthritis *(continued)*
- generalized *(continued)*
  - primary M15.0
  - specified NEC M15.8
- hand joint M19.04-
  - first carpometacarpal joint M18.9
- hip M16.1-
  - bilateral M16.0
  - due to hip dysplasia (unilateral) M16.3-
    - bilateral M16.2
- interphalangeal
  - distal (Heberden) M15.1
  - proximal (Bouchard) M15.2
- knee M17.9
  - bilateral M17.0
- shoulder M19.01-
- spine *—see* Spondylosis
- wrist M19.03-
- post-traumatic NEC M19.92
  - ankle M19.17-
  - elbow M19.12-
  - foot joint M19.17-
  - hand joint M19.14-
    - first carpometacarpal joint M18.3-
      - bilateral M18.2
  - hip M16.5-
    - bilateral M16.4
  - knee M17.3-
    - bilateral M17.2
  - shoulder M19.11-
  - wrist M19.13-
- primary M19.91
  - ankle M19.07-
  - elbow M19.02-
  - foot joint M19.07-
  - hand joint M19.04-
    - first carpometacarpal joint M18.1-
      - bilateral M18.0
  - hip M16.1-
    - bilateral M16.0
  - knee M17.1-
    - bilateral M17.0
  - shoulder M19.01-
  - spine *—see* Spondylosis
  - wrist M19.03-
- secondary M19.93
  - ankle M19.27-
  - elbow M19.22-
  - foot joint M19.27-
  - hand joint M19.24-
    - first carpometacarpal joint M18.5-
      - bilateral M18.4
  - hip M16.7
    - bilateral M16.6
  - knee M17.5
    - bilateral M17.4
  - multiple M15.3
  - shoulder M19.21-
  - spine *—see* Spondylosis
  - wrist M19.23-

Osteoarthropathy (hypertrophic) M19.90
- ankle *—see* Osteoarthritis, primary, ankle
- elbow *—see* Osteoarthritis, primary, elbow
- foot joint *—see* Osteoarthritis, primary, foot
- hand joint *—see* Osteoarthritis, primary, hand joint
- knee joint *—see* Osteoarthritis, primary, knee
- multiple site *—see* Osteoarthritis, primary, multiple joint
- pulmonary *—see also* Osteoarthropathy, specified type NEC
  - hypertrophic *—see* Osteoarthropathy, hypertrophic, specified type NEC

Osteoarthropathy *(continued)*
- secondary hypertrophic *—see* Osteoarthropathy, specified type NEC
- shoulder *—see* Osteoarthritis, primary, shoulder
- specified joint NEC *—see* Osteoarthritis, primary, specified joint NEC
- specified type NEC M89.40
  - carpus M89.44-
  - clavicle M89.41-
  - femur M89.45-
  - fibula M89.46-
  - finger M89.44-
  - humerus M89.42-
  - ilium M89.459
  - ischium M89.459
  - metacarpus M89.44-
  - metatarsus M89.47-
  - multiple sites M89.49
  - neck M89.48
  - radius M89.43-
  - rib M89.48
  - scapula M89.41-
  - skull M89.48
  - tarsus M89.47-
  - tibia M89.46-
  - toe M89.47-
  - ulna M89.43-
  - vertebra M89.48
- secondary *—see* Osteoarthropathy, specified type NEC
- spine *—see* Spondylosis
- wrist *—see* Osteoarthritis, primary, wrist

Osteoarthrosis (degenerative) (hypertrophic) (joint) *—see also* Osteoarthritis
- deformans alkaptonurica E70.29 *[M36.8]*
- erosive M15.4
- generalized M15.9
  - primary M15.0
- polyarticular M15.9
- spine *—see* Spondylosis

Osteoblastoma *—see* Neoplasm, bone, benign
- aggressive *—see* Neoplasm, bone, uncertain behavior

Osteochondroarthrosis deformans endemica *—see* Disease, Kaschin-Beck

Osteochondritis *—see also* Osteochondropathy, by site
- Brailsford's *—see* Osteochondrosis, juvenile, radius
- dissecans M93.20
  - ankle M93.27-
  - elbow M93.22-
  - foot M93.27-
  - hand M93.24-
  - hip M93.25-
  - knee M93.26-
  - multiple sites M93.29
  - shoulder joint M93.21-
  - specified site NEC M93.28
  - wrist M93.23-
- juvenile M92.9
  - patellar *—see* Osteochondrosis, juvenile, patella
- syphilitic (congenital) (early) A50.02 *[M90.80]*
  - ankle A50.02 *[M90.87]*-
  - elbow A50.02 *[M90.82]*-
  - foot A50.02 *[M90.87]*-
  - forearm A50.02 *[M90.83]*-
  - hand A50.02 *[M90.84]*-
  - hip A50.02 *[M90.85]*-
  - knee A50.02 *[M90.86]*-

Osteochondritis *(continued)*
- syphilitic *(continued)*
  - multiple sites A50.02 *[M90.89]*
  - shoulder joint A50.02 *[M90.81]*-
  - specified site NEC A50.02 *[M90.88]*

Osteochondrodysplasia Q78.9
- with defects of growth of tubular bones and spine Q77.9
  - specified NEC Q77.8
- specified NEC Q78.8

Osteochondrodystrophy E78.9

Osteochondrolysis *—see* Osteochondritis, dissecans

Osteochondroma *—see* Neoplasm, bone, benign

Osteochondromatosis D48.0
- syndrome Q78.4

Osteochondromyxosarcoma *—see* Neoplasm, bone, malignant

Osteochondropathy M93.90
- ankle M93.97-
- elbow M93.92-
- foot M93.97-
- hand M93.94-
- hip M93.95-
- Kienböck's disease of adults M93.1
- knee M93.96-
- multiple joints M93.99
- osteochondritis dissecans *—see* Osteochondritis, dissecans
- osteochondrosis *—see* Osteochondrosis
- shoulder region M93.91-
- slipped upper femoral epiphysis *—see* Slipped, epiphysis, upper femoral
- specified joint NEC M93.98
- specified type NEC M93.80
  - ankle M93.87-
  - elbow M93.82-
  - foot M93.87-
  - hand M93.84-
  - hip M93.85-
  - knee M93.86-
  - multiple joints M93.89
  - shoulder region M93.81-
  - specified joint NEC M93.88
  - wrist M93.83-
- syphilitic, congenital
  - early A50.02 *[M90.80]*
  - late A50.56 *[M90.80]*
- wrist M93.93-

Osteochondrosarcoma *—see* Neoplasm, bone, malignant

Osteochondrosis *—see also* Osteochondropathy, by site
- acetabulum (juvenile) M91.0
- adult *—see* Osteochondropathy, specified type NEC, by site
- astragalus (juvenile) *—see* Osteochondrosis, juvenile, tarsus
- Blount's *—see* Osteochondrosis, juvenile, tibia
- Buchanan's M91.0
- Burns' *—see* Osteochondrosis, juvenile, ulna
- calcaneus (juvenile) *—see* Osteochondrosis, juvenile, tarsus
- capitular epiphysis (femur) (juvenile) *—see* Legg-Calvé-Perthes disease
- carpal (juvenile) (lunate) (scaphoid) *—see* Osteochondrosis, juvenile, hand, carpal lunate
  - adult M93.1
- coxae juvenilis *—see* Legg-Calvé-Perthes disease
- deformans juvenilis, coxae *—see* Legg-Calvé-Perthes disease

Osteochondrosis *(continued)*
- Diaz's *—see* Osteochondrosis, juvenile, tarsus
- dissecans (knee) (shoulder) *—see* Osteochondritis, dissecans
- femoral capital epiphysis (juvenile) *—see* Legg-Calvé-Perthes disease
- femur (head), juvenile *—see* Legg-Calvé-Perthes disease
- fibula (juvenile) *—see* Osteochondrosis, juvenile, fibula
- foot NEC (juvenile) M92.8
- Freiberg's *—see* Osteochondrosis, juvenile, metatarsus
- Haas' (juvenile) *—see* Osteochondrosis, juvenile, humerus
- Haglund's *—see* Osteochondrosis, juvenile, tarsus
- hip (juvenile) *—see* Legg-Calvé-Perthes disease
- humerus (capitulum) (head) (juvenile) *—see* Osteochondrosis, juvenile, humerus
- ilium, iliac crest (juvenile) M91.0
- ischiopubic synchondrosis M91.0
- Iselin's *—see* Osteochondrosis, juvenile, metatarsus
- juvenile, juvenilis M92.9
  - after congenital dislocation of hip reduction *—see* Osteochondrosis, juvenile, hip, specified NEC
  - arm *—see* Osteochondrosis, juvenile, upper limb NEC
  - capitular epiphysis (femur) *—see* Legg-Calvé-Perthes disease
  - clavicle, sternal epiphysis *—see* Osteochondrosis, juvenile, upper limb NEC
  - coxae *—see* Legg-Calvé-Perthes disease
  - deformans M92.9
  - fibula M92.5-
  - foot NEC M92.8
  - hand M92.20-
    - carpal lunate M92.21-
    - metacarpal head M92.22-
    - specified site NEC M92.29-
  - head of femur *—see* Legg-Calvé-Perthes disease
  - hip and pelvis M91.9-
    - coxa plana *—see* Coxa, plana
    - femoral head *—see* Legg-Calvé-Perthes disease
    - pelvis M91.0
    - pseudocoxalgia *—see* Pseudocoxalgia
    - specified NEC M91.8-
  - humerus M92.0-
  - limb
    - lower NEC M92.8
    - upper NEC *—see* Osteochondrosis, juvenile, upper limb NEC
  - medial cuneiform bone *—see* Osteochondrosis, juvenile, tarsus
  - metatarsus M92.7-
  - patella M92.4-
  - radius M92.1-
  - specified site NEC M92.8
  - spine M42.00
    - cervical region M42.02
    - cervicothoracic region M42.03
    - lumbar region M42.06
    - lumbosacral region M42.07
    - multiple sites M42.09
    - occipito-atlanto-axial region M42.01
    - sacrococcygeal region M42.08
    - thoracic region M42.04
    - thoracolumbar region M42.05

Osteochondrosis *(continued)*
juvenile, juvenilis *(continued)*
tarsus M92.6-
tibia M92.5-
ulna M92.1-
upper limb NEC M92.3-
vertebra (body) (epiphyseal plates) (Calvé's) (Scheuermann's) —*see* Osteochondrosis, juvenile, spine
Kienböck's —*see* Osteochondrosis, juvenile, hand, carpal lunate
adult M93.1
Köhler's
patellar —*see* Osteochondrosis, juvenile, patella
tarsal navicular —*see* Osteochondrosis, juvenile, tarsus
Legg-Perthes (-Calvé)(-Waldenström) —*see* Legg-Calvé-Perthes disease
limb
lower NEC (juvenile) M92.8
upper NEC (juvenile) —*see* Osteochondrosis, juvenile, upper limb NEC
lunate bone (carpal) (juvenile) —*see also* Osteochondrosis, juvenile, hand, carpal lunate
adult M93.1
Mauclaire's —*see* Osteochondrosis, juvenile, hand, metacarpal
metacarpal (head) (juvenile) —*see* Osteochondrosis, juvenile, hand, metacarpal
metatarsus (fifth) (head) (juvenile) (second) —*see* Osteochondrosis, juvenile, metatarsus
navicular (juvenile) —*see* Osteochondrosis, juvenile, tarsus
os
calcis (juvenile) —*see* Osteochondrosis, juvenile, tarsus
tibiale externum (juvenile) —*see* Osteochondrosis, juvenile, tarsus
Osgood-Schlatter —*see* Osteochondrosis, juvenile, tibia
Panner's —*see* Osteochondrosis, juvenile, humerus
patellar center (juvenile) (primary) (secondary) —*see* Osteochondrosis, juvenile, patella
pelvis (juvenile) M91.0
Pierson's M91.0
radius (head) (juvenile) —*see* Osteochondrosis, juvenile, radius
Scheuermann's —*see* Osteochondrosis, juvenile, spine
Sever's —*see* Osteochondrosis, juvenile, tarsus
Sinding-Larsen —*see* Osteochondrosis, juvenile, patella
spine M42.9
adult M42.10
cervical region M42.12
cervicothoracic region M42.13
lumbar region M42.16
lumbosacral region M42.17
multiple sites M42.19
occipito-atlanto-axial region M42.11
sacrococcygeal region M42.18
thoracic region M42.14
thoracolumbar region M42.15
juvenile —*see* Osteochondrosis, juvenile, spine
symphysis pubis (juvenile) M91.0
syphilitic (congenital) A50.02
talus (juvenile) —*see* Osteochondrosis, juvenile, tarsus
tarsus (navicular) (juvenile) —*see* Osteochondrosis, juvenile, tarsus

Osteochondrosis *(continued)*
tibia (proximal) (tubercle) (juvenile) —*see* Osteochondrosis, juvenile, tibia
tuberculous —*see* Tuberculosis, bone
ulna (lower) (juvenile) —*see* Osteochondrosis, juvenile, ulna
van Neck's M91.0
vertebral —*see* Osteochondrosis, spine

Osteoclastoma D48.0
malignant —*see* Neoplasm, bone, malignant

Osteodynia —*see* Disorder, bone, specified type NEC

Osteodystrophy Q78.9
azotemic N25.0
congenital Q78.9
parathyroid, secondary E21.1
renal N25.0

Osteofibroma —*see* Neoplasm, bone, benign

Osteofibrosarcoma —*see* Neoplasm, bone, malignant

Osteogenesis imperfecta Q78.0

Osteogenic —*see* condition

Osteolysis M89.50
carpus M89.54-
clavicle M89.51-
femur M89.55-
fibula M89.56-
finger M89.54-
humerus M89.52-
ilium M89.559
ischium M89.559
joint prosthesis (periprosthetic) —*see* Complications, joint prosthesis, mechanical, periprosthetic, osteolysis, by site
metacarpus M89.54-
metatarsus M89.57-
multiple sites M89.59
neck M89.58
periprosthetic —*see* Complications, joint prosthesis, mechanical, periprosthetic, osteolysis, by site
radius M89.53-
rib M89.58
scapula M89.51-
skull M89.58
tarsus M89.57-
tibia M89.56-
toe M89.57-
ulna M89.53-
vertebra M89.58

Osteoma —*see also* Neoplasm, bone, benign
osteoid —*see also* Neoplasm, bone, benign
giant —*see* Neoplasm, bone, benign

Osteomalacia M83.9
adult M83.9
drug-induced NEC M83.5
due to
malabsorption (postsurgical) M83.2
malnutrition M83.3
specified NEC M83.8
aluminium-induced M83.4
infantile —*see* Rickets
juvenile —*see* Rickets
oncogenic E83.89
pelvis M83.8
puerperal M83.0
senile M83.1
vitamin-D-resistant in adults E83.31 *[M90.8]-*
carpus E83.31 *[M90.84]-*

Osteomalacia *(continued)*
vitamin-D-resistant in adults *(continued)*
clavicle E83.31 *[M90.81]-*
femur E83.31 *[M90.85]-*
fibula E83.31 *[M90.86]-*
finger E83.31 *[M90.84]-*
humerus E83.31 *[M90.82]-*
ilium E83.31 *[M90.859]*
ischium E83.31 *[M90.859]*
metacarpus E83.31 *[M90.84]-*
metatarsus E83.31 *[M90.87]-*
multiple sites E83.31 *[M90.89]*
neck E83.31 *[M90.88]*
radius E83.31 *[M90.83]-*
rib E83.31 *[M90.88]*
scapula E83.31 *[M90.819]*
skull E83.31 *[M90.88]*
tarsus E83.31 *[M90.879]*
tibia E83.31 *[M90.869]*
toe E83.31 *[M90.879]*
ulna E83.31 *[M90.839]*
vertebra E83.31 *[M90.88]*

Osteomyelitis (general) (infective) (localized) (neonatal) (purulent) (septic) (staphylococcal) (streptococcal) (suppurative) (with periostitis) M86.9
acute M86.10
carpus M86.14-
clavicle M86.11-
femur M86.15-
fibula M86.16-
finger M86.14-
hematogenous M86.00
carpus M86.04-
clavicle M86.01-
femur M86.05-
fibula M86.06-
finger M86.04-
humerus M86.02-
ilium M86.059
ischium M86.059
mandible M27.2
metacarpus M86.04-
metatarsus M86.07-
multiple sites M86.09
neck M86.08
orbit H05.02-
petrous bone —*see* Petrositis
radius M86.03-
rib M86.08
scapula M86.01-
skull M86.08
tarsus M86.07-
tibia M86.06-
toe M86.07-
ulna M86.03-
vertebra —*see* Osteomyelitis, vertebra
humerus M86.12-
ilium M86.159
ischium M86.159
mandible M27.2
metacarpus M86.14-
metatarsus M86.17-
multiple sites M86.19
neck M86.18
orbit H05.02-
petrous bone —*see* Petrositis
radius M86.13-
rib M86.18
scapula M86.11-
skull M86.18
tarsus M86.17-
tibia M86.16-
toe M86.17-
ulna M86.13-
vertebra —*see* Osteomyelitis, vertebra

Osteomyelitis *(continued)*
chronic (or old) M86.60
with draining sinus M86.40
carpus M86.44-
clavicle M86.41-
femur M86.45-
fibula M86.46-
finger M86.44-
humerus M86.42-
ilium M86.459
ischium M86.459
mandible M27.2
metacarpus M86.44-
metatarsus M86.47-
multiple sites M86.49
neck M86.48
orbit H05.02-
petrous bone —*see* Petrositis
radius M86.43-
rib M86.48
scapula M86.41-
skull M86.48
tarsus M86.47-
tibia M86.46-
toe M86.47-
ulna M86.43-
vertebra —*see* Osteomyelitis, vertebra
carpus M86.64-
clavicle M86.61-
femur M86.65-
fibula M86.66-
finger M86.64-
hematogenous NEC M86.50
carpus M86.54-
clavicle M86.51-
femur M86.55-
fibula M86.56-
finger M86.54-
humerus M86.52-
ilium M86.559
ischium M86.559
mandible M27.2
metacarpus M86.54-
metatarsus M86.57-
multifocal M86.30
carpus M86.34-
clavicle M86.31-
femur M86.35-
fibula M86.36-
finger M86.34-
humerus M86.32-
ilium M86.359
ischium M86.359
metacarpus M86.34-
metatarsus M86.37-
multiple sites M86.39
neck M86.38
radius M86.33-
rib M86.38
scapula M86.31-
skull M86.38
tarsus M86.37-
tibia M86.36-
toe M86.37-
ulna M86.33-
vertebra —*see* Osteomyelitis, vertebra
multiple sites M86.59
neck M86.58
orbit H05.02-
petrous bone —*see* Petrositis
radius M86.53-
rib M86.58
scapula M86.51-
skull M86.58
tarsus M86.57-
tibia M86.56-
toe M86.57-
ulna M86.53-
vertebra —*see* Osteomyelitis, vertebra

rrhea H92.1-
erebrospinal G96.0
sclerosis (general) H80.9-
ochlear (endosteal) H80.2-
nvolving
  otic capsule —*see* Otosclerosis, cochlear
  oval window
    nonobliterative H80.0-
    obliterative H80.1-
  round window —*see* Otosclerosis, cochlear
onobliterative —*see* Otosclerosis, involving, oval window, nonobliterative
bliterative —*see* Otosclerosis, involving, oval window, obliterative
pecified NEC H80.8-
spongiosis —*see* Otosclerosis
to's disease or pelvis M24.7
tcome of delivery Z37.9
nultiple births Z37.9
  all liveborn Z37.50
    quadruplets Z37.52
    quintuplets Z37.53
    sextuplets Z37.54
    specified number NEC Z37.59
    triplets Z37.51
  all stillborn Z37.7
  some liveborn Z37.60
    quadruplets Z37.62
    quintuplets Z37.63
    sextuplets Z37.64
    specified number NEC Z37.69
    triplets Z37.61
ingle NEC Z37.9
  liveborn Z37.0
  stillborn Z37.1
wins NEC Z37.9
  both liveborn Z37.2
  both stillborn Z37.4
  one liveborn, one stillborn Z37.3
tlet —*see* condition
alocytosis (congenital) (hereditary) —*see* Elliptocytosis
arian —*see* Condition
ariocele N83.4
aritis (cystic) —*see* Oophoritis
ary, ovarian —*see also* condition
resistant syndrome E28.39
vein syndrome N13.8
eractive —*see also* Hyperfunction
adrenal cortex NEC E27.0
bladder N32.81
hypothalamus E23.3
thyroid —*see* Hyperthyroidism
eractivity R46.3
child —*see* Disorder, attention-deficit hyperactivity
verbite (deep) (excessive) (horizontal) (vertical) M26.29
verbreathing —*see* Hyperventilation
verconscientious personality F60.5
verdevelopment —*see* Hypertrophy
verdistension —*see* Distension
verdose, overdosage (drug) —*see* Table of Drugs and Chemicals, by drug, poisoning
vereating R63.2
nonorganic origin F50.8
psychogenic F50.8
verexertion (effects) (exhaustion) T73.3

Overexposure (effects) T73.9
  exhaustion T73.2
Overfeeding —*see* Overeating
  newborn P92.4
Overfill, endodontic M27.52
Overgrowth, bone —*see* Hypertrophy, bone
Overhanging of dental restorative material (unrepairable) K08.52
Overheated (places) (effects) —*see* Heat
Overjet (excessive horizontal) M26.23
Overlaid, overlying (suffocation) —*see* Asphyxia, traumatic, due to mechanical threat
Overlap, excessive horizontal (teeth) M26.23
Overlapping toe (acquired) —*see also* Deformity, toe, specified NEC
  congenital (fifth toe) Q66.89
Overload
  circulatory, due to transfusion (blood) (blood components) (TACO) E87.71
  fluid E87.70
    due to transfusion (blood) (blood components) E87.71
    specified NEC E87.79
  iron, due to repeated red blood cell transfusions E83.111
  potassium (K) E87.5
  sodium (Na) E87.0
Overnutrition —*see* Hyperalimentation
Overproduction —*see also* Hypersecretion
  ACTH E27.0
  catecholamine E27.5
  growth hormone E22.0
Overprotection, child by parent Z62.1
Overriding
  aorta Q25.4
  finger (acquired) —*see* Deformity, finger
    congenital Q68.1
  toe (acquired) —*see also* Deformity, toe, specified NEC
    congenital Q66.89
Overstrained R53.83
  heart —*see* Hypertrophy, cardiac
Overuse, muscle NEC M70.8-
Overweight E66.3
Overworked R53.83
Oviduct —*see* condition
Ovotestis Q56.0
Ovulation (cycle)
  failure or lack of N97.0
  pain N94.0
Ovum —*see* condition
Owren's disease or syndrome (parahemophilia) D68.2
Ox heart —*see* Hypertrophy, cardiac
Oxalosis E72.53
Oxaluria E72.53
Oxycephaly, oxycephalic Q75.0
  syphilitic, congenital A50.02
Oxyuriasis B80
Oxyuris vermicularis (infestation) B80
Ozena J31.0

P

Pachyderma, pachydermia L85.9
  larynx (verrucosa) J38.7
Pachydermatocele (congenital) Q82.8
Pachydermoperiostosis —*see also* Osteoarthropathy, hypertrophic, specified type NEC
  clubbed nail M89.40 *[L62]*
Pachygyria Q04.3
Pachymeningitis (adhesive) (basal) (brain) (cervical) (chronic) (circumscribed) (external) (fibrous) (hemorrhagic) (hypertrophic) (internal) (purulent) (spinal) (suppurative) —*see* Meningitis
Pachyonychia (congenital) Q84.5
Pacinian tumor —*see* Neoplasm, skin, benign
Pad, knuckle or Garrod's M72.1
Paget-Schroetter syndrome I82.890
Paget's disease
  with infiltrating duct carcinoma —*see* Neoplasm, breast, malignant
  bone M88.9
    carpus M88.84-
    clavicle M88.81-
    femur M88.85-
    fibula M88.86-
    finger M88.84-
    humerus M88.82-
    ilium M88.85-
    in neoplastic disease —*see* Osteitis, deformans, in neoplastic disease
    ischium M88.85-
    metacarpus M88.84-
    metatarsus M88.87-
    multiple sites M88.89
    neck M88.88
    radius M88.83-
    rib M88.88
    scapula M88.81-
    skull M88.0
    tarsus M88.87-
    tibia M88.86-
    toe M88.87-
    ulna M88.83-
    vertebra M88.88
  breast (female) C50.01-
    male C50.02-
  extramammary —*see also* Neoplasm, skin, malignant
    anus C21.0
      margin C44.590
      skin C44.590
  intraductal carcinoma —*see* Neoplasm, breast, malignant
  malignant —*see* Neoplasm, skin, malignant
    breast (female) C50.01-
      male C50.02-
    unspecified site (female) C50.01-
      male C50.02-
  mammary —*see* Paget's disease, breast
  nipple —*see* Paget's disease, breast
  osteitis deformans —*see* Paget's disease, bone
Pain (s) —*see also* Painful R52
  abdominal R10.9
    colic R10.83
    generalized R10.84
      with acute abdomen R10.0
    lower R10.30
      left quadrant R10.32
      pelvic or perineal R10.2
      periumbilical R10.33
      right quadrant R10.31

Pain *(continued)*
  abdominal *(continued)*
    rebound —*see* Tenderness, abdominal, rebound
    severe with abdominal rigidity R10.0
    tenderness —*see* Tenderness, abdominal
    upper R10.10
      epigastric R10.13
      left quadrant R10.12
      right quadrant R10.11
  acute R52
    due to trauma G89.11
    neoplasm related G89.3
    postprocedural NEC G89.18
    post-thoracotomy G89.12
    specified by site - code to Pain, by site
  adnexa (uteri) R10.2
  anginoid —*see* Pain, precordial
  anus K62.89
  arm —*see* Pain, limb, upper
  axillary (axilla) M79.62-
  back (postural) M54.9
  bladder R39.89
    associated with micturition —*see* Micturition, painful
  bone —*see* Disorder, bone, specified type NEC
  breast N64.4
  broad ligament R10.2
  cancer associated (acute) (chronic) G89.3
  cecum —*see* Pain, abdominal
  cervicobrachial M53.1
  chest (central) R07.9
    anterior wall R07.89
    atypical R07.89
    ischemic I20.9
    musculoskeletal R07.89
    non-cardiac R07.89
    on breathing R07.1
    pleurodynia R07.81
    precordial R07.2
    wall (anterior) R07.89
  chronic G89.29
    associated with significant psychosocial dysfunction G89.4
    due to trauma G89.21
    neoplasm related G89.3
    postoperative NEC G89.28
    postprocedural NEC G89.28
    post-thoracotomy G89.22
    specified NEC G89.29
  coccyx M53.3
  colon —*see* Pain, abdominal
  coronary —*see* Angina
  costochondral R07.1
  diaphragm R07.1
  due to cancer G89.3
  due to device, implant or graft —*see also* Complications, by site and type, specified NEC T85.84
    arterial graft NEC T82.848
    breast (implant) T85.84
    catheter NEC T85.84
      dialysis (renal) T82.848
        intraperitoneal T85.84
      infusion NEC T82.848
        spinal (epidural) (subdural) T85.84
      urinary (indwelling) T83.84
    electronic (electrode) (pulse generator) (stimulator)
      bone T84.84
      cardiac T82.847
      nervous system (brain) (peripheral nerve) (spinal) T85.84
      urinary T83.84

Pain *(continued)*
due to device, implant or graft —*see also* Complications, by site and type, specified NEC *(continued)*
fixation, internal (orthopedic) NEC T84.84
gastrointestinal (bile duct) (esophagus) T85.84
genital NEC T83.84
heart NEC T82.847
infusion NEC T85.84
joint prosthesis T84.84
ocular (corneal graft) (orbital implant) NEC T85.84
orthopedic NEC T84.84
specified NEC T85.84
urinary NEC T83.84
vascular NEC T82.848
ventricular intracranial shunt T85.84
due to malignancy (primary) (secondary) G89.3
ear —*see* subcategory H92.0
epigastric, epigastrium R10.13
eye —*see* Pain, ocular
face, facial R51
atypical G50.1
female genital organs NEC N94.89
finger —*see* Pain, limb, upper
flank —*see* Pain, abdominal
foot —*see* Pain, limb, lower
gallbladder K82.9
gas (intestinal) R14.1
gastric —*see* Pain, abdominal
generalized NOS R52
genital organ
female N94.89
male N50.8
groin —*see* Pain, abdominal, lower
hand —*see* Pain, limb, upper
head —*see* Headache
heart —*see* Pain, precordial
infra-orbital —*see* Neuralgia, trigeminal
intercostal R07.82
intermenstrual N94.0
jaw R68.84
joint M25.50
ankle M25.57-
elbow M25.52-
finger M79.64-
foot M25.57-
hand M79.64-
hip M25.55-
knee M25.56-
shoulder M25.51-
toe M25.57-
wrist M25.53-
kidney N23
laryngeal R07.0
leg —*see* Pain, limb, lower
limb M79.609
lower M79.60-
foot M79.67-
lower leg M79.66-
thigh M79.65-
toe M79.67-
upper M79.60-
axilla M79.62-
finger M79.64-
forearm M79.63-
hand M79.64-
upper arm M79.62-
loin M54.5
low back M54.5
lumbar region M54.5
mandibular R68.84
mastoid —*see* subcategory H92.0
maxilla R68.84
menstrual —*see also* Dysmenorrhea N94.6

Pain *(continued)*
metacarpophalangeal (joint) —*see* Pain, joint, hand
metatarsophalangeal (joint) —*see* Pain, joint, foot
mouth K13.79
muscle —*see* Myalgia
musculoskeletal —*see also* Pain, by site M79.1
myofascial M79.1
nasal J34.89
nasopharynx J39.2
neck NEC M54.2
nerve NEC —*see* Neuralgia
neuromuscular —*see* Neuralgia
nose J34.89
ocular H57.1-
ophthalmic —*see* Pain, ocular
orbital region —*see* Pain, ocular
ovary N94.89
over heart —*see* Pain, precordial
ovulation N94.0
pelvic (female) R10.2
penis N48.89
pericardial —*see* Pain, precordial
perineal, perineum R10.2
pharynx J39.2
pleura, pleural, pleuritic R07.81
postoperative NOS G89.18
postprocedural NOS G89.18
post-thoracotomy G89.12
precordial (region) R07.2
premenstrual N94.3
psychogenic (persistent) (any site) F45.41
radicular (spinal) —*see* Radiculopathy
rectum K62.89
respiration R07.1
retrosternal R07.2
rheumatoid, muscular —*see* Myalgia
rib R07.81
root (spinal) —*see* Radiculopathy
round ligament (stretch) R10.2
sacroiliac M53.3
sciatic —*see* Sciatica
scrotum N50.8
seminal vesicle N50.8
shoulder M25.51-
spermatic cord N50.8
spinal root —*see* Radiculopathy
spine M54.9
cervical M54.2
low back M54.5
with sciatica M54.4-
thoracic M54.6
stomach —*see* Pain, abdominal
substernal R07.2
temporomandibular (joint) M26.62
testis N50.8
thoracic spine M54.6
with radicular and visceral pain M54.14
throat R07.0
tibia —*see* Pain, limb, lower
toe —*see* Pain, limb, lower
tongue K14.6
tooth K08.8
trigeminal —*see* Neuralgia, trigeminal
tumor associated G89.3
ureter N23
urinary (organ) (system) N23
uterus NEC N94.89
vagina R10.2
vertebrogenic (syndrome) M54.89
vesical R39.89
associated with micturition —*see* Micturition, painful
vulva R10.2

Painful —*see also* Pain
coitus
female N94.1
male N53.12
psychogenic F52.6
ejaculation (semen) N53.12
psychogenic F52.6
erection —*see* Priapism
feet syndrome E53.8
joint replacement (hip) (knee) T84.84
menstruation —*see* Dysmenorrhea
psychogenic F45.8
micturition —*see* Micturition, painful
respiration R07.1
scar NEC L90.5
wire sutures T81.89

Painter's colic —*see* subcategory T56.0

Palate —*see* condition

Palatoplegia K13.79

Palatoschisis —*see* Cleft, palate

Palilalia R48.8

Palliative care Z51.5

Pallor R23.1
optic disc, temporal —*see* Atrophy, optic

Palmar —*see also* condition
fascia —*see* condition

Palpable
cecum K63.89
kidney N28.89
ovary N83.8
prostate N42.9
spleen —*see* Splenomegaly

Palpitations (heart) R00.2
psychogenic F45.8

Palsy —*see also* Paralysis G83.9
atrophic diffuse (progressive) G12.22
Bell's —*see also* Palsy, facial
newborn P11.3
brachial plexus NEC G54.0
newborn (birth injury) P14.3
brain —*see* Palsy, cerebral
bulbar (progressive) (chronic) G12.22
of childhood (Fazio-Londe) G12.1
pseudo NEC G12.29
supranuclear (progressive) G23.1
cerebral (congenital) G80.9
ataxic G80.4
athetoid G80.3
choreathetoid G80.3
diplegic G80.8
spastic G80.1
dyskinetic G80.3
athetoid G80.3
choreathetoid G80.3
distonic G80.3
dystonic G80.3
hemiplegic G80.8
spastic G80.2
mixed G80.8
monoplegic G80.8
spastic G80.1
paraplegic G80.8
spastic G80.1
quadriplegic G80.8
spastic G80.0
spastic G80.1
diplegic G80.1
hemiplegic G80.2
monoplegic G80.1
quadriplegic G80.0
specified NEC G80.1
tetrapelgic G80.0
specified NEC G80.8
syphilitic A52.12
congenital A50.49
tetraplegic G80.8
spastic G80.0

Palsy *(continued)*
cranial nerve —*see also* Disorder, nerve, cranial
multiple G52.7
in
infectious disease B99 *[G5*
neoplastic disease —*see al*
Neoplasm D49.9 *[G53]*
parasitic disease B89 *[G53*
sarcoidosis D86.82
creeping G12.22
diver's T70.3
Erb's P14.0
facial G51.0
newborn (birth injury) P11.3
glossopharyngeal G52.1
Klumpke (-Déjérine) P14.1
lead —*see* subcategory T56.0
median nerve (tardy) G56.1-
nerve G58.9
specified NEC G58.8
peroneal nerve (acute) (tardy) G57.
progressive supranuclear G23.1
pseudobulbar NEC G12.29
radial nerve (acute) G56.3-
seventh nerve —*see also* Palsy, faci
newborn P11.3
shaking —*see* Parkinsonism
spastic (cerebral) (spinal) G80.1
ulnar nerve (tardy) G56.2-
wasting G12.29

Paludism —*see* Malaria

Panangiitis M30.0

Panaris, panaritium —*see also* Cellulitis, digit
with lymphangitis —*see* Lymphangitis, acute, digit

Panarteritis nodosa M30.0
brain or cerebral I67.7

Pancake heart R93.1
with cor pulmonale (chronic) I27.8

Pancarditis (acute) (chronic) I51.89
rheumatic I09.89
active or acute I01.8

Pancoast's syndrome or tumor C34.

Pancolitis, ulcerative (chronic) K51.0
with
complication K51.019
abscess K51.014
fistula K51.013
obstruction K51.012
rectal bleeding K51.011
specified complication NEC K51.018

Pancreas, pancreatic —*see* condition

Pancreatitis (annular) (apoplectic) (calcareous) (edematous) (hemorrhagic) (malignant) (recurren (subacute) (suppurative) K85.9
acute K85.9
alcohol induced K85.2
biliary K85.1
drug induced K85.3
gallstone K85.1
idiopathic K85.0
specified NEC K85.8
chronic (infectious) K86.1
alcohol-induced K86.0
recurrent K86.1
relapsing K86.1
cystic (chronic) K86.1
cytomegaloviral B25.2
fibrous (chronic) K86.1
gangrenous K85.8
gallstone K85.1
interstitial (chronic) K86.1
acute K85.8
mumps B26.3

- **ncreatitis** *(continued)*
  - ecurrent (chronic) K86.1
  - elapsing, chronic K86.1
  - yphilitic A52.74
- **ncreatoblastoma** —*see* Neoplasm, ancreas, malignant
- **ncreolithiasis** K86.8
- **ncytolysis** D75.89
- **ncytopenia** (acquired) D61.818
  - ith
    - malformations D61.09
    - myelodysplastic syndrome —*see* Syndrome, myelodysplastic
  - ntineoplastic chemotherapy induced D61.810
  - ongenital D61.09
  - rug-induced NEC D61.811
- **nencephalitis, subacute, sclerosing** A81.1
- **nhematopenia** D61.9
  - ongenital D61.09
  - onstitutional D61.09
  - plenic, primary D73.1
- **nhemocytopenia** D61.9
  - ongenital D61.09
  - onstitutional D61.09
- **nhypogonadism** E29.1
- **nhypopituitarism** E23.0
  - repubertal E23.0
- **nic** (attack) (state) F41.0
  - eaction to exceptional stress (transient) F43.0
- **nmyelopathy, familial, onstitutional** D61.09
- **nmyelophthisis** D61.82
  - ongenital D61.09
- **nmyelosis** (acute) (with nyelofibrosis) C94.4-
- **nner's disease** —*see* Osteochondrosis, juvenile, humerus
- **nneuritis endemica** E51.11
- **nniculitis** (nodular) (nonsuppurative) M79.3
  - ack M54.00
    - cervical region M54.02
    - cervicothoracic region M54.03
    - lumbar region M54.06
    - lumbosacral region M54.07
    - multiple sites M54.09
    - occipito-atlanto-axial region M54.01
    - sacrococcygeal region M54.08
    - thoracic region M54.04
    - thoracolumbar region M54.05
  - upus L93.2
  - nesenteric K65.4
  - eck M54.02
    - cervicothoracic region M54.03
    - occipito-atlanto-axial region M54.01
  - elapsing M35.6
- **nniculus adiposus** (abdominal) E65
- **nnus** (allergic) (cornea) (degenerativus) (keratic) H16.42-
  - bdominal (symptomatic) E65
  - rachomatosus, trachomatous (active) A71.1
- **nophthalmitis** H44.01-
- **nsinusitis** (chronic) (hyperplastic) (nonpurulent) (purulent) J32.4
  - cute J01.40
    - recurrent J01.41
  - uberculous A15.8
- **nuveitis** (sympathetic) H44.11-
- **Panvalvular disease** I08.9
  - specified NEC I08.8
- **Papanicolaou smear, cervix** Z12.4
  - as part of routine gynecological examination Z01.419
    - with abnormal findings Z01.411
  - for suspected neoplasm Z12.4
  - nonspecific abnormal finding R87.619
  - routine Z01.419
    - with abnormal findings Z01.411
- **Papilledema** (choked disc) H47.10
  - associated with
    - decreased ocular pressure H47.12
    - increased intracranial pressure H47.11
    - retinal disorder H47.13
  - Foster-Kennedy syndrome H47.14-
- **Papillitis** H46.00
  - anus K62.89
  - chronic lingual K14.4
  - necrotizing, kidney N17.2
  - optic H46.0-
  - rectum K62.89
  - renal, necrotizing N17.2
  - tongue K14.0
- **Papilloma** —*see also* Neoplasm, benign, by site
  - acuminatum (female) (male) (anogenital) A63.0
  - benign pinta (primary) A67.0
  - bladder (urinary) (transitional cell) D41.4
  - choroid plexus (lateral ventricle) (third ventricle) D33.0
    - anaplastic C71.5
    - fourth ventricle D33.1
    - malignant C71.5
  - renal pelvis (transitional cell) D41.1-
    - benign D30.1-
  - Schneiderian
    - specified site —*see* Neoplasm, benign, by site
    - unspecified site D14.0
  - serous surface
    - borderline malignancy
      - specified site —*see* Neoplasm, uncertain behavior, by site
      - unspecified site D39.10
    - specified site —*see* Neoplasm, benign, by site
    - unspecified site D27.9
  - transitional (cell)
    - bladder (urinary) D41.4
    - inverted type —*see* Neoplasm, uncertain behavior, by site
    - renal pelvis D41.1-
    - ureter D41.2-
  - ureter (transitional cell) D41.2-
    - benign D30.2-
  - urothelial —*see* Neoplasm, uncertain behavior, by site
  - villous —*see* Neoplasm, uncertain behavior, by site
    - adenocarcinoma in —*see* Neoplasm, malignant, by site
      - in situ —*see* Neoplasm, in situ
  - yaws, plantar or palmar A66.1
- **Papillomata, multiple, of yaws** A66.1
- **Papillomatosis** —*see also* Neoplasm, benign, by site
  - confluent and reticulated L83
  - cystic, breast —*see* Mastopathy, cystic
  - ductal, breast —*see* Mastopathy, cystic
  - intraductal (diffuse) —*see* Neoplasm, benign, by site
  - subareolar duct D24-
- **Papillomavirus, as cause of disease classified elsewhere** B97.7
- **Papillon-Léage and Psaume syndrome** Q87.0
- **Papule** (s) R23.8
  - carate (primary) A67.0
  - fibrous, of nose D22.39
  - Gottron's L94.4
  - pinta (primary) A67.0
- **Papulosis**
  - lymphomatoid C86.6
  - malignant I77.89
- **Papyraceous fetus** O31.0-
- **Para-albuminemia** E88.09
- **Paracephalus** Q89.7
- **Parachute mitral valve** Q23.2
- **Paracoccidioidomycosis** B41.9
  - disseminated B41.7
  - generalized B41.7
  - mucocutaneous-lymphangitic B41.8
  - pulmonary B41.0
  - specified NEC B41.8
  - visceral B41.8
- **Paradentosis** K05.4
- **Paraffinoma** T88.8
- **Paraganglioma** D44.7
  - adrenal D35.0-
    - malignant C74.1-
  - aortic body D44.7
    - malignant C75.5
  - carotid body D44.6
    - malignant C75.4
  - chromaffin —*see also* Neoplasm, benign, by site
    - malignant —*see* Neoplasm, malignant, by site
  - extra-adrenal D44.7
    - malignant C75.5
      - specified site —*see* Neoplasm, malignant, by site
      - unspecified site C75.5
    - specified site —*see* Neoplasm, uncertain behavior, by site
    - unspecified site D44.7
  - gangliocytic D13.2
    - specified site —*see* Neoplasm, benign, by site
    - unspecified site D13.2
  - glomus jugulare D44.7
    - malignant C75.5
  - jugular D44.7
  - malignant C75.5
    - specified site —*see* Neoplasm, malignant, by site
    - unspecified site C75.5
  - nonchromaffin D44.7
    - malignant C75.5
      - specified site —*see* Neoplasm, malignant, by site
      - unspecified site C75.5
    - specified site —*see* Neoplasm, uncertain behavior, by site
    - unspecified site D44.7
  - parasympathetic D44.7
    - specified site —*see* Neoplasm, uncertain behavior, by site
    - unspecified site D44.7
  - specified site —*see* Neoplasm, uncertain behavior, by site
  - sympathetic D44.7
    - specified site —*see* Neoplasm, uncertain behavior, by site
    - unspecified site D44.7
  - unspecified site D44.7
- **Parageusia** R43.2
  - psychogenic F45.8
- **Paragonimiasis** B66.4
- **Paragranuloma, Hodgkin** —*see* Lymphoma, Hodgkin, classical, specified NEC
- **Parahemophilia** —*see also* Defect, coagulation D68.2
- **Parakeratosis** R23.4
  - variegata L41.0
- **Paralysis, paralytic** (complete) (incomplete) G83.9
  - with
    - syphilis A52.17
  - abducens, abducent (nerve) —*see* Strabismus, paralytic, sixth nerve
  - abductor, lower extremity G57.9-
  - accessory nerve G52.8
  - accommodation —*see also* Paresis, of accommodation
    - hysterical F44.89
  - acoustic nerve (except Deafness) —*see* subcategory H93.3
  - agitans —*see also* Parkinsonism G20
    - arteriosclerotic G21.4
  - alternating (oculomotor) G83.89
  - amyotrophic G12.21
  - ankle G57.9-
  - anus (sphincter) K62.89
  - arm —*see* Monoplegia, upper limb
  - ascending (spinal), acute G61.0
  - association G12.29
  - asthenic bulbar G70.00
    - with exacerbation (acute) G70.01
    - in crisis G70.01
  - ataxic (hereditary) G11.9
    - general (syphilitic) A52.17
  - atrophic G58.9
    - infantile, acute —*see* Poliomyelitis, paralytic
    - progressive G12.22
    - spinal (acute) —*see* Poliomyelitis, paralytic
  - axillary G54.0
  - Babinski-Nageotte's G83.89
  - Bell's G51.0
    - newborn P11.3
  - Benedikt's G46.3
  - birth injury P14.9
    - spinal cord P11.5
  - bladder (neurogenic) (sphincter) N31.2
  - bowel, colon or intestine K56.0
  - brachial plexus G54.0
    - birth injury P14.3
    - newborn (birth injury) P14.3
  - brain G83.9
    - diplegia G83.0
    - triplegia G83.89
  - bronchial J98.09
  - Brown-Séquard G83.81
  - bulbar (chronic) (progressive) G12.22
    - infantile —*see* Poliomyelitis, paralytic
    - poliomyelitic —*see* Poliomyelitis, paralytic
    - pseudo G12.29
  - bulbospinal G70.00
    - with exacerbation (acute) G70.01
    - in crisis G70.01
  - cardiac —*see also* Failure, heart I50.9
  - cerebrocerebellar, diplegic G80.1
  - cervical
    - plexus G54.2
    - sympathetic G90.09
  - Céstan-Chenais G46.3
  - Charcot-Marie-Tooth type G60.0
  - Clark's G80.9
  - colon K56.0
  - compressed air T70.3
  - compression
    - arm G56.9-
    - leg G57.9-
    - lower extremity G57.9-
    - upper extremity G56.9-

- **Pause, sinoatrial** I49.5
- **Paxton's disease** B36.2
- **Pearl** (s)
  - enamel K00.2
  - Epstein's K09.8
- **Pearl-worker's disease** —*see* Osteomyelitis, specified type NEC
- **Pectenosis** K62.4
- **Pectoral** —*see* condition
- **Pectus**
  - carinatum (congenital) Q67.7
    - acquired M95.4
    - rachitic sequelae (late effect) E64.3
  - excavatum (congenital) Q67.6
    - acquired M95.4
    - rachitic sequelae (late effect) E64.3
  - recurvatum (congenital) Q67.6
- **Pedatrophia** E41
- **Pederosis** F65.4
- **Pediculosis** (infestation) B85.2
  - capitis (head-louse) (any site) B85.0
  - corporis (body-louse) (any site) B85.1
  - eyelid B85.0
  - mixed (classifiable to more than one of the titles B85.0-B85.3) B85.4
  - pubis (pubic louse) (any site) B85.3
  - vestimenti B85.1
  - vulvae B85.3
- **Pediculus** (infestation) —*see* Pediculosis
- **Pedophilia** F65.4
- **Peg-shaped teeth** K00.2
- **Pelade** —*see* Alopecia, areata
- **Pelger-Huët anomaly or syndrome** D72.0
- **Peliosis** (rheumatica) D69.0
  - hepatis K76.4
    - with toxic liver disease K71.8
- **Pelizaeus-Merzbacher disease** E75.29
- **Pellagra** (alcoholic) (with polyneuropathy) E52
- **Pellagra-cerebellar-ataxia-renal aminoaciduria syndrome** E72.02
- **Pellegrini** (-Stieda) **disease or syndrome** —*see* Bursitis, tibial collateral
- **Pellizzi's syndrome** E34.8
- **Pel's crisis** A52.11
- **Pelvic** —*see also* condition
  - examination (periodic) (routine) Z01.419
    - with abnormal findings Z01.411
  - kidney, congenital Q63.2
- **Pelviolithiasis** —*see* Calculus, kidney
- **Pelviperitonitis** —*see also* Peritonitis, pelvic
  - gonococcal A54.24
  - puerperal O85
- **Pelvis** —*see* condition or type
- **Pemphigoid** L12.9
  - benign, mucous membrane L12.1
  - bullous L12.0
  - cicatricial L12.1
  - juvenile L12.2
  - ocular L12.1
  - specified NEC L12.8
- **Pemphigus** L10.9
  - benign familial (chronic) Q82.8
  - Brazilian L10.3
  - circinatus L13.0
  - conjunctiva L12.1
  - drug-induced L10.5
  - erythematosus L10.4
- **Pemphigus** *(continued)*
  - foliaceous L10.2
  - gangrenous —*see* Gangrene
  - neonatorum L01.03
  - ocular L12.1
  - paraneoplastic L10.81
  - specified NEC L10.89
  - syphilitic (congenital) A50.06
  - vegetans L10.1
  - vulgaris L10.0
  - wildfire L10.3
- **Pendred's syndrome** E07.1
- **Pendulous**
  - abdomen, in pregnancy —*see* Pregnancy, complicated by, abnormal, pelvic organs or tissues NEC
  - breast N64.89
- **Penetrating wound** —*see also* Puncture
  - with internal injury —*see* Injury, by site
  - eyeball —*see* Puncture, eyeball
  - orbit (with or without foreign body) —*see* Puncture, orbit
  - uterus by instrument with or following ectopic or molar pregnancy O08.6
- **Penicillosis** B48.4
- **Penis** —*see* condition
- **Penitis** N48.29
- **Pentalogy of Fallot** Q21.8
- **Pentasomy X syndrome** Q97.1
- **Pentosuria** (essential) E74.8
- **Percreta placenta** O43.23-
- **Peregrinating patient** —*see* Disorder, factitious
- **Perforation, perforated** (nontraumatic) (of)
  - accidental during procedure (blood vessel) (nerve) (organ) —*see* Complication, accidental puncture or laceration
  - antrum —*see* Sinusitis, maxillary
  - appendix K35.2
  - atrial septum, multiple Q21.1
  - attic, ear —*see* Perforation, tympanum, attic
  - bile duct (common) (hepatic) K83.2
    - cystic K82.2
  - bladder (urinary)
    - with or following ectopic or molar pregnancy O08.6
    - obstetrical trauma O71.5
    - traumatic S37.29
      - at delivery O71.5
  - bowel K63.1
    - with or following ectopic or molar pregnancy O08.6
    - newborn P78.0
    - obstetrical trauma O71.5
    - traumatic —*see* Laceration, intestine
  - broad ligament N83.8
    - with or following ectopic or molar pregnancy O08.6
    - obstetrical trauma O71.6
  - by
    - device, implant or graft —*see also* Complications, by site and type, mechanical T85.628
      - arterial graft NEC —*see* Complication, cardiovascular device, mechanical, vascular
      - breast (implant) T85.49
      - catheter NEC T85.698
        - cystostomy T83.090
- **Perforation, perforated** *(continued)*
  - by *(continued)*
    - device, implant or graft —*see also* Complications, by site and type, mechanical *(continued)*
      - catheter *(continued)*
        - dialysis (renal) T82.49
          - intraperitoneal T85.691
        - infusion NEC T82.594
          - spinal (epidural) (subdural) T85.690
        - urinary, indwelling T83.098
      - electronic (electrode) (pulse generator) (stimulator)
        - bone T84.390
        - cardiac T82.199
          - electrode T82.190
          - pulse generator T82.191
          - specified type NEC T82.198
        - nervous system —*see* Complication, prosthetic device, mechanical, electronic nervous system stimulator
        - urinary —*see* Complication, genitourinary, device, urinary, mechanical
      - fixation, internal (orthopedic) NEC —*see* Complication, fixation device, mechanical
      - gastrointestinal —*see* Complications, prosthetic device, mechanical, gastrointestinal device
      - genital NEC T83.498
        - intrauterine contraceptive device T83.39
        - penile prosthesis T83.490
      - heart NEC —*see* Complication, cardiovascular device, mechanical
      - joint prosthesis —*see* Complications, joint prosthesis, mechanical, specified NEC, by site
      - ocular NEC —*see* Complications, prosthetic device, mechanical, ocular device
      - orthopedic NEC —*see* Complication, orthopedic, device, mechanical
      - specified NEC T85.628
      - urinary NEC —*see also* Complication, genitourinary, device, urinary, mechanical
        - graft T83.29
      - vascular NEC —*see* Complication, cardiovascular device, mechanical
      - ventricular intracranial shunt T85.09
    - foreign body left accidentally in operative wound T81.539
    - instrument (any) during a procedure, accidental —*see* Puncture, accidental complicating surgery
  - cecum K35.2
  - cervix (uteri) N88.8
    - with or following ectopic or molar pregnancy O08.6
    - obstetrical trauma O71.3
  - colon K63.1
    - newborn P78.0
    - obstetrical trauma O71.5
    - traumatic —*see* Laceration, intestine, large
  - common duct (bile) K83.2
  - cornea (due to ulceration) —*see* Ulcer, cornea, perforated
- **Perforation, perforated** *(continued)*
  - cystic duct K82.2
  - diverticulum (intestine) K57.80
    - with bleeding K57.81
    - large intestine K57.20
      - with
        - bleeding K57.21
        - small intestine K57.40
          - with bleeding K57.41
    - small intestine K57.00
      - with
        - bleeding K57.01
        - large intestine K57.40
          - with bleeding K57.41
  - ear drum —*see* Perforation, tympanum
  - esophagus K22.3
  - ethmoidal sinus —*see* Sinusitis, ethmoidal
  - frontal sinus —*see* Sinusitis, front
  - gallbladder K82.2
  - heart valve —*see* Endocarditis
  - ileum K63.1
    - newborn P78.0
    - obstetrical trauma O71.5
    - traumatic —*see* Laceration, intestine, small
  - instrumental, surgical (accidental) (blood vessel) (nerve) (organ) —*see* Puncture, accidental complicating surgery
  - intestine NEC K63.1
    - with ectopic or molar pregnancy O08.6
    - newborn P78.0
    - obstetrical trauma O71.5
    - traumatic —*see* Laceration, intestine
    - ulcerative NEC K63.1
      - newborn P78.0
  - jejunum, jejunal K63.1
    - obstetrical trauma O71.5
    - traumatic —*see* Laceration, intestine, small
    - ulcer —*see* Ulcer, gastrojejunal, with perforation
  - joint prosthesis —*see* Complicatio joint prosthesis, mechanical, specified NEC, by site
  - mastoid (antrum) (cell) —*see* Disorder, mastoid, specified NE
  - maxillary sinus —*see* Sinusitis, maxillary
  - membrana tympani —*see* Perforati tympanum
  - nasal
    - septum J34.89
      - congenital Q30.3
      - syphilitic A52.73
    - sinus J34.89
      - congenital Q30.8
      - due to sinusitis —*see* Sinusiti
  - palate —*see also* Cleft, palate Q35
    - syphilitic A52.79
  - palatine vault —*see also* Cleft, pal hard Q35.1
    - syphilitic A52.79
      - congenital A50.59
  - pars flaccida (ear drum) —*see* Perforation, tympanum, attic
  - pelvic
    - floor S31.030
      - with
        - ectopic or molar pregnancy O08.6
        - penetration into retroperitoneal space S31.031
        - retained foreign body S31.0
          - with penetration into retroperitoneal space S31.041

oration, perforated *(continued)*
- lvic *(continued)*
  - floor *(continued)*
    - following ectopic or molar pregnancy O08.6
    - obstetrical trauma O70.1
  - organ S37.99
    - adrenal gland S37.818
    - bladder —*see* Perforation, bladder
    - fallopian tube S37.599
      - bilateral S37.592
      - unilateral S37.591
    - kidney S37.09-
    - obstetrical trauma O71.5
    - ovary S37.499
      - bilateral S37.492
      - unilateral S37.491
    - prostate S37.828
    - specified organ NEC S37.898
    - ureter —*see* Perforation, ureter
    - urethra —*see* Perforation, urethra
    - uterus —*see* Perforation, uterus
- rineum —*see* Laceration, perineum
- harynx J39.2
- ctum K63.1
  - newborn P78.0
  - obstetrical trauma O71.5
  - traumatic S36.63
- ot canal space due to endodontic treatment M27.51
- gmoid K63.1
  - newborn P78.0
  - obstetrical trauma O71.5
  - traumatic S36.533
- nus (accessory) (chronic) (nasal) J34.89
- henoidal sinus —*see* Sinusitis, sphenoidal
- rgical (accidental) (by instrument) (blood vessel) (nerve) (organ) —*see* Puncture, accidental complicating surgery
- aumatic
  - external —*see* Puncture
  - eye —*see* Puncture, eyeball
  - internal organ —*see* Injury, by site
- mpanum, tympanic (membrane) (persistent post-traumatic) (postinflammatory) H72.9-
  - attic H72.1-
    - multiple —*see* Perforation, tympanum, multiple
    - total —*see* Perforation, tympanum, total
  - central H72.0-
    - multiple —*see* Perforation, tympanum, multiple
    - total —*see* Perforation, tympanum, total
  - marginal NEC —*see* subcategory H72.2
  - multiple H72.81-
  - pars flaccida —*see* Perforation, tympanum, attic
  - total H72.82-
  - traumatic, current episode S09.2-
- phoid, gastrointestinal —*see* Typhoid
- lcer —*see* Ulcer, by site, with perforation
- reter N28.89
  - traumatic S37.19
- rethra N36.8
  - with ectopic or molar pregnancy O08.6
  - following ectopic or molar pregnancy O08.6
  - obstetrical trauma O71.5
  - traumatic S37.39
    - at delivery O71.5

Perforation, perforated *(continued)*
- uterus
  - with ectopic or molar pregnancy O08.6
  - by intrauterine contraceptive device T83.39
  - following ectopic or molar pregnancy O08.6
  - obstetrical trauma O71.1
  - traumatic S37.69
    - obstetric O71.1
- uvula K13.79
  - syphilitic A52.79
- vagina
  - obstetrical trauma O71.4
  - other trauma —*see* Puncture, vagina

Periadenitis mucosa necrotica recurrens K12.0

Periappendicitis (acute) —*see* Appendicitis

Periarteritis nodosa (disseminated) (infectious) (necrotizing) M30.0

Periarthritis (joint) —*see also* Enthesopathy
- Duplay's M75.0-
- gonococcal A54.42
- humeroscapularis —*see* Capsulitis, adhesive
- scapulohumeral —*see* Capsulitis, adhesive
- shoulder —*see* Capsulitis, adhesive
- wrist M77.2-

Periarthrosis (angioneural) —*see* Enthesopathy

Pericapsulitis, adhesive (shoulder) —*see* Capsulitis, adhesive

Pericarditis (with decompensation) (with effusion) I31.9
- with rheumatic fever (conditions in I00)
  - active —*see* Pericarditis, rheumatic
  - inactive or quiescent I09.2
- acute (hemorrhagic) (nonrheumatic) (Sicca) I30.9
  - with chorea (acute) (rheumatic) (Sydenham's) I02.0
  - benign I30.8
  - nonspecific I30.0
  - rheumatic I01.0
    - with chorea (acute) (Sydenham's) I02.0
- adhesive or adherent (chronic) (external) (internal) I31.0
  - acute —*see* Pericarditis, acute
  - rheumatic I09.2
- bacterial (acute) (subacute) (with serous or seropurulent effusion) I30.1
- calcareous I31.1
- cholesterol (chronic) I31.8
  - acute I30.9
- chronic (nonrheumatic) I31.9
  - rheumatic I09.2
- constrictive (chronic) I31.1
- coxsackie B33.23
- fibrinocaseous (tuberculous) A18.84
- fibrinopurulent I30.1
- fibrinous I30.8
- fibrous I31.0
- gonococcal A54.83
- idiopathic I30.0
- in systemic lupus erythematosus M32.12
- infective I30.1
- meningococcal A39.53
- neoplastic (chronic) I31.8
  - acute I30.9
- obliterans, obliterating I31.0

Pericarditis *(continued)*
- plastic I31.0
- pneumococcal I30.1
- postinfarction I24.1
- purulent I30.1
- rheumatic (active) (acute) (with effusion) (with pneumonia) I01.0
  - with chorea (acute) (rheumatic) (Sydenham's) I02.0
  - chronic or inactive (with chorea) I09.2
- rheumatoid —*see* Rheumatoid, carditis
- septic I30.1
- serofibrinous I30.8
- staphylococcal I30.1
- streptococcal I30.1
- suppurative I30.1
- syphilitic A52.06
- tuberculous A18.84
- uremic N18.9 *[I32]*
- viral I30.1

Pericardium, pericardial —*see* condition

Pericellulitis —*see* Cellulitis

Pericementitis (chronic) (suppurative) —*see also* Periodontitis
- acute K05.20
  - generalized K05.22
  - localized K05.21

Perichondritis
- auricle —*see* Perichondritis, ear
- bronchus J98.09
- ear (external) H61.00-
  - acute H61.01-
  - chronic H61.02-
- external auditory canal —*see* Perichondritis, ear
- larynx J38.7
  - syphilitic A52.73
  - typhoid A01.09
- nose J34.89
- pinna —*see* Perichondritis, ear
- trachea J39.8

Periclasia K05.4

Pericoronitis —*see* Periodontitis

Pericystitis N30.90
- with hematuria N30.91

Peridiverticulitis (intestine) K57.92
- cecum —*see* Diverticulitis, intestine, large
- colon —*see* Diverticulitis, intestine, large
- duodenum —*see* Diverticulitis, intestine, small
- intestine —*see* Diverticulitis, intestine
- jejunum —*see* Diverticulitis, intestine, small
- rectosigmoid —*see* Diverticulitis, intestine, large
- rectum —*see* Diverticulitis, intestine, large
- sigmoid —*see* Diverticulitis, intestine, large

Periendocarditis —*see* Endocarditis

Periepididymitis N45.1

Perifolliculitis L01.02
- abscedens, caput, scalp L66.3
- capitis, abscedens (et suffodiens) L66.3
- superficial pustular L01.02

Perihepatitis K65.8

Perilabyrinthitis (acute) —*see* subcategory H83.0

Perimeningitis —*see* Meningitis

Perimetritis —*see* Endometritis

Perimetrosalpingitis —*see* Salpingo-oophoritis

Perineocele N81.81

Perinephric, perinephritic —*see* condition

Perinephritis —*see also* Infection, kidney
- purulent —*see* Abscess, kidney

Perineum, perineal —*see* condition

Perineuritis NEC —*see* Neuralgia

Periodic —*see* condition

Periodontitis (chronic) (complex) (compound) (local) (simplex) K05.30
- acute K05.20
  - generalized K05.22
  - localized K05.21
- apical K04.5
  - acute (pulpal origin) K04.4
- generalized K05.32
- localized K05.31

Periodontoclasia K05.4

Periodontosis (juvenile) K05.4

Periods —*see also* Menstruation
- heavy N92.0
- irregular N92.6
- shortened intervals (irregular) N92.1

Perionychia —*see also* Cellulitis, digit
- with lymphangitis —*see* Lymphangitis, acute, digit

Perioophoritis —*see* Salpingo-oophoritis

Periorchitis N45.2

Periosteum, periosteal —*see* condition

Periostitis (albuminosa) (circumscribed) (diffuse) (infective) (monomelic) —*see also* Osteomyelitis
- alveolar M27.3
- alveolodental M27.3
- dental M27.3
- gonorrheal A54.43
- jaw (lower) (upper) M27.2
- orbit H05.03-
- syphilitic A52.77
  - congenital (early) A50.02 *[M90.80]*
  - secondary A51.46
- tuberculous —*see* Tuberculosis, bone
- yaws (hypertrophic) (early) (late) A66.6 *[M90.80]*

Periostosis (hyperplastic) —*see also* Disorder, bone, specified type NEC
- with osteomyelitis —*see* Osteomyelitis, specified type NEC

Peripartum
- cardiomyopathy O90.3

Periphlebitis —*see* Phlebitis

Periproctitis K62.89

Periprostatitis —*see* Prostatitis

Perirectal —*see* condition

Perirenal —*see* condition

Perisalpingitis —*see* Salpingo-oophoritis

Perisplenitis (infectional) D73.89

Peristalsis, visible or reversed R19.2

Peritendinitis —*see* Enthesopathy

Peritoneum, peritoneal —*see* condition

Peritonitis (adhesive) (bacterial) (fibrinous) (hemorrhagic) (idiopathic) (localized) (perforative) (primary) (with adhesions) (with effusion) K65.9
- with or following
  - abscess K65.1

Peritonitis *(continued)*
  with or following *(continued)*
    appendicitis K35.2
      with perforation or rupture K35.2
      generalized K35.2
      localized K35.3
    diverticular disease (intestine) K57.80
      with bleeding K57.81
      large intestine K57.20
        with
          bleeding K57.21
          small intestine K57.40
            with bleeding K57.41
      small intestine K57.00
        with
          bleeding K57.01
          large intestine K57.40
            with bleeding K57.41
      ectopic or molar pregnancy O08.0
  acute (generalized) K65.0
  aseptic T81.61
  bile, biliary K65.3
  chemical T81.61
  chlamydial A74.81
  complicating abortion —*see* Abortion, by type, complicated by, pelvic peritonitis
  congenital P78.1
  chronic proliferative K65.8
  diaphragmatic K65.0
  diffuse K65.0
  diphtheritic A36.89
  disseminated K65.0
  due to
    bile K65.3
    foreign
      body or object accidentally left during a procedure (instrument) (sponge) (swab) T81.599
      substance accidentally left during a procedure (chemical) (powder) (talc) T81.61
    talc T81.61
    urine K65.8
  eosinophilic K65.8
    acute K65.0
  fibrocaseous (tuberculous) A18.31
  fibropurulent K65.0
  following ectopic or molar pregnancy O08.0
  general (ized) K65.0
  gonococcal A54.85
  meconium (newborn) P78.0
  neonatal P78.1
    meconium P78.0
  pancreatic K65.0
  paroxysmal, familial E85.0
    benign E85.0
  pelvic
    female N73.5
      acute N73.3
      chronic N73.4
        with adhesions N73.6
    male K65.0
  periodic, familial E85.0
  proliferative, chronic K65.8
  puerperal, postpartum, childbirth O85
  purulent K65.0
  septic K65.0
  specified NEC K65.8
  spontaneous bacterial K65.2
  subdiaphragmatic K65.0
  subphrenic K65.0
  suppurative K65.0
  syphilitic A52.74
    congenital (early) A50.08 *[K67]*
  talc T81.61
  tuberculous A18.31
  urine K65.8

Peritonsillar —*see* condition

Peritonsillitis J36

Perityphlitis K37

Periureteritis N28.89

Periurethral —*see* condition

Periurethritis (gangrenous) —*see* Urethritis

Periuterine —*see* condition

Perivaginitis —*see* Vaginitis

Perivasculitis, retinal H35.06-

Perivasitis (chronic) N49.1

Perivesiculitis (seminal) —*see* Vesiculitis

Perlèche NEC K13.0
  due to
    candidiasis B37.83
    moniliasis B37.83
    riboflavin deficiency E53.0
    vitamin B2 (riboflavin) deficiency E53.0

Pernicious —*see* condition

Pernio, perniosis T69.1

Perpetrator (of abuse) —*see* Index to External Causes of Injury, Perpetrator

Persecution
  delusion F22
  social Z60.5

Perseveration (tonic) R48.8

Persistence, persistent (congenital)
  anal membrane Q42.3
    with fistula Q42.2
  arteria stapedia Q16.3
  atrioventricular canal Q21.2
  branchial cleft Q18.0
  bulbus cordis in left ventricle Q21.8
  canal of Cloquet Q14.0
  capsule (opaque) Q12.8
  cilioretinal artery or vein Q14.8
  cloaca Q43.7
  communication —*see* Fistula, congenital
  convolutions
    aortic arch Q25.4
    fallopian tube Q50.6
    oviduct Q50.6
    uterine tube Q50.6
  double aortic arch Q25.4
  ductus arteriosus (Botalli) Q25.0
  fetal
    circulation P29.3
    form of cervix (uteri) Q51.828
    hemoglobin, hereditary (HPFH) D56.4
  foramen
    Botalli Q21.1
    ovale Q21.1
  Gartner's duct Q52.4
  hemoglobin, fetal (hereditary) (HPFH) D56.4
  hyaloid
    artery (generally incomplete) Q14.0
    system Q14.8
  hymen, in pregnancy or childbirth —*see* Pregnancy, complicated by, abnormal, vulva
  lanugo Q84.2
  left
    posterior cardinal vein Q26.8
    root with right arch of aorta Q25.4
    superior vena cava Q26.1
  Meckel's diverticulum Q43.0
    malignant —*see* Table of Neoplasms, small intestine, malignant

Persistence, persistent *(continued)*
  mucosal disease (middle ear) —*see* Otitis, media, suppurative, chronic, tubotympanic
  nail (s), anomalous Q84.6
  omphalomesenteric duct Q43.0
  organ or site not listed —*see* Anomaly, by site
  ostium
    atrioventriculare commune Q21.2
    primum Q21.2
    secundum Q21.1
  ovarian rests in fallopian tube Q50.6
  pancreatic tissue in intestinal tract Q43.8
  primary (deciduous)
    teeth K00.6
    vitreous hyperplasia Q14.0
  pupillary membrane Q13.89
  right aortic arch Q25.4
  rhesus (Rh) titer —*see* Complication (s), transfusion, incompatibility reaction, Rh (factor)
  sinus
    urogenitalis
      female Q52.8
      male Q55.8
    venosus with imperfect incorporation in right auricle Q26.8
  thymus (gland) (hyperplasia) E32.0
  thyroglossal duct Q89.2
  thyrolingual duct Q89.2
  truncus arteriosus or communis Q20.0
  tunica vasculosa lentis Q12.2
  umbilical sinus Q64.4
  urachus Q64.4
  vitelline duct Q43.0

Person (with)
  admitted for clinical research, as a control subject (normal comparison) (participant) Z00.6
  awaiting admission to adequate facility elsewhere Z75.1
  concern (normal) about sick person in family Z63.6
  consulting on behalf of another Z71.0
  feigning illness Z76.5
  living (in)
    alone Z60.2
    boarding school Z59.3
    residential institution Z59.3
    without
      adequate housing (heating) (space) Z59.1
      housing (permanent) (temporary) Z59.0
      person able to render necessary care Z74.2
      shelter Z59.0
  on waiting list Z75.1
  sick or handicapped in family Z63.6

Personality (disorder) F60.9
  accentuation of traits (type A pattern) Z73.1
  affective F34.0
  aggressive F60.3
  amoral F60.2
  anacastic, anankastic F60.5
  antisocial F60.2
  anxious F60.6
  asocial F60.2
  asthenic F60.7
  avoidant F60.6
  borderline F60.3
  change due to organic condition (enduring) F07.0
  compulsive F60.5
  cycloid F34.0
  cyclothymic F34.0
  dependent F60.7

Personality *(continued)*
  depressive F34.1
  dissocial F60.2
  dual F44.81
  eccentric F60.89
  emotionally unstable F60.3
  expansive paranoid F60.0
  explosive F60.3
  fanatic F60.0
  haltlose type F60.89
  histrionic F60.4
  hyperthymic F34.0
  hypothymic F34.1
  hysterical F60.4
  immature F60.89
  inadequate F60.7
  labile (emotional) F60.3
  mixed (nonspecific) F60.81
  morally defective F60.2
  multiple F44.81
  narcissistic F60.81
  obsessional F60.5
  obsessive (-compulsive) F60.5
  organic F07.0
  overconscientious F60.5
  paranoid F60.0
  passive (-dependent) F60.7
  passive-aggressive F60.89
  pathologic F60.9
  pattern defect or disturbance F60.9
  pseudopsychopathic (organic) F07
  pseudoretarded (organic) F07.0
  psychoinfantile F60.4
  psychoneurotic NEC F60.89
  psychopathic F60.2
  querulant F60.0
  sadistic F60.89
  schizoid F60.1
  self-defeating F60.7
  sensitive paranoid F60.0
  sociopathic (amoral) (antisocial) (asocial) (dissocial) F60.2
  specified NEC F60.89
  type A Z73.1
  unstable (emotional) F60.3

Perthes' disease —*see* Legg-Calvé-Perthes disease

Pertussis —*see also* Whooping coug
  A37.90

Perversion, perverted
  appetite F50.8
    psychogenic F50.8
  function
    pituitary gland E23.2
      posterior lobe E22.2
  sense of smell and taste R43.8
    psychogenic F45.8
  sexual —*see* Deviation, sexual

Pervious, congenital —*see also* Imperfect, closure
  ductus arteriosus Q25.0

Pes (congenital) —*see also* Talipes
  acquired —*see also* Deformity, lim
    foot, specified NEC
    planus —*see* Deformity, limb, fl
      foot
  adductus Q66.89
  cavus Q66.7
  deformity NEC, acquired —*see* Deformity, limb, foot, specified NEC
  planus (acquired) (any degree) —*s*
    also Deformity, limb, flat foot
    rachitic sequelae (late effect) E6
  valgus Q66.6

Pest, pestis —*see* Plague

Petechia, petechiae R23.3
  newborn P54.5

Petechial typhus A75.9

- **Pick's**
  - cerebral atrophy G31.01 *[F02.80]*
    - with behavioral disturbance G31.01 *[F02.81]*
  - disease or syndrome (brain) G31.01 *[F02.80]*
    - with behavioral disturbance G31.01 *[F02.81]*
- **Pickwickian syndrome** E66.2
- **Piebaldism** E70.39
- **Piedra** (beard) (scalp) B36.8
  - black B36.3
  - white B36.2
- **Pierre Robin deformity or syndrome** Q87.0
- **Pierson's disease or osteochondrosis** M91.0
- **Pig-bel** A05.2
- **Pigeon**
  - breast or chest (acquired) M95.4
    - congenital Q67.7
    - rachitic sequelae (late effect) E64.3
  - breeder's disease or lung J67.2
  - fancier's disease or lung J67.2
  - toe —*see* Deformity, toe, specified NEC
- **Pigmentation** (abnormal) (anomaly) L81.9
  - conjunctiva H11.13-
  - cornea (anterior) H18.01-
    - posterior H18.05-
    - stromal H18.06-
  - diminished melanin formation NEC L81.6
  - iron L81.8
  - lids, congenital Q82.8
  - limbus corneae —*see* Pigmentation, cornea
  - metals L81.8
  - optic papilla, congenital Q14.2
  - retina, congenital (grouped) (nevoid) Q14.1
  - scrotum, congenital Q82.8
  - tattoo L81.8
- **Piles** —*see also* Hemorrhoids K64.9
- **Pili**
  - annulati or torti (congenital) Q84.1
  - incarnati L73.1
- **Pill roller hand** (intrinsic) —*see* Parkinsonism
- **Pilomatrixoma** —*see* Neoplasm, skin, benign
  - malignant —*see* Neoplasm, skin, malignant
- **Pilonidal** —*see* condition
- **Pimple** R23.8
- **Pinched nerve** —*see* Neuropathy, entrapment
- **Pindborg tumor** —*see* Cyst, calcifying odontogenic
- **Pineal body or gland** —*see* condition
- **Pinealoblastoma** C75.3
- **Pinealoma** D44.5
  - malignant C75.3
- **Pineoblastoma** C75.3
- **Pineocytoma** D44.5
- **Pinguecula** H11.15-
- **Pingueculitis** H10.81-
- **Pinhole meatus** —*see also* Stricture, urethra N35.9
- **Pink**
  - disease —*see* subcategory T56.1
  - eye —*see* Conjunctivitis, acute, mucopurulent
- **Pinkus' disease** (lichen nitidus) L44.1
- **Pinpoint**
  - meatus —*see* Stricture, urethra
  - os (uteri) —*see* Stricture, cervix
- **Pins and needles** R20.2
- **Pinta** A67.9
  - cardiovascular lesions A67.2
  - chancre (primary) A67.0
  - erythematous plaques A67.1
  - hyperchromic lesions A67.1
  - hyperkeratosis A67.1
  - lesions A67.9
    - cardiovascular A67.2
    - hyperchromic A67.1
    - intermediate A67.1
    - late A67.2
    - mixed A67.3
    - primary A67.0
    - skin (achromic) (cicatricial) (dyschromic) A67.2
      - hyperchromic A67.1
      - mixed (achromic and hyperchromic) A67.3
  - papule (primary) A67.0
  - skin lesions (achromic) (cicatricial) (dyschromic) A67.2
    - hyperchromic A67.1
    - mixed (achromic and hyperchromic) A67.3
  - vitiligo A67.2
- **Pintids** A67.1
- **Pinworm** (disease) (infection) (infestation) B80
- **Piroplasmosis** B60.0
- **Pistol wound** —*see* Gunshot wound
- **Pitchers' elbow** —*see* Derangement, joint, specified type NEC, elbow
- **Pithecoid pelvis** Q74.2
  - with disproportion (fetopelvic) O33.0
    - causing obstructed labor O65.0
- **Pithiatism** F48.8
- **Pitted** —*see* Pitting
- **Pitting** —*see also* Edema R60.9
  - lip R60.0
  - nail L60.8
  - teeth K00.4
- **Pituitary gland** —*see* condition
- **Pituitary-snuff-taker's disease** J67.8
- **Pityriasis** (capitis) L21.0
  - alba L30.5
  - circinata (et maculata) L42
  - furfuracea L21.0
  - Hebra's L26
  - lichenoides L41.0
    - chronica L41.1
    - et varioliformis (acuta) L41.0
  - maculata (et circinata) L30.5
  - nigra B36.1
  - pilaris, Hebra's L44.0
  - rosea L42
  - rotunda L44.8
  - rubra (Hebra) pilaris L44.0
  - simplex L30.5
  - specified type NEC L30.5
  - streptogenes L30.5
  - versicolor (scrotal) B36.0
- **Placenta, placental** —*see* Pregnancy, complicated by (care of) (management affected by), specified condition
- **Placentitis** O41.14-
- **Plagiocephaly** Q67.3
- **Plague** A20.9
  - abortive A20.8
  - ambulatory A20.8
  - asymptomatic A20.8
  - bubonic A20.0
  - cellulocutaneous A20.1
  - cutaneobubonic A20.1
  - lymphatic gland A20.0
  - meningitis A20.3
  - pharyngeal A20.8
  - pneumonic (primary) (secondary) A20.2
  - pulmonary, pulmonic A20.2
  - septicemic A20.7
  - tonsillar A20.8
    - septicemic A20.7
- **Planning, family**
  - contraception Z30.9
  - procreation Z31.69
- **Plaque** (s)
  - artery, arterial —*see* Arteriosclerosis
  - calcareous —*see* Calcification
  - coronary, lipid rich I25.83
  - epicardial I31.8
  - erythematous, of pinta A67.1
  - Hollenhorst's —*see* Occlusion, artery, retina
  - lipid rich, coronary I25.83
  - pleural (without asbestos) J92.9
    - with asbestos J92.0
  - tongue K13.29
- **Plasmacytoma** C90.3-
  - extramedullary C90.2-
  - medullary C90.0-
  - solitary C90.3-
- **Plasmacytopenia** D72.818
- **Plasmacytosis** D72.822
- **Plaster ulcer** —*see* Ulcer, pressure, by site
- **Plateau iris syndrome** (post-iridectomy) (postprocedural) (without glaucoma) H21.82
  - with glaucoma H40.22-
- **Platybasia** Q75.8
- **Platyonychia** (congenital) Q84.6
  - acquired L60.8
- **Platypelloid pelvis** M95.5
  - with disproportion (fetopelvic) O33.0
    - causing obstructed labor O65.0
  - congenital Q74.2
- **Platyspondylisis** Q76.49
- **Plaut** (-Vincent) **disease** —*see also* Vincent's A69.1
- **Plethora** R23.2
  - newborn P61.1
- **Pleura, pleural** —*see* condition
- **Pleuralgia** R07.81
- **Pleurisy** (acute) (adhesive) (chronic) (costal) (diaphragmatic) (double) (dry) (fibrinous) (fibrous) (interlobar) (latent) (plastic) (primary) (residual) (sicca) (sterile) (subacute) (unresolved) R09.1
  - with
    - adherent pleura J86.0
    - effusion J90
      - chylous, chyliform J94.0
      - tuberculous (non primary) A15.6
        - primary (progressive) A15.7
    - tuberculosis —*see* Pleurisy, tuberculous (non primary)
  - encysted —*see* Pleurisy, with effusion
  - exudative —*see* Pleurisy, with effusion

Pleurisy *(continued)*

  - fibrinopurulent, fibropurulent —*se* Pyothorax
  - hemorrhagic —*see* Hemothorax
  - pneumococcal J90
  - purulent —*see* Pyothorax
  - septic —*see* Pyothorax
  - serofibrinous —*see* Pleurisy, with effusion
  - seropurulent —*see* Pyothorax
  - serous —*see* Pleurisy, with effusic
  - staphylococcal J86.9
  - streptococcal J90
  - suppurative —*see* Pyothorax
  - traumatic (post) (current) —*see* Injury, intrathoracic, pleura
  - tuberculous (with effusion) (non primary) A15.6
    - primary (progressive) A15.7
- **Pleuritis sicca** —*see* Pleurisy
- **Pleurobronchopneumonia** —*see* Pneumonia, broncho-
- **Pleurodynia** R07.81
  - epidemic B33.0
  - viral B33.0
- **Pleuropericarditis** —*see also* Pericarditis
  - acute I30.9
- **Pleuropneumonia** (acute) (bilateral) (double) (septic) —*see also* Pneumonia J18.8
  - chronic —*see* Fibrosis, lung
- **Pleuro-pneumonia-like-organism (PPLO), as cause of disease classified elsewhere** B96.0
- **Pleurorrhea** —*see* Pleurisy, with effusion
- **Plexitis, brachial** G54.0
- **Plica**
  - polonica B85.0
  - syndrome, knee M67.5-
  - tonsil J35.8
- **Plicated tongue** K14.5
- **Plug**
  - bronchus NEC J98.09
  - meconium (newborn) NEC syndro P76.0
  - mucus —*see* Asphyxia, mucus
- **Plumbism** —*see* subcategory T56.0
- **Plummer's disease** E05.20
  - with thyroid storm E05.21
- **Plummer-Vinson syndrome** D50.1
- **Pluricarential syndrome of infancy** E40
- **Plus** (and minus) hand (intrinsic) —*s* Deformity, limb, specified type NE forearm
- **Pneumathemia** —*see* Air, embolism
- **Pneumatic hammer** (drill) **syndrom** T75.21
- **Pneumatocele** (lung) J98.4
  - intracranial G93.89
  - tension J44.9
- **Pneumatosis**
  - cystoides intestinalis K63.89
  - intestinalis K63.89
  - peritonei K66.8
- **Pneumaturia** R39.89
- **Pneumoblastoma** —*see* Neoplasm, lung, malignant
- **Pneumocephalus** G93.89
- **Pneumococcemia** A40.3
- **Pneumococcus, pneumococcal** —*see* condition

umoconiosis (due to) (inhalation
) J64
ith tuberculosis (any type in A15)
J65
uminum J63.0
sbestos J61
agasse, bagassosis J67.1
auxite J63.1
eryllium J63.2
oal miners' (simple) J60
oalworkers' (simple) J60
ollier's J60
otton dust J66.0
iatomite (diatomaceous earth) J62.8
ust
inorganic NEC J63.6
lime J62.8
marble J62.8
organic NEC J66.8
umes or vapors (from silo) J68.9
raphite J63.3
rinder's J62.8
aolin J62.8
ica J62.8
illstone maker's J62.8
ineral fibers NEC J61
iner's J60
oldy hay J67.0
otter's J62.8
eumatoid —*see* Rheumatoid, lung
andblaster's J62.8
lica, silicate NEC J62.8
with carbon J60
onemason's J62.8
lc (dust) J62.0

umocystis carinii pneumonia B59

umocystis jiroveci (pneumonia)
59

umocystosis (with pneumonia) B59

umohemopericardium I31.2

umohemothorax J94.2
aumatic S27.2

umohydropericardium —*see*
ericarditis

umohydrothorax —*see*
Iydrothorax

umomediastinum J98.2
ongenital or perinatal P25.2

umomycosis B49 *[J99]*

eumonia (acute) (double)
migratory) (purulent) (septic)
unresolved) J18.9
ith
lung abscess J85.1
due to specified organism —*see*
Pneumonia, in (due to)
influenza —*see* Influenza, with,
pneumonia
denoviral J12.0
dynamic J18.2
lba A50.04
llergic (eosinophilic) J82
lveolar —*see* Pneumonia, lobar
naerobes J15.8
nthrax A22.1
pex, apical —*see* Pneumonia, lobar
Ascaris B77.81
spiration J69.0
due to
aspiration of microorganisms
bacterial J15.9
viral J12.9
food (regurgitated) J69.0
gastric secretions J69.0
milk (regurgitated) J69.0
oils, essences J69.1
solids, liquids NEC J69.8
vomitus J69.0

Pneumonia *(continued)*
aspiration *(continued)*
newborn P24.81
amniotic fluid (clear) P24.11
blood P24.21
liquor (amnii) P24.11
meconium P24.01
milk P24.31
mucus P24.11
food (regurgitated) P24.31
specified NEC P24.81
stomach contents P24.31
postprocedural J95.4
atypical NEC J18.9
bacillus J15.9
specified NEC J15.8
bacterial J15.9
specified NEC J15.8
Bacteroides (fragilis) (oralis)
(melaninogenicus) J15.8
basal, basic, basilar —*see* Pneumonia,
by type
bronchiolitis obliterans organized
(BOOP) J84.89
broncho-, bronchial (confluent)
(croupous) (diffuse) (disseminated)
(hemorrhagic) (involving lobes)
(lobar) (terminal) J18.0
allergic (eosinophilic) J82
aspiration —*see* Pneumonia,
aspiration
bacterial J15.9
specified NEC J15.8
chronic —*see* Fibrosis, lung
diplococcal J13
Eaton's agent J15.7
Escherichia coli (E. coli) J15.5
Friedländer's bacillus J15.0
Hemophilus influenzae J14
hypostatic J18.2
inhalation —*see also* Pneumonia,
aspiration
due to fumes or vapors
(chemical) J68.0
of oils or essences J69.1
Klebsiella (pneumoniae) J15.0
lipid, lipoid J69.1
endogenous J84.89
Mycoplasma (pneumoniae) J15.7
pleuro-pneumonia-like-organisms
(PPLO) J15.7
pneumococcal J13
Proteus J15.6
Pseudomonas J15.1
Serratia marcescens J15.6
specified organism NEC J16.8
staphylococcal —*see* Pneumonia,
staphylococcal
streptococcal NEC J15.4
group B J15.3
pneumoniae J13
viral, virus —*see* Pneumonia, viral
Butyrivibrio (fibriosolvens) J15.8
Candida B37.1
caseous —*see* Tuberculosis,
pulmonary
catarrhal —*see* Pneumonia, broncho
chlamydial J16.0
congenital P23.1
cholesterol J84.89
cirrhotic (chronic) —*see* Fibrosis,
lung
Clostridium (haemolyticum) (novyi)
J15.8
confluent —*see* Pneumonia, broncho
congenital (infective) P23.9
due to
bacterium NEC P23.6
Chlamydia P23.1
Escherichia coli P23.4
Haemophilus influenzae P23.6
infective organism NEC P23.8

Pneumonia *(continued)*
congenital *(continued)*
due to *(continued)*
Klebsiella pneumoniae P23.6
Mycoplasma P23.6
Pseudomonas P23.5
Staphylococcus P23.2
Streptococcus (except group B)
P23.6
group B P23.3
viral agent P23.0
specified NEC P23.8
croupous —*see* Pneumonia, lobar
cryptogenic organizing J84.116
cytomegalic inclusion B25.0
cytomegaloviral B25.0
deglutition —*see* Pneumonia,
aspiration
desquamative interstitial J84.117
diffuse —*see* Pneumonia, broncho
diplococcal, diplococcus (broncho-)
(lobar) J13
disseminated (focal) —*see*
Pneumonia, broncho
Eaton's agent J15.7
embolic, embolism —*see* Embolism,
pulmonary
Enterobacter J15.6
eosinophilic J82
Escherichia coli (E. coli) J15.5
Eubacterium J15.8
fibrinous —*see* Pneumonia, lobar
fibroid, fibrous (chronic) —*see*
Fibrosis, lung
Friedländer's bacillus J15.0
Fusobacterium (nucleatum) J15.8
gangrenous J85.0
giant cell (measles) B05.2
gonococcal A54.84
gram-negative bacteria NEC J15.6
anaerobic J15.8
Hemophilus influenzae (broncho)
(lobar) J14
human metapneumovirus J12.3
hypostatic (broncho) (lobar) J18.2
in (due to)
actinomycosis A42.0
adenovirus J12.0
anthrax A22.1
ascariasis B77.81
aspergillosis B44.9
Bacillus anthracis A22.1
Bacterium anitratum J15.6
candidiasis B37.1
chickenpox B01.2
Chlamydia J16.0
neonatal P23.1
coccidioidomycosis B38.2
acute B38.0
chronic B38.1
cytomegalovirus disease B25.0
Diplococcus (pneumoniae) J13
Eaton's agent J15.7
Enterobacter J15.6
Escherichia coli (E. coli) J15.5
Friedländer's bacillus J15.0
fumes and vapors (chemical)
(inhalation) J68.0
gonorrhea A54.84
Hemophilus influenzae (H.
influenzae) J14
Herellea J15.6
histoplasmosis B39.2
acute B39.0
chronic B39.1
human metapneumovirus J12.3
Klebsiella (pneumoniae) J15.0
measles B05.2
Mycoplasma (pneumoniae) J15.7
nocardiosis, nocardiasis A43.0
ornithosis A70
parainfluenza virus J12.2

Pneumonia *(continued)*
in *(continued)*
pleuro-pneumonia-like-organism
(PPLO) J15.7
pneumococcus J13
pneumocystosis (Pneumocystis
carinii) (Pneumocystis jiroveci)
B59
Proteus J15.6
Pseudomonas NEC J15.1
pseudomallei A24.1
psittacosis A70
Q fever A78
respiratory syncytial virus J12.1
rheumatic fever I00 *[J17]*
rubella B06.81
Salmonella (infection) A02.22
typhi A01.03
schistosomiasis B65.9 *[J17]*
Serratia marcescens J15.6
specified
bacterium NEC J15.8
organism NEC J16.8
spirochetal NEC A69.8
Staphylococcus J15.20
aureus (methicillin susceptible)
(MSSA) J15.211
methicillin resistant (MRSA)
J15.212
specified NEC J15.29
Streptococcus J15.4
group B J15.3
pneumoniae J13
specified NEC J15.4
toxoplasmosis B58.3
tularemia A21.2
typhoid (fever) A01.03
varicella B01.2
virus —*see* Pneumonia, viral
whooping cough A37.91
due to
Bordetella parapertussis
A37.11
Bordetella pertussis A37.01
specified NEC A37.81
Yersinia pestis A20.2
inhalation of food or vomit —*see*
Pneumonia, aspiration
interstitial J84.9
chronic J84.111
desquamative J84.117
due to
collagen vascular disease
J84.17
known underlying cause J84.17
idiopathic NOS J84.111
in disease classified elsewhere
J84.17
lymphocytic (due to collagen
vascular disease) (in diseases
classified elsewhere) J84.17
lymphoid J84.2
non-specific J84.89
due to
collagen vascular disease
J84.17
known underlying cause
J84.17
idiopathic J84.113
in diseases classified elsewhere
J84.17
plasma cell B59
pseudomonas J15.1
usual J84.112
due to collagen vascular disease
J84.17
idiopathic J84.112
in diseases classified elsewhere
J84.17
Klebsiella (pneumoniae) J15.0
lipid, lipoid (exogenous) J69.1
endogenous J84.89

Pneumonia *(continued)*
lobar (disseminated) (double) (interstitial) J18.1
bacterial J15.9
specified NEC J15.8
chronic —*see* Fibrosis, lung
Escherichia coli (E. coli) J15.5
Friedländer's bacillus J15.0
Hemophilus influenzae J14
hypostatic J18.2
Klebsiella (pneumoniae) J15.0
pneumococcal J13
Proteus J15.6
Pseudomonas J15.1
specified organism NEC J16.8
staphylococcal —*see* Pneumonia, staphylococcal
streptococcal NEC J15.4
Streptococcus pneumoniae J13
viral, virus —*see* Pneumonia, viral
lobular —*see* Pneumonia, broncho
Löffler's J82
lymphoid interstitial J84.2
massive —*see* Pneumonia, lobar
meconium P24.01
MSSA (methicillin susceptible Staphylococcus aureus) J15.211
multilobar —*see* Pneumonia, by type
Mycoplasma (pneumoniae) J15.7
necrotic J85.0
neonatal P23.9
aspiration —*see* Aspiration, by substance, with pneumonia
nitrogen dioxide J68.9
organizing J84.89
due to
collagen vascular disease J84.17
known underlying cause J84.17
in diseases classified elsewhere J84.17
orthostatic J18.2
parainfluenza virus J12.2
parenchymatous —*see* Fibrosis, lung
passive J18.2
patchy —*see* Pneumonia, broncho
Peptococcus J15.8
Peptostreptococcus J15.8
plasma cell (of infants) B59
pleurolobar —*see* Pneumonia, lobar
pleuro-pneumonia-like organism (PPLO) J15.7
pneumococcal (broncho) (lobar) J13
Pneumocystis (carinii) (jiroveci) B59
postinfectional NEC B99 *[J17]*
postmeasles B05.2
Proteus J15.6
Pseudomonas J15.1
psittacosis A70
radiation J70.0
respiratory syncytial virus J12.1
resulting from a procedure J95.89
rheumatic I00 *[J17]*
Salmonella (arizonae) (cholerae-suis) (enteritidis) (typhimurium) A02.22
typhi A01.03
typhoid fever A01.03
SARS-associated coronavirus J12.81
segmented, segmental —*see* Pneumonia, broncho-
Serratia marcescens J15.6
specified NEC J18.8
bacterium NEC J15.8
organism NEC J16.8
virus NEC J12.89
spirochetal NEC A69.8
staphylococcal (broncho) (lobar) J15.20
aureus (methicillin susceptible) (MSSA) J15.211
methicillin resistant (MRSA) J15.212
specified NEC J15.29

Pneumonia *(continued)*
static, stasis J18.2
streptococcal NEC (broncho) (lobar) J15.4
group
A J15.4
B J15.3
specified NEC J15.4
Streptococcus pneumoniae J13
syphilitic, congenital (early) A50.04
traumatic (complication) (early) (secondary) T79.8
tuberculous (any) —*see* Tuberculosis, pulmonary
tularemic A21.2
varicella B01.2
Veillonella J15.8
ventilator associated J95.851
viral, virus (broncho) (interstitial) (lobar) J12.9
adenoviral J12.0
congenital P23.0
human metapneumovirus J12.3
parainfluenza J12.2
respiratory syncytial J12.1
SARS-associated coronavirus J12.81
specified NEC J12.89
white (congenital) A50.04

Pneumonic —*see* condition

Pneumonitis (acute) (primary) —*see also* Pneumonia
air-conditioner J67.7
allergic (due to) J67.9
organic dust NEC J67.8
red cedar dust J67.8
sequoiosis J67.8
wood dust J67.8
aspiration J69.0
due to
anesthesia J95.4
during
labor and delivery O74.0
pregnancy O29.01-
puerperium O89.01
fumes or gases J68.0
obstetric O74.0
chemical (due to gases, fumes or vapors) (inhalation) J68.0
due to anesthesia J95.4
cholesterol J84.89
crack (cocaine) J68.0
chronic —*see* Fibrosis, lung
congenital rubella P35.0
due to
beryllium J68.0
cadmium J68.0
crack (cocaine) J68.0
detergent J69.8
fluorocarbon-polymer J68.0
food, vomit (aspiration) J69.0
fumes or vapors J68.0
gases, fumes or vapors (inhalation) J68.0
inhalation
blood J69.8
essences J69.1
food (regurgitated), milk, vomit J69.0
oils, essences J69.1
saliva J69.0
solids, liquids NEC J69.8
manganese J68.0
nitrogen dioxide J68.0
oils, essences J69.1
solids, liquids NEC J69.8
toxoplasmosis (acquired) B58.3
congenital P37.1
vanadium J68.0
ventilator J95.851
eosinophilic J82

Pneumonitis *(continued)*
hypersensitivity J67.9
air conditioner lung J67.7
bagassosis J67.1
bird fancier's lung J67.2
farmer's lung J67.0
maltworker's lung J67.4
maple bark-stripper's lung J67.6
mushroom worker's lung J67.5
specified organic dust NEC J67.8
suberosis J67.3
interstitial (chronic) J84.89
acute J84.114
lymphoid J84.2
non-specific J84.89
idiopathic J84.113
lymphoid, interstitial J84.2
meconium P24.01
postanesthetic J95.4
correct substance properly administered —*see* Table of Drugs and Chemicals, by drug, adverse effect
in labor and delivery O74.0
in pregnancy O29.01-
obstetric O74.0
overdose or wrong substance given or taken (by accident) —*see* Table of Drugs and Chemicals, by drug, poisoning
postpartum, puerperal O89.01
postoperative J95.4
obstetric O74.0
radiation J70.0
rubella, congenital P35.0
ventilation (air-conditioning) J67.7
ventilator associated J95.851
wood-dust J67.8

Pneumonoconiosis —*see* Pneumoconiosis

Pneumoparotid K11.8

Pneumopathy NEC J98.4
alveolar J84.09
due to organic dust NEC J66.8
parietoalveolar J84.09

Pneumopericarditis —*see also* Pericarditis
acute I30.9

Pneumopericardium —*see also* Pericarditis
congenital P25.3
newborn P25.3
traumatic (post) —*see* Injury, heart

Pneumophagia (psychogenic) F45.8

Pneumopleurisy, pneumopleuritis —*see also* Pneumonia J18.8

Pneumopyopericardium I30.1

Pneumopyothorax —*see* Pyopneumothorax
with fistula J86.0

Pneumorrhagia —*see also* Hemorrhage, lung
tuberculous —*see* Tuberculosis, pulmonary

Pneumothorax NOS J93.9
acute J93.83
chronic J93.81
congenital P25.1
perinatal period P25.1
postprocedural J95.811
specified NEC J93.83
spontaneous NOS J93.83
newborn P25.1
primary J93.11
secondary J93.12
tension J93.0
tense valvular, infectional J93.0
tension (spontaneous) J93.0

Pneumothorax NOS *(continued)*
traumatic S27.0
with hemothorax S27.2
tuberculous —*see* Tuberculosis, pulmonary

Podagra —*see also* Gout M10.9

Podencephalus Q01.9

Poikilocytosis R71.8

Poikiloderma L81.6
Civatte's L57.3
congenital Q82.8
vasculare atrophicans L94.5

Poikilodermatomyositis M33.10
with
myopathy M33.12
respiratory involvement M33.1
specified organ involvement NE M33.19

Pointed ear (congenital) Q17.3

Poison ivy, oak, sumac or other pla dermatitis (allergic) (contact) L2

Poisoning (acute) —*see also* Table c Drugs and Chemicals
algae and toxins T65.82-
Bacillus B (aertrycke) (cholerae (s (paratyphosus) (suipestifer) A02
botulinus A05.1
bacterial toxins A05.9
berries, noxious —*see* Poisoning, food, noxious, berries
botulism A05.1
ciguatera fish T61.0-
Clostridium botulinum A05.1
death-cap (Amanita phalloides) (Amanita verna) —*see* Poisonin food, noxious, mushrooms
drug —*see* Table of Drugs and Chemicals, by drug, poisoning
epidemic, fish (noxious) —*see* Poisoning, seafood
bacterial A05.9
fava bean D55.0
fish (noxious) T61.9-
bacterial —*see* Intoxication, foodborne, by agent
ciguatera fish —*see* Poisoning, ciguatera fish
scombroid fish —*see* Poisoning, scombroid fish
specified type NEC T61.77-
food (acute) (diseased) (infected) (noxious) NEC T62.9-
bacterial —*see* Intoxication, foodborne, by agent
due to
Bacillus (aertrycke) (choleraesuis) (paratyphosu (suipestifer) A02.9
botulinus A05.1
Clostridium (perfringens) (Welchii) A05.2
salmonella (aertrycke) (callinarum) (choleraesuis) (enteritidis) (paratyphi) (suipestifer) A02.9
with
gastroenteritis A02.0
sepsis A02.1
staphylococcus A05.0
Vibrio
parahaemolyticus A05.3
vulnificus A05.5
noxious or naturally toxic T62.9-
berries —*see* subcategory T62
fish —*see* Poisoning, seafood
mushrooms —*see* subcategory T62.0X-
plants NEC —*see* subcategory T62.2X-

Polyneuropathy *(continued)*
- toxic agent NEC (*continued*)
  - sequelae G65.2
  - triorthocresyl phosphate G62.2
    - sequelae G65.2
  - tuberculosis A17.89
  - uremia N18.9 *[G63]*
  - vitamin B12 deficiency E53.8 *[G63]*
    - with anemia (pernicious) D51.0 *[G63]*
      - due to dietary deficiency D51.3 *[G63]*
  - zoster B02.23
- inflammatory G61.9
  - chronic demyelinating (CIDP) G61.81
  - sequelae G65.1
  - specified NEC G61.89
- lead G62.2
  - sequelae G65.2
- nutritional NEC E63.9 *[G63]*
- postherpetic (zoster) B02.23
- progressive G60.3
- radiation-induced G62.82
- sensory (hereditary) (idiopathic) G60.8
- specified NEC G62.89
- syphilitic (late) A52.15
  - congenital A50.43

Polyopia H53.8

Polyorchism, polyorchidism Q55.21

Polyosteoarthritis —*see also* Osteoarthritis, generalized M15.9-
- post-traumatic M15.3
- specified NEC M15.8

Polyostotic fibrous dysplasia Q78.1

Polyotia Q17.0

Polyp, polypus
- accessory sinus J33.8
- adenocarcinoma in —*see* Neoplasm, malignant, by site
- adenocarcinoma in situ in —*see* Neoplasm, in situ, by site
- adenoid tissue J33.0
- adenomatous —*see also* Neoplasm, benign, by site
  - adenocarcinoma in —*see* Neoplasm, malignant, by site
  - adenocarcinoma in situ in —*see* Neoplasm, in situ, by site
  - carcinoma in —*see* Neoplasm, malignant, by site
  - carcinoma in situ in —*see* Neoplasm, in situ, by site
  - multiple —*see* Neoplasm, benign
    - adenocarcinoma in —*see* Neoplasm, malignant, by site
    - adenocarcinoma in situ in —*see* Neoplasm, in situ, by site
- antrum J33.8
- anus, anal (canal) K62.0
- Bartholin's gland N84.3
- bladder D41.4
- carcinoma in —*see* Neoplasm, malignant, by site
- carcinoma in situ in —*see* Neoplasm, in situ, by site
- cecum D12.0
- cervix (uteri) N84.1
  - in pregnancy or childbirth —*see* Pregnancy, complicated by, abnormal, cervix
  - mucous N84.1
  - nonneoplastic N84.1
- choanal J33.0
- cholesterol K82.4
- clitoris N84.3

Polyp, polypus *(continued)*
- colon K63.5
  - adenomatous D12.6
  - ascending D12.2
  - cecum D12.0
  - descending D12.4
  - inflammatory K51.40
    - with
      - abscess K51.414
      - complication K51.419
        - specified NEC K51.418
      - fistula K51.413
      - intestinal obstruction K51.412
      - rectal bleeding K51.411
  - sigmoid D12.5
  - transverse D12.3
- corpus uteri N84.0
- dental K04.0
- duodenum K31.7
- ear (middle) H74.4-
- endometrium N84.0
- ethmoidal (sinus) J33.8
- fallopian tube N84.8
- female genital tract N84.9
  - specified NEC N84.8
- frontal (sinus) J33.8
- gallbladder K82.4
- gingiva, gum K06.8
- labia, labium (majus) (minus) N84.3
- larynx (mucous) J38.1
  - adenomatous D14.1
- malignant —*see* Neoplasm, malignant, by site
- maxillary (sinus) J33.8
- middle ear —*see* Polyp, ear (middle)
- myometrium N84.0
- nares
  - anterior J33.9
  - posterior J33.0
- nasal (mucous) J33.9
  - cavity J33.0
  - septum J33.0
- nasopharyngeal J33.0
- nose (mucous) J33.9
- oviduct N84.8
- pharynx J39.2
- placenta O90.89
- prostate —*see* Enlargement, enlarged, prostate
- pudenda, pudendum N84.3
- pulpal (dental) K04.0
- rectum (nonadenomatous) K62.1
  - adenomatous —*see* Polyp, adenomatous
- septum (nasal) J33.0
- sinus (accessory) (ethmoidal) (frontal) (maxillary) (sphenoidal) J33.8
- sphenoidal (sinus) J33.8
- stomach K31.7
  - adenomatous D13.1
- tube, fallopian N84.8
- turbinate, mucous membrane J33.8
- umbilical, newborn P83.6
- ureter N28.89
- urethra N36.2
- uterus (body) (corpus) (mucous) N84.0
  - cervix N84.1
  - in pregnancy or childbirth —*see* Pregnancy, complicated by, tumor, uterus
- vagina N84.2
- vocal cord (mucous) J38.1
- vulva N84.3

Polyphagia R63.2

Polyploidy Q92.7

Polypoid —*see* condition

Polyposis —*see also* Polyp
- coli (adenomatous) D12.6
  - adenocarcinoma in C18.9
  - adenocarcinoma in situ in —*see* Neoplasm, in situ, by site
  - carcinoma in C18.9
- colon (adenomatous) D12.6
- familial D12.6
  - adenocarcinoma in situ in —*see* Neoplasm, in situ, by site
- intestinal (adenomatous) D12.6
- malignant lymphomatous C83.1-
- multiple, adenomatous —*see also* Neoplasm, benign D36.9

Polyradiculitis —*see* Polyneuropathy

Polyradiculoneuropathy (acute) (postinfective) (segmentally demyelinating) G61.0

Polyserositis
- due to pericarditis I31.1
- pericardial I31.1
- periodic, familial E85.0
- tuberculous A19.9
  - acute A19.1
  - chronic A19.8

Polysplenia syndrome Q89.09

Polysyndactyly —*see also* Syndactylism, syndactyly Q70.4

Polytrichia L68.3

Polyunguia Q84.6

Polyuria R35.8
- nocturnal R35.1
- psychogenic F45.8

Pompe's disease (glycogen storage) E74.02

Pompholyx L30.1

Poncet's disease (tuberculous rheumatism) A18.09

Pond fracture —*see* Fracture, skull

Ponos B55.0

Pons, pontine —*see* condition

Poor
- aesthetic of existing restoration of tooth K08.56
- contractions, labor O62.2
- gingival margin to tooth restoration K08.51
- personal hygiene R46.0
- prenatal care, affecting management of pregnancy —*see* Pregnancy, complicated by, insufficient, prenatal care
- sucking reflex (newborn) R29.2
- urinary stream R39.12
- vision NEC H54.7

Poradenitis, nostras inguinalis or venerea A55

Porencephaly (congenital) (developmental) (true) Q04.6
- acquired G93.0
- nondevelopmental G93.0
- traumatic (post) F07.89

Porocephaliasis B88.8

Porokeratosis Q82.8

Poroma, eccrine —*see* Neoplasm, skin, benign

Porphyria (South African) E80.20
- acquired E80.20
- acute intermittent (hepatic) (Swedish) E80.21
- cutanea tarda (hereditary) (symptomatic) E80.1

Porphyria *(continued)*
- due to drugs E80.20
  - correct substance properly administered —*see* Table of Drugs and Chemicals, by dr adverse effect
  - overdose or wrong substance given or taken —*see* Table o Drugs and Chemicals, by dr poisoning
- erythropoietic (congenital) (hereditary) E80.0
- hepatocutaneous type E80.1
- secondary E80.20
- toxic NEC E80.20
- variegata E80.20

Porphyrinuria —*see* Porphyria

Porphyruria —*see* Porphyria

Portal —*see* condition

Port wine nevus, mark, or stain Q

Posadas-Wernicke disease B38.9

Positive
- culture (nonspecific)
  - blood R78.81
  - bronchial washings R84.5
  - cerebrospinal fluid R83.5
  - cervix uteri R87.5
  - nasal secretions R84.5
  - nipple discharge R89.5
  - nose R84.5
    - staphylococcus (Methicillin susceptible) Z22.321
      - Methicillin resistant Z22.3
  - peritoneal fluid R85.5
  - pleural fluid R84.5
  - prostatic secretions R86.5
  - saliva R85.5
  - seminal fluid R86.5
  - sputum R84.5
  - synovial fluid R89.5
  - throat scrapings R84.5
  - urine R82.7
  - vagina R87.5
  - vulva R87.5
  - wound secretions R89.5
- PPD (skin test) R76.11
- serology for syphilis A53.0
  - false R76.8
  - with signs or symptoms - code Syphilis, by site and stage
- skin test, tuberculin (without activ tuberculosis) R76.11
- test, human immunodeficiency vir (HIV) R75
- VDRL A53.0
  - with signs or symptoms - code site and stage under Syphilis A53.9
- Wassermann reaction A53.0

Postcardiotomy syndrome I97.0

Postcaval ureter Q62.62

Postcholecystectomy syndrome K9

Postclimacteric bleeding N95.0

Postcommissurotomy syndrome I9

Postconcussional syndrome F07.81

Postcontusional syndrome F07.81

Postcricoid region —*see* condition

Post-dates (40-42 weeks) (pregnanc (mother) O48.0
- more than 42 weeks gestation O48

Postencephalitic syndrome F07.89

Posterior —*see* condition

Posterolateral sclerosis (spinal cord —*see* Degeneration, combined

Postexanthematous —*see* condition

febrile —*see* condition

gastrectomy dumping syndrome
91.1

hemiplegic chorea —*see*
onoplegia

hemorrhagic anemia (chronic)
50.0
ute D62
wborn P61.3

herpetic neuralgia (zoster)
02.29
geminal B02.22

hitis N47.7

immunization complication
reaction —*see* Complications,
ccination

infectious —*see* condition

laminectomy syndrome NEC
96.1

leukotomy syndrome F07.0

mastectomy lymphedema
yndrome) I97.2

maturity, postmature (over 42
eeks)
aternal (over 42 weeks gestation)
O48.1
wborn P08.22

measles complication NEC —*see*
so condition B05.89

menopausal
ndometrium (atrophic) N95.8
suppurative —*see also*
Endometritis N71.9
steoporosis —*see* Osteoporosis,
postmenopausal

nasal drip R09.82
e to
allergic rhinitis —*see* Rhinitis,
allergic
common cold J00
gastroesophageal reflux —*see*
Reflux, gastroesophageal
nasopharyngitis —*see*
Nasopharyngitis
other know condition - code to
condition
sinusitis —*see* Sinusitis

natal —*see* condition

operative (postprocedural) —*see*
omplication, postoperative
neumothorax, therapeutic Z98.3
ate NEC Z98.89

pancreatectomy hyperglycemia
89.1

partum —*see* Puerperal

phlebitic syndrome —*see*
yndrome, postthrombotic

poliomyelitic —*see also* condition
steopathy —*see* Osteopathy, after
poliomyelitis

polio (myelitic) **syndrome** G14

procedural —*see also*
ostoperative
ypoinsulinemia E89.1

schizophrenic depression F32.8

surgery status —*see also* Status
post)
neumothorax, therapeutic Z98.3

t-term (40-42 weeks) (pregnancy)
mother) O48.0
nfant P08.21
ore than 42 weeks gestation
(mother) O48.1

Post-traumatic brain syndrome, nonpsychotic F07.81

Post-typhoid abscess A01.09

Postures, hysterical F44.2

Postvaccinal reaction or complication —*see* Complications, vaccination

Postvalvulotomy syndrome I97.0

Potain's
disease (pulmonary edema) —*see* Edema, lung
syndrome (gastrectasis with dyspepsia) K31.0

Potter's
asthma J62.8
facies Q60.6
lung J62.8
syndrome (with renal agenesis) Q60.6

Pott's
curvature (spinal) A18.01
disease or paraplegia A18.01
spinal curvature A18.01
tumor, puffy —*see* Osteomyelitis, specified type NEC

Pouch
bronchus Q32.4
Douglas' —*see* condition
esophagus, esophageal, congenital Q39.6
acquired K22.5
gastric K31.4
Hartmann's K82.8
pharynx, pharyngeal (congenital) Q38.7

Pouchitis K91.850

Poultrymen's itch B88.0

Poverty NEC Z59.6
extreme Z59.5

Poxvirus NEC B08.8

Prader-Willi syndrome Q87.1

Preauricular appendage or tag Q17.0

Prebetalipoproteinemia (acquired) (essential) (familial) (hereditary) (primary) (secondary) E78.1
with chylomicronemia E78.3

Precipitate labor or delivery O62.3

Preclimacteric bleeding (menorrhagia) N92.4

Precocious
adrenarche E30.1
menarche E30.1
menstruation E30.1
pubarche E30.1
puberty E30.1
central E22.8
sexual development NEC E30.1
thelarche E30.8

Precocity, sexual (constitutional) (cryptogenic) (female) (idiopathic) (male) E30.1
with adrenal hyperplasia E25.9
congenital E25.0

Precordial pain R07.2

Predeciduous teeth K00.2

Prediabetes, prediabetic R73.09
complicating
pregnancy —*see* Pregnancy, complicated by, diseases of, specified type or system NEC
puerperium O99.89

Predislocation status of hip at birth Q65.6

Pre-eclampsia O14.9-
with pre-existing hypertension — *see* Hypertension, complicating pregnancy, pre-existing, with, pre-eclampsia
mild O14.0-
moderate O14.0-
severe O14.1-
with hemolysis, elevated liver enzymes and low platelet count (HELLP) O14.2-

Pre-eruptive color change, teeth, tooth K00.8

Pre-excitation atrioventricular conduction I45.6

Preglaucoma H40.00-

Pregnancy (single) (uterine) —*see also* Delivery and Puerperal
Note: The Tabular must be reviewed for assignment of the appropriate character indicating the trimester of the pregnancy
Note: The Tabular must be reviewed for assignment of appropriate seventh character for multiple gestation codes in Chapter 15
abdominal (ectopic) O00.0
with viable fetus O36.7-
ampullar O00.1
biochemical O02.81
broad ligament O00.8
cervical O00.8
chemical O02.81
complicated NOS O26.9-
complicated by (care of) (management affected by)
abnormal, abnormality
cervix O34.4-
causing obstructed labor O65.5
cord (umbilical) O69.9
findings on antenatal screening of mother O28.9
biochemical O28.1
cytological O28.2
chromosomal O28.5
genetic O28.5
hematological O28.0
radiological O28.4
specified NEC O28.8
ultrasonic O28.3
glucose (tolerance) NEC O99.810
pelvic organs O34.9-
specified NEC O34.8-
causing obstructed labor O65.5
pelvis (bony) (major) NEC O33.0
perineum O34.7-
position
placenta O44.1-
without hemorrhage O44.0-
uterus O34.59-
uterus O34.59-
causing obstructed labor O65.5
congenital O34.0-
vagina O34.6-
causing obstructed labor O65.5
vulva O34.7-
causing obstructed labor O65.5
abruptio placentae —*see* Abruptio placentae
abscess or cellulitis
bladder O23.1-
breast O91.11-
genital organ or tract O23.9-

Pregnancy *(continued)*
complicated by *(continued)*
abuse
physical O9A.31-
psychological O9A.51-
sexual O9A.41-
adverse effect anesthesia O29.9-
aspiration pneumonitis O29.01-
cardiac arrest O29.11-
cardiac complication NEC O29.19-
cardiac failure O29.12-
central nervous system complication NEC O29.29-
cerebral anoxia O29.21-
failed or difficult intubation O29.6-
inhalation of stomach contents or secretions NOS O29.01-
local, toxic reaction O29.3X
Mendelson's syndrome O29.01-
pressure collapse of lung O29.02-
pulmonary complications NEC O29.09-
specified NEC O29.8X-
spinal and epidural type NEC O29.5X
induced headache O29.4-
albuminuria O12.1-
alcohol use O99.31-
amnionitis O41.12-
anaphylactoid syndrome of pregnancy O88.01-
anemia (conditions in D50-D64) (pre-existing) O99.01-
complicating the puerperium O99.03
antepartum hemorrhage O46.9-
with coagulation defect —*see* Hemorrhage, antepartum, with coagulation defect
specified NEC O46.8X-
appendicitis O99.61-
atrophy (yellow) (acute) liver (subacute) O26.61-
bariatric surgery status O99.84-
bicornis or bicornuate uterus O34.59-
biliary tract problems O26.61-
breech presentation O32.1
cardiovascular diseases (conditions in I00-I09, I20-I52, I70-I99) O99.41-
cerebrovascular disorders (conditions in I60-I69) O99.41-
cervical shortening O26.87-
cervicitis O23.51-
chloasma (gravidarum) O26.89-
cholestasis (intrahepatic) O26.61-
cholecystitis O99.61-
chorioamnionitis O41.12-
circulatory system disorder (conditions in I00-I09, I20-I99, O99.41-)
compound presentation O32.6
conjoined twins O30.02-
connective system disorders (conditions in M00-M99) O99.89
contracted pelvis (general) O33.1
inlet O33.2
outlet O33.3
convulsions (eclamptic) (uremic) —*see also* Eclampsia O15.9-
cracked nipple O92.11-
cystitis O23.1-
cystocele O34.8-
death of fetus (near term) O36.4
early pregnancy O02.1
of one fetus or more in multiple gestation O31.2-

Pregnancy *(continued)*
complicated by *(continued)*
deciduitis O41.14-
decreased fetal movement O36.81-
dental problems O99.61-
diabetes (mellitus) O24.91-
gestational (pregnancy induced) —*see* - Diabetes, gestational
pre-existing O24.31-
specified NEC O24.81-
type 1 O24.01-
type 2 O24.11-
digestive system disorders (conditions in K00-K93) O99.61-
diseases of —*see* Pregnancy, complicated by, specified body system disease
biliary tract O26.61-
blood NEC (conditions in D65-D77) O99.11-
liver O26.61-
specified NEC O99.89
disorders of —*see* Pregnancy, complicated by, specified body system disorder
amniotic fluid and membranes O41.9-
specified NEC O41.8X-
biliary tract O26.61-
ear and mastoid process (conditions in H60-H95) O99.89
eye and adnexa (conditions in H00-H59) O99.89
liver O26.61-
skin (conditions in L00-L99) O99.71-
specified NEC O99.89
displacement, uterus NEC O34.59-
causing obstructed labor O65.5
disproportion (due to) O33.9
fetal deformities NEC O33.7
generally contracted pelvis O33.1
hydrocephalic fetus O33.6
inlet contraction of pelvis O33.2
mixed maternal and fetal origin O33.4
specified NEC O33.8
double uterus O34.59-
causing obstructed labor O65.5
drug use (conditions in F11-F19) O99.32-
eclampsia, eclamptic (coma) (convulsions) (delirium) (nephritis) (uremia) —*see also* Eclampsia O15.-
ectopic pregnancy —*see* Pregnancy, ectopic
edema O12.0-
with
gestational hypertension, mild —*see also* Pre-eclampsia O14.0-
proteinuria O12.2-
effusion, amniotic fluid —*see* Pregnancy, complicated by, premature rupture of membranes
elderly
multigravida O09.52-
primigravida O09.51-
embolism —*see also* Embolism, obstetric, pregnancy O88.-
endocrine diseases NEC O99.28-
endometritis O86.12
excessive weight gain O26.0-
exhaustion O26.81-
during labor and delivery O75.81
face presentation O32.3

Pregnancy *(continued)*
complicated by *(continued)*
failed induction of labor O61.9
instrumental O61.1
mechanical O61.1
medical O61.0
specified NEC O61.8
surgical O61.1
failed or difficult intubation for anesthesia O29.6-
false labor (pains) O47.9
at or after 37 completed weeks of pregnancy O47.1
before 37 completed weeks of pregnancy O47.0-
fatigue O26.81-
during labor and delivery O75.81
fatty metamorphosis of liver O26.61-
female genital mutilation O34.8- *[N90.81-]*
fetal (maternal care for)
abnormality or damage O35.9
acid-base balance O68
specified type NEC O35.8
acidemia O68
acidosis O68
alkalosis O68
anemia and thrombocytopenia O36.82-
anencephaly O35.0
chromosomal abnormality (conditions in Q90-Q99) O35.1
conjoined twins O30.02-
damage from
amniocentesis O35.7
biopsy procedures O35.7
drug addiction O35.5
hematological investigation O35.7
intrauterine contraceptive device O35.7
maternal
alcohol addiction O35.4
cytomegalovirus infection O35.3
disease NEC O35.8
drug addiction O35.5
listeriosis O35.8
rubella O35.3
toxoplasmosis O35.8
viral infection O35.3
medical procedure NEC O35.7
radiation O35.6
death (near term) O36.4
early pregnancy O02.1
decreased movement O36.81-
disproportion due to deformity (fetal) O33.7
excessive growth (large for dates) O36.6-
growth retardation O36.59-
light for dates O36.59-
small for dates O36.59-
heart rate irregularity (bradycardia) (decelerations) (tachycardia) O76
hereditary disease O35.2
hydrocephalus O35.0
intrauterine death O36.4
poor growth O36.59-
light for dates O36.59-
small for dates O36.59-
problem O36.9-
specified NEC O36.89-
reduction (elective) O31.3-
selective termination O31.3-
spina bifida O35.0
thrombocytopenia O36.82-
fibroid (tumor) (uterus) O34.1-

Pregnancy *(continued)*
complicated by *(continued)*
fissure of nipple O92.11-
gallstones O99.61-
gastric banding status O99.84-
gastric bypass status O99.84-
genital herpes (asymptomatic) (history of) (inactive) O98.51-
genital tract infection O23.9-
glomerular diseases (conditions in N00-N07) O26.83-
with hypertension, pre-existing —*see* Hypertension, complicating, pregnancy, pre-existing, with, renal disease
gonorrhea O98.21-
grand multiparity O09.4
habitual aborter —*see* Pregnancy, complicated by, recurrent pregnancy loss
HELLP syndrome (hemolysis, elevated liver enzymes and low platelet count) O14.2-
hemorrhage
antepartum —*see* Hemorrhage, antepartum
before 20 completed weeks gestation O20.9
specified NEC O20.8
due to premature separation, placenta —*see also* Abruptio placentae O45.9-
early O20.9
specified NEC O20.8
threatened abortion O20.0
hemorrhoids O22.4-
hepatitis (viral) O98.41-
herniation of uterus O34.59-
high
head at term O32.4
risk —*see* Supervision (of) (for), high-risk
history of in utero procedure during previous pregnancy O09.82-
HIV O98.71-
human immunodeficiency virus (HIV) disease O98.71-
hydatidiform mole —*see also* Mole, hydatidiform O01.9-
hydramnios O40.-
hydrocephalic fetus (disproportion) O33.6
hydrops
amnii O40.-
fetalis O36.2-
associated with
isoimmunization —*see also* Pregnancy, complicated by, isoimmunization O36.11-
hydrorrhea O42.90
hyperemesis (gravidarum) (mild) —*see also* Hyperemesis, gravidarum O21.0-
hypertension —*see* Hypertension, complicating pregnancy
hypertensive
heart and renal disease, pre-existing —*see* Hypertension, complicating, pregnancy, pre-existing, with, heart disease, with renal disease
heart disease, pre-existing —*see* Hypertension, complicating, pregnancy, pre-existing, with, heart disease
renal disease, pre-existing —*see* Hypertension, complicating, pregnancy, pre-existing, with, renal disease
hypotension O26.5-
immune disorders NEC (conditions in D80-D89) O99.11-

Pregnancy *(continued)*
complicated by *(continued)*
incarceration, uterus O34.51-
incompetent cervix O34.3-
inconclusive fetal viability O36.80
infection (s) O98.91-
amniotic fluid or sac O41.10-
bladder O23.1-
carrier state NEC O99.830
streptococcus B O99.820
genital organ or tract O23.9-
specified NEC O23.59-
genitourinary tract O23.9-
gonorrhea O98.21-
hepatitis (viral) O98.41-
HIV O98.71-
human immunodeficiency vir
(HIV) O98.71-
kidney O23.0-
nipple O91.01-
parasitic disease O98.91-
specified NEC O98.81-
protozoal disease O98.61-
sexually transmitted NEC O98.31-
specified type NEC O98.81-
syphilis O98.11-
tuberculosis O98.01-
urethra O23.2-
urinary (tract) O23.4-
specified NEC O23.3-
viral disease O98.51-
injury or poisoning (conditions i
S00-T88) O9A.21-
due to abuse
physical O9A.31-
psychological O9A.51-
sexual O9A.41-
insufficient
prenatal care O09.3-
weight gain O26.1-
insulin resistance O26.89
intrauterine fetal death (near terr
O36.4
early pregnancy O02.1
multiple gestation (one fetus c
more) O31.2-
isoimmunization O36.11-
anti-A sensitization O36.11-
anti-B sensitization O36.19-
Rh O36.09-
anti-D antibody O36.01-
specified NEC O36.19-
laceration of uterus NEC O71.81
malformation
placenta, placental (vessel) O43.10-
specified NEC O43.19-
uterus (congenital) O34.0-
malnutrition (conditions in E40-E46) O25.1-
maternal hypotension syndrome O26.5-
mental disorders (conditions in F01-F09, F20-F99) O99.34-
alcohol use O99.31-
drug use O99.32-
smoking O99.33-
mentum presentation O32.3
metabolic disorders O99.28-
missed
abortion O02.1
delivery O36.4
multiple gestations O30.9-
conjoined twins O30.02-
specified number of multiples
NEC —*see* Pregnancy, multiple (gestation), specifie
NEC
quadruplet —*see* Pregnancy, quadruplet

- **ːS** (posterior reversible ɪcephalopathy syndrome) I67.83
- **sbycardia** R54
- **sbycusis, presbyacusia** H91.1-
- **sbyesophagus** K22.8
- **sbyophrenia** F03
- **sbyopia** H52.4
- **scription of contraceptives** (initial) 30.019
  - mergency (postcoital) Z30.012
  - nplantable subdermal Z30.019
  - ɪjectable Z30.013
  - ɪtrauterine contraceptive device Z30.014
  - ills Z30.011
  - ostcoital (emergency) Z30.012
  - ɛpeat Z30.40
    - implantable subdermal Z30.49
    - injectable Z30.42
    - pills Z30.41
    - specified type NEC Z30.49
  - ɔecified type NEC Z30.018
- **sence** (of)
  - nkle-joint implant (functional) (prosthesis) Z96.66-
  - ɔrtocoronary (bypass) graft Z95.1
  - rterial-venous shunt (dialysis) Z99.2
  - rtificial
    - eye (globe) Z97.0
    - heart (fully implantable) (mechanical) Z95.812
      - valve Z95.2
    - larynx Z96.3
    - lens (intraocular) Z96.1
    - limb (complete) (partial) Z97.1-
      - arm Z97.1-
        - bilateral Z97.15
      - leg Z97.1-
        - bilateral Z97.16
  - udiological implant (functional) Z96.29
  - ladder implant (functional) Z96.0
  - one
    - conduction hearing device Z96.29
    - implant (functional) NEC Z96.7
    - joint (prosthesis) —*see* Presence, joint implant
  - ardiac
    - defibrillator (functional) (with synchronous cardiac pacemaker) Z95.810
    - implant or graft Z95.9
      - specified type NEC Z95.818
    - pacemaker Z95.0
  - erebrospinal fluid drainage device Z98.2
  - ochlear implant (functional) Z96.21
  - ontact lens (es) Z97.3
  - oronary artery graft or prosthesis Z95.5
  - ːSF shunt Z98.2
  - ental prosthesis device Z97.2
  - entures Z97.2
  - evice (external) NEC Z97.8
    - cardiac NEC Z95.818
    - heart assist Z95.811
    - implanted (functional) Z96.9
      - specified NEC Z96.89
    - prosthetic Z97.8
  - ar implant Z96.20
    - cochlear implant Z96.21
    - myringotomy tube Z96.22
    - specified type NEC Z96.29
  - lbow-joint implant (functional) (prosthesis) Z96.62-
  - ndocrine implant (functional) NEC Z96.49
  - ustachian tube stent or device (functional) Z96.29

Presence *(continued)*

- external hearing-aid or device Z97.4
- finger-joint implant (functional) (prosthetic) Z96.69-
- functional implant Z96.9
  - specified NEC Z96.89
- graft
  - cardiac NEC Z95.818
  - vascular NEC Z95.828
- hearing-aid or device (external) Z97.4
  - implant (bone) (cochlear) (functional) Z96.21
- heart assist device Z95.811
- heart valve implant (functional) Z95.2
  - prosthetic Z95.2
  - specified type NEC Z95.4
  - xenogenic Z95.3
- hip-joint implant (functional) (prosthesis) Z96.64-
- implanted device (artificial) (functional) (prosthetic) Z96.9
  - automatic cardiac defibrillator (with synchronous cardiac pacemaker) Z95.810
  - cardiac pacemaker Z95.0
  - cochlear Z96.21
  - dental Z96.5
  - heart Z95.812
  - heart valve Z95.2
    - prosthetic Z95.2
    - specified NEC Z95.4
    - xenogenic Z95.3
  - insulin pump Z96.41
  - intraocular lens Z96.1
  - joint Z96.60
    - ankle Z96.66-
    - elbow Z96.62-
    - finger Z96.69-
    - hip Z96.64-
    - knee Z96.65-
    - shoulder Z96.61-
    - specified NEC Z96.698
    - wrist Z96.63-
  - larynx Z96.3
  - myringotomy tube Z96.22
  - otological Z96.20
    - cochlear Z96.21
    - eustachian stent Z96.29
    - myringotomy Z96.22
    - specified NEC Z96.29
    - stapes Z96.29
  - skin Z96.81
  - skull plate Z96.7
  - specified NEC Z96.89
  - urogenital Z96.0
- insulin pump (functional) Z96.41
- intestinal bypass or anastomosis Z98.0
- intraocular lens (functional) Z96.1
- intrauterine contraceptive device (IUD) Z97.5
- intravascular implant (functional) (prosthetic) NEC Z95.9
  - coronary artery Z95.5
  - defibrillator (with synchronous cardiac pacemaker) Z95.810
  - peripheral vessel (with angioplasty) Z95.820
- joint implant (prosthetic) (any) Z96.60
  - ankle —*see* Presence, ankle joint implant
  - elbow —*see* Presence, elbow joint implant
  - finger —*see* Presence, finger joint implant
  - hip —*see* Presence, hip joint implant
  - knee —*see* Presence, knee joint implant
  - shoulder —*see* Presence, shoulder joint implant

Presence *(continued)*

- joint implant *(continued)*
  - specified joint NEC Z96.698
  - wrist —*see* Presence, wrist joint implant
- knee-joint implant (functional) (prosthesis) Z96.65-
- laryngeal implant (functional) Z96.3
- mandibular implant (dental) Z96.5
- myringotomy tube (s) Z96.22
- orthopedic-joint implant (prosthetic) (any) —*see* Presence, joint implant
- otological implant (functional) Z96.29
- shoulder-joint implant (functional) (prosthesis) Z96.61-
- skull-plate implant Z96.7
- spectacles Z97.3
- stapes implant (functional) Z96.29
- systemic lupus erythematosus [SLE] inhibitor D68.62
- tendon implant (functional) (graft) Z96.7
- tooth root (s) implant Z96.5
- ureteral stent Z96.0
- urethral stent Z96.0
- urogenital implant (functional) Z96.0
- vascular implant or device Z95.9
  - access port device Z95.828
  - specified type NEC Z95.828
- wrist-joint implant (functional) (prosthesis) Z96.63-

Presenile —*see also* condition
- dementia F03
- premature aging E34.8

Presentation, fetal —*see* Delivery, complicated by, malposition

Prespondylolisthesis (congenital) Q76.2

Pressure
- area, skin —*see* Ulcer, pressure, by site
- brachial plexus G54.0
- brain G93.5
  - injury at birth NEC P11.1
- cerebral —*see* Pressure, brain
- chest R07.89
- cone, tentorial G93.5
- hyposystolic —*see also* Hypotension
  - incidental reading, without diagnosis of hypotension R03.1
- increased
  - intracranial (benign) G93.2
    - injury at birth P11.0
  - intraocular H40.05-
- lumbosacral plexus G54.1
- mediastinum J98.5
- necrosis (chronic) —*see* Ulcer, pressure, by site
- parental, inappropriate (excessive) Z62.6
- sore (chronic) —*see* Ulcer, pressure, by site
- spinal cord G95.20
- ulcer (chronic) —*see* Ulcer, pressure, by site
- venous, increased I87.8

Pre-syncope R55

Preterm
- delivery —*see also* Pregnancy, complicated by, preterm labor O60.10
- labor —*see* Pregnancy, complicated by, preterm labor
- newborn (infant) P07.30
  - gestational age
    - 28 completed weeks (28 weeks, 0 days through 28 weeks, 6 days) P07.31

Preterm *(continued)*
- newborn *(continued)*
  - gestational age *(continued)*
    - 29 completed weeks (29 weeks, 0 days through 29 weeks, 6 days) P07.32
    - 30 completed weeks (30 weeks, 0 days through 30 weeks, 6 days) P07.33
    - 31 completed weeks (31 weeks, 0 days through 31 weeks, 6 days) P07.34
    - 32 completed weeks (32 weeks, 0 days through 32 weeks, 6 days) P07.35
    - 33 completed weeks (33 weeks, 0 days through 33 weeks, 6 days) P07.36
    - 34 completed weeks (34 weeks, 0 days through 34 weeks, 6 days) P07.37
    - 35 completed weeks (35 weeks, 0 days through 35 weeks, 6 days) P07.38
    - 36 completed weeks (36 weeks, 0 days through 36 weeks, 6 days) P07.39

Previa
- placenta (low) (marginal) (partial) (total) (with hemorrhage) O44.1-
  - without hemorrhage O44.0-
- vasa O69.4

Priapism N48.30
- due to
  - disease classified elsewhere N48.32
  - drug N48.33
  - specified cause NEC N48.39
  - trauma N48.31

Prickling sensation (skin) R20.2

Prickly heat L74.0

Primary —*see* condition

Primigravida
- elderly, affecting management of pregnancy, labor and delivery (supervision only) —*see* Pregnancy, complicated by, elderly, primigravida
- older, affecting management of pregnancy, labor and delivery (supervision only) —*see* Pregnancy, complicated by, elderly, primigravida
- very young, affecting management of pregnancy, labor and delivery (supervision only) —*see* Pregnancy, complicated by, young mother, primigravida

Primipara
- elderly, affecting management of pregnancy, labor and delivery (supervision only) —*see* Pregnancy, complicated by, elderly, primigravida
- older, affecting management of pregnancy, labor and delivery (supervision only) —*see* Pregnancy, complicated by, elderly, primigravida
- very young, affecting management of pregnancy, labor and delivery (supervision only) —*see* Pregnancy, complicated by, young mother, primigravida

Primus varus (bilateral) Q66.2

PRIND (Prolonged reversible ischemic neurologic deficit) I63.9

Pringle's disease (tuberous sclerosis) Q85.1

Prinzmetal angina I20.1

Prizefighter ear —*see* Cauliflower ear

Problem (with) (related to)
- academic Z55.8
- acculturation Z60.3
- adjustment (to)
  - change of job Z56.1
  - life-cycle transition Z60.0
  - pension Z60.0
  - retirement Z60.0
- adopted child Z62.821
- alcoholism in family Z63.72
- atypical parenting situation Z62.9
- bankruptcy Z59.8
- behavioral (adult) F69
  - drug *see*king Z72.89
- birth of sibling affecting child Z62.898
- care (of)
  - provider dependency Z74.9
    - specified NEC Z74.8
  - sick or handicapped person in family or household Z63.6
- child
  - abuse (affecting the child) —*see* Maltreatment, child
  - custody or support proceedings Z65.3
  - in welfare custody Z62.21
  - in care of non-parental family member Z62.21
  - in foster care Z62.21
  - living in orphanage or group home Z62.22
- child-rearing Z62.9
  - specified NEC Z62.898
- communication (developmental) F80.9
- conflict or discord (with)
  - boss Z56.4
  - classmates Z55.4
  - counselor Z64.4
  - employer Z56.4
  - family Z63.9
    - specified NEC Z63.8
  - probation officer Z64.4
  - social worker Z64.4
  - teachers Z55.4
  - workmates Z56.4
- conviction in legal proceedings Z65.0
  - with imprisonment Z65.1
- counselor Z64.4
- creditors Z59.8
- digestive K92.9
- drug addict in family Z63.72
- ear —*see* Disorder, ear
- economic Z59.9
  - affecting care Z59.9
  - specified NEC Z59.8
- education Z55.9
  - specified NEC Z55.8
- employment Z56.9
  - change of job Z56.1
  - discord Z56.4
  - environment Z56.5
  - sexual harassment Z56.81
  - specified NEC Z56.89
  - stress NEC Z56.6
  - stressful schedule Z56.3
  - threat of job loss Z56.2
  - unemployment Z56.0
- enuresis, child F98.0
- eye H57.9
- failed examinations (school) Z55.2
- falling Z91.81
- family —*see also* Disruption, family Z63.9-
  - specified NEC Z63.8
- feeding (elderly) (infant) R63.3
  - newborn P92.9
    - breast P92.5

Problem *(continued)*
- feeding *(continued)*
  - newborn *(continued)*
    - overfeeding P92.4
    - slow P92.2
    - specified NEC P92.8
    - underfeeding P92.3
  - nonorganic F50.8
- finance Z59.9
  - specified NEC Z59.8
- foreclosure on loan Z59.8
- foster child Z62.822
- frightening experience (s) in childhood Z62.898
- genital NEC
  - female N94.9
  - male N50.9
- health care Z75.9
  - specified NEC Z75.8
- hearing —*see* Deafness
- homelessness Z59.0
- housing Z59.9
  - inadequate Z59.1
  - isolated Z59.8
  - specified NEC Z59.8
- identity (of childhood) F93.8
- illegitimate pregnancy (unwanted) Z64.0
- illiteracy Z55.0
- impaired mobility Z74.09
- imprisonment or incarceration Z65.1
- inadequate teaching affecting education Z55.8
- inappropriate (excessive) parental pressure Z62.6
- influencing health status NEC Z78.9
- in-law Z63.1
- institutionalization, affecting child Z62.22
- intrafamilial communication Z63.8
- jealousy, child F93.8
- landlord Z59.2
- language (developmental) F80.9
- learning (developmental) F81.9
- legal Z65.3
  - conviction without imprisonment Z65.0
  - imprisonment Z65.1
  - release from prison Z65.2
- life-management Z73.9
  - specified NEC Z73.89
- life-style Z72.9
  - gambling Z72.6
  - high-risk sexual behavior (heterosexual) Z72.51
    - bisexual Z72.53
    - homosexual Z72.52
  - inappropriate eating habits Z72.4
  - self-damaging behavior NEC Z72.89
  - specified NEC Z72.89
  - tobacco use Z72.0
- literacy Z55.9
  - low level Z55.0
  - specified NEC Z55.8
- living alone Z60.2
- lodgers Z59.2
- loss of love relationship in childhood Z62.898
- marital Z63.0
  - involving
    - divorce Z63.5
    - estrangement Z63.5
    - gender identity F66
- mastication K08.8
- medical
  - care, within family Z63.6
  - facilities Z75.9
    - specified NEC Z75.8
- mental F48.9

Problem *(continued)*
- multiparity Z64.1
- negative life events in childhood Z62.9
  - altered pattern of family relationships Z62.898
  - frightening experience Z62.898
  - loss of
    - love relationship Z62.898
    - self-esteem Z62.898
  - physical abuse (alleged) —*see* Maltreatment, child
  - removal from home Z62.29
  - specified event NEC Z62.898
- neighbor Z59.2
- neurological NEC R29.818
- new step-parent affecting child Z62.898
- none (feared complaint unfounded) Z71.1
- occupational NEC Z56.89
- parent-child —*see* Conflict, parent-child
- personal hygiene Z91.89
- personality F69
- phase-of-life transition, adjustment Z60.0
- presence of sick or disabled person in family or household Z63.79
  - needing care Z63.6
- primary support group (family) Z63.9
  - specified NEC Z63.8
- probation officer Z64.4
- psychiatric F99
- psychosexual (development) F66
- psychosocial Z65.9
  - specified NEC Z65.8
- relationship Z63.9
  - childhood F93.8
- release from prison Z65.2
- removal from home affecting child Z62.29
- *see*king and accepting known hazardous and harmful
  - behavioral or psychological interventions Z65.8
  - chemical, nutritional or physical interventions Z65.8
- sexual function (nonorganic) F52.9
- sight H54.7
- sleep disorder, child F51.9
- smell —*see* Disturbance, sensation, smell
- social
  - environment Z60.9
    - specified NEC Z60.8
  - exclusion and rejection Z60.4
  - worker Z64.4
- speech R47.9
  - developmental F80.9
  - specified NEC R47.89
- swallowing —*see* Dysphagia
- taste —*see* Disturbance, sensation, taste
- tic, child F95.0
- underachievement in school Z55.3
- unemployment Z56.0
  - threatened Z56.2
- unwanted pregnancy Z64.0
- upbringing Z62.9
  - specified NEC Z62.898
- urinary N39.9
- voice production R47.89
- work schedule (stressful) Z56.3

Procedure (surgical)
- for purpose other than remedying health state Z41.9
  - specified NEC Z41.8

Procedure *(continued)*
- not done Z53.9
  - because of
    - administrative reasons Z53.8
    - contraindication Z53.09
      - smoking Z53.01
    - patient's decision Z53.20
      - for reasons of belief or grou pressure Z53.1
      - left against medical advice (AMA) Z53.21
      - specified reason NEC Z53.29
    - specified reason NEC Z53.8

Procidentia (uteri) N81.3

Proctalgia K62.89
- fugax K59.4
- spasmodic K59.4

Proctitis K62.89
- amebic (acute) A06.0
- chlamydial A56.3
- gonococcal A54.6
- granulomatous —*see* Enteritis, regional, large intestine
- herpetic A60.1
- radiation K62.7
- tuberculous A18.32
- ulcerative (chronic) K51.20
  - with
    - complication K51.219
      - abscess K51.214
      - fistula K51.213
      - obstruction K51.212
      - rectal bleeding K51.211
      - specified NEC K51.218

Proctocele
- female (without uterine prolapse) N81.6
  - with uterine prolapse N81.2
    - complete N81.3
- male K62.3

Proctocolitis, mucosal —*see* Rectosigmoiditis, ulcerative

Proctoptosis K62.3

Proctorrhagia K62.5

Proctosigmoiditis K63.89
- ulcerative (chronic) —*see* Rectosigmoiditis, ulcerative

Proctospasm K59.4
- psychogenic F45.8

Profichet's disease —*see* Disorder, s tissue, specified type NEC

Progeria E34.8

Prognathism (mandibular) (maxillary M26.19

Progonoma (melanotic) —*see* Neoplasm, benign, by site

Progressive —*see* condition

Prolactinoma
- specified site —*see* Neoplasm, benign, by site
- unspecified site D35.2

Prolapse, prolapsed
- anus, anal (canal) (sphincter) K62.2
- arm or hand O32.2
  - causing obstructed labor O64.4
- bladder (mucosa) (sphincter) (acquired)
  - congenital Q79.4
  - female —*see* Cystocele
  - male N32.89
- breast implant (prosthetic) T85.49
- cecostomy K94.09
- cecum K63.4

apse, prolapsed *(continued)*
- ervix, cervical (hypertrophied) N81.2
  - anterior lip, obstructing labor O65.5
  - congenital Q51.828
  - postpartal, old N81.2
  - stump N81.85
- liary body (traumatic) *—see* Laceration, eye (ball), with prolapse or loss of interocular tissue
- olon (pedunculated) K63.4
- olostomy K94.09
- sc (intervertebral) *—see* Displacement, intervertebral disc
- ve implant (orbital) T85.398
  - lens (ocular) *—see* Complications, intraocular lens
- llopian tube N83.4
- astric (mucosa) K31.89
- enital, female N81.9
  - specified NEC N81.89
- obe, nontraumatic *—see* Luxation, globe
- eostomy bud K94.19
- tervertebral disc *—see* Displacement, intervertebral disc
- testine (small) K63.4
- is (traumatic) *—see* Laceration, eye (ball), with prolapse or loss of interocular tissue
  - nontraumatic H21.89
- dney N28.83
  - congenital Q63.2
- ryngeal muscles or ventricle J38.7
- ver K76.89
- eatus urinarius N36.8
- itral (valve) I34.1
- cular lens implant *—see* Complications, intraocular lens
- rgan or site, congenital NEC *—see* Malposition, congenital
- vary N83.4
- elvic floor, female N81.89
- erineum, female N81.89
- ectum (mucosa) (sphincter) K62.3
  - due to trichuris trichuria B79
- pleen D73.89
- omach K31.89
- mbilical cord
  - complicating delivery O69.0
- rachus, congenital Q64.4
- reter N28.89
  - with obstruction N13.5
    - with infection N13.6
- reterovesical orifice N28.89
- rethra (acquired) (infected) (mucosa) N36.8
  - congenital Q64.71
- rinary meatus N36.8
  - congenital Q64.72
- terovaginal N81.4
  - complete N81.3
  - incomplete N81.2
- terus (with prolapse of vagina) N81.4
  - complete N81.3
  - congenital Q51.818
  - first degree N81.2
  - in pregnancy or childbirth *—see* Pregnancy, complicated by, abnormal, uterus
  - incomplete N81.2
  - postpartal (old) N81.4
  - second degree N81.2
  - third degree N81.3
- veal (traumatic) *—see* Laceration, eye (ball), with prolapse or loss of interocular tissue

Prolapse, prolapsed *(continued)*
- vagina (anterior) (wall) *—see* Cystocele
  - with prolapse of uterus N81.4
    - complete N81.3
    - incomplete N81.2
  - posterior wall N81.6
  - posthysterectomy N99.3
- vitreous (humor) H43.0-
  - in wound *—see* Laceration, eye (ball), with prolapse or loss of interocular tissue
- womb *—see* Prolapse, uterus

Prolapsus, female N81.9
- specified NEC N81.89

Proliferation (s)
- primary cutaneous CD30-positive large T-cell C86.6

Proliferative *—see* condition

Prolonged, prolongation (of)
- bleeding (time) (idiopathic) R79.1
- coagulation (time) R79.1
- gestation (over 42 completed weeks)
  - mother O48.1
  - newborn P08.22
- interval I44.0
- labor O63.9
  - first stage O63.0
  - second stage O63.1
- partial thromboplastin time (PTT) R79.1
- pregnancy (more than 42 weeks gestation) O48.1
- prothrombin time R79.1
- QT interval I45.81
- uterine contractions in labor O62.4

Prominence, prominent
- auricle (congenital) (ear) Q17.5
- ischial spine or sacral promontory
- with disproportion (fetopelvic) O33.0
  - causing obstructed labor O65.0
- nose (congenital) acquired M95.0

Promiscuity *—see* High, risk, sexual behavior

Pronation
- ankle *—see* Deformity, limb, foot, specified NEC
- foot *—see also* Deformity, limb, foot, specified NEC
  - congenital Q74.2

Prophylactic
- administration of
  - antibiotics, long-term Z79.2
    - short-term use - omit code
  - drug *—see also* Long-term (current) drug therapy (use of) Z79.899-
- medication Z79.899
- organ removal (for neoplasia management) Z40.00
  - breast Z40.01
  - ovary Z40.02
  - specified site NEC Z40.09
- surgery Z40.9
  - for risk factors related to malignant neoplasm *—see* Prophylactic, organ removal
  - specified NEC Z40.8
- vaccination Z23

Propionic acidemia E71.121

Proptosis (ocular) *—see also* Exophthalmos
- thyroid *—see* Hyperthyroidism, with goiter

Prosecution, anxiety concerning Z65.3

Prosopagnosia R48.3

Prostadynia N42.81

Prostate, prostatic *—see* condition

Prostatism *—see* Hyperplasia, prostate

Prostatitis (congestive) (suppurative) (with cystitis) N41.9
- acute N41.0
- cavitary N41.8
- chronic N41.1
- diverticular N41.8
- due to Trichomonas (vaginalis) A59.02
- fibrous N41.1
- gonococcal (acute) (chronic) A54.22
- granulomatous N41.4
- hypertrophic N41.1
- subacute N41.1
- trichomonal A59.02
- tuberculous A18.14

Prostatocystitis N41.3

Prostatorrhea N42.89

Prostatosis N42.82

Prostration R53.83
- heat *—see also* Heat, exhaustion
  - anhydrotic T67.3
  - due to
    - salt (and water) depletion T67.4
    - water depletion T67.3
- nervous F48.8
- senile R54

Protanomaly (anomalous trichromat) H53.54

Protanopia (complete) (incomplete) H53.54

Protection (against) (from) *—see* Prophylactic

Protein
- deficiency NEC *—see* Malnutrition
- malnutrition *—see* Malnutrition
- sickness *—see also* Reaction, serum T80.69

Proteinemia R77.9

Proteinosis
- alveolar (pulmonary) J84.01
- lipid or lipoid (of Urbach) E78.89

Proteinuria R80.9
- Bence Jones R80.3
- complicating pregnancy *—see* Proteinuria, gestational
- gestational O12.1-
  - with edema O12.2-
- idiopathic R80.0
- isolated R80.0
  - with glomerular lesion N06.9
    - dense deposit disease N06.6
    - diffuse
      - crescentic glomerulonephritis N06.7
      - endocapillary proliferative glomerulonephritis N06.4
      - mesangiocapillary glomerulonephritis N06.5
    - focal and segmental hyalinosis or sclerosis N06.1
    - membranous (diffuse) N06.2
    - mesangial proliferative (diffuse) N06.3
    - minimal change N06.0
    - specified pathology NEC N06.8
- orthostatic R80.2
  - with glomerular lesion *—see* Proteinuria, isolated, with glomerular lesion
- persistent R80.1
  - with glomerular lesion *—see* Proteinuria, isolated, with glomerular lesion
- postural R80.2
  - with glomerular lesion *—see* Proteinuria, isolated, with glomerular lesion

Proteinuria *(continued)*
- pre-eclamptic *—see* Pre-eclampsia
- specified type NEC R80.8

Proteolysis, pathologic D65

Proteus (mirabilis) (morganii)**, as cause of disease classified elsewhere** B96.4

Prothrombin gene mutation D68.52

Protoporphyria, erythropoietic E80.0

Protozoal *—see also* condition
- disease B64
  - specified NEC B60.8

Protrusion, protrusio
- acetabuli M24.7
- acetabulum (into pelvis) M24.7
- device, implant or graft *—see also* Complications, by site and type, mechanical T85.698
  - arterial graft NEC *—see* Complication, cardiovascular device, mechanical, vascular
  - breast (implant) T85.49
  - catheter NEC T85.698
    - cystostomy T83.090
    - dialysis (renal) T82.49
      - intraperitoneal T85.691
    - infusion NEC T82.594
      - spinal (epidural) (subdural) T85.690
    - urinary, indwelling T83.098
  - electronic (electrode) (pulse generator) (stimulator)
    - bone T84.390
    - nervous system *—see* Complication, prosthetic device, mechanical, electronic nervous system stimulator
  - fixation, internal (orthopedic) NEC *—see* Complication, fixation device, mechanical
  - gastrointestinal *—see* Complications, prosthetic device, mechanical, gastrointestinal device
  - genital NEC T83.498
    - intrauterine contraceptive device T83.39
    - penile prosthesis T83.490
  - heart NEC *—see* Complication, cardiovascular device, mechanical
  - joint prosthesis *—see* Complications, joint prosthesis, mechanical, specified NEC, by site
  - ocular NEC *—see* Complications, prosthetic device, mechanical, ocular device
  - orthopedic NEC *—see* Complication, orthopedic, device, mechanical
  - specified NEC T85.628
  - urinary NEC *—see also* Complication, genitourinary, device, urinary, mechanical
    - graft T83.29
  - vascular NEC *—see* Complication, cardiovascular device, mechanical
  - ventricular intracranial shunt T85.09
- intervertebral disc *—see* Displacement, intervertebral disc
- joint prosthesis *—see* Complications, joint prosthesis, mechanical, specified NEC, by site
- nucleus pulposus *—see* Displacement, intervertebral disc

Prune belly (syndrome) Q79.4

- **Puerperal, puerperium** *(continued)*
  - infection *(continued)*
    - maternal *(continued)*
      - viral hepatitis O98.43
      - viral NEC O98.53
    - nipple O91.02
      - associated with lactation O91.03
    - peritoneum O85
    - renal O86.21
    - specified NEC O86.89
    - urinary (asymptomatic) (tract) NEC O86.20
      - bladder O86.22
      - kidney O86.21
      - specified site NEC O86.29
      - urethra O86.22
    - vagina O86.13
    - vein —*see* Puerperal, phlebitis
  - ischemia, cerebral O99.43
  - lymphangitis O86.89
    - breast O91.22
      - associated with lactation O91.23
  - malignancy O9A.13
  - malnutrition O25.3
  - mammillitis O91.02
    - associated with lactation O91.03
  - mammitis O91.22
    - associated with lactation O91.23
  - mania F30.8
  - mastitis O91.22
    - associated with lactation O91.23
    - purulent O91.12
      - associated with lactation O91.13
  - melancholia —*see* Disorder, depressive
  - mental disorder NEC O99.345
  - metroperitonitis O85
  - metrorrhagia —*see* Hemorrhage, postpartum
  - metrosalpingitis O86.19
  - metrovaginitis O86.13
  - milk leg O87.1
  - monoplegia, cerebral O99.43
  - mood disturbance O90.6
  - necrosis, liver (acute) (subacute) (conditions in subcategory K72.0) O26.63
    - with renal failure O90.4
  - nervous system disorder O99.355
  - neuritis O90.89
  - obesity (pre-existing prior to pregnancy) O99.215
  - obesity surgery status O99.845
  - occlusion, precerebral artery O99.43
  - paralysis
    - bladder (sphincter) O90.89
    - cerebral O99.43
  - paralytic stroke O99.43
  - parametritis O85
  - paravaginitis O86.13
  - pelviperitonitis O85
  - perimetritis O86.12
  - perimetrosalpingitis O86.19
  - perinephritis O86.21
  - periphlebitis —*see* Puerperal phlebitis
  - peritoneal infection O85
  - peritonitis (pelvic) O85
  - perivaginitis O86.13
  - phlebitis O87.0
    - deep O87.1
    - pelvic O87.1
    - superficial O87.0
  - phlebothrombosis, deep O87.1
  - phlegmasia alba dolens O87.1
  - placental polyp O90.89
  - pneumonia, embolic —*see* Embolism, obstetric, puerperal
  - pre-eclampsia —*see* Pre-eclampsia
  - psychosis F53
  - pyelitis O86.21
  - pyelocystitis O86.29
  - pyelonephritis O86.21
  - pyelonephrosis O86.21
  - pyemia O85
  - pyocystitis O86.29
  - pyohemia O85
  - pyometra O86.12
  - pyonephritis O86.21
  - pyosalpingitis O86.19
  - pyrexia (of unknown origin) O86.4
  - renal
    - disease NEC O90.89
    - failure O90.4
  - respiratory disease NEC O99.53
  - retention
    - decidua —*see* Retention, decidua
    - placenta O72.0
    - secundines —*see* Retention, secundines
  - retrated nipple O92.02
  - salpingo-ovaritis O86.19
  - salpingoperitonitis O85
  - secondary perineal tear O90.1
  - sepsis (pelvic) O85
  - sepsis O85
  - septic thrombophlebitis O86.81
  - skin disorder NEC O99.73
  - specified condition NEC O99.89
  - stroke O99.43
  - subinvolution (uterus) O90.89
  - subluxation of symphysis (pubis) O26.73
  - suppuration —*see* Puerperal, abscess
  - tetanus A34
  - thelitis O91.02
    - associated with lactation O91.03
  - thrombocytopenia O72.3
  - thrombophlebitis (superficial) O87.0
    - deep O87.1
    - pelvic O87.1
    - septic O86.81
  - thrombosis (venous) —*see* Thrombosis, puerperal
  - thyroiditis O90.5
  - toxemia (eclamptic) (pre-eclamptic) (with convulsions) O15.2
  - trauma, non-obstetric O9A.23
    - caused by abuse (physical) (suspected) O9A.33
      - confirmed O9A.33
      - psychological (suspected) O9A.53
        - confirmed O9A.53
      - sexual (suspected) O9A.43
        - confirmed O9A.43
  - uremia (due to renal failure) O90.4
  - urethritis O86.22
  - vaginitis O86.13
  - varicose veins (legs) O87.4
    - vulva or perineum O87.8
  - venous O87.9
  - vulvitis O86.19
  - vulvovaginitis O86.13
  - white leg O87.1

Puerperium —*see* Puerperal

Pulmolithiasis J98.4

Pulmonary —*see* condition

Pulpitis (acute) (anachoretic) (chronic) (hyperplastic) (irreversible) (putrescent) (reversible) (suppurative) (ulcerative) K04.0

Pulpless tooth K04.99

- **Pulse**
  - alternating R00.8
  - bigeminal R00.8
  - fast R00.0
  - feeble, rapid due to shock following injury T79.4
  - rapid R00.0
  - weak R09.89

Pulsus alternans or trigeminus R00.8

Punch drunk F07.81

Punctum lacrimale occlusion —*see* Obstruction, lacrimal

- **Puncture**
  - abdomen, abdominal
    - wall S31.139
      - with
        - foreign body S31.149
        - penetration into peritoneal cavity S31.639
          - with foreign body S31.649
      - epigastric region S31.132
        - with
          - foreign body S31.142
          - penetration into peritoneal cavity S31.632
            - with foreign body S31.642
      - left
        - lower quadrant S31.134
          - with
            - foreign body S31.144
            - penetration into peritoneal cavity S31.634
              - with foreign body S31.644
        - upper quadrant S31.131
          - with
            - foreign body S31.141
            - penetration into peritoneal cavity S31.631
              - with foreign body S31.641
      - periumbilic region S31.135
        - with
          - foreign body S31.145
          - penetration into peritoneal cavity S31.635
            - with foreign body S31.645
      - right
        - lower quadrant S31.133
          - with
            - foreign body S31.143
            - penetration into peritoneal cavity S31.633
              - with foreign body S31.643
        - upper quadrant S31.130
          - with
            - foreign body S31.140
            - penetration into peritoneal cavity S31.630
              - with foreign body S31.640
  - accidental, complicating surgery —*see* Complication, accidental puncture or laceration
  - alveolar (process) —*see* Puncture, oral cavity
  - ankle S91.039
    - with
      - foreign body S91.049
    - left S91.032
      - with
        - foreign body S91.042
    - right S91.031
      - with
        - foreign body S91.041
  - anus S31.833
    - with foreign body S31.834
  - arm (upper) S41.139
    - with foreign body S41.149
    - left S41.132
      - with foreign body S41.142
    - lower —*see* Puncture, forearm

- **Puncture** *(continued)*
  - arm *(continued)*
    - right S41.131
      - with foreign body S41.141
  - auditory canal (external) (meatus) *see* Puncture, ear
  - auricle, ear —*see* Puncture, ear
  - axilla —*see* Puncture, arm
  - back —*see also* Puncture, thorax, back
    - lower S31.030
      - with
        - foreign body S31.040
          - with penetration into retroperitoneal space S31.041
        - penetration into retroperitoneal space S31.031
  - bladder (traumatic) S37.29
    - nontraumatic N32.89
  - breast S21.039
    - with foreign body S21.049
    - left S21.032
      - with foreign body S21.042
    - right S21.031
      - with foreign body S21.041
  - buttock S31.803
    - with foreign body S31.804
    - left S31.823
      - with foreign body S31.824
    - right S31.813
      - with foreign body S31.814
  - by
    - device, implant or graft —*see* Complications, by site and ty mechanical
    - foreign body left accidentally in operative wound T81.539
    - instrument (any) during a procedure, accidental —*see* Puncture, accidental complicating surgery
  - calf —*see* Puncture, leg
  - canaliculus lacrimalis —*see* Punct eyelid
  - canthus, eye —*see* Puncture, eyeli
  - cervical esophagus S11.23
    - with foreign body S11.24
  - cheek (external) S01.439
    - with foreign body S01.449
    - left S01.432
      - with foreign body S01.442
    - right S01.431
      - with foreign body S01.441
    - internal —*see* Puncture, oral cav
  - chest wall —*see* Puncture, thorax
  - chin —*see* Puncture, head, specifie site NEC
  - clitoris —*see* Puncture, vulva
  - costal region —*see* Puncture, thora
  - digit (s)
    - hand —*see* Puncture, finger
    - foot —*see* Puncture, toe
  - ear (canal) (external) S01.339
    - with foreign body S01.349
    - left S01.332
      - with foreign body S01.342
    - right S01.331
      - with foreign body S01.341
    - drum S09.2-
  - elbow S51.039
    - with
      - foreign body S51.049
    - left S51.032
      - with
        - foreign body S51.042
    - right S51.031
      - with
        - foreign body S51.041
  - epididymis —*see* Puncture, testis

Puncture *(continued)*
subungual
finger (s) —*see* Puncture, finger, with damage to nail
toe —*see* Puncture, toe, with damage to nail
supraclavicular fossa —*see* Puncture, neck, specified site NEC
temple, temporal region —*see* Puncture, head, specified site NEC
temporomandibular area —*see* Puncture, cheek
testis S31.33
with foreign body S31.34
thigh S71.139
with foreign body S71.149
left S71.132
with foreign body S71.142
right S71.131
with foreign body S71.141
thorax, thoracic (wall) S21.93
with foreign body S21.94
back S21.23-
with
foreign body S21.24-
with penetration S21.44
penetration S21.43
breast —*see* Puncture, breast
front S21.13-
with
foreign body S21.14-
with penetration S21.34
penetration S21.33
throat —*see* Puncture, neck
thumb S61.039
with
damage to nail S61.139
with
foreign body S61.149
foreign body S61.049
left S61.032
with
damage to nail S61.132
with
foreign body S61.142
foreign body S61.042
right S61.031
with
damage to nail S61.131
with
foreign body S61.141
foreign body S61.041
thyroid gland S11.13
with foreign body S11.14
toe (s) S91.139
with
damage to nail S91.239
with
foreign body S91.249
foreign body S91.149
great S91.133
with
damage to nail S91.233
with
foreign body S91.243
foreign body S91.143
left S91.132
with
damage to nail S91.232
with
foreign body S91.242
foreign body S91.142
right S91.131
with
damage to nail S91.231
with
foreign body S91.241
foreign body S91.141

Puncture *(continued)*
toe *(continued)*
lesser S91.136
with
damage to nail S91.236
with
foreign body S91.246
foreign body S91.146
left S91.135
with
damage to nail S91.235
with
foreign body S91.245
foreign body S91.145
right S91.134
with
damage to nail S91.234
with
foreign body S91.244
foreign body S91.144
tongue —*see* Puncture, oral cavity
trachea S11.023
with foreign body S11.024
tunica vaginalis —*see* Puncture, testis
tympanum, tympanic membrane S09.2-
umbilical region S31.135
with foreign body S31.145
uvula —*see* Puncture, oral cavity
vagina S31.43
with foreign body S31.44
vocal cords S11.033
with foreign body S11.034
vulva S31.43
with foreign body S31.44
wrist S61.539
with
foreign body S61.549
left S61.532
with
foreign body S61.542
right S61.531
with
foreign body S61.541

PUO(pyrexia of unknown origin) R50.9

Pupillary membrane (persistent) Q13.89

Pupillotonia —*see* Anomaly, pupil, function, tonic pupil

Purpura D69.2
abdominal D69.0
allergic D69.0
anaphylactoid D69.0
annularis telangiectodes L81.7
arthritic D69.0
autoerythrocyte sensitization D69.2
autoimmune D69.0
bacterial D69.0
Bateman's (senile) D69.2
capillary fragility (hereditary) (idiopathic) D69.8
cryoglobulinemic D89.1
Devil's pinches D69.2
fibrinolytic —*see* Fibrinolysis
fulminans, fulminous D65
gangrenous D65
hemorrhagic, hemorrhagica D69.3
not due to thrombocytopenia D69.0
Henoch (-Schönlein) (allergic) D69.0
hypergammaglobulinemic (benign) (Waldenström) D89.0
idiopathic (thrombocytopenic) D69.3
nonthrombocytopenic D69.0
immune thrombocytopenic D69.3
infectious D69.0
malignant D69.0
neonatorum P54.5
nervosa D69.0

Purpura *(continued)*
newborn P54.5
nonthrombocytopenic D69.2
hemorrhagic D69.0
idiopathic D69.0
nonthrombopenic D69.2
peliosis rheumatica D69.0
posttransfusion (post-transfusion) (from (fresh) whole blood or blood products) D69.51
primary D69.49
red cell membrane sensitivity D69.2
rheumatica D69.0
Schönlein (-Henoch) (allergic) D69.0
scorbutic E54 *[D77]*
senile D69.2
simplex D69.2
symptomatica D69.0
telangiectasia annularis L81.7
thrombocytopenic D69.49
congenital D69.42
hemorrhagic D69.3
hereditary D69.42
idiopathic D69.3
immune D69.3
neonatal, transitory P61.0
thrombotic M31.1
thrombohemolytic —*see* Fibrinolysis
thrombolytic —*see* Fibrinolysis
thrombopenic D69.49
thrombotic, thrombocytopenic M31.1
toxic D69.0
vascular D69.0
visceral symptoms D69.0

Purpuric spots R23.3

Purulent —*see* condition

Pus
in
stool R19.5
urine N39.0
tube (rupture) —*see* Salpingo-oophoritis

Pustular rash L08.0

Pustule (nonmalignant) L08.9
malignant A22.0

Pustulosis palmaris et plantaris L40.3

Putnam (-Dana) **disease or syndrome** —*see* Degeneration, combined

Putrescent pulp (dental) K04.1

Pyarthritis, pyarthrosis —*see* Arthritis, pyogenic or pyemic
tuberculous —*see* Tuberculosis, joint

Pyelectasis —*see* Hydronephrosis

Pyelitis (congenital) (uremic) —*see also* Pyelonephritis
with
calculus —*see* category N20
with hydronephrosis N13.2
contracted kidney N11.9
acute N10
chronic N11.9
with calculus —*see* category N20
with hydronephrosis N13.2
cystica N28.84
puerperal (postpartum) O86.21
tuberculous A18.11

Pyelocystitis —*see* Pyelonephritis

Pyelonephritis —*see also* Nephritis, tubulo-interstitial
with
calculus —*see* category N20
with hydronephrosis N13.2
contracted kidney N11.9
acute N10
calculous —*see* category N20
with hydronephrosis N13.2

Pyelonephritis *(continued)*
chronic N11.9
with calculus —*see* category N2
with hydronephrosis N13.2
associated with ureteral obstruc or stricture N11.1
nonobstructive N11.8
with reflux (vesicoureteral) N11.0
obstructive N11.1
specified NEC N11.8
in (due to)
brucellosis A23.9 *[N16]*
cryoglobulinemia (mixed) D89. *[N16]*
cystinosis E72.04
diphtheria A36.84
glycogen storage disease E74.0 *[N16]*
leukemia NEC C95.9- *[N16]*
lymphoma NEC C85.90 *[N16]*
multiple myeloma C90.0- *[N16*
obstruction N11.1
Salmonella infection A02.25
sarcoidosis D86.84
sepsis A41.9 *[N16]*
Sjögren's disease M35.04
toxoplasmosis B58.83
transplant rejection T86.91 *[N1*
Wilson's disease E83.01 *[N16]*
nonobstructive N12
with reflux (vesicoureteral) N11
chronic N11.8
syphilitic A52.75

Pyelonephrosis (obstructive) N11.1
chronic N11.9

Pyelophlebitis I80.8

Pyeloureteritis cystica N28.85

Pyemia, pyemic (fever) (infection) (purulent) —*see also* Sepsis
joint —*see* Arthritis, pyogenic or pyemic
liver K75.1
pneumococcal A40.3
portal K75.1
postvaccinal T88.0
puerperal, postpartum, childbirth C
specified organism NEC A41.89
tuberculous —*see* Tuberculosis, miliary

Pygopagus Q89.4

Pyknoepilepsy (idiopathic) —*see* Pyknolepsy

Pyknolepsy G40.A09
intractable G40.A19
with status epilepticus G40.A11
without status epilepticus G40.A
not intractable G40.A09
with status epilepticus G40.A01
without status epilepticus G40.A

Pylephlebitis K75.1

Pyle's syndrome Q78.5

Pylethrombophlebitis K75.1

Pylethrombosis K75.1

Pyloritis K29.90
with bleeding K29.91

Pylorospasm (reflex) **NEC** K31.3
congenital or infantile Q40.0
newborn Q40.0
neurotic F45.8
psychogenic F45.8

Pylorus, pyloric —*see* condition

Pyoarthrosis —*see* Arthritis, pyogeni or pyemic

Pyocele
mastoid —*see* Mastoiditis, acute

cele *(continued)*
nus (accessory) —*see* Sinusitis
rbinate (bone) J32.9
rethra —*see also* Urethritis N34.0

colpos —*see* Vaginitis

cystitis N30.80
ith hematuria N30.81

derma, pyodermia L08.0
angrenosum L88
ewborn P39.4
hagedenic L88
egetans L08.81

dermatitis L08.0
egetans L08.81

genic —*see* condition

hydronephrosis N13.6

metra, pyometrium, pyometritis —*see* Endometritis

myositis (tropical) —*see* Myositis, nfective

nephritis N12

nephrosis N13.6
uberculous A18.11

-oophoritis —*see* Salpingo-oophoritis

-ovarium —*see* Salpingo-oophoritis

pericarditis, pyopericardium I30.1

phlebitis —*see* Phlebitis

pneumopericardium I30.1

pneumothorax (infective) J86.9
vith fistula J86.0
uberculous NEC A15.6

salpinx, pyosalpingitis —*see also* Salpingo-oophoritis

thorax J86.9
vith fistula J86.0
uberculous NEC A15.6

ureter N28.89
uberculous A18.11

ramidopallidonigral syndrome G20

rexia (of unknown origin) R50.9
tmospheric T67.0
uring labor NEC O75.2
eat T67.0
ewborn P81.9
environmentally-induced P81.0
ersistent R50.9
uerperal O86.4

roglobulinemia NEC E88.09

romania F63.1

rosis R12

uria (bacterial) N39.0

fever A78
with pneumonia A78

adricuspid aortic valve Q23.8

adrilateral fever A78

adriparesis —*see* Quadriplegia
meaning muscle weakness M62.81

adriplegia G82.50
complete
C1-C4 level G82.51
C5-C7 level G82.53
congenital (cerebral) (spinal) G80.8
spastic G80.0
embolic (current episode) I63.4
functional R53.2
incomplete
C1-C4 level G82.52
C5-C7 level G82.54

Quadriplegia *(continued)*
thrombotic (current episode) I63.3
traumatic -- code to injury with seventh character S
current episode —*see* Injury, spinal (cord), cervical

Quadruplet, pregnancy —*see* Pregnancy, quadruplet

Quarrelsomeness F60.3

Queensland fever A77.3

Quervain's disease M65.4
thyroid E06.1

Queyrat's erythroplasia D07.4
penis D07.4
specified site —*see* Neoplasm, skin, in situ
unspecified site D07.4

Quincke's disease or edema T78.3
hereditary D84.1

Quinsy (gangrenous) J36

Quintan fever A79.0

Quintuplet, pregnancy —*see* Pregnancy, quintuplet

R

Rabbit fever —*see* Tularemia

Rabies A82.9
contact Z20.3
exposure to Z20.3
inoculation reaction —*see* Complications, vaccination
sylvatic A82.0
urban A82.1

Rachischisis —*see* Spina bifida

Rachitic —*see also* condition
deformities of spine (late effect) (sequelae) E64.3
pelvis (late effect) (sequelae) E64.3
with disproportion (fetopelvic) O33.0
causing obstructed labor O65.0

Rachitis, rachitism (acute) (tarda) —*see also* Rickets
renalis N25.0
sequelae E64.3

Radial nerve —*see* condition

Radiation
burn —*see* Burn
effects NOS T66
sickness NOS T66
therapy, encounter for Z51.0

Radiculitis (pressure) (vertebrogenic) —*see* Radiculopathy

Radiculomyelitis —*see also* Encephalitis
toxic, due to
Clostridium tetani A35
Corynebacterium diphtheriae A36.82

Radiculopathy M54.10
cervical region M54.12
cervicothoracic region M54.13
due to
disc disorder
C3 M50.11
C4 M50.11
C5 M50.12
C6 M50.12
C7 M50.12
C8 M50.13
displacement of intervertebral disc —*see* Disorder, disc, with, radiculopathy
leg M54.1-

Radiculopathy *(continued)*
lumbar region M54.16
lumbosacral region M54.17
occipito-atlanto-axial region M54.11
postherpetic B02.29
sacrococcygeal region M54.18
syphilitic A52.11
thoracic region (with visceral pain) M54.14
thoracolumbar region M54.15

Radiodermal burns (acute, chronic, or occupational) —*see* Burn

Radiodermatitis L58.9
acute L58.0
chronic L58.1

Radiotherapy session Z51.0

Rage, meaning rabies —*see* Rabies

Ragpicker's disease A22.1

Ragsorter's disease A22.1

Raillietiniasis B71.8

Railroad neurosis F48.8

Railway spine F48.8

Raised —*see also* Elevated
antibody titer R76.0

Rake teeth, tooth M26.39

Rales R09.89

Ramifying renal pelvis Q63.8

Ramsay-Hunt disease or syndrome —*see also* Hunt's disease B02.21
meaning dyssynergia cerebellaris myoclonica G11.1

Ranula K11.6
congenital Q38.4

Rape
adult
confirmed T74.21
suspected T76.21
alleged, observation or examination, ruled out
adult Z04.41
child Z04.42
child
confirmed T74.22
suspected T76.22

Rapid
feeble pulse, due to shock, following injury T79.4
heart (beat) R00.0
psychogenic F45.8
second stage (delivery) O62.3
time-zone change syndrome —*see* Disorder, sleep, circadian rhythm, psychogenic

Rarefaction, bone —*see* Disorder, bone, density and structure, specified NEC

Rash (toxic) R21
canker A38.9
diaper L22
drug (internal use) L27.0
contact —*see also* Dermatitis, due to, drugs, external L25.1
following immunization T88.1
food —*see* Dermatitis, due to, food
heat L74.0
napkin (psoriasiform) L22
nettle —*see* Urticaria
pustular L08.0
rose R21
epidemic B06.9
scarlet A38.9
serum —*see also* Reaction, serum T80.69
wandering tongue K14.1

Rasmussen aneurysm —*see* Tuberculosis, pulmonary

Rasmussen encephalitis G04.81

Rat-bite fever A25.9
due to Streptobacillus moniliformis A25.1
spirochetal (morsus muris) A25.0

Rathke's pouch tumor D44.3

Raymond (-Céstan) **syndrome** I65.8

Raynaud's disease, phenomenon or syndrome (secondary) I73.00
with gangrene (symmetric) I73.01

RDS (newborn) (type I) P22.0
type II P22.1

Reaction —*see also* Disorder
adaptation —*see* Disorder, adjustment
adjustment (anxiety) (conduct disorder) (depressiveness) (distress) —*see* Disorder, adjustment
with
mutism, elective (child) (adolescent) F94.0
adverse
food (any) (ingested) NEC T78.1
anaphylactic —*see* Shock, anaphylactic, due to food
affective —*see* Disorder, mood
allergic —*see* Allergy
anaphylactic —*see* Shock, anaphylactic
anaphylactoid —*see* Shock, anaphylactic
anesthesia —*see* Anesthesia, complication
antitoxin (prophylactic) (therapeutic) —*see* Complications, vaccination
anxiety F41.1
Arthus —*see* Arthus' phenomenon
asthenic F48.8
combat and operational stress F43.0
compulsive F42
conversion F44.9
crisis, acute F43.0
deoxyribonuclease (DNA) (DNase) hypersensitivity D69.2
depressive (single episode) F32.9
affective (single episode) F31.4
recurrent episode F33.9
neurotic F34.1
psychoneurotic F34.1
psychotic F32.3
recurrent —*see* Disorder, depressive, recurrent
dissociative F44.9
drug NEC T88.7
addictive —*see* Dependence, drug
transmitted via placenta or breast milk —*see* Absorption, drug, addictive, through placenta
allergic —*see* Allergy, drug
lichenoid L43.2
newborn P93.8
gray baby syndrome P93.0
overdose or poisoning (by accident) —*see* Table of Drugs and Chemicals, by drug, poisoning
photoallergic L56.1
phototoxic L56.0
withdrawal —*see* Dependence, by drug, with, withdrawal
infant of dependent mother P96.1
newborn P96.1
wrong substance given or taken (by accident) —*see* Table of Drugs and Chemicals, by drug, poisoning

- **Reaction** *(continued)*
  - fear F40.9
    - child (abnormal) F93.8
  - febrile nonhemolytic transfusion (FNHTR) R50.84
  - fluid loss, cerebrospinal G97.1
  - foreign
    - body NEC *—see* Granuloma, foreign body
      - in operative wound (inadvertently left) *—see* Foreign body, accidentally left during a procedure
    - substance accidentally left during a procedure (chemical) (powder) (talc) T81.60
      - aseptic peritonitis T81.61
      - body or object (instrument) (sponge) (swab) *—see* Foreign body, accidentally left during a procedure
      - specified reaction NEC T81.69
  - grief *—see* Disorder, adjustment
  - Herxheimer's R68.89
  - hyperkinetic *—see* Hyperkinesia
  - hypochondriacal F45.20
  - hypoglycemic, due to insulin E16.0
    - with coma (diabetic) *—see* Diabetes, coma
      - nondiabetic E15
    - therapeutic misadventure *—see* subcategory T38.3
  - hypomanic F30.8
  - hysterical F44.9
  - immunization *—see* Complications, vaccination
  - incompatibility
    - ABO blood group (infusion) (transfusion) *—see* Complication (s), transfusion, incompatibility reaction, ABO
      - delayed serologic T80.39
    - minor blood group (Duffy) (E) (K (ell)) (Kidd) (Lewis) (M) (N) (P) (S) T80.89
    - Rh (factor) (infusion) (transfusion) *—see* Complication (s), transfusion, incompatibility reaction, Rh (factor)
  - inflammatory *—see* Infection
  - infusion *—see* Complications, infusion
  - inoculation (immune serum) *—see* Complications, vaccination
  - insulin T38.3-
  - involutional psychotic *—see* Disorder, depressive
  - leukemoid D72.823
    - basophilic D72.823
    - lymphocytic D72.823
    - monocytic D72.823
    - myelocytic D72.823
    - neutrophilic D72.823
  - LSD (acute)
    - due to drug abuse *—see* Abuse, drug, hallucinogen
    - due to drug dependence *—see* Dependence, drug, hallucinogen
  - lumbar puncture G97.1
  - manic-depressive *—see* Disorder, bipolar
  - neurasthenic F48.8
  - neurogenic *—see* Neurosis
  - neurotic F48.9
  - neurotic-depressive F34.1
  - nitritoid *—see* Crisis, nitritoid
  - nonspecific
    - to
      - cell mediated immunity measurement of gamma interferon antigen response without active tuberculosis R76.12

- **Reaction** *(continued)*
  - nonspecific *(continued)*
    - to *(continued)*
      - QuantiFERON-TB test (QFT) without active tuberculosis R76.12
      - tuberculin test *—see also* Reaction, tuberculin skin test R76.11
  - obsessive-compulsive F42
  - organic, acute or subacute *—see* Delirium
  - paranoid (acute) F23
    - chronic F22
    - senile F03
  - passive dependency F60.7
  - phobic F40.9
  - post-traumatic stress, uncomplicated Z73.3
  - psychogenic F99
  - psychoneurotic *—see also* Neurosis
    - compulsive F42
    - depersonalization F48.1
    - depressive F34.1
    - hypochondriacal F45.20
    - neurasthenic F48.8
    - obsessive F42
  - psychophysiologic *—see* Disorder, somatoform
  - psychosomatic *—see* Disorder, somatoform
  - psychotic *—see* Psychosis
  - scarlet fever toxin *—see* Complications, vaccination
  - schizophrenic F23
    - acute (brief) (undifferentiated) F23
    - latent F21
    - undifferentiated (acute) (brief) F23
  - serological for syphilis *—see* Serology for syphilis
  - serum T80.69
    - anaphylactic (immediate) *—see also* Shock, anaphylactic T80.59
    - specified reaction NEC
      - due to
        - administration of blood and blood products T80.61
        - immunization T80.62
        - serum specified NEC T80.69
        - vaccination T80.62
  - situational *—see* Disorder, adjustment
  - somatization *—see* Disorder, somatoform
  - spinal puncture G97.1
  - stress (severe) F43.9
    - acute (agitation) ("daze") (disorientation) (disturbance of consciousness) (flight reaction) (fugue) F43.0
    - specified NEC F43.8
  - surgical procedure *—see* Complications, surgical procedure
  - tetanus antitoxin *—see* Complications, vaccination
  - toxic, to local anesthesia T81.89
    - in labor and delivery O74.4
    - in pregnancy O29.3X-
    - postpartum, puerperal O89.3
  - toxin-antitoxin *—see* Complications, vaccination
  - transfusion (blood) (bone marrow) (lymphocytes) (allergic) *—see* Complications, transfusion
  - tuberculin skin test, abnormal R76.11
  - vaccination (any) *—see* Complications, vaccination
  - withdrawing, child or adolescent F93.8

- **Reactive airway disease** *—see* Asthma

- **Reactive depression** *—see* Reaction, depressive

- **Rearrangement**
  - chromosomal
    - balanced (in) Q95.9
      - abnormal individual (autosomal) Q95.2
        - non-sex (autosomal) chromosomes Q95.2
        - sex/non-sex chromosomes Q95.3
      - specified NEC Q95.8

- **Recalcitrant patient** *—see* Noncompliance

- **Recanalization, thrombus** *—see* Thrombosis

- **Recession, receding**
  - chamber angle (eye) H21.55-
  - chin M26.09
  - gingival (generalized) (localized) (postinfective) (postoperative) K06.0

- **Recklinghausen disease** Q85.01
  - bones E21.0

- **Reclus' disease** (cystic) *—see* Mastopathy, cystic

- **Recrudescent typhus** (fever) A75.1

- **Recruitment, auditory** H93.21-

- **Rectalgia** K62.89

- **Rectitis** K62.89

- **Rectocele**
  - female (without uterine prolapse) N81.6
    - with uterine prolapse N81.4
      - incomplete N81.2
  - in pregnancy *—see* Pregnancy, complicated by, abnormal, pelvic organs or tissues NEC
  - male K62.3

- **Rectosigmoid junction** *—see* condition

- **Rectosigmoiditis** K63.89
  - ulcerative (chronic) K51.30
    - with
      - complication K51.319
        - abscess K51.314
        - fistula K51.313
        - obstruction K51.312
        - rectal bleeding K51.311
        - specified NEC K51.318

- **Rectourethral** *—see* condition

- **Rectovaginal** *—see* condition

- **Rectovesical** *—see* condition

- **Rectum, rectal** *—see* condition

- **Recurrent** *—see* condition
  - pregnancy loss *—see* Loss (of), pregnancy, recurrent

- **Red bugs** B88.0

- **Red-cedar lung or pneumonitis** J67.8

- **Red tide** *—see also* Table of Drugs and Chemicals T65.82-

- **Reduced**
  - mobility Z74.09
  - ventilatory or vital capacity R94.2

- **Redundant, redundancy**
  - anus (congenital) Q43.8
  - clitoris N90.89
  - colon (congenital) Q43.8
  - foreskin (congenital) N47.8
  - intestine (congenital) Q43.8
  - labia N90.6
  - organ or site, congenital NEC *—see* Accessory
  - panniculus (abdominal) E65
  - prepuce (congenital) N47.8
  - pylorus K31.89
  - rectum (congenital) Q43.8

- **Redundant, redundancy** *(continued)*
  - scrotum N50.8
  - sigmoid (congenital) Q43.8
  - skin (of face) L57.4
    - eyelids *—see* Blepharochalasis
  - stomach K31.89

- **Reduplication** *—see* Duplication

- **Reflex** R29.2
  - hyperactive gag J39.2
  - pupillary, abnormal *—see* Anomal[y], pupil, function
  - vasoconstriction I73.9
  - vasovagal R55

- **Reflux** K21.9
  - acid K21.9
  - esophageal K21.9
    - with esophagitis K21.0
    - newborn P78.83
  - gastroesophageal K21.9
    - with esophagitis K21.0
  - mitral *—see* Insufficiency, mitral
  - ureteral *—see* Reflux, vesicouteter[al]
  - vesicoureteral (with scarring) N13[.70]
    - with
      - nephropathy N13.729
        - with hydroureter N13.739
          - bilateral N13.732
          - unilateral N13.731
        - bilateral N13.722
        - unilateral N13.721
        - without hydroureter N13.7[2]
          - bilateral N13.722
          - unilateral N13.721
      - pyelonephritis (chronic) N11.[0]
    - congenital Q62.7
    - without nephropathy N13.71

- **Reforming, artificial openings** *—see* Attention to, artificial, opening

- **Refractive error** *—see* Disorder, refraction

- **Refsum's disease or syndrome** G60.[1]

- **Refusal of**
  - food, psychogenic F50.8
  - treatment (because of) Z53.20
    - left against medical advice (AM[A]) Z53.21
    - patient's decision NEC Z53.29
    - reasons of belief or group pressu[re] Z53.1

- **Regional** *—see* condition

- **Regurgitation** R11.10
  - aortic (valve) *—see* Insufficiency, aortic
  - food *—see also* Vomiting
    - with reswallowing *—see* Rumination
    - newborn P92.1
  - gastric contents *—see* Vomiting
  - heart *—see* Endocarditis
  - mitral (valve) *—see* Insufficiency, mitral
    - congenital Q23.3
  - myocardial *—see* Endocarditis
  - pulmonary (valve) (heart) I37.1
    - congenital Q22.2
    - syphilitic A52.03
  - tricuspid *—see* Insufficiency, tricuspid
  - valve, valvular *—see* Endocarditis
    - congenital Q24.8
  - vesicoureteral *—see* Reflux, vesicoureteral

- **Reifenstein syndrome** E34.52

- **Reinsertion, contraceptive device** Z30.433

- **Reiter's disease, syndrome, or urethritis** M02.30
  - ankle M02.37-

er's disease, syndrome, or
ethritis *(continued)*
ow M02.32-
ot joint M02.37-
nd joint M02.34-
p M02.35-
ee M02.36-
ultiple site M02.39
oulder M02.31-
rtebra M02.38
ist M02.33-
hmann's disease or syndrome
31.89
ction
od, psychogenic F50.8
nsplant T86.91
bone T86.830
marrow T86.01
cornea T86.840
heart T86.21
with lung (s) T86.31
intestine T86.850
kidney T86.11
liver T86.41
lung (s) T86.810
with heart T86.31
organ (immune or nonimmune cause) T86.91
pancreas T86.890
skin (allograft) (autograft) T86.820
specified NEC T86.890
stem cell (peripheral blood) (umbilical cord) T86.5
psing fever A68.9
arter's (Asiatic) A68.1
utton's (West African) A68.1
och's A68.9
use-borne (epidemic) A68.0
ovy's (American) A68.1
bermeyers's (European) A68.0
pirillum A68.9
k-borne (endemic) A68.1
ationship
cclusal
open anterior M26.220
open posterior M26.221
axation
nus (sphincter) K62.89
psychogenic F45.8
ch (foot) —*see also* Deformity, limb, flat foot
ack ligaments —*see* Instability, joint, spine
ladder (sphincter) N31.2
ardioesophageal K21.9
ervix —*see* Incompetency, cervix
iaphragm J98.6
oint (capsule) (ligament) (paralytic) —*see* Flail, joint
congenital NEC Q74.8
umbosacral (joint) —*see* subcategory M53.2
elvic floor N81.89
erineum N81.89
osture R29.3
ectum (sphincter) K62.89
acroiliac (joint) —*see* subcategory M53.2
crotum N50.8
rethra (sphincter) N36.44
esical N31.2
ease from prison, anxiety concerning Z65.2
mains
anal of Cloquet Q14.0
apsule (opaque) Q14.8
mittent fever (malarial) B54
nnant
anal of Cloquet Q14.0
apsule (opaque) Q14.8

Remnant *(continued)*
cervix, cervical stump (acquired) (postoperative) N88.8
cystic duct, postcholecystectomy K91.5
fingernail L60.8
congenital Q84.6
meniscus, knee —*see* Derangement, knee, meniscus, specified NEC
thyroglossal duct Q89.2
tonsil J35.8
infected (chronic) J35.01
urachus Q64.4

Removal (from) (of)
artificial
arm Z44.00-
complete Z44.01-
partial Z44.02-
eye Z44.2-
leg Z44.10-
complete Z44.11-
partial Z44.12-
breast implant Z45.81
cardiac pulse generator (battery) (end-of-life) Z45.010
catheter (urinary) (indwelling) Z46.6
from artificial opening —*see* Attention to, artificial, opening
non-vascular Z46.82
vascular NEC Z45.2
drains Z48.03
device Z46.9
contraceptive Z30.432
implanted NEC Z45.89
specified NEC Z46.89
dressing (nonsurgical) Z48.00
surgical Z48.01
external
fixation device - code to fracture with seventh character D
prosthesis, prosthetic device Z44.9
breast Z44.3-
specified NEC Z44.8
home in childhood (to foster home or institution) Z62.29
ileostomy Z43.2
insulin pump Z46.81
myringotomy device (stent) (tube) Z45.82
nervous system device NEC Z46.2
brain neuropacemaker Z46.2
visual substitution device Z46.2
implanted Z45.31
non-vascular catheter Z46.82
orthodontic device Z46.4
organ, prophylactic (for neoplasia management) —*see* Prophylactic, organ removal
staples Z48.02
stent
ureteral Z46.6
suture Z48.02
urinary device Z46.6
vascular access device or catheter Z45.2

Ren
arcuatus Q63.1
mobile, mobilis N28.89
congenital Q63.8
unguliformis Q63.1

Renal —*see* condition

Rendu-Osler-Weber disease or syndrome I78.0

Reninoma D41.0-

Renon-Delille syndrome E23.3

Reovirus, as cause of disease classified elsewhere B97.5

Repeated falls NEC R29.6

Replaced chromosome by dicentric ring Q93.2

Replacement by artificial or mechanical device or prosthesis of
bladder Z96.0
blood vessel NEC Z95.828
bone NEC Z96.7
cochlea Z96.21
coronary artery Z95.5
eustachian tube Z96.29
eye globe Z97.0
heart Z95.812
valve Z95.2
prosthetic Z95.2
specified NEC Z95.4
xenogenic Z95.3
intestine Z96.89
joint Z96.60
hip —*see* Presence, hip joint implant
knee —*see* Presence, knee joint implant
specified site NEC Z96.698
larynx Z96.3
lens Z96.1
limb (s) —*see* Presence, artificial, limb
mandible NEC (for tooth root implant (s)) Z96.5
organ NEC Z96.89
peripheral vessel NEC Z95.828
stapes Z96.29
teeth Z97.2
tendon Z96.7
tissue NEC Z96.89
tooth root (s) Z96.5
vessel NEC Z95.828
coronary (artery) Z95.5

Request for expert evidence Z04.8

Reserve, decreased or low
cardiac —*see* Disease, heart
kidney N28.89

Residual —*see also* condition
ovary syndrome N99.83
state, schizophrenic F20.5
urine R39.19

Resistance, resistant (to)
activated protein C D68.51
complicating pregnancy O26.89
insulin E88.81
organism (s)
to
drug
aminoglycosides Z16.29
amoxicillin Z16.11
ampicillin Z16.11
antibiotic (s) Z16.20
multiple Z16.24
specified NEC Z16.29
antifungal Z16.32
antimicrobial (single) Z16.30
multiple Z16.35
specified NEC Z16.39
antimycbacterial (single) Z16.341
multiple Z16.342
antiparasitic Z16.31
antiviral Z16.33
beta lactam antibiotics Z16.10
specified NEC Z16.19
cephalosporins Z16.19
extended beta lactamase (ESBL) Z16.12
fluoroquinolones Z16.23
macrolides Z16.29
methicillin —*see* MRSA
multiple drugs (MDRO) antibiotics Z16.24
penicillins Z16.11

Resistance, resistant *(continued)*
organism *(continued)*
to *(continued)*
drug *(continued)*
quinine (and related compounds) Z16.31
quinolones Z16.23
sulfonamides Z16.29
tetracyclines Z16.29
tuberculostatics (single) Z16.341
multiple Z16.342
vancomycin Z16.21
related antibiotics Z16.22
thyroid hormone E07.89

Resorption
dental (roots) K03.3
alveoli M26.79
teeth (external) (internal) (pathological) (roots) K03.3

Respiration
Cheyne-Stokes R06.3
decreased due to shock, following injury T79.4
disorder of, psychogenic F45.8
insufficient, or poor R06.89
newborn P28.5
painful R07.1
sighing, psychogenic F45.8

Respiratory —*see also* condition
distress syndrome (newborn) (type I) P22.0
type II P22.1
syncytial virus, as cause of disease classified elsewhere B97.4

Respite care Z75.5

Response (drug)
photoallergic L56.1
phototoxic L56.0

Restless legs (syndrome) G25.81

Restlessness R45.1

Restriction of housing space Z59.1

Restoration (of)
dental
aesthetically inadequate or displeasing K08.56
defective K08.50
specified NEC K08.59
failure of marginal integrity K08.51
failure of periodontal anatomical intergrity K08.54
organ continuity from previous sterilization (tuboplasty) (vasoplasty) Z31.0
aftercare Z31.42
tooth (existing)
contours biologically incompatible with oral health K08.54
open margins K08.51
overhanging K08.52
poor aesthetic K08.56
poor gingival margins K08.51
unsatisfactory, of tooth K08.50
specified NEC K08.59

Restorative material (dental)
allergy to K08.55
fractured K08.539
with loss of material K08.531
without loss of material K08.530
unrepairable overhanging of K08.52

Rests, ovarian, in fallopian tube Q50.6

Restzustand (schizophrenic) F20.5

Retained —*see also* Retention
cholelithiasis following cholecystectomy K91.86

Retained *(continued)*
  foreign body fragments (type of) Z18.9
    acrylics Z18.2
    animal quill (s) or spines Z18.31
    cement Z18.83
    concrete Z18.83
    crystalline Z18.83
    depleted isotope Z18.09
    depleted uranium Z18.01
    diethylhexylphthalates Z18.2
    glass Z18.81
    isocyanate Z18.2
    magnetic metal Z18.11
    metal Z18.10
    nonmagnectic metal Z18.12
    nontherapeutic radioactive Z18.09
    organic NEC Z18.39
    plastic Z18.2
    quill (s) (animal) Z18.31
    radioactive (nontherapeutic) NEC Z18.09
    specified NEC Z18.89
    spine (s) (animal) Z18.31
    stone Z18.83
    tooth (teeth) Z18.32
    wood Z18.33
  fragments (type of) Z18.9
    acrylics Z18.2
    animal quill (s) or spines Z18.31
    cement Z18.83
    concrete Z18.83
    crystalline Z18.83
    depleted isotope Z18.09
    depleted uranium Z18.01
    diethylhexylphthalates Z18.2
    glass Z18.81
    isocyanate Z18.2
    magnetic metal Z18.11
    metal Z18.10
    nonmagnectic metal Z18.12
    nontherapeutic radioactive Z18.09
    organic NEC Z18.39
    plastic Z18.2
    quill (s) (animal) Z18.31
    radioactive (nontherapeutic) NEC Z18.09
    specified NEC Z18.89
    spine (s) (animal) Z18.31
    stone Z18.83
    tooth (teeth) Z18.32
    wood Z18.33
  gallstones, following cholecystectomy K91.86

Retardation
  development, developmental, specific —*see* Disorder, developmental
  endochondral bone growth —*see* Disorder, bone, development or growth
  growth R62.50
    due to malnutrition E45
  mental —*see* Disability, intellectual
  motor function, specific F82
  physical (child) R62.52
    due to malnutrition E45
  reading (specific) F81.0
  spelling (specific) (without reading disorder) F81.81

Retching —*see* Vomiting

Retention —*see also* Retained
  bladder —*see* Retention, urine
  carbon dioxide E87.2
  cholelithiasis following cholecystectomy K91.86
  cyst —*see* Cyst
  dead
    fetus (at or near term) (mother) O36.4
      early fetal death O02.1
    ovum O02.0

Retention *(continued)*
  decidua (fragments) (following delivery) (with hemorrhage) O72.2
    without hemorrhage O73.1
  deciduous tooth K00.6
  dental root K08.3
  fecal —*see* Constipation
  fetus
    dead O36.4
      early O02.1
  fluid R60.9
  foreign body —*see also* Foreign body, retained
    current trauma - code as Foreign body, by site or type
  gallstones, following cholecystectomy K91.86
  gastric K31.89
  intrauterine contraceptive device, in pregnancy —*see* Pregnancy, complicated by, retention, intrauterine device
  membranes (complicating delivery) (with hemorrhage) O72.2
    with abortion —*see* Abortion, by type
    without hemorrhage O73.1
  meniscus —*see* Derangement, meniscus
  menses N94.89
  milk (puerperal, postpartum) O92.79
  nitrogen, extrarenal R39.2
  ovary syndrome N99.83
  placenta (total) (with hemorrhage) O72.0
    without hemorrhage O73.0
    portions or fragments (with hemorrhage) O72.2
      without hemorrhage O73.1
  products of conception
    early pregnancy (dead fetus) O02.1
    following
      delivery (with hemorrhage) O72.2
        without hemorrhage O73.1
  secundines (following delivery) (with hemorrhage) O72.0
    without hemorrhage O73.0
    complicating puerperium (delayed hemorrhage) O72.2
    partial O72.2
      without hemorrhage O73.1
  smegma, clitoris N90.89
  urine R33.9
    due to hyperplasia (hypertrophy) of prostate —*see* Hyperplasia, prostate
    drug-induced R33.0
    organic R33.8
      drug-induced R33.0
    psychogenic F45.8
    specified NEC R33.8
  water (in tissues) —*see* Edema

Reticular erythematous mucinosis L98.5

Reticulation, dust —*see* Pneumoconiosis

Reticulocytosis R70.1

Reticuloendotheliosis
  acute infantile C96.0
  leukemic C91.4-
  malignant C96.9
  nonlipid C96.0

Reticulohistiocytoma (giant-cell) D76.3

Reticuloid, actinic L57.1

Reticulosis (skin)
  acute of infancy C96.0
  hemophagocytic, familial D76.1

Reticulosis *(continued)*
  histiocytic medullary C96.9
  lipomelanotic I89.8
  malignant (midline) C86.0
  nonlipid C96.0
  polymorphic C86.0
  Sézary —*see* Sézary disease

Retina, retinal —*see also* condition
  dark area D49.81

Retinitis —*see also* Inflammation, chorioretinal
  albuminurica N18.9 *[H32]*
  diabetic —*see* Diabetes, retinitis
  disciformis —*see* Degeneration, macula
  focal —*see* Inflammation, chorioretinal, focal
  gravidarum —*see* Pregnancy, complicated by, specified pregnancy-related condition NEC
  juxtapapillaris —*see* Inflammation, chorioretinal, focal, juxtapapillary
  luetic —*see* Retinitis, syphilitic
  pigmentosa H35.52
  proliferans —*see* Disorder, globe, degenerative, specified type NEC
  proliferating —*see* Disorder, globe, degenerative, specified type NEC
  renal N18.9 *[H32]*
  syphilitic (early) (secondary) A51.43
    central, recurrent A52.71
    congenital (early) A50.01 *[H32]*
    late A52.71
  tuberculous A18.53

Retinoblastoma C69.2-
  differentiated C69.2-
  undifferentiated C69.2-

Retinochoroiditis —*see also* Inflammation, chorioretinal
  disseminated —*see* Inflammation, chorioretinal, disseminated
    syphilitic A52.71
  focal —*see* Inflammation, chorioretinal
  juxtapapillaris —*see* Inflammation, chorioretinal, focal, juxtapapillary

Retinopathy (background) H35.00
  arteriosclerotic I70.8 *[H35.0]*-
  atherosclerotic I70.8 *[H35.0]*-
  central serous —*see* Chorioretinopathy, central serous
  Coats H35.02-
  diabetic —*see* Diabetes, retinopathy
  exudative H35.02-
  hypertensive H35.03-
  in (due to)
    diabetes —*see* Diabetes, retinopathy
    sickle-cell disorders D57.- H36
  of prematurity H35.10-
    stage 0 H35.11-
    stage 1 H35.12-
    stage 2 H35.13-
    stage 3 H35.14-
    stage 4 H35.15-
    stage 5 H35.16-
  pigmentary, congenital —*see* Dystrophy, retina
  proliferative NEC H35.2-
    diabetic —*see* Diabetes, retinopathy, proliferative
    sickle-cell D57.- H36
  solar H31.02-

Retinoschisis H33.10-
  congenital Q14.1
  specified type NEC H33.19-

Retortamoniasis A07.8

Retractile testis Q55.22

Retraction
  cervix —*see* Retroversion, uterus
  drum (membrane) —*see* Disorde
    tympanic membrane, specified NEC
  finger —*see* Deformity, finger
  lid H02.539
    left H02.536
      lower H02.535
      upper H02.534
    right H02.533
      lower H02.532
      upper H02.531
  lung J98.4
  mediastinum J98.5
  nipple N64.53
    associated with
      lactation O92.03
      pregnancy O92.01-
      puerperium O92.02
    congenital Q83.8
  palmar fascia M72.0
  pleura —*see* Pleurisy
  ring, uterus (Bandl's) (pathologic
    O62.4
  sternum (congenital) Q76.7
    acquired M95.4
  uterus —*see* Retroversion, uterus
  valve (heart) —*see* Endocarditis

Retrobulbar —*see* condition

Retrocecal —*see* condition

Retrocession —*see* Retroversion

Retrodisplacement —*see* Retrovers

Retroflection, retroflexion —*see* Retroversion

Retrognathia, retrognathism (mandibular) (maxillary) M26.19

Retrograde menstruation N92.5

Retroperineal —*see* condition

Retroperitoneal —*see* condition

Retroperitonitis K68.9

Retropharyngeal —*see* condition

Retroplacental —*see* condition

Retroposition —*see* Retroversion

Retroprosthetic membrane T85.39

Retrosternal thyroid (congenital) Q89.2

Retroversion, retroverted
  cervix —*see* Retroversion, uterus
  female NEC —*see* Retroversion, uterus
  iris H21.89
  testis (congenital) Q55.29
  uterus (acquired) (acute) (any degree) (asymptomatic) (cervix) (postinfectional) (postpartal, old N85.4
    congenital Q51.818
    in pregnancy O34.53-

Retrovirus, as cause of disease classified elsewhere B97.30
  human
    immunodeficiency, type 2 (HIV B97.35
    T-cell lymphotropic
      type I (HTLV-I) B97.33
      type II (HTLV-II) B97.34
  lentivirus B97.31
  oncovirus B97.32
  specified NEC B97.39

Retrusion, premaxilla (development M26.09

Rett's disease or syndrome F84.2

Reverse peristalsis R19.2

Reye's syndrome G93.7

(factor)
emolytic disease (newborn) P55.0
compatibility, immunization or sensitization
affecting management of pregnancy NEC O36.09-
anti-D antibody O36.01-
newborn P55.0
transfusion reaction —*see* Complication (s), transfusion, incompatibility reaction, Rh (factor)
egative mother affecting newborn P55.0
ter elevated —*see* Complication (s), transfusion, incompatibility reaction, Rh (factor)
ansfusion reaction —*see* Complication (s), transfusion, incompatibility reaction, Rh (factor)

abdomyolysis (idiopathic) **NEC** M62.82
raumatic T79.6

abdomyoma —*see also* Neoplasm, onnective tissue, benign
dult —*see* Neoplasm, connective tissue, benign
etal —*see* Neoplasm, connective tissue, benign
lycogenic —*see* Neoplasm, connective tissue, benign

abdomyosarcoma (any type) — *ee* Neoplasm, connective tissue, nalignant

abdosarcoma —*see* Rhabdomyosarcoma

esus (factor) **incompatibility** —*see* Rh, incompatibility

eumatic (acute) (subacute) chronic)
dherent pericardium I09.2
oronary arteritis I01.9
egeneration, myocardium I09.0
ever (acute) —*see* Fever, rheumatic
eart —*see* Disease, heart, rheumatic
nyocardial degeneration —*see* Degeneration, myocardium
nyocarditis (chronic) (inactive) (with chorea) I09.0
active or acute I01.2
with chorea (acute) (rheumatic) (Sydenham's) I02.0
ancarditis, acute I01.8
with chorea (acute (rheumatic) Sydenham's) I02.0
pericarditis (active) (acute) (with effusion) (with pneumonia) I01.0
with chorea (acute) (rheumatic) (Sydenham's) I02.0
chronic or inactive I09.2
pneumonia I00 *[J17]*
torticollis M43.6
typhoid fever A01.09

eumatism (articular) (neuralgic) (nonarticular) M79.0
gout —*see* Arthritis, rheumatoid
intercostal, meaning Tietze's disease M94.0
palindromic (any site) M12.30
ankle M12.37-
elbow M12.32-
foot joint M12.37-
hand joint M12.34-
hip M12.35-
knee M12.36-
multiple site M12.39
shoulder M12.31-
specified joint NEC M12.38

Rheumatism *(continued)*
vertebrae M12.38
wrist M12.33-
sciatic M54.4-

Rheumatoid —*see also* condition
arthritis —*see also* Arthritis, rheumatoid
with involvement of organs NEC M05.60
ankle M05.67-
elbow M05.62-
foot joint M05.67-
hand joint M05.64-
hip M05.65-
knee M05.66-
multiple site M05.69
shoulder M05.61-
vertebra —*see* Spondylitis, ankylosing
wrist M05.63-
seronegative —*see* Arthritis, rheumatoid, seronegative
seropositive —*see* Arthritis, rheumatoid, seropositive
carditis M05.30
ankle M05.37-
elbow M05.32-
foot joint M05.37-
hand joint M05.34-
hip M05.35-
knee M05.36-
multiple site M05.39
shoulder M05.31-
vertebra —*see* Spondylitis, ankylosing
wrist M05.33-
endocarditis —*see* Rheumatoid, carditis
lung (disease) M05.10
ankle M05.17-
elbow M05.12-
foot joint M05.17-
hand joint M05.14-
hip M05.15-
knee M05.16-
multiple site M05.19
shoulder M05.11-
vertebra —*see* Spondylitis, ankylosing
wrist M05.13-
myocarditis —*see* Rheumatoid, carditis
myopathy M05.40
ankle M05.47-
elbow M05.42-
foot joint M05.47-
hand joint M05.44-
hip M05.45-
knee M05.46-
multiple site M05.49
shoulder M05.41-
vertebra —*see* Spondylitis, ankylosing
wrist M05.43-
pericarditis —*see* Rheumatoid, carditis
polyarthritis —*see* Arthritis, rheumatoid
polyneuropathy M05.50
ankle M05.57-
elbow M05.52-
foot joint M05.57-
hand joint M05.54-
hip M05.55-
knee M05.56-
multiple site M05.59
shoulder M05.51-
vertebra —*see* Spondylitis, ankylosing
wrist M05.53-
vasculitis M05.20
ankle M05.27-

Rheumatoid *(continued)*
vasculitis *(continued)*
elbow M05.22-
foot joint M05.27-
hand joint M05.24-
hip M05.25-
knee M05.26-
multiple site M05.29
shoulder M05.21-
vertebra —*see* Spondylitis, ankylosing
wrist M05.23-

Rhinitis (atrophic) (catarrhal) (chronic) (croupous) (fibrinous) (granulomatous) (hyperplastic) (hypertrophic) (membranous) (obstructive) (purulent) (suppurative) (ulcerative) J31.0
with
sore throat —*see* Nasopharyngitis
acute J00
allergic J30.9
with asthma J45.909
with
exacerbation (acute) J45.901
status asthmaticus J45.902
due to
food J30.5
pollen J30.1
nonseasonal J30.89
perennial J30.89
seasonal NEC J30.2
specified NEC J30.89
infective J00
pneumococcal J00
syphilitic A52.73
congenital A50.05 *[J99]*
tuberculous A15.8
vasomotor J30.0

Rhinoantritis (chronic) —*see* Sinusitis, maxillary

Rhinodacryolith —*see* Dacryolith

Rhinolith (nasal sinus) J34.89

Rhinomegaly J34.89

Rhinopharyngitis (acute) (subacute) — *see also* Nasopharyngitis
chronic J31.1
destructive ulcerating A66.5
mutilans A66.5

Rhinophyma L71.1

Rhinorrhea J34.89
cerebrospinal (fluid) G96.0
paroxysmal —*see* Rhinitis, allergic
spasmodic —*see* Rhinitis, allergic

Rhinosalpingitis —*see* Salpingitis, eustachian

Rhinoscleroma A48.8

Rhinosporidiosis B48.1

Rhinovirus infection NEC B34.8

Rhizomelic chondrodysplasia punctata E71.540

Rhythm
atrioventricular nodal I49.8
disorder I49.9
coronary sinus I49.8
ectopic I49.8
nodal I49.8
escape I49.9
heart, abnormal I49.9
idioventricular I44.2
nodal I49.8
sleep, inversion G47.2-
nonorganic origin —*see* Disorder, sleep, circadian rhythm, psychogenic

Rhytidosis facialis L98.8

Rib —*see also* condition
cervical Q76.5

Riboflavin deficiency E53.0

Rice bodies —*see also* Loose, body, joint
knee M23.4-

Richter syndrome —*see* Leukemia, chronic lymphocytic, B-cell type

Richter's hernia —*see* Hernia, abdomen, with obstruction

Ricinism —*see* Poisoning, food, noxious, plant

Rickets (active) (acute) (adolescent) (chest wall) (congenital) (current) (infantile) (intestinal) E55.0
adult —*see* Osteomalacia
celiac K90.0
hypophosphatemic with nephrotic-glycosuric dwarfism E72.09
inactive E64.3
kidney N25.0
renal N25.0
sequelae, any E64.3
vitamin-D-resistant E83.31 *[M90.80]*

Rickettsial disease A79.9
specified type NEC A79.89

Rickettsialpox (Rickettsia akari) A79.1

Rickettsiosis A79.9
due to
Ehrlichia sennetsu A79.81
Rickettsia akari (rickettsialpox) A79.1
specified type NEC A79.89
tick-borne A77.9
vesicular A79.1

Rider's bone —*see* Ossification, muscle, specified NEC

Ridge, alveolus —*see also* condition
flabby K06.8

Ridged ear, congenital Q17.3

Riedel's
lobe, liver Q44.7
struma, thyroiditis or disease E06.5

Rieger's anomaly or syndrome Q13.81

Riehl's melanosis L81.4

Rietti-Greppi-Micheli anemia D56.9

Rieux's hernia —*see* Hernia, abdomen, specified site NEC

Riga (-Fede) **disease** K14.0

Riggs' disease —*see* Periodontitis

Right middle lobe syndrome J98.11

Rigid, rigidity —*see also* condition
abdominal R19.30
with severe abdominal pain R10.0
epigastric R19.36
generalized R19.37
left lower quadrant R19.34
left upper quadrant R19.32
periumbilic R19.35
right lower quadrant R19.33
right upper quadrant R19.31
articular, multiple, congenital Q68.8
cervix (uteri) in pregnancy —*see* Pregnancy, complicated by, abnormal, cervix
hymen (acquired) (congenital) N89.6
nuchal R29.1
pelvic floor in pregnancy —*see* Pregnancy, complicated by, abnormal, pelvic organs or tissues NEC
perineum or vulva in pregnancy — *see* Pregnancy, complicated by, abnormal, vulva
spine —*see* Dorsopathy, specified NEC

Rigid, rigidity *(continued)*
vagina in pregnancy —*see* Pregnancy, complicated by, abnormal, vagina
Rigors R68.89
with fever R50.9
Riley-Day syndrome G90.1
RIND (reversible ischemic neurologic deficit) I63.9
Ring (s)
aorta (vascular) Q25.4
Bandl's O62.4
contraction, complicating delivery O62.4
esophageal, lower (muscular) K22.2
Fleischer's (cornea) H18.04-
hymenal, tight (acquired) (congenital) N89.6
Kayser-Fleischer (cornea) H18.04-
retraction, uterus, pathological O62.4
Schatzki's (esophagus) (lower) K22.2
congenital Q39.3
Soemmerring's —*see* Cataract, secondary
vascular (congenital) Q25.8
aorta Q25.4
Ringed hair (congenital) Q84.1
Ringworm B35.9
beard B35.0
black dot B35.0
body B35.4
Burmese B35.5
corporeal B35.4
foot B35.3
groin B35.6
hand B35.2
honeycomb B35.0
nails B35.1
perianal (area) B35.6
scalp B35.0
specified NEC B35.8
Tokelau B35.5
Rise, venous pressure I87.8
Risk, suicidal
meaning personal history of attempted suicide Z91.5
meaning suicidal ideation —*see* Ideation, suicidal
Ritter's disease L00
Rivalry, sibling Z62.891
Rivalta's disease A42.2
River blindness B73.01
Robert's pelvis Q74.2
with disproportion (fetopelvic) O33.0
causing obstructed labor O65.0
Robin (-Pierre) **syndrome** Q87.0
Robinow-Silvermann-Smith syndrome Q87.1
Robinson's (hidrotic) **ectodermal dysplasia or syndrome** Q82.4
Robles' disease B73.01
Rocky Mountain (spotted) **fever** A77.0
Roetheln —*see* Rubella
Roger's disease Q21.0
Rokitansky-Aschoff sinuses (gallbladder) K82.8
Rolando's fracture (displaced) S62.22-
nondisplaced S62.22-
Romano-Ward (prolonged QT interval) **syndrome** I45.81
Romberg's disease or syndrome G51.8
Roof, mouth —*see* condition

Rosacea L71.9
acne L71.9
keratitis L71.8
specified NEC L71.8
Rosary, rachitic E55.0
Rose
cold J30.1
fever J30.1
rash R21
epidemic B06.9
Rosenbach's erysipeloid A26.0
Rosenthal's disease or syndrome D68.1
Roseola B09
infantum B08.20
due to human herpesvirus 6 B08.21
due to human herpesvirus 7 B08.22
Rossbach's disease K31.89
psychogenic F45.8
Ross River disease or fever B33.1
Rostan's asthma (cardiac) —*see* Failure, ventricular, left
Rotation
anomalous, incomplete or insufficient, intestine Q43.3
cecum (congenital) Q43.3
colon (congenital) Q43.3
spine, incomplete or insufficient —*see* Dorsopathy, deforming, specified NEC
tooth, teeth, fully erupted M26.35
vertebra, incomplete or insufficient —*see* Dorsopathy, deforming, specified NEC
Rotes Quérol disease or syndrome — *see* Hyperostosis, ankylosing
Roth (-Bernhardt) **disease or syndrome** —*see* Meralgia paraesthetica
Rothmund (-Thomson) **syndrome** Q82.8
Rotor's disease or syndrome E80.6
Round
back (with wedging of vertebrae) — *see* Kyphosis
sequelae (late effect) of rickets E64.3
worms (large) (infestation) NEC B82.0
Ascariasis —*see also* Ascariasis B77.9
Roussy-Lévy syndrome G60.0
Rubella (German measles) B06.9
complication NEC B06.09
neurological B06.00
congenital P35.0
contact Z20.4
exposure to Z20.4
maternal
manifest rubella in infant P35.0
care for (suspected) damage to fetus O35.3
suspected damage to fetus affecting management of pregnancy O35.3
specified complications NEC B06.89
Rubeola (meaning measles) —*see* Measles
meaning rubella —*see* Rubella
Rubeosis, iris —*see* Disorder, iris, vascular
Rubinstein-Taybi syndrome Q87.2
Rudimentary (congenital) —*see also* Agenesis
arm —*see* Defect, reduction, upper limb
bone Q79.9

Rudimentary *(continued)*
cervix uteri Q51.828
eye Q11.2
lobule of ear Q17.3
patella Q74.1
respiratory organs in thoracopagus Q89.4
tracheal bronchus Q32.4
uterus Q51.818
in male Q56.1
vagina Q52.0
Ruled out condition —*see* Observation, suspected
Rumination R11.10
with nausea R11.2
disorder of infancy F98.21
neurotic F42
newborn P92.1
obsessional F42
psychogenic F42
Runeberg's disease D51.0
Runny nose R09.89
Rupia (syphilitic) A51.39
congenital A50.06
tertiary A52.79
Rupture, ruptured
abscess (spontaneous) - code by site under Abscess
aneurysm —*see* Aneurysm
anus (sphincter) —*see* Laceration, anus
aorta, aortic I71.8
abdominal I71.3
arch I71.1
ascending I71.1
descending I71.8
abdominal I71.3
thoracic I71.1
syphilitic A52.01
thoracoabdominal I71.5
thorax, thoracic I71.1
transverse I71.1
traumatic —*see* Injury, aorta, laceration, major
valve or cusp —*see also* Endocarditis, aortic I35.8
appendix (with peritonitis) K35.2
arteriovenous fistula, brain I60.8
artery I77.2
brain —*see* Hemorrhage, intracranial, intracerebral
coronary —*see* Infarct, myocardium
heart —*see* Infarct, myocardium
pulmonary I28.8
traumatic (complication) —*see* Injury, blood vessel
bile duct (common) (hepatic) K83.2
cystic K82.2
bladder (sphincter) (nontraumatic) (spontaneous) N32.89
following ectopic or molar pregnancy O08.6
obstetrical trauma O71.5
traumatic S37.29
blood vessel —*see also* Hemorrhage
brain —*see* Hemorrhage, intracranial, intracerebral
heart —*see* Infarct, myocardium
traumatic (complication) —*see* Injury, blood vessel, laceration, major, by site
bone —*see* Fracture
bowel (nontraumatic) K63.1
brain
aneurysm (congenital) —*see also* Hemorrhage, intracranial, subarachnoid
syphilitic A52.05
hemorrhagic —*see* Hemorrhage, intracranial, intracerebral

Rupture, ruptured *(continued)*
capillaries I78.8
cardiac (auricle) (ventricle) (wall) I23.3
with hemopericardium I23.0
infectional I40.9
traumatic —*see* Injury, heart
cartilage (articular) (current) —*see also* Sprain
knee S83.3-
semilunar —*see* Tear, meniscus
cecum (with peritonitis) K65.0
with peritoneal abscess K35.3
traumatic S36.598
celiac artery, traumatic —*see* Injury, blood vessel, celiac artery, laceration, major
cerebral aneurysm (congenital) (*see* Hemorrhage, intracranial, subarachnoid)
cervix (uteri)
with ectopic or molar pregnancy O08.6
following ectopic or molar pregnancy O08.6
obstetrical trauma O71.3
traumatic S37.69
chordae tendineae NEC I51.1
concurrent with acute myocardial infarction —*see* Infarct, myocardium
following acute myocardial infarction (current complication) I23.4
choroid (direct) (indirect) (traumatic) H31.32-
circle of Willis I60.6
colon (nontraumatic) K63.1
traumatic —*see* Injury, intestine, large
cornea (traumatic) —*see* Injury, eye, laceration
coronary (artery) (thrombotic) —*see* Infarct, myocardium
corpus luteum (infected) (ovary) N8
cyst —*see* Cyst
cystic duct K82.2
Descemet's membrane —*see* Change, corneal membrane, Descemet's, rupture
traumatic —*see* Injury, eye, laceration
diaphragm, traumatic —*see* Injury, intrathoracic, diaphragm
disc —*see* Rupture, intervertebral disc
diverticulum (intestine) K57.80
with bleeding K57.81
bladder N32.3
large intestine K57.20
with
bleeding K57.21
small intestine K57.40
with bleeding K57.41
small intestine K57.00
with
bleeding K57.01
large intestine K57.40
with bleeding K57.41
duodenal stump K31.89
ear drum (nontraumatic) —*see also* Perforation, tympanum
traumatic S09.2-
due to blast injury —*see* Injury, blast, ear
esophagus K22.3
eye (without prolapse or loss of intraocular tissue) —*see* Injury, eye, laceration
fallopian tube NEC (nonobstetric) (nontraumatic) N83.8
due to pregnancy O00.1

Rupture, ruptured *(continued)*
  uterus (traumatic) S37.69
    before labor O71.0-
    during or after labor O71.1
    nonpuerperal, nontraumatic N85.8
    pregnant (during labor) O71.1
      before labor O71.0-
  vagina —*see* Injury, vagina
  valve, valvular (heart) —*see* Endocarditis
  varicose vein —*see* Varix
  varix —*see* Varix
  vena cava R58
    traumatic —*see* Injury, vena cava, laceration, major
  vesical (urinary) N32.89
  vessel (blood) R58
    pulmonary I28.8
    traumatic —*see* Injury, blood vessel
  viscus R19.8
  vulva complicating delivery O70.0

Russell-Silver syndrome Q87.1

Russian spring-summer type encephalitis A84.0

Rust's disease (tuberculous cervical spondylitis) A18.01

Ruvalcaba-Myhre-Smith syndrome E71.440

Rytand-Lipsitch syndrome I44.2

S

Saber, sabre shin or tibia (syphilitic) A50.56 *[M90.8-]*

Sac lacrimal —*see* condition

Saccharomyces infection B37.9

Saccharopinuria E72.3

Saccular —*see* condition

Sacculation
  aorta (nonsyphilitic) —*see* Aneurysm, aorta
  bladder N32.3
  intralaryngeal (congenital) (ventricular) Q31.3
  larynx (congenital) (ventricular) Q31.3
  organ or site, congenital —*see* Distortion
  pregnant uterus —*see* Pregnancy, complicated by, abnormal, uterus
  ureter N28.89
  urethra N36.1
  vesical N32.3

Sachs' amaurotic familial idiocy or disease E75.02

Sachs-Tay disease E75.02

Sacks-Libman disease M32.11

Sacralgia M53.3

Sacralization Q76.49

Sacrodynia M53.3

Sacroiliac joint —*see* condition

Sacroiliitis NEC M46.1

Sacrum —*see* condition

Saddle
  back —*see* Lordosis
  embolus
    abdominal aorta I74.01
    pulmonary artery I26.92
      with acute cor pulmonale I26.02
  injury - code to condition
  nose M95.0
    due to syphilis A50.57

Sadism (sexual) F65.52

Sadness, postpartal O90.6

Sadomasochism F65.50

Saemisch's ulcer (cornea) —*see* Ulcer, cornea, central

Sahib disease B55.0

Sailors' skin L57.8

Saint
  Anthony's fire —*see* Erysipelas
  triad —*see* Hernia, diaphragm
  Vitus' dance —*see* Chorea, Sydenham's

Salaam
  attack (s) —*see* Epilepsy, spasms
  tic R25.8

Salicylism
  abuse F55.8
  overdose or wrong substance given —*see* Table of Drugs and Chemicals, by drug, poisoning

Salivary duct or gland —*see* condition

Salivation, excessive K11.7

Salmonella —*see* Infection, Salmonella

Salmonellosis A02.0

Salpingitis (catarrhal) (fallopian tube) (nodular) (pseudofollicular) (purulent) (septic) N70.91
  with oophoritis N70.93
  acute N70.01
    with oophoritis N70.03
  chlamydial A56.11
  chronic N70.11
    with oophoritis N70.13
  complicating abortion —*see* Abortion, by type, complicated by, salpingitis
  ear —*see* Salpingitis, eustachian
  eustachian (tube) H68.00-
    acute H68.01-
    chronic H68.02-
  follicularis N70.11
    with oophoritis N70.13
  gonococcal (acute) (chronic) A54.24
  interstitial, chronic N70.11
    with oophoritis N70.13
  isthmica nodosa N70.11
    with oophoritis N70.13
  specific (gonococcal) (acute) (chronic) A54.24
  tuberculous (acute) (chronic) A18.17
  venereal (gonococcal) (acute) (chronic) A54.24

Salpingocele N83.4

Salpingo-oophoritis (catarrhal) (purulent) (ruptured) (septic) (suppurative) N70.93
  acute N70.03
    with ectopic or molar pregnancy O08.0
    following ectopic or molar pregnancy O08.0
    gonococcal A54.24
  chronic N70.13
  following ectopic or molar pregnancy O08.0
  gonococcal (acute) (chronic) A54.24
  puerperal O86.19
  specific (gonococcal) (acute) (chronic) A54.24
  subacute N70.03
  tuberculous (acute) (chronic) A18.17
  venereal (gonococcal) (acute) (chronic) A54.24

Salpingo-ovaritis —*see* Salpingo-oophoritis

Salpingoperitonitis —*see* Salpingo-oophoritis

Salzmann's nodular dystrophy —*see* Degeneration, cornea, nodular

Sampson's cyst or tumor N80.1

San Joaquin (Valley) **fever** B38.0

Sandblaster's asthma, lung or pneumoconiosis J62.8

Sander's disease (paranoia) F22

Sandfly fever A93.1

Sandhoff's disease E75.01

Sanfilippo (Type B) (Type C) (Type D) **syndrome** E76.22

Sanger-Brown ataxia G11.2

Sao Paulo fever or typhus A77.0

Saponification, mesenteric K65.8

Sarcocele (benign)
  syphilitic A52.76
    congenital A50.59

Sarcocystosis A07.8

Sarcoepiplocele —*see* Hernia

Sarcoepiplomphalocele Q79.2

Sarcoid —*see also* Sarcoidosis
  arthropathy D86.86
  Boeck's D86.9
  Darier-Roussy D86.3
  iridocyclitis D86.83
  meningitis D86.81
  myocarditis D86.85
  myositis D86.87
  pyelonephritis D86.84
  Spiegler-Fendt L08.89

Sarcoidosis D86.9
  with
    cranial nerve palsies D86.82
    hepatic granuloma D86.89
    polyarthritis D86.86
    tubulo-interstitial nephropathy D86.84
  combined sites NEC D86.89
  lung D86.0
    and lymph nodes D86.2
  lymph nodes D86.1
    and lung D86.2
  meninges D86.81
  skin D86.3
  specified type NEC D86.89

Sarcoma (of) —*see also* Neoplasm, connective tissue, malignant
  alveolar soft part —*see* Neoplasm, connective tissue, malignant
  ameloblastic C41.1
    upper jaw (bone) C41.0
  botryoid —*see* Neoplasm, connective tissue, malignant
  botryoides —*see* Neoplasm, connective tissue, malignant
  cerebellar C71.6
    circumscribed (arachnoidal) C71.6
  circumscribed (arachnoidal) cerebellar C71.6
  clear cell —*see also* Neoplasm, connective tissue, malignant
    kidney C64.-
  dendritic cells (accessory cells) C96.4
  embryonal —*see* Neoplasm, connective tissue, malignant
  endometrial (stromal) C54.1
    isthmus C54.0
  epithelioid (cell) —*see* Neoplasm, connective tissue, malignant
  Ewing's —*see* Neoplasm, bone, malignant
  follicular dendritic cell C96.4
  germinoblastic (diffuse) —*see* Lymphoma, diffuse large cell
    follicular —*see* Lymphoma, follicular, specified NEC

Sarcoma *(continued)*
  giant cell (except of bone) —*see also* Neoplasm, connective tissu malignant
    bone —*see* Neoplasm, bone, malignant
  glomoid —*see* Neoplasm, connect tissue, malignant
  granulocytic C92.3-
  hemangioendothelial —*see* Neoplasm, connective tissue, malignant
  hemorrhagic, multiple —*see* Sarcoma, Kaposi's
  histiocytic C96.A
  Hodgkin —*see* Lymphoma, Hodgkin
  immunoblastic (diffuse) —*see* Lymphoma, diffuse large cell
  interdigitating dendritic cell C96.4
  Kaposi's
    colon C46.4
    connective tissue C46.1
    gastrointestinal organ C46.4
    lung C46.5-
    lymph node (s) C46.3
    palate (hard) (soft) C46.2
    rectum C46.4
    skin C46.0
    specified site NEC C46.7
    stomach C46.4
    unspecified site C46.9
  Kupffer cell C22.3
  Langerhans cell C96.4
  leptomeningeal —*see* Neoplasm, meninges, malignant
  liver NEC C22.4
  lymphangioendothelial —*see* Neoplasm, connective tissue, malignant
  lymphoblastic —*see* Lymphoma, lymphoblastic (diffuse)
  lymphocytic —*see* Lymphoma, sn cell B-cell
  mast cell C96.2
  melanotic —*see* Melanoma
  meningeal —*see* Neoplasm, meninges, malignant
  meningothelial —*see* Neoplasm, meninges, malignant
  mesenchymal —*see also* Neoplas connective tissue, malignant
    mixed —*see* Neoplasm, connec tissue, malignant
  mesothelial —*see* Mesothelioma
  monstrocellular
    specified site —*see* Neoplasm, malignant, by site
    unspecified site C71.9
  myeloid C92.3-
  neurogenic —*see* Neoplasm, nerv malignant
  odontogenic C41.1
    upper jaw (bone) C41.0
  osteoblastic —*see* Neoplasm, bon malignant
  osteogenic —*see also* Neoplasm, bone, malignant
    juxtacortical —*see* Neoplasm, bone, malignant
    periosteal —*see* Neoplasm, bor malignant
  periosteal —*see also* Neoplasm, bone, malignant
    osteogenic —*see* Neoplasm, bo malignant
  pleomorphic cell —*see* Neoplasm connective tissue, malignant
  reticulum cell (diffuse) —*see* Lymphoma, diffuse large cell
    nodular —*see* Lymphoma, follicular

Seizure *(continued)*
post traumatic R56.1
recurrent G40.909
specified NEC G40.89
uncinate —*see* Epilepsy, localization-related, symptomatic, with complex partial seizures

Selenium deficiency, dietary E59

Self-damaging behavior (life-style) Z72.89

Self-harm (attempted)
history (personal) Z91.5
in family Z81.8

Self-mutilation (attempted)
history (personal) Z91.5
in family Z81.8

Self-poisoning
history (personal) Z91.5
in family Z81.8
observation following (alleged) attempt Z03.6

Semicoma R40.1

Seminal vesiculitis N49.0

Seminoma C62.9-
specified site —*see* Neoplasm, malignant, by site

Senear-Usher disease or syndrome L10.4

Senectus R54

Senescence (without mention of psychosis) R54

Senile, senility —*see also* condition R41.81
with
acute confusional state F05
mental changes NOS F03
psychosis NEC —*see* Psychosis, senile
asthenia R54
cervix (atrophic) N88.8
debility R54
endometrium (atrophic) N85.8
fallopian tube (atrophic) —*see* Atrophy, fallopian tube
heart (failure) R54
ovary (atrophic) —*see* Atrophy, ovary
premature E34.8
vagina, vaginitis (atrophic) N95.2
wart L82.1

Sensation
burning (skin) R20.8
tongue K14.6
loss of R20.8
prickling (skin) R20.2
tingling (skin) R20.2

Sense loss
smell —*see* Disturbance, sensation, smell
taste —*see* Disturbance, sensation, taste
touch R20.8

Sensibility disturbance (cortical) (deep) (vibratory) R20.9

Sensitive, sensitivity —*see also* Allergy
carotid sinus G90.01
child (excessive) F93.8
cold, autoimmune D59.1
dentin K03.89
latex Z91.040
methemoglobin D74.8
tuberculin, without clinical or radiological symptoms R76.11
visual
glare H53.71
impaired contrast H53.72

Sensitiver Beziehungswahn F22

Sensitization, auto-erythrocytic D69.2

Separation
anxiety, abnormal (of childhood) F93.0
apophysis, traumatic - code as Fracture, by site
choroid —*see* Detachment, choroid
epiphysis, epiphyseal
nontraumatic —*see also* Osteochondropathy, specified type NEC
upper femoral —*see* Slipped, epiphysis, upper femoral
traumatic - code as Fracture, by site
fracture —*see* Fracture
infundibulum cardiac from right ventricle by a partition Q24.3
joint (traumatic) (current) - code by site under Dislocation
pubic bone, obstetrical trauma O71.6
retina, retinal —*see* Detachment, retina
symphysis pubis, obstetrical trauma O71.6
tracheal ring, incomplete, congenital Q32.1

Sepsis (generalized) (unspecified organism) A41.9
with
organ dysfunction (acute) (multiple) R65.20
with septic shock R65.21
actinomycotic A42.7
adrenal hemorrhage syndrome (meningococcal) A39.1
anaerobic A41.4
Bacillus anthracis A22.7
Brucella —*see also* Brucellosis A23.9
candidal B37.7
cryptogenic A41.9
due to device, implant or graft T85.79
arterial graft NEC T82.7
breast (implant) T85.79
catheter NEC T85.79
dialysis (renal) T82.7
intraperitoneal T85.71
infusion NEC T82.7
spinal (epidural) (subdural) T85.79
urinary (indwelling) T83.51
ectopic or molar pregnancy O08.82
electronic (electrode) (pulse generator) (stimulator)
bone T84.7
cardiac T82.7
nervous system (brain) (peripheral nerve) (spinal) T85.79
urinary T83.59
fixation, internal (orthopedic) —*see* Complication, fixation device, infection
gastrointestinal (bile duct) (esophagus) T85.79
genital T83.6
heart NEC T82.7
valve (prosthesis) T82.6
graft T82.7
joint prosthesis —*see* Complication, joint prosthesis, infection
ocular (corneal graft) (orbital implant) T85.79
orthopedic NEC T84.7
fixation device, internal —*see* Complication, fixation device, infection
specified NEC T85.79
vascular T82.7
ventricular intracranial shunt T85.79

Sepsis *(continued)*
during labor O75.3
Enterococcus A41.81
Erysipelothrix (rhusiopathiae) (erysipeloid) A26.7
Escherichia coli (E. coli) A41.5
extraintestinal yersiniosis A28.2
following
abortion (subsequent episode) O08.0
current episode —*see* Abortion
ectopic or molar pregnancy O08.82
immunization T88.0
infusion, therapeutic injection or transfusion NEC T80.29
gangrenous A41.9
gonococcal A54.86
Gram-negative (organism) A41.5
anaerobic A41.4
Haemophilus influenzae A41.3
herpesviral B00.7
intra-abdominal K65.1
intraocular —*see* Endophthalmitis, purulent
Listeria monocytogenes A32.7
localized - code to specific localized infection
in operation wound T81.4
skin —*see* Abscess
malleus A24.0
melioidosis A24.1
meningeal —*see* Meningitis
meningococcal A39.4
acute A39.2
chronic A39.3
MSSA (Methicillin susceptible Staphylococcus aureus) A41.01
newborn P36.9
due to
anaerobes NEC P36.5
Escherichia coli P36.4
Staphylococcus P36.30
aureus P36.2
specified NEC P36.39
Streptococcus P36.10
group B P36.0
specified NEC P36.19
specified NEC P36.8
Pasteurella multocida A28.0
pelvic, puerperal, postpartum, childbirth O85
postprocedural T81.4
pneumococcal A40.3
puerperal, postpartum, childbirth (pelvic) O85
Salmonella (arizonae) (cholerae-suis) (enteritidis) (typhimurium) A02.1
severe R65.20
with septic shock R65.21
skin, localized —*see* Abscess
Shigella —*see also* Dysentery, bacillary A03.9
specified organism NEC A41.89
Staphylococcus, staphylococcal A41.2
aureus (methicillin susceptible) (MSSA) A41.01
methicillin resistant (MRSA) A41.02
coagulase-negative A41.1
specified NEC A41.1
Streptococcus, streptococcal A40.9
agalactiae A40.1
group
A A40.0
B A40.1
D A41.81
neonatal P36.10
group B P36.0
specified NEC P36.19
pneumoniae A40.3
pyogenes A40.0
specified NEC A40.8

Sepsis *(continued)*
tracheostomy stoma J95.02
tularemic A21.7
umbilical, umbilical cord (newborn) —*see* Sepsis, newborn
Yersinia pestis A20.7

Septate —*see* Septum

Septic —*see* condition
arm —*see* Cellulitis, upper limb
with lymphangitis —*see* Lymphangitis, acute, upper lim
embolus —*see* Embolism
finger —*see* Cellulitis, digit
with lymphangitis —*see* Lymphangitis, acute, digit
foot —*see* Cellulitis, lower limb
with lymphangitis —*see* Lymphangitis, acute, lower limb
gallbladder (acute) K81.0
hand —*see* Cellulitis, upper limb
with lymphangitis —*see* Lymphangitis, acute, upper limb
joint —*see* Arthritis, pyogenic or pyemic
leg —*see* Cellulitis, lower limb
with lymphangitis —*see* Lymphangitis, acute, lower lim
nail —*see also* Cellulitis, digit
with lymphangitis —*see* Lymphangitis, acute, digit
sore —*see also* Abscess
throat J02.0
streptococcal J02.0
spleen (acute) D73.89
teeth, tooth (pulpal origin) K04.4
throat —*see* Pharyngitis
thrombus —*see* Thrombosis
toe —*see* Cellulitis, digit
with lymphangitis —*see* Lymphangitis, acute, digit
tonsils, chronic J35.01
with adenoiditis J35.03
uterus —*see* Endometritis

Septicemia A41.9
meaning sepsis —*see* Sepsis

Septum, septate (congenital) —*see als* Anomaly, by site
anal Q42.3
with fistula Q42.2
aqueduct of Sylvius Q03.0
with spina bifida —*see* Spina bifida, by site, with hydrocephalus
uterus (complete) (partial) Q51.2
vagina Q52.10
in pregnancy —*see* Pregnancy, complicated by, abnormal vagina causing obstructed labor O65.5
longitudinal (with or without obstruction) Q52.12
transverse Q52.11

Sequelae (of) —*see also* condition
abscess, intracranial or intraspinal (conditions in G06) G09
amputation -- code to injury with seventh character S
burn and corrosion -- code to injury with seventh character S
calcium deficiency E64.8
cerebrovascular disease —*see* Sequelae, disease, cerebrovascular
childbirth O94
contusion -- code to injury with seventh character S
corrosion —*see* Sequelae, burn and corrosion
crushing injury -- code to injury with seventh character S

Sequelae *(continued)*
- disease
  - cerebrovascular I69.90
    - alteration of sensation I69.998
    - aphasia I69.920
    - apraxia I69.990
    - ataxia I69.993
    - cognitive deficits I69.91
    - disturbance of vision I69.998
    - dysarthria I69.922
    - dysphagia I69.991
    - dysphasia I69.921
    - facial droop I69.992
    - facial weakness I69.992
    - fluency disorder I69.923
    - hemiplegia I69.95-
    - hemorrhage
      - intracerebral —*see* Sequelae, hemorrhage, intracerebral
      - intracranial, nontraumatic NEC —*see* Sequelae, hemorrhage, intracranial, nontraumatic
      - subarachnoid —*see* Sequelae, hemorrhage, subarachnoid
    - language deficit I69.928
    - monoplegia
      - lower limb I69.84-
      - upper limb I69.93-
    - paralytic syndrome I69.96-
    - specified effect NEC I69.998
    - specified type NEC I69.80
      - alteration of sensation I69.898
      - aphasia I69.820
      - apraxia I69.890
      - ataxia I69.893
      - cognitive deficits I69.81
      - disturbance of vision I69.898
      - dysarthria I69.822
      - dysphagia I69.891
      - dysphasia I69.821
      - facial droop I69.892
      - facial weakness I69.892
      - fluency disorder I69.823
      - hemiplegia I69.85-
      - language deficit I69.828
      - monoplegia
        - lower limb I69.84-
        - upper limb I69.83-
      - paralytic syndrome I69.86-
      - specified effect NEC I69.898
    - speech deficit I69.928
      - speech deficit I69.828
    - stroke NOS —*see* Sequelae, stroke NOS
- dislocation -- code to injury with seventh character S
- encephalitis or encephalomyelitis (conditions in G04) G09
  - in infectious disease NEC B94.8
  - viral B94.1
- external cause -- code to injury with seventh character S
- foreign body entering natural orifice -- code to injury with seventh character S
- fracture -- code to injury with seventh character S
- frostbite -- code to injury with seventh character S
- Hansen's disease B92
- hemorrhage
  - intracerebral I69.10
    - alteration of sensation I69.198
    - aphasia I69.120
    - apraxia I69.190
    - ataxia I69.193
    - cognitive deficits I69.11
    - disturbance of vision I69.198
    - dysarthria I69.122
    - dysphagia I69.191
    - dysphasia I69.121

Sequelae *(continued)*
- hemorrhage *(continued)*
  - intracerebral *(continued)*
    - facial droop I69.192
    - facial weakness I69.192
    - fluency disorder I69.123
    - hemiplegia I69.15-
    - language deficit NEC I69.128
    - monoplegia
      - lower limb I69.14-
      - upper limb I69.13-
    - paralytic syndrome I69.16-
    - specified effect NEC I69.198
    - speech deficit NEC I69.128
  - intracranial, nontraumatic NEC I69.20
    - alteration of sensation I69.298
    - aphasia I69.220
    - apraxia I69.290
    - ataxia I69.293
    - cognitive deficits I69.21
    - disturbance of vision I69.298
    - dysarthria I69.222
    - dysphagia I69.291
    - dysphasia I69.221
    - facial droop I69.292
    - facial weakness I69.292
    - fluency disorder I69.223
    - hemiplegia I69.25-
    - language deficit NEC I69.228
    - monoplegia
      - lower limb I69.24-
      - upper limb I69.23-
    - paralytic syndrome I69.26-
    - specified effect NEC I69.298
    - speech deficit NEC I69.228
  - subarachnoid I69.00
    - alteration of sensation I69.098
    - aphasia I69.020
    - apraxia I69.090
    - ataxia I69.093
    - cognitive deficits I69.01
    - disturbance of vision I69.098
    - dysarthria I69.022
    - dysphagia I69.091
    - dysphasia I69.021
    - facial droop I69.092
    - facial weakness I69.092
    - fluency disorder I69.023
    - hemiplegia I69.05-
    - language deficit NEC I69.028
    - monoplegia
      - lower limb I69.04-
      - upper limb I69.03-
    - paralytic syndrome I69.06-
    - specified effect NEC I69.098
    - speech deficit NEC I69.028
- hepatitis, viral B94.2
- hyperalimentation E68
- infarction
  - cerebral I69.30
    - alteration of sensation I69.398
    - aphasia I69.320
    - apraxia I69.390
    - ataxia I69.393
    - cognitive deficits I69.31
    - disturbance of vision I69.398
    - dysarthria I69.322
    - dysphagia I69.391
    - dysphasia I69.321
    - facial droop I69.392
    - facial weakness I69.392
    - fluency disorder I69.323
    - hemiplegia I69.35-
    - language deficit NEC I69.328
    - monoplegia
      - lower limb I69.34-
      - upper limb I69.33-
    - paralytic syndrome I69.36-
    - specified effect NEC I69.398
    - speech deficit NEC I69.328

Sequelae *(continued)*
- infection, pyogenic, intracranial or intraspinal G09
- infectious disease B94.9
  - specified NEC B94.8
- injury -- code to injury with seventh character S
- leprosy B92
- meningitis
  - bacterial (conditions in G00) G09
  - other or unspecified cause (conditions in G03) G09
- muscle (and tendon) injury -- code to injury with seventh character S
- myelitis —*see* Sequelae, encephalitis
- niacin deficiency E64.8
- nutritional deficiency E64.9
  - specified NEC E64.8
- obstetrical condition O94
- parasitic disease B94.9
- phlebitis or thrombophlebitis of intracranial or intraspinal venous sinuses and veins (conditions in G08) G09
- poisoning -- code to poisoning with seventh character S
  - nonmedicinal substance — *see* Sequelae, toxic effect, nonmedicinal substance
- poliomyelitis (acute) B91
- pregnancy O94
- protein-energy malnutrition E64.0
- puerperium O94
- rickets E64.3
- selenium deficiency E64.8
- sprain and strain -- code to injury with seventh character S
- stroke NOS I69.30
  - alteration in sensation I69.398
  - aphasia I69.320
  - apraxia I69.390
  - ataxia I69.393
  - cognitive deficits I69.31
  - disturbance of vision I69.398
  - dysarthria I69.322
  - dysphagia I69.391
  - dysphasia I69.321
  - facial droop I69.392
  - facial weakness I69.392
  - hemiplegia I69.35-
  - language deficit NEC I69.328
  - monoplegia
    - lower limb I69.34-
    - upper limb I69.33-
  - paralytic syndrome I69.36-
  - specified effect NEC I69.398
  - speech deficit NEC I69.328
- tendon and muscle injury -- code to injury with seventh character S
- thiamine deficiency E64.8
- trachoma B94.0
- tuberculosis B90.9
  - bones and joints B90.2
  - central nervous system B90.0
  - genitourinary B90.1
  - pulmonary (respiratory) B90.9
  - specified organs NEC B90.8
- viral
  - encephalitis B94.1
  - hepatitis B94.2
- vitamin deficiency NEC E64.8
  - A E64.1
  - B E64.8
  - C E64.2
- wound, open -- code to injury with seventh character S

Sequestration —*see also* Sequestrum
- lung, congenital Q33.2

Sequestrum
- bone —*see* Osteomyelitis, chronic
- dental M27.2

Sequestrum *(continued)*
- jaw bone M27.2
- orbit —*see* Osteomyelitis, orbit
- sinus (accessory) (nasal) —*see* Sinusitis

Sequoiosis lung or pneumonitis J67.8

Serology for syphilis
- doubtful
  - with signs or symptoms - code by site and stage under Syphilis
  - follow-up of latent syphilis —*see* Syphilis, latent
- negative, with signs or symptoms - code by site and stage under Syphilis
- positive A53.0
  - with signs or symptoms - code by site and stage under Syphilis
- reactivated A53.0

Seroma —*see also* Hematoma
- traumatic, secondary and recurrent T79.2

Seropurulent —*see* condition

Serositis, multiple K65.8
- pericardial I31.1
- peritoneal K65.8

Serous —*see* condition

Sertoli cell
- adenoma
  - specified site —*see* Neoplasm, benign, by site
  - unspecified site
    - female D27.9
    - male D29.20
- carcinoma
  - specified site —*see* Neoplasm, malignant, by site
  - unspecified site (male) C62.9-
    - female C56.9
- tumor
  - with lipid storage
    - specified site —*see* Neoplasm, benign, by site
    - unspecified site
      - female D27.9
      - male D29.20
  - specified site —*see* Neoplasm, benign, by site
  - unspecified site
    - female D27.9
    - male D29.20

Sertoli-Leydig cell tumor —*see* Neoplasm, benign, by site
- specified site —*see* Neoplasm, benign, by site
- unspecified site
  - female D27.9
  - male D29.20

Serum
- allergy, allergic reaction —*see also* Reaction, serum T80.69
  - shock —*see also* Shock, anaphylactic T80.59
- arthritis —*see also* Reaction, serum T80.69
- complication or reaction NEC —*see also* Reaction, serum T80.69
- disease NEC —*see also* Reaction, serum T80.69
- hepatitis —*see also* Hepatitis, viral, type B
  - carrier (suspected) of Z22.51
- intoxication —*see also* Reaction, serum T80.69
- neuritis —*see also* Reaction, serum T80.69
- neuropathy G61.1
- poisoning NEC —*see also* Reaction, serum T80.69

Serum *(continued)*
- rash NEC —*see also* Reaction, serum T80.69
- reaction NEC —*see also* Reaction, serum T80.69
- sickness NEC —*see also* Reaction, serum T80.69
- urticaria —*see also* Reaction, serum T80.69

Sesamoiditis M25.8-

Sever's disease or osteochondrosis —*see* Osteochondrosis, juvenile, tarsus

Severe sepsis R65.20
- with septic shock R65.21

Sex
- chromosome mosaics Q97.8
  - lines with various numbers of X chromosomes Q97.2
- education Z70.8
- reassignment surgery status Z87.890

Sextuplet pregnancy —*see* Pregnancy, sextuplet

Sexual
- function, disorder of (psychogenic) F52.9
- immaturity (female) (male) E30.0
- impotence (psychogenic) organic origin NEC —*see* Dysfunction, sexual, male
- precocity (constitutional) (cryptogenic)(female) (idiopathic) (male) E30.1

Sexuality, pathologic —*see* Deviation, sexual

Sézary disease C84.1-

Shadow, lung R91.8

Shaking palsy or paralysis —*see* Parkinsonism

Shallowness, acetabulum —*see* Derangement, joint, specified type NEC, hip

Shaver's disease J63.1

Sheath (tendon) —*see* condition

Sheathing, retinal vessels H35.01-

Shedding
- nail L60.8
- premature, primary (deciduous) teeth K00.6

Sheehan's disease or syndrome E23.0

Shelf, rectal K62.89

Shell teeth K00.5

Shellshock (current) F43.0
- lasting state —*see* Disorder, post-traumatic stress

Shield kidney Q63.1

Shift
- auditory threshold (temporary) H93.24-
- mediastinal R93.8

Shifting sleep-work schedule (affecting sleep) G47.26

Shiga (-Kruse) **dysentery** A03.0

Shiga's bacillus A03.0

Shigella (dysentery) —*see* Dysentery, bacillary

Shigellosis A03.9
- Group A A03.0
- Group B A03.1
- Group C A03.2
- Group D A03.3

Shin splints S86.89

Shingles —*see* Herpes, zoster

Shipyard disease or eye B30.0

Shirodkar suture, in pregnancy —*see* Pregnancy, complicated by, incompetent cervix

Shock R57.9
- with ectopic or molar pregnancy O08.3
- adrenal (cortical) (Addisonian) E27.2
- adverse food reaction (anaphylactic) —*see* Shock, anaphylactic, due to food
- allergic —*see* Shock, anaphylactic
- anaphylactic T78.2
  - chemical —*see* Table of Drugs and Chemicals
  - due to drug or medicinal substance
    - correct substance properly administered T88.6
    - overdose or wrong substance given or taken (by accident) —*see* Table of Drugs and Chemicals, by drug, poisoning
  - due to food (nonpoisonous) T78.00
    - additives T78.06
    - dairy products T78.07
    - eggs T78.08
    - fish T78.03
      - shellfish T78.02
    - fruit T78.04
    - milk T78.07
    - nuts T78.05
      - peanuts T78.01
    - peanuts T78.01
    - *see*ds T78.05
    - specified type NEC T78.09
    - vegetable T78.04
  - following sting (s) —*see* Venom
  - immunization T80.52
  - serum T80.59
    - blood and blood products T80.51
    - immunization T80.52
    - specified NEC T80.59
    - vaccination T80.52
- anaphylactoid —*see* Shock, anaphylactic
- anesthetic
  - correct substance properly administered T88.2
  - overdose or wrong substance given or taken —*see* Table of Drugs and Chemicals, by drug, poisoning
    - specified anesthetic —*see* Table of Drugs and Chemicals, by drug, poisoning
- cardiogenic R57.0
- chemical substance —*see* Table of Drugs and Chemicals
- complicating ectopic or molar pregnancy O08.3
- culture —*see* Disorder, adjustment
- drug
  - due to correct substance properly administered T88.6
  - overdose or wrong substance given or taken (by accident) —*see* Table of Drugs and Chemicals, by drug, poisoning
- during or after labor and delivery O75.1
- electric T75.4
- (taser) T75.4
- endotoxic R65.21
  - postprocedural (during or resulting from a procedure, not elsewhere classified) T81.12
- following
  - ectopic or molar pregnancy O08.3
  - injury (immediate) (delayed) T79.4
  - labor and delivery O75.1

Shock *(continued)*
- food (anaphylactic) —*see* Shock, anaphylactic, due to food
- from electroshock gun (taser) T75.4
- gram-negative R65.21
  - postprocedural (during or resulting from a procedure, not elsewhere classified) T81.12
- hematologic R57.8
- hemorrhagic
  - surgery (intraoperative) (postoperative) T81.19
  - trauma T79.4
- hypovolemic R57.1
  - surgical T81.19
  - traumatic T79.4
- insulin E15
  - therapeutic misadventure —*see* subcategory T38.3
- kidney N17.0
  - traumatic (following crushing) T79.5
- lightning T75.01
- lung J80
- obstetric O75.1
  - with ectopic or molar pregnancy O08.3
  - following ectopic or molar pregnancy O08.3
- pleural (surgical) T81.19
  - due to trauma T79.4
- postprocedural (postoperative) T81.10
  - with ectopic or molar pregnancy O08.3
  - cardiogenic T81.11
  - endotoxic T81.12
  - following ectopic or molar pregnancy O08.3
  - gram-negative T81.12
  - hypovolemic T81.19
  - septic T81.12
  - specified type NEC T81.19
- psychic F43.0
- septic (due to severe sepsis) R65.21
- specified NEC R57.8
- surgical T81.10
- taser gun (taser) T75.4
- therapeutic misadventure NEC T81.10
- thyroxin
  - overdose or wrong substance given or taken —*see* Table of Drugs and Chemicals, by drug, poisoning
- toxic, syndrome A48.3
- transfusion —*see* Complications, transfusion
- traumatic (immediate) (delayed) T79.4

Shoemaker's chest M95.4

Short, shortening, shortness
- arm (acquired) —*see also* Deformity, limb, unequal length
  - congenital Q71.81-
  - forearm —*see* Deformity, limb, unequal length
- bowel syndrome K91.2
- breath R06.02
- cervical (complicating pregnancy) O26.87-
  - non-gravid uterus N88.3
- common bile duct, congenital Q44.5
- cord (umbilical), complicating delivery O69.3
- cystic duct, congenital Q44.5
- esophagus (congenital) Q39.8
- femur (acquired) —*see* Deformity, limb, unequal length, femur
  - congenital —*see* Defect, reduction, lower limb, longitudinal, femur
- frenum, frenulum, linguae (congenital) Q38.1

Short, shortening, shortness *(continued)*
- hip (acquired) —*see also* Deformity, limb, unequal length
  - congenital Q65.89
- leg (acquired) —*see also* Deformity, limb, unequal length
  - congenital Q72.81-
  - lower leg —*see also* Deformity, limb, unequal length
- limbed stature, with immunodeficiency D82.2
- lower limb (acquired) —*see also* Deformity, limb, unequal length
  - congenital Q72.81-
- organ or site, congenital NEC —*see* Distortion
- palate, congenital Q38.5
- radius (acquired) —*see also* Deformity, limb, unequal length
  - congenital —*see* Defect, reduction, upper limb, longitudinal, radius
- rib syndrome Q77.2
- stature (child) (hereditary) (idiopathic) NEC R62.52
  - constitutional E34.3
  - due to endocrine disorder E34.3
  - Laron-type E34.3
- tendon —*see also* Contraction, tendon
  - with contracture of joint —*see* Contraction, joint
  - Achilles (acquired) M67.0-
    - congenital Q66.89
  - congenital Q79.8
- thigh (acquired) —*see also* Deformity, limb, unequal length, femur
  - congenital —*see* Defect, reduction, lower limb, longitudinal, femur
- tibialis anterior (tendon) —*see* Contraction, tendon
- umbilical cord
  - complicating delivery O69.3
- upper limb, congenital —*see* Defect, reduction, upper limb, specified type NEC
- urethra N36.8
- uvula, congenital Q38.5
- vagina (congenital) Q52.4

Shortsightedness —*see* Myopia

Shoshin (acute fulminating beriberi) E51.11

Shoulder —*see* condition

Shovel-shaped incisors K00.2

Shower, thromboembolic —*see* Embolism

Shunt
- arterial-venous (dialysis) Z99.2
- arteriovenous, pulmonary (acquired) I28.0
  - congenital Q25.72
- cerebral ventricle (communicating) in situ Z98.2
- surgical, prosthetic, with complications —*see* Complications, cardiovascular, device or implant

Shutdown, renal N28.9

Shy-Drager syndrome G90.3

Sialadenitis, sialadenosis (any gland) (chronic) (periodic) (suppurative) —*see* Sialoadenitis

Sialectasia K11.8

Sialidosis E77.1

Sialitis, silitis (any gland) (chronic) (suppurative) —*see* Sialoadenitis

aloadenitis (any gland) (periodic) (suppurative) K11.20
- acute K11.21
  - recurrent K11.22
- chronic K11.23

aloadenopathy K11.9

aloangitis —*see* Sialoadenitis

alodochitis (fibrinosa) —*see* Sialoadenitis

alodocholithiasis K11.5

alolithiasis K11.5

alometaplasia, necrotizing K11.8

alorrhea —*see also* Ptyalism
- periodic —*see* Sialoadenitis

alosis K11.7

amese twin Q89.4

bling rivalry Z62.891

card's syndrome G52.7

cca syndrome M35.00
- with
  - keratoconjunctivitis M35.01
  - lung involvement M35.02
  - myopathy M35.03
  - renal tubulo-interstitial disorders M35.04
- specified organ involvement NEC M35.09

ick R69
- or handicapped person in family Z63.79
  - needing care at home Z63.6
- sinus (syndrome) I49.5

ick-euthyroid syndrome E07.81

ickle-cell
- anemia —*see* Disease, sickle-cell
- trait D57.3

icklemia —*see also* Disease, sickle-cell
- trait D57.3

ickness
- air (travel) T75.3
- airplane T75.3
- alpine T70.29
- altitude T70.20
- Andes T70.29
- aviator's T70.29
- balloon T70.29
- car T75.3
- compressed air T70.3
- decompression T70.3
- green D50.8
- milk —*see* Poisoning, food, noxious
- motion T75.3
- mountain T70.29
  - acute D75.1
- protein —*see also* Reaction, serum T80.69
- radiation T66
- roundabout (motion) T75.3
- sea T75.3
- serum NEC —*see also* Reaction, serum T80.69
- sleeping (African) B56.9
  - by Trypanosoma B56.9
    - brucei
      - gambiense B56.0
      - rhodesiense B56.1
  - East African B56.1
  - Gambian B56.0
  - Rhodesian B56.1
  - West African B56.0
- swing (motion) T75.3
- train (railway) (travel) T75.3
- travel (any vehicle) T75.3

Sideropenia —*see* Anemia, iron deficiency

Siderosilicosis J62.8

Siderosis (lung) J63.4
- eye (globe) —*see* Disorder, globe, degenerative, siderosis

Siemens' syndrome (ectodermal dysplasia) Q82.8

Sighing R06.89
- psychogenic F45.8

Sigmoid —*see also* condition
- flexure —*see* condition
- kidney Q63.1

Sigmoiditis —*see also* Enteritis K52.9
- infectious A09
- noninfectious K52.9

Silfverskiöld's syndrome Q78.9

Silicosiderosis J62.8

Silicosis, silicotic (simple) (complicated) J62.8
- with tuberculosis J65

Silicotuberculosis J65

Silo-fillers' disease J68.8
- bronchitis J68.0
- pneumonitis J68.0
- pulmonary edema J68.1

Silver's syndrome Q87.1

Simian malaria B53.1

Simmonds' cachexia or disease E23.0

Simons' disease or syndrome (progressive lipodystrophy) E88.1

Simple, simplex —*see* condition

Simulation, conscious (of illness) Z76.5

Simultanagnosia (asimultagnosia) R48.3

Sin Nombre virus disease (Hantavirus) (cardio)-**pulmonary syndrome)** B33.4

Sinding-Larsen disease or osteochondrosis —*see* Osteochondrosis, juvenile, patella

Singapore hemorrhagic fever A91

Singer's node or nodule J38.2

Single
- atrium Q21.2
- coronary artery Q24.5
- umbilical artery Q27.0
- ventricle Q20.4

Singultus R06.6
- epidemicus B33.0

Sinus —*see also* Fistula
- abdominal K63.89
- arrest I45.5
- arrhythmia I49.8
- bradycardia R00.1
- branchial cleft (internal) (external) Q18.0
- coccygeal —*see* Sinus, pilonidal
- dental K04.6
- dermal (congenital) Q06.8
  - with abscess Q06.8
  - coccygeal, pilonidal —*see* Sinus, coccygeal
- infected, skin NEC L08.89
- marginal, ruptured or bleeding —*see* Hemorrhage, antepartum, specified cause NEC
- medial, face and neck Q18.8
- pause I45.5
- pericranii Q01.9
- pilonidal (infected) (rectum) L05.92
  - with abscess L05.02
- preauricular Q18.1
- rectovaginal N82.3

Sinus *(continued)*
- Rokitansky-Aschoff (gallbladder) K82.8
- sacrococcygeal (dermoid) (infected) —*see* Sinus, pilonidal
- tachycardia R00.0
  - paroxysmal I47.1
- tarsi syndrome - M25.57-
- testis N50.8
- tract (postinfective) —*see* Fistula
- urachus Q64.4

Sinusitis (accessory) (chronic) (hyperplastic) (nasal) (nonpurulent) (purulent) J32.9
- acute J01.90
  - ethmoidal J01.20
    - recurrent J01.21
  - frontal J01.10
    - recurrent J01.11
  - involving more than one sinus, other than pansinusitis J01.80
    - recurrent J01.81
  - maxillary J01.00
    - recurrent J01.01
  - pansinusitis J01.40
    - recurrent J01.41
  - recurrent J01.91
  - specified NEC J01.80
    - recurrent J01.81
  - sphenoidal J01.30
    - recurrent J01.31
- allergic —*see* Rhinitis, allergic
- due to high altitude T70.1
- ethmoidal J32.2
  - acute J01.20
    - recurrent J01.21
- frontal J32.1
  - acute J01.10
    - recurrent J01.11
- influenzal —*see* Influenza, with, respiratory manifestations NEC
- involving more than one sinus but not pansinusitis J32.8
  - acute J01.80
    - recurrent J01.81
- maxillary J32.0
  - acute J01.00
    - recurrent J01.01
- sphenoidal J32.3
  - acute J01.30
    - recurrent J01.31
- tuberculous, any sinus A15.8

Sinusitis-bronchiectasis-situs inversus (syndrome) (triad) Q89.3

Sipple's syndrome E31.22

Sirenomelia (syndrome) Q87.2

Siriasis T67.0

Sirkari's disease B55.0

Siti A65

Situation, psychiatric F99

Situational
- disturbance (transient) —*see* Disorder, adjustment
  - acute F43.0
- maladjustment —*see* Disorder, adjustment
- reaction —*see* Disorder, adjustment
  - acute F43.0

Situs inversus or transversus (abdominalis) (thoracis) Q89.3

Sixth disease B08.20
- due to human herpesvirus 6 B08.21
- due to human herpesvirus 7 B08.22

Sjögren-Larsson syndrome Q87.1

Sjögren's syndrome or disease —*see* Sicca syndrome

Skeletal —*see* condition

Skene's gland —*see* condition

Skenitis —*see* Urethritis

Skerljevo A65

Skevas-Zerfus disease —*see* Toxicity, venom, marine animal, sea anemone

Skin —*see also* condition
- clammy R23.1
- donor —*see* Donor, skin
- hidebound M35.9

Slate-dressers' or slate-miners' lung J62.8

Sleep
- apnea —*see* Apnea, sleep
- deprivation Z72.820
- disorder or disturbance G47.9
  - child F51.9
  - nonorganic origin F51.9
  - specified NEC G47.8
- disturbance G47.9
  - nonorganic origin F51.9
- drunkenness F51.9
- rhythm inversion G47.2-
- terrors F51.4
- walking F51.3
  - hysterical F44.89

Sleep hygiene
- abuse Z72.821
- inadequate Z72.821
- poor Z72.821

Sleeping sickness —*see* Sickness, sleeping

Sleeplessness —*see* Insomnia
- menopausal N95.1

Sleep-wake schedule disorder G47.20

Slim disease (in HIV infection) B20

Slipped, slipping
- epiphysis (traumatic) —*see also* Osteochondropathy, specified type NEC
  - capital femoral (traumatic)
    - acute (on chronic) S79.01-
  - current traumatic - code as Fracture, by site
  - upper femoral (nontraumatic) M93.00-
    - acute M93.01-
      - on chronic M93.03-
    - chronic M93.02-
- intervertebral disc —*see* Displacement, intervertebral disc
- ligature, umbilical P51.8
- patella —*see* Disorder, patella, derangement NEC
- rib M89.8X8
- sacroiliac joint —*see* subcategory M53.2
- tendon —*see* Disorder, tendon
- ulnar nerve, nontraumatic —*see* Lesion, nerve, ulnar
- vertebra NEC —*see* Spondylolisthesis

Slocumb's syndrome E27.0

Sloughing (multiple) (phagedena) (skin) —*see also* Gangrene
- abscess —*see* Abscess
- appendix K38.8
- fascia —*see* Disorder, soft tissue, specified type NEC
- scrotum N50.8
- tendon —*see* Disorder, tendon
- transplanted organ —*see* Rejection, transplant
- ulcer —*see* Ulcer, skin

Slow
- feeding, newborn P92.2
- flow syndrome, coronary I20.8
- heart (beat) R00.1

Slowing, urinary stream R39.19

Sluder's neuralgia (syndrome) G44.89
Slurred, slurring speech R47.81
Small (ness)
for gestational age —*see* Small for dates
introitus, vagina N89.6
kidney (unknown cause) N27.9
bilateral N27.1
unilateral N27.0
ovary (congenital) Q50.39
pelvis
with disproportion (fetopelvic) O33.1
causing obstructed labor O65.1
uterus N85.8
white kidney N03.9
Small-and-light-for-dates —*see* Small for dates
Small-for-dates (infant) P05.10
with weight of
499 grams or less P05.11
500-749 grams P05.12
750-999 grams P05.13
1000-1249 grams P05.14
1250-1499 grams P05.15
1500-1749 grams P05.16
1750-1999 grams P05.17
2000-2499 grams P05.18
Smallpox B03
Smearing, fecal R15.1
Smith-Lemli-Opitz syndrome E78.72
Smith's fracture S52.54-
Smoker —*see* Dependence, drug, nicotine
Smoker's
bronchitis J41.0
cough J41.0
palate K13.24
throat J31.2
tongue K13.24
Smoking
passive Z77.22
Smothering spells R06.81
Snaggle teeth, tooth M26.39
Snapping
finger —*see* Trigger finger
hip —*see* Derangement, joint, specified type NEC, hip
involving the iliotiblial band M76.3-
knee —*see* Derangement, knee
involving the iliotiblial band M76.3-
Sneddon-Wilkinson disease or syndrome (sub-corneal pustular dermatosis) L13.1
Sneezing (intractable) R06.7
Sniffing
cocaine
abuse —*see* Abuse, drug, cocaine
dependence —*see* Dependence, drug, cocaine
gasoline
abuse —*see* Abuse, drug, inhalant
dependence —*see* Dependence, drug, inhalant
glue (airplane)
abuse —*see* Abuse, drug, inhalant
drug dependence —*see* Dependence, drug, inhalant
Sniffles
newborn P28.89
Snoring R06.83
Snow blindness —*see* Photokeratitis
Snuffles (non-syphilitic) R06.5
newborn P28.89
syphilitic (infant) A50.05 *[J99]*
Social
exclusion Z60.4
due to discrimination or persecution (perceived) Z60.5
migrant Z59.0
acculturation difficulty Z60.3
rejection Z60.4
due to discrimination or persecution Z60.5
role conflict NEC Z73.5
skills inadequacy NEC Z73.4
transplantation Z60.3
Sodoku A25.0
Soemmerring's ring —*see* Cataract, secondary
Soft —*see also* condition
nails L60.3
Softening
bone —*see* Osteomalacia
brain (necrotic) (progressive) G93.89
congenital Q04.8
embolic I63.4
hemorrhagic —*see* Hemorrhage, intracranial, intracerebral
occlusive I63.5
thrombotic I63.3
cartilage M94.2-
patella M22.4-
cerebellar —*see* Softening, brain
cerebral —*see* Softening, brain
cerebrospinal —*see* Softening, brain
myocardial, heart —*see* Degeneration, myocardial
spinal cord G95.89
stomach K31.89
Soldier's
heart F45.8
patches I31.0
Solitary
cyst, kidney N28.1
kidney, congenital Q60.0
Solvent abuse —*see* Abuse, drug, inhalant
dependence —*see* Dependence, drug, inhalant
Somatization reaction, somatic reaction —*see* Disorder, somatoform
Somnambulism F51.3
hysterical F44.89
Somnolence R40.0
nonorganic origin F51.11
Sonne dysentery A03.3
Soor B37.0
Sore
bed —*see* Ulcer, pressure, by site
chiclero B55.1
Delhi B55.1
desert —*see* Ulcer, skin
eye H57.1-
Lahore B55.1
mouth K13.79
canker K12.0
muscle M79.1
Naga —*see* Ulcer, skin
of skin —*see* Ulcer, skin
oriental B55.1
pressure —*see* Ulcer, pressure, by site
skin L98.9
soft A57
throat (acute) —*see also* Pharyngitis
with influenza, flu, or grippe —*see* Influenza, with, respiratory manifestations NEC
chronic J31.2
Sore *(continued)*
throat *(continued)*
coxsackie (virus) B08.5
diphtheritic A36.0
herpesviral B00.2
influenzal —*see* Influenza, with, respiratory manifestations NEC
septic J02.0
streptococcal (ulcerative) J02.0
viral NEC J02.8
coxsackie B08.5
tropical —*see* Ulcer, skin
veldt —*see* Ulcer, skin
Soto's syndrome (cerebral gigantism) Q87.3
South African cardiomyopathy syndrome I42.8
Southeast Asian hemorrhagic fever A91
Spacing
abnormal, tooth, teeth, fully erupted M26.30
excessive, tooth, fully erupted M26.32
Spade-like hand (congenital) Q68.1
Spading nail L60.8
congenital Q84.6
Spanish collar N47.1
Sparganosis B70.1
Spasm (s), **spastic, spasticity** —*see also* condition R25.2
accommodation —*see* Spasm, of accommodation
ampulla of Vater K83.4
anus, ani (sphincter) (reflex) K59.4
psychogenic F45.8
artery I73.9
cerebral G45.9
Bell's G51.3
bladder (sphincter, external or internal) N32.89
psychogenic F45.8
bronchus, bronchiole J98.01
cardia K22.0
cardiac I20.1
carpopedal —*see* Tetany
cerebral (arteries) (vascular) G45.9
cervix, complicating delivery O62.4
ciliary body (of accommodation) —*see* Spasm, of accommodation
colon K58.9
with diarrhea K58.0
psychogenic F45.8
common duct K83.8
compulsive —*see* Tic
conjugate H51.8
coronary (artery) I20.1
diaphragm (reflex) R06.6
epidemic B33.0
psychogenic F45.8
duodenum K59.8
epidemic diaphragmatic (transient) B33.0
esophagus (diffuse) K22.4
psychogenic F45.8
facial G51.3
fallopian tube N83.8
gastrointestinal (tract) K31.89
psychogenic F45.8
glottis J38.5
hysterical F44.4
psychogenic F45.8
conversion reaction F44.4
reflex through recurrent laryngeal nerve J38.5
habit —*see* Tic
heart I20.1
hemifacial (clonic) G51.3
hourglass —*see* Contraction, hourglass
Spasm (s), **spastic, spasticity** *(continued)*
hysterical F44.4
infantile —*see* Epilepsy, spasms
inferior oblique, eye H51.8
intestinal —*see also* Syndrome, irritable bowel K58.9
psychogenic F45.8
larynx, laryngeal J38.5
hysterical F44.4
psychogenic F45.8
conversion reaction F44.4
levator palpebrae superioris —*see* Disorder, eyelid function
muscle NEC M62.838
back M62.830
nerve, trigeminal G51.0
nervous F45.8
nodding F98.4
occupational F48.8
oculogyric H51.8
psychogenic F45.8
of accommodation H52.53-
ophthalmic artery —*see* Occlusion, artery, retina
perineal, female N94.89
peroneo-extensor —*see also* Deformity, limb, flat foot
pharynx (reflex) J39.2
hysterical F45.8
psychogenic F45.8
psychogenic F45.8
pylorus NEC K31.3
adult hypertrophic K31.89
congenital or infantile Q40.0
psychogenic F45.8
rectum (sphincter) K59.4
psychogenic F45.8
retinal (artery) —*see* Occlusion, artery, retina
sigmoid —*see also* Syndrome, irritable bowel K58.9
psychogenic F45.8
sphincter of Oddi K83.4
stomach K31.89
neurotic F45.8
throat J39.2
hysterical F45.8
psychogenic F45.8
tic F95.9
chronic F95.1
transient of childhood F95.0
tongue K14.8
torsion (progressive) G24.1
trigeminal nerve —*see* Neuralgia, trigeminal
ureter N13.5
urethra (sphincter) N35.9
uterus N85.8
complicating labor O62.4
vagina N94.2
psychogenic F52.5
vascular I73.9
vasomotor I73.9
vein NEC I87.8
viscera —*see* Pain, abdominal
Spasmodic —*see* condition
Spasmophilia —*see* Tetany
Spasmus nutans F98.4
Spastic, spasticity —*see also* Spasm
child (cerebral) (congenital) (paralysis) G80.1
Speaker's throat R49.8
Specific, specified —*see* condition
Speech
defect, disorder, disturbance, impediment R47.9
psychogenic, in childhood and adolescence F98.8
slurring R47.81
specified NEC R47.89

encer's disease A08.19

ens' syndrome (syncope with heart block) I45.9

erm counts (fertility testing) Z31.41
- postvasectomy Z30.8
  - reversal Z31.42

ermatic cord —*see* condition

ermatocele N43.40
- congenital Q55.4
- multiple N43.42
- single N43.41

ermatocystitis N49.0

ermatocytoma C62.9-
- specified site —*see* Neoplasm, malignant, by site

ermatorrhea N50.8

hacelus —*see* Gangrene

henoidal —*see* condition

henoiditis (chronic) —*see* Sinusitis, sphenoidal

henopalatine ganglion neuralgia G90.09

hericity, increased, lens (congenital) Q12.4

pherocytosis (congenital) (familial) (hereditary) D58.0
- hemoglobin disease D58.0
- sickle-cell (disease) D57.8-

pherophakia Q12.4

phincter —*see* condition

phincteritis, sphincter of Oddi —*see* Cholangitis

phingolipidosis E75.3
- specified NEC E75.29

phingomyelinosis E75.3

picule tooth K00.2

pider
- bite —*see* Toxicity, venom, spider
- fingers —*see* Syndrome, Marfan's
- nevus I78.1
- toes —*see* Syndrome, Marfan's
- vascular I78.1

piegler-Fendt
- benign lymphocytoma L98.8
- sarcoid L08.89

pielmeyer-Vogt disease E75.4

pina bifida (aperta) Q05.9
- with hydrocephalus NEC Q05.4
- cervical Q05.5
  - with hydrocephalus Q05.0
- dorsal Q05.6
  - with hydrocephalus Q05.1
- lumbar Q05.7
  - with hydrocephalus Q05.2
- lumbosacral Q05.7
  - with hydrocephalus Q05.2
- occulta Q76.0
- sacral Q05.8
  - with hydrocephalus Q05.3
- thoracic Q05.6
  - with hydrocephalus Q05.1
- thoracolumbar Q05.6
  - with hydrocephalus Q05.1

Spindle, Krukenberg's —*see* Pigmentation, cornea, posterior

Spine, spinal —*see* condition

Spiradenoma (eccrine) —*see* Neoplasm, skin, benign

Spirillosis A25.0

Spirillum
- minus A25.0
- obermeieri infection A68.0

Spirochetal —*see* condition

Spirochetosis A69.9
- arthritic, arthritica A69.9
- bronchopulmonary A69.8
- icterohemorrhagic A27.0
- lung A69.8

Spirometrosis B70.1

Spitting blood —*see* Hemoptysis

Splanchnoptosis K63.4

Spleen, splenic —*see* condition

Splenectasis —*see* Splenomegaly

Splenitis (interstitial) (malignant) (nonspecific) D73.89
- malarial —*see also* Malaria B54 *[D77]*
- tuberculous A18.85

Splenocele D73.89

Splenomegaly, splenomegalia (Bengal) (cryptogenic) (idiopathic) (tropical) R16.1
- with hepatomegaly R16.2
- cirrhotic D73.2
- congenital Q89.09
- congestive, chronic D73.2
- Egyptian B65.1
- Gaucher's E75.22
- malarial —*see also* Malaria B54 *[D77]*
- neutropenic D73.81
- Niemann-Pick —*see* Niemann-Pick disease or syndrome
- siderotic D73.2
- syphilitic A52.79
  - congenital (early) A50.08 *[D77]*

Splenopathy D73.9

Splenoptosis D73.89

Splenosis D73.89

Splinter —*see* Foreign body, superficial, by site

Split, splitting
- foot Q72.7-
- heart sounds R01.2
- lip, congenital —*see* Cleft, lip
- nails L60.3
- urinary stream R39.13

Spondylarthrosis —*see* Spondylosis

Spondylitis (chronic) —*see also* Spondylopathy, inflammatory
- ankylopoietica —*see* Spondylitis, ankylosing
- ankylosing (chronic) M45.9
  - with lung involvement M45.9 *[J99]*
  - cervical region M45.2
  - cervicothoracic region M45.3
  - juvenile M08.1
  - lumbar region M45.6
  - lumbosacral region M45.7
  - multiple sites M45.0
  - occipito-atlanto-axial region M45.1
  - sacrococcygeal region M45.8
  - thoracic region M45.4
  - thoracolumbar region M45.5
- atrophic (ligamentous) —*see* Spondylitis, ankylosing
- deformans (chronic) —*see* Spondylosis
- gonococcal A54.41
- gouty M10.08
- in (due to)
  - brucellosis A23.9 *[M49.80]*
    - cervical region A23.9 *[M49.82]*
    - cervicothoracic region A23.9 *[M49.83]*
    - lumbar region A23.9 *[M49.86]*

Spondylitis *(continued)*
- in *(continued)*
  - brucellosis *(continued)*
    - lumbosacral region A23.9 *[M49.87]*
    - multiple sites A23.9 *[M49.89]*
    - occipito-atlanto-axial region A23.9 *[M49.81]*
    - sacrococcygeal region A23.9 *[M49.88]*
    - thoracic region A23.9 *[M49.84]*
    - thoracolumbar region A23.9 *[M49.85]*
  - enterobacteria —*see also* subcategory M49.8 *[A04.9]*
  - tuberculosis A18.01
- infectious NEC —*see* Spondylopathy, infective
- juvenile ankylosing (chronic) M08.1
- Kümmell's —*see* Spondylopathy, traumatic
- Marie-Strümpell —*see* Spondylitis, ankylosing
- muscularis —*see* Spondylopathy, specified NEC
- psoriatic L40.53
- rheumatoid —*see* Spondylitis, ankylosing
- rhizomelica —*see* Spondylitis, ankylosing
- sacroiliac NEC M46.1
- senescent, senile —*see* Spondylosis
- traumatic (chronic) or post-traumatic —*see* Spondylopathy, traumatic
- tuberculous A18.01
- typhosa A01.05

Spondylolisthesis (acquired) (degenerative) M43.10
- with disproportion (fetopelvic) O33.0
  - causing obstructed labor O65.0
- cervical region M43.12
- cervicothoracic region M43.13
- congenital Q76.2
- lumbar region M43.16
- lumbosacral region M43.17
- multiple sites M43.19
- occipito-atlanto-axial region M43.11
- sacrococcygeal region M43.18
- thoracic region M43.14
- thoracolumbar region M43.15
- traumatic (old) M43.10
  - acute
    - fifth cervical (displaced) S12.430
      - nondisplaced S12.431
      - specified type NEC (displaced) S12.450
        - nondisplaced S12.451
      - type III S12.44
    - fourth cervical (displaced) S12.330
      - nondisplaced S12.331
      - specified type NEC (displaced) S12.350
        - nondisplaced S12.351
      - type III S12.34
    - second cervical (displaced) S12.130
      - nondisplaced S12.131
      - specified type NEC (displaced) S12.150
        - nondisplaced S12.151
      - type III S12.14
    - seventh cervical (displaced) S12.630
      - nondisplaced S12.631
      - specified type NEC (displaced) S12.650
        - nondisplaced S12.651
      - type III S12.64

Spondylolisthesis *(continued)*
- traumatic *(continued)*
  - acute *(continued)*
    - sixth cervical (displaced) S12.530
      - nondisplaced S12.531
      - specified type NEC (displaced) S12.550
        - nondisplaced S12.551
      - type III S12.54
    - third cervical (displaced) S12.230
      - nondisplaced S12.231
      - specified type NEC (displaced) S12.250
        - nondisplaced S12.251
      - type III S12.24

Spondylolysis (acquired) M43.00
- cervical region M43.02
- cervicothoracic region M43.03
- congenital Q76.2
- lumbar region M43.06
- lumbosacral region M43.07
  - with disproportion (fetopelvic) O33.0
    - causing obstructed labor O65.8
- multiple sites M43.09
- occipito-atlanto-axial region M43.01
- sacrococcygeal region M43.08
- thoracic region M43.04
- thoracolumbar region M43.05

Spondylopathy M48.9
- infective NEC M46.50
  - cervical region M46.52
  - cervicothoracic region M46.53
  - lumbar region M46.56
  - lumbosacral region M46.57
  - multiple sites M46.59
  - occipito-atlanto-axial region M46.51
  - sacrococcygeal region M46.58
  - thoracic region M46.54
  - thoracolumbar region M46.55
- inflammatory M46.90
  - cervical region M46.92
  - cervicothoracic region M46.93
  - lumbar region M46.96
  - lumbosacral region M46.97
  - multiple sites M46.99
  - occipito-atlanto-axial region M46.91
  - sacrococcygeal region M46.98
  - specified type NEC M46.80
    - cervical region M46.82
    - cervicothoracic region M46.83
    - lumbar region M46.86
    - lumbosacral region M46.87
    - multiple sites M46.89
    - occipito-atlanto-axial region M46.81
    - sacrococcygeal region M46.88
    - thoracic region M46.84
    - thoracolumbar region M46.85
  - thoracic region M46.94
  - thoracolumbar region M46.95
- neuropathic, in
  - syringomyelia and syringobulbia G95.0
  - tabes dorsalis A52.11
- specified NEC M48.8
- traumatic M48.30
  - cervical region M48.32
  - cervicothoracic region M48.33
  - lumbar region M48.36
  - lumbosacral region M48.37
  - occipito-atlanto-axial region M48.31
  - sacrococcygeal region M48.38
  - thoracic region M48.34
  - thoracolumbar region M48.35

Spondylosis M47.9
with
disproportion (fetopelvic) O33.0
causing obstructed labor O65.0
myelopathy NEC M47.10
cervical region M47.12
cervicothoracic region M47.13
lumbar region M47.16
occipito-atlanto-axial region M47.11
thoracic region M47.14
thoracolumbar region M47.15
radiculopathy M47.20
cervical region M47.22
cervicothoracic region M47.23
lumbar region M47.26
lumbosacral region M47.27
occipito-atlanto-axial region M47.21
sacrococcygeal region M47.28
thoracic region M47.24
thoracolumbar region M47.25
specified NEC M47.899
cervical region M47.892
cervicothoracic region M47.893
lumbar region M47.896
lumbosacral region M47.897
occipito-atlanto-axial region M47.891
sacrococcygeal region M47.898
thoracic region M47.894
thoracolumbar region M47.895
traumatic —*see* Spondylopathy, traumatic
without myelopathy or radiculopathy M47.819
cervical region M47.812
cervicothoracic region M47.813
lumbar region M47.816
lumbosacral region M47.817
occipito-atlanto-axial region M47.811
sacrococcygeal region M47.818
thoracic region M47.814
thoracolumbar region M47.815

Sponge
inadvertently left in operation wound —*see* Foreign body, accidentally left during a procedure
kidney (medullary) Q61.5

Sponge-diver's disease —*see* Toxicity, venom, marine animal, sea anemone

Spongioblastoma (any type) —*see* Neoplasm, malignant, by site
specified site —*see* Neoplasm, malignant, by site
unspecified site C71.9

Spongioneuroblastoma —*see* Neoplasm, malignant, by site

Spontaneous —*see also* condition
fracture (cause unknown) —*see* Fracture, pathological

Spoon nail L60.3
congenital Q84.6

Sporadic —*see* condition

Sporothrix schenckii infection —*see* Sporotrichosis

Sporotrichosis B42.9
arthritis B42.82
disseminated B42.7
generalized B42.7
lymphocutaneous (fixed) (progressive) B42.1
pulmonary B42.0
specified NEC B42.89

Spots, spotting (in) (of)
Bitot's —*see also* Pigmentation, conjunctiva
in the young child E50.1
vitamin A deficiency E50.1
café, au lait L81.3
Cayenne pepper I78.1
cotton wool, retina —*see* Occlusion, artery, retina
de Morgan's (senile angiomas) I78.1
Fuchs' black (myopic) H44.2-
intermenstrual (regular) N92.0
irregular N92.1
Koplik's B05.9
liver L81.4
pregnancy O26.85-
purpuric R23.3
ruby I78.1

Spotted fever —*see* Fever, spotted N92.3

Sprain (joint) (ligament)
acromioclavicular joint or ligament S43.5-
ankle S93.40-
calcaneofibular ligament S93.41-
deltoid ligament S93.42-
internal collateral ligament —*see* Sprain, ankle, specified ligament NEC
specified ligament NEC S93.49-
talofibular ligament —*see* Sprain, ankle, specified ligament NEC
tibiofibular ligament S93.43-
anterior longitudinal, cervical S13.4
atlas, atlanto-axial, atlanto-occipital S13.4
breast bone —*see* Sprain, sternum
calcaneofibular —*see* Sprain, ankle
carpal —*see* Sprain, wrist
carpometacarpal —*see* Sprain, hand, specified site NEC
cartilage
costal S23.41
semilunar (knee) —*see* Sprain, knee, specified site NEC
with current tear —*see* Tear, meniscus
thyroid region S13.5
xiphoid —*see* Sprain, sternum
cervical, cervicodorsal, cervicothoracic S13.4
chondrosternal S23.421
coracoclavicular S43.8-
coracohumeral S43.41-
coronary, knee —*see* Sprain, knee, specified site NEC
costal cartilage S23.41
cricoarytenoid articulation or ligament S13.5
cricothyroid articulation S13.5
cruciate, knee —*see* Sprain, knee, cruciate
deltoid, ankle —*see* Sprain, ankle
dorsal (spine) S23.3
elbow S53.40-
radial collateral ligament S53.43-
radiohumeral S53.41-
rupture
radial collateral ligament —*see* Rupture, traumatic, ligament, radial collateral
ulnar collateral ligament —*see* Rupture, traumatic, ligament, ulnar collateral
specified type NEC S53.49-
ulnar collateral ligament S53.44-
ulnohumeral S53.42-
femur, head —*see* Sprain, hip
fibular collateral, knee —*see* Sprain, knee, collateral
fibulocalcaneal —*see* Sprain, ankle

Sprain *(continued)*
finger (s) S63.61-
index S63.61-
interphalangeal (joint) S63.63-
index S63.63-
little S63.63-
middle S63.63-
ring S63.63-
little S63.61-
middle S63.61-
ring S63.61-
metacarpophalangeal (joint) S63.65-
specified site NEC S63.69-
index S63.69-
little S63.69-
middle S63.69-
ring S63.69-
foot S93.60-
specified ligament NEC S93.69-
tarsal ligament S93.61-
tarsometatarsal ligament S93.62-
toe —*see* Sprain, toe
hand S63.9-
finger —*see* Sprain, finger
specified site NEC S63.8
thumb —*see* Sprain, thumb
head S03.9
hip S73.10-
iliofemoral ligament S73.11-
ischiocapsular (ligament) S73.12-
specified NEC S73.19-
iliofemoral —*see* Sprain, hip
innominate
acetabulum —*see* Sprain, hip
sacral junction S33.6
internal
collateral, ankle —*see* Sprain, ankle
semilunar cartilage —*see* Sprain, knee, specified site NEC
interphalangeal
finger —*see* Sprain, finger, interphalangeal (joint)
toe —*see* Sprain, toe, interphalangeal joint
ischiocapsular —*see* Sprain, hip
ischiofemoral —*see* Sprain, hip
jaw (articular disc) (cartilage) (meniscus) S03.4
old M26.69
knee S83.9-
collateral ligament S83.40-
lateral (fibular) S83.42-
medial (tibial) S83.41-
cruciate ligament S83.50-
anterior S83.51-
posterior S83.52-
lateral (fibular) collateral ligament S83.42-
medial (tibial) collateral ligament S83.41-
patellar ligament S76.11-
specified site NEC S83.8X-
superior tibiofibular joint (ligament) S83.6-
lateral collateral, knee —*see* Sprain, knee, collateral
lumbar (spine) S33.5
lumbosacral S33.9
mandible (articular disc) S03.4
old M26.69
medial collateral, knee —*see* Sprain, knee, collateral
meniscus
jaw S03.4
old M26.69
knee —*see* Sprain, knee, specified site NEC
with current tear —*see* Tear, meniscus
old —*see* Derangement, knee, meniscus, due to old tear

Sprain *(continued)*
meniscus *(continued)*
mandible S03.4
old M26.69
metacarpal (distal) (proximal) —*se*
Sprain, hand, specified site NEC
metacarpophalangeal —*see* Sprain, finger, metacarpophalangeal (join
metatarsophalangeal —*see* Sprain, toe, metatarsophalangeal joint
midcarpal —*see* Sprain, hand, specified site NEC
midtarsal —*see* Sprain, foot, specifi site NEC
neck S13.9
anterior longitudinal cervical ligament S13.4
atlanto-axial joint S13.4
atlanto-occipital joint S13.4
cervical spine S13.4
cricoarytenoid ligament S13.5
cricothyroid ligament S13.5
specified site NEC S13.8
thyroid region (cartilage) S13.5
nose S03.8
orbicular, hip —*see* Sprain, hip
patella —*see* Sprain, knee, specified site NEC
patellar ligament S76.11-
pelvis NEC S33.8
phalanx
finger —*see* Sprain, finger
toe —*see* Sprain, toe
pubofemoral —*see* Sprain, hip
radiocarpal —*see* Sprain, wrist
radiohumeral —*see* Sprain, elbow
radius, collateral —*see* Rupture, traumatic, ligament, radial collateral
rib (cage) S23.41
rotator cuff (capsule) S43.42-
sacroiliac (region)
chronic or old —*see* subcategory M53.2
joint S33.6
scaphoid (hand) —*see* Sprain, hand, specified site NEC
scapula (r) —*see* Sprain, shoulder girdle, specified site NEC
semilunar cartilage (knee) —*see* Sprain, knee, specified site NEC
with current tear —*see* Tear, meniscus
old —*see* Derangement, knee, meniscus, due to old tear
shoulder joint S43.40-
acromioclavicular joint (ligament) —*see* Sprain, acromioclavicular joint
blade —*see* Sprain, shoulder, girdle, specified site NEC
coracoclavicular joint (ligament) —*see* Sprain, coracoclavicular joint
coracohumeral ligament —*see* Sprain, coracohumeral joint
girdle S43.9-
specified site NEC S43.8-
rotator cuff —*see* Sprain, rotator cuf
specified site NEC S43.49-
sternoclavicular joint (ligament) —*see* Sprain, sternoclavicular joint
spine
cervical S13.4
lumbar S33.5
thoracic S23.3
sternoclavicular joint S43.6-
sternum S23.429
chondrosternal joint S23.421
specified site NEC S23.428
sternoclavicular (joint) (ligament) S23.420

- **Sprain** *(continued)*
  - symphysis
    - jaw S03.4
      - old M26.69
    - mandibular S03.4
      - old M26.69
  - talofibular —*see* Sprain, ankle
  - tarsal —*see* Sprain, foot, specified site NEC
  - tarsometatarsal —*see* Sprain, foot, specified site NEC
  - temporomandibular S03.4
    - old M26.69
  - thorax S23.9
    - ribs S23.41
    - specified site NEC S23.8
    - spine S23.3
    - sternum —*see* Sprain, sternum
  - thumb S63.60-
    - interphalangeal (joint) S63.62-
    - metacarpophalangeal (joint) S63.64-
    - specified site NEC S63.68-
  - thyroid cartilage or region S13.5
  - tibia (proximal end) —*see* Sprain, knee, specified site NEC
  - tibial collateral, knee —*see* Sprain, knee, collateral
  - tibiofibular
    - distal —*see* Sprain, ankle
    - superior —*see* Sprain, knee, specified site NEC
  - toe (s) S93.50-
    - great S93.50-
    - interphalangeal joint S93.51-
      - great S93.51-
      - lesser S93.51-
    - lesser S93.50-
    - metatarsophalangeal joint S93.52-
      - great S93.52-
      - lesser S93.52-
  - ulna, collateral —*see* Rupture, traumatic, ligament, ulnar collateral
  - ulnohumeral —*see* Sprain, elbow
  - wrist S63.50-
    - carpal S63.51-
    - radiocarpal S63.52-
    - specified site NEC S63.59-
  - xiphoid cartilage —*see* Sprain, sternum
- **Sprengel's deformity** (congenital) Q74.0
- **Sprue** (tropical) K90.1
  - celiac K90.0
  - idiopathic K90.0
  - meaning thrush B37.0
  - nontropical K90.0
- **Spur, bone** —*see also* Enthesopathy
  - calcaneal M77.3-
  - iliac crest M76.2-
  - nose (septum) J34.89
- **Spurway's syndrome** Q78.0
- **Sputum**
  - abnormal (amount) (color) (odor) (purulent) R09.3
  - blood-stained R04.2
  - excessive (cause unknown) R09.3
- **Squamous** —*see also* condition
  - epithelium in
    - cervical canal (congenital) Q51.828
    - uterine mucosa (congenital) Q51.818
- **Squashed nose** M95.0
  - congenital Q67.4
- **Squeeze, diver's** T70.3
- **Squint** —*see also* Strabismus
  - accommodative —*see* Strabismus, convergent concomitant
- **St. Hubert's disease** A82.9
- **Stab** —*see also* Laceration
  - internal organs —*see* Injury, by site
- **Stafne's cyst or cavity** M27.0
- **Staggering gait** R26.0
  - hysterical F44.4
- **Staghorn calculus** —*see* Calculus, kidney
- **Stähli's line** (cornea) (pigment) —*see* Pigmentation, cornea, anterior
- **Stain, staining**
  - meconium (newborn) P96.83
  - port wine Q82.5
  - tooth, teeth (hard tissues) (extrinsic) K03.6
    - due to
      - accretions K03.6
      - deposits (betel) (black) (green) (materia alba) (orange) (soft) (tobacco) K03.6
      - metals (copper) (silver) K03.7
      - nicotine K03.6
      - pulpal bleeding K03.7
      - tobacco K03.6
    - intrinsic K00.8
- **Stammering** —*see also* Disorder, fluency F80.81
- **Standstill**
  - auricular I45.5
  - cardiac —*see* Arrest, cardiac
  - sinoatrial I45.5
  - ventricular —*see* Arrest, cardiac
- **Stannosis** J63.5
- **Stanton's disease** —*see* Melioidosis
- **Staphylitis** (acute) (catarrhal) (chronic) (gangrenous) (membranous) (suppurative) (ulcerative) K12.2
- **Staphylococcal scalded skin syndrome** L00
- **Staphylococcemia** A41.2
- **Staphylococcus, staphylococcal** —*see also* condition
  - as cause of disease classified elsewhere B95.8
    - aureus (methicillin susceptible) (MSSA) B95.61
      - methicillin resistant (MRSA) B95.62
  - specified NEC, as cause of disease classified elsewhere B95.7
- **Staphyloma** (sclera)
  - cornea H18.72-
  - equatorial H15.81-
  - localized (anterior) H15.82-
  - posticum H15.83-
  - ring H15.85-
- **Stargardt's disease** —*see* Dystrophy, retina
- **Starvation** (inanition) (due to lack of food) T73.0
  - edema —*see* Malnutrition, severe
- **Stasis**
  - bile (noncalculous) K83.1
  - bronchus J98.09
    - with infection —*see* Bronchitis
  - cardiac —*see* Failure, heart, congestive
  - cecum K59.8
  - colon K59.8
  - dermatitis —*see* Varix, leg, with, inflammation
  - duodenal K31.5
  - eczema —*see* Varix, leg, with, inflammation
- **Stasis** *(continued)*
  - edema —*see* Hypertension, venous (chronic), idiopathic
  - foot T69.0-
  - ileocecal coil K59.8
  - ileum K59.8
  - intestinal K59.8
  - jejunum K59.8
  - kidney N19
  - liver (cirrhotic) K76.1
  - lymphatic I89.8
  - pneumonia J18.2
  - pulmonary —*see* Edema, lung
  - rectal K59.8
  - renal N19
    - tubular N17.0
  - ulcer —*see* Varix, leg, with, ulcer
    - without varicose veins I87.2
  - urine —*see* Retention, urine
  - venous I87.8
- **State** (of)
  - affective and paranoid, mixed, organic psychotic F06.8
  - agitated R45.1
    - acute reaction to stress F43.0
  - anxiety (neurotic) F41.1
  - apprehension F41.1
  - burn-out Z73.0
  - climacteric, female Z78.0
    - symptomatic N95.1
  - compulsive F42
    - mixed with obsessional thoughts F42
  - confusional (psychogenic) F44.89
    - acute —*see also* Delirium
      - with
        - arteriosclerotic dementia F01.50
          - with behavioral disturbance F01.51
        - senility or dementia F05
      - alcoholic F10.231
    - epileptic F05
    - reactive (from emotional stress, psychological trauma) F44.89
    - subacute —*see* Delirium
  - convulsive —*see* Convulsions
  - crisis F43.0
  - depressive F32.9
    - neurotic F34.1
  - dissociative F44.9
  - emotional shock (stress) R45.7
  - hypercoagulation —*see* Hypercoagulable
  - locked-in G83.5
  - menopausal Z78.0
    - symptomatic N95.1
  - neurotic F48.9
    - with depersonalization F48.1
  - obsessional F42
  - oneiroid (schizophrenia-like) F23
  - organic
    - hallucinatory (nonalcoholic) F06.0
    - paranoid (-hallucinatory) F06.2
  - panic F41.0
  - paranoid F22
    - climacteric F22
    - involutional F22
    - menopausal F22
    - organic F06.2
    - senile F03
    - simple F22
  - persistent vegetative R40.3
  - phobic F40.9
  - postleukotomy F07.0
  - pregnant, incidental Z33.1
  - psychogenic, twilight F44.89
  - psychopathic (constitutional) F60.2
  - psychotic, organic —*see also* Psychosis, organic
    - mixed paranoid and affective F06.8
- **State** *(continued)*
  - psychotic, organic —*see also* Psychosis, organic *(continued)*
    - senile or presenile F03
    - transient NEC F06.8
      - with
        - hallucinations F06.0
        - depression F06.31
  - residual schizophrenic F20.5
  - restlessness R45.1
  - stress (emotional) R45.7
  - tension (mental) F48.9
    - specified NEC F48.8
  - transient organic psychotic NEC F06.8
    - depressive type F06.31
    - hallucinatory type F06.30
  - twilight
    - epileptic F05
    - psychogenic F44.89
  - vegetative, persistent R40.3
  - vital exhaustion Z73.0
  - withdrawal, —*see* Withdrawal, state
- **Status** (post) —*see also* Presence (of)
  - absence, epileptic —*see* Epilepsy, by type, with status epilepticus
  - administration of tPA (rtPA) in a different facility within the last 24 hours prior to admission to current facility Z92.82
  - adrenalectomy (unilateral) (bilateral) E89.6
  - anastomosis Z98.0
  - angioplasty (peripheral) Z98.62
    - with implant Z95.820
    - coronary artery Z98.61
      - with implant Z95.5
  - anginosus I20.9
  - aortocoronary bypass Z95.1
  - arthrodesis Z98.1
  - artificial opening (of) Z93.9
    - gastrointestinal tract Z93.4
    - specified NEC Z93.8
    - urinary tract Z93.6
    - vagina Z93.8
  - asthmaticus —*see* Asthma, by type, with status asthmaticus
  - awaiting organ transplant Z76.82
  - bariatric surgery Z98.84
  - bed confinement Z74.01
  - bleb, filtering (vitreous), after glaucoma surgery Z98.83
  - breast implant Z98.82
    - removal Z98.86
  - cataract extraction Z98.4-
  - cholecystectomy Z90.49
  - clitorectomy N90.811
    - with excision of labia minora N90.812
  - colectomy (complete) (partial) Z90.49
  - colonization —*see* Carrier (suspected) of
  - colostomy Z93.3
  - convulsivus idiopathicus —*see* Epilepsy, by type, with status epilepticus
  - coronary artery angioplasty —*see* Status, angioplasty, coronary artery
  - cystectomy (urinary bladder) Z90.6
  - cystostomy Z93.50
    - appendico-vesicostomy Z93.52
    - cutaneous Z93.51
    - specified NEC Z93.59
  - delinquent immunization Z28.3
  - dental Z98.818
    - crown Z98.811
    - fillings Z98.811
    - restoration Z98.811
    - sealant Z98.810
    - specified NEC Z98.818

Status *(continued)*
- deployment (current) (military) Z56.82
- dialysis (hemodialysis) (peritoneal) Z99.2
- do not resuscitate (DNR) Z66
- donor —*see* Donor
- embedded fragments —*see* Retained, foreign body fragments (type of)
- embedded splinter —*see* Retained, foreign body fragments (type of)
- enterostomy Z93.4
- epileptic, epilepticus —*see also* Epilepsy, by type, with status epilepticus G40.901
- estrogen receptor
  - negative Z17.1
  - positive Z17.0
- female genital cutting —*see* Female genital mutilation status
- female genital mutilation —*see* Female genital mutilation status
- filtering (vitreous) bleb after glaucoma surgery Z98.83
- gastrectomy (complete) (partial) Z90.3
- gastric banding Z98.84
- gastric bypass for obesity Z98.84
- gastrostomy Z93.1
- human immunodeficiency virus (HIV) infection, asymptomatic Z21
- hysterectomy (complete) (total) Z90.710
  - partial (with remaining cervial stump) Z90.711
- ileostomy Z93.2
- implant
  - breast Z98.82
- infibulation N90.813
- intestinal bypass Z98.0
- jejunostomy Z93.4
- laryngectomy Z90.02
- lapsed immunization schedule Z28.3
- lymphaticus E32.8
- marmoratus G80.3
- mastectomy (unilateral) (bilateral) Z90.1-
- military deployment status (current) Z56.82
  - in theater or in support of military war, peacekeeping and humanitarian operations Z56.82
- nephrectomy (unilateral) (bilateral) Z90.5
- nephrostomy Z93.6
- obesity surgery Z98.84
- oophorectomy
  - bilateral Z90.722
  - unilateral Z90.721
- organ replacement
  - by artificial or mechanical device or prosthesis of
    - artery Z95.828
    - bladder Z96.0
    - blood vessel Z95.828
    - breast Z97.8
    - eye globe Z97.0
    - heart Z95.812
      - valve Z95.2
    - intestine Z97.8
    - joint Z96.60
      - hip —*see* Presence, hip joint implant
      - knee —*see* Presence, knee joint implant
      - specified site NEC Z96.698
    - kidney Z97.8
    - larynx Z96.3
    - lens Z96.1
    - limbs —*see* Presence, artificial, limb
    - liver Z97.8

Status *(continued)*
- organ replacement *(continued)*
  - by artificial or mechanical device or prosthesis of *(continued)*
    - lung Z97.8
    - pancreas Z97.8
  - by organ transplant (heterologous) (homologous) —*see* Transplant
- pacemaker
  - brain Z96.89
  - cardiac Z95.0
  - specified NEC Z96.89
- pancreatectomy Z90.410
  - complete Z90.410
  - partial Z90.411
  - total Z90.410
- physical restraint Z78.1
- pneumonectomy (complete) (partial) Z90.2
- pneumothorax, therapeutic Z98.3
- postcommotio cerebri F07.81
- postoperative (postprocedural) NEC Z98.89
  - breast implant Z98.82
  - dental Z98.818
    - crown Z98.811
    - fillings Z98.811
    - restoration Z98.811
    - sealant Z98.810
    - specified NEC Z98.818
  - pneumothorax, therapeutic Z98.3
- postpartum (routine follow-up) Z39.2
  - care immediately after delivery Z39.0
- postsurgical (postprocedural) NEC Z98.89
  - pneumothorax, therapeutic Z98.3
- pregnancy, incidental Z33.1
- prosthesis coronary angioplasty Z95.5
- pseudophakia Z96.1
- renal dialysis (hemodialysis) (peritoneal) Z99.2
- retained foreign body —*see* Retained, foreign body fragments (type of)
- reversed jejunal transposition (for bypass) Z98.0
- salpingo-oophorectomy
  - bilateral Z90.722
  - unilateral Z90.721
- sex reassignment surgery status Z87.890
- shunt
  - arteriovenous (for dialysis) Z99.2
  - cerebrospinal fluid Z98.2
  - ventricular (communicating) (for drainage) Z98.2
- splenectomy Z90.81
- thymicolymphaticus E32.8
- thymicus E32.8
- thymolymphaticus E32.8
- thyroidectomy (hypothyroidism) E89.0
- tooth (teeth) extraction —*see also* Absence, teeth, acquired K08.409
- tPA (rtPA) administration in a different facility within the last 24 hours prior to admission to current facility Z92.82
- tracheostomy Z93.0
- transplant —*see* Transplant
  - organ removed Z98.85
- tubal ligation Z98.51
- underimmunization Z28.3
- ureterostomy Z93.6
- urethrostomy Z93.6
- vagina, artificial Z93.8
- vasectomy Z98.52
- wheelchair confinement Z99.3

Stealing
- child problem F91.8
  - in company with others Z72.810
- pathological (compulsive) F63.2

Steam burn —*see* Burn

Steatocystoma multiplex L72.2

Steatohepatitis (nonalcoholic) (NASH) K75.81

Steatoma L72.3
- eyelid (cystic) —*see* Dermatosis, eyelid
  - infected —*see* Hordeolum

Steatorrhea (chronic) K90.4
- with lacteal obstruction K90.2
- idiopathic (adult) (infantile) K90.0
- pancreatic K90.3
- primary K90.0
- tropical K90.1

Steatosis E88.89
- heart —*see* Degeneration, myocardial
- kidney N28.89
- liver NEC K76.0

Steele-Richardson-Olszewski disease or syndrome G23.1

Steinbrocker's syndrome G90.8

Steinert's disease G71.11

Stein-Leventhal syndrome E28.2

Stein's syndrome E28.2

STEMI —*see also* - Infarct, myocardium, ST elevation I21.3

Stenocardia I20.8

Stenocephaly Q75.8

Stenosis, stenotic (cicatricial) —*see also* Stricture
- ampulla of Vater K83.1
- anus, anal (canal) (sphincter) K62.4
  - and rectum K62.4
  - congenital Q42.3
    - with fistula Q42.2
- aorta (ascending) (supraventricular) (congenital) Q25.3
  - arteriosclerotic I70.0
  - calcified I70.0
- aortic (valve) I35.0
  - with insufficiency I35.2
  - congenital Q23.0
  - rheumatic I06.0
    - with
      - incompetency, insufficiency or regurgitation I06.2
        - with mitral (valve) disease I08.0
          - with tricuspid (valve) disease I08.3
      - mitral (valve) disease I08.0
        - with tricuspid (valve) disease I08.3
      - tricuspid (valve) disease I08.2
        - with mitral (valve) disease I08.3
  - specified cause NEC I35.0
  - syphilitic A52.03
- aqueduct of Sylvius (congenital) Q03.0
  - with spina bifida —*see* Spina bifida, by site, with hydrocephalus
  - acquired G91.1
- artery NEC —*see also* Arteriosclerosis I77.1
  - celiac I77.4
  - cerebral —*see* Occlusion, artery, cerebral
  - extremities —*see* Arteriosclerosis, extremities
  - precerebral —*see* Occlusion, artery, precerebral
  - pulmonary (congenital) Q25.6
    - acquired I28.8
  - renal I70.1

Stenosis, stenotic *(continued)*
- bile duct (common) (hepatic) K83.1
  - congenital Q44.3
- bladder-neck (acquired) N32.0
  - congenital Q64.31
- brain G93.89
- bronchus J98.09
  - congenital Q32.3
  - syphilitic A52.72
- cardia (stomach) K22.2
  - congenital Q39.3
- cardiovascular —*see* Disease, cardiovascular
- caudal M48.08
- cervix, cervical (canal) N88.2
  - congenital Q51.828
  - in pregnancy or childbirth —*see* Pregnancy, complicated by, abnormal cervix
- colon —*see also* Obstruction, intestine
  - congenital Q42.9
    - specified NEC Q42.8
- colostomy K94.03
- common (bile) duct K83.1
  - congenital Q44.3
- coronary (artery) —*see* Disease, heart, ischemic, atherosclerotic
- cystic duct —*see* Obstruction, gallbladder
- due to presence of device, implant or graft —*see also* Complications, by site and type, specified NEC T85.85
  - arterial graft NEC T82.858
  - breast (implant) T85.85
  - catheter T85.85
    - dialysis (renal) T82.858
      - intraperitoneal T85.85
    - infusion NEC T82.858
      - spinal (epidural) (subdural) T85.85
    - urinary (indwelling) T83.85
  - fixation, internal (orthopedic) NEC T84.85
  - gastrointestinal (bile duct) (esophagus) T85.85
  - genital NEC T83.85
  - heart NEC T82.857
  - joint prosthesis T84.85
  - ocular (corneal graft) (orbital implant) NEC T85.85
  - orthopedic NEC T84.85
  - specified NEC T85.85
  - urinary NEC T83.85
  - vascular NEC T82.858
  - ventricular intracranial shunt T85.85
- duodenum K31.5
  - congenital Q41.0
- ejaculatory duct NEC N50.8
- endocervical os —*see* Stenosis, cervix
- enterostomy K94.13
- esophagus K22.2
  - congenital Q39.3
  - syphilitic A52.79
    - congenital A50.59 *[K23]*
- eustachian tube —*see* Obstruction, eustachian tube
- external ear canal (acquired) H61.30-
  - congenital Q16.1
  - due to
    - inflammation H61.32-
    - trauma H61.31-
  - postprocedural H95.81-
  - specified cause NEC H61.39-
- gallbladder —*see* Obstruction, gallbladder
- glottis J38.6

Stenosis, stenotic *(continued)*
- heart valve (congenital) Q24.8
  - aortic Q23.0
  - mitral Q23.2
  - pulmonary Q22.1
  - tricuspid Q22.4
- hepatic duct K83.1
- hymen N89.6
- hypertrophic subaortic (idiopathic) I42.1
- ileum K56.69
  - congenital Q41.2
- infundibulum cardia Q24.3
- intervertebral foramina *—see also* Lesion, biomechanical, specified NEC
  - connective tissue M99.79
    - abdomen M99.79
    - cervical region M99.71
    - cervicothoracic M99.71
    - head region M99.70
    - lumbar region M99.73
    - lumbosacral M99.73
    - occipitocervical M99.70
    - sacral region M99.74
    - sacrococcygeal M99.74
    - sacroiliac M99.74
    - specified NEC M99.79
    - thoracic region M99.72
    - thoracolumbar M99.72
  - disc M99.79
    - abdomen M99.79
    - cervical region M99.71
    - cervicothoracic M99.71
    - head region M99.70
    - lower extremity M99.76
    - lumbar region M99.73
    - lumbosacral M99.73
    - occipitocervical M99.70
    - pelvic M99.75
    - rib cage M99.78
    - sacral region M99.74
    - sacrococcygeal M99.74
    - sacroiliac M99.74
    - specified NEC M99.79
    - thoracic region M99.72
    - thoracolumbar M99.72
    - upper extremity M99.77
  - osseous M99.69
    - abdomen M99.69
    - cervical region M99.61
    - cervicothoracic M99.61
    - head region M99.60
    - lower extremity M99.66
    - lumbar region M99.63
    - lumbosacral M99.63
    - occipitocervical M99.60
    - pelvic M99.65
    - rib cage M99.68
    - sacral region M99.64
    - sacrococcygeal M99.64
    - sacroiliac M99.64
    - specified NEC M99.69
    - thoracic region M99.62
    - thoracolumbar M99.62
    - upper extremity M99.67
  - subluxation *—see* Stenosis, intervertebral foramina, osseous
- intestine *—see also* Obstruction, intestine
  - congenital (small) Q41.9
    - large Q42.9
      - specified NEC Q42.8
    - specified NEC Q41.8
- jejunum K56.69
  - congenital Q41.1
- lacrimal (passage)
  - canaliculi H04.54-
  - congenital Q10.5
  - duct H04.55-
  - punctum H04.56-
  - sac H04.57-

Stenosis, stenotic *(continued)*
- lacrimonasal duct *—see* Stenosis, lacrimal, duct
  - congenital Q10.5
- larynx J38.6
  - congenital NEC Q31.8
    - subglottic Q31.1
  - syphilitic A52.73
    - congenital A50.59 *[J99]*
- mitral (chronic) (inactive) (valve) I05.0
  - with
    - aortic valve disease I08.0
    - incompetency, insufficiency or regurgitation I05.2
  - active or acute I01.1
    - with rheumatic or Sydenham's chorea I02.0
  - congenital Q23.2
  - specified cause, except rheumatic I34.2
  - syphilitic A52.03
- myocardium, myocardial *—see also* Degeneration, myocardial
  - hypertrophic subaortic (idiopathic) I42.1
- nares (anterior) (posterior) J34.89
  - congenital Q30.0
- nasal duct *—see also* Stenosis, lacrimal, duct
  - congenital Q10.5
- nasolacrimal duct *—see also* Stenosis, lacrimal, duct
  - congenital Q10.5
- neural canal *—see also* Lesion, biomechanical, specified NEC
  - connective tissue M99.49
    - abdomen M99.49
    - cervical region M99.41
    - cervicothoracic M99.41
    - head region M99.40
    - lower extremity M99.46
    - lumbar region M99.43
    - lumbosacral M99.43
    - occipitocervical M99.40
    - pelvic M99.45
    - rib cage M99.48
    - sacral region M99.44
    - sacrococcygeal M99.44
    - sacroiliac M99.44
    - specified NEC M99.49
    - thoracic region M99.42
    - thoracolumbar M99.42
    - upper extremity M99.47
  - intervertebral disc M99.59
    - abdomen M99.59
    - cervical region M99.51
    - cervicothoracic M99.51
    - head region M99.50
    - lower extremity M99.56
    - lumbar region M99.53
    - lumbosacral M99.53
    - occipitocervical M99.50
    - pelvic M99.55
    - rib cage M99.58
    - sacral region M99.54
    - sacrococcygeal M99.54
    - sacroiliac M99.54
    - specified NEC M99.59
    - thoracic region M99.52
    - thoracolumbar M99.52
    - upper extremity M99.57
  - osseous M99.39
    - abdomen M99.39
    - cervical region M99.31
    - cervicothoracic M99.31
    - head region M99.30
    - lower extremity M99.36
    - lumbar region M99.33
    - lumbosacral M99.33
    - pelvic M99.35
    - rib cage M99.38

Stenosis, stenotic *(continued)*
- neural canal *—see also* Lesion, biomechanical, specified NEC *(continued)*
  - osseous *(continued)*
    - occipitocervical M99.30
    - sacral region M99.34
    - sacrococcygeal M99.34
    - sacroiliac M99.34
    - specified NEC M99.39
    - thoracic region M99.32
    - thoracolumbar M99.32
    - upper extremity M99.37
  - subluxation M99.29
    - cervical region M99.21
    - cervicothoracic M99.21
    - head region M99.20
    - lower extremity M99.26
    - lumbar region M99.23
    - lumbosacral M99.23
    - occipitocervical M99.20
    - pelvic M99.25
    - rib cage M99.28
    - sacral region M99.24
    - sacrococcygeal M99.24
    - sacroiliac M99.24
    - specified NEC M99.29
    - thoracic region M99.22
    - thoracolumbar M99.22
    - upper extremity M99.27
- organ or site, congenital NEC *—see* Atresia, by site
- papilla of Vater K83.1
- pulmonary (artery) (congenital) Q25.6
  - with ventricular septal defect, transposition of aorta, and hypertrophy of right ventricle Q21.3
  - acquired I28.8
  - in tetralogy of Fallot Q21.3
  - infundibular Q24.3
  - subvalvular Q24.3
  - supravalvular Q25.6
  - valve I37.0
    - with insufficiency I37.2
    - congenital Q22.1
    - rheumatic I09.89
      - with aortic, mitral or tricuspid (valve) disease I08.8
  - vein, acquired I28.8
  - vessel NEC I28.8
- pulmonic (congenital) Q22.1
  - infundibular Q24.3
  - subvalvular Q24.3
- pylorus (hypertrophic) (acquired) K31.1
  - adult K31.1
  - congenital Q40.0
  - infantile Q40.0
- rectum (sphincter) *—see* Stricture, rectum
- renal artery I70.1
  - congenital Q27.1
- salivary duct (any) K11.8
- sphincter of Oddi K83.1
- spinal M48.00
  - cervical region M48.02
  - cervicothoracic region M48.03
  - lumbar region M48.06
  - lumbosacral region M48.07
  - occipito-atlanto-axial region M48.01
  - sacrococcygeal region M48.08
  - thoracic region M48.04
  - thoracolumbar region M48.05
- stomach, hourglass K31.2
- subaortic (congenital) Q24.4
  - hypertrophic (idiopathic) I42.1
- subglottic J38.6
  - congenital Q31.1
  - postprocedural J95.5

Stenosis, stenotic *(continued)*
- trachea J39.8
  - congenital Q32.1
  - syphilitic A52.73
  - tuberculous NEC A15.5
- tracheostomy J95.03
- tricuspid (valve) I07.0
  - with
    - aortic (valve) disease I08.2
    - incompetency, insufficiency or regurgitation I07.2
      - with aortic (valve) disease I08.2
        - with mitral (valve) disease I08.3
    - mitral (valve) disease I08.1
      - with aortic (valve) disease I08.3
  - congenital Q22.4
  - nonrheumatic I36.0
    - with insufficiency I36.2
- tubal N97.1
- ureter *—see* Atresia, ureter
- ureteropelvic junction, congenital Q62.11
- ureterovesical orifice, congenital Q62.12
- urethra (valve) *—see also* Stricture, urethra
  - congenital Q64.32
- urinary meatus, congenital Q64.33
- vagina N89.5
  - congenital Q52.4
  - in pregnancy *—see* Pregnancy, complicated by, abnormal vagina causing obstructed labor O65.5
- valve (cardiac) (heart) *—see also* Endocarditis I38
  - congenital Q24.8
    - aortic Q23.0
    - mitral Q23.2
    - pulmonary Q22.1
    - tricuspid Q22.4
- vena cava (inferior) (superior) I87.1
  - congenital Q26.0
- vesicourethral orifice Q64.31
- vulva N90.5

Stent jail T82.897

Stercolith (impaction) K56.41
- appendix K38.1

Stercoraceous, stercoral ulcer K63.3
- anus or rectum K62.6

Stereotypies NEC F98.4

Sterility *—see* Infertility

Sterilization *—see* Encounter (for), sterilization

Sternalgia *—see* Angina

Sternopagus Q89.4

Sternum bifidum Q76.7

Steroid
- effects (adverse) (adrenocortical) (iatrogenic)
  - cushingoid E24.2
    - correct substance properly administered *—see* Table of Drugs and Chemicals, by drug, adverse effect
    - overdose or wrong substance given or taken *—see* Table of Drugs and Chemicals, by drug, poisoning
  - diabetes *—see* category E09
    - correct substance properly administered *—see* Table of Drugs and Chemicals, by drug, adverse effect
    - overdose or wrong substance given or taken *—see* Table of Drugs and Chemicals, by drug, poisoning

Steroid *(continued)*
- effects *(continued)*
  - fever R50.2
  - insufficiency E27.3
    - correct substance properly administered —*see* Table of Drugs and Chemicals, by drug, adverse effect
    - overdose or wrong substance given or taken —*see* Table of Drugs and Chemicals, by drug, poisoning
- responder H40.04-

Stevens-Johnson disease or syndrome L51.1
- toxic epidermal necrolysis overlap L51.3

Stewart-Morel syndrome M85.2

Sticker's disease B08.3

Sticky eye —*see* Conjunctivitis, acute, mucopurulent

Stieda's disease —*see* Bursitis, tibial collateral

Stiff neck —*see* Torticollis

Stiff-man syndrome G25.82

Stiffness, joint NEC M25.60-
- ankle M25.67-
- ankylosis —*see* Ankylosis, joint
- contracture —*see* Contraction, joint
- elbow M25.62-
- foot M25.67-
- hand M25.64-
- hip M25.65-
- knee M25.66-
- shoulder M25.61-
- wrist M25.63-

Stigmata congenital syphilis A50.59

Stillbirth P95

Still-Felty syndrome —*see* Felty's syndrome

Still's disease or syndrome (juvenile) M08.20
- adult-onset M06.1
- ankle M08.27-
- elbow M08.22-
- foot joint M08.27-
- hand joint M08.24-
- hip M08.25-
- knee M08.26-
- multiple site M08.29
- shoulder M08.21-
- vertebra M08.28
- wrist M08.23-

Stimulation, ovary E28.1

Sting (venomous) (with allergic or anaphylactic shock) —*see* Table of Drugs and Chemicals, by animal or substance, poisoning

Stippled epiphyses Q78.8

Stitch
- abscess T81.4
- burst (in operation wound) —*see* Disruption, wound, operation

Stokes-Adams disease or syndrome I45.9

Stokes' disease E05.00
- with thyroid storm E05.01

Stokvis (-Talma) **disease** D74.8

Stoma malfunction
- colostomy K94.03
- enterostomy K94.13
- gastrostomy K94.23
- ileostomy K94.13
- tracheostomy J95.03

Stomach —*see* condition

Stomatitis (denture) (ulcerative) K12.1
- angular K13.0
  - due to dietary or vitamin deficiency E53.0
- aphthous K12.0
- bovine B08.61
- candidal B37.0
- catarrhal K12.1
- diphtheritic A36.89
- due to
  - dietary deficiency E53.0
  - thrush B37.0
  - vitamin deficiency
    - B group NEC E53.9
    - B2(riboflavin) E53.0
- epidemic B08.8
- epizootic B08.8
- follicular K12.1
- gangrenous A69.0
- Geotrichum B48.3
- herpesviral, herpetic B00.2
- herpetiformis K12.0
- malignant K12.1
- membranous acute K12.1
- monilial B37.0
- mycotic B37.0
- necrotizing ulcerative A69.0
- parasitic B37.0
- septic K12.1
- spirochetal A69.1
- suppurative (acute) K12.2
- ulceromembranous A69.1
- vesicular K12.1
  - with exanthem (enteroviral) B08.4
  - virus disease A93.8
- Vincent's A69.1

Stomatocytosis D58.8

Stomatomycosis B37.0

Stomatorrhagia K13.79

Stone (s) —*see also* Calculus
- bladder (diverticulum) N21.0
- cystine E72.09
- heart syndrome I50.1
- kidney N20.0
- prostate N42.0
- pulpal (dental) K04.2
- renal N20.0
- salivary gland or duct (any) K11.5
- urethra (impacted) N21.1
- urinary (duct) (impacted) (passage) N20.9
  - bladder (diverticulum) N21.0
  - lower tract N21.9
  - specified NEC N21.8
- xanthine E79.8 *[N22]*

Stonecutter's lung J62.8

Stonemason's asthma, disease, lung or pneumoconiosis J62.8

Stoppage
- heart —*see* Arrest, cardiac
- urine —*see* Retention, urine

Storm, thyroid —*see* Thyrotoxicosis

Strabismus (congenital) (nonparalytic) H50.9
- concomitant H50.40
  - convergent —*see* Strabismus, convergent concomitant
  - divergent —*see* Strabismus, divergent concomitant
- convergent concomitant H50.00
  - accommodative component H50.43
  - alternating H50.05
    - with
      - A pattern H50.06
      - specified nonconcomitances NEC H50.08
      - V pattern H50.07

Strabismus *(continued)*
- convergent concomitant *(continued)*
  - monocular H50.01-
    - with
      - A pattern H50.02-
      - specified nonconcomitances NEC H50.04-
      - V pattern H50.03-
  - intermittent H50.31-
    - alternating H50.32
- cyclotropia H50.1-
- divergent concomitant H50.10
  - alternating H50.15
    - with
      - A pattern H50.16
      - specified noncomitances NEC H50.18
      - V pattern H50.17
  - monocular H50.11-
    - with
      - A pattern H50.12-
      - specified noncomitances NEC H50.14-
      - V pattern H50.13-
  - intermittent H50.33
    - alternating H50.34
- Duane's syndrome H50.81-
- due to adhesions, scars H50.69
- heterophoria H50.50
  - alternating H50.55
  - cyclophoria H50.54
  - esophoria H50.51
  - exophoria H50.52
  - vertical H50.53
- heterotropia H50.40
  - intermittent H50.30
- hypertropia H50.2-
- hypotropia —*see* Hypertropia
- latent H50.50
- mechanical H50.60
  - Brown's sheath syndrome H50.61-
  - specified type NEC H50.69
- monofixation syndrome H50.42
- paralytic H49.9
  - abducens nerve H49.2-
  - fourth nerve H49.1-
  - Kearns-Sayre syndrome H49.81-
  - ophthalmoplegia (external)
    - progressive H49.4-
      - with pigmentary retinopathy H49.81-
    - total H49.3-
  - sixth nerve H49.2-
  - specified type NEC H49.88-
  - third nerve H49.0-
  - trochlear nerve H49.1-
- specified type NEC H50.89
- vertical H50.2-

Strain
- back S39.012
- cervical S16.1
- eye NEC —*see* Disturbance, vision, subjective
- heart —*see* Disease, heart
- low back S39.012
- mental NOS Z73.3
  - work-related Z56.6
- muscle (tendon) —*see* Injury, muscle, by site, strain
- neck S16.1
- postural —*see also* Disorder, soft tissue, due to use
- physical NOS Z73.3
  - work-related Z56.6
- psychological NEC Z73.3
- tendon —*see* Injury, muscle, by site, strain

Straining, on urination R39.16

Strand, vitreous —*see* Opacity, vitreous, membranes and strands

Strangulation, strangulated —*see al*
- Asphyxia, traumatic
- appendix K38.8
- bladder-neck N32.0
- bowel or colon K56.2
- food or foreign body —*see* Foreign body, by site
- hemorrhoids —*see* Hemorrhoids, with complication
- hernia —*see also* Hernia, by site, with obstruction
  - with gangrene —*see* Hernia, by site, with gangrene
- intestine (large) (small) K56.2
  - with hernia —*see also* Hernia, by site, with obstruction
    - with gangrene —*see* Hernia, by site, with gangrene
- mesentery K56.2
- mucus —*see* Asphyxia, mucus
- omentum K56.2
- organ or site, congenital NEC —*see* Atresia, by site
- ovary —*see* Torsion, ovary
- penis N48.89
  - foreign body T19.4
- rupture —*see* Hernia, by site, with obstruction
- stomach due to hernia —*see also* Hernia, by site, with obstruction
  - with gangrene —*see* Hernia, by site, with gangrene
- vesicourethral orifice N32.0

Strangury R30.0

Straw itch B88.0

Strawberry
- gallbladder K82.4
- mark Q82.5
- tongue (red) (white) K14.3

Streak (s)
- macula, angioid H35.33
- ovarian Q50.32

Strephosymbolia F81.0
- secondary to organic lesion R48.8

Streptobacillary fever A25.1

Streptobacillosis A25.1

Streptobacillus moniliformis A25.1

Streptococcus, streptococcal —*see also* condition
- as cause of disease classified elsewhere B95.5
- group
  - A, as cause of disease classified elsewhere B95.0
  - B, as cause of disease classified elsewhere B95.1
  - D, as cause of disease classified elsewhere B95.2
- pneumoniae, as cause of disease classified elsewhere B95.3
- specified NEC, as cause of disease classified elsewhere B95.4

Streptomycosis B47.1

Streptotrichosis A48.8

Stress F43.9
- family —*see* Disruption, family
- fetal P84
  - complicating pregnancy O77.9
    - due to drug administration O77.1
- mental NEC Z73.3
  - work-related Z56.6
- physical NEC Z73.3
  - work-related Z56.6
- polycythemia D75.1
- reaction —*see also* Reaction, stress F43.9
- work schedule Z56.3

- **retching, nerve** —*see* Injury, nerve
- **riae albicantes, atrophicae or distensae** (cutis) L90.6
- **ricture** —*see also* Stenosis
  - ampulla of Vater K83.1
  - anus (sphincter) K62.4
    - congenital Q42.3
      - with fistula Q42.2
    - infantile Q42.3
      - with fistula Q42.2
  - aorta (ascending) (congenital) Q25.3
    - arteriosclerotic I70.0
    - calcified I70.0
    - supravalvular, congenital Q25.3
  - aortic (valve) —*see* Stenosis, aortic
  - aqueduct of Sylvius (congenital) Q03.0
    - with spina bifida —*see* Spina bifida, by site, with hydrocephalus
    - acquired G91.1
  - artery I77.1
    - basilar —*see* Occlusion, artery, basilar
    - carotid —*see* Occlusion, artery, carotid
    - celiac I77.4
    - congenital (peripheral) Q27.8
      - cerebral Q28.3
      - coronary Q24.5
      - digestive system Q27.8
      - lower limb Q27.8
      - retinal Q14.1
      - specified site NEC Q27.8
      - umbilical Q27.0
      - upper limb Q27.8
    - coronary —*see* Disease, heart, ischemic, atherosclerotic
      - congenital Q24.5
    - precerebral —*see* Occlusion, artery, precerebral
    - pulmonary (congenital) Q25.6
      - acquired I28.8
    - renal I70.1
    - vertebral —*see* Occlusion, artery, vertebral
  - auditory canal (external) (congenital)
    - acquired —*see* Stenosis, external ear canal
  - bile duct (common) (hepatic) K83.1
    - congenital Q44.3
    - postoperative K91.89
  - bladder N32.89
    - neck N32.0
  - bowel —*see* Obstruction, intestine
  - brain G93.89
  - bronchus J98.09
    - congenital Q32.3
    - syphilitic A52.72
  - cardia (stomach) K22.2
    - congenital Q39.3
  - cardiac —*see also* Disease, heart
    - orifice (stomach) K22.2
  - cecum —*see* Obstruction, intestine
  - cervix, cervical (canal) N88.2
    - congenital Q51.828
    - in pregnancy —*see* Pregnancy, complicated by, abnormal cervix
      - causing obstructed labor O65.5
  - colon —*see also* Obstruction, intestine
    - congenital Q42.9
      - specified NEC Q42.8
  - colostomy K94.03
  - common (bile) duct K83.1
  - coronary (artery) —*see* Disease, heart, ischemic, atherosclerotic
  - cystic duct —*see* Obstruction, gallbladder
  - digestive organs NEC, congenital Q45.8

Stricture *(continued)*

- duodenum K31.5
  - congenital Q41.0
- ear canal (external) (congenital) Q16.1
  - acquired —*see* Stricture, auditory canal, acquired
- ejaculatory duct N50.8
- enterostomy K94.13
- esophagus K22.2
  - congenital Q39.3
  - syphilitic A52.79
    - congenital A50.59 *[K23]*
- eustachian tube —*see also* Obstruction, eustachian tube
  - congenital Q17.8
- fallopian tube N97.1
  - gonococcal A54.24
  - tuberculous A18.17
- gallbladder —*see* Obstruction, gallbladder
- glottis J38.6
- heart —*see also* Disease, heart
  - valve —*see also* Endocarditis I38
    - aortic Q23.0
    - mitral Q23.4
    - pulmonary Q22.1
    - tricuspid Q22.4
- hepatic duct K83.1
- hourglass, of stomach K31.2
- hymen N89.6
- hypopharynx J39.2
- ileum K56.69
  - congenital Q41.2
- intestine —*see also* Obstruction, intestine
  - congenital (small) Q41.9
    - large Q42.9
      - specified NEC Q42.8
    - specified NEC Q41.8
  - ischemic K55.1
- jejunum K56.69
  - congenital Q41.1
- lacrimal passages —*see also* Stenosis, lacrimal
  - congenital Q10.5
- larynx J38.6
  - congenital NEC Q31.8
    - subglottic Q31.1
  - syphilitic A52.73
    - congenital A50.59 *[J99]*
- meatus
  - ear (congenital) Q16.1
    - acquired —*see* Stricture, auditory canal, acquired
  - osseous (ear) (congenital) Q16.1
    - acquired —*see* Stricture, auditory canal, acquired
  - urinarius —*see also* Stricture, urethra
    - congenital Q64.33
- mitral (valve) —*see* Stenosis, mitral
- myocardium, myocardial I51.5
  - hypertrophic subaortic (idiopathic) I42.1
- nares (anterior) (posterior) J34.89
  - congenital Q30.0
- nasal duct —*see also* Stenosis, lacrimal, duct
  - congenital Q10.5
- nasolacrimal duct —*see also* Stenosis, lacrimal, duct
  - congenital Q10.5
- nasopharynx J39.2
  - syphilitic A52.73
- nose J34.89
  - congenital Q30.0
- nostril (anterior) (posterior) J34.89
  - congenital Q30.0
  - syphilitic A52.73
    - congenital A50.59 *[J99]*

Stricture *(continued)*

- organ or site, congenital NEC —*see* Atresia, by site
- os uteri —*see* Stricture, cervix
- osseous meatus (ear) (congenital) Q16.1
  - acquired —*see* Stricture, auditory canal, acquired
- oviduct —*see* Stricture, fallopian tube
- pelviureteric junction (congenital) Q62.11
- penis, by foreign body T19.4
- pharynx J39.2
- prostate N42.89
- pulmonary, pulmonic
  - artery (congenital) Q25.6
    - acquired I28.8
    - noncongenital I28.8
  - infundibulum (congenital) Q24.3
  - valve I37.0
    - congenital Q22.1
  - vein, acquired I28.8
  - vessel NEC I28.8
- punctum lacrimale —*see also* Stenosis, lacrimal, punctum
  - congenital Q10.5
- pylorus (hypertrophic) K31.1
  - adult K31.1
  - congenital Q40.0
  - infantile Q40.0
- rectosigmoid K56.69
- rectum (sphincter) K62.4
  - congenital Q42.1
    - with fistula Q42.0
  - due to
    - chlamydial lymphogranuloma A55
    - irradiation K91.89
    - lymphogranuloma venereum A55
  - gonococcal A54.6
  - inflammatory (chlamydial) A55
  - syphilitic A52.74
  - tuberculous A18.32
- renal artery I70.1
  - congenital Q27.1
- salivary duct or gland (any) K11.8
- sigmoid (flexure) —*see* Obstruction, intestine
- spermatic cord N50.8
- stoma (following) (of)
  - colostomy K94.03
  - enterostomy K94.13
  - gastrostomy K94.23
  - ileostomy K94.13
  - tracheostomy J95.03
- stomach K31.89
  - congenital Q40.2
  - hourglass K31.2
- subaortic Q24.4
  - hypertrophic (acquired) (idiopathic) I42.1
- subglottic J38.6
- syphilitic NEC A52.79
- trachea J39.8
  - congenital Q32.1
  - syphilitic A52.73
  - tuberculous NEC A15.5
- tracheostomy J95.03
- tricuspid (valve) —*see* Stenosis, tricuspid
- tunica vaginalis N50.8
- ureter (postoperative) N13.5
  - with
    - hydronephrosis N13.1
      - with infection N13.6
    - pyelonephritis (chronic) N11.1
  - congenital —*see* Atresia, ureter
  - tuberculous A18.11
- ureteropelvic junction (congenital) Q62.11
- ureterovesical orifice N13.5
  - with infection N13.6

Stricture *(continued)*

- urethra (organic) (spasmodic) N35.9
  - associated with schistosomiasis B65.0 *[N37]*
  - congenital Q64.39
    - valvular (posterior) Q64.2
  - due to
    - infection —*see* Stricture, urethra, postinfective
    - trauma —*see* Stricture, urethra, post-traumatic
  - gonococcal, gonorrheal A54.01
  - infective NEC —*see* Stricture, urethra, postinfective
  - late effect (sequelae) of injury —*see* Stricture, urethra, post-traumatic
  - postcatheterization —*see* Stricture, urethra, postprocedural
  - postinfective NEC
    - female N35.12
    - male N35.119
      - anterior urethra N35.114
      - bulbous urethra N35.112
      - meatal N35.111
      - membranous urethra N35.113
  - postobstetric N35.021
  - postoperative —*see* Stricture, urethra, postprocedural
  - postprocedural
    - female N99.12
    - male N99.114
      - anterior urethra N99.113
      - bulbous urethra N99.111
      - meatal N99.110
      - membranous urethra N99.112
  - post-traumatic
    - female N35.028
      - due to childbirth N35.021
    - male N35.014
      - anterior urethra N35.013
      - bulbous urethra N35.011
      - meatal N35.010
      - membranous urethra N35.012
  - sequela (late effect) of
    - childbirth N35.021
    - injury —*see* Stricture, urethra, post-traumatic
  - specified cause NEC N35.8
  - syphilitic A52.76
  - traumatic —*see* Stricture, urethra, post-traumatic
  - valvular (posterior), congenital Q64.2
- urinary meatus —*see* Stricture, urethra
- uterus, uterine (synechiae) N85.6
  - os (external) (internal) —*see* Stricture, cervix
- vagina (outlet) —*see* Stenosis, vagina
- valve (cardiac) (heart) —*see also* Endocarditis
  - congenital
    - aortic Q23.0
    - mitral Q23.2
    - pulmonary Q22.1
    - tricuspid Q22.4
- vas deferens N50.8
  - congenital Q55.4
- vein I87.1
- vena cava (inferior) (superior) NEC I87.1
  - congenital Q26.0
- vesicourethral orifice N32.0
  - congenital Q64.31
- vulva (acquired) N90.5

Stridor R06.1
- congenital (larynx) P28.89

Stridulous —*see* condition

- **Stroke** (apoplectic) (brain) (embolic) (ischemic) (paralytic) (thrombotic) I63.9
  - epileptic —*see* Epilepsy
  - heat T67.0
  - in evolution I63.9
  - intraoperative
    - during cardiac surgery I97.810
    - during other surgery I97.811
  - lightning —*see* Lightning
  - meaning
    - cerebral hemorrhage - code to Hemorrhage, intracranial
    - cerebral infarction - code to Infarction, cerebral
  - postprocedural
    - following cardiac surgery I97.820
    - following other surgery I97.821
  - unspecified (NOS) I63.9
- **Stromatosis, endometrial** D39.0
- **Strongyloidiasis, strongyloidosis** B78.9
  - cutaneous B78.1
  - disseminated B78.7
  - intestinal B78.0
- **Strophulus pruriginosus** L28.2
- **Struck by lightning** —*see* Lightning
- **Struma** —*see also* Goiter
  - Hashimoto E06.3
  - lymphomatosa E06.3
  - nodosa (simplex) E04.9
    - endemic E01.2
      - multinodular E01.1
    - multinodular E04.2
      - iodine-deficiency related E01.1
    - toxic or with hyperthyroidism E05.20
      - with thyroid storm E05.21
      - multinodular E05.20
        - with thyroid storm E05.21
      - uninodular E05.10
        - with thyroid storm E05.11
    - toxicosa E05.20
      - with thyroid storm E05.21
      - multinodular E05.20
        - with thyroid storm E05.21
      - uninodular E05.10
        - with thyroid storm E05.11
    - uninodular E04.1
  - ovarii D27.-
  - Riedel's E06.5
- **Strumipriva cachexia** E03.4
- **Strümpell-Marie spine** —*see* Spondylitis, ankylosing
- **Strümpell-Westphal pseudosclerosis** E83.01
- **Stuart deficiency disease** (factor X) D68.2
- **Stuart-Prower factor deficiency** (factor X) D68.2
- **Student's elbow** —*see* Bursitis, elbow, olecranon
- **Stump** —*see* Amputation
- **Stunting, nutritional** E45
- **Stupor** (catatonic) R40.1
  - depressive F32.8
  - dissociative F44.2
  - manic F30.2
  - manic-depressive F31.89
  - psychogenic (anergic) F44.2
  - reaction to exceptional stress (transient) F43.0
- **Sturge** (-Weber) (-Dimitri) (-Kalischer) **disease or syndrome** Q85.8
- **Stuttering** F80.81
  - adult onset F98.5
  - childhood onset F80.81
  - following cerebrovascular disease —*see* Disorder, fluency. following cerebrovascular disease
  - in conditions classified elsewhere R47.82
- **Sty, stye** (external) (internal) (meibomian) (zeisian) —*see* Hordeolum
- **Subacidity, gastric** K31.89
  - psychogenic F45.8
- **Subacute** —*see* condition
- **Subarachnoid** —*see* condition
- **Subcortical** —*see* condition
- **Subcostal syndrome, nerve compression** —*see* Mononeuropathy, upper limb, specified site NEC
- **Subcutaneous, subcuticular** —*see* condition
- **Subdural** —*see* condition
- **Subendocardium** —*see* condition
- **Subependymoma**
  - specified site —*see* Neoplasm, uncertain behavior, by site
  - unspecified site D43.2
- **Suberosis** J67.3
- **Subglossitis** —*see* Glossitis
- **Subhemophilia** D66
- **Subinvolution**
  - breast (postlactational) (postpuerperal) N64.89
  - puerperal O90.89
  - uterus (chronic) (nonpuerperal) N85.3
    - puerperal O90.89
- **Sublingual** —*see* condition
- **Sublinguitis** —*see* Sialoadenitis
- **Subluxatable hip** Q65.6
- **Subluxation** —*see also* Dislocation
  - acromioclavicular S43.11-
  - ankle S93.0-
  - atlantoaxial, recurrent M43.4
    - with myelopathy M43.3
  - carpometacarpal (joint) NEC S63.05-
    - thumb S63.04-
  - complex, vertebral —*see* Complex, subluxation
  - congenital —*see also* Malposition, congenital
    - hip —*see* Dislocation, hip, congenital, partial
    - joint (excluding hip)
      - lower limb Q68.8
      - shoulder Q68.8
      - upper limb Q68.8
  - elbow (traumatic) S53.10-
    - anterior S53.11-
    - lateral S53.14-
    - medial S53.13-
    - posterior S53.12-
    - specified type NEC S53.19-
  - finger S63.20-
    - index S63.20-
    - interphalangeal S63.22-
      - distal S63.24-
        - index S63.24-
        - little S63.24-
        - middle S63.24-
        - ring S63.24-
      - index S63.22-
      - little S63.22-
      - middle S63.22-
      - proximal S63.23-
        - index S63.23-
        - little S63.23-
        - middle S63.23-
        - ring S63.23-
      - ring S63.22-
    - little S63.20-
    - metacarpophalangeal S63.21-
      - index S63.21-
      - little S63.21-
      - middle S63.21-
      - ring S63.21-
    - middle S63.20-
    - ring S63.20-
  - foot S93.30-
    - specified site NEC S93.33-
    - tarsal joint S93.31-
    - tarsometatarsal joint S93.32-
    - toe —*see* Subluxation, toe
  - hip S73.00-
    - anterior S73.03-
      - obturator S73.02-
    - central S73.04-
    - posterior S73.01-
  - interphalangeal (joint)
    - finger S63.22-
      - distal joint S63.24-
        - index S63.24-
        - little S63.24-
        - middle S63.24-
        - ring S63.24-
      - index S63.22-
      - little S63.22-
      - middle S63.22-
      - proximal joint S63.23-
        - index S63.23-
        - little S63.23-
        - middle S63.23-
        - ring S63.23-
      - ring S63.22-
    - thumb S63.12-
      - distal joint S63.14-
      - proximal joint S63.13-
    - toe S93.13-
      - great S93.13-
      - lesser S93.13-
  - joint prosthesis —*see* Complications, joint prosthesis, mechanical, displacement, by site
  - knee S83.10-
    - cap —*see* Subluxation, patella
    - patella —*see* Subluxation, patella
    - proximal tibia
      - anteriorly S83.11-
      - laterally S83.14-
      - medially S83.13-
      - posteriorly S83.12-
    - specified type NEC S83.19-
  - lens —*see* Dislocation, lens, partial
  - ligament, traumatic —*see* Sprain, by site
  - metacarpal (bone)
    - proximal end S63.06-
  - metacarpophalangeal (joint)
    - finger S63.21-
      - index S63.21-
      - little S63.21-
      - middle S63.21-
      - ring S63.21-
    - thumb S63.11-
  - metatarsophalangeal joint S93.14-
    - great toe S93.14-
    - lesser toe S93.14-
  - midcarpal (joint) S63.03-
  - patella S83.00-
    - lateral S83.01-
    - recurrent (nontraumatic) —*see* Dislocation, patella, recurrent, incomplete
    - specified type NEC S83.09-
  - pathological —*see* Dislocation, pathological
  - radial head S53.00-
    - anterior S53.01-
    - nursemaid's elbow S53.03-
    - posterior S53.02-
    - specified type NEC S53.09-
  - radiocarpal (joint) S63.02-
  - radioulnar (joint)
    - distal S63.01-
    - proximal —*see* Subluxation, elbow
  - shoulder
    - congenital Q68.8
    - girdle S43.30-
      - scapula S43.31-
      - specified site NEC S43.39-
    - traumatic S43.00-
      - anterior S43.01-
      - inferior S43.03-
      - posterior S43.02-
      - specified type NEC S43.08-
  - sternoclavicular (joint) S43.20-
    - anterior S43.21-
    - posterior S43.22-
  - symphysis (pubis)
  - thumb S63.103
    - interphalangeal joint —*see* Subluxation, interphalangeal (joint), thumb
    - metacarpophalangeal joint —*see* Subluxation, metacarpophalangeal (joint), thumb
  - toe (s) S93.10-
    - great S93.10-
      - interphalangeal joint S93.13-
      - metatarsophalangeal joint S93.14-
    - interphalangeal joint S93.13-
    - lesser S93.10-
      - interphalangeal joint S93.13-
      - metatarsophalangeal joint S93.14-
    - metatarsophalangeal joint S93.149
  - ulna
    - distal end S63.07-
    - proximal end —*see* Subluxation, elbow
  - ulnohumeral joint —*see* Subluxation, elbow
  - vertebral
    - recurrent NEC —*see* subcategory M43.5
    - traumatic
      - cervical S13.100
        - atlantoaxial joint S13.120
        - atlantooccipital joint S13.110
        - atloidooccipital joint S13.110
        - joint between
          - C0 and C1 S13.110
          - C1 and C2 S13.120
          - C2 and C3 S13.130
          - C3 and C4 S13.140
          - C4 and C5 S13.150
          - C5and C6 S13.160
          - C6and C7 S13.170
          - C7and T1 S13.180
        - occipitoatloid joint S13.110
      - lumbar S33.100
        - joint between
          - L1and L2 S33.110
          - L2and L3 S33.120
          - L3 and L4 S33.130
          - L4and L5 S33.140
      - thoracic S23.100
        - joint between
          - T1and T2 S23.110
          - T2and T3 S23.120
          - T3 and T4 S23.122
          - T4 and T5 S23.130
          - T5 and T6 S23.132
          - T6 and T7 S23.140
          - T7 and T8 S23.142
          - T8 and T9 S23.150
          - T9 and T10 S23.152
          - T10 and T11 S23.160
          - T11 and T12 S23.162
          - T12 and L1 S23.170

- **[S]ubluxation** *(continued)*
  - [w]rist (carpal bone) S63.00-
    - carpometacarpal joint —*see* Subluxation, carpometacarpal (joint)
    - distal radioulnar joint —*see* Subluxation, radioulnar (joint), distal
    - metacarpal bone, proximal —*see* Subluxation, metacarpal (bone), proximal end
    - midcarpal —*see* Subluxation, midcarpal (joint)
    - radiocarpal joint —*see* Subluxation, radiocarpal (joint)
    - recurrent —*see* Dislocation, recurrent, wrist
    - specified site NEC S63.09-
    - ulna —*see* Subluxation, ulna, distal end
- **[Su]bmaxillary** —*see* condition
- **[Su]bmersion** (fatal) (nonfatal) T75.1
- **[Su]bmucous** —*see* condition
- **[Su]bnormal, subnormality**
  - [a]ccommodation (old age) H52.4
  - [m]ental —*see* Disability, intellectual
  - [t]emperature (accidental) T68
- **[Su]bphrenic** —*see* condition
- **[Su]bscapular nerve** —*see* condition
- **[Su]bseptus uterus** Q51.2
- **[Su]bsiding appendicitis** K36
- **[Su]bsternal thyroid** E04.9
  - [c]ongenital Q89.2
- **[Su]bstitution disorder** F44.9
- **[Su]btentorial** —*see* condition
- **[Su]bthyroidism** (acquired) —*see also* Hypothyroidism
  - congenital E03.1
- **[Su]ccenturiate placenta** O43.19-
- **[Su]cking thumb, child** (excessive) F98.8
- **[Su]damen, sudamina** L74.1
- **[Su]danese kala-azar** B55.0
- **[Su]dden**
  - heart failure —*see* Failure, heart
  - hearing loss —*see* Deafness, sudden
- **[Su]deck's atrophy, disease, or syndrome** —*see* Algoneurodystrophy
- **[Su]ffocation** —*see* Asphyxia, traumatic
- **[S]ugar**
  - blood
    - high (transient) R73.9
    - low (transient) E16.2
  - in urine R81
- **[S]uicide, suicidal** (attempted) T14.91
  - by poisoning —*see* Table of Drugs and Chemicals
  - history of (personal) Z91.5
    - in family Z81.8
  - ideation —*see* Ideation, suicidal
  - risk
    - meaning personal history of attempted suicide Z91.5
    - meaning suicidal ideation —*see* Ideation, suicidal
  - tendencies
    - meaning personal history of attempted suicide Z91.5
    - meaning suicidal ideation —*see* Ideation, suicidal
  - trauma —*see* nature of injury by site
- **Suipestifer infection** —*see* Infection, salmonella
- **Sulfhemoglobinemia, sulphemoglobinemia** (acquired) (with methemoglobinemia) D74.8
- **Sumatran mite fever** A75.3
- **Summer** —*see* condition
- **Sunburn** L55.9
  - first degree L55.0
  - second degree L55.1
  - third degree L55.2
- **SUNCT** (short lasting unilateral neuralgiform headache with conjunctival injection and tearing) G44.059
  - intractable G44.051
  - not intractable G44.059
- **Sunken acetabulum** —*see* Derangement, joint, specified type NEC, hip
- **Sunstroke** T67.0
- **Superfecundation** —*see* Pregnancy, multiple
- **Superfetation** —*see* Pregnancy, multiple
- **Superinvolution** (uterus) N85.8
- **Supernumerary** (congenital)
  - aortic cusps Q23.8
  - auditory ossicles Q16.3
  - bone Q79.8
  - breast Q83.1
  - carpal bones Q74.0
  - cusps, heart valve NEC Q24.8
    - aortic Q23.8
    - mitral Q23.2
    - pulmonary Q22.3
  - digit (s) Q69.9
  - ear (lobule) Q17.0
  - fallopian tube Q50.6
  - finger Q69.0
  - hymen Q52.4
  - kidney Q63.0
  - lacrimonasal duct Q10.6
  - lobule (ear) Q17.0
  - mitral cusps Q23.2
  - muscle Q79.8
  - nipple (s) Q83.3
  - organ or site not listed —*see* Accessory
  - ossicles, auditory Q16.3
  - ovary Q50.31
  - oviduct Q50.6
  - pulmonary, pulmonic cusps Q22.3
  - rib Q76.6
    - cervical or first (syndrome) Q76.5
  - roots (of teeth) K00.2
  - spleen Q89.09
  - tarsal bones Q74.2
  - teeth K00.1
  - testis Q55.29
  - thumb Q69.1
  - toe Q69.2
  - uterus Q51.2
  - vagina Q52.1
  - vertebra Q76.49
- **Supervision** (of)
  - contraceptive —*see* Prescription, contraceptives
  - dietary (for) Z71.3
    - allergy (food) Z71.3
    - colitis Z71.3
    - diabetes mellitus Z71.3
    - food allergy or intolerance Z71.3
    - gastritis Z71.3
    - hypercholesterolemia Z71.3
    - hypoglycemia Z71.3
    - intolerance (food) Z71.3
    - obesity Z71.3
    - specified NEC Z71.3
- **Supervision** *(continued)*
  - healthy infant or child Z76.2
    - foundling Z76.1
  - high-risk pregnancy —*see* Pregnancy, complicated by, high, risk
  - lactation Z39.1
  - pregnancy —*see* Pregnancy, supervision of
- **Supplemental teeth** K00.1
- **Suppression**
  - binocular vision H53.34
  - lactation O92.5
  - menstruation N94.89
  - ovarian secretion E28.39
  - renal N28.9
  - urine, urinary secretion R34
- **Suppuration, suppurative** —*see also* condition
  - accessory sinus (chronic) —*see* Sinusitis
  - adrenal gland
  - antrum (chronic) —*see* Sinusitis, maxillary
  - bladder —*see* Cystitis
  - brain G06.0
    - sequelae G09
  - breast N61
    - puerperal, postpartum or gestational —*see* Mastitis, obstetric, purulent
  - dental periosteum M27.3
  - ear (middle) —*see also* Otitis, media
    - external NEC —*see* Otitis, externa, infective
    - internal —*see* subcategory H83.0
  - ethmoidal (chronic) (sinus) —*see* Sinusitis, ethmoidal
  - fallopian tube —*see* Salpingo-oophoritis
  - frontal (chronic) (sinus) —*see* Sinusitis, frontal
  - gallbladder (acute) K81.0
  - gum K05.20
    - generalized K05.22
    - localized K05.21
  - intracranial G06.0
  - joint —*see* Arthritis, pyogenic or pyemic
  - labyrinthine —*see* subcategory H83.0
  - lung —*see* Abscess, lung
  - mammary gland N61
    - puerperal, postpartum O91.12
      - associated with lactation O91.13
  - maxilla, maxillary M27.2
    - sinus (chronic) —*see* Sinusitis, maxillary
  - muscle —*see* Myositis, infective
  - nasal sinus (chronic) —*see* Sinusitis
  - pancreas, acute K85.8
  - parotid gland —*see* Sialoadenitis
  - pelvis, pelvic
    - female —*see* Disease, pelvis, inflammatory
    - male K65.0
  - pericranial —*see* Osteomyelitis
  - salivary duct or gland (any) —*see* Sialoadenitis
  - sinus (accessory) (chronic) (nasal) —*see* Sinusitis
  - sphenoidal sinus (chronic) —*see* Sinusitis, sphenoidal
  - thymus (gland) E32.1
  - thyroid (gland) E06.0
  - tonsil —*see* Tonsillitis
  - uterus —*see* Endometritis
- **Supraeruption of tooth** (teeth) M26.34
- **Supraglottitis** J04.30
  - with obstruction J04.31
- **Suprarenal** (gland) —*see* condition
- **Suprascapular nerve** —*see* condition
- **Suprasellar** —*see* condition
- **Surfer's knots or nodules** S89.8-
- **Surgical**
  - emphysema T81.82
  - procedures, complication or misadventure —*see* Complications, surgical procedures
  - shock T81.10
- **Surveillance** (of) (for) —*see also* Observation
  - alcohol abuse Z71.41
  - contraceptive —*see* Prescription, contraceptives
  - dietary Z71.3
  - drug abuse Z71.51
- **Susceptibility to disease, genetic** Z15.89
  - malignant neoplasm Z15.09
    - breast Z15.01
    - endometrium Z15.04
    - ovary Z15.02
    - prostate Z15.03
    - specified NEC Z15.09
  - multiple endocrine neoplasia Z15.81
- **Suspected condition, ruled out** —*see also* Observation, suspected
  - amniotic cavity and membrane Z03.71
  - cervical shortening Z03.75
  - fetal anomaly Z03.73
  - fetal growth Z03.74
  - maternal and fetal conditions NEC Z03.79
  - oligohydramnios Z03.71
  - placental problem Z03.72
  - polyhydramnios Z03.71
- **Suspended uterus**
  - in pregnancy or childbirth —*see* Pregnancy, complicated by, abnormal uterus
- **Sutton's nevus** D22.9
- **Suture**
  - burst (in operation wound) T81.31
    - external operation wound T81.31
    - internal operation wound T81.32
  - inadvertently left in operation wound —*see* Foreign body, accidentally left during a procedure
  - removal Z48.02
- **Swab inadvertently left in operation wound** —*see* Foreign body, accidentally left during a procedure
- **Swallowed, swallowing**
  - difficulty —*see* Dysphagia
  - foreign body —*see* Foreign body, alimentary tract
- **Swan-neck deformity** (finger) —*see* Deformity, finger, swan-neck
- **Swearing, compulsive** F42
  - in Gilles de la Tourette's syndrome F95.2
- **Sweat, sweats**
  - fetid L75.0
  - night R61
- **Sweating, excessive** R61
- **Sweeley-Klionsky disease** E75.21
- **Sweet's disease or dermatosis** L98.2
- **Swelling** (of) R60.9
  - abdomen, abdominal (not referable to any particular organ) —*see* Mass, abdominal
  - ankle —*see* Effusion, joint, ankle
  - arm M79.89
    - forearm M79.89
  - breast N63

Swelling *(continued)*
Calabar B74.3
cervical gland R59.0
chest, localized R22.2
ear H93.8-
extremity (lower) (upper) —*see* Disorder, soft tissue, specified type NEC
finger M79.89
foot M79.89
glands R59.9
generalized R59.1
localized R59.0
hand M79.89
head (localized) R22.0
inflammatory —*see* Inflammation
intra-abdominal —*see* Mass, abdominal
joint —*see* Effusion, joint
leg M79.89
lower M79.89
limb —*see* Disorder, soft tissue, specified type NEC
localized (skin) R22.9
chest R22.2
head R22.0
limb
lower —*see* Mass, localized, limb, lower
upper —*see* Mass, localized, limb, upper
neck R22.1
trunk R22.2
neck (localized) R22.1
pelvic —*see* Mass, abdominal
scrotum N50.8
splenic —*see* Splenomegaly
testis N50.8
toe M79.89
umbilical R19.09
wandering, due to Gnathostoma (spinigerum) B83.1
white —*see* Tuberculosis, arthritis

Swift (-Feer) **disease**
overdose or wrong substance given or taken —*see* Table of Drugs and Chemicals, by drug, poisoning

Swimmer's
cramp T75.1
ear H60.33-
itch B65.3

Swimming in the head R42

Swollen —*see* Swelling

Swyer syndrome Q99.1

Sycosis L73.8
barbae (not parasitic) L73.8
contagiosa (mycotic) B35.0
lupoides L73.8
mycotic B35.0
parasitic B35.0
vulgaris L73.8

Sydenham's chorea —*see* Chorea, Sydenham's

Sylvatic yellow fever A95.0

Sylvest's disease B33.0

Symblepharon H11.23-
congenital Q10.3

Symond's syndrome G93.2

Sympathetic —*see* condition

Sympatheticotonia G90.8

Sympathicoblastoma
specified site —*see* Neoplasm, malignant, by site
unspecified site C74.90

Sympathogonioma —*see* Sympathicoblastoma

Symphalangy (fingers) (toes) Q70.9

Symptoms NEC R68.89
breast NEC N64.59
development NEC R63.8
factitious, self-induced —*see* Disorder, factitious
genital organs, female R10.2
involving
abdomen NEC R19.8
appearance NEC R46.89
awareness R41.9
altered mental status R41.82
amnesia —*see* Amnesia
borderline intellectual functioning R41.83
coma —*see* Coma
disorientation R41.0
neurologic neglect syndrome R41.4
senile cognitive decline R41.81
specified symptom NEC R41.89
behavior NEC R46.89
cardiovascular system NEC R09.89
chest NEC R09.89
circulatory system NEC R09.89
cognitive functions R41.9
altered mental status R41.82
amnesia —*see* Amnesia
borderline intellectual functioning R41.83
coma —*see* Coma
disorientation R41.0
neurologic neglect syndrome R41.4
senile cognitive decline R41.81
specified symptom NEC R41.89
development NEC R62.50
digestive system NEC R19.8
emotional state NEC R45.89
emotional lability R45.86
food and fluid intake R63.8
general perceptions and sensations R44.9
specified NEC R44.8
musculoskeletal system R29.91
specified NEC R29.898
nervous system R29.90
specified NEC R29.818
pelvis NEC R19.8
respiratory system NEC R09.89
skin and integument R23.9
urinary system R39.9
menopausal N95.1
metabolism NEC R63.8
neurotic F48.8
of infancy R68.19
pelvis NEC, female R10.2
skin and integument NEC R23.9
subcutaneous tissue NEC R23.9

Sympus Q74.2

Syncephalus Q89.4

Synchondrosis
abnormal (congenital) Q78.8
ischiopubic M91.0

Synchysis (scintillans) (senile) (vitreous body) H43.89

Syncope (near) (pre-) R55
anginosa I20.8
bradycardia R00.1
cardiac R55
carotid sinus G90.01
due to spinal (lumbar) puncture G97.1
heart R55
heat T67.1
laryngeal R05
psychogenic F48.8
tussive R05
vasoconstriction R55
vasodepressor R55

Syncope *(continued)*
vasomotor R55
vasovagal R55

Syndactylism, syndactyly Q70.9
complex (with synostosis)
fingers Q70.0-
toes Q70.2-
simple (without synostosis)
fingers Q70.1-
toes Q70.3-

Syndrome —*see also* Disease
5q minus NOS D46.C
48, XXXX Q97.1
49, XXXXX Q97.1
abdominal
acute R10.0
muscle deficiency Q79.4
abnormal innervation H02.519
left H02.516
lower H02.515
upper H02.514
right H02.513
lower H02.512
upper H02.511
abstinence, neonatal P96.1
acid pulmonary aspiration, obstetric O74.0
acquired immunodeficiency —*see* Human, immunodeficiency virus (HIV) disease
acute abdominal R10.0
acute respiratory distress (adult) (child) J80
Adair-Dighton Q78.0
Adams-Stokes (-Morgagni) I45.9
adiposogenital E23.6
adrenal
hemorrhage (meningococcal) A39.1
meningococcic A39.1
adrenocortical —*see* Cushing's, syndrome
adrenogenital E25.9
congenital, associated with enzyme deficiency E25.0
afferent loop NEC K91.89
Alagille's Q44.7
alcohol withdrawal (without convulsions) —*see* Dependence, alcohol, with, withdrawal
Alder's D72.0
Aldrich (-Wiskott) D82.0
alien hand R41.4
Alport Q87.81
alveolar hypoventilation E66.2
alveolocapillary block J84.10
amnesic, amnestic (confabulatory) (due to) —*see* Disorder, amnesic
amyostatic (Wilson's disease) E83.01
androgen insensitivity E34.50
complete E34.51
partial E34.52
androgen resistance —*see also* Syndrome, androgen insensitivity E34.50
Angelman Q93.5
anginal —*see* Angina
ankyloglossia superior Q38.1
anterior
chest wall R07.89
cord G83.82
spinal artery G95.19
compression M47.019
cervical region M47.012
cervicothoracic region M47.013
lumbar region M47.016
occipito-atlanto-axial region M47.011
thoracic region M47.014
thoracolumbar region M47.015
tibial M76.81-

Syndrome *(continued)*
antibody deficiency D80.9
agammaglobulinemic D80.1
hereditary D80.0
congenital D80.0
hypogammaglobulinemic D80.1
hereditary D80.0
anticardiolipin (-antibody) D68.61
antiphospholipid (-antibody) D68.
aortic
arch M31.4
bifurcation I74.09
aortomesenteric duodenum occlusi K31.5
apical ballooning (transient left ventricular) I51.81
arcuate ligament I77.4
argentaffin, argintaffinoma E34.0
Arnold-Chiari —*see* Arnold-Chiari disease
Arrillaga-Ayerza I27.0
Asherman's N85.6
aspiration, of newborn —*see* Aspiration, by substance, with pneumonia
meconium P24.01
ataxia-telangiectasia G11.3
auriculotemporal G50.8
autoerythrocyte sensitization (Gardner-Diamond) D69.2
autoimmune polyglandular E31.0
autoimmune lymphoproliferative [ALPS] D89.82
autosomal —*see* Abnormal, autosomes
Avellis' G46.8
Ayerza (-Arrillaga) I27.0
Babinski-Nageotte G83.89
Bakwin-Krida Q79.8
bare lymphocyte D81.6
Barré-Guillain G61.0
Barré-Liéou M53.0
Barrett's —*see* Barrett's, esophagus
Barsony-Polgar K22.4
Barsony-Teschendorf K22.4
Barth E78.71
Bartter's E26.81
basal cell nevus Q87.89
Basedow's E05.00
with thyroid storm E05.01
basilar artery G45.0
Batten-Steinert G71.11
battered
baby or child —*see* Maltreatment, child, physical abuse
spouse —*see* Maltreatment, adult physical abuse
Beals Q87.40
Beau's I51.5
Beck's I65.8
Benedikt's G46.3
Béquez César (-Steinbrinck-Chédiak Higashi) E70.330
Bernhardt-Roth —*see* Meralgia paresthetica
Bernheim's I50.9
big spleen D73.1
bilateral polycystic ovarian E28.2
Bing-Horton's —*see* Horton's headache
Birt-Hogg-Dube syndrome Q87.89
Björck (-Thorsen) E34.0
black
lung J60
widow spider bite —*see* Toxicity, venom, spider, black widow
Blackfan-Diamond D61.01
blind loop K90.2
congenital Q43.8
postsurgical K91.2
blue sclera Q78.0
blue toe I75.02-

Syndrome *(continued)*
- Boder-Sedgewick G11.3
- Boerhaave's K22.3
- Borjeson Forssman Lehmann Q89.8
- Bouillaud's I01.9
- Bourneville (-Pringle) Q85.1
- Bouveret (-Hoffman) I47.9
- brachial plexus G54.0
- bradycardia-tachycardia I49.5
- brain (nonpsychotic) F09
  - with psychosis, psychotic reaction F09
  - acute or subacute —*see* Delirium
  - congenital —*see* Disability, intellectual
  - organic F09
    - post-traumatic (nonpsychotic) F07.81
      - psychotic F09
  - personality change F07.0
  - postcontusional F07.81
  - post-traumatic, nonpsychotic F07.81
  - psycho-organic F09
  - psychotic F06.8
- brain stem stroke G46.3
- Brandt's (acrodermatitis enteropathica) E83.2
- broad ligament laceration N83.8
- Brock's J98.11
- bronze baby P83.8
- Brown-Sequard G83.81
- bubbly lung P27.0
- Buchem's M85.2
- Budd-Chiari I82.0
- bulbar (progressive) G12.22
- Bürger-Grütz E78.3
- Burke's K86.8
- Burnett's (milk-alkali) E83.52
- burning feet E53.9
- Bywaters' T79.5
- Call-Fleming I67.841
- carbohydrate-deficient glycoprotein (CDGS) E77.8
- carcinogenic thrombophlebitis I82.1
- carcinoid E34.0
- cardiac asthma I50.1
- cardiacos negros I27.0
- cardiofaciocutaneous Q87.89
- cardiopulmonary-obesity E66.2
- cardiorenal —*see* Hypertension, cardiorenal
- cardiorespiratory distress (idiopathic), newborn P22.0
- cardiovascular renal —*see* Hypertension, cardiorenal
- carotid
  - artery (hemispheric) (internal) G45.1
  - body G90.01
  - sinus G90.01
- carpal tunnel G56.0-
- Cassidy (-Scholte) E34.0
- cat cry Q93.4
- cat eye Q92.8
- cauda equina G83.4
- causalgia —*see* Causalgia
- celiac K90.0
  - artery compression I77.4
  - axis I77.4
- central pain G89.0
- cerebellar
  - hereditary G11.9
  - stroke G46.4
- cerebellomedullary malformation —*see* Spina bifida
- cerebral
  - artery
    - anterior G46.1
    - middle G46.0
    - posterior G46.2
  - gigantism E22.0

Syndrome *(continued)*
- cervical (root) M53.1
  - disc —*see* Disorder, disc, cervical, with neuritis
  - fusion Q76.1
  - posterior, sympathicus M53.0
  - rib Q76.5
  - sympathetic paralysis G90.2
- cervicobrachial (diffuse) M53.1
- cervicocranial M53.0
- cervicodorsal outlet G54.2
- cervicothoracic outlet G54.0
- Céstan (-Raymond) I65.8
- Charcot's (angina cruris) (intermittent claudication) I73.9
- Charcot-Weiss-Baker G90.09
- CHARGE Q89.8
- Chédiak-Higashi (-Steinbrinck) E70.330
- chest wall R07.1
- Chiari's (hepatic vein thrombosis) I82.0
- Chilaiditi's Q43.3
- child maltreatment —*see* Maltreatment, child
- chondrocostal junction M94.0
- chondroectodermal dysplasia Q77.6
- chromosome 4 short arm deletion Q93.3
- chromosome 5 short arm deletion Q93.4
- chronic
  - pain G89.4
    - personality F68.8
- Clarke-Hadfield K86.8
- Clerambault's automatism G93.89
- Clouston's (hidrotic ectodermal dysplasia) Q82.4
- clumsiness, clumsy child F82
- cluster headache G44.009
  - intractable G44.001
  - not intractable G44.009
- Coffin-Lowry Q89.8
- cold injury (newborn) P80.0
- combined immunity deficiency D81.9
- compartment (deep) (posterior) (traumatic) T79.A0
  - abdomen T79.A3
  - lower extremity (hip, buttock, thigh, leg, foot, toes) T79.A2
  - nontraumatic
    - abdomen M79.A3
    - lower extremity (hip, buttock, thigh, leg, foot, toes) M79.A2-
    - specified site NEC M79.A9
    - upper extremity (shoulder, arm, forearm, wrist, hand, fingers) M79.A1-
  - postprocedural —*see* Syndrome, compartment, nontraumatic
  - specified site NEC T79.A9
  - upper extremity (shoulder, arm, forearm, wrist, hand, fingers) T79.A1
- complex regional pain —*see* Syndrome, pain, complex regional
- compression T79.5
  - anterior spinal —*see* Syndrome, anterior, spinal artery, compression
  - cauda equina G83.4
  - celiac artery I77.4
  - vertebral artery M47.029
    - occipito-atlanto-axial region M47.021
    - cervical region M47.022
- concussion F07.81
- congenital
  - affecting multiple systems NEC Q87.89
  - central alveolar hypoventilation G47.35

Syndrome *(continued)*
- congenital *(continued)*
  - facial diplegia Q87.0
  - muscular hypertrophy-cerebral Q87.89
  - oculo-auriculovertebral Q87.0
  - oculofacial diplegia (Moebius) Q87.0
  - rubella (manifest) P35.0
- congestion-fibrosis (pelvic), female N94.89
- congestive dysmenorrhea N94.6
- Conn's E26.01
- connective tissue M35.9
  - overlap NEC M35.1
- conus medullaris G95.81
- cord
  - anterior G83.82
  - posterior G83.83
- coronary
  - acute NEC I24.9
  - insufficiency or intermediate I20.0
  - slow flow I20.8
- Costen's (complex) M26.69
- costochondral junction M94.0
- costoclavicular G54.0
- costovertebral E22.0
- Cowden Q85.8
- craniovertebral M53.0
- Creutzfeldt-Jakob —*see* Creutzfeldt-Jakob disease or syndrome
- cri-du-chat Q93.4
- crib death R99
- cricopharyngeal —*see* Dysphagia
- croup J05.0
- CRPS I —*see* Syndrome, pain, complex regional I
- crush T79.5
- cubital tunnel —*see* Lesion, nerve, ulnar
- Curschmann (-Batten) (-Steinert) G71.11
- Cushing's E24.9
  - alcohol-induced E24.4
  - due to
    - alcohol
    - drugs E24.2
    - ectopic ACTH E24.3
    - overproduction of pituitary ACTH E24.0
  - drug-induced E24.2
  - overdose or wrong substance given or taken —*see* Table of Drugs and Chemicals, by drug, poisoning
  - pituitary-dependent E24.0
  - specified type NEC E24.8
- cryptophthalmos Q87.0
- cystic duct stump K91.5
- Dana-Putnam D51.0
- Danbolt (-Cross) (acrodermatitis enteropathica) E83.2
- Dandy-Walker Q03.1
  - with spina bifida Q07.01
- Danlos' Q79.8
- defibrination —*see also* Fibrinolysis
  - with
    - antepartum hemorrhage —*see* Hemorrhage, antepartum, with coagulation defect
    - intrapartum hemorrhage —*see* Hemorrhage, complicating, delivery
  - newborn P60
  - postpartum O72.3
- Degos' I77.89
- Déjérine-Roussy G89.0
- delayed sleep phase G47.21
- demyelinating G37.9
- dependence —*see* F10-F19 with fourth character .2

Syndrome *(continued)*
- depersonalization (-derealization) F48.1
- De Quervain E34.51
- de Toni-Fanconi (-Debré) E72.09
  - with cystinosis E72.04
- diabetes mellitus-hypertension-nephrosis —*see* Diabetes, nephrosis
- diabetes mellitus in newborn infant P70.2
- diabetes-nephrosis —*see* Diabetes, nephrosis
- diabetic amyotrophy —*see* Diabetes, amyotrophy
- Diamond-Blackfan D61.01
- Diamond-Gardener D69.2
- DIC (diffuse or disseminated intravascular coagulopathy) D65
- di George's D82.1
- Dighton's Q78.0
- disequilibrium E87.8
- Döhle body-panmyelopathic D72.0
- dorsolateral medullary G46.4
- double athetosis G80.3
- Down —*see also* Down syndrome Q90.9
- Dresbach's (elliptocytosis) D58.1
- Dressler's (postmyocardial infarction) I24.1
  - postcardiotomy I97.0
- drug withdrawal, infant of dependent mother P96.1
- dry eye H04.12-
- due to abnormality
  - chromosomal Q99.9
    - sex
      - female phenotype Q97.9
      - male phenotype Q98.9
    - specified NEC Q99.8
- dumping (postgastrectomy) K91.1
  - nonsurgical K31.89
- Dupré's (meningism) R29.1
- dysmetabolic X E88.81
- dyspraxia, developmental F82
- Eagle-Barrett Q79.4
- Eaton-Lambert —*see* Syndrome, Lambert-Eaton
- Ebstein's Q22.5
- ectopic ACTH E24.3
- eczema-thrombocytopenia D82.0
- Eddowes' Q78.0
- effort (psychogenic) F45.8
- Eisenmenger's I27.89
- Ehlers-Danlos Q79.6
- Ekman's Q78.0
- electric feet E53.8
- Ellis-van Creveld Q77.6
- empty nest Z60.0
- endocrine-hypertensive E27.0
- entrapment —*see* Neuropathy, entrapment
- eosinophilia-myalgia M35.8
- epileptic —*see also* Epilepsy, by type
  - absence G40.A09
    - intractable G40.A19
      - with status epilepticus G40.A11
      - without status epilepticus G40.A19
    - not intractable G40.A09
      - with status epilepticus G40.A01
      - without status epilepticus G40.A09
- Erdheim-Chester (ECD) E88.89
- Erdheim's E22.0
- erythrocyte fragmentation D59.4
- Evans D69.41
- exhaustion F48.8
- extrapyramidal G25.9
  - specified NEC G25.89

Syndrome *(continued)*
- Reifenstein E34.52
- renal glomerulohyalinosis-diabetic — *see* Diabetes, nephrosis
- Rendu-Osler-Weber I78.0
- residual ovary N99.83
- resistant ovary E28.39
- respiratory
  - distress
    - acute J80
      - adult J80
      - child J80
    - newborn (idiopathic) (type I) P22.0
      - type II P22.1
- restless legs G25.81
- retinoblastoma (familial) C69.2
- retroperitoneal fibrosis N13.5
- retroviral seroconversion (acute) Z21
- Reye's G93.7
- Richter —*see* Leukemia, chronic lymphocytic, B-cell type
- Ridley's I50.1
- right
  - heart, hypoplastic Q22.6
  - ventricular obstruction —*see* Failure, heart, congestive
- Romano-Ward (prolonged QT interval) I45.81
- rotator cuff, shoulder —*see also* Tear, rotator cuff M75.10-
- Rotes Quérol —*see* Hyperostosis, ankylosing
- Roth —*see* Meralgia paresthetica
- rubella (congenital) P35.0
- Ruvalcaba-Myhre-Smith E71.440
- Rytand-Lipsitch I44.2
- salt
  - depletion E87.1
    - due to heat NEC T67.8
      - causing heat exhaustion or prostration T67.4
  - low E87.1
- salt-losing N28.89
- Scaglietti-Dagnini E22.0
- scalenus anticus (anterior) G54.0
- scapulocostal —*see* Mononeuropathy, upper limb, specified site NEC
- scapuloperoneal G71.0
- schizophrenic, of childhood NEC F84.5
- Schnitzler D47.2
- Scholte's E34.0
- Schroeder's E27.0
- Schüller-Christian C96.5
- Schwachman's —*see* Syndrome, Shwachman's
- Schwartz (-Jampel) G71.13
- Schwartz-Bartter E22.2
- scimitar Q26.8
- sclerocystic ovary E28.2
- Seitelberger's G31.89
- septicemic adrenal hemorrhage A39.1
- seroconversion, retroviral (acute) Z21
- serous meningitis G93.2
- severe acute respiratory (SARS) J12.81
- shaken infant T74.4
- shock (traumatic) T79.4
  - kidney N17.0
    - following crush injury T79.5
  - toxic A48.3
- shock-lung J80
- Shone's - code to specific anomalies
- short
  - bowel K91.2
  - rib Q77.2
- shoulder-hand —*see* Algoneurodystrophy
- Shwachman's D70.4
- sicca —*see* Sicca syndrome

Syndrome *(continued)*
- sick
  - cell E87.1
  - sinus I49.5
- sick-euthyroid E07.81
- sideropenic D50.1
- Siemens' ectodermal dysplasia Q82.4
- Silfverskiöld's Q78.9
- Simons' E88.1
- sinus tarsi - M25.57-
- sinusitis-bronchiectasis-situs inversus Q89.3
- Sipple's E31.22
- sirenomelia Q87.2
- Slocumb's E27.0
- slow flow, coronary I20.8
- Sluder's G44.89
- Smith-Magenis Q93.88
- Sneddon-Wilkinson L13.1
- Sotos' E22.0
- South African cardiomyopathy I42.8
- spasmodic
  - upward movement, eyes H51.8
  - winking F95.8
- Spen's I45.9
- splenic
  - agenesis Q89.01
  - flexure K59.8
  - neutropenia D73.81
- Spurway's Q78.0
- staphylococcal scalded skin L00
- Stein-Leventhal E28.2
- Stein's E28.2
- Stevens-Johnson syndrome L51.1
  - toxic epidermal necrolysis overlap L51.3
- Stewart-Morel M85.2
- Stickler Q89.8
- stiff baby Q89.8
- stiff man G25.82
- Still-Felty —*see* Felty's syndrome
- Stokes (-Adams) I45.9
- stone heart I50.1
- straight back, congenital Q76.49
- subclavian steal G45.8
- subcoracoid-pectoralis minor G54.0
- subcostal nerve compression I77.89
- subphrenic interposition Q43.3
- superior
  - cerebellar artery I63.8
  - mesenteric artery K55.1
  - semi-circular canal dehiscence H83.8X-
  - vena cava I87.1
- supine hypotensive (maternal) —*see* Syndrome, hypotension, maternal
- suprarenal cortical E27.0
- supraspinatus —*see also* Tear, rotator cuff M75.10-
- Susac G93.49
- swallowed blood P78.2
- sweat retention L74.0
- Swyer Q99.1
- Symond's G93.2
- sympathetic
  - cervical paralysis G90.2
  - pelvic, female N94.89
- systemic inflammatory response (SIRS), of non-infectious origin (without organ dysfunction) R65.10
  - with acute organ dysfunction R65.11
- tachycardia-bradycardia I49.5
- takotsubo I51.81
- TAR (thrombocytopenia with absent radius) Q87.2
- tarsal tunnel G57.5-
- teething K00.7
- tegmental G93.89
- telangiectasic-pigmentation-cataract Q82.8

Syndrome *(continued)*
- temporal pyramidal apex —*see* Otitis, media, suppurative, acute
- temporomandibular joint-pain-dysfunction M26.62
- Terry's H44.2-
- testicular feminization —*see also* Syndrome, androgen insensitivity E34.51
- thalamic pain (hyperesthetic) G89.0
- thoracic outlet (compression) G54.0
- Thorson-Björck E34.0
- thrombocytopenia with absent radius (TAR) Q87.2
- thyroid-adrenocortical insufficiency E31.0
- tibial
  - anterior M76.81-
  - posterior M76.82-
- Tietze's M94.0
- time-zone (rapid) G47.25
- Toni-Fanconi E72.09
  - with cystinosis E72.04
- Touraine's Q79.8
- tourniquet —*see* Constriction, external, by site
- toxic shock A48.3
- transient left ventricular apical ballooning I51.81
- traumatic vasospastic T75.22
- Treacher Collins Q75.4
- triple X, female Q97.0
- trisomy Q92.9
  - 13 Q91.7
    - meiotic nondisjunction Q91.4
    - mitotic nondisjunction Q91.5
    - mosaicism Q91.5
    - translocation Q91.6
  - 18 Q91.3
    - meiotic nondisjunction Q91.0
    - mitotic nondisjunction Q91.1
    - mosaicism Q91.1
    - translocation Q91.2
  - 20 (q)(p) Q92.8
  - 21 Q90.9
    - meiotic nondisjunction Q90.0
    - mitotic nondisjunction Q90.1
    - mosaicism Q90.1
    - translocation Q90.2
  - 22 Q92.8
- tropical wet feet T69.0-
- Trousseau's I82.1
- tumor lysis (following antineoplastic chemotherapy) (spontaneous) NEC E88.3
- Twiddler's (due to)
  - automatic implantable defibrillator T82.198
  - cardiac pacemaker T82.198
- Unverricht (-Lundborg) —*see* Epilepsy, generalized, idiopathic
- upward gaze H51.8
- uremia, chronic —*see also* Disease, kidney, chronic N18.9
- urethral N34.3
- urethro-oculo-articular —*see* Reiter's disease
- urohepatic K76.7
- vago-hypoglossal G52.7
- vascular NEC in cerebrovascular disease G46.8
- vasoconstriction, reversible cerebrovascular I67.841
- vasomotor I73.9
- vasospastic (traumatic) T75.22
- vasovagal R55
- van Buchem's M85.2
- van der Hoeve's Q78.0
- VATER Q87.2
- velo-cardio-facial Q93.81
- vena cava (inferior) (superior) (obstruction) I87.1

Syndrome *(continued)*
- vertebral
  - artery G45.0
    - compression —*see* Syndrome, anterior, spinal artery, compression
  - steal G45.0
- vertebro-basilar artery G45.0
- vertebrogenic (pain) M54.89
- vertiginous —*see* Disorder, vestibular function
- Vinson-Plummer D50.1
- virus B34.9
- visceral larva migrans B83.0
- visual disorientation H53.8
- vitamin B6 deficiency E53.1
- vitreal corneal H59.01-
- vitreous (touch) H59.01-
- Vogt-Koyanagi H20.82-
- Volkmann's T79.6
- von Schroetter's I82.890
- von Willebrand (-Jürgen) D68.0
- Waldenström-Kjellberg D50.1
- Wallenberg's G46.3
- water retention E87.79
- Waterhouse (-Friderichsen) A39.1
- Weber-Gubler G46.3
- Weber-Leyden G46.3
- Weber's G46.3
- Wegener's M31.30
  - with
    - kidney involvement M31.31
    - lung involvement M31.30
      - with kidney involvement M31.31
- Weingarten's (tropical eosinophilia) J82
- Weiss-Baker G90.09
- Werdnig-Hoffman G12.0
- Wermer's E31.21
- Werner's E34.8
- Wernicke-Korsakoff (nonalcoholic) F04
  - alcoholic F10.26
- West's —*see* Epilepsy, spasms
- Westphal-Strümpell E83.01
- wet
  - feet (maceration) (tropical) T69.0-
  - lung, newborn P22.1
- whiplash S13.4
- whistling face Q87.0
- Wilkie's K55.1
- Wilkinson-Sneddon L13.1
- Willebrand (-Jürgens) D68.0
- Wilson's (hepatolenticular degeneration) E83.01
- Wiskott-Aldrich D82.0
- withdrawal —*see* Withdrawal, state
  - drug
    - infant of dependent mother P96.1
    - therapeutic use, newborn P96.2
- Woakes' (ethmoiditis) J33.1
- Wright's (hyperabduction) I77.89
- X I20.9
- XXXX Q97.1
- XXXXX Q97.1
- XXXXY Q98.1
- XXY Q98.0
- yellow nail L60.5
- Zahorsky's B08.5
- Zellweger syndrome E71.510
- Zellweger-like syndrome E71.541

Synechia (anterior) (iris) (posterior) (pupil) —*see also* Adhesions, iris
- intra-uterine (traumatic) N85.6

Synesthesia R20.8

Syngamiasis, syngamosis B83.3

Synodontia K00.2

Synorchidism, synorchism Q55.1

ostosis (congenital) Q78.8
stragalo-scaphoid Q74.2
adioulnar Q74.0
ovial sarcoma —*see* Neoplasm, connective tissue, malignant
ovioma (malignant) —*see also* Neoplasm, connective tissue, malignant
benign —*see* Neoplasm, connective tissue, benign
noviosarcoma —*see* Neoplasm, connective tissue, malignant
novitis —*see also* Tenosynovitis
crepitant
hand M70.0-
wrist M70.03-
gonococcal A54.49
gouty —*see* Gout, idiopathic
in (due to)
crystals M65.8-
gonorrhea A54.49
syphilis (late) A52.78
use, overuse, pressure —*see* Disorder, soft tissue, due to use
infective NEC —*see* Tenosynovitis, infective NEC
specified NEC —*see* Tenosynovitis, specified type NEC
syphilitic A52.78
congenital (early) A50.02
toxic —*see* Synovitis, transient
transient M67.3-
ankle M67.37-
elbow M67.32-
foot joint M67.37-
hand joint M67.34-
hip M67.35-
knee M67.36-
multiple site M67.39
pelvic region M67.35-
shoulder M67.31-
specified joint NEC M67.38
wrist M67.33-
traumatic, current —*see* Sprain
tuberculous —*see* Tuberculosis, synovitis
villonodular (pigmented) M12.2-
ankle M12.27-
elbow M12.22-
foot joint M12.27-
hand joint M12.24-
hip M12.25-
knee M12.26-
multiple site M12.29
pelvic region M12.25-
shoulder M12.21-
specified joint NEC M12.28
vertebrae M12.28
wrist M12.23-
yphilid A51.39
congenital A50.06
newborn A50.06
tubercular (late) A52.79
yphilis, syphilitic (acquired) A53.9
abdomen (late) A52.79
acoustic nerve A52.15
adenopathy (secondary) A51.49
adrenal (gland) (with cortical hypofunction) A52.79
age under 2 years NOS —*see also* Syphilis, congenital, early
acquired A51.9
alopecia (secondary) A51.32
anemia (late) A52.79 *[D63.8]*
aneurysm (aorta) (ruptured) A52.01
central nervous system A52.05
congenital A50.54 *[I79.0]*
anus (late) A52.74
primary A51.1
secondary A51.39

Syphilis, syphilitic *(continued)*
aorta (arch) (abdominal) (thoracic) A52.02
aneurysm A52.01
aortic (insufficiency) (regurgitation) (stenosis) A52.03
aneurysm A52.01
arachnoid (adhesive) (cerebral) (spinal) A52.13
asymptomatic —*see* Syphilis, latent
ataxia (locomotor) A52.11
atrophoderma maculatum A51.39
auricular fibrillation A52.06
bladder (late) A52.76
bone A52.77
secondary A51.46
brain A52.17
breast (late) A52.79
bronchus (late) A52.72
bubo (primary) A51.0
bulbar palsy A52.19
bursa (late) A52.78
cardiac decompensation A52.06
cardiovascular A52.00
central nervous system (late) (recurrent) (relapse) (tertiary) A52.3
with
ataxia A52.11
general paralysis A52.17
juvenile A50.45
paresis (general) A52.17
juvenile A50.45
tabes (dorsalis) A52.11
juvenile A50.45
taboparesis A52.17
juvenile A50.45
aneurysm A52.05
congenital A50.40
juvenile A50.40
remission in (sustained) A52.3
serology doubtful, negative, or positive A52.3
specified nature or site NEC A52.19
vascular A52.05
cerebral A52.17
meningovascular A52.13
nerves (multiple palsies) A52.15
sclerosis A52.17
thrombosis A52.05
cerebrospinal (tabetic type) A52.12
cerebrovascular A52.05
cervix (late) A52.76
chancre (multiple) A51.0
extragenital A51.2
Rollet's A51.0
Charcot's joint A52.16
chorioretinitis A51.43
congenital A50.01
late A52.71
prenatal A50.01
choroiditis —*see* Syphilitic chorioretinitis
choroidoretinitis —*see* Syphilitic chorioretinitis
ciliary body (secondary) A51.43
late A52.71
colon (late) A52.74
combined spinal sclerosis A52.11
condyloma (latum) A51.31
congenital A50.9
with
paresis (general) A50.45
tabes (dorsalis) A50.45
taboparesis A50.45
chorioretinitis, choroiditis A50.01 *[H32]*
early, or less than 2 years after birth NEC A50.2
with manifestations —*see* Syphilis, congenital, early, symptomatic

Syphilis, syphilitic *(continued)*
congenital *(continued)*
early, or less than 2 years after birth NEC *(continued)*
latent (without manifestations) A50.1
negative spinal fluid test A50.1
serology positive A50.1
symptomatic A50.09
cutaneous A50.06
mucocutaneous A50.07
oculopathy A50.01
osteochondropathy A50.02
pharyngitis A50.03
pneumonia A50.04
rhinitis A50.05
visceral A50.08
interstitial keratitis A50.31
juvenile neurosyphilis A50.45
late, or 2 years or more after birth NEC A50.7
chorioretinitis, choroiditis A50.32
interstitial keratitis A50.31
juvenile neurosyphilis A50.45
latent (without manifestations) A50.6
negative spinal fluid test A50.6
serology positive A50.6
symptomatic or with manifestations NEC A50.59
arthropathy A50.55
cardiovascular A50.54
Clutton's joints A50.51
Hutchinson's teeth A50.52
Hutchinson's triad A50.53
osteochondropathy A50.56
saddle nose A50.57
conjugal A53.9
tabes A52.11
conjunctiva (late) A52.71
contact Z20.2
cord bladder A52.19
cornea, late A52.71
coronary (artery) (sclerosis) A52.06
coryza, congenital A50.05
cranial nerve A52.15
multiple palsies A52.15
cutaneous —*see* Syphilis, skin
dacryocystitis (late) A52.71
degeneration, spinal cord A52.12
dementia paralytica A52.17
juvenilis A50.45
destruction of bone A52.77
dilatation, aorta A52.01
due to blood transfusion A53.9
dura mater A52.13
ear A52.79
inner A52.79
nerve (eighth) A52.15
neurorecurrence A52.15
early A51.9
cardiovascular A52.00
central nervous system A52.3
latent (without manifestations) (less than 2 years after infection) A51.5
negative spinal fluid test A51.5
serological relapse after treatment A51.5
serology positive A51.5
relapse (treated, untreated) A51.9
skin A51.39
symptomatic A51.9
extragenital chancre A51.2
primary, except extragenital chancre A51.0
secondary —*see also* Syphilis, secondary A51.39
relapse (treated, untreated) A51.49
ulcer A51.39

Syphilis, syphilitic *(continued)*
eighth nerve (neuritis) A52.15
endemic A65
endocarditis A52.03
aortic A52.03
pulmonary A52.03
epididymis (late) A52.76
epiglottis (late) A52.73
epiphysitis (congenital) (early) A50.02
episcleritis (late) A52.71
esophagus A52.79
eustachian tube A52.73
exposure to Z20.2
eye A52.71
eyelid (late) (with gumma) A52.71
fallopian tube (late) A52.76
fracture A52.77
gallbladder (late) A52.74
gastric (polyposis) (late) A52.74
general A53.9
paralysis A52.17
juvenile A50.45
genital (primary) A51.0
glaucoma A52.71
gumma NEC A52.79
cardiovascular system A52.00
central nervous system A52.3
congenital A50.59
heart (block) (decompensation) (disease) (failure) A52.06 *[I52]*
valve NEC A52.03
hemianesthesia A52.19
hemianopsia A52.71
hemiparesis A52.17
hemiplegia A52.17
hepatic artery A52.09
hepatis A52.74
hepatomegaly, congenital A50.08
hereditaria tarda —*see* Syphilis, congenital, late
hereditary —*see* Syphilis, congenital
Hutchinson's teeth A50.52
hyalitis A52.71
inactive —*see* Syphilis, latent
infantum —*see* Syphilis, congenital
inherited —*see* Syphilis, congenital
internal ear A52.79
intestine (late) A52.74
iris, iritis (secondary) A51.43
late A52.71
joint (late) A52.77
keratitis (congenital) (interstitial) (late) A50.31
kidney (late) A52.75
lacrimal passages (late) A52.71
larynx (late) A52.73
late A52.9
cardiovascular A52.00
central nervous system A52.3
kidney A52.75
latent or 2 years or more after infection (without manifestations) A52.8
negative spinal fluid test A52.8
serology positive A52.8
paresis A52.17
specified site NEC A52.79
symptomatic or with manifestations A52.79
tabes A52.11
latent A53.0
with signs or symptoms - code by site and stage under Syphilis
central nervous system A52.2
date of infection unspecified A53.0
early, or less than 2 years after infection A51.5
follow-up of latent syphilis A53.0
date of infection unspecified A53.0
late, or 2 years or more after infection A52.8

Syphilis, syphilitic *(continued)*
latent *(continued)*
late, or 2 years or more after infection A52.8
positive serology (only finding) A53.0
date of infection unspecified A53.0
early, or less than 2 years after infection A51.5
late, or 2 years or more after infection A52.8
lens (late) A52.71
leukoderma A51.39
late A52.79
lienitis A52.79
lip A51.39
chancre (primary) A51.2
late A52.79
Lissauer's paralysis A52.17
liver A52.74
locomotor ataxia A52.11
lung A52.72
lymph gland (early) (secondary) A51.49
late A52.79
lymphadenitis (secondary) A51.49
macular atrophy of skin A51.39
striated A52.79
mediastinum (late) A52.73
meninges (adhesive) (brain) (spinal cord) A52.13
meningitis A52.13
acute (secondary) A51.41
congenital A50.41
meningoencephalitis A52.14
meningovascular A52.13
congenital A50.41
mesarteritis A52.09
brain A52.04
middle ear A52.77
mitral stenosis A52.03
monoplegia A52.17
mouth (secondary) A51.39
late A52.79
mucocutaneous (secondary) A51.39
late A52.79
mucous
membrane (secondary) A51.39
late A52.79
patches A51.39
congenital A50.07
mulberry molars A50.52
muscle A52.78
myocardium A52.06
nasal sinus (late) A52.73
neonatorum —*see* Syphilis, congenital
nephrotic syndrome (secondary) A51.44
nerve palsy (any cranial nerve) A52.15
multiple A52.15
nervous system, central A52.3
neuritis A52.15
acoustic A52.15
neurorecidive of retina A52.19
neuroretinitis A52.19
newborn —*see* Syphilis, congenital
nodular superficial (late) A52.79
nonvenereal A65
nose (late) A52.73
saddle back deformity A50.57
occlusive arterial disease A52.09
oculopathy A52.71
ophthalmic (late) A52.71
optic nerve (atrophy) (neuritis) (papilla) A52.15
orbit (late) A52.71
organic A53.9
osseous (late) A52.77

Syphilis, syphilitic *(continued)*
osteochondritis (congenital) (early) A50.02 *[M90.80]*
osteoporosis A52.77
ovary (late) A52.76
oviduct (late) A52.76
palate (late) A52.79
pancreas (late) A52.74
paralysis A52.17
general A52.17
juvenile A50.45
paresis (general) A52.17
juvenile A50.45
paresthesia A52.19
Parkinson's disease or syndrome A52.19
paroxysmal tachycardia A52.06
pemphigus (congenital) A50.06
penis (chancre) A51.0
late A52.76
pericardium A52.06
perichondritis, larynx (late) A52.73
periosteum (late) A52.77
congenital (early) A50.02 *[M90.80]*
early (secondary) A51.46
peripheral nerve A52.79
petrous bone (late) A52.77
pharynx (late) A52.73
secondary A51.39
pituitary (gland) A52.79
pleura (late) A52.73
pneumonia, white A50.04
pontine lesion A52.17
portal vein A52.09
primary A51.0
anal A51.1
and secondary —*see* Syphilis, secondary
central nervous system A52.3
extragenital chancre NEC A51.2
fingers A51.2
genital A51.0
lip A51.2
specified site NEC A51.2
tonsils A51.2
prostate (late) A52.76
ptosis (eyelid) A52.71
pulmonary (late) A52.72
artery A52.09
pyelonephritis (late) A52.75
recently acquired, symptomatic A51.9
rectum (late) A52.74
respiratory tract (late) A52.73
retina, late A52.71
retrobulbar neuritis A52.15
salpingitis A52.76
sclera (late) A52.71
sclerosis
cerebral A52.17
coronary A52.06
multiple A52.11
scotoma (central) A52.71
scrotum (late) A52.76
secondary (and primary) A51.49
adenopathy A51.49
anus A51.39
bone A51.46
chorioretinitis, choroiditis A51.43
hepatitis A51.45
liver A51.45
lymphadenitis A51.49
meningitis (acute) A51.41
mouth A51.39
mucous membranes A51.39
periosteum, periostitis A51.46
pharynx A51.39
relapse (treated, untreated) A51.49
skin A51.39
specified form NEC A51.49
tonsil A51.39
ulcer A51.39

Syphilis, syphilitic *(continued)*
secondary *(continued)*
viscera NEC A51.49
vulva A51.39
seminal vesicle (late) A52.76
seronegative with signs or symptoms - code by site and stage under Syphilis
seropositive
with signs or symptoms - code by site and stage under Syphilis
follow-up of latent syphilis —*see* Syphilis, latent
only finding —*see* Syphilis, latent
seventh nerve (paralysis) A52.15
sinus, sinusitis (late) A52.73
skeletal system A52.77
skin (with ulceration) (early) (secondary) A51.39
late or tertiary A52.79
small intestine A52.74
spastic spinal paralysis A52.17
spermatic cord (late) A52.76
spinal (cord) A52.12
spleen A52.79
splenomegaly A52.79
spondylitis A52.77
staphyloma A52.71
stigmata (congenital) A50.59
stomach A52.74
synovium A52.78
tabes dorsalis (late) A52.11
juvenile A50.45
tabetic type A52.11
juvenile A50.45
taboparesis A52.17
juvenile A50.45
tachycardia A52.06
tendon (late) A52.78
tertiary A52.9
with symptoms NEC A52.79
cardiovascular A52.00
central nervous system A52.3
multiple NEC A52.79
specified site NEC A52.79
testis A52.76
thorax A52.73
throat A52.73
thymus (gland) (late) A52.79
thyroid (late) A52.79
tongue (late) A52.79
tonsil (lingual) (late) A52.73
primary A51.2
secondary A51.39
trachea (late) A52.73
tunica vaginalis (late) A52.76
ulcer (any site) (early) (secondary) A51.39
late A52.79
perforating A52.79
foot A52.11
urethra (late) A52.76
urogenital (late) A52.76
uterus (late) A52.76
uveal tract (secondary) A51.43
late A52.71
uveitis (secondary) A51.43
late A52.71
uvula (late) (perforated) A52.79
vagina A51.0
late A52.76
valvulitis NEC A52.03
vascular A52.00
brain (cerebral) A52.05
ventriculi A52.74
vesicae urinariae (late) A52.76
viscera (abdominal) (late) A52.74
secondary A51.49
vitreous (opacities) (late) A52.71
hemorrhage A52.71

Syphilis, syphilitic *(continued)*
vulva A51.0
late A52.76
secondary A51.39

Syphiloma A52.79
cardiovascular system A52.00
central nervous system A52.3
circulatory system A52.00
congenital A50.59

Syphilophobia F45.29

Syringadenoma —*see also* Neoplas
skin, benign
papillary —*see* Neoplasm, skin, benign

Syringobulbia G95.0

Syringocystadenoma —*see* Neoplas
skin, benign
papillary —*see* Neoplasm, skin, benign

Syringoma —*see also* Neoplasm, ski
benign
chondroid —*see* Neoplasm, skin, benign

Syringomyelia G95.0

Syringomyelitis —*see* Encephalitis

Syringomyelocele —*see* Spina bifida

Syringopontia G95.0

System, systemic —*see also* conditic
disease, combined —*see* Degeneration, combined
inflammatory response syndrome (SIRS) of non-infectious origin (without organ dysfunction) R65
with acute organ dysfunction R65.11
lupus erythematosus M32.9
inhibitor present D68.62

T

Tabacism, tabacosis, tabagism —*see also* Poisoning, tobacco
meaning dependence (without remission) F17.200
with
disorder F17.299
remission F17.211
specified disorder NEC F17.298
withdrawal F17.203

Tabardillo A75.9
flea-borne A75.2
louse-borne A75.0

Tabes, tabetic A52.10
with
central nervous system syphilis A52.10
Charcot's joint A52.16
cord bladder A52.19
crisis, viscera (any) A52.19
paralysis, general A52.17
paresis (general) A52.17
perforating ulcer (foot) A52.19
arthropathy (Charcot) A52.16
bladder A52.19
bone A52.11
cerebrospinal A52.12
congenital A50.45
conjugal A52.10
dorsalis A52.11
juvenile A50.49
juvenile A50.49
latent A52.19
mesenterica A18.39
paralysis, insane, general A52.17
spasmodic A52.17
syphilis (cerebrospinal) A52.12

Tenderness, abdominal *(continued)*
left upper quadrant R10.812
periumbilic R10.815
right lower quadrant R10.813
right upper quadrant R10.811
rebound R10.829
epigastric R10.826
generalized R10.827
left lower quadrant R10.824
left upper quadrant R10.822
periumbilic R10.825
right lower quadrant R10.823
right upper quadrant R10.821

Tendinitis, tendonitis —*see also* Enthesopathy
Achilles M76.6-
adhesive —*see* Tenosynovitis, specified type NEC
shoulder —*see* Capsulitis, adhesive
bicipital M75.2-
calcific M65.2-
ankle M65.27-
foot M65.27-
forearm M65.23-
hand M65.24-
lower leg M65.26-
multiple sites M65.29
pelvic region M65.25-
shoulder M75.3-
specified site NEC M65.28
thigh M65.25-
upper arm M65.22-
due to use, overuse, pressure —*see also* Disorder, soft tissue, due to use
specified NEC —*see* Disorder, soft tissue, due to use, specified NEC
gluteal M76.0-
patellar M76.5-
peroneal M76.7-
psoas M76.1-
tibial (posterior) M76.82-
anterior M76.81-
trochanteric —*see* Bursitis, hip, trochanteric

Tendon —*see* condition

Tendosynovitis —*see* Tenosynovitis

Tenesmus (rectal) R19.8
vesical R30.1

Tennis elbow —*see* Epicondylitis, lateral

Tenonitis —*see also* Tenosynovitis
eye (capsule) H05.04-

Tenontosynovitis —*see* Tenosynovitis

Tenontothecitis —*see* Tenosynovitis

Tenophyte —*see* Disorder, synovium, specified type NEC

Tenosynovitis —*see also* Synovitis M65.9
adhesive —*see* Tenosynovitis, specified type NEC
shoulder —*see* Capsulitis, adhesive
bicipital (calcifying) —*see* Tendinitis, bicipital
gonococcal A54.49
in (due to)
crystals M65.8-
gonorrhea A54.49
syphilis (late) A52.78
use, overuse, pressure —*see also* Disorder, soft tissue, due to use
specified NEC —*see* Disorder, soft tissue, due to use, specified NEC
infective NEC M65.1-
ankle M65.17-
foot M65.17-
forearm M65.13-

Tenosynovitis *(continued)*
infective *(continued)*
hand M65.14-
lower leg M65.16-
multiple sites M65.19
pelvic region M65.15-
shoulder region M65.11-
specified site NEC M65.18
thigh M65.15-
upper arm M65.12-
radial styloid M65.4
shoulder region M65.81-
adhesive —*see* Capsulitis, adhesive
specified type NEC M65.88
ankle M65.87-
foot M65.87-
forearm M65.83-
hand M65.84-
lower leg M65.86-
multiple sites M65.89
pelvic region M65.85-
shoulder region M65.81-
specified site NEC M65.88
thigh M65.85-
upper arm M65.82-
tuberculous —*see* Tuberculosis, tenosynovitis

Tenovaginitis —*see* Tenosynovitis

Tension
arterial, high —*see also* Hypertension
without diagnosis of hypertension R03.0
headache G44.209
intractable G44.201
not intractable G44.209
nervous R45.0
pneumothorax J93.0
premenstrual N94.3
state (mental) F48.9

Tentorium —*see* condition

Teratencephalus Q89.8

Teratism Q89.7

Teratoblastoma (malignant) —*see* Neoplasm, malignant, by site

Teratocarcinoma —*see also* Neoplasm, malignant, by site
liver C22.7

Teratoma (solid) —*see also* Neoplasm, uncertain behavior, by site
with embryonal carcinoma, mixed —*see* Neoplasm, malignant, by site
with malignant transformation —*see* Neoplasm, malignant, by site
adult (cystic) —*see* Neoplasm, benign, by site
benign —*see* Neoplasm, benign, by site
combined with choriocarcinoma —*see* Neoplasm, malignant, by site
cystic (adult) —*see* Neoplasm, benign, by site
differentiated —*see* Neoplasm, benign, by site
embryonal —*see also* Neoplasm, malignant, by site
liver C22.7
immature —*see* Neoplasm, malignant, by site
liver C22.7
adult, benign, cystic, differentiated type or mature D13.4
malignant —*see also* Neoplasm, malignant, by site
anaplastic —*see* Neoplasm, malignant, by site
intermediate —*see* Neoplasm, malignant, by site
specified site —*see* Neoplasm, malignant, by site
unspecified site C62.90

Teratoma *(continued)*
malignant —*see also* Neoplasm, malignant, by site *(continued)*
undifferentiated —*see* Neoplasm, malignant, by site
mature —*see* Neoplasm, uncertain behavior, by site
malignant —*see* Neoplasm, by site, malignant, by site
ovary D27.-
embryonal, immature or malignant C56-
solid —*see* Neoplasm, uncertain behavior, by site
testis C62.9-
adult, benign, cystic, differentiated type or mature D29.2-
scrotal C62.1-
undescended C62.0-

Termination
anomalous —*see also* Malposition, congenital
right pulmonary vein Q26.3
pregnancy, elective Z33.2

Ternidens diminutus infestation B81.8

Ternidensiasis B81.8

Terror (s) **night** (child) F51.4

Terrorism, victim of Z65.4

Terry's syndrome H44.2-

Tertiary —*see* condition

Test, tests, testing (for)
adequacy (for dialysis)
hemodialysis Z49.31
peritoneal Z49.32
blood pressure Z01.30
abnormal reading —*see* Blood, pressure
blood-alcohol Z04.8
positive —*see* Findings, abnormal, in blood
blood-drug Z04.8
positive —*see* Findings, abnormal, in blood
blood typing Z01.83
Rh typing Z01.83
cardiac pulse generator (battery) Z45.010
fertility Z31.41
genetic
disease carrier status for
procreative management
female Z31.430
male Z31.440
male partner of patient with recurrent pregnancy loss Z31.441
procreative management NEC
female Z31.438
male Z31.448
hearing Z01.10
with abnormal findings NEC Z01.118
HIV (human immunodeficiency virus)
nonconclusive (in infants) R75
positive Z21
seropositive Z21
immunity status Z01.84
intelligence NEC Z01.89
laboratory (as part of a general medical examination) Z00.00
with abnormal finding Z00.01
for medicolegal reason NEC Z04.8
male partner of patient with recurrent pregnancy loss Z31.441
Mantoux (for tuberculosis) Z11.1
abnormal result R76.11
pregnancy, positive first pregnancy —*see* Pregnancy, normal, first

Test, tests, testing *(continued)*
procreative Z31.49
fertility Z31.41
skin, diagnostic
allergy Z01.82
special screening examination —*see* Screening, by name of disease
Mantoux Z11.1
tuberculin Z11.1
specified NEC Z01.89
tuberculin Z11.1
abnormal result R76.11
vision Z01.00
with abnormal findings Z01.01
Wassermann Z11.3
positive —*see* Serology for syphilis, positive

Testicle, testicular, testis —*see also* condition
feminization syndrome —*see also* Syndrome, androgen insensitivity E34.51
migrans Q55.29

Tetanus, tetanic (cephalic) (convulsions) A35
with
abortion A34
ectopic or molar pregnancy O08
following ectopic or molar pregnancy O08.0
inoculation reaction (due to serum) —*see* Complications, vaccination
neonatorum A33
obstetrical A34
puerperal, postpartum, childbirth A

Tetany (due to) R29.0
alkalosis E87.3
associated with rickets E55.0
convulsions R29.0
hysterical F44.5
functional (hysterical) F44.5
hyperkinetic R29.0
hysterical F44.5
hyperpnea R06.4
hysterical F44.5
psychogenic F45.8
hyperventilation —*see also* Hyperventilation R06.4
hysterical F44.5
neonatal (without calcium or magnesium deficiency) P71.3
parathyroid (gland) E20.9
parathyroprival E89.2
post- (para)thyroidectomy E89.2
postoperative E89.2
pseudotetany R29.0
psychogenic (conversion reaction) F44.5

Tetralogy of Fallot Q21.3

Tetraplegia (chronic) —*see also* Quadriplegia G82.50

Thailand hemorrhagic fever A91

Thalassanemia —*see* Thalassemia

Thalassemia (anemia) (disease) D56.9
with other hemoglobinopathy D56.8
alpha (major) (severe) (triple gene defect) D56.0
minor D56.3
silent carrier D56.3
trait D56.3
beta (severe) D56.1
homozygous D56.1
major D56.1
minor D56.3
trait D56.3
delta-beta (homozygous) D56.2
minor D56.3
trait D56.3

alassemia *(continued)*
dominant D56.8
hemoglobin
C D56.8
E-beta D56.5
intermedia D56.1
major D56.1
minor D56.3
mixed D56.8
sickle-cell —*see* Disease, sickle-cell, thalassemia
specified type NEC D56.8
trait D56.3
variants D56.8

hanatophoric dwarfism or short stature Q77.1

haysen-Gee disease (nontropical sprue) K90.0

haysen's disease K90.0

hecoma D27-
luteinized D27-
malignant C56-

helarche, premature E30.8

helaziasis B83.8

helitis N61
puerperal, postpartum or gestational —*see* Infection, nipple

herapeutic —*see* condition

herapy
drug, long-term (current) (prophylactic)
agents affecting estrogen receptors and estrogen levels NEC Z79.818
anastrozole (Arimidex) Z79.811
antibiotics Z79.2
short-term use - omit code
anticoagulants Z79.01
anti-inflammatory Z79.1
antiplatelet Z79.02
antithrombotics Z79.02
aromatase inhibitors Z79.811
aspirin Z79.82
birth control pill or patch Z79.3
bisphosphonates Z79.83
contraceptive, oral Z79.3
drug, specified NEC Z79.899
estrogen receptor downregulators Z79.818
Evista Z79.810
exemestane (Aromasin) Z79.811
Fareston Z79.810
fulvestrant (Faslodex) Z79.818
gonadotropin-releasing hormone (GnRH) agonist Z79.818
goserelin acetate (Zoladex) Z79.818
hormone replacement (postmenopausal) Z79.890
insulin Z79.4
letrozole (Femara) Z79.811
leuprolide acetate (leuprorelin) (Lupron) Z79.818
megestrol acetate (Megace) Z79.818
methadone
for pain management Z79.891
maintenance therapy F11.20
Nolvadex Z79.810
opiate analgesic Z79.891
oral contraceptive Z79.3
raloxifene (Evista) Z79.810
selective estrogen receptor modulators (SERMs) Z79.810
short term - omit code
steroids
inhaled Z79.51
systemic Z79.52
tamoxifen (Nolvadex) Z79.810
toremifene (Fareston) Z79.810

Thermic —*see* condition

Thermography (abnormal) —*see also* Abnormal, diagnostic imaging R93.8
breast R92.8

Thermoplegia T67.0

Thesaurismosis, glycogen —*see* Disease, glycogen storage

Thiamin deficiency E51.9
specified NEC E51.8

Thiaminic deficiency with beriberi E51.11

Thibierge-Weissenbach syndrome — *see* Sclerosis, systemic

Thickening
bone —*see* Hypertrophy, bone
breast N64.59
endometrium R93.8
epidermal L85.9
specified NEC L85.8
hymen N89.6
larynx J38.7
nail L60.2
congenital Q84.5
periosteal —*see* Hypertrophy, bone
pleura J92.9
with asbestos J92.0
skin R23.4
subepiglottic J38.7
tongue K14.8
valve, heart —*see* Endocarditis

Thigh —*see* condition

Thinning vertebra —*see* Spondylopathy, specified NEC

Thirst, excessive R63.1
due to deprivation of water T73.1

Thomsen disease G71.12

Thoracic —*see also* condition
kidney Q63.2
outlet syndrome G54.0

Thoracogastroschisis (congenital) Q79.8

Thoracopagus Q89.4

Thorax —*see* condition

Thorn's syndrome N28.89

Thorson-Björck syndrome E34.0

Threadworm (infection) (infestation) B80

Threatened
abortion O20.0
with subsequent abortion O03.9
job loss, anxiety concerning Z56.2
labor (without delivery) O47.9
after 37 completed weeks of gestation O47.1
before 37 completed weeks of gestation O47.0-
loss of job, anxiety concerning Z56.2
miscarriage O20.0
unemployment, anxiety concerning Z56.2

Three-day fever A93.1

Threshers' lung J67.0

Thrix annulata (congenital) Q84.1

Throat —*see* condition

Thrombasthenia (Glanzmann) (hemorrhagic) (hereditary) D69.1

Thromboangiitis I73.1
obliterans (general) I73.1
cerebral I67.89
vessels
brain I67.89
spinal cord I67.89

Thromboarteritis —*see* Arteritis

Thromboasthenia (Glanzmann) (hemorrhagic) (hereditary) D69.1

Thrombocytasthenia (Glanzmann) D69.1

Thrombocythemia (essential) (hemorrhagic) (idiopathic) (primary) D47.3

Thrombocytopathy (dystrophic) (granulopenic) D69.1

Thrombocytopenia, thrombocytopenic D69.6
with absent radius (TAR) Q87.2
congenital D69.42
dilutional D69.59
due to
drugs D69.59
extracorporeal circulation of blood D69.59
(massive) blood transfusion D69.59
platelet alloimmunization D69.59
essential D69.3
heparin induced (HIT) D75.82
hereditary D69.42
idiopathic D69.3
neonatal, transitory P61.0
due to
exchange transfusion P61.0
idiopathic maternal thrombocytopenia P61.0
isoimmunization P61.0
primary NEC D69.49
idiopathic D69.3
puerperal, postpartum O72.3
secondary D69.59
transient neonatal P61.0

Thrombocytosis, essential D47.3
primary D47.3

Thromboembolism —*see* Embolism

Thrombopathy (Bernard-Soulier) D69.1
constitutional D68.0
Willebrand-Jurgens D68.0

Thrombopenia —*see* Thrombocytopenia

Thrombophilia D68.59
primary NEC D68.59
secondary NEC D68.69
specified NEC D68.69

Thrombophlebitis I80.9
antepartum O22.2-
deep O22.3-
superficial O22.2-
cavernous (venous) sinus G08
complicating pregnancy O22.5-
nonpyogenic I67.6
cerebral (sinus) (vein) G08
nonpyogenic I67.6
sequelae G09
due to implanted device —*see* Complications, by site and type, specified NEC
during or resulting from a procedure NEC T81.72
femoral vein (superficial) I80.1-
femoropopliteal vein I80.0-
hepatic (vein) I80.8
idiopathic, recurrent I82.1
iliofemoral I80.1-
intracranial venous sinus (any) G08
nonpyogenic I67.6
sequelae G09
intraspinal venous sinuses and veins G08
nonpyogenic G95.19
lateral (venous) sinus G08
nonpyogenic I67.6
leg I80.299
superficial I80.0-

Thrombophlebitis *(continued)*
longitudinal (venous) sinus G08
nonpyogenic I67.6
lower extremity I80.299
migrans, migrating I82.1
pelvic
with ectopic or molar pregnancy O08.0
following ectopic or molar pregnancy O08.0
puerperal O87.1
popliteal vein —*see* Phlebitis, leg, deep, popliteal
portal (vein) K75.1
postoperative T81.72
pregnancy —*see* Thrombophlebitis, antepartum
puerperal, postpartum, childbirth O87.0
deep O87.1
pelvic O87.1
septic O86.81
superficial O87.0
saphenous (greater) (lesser) I80.0-
sinus (intracranial) G08
nonpyogenic I67.6
specified site NEC I80.8
tibial vein I80.23-

Thrombosis, thrombotic (bland) (multiple) (progressive) (silent) (vessel) I82.90
anal K64.5
antepartum —*see* Thrombophlebitis, antepartum
aorta, aortic I74.10
abdominal I74.09
saddle I74.01
bifurcation I74.09
saddle I74.01
specified site NEC I74.19
terminal I74.09
thoracic I74.11
valve —*see* Endocarditis, aortic
apoplexy I63.3
artery, arteries (postinfectional) I74.9
auditory, internal —*see* Occlusion, artery, precerebral, specified NEC
basilar —*see* Occlusion, artery, basilar
carotid (common) (internal) —*see* Occlusion, artery, carotid
cerebellar (anterior inferior) (posterior inferior) (superior) — *see* Occlusion, artery, cerebellar
cerebral —*see* Occlusion, artery, cerebral
choroidal (anterior) —*see* Occlusion, artery, cerebral, specified NEC
communicating, posterior —*see* Occlusion, artery, cerebral, specified NEC
coronary —*see also* Infarct, myocardium
not resulting in infarction I24.0
hepatic I74.8
hypophyseal —*see* Occlusion, artery, cerebral, specified NEC
iliac I74.5
limb I74.4
lower I74.3
upper I74.2
meningeal, anterior or posterior — *see* Occlusion, artery, cerebral, specified NEC
mesenteric (with gangrene) K55.0
ophthalmic —*see* Occlusion, artery, retina
pontine —*see* Occlusion, artery, cerebral, specified NEC

Thrombosis, thrombotic *(continued)*
- artery, arteries *(continued)*
  - precerebral —*see* Occlusion, artery, precerebral
  - pulmonary (iatrogenic) —*see* Embolism, pulmonary
  - renal N28.0
  - retinal —*see* Occlusion, artery, retina
  - spinal, anterior or posterior G95.11
  - traumatic NEC T14.8
  - vertebral —*see* Occlusion, artery, vertebral
- atrium, auricular —*see also* Infarct, myocardium
  - following acute myocardial infarction (current complication) I23.6
  - not resulting in infarction I24.0
- basilar (artery) —*see* Occlusion, artery, basilar
- brain (artery) (stem) —*see also* Occlusion, artery, cerebral
  - due to syphilis A52.05
  - puerperal O99.43
  - sinus —*see* Thrombosis, intracranial venous sinus
- capillary I78.8
- cardiac —*see also* Infarct, myocardium
  - not resulting in infarction I24.0
  - valve —*see* Endocarditis
- carotid (artery) (common) (internal) —*see* Occlusion, artery, carotid
- cavernous (venous) sinus —*see* Thrombosis, intracranial venous sinus
- cerebellar artery (anterior inferior) (posterior inferior) (superior) I66.3
- cerebral (artery) —*see* Occlusion, artery, cerebral
- cerebrovenous sinus —*see also* Thrombosis, intracranial venous sinus
  - puerperium O87.3
- chronic I82.91
- coronary (artery) (vein) —*see also* Infarct, myocardium
  - not resulting in infarction I24.0
- corpus cavernosum N48.89
- cortical I66.9
- deep —*see* Embolism, vein, lower extremity
- due to device, implant or graft —*see also* Complications, by site and type, specified NEC T85.86
  - arterial graft NEC T82.868
  - breast (implant) T85.86
  - catheter NEC T85.86
    - dialysis (renal) T82.868
      - intraperitoneal T85.86
    - infusion NEC T82.868
      - spinal (epidural) (subdural) T85.86
    - urinary (indwelling) T83.86
  - electronic (electrode) (pulse generator) (stimulator)
    - bone T84.86
    - cardiac T82.867
    - nervous system (brain) (peripheral nerve) (spinal) T85.86
    - urinary T83.86
  - fixation, internal (orthopedic) NEC T84.86
  - gastrointestinal (bile duct) (esophagus) T85.86
  - genital NEC T83.86
  - heart T82.867
  - joint prosthesis T84.86
  - ocular (corneal graft) (orbital implant) NEC T85.86

Thrombosis, thrombotic *(continued)*
- due to device, implant or graft —*see also* Complications, by site and type, specified NEC *(continued)*
  - orthopedic NEC T84.86
  - specified NEC T85.86
  - urinary NEC T83.86
  - vascular NEC T82.868
  - ventricular intracranial shunt T85.86
- during the puerperium —*see* Thrombosis, puerperal
- endocardial —*see also* Infarct, myocardium
  - not resulting in infarction I24.0
- eye —*see* Occlusion, retina
- genital organ
  - female NEC N94.89
    - pregnancy —*see* Thrombophlebitis, antepartum
  - male N50.1
- gestational —*see* Phlebopathy, gestational
- heart (chamber) —*see also* Infarct, myocardium
  - not resulting in infarction I24.0
- hepatic (vein) I82.0
  - artery I74.8
- history (of) Z86.718
- intestine (with gangrene) K55.0
- intracardiac NEC (apical) (atrial) (auricular) (ventricular) (old) I51.3
- intracranial (arterial) I66.9
  - venous sinus (any) G08
    - nonpyogenic origin I67.6
    - puerperium O87.3
- intramural —*see also* Infarct, myocardium
  - not resulting in infarction I24.0
- intraspinal venous sinuses and veins G08
  - nonpyogenic G95.19
- kidney (artery) N28.0
- lateral (venous) sinus —*see* Thrombosis, intracranial venous sinus
- leg —*see* Thrombosis, vein, lower extremity
  - arterial I74.3
- liver (venous) I82.0
  - artery I74.8
  - portal vein I81
- longitudinal (venous) sinus —*see* Thrombosis, intracranial venous sinus
- lower limb —*see* Thrombosis, vein, lower extremity
- lung (iatrogenic) (postoperative) —*see* Embolism, pulmonary
- meninges (brain) (arterial) I66.8
- mesenteric (artery) (with gangrene) K55.0
  - vein (inferior) (superior) I81
- mitral I34.8
- mural —*see also* Infarct, myocardium
  - due to syphilis A52.06
  - not resulting in infarction I24.0
- omentum (with gangrene) K55.0
- ophthalmic —*see* Occlusion, retina
- pampiniform plexus (male) N50.1
- parietal —*see also* Infarct, myocardium
  - not resulting in infarction I24.0
- penis, superficial vein N48.81
- perianal venous K64.5
- peripheral arteries I74.4
  - upper I74.2
- personal history (of) Z86.718
- portal I81
  - due to syphilis A52.09
- precerebral artery —*see* Occlusion, artery, precerebral

Thrombosis, thrombotic *(continued)*
- puerperal, postpartum O87.0
  - brain (artery) O99.43
    - venous (sinus) O87.3
  - cardiac O99.43
  - cerebral (artery) O99.43
    - venous (sinus) O87.3
  - superficial O87.0
- pulmonary (artery) (iatrogenic) (postoperative) (vein) —*see* Embolism, pulmonary
- renal (artery) N28.0
  - vein I82.3
- resulting from presence of device, implant or graft —*see* Complications, by site and type, specified NEC
- retina, retinal —*see* Occlusion, retina
- scrotum N50.1
- seminal vesicle N50.1
- sigmoid (venous) sinus —*see* Thrombosis, intracranial venous sinus
- sinus, intracranial (any) —*see* Thrombosis, intracranial venous sinus
- specified site NEC I82.890
  - chronic I82.891
- spermatic cord N50.1
- spinal cord (arterial) G95.11
  - due to syphilis A52.09
  - pyogenic origin G06.1
- spleen, splenic D73.5
  - artery I74.8
- testis N50.1
- tumor —*see* Neoplasm, unspecified behavior, by site
- traumatic NEC T14.8
- tricuspid I07.8
- tunica vaginalis N50.1
- umbilical cord (vessels), complicating delivery O69.5
- vas deferens N50.1
- vein (acute) I82.90
  - antecubital I82.61-
    - chronic I82.71-
  - axillary I82.A1-
    - chronic I82.A2-
  - basilic I82.61-
    - chronic I82.71-
  - brachial I82.62-
    - chronic I82.72-
  - brachiocephalic (innominate) I82.290
    - chronic I82.291
  - cerebral, nonpyogenic I67.6
  - cephalic I82.61-
    - chronic I82.71-
  - chronic I82.91
  - deep (DVT) I82.40-
    - calf I82.4Z-
      - chronic I82.5Z-
    - lower leg I82.4Z-
      - chronic I82.5Z-
    - thigh I82.4Y-
      - chronic I82.5Y-
    - upper leg I82.4Y
      - chronic I82.5y--
  - femoral I82.41-
    - chronic I82.51-
  - iliac (iliofemoral) I82.42-
    - chronic I82.52-
  - innominate I82.290
    - chronic I82.291
  - internal jugular I82.C1-
    - chronic I82.C2-
  - lower extremity
    - deep I82.40-
      - chronic I82.50-
      - specified NEC I82.49-
        - chronic NEC I82.59-

Thrombosis, thrombotic *(continued)*
- vein *(continued)*
  - lower extremity *(continued)*
    - distal
      - deep I82.4Z-
    - proximal
      - deep I82.4Y-
        - chronic I82.5Y-
    - superficial I82.81-
  - perianal K64.5
  - popliteal I82.43-
    - chronic I82.53-
  - radial I82.62-
    - chronic I82.72-
  - renal I82.3
  - saphenous (greater) (lesser) I82.8
  - specified NEC I82.890
    - chronic NEC I82.891
  - subclavian I82.B1-
    - chronic I82.B2-
  - thoracic NEC I82.290
    - chronic I82.291
  - tibial I82.44-
    - chronic I82.54-
  - ulnar I82.62-
    - chronic I82.72-
  - upper extremity I82.60-
    - chronic I82.70-
    - deep I82.62-
      - chronic I82.72-
    - superficial I82.61-
      - chronic I82.71-
  - vena cava
    - inferior I82.220
      - chronic I82.221
    - superior I82.210
      - chronic I82.211
- venous, perianal K64.5
- ventricle —*see also* Infarct, myocardium
  - following acute myocardial infarction (current complication I23.6
  - not resulting in infarction I24.0

Thrombus —*see* Thrombosis

Thrush —*see also* Candidiasis
- oral B37.0
- newborn P37.5
- vaginal B37.3

Thumb —*see also* condition
- sucking (child problem) F98.8

Thymitis E32.8

Thymoma (benign) D15.0
- malignant C37

Thymus, thymic (gland) —*see* condition

Thyrocele —*see* Goiter

Thyroglossal —*see also* condition
- cyst Q89.2
- duct, persistent Q89.2

Thyroid (gland) (body) —*see also* condition
- hormone resistance E07.89
- lingual Q89.2
- nodule (cystic) (nontoxic) (single) E04.1

Thyroiditis E06.9
- acute (nonsuppurative) (pyogenic) (suppurative) E06.0
- autoimmune E06.3
- chronic (nonspecific) (sclerosing) E06.5
  - with thyrotoxicosis, transient E06.2
  - fibrous E06.5
  - lymphadenoid E06.3
  - lymphocytic E06.3
  - lymphoid E06.3

- **Thyroiditis** *(continued)*
  - de Quervain's E06.1
  - drug-induced E06.4
  - fibrous (chronic) E06.5
  - giant-cell (follicular) E06.1
  - granulomatous (de Quervain) (subacute) E06.1
  - Hashimoto's (struma lymphomatosa) E06.3
  - iatrogenic E06.4
  - ligneous E06.5
  - lymphocytic (chronic) E06.3
  - lymphoid E06.3
  - lymphomatous E06.3
  - nonsuppurative E06.1
  - postpartum, puerperal O90.5
  - pseudotuberculous E06.1
  - pyogenic E06.0
  - radiation E06.4
  - Riedel's E06.5
  - subacute (granulomatous) E06.1
  - suppurative E06.0
  - tuberculous A18.81
  - viral E06.1
  - woody E06.5
- **Thyrolingual duct, persistent** Q89.2
- **Thyromegaly** E01.0
- **Thyrotoxic**
  - crisis —*see* Thyrotoxicosis
  - heart disease or failure —*see also* Thyrotoxicosis E05.90 *[I43]*
    - with thyroid storm E05.91 *[I43]*
  - storm —*see* Thyrotoxicosis
- **Thyrotoxicosis** (recurrent) E05.90
  - with
    - goiter (diffuse) E05.00
      - with thyroid storm E05.01
      - adenomatous uninodular E05.10
        - with thyroid storm E05.11
      - multinodular E05.20
        - with thyroid storm E05.21
      - nodular E05.20
        - with thyroid storm E05.21
      - uninodular E05.10
        - with thyroid storm E05.11
    - infiltrative
      - dermopathy E05.00
        - with thyroid storm E05.01
      - ophthalmopathy E05.00
        - with thyroid storm E05.01
    - single thyroid nodule E05.10
      - with thyroid storm E05.11
    - thyroid storm E05.91
  - due to
    - ectopic thyroid nodule or tissue E05.30
      - with thyroid storm E05.31
    - ingestion of (excessive) thyroid material E05.40
      - with thyroid storm E05.41
    - overproduction of thyroid-stimulating hormone E05.80
      - with thyroid storm E05.81
    - specified cause NEC E05.80
      - with thyroid storm E05.81
  - factitia E05.40
    - with thyroid storm E05.41
  - heart E05.90 *[I43]*
    - with thyroid storm E05.91 *[I43]*
    - failure E05.90 *[I43]*
  - neonatal (transient) P72.1
  - transient with chronic thyroiditis E06.2
- **Tibia vara** —*see* Osteochondrosis, juvenile, tibia
- **Tic** (disorder) F95.9
  - breathing F95.8
  - child problem F95.0
  - compulsive F95.1
  - de la Tourette F95.2
- **Tic** *(continued)*
  - degenerative (generalized) (localized) G25.69
    - facial G25.69
  - disorder
    - chronic
      - motor F95.1
      - vocal F95.1
    - combined vocal and multiple motor F95.2
    - transient F95.0
  - douloureux G50.0
    - atypical G50.1
    - postherpetic, postzoster B02.22
  - drug-induced G25.61
  - eyelid F95.8
  - habit F95.9
    - chronic F95.1
    - transient of childhood F95.0
  - lid, transient of childhood F95.0
  - motor-verbal F95.2
  - occupational F48.8
  - orbicularis F95.8
    - transient of childhood F95.0
  - organic origin G25.69
  - postchoreic G25.69
  - psychogenic, compulsive F95.1
  - salaam R25.8
  - spasm (motor or vocal) F95.9
    - chronic F95.1
    - transient of childhood F95.0
  - specified NEC F95.8
- **Tick-borne** —*see* condition
- **Tietze's disease or syndrome** M94.0
- **Tight, tightness**
  - anus K62.89
  - chest R07.89
  - fascia (lata) M62.89
  - foreskin (congenital) N47.1
  - hymen, hymenal ring N89.6
  - introitus (acquired) (congenital) N89.6
  - rectal sphincter K62.89
  - tendon —*see* Short, tendon
  - urethral sphincter N35.9
- **Tilting vertebra** —*see* Dorsopathy, deforming, specified NEC
- **Timidity, child** F93.8
- **Tin-miner's lung** J63.5
- **Tinea** (intersecta) (tarsi) B35.9
  - amiantacea L44.8
  - asbestina B35.0
  - barbae B35.0
  - beard B35.0
  - black dot B35.0
  - blanca B36.2
  - capitis B35.0
  - corporis B35.4
  - cruris B35.6
  - flava B36.0
  - foot B35.3
  - furfuracea B36.0
  - imbricata (Tokelau) B35.5
  - kerion B35.0
  - manuum B35.2
  - microsporic —*see* Dermatophytosis
  - nigra B36.1
  - nodosa —*see* Piedra
  - pedis B35.3
  - scalp B35.0
  - specified site NEC B35.8
  - sycosis B35.0
  - tonsurans B35.0
  - trichophytic —*see* Dermatophytosis
  - unguium B35.1
  - versicolor B36.0
- **Tingling sensation** (skin) R20.2
- **Tinnitus** (audible) (aurium) (subjective) —*see* subcategory H93.1
- **Tipped tooth** (teeth) M26.33
- **Tipping**
  - pelvis M95.5
    - with disproportion (fetopelvic) O33.0
      - causing obstructed labor O65.0
  - tooth (teeth), fully erupted M26.33
- **Tiredness** R53.83
- **Tissue** —*see* condition
- **Tobacco** (nicotine)
  - dependence —*see* Dependence, drug, nicotine
  - harmful use Z72.0
  - heart —*see* Tobacco, toxic effect
  - maternal use, affecting newborn P04.2
  - toxic effect —*see* Table of Drugs and Chemicals, by substance, poisoning
    - chewing tobacco —*see* Table of Drugs and Chemicals, by substance, poisoning
    - cigarettes —*see* Table of Drugs and Chemicals, by substance, poisoning
  - use Z72.0
    - complicating
      - childbirth O99.334
      - pregnancy O99.33-
      - puerperium O99.335
    - counseling and surveillance Z71.6
  - withdrawal state —*see* Dependence, drug, nicotine
- **Tocopherol deficiency** E56.0
- **Todd's**
  - cirrhosis K74.3
  - paralysis (postepileptic) (transitory) G83.84
- **Toe** —*see* condition
- **Toilet, artificial opening** —*see* Attention to, artificial, opening
- **Tokelau** (ringworm) B35.5
- **Tollwut** —*see* Rabies
- **Tommaselli's disease** R31.9
  - correct substance properly administered —*see* Table of Drugs and Chemicals, by drug, adverse effect
  - overdose or wrong substance given or taken —*see* Table of Drugs and Chemicals, by drug, poisoning
- **Tongue** —*see also* condition
  - tie Q38.1
- **Tonic pupil** —*see* Anomaly, pupil, function, tonic pupil
- **Toni-Fanconi syndrome** (cystinosis) E72.09
  - with cystinosis E72.04
- **Tonsil** —*see* condition
- **Tonsillitis** (acute) (catarrhal) (croupous) (follicular) (gangrenous) (infective) (lacunar) (lingual) (malignant) (membranous) (parenchymatous) (phlegmonous) (pseudomembranous) (purulent) (septic) (subacute) (suppurative) (toxic) (ulcerative) (vesicular) (viral) J03.90
  - chronic J35.01
    - with adenoiditis J35.03
  - diphtheritic A36.0
  - hypertrophic J35.01
    - with adenoiditis J35.03
  - recurrent J03.91
  - specified organism NEC J03.80
    - recurrent J03.81
  - staphylococcal J03.80
    - recurrent J03.81
- **Tonsillitis** *(continued)*
  - streptococcal J03.00
    - recurrent J03.01
  - tuberculous A15.8
  - Vincent's A69.1
- **Tooth, teeth** —*see* condition
- **Toothache** K08.8
- **Topagnosis** R20.8
- **Tophi** —*see* Gout, chronic
- **TORCH infection** —*see* Infection, congenital
  - without active infection P00.2
- **Torn** —*see* Tear
- **Tornwaldt's cyst or disease** J39.2
- **Torsion**
  - accessory tube —*see* Torsion, fallopian tube
  - adnexa (female) —*see* Torsion, fallopian tube
  - aorta, acquired I77.1
  - appendix epididymis N44.04
  - appendix testis N44.03
  - bile duct (common) (hepatic) K83.8
    - congenital Q44.5
  - bowel, colon or intestine K56.2
  - cervix —*see* Malposition, uterus
  - cystic duct K82.8
  - dystonia —*see* Dystonia, torsion
  - epididymis (appendix) N44.04
  - fallopian tube N83.52
    - with ovary N83.53
  - gallbladder K82.8
    - congenital Q44.1
  - hydatid of Morgagni
    - female N83.52
    - male N44.03
  - kidney (pedicle) (leading to infarction) N28.0
  - Meckel's diverticulum (congenital) Q43.0
    - malignant —*see* Table of Neoplasms, small intestine, malignant
  - mesentery K56.2
  - omentum K56.2
  - organ or site, congenital NEC —*see* Anomaly, by site
  - ovary (pedicle) N83.51
    - with fallopian tube N83.53
    - congenital Q50.2
  - oviduct —*see* Torsion, fallopian tube
  - penis (acquired) N48.82
    - congenital Q55.63
  - spasm —*see* Dystonia, torsion
  - spermatic cord N44.02
    - extravaginal N44.01
    - intravaginal N44.02
  - spleen D73.5
  - testis, testicle N44.00
    - appendix N44.03
  - tibia —*see* Deformity, limb, specified type NEC, lower leg
  - uterus —*see* Malposition, uterus
- **Torticollis** (intermittent) (spastic) M43.6
  - congenital (sternomastoid) Q68.0
  - due to birth injury P15.8
  - hysterical F44.4
  - ocular R29.891
  - psychogenic F45.8
    - conversion reaction F44.4
  - rheumatic M43.6
  - rheumatoid M06.88
  - spasmodic G24.3
  - traumatic, current S13.4
- **Tortipelvis** G24.1
- **Tortuous**
  - artery I77.1

Tortuous *(continued)*
organ or site, congenital NEC —*see* Distortion
retinal vessel, congenital Q14.1
ureter N13.8
urethra N36.8
vein —*see* Varix

Torture, victim of Z65.4

Torula, torular (histolytica) (infection) —*see* Cryptococcosis

Torulosis —*see* Cryptococcosis

Torus (mandibularis) (palatinus) M27.0
fracture —*see* Fracture, by site, torus

Touraine's syndrome Q79.8

Tourette's syndrome F95.2

Tourniquet syndrome —*see* Constriction, external, by site

Tower skull Q75.0
with exophthalmos Q87.0

Toxemia R68.89
bacterial —*see* Sepsis
burn —*see* Burn
eclamptic (with pre-existing hypertension) —*see* Eclampsia
erysipelatous —*see* Erysipelas
fatigue R68.89
food —*see* Poisoning, food
gastrointestinal K52.1
intestinal K52.1
kidney —*see* Uremia
malarial —*see* Malaria
myocardial —*see* Myocarditis, toxic
of pregnancy —*see* Pre-eclampsia
pre-eclamptic —*see* Pre-eclampsia
small intestine K52.1
staphylococcal, due to food A05.0
stasis R68.89
uremic —*see* Uremia
urinary —*see* Uremia

Toxemica cerebropathia psychica (nonalcoholic) F04
alcoholic —*see* Alcohol, amnestic disorder

Toxic (poisoning) —*see also* condition T65.91
effect —*see* Table of Drugs and Chemicals, by substance, poisoning
shock syndrome A48.3
thyroid (gland) —*see* Thyrotoxicosis

Toxicemia —*see* Toxemia

Toxicity —*see* Table of Drugs and Chemicals, by substance, poisoning
fava bean D55.0
food, noxious —*see* Poisoning, food
from drug or nonmedicinal substance —*see* Table of Drugs and Chemicals, by drug

Toxicosis —*see also* Toxemia
capillary, hemorrhagic D69.0

Toxinfection, gastrointestinal K52.1

Toxocariasis B83.0

Toxoplasma, toxoplasmosis (acquired) B58.9
with
hepatitis B58.1
meningoencephalitis B58.2
ocular involvement B58.00
other organ involvement B58.89
pneumonia, pneumonitis B58.3
congenital (acute) (subacute) (chronic) P37.1
maternal, manifest toxoplasmosis in infant (acute) (subacute) (chronic) P37.1

tPA (rtPA) **administation in a different facility within the last 24 hours prior to admission to current facility** Z92.82

Trabeculation, bladder N32.89

Trachea —*see* condition

Tracheitis (catarrhal) (infantile) (membranous) (plastic) (septal) (suppurative) (viral) J04.10
with
bronchitis (15 years of age and above) J40
acute or subacute —*see* Bronchitis, acute
chronic J42
tuberculous NEC A15.5
under 15 years of age J20.9
laryngitis (acute) J04.2
chronic J37.1
tuberculous NEC A15.5
acute J04.10
with obstruction J04.11
chronic J42
with
bronchitis (chronic) J42
laryngitis (chronic) J37.1
diphtheritic (membranous) A36.89
due to external agent —*see* Inflammation, respiratory, upper, due to
syphilitic A52.73
tuberculous A15.5

Trachelitis (nonvenereal) —*see* Cervicitis

Tracheobronchial —*see* condition

Tracheobronchitis (15 years of age and above) —*see also* Bronchitis
due to
Bordetella bronchiseptica A37.80
with pneumonia A37.81
Francisella tularensis A21.8

Tracheobronchomegaly Q32.4
with bronchiectasis J47.9
with
exacerbation (acute) J47.1
lower respiratory infection J47.0
acquired J98.09
with bronchiectasis J47.9
with
exacerbation (acute) J47.1
lower respiratory infection J47.0

Tracheobronchopneumonitis —*see* Pneumonia, broncho-

Tracheocele (external) (internal) J39.8
congenital Q32.1

Tracheomalacia J39.8
congenital Q32.0

Tracheopharyngitis (acute) J06.9
chronic J42
due to external agent —*see* Inflammation, respiratory, upper, due to

Tracheostenosis J39.8

Tracheostomy
complication —*see* Complication, tracheostomy
status Z93.0
attention to Z43.0
malfunctioning J95.03

Trachoma, trachomatous A71.9
active (stage) A71.1
contraction of conjunctiva A71.1
dubium A71.0
initial (stage) A71.0
healed or sequelae B94.0
pannus A71.1
Türck's J37.0

Traction, vitreomacular H43.82-

Train sickness T75.3

Trait (s)
Hb-S D57.3
hemoglobin
abnormal NEC D58.2
with thalassemia D56.3
C —*see* Disease, hemoglobin C
S(Hb-S) D57.3
Lepore D56.3
personality, accentuated Z73.1
sickle-cell D57.3
with elliptocytosis or spherocytosis D57.3
type A personality Z73.1

Tramp Z59.0

Trance R41.89
hysterical F44.89

Transection
abdomen (partial) S38.3
aorta (incomplete) —*see also* Injury, aorta
complete —*see* Injury, aorta, laceration, major
carotid artery (incomplete) —*see also* Injury, blood vessel, carotid, laceration
complete —*see* Injury, blood vessel, carotid, laceration, major
celiac artery (incomplete) S35.211
branch (incomplete) S35.291
complete S35.292
complete S35.212
innominate
artery (incomplete) —*see also* Injury, blood vessel, thoracic, innominate, artery, laceration
complete —*see* Injury, blood vessel, thoracic, innominate, artery, laceration, major
vein (incomplete) —*see also* Injury, blood vessel, thoracic, innominate, vein, laceration
complete —*see* Injury, blood vessel, thoracic, innominate, vein, laceration, major
jugular vein (external) (incomplete) —*see also* Injury, blood vessel, jugular vein, laceration
complete —*see* Injury, blood vessel, jugular vein, laceration, major
internal (incomplete) —*see also* Injury, blood vessel, jugular vein, internal, laceration
complete —*see* Injury, blood vessel, jugular vein, internal, laceration, major
mesenteric artery (incomplete) —*see also* Injury, mesenteric, artery, laceration
complete —*see* Injury, mesenteric artery, laceration, major
pulmonary vessel (incomplete) —*see also* Injury, blood vessel, thoracic, pulmonary, laceration
complete —*see* Injury, blood vessel, thoracic, pulmonary, laceration, major
subclavian —*see* Transection, innominate
vena cava (incomplete) —*see also* Injury, vena cava
complete —*see* Injury, vena cava, laceration, major
vertebral artery (incomplete) —*see also* Injury, blood vessel, vertebral, laceration
complete —*see* Injury, blood vessel, vertebral, laceration, major

Transaminasemia R74.0

Transfusion
associated (red blood cell) hemochromatosis E83.111
blood
ABO incompatible —*see* Complication (s), transfusion, incompatibility reaction, ABO
minor blood group (Duffy) (E) (ell)) (Kidd) (Lewis) (M) (N) (S) T80.89
reaction or complication —*see* Complications, transfusion
fetomaternal (mother) —*see* Pregnancy, complicated by, placenta, transfusion syndrome
maternofetal (mother) —*see* Pregnancy, complicated by, placenta, transfusion syndrome
placental (syndrome) (mother) —*see* Pregnancy, complicated by, placenta, transfusion syndrome
reaction (adverse) —*see* Complications, transfusion
related acute lung injury (TRALI) J95.84
twin-to-twin —*see* Pregnancy, complicated by, placenta, transfusion syndrome, fetus to fe

Transient (meaning homeless) —*see also* condition Z59.0

Translocation
balanced autosomal Q95.9
in normal individual Q95.0
chromosomes NEC Q99.8
balanced and insertion in normal individual Q95.0
Down syndrome Q90.2
trisomy
13 Q91.6
18 Q91.2
21 Q90.2

Translucency, iris —*see* Degeneration, iris

Transmission of chemical substances through the placenta —*see* Absorption, chemical, through placenta

Transparency, lung, unilateral J43.0

Transplant (ed) (status) Z94.9
awaiting organ Z76.82
bone Z94.6
marrow Z94.81
candidate Z76.82
complication —*see* Complication, transplant
cornea Z94.7
heart Z94.1
and lung (s) Z94.3
valve Z95.2
prosthetic Z95.2
specified NEC Z95.4
xenogenic Z95.3
intestine Z94.82
kidney Z94.0
liver Z94.4
lung (s) Z94.2
and heart Z94.3
organ (failure) (infection) (rejection) Z94.9
removal status Z98.85
pancreas Z94.83
skin Z94.5
social Z60.3
specified organ or tissue NEC Z94.89
stem cells Z94.84
tissue Z94.9

Transplants, ovarian, endometrial N80.1

sposed —*see* Transposition

sposition (congenital) —*see also* alposition, congenital
dominal viscera Q89.3
rta (dextra) Q20.3
pendix Q43.8
lon Q43.8
rrected Q20.5
eat vessels (complete) (partial) Q20.3
art Q24.0
with complete transposition of viscera Q89.3
testine (large) (small) Q43.8
versed jejunal (for bypass) (status) Z98.0
rotum Q55.23
omach Q40.2
with general transposition of viscera Q89.3
oth, teeth, fully erupted M26.30
essels, great (complete) (partial) Q20.3
iscera (abdominal) (thoracic) Q89.3

nssexualism F64.1

nsverse —*see also* condition
rrest (deep), in labor O64.0
e (mother) O32.2
causing obstructed labor O64.8

nsvestism, transvestitism (dual-ole) F64.1
etishistic F65.1

pped placenta (with hemorrhage))72.0
vithout hemorrhage O73.0

uma, traumatism —*see also* Injury
coustic —*see* subcategory H83.3
irth —*see* Birth, injury
omplicating ectopic or molar pregnancy O08.6
luring delivery O71.9
ollowing ectopic or molar pregnancy O08.6
bstetric O71.9
specified NEC O71.89

umatic —*see also* condition
rain injury —*see* category S06

eacher Collins syndrome Q75.4

eitz's hernia —*see* Hernia, abdomen, specified site NEC

ematode infestation —*see* Infestation, fluke

ematodiasis —*see* Infestation, fluke

embling paralysis —*see* Parkinsonism

emor (s) R25.1
drug induced G25.1
essential (benign) G25.0
familial G25.0
hereditary G25.0
hysterical F44.4
intention G25.2
medication induced postural G25.1
mercurial —*see* subcategory T56.1
Parkinson's —*see* Parkinsonism
psychogenic (conversion reaction) F44.4
senilis R54
specified type NEC G25.2

ench
fever A79.0
foot —*see* Immersion, foot
mouth A69.1

eponema pallidum infection —*see* Syphilis

Treponematosis
due to
T. pallidum —*see* Syphilis
T. pertenue —*see* Yaws

Triad
Hutchinson's (congenital syphilis) A50.53
Kartagener's Q89.3
Saint's —*see* Hernia, diaphragm

Trichiasis (eyelid) H02.059
with entropion —*see* Entropion
left H02.056
lower H02.055
upper H02.054
right H02.053
lower H02.052
upper H02.051

Trichinella spiralis (infection) (infestation) B75

Trichinellosis, trichiniasis, trichinelliasis, trichinosis B75
with muscle disorder B75 *[M63.80]*
ankle B75 *[M63.87]*-
foot B75 *[M63.87]*-
forearm B75 *[M63.83]*-
hand B75 *[M63.84]*-
lower leg B75 *[M63.86]*-
multiple sites B75 *[M63.89]*
pelvic region B75 *[M63.85]*-
shoulder region B75 *[M63.81]*-
specified site NEC B75 *[M63.88]*
thigh B75 *[M63.85]*-
upper arm B75 *[M63.82]*-

Trichobezoar T18.9
intestine T18.3
stomach T18.2

Trichocephaliasis, trichocephalosis B79

Trichocephalus infestation B79

Trichoclasis L67.8

Trichoepithelioma —*see also* Neoplasm, skin, benign
malignant —*see* Neoplasm, skin, malignant

Trichofolliculoma —*see* Neoplasm, skin, benign

Tricholemmoma —*see* Neoplasm, skin, benign

Trichomoniasis A59.9
bladder A59.03
cervix A59.09
intestinal A07.8
prostate A59.02
seminal vesicles A59.09
specified site NEC A59.8
urethra A59.03
urogenitalis A59.00
vagina A59.01
vulva A59.01

Trichomycosis
axillaris A48.8
nodosa, nodularis B36.8

Trichonodosis L67.8

Trichophytid, trichophyton infection —*see* Dermatophytosis

Trichophytobezoar T18.9
intestine T18.3
stomach T18.2

Trichophytosis —*see* Dermatophytosis

Trichoptilosis L67.8

Trichorrhexis (nodosa) (invaginata) L67.0

Trichosis axillaris A48.8

Trichosporosis nodosa B36.2

Trichostasis spinulosa (congenital) Q84.1

Trichostrongyliasis, trichostrongylosis (small intestine) B81.2

Trichostrongylus infection B81.2

Trichotillomania F63.3

Trichromat, trichromatopsia, anomalous (congenital) H53.55

Trichuriasis B79

Trichuris trichiura (infection) (infestation) (any site) B79

Tricuspid (valve) —*see* condition

Trifid —*see also* Accessory
kidney (pelvis) Q63.8
tongue Q38.3

Trigeminal neuralgia —*see* Neuralgia, trigeminal

Trigeminy R00.8

Trigger finger (acquired) M65.30
congenital Q74.0
index finger M65.32-
little finger M65.35-
middle finger M65.33-
ring finger M65.34-
thumb M65.31-

Trigonitis (bladder) (chronic) (pseudomembranous) N30.30
with hematuria N30.31

Trigonocephaly Q75.0

Trilocular heart —*see* Cor triloculare

Trimethylaminuria E72.52

Tripartite placenta O43.19-

Triphalangeal thumb Q74.0

Triple —*see also* Accessory
kidneys Q63.0
uteri Q51.818
X, female Q97.0

Triplegia G83.89
congenital G80.8

Triplet (newborn) —*see also* Newborn, triplet
complicating pregnancy —*see* Pregnancy, triplet

Triplication —*see* Accessory

Triploidy Q92.7

Trismus R25.2
neonatorum A33
newborn A33

Trisomy (syndrome) Q92.9
autosomes Q92.9
chromosome specified NEC Q92.8
partial Q92.2
due to unbalanced translocation Q92.5
whole (nonsex chromosome)
meiotic nondisjunction Q92.0
mitotic nondisjunction Q92.1
mosaicism Q92.1
specified NEC Q92.8
due to
dicentrics —*see* Extra, marker chromosomes
extra rings —*see* Extra, marker chromosomes
isochromosomes —*see* Extra, marker chromosomes
specified NEC Q92.8
whole chromosome Q92.9
meiotic nondisjunction Q92.0
mitotic nondisjunction Q92.1
mosaicism Q92.1
partial Q92.9
specified NEC Q92.8

Trisomy *(continued)*
13 (partial) Q91.7
meiotic nondisjunction Q91.4
mitotic nondisjunction Q91.5
mosaicism Q91.5
translocation Q91.6
18 (partial) Q91.3
meiotic nondisjunction Q91.0
mitotic nondisjunction Q91.1
mosaicism Q91.1
translocation Q91.2
20 Q92.8
21 (partial) Q90.9
meiotic nondisjunction Q90.0
mitotic nondisjunction Q90.1
mosaicism Q90.1
translocation Q90.2
22 Q92.8

Tritanomaly, tritanopia H53.55

Trombiculosis, trombiculiasis, trombidiosis B88.0

Trophedema (congenital) (hereditary) Q82.0

Trophoblastic disease —*see also* Mole, hydatidiform O01.9

Tropholymphedema Q82.0

Trophoneurosis NEC G96.8
disseminated M34.9

Tropical —*see* condition

Trouble —*see also* Disease
heart —*see* Disease, heart
kidney —*see* Disease, renal
nervous R45.0
sinus —*see* Sinusitis

Trousseau's syndrome (thrombophlebitis migrans) I82.1

Truancy, childhood
from school Z72.810

Truncus
arteriosus (persistent) Q20.0
communis Q20.0

Trunk —*see* condition

Trypanosomiasis
African B56.9
by Trypanosoma brucei
gambiense B56.0
rhodesiense B56.1
American —*see* Chagas' disease
Brazilian —*see* Chagas' disease
by Trypanosoma
brucei gambiense B56.0
brucei rhodesiense B56.1
cruzi —*see* Chagas' disease
gambiensis, Gambian B56.0
rhodesiensis, Rhodesian B56.1
South American —*see* Chagas' disease
where
African trypanosomiasis is prevalent B56.9
Chagas' disease is prevalent B57.2

T-shaped incisors K00.2

Tsutsugamushi (disease) (fever) A75.3

Tube, tubal, tubular —*see* condition

Tubercle —*see also* Tuberculosis
brain, solitary A17.81
Darwin's Q17.8
Ghon, primary infection A15.7

Tuberculid, tuberculide (indurating, subcutaneous) (lichenoid) (miliary) (papulonecrotic) (primary) (skin) A18.4

Tuberculoma —*see also* Tuberculosis
brain A17.81
meninges (cerebral) (spinal) A17.1
spinal cord A17.81

Tuberculosis, tubercular, tuberculous (calcification) (calcified) (caseous) (chromogenic acid-fast bacilli) (degeneration) (fibrocaseous) (fistula) (interstitial) (isolated circumscribed lesions) (necrosis) (parenchymatous) (ulcerative) A15.9
- with pneumoconiosis (any condition in J60-J64) J65
- abdomen (lymph gland) A18.39
- abscess (respiratory) A15.9
  - bone A18.03
    - hip A18.02
    - knee A18.02
    - sacrum A18.01
    - specified site NEC A18.03
    - spinal A18.01
    - vertebra A18.01
  - brain A17.81
  - breast A18.89
  - Cowper's gland A18.15
  - dura (mater) (cerebral) (spinal) A17.81
  - epidural (cerebral) (spinal) A17.81
  - female pelvis A18.17
  - frontal sinus A15.8
  - genital organs NEC A18.10
  - genitourinary A18.10
  - gland (lymphatic) —*see* Tuberculosis, lymph gland
  - hip A18.02
  - intestine A18.32
  - ischiorectal A18.32
  - joint NEC A18.02
    - hip A18.02
    - knee A18.02
    - specified NEC A18.02
    - vertebral A18.01
  - kidney A18.11
  - knee A18.02
  - latent R76.11
  - lumbar (spine) A18.01
  - lung —*see* Tuberculosis, pulmonary
  - meninges (cerebral) (spinal) A17.0
  - muscle A18.09
  - perianal (fistula) A18.32
  - perinephritic A18.11
  - perirectal A18.32
  - rectum A18.32
  - retropharyngeal A15.8
  - sacrum A18.01
  - scrofulous A18.2
  - scrotum A18.15
  - skin (primary) A18.4
  - spinal cord A17.81
  - spine or vertebra (column) A18.01
  - subdiaphragmatic A18.31
  - testis A18.15
  - urinary A18.13
  - uterus A18.17
- accessory sinus —*see* Tuberculosis, sinus
- Addison's disease A18.7
- adenitis —*see* Tuberculosis, lymph gland
- adenoids A15.8
- adenopathy —*see* Tuberculosis, lymph gland
- adherent pericardium A18.84
- adnexa (uteri) A18.17
- adrenal (capsule) (gland) A18.7
- alimentary canal A18.32
- anemia A18.89
- ankle (joint) (bone) A18.02
- anus A18.32
- apex, apical —*see* Tuberculosis, pulmonary
- appendicitis, appendix A18.32
- arachnoid A17.0
- artery, arteritis A18.89
  - cerebral A18.89

Tuberculosis, tubercular, tuberculous *(continued)*
- arthritis (chronic) (synovial) A18.02
  - spine or vertebra (column) A18.01
- articular —*see* Tuberculosis, joint
- ascites A18.31
- asthma —*see* Tuberculosis, pulmonary
- axilla, axillary (gland) A18.2
- bladder A18.12
- bone A18.03
  - hip A18.02
  - knee A18.02
  - limb NEC A18.03
  - sacrum A18.01
  - spine or vertebral column A18.01
- bowel (miliary) A18.32
- brain A17.81
- breast A18.89
- broad ligament A18.17
- bronchi, bronchial, bronchus A15.5
  - ectasia, ectasis (bronchiectasis) —*see* Tuberculosis, pulmonary
  - fistula A15.5
    - primary (progressive) A15.7
  - gland or node A15.4
    - primary (progressive) A15.7
  - lymph gland or node A15.4
    - primary (progressive) A15.7
- bronchiectasis —*see* Tuberculosis, pulmonary
- bronchitis A15.5
- bronchopleural A15.6
- bronchopneumonia, bronchopneumonic —*see* Tuberculosis, pulmonary
- bronchorrhagia A15.5
- bronchotracheal A15.5
- bronze disease A18.7
- buccal cavity A18.83
- bulbourethral gland A18.15
- bursa A18.09
- cachexia A15.9
- cardiomyopathy A18.84
- caries —*see* Tuberculosis, bone
- cartilage A18.02
  - intervertebral A18.01
- catarrhal —*see* Tuberculosis, respiratory
- cecum A18.32
- cellulitis (primary) A18.4
- cerebellum A17.81
- cerebral, cerebrum A17.81
- cerebrospinal A17.81
  - meninges A17.0
- cervical (lymph gland or node) A18.2
- cervicitis, cervix (uteri) A18.16
- chest —*see* Tuberculosis, respiratory
- chorioretinitis A18.53
- choroid, choroiditis A18.53
- ciliary body A18.54
- colitis A18.32
- collier's J65
- colliquativa (primary) A18.4
- colon A18.32
- complex, primary A15.7
- congenital P37.0
- conjunctiva A18.59
- connective tissue (systemic) A18.89
- contact Z20.1
- cornea (ulcer) A18.52
- Cowper's gland A18.15
- coxae A18.02
- coxalgia A18.02
- cul-de-sac of Douglas A18.17
- curvature, spine A18.01
- cutis (colliquativa) (primary) A18.4
- cyst, ovary A18.18
- cystitis A18.12
- dactylitis A18.03
- diarrhea A18.32
- diffuse —*see* Tuberculosis, miliary

Tuberculosis, tubercular, tuberculous *(continued)*
- digestive tract A18.32
- disseminated —*see* Tuberculosis, miliary
- duodenum A18.32
- dura (mater) (cerebral) (spinal) A17.0
  - abscess (cerebral) (spinal) A17.81
- dysentery A18.32
- ear (inner) (middle) A18.6
  - bone A18.03
  - external (primary) A18.4
  - skin (primary) A18.4
- elbow A18.02
- emphysema —*see* Tuberculosis, pulmonary
- empyema A15.6
- encephalitis A17.82
- endarteritis A18.89
- endocarditis A18.84
  - aortic A18.84
  - mitral A18.84
  - pulmonary A18.84
  - tricuspid A18.84
- endocrine glands NEC A18.82
- endometrium A18.17
- enteric, enterica, enteritis A18.32
- enterocolitis A18.32
- epididymis, epididymitis A18.15
- epidural abscess (cerebral) (spinal) A17.81
- epiglottis A15.5
- episcleritis A18.51
- erythema (induratum) (nodosum) (primary) A18.4
- esophagus A18.83
- eustachian tube A18.6
- exposure (to) Z20.1
- exudative —*see* Tuberculosis, pulmonary
- eye A18.50
- eyelid (primary) (lupus) A18.4
- fallopian tube (acute) (chronic) A18.17
- fascia A18.09
- fauces A15.8
- female pelvic inflammatory disease A18.17
- finger A18.03
- first infection A15.7
- gallbladder A18.83
- ganglion A18.09
- gastritis A18.83
- gastrocolic fistula A18.32
- gastroenteritis A18.32
- gastrointestinal tract A18.32
- general, generalized —*see* Tuberculosis, miliary
- genital organs A18.10
- genitourinary A18.10
- genu A18.02
- glandula suprarenalis A18.7
- glandular, general A18.2
- glottis A15.5
- grinder's J65
- gum A18.83
- hand A18.03
- heart A18.84
- hematogenous —*see* Tuberculosis, miliary
- hemoptysis —*see* Tuberculosis, pulmonary
- hemorrhage NEC —*see* Tuberculosis, pulmonary
- hemothorax A15.6
- hepatitis A18.83
- hilar lymph nodes A15.4
  - primary (progressive) A15.7
- hip (joint) (disease) (bone) A18.02
- hydropneumothorax A15.6
- hydrothorax A15.6
- hypoadrenalism A18.7

Tuberculosis, tubercular, tubercul *(continued)*
- hypopharynx A15.8
- ileocecal (hyperplastic) A18.32
- ileocolitis A18.32
- ileum A18.32
- iliac spine (superior) A18.03
- immunological findings only A15.7
- indurativa (primary) A18.4
- infantile A15.7
- infection A15.9
  - without clinical manifestations A15.7
- infraclavicular gland A18.2
- inguinal gland A18.2
- inguinalis A18.2
- intestine (any part) A18.32
- iridocyclitis A18.54
- iris, iritis A18.54
- ischiorectal A18.32
- jaw A18.03
- jejunum A18.32
- joint A18.02
  - vertebral A18.01
- keratitis (interstitial) A18.52
- keratoconjunctivitis A18.52
- kidney A18.11
- knee (joint) A18.02
- kyphosis, kyphoscoliosis A18.01
- laryngitis A15.5
- larynx A15.5
- latent R76.11
- leptomeninges, leptomeningitis (cerebral) (spinal) A17.0
- lichenoides (primary) A18.4
- linguae A18.83
- lip A18.83
- liver A18.83
- lordosis A18.01
- lung —*see* Tuberculosis, pulmonar
- lupus vulgaris A18.4
- lymph gland or node (peripheral) A18.2
  - abdomen A18.39
  - bronchial A15.4
    - primary (progressive) A15.7
  - cervical A18.2
  - hilar A15.4
    - primary (progressive) A15.7
  - intrathoracic A15.4
    - primary (progressive) A15.7
  - mediastinal A15.4
    - primary (progressive) A15.7
  - mesenteric A18.39
  - retroperitoneal A18.39
  - tracheobronchial A15.4
    - primary (progressive) A15.7
- lymphadenitis —*see* Tuberculosis, lymph gland
- lymphangitis —*see* Tuberculosis, lymph gland
- lymphatic (gland) (vessel) —*see* Tuberculosis, lymph gland
- mammary gland A18.89
- marasmus A15.9
- mastoiditis A18.03
- mediastinal lymph gland or node A15.4
  - primary (progressive) A15.7
- mediastinitis A15.8
  - primary (progressive) A15.7
- mediastinum A15.8
  - primary (progressive) A15.7
- medulla A17.81
- melanosis, Addisonian A18.7
- meninges, meningitis (basilar) (cerebral) (cerebrospinal) (spinal) A17.0
- meningoencephalitis A17.82
- mesentery, mesenteric (gland or nod A18.39

Tumor *(continued)*
carcinoid *(continued)*
malignant C7A.00
appendix C7A.020
ascending colon C7A.022
bronchus (lung) C7A.090
cecum C7A.021
colon C7A.029
descending colon C7A.024
duodenum C7A.010
foregut NOS C7A.094
hindgut NOS C7A.096
ileum C7A.012
jejunum C7A.011
kidney C7A.093
large intestine C7A.029
lung (bronchus) C7A.090
midgut NOS C7A.095
rectum C7A.026
sigmoid colon C7A.025
small intestine C7A.019
specified NEC C7A.098
stomach C7A.092
thymus C7A.091
transverse colon C7A.023
mesentary metastasis C7B.04
secondary C7B.00
bone C7B.03
distant lymph nodes C7B.01
liver C7B.02
peritoneum C7B.04
specified NEC C7B.09
carotid body D44.6
malignant C75.4
cells —*see also* Neoplasm, unspecified behavior, by site
benign —*see* Neoplasm, benign, by site
malignant —*see* Neoplasm, malignant, by site
uncertain whether benign or malignant —*see* Neoplasm, uncertain behavior, by site
cervix, in pregnancy or childbirth —*see* Pregnancy, complicated by, tumor, cervix
chondromatous giant cell —*see* Neoplasm, bone, benign
chromaffin —*see also* Neoplasm, benign, by site
malignant —*see* Neoplasm, malignant, by site
Cock's peculiar L72.3
Codman's —*see* Neoplasm, bone, benign
dentigerous, mixed —*see* Cyst, calcifying odontogenic
dermoid —*see* Neoplasm, benign, by site
with malignant transformation C56-
desmoid (extra-abdominal) —*see also* Neoplasm, connective tissue, uncertain behavior
abdominal —*see* Neoplasm, connective tissue, uncertain behavior
embolus —*see* Neoplasm, secondary, by site
embryonal (mixed) —*see also* Neoplasm, uncertain behavior, by site
liver C22.7
endodermal sinus
specified site —*see* Neoplasm, malignant, by site
unspecified site
female C56.-
male C62.90
epithelial
benign —*see* Neoplasm, benign, by site

Tumor *(continued)*
epithelial *(continued)*
malignant —*see* Neoplasm, malignant, by site
Ewing's —*see* Neoplasm, bone, malignant, by site
fatty —*see* Lipoma
fibroid —*see* Leiomyoma
G cell
malignant
pancreas C25.4
specified site NEC —*see* Neoplasm, malignant, by site
unspecified site C25.4
specified site —*see* Neoplasm, uncertain behavior, by site
unspecified site D37.8
germ cell —*see also* Neoplasm, malignant, by site
mixed —*see* Neoplasm, malignant, by site
ghost cell, odontogenic —*see* Cyst, calcifying odontogenic
giant cell —*see also* Neoplasm, uncertain behavior, by site
bone D48.0
malignant —*see* Neoplasm, bone, malignant
chondromatous —*see* Neoplasm, bone, benign
malignant —*see* Neoplasm, malignant, by site
soft parts —*see* Neoplasm, connective tissue, uncertain behavior
malignant —*see* Neoplasm, connective tissue, malignant
glomus D18.00
intra-abdominal D18.03
intracranial D18.02
jugulare D44.7
malignant C75.5
skin D18.01
specified site NEC D18.09
gonadal stromal —*see* Neoplasm, uncertain behavior, by site
granular cell —*see also* Neoplasm, connective tissue, benign
malignant —*see* Neoplasm, connective tissue, malignant
granulosa cell D39.1-
juvenile D39.1-
malignant C56-
granulosa cell-theca cell D39.1-
malignant C56-
Grawitz's C64-
hemorrhoidal —*see* Hemorrhoids
hilar cell D27-
hilus cell D27-
Hurthle cell (benign) D34
malignant C73
hydatid —*see* Echinococcus
hypernephroid —*see also* Neoplasm, uncertain behavior, by site
interstitial cell —*see also* Neoplasm, uncertain behavior, by site
benign —*see* Neoplasm, benign, by site
malignant —*see* Neoplasm, malignant, by site
intravascular bronchial alveolar D38.1
islet cell —*see* Neoplasm, benign, by site
malignant —*see* Neoplasm, malignant, by site
pancreas C25.4
specified site NEC —*see* Neoplasm, malignant, by site
unspecified site C25.4
pancreas D13.7

Tumor *(continued)*
islet cell —*see* Neoplasm, benign, by site *(continued)*
specified site NEC —*see* Neoplasm, benign, by site
unspecified site D13.7
juxtaglomerular D41.0-
Klatskin's C24.0
Krukenberg's C79.6-
Leydig cell —*see* Neoplasm, uncertain behavior, by site
benign —*see* Neoplasm, benign, by site
specified site —*see* Neoplasm, benign, by site
unspecified site
female D27.9
male D29.20
malignant —*see* Neoplasm, malignant, by site
specified site —*see* Neoplasm, malignant, by site
unspecified site
female C56.9
male C62.90
specified site —*see* Neoplasm, uncertain behavior, by site
unspecified site
female D39.10
male D40.10
lipid cell, ovary D27-
lipoid cell, ovary D27-
malignant —*see also* Neoplasm, malignant, by site C80.1
fusiform cell (type) C80.1
giant cell (type) C80.1
localized, plasma cell —*see* Plasmacytoma, solitary
mixed NEC C80.1
small cell (type) C80.1
spindle cell (type) C80.1
unclassified C80.1
mast cell D47.0
malignant C96.2
melanotic, neuroectodermal —*see* Neoplasm, benign, by site
Merkel cell —*see* Carcinoma, Merkel cell
mesenchymal
malignant —*see* Neoplasm, connective tissue, malignant
mixed —*see* Neoplasm, connective tissue, uncertain behavior
mesodermal, mixed —*see also* Neoplasm, malignant, by site
liver C22.4
mesonephric —*see also* Neoplasm, uncertain behavior, by site
malignant —*see* Neoplasm, malignant, by site
metastatic
from specified site —*see* Neoplasm, malignant, by site
of specified site —*see* Neoplasm, malignant, by site
to specified site —*see* Neoplasm, secondary, by site
mixed NEC —*see also* Neoplasm, benign, by site
malignant —*see* Neoplasm, malignant, by site
mucinous of low malignant potential
specified site —*see* Neoplasm, malignant, by site
unspecified site C56.9
mucocarcinoid
specified site —*see* Neoplasm, malignant, by site
unspecified site C18.1
mucoepidermoid —*see* Neoplasm, uncertain behavior, by site

Tumor *(continued)*
Müllerian, mixed
specified site —*see* Neoplasm, malignant, by site
unspecified site C54.9
myoepithelial —*see* Neoplasm, benign, by site
neuroectodermal (peripheral) —*s* Neoplasm, malignant, by site
primitive
specified site —*see* Neoplas malignant, by site
unspecified site C71.9
neuroendocrine D3A.8
malignant poorly differentiated C7A.1
secondary NEC C7B.8
specified NEC C7A.8
neurogenic olfactory C30.0
nonencapsulated sclerosing C73
odontogenic (adenomatoid) (benign) (calcifying epithelial) (keratocystic) (squamous) —*se* Cyst, calcifying odontogenic
malignant C41.1
upper jaw (bone) C41.0
ovarian stromal D39.1-
ovary, in pregnancy —*see* Pregna complicated by
pacinian —*see* Neoplasm, skin, benign
Pancoast's —*see* Pancoast's syndrome
papillary —*see also* Papilloma
cystic D37.9
mucinous of low malignant potential C56-
specified site —*see* Neoplas malignant, by site
unspecified site C56.9
serous of low malignant potenti
specified site —*see* Neoplas malignant, by site
unspecified site C56.9
pelvic, in pregnancy or childbirth *see* Pregnancy, complicated by
phantom F45.8
phyllodes D48.6-
benign D24-
malignant —*see* Neoplasm, bre malignant
Pindborg —*see* Cyst, calcifying odontogenic
placental site trophoblastic D39.2
plasma cell (malignant) (localized *see* Plasmacytoma, solitary
polyvesicular vitelline
specified site —*see* Neoplasm, malignant, by site
unspecified site
female C56.9
male C62.90
Pott's puffy —*see* Osteomyelitis, specified NEC
Rathke's pouch D44.3
retinal anlage —*see* Neoplasm, benign, by site
salivary gland type, mixed —*see* Neoplasm, salivary gland, benig
malignant —*see* Neoplasm, salivary gland, malignant
Sampson's N80.1
Schmincke's —*see* Neoplasm, nasopharynx, malignant
sclerosing stromal D27-
sebaceous —*see* Cyst, sebaceous
secondary —*see* Neoplasm, secondary, by site
carcinoid C7B.00
bone C7B.03
distant lymph nodes C7B.01
liver C7B.02

Ulcer, ulcerated, ulcerating, ulceration, ulcerative *(continued)*
Curling's —*see* Ulcer, peptic, acute
Cushing's —*see* Ulcer, peptic, acute
cystic duct K82.8
cystitis (interstitial) —*see* Cystitis, interstitial
decubitus —*see* Ulcer, pressure, by site
dendritic, cornea (herpes simplex) B00.52
diabetes, diabetic —*see* Diabetes, ulcer
Dieulafoy's K25.0
due to
infection NEC —*see* Ulcer, skin
radiation NEC L59.8
trophic disturbance (any region) —*see* Ulcer, skin
X-ray L58.1
duodenum, duodenal (eroded) (peptic) K26.9
with
hemorrhage K26.4
and perforation K26.6
perforation K26.5
acute K26.3
with
hemorrhage K26.0
and perforation K26.2
perforation K26.1
chronic K26.7
with
hemorrhage K26.4
and perforation K26.6
perforation K26.5
dysenteric A09
elusive —*see* Cystitis, interstitial
endocarditis (acute) (chronic) (subacute) I28.8
epiglottis J38.7
esophagus (peptic) K22.10
with bleeding K22.11
due to
aspirin K22.10
with bleeding K22.11
gastrointestinal reflux disease K21.0
ingestion of chemical or medicament K22.10
with bleeding K22.11
fungal K22.10
with bleeding K22.11
infective K22.10
with bleeding K22.11
varicose —*see* Varix, esophagus
eyelid (region) H01.8
fauces J39.2
Fenwick (-Hunner) (solitary) —*see* Cystitis, interstitial
fistulous —*see* Ulcer, skin
foot (indolent) (trophic) —*see* Ulcer, lower limb
frambesial, initial A66.0
frenum (tongue) K14.0
gallbladder or duct K82.8
gangrenous —*see* Gangrene
gastric —*see* Ulcer, stomach
gastrocolic —*see* Ulcer, gastrojejunal
gastroduodenal —*see* Ulcer, peptic
gastroesophageal —*see* Ulcer, stomach
gastrointestinal —*see* Ulcer, gastrojejunal
gastrojejunal (peptic) K28.9
with
hemorrhage K28.4
and perforation K28.6
perforation K28.5

Ulcer, ulcerated, ulcerating, ulceration, ulcerative *(continued)*
gastrojejunal *(continued)*
acute K28.3
with
hemorrhage K28.0
and perforation K28.2
perforation K28.1
chronic K28.7
with
hemorrhage K28.4
and perforation K28.6
perforation K28.5
gastrojejunocolic —*see* Ulcer, gastrojejunal
gingiva K06.8
gingivitis K05.10
nonplaque induced K05.11
plaque induced K05.10
glottis J38.7
granuloma of pudenda A58
gum K06.8
gumma, due to yaws A66.4
heel —*see* Ulcer, lower limb
hemorrhoid —*see also* Hemorrhoids, by degree K64.8
Hunner's —*see* Cystitis, interstitial
hypopharynx J39.2
hypopyon (chronic) (subacute) —*see* Ulcer, cornea, with hypopyon
hypostaticum —*see* Ulcer, varicose
ileum —*see* Ulcer, intestine
intestine, intestinal K63.3
with perforation K63.1
amebic A06.1
duodenal —*see* Ulcer, duodenum
granulocytopenic (with hemorrhage) —*see* Neutropenia
marginal —*see* Ulcer, gastrojejunal
perforating K63.1
newborn P78.0
primary, small intestine K63.3
rectum K62.6
stercoraceous, stercoral K63.3
tuberculous A18.32
typhoid (fever) —*see* Typhoid
varicose I86.8
jejunum, jejunal —*see* Ulcer, gastrojejunal
keratitis —*see* Ulcer, cornea
knee —*see* Ulcer, lower limb
labium (majus) (minus) N76.6
laryngitis —*see* Laryngitis
larynx (aphthous) (contact) J38.7
diphtheritic A36.2
leg —*see* Ulcer, lower limb
lip K13.0
Lipschütz's N76.6
lower limb (atrophic) (chronic) (neurogenic) (perforating) (pyogenic) (trophic) (tropical) L97.909
with
bone necrosis L97.904
exposed fat layer L97.902
muscle necrosis L97.903
skin breakdown only L97.901
ankle L97.309
with
bone necrosis L97.304
exposed fat layer L97.302
muscle necrosis L97.303
skin breakdown only L97.301
left L97.329
with
bone necrosis L97.324
exposed fat layer L97.322
muscle necrosis L97.323
skin breakdown only L97.321
right L97.319

Ulcer, ulcerated, ulcerating, ulceration, ulcerative *(continued)*
lower limb *(continued)*
ankle *(continued)*
right *(continued)*
with
bone necrosis L97.314
exposed fat layer L97.312
muscle necrosis L97.313
skin breakdown only L97.311
calf L97.209
with
bone necrosis L97.204
exposed fat layer L97.202
muscle necrosis L97.203
skin breakdown only L97.201
left L97.229
with
bone necrosis L97.224
exposed fat layer L97.222
muscle necrosis L97.223
skin breakdown only L97.221
right L97.219
with
bone necrosis L97.214
exposed fat layer L97.212
muscle necrosis L97.213
skin breakdown only L97.211
decubitus —*see* Ulcer, pressure, by site
foot specified NEC L97.509
with
bone necrosis L97.504
exposed fat layer L97.502
muscle necrosis L97.503
skin breakdown only L97.501
left L97.529
with
bone necrosis L97.524
exposed fat layer L97.522
muscle necrosis L97.523
skin breakdown only L97.521
right L97.519
with
bone necrosis L97.514
exposed fat layer L97.512
muscle necrosis L97.513
skin breakdown only L97.511
heel L97.409
with
bone necrosis L97.404
exposed fat layer L97.402
muscle necrosis L97.403
skin breakdown only L97.401
left L97.429
with
bone necrosis L97.424
exposed fat layer L97.422
muscle necrosis L97.423
skin breakdown only L97.421
right L97.419
with
bone necrosis L97.414
exposed fat layer L97.412
muscle necrosis L97.413
skin breakdown only L97.411
left L97.929
with
bone necrosis L97.924
exposed fat layer L97.922
muscle necrosis L97.923
skin breakdown only L97.921

Ulcer, ulcerated, ulcerating, ulceration, ulcerative *(continued)*
lower limb *(continued)*
lower leg NOS L97.909
with
bone necrosis L97.904
exposed fat layer L97.902
muscle necrosis L97.903
skin breakdown only L97.901
left L97.929
with
bone necrosis L97.924
exposed fat layer L97.9
muscle necrosis L97.92
skin breakdown only L97.921
right L97.919
with
bone necrosis L97.914
exposed fat layer L97.9
muscle necrosis L97.91
skin breakdown only L97.911
specified site NEC L97.809
with
bone necrosis L97.804
exposed fat layer L97.8
muscle necrosis L97.80
skin breakdown only L97.801
left L97.829
with
bone necrosis L97.82
exposed fat layer L97.822
muscle necrosis L97.823
skin breakdown only L97.821
right L97.819
with
bone necrosis L97.81
exposed fat layer L97.812
muscle necrosis L97.813
skin breakdown only L97.811
midfoot L97.409
with
bone necrosis L97.404
exposed fat layer L97.402
muscle necrosis L97.403
skin breakdown only L97.401
left L97.429
with
bone necrosis L97.424
exposed fat layer L97.4
muscle necrosis L97.42
skin breakdown only L97.421
right L97.419
with
bone necrosis L97.414
exposed fat layer L97.4
muscle necrosis L97.41
skin breakdown only L97.411
right L97.919
with
bone necrosis L97.914
exposed fat layer L97.912
muscle necrosis L97.913
skin breakdown only L97.
thigh L97.109
with
bone necrosis L97.104
exposed fat layer L97.102
muscle necrosis L97.103
skin breakdown only L97.

r, ulcerated, ulcerating,
ceration, ulcerative *(continued)*
wer limb *(continued)*
thigh *(continued)*
left L97.129
with
bone necrosis L97.124
exposed fat layer L97.122
muscle necrosis L97.123
skin breakdown only L97.121
right L97.119
with
bone necrosis L97.114
exposed fat layer L97.112
muscle necrosis L97.113
skin breakdown only L97.111
toe L97.509
with
bone necrosis L97.504
exposed fat layer L97.502
muscle necrosis L97.503
skin breakdown only L97.501
left L97.529
with
bone necrosis L97.524
exposed fat layer L97.522
muscle necrosis L97.523
skin breakdown only L97.521
right L97.519
with
bone necrosis L97.514
exposed fat layer L97.512
muscle necrosis L97.513
skin breakdown only L97.511
leprous A30.1
syphilitic A52.19
varicose —*see* Varix, leg, with, ulcer
etic —*see* Ulcer, syphilitic
ng J98.4
tuberculous —*see* Tuberculosis, pulmonary
alignant —*see* Neoplasm, malignant, by site
arginal NEC —*see* Ulcer, gastrojejunal
eatus (urinarius) N34.2
eckel's diverticulum Q43.0
malignant —*see* Table of Neoplasms, small intestine, malignant
eleney's (chronic undermining) —*see* Ulcer, skin
ooren's (cornea) —*see* Ulcer, cornea, Mooren's
ycobacterial (skin) A31.1
asopharynx J39.2
eck, uterus N86
eurogenic NEC —*see* Ulcer, skin
ose, nasal (passage) (infective) (septum) J34.0
skin —*see* Ulcer, skin
spirochetal A69.8
varicose (bleeding) I86.8
ral mucosa (traumatic) K12.1
alate (soft) K12.1
enis (chronic) N48.5
eptic (site unspecified) K27.9
with
hemorrhage K27.4
and perforation K27.6
perforation K27.5
acute K27.3
with
hemorrhage K27.0
and perforation K27.2
perforation K27.1

Ulcer, ulcerated, ulcerating,
ulceration, ulcerative *(continued)*
peptic *(continued)*
chronic K27.7
with
hemorrhage K27.4
and perforation K27.6
perforation K27.5
esophagus K22.10
with bleeding K22.11
newborn P78.82
perforating K27.5
skin —*see* Ulcer, skin
peritonsillar J35.8
phagedenic (tropical) —*see* Ulcer, skin
pharynx J39.2
phlebitis —*see* Phlebitis
plaster —*see* Ulcer, pressure, by site
popliteal space —*see* Ulcer, lower limb
postpyloric —*see* Ulcer, duodenum
prepuce N47.7
prepyloric —*see* Ulcer, stomach
pressure (pressure area) L89.9-
ankle L89.5-
back L89.1-
buttock L89.3-
coccyx L89.15-
contiguous site of back, buttock, hip L89.4-
elbow L89.0-
face L89.81-
head L89.81-
heel L89.6-
hip L89.2-
sacral region (tailbone) L89.15-
specified site NEC L89.89-
stage 1 (healing) (pre-ulcer skin changes limited to persistent focal edema)
ankle L89.5-
back L89.1-
buttock L89.3-
coccyx L89.15-
contiguous site of back, buttock, hip L89.4-
elbow L89.0-
face L89.81-
head L89.81-
heel L89.6-
hip L89.2-
sacral region (tailbone) L89.15-
specified site NEC L89.89-
stage 2 (healing) (abrasion, blister, partial thickness skin loss involving epidermis and/or dermis)
ankle L89.5-
back L89.1-
buttock L89.3-
coccyx L89.15-
contiguous site of back, buttock, hip L89.4-
elbow L89.0-
face L89.81-
head L89.81-
heel L89.6-
hip L89.2-
sacral region (tailbone) L89.15-
specified site NEC L89.89-
stage 3 (healing) (full thickness skin loss involving damage or necrosis of subcutaneous tissue)
ankle L89.5-
back L89.1-
buttock L89.3-
coccyx L89.15-
contiguous site of back, buttock, hip L89.4-
elbow L89.0-
face L89.81-

Ulcer, ulcerated, ulcerating,
ulceration, ulcerative *(continued)*
pressure *(continued)*
stage 3 *(continued)*
head L89.81-
heel L89.6-
hip L89.2-
sacral region (tailbone) L89.15-
specified site NEC L89.89-
stage 4 (healing) (necrosis of soft tissues through to underlying muscle, tendon, or bone)
ankle L89.5-
back L89.1-
buttock L89.3-
coccyx L89.15-
contiguous site of back, buttock, hip L89.4-
elbow L89.0-
face L89.81-
head L89.81-
heel L89.6-
hip L89.2-
sacral region (tailbone) L89.15-
specified site NEC L89.89-
unspecified stage
ankle L89.5-
back L89.1-
buttock L89.3-
coccyx L89.15-
contiguous site of back, buttock, hip L89.4-
elbow L89.0-
face L89.81-
head L89.81-
heel L89.6-
hip L89.2-
sacral region (tailbone) L89.15-
specified site NEC L89.89-
unstageable
ankle L89.5-
back L89.1-
buttock L89.3-
coccyx L89.15-
contiguous site of back, buttock, hip L89.4-
elbow L89.0-
face L89.81-
head L89.81-
heel L89.6-
hip L89.2-
sacral region (tailbone) L89.15-
specified site NEC L89.89-
primary of intestine K63.3
with perforation K63.1
prostate N41.9
pyloric —*see* Ulcer, stomach
rectosigmoid K63.3
with perforation K63.1
rectum (sphincter) (solitary) K62.6
stercoraceous, stercoral K62.6
retina —*see* Inflammation, chorioretinal
rodent —*see also* Neoplasm, skin, malignant
sclera —*see* Scleritis
scrofulous (tuberculous) A18.2
scrotum N50.8
tuberculous A18.15
varicose I86.1
seminal vesicle N50.8
sigmoid —*see* Ulcer, intestine
skin (atrophic) (chronic) (neurogenic) (non-healing) (perforating) (pyogenic) (trophic) (tropical) L98.499
with gangrene —*see* Gangrene
amebic A06.7
back —*see* Ulcer, back
buttock —*see* Ulcer, buttock
decubitus —*see* Ulcer, pressure
lower limb —*see* Ulcer, lower limb

Ulcer, ulcerated, ulcerating,
ulceration, ulcerative *(continued)*
skin *(continued)*
mycobacterial A31.1
specified site NEC L98.499
with
bone necrosis L98.494
exposed fat layer L98.492
muscle necrosis L98.493
skin breakdown only L98.491
tuberculous (primary) A18.4
varicose —*see* Ulcer, varicose
sloughing —*see* Ulcer, skin
solitary, anus or rectum (sphincter) K62.6
sore throat J02.9
streptococcal J02.0
spermatic cord N50.8
spine (tuberculous) A18.01
stasis (venous) —*see* Varix, leg, with, ulcer
without varicose veins I87.2
stercoraceous, stercoral K63.3
with perforation K63.1
anus or rectum K62.6
stoma, stomal —*see* Ulcer, gastrojejunal
stomach (eroded) (peptic) (round) K25.9
with
hemorrhage K25.4
and perforation K25.6
perforation K25.5
acute K25.3
with
hemorrhage K25.0
and perforation K25.2
perforation K25.1
chronic K25.7
with
hemorrhage K25.4
and perforation K25.6
perforation K25.5
stomal —*see* Ulcer, gastrojejunal
stomatitis K12.1
stress —*see* Ulcer, peptic
strumous (tuberculous) A18.2
submucosal, bladder —*see* Cystitis, interstitial
syphilitic (any site) (early) (secondary) A51.39
late A52.79
perforating A52.79
foot A52.11
testis N50.8
thigh —*see* Ulcer, lower limb
throat J39.2
diphtheritic A36.0
toe —*see* Ulcer, lower limb
tongue (traumatic) K14.0
tonsil J35.8
diphtheritic A36.0
trachea J39.8
trophic —*see* Ulcer, skin
tropical —*see* Ulcer, skin
tuberculous —*see* Tuberculosis, ulcer
tunica vaginalis N50.8
turbinate J34.89
typhoid (perforating) —*see* Typhoid
unspecified site —*see* Ulcer, skin
urethra (meatus) —*see* Urethritis
uterus N85.8
cervix N86
with cervicitis N72
neck N86
with cervicitis N72
vagina N76.5
in Behçet's disease M35.2 *[N77.0]*
pessary N89.8
valve, heart I33.0

V

Vaginitis *(continued)*
puerperal (postpartum) O86.13
senile (atrophic) N95.2
subacute or chronic N76.1
syphilitic (early) A51.0
late A52.76
trichomonal A59.01
tuberculous A18.18

Vaginosis —*see* Vaginitis

Vagotonia G52.2

Vagrancy Z59.0

VAIN —*see* Neoplasia, intraepithelial, vagina

Vallecula —*see* condition

Valley fever B38.0

Valsuani's disease —*see* Anemia, obstetric

Valve, valvular (formation) —*see also* condition
cerebral ventricle (communicating) in situ Z98.2
cervix, internal os Q51.828
congenital NEC —*see* Atresia, by site
ureter (pelvic junction) (vesical orifice) Q62.39
urethra (congenital) (posterior) Q64.2

Valvulitis (chronic) —*see* Endocarditis

Valvulopathy —*see* Endocarditis

Van Bogaert's leukoencephalopathy (sclerosing) (subacute) A81.1

Van Bogaert-Scherer-Epstein disease or syndrome E75.5

Van Buchem's syndrome M85.2

Van Creveld-von Gierke disease E74.01

Van der Hoeve (-de Kleyn) **syndrome** Q78.0

Van der Woude's syndrome Q38.0

Van Neck's disease or osteochondrosis M91.0

Vanishing lung J44.9

Vapor asphyxia or suffocation T59.9
specified agent —*see* Table of Drugs and Chemicals

Variance, lethal ball, prosthetic heart valve T82.09

Variants, thalassemic D56.8

Variations in hair color L67.1

Varicella B01.9
with
complications NEC B01.89
encephalitis B01.11
encephalomyelitis B01.11
meningitis B01.0
myelitis B01.12
pneumonia B01.2
congenital P35.8

Varices —*see* Varix

Varicocele (scrotum) (thrombosed) I86.1
ovary I86.2
perineum I86.3
spermatic cord (ulcerated) I86.1

Varicose
aneurysm (ruptured) I77.0
dermatitis —*see* Varix, leg, with, inflammation
eczema —*see* Varix, leg, with, inflammation
phlebitis —*see* Varix, with, inflammation
tumor —*see* Varix

Varicose *(continued)*
ulcer (lower limb, any part) —*see also* Varix, leg, with, ulcer
anus —*see also* Hemorrhoids K64.8
esophagus —*see* Varix, esophagus
inflamed or infected —*see* Varix, leg, with ulcer, with inflammation
nasal septum I86.8
perineum I86.3
scrotum I86.1
specified site NEC I86.8
vein —*see* Varix
vessel —*see* Varix, leg

Varicosis, varicosities, varicosity —*see* Varix

Variola (major) (minor) B03

Varioloid B03

Varix (lower limb) (ruptured) I83.90
with
edema I83.899
inflammation I83.10
with ulcer (venous) I83.209
pain I83.819
specified complication NEC I83.899
stasis dermatitis I83.10
with ulcer (venous) I83.209
swelling I83.899
ulcer I83.009
with inflammation I83.209
aneurysmal I77.0
asymptomatic I83.9-
bladder I86.2
broad ligament I86.2
complicating
childbirth (lower extremity) O87.4
anus or rectum O87.2
genital (vagina, vulva or perineum) O87.8
pregnancy (lower extremity) O22.0-
anus or rectum O22.4-
genital (vagina, vulva or perineum) O22.1-
puerperium (lower extremity) O87.4
anus or rectum O87.2
genital (vagina, vulva, perineum) O87.8
congenital (any site) Q27.8
esophagus (idiopathic) (primary) (ulcerated) I85.00
bleeding I85.01
congenital Q27.8
in (due to)
alcoholic liver disease I85.10
bleeding I85.11
cirrhosis of liver I85.10
bleeding I85.11
portal hypertension I85.10
bleeding I85.11
schistosomiasis I85.10
bleeding I85.11
toxic liver disease I85.10
bleeding I85.11
secondary I85.10
bleeding I85.11
gastric I86.4
inflamed or infected I83.10
ulcerated I83.209
labia (majora) I86.3
leg (asymptomatic) I83.90
with
edema I83.899
inflammation I83.10
with ulcer —*see* Varix, leg, with, ulcer, with inflammation by site

Varix *(continued)*
leg *(continued)*
with *(continued)*
pain I83.819
specified complication NEC I83.899
swelling I83.899
ulcer I83.009
with inflammation I83.209
ankle I83.003
with inflammation I83.203
calf I83.002
with inflammation I83.202
foot NEC I83.005
with inflammation I83.205
heel I83.004
with inflammation I83.204
lower leg NEC I83.008
with inflammation I83.208
midfoot I83.004
with inflammation I83.204
thigh I83.001
with inflammation I83.201
bilateral (asymptomatic) I83.93
with
edema I83.893
pain I83.813
specified complication NEC I83.893
swelling I83.893
ulcer I83.009
with inflammation I83.209
left (asymptomatic) I83.92
with
edema I83.892
pain I83.812
specified complication NEC I83.892
swelling I83.892
inflammation I83.12
with ulcer —*see* Varix, leg, with, ulcer, with inflammation by site
ulcer I83.029
with inflammation I83.229
ankle I83.023
with inflammation I83.223
calf I83.022
with inflammation I83.222
foot NEC I83.025
with inflammation I83.225
heel I83.024
with inflammation I83.224
lower leg NEC I83.028
with inflammation I83.228
midfoot I83.024
with inflammation I83.224
thigh I83.021
with inflammation I83.221
right (asymptomatic) I83.91
with
edema I83.891
pain I83.811
specified complication NEC I83.891
swelling I83.891
inflammation I83.11
with ulcer —*see* Varix, leg, with, ulcer, with inflammation by site
ulcer I83.019
with inflammation I83.219
ankle I83.013
with inflammation I83.213

Varix *(continued)*
leg *(continued)*
right *(continued)*
with *(continued)*
ulcer *(continued)*
calf I83.012
with inflammation I83.212
foot NEC I83.015
with inflammation I83.215
heel I83.014
with inflammation I83.214
lower leg NEC I83.018
with inflammation I83.218
midfoot I83.014
with inflammation I83.214
thigh I83.011
with inflammation I83.211
nasal septum I86.8
orbit I86.8
congenital Q27.8
ovary I86.2
papillary I78.1
pelvis I86.2
perineum I86.3
pharynx I86.8
placenta O43.89-
renal papilla I86.8
retina H35.09
scrotum (ulcerated) I86.1
sigmoid colon I86.8
specified site NEC I86.8
spinal (cord) (vessels) I86.8
spleen, splenic (vein) (with phlebolith) I86.8
stomach I86.4
sublingual I86.0
ulcerated I83.009
inflamed or infected I83.209
uterine ligament I86.2
vagina I86.8
vocal cord I86.8
vulva I86.3

Vas deferens —*see* condition

Vas deferentitis N49.1

Vasa previa O69.4
hemorrhage from, affecting newbo P50.0

Vascular —*see also* condition
loop on optic papilla Q14.2
spasm I73.9
spider I78.1

Vascularization, cornea —*see* Neovascularization, cornea

Vasculitis I77.6
allergic D69.0
cryoglobulinemic D89.1
disseminated I77.6
hypocomplementemic M31.8
kidney I77.89
livedoid L95.0
nodular L95.8
retina H35.06-
rheumatic —*see* Fever, rheumatic
rheumatoid —*see* Rheumatoid, vasculitis
skin (limited to) L95.9
specified NEC L95.8

Vasculopathy, necrotizing M31.9
cardiac allograft T86.290
specified NEC M31.8

Vasitis (nodosa) N49.1
tuberculous A18.15

Vasodilation I73.9

motor —*see* condition
plasty, after previous sterilization
1.0
ercare Z31.42
spasm (vasoconstriction) I73.9
rebral (cerebrovascular) (artery)
I67.848
reversible I67.841
ronary I20.1
rve
arm —*see* Mononeuropathy, upper limb
brachial plexus G54.0
cervical plexus G54.2
leg —*see* Mononeuropathy, lower limb
ripheral NOS I73.9
tina (artery) —*see* Occlusion, artery, retina
spastic —*see* condition
vagal attack (paroxysmal) R55
ychogenic F45.8
ER syndrome Q87.2
r's ampulla —*see* condition
tation, vegetative
lenoid (nasal fossa) J35.8
docarditis (acute) (any valve)
(subacute) I33.0
art (mycotic) (valve) I33.0

ckson's Q43.3
, venous —*see* condition
t sore —*see* Ulcer, skin
eau's hernia —*see* Hernia, moral
ereal
bo A55
sease A64
anuloma inguinale A58
mphogranuloma (Durand-Nicolas-Favre) A55
ofibrosis I87.8
om, venomous —*see* Table of rugs and Chemicals, by animal or ubstance, poisoning
ous —*see* condition
tilator lung, newborn P27.8
tral —*see* condition
tricle, ventricular —*see also* ondition
scape I49.3
version Q20.5
triculitis (cerebral) —*see also* ncephalitis G04.90
triculostomy status Z98.2
net's syndrome G52.7
neuil's disease (syphilitic bursitis)
52.78
ruca (due to HPV) (filiformis)
simplex) (viral) (vulgaris) B07.9
cuminata A63.0
ecrogenica (primary) (tuberculosa)
A18.4
lana B07.8
lantaris B07.0
eborrheica L82.1
inflamed L82.0
enile (seborrheic) L82.1
inflamed L82.0
berculosa (primary) A18.4
enereal A63.0
rucosities —*see* Verruca
ruga peruana, peruviana A44.1

Version
with extraction
cervix —*see* Malposition, uterus
uterus (postinfectional) (postpartal, old) —*see* Malposition, uterus
Vertebra, vertebral —*see* condition
Vertical talus (congenital) Q66.80
left foot Q66.82
right foot Q66.81
Vertigo R42
auditory —*see* Vertigo, aural
aural H81.31-
benign paroxysmal (positional) H81.1-
central (origin) H81.4-
cerebral H81.4-
Dix and Hallpike (epidemic) —*see* Neuronitis, vestibular
due to infrasound T75.23
epidemic A88.1
Dix and Hallpike —*see* Neuronitis, vestibular
Pedersen's —*see* Neuronitis, vestibular
vestibular neuronitis —*see* Neuronitis, vestibular
hysterical F44.89
infrasound —*see* subcategory T75.23
labyrinthine H81.0
laryngeal R05
malignant positional H81.4-
Ménière's —*see* subcategory H81.0
menopausal N95.1
otogenic —*see* Vertigo, aural
paroxysmal positional, benign —*see* Vertigo, benign paroxysmal
Pedersen's (epidemic) —*see* Neuronitis, vestibular
peripheral NEC H81.39-
positional
benign paroxysmal —*see* Vertigo, benign paroxysmal
malignant H81.4-
Very-low-density-lipoprotein-type (VLDL) hyperlipoproteinemia E78.1
Vesania —*see* Psychosis
Vesical —*see* condition
Vesicle
cutaneous R23.8
seminal —*see* condition
skin R23.8
Vesicocolic —*see* condition
Vesicoperineal —*see* condition
Vesicorectal —*see* condition
Vesicourethrorectal —*see* condition
Vesicovaginal —*see* condition
Vesicular —*see* condition
Vesiculitis (seminal) N49.0
amebic A06.82
gonorrheal (acute) (chronic) A54.23
trichomonal A59.09
tuberculous A18.15
Vestibulitis (ear) —*see also* subcategory H83.0
nose (external) J34.89
vulvar N94.810
Vestibulopathy , acute peripheral (recurrent) —*see* Neuronitis, vestibular
Vestige, vestigial —*see also* Persistence
branchial Q18.0
structures in vitreous Q14.0
Vibration
adverse effects T75.20
pneumatic hammer syndrome T75.21

Vibration *(continued)*
adverse effects *(continued)*
specified effect NEC T75.29
vasospastic syndrome T75.22
vertigo from infrasound T75.23
exposure (occupational) Z57.7
vertigo T75.23
Vibriosis A28.9
Victim (of)
crime Z65.4
disaster Z65.5
terrorism Z65.4
torture Z65.4
war Z65.5
Vidal's disease L28.0
Villaret's syndrome G52.7
Villous —*see* condition
VIN —*see* Neoplasia, intraepithelial, vulva
Vincent's infection (angina) (gingivitis) A69.1
stomatitis NEC A69.1
Vinson-Plummer syndrome D50.1
Violence, physical R45.6
Viosterol deficiency —*see* Deficiency, calciferol
Vipoma —*see* Neoplasm, malignant, by site
Viremia B34.9
Virilism (adrenal) E25.9
congenital E25.0
Virilization (female) (suprarenal) E25.9
congenital E25.0
isosexual E28.2
Virulent bubo A57
Virus, viral —*see also* condition
as cause of disease classified elsewhere B97.89
cytomegalovirus B25.9
human immunodeficiency (HIV) —*see* Human, immunodeficiency virus (HIV) disease
infection —*see* Infection, virus
specified NEC B34.8
swine influneza (viruses that normally cause infections in pigs) —*see also* Influenza, due to, identified novel influenza A virus J09.X2
West Nile (fever) A92.30
with
complications NEC A92.39
cranial nerve disorders A92.32
encephalitis A92.31
encephalomyelitis A92.31
neurologic manifestation NEC A92.32
optic neuritis A92.32
polyradiculitis A92.32
Viscera, visceral —*see* condition
Visceroptosis K63.4
Visible peristalsis R19.2
Vision, visual
binocular, suppression H53.34
blurred, blurring H53.8
hysterical F44.6
defect, defective NEC H54.7
disorientation (syndrome) H53.8
disturbance H53.9
hysterical F44.6
double H53.2
examination Z01.00
with abnormal findings Z01.01
field, limitation (defect) —*see* Defect, visual field
hallucinations R44.1

Vision, visual *(continued)*
halos H53.19
loss —*see* Loss, vision
sudden —*see* Disturbance, vision, subjective, loss, sudden
low (both eyes) —*see* Low, vision
perception, simultaneous without fusion H53.33
Vitality, lack or want of R53.83
newborn P96.89
Vitamin deficiency —*see* Deficiency, vitamin
Vitelline duct, persistent Q43.0
Vitiligo L80
eyelid H02.739
left H02.736
lower H02.735
upper H02.734
right H02.733
lower H02.732
upper H02.731
pinta A67.2
vulva N90.89
Vitreal corneal syndrome H59.01-
Vitreoretinopathy, proliferative —*see also* Retinopathy, proliferative
with retinal detachment —*see* Detachment, retina, traction
Vitreous —*see also* condition
touch syndrome —*see* Complication, postprocedural, following cataract surgery
Vocal cord —*see* condition
Vogt-Koyanagi syndrome H20.82-
Vogt's disease or syndrome G80.3
Vogt-Spielmeyer amaurotic idiocy or disease E75.4
Voice
change R49.9
specified NEC R49.8
loss —*see* Aphonia
Volhynian fever A79.0
Volkmann's ischemic contracture or paralysis (complicating trauma) T79.6
Volvulus (bowel) (colon) (duodenum) (intestine) K56.2
with perforation K56.2
congenital Q43.8
fallopian tube —*see* Torsion, fallopian tube
oviduct —*see* Torsion, fallopian tube
stomach (due to absence of gastrocolic ligament) K31.89
Vomiting R11.10
with nausea R11.2
asphyxia —*see* Foreign body, by site, causing asphyxia, gastric contents
bilious (cause unknown) R11.14
in newborn P92.01
following gastro-intestinal surgery K91.0
blood —*see* Hematemesis
causing asphyxia, choking, or suffocation —*see* Foreign body, by site
cyclical G43.A0
with refractory migraine G43.A1
intractable G43.A1
not intractable G43.A0
psychogenic F50.8
without refractory migraine G43.A0
fecal mater R11.13
following gastrointestinal surgery K91.0
psychogenic F50.8

Vomiting *(continued)*
functional K31.89
hysterical F50.8
nervous F50.8
neurotic F50.8
newborn NEC P92.09
bilious P92.01
periodic R11.10
psychogenic F50.8
projectile R11.12
psychogenic F50.8
uremic —*see* Uremia
without nausea R11.11

Vomito negro —*see* Fever, yellow

Von Bezold's abscess —*see* Mastoiditis, acute

Von Economo-Cruchet disease A85.8

Von Eulenburg's disease G71.19

Von Gierke's disease E74.01

Von Hippel (-Lindau) **disease or syndrome** Q85.8

Von Jaksch's anemia or disease D64.89

Von Recklinghausen
disease (neurofibromatosis) Q85.01
bones E21.0

Von Schroetter's syndrome I82.890

Von Willebrand (-Jurgens) (-Minot) **disease or syndrome** D68.0

Von Zumbusch's disease L40.1

Voyeurism F65.3

Vrolik's disease Q78.0

Vulva —*see* condition

Vulvismus N94.2

Vulvitis (acute) (allergic) (atrophic) (hypertrophic) (intertriginous) (senile) N76.2
with ectopic or molar pregnancy O08.0
adhesive, congenital Q52.79
blennorrhagic (gonococcal) A54.02
candidal B37.3
chlamydial A56.02
due to Haemophilus ducreyi A57
following ectopic or molar pregnancy O08.0
gonococcal A54.02
with abscess (accessory gland) (periurethral) A54.1
herpesviral A60.04
leukoplakic N90.4
monilial B37.3
puerperal (postpartum) O86.19
subacute or chronic N76.3
syphilitic (early) A51.0
late A52.76
trichomonal A59.01
tuberculous A18.18

Vulvodynia N94.819
specified NEC N94.818

Vulvorectal —*see* condition

Vulvovaginitis (acute) —*see* Vaginitis

W

Waiting list, person on Z75.1
for organ transplant Z76.82
undergoing social agency investigation Z75.2

Waldenström-Kjellberg syndrome D50.1

Waldenström
hypergammaglobulinemia D89.0
syndrome or macroglobulinemia C88.0

Walking
difficulty R26.2
psychogenic F44.4
sleep F51.3
hysterical F44.89

Wall, abdominal —*see* condition

Wallenberg's disease or syndrome G46.3

Wallgren's disease I87.8

Wandering
gallbladder, congenital Q44.1
in diseases classified elsewhere Z91.83
kidney, congenital Q63.8
organ or site, congenital NEC —*see* Malposition, congenital, by site
pacemaker (heart) I49.8
spleen D73.89

War neurosis F48.8

Wart (due to HPV) (filiform) (infectious) (viral) B07.9
anogenital region (venereal) A63.0
common B07.8
external genital organs (venereal) A63.0
flat B07.8
Hassal-Henle's (of cornea) H18.49
Peruvian A44.1
plantar B07.0
prosector (tuberculous) A18.4
seborrheic L82.1
inflamed L82.0
senile (seborrheic) L82.1
inflamed L82.0
tuberculous A18.4
venereal A63.0

Warthin's tumor —*see* Neoplasm, salivary gland, benign

Wassilieff's disease A27.0

Wasting
disease R64
due to malnutrition E41
extreme (due to malnutrition) E41
muscle NEC —*see* Atrophy, muscle

Water
clefts (senile cataract) —*see* Cataract, senile, incipient
deprivation of T73.1
intoxication E87.79
itch B76.9
lack of T73.1
loading E87.70
on
brain —*see* Hydrocephalus
chest J94.8
poisoning E87.79

Waterbrash R12

Waterhouse (-Friderichsen) **syndrome or disease** (meningococcal) A39.1

Water-losing nephritis N25.89

Watermelon stomach K31.819
with hemorrhage K31.811
without hemorrhage K31.819

Watsoniasis B66.8

Wax in ear —*see* Impaction, cerumen

Weak, weakening, weakness (generalized) R53.1
arches (acquired) —*see also* Deformity, limb, flat foot
bladder (sphincter) R32
facial R29.810
following
cerebrovascular disease I69.992
cerebral infarction I69.392
intracerebral hemorrhage I69.192

Weak, weakening, weakness *(continued)*
facial *(continued)*
following *(continued)*
cerebrovascular disease *(continued)*
nontraumatic intracranial hemorrhage NEC I69.292
specified disease NEC I69.892
stroke I69.392
subarachnoid hemorrhage I69.092
foot (double) —*see* Weak, arches
heart, cardiac —*see* Failure, heart
mind F70
muscle M62.81
myocardium —*see* Failure, heart
newborn P96.89
pelvic fundus N81.89
pubocervical tissue N81.82
senile R54
rectovaginal tissue N81.83
urinary stream R39.12
valvular —*see* Endocarditis

Wear, worn (with normal or routine use)
articular bearing surface of internal joint prosthesis —*see* Complications, joint prosthesis, mechanical, wear of articular bearing surfaces, by site
device, implant or graft —*see* Complications, by site, mechanical complication
tooth, teeth (approximal) (hard tissues) (interproximal) (occlusal) K03.0

Weather, weathered
effects of
cold T69.9
specified effect NEC T69.8
hot —*see* Heat
skin L57.8

Weaver's syndrome Q87.3

Web, webbed (congenital)
duodenal Q43.8
esophagus Q39.4
fingers Q70.1-
larynx (glottic) (subglottic) Q31.0
neck (pterygium colli) Q18.3
Paterson-Kelly D50.1
popliteal syndrome Q87.89
toes Q70.3-

Weber-Christian disease M35.6

Weber-Cockayne syndrome (epidermolysis bullosa) Q81.8

Weber-Gubler syndrome G46.3

Weber-Leyden syndrome G46.3

Weber-Osler syndrome I78.0

Weber's paralysis or syndrome G46.3

Wedge-shaped or wedging vertebra —*see* Collapse, vertebra NEC

Wegener's granulomatosis or syndrome M31.30
with
kidney involvement M31.31
lung involvement M31.30
with kidney involvement M31.31

Wegner's disease A50.02

Weight
1000-2499 grams at birth (low) —*see* Low, birthweight
999 grams or less at birth (extremely low) —*see* Low, birthweight, extreme

Weight *(continued)*
gain (abnormal) (excessive) R63.
in pregnancy —*see* Pregnancy, complicated by, excessive weight gain
low —*see* Pregnancy, complicated by, insufficie weight gain
loss (abnormal) (cause unknown) R63.4

Weightlessness (effect of) T75.82

Weil (I)-**Marchesani syndrome** Q8

Weil's disease A27.0

Weingarten's syndrome J82

Weir Mitchell's disease I73.81

Weiss-Baker syndrome G90.09

Wells' disease L98.3

Wen —*see* Cyst, sebaceous

Wenckebach's block or phenomen I44.1

Werdnig-Hoffmann syndrome (muscular atrophy) G12.0

Werlhof's disease D69.3

Wermer's disease or syndrome E3

Werner-His disease A79.0

Werner's disease or syndrome E34

Wernicke-Korsakoff's syndrome o psychosis (alcoholic) F10.96
with dependence F10.26
drug-induced
due to drug abuse —*see* Abuse, drug, by type, with amnestic disorder
due to drug dependence —*see* Dependence, drug, by type, w amnestic disorder
nonalcoholic F04

Wernicke-Posadas disease B38.9

Wernicke's
developmental aphasia F80.2
disease or syndrome E51.2
encephalopathy E51.2
polioencephalitis, superior E51.2

West African fever B50.8

Westphal-Strümpell syndrome E83

West's syndrome —*see* Epilepsy, spasms

Wet
feet, tropical (maceration) (syndro —*see* Immersion, foot
lung (syndrome), newborn P22.1

Wharton's duct —*see* condition

Wheal —*see* Urticaria

Wheezing R06.2

Whiplash injury S13.4

Whipple's disease —*see also* subcategory M14.8- K90.81

Whipworm (disease) (infection) (infestation) B79

Whistling face Q87.0

White —*see also* condition
kidney, small N03.9
leg, puerperal, postpartum, childbi O87.1
mouth B37.0
patches of mouth K13.29
spot lesions, teeth
chewing surface K02.51
pit and fissure surface K02.51
smooth surface K02.61

Whitehead L70.0

tlow —*see also* Cellulitis, digit
th lymphangitis —*see* Lymphangitis, acute, digit
rpesviral B00.89

tmore's disease or fever —*see* elioidosis

oping cough A37.90
th pneumonia A37.91
due to Bordetella
bronchiseptica A37.81
parapertussis A37.11
pertussis A37.01
specified organism NEC A37.81
e to
Bordetella
bronchiseptica A37.80
with pneumonia A37.81
parapertussis A37.10
with pneumonia A37.11
pertussis A37.00
with pneumonia A37.01
specified NEC A37.80
with pneumonia A37.81

hman's asthma J38.5

e cranial sutures, newborn 96.3

ening aorta —*see* Ectasia, aorta
ith aneurysm —*see* Aneurysm, aorta

kie's disease or syndrome K55.1

kinson-Sneddon disease or ndrome L13.1

ebrand (-Jürgens) **thrombopathy** 68.0

ige-Hunt disease or syndrome 23.1

ms' tumor C64-

son-Mikity syndrome P27.0

son's
sease or syndrome E83.01
epatolenticular degeneration E83.01
chen ruber L43.9

dow —*see also* Imperfect, closure
orticopulmonary Q21.4

ter —*see* condition

kott-Aldrich syndrome D82.0

hdrawal state —*see also* ependence, drug by type, with ithdrawal
ewborn
correct therapeutic substance properly administered P96.2
infant of dependent mother P96.1
erapeutic substance, neonatal P96.2

ts' anemia D50.8

zelsucht F07.0

akes' ethmoiditis or syndrome 33.1

ff-Hirschorn syndrome Q93.3

ff-Parkinson-White syndrome 45.6

hynian fever A79.0

man's disease E75.5

od lung or pneumonitis J67.8

olly, wooly hair (congenital) (nevus) 84.1

olsorter's disease A22.1

rd
lindness (congenital) (developmental) F81.0
eafness (congenital) (developmental) H93.25

Worm (s) (infection) (infestation) —*see also* Infestation, helminth
guinea B72
in intestine NEC B82.0

Worm-eaten soles A66.3

Worn out —*see* Exhaustion
cardiac
defibrillator (with synchronous cardiace pacemaker) Z45.02
pacemaker
battery Z45.010
lead Z45.018
device, implant or graft —*see* Complications, by site, mechanical

Worried well Z71.1

Worries R45.82

Wound, open
abdomen, abdominal
wall S31.109
with penetration into peritoneal cavity S31.609
bite —*see* Bite, abdomen, wall
epigastric region S31.102
with penetration into peritoneal cavity S31.602
bite —*see* Bite, abdomen, wall, epigastric region
laceration —*see* Laceration, abdomen, wall, epigastric region
puncture —*see* Puncture, abdomen, wall, epigastric region
laceration —*see* Laceration, abdomen, wall
left
lower quadrant S31.104
with penetration into peritoneal cavity S31.604
bite —*see* Bite, abdomen, wall, left, lower quadrant
laceration —*see* Laceration, abdomen, wall, left, lower quadrant
puncture —*see* Puncture, abdomen, wall, left, lower quadrant
upper quadrant S31.101
with penetration into peritoneal cavity S31.601
bite —*see* Bite, abdomen, wall, left, upper quadrant
laceration —*see* Laceration, abdomen, wall, left, upper quadrant
puncture —*see* Puncture, abdomen, wall, left, upper quadrant
periumbilic region S31.105
with penetration into peritoneal cavity S31.605
bite —*see* Bite, abdomen, wall, periumbilic region
laceration —*see* Laceration, abdomen, wall, periumbilic region
puncture —*see* Puncture, abdomen, wall, periumbilic region
puncture —*see* Puncture, abdomen, wall
right
lower quadrant S31.103
with penetration into peritoneal cavity S31.603
bite —*see* Bite, abdomen, wall, right, lower quadrant

Wound, open *(continued)*
abdomen, abdominal *(continued)*
wall *(continued)*
right *(continued)*
lower quadrant *(continued)*
laceration —*see* Laceration, abdomen, wall, right, lower quadrant
puncture —*see* Puncture, abdomen, wall, right, lower quadrant
upper quadrant S31.100
with penetration into peritoneal cavity S31.600
bite —*see* Bite, abdomen, wall, right, upper quadrant
laceration —*see* Laceration, abdomen, wall, right, upper quadrant
puncture —*see* Puncture, abdomen, wall, right, upper quadrant
alveolar (process) —*see* Wound, open, oral cavity
ankle S91.00-
bite —*see* Bite, ankle
laceration —*see* Laceration, ankle
puncture —*see* Puncture, ankle
antecubital space —*see* Wound, open, elbow
anterior chamber, eye —*see* Wound, open, ocular
anus S31.839
bite S31.835
laceration —*see* Laceration, anus
puncture —*see* Puncture, anus
arm (upper) S41.10-
with amputation —*see* Amputation, traumatic, arm
bite —*see* Bite, arm
forearm —*see* Wound, open, forearm
laceration —*see* Laceration, arm
puncture —*see* Puncture, arm
auditory canal (external) (meatus) —*see* Wound, open, ear
auricle, ear —*see* Wound, open, ear
axilla —*see* Wound, open, arm
back —*see also* Wound, open, thorax, back
lower S31.000
with penetration into retroperitoneal space S31.001
bite —*see* Bite, back, lower
laceration —*see* Laceration, back, lower
puncture —*see* Puncture, back, lower
bite —*see* Bite
blood vessel —*see* Injury, blood vessel
breast S21.00-
with amputation —*see* Amputation, traumatic, breast
bite —*see* Bite, breast
laceration —*see* Laceration, breast
puncture —*see* Puncture, breast
buttock S31.809
bite —*see* Bite, buttock
laceration —*see* Laceration, buttock
left S31.829
puncture —*see* Puncture, buttock
right S31.819
calf —*see* Wound, open, leg
canaliculus lacrimalis —*see* Wound, open, eyelid
canthus, eye —*see* Wound, open, eyelid

Wound, open *(continued)*
cervical esophagus S11.20
bite S11.25
laceration —*see* Laceration, esophagus, traumatic, cervical
puncture —*see* Puncture, cervical esophagus
cheek (external) S01.40-
bite —*see* Bite, cheek
laceration —*see* Laceration, cheek
puncture —*see* Puncture, cheek
internal —*see* Wound, open, oral cavity
chest wall —*see* Wound, open, thorax
chin —*see* Wound, open, head, specified site NEC
choroid —*see* Wound, open, ocular
ciliary body (eye) —*see* Wound, open, ocular
clitoris S31.40
with amputation —*see* Amputation, traumatic, clitoris
bite S31.45
laceration —*see* Laceration, vulva
puncture —*see* Puncture, vulva
conjunctiva —*see* Wound, open, ocular
cornea —*see* Wound, open, ocular
costal region —*see* Wound, open, thorax
Descemet's membrane —*see* Wound, open, ocular
digit (s)
foot —*see* Wound, open, toe
hand —*see* Wound, open, finger
ear (canal) (external) S01.30-
with amputation —*see* Amputation, traumatic, ear
bite —*see* Bite, ear
laceration —*see* Laceration, ear
puncture —*see* Puncture, ear
drum S09.2-
elbow S51.00-
bite —*see* Bite, elbow
laceration —*see* Laceration, elbow
puncture —*see* Puncture, elbow
epididymis —*see* Wound, open, testis
epigastric region S31.102
with penetration into peritoneal cavity S31.602
bite —*see* Bite, abdomen, wall, epigastric region
laceration —*see* Laceration, abdomen, wall, epigastric region
puncture —*see* Puncture, abdomen, wall, epigastric region
epiglottis —*see* Wound, open, neck, specified site NEC
esophagus (thoracic) S27.819
cervical —*see* Wound, open, cervical esophagus
laceration S27.813
specified type NEC S27.818
eye —*see* Wound, open, ocular
eyeball —*see* Wound, open, ocular
eyebrow —*see* Wound, open, eyelid
eyelid S01.10-
bite —*see* Bite, eyelid
laceration —*see* Laceration, eyelid
puncture —*see* Puncture, eyelid
face NEC —*see* Wound, open, head, specified site NEC
finger (s) S61.209
with
amputation —*see* Amputation, traumatic, finger
damage to nail S61.309
bite —*see* Bite, finger
index S61.208
with
damage to nail S61.308

Wound, open *(continued)*
- finger *(continued)*
  - index *(continued)*
    - left S61.201
      - with
        - damage to nail S61.301
    - right S61.200
      - with
        - damage to nail S61.300
  - laceration *—see* Laceration, finger
  - little S61.208
    - with
      - damage to nail S61.308
    - left S61.207
      - with damage to nail S61.307
    - right S61.206
      - with damage to nail S61.306
  - middle S61.208
    - with
      - damage to nail S61.308
    - left S61.203
      - with damage to nail S61.303
    - right S61.202
      - with damage to nail S61.302
  - puncture *—see* Puncture, finger
  - ring S61.208
    - with
      - damage to nail S61.308
    - left S61.205
      - with damage to nail S61.305
    - right S61.204
      - with damage to nail S61.304
- flank *—see* Wound, open, abdomen, wall
- foot (except toe(s) alone) S91.30-
  - with amputation *—see* Amputation, traumatic, foot
  - bite *—see* Bite, foot
  - laceration *—see* Laceration, foot
  - puncture *—see* Puncture, foot
  - toe *—see* Wound, open, toe
- forearm S51.80-
  - with
    - amputation *—see* Amputation, traumatic, forearm
  - bite *—see* Bite, forearm
  - elbow only *—see* Wound, open, elbow
  - laceration *—see* Laceration, forearm
  - puncture *—see* Puncture, forearm
- forehead *—see* Wound, open, head, specified site NEC
- genital organs, external
  - with amputation *—see* Amputation, traumatic, genital organs
  - bite *—see* Bite, genital organ
  - female S31.502
    - vagina S31.40
    - vulva S31.40
  - laceration *—see* Laceration, genital organ
  - male S31.501
    - penis S31.20
    - scrotum S31.30
    - testes S31.30
  - puncture *—see* Puncture, genital organ
- globe (eye) *—see* Wound, open, ocular
- groin *—see* Wound, open, abdomen, wall
- gum *—see* Wound, open, oral cavity
- hand S61.40-
  - with
    - amputation *—see* Amputation, traumatic, hand
  - bite *—see* Bite, hand
  - finger (s) *—see* Wound, open, finger
  - laceration *—see* Laceration, hand
  - puncture *—see* Puncture, hand
  - thumb *—see* Wound, open, thumb

Wound, open *(continued)*
- head S01.90
  - bite *—see* Bite, head
  - cheek *—see* Wound, open, cheek
  - ear *—see* Wound, open, ear
  - eyelid *—see* Wound, open, eyelid
  - laceration *—see* Laceration, head
  - lip *—see* Wound, open, lip
  - nose S01.20
  - oral cavity *—see* Wound, open, oral cavity
  - puncture *—see* Puncture, head
  - scalp *—see* Wound, open, scalp
  - specified site NEC S01.80
  - temporomandibular area *—see* Wound, open, cheek
- heel *—see* Wound, open, foot
- hip S71.00-
  - with amputation *—see* Amputation, traumatic, hip
  - bite *—see* Bite, hip
  - laceration *—see* Laceration, hip
  - puncture *—see* Puncture, hip
- hymen S31.40
  - bite *—see* Bite, vulva
  - laceration *—see* Laceration, vagina
  - puncture *—see* Puncture, vagina
- hypochondrium S31.109
  - bite *—see* Bite, hypochondrium
  - laceration *—see* Laceration, hypochondrium
  - puncture *—see* Puncture, hypochondrium
- hypogastric region S31.109
  - bite *—see* Bite, hypogastric region
  - laceration *—see* Laceration, hypogastric region
  - puncture *—see* Puncture, hypogastric region
- iliac (region) *—see* Wound, open, inguinal region
- inguinal region S31.109
  - bite *—see* Bite, abdomen, wall, lower quadrant
  - laceration *—see* Laceration, inguinal region
  - puncture *—see* Puncture, inguinal region
- instep *—see* Wound, open, foot
- interscapular region *—see* Wound, open, thorax, back
- intraocular *—see* Wound, open, ocular
- iris *—see* Wound, open, ocular
- jaw *—see* Wound, open, head, specified site NEC
- knee S81.00-
  - bite *—see* Bite, knee
  - laceration *—see* Laceration, knee
  - puncture *—see* Puncture, knee
- labium (majus) (minus) *—see* Wound, open, vulva
- laceration *—see* Laceration, by site
- lacrimal duct *—see* Wound, open, eyelid
- larynx S11.019
  - bite *—see* Bite, larynx
  - laceration *—see* Laceration, larynx
  - puncture *—see* Puncture, larynx
- left
  - lower quadrant S31.104
    - with penetration into peritoneal cavity S31.604
    - bite *—see* Bite, abdomen, wall, left, lower quadrant
    - laceration *—see* Laceration, abdomen, wall, left, lower quadrant
    - puncture *—see* Puncture, abdomen, wall, left, lower quadrant

Wound, open *(continued)*
- left *(continued)*
  - upper quadrant S31.101
    - with penetration into peritoneal cavity S31.601
    - bite *—see* Bite, abdomen, wall, left, upper quadrant
    - laceration *—see* Laceration, abdomen, wall, left, upper quadrant
    - puncture *—see* Puncture, abdomen, wall, left, upper quadrant
- leg (lower) S81.80-
  - with amputation *—see* Amputation, traumatic, leg
  - ankle *—see* Wound, open, ankle
  - bite *—see* Bite, leg
  - foot *—see* Wound, open, foot
  - knee *—see* Wound, open, knee
  - laceration *—see* Laceration, leg
  - puncture *—see* Puncture, leg
  - toe *—see* Wound, open, toe
  - upper *—see* Wound, open, thigh
- lip S01.501
  - bite *—see* Bite, lip
  - laceration *—see* Laceration, lip
  - puncture *—see* Puncture, lip
- loin S31.109
  - bite *—see* Bite, abdomen, wall
  - laceration *—see* Laceration, loin
  - puncture *—see* Puncture, loin
- lower back *—see* Wound, open, back, lower
- lumbar region *—see* Wound, open, back, lower
- malar region *—see* Wound, open, head, specified site NEC
- mammary *—see* Wound, open, breast
- mastoid region *—see* Wound, open, head, specified site NEC
- mouth *—see* Wound, open, oral cavity
- nail
  - finger *—see* Wound, open, finger, with damage to nail
  - toe *—see* Wound, open, toe, with damage to nail
- nape (neck) *—see* Wound, open, neck
- nasal (septum) (sinus) *—see* Wound, open, nose
- nasopharynx *—see* Wound, open, head, specified site NEC
- neck S11.90
  - bite *—see* Bite, neck
  - involving
    - cervical esophagus S11.20
    - larynx *—see* Wound, open, larynx
    - pharynx S11.20
    - thyroid S11.10
    - trachea (cervical) S11.029
      - bite *—see* Bite, trachea
      - laceration S11.021
        - with foreign body S11.022
      - puncture S11.023
        - with foreign body S11.024
  - laceration *—see* Laceration, neck
  - puncture *—see* Puncture, neck
  - specified site NEC S11.80
    - specified type NEC S11.89
- nose (septum) (sinus) S01.20
  - with amputation *—see* Amputation, traumatic, nose
  - bite *—see* Bite, nose
  - laceration *—see* Laceration, nose
  - puncture *—see* Puncture, nose
- ocular S05.90
  - avulsion (traumatic enucleation) S05.7-
  - eyeball S05.6-
    - with foreign body S05.5-

Wound, open *(continued)*
- ocular *(continued)*
  - eyelid *—see* Wound, open, eye
  - laceration and rupture S05.3-
    - with prolapse or loss of intraocular tissue S05.2-
  - orbit (penetrating) (with or wit foreign body) S05.4-
  - periocular area *—see* Wound, o eyelid
  - specified NEC S05.8X-
- oral cavity S01.502
  - bite S01.552
  - laceration *—see* Laceration, or cavity
  - puncture *—see* Puncture, oral cavity
- orbit *—see* Wound, open, ocular,
- palate *—see* Wound, open, oral ca
- palm *—see* Wound, open, hand
- pelvis, pelvic *—see also* Wound, open, back, lower
  - girdle *—see* Wound, open, hip
- penetrating *—see* Puncture, by sit
- penis S31.20
  - with amputation *—see* Amputa traumatic, penis
  - bite S31.25
  - laceration *—see* Laceration, pe
  - puncture *—see* Puncture, penis
- perineum
  - bite *—see* Bite, perineum
  - female S31.502
  - laceration *—see* Laceration, perineum
  - male S31.501
  - puncture *—see* Puncture, perin
- periocular area (with or without lacrimal passages) *—see* Woun open, eyelid
- periumbilic region S31.105
  - with penetration into peritoneal cavity S31.605
  - bite *—see* Bite, abdomen, wall, periumbilic region
  - laceration *—see* Laceration, abdomen, wall, periumbilic region
  - puncture *—see* Puncture, abdon wall, periumbilic region
- phalanges
  - finger *—see* Wound, open, finge
  - toe *—see* Wound, open, toe
- pharynx S11.20
- pinna *—see* Wound, open, ear
- popliteal space *—see* Wound, ope knee
- prepuce *—see* Wound, open, penis
- pubic region *—see* Wound, open, back, lower
- pudendum *—see* Wound, open, genital organs, external
- puncture wound *—see* Puncture
- rectovaginal septum *—see* Wound, open, vagina
- right
  - lower quadrant S31.103
    - with penetration into peritone cavity S31.603
    - bite *—see* Bite, abdomen, wa right, lower quadrant
    - laceration *—see* Laceration, abdomen, wall, right, lowe quadrant
    - puncture *—see* Puncture, abdomen, wall, right, lowe quadrant
  - upper quadrant S31.100
    - with penetration into peritone cavity S31.600
    - bite *—see* Bite, abdomen, wa right, upper quadrant

X

Y

Yeast infection —*see also* Candidiasis B37.9
Yellow
- atrophy (liver) —*see* Failure, hepatic
- fever —*see* Fever, yellow
- jack —*see* Fever, yellow
- jaundice —*see* Jaundice
- nail syndrome L60.5

Yersiniosis —*see also* Infection, Yersinia
- extraintestinal A28.2
- intestinal A04.6

Z

Zahorsky's syndrome (herpangina) B08.5
Zellweger's syndrome Q87.89
Zenker's diverticulum (esophagus) K22.5
Ziehen-Oppenheim disease G24.1
Zieve's syndrome K70.0
Zinc
- deficiency, dietary E60
- metabolism disorder E83.2

Zollinger-Ellison syndrome E16.4
Zona —*see* Herpes, zoster
Zoophobia F40.218
Zoster (herpes) —*see* Herpes, zoste
Zygomycosis B46.9
- specified NEC B46.8

Zymotic —*see* condition

Neoplasm Table Guidance

The list below gives the code numbers for neoplasms by anatomical site. For each site there are six possible code numbers according to whe the neoplasm in question is malignant, benign, in situ, of uncertain behavior, or of unspecified nature. The description of the neoplasm will o indicate which of the six columns is appropriate; e.g., malignant melanoma of skin, benign fibroadenoma of breast, carcinoma in situ of cervix u

Where such descriptors are not present, the remainder of the Index should be consulted where guidance is given to the appropriate colu for each morphological (histological) variety listed; e.g., Mesonephroma—see Neoplasm, malignant; Embryoma—see also Neoplasm, uncer behavior; Disease, Bowen's—see Neoplasm, skin, in situ. However, the guidance in the Index can be overridden if one of the descriptors mentio above is present; e.g., malignant adenoma of colon is coded to C18.9 and not to D12.6 as the adjective "malignant" overrides the Index e "Adenoma—see also Neoplasm, benign."

Codes listed with a dash -, following the code have a required additional character for laterality. The tabular must be reviewed for the comp code.

Table of Neoplasms

	Malignant Primary	Malignant Secondary	Ca in situ	Benign	Uncertain Behavior	Unspecified Behavior
plasm, neoplastic	C80.1	C79.9	D09.9	D36.9	D48.9	D49.9
A						
domen, abdominal	C76.2	C79.8-	D09.8	D36.7	D48.7	D49.89
cavity	C76.2	C79.8-	D09.8	D36.7	D48.7	D49.89
organ	C76.2	C79.8-	D09.8	D36.7	D48.7	D49.89
viscera	C76.2	C79.8-	D09.8	D36.7	D48.7	D49.89
wall—see also Neoplasm, abdomen, wall, skin	C44.509	C79.2	D04.5	D23.5	D48.5	D49.2
connective tissue	C49.4	C79.8-	-	D21.4	D48.1	D49.2
skin	C44.509					
basal cell carcinoma	C44.519	-	-	-	-	-
specified type NEC	C44.599	-	-	-	-	-
squamous cell carcinoma	C44.529	-	-	-	-	-
dominopelvic	C76.8	C79.8-	-	D36.7	D48.7	D49.89
cessory sinus—see eoplasm, sinus						
oustic nerve	C72.4-	C79.49	-	D33.3	D43.3	D49.7
lenoid(pharynx) (tissue)	C11.1	C79.89	D00.08	D10.6	D37.05	D49.0
lipose tissue —see also eoplasm, connective tissue	C49.4	C79.89	-	D21.9	D48.1	D49.2
lnexa(uterine)	C57.4	C79.89	D07.39	D28.7	D39.8	D49.5
lrenal	C74.9-	C79.7-	D09.3	D35.0-	D44.1-	D49.7
capsule	C74.9-	C79.7-	D09.3	D35.0-	D44.1-	D49.7
cortex	C74.0-	C79.7-	D09.3	D35.0-	D44.1-	D49.7
gland	C74.9-	C79.7-	D09.3	D35.0-	D44.1-	D49.7
medulla	C74.1-	C79.7-	D09.3	D35.0-	D44.1-	D49.7
a nasi(external)—see also eoplasm, skin, nose	C44.301	C79.2	D04.39	D23.39	D48.5	D49.2
limentary canal or tract EC	C26.9	C78.80	D01.9	D13.9	D37.9	D49.0
veolar	C03.9	C79.89	D00.03	D10.39	D37.09	D49.0
mucosa	C03.9	C79.89	D00.03	D10.39	D37.09	D49.0
lower	C03.1	C79.89	D00.03	D10.39	D37.09	D49.0
upper	C03.0	C79.89	D00.03	D10.39	D37.09	D49.0
ridge or process	C41.1	C79.51	-	D16.5	D48.0	D49.2
carcinoma	C03.9	C79.8-	-	-	-	-
lower	C03.1	C79.8-	-	-	-	-
upper	C03.0	C79.8-	-	-	-	-
lower	C41.1	C79.51	-	D16.5-	D48.0	D49.2
mucosa	C03.9	C79.89	D00.03	D10.39	D37.09	D49.0
lower	C03.1	C79.89	D00.03	D10.39	D37.09	D49.0
upper	C03.0	C79.89	D00.03	D10.39	D37.09	D49.0
upper	C41.0	C79.51	-	D16.4-	D48.0	D49.2
sulcus	C06.1	C79.89	D00.02	D10.39	D37.09	D49.0
lveolus	C03.9	C79.89	D00.03	D10.39	D37.09	D49.0
lower	C03.1	C79.89	D00.03	D10.39	D37.09	D49.0
upper	C03.0	C79.89	D00.03	D10.39	D37.09	D49.0
mpulla of Vater	C24.1	C78.89	D01.5	D13.5	D37.6	D49.0
nkle NEC	C76.5-	C79.89	D04.7-	D36.7	D48.7	D49.89
norectum, norectal(junction)	C21.8	C78.5	D01.3	D12.9	D37.8	D49.0

	Malignant Primary	Malignant Secondary	Ca in situ	Benign	Uncertain Behavior	Unspecified Behavior
antecubital fossa or space	C76.4-	C79.89	D04.6-	D36.7	D48.7	D49.89
antrum(Highmore) (maxillary)	C31.0	C78.39	D02.3	D14.0	D38.5	D49.1
pyloric	C16.3	C78.89	D00.2	D13.1	D37.1	D49.0
tympanicum	C30.1	C78.39	D02.3	D14.0	D38.5	D49.1
anus, anal	C21.0	C78.5	D01.3	D12.9	D37.8	D49.0
canal	C21.1	C78.5	D01.3	D12.9	D37.8	D49.0
cloacogenic zone	C21.2	C78.5	D01.3	D12.9	D37.8	D49.0
margin—see also Neoplasm, anus, skin	C44.500	C79.2	D04.5	D23.5	D48.5	D49.2
overlapping lesion with rectosigmoid junction or rectum	C21.8	-	-	-	-	-
skin	C44.500	C79.2	D04.5	D23.5	D48.5	D49.2
basal cell carcinoma	C44.510	-	-	-	-	-
specified type NEC	C44.590	-	-	-	-	-
squamous cell carcinoma	C44.520	-	-	-	-	-
sphincter	C21.1	C78.5	D01.3	D12.9	D37.8	D49.0
aorta(thoracic)	C49.3	C79.89	-	D21.3	D48.1	D49.2
abdominal	C49.4	C79.89	-	D21.4	D48.1	D49.2
aortic body	C75.5	C79.89	-	D35.6	D44.7	D49.7
aponeurosis	C49.9	C79.89	-	D21.9	D48.1	D49.2
palmar	C49.1-	C79.89	-	D21.1-	D48.1	D49.2
plantar	C49.2-	C79.89	-	D21.2-	D48.1	D49.2
appendix	C18.1	C78.5	D01.0	D12.1	D37.3	D49.0
arachnoid	C70.9	C79.49	-	D32.9	D42.9	D49.7
cerebral	C70.0	C79.32	-	D32.0	D42.0	D49.7
spinal	C70.1	C79.49	-	D32.1	D42.1	D49.7
areola	C50.0-	C79.81	D05.-	D24.-	D48.6-	D49.3
arm NEC	C76.4-	C79.89	D04.6-	D36.7	D48.7	D49.89
artery—see Neoplasm, connective tissue						
aryepiglottic fold	C13.1	C79.89	D00.08	D10.7	D37.05	D49.0
hypopharyngeal aspect	C13.1	C79.89	D00.08	D10.7	D37.05	D49.0
laryngeal aspect	C32.1	C78.39	D02.0	D14.1	D38.0	D49.1
marginal zone	C13.1	C79.89	D00.08	D10.7	D37.05	D49.0
arytenoid(cartilage)	C32.3	C78.39	D02.0	D14.1	D38.0	D49.1
fold—see Neoplasm, aryepiglottic						
associated with transplanted organ	C80.2	-	-	-	-	-
atlas	C41.2	C79.51	-	D16.6	D48.0	D49.2
atrium, cardiac	C38.0	C79.89	-	D15.1	D48.7	D49.89
auditory						
canal(external) (skin) A81	C44.20-	C79.2	D04.2-	D23.2-	D48.5	D49.2
internal	C30.1	C78.39	D02.3	D14.0	D38.5	D49.1
nerve	C72.4-	C79.49	-	D33.3	D43.3	D49.7
tube	C30.1	C78.39	D02.3	D14.0	D38.5	D49.1
opening	C11.2	C79.89	D00.08	D10.6	D37.05	D49.0
auricle, ear—see also Neoplasm, skin, ear	C44.20-	C79.2	D04.2-	D23.2-	D48.5	D49.2

	Malignant Primary	Malignant Secondary	Ca in situ	Benign	Uncertain Behavior	Unspecified Behavior
auricular canal (external)—see also Neoplasm, skin, ear	C44.20-	C79.2	D04.2-	D23.2-	D48.5	D49.2
internal	C30.1	C78.39	D02.3	D14.0	D38.5	D49.2
autonomic nerve or nervous system NEC (see Neoplasm, nerve, peripheral)						
axilla, axillary	C76.1	C79.89	D09.8	D36.7	D48.7	D49.89
fold—see also Neoplasm, skin, trunk	C44.509	C79.2	D04.5	D23.5	D48.5	D49.2
B						
back NEC	C76.8	C79.89	D04.5	D36.7	D48.7	D49.89
Bartholin's gland	C51.0	C79.82	D07.1	D28.0	D39.8	D49.5
basal ganglia	C71.0	C79.31	-	D33.0	D43.0	D49.6
basis pedunculi	C71.7	C79.31	-	D33.1	D43.1	D49.6
bile or biliary(tract)	C24.9	C78.89	D01.5	D13.5	D37.6	D49.0
canaliculi(biliferi) (intrahepatic)	C22.1	C78.7	D01.5	D13.4	D37.6	D49.0
canals, interlobular	C22.1	C78.89	D01.5	D13.4	D37.6	D49.0
duct or passage(common) (cystic) (extrahepatic)	C24.0	C78.89	D01.5	D13.5	D37.6	D49.0
interlobular	C22.1	C78.89	D01.5	D13.4	D37.6	D49.0
intrahepatic	C22.1	C78.7	D01.5	D13.4	D37.6	D49.0
and extrahepatic	C24.8	C78.89	D01.5	D13.5	D37.6	D49.0
bladder(urinary)	C67.9	C79.11	D09.0	D30.3	D41.4	D49.4
dome	C67.1	C79.11	D09.0	D30.3	D41.4	D49.4
neck	C67.5	C79.11	D09.0	D30.3	D41.4	D49.4
orifice	C67.9	C79.11	D09.0	D30.3	D41.4	D49.4
ureteric	C67.6	C79.11	D09.0	D30.3	D41.4	D49.4
urethral	C67.5	C79.11	D09.0	D30.3	D41.4	D49.4
overlapping lesion	C67.8	-	-	-	-	-
sphincter	C67.8	C79.11	D09.0	D30.3	D41.4	D49.4
trigone	C67.0	C79.11	D09.0	D30.3	D41.4	D49.4
urachus	C67.7	C79.11	D09.0	D30.3	D41.4	D49.4
wall	C67.9	C79.11	D09.0	D30.3	D41.4	D49.4
anterior	C67.3	C79.11	D09.0	D30.3	D41.4	D49.4
lateral	C67.2	C79.11	D09.0	D30.3	D41.4	D49.4
posterior	C67.4	C79.11	D09.0	D30.3	D41.4	D49.4
blood vessel—see Neoplasm, connective tissue						
bone(periosteum)	C41.9	C79.51	-	D16.9	D48.0	D49.2
acetabulum	C41.4	C79.51	-	D16.8	D48.0	D49.2
ankle	C40.3-	C79.51	-	D16.3-	-	-
arm NEC	C40.0-	C79.51	-	D16.0-	-	-
astragalus	C40.3-	C79.51	-	D16.3-	-	-
atlas	C41.2	C79.51	-	D16.6	D48.0	D49.2
axis	C41.2	C79.51	-	D16.6	D48.0	D49.2
back NEC	C41.2	C79.51	-	D16.6	D48.0	D49.2
calcaneus	C40.3-	C79.51	-	D16.3-	-	-
calvarium	C41.0	C79.51	-	D16.4	D48.0	D49.2
carpus(any)	C40.1-	C79.51	-	D16.1-	-	-
cartilage NEC	C41.9	C79.51	-	D16.9	D48.0	D49.2
clavicle	C41.3	C79.51	-	D16.7	D48.0	D49.2
clivus	C41.0	C79.51	-	D16.4	D48.0	D49.2
coccygeal vertebra	C41.4	C79.51	-	D16.8	D48.0	D49.2

	Malignant Primary	Malignant Secondary	Ca in situ	Benign	Uncertain Behavior	Unspecified
bone(periosteum) — *continued*						
coccyx	C41.4	C79.51	-	D16.8	D48.0	D49
costal cartilage	C41.3	C79.51	-	D16.7	D48.0	D49
costovertebral joint	C41.3	C79.51	-	D16.7	D48.0	D49
cranial	C41.0	C79.51	-	D16.4	D48.0	D49
cuboid	C40.3-	C79.51	-	D16.3-	-	-
cuneiform	C41.9	C79.51	-	D16.9	D48.0	D49
elbow	C40.0-	C79.51	-	D16.0-	-	-
ethmoid(labyrinth)	C41.0	C79.51	-	D16.4	D48.0	D49
face	C41.0	C79.51	-	D16.4	D48.0	D49
femur(any part)	C40.2-	C79.51	-	D16.2-	-	-
fibula(any part)	C40.2-	C79.51	-	D16.2-	-	-
finger(any)	C40.1-	C79.51	-	D16.1-	-	-
foot	C40.3-	C79.51	-	D16.3-	-	-
forearm	C40.0-	C79.51	-	D16.0-	-	-
frontal	C41.0	C79.51	-	D16.4	D48.0	D49
hand	C40.1-	C79.51	-	D16.1-	-	-
heel	C40.3-	C79.51	-	D16.3-	-	-
hip	C41.4	C79.51	-	D16.8	D48.0	D49
humerus(any part)	C40.0-	C79.51	-	D16.0-	-	-
hyoid	C41.0	C79.51	-	D16.4	D48.0	D49
ilium	C41.4	C79.51	-	D16.8	D48.0	D49
innominate	C41.4	C79.51	-	D16.8	D48.0	D49
intervertebral cartilage or disc	C41.2	C79.51	-	D16.6	D48.0	D49
ischium	C41.4	C79.51	-	D16.8	D48.0	D49
jaw(lower)	C41.1	C79.51	-	D16.5	D48.0	D49
knee	C40.2-	C79.51	-	D16.2-	-	-
leg NEC	C40.2-	C79.51	-	D16.2-	-	-
limb NEC	C40.9-	C79.51	-	D16.9	-	-
lower(long bones)	C40.2-	C79.51	-	D16.2-	-	-
short bones	C40.3-	C79.51	-	D16.3-	-	-
upper(long bones)	C40.0-	C79.51	-	D16.0-	-	-
short bones	C40.1-	C79.51	-	D16.1-	-	-
malar	C41.0	C79.51	-	D16.4	D48.0	D49
mandible	C41.1	C79.51	-	D16.5	D48.0	D49
marrow NEC (any bone)	C96.9	C79.52	-	-	D47.9	D49.
mastoid	C41.0	C79.51	-	D16.4	D48.0	D49
maxilla, maxillary(superior)	C41.0	C79.51	-	D16.4	D48.0	D49
inferior	C41.1	C79.51	-	D16.4	D48.0	D49
metacarpus(any)	C40.1-	C79.51	-	D16.1-	-	-
metatarsus(any)	C40.3-	C79.51	-	D16.3-	-	-
navicular						
ankle	C40.3-	C79.51	-	-	-	-
hand	C40.1-	C79.51	-	-	-	-
nose, nasal	C41.0	C79.51	-	D16.4	D48.0	D49.
occipital	C41.0	C79.51	-	D16.4	D48.0	D49.
orbit	C41.0	C79.51	-	D16.4	D48.0	D49.
overlapping sites	C40.8-	-	-	-	-	-
parietal	C41.0	C79.51	-	D16.4	D48.0	D49.
patella	C40.2-	C79.51	-	-	-	-
pelvic	C41.4	C79.51	-	D16.8	D48.0	D49.

	Malignant Primary	Malignant Secondary	Ca in situ	Benign	Uncertain Behavior	Unspecified Behavior
ne(periosteum) — *ntinued*						
phalanges						
foot	C40.3-	C79.51	-	-	-	-
hand	C40.1-	C79.51	-	-	-	-
pubic	C41.4	C79.51	-	D16.8	D48.0	D49.2
radius(any part)	C40.0-	C79.51	-	D16.0-	-	-
rib	C41.3	C79.51	-	D16.7	D48.0	D49.2
sacral vertebra	C41.4	C79.51	-	D16.8	D48.0	D49.2
sacrum	C41.4	C79.51	-	D16.8	D48.0	D49.2
scaphoid					-	-
of ankle	C40.3-	C79.51	-	-	-	-
of hand	C40.1-	C79.51	-	-	-	-
scapula(any part)	C40.0-	C79.51	-	D16.0-	-	-
sella turcica	C41.0	C79.51	-	D16.4	D48.0	D49.2
shoulder	C40.0-	C79.51	-	D16.0-	-	-
skull	C41.0	C79.51	-	D16.4	D48.0	D49.2
sphenoid	C41.0	C79.51	-	D16.4	D48.0	D49.2
spine, spinal(column)	C41.2	C79.51	-	D16.6	D48.0	D49.2
coccyx	C41.4	C79.51	-	D16.8	D48.0	D49.2
sacrum	C41.4	C79.51	-	D16.8	D48.0	D49.2
sternum	C41.3	C79.51	-	D16.7	D48.0	D49.2
tarsus(any)	C40.3-	C79.51	-	-	-	-
temporal	C41.0	C79.51	-	D16.4	D48.0	D49.2
thumb	C40.1-	C79.51	-	-	-	-
tibia(any part)	C40.2-	C79.51	-	-	-	-
toe(any)	C40.3-	C79.51	-	-	-	-
trapezium	C40.1-	C79.51	-	-	-	-
trapezoid	C40.1-	C79.51	-	-	-	-
turbinate	C41.0	C79.51	-	D16.4	D48.0	D49.2
ulna(any part)	C40.0-	C79.51	-	D16.0-	-	-
unciform	C40.1-	C79.51	-	-	-	-
vertebra(column)	C41.2	C79.51	-	D16.6	D48.0	D49.2
coccyx	C41.4	C79.51	-	D16.8	D48.0	D49.2
sacrum	C41.4	C79.51	-	D16.8	D48.0	D49.2
vomer	C41.0	C79.51	-	D16.4	D48.0	D49.2
wrist	C40.1-	C79.51	-	-	-	-
xiphoid process	C41.3	C79.51	-	D16.7	D48.0	D49.2
zygomatic	C41.0	C79.51	-	D16.4	D48.0	D49.2
ook-leaf(mouth)	C06.89	C79.89	D00.00	D10.39	D37.09	D49.0
owel—see Neoplasm, ntestine						
rachial plexus	C47.1-	C79.89	-	D36.12	D48.2	D49.2
rain NEC	C71.9	C79.31	-	D33.2	D43.2	D49.6
basal ganglia	C71.0	C79.31	-	D33.0	D43.0	D49.6
cerebellopontine angle	C71.6	C79.31	-	D33.1	D43.1	D49.6
cerebellum NOS	C71.6	C79.31	-	D33.1	D43.1	D49.6
cerebrum	C71.0	C79.31	-	D33.0	D43.0	D49.6
choroid plexus	C71.7	C79.31	-	D33.1	D43.1	D49.6
corpus callosum	C71.8	C79.31	-	D33.2	D43.2	D49.6
corpus striatum	C71.0	C79.31	-	D33.0	D43.0	D49.6
cortex(cerebral)	C71.0	C79.31	-	D33.0	D43.0	D49.6
frontal lobe	C71.1	C79.31	-	D33.0	D43.0	D49.6
globus pallidus	C71.0	C79.31	-	D33.0	D43.0	D49.6
hippocampus	C71.2	C79.31	-	D33.0	D43.0	D49.6

	Malignant Primary	Malignant Secondary	Ca in situ	Benign	Uncertain Behavior	Unspecified Behavior
brain NEC — *continued*						
hypothalamus	C71.0	C79.31	-	D33.0	D43.0	D49.6
internal capsule	C71.0	C79.31	-	D33.0	D43.0	D49.6
medulla oblongata	C71.7	C79.31	-	D33.1	D43.1	D49.6
meninges	C70.0	C79.32	-	D32.0	D42.0	D49.7
midbrain	C71.7	C79.31	-	D33.1	D43.1	D49.6
occipital lobe	C71.4	C79.31	-	D33.0	D43.0	D49.6
overlapping lesion	C71.8	C79.31	-	-	-	-
parietal lobe	C71.3	C79.31	-	D33.0	D43.0	D49.6
peduncle	C71.7	C79.31	-	D33.1	D43.1	D49.6
pons	C71.7	C79.31	-	D33.1	D43.1	D49.6
stem	C71.7	C79.31	-	D33.1	D43.1	D49.6
tapetum	C71.8	C79.31	-	D33.2	D43.2	D49.6
temporal lobe	C71.2	C79.31	-	D33.0	D43.0	D49.6
thalamus	C71.0	C79.31	-	D33.0	D43.0	D49.6
uncus	C71.2	C79.31	-	D33.0	D43.0	D49.6
ventricle(floor)	C71.5	C79.31	-	D33.0	D43.0	D49.6
fourth	C71.7	C79.31	-	D33.1	D43.1	D49.6
branchial(cleft) (cyst) (vestiges)	C10.4	C79.89	D00.08	D10.5	D37.05	D49.0
breast(connective tissue) (glandular tissue) (soft parts)	C50.9-	C79.81	D05.-	D24.-	D48.6-	D49.3
areola	C50.0-	C79.81	D05.-	D24.-	D48.6-	D49.3
axillary tail	C50.6-	C79.81	D05.-	D24.-	D48.6-	D49.3
central portion	C50.1-	C79.81	D05.-	D24.-	D48.6-	D49.3
inner	C50.8-	C79.81	D05.-	D24.-	D48.6-	D49.3
lower	C50.8-	C79.81	D05.-	D24.-	D48.6-	D49.3
lower-inner quadrant	C50.3-	C79.81	D05.-	D24.-	D48.6-	D49.3
lower-outer quadrant	C50.5-	C79.81	D05.-	D24.-	D48.6-	D49.3
mastectomy site(skin)—see also Neoplasm, breast, skin	C44.501	C79.2	-	-	-	-
specified as breast tissue	C50.8-	C79.81	-	-	-	-
midline	C50.8-	C79.81	D05.-	D24.-	D48.6-	D49.3
nipple	C50.0-	C79.81	D05.-	D24.-	D48.6-	D49.3
outer	C50.8-	C79.81	D05.-	D24.-	D48.6-	D49.3
overlapping lesion	C50.8-	-	-	-	-	-
skin	C44.501	C79.2	D04.5	D23.5	D48.5	D49.2
basal cell carcinoma	C44.511	-	-	-	-	-
specified type NEC	C44.591	-	-	-	-	-
squamous cell carcinoma	C44.521	-	-	-	-	-
tail(axillary)	C50.6-	C79.81	D05.-	D24.-	D48.6-	D49.3
upper	C50.8-	C79.81	D05.-	D24.-	D48.6-	D49.3
upper-inner quadrant	C50.2-	C79.81	D05.-	D24.-	D48.6-	D49.3
upper-outer quadrant	C50.4-	C79.81	D05.-	D24.-	D48.6-	D49.3
broad ligament	C57.1-	C79.82	D07.39	D28.2	D39.8	D49.5
bronchiogenic, bronchogenic(lung)	C34.9-	C78.0-	D02.2-	D14.3-	D38.1	D49.1
bronchiole	C34.9-	C78.0-	D02.2-	D14.3-	D38.1	D49.1
bronchus	C34.9-	C78.0-	D02.2-	D14.3-	D38.1	D49.1
carina	C34.0-	C78.0-	D02.2-	D14.3-	D38.1	D49.1
lower lobe of lung	C34.3-	C78.0-	D02.2-	D14.3-	D38.1	D49.1
main	C34.0-	C78.0-	D02.2-	D14.3-	D38.1	D49.1

	Malignant Primary	Malignant Secondary	Ca in situ	Benign	Uncertain Behavior	Unspecified Behavior
bronchus — *continued*						
middle lobe of lung	C34.2	C78.0-	D02.21	D14.31	D38.1	D49.1
overlapping lesion	C34.8-	-	-	-	-	-
upper lobe of lung	C34.1-	C78.0-	D02.2-	D14.3-	D38.1	D49.1
brow	C44.309	C79.2	D04.39	D23.39	D48.5	D49.2
basal cell carcinoma	C44.319	-	-	-	-	-
specified type NEC	C44.399	-	-	-	-	-
squamous cell carcinoma	C44.329	-	-	-	-	-
buccal(cavity)	C06.9	C79.89	D00.00	D10.39	D37.09	D49.0
commissure	C06.0	C79.89	D00.02	D10.39	D37.09	D49.0
groove(lower) (upper)	C06.1	C79.89	D00.02	D10.39	D37.09	D49.0
mucosa	C06.0	C79.89	D00.02	D10.39	D37.09	D49.0
sulcus(lower) (upper)	C06.1	C79.89	D00.02	D10.39	D37.09	D49.0
bulbourethral gland	C68.0	C79.19	D09.19	D30.4	D41.3	D49.5
bursa—see Neoplasm, connective tissue						
buttock NEC	C76.3	C79.89	D04.5	D36.7	D48.7	D49.89
C						
calf	C76.5-	C79.89	D04.7-	D36.7	D48.7	D49.89
calvarium	C41.0	C79.51	-	D16.4	D48.0	D49.2
calyx, renal	C65.-	C79.0-	D09.19	D30.1-	D41.1-	D49.5
canal						
anal	C21.1	C78.5	D01.3	D12.9	D37.8	D49.0
auditory(external)—see also Neoplasm, skin, ear	C44.20-	C79.2	D04.2-	D23.2-	D48.5	D49.2
auricular(external)—see also Neoplasm, skin, ear	C44.20-	C79.2	D04.2-	D23.2-	D48.5	D49.2
canaliculi, biliary(biliferi) (intrahepatic)	C22.1	C78.7	D01.5	D13.4	D37.6	D49.0
canthus(eye) (inner) (outer)	C44.10-	C79.2	D04.1-	D23.1-	D48.5	D49.2
basal cell carcinoma	C44.11-	-	-	-	-	-
specified type NEC	C44.19-	-	-	-	-	-
squamous cell carcinoma	C44.12-	-	-	-	-	-
capillary—see Neoplasm, connective tissue						
caput coli	C18.0	C78.5	D01.0	D12.0	D37.4	D49.0
carcinoid—see Tumor, carcinoid						
cardia(gastric)	C16.0	C78.89	D00.2	D13.1	D37.1	D49.0
cardiac orifice(stomach)	C16.0	C78.89	D00.2	D13.1	D37.1	D49.0
cardio-esophageal junction	C16.0	C78.89	D00.2	D13.1	D37.1	D49.0
cardio-esophagus	C16.0	C78.89	D00.2	D13.1	D37.1	D49.0
carina(bronchus)	C34.0-	C78.0-	D02.2-	D14.3-	D38.1	D49.1
carotid(artery)	C49.0	C79.89	-	D21.0	D48.1	D49.2
body	C75.4	C79.89	-	D35.5	D44.6	D49.7
carpus(any bone)	C40.1-	C79.51	-	D16.1-	-	-
cartilage(articular) (joint) NEC—see also Neoplasm, bone	C41.9	C79.51	-	D16.9	D48.0	D49.2
arytenoid	C32.3	C78.39	D02.0	D14.1	D38.0	D49.1
auricular	C49.0	C79.89	-	D21.0	D48.1	D49.2
bronchi	C34.0-	C78.39	-	D14.3-	D38.1	D49.1
costal	C41.3	C79.51	-	D16.7	D48.0	D49.2
cricoid	C32.3	C78.39	D02.0	D14.1	D38.0	D49.1
cuneiform	C32.3	C78.39	D02.0	D14.1	D38.0	D49.1
ear(external)	C49.0	C79.89	-	D21.0	D48.1	D49.2

	Malignant Primary	Malignant Secondary	Ca in situ	Benign	Uncertain Behavior	Unspecified Behavior
cartilage(articular) (joint) NEC—see also Neoplasm, bone — *continued*						
ensiform	C41.3	C79.51	-	D16.7	D48.0	D49
epiglottis	C32.1	C78.39	D02.0	D14.1	D38.0	D49
anterior surface	C10.1	C79.89	D00.08	D10.5	D37.05	D49
eyelid	C49.0	C79.89	-	D21.0	D48.1	D49
intervertebral	C41.2	C79.51	-	D16.6	D48.0	D49
larynx, laryngeal	C32.3	C78.39	D02.0	D14.1	D38.0	D49
nose, nasal	C30.0	C78.39	D02.3	D14.0	D38.5	D49
pinna	C49.0	C79.89	-	D21.0	D48.1	D49
rib	C41.3	C79.51	-	D16.7	D48.0	D49
semilunar(knee)	C40.2-	C79.51	-	D16.2-	D48.0	D49
thyroid	C32.3	C78.39	D02.0	D14.1	D38.0	D49
trachea	C33	C78.39	D02.1	D14.2	D38.1	D49
cauda equina	C72.1	C79.49	-	D33.4	D43.4	D49
cavity						
buccal	C06.9	C79.89	D00.00	D10.30	D37.09	D49
nasal	C30.0	C78.39	D02.3	D14.0	D38.5	D49
oral	C06.9	C79.89	D00.00	D10.30	D37.09	D49
peritoneal	C48.2	C78.6	-	D20.1	D48.4	D49
tympanic	C30.1	C78.39	D02.3	D14.0	D38.5	D49
cecum	C18.0	C78.5	D01.0	D12.0	D37.4	D49
central nervous system	C72.9	C79.40	-	-	-	-
cerebellopontine (angle)	C71.6	C79.31	-	D33.1	D43.1	D49
cerebellum, cerebellar	C71.6	C79.31	-	D33.1	D43.1	D49
cerebrum, cerebral(cortex) (hemisphere) (white matter)	C71.0	C79.31	-	D33.0	D43.0	D49
meninges	C70.0	C79.32	-	D32.0	D42.0	D49
peduncle	C71.7	C79.31	-	D33.1	D43.1	D49
ventricle	C71.5	C79.31	-	D33.0	D43.0	D49
fourth	C71.7	C79.31	-	D33.1	D43.1	D49
cervical region	C76.0	C79.89	D09.8	D36.7	D48.7	D49.8
cervix(cervical) (uteri) (uterus)	C53.9	C79.82	D06.9	D26.0	D39.0	D49.
canal	C53.0	C79.82	D06.0	D26.0	D39.0	D49.
endocervix(canal) (gland)	C53.0	C79.82	D06.0	D26.0	D39.0	D49.
exocervix	C53.1	C79.82	D06.1	D26.0	D39.0	D49.
external os	C53.1	C79.82	D06.1	D26.0	D39.0	D49.
internal os	C53.0	C79.82	D06.0	D26.0	D39.0	D49.
nabothian gland	C53.0	C79.82	D06.0	D26.0	D39.0	D49.
overlapping lesion	C53.8	-	-	-	-	-
squamocolumnar junction	C53.8	C79.82	D06.7	D26.0	D39.0	D49.
stump	C53.8	C79.82	D06.7	D26.0	D39.0	D49.
cheek	C76.0	C79.89	D09.8	D36.7	D48.7	D49.8
external	C44.309	C79.2	D04.39	D23.39	D48.5	D49.
basal cell carcinoma	C44.319	-	-	-	-	-
specified type NEC	C44.399	-	-	-	-	-
squamous cell carcinoma	C44.329	-	-	-	-	-
inner aspect	C06.0	C79.89	D00.02	D10.39	D37.09	D49.
internal	C06.0	C79.89	D00.02	D10.39	D37.09	D49.
mucosa	C06.0	C79.89	D00.02	D10.39	D37.09	D49.
chest(wall) NEC	C76.1	C79.89	D09.8	D36.7	D48.7	D49.8

	Malignant Primary	Malignant Secondary	Ca in situ	Benign	Uncertain Behavior	Unspecified Behavior
iasma opticum	C72.3-	C79.49	-	D33.3	D43.3	D49.7
in	C44.309	C79.2	D04.39	D23.39	D48.5	D49.2
basal cell carcinoma	C44.319	-	-	-	-	-
specified type NEC	C44.399	-	-	-	-	-
squamous cell carcinoma	C44.329	-	-	-	-	-
oana	C11.3	C79.89	D00.08	D10.6	D37.05	D49.0
olangiole	C22.1	C78.89	D01.5	D13.4	D37.6	D49.0
oledochal duct	C24.0	C78.89	D01.5	D13.5	D37.6	D49.0
oroid	C69.3-	C79.49	D09.2-	D31.3-	D48.7	D49.81
plexus	C71.5	C79.31	-	D33.0	D43.0	D49.6
iary body	C69.4-	C79.49	D09.2-	D31.4-	D48.7	D49.89
avicle	C41.3	C79.51	-	D16.7	D48.0	D49.2
toris	C51.2	C79.82	D07.1	D28.0	D39.8	D49.5
ivus	C41.0	C79.51	-	D16.4-	D48.0	D49.2
oacogenic zone	C21.2	C78.5	D01.3	D12.9	D37.8	D49.0
ccygeal						
body or glomus	C49.5	C79.89	-	D21.5	D48.1	D49.2
vertebra	C41.4	C79.51	-	D16.8	D48.0	D49.2
ccyx	C41.4	C79.51	-	D16.8	D48.0	D49.2
lon—see also Neoplasm, testine, large	C18.9	C78.5	-	-	-	-
with rectum	C19	C78.5	D01.1	D12.7	D37.5	D49.0
lumn, spinal—see eoplasm, spine						
lumnella—see also eoplasm, skin, face	C44.390	C79.2	D04.39	D23.39	D48.5	D49.2
mmissure						
labial, lip	C00.6	C79.89	D00.01	D10.39	D37.01	D49.0
laryngeal	C32.0	C78.39	D02.0	D14.1	D38.0	D49.1
mmon(bile) duct	C24.0	C78.89	D01.5	D13.5	D37.6	D49.0
ncha—see also eoplasm, skin, ear	C44.20-	C79.2	D04.2-	D23.2-	D48.5	D49.2
nose	C30.0	C78.39	D02.3	D14.0	D38.5	D49.1
njunctiva	C69.0-	C79.49	D09.2-	D31.0-	D48.7	D49.89
nnective tissue NEC	C49.9	C79.89	-	D21.9	D48.1	D49.2
Note: For neoplasms of connective tissue(blood vessel, bursa, fascia, ligament, muscle, peripheral nerves, sympathetic and parasympathetic nerves and ganglia, synovia, tendon, etc.) or of morphological types that indicate connective tissue, code according to the list under "Neoplasm, connective tissue". For sites that do not appear in this list, code to neoplasm of that site; e.g., fibrosarcoma, pancreas (C25.9)						
Note: Morphological types that indicate connective tissue appear in their proper place in the alphabetic index with the instruction "see Neoplasm, connective tissue …"						

	Malignant Primary	Malignant Secondary	Ca in situ	Benign	Uncertain Behavior	Unspecified Behavior
connective tissue NEC — *continued*						
abdomen	C49.4	C79.89	-	D21.4	D48.1	D49.2
abdominal wall	C49.4	C79.89	-	D21.4	D48.1	D49.2
ankle	C49.2-	C79.89	-	D21.2-	D48.1	D49.2
antecubital fossa or space	C49.1-	C79.89	-	D21.1-	D48.1	D49.2
arm	C49.1-	C79.89	-	D21.1-	D48.1	D49.2
auricle(ear)	C49.0	C79.89	-	D21.0	D48.1	D49.2
axilla	C49.3	C79.89	-	D21.3	D48.1	D49.2
back	C49.6	C79.89	-	D21.6	D48.1	D49.2
breast—see Neoplasm, breast						
buttock	C49.5	C79.89	-	D21.5	D48.1	D49.2
calf	C49.2-	C79.89	-	D21.2-	D48.1	D49.2
cervical region	C49.0	C79.89	-	D21.0	D48.1	D49.2
cheek	C49.0	C79.89	-	D21.0	D48.1	D49.2
chest(wall)	C49.3	C79.89	-	D21.3	D48.1	D49.2
chin	C49.0	C79.89	-	D21.0	D48.1	D49.2
diaphragm	C49.3	C79.89	-	D21.3	D48.1	D49.2
ear(external)	C49.0	C79.89	-	D21.0	D48.1	D49.2
elbow	C49.1-	C79.89	-	D21.1-	D48.1	D49.2
extrarectal	C49.5	C79.89	-	D21.5	D48.1	D49.2
extremity	C49.9	C79.89	-	D21.9	D48.1	D49.2
lower	C49.2-	C79.89	-	D21.2-	D48.1	D49.2
upper	C49.1-	C79.89	-	D21.1-	D48.1	D49.2
eyelid	C49.0	C79.89	-	D21.0	D48.1	D49.2
face	C49.0	C79.89	-	D21.0	D48.1	D49.2
finger	C49.1-	C79.89	-	D21.1-	D48.1	D49.2
flank	C49.6	C79.89	-	D21.6	D48.1	D49.2
foot	C49.2-	C79.89	-	D21.2-	D48.1	D49.2
forearm	C49.1-	C79.89	-	D21.1-	D48.1	D49.2
forehead	C49.0	C79.89	-	D21.0	D48.1	D49.2
gastric	C49.4	C79.89	-	D21.4	D48.1	D49.2
gastrointestinal	C49.4	C79.89	-	D21.4	D48.1	D49.2
gluteal region	C49.5	C79.89	-	D21.5	D48.1	D49.2
great vessels NEC	C49.3	C79.89	-	D21.3	D48.1	D49.2
groin	C49.5	C79.89	-	D21.5	D48.1	D49.2
hand	C49.1-	C79.89	-	D21.1-	D48.1	D49.2
head	C49.0	C79.89	-	D21.0	D48.1	D49.2
heel	C49.2-	C79.89	-	D21.2-	D48.1	D49.2
hip	C49.2-	C79.89	-	D21.2-	D48.1	D49.2
hypochondrium	C49.4	C79.89	-	D21.4	D48.1	D49.2
iliopsoas muscle	C49.5	C79.89	-	D21.5	D48.1	D49.2
infraclavicular region	C49.3	C79.89	-	D21.3	D48.1	D49.2
inguinal(canal) (region)	C49.5	C79.89	-	D21.5	D48.1	D49.2
intestinal	C49.4	C79.89	-	D21.4	D48.1	D49.2
intrathoracic	C49.3	C79.89	-	D21.3	D48.1	D49.2
ischiorectal fossa	C49.5	C79.89	-	D21.5	D48.1	D49.2
jaw	C03.9	C79.89	D00.03	D10.39	D48.1	D49.0
knee	C49.2-	C79.89	-	D21.2-	D48.1	D49.2
leg	C49.2-	C79.89	-	D21.2-	D48.1	D49.2
limb NEC	C49.9	C79.89	-	D21.9	D48.1	D49.2
lower	C49.2-	C79.89	-	D21.2-	D48.1	D49.2
upper	C49.1-	C79.89	-	D21.1-	D48.1	D49.2

	Malignant Primary	Malignant Secondary	Ca in situ	Benign	Uncertain Behavior	Unspecified Behavior
connective tissue NEC— *continued*						
nates	C49.5	C79.89	-	D21.5	D48.1	D49.2
neck	C49.0	C79.89	-	D21.0	D48.1	D49.2
orbit	C69.6-	C79.49	D09.2-	D31.6-	D48.1	D49.89
overlapping lesion	C49.8	-	-	-	-	-
pararectal	C49.5	C79.89	-	D21.5	D48.1	D49.2
para-urethral	C49.5	C79.89	-	D21.5	D48.1	D49.2
paravaginal	C49.5	C79.89	-	D21.5	D48.1	D49.2
pelvis(floor)	C49.5	C79.89	-	D21.5	D48.1	D49.2
pelvo-abdominal	C49.8	C79.89	-	D21.6	D48.1	D49.2
perineum	C49.5	C79.89	-	D21.5	D48.1	D49.2
perirectal(tissue)	C49.5	C79.89	-	D21.5	D48.1	D49.2
periurethral(tissue)	C49.5	C79.89	-	D21.5	D48.1	D49.2
popliteal fossa or space	C49.2-	C79.89	-	D21.2-	D48.1	D49.2
presacral	C49.5	C79.89	-	D21.5	D48.1	D49.2
psoas muscle	C49.4	C79.89	-	D21.4	D48.1	D49.2
pterygoid fossa	C49.0	C79.89	-	D21.0	D48.1	D49.2
rectovaginal septum or wall	C49.5	C79.89	-	D21.5	D48.1	D49.2
rectovesical	C49.5	C79.89	-	D21.5	D48.1	D49.2
retroperitoneum	C48.0	C78.6	-	D20.0	D48.3	D49.0
sacrococcygeal region	C49.5	C79.89	-	D21.5	D48.1	D49.2
scalp	C49.0	C79.89	-	D21.0	D48.1	D49.2
scapular region	C49.3	C79.89	-	D21.3	D48.1	D49.2
shoulder	C49.1-	C79.89	-	D21.1-	D48.1	D49.2
skin(dermis) NEC—see also Neoplasm, skin, by site	C44.90	C79.2	D04.9	D23.9	D48.5	D49.2
stomach	C49.4	C79.89	-	D21.4	D48.1	D49.2
submental	C49.0	C79.89	-	D21.0	D48.1	D49.2
supraclavicular region	C49.0	C79.89	-	D21.0	D48.1	D49.2
temple	C49.0	C79.89	-	D21.0	D48.1	D49.2
temporal region	C49.0	C79.89	-	D21.0	D48.1	D49.2
thigh	C49.2-	C79.89	-	D21.2-	D48.1	D49.2
thoracic(duct) (wall)	C49.3	C79.89	-	D21.3	D48.1	D49.2
thorax	C49.3	C79.89	-	D21.3	D48.1	D49.2
thumb	C49.1-	C79.89	-	D21.1-	D48.1	D49.2
toe	C49.2-	C79.89	-	D21.2-	D48.1	D49.2
trunk	C49.6	C79.89	-	D21.6	D48.1	D49.2
umbilicus	C49.4	C79.89	-	D21.4	D48.1	D49.2
vesicorectal	C49.5	C79.89	-	D21.5	D48.1	D49.2
wrist	C49.1-	C79.89	-	D21.1-	D48.1	D49.2
conus medullaris	C72.0	C79.49	-	D33.4	D43.4	D49.7
cord(true) (vocal)	C32.0	C78.39	D02.0	D14.1	D38.0	D49.1
false	C32.1	C78.39	D02.0	D14.1	D38.0	D49.1
spermatic	C63.1-	C79.82	D07.69	D29.8	D40.8	D49.5
spinal(cervical) (lumbar) (thoracic)	C72.0	C79.49	-	D33.4	D43.4	D49.7
cornea(limbus)	C69.1-	C79.49	D09.2-	D31.1-	D48.7	D49.89
corpus						
albicans	C56.-	C79.6-	D07.39	D27.-	D39.1-	D49.5
callosum, brain	C71.0	C79.31	-	D33.2	D43.2	D49.6
cavernosum	C60.2	C79.82	D07.4	D29.0	D40.8	D49.5
gastric	C16.2	C78.89	D00.2	D13.1	D37.1	D49.0

	Malignant Primary	Malignant Secondary	Ca in situ	Benign	Uncertain Behavior	Unspecified
corpus — *continued*						
overlapping sites	C54.8	-	-	-	-	-
penis	C60.2	C79.82	D07.4	D29.0	D40.8	D4
striatum, cerebrum	C71.0	C79.31	-	D33.0	D43.0	D4
uteri	C54.9	C79.82	D07.0	D26.1	D39.0	D4
isthmus	C54.0	C79.82	D07.0	D26.1	D39.0	D4
cortex						
adrenal	C74.0-	C79.7-	D09.3	D35.0-	D44.1-	D4
cerebral	C71.0	C79.31	-	D33.0	D43.0	D4
costal cartilage	C41.3	C79.51	-	D16.7	D48.0	D4
costovertebral joint	C41.3	C79.51	-	D16.7	D48.0	D4
Cowper's gland	C68.0	C79.19	D09.19	D30.4	D41.3	D4
cranial(fossa, any)	C71.9	C79.31	-	D33.2	D43.2	D4
meninges	C70.0	C79.32	-	D32.0	D42.0	D4
nerve	C72.50	C79.49	-	D33.3	D43.3	D4
specified NEC	C72.59	C79.49	-	D33.3	D43.3	D4
craniobuccal pouch	C75.2	C79.89	D09.3	D35.2	D44.3	D4
craniopharyngeal(duct) (pouch)	C75.2	C79.89	D09.3	D35.3	D44.4	D4
cricoid	C13.0	C79.89	D00.08	D10.7	D37.05	D4
cartilage	C32.3	C78.39	D02.0	D14.1	D38.0	D4
cricopharynx	C13.0	C79.89	D00.08	D10.7	D37.05	D4
crypt of Morgagni	C21.8	C78.5	D01.3	D12.9	D37.8	D4
crystalline lens	C69.4-	C79.49	D09.2-	D31.4-	D48.7	D49
cul-de-sac(Douglas')	C48.1	C78.6	-	D20.1	D48.4	D4
cuneiform cartilage	C32.3	C78.39	D02.0	D14.1	D38.0	D4
cutaneous—see Neoplasm, skin						
cutis—see Neoplasm, skin						
cystic(bile) duct (common)	C24.0	C78.89	D01.5	D13.5	D37.6	D4
D						
dermis—see Neoplasm, skin						
diaphragm	C49.3	C79.89	-	D21.3	D48.1	D49
digestive organs, system, tube, or tract NEC	C26.9	C78.89	D01.9	D13.9	D37.9	D49
disc, intervertebral	C41.2	C79.51	-	D16.6	D48.0	D49
disease, generalized	C80.0	-	-	-	-	-
disseminated	C80.0	-	-	-	-	-
Douglas' cul-de-sac or pouch	C48.1	C78.6	-	D20.1	D48.4	D49
duodenojejunal junction	C17.8	C78.4	D01.49	D13.39	D37.2	D49
duodenum	C17.0	C78.4	D01.49	D13.2	D37.2	D49
dura(cranial) (mater)	C70.9	C79.49	-	D32.9	D42.9	D49
cerebral	C70.0	C79.32	-	D32.0	D42.0	D49
spinal	C70.1	C79.49	-	D32.1	D42.1	D49
E						
ear(external)—see also Neoplasm, skin, ear	C44.20-	C79.2	D04.2-	D23.2-	D48.5	D49
auricle or auris—see also Neoplasm, skin, ear	C44.20-	C79.2	D04.2-	D23.2-	D48.5	D49
canal, external—see also Neoplasm, skin, ear	C44.20-	C79.2	D04.2-	D23.2-	D48.5	D49
cartilage	C49.0	C79.89	-	D21.0	D48.1	D49
external meatus—see also Neoplasm, skin, ear	C44.20-	C79.2	D04.2-	D23.2-	D48.5	D49

	Malignant Primary	Malignant Secondary	Ca in situ	Benign	Uncertain Behavior	Unspecified Behavior
r — *continued*						
nner	C30.1	C78.39	D02.3	D14.0	D38.5	D49.1
obule—see also Neoplasm, skin, ear	C44.20-	C79.2	D04.2-	D23.2-	D48.5	D49.2
niddle	C30.1	C78.39	D02.3	D14.0	D38.5	D49.1
overlapping lesion with accessory sinuses	C31.8	-	-	-	-	-
skin	C44.20-	C79.2	D04.2-	D23.2-	D48.5	D49.2
basal cell carcinoma	C44.21-	-	-	-	-	-
specified type NEC	C44.29-	-	-	-	-	-
squamous cell carcinoma	C44.22-	-	-	-	-	-
rlobe	C44.20-	C79.2	D04.2-	D23.2-	D48.5	D49.2
basal cell carcinoma	C44.21-	-	-	-	-	-
specified type NEC	C44.29-	-	-	-	-	-
squamous cell carcinoma	C44.22-	-	-	-	-	-
aculatory duct	C63.7	C79.82	D07.69	D29.8	D40.8	D49.5
bow NEC	C76.4-	C79.89	D04.6-	D36.7	D48.7	D49.89
docardium	C38.0	C79.89	-	D15.1	D48.7	D49.89
docervix(canal) (gland)	C53.0	C79.82	D06.0	D26.0	D39.0	D49.5
docrine gland NEC	C75.9	C79.89	D09.3	D35.9	D44.9	D49.7
pluriglandular	C75.8	C79.89	D09.3	D35.7	D44.9	D49.7
dometrium(gland) (stroma)	C54.1	C79.82	D07.0	D26.1	D39.0	D49.5
siform cartilage	C41.3	C79.51	-	D16.7	D48.0	D49.2
teric—see Neoplasm, testine						
endyma(brain)	C71.5	C79.31	-	D33.0	D43.0	D49.6
fourth ventricle	C71.7	C79.31	-	D33.1	D43.1	D49.6
icardium	C38.0	C79.89	-	D15.1	D48.7	D49.89
ididymis	C63.0-	C79.82	D07.69	D29.3-	D40.8	D49.5
idural	C72.9	C79.49	-	D33.9	D43.9	D49.7
iglottis	C32.1	C78.39	D02.0	D14.1	D38.0	D49.1
anterior aspect or surface	C10.1	C79.89	D00.08	D10.5	D37.05	D49.0
cartilage	C32.3	C78.39	D02.0	D14.1	D38.0	D49.1
free border(margin)	C10.1	C79.89	D00.08	D10.5	D37.05	D49.0
junctional region	C10.8	C79.89	D00.08	D10.5	D37.05	D49.0
posterior(laryngeal) surface	C32.1	C78.39	D02.0	D14.1	D38.0	D49.1
suprahyoid portion	C32.1	C78.39	D02.0	D14.1	D38.0	D49.1
sophagogastric junction	C16.0	C78.89	D00.2	D13.1	D37.1	D49.0
sophagus	C15.9	C78.89	D00.1	D13.0	D37.8	D49.0
abdominal	C15.5	C78.89	D00.1	D13.0	D37.8	D49.0
cervical	C15.3	C78.89	D00.1	D13.0	D37.8	D49.0
distal(third)	C15.5	C78.89	D00.1	D13.0	D37.8	D49.0
lower(third)	C15.5	C78.89	D00.1	D13.0	D37.8	D49.0
middle(third)	C15.4	C78.89	D00.1	D13.0	D37.8	D49.0
overlapping lesion	C15.8	-	-	-	-	-
proximal(third)	C15.3	C78.89	D00.1	D13.0	D37.8	D49.0
thoracic	C15.4	C78.89	D00.1	D13.0	D37.8	D49.0
upper(third)	C15.3	C78.89	D00.1	D13.0	D37.8	D49.0
thmoid(sinus)	C31.1	C78.39	D02.3	D14.0	D38.5	D49.1
bone or labyrinth	C41.0	C79.51	-	D16.4-	D48.0	D49.2
ustachian tube	C30.1	C78.39	D02.3	D14.0	D38.5	D49.1
xocervix	C53.1	C79.82	D06.1	D26.0	D39.0	D49.5

	Malignant Primary	Malignant Secondary	Ca in situ	Benign	Uncertain Behavior	Unspecified Behavior
external						
meatus(ear)—see also Neoplasm, skin, ear	C44.20-	C79.2	D04.2-	D23.2-	D48.5	D49.2
os, cervix uteri	C53.1	C79.82	D06.1	D26.0	D39.0	D49.5
extradural	C72.9	C79.49	-	D33.9	D43.9	D49.7
extrahepatic(bile) duct	C24.0	C78.89	D01.5	D13.5	D37.6	D49.0
overlapping lesion with gallbladder	C24.8	-	-	-	-	-
extraocular muscle	C69.6-	C79.49	D09.2-	D31.6-	D48.7	D49.89
extrarectal	C76.3	C79.89	D09.8	D36.7	D48.7	D49.89
extremity	C76.8	C79.89	D04.8	D36.7	D48.7	D49.89
lower	C76.5-	C79.89	D04.7-	D36.7	D48.7	D49.89
upper	C76.4-	C79.89	D04.6-	D36.7	D48.7	D49.89
eye NEC	C69.9-	C79.49	D09.2-	D31.9	D48.7	D49.89
overlapping sites	C69.8-	-	-	-	-	-
eyeball	C69.9-	C79.49	D09.2-	D31.9-	D48.7	D49.89
eyebrow	C44.309	C79.2	D04.39	D23.39	D48.5	D49.2
basal cell carcinoma	C44.319	-	-	-	-	-
specified type NEC	C44.399	-	-	-	-	-
squamous cell carcinoma	C44.329	-	-	-	-	-
eyelid(lower) (skin) (upper)	C44.10-	-	-	-	-	-
basal cell carcinoma	C44.11-	-	-	-	-	-
specified type NEC	C44.19-	-	-	-	-	-
squamous cell carcinoma	C44.12-	-	-	-	-	-
cartilage	C49.0	C79.89	-	D21.0	D48.1	D49.2
F						
face NEC	C76.0	C79.89	D04.39	D36.7	D48.7	D49.89
fallopian tube(accessory)	C57.0-	C79.82	D07.39	D28.2	D39.8	D49.5
falx(cerebella) (cerebri)	C70.0	C79.32	-	D32.0	D42.0	D49.7
fascia—see also Neoplasm, connective tissue						
palmar	C49.1-	C79.89	-	D21.1-	D48.1	D49.2
plantar	C49.2-	C79.89	-	D21.2-	D48.1	D49.2
fatty tissue—see Neoplasm, connective tissue						
fauces, faucial NEC	C10.9	C79.89	D00.08	D10.5	D37.05	D49.0
pillars	C09.1	C79.89	D00.08	D10.5	D37.05	D49.0
tonsil	C09.9	C79.89	D00.08	D10.4	D37.05	D49.0
femur(any part)	C40.2-	-	-	D16.2-	-	-
fetal membrane	C58	C79.82	D07.0	D26.7	D39.2	D49.5
fibrous tissue—see Neoplasm, connective tissue						
fibula(any part)	C40.2-	C79.51	-	D16.2-	-	-
filum terminale	C72.0	C79.49	-	D33.4	D43.4	D49.7
finger NEC	C76.4-	C79.89	D04.6-	D36.7	D48.7	D49.89
flank NEC	C76.8	C79.89	D04.5	D36.7	D48.7	D49.89
follicle, nabothian	C53.0	C79.82	D06.0	D26.0	D39.0	D49.5
foot NEC	C76.5-	C79.89	D04.7-	D36.7	D48.7	D49.89
forearm NEC	C76.4-	C79.89	D04.6-	D36.7	D48.7	D49.89
forehead(skin)	C44.309	C79.2	D04.39	D23.39	D48.5	D49.2
basal cell carcinoma	C44.319	-	-	-	-	-
specified type NEC	C44.399	-	-	-	-	-
squamous cell carcinoma	C44.329	-	-	-	-	-
foreskin	C60.0	C79.82	D07.4	D29.0	D40.8	D49.5

	Malignant Primary	Malignant Secondary	Ca in situ	Benign	Uncertain Behavior	Unspecified Behavior
fornix						
pharyngeal	C11.3	C79.89	D00.08	D10.6	D37.05	D49.0
vagina	C52	C79.82	D07.2	D28.1	D39.8	D49.5
fossa(of)						
anterior(cranial)	C71.9	C79.31	-	D33.2	D43.2	D49.6
cranial	C71.9	C79.31	-	D33.2	D43.2	D49.6
ischiorectal	C76.3	C79.89	D09.8	D36.7	D48.7	D49.89
middle(cranial)	C71.9	C79.31	-	D33.2	D43.2	D49.6
piriform	C12	C79.89	D00.08	D10.7	D37.05	D49.0
pituitary	C75.1	C79.89	D09.3	D35.2	D44.3	D49.7
posterior(cranial)	C71.9	C79.31	-	D33.2	D43.2	D49.6
pterygoid	C49.0	C79.89	-	D21.0	D48.1	D49.2
pyriform	C12	C79.89	D00.08	D10.7	D37.05	D49.0
Rosenmuller	C11.2	C79.89	D00.08	D10.6	D37.05	D49.0
tonsillar	C09.0	C79.89	D00.08	D10.5	D37.05	D49.0
fourchette	C51.9	C79.82	D07.1	D28.0	D39.8	D49.5
frenulum						
labii—see Neoplasm, lip, internal						
linguae	C02.2	C79.89	D00.07	D10.1	D37.02	D49.0
frontal						
bone	C41.0	C79.51	-	D16.4	D48.0	D49.2
lobe, brain	C71.1	C79.31	-	D33.0	D43.0	D49.6
pole	C71.1	C79.31	-	D33.0	D43.0	D49.6
sinus	C31.2	C78.39	D02.3	D14.0	D38.5	D49.1
fundus						
stomach	C16.1	C78.89	D00.2	D13.1	D37.1	D49.0
uterus	C54.3	C79.82	D07.0	D26.1	D39.0	D49.5
G						
gall duct(extrahepatic)	C24.0	C78.89	D01.5	D13.5	D37.6	D49.0
intrahepatic	C22.1	C78.7	D01.5	D13.4	D37.6	D49.0
gallbladder	C23	C78.89	D01.5	D13.5	D37.6	D49.0
overlapping lesion with extrahepatic bile ducts	C24.8	-	-	-	-	-
ganglia—see also Neoplasm, nerve, peripheral	C47.9	C79.89	-	D36.10	D48.2	D49.2
basal	C71.0	C79.31	-	D33.0	D43.0	D49.6
cranial nerve	C72.50	C79.49	-	D33.3	D43.3	D49.7
Gartner's duct	C52	C79.82	D07.2	D28.1	D39.8	D49.5
gastric—see Neoplasm, stomach						
gastrocolic	C26.9	C78.89	D01.9	D13.9	D37.9	D49.0
gastroesophageal junction	C16.0	C78.89	D00.2	D13.1	D37.1	D49.0
gastrointestinal(tract) NEC	C26.9	C78.89	D01.9	D13.9	D37.9	D49.0
generalized	C80.0	-	-	-	-	-
genital organ or tract						
female NEC	C57.9	C79.82	D07.30	D28.9	D39.9	D49.5
overlapping lesion	C57.8	-	-	-	-	-
specified site NEC	C57.7	C79.82	D07.39	D28.7	D39.8	D49.5
male NEC	C63.9	C79.82	D07.60	D29.9	D40.9	D49.5
overlapping lesion	C63.8	-	-	-	-	-
specified site NEC	C63.7	C79.82	D07.69	D29.8	D40.8	D49.5
genitourinary tract						
female	C57.9	C79.82	D07.30	D28.9	D39.9	D49.5
male	C63.9	C79.82	D07.60	D29.9	D40.9	D49.5

	Malignant Primary	Malignant Secondary	Ca in situ	Benign	Uncertain Behavior	Unspecified
gingiva(alveolar) (marginal)	C03.9	C79.89	D00.03	D10.39	D37.09	D4
lower	C03.1	C79.89	D00.03	D10.39	D37.09	D4
mandibular	C03.1	C79.89	D00.03	D10.39	D37.09	D4
maxillary	C03.0	C79.89	D00.03	D10.39	D37.09	D4
upper	C03.0	C79.89	D00.03	D10.39	D37.09	D4
gland, glandular (lymphatic) (system)—see also Neoplasm, lymph gland						
endocrine NEC	C75.9	C79.89	D09.3	D35.9	D44.9	D4
salivary—see Neoplasm, salivary gland						
glans penis	C60.1	C79.82	D07.4	D29.0	D40.8	D4
globus pallidus	C71.0	C79.31	-	D33.0	D43.0	D4
glomus						
coccygeal	C49.5	C79.89	-	D21.5	D48.1	D4
jugularis	C75.5	C79.89	-	D35.6	D44.7	D4
glosso-epiglottic fold(s)	C10.1	C79.89	D00.08	D10.5	D37.05	D4
glossopalatine fold	C09.1	C79.89	D00.08	D10.5	D37.05	D4
glossopharyngeal sulcus	C09.0	C79.89	D00.08	D10.5	D37.05	D4
glottis	C32.0	C78.39	D02.0	D14.1	D38.0	D4
gluteal region	C76.3	C79.89	D04.5	D36.7	D48.7	D49
great vessels NEC	C49.3	C79.89	-	D21.3	D48.1	D4
groin NEC	C76.3	C79.89	D04.5	D36.7	D48.7	D49
gum	C03.9	C79.89	D00.03	D10.39	D37.09	D4
lower	C03.1	C79.89	D00.03	D10.39	D37.09	D4
upper	C03.0	C79.89	D00.03	D10.39	D37.09	D4
H						
hand NEC	C76.4-	C79.89	D04.6-	D36.7	D48.7	D49
head NEC	C76.0	C79.89	D04.4	D36.7	D48.7	D49
heart	C38.0	C79.89	-	D15.1	D48.7	D49
heel NEC	C76.5-	C79.89	D04.7-	D36.7	D48.7	D49
helix—see also Neoplasm, skin, ear	C44.20-	C79.2	D04.2-	D23.2-	D48.5	D49
hematopoietic, hemopoietic tissue NEC	C96.9	-	-	-	-	-
specified NEC	C96.Z	-	-	-	-	-
hemisphere, cerebral	C71.0	C79.31	-	D33.0	D43.0	D49
hemorrhoidal zone	C21.1	C78.5	D01.3	D12.9	D37.8	D49
hepatic—see also Index to disease, by histology	C22.9	C78.7	D01.5	D13.4	D37.6	D49
duct(bile)	C24.0	C78.89	D01.5	D13.5	D37.6	D49
flexure(colon)	C18.3	C78.5	D01.0	D12.3	D37.4	D49
primary	C22.8	C78.7	D01.5	D13.4	D37.6	D49
hepatobiliary	C24.9	C78.89	D01.5	D13.5	D37.6	D49
hepatoblastoma	C22.2	C78.7	D01.5	D13.4	D37.6	D49
hepatoma	C22.0	C78.7	D01.5	D13.4	D37.6	D49
hilus of lung	C34.0-	C78.0-	D02.2-	D14.3-	D38.1	D49
hip NEC	C76.5-	C79.89	D04.7-	D36.7	D48.7	D49.
hippocampus, brain	C71.2	C79.31	-	D33.0	D43.0	D49
humerus(any part)	C40.0-	C79.51	-	D16.0-	-	-
hymen	C52	C79.82	D07.2	D28.1	D39.8	D49
hypopharynx, hypopharyngeal NEC	C13.9	C79.89	D00.08	D10.7	D37.05	D49.
overlapping lesion	C13.8	-	-	-	-	-
postcricoid region	C13.0	C79.89	D00.08	D10.7	D37.05	D49

	Malignant Primary	Malignant Secondary	Ca in situ	Benign	Uncertain Behavior	Unspecified Behavior
popharynx, popharyngeal NEC — *ntinued*						
posterior wall	C13.2	C79.89	D00.08	D10.7	D37.05	D49.0
pyriform fossa(sinus)	C12	C79.89	D00.08	D10.7	D37.05	D49.0
pophysis	C75.1	C79.89	D09.3	D35.2	D44.3	D49.7
pothalamus	C71.0	C79.31	-	D33.0	D43.0	D49.6
I						
ocecum, ileocecal(coil) inction) (valve)	C18.0	C78.5	D01.0	D12.0	D37.4	D49.0
um	C17.2	C78.4	D01.49	D13.39	D37.2	D49.0
um	C41.4	C79.51	-	D16.8	D48.0	D49.2
nmunoproliferative NEC	C88.9	-	-	-	-	-
fraclavicular(region)	C76.1	C79.89	D04.5	D36.7	D48.7	D49.89
guinal(region)	C76.3	C79.89	D04.5	D36.7	D48.7	D49.89
sula	C71.0	C79.31	-	D33.0	D43.0	D49.6
sular tissue ancreas)	C25.4	C78.89	D01.7	D13.7	D37.8	D49.0
brain	C71.0	C79.31	-	D33.0	D43.0	D49.6
terarytenoid fold	C13.1	C79.89	D00.08	D10.7	D37.05	D49.0
hypopharyngeal aspect	C13.1	C79.89	D00.08	D10.7	D37.05	D49.0
laryngeal aspect	C32.1	C78.39	D02.0	D14.1	D38.0	D49.1
marginal zone	C13.1	C79.89	D00.08	D10.7	D37.05	D49.0
terdental papillae	C03.9	C79.89	D00.03	D10.39	D37.09	D49.0
lower	C03.1	C79.89	D00.03	D10.39	D37.09	D49.0
upper	C03.0	C79.89	D00.03	D10.39	D37.09	D49.0
ternal						
capsule	C71.0	C79.31	-	D33.0	D43.0	D49.6
os(cervix)	C53.0	C79.82	D06.0	D26.0	D39.0	D49.5
tervertebral cartilage r disc	C41.2	C79.51	-	D16.6	D48.0	D49.2
ntestine, intestinal	C26.0	C78.80	D01.40	D13.9	D37.8	D49.0
large	C18.9	C78.5	D01.0	D12.6	D37.4	D49.0
appendix	C18.1	C78.5	D01.0	D12.1	D37.3	D49.0
caput coli	C18.0	C78.5	D01.0	D12.0	D37.4	D49.0
cecum	C18.0	C78.5	D01.0	D12.0	D37.4	D49.0
colon	C18.9	C78.5	D01.0	D12.6	D37.4	D49.0
and rectum	C19	C78.5	D01.1	D12.7	D37.5	D49.0
ascending	C18.2	C78.5	D01.0	D12.2	D37.4	D49.0
caput	C18.0	C78.5	D01.0	D12.0	D37.4	D49.0
descending	C18.6	C78.5	D01.0	D12.4	D37.4	D49.0
distal	C18.6	C78.5	D01.0	D12.4	D37.4	D49.0
left	C18.6	C78.5	D01.0	D12.4	D37.4	D49.0
overlapping lesion	C18.8	-	-	-	-	-
pelvic	C18.7	C78.5	D01.0	D12.5	D37.4	D49.0
right	C18.2	C78.5	D01.0	D12.2	D37.4	D49.0
sigmoid (flexure)	C18.7	C78.5	D01.0	D12.5	D37.4	D49.0
transverse	C18.4	C78.5	D01.0	D12.3	D37.4	D49.0
hepatic flexure	C18.3	C78.5	D01.0	D12.3	D37.4	D49.0
ileocecum, ileocecal(coil) (valve)	C18.0	C78.5	D01.0	D12.0	D37.4	D49.0
overlapping lesion	C18.8	-	-	-	-	-
sigmoid flexure(lower) (upper)	C18.7	C78.5	D01.0	D12.5	D37.4	D49.0
splenic flexure	C18.5	C78.5	D01.0	D12.3	D37.4	D49.0

	Malignant Primary	Malignant Secondary	Ca in situ	Benign	Uncertain Behavior	Unspecified Behavior
intestine, intestinal — *continued*						
small	C17.9	C78.4	D01.40	D13.30	D37.2	D49.0
duodenum	C17.0	C78.4	D01.49	D13.2	D37.2	D49.0
ileum	C17.2	C78.4	D01.49	D13.39	D37.2	D49.0
jejunum	C17.1	C78.4	D01.49	D13.39	D37.2	D49.0
overlapping lesion	C17.8	-	-	-	-	-
tract NEC	C26.0	C78.89	D01.40	D13.9	D37.8	D49.0
intra-abdominal	C76.2	C79.89	D09.8	D36.7	D48.7	D49.89
intracranial NEC	C71.9	C79.31	-	D33.2	D43.2	D49.6
intrahepatic(bile) duct	C22.1	C78.7	D01.5	D13.4	D37.6	D49.0
intraocular	C69.9-	C79.49	D09.2-	D31.9-	D48.7	D49.89
intraorbital	C69.6-	C79.49	D09.2-	D31.6-	D48.7	D49.89
intrasellar	C75.1	C79.89	D09.3	D35.2	D44.3	D49.7
intrathoracic(cavity) (organs)	C76.1	C79.89	D09.8	D15.9	D48.7	D49.89
specified NEC	C76.1	C79.89	D09.8	D15.7	-	-
iris	C69.4-	C79.49	D09.2-	D31.4-	D48.7	D49.89
ischiorectal(fossa)	C76.3	C79.89	D09.8	D36.7	D48.7	D49.89
ischium	C41.4	C79.51	-	D16.8	D48.0	D49.2
island of Reil	C71.0	C79.31	-	D33.0	D43.0	D49.6
islands or islets of Langerhans	C25.4	C78.89	D01.7	D13.7	D37.8	D49.0
isthmus uteri	C54.0	C79.82	D07.0	D26.1	D39.0	D49.5
J						
jaw	C76.0	C79.89	D09.8	D36.7	D48.7	D49.89
bone	C41.1	C79.51	-	D16.5	D48.0	D49.2
lower	C41.1	C79.51	-	D16.5	-	-
upper	C41.0	C79.51	-	D16.4	-	-
carcinoma(any type) (lower) (upper)	C76.0	C79.89	-	-	-	-
skin—see also Neoplasm, skin, face	C44.309	C79.2	D04.39	D23.39	D48.5	D49.2
soft tissues	C03.9	C79.89	D00.03	D10.39	D37.09	D49.0
lower	C03.1	C79.89	D00.03	D10.39	D37.09	D49.0
upper	C03.0	C79.89	D00.03	D10.39	D37.09	D49.0
jejunum	C17.1	C78.4	D01.49	D13.39	D37.2	D49.0
joint NEC—see also Neoplasm, bone	C41.9	C79.51	-	D16.9	D48.0	D49.2
acromioclavicular	C40.0-	C79.51	-	D16.0-	-	-
bursa or synovial membrane—see Neoplasm, connective tissue						
costovertebral	C41.3	C79.51	-	D16.7	D48.0	D49.2
sternocostal	C41.3	C79.51	-	D16.7	D48.0	D49.2
temporomandibular	C41.1	C79.51	-	D16.5	D48.0	D49.2
junction						
anorectal	C21.8	C78.5	D01.3	D12.9	D37.8	D49.0
cardioesophageal	C16.0	C78.89	D00.2	D13.1	D37.1	D49.0
esophagogastric	C16.0	C78.89	D00.2	D13.1	D37.1	D49.0
gastroesophageal	C16.0	C78.89	D00.2	D13.1	D37.1	D49.0
hard and soft palate	C05.9	C79.89	D00.00	D10.39	D37.09	D49.0
ileocecal	C18.0	C78.5	D01.0	D12.0	D37.4	D49.0
pelvirectal	C19	C78.5	D01.1	D12.7	D37.5	D49.0
pelviureteric	C65.-	C79.0-	D09.19	D30.1-	D41.1-	D49.5

	Malignant Primary	Malignant Secondary	Ca in situ	Benign	Uncertain Behavior	Unspecified Behavior
junction — *continued*						
rectosigmoid	C19	C78.5	D01.1	D12.7	D37.5	D49.0
squamocolumnar, of cervix	C53.8	C79.82	D06.7	D26.0	D39.0	D49.5
K						
Kaposi's sarcoma—see Kaposi's, sarcoma						
kidney(parenchymal)	C64.-	C79.0-	D09.19	D30.0-	D41.0-	D49.5
calyx	C65.-	C79.0-	D09.19	D30.1-	D41.1-	D49.5
hilus	C65.-	C79.0-	D09.19	D30.1-	D41.1-	D49.5
pelvis	C65.-	C79.0-	D09.19	D30.1-	D41.1-	D49.5
knee NEC	C76.5-	C79.89	D04.7-	D36.7	D48.7	D49.89
L						
labia(skin)	C51.9	C79.82	D07.1	D28.0	D39.8	D49.5
majora	C51.0	C79.82	D07.1	D28.0	D39.8	D49.5
minora	C51.1	C79.82	D07.1	D28.0	D39.8	D49.5
labial—see also Neoplasm, lip	C00.9	C79.89	D00.01	D10.0	D37.01	D49.0
sulcus(lower) (upper)	C06.1	C79.89	D00.02	D10.39	D37.09	D49.0
labium(skin)	C51.9	C79.82	D07.1	D28.0	D39.8	D49.5
majus	C51.0	C79.82	D07.1	D28.0	D39.8	D49.5
minus	C51.1	C79.82	D07.1	D28.0	D39.8	D49.5
lacrimal						
canaliculi	C69.5-	C79.49	D09.2-	D31.5-	D48.7	D49.89
duct(nasal)	C69.5-	C79.49	D09.2-	D31.5-	D48.7	D49.89
gland	C69.5-	C79.49	D09.2-	D31.5-	D48.7	D49.89
punctum	C69.5-	C79.49	D09.2-	D31.5-	D48.7	D49.89
sac	C69.5-	C79.49	D09.2-	D31.5-	D48.7	D49.89
Langerhans, islands or islets	C25.4	C78.89	D01.7	D13.7	D37.8	D49.0
laryngopharynx	C13.9	C79.89	D00.08	D10.7	D37.05	D49.0
larynx, laryngeal NEC	C32.9	C78.39	D02.0	D14.1	D38.0	D49.1
aryepiglottic fold	C32.1	C78.39	D02.0	D14.1	D38.0	D49.1
cartilage(arytenoid) (cricoid) (cuneiform) (thyroid)	C32.3	C78.39	D02.0	D14.1	D38.0	D49.1
commissure(anterior) (posterior)	C32.0	C78.39	D02.0	D14.1	D38.0	D49.1
extrinsic NEC	C32.1	C78.39	D02.0	D14.1	D38.0	D49.1
meaning hypopharynx	C13.9	C79.89	D00.08	D10.7	D37.05	D49.0
interarytenoid fold	C32.1	C78.39	D02.0	D14.1	D38.0	D49.1
intrinsic	C32.0	C78.39	D02.0	D14.1	D38.0	D49.1
overlapping lesion	C32.8	-	-	-	-	-
ventricular band	C32.1	C78.39	D02.0	D14.1	D38.0	D49.1
leg NEC	C76.5-	C79.89	D04.7-	D36.7	D48.7	D49.89
lens, crystalline	C69.4-	C79.49	D09.2-	D31.4-	D48.7	D49.89
lid(lower) (upper)	C44.10-	C79.2	D04.1-	D23.1-	D48.5	D49.2
basal cell carcinoma	C44.11-	-	-	-	-	-
specified type NEC	C44.19-	-	-	-	-	-
squamous cell carcinoma	C44.12-	-	-	-	-	-
ligament—see also Neoplasm, connective tissue						
broad	C57.1-	C79.82	D07.39	D28.2	D39.8	D49.5
Mackenrodt's	C57.7	C79.82	D07.39	D28.7	D39.8	D49.5

	Malignant Primary	Malignant Secondary	Ca in situ	Benign	Uncertain Behavior	Unspecified
ligament — *continued*						
non-uterine—see Neoplasm, connective tissue						
round	C57.2-	C79.82	-	D28.2	D39.8	D49
sacro-uterine	C57.3	C79.82	-	D28.2	D39.8	D49
uterine	C57.3	C79.82	-	D28.2	D39.8	D49
utero-ovarian	C57.7	C79.82	D07.39	D28.2	D39.8	D49
uterosacral	C57.3	C79.82	-	D28.2	D39.8	D49
limb	C76.8	C79.89	D04.8	D36.7	D48.7	D49
lower	C76.5-	C79.89	D04.7-	D36.7	D48.7	D49
upper	C76.4-	C79.89	D04.6-	D36.7	D48.7	D49
limbus of cornea	C69.1-	C79.49	D09.2-	D31.1-	D48.7	D49
lingual NEC—see also Neoplasm, tongue	C02.9	C79.89	D00.07	D10.1	D37.02	D49
lingula, lung	C34.1-	C78.0-	D02.2-	D14.3-	D38.1	D49
lip	C00.9	C79.89	D00.01	D10.0	D37.01	D49
buccal aspect—see Neoplasm, lip, internal						
commissure	C00.6	C79.89	D00.01	D10.0	D37.01	D49
external	C00.2	C79.89	D00.01	D10.0	D37.01	D49
lower	C00.1	C79.89	D00.01	D10.0	D37.01	D49
upper	C00.0	C79.89	D00.01	D10.0	D37.01	D49
frenulum—see Neoplasm, lip, internal						
inner aspect—see Neoplasm, lip, internal						
internal	C00.5	C79.89	D00.01	D10.0	D37.01	D49
lower	C00.4	C79.89	D00.01	D10.0	D37.01	D49
upper	C00.3	C79.89	D00.01	D10.0	D37.01	D49
lipstick area	C00.2	C79.89	D00.01	D10.0	D37.01	D49
lower	C00.1	C79.89	D00.01	D10.0	D37.01	D49
upper	C00.0	C79.89	D00.01	D10.0	D37.01	D49
lower	C00.1	C79.89	D00.01	D10.0	D37.01	D49
internal	C00.4	C79.89	D00.01	D10.0	D37.01	D49
mucosa—see Neoplasm, lip, intervnal						
oral aspect—see Neoplasm, lip, internal						
overlapping lesion	C00.8	-	-	-	-	-
with oral cavity or pharynx	C14.8	-	-	-	-	-
skin(commissure) (lower) (upper)	C44.00	C79.2	D04.0	D23.0	D48.5	D49
basal cell carcinoma	C44.01	-	-	-	-	-
specified type NEC	C44.09	-	-	-	-	-
squamous cell carcinoma	C44.02	-	-	-	-	-
upper	C00.0	C79.89	D00.01	D10.0	D37.01	D49
internal	C00.3	C79.89	D00.01	D10.0	D37.01	D49
vermilion border	C00.2	C79.89	D00.01	D10.0	D37.01	D49
lower	C00.1	C79.89	D00.01	D10.0	D37.01	D49
upper	C00.0	C79.89	D00.01	D10.0	D37.01	D49
lipomatous—see Lipoma, by site						
liver—see also Index to disease, by histology	C22.9	C78.7	D01.5	D13.4	D37.6	D49
primary	C22.8	C78.7	D01.5	D13.4	D37.6	D49

	Malignant Primary	Malignant Secondary	Ca in situ	Benign	Uncertain Behavior	Unspecified Behavior
mbosacral plexus	C47.5	C79.89	-	D36.16	D48.2	D49.2
ng	C34.9-	C78.0-	D02.2-	D14.3-	D38.1	D49.1
azygos lobe	C34.1-	C78.0-	D02.2-	D14.3-	D38.1	D49.1
carina	C34.0-	C78.0-	D02.2-	D14.3-	D38.1	D49.1
hilus	C34.0-	C78.0-	D02.2-	D14.3-	D38.1	D49.1
linqula	C34.1-	C78.0-	D02.2-	D14.3-	D38.1	D49.1
lobe NEC	C34.9-	C78.0-	D02.2-	D14.3-	D38.1	D49.1
lower lobe	C34.3-	C78.0-	D02.2-	D14.3-	D38.1	D49.1
main bronchus	C34.0-	C78.0-	D02.2-	D14.3-	D38.1	D49.1
mesothelioma—see Mesothelioma						
middle lobe	C34.2	C78.0-	D02.21	D14.31	D38.1	D49.1
overlapping lesion	C34.8-	-	-	-	-	-
upper lobe	C34.1-	C78.0-	D02.2-	D14.3-	D38.1	D49.1
mph, lymphatic channel EC	C49.9	C79.89	-	D21.9	D48.1	D49.2
gland(secondary)	-	C77.9	-	D36.0	D48.7	D49.89
abdominal	-	C77.2	-	D36.0	D48.7	D49.89
aortic	-	C77.2	-	D36.0	D48.7	D49.89
arm	-	C77.3	-	D36.0	D48.7	D49.89
auricular(anterior) (posterior)	-	C77.0	-	D36.0	D48.7	D49.89
axilla, axillary	-	C77.3	-	D36.0	D48.7	D49.89
brachial	-	C77.3	-	D36.0	D48.7	D49.89
bronchial	-	C77.1	-	D36.0	D48.7	D49.89
bronchopulmonary	-	C77.1	-	D36.0	D48.7	D49.89
celiac	-	C77.2	-	D36.0	D48.7	D49.89
cervical	-	C77.0	-	D36.0	D48.7	D49.89
cervicofacial	-	C77.0	-	D36.0	D48.7	D49.89
Cloquet	-	C77.4	-	D36.0	D48.7	D49.89
colic	-	C77.2	-	D36.0	D48.7	D49.89
common duct	-	C77.2	-	D36.0	D48.7	D49.89
cubital	-	C77.3	-	D36.0	D48.7	D49.89
diaphragmatic	-	C77.1	-	D36.0	D48.7	D49.89
epigastric, inferior	-	C77.1	-	D36.0	D48.7	D49.89
epitrochlear	-	C77.3	-	D36.0	D48.7	D49.89
esophageal	-	C77.1	-	D36.0	D48.7	D49.89
face	-	C77.0	-	D36.0	D48.7	D49.89
femoral	-	C77.4	-	D36.0	D48.7	D49.89
gastric	-	C77.2	-	D36.0	D48.7	D49.89
groin	-	C77.4	-	D36.0	D48.7	D49.89
head	-	C77.0	-	D36.0	D48.7	D49.89
hepatic	-	C77.2	-	D36.0	D48.7	D49.89
hilar(pulmonary)	-	C77.1	-	D36.0	D48.7	D49.89
splenic	-	C77.2	-	D36.0	D48.7	D49.89
hypogastric	-	C77.5	-	D36.0	D48.7	D49.89
ileocolic	-	C77.2	-	D36.0	D48.7	D49.89
iliac	-	C77.5	-	D36.0	D48.7	D49.89
infraclavicular	-	C77.3	-	D36.0	D48.7	D49.89
inguina, inguinal	-	C77.4	-	D36.0	D48.7	D49.89
innominate	-	C77.1	-	D36.0	D48.7	D49.89
intercostal	-	C77.1	-	D36.0	D48.7	D49.89
intestinal	-	C77.2	-	D36.0	D48.7	D49.89
intrabdominal	-	C77.2	-	D36.0	D48.7	D49.89
intrapelvic	-	C77.5	-	D36.0	D48.7	D49.89

	Malignant Primary	Malignant Secondary	Ca in situ	Benign	Uncertain Behavior	Unspecified Behavior
lymph, lymphatic channel NEC, gland — *continued*						
intrathoracic	-	C77.1	-	D36.0	D48.7	D49.89
jugular	-	C77.0	-	D36.0	D48.7	D49.89
leg	-	C77.4	-	D36.0	D48.7	D49.89
limb						
lower	-	C77.4	-	D36.0	D48.7	D49.89
upper	-	C77.3	-	D36.0	D48.7	D49.89
lower limb	-	C77.4	-	D36.0	D48.7	D49.89
lumbar	-	C77.2	-	D36.0	D48.7	D49.89
mandibular	-	C77.0	-	D36.0	D48.7	D49.89
mediastinal	-	C77.1	-	D36.0	D48.7	D49.89
mesenteric(inferior) (superior)	-	C77.2	-	D36.0	D48.7	D49.89
midcolic	-	C77.2	-	D36.0	D48.7	D49.89
multiple sites in categories C77.0 - C77.5	-	C77.8	-	D36.0	D48.7	D49.89
neck	-	C77.0	-	D36.0	D48.7	D49.89
obturator	-	C77.5	-	D36.0	D48.7	D49.89
occipital	-	C77.0	-	D36.0	D48.7	D49.89
pancreatic	-	C77.2	-	D36.0	D48.7	D49.89
para-aortic	-	C77.2	-	D36.0	D48.7	D49.89
paracervical	-	C77.5	-	D36.0	D48.7	D49.89
parametrial	-	C77.5	-	D36.0	D48.7	D49.89
parasternal	-	C77.1	-	D36.0	D48.7	D49.89
parotid	-	C77.0	-	D36.0	D48.7	D49.89
pectoral	-	C77.3	-	D36.0	D48.7	D49.89
pelvic	-	C77.5	-	D36.0	D48.7	D49.89
peri-aortic	-	C77.2	-	D36.0	D48.7	D49.89
peripancreatic	-	C77.2	-	D36.0	D48.7	D49.89
popliteal	-	C77.4	-	D36.0	D48.7	D49.89
porta hepatis	-	C77.2	-	D36.0	D48.7	D49.89
portal	-	C77.2	-	D36.0	D48.7	D49.89
preauricular	-	C77.0	-	D36.0	D48.7	D49.89
prelaryngeal	-	C77.0	-	D36.0	D48.7	D49.89
presymphysial	-	C77.5	-	D36.0	D48.7	D49.89
pretracheal	-	C77.0	-	D36.0	D48.7	D49.89
primary(any site) NEC	C96.9	-	-	-	-	-
pulmonary(hiler)	-	C77.1	-	D36.0	D48.7	D49.89
pyloric	-	C77.2	-	D36.0	D48.7	D49.89
retroperitoneal	-	C77.2	-	D36.0	D48.7	D49.89
retropharyngeal	-	C77.0	-	D36.0	D48.7	D49.89
Rosenmuller's	-	C77.4	-	D36.0	D48.7	D49.89
sacral	-	C77.5	-	D36.0	D48.7	D49.89
scalene	-	C77.0	-	D36.0	D48.7	D49.89
site NEC	-	C77.9	-	D36.0	D48.7	D49.89
splenic(hilar)	-	C77.2	-	D36.0	D48.7	D49.89
subclavicular	-	C77.3	-	D36.0	D48.7	D49.89
subinguinal	-	C77.4	-	D36.0	D48.7	D49.89
sublingual	-	C77.0	-	D36.0	D48.7	D49.89
submandibular	-	C77.0	-	D36.0	D48.7	D49.89
submaxillary	-	C77.0	-	D36.0	D48.7	D49.89
submental	-	C77.0	-	D36.0	D48.7	D49.89
subscapular	-	C77.3	-	D36.0	D48.7	D49.89

	Malignant Primary	Malignant Secondary	Ca in situ	Benign	Uncertain Behavior	Unspecified Behavior
lymph, lymphatic channel NEC, gland — *continued*						
supraclavicular	-	C77.0	-	D36.0	D48.7	D49.89
thoracic	-	C77.1	-	D36.0	D48.7	D49.89
tibial	-	C77.4	-	D36.0	D48.7	D49.89
tracheal	-	C77.1	-	D36.0	D48.7	D49.89
tracheobronchial	-	C77.1	-	D36.0	D48.7	D49.89
upper limb	-	C77.3	-	D36.0	D48.7	D49.89
Virchow's	-	C77.0	-	D36.0	D48.7	D49.89
node—see also Neoplasm, lymph gland						
primary NEC	C96.9	-	-	-	-	-
vessel—see also Neoplasm, connective tissue	C49.9	C79.89	-	D21.9	D48.1	D49.2
M						
Mackenrodt's ligament	C57.7	C79.82	D07.39	D28.7	D39.8	D49.5
malar	C41.0	C79.51	-	D16.4	D48.0	D49.2
region—see Neoplasm, cheek						
mammary gland—see Neoplasm, breast						
mandible	C41.1	C79.51	-	D16.5	D48.0	D49.2
alveolar						
mucosa (carcinoma)	C03.1	C79.89	D00.03	D10.39	D37.09	D49.0
ridge or process	C41.1	C79.51	-	D16.5	D48.0	D49.2
marrow(bone) NEC	C96.9	C79.52	-	-	D47.9	D49.89
mastectomy site(skin)—see also Neoplasm, breast, skin	C44.501	C79.2	-	-	-	-
specified as breast tissue	C50.8-	C79.81	-	-	-	-
mastoid(air cells) (antrum) (cavity)	C30.1	C78.39	D02.3	D14.0	D38.5	D49.1
bone or process	C41.0	C79.51	-	D16.4	D48.0	D49.2
maxilla, maxillary(superior)	C41.0	C79.51	-	D16.4	D48.0	D49.2
alveolar						
mucosa	C03.0	C79.89	D00.03	D10.39	D37.09	D49.0
ridge or process(carcinoma)	C41.0	C79.51	-	D16.4	D48.0	D49.2
antrum	C31.0	C78.39	D02.3	D14.0	D38.5	D49.1
carcinoma	C03.0	C79.51	-	-	-	-
inferior—see Neoplasm, mandible						
sinus	C31.0	C78.39	D02.3	D14.0	D38.5	D49.1
meatus external (ear)—see also Neoplasm, skin, ear	C44.20-	C79.2	D04.2-	D23.2-	D48.5	D49.2
Meckel diverticulum, malignant	C17.3	C78.4	D01.49	D13.39	D37.2	D49.0
mediastinum, mediastinal	C38.3	C78.1	-	D15.2	D38.3	D49.89
anterior	C38.1	C78.1	-	D15.2	D38.3	D49.89
posterior	C38.2	C78.1	-	D15.2	D38.3	D49.89
medulla						
adrenal	C74.1-	C79.7-	D09.3	D35.0-	D44.1-	D49.7
oblongata	C71.7	C79.31	-	D33.1	D43.1	D49.6
meibomian gland	C44.10-	C79.2	D04.1-	D23.1-	D48.5	D49.2
basal cell carcinoma	C44.11-	-	-	-	-	-
specified type NEC	C44.19-	-	-	-	-	-
squamous cell carcinoma	C44.12-	-	-	-	-	-

	Malignant Primary	Malignant Secondary	Ca in situ	Benign	Uncertain Behavior	Unspecified
melanoma—see Melanoma						
meninges	C70.9	C79.49	-	D32.9	D42.9	D49
brain	C70.0	C79.32	-	D32.0	D42.0	D49
cerebral	C70.0	C79.32	-	D32.0	D42.0	D49
crainial	C70.0	C79.32	-	D32.0	D42.0	D49
intracranial	C70.0	C79.32	-	D32.0	D42.0	D49
spinal(cord)	C70.1	C79.49	-	D32.1	D42.1	D49
meniscus, knee joint(lateral) (medial)	C40.2-	C79.51	-	D16.2-	D48.0	D49
Merkel cell—see Carcinoma, Merkel cell						
mesentery, mesenteric	C48.1	C78.6	-	D20.1	D48.4	D49
mesoappendix	C48.1	C78.6	-	D20.1	D48.4	D49
mesocolon	C48.1	C78.6	-	D20.1	D48.4	D49
mesopharynx—see Neoplasm, oropharynx						
mesosalpinx	C57.1-	C79.82	D07.39	D28.2	D39.8	D49
mesothelial tissue—see Mesothelioma						
mesothelioma—see Mesothelioma						
mesovarium	C57.1-	C79.82	D07.39	D28.2	D39.8	D49
metacarpus(any bone)	C40.1-	C79.51	-	D16.1-	-	-
metastatic NEC—see also Neoplasm, by site, secondary	-	C79.9	-	-	-	-
metatarsus(any bone)	C40.3-	C79.51	-	D16.3-	-	-
midbrain	C71.7	C79.31	-	D33.1	D43.1	D49
milk duct—see Neoplasm, breast						
mons						
pubis	C51.9	C79.82	D07.1	D28.0	D39.8	D49.
veneris	C51.9	C79.82	D07.1	D28.0	D39.8	D49.
motor tract	C72.9	C79.49	-	D33.9	D43.9	D49.
brain	C71.9	C79.31	-	D33.2	D43.2	D49.
cauda equina	C72.1	C79.49	-	D33.4	D43.4	D49.
spinal	C72.0	C79.49	-	D33.4	D43.4	D49.
mouth	C06.9	C79.89	D00.00	D10.30	D37.09	D49.
book-leaf	C06.89	C79.89	-	-	-	-
floor	C04.9	C79.89	D00.06	D10.2	D37.09	D49.
anterior portion	C04.0	C79.89	D00.06	D10.2	D37.09	D49.
lateral portion	C04.1	C79.89	D00.06	D10.2	D37.09	D49.
overlapping lesion	C04.8	-	-	-	-	-
overlapping NEC	C06.80	-	-	-	-	-
roof	C05.9	C79.89	D00.00	D10.39	D37.09	D49.
specified part NEC	C06.89	C79.89	D00.00	D10.39	D37.09	D49.
vestibule	C06.1	C79.89	D00.00	D10.39	D37.09	D49.
mucosa						
alveolar(ridge or process)	C03.9	C79.89	D00.03	D10.39	D37.09	D49.
lower	C03.1	C79.89	D00.03	D10.39	D37.09	D49.
upper	C03.0	C79.89	D00.03	D10.39	D37.09	D49.
buccal	C06.0	C79.89	D00.02	D10.39	D37.09	D49.(
cheek	C06.0	C79.89	D00.02	D10.39	D37.09	D49.
lip—see Neoplasm, lip, internal						
nasal	C30.0	C78.39	D02.3	D14.0	D38.5	D49.1
oral	C06.0	C79.89	D00.02	D10.39	D37.09	D49.(

	Malignant Primary	Malignant Secondary	Ca in situ	Benign	Uncertain Behavior	Unspecified Behavior
ıllerian duct						
'emale	C57.7	C79.82	D07.39	D28.7	D39.8	D49.5
nale	C63.7	C79.82	D07.69	D29.8	D40.8	D49.5
ıscle—see also ›oplasm, connective tissue						
›xtraocular	C69.6-	C79.49	D09.2-	D31.6-	D48.7	D49.89
›ocardium	C38.0	C79.89	-	D15.1	D48.7	D49.89
›ometrium	C54.2	C79.82	D07.0	D26.1	D39.0	D49.5
›opericardium	C38.0	C79.89	-	D15.1	D48.7	D49.89
N						
bothian gland(follicle)	C53.0	C79.82	D06.0	D26.0	D39.0	D49.5
il—see also Neoplasm, ‹in, limb	C44.90	C79.2	D04.9	D23.9	D48.5	D49.2
finger—see also Neoplasm, skin, limb, upper	C44.60-	C79.2	D04.6-	D23.6-	D48.5	D49.2
toe—see also Neoplasm, skin, limb, lower	C44.70-	C79.2	D04.7-	D23.7-	D48.5	D49.2
ıres, naris(anterior) osterior)	C30.0	C78.39	D02.3	D14.0	D38.5	D49.1
ısal—see Neoplasm, nose						
ısolabial groove—see so Neoplasm, skin, face	C44.309	C79.2	D04.39	D23.39	D48.5	D49.2
ısolacrimal duct	C69.5-	C79.49	D09.2-	D31.5-	D48.7	D49.89
ısopharynx, ısopharyngeal	C11.9	C79.89	D00.08	D10.6	D37.05	D49.0
floor	C11.3	C79.89	D00.08	D10.6	D37.05	D49.0
overlapping lesion	C11.8	-	-	-	-	-
roof	C11.0	C79.89	D00.08	D10.6	D37.05	D49.0
wall	C11.9	C79.89	D00.08	D10.6	D37.05	D49.0
anterior	C11.3	C79.89	D00.08	D10.6	D37.05	D49.0
lateral	C11.2	C79.89	D00.08	D10.6	D37.05	D49.0
posterior	C11.1	C79.89	D00.08	D10.6	D37.05	D49.0
superior	C11.0	C79.89	D00.08	D10.6	D37.05	D49.0
ıtes—see also Neoplasm, ‹in, trunk	C44.509	C79.2	D04.5	D23.5	D48.5	D49.2
eck NEC	C76.0	C79.89	D09.8	D36.7	D48.7	D49.89
skin	C44.40	-	-	-	-	-
basal cell carcinoma	C44.41	-	-	-	-	-
specified type NEC	C44.49	-	-	-	-	-
squamous cell carcinoma	C44.42	-	-	-	-	-
erve(ganglion)	C47.9	C79.89	-	D36.10	D48.2	D49.2
abducens	C72.59	C79.49	-	D33.3	D43.3	D49.7
accessory(spinal)	C72.59	C79.49	-	D33.3	D43.3	D49.7
acoustic	C72.4-	C79.49	-	D33.3	D43.3	D49.7
auditory	C72.4-	C79.49	-	D33.3	D43.3	D49.7
autonomic NEC—see also Neoplasm, nerve, peripheral	C47.9	C79.89	-	D36.10	D48.2	D49.2
brachial	C47.1-	C79.89	-	D36.12	D48.2	D49.2
cranial	C72.50	C79.49	-	D33.3	D43.3	D49.7
specified NEC	C72.59	C79.49	-	D33.3	D43.3	D49.7
facial	C72.59	C79.49	-	D33.3	D43.3	D49.7
femoral	C47.2-	C79.89	-	D36.13	D48.2	D49.2
ganglion NEC—see also Neoplasm, nerve, peripheral	C47.9	C79.89	-	D36.10	D48.2	D49.2
nerve(ganglion) — *continued*						
glossopharyngeal	C72.59	C79.49	-	D33.3	D43.3	D49.7
hypoglossal	C72.59	C79.49	-	D33.3	D43.3	D49.7
intercostal	C47.3	C79.89	-	D36.14	D48.2	D49.2
lumbar	C47.6	C79.89	-	D36.17	D48.2	D49.2
median	C47.1-	C79.89	-	D36.12	D48.2	D49.2
obturator	C47.2-	C79.89	-	D36.13	D48.2	D49.2
oculomotor	C72.59	C79.49	-	D33.3	D43.3	D49.7
olfactory	C47.2-	C79.49	-	D33.3	D43.3	D49.7
optic	C72.3-	C79.49	-	D33.3	D43.3	D49.7
parasympathetic NEC	C47.9	C79.89	-	D36.10	D48.2	D49.2
peripheral NEC	C47.9	C79.89	-	D36.10	D48.2	D49.2
abdomen	C47.4	C79.89	-	D36.15	D48.2	D49.2
abdominal wall	C47.4	C79.89	-	D36.15	D48.2	D49.2
ankle	C47.2-	C79.89	-	D36.13	D48.2	D49.2
antecubital fossa or space	C47.1-	C79.89	-	D36.12	D48.2	D49.2
arm	C47.1-	C79.89	-	D36.12	D48.2	D49.2
auricle(ear)	C47.0	C79.89	-	D36.11	D48.2	D49.2
axilla	C47.3	C79.89	-	D36.12	D48.2	D49.2
back	C47.6	C79.89	-	D36.17	D48.2	D49.2
buttock	C47.5	C79.89	-	D36.16	D48.2	D49.2
calf	C47.2-	C79.89	-	D36.13	D48.2	D49.2
cervical region	C47.0	C79.89	-	D36.11	D48.2	D49.2
cheek	C47.0	C79.89	-	D36.11	D48.2	D49.2
chest(wall)	C47.3	C79.89	-	D36.14	D48.2	D49.2
chin	C47.0	C79.89	-	D36.11	D48.2	D49.2
ear(external)	C47.0	C79.89	-	D36.11	D48.2	D49.2
elbow	C47.1-	C79.89	-	D36.12	D48.2	D49.2
extrarectal	C47.5	C79.89	-	D36.16	D48.2	D49.2
extremity	C47.9	C79.89	-	D36.10	D48.2	D49.2
lower	C47.2-	C79.89	-	D36.13	D48.2	D49.2
upper	C47.1-	C79.89	-	D36.12	D48.2	D49.2
eyelid	C47.0	C79.89	-	D36.11	D48.2	D49.2
face	C47.0	C79.89	-	D36.11	D48.2	D49.2
finger	C47.1-	C79.89	-	D36.12	D48.2	D49.2
flank	C47.6	C79.89	-	D36.17	D48.2	D49.2
foot	C47.2-	C79.89	-	D36.13	D48.2	D49.2
forearm	C47.1-	C79.89	-	D36.12	D48.2	D49.2
forehead	C47.0	C79.89	-	D36.11	D48.2	D49.2
gluteal region	C47.5	C79.89	-	D36.16	D48.2	D49.2
groin	C47.5	C79.89	-	D36.16	D48.2	D49.2
hand	C47.1-	C79.89	-	D36.12	D48.2	D49.2
head	C47.0	C79.89	-	D36.11	D48.2	D49.2
heel	C47.2-	C79.89	-	D36.13	D48.2	D49.2
hip	C47.2-	C79.89	-	D36.13	D48.2	D49.2
infraclavicular region	C47.3	C79.89	-	D36.14	D48.2	D49.2
inguinal(canal) (region)	C47.5	C79.89	-	D36.16	D48.2	D49.2
intrathoracic	C47.3	C79.89	-	D36.14	D48.2	D49.2
ischiorectal fossa	C47.5	C79.89	-	D36.16	D48.2	D49.2
knee	C47.2-	C79.89	-	D36.13	D48.2	D49.2
leg	C47.2-	C79.89	-	D36.13	D48.2	D49.2

	Malignant Primary	Malignant Secondary	Ca in situ	Benign	Uncertain Behavior	Unspecified Behavior
nerve(ganglion), peripheral NEC —*continued*						
limb NEC	C47.9	C79.89	-	D36.10	D48.2	D49.2
lower	C47.2-	C79.89	-	D36.13	D48.2	D49.2
upper	C47.1-	C79.89	-	D36.12	D48.2	D49.2
nates	C47.5	C79.89	-	D36.16	D48.2	D49.2
neck	C47.0	C79.89	-	D36.11	D48.2	D49.2
orbit	C69.6-	C79.49	-	D31.6-	D48.7	D49.2
pararectal	C47.5	C79.89	-	D36.16	D48.2	D49.2
paraurethral	C47.5	C79.89	-	D36.16	D48.2	D49.2
paravaginal	C47.5	C79.89	-	D36.16	D48.2	D49.2
pelvis(floor)	C47.5	C79.89	-	D36.16	D48.2	D49.2
pelvoabdominal	C47.8	C79.89	-	D36.17	D48.2	D49.2
perineum	C47.5	C79.89	-	D36.16	D48.2	D49.2
perirectal(tissue)	C47.5	C79.89	-	D36.16	D48.2	D49.2
periurethral(tissue)	C47.5	C79.89	-	D36.16	D48.2	D49.2
popliteal fossa or space	C47.2-	C79.89	-	D36.13	D48.2	D49.2
presacral	C47.5	C79.89	-	D36.16	D48.2	D49.2
pterygoid fossa	C47.0	C79.89	-	D36.11	D48.2	D49.2
rectovaginal septum or wall	C47.5	C79.89	-	D36.16	D48.2	D49.2
rectovesical	C47.5	C79.89	-	D36.16	D48.2	D49.2
sacrococcygeal region	C47.5	C79.89	-	D36.16	D48.2	D49.2
scalp	C47.0	C79.89	-	D36.11	D48.2	D49.2
scapular region	C47.3	C79.89	-	D36.14	D48.2	D49.2
shoulder	C47.1-	C79.89	-	D36.12	D48.2	D49.2
submental	C47.0	C79.89	-	D36.11	D48.2	D49.2
supraclavicular region	C47.0	C79.89	-	D36.11	D48.2	D49.2
temple	C47.0	C79.89	-	D36.11	D48.2	D49.2
temporal region	C47.0	C79.89	-	D36.11	D48.2	D49.2
thigh	C47.2-	C79.89	-	D36.13	D48.2	D49.2
thoracic(duct) (wall)	C47.3	C79.89	-	D36.14	D48.2	D49.2
thorax	C47.3	C79.89	-	D36.14	D48.2	D49.2
thumb	C47.1-	C79.89	-	D36.12	D48.2	D49.2
toe	C47.2-	C79.89	-	D36.13	D48.2	D49.2
trunk	C47.6	C79.89	-	D36.17	D48.2	D49.2
umbilicus	C47.4	C79.89	-	D36.15	D48.2	D49.2
vesicorectal	C47.5	C79.89	-	D36.16	D48.2	D49.2
wrist	C47.1-	C79.89	-	D36.12	D48.2	D49.2
radial	C47.1-	C79.89	-	D36.12	D48.2	D49.2
sacral	C47.5	C79.89	-	D36.16	D48.2	D49.2
sciatic	C47.2-	C79.89	-	D36.13	D48.2	D49.2
spinal NEC	C47.9	C79.89	-	D36.10	D48.2	D49.2
accessory	C72.59	C79.49	-	D33.3	D43.3	D49.7
sympathetic NEC—see also Neoplasm, nerve, peripheral	C47.9	C79.89	-	D36.10	D48.2	D49.2
trigeminal	C72.59	C79.49	-	D33.3	D43.3	D49.7
trochlear	C72.59	C79.49	-	D33.3	D43.3	D49.7
ulnar	C47.1-	C79.89	-	D36.12	D48.2	D49.2
vagus	C72.59	C79.49	-	D33.3	D43.3	D49.7
nervous system(central)	C72.9	C79.40	-	D33.9	D43.9	D49.7
autonomic—see Neoplasm, nerve, peripheral						

	Malignant Primary	Malignant Secondary	Ca in situ	Benign	Uncertain Behavior	Unspecified
nervous system(central) —*continued*						
parasympathetic—see Neoplasm, nerve, peripheral						
specified site NEC	-	C79.49	-	D33.7	D43.8	-
sympathetic—see Neoplasm, nerve, peripheral						
nevus—see Nevus						
nipple	C50.0-	C79.81	D05.-	D24.-	-	-
nose, nasal	C76.0	C79.89	D09.8	D36.7	D48.7	D49
ala(external) (nasi)—see also Neoplasm, nose, skin	C44.301	C79.2	D04.39	D23.39	D48.5	D49
bone	C41.0	C79.51	-	D16.4	D48.0	D49
cartilage	C30.0	C78.39	D02.3	D14.0	D38.5	D49
cavity	C30.0	C78.39	D02.3	D14.0	D38.5	D49
choana	C11.3	C79.89	D00.08	D10.6	D37.05	D49
external(skin)—see also Neoplasm, nose, skin	C44.301	C79.2	D04.39	D23.39	D48.5	D49
fossa	C30.0	C78.39	D02.3	D14.0	D38.5	D49
internal	C30.0	C78.39	D02.3	D14.0	D38.5	D49
mucosa	C30.0	C78.39	D02.3	D14.0	D38.5	D49
septum	C30.0	C78.39	D02.3	D14.0	D38.5	D49
posterior margin	C11.3	C79.89	D00.08	D10.6	D37.05	D49
sinus—see Neoplasm, sinus						
skin	C44.301	C79.2	D04.39	D23.39	D48.5	D49
basal cell carcinoma	C44.311	-	-	-	-	-
specified type NEC	C44.391	-	-	-	-	-
squamous cell carcinoma	C44.321	-	-	-	-	-
turbinate(mucosa)	C30.0	C78.39	D02.3	D14.0	D38.5	D49
bone	C41.0	C79.51	-	D16.4	D48.0	D49
vestibule	C30.0	C78.39	D02.3	D14.0	D38.5	D49
nostril	C30.0	C78.39	D02.3	D14.0	D38.5	D49
nucleus pulposus	C41.2	C79.51	-	D16.6	D48.0	D49
O						
occipital						
bone	C41.0	C79.51	-	D16.4	D48.0	D49
lobe or pole, brain	C71.4	C79.31	-	D33.0	D43.0	D49
odontogenic—see Neoplasm, jaw bone						
olfactory nerve or bulb	C72.2-	C79.49	-	D33.3	D43.3	D49
olive(brain)	C71.7	C79.31	-	D33.1	D43.1	D49
omentum	C48.1	C78.6	-	D20.1	D48.4	D49
operculum(brain)	C71.0	C79.31	-	D33.0	D43.0	D49
optic nerve, chiasm, or tract	C72.3-	C79.49	-	D33.3	D43.3	D49
oral(cavity)	C06.9	C79.89	D00.00	D10.30	D37.09	D49
ill-defined	C14.8	C79.89	D00.00	D10.30	D37.09	D49
mucosa	C06.0	C79.89	D00.02	D10.39	D37.09	D49
orbit	C69.6-	C79.49	D09.2-	D31.6-	D48.7	D49.
autonomic nerve	C69.6-	C79.49	-	D31.6-	D48.7	D49
bone	C41.0	C79.51	-	D16.4	D48.0	D49
eye	C69.6-	C79.49	D09.2-	D31.6-	D48.7	D49.
peripheral nerves	C69.6-	C79.49	-	D31.6-	D48.7	D49
soft parts	C69.6-	C79.49	D09.2-	D31.6-	D48.7	D49.

	Malignant Primary	Malignant Secondary	Ca in situ	Benign	Uncertain Behavior	Unspecified Behavior
gan of Zuckerkandl	C75.5	C79.89	-	D35.6	D44.7	D49.7
opharynx	C10.9	C79.89	D00.08	D10.5	D37.05	D49.0
branchial cleft (vestige)	C10.4	C79.89	D00.08	D10.5	D37.05	D49.0
junctional region	C10.8	C79.89	D00.08	D10.5	D37.05	D49.0
lateral wall	C10.2	C79.89	D00.08	D10.5	D37.05	D49.0
overlapping lesion	C10.8	-	-	-	-	-
pillars or fauces	C09.1	C79.89	D00.08	D10.5	D37.05	D49.0
posterior wall	C10.3	C79.89	D00.08	D10.5	D37.05	D49.0
vallecula	C10.0	C79.89	D00.08	D10.5	D37.05	D49.0
s						
external	C53.1	C79.82	D06.1	D26.0	D39.0	D49.5
internal	C53.0	C79.82	D06.0	D26.0	D39.0	D49.5
ary	C56.-	C79.6-	D07.39	D27.-	D39.1-	D49.5
iduct	C57.0-	C79.82	D07.39	D28.2	D39.8	D49.5
P						
alate	C05.9	C79.89	D00.00	D10.39	D37.09	D49.0
hard	C05.0	C79.89	D00.05	D10.39	D37.09	D49.0
junction of hard and soft palate	C05.9	C79.89	D00.00	D10.39	D37.09	D49.0
overlapping lesions	C05.8	-	-	-	-	-
soft	C05.1	C79.89	D00.04	D10.39	D37.09	D49.0
nasopharyngeal surface	C11.3	C79.89	D00.08	D10.6	D37.05	D49.0
posterior surface	C11.3	C79.89	D00.08	D10.6	D37.05	D49.0
superior surface	C11.3	C79.89	D00.08	D10.6	D37.05	D49.0
alatoglossal arch	C09.1	C79.89	D00.00	D10.5	D37.09	D49.0
alatopharyngeal arch	C09.1	C79.89	D00.00	D10.5	D37.09	D49.0
allium	C71.0	C79.31	-	D33.0	D43.0	D49.6
alpebra	C44.10-	C79.2	D04.1-	D23.1-	D48.5	D49.2
basal cell carcinoma	C44.11-	-	-	-	-	-
specified type NEC	C44.19-	-	-	-	-	-
squamous cell carcinoma	C44.12-	-	-	-	-	-
ancreas	C25.9	C78.89	D01.7	D13.6	D37.8	D49.0
body	C25.1	C78.89	D01.7	D13.6	D37.8	D49.0
duct(of Santorini) (of Wirsung)	C25.3	C78.89	D01.7	D13.6	D37.8	D49.0
ectopic tissue	C25.7	C78.89	-	D13.6	D37.8	D49.0
head	C25.0	C78.89	D01.7	D13.6	D37.8	D49.0
islet cells	C25.4	C78.89	D01.7	D13.7	D37.8	D49.0
neck	C25.7	C78.89	D01.7	D13.6	D37.8	D49.0
overlapping lesion	C25.8	-	-	-	-	-
tail	C25.2	C78.89	D01.7	D13.6	D37.8	D49.0
ara-aortic body	C75.5	C79.89	-	D35.6	D44.7	D49.7
araganglion NEC	C75.5	C79.89	-	D35.6	D44.7	D49.7
arametrium	C57.3	C79.82	-	D28.2	D39.8	D49.5
aranephric	C48.0	C78.6	-	D20.0	D48.3	D49.0
ararectal	C76.3	C79.89	-	D36.7	D48.7	D49.89
arasagittal(region)	C76.0	C79.89	D09.8	D36.7	D48.7	D49.89
arasellar	C72.9	C79.49	-	D33.9	D43.8	D49.7
arathyroid(gland)	C75.0	C79.89	D09.3	D35.1	D44.2	D49.7
paraurethral	C76.3	C79.89	-	D36.7	D48.7	D49.89
gland	C68.1	C79.19	D09.19	D30.8	D41.8	D49.5
paravaginal	C76.3	C79.89	-	D36.7	D48.7	D49.89
parenchyma, kidney	C64.-	C79.0-	D09.19	D30.0-	D41.0-	D49.5

	Malignant Primary	Malignant Secondary	Ca in situ	Benign	Uncertain Behavior	Unspecified Behavior
parietal						
bone	C41.0	C79.51	-	D16.4	D48.0	D49.2
lobe, brain	C71.3	C79.31	-	D33.0	D43.0	D49.6
paroophoron	C57.1-	C79.82	D07.39	D28.2	D39.8	D49.5
parotid(duct) (gland)	C07	C79.89	D00.00	D11.0	D37.030	D49.0
parovarium	C57.1-	C79.82	D07.39	D28.2	D39.8	D49.5
patella	C40.20	C79.51	-	-	-	-
peduncle, cerebral	C71.7	C79.31	-	D33.1	D43.1	D49.6
pelvirectal junction	C19	C78.5	D01.1	D12.7	D37.5	D49.0
pelvis, pelvic	C76.3	C79.89	D09.8	D36.7	D48.7	D49.89
bone	C41.4	C79.51	-	D16.8	D48.0	D49.2
floor	C76.3	C79.89	D09.8	D36.7	D48.7	D49.89
renal	C65.-	C79.0-	D09.19	D30.1-	D41.1-	D49.5
viscera	C76.3	C79.89	D09.8	D36.7	D48.7	D49.89
wall	C76.3	C79.89	D09.8	D36.7	D48.7	D49.89
pelvo-abdominal	C76.8	C79.89	D09.8	D36.7	D48.7	D49.89
penis	C60.9	C79.82	D07.4	D29.0	D40.8	D49.5
body	C60.2	C79.82	D07.4	D29.0	D40.8	D49.5
corpus(cavernosum)	C60.2	C79.82	D07.4	D29.0	D40.8	D49.5
glans	C60.1	C79.82	D07.4	D29.0	D40.8	D49.5
overlapping sites	C60.8	-	-	-	-	-
skin NEC	C60.9	C79.82	D07.4	D29.0	D40.8	D49.5
periadrenal(tissue)	C48.0	C78.6	-	D20.0	D48.3	D49.0
perianal(skin)—see also Neoplasm, anus, skin	C44.500	C79.2	D04.5	D23.5	D48.5	D49.2
pericardium	C38.0	C79.89	-	D15.1	D48.7	D49.89
perinephric	C48.0	C78.6	-	D20.0	D48.3	D49.0
perineum	C76.3	C79.89	D09.8	D36.7	D48.7	D49.89
periodontal tissue NEC	C03.9	C79.89	D00.03	D10.39	D37.09	D49.0
periosteum—see Neoplasm, bone						
peripancreatic	C48.0	C78.6	-	D20.0	D48.3	D49.0
peripheral nerve NEC	C47.9	C79.89	-	D36.10	D48.2	D49.2
perirectal(tissue)	C76.3	C79.89	-	D36.7	D48.7	D49.89
perirenal(tissue)	C48.0	C78.6	-	D20.0	D48.3	D49.0
peritoneum, peritoneal(cavity)	C48.2	C78.6	-	D20.1	D48.4	D49.0
benign mesothelial tissue—see Mesothelioma, benign						
overlapping lesion	C48.8	-	-	-	-	-
with digestive organs	C26.9	-	-	-	-	-
parietal	C48.1	C78.6	-	D20.1	D48.4	D49.0
pelvic	C48.1	C78.6	-	D20.1	D48.4	D49.0
specified part NEC	C48.1	C78.6	-	D20.1	D48.4	D49.0
peritonsillar(tissue)	C76.0	C79.89	D09.8	D36.7	D48.7	D49.89
periurethral tissue	C76.3	C79.89	-	D36.7	D48.7	D49.89
phalanges						
foot	C40.3-	C79.51	-	D16.3-	-	-
hand	C40.1-	C79.51	-	D16.1-	-	-
pharynx, pharyngeal	C14.0	C79.89	D00.08	D10.9	D37.05	D49.0
bursa	C11.1	C79.89	D00.08	D10.6	D37.05	D49.0
fornix	C11.3	C79.89	D00.08	D10.6	D37.05	D49.0
recess	C11.2	C79.89	D00.08	D10.6	D37.05	D49.0
region	C14.0	C79.89	D00.08	D10.9	D37.05	D49.0

	Malignant Primary	Malignant Secondary	Ca in situ	Benign	Uncertain Behavior	Unspecified Behavior
pharynx, pharyngeal — *continued*						
tonsil	C11.1	C79.89	D00.08	D10.6	D37.05	D49.0
wall(lateral) (posterior)	C14.0	C79.89	D00.08	D10.9	D37.05	D49.0
pia mater	C70.9	C79.40	-	D32.9	D42.9	D49.7
cerebral	C70.0	C79.32	-	D32.0	D42.0	D49.7
cranial	C70.0	C79.32	-	D32.0	D42.0	D49.7
spinal	C70.1	C79.49	-	D32.1	D42.1	D49.7
pillars of fauces	C09.1	C79.89	D00.08	D10.5	D37.05	D49.0
pineal(body) (gland)	C75.3	C79.89	D09.3	D35.4	D44.5	D49.7
pinna(ear) NEC—see also Neoplasm, skin, ear	C44.20-	C79.2	D04.2-	D23.2-	D48.5	D49.2
piriform fossa or sinus	C12	C79.89	D00.08	D10.7	D37.05	D49.0
pituitary(body) (fossa) (gland) (lobe)	C75.1	C79.89	D09.3	D35.2	D44.3	D49.7
placenta	C58	C79.82	D07.0	D26.7	D39.2	D49.5
pleura, pleural(cavity)	C38.4	C78.2	-	D19.0	D38.2	D49.1
overlapping lesion with heart or mediastinum	C38.8	-	-	-	-	-
parietal	C38.4	C78.2	-	D19.0	D38.2	D49.1
visceral	C38.4	C78.2	-	D19.0	D38.2	D49.1
plexus						
brachial	C47.1-	C79.89	-	D36.12	D48.2	D49.2
cervical	C47.0	C79.89	-	D36.11	D48.2	D49.2
choroid	C71.5	C79.31	-	D33.0	D43.0	D49.6
lumbosacral	C47.5	C79.89	-	D36.16	D48.2	D49.2
sacral	C47.5	C79.89	-	D36.16	D48.2	D49.2
pluriendocrine	C75.8	C79.89	D09.3	D35.7	D44.9	D49.7
pole						
frontal	C71.1	C79.31	-	D33.0	D43.0	D49.6
occipital	C71.4	C79.31	-	D33.0	D43.0	D49.6
pons(varolii)	C71.7	C79.31	-	D33.1	D43.1	D49.6
popliteal fossa or space	C76.5-	C79.89	D04.7-	D36.7	D48.7	D49.89
postcricoid(region)	C13.0	C79.89	D00.08	D10.7	D37.05	D49.0
posterior fossa(cranial)	C71.9	C79.31	-	D33.2	D43.2	D49.6
postnasal space	C11.9	C79.89	D00.08	D10.6	D37.05	D49.0
prepuce	C60.0	C79.82	D07.4	D29.0	D40.8	D49.5
prepylorus	C16.4	C78.89	D00.2	D13.1	D37.1	D49.0
presacral(region)	C76.3	C79.89	-	D36.7	D48.7	D49.89
prostate(gland)	C61	C79.82	D07.5	D29.1	D40.0	D49.5
utricle	C68.0	C79.19	D09.19	D30.4	D41.3	D49.5
pterygoid fossa	C49.0	C79.89	-	D21.0	D48.1	D49.2
pubic bone	C41.4	C79.51	-	D16.8	D48.0	D49.2
pudenda, pudendum(femaie)	C51.9	C79.82	D07.1	D28.0	D39.8	D49.5
pulmonary—see also Neoplasm, lung	C34.9-	C78.0-	D02.2-	D14.3-	D38.1	D49.1
putamen	C71.0	C79.31	-	D33.0	D43.0	D49.6
pyloric						
antrum	C16.3	C78.89	D00.2	D13.1	D37.1	D49.0
canal	C16.4	C78.89	D00.2	D13.1	D37.1	D49.0
pylorus	C16.4	C78.89	D00.2	D13.1	D37.1	D49.0
pyramid(brain)	C71.7	C79.31	-	D33.1	D43.1	D49.6
pyriform fossa or sinus	C12	C79.89	D00.08	D10.7	D37.05	D49.0

	Malignant Primary	Malignant Secondary	Ca in situ	Benign	Uncertain Behavior	Unspecified
		R				
radius(any part)	C40.0-	C79.51	-	D16.0-	-	-
Rathke's pouch	C75.1	C79.89	D09.3	D35.2	D44.3	D49
rectosigmoid(junction)	C19	C78.5	D01.1	D12.7	D37.5	D49
overlapping lesion with anus or rectum	C21.8	-	-	-	-	-
rectouterine pouch	C48.1	C78.6	-	D20.1	D48.4	D49
rectovaginal septum or wall	C76.3	C79.89	D09.8	D36.7	D48.7	D49
rectovesical septum	C76.3	C79.89	D09.8	D36.7	D48.7	D49
rectum(ampulla)	C20	C78.5	D01.2	D12.8	D37.5	D49
and colon	C19	C78.5	D01.1	D12.7	D37.5	D49
overlapping lesion with anus or rectosigmoid junction	C21.8	-	-	-	-	-
renal	C64.-	C79.0-	D09.19	D30.0-	D41.0-	D49
calyx	C65.-	C79.0-	D09.19	D30.1-	D41.1-	D49
hilus	C65.-	C79.0-	D09.19	D30.1-	D41.1-	D49
parenchyma	C64.-	C79.0-	D09.19	D30.0-	D41.0-	D49
pelvis	C65.-	C79.0-	D09.19	D30.1-	D41.1-	D49
respiratory						
organs or system NEC	C39.9	C78.30	D02.4	D14.4	D38.6	D49
tract NEC	C39.9	C78.30	D02.4	D14.4	D38.5	D49
upper	C39.0	C78.30	D02.4	D14.4	D38.5	D49
retina	C69.2-	C79.49	D09.2-	D31.2-	D48.7	D49
retrobulbar	C69.6-	C79.49	-	D31.6-	D48.7	D49
retrocecal	C48.0	C78.6	-	D20.0	D48.3	D49
retromolar(area) (triangle) (trigone)	C06.2	C79.89	D00.00	D10.39	D37.09	D49
retro-orbital	C76.0	C79.89	D09.8	D36.7	D48.7	D49
retroperitoneal(space) (tissue)	C48.0	C78.6	-	D20.0	D48.3	D49
retroperitoneum	C48.0	C78.6	-	D20.0	D48.3	D49
retropharyngeal	C14.0	C79.89	D00.08	D10.9	D37.05	D49
retrovesical(septum)	C76.3	C79.89	D09.8	D36.7	D48.7	D49
rhinencephalon	C71.0	C79.31	-	D33.0	D43.0	D49
rib	C41.3	C79.51	-	D16.7	D48.0	D49
Rosenmuller's fossa	C11.2	C79.89	D00.08	D10.6	D37.05	D49
round ligament	C57.2-	C79.82	-	D28.2	D39.8	D49
		S				
sacrococcyx, sacrococcygeal	C41.4	C79.51		D16.8	D48.0	D49
region	C76.3	C79.89	D09.8	D36.7	D48.7	D49
sacrouterine ligament	C57.3	C79.82	-	D28.2	D39.8	D49
sacrum, sacral(vertebra)	C41.4	C79.51	-	D16.8	D48.0	D49
salivary gland or duct(major)	C08.9	C79.89	D00.00	D11.9	D37.039	D49
minor NEC	C06.9	C79.89	D00.00	D10.39	D37.04	D49
overlapping lesion	C08.9	-	-	-	-	-
parotid	C07	C79.89	D00.00	D11.0	D37.030	D49
pluriglandular	C08.9	C79.89	D00.00	D11.9	D37.039	D49
sublingual	C08.1	C79.89	D00.00	D11.7	D37.031	D49
submandibular	C08.0	C79.89	D00.00	D11.7	D37.032	D49
submaxillary	C08.0	C79.89	D00.00	D11.7	D37.032	D49
salpinx(uterine)	C57.0-	C79.82	D07.39	D28.2	D39.8	D49
Santorini's duct	C25.3	C78.89	D01.7	D13.6	D37.8	D49

	Malignant Primary	Malignant Secondary	Ca in situ	Benign	Uncertain Behavior	Unspecified Behavior
calp	C44.40	C79.2	D04.4	D23.4	D48.5	D49.2
basal cell carcinoma	C44.41	-	-	-	-	-
specified type NEC	C44.49	-	-	-	-	-
squamous cell carcinoma	C44.42	-	-	-	-	-
apula(any part)	C40.0-	C79.51	-	D16.0-	-	-
apular region	C76.1	C79.89	D09.8	D36.7	D48.7	D49.89
ar NEC—see *also* eoplasm, skin, by site	C44.90	C79.2	D04.9	D23.9	D48.5	D49.2
ciatic nerve	C47.2-	C79.89	-	D36.13	D48.2	D49.2
clera	C69.4-	C79.49	D09.2-	D31.4-	D48.7	D49.89
crotum(skin)	C63.2	C79.82	D07.61	D29.4	D40.8	D49.5
ebaceous gland—see eoplasm, skin						
ella turcica	C75.1	C79.89	D09.3	D35.2	D44.3	D49.7
bone	C41.0	C79.51	-	D16.4	D48.0	D49.2
emilunar cartilage(knee)	C40.2-	C79.51	-	D16.2-	D48.0	D49.2
eminal vesicle	C63.7	C79.82	D07.69	D29.8	D40.8	D49.5
eptum						
nasal	C30.0	C78.39	D02.3	D14.0	D38.5	D49.1
posterior margin	C11.3	C79.89	D00.08	D10.6	D37.05	D49.0
rectovaginal	C76.3	C79.89	D09.8	D36.7	D48.7	D49.89
rectovesical	C76.3	C79.89	D09.8	D36.7	D48.7	D49.89
urethrovaginal	C57.9	C79.82	D07.30	D28.9	D39.9	D49.5
vesicovaginal	C57.9	C79.82	D07.30	D28.9	D39.9	D49.5
houlder NEC	C76.4-	C79.89	D04.6-	D36.7	D48.7	D49.89
igmoid flexure(lower) upper)	C18.7	C78.5	D01.0	D12.5	D37.4	D49.0
inus(accessory)	C31.9	C78.39	D02.3	D14.0	D38.5	D49.1
bone(any)	C41.0	C79.51	-	D16.4	D48.0	D49.2
ethmoidal	C31.1	C78.39	D02.3	D14.0	D38.5	D49.1
frontal	C31.2	C78.39	D02.3	D14.0	D38.5	D49.1
maxillary	C31.0	C78.39	D02.3	D14.0	D38.5	D49.1
nasal, paranasal NEC	C31.9	C78.39	D02.3	D14.0	D38.5	D49.1
overlapping lesion	C31.8	-	-	-	-	-
pyriform	C12	C79.89	D00.08	D10.7	D37.05	D49.0
sphenoid	C31.3	C78.39	D02.3	D14.0	D38.5	D49.1
skeleton, skeletal NEC	C41.9	C79.51	-	D16.9	D48.0	D49.2
Skene's gland	C68.1	C79.19	D09.19	D30.8	D41.8	D49.5
skin NOS	C44.90	C79.2	D04.9	D23.9	D48.5	D49.2
abdominal wall	C44.509	C79.2	D04.5	D23.5	D48.5	D49.2
basal cell carcinoma	C44.519	-	-	-	-	-
specified type NEC	C44.599	-	-	-	-	-
squamous cell carcinoma	C44.529	-	-	-	-	-
ala nasi—see also Neoplasm, nose, skin	C44.301	C79.2	D04.39	D23.39	D48.5	D49.2
ankle—see also Neoplasm, skin, limb, lower	C44.70-	C79.2	D04.7-	D23.7-	D48.5	D49.2
antecubital space—see also Neoplasm, skin, limb, upper	C44.60-	C79.2	D04.6-	D23.6-	D48.5	D49.2
anus	C44.500	C79.2	D04.5	D23.5	D48.5	D49.2
basal cell carcinoma	C44.510	-	-	-	-	-
specified type NEC	C44.590	-	-	-	-	-
squamous cell carcinoma	C44.520	-	-	-	-	-

	Malignant Primary	Malignant Secondary	Ca in situ	Benign	Uncertain Behavior	Unspecified Behavior
skin NOS — *continued*						
arm—see also Neoplasm, skin, limb, upper	C44.60-	C79.2	D04.6-	D23.6-	D48.5	D49.2
auditory canal(external)—see also Neoplasm, skin, ear	C44.20-	C79.2	D04.2-	D23.2-	D48.5	D49.2
auricle(ear)—see also Neoplasm, skin, ear	C44.20-	C79.2	D04.2-	D23.2-	D48.5	D49.2
auricular canal(external)—see also Neoplasm, skin, ear	C44.20-	C79.2	D04.2-	D23.2-	D48.5	D49.2
axilla, axillary fold—see also Neoplasm, skin, trunk	C44.509	C79.2	D04.5	D23.5	D48.5	D49.2
back—see also Neoplasm, skin, trunk	C44.509	C79.2	D04.5	D23.5	D48.5	D49.2
basal cell carcinoma	C44.91					
breast	C44.501	C79.2	D04.5	D23.5	D48.5	D49.2
basal cell carcinoma	C44.511	-	-	-	-	-
specified type NEC	C44.591	-	-	-	-	-
squamous cell carcinoma	C44.521	-	-	-	-	-
brow—see also Neoplasm, skin, face	C44.309	C79.2	D04.39	D23.39	D48.5	D49.2
buttock—see also Neoplasm, skin, trunk	C44.509	C79.2	D04.5	D23.5	D48.5	D49.2
calf—see also Neoplasm, skin, limb, lower	C44.70-	C79.2	D04.7-	D23.7-	D48.5	D49.2
canthus(eye) (inner) (outer)	C44.10-	C79.2	D04.1-	D23.1-	D48.5	D49.2
basal cell carcinoma	C44.11-	-	-	-	-	-
specified type NEC	C44.19-	-	-	-	-	-
squamous cell carcinoma	C44.12-	-	-	-	-	-
cervical region—see also Neoplasm, skin, neck	C44.40	C79.2	D04.4	D23.4	D48.5	D49.2
cheek(external) —see also Neoplasm, skin, face	C44.309	C79.2	D04.39	D23.39	D48.5	D49.2
chest(wall)—see also Neoplasm, skin, trunk	C44.509	C79.2	D04.5	D23.5	D48.5	D49.2
chin—see also Neoplasm, skin, face	C44.309	C79.2	D04.39	D23.39	D48.5	D49.2
clavicular area—see also Neoplasm, skin, trunk	C44.509	C79.2	D04.5	D23.5	D48.5	D49.2
clitoris	C51.2	C79.82	D07.1	D28.0	D39.8	D49.5
columnella—see also Neoplasm, skin, face	C44.309	C79.2	D04.39	D23.39	D48.5	D49.2
concha—see also Neoplasm, skin, ear	C44.20-	C79.2	D04.2-	D23.2-	D48.5	D49.2
ear(external)	C44.20-	C79.2	D04.2-	D23.2-	D48.5	D49.2
basal cell carcinoma	C44.21-	-	-	-	-	-
specified type NEC	C44.29-	-	-	-	-	-
squamous cell carcinoma	C44.22-	-	-	-	-	-
elbow—see also Neoplasm, skin, limb, upper	C44.60-	C79.2	D04.6-	D23.6-	D48.5	D49.2
eyebrow—see also Neoplasm, skin, face	C44.309	C79.2	D04.39	D23.39	D48.5	D49.2

	Malignant Primary	Malignant Secondary	Ca in situ	Benign	Uncertain Behavior	Unspecified Behavior
skin NOS — *continued*						
eyelid	C44.10-	C79.2	D04.1-	D23.1-	D48.5	D49.2
basal cell carcinoma	C44.11-	-	-	-	-	-
specified type NEC	C44.19-	-	-	-	-	-
squamous cell carcinoma	C44.12-	-	-	-	-	-
face NOS	C44.300	C79.2	D04.30	D23.30	D48.5	D49.2
basal cell carcinoma	C44.310	-	-	-	-	-
specified type NEC	C44.390	-	-	-	-	-
squamous cell carcinoma	C44.320	-	-	-	-	-
female genital organs(external)	C51.9	C79.82	D07.1	D28.0	D39.8	D49.5
clitoris	C51.2	C79.82	D07.1	D28.0	D39.8	D49.5
labium NEC	C51.9	C79.82	D07.1	D28.0	D39.8	D49.5
majus	C51.0	C79.82	D07.1	D28.0	D39.8	D49.5
minus	C51.1	C79.82	D07.1	D28.0	D39.8	D49.5
pudendum	C51.9	C79.82	D07.1	D28.0	D39.8	D49.5
vulva	C51.9	C79.82	D07.1	D28.0	D39.8	D49.5
finger—see also Neoplasm, skin, limb, upper	C44.60-	C79.2	D04.6-	D23.6-	D48.5	D49.2
flank—see also Neoplasm, skin, trunk	C44.509	C79.2	D04.5	D23.5	D48.5	D49.2
foot—see also Neoplasm, skin, limb, lower	C44.70-	C79.2	D04.7-	D23.7-	D48.5	D49.2
forearm—see also Neoplasm, skin, limb, upper	C44.60-	C79.2	D04.6-	D23.6-	D48.5	D49.2
forehead—see also *Neoplasm, skin, face*	C44.309	C79.2	D04.39	D23.39	D48.5	D49.2
glabella—see also Neoplasm, skin, face	C44.309	C79.2	D04.39	D23.39	D48.5	D49.2
gluteal region—see also Neoplasm, skin, trunk	C44.509	C79.2	D04.5	D23.5	D48.5	D49.2
groin—see also Neoplasm, skin, trunk	C44.509	C79.2	D04.5	D23.5	D48.5	D49.2
hand—see also Neoplasm, skin, limb, upper	C44.60-	C79.2	D04.6-	D23.6-	D48.5	D49.2
head NEC—see also Neoplasm, skin, scalp	C44.40	C79.2	D04.4	D23.4	D48.5	D49.2
heel—see also Neoplasm, skin, limb, lower	C44.70-	C79.2	D04.7-	D23.7-	D48.5	D49.2
helix—see also Neoplasm, skin, ear	C44.20-	C79.2	D04.2-	D23.2-	D48.5	D49.2
hip—see also Neoplasm, skin, limb, lower	C44.70-	C79.2	D04.7-	D23.7-	D48.5	D49.2
infraclavicular region—see also Neoplasm, skin, trunk	C44.509	C79.2	D04.5	D23.5	D48.5	D49.2
inguinal region—see also Neoplasm, skin, trunk	C44.509	C79.2	D04.5	D23.5	D48.5	D49.2
jaw—see also Neoplasm, skin, face	C44.309	C79.2	D04.39	D23.39	D48.5	D49.2
Kaposi's sarcoma—see Kaposi's, sarcoma, skin						
knee—see also Neoplasm, skin, limb, lower	C44.70-	C79.2	D04.7-	D23.7-	D48.5	D49.2

	Malignant Primary	Malignant Secondary	Ca in situ	Benign	Uncertain Behavior	Unspecified Behavior
skin NOS — *continued*						
labia						
majora	C51.0	C79.82	D07.1	D28.0	D39.8	D49
minora	C51.1	C79.82	D07.1	D28.0	D39.8	D49
leg—see also Neoplasm, skin, limb, lower	C44.70-	C79.2	D04.7-	D23.7-	D48.5	D49
lid(lower) (upper)	C44.10-	C79.2	D04.1-	D23.1-	D48.5	D49
basal cell carcinoma	C44.11-	-	-	-	-	-
specified type NEC	C44.19-	-	-	-	-	-
squamous cell carcinoma	C44.12-	-	-	-	-	-
limb NEC	C44.90	C79.2	D04.9	D23.9	D48.5	D49
basal cell carcinoma	C44.91					
lower	C44.70-	C79.2	D04.7-	D23.7-	D48.5	D49
basal cell carcinoma	C44.71-	-	-	-	-	-
specified type NEC	C44.79-	-	-	-	-	-
squamous cell carcinoma	C44.72-	-	-	-	-	-
upper	C44.60-	C79.2	D04.6-	D23.6-	D48.5	D49
basal cell carcinoma	C44.61-	-	-	-	-	-
specified type NEC	C44.69-	-	-	-	-	-
squamous cell carcinoma	C44.62-	-	-	-	-	-
lip(lower) (upper)	C44.00	C79.2	D04.0	D23.0	D48.5	D49
basal cell carcinoma	C44.01	-	-	-	-	-
specified type NEC	C44.09	-	-	-	-	-
squamous cell carcinoma	C44.02	-	-	-	-	-
male genital organs	C63.9	C79.82	D07.60	D29.9	D40.8	D49
penis	C60.9	C79.82	D07.4	D29.0	D40.8	D49
prepuce	C60.0	C79.82	D07.4	D29.0	D40.8	D49
scrotum	C63.2	C79.82	D07.61	D29.4	D40.8	D49
mastectomy site(skin)—see also Neoplasm, skin, breast	C44.501	C79.2	-	-	-	-
specified as breast tissue	C50.8-	C79.81	-	-	-	-
meatus, acoustic(external)—see also Neoplasm, skin, ear	C44.20-	C79.2	D04.2-	D23.2-	D48.5	D49.
melanotic—see Melanoma						
Merkel cell—see Carcinoma, Merkel cell						
nates—see also Neoplasm, skin, trunk	C44.509	C79.2	D04.5	D23.5	D48.5	D49.
neck	C44.40	C79.2	D04.4	D23.4	D48.5	D49.
basal cell carcinoma	C44.41	-	-	-	-	-
specified type NEC	C44.49	-	-	-	-	-
squamous cell carcinoma	C44.42	-	-	-	-	-
nevus—see Nevus, skin						
nose(external)—see also Neoplasm, nose, skin	C44.301	C79.2	D04.39	D23.39	D48.5	D49.
overlapping lesion	C44.80	-	-	-	-	-
basal cell carcinoma	C44.81	-	-	-	-	-
specified type NEC	C44.89	-	-	-	-	-
squamous cell carcinoma	C44.82	-	-	-	-	-

	Malignant Primary	Malignant Secondary	Ca in situ	Benign	Uncertain Behavior	Unspecified Behavior
kin NOS — *continued*						
palm—see also Neoplasm, skin, limb, upper	C44.60-	C79.2	D04.6-	D23.6-	D48.5	D49.2
palpebra	C44.10-	C79.2	D04.1-	D23.1-	D48.5	D49.2
basal cell carcinoma	C44.11-	-	-	-	-	-
specified type NEC	C44.19-	-	-	-	-	-
squamous cell carcinoma	C44.12-	-	-	-	-	-
penis NEC	C60.9	C79.82	D07.4	D29.0	D40.8	D49.5
perianal—see also Neoplasm, skin, anus	C44.500	C79.2	D04.5	D23.5	D48.5	D49.2
perineum—see also Neoplasm, skin, anus	C44.500	C79.2	D04.5	D23.5	D48.5	D49.2
pinna—see also Neoplasm, skin, ear	C44.20-	C79.2	D04.2-	D23.2-	D48.5	D49.2
plantar—see also Neoplasm, skin, limb, lower	C44.70-	C79.2	D04.7-	D23.7-	D48.5	D49.2
popliteal fossa or space—see also Neoplasm, skin, limb, lower	C44.70-	C79.2	D04.7-	D23.7-	D48.5	D49.2
prepuce	C60.0	C79.82	D07.4	D29.0	D40.8	D49.5
pubes—see also Neoplasm, skin, trunk	C44.509	C79.2	D04.5	D23.5	D48.5	D49.2
sacrococcygeal region—see also Neoplasm, skin, trunk	C44.509	C79.2	D04.5	D23.5	D48.5	D49.2
scalp	C44.40	C79.2	D04.4	D23.4	D48.5	D49.2
basal cell carcinoma	C44.41	-	-	-	-	-
specified type NEC	C44.49	-	-	-	-	-
squamous cell carcinoma	C44.42	-	-	-	-	-
scapular region—see also Neoplasm, skin, trunk	C44.509	C79.2	D04.5	D23.5	D48.5	D49.2
scrotum	C63.2	C79.82	D07.61	D29.4	D40.8	D49.5
shoulder—see also Neoplasm, skin, limb, upper	C44.60-	C79.2	D04.6-	D23.6-	D48.5	D49.2
sole(foot)—see also Neoplasm, skin, limb, lower	C44.70-	C79.2	D04.7-	D23.7-	D48.5	D49.2
specified sites NEC	C44.80	C79.2	D04.8	D23.9	D48.5	D49.2
basal cell carcinoma	C44.81	-	-	-	-	-
specified type NEC	C44.89	-	-	-	-	-
squamous cell carcinoma	C44.82	-	-	-	-	-
specified type NEC	C44.99	-	-	-	-	-
squamous cell carcinoma	C44.92	-	-	-	-	-
submammary fold—see also Neoplasm, skin, trunk	C44.509	C79.2	D04.5	D23.5	D48.5	D49.2
supraclavicular region—see also Neoplasm, skin, neck	C44.40	C79.2	D04.4	D23.4	D48.5	D49.2
temple—see also Neoplasm, skin, face	C44.309	C79.2	D04.39	D23.39	D48.5	D49.2
thigh—see also Neoplasm, skin, limb, lower	C44.70-	C79.2	D04.7-	D23.7-	D48.5	D49.2
thoracic wall—see also Neoplasm, skin, trunk	C44.509	C79.2	D04.5	D23.5	D48.5	D49.2

	Malignant Primary	Malignant Secondary	Ca in situ	Benign	Uncertain Behavior	Unspecified Behavior
skin NOS — *continued*						
thumb—see also Neoplasm, skin, limb, upper	C44.60-	C79.2	D04.6-	D23.6-	D48.5	D49.2
toe—see also Neoplasm, skin, limb, lower	C44.70-	C79.2	D04.7-	D23.7-	D48.5	D49.2
tragus—see also Neoplasm, skin, ear	C44.20-	C79.2	D04.2-	D23.2-	D48.5	D49.2
trunk	C44.509	C79.2	D04.5	D23.5	D48.5	D49.2
basal cell carcinoma	C44.519	-	-	-	-	-
specified type NEC	C44.599	-	-	-	-	-
squamous cell carcinoma	C44.529	-	-	-	-	-
umbilicus—see also Neoplasm, skin, trunk	C44.509	C79.2	D04.5	D23.5	D48.5	D49.2
vulva	C51.9	C79.82	D07.1	D28.0	D39.8	D49.5
overlapping lesion	C51.8	-	-	-	-	-
wrist—see also Neoplasm, skin, limb, upper	C44.60-	C79.2	D04.6-	D23.6-	D48.5	D49.2
skull	C41.0	C79.51	-	D16.4	D48.0	D49.2
soft parts or tissues—see Neoplasm, connective tissue						
specified site NEC	C76.8	C79.89	D09.8	D36.7	D48.7	D49.89
spermatic cord	C63.1-	C79.82	D07.69	D29.8	D40.8	D49.5
sphenoid	C31.3	C78.39	D02.3	D14.0	D38.5	D49.1
bone	C41.0	C79.51	-	D16.4	D48.0	D49.2
sinus	C31.3	C78.39	D02.3	D14.0	D38.5	D49.1
sphincter						
anal	C21.1	C78.5	D01.3	D12.9	D37.8	D49.0
of Oddi	C24.0	C78.89	D01.5	D13.5	D37.6	D49.0
spine, spinal(column)	C41.2	C79.51	-	D16.6	D48.0	D49.2
bulb	C71.7	C79.31	-	D33.1	D43.1	D49.6
coccyx	C41.4	C79.51	-	D16.8	D48.0	D49.2
cord(cervical) (lumbar) (sacral) (thoracic)	C72.0	C79.49	-	D33.4	D43.4	D49.7
dura mater	C70.1	C79.49	-	D32.1	D42.1	D49.7
lumbosacral	C41.2	C79.51	-	D16.6	D48.0	D49.2
marrow NEC	C96.9	C79.52	-	-	D47.9	D49.89
membrane	C70.1	C79.49	-	D32.1	D42.1	D49.7
meninges	C70.1	C79.49	-	D32.1	D42.1	D49.7
nerve(root)	C47.9	C79.89	-	D36.10	D48.2	D49.2
pia mater	C70.1	C79.49	-	D32.1	D42.1	D49.7
root	C47.9	C79.89	-	D36.10	D48.2	D49.2
sacrum	C41.4	C79.51	-	D16.8	D48.0	D49.2
spleen, splenic NEC	C26.1	C78.89	D01.7	D13.9	D37.8	D49.0
flexure(colon)	C18.5	C78.5	D01.0	D12.3	D37.4	D49.0
stem, brain	C71.7	C79.31	-	D33.1	D43.1	D49.6
Stensen's duct	C07	C79.89	D00.00	D11.0	D37.030	D49.0
sternum	C41.3	C79.51	-	D16.7	D48.0	D49.2
stomach	C16.9	C78.89	D00.2	D13.1	D37.1	D49.0
antrum(pyloric)	C16.3	C78.89	D00.2	D13.1	D37.1	D49.0
body	C16.2	C78.89	D00.2	D13.1	D37.1	D49.0
cardia	C16.0	C78.89	D00.2	D13.1	D37.1	D49.0
cardiac orifice	C16.0	C78.89	D00.2	D13.1	D37.1	D49.0
corpus	C16.2	C78.89	D00.2	D13.1	D37.1	D49.0

	Malignant Primary	Malignant Secondary	Ca in situ	Benign	Uncertain Behavior	Unspecified Behavior
stomach — *continued*						
fundus	C16.1	C78.89	D00.2	D13.1	D37.1	D49.0
greater curvature NEC	C16.6	C78.89	D00.2	D13.1	D37.1	D49.0
lesser curvature NEC	C16.5	C78.89	D00.2	D13.1	D37.1	D49.0
overlapping lesion	C16.8	-	-	-	-	-
prepylorus	C16.4	C78.89	D00.2	D13.1	D37.1	D49.0
pylorus	C16.4	C78.89	D00.2	D13.1	D37.1	D49.0
wall NEC	C16.9	C78.89	D00.2	D13.1	D37.1	D49.0
anterior NEC	C16.8	C78.89	D00.2	D13.1	D37.1	D49.0
posterior NEC	C16.8	C78.89	D00.2	D13.1	D37.1	D49.0
stroma, endometrial	C54.1	C79.82	D07.0	D26.1	D39.0	D49.5
stump, cervical	C53.8	C79.82	D06.7	D26.0	D39.0	D49.5
subcutaneous(nodule) (tissue) NEC—see Neoplasm, connective tissue						
subdural	C70.9	C79.32	-	D32.9	D42.9	D49.7
subglottis, subglottic	C32.2	C78.39	D02.0	D14.1	D38.0	D49.1
sublingual	C04.9	C79.89	D00.06	D10.2	D37.09	D49.0
gland or duct	C08.1	C79.89	D00.00	D11.7	D37.031	D49.0
submandibular gland	C08.0	C79.89	D00.00	D11.7	D37.032	D49.0
submaxillary gland or duct	C08.0	C79.89	D00.00	D11.7	D37.032	D49.0
submental	C76.0	C79.89	D09.8	D36.7	D48.7	D49.89
subpleural	C34.9-	C78.0-	D02.2-	D14.3-	D38.1	D49.1
substernal	C38.1	C78.1	-	D15.2	D38.3	D49.89
sudoriferous, sudoriparous gland, site unspecified	C44.90	C79.2	D04.9	D23.9	D48.5	D49.2
specified site—see Neoplasm, skin						
supraclavicular region	C76.0	C79.89	D09.8	D36.7	D48.7	D49.89
supraglottis	C32.1	C78.39	D02.0	D14.1	D38.0	D49.1
suprarenal	C74.9-	C79.7-	D09.3	D35.0-	D44.1-	D49.7
capsule	C74.9-	C79.7-	D09.3	D35.0-	D44.1-	D49.7
cortex	C74.0-	C79.7-	D09.3	D35.0-	D44.1-	D49.7
gland	C74.9-	C79.7-	D09.3	D35.0-	D44.1-	D49.7
medulla	C74.1-	C79.7-	D09.3	D35.0-	D44.1-	D49.7
suprasellar(region)	C71.9	C79.31	-	D33.2	D43.2	D49.6
supratentorial(brain) NEC	C71.0	C79.31	-	D33.0	D43.0	D49.6
sweat gland(apocrine) (eccrine), site unspecified	C44.90	C79.2	D04.9	D23.9	D48.5	D49.2
specified site—see Neoplasm, skin						
sympathetic nerve or nervous system NEC	C47.9	C79.89	-	D36.10	D48.2	D49.2
symphysis pubis	C41.4	C79.51	-	D16.8	D48.0	D49.2
synovial membrane—see Neoplasm, connective tissue						
T						
tapetum, brain	C71.8	C79.31	-	D33.2	D43.2	D49.6
tarsus(any bone)	C40.3-	C79.51	-	D16.3-	-	-
temple(skin)—see also Neoplasm, skin, face	C44.309	C79.2	D04.39	D23.39	D48.5	D49.2
temporal						
bone	C41.0	C79.51	-	D16.4	D48.0	D49.2
lobe or pole	C71.2	C79.31	-	D33.0	D43.0	D49.6
region	C76.0	C79.89	D09.8	D36.7	D48.7	D49.89
skin—see also Neoplasm, skin, face	C44.309	C79.2	D04.39	D23.39	D48.5	D49.2

	Malignant Primary	Malignant Secondary	Ca in situ	Benign	Uncertain Behavior	Unspecified Behavior
tendon(sheath)—see Neoplasm, connective tissue						
tentorium(cerebelli)	C70.0	C79.32	-	D32.0	D42.0	D49.
testis, testes	C62.9-	C79.82	D07.69	D29.2-	D40.1-	D49.
descended	C62.1-	C79.82	D07.69	D29.2-	D40.1-	D49.
ectopic	C62.0-	C79.82	D07.69	D29.2-	D40.1-	D49.
retained	C62.0-	C79.82	D07.69	D29.2-	D40.1-	D49.
scrotal	C62.1-	C79.82	D07.69	D29.2-	D40.1-	D49.
undescended	C62.0-	C79.82	D07.69	D29.2-	D40.1-	D49.
unspecified whether descended or undescended	C62.9-	C79.82	D07.69	D29.2-	D40.1-	D49.
thalamus	C71.0	C79.31	-	D33.0	D43.0	D49.
thigh NEC	C76.5-	C79.89	D04.7-	D36.7	D48.7	D49.8
thorax, thoracic(cavity) (organs NEC)	C76.1	C79.89	D09.8	D36.7	D48.7	D49.8
duct	C49.3	C79.89	-	D21.3	D48.1	D49.
wall NEC	C76.1	C79.89	D09.8	D36.7	D48.7	D49.8
throat	C14.0	C79.89	D00.08	D10.9	D37.05	D49.
thumb NEC	C76.4-	C79.89	D04.6-	D36.7	D48.7	D49.8
thymus(gland)	C37	C79.89	D09.3	D15.0	D38.4	D49.8
thyroglossal duct	C73	C79.89	D09.3	D34	D44.0	D49.
thyroid(gland)	C73	C79.89	D09.3	D34	D44.0	D49.
cartilage	C32.3	C78.39	D02.0	D14.1	D38.0	D49.
tibia(any part)	C40.2-	C79.51	-	D16.2-	-	-
toe NEC	C76.5-	C79.89	D04.7-	D36.7	D48.7	D49.8
tongue	C02.9	C79.89	D00.07	D10.1	D37.02	D49.
anterior(two-thirds) NEC	C02.3	C79.89	D00.07	D10.1	D37.02	D49.
dorsal surface	C02.0	C79.89	D00.07	D10.1	D37.02	D49.
ventral surface	C02.2	C79.89	D00.07	D10.1	D37.02	D49.
base(dorsal surface)	C01	C79.89	D00.07	D10.1	D37.02	D49.
border(lateral)	C02.1	C79.89	D00.07	D10.1	D37.02	D49.0
dorsal surface NEC	C02.0	C79.89	D00.07	D10.1	D37.02	D49.0
fixed part NEC	C01	C79.89	D00.07	D10.1	D37.02	D49.0
foreamen cecum	C02.0	C79.89	D00.07	D10.1	D37.02	D49.0
frenulum linguae	C02.2	C79.89	D00.07	D10.1	D37.02	D49.0
junctional zone	C02.8	C79.89	D00.07	D10.1	D37.02	D49.0
margin(lateral)	C02.1	C79.89	D00.07	D10.1	D37.02	D49.0
midline NEC	C02.0	C79.89	D00.07	D10.1	D37.02	D49.0
mobile part NEC	C02.3	C79.89	D00.07	D10.1	D37.02	D49.0
overlapping lesion	C02.8	-	-	-	-	-
posterior(third)	C01	C79.89	D00.07	D10.1	D37.02	D49.0
root	C01	C79.89	D00.07	D10.1	D37.02	D49.0
surface(dorsal)	C02.0	C79.89	D00.07	D10.1	D37.02	D49.0
base	C01	C79.89	D00.07	D10.1	D37.02	D49.0
ventral	C02.2	C79.89	D00.07	D10.1	D37.02	D49.0
tip	C02.1	C79.89	D00.07	D10.1	D37.02	D49.0
tonsil	C02.4	C79.89	D00.07	D10.1	D37.02	D49.0
tonsil	C09.9	C79.89	D00.08	D10.4	D37.05	D49.0
fauces, faucial	C09.9	C79.89	D00.08	D10.4	D37.05	D49.0
lingual	C02.4	C79.89	D00.07	D10.1	D37.02	D49.0
overlapping sites	C09.8	-	-	-	-	-
palatine	C09.9	C79.89	D00.08	D10.4	D37.05	D49.0

	Malignant Primary	Malignant Secondary	Ca in situ	Benign	Uncertain Behavior	Unspecified Behavior
tonsil — *continued*						
pharyngeal	C11.1	C79.89	D00.08	D10.6	D37.05	D49.0
pillar(anterior) (posterior)	C09.1	C79.89	D00.08	D10.5	D37.05	D49.0
tonsillar fossa	C09.0	C79.89	D00.08	D10.5	D37.05	D49.0
tooth socket NEC	C03.9	C79.89	D00.03	D10.39	D37.09	D49.0
trachea(cartilage) (mucosa)	C33	C78.39	D02.1	D14.2	D38.1	D49.1
overlapping lesion with bronchus or lung	C34.8-	-	-	-	-	-
tracheobronchial	C34.8-	C78.39	D02.1	D14.2	D38.1	D49.1
overlapping lesion with lung	C34.8-	-	-	-	-	-
tragus—see also Neoplasm, skin, ear	C44.20-	C79.2	D04.2-	D23.2-	D48.5	D49.2
trunk NEC	C76.8	C79.89	D04.5	D36.7	D48.7	D49.89
tubo-ovarian	C57.8	C79.82	D07.39	D28.7	D39.8	D49.5
tunica vaginalis	C63.7	C79.82	D07.69	D29.8	D40.8	D49.5
turbinate(bone)	C41.0	C79.51	-	D16.4	D48.0	D49.2
nasal	C30.0	C78.39	D02.3	D14.0	D38.5	D49.1
tympanic cavity	C30.1	C78.39	D02.3	D14.0	D38.5	D49.1
U						
ulna(any part)	C40.0-	C79.51	-	D16.0-	-	-
umbilicus, umbilical—see also Neoplasm, skin, trunk	C44.509	C79.2	D04.5	D23.5	D48.5	D49.2
uncus, brain	C71.2	C79.31	-	D33.0	D43.0	D49.6
unknown site or unspecified	C80.1	C79.9	D09.9	D36.9	D48.9	D49.9
urachus	C67.7	C79.11	D09.0	D30.3	D41.4	D49.4
ureter, ureteral	C66.-	C79.19	D09.19	D30.2-	D41.2-	D49.5
orifice(bladder)	C67.6	C79.11	D09.0	D30.3	D41.4	D49.4
ureter-bladder (junction)	C67.6	C79.11	D09.0	D30.3	D41.4	D49.4
urethra, urethral (gland)	C68.0	C79.19	D09.19	D30.4	D41.3	D49.5
orifice, internal	C67.5	C79.11	D09.0	D30.3	D41.4	D49.4
urethrovaginal(septum)	C57.9	C79.82	D07.30	D28.9	D39.8	D49.5
urinary organ or system	C68.9	C79.10	D09.10	D30.9	D41.9	D49.5
bladder—see Neoplasm, bladder						
overlapping lesion	C68.8	-	-	-	-	-
specified sites NEC	C68.8	C79.19	D09.19	D30.8	D41.8	D49.5
utero-ovarian	C57.8	C79.82	D07.39	D28.7	D39.8	D49.5
ligament	C57.1	C79.82	D07.39	D28.2	D39.8	D49.5
uterosacral ligament	C57.3	C79.82	-	D28.2	D39.8	D49.5
uterus, uteri, uterine	C55	C79.82	D07.0	D26.9	D39.0	D49.5
adnexa NEC	C57.4	C79.82	D07.39	D28.7	D39.8	D49.5
body	C54.9	C79.82	D07.0	D26.1	D39.0	D49.5
cervix	C53.9	C79.82	D06.9	D26.0	D39.0	D49.5
cornu	C54.9	C79.82	D07.0	D26.1	D39.0	D49.5
corpus	C54.9	C79.82	D07.0	D26.1	D39.0	D49.5
endocervix(canal) (gland)	C53.0	C79.82	D06.0	D26.0	D39.0	D49.5
endometrium	C54.1	C79.82	D07.0	D26.1	D39.0	D49.5
exocervix	C53.1	C79.82	D06.1	D26.0	D39.0	D49.5
external os	C53.1	C79.82	D06.1	D26.0	D39.0	D49.5
fundus	C54.3	C79.82	D07.0	D26.1	D39.0	D49.5
internal os	C53.0	C79.82	D06.0	D26.0	D39.0	D49.5
isthmus	C54.0	C79.82	D07.0	D26.1	D39.0	D49.5

	Malignant Primary	Malignant Secondary	Ca in situ	Benign	Uncertain Behavior	Unspecified Behavior
uterus, uteri, uterine — *continued*						
ligament	C57.3	C79.82	-	D28.2	D39.8	D49.5
broad	C57.1	C79.82	D07.39	D28.2	D39.8	D49.5
round	C57.2	C79.82	-	D28.2	D39.8	D49.5
lower segment	C54.0	C79.82	D07.0	D26.1	D39.0	D49.5
myometrium	C54.2	C79.82	D07.0	D26.1	D39.0	D49.5
overlapping sites	C54.8	-	-	-	-	-
squamocolumnar junction	C53.8	C79.82	D06.7	D26.0	D39.0	D49.5
tube	C57.0-	C79.82	D07.39	D28.2	D39.8	D49.5
utricle, prostatic	C68.0	C79.19	D09.19	D30.4	D41.3	D49.5
uveal tract	C69.4-	C79.49	D09.2-	D31.4-	D48.7	D49.89
uvula	C05.2	C79.89	D00.04	D10.39	D37.09	D49.0
V						
vagina, vaginal(fornix) (vault) (wall)	C52	C79.82	D07.2	D28.1	D39.8	D49.5
vaginovesical	C57.9	C79.82	D07.30	D28.9	D39.9	D49.5
septum	C57.9	C79.82	D07.30	D28.9	D39.9	D49.5
vallecula(epigiottis)	C10.0	C79.89	D00.08	D10.5	D37.05	D49.0
vas deferens	C63.1-	C79.82	D07.69	D29.8	D40.8	D49.5
vascular—see Neoplasm, connective tissue						
Vater's ampulla	C24.1	C78.89	D01.5	D13.5	D37.6	D49.0
vein, venous—see Neoplasm, connective tissue						
vena cava(abdominal) (inferior)	C49.4	C79.89	-	D21.4	D48.1	D49.2
superior	C49.3	C79.89	-	D21.3	D48.1	D49.2
ventricle(cerebral) (floor) (lateral) (third)	C71.5	C79.31	-	D33.0	D43.0	D49.6
cardiac(left) (right)	C38.0	C79.89	-	D15.1	D48.7	D49.89
fourth	C71.7	C79.31	-	D33.1	D43.1	D49.6
ventricular band of larynx	C32.1	C78.39	D02.0	D14.1	D38.0	D49.1
ventriculus—see Neoplasm, stomach						
vermillion border—see Neoplasm, lip						
vermis, cerebellum	C71.6	C79.31	-	D33.1	D43.1	D49.6
vertebra(column)	C41.2	C79.51	-	D16.6	D48.0	D49.2
coccyx	C41.4	C79.51	-	D16.8	D48.0	D49.2
marrow NEC	C96.9	C79.52	-	-	D47.9	D49.89
sacrum	C41.4	C79.51	-	D16.8	D48.0	D49.2
vesical—see Neoplasm, bladder						
vesicle, seminal	C63.7	C79.82	D07.69	D29.8	D40.8	D49.5
vesicocervical tissue	C57.9	C79.82	D07.30	D28.9	D39.9	D49.5
vesicorectal	C76.3	C79.82	D09.8	D36.7	D48.7	D49.89
vesicovaginal	C57.9	C79.82	D07.30	D28.9	D39.9	D49.5
septum	C57.9	C79.82	D07.30	D28.9	D39.8	D49.5
vessel(blood)—see Neoplasm, connective tissue						
vestibular gland, greater	C51.0	C79.82	D07.1	D28.0	D39.8	D49.5
vestibule						
mouth	C06.1	C79.89	D00.00	D10.39	D37.09	D49.0
nose	C30.0	C78.39	D02.3	D14.0	D38.5	D49.1
Virchow's gland	C77.0	C77.0	-	D36.0	D48.7	D49.89

	Malignant Primary	Malignant Secondary	Ca in situ	Benign	Uncertain Behavior	Unspecified Behavior
viscera NEC	C76.8	C79.89	D09.8	D36.7	D48.7	D49.89
vocal cords(true)	C32.0	C78.39	D02.0	D14.1	D38.0	D49.1
false	C32.1	C78.39	D02.0	D14.1	D38.0	D49.1
vomer	C41.0	C79.51	-	D16.4	D48.0	D49.2
vulva	C51.9	C79.82	D07.1	D28.0	D39.8	D49.5
vulvovaginal gland	C51.0	C79.82	D07.1	D28.0	D39.8	D49.5
W						
Waldeyer's ring	C14.2	C79.89	D00.08	D10.9	D37.05	D49.0
Wharton's duct	C08.0	C79.89	D00.00	D11.7	D37.032	D49.0
white matter(central) (cerebral)	C71.0	C79.31	-	D33.0	D43.0	D49.6
windpipe	C33	C78.39	D02.1	D14.2	D38.1	D49.1

	Malignant Primary	Malignant Secondary	Ca in situ	Benign	Uncertain Behavior	Unspecified Behavior
Wirsung's duct	C25.3	C78.89	D01.7	D13.6	D37.8	D49.0
wolffian(body) (duct)						
female	C57.7	C79.82	D07.39	D28.7	D39.8	D49.5
male	C63.7	C79.82	D07.69	D29.8	D40.8	D49.5
womb—see Neoplasm, uterus						
wrist NEC	C76.4-	C79.89	D04.6-	D36.7	D48.7	D49.8
X						
xiphoid process	C41.3	C79.51	-	D16.7	D48.0	D49.2
Z						
Zuckerkandl organ	C75.5	C79.89	-	D35.6	D44.7	D49.7

Table of Drugs and Chemicals

Substance	Poisoning, Accidental (unintentional)	Poisoning, Intentional self-harm	Poisoning, Assault	Poisoning, Undetermined	Adverse effect	Underdosing
-propanol	T51.3X1	T51.3X2	T51.3X3	T51.3X4	—	—
-propanol	T51.2X1	T51.2X2	T51.2X3	T51.2X4	—	—
,4-D(dichlorophen-xyacetic acid)	T60.3X1	T60.3X2	T60.3X3	T60.3X4	—	—
,4-toluene diisocyanate	T65.0X1	T65.0X2	T65.0X3	T65.0X4	—	—
,4,5-T(trichloro-henoxyacetic acid)	T60.1X1	T60.1X2	T60.1X3	T60.1X4	—	—
4-hydroxydihydro-norphinone	T40.2X1	T40.2X2	T40.2X3	T40.2X4	T40.2X5	T40.2X6
A						
BOB	T37.5X1	T37.5X2	T37.5X3	T37.5X4	T37.5X5	T37.5X6
brine	T62.2X1	T62.2X2	T62.2X3	T62.2X4	—	—
brus(seed)	T62.2X1	T62.2X2	T62.2X3	T62.2X4	—	—
bsinthe	T51.0X1	T51.0X2	T51.0X3	T51.0X4	—	—
beverage	T51.0X1	T51.0X2	T51.0X3	T51.0X4	—	—
caricide	T60.8X1	T60.8X2	T60.8X3	T60.8X4	—	—
cebutolol	T44.7X1	T44.7X2	T44.7X3	T44.7X4	T44.7X5	T44.7X6
cecarbromal	T42.6X1	T42.6X2	T42.6X3	T42.6X4	T42.6X5	T42.6X6
ceclidine	T44.1X1	T44.1X2	T44.1X3	T44.1X4	T44.1X5	T44.1X6
cedapsone	T37.0X1	T37.0X2	T37.0X3	T37.0X4	T37.0X5	T37.0X6
cefylline piperazine	T48.6X1	T48.6X2	T48.6X3	T48.6X4	T48.6X5	T48.6X6
cemorphan	T40.2X1	T40.2X2	T40.2X3	T40.2X4	T40.2X5	T40.2X6
cenocoumarin	T45.511	T45.512	T45.513	T45.514	T45.515	T45.516
cenocoumarol	T45.511	T45.512	T45.513	T45.514	T45.515	T45.516
cepifylline	T48.6X1	T48.6X2	T48.6X3	T48.6X4	T48.6X5	T48.6X6
cepromazine	T43.3X1	T43.3X2	T43.3X3	T43.3X4	T43.3X5	T43.3X6
cesulfamethoxy-pyridazine	T37.0X1	T37.0X2	T37.0X3	T37.0X4	T37.0X5	T37.0X6
Acetal	T52.8X1	T52.8X2	T52.8X3	T52.8X4	—	—
Acetaldehyde(vapor)	T52.8X1	T52.8X2	T52.8X3	T52.8X4	—	—
liquid	T65.891	T65.892	T65.893	T65.894	—	—
P-Acetamidophenol	T39.1X1	T39.1X2	T39.1X3	T39.1X4	T39.1X5	T39.1X6
Acetaminophen	T39.1X1	T39.1X2	T39.1X3	T39.1X4	T39.1X5	T39.1X6
Acetaminosalol	T39.1X1	T39.1X2	T39.1X3	T39.1X4	T39.1X5	T39.1X6
Acetanilide	T39.1X1	T39.1X2	T39.1X3	T39.1X4	T39.1X5	T39.1X6
Acetarsol	T37.3X1	T37.3X2	T37.3X3	T37.3X4	T37.3X5	T37.3X6
Acetazolamide	T50.2X1	T50.2X2	T50.2X3	T50.2X4	T50.2X5	T50.2X6
Acetiamine	T45.2X1	T45.2X2	T45.2X3	T45.2X4	T45.2X5	T45.2X6
Acetic						
acid	T54.2X1	T54.2X2	T54.2X3	T54.2X4	—	—
with sodium acetate(ointment)	T49.3X1	T49.3X2	T49.3X3	T49.3X4	T49.3X5	T49.3X6
ester(solvent)(vapor)	T52.8X1	T52.8X2	T52.8X3	T52.8X4	—	—
irrigating solution	T50.3X1	T50.3X2	T50.3X3	T50.3X4	T50.3X5	T50.3X6
medicinal(lotion)	T49.2X1	T49.2X2	T49.2X3	T49.2X4	T49.2X5	T49.2X6
anhydride	T65.891	T65.892	T65.893	T65.894	—	—
ether(vapor)	T52.8X1	T52.8X2	T52.8X3	T52.8X4	—	—
Acetohexamide	T38.3X1	T38.3X2	T38.3X3	T38.3X4	T38.3X5	T38.3X6

Substance	Poisoning, Accidental (unintentional)	Poisoning, Intentional self-harm	Poisoning, Assault	Poisoning, Undetermined	Adverse effect	Underdosing
Acetohydroxamic acid	T50.991	T50.992	T50.993	T50.994	T50.995	T50.996
Acetomenaphthone	T45.7X1	T45.7X2	T45.7X3	T45.7X4	T45.7X5	T45.7X6
Acetomorphine	T40.1X1	T40.1X2	T40.1X3	T40.1X4	—	—
Acetone(oils)	T52.4X1	T52.4X2	T52.4X3	T52.4X4	—	—
chlorinated	T52.4X1	T52.4X2	T52.4X3	T52.4X4	—	—
vapor	T52.4X1	T52.4X2	T52.4X3	T52.4X4	—	—
Acetonitrile	T52.8X1	T52.8X2	T52.8X3	T52.8X4	—	—
Acetophenazine	T43.3X1	T43.3X2	T43.3X3	T43.3X4	T43.3X5	T43.3X6
Acetophenetedin	T39.1X1	T39.1X2	T39.1X3	T39.1X4	T39.1X5	T39.1X6
Acetophenone	T52.4X1	T52.4X2	T52.4X3	T52.4X4	—	—
Acetorphine	T40.2X1	T40.2X2	T40.2X3	T40.2X4	—	—
Acetosulfone(sodium)	T37.1X1	T37.1X2	T37.1X3	T37.1X4	T37.1X5	T37.1X6
Acetrizoate(sodium)	T50.8X1	T50.8X2	T50.8X3	T50.8X4	T50.8X5	T50.8X6
Acetrizoic acid	T50.8X1	T50.8X2	T50.8X3	T50.8X4	T50.8X5	T50.8X6
Acetyl						
bromide	T53.6X1	T53.6X2	T53.6X3	T53.6X4	—	—
chloride	T53.6X1	T53.6X2	T53.6X3	T53.6X4	—	—
Acetylcarbromal	T42.6X1	T42.6X2	T42.6X3	T42.6X4	T42.6X5	T42.6X6
Acetylcholine						
chloride	T44.1X1	T44.1X2	T44.1X3	T44.1X4	T44.1X5	T44.1X6
derivative	T44.1X1	T44.1X2	T44.1X3	T44.1X4	T44.1X5	T44.1X6
Acetylcysteine	T48.4X1	T48.4X2	T48.4X3	T48.4X4	T48.4X5	T48.4X6
Acetyldigitoxin	T46.0X1	T46.0X2	T46.0X3	T46.0X4	T46.0X5	T46.0X6
Acetyldigoxin	T46.0X1	T46.0X2	T46.0X3	T46.0X4	T46.0X5	T46.0X6
Acetyldihydrocodeine	T40.2X1	T40.2X2	T40.2X3	T40.2X4	—	—
Acetyldihydroco-deinone	T40.2X1	T40.2X2	T40.2X3	T40.2X4	—	—
Acetylene(gas)	T59.891	T59.892	T59.893	T59.894	—	—
dichloride	T53.6X1	T53.6X2	T53.6X3	T53.6X4	—	—
incomplete combustion of	T58.11	T58.12	T58.13	T58.14	—	—
industrial	T59.891	T59.892	T59.893	T59.894	—	—
tetrachloride	T53.6X1	T53.6X2	T53.6X3	T53.6X4	—	—
vapor	T53.6X1	T53.6X2	T53.6X3	T53.6X4	—	—
Acetylpheneturide	T42.6X1	T42.6X2	T42.6X3	T42.6X4	T42.6X5	T42.6X6
Acetylphenylhydra-zine	T39.8X1	T39.8X2	T39.8X3	T39.8X4	T39.8X5	T39.8X6
Acetylsalicylic acid(salts)	T39.011	T39.012	T39.013	T39.014	T39.015	T39.016
enteric coated	T39.011	T39.012	T39.013	T39.014	T39.015	T39.016
Acetylsulfamethoxy-pyridazine	T37.0X1	T37.0X2	T37.0X3	T37.0X4	T37.0X5	T37.0X6
Achromycin	T36.4X1	T36.4X2	T36.4X3	T36.4X4	T36.4X5	T36.4X6
ophthalmic preparation	T49.5X1	T49.5X2	T49.5X3	T49.5X4	T49.5X5	T49.5X6
topical NEC	T49.0X1	T49.0X2	T49.0X3	T49.0X4	T49.0X5	T49.0X6
Aciclovir	T37.5X1	T37.5X2	T37.5X3	T37.5X4	T37.5X5	T37.5X6
Acid(corrosive) NEC	T54.2X1	T54.2X2	T54.2X3	T54.2X4	—	—
Acidifying agent NEC	T50.901	T50.902	T50.903	T50.904	T50.905	T50.906
Acipimox	T46.6X1	T46.6X2	T46.6X3	T46.6X4	T46.6X5	T46.6X6
Acitretin	T50.991	T50.992	T50.993	T50.994	T50.995	T50.996
Aclarubicin	T45.1X1	T45.1X2	T45.1X3	T45.1X4	T45.1X5	T45.1X6

Substance	Poisoning, Accidental (unintentional)	Poisoning, Intentional self-harm	Poisoning, Assault	Poisoning, Undetermined	Adverse effect	Underdosing
Aclatonium napadisilate	T48.1X1	T48.1X2	T48.1X3	T48.1X4	T48.1X5	T48.1X6
Aconite(wild)	T46.991	T46.992	T46.993	T46.994	T46.995	T46.996
Aconitine	T46.991	T46.992	T46.993	T46.994	T46.995	T46.996
Aconitum ferox	T46.991	T46.992	T46.993	T46.994	T46.995	T46.996
Acridine	T65.6X1	T65.6X2	T65.6X3	T65.6X4	—	—
vapor	T59.891	T59.892	T59.893	T59.894	—	—
Acriflavine	T37.91	T37.92	T37.93	T37.94	T37.95	T37.96
Acriflavinium chloride	T49.0X1	T49.0X2	T49.0X3	T49.0X4	T49.0X5	T49.0X6
Acrinol	T49.0X1	T49.0X2	T49.0X3	T49.0X4	T49.0X5	T49.0X6
Acrisorcin	T49.0X1	T49.0X2	T49.0X3	T49.0X4	T49.0X5	T49.0X6
Acrivastine	T45.0X1	T45.0X2	T45.0X3	T45.0X4	T45.0X5	T45.0X6
Acrolein(gas)	T59.891	T59.892	T59.893	T59.894	—	—
liquid	T54.1X1	T54.1X2	T54.1X3	T54.1X4	—	—
Acrylamide	T65.891	T65.892	T65.893	T65.894	—	—
Acrylic resin	T49.3X1	T49.3X2	T49.3X3	T49.3X4	T49.3X5	T49.3X6
Acrylonitrile	T65.891	T65.892	T65.893	T65.894	—	—
Actaea spicata	T62.2X1	T62.2X2	T62.2X3	T62.2X4	—	—
berry	T62.1X1	T62.1X2	T62.1X3	T62.1X4	—	—
Acterol	T37.3X1	T37.3X2	T37.3X3	T37.3X4	T37.3X5	T37.3X6
ACTH	T38.811	T38.812	T38.813	T38.814	T38.815	T38.816
Actinomycin C	T45.1X1	T45.1X2	T45.1X3	T45.1X4	T45.1X5	T45.1X6
Actinomycin D	T45.1X1	T45.1X2	T45.1X3	T45.1X4	T45.1X5	T45.1X6
Activated charcoal—see also Charcoal, medicinal	T47.6X1	T47.6X2	T47.6X3	T47.6X4	T47.6X5	T47.6X6
Acyclovir	T37.5X1	T37.5X2	T37.5X3	T37.5X4	T37.5X5	T37.5X6
Adenine	T45.2X1	T45.2X2	T45.2X3	T45.2X4	T45.2X5	T45.2X6
arabinoside	T37.5X1	T37.5X2	T37.5X3	T37.5X4	T37.5X5	T37.5X6
Adenosine (phosphate)	T46.2X1	T46.2X2	T46.2X3	T46.2X4	T46.2X5	T46.2X6
ADH	T38.891	T38.892	T38.893	T38.894	T38.895	T38.896
Adhesive NEC	T65.891	T65.892	T65.893	T65.894	—	—
Adicillin	T36.0X1	T36.0X2	T36.0X3	T36.0X4	T36.0X5	T36.0X6
Adiphenine	T44.3X1	T44.3X2	T44.3X3	T44.3X4	T44.3X5	T44.3X6
Adipiodone	T50.8X1	T50.8X2	T50.8X3	T50.8X4	T50.8X5	T50.8X6
Adjunct, pharmaceutical	T50.901	T50.902	T50.903	T50.904	T50.905	T50.906
Adrenal(extract, cortex or medulla)(glucocorticoids)(hormones)(mineralocorticoids)	T38.0X1	T38.0X2	T38.0X3	T38.0X4	T38.0X5	T38.0X6
ENT agent	T49.6X1	T49.6X2	T49.6X3	T49.6X4	T49.6X5	T49.6X6
ophthalmic preparation	T49.5X1	T49.5X2	T49.5X3	T49.5X4	T49.5X5	T49.5X6
topical NEC	T49.0X1	T49.0X2	T49.0X3	T49.0X4	T49.0X5	T49.0X6
Adrenaline	T44.5X1	T44.5X2	T44.5X3	T44.5X4	T44.5X5	T44.5X6
Adrenalin—see Adrenaline						
Adrenergic NEC	T44.901	T44.902	T44.903	T44.904	T44.905	T44.906
blocking agent NEC	T44.8X1	T44.8X2	T44.8X3	T44.8X4	T44.8X5	T44.8X6
beta, heart	T44.7X1	T44.7X2	T44.7X3	T44.7X4	T44.7X5	T44.7X6
specified NEC	T44.991	T44.992	T44.993	T44.994	T44.995	T44.996
Adrenochrome						
(mono) semicarbazone	T46.991	T46.992	T46.993	T46.994	T46.995	T46.996
derivative	T46.991	T46.992	T46.993	T46.994	T46.995	T46.996
Adrenocorticotrophic hormone	T38.811	T38.812	T38.813	T38.814	T38.815	T38.816

Substance	Poisoning, Accidental (unintentional)	Poisoning, Intentional self-harm	Poisoning, Assault	Poisoning, Undetermined	Adverse effect	Underdosing
Adrenocorticotro-phin	T38.811	T38.812	T38.813	T38.814	T38.815	T38.81
Adriamycin	T45.1X1	T45.1X2	T45.1X3	T45.1X4	T45.1X5	T45.1X
Aerosol spray NEC	T65.91	T65.92	T65.93	T65.94	—	—
Aerosporin	T36.8X1	T36.8X2	T36.8X3	T36.8X4	T36.8X5	T36.8X
ENT agent	T49.6X1	T49.6X2	T49.6X3	T49.6X4	T49.6X5	T49.6X
ophthalmic preparation	T49.5X1	T49.5X2	T49.5X3	T49.5X4	T49.5X5	T49.5X
topical NEC	T49.0X1	T49.0X2	T49.0X3	T49.0X4	T49.0X5	T49.0X
Aethusa cynapium	T62.2X1	T62.2X2	T62.2X3	T62.2X4	—	—
Afghanistan black	T40.7X1	T40.7X2	T40.7X3	T40.7X4	T40.7X5	T40.7X
Aflatoxin	T64.01	T64.02	T64.03	T64.04	—	—
Afloqualone	T42.8X1	T42.8X2	T42.8X3	T42.8X4	T42.8X5	T42.8X
African boxwood	T62.2X1	T62.2X2	T62.2X3	T62.2X4	—	—
Agar	T47.4X1	T47.4X2	T47.4X3	T47.4X4	T47.4X5	T47.4X
Agonist						
predominantly						
alpha-adrenoreceptor	T44.4X1	T44.4X2	T44.4X3	T44.4X4	T44.4X5	T44.4X
beta-adrenoreceptor	T44.5X1	T44.5X2	T44.5X3	T44.5X4	T44.5X5	T44.5X
Agricultural agent NEC	T65.91	T65.92	T65.93	T65.94	—	—
Agrypnal	T42.3X1	T42.3X2	T42.3X3	T42.3X4	T42.3X5	T42.3X
AHLG	T50.Z11	T50.Z12	T50.Z13	T50.Z14	T50.Z15	T50.Z1
Air contaminant(s), source/type NOS	T65.91	T65.92	T65.93	T65.94	—	—
Ajmaline	T46.2X1	T46.2X2	T46.2X3	T46.2X4	T46.2X5	T46.2X
Akee	T62.1X1	T62.1X2	T62.1X3	T62.1X4	—	—
Akrinol	T49.0X1	T49.0X2	T49.0X3	T49.0X4	T49.0X5	T49.0X
Akritoin	T37.8X1	T37.8X2	T37.8X3	T37.8X4	T37.8X5	T37.8X
Alacepril	T46.4X1	T46.4X2	T46.4X3	T46.4X4	T46.4X5	T46.4X
Alantolactone	T37.4X1	T37.4X2	T37.4X3	T37.4X4	T37.4X5	T37.4X
Albamycin	T36.8X1	T36.8X2	T36.8X3	T36.8X4	T36.8X5	T36.8X
Albendazole	T37.4X1	T37.4X2	T37.4X3	T37.4X4	T37.4X5	T37.4X
Albumin						
bovine	T45.8X1	T45.8X2	T45.8X3	T45.8X4	T45.8X5	T45.8X
human serum	T45.8X1	T45.8X2	T45.8X3	T45.8X4	T45.8X5	T45.8X
salt-poor	T45.8X1	T45.8X2	T45.8X3	T45.8X4	T45.8X5	T45.8X
normal human serum	T45.8X1	T45.8X2	T45.8X3	T45.8X4	T45.8X5	T45.8X
Albuterol	T48.6X1	T48.6X2	T48.6X3	T48.6X4	T48.6X5	T48.6X
Albutoin	T42.0X1	T42.0X2	T42.0X3	T42.0X4	T42.0X5	T42.0X
Alclometasone	T49.0X1	T49.0X2	T49.0X3	T49.0X4	T49.0X5	T49.0X
Alcohol	T51.91	T51.92	T51.93	T51.94	—	—
absolute	T51.0X1	T51.0X2	T51.0X3	T51.0X4	—	—
beverage	T51.0X1	T51.0X2	T51.0X3	T51.0X4	—	—
allyl	T51.8X1	T51.8X2	T51.8X3	T51.8X4	—	—
amyl	T51.3X1	T51.3X2	T51.3X3	T51.3X4	—	—
antifreeze	T51.1X1	T51.1X2	T51.1X3	T51.1X4	—	—
beverage	T51.0X1	T51.0X2	T51.0X3	T51.0X4	—	—
butyl	T51.3X1	T51.3X2	T51.3X3	T51.3X4	—	—
dehydrated	T51.0X1	T51.0X2	T51.0X3	T51.0X4	—	—
beverage	T51.0X1	T51.0X2	T51.0X3	T51.0X4	—	—
denatured	T51.0X1	T51.0X2	T51.0X3	T51.0X4	—	—
deterrent NEC	T50.6X1	T50.6X2	T50.6X3	T50.6X4	T50.6X5	T50.6X6

Substance	Poisoning, Accidental (unintentional)	Poisoning, Intentional self-harm	Poisoning, Assault	Poisoning, Undetermined	Adverse effect	Underdosing
lcohol — *Continued*						
diagnostic(gastric function)	T50.8X1	T50.8X2	T50.8X3	T50.8X4	T50.8X5	T50.8X6
ethyl	T51.0X1	T51.0X2	T51.0X3	T51.0X4	—	—
beverage	T51.0X1	T51.0X2	T51.0X3	T51.0X4	—	—
grain	T51.0X1	T51.0X2	T51.0X3	T51.0X4	—	—
beverage	T51.0X1	T51.0X2	T51.0X3	T51.0X4	—	—
industrial	T51.0X1	T51.0X2	T51.0X3	T51.0X4	—	—
isopropyl	T51.2X1	T51.2X2	T51.2X3	T51.2X4	—	—
methyl	T51.1X1	T51.1X2	T51.1X3	T51.1X4	—	—
preparation for consumption	T51.0X1	T51.0X2	T51.0X3	T51.0X4	—	—
propyl	T51.3X1	T51.3X2	T51.3X3	T51.3X4	—	—
secondary	T51.2X1	T51.2X2	T51.2X3	T51.2X4	—	—
radiator	T51.1X1	T51.1X2	T51.1X3	T51.1X4	—	—
rubbing	T51.2X1	T51.2X2	T51.2X3	T51.2X4	—	—
specified type NEC	T51.8X1	T51.8X2	T51.8X3	T51.8X4	—	—
surgical	T51.0X1	T51.0X2	T51.0X3	T51.0X4	—	—
vapor(from any type of Alcohol)	T59.891	T59.892	T59.893	T59.894	—	—
wood	T51.1X1	T51.1X2	T51.1X3	T51.1X4	—	—
lcuronium(chloride)	T48.1X1	T48.1X2	T48.1X3	T48.1X4	T48.1X5	T48.1X6
ldactone	T50.0X1	T50.0X2	T50.0X3	T50.0X4	T50.0X5	T50.0X6
ldesulfone sodium	T37.1X1	T37.1X2	T37.1X3	T37.1X4	T37.1X5	T37.1X6
ldicarb	T60.0X1	T60.0X2	T60.0X3	T60.0X4	—	—
ldomet	T46.5X1	T46.5X2	T46.5X3	T46.5X4	T46.5X5	T46.5X6
ldosterone	T50.0X1	T50.0X2	T50.0X3	T50.0X4	T50.0X5	T50.0X6
ldrin(dust)	T60.1X1	T60.1X2	T60.1X3	T60.1X4	—	—
leve—see Naproxen						
lexitol sodium	T47.1X1	T47.1X2	T47.1X3	T47.1X4	T47.1X5	T47.1X6
lfacalcidol	T45.2X1	T45.2X2	T45.2X3	T45.2X4	T45.2X5	T45.2X6
lfadolone	T41.1X1	T41.1X2	T41.1X3	T41.1X4	T41.1X5	T41.1X6
lfaxalone	T41.1X1	T41.1X2	T41.1X3	T41.1X4	T41.1X5	T41.1X6
lfentanil	T40.4X1	T40.4X2	T40.4X3	T40.4X4	T40.4X5	T40.4X6
lfuzosin (hydrochloride)	T44.8X1	T44.8X2	T44.8X3	T44.8X4	T44.8X5	T44.8X6
lgae(harmful) (toxin)	T65.821	T65.822	T65.823	T65.824	—	—
lgeldrate	T47.1X1	T47.1X2	T47.1X3	T47.1X4	T47.1X5	T47.1X6
lgin	T47.8X1	T47.8X2	T47.8X3	T47.8X4	T47.8X5	T47.8X6
lglucerase	T45.3X1	T45.3X2	T45.3X3	T45.3X4	T45.3X5	T45.3X6
lidase	T45.3X1	T45.3X2	T45.3X3	T45.3X4	T45.3X5	T45.3X6
limemazine	T43.3X1	T43.3X2	T43.3X3	T43.3X4	T43.3X5	T43.3X6
liphatic thiocyanates	T65.0X1	T65.0X2	T65.0X3	T65.0X4	—	—
lizapride	T45.0X1	T45.0X2	T45.0X3	T45.0X4	T45.0X5	T45.0X6
lkali(caustic)	T54.3X1	T54.3X2	T54.3X3	T54.3X4	—	—
lkaline antiseptic solution(aromatic)	T49.6X1	T49.6X2	T49.6X3	T49.6X4	T49.6X5	T49.6X6
lkalinizing agents(medicinal)	T50.901	T50.902	T50.903	T50.904	T50.905	T50.906
Alkalizing agent NEC	T50.901	T50.902	T50.903	T50.904	T50.905	T50.906
Alka-seltzer	T39.011	T39.012	T39.013	T39.014	T39.015	T39.016
Alkavervir	T46.5X1	T46.5X2	T46.5X3	T46.5X4	T46.5X5	T46.5X6
Alkonium(bromide)	T49.0X1	T49.0X2	T49.0X3	T49.0X4	T49.0X5	T49.0X6

Substance	Poisoning, Accidental (unintentional)	Poisoning, Intentional self-harm	Poisoning, Assault	Poisoning, Undetermined	Adverse effect	Underdosing
Alkylating drug NEC	T45.1X1	T45.1X2	T45.1X3	T45.1X4	T45.1X5	T45.1X6
antimyeloprolifera-tive	T45.1X1	T45.1X2	T45.1X3	T45.1X4	T45.1X5	T45.1X6
lymphatic	T45.1X1	T45.1X2	T45.1X3	T45.1X4	T45.1X5	T45.1X6
Alkylisocyanate	T65.0X1	T65.0X2	T65.0X3	T65.0X4	—	—
Allantoin	T49.4X1	T49.4X2	T49.4X3	T49.4X4	T49.4X5	T49.4X6
Allegron	T43.011	T43.012	T43.013	T43.014	T43.015	T43.016
Allethrin	T49.0X1	T49.0X2	T49.0X3	T49.0X4	T49.0X5	T49.0X6
Allobarbital	T42.3X1	T42.3X2	T42.3X3	T42.3X4	T42.3X5	T42.3X6
Allopurinol	T50.4X1	T50.4X2	T50.4X3	T50.4X4	T50.4X5	T50.4X6
Allyl						
Alcohol	T51.8X1	T51.8X2	T51.8X3	T51.8X4	—	—
disulfide	T46.6X1	T46.6X2	T46.6X3	T46.6X4	T46.6X5	T46.6X6
Allylestrenol	T38.5X1	T38.5X2	T38.5X3	T38.5X4	T38.5X5	T38.5X6
Allylisopropyl-acetylurea	T42.6X1	T42.6X2	T42.6X3	T42.6X4	T42.6X5	T42.6X6
Allylisopropyl-malonylurea	T42.3X1	T42.3X2	T42.3X3	T42.3X4	T42.3X5	T42.3X6
Allylthiourea	T49.3X1	T49.3X2	T49.3X3	T49.3X4	T49.3X5	T49.3X6
Allyltribromide	T42.6X1	T42.6X2	T42.6X3	T42.6X4	T42.6X5	T42.6X6
Allypropymal	T42.3X1	T42.3X2	T42.3X3	T42.3X4	T42.3X5	T42.3X6
Almagate	T47.1X1	T47.1X2	T47.1X3	T47.1X4	T47.1X5	T47.1X6
Almasilate	T47.1X1	T47.1X2	T47.1X3	T47.1X4	T47.1X5	T47.1X6
Almitrine	T50.7X1	T50.7X2	T50.7X3	T50.7X4	T50.7X5	T50.7X6
Aloes	T47.2X1	T47.2X2	T47.2X3	T47.2X4	T47.2X5	T47.2X6
Aloglutamol	T47.1X1	T47.1X2	T47.1X3	T47.1X4	T47.1X5	T47.1X6
Aloin	T47.2X1	T47.2X2	T47.2X3	T47.2X4	T47.2X5	T47.2X6
Aloxidone	T42.2X1	T42.2X2	T42.2X3	T42.2X4	T42.2X5	T42.2X6
Alpha						
acetyldigoxin	T46.0X1	T46.0X2	T46.0X3	T46.0X4	T46.0X5	T46.0X6
adrenergic blocking drug	T44.6X1	T44.6X2	T44.6X3	T44.6X4	T44.6X5	T44.6X6
amylase	T45.3X1	T45.3X2	T45.3X3	T45.3X4	T45.3X5	T45.3X6
tocoferol(acetate)	T45.2X1	T45.2X2	T45.2X3	T45.2X4	T45.2X5	T45.2X6
tocopherol	T45.2X1	T45.2X2	T45.2X3	T45.2X4	T45.2X5	T45.2X6
Alphadolone	T41.1X1	T41.1X2	T41.1X3	T41.1X4	T41.1X5	T41.1X6
Alphaprodine	T40.4X1	T40.4X2	T40.4X3	T40.4X4	T40.4X5	T40.4X6
Alphaxalone	T41.1X1	T41.1X2	T41.1X3	T41.1X4	T41.1X5	T41.1X6
Alprazolam	T42.4X1	T42.4X2	T42.4X3	T42.4X4	T42.4X5	T42.4X6
Alprenolol	T44.7X1	T44.7X2	T44.7X3	T44.7X4	T44.7X5	T44.7X6
Alprostadil	T46.7X1	T46.7X2	T46.7X3	T46.7X4	T46.7X5	T46.7X6
Alsactide	T38.811	T38.812	T38.813	T38.814	T38.815	T38.816
Alseroxylon	T46.5X1	T46.5X2	T46.5X3	T46.5X4	T46.5X5	T46.5X6
Alteplase	T45.611	T45.612	T45.613	T45.614	T45.615	T45.616
Altizide	T50.2X1	T50.2X2	T50.2X3	T50.2X4	T50.2X5	T50.2X6
Altretamine	T45.1X1	T45.1X2	T45.1X3	T45.1X4	T45.1X5	T45.1X6
Alum(medicinal)	T49.4X1	T49.4X2	T49.4X3	T49.4X4	T49.4X5	T49.4X6
nonmedicinal (ammonium) (potassium)	T56.891	T56.892	T56.893	T56.894	—	—
Aluminium, aluminum						
acetate	T49.2X1	T49.2X2	T49.2X3	T49.2X4	T49.2X5	T49.2X6
solution	T49.0X1	T49.0X2	T49.0X3	T49.0X4	T49.0X5	T49.0X6
aspirin	T39.011	T39.012	T39.013	T39.014	T39.015	T39.016

Substance	Poisoning, Accidental (unintentional)	Poisoning, Intentional self-harm	Poisoning, Assault	Poisoning, Undetermined	Adverse effect	Underdosing
Aluminium, aluminum — *Continued*						
bis(acetylsalicylate)	T39.011	T39.012	T39.013	T39.014	T39.015	T39.016
carbonate(gel, basic)	T47.1X1	T47.1X2	T47.1X3	T47.1X4	T47.1X5	T47.1X6
chlorhydroxide-complex	T47.1X1	T47.1X2	T47.1X3	T47.1X4	T47.1X5	T47.1X6
chloride	T49.2X1	T49.2X2	T49.2X3	T49.2X4	T49.2X5	T49.2X6
clofibrate	T46.6X1	T46.6X2	T46.6X3	T46.6X4	T46.6X5	T46.6X6
diacetate	T49.2X1	T49.2X2	T49.2X3	T49.2X4	T49.2X5	T49.2X6
glycinate	T47.1X1	T47.1X2	T47.1X3	T47.1X4	T47.1X5	T47.1X6
hydroxide(gel)	T47.1X1	T47.1X2	T47.1X3	T47.1X4	T47.1X5	T47.1X6
hydroxide-magnesium carb. gel	T47.1X1	T47.1X2	T47.1X3	T47.1X4	T47.1X5	T47.1X6
magnesium silicate	T47.1X1	T47.1X2	T47.1X3	T47.1X4	T47.1X5	T47.1X6
nicotinate	T46.7X1	T46.7X2	T46.7X3	T46.7X4	T46.7X5	T46.7X6
ointment(surgical) (topical)	T49.3X1	T49.3X2	T49.3X3	T49.3X4	T49.3X5	T49.3X6
phosphate	T47.1X1	T47.1X2	T47.1X3	T47.1X4	T47.1X5	T47.1X6
salicylate	T39.091	T39.092	T39.093	T39.094	T39.095	T39.096
silicate	T47.1X1	T47.1X2	T47.1X3	T47.1X4	T47.1X5	T47.1X6
sodium silicate	T47.1X1	T47.1X2	T47.1X3	T47.1X4	T47.1X5	T47.1X6
subacetate	T49.2X1	T49.2X2	T49.2X3	T49.2X4	T49.2X5	T49.2X6
sulfate	T49.0X1	T49.0X2	T49.0X3	T49.0X4	T49.0X5	T49.0X6
tannate	T47.6X1	T47.6X2	T47.6X3	T47.6X4	T47.6X5	T47.6X6
topical NEC	T49.3X1	T49.3X2	T49.3X3	T49.3X4	T49.3X5	T49.3X6
Alurate	T42.3X1	T42.3X2	T42.3X3	T42.3X4	T42.3X5	T42.3X6
Alverine	T44.3X1	T44.3X2	T44.3X3	T44.3X4	T44.3X5	T44.3X6
Alvodine	T40.2X1	T40.2X2	T40.2X3	T40.2X4	T40.2X5	T40.2X6
Amanita phalloides	T62.0X1	T62.0X2	T62.0X3	T62.0X4	—	—
Amanitine	T62.0X1	T62.0X2	T62.0X3	T62.0X4	—	—
Amantadine	T42.8X1	T42.8X2	T42.8X3	T42.8X4	T42.8X5	T42.8X6
Ambazone	T49.6X1	T49.6X2	T49.6X3	T49.6X4	T49.6X5	T49.6X6
Ambenonium (chloride)	T44.0X1	T44.0X2	T44.0X3	T44.0X4	T44.0X5	T44.0X6
Ambroxol	T48.4X1	T48.4X2	T48.4X3	T48.4X4	T48.4X5	T48.4X6
Ambuphylline	T48.6X1	T48.6X2	T48.6X3	T48.6X4	T48.6X5	T48.6X6
Ambutonium bromide	T44.3X1	T44.3X2	T44.3X3	T44.3X4	T44.3X5	T44.3X6
Amcinonide	T49.0X1	T49.0X2	T49.0X3	T49.0X4	T49.0X5	T49.0X6
Amdinocilline	T36.0X1	T36.0X2	T36.0X3	T36.0X4	T36.0X5	T36.0X6
Ametazole	T50.8X1	T50.8X2	T50.8X3	T50.8X4	T50.8X5	T50.8X6
Amethocaine	T41.3X1	T41.3X2	T41.3X3	T41.3X4	T41.3X5	T41.3X6
regional	T41.3X1	T41.3X2	T41.3X3	T41.3X4	T41.3X5	T41.3X6
spinal	T41.3X1	T41.3X2	T41.3X3	T41.3X4	T41.3X5	T41.3X6
Amethopterin	T45.1X1	T45.1X2	T45.1X3	T45.1X4	T45.1X5	T45.1X6
Amezinium metilsulfate	T44.991	T44.992	T44.993	T44.994	T44.995	T44.996
Amfebutamone	T43.291	T43.292	T43.293	T43.294	T43.295	T43.296
Amfepramone	T50.5X1	T50.5X2	T50.5X3	T50.5X4	T50.5X5	T50.5X6
Amfetamine	T43.621	T43.622	T43.623	T43.624	T43.625	T43.626
Amfetaminil	T43.621	T43.622	T43.623	T43.624	T43.625	T43.626
Amfomycin	T36.8X1	T36.8X2	T36.8X3	T36.8X4	T36.8X5	T36.8X6
Amidefrine mesilate	T48.5X1	T48.5X2	T48.5X3	T48.5X4	T48.5X5	T48.5X6
Amidone	T40.3X1	T40.3X2	T40.3X3	T40.3X4	T40.3X5	T40.3X6

Substance	Poisoning, Accidental (unintentional)	Poisoning, Intentional self-harm	Poisoning, Assault	Poisoning, Undetermined	Adverse effect	Underdosing
Amidopyrine	T39.2X1	T39.2X2	T39.2X3	T39.2X4	T39.2X5	T39.2
Amidotrizoate	T50.8X1	T50.8X2	T50.8X3	T50.8X4	T50.8X5	T50.8
Amiflamine	T43.1X1	T43.1X2	T43.1X3	T43.1X4	T43.1X5	T43.1
Amikacin	T36.5X1	T36.5X2	T36.5X3	T36.5X4	T36.5X5	T36.5
Amikhelline	T46.3X1	T46.3X2	T46.3X3	T46.3X4	T46.3X5	T46.3
Amiloride	T50.2X1	T50.2X2	T50.2X3	T50.2X4	T50.2X5	T50.2
Aminacrine	T49.0X1	T49.0X2	T49.0X3	T49.0X4	T49.0X5	T49.0
Amineptine	T43.011	T43.012	T43.013	T43.014	T43.015	T43.0
Aminitrozole	T37.3X1	T37.3X2	T37.3X3	T37.3X4	T37.3X5	T37.3
Amino acids	T50.3X1	T50.3X2	T50.3X3	T50.3X4	T50.3X5	T50.3
Aminoacetic acid(derivatives)	T50.3X1	T50.3X2	T50.3X3	T50.3X4	T50.3X5	T50.3
Aminoacridine	T49.0X1	T49.0X2	T49.0X3	T49.0X4	T49.0X5	T49.0
Aminobenzoic acid(-p)	T49.3X1	T49.3X2	T49.3X3	T49.3X4	T49.3X5	T49.3
4-Aminobutyric acid	T43.8X1	T43.8X2	T43.8X3	T43.8X4	T43.8X5	T43.8
Aminocaproic acid	T45.621	T45.622	T45.623	T45.624	T45.625	T45.62
Aminoethyl-isothiourium	T45.8X1	T45.8X2	T45.8X3	T45.8X4	T45.8X5	T45.8X
Aminofenazone	T39.2X1	T39.2X2	T39.2X3	T39.2X4	T39.2X5	T39.2X
Aminoglutethimide	T45.1X1	T45.1X2	T45.1X3	T45.1X4	T45.1X5	T45.1X
Aminohippuric acid	T50.8X1	T50.8X2	T50.8X3	T50.8X4	T50.8X5	T50.8X
Aminomethylbenzoic acid	T45.691	T45.692	T45.693	T45.694	T45.695	T45.69
Aminometradine	T50.2X1	T50.2X2	T50.2X3	T50.2X4	T50.2X5	T50.2X
Aminopentamide	T44.3X1	T44.3X2	T44.3X3	T44.3X4	T44.3X5	T44.3X
Aminophenazone	T39.2X1	T39.2X2	T39.2X3	T39.2X4	T39.2X5	T39.2X
Aminophenol	T54.0X1	T54.0X2	T54.0X3	T54.0X4	—	—
4-Aminophenol derivatives	T39.1X1	T39.1X2	T39.1X3	T39.1X4	T39.1X5	T39.1X
Aminophenylpyri-done	T43.591	T43.592	T43.593	T43.594	T43.595	T43.59
Aminophylline	T48.6X1	T48.6X2	T48.6X3	T48.6X4	T48.6X5	T48.6X
Aminopterin sodium	T45.1X1	T45.1X2	T45.1X3	T45.1X4	T45.1X5	T45.1X
Aminopyrine	T39.2X1	T39.2X2	T39.2X3	T39.2X4	T39.2X5	T39.2X
8-Aminoquinoline drugs	T37.2X1	T37.2X2	T37.2X3	T37.2X4	T37.2X5	T37.2X
Aminorex	T50.5X1	T50.5X2	T50.5X3	T50.5X4	T50.5X5	T50.5X
Aminosalicylic acid	T37.1X1	T37.1X2	T37.1X3	T37.1X4	T37.1X5	T37.1X
Aminosalylum	T37.1X1	T37.1X2	T37.1X3	T37.1X4	T37.1X5	T37.1X
Amiodarone	T46.2X1	T46.2X2	T46.2X3	T46.2X4	T46.2X5	T46.2X
Amiphenazole	T50.7X1	T50.7X2	T50.7X3	T50.7X4	T50.7X5	T50.7X
Amiquinsin	T46.5X1	T46.5X2	T46.5X3	T46.5X4	T46.5X5	T46.5X
Amisometradine	T50.2X1	T50.2X2	T50.2X3	T50.2X4	T50.2X5	T50.2X
Amisulpride	T43.591	T43.592	T43.593	T43.594	T43.595	T43.59
Amitriptyline	T43.011	T43.012	T43.013	T43.014	T43.015	T43.01
Amitriptylinoxide	T43.011	T43.012	T43.013	T43.014	T43.015	T43.01
Amlexanox	T48.6X1	T48.6X2	T48.6X3	T48.6X4	T48.6X5	T48.6X
Ammonia(fumes) (gas) (vapor)	T59.891	T59.892	T59.893	T59.894	—	—
aromatic spirit	T48.991	T48.992	T48.993	T48.994	T48.995	T48.99
liquid(household)	T54.3X1	T54.3X2	T54.3X3	T54.3X4	—	—
Ammoniated mercury	T49.0X1	T49.0X2	T49.0X3	T49.0X4	T49.0X5	T49.0X
Ammonium						
acid tartrate	T49.5X1	T49.5X2	T49.5X3	T49.5X4	T49.5X5	T49.5X
bromide	T42.6X1	T42.6X2	T42.6X3	T42.6X4	T42.6X5	T42.6X
carbonate	T54.3X1	T54.3X2	T54.3X3	T54.3X4	—	—

Substance	Poisoning, Accidental (unintentional)	Poisoning, Intentional self-harm	Poisoning, Assault	Poisoning, Undetermined	Adverse effect	Underdosing
nmonium — *Continued*						
chloride	T50.991	T50.992	T50.993	T50.994	T50.995	T50.996
expectorant	T48.4X1	T48.4X2	T48.4X3	T48.4X4	T48.4X5	T48.4X6
compounds (household) NEC	T54.3X1	T54.3X2	T54.3X3	T54.3X4	—	—
fumes(any usage)	T59.891	T59.892	T59.893	T59.894	—	—
industrial	T54.3X1	T54.3X2	T54.3X3	T54.3X4	—	—
ichthyosulronate	T49.4X1	T49.4X2	T49.4X3	T49.4X4	T49.4X5	T49.4X6
mandelate	T37.91	T37.92	T37.93	T37.94	T37.95	T37.96
sulfamate	T60.3X1	T60.3X2	T60.3X3	T60.3X4	—	—
sulfonate resin	T47.8X1	T47.8X2	T47.8X3	T47.8X4	T47.8X5	T47.8X6
nobarbital(sodium)	T42.3X1	T42.3X2	T42.3X3	T42.3X4	T42.3X5	T42.3X6
nodiaquine	T37.2X1	T37.2X2	T37.2X3	T37.2X4	T37.2X5	T37.2X6
nopyroquin(e)	T37.2X1	T37.2X2	T37.2X3	T37.2X4	T37.2X5	T37.2X6
noxapine	T43.011	T43.012	T43.013	T43.014	T43.015	T43.016
noxicillin	T36.0X1	T36.0X2	T36.0X3	T36.0X4	T36.0X5	T36.0X6
nperozide	T43.591	T43.592	T43.593	T43.594	T43.595	T43.596
nphenidone	T43.591	T43.592	T43.593	T43.594	T43.595	T43.596
nphetamine NEC	T43.621	T43.622	T43.623	T43.624	T43.625	T43.626
nphomycin	T36.8X1	T36.8X2	T36.8X3	T36.8X4	T36.8X5	T36.8X6
mphotalide	T37.4X1	T37.4X2	T37.4X3	T37.4X4	T37.4X5	T37.4X6
mphotericin B	T36.7X1	T36.7X2	T36.7X3	T36.7X4	T36.7X5	T36.7X6
topical	T49.0X1	T49.0X2	T49.0X3	T49.0X4	T49.0X5	T49.0X6
mpicillin	T36.0X1	T36.0X2	T36.0X3	T36.0X4	T36.0X5	T36.0X6
mprotropine	T44.3X1	T44.3X2	T44.3X3	T44.3X4	T44.3X5	T44.3X6
msacrine	T45.1X1	T45.1X2	T45.1X3	T45.1X4	T45.1X5	T45.1X6
mygdaline	T62.2X1	T62.2X2	T62.2X3	T62.2X4	—	—
myl						
acetate	T52.8X1	T52.8X2	T52.8X3	T52.8X4	—	—
vapor	T59.891	T59.892	T59.893	T59.894	—	—
alcohol	T51.3X1	T51.3X2	T51.3X3	T51.3X4	—	—
chloride	T53.6X1	T53.6X2	T53.6X3	T53.6X4	—	—
formate	T52.8X1	T52.8X2	T52.8X3	T52.8X4	—	—
nitrite	T46.3X1	T46.3X2	T46.3X3	T46.3X4	T46.3X5	T46.3X6
propionate	T65.891	T65.892	T65.893	T65.894	—	—
mylase	T47.5X1	T47.5X2	T47.5X3	T47.5X4	T47.5X5	T47.5X6
myleine, regional	T41.3X1	T41.3X2	T41.3X3	T41.3X4	T41.3X5	T41.3X6
mylene						
dichloride	T53.6X1	T53.6X2	T53.6X3	T53.6X4	—	—
hydrate	T51.3X1	T51.3X2	T51.3X3	T51.3X4	—	—
Amylmetacresol	T49.6X1	T49.6X2	T49.6X3	T49.6X4	T49.6X5	T49.6X6
Amylobarbitone	T42.3X1	T42.3X2	T42.3X3	T42.3X4	T42.3X5	T42.3X6
Amylocaine, regional	T41.3X1	T41.3X2	T41.3X3	T41.3X4	T41.3X5	T41.3X6
infiltration (subcutaneous)	T41.3X1	T41.3X2	T41.3X3	T41.3X4	T41.3X5	T41.3X6
nerve block(peripheral) (plexus)	T41.3X1	T41.3X2	T41.3X3	T41.3X4	T41.3X5	T41.3X6
spinal	T41.3X1	T41.3X2	T41.3X3	T41.3X4	T41.3X5	T41.3X6
topical(surface)	T41.3X1	T41.3X2	T41.3X3	T41.3X4	T41.3X5	T41.3X6
Amylopectin	T47.6X1	T47.6X2	T47.6X3	T47.6X4	T47.6X5	T47.6X6
Amytal(sodium)	T42.3X1	T42.3X2	T42.3X3	T42.3X4	T42.3X5	T42.3X6
Anabolic steroid	T38.7X1	T38.7X2	T38.7X3	T38.7X4	T38.7X5	T38.7X6

Substance	Poisoning, Accidental (unintentional)	Poisoning, Intentional self-harm	Poisoning, Assault	Poisoning, Undetermined	Adverse effect	Underdosing
Analeptic NEC	T50.7X1	T50.7X2	T50.7X3	T50.7X4	T50.7X5	T50.7X6
Analgesic	T39.91	T39.92	T39.93	T39.94	T39.95	T39.96
anti-inflammatory NEC	T39.91	T39.92	T39.93	T39.94	T39.95	T39.96
propionic acid derivative	T39.311	T39.312	T39.313	T39.314	T39.315	T39.316
antirheumatic NEC	T39.4X1	T39.4X2	T39.4X3	T39.4X4	T39.4X5	T39.4X6
aromatic NEC	T39.1X1	T39.1X2	T39.1X3	T39.1X4	T39.1X5	T39.1X6
narcotic NEC	T40.601	T40.602	T40.603	T40.604	T40.605	T40.606
combination	T40.601	T40.602	T40.603	T40.604	T40.605	T40.606
obstetric	T40.601	T40.602	T40.603	T40.604	T40.605	T40.606
non-narcotic NEC	T39.91	T39.92	T39.93	T39.94	T39.95	T39.96
combination	T39.91	T39.92	T39.93	T39.94	T39.95	T39.96
pyrazole	T39.2X1	T39.2X2	T39.2X3	T39.2X4	T39.2X5	T39.2X6
specified NEC	T39.8X1	T39.8X2	T39.8X3	T39.8X4	T39.8X5	T39.8X6
Analgin	T39.2X1	T39.2X2	T39.2X3	T39.2X4	T39.2X5	T39.2X6
Anamirta cocculus	T62.1X1	T62.1X2	T62.1X3	T62.1X4	—	—
Ancillin	T36.0X1	T36.0X2	T36.0X3	T36.0X4	T36.0X5	T36.0X6
Ancrod	T45.691	T45.692	T45.693	T45.694	T45.695	T45.696
Androgen	T38.7X1	T38.7X2	T38.7X3	T38.7X4	T38.7X5	T38.7X6
Androgen-estrogen mixture	T38.7X1	T38.7X2	T38.7X3	T38.7X4	T38.7X5	T38.7X6
Androstalone	T38.7X1	T38.7X2	T38.7X3	T38.7X4	T38.7X5	T38.7X6
Androstanolone	T38.7X1	T38.7X2	T38.7X3	T38.7X4	T38.7X5	T38.7X6
Androsterone	T38.7X1	T38.7X2	T38.7X3	T38.7X4	T38.7X5	T38.7X6
Anemone pulsatilla	T62.2X1	T62.2X2	T62.2X3	T62.2X4	—	—
Anesthesia						
caudal	T41.3X1	T41.3X2	T41.3X3	T41.3X4	T41.3X5	T41.3X6
endotracheal	T41.0X1	T41.0X2	T41.0X3	T41.0X4	T41.0X5	T41.0X6
epidural	T41.3X1	T41.3X2	T41.3X3	T41.3X4	T41.3X5	T41.3X6
inhalation	T41.0X1	T41.0X2	T41.0X3	T41.0X4	T41.0X5	T41.0X6
local	T41.3X1	T41.3X2	T41.3X3	T41.3X4	T41.3X5	T41.3X6
mucosal	T41.3X1	T41.3X2	T41.3X3	T41.3X4	T41.3X5	T41.3X6
muscle relaxation	T48.1X1	T48.1X2	T48.1X3	T48.1X4	T48.1X5	T48.1X6
nerve blocking	T41.3X1	T41.3X2	T41.3X3	T41.3X4	T41.3X5	T41.3X6
plexus blocking	T41.3X1	T41.3X2	T41.3X3	T41.3X4	T41.3X5	T41.3X6
potentiated	T41.201	T41.202	T41.203	T41.204	T41.205	T41.206
rectal	T41.201	T41.202	T41.203	T41.204	T41.205	T41.206
general	T41.201	T41.202	T41.203	T41.204	T41.205	T41.206
local	T41.3X1	T41.3X2	T41.3X3	T41.3X4	T41.3X5	T41.3X6
regional	T41.3X1	T41.3X2	T41.3X3	T41.3X4	T41.3X5	T41.3X6
surface	T41.3X1	T41.3X2	T41.3X3	T41.3X4	T41.3X5	T41.3X6
Anesthetic NEC —see also Anesthesia	T41.41	T41.42	T41.43	T41.44	T41.45	T41.46
with muscle relaxant	T41.201	T41.202	T41.203	T41.204	T41.205	T41.206
general	T41.201	T41.202	T41.203	T41.204	T41.205	T41.206
local	T41.3X1	T41.3X2	T41.3X3	T41.3X4	T41.3X5	T41.3X6
gaseous NEC	T41.0X1	T41.0X2	T41.0X3	T41.0X4	T41.0X5	T41.0X6
general NEC	T41.201	T41.202	T41.203	T41.204	T41.205	T41.206
halogenated hydrocarbon derivatives NEC	T41.0X1	T41.0X2	T41.0X3	T41.0X4	T41.0X5	T41.0X6
infiltration NEC	T41.3X1	T41.3X2	T41.3X3	T41.3X4	T41.3X5	T41.3X6
intravenous NEC	T41.1X1	T41.1X2	T41.1X3	T41.1X4	T41.1X5	T41.1X6

Substance	Poisoning, Accidental (unintentional)	Poisoning, Intentional self-harm	Poisoning, Assault	Poisoning, Undetermined	Adverse effect	Underdosing
Anesthetic NEC — *Continued*						
local NEC	T41.3X1	T41.3X2	T41.3X3	T41.3X4	T41.3X5	T41.3X6
rectal	T41.201	T41.202	T41.203	T41.204	T41.205	T41.206
general	T41.201	T41.202	T41.203	T41.204	T41.205	T41.206
local	T41.3X1	T41.3X2	T41.3X3	T41.3X4	T41.3X5	T41.3X6
regional NEC	T41.3X1	T41.3X2	T41.3X3	T41.3X4	T41.3X5	T41.3X6
spinal NEC	T41.3X1	T41.3X2	T41.3X3	T41.3X4	T41.3X5	T41.3X6
thiobarbiturate	T41.1X1	T41.1X2	T41.1X3	T41.1X4	T41.1X5	T41.1X6
topical	T41.3X1	T41.3X2	T41.3X3	T41.3X4	T41.3X5	T41.3X6
Aneurine	T45.2X1	T45.2X2	T45.2X3	T45.2X4	T45.2X5	T45.2X6
Angio-Conray	T50.8X1	T50.8X2	T50.8X3	T50.8X4	T50.8X5	T50.8X6
Angiotensin	T44.5X1	T44.5X2	T44.5X3	T44.5X4	T44.5X5	T44.5X6
Angiotensinamide	T44.991	T44.992	T44.993	T44.994	T44.995	T44.996
Anhydrohydroxy-progesterone	T38.5X1	T38.5X2	T38.5X3	T38.5X4	T38.5X5	T38.5X6
Anhydron	T50.2X1	T50.2X2	T50.2X3	T50.2X4	T50.2X5	T50.2X6
Anileridine	T40.4X1	T40.4X2	T40.4X3	T40.4X4	T40.4X5	T40.4X6
Aniline(dye) (liquid)	T65.3X1	T65.3X2	T65.3X3	T65.3X4	—	—
analgesic	T39.1X1	T39.1X2	T39.1X3	T39.1X4	T39.1X5	T39.1X6
derivatives, therapeutic NEC	T39.1X1	T39.1X2	T39.1X3	T39.1X4	T39.1X5	T39.1X6
vapor	T65.3X1	T65.3X2	T65.3X3	T65.3X4	—	—
Aniscoropine	T44.3X1	T44.3X2	T44.3X3	T44.3X4	T44.3X5	T44.3X6
Anise oil	T47.5X1	T47.5X2	T47.5X3	T47.5X4	T47.5X5	T47.5X6
Anisidine	T65.3X1	T65.3X2	T65.3X3	T65.3X4	—	—
Anisindione	T45.511	T45.512	T45.513	T45.514	T45.515	T45.516
Anisotropine methyl-bromide	T44.3X1	T44.3X2	T44.3X3	T44.3X4	T44.3X5	T44.3X6
Anistreplase	T45.611	T45.612	T45.613	T45.614	T45.615	T45.616
Anorexiant(central)	T50.5X1	T50.5X2	T50.5X3	T50.5X4	T50.5X5	T50.5X6
Anorexic agents	T50.5X1	T50.5X2	T50.5X3	T50.5X4	T50.5X5	T50.5X6
Ansamycin	T36.6X1	T36.6X2	T36.6X3	T36.6X4	T36.6X5	T36.6X6
Ant(bite) (sting)	T63.421	T63.422	T63.423	T63.424	—	—
Ant poison—see Insecticide						
Antabuse	T50.6X1	T50.6X2	T50.6X3	T50.6X4	T50.6X5	T50.6X6
Antacid NEC	T47.1X1	T47.1X2	T47.1X3	T47.1X4	T47.1X5	T47.1X6
Antagonist						
Aldosterone	T50.0X1	T50.0X2	T50.0X3	T50.0X4	T50.0X5	T50.0X6
alpha-adrenoreceptor	T44.6X1	T44.6X2	T44.6X3	T44.6X4	T44.6X5	T44.6X6
anticoagulant	T45.7X1	T45.7X2	T45.7X3	T45.7X4	T45.7X5	T45.7X6
beta-adrenoreceptor	T44.7X1	T44.7X2	T44.7X3	T44.7X4	T44.7X5	T44.7X6
extrapyramidal NEC	T44.3X1	T44.3X2	T44.3X3	T44.3X4	T44.3X5	T44.3X6
folic acid	T45.1X1	T45.1X2	T45.1X3	T45.1X4	T45.1X5	T45.1X6
H2 receptor	T47.0X1	T47.0X2	T47.0X3	T47.0X4	T47.0X5	T47.0X6
heavy metal	T45.8X1	T45.8X2	T45.8X3	T45.8X4	T45.8X5	T45.8X6
narcotic analgesic	T50.7X1	T50.7X2	T50.7X3	T50.7X4	T50.7X5	T50.7X6
opiate	T50.7X1	T50.7X2	T50.7X3	T50.7X4	T50.7X5	T50.7X6
pyrimidine	T45.1X1	T45.1X2	T45.1X3	T45.1X4	T45.1X5	T45.1X6
serotonin	T46.5X1	T46.5X2	T46.5X3	T46.5X4	T46.5X5	T46.5X6
Antazolin(e)	T45.0X1	T45.0X2	T45.0X3	T45.0X4	T45.0X5	T45.0X6

Substance	Poisoning, Accidental (unintentional)	Poisoning, Intentional self-harm	Poisoning, Assault	Poisoning, Undetermined	Adverse effect	Underdosing
Anterior pituitary hormone NEC	T38.811	T38.812	T38.813	T38.814	T38.815	T38.8
Anthelmintic NEC	T37.4X1	T37.4X2	T37.4X3	T37.4X4	T37.4X5	T37.4
Anthiolimine	T37.4X1	T37.4X2	T37.4X3	T37.4X4	T37.4X5	T37.4
Anthralin	T49.4X1	T49.4X2	T49.4X3	T49.4X4	T49.4X5	T49.4
Anthramycin	T45.1X1	T45.1X2	T45.1X3	T45.1X4	T45.1X5	T45.1
Antiadrenergic NEC	T44.8X1	T44.8X2	T44.8X3	T44.8X4	T44.8X5	T44.8
Antiallergic NEC	T45.0X1	T45.0X2	T45.0X3	T45.0X4	T45.0X5	T45.0
Anti-anemic(drug) (preparation)	T45.8X1	T45.8X2	T45.8X3	T45.8X4	T45.8X5	T45.8
Antiandrogen NEC	T38.6X1	T38.6X2	T38.6X3	T38.6X4	T38.6X5	T38.6
Antianxiety drug NEC	T43.501	T43.502	T43.503	T43.504	T43.505	T43.5
Antiaris toxicaria	T65.891	T65.892	T65.893	T65.894	—	—
Antiarteriosclerotic drug	T46.6X1	T46.6X2	T46.6X3	T46.6X4	T46.6X5	T46.6
Antiasthmatic drug NEC	T48.6X1	T48.6X2	T48.6X3	T48.6X4	T48.6X5	T48.6
Antibiotic NEC	T36.91	T36.92	T36.93	T36.94	T36.95	T36.9
aminoglycoside	T36.5X1	T36.5X2	T36.5X3	T36.5X4	T36.5X5	T36.5
anticancer	T45.1X1	T45.1X2	T45.1X3	T45.1X4	T45.1X5	T45.1
antifungal	T36.7X1	T36.7X2	T36.7X3	T36.7X4	T36.7X5	T36.7
antimycobacterial	T36.5X1	T36.5X2	T36.5X3	T36.5X4	T36.5X5	T36.5
antineoplastic	T45.1X1	T45.1X2	T45.1X3	T45.1X4	T45.1X5	T45.1
cephalosporin (group)	T36.1X1	T36.1X2	T36.1X3	T36.1X4	T36.1X5	T36.1
chloramphenicol (group)	T36.2X1	T36.2X2	T36.2X3	T36.2X4	T36.2X5	T36.2
ENT	T49.6X1	T49.6X2	T49.6X3	T49.6X4	T49.6X5	T49.6
eye	T49.5X1	T49.5X2	T49.5X3	T49.5X4	T49.5X5	T49.5
fungicidal(local)	T49.0X1	T49.0X2	T49.0X3	T49.0X4	T49.0X5	T49.0
intestinal	T36.8X1	T36.8X2	T36.8X3	T36.8X4	T36.8X5	T36.8
b-lactam NEC	T36.1X1	T36.1X2	T36.1X3	T36.1X4	T36.1X5	T36.1
local	T49.0X1	T49.0X2	T49.0X3	T49.0X4	T49.0X5	T49.0
macrolides	T36.3X1	T36.3X2	T36.3X3	T36.3X4	T36.3X5	T36.3
polypeptide	T36.8X1	T36.8X2	T36.8X3	T36.8X4	T36.8X5	T36.8
specified NEC	T36.8X1	T36.8X2	T36.8X3	T36.8X4	T36.8X5	T36.8
tetracycline(group)	T36.4X1	T36.4X2	T36.4X3	T36.4X4	T36.4X5	T36.4
throat	T49.6X1	T49.6X2	T49.6X3	T49.6X4	T49.6X5	T49.6
Anticancer agents NEC	T45.1X1	T45.1X2	T45.1X3	T45.1X4	T45.1X5	T45.1
Anticholesterolemic drug NEC	T46.6X1	T46.6X2	T46.6X3	T46.6X4	T46.6X5	T46.6
Anticholinergic NEC	T44.3X1	T44.3X2	T44.3X3	T44.3X4	T44.3X5	T44.3
Anticholinesterase	T44.0X1	T44.0X2	T44.0X3	T44.0X4	T44.0X5	T44.0
organophosphorus	T44.0X1	T44.0X2	T44.0X3	T44.0X4	T44.0X5	T44.0
insecticide	T60.0X1	T60.0X2	T60.0X3	T60.0X4	—	—
nerve gas	T59.891	T59.892	T59.893	T59.894	—	—
reversible	T44.0X1	T44.0X2	T44.0X3	T44.0X4	T44.0X5	T44.0
ophthalmological	T49.5X1	T49.5X2	T49.5X3	T49.5X4	T49.5X5	T49.5
Anticoagulant NEC	T45.511	T45.512	T45.513	T45.514	T45.515	T45.5
Antagonist	T45.7X1	T45.7X2	T45.7X3	T45.7X4	T45.7X5	T45.7
Anti-common-cold drug NEC	T48.5X1	T48.5X2	T48.5X3	T48.5X4	T48.5X5	T48.5

Substance	Poisoning, Accidental (unintentional)	Poisoning, Intentional self-harm	Poisoning, Assault	Poisoning, Undetermined	Adverse effect	Underdosing
nticonvulsant	T42.71	T42.72	T42.73	T42.74	T42.75	T42.76
barbiturate	T42.3X1	T42.3X2	T42.3X3	T42.3X4	T42.3X5	T42.3X6
combination(with barbiturate)	T42.3X1	T42.3X2	T42.3X3	T42.3X4	T42.3X5	T42.3X6
hydantoin	T42.0X1	T42.0X2	T42.0X3	T42.0X4	T42.0X5	T42.0X6
hypnotic NEC	T42.6X1	T42.6X2	T42.6X3	T42.6X4	T42.6X5	T42.6X6
oxazolidinedione	T42.2X1	T42.2X2	T42.2X3	T42.2X4	T42.2X5	T42.2X6
pyrimidinedione	T42.6X1	T42.6X2	T42.6X3	T42.6X4	T42.6X5	T42.6X6
specified NEC	T42.6X1	T42.6X2	T42.6X3	T42.6X4	T42.6X5	T42.6X6
succinimide	T42.2X1	T42.2X2	T42.2X3	T42.2X4	T42.2X5	T42.2X6
nti-D immuno- lobulin(human)	T50.Z11	T50.Z12	T50.Z13	T50.Z14	T50.Z15	T50.Z16
ntidepressant	T43.201	T43.202	T43.203	T43.204	T43.205	T43.206
monoamine oxidase inhibitor	T43.1X1	T43.1X2	T43.1X3	T43.1X4	T43.1X5	T43.1X6
selective serotonin norepinephrine reuptake inhibitor	T43.211	T43.212	T43.213	T43.214	T43.215	T43.216
selective serotonin reuptake inhibitor	T43.221	T43.222	T43.223	T43.224	T43.225	T43.226
specified NEC	T43.291	T43.292	T43.293	T43.294	T43.295	T43.296
tetracyclic	T43.021	T43.022	T43.023	T43.024	T43.025	T43.026
triazolopyridine	T43.211	T43.212	T43.213	T43.214	T43.215	T43.216
tricyclic	T43.011	T43.012	T43.013	T43.014	T43.015	T43.016
Antidiabetic NEC	T38.3X1	T38.3X2	T38.3X3	T38.3X4	T38.3X5	T38.3X6
biguanide	T38.3X1	T38.3X2	T38.3X3	T38.3X4	T38.3X5	T38.3X6
and sulfonyl combined	T38.3X1	T38.3X2	T38.3X3	T38.3X4	T38.3X5	T38.3X6
combined	T38.3X1	T38.3X2	T38.3X3	T38.3X4	T38.3X5	T38.3X6
sulfonylurea	T38.3X1	T38.3X2	T38.3X3	T38.3X4	T38.3X5	T38.3X6
Antidiarrheal drug NEC	T47.6X1	T47.6X2	T47.6X3	T47.6X4	T47.6X5	T47.6X6
absorbent	T47.6X1	T47.6X2	T47.6X3	T47.6X4	T47.6X5	T47.6X6
Antidiphtheria serum	T50.Z11	T50.Z12	T50.Z13	T50.Z14	T50.Z15	T50.Z16
Antidiuretic hormone	T38.891	T38.892	T38.893	T38.894	T38.895	T38.896
Antidote NEC	T50.6X1	T50.6X2	T50.6X3	T50.6X4	T50.6X5	T50.6X6
heavy metal	T45.8X1	T45.8X2	T45.8X3	T45.8X4	T45.8X5	T45.8X6
Antidysrhythmic NEC	T46.2X1	T46.2X2	T46.2X3	T46.2X4	T46.2X5	T46.2X6
Antiemetic drug	T45.0X1	T45.0X2	T45.0X3	T45.0X4	T45.0X5	T45.0X6
Antiepilepsy agent	T42.71	T42.72	T42.73	T42.74	T42.75	T42.76
combination	T42.5X1	T42.5X2	T42.5X3	T42.5X4	T42.5X5	T42.5X6
mixed	T42.5X1	T42.5X2	T42.5X3	T42.5X4	T42.5X5	T42.5X6
specified, NEC	T42.6X1	T42.6X2	T42.6X3	T42.6X4	T42.6X5	T42.6X6
Antiestrogen NEC	T38.6X1	T38.6X2	T38.6X3	T38.6X4	T38.6X5	T38.6X6
Antifertility pill	T38.4X1	T38.4X2	T38.4X3	T38.4X4	T38.4X5	T38.4X6
Antifibrinolytic drug	T45.621	T45.622	T45.623	T45.624	T45.625	T45.626
Antifilarial drug	T37.4X1	T37.4X2	T37.4X3	T37.4X4	T37.4X5	T37.4X6
Antiflatulent	T47.5X1	T47.5X2	T47.5X3	T47.5X4	T47.5X5	T47.5X6
Antifreeze	T65.91	T65.92	T65.93	T65.94	—	—
alcohol	T51.1X1	T51.1X2	T51.1X3	T51.1X4	—	—
ethylene glycol	T51.8X1	T51.8X2	T51.8X3	T51.8X4	—	—
Antifungal						
antibiotic(systemic)	T36.7X1	T36.7X2	T36.7X3	T36.7X4	T36.7X5	T36.7X6
anti-infective NEC	T37.91	T37.92	T37.93	T37.94	T37.95	T37.96

Substance	Poisoning, Accidental (unintentional)	Poisoning, Intentional self-harm	Poisoning, Assault	Poisoning, Undetermined	Adverse effect	Underdosing
Antifungal — *Continued*						
disinfectant, local	T49.0X1	T49.0X2	T49.0X3	T49.0X4	T49.0X5	T49.0X6
nonmedicinal(spray)	T60.3X1	T60.3X2	T60.3X3	T60.3X4	—	—
topical	T49.0X1	T49.0X2	T49.0X3	T49.0X4	T49.0X5	T49.0X6
Anti-gastric-secretion drug NEC	T47.1X1	T47.1X2	T47.1X3	T47.1X4	T47.1X5	T47.1X6
Antigonadotrophin NEC	T38.6X1	T38.6X2	T38.6X3	T38.6X4	T38.6X5	T38.6X6
Antihallucinogen	T43.501	T43.502	T43.503	T43.504	T43.505	T43.506
Antihelmintics	T37.4X1	T37.4X2	T37.4X3	T37.4X4	T37.4X5	T37.4X6
Antihemophilic						
factor	T45.8X1	T45.8X2	T45.8X3	T45.8X4	T45.8X5	T45.8X6
fraction	T45.8X1	T45.8X2	T45.8X3	T45.8X4	T45.8X5	T45.8X6
globulin concentrate	T45.7X1	T45.7X2	T45.7X3	T45.7X4	T45.7X5	T45.7X6
human plasma	T45.8X1	T45.8X2	T45.8X3	T45.8X4	T45.8X5	T45.8X6
plasma, dried	T45.7X1	T45.7X2	T45.7X3	T45.7X4	T45.7X5	T45.7X6
Antihemorrhoidal preparation	T49.2X1	T49.2X2	T49.2X3	T49.2X4	T49.2X5	T49.2X6
Antiheparin drug	T45.7X1	T45.7X2	T45.7X3	T45.7X4	T45.7X5	T45.7X6
Antihistamine	T45.0X1	T45.0X2	T45.0X3	T45.0X4	T45.0X5	T45.0X6
Antihookworm drug	T37.4X1	T37.4X2	T37.4X3	T37.4X4	T37.4X5	T37.4X6
Anti-human lymphocytic globulin	T50.Z11	T50.Z12	T50.Z13	T50.Z14	T50.Z15	T50.Z16
Antihyperlipidemic drug	T46.6X1	T46.6X2	T46.6X3	T46.6X4	T46.6X5	T46.6X6
Antihypertensive drug NEC	T46.5X1	T46.5X2	T46.5X3	T46.5X4	T46.5X5	T46.5X6
Anti-infective NEC	T37.91	T37.92	T37.93	T37.94	T37.95	T37.96
anthelmintic	T37.4X1	T37.4X2	T37.4X3	T37.4X4	T37.4X5	T37.4X6
antibiotics	T36.91	T36.92	T36.93	T36.94	T36.95	T36.96
specified NEC	T36.8X1	T36.8X2	T36.8X3	T36.8X4	T36.8X5	T36.8X6
antimalarial	T37.2X1	T37.2X2	T37.2X3	T37.2X4	T37.2X5	T37.2X6
antimycobacterial NEC	T37.1X1	T37.1X2	T37.1X3	T37.1X4	T37.1X5	T37.1X6
antibiotics	T36.5X1	T36.5X2	T36.5X3	T36.5X4	T36.5X5	T36.5X6
antiprotozoal NEC	T37.3X1	T37.3X2	T37.3X3	T37.3X4	T37.3X5	T37.3X6
blood	T37.2X1	T37.2X2	T37.2X3	T37.2X4	T37.2X5	T37.2X6
antiviral	T37.5X1	T37.5X2	T37.5X3	T37.5X4	T37.5X5	T37.5X6
arsenical	T37.8X1	T37.8X2	T37.8X3	T37.8X4	T37.8X5	T37.8X6
bismuth, local	T49.0X1	T49.0X2	T49.0X3	T49.0X4	T49.0X5	T49.0X6
ENT	T49.6X1	T49.6X2	T49.6X3	T49.6X4	T49.6X5	T49.6X6
eye NEC	T49.5X1	T49.5X2	T49.5X3	T49.5X4	T49.5X5	T49.5X6
heavy metals NEC	T37.8X1	T37.8X2	T37.8X3	T37.8X4	T37.8X5	T37.8X6
local NEC	T49.0X1	T49.0X2	T49.0X3	T49.0X4	T49.0X5	T49.0X6
specified NEC	T49.0X1	T49.0X2	T49.0X3	T49.0X4	T49.0X5	T49.0X6
mixed	T37.91	T37.92	T37.93	T37.94	T37.95	T37.96
ophthalmic preparation	T49.5X1	T49.5X2	T49.5X3	T49.5X4	T49.5X5	T49.5X6
topical NEC	T49.0X1	T49.0X2	T49.0X3	T49.0X4	T49.0X5	T49.0X6
Anti-inflammatory drug NEC	T39.391	T39.392	T39.393	T39.394	T39.395	T39.396
local	T49.0X1	T49.0X2	T49.0X3	T49.0X4	T49.0X5	T49.0X6
nonsteroidal NEC	T39.391	T39.392	T39.393	T39.394	T39.395	T39.396
propionic acid derivative	T39.311	T39.312	T39.313	T39.314	T39.315	T39.316
specified NEC	T39.391	T39.392	T39.393	T39.394	T39.395	T39.396

Substance	Poisoning, Accidental (unintentional)	Poisoning, Intentional self-harm	Poisoning, Assault	Poisoning, Undetermined	Adverse effect	Underdosing
Antikaluretic	T50.3X1	T50.3X2	T50.3X3	T50.3X4	T50.3X5	T50.3X6
Antiknock(tetraethyl lead)	T56.0X1	T56.0X2	T56.0X3	T56.0X4	—	—
Antilipemic drug NEC	T46.6X1	T46.6X2	T46.6X3	T46.6X4	T46.6X5	T46.6X6
Antimalarial	T37.2X1	T37.2X2	T37.2X3	T37.2X4	T37.2X5	T37.2X6
prophylactic NEC	T37.2X1	T37.2X2	T37.2X3	T37.2X4	T37.2X5	T37.2X6
pyrimidine derivative	T37.2X1	T37.2X2	T37.2X3	T37.2X4	T37.2X5	T37.2X6
Antimetabolite	T45.1X1	T45.1X2	T45.1X3	T45.1X4	T45.1X5	T45.1X6
Antimitotic agent	T45.1X1	T45.1X2	T45.1X3	T45.1X4	T45.1X5	T45.1X6
Antimony (compounds) (vapor)NEC	T56.891	T56.892	T56.893	T56.894	—	—
anti-infectives	T37.8X1	T37.8X2	T37.8X3	T37.8X4	T37.8X5	T37.8X6
dimercaptosuccinate	T37.3X1	T37.3X2	T37.3X3	T37.3X4	T37.3X5	T37.3X6
hydride	T56.891	T56.892	T56.893	T56.894	—	—
pesticide(vapor)	T60.8X1	T60.8X2	T60.8X3	T60.8X4	—	—
potassium(sodium) tartrate	T37.8X1	T37.8X2	T37.8X3	T37.8X4	T37.8X5	T37.8X6
sodium dimercaptosuccinate	T37.3X1	T37.3X2	T37.3X3	T37.3X4	T37.3X5	T37.3X6
tartrated	T37.8X1	T37.8X2	T37.8X3	T37.8X4	T37.8X5	T37.8X6
Antimuscarinic NEC	T44.3X1	T44.3X2	T44.3X3	T44.3X4	T44.3X5	T44.3X6
Antimycobacterial drug NEC	T37.1X1	T37.1X2	T37.1X3	T37.1X4	T37.1X5	T37.1X6
antibiotics	T36.5X1	T36.5X2	T36.5X3	T36.5X4	T36.5X5	T36.5X6
combination	T37.1X1	T37.1X2	T37.1X3	T37.1X4	T37.1X5	T37.1X6
Antinausea drug	T45.0X1	T45.0X2	T45.0X3	T45.0X4	T45.0X5	T45.0X6
Antinematode drug	T37.4X1	T37.4X2	T37.4X3	T37.4X4	T37.4X5	T37.4X6
Antineoplastic NEC	T45.1X1	T45.1X2	T45.1X3	T45.1X4	T45.1X5	T45.1X6
alkaloidal	T45.1X1	T45.1X2	T45.1X3	T45.1X4	T45.1X5	T45.1X6
antibiotics	T45.1X1	T45.1X2	T45.1X3	T45.1X4	T45.1X5	T45.1X6
combination	T45.1X1	T45.1X2	T45.1X3	T45.1X4	T45.1X5	T45.1X6
estrogen	T38.5X1	T38.5X2	T38.5X3	T38.5X4	T38.5X5	T38.5X6
steroid	T38.7X1	T38.7X2	T38.7X3	T38.7X4	T38.7X5	T38.7X6
Antiparasitic drug(systemic)	T37.91	T37.92	T37.93	T37.94	T37.95	T37.96
local	T49.0X1	T49.0X2	T49.0X3	T49.0X4	T49.0X5	T49.0X6
specified NEC	T37.8X1	T37.8X2	T37.8X3	T37.8X4	T37.8X5	T37.8X6
Antiparkinsonism drug NEC	T42.8X1	T42.8X2	T42.8X3	T42.8X4	T42.8X5	T42.8X6
Antiperspirant NEC	T49.2X1	T49.2X2	T49.2X3	T49.2X4	T49.2X5	T49.2X6
Antiphlogistic NEC	T39.4X1	T39.4X2	T39.4X3	T39.4X4	T39.4X5	T39.4X6
Antiplatyhelmintic drug	T37.4X1	T37.4X2	T37.4X3	T37.4X4	T37.4X5	T37.4X6
Antiprotozoal drug NEC	T37.3X1	T37.3X2	T37.3X3	T37.3X4	T37.3X5	T37.3X6
blood	T37.2X1	T37.2X2	T37.2X3	T37.2X4	T37.2X5	T37.2X6
local	T49.0X1	T49.0X2	T49.0X3	T49.0X4	T49.0X5	T49.0X6
Antipruritic drug NEC	T49.1X1	T49.1X2	T49.1X3	T49.1X4	T49.1X5	T49.1X6
Antipsychotic drug	T43.501	T43.502	T43.503	T43.504	T43.505	T43.506
specified NEC	T43.591	T43.592	T43.593	T43.594	T43.595	T43.596
Antipyretic	T39.91	T39.92	T39.93	T39.94	T39.95	T39.96
specified NEC	T39.8X1	T39.8X2	T39.8X3	T39.8X4	T39.8X5	T39.8X6
Antipyrine	T39.2X1	T39.2X2	T39.2X3	T39.2X4	T39.2X5	T39.2X6
Antirabies hyperimmune serum	T50.Z11	T50.Z12	T50.Z13	T50.Z14	T50.Z15	T50.Z16
Antirheumatic NEC	T39.4X1	T39.4X2	T39.4X3	T39.4X4	T39.4X5	T39.4X6

Substance	Poisoning, Accidental (unintentional)	Poisoning, Intentional self-harm	Poisoning, Assault	Poisoning, Undetermined	Adverse effect	Underdosing
Antirigidity drug NEC	T42.8X1	T42.8X2	T42.8X3	T42.8X4	T42.8X5	T42.8X
Antischistosomal drug	T37.4X1	T37.4X2	T37.4X3	T37.4X4	T37.4X5	T37.4X
Antiscorpion sera	T50.Z11	T50.Z12	T50.Z13	T50.Z14	T50.Z15	T50.Z
Antiseborrheics	T49.4X1	T49.4X2	T49.4X3	T49.4X4	T49.4X5	T49.4X
Antiseptics(external) (medicinal)	T49.0X1	T49.0X2	T49.0X3	T49.0X4	T49.0X5	T49.0X
Antistine	T45.0X1	T45.0X2	T45.0X3	T45.0X4	T45.0X5	T45.0X
Antitapeworm drug	T37.4X1	T37.4X2	T37.4X3	T37.4X4	T37.4X5	T37.4X
Antitetanus immunoglobulin	T50.Z11	T50.Z12	T50.Z13	T50.Z14	T50.Z15	T50.Z
Antithyroid drug NEC	T38.2X1	T38.2X2	T38.2X3	T38.2X4	T38.2X5	T38.2X
Antitoxin	T50.Z11	T50.Z12	T50.Z13	T50.Z14	T50.Z15	T50.Z
diphtheria	T50.Z11	T50.Z12	T50.Z13	T50.Z14	T50.Z15	T50.Z
gas gangrene	T50.Z11	T50.Z12	T50.Z13	T50.Z14	T50.Z15	T50.Z
tetanus	T50.Z11	T50.Z12	T50.Z13	T50.Z14	T50.Z15	T50.Z
Antitrichomonal drug	T37.3X1	T37.3X2	T37.3X3	T37.3X4	T37.3X5	T37.3X
Antituberculars	T37.1X1	T37.1X2	T37.1X3	T37.1X4	T37.1X5	T37.1X
antibiotics	T36.5X1	T36.5X2	T36.5X3	T36.5X4	T36.5X5	T36.5X
Antitussive NEC	T48.3X1	T48.3X2	T48.3X3	T48.3X4	T48.3X5	T48.3X
codeine mixture	T40.2X1	T40.2X2	T40.2X3	T40.2X4	T40.2X5	T40.2X
opiate	T40.2X1	T40.2X2	T40.2X3	T40.2X4	T40.2X5	T40.2X
Antivaricose drug	T46.8X1	T46.8X2	T46.8X3	T46.8X4	T46.8X5	T46.8X
Antivenin, antivenom(sera)	T50.Z11	T50.Z12	T50.Z13	T50.Z14	T50.Z15	T50.Z
crotaline	T50.Z11	T50.Z12	T50.Z13	T50.Z14	T50.Z15	T50.Z
spider bite	T50.Z11	T50.Z12	T50.Z13	T50.Z14	T50.Z15	T50.Z
Antivertigo drug	T45.0X1	T45.0X2	T45.0X3	T45.0X4	T45.0X5	T45.0X
Antiviral drug NEC	T37.5X1	T37.5X2	T37.5X3	T37.5X4	T37.5X5	T37.5X
eye	T49.5X1	T49.5X2	T49.5X3	T49.5X4	T49.5X5	T49.5X
Antiwhipworm drug	T37.4X1	T37.4X2	T37.4X3	T37.4X4	T37.4X5	T37.4X
Antrol—see also by specific chemical substance	T60.91	T60.92	T60.93	T60.94	—	—
fungicide	T60.91	T60.92	T60.93	T60.94	—	—
ANTU(alpha naphthylthiourea)	T60.4X1	T60.4X2	T60.4X3	T60.4X4	—	—
Apalcillin	T36.0X1	T36.0X2	T36.0X3	T36.0X4	T36.0X5	T36.0X
APC	T48.5X1	T48.5X2	T48.5X3	T48.5X4	T48.5X5	T48.5X
Aplonidine	T44.4X1	T44.4X2	T44.4X3	T44.4X4	T44.4X5	T44.4X
Apomorphine	T47.7X1	T47.7X2	T47.7X3	T47.7X4	T47.7X5	T47.7X
Appetite depressants, central	T50.5X1	T50.5X2	T50.5X3	T50.5X4	T50.5X5	T50.5X
Apraclonidine (hydrochloride)	T44.4X1	T44.4X2	T44.4X3	T44.4X4	T44.4X5	T44.4X
Apresoline	T46.5X1	T46.5X2	T46.5X3	T46.5X4	T46.5X5	T46.5X
Aprindine	T46.2X1	T46.2X2	T46.2X3	T46.2X4	T46.2X5	T46.2X
Aprobarbital	T42.3X1	T42.3X2	T42.3X3	T42.3X4	T42.3X5	T42.3X
Apronalide	T42.6X1	T42.6X2	T42.6X3	T42.6X4	T42.6X5	T42.6X
Aprotinin	T45.621	T45.622	T45.623	T45.624	T45.625	T45.62
Aptocaine	T41.3X1	T41.3X2	T41.3X3	T41.3X4	T41.3X5	T41.3X
Aqua fortis	T54.2X1	T54.2X2	T54.2X3	T54.2X4	—	—
Ara-A	T37.5X1	T37.5X2	T37.5X3	T37.5X4	T37.5X5	T37.5X
Ara-C	T45.1X1	T45.1X2	T45.1X3	T45.1X4	T45.1X5	T45.1X
Arachis oil	T49.3X1	T49.3X2	T49.3X3	T49.3X4	T49.3X5	T49.3X
cathartic	T47.4X1	T47.4X2	T47.4X3	T47.4X4	T47.4X5	T47.4X

Substance	Poisoning, Accidental (unintentional)	Poisoning, Intentional self-harm	Poisoning, Assault	Poisoning, Undetermined	Adverse effect	Underdosing
ralen	T37.2X1	T37.2X2	T37.2X3	T37.2X4	T37.2X5	T37.2X6
ecoline	T44.1X1	T44.1X2	T44.1X3	T44.1X4	T44.1X5	T44.1X6
ginine	T50.991	T50.992	T50.993	T50.994	T50.995	T50.996
glutamate	T50.991	T50.992	T50.993	T50.994	T50.995	T50.996
gyrol	T49.0X1	T49.0X2	T49.0X3	T49.0X4	T49.0X5	T49.0X6
ENT agent	T49.6X1	T49.6X2	T49.6X3	T49.6X4	T49.6X5	T49.6X6
ophthalmic preparation	T49.5X1	T49.5X2	T49.5X3	T49.5X4	T49.5X5	T49.5X6
istocort	T38.0X1	T38.0X2	T38.0X3	T38.0X4	T38.0X5	T38.0X6
ENT agent	T49.6X1	T49.6X2	T49.6X3	T49.6X4	T49.6X5	T49.6X6
ophthalmic preparation	T49.5X1	T49.5X2	T49.5X3	T49.5X4	T49.5X5	T49.5X6
topical NEC	T49.0X1	T49.0X2	T49.0X3	T49.0X4	T49.0X5	T49.0X6
romatics, corrosive	T54.1X1	T54.1X2	T54.1X3	T54.1X4	—	—
disinfectants	T54.1X1	T54.1X2	T54.1X3	T54.1X4	—	—
senate of lead	T57.0X1	T57.0X2	T57.0X3	T57.0X4	—	—
herbicide	T57.0X1	T57.0X2	T57.0X3	T57.0X4	—	—
rsenic, arsenicals ompounds)(dust) apor) NEC	T57.0X1	T57.0X2	T57.0X3	T57.0X4	—	—
anti-infectives	T37.8X1	T37.8X2	T37.8X3	T37.8X4	T37.8X5	T37.8X6
pesticide(dust) (fumes)	T57.0X1	T57.0X2	T57.0X3	T57.0X4	—	—
rsine(gas)	T57.0X1	T57.0X2	T57.0X3	T57.0X4	—	—
rsphenamine(silver)	T37.8X1	T37.8X2	T37.8X3	T37.8X4	T37.8X5	T37.8X6
rsthinol	T37.3X1	T37.3X2	T37.3X3	T37.3X4	T37.3X5	T37.3X6
rtane	T44.3X1	T44.3X2	T44.3X3	T44.3X4	T44.3X5	T44.3X6
rthropod en omous) NEC	T63.481	T63.482	T63.483	T63.484	—	—
rticaine	T41.3X1	T41.3X2	T41.3X3	T41.3X4	T41.3X5	T41.3X6
sbestos	T57.8X1	T57.8X2	T57.8X3	T57.8X4	—	—
scaridole	T37.4X1	T37.4X2	T37.4X3	T37.4X4	T37.4X5	T37.4X6
scorbic acid	T45.2X1	T45.2X2	T45.2X3	T45.2X4	T45.2X5	T45.2X6
siaticoside	T49.0X1	T49.0X2	T49.0X3	T49.0X4	T49.0X5	T49.0X6
sparaginase	T45.1X1	T45.1X2	T45.1X3	T45.1X4	T45.1X5	T45.1X6
spidium(oleoresin)	T37.4X1	T37.4X2	T37.4X3	T37.4X4	T37.4X5	T37.4X6
spirin(aluminum) soluble)	T39.011	T39.012	T39.013	T39.014	T39.015	T39.016
spoxicillin	T36.0X1	T36.0X2	T36.0X3	T36.0X4	T36.0X5	T36.0X6
stemizole	T45.0X1	T45.0X2	T45.0X3	T45.0X4	T45.0X5	T45.0X6
stringent(local)	T49.2X1	T49.2X2	T49.2X3	T49.2X4	T49.2X5	T49.2X6
specified NEC	T49.2X1	T49.2X2	T49.2X3	T49.2X4	T49.2X5	T49.2X6
stromicin	T36.5X1	T36.5X2	T36.5X3	T36.5X4	T36.5X5	T36.5X6
taractic drug NEC	T43.501	T43.502	T43.503	T43.504	T43.505	T43.506
tenolol	T44.7X1	T44.7X2	T44.7X3	T44.7X4	T44.7X5	T44.7X6
tonia drug, intestinal	T47.4X1	T47.4X2	T47.4X3	T47.4X4	T47.4X5	T47.4X6
tophan	T50.4X1	T50.4X2	T50.4X3	T50.4X4	T50.4X5	T50.4X6
tracurium besilate	T48.1X1	T48.1X2	T48.1X3	T48.1X4	T48.1X5	T48.1X6
tropine	T44.3X1	T44.3X2	T44.3X3	T44.3X4	T44.3X5	T44.3X6
derivative	T44.3X1	T44.3X2	T44.3X3	T44.3X4	T44.3X5	T44.3X6
methonitrate	T44.3X1	T44.3X2	T44.3X3	T44.3X4	T44.3X5	T44.3X6
ttapulgite	T47.6X1	T47.6X2	T47.6X3	T47.6X4	T47.6X5	T47.6X6
uramine	T65.891	T65.892	T65.893	T65.894	—	—
dye	T65.6X1	T65.6X2	T65.6X3	T65.6X4	—	—
fungicide	T60.3X1	T60.3X2	T60.3X3	T60.3X4	—	—
Auranofin	T39.4X1	T39.4X2	T39.4X3	T39.4X4	T39.4X5	T39.4X6
Aurantiin	T46.991	T46.992	T46.993	T46.994	T46.995	T46.996
Aureomycin	T36.4X1	T36.4X2	T36.4X3	T36.4X4	T36.4X5	T36.4X6
ophthalmic preparation	T49.5X1	T49.5X2	T49.5X3	T49.5X4	T49.5X5	T49.5X6
topical NEC	T49.0X1	T49.0X2	T49.0X3	T49.0X4	T49.0X5	T49.0X6
Aurothioglucose	T39.4X1	T39.4X2	T39.4X3	T39.4X4	T39.4X5	T39.4X6
Aurothioglycanide	T39.4X1	T39.4X2	T39.4X3	T39.4X4	T39.4X5	T39.4X6
Aurothiomalate sodium	T39.4X1	T39.4X2	T39.4X3	T39.4X4	T39.4X5	T39.4X6
Aurotioprol	T39.4X1	T39.4X2	T39.4X3	T39.4X4	T39.4X5	T39.4X6
Automobile fuel	T52.0X1	T52.0X2	T52.0X3	T52.0X4	—	—
Autonomic nervous system agent NEC	T44.901	T44.902	T44.903	T44.904	T44.905	T44.906
Avlosulfon	T37.1X1	T37.1X2	T37.1X3	T37.1X4	T37.1X5	T37.1X6
Avomine	T42.6X1	T42.6X2	T42.6X3	T42.6X4	T42.6X5	T42.6X6
Axerophthol	T45.2X1	T45.2X2	T45.2X3	T45.2X4	T45.2X5	T45.2X6
Azacitidine	T45.1X1	T45.1X2	T45.1X3	T45.1X4	T45.1X5	T45.1X6
Azacyclonol	T43.591	T43.592	T43.593	T43.594	T43.595	T43.596
Azadirachta	T60.2X1	T60.2X2	T60.2X3	T60.2X4	—	—
Azanidazole	T37.3X1	T37.3X2	T37.3X3	T37.3X4	T37.3X5	T37.3X6
Azapetine	T46.7X1	T46.7X2	T46.7X3	T46.7X4	T46.7X5	T46.7X6
Azapropazone	T39.2X1	T39.2X2	T39.2X3	T39.2X4	T39.2X5	T39.2X6
Azaribine	T45.1X1	T45.1X2	T45.1X3	T45.1X4	T45.1X5	T45.1X6
Azaserine	T45.1X1	T45.1X2	T45.1X3	T45.1X4	T45.1X5	T45.1X6
Azatadine	T45.0X1	T45.0X2	T45.0X3	T45.0X4	T45.0X5	T45.0X6
Azatepa	T45.1X1	T45.1X2	T45.1X3	T45.1X4	T45.1X5	T45.1X6
Azathioprine	T45.1X1	T45.1X2	T45.1X3	T45.1X4	T45.1X5	T45.1X6
Azelaic acid	T49.0X1	T49.0X2	T49.0X3	T49.0X4	T49.0X5	T49.0X6
Azelastine	T45.0X1	T45.0X2	T45.0X3	T45.0X4	T45.0X5	T45.0X6
Azidocillin	T36.0X1	T36.0X2	T36.0X3	T36.0X4	T36.0X5	T36.0X6
Azidothymidine	T37.5X1	T37.5X2	T37.5X3	T37.5X4	T37.5X5	T37.5X6
Azinphos(ethyl) (methyl)	T60.0X1	T60.0X2	T60.0X3	T60.0X4	—	—
Aziridine (chelating)	T54.1X1	T54.1X2	T54.1X3	T54.1X4	—	—
Azithromycin	T36.3X1	T36.3X2	T36.3X3	T36.3X4	T36.3X5	T36.3X6
Azlocillin	T36.0X1	T36.0X2	T36.0X3	T36.0X4	T36.0X5	T36.0X6
Azobenzene smoke	T65.3X1	T65.3X2	T65.3X3	T65.3X4	—	—
acaricide	T60.8X1	T60.8X2	T60.8X3	T60.8X4	—	—
Azosulfamide	T37.0X1	T37.0X2	T37.0X3	T37.0X4	T37.0X5	T37.0X6
AZT	T37.5X1	T37.5X2	T37.5X3	T37.5X4	T37.5X5	T37.5X6
Aztreonam	T36.1X1	T36.1X2	T36.1X3	T36.1X4	T36.1X5	T36.1X6
Azulfidine	T37.0X1	T37.0X2	T37.0X3	T37.0X4	T37.0X5	T37.0X6
Azuresin	T50.8X1	T50.8X2	T50.8X3	T50.8X4	T50.8X5	T50.8X6
B						
Bacampicillin	T36.0X1	T36.0X2	T36.0X3	T36.0X4	T36.0X5	T36.0X6
Bacillus						
lactobacillus	T47.8X1	T47.8X2	T47.8X3	T47.8X4	T47.8X5	T47.8X6
subtilis	T47.6X1	T47.6X2	T47.6X3	T47.6X4	T47.6X5	T47.6X6
Bacimycin	T49.0X1	T49.0X2	T49.0X3	T49.0X4	T49.0X5	T49.0X6
ophthalmic preparation	T49.5X1	T49.5X2	T49.5X3	T49.5X4	T49.5X5	T49.5X6

Substance	Poisoning, Accidental (unintentional)	Poisoning, Intentional self-harm	Poisoning, Assault	Poisoning, Undetermined	Adverse effect	Underdosing
Bacitracin zinc	T49.0X1	T49.0X2	T49.0X3	T49.0X4	T49.0X5	T49.0X6
with neomycin	T49.0X1	T49.0X2	T49.0X3	T49.0X4	T49.0X5	T49.0X6
ENT agent	T49.6X1	T49.6X2	T49.6X3	T49.6X4	T49.6X5	T49.6X6
ophthalmic preparation	T49.5X1	T49.5X2	T49.5X3	T49.5X4	T49.5X5	T49.5X6
topical NEC	T49.0X1	T49.0X2	T49.0X3	T49.0X4	T49.0X5	T49.0X6
Baclofen	T42.8X1	T42.8X2	T42.8X3	T42.8X4	T42.8X5	T42.8X6
Baking soda	T50.991	T50.992	T50.993	T50.994	T50.995	T50.996
BAL	T45.8X1	T45.8X2	T45.8X3	T45.8X4	T45.8X5	T45.8X6
Bambuterol	T48.6X1	T48.6X2	T48.6X3	T48.6X4	T48.6X5	T48.6X6
Bamethan(sulfate)	T46.7X1	T46.7X2	T46.7X3	T46.7X4	T46.7X5	T46.7X6
Bamifylline	T48.6X1	T48.6X2	T48.6X3	T48.6X4	T48.6X5	T48.6X6
Bamipine	T45.0X1	T45.0X2	T45.0X3	T45.0X4	T45.0X5	T45.0X6
Baneberry—see Actauseea spicata						
Banewort—see Belladonna						
Barbenyl	T42.3X1	T42.3X2	T42.3X3	T42.3X4	T42.3X5	T42.3X6
Barbexaclone	T42.6X1	T42.6X2	T42.6X3	T42.6X4	T42.6X5	T42.6X6
Barbital	T42.3X1	T42.3X2	T42.3X3	T42.3X4	T42.3X5	T42.3X6
sodium	T42.3X1	T42.3X2	T42.3X3	T42.3X4	T42.3X5	T42.3X6
Barbitone	T42.3X1	T42.3X2	T42.3X3	T42.3X4	T42.3X5	T42.3X6
Barbiturate NEC	T42.3X1	T42.3X2	T42.3X3	T42.3X4	T42.3X5	T42.3X6
with tranquilizer	T42.3X1	T42.3X2	T42.3X3	T42.3X4	T42.3X5	T42.3X6
anesthetic (intravenous)	T41.1X1	T41.1X2	T41.1X3	T41.1X4	T41.1X5	T41.1X6
Barium(carbonate) (chloride) (sulfite)	T57.8X1	T57.8X2	T57.8X3	T57.8X4	—	—
diagnostic agent	T50.8X1	T50.8X2	T50.8X3	T50.8X4	T50.8X5	T50.8X6
pesticide	T60.4X1	T60.4X2	T60.4X3	T60.4X4	—	—
rodenticide	T60.4X1	T60.4X2	T60.4X3	T60.4X4	—	—
sulfate(medicinal)	T50.8X1	T50.8X2	T50.8X3	T50.8X4	T50.8X5	T50.8X6
Barrier cream	T49.3X1	T49.3X2	T49.3X3	T49.3X4	T49.3X5	T49.3X6
Basic fuchsin	T49.0X1	T49.0X2	T49.0X3	T49.0X4	T49.0X5	T49.0X6
Battery acid or fluid	T54.2X1	T54.2X2	T54.2X3	T54.2X4	—	—
Bay rum	T51.8X1	T51.8X2	T51.8X3	T51.8X4	—	—
BCG(vaccine)	T50.A91	T50.A92	T50.A93	T50.A94	T50.A95	T50.A96
BCNU	T45.1X1	T45.1X2	T45.1X3	T45.1X4	T45.1X5	T45.1X6
Bearsfoot	T62.2X1	T62.2X2	T62.2X3	T62.2X4	—	—
Beclamide	T42.6X1	T42.6X2	T42.6X3	T42.6X4	T42.6X5	T42.6X6
Beclomethasone	T44.5X1	T44.5X2	T44.5X3	T44.5X4	T44.5X5	T44.5X6
Bee(sting) (venom)	T63.441	T63.442	T63.443	T63.444	—	—
Befunolol	T49.5X1	T49.5X2	T49.5X3	T49.5X4	T49.5X5	T49.5X6
Bekanamycin	T36.5X1	T36.5X2	T36.5X3	T36.5X4	T36.5X5	T36.5X6
Belladonna—see also Nightshade						
alkaloids	T44.3X1	T44.3X2	T44.3X3	T44.3X4	T44.3X5	T44.3X6
extract	T44.3X1	T44.3X2	T44.3X3	T44.3X4	T44.3X5	T44.3X6
herb	T44.3X1	T44.3X2	T44.3X3	T44.3X4	T44.3X5	T44.3X6
Bemegride	T50.7X1	T50.7X2	T50.7X3	T50.7X4	T50.7X5	T50.7X6
Benactyzine	T44.3X1	T44.3X2	T44.3X3	T44.3X4	T44.3X5	T44.3X6
Benadryl	T45.0X1	T45.0X2	T45.0X3	T45.0X4	T45.0X5	T45.0X6
Benaprizine	T44.3X1	T44.3X2	T44.3X3	T44.3X4	T44.3X5	T44.3X6

Substance	Poisoning, Accidental (unintentional)	Poisoning, Intentional self-harm	Poisoning, Assault	Poisoning, Undetermined	Adverse effect	Underdosing
Benazepril	T46.4X1	T46.4X2	T46.4X3	T46.4X4	T46.4X5	T46.4
Bencyclane	T46.7X1	T46.7X2	T46.7X3	T46.7X4	T46.7X5	T46.7
Bendazol	T46.3X1	T46.3X2	T46.3X3	T46.3X4	T46.3X5	T46.3X
Bendrofluazide	T50.2X1	T50.2X2	T50.2X3	T50.2X4	T50.2X5	T50.2X
Bendroflumethiazide	T50.2X1	T50.2X2	T50.2X3	T50.2X4	T50.2X5	T50.2X
Benemid	T50.4X1	T50.4X2	T50.4X3	T50.4X4	T50.4X5	T50.4X
Benethamine penicillin	T36.0X1	T36.0X2	T36.0X3	T36.0X4	T36.0X5	T36.0X
Benexate	T47.1X1	T47.1X2	T47.1X3	T47.1X4	T47.1X5	T47.1X
Benfluorex	T46.6X1	T46.6X2	T46.6X3	T46.6X4	T46.6X5	T46.6X
Benfotiamine	T45.2X1	T45.2X2	T45.2X3	T45.2X4	T45.2X5	T45.2X
Benisone	T49.0X1	T49.0X2	T49.0X3	T49.0X4	T49.0X5	T49.0X
Benomyl	T60.0X1	T60.0X2	T60.0X3	T60.0X4	—	—
Benoquin	T49.8X1	T49.8X2	T49.8X3	T49.8X4	T49.8X5	T49.8X
Benoxinate	T41.3X1	T41.3X2	T41.3X3	T41.3X4	T41.3X5	T41.3X
Benperidol	T43.4X1	T43.4X2	T43.4X3	T43.4X4	T43.4X5	T43.4X
Benproperine	T48.3X1	T48.3X2	T48.3X3	T48.3X4	T48.3X5	T48.3X
Benserazide	T42.8X1	T42.8X2	T42.8X3	T42.8X4	T42.8X5	T42.8X
Bentazepam	T42.4X1	T42.4X2	T42.4X3	T42.4X4	T42.4X5	T42.4X
Bentiromide	T50.8X1	T50.8X2	T50.8X3	T50.8X4	T50.8X5	T50.8X
Bentonite	T49.3X1	T49.3X2	T49.3X3	T49.3X4	T49.3X5	T49.3X
Benzalbutyramide	T46.6X1	T46.6X2	T46.6X3	T46.6X4	T46.6X5	T46.6X
Benzalkonium (chloride)	T49.0X1	T49.0X2	T49.0X3	T49.0X4	T49.0X5	T49.0X
ophthalmic preparation	T49.5X1	T49.5X2	T49.5X3	T49.5X4	T49.5X5	T49.5X
Benzamidosali cylate(calcium)	T37.1X1	T37.1X2	T37.1X3	T37.1X4	T37.1X5	T37.1X
Benzamine	T41.3X1	T41.3X2	T41.3X3	T41.3X4	T41.3X5	T41.3X
lactate	T49.1X1	T49.1X2	T49.1X3	T49.1X4	T49.1X5	T49.1X
Benzamphetamine	T50.5X1	T50.5X2	T50.5X3	T50.5X4	T50.5X5	T50.5X
Benzapril hydrochloride	T46.5X1	T46.5X2	T46.5X3	T46.5X4	T46.5X5	T46.5X
Benzathine benzylpenicillin	T36.0X1	T36.0X2	T36.0X3	T36.0X4	T36.0X5	T36.0X
Benzathine penicillin	T36.0X1	T36.0X2	T36.0X3	T36.0X4	T36.0X5	T36.0X
Benzatropine	T42.8X1	T42.8X2	T42.8X3	T42.8X4	T42.8X5	T42.8X
Benzbromarone	T50.4X1	T50.4X2	T50.4X3	T50.4X4	T50.4X5	T50.4X
Benzcarbimine	T45.1X1	T45.1X2	T45.1X3	T45.1X4	T45.1X5	T45.1X
Benzedrex	T44.991	T44.992	T44.993	T44.994	T44.995	T44.99
Benzedrine (amphetamine)	T43.621	T43.622	T43.623	T43.624	T43.625	T43.62
Benzenamine	T65.3X1	T65.3X2	T65.3X3	T65.3X4	—	—
Benzene	T52.1X1	T52.1X2	T52.1X3	T52.1X4	—	—
homologues(acetyl) (dimethyl)(methyl) (solvent)	T52.2X1	T52.2X2	T52.2X3	T52.2X4	—	—
Benzethonium (chloride)	T49.0X1	T49.0X2	T49.0X3	T49.0X4	T49.0X5	T49.0X
Benzfetamine	T50.5X1	T50.5X2	T50.5X3	T50.5X4	T50.5X5	T50.5X
Benzhexol	T44.3X1	T44.3X2	T44.3X3	T44.3X4	T44.3X5	T44.3X
Benzhydramine (chloride)	T45.0X1	T45.0X2	T45.0X3	T45.0X4	T45.0X5	T45.0X
Benzidine	T65.891	T65.892	T65.893	T65.894	—	—
Benzilonium bromide	T44.3X1	T44.3X2	T44.3X3	T44.3X4	T44.3X5	T44.3X
Benzimidazole	T60.3X1	T60.3X2	T60.3X3	T60.3X4	—	—
Benzin(e)—see Ligroin						

Substance	Poisoning, Accidental (unintentional)	Poisoning, Intentional self-harm	Poisoning, Assault	Poisoning, Undetermined	Adverse effect	Underdosing
nziodarone	T46.3X1	T46.3X2	T46.3X3	T46.3X4	T46.3X5	T46.3X6
nznidazole	T37.3X1	T37.3X2	T37.3X3	T37.3X4	T37.3X5	T37.3X6
nzocaine	T41.3X1	T41.3X2	T41.3X3	T41.3X4	T41.3X5	T41.3X6
nzodiapin	T42.4X1	T42.4X2	T42.4X3	T42.4X4	T42.4X5	T42.4X6
nzodiazepine NEC	T42.4X1	T42.4X2	T42.4X3	T42.4X4	T42.4X5	T42.4X6
nzoic acid	T49.0X1	T49.0X2	T49.0X3	T49.0X4	T49.0X5	T49.0X6
vith salicylic acid	T49.0X1	T49.0X2	T49.0X3	T49.0X4	T49.0X5	T49.0X6
nzoin(tincture)	T48.5X1	T48.5X2	T48.5X3	T48.5X4	T48.5X5	T48.5X6
nzol(benzene)	T52.1X1	T52.1X2	T52.1X3	T52.1X4	—	—
vapor	T52.0X1	T52.0X2	T52.0X3	T52.0X4	—	—
nzomorphan	T40.2X1	T40.2X2	T40.2X3	T40.2X4	T40.2X5	T40.2X6
nzonatate	T48.3X1	T48.3X2	T48.3X3	T48.3X4	T48.3X5	T48.3X6
nzophenones	T49.3X1	T49.3X2	T49.3X3	T49.3X4	T49.3X5	T49.3X6
nzopyrone	T46.991	T46.992	T46.993	T46.994	T46.995	T46.996
nzothiadiazides	T50.2X1	T50.2X2	T50.2X3	T50.2X4	T50.2X5	T50.2X6
nzoxonium chloride	T49.0X1	T49.0X2	T49.0X3	T49.0X4	T49.0X5	T49.0X6
nzoyl peroxide	T49.0X1	T49.0X2	T49.0X3	T49.0X4	T49.0X5	T49.0X6
nzoylpas calcium	T37.1X1	T37.1X2	T37.1X3	T37.1X4	T37.1X5	T37.1X6
nzperidin	T43.591	T43.592	T43.593	T43.594	T43.595	T43.596
nzperidol	T43.591	T43.592	T43.593	T43.594	T43.595	T43.596
nzphetamine	T50.5X1	T50.5X2	T50.5X3	T50.5X4	T50.5X5	T50.5X6
nzpyrinium bromide	T44.1X1	T44.1X2	T44.1X3	T44.1X4	T44.1X5	T44.1X6
nzquinamide	T45.0X1	T45.0X2	T45.0X3	T45.0X4	T45.0X5	T45.0X6
nzthiazide	T50.2X1	T50.2X2	T50.2X3	T50.2X4	T50.2X5	T50.2X6
nztropine						
anticholinergic	T44.3X1	T44.3X2	T44.3X3	T44.3X4	T44.3X5	T44.3X6
antiparkinson	T42.8X1	T42.8X2	T42.8X3	T42.8X4	T42.8X5	T42.8X6
enzydamine	T49.0X1	T49.0X2	T49.0X3	T49.0X4	T49.0X5	T49.0X6
enzyl						
acetate	T52.8X1	T52.8X2	T52.8X3	T52.8X4	—	—
alcohol	T49.0X1	T49.0X2	T49.0X3	T49.0X4	T49.0X5	T49.0X6
benzoate	T49.0X1	T49.0X2	T49.0X3	T49.0X4	T49.0X5	T49.0X6
Benzoic acid	T49.0X1	T49.0X2	T49.0X3	T49.0X4	T49.0X5	T49.0X6
morphine	T40.2X1	T40.2X2	T40.2X3	T40.2X4	—	—
nicotinate	T46.6X1	T46.6X2	T46.6X3	T46.6X4	T46.6X5	T46.6X6
penicillin	T36.0X1	T36.0X2	T36.0X3	T36.0X4	T36.0X5	T36.0X6
enzylhydrochl-orthia-zide	T50.2X1	T50.2X2	T50.2X3	T50.2X4	T50.2X5	T50.2X6
enzylpenicillin	T36.0X1	T36.0X2	T36.0X3	T36.0X4	T36.0X5	T36.0X6
enzylthiouracil	T38.2X1	T38.2X2	T38.2X3	T38.2X4	T38.2X5	T38.2X6
ephenium hydroxy-aphthoate	T37.4X1	T37.4X2	T37.4X3	T37.4X4	T37.4X5	T37.4X6
epridil	T46.1X1	T46.1X2	T46.1X3	T46.1X4	T46.1X5	T46.1X6
ergamot oil	T65.891	T65.892	T65.893	T65.894	—	—
ergapten	T50.991	T50.992	T50.993	T50.994	T50.995	T50.996
erries, poisonous	T62.1X1	T62.1X2	T62.1X3	T62.1X4	—	—
eryllium compounds)	T56.7X1	T56.7X2	T56.7X3	T56.7X4	—	—
-acetyldigoxin	T46.0X1	T46.0X2	T46.0X3	T46.0X4	T46.0X5	T46.0X6
eta adrenergic blocking gent, heart	T44.7X1	T44.7X2	T44.7X3	T44.7X4	T44.7X5	T44.7X6
-benzalbutyramide	T46.6X1	T46.6X2	T46.6X3	T46.6X4	T46.6X5	T46.6X6
etacarotene	T45.2X1	T45.2X2	T45.2X3	T45.2X4	T45.2X5	T45.2X6

Substance	Poisoning, Accidental (unintentional)	Poisoning, Intentional self-harm	Poisoning, Assault	Poisoning, Undetermined	Adverse effect	Underdosing
b-eucaine	T49.1X1	T49.1X2	T49.1X3	T49.1X4	T49.1X5	T49.1X6
Beta-Chlor	T42.6X1	T42.6X2	T42.6X3	T42.6X4	T42.6X5	T42.6X6
b-galactosidase	T47.5X1	T47.5X2	T47.5X3	T47.5X4	T47.5X5	T47.5X6
Betahistine	T46.7X1	T46.7X2	T46.7X3	T46.7X4	T46.7X5	T46.7X6
Betaine	T47.5X1	T47.5X2	T47.5X3	T47.5X4	T47.5X5	T47.5X6
Betamethasone	T49.0X1	T49.0X2	T49.0X3	T49.0X4	T49.0X5	T49.0X6
topical	T49.0X1	T49.0X2	T49.0X3	T49.0X4	T49.0X5	T49.0X6
Betamicin	T36.8X1	T36.8X2	T36.8X3	T36.8X4	T36.8X5	T36.8X6
Betanidine	T46.5X1	T46.5X2	T46.5X3	T46.5X4	T46.5X5	T46.5X6
b-sitosterol(s)	T46.6X1	T46.6X2	T46.6X3	T46.6X4	T46.6X5	T46.6X6
Betaxolol	T44.7X1	T44.7X2	T44.7X3	T44.7X4	T44.7X5	T44.7X6
Betazole	T50.8X1	T50.8X2	T50.8X3	T50.8X4	T50.8X5	T50.8X6
Bethanechol	T44.1X1	T44.1X2	T44.1X3	T44.1X4	T44.1X5	T44.1X6
chloride	T44.1X1	T44.1X2	T44.1X3	T44.1X4	T44.1X5	T44.1X6
Bethanidine	T46.5X1	T46.5X2	T46.5X3	T46.5X4	T46.5X5	T46.5X6
Betoxycaine	T41.3X1	T41.3X2	T41.3X3	T41.3X4	T41.3X5	T41.3X6
Betula oil	T49.3X1	T49.3X2	T49.3X3	T49.3X4	T49.3X5	T49.3X6
Bevantolol	T44.7X1	T44.7X2	T44.7X3	T44.7X4	T44.7X5	T44.7X6
Bevonium metilsulfate	T44.3X1	T44.3X2	T44.3X3	T44.3X4	T44.3X5	T44.3X6
Bezafibrate	T46.6X1	T46.6X2	T46.6X3	T46.6X4	T46.6X5	T46.6X6
Bezitramide	T40.4X1	T40.4X2	T40.4X3	T40.4X4	T40.4X5	T40.4X6
BHA	T50.991	T50.992	T50.993	T50.994	T50.995	T50.996
Bhang	T40.7X1	T40.7X2	T40.7X3	T40.7X4	T40.7X5	T40.7X6
BHC(medicinal)	T49.0X1	T49.0X2	T49.0X3	T49.0X4	T49.0X5	T49.0X6
nonmedicinal(vapor)	T53.6X1	T53.6X2	T53.6X3	T53.6X4	—	—
Bialamicol	T37.3X1	T37.3X2	T37.3X3	T37.3X4	T37.3X5	T37.3X6
Bibenzonium bromide	T48.3X1	T48.3X2	T48.3X3	T48.3X4	T48.3X5	T48.3X6
Bibrocathol	T49.5X1	T49.5X2	T49.5X3	T49.5X4	T49.5X5	T49.5X6
Bichloride of mercury—see Mercury, chloride						
Bichromates (calcium) (potassium)(sodium) (crystals)	T57.8X1	T57.8X2	T57.8X3	T57.8X4	—	—
fumes	T56.2X1	T56.2X2	T56.2X3	T56.2X4	—	—
Biclotymol	T49.6X1	T49.6X2	T49.6X3	T49.6X4	T49.6X5	T49.6X6
Bicucculine	T50.7X1	T50.7X2	T50.7X3	T50.7X4	T50.7X5	T50.7X6
Bifemelane	T43.291	T43.292	T43.293	T43.294	T43.295	T43.296
Biguanide derivatives, oral	T38.3X1	T38.3X2	T38.3X3	T38.3X4	T38.3X5	T38.3X6
Bile salts	T47.5X1	T47.5X2	T47.5X3	T47.5X4	T47.5X5	T47.5X6
Biligrafin	T50.8X1	T50.8X2	T50.8X3	T50.8X4	T50.8X5	T50.8X6
Bilopaque	T50.8X1	T50.8X2	T50.8X3	T50.8X4	T50.8X5	T50.8X6
Binifibrate	T46.6X1	T46.6X2	T46.6X3	T46.6X4	T46.6X5	T46.6X6
Binitrobenzol	T65.3X1	T65.3X2	T65.3X3	T65.3X4	—	—
Bioflavonoid(s)	T46.991	T46.992	T46.993	T46.994	T46.995	T46.996
Biological substance NEC	T50.901	T50.902	T50.903	T50.904	T50.905	T50.906
Biotin	T45.2X1	T45.2X2	T45.2X3	T45.2X4	T45.2X5	T45.2X6
Biperiden	T44.3X1	T44.3X2	T44.3X3	T44.3X4	T44.3X5	T44.3X6
Bisacodyl	T47.2X1	T47.2X2	T47.2X3	T47.2X4	T47.2X5	T47.2X6
Bisbentiamine	T45.2X1	T45.2X2	T45.2X3	T45.2X4	T45.2X5	T45.2X6
Bisbutiamine	T45.2X1	T45.2X2	T45.2X3	T45.2X4	T45.2X5	T45.2X6
Bisdequalinium(salts) (diacetate)	T49.6X1	T49.6X2	T49.6X3	T49.6X4	T49.6X5	T49.6X6

Substance	Poisoning, Accidental (unintentional)	Poisoning, Intentional self-harm	Poisoning, Assault	Poisoning, Undetermined	Adverse effect	Underdosing
Bishydroxycoumarin	T45.511	T45.512	T45.513	T45.514	T45.515	T45.516
Bismarsen	T37.8X1	T37.8X2	T37.8X3	T37.8X4	T37.8X5	T37.8X6
Bismuth salts	T47.6X1	T47.6X2	T47.6X3	T47.6X4	T47.6X5	T47.6X6
aluminate	T47.1X1	T47.1X2	T47.1X3	T47.1X4	T47.1X5	T47.1X6
anti-infectives	T37.8X1	T37.8X2	T37.8X3	T37.8X4	T37.8X5	T37.8X6
formic iodide	T49.0X1	T49.0X2	T49.0X3	T49.0X4	T49.0X5	T49.0X6
glycolylarsenate	T49.0X1	T49.0X2	T49.0X3	T49.0X4	T49.0X5	T49.0X6
nonmedicinal (compounds) NEC	T65.91	T65.92	T65.93	T65.94	—	—
subcarbonate	T47.6X1	T47.6X2	T47.6X3	T47.6X4	T47.6X5	T47.6X6
subsalicylate	T37.8X1	T37.8X2	T37.8X3	T37.8X4	T37.8X5	T37.8X6
sulfarsphenamine	T37.8X1	T37.8X2	T37.8X3	T37.8X4	T37.8X5	T37.8X6
Bisoprolol	T44.7X1	T44.7X2	T44.7X3	T44.7X4	T44.7X5	T44.7X6
Bisoxatin	T47.2X1	T47.2X2	T47.2X3	T47.2X4	T47.2X5	T47.2X6
Bisulepin(hydro-chloride)	T45.0X1	T45.0X2	T45.0X3	T45.0X4	T45.0X5	T45.0X6
Bithionol	T37.8X1	T37.8X2	T37.8X3	T37.8X4	T37.8X5	T37.8X6
anthelminthic	T37.4X1	T37.4X2	T37.4X3	T37.4X4	T37.4X5	T37.4X6
Bitolterol	T48.6X1	T48.6X2	T48.6X3	T48.6X4	T48.6X5	T48.6X6
Bitoscanate	T37.4X1	T37.4X2	T37.4X3	T37.4X4	T37.4X5	T37.4X6
Bitter almond oil	T62.8X1	T62.8X2	T62.8X3	T62.8X4	—	—
Bittersweet	T62.2X1	T62.2X2	T62.2X3	T62.2X4	—	—
Black						
flag	T60.91	T60.92	T60.93	T60.94	—	—
henbane	T62.2X1	T62.2X2	T62.2X3	T62.2X4	—	—
leaf(40)	T60.91	T60.92	T60.93	T60.94	—	—
widow spider(bite)	T63.311	T63.312	T63.313	T63.314	—	—
antivenin	T50.Z11	T50.Z12	T50.Z13	T50.Z14	T50.Z15	T50.Z16
Blast furnace gas(carbon monoxide from)	T58.8X1	T58.8X2	T58.8X3	T58.8X4	—	—
Bleach	T54.91	T54.92	T54.93	T54.94	—	—
Bleaching agent(medicinal)	T49.4X1	T49.4X2	T49.4X3	T49.4X4	T49.4X5	T49.4X6
Bleomycin	T45.1X1	T45.1X2	T45.1X3	T45.1X4	T45.1X5	T45.1X6
Blockain	T41.3X1	T41.3X2	T41.3X3	T41.3X4	T41.3X5	T41.3X6
infiltration (subcutaneous)	T41.3X1	T41.3X2	T41.3X3	T41.3X4	T41.3X5	T41.3X6
nerve block(peripheral) (plexus)	T41.3X1	T41.3X2	T41.3X3	T41.3X4	T41.3X5	T41.3X6
topical(surface)	T41.3X1	T41.3X2	T41.3X3	T41.3X4	T41.3X5	T41.3X6
Blockers, calcium channel	T46.1X1	T46.1X2	T46.1X3	T46.1X4	T46.1X5	T46.1X6
Blood(derivatives) (natural) (plasma) (whole)	T45.8X1	T45.8X2	T45.8X3	T45.8X4	T45.8X5	T45.8X6
dried	T45.8X1	T45.8X2	T45.8X3	T45.8X4	T45.8X5	T45.8X6
drug affecting NEC	T45.91	T45.92	T45.93	T45.94	T45.95	T45.96
expander NEC	T45.8X1	T45.8X2	T45.8X3	T45.8X4	T45.8X5	T45.8X6
fraction NEC	T45.8X1	T45.8X2	T45.8X3	T45.8X4	T45.8X5	T45.8X6
substitute (macromolecular)	T45.8X1	T45.8X2	T45.8X3	T45.8X4	T45.8X5	T45.8X6
Blue velvet	T40.2X1	T40.2X2	T40.2X3	T40.2X4	—	—
Bone meal	T62.8X1	T62.8X2	T62.8X3	T62.8X4	—	—
Bonine	T45.0X1	T45.0X2	T45.0X3	T45.0X4	T45.0X5	T45.0X6
Bopindolol	T44.7X1	T44.7X2	T44.7X3	T44.7X4	T44.7X5	T44.7X6

Substance	Poisoning, Accidental (unintentional)	Poisoning, Intentional self-harm	Poisoning, Assault	Poisoning, Undetermined	Adverse effect	Underdosing
Boracic acid	T49.0X1	T49.0X2	T49.0X3	T49.0X4	T49.0X5	T49.0
ENT agent	T49.6X1	T49.6X2	T49.6X3	T49.6X4	T49.6X5	T49.6
ophthalmic preparation	T49.5X1	T49.5X2	T49.5X3	T49.5X4	T49.5X5	T49.5
Borane complex	T57.8X1	T57.8X2	T57.8X3	T57.8X4	—	—
Borate(s)	T57.8X1	T57.8X2	T57.8X3	T57.8X4	—	—
buffer	T50.991	T50.992	T50.993	T50.994	T50.995	T50.9
cleanser	T54.91	T54.92	T54.93	T54.94	—	—
sodium	T57.8X1	T57.8X2	T57.8X3	T57.8X4	—	—
Borax(cleanser)	T54.91	T54.92	T54.93	T54.94	—	—
Bordeaux mixture	T60.3X1	T60.3X2	T60.3X3	T60.3X4	—	—
Boric acid	T49.0X1	T49.0X2	T49.0X3	T49.0X4	T49.0X5	T49.0
ENT agent	T49.6X1	T49.6X2	T49.6X3	T49.6X4	T49.6X5	T49.6
ophthalmic preparation	T49.5X1	T49.5X2	T49.5X3	T49.5X4	T49.5X5	T49.5
Bornaprine	T44.3X1	T44.3X2	T44.3X3	T44.3X4	T44.3X5	T44.3
Boron	T57.8X1	T57.8X2	T57.8X3	T57.8X4	—	—
hydride NEC	T57.8X1	T57.8X2	T57.8X3	T57.8X4	—	—
fumes or gas	T57.8X1	T57.8X2	T57.8X3	T57.8X4	—	—
trifluoride	T59.891	T59.892	T59.893	T59.894	—	—
Botox	T48.291	T48.292	T48.293	T48.294	T48.295	T48.2
Botulinus anti-toxin (type A, B)	T50.Z11	T50.Z12	T50.Z13	T50.Z14	T50.Z15	T50.Z
Brake fluid vapor	T59.891	T59.892	T59.893	T59.894	—	—
Brallobarbital	T42.3X1	T42.3X2	T42.3X3	T42.3X4	T42.3X5	T42.3
Bran(wheat)	T47.4X1	T47.4X2	T47.4X3	T47.4X4	T47.4X5	T47.4
Brass(fumes)	T56.891	T56.892	T56.893	T56.894	—	—
Brasso	T52.0X1	T52.0X2	T52.0X3	T52.0X4	—	—
Bretylium tosilate	T46.2X1	T46.2X2	T46.2X3	T46.2X4	T46.2X5	T46.2
Brevital(sodium)	T41.1X1	T41.1X2	T41.1X3	T41.1X4	T41.1X5	T41.1
Brinase	T45.3X1	T45.3X2	T45.3X3	T45.3X4	T45.3X5	T45.3
British antilewisite	T45.8X1	T45.8X2	T45.8X3	T45.8X4	T45.8X5	T45.8
Brodifacoum	T60.4X1	T60.4X2	T60.4X3	T60.4X4	—	—
Bromal(hydrate)	T42.6X1	T42.6X2	T42.6X3	T42.6X4	T42.6X5	T42.6
Bromazepam	T42.4X1	T42.4X2	T42.4X3	T42.4X4	T42.4X5	T42.4
Bromazine	T45.0X1	T45.0X2	T45.0X3	T45.0X4	T45.0X5	T45.0
Brombenzylcyanide	T59.3X1	T59.3X2	T59.3X3	T59.3X4	—	—
Bromelains	T45.3X1	T45.3X2	T45.3X3	T45.3X4	T45.3X5	T45.3
Bromethalin	T60.4X1	T60.4X2	T60.4X3	T60.4X4	—	—
Bromhexine	T48.4X1	T48.4X2	T48.4X3	T48.4X4	T48.4X5	T48.4
Bromide salts	T42.6X1	T42.6X2	T42.6X3	T42.6X4	T42.6X5	T42.6
Bromindione	T45.511	T45.512	T45.513	T45.514	T45.515	T45.5
Bromine						
compounds (medicinal)	T42.6X1	T42.6X2	T42.6X3	T42.6X4	T42.6X5	T42.6
sedative	T42.6X1	T42.6X2	T42.6X3	T42.6X4	T42.6X5	T42.6
vapor	T59.891	T59.892	T59.893	T59.894	—	—
Bromisoval	T42.6X1	T42.6X2	T42.6X3	T42.6X4	T42.6X5	T42.6
Bromisovalum	T42.6X1	T42.6X2	T42.6X3	T42.6X4	T42.6X5	T42.6
Bromobenzylcyanide	T59.3X1	T59.3X2	T59.3X3	T59.3X4	—	—
Bromochloro-salicylani-lide	T49.0X1	T49.0X2	T49.0X3	T49.0X4	T49.0X5	T49.0
Bromocriptine	T42.8X1	T42.8X2	T42.8X3	T42.8X4	T42.8X5	T42.8
Bromodiphenhy-dramine	T45.0X1	T45.0X2	T45.0X3	T45.0X4	T45.0X5	T45.0
Bromoform	T42.6X1	T42.6X2	T42.6X3	T42.6X4	T42.6X5	T42.6

Substance	Poisoning, Accidental (unintentional)	Poisoning, Intentional self-harm	Poisoning, Assault	Poisoning, Undetermined	Adverse effect	Underdosing
mophenol blue reagent	T50.991	T50.992	T50.993	T50.994	T50.995	T50.996
mopride	T47.8X1	T47.8X2	T47.8X3	T47.8X4	T47.8X5	T47.8X6
mosalicyl chloranitide	T49.0X1	T49.0X2	T49.0X3	T49.0X4	T49.0X5	T49.0X6
mosalicyl hydroxamic d	T37.1X1	T37.1X2	T37.1X3	T37.1X4	T37.1X5	T37.1X6
mo-seltzer	T39.1X1	T39.1X2	T39.1X3	T39.1X4	T39.1X5	T39.1X6
moxynil	T60.3X1	T60.3X2	T60.3X3	T60.3X4	—	—
mperidol	T43.4X1	T43.4X2	T43.4X3	T43.4X4	T43.4X5	T43.4X6
mpheniramine	T45.0X1	T45.0X2	T45.0X3	T45.0X4	T45.0X5	T45.0X6
msulfophthalein	T50.8X1	T50.8X2	T50.8X3	T50.8X4	T50.8X5	T50.8X6
mural	T42.6X1	T42.6X2	T42.6X3	T42.6X4	T42.6X5	T42.6X6
mvaletone	T42.6X1	T42.6X2	T42.6X3	T42.6X4	T42.6X5	T42.6X6
nchodilator NEC	T48.6X1	T48.6X2	T48.6X3	T48.6X4	T48.6X5	T48.6X6
tizolam	T42.4X1	T42.4X2	T42.4X3	T42.4X4	T42.4X5	T42.4X6
vincamine	T46.7X1	T46.7X2	T46.7X3	T46.7X4	T46.7X5	T46.7X6
wn recluse spider(bite) nom)	T63.331	T63.332	T63.333	T63.334	—	—
wn spider(bite) (venom)	T63.391	T63.392	T63.393	T63.394	—	—
xaterol	T48.6X1	T48.6X2	T48.6X3	T48.6X4	T48.6X5	T48.6X6
xuridine	T45.1X1	T45.1X2	T45.1X3	T45.1X4	T45.1X5	T45.1X6
xyquinoline	T37.8X1	T37.8X2	T37.8X3	T37.8X4	T37.8X5	T37.8X6
uceine	T48.291	T48.292	T48.293	T48.294	T48.295	T48.296
ucia	T62.2X1	T62.2X2	T62.2X3	T62.2X4	—	—
ucine	T65.1X1	T65.1X2	T65.1X3	T65.1X4	—	—
unswick green—see pper						
uten—see Ibuprofen						
yonia	T47.2X1	T47.2X2	T47.2X3	T47.2X4	T47.2X5	T47.2X6
clizine	T45.0X1	T45.0X2	T45.0X3	T45.0X4	T45.0X5	T45.0X6
closamide	T49.0X1	T49.0X2	T49.0X3	T49.0X4	T49.0X5	T49.0X6
desonide	T44.5X1	T44.5X2	T44.5X3	T44.5X4	T44.5X5	T44.5X6
dralazine	T46.5X1	T46.5X2	T46.5X3	T46.5X4	T46.5X5	T46.5X6
fferin	T39.011	T39.012	T39.013	T39.014	T39.015	T39.016
flomedil	T46.7X1	T46.7X2	T46.7X3	T46.7X4	T46.7X5	T46.7X6
formin	T38.3X1	T38.3X2	T38.3X3	T38.3X4	T38.3X5	T38.3X6
fotenine	T40.991	T40.992	T40.993	T40.994	—	—
frolin	T48.6X1	T48.6X2	T48.6X3	T48.6X4	T48.6X5	T48.6X6
fylline	T48.6X1	T48.6X2	T48.6X3	T48.6X4	T48.6X5	T48.6X6
lk filler	T50.5X1	T50.5X2	T50.5X3	T50.5X4	T50.5X5	T50.5X6
cathartic	T47.4X1	T47.4X2	T47.4X3	T47.4X4	T47.4X5	T47.4X6
metanide	T50.1X1	T50.1X2	T50.1X3	T50.1X4	T50.1X5	T50.1X6
naftine	T46.2X1	T46.2X2	T46.2X3	T46.2X4	T46.2X5	T46.2X6
namiodyl	T50.8X1	T50.8X2	T50.8X3	T50.8X4	T50.8X5	T50.8X6
nazosin	T44.6X1	T44.6X2	T44.6X3	T44.6X4	T44.6X5	T44.6X6
nitrolol	T44.7X1	T44.7X2	T44.7X3	T44.7X4	T44.7X5	T44.7X6
phenine	T46.7X1	T46.7X2	T46.7X3	T46.7X4	T46.7X5	T46.7X6
pivacaine	T41.3X1	T41.3X2	T41.3X3	T41.3X4	T41.3X5	T41.3X6
infiltration (subcutaneous)	T41.3X1	T41.3X2	T41.3X3	T41.3X4	T41.3X5	T41.3X6
nerve block(peripheral) (plexus)	T41.3X1	T41.3X2	T41.3X3	T41.3X4	T41.3X5	T41.3X6
spinal	T41.3X1	T41.3X2	T41.3X3	T41.3X4	T41.3X5	T41.3X6

Substance	Poisoning, Accidental (unintentional)	Poisoning, Intentional self-harm	Poisoning, Assault	Poisoning, Undetermined	Adverse effect	Underdosing
Bupranolol	T44.7X1	T44.7X2	T44.7X3	T44.7X4	T44.7X5	T44.7X6
Buprenorphine	T40.4X1	T40.4X2	T40.4X3	T40.4X4	T40.4X5	T40.4X6
Bupropion	T43.291	T43.292	T43.293	T43.294	T43.295	T43.296
Burimamide	T47.1X1	T47.1X2	T47.1X3	T47.1X4	T47.1X5	T47.1X6
Buserelin	T38.891	T38.892	T38.893	T38.894	T38.895	T38.896
Buspirone	T43.591	T43.592	T43.593	T43.594	T43.595	T43.596
Busulfan, busulphan	T45.1X1	T45.1X2	T45.1X3	T45.1X4	T45.1X5	T45.1X6
Butabarbital(sodium)	T42.3X1	T42.3X2	T42.3X3	T42.3X4	T42.3X5	T42.3X6
Butabarbitone	T42.3X1	T42.3X2	T42.3X3	T42.3X4	T42.3X5	T42.3X6
Butabarpal	T42.3X1	T42.3X2	T42.3X3	T42.3X4	T42.3X5	T42.3X6
Butacaine	T41.3X1	T41.3X2	T41.3X3	T41.3X4	T41.3X5	T41.3X6
Butalamine	T46.7X1	T46.7X2	T46.7X3	T46.7X4	T46.7X5	T46.7X6
Butalbital	T42.3X1	T42.3X2	T42.3X3	T42.3X4	T42.3X5	T42.3X6
Butallylonal	T42.3X1	T42.3X2	T42.3X3	T42.3X4	T42.3X5	T42.3X6
Butamben	T41.3X1	T41.3X2	T41.3X3	T41.3X4	T41.3X5	T41.3X6
Butamirate	T48.3X1	T48.3X2	T48.3X3	T48.3X4	T48.3X5	T48.3X6
Butane(distributed in mobile container)	T59.891	T59.892	T59.893	T59.894	—	—
distributed through pipes	T59.891	T59.892	T59.893	T59.894	—	—
incomplete combustion	T58.11	T58.12	T58.13	T58.14	—	—
Butanilicaine	T41.3X1	T41.3X2	T41.3X3	T41.3X4	T41.3X5	T41.3X6
Butanol	T51.3X1	T51.3X2	T51.3X3	T51.3X4	—	—
Butanone, 2-butanone	T52.4X1	T52.4X2	T52.4X3	T52.4X4	—	—
Butantrone	T49.4X1	T49.4X2	T49.4X3	T49.4X4	T49.4X5	T49.4X6
Butaperazine	T43.3X1	T43.3X2	T43.3X3	T43.3X4	T43.3X5	T43.3X6
Butazolidin	T39.2X1	T39.2X2	T39.2X3	T39.2X4	T39.2X5	T39.2X6
Butetamate	T48.6X1	T48.6X2	T48.6X3	T48.6X4	T48.6X5	T48.6X6
Butethal	T42.3X1	T42.3X2	T42.3X3	T42.3X4	T42.3X5	T42.3X6
Butethamate	T44.3X1	T44.3X2	T44.3X3	T44.3X4	T44.3X5	T44.3X6
Buthalitone(sodium)	T41.1X1	T41.1X2	T41.1X3	T41.1X4	T41.1X5	T41.1X6
Butisol(sodium)	T42.3X1	T42.3X2	T42.3X3	T42.3X4	T42.3X5	T42.3X6
Butizide	T50.2X1	T50.2X2	T50.2X3	T50.2X4	T50.2X5	T50.2X6
Butobarbital	T42.3X1	T42.3X2	T42.3X3	T42.3X4	T42.3X5	T42.3X6
sodium	T42.3X1	T42.3X2	T42.3X3	T42.3X4	T42.3X5	T42.3X6
Butobarbitone	T42.3X1	T42.3X2	T42.3X3	T42.3X4	T42.3X5	T42.3X6
Butoconazole(nitrate)	T49.0X1	T49.0X2	T49.0X3	T49.0X4	T49.0X5	T49.0X6
Butorphanol	T40.4X1	T40.4X2	T40.4X3	T40.4X4	T40.4X5	T40.4X6
Butriptyline	T43.011	T43.012	T43.013	T43.014	T43.015	T43.016
Butropium bromide	T44.3X1	T44.3X2	T44.3X3	T44.3X4	T44.3X5	T44.3X6
Butter of antimony—see Antimony						
Buttercups	T62.2X1	T62.2X2	T62.2X3	T62.2X4	—	—
Butyl						
acetate(secondary)	T52.8X1	T52.8X2	T52.8X3	T52.8X4	—	—
alcohol	T51.3X1	T51.3X2	T51.3X3	T51.3X4	—	—
aminobenzoate	T41.3X1	T41.3X2	T41.3X3	T41.3X4	T41.3X5	T41.3X6
butyrate	T52.8X1	T52.8X2	T52.8X3	T52.8X4	—	—
carbinol	T51.3X1	T51.3X2	T51.3X3	T51.3X4	—	—
carbitol	T52.3X1	T52.3X2	T52.3X3	T52.3X4	—	—
cellosolve	T52.3X1	T52.3X2	T52.3X3	T52.3X4	—	—
chloral(hydrate)	T42.6X1	T42.6X2	T42.6X3	T42.6X4	T42.6X5	T42.6X6

Substance	Poisoning, Accidental (unintentional)	Poisoning, Intentional self-harm	Poisoning, Assault	Poisoning, Undetermined	Adverse effect	Underdosing
Butyl — *Continued*						
formate	T52.8X1	T52.8X2	T52.8X3	T52.8X4	—	—
lactate	T52.8X1	T52.8X2	T52.8X3	T52.8X4	—	—
propionate	T52.8X1	T52.8X2	T52.8X3	T52.8X4	—	—
scopolamine bromide	T44.3X1	T44.3X2	T44.3X3	T44.3X4	T44.3X5	T44.3X6
thiobarbital sodium	T41.1X1	T41.1X2	T41.1X3	T41.1X4	T41.1X5	T41.1X6
Butylated hydroxy-anisole	T50.991	T50.992	T50.993	T50.994	T50.995	T50.996
Butylchloral hydrate	T42.6X1	T42.6X2	T42.6X3	T42.6X4	T42.6X5	T42.6X6
Butyltoluene	T52.2X1	T52.2X2	T52.2X3	T52.2X4	—	—
Butyn	T41.3X1	T41.3X2	T41.3X3	T41.3X4	T41.3X5	T41.3X6
Butyrophenone(-based tranquilizers)	T43.4X1	T43.4X2	T43.4X3	T43.4X4	T43.4X5	T43.4X6
C						
Cabergoline	T42.8X1	T42.8X2	T42.8X3	T42.8X4	T42.8X5	T42.8X6
Cacodyl, cacodylic acid	T57.0X1	T57.0X2	T57.0X3	T57.0X4	—	—
Cactinomycin	T45.1X1	T45.1X2	T45.1X3	T45.1X4	T45.1X5	T45.1X6
Cade oil	T49.4X1	T49.4X2	T49.4X3	T49.4X4	T49.4X5	T49.4X6
Cadexomer iodine	T49.0X1	T49.0X2	T49.0X3	T49.0X4	T49.0X5	T49.0X6
Cadmium(chloride) (fumes) (oxide)	T56.3X1	T56.3X2	T56.3X3	T56.3X4	—	—
sulfide(medicinal) NEC	T49.4X1	T49.4X2	T49.4X3	T49.4X4	T49.4X5	T49.4X6
Cadralazine	T46.5X1	T46.5X2	T46.5X3	T46.5X4	T46.5X5	T46.5X6
Caffeine	T43.611	T43.612	T43.613	T43.614	T43.615	T43.616
Calabar bean	T62.2X1	T62.2X2	T62.2X3	T62.2X4	—	—
Caladium seguinum	T62.2X1	T62.2X2	T62.2X3	T62.2X4	—	—
Calamine(lotion)	T49.3X1	T49.3X2	T49.3X3	T49.3X4	T49.3X5	T49.3X6
Calcifediol	T45.2X1	T45.2X2	T45.2X3	T45.2X4	T45.2X5	T45.2X6
Calciferol	T45.2X1	T45.2X2	T45.2X3	T45.2X4	T45.2X5	T45.2X6
Calcitonin	T50.991	T50.992	T50.993	T50.994	T50.995	T50.996
Calcitriol	T45.2X1	T45.2X2	T45.2X3	T45.2X4	T45.2X5	T45.2X6
Calcium	T50.3X1	T50.3X2	T50.3X3	T50.3X4	T50.3X5	T50.3X6
actylsalicylate	T39.011	T39.012	T39.013	T39.014	T39.015	T39.016
benzamidosalicylate	T37.1X1	T37.1X2	T37.1X3	T37.1X4	T37.1X5	T37.1X6
bromide	T42.6X1	T42.6X2	T42.6X3	T42.6X4	T42.6X5	T42.6X6
bromolactobionate	T42.6X1	T42.6X2	T42.6X3	T42.6X4	T42.6X5	T42.6X6
carbaspirin	T39.011	T39.012	T39.013	T39.014	T39.015	T39.016
carbimide	T50.6X1	T50.6X2	T50.6X3	T50.6X4	T50.6X5	T50.6X6
carbonate	T47.1X1	T47.1X2	T47.1X3	T47.1X4	T47.1X5	T47.1X6
chloride	T50.991	T50.992	T50.993	T50.994	T50.995	T50.996
anhydrous	T50.991	T50.992	T50.993	T50.994	T50.995	T50.996
cyanide	T57.8X1	T57.8X2	T57.8X3	T57.8X4	—	—
dioctyl sulfosuccinate	T47.4X1	T47.4X2	T47.4X3	T47.4X4	T47.4X5	T47.4X6
disodium edathamil	T45.8X1	T45.8X2	T45.8X3	T45.8X4	T45.8X5	T45.8X6
disodium edetate	T45.8X1	T45.8X2	T45.8X3	T45.8X4	T45.8X5	T45.8X6
dobesilate	T46.991	T46.992	T46.993	T46.994	T46.995	T46.996
EDTA	T45.8X1	T45.8X2	T45.8X3	T45.8X4	T45.8X5	T45.8X6
ferrous citrate	T45.4X1	T45.4X2	T45.4X3	T45.4X4	T45.4X5	T45.4X6
folinate	T45.8X1	T45.8X2	T45.8X3	T45.8X4	T45.8X5	T45.8X6
glubionate	T50.3X1	T50.3X2	T50.3X3	T50.3X4	T50.3X5	T50.3X6
gluconate	T50.3X1	T50.3X2	T50.3X3	T50.3X4	T50.3X5	T50.3X6
gluconoga-lactogluconate	T50.3X1	T50.3X2	T50.3X3	T50.3X4	T50.3X5	T50.3X6

Substance	Poisoning, Accidental (unintentional)	Poisoning, Intentional self-harm	Poisoning, Assault	Poisoning, Undetermined	Adverse effect	Underdosing
Calcium — *Continued*						
hydrate, hydroxide	T54.3X1	T54.3X2	T54.3X3	T54.3X4	—	—
hypochlorite	T54.3X1	T54.3X2	T54.3X3	T54.3X4	—	—
iodide	T48.4X1	T48.4X2	T48.4X3	T48.4X4	T48.4X5	T48.4
ipodate	T50.8X1	T50.8X2	T50.8X3	T50.8X4	T50.8X5	T50.8
lactate	T50.3X1	T50.3X2	T50.3X3	T50.3X4	T50.3X5	T50.3
leucovorin	T45.8X1	T45.8X2	T45.8X3	T45.8X4	T45.8X5	T45.8
mandelate	T37.91	T37.92	T37.93	T37.94	T37.95	T37.9
oxide	T54.3X1	T54.3X2	T54.3X3	T54.3X4	—	—
pantothenate	T45.2X1	T45.2X2	T45.2X3	T45.2X4	T45.2X5	T45.2
phosphate	T50.3X1	T50.3X2	T50.3X3	T50.3X4	T50.3X5	T50.3
salicylate	T39.091	T39.092	T39.093	T39.094	T39.095	T39.0
salts	T50.3X1	T50.3X2	T50.3X3	T50.3X4	T50.3X5	T50.3
Calculus-dissolving drug	T50.991	T50.992	T50.993	T50.994	T50.995	T50.9
Calomel	T49.0X1	T49.0X2	T49.0X3	T49.0X4	T49.0X5	T49.0
Caloric agent	T50.3X1	T50.3X2	T50.3X3	T50.3X4	T50.3X5	T50.3
Calusterone	T38.7X1	T38.7X2	T38.7X3	T38.7X4	T38.7X5	T38.7
Camazepam	T42.4X1	T42.4X2	T42.4X3	T42.4X4	T42.4X5	T42.4
Camomile	T49.0X1	T49.0X2	T49.0X3	T49.0X4	T49.0X5	T49.0
Camoquin	T37.2X1	T37.2X2	T37.2X3	T37.2X4	T37.2X5	T37.2
Camphor						
insecticide	T60.2X1	T60.2X2	T60.2X3	T60.2X4	—	—
medicinal	T49.8X1	T49.8X2	T49.8X3	T49.8X4	T49.8X5	T49.8
Camylofin	T44.3X1	T44.3X2	T44.3X3	T44.3X4	T44.3X5	T44.3
Cancer chemotherapy drug regimen	T45.1X1	T45.1X2	T45.1X3	T45.1X4	T45.1X5	T45.1
Candeptin	T49.0X1	T49.0X2	T49.0X3	T49.0X4	T49.0X5	T49.0
Candicidin	T49.0X1	T49.0X2	T49.0X3	T49.0X4	T49.0X5	T49.0
Cannabinol	T40.7X1	T40.7X2	T40.7X3	T40.7X4	T40.7X5	T40.7
Cannabis (derivatives)	T40.7X1	T40.7X2	T40.7X3	T40.7X4	T40.7X5	T40.7
Canned heat	T51.1X1	T51.1X2	T51.1X3	T51.1X4	—	—
Canrenoic acid	T50.0X1	T50.0X2	T50.0X3	T50.0X4	T50.0X5	T50.0
Canrenone	T50.0X1	T50.0X2	T50.0X3	T50.0X4	T50.0X5	T50.0
Cantharides, cantharidin, cantharis	T49.8X1	T49.8X2	T49.8X3	T49.8X4	T49.8X5	T49.8
Canthaxanthin	T50.991	T50.992	T50.993	T50.994	T50.995	T50.9
Capillary-active drug NEC	T46.901	T46.902	T46.903	T46.904	T46.905	T46.9
Capreomycin	T36.8X1	T36.8X2	T36.8X3	T36.8X4	T36.8X5	T36.8
Capsicum	T49.4X1	T49.4X2	T49.4X3	T49.4X4	T49.4X5	T49.4
Captafol	T60.3X1	T60.3X2	T60.3X3	T60.3X4	—	—
Captan	T60.3X1	T60.3X2	T60.3X3	T60.3X4	—	—
Captodiame, captodiamine	T43.591	T43.592	T43.593	T43.594	T43.595	T43.59
Captopril	T46.4X1	T46.4X2	T46.4X3	T46.4X4	T46.4X5	T46.4X
Caramiphen	T44.3X1	T44.3X2	T44.3X3	T44.3X4	T44.3X5	T44.3X
Carazolol	T44.7X1	T44.7X2	T44.7X3	T44.7X4	T44.7X5	T44.7X
Carbachol	T44.1X1	T44.1X2	T44.1X3	T44.1X4	T44.1X5	T44.1X
Carbacrylamine (resin)	T50.3X1	T50.3X2	T50.3X3	T50.3X4	T50.3X5	T50.3X
Carbamate(insecticide)	T60.0X1	T60.0X2	T60.0X3	T60.0X4	—	—
Carbamate(sedative)	T42.6X1	T42.6X2	T42.6X3	T42.6X4	T42.6X5	T42.6X
herbicide	T60.0X1	T60.0X2	T60.0X3	T60.0X4	—	—
insecticide	T60.0X1	T60.0X2	T60.0X3	T60.0X4	—	—

Substance	Poisoning, Accidental (unintentional)	Poisoning, Intentional self-harm	Poisoning, Assault	Poisoning, Undetermined	Adverse effect	Underdosing
rbamazepine	T42.1X1	T42.1X2	T42.1X3	T42.1X4	T42.1X5	T42.1X6
rbamide	T47.3X1	T47.3X2	T47.3X3	T47.3X4	T47.3X5	T47.3X6
eroxide	T49.0X1	T49.0X2	T49.0X3	T49.0X4	T49.0X5	T49.0X6
opical	T49.8X1	T49.8X2	T49.8X3	T49.8X4	T49.8X5	T49.8X6
rbamylcholine chloride	T44.1X1	T44.1X2	T44.1X3	T44.1X4	T44.1X5	T44.1X6
rbaril	T60.0X1	T60.0X2	T60.0X3	T60.0X4	—	—
rbarsone	T37.3X1	T37.3X2	T37.3X3	T37.3X4	T37.3X5	T37.3X6
rbaryl	T60.0X1	T60.0X2	T60.0X3	T60.0X4	—	—
rbaspirin	T39.011	T39.012	T39.013	T39.014	T39.015	T39.016
rbazochrome licylate) dium sulfonate)	T49.4X1	T49.4X2	T49.4X3	T49.4X4	T49.4X5	T49.4X6
rbenicillin	T36.0X1	T36.0X2	T36.0X3	T36.0X4	T36.0X5	T36.0X6
rbenoxolone	T47.1X1	T47.1X2	T47.1X3	T47.1X4	T47.1X5	T47.1X6
rbetapentane	T48.3X1	T48.3X2	T48.3X3	T48.3X4	T48.3X5	T48.3X6
rbethyl salicylate	T39.091	T39.092	T39.093	T39.094	T39.095	T39.096
rbidopa(with levodopa)	T42.8X1	T42.8X2	T42.8X3	T42.8X4	T42.8X5	T42.8X6
rbimazole	T38.2X1	T38.2X2	T38.2X3	T38.2X4	T38.2X5	T38.2X6
rbinol	T51.1X1	T51.1X2	T51.1X3	T51.1X4	—	—
rbinoxamine	T45.0X1	T45.0X2	T45.0X3	T45.0X4	T45.0X5	T45.0X6
rbiphene	T39.8X1	T39.8X2	T39.8X3	T39.8X4	T39.8X5	T39.8X6
rbitol	T52.3X1	T52.3X2	T52.3X3	T52.3X4	—	—
rbo medicinalis	T47.6X1	T47.6X2	T47.6X3	T47.6X4	T47.6X5	T47.6X6
rbocaine	T41.3X1	T41.3X2	T41.3X3	T41.3X4	T41.3X5	T41.3X6
infiltration (subcutaneous)	T41.3X1	T41.3X2	T41.3X3	T41.3X4	T41.3X5	T41.3X6
nerve block(peripheral) (plexus)	T41.3X1	T41.3X2	T41.3X3	T41.3X4	T41.3X5	T41.3X6
topical(surface)	T41.3X1	T41.3X2	T41.3X3	T41.3X4	T41.3X5	T41.3X6
rbocisteine	T48.4X1	T48.4X2	T48.4X3	T48.4X4	T48.4X5	T48.4X6
rbocromen	T46.3X1	T46.3X2	T46.3X3	T46.3X4	T46.3X5	T46.3X6
rbol fuchsin	T49.0X1	T49.0X2	T49.0X3	T49.0X4	T49.0X5	T49.0X6
rbolic acid—see also henol	T54.0X1	T54.0X2	T54.0X3	T54.0X4	—	—
rbolonium romide)	T48.1X1	T48.1X2	T48.1X3	T48.1X4	T48.1X5	T48.1X6
rbomycin	T36.8X1	T36.8X2	T36.8X3	T36.8X4	T36.8X5	T36.8X6
rbon						
bisulfide(liquid)	T65.4X1	T65.4X2	T65.4X3	T65.4X4	—	—
vapor	T65.4X1	T65.4X2	T65.4X3	T65.4X4	—	—
dioxide(gas)	T59.7X1	T59.7X2	T59.7X3	T59.7X4	—	—
medicinal	T41.5X1	T41.5X2	T41.5X3	T41.5X4	T41.5X5	T41.5X6
nonmedicinal	T59.7X1	T59.7X2	T59.7X3	T59.7X4	—	—
snow	T49.4X1	T49.4X2	T49.4X3	T49.4X4	T49.4X5	T49.4X6
disulfide(liquid)	T65.4X1	T65.4X2	T65.4X3	T65.4X4	—	—
vapor	T65.4X1	T65.4X2	T65.4X3	T65.4X4	—	—
monoxide(from incomplete combustion)	T58.91	T58.92	T58.93	T58.94	—	—
blast furnace gas	T58.8X1	T58.8X2	T58.8X3	T58.8X4	—	—
butane(distributed in mobile container)	T58.11	T58.12	T58.13	T58.14	—	—
distributed through pipes	T58.11	T58.12	T58.13	T58.14	—	—
Carbon — *Continued*						
charcoal fumes	T58.2X1	T58.2X2	T58.2X3	T58.2X4	—	—
coal	T58.2X1	T58.2X2	T58.2X3	T58.2X4	—	—
coke(in domestic stoves, fireplaces)	T58.2X1	T58.2X2	T58.2X3	T58.2X4	—	—
gas(piped)	T58.11	T58.12	T58.13	T58.14	—	—
solid(in domestic stoves, fireplaces)	T58.2X1	T58.2X2	T58.2X3	T58.2X4	—	—
exhaust gas(motor) not in transit	T58.01	T58.02	T58.03	T58.04	—	—
combustion engine, any not in watercraft	T58.01	T58.02	T58.03	T58.04	—	—
farm tractor, not in transit	T58.01	T58.02	T58.03	T58.04	—	—
gas engine	T58.01	T58.02	T58.03	T58.04	—	—
motor pump	T58.01	T58.02	T58.03	T58.04	—	—
motor vehicle, not in transit	T58.01	T58.02	T58.03	T58.04	—	—
fuel(in domestic use)	T58.2X1	T58.2X2	T58.2X3	T58.2X4	—	—
gas(piped)	T58.11	T58.12	T58.13	T58.14	—	—
in mobile container	T58.11	T58.12	T58.13	T58.14	—	—
piped(natural)	T58.11	T58.12	T58.13	T58.14	—	—
utility	T58.11	T58.12	T58.13	T58.14	—	—
in mobile container	T58.11	T58.12	T58.13	T58.14	—	—
illuminating gas	T58.11	T58.12	T58.13	T58.14	—	—
industrial fuels or gases, any	T58.8X1	T58.8X2	T58.8X3	T58.8X4	—	—
kerosene(in domestic stoves, fireplaces)	T58.2X1	T58.2X2	T58.2X3	T58.2X4	—	—
kiln gas or vapor	T58.8X1	T58.8X2	T58.8X3	T58.8X4	—	—
motor exhaust gas, not in transit	T58.01	T58.02	T58.03	T58.04	—	—
piped gas(manufactured) (natural)	T58.11	T58.12	T58.13	T58.14	—	—
producer gas	T58.8X1	T58.8X2	T58.8X3	T58.8X4	—	—
propane (distributedin mobilecontainer)	T58.11	T58.12	T58.13	T58.14	—	—
distributed through pipes	T58.11	T58.12	T58.13	T58.14	—	—
specified source NEC	T58.8X1	T58.8X2	T58.8X3	T58.8X4	—	—
stove gas	T58.11	T58.12	T58.13	T58.14	—	—
piped	T58.11	T58.12	T58.13	T58.14	—	—
utility gas	T58.11	T58.12	T58.13	T58.14	—	—
piped	T58.11	T58.12	T58.13	T58.14	—	—
water gas	T58.11	T58.12	T58.13	T58.14	—	—
wood(in domestic stoves, fireplaces)	T58.2X1	T58.2X2	T58.2X3	T58.2X4	—	—
tetrachloride(vapor) NEC	T53.0X1	T53.0X2	T53.0X3	T53.0X4	—	—
liquid(cleansing agent) NEC	T53.0X1	T53.0X2	T53.0X3	T53.0X4	—	—
solvent	T53.0X1	T53.0X2	T53.0X3	T53.0X4	—	—
Carbonic acid gas	T59.7X1	T59.7X2	T59.7X3	T59.7X4	—	—
anhydrase inhibitor NEC	T50.2X1	T50.2X2	T50.2X3	T50.2X4	T50.2X5	T50.2X6

Substance	Poisoning, Accidental (unintentional)	Poisoning, Intentional self-harm	Poisoning, Assault	Poisoning, Undetermined	Adverse effect	Underdosing
Carbophenothion	T60.0X1	T60.0X2	T60.0X3	T60.0X4	—	—
Carboplatin	T45.1X1	T45.1X2	T45.1X3	T45.1X4	T45.1X5	T45.1X6
Carboprost	T48.0X1	T48.0X2	T48.0X3	T48.0X4	T48.0X5	T48.0X6
Carboquone	T45.1X1	T45.1X2	T45.1X3	T45.1X4	T45.1X5	T45.1X6
Carbowax	T49.3X1	T49.3X2	T49.3X3	T49.3X4	T49.3X5	T49.3X6
Carboxymethyl-cellulose	T47.4X1	T47.4X2	T47.4X3	T47.4X4	T47.4X5	T47.4X6
S-Carboxymethyl-cysteine	T48.4X1	T48.4X2	T48.4X3	T48.4X4	T48.4X5	T48.4X6
Carbrital	T42.3X1	T42.3X2	T42.3X3	T42.3X4	T42.3X5	T42.3X6
Carbromal	T42.6X1	T42.6X2	T42.6X3	T42.6X4	T42.6X5	T42.6X6
Carbutamide	T38.3X1	T38.3X2	T38.3X3	T38.3X4	T38.3X5	T38.3X6
Carbuterol	T48.6X1	T48.6X2	T48.6X3	T48.6X4	T48.6X5	T48.6X6
Cardiac						
depressants	T46.2X1	T46.2X2	T46.2X3	T46.2X4	T46.2X5	T46.2X6
rhythm regulator	T46.2X1	T46.2X2	T46.2X3	T46.2X4	T46.2X5	T46.2X6
specified NEC	T46.2X1	T46.2X2	T46.2X3	T46.2X4	T46.2X5	T46.2X6
Cardiografin	T50.8X1	T50.8X2	T50.8X3	T50.8X4	T50.8X5	T50.8X6
Cardio-green	T50.8X1	T50.8X2	T50.8X3	T50.8X4	T50.8X5	T50.8X6
Cardiotonic (glycoside)NEC	T46.0X1	T46.0X2	T46.0X3	T46.0X4	T46.0X5	T46.0X6
Cardiovascular drug NEC	T46.901	T46.902	T46.903	T46.904	T46.905	T46.906
Cardrase	T50.2X1	T50.2X2	T50.2X3	T50.2X4	T50.2X5	T50.2X6
Carfecillin	T36.0X1	T36.0X2	T36.0X3	T36.0X4	T36.0X5	T36.0X6
Carfenazine	T43.3X1	T43.3X2	T43.3X3	T43.3X4	T43.3X5	T43.3X6
Carfusin	T49.0X1	T49.0X2	T49.0X3	T49.0X4	T49.0X5	T49.0X6
Carindacillin	T36.0X1	T36.0X2	T36.0X3	T36.0X4	T36.0X5	T36.0X6
Carisoprodol	T42.8X1	T42.8X2	T42.8X3	T42.8X4	T42.8X5	T42.8X6
Carmellose	T47.4X1	T47.4X2	T47.4X3	T47.4X4	T47.4X5	T47.4X6
Carminative	T47.5X1	T47.5X2	T47.5X3	T47.5X4	T47.5X5	T47.5X6
Carmofur	T45.1X1	T45.1X2	T45.1X3	T45.1X4	T45.1X5	T45.1X6
Carmustine	T45.1X1	T45.1X2	T45.1X3	T45.1X4	T45.1X5	T45.1X6
Carotene	T45.2X1	T45.2X2	T45.2X3	T45.2X4	T45.2X5	T45.2X6
Carphenazine	T43.3X1	T43.3X2	T43.3X3	T43.3X4	T43.3X5	T43.3X6
Carpipramine	T42.4X1	T42.4X2	T42.4X3	T42.4X4	T42.4X5	T42.4X6
Carprofen	T39.311	T39.312	T39.313	T39.314	T39.315	T39.316
Carpronium chloride	T44.3X1	T44.3X2	T44.3X3	T44.3X4	T44.3X5	T44.3X6
Carrageenan	T47.8X1	T47.8X2	T47.8X3	T47.8X4	T47.8X5	T47.8X6
Carteolol	T44.7X1	T44.7X2	T44.7X3	T44.7X4	T44.7X5	T44.7X6
Carter's Little Pills	T47.2X1	T47.2X2	T47.2X3	T47.2X4	T47.2X5	T47.2X6
Cascara(sagrada)	T47.2X1	T47.2X2	T47.2X3	T47.2X4	T47.2X5	T47.2X6
Cassava	T62.2X1	T62.2X2	T62.2X3	T62.2X4	—	—
Castellani's paint	T49.0X1	T49.0X2	T49.0X3	T49.0X4	T49.0X5	T49.0X6
Castor						
bean	T62.2X1	T62.2X2	T62.2X3	T62.2X4	—	—
oil	T47.2X1	T47.2X2	T47.2X3	T47.2X4	T47.2X5	T47.2X6
Catalase	T45.3X1	T45.3X2	T45.3X3	T45.3X4	T45.3X5	T45.3X6
Caterpillar(sting)	T63.431	T63.432	T63.433	T63.434	—	—
Catha(edulis) (tea)	T43.691	T43.692	T43.693	T43.694	—	—
Cathartic NEC	T47.4X1	T47.4X2	T47.4X3	T47.4X4	T47.4X5	T47.4X6
anthacene derivative	T47.2X1	T47.2X2	T47.2X3	T47.2X4	T47.2X5	T47.2X6
bulk	T47.4X1	T47.4X2	T47.4X3	T47.4X4	T47.4X5	T47.4X6
contact	T47.2X1	T47.2X2	T47.2X3	T47.2X4	T47.2X5	T47.2X6
emollient NEC	T47.4X1	T47.4X2	T47.4X3	T47.4X4	T47.4X5	T47.4X6

Substance	Poisoning, Accidental (unintentional)	Poisoning, Intentional self-harm	Poisoning, Assault	Poisoning, Undetermined	Adverse effect	Underdosing
Cathartic NEC — *Continued*						
irritant NEC	T47.2X1	T47.2X2	T47.2X3	T47.2X4	T47.2X5	T47.2
mucilage	T47.4X1	T47.4X2	T47.4X3	T47.4X4	T47.4X5	T47.4
saline	T47.3X1	T47.3X2	T47.3X3	T47.3X4	T47.3X5	T47.3
vegetable	T47.2X1	T47.2X2	T47.2X3	T47.2X4	T47.2X5	T47.2
Cathine	T50.5X1	T50.5X2	T50.5X3	T50.5X4	T50.5X5	T50.5
Cathomycin	T36.8X1	T36.8X2	T36.8X3	T36.8X4	T36.8X5	T36.8
Cation exchange resin	T50.3X1	T50.3X2	T50.3X3	T50.3X4	T50.3X5	T50.3
Caustic(s) NEC	T54.91	T54.92	T54.93	T54.94	—	—
alkali	T54.3X1	T54.3X2	T54.3X3	T54.3X4	—	—
hydroxide	T54.3X1	T54.3X2	T54.3X3	T54.3X4	—	—
potash	T54.3X1	T54.3X2	T54.3X3	T54.3X4	—	—
soda	T54.3X1	T54.3X2	T54.3X3	T54.3X4	—	—
specified NEC	T54.91	T54.92	T54.93	T54.94	—	—
Ceepryn	T49.0X1	T49.0X2	T49.0X3	T49.0X4	T49.0X5	T49.0
ENT agent	T49.6X1	T49.6X2	T49.6X3	T49.6X4	T49.6X5	T49.6
lozenges	T49.6X1	T49.6X2	T49.6X3	T49.6X4	T49.6X5	T49.6
Cefacetrile	T36.1X1	T36.1X2	T36.1X3	T36.1X4	T36.1X5	T36.1
Cefaclor	T36.1X1	T36.1X2	T36.1X3	T36.1X4	T36.1X5	T36.1
Cefadroxil	T36.1X1	T36.1X2	T36.1X3	T36.1X4	T36.1X5	T36.1
Cefalexin	T36.1X1	T36.1X2	T36.1X3	T36.1X4	T36.1X5	T36.1
Cefaloglycin	T36.1X1	T36.1X2	T36.1X3	T36.1X4	T36.1X5	T36.1
Cefaloridine	T36.1X1	T36.1X2	T36.1X3	T36.1X4	T36.1X5	T36.1
Cefalosporins	T36.1X1	T36.1X2	T36.1X3	T36.1X4	T36.1X5	T36.1
Cefalotin	T36.1X1	T36.1X2	T36.1X3	T36.1X4	T36.1X5	T36.1
Cefamandole	T36.1X1	T36.1X2	T36.1X3	T36.1X4	T36.1X5	T36.1X
Cefamycin antibiotic	T36.1X1	T36.1X2	T36.1X3	T36.1X4	T36.1X5	T36.1X
Cefapirin	T36.1X1	T36.1X2	T36.1X3	T36.1X4	T36.1X5	T36.1
Cefatrizine	T36.1X1	T36.1X2	T36.1X3	T36.1X4	T36.1X5	T36.1
Cefazedone	T36.1X1	T36.1X2	T36.1X3	T36.1X4	T36.1X5	T36.1X
Cefazolin	T36.1X1	T36.1X2	T36.1X3	T36.1X4	T36.1X5	T36.1
Cefbuperazone	T36.1X1	T36.1X2	T36.1X3	T36.1X4	T36.1X5	T36.1
Cefetamet	T36.1X1	T36.1X2	T36.1X3	T36.1X4	T36.1X5	T36.1X
Cefixime	T36.1X1	T36.1X2	T36.1X3	T36.1X4	T36.1X5	T36.1X
Cefmenoxime	T36.1X1	T36.1X2	T36.1X3	T36.1X4	T36.1X5	T36.1X
Cefmetazole	T36.1X1	T36.1X2	T36.1X3	T36.1X4	T36.1X5	T36.1X
Cefminox	T36.1X1	T36.1X2	T36.1X3	T36.1X4	T36.1X5	T36.1X
Cefonicid	T36.1X1	T36.1X2	T36.1X3	T36.1X4	T36.1X5	T36.1X
Cefoperazone	T36.1X1	T36.1X2	T36.1X3	T36.1X4	T36.1X5	T36.1X
Ceforanide	T36.1X1	T36.1X2	T36.1X3	T36.1X4	T36.1X5	T36.1X
Cefotaxime	T36.1X1	T36.1X2	T36.1X3	T36.1X4	T36.1X5	T36.1X
Cefotetan	T36.1X1	T36.1X2	T36.1X3	T36.1X4	T36.1X5	T36.1X
Cefotiam	T36.1X1	T36.1X2	T36.1X3	T36.1X4	T36.1X5	T36.1X
Cefoxitin	T36.1X1	T36.1X2	T36.1X3	T36.1X4	T36.1X5	T36.1X
Cefpimizole	T36.1X1	T36.1X2	T36.1X3	T36.1X4	T36.1X5	T36.1X
Cefpiramide	T36.1X1	T36.1X2	T36.1X3	T36.1X4	T36.1X5	T36.1X
Cefradine	T36.1X1	T36.1X2	T36.1X3	T36.1X4	T36.1X5	T36.1X
Cefroxadine	T36.1X1	T36.1X2	T36.1X3	T36.1X4	T36.1X5	T36.1X
Cefsulodin	T36.1X1	T36.1X2	T36.1X3	T36.1X4	T36.1X5	T36.1X
Ceftazidime	T36.1X1	T36.1X2	T36.1X3	T36.1X4	T36.1X5	T36.1X
Cefteram	T36.1X1	T36.1X2	T36.1X3	T36.1X4	T36.1X5	T36.1X

Substance	Poisoning, Accidental (unintentional)	Poisoning, Intentional self-harm	Poisoning, Assault	Poisoning, Undetermined	Adverse effect	Underdosing
ftezole	T36.1X1	T36.1X2	T36.1X3	T36.1X4	T36.1X5	T36.1X6
ftizoxime	T36.1X1	T36.1X2	T36.1X3	T36.1X4	T36.1X5	T36.1X6
ftriaxone	T36.1X1	T36.1X2	T36.1X3	T36.1X4	T36.1X5	T36.1X6
furoxime	T36.1X1	T36.1X2	T36.1X3	T36.1X4	T36.1X5	T36.1X6
fuzonam	T36.1X1	T36.1X2	T36.1X3	T36.1X4	T36.1X5	T36.1X6
lestone	T38.0X1	T38.0X2	T38.0X3	T38.0X4	T38.0X5	T38.0X6
topical	T49.0X1	T49.0X2	T49.0X3	T49.0X4	T49.0X5	T49.0X6
liprolol	T44.7X1	T44.7X2	T44.7X3	T44.7X4	T44.7X5	T44.7X6
ll stimulants and oliferants	T49.8X1	T49.8X2	T49.8X3	T49.8X4	T49.8X5	T49.8X6
llosolve	T52.91	T52.92	T52.93	T52.94	—	—
llulose						
cathartic	T47.4X1	T47.4X2	T47.4X3	T47.4X4	T47.4X5	T47.4X6
hydroxyethyl	T47.4X1	T47.4X2	T47.4X3	T47.4X4	T47.4X5	T47.4X6
nitrates(topical)	T49.3X1	T49.3X2	T49.3X3	T49.3X4	T49.3X5	T49.3X6
oxidized	T49.4X1	T49.4X2	T49.4X3	T49.4X4	T49.4X5	T49.4X6
entipede(bite)	T63.411	T63.412	T63.413	T63.414	—	—
entral nervous stem						
depressants	T42.71	T42.72	T42.73	T42.74	T42.75	T42.76
anesthetic(general) NEC	T41.201	T41.202	T41.203	T41.204	T41.205	T41.206
gases NEC	T41.0X1	T41.0X2	T41.0X3	T41.0X4	T41.0X5	T41.0X6
intravenous	T41.1X1	T41.1X2	T41.1X3	T41.1X4	T41.1X5	T41.1X6
barbiturates	T42.3X1	T42.3X2	T42.3X3	T42.3X4	T42.3X5	T42.3X6
benzodiazepines	T42.4X1	T42.4X2	T42.4X3	T42.4X4	T42.4X5	T42.4X6
bromides	T42.6X1	T42.6X2	T42.6X3	T42.6X4	T42.6X5	T42.6X6
cannabis sativa	T40.7X1	T40.7X2	T40.7X3	T40.7X4	T40.7X5	T40.7X6
chloral hydrate	T42.6X1	T42.6X2	T42.6X3	T42.6X4	T42.6X5	T42.6X6
ethanol	T51.0X1	T51.0X2	T51.0X3	T51.0X4	—	—
hallucinogenics	T40.901	T40.902	T40.903	T40.904	T40.905	T40.906
hypnotics	T42.71	T42.72	T42.73	T42.74	T42.75	T42.76
specified NEC	T42.6X1	T42.6X2	T42.6X3	T42.6X4	T42.6X5	T42.6X6
muscle relaxants	T42.8X1	T42.8X2	T42.8X3	T42.8X4	T42.8X5	T42.8X6
paraldehyde	T42.6X1	T42.6X2	T42.6X3	T42.6X4	T42.6X5	T42.6X6
sedatives; sedative-hypnotics	T42.71	T42.72	T42.73	T42.74	T42.75	T42.76
mixed NEC	T42.6X1	T42.6X2	T42.6X3	T42.6X4	T42.6X5	T42.6X6
specified NEC	T42.6X1	T42.6X2	T42.6X3	T42.6X4	T42.6X5	T42.6X6
muscle-tone depressants	T42.8X1	T42.8X2	T42.8X3	T42.8X4	T42.8X5	T42.8X6
stimulants	T43.601	T43.602	T43.603	T43.604	T43.605	T43.606
amphetamines	T43.621	T43.622	T43.623	T43.624	T43.625	T43.626
analeptics	T50.7X1	T50.7X2	T50.7X3	T50.7X4	T50.7X5	T50.7X6
antidepressants	T43.201	T43.202	T43.203	T43.204	T43.205	T43.206
opiate antagonists	T50.7X1	T50.7X2	T50.7X3	T50.7X4	T50.7X5	T50.7X6
specified NEC	T43.691	T43.692	T43.693	T43.694	T43.695	T43.696
Cephalexin	T36.1X1	T36.1X2	T36.1X3	T36.1X4	T36.1X5	T36.1X6
Cephaloglycin	T36.1X1	T36.1X2	T36.1X3	T36.1X4	T36.1X5	T36.1X6
Cephaloridine	T36.1X1	T36.1X2	T36.1X3	T36.1X4	T36.1X5	T36.1X6
Cephalosporins	T36.1X1	T36.1X2	T36.1X3	T36.1X4	T36.1X5	T36.1X6
N(adicillin)	T36.0X1	T36.0X2	T36.0X3	T36.0X4	T36.0X5	T36.0X6
Cephalothin	T36.1X1	T36.1X2	T36.1X3	T36.1X4	T36.1X5	T36.1X6
Cephalotin	T36.1X1	T36.1X2	T36.1X3	T36.1X4	T36.1X5	T36.1X6
Cephradine	T36.1X1	T36.1X2	T36.1X3	T36.1X4	T36.1X5	T36.1X6
Cerbera(odallam)	T62.2X1	T62.2X2	T62.2X3	T62.2X4	—	—
Cerberin	T46.0X1	T46.0X2	T46.0X3	T46.0X4	T46.0X5	T46.0X6
Cerebral stimulants	T43.601	T43.602	T43.603	T43.604	T43.605	T43.606
psychotherapeutic	T43.601	T43.602	T43.603	T43.604	T43.605	T43.606
specified NEC	T43.691	T43.692	T43.693	T43.694	T43.695	T43.696
Cerium oxalate	T45.0X1	T45.0X2	T45.0X3	T45.0X4	T45.0X5	T45.0X6
Cerous oxalate	T45.0X1	T45.0X2	T45.0X3	T45.0X4	T45.0X5	T45.0X6
Ceruletide	T50.8X1	T50.8X2	T50.8X3	T50.8X4	T50.8X5	T50.8X6
Cetalkonium (chloride)	T49.0X1	T49.0X2	T49.0X3	T49.0X4	T49.0X5	T49.0X6
Cethexonium chloride	T49.0X1	T49.0X2	T49.0X3	T49.0X4	T49.0X5	T49.0X6
Cetiedil	T46.7X1	T46.7X2	T46.7X3	T46.7X4	T46.7X5	T46.7X6
Cetirizine	T45.0X1	T45.0X2	T45.0X3	T45.0X4	T45.0X5	T45.0X6
Cetomacrogol	T50.991	T50.992	T50.993	T50.994	T50.995	T50.996
Cetotiamine	T45.2X1	T45.2X2	T45.2X3	T45.2X4	T45.2X5	T45.2X6
Cetoxime	T45.0X1	T45.0X2	T45.0X3	T45.0X4	T45.0X5	T45.0X6
Cetraxate	T47.1X1	T47.1X2	T47.1X3	T47.1X4	T47.1X5	T47.1X6
Cetrimide	T49.0X1	T49.0X2	T49.0X3	T49.0X4	T49.0X5	T49.0X6
Cetrimonium (bromide)	T49.0X1	T49.0X2	T49.0X3	T49.0X4	T49.0X5	T49.0X6
Cetylpyridinium chloride	T49.0X1	T49.0X2	T49.0X3	T49.0X4	T49.0X5	T49.0X6
ENT agent	T49.6X1	T49.6X2	T49.6X3	T49.6X4	T49.6X5	T49.6X6
lozenges	T49.6X1	T49.6X2	T49.6X3	T49.6X4	T49.6X5	T49.6X6
Cevadilla—see Sabadilla						
Cevitamic acid	T45.2X1	T45.2X2	T45.2X3	T45.2X4	T45.2X5	T45.2X6
Chalk, precipitated	T47.1X1	T47.1X2	T47.1X3	T47.1X4	T47.1X5	T47.1X6
Chamomile	T49.0X1	T49.0X2	T49.0X3	T49.0X4	T49.0X5	T49.0X6
Ch'an su	T46.0X1	T46.0X2	T46.0X3	T46.0X4	T46.0X5	T46.0X6
Charcoal	T47.6X1	T47.6X2	T47.6X3	T47.6X4	T47.6X5	T47.6X6
activated—see also Charcoal, medicinal	T47.6X1	T47.6X2	T47.6X3	T47.6X4	T47.6X5	T47.6X6
fumes(Carbon monoxide)	T58.2X1	T58.2X2	T58.2X3	T58.2X4	—	—
industrial	T58.8X1	T58.8X2	T58.8X3	T58.8X4	—	—
medicinal (activated)	T47.6X1	T47.6X2	T47.6X3	T47.6X4	T47.6X5	T47.6X6
antidiarrheal	T47.6X1	T47.6X2	T47.6X3	T47.6X4	T47.6X5	T47.6X6
poison control	T47.8X1	T47.8X2	T47.8X3	T47.8X4	T47.8X5	T47.8X6
specified use other than for diarrhea	T47.8X1	T47.8X2	T47.8X3	T47.8X4	T47.8X5	T47.8X6
topical	T49.8X1	T49.8X2	T49.8X3	T49.8X4	T49.8X5	T49.8X6
Chaulmosulfone	T37.1X1	T37.1X2	T37.1X3	T37.1X4	T37.1X5	T37.1X6
Chelating agent NEC	T50.6X1	T50.6X2	T50.6X3	T50.6X4	T50.6X5	T50.6X6
Chelidonium majus	T62.2X1	T62.2X2	T62.2X3	T62.2X4	—	—
Chemical substance NEC	T65.91	T65.92	T65.93	T65.94	—	—
Chenodeoxycholic acid	T47.5X1	T47.5X2	T47.5X3	T47.5X4	T47.5X5	T47.5X6
Chenodiol	T47.5X1	T47.5X2	T47.5X3	T47.5X4	T47.5X5	T47.5X6
Chenopodium	T37.4X1	T37.4X2	T37.4X3	T37.4X4	T37.4X5	T37.4X6
Cherry laurel	T62.2X1	T62.2X2	T62.2X3	T62.2X4	—	—
Chinidin(e)	T46.2X1	T46.2X2	T46.2X3	T46.2X4	T46.2X5	T46.2X6
Chiniofon	T37.8X1	T37.8X2	T37.8X3	T37.8X4	T37.8X5	T37.8X6

Substance	Poisoning, Accidental (unintentional)	Poisoning, Intentional self-harm	Poisoning, Assault	Poisoning, Undetermined	Adverse effect	Underdosing
Chlophedianol	T48.3X1	T48.3X2	T48.3X3	T48.3X4	T48.3X5	T48.3X6
Chloral	T42.6X1	T42.6X2	T42.6X3	T42.6X4	T42.6X5	T42.6X6
derivative	T42.6X1	T42.6X2	T42.6X3	T42.6X4	T42.6X5	T42.6X6
hydrate	T42.6X1	T42.6X2	T42.6X3	T42.6X4	T42.6X5	T42.6X6
Chloralamide	T42.6X1	T42.6X2	T42.6X3	T42.6X4	T42.6X5	T42.6X6
Chloralodol	T42.6X1	T42.6X2	T42.6X3	T42.6X4	T42.6X5	T42.6X6
Chloralose	T60.4X1	T60.4X2	T60.4X3	T60.4X4	—	—
Chlorambucil	T45.1X1	T45.1X2	T45.1X3	T45.1X4	T45.1X5	T45.1X6
Chloramine	T57.8X1	T57.8X2	T57.8X3	T57.8X4	—	—
T	T49.0X1	T49.0X2	T49.0X3	T49.0X4	T49.0X5	T49.0X6
topical	T49.0X1	T49.0X2	T49.0X3	T49.0X4	T49.0X5	T49.0X6
Chloramphenicol	T36.2X1	T36.2X2	T36.2X3	T36.2X4	T36.2X5	T36.2X6
ENT agent	T49.6X1	T49.6X2	T49.6X3	T49.6X4	T49.6X5	T49.6X6
ophthalmic preparation	T49.5X1	T49.5X2	T49.5X3	T49.5X4	T49.5X5	T49.5X6
topical NEC	T49.0X1	T49.0X2	T49.0X3	T49.0X4	T49.0X5	T49.0X6
Chlorate (potassium) (sodium) NEC	T60.3X1	T60.3X2	T60.3X3	T60.3X4	—	—
herbicide	T60.3X1	T60.3X2	T60.3X3	T60.3X4	—	—
Chlorazanil	T50.2X1	T50.2X2	T50.2X3	T50.2X4	T50.2X5	T50.2X6
Chlorbenzene, chlorbenzol	T53.7X1	T53.7X2	T53.7X3	T53.7X4	—	—
Chlorbenzoxamine	T44.3X1	T44.3X2	T44.3X3	T44.3X4	T44.3X5	T44.3X6
Chlorbutol	T42.6X1	T42.6X2	T42.6X3	T42.6X4	T42.6X5	T42.6X6
Chlorcyclizine	T45.0X1	T45.0X2	T45.0X3	T45.0X4	T45.0X5	T45.0X6
Chlordan(e) (dust)	T60.1X1	T60.1X2	T60.1X3	T60.1X4	—	—
Chlordantoin	T49.0X1	T49.0X2	T49.0X3	T49.0X4	T49.0X5	T49.0X6
Chlordiazepoxide	T42.4X1	T42.4X2	T42.4X3	T42.4X4	T42.4X5	T42.4X6
Chlordiethyl benzamide	T49.3X1	T49.3X2	T49.3X3	T49.3X4	T49.3X5	T49.3X6
Chloresium	T49.8X1	T49.8X2	T49.8X3	T49.8X4	T49.8X5	T49.8X6
Chlorethiazol	T42.6X1	T42.6X2	T42.6X3	T42.6X4	T42.6X5	T42.6X6
Chlorethyl—see Ethyl chloride						
Chloretone	T42.6X1	T42.6X2	T42.6X3	T42.6X4	T42.6X5	T42.6X6
Chlorex	T53.6X1	T53.6X2	T53.6X3	T53.6X4	—	—
insecticide	T60.1X1	T60.1X2	T60.1X3	T60.1X4	—	—
Chlorfenvinphos	T60.0X1	T60.0X2	T60.0X3	T60.0X4	—	—
Chlorhexadol	T42.6X1	T42.6X2	T42.6X3	T42.6X4	T42.6X5	T42.6X6
Chlorhexamide	T45.1X1	T45.1X2	T45.1X3	T45.1X4	T45.1X5	T45.1X6
Chlorhexidine	T49.0X1	T49.0X2	T49.0X3	T49.0X4	T49.0X5	T49.0X6
Chlorhydro-xyquinolin	T49.0X1	T49.0X2	T49.0X3	T49.0X4	T49.0X5	T49.0X6
Chloride of lime(bleach)	T54.3X1	T54.3X2	T54.3X3	T54.3X4	—	—
Chlorimipramine	T43.011	T43.012	T43.013	T43.014	T43.015	T43.016
Chlorinated						
camphene	T53.6X1	T53.6X2	T53.6X3	T53.6X4	—	—
diphenyl	T53.7X1	T53.7X2	T53.7X3	T53.7X4	—	—
hydrocarbons NEC	T53.91	T53.92	T53.93	T53.94	—	—
solvents	T53.91	T53.92	T53.93	T53.94	—	—
lime(bleach)	T54.3X1	T54.3X2	T54.3X3	T54.3X4	—	—
and boric acid solution	T49.0X1	T49.0X2	T49.0X3	T49.0X4	T49.0X5	T49.0X6
naphthalene (insecticide)	T60.1X1	T60.1X2	T60.1X3	T60.1X4	—	—
industrial(non-pesticide)	T53.7X1	T53.7X2	T53.7X3	T53.7X4	—	—
Chlorinated — *Continued*						
pesticide NEC	T60.8X1	T60.8X2	T60.8X3	T60.8X4	—	—
soda—see also sodium hypochlorite						
solution	T49.0X1	T49.0X2	T49.0X3	T49.0X4	T49.0X5	T49.0X
Chlorine(fumes) (gas)	T59.4X1	T59.4X2	T59.4X3	T59.4X4	—	—
bleach	T54.3X1	T54.3X2	T54.3X3	T54.3X4	—	—
compound gas NEC	T59.4X1	T59.4X2	T59.4X3	T59.4X4	—	—
disinfectant	T59.4X1	T59.4X2	T59.4X3	T59.4X4	—	—
releasing agents NEC	T59.4X1	T59.4X2	T59.4X3	T59.4X4	—	—
Chlorisondamine chloride	T46.991	T46.992	T46.993	T46.994	T46.995	T46.9
Chlormadinone	T38.5X1	T38.5X2	T38.5X3	T38.5X4	T38.5X5	T38.5X
Chlormephos	T60.0X1	T60.0X2	T60.0X3	T60.0X4	—	—
Chlormerodrin	T50.2X1	T50.2X2	T50.2X3	T50.2X4	T50.2X5	T50.2X
Chlormethiazole	T42.6X1	T42.6X2	T42.6X3	T42.6X4	T42.6X5	T42.6X
Chlormethine	T45.1X1	T45.1X2	T45.1X3	T45.1X4	T45.1X5	T45.1X
Chlormethyle-necycline	T36.4X1	T36.4X2	T36.4X3	T36.4X4	T36.4X5	T36.4X
Chlormezanone	T42.6X1	T42.6X2	T42.6X3	T42.6X4	T42.6X5	T42.6X
Chloroacetic acid	T60.3X1	T60.3X2	T60.3X3	T60.3X4	—	—
Chloroacetone	T59.3X1	T59.3X2	T59.3X3	T59.3X4	—	—
Chloroacetophenone	T59.3X1	T59.3X2	T59.3X3	T59.3X4	—	—
Chloroaniline	T53.7X1	T53.7X2	T53.7X3	T53.7X4	—	—
Chlorobenzene, chlorobenzol	T53.7X1	T53.7X2	T53.7X3	T53.7X4	—	—
Chlorobromo methane(fire extinguisher)	T53.6X1	T53.6X2	T53.6X3	T53.6X4	—	—
Chlorobutanol	T49.0X1	T49.0X2	T49.0X3	T49.0X4	T49.0X5	T49.0X
Chlorocresol	T49.0X1	T49.0X2	T49.0X3	T49.0X4	T49.0X5	T49.0X
Chlorodehydro-methyltestosterone	T38.7X1	T38.7X2	T38.7X3	T38.7X4	T38.7X5	T38.7X
Chlorodinitro-benzene	T53.7X1	T53.7X2	T53.7X3	T53.7X4	—	—
dust or vapor	T53.7X1	T53.7X2	T53.7X3	T53.7X4	—	—
Chlorodiphenyl	T53.7X1	T53.7X2	T53.7X3	T53.7X4	—	—
Chloroethane—see Ethyl chloride						
Chloroethylene	T53.6X1	T53.6X2	T53.6X3	T53.6X4	—	—
Chlorofluorocarbons	T53.5X1	T53.5X2	T53.5X3	T53.5X4	—	—
Chloroform(fumes) (vapor)	T53.1X1	T53.1X2	T53.1X3	T53.1X4	—	—
anesthetic	T41.0X1	T41.0X2	T41.0X3	T41.0X4	T41.0X5	T41.0X
solvent	T53.1X1	T53.1X2	T53.1X3	T53.1X4	—	—
water, concentrated	T41.0X1	T41.0X2	T41.0X3	T41.0X4	T41.0X5	T41.0X
Chloroguanide	T37.2X1	T37.2X2	T37.2X3	T37.2X4	T37.2X5	T37.2X
Chloromycetin	T36.2X1	T36.2X2	T36.2X3	T36.2X4	T36.2X5	T36.2X
ENT agent	T49.6X1	T49.6X2	T49.6X3	T49.6X4	T49.6X5	T49.6X
ophthalmic preparation	T49.5X1	T49.5X2	T49.5X3	T49.5X4	T49.5X5	T49.5X
otic solution	T49.6X1	T49.6X2	T49.6X3	T49.6X4	T49.6X5	T49.6X
topical NEC	T49.0X1	T49.0X2	T49.0X3	T49.0X4	T49.0X5	T49.0X
Chloronitrobenzene	T53.7X1	T53.7X2	T53.7X3	T53.7X4	—	—
dust or vapor	T53.7X1	T53.7X2	T53.7X3	T53.7X4	—	—
Chlorophacinone	T60.4X1	T60.4X2	T60.4X3	T60.4X4	—	—
Chlorophenol	T53.7X1	T53.7X2	T53.7X3	T53.7X4	—	—
Chlorophenothane	T60.1X1	T60.1X2	T60.1X3	T60.1X4	—	—
Chlorophyll	T50.991	T50.992	T50.993	T50.994	T50.995	T50.996

Substance	Poisoning, Accidental (unintentional)	Poisoning, Intentional self-harm	Poisoning, Assault	Poisoning, Undetermined	Adverse effect	Underdosing
loropicrin(fumes)	T53.6X1	T53.6X2	T53.6X3	T53.6X4	—	—
umigant	T60.8X1	T60.8X2	T60.8X3	T60.8X4	—	—
ungicide	T60.3X1	T60.3X2	T60.3X3	T60.3X4	—	—
esticide	T60.8X1	T60.8X2	T60.8X3	T60.8X4	—	—
loroprocaine	T41.3X1	T41.3X2	T41.3X3	T41.3X4	T41.3X5	T41.3X6
nfiltration (subcutaneous)	T41.3X1	T41.3X2	T41.3X3	T41.3X4	T41.3X5	T41.3X6
erve block(peripheral) (plexus)	T41.3X1	T41.3X2	T41.3X3	T41.3X4	T41.3X5	T41.3X6
spinal	T41.3X1	T41.3X2	T41.3X3	T41.3X4	T41.3X5	T41.3X6
loroptic	T49.5X1	T49.5X2	T49.5X3	T49.5X4	T49.5X5	T49.5X6
loropurine	T45.1X1	T45.1X2	T45.1X3	T45.1X4	T45.1X5	T45.1X6
loropyramine	T45.0X1	T45.0X2	T45.0X3	T45.0X4	T45.0X5	T45.0X6
loropyrifos	T60.0X1	T60.0X2	T60.0X3	T60.0X4	—	—
loropyrilene	T45.0X1	T45.0X2	T45.0X3	T45.0X4	T45.0X5	T45.0X6
loroquine	T37.2X1	T37.2X2	T37.2X3	T37.2X4	T37.2X5	T37.2X6
lorothalonil	T60.3X1	T60.3X2	T60.3X3	T60.3X4	—	—
hlorothen	T45.0X1	T45.0X2	T45.0X3	T45.0X4	T45.0X5	T45.0X6
hlorothiazide	T50.2X1	T50.2X2	T50.2X3	T50.2X4	T50.2X5	T50.2X6
hlorothymol	T49.4X1	T49.4X2	T49.4X3	T49.4X4	T49.4X5	T49.4X6
hlorotrianisene	T38.5X1	T38.5X2	T38.5X3	T38.5X4	T38.5X5	T38.5X6
hlorovinyldichloro-arsine, t in war	T57.0X1	T57.0X2	T57.0X3	T57.0X4	—	—
hloroxine	T49.4X1	T49.4X2	T49.4X3	T49.4X4	T49.4X5	T49.4X6
hloroxylenol	T49.0X1	T49.0X2	T49.0X3	T49.0X4	T49.0X5	T49.0X6
hlorphenamine	T45.0X1	T45.0X2	T45.0X3	T45.0X4	T45.0X5	T45.0X6
hlorphenesin	T42.8X1	T42.8X2	T42.8X3	T42.8X4	T42.8X5	T42.8X6
topical(antifungal)	T49.0X1	T49.0X2	T49.0X3	T49.0X4	T49.0X5	T49.0X6
hlorpheniramine	T45.0X1	T45.0X2	T45.0X3	T45.0X4	T45.0X5	T45.0X6
hlorphenoxamine	T45.0X1	T45.0X2	T45.0X3	T45.0X4	T45.0X5	T45.0X6
hlorphentermine	T50.5X1	T50.5X2	T50.5X3	T50.5X4	T50.5X5	T50.5X6
hlorprocaine—see hloroprocaine						
hlorproguanil	T37.2X1	T37.2X2	T37.2X3	T37.2X4	T37.2X5	T37.2X6
hlorpromazine	T43.3X1	T43.3X2	T43.3X3	T43.3X4	T43.3X5	T43.3X6
hlorpropamide	T38.3X1	T38.3X2	T38.3X3	T38.3X4	T38.3X5	T38.3X6
hlorprothixene	T43.4X1	T43.4X2	T43.4X3	T43.4X4	T43.4X5	T43.4X6
hlorquinaldol	T49.0X1	T49.0X2	T49.0X3	T49.0X4	T49.0X5	T49.0X6
hlorquinol	T49.0X1	T49.0X2	T49.0X3	T49.0X4	T49.0X5	T49.0X6
hlortalidone	T50.2X1	T50.2X2	T50.2X3	T50.2X4	T50.2X5	T50.2X6
hlortetracycline	T36.4X1	T36.4X2	T36.4X3	T36.4X4	T36.4X5	T36.4X6
hlorthalidone	T50.2X1	T50.2X2	T50.2X3	T50.2X4	T50.2X5	T50.2X6
hlorthiophos	T60.0X1	T60.0X2	T60.0X3	T60.0X4	—	—
hlortrianisene	T38.5X1	T38.5X2	T38.5X3	T38.5X4	T38.5X5	T38.5X6
hlor-Trimeton	T45.0X1	T45.0X2	T45.0X3	T45.0X4	T45.0X5	T45.0X6
hlorthion	T60.0X1	T60.0X2	T60.0X3	T60.0X4	—	—
hlorzoxazone	T42.8X1	T42.8X2	T42.8X3	T42.8X4	T42.8X5	T42.8X6
hoke damp	T59.7X1	T59.7X2	T59.7X3	T59.7X4	—	—
holagogues	T47.5X1	T47.5X2	T47.5X3	T47.5X4	T47.5X5	T47.5X6
holebrine	T50.8X1	T50.8X2	T50.8X3	T50.8X4	T50.8X5	T50.8X6
holecalciferol	T45.2X1	T45.2X2	T45.2X3	T45.2X4	T45.2X5	T45.2X6
holecystokinin	T50.8X1	T50.8X2	T50.8X3	T50.8X4	T50.8X5	T50.8X6

Substance	Poisoning, Accidental (unintentional)	Poisoning, Intentional self-harm	Poisoning, Assault	Poisoning, Undetermined	Adverse effect	Underdosing
Cholera vaccine	T50.A91	T50.A92	T50.A93	T50.A94	T50.A95	T50.A96
Choleretic	T47.5X1	T47.5X2	T47.5X3	T47.5X4	T47.5X5	T47.5X6
Cholesterol-lowering agents	T46.6X1	T46.6X2	T46.6X3	T46.6X4	T46.6X5	T46.6X6
Cholestyramine (resin)	T46.6X1	T46.6X2	T46.6X3	T46.6X4	T46.6X5	T46.6X6
Cholic acid	T47.5X1	T47.5X2	T47.5X3	T47.5X4	T47.5X5	T47.5X6
Choline	T48.6X1	T48.6X2	T48.6X3	T48.6X4	T48.6X5	T48.6X6
chloride	T50.991	T50.992	T50.993	T50.994	T50.995	T50.996
dihydrogen citrate	T50.991	T50.992	T50.993	T50.994	T50.995	T50.996
salicylate	T39.091	T39.092	T39.093	T39.094	T39.095	T39.096
theophyllinate	T48.6X1	T48.6X2	T48.6X3	T48.6X4	T48.6X5	T48.6X6
Cholinergic(drug) NEC	T44.1X1	T44.1X2	T44.1X3	T44.1X4	T44.1X5	T44.1X6
muscle tone enhancer	T44.1X1	T44.1X2	T44.1X3	T44.1X4	T44.1X5	T44.1X6
organophosphorus	T44.0X1	T44.0X2	T44.0X3	T44.0X4	T44.0X5	T44.0X6
insecticide	T60.0X1	T60.0X2	T60.0X3	T60.0X4	—	—
nerve gas	T59.891	T59.892	T59.893	T59.894	—	—
trimethyl ammonium propanediol	T44.1X1	T44.1X2	T44.1X3	T44.1X4	T44.1X5	T44.1X6
Cholinesterase reactivator	T50.6X1	T50.6X2	T50.6X3	T50.6X4	T50.6X5	T50.6X6
Cholografin	T50.8X1	T50.8X2	T50.8X3	T50.8X4	T50.8X5	T50.8X6
Chorionic gonadotropin	T38.891	T38.892	T38.893	T38.894	T38.895	T38.896
Chromate	T56.2X1	T56.2X2	T56.2X3	T56.2X4	—	—
dust or mist	T56.2X1	T56.2X2	T56.2X3	T56.2X4	—	—
lead—see also lead	T56.0X1	T56.0X2	T56.0X3	T56.0X4	—	—
paint	T56.0X1	T56.0X2	T56.0X3	T56.0X4	—	—
Chromic						
acid	T56.2X1	T56.2X2	T56.2X3	T56.2X4	—	—
dust or mist	T56.2X1	T56.2X2	T56.2X3	T56.2X4	—	—
phosphate 32P	T45.1X1	T45.1X2	T45.1X3	T45.1X4	T45.1X5	T45.1X6
Chromium	T56.2X1	T56.2X2	T56.2X3	T56.2X4	—	—
compounds—see Chromate						
sesquioxide	T50.8X1	T50.8X2	T50.8X3	T50.8X4	T50.8X5	T50.8X6
Chromomycin A3	T45.1X1	T45.1X2	T45.1X3	T45.1X4	T45.1X5	T45.1X6
Chromonar	T46.3X1	T46.3X2	T46.3X3	T46.3X4	T46.3X5	T46.3X6
Chromyl chloride	T56.2X1	T56.2X2	T56.2X3	T56.2X4	—	—
Chrysarobin	T49.4X1	T49.4X2	T49.4X3	T49.4X4	T49.4X5	T49.4X6
Chrysazin	T47.2X1	T47.2X2	T47.2X3	T47.2X4	T47.2X5	T47.2X6
Chymar	T45.3X1	T45.3X2	T45.3X3	T45.3X4	T45.3X5	T45.3X6
ophthalmic preparation	T49.5X1	T49.5X2	T49.5X3	T49.5X4	T49.5X5	T49.5X6
Chymopapain	T45.3X1	T45.3X2	T45.3X3	T45.3X4	T45.3X5	T45.3X6
Chymotrypsin	T45.3X1	T45.3X2	T45.3X3	T45.3X4	T45.3X5	T45.3X6
ophthalmic preparation	T49.5X1	T49.5X2	T49.5X3	T49.5X4	T49.5X5	T49.5X6
Cianidanol	T50.991	T50.992	T50.993	T50.994	T50.995	T50.996
Cianopramine	T43.011	T43.012	T43.013	T43.014	T43.015	T43.016
Cibenzoline	T46.2X1	T46.2X2	T46.2X3	T46.2X4	T46.2X5	T46.2X6
Ciclacillin	T36.0X1	T36.0X2	T36.0X3	T36.0X4	T36.0X5	T36.0X6
Ciclobarbital—see Hexobarbital						
Ciclonicate	T46.7X1	T46.7X2	T46.7X3	T46.7X4	T46.7X5	T46.7X6
Ciclopirox(olamine)	T49.0X1	T49.0X2	T49.0X3	T49.0X4	T49.0X5	T49.0X6
Ciclosporin	T45.1X1	T45.1X2	T45.1X3	T45.1X4	T45.1X5	T45.1X6

Substance	Poisoning, Accidental (unintentional)	Poisoning, Intentional self-harm	Poisoning, Assault	Poisoning, Undetermined	Adverse effect	Underdosing
Cicuta maculata or virosa	T62.2X1	T62.2X2	T62.2X3	T62.2X4	—	—
Cicutoxin	T62.2X1	T62.2X2	T62.2X3	T62.2X4	—	—
Cigarette lighter fluid	T52.0X1	T52.0X2	T52.0X3	T52.0X4	—	—
Cigarettes (tobacco)	T65.221	T65.222	T65.223	T65.224	—	—
Ciguatoxin	T61.01	T61.02	T61.03	T61.04	—	—
Cilazapril	T46.4X1	T46.4X2	T46.4X3	T46.4X4	T46.4X5	T46.4X6
Cimetidine	T47.0X1	T47.0X2	T47.0X3	T47.0X4	T47.0X5	T47.0X6
Cimetropium bromide	T44.3X1	T44.3X2	T44.3X3	T44.3X4	T44.3X5	T44.3X6
Cinchocaine	T41.3X1	T41.3X2	T41.3X3	T41.3X4	T41.3X5	T41.3X6
topical(surface)	T41.3X1	T41.3X2	T41.3X3	T41.3X4	T41.3X5	T41.3X6
Cinchona	T37.2X1	T37.2X2	T37.2X3	T37.2X4	T37.2X5	T37.2X6
Cinchonine alkaloids	T37.2X1	T37.2X2	T37.2X3	T37.2X4	T37.2X5	T37.2X6
Cinchophen	T50.4X1	T50.4X2	T50.4X3	T50.4X4	T50.4X5	T50.4X6
Cinepazide	T46.7X1	T46.7X2	T46.7X3	T46.7X4	T46.7X5	T46.7X6
Cinnamedrine	T48.5X1	T48.5X2	T48.5X3	T48.5X4	T48.5X5	T48.5X6
Cinnarizine	T45.0X1	T45.0X2	T45.0X3	T45.0X4	T45.0X5	T45.0X6
Cinoxacin	T37.8X1	T37.8X2	T37.8X3	T37.8X4	T37.8X5	T37.8X6
Ciprofibrate	T46.6X1	T46.6X2	T46.6X3	T46.6X4	T46.6X5	T46.6X6
Ciprofloxacin	T36.8X1	T36.8X2	T36.8X3	T36.8X4	T36.8X5	T36.8X6
Cisapride	T47.8X1	T47.8X2	T47.8X3	T47.8X4	T47.8X5	T47.8X6
Cisplatin	T45.1X1	T45.1X2	T45.1X3	T45.1X4	T45.1X5	T45.1X6
Citalopram	T43.221	T43.222	T43.223	T43.224	T43.225	T43.226
Citanest	T41.3X1	T41.3X2	T41.3X3	T41.3X4	T41.3X5	T41.3X6
infiltration (subcutaneous)	T41.3X1	T41.3X2	T41.3X3	T41.3X4	T41.3X5	T41.3X6
nerve block(peripheral) (plexus)	T41.3X1	T41.3X2	T41.3X3	T41.3X4	T41.3X5	T41.3X6
Citric acid	T47.5X1	T47.5X2	T47.5X3	T47.5X4	T47.5X5	T47.5X6
Citrovorum(factor)	T45.8X1	T45.8X2	T45.8X3	T45.8X4	T45.8X5	T45.8X6
Claviceps purpurea	T62.2X1	T62.2X2	T62.2X3	T62.2X4	—	—
Clavulanic acid	T36.1X1	T36.1X2	T36.1X3	T36.1X4	T36.1X5	T36.1X6
Cleaner, cleansing agent, type not specified	T65.891	T65.892	T65.893	T65.894	—	—
of paint or varnish	T52.91	T52.92	T52.93	T52.94	—	—
specified type NEC	T65.891	T65.892	T65.893	T65.894	—	—
Clebopride	T47.8X1	T47.8X2	T47.8X3	T47.8X4	T47.8X5	T47.8X6
Clefamide	T37.3X1	T37.3X2	T37.3X3	T37.3X4	T37.3X5	T37.3X6
Clemastine	T45.0X1	T45.0X2	T45.0X3	T45.0X4	T45.0X5	T45.0X6
Clematis vitalba	T62.2X1	T62.2X2	T62.2X3	T62.2X4	—	—
Clemizole	T45.0X1	T45.0X2	T45.0X3	T45.0X4	T45.0X5	T45.0X6
penicillin	T36.0X1	T36.0X2	T36.0X3	T36.0X4	T36.0X5	T36.0X6
Clenbuterol	T48.6X1	T48.6X2	T48.6X3	T48.6X4	T48.6X5	T48.6X6
Clidinium bromide	T44.3X1	T44.3X2	T44.3X3	T44.3X4	T44.3X5	T44.3X6
Clindamycin	T36.8X1	T36.8X2	T36.8X3	T36.8X4	T36.8X5	T36.8X6
Clinofibrate	T46.6X1	T46.6X2	T46.6X3	T46.6X4	T46.6X5	T46.6X6
Clioquinol	T37.8X1	T37.8X2	T37.8X3	T37.8X4	T37.8X5	T37.8X6
Cliradon	T40.2X1	T40.2X2	T40.2X3	T40.2X4	—	—
Clobazam	T42.4X1	T42.4X2	T42.4X3	T42.4X4	T42.4X5	T42.4X6
Clobenzorex	T50.5X1	T50.5X2	T50.5X3	T50.5X4	T50.5X5	T50.5X6
Clobetasol	T49.0X1	T49.0X2	T49.0X3	T49.0X4	T49.0X5	T49.0X6

Substance	Poisoning, Accidental (unintentional)	Poisoning, Intentional self-harm	Poisoning, Assault	Poisoning, Undetermined	Adverse effect	Underdosing
Clobetasone	T49.0X1	T49.0X2	T49.0X3	T49.0X4	T49.0X5	T49.0
Clobutinol	T48.3X1	T48.3X2	T48.3X3	T48.3X4	T48.3X5	T48.3
Clocortolone	T38.0X1	T38.0X2	T38.0X3	T38.0X4	T38.0X5	T38.0
Clodantoin	T49.0X1	T49.0X2	T49.0X3	T49.0X4	T49.0X5	T49.0
Clodronic acid	T50.991	T50.992	T50.993	T50.994	T50.995	T50.9
Clofazimine	T37.1X1	T37.1X2	T37.1X3	T37.1X4	T37.1X5	T37.1
Clofedanol	T48.3X1	T48.3X2	T48.3X3	T48.3X4	T48.3X5	T48.3
Clofenamide	T50.2X1	T50.2X2	T50.2X3	T50.2X4	T50.2X5	T50.2
Clofenotane	T49.0X1	T49.0X2	T49.0X3	T49.0X4	T49.0X5	T49.0
Clofezone	T39.2X1	T39.2X2	T39.2X3	T39.2X4	T39.2X5	T39.2
Clofibrate	T46.6X1	T46.6X2	T46.6X3	T46.6X4	T46.6X5	T46.6
Clofibride	T46.6X1	T46.6X2	T46.6X3	T46.6X4	T46.6X5	T46.6
Cloforex	T50.5X1	T50.5X2	T50.5X3	T50.5X4	T50.5X5	T50.5
Clomethiazole	T42.6X1	T42.6X2	T42.6X3	T42.6X4	T42.6X5	T42.6
Clometocillin	T36.0X1	T36.0X2	T36.0X3	T36.0X4	T36.0X5	T36.0
Clomifene	T38.5X1	T38.5X2	T38.5X3	T38.5X4	T38.5X5	T38.5
Clomiphene	T38.5X1	T38.5X2	T38.5X3	T38.5X4	T38.5X5	T38.5
Clomipramine	T43.011	T43.012	T43.013	T43.014	T43.015	T43.0
Clomocycline	T36.4X1	T36.4X2	T36.4X3	T36.4X4	T36.4X5	T36.4
Clonazepam	T42.4X1	T42.4X2	T42.4X3	T42.4X4	T42.4X5	T42.4
Clonidine	T46.5X1	T46.5X2	T46.5X3	T46.5X4	T46.5X5	T46.5
Clonixin	T39.8X1	T39.8X2	T39.8X3	T39.8X4	T39.8X5	T39.8
Clopamide	T50.2X1	T50.2X2	T50.2X3	T50.2X4	T50.2X5	T50.2
Clopenthixol	T43.4X1	T43.4X2	T43.4X3	T43.4X4	T43.4X5	T43.4
Cloperastine	T48.3X1	T48.3X2	T48.3X3	T48.3X4	T48.3X5	T48.3
Clophedianol	T48.3X1	T48.3X2	T48.3X3	T48.3X4	T48.3X5	T48.3
Cloponone	T36.2X1	T36.2X2	T36.2X3	T36.2X4	T36.2X5	T36.2
Cloprednol	T38.0X1	T38.0X2	T38.0X3	T38.0X4	T38.0X5	T38.0
Cloral betaine	T42.6X1	T42.6X2	T42.6X3	T42.6X4	T42.6X5	T42.6X
Cloramfenicol	T36.2X1	T36.2X2	T36.2X3	T36.2X4	T36.2X5	T36.2X
Clorazepate (dipotassium)	T42.4X1	T42.4X2	T42.4X3	T42.4X4	T42.4X5	T42.4X
Clorexolone	T50.2X1	T50.2X2	T50.2X3	T50.2X4	T50.2X5	T50.2X
Clorfenamine	T45.0X1	T45.0X2	T45.0X3	T45.0X4	T45.0X5	T45.0X
Clorgiline	T43.1X1	T43.1X2	T43.1X3	T43.1X4	T43.1X5	T43.1X
Clorotepine	T44.3X1	T44.3X2	T44.3X3	T44.3X4	T44.3X5	T44.3X
Clorox(bleach)	T54.91	T54.92	T54.93	T54.94	—	—
Clorprenaline	T48.6X1	T48.6X2	T48.6X3	T48.6X4	T48.6X5	T48.6X
Clortermine	T50.5X1	T50.5X2	T50.5X3	T50.5X4	T50.5X5	T50.5X
Clotiapine	T43.591	T43.592	T43.593	T43.594	T43.595	T43.59
Clotiazepam	T42.4X1	T42.4X2	T42.4X3	T42.4X4	T42.4X5	T42.4X
Clotibric acid	T46.6X1	T46.6X2	T46.6X3	T46.6X4	T46.6X5	T46.6X
Clotrimazole	T49.0X1	T49.0X2	T49.0X3	T49.0X4	T49.0X5	T49.0X
Cloxacillin	T36.0X1	T36.0X2	T36.0X3	T36.0X4	T36.0X5	T36.0X
Cloxazolam	T42.4X1	T42.4X2	T42.4X3	T42.4X4	T42.4X5	T42.4X
Cloxiquine	T49.0X1	T49.0X2	T49.0X3	T49.0X4	T49.0X5	T49.0X
Clozapine	T42.4X1	T42.4X2	T42.4X3	T42.4X4	T42.4X5	T42.4X
Coagulant NEC	T45.7X1	T45.7X2	T45.7X3	T45.7X4	T45.7X5	T45.7X
Coal(carbon monoxide from)—see also Carbon, monoxide, coal	T58.2X1	T58.2X2	T58.2X3	T58.2X4	—	—
oil—see Kerosene						
tar	T49.1X1	T49.1X2	T49.1X3	T49.1X4	T49.1X5	T49.1X

Substance	Poisoning, Accidental (unintentional)	Poisoning, Intentional self-harm	Poisoning, Assault	Poisoning, Undetermined	Adverse effect	Underdosing
al(carbon monoxide m)—see also Carbon, noxide, coal — *Continued*						
fumes	T59.891	T59.892	T59.893	T59.894	—	—
medicinal (ointment)	T49.4X1	T49.4X2	T49.4X3	T49.4X4	T49.4X5	T49.4X6
analgesics NEC	T39.2X1	T39.2X2	T39.2X3	T39.2X4	T39.2X5	T39.2X6
naphtha(solvent)	T52.0X1	T52.0X2	T52.0X3	T52.0X4	—	—
balamine	T45.2X1	T45.2X2	T45.2X3	T45.2X4	T45.2X5	T45.2X6
balt(nonmedicinal) mes) (industrial)	T56.891	T56.892	T56.893	T56.894	—	—
nedicinal(trace) (chloride)	T45.8X1	T45.8X2	T45.8X3	T45.8X4	T45.8X5	T45.8X6
bra(venom)	T63.041	T63.042	T63.043	T63.044	—	—
ca(leaf)	T40.5X1	T40.5X2	T40.5X3	T40.5X4	T40.5X5	T40.5X6
caine	T40.5X1	T40.5X2	T40.5X3	T40.5X4	T40.5X5	T40.5X6
opical anesthetic	T41.3X1	T41.3X2	T41.3X3	T41.3X4	T41.3X5	T41.3X6
carboxylase	T45.3X1	T45.3X2	T45.3X3	T45.3X4	T45.3X5	T45.3X6
ccidioidin	T50.8X1	T50.8X2	T50.8X3	T50.8X4	T50.8X5	T50.8X6
cculus indicus	T62.1X1	T62.1X2	T62.1X3	T62.1X4	—	—
chineal	T65.6X1	T65.6X2	T65.6X3	T65.6X4	—	—
nedicinal products	T50.991	T50.992	T50.993	T50.994	T50.995	T50.996
deine	T40.2X1	T40.2X2	T40.2X3	T40.2X4	T40.2X5	T40.2X6
d-liver oil	T45.2X1	T45.2X2	T45.2X3	T45.2X4	T45.2X5	T45.2X6
enzyme A	T50.991	T50.992	T50.993	T50.994	T50.995	T50.996
ffee	T62.8X1	T62.8X2	T62.8X3	T62.8X4	—	—
galactoiso-merase	T50.991	T50.992	T50.993	T50.994	T50.995	T50.996
gentin	T44.3X1	T44.3X2	T44.3X3	T44.3X4	T44.3X5	T44.3X6
ke fumes or gas(carbon noxide)	T58.2X1	T58.2X2	T58.2X3	T58.2X4	—	—
ndustrial use	T58.8X1	T58.8X2	T58.8X3	T58.8X4	—	—
lace	T47.4X1	T47.4X2	T47.4X3	T47.4X4	T47.4X5	T47.4X6
laspase	T45.1X1	T45.1X2	T45.1X3	T45.1X4	T45.1X5	T45.1X6
lchicine	T50.4X1	T50.4X2	T50.4X3	T50.4X4	T50.4X5	T50.4X6
lchicum	T62.2X1	T62.2X2	T62.2X3	T62.2X4	—	—
ld cream	T49.3X1	T49.3X2	T49.3X3	T49.3X4	T49.3X5	T49.3X6
lecalciferol	T45.2X1	T45.2X2	T45.2X3	T45.2X4	T45.2X5	T45.2X6
lestipol	T46.6X1	T46.6X2	T46.6X3	T46.6X4	T46.6X5	T46.6X6
lestyramine	T46.6X1	T46.6X2	T46.6X3	T46.6X4	T46.6X5	T46.6X6
limycin	T36.8X1	T36.8X2	T36.8X3	T36.8X4	T36.8X5	T36.8X6
listimethate	T36.8X1	T36.8X2	T36.8X3	T36.8X4	T36.8X5	T36.8X6
listin	T36.8X1	T36.8X2	T36.8X3	T36.8X4	T36.8X5	T36.8X6
ulfate(eye preparation)	T49.5X1	T49.5X2	T49.5X3	T49.5X4	T49.5X5	T49.5X6
llagen	T50.991	T50.992	T50.993	T50.994	T50.995	T50.996
llagenase	T49.4X1	T49.4X2	T49.4X3	T49.4X4	T49.4X5	T49.4X6
llodion	T49.3X1	T49.3X2	T49.3X3	T49.3X4	T49.3X5	T49.3X6
locynth	T47.2X1	T47.2X2	T47.2X3	T47.2X4	T47.2X5	T47.2X6
lophony adhesive	T49.3X1	T49.3X2	T49.3X3	T49.3X4	T49.3X5	T49.3X6
lorant—see also Dye	T50.991	T50.992	T50.993	T50.994	T50.995	T50.996
loring matter—see e(s)						
mbustion gas(after mbustion)—see Carbon, noxide						
rior to combustion	T59.891	T59.892	T59.893	T59.894	—	—

Substance	Poisoning, Accidental (unintentional)	Poisoning, Intentional self-harm	Poisoning, Assault	Poisoning, Undetermined	Adverse effect	Underdosing
Compazine	T43.3X1	T43.3X2	T43.3X3	T43.3X4	T43.3X5	T43.3X6
Compound						
42(warfarin)	T60.4X1	T60.4X2	T60.4X3	T60.4X4	—	—
269(endrin)	T60.1X1	T60.1X2	T60.1X3	T60.1X4	—	—
497(dieldrin)	T60.1X1	T60.1X2	T60.1X3	T60.1X4	—	—
1080(sodium fluoroacetate)	T60.4X1	T60.4X2	T60.4X3	T60.4X4	—	—
3422(parathion)	T60.0X1	T60.0X2	T60.0X3	T60.0X4	—	—
3911(phorate)	T60.0X1	T60.0X2	T60.0X3	T60.0X4	—	—
3956(toxaphene)	T60.1X1	T60.1X2	T60.1X3	T60.1X4	—	—
4049(malathion)	T60.0X1	T60.0X2	T60.0X3	T60.0X4	—	—
4069(malathion)	T60.0X1	T60.0X2	T60.0X3	T60.0X4	—	—
4124(dicapthon)	T60.0X1	T60.0X2	T60.0X3	T60.0X4	—	—
E(cortisone)	T38.0X1	T38.0X2	T38.0X3	T38.0X4	T38.0X5	T38.0X6
F(hydrocortisone)	T38.0X1	T38.0X2	T38.0X3	T38.0X4	T38.0X5	T38.0X6
Congener, avwnabolic	T38.7X1	T38.7X2	T38.7X3	T38.7X4	T38.7X5	T38.7X6
Congo red	T50.8X1	T50.8X2	T50.8X3	T50.8X4	T50.8X5	T50.8X6
Coniine, conine	T62.2X1	T62.2X2	T62.2X3	T62.2X4	—	—
Conium(maculatum)	T62.2X1	T62.2X2	T62.2X3	T62.2X4	—	—
Conjugated estrogenic substances	T38.5X1	T38.5X2	T38.5X3	T38.5X4	T38.5X5	T38.5X6
Contac	T48.5X1	T48.5X2	T48.5X3	T48.5X4	T48.5X5	T48.5X6
Contact lens solution	T49.5X1	T49.5X2	T49.5X3	T49.5X4	T49.5X5	T49.5X6
Contraceptive(oral)	T38.4X1	T38.4X2	T38.4X3	T38.4X4	T38.4X5	T38.4X6
vaginal	T49.8X1	T49.8X2	T49.8X3	T49.8X4	T49.8X5	T49.8X6
Contrast medium, radiography	T50.8X1	T50.8X2	T50.8X3	T50.8X4	T50.8X5	T50.8X6
Convallaria glycosides	T46.0X1	T46.0X2	T46.0X3	T46.0X4	T46.0X5	T46.0X6
Convallaria majalis	T62.2X1	T62.2X2	T62.2X3	T62.2X4	—	—
berry	T62.1X1	T62.1X2	T62.1X3	T62.1X4	—	—
Copper(dust) (fumes) (nonmedicinal) NEC	T56.4X1	T56.4X2	T56.4X3	T56.4X4	—	—
arsenate, arsenite	T57.0X1	T57.0X2	T57.0X3	T57.0X4	—	—
insecticide	T60.2X1	T60.2X2	T60.2X3	T60.2X4	—	—
emetic	T47.7X1	T47.7X2	T47.7X3	T47.7X4	T47.7X5	T47.7X6
fungicide	T60.3X1	T60.3X2	T60.3X3	T60.3X4	—	—
gluconate	T49.0X1	T49.0X2	T49.0X3	T49.0X4	T49.0X5	T49.0X6
insecticide	T60.2X1	T60.2X2	T60.2X3	T60.2X4	—	—
medicinal(trace)	T45.8X1	T45.8X2	T45.8X3	T45.8X4	T45.8X5	T45.8X6
oleate	T49.0X1	T49.0X2	T49.0X3	T49.0X4	T49.0X5	T49.0X6
sulfate	T56.4X1	T56.4X2	T56.4X3	T56.4X4	—	—
cupric	T56.4X1	T56.4X2	T56.4X3	T56.4X4	—	—
fungicide	T60.3X1	T60.3X2	T60.3X3	T60.3X4	—	—
medicinal						
ear	T49.6X1	T49.6X2	T49.6X3	T49.6X4	T49.6X5	T49.6X6
emetic	T47.7X1	T47.7X2	T47.7X3	T47.7X4	T47.7X5	T47.7X6
eye	T49.5X1	T49.5X2	T49.5X3	T49.5X4	T49.5X5	T49.5X6
cuprous	T56.4X1	T56.4X2	T56.4X3	T56.4X4	—	—
fungicide	T60.3X1	T60.3X2	T60.3X3	T60.3X4	—	—
medicinal						
ear	T49.6X1	T49.6X2	T49.6X3	T49.6X4	T49.6X5	T49.6X6

Substance	Poisoning, Accidental (unintentional)	Poisoning, Intentional self-harm	Poisoning, Assault	Poisoning, Undetermined	Adverse effect	Underdosing
Copper(dust) (fumes) (nonmedicinal) NEC — *Continued*						
emetic	T47.7X1	T47.7X2	T47.7X3	T47.7X4	T47.7X5	T47.7X6
eye	T49.5X1	T49.5X2	T49.5X3	T49.5X4	T49.5X5	T49.5X6
Copperhead snake(bite) (venom)	T63.061	T63.062	T63.063	T63.064	—	—
Coral(sting)	T63.691	T63.692	T63.693	T63.694	—	—
snake(bite) (venom)	T63.021	T63.022	T63.023	T63.024	—	—
Corbadrine	T49.6X1	T49.6X2	T49.6X3	T49.6X4	T49.6X5	T49.6X6
Cordite	T65.891	T65.892	T65.893	T65.894	—	—
vapor	T59.891	T59.892	T59.893	T59.894	—	—
Cordran	T49.0X1	T49.0X2	T49.0X3	T49.0X4	T49.0X5	T49.0X6
Corn cures	T49.4X1	T49.4X2	T49.4X3	T49.4X4	T49.4X5	T49.4X6
Corn starch	T49.3X1	T49.3X2	T49.3X3	T49.3X4	T49.3X5	T49.3X6
Cornhusker's lotion	T49.3X1	T49.3X2	T49.3X3	T49.3X4	T49.3X5	T49.3X6
Coronary vasodilator NEC	T46.3X1	T46.3X2	T46.3X3	T46.3X4	T46.3X5	T46.3X6
Corrosive NEC	T54.91	T54.92	T54.93	T54.94	—	—
acid NEC	T54.2X1	T54.2X2	T54.2X3	T54.2X4	—	—
aromatics	T54.1X1	T54.1X2	T54.1X3	T54.1X4	—	—
disinfectant	T54.1X1	T54.1X2	T54.1X3	T54.1X4	—	—
fumes NEC	T54.91	T54.92	T54.93	T54.94	—	—
specified NEC	T54.91	T54.92	T54.93	T54.94	—	—
sublimate	T56.1X1	T56.1X2	T56.1X3	T56.1X4	—	—
Cortate	T38.0X1	T38.0X2	T38.0X3	T38.0X4	T38.0X5	T38.0X6
Cort-Dome	T38.0X1	T38.0X2	T38.0X3	T38.0X4	T38.0X5	T38.0X6
ENT agent	T49.6X1	T49.6X2	T49.6X3	T49.6X4	T49.6X5	T49.6X6
ophthalmic preparation	T49.5X1	T49.5X2	T49.5X3	T49.5X4	T49.5X5	T49.5X6
topical NEC	T49.0X1	T49.0X2	T49.0X3	T49.0X4	T49.0X5	T49.0X6
Cortef	T38.0X1	T38.0X2	T38.0X3	T38.0X4	T38.0X5	T38.0X6
ENT agent	T49.6X1	T49.6X2	T49.6X3	T49.6X4	T49.6X5	T49.6X6
ophthalmic preparation	T49.5X1	T49.5X2	T49.5X3	T49.5X4	T49.5X5	T49.5X6
topical NEC	T49.0X1	T49.0X2	T49.0X3	T49.0X4	T49.0X5	T49.0X6
Corticosteroid	T38.0X1	T38.0X2	T38.0X3	T38.0X4	T38.0X5	T38.0X6
ENT agent	T49.6X1	T49.6X2	T49.6X3	T49.6X4	T49.6X5	T49.6X6
mineral	T50.0X1	T50.0X2	T50.0X3	T50.0X4	T50.0X5	T50.0X6
ophthalmic	T49.5X1	T49.5X2	T49.5X3	T49.5X4	T49.5X5	T49.5X6
topical NEC	T49.0X1	T49.0X2	T49.0X3	T49.0X4	T49.0X5	T49.0X6
Corticotropin	T38.811	T38.812	T38.813	T38.814	T38.815	T38.816
Cortisol	T49.0X1	T49.0X2	T49.0X3	T49.0X4	T49.0X5	T49.0X6
ENT agent	T49.6X1	T49.6X2	T49.6X3	T49.6X4	T49.6X5	T49.6X6
ophthalmic preparation	T49.5X1	T49.5X2	T49.5X3	T49.5X4	T49.5X5	T49.5X6
topical NEC	T49.0X1	T49.0X2	T49.0X3	T49.0X4	T49.0X5	T49.0X6
Cortisone(acetate)	T38.0X1	T38.0X2	T38.0X3	T38.0X4	T38.0X5	T38.0X6
ENT agent	T49.6X1	T49.6X2	T49.6X3	T49.6X4	T49.6X5	T49.6X6
ophthalmic preparation	T49.5X1	T49.5X2	T49.5X3	T49.5X4	T49.5X5	T49.5X6
topical NEC	T49.0X1	T49.0X2	T49.0X3	T49.0X4	T49.0X5	T49.0X6
Cortivazol	T38.0X1	T38.0X2	T38.0X3	T38.0X4	T38.0X5	T38.0X6
Cortogen	T38.0X1	T38.0X2	T38.0X3	T38.0X4	T38.0X5	T38.0X6
ENT agent	T49.6X1	T49.6X2	T49.6X3	T49.6X4	T49.6X5	T49.6X6
ophthalmic preparation	T49.5X1	T49.5X2	T49.5X3	T49.5X4	T49.5X5	T49.5X6

Substance	Poisoning, Accidental (unintentional)	Poisoning, Intentional self-harm	Poisoning, Assault	Poisoning, Undetermined	Adverse effect	Underdosing
Cortone	T38.0X1	T38.0X2	T38.0X3	T38.0X4	T38.0X5	T38.0
ENT agent	T49.6X1	T49.6X2	T49.6X3	T49.6X4	T49.6X5	T49.6
ophthalmic preparation	T49.5X1	T49.5X2	T49.5X3	T49.5X4	T49.5X5	T49.5
Cortril	T38.0X1	T38.0X2	T38.0X3	T38.0X4	T38.0X5	T38.0
ENT agent	T49.6X1	T49.6X2	T49.6X3	T49.6X4	T49.6X5	T49.6
ophthalmic preparation	T49.5X1	T49.5X2	T49.5X3	T49.5X4	T49.5X5	T49.5
topical NEC	T49.0X1	T49.0X2	T49.0X3	T49.0X4	T49.0X5	T49.0
Corynebacterium parvum	T45.1X1	T45.1X2	T45.1X3	T45.1X4	T45.1X5	T45.1
Cosmetic preparation	T49.8X1	T49.8X2	T49.8X3	T49.8X4	T49.8X5	T49.8
Cosmetics	T49.8X1	T49.8X2	T49.8X3	T49.8X4	T49.8X5	T49.8
Cosyntropin	T38.811	T38.812	T38.813	T38.814	T38.815	T38.8
Cotarnine	T45.7X1	T45.7X2	T45.7X3	T45.7X4	T45.7X5	T45.7
Co-trimoxazole	T36.8X1	T36.8X2	T36.8X3	T36.8X4	T36.8X5	T36.8
Cottonseed oil	T49.3X1	T49.3X2	T49.3X3	T49.3X4	T49.3X5	T49.3
Cough mixture(syrup)	T48.4X1	T48.4X2	T48.4X3	T48.4X4	T48.4X5	T48.4
containing opiates	T40.2X1	T40.2X2	T40.2X3	T40.2X4	T40.2X5	T40.2
expectorants	T48.4X1	T48.4X2	T48.4X3	T48.4X4	T48.4X5	T48.4
Coumadin	T45.511	T45.512	T45.513	T45.514	T45.515	T45.5
rodenticide	T60.4X1	T60.4X2	T60.4X3	T60.4X4	—	—
Coumaphos	T60.0X1	T60.0X2	T60.0X3	T60.0X4	—	—
Coumarin	T45.511	T45.512	T45.513	T45.514	T45.515	T45.5
Coumetarol	T45.511	T45.512	T45.513	T45.514	T45.515	T45.5
Cowbane	T62.2X1	T62.2X2	T62.2X3	T62.2X4	—	—
Cozyme	T45.2X1	T45.2X2	T45.2X3	T45.2X4	T45.2X5	T45.2
Crack	T40.5X1	T40.5X2	T40.5X3	T40.5X4	—	—
Crataegus extract	T46.0X1	T46.0X2	T46.0X3	T46.0X4	T46.0X5	T46.0
Creolin	T54.1X1	T54.1X2	T54.1X3	T54.1X4	—	—
disinfectant	T54.1X1	T54.1X2	T54.1X3	T54.1X4	—	—
Creosol(compound)	T49.0X1	T49.0X2	T49.0X3	T49.0X4	T49.0X5	T49.0X
Creosote(coal tar) (beechwood)	T49.0X1	T49.0X2	T49.0X3	T49.0X4	T49.0X5	T49.0X
medicinal (expectorant)	T48.4X1	T48.4X2	T48.4X3	T48.4X4	T48.4X5	T48.4X
syrup	T48.4X1	T48.4X2	T48.4X3	T48.4X4	T48.4X5	T48.4X
Cresol(s)	T49.0X1	T49.0X2	T49.0X3	T49.0X4	T49.0X5	T49.0X
and soap solution	T49.0X1	T49.0X2	T49.0X3	T49.0X4	T49.0X5	T49.0X
Cresyl acetate	T49.0X1	T49.0X2	T49.0X3	T49.0X4	T49.0X5	T49.0X
Cresylic acid	T49.0X1	T49.0X2	T49.0X3	T49.0X4	T49.0X5	T49.0X
Crimidine	T60.4X1	T60.4X2	T60.4X3	T60.4X4	—	—
Croconazole	T37.8X1	T37.8X2	T37.8X3	T37.8X4	T37.8X5	T37.8X
Cromoglicic acid	T48.6X1	T48.6X2	T48.6X3	T48.6X4	T48.6X5	T48.6X
Cromolyn	T48.6X1	T48.6X2	T48.6X3	T48.6X4	T48.6X5	T48.6X
Cromonar	T46.3X1	T46.3X2	T46.3X3	T46.3X4	T46.3X5	T46.3X
Cropropamide	T39.8X1	T39.8X2	T39.8X3	T39.8X4	T39.8X5	T39.8X
with crotethamide	T50.7X1	T50.7X2	T50.7X3	T50.7X4	T50.7X5	T50.7X
Crotamiton	T49.0X1	T49.0X2	T49.0X3	T49.0X4	T49.0X5	T49.0X
Crotethamide	T39.8X1	T39.8X2	T39.8X3	T39.8X4	T39.8X5	T39.8X
with cropropamide	T50.7X1	T50.7X2	T50.7X3	T50.7X4	T50.7X5	T50.7X
Croton(oil)	T47.2X1	T47.2X2	T47.2X3	T47.2X4	T47.2X5	T47.2X
chloral	T42.6X1	T42.6X2	T42.6X3	T42.6X4	T42.6X5	T42.6X
Crude oil	T52.0X1	T52.0X2	T52.0X3	T52.0X4	—	—

Substance	Poisoning, Accidental (unintentional)	Poisoning, Intentional self-harm	Poisoning, Assault	Poisoning, Undetermined	Adverse effect	Underdosing
yogenine	T39.8X1	T39.8X2	T39.8X3	T39.8X4	T39.8X5	T39.8X6
yolite(vapor)	T60.1X1	T60.1X2	T60.1X3	T60.1X4	—	—
nsecticide	T60.1X1	T60.1X2	T60.1X3	T60.1X4	—	—
yptenamine nnates)	T46.5X1	T46.5X2	T46.5X3	T46.5X4	T46.5X5	T46.5X6
ystal violet	T49.0X1	T49.0X2	T49.0X3	T49.0X4	T49.0X5	T49.0X6
ckoopint	T62.2X1	T62.2X2	T62.2X3	T62.2X4	—	—
metharol	T45.511	T45.512	T45.513	T45.514	T45.515	T45.516
pric						
acetate	T60.3X1	T60.3X2	T60.3X3	T60.3X4	—	—
acetoarsenite	T57.0X1	T57.0X2	T57.0X3	T57.0X4	—	—
arsenate	T57.0X1	T57.0X2	T57.0X3	T57.0X4	—	—
gluconate	T49.0X1	T49.0X2	T49.0X3	T49.0X4	T49.0X5	T49.0X6
oleate	T49.0X1	T49.0X2	T49.0X3	T49.0X4	T49.0X5	T49.0X6
sulfate	T56.4X1	T56.4X2	T56.4X3	T56.4X4	—	—
uprous sulfate—see also opper sulfate	T56.4X1	T56.4X2	T56.4X3	T56.4X4	—	—
urare, curarine	T48.1X1	T48.1X2	T48.1X3	T48.1X4	T48.1X5	T48.1X6
yamemazine	T43.3X1	T43.3X2	T43.3X3	T43.3X4	T43.3X5	T43.3X6
yamopsis tragono-loba	T46.6X1	T46.6X2	T46.6X3	T46.6X4	T46.6X5	T46.6X6
yanacetyl hydrazide	T37.1X1	T37.1X2	T37.1X3	T37.1X4	T37.1X5	T37.1X6
yanic acid(gas)	T59.891	T59.892	T59.893	T59.894	—	—
yanide(s) (compounds) otassium) (sodium) EC	T65.0X1	T65.0X2	T65.0X3	T65.0X4	—	—
dust or gas(inhalation) NEC	T57.3X1	T57.3X2	T57.3X3	T57.3X4	—	—
fumigant	T65.0X1	T65.0X2	T65.0X3	T65.0X4	—	—
hydrogen	T57.3X1	T57.3X2	T57.3X3	T57.3X4	—	—
ercuric—see Mercury						
pesticide(dust) (fumes)	T65.0X1	T65.0X2	T65.0X3	T65.0X4	—	—
yanoacrylate adhesive	T49.3X1	T49.3X2	T49.3X3	T49.3X4	T49.3X5	T49.3X6
yanocobalamin	T45.8X1	T45.8X2	T45.8X3	T45.8X4	T45.8X5	T45.8X6
yanogen(chloride) gas) NEC	T59.891	T59.892	T59.893	T59.894	—	—
yclacillin	T36.0X1	T36.0X2	T36.0X3	T36.0X4	T36.0X5	T36.0X6
yclaine	T41.3X1	T41.3X2	T41.3X3	T41.3X4	T41.3X5	T41.3X6
yclamate	T50.991	T50.992	T50.993	T50.994	T50.995	T50.996
yclamen europaeum	T62.2X1	T62.2X2	T62.2X3	T62.2X4	—	—
yclandelate	T46.7X1	T46.7X2	T46.7X3	T46.7X4	T46.7X5	T46.7X6
yclazocine	T50.7X1	T50.7X2	T50.7X3	T50.7X4	T50.7X5	T50.7X6
yclizine	T45.0X1	T45.0X2	T45.0X3	T45.0X4	T45.0X5	T45.0X6
yclobarbital	T42.3X1	T42.3X2	T42.3X3	T42.3X4	T42.3X5	T42.3X6
yclobarbitone	T42.3X1	T42.3X2	T42.3X3	T42.3X4	T42.3X5	T42.3X6
yclobenzaprine	T48.1X1	T48.1X2	T48.1X3	T48.1X4	T48.1X5	T48.1X6
yclodrine	T44.3X1	T44.3X2	T44.3X3	T44.3X4	T44.3X5	T44.3X6
ycloguanil embonate	T37.2X1	T37.2X2	T37.2X3	T37.2X4	T37.2X5	T37.2X6
yclohexane	T52.8X1	T52.8X2	T52.8X3	T52.8X4	—	—
Cyclohexanol	T51.8X1	T51.8X2	T51.8X3	T51.8X4	—	—
Cyclohexanone	T52.4X1	T52.4X2	T52.4X3	T52.4X4	—	—
Cycloheximide	T60.3X1	T60.3X2	T60.3X3	T60.3X4	—	—

Substance	Poisoning, Accidental (unintentional)	Poisoning, Intentional self-harm	Poisoning, Assault	Poisoning, Undetermined	Adverse effect	Underdosing
Cyclohexyl acetate	T52.8X1	T52.8X2	T52.8X3	T52.8X4	—	—
Cycloleucin	T45.1X1	T45.1X2	T45.1X3	T45.1X4	T45.1X5	T45.1X6
Cyclomethycaine	T41.3X1	T41.3X2	T41.3X3	T41.3X4	T41.3X5	T41.3X6
Cyclopentamine	T44.4X1	T44.4X2	T44.4X3	T44.4X4	T44.4X5	T44.4X6
Cyclopenthiazide	T50.2X1	T50.2X2	T50.2X3	T50.2X4	T50.2X5	T50.2X6
Cyclopentolate	T44.3X1	T44.3X2	T44.3X3	T44.3X4	T44.3X5	T44.3X6
Cyclophosphamide	T45.1X1	T45.1X2	T45.1X3	T45.1X4	T45.1X5	T45.1X6
Cycloplegic drug	T49.5X1	T49.5X2	T49.5X3	T49.5X4	T49.5X5	T49.5X6
Cyclopropane	T41.291	T41.292	T41.293	T41.294	T41.295	T41.296
Cyclopyrabital	T39.8X1	T39.8X2	T39.8X3	T39.8X4	T39.8X5	T39.8X6
Cycloserine	T37.1X1	T37.1X2	T37.1X3	T37.1X4	T37.1X5	T37.1X6
Cyclosporin	T45.1X1	T45.1X2	T45.1X3	T45.1X4	T45.1X5	T45.1X6
Cyclothiazide	T50.2X1	T50.2X2	T50.2X3	T50.2X4	T50.2X5	T50.2X6
Cycrimine	T44.3X1	T44.3X2	T44.3X3	T44.3X4	T44.3X5	T44.3X6
Cyhalothrin	T60.1X1	T60.1X2	T60.1X3	T60.1X4	—	—
Cymarin	T46.0X1	T46.0X2	T46.0X3	T46.0X4	T46.0X5	T46.0X6
Cypermethrin	T60.1X1	T60.1X2	T60.1X3	T60.1X4	—	—
Cyphenothrin	T60.2X1	T60.2X2	T60.2X3	T60.2X4	—	—
Cyproheptadine	T45.0X1	T45.0X2	T45.0X3	T45.0X4	T45.0X5	T45.0X6
Cyproterone	T38.6X1	T38.6X2	T38.6X3	T38.6X4	T38.6X5	T38.6X6
Cysteamine	T50.6X1	T50.6X2	T50.6X3	T50.6X4	T50.6X5	T50.6X6
Cytarabine	T45.1X1	T45.1X2	T45.1X3	T45.1X4	T45.1X5	T45.1X6
Cytisus						
laburnum	T62.2X1	T62.2X2	T62.2X3	T62.2X4	—	—
scoparius	T62.2X1	T62.2X2	T62.2X3	T62.2X4	—	—
Cytochrome C	T47.5X1	T47.5X2	T47.5X3	T47.5X4	T47.5X5	T47.5X6
Cytomel	T38.1X1	T38.1X2	T38.1X3	T38.1X4	T38.1X5	T38.1X6
Cytosine arabinoside	T45.1X1	T45.1X2	T45.1X3	T45.1X4	T45.1X5	T45.1X6
Cytoxan	T45.1X1	T45.1X2	T45.1X3	T45.1X4	T45.1X5	T45.1X6
Cytozyme	T45.7X1	T45.7X2	T45.7X3	T45.7X4	T45.7X5	T45.7X6
2,4-D	T60.3X1	T60.3X2	T60.3X3	T60.3X4	—	—
D						
Dacarbazine	T45.1X1	T45.1X2	T45.1X3	T45.1X4	T45.1X5	T45.1X6
Dactinomycin	T45.1X1	T45.1X2	T45.1X3	T45.1X4	T45.1X5	T45.1X6
DADPS	T37.1X1	T37.1X2	T37.1X3	T37.1X4	T37.1X5	T37.1X6
Dakin's solution	T49.0X1	T49.0X2	T49.0X3	T49.0X4	T49.0X5	T49.0X6
Dalapon(sodium)	T60.3X1	T60.3X2	T60.3X3	T60.3X4	—	—
Dalmane	T42.4X1	T42.4X2	T42.4X3	T42.4X4	T42.4X5	T42.4X6
Danazol	T38.6X1	T38.6X2	T38.6X3	T38.6X4	T38.6X5	T38.6X6
Danilone	T45.511	T45.512	T45.513	T45.514	T45.515	T45.516
Danthron	T47.2X1	T47.2X2	T47.2X3	T47.2X4	T47.2X5	T47.2X6
Dantrolene	T42.8X1	T42.8X2	T42.8X3	T42.8X4	T42.8X5	T42.8X6
Dantron	T47.2X1	T47.2X2	T47.2X3	T47.2X4	T47.2X5	T47.2X6
Daphne(gnidium) (mezereum)	T62.2X1	T62.2X2	T62.2X3	T62.2X4	—	—
berry	T62.1X1	T62.1X2	T62.1X3	T62.1X4	—	—
Dapsone	T37.1X1	T37.1X2	T37.1X3	T37.1X4	T37.1X5	T37.1X6
Daraprim	T37.2X1	T37.2X2	T37.2X3	T37.2X4	T37.2X5	T37.2X6
Darnel	T62.2X1	T62.2X2	T62.2X3	T62.2X4	—	—
Darvon	T39.8X1	T39.8X2	T39.8X3	T39.8X4	T39.8X5	T39.8X6

Substance	Poisoning, Accidental (unintentional)	Poisoning, Intentional self-harm	Poisoning, Assault	Poisoning, Undetermined	Adverse effect	Underdosing
Daunomycin	T45.1X1	T45.1X2	T45.1X3	T45.1X4	T45.1X5	T45.1X6
Daunorubicin	T45.1X1	T45.1X2	T45.1X3	T45.1X4	T45.1X5	T45.1X6
DBI	T38.3X1	T38.3X2	T38.3X3	T38.3X4	T38.3X5	T38.3X6
D-Con	T60.91	T60.92	T60.93	T60.94	—	—
insecticide	T60.2X1	T60.2X2	T60.2X3	T60.2X4	—	—
rodenticide	T60.4X1	T60.4X2	T60.4X3	T60.4X4	—	—
DDAVP	T38.891	T38.892	T38.893	T38.894	T38.895	T38.896
DDE(bis (chlorophenyl)-dichloroethylene)	T60.2X1	T60.2X2	T60.2X3	T60.2X4	—	—
DDS	T37.1X1	T37.1X2	T37.1X3	T37.1X4	T37.1X5	T37.1X6
DDT(dust)	T60.1X1	T60.1X2	T60.1X3	T60.1X4	—	—
Deadly nightshade—see also Belladonna	T62.2X1	T62.2X2	T62.2X3	T62.2X4	—	—
berry	T62.1X1	T62.1X2	T62.1X3	T62.1X4	—	—
Deamino-D-arginine vasopressin	T38.891	T38.892	T38.893	T38.894	T38.895	T38.896
Deanol(aceglumate)	T50.991	T50.992	T50.993	T50.994	T50.995	T50.996
Debrisoquine	T46.5X1	T46.5X2	T46.5X3	T46.5X4	T46.5X5	T46.5X6
Decaborane	T57.8X1	T57.8X2	T57.8X3	T57.8X4	—	—
fumes	T59.891	T59.892	T59.893	T59.894	—	—
Decadron	T38.0X1	T38.0X2	T38.0X3	T38.0X4	T38.0X5	T38.0X6
ENT agent	T49.6X1	T49.6X2	T49.6X3	T49.6X4	T49.6X5	T49.6X6
ophthalmic preparation	T49.5X1	T49.5X2	T49.5X3	T49.5X4	T49.5X5	T49.5X6
topical NEC	T49.0X1	T49.0X2	T49.0X3	T49.0X4	T49.0X5	T49.0X6
Decahydro-naphthalene	T52.8X1	T52.8X2	T52.8X3	T52.8X4	—	—
Decalin	T52.8X1	T52.8X2	T52.8X3	T52.8X4	—	—
Decametho-nium(bromide)	T48.1X1	T48.1X2	T48.1X3	T48.1X4	T48.1X5	T48.1X6
Decholin	T47.5X1	T47.5X2	T47.5X3	T47.5X4	T47.5X5	T47.5X6
Declomycin	T36.4X1	T36.4X2	T36.4X3	T36.4X4	T36.4X5	T36.4X6
Decongestant, nasal(mucosa)	T48.5X1	T48.5X2	T48.5X3	T48.5X4	T48.5X5	T48.5X6
combination	T48.5X1	T48.5X2	T48.5X3	T48.5X4	T48.5X5	T48.5X6
Deet	T60.8X1	T60.8X2	T60.8X3	T60.8X4	—	—
Deferoxamine	T45.8X1	T45.8X2	T45.8X3	T45.8X4	T45.8X5	T45.8X6
Deflazacort	T38.0X1	T38.0X2	T38.0X3	T38.0X4	T38.0X5	T38.0X6
Deglycyrrhizinized extract of licorice	T48.4X1	T48.4X2	T48.4X3	T48.4X4	T48.4X5	T48.4X6
Dehydrocholic acid	T47.5X1	T47.5X2	T47.5X3	T47.5X4	T47.5X5	T47.5X6
Dehydroemetine	T37.3X1	T37.3X2	T37.3X3	T37.3X4	T37.3X5	T37.3X6
Dekalin	T52.8X1	T52.8X2	T52.8X3	T52.8X4	—	—
Delalutin	T38.5X1	T38.5X2	T38.5X3	T38.5X4	T38.5X5	T38.5X6
Delorazepam	T42.4X1	T42.4X2	T42.4X3	T42.4X4	T42.4X5	T42.4X6
Delphinium	T62.2X1	T62.2X2	T62.2X3	T62.2X4	—	—
Deltamethrin	T60.1X1	T60.1X2	T60.1X3	T60.1X4	—	—
Deltasone	T38.0X1	T38.0X2	T38.0X3	T38.0X4	T38.0X5	T38.0X6
Deltra	T38.0X1	T38.0X2	T38.0X3	T38.0X4	T38.0X5	T38.0X6
Delvinal	T42.3X1	T42.3X2	T42.3X3	T42.3X4	T42.3X5	T42.3X6
Demecarium (bromide)	T49.5X1	T49.5X2	T49.5X3	T49.5X4	T49.5X5	T49.5X6
Demeclocycline	T36.4X1	T36.4X2	T36.4X3	T36.4X4	T36.4X5	T36.4X6
Demecolcine	T45.1X1	T45.1X2	T45.1X3	T45.1X4	T45.1X5	T45.1X6
Demegestone	T38.5X1	T38.5X2	T38.5X3	T38.5X4	T38.5X5	T38.5X6

Substance	Poisoning, Accidental (unintentional)	Poisoning, Intentional self-harm	Poisoning, Assault	Poisoning, Undetermined	Adverse effect	Underdosing
Demelanizing agents	T49.8X1	T49.8X2	T49.8X3	T49.8X4	T49.8X5	T49.8
Demephion -O and -S	T60.0X1	T60.0X2	T60.0X3	T60.0X4	—	—
Demerol	T40.2X1	T40.2X2	T40.2X3	T40.2X4	T40.2X5	T40.2
Demethylchlor-tetracycline	T36.4X1	T36.4X2	T36.4X3	T36.4X4	T36.4X5	T36.4
Demethyltetracycline	T36.4X1	T36.4X2	T36.4X3	T36.4X4	T36.4X5	T36.4
Demeton -O and -S	T60.0X1	T60.0X2	T60.0X3	T60.0X4	—	—
Demulcent(external)	T49.3X1	T49.3X2	T49.3X3	T49.3X4	T49.3X5	T49.3
specified NEC	T49.3X1	T49.3X2	T49.3X3	T49.3X4	T49.3X5	T49.3
Demulen	T38.4X1	T38.4X2	T38.4X3	T38.4X4	T38.4X5	T38.4
Denatured alcohol	T51.0X1	T51.0X2	T51.0X3	T51.0X4	—	—
Dendrid	T49.5X1	T49.5X2	T49.5X3	T49.5X4	T49.5X5	T49.5
Dental drug, topical application NEC	T49.7X1	T49.7X2	T49.7X3	T49.7X4	T49.7X5	T49.7
Dentifrice	T49.7X1	T49.7X2	T49.7X3	T49.7X4	T49.7X5	T49.7
Deodorant spray(feminine hygiene)	T49.8X1	T49.8X2	T49.8X3	T49.8X4	T49.8X5	T49.8
Deoxycortone	T50.0X1	T50.0X2	T50.0X3	T50.0X4	T50.0X5	T50.0
2-Deoxy-5-fluorouridine	T45.1X1	T45.1X2	T45.1X3	T45.1X4	T45.1X5	T45.1
5-Deoxy-5-fluorouridine	T45.1X1	T45.1X2	T45.1X3	T45.1X4	T45.1X5	T45.1
Deoxyribonuclease (pancreatic)	T45.3X1	T45.3X2	T45.3X3	T45.3X4	T45.3X5	T45.3
Depilatory	T49.4X1	T49.4X2	T49.4X3	T49.4X4	T49.4X5	T49.4
Deprenalin	T42.8X1	T42.8X2	T42.8X3	T42.8X4	T42.8X5	T42.8
Deprenyl	T42.8X1	T42.8X2	T42.8X3	T42.8X4	T42.8X5	T42.8
Depressant, appetite	T50.5X1	T50.5X2	T50.5X3	T50.5X4	T50.5X5	T50.5
Depressant						
appetite(central)	T50.5X1	T50.5X2	T50.5X3	T50.5X4	T50.5X5	T50.5
cardiac	T46.2X1	T46.2X2	T46.2X3	T46.2X4	T46.2X5	T46.2
central nervous system(anesthetic)—see also Central nervous system, depressants	T42.71	T42.72	T42.73	T42.74	T42.75	T42.7
general anesthetic	T41.201	T41.202	T41.203	T41.204	T41.205	T41.2
muscle tone	T42.8X1	T42.8X2	T42.8X3	T42.8X4	T42.8X5	T42.8
muscle tone, central	T42.8X1	T42.8X2	T42.8X3	T42.8X4	T42.8X5	T42.8
psychotherapeutic	T43.501	T43.502	T43.503	T43.504	T43.505	T43.5
Deptropine	T45.0X1	T45.0X2	T45.0X3	T45.0X4	T45.0X5	T45.0
Dequalinium (chloride)	T49.0X1	T49.0X2	T49.0X3	T49.0X4	T49.0X5	T49.0
Derris root	T60.2X1	T60.2X2	T60.2X3	T60.2X4	—	—
Deserpidine	T46.5X1	T46.5X2	T46.5X3	T46.5X4	T46.5X5	T46.5
Desferrioxamine	T45.8X1	T45.8X2	T45.8X3	T45.8X4	T45.8X5	T45.8
Desipramine	T43.011	T43.012	T43.013	T43.014	T43.015	T43.0
Deslanoside	T46.0X1	T46.0X2	T46.0X3	T46.0X4	T46.0X5	T46.0
Desloughing agent	T49.4X1	T49.4X2	T49.4X3	T49.4X4	T49.4X5	T49.4
Desmethy-limipramine	T43.011	T43.012	T43.013	T43.014	T43.015	T43.0
Desmopressin	T38.891	T38.892	T38.893	T38.894	T38.895	T38.8
Desocodeine	T40.2X1	T40.2X2	T40.2X3	T40.2X4	T40.2X5	T40.2
Desogestrel	T38.5X1	T38.5X2	T38.5X3	T38.5X4	T38.5X5	T38.5
Desomorphine	T40.2X1	T40.2X2	T40.2X3	T40.2X4	—	—
Desonide	T49.0X1	T49.0X2	T49.0X3	T49.0X4	T49.0X5	T49.0
Desoximetasone	T49.0X1	T49.0X2	T49.0X3	T49.0X4	T49.0X5	T49.0
Desoxycorticosteroid	T50.0X1	T50.0X2	T50.0X3	T50.0X4	T50.0X5	T50.0
Desoxycortone	T50.0X1	T50.0X2	T50.0X3	T50.0X4	T50.0X5	T50.0

Substance	Poisoning, Accidental (unintentional)	Poisoning, Intentional self-harm	Poisoning, Assault	Poisoning, Undetermined	Adverse effect	Underdosing
oxyephedrine	T43.621	T43.622	T43.623	T43.624	T43.625	T43.626
axtran	T46.6X1	T46.6X2	T46.6X3	T46.6X4	T46.6X5	T46.6X6
ergent	T49.2X1	T49.2X2	T49.2X3	T49.2X4	T49.2X5	T49.2X6
xternal medication	T49.2X1	T49.2X2	T49.2X3	T49.2X4	T49.2X5	T49.2X6
cal	T49.2X1	T49.2X2	T49.2X3	T49.2X4	T49.2X5	T49.2X6
edicinal	T49.2X1	T49.2X2	T49.2X3	T49.2X4	T49.2X5	T49.2X6
onmedicinal	T55.1X1	T55.1X2	T55.1X3	T55.1X4	—	—
ecified NEC	T55.1X1	T55.1X2	T55.1X3	T55.1X4	—	—
errent, alcohol	T50.6X1	T50.6X2	T50.6X3	T50.6X4	T50.6X5	T50.6X6
oxifying agent	T50.6X1	T50.6X2	T50.6X3	T50.6X4	T50.6X5	T50.6X6
rothyronine	T38.1X1	T38.1X2	T38.1X3	T38.1X4	T38.1X5	T38.1X6
tol(external medication)	T49.0X1	T49.0X2	T49.0X3	T49.0X4	T49.0X5	T49.0X6
amethasone	T38.0X1	T38.0X2	T38.0X3	T38.0X4	T38.0X5	T38.0X6
NT agent	T49.6X1	T49.6X2	T49.6X3	T49.6X4	T49.6X5	T49.6X6
phthalmic preparation	T49.5X1	T49.5X2	T49.5X3	T49.5X4	T49.5X5	T49.5X6
opical NEC	T49.0X1	T49.0X2	T49.0X3	T49.0X4	T49.0X5	T49.0X6
amfetamine	T43.621	T43.622	T43.623	T43.624	T43.625	T43.626
amphetamine	T43.621	T43.622	T43.623	T43.624	T43.625	T43.626
brom-pheniramine	T45.0X1	T45.0X2	T45.0X3	T45.0X4	T45.0X5	T45.0X6
chlorpheniramine	T45.0X1	T45.0X2	T45.0X3	T45.0X4	T45.0X5	T45.0X6
edrine	T43.621	T43.622	T43.623	T43.624	T43.625	T43.626
etimide	T44.3X1	T44.3X2	T44.3X3	T44.3X4	T44.3X5	T44.3X6
fenfluramine	T50.5X1	T50.5X2	T50.5X3	T50.5X4	T50.5X5	T50.5X6
panthenol	T45.2X1	T45.2X2	T45.2X3	T45.2X4	T45.2X5	T45.2X6
tran(40) (70) (150)	T45.8X1	T45.8X2	T45.8X3	T45.8X4	T45.8X5	T45.8X6
triferron	T45.4X1	T45.4X2	T45.4X3	T45.4X4	T45.4X5	T45.4X6
tro calcium tothenate	T45.2X1	T45.2X2	T45.2X3	T45.2X4	T45.2X5	T45.2X6
tro pantothenyl alcohol	T45.2X1	T45.2X2	T45.2X3	T45.2X4	T45.2X5	T45.2X6
troamphetamine	T43.621	T43.622	T43.623	T43.624	T43.625	T43.626
tromethorphan	T48.3X1	T48.3X2	T48.3X3	T48.3X4	T48.3X5	T48.3X6
tromoramide	T40.4X1	T40.4X2	T40.4X3	T40.4X4	—	—
opical	T49.8X1	T49.8X2	T49.8X3	T49.8X4	T49.8X5	T49.8X6
tropropoxyphene	T40.4X1	T40.4X2	T40.4X3	T40.4X4	T40.4X5	T40.4X6
trorphan	T40.2X1	T40.2X2	T40.2X3	T40.2X4	T40.2X5	T40.2X6
trose	T50.3X1	T50.3X2	T50.3X3	T50.3X4	T50.3X5	T50.3X6
oncentrated solution, travenous	T46.8X1	T46.8X2	T46.8X3	T46.8X4	T46.8X5	T46.8X6
trothyroxin	T38.1X1	T38.1X2	T38.1X3	T38.1X4	T38.1X5	T38.1X6
trothyroxine sodium	T38.1X1	T38.1X2	T38.1X3	T38.1X4	T38.1X5	T38.1X6
P	T44.0X1	T44.0X2	T44.0X3	T44.0X4	T44.0X5	T44.0X6
E	T37.3X1	T37.3X2	T37.3X3	T37.3X4	T37.3X5	T37.3X6
5	T46.5X1	T46.5X2	T46.5X3	T46.5X4	T46.5X5	T46.5X6
binese	T38.3X1	T38.3X2	T38.3X3	T38.3X4	T38.3X5	T38.3X6
cetone alcohol	T52.4X1	T52.4X2	T52.4X3	T52.4X4	—	—
cetyl monoxime	T50.991	T50.992	T50.993	T50.994	—	—
cetylmorphine	T40.1X1	T40.1X2	T40.1X3	T40.1X4	—	—
chylon plaster	T49.4X1	T49.4X2	T49.4X3	T49.4X4	T49.4X5	T49.4X6
ethylst-ilboestrolum	T38.5X1	T38.5X2	T38.5X3	T38.5X4	T38.5X5	T38.5X6
gnostic agent NEC	T50.8X1	T50.8X2	T50.8X3	T50.8X4	T50.8X5	T50.8X6
l(soap)	T49.2X1	T49.2X2	T49.2X3	T49.2X4	T49.2X5	T49.2X6
edative	T42.3X1	T42.3X2	T42.3X3	T42.3X4	T42.3X5	T42.3X6

Substance	Poisoning, Accidental (unintentional)	Poisoning, Intentional self-harm	Poisoning, Assault	Poisoning, Undetermined	Adverse effect	Underdosing
Dialkyl carbonate	T52.91	T52.92	T52.93	T52.94	—	—
Diallylbarbituric acid	T42.3X1	T42.3X2	T42.3X3	T42.3X4	T42.3X5	T42.3X6
Diallymal	T42.3X1	T42.3X2	T42.3X3	T42.3X4	T42.3X5	T42.3X6
Dialysis solution (intraperitoneal)	T50.3X1	T50.3X2	T50.3X3	T50.3X4	T50.3X5	T50.3X6
Diaminodi-phenylsulfone	T37.1X1	T37.1X2	T37.1X3	T37.1X4	T37.1X5	T37.1X6
Diamorphine	T40.1X1	T40.1X2	T40.1X3	T40.1X4	—	—
Diamox	T50.2X1	T50.2X2	T50.2X3	T50.2X4	T50.2X5	T50.2X6
Diamthazole	T49.0X1	T49.0X2	T49.0X3	T49.0X4	T49.0X5	T49.0X6
Dianthone	T47.2X1	T47.2X2	T47.2X3	T47.2X4	T47.2X5	T47.2X6
Diaphenylsulfone	T37.0X1	T37.0X2	T37.0X3	T37.0X4	T37.0X5	T37.0X6
Diasone(sodium)	T37.1X1	T37.1X2	T37.1X3	T37.1X4	T37.1X5	T37.1X6
Diastase	T47.5X1	T47.5X2	T47.5X3	T47.5X4	T47.5X5	T47.5X6
Diatrizoate	T50.8X1	T50.8X2	T50.8X3	T50.8X4	T50.8X5	T50.8X6
Diazepam	T42.4X1	T42.4X2	T42.4X3	T42.4X4	T42.4X5	T42.4X6
Diazinon	T60.0X1	T60.0X2	T60.0X3	T60.0X4	—	—
Diazomethane(gas)	T59.891	T59.892	T59.893	T59.894	—	—
Diazoxide	T46.5X1	T46.5X2	T46.5X3	T46.5X4	T46.5X5	T46.5X6
Dibekacin	T36.5X1	T36.5X2	T36.5X3	T36.5X4	T36.5X5	T36.5X6
Dibenamine	T44.6X1	T44.6X2	T44.6X3	T44.6X4	T44.6X5	T44.6X6
Dibenzepin	T43.011	T43.012	T43.013	T43.014	T43.015	T43.016
Dibenzheptropine	T45.0X1	T45.0X2	T45.0X3	T45.0X4	T45.0X5	T45.0X6
Dibenzyline	T44.6X1	T44.6X2	T44.6X3	T44.6X4	T44.6X5	T44.6X6
Diborane(gas)	T59.891	T59.892	T59.893	T59.894	—	—
Dibromoch-loropropane	T60.8X1	T60.8X2	T60.8X3	T60.8X4	—	—
Dibromodulcitol	T45.1X1	T45.1X2	T45.1X3	T45.1X4	T45.1X5	T45.1X6
Dibromoethane	T53.6X1	T53.6X2	T53.6X3	T53.6X4	—	—
Dibromomannitol	T45.1X1	T45.1X2	T45.1X3	T45.1X4	T45.1X5	T45.1X6
Dibromopropamidine isethionate	T49.0X1	T49.0X2	T49.0X3	T49.0X4	T49.0X5	T49.0X6
Dibrompropamidine	T49.0X1	T49.0X2	T49.0X3	T49.0X4	T49.0X5	T49.0X6
Dibucaine	T41.3X1	T41.3X2	T41.3X3	T41.3X4	T41.3X5	T41.3X6
topical(surface)	T41.3X1	T41.3X2	T41.3X3	T41.3X4	T41.3X5	T41.3X6
Dibunate sodium	T48.3X1	T48.3X2	T48.3X3	T48.3X4	T48.3X5	T48.3X6
Dibutoline sulfate	T44.3X1	T44.3X2	T44.3X3	T44.3X4	T44.3X5	T44.3X6
Dicamba	T60.3X1	T60.3X2	T60.3X3	T60.3X4	—	—
Dicapthon	T60.0X1	T60.0X2	T60.0X3	T60.0X4	—	—
Dichlobenil	T60.3X1	T60.3X2	T60.3X3	T60.3X4	—	—
Dichlone	T60.3X1	T60.3X2	T60.3X3	T60.3X4	—	—
Dichloralphenozone	T42.6X1	T42.6X2	T42.6X3	T42.6X4	T42.6X5	T42.6X6
Dichlorbenzidine	T65.3X1	T65.3X2	T65.3X3	T65.3X4	—	—
Dichlorhydrin	T52.8X1	T52.8X2	T52.8X3	T52.8X4	—	—
Dichlorhydroxy-quinoline	T37.8X1	T37.8X2	T37.8X3	T37.8X4	T37.8X5	T37.8X6
Dichlorobenzene	T53.7X1	T53.7X2	T53.7X3	T53.7X4	—	—
Dichlorobenzyl alcohol	T49.6X1	T49.6X2	T49.6X3	T49.6X4	T49.6X5	T49.6X6
Dichlorodifluoro-methane	T53.5X1	T53.5X2	T53.5X3	T53.5X4	—	—
Dichloroethane	T52.8X1	T52.8X2	T52.8X3	T52.8X4	—	—
Sym-Dichloroethyl ether	T53.6X1	T53.6X2	T53.6X3	T53.6X4	—	—
Dichloroethyl sulfide, not in war	T59.891	T59.892	T59.893	T59.894	—	—

Substance	Poisoning, Accidental (unintentional)	Poisoning, Intentional self-harm	Poisoning, Assault	Poisoning, Undetermined	Adverse effect	Underdosing
Dichloroethylene	T53.6X1	T53.6X2	T53.6X3	T53.6X4	—	—
Dichloroformoxine, not in war	T59.891	T59.892	T59.893	T59.894	—	—
Dichlorohydrin, alpha-dichlorohydrin	T52.8X1	T52.8X2	T52.8X3	T52.8X4	—	—
Dichloromethane (solvent)	T53.4X1	T53.4X2	T53.4X3	T53.4X4	—	—
vapor	T53.4X1	T53.4X2	T53.4X3	T53.4X4	—	—
Dichloronaphtho-quinone	T60.3X1	T60.3X2	T60.3X3	T60.3X4	—	—
Dichlorophen	T37.4X1	T37.4X2	T37.4X3	T37.4X4	T37.4X5	T37.4X6
2,4-Dichlorophenoxy-acetic acid	T60.3X1	T60.3X2	T60.3X3	T60.3X4	—	—
Dichloropropene	T60.3X1	T60.3X2	T60.3X3	T60.3X4	—	—
Dichloropropionic acid	T60.3X1	T60.3X2	T60.3X3	T60.3X4	—	—
Dichlorphenamide	T50.2X1	T50.2X2	T50.2X3	T50.2X4	T50.2X5	T50.2X6
Dichlorvos	T60.0X1	T60.0X2	T60.0X3	T60.0X4	—	—
Diclofenac	T39.391	T39.392	T39.393	T39.394	T39.395	T39.396
Diclofenamide	T50.2X1	T50.2X2	T50.2X3	T50.2X4	T50.2X5	T50.2X6
Diclofensine	T43.291	T43.292	T43.293	T43.294	T43.295	T43.296
Diclonixine	T39.8X1	T39.8X2	T39.8X3	T39.8X4	T39.8X5	T39.8X6
Dicloxacillin	T36.0X1	T36.0X2	T36.0X3	T36.0X4	T36.0X5	T36.0X6
Dicophane	T49.0X1	T49.0X2	T49.0X3	T49.0X4	T49.0X5	T49.0X6
Dicoumarol, dicoumarin, dicumarol	T45.511	T45.512	T45.513	T45.514	T45.515	T45.516
Dicrotophos	T60.0X1	T60.0X2	T60.0X3	T60.0X4	—	—
Dicyanogen(gas)	T65.0X1	T65.0X2	T65.0X3	T65.0X4	—	—
Dicyclomine	T44.3X1	T44.3X2	T44.3X3	T44.3X4	T44.3X5	T44.3X6
Dicycloverine	T44.3X1	T44.3X2	T44.3X3	T44.3X4	T44.3X5	T44.3X6
Dideoxycytidine	T37.5X1	T37.5X2	T37.5X3	T37.5X4	T37.5X5	T37.5X6
Dideoxyinosine	T37.5X1	T37.5X2	T37.5X3	T37.5X4	T37.5X5	T37.5X6
Dieldrin(vapor)	T60.1X1	T60.1X2	T60.1X3	T60.1X4	—	—
Diemal	T42.3X1	T42.3X2	T42.3X3	T42.3X4	T42.3X5	T42.3X6
Dienestrol	T38.5X1	T38.5X2	T38.5X3	T38.5X4	T38.5X5	T38.5X6
Dienoestrol	T38.5X1	T38.5X2	T38.5X3	T38.5X4	T38.5X5	T38.5X6
Dietetic drug NEC	T50.901	T50.902	T50.903	T50.904	T50.905	T50.906
Diethazine	T42.8X1	T42.8X2	T42.8X3	T42.8X4	T42.8X5	T42.8X6
Diethyl						
barbituric acid	T42.3X1	T42.3X2	T42.3X3	T42.3X4	T42.3X5	T42.3X6
carbamazine	T37.4X1	T37.4X2	T37.4X3	T37.4X4	T37.4X5	T37.4X6
carbinol	T51.3X1	T51.3X2	T51.3X3	T51.3X4	—	—
carbonate	T52.8X1	T52.8X2	T52.8X3	T52.8X4	—	—
ether(vapor)—see also ether	T41.0X1	T41.0X2	T41.0X3	T41.0X4	T41.0X5	T41.0X6
oxide	T52.8X1	T52.8X2	T52.8X3	T52.8X4	—	—
propion	T50.5X1	T50.5X2	T50.5X3	T50.5X4	T50.5X5	T50.5X6
stilbestrol	T38.5X1	T38.5X2	T38.5X3	T38.5X4	T38.5X5	T38.5X6
toluamide (nonmedicinal)	T60.8X1	T60.8X2	T60.8X3	T60.8X4	—	—
medicinal	T49.3X1	T49.3X2	T49.3X3	T49.3X4	T49.3X5	T49.3X6
Diethylcarbamazine	T37.4X1	T37.4X2	T37.4X3	T37.4X4	T37.4X5	T37.4X6
Diethylene						
dioxide	T52.8X1	T52.8X2	T52.8X3	T52.8X4	—	—
glycol(monoacetate) (monobutyl ether) (monoethyl ether)	T52.3X1	T52.3X2	T52.3X3	T52.3X4	—	—

Substance	Poisoning, Accidental (unintentional)	Poisoning, Intentional self-harm	Poisoning, Assault	Poisoning, Undetermined	Adverse effect	Underdosing
Diethylhexy-lphthalate	T65.891	T65.892	T65.893	T65.894	—	—
Diethylpropion	T50.5X1	T50.5X2	T50.5X3	T50.5X4	T50.5X5	T50.5
Diethylstilbestrol	T38.5X1	T38.5X2	T38.5X3	T38.5X4	T38.5X5	T38.5
Diethylstilboestrol	T38.5X1	T38.5X2	T38.5X3	T38.5X4	T38.5X5	T38.5
Diethylsulfone-diethylmethane	T42.6X1	T42.6X2	T42.6X3	T42.6X4	T42.6X5	T42.6
Diethyltoluamide	T49.0X1	T49.0X2	T49.0X3	T49.0X4	T49.0X5	T49.0
Diethyltryptamine (DET)	T40.991	T40.992	T40.993	T40.994	—	—
Difebarbamate	T42.3X1	T42.3X2	T42.3X3	T42.3X4	T42.3X5	T42.3
Difencloxazine	T40.2X1	T40.2X2	T40.2X3	T40.2X4	T40.2X5	T40.2
Difenidol	T45.0X1	T45.0X2	T45.0X3	T45.0X4	T45.0X5	T45.0
Difenoxin	T47.6X1	T47.6X2	T47.6X3	T47.6X4	T47.6X5	T47.6
Difetarsone	T37.3X1	T37.3X2	T37.3X3	T37.3X4	T37.3X5	T37.3
Diffusin	T45.3X1	T45.3X2	T45.3X3	T45.3X4	T45.3X5	T45.3
Diflorasone	T49.0X1	T49.0X2	T49.0X3	T49.0X4	T49.0X5	T49.0
Diflos	T44.0X1	T44.0X2	T44.0X3	T44.0X4	T44.0X5	T44.0
Diflubenzuron	T60.1X1	T60.1X2	T60.1X3	T60.1X4	—	—
Diflucortolone	T49.0X1	T49.0X2	T49.0X3	T49.0X4	T49.0X5	T49.0
Diflunisal	T39.091	T39.092	T39.093	T39.094	T39.095	T39.0
Difluoromethyldopa	T42.8X1	T42.8X2	T42.8X3	T42.8X4	T42.8X5	T42.8
Difluorophate	T44.0X1	T44.0X2	T44.0X3	T44.0X4	T44.0X5	T44.0
Digestant NEC	T47.5X1	T47.5X2	T47.5X3	T47.5X4	T47.5X5	T47.5
Digitalin(e)	T46.0X1	T46.0X2	T46.0X3	T46.0X4	T46.0X5	T46.0
Digitalis(leaf)(glycoside)	T46.0X1	T46.0X2	T46.0X3	T46.0X4	T46.0X5	T46.0
lanata	T46.0X1	T46.0X2	T46.0X3	T46.0X4	T46.0X5	T46.0
purpurea	T46.0X1	T46.0X2	T46.0X3	T46.0X4	T46.0X5	T46.0
Digitoxin	T46.0X1	T46.0X2	T46.0X3	T46.0X4	T46.0X5	T46.0
Digitoxose	T46.0X1	T46.0X2	T46.0X3	T46.0X4	T46.0X5	T46.0
Digoxin	T46.0X1	T46.0X2	T46.0X3	T46.0X4	T46.0X5	T46.0
Digoxine	T46.0X1	T46.0X2	T46.0X3	T46.0X4	T46.0X5	T46.0
Dihydralazine	T46.5X1	T46.5X2	T46.5X3	T46.5X4	T46.5X5	T46.5
Dihydrazine	T46.5X1	T46.5X2	T46.5X3	T46.5X4	T46.5X5	T46.5
Dihydrocodeine	T40.2X1	T40.2X2	T40.2X3	T40.2X4	T40.2X5	T40.2
Dihydrocodeinone	T40.2X1	T40.2X2	T40.2X3	T40.2X4	T40.2X5	T40.2
Dihydroergocornine	T46.7X1	T46.7X2	T46.7X3	T46.7X4	T46.7X5	T46.7
Dihydroergocristine (mesilate)	T46.7X1	T46.7X2	T46.7X3	T46.7X4	T46.7X5	T46.7
Dihydroergokryptine	T46.7X1	T46.7X2	T46.7X3	T46.7X4	T46.7X5	T46.7
Dihydroergotamine	T46.5X1	T46.5X2	T46.5X3	T46.5X4	T46.5X5	T46.5
Dihydroergotoxine	T46.7X1	T46.7X2	T46.7X3	T46.7X4	T46.7X5	T46.7
mesilate	T46.7X1	T46.7X2	T46.7X3	T46.7X4	T46.7X5	T46.7
Dihydrohydroxy-codeinone	T40.2X1	T40.2X2	T40.2X3	T40.2X4	T40.2X5	T40.2
Dihydrohydroxy-morphinone	T40.2X1	T40.2X2	T40.2X3	T40.2X4	T40.2X5	T40.2
Dihydroisocodeine	T40.2X1	T40.2X2	T40.2X3	T40.2X4	T40.2X5	T40.2
Dihydromorphine	T40.2X1	T40.2X2	T40.2X3	T40.2X4	—	—
Dihydromorphinone	T40.2X1	T40.2X2	T40.2X3	T40.2X4	T40.2X5	T40.2
Dihydrostreptomycin	T36.5X1	T36.5X2	T36.5X3	T36.5X4	T36.5X5	T36.5
Dihydrotachysterol	T45.2X1	T45.2X2	T45.2X3	T45.2X4	T45.2X5	T45.2
Dihydroxyaluminum aminoacetate	T47.1X1	T47.1X2	T47.1X3	T47.1X4	T47.1X5	T47.1
Dihydroxyaluminum sodium carbonate	T47.1X1	T47.1X2	T47.1X3	T47.1X4	T47.1X5	T47.1

Substance	Poisoning, Accidental (unintentional)	Poisoning, Intentional self-harm	Poisoning, Assault	Poisoning, Undetermined	Adverse effect	Underdosing
ydroxyanthra-quinone	T47.2X1	T47.2X2	T47.2X3	T47.2X4	T47.2X5	T47.2X6
ydroxycodeinone	T40.2X1	T40.2X2	T40.2X3	T40.2X4	T40.2X5	T40.2X6
ydroxypropyl phylline	T50.2X1	T50.2X2	T50.2X3	T50.2X4	T50.2X5	T50.2X6
odohydroxyquin	T37.8X1	T37.8X2	T37.8X3	T37.8X4	T37.8X5	T37.8X6
pical	T49.0X1	T49.0X2	T49.0X3	T49.0X4	T49.0X5	T49.0X6
odo-hydroxyquinoline	T37.8X1	T37.8X2	T37.8X3	T37.8X4	T37.8X5	T37.8X6
odotyrosine	T38.2X1	T38.2X2	T38.2X3	T38.2X4	T38.2X5	T38.2X6
sopromine	T44.3X1	T44.3X2	T44.3X3	T44.3X4	T44.3X5	T44.3X6
sopropylamine	T46.3X1	T46.3X2	T46.3X3	T46.3X4	T46.3X5	T46.3X6
sopropyl-fluorophos-nate	T44.0X1	T44.0X2	T44.0X3	T44.0X4	T44.0X5	T44.0X6
antin	T42.0X1	T42.0X2	T42.0X3	T42.0X4	T42.0X5	T42.0X6
audid	T40.2X1	T40.2X2	T40.2X3	T40.2X4	T40.2X5	T40.2X6
azep	T46.3X1	T46.3X2	T46.3X3	T46.3X4	T46.3X5	T46.3X6
l	T47.5X1	T47.5X2	T47.5X3	T47.5X4	T47.5X5	T47.5X6
oxanide	T37.3X1	T37.3X2	T37.3X3	T37.3X4	T37.3X5	T37.3X6
tiazem	T46.1X1	T46.1X2	T46.1X3	T46.1X4	T46.1X5	T46.1X6
nazole	T49.0X1	T49.0X2	T49.0X3	T49.0X4	T49.0X5	T49.0X6
nefline	T50.7X1	T50.7X2	T50.7X3	T50.7X4	T50.7X5	T50.7X6
nefox	T60.0X1	T60.0X2	T60.0X3	T60.0X4	—	—
memorfan	T48.3X1	T48.3X2	T48.3X3	T48.3X4	T48.3X5	T48.3X6
menhydrinate	T45.0X1	T45.0X2	T45.0X3	T45.0X4	T45.0X5	T45.0X6
mercaprol(British anti-visite)	T45.8X1	T45.8X2	T45.8X3	T45.8X4	T45.8X5	T45.8X6
mercaptopropanol	T45.8X1	T45.8X2	T45.8X3	T45.8X4	T45.8X5	T45.8X6
mestrol	T38.5X1	T38.5X2	T38.5X3	T38.5X4	T38.5X5	T38.5X6
metane	T45.0X1	T45.0X2	T45.0X3	T45.0X4	T45.0X5	T45.0X6
methicone	T47.1X1	T47.1X2	T47.1X3	T47.1X4	T47.1X5	T47.1X6
methindene	T45.0X1	T45.0X2	T45.0X3	T45.0X4	T45.0X5	T45.0X6
methisoquin	T49.1X1	T49.1X2	T49.1X3	T49.1X4	T49.1X5	T49.1X6
methisterone	T38.5X1	T38.5X2	T38.5X3	T38.5X4	T38.5X5	T38.5X6
methoate	T60.0X1	T60.0X2	T60.0X3	T60.0X4	—	—
methocaine	T41.3X1	T41.3X2	T41.3X3	T41.3X4	T41.3X5	T41.3X6
methoxanate	T48.3X1	T48.3X2	T48.3X3	T48.3X4	T48.3X5	T48.3X6
methyl						
arsine, arsinic acid	T57.0X1	T57.0X2	T57.0X3	T57.0X4	—	—
carbinol	T51.2X1	T51.2X2	T51.2X3	T51.2X4	—	—
carbonate	T52.8X1	T52.8X2	T52.8X3	T52.8X4	—	—
diguanide	T38.3X1	T38.3X2	T38.3X3	T38.3X4	T38.3X5	T38.3X6
ketone	T52.4X1	T52.4X2	T52.4X3	T52.4X4	—	—
vapor	T52.4X1	T52.4X2	T52.4X3	T52.4X4	—	—
meperidine	T40.2X1	T40.2X2	T40.2X3	T40.2X4	T40.2X5	T40.2X6
parathion	T60.0X1	T60.0X2	T60.0X3	T60.0X4	—	—
phthlate	T49.3X1	T49.3X2	T49.3X3	T49.3X4	T49.3X5	T49.3X6
polysiloxane	T47.8X1	T47.8X2	T47.8X3	T47.8X4	T47.8X5	T47.8X6
sulfate(fumes)	T59.891	T59.892	T59.893	T59.894	—	—
liquid	T65.891	T65.892	T65.893	T65.894	—	—
sulfoxide (nonmedicinal)	T52.8X1	T52.8X2	T52.8X3	T52.8X4	—	—
medicinal	T49.4X1	T49.4X2	T49.4X3	T49.4X4	T49.4X5	T49.4X6
tryptamine	T40.991	T40.992	T40.993	T40.994	—	—
tubocurarine	T48.1X1	T48.1X2	T48.1X3	T48.1X4	T48.1X5	T48.1X6

Substance	Poisoning, Accidental (unintentional)	Poisoning, Intentional self-harm	Poisoning, Assault	Poisoning, Undetermined	Adverse effect	Underdosing
Dimethylamine sulfate	T49.4X1	T49.4X2	T49.4X3	T49.4X4	T49.4X5	T49.4X6
Dimethylformamide	T52.8X1	T52.8X2	T52.8X3	T52.8X4	—	—
Dimethyltubocurari-nium chloride	T48.1X1	T48.1X2	T48.1X3	T48.1X4	T48.1X5	T48.1X6
Dimeticone	T47.1X1	T47.1X2	T47.1X3	T47.1X4	T47.1X5	T47.1X6
Dimetilan	T60.0X1	T60.0X2	T60.0X3	T60.0X4	—	—
Dimetindene	T45.0X1	T45.0X2	T45.0X3	T45.0X4	T45.0X5	T45.0X6
Dimetotiazine	T43.3X1	T43.3X2	T43.3X3	T43.3X4	T43.3X5	T43.3X6
Dimorpholamine	T50.7X1	T50.7X2	T50.7X3	T50.7X4	T50.7X5	T50.7X6
Dimoxyline	T46.3X1	T46.3X2	T46.3X3	T46.3X4	T46.3X5	T46.3X6
Dinitrobenzene	T65.3X1	T65.3X2	T65.3X3	T65.3X4	—	—
vapor	T59.891	T59.892	T59.893	T59.894	—	—
Dinitrobenzol	T65.3X1	T65.3X2	T65.3X3	T65.3X4	—	—
vapor	T59.891	T59.892	T59.893	T59.894	—	—
Dinitrobutylphenol	T65.3X1	T65.3X2	T65.3X3	T65.3X4	—	—
Dinitro(-ortho-)cresol (pesticide) (spray)	T65.3X1	T65.3X2	T65.3X3	T65.3X4	—	—
Dinitro-cyclohexylphenol	T65.3X1	T65.3X2	T65.3X3	T65.3X4	—	—
Dinitrophenol	T65.3X1	T65.3X2	T65.3X3	T65.3X4	—	—
Dinoprost	T48.0X1	T48.0X2	T48.0X3	T48.0X4	T48.0X5	T48.0X6
Dinoprostone	T48.0X1	T48.0X2	T48.0X3	T48.0X4	T48.0X5	T48.0X6
Dinoseb	T60.3X1	T60.3X2	T60.3X3	T60.3X4	—	—
Dioctyl sulfosuccinate (calcium) (sodium)	T47.4X1	T47.4X2	T47.4X3	T47.4X4	T47.4X5	T47.4X6
Diodone	T50.8X1	T50.8X2	T50.8X3	T50.8X4	T50.8X5	T50.8X6
Diodoquin	T37.8X1	T37.8X2	T37.8X3	T37.8X4	T37.8X5	T37.8X6
Dionin	T40.2X1	T40.2X2	T40.2X3	T40.2X4	T40.2X5	T40.2X6
Diosmin	T46.991	T46.992	T46.993	T46.994	T46.995	T46.996
Dioxane	T52.8X1	T52.8X2	T52.8X3	T52.8X4	—	—
Dioxathion	T60.0X1	T60.0X2	T60.0X3	T60.0X4	—	—
Dioxin	T53.7X1	T53.7X2	T53.7X3	T53.7X4	—	—
Dioxopromethazine	T43.3X1	T43.3X2	T43.3X3	T43.3X4	T43.3X5	T43.3X6
Dioxyline	T46.3X1	T46.3X2	T46.3X3	T46.3X4	T46.3X5	T46.3X6
Dipentene	T52.8X1	T52.8X2	T52.8X3	T52.8X4	—	—
Diperodon	T41.3X1	T41.3X2	T41.3X3	T41.3X4	T41.3X5	T41.3X6
Diphacinone	T60.4X1	T60.4X2	T60.4X3	T60.4X4	—	—
Diphemanil	T44.3X1	T44.3X2	T44.3X3	T44.3X4	T44.3X5	T44.3X6
metilsulfate	T44.3X1	T44.3X2	T44.3X3	T44.3X4	T44.3X5	T44.3X6
Diphenadione	T45.511	T45.512	T45.513	T45.514	T45.515	T45.516
rodenticide	T60.4X1	T60.4X2	T60.4X3	T60.4X4	—	—
Diphenhydramine	T45.0X1	T45.0X2	T45.0X3	T45.0X4	T45.0X5	T45.0X6
Diphenidol	T45.0X1	T45.0X2	T45.0X3	T45.0X4	T45.0X5	T45.0X6
Diphenoxylate	T47.6X1	T47.6X2	T47.6X3	T47.6X4	T47.6X5	T47.6X6
Diphenylamine	T65.3X1	T65.3X2	T65.3X3	T65.3X4	—	—
Diphenylbutazone	T39.2X1	T39.2X2	T39.2X3	T39.2X4	T39.2X5	T39.2X6
Diphenyl-chloroarsine, not in war	T57.0X1	T57.0X2	T57.0X3	T57.0X4	—	—
Diphenylhydantoin	T42.0X1	T42.0X2	T42.0X3	T42.0X4	T42.0X5	T42.0X6
Diphenylmethane dye	T52.1X1	T52.1X2	T52.1X3	T52.1X4	—	—
Diphenylpyraline	T45.0X1	T45.0X2	T45.0X3	T45.0X4	T45.0X5	T45.0X6
Diphtheria						
antitoxin	T50.Z11	T50.Z12	T50.Z13	T50.Z14	T50.Z15	T50.Z16

Substance	Poisoning, Accidental (unintentional)	Poisoning, Intentional self-harm	Poisoning, Assault	Poisoning, Undetermined	Adverse effect	Underdosing
Diphtheria — *Continued*						
toxoid	T50.A91	T50.A92	T50.A93	T50.A94	T50.A95	T50.A96
with tetanus toxoid	T50.A21	T50.A22	T50.A23	T50.A24	T50.A25	T50.A26
with pertussis component	T50.A11	T50.A12	T50.A13	T50.A14	T50.A15	T50.A16
vaccine	T50.A91	T50.A92	T50.A93	T50.A94	T50.A95	T50.A96
combination						
including pertussis	T50.A11	T50.A12	T50.A13	T50.A14	T50.A15	T50.A16
without pertussis	T50.A21	T50.A22	T50.A23	T50.A24	T50.A25	T50.A26
Diphylline	T50.2X1	T50.2X2	T50.2X3	T50.2X4	T50.2X5	T50.2X6
Dipipanone	T40.4X1	T40.4X2	T40.4X3	T40.4X4	—	—
Dipivefrine	T49.5X1	T49.5X2	T49.5X3	T49.5X4	T49.5X5	T49.5X6
Diplovax	T50.B91	T50.B92	T50.B93	T50.B94	T50.B95	T50.B96
Diprophylline	T50.2X1	T50.2X2	T50.2X3	T50.2X4	T50.2X5	T50.2X6
Dipropyline	T48.291	T48.292	T48.293	T48.294	T48.295	T48.296
Dipyridamole	T46.3X1	T46.3X2	T46.3X3	T46.3X4	T46.3X5	T46.3X6
Dipyrone	T39.2X1	T39.2X2	T39.2X3	T39.2X4	T39.2X5	T39.2X6
Diquat(dibromide)	T60.3X1	T60.3X2	T60.3X3	T60.3X4	—	—
Disinfectant	T65.891	T65.892	T65.893	T65.894	—	—
alkaline	T54.3X1	T54.3X2	T54.3X3	T54.3X4	—	—
aromatic	T54.1X1	T54.1X2	T54.1X3	T54.1X4	—	—
intestinal	T37.8X1	T37.8X2	T37.8X3	T37.8X4	T37.8X5	T37.8X6
Disipal	T42.8X1	T42.8X2	T42.8X3	T42.8X4	T42.8X5	T42.8X6
Disodium edetate	T50.6X1	T50.6X2	T50.6X3	T50.6X4	T50.6X5	T50.6X6
Disoprofol	T41.291	T41.292	T41.293	T41.294	T41.295	T41.296
Disopyramide	T46.2X1	T46.2X2	T46.2X3	T46.2X4	T46.2X5	T46.2X6
Distigmine(bromide)	T44.0X1	T44.0X2	T44.0X3	T44.0X4	T44.0X5	T44.0X6
Disulfamide	T50.2X1	T50.2X2	T50.2X3	T50.2X4	T50.2X5	T50.2X6
Disulfanilamide	T37.0X1	T37.0X2	T37.0X3	T37.0X4	T37.0X5	T37.0X6
Disulfiram	T50.6X1	T50.6X2	T50.6X3	T50.6X4	T50.6X5	T50.6X6
Disulfoton	T60.0X1	T60.0X2	T60.0X3	T60.0X4	—	—
Dithiazanine iodide	T37.4X1	T37.4X2	T37.4X3	T37.4X4	T37.4X5	T37.4X6
Dithiocarbamate	T60.0X1	T60.0X2	T60.0X3	T60.0X4	—	—
Dithranol	T49.4X1	T49.4X2	T49.4X3	T49.4X4	T49.4X5	T49.4X6
Diucardin	T50.2X1	T50.2X2	T50.2X3	T50.2X4	T50.2X5	T50.2X6
Diupres	T50.2X1	T50.2X2	T50.2X3	T50.2X4	T50.2X5	T50.2X6
Diuretic NEC	T50.2X1	T50.2X2	T50.2X3	T50.2X4	T50.2X5	T50.2X6
benzothiadiazine	T50.2X1	T50.2X2	T50.2X3	T50.2X4	T50.2X5	T50.2X6
carbonic acid anhydrase inhibitors	T50.2X1	T50.2X2	T50.2X3	T50.2X4	T50.2X5	T50.2X6
furfuryl NEC	T50.2X1	T50.2X2	T50.2X3	T50.2X4	T50.2X5	T50.2X6
loop(high-ceiling)	T50.1X1	T50.1X2	T50.1X3	T50.1X4	T50.1X5	T50.1X6
mercurial NEC	T50.2X1	T50.2X2	T50.2X3	T50.2X4	T50.2X5	T50.2X6
osmotic	T50.2X1	T50.2X2	T50.2X3	T50.2X4	T50.2X5	T50.2X6
purine NEC	T50.2X1	T50.2X2	T50.2X3	T50.2X4	T50.2X5	T50.2X6
saluretic NEC	T50.2X1	T50.2X2	T50.2X3	T50.2X4	T50.2X5	T50.2X6
sulfonamide	T50.2X1	T50.2X2	T50.2X3	T50.2X4	T50.2X5	T50.2X6
thiazide NEC	T50.2X1	T50.2X2	T50.2X3	T50.2X4	T50.2X5	T50.2X6
xanthine	T50.2X1	T50.2X2	T50.2X3	T50.2X4	T50.2X5	T50.2X6
Diurgin	T50.2X1	T50.2X2	T50.2X3	T50.2X4	T50.2X5	T50.2X6
Diuril	T50.2X1	T50.2X2	T50.2X3	T50.2X4	T50.2X5	T50.2X6

Substance	Poisoning, Accidental (unintentional)	Poisoning, Intentional self-harm	Poisoning, Assault	Poisoning, Undetermined	Adverse effect	Underdosing
Diuron	T60.3X1	T60.3X2	T60.3X3	T60.3X4	—	—
Divalproex	T42.6X1	T42.6X2	T42.6X3	T42.6X4	T42.6X5	T42.
Divinyl ether	T41.0X1	T41.0X2	T41.0X3	T41.0X4	T41.0X5	T41.
Dixanthogen	T49.0X1	T49.0X2	T49.0X3	T49.0X4	T49.0X5	T49.
Dixyrazine	T43.3X1	T43.3X2	T43.3X3	T43.3X4	T43.3X5	T43.
D-lysergic acid diethylamide	T40.8X1	T40.8X2	T40.8X3	T40.8X4	—	—
DMCT	T36.4X1	T36.4X2	T36.4X3	T36.4X4	T36.4X5	T36.
DMSO—see Dimethyl sulfoxide						
DNBP	T60.3X1	T60.3X2	T60.3X3	T60.3X4	—	—
DNOC	T65.3X1	T65.3X2	T65.3X3	T65.3X4	—	—
Dobutamine	T44.5X1	T44.5X2	T44.5X3	T44.5X4	T44.5X5	T44.
DOCA	T38.0X1	T38.0X2	T38.0X3	T38.0X4	T38.0X5	T38.
Docusate sodium	T47.4X1	T47.4X2	T47.4X3	T47.4X4	T47.4X5	T47.
Dodicin	T49.0X1	T49.0X2	T49.0X3	T49.0X4	T49.0X5	T49.0
Dofamium chloride	T49.0X1	T49.0X2	T49.0X3	T49.0X4	T49.0X5	T49.0
Dolophine	T40.3X1	T40.3X2	T40.3X3	T40.3X4	T40.3X5	T40.3
Doloxene	T39.8X1	T39.8X2	T39.8X3	T39.8X4	T39.8X5	T39.8
Domestic gas(after combustion)—see Gas, utility						
prior to combustion	T59.891	T59.892	T59.893	T59.894	—	—
Domiodol	T48.4X1	T48.4X2	T48.4X3	T48.4X4	T48.4X5	T48.4
Domiphen(bromide)	T49.0X1	T49.0X2	T49.0X3	T49.0X4	T49.0X5	T49.0
Domperidone	T45.0X1	T45.0X2	T45.0X3	T45.0X4	T45.0X5	T45.0
Dopa	T42.8X1	T42.8X2	T42.8X3	T42.8X4	T42.8X5	T42.8
Dopamine	T44.991	T44.992	T44.993	T44.994	T44.995	T44.9
Doriden	T42.6X1	T42.6X2	T42.6X3	T42.6X4	T42.6X5	T42.6
Dormiral	T42.3X1	T42.3X2	T42.3X3	T42.3X4	T42.3X5	T42.3
Dormison	T42.6X1	T42.6X2	T42.6X3	T42.6X4	T42.6X5	T42.6
Dornase	T48.4X1	T48.4X2	T48.4X3	T48.4X4	T48.4X5	T48.4
Dorsacaine	T41.3X1	T41.3X2	T41.3X3	T41.3X4	T41.3X5	T41.3
Dosulepin	T43.011	T43.012	T43.013	T43.014	T43.015	T43.0
Dothiepin	T43.011	T43.012	T43.013	T43.014	T43.015	T43.0
Doxantrazole	T48.6X1	T48.6X2	T48.6X3	T48.6X4	T48.6X5	T48.6
Doxapram	T50.7X1	T50.7X2	T50.7X3	T50.7X4	T50.7X5	T50.7
Doxazosin	T44.6X1	T44.6X2	T44.6X3	T44.6X4	T44.6X5	T44.6
Doxepin	T43.011	T43.012	T43.013	T43.014	T43.015	T43.0
Doxifluridine	T45.1X1	T45.1X2	T45.1X3	T45.1X4	T45.1X5	T45.1
Doxorubicin	T45.1X1	T45.1X2	T45.1X3	T45.1X4	T45.1X5	T45.1
Doxycycline	T36.4X1	T36.4X2	T36.4X3	T36.4X4	T36.4X5	T36.4
Doxylamine	T45.0X1	T45.0X2	T45.0X3	T45.0X4	T45.0X5	T45.0
Dramamine	T45.0X1	T45.0X2	T45.0X3	T45.0X4	T45.0X5	T45.0
Drano(drain cleaner)	T54.3X1	T54.3X2	T54.3X3	T54.3X4	—	—
Dressing, live pulp	T49.7X1	T49.7X2	T49.7X3	T49.7X4	T49.7X5	T49.7
Drocode	T40.2X1	T40.2X2	T40.2X3	T40.2X4	T40.2X5	T40.2
Dromoran	T40.2X1	T40.2X2	T40.2X3	T40.2X4	T40.2X5	T40.2
Dromostanolone	T38.7X1	T38.7X2	T38.7X3	T38.7X4	T38.7X5	T38.7
Dronabinol	T40.7X1	T40.7X2	T40.7X3	T40.7X4	T40.7X5	T40.7
Droperidol	T43.591	T43.592	T43.593	T43.594	T43.595	T43.5
Dropropizine	T48.3X1	T48.3X2	T48.3X3	T48.3X4	T48.3X5	T48.3

Substance	Poisoning, Accidental (unintentional)	Poisoning, Intentional self-harm	Poisoning, Assault	Poisoning, Undetermined	Adverse effect	Underdosing
tanolone	T38.7X1	T38.7X2	T38.7X3	T38.7X4	T38.7X5	T38.7X6
averine	T44.3X1	T44.3X2	T44.3X3	T44.3X4	T44.3X5	T44.3X6
recogin alfa	T45.511	T45.512	T45.513	T45.514	T45.515	T45.516
NEC	T50.901	T50.902	T50.903	T50.904	T50.905	T50.906
cified NEC	T50.991	T50.992	T50.993	T50.994	T50.995	T50.996
	T45.1X1	T45.1X2	T45.1X3	T45.1X4	T45.1X5	T45.1X6
isine	T44.3X1	T44.3X2	T44.3X3	T44.3X4	T44.3X5	T44.3X6
lax	T47.2X1	T47.2X2	T47.2X3	T47.2X4	T47.2X5	T47.2X6
nol(C) (EP)	T49.2X1	T49.2X2	T49.2X3	T49.2X4	T49.2X5	T49.2X6
bolin	T38.7X1	T38.7X2	T38.7X3	T38.7X4	T38.7X5	T38.7X6
ne	T41.3X1	T41.3X2	T41.3X3	T41.3X4	T41.3X5	T41.3X6
nine	T41.3X1	T41.3X2	T41.3X3	T41.3X4	T41.3X5	T41.3X6
ogesterone	T38.5X1	T38.5X2	T38.5X3	T38.5X4	T38.5X5	T38.5X6
NEC	T65.6X1	T65.6X2	T65.6X3	T65.6X4	—	—
septic	T49.0X1	T49.0X2	T49.0X3	T49.0X4	T49.0X5	T49.0X6
gnostic agents	T50.8X1	T50.8X2	T50.8X3	T50.8X4	T50.8X5	T50.8X6
rmaceutical NEC	T50.901	T50.902	T50.903	T50.904	T50.905	T50.906
s	T44.0X1	T44.0X2	T44.0X3	T44.0X4	T44.0X5	T44.0X6
lor	T38.3X1	T38.3X2	T38.3X3	T38.3X4	T38.3X5	T38.3X6
mite	T65.3X1	T65.3X2	T65.3X3	T65.3X4	—	—
es	T59.891	T59.892	T59.893	T59.894	—	—
ylline	T44.3X1	T44.3X2	T44.3X3	T44.3X4	T44.3X5	T44.3X6
E						
rug NEC	T49.6X1	T49.6X2	T49.6X3	T49.6X4	T49.6X5	T49.6X6
reparations	T49.6X1	T49.6X2	T49.6X3	T49.6X4	T49.6X5	T49.6X6
hiophate, hiopate, iopate	T49.5X1	T49.5X2	T49.5X3	T49.5X4	T49.5X5	T49.5X6
azole	T49.0X1	T49.0X2	T49.0X3	T49.0X4	T49.0X5	T49.0X6
iopate iodide	T49.5X1	T49.5X2	T49.5X3	T49.5X4	T49.5X5	T49.5X6
sy	T43.621	T43.622	T43.623	T43.624	T43.625	T43.626
urea	T42.6X1	T42.6X2	T42.6X3	T42.6X4	T42.6X5	T42.6X6
amil disodium	T45.8X1	T45.8X2	T45.8X3	T45.8X4	T45.8X5	T45.8X6
in	T50.1X1	T50.1X2	T50.1X3	T50.1X4	T50.1X5	T50.1X6
te, disodium(calcium)	T45.8X1	T45.8X2	T45.8X3	T45.8X4	T45.8X5	T45.8X6
idine	T49.5X1	T49.5X2	T49.5X3	T49.5X4	T49.5X5	T49.5X6
honium	T44.0X1	T44.0X2	T44.0X3	T44.0X4	T44.0X5	T44.0X6
ride	T44.0X1	T44.0X2	T44.0X3	T44.0X4	T44.0X5	T44.0X6
	T50.6X1	T50.6X2	T50.6X3	T50.6X4	T50.6X5	T50.6X6
ithine	T37.2X1	T37.2X2	T37.2X3	T37.2X4	T37.2X5	T37.2X6
ate	T46.3X1	T46.3X2	T46.3X3	T46.3X4	T46.3X5	T46.3X6
	T49.8X1	T49.8X2	T49.8X3	T49.8X4	T49.8X5	T49.8X6
se	T47.5X1	T47.5X2	T47.5X3	T47.5X4	T47.5X5	T47.5X6
rium	T47.2X1	T47.2X2	T47.2X3	T47.2X4	T47.2X5	T47.2X6
nin	T50.991	T50.992	T50.993	T50.994	T50.995	T50.996
	T62.2X1	T62.2X2	T62.2X3	T62.2X4	—	—
y,(unripe)	T62.1X1	T62.1X2	T62.1X3	T62.1X4	—	—
olyte balance	T50.3X1	T50.3X2	T50.3X3	T50.3X4	T50.3X5	T50.3X6
olytes NEC	T50.3X1	T50.3X2	T50.3X3	T50.3X4	T50.3X5	T50.3X6
olytic agent NEC	T50.3X1	T50.3X2	T50.3X3	T50.3X4	T50.3X5	T50.3X6
ntal diet	T50.901	T50.902	T50.903	T50.904	T50.905	T50.906

Substance	Poisoning, Accidental (unintentional)	Poisoning, Intentional self-harm	Poisoning, Assault	Poisoning, Undetermined	Adverse effect	Underdosing
Elliptinium acetate	T45.1X1	T45.1X2	T45.1X3	T45.1X4	T45.1X5	T45.1X6
Embramine	T45.0X1	T45.0X2	T45.0X3	T45.0X4	T45.0X5	T45.0X6
Emepronium(salts)	T44.3X1	T44.3X2	T44.3X3	T44.3X4	T44.3X5	T44.3X6
bromide	T44.3X1	T44.3X2	T44.3X3	T44.3X4	T44.3X5	T44.3X6
Emetic NEC	T47.7X1	T47.7X2	T47.7X3	T47.7X4	T47.7X5	T47.7X6
Emetine	T37.3X1	T37.3X2	T37.3X3	T37.3X4	T37.3X5	T37.3X6
Emollient NEC	T49.3X1	T49.3X2	T49.3X3	T49.3X4	T49.3X5	T49.3X6
Emorfazone	T39.8X1	T39.8X2	T39.8X3	T39.8X4	T39.8X5	T39.8X6
Emylcamate	T43.591	T43.592	T43.593	T43.594	T43.595	T43.596
Enalapril	T46.4X1	T46.4X2	T46.4X3	T46.4X4	T46.4X5	T46.4X6
Enalaprilat	T46.4X1	T46.4X2	T46.4X3	T46.4X4	T46.4X5	T46.4X6
Encainide	T46.2X1	T46.2X2	T46.2X3	T46.2X4	T46.2X5	T46.2X6
Endocaine	T41.3X1	T41.3X2	T41.3X3	T41.3X4	T41.3X5	T41.3X6
Endosulfan	T60.2X1	T60.2X2	T60.2X3	T60.2X4	—	—
Endothall	T60.3X1	T60.3X2	T60.3X3	T60.3X4	—	—
Endralazine	T46.5X1	T46.5X2	T46.5X3	T46.5X4	T46.5X5	T46.5X6
Endrin	T60.1X1	T60.1X2	T60.1X3	T60.1X4	—	—
Enflurane	T41.0X1	T41.0X2	T41.0X3	T41.0X4	T41.0X5	T41.0X6
Enhexymal	T42.3X1	T42.3X2	T42.3X3	T42.3X4	T42.3X5	T42.3X6
Enocitabine	T45.1X1	T45.1X2	T45.1X3	T45.1X4	T45.1X5	T45.1X6
Enovid	T38.4X1	T38.4X2	T38.4X3	T38.4X4	T38.4X5	T38.4X6
Enoxacin	T36.8X1	T36.8X2	T36.8X3	T36.8X4	T36.8X5	T36.8X6
Enoxaparin(sodium)	T45.511	T45.512	T45.513	T45.514	T45.515	T45.516
Enpiprazole	T43.591	T43.592	T43.593	T43.594	T43.595	T43.596
Enprofylline	T48.6X1	T48.6X2	T48.6X3	T48.6X4	T48.6X5	T48.6X6
Enprostil	T47.1X1	T47.1X2	T47.1X3	T47.1X4	T47.1X5	T47.1X6
ENT preparations (anti-infectives)	T49.6X1	T49.6X2	T49.6X3	T49.6X4	T49.6X5	T49.6X6
Enterogastrone	T38.891	T38.892	T38.893	T38.894	T38.895	T38.896
Enviomycin	T36.8X1	T36.8X2	T36.8X3	T36.8X4	T36.8X5	T36.8X6
Enzodase	T45.3X1	T45.3X2	T45.3X3	T45.3X4	T45.3X5	T45.3X6
Enzyme NEC	T45.3X1	T45.3X2	T45.3X3	T45.3X4	T45.3X5	T45.3X6
depolymerizing	T49.8X1	T49.8X2	T49.8X3	T49.8X4	T49.8X5	T49.8X6
fibrolytic	T45.3X1	T45.3X2	T45.3X3	T45.3X4	T45.3X5	T45.3X6
gastric	T47.5X1	T47.5X2	T47.5X3	T47.5X4	T47.5X5	T47.5X6
intestinal	T47.5X1	T47.5X2	T47.5X3	T47.5X4	T47.5X5	T47.5X6
local action	T49.4X1	T49.4X2	T49.4X3	T49.4X4	T49.4X5	T49.4X6
proteolytic	T49.4X1	T49.4X2	T49.4X3	T49.4X4	T49.4X5	T49.4X6
thrombolytic	T45.3X1	T45.3X2	T45.3X3	T45.3X4	T45.3X5	T45.3X6
EPAB	T41.3X1	T41.3X2	T41.3X3	T41.3X4	T41.3X5	T41.3X6
Epanutin	T42.0X1	T42.0X2	T42.0X3	T42.0X4	T42.0X5	T42.0X6
Ephedra	T44.991	T44.992	T44.993	T44.994	T44.995	T44.996
Ephedrine	T44.991	T44.992	T44.993	T44.994	T44.995	T44.996
Epichlorhydrin, epichlorohydrin	T52.8X1	T52.8X2	T52.8X3	T52.8X4	—	—
Epicillin	T36.0X1	T36.0X2	T36.0X3	T36.0X4	T36.0X5	T36.0X6
Epiestriol	T38.5X1	T38.5X2	T38.5X3	T38.5X4	T38.5X5	T38.5X6
Epilim—see Sodium valproate						
Epimestrol	T38.5X1	T38.5X2	T38.5X3	T38.5X4	T38.5X5	T38.5X6
Epinephrine	T44.5X1	T44.5X2	T44.5X3	T44.5X4	T44.5X5	T44.5X6
Epirubicin	T45.1X1	T45.1X2	T45.1X3	T45.1X4	T45.1X5	T45.1X6

Substance	Poisoning, Accidental (unintentional)	Poisoning, Intentional self-harm	Poisoning, Assault	Poisoning, Undetermined	Adverse effect	Underdosing
Epitiostanol	T38.7X1	T38.7X2	T38.7X3	T38.7X4	T38.7X5	T38.7X6
Epitizide	T50.2X1	T50.2X2	T50.2X3	T50.2X4	T50.2X5	T50.2X6
EPN	T60.0X1	T60.0X2	T60.0X3	T60.0X4	—	—
EPO	T45.8X1	T45.8X2	T45.8X3	T45.8X4	T45.8X5	T45.8X6
Epoetin alpha	T45.8X1	T45.8X2	T45.8X3	T45.8X4	T45.8X5	T45.8X6
Epomediol	T50.991	T50.992	T50.993	T50.994	T50.995	T50.996
Epoprostenol	T45.521	T45.522	T45.523	T45.524	T45.525	T45.526
Epoxy resin	T65.891	T65.892	T65.893	T65.894	—	—
Eprazinone	T48.4X1	T48.4X2	T48.4X3	T48.4X4	T48.4X5	T48.4X6
Epsilon amino-caproic acid	T45.621	T45.622	T45.623	T45.624	T45.625	T45.626
Epsom salt	T47.3X1	T47.3X2	T47.3X3	T47.3X4	T47.3X5	T47.3X6
Eptazocine	T40.4X1	T40.4X2	T40.4X3	T40.4X4	T40.4X5	T40.4X6
Equanil	T43.591	T43.592	T43.593	T43.594	T43.595	T43.596
Equisetum	T62.2X1	T62.2X2	T62.2X3	T62.2X4	—	—
diuretic	T50.2X1	T50.2X2	T50.2X3	T50.2X4	T50.2X5	T50.2X6
Ergobasine	T48.0X1	T48.0X2	T48.0X3	T48.0X4	T48.0X5	T48.0X6
Ergocalciferol	T45.2X1	T45.2X2	T45.2X3	T45.2X4	T45.2X5	T45.2X6
Ergoloid mesylates	T46.7X1	T46.7X2	T46.7X3	T46.7X4	T46.7X5	T46.7X6
Ergometrine	T48.0X1	T48.0X2	T48.0X3	T48.0X4	T48.0X5	T48.0X6
Ergonovine	T48.0X1	T48.0X2	T48.0X3	T48.0X4	T48.0X5	T48.0X6
Ergot NEC	T64.81	T64.82	T64.83	T64.84	—	—
derivative	T48.0X1	T48.0X2	T48.0X3	T48.0X4	T48.0X5	T48.0X6
medicinal(alkaloids)	T48.0X1	T48.0X2	T48.0X3	T48.0X4	T48.0X5	T48.0X6
prepared	T48.0X1	T48.0X2	T48.0X3	T48.0X4	T48.0X5	T48.0X6
Ergotamine	T46.5X1	T46.5X2	T46.5X3	T46.5X4	T46.5X5	T46.5X6
Ergotocine	T48.0X1	T48.0X2	T48.0X3	T48.0X4	T48.0X5	T48.0X6
Ergotrate	T48.0X1	T48.0X2	T48.0X3	T48.0X4	T48.0X5	T48.0X6
Eritrityl tetranitrate	T46.3X1	T46.3X2	T46.3X3	T46.3X4	T46.3X5	T46.3X6
Erythrityl tetranitrate	T46.3X1	T46.3X2	T46.3X3	T46.3X4	T46.3X5	T46.3X6
Erythrol tetranitrate	T46.3X1	T46.3X2	T46.3X3	T46.3X4	T46.3X5	T46.3X6
Erythromycin(salts)	T36.3X1	T36.3X2	T36.3X3	T36.3X4	T36.3X5	T36.3X6
ophthalmic preparation	T49.5X1	T49.5X2	T49.5X3	T49.5X4	T49.5X5	T49.5X6
topical NEC	T49.0X1	T49.0X2	T49.0X3	T49.0X4	T49.0X5	T49.0X6
Erythropoietin	T45.8X1	T45.8X2	T45.8X3	T45.8X4	T45.8X5	T45.8X6
human	T45.8X1	T45.8X2	T45.8X3	T45.8X4	T45.8X5	T45.8X6
Escin	T46.991	T46.992	T46.993	T46.994	T46.995	T46.996
Esculin	T45.2X1	T45.2X2	T45.2X3	T45.2X4	T45.2X5	T45.2X6
Esculoside	T45.2X1	T45.2X2	T45.2X3	T45.2X4	T45.2X5	T45.2X6
ESDT(ether-soluble tar distillate)	T49.1X1	T49.1X2	T49.1X3	T49.1X4	T49.1X5	T49.1X6
Eserine	T49.5X1	T49.5X2	T49.5X3	T49.5X4	T49.5X5	T49.5X6
Esflurbiprofen	T39.311	T39.312	T39.313	T39.314	T39.315	T39.316
Eskabarb	T42.3X1	T42.3X2	T42.3X3	T42.3X4	T42.3X5	T42.3X6
Eskalith	T43.8X1	T43.8X2	T43.8X3	T43.8X4	T43.8X5	T43.8X6
Esmolol	T44.7X1	T44.7X2	T44.7X3	T44.7X4	T44.7X5	T44.7X6
Estanozolol	T38.7X1	T38.7X2	T38.7X3	T38.7X4	T38.7X5	T38.7X6
Estazolam	T42.4X1	T42.4X2	T42.4X3	T42.4X4	T42.4X5	T42.4X6
Estradiol	T38.5X1	T38.5X2	T38.5X3	T38.5X4	T38.5X5	T38.5X6
with testosterone	T38.7X1	T38.7X2	T38.7X3	T38.7X4	T38.7X5	T38.7X6
benzoate	T38.5X1	T38.5X2	T38.5X3	T38.5X4	T38.5X5	T38.5X6

Substance	Poisoning, Accidental (unintentional)	Poisoning, Intentional self-harm	Poisoning, Assault	Poisoning, Undetermined	Adverse effect	
Estramustine	T45.1X1	T45.1X2	T45.1X3	T45.1X4	T45.1X5	T45
Estriol	T38.5X1	T38.5X2	T38.5X3	T38.5X4	T38.5X5	T38
Estrogen	T38.5X1	T38.5X2	T38.5X3	T38.5X4	T38.5X5	T38
with progesterone	T38.5X1	T38.5X2	T38.5X3	T38.5X4	T38.5X5	T38
conjugated	T38.5X1	T38.5X2	T38.5X3	T38.5X4	T38.5X5	T38
Estrone	T38.5X1	T38.5X2	T38.5X3	T38.5X4	T38.5X5	T38
Estropipate	T38.5X1	T38.5X2	T38.5X3	T38.5X4	T38.5X5	T38
Etacrynate sodium	T50.1X1	T50.1X2	T50.1X3	T50.1X4	T50.1X5	T50
Etacrynic acid	T50.1X1	T50.1X2	T50.1X3	T50.1X4	T50.1X5	T50
Etafedrine	T48.6X1	T48.6X2	T48.6X3	T48.6X4	T48.6X5	T48
Etafenone	T46.3X1	T46.3X2	T46.3X3	T46.3X4	T46.3X5	T46
Etambutol	T37.1X1	T37.1X2	T37.1X3	T37.1X4	T37.1X5	T37
Etamiphyllin	T48.6X1	T48.6X2	T48.6X3	T48.6X4	T48.6X5	T48
Etamivan	T50.7X1	T50.7X2	T50.7X3	T50.7X4	T50.7X5	T50
Etamsylate	T45.7X1	T45.7X2	T45.7X3	T45.7X4	T45.7X5	T45
Etebenecid	T50.4X1	T50.4X2	T50.4X3	T50.4X4	T50.4X5	T50
Ethacridine	T49.0X1	T49.0X2	T49.0X3	T49.0X4	T49.0X5	T49
Ethacrynic acid	T50.1X1	T50.1X2	T50.1X3	T50.1X4	T50.1X5	T50
Ethadione	T42.2X1	T42.2X2	T42.2X3	T42.2X4	T42.2X5	T42
Ethambutol	T37.1X1	T37.1X2	T37.1X3	T37.1X4	T37.1X5	T37
Ethamide	T50.2X1	T50.2X2	T50.2X3	T50.2X4	T50.2X5	T50
Ethamivan	T50.7X1	T50.7X2	T50.7X3	T50.7X4	T50.7X5	T50
Ethamsylate	T45.7X1	T45.7X2	T45.7X3	T45.7X4	T45.7X5	T45
Ethanol	T51.0X1	T51.0X2	T51.0X3	T51.0X4	—	—
beverage	T51.0X1	T51.0X2	T51.0X3	T51.0X4	—	—
Ethanolamine oleate	T46.8X1	T46.8X2	T46.8X3	T46.8X4	T46.8X5	T46
Ethaverine	T44.3X1	T44.3X2	T44.3X3	T44.3X4	T44.3X5	T44
Ethchlorvynol	T42.6X1	T42.6X2	T42.6X3	T42.6X4	T42.6X5	T42
Ethebenecid	T50.4X1	T50.4X2	T50.4X3	T50.4X4	T50.4X5	T50
Ether(vapor)	T41.0X1	T41.0X2	T41.0X3	T41.0X4	T41.0X5	T41
anesthetic	T41.0X1	T41.0X2	T41.0X3	T41.0X4	T41.0X5	T41
divinyl	T41.0X1	T41.0X2	T41.0X3	T41.0X4	T41.0X5	T41
ethyl(medicinal)	T41.0X1	T41.0X2	T41.0X3	T41.0X4	T41.0X5	T41
nonmedicinal	T52.8X1	T52.8X2	T52.8X3	T52.8X4	—	
petroleum—see Ligroin						
solvent	T52.8X1	T52.8X2	T52.8X3	T52.8X4	—	
Ethiazide	T50.2X1	T50.2X2	T50.2X3	T50.2X4	T50.2X5	T50
Ethidium chloride (vapor)	T59.891	T59.892	T59.893	T59.894	—	
Ethinamate	T42.6X1	T42.6X2	T42.6X3	T42.6X4	T42.6X5	T42
Ethinylestradiol, ethinyloestradiol	T38.5X1	T38.5X2	T38.5X3	T38.5X4	T38.5X5	T38
with						
levonorgestrel	T38.4X1	T38.4X2	T38.4X3	T38.4X4	T38.4X5	T38
norethisterone	T38.4X1	T38.4X2	T38.4X3	T38.4X4	T38.4X5	T38
Ethiodized oil(131 I)	T50.8X1	T50.8X2	T50.8X3	T50.8X4	T50.8X5	T50
Ethion	T60.0X1	T60.0X2	T60.0X3	T60.0X4	—	
Ethionamide	T37.1X1	T37.1X2	T37.1X3	T37.1X4	T37.1X5	T37
Ethioniamide	T37.1X1	T37.1X2	T37.1X3	T37.1X4	T37.1X5	T37
Ethisterone	T38.5X1	T38.5X2	T38.5X3	T38.5X4	T38.5X5	T38
Ethobral	T42.3X1	T42.3X2	T42.3X3	T42.3X4	T42.3X5	T4

Substance	Poisoning, Accidental (unintentional)	Poisoning, Intentional self-harm	Poisoning, Assault	Poisoning, Undetermined	Adverse effect	Underdosing
caine tration) (topical)	T41.3X1	T41.3X2	T41.3X3	T41.3X4	T41.3X5	T41.3X6
ve block(peripheral) exus)	T41.3X1	T41.3X2	T41.3X3	T41.3X4	T41.3X5	T41.3X6
nal	T41.3X1	T41.3X2	T41.3X3	T41.3X4	T41.3X5	T41.3X6
heptazine	T40.4X1	T40.4X2	T40.4X3	T40.4X4	T40.4X5	T40.4X6
propazine	T44.3X1	T44.3X2	T44.3X3	T44.3X4	T44.3X5	T44.3X6
suximide	T42.2X1	T42.2X2	T42.2X3	T42.2X4	T42.2X5	T42.2X6
toin	T42.0X1	T42.0X2	T42.0X3	T42.0X4	T42.0X5	T42.0X6
xazene	T37.91	T37.92	T37.93	T37.94	T37.95	T37.96
xazorutoside	T46.991	T46.992	T46.993	T46.994	T46.995	T46.996
oxyethanol	T52.3X1	T52.3X2	T52.3X3	T52.3X4	—	—
xzolamide	T50.2X1	T50.2X2	T50.2X3	T50.2X4	T50.2X5	T50.2X6
l						
tate	T52.8X1	T52.8X2	T52.8X3	T52.8X4	—	—
ohol	T51.0X1	T51.0X2	T51.0X3	T51.0X4	—	—
everage	T51.0X1	T51.0X2	T51.0X3	T51.0X4	—	—
ehyde(vapor)	T59.891	T59.892	T59.893	T59.894	—	—
iquid	T52.8X1	T52.8X2	T52.8X3	T52.8X4	—	—
inobenzoate	T41.3X1	T41.3X2	T41.3X3	T41.3X4	T41.3X5	T41.3X6
inophenothiazine	T43.3X1	T43.3X2	T43.3X3	T43.3X4	T43.3X5	T43.3X6
nzoate	T52.8X1	T52.8X2	T52.8X3	T52.8X4	—	—
coumacetate	T45.511	T45.512	T45.513	T45.514	T45.515	T45.516
mide(anesthetic)	T41.0X1	T41.0X2	T41.0X3	T41.0X4	T41.0X5	T41.0X6
bamate	T45.1X1	T45.1X2	T45.1X3	T45.1X4	T45.1X5	T45.1X6
binol	T51.3X1	T51.3X2	T51.3X3	T51.3X4	—	—
bonate	T52.8X1	T52.8X2	T52.8X3	T52.8X4	—	—
aulmoograte	T37.1X1	T37.1X2	T37.1X3	T37.1X4	T37.1X5	T37.1X6
loride(anesthetic)	T41.0X1	T41.0X2	T41.0X3	T41.0X4	T41.0X5	T41.0X6
nesthetic(local)	T41.3X1	T41.3X2	T41.3X3	T41.3X4	T41.3X5	T41.3X6
inhaled	T41.0X1	T41.0X2	T41.0X3	T41.0X4	T41.0X5	T41.0X6
ocal	T49.4X1	T49.4X2	T49.4X3	T49.4X4	T49.4X5	T49.4X6
solvent	T53.6X1	T53.6X2	T53.6X3	T53.6X4	—	—
unate	T48.3X1	T48.3X2	T48.3X3	T48.3X4	T48.3X5	T48.3X6
chloroarsine apor)	T57.0X1	T57.0X2	T57.0X3	T57.0X4	—	—
ranol	T38.7X1	T38.7X2	T38.7X3	T38.7X4	T38.7X5	T38.7X6
er—see also ether	T52.8X1	T52.8X2	T52.8X3	T52.8X4	—	—
mate NEC olvent)	T52.0X1	T52.0X2	T52.0X3	T52.0X4	—	—
marate	T49.4X1	T49.4X2	T49.4X3	T49.4X4	T49.4X5	T49.4X6
droxyisobutyrate EC(solvent)	T52.8X1	T52.8X2	T52.8X3	T52.8X4	—	—
doacetate	T59.3X1	T59.3X2	T59.3X3	T59.3X4	—	—
tate NEC(lvent)	T52.8X1	T52.8X2	T52.8X3	T52.8X4	—	—
lazepate	T42.4X1	T42.4X2	T42.4X3	T42.4X4	T42.4X5	T42.4X6
ercuric chloride	T56.1X1	T56.1X2	T56.1X3	T56.1X4	—	—
ethylcarbinol	T51.8X1	T51.8X2	T51.8X3	T51.8X4	—	—
orphine	T40.2X1	T40.2X2	T40.2X3	T40.2X4	T40.2X5	T40.2X6
radrenaline	T48.6X1	T48.6X2	T48.6X3	T48.6X4	T48.6X5	T48.6X6
ybutyrate NEC(solvent)	T52.8X1	T52.8X2	T52.8X3	T52.8X4	—	—

Substance	Poisoning, Accidental (unintentional)	Poisoning, Intentional self-harm	Poisoning, Assault	Poisoning, Undetermined	Adverse effect	Underdosing
Ethylene(gas)	T59.891	T59.892	T59.893	T59.894	—	—
anesthetic(general)	T41.0X1	T41.0X2	T41.0X3	T41.0X4	T41.0X5	T41.0X6
chlorohydrin	T52.8X1	T52.8X2	T52.8X3	T52.8X4	—	—
vapor	T53.6X1	T53.6X2	T53.6X3	T53.6X4	—	—
dichloride	T52.8X1	T52.8X2	T52.8X3	T52.8X4	—	—
vapor	T53.6X1	T53.6X2	T53.6X3	T53.6X4	—	—
dinitrate	T52.3X1	T52.3X2	T52.3X3	T52.3X4	—	—
glycol(s)	T52.8X1	T52.8X2	T52.8X3	T52.8X4	—	—
dinitrate	T52.3X1	T52.3X2	T52.3X3	T52.3X4	—	—
monobutyl ether	T52.3X1	T52.3X2	T52.3X3	T52.3X4	—	—
imine	T54.1X1	T54.1X2	T54.1X3	T54.1X4	—	—
oxide(fumigant) (nonmedicinal)	T59.891	T59.892	T59.893	T59.894	—	—
medicinal	T49.0X1	T49.0X2	T49.0X3	T49.0X4	T49.0X5	T49.0X6
Ethylenediamine theophylline	T48.6X1	T48.6X2	T48.6X3	T48.6X4	T48.6X5	T48.6X6
Ethylenediaminetetra-acetic acid	T50.6X1	T50.6X2	T50.6X3	T50.6X4	T50.6X5	T50.6X6
Ethylen-edinitrilotetra-acetate	T50.6X1	T50.6X2	T50.6X3	T50.6X4	T50.6X5	T50.6X6
Ethylestrenol	T38.7X1	T38.7X2	T38.7X3	T38.7X4	T38.7X5	T38.7X6
Ethylhydro-xycellulose	T47.4X1	T47.4X2	T47.4X3	T47.4X4	T47.4X5	T47.4X6
Ethylidene						
chloride NEC	T53.6X1	T53.6X2	T53.6X3	T53.6X4	—	—
diacetate	T60.3X1	T60.3X2	T60.3X3	T60.3X4	—	—
dicoumarin	T45.511	T45.512	T45.513	T45.514	T45.515	T45.516
dicoumarol	T45.511	T45.512	T45.513	T45.514	T45.515	T45.516
diethyl ether	T52.0X1	T52.0X2	T52.0X3	T52.0X4	—	—
Ethylmorphine	T40.2X1	T40.2X2	T40.2X3	T40.2X4	T40.2X5	T40.2X6
Ethylnorepinephrine	T48.6X1	T48.6X2	T48.6X3	T48.6X4	T48.6X5	T48.6X6
Ethylparachloro-phenoxyisobutyrate	T46.6X1	T46.6X2	T46.6X3	T46.6X4	T46.6X5	T46.6X6
Ethynodiol	T38.4X1	T38.4X2	T38.4X3	T38.4X4	T38.4X5	T38.4X6
with mestranol diacetate	T38.4X1	T38.4X2	T38.4X3	T38.4X4	T38.4X5	T38.4X6
Etidocaine	T41.3X1	T41.3X2	T41.3X3	T41.3X4	T41.3X5	T41.3X6
infiltration (subcutaneous)	T41.3X1	T41.3X2	T41.3X3	T41.3X4	T41.3X5	T41.3X6
nerve(peripheral) (plexus)	T41.3X1	T41.3X2	T41.3X3	T41.3X4	T41.3X5	T41.3X6
Etidronate	T50.991	T50.992	T50.993	T50.994	T50.995	T50.996
Etidronic acid(disodium salt)	T50.991	T50.992	T50.993	T50.994	T50.995	T50.996
Etifoxine	T42.6X1	T42.6X2	T42.6X3	T42.6X4	T42.6X5	T42.6X6
Etilefrine	T44.4X1	T44.4X2	T44.4X3	T44.4X4	T44.4X5	T44.4X6
Etilfen	T42.3X1	T42.3X2	T42.3X3	T42.3X4	T42.3X5	T42.3X6
Etinodiol	T38.4X1	T38.4X2	T38.4X3	T38.4X4	T38.4X5	T38.4X6
Etiroxate	T46.6X1	T46.6X2	T46.6X3	T46.6X4	T46.6X5	T46.6X6
Etizolam	T42.4X1	T42.4X2	T42.4X3	T42.4X4	T42.4X5	T42.4X6
Etodolac	T39.391	T39.392	T39.393	T39.394	T39.395	T39.396
Etofamide	T37.3X1	T37.3X2	T37.3X3	T37.3X4	T37.3X5	T37.3X6
Etofibrate	T46.6X1	T46.6X2	T46.6X3	T46.6X4	T46.6X5	T46.6X6
Etofylline	T46.7X1	T46.7X2	T46.7X3	T46.7X4	T46.7X5	T46.7X6
clofibrate	T46.6X1	T46.6X2	T46.6X3	T46.6X4	T46.6X5	T46.6X6

Substance	Poisoning, Accidental (unintentional)	Poisoning, Intentional self-harm	Poisoning, Assault	Poisoning, Undetermined	Adverse effect	Underdosing
Etoglucid	T45.1X1	T45.1X2	T45.1X3	T45.1X4	T45.1X5	T45.1X6
Etomidate	T41.1X1	T41.1X2	T41.1X3	T41.1X4	T41.1X5	T41.1X6
Etomide	T39.8X1	T39.8X2	T39.8X3	T39.8X4	T39.8X5	T39.8X6
Etomidoline	T44.3X1	T44.3X2	T44.3X3	T44.3X4	T44.3X5	T44.3X6
Etoposide	T45.1X1	T45.1X2	T45.1X3	T45.1X4	T45.1X5	T45.1X6
Etorphine	T40.2X1	T40.2X2	T40.2X3	T40.2X4	T40.2X5	T40.2X6
Etoval	T42.3X1	T42.3X2	T42.3X3	T42.3X4	T42.3X5	T42.3X6
Etozolin	T50.1X1	T50.1X2	T50.1X3	T50.1X4	T50.1X5	T50.1X6
Etretinate	T50.991	T50.992	T50.993	T50.994	T50.995	T50.996
Etryptamine	T43.691	T43.692	T43.693	T43.694	T43.695	T43.696
Etybenzatropine	T44.3X1	T44.3X2	T44.3X3	T44.3X4	T44.3X5	T44.3X6
Etynodiol	T38.4X1	T38.4X2	T38.4X3	T38.4X4	T38.4X5	T38.4X6
Eucaine	T41.3X1	T41.3X2	T41.3X3	T41.3X4	T41.3X5	T41.3X6
Eucalyptus oil	T49.7X1	T49.7X2	T49.7X3	T49.7X4	T49.7X5	T49.7X6
Eucatropine	T49.5X1	T49.5X2	T49.5X3	T49.5X4	T49.5X5	T49.5X6
Eucodal	T40.2X1	T40.2X2	T40.2X3	T40.2X4	T40.2X5	T40.2X6
Euneryl	T42.3X1	T42.3X2	T42.3X3	T42.3X4	T42.3X5	T42.3X6
Euphthalmine	T44.3X1	T44.3X2	T44.3X3	T44.3X4	T44.3X5	T44.3X6
Eurax	T49.0X1	T49.0X2	T49.0X3	T49.0X4	T49.0X5	T49.0X6
Euresol	T49.4X1	T49.4X2	T49.4X3	T49.4X4	T49.4X5	T49.4X6
Euthroid	T38.1X1	T38.1X2	T38.1X3	T38.1X4	T38.1X5	T38.1X6
Evans blue	T50.8X1	T50.8X2	T50.8X3	T50.8X4	T50.8X5	T50.8X6
Evipal	T42.3X1	T42.3X2	T42.3X3	T42.3X4	T42.3X5	T42.3X6
sodium	T41.1X1	T41.1X2	T41.1X3	T41.1X4	T41.1X5	T41.1X6
Evipan	T42.3X1	T42.3X2	T42.3X3	T42.3X4	T42.3X5	T42.3X6
sodium	T41.1X1	T41.1X2	T41.1X3	T41.1X4	T41.1X5	T41.1X6
Exalamide	T49.0X1	T49.0X2	T49.0X3	T49.0X4	T49.0X5	T49.0X6
Exalgin	T39.1X1	T39.1X2	T39.1X3	T39.1X4	T39.1X5	T39.1X6
Excipients, pharmaceutical	T50.901	T50.902	T50.903	T50.904	T50.905	T50.906
Exhaust gas(engine) (motor vehicle)	T58.01	T58.02	T58.03	T58.04	—	—
Ex-Lax(phenolphthalein)	T47.2X1	T47.2X2	T47.2X3	T47.2X4	T47.2X5	T47.2X6
Expectorant NEC	T48.4X1	T48.4X2	T48.4X3	T48.4X4	T48.4X5	T48.4X6
Extended insulin zinc suspension	T38.3X1	T38.3X2	T38.3X3	T38.3X4	T38.3X5	T38.3X6
External medications(skin) (mucous membrane)	T49.91	T49.92	T49.93	T49.94	T49.95	T49.96
dental agent	T49.7X1	T49.7X2	T49.7X3	T49.7X4	T49.7X5	T49.7X6
ENT agent	T49.6X1	T49.6X2	T49.6X3	T49.6X4	T49.6X5	T49.6X6
ophthalmic preparation	T49.5X1	T49.5X2	T49.5X3	T49.5X4	T49.5X5	T49.5X6
specified NEC	T49.8X1	T49.8X2	T49.8X3	T49.8X4	T49.8X5	T49.8X6
Extrapyramidal antagonist NEC	T44.3X1	T44.3X2	T44.3X3	T44.3X4	T44.3X5	T44.3X6
Eye agents(anti-infective)	T49.5X1	T49.5X2	T49.5X3	T49.5X4	T49.5X5	T49.5X6
Eye drug NEC	T49.5X1	T49.5X2	T49.5X3	T49.5X4	T49.5X5	T49.5X6
F						
FAC(fluorouracil + doxorubicin + cyclophosphamide)	T45.1X1	T45.1X2	T45.1X3	T45.1X4	T45.1X5	T45.1X6
Factor						
I(fibrinogen)	T45.8X1	T45.8X2	T45.8X3	T45.8X4	T45.8X5	T45.8X6
III(thromboplastin)	T45.8X1	T45.8X2	T45.8X3	T45.8X4	T45.8X5	T45.8X6

Substance	Poisoning, Accidental (unintentional)	Poisoning, Intentional self-harm	Poisoning, Assault	Poisoning, Undetermined	Adverse effect	
Factor — *Continued*						
VIII(antihemophilic Factor) (concentrate)	T45.8X1	T45.8X2	T45.8X3	T45.8X4	T45.8X5	T45
IX complex	T45.7X1	T45.7X2	T45.7X3	T45.7X4	T45.7X5	T45
human	T45.8X1	T45.8X2	T45.8X3	T45.8X4	T45.8X5	T45
Famotidine	T47.0X1	T47.0X2	T47.0X3	T47.0X4	T47.0X5	T47
Fat suspension, intravenous	T50.991	T50.992	T50.993	T50.994	T50.995	T5
Fazadinium bromide	T48.1X1	T48.1X2	T48.1X3	T48.1X4	T48.1X5	T48
Febarbamate	T42.3X1	T42.3X2	T42.3X3	T42.3X4	T42.3X5	T42
Fecal softener	T47.4X1	T47.4X2	T47.4X3	T47.4X4	T47.4X5	T47
Fedrilate	T48.3X1	T48.3X2	T48.3X3	T48.3X4	T48.3X5	T48
Felodipine	T46.1X1	T46.1X2	T46.1X3	T46.1X4	T46.1X5	T46
Felypressin	T38.891	T38.892	T38.893	T38.894	T38.895	T38
Femoxetine	T43.221	T43.222	T43.223	T43.224	T43.225	T43
Fenalcomine	T46.3X1	T46.3X2	T46.3X3	T46.3X4	T46.3X5	T46
Fenamisal	T37.1X1	T37.1X2	T37.1X3	T37.1X4	T37.1X5	T37
Fenazone	T39.2X1	T39.2X2	T39.2X3	T39.2X4	T39.2X5	T39
Fenbendazole	T37.4X1	T37.4X2	T37.4X3	T37.4X4	T37.4X5	T37
Fenbutrazate	T50.5X1	T50.5X2	T50.5X3	T50.5X4	T50.5X5	T50
Fencamfamine	T43.691	T43.692	T43.693	T43.694	T43.695	T43
Fendiline	T46.1X1	T46.1X2	T46.1X3	T46.1X4	T46.1X5	T46
Fenetylline	T43.691	T43.692	T43.693	T43.694	T43.695	T43
Fenflumizole	T39.391	T39.392	T39.393	T39.394	T39.395	T39
Fenfluramine	T50.5X1	T50.5X2	T50.5X3	T50.5X4	T50.5X5	T50
Fenobarbital	T42.3X1	T42.3X2	T42.3X3	T42.3X4	T42.3X5	T42
Fenofibrate	T46.6X1	T46.6X2	T46.6X3	T46.6X4	T46.6X5	T46.
Fenoprofen	T39.311	T39.312	T39.313	T39.314	T39.315	T39
Fenoterol	T48.6X1	T48.6X2	T48.6X3	T48.6X4	T48.6X5	T48.
Fenoverine	T44.3X1	T44.3X2	T44.3X3	T44.3X4	T44.3X5	T44.
Fenoxazoline	T48.5X1	T48.5X2	T48.5X3	T48.5X4	T48.5X5	T48.
Fenproporex	T50.5X1	T50.5X2	T50.5X3	T50.5X4	T50.5X5	T50.
Fenquizone	T50.2X1	T50.2X2	T50.2X3	T50.2X4	T50.2X5	T50.
Fentanyl	T40.4X1	T40.4X2	T40.4X3	T40.4X4	T40.4X5	T40.
Fentazin	T43.3X1	T43.3X2	T43.3X3	T43.3X4	T43.3X5	T43.
Fenthion	T60.0X1	T60.0X2	T60.0X3	T60.0X4	—	–
Fenticlor	T49.0X1	T49.0X2	T49.0X3	T49.0X4	T49.0X5	T49.
Fenylbutazone	T39.2X1	T39.2X2	T39.2X3	T39.2X4	T39.2X5	T39.
Feprazone	T39.2X1	T39.2X2	T39.2X3	T39.2X4	T39.2X5	T39.
Fer de lance(bite) (venom)	T63.061	T63.062	T63.063	T63.064	—	–
Ferric—see also Iron						
chloride	T45.4X1	T45.4X2	T45.4X3	T45.4X4	T45.4X5	T45.
citrate	T45.4X1	T45.4X2	T45.4X3	T45.4X4	T45.4X5	T45.
hydroxide						
colloidal	T45.4X1	T45.4X2	T45.4X3	T45.4X4	T45.4X5	T45.
polymaltose	T45.4X1	T45.4X2	T45.4X3	T45.4X4	T45.4X5	T45.
pyrophosphate	T45.4X1	T45.4X2	T45.4X3	T45.4X4	T45.4X5	T45.
Ferritin	T45.4X1	T45.4X2	T45.4X3	T45.4X4	T45.4X5	T45.
Ferrocholinate	T45.4X1	T45.4X2	T45.4X3	T45.4X4	T45.4X5	T45.
Ferrodextrane	T45.4X1	T45.4X2	T45.4X3	T45.4X4	T45.4X5	T45.
Ferropolimaler	T45.4X1	T45.4X2	T45.4X3	T45.4X4	T45.4X5	T45.

Substance	Poisoning, Accidental (unintentional)	Poisoning, Intentional self-harm	Poisoning, Assault	Poisoning, Undetermined	Adverse effect	Underdosing
ous—see also Iron						
osphate	T45.4X1	T45.4X2	T45.4X3	T45.4X4	T45.4X5	T45.4X6
:	T45.4X1	T45.4X2	T45.4X3	T45.4X4	T45.4X5	T45.4X6
vith folic acid	T45.4X1	T45.4X2	T45.4X3	T45.4X4	T45.4X5	T45.4X6
ous fumerate, onate, lactate, salt ', sulfate(medicinal)	T45.4X1	T45.4X2	T45.4X3	T45.4X4	T45.4X5	T45.4X6
ovanadium es)	T59.891	T59.892	T59.893	T59.894	—	—
um—see Iron						
ilizers NEC	T65.891	T65.892	T65.893	T65.894	—	—
th herbicide mixture	T60.3X1	T60.3X2	T60.3X3	T60.3X4	—	—
xilate	T47.6X1	T47.6X2	T47.6X3	T47.6X4	T47.6X5	T47.6X6
r, dietary	T47.4X1	T47.4X2	T47.4X3	T47.4X4	T47.4X5	T47.4X6
rglass	T65.831	T65.832	T65.833	T65.834	—	—
inogen(human)	T45.8X1	T45.8X2	T45.8X3	T45.8X4	T45.8X5	T45.8X6
inolysin (human)	T45.691	T45.692	T45.693	T45.694	T45.695	T45.696
inolysis						
ecting drug	T45.601	T45.602	T45.603	T45.604	T45.605	T45.606
ibitor NEC	T45.621	T45.622	T45.623	T45.624	T45.625	T45.626
inolytic drug	T45.611	T45.612	T45.613	T45.614	T45.615	T45.616
mas	T37.4X1	T37.4X2	T37.4X3	T37.4X4	T37.4X5	T37.4X6
ring cream	T49.3X1	T49.3X2	T49.3X3	T49.3X4	T49.3X5	T49.3X6
inal	T39.011	T39.012	T39.013	T39.014	T39.015	T39.016
damp	T59.891	T59.892	T59.893	T59.894	—	—
, noxious, nonbacterial	T61.91	T61.92	T61.93	T61.94	—	—
guatera	T61.01	T61.02	T61.03	T61.04	—	—
ombroid	T61.11	T61.12	T61.13	T61.14	—	—
ell	T61.781	T61.782	T61.783	T61.784	—	—
ecified NEC	T61.771	T61.772	T61.773	T61.774	—	—
yl	T37.3X1	T37.3X2	T37.3X3	T37.3X4	T37.3X5	T37.3X6
ine adenine cleotide	T45.2X1	T45.2X2	T45.2X3	T45.2X4	T45.2X5	T45.2X6
odic acid	T46.991	T46.992	T46.993	T46.994	T46.995	T46.996
oxate	T44.3X1	T44.3X2	T44.3X3	T44.3X4	T44.3X5	T44.3X6
edil	T48.1X1	T48.1X2	T48.1X3	T48.1X4	T48.1X5	T48.1X6
seed(medicinal)	T49.3X1	T49.3X2	T49.3X3	T49.3X4	T49.3X5	T49.3X6
ainide	T46.2X1	T46.2X2	T46.2X3	T46.2X4	T46.2X5	T46.2X6
oxacin	T36.8X1	T36.8X2	T36.8X3	T36.8X4	T36.8X5	T36.8X6
tafenine	T39.8X1	T39.8X2	T39.8X3	T39.8X4	T39.8X5	T39.8X6
nax	T44.6X1	T44.6X2	T44.6X3	T44.6X4	T44.6X5	T44.6X6
noxef	T36.1X1	T36.1X2	T36.1X3	T36.1X4	T36.1X5	T36.1X6
propione	T44.3X1	T44.3X2	T44.3X3	T44.3X4	T44.3X5	T44.3X6
antyrone	T47.5X1	T47.5X2	T47.5X3	T47.5X4	T47.5X5	T47.5X6
aquin	T37.8X1	T37.8X2	T37.8X3	T37.8X4	T37.8X5	T37.8X6
inef	T38.0X1	T38.0X2	T38.0X3	T38.0X4	T38.0X5	T38.0X6
NT agent	T49.6X1	T49.6X2	T49.6X3	T49.6X4	T49.6X5	T49.6X6
ophthalmic preparation	T49.5X1	T49.5X2	T49.5X3	T49.5X4	T49.5X5	T49.5X6
opical NEC	T49.0X1	T49.0X2	T49.0X3	T49.0X4	T49.0X5	T49.0X6
wers of sulfur	T49.4X1	T49.4X2	T49.4X3	T49.4X4	T49.4X5	T49.4X6
xuridine	T45.1X1	T45.1X2	T45.1X3	T45.1X4	T45.1X5	T45.1X6
anisone	T43.4X1	T43.4X2	T43.4X3	T43.4X4	T43.4X5	T43.4X6

Substance	Poisoning, Accidental (unintentional)	Poisoning, Intentional self-harm	Poisoning, Assault	Poisoning, Undetermined	Adverse effect	Underdosing
Flubendazole	T37.4X1	T37.4X2	T37.4X3	T37.4X4	T37.4X5	T37.4X6
Fluclorolone acetonide	T49.0X1	T49.0X2	T49.0X3	T49.0X4	T49.0X5	T49.0X6
Flucloxacillin	T36.0X1	T36.0X2	T36.0X3	T36.0X4	T36.0X5	T36.0X6
Fluconazole	T37.8X1	T37.8X2	T37.8X3	T37.8X4	T37.8X5	T37.8X6
Flucytosine	T37.8X1	T37.8X2	T37.8X3	T37.8X4	T37.8X5	T37.8X6
Fludeoxyglucose(18F)	T50.8X1	T50.8X2	T50.8X3	T50.8X4	T50.8X5	T50.8X6
Fludiazepam	T42.4X1	T42.4X2	T42.4X3	T42.4X4	T42.4X5	T42.4X6
Fludrocortisone	T50.0X1	T50.0X2	T50.0X3	T50.0X4	T50.0X5	T50.0X6
ENT agent	T49.6X1	T49.6X2	T49.6X3	T49.6X4	T49.6X5	T49.6X6
ophthalmic preparation	T49.5X1	T49.5X2	T49.5X3	T49.5X4	T49.5X5	T49.5X6
topical NEC	T49.0X1	T49.0X2	T49.0X3	T49.0X4	T49.0X5	T49.0X6
Fludroxycortide	T49.0X1	T49.0X2	T49.0X3	T49.0X4	T49.0X5	T49.0X6
Flufenamic acid	T39.391	T39.392	T39.393	T39.394	T39.395	T39.396
Fluindione	T45.511	T45.512	T45.513	T45.514	T45.515	T45.516
Flumequine	T37.8X1	T37.8X2	T37.8X3	T37.8X4	T37.8X5	T37.8X6
Flumethasone	T49.0X1	T49.0X2	T49.0X3	T49.0X4	T49.0X5	T49.0X6
Flumethiazide	T50.2X1	T50.2X2	T50.2X3	T50.2X4	T50.2X5	T50.2X6
Flumidin	T37.5X1	T37.5X2	T37.5X3	T37.5X4	T37.5X5	T37.5X6
Flunarizine	T46.7X1	T46.7X2	T46.7X3	T46.7X4	T46.7X5	T46.7X6
Flunidazole	T37.8X1	T37.8X2	T37.8X3	T37.8X4	T37.8X5	T37.8X6
Flunisolide	T48.6X1	T48.6X2	T48.6X3	T48.6X4	T48.6X5	T48.6X6
Flunitrazepam	T42.4X1	T42.4X2	T42.4X3	T42.4X4	T42.4X5	T42.4X6
Fluocinolone (acetonide)	T49.0X1	T49.0X2	T49.0X3	T49.0X4	T49.0X5	T49.0X6
Fluocinonide	T49.0X1	T49.0X2	T49.0X3	T49.0X4	T49.0X5	T49.0X6
Fluocortin(butyl)	T49.0X1	T49.0X2	T49.0X3	T49.0X4	T49.0X5	T49.0X6
Fluocortolone	T49.0X1	T49.0X2	T49.0X3	T49.0X4	T49.0X5	T49.0X6
Fluohydrocortisone	T38.0X1	T38.0X2	T38.0X3	T38.0X4	T38.0X5	T38.0X6
ENT agent	T49.6X1	T49.6X2	T49.6X3	T49.6X4	T49.6X5	T49.6X6
ophthalmic preparation	T49.5X1	T49.5X2	T49.5X3	T49.5X4	T49.5X5	T49.5X6
topical NEC	T49.0X1	T49.0X2	T49.0X3	T49.0X4	T49.0X5	T49.0X6
Fluonid	T49.0X1	T49.0X2	T49.0X3	T49.0X4	T49.0X5	T49.0X6
Fluopromazine	T43.3X1	T43.3X2	T43.3X3	T43.3X4	T43.3X5	T43.3X6
Fluoracetate	T60.8X1	T60.8X2	T60.8X3	T60.8X4	—	—
Fluorescein	T50.8X1	T50.8X2	T50.8X3	T50.8X4	T50.8X5	T50.8X6
Fluorhydrocortisone	T50.0X1	T50.0X2	T50.0X3	T50.0X4	T50.0X5	T50.0X6
Fluoride(nonmedicin al) (pesticide) (sodium) NEC	T60.8X1	T60.8X2	T60.8X3	T60.8X4	—	—
hydrogen—see Hydrofluoric acid						
medicinal NEC	T50.991	T50.992	T50.993	T50.994	T50.995	T50.996
dental use	T49.7X1	T49.7X2	T49.7X3	T49.7X4	T49.7X5	T49.7X6
not pesticide NEC	T54.91	T54.92	T54.93	T54.94	—	—
stannous	T49.7X1	T49.7X2	T49.7X3	T49.7X4	T49.7X5	T49.7X6
Fluorinated corticosteroids	T38.0X1	T38.0X2	T38.0X3	T38.0X4	T38.0X5	T38.0X6
Fluorine(gas)	T59.5X1	T59.5X2	T59.5X3	T59.5X4	—	—
salt—see Fluoride(s)						
Fluoristan	T49.7X1	T49.7X2	T49.7X3	T49.7X4	T49.7X5	T49.7X6
Fluormetholone	T49.0X1	T49.0X2	T49.0X3	T49.0X4	T49.0X5	T49.0X6
Fluoroacetate	T60.8X1	T60.8X2	T60.8X3	T60.8X4	—	—
Fluorocarbon monomer	T53.6X1	T53.6X2	T53.6X3	T53.6X4	—	—
Fluorocytosine	T37.8X1	T37.8X2	T37.8X3	T37.8X4	T37.8X5	T37.8X6

Substance	Poisoning, Accidental (unintentional)	Poisoning, Intentional self-harm	Poisoning, Assault	Poisoning, Undetermined	Adverse effect	Underdosing
Fluorodeoxyuridine	T45.1X1	T45.1X2	T45.1X3	T45.1X4	T45.1X5	T45.1X6
Fluorometholone	T49.0X1	T49.0X2	T49.0X3	T49.0X4	T49.0X5	T49.0X6
ophthalmic preparation	T49.5X1	T49.5X2	T49.5X3	T49.5X4	T49.5X5	T49.5X6
Fluorophosphate insecticide	T60.0X1	T60.0X2	T60.0X3	T60.0X4	—	—
Fluorosol	T46.3X1	T46.3X2	T46.3X3	T46.3X4	T46.3X5	T46.3X6
Fluorouracil	T45.1X1	T45.1X2	T45.1X3	T45.1X4	T45.1X5	T45.1X6
Fluorphenylalanine	T49.5X1	T49.5X2	T49.5X3	T49.5X4	T49.5X5	T49.5X6
Fluothane	T41.0X1	T41.0X2	T41.0X3	T41.0X4	T41.0X5	T41.0X6
Fluoxetine	T43.221	T43.222	T43.223	T43.224	T43.225	T43.226
Fluoxymesterone	T38.7X1	T38.7X2	T38.7X3	T38.7X4	T38.7X5	T38.7X6
Flupenthixol	T43.4X1	T43.4X2	T43.4X3	T43.4X4	T43.4X5	T43.4X6
Flupentixol	T43.4X1	T43.4X2	T43.4X3	T43.4X4	T43.4X5	T43.4X6
Fluphenazine	T43.3X1	T43.3X2	T43.3X3	T43.3X4	T43.3X5	T43.3X6
Fluprednidene	T49.0X1	T49.0X2	T49.0X3	T49.0X4	T49.0X5	T49.0X6
Fluprednisolone	T38.0X1	T38.0X2	T38.0X3	T38.0X4	T38.0X5	T38.0X6
Fluradoline	T39.8X1	T39.8X2	T39.8X3	T39.8X4	T39.8X5	T39.8X6
Flurandrenolide	T49.0X1	T49.0X2	T49.0X3	T49.0X4	T49.0X5	T49.0X6
Flurandrenolone	T49.0X1	T49.0X2	T49.0X3	T49.0X4	T49.0X5	T49.0X6
Flurazepam	T42.4X1	T42.4X2	T42.4X3	T42.4X4	T42.4X5	T42.4X6
Flurbiprofen	T39.311	T39.312	T39.313	T39.314	T39.315	T39.316
Flurobate	T49.0X1	T49.0X2	T49.0X3	T49.0X4	T49.0X5	T49.0X6
Fluroxene	T41.0X1	T41.0X2	T41.0X3	T41.0X4	T41.0X5	T41.0X6
Fluspirilene	T43.591	T43.592	T43.593	T43.594	T43.595	T43.596
Flutamide	T38.6X1	T38.6X2	T38.6X3	T38.6X4	T38.6X5	T38.6X6
Flutazolam	T42.4X1	T42.4X2	T42.4X3	T42.4X4	T42.4X5	T42.4X6
Fluticasone propionate	T49.1X1	T49.1X2	T49.1X3	T49.1X4	T49.1X5	T49.1X6
Flutoprazepam	T42.4X1	T42.4X2	T42.4X3	T42.4X4	T42.4X5	T42.4X6
Flutropium bromide	T48.6X1	T48.6X2	T48.6X3	T48.6X4	T48.6X5	T48.6X6
Fluvoxamine	T43.221	T43.222	T43.223	T43.224	T43.225	T43.226
Folacin	T45.8X1	T45.8X2	T45.8X3	T45.8X4	T45.8X5	T45.8X6
Folic acid	T45.8X1	T45.8X2	T45.8X3	T45.8X4	T45.8X5	T45.8X6
with ferrous salt	T45.2X1	T45.2X2	T45.2X3	T45.2X4	T45.2X5	T45.2X6
antagonist	T45.1X1	T45.1X2	T45.1X3	T45.1X4	T45.1X5	T45.1X6
Folinic acid	T45.8X1	T45.8X2	T45.8X3	T45.8X4	T45.8X5	T45.8X6
Folium stramoniae	T48.6X1	T48.6X2	T48.6X3	T48.6X4	T48.6X5	T48.6X6
Follicle-stimulating hormone, human	T38.811	T38.812	T38.813	T38.814	T38.815	T38.816
Folpet	T60.3X1	T60.3X2	T60.3X3	T60.3X4	—	—
Fominoben	T48.3X1	T48.3X2	T48.3X3	T48.3X4	T48.3X5	T48.3X6
Food, foodstuffs, noxious, nonbacterial, NEC	T62.91	T62.92	T62.93	T62.94	—	—
berries	T62.1X1	T62.1X2	T62.1X3	T62.1X4	—	—
fish—see also Fish	T61.91	T61.92	T61.93	T61.94	—	—
mushrooms	T62.0X1	T62.0X2	T62.0X3	T62.0X4	—	—
plants	T62.2X1	T62.2X2	T62.2X3	T62.2X4	—	—
seafood	T61.91	T61.92	T61.93	T61.94	—	—
specified NEC	T61.8X1	T61.8X2	T61.8X3	T61.8X4	—	—
seeds	T62.2X1	T62.2X2	T62.2X3	T62.2X4	—	—
shellfish	T61.781	T61.782	T61.783	T61.784	—	—
specified NEC	T62.8X1	T62.8X2	T62.8X3	T62.8X4	—	—

Substance	Poisoning, Accidental (unintentional)	Poisoning, Intentional self-harm	Poisoning, Assault	Poisoning, Undetermined	Adverse effect	Underdosing
Fool's parsley	T62.2X1	T62.2X2	T62.2X3	T62.2X4	—	—
Formaldehyde (solution), gas or vapor	T59.2X1	T59.2X2	T59.2X3	T59.2X4	—	—
fungicide	T60.3X1	T60.3X2	T60.3X3	T60.3X4	—	—
Formalin	T59.2X1	T59.2X2	T59.2X3	T59.2X4	—	—
fungicide	T60.3X1	T60.3X2	T60.3X3	T60.3X4	—	—
vapor	T59.2X1	T59.2X2	T59.2X3	T59.2X4	—	—
Formic acid	T54.2X1	T54.2X2	T54.2X3	T54.2X4	—	—
vapor	T59.891	T59.892	T59.893	T59.894	—	—
Foscarnet sodium	T37.5X1	T37.5X2	T37.5X3	T37.5X4	T37.5X5	T37
Fosfestrol	T38.5X1	T38.5X2	T38.5X3	T38.5X4	T38.5X5	T38
Fosfomycin	T36.8X1	T36.8X2	T36.8X3	T36.8X4	T36.8X5	T36
Fosfonet sodium	T37.5X1	T37.5X2	T37.5X3	T37.5X4	T37.5X5	T37
Fosinopril	T46.4X1	T46.4X2	T46.4X3	T46.4X4	T46.4X5	T46
sodium	T46.4X1	T46.4X2	T46.4X3	T46.4X4	T46.4X5	T46
Fowler's solution	T57.0X1	T57.0X2	T57.0X3	T57.0X4	—	—
Foxglove	T62.2X1	T62.2X2	T62.2X3	T62.2X4	—	—
Framycetin	T36.5X1	T36.5X2	T36.5X3	T36.5X4	T36.5X5	T36
Frangula	T47.2X1	T47.2X2	T47.2X3	T47.2X4	T47.2X5	T47
extract	T47.2X1	T47.2X2	T47.2X3	T47.2X4	T47.2X5	T47
Frei antigen	T50.8X1	T50.8X2	T50.8X3	T50.8X4	T50.8X5	T50
Freon	T53.5X1	T53.5X2	T53.5X3	T53.5X4	—	—
Fructose	T50.3X1	T50.3X2	T50.3X3	T50.3X4	T50.3X5	T50
Frusemide	T50.1X1	T50.1X2	T50.1X3	T50.1X4	T50.1X5	T50
FSH	T38.811	T38.812	T38.813	T38.814	T38.815	T38
Ftorafur	T45.1X1	T45.1X2	T45.1X3	T45.1X4	T45.1X5	T45
Fuel						
automobile	T52.0X1	T52.0X2	T52.0X3	T52.0X4	—	—
exhaust gas, not in transit	T58.01	T58.02	T58.03	T58.04	—	—
vapor NEC	T52.0X1	T52.0X2	T52.0X3	T52.0X4	—	—
gas(domestic use)—see also Carbon, monoxide, fuel, utility	T59.891	T59.892	T59.893	T59.894	—	—
utility	T59.891	T59.892	T59.893	T59.894	—	—
in mobile container	T59.891	T59.892	T59.893	T59.894	—	—
incomplete combustion of—see Carbon, monoxide, fuel, utility						
piped(natural)	T59.891	T59.892	T59.893	T59.894	—	—
industrial, incomplete combustion	T58.8X1	T58.8X2	T58.8X3	T58.8X4	—	—
Fugillin	T36.8X1	T36.8X2	T36.8X3	T36.8X4	T36.8X5	T36
Fulminate of mercury	T56.1X1	T56.1X2	T56.1X3	T56.1X4	—	—
Fulvicin	T36.7X1	T36.7X2	T36.7X3	T36.7X4	T36.7X5	T36
Fumadil	T36.8X1	T36.8X2	T36.8X3	T36.8X4	T36.8X5	T36
Fumagillin	T36.8X1	T36.8X2	T36.8X3	T36.8X4	T36.8X5	T36
Fumaric acid	T49.4X1	T49.4X2	T49.4X3	T49.4X4	T49.4X5	T49
Fumes(from)	T59.91	T59.92	T59.93	T59.94	—	—
carbon monoxide—see Carbon, monoxide						
charcoal(domestic use)—see Charcoal, fumes						

Substance	Poisoning, Accidental (unintentional)	Poisoning, Intentional self-harm	Poisoning, Assault	Poisoning, Undetermined	Adverse effect	Underdosing
es(from) — *Continued*						
oroform—see loroform						
e(in domestic stoves, places)—see Coke nes						
rosive NEC	T54.91	T54.92	T54.93	T54.94	—	—
—see ether						
ons	T53.5X1	T53.5X2	T53.5X3	T53.5X4	—	—
lrocarbons	T59.891	T59.892	T59.893	T59.894	—	—
etroleum (liquefied)	T59.891	T59.892	T59.893	T59.894	—	—
distributed through pipes(pure or mixed with air)	T59.891	T59.892	T59.893	T59.894	—	—
d—see lead						
tal—see Metals, or the cified metal						
ogen dioxide	T59.0X1	T59.0X2	T59.0X3	T59.0X4	—	—
ticides—see Pesticides						
roleum uefied)	T59.891	T59.892	T59.893	T59.894	—	—
istributed through ipes(pure or mixed ith air)	T59.891	T59.892	T59.893	T59.894	—	—
yester	T59.891	T59.892	T59.893	T59.894	—	—
cified source NEC—see substance cified	T59.891	T59.892	T59.893	T59.894	—	—
fur dioxide	T59.1X1	T59.1X2	T59.1X3	T59.1X4	—	—
igant NEC	T60.91	T60.92	T60.93	T60.94	—	—
i, noxious, used as	T62.0X1	T62.0X2	T62.0X3	T62.0X4	—	—
icide (nonmedicinal)	T60.3X1	T60.3X2	T60.3X3	T60.3X4	—	—
izone	T36.7X1	T36.7X2	T36.7X3	T36.7X4	T36.7X5	T36.7X6
ical	T49.0X1	T49.0X2	T49.0X3	T49.0X4	T49.0X5	T49.0X6
cin	T49.0X1	T49.0X2	T49.0X3	T49.0X4	T49.0X5	T49.0X6
dantin	T37.91	T37.92	T37.93	T37.94	T37.95	T37.96
zolidone	T37.8X1	T37.8X2	T37.8X3	T37.8X4	T37.8X5	T37.8X6
zolium ide	T49.0X1	T49.0X2	T49.0X3	T49.0X4	T49.0X5	T49.0X6
ural	T52.8X1	T52.8X2	T52.8X3	T52.8X4	—	—
ace(coal burning) estic), gas from	T58.2X1	T58.2X2	T58.2X3	T58.2X4	—	—
ustrial	T58.8X1	T58.8X2	T58.8X3	T58.8X4	—	—
iture polish	T65.891	T65.892	T65.893	T65.894	—	—
semide	T50.1X1	T50.1X2	T50.1X3	T50.1X4	T50.1X5	T50.1X6
xone	T37.91	T37.92	T37.93	T37.94	T37.95	T37.96
ltiamine	T45.2X1	T45.2X2	T45.2X3	T45.2X4	T45.2X5	T45.2X6
fungine	T36.8X1	T36.8X2	T36.8X3	T36.8X4	T36.8X5	T36.8X6
oil(any) (amyl) l) (propyl), vapor	T51.3X1	T51.3X2	T51.3X3	T51.3X4	—	—
date nolamine) (sodium)	T36.8X1	T36.8X2	T36.8X3	T36.8X4	T36.8X5	T36.8X6
dic acid	T36.8X1	T36.8X2	T36.8X3	T36.8X4	T36.8X5	T36.8X6
acid, nonasodium	T50.6X1	T50.6X2	T50.6X3	T50.6X4	T50.6X5	T50.6X6

Substance	Poisoning, Accidental (unintentional)	Poisoning, Intentional self-harm	Poisoning, Assault	Poisoning, Undetermined	Adverse effect	Underdosing
G						
GABA	T43.8X1	T43.8X2	T43.8X3	T43.8X4	T43.8X5	T43.8X6
Gadopentetic acid	T50.8X1	T50.8X2	T50.8X3	T50.8X4	T50.8X5	T50.8X6
Galactose	T50.3X1	T50.3X2	T50.3X3	T50.3X4	T50.3X5	T50.3X6
b-Galactosidase	T47.5X1	T47.5X2	T47.5X3	T47.5X4	T47.5X5	T47.5X6
Galantamine	T44.0X1	T44.0X2	T44.0X3	T44.0X4	T44.0X5	T44.0X6
Gallamine (triethiodide)	T48.1X1	T48.1X2	T48.1X3	T48.1X4	T48.1X5	T48.1X6
Gallium citrate	T50.991	T50.992	T50.993	T50.994	T50.995	T50.996
Gallopamil	T46.1X1	T46.1X2	T46.1X3	T46.1X4	T46.1X5	T46.1X6
Gamboge	T47.2X1	T47.2X2	T47.2X3	T47.2X4	T47.2X5	T47.2X6
Gamimune	T50.Z11	T50.Z12	T50.Z13	T50.Z14	T50.Z15	T50.Z16
Gamma globulin	T50.Z11	T50.Z12	T50.Z13	T50.Z14	T50.Z15	T50.Z16
Gamma-aminobutyric acid	T43.8X1	T43.8X2	T43.8X3	T43.8X4	T43.8X5	T43.8X6
Gamma-benzene hexachloride (medicinal)	T49.0X1	T49.0X2	T49.0X3	T49.0X4	T49.0X5	T49.0X6
nonmedicinal, vapor	T53.6X1	T53.6X2	T53.6X3	T53.6X4	—	—
Gamma-BHC(medicinal)—see also Gamma-benzene hexachloride	T49.0X1	T49.0X2	T49.0X3	T49.0X4	T49.0X5	T49.0X6
Gamulin	T50.Z11	T50.Z12	T50.Z13	T50.Z14	T50.Z15	T50.Z16
Ganciclovir(sodium)	T37.5X1	T37.5X2	T37.5X3	T37.5X4	T37.5X5	T37.5X6
Ganglionic blocking drug NEC	T44.2X1	T44.2X2	T44.2X3	T44.2X4	T44.2X5	T44.2X6
specified NEC	T44.2X1	T44.2X2	T44.2X3	T44.2X4	T44.2X5	T44.2X6
Ganja	T40.7X1	T40.7X2	T40.7X3	T40.7X4	T40.7X5	T40.7X6
Garamycin	T36.5X1	T36.5X2	T36.5X3	T36.5X4	T36.5X5	T36.5X6
ophthalmic preparation	T49.5X1	T49.5X2	T49.5X3	T49.5X4	T49.5X5	T49.5X6
topical NEC	T49.0X1	T49.0X2	T49.0X3	T49.0X4	T49.0X5	T49.0X6
Gardenal	T42.3X1	T42.3X2	T42.3X3	T42.3X4	T42.3X5	T42.3X6
Gardepanyl	T42.3X1	T42.3X2	T42.3X3	T42.3X4	T42.3X5	T42.3X6
Gas	T59.91	T59.92	T59.93	T59.94	—	—
acetylene	T59.891	T59.892	T59.893	T59.894	—	—
incomplete combustion of	T58.11	T58.12	T58.13	T58.14	—	—
air contaminants, source or type not specified	T59.91	T59.92	T59.93	T59.94	—	—
anesthetic	T41.0X1	T41.0X2	T41.0X3	T41.0X4	T41.0X5	T41.0X6
blast furnace	T58.8X1	T58.8X2	T58.8X3	T58.8X4	—	—
butane—see butane						
carbon monoxide—see Carbon, monoxide						
chlorine	T59.4X1	T59.4X2	T59.4X3	T59.4X4	—	—
coal	T58.2X1	T58.2X2	T58.2X3	T58.2X4	—	—
cyanide	T57.3X1	T57.3X2	T57.3X3	T57.3X4	—	—
dicyanogen	T65.0X1	T65.0X2	T65.0X3	T65.0X4	—	—
domestic—see Domestic gas						
exhaust	T58.01	T58.02	T58.03	T58.04	—	—
from utility(for cooking, heating, or lighting) (after combustion)—see Carbon, monoxide, fuel, utility						

Substance	Poisoning, Accidental (unintentional)	Poisoning, Intentional self-harm	Poisoning, Assault	Poisoning, Undetermined	Adverse effect	Underdosing
Gas — *Continued*						
prior to combustion	T59.891	T59.892	T59.893	T59.894	—	—
from wood- or coal-burning stove or fireplace	T58.2X1	T58.2X2	T58.2X3	T58.2X4	—	—
fuel(domestic use) (after combustion)—see also Carbon, monoxide, fuel						
industrial use	T58.8X1	T58.8X2	T58.8X3	T58.8X4	—	—
prior to combustion	T59.891	T59.892	T59.893	T59.894	—	—
utility	T59.891	T59.892	T59.893	T59.894	—	—
in mobile container	T59.891	T59.892	T59.893	T59.894	—	—
incomplete combustion of—see Carbon, monoxide, fuel, utility						
piped(natural)	T59.891	T59.892	T59.893	T59.894	—	—
garage	T58.01	T58.02	T58.03	T58.04	—	—
hydrocarbon NEC	T59.891	T59.892	T59.893	T59.894	—	—
incomplete combustion of—see Carbon, monoxide, fuel, utility						
liquefied—see butane						
piped	T59.891	T59.892	T59.893	T59.894	—	—
hydrocyanic acid	T65.0X1	T65.0X2	T65.0X3	T65.0X4	—	—
illuminating(after combustion)	T58.11	T58.12	T58.13	T58.14	—	—
prior to combustion	T59.891	T59.892	T59.893	T59.894	—	—
incomplete combustion, any—see Carbon, monoxide						
kiln	T58.8X1	T58.8X2	T58.8X3	T58.8X4	—	—
lacrimogenic	T59.3X1	T59.3X2	T59.3X3	T59.3X4	—	—
liquefied petroleum—see butane						
marsh	T59.891	T59.892	T59.893	T59.894	—	—
motor exhaust, not in transit	T58.01	T58.02	T58.03	T58.04	—	—
mustard, not in war	T59.891	T59.892	T59.893	T59.894	—	—
natural	T59.891	T59.892	T59.893	T59.894	—	—
nerve, not in war	T59.91	T59.92	T59.93	T59.94	—	—
oil	T52.0X1	T52.0X2	T52.0X3	T52.0X4	—	—
petroleum(liquefied) (distributed in mobile containers)	T59.891	T59.892	T59.893	T59.894	—	—
piped(pure or mixed with air)	T59.891	T59.892	T59.893	T59.894	—	—
piped(manufactured) (natural) NEC	T59.891	T59.892	T59.893	T59.894	—	—
producer	T58.8X1	T58.8X2	T58.8X3	T58.8X4	—	—
propane—see propane						
refrigerant (chlorofluoro-carbon)	T53.5X1	T53.5X2	T53.5X3	T53.5X4	—	—
not chlorofluoro-carbon	T59.891	T59.892	T59.893	T59.894	—	—
sewer	T59.91	T59.92	T59.93	T59.94	—	—
specified source NEC	T59.91	T59.92	T59.93	T59.94	—	—
stove(after combustion)	T58.11	T58.12	T58.13	T58.14	—	—
prior to combustion	T59.891	T59.892	T59.893	T59.894	—	—

Substance	Poisoning, Accidental (unintentional)	Poisoning, Intentional self-harm	Poisoning, Assault	Poisoning, Undetermined	Adverse effect	Underdosing
Gas — *Continued*						
tear	T59.3X1	T59.3X2	T59.3X3	T59.3X4	—	—
therapeutic	T41.5X1	T41.5X2	T41.5X3	T41.5X4	T41.5X5	T41
utility(for cooking, heating, or lighting) (piped) NEC	T59.891	T59.892	T59.893	T59.894	—	—
in mobile container	T59.891	T59.892	T59.893	T59.894	—	—
incomplete combustion of—see Carbon, monoxide, fuel, utilty						
piped(natural)	T59.891	T59.892	T59.893	T59.894	—	—
water	T58.11	T58.12	T58.13	T58.14	—	—
incomplete combustion of—see Carbon, monoxide, fuel, utility						
Gaseous substance—see Gas						
Gasoline	T52.0X1	T52.0X2	T52.0X3	T52.0X4	—	—
vapor	T52.0X1	T52.0X2	T52.0X3	T52.0X4	—	—
Gastric enzymes	T47.5X1	T47.5X2	T47.5X3	T47.5X4	T47.5X5	T47.
Gastrografin	T50.8X1	T50.8X2	T50.8X3	T50.8X4	T50.8X5	T50.
Gastrointestinal drug	T47.91	T47.92	T47.93	T47.94	T47.95	T47
biological	T47.8X1	T47.8X2	T47.8X3	T47.8X4	T47.8X5	T47.
specified NEC	T47.8X1	T47.8X2	T47.8X3	T47.8X4	T47.8X5	T47.
Gaultheria procumbens	T62.2X1	T62.2X2	T62.2X3	T62.2X4	—	—
Gefarnate	T44.3X1	T44.3X2	T44.3X3	T44.3X4	T44.3X5	T44.
Gelatin(intravenous)	T45.8X1	T45.8X2	T45.8X3	T45.8X4	T45.8X5	T45.
absorbable(sponge)	T45.7X1	T45.7X2	T45.7X3	T45.7X4	T45.7X5	T45.
Gelfilm	T49.8X1	T49.8X2	T49.8X3	T49.8X4	T49.8X5	T49.
Gelfoam	T45.7X1	T45.7X2	T45.7X3	T45.7X4	T45.7X5	T45.
Gelsemine	T50.991	T50.992	T50.993	T50.994	T50.995	T50.
Gelsemium (sempervirens)	T62.2X1	T62.2X2	T62.2X3	T62.2X4	—	—
Gemeprost	T48.0X1	T48.0X2	T48.0X3	T48.0X4	T48.0X5	T48.
Gemfibrozil	T46.6X1	T46.6X2	T46.6X3	T46.6X4	T46.6X5	T46.
Gemonil	T42.3X1	T42.3X2	T42.3X3	T42.3X4	T42.3X5	T42.
Gentamicin	T36.5X1	T36.5X2	T36.5X3	T36.5X4	T36.5X5	T36.
ophthalmic preparation	T49.5X1	T49.5X2	T49.5X3	T49.5X4	T49.5X5	T49.
topical NEC	T49.0X1	T49.0X2	T49.0X3	T49.0X4	T49.0X5	T49.0
Gentian	T47.5X1	T47.5X2	T47.5X3	T47.5X4	T47.5X5	T47.
violet	T49.0X1	T49.0X2	T49.0X3	T49.0X4	T49.0X5	T49.0
Gepefrine	T44.4X1	T44.4X2	T44.4X3	T44.4X4	T44.4X5	T44.
Gestonorone caproate	T38.5X1	T38.5X2	T38.5X3	T38.5X4	T38.5X5	T38.
Gexane	T49.0X1	T49.0X2	T49.0X3	T49.0X4	T49.0X5	T49.0
Gila monster(venom)	T63.111	T63.112	T63.113	T63.114	—	—
Ginger	T47.5X1	T47.5X2	T47.5X3	T47.5X4	T47.5X5	T47.
Jamaica—see Jamaica, ginger						
Gitalin	T46.0X1	T46.0X2	T46.0X3	T46.0X4	T46.0X5	T46.0
amorphous	T46.0X1	T46.0X2	T46.0X3	T46.0X4	T46.0X5	T46.0
Gitaloxin	T46.0X1	T46.0X2	T46.0X3	T46.0X4	T46.0X5	T46.0
Gitoxin	T46.0X1	T46.0X2	T46.0X3	T46.0X4	T46.0X5	T46.0
Glafenine	T39.8X1	T39.8X2	T39.8X3	T39.8X4	T39.8X5	T39.8

Substance	Poisoning, Accidental (unintentional)	Poisoning, Intentional self-harm	Poisoning, Assault	Poisoning, Undetermined	Adverse effect	Underdosing
dular ct(medicinal) NEC	T50.Z91	T50.Z92	T50.Z93	T50.Z94	T50.Z95	T50.Z96
carubin	T37.3X1	T37.3X2	T37.3X3	T37.3X4	T37.3X5	T37.3X6
enclamide	T38.3X1	T38.3X2	T38.3X3	T38.3X4	T38.3X5	T38.3X6
ornuride	T38.3X1	T38.3X2	T38.3X3	T38.3X4	T38.3X5	T38.3X6
azide	T38.3X1	T38.3X2	T38.3X3	T38.3X4	T38.3X5	T38.3X6
idine	T38.3X1	T38.3X2	T38.3X3	T38.3X4	T38.3X5	T38.3X6
izide	T38.3X1	T38.3X2	T38.3X3	T38.3X4	T38.3X5	T38.3X6
uidone	T38.3X1	T38.3X2	T38.3X3	T38.3X4	T38.3X5	T38.3X6
olamide	T38.3X1	T38.3X2	T38.3X3	T38.3X4	T38.3X5	T38.3X6
oxepide	T38.3X1	T38.3X2	T38.3X3	T38.3X4	T38.3X5	T38.3X6
in zinc insulin	T38.3X1	T38.3X2	T38.3X3	T38.3X4	T38.3X5	T38.3X6
ulin						
ilymphocytic	T50.Z11	T50.Z12	T50.Z13	T50.Z14	T50.Z15	T50.Z16
irhesus	T50.Z11	T50.Z12	T50.Z13	T50.Z14	T50.Z15	T50.Z16
ivenin	T50.Z11	T50.Z12	T50.Z13	T50.Z14	T50.Z15	T50.Z16
iviral	T50.Z11	T50.Z12	T50.Z13	T50.Z14	T50.Z15	T50.Z16
agon	T38.3X1	T38.3X2	T38.3X3	T38.3X4	T38.3X5	T38.3X6
ocorticoids	T38.0X1	T38.0X2	T38.0X3	T38.0X4	T38.0X5	T38.0X6
ocorticosteroid	T38.0X1	T38.0X2	T38.0X3	T38.0X4	T38.0X5	T38.0X6
onic acid	T50.991	T50.992	T50.993	T50.994	T50.995	T50.996
osamine sulfate	T39.4X1	T39.4X2	T39.4X3	T39.4X4	T39.4X5	T39.4X6
ose	T50.3X1	T50.3X2	T50.3X3	T50.3X4	T50.3X5	T50.3X6
h sodium oride	T50.3X1	T50.3X2	T50.3X3	T50.3X4	T50.3X5	T50.3X6
osulfone sodium	T37.1X1	T37.1X2	T37.1X3	T37.1X4	T37.1X5	T37.1X6
urolactone	T47.8X1	T47.8X2	T47.8X3	T47.8X4	T47.8X5	T47.8X6
NEC	T52.8X1	T52.8X2	T52.8X3	T52.8X4	—	—
amic acid	T47.5X1	T47.5X2	T47.5X3	T47.5X4	T47.5X5	T47.5X6
aral(medicinal)	T49.0X1	T49.0X2	T49.0X3	T49.0X4	T49.0X5	T49.0X6
nmedicinal	T65.891	T65.892	T65.893	T65.894	—	—
araldehyde medicinal)	T65.891	T65.892	T65.893	T65.894	—	—
dicinal	T49.0X1	T49.0X2	T49.0X3	T49.0X4	T49.0X5	T49.0X6
athione	T50.6X1	T50.6X2	T50.6X3	T50.6X4	T50.6X5	T50.6X6
ethimide	T42.6X1	T42.6X2	T42.6X3	T42.6X4	T42.6X5	T42.6X6
uride	T38.3X1	T38.3X2	T38.3X3	T38.3X4	T38.3X5	T38.3X6
erin	T47.4X1	T47.4X2	T47.4X3	T47.4X4	T47.4X5	T47.4X6
erol	T47.4X1	T47.4X2	T47.4X3	T47.4X4	T47.4X5	T47.4X6
ax	T49.6X1	T49.6X2	T49.6X3	T49.6X4	T49.6X5	T49.6X6
ravenous	T50.3X1	T50.3X2	T50.3X3	T50.3X4	T50.3X5	T50.3X6
linated	T48.4X1	T48.4X2	T48.4X3	T48.4X4	T48.4X5	T48.4X6
erophosphate	T50.991	T50.992	T50.993	T50.994	T50.995	T50.996
eryl						
alacolate	T48.4X1	T48.4X2	T48.4X3	T48.4X4	T48.4X5	T48.4X6
rate	T46.3X1	T46.3X2	T46.3X3	T46.3X4	T46.3X5	T46.3X6
acetate(topical)	T49.0X1	T49.0X2	T49.0X3	T49.0X4	T49.0X5	T49.0X6
nitrate	T46.3X1	T46.3X2	T46.3X3	T46.3X4	T46.3X5	T46.3X6
ine	T50.3X1	T50.3X2	T50.3X3	T50.3X4	T50.3X5	T50.3X6
lopyramide	T38.3X1	T38.3X2	T38.3X3	T38.3X4	T38.3X5	T38.3X6
obiarsol	T37.3X1	T37.3X2	T37.3X3	T37.3X4	T37.3X5	T37.3X6
ols(ether)	T52.3X1	T52.3X2	T52.3X3	T52.3X4	—	—

Substance	Poisoning, Accidental (unintentional)	Poisoning, Intentional self-harm	Poisoning, Assault	Poisoning, Undetermined	Adverse effect	Underdosing
Glyconiazide	T37.1X1	T37.1X2	T37.1X3	T37.1X4	T37.1X5	T37.1X6
Glycopyrrolate	T44.3X1	T44.3X2	T44.3X3	T44.3X4	T44.3X5	T44.3X6
Glycopyrronium	T44.3X1	T44.3X2	T44.3X3	T44.3X4	T44.3X5	T44.3X6
bromide	T44.3X1	T44.3X2	T44.3X3	T44.3X4	T44.3X5	T44.3X6
Glycoside, cardiac(stimulant)	T46.0X1	T46.0X2	T46.0X3	T46.0X4	T46.0X5	T46.0X6
Glycyclamide	T38.3X1	T38.3X2	T38.3X3	T38.3X4	T38.3X5	T38.3X6
Glycyrrhiza extract	T48.4X1	T48.4X2	T48.4X3	T48.4X4	T48.4X5	T48.4X6
Glycyrrhizic acid	T48.4X1	T48.4X2	T48.4X3	T48.4X4	T48.4X5	T48.4X6
Glycyrrhizinate potassium	T48.4X1	T48.4X2	T48.4X3	T48.4X4	T48.4X5	T48.4X6
Glymidine sodium	T38.3X1	T38.3X2	T38.3X3	T38.3X4	T38.3X5	T38.3X6
Glyphosate	T60.3X1	T60.3X2	T60.3X3	T60.3X4	—	—
Glyphylline	T48.6X1	T48.6X2	T48.6X3	T48.6X4	T48.6X5	T48.6X6
Gold						
colloidal(198Au)	T45.1X1	T45.1X2	T45.1X3	T45.1X4	T45.1X5	T45.1X6
salts	T39.4X1	T39.4X2	T39.4X3	T39.4X4	T39.4X5	T39.4X6
Golden sulfide of antimony	T56.891	T56.892	T56.893	T56.894	—	—
Goldylocks	T62.2X1	T62.2X2	T62.2X3	T62.2X4	—	—
Gonadal tissue extract	T38.901	T38.902	T38.903	T38.904	T38.905	T38.906
female	T38.5X1	T38.5X2	T38.5X3	T38.5X4	T38.5X5	T38.5X6
male	T38.7X1	T38.7X2	T38.7X3	T38.7X4	T38.7X5	T38.7X6
Gonadorelin	T38.891	T38.892	T38.893	T38.894	T38.895	T38.896
Gonadotropin	T38.891	T38.892	T38.893	T38.894	T38.895	T38.896
chorionic	T38.891	T38.892	T38.893	T38.894	T38.895	T38.896
pituitary	T38.811	T38.812	T38.813	T38.814	T38.815	T38.816
Goserelin	T45.1X1	T45.1X2	T45.1X3	T45.1X4	T45.1X5	T45.1X6
Grain alcohol	T51.0X1	T51.0X2	T51.0X3	T51.0X4	—	—
Gramicidin	T49.0X1	T49.0X2	T49.0X3	T49.0X4	T49.0X5	T49.0X6
Granisetron	T45.0X1	T45.0X2	T45.0X3	T45.0X4	T45.0X5	T45.0X6
Gratiola officinalis	T62.2X1	T62.2X2	T62.2X3	T62.2X4	—	—
Grease	T65.891	T65.892	T65.893	T65.894	—	—
Green hellebore	T62.2X1	T62.2X2	T62.2X3	T62.2X4	—	—
Green soap	T49.2X1	T49.2X2	T49.2X3	T49.2X4	T49.2X5	T49.2X6
Grifulvin	T36.7X1	T36.7X2	T36.7X3	T36.7X4	T36.7X5	T36.7X6
Griseofulvin	T36.7X1	T36.7X2	T36.7X3	T36.7X4	T36.7X5	T36.7X6
Growth hormone	T38.811	T38.812	T38.813	T38.814	T38.815	T38.816
Guaiac reagent	T50.991	T50.992	T50.993	T50.994	T50.995	T50.996
Guaiacol derivatives	T48.4X1	T48.4X2	T48.4X3	T48.4X4	T48.4X5	T48.4X6
Guaifenesin	T48.4X1	T48.4X2	T48.4X3	T48.4X4	T48.4X5	T48.4X6
Guaimesal	T48.4X1	T48.4X2	T48.4X3	T48.4X4	T48.4X5	T48.4X6
Guaiphenesin	T48.4X1	T48.4X2	T48.4X3	T48.4X4	T48.4X5	T48.4X6
Guamecycline	T36.4X1	T36.4X2	T36.4X3	T36.4X4	T36.4X5	T36.4X6
Guanabenz	T46.5X1	T46.5X2	T46.5X3	T46.5X4	T46.5X5	T46.5X6
Guanacline	T46.5X1	T46.5X2	T46.5X3	T46.5X4	T46.5X5	T46.5X6
Guanadrel	T46.5X1	T46.5X2	T46.5X3	T46.5X4	T46.5X5	T46.5X6
Guanatol	T37.2X1	T37.2X2	T37.2X3	T37.2X4	T37.2X5	T37.2X6
Guanethidine	T46.5X1	T46.5X2	T46.5X3	T46.5X4	T46.5X5	T46.5X6
Guanfacine	T46.5X1	T46.5X2	T46.5X3	T46.5X4	T46.5X5	T46.5X6
Guano	T65.891	T65.892	T65.893	T65.894	—	—
Guanochlor	T46.5X1	T46.5X2	T46.5X3	T46.5X4	T46.5X5	T46.5X6
Guanoclor	T46.5X1	T46.5X2	T46.5X3	T46.5X4	T46.5X5	T46.5X6

Substance	Poisoning, Accidental (unintentional)	Poisoning, Intentional self-harm	Poisoning, Assault	Poisoning, Undetermined	Adverse effect	Underdosing
Guanoctine	T46.5X1	T46.5X2	T46.5X3	T46.5X4	T46.5X5	T46.5X6
Guanoxabenz	T46.5X1	T46.5X2	T46.5X3	T46.5X4	T46.5X5	T46.5X6
Guanoxan	T46.5X1	T46.5X2	T46.5X3	T46.5X4	T46.5X5	T46.5X6
Guar gum(medicinal)	T46.6X1	T46.6X2	T46.6X3	T46.6X4	T46.6X5	T46.6X6
H						
Hachimycin	T36.7X1	T36.7X2	T36.7X3	T36.7X4	T36.7X5	T36.7X6
Hair						
dye	T49.4X1	T49.4X2	T49.4X3	T49.4X4	T49.4X5	T49.4X6
preparation NEC	T49.4X1	T49.4X2	T49.4X3	T49.4X4	T49.4X5	T49.4X6
Halazepam	T42.4X1	T42.4X2	T42.4X3	T42.4X4	T42.4X5	T42.4X6
Halcinolone	T49.0X1	T49.0X2	T49.0X3	T49.0X4	T49.0X5	T49.0X6
Halcinonide	T49.0X1	T49.0X2	T49.0X3	T49.0X4	T49.0X5	T49.0X6
Halethazole	T49.0X1	T49.0X2	T49.0X3	T49.0X4	T49.0X5	T49.0X6
Hallucinogen NEC	T40.901	T40.902	T40.903	T40.904	T40.905	T40.906
Halofantrine	T37.2X1	T37.2X2	T37.2X3	T37.2X4	T37.2X5	T37.2X6
Halofenate	T46.6X1	T46.6X2	T46.6X3	T46.6X4	T46.6X5	T46.6X6
Halometasone	T49.0X1	T49.0X2	T49.0X3	T49.0X4	T49.0X5	T49.0X6
Haloperidol	T43.4X1	T43.4X2	T43.4X3	T43.4X4	T43.4X5	T43.4X6
Haloprogin	T49.0X1	T49.0X2	T49.0X3	T49.0X4	T49.0X5	T49.0X6
Halotex	T49.0X1	T49.0X2	T49.0X3	T49.0X4	T49.0X5	T49.0X6
Halothane	T41.0X1	T41.0X2	T41.0X3	T41.0X4	T41.0X5	T41.0X6
Haloxazolam	T42.4X1	T42.4X2	T42.4X3	T42.4X4	T42.4X5	T42.4X6
Halquinols	T49.0X1	T49.0X2	T49.0X3	T49.0X4	T49.0X5	T49.0X6
Hamamelis	T49.2X1	T49.2X2	T49.2X3	T49.2X4	T49.2X5	T49.2X6
Haptendextran	T45.8X1	T45.8X2	T45.8X3	T45.8X4	T45.8X5	T45.8X6
Harmonyl	T46.5X1	T46.5X2	T46.5X3	T46.5X4	T46.5X5	T46.5X6
Hartmann's solution	T50.3X1	T50.3X2	T50.3X3	T50.3X4	T50.3X5	T50.3X6
Hashish	T40.7X1	T40.7X2	T40.7X3	T40.7X4	T40.7X5	T40.7X6
Hawaiian Woodrose seeds	T40.991	T40.992	T40.993	T40.994	—	—
HCB	T60.3X1	T60.3X2	T60.3X3	T60.3X4	—	—
HCH	T53.6X1	T53.6X2	T53.6X3	T53.6X4	—	—
medicinal	T49.0X1	T49.0X2	T49.0X3	T49.0X4	T49.0X5	T49.0X6
HCN	T57.3X1	T57.3X2	T57.3X3	T57.3X4	—	—
Headache cures, drugs, powders NEC	T50.901	T50.902	T50.903	T50.904	T50.905	T50.906
Heavenly Blue(morning glory)	T40.991	T40.992	T40.993	T40.994	—	—
Heavy metal antidote	T45.8X1	T45.8X2	T45.8X3	T45.8X4	T45.8X5	T45.8X6
Hedaquinium	T49.0X1	T49.0X2	T49.0X3	T49.0X4	T49.0X5	T49.0X6
Hedge hyssop	T62.2X1	T62.2X2	T62.2X3	T62.2X4	—	—
Heet	T49.8X1	T49.8X2	T49.8X3	T49.8X4	T49.8X5	T49.8X6
Helenin	T37.4X1	T37.4X2	T37.4X3	T37.4X4	T37.4X5	T37.4X6
Helium (nonmedicinal) NEC	T59.891	T59.892	T59.893	T59.894	—	—
medicinal	T48.991	T48.992	T48.993	T48.994	T48.995	T48.996
Hellebore(black) (green) (white)	T62.2X1	T62.2X2	T62.2X3	T62.2X4	—	—
Hematin	T45.8X1	T45.8X2	T45.8X3	T45.8X4	T45.8X5	T45.8X6
Hematinic preparation	T45.8X1	T45.8X2	T45.8X3	T45.8X4	T45.8X5	T45.8X6
Hematological agent	T45.91	T45.92	T45.93	T45.94	T45.95	T45.96
specified NEC	T45.8X1	T45.8X2	T45.8X3	T45.8X4	T45.8X5	T45.8X6
Hemlock	T62.2X1	T62.2X2	T62.2X3	T62.2X4	—	—

Substance	Poisoning, Accidental (unintentional)	Poisoning, Intentional self-harm	Poisoning, Assault	Poisoning, Undetermined	Adverse effect	[Underdosing]
Hemostatic	T45.621	T45.622	T45.623	T45.624	T45.625	T45
drug, systemic	T45.621	T45.622	T45.623	T45.624	T45.625	T45
Hemostyptic	T49.4X1	T49.4X2	T49.4X3	T49.4X4	T49.4X5	T49
Henbane	T62.2X1	T62.2X2	T62.2X3	T62.2X4	—	—
Heparin(sodium)	T45.511	T45.512	T45.513	T45.514	T45.515	T45
action reverser	T45.7X1	T45.7X2	T45.7X3	T45.7X4	T45.7X5	T45
Heparin-fraction	T45.511	T45.512	T45.513	T45.514	T45.515	T45
Heparinoid(systemic)	T45.511	T45.512	T45.513	T45.514	T45.515	T45
Hepatic secretion stimulant	T47.8X1	T47.8X2	T47.8X3	T47.8X4	T47.8X5	T47.
Hepatitis B						
immune globulin	T50.Z11	T50.Z12	T50.Z13	T50.Z14	T50.Z15	T50
vaccine	T50.B91	T50.B92	T50.B93	T50.B94	T50.B95	T50.
Hepronicate	T46.7X1	T46.7X2	T46.7X3	T46.7X4	T46.7X5	T46.
Heptabarb	T42.3X1	T42.3X2	T42.3X3	T42.3X4	T42.3X5	T42.
Heptabarbital	T42.3X1	T42.3X2	T42.3X3	T42.3X4	T42.3X5	T42.
Heptabarbitone	T42.3X1	T42.3X2	T42.3X3	T42.3X4	T42.3X5	T42.
Heptachlor	T60.1X1	T60.1X2	T60.1X3	T60.1X4	—	—
Heptalgin	T40.2X1	T40.2X2	T40.2X3	T40.2X4	T40.2X5	T40.
Heptaminol	T46.3X1	T46.3X2	T46.3X3	T46.3X4	T46.3X5	T46.
Herbicide NEC	T60.3X1	T60.3X2	T60.3X3	T60.3X4	—	—
Heroin	T40.1X1	T40.1X2	T40.1X3	T40.1X4	—	—
Herplex	T49.5X1	T49.5X2	T49.5X3	T49.5X4	T49.5X5	T49.
HES	T45.8X1	T45.8X2	T45.8X3	T45.8X4	T45.8X5	T45.
Hesperidin	T46.991	T46.992	T46.993	T46.994	T46.995	T46.
Hetacillin	T36.0X1	T36.0X2	T36.0X3	T36.0X4	T36.0X5	T36.
Hetastarch	T45.8X1	T45.8X2	T45.8X3	T45.8X4	T45.8X5	T45.
HETP	T60.0X1	T60.0X2	T60.0X3	T60.0X4	—	—
Hexachlorobenzene (vapor)	T60.3X1	T60.3X2	T60.3X3	T60.3X4	—	—
Hexachlorocyclohexane	T53.6X1	T53.6X2	T53.6X3	T53.6X4	—	—
Hexachlorophene	T49.0X1	T49.0X2	T49.0X3	T49.0X4	T49.0X5	T49.(
Hexadiline	T46.3X1	T46.3X2	T46.3X3	T46.3X4	T46.3X5	T46.
Hexadimethrine (bromide)	T45.7X1	T45.7X2	T45.7X3	T45.7X4	T45.7X5	T45.
Hexadylamine	T46.3X1	T46.3X2	T46.3X3	T46.3X4	T46.3X5	T46.
Hexaethyl tetraphosphate	T60.0X1	T60.0X2	T60.0X3	T60.0X4	—	—
Hexafluorenium bromide	T48.1X1	T48.1X2	T48.1X3	T48.1X4	T48.1X5	T48.
Hexafluronium (bromide)	T48.1X1	T48.1X2	T48.1X3	T48.1X4	T48.1X5	T48.
Hexa-germ	T49.2X1	T49.2X2	T49.2X3	T49.2X4	T49.2X5	T49.
Hexahydrobenzol	T52.8X1	T52.8X2	T52.8X3	T52.8X4	—	—
Hexahydrocresol(s)	T51.8X1	T51.8X2	T51.8X3	T51.8X4	—	—
arsenide	T57.0X1	T57.0X2	T57.0X3	T57.0X4	—	—
arseniurated	T57.0X1	T57.0X2	T57.0X3	T57.0X4	—	—
cyanide	T57.3X1	T57.3X2	T57.3X3	T57.3X4	—	—
gas	T59.891	T59.892	T59.893	T59.894	—	—
Fluoride(liquid)	T57.8X1	T57.8X2	T57.8X3	T57.8X4	—	—
vapor	T59.891	T59.892	T59.893	T59.894	—	—
phophorated	T60.0X1	T60.0X2	T60.0X3	T60.0X4	—	—
sulfate	T57.8X1	T57.8X2	T57.8X3	T57.8X4	—	—
sulfide(gas)	T59.6X1	T59.6X2	T59.6X3	T59.6X4	—	—
arseniurated	T57.0X1	T57.0X2	T57.0X3	T57.0X4	—	—
sulfurated	T57.8X1	T57.8X2	T57.8X3	T57.8X4	—	—

Substance	Poisoning, Accidental (unintentional)	Poisoning, Intentional self-harm	Poisoning, Assault	Poisoning, Undetermined	Adverse effect	Underdosing
hydrophenol	T51.8X1	T51.8X2	T51.8X3	T51.8X4	—	—
len	T51.8X1	T51.8X2	T51.8X3	T51.8X4	—	—
methonium bromide	T44.2X1	T44.2X2	T44.2X3	T44.2X4	T44.2X5	T44.2X6
methylene	T52.8X1	T52.8X2	T52.8X3	T52.8X4	—	—
methylmelamine	T45.1X1	T45.1X2	T45.1X3	T45.1X4	T45.1X5	T45.1X6
midine	T49.0X1	T49.0X2	T49.0X3	T49.0X4	T49.0X5	T49.0X6
mine ndelate)	T37.8X1	T37.8X2	T37.8X3	T37.8X4	T37.8X5	T37.8X6
none, 2-hexanone	T52.4X1	T52.4X2	T52.4X3	T52.4X4	—	—
nuorenium	T48.1X1	T48.1X2	T48.1X3	T48.1X4	T48.1X5	T48.1X6
propymate	T42.6X1	T42.6X2	T42.6X3	T42.6X4	T42.6X5	T42.6X6
sonium iodide	T44.3X1	T44.3X2	T44.3X3	T44.3X4	T44.3X5	T44.3X6
carbacholine bromide	T48.1X1	T48.1X2	T48.1X3	T48.1X4	T48.1X5	T48.1X6
emal	T42.3X1	T42.3X2	T42.3X3	T42.3X4	T42.3X5	T42.3X6
estrol	T38.5X1	T38.5X2	T38.5X3	T38.5X4	T38.5X5	T38.5X6
ethal(sodium)	T42.3X1	T42.3X2	T42.3X3	T42.3X4	T42.3X5	T42.3X6
etidine	T37.8X1	T37.8X2	T37.8X3	T37.8X4	T37.8X5	T37.8X6
obarbital	T42.3X1	T42.3X2	T42.3X3	T42.3X4	T42.3X5	T42.3X6
ctal	T41.291	T41.292	T41.293	T41.294	T41.295	T41.296
dium	T41.1X1	T41.1X2	T41.1X3	T41.1X4	T41.1X5	T41.1X6
obendine	T46.3X1	T46.3X2	T46.3X3	T46.3X4	T46.3X5	T46.3X6
ocyclium	T44.3X1	T44.3X2	T44.3X3	T44.3X4	T44.3X5	T44.3X6
etilsulfate	T44.3X1	T44.3X2	T44.3X3	T44.3X4	T44.3X5	T44.3X6
oestrol	T38.5X1	T38.5X2	T38.5X3	T38.5X4	T38.5X5	T38.5X6
one	T52.4X1	T52.4X2	T52.4X3	T52.4X4	—	—
oprenaline	T48.6X1	T48.6X2	T48.6X3	T48.6X4	T48.6X5	T48.6X6
ylcaine	T41.3X1	T41.3X2	T41.3X3	T41.3X4	T41.3X5	T41.3X6
ylresorcinol	T52.2X1	T52.2X2	T52.2X3	T52.2X4	—	—
H(human growth mone)	T38.811	T38.812	T38.813	T38.814	T38.815	T38.816
kle's pills	T47.2X1	T47.2X2	T47.2X3	T47.2X4	T47.2X5	T47.2X6
alog	T50.8X1	T50.8X2	T50.8X3	T50.8X4	T50.8X5	T50.8X6
amine (phosphate)	T50.8X1	T50.8X2	T50.8X3	T50.8X4	T50.8X5	T50.8X6
oplasmin	T50.8X1	T50.8X2	T50.8X3	T50.8X4	T50.8X5	T50.8X6
y berries	T62.2X1	T62.2X2	T62.2X3	T62.2X4	—	—
natropine	T44.3X1	T44.3X2	T44.3X3	T44.3X4	T44.3X5	T44.3X6
ethylbromide	T44.3X1	T44.3X2	T44.3X3	T44.3X4	T44.3X5	T44.3X6
nochlorcyclizine	T45.0X1	T45.0X2	T45.0X3	T45.0X4	T45.0X5	T45.0X6
nosalate	T49.3X1	T49.3X2	T49.3X3	T49.3X4	T49.3X5	T49.3X6
no-tet	T50.Z11	T50.Z12	T50.Z13	T50.Z14	T50.Z15	T50.Z16
mone	T38.801	T38.802	T38.803	T38.804	T38.805	T38.806
drenal cortical steroids	T38.0X1	T38.0X2	T38.0X3	T38.0X4	T38.0X5	T38.0X6
ndrogenic	T38.7X1	T38.7X2	T38.7X3	T38.7X4	T38.7X5	T38.7X6
nterior pituitary NEC	T38.811	T38.812	T38.813	T38.814	T38.815	T38.816
ntidiabetic agents	T38.3X1	T38.3X2	T38.3X3	T38.3X4	T38.3X5	T38.3X6
ntidiuretic	T38.891	T38.892	T38.893	T38.894	T38.895	T38.896
ancer therapy	T45.1X1	T45.1X2	T45.1X3	T45.1X4	T45.1X5	T45.1X6
ollicle stimulating	T38.811	T38.812	T38.813	T38.814	T38.815	T38.816
onadotropic	T38.891	T38.892	T38.893	T38.894	T38.895	T38.896
pituitary	T38.811	T38.812	T38.813	T38.814	T38.815	T38.816
rowth	T38.811	T38.812	T38.813	T38.814	T38.815	T38.816
uteinizing	T38.811	T38.812	T38.813	T38.814	T38.815	T38.816

Substance	Poisoning, Accidental (unintentional)	Poisoning, Intentional self-harm	Poisoning, Assault	Poisoning, Undetermined	Adverse effect	Underdosing
Hormone — *Continued*						
ovarian	T38.5X1	T38.5X2	T38.5X3	T38.5X4	T38.5X5	T38.5X6
oxytocic	T48.0X1	T48.0X2	T48.0X3	T48.0X4	T48.0X5	T48.0X6
parathyroid (derivatives)	T50.991	T50.992	T50.993	T50.994	T50.995	T50.996
pituitary(posterior) NEC	T38.891	T38.892	T38.893	T38.894	T38.895	T38.896
anterior	T38.811	T38.812	T38.813	T38.814	T38.815	T38.816
specified, NEC	T38.891	T38.892	T38.893	T38.894	T38.895	T38.896
thyroid	T38.1X1	T38.1X2	T38.1X3	T38.1X4	T38.1X5	T38.1X6
Hornet(sting)	T63.451	T63.452	T63.453	T63.454	—	—
Horse anti-human lymphocytic serum	T50.Z11	T50.Z12	T50.Z13	T50.Z14	T50.Z15	T50.Z16
Horticulture agent NEC	T65.91	T65.92	T65.93	T65.94	—	—
with pesticide	T60.91	T60.92	T60.93	T60.94	—	—
Human						
albumin	T45.8X1	T45.8X2	T45.8X3	T45.8X4	T45.8X5	T45.8X6
growth hormone(HGH)	T38.811	T38.812	T38.813	T38.814	T38.815	T38.816
immune serum	T50.Z11	T50.Z12	T50.Z13	T50.Z14	T50.Z15	T50.Z16
Hyaluronidase	T45.3X1	T45.3X2	T45.3X3	T45.3X4	T45.3X5	T45.3X6
Hyazyme	T45.3X1	T45.3X2	T45.3X3	T45.3X4	T45.3X5	T45.3X6
Hycodan	T40.2X1	T40.2X2	T40.2X3	T40.2X4	T40.2X5	T40.2X6
Hydantoin derivative NEC	T42.0X1	T42.0X2	T42.0X3	T42.0X4	T42.0X5	T42.0X6
Hydeltra	T38.0X1	T38.0X2	T38.0X3	T38.0X4	T38.0X5	T38.0X6
Hydergine	T44.6X1	T44.6X2	T44.6X3	T44.6X4	T44.6X5	T44.6X6
Hydrabamine penicillin	T36.0X1	T36.0X2	T36.0X3	T36.0X4	T36.0X5	T36.0X6
Hydralazine	T46.5X1	T46.5X2	T46.5X3	T46.5X4	T46.5X5	T46.5X6
Hydrargaphen	T49.0X1	T49.0X2	T49.0X3	T49.0X4	T49.0X5	T49.0X6
Hydrargyri amino-chloridum	T49.0X1	T49.0X2	T49.0X3	T49.0X4	T49.0X5	T49.0X6
Hydrastine	T48.291	T48.292	T48.293	T48.294	T48.295	T48.296
Hydrazine	T54.1X1	T54.1X2	T54.1X3	T54.1X4	—	—
monoamine oxidase inhibitors	T43.1X1	T43.1X2	T43.1X3	T43.1X4	T43.1X5	T43.1X6
Hydrazoic acid, azides	T54.2X1	T54.2X2	T54.2X3	T54.2X4	—	—
Hydriodic acid	T48.4X1	T48.4X2	T48.4X3	T48.4X4	T48.4X5	T48.4X6
Hydrocarbon gas	T59.891	T59.892	T59.893	T59.894	—	—
incomplete combustion of—see Carbon, monoxide, fuel, utility						
liquefied(mobile container)	T59.891	T59.892	T59.893	T59.894	—	—
piped(natural)	T59.891	T59.892	T59.893	T59.894	—	—
Hydrochloric acid(liquid)	T54.2X1	T54.2X2	T54.2X3	T54.2X4	—	—
medicinal (digestant)	T47.5X1	T47.5X2	T47.5X3	T47.5X4	T47.5X5	T47.5X6
vapor	T59.891	T59.892	T59.893	T59.894	—	—
Hydrochlorothiazide	T50.2X1	T50.2X2	T50.2X3	T50.2X4	T50.2X5	T50.2X6
Hydrocodone	T40.2X1	T40.2X2	T40.2X3	T40.2X4	T40.2X5	T40.2X6
Hydrocortisone (derivatives)	T49.0X1	T49.0X2	T49.0X3	T49.0X4	T49.0X5	T49.0X6
aceponate	T49.0X1	T49.0X2	T49.0X3	T49.0X4	T49.0X5	T49.0X6
ENT agent	T49.6X1	T49.6X2	T49.6X3	T49.6X4	T49.6X5	T49.6X6
ophthalmic preparation	T49.5X1	T49.5X2	T49.5X3	T49.5X4	T49.5X5	T49.5X6
topical NEC	T49.0X1	T49.0X2	T49.0X3	T49.0X4	T49.0X5	T49.0X6

Substance	Poisoning, Accidental (unintentional)	Poisoning, Intentional self-harm	Poisoning, Assault	Poisoning, Undetermined	Adverse effect	Underdosing
Hydrocortone	T38.0X1	T38.0X2	T38.0X3	T38.0X4	T38.0X5	T38.0X6
ENT agent	T49.6X1	T49.6X2	T49.6X3	T49.6X4	T49.6X5	T49.6X6
ophthalmic preparation	T49.5X1	T49.5X2	T49.5X3	T49.5X4	T49.5X5	T49.5X6
topical NEC	T49.0X1	T49.0X2	T49.0X3	T49.0X4	T49.0X5	T49.0X6
Hydrocyanic acid(liquid)	T57.3X1	T57.3X2	T57.3X3	T57.3X4	—	—
gas	T65.0X1	T65.0X2	T65.0X3	T65.0X4	—	—
Hydroflumethiazide	T50.2X1	T50.2X2	T50.2X3	T50.2X4	T50.2X5	T50.2X6
Hydrofluoric acid(liquid)	T54.2X1	T54.2X2	T54.2X3	T54.2X4	—	—
vapor	T59.891	T59.892	T59.893	T59.894	—	—
Hydrogen	T59.891	T59.892	T59.893	T59.894	—	—
arsenide	T57.0X1	T57.0X2	T57.0X3	T57.0X4	—	—
arseniureted	T57.0X1	T57.0X2	T57.0X3	T57.0X4	—	—
chloride	T57.8X1	T57.8X2	T57.8X3	T57.8X4	—	—
cyanide(salts)	T57.3X1	T57.3X2	T57.3X3	T57.3X4	—	—
gas	T57.3X1	T57.3X2	T57.3X3	T57.3X4	—	—
Fluoride	T59.5X1	T59.5X2	T59.5X3	T59.5X4	—	—
vapor	T59.5X1	T59.5X2	T59.5X3	T59.5X4	—	—
peroxide	T49.0X1	T49.0X2	T49.0X3	T49.0X4	T49.0X5	T49.0X6
phosphureted	T57.1X1	T57.1X2	T57.1X3	T57.1X4	—	—
sulfide	T59.6X1	T59.6X2	T59.6X3	T59.6X4	—	—
arseniureted	T57.0X1	T57.0X2	T57.0X3	T57.0X4	—	—
sulfureted	T59.6X1	T59.6X2	T59.6X3	T59.6X4	—	—
Hydromethylpyridine	T46.7X1	T46.7X2	T46.7X3	T46.7X4	T46.7X5	T46.7X6
Hydromorphinol	T40.2X1	T40.2X2	T40.2X3	T40.2X4	—	—
Hydromorphinone	T40.2X1	T40.2X2	T40.2X3	T40.2X4	T40.2X5	T40.2X6
Hydromorphone	T40.2X1	T40.2X2	T40.2X3	T40.2X4	T40.2X5	T40.2X6
Hydromox	T50.2X1	T50.2X2	T50.2X3	T50.2X4	T50.2X5	T50.2X6
Hydrophilic lotion	T49.3X1	T49.3X2	T49.3X3	T49.3X4	T49.3X5	T49.3X6
Hydroquinidine	T46.2X1	T46.2X2	T46.2X3	T46.2X4	T46.2X5	T46.2X6
Hydroquinone	T52.2X1	T52.2X2	T52.2X3	T52.2X4	—	—
vapor	T59.891	T59.892	T59.893	T59.894	—	—
Hydrosulfuric acid(gas)	T59.6X1	T59.6X2	T59.6X3	T59.6X4	—	—
Hydrotalcite	T47.1X1	T47.1X2	T47.1X3	T47.1X4	T47.1X5	T47.1X6
Hydrous wool fat	T49.3X1	T49.3X2	T49.3X3	T49.3X4	T49.3X5	T49.3X6
Hydroxide, caustic	T54.3X1	T54.3X2	T54.3X3	T54.3X4	—	—
Hydroxocobalamin	T45.8X1	T45.8X2	T45.8X3	T45.8X4	T45.8X5	T45.8X6
Hydroxyamp-hetamine	T49.5X1	T49.5X2	T49.5X3	T49.5X4	T49.5X5	T49.5X6
Hydroxycarbamide	T45.1X1	T45.1X2	T45.1X3	T45.1X4	T45.1X5	T45.1X6
Hydroxychloroquine	T37.8X1	T37.8X2	T37.8X3	T37.8X4	T37.8X5	T37.8X6
Hydroxydihydro-codeinone	T40.2X1	T40.2X2	T40.2X3	T40.2X4	T40.2X5	T40.2X6
Hydroxyestrone	T38.5X1	T38.5X2	T38.5X3	T38.5X4	T38.5X5	T38.5X6
Hydroxyethyl starch	T45.8X1	T45.8X2	T45.8X3	T45.8X4	T45.8X5	T45.8X6
Hydroxyme-thylpentanone	T52.4X1	T52.4X2	T52.4X3	T52.4X4	—	—
Hydroxyphenamate	T43.591	T43.592	T43.593	T43.594	T43.595	T43.596
Hydroxypheny-lbutazone	T39.2X1	T39.2X2	T39.2X3	T39.2X4	T39.2X5	T39.2X6
Hydroxyprogesterone	T38.5X1	T38.5X2	T38.5X3	T38.5X4	T38.5X5	T38.5X6
caproate	T38.5X1	T38.5X2	T38.5X3	T38.5X4	T38.5X5	T38.5X6
Hydroxyquinoline (derivatives) NEC	T37.8X1	T37.8X2	T37.8X3	T37.8X4	T37.8X5	T37.8X6
Hydroxystilbamidine	T37.3X1	T37.3X2	T37.3X3	T37.3X4	T37.3X5	T37.3X6

Substance	Poisoning, Accidental (unintentional)	Poisoning, Intentional self-harm	Poisoning, Assault	Poisoning, Undetermined	Adverse effect	U[illegible]
Hydroxytoluene (nonmedicinal)	T54.0X1	T54.0X2	T54.0X3	T54.0X4	—	–
medicinal	T49.0X1	T49.0X2	T49.0X3	T49.0X4	T49.0X5	T49
Hydroxyurea	T45.1X1	T45.1X2	T45.1X3	T45.1X4	T45.1X5	T45
Hydroxyzine	T43.591	T43.592	T43.593	T43.594	T43.595	T43
Hyoscine	T44.3X1	T44.3X2	T44.3X3	T44.3X4	T44.3X5	T44
Hyoscyamine	T44.3X1	T44.3X2	T44.3X3	T44.3X4	T44.3X5	T44
Hyoscyamus	T44.3X1	T44.3X2	T44.3X3	T44.3X4	T44.3X5	T44
dry extract	T44.3X1	T44.3X2	T44.3X3	T44.3X4	T44.3X5	T44
Hypaque	T50.8X1	T50.8X2	T50.8X3	T50.8X4	T50.8X5	T50
Hypertussis	T50.Z11	T50.Z12	T50.Z13	T50.Z14	T50.Z15	T50
Hypnotic	T42.71	T42.72	T42.73	T42.74	T42.75	T42
anticonvulsant	T42.71	T42.72	T42.73	T42.74	T42.75	T42
specified NEC	T42.6X1	T42.6X2	T42.6X3	T42.6X4	T42.6X5	T42
Hypochlorite	T49.0X1	T49.0X2	T49.0X3	T49.0X4	T49.0X5	T49
Hypophysis, posterior	T38.891	T38.892	T38.893	T38.894	T38.895	T38
Hypotensive NEC	T46.5X1	T46.5X2	T46.5X3	T46.5X4	T46.5X5	T46
Hypromellose	T49.5X1	T49.5X2	T49.5X3	T49.5X4	T49.5X5	T49
I						
Ibacitabine	T37.5X1	T37.5X2	T37.5X3	T37.5X4	T37.5X5	T37.
Ibopamine	T44.991	T44.992	T44.993	T44.994	T44.995	T44
Ibufenac	T39.311	T39.312	T39.313	T39.314	T39.315	T39
Ibuprofen	T39.311	T39.312	T39.313	T39.314	T39.315	T39
Ibuproxam	T39.311	T39.312	T39.313	T39.314	T39.315	T39
Ibuterol	T48.6X1	T48.6X2	T48.6X3	T48.6X4	T48.6X5	T48.
Ichthammol	T49.0X1	T49.0X2	T49.0X3	T49.0X4	T49.0X5	T49.
Ichthyol	T49.4X1	T49.4X2	T49.4X3	T49.4X4	T49.4X5	T49.
Idarubicin	T45.1X1	T45.1X2	T45.1X3	T45.1X4	T45.1X5	T45.
Idrocilamide	T42.8X1	T42.8X2	T42.8X3	T42.8X4	T42.8X5	T42.
Ifenprodil	T46.7X1	T46.7X2	T46.7X3	T46.7X4	T46.7X5	T46.
Ifosfamide	T45.1X1	T45.1X2	T45.1X3	T45.1X4	T45.1X5	T45.
Iletin	T38.3X1	T38.3X2	T38.3X3	T38.3X4	T38.3X5	T38.
Ilex	T62.2X1	T62.2X2	T62.2X3	T62.2X4	—	–
Illuminating gas(after combustion)	T58.11	T58.12	T58.13	T58.14	—	–
prior to combustion	T59.891	T59.892	T59.893	T59.894	—	–
Ilopan	T45.2X1	T45.2X2	T45.2X3	T45.2X4	T45.2X5	T45.
Iloprost	T46.7X1	T46.7X2	T46.7X3	T46.7X4	T46.7X5	T46.
Ilotycin	T36.3X1	T36.3X2	T36.3X3	T36.3X4	T36.3X5	T36.
ophthalmic preparation	T49.5X1	T49.5X2	T49.5X3	T49.5X4	T49.5X5	T49.
topical NEC	T49.0X1	T49.0X2	T49.0X3	T49.0X4	T49.0X5	T49.
Imidazole-4-carboxamide	T45.1X1	T45.1X2	T45.1X3	T45.1X4	T45.1X5	T45.
Imipenem	T36.0X1	T36.0X2	T36.0X3	T36.0X4	T36.0X5	T36.
Imipramine	T43.011	T43.012	T43.013	T43.014	T43.015	T43.
Iminostilbene	T42.1X1	T42.1X2	T42.1X3	T42.1X4	T42.1X5	T42.
Immu-G	T50.Z11	T50.Z12	T50.Z13	T50.Z14	T50.Z15	T50.
Immuglobin	T50.Z11	T50.Z12	T50.Z13	T50.Z14	T50.Z15	T50.
Immune						
globulin	T50.Z11	T50.Z12	T50.Z13	T50.Z14	T50.Z15	T50.
serum globulin	T50.Z11	T50.Z12	T50.Z13	T50.Z14	T50.Z15	T50.

Substance	Poisoning, Accidental (unintentional)	Poisoning, Intentional self-harm	Poisoning, Assault	Poisoning, Undetermined	Adverse effect	Underdosing
unoglobin an(intravenous) mal)	T50.Z11	T50.Z12	T50.Z13	T50.Z14	T50.Z15	T50.Z16
modified	T50.Z11	T50.Z12	T50.Z13	T50.Z14	T50.Z15	T50.Z16
unosuppressive drug	T45.1X1	T45.1X2	T45.1X3	T45.1X4	T45.1X5	T45.1X6
u-tetanus	T50.Z11	T50.Z12	T50.Z13	T50.Z14	T50.Z15	T50.Z16
lpine	T43.221	T43.222	T43.223	T43.224	T43.225	T43.226
nazoline	T48.5X1	T48.5X2	T48.5X3	T48.5X4	T48.5X5	T48.5X6
ndione ivatives)	T45.511	T45.512	T45.513	T45.514	T45.515	T45.516
pamide	T46.5X1	T46.5X2	T46.5X3	T46.5X4	T46.5X5	T46.5X6
ndione ivatives)	T45.511	T45.512	T45.513	T45.514	T45.515	T45.516
nolol	T44.7X1	T44.7X2	T44.7X3	T44.7X4	T44.7X5	T44.7X6
ral	T44.7X1	T44.7X2	T44.7X3	T44.7X4	T44.7X5	T44.7X6
an						
mp	T40.7X1	T40.7X2	T40.7X3	T40.7X4	T40.7X5	T40.7X6
bacco	T62.2X1	T62.2X2	T62.2X3	T62.2X4	—	—
go carmine	T50.8X1	T50.8X2	T50.8X3	T50.8X4	T50.8X5	T50.8X6
bufen	T45.521	T45.522	T45.523	T45.524	T45.525	T45.526
ocin	T39.2X1	T39.2X2	T39.2X3	T39.2X4	T39.2X5	T39.2X6
ocyanine green	T50.8X1	T50.8X2	T50.8X3	T50.8X4	T50.8X5	T50.8X6
ometacin	T39.391	T39.392	T39.393	T39.394	T39.395	T39.396
omethacin	T39.391	T39.392	T39.393	T39.394	T39.395	T39.396
rnesil	T39.4X1	T39.4X2	T39.4X3	T39.4X4	T39.4X5	T39.4X6
oramin	T44.6X1	T44.6X2	T44.6X3	T44.6X4	T44.6X5	T44.6X6
ustrial						
cohol	T51.0X1	T51.0X2	T51.0X3	T51.0X4	—	—
mes	T59.891	T59.892	T59.893	T59.894	—	—
lvents(fumes) (vapors)	T52.91	T52.92	T52.93	T52.94	—	—
uenza vaccine	T50.B91	T50.B92	T50.B93	T50.B94	T50.B95	T50.B96
ested substance NEC	T65.91	T65.92	T65.93	T65.94	—	—
l	T37.1X1	T37.1X2	T37.1X3	T37.1X4	T37.1X5	T37.1X6
alation, gas(noxious)— Gas						
ibitor						
ngiotensin-converting nzyme	T46.4X1	T46.4X2	T46.4X3	T46.4X4	T46.4X5	T46.4X6
arbonic anhydrase	T50.2X1	T50.2X2	T50.2X3	T50.2X4	T50.2X5	T50.2X6
brinolysis	T45.621	T45.622	T45.623	T45.624	T45.625	T45.626
onoamine oxidase NEC	T43.1X1	T43.1X2	T43.1X3	T43.1X4	T43.1X5	T43.1X6
hydrazine	T43.1X1	T43.1X2	T43.1X3	T43.1X4	T43.1X5	T43.1X6
ostsynaptic	T43.8X1	T43.8X2	T43.8X3	T43.8X4	T43.8X5	T43.8X6
rothrombin synthesis	T45.511	T45.512	T45.513	T45.514	T45.515	T45.516
	T65.891	T65.892	T65.893	T65.894	—	—
rganic substance NEC	T57.91	T57.92	T57.93	T57.94	—	—
sine pranobex	T37.5X1	T37.5X2	T37.5X3	T37.5X4	T37.5X5	T37.5X6
sitol	T50.991	T50.992	T50.993	T50.994	T50.995	T50.996
icotinate	T46.7X1	T46.7X2	T46.7X3	T46.7X4	T46.7X5	T46.7X6
roquone	T45.1X1	T45.1X2	T45.1X3	T45.1X4	T45.1X5	T45.1X6
ect(sting), venomous	T63.481	T63.482	T63.483	T63.484	—	—
nt	T63.421	T63.422	T63.423	T63.424	—	—
ee	T63.441	T63.442	T63.443	T63.444	—	—

Substance	Poisoning, Accidental (unintentional)	Poisoning, Intentional self-harm	Poisoning, Assault	Poisoning, Undetermined	Adverse effect	Underdosing
Insect(sting), venomous — *Continued*						
caterpillar	T63.431	T63.432	T63.433	T63.434	—	—
hornet	T63.451	T63.452	T63.453	T63.454	—	—
wasp	T63.461	T63.462	T63.463	T63.464	—	—
Insecticide NEC	T60.91	T60.92	T60.93	T60.94	—	—
carbamate	T60.0X1	T60.0X2	T60.0X3	T60.0X4	—	—
chlorinated	T60.1X1	T60.1X2	T60.1X3	T60.1X4	—	—
mixed	T60.91	T60.92	T60.93	T60.94	—	—
organochlorine	T60.1X1	T60.1X2	T60.1X3	T60.1X4	—	—
organophosphorus	T60.0X1	T60.0X2	T60.0X3	T60.0X4	—	—
Insular tissue extract	T38.3X1	T38.3X2	T38.3X3	T38.3X4	T38.3X5	T38.3X6
Insulin(amorphous) (globin) (isophane) (Lente) (NPH) (Semilente) (Ultralente)	T38.3X1	T38.3X2	T38.3X3	T38.3X4	T38.3X5	T38.3X6
defalan	T38.3X1	T38.3X2	T38.3X3	T38.3X4	T38.3X5	T38.3X6
human	T38.3X1	T38.3X2	T38.3X3	T38.3X4	T38.3X5	T38.3X6
injection, soluble	T38.3X1	T38.3X2	T38.3X3	T38.3X4	T38.3X5	T38.3X6
biphasic	T38.3X1	T38.3X2	T38.3X3	T38.3X4	T38.3X5	T38.3X6
intermediate acting	T38.3X1	T38.3X2	T38.3X3	T38.3X4	T38.3X5	T38.3X6
protamine zinc	T38.3X1	T38.3X2	T38.3X3	T38.3X4	T38.3X5	T38.3X6
slow acting	T38.3X1	T38.3X2	T38.3X3	T38.3X4	T38.3X5	T38.3X6
zinc						
protamine injection	T38.3X1	T38.3X2	T38.3X3	T38.3X4	T38.3X5	T38.3X6
suspension (amorphous) (crystalline)	T38.3X1	T38.3X2	T38.3X3	T38.3X4	T38.3X5	T38.3X6
Interferon (alpha) (beta) (gamma)	T37.5X1	T37.5X2	T37.5X3	T37.5X4	T37.5X5	T37.5X6
Intestinal motility control drug	T47.6X1	T47.6X2	T47.6X3	T47.6X4	T47.6X5	T47.6X6
biological	T47.8X1	T47.8X2	T47.8X3	T47.8X4	T47.8X5	T47.8X6
Intranarcon	T41.1X1	T41.1X2	T41.1X3	T41.1X4	T41.1X5	T41.1X6
Intravenous						
amino acids	T50.991	T50.992	T50.993	T50.994	T50.995	T50.996
fat suspension	T50.991	T50.992	T50.993	T50.994	T50.995	T50.996
Inulin	T50.8X1	T50.8X2	T50.8X3	T50.8X4	T50.8X5	T50.8X6
Invert sugar	T50.3X1	T50.3X2	T50.3X3	T50.3X4	T50.3X5	T50.3X6
Inza—see Naproxen						
Iobenzamic acid	T50.8X1	T50.8X2	T50.8X3	T50.8X4	T50.8X5	T50.8X6
Iocarmic acid	T50.8X1	T50.8X2	T50.8X3	T50.8X4	T50.8X5	T50.8X6
Iocetamic acid	T50.8X1	T50.8X2	T50.8X3	T50.8X4	T50.8X5	T50.8X6
Iodamide	T50.8X1	T50.8X2	T50.8X3	T50.8X4	T50.8X5	T50.8X6
Iodide NEC—see also Iodine	T49.0X1	T49.0X2	T49.0X3	T49.0X4	T49.0X5	T49.0X6
mercury(ointment)	T49.0X1	T49.0X2	T49.0X3	T49.0X4	T49.0X5	T49.0X6
methylate	T49.0X1	T49.0X2	T49.0X3	T49.0X4	T49.0X5	T49.0X6
potassium (expectorant) NEC	T48.4X1	T48.4X2	T48.4X3	T48.4X4	T48.4X5	T48.4X6
Iodinated						
contrast medium	T50.8X1	T50.8X2	T50.8X3	T50.8X4	T50.8X5	T50.8X6
glycerol	T48.4X1	T48.4X2	T48.4X3	T48.4X4	T48.4X5	T48.4X6
human serum albumin(131I)	T50.8X1	T50.8X2	T50.8X3	T50.8X4	T50.8X5	T50.8X6

Substance	Poisoning, Accidental (unintentional)	Poisoning, Intentional self-harm	Poisoning, Assault	Poisoning, Undetermined	Adverse effect	Underdosing
Iodine(antiseptic, external) (tincture) NEC	T49.0X1	T49.0X2	T49.0X3	T49.0X4	T49.0X5	T49.0X6
125—see also Radiation sickness, and Exposure to radioactivce isotopes	T50.8X1	T50.8X2	T50.8X3	T50.8X4	T50.8X5	T50.8X6
therapeutic	T50.991	T50.992	T50.993	T50.994	T50.995	T50.996
131—see also Radiation sickness, and Exposure to radioactivce isotopes	T50.8X1	T50.8X2	T50.8X3	T50.8X4	T50.8X5	T50.8X6
therapeutic	T38.2X1	T38.2X2	T38.2X3	T38.2X4	T38.2X5	T38.2X6
diagnostic	T50.8X1	T50.8X2	T50.8X3	T50.8X4	T50.8X5	T50.8X6
for thyroid conditions (antithyroid)	T38.2X1	T38.2X2	T38.2X3	T38.2X4	T38.2X5	T38.2X6
solution	T49.0X1	T49.0X2	T49.0X3	T49.0X4	T49.0X5	T49.0X6
vapor	T59.891	T59.892	T59.893	T59.894	—	—
Iodipamide	T50.8X1	T50.8X2	T50.8X3	T50.8X4	T50.8X5	T50.8X6
Iodized(poppy seed) oil	T50.8X1	T50.8X2	T50.8X3	T50.8X4	T50.8X5	T50.8X6
Iodobismitol	T37.8X1	T37.8X2	T37.8X3	T37.8X4	T37.8X5	T37.8X6
Iodochlorhyd-roxyquin	T37.8X1	T37.8X2	T37.8X3	T37.8X4	T37.8X5	T37.8X6
topical	T49.0X1	T49.0X2	T49.0X3	T49.0X4	T49.0X5	T49.0X6
Iodochlorhydroxy-quinoline	T37.8X1	T37.8X2	T37.8X3	T37.8X4	T37.8X5	T37.8X6
Iodocholesterol(131I)	T50.8X1	T50.8X2	T50.8X3	T50.8X4	T50.8X5	T50.8X6
Iodoform	T49.0X1	T49.0X2	T49.0X3	T49.0X4	T49.0X5	T49.0X6
Iodohippuric acid	T50.8X1	T50.8X2	T50.8X3	T50.8X4	T50.8X5	T50.8X6
Iodopanoic acid	T50.8X1	T50.8X2	T50.8X3	T50.8X4	T50.8X5	T50.8X6
Iodophthalein (sodium)	T50.8X1	T50.8X2	T50.8X3	T50.8X4	T50.8X5	T50.8X6
Iodopyracet	T50.8X1	T50.8X2	T50.8X3	T50.8X4	T50.8X5	T50.8X6
Iodoquinol	T37.8X1	T37.8X2	T37.8X3	T37.8X4	T37.8X5	T37.8X6
Iodoxamic acid	T50.8X1	T50.8X2	T50.8X3	T50.8X4	T50.8X5	T50.8X6
Iofendylate	T50.8X1	T50.8X2	T50.8X3	T50.8X4	T50.8X5	T50.8X6
Ioglycamic acid	T50.8X1	T50.8X2	T50.8X3	T50.8X4	T50.8X5	T50.8X6
Iohexol	T50.8X1	T50.8X2	T50.8X3	T50.8X4	T50.8X5	T50.8X6
Ion exchange resin						
anion	T47.8X1	T47.8X2	T47.8X3	T47.8X4	T47.8X5	T47.8X6
cation	T50.3X1	T50.3X2	T50.3X3	T50.3X4	T50.3X5	T50.3X6
cholestyramine	T46.6X1	T46.6X2	T46.6X3	T46.6X4	T46.6X5	T46.6X6
intestinal	T47.8X1	T47.8X2	T47.8X3	T47.8X4	T47.8X5	T47.8X6
Iopamidol	T50.8X1	T50.8X2	T50.8X3	T50.8X4	T50.8X5	T50.8X6
Iopanoic acid	T50.8X1	T50.8X2	T50.8X3	T50.8X4	T50.8X5	T50.8X6
Iophenoic acid	T50.8X1	T50.8X2	T50.8X3	T50.8X4	T50.8X5	T50.8X6
Iopodate, sodium	T50.8X1	T50.8X2	T50.8X3	T50.8X4	T50.8X5	T50.8X6
Iopodic acid	T50.8X1	T50.8X2	T50.8X3	T50.8X4	T50.8X5	T50.8X6
Iopromide	T50.8X1	T50.8X2	T50.8X3	T50.8X4	T50.8X5	T50.8X6
Iopydol	T50.8X1	T50.8X2	T50.8X3	T50.8X4	T50.8X5	T50.8X6
Iotalamic acid	T50.8X1	T50.8X2	T50.8X3	T50.8X4	T50.8X5	T50.8X6
Iothalamate	T50.8X1	T50.8X2	T50.8X3	T50.8X4	T50.8X5	T50.8X6
Iothiouracil	T38.2X1	T38.2X2	T38.2X3	T38.2X4	T38.2X5	T38.2X6
Iotrol	T50.8X1	T50.8X2	T50.8X3	T50.8X4	T50.8X5	T50.8X6
Iotrolan	T50.8X1	T50.8X2	T50.8X3	T50.8X4	T50.8X5	T50.8X6
Iotroxate	T50.8X1	T50.8X2	T50.8X3	T50.8X4	T50.8X5	T50.8X6
Iotroxic acid	T50.8X1	T50.8X2	T50.8X3	T50.8X4	T50.8X5	T50.8X6
Ioversol	T50.8X1	T50.8X2	T50.8X3	T50.8X4	T50.8X5	T50.8X6

Substance	Poisoning, Accidental (unintentional)	Poisoning, Intentional self-harm	Poisoning, Assault	Poisoning, Undetermined	Adverse effect	
Ioxaglate	T50.8X1	T50.8X2	T50.8X3	T50.8X4	T50.8X5	T50
Ioxaglic acid	T50.8X1	T50.8X2	T50.8X3	T50.8X4	T50.8X5	T50
Ioxitalamic acid	T50.8X1	T50.8X2	T50.8X3	T50.8X4	T50.8X5	T50
Ipecac	T47.7X1	T47.7X2	T47.7X3	T47.7X4	T47.7X5	T47
Ipecacuanha	T48.4X1	T48.4X2	T48.4X3	T48.4X4	T48.4X5	T48.
Ipodate, calcium	T50.8X1	T50.8X2	T50.8X3	T50.8X4	T50.8X5	T50.
Ipral	T42.3X1	T42.3X2	T42.3X3	T42.3X4	T42.3X5	T42.
Ipratropium (bromide)	T48.6X1	T48.6X2	T48.6X3	T48.6X4	T48.6X5	T48
Ipriflavone	T46.3X1	T46.3X2	T46.3X3	T46.3X4	T46.3X5	T46.
Iprindole	T43.011	T43.012	T43.013	T43.014	T43.015	T43
Iproclozide	T43.1X1	T43.1X2	T43.1X3	T43.1X4	T43.1X5	T43.
Iprofenin	T50.8X1	T50.8X2	T50.8X3	T50.8X4	T50.8X5	T50
Iproheptine	T49.2X1	T49.2X2	T49.2X3	T49.2X4	T49.2X5	T49
Iproniazid	T43.1X1	T43.1X2	T43.1X3	T43.1X4	T43.1X5	T43.
Iproplatin	T45.1X1	T45.1X2	T45.1X3	T45.1X4	T45.1X5	T45
Iproveratril	T46.1X1	T46.1X2	T46.1X3	T46.1X4	T46.1X5	T46
Iron(compounds) (medicinal) NEC	T45.4X1	T45.4X2	T45.4X3	T45.4X4	T45.4X5	T45
ammonium	T45.4X1	T45.4X2	T45.4X3	T45.4X4	T45.4X5	T45
dextran injection	T45.4X1	T45.4X2	T45.4X3	T45.4X4	T45.4X5	T45
nonmedicinal	T56.891	T56.892	T56.893	T56.894	—	–
salts	T45.4X1	T45.4X2	T45.4X3	T45.4X4	T45.4X5	T45
sorbitex	T45.4X1	T45.4X2	T45.4X3	T45.4X4	T45.4X5	T45.
sorbitol citric acid complex	T45.4X1	T45.4X2	T45.4X3	T45.4X4	T45.4X5	T45.
Irrigating fluid(vaginal)	T49.8X1	T49.8X2	T49.8X3	T49.8X4	T49.8X5	T49.
eye	T49.5X1	T49.5X2	T49.5X3	T49.5X4	T49.5X5	T49
Isepamicin	T36.5X1	T36.5X2	T36.5X3	T36.5X4	T36.5X5	T36
Isoaminile(citrate)	T48.3X1	T48.3X2	T48.3X3	T48.3X4	T48.3X5	T48.
Isoamyl nitrite	T46.3X1	T46.3X2	T46.3X3	T46.3X4	T46.3X5	T46
Isobenzan	T60.1X1	T60.1X2	T60.1X3	T60.1X4	—	–
Isobutyl acetate	T52.8X1	T52.8X2	T52.8X3	T52.8X4	—	–
Isocarboxazid	T43.1X1	T43.1X2	T43.1X3	T43.1X4	T43.1X5	T43
Isoconazole	T49.0X1	T49.0X2	T49.0X3	T49.0X4	T49.0X5	T49
Isocyanate	T65.0X1	T65.0X2	T65.0X3	T65.0X4	—	–
Isoephedrine	T44.991	T44.992	T44.993	T44.994	T44.995	T44
Isoetarine	T48.6X1	T48.6X2	T48.6X3	T48.6X4	T48.6X5	T48
Isoethadione	T42.2X1	T42.2X2	T42.2X3	T42.2X4	T42.2X5	T42
Isoetharine	T44.5X1	T44.5X2	T44.5X3	T44.5X4	T44.5X5	T44.
Isoflurane	T41.0X1	T41.0X2	T41.0X3	T41.0X4	T41.0X5	T41.
Isoflurophate	T44.0X1	T44.0X2	T44.0X3	T44.0X4	T44.0X5	T44.
Isomaltose, ferric complex	T45.4X1	T45.4X2	T45.4X3	T45.4X4	T45.4X5	T45.
Isometheptene	T44.3X1	T44.3X2	T44.3X3	T44.3X4	T44.3X5	T44.
Isoniazid	T37.1X1	T37.1X2	T37.1X3	T37.1X4	T37.1X5	T37.
with						
rifampicin	T36.6X1	T36.6X2	T36.6X3	T36.6X4	T36.6X5	T36
thioacetazone	T37.1X1	T37.1X2	T37.1X3	T37.1X4	T37.1X5	T37.
Isonicotinic acid hydrazide	T37.1X1	T37.1X2	T37.1X3	T37.1X4	T37.1X5	T37.
Isonipecaine	T40.4X1	T40.4X2	T40.4X3	T40.4X4	T40.4X5	T40.
Isopentaquine	T37.2X1	T37.2X2	T37.2X3	T37.2X4	T37.2X5	T37.
Isophane insulin	T38.3X1	T38.3X2	T38.3X3	T38.3X4	T38.3X5	T38.
Isophorone	T65.891	T65.892	T65.893	T65.894	—	–
Isophosphamide	T45.1X1	T45.1X2	T45.1X3	T45.1X4	T45.1X5	T45.

Substance	Poisoning, Accidental (unintentional)	Poisoning, Intentional self-harm	Poisoning, Assault	Poisoning, Undetermined	Adverse effect	Underdosing
regnenone	T38.5X1	T38.5X2	T38.5X3	T38.5X4	T38.5X5	T38.5X6
renaline	T48.6X1	T48.6X2	T48.6X3	T48.6X4	T48.6X5	T48.6X6
romethazine	T43.3X1	T43.3X2	T43.3X3	T43.3X4	T43.3X5	T43.3X6
ropamide	T44.3X1	T44.3X2	T44.3X3	T44.3X4	T44.3X5	T44.3X6
ide	T44.3X1	T44.3X2	T44.3X3	T44.3X4	T44.3X5	T44.3X6
ropanol	T51.2X1	T51.2X2	T51.2X3	T51.2X4	—	—
ropyl						
etate	T52.8X1	T52.8X2	T52.8X3	T52.8X4	—	—
ohol	T51.2X1	T51.2X2	T51.2X3	T51.2X4	—	—
nedicinal	T49.4X1	T49.4X2	T49.4X3	T49.4X4	T49.4X5	T49.4X6
er	T52.8X1	T52.8X2	T52.8X3	T52.8X4	—	—
ropylamino- azone	T39.2X1	T39.2X2	T39.2X3	T39.2X4	T39.2X5	T39.2X6
roterenol	T48.6X1	T48.6X2	T48.6X3	T48.6X4	T48.6X5	T48.6X6
rbide dinitrate	T46.3X1	T46.3X2	T46.3X3	T46.3X4	T46.3X5	T46.3X6
ipendyl	T45.0X1	T45.0X2	T45.0X3	T45.0X4	T45.0X5	T45.0X6
etinoin	T50.991	T50.992	T50.993	T50.994	T50.995	T50.996
azolyl penicillin	T36.0X1	T36.0X2	T36.0X3	T36.0X4	T36.0X5	T36.0X6
cam	T39.391	T39.392	T39.393	T39.394	T39.395	T39.396
suprine	T46.7X1	T46.7X2	T46.7X3	T46.7X4	T46.7X5	T46.7X6
gula	T47.4X1	T47.4X2	T47.4X3	T47.4X4	T47.4X5	T47.4X6
sk	T47.4X1	T47.4X2	T47.4X3	T47.4X4	T47.4X5	T47.4X6
dipine	T46.1X1	T46.1X2	T46.1X3	T46.1X4	T46.1X5	T46.1X6
roxine sodium	T38.1X1	T38.1X2	T38.1X3	T38.1X4	T38.1X5	T38.1X6
onazole	T37.8X1	T37.8X2	T37.8X3	T37.8X4	T37.8X5	T37.8X6
nin tosilate	T46.3X1	T46.3X2	T46.3X3	T46.3X4	T46.3X5	T46.3X6
mectin	T37.4X1	T37.4X2	T37.4X3	T37.4X4	T37.4X5	T37.4X6
iazid	T37.1X1	T37.1X2	T37.1X3	T37.1X4	T37.1X5	T37.1X6
th thioacetazone	T37.1X1	T37.1X2	T37.1X3	T37.1X4	T37.1X5	T37.1X6
J						
p	T47.2X1	T47.2X2	T47.2X3	T47.2X4	T47.2X5	T47.2X6
aica						
gwood(bark)	T39.8X1	T39.8X2	T39.8X3	T39.8X4	T39.8X5	T39.8X6
ger	T65.891	T65.892	T65.893	T65.894	—	—
root	T62.2X1	T62.2X2	T62.2X3	T62.2X4	—	—
pha	T62.2X1	T62.2X2	T62.2X3	T62.2X4	—	—
rcas	T62.2X1	T62.2X2	T62.2X3	T62.2X4	—	—
fer	T45.4X1	T45.4X2	T45.4X3	T45.4X4	T45.4X5	T45.4X6
fish(sting)	T63.621	T63.622	T63.623	T63.624	—	—
irity(bean)	T62.2X1	T62.2X2	T62.2X3	T62.2X4	—	—
on weed(stramonium)	T62.2X1	T62.2X2	T62.2X3	T62.2X4	—	—
eds	T62.2X1	T62.2X2	T62.2X3	T62.2X4	—	—
mycin	T36.3X1	T36.3X2	T36.3X3	T36.3X4	T36.3X5	T36.3X6
per tar	T49.1X1	T49.1X2	T49.1X3	T49.1X4	T49.1X5	T49.1X6
K						
dinogenase	T46.7X1	T46.7X2	T46.7X3	T46.7X4	T46.7X5	T46.7X6
krein	T46.7X1	T46.7X2	T46.7X3	T46.7X4	T46.7X5	T46.7X6
amycin	T36.5X1	T36.5X2	T36.5X3	T36.5X4	T36.5X5	T36.5X6
trex	T36.5X1	T36.5X2	T36.5X3	T36.5X4	T36.5X5	T36.5X6
in	T47.6X1	T47.6X2	T47.6X3	T47.6X4	T47.6X5	T47.6X6
ht	T47.6X1	T47.6X2	T47.6X3	T47.6X4	T47.6X5	T47.6X6
aya(gum)	T47.4X1	T47.4X2	T47.4X3	T47.4X4	T47.4X5	T47.4X6

Substance	Poisoning, Accidental (unintentional)	Poisoning, Intentional self-harm	Poisoning, Assault	Poisoning, Undetermined	Adverse effect	Underdosing
Kebuzone	T39.2X1	T39.2X2	T39.2X3	T39.2X4	T39.2X5	T39.2X6
Kelevan	T60.1X1	T60.1X2	T60.1X3	T60.1X4	—	—
Kemithal	T41.1X1	T41.1X2	T41.1X3	T41.1X4	T41.1X5	T41.1X6
Kenacort	T38.0X1	T38.0X2	T38.0X3	T38.0X4	T38.0X5	T38.0X6
Keratolytic drug NEC	T49.4X1	T49.4X2	T49.4X3	T49.4X4	T49.4X5	T49.4X6
anthracene	T49.4X1	T49.4X2	T49.4X3	T49.4X4	T49.4X5	T49.4X6
Keratoplastic NEC	T49.4X1	T49.4X2	T49.4X3	T49.4X4	T49.4X5	T49.4X6
Kerosene, kerosine(fuel) (solvent) NEC	T52.0X1	T52.0X2	T52.0X3	T52.0X4	—	—
insecticide	T52.0X1	T52.0X2	T52.0X3	T52.0X4	—	—
vapor	T52.0X1	T52.0X2	T52.0X3	T52.0X4	—	—
Ketamine	T41.291	T41.292	T41.293	T41.294	T41.295	T41.296
Ketazolam	T42.4X1	T42.4X2	T42.4X3	T42.4X4	T42.4X5	T42.4X6
Ketazon	T39.2X1	T39.2X2	T39.2X3	T39.2X4	T39.2X5	T39.2X6
Ketobemidone	T40.4X1	T40.4X2	T40.4X3	T40.4X4	—	—
Ketoconazole	T49.0X1	T49.0X2	T49.0X3	T49.0X4	T49.0X5	T49.0X6
Ketols	T52.4X1	T52.4X2	T52.4X3	T52.4X4	—	—
Ketone oils	T52.4X1	T52.4X2	T52.4X3	T52.4X4	—	—
Ketoprofen	T39.311	T39.312	T39.313	T39.314	T39.315	T39.316
Ketorolac	T39.8X1	T39.8X2	T39.8X3	T39.8X4	T39.8X5	T39.8X6
Ketotifen	T45.0X1	T45.0X2	T45.0X3	T45.0X4	T45.0X5	T45.0X6
Khat	T43.691	T43.692	T43.693	T43.694	—	—
Khellin	T46.3X1	T46.3X2	T46.3X3	T46.3X4	T46.3X5	T46.3X6
Khelloside	T46.3X1	T46.3X2	T46.3X3	T46.3X4	T46.3X5	T46.3X6
Kiln gas or vapor(carbon monoxide)	T58.8X1	T58.8X2	T58.8X3	T58.8X4	—	—
Kitasamycin	T36.3X1	T36.3X2	T36.3X3	T36.3X4	T36.3X5	T36.3X6
Konsyl	T47.4X1	T47.4X2	T47.4X3	T47.4X4	T47.4X5	T47.4X6
Kosam seed	T62.2X1	T62.2X2	T62.2X3	T62.2X4	—	—
Krait(venom)	T63.091	T63.092	T63.093	T63.094	—	—
Kwell(insecticide)	T60.1X1	T60.1X2	T60.1X3	T60.1X4	—	—
anti-infective(topical)	T49.0X1	T49.0X2	T49.0X3	T49.0X4	T49.0X5	T49.0X6
L						
Labetalol	T44.8X1	T44.8X2	T44.8X3	T44.8X4	T44.8X5	T44.8X6
Laburnum(seeds)	T62.2X1	T62.2X2	T62.2X3	T62.2X4	—	—
leaves	T62.2X1	T62.2X2	T62.2X3	T62.2X4	—	—
Lachesine	T49.5X1	T49.5X2	T49.5X3	T49.5X4	T49.5X5	T49.5X6
Lacidipine	T46.5X1	T46.5X2	T46.5X3	T46.5X4	T46.5X5	T46.5X6
Lacquer	T65.6X1	T65.6X2	T65.6X3	T65.6X4	—	—
Lacrimogenic gas	T59.3X1	T59.3X2	T59.3X3	T59.3X4	—	—
Lactated potassic saline	T50.3X1	T50.3X2	T50.3X3	T50.3X4	T50.3X5	T50.3X6
Lactic acid	T49.8X1	T49.8X2	T49.8X3	T49.8X4	T49.8X5	T49.8X6
Lactobacillus						
acidophilus	T47.6X1	T47.6X2	T47.6X3	T47.6X4	T47.6X5	T47.6X6
compound	T47.6X1	T47.6X2	T47.6X3	T47.6X4	T47.6X5	T47.6X6
bifidus, lyophilized	T47.6X1	T47.6X2	T47.6X3	T47.6X4	T47.6X5	T47.6X6
bulgaricus	T47.6X1	T47.6X2	T47.6X3	T47.6X4	T47.6X5	T47.6X6
sporogenes	T47.6X1	T47.6X2	T47.6X3	T47.6X4	T47.6X5	T47.6X6
Lactoflavin	T45.2X1	T45.2X2	T45.2X3	T45.2X4	T45.2X5	T45.2X6
Lactose(as excipient)	T50.901	T50.902	T50.903	T50.904	T50.905	T50.906
Lactuca(virosa) (extract)	T42.6X1	T42.6X2	T42.6X3	T42.6X4	T42.6X5	T42.6X6
Lactucarium	T42.6X1	T42.6X2	T42.6X3	T42.6X4	T42.6X5	T42.6X6

Substance	Poisoning, Accidental (unintentional)	Poisoning, Intentional self-harm	Poisoning, Assault	Poisoning, Undetermined	Adverse effect	Underdosing
Lactulose	T47.3X1	T47.3X2	T47.3X3	T47.3X4	T47.3X5	T47.3X6
Laevo—see Levo-						
Lanatosides	T46.0X1	T46.0X2	T46.0X3	T46.0X4	T46.0X5	T46.0X6
Lanolin	T49.3X1	T49.3X2	T49.3X3	T49.3X4	T49.3X5	T49.3X6
Largactil	T43.3X1	T43.3X2	T43.3X3	T43.3X4	T43.3X5	T43.3X6
Larkspur	T62.2X1	T62.2X2	T62.2X3	T62.2X4	—	—
Laroxyl	T43.011	T43.012	T43.013	T43.014	T43.015	T43.016
Lasix	T50.1X1	T50.1X2	T50.1X3	T50.1X4	T50.1X5	T50.1X6
Lassar's paste	T49.4X1	T49.4X2	T49.4X3	T49.4X4	T49.4X5	T49.4X6
Latamoxef	T36.1X1	T36.1X2	T36.1X3	T36.1X4	T36.1X5	T36.1X6
Latex	T65.811	T65.812	T65.813	T65.814	—	—
Lathyrus(seed)	T62.2X1	T62.2X2	T62.2X3	T62.2X4	—	—
Laudanum	T40.0X1	T40.0X2	T40.0X3	T40.0X4	T40.0X5	T40.0X6
Laudexium	T48.1X1	T48.1X2	T48.1X3	T48.1X4	T48.1X5	T48.1X6
Laughing gas	T41.0X1	T41.0X2	T41.0X3	T41.0X4	T41.0X5	T41.0X6
Laurel, black or cherry	T62.2X1	T62.2X2	T62.2X3	T62.2X4	—	—
Laurolinium	T49.0X1	T49.0X2	T49.0X3	T49.0X4	T49.0X5	T49.0X6
Lauryl sulfoacetate	T49.2X1	T49.2X2	T49.2X3	T49.2X4	T49.2X5	T49.2X6
Laxative NEC	T47.4X1	T47.4X2	T47.4X3	T47.4X4	T47.4X5	T47.4X6
osmotic	T47.3X1	T47.3X2	T47.3X3	T47.3X4	T47.3X5	T47.3X6
saline	T47.3X1	T47.3X2	T47.3X3	T47.3X4	T47.3X5	T47.3X6
stimulant	T47.2X1	T47.2X2	T47.2X3	T47.2X4	T47.2X5	T47.2X6
L-dopa	T42.8X1	T42.8X2	T42.8X3	T42.8X4	T42.8X5	T42.8X6
Lead(dust) (fumes) (vapor) NEC	T56.0X1	T56.0X2	T56.0X3	T56.0X4	—	—
acetate	T49.2X1	T49.2X2	T49.2X3	T49.2X4	T49.2X5	T49.2X6
alkyl(fuel additive)	T56.0X1	T56.0X2	T56.0X3	T56.0X4	—	—
anti-infectives	T37.8X1	T37.8X2	T37.8X3	T37.8X4	T37.8X5	T37.8X6
antiknock compound (tetraethyl)	T56.0X1	T56.0X2	T56.0X3	T56.0X4	—	—
arsenate, arsenite(dust) (herbicide) (insecticide) (vapor)	T57.0X1	T57.0X2	T57.0X3	T57.0X4	—	—
carbonate	T56.0X1	T56.0X2	T56.0X3	T56.0X4	—	—
paint	T56.0X1	T56.0X2	T56.0X3	T56.0X4	—	—
chromate	T56.0X1	T56.0X2	T56.0X3	T56.0X4	—	—
paint	T56.0X1	T56.0X2	T56.0X3	T56.0X4	—	—
dioxide	T56.0X1	T56.0X2	T56.0X3	T56.0X4	—	—
inorganic	T56.0X1	T56.0X2	T56.0X3	T56.0X4	—	—
iodide	T56.0X1	T56.0X2	T56.0X3	T56.0X4	—	—
pigment(paint)	T56.0X1	T56.0X2	T56.0X3	T56.0X4	—	—
monoxide(dust)	T56.0X1	T56.0X2	T56.0X3	T56.0X4	—	—
paint	T56.0X1	T56.0X2	T56.0X3	T56.0X4	—	—
organic	T56.0X1	T56.0X2	T56.0X3	T56.0X4	—	—
oxide	T56.0X1	T56.0X2	T56.0X3	T56.0X4	—	—
paint	T56.0X1	T56.0X2	T56.0X3	T56.0X4	—	—
paint	T56.0X1	T56.0X2	T56.0X3	T56.0X4	—	—
salts	T56.0X1	T56.0X2	T56.0X3	T56.0X4	—	—
specified compound NEC	T56.0X1	T56.0X2	T56.0X3	T56.0X4	—	—
tetra-ethyl	T56.0X1	T56.0X2	T56.0X3	T56.0X4	—	—
Lebanese red	T40.7X1	T40.7X2	T40.7X3	T40.7X4	T40.7X5	T40.7X6
Lefetamine	T39.8X1	T39.8X2	T39.8X3	T39.8X4	T39.8X5	T39.8X6

Substance	Poisoning, Accidental (unintentional)	Poisoning, Intentional self-harm	Poisoning, Assault	Poisoning, Undetermined	Adverse effect	U…
Lenperone	T43.4X1	T43.4X2	T43.4X3	T43.4X4	T43.4X5	T43.
Lente lietin(insulin)	T38.3X1	T38.3X2	T38.3X3	T38.3X4	T38.3X5	T38.
Leptazol	T50.7X1	T50.7X2	T50.7X3	T50.7X4	T50.7X5	T50.
Leptophos	T60.0X1	T60.0X2	T60.0X3	T60.0X4	—	–
Leritine	T40.2X1	T40.2X2	T40.2X3	T40.2X4	T40.2X5	T40.
Letosteine	T48.4X1	T48.4X2	T48.4X3	T48.4X4	T48.4X5	T48.
Letter	T38.1X1	T38.1X2	T38.1X3	T38.1X4	T38.1X5	T38.
Lettuce opium	T42.6X1	T42.6X2	T42.6X3	T42.6X4	T42.6X5	T42.
Leucinocaine	T41.3X1	T41.3X2	T41.3X3	T41.3X4	T41.3X5	T41.
Leucocianidol	T46.991	T46.992	T46.993	T46.994	T46.995	T46
Leucovorin(factor)	T45.8X1	T45.8X2	T45.8X3	T45.8X4	T45.8X5	T45.
Leukeran	T45.1X1	T45.1X2	T45.1X3	T45.1X4	T45.1X5	T45.
Leuprolide	T38.891	T38.892	T38.893	T38.894	T38.895	T38
Levalbuterol	T48.6X1	T48.6X2	T48.6X3	T48.6X4	T48.6X5	T48.
Levallorphan	T50.7X1	T50.7X2	T50.7X3	T50.7X4	T50.7X5	T50.
Levamisole	T37.4X1	T37.4X2	T37.4X3	T37.4X4	T37.4X5	T37.
Levanil	T42.6X1	T42.6X2	T42.6X3	T42.6X4	T42.6X5	T42.
Levarterenol	T44.4X1	T44.4X2	T44.4X3	T44.4X4	T44.4X5	T44.
Levdropropizine	T48.3X1	T48.3X2	T48.3X3	T48.3X4	T48.3X5	T48.
Levobunolol	T49.5X1	T49.5X2	T49.5X3	T49.5X4	T49.5X5	T49.
Levocabastine (hydrochloride)	T45.0X1	T45.0X2	T45.0X3	T45.0X4	T45.0X5	T45.
Levocarnitine	T50.991	T50.992	T50.993	T50.994	T50.995	T50
Levodopa	T42.8X1	T42.8X2	T42.8X3	T42.8X4	T42.8X5	T42.
with carbidopa	T42.8X1	T42.8X2	T42.8X3	T42.8X4	T42.8X5	T42.
Levo-dromoran	T40.2X1	T40.2X2	T40.2X3	T40.2X4	T40.2X5	T40.
Levoglutamide	T50.991	T50.992	T50.993	T50.994	T50.995	T50
Levoid	T38.1X1	T38.1X2	T38.1X3	T38.1X4	T38.1X5	T38.
Levo-iso-methadone	T40.3X1	T40.3X2	T40.3X3	T40.3X4	T40.3X5	T40.
Levomepromazine	T43.3X1	T43.3X2	T43.3X3	T43.3X4	T43.3X5	T43.
Levonordefrin	T49.6X1	T49.6X2	T49.6X3	T49.6X4	T49.6X5	T49.
Levonorgestrel	T38.4X1	T38.4X2	T38.4X3	T38.4X4	T38.4X5	T38.
with ethinylestradiol	T38.5X1	T38.5X2	T38.5X3	T38.5X4	T38.5X5	T38.
Levopromazine	T43.3X1	T43.3X2	T43.3X3	T43.3X4	T43.3X5	T43.
Levoprome	T42.6X1	T42.6X2	T42.6X3	T42.6X4	T42.6X5	T42.
Levopropoxyphene	T40.4X1	T40.4X2	T40.4X3	T40.4X4	T40.4X5	T40.
Levopropylhexedrine	T50.5X1	T50.5X2	T50.5X3	T50.5X4	T50.5X5	T50.
Levoproxyphylline	T48.6X1	T48.6X2	T48.6X3	T48.6X4	T48.6X5	T48.
Levorphanol	T40.4X1	T40.4X2	T40.4X3	T40.4X4	T40.4X5	T40.
Levothyroxine	T38.1X1	T38.1X2	T38.1X3	T38.1X4	T38.1X5	T38.
sodium	T38.1X1	T38.1X2	T38.1X3	T38.1X4	T38.1X5	T38.
Levsin	T44.3X1	T44.3X2	T44.3X3	T44.3X4	T44.3X5	T44.
Levulose	T50.3X1	T50.3X2	T50.3X3	T50.3X4	T50.3X5	T50.
Lewisite(gas), not in war	T57.0X1	T57.0X2	T57.0X3	T57.0X4	—	—
Librium	T42.4X1	T42.4X2	T42.4X3	T42.4X4	T42.4X5	T42.
Lidex	T49.0X1	T49.0X2	T49.0X3	T49.0X4	T49.0X5	T49.
Lidocaine	T41.3X1	T41.3X2	T41.3X3	T41.3X4	T41.3X5	T41.
regional	T41.3X1	T41.3X2	T41.3X3	T41.3X4	T41.3X5	T41.
spinal	T41.3X1	T41.3X2	T41.3X3	T41.3X4	T41.3X5	T41.
Lidofenin	T50.8X1	T50.8X2	T50.8X3	T50.8X4	T50.8X5	T50.
Lidoflazine	T46.1X1	T46.1X2	T46.1X3	T46.1X4	T46.1X5	T46.

Substance	Poisoning, Accidental (unintentional)	Poisoning, Intentional self-harm	Poisoning, Assault	Poisoning, Undetermined	Adverse effect	Underdosing
r fluid	T52.0X1	T52.0X2	T52.0X3	T52.0X4	—	—
hemicellulose	T47.6X1	T47.6X2	T47.6X3	T47.6X4	T47.6X5	T47.6X6
caine	T41.3X1	T41.3X2	T41.3X3	T41.3X4	T41.3X5	T41.3X6
onal	T41.3X1	T41.3X2	T41.3X3	T41.3X4	T41.3X5	T41.3X6
l	T41.3X1	T41.3X2	T41.3X3	T41.3X4	T41.3X5	T41.3X6
n(e) (solvent)	T52.0X1	T52.0X2	T52.0X3	T52.0X4	—	—
r	T59.891	T59.892	T59.893	T59.894	—	—
rum vulgare	T62.2X1	T62.2X2	T62.2X3	T62.2X4	—	—
the valley	T62.2X1	T62.2X2	T62.2X3	T62.2X4	—	—
chloride)	T54.3X1	T54.3X2	T54.3X3	T54.3X4	—	—
ene	T52.8X1	T52.8X2	T52.8X3	T52.8X4	—	—
nycin	T36.8X1	T36.8X2	T36.8X3	T36.8X4	T36.8X5	T36.8X6
ne(insecticide) edicinal) (vapor)	T53.6X1	T53.6X2	T53.6X3	T53.6X4	—	—
cinal	T49.0X1	T49.0X2	T49.0X3	T49.0X4	T49.0X5	T49.0X6
ents NEC	T49.91	T49.92	T49.93	T49.94	T49.95	T49.96
ic acid	T46.6X1	T46.6X2	T46.6X3	T46.6X4	T46.6X5	T46.6X6
nic acid	T46.6X1	T46.6X2	T46.6X3	T46.6X4	T46.6X5	T46.6X6
d	T47.4X1	T47.4X2	T47.4X3	T47.4X4	T47.4X5	T47.4X6
ronine	T38.1X1	T38.1X2	T38.1X3	T38.1X4	T38.1X5	T38.1X6
x	T38.1X1	T38.1X2	T38.1X3	T38.1X4	T38.1X5	T38.1X6
creatin	T47.5X1	T47.5X2	T47.5X3	T47.5X4	T47.5X5	T47.5X6
lprostadil	T46.7X1	T46.7X2	T46.7X3	T46.7X4	T46.7X5	T46.7X6
utin	T38.5X1	T38.5X2	T38.5X3	T38.5X4	T38.5X5	T38.5X6
opic drug NEC	T50.901	T50.902	T50.903	T50.904	T50.905	T50.906
ied petroleum gases	T59.891	T59.892	T59.893	T59.894	—	—
l(pure or mixed with	T59.891	T59.892	T59.893	T59.894	—	—
l						
ffin	T47.4X1	T47.4X2	T47.4X3	T47.4X4	T47.4X5	T47.4X6
latum	T47.4X1	T47.4X2	T47.4X3	T47.4X4	T47.4X5	T47.4X6
ical	T49.3X1	T49.3X2	T49.3X3	T49.3X4	T49.3X5	T49.3X6
ified NEC	T65.891	T65.892	T65.893	T65.894	—	—
tance	T65.91	T65.92	T65.93	T65.94	—	—
creosolis situs	T65.891	T65.892	T65.893	T65.894	—	—
rice	T48.4X1	T48.4X2	T48.4X3	T48.4X4	T48.4X5	T48.4X6
ct	T47.8X1	T47.8X2	T47.8X3	T47.8X4	T47.8X5	T47.8X6
pril	T46.4X1	T46.4X2	T46.4X3	T46.4X4	T46.4X5	T46.4X6
de	T42.8X1	T42.8X2	T42.8X3	T42.8X4	T42.8X5	T42.8X6
e	T43.8X1	T43.8X2	T43.8X3	T43.8X4	T43.8X5	T43.8X6
m	T56.891	T56.892	T56.893	T56.894	—	—
onate	T43.591	T43.592	T43.593	T43.594	T43.595	T43.596
(carbonate)	T43.591	T43.592	T43.593	T43.594	T43.595	T43.596
ate	T43.8X1	T43.8X2	T43.8X3	T43.8X4	T43.8X5	T43.8X6
ct	T45.8X1	T45.8X2	T45.8X3	T45.8X4	T45.8X5	T45.8X6
parenteral use	T45.8X1	T45.8X2	T45.8X3	T45.8X4	T45.8X5	T45.8X6
ion 1	T45.8X1	T45.8X2	T45.8X3	T45.8X4	T45.8X5	T45.8X6
olysate	T45.8X1	T45.8X2	T45.8X3	T45.8X4	T45.8X5	T45.8X6
(bite) (venom)	T63.121	T63.122	T63.123	T63.124	—	—
	T45.8X1	T45.8X2	T45.8X3	T45.8X4	T45.8X5	T45.8X6

Substance	Poisoning, Accidental (unintentional)	Poisoning, Intentional self-harm	Poisoning, Assault	Poisoning, Undetermined	Adverse effect	Underdosing
Lobelia	T62.2X1	T62.2X2	T62.2X3	T62.2X4	—	—
Lobeline	T50.7X1	T50.7X2	T50.7X3	T50.7X4	T50.7X5	T50.7X6
Local action drug NEC	T49.8X1	T49.8X2	T49.8X3	T49.8X4	T49.8X5	T49.8X6
Locorten	T49.0X1	T49.0X2	T49.0X3	T49.0X4	T49.0X5	T49.0X6
Lofepramine	T43.011	T43.012	T43.013	T43.014	T43.015	T43.016
Lolium temulentum	T62.2X1	T62.2X2	T62.2X3	T62.2X4	—	—
Lomotil	T47.6X1	T47.6X2	T47.6X3	T47.6X4	T47.6X5	T47.6X6
Lomustine	T45.1X1	T45.1X2	T45.1X3	T45.1X4	T45.1X5	T45.1X6
Lonidamine	T45.1X1	T45.1X2	T45.1X3	T45.1X4	T45.1X5	T45.1X6
Loperamide	T47.6X1	T47.6X2	T47.6X3	T47.6X4	T47.6X5	T47.6X6
Loprazolam	T42.4X1	T42.4X2	T42.4X3	T42.4X4	T42.4X5	T42.4X6
Lorajmine	T46.2X1	T46.2X2	T46.2X3	T46.2X4	T46.2X5	T46.2X6
Loratidine	T45.0X1	T45.0X2	T45.0X3	T45.0X4	T45.0X5	T45.0X6
Lorazepam	T42.4X1	T42.4X2	T42.4X3	T42.4X4	T42.4X5	T42.4X6
Lorcainide	T46.2X1	T46.2X2	T46.2X3	T46.2X4	T46.2X5	T46.2X6
Lormetazepam	T42.4X1	T42.4X2	T42.4X3	T42.4X4	T42.4X5	T42.4X6
Lotions NEC	T49.91	T49.92	T49.93	T49.94	T49.95	T49.96
Lotusate	T42.3X1	T42.3X2	T42.3X3	T42.3X4	T42.3X5	T42.3X6
Lovastatin	T46.6X1	T46.6X2	T46.6X3	T46.6X4	T46.6X5	T46.6X6
Lowila	T49.2X1	T49.2X2	T49.2X3	T49.2X4	T49.2X5	T49.2X6
Loxapine	T43.591	T43.592	T43.593	T43.594	T43.595	T43.596
Lozenges(throat)	T49.6X1	T49.6X2	T49.6X3	T49.6X4	T49.6X5	T49.6X6
LSD	T40.8X1	T40.8X2	T40.8X3	T40.8X4	—	—
L-Tryptophan—see amino acid						
Lubricant, eye	T49.5X1	T49.5X2	T49.5X3	T49.5X4	T49.5X5	T49.5X6
Lubricating oil NEC	T52.0X1	T52.0X2	T52.0X3	T52.0X4	—	—
Lucanthone	T37.4X1	T37.4X2	T37.4X3	T37.4X4	T37.4X5	T37.4X6
Luminal	T42.3X1	T42.3X2	T42.3X3	T42.3X4	T42.3X5	T42.3X6
Lung irritant(gas) NEC	T59.91	T59.92	T59.93	T59.94	—	—
Luteinizing hormone	T38.811	T38.812	T38.813	T38.814	T38.815	T38.816
Lutocylol	T38.5X1	T38.5X2	T38.5X3	T38.5X4	T38.5X5	T38.5X6
Lutromone	T38.5X1	T38.5X2	T38.5X3	T38.5X4	T38.5X5	T38.5X6
Lututrin	T48.291	T48.292	T48.293	T48.294	T48.295	T48.296
Lye(concentrated)	T54.3X1	T54.3X2	T54.3X3	T54.3X4	—	—
Lygranum(skin test)	T50.8X1	T50.8X2	T50.8X3	T50.8X4	T50.8X5	T50.8X6
Lymecycline	T36.4X1	T36.4X2	T36.4X3	T36.4X4	T36.4X5	T36.4X6
Lymphogranuloma venereum antigen	T50.8X1	T50.8X2	T50.8X3	T50.8X4	T50.8X5	T50.8X6
Lynestrenol	T38.4X1	T38.4X2	T38.4X3	T38.4X4	T38.4X5	T38.4X6
Lyovac Sodium Edecrin	T50.1X1	T50.1X2	T50.1X3	T50.1X4	T50.1X5	T50.1X6
Lypressin	T38.891	T38.892	T38.893	T38.894	T38.895	T38.896
Lysergic acid diethylamide	T40.8X1	T40.8X2	T40.8X3	T40.8X4	—	—
Lysergide	T40.8X1	T40.8X2	T40.8X3	T40.8X4	—	—
Lysine vasopressin	T38.891	T38.892	T38.893	T38.894	T38.895	T38.896
Lysol	T54.1X1	T54.1X2	T54.1X3	T54.1X4	—	—
Lysozyme	T49.0X1	T49.0X2	T49.0X3	T49.0X4	T49.0X5	T49.0X6
Lytta(vitatta)	T49.8X1	T49.8X2	T49.8X3	T49.8X4	T49.8X5	T49.8X6
M						
Mace	T59.3X1	T59.3X2	T59.3X3	T59.3X4	—	—
Macrogol	T50.991	T50.992	T50.993	T50.994	T50.995	T50.996

Substance	Poisoning, Accidental (unintentional)	Poisoning, Intentional self-harm	Poisoning, Assault	Poisoning, Undetermined	Adverse effect	Underdosing
Macrolide						
anabolic drug	T38.7X1	T38.7X2	T38.7X3	T38.7X4	T38.7X5	T38.7X6
antibiotic	T36.3X1	T36.3X2	T36.3X3	T36.3X4	T36.3X5	T36.3X6
Mafenide	T49.0X1	T49.0X2	T49.0X3	T49.0X4	T49.0X5	T49.0X6
Magaldrate	T47.1X1	T47.1X2	T47.1X3	T47.1X4	T47.1X5	T47.1X6
Magic mushroom	T40.991	T40.992	T40.993	T40.994	—	—
Magnamycin	T36.8X1	T36.8X2	T36.8X3	T36.8X4	T36.8X5	T36.8X6
Magnesia magna	T47.1X1	T47.1X2	T47.1X3	T47.1X4	T47.1X5	T47.1X6
Magnesium NEC	T56.891	T56.892	T56.893	T56.894	—	—
carbonate	T47.1X1	T47.1X2	T47.1X3	T47.1X4	T47.1X5	T47.1X6
citrate	T47.4X1	T47.4X2	T47.4X3	T47.4X4	T47.4X5	T47.4X6
hydroxide	T47.1X1	T47.1X2	T47.1X3	T47.1X4	T47.1X5	T47.1X6
oxide	T47.1X1	T47.1X2	T47.1X3	T47.1X4	T47.1X5	T47.1X6
peroxide	T49.0X1	T49.0X2	T49.0X3	T49.0X4	T49.0X5	T49.0X6
salicylate	T39.091	T39.092	T39.093	T39.094	T39.095	T39.096
silicofluoride	T50.3X1	T50.3X2	T50.3X3	T50.3X4	T50.3X5	T50.3X6
sulfate	T47.4X1	T47.4X2	T47.4X3	T47.4X4	T47.4X5	T47.4X6
thiosulfate	T45.0X1	T45.0X2	T45.0X3	T45.0X4	T45.0X5	T45.0X6
trisilicate	T47.1X1	T47.1X2	T47.1X3	T47.1X4	T47.1X5	T47.1X6
Malathion(medicinal)	T49.0X1	T49.0X2	T49.0X3	T49.0X4	T49.0X5	T49.0X6
insecticide	T60.0X1	T60.0X2	T60.0X3	T60.0X4	—	—
Male fern extract	T37.4X1	T37.4X2	T37.4X3	T37.4X4	T37.4X5	T37.4X6
M-AMSA	T45.1X1	T45.1X2	T45.1X3	T45.1X4	T45.1X5	T45.1X6
Mandelic acid	T37.8X1	T37.8X2	T37.8X3	T37.8X4	T37.8X5	T37.8X6
Manganese(dioxide) (salts)	T57.2X1	T57.2X2	T57.2X3	T57.2X4	—	—
medicinal	T50.991	T50.992	T50.993	T50.994	T50.995	T50.996
Mannitol	T47.3X1	T47.3X2	T47.3X3	T47.3X4	T47.3X5	T47.3X6
hexanitrate	T46.3X1	T46.3X2	T46.3X3	T46.3X4	T46.3X5	T46.3X6
Mannomustine	T45.1X1	T45.1X2	T45.1X3	T45.1X4	T45.1X5	T45.1X6
MAO inhibitors	T43.1X1	T43.1X2	T43.1X3	T43.1X4	T43.1X5	T43.1X6
Mapharsen	T37.8X1	T37.8X2	T37.8X3	T37.8X4	T37.8X5	T37.8X6
Maphenide	T49.0X1	T49.0X2	T49.0X3	T49.0X4	T49.0X5	T49.0X6
Maprotiline	T43.021	T43.022	T43.023	T43.024	T43.025	T43.026
Marcaine	T41.3X1	T41.3X2	T41.3X3	T41.3X4	T41.3X5	T41.3X6
infiltration (subcutaneous)	T41.3X1	T41.3X2	T41.3X3	T41.3X4	T41.3X5	T41.3X6
nerve block(peripheral) (plexus)	T41.3X1	T41.3X2	T41.3X3	T41.3X4	T41.3X5	T41.3X6
Marezine	T45.0X1	T45.0X2	T45.0X3	T45.0X4	T45.0X5	T45.0X6
Marihuana	T40.7X1	T40.7X2	T40.7X3	T40.7X4	T40.7X5	T40.7X6
Marijuana	T40.7X1	T40.7X2	T40.7X3	T40.7X4	T40.7X5	T40.7X6
Marine(sting)	T63.691	T63.692	T63.693	T63.694	—	—
animals(sting)	T63.691	T63.692	T63.693	T63.694	—	—
plants(sting)	T63.711	T63.712	T63.713	T63.714	—	—
Marplan	T43.1X1	T43.1X2	T43.1X3	T43.1X4	T43.1X5	T43.1X6
Marsh gas	T59.891	T59.892	T59.893	T59.894	—	—
Marsilid	T43.1X1	T43.1X2	T43.1X3	T43.1X4	T43.1X5	T43.1X6
Matulane	T45.1X1	T45.1X2	T45.1X3	T45.1X4	T45.1X5	T45.1X6
Mazindol	T50.5X1	T50.5X2	T50.5X3	T50.5X4	T50.5X5	T50.5X6
MCPA	T60.3X1	T60.3X2	T60.3X3	T60.3X4	—	—
MDMA	T43.621	T43.622	T43.623	T43.624	T43.625	T43.626

Substance	Poisoning, Accidental (unintentional)	Poisoning, Intentional self-harm	Poisoning, Assault	Poisoning, Undetermined	Adverse effect
Meadow saffron	T62.2X1	T62.2X2	T62.2X3	T62.2X4	—
Measles virus vaccine(attenuated)	T50.B91	T50.B92	T50.B93	T50.B94	T50.B95
Meat, noxious	T62.8X1	T62.8X2	T62.8X3	T62.8X4	—
Meballymal	T42.3X1	T42.3X2	T42.3X3	T42.3X4	T42.3X5
Mebanazine	T43.1X1	T43.1X2	T43.1X3	T43.1X4	T43.1X5
Mebaral	T42.3X1	T42.3X2	T42.3X3	T42.3X4	T42.3X5
Mebendazole	T37.4X1	T37.4X2	T37.4X3	T37.4X4	T37.4X5
Mebeverine	T44.3X1	T44.3X2	T44.3X3	T44.3X4	T44.3X5
Mebhydrolin	T45.0X1	T45.0X2	T45.0X3	T45.0X4	T45.0X5
Mebumal	T42.3X1	T42.3X2	T42.3X3	T42.3X4	T42.3X5
Mebutamate	T43.591	T43.592	T43.593	T43.594	T43.595
Mecamylamine	T44.2X1	T44.2X2	T44.2X3	T44.2X4	T44.2X5
Mechlorethamine	T45.1X1	T45.1X2	T45.1X3	T45.1X4	T45.1X5
Mecillinam	T36.0X1	T36.0X2	T36.0X3	T36.0X4	T36.0X5
Meclizine (hydrochloride)	T45.0X1	T45.0X2	T45.0X3	T45.0X4	T45.0X5
Meclocycline	T36.4X1	T36.4X2	T36.4X3	T36.4X4	T36.4X5
Meclofenamate	T39.391	T39.392	T39.393	T39.394	T39.395
Meclofenamic acid	T39.391	T39.392	T39.393	T39.394	T39.395
Meclofenoxate	T43.691	T43.692	T43.693	T43.694	T43.695
Meclozine	T45.0X1	T45.0X2	T45.0X3	T45.0X4	T45.0X5
Mecobalamin	T45.8X1	T45.8X2	T45.8X3	T45.8X4	T45.8X5
Mecoprop	T60.3X1	T60.3X2	T60.3X3	T60.3X4	—
Mecrilate	T49.3X1	T49.3X2	T49.3X3	T49.3X4	T49.3X5
Mecysteine	T48.4X1	T48.4X2	T48.4X3	T48.4X4	T48.4X5
Medazepam	T42.4X1	T42.4X2	T42.4X3	T42.4X4	T42.4X5
Medicament NEC	T50.901	T50.902	T50.903	T50.904	T50.905
Medinal	T42.3X1	T42.3X2	T42.3X3	T42.3X4	T42.3X5
Medomin	T42.3X1	T42.3X2	T42.3X3	T42.3X4	T42.3X5
Medrogestone	T38.5X1	T38.5X2	T38.5X3	T38.5X4	T38.5X5
Medroxalol	T44.8X1	T44.8X2	T44.8X3	T44.8X4	T44.8X5
Medroxyprogesteron eacetate(depot)	T38.5X1	T38.5X2	T38.5X3	T38.5X4	T38.5X5
Medrysone	T49.0X1	T49.0X2	T49.0X3	T49.0X4	T49.0X5
Mefenamic acid	T39.391	T39.392	T39.393	T39.394	T39.395
Mefenorex	T50.5X1	T50.5X2	T50.5X3	T50.5X4	T50.5X5
Mefloquine	T37.2X1	T37.2X2	T37.2X3	T37.2X4	T37.2X5
Mefruside	T50.2X1	T50.2X2	T50.2X3	T50.2X4	T50.2X5
Megahallucinogen	T40.901	T40.902	T40.903	T40.904	T40.905
Megestrol	T38.5X1	T38.5X2	T38.5X3	T38.5X4	T38.5X5
Meglumine					
antimoniate	T37.8X1	T37.8X2	T37.8X3	T37.8X4	T37.8X5
diatrizoate	T50.8X1	T50.8X2	T50.8X3	T50.8X4	T50.8X5
iodipamide	T50.8X1	T50.8X2	T50.8X3	T50.8X4	T50.8X5
iotroxate	T50.8X1	T50.8X2	T50.8X3	T50.8X4	T50.8X5
MEK(methyl ethyl ketone)	T52.4X1	T52.4X2	T52.4X3	T52.4X4	—
Meladinin	T49.3X1	T49.3X2	T49.3X3	T49.3X4	T49.3X5
Meladrazine	T44.3X1	T44.3X2	T44.3X3	T44.3X4	T44.3X5
Melaleuca alternifolia oil	T49.0X1	T49.0X2	T49.0X3	T49.0X4	T49.0X5

Substance	Poisoning, Accidental (unintentional)	Poisoning, Intentional self-harm	Poisoning, Assault	Poisoning, Undetermined	Adverse effect	Underdosing
anizing agents	T49.3X1	T49.3X2	T49.3X3	T49.3X4	T49.3X5	T49.3X6
anocyte-stimulating none	T38.891	T38.892	T38.893	T38.894	T38.895	T38.896
arsonyl potassium	T37.3X1	T37.3X2	T37.3X3	T37.3X4	T37.3X5	T37.3X6
arsoprol	T37.3X1	T37.3X2	T37.3X3	T37.3X4	T37.3X5	T37.3X6
ia azedarach	T62.2X1	T62.2X2	T62.2X3	T62.2X4	—	—
itracen	T43.011	T43.012	T43.013	T43.014	T43.015	T43.016
laril	T43.3X1	T43.3X2	T43.3X3	T43.3X4	T43.3X5	T43.3X6
oxine	T49.3X1	T49.3X2	T49.3X3	T49.3X4	T49.3X5	T49.3X6
perone	T43.4X1	T43.4X2	T43.4X3	T43.4X4	T43.4X5	T43.4X6
phalan	T45.1X1	T45.1X2	T45.1X3	T45.1X4	T45.1X5	T45.1X6
nantine	T43.8X1	T43.8X2	T43.8X3	T43.8X4	T43.8X5	T43.8X6
nadiol	T45.7X1	T45.7X2	T45.7X3	T45.7X4	T45.7X5	T45.7X6
dium sulfate	T45.7X1	T45.7X2	T45.7X3	T45.7X4	T45.7X5	T45.7X6
nadione	T45.7X1	T45.7X2	T45.7X3	T45.7X4	T45.7X5	T45.7X6
dium bisulfite	T45.7X1	T45.7X2	T45.7X3	T45.7X4	T45.7X5	T45.7X6
naphthone	T45.7X1	T45.7X2	T45.7X3	T45.7X4	T45.7X5	T45.7X6
naquinone	T45.7X1	T45.7X2	T45.7X3	T45.7X4	T45.7X5	T45.7X6
natetrenone	T45.7X1	T45.7X2	T45.7X3	T45.7X4	T45.7X5	T45.7X6
ningococcal vaccine	T50.A91	T50.A92	T50.A93	T50.A94	T50.A95	T50.A96
nningovax(-AC) (-C)	T50.A91	T50.A92	T50.A93	T50.A94	T50.A95	T50.A96
notropins	T38.811	T38.812	T38.813	T38.814	T38.815	T38.816
nthol	T48.5X1	T48.5X2	T48.5X3	T48.5X4	T48.5X5	T48.5X6
pacrine	T37.2X1	T37.2X2	T37.2X3	T37.2X4	T37.2X5	T37.2X6
parfynol	T42.6X1	T42.6X2	T42.6X3	T42.6X4	T42.6X5	T42.6X6
partricin	T36.7X1	T36.7X2	T36.7X3	T36.7X4	T36.7X5	T36.7X6
pazine	T43.3X1	T43.3X2	T43.3X3	T43.3X4	T43.3X5	T43.3X6
penzolate	T44.3X1	T44.3X2	T44.3X3	T44.3X4	T44.3X5	T44.3X6
romide	T44.3X1	T44.3X2	T44.3X3	T44.3X4	T44.3X5	T44.3X6
peridine	T40.4X1	T40.4X2	T40.4X3	T40.4X4	T40.4X5	T40.4X6
phebarbital	T42.3X1	T42.3X2	T42.3X3	T42.3X4	T42.3X5	T42.3X6
phenamin(e)	T42.8X1	T42.8X2	T42.8X3	T42.8X4	T42.8X5	T42.8X6
phenesin	T42.8X1	T42.8X2	T42.8X3	T42.8X4	T42.8X5	T42.8X6
phenhydramine	T45.0X1	T45.0X2	T45.0X3	T45.0X4	T45.0X5	T45.0X6
phenoxalone	T42.8X1	T42.8X2	T42.8X3	T42.8X4	T42.8X5	T42.8X6
phentermine	T44.991	T44.992	T44.993	T44.994	T44.995	T44.996
phenytoin	T42.0X1	T42.0X2	T42.0X3	T42.0X4	T42.0X5	T42.0X6
ith phenobarbital	T42.3X1	T42.3X2	T42.3X3	T42.3X4	T42.3X5	T42.3X6
phobarbital	T42.3X1	T42.3X2	T42.3X3	T42.3X4	T42.3X5	T42.3X6
phosfolan	T60.0X1	T60.0X2	T60.0X3	T60.0X4	—	—
pindolol	T44.7X1	T44.7X2	T44.7X3	T44.7X4	T44.7X5	T44.7X6
piperphenidol	T44.3X1	T44.3X2	T44.3X3	T44.3X4	T44.3X5	T44.3X6
pitiostane	T38.7X1	T38.7X2	T38.7X3	T38.7X4	T38.7X5	T38.7X6
pivacaine	T41.3X1	T41.3X2	T41.3X3	T41.3X4	T41.3X5	T41.3X6
pidural	T41.3X1	T41.3X2	T41.3X3	T41.3X4	T41.3X5	T41.3X6
prednisone	T38.0X1	T38.0X2	T38.0X3	T38.0X4	T38.0X5	T38.0X6
eprobam	T43.591	T43.592	T43.593	T43.594	T43.595	T43.596
eprobamate	T43.591	T43.592	T43.593	T43.594	T43.595	T43.596
eproscillarin	T46.0X1	T46.0X2	T46.0X3	T46.0X4	T46.0X5	T46.0X6
eprylcaine	T41.3X1	T41.3X2	T41.3X3	T41.3X4	T41.3X5	T41.3X6
eptazinol	T39.8X1	T39.8X2	T39.8X3	T39.8X4	T39.8X5	T39.8X6

Substance	Poisoning, Accidental (unintentional)	Poisoning, Intentional self-harm	Poisoning, Assault	Poisoning, Undetermined	Adverse effect	Underdosing
Mepyramine	T45.0X1	T45.0X2	T45.0X3	T45.0X4	T45.0X5	T45.0X6
Mequitazine	T43.3X1	T43.3X2	T43.3X3	T43.3X4	T43.3X5	T43.3X6
Meralluride	T50.2X1	T50.2X2	T50.2X3	T50.2X4	T50.2X5	T50.2X6
Merbaphen	T50.2X1	T50.2X2	T50.2X3	T50.2X4	T50.2X5	T50.2X6
Merbromin	T49.0X1	T49.0X2	T49.0X3	T49.0X4	T49.0X5	T49.0X6
Mercaptoben-zothiazole salts	T49.0X1	T49.0X2	T49.0X3	T49.0X4	T49.0X5	T49.0X6
Mercaptomerin	T50.2X1	T50.2X2	T50.2X3	T50.2X4	T50.2X5	T50.2X6
Mercaptopurine	T45.1X1	T45.1X2	T45.1X3	T45.1X4	T45.1X5	T45.1X6
Mercumatilin	T50.2X1	T50.2X2	T50.2X3	T50.2X4	T50.2X5	T50.2X6
Mercuramide	T50.2X1	T50.2X2	T50.2X3	T50.2X4	T50.2X5	T50.2X6
Mercurochrome	T49.0X1	T49.0X2	T49.0X3	T49.0X4	T49.0X5	T49.0X6
Mercurophylline	T50.2X1	T50.2X2	T50.2X3	T50.2X4	T50.2X5	T50.2X6
Mercury, mercurial, mercuric, mercurous (compounds)(cyanide) (fumes) (nonmedicinal) (vapor) NEC	T56.1X1	T56.1X2	T56.1X3	T56.1X4	—	—
ammoniated	T49.0X1	T49.0X2	T49.0X3	T49.0X4	T49.0X5	T49.0X6
anti-infective						
local	T49.0X1	T49.0X2	T49.0X3	T49.0X4	T49.0X5	T49.0X6
systemic	T37.8X1	T37.8X2	T37.8X3	T37.8X4	T37.8X5	T37.8X6
topical	T49.0X1	T49.0X2	T49.0X3	T49.0X4	T49.0X5	T49.0X6
chloride (ammoniated)	T49.0X1	T49.0X2	T49.0X3	T49.0X4	T49.0X5	T49.0X6
fungicide	T56.1X1	T56.1X2	T56.1X3	T56.1X4	—	—
diuretic NEC	T50.2X1	T50.2X2	T50.2X3	T50.2X4	T50.2X5	T50.2X6
fungicide	T56.1X1	T56.1X2	T56.1X3	T56.1X4	—	—
organic(fungicide)	T56.1X1	T56.1X2	T56.1X3	T56.1X4	—	—
oxide, yellow	T49.0X1	T49.0X2	T49.0X3	T49.0X4	T49.0X5	T49.0X6
Mersalyl	T50.2X1	T50.2X2	T50.2X3	T50.2X4	T50.2X5	T50.2X6
Merthiolate	T49.0X1	T49.0X2	T49.0X3	T49.0X4	T49.0X5	T49.0X6
ophthalmic preparation	T49.5X1	T49.5X2	T49.5X3	T49.5X4	T49.5X5	T49.5X6
Meruvax	T50.B91	T50.B92	T50.B93	T50.B94	T50.B95	T50.B96
Mesalazine	T47.8X1	T47.8X2	T47.8X3	T47.8X4	T47.8X5	T47.8X6
Mescal buttons	T40.991	T40.992	T40.993	T40.994	—	—
Mescaline	T40.991	T40.992	T40.993	T40.994	—	—
Mesna	T48.4X1	T48.4X2	T48.4X3	T48.4X4	T48.4X5	T48.4X6
Mesoglycan	T46.6X1	T46.6X2	T46.6X3	T46.6X4	T46.6X5	T46.6X6
Mesoridazine	T43.3X1	T43.3X2	T43.3X3	T43.3X4	T43.3X5	T43.3X6
Mestanolone	T38.7X1	T38.7X2	T38.7X3	T38.7X4	T38.7X5	T38.7X6
Mesterolone	T38.7X1	T38.7X2	T38.7X3	T38.7X4	T38.7X5	T38.7X6
Mestranol	T38.5X1	T38.5X2	T38.5X3	T38.5X4	T38.5X5	T38.5X6
Mesulergine	T42.8X1	T42.8X2	T42.8X3	T42.8X4	T42.8X5	T42.8X6
Mesulfen	T49.0X1	T49.0X2	T49.0X3	T49.0X4	T49.0X5	T49.0X6
Mesuximide	T42.2X1	T42.2X2	T42.2X3	T42.2X4	T42.2X5	T42.2X6
Metabutethamine	T41.3X1	T41.3X2	T41.3X3	T41.3X4	T41.3X5	T41.3X6
Metactesylacetate	T49.0X1	T49.0X2	T49.0X3	T49.0X4	T49.0X5	T49.0X6
Metacycline	T36.4X1	T36.4X2	T36.4X3	T36.4X4	T36.4X5	T36.4X6
Metaldehyde(snail killer) NEC	T60.8X1	T60.8X2	T60.8X3	T60.8X4	—	—

Substance	Poisoning, Accidental (unintentional)	Poisoning, Intentional self-harm	Poisoning, Assault	Poisoning, Undetermined	Adverse effect	Underdosing
Metals(heavy) (nonmedicinal)	T56.91	T56.92	T56.93	T56.94	—	—
dust, fumes, or vapor NEC	T56.91	T56.92	T56.93	T56.94	—	—
light NEC	T56.91	T56.92	T56.93	T56.94	—	—
dust, fumes, or vapor NEC	T56.91	T56.92	T56.93	T56.94	—	—
specified NEC	T56.891	T56.892	T56.893	T56.894	—	—
thallium	T56.811	T56.812	T56.813	T56.814	—	—
Metamfetamine	T43.621	T43.622	T43.623	T43.624	T43.625	T43.626
Metamizole sodium	T39.2X1	T39.2X2	T39.2X3	T39.2X4	T39.2X5	T39.2X6
Metampicillin	T36.0X1	T36.0X2	T36.0X3	T36.0X4	T36.0X5	T36.0X6
Metamucil	T47.4X1	T47.4X2	T47.4X3	T47.4X4	T47.4X5	T47.4X6
Metandienone	T38.7X1	T38.7X2	T38.7X3	T38.7X4	T38.7X5	T38.7X6
Metandrostenolone	T38.7X1	T38.7X2	T38.7X3	T38.7X4	T38.7X5	T38.7X6
Metaphen	T49.0X1	T49.0X2	T49.0X3	T49.0X4	T49.0X5	T49.0X6
Metaphos	T60.0X1	T60.0X2	T60.0X3	T60.0X4	—	—
Metapramine	T43.011	T43.012	T43.013	T43.014	T43.015	T43.016
Metaproterenol	T48.291	T48.292	T48.293	T48.294	T48.295	T48.296
Metaraminol	T44.4X1	T44.4X2	T44.4X3	T44.4X4	T44.4X5	T44.4X6
Metaxalone	T42.8X1	T42.8X2	T42.8X3	T42.8X4	T42.8X5	T42.8X6
Metenolone	T38.7X1	T38.7X2	T38.7X3	T38.7X4	T38.7X5	T38.7X6
Metergoline	T42.8X1	T42.8X2	T42.8X3	T42.8X4	T42.8X5	T42.8X6
Metescufylline	T46.991	T46.992	T46.993	T46.994	T46.995	T46.996
Metetoin	T42.0X1	T42.0X2	T42.0X3	T42.0X4	T42.0X5	T42.0X6
Metformin	T38.3X1	T38.3X2	T38.3X3	T38.3X4	T38.3X5	T38.3X6
Methacholine	T44.1X1	T44.1X2	T44.1X3	T44.1X4	T44.1X5	T44.1X6
Methacycline	T36.4X1	T36.4X2	T36.4X3	T36.4X4	T36.4X5	T36.4X6
Methadone	T40.3X1	T40.3X2	T40.3X3	T40.3X4	T40.3X5	T40.3X6
Methallenestril	T38.5X1	T38.5X2	T38.5X3	T38.5X4	T38.5X5	T38.5X6
Methallenoestril	T38.5X1	T38.5X2	T38.5X3	T38.5X4	T38.5X5	T38.5X6
Methamphetamine	T43.621	T43.622	T43.623	T43.624	T43.625	T43.626
Methampyrone	T39.2X1	T39.2X2	T39.2X3	T39.2X4	T39.2X5	T39.2X6
Methandienone	T38.7X1	T38.7X2	T38.7X3	T38.7X4	T38.7X5	T38.7X6
Methandriol	T38.7X1	T38.7X2	T38.7X3	T38.7X4	T38.7X5	T38.7X6
Methandrostenolone	T38.7X1	T38.7X2	T38.7X3	T38.7X4	T38.7X5	T38.7X6
Methane	T59.891	T59.892	T59.893	T59.894	—	—
Methanethiol	T59.891	T59.892	T59.893	T59.894	—	—
Methaniazide	T37.1X1	T37.1X2	T37.1X3	T37.1X4	T37.1X5	T37.1X6
Methanol(vapor)	T51.1X1	T51.1X2	T51.1X3	T51.1X4	—	—
Methantheline	T44.3X1	T44.3X2	T44.3X3	T44.3X4	T44.3X5	T44.3X6
Methanthelinium bromide	T44.3X1	T44.3X2	T44.3X3	T44.3X4	T44.3X5	T44.3X6
Methaphenilene	T45.0X1	T45.0X2	T45.0X3	T45.0X4	T45.0X5	T45.0X6
Methapyrilene	T45.0X1	T45.0X2	T45.0X3	T45.0X4	T45.0X5	T45.0X6
Methaqualone (compound)	T42.6X1	T42.6X2	T42.6X3	T42.6X4	T42.6X5	T42.6X6
Metharbital	T42.3X1	T42.3X2	T42.3X3	T42.3X4	T42.3X5	T42.3X6
Methazolamide	T50.2X1	T50.2X2	T50.2X3	T50.2X4	T50.2X5	T50.2X6
Methdilazine	T43.3X1	T43.3X2	T43.3X3	T43.3X4	T43.3X5	T43.3X6
Methedrine	T43.621	T43.622	T43.623	T43.624	T43.625	T43.626
Methenamine (mandelate)	T37.8X1	T37.8X2	T37.8X3	T37.8X4	T37.8X5	T37.8X6
Methenolone	T38.7X1	T38.7X2	T38.7X3	T38.7X4	T38.7X5	T38.7X6
Methergine	T48.0X1	T48.0X2	T48.0X3	T48.0X4	T48.0X5	T48.0X6

Substance	Poisoning, Accidental (unintentional)	Poisoning, Intentional self-harm	Poisoning, Assault	Poisoning, Undetermined	Adverse effect	Und
Methetoin	T42.0X1	T42.0X2	T42.0X3	T42.0X4	T42.0X5	T42.
Methiacil	T38.2X1	T38.2X2	T38.2X3	T38.2X4	T38.2X5	T38.
Methicillin	T36.0X1	T36.0X2	T36.0X3	T36.0X4	T36.0X5	T36.
Methimazole	T38.2X1	T38.2X2	T38.2X3	T38.2X4	T38.2X5	T38.
Methiodal sodium	T50.8X1	T50.8X2	T50.8X3	T50.8X4	T50.8X5	T50.
Methionine	T50.991	T50.992	T50.993	T50.994	T50.995	T50
Methisazone	T37.5X1	T37.5X2	T37.5X3	T37.5X4	T37.5X5	T37.
Methisoprinol	T37.5X1	T37.5X2	T37.5X3	T37.5X4	T37.5X5	T37.
Methitural	T42.3X1	T42.3X2	T42.3X3	T42.3X4	T42.3X5	T42.
Methixene	T44.3X1	T44.3X2	T44.3X3	T44.3X4	T44.3X5	T44.
Methobarbital, methobarbitone	T42.3X1	T42.3X2	T42.3X3	T42.3X4	T42.3X5	T42.
Methocarbamol	T42.8X1	T42.8X2	T42.8X3	T42.8X4	T42.8X5	T42.
skeletal muscle relaxant	T48.1X1	T48.1X2	T48.1X3	T48.1X4	T48.1X5	T48.
Methohexital	T41.1X1	T41.1X2	T41.1X3	T41.1X4	T41.1X5	T41.
Methohexitone	T41.1X1	T41.1X2	T41.1X3	T41.1X4	T41.1X5	T41.
Methoin	T42.0X1	T42.0X2	T42.0X3	T42.0X4	T42.0X5	T42.
Methopholine	T39.8X1	T39.8X2	T39.8X3	T39.8X4	T39.8X5	T39.
Methopromazine	T43.3X1	T43.3X2	T43.3X3	T43.3X4	T43.3X5	T43.
Methorate	T48.3X1	T48.3X2	T48.3X3	T48.3X4	T48.3X5	T48.
Methoserpidine	T46.5X1	T46.5X2	T46.5X3	T46.5X4	T46.5X5	T46.5
Methotrexate	T45.1X1	T45.1X2	T45.1X3	T45.1X4	T45.1X5	T45.
Methotrimeprazine	T43.3X1	T43.3X2	T43.3X3	T43.3X4	T43.3X5	T43.3
Methoxa-Dome	T49.3X1	T49.3X2	T49.3X3	T49.3X4	T49.3X5	T49.3
Methoxamine	T44.4X1	T44.4X2	T44.4X3	T44.4X4	T44.4X5	T44.4
Methoxsalen	T50.991	T50.992	T50.993	T50.994	T50.995	T50.9
Methoxyaniline	T65.3X1	T65.3X2	T65.3X3	T65.3X4	—	—
Methoxybenzyl penicillin	T36.0X1	T36.0X2	T36.0X3	T36.0X4	T36.0X5	T36.0
Methoxychlor	T53.7X1	T53.7X2	T53.7X3	T53.7X4	—	—
Methoxy-DDT	T53.7X1	T53.7X2	T53.7X3	T53.7X4	—	—
2-Methoxyethanol	T52.3X1	T52.3X2	T52.3X3	T52.3X4	—	—
Methoxyflurane	T41.0X1	T41.0X2	T41.0X3	T41.0X4	T41.0X5	T41.0
Methoxyphenamine	T48.6X1	T48.6X2	T48.6X3	T48.6X4	T48.6X5	T48.6
Methoxypromazine	T43.3X1	T43.3X2	T43.3X3	T43.3X4	T43.3X5	T43.3
5-Methoxypsoralen (5-MOP)	T50.991	T50.992	T50.993	T50.994	T50.995	T50.9
8-Methoxypsoralen (8-MOP)	T50.991	T50.992	T50.993	T50.994	T50.995	T50.9
Methscopolamine bromide	T44.3X1	T44.3X2	T44.3X3	T44.3X4	T44.3X5	T44.3
Methsuximide	T42.2X1	T42.2X2	T42.2X3	T42.2X4	T42.2X5	T42.2
Methyclothiazide	T50.2X1	T50.2X2	T50.2X3	T50.2X4	T50.2X5	T50.2
Methyl						
acetate	T52.4X1	T52.4X2	T52.4X3	T52.4X4	—	—
acetone	T52.4X1	T52.4X2	T52.4X3	T52.4X4	—	—
acrylate	T65.891	T65.892	T65.893	T65.894	—	—
alcohol	T51.1X1	T51.1X2	T51.1X3	T51.1X4	—	—
aminophenol	T65.3X1	T65.3X2	T65.3X3	T65.3X4	—	—
amphetamine	T43.621	T43.622	T43.623	T43.624	T43.625	T43.6
androstanolone	T38.7X1	T38.7X2	T38.7X3	T38.7X4	T38.7X5	T38.7
atropine	T44.3X1	T44.3X2	T44.3X3	T44.3X4	T44.3X5	T44.3
benzene	T52.2X1	T52.2X2	T52.2X3	T52.2X4	—	—

Substance	Poisoning, Accidental (unintentional)	Poisoning, Intentional self-harm	Poisoning, Assault	Poisoning, Undetermined	Adverse effect	Underdosing
yl — *Continued*						
nzoate	T52.8X1	T52.8X2	T52.8X3	T52.8X4	—	—
nzol	T52.2X1	T52.2X2	T52.2X3	T52.2X4	—	—
mide(gas)	T59.891	T59.892	T59.893	T59.894	—	—
umigant	T60.8X1	T60.8X2	T60.8X3	T60.8X4	—	—
anol	T51.3X1	T51.3X2	T51.3X3	T51.3X4	—	—
binol	T51.1X1	T51.1X2	T51.1X3	T51.1X4	—	—
bonate	T52.8X1	T52.8X2	T52.8X3	T52.8X4	—	—
NU	T45.1X1	T45.1X2	T45.1X3	T45.1X4	T45.1X5	T45.1X6
losolve	T52.91	T52.92	T52.93	T52.94	—	—
llulose	T47.4X1	T47.4X2	T47.4X3	T47.4X4	T47.4X5	T47.4X6
oride(gas)	T59.891	T59.892	T59.893	T59.894	—	—
loroformate	T59.3X1	T59.3X2	T59.3X3	T59.3X4	—	—
clohexane	T52.8X1	T52.8X2	T52.8X3	T52.8X4	—	—
clohexanol	T51.8X1	T51.8X2	T51.8X3	T51.8X4	—	—
clohexanone	T52.8X1	T52.8X2	T52.8X3	T52.8X4	—	—
clohexyl acetate	T52.8X1	T52.8X2	T52.8X3	T52.8X4	—	—
meton	T60.0X1	T60.0X2	T60.0X3	T60.0X4	—	—
ydromorphinone	T40.2X1	T40.2X2	T40.2X3	T40.2X4	T40.2X5	T40.2X6
gometrine	T48.0X1	T48.0X2	T48.0X3	T48.0X4	T48.0X5	T48.0X6
gonovine	T48.0X1	T48.0X2	T48.0X3	T48.0X4	T48.0X5	T48.0X6
yl ketone	T52.4X1	T52.4X2	T52.4X3	T52.4X4	—	—
icamine antimonate	T37.8X1	T37.8X2	T37.8X3	T37.8X4	T37.8X5	T37.8X6
drazine	T65.891	T65.892	T65.893	T65.894	—	—
dide	T65.891	T65.892	T65.893	T65.894	—	—
butyl ketone	T52.4X1	T52.4X2	T52.4X3	T52.4X4	—	—
othiocyanate	T60.3X1	T60.3X2	T60.3X3	T60.3X4	—	—
ercaptan	T59.891	T59.892	T59.893	T59.894	—	—
orphine NEC	T40.2X1	T40.2X2	T40.2X3	T40.2X4	T40.2X5	T40.2X6
cotinate	T49.4X1	T49.4X2	T49.4X3	T49.4X4	T49.4X5	T49.4X6
raben	T49.0X1	T49.0X2	T49.0X3	T49.0X4	T49.0X5	T49.0X6
rafynol	T42.6X1	T42.6X2	T42.6X3	T42.6X4	T42.6X5	T42.6X6
rathion	T60.0X1	T60.0X2	T60.0X3	T60.0X4	—	—
ridol	T43.4X1	T43.4X2	T43.4X3	T43.4X4	T43.4X5	T43.4X6
nenidate	T43.631	T43.632	T43.633	T43.634	T43.635	T43.636
ednisolone	T38.0X1	T38.0X2	T38.0X3	T38.0X4	T38.0X5	T38.0X6
ENT agent	T49.6X1	T49.6X2	T49.6X3	T49.6X4	T49.6X5	T49.6X6
ophthalmic preparation	T49.5X1	T49.5X2	T49.5X3	T49.5X4	T49.5X5	T49.5X6
topical NEC	T49.0X1	T49.0X2	T49.0X3	T49.0X4	T49.0X5	T49.0X6
opylcarbinol	T51.3X1	T51.3X2	T51.3X3	T51.3X4	—	—
saniline NEC	T49.0X1	T49.0X2	T49.0X3	T49.0X4	T49.0X5	T49.0X6
licylate	T49.2X1	T49.2X2	T49.2X3	T49.2X4	T49.2X5	T49.2X6
lfate(fumes)	T59.891	T59.892	T59.893	T59.894	—	—
liquid	T52.8X1	T52.8X2	T52.8X3	T52.8X4	—	—
lfonal	T42.6X1	T42.6X2	T42.6X3	T42.6X4	T42.6X5	T42.6X6
stosterone	T38.7X1	T38.7X2	T38.7X3	T38.7X4	T38.7X5	T38.7X6
iouracil	T38.2X1	T38.2X2	T38.2X3	T38.2X4	T38.2X5	T38.2X6
thylamphetamine	T43.621	T43.622	T43.623	T43.624	T43.625	T43.626
thylated spirit	T51.1X1	T51.1X2	T51.1X3	T51.1X4	—	—
thylatropine nitrate	T44.3X1	T44.3X2	T44.3X3	T44.3X4	T44.3X5	T44.3X6
thylbenactyzium mide	T44.3X1	T44.3X2	T44.3X3	T44.3X4	T44.3X5	T44.3X6

Substance	Poisoning, Accidental (unintentional)	Poisoning, Intentional self-harm	Poisoning, Assault	Poisoning, Undetermined	Adverse effect	Underdosing
Methylbenzethonium chloride	T49.0X1	T49.0X2	T49.0X3	T49.0X4	T49.0X5	T49.0X6
Methylcellulose	T47.4X1	T47.4X2	T47.4X3	T47.4X4	T47.4X5	T47.4X6
laxative	T47.4X1	T47.4X2	T47.4X3	T47.4X4	T47.4X5	T47.4X6
Methylchlorophenoxy-acetic acid	T60.3X1	T60.3X2	T60.3X3	T60.3X4	—	—
Methyldopa	T46.5X1	T46.5X2	T46.5X3	T46.5X4	T46.5X5	T46.5X6
Methyldopate	T46.5X1	T46.5X2	T46.5X3	T46.5X4	T46.5X5	T46.5X6
Methylene						
blue	T50.6X1	T50.6X2	T50.6X3	T50.6X4	T50.6X5	T50.6X6
chloride or dichloride(solvent) NEC	T53.4X1	T53.4X2	T53.4X3	T53.4X4	—	—
Methylenedioxy-amphetamine	T43.621	T43.622	T43.623	T43.624	T43.625	T43.626
Methylenedioxy-methamphetamine	T43.621	T43.622	T43.623	T43.624	T43.625	T43.626
Methylergometrine	T48.0X1	T48.0X2	T48.0X3	T48.0X4	T48.0X5	T48.0X6
Methylergonovine	T48.0X1	T48.0X2	T48.0X3	T48.0X4	T48.0X5	T48.0X6
Methylestrenolone	T38.5X1	T38.5X2	T38.5X3	T38.5X4	T38.5X5	T38.5X6
Methylethyl cellulose	T50.991	T50.992	T50.993	T50.994	T50.995	T50.996
Methylhexabital	T42.3X1	T42.3X2	T42.3X3	T42.3X4	T42.3X5	T42.3X6
Methylmorphine	T40.2X1	T40.2X2	T40.2X3	T40.2X4	T40.2X5	T40.2X6
Methylparaben (ophthalmic)	T49.5X1	T49.5X2	T49.5X3	T49.5X4	T49.5X5	T49.5X6
Methylparafynol	T42.6X1	T42.6X2	T42.6X3	T42.6X4	T42.6X5	T42.6X6
Methylpentynol, methylpenthynol	T42.6X1	T42.6X2	T42.6X3	T42.6X4	T42.6X5	T42.6X6
Methylphenidate	T43.631	T43.632	T43.633	T43.634	T43.635	T43.636
Methylphenobarbital	T42.3X1	T42.3X2	T42.3X3	T42.3X4	T42.3X5	T42.3X6
Methylpolysiloxane	T47.1X1	T47.1X2	T47.1X3	T47.1X4	T47.1X5	T47.1X6
Methylprednisolone— see Methyl, prednisolone						
Methylrosaniline	T49.0X1	T49.0X2	T49.0X3	T49.0X4	T49.0X5	T49.0X6
Methylrosanilinium chloride	T49.0X1	T49.0X2	T49.0X3	T49.0X4	T49.0X5	T49.0X6
Methyltestosterone	T38.7X1	T38.7X2	T38.7X3	T38.7X4	T38.7X5	T38.7X6
Methylthionine chloride	T50.6X1	T50.6X2	T50.6X3	T50.6X4	T50.6X5	T50.6X6
Methylthioninium chloride	T50.6X1	T50.6X2	T50.6X3	T50.6X4	T50.6X5	T50.6X6
Methylthiouracil	T38.2X1	T38.2X2	T38.2X3	T38.2X4	T38.2X5	T38.2X6
Methyprylon	T42.6X1	T42.6X2	T42.6X3	T42.6X4	T42.6X5	T42.6X6
Methysergide	T46.5X1	T46.5X2	T46.5X3	T46.5X4	T46.5X5	T46.5X6
Metiamide	T47.1X1	T47.1X2	T47.1X3	T47.1X4	T47.1X5	T47.1X6
Meticillin	T36.0X1	T36.0X2	T36.0X3	T36.0X4	T36.0X5	T36.0X6
Meticrane	T50.2X1	T50.2X2	T50.2X3	T50.2X4	T50.2X5	T50.2X6
Metildigoxin	T46.0X1	T46.0X2	T46.0X3	T46.0X4	T46.0X5	T46.0X6
Metipranolol	T49.5X1	T49.5X2	T49.5X3	T49.5X4	T49.5X5	T49.5X6
Metirosine	T46.5X1	T46.5X2	T46.5X3	T46.5X4	T46.5X5	T46.5X6
Metisazone	T37.5X1	T37.5X2	T37.5X3	T37.5X4	T37.5X5	T37.5X6
Metixene	T44.3X1	T44.3X2	T44.3X3	T44.3X4	T44.3X5	T44.3X6
Metizoline	T48.5X1	T48.5X2	T48.5X3	T48.5X4	T48.5X5	T48.5X6
Metoclopramide	T45.0X1	T45.0X2	T45.0X3	T45.0X4	T45.0X5	T45.0X6
Metofenazate	T43.3X1	T43.3X2	T43.3X3	T43.3X4	T43.3X5	T43.3X6
Metofoline	T39.8X1	T39.8X2	T39.8X3	T39.8X4	T39.8X5	T39.8X6
Metolazone	T50.2X1	T50.2X2	T50.2X3	T50.2X4	T50.2X5	T50.2X6

Substance	Poisoning, Accidental (unintentional)	Poisoning, Intentional self-harm	Poisoning, Assault	Poisoning, Undetermined	Adverse effect	Underdosing
Metopon	T40.2X1	T40.2X2	T40.2X3	T40.2X4	T40.2X5	T40.2X6
Metoprine	T45.1X1	T45.1X2	T45.1X3	T45.1X4	T45.1X5	T45.1X6
Metoprolol	T44.7X1	T44.7X2	T44.7X3	T44.7X4	T44.7X5	T44.7X6
Metrifonate	T60.0X1	T60.0X2	T60.0X3	T60.0X4	—	—
Metrizamide	T50.8X1	T50.8X2	T50.8X3	T50.8X4	T50.8X5	T50.8X6
Metrizoic acid	T50.8X1	T50.8X2	T50.8X3	T50.8X4	T50.8X5	T50.8X6
Metronidazole	T37.8X1	T37.8X2	T37.8X3	T37.8X4	T37.8X5	T37.8X6
Metycaine	T41.3X1	T41.3X2	T41.3X3	T41.3X4	T41.3X5	T41.3X6
infiltration (subcutaneous)	T41.3X1	T41.3X2	T41.3X3	T41.3X4	T41.3X5	T41.3X6
nerve block(peripheral) (plexus)	T41.3X1	T41.3X2	T41.3X3	T41.3X4	T41.3X5	T41.3X6
topical(surface)	T41.3X1	T41.3X2	T41.3X3	T41.3X4	T41.3X5	T41.3X6
Metyrapone	T50.8X1	T50.8X2	T50.8X3	T50.8X4	T50.8X5	T50.8X6
Mevinphos	T60.0X1	T60.0X2	T60.0X3	T60.0X4	—	—
Mexazolam	T42.4X1	T42.4X2	T42.4X3	T42.4X4	T42.4X5	T42.4X6
Mexenone	T49.3X1	T49.3X2	T49.3X3	T49.3X4	T49.3X5	T49.3X6
Mexiletine	T46.2X1	T46.2X2	T46.2X3	T46.2X4	T46.2X5	T46.2X6
Mezereon	T62.2X1	T62.2X2	T62.2X3	T62.2X4	—	—
berries	T62.1X1	T62.1X2	T62.1X3	T62.1X4	—	—
Mezlocillin	T36.0X1	T36.0X2	T36.0X3	T36.0X4	T36.0X5	T36.0X6
Mianserin	T43.021	T43.022	T43.023	T43.024	T43.025	T43.026
Micatin	T49.0X1	T49.0X2	T49.0X3	T49.0X4	T49.0X5	T49.0X6
Miconazole	T49.0X1	T49.0X2	T49.0X3	T49.0X4	T49.0X5	T49.0X6
Micronomicin	T36.5X1	T36.5X2	T36.5X3	T36.5X4	T36.5X5	T36.5X6
Midazolam	T42.4X1	T42.4X2	T42.4X3	T42.4X4	T42.4X5	T42.4X6
Midecamycin	T36.3X1	T36.3X2	T36.3X3	T36.3X4	T36.3X5	T36.3X6
Mifepristone	T38.6X1	T38.6X2	T38.6X3	T38.6X4	T38.6X5	T38.6X6
Milk of magnesia	T47.1X1	T47.1X2	T47.1X3	T47.1X4	T47.1X5	T47.1X6
Millipede(tropical) (venomous)	T63.411	T63.412	T63.413	T63.414	—	—
Miltown	T43.591	T43.592	T43.593	T43.594	T43.595	T43.596
Milverine	T44.3X1	T44.3X2	T44.3X3	T44.3X4	T44.3X5	T44.3X6
Minaprine	T43.291	T43.292	T43.293	T43.294	T43.295	T43.296
Minaxolone	T41.291	T41.292	T41.293	T41.294	T41.295	T41.296
Mineral						
acids	T54.2X1	T54.2X2	T54.2X3	T54.2X4	—	—
oil(laxative)(medicinal)	T47.4X1	T47.4X2	T47.4X3	T47.4X4	T47.4X5	T47.4X6
emulsion	T47.2X1	T47.2X2	T47.2X3	T47.2X4	T47.2X5	T47.2X6
nonmedicinal	T52.0X1	T52.0X2	T52.0X3	T52.0X4	—	—
topical	T49.3X1	T49.3X2	T49.3X3	T49.3X4	T49.3X5	T49.3X6
salt NEC	T50.3X1	T50.3X2	T50.3X3	T50.3X4	T50.3X5	T50.3X6
spirits	T52.0X1	T52.0X2	T52.0X3	T52.0X4	—	—
Mineralocorticosteroid	T50.0X1	T50.0X2	T50.0X3	T50.0X4	T50.0X5	T50.0X6
Minocycline	T36.4X1	T36.4X2	T36.4X3	T36.4X4	T36.4X5	T36.4X6
Minoxidil	T46.7X1	T46.7X2	T46.7X3	T46.7X4	T46.7X5	T46.7X6
Miokamycin	T36.3X1	T36.3X2	T36.3X3	T36.3X4	T36.3X5	T36.3X6
Miotic drug	T49.5X1	T49.5X2	T49.5X3	T49.5X4	T49.5X5	T49.5X6
Mipafox	T60.0X1	T60.0X2	T60.0X3	T60.0X4	—	—
Mirex	T60.1X1	T60.1X2	T60.1X3	T60.1X4	—	—
Mirtazapine	T43.021	T43.022	T43.023	T43.024	T43.025	T43.026
Misonidazole	T37.3X1	T37.3X2	T37.3X3	T37.3X4	T37.3X5	T37.3X6

Substance	Poisoning, Accidental (unintentional)	Poisoning, Intentional self-harm	Poisoning, Assault	Poisoning, Undetermined	Adverse effect	Underdosing
Misoprostol	T47.1X1	T47.1X2	T47.1X3	T47.1X4	T47.1X5	T47
Mithramycin	T45.1X1	T45.1X2	T45.1X3	T45.1X4	T45.1X5	T45
Mitobronitol	T45.1X1	T45.1X2	T45.1X3	T45.1X4	T45.1X5	T45
Mitoguazone	T45.1X1	T45.1X2	T45.1X3	T45.1X4	T45.1X5	T45
Mitolactol	T45.1X1	T45.1X2	T45.1X3	T45.1X4	T45.1X5	T45
Mitomycin	T45.1X1	T45.1X2	T45.1X3	T45.1X4	T45.1X5	T45
Mitopodozide	T45.1X1	T45.1X2	T45.1X3	T45.1X4	T45.1X5	T45.
Mitotane	T45.1X1	T45.1X2	T45.1X3	T45.1X4	T45.1X5	T45.
Mitoxantrone	T45.1X1	T45.1X2	T45.1X3	T45.1X4	T45.1X5	T45.
Mivacurium chloride	T48.1X1	T48.1X2	T48.1X3	T48.1X4	T48.1X5	T48.
Miyari bacteria	T47.6X1	T47.6X2	T47.6X3	T47.6X4	T47.6X5	T47.
Moclobemide	T43.1X1	T43.1X2	T43.1X3	T43.1X4	T43.1X5	T43.
Moderil	T46.5X1	T46.5X2	T46.5X3	T46.5X4	T46.5X5	T46.
Mofebutazone	T39.2X1	T39.2X2	T39.2X3	T39.2X4	T39.2X5	T39.
Mogadon—see Nitrazepam						
Molindone	T43.591	T43.592	T43.593	T43.594	T43.595	T43.
Molsidomine	T46.3X1	T46.3X2	T46.3X3	T46.3X4	T46.3X5	T46.
Mometasone	T49.0X1	T49.0X2	T49.0X3	T49.0X4	T49.0X5	T49.
Monistat	T49.0X1	T49.0X2	T49.0X3	T49.0X4	T49.0X5	T49.
Monkshood	T62.2X1	T62.2X2	T62.2X3	T62.2X4	—	—
Monoamine oxidase inhibitor NEC	T43.1X1	T43.1X2	T43.1X3	T43.1X4	T43.1X5	T43.
hydrazine	T43.1X1	T43.1X2	T43.1X3	T43.1X4	T43.1X5	T43.
Monobenzone	T49.4X1	T49.4X2	T49.4X3	T49.4X4	T49.4X5	T49.
Monochloroacetic acid	T60.3X1	T60.3X2	T60.3X3	T60.3X4	—	—
Monochlorobenzene	T53.7X1	T53.7X2	T53.7X3	T53.7X4	—	—
Monoethanolamine	T46.8X1	T46.8X2	T46.8X3	T46.8X4	T46.8X5	T46.
oleate	T46.8X1	T46.8X2	T46.8X3	T46.8X4	T46.8X5	T46.
Monooctanoin	T50.991	T50.992	T50.993	T50.994	T50.995	T50.
Monophenylbutazone	T39.2X1	T39.2X2	T39.2X3	T39.2X4	T39.2X5	T39.
Monosodium glutamate	T65.891	T65.892	T65.893	T65.894	—	—
Monosulfiram	T49.0X1	T49.0X2	T49.0X3	T49.0X4	T49.0X5	T49.
Monoxide, carbon—see Carbon, monoxide						
Monoxidine hydrochloride	T46.1X1	T46.1X2	T46.1X3	T46.1X4	T46.1X5	T46.
Monuron	T60.3X1	T60.3X2	T60.3X3	T60.3X4	—	—
Moperone	T43.4X1	T43.4X2	T43.4X3	T43.4X4	T43.4X5	T43.4
Mopidamol	T45.1X1	T45.1X2	T45.1X3	T45.1X4	T45.1X5	T45.1
MOPP(mechloreth-amine + vincristine + prednisone + procarba-zine)	T45.1X1	T45.1X2	T45.1X3	T45.1X4	T45.1X5	T45.1
Morfin	T40.2X1	T40.2X2	T40.2X3	T40.2X4	T40.2X5	T40.2
Morinamide	T37.1X1	T37.1X2	T37.1X3	T37.1X4	T37.1X5	T37.1
Morning glory seeds	T40.991	T40.992	T40.993	T40.994	—	—
Moroxydine	T37.5X1	T37.5X2	T37.5X3	T37.5X4	T37.5X5	T37.5
Morphazinamide	T37.1X1	T37.1X2	T37.1X3	T37.1X4	T37.1X5	T37.1
Morphine	T40.2X1	T40.2X2	T40.2X3	T40.2X4	T40.2X5	T40.2
antagonist	T50.7X1	T50.7X2	T50.7X3	T50.7X4	T50.7X5	T50.7
Morpholinylethyl-morphine	T40.2X1	T40.2X2	T40.2X3	T40.2X4	—	—
Morsuximide	T42.2X1	T42.2X2	T42.2X3	T42.2X4	T42.2X5	T42.2

Substance	Poisoning, Accidental (unintentional)	Poisoning, Intentional self-harm	Poisoning, Assault	Poisoning, Undetermined	Adverse effect	Underdosing
osapramine	T43.591	T43.592	T43.593	T43.594	T43.595	T43.596
oth balls—see also sticides	T60.2X1	T60.2X2	T60.2X3	T60.2X4	—	—
naphthalene	T60.2X1	T60.2X2	T60.2X3	T60.2X4	—	—
paradichlorobenzene	T60.1X1	T60.1X2	T60.1X3	T60.1X4	—	—
otor exhaust gas	T58.01	T58.02	T58.03	T58.04	—	—
outhwash (antiseptic) incchloride)	T49.6X1	T49.6X2	T49.6X3	T49.6X4	T49.6X5	T49.6X6
oxastine	T45.0X1	T45.0X2	T45.0X3	T45.0X4	T45.0X5	T45.0X6
oxaverine	T44.3X1	T44.3X2	T44.3X3	T44.3X4	T44.3X5	T44.3X6
oxisylyte	T46.7X1	T46.7X2	T46.7X3	T46.7X4	T46.7X5	T46.7X6
ucilage, plant	T47.4X1	T47.4X2	T47.4X3	T47.4X4	T47.4X5	T47.4X6
ucolytic drug	T48.4X1	T48.4X2	T48.4X3	T48.4X4	T48.4X5	T48.4X6
ucomyst	T48.4X1	T48.4X2	T48.4X3	T48.4X4	T48.4X5	T48.4X6
ucous membrane gents(external)	T49.91	T49.92	T49.93	T49.94	T49.95	T49.96
specified NEC	T49.8X1	T49.8X2	T49.8X3	T49.8X4	T49.8X5	T49.8X6
lumps						
immune globulin (human)	T50.Z11	T50.Z12	T50.Z13	T50.Z14	T50.Z15	T50.Z16
skin test antigen	T50.8X1	T50.8X2	T50.8X3	T50.8X4	T50.8X5	T50.8X6
vaccine	T50.B91	T50.B92	T50.B93	T50.B94	T50.B95	T50.B96
lumpsvax	T50.B91	T50.B92	T50.B93	T50.B94	T50.B95	T50.B96
lupirocin	T49.0X1	T49.0X2	T49.0X3	T49.0X4	T49.0X5	T49.0X6
luriatic acid—see ydrochloric acid						
luromonab-CD3	T45.1X1	T45.1X2	T45.1X3	T45.1X4	T45.1X5	T45.1X6
luscle-action drug NEC	T48.201	T48.202	T48.203	T48.204	T48.205	T48.206
luscle affecting agents EC	T48.201	T48.202	T48.203	T48.204	T48.205	T48.206
oxytocic	T48.0X1	T48.0X2	T48.0X3	T48.0X4	T48.0X5	T48.0X6
relaxants	T48.201	T48.202	T48.203	T48.204	T48.205	T48.206
central nervous system	T42.8X1	T42.8X2	T42.8X3	T42.8X4	T42.8X5	T42.8X6
skeletal	T48.1X1	T48.1X2	T48.1X3	T48.1X4	T48.1X5	T48.1X6
smooth	T44.3X1	T44.3X2	T44.3X3	T44.3X4	T44.3X5	T44.3X6
luscle relaxant—see elaxant, muscle						
luscle-tone depressant, entral NEC	T42.8X1	T42.8X2	T42.8X3	T42.8X4	T42.8X5	T42.8X6
specified NEC	T42.8X1	T42.8X2	T42.8X3	T42.8X4	T42.8X5	T42.8X6
lushroom, noxious	T62.0X1	T62.0X2	T62.0X3	T62.0X4	—	—
lussel, noxious	T61.781	T61.782	T61.783	T61.784	—	—
lustard(emetic)	T47.7X1	T47.7X2	T47.7X3	T47.7X4	T47.7X5	T47.7X6
black	T47.7X1	T47.7X2	T47.7X3	T47.7X4	T47.7X5	T47.7X6
gas, not in war	T59.91	T59.92	T59.93	T59.94	—	—
nitrogen	T45.1X1	T45.1X2	T45.1X3	T45.1X4	T45.1X5	T45.1X6
lustine	T45.1X1	T45.1X2	T45.1X3	T45.1X4	T45.1X5	T45.1X6
M-vac	T45.1X1	T45.1X2	T45.1X3	T45.1X4	T45.1X5	T45.1X6
Mycifradin	T36.5X1	T36.5X2	T36.5X3	T36.5X4	T36.5X5	T36.5X6
topical	T49.0X1	T49.0X2	T49.0X3	T49.0X4	T49.0X5	T49.0X6
Mycitracin	T36.8X1	T36.8X2	T36.8X3	T36.8X4	T36.8X5	T36.8X6
ophthalmic preparation	T49.5X1	T49.5X2	T49.5X3	T49.5X4	T49.5X5	T49.5X6
Mycostatin	T36.7X1	T36.7X2	T36.7X3	T36.7X4	T36.7X5	T36.7X6
topical	T49.0X1	T49.0X2	T49.0X3	T49.0X4	T49.0X5	T49.0X6

Substance	Poisoning, Accidental (unintentional)	Poisoning, Intentional self-harm	Poisoning, Assault	Poisoning, Undetermined	Adverse effect	Underdosing
Mycotoxins	T64.81	T64.82	T64.83	T64.84	—	—
aflatoxin	T64.01	T64.02	T64.03	T64.04	—	—
specified NEC	T64.81	T64.82	T64.83	T64.84	—	—
Mydriacyl	T44.3X1	T44.3X2	T44.3X3	T44.3X4	T44.3X5	T44.3X6
Mydriatic drug	T49.5X1	T49.5X2	T49.5X3	T49.5X4	T49.5X5	T49.5X6
Myelobromal	T45.1X1	T45.1X2	T45.1X3	T45.1X4	T45.1X5	T45.1X6
Myleran	T45.1X1	T45.1X2	T45.1X3	T45.1X4	T45.1X5	T45.1X6
Myochrysin(e)	T39.2X1	T39.2X2	T39.2X3	T39.2X4	T39.2X5	T39.2X6
Myoneural blocking agents	T48.1X1	T48.1X2	T48.1X3	T48.1X4	T48.1X5	T48.1X6
Myralact	T49.0X1	T49.0X2	T49.0X3	T49.0X4	T49.0X5	T49.0X6
Myristica fragrans	T62.2X1	T62.2X2	T62.2X3	T62.2X4	—	—
Myristicin	T65.891	T65.892	T65.893	T65.894	—	—
Mysoline	T42.3X1	T42.3X2	T42.3X3	T42.3X4	T42.3X5	T42.3X6
N						
Nabilone	T40.7X1	T40.7X2	T40.7X3	T40.7X4	T40.7X5	T40.7X6
Nabumetone	T39.391	T39.392	T39.393	T39.394	T39.395	T39.396
Nadolol	T44.7X1	T44.7X2	T44.7X3	T44.7X4	T44.7X5	T44.7X6
Nafcillin	T36.0X1	T36.0X2	T36.0X3	T36.0X4	T36.0X5	T36.0X6
Nafoxidine	T38.6X1	T38.6X2	T38.6X3	T38.6X4	T38.6X5	T38.6X6
Naftazone	T46.991	T46.992	T46.993	T46.994	T46.995	T46.996
Naftidrofuryl (oxalate)	T46.7X1	T46.7X2	T46.7X3	T46.7X4	T46.7X5	T46.7X6
Naftifine	T49.0X1	T49.0X2	T49.0X3	T49.0X4	T49.0X5	T49.0X6
Nail polish remover	T52.91	T52.92	T52.93	T52.94	—	—
Nalbuphine	T40.4X1	T40.4X2	T40.4X3	T40.4X4	T40.4X5	T40.4X6
Naled	T60.0X1	T60.0X2	T60.0X3	T60.0X4	—	—
Nalidixic acid	T37.8X1	T37.8X2	T37.8X3	T37.8X4	T37.8X5	T37.8X6
Nalorphine	T50.7X1	T50.7X2	T50.7X3	T50.7X4	T50.7X5	T50.7X6
Naloxone	T50.7X1	T50.7X2	T50.7X3	T50.7X4	T50.7X5	T50.7X6
Naltrexone	T50.7X1	T50.7X2	T50.7X3	T50.7X4	T50.7X5	T50.7X6
Namenda	T43.8X1	T43.8X2	T43.8X3	T43.8X4	T43.8X5	T43.8X6
Nandrolone	T38.7X1	T38.7X2	T38.7X3	T38.7X4	T38.7X5	T38.7X6
Naphazoline	T48.5X1	T48.5X2	T48.5X3	T48.5X4	T48.5X5	T48.5X6
Naphtha(painters') (petroleum)	T52.0X1	T52.0X2	T52.0X3	T52.0X4	—	—
solvent	T52.0X1	T52.0X2	T52.0X3	T52.0X4	—	—
vapor	T52.0X1	T52.0X2	T52.0X3	T52.0X4	—	—
Naphthalene(non-chlorinated)	T60.2X1	T60.2X2	T60.2X3	T60.2X4	—	—
chlorinated	T60.1X1	T60.1X2	T60.1X3	T60.1X4	—	—
vapor	T60.1X1	T60.1X2	T60.1X3	T60.1X4	—	—
insecticide or moth repellent	T60.2X1	T60.2X2	T60.2X3	T60.2X4	—	—
chlorinated	T60.1X1	T60.1X2	T60.1X3	T60.1X4	—	—
vapor	T60.2X1	T60.2X2	T60.2X3	T60.2X4	—	—
chlorinated	T60.1X1	T60.1X2	T60.1X3	T60.1X4	—	—
Naphthol	T65.891	T65.892	T65.893	T65.894	—	—
Naphthylamine	T65.891	T65.892	T65.893	T65.894	—	—
Naphthylthiourea (ANTU)	T60.4X1	T60.4X2	T60.4X3	T60.4X4	—	—
Naprosyn—see Naproxen						
Naproxen	T39.311	T39.312	T39.313	T39.314	T39.315	T39.316

Substance	Poisoning, Accidental (unintentional)	Poisoning, Intentional self-harm	Poisoning, Assault	Poisoning, Undetermined	Adverse effect	Underdosing
Narcotic(drug)	T40.601	T40.602	T40.603	T40.604	T40.605	T40.606
analgesic NEC	T40.601	T40.602	T40.603	T40.604	T40.605	T40.606
antagonist	T50.7X1	T50.7X2	T50.7X3	T50.7X4	T50.7X5	T50.7X6
specified NEC	T40.691	T40.692	T40.693	T40.694	T40.695	T40.696
synthetic	T40.4X1	T40.4X2	T40.4X3	T40.4X4	T40.4X5	T40.4X6
Narcotine	T48.3X1	T48.3X2	T48.3X3	T48.3X4	T48.3X5	T48.3X6
Nardil	T43.1X1	T43.1X2	T43.1X3	T43.1X4	T43.1X5	T43.1X6
Nasal drug NEC	T49.6X1	T49.6X2	T49.6X3	T49.6X4	T49.6X5	T49.6X6
Natamycin	T49.0X1	T49.0X2	T49.0X3	T49.0X4	T49.0X5	T49.0X6
Natrium cyanide—see Cyanide(s)						
Natural						
blood(product)	T45.8X1	T45.8X2	T45.8X3	T45.8X4	T45.8X5	T45.8X6
gas(piped)	T59.891	T59.892	T59.893	T59.894	—	—
incomplete combustion	T58.11	T58.12	T58.13	T58.14	—	—
Nealbarbital	T42.3X1	T42.3X2	T42.3X3	T42.3X4	T42.3X5	T42.3X6
Nectadon	T48.3X1	T48.3X2	T48.3X3	T48.3X4	T48.3X5	T48.3X6
Nedocromil	T48.6X1	T48.6X2	T48.6X3	T48.6X4	T48.6X5	T48.6X6
Nefopam	T39.8X1	T39.8X2	T39.8X3	T39.8X4	T39.8X5	T39.8X6
Nematocyst(sting)	T63.691	T63.692	T63.693	T63.694	—	—
Nembutal	T42.3X1	T42.3X2	T42.3X3	T42.3X4	T42.3X5	T42.3X6
Nemonapride	T43.591	T43.592	T43.593	T43.594	T43.595	T43.596
Neoarsphenamine	T37.8X1	T37.8X2	T37.8X3	T37.8X4	T37.8X5	T37.8X6
Neocinchophen	T50.4X1	T50.4X2	T50.4X3	T50.4X4	T50.4X5	T50.4X6
Neomycin (derivatives)	T36.5X1	T36.5X2	T36.5X3	T36.5X4	T36.5X5	T36.5X6
with						
bacitracin	T49.0X1	T49.0X2	T49.0X3	T49.0X4	T49.0X5	T49.0X6
neostigmine	T44.0X1	T44.0X2	T44.0X3	T44.0X4	T44.0X5	T44.0X6
ENT agent	T49.6X1	T49.6X2	T49.6X3	T49.6X4	T49.6X5	T49.6X6
ophthalmic preparation	T49.5X1	T49.5X2	T49.5X3	T49.5X4	T49.5X5	T49.5X6
topical NEC	T49.0X1	T49.0X2	T49.0X3	T49.0X4	T49.0X5	T49.0X6
Neonal	T42.3X1	T42.3X2	T42.3X3	T42.3X4	T42.3X5	T42.3X6
Neoprontosil	T37.0X1	T37.0X2	T37.0X3	T37.0X4	T37.0X5	T37.0X6
Neosalvarsan	T37.8X1	T37.8X2	T37.8X3	T37.8X4	T37.8X5	T37.8X6
Neosilversalvarsan	T37.8X1	T37.8X2	T37.8X3	T37.8X4	T37.8X5	T37.8X6
Neosporin	T36.8X1	T36.8X2	T36.8X3	T36.8X4	T36.8X5	T36.8X6
ENT agent	T49.6X1	T49.6X2	T49.6X3	T49.6X4	T49.6X5	T49.6X6
opthalmic preparation	T49.5X1	T49.5X2	T49.5X3	T49.5X4	T49.5X5	T49.5X6
topical NEC	T49.0X1	T49.0X2	T49.0X3	T49.0X4	T49.0X5	T49.0X6
Neostigmine bromide	T44.0X1	T44.0X2	T44.0X3	T44.0X4	T44.0X5	T44.0X6
Neraval	T42.3X1	T42.3X2	T42.3X3	T42.3X4	T42.3X5	T42.3X6
Neravan	T42.3X1	T42.3X2	T42.3X3	T42.3X4	T42.3X5	T42.3X6
Nerium oleander	T62.2X1	T62.2X2	T62.2X3	T62.2X4	—	—
Nerve gas, not in war	T59.91	T59.92	T59.93	T59.94	—	—
Nesacaine	T41.3X1	T41.3X2	T41.3X3	T41.3X4	T41.3X5	T41.3X6
infiltration (subcutaneous)	T41.3X1	T41.3X2	T41.3X3	T41.3X4	T41.3X5	T41.3X6
nerve block(peripheral) (plexus)	T41.3X1	T41.3X2	T41.3X3	T41.3X4	T41.3X5	T41.3X6
Netilmicin	T36.5X1	T36.5X2	T36.5X3	T36.5X4	T36.5X5	T36.5X6
Neurobarb	T42.3X1	T42.3X2	T42.3X3	T42.3X4	T42.3X5	T42.3X6

Substance	Poisoning, Accidental (unintentional)	Poisoning, Intentional self-harm	Poisoning, Assault	Poisoning, Undetermined	Adverse effect	Underdosing
Neuroleptic drug NEC	T43.501	T43.502	T43.503	T43.504	T43.505	T43.5
Neuromuscular blocking drug	T48.1X1	T48.1X2	T48.1X3	T48.1X4	T48.1X5	T48.1
Neutral insulin injection	T38.3X1	T38.3X2	T38.3X3	T38.3X4	T38.3X5	T38.3
Neutral spirits	T51.0X1	T51.0X2	T51.0X3	T51.0X4	—	—
beverage	T51.0X1	T51.0X2	T51.0X3	T51.0X4	—	—
Niacin	T46.7X1	T46.7X2	T46.7X3	T46.7X4	T46.7X5	T46.7
Niacinamide	T45.2X1	T45.2X2	T45.2X3	T45.2X4	T45.2X5	T45.2
Nialamide	T43.1X1	T43.1X2	T43.1X3	T43.1X4	T43.1X5	T43.1
Niaprazine	T42.6X1	T42.6X2	T42.6X3	T42.6X4	T42.6X5	T42.6
Nicametate	T46.7X1	T46.7X2	T46.7X3	T46.7X4	T46.7X5	T46.7
Nicardipine	T46.1X1	T46.1X2	T46.1X3	T46.1X4	T46.1X5	T46.1
Nicergoline	T46.7X1	T46.7X2	T46.7X3	T46.7X4	T46.7X5	T46.7
Nickel(carbonyl) (tetra-carbonyl)(fumes) (vapor)	T56.891	T56.892	T56.893	T56.894	—	—
Nickelocene	T56.891	T56.892	T56.893	T56.894	—	—
Niclosamide	T37.4X1	T37.4X2	T37.4X3	T37.4X4	T37.4X5	T37.4
Nicofuranose	T46.7X1	T46.7X2	T46.7X3	T46.7X4	T46.7X5	T46.7
Nicomorphine	T40.2X1	T40.2X2	T40.2X3	T40.2X4	—	—
Nicorandil	T46.3X1	T46.3X2	T46.3X3	T46.3X4	T46.3X5	T46.3
Nicotiana(plant)	T62.2X1	T62.2X2	T62.2X3	T62.2X4	—	—
Nicotinamide	T45.2X1	T45.2X2	T45.2X3	T45.2X4	T45.2X5	T45.2
Nicotine(insecticide) (spray) (sulfate) NEC	T60.2X1	T60.2X2	T60.2X3	T60.2X4	—	—
from tobacco	T65.291	T65.292	T65.293	T65.294	—	—
cigarettes	T65.221	T65.222	T65.223	T65.224	—	—
not insecticide	T65.291	T65.292	T65.293	T65.294	—	—
Nicotinic acid	T46.7X1	T46.7X2	T46.7X3	T46.7X4	T46.7X5	T46.7
Nicotinyl alcohol	T46.7X1	T46.7X2	T46.7X3	T46.7X4	T46.7X5	T46.7
Nicoumalone	T45.511	T45.512	T45.513	T45.514	T45.515	T45.5
Nifedipine	T46.1X1	T46.1X2	T46.1X3	T46.1X4	T46.1X5	T46.1
Nifenazone	T39.2X1	T39.2X2	T39.2X3	T39.2X4	T39.2X5	T39.2
Nifuraldezone	T37.91	T37.92	T37.93	T37.94	T37.95	T37.9
Nifuratel	T37.8X1	T37.8X2	T37.8X3	T37.8X4	T37.8X5	T37.8
Nifurtimox	T37.3X1	T37.3X2	T37.3X3	T37.3X4	T37.3X5	T37.3
Nifurtoinol	T37.8X1	T37.8X2	T37.8X3	T37.8X4	T37.8X5	T37.8
Nightshade, deadly(solanum)—see also Belladonna	T62.2X1	T62.2X2	T62.2X3	T62.2X4	—	—
berry	T62.1X1	T62.1X2	T62.1X3	T62.1X4	—	—
Nikethamide	T50.7X1	T50.7X2	T50.7X3	T50.7X4	T50.7X5	T50.7
Nilstat	T36.7X1	T36.7X2	T36.7X3	T36.7X4	T36.7X5	T36.7
topical	T49.0X1	T49.0X2	T49.0X3	T49.0X4	T49.0X5	T49.0
Nilutamide	T38.6X1	T38.6X2	T38.6X3	T38.6X4	T38.6X5	T38.6
Nimesulide	T39.391	T39.392	T39.393	T39.394	T39.395	T39.39
Nimetazepam	T42.4X1	T42.4X2	T42.4X3	T42.4X4	T42.4X5	T42.4
Nimodipine	T46.1X1	T46.1X2	T46.1X3	T46.1X4	T46.1X5	T46.1
Nimorazole	T37.3X1	T37.3X2	T37.3X3	T37.3X4	T37.3X5	T37.3
Nimustine	T45.1X1	T45.1X2	T45.1X3	T45.1X4	T45.1X5	T45.1
Niridazole	T37.4X1	T37.4X2	T37.4X3	T37.4X4	T37.4X5	T37.4

Substance	Poisoning, Accidental (unintentional)	Poisoning, Intentional self-harm	Poisoning, Assault	Poisoning, Undetermined	Adverse effect	Underdosing
sentil	T40.2X1	T40.2X2	T40.2X3	T40.2X4	T40.2X5	T40.2X6
soldipine	T46.1X1	T46.1X2	T46.1X3	T46.1X4	T46.1X5	T46.1X6
itramine	T65.3X1	T65.3X2	T65.3X3	T65.3X4	—	—
itrate, organic	T46.3X1	T46.3X2	T46.3X3	T46.3X4	T46.3X5	T46.3X6
itrazepam	T42.4X1	T42.4X2	T42.4X3	T42.4X4	T42.4X5	T42.4X6
itrefazole	T50.6X1	T50.6X2	T50.6X3	T50.6X4	T50.6X5	T50.6X6
itrendipine	T46.1X1	T46.1X2	T46.1X3	T46.1X4	T46.1X5	T46.1X6
itric						
acid(liquid)	T54.2X1	T54.2X2	T54.2X3	T54.2X4	—	—
vapor	T59.891	T59.892	T59.893	T59.894	—	—
oxide(gas)	T59.0X1	T59.0X2	T59.0X3	T59.0X4	—	—
itrimidazine	T37.3X1	T37.3X2	T37.3X3	T37.3X4	T37.3X5	T37.3X6
itrite, amyl(medicinal) apor)	T46.3X1	T46.3X2	T46.3X3	T46.3X4	T46.3X5	T46.3X6
itroaniline	T65.3X1	T65.3X2	T65.3X3	T65.3X4	—	—
vapor	T59.891	T59.892	T59.893	T59.894	—	—
itrobenzene, nitrobenzol	T65.3X1	T65.3X2	T65.3X3	T65.3X4	—	—
vapor	T65.3X1	T65.3X2	T65.3X3	T65.3X4	—	—
itrocellulose	T65.891	T65.892	T65.893	T65.894	—	—
lacquer	T65.891	T65.892	T65.893	T65.894	—	—
itrodiphenyl	T65.3X1	T65.3X2	T65.3X3	T65.3X4	—	—
itrofural	T49.0X1	T49.0X2	T49.0X3	T49.0X4	T49.0X5	T49.0X6
itrofurantoin	T37.8X1	T37.8X2	T37.8X3	T37.8X4	T37.8X5	T37.8X6
itrofurazone	T49.0X1	T49.0X2	T49.0X3	T49.0X4	T49.0X5	T49.0X6
itrogen	T59.0X1	T59.0X2	T59.0X3	T59.0X4	—	—
mustard	T45.1X1	T45.1X2	T45.1X3	T45.1X4	T45.1X5	T45.1X6
itroglycerin, nitro-lycerol(medicinal)	T46.3X1	T46.3X2	T46.3X3	T46.3X4	T46.3X5	T46.3X6
nonmedicinal	T65.5X1	T65.5X2	T65.5X3	T65.5X4	—	—
fumes	T65.5X1	T65.5X2	T65.5X3	T65.5X4	—	—
Nitroglycol	T52.3X1	T52.3X2	T52.3X3	T52.3X4	—	—
Nitrohydrochloric acid	T54.2X1	T54.2X2	T54.2X3	T54.2X4	—	—
Nitromersol	T49.0X1	T49.0X2	T49.0X3	T49.0X4	T49.0X5	T49.0X6
Nitronaphthalene	T65.891	T65.892	T65.893	T65.894	—	—
Nitrophenol	T54.0X1	T54.0X2	T54.0X3	T54.0X4	—	—
Nitropropane	T52.8X1	T52.8X2	T52.8X3	T52.8X4	—	—
Nitroprusside	T46.5X1	T46.5X2	T46.5X3	T46.5X4	T46.5X5	T46.5X6
Nitrosodimethylamine	T65.3X1	T65.3X2	T65.3X3	T65.3X4	—	—
Nitrothiazol	T37.4X1	T37.4X2	T37.4X3	T37.4X4	T37.4X5	T37.4X6
Nitrotoluene, nitrotoluol	T65.3X1	T65.3X2	T65.3X3	T65.3X4	—	—
vapor	T65.3X1	T65.3X2	T65.3X3	T65.3X4	—	—
Nitrous						
acid(liquid)	T54.2X1	T54.2X2	T54.2X3	T54.2X4	—	—
fumes	T59.891	T59.892	T59.893	T59.894	—	—
ether spirit	T46.3X1	T46.3X2	T46.3X3	T46.3X4	T46.3X5	T46.3X6
oxide	T41.0X1	T41.0X2	T41.0X3	T41.0X4	T41.0X5	T41.0X6
Nitroxoline	T37.8X1	T37.8X2	T37.8X3	T37.8X4	T37.8X5	T37.8X6
Nitrozone	T49.0X1	T49.0X2	T49.0X3	T49.0X4	T49.0X5	T49.0X6
Nizatidine	T47.0X1	T47.0X2	T47.0X3	T47.0X4	T47.0X5	T47.0X6
Nizofenone	T43.8X1	T43.8X2	T43.8X3	T43.8X4	T43.8X5	T43.8X6
Noctec	T42.6X1	T42.6X2	T42.6X3	T42.6X4	T42.6X5	T42.6X6
Noludar	T42.6X1	T42.6X2	T42.6X3	T42.6X4	T42.6X5	T42.6X6
Nomegestrol	T38.5X1	T38.5X2	T38.5X3	T38.5X4	T38.5X5	T38.5X6
Nomifensine	T43.291	T43.292	T43.293	T43.294	T43.295	T43.296
Nonoxinol	T49.8X1	T49.8X2	T49.8X3	T49.8X4	T49.8X5	T49.8X6
Nonylphenoxy (polyethoxy-ethanol)	T49.8X1	T49.8X2	T49.8X3	T49.8X4	T49.8X5	T49.8X6
Noptil	T42.3X1	T42.3X2	T42.3X3	T42.3X4	T42.3X5	T42.3X6
Noradrenaline	T44.4X1	T44.4X2	T44.4X3	T44.4X4	T44.4X5	T44.4X6
Noramidopyrine	T39.2X1	T39.2X2	T39.2X3	T39.2X4	T39.2X5	T39.2X6
methanesulfonate sodium	T39.2X1	T39.2X2	T39.2X3	T39.2X4	T39.2X5	T39.2X6
Norbormide	T60.4X1	T60.4X2	T60.4X3	T60.4X4	—	—
Nordazepam	T42.4X1	T42.4X2	T42.4X3	T42.4X4	T42.4X5	T42.4X6
Norepinephrine	T44.4X1	T44.4X2	T44.4X3	T44.4X4	T44.4X5	T44.4X6
Norethandrolone	T38.7X1	T38.7X2	T38.7X3	T38.7X4	T38.7X5	T38.7X6
Norethindrone	T38.4X1	T38.4X2	T38.4X3	T38.4X4	T38.4X5	T38.4X6
Norethisterone (acetate) (enantate)	T38.4X1	T38.4X2	T38.4X3	T38.4X4	T38.4X5	T38.4X6
with ethinylestradiol	T38.5X1	T38.5X2	T38.5X3	T38.5X4	T38.5X5	T38.5X6
Noretynodrel	T38.5X1	T38.5X2	T38.5X3	T38.5X4	T38.5X5	T38.5X6
Norfenefrine	T44.4X1	T44.4X2	T44.4X3	T44.4X4	T44.4X5	T44.4X6
Norfloxacin	T36.8X1	T36.8X2	T36.8X3	T36.8X4	T36.8X5	T36.8X6
Norgestrel	T38.4X1	T38.4X2	T38.4X3	T38.4X4	T38.4X5	T38.4X6
Norgestrienone	T38.4X1	T38.4X2	T38.4X3	T38.4X4	T38.4X5	T38.4X6
Norlestrin	T38.4X1	T38.4X2	T38.4X3	T38.4X4	T38.4X5	T38.4X6
Norlutin	T38.4X1	T38.4X2	T38.4X3	T38.4X4	T38.4X5	T38.4X6
Normal serum albumin(human), salt-poor	T45.8X1	T45.8X2	T45.8X3	T45.8X4	T45.8X5	T45.8X6
Normethandrone	T38.5X1	T38.5X2	T38.5X3	T38.5X4	T38.5X5	T38.5X6
Normison—see Benzodiazepines						
Normorphine	T40.2X1	T40.2X2	T40.2X3	T40.2X4	—	—
Norpseudoephedrine	T50.5X1	T50.5X2	T50.5X3	T50.5X4	T50.5X5	T50.5X6
Nortestosterone (furanpro pionate)	T38.7X1	T38.7X2	T38.7X3	T38.7X4	T38.7X5	T38.7X6
Nortriptyline	T43.011	T43.012	T43.013	T43.014	T43.015	T43.016
Noscapine	T48.3X1	T48.3X2	T48.3X3	T48.3X4	T48.3X5	T48.3X6
Nose preparations	T49.6X1	T49.6X2	T49.6X3	T49.6X4	T49.6X5	T49.6X6
Novobiocin	T36.5X1	T36.5X2	T36.5X3	T36.5X4	T36.5X5	T36.5X6
Novocain(infiltration) (topical)	T41.3X1	T41.3X2	T41.3X3	T41.3X4	T41.3X5	T41.3X6
nerve block(peripheral) (plexus)	T41.3X1	T41.3X2	T41.3X3	T41.3X4	T41.3X5	T41.3X6
spinal	T41.3X1	T41.3X2	T41.3X3	T41.3X4	T41.3X5	T41.3X6
Noxious foodstuff	T62.91	T62.92	T62.93	T62.94	—	—
specified NEC	T62.8X1	T62.8X2	T62.8X3	T62.8X4	—	—
Noxiptiline	T43.011	T43.012	T43.013	T43.014	T43.015	T43.016
Noxytiolin	T49.0X1	T49.0X2	T49.0X3	T49.0X4	T49.0X5	T49.0X6
NPH Iletin(insulin)	T38.3X1	T38.3X2	T38.3X3	T38.3X4	T38.3X5	T38.3X6
Numorphan	T40.2X1	T40.2X2	T40.2X3	T40.2X4	T40.2X5	T40.2X6
Nunol	T42.3X1	T42.3X2	T42.3X3	T42.3X4	T42.3X5	T42.3X6

Substance	Poisoning, Accidental (unintentional)	Poisoning, Intentional self-harm	Poisoning, Assault	Poisoning, Undetermined	Adverse effect	Underdosing
Nupercaine(spinal anesthetic)	T41.3X1	T41.3X2	T41.3X3	T41.3X4	T41.3X5	T41.3X6
topical(surface)	T41.3X1	T41.3X2	T41.3X3	T41.3X4	T41.3X5	T41.3X6
Nutmeg oil(liniment)	T49.3X1	T49.3X2	T49.3X3	T49.3X4	T49.3X5	T49.3X6
Nutritional supplement	T50.901	T50.902	T50.903	T50.904	T50.905	T50.906
Nux vomica	T65.1X1	T65.1X2	T65.1X3	T65.1X4	—	—
Nydrazid	T37.1X1	T37.1X2	T37.1X3	T37.1X4	T37.1X5	T37.1X6
Nylidrin	T46.7X1	T46.7X2	T46.7X3	T46.7X4	T46.7X5	T46.7X6
Nystatin	T36.7X1	T36.7X2	T36.7X3	T36.7X4	T36.7X5	T36.7X6
topical	T49.0X1	T49.0X2	T49.0X3	T49.0X4	T49.0X5	T49.0X6
Nytol	T45.0X1	T45.0X2	T45.0X3	T45.0X4	T45.0X5	T45.0X6
O						
Obidoxime chloride	T50.6X1	T50.6X2	T50.6X3	T50.6X4	T50.6X5	T50.6X6
Octafonium(chloride)	T49.3X1	T49.3X2	T49.3X3	T49.3X4	T49.3X5	T49.3X6
Octamethyl pyrophos-phoramide	T60.0X1	T60.0X2	T60.0X3	T60.0X4	—	—
Octanoin	T50.991	T50.992	T50.993	T50.994	T50.995	T50.996
Octatropine methyl-bromide	T44.3X1	T44.3X2	T44.3X3	T44.3X4	T44.3X5	T44.3X6
Octotiamine	T45.2X1	T45.2X2	T45.2X3	T45.2X4	T45.2X5	T45.2X6
Octoxinol(9)	T49.8X1	T49.8X2	T49.8X3	T49.8X4	T49.8X5	T49.8X6
Octreotide	T38.991	T38.992	T38.993	T38.994	T38.995	T38.996
Octyl nitrite	T46.3X1	T46.3X2	T46.3X3	T46.3X4	T46.3X5	T46.3X6
Oestradiol	T38.5X1	T38.5X2	T38.5X3	T38.5X4	T38.5X5	T38.5X6
Oestriol	T38.5X1	T38.5X2	T38.5X3	T38.5X4	T38.5X5	T38.5X6
Oestrogen	T38.5X1	T38.5X2	T38.5X3	T38.5X4	T38.5X5	T38.5X6
Oestrone	T38.5X1	T38.5X2	T38.5X3	T38.5X4	T38.5X5	T38.5X6
Ofloxacin	T36.8X1	T36.8X2	T36.8X3	T36.8X4	T36.8X5	T36.8X6
Oil(of)	T65.891	T65.892	T65.893	T65.894	—	—
bitter almond	T62.8X1	T62.8X2	T62.8X3	T62.8X4	—	—
cloves	T49.7X1	T49.7X2	T49.7X3	T49.7X4	T49.7X5	T49.7X6
colors	T65.6X1	T65.6X2	T65.6X3	T65.6X4	—	—
fumes	T59.891	T59.892	T59.893	T59.894	—	—
lubricating	T52.0X1	T52.0X2	T52.0X3	T52.0X4	—	—
Niobe	T52.8X1	T52.8X2	T52.8X3	T52.8X4	—	—
vitriol(liquid)	T54.2X1	T54.2X2	T54.2X3	T54.2X4	—	—
fumes	T54.2X1	T54.2X2	T54.2X3	T54.2X4	—	—
wintergreen(bitter) NEC	T49.3X1	T49.3X2	T49.3X3	T49.3X4	T49.3X5	T49.3X6
Oily preparation(for skin)	T49.3X1	T49.3X2	T49.3X3	T49.3X4	T49.3X5	T49.3X6
Ointment NEC	T49.3X1	T49.3X2	T49.3X3	T49.3X4	T49.3X5	T49.3X6
Olanzapine	T43.591	T43.592	T43.593	T43.594	T43.595	T43.596
Oleander	T62.2X1	T62.2X2	T62.2X3	T62.2X4	—	—
Oleandomycin	T36.3X1	T36.3X2	T36.3X3	T36.3X4	T36.3X5	T36.3X6
Oleandrin	T46.0X1	T46.0X2	T46.0X3	T46.0X4	T46.0X5	T46.0X6
Oleic acid	T46.6X1	T46.6X2	T46.6X3	T46.6X4	T46.6X5	T46.6X6
Oleovitamin A	T45.2X1	T45.2X2	T45.2X3	T45.2X4	T45.2X5	T45.2X6
Oleum ricini	T47.2X1	T47.2X2	T47.2X3	T47.2X4	T47.2X5	T47.2X6
Olive oil(medicinal) NEC	T47.4X1	T47.4X2	T47.4X3	T47.4X4	T47.4X5	T47.4X6
Olivomycin	T45.1X1	T45.1X2	T45.1X3	T45.1X4	T45.1X5	T45.1X6
Olsalazine	T47.8X1	T47.8X2	T47.8X3	T47.8X4	T47.8X5	T47.8X6
Omeprazole	T47.1X1	T47.1X2	T47.1X3	T47.1X4	T47.1X5	T47.1X6
OMPA	T60.0X1	T60.0X2	T60.0X3	T60.0X4	—	—

Substance	Poisoning, Accidental (unintentional)	Poisoning, Intentional self-harm	Poisoning, Assault	Poisoning, Undetermined	Adverse effect	Underdosing
Oncovin	T45.1X1	T45.1X2	T45.1X3	T45.1X4	T45.1X5	T45.1
Ondansetron	T45.0X1	T45.0X2	T45.0X3	T45.0X4	T45.0X5	T45.0
Ophthaine	T41.3X1	T41.3X2	T41.3X3	T41.3X4	T41.3X5	T41.3
Ophthetic	T41.3X1	T41.3X2	T41.3X3	T41.3X4	T41.3X5	T41.3
Opiate NEC	T40.601	T40.602	T40.603	T40.604	T40.605	T40.6
antagonists	T50.7X1	T50.7X2	T50.7X3	T50.7X4	T50.7X5	T50.7
Opioid NEC	T40.2X1	T40.2X2	T40.2X3	T40.2X4	T40.2X5	T40.2
Opipramol	T43.011	T43.012	T43.013	T43.014	T43.015	T43.0
Opium alkaloids(total)	T40.0X1	T40.0X2	T40.0X3	T40.0X4	T40.0X5	T40.0
standardized powdered	T40.0X1	T40.0X2	T40.0X3	T40.0X4	T40.0X5	T40.0
tincture (camphorated)	T40.0X1	T40.0X2	T40.0X3	T40.0X4	T40.0X5	T40.0
Oracon	T38.4X1	T38.4X2	T38.4X3	T38.4X4	T38.4X5	T38.4
Oragrafin	T50.8X1	T50.8X2	T50.8X3	T50.8X4	T50.8X5	T50.8
Oral contraceptives	T38.4X1	T38.4X2	T38.4X3	T38.4X4	T38.4X5	T38.4
Oral rehydration salts	T50.3X1	T50.3X2	T50.3X3	T50.3X4	T50.3X5	T50.3
Orazamide	T50.991	T50.992	T50.993	T50.994	T50.995	T50.9
Orciprenaline	T48.291	T48.292	T48.293	T48.294	T48.295	T48.2
Organidin	T48.4X1	T48.4X2	T48.4X3	T48.4X4	T48.4X5	T48.4
Organonitrate NEC	T46.3X1	T46.3X2	T46.3X3	T46.3X4	T46.3X5	T46.3
Organophosphates	T60.0X1	T60.0X2	T60.0X3	T60.0X4	—	—
Orimune	T50.B91	T50.B92	T50.B93	T50.B94	T50.B95	T50.B
Orinase	T38.3X1	T38.3X2	T38.3X3	T38.3X4	T38.3X5	T38.3X
Ormeloxifene	T38.6X1	T38.6X2	T38.6X3	T38.6X4	T38.6X5	T38.6X
Ornidazole	T37.3X1	T37.3X2	T37.3X3	T37.3X4	T37.3X5	T37.3X
Ornithine aspartate	T50.991	T50.992	T50.993	T50.994	T50.995	T50.9
Ornoprostil	T47.1X1	T47.1X2	T47.1X3	T47.1X4	T47.1X5	T47.1X
Orphenadrine (hydrochloride)	T42.8X1	T42.8X2	T42.8X3	T42.8X4	T42.8X5	T42.8X
Ortal(sodium)	T42.3X1	T42.3X2	T42.3X3	T42.3X4	T42.3X5	T42.3X
Orthoboric acid	T49.0X1	T49.0X2	T49.0X3	T49.0X4	T49.0X5	T49.0X
ENT agent	T49.6X1	T49.6X2	T49.6X3	T49.6X4	T49.6X5	T49.6X
ophthalmic preparation	T49.5X1	T49.5X2	T49.5X3	T49.5X4	T49.5X5	T49.5X
Orthocaine	T41.3X1	T41.3X2	T41.3X3	T41.3X4	T41.3X5	T41.3X
Orthodichlorobenzene	T53.7X1	T53.7X2	T53.7X3	T53.7X4	—	—
Ortho-Novum	T38.4X1	T38.4X2	T38.4X3	T38.4X4	T38.4X5	T38.4X
Orthotolidine (reagent)	T54.2X1	T54.2X2	T54.2X3	T54.2X4	—	—
Osmic acid(liquid)	T54.2X1	T54.2X2	T54.2X3	T54.2X4	—	—
fumes	T54.2X1	T54.2X2	T54.2X3	T54.2X4	—	—
Osmotic diuretics	T50.2X1	T50.2X2	T50.2X3	T50.2X4	T50.2X5	T50.2X
Otilonium bromide	T44.3X1	T44.3X2	T44.3X3	T44.3X4	T44.3X5	T44.3X
Otorhinolaryngological drug NEC	T49.6X1	T49.6X2	T49.6X3	T49.6X4	T49.6X5	T49.6X
Ouabain(e)	T46.0X1	T46.0X2	T46.0X3	T46.0X4	T46.0X5	T46.0X
Ovarian						
hormone	T38.5X1	T38.5X2	T38.5X3	T38.5X4	T38.5X5	T38.5X
stimulant	T38.5X1	T38.5X2	T38.5X3	T38.5X4	T38.5X5	T38.5X
Ovral	T38.4X1	T38.4X2	T38.4X3	T38.4X4	T38.4X5	T38.4X
Ovulen	T38.4X1	T38.4X2	T38.4X3	T38.4X4	T38.4X5	T38.4X
Oxacillin	T36.0X1	T36.0X2	T36.0X3	T36.0X4	T36.0X5	T36.0X
Oxalic acid	T54.2X1	T54.2X2	T54.2X3	T54.2X4	—	—
ammonium salt	T50.991	T50.992	T50.993	T50.994	T50.995	T50.99

Substance	Poisoning, Accidental (unintentional)	Poisoning, Intentional self-harm	Poisoning, Assault	Poisoning, Undetermined	Adverse effect	Underdosing
mniquine	T37.4X1	T37.4X2	T37.4X3	T37.4X4	T37.4X5	T37.4X6
namide	T43.591	T43.592	T43.593	T43.594	T43.595	T43.596
ndrolone	T38.7X1	T38.7X2	T38.7X3	T38.7X4	T38.7X5	T38.7X6
ntel	T37.4X1	T37.4X2	T37.4X3	T37.4X4	T37.4X5	T37.4X6
pium iodide	T44.3X1	T44.3X2	T44.3X3	T44.3X4	T44.3X5	T44.3X6
protiline	T43.021	T43.022	T43.023	T43.024	T43.025	T43.026
prozin	T39.311	T39.312	T39.313	T39.314	T39.315	T39.316
tomide	T45.0X1	T45.0X2	T45.0X3	T45.0X4	T45.0X5	T45.0X6
zepam	T42.4X1	T42.4X2	T42.4X3	T42.4X4	T42.4X5	T42.4X6
zimedrine	T50.5X1	T50.5X2	T50.5X3	T50.5X4	T50.5X5	T50.5X6
zolam	T42.4X1	T42.4X2	T42.4X3	T42.4X4	T42.4X5	T42.4X6
zolidine derivatives	T42.2X1	T42.2X2	T42.2X3	T42.2X4	T42.2X5	T42.2X6
zolidinedione ivative)	T42.2X1	T42.2X2	T42.2X3	T42.2X4	T42.2X5	T42.2X6
bile extract	T47.5X1	T47.5X2	T47.5X3	T47.5X4	T47.5X5	T47.5X6
arbazepine	T42.1X1	T42.1X2	T42.1X3	T42.1X4	T42.1X5	T42.1X6
drine	T44.4X1	T44.4X2	T44.4X3	T44.4X4	T44.4X5	T44.4X6
ladin(citrate)	T48.3X1	T48.3X2	T48.3X3	T48.3X4	T48.3X5	T48.3X6
ndolone	T38.5X1	T38.5X2	T38.5X3	T38.5X4	T38.5X5	T38.5X6
tacaine	T41.3X1	T41.3X2	T41.3X3	T41.3X4	T41.3X5	T41.3X6
thazine	T41.3X1	T41.3X2	T41.3X3	T41.3X4	T41.3X5	T41.3X6
torone	T39.8X1	T39.8X2	T39.8X3	T39.8X4	T39.8X5	T39.8X6
conazole	T49.0X1	T49.0X2	T49.0X3	T49.0X4	T49.0X5	T49.0X6
dizing agent NEC	T54.91	T54.92	T54.93	T54.94	—	—
purinol	T50.4X1	T50.4X2	T50.4X3	T50.4X4	T50.4X5	T50.4X6
triptan	T43.291	T43.292	T43.293	T43.294	T43.295	T43.296
tropium bromide	T48.6X1	T48.6X2	T48.6X3	T48.6X4	T48.6X5	T48.6X6
odipine	T46.1X1	T46.1X2	T46.1X3	T46.1X4	T46.1X5	T46.1X6
olamine	T48.3X1	T48.3X2	T48.3X3	T48.3X4	T48.3X5	T48.3X6
olinic acid	T37.8X1	T37.8X2	T37.8X3	T37.8X4	T37.8X5	T37.8X6
omemazine	T43.3X1	T43.3X2	T43.3X3	T43.3X4	T43.3X5	T43.3X6
ophenarsine	T37.3X1	T37.3X2	T37.3X3	T37.3X4	T37.3X5	T37.3X6
prenolol	T44.7X1	T44.7X2	T44.7X3	T44.7X4	T44.7X5	T44.7X6
soralen	T49.3X1	T49.3X2	T49.3X3	T49.3X4	T49.3X5	T49.3X6
triphylline	T48.6X1	T48.6X2	T48.6X3	T48.6X4	T48.6X5	T48.6X6
ybate sodium	T41.291	T41.292	T41.293	T41.294	T41.295	T41.296
ybuprocaine	T41.3X1	T41.3X2	T41.3X3	T41.3X4	T41.3X5	T41.3X6
ybutynin	T44.3X1	T44.3X2	T44.3X3	T44.3X4	T44.3X5	T44.3X6
ychlorosene	T49.0X1	T49.0X2	T49.0X3	T49.0X4	T49.0X5	T49.0X6
ycodone	T40.2X1	T40.2X2	T40.2X3	T40.2X4	T40.2X5	T40.2X6
yfedrine	T46.3X1	T46.3X2	T46.3X3	T46.3X4	T46.3X5	T46.3X6
ygen	T41.5X1	T41.5X2	T41.5X3	T41.5X4	T41.5X5	T41.5X6
ylone	T49.0X1	T49.0X2	T49.0X3	T49.0X4	T49.0X5	T49.0X6
phthalmic preparation	T49.5X1	T49.5X2	T49.5X3	T49.5X4	T49.5X5	T49.5X6
ymesterone	T38.7X1	T38.7X2	T38.7X3	T38.7X4	T38.7X5	T38.7X6
ymetazoline	T48.5X1	T48.5X2	T48.5X3	T48.5X4	T48.5X5	T48.5X6
ymetholone	T38.7X1	T38.7X2	T38.7X3	T38.7X4	T38.7X5	T38.7X6
ymorphone	T40.2X1	T40.2X2	T40.2X3	T40.2X4	T40.2X5	T40.2X6
ypertine	T43.591	T43.592	T43.593	T43.594	T43.595	T43.596
yphenbutazone	T39.2X1	T39.2X2	T39.2X3	T39.2X4	T39.2X5	T39.2X6
yphencyclimine	T44.3X1	T44.3X2	T44.3X3	T44.3X4	T44.3X5	T44.3X6

Substance	Poisoning, Accidental (unintentional)	Poisoning, Intentional self-harm	Poisoning, Assault	Poisoning, Undetermined	Adverse effect	Underdosing
Oxyphenisatine	T47.2X1	T47.2X2	T47.2X3	T47.2X4	T47.2X5	T47.2X6
Oxyphenonium bromide	T44.3X1	T44.3X2	T44.3X3	T44.3X4	T44.3X5	T44.3X6
Oxypolygelatin	T45.8X1	T45.8X2	T45.8X3	T45.8X4	T45.8X5	T45.8X6
Oxyquinoline (derivatives)	T37.8X1	T37.8X2	T37.8X3	T37.8X4	T37.8X5	T37.8X6
Oxytetracycline	T36.4X1	T36.4X2	T36.4X3	T36.4X4	T36.4X5	T36.4X6
Oxytocic drug NEC	T48.0X1	T48.0X2	T48.0X3	T48.0X4	T48.0X5	T48.0X6
Oxytocin(synthetic)	T48.0X1	T48.0X2	T48.0X3	T48.0X4	T48.0X5	T48.0X6
Ozone	T59.891	T59.892	T59.893	T59.894	—	—
P						
PABA	T49.3X1	T49.3X2	T49.3X3	T49.3X4	T49.3X5	T49.3X6
Packed red cells	T45.8X1	T45.8X2	T45.8X3	T45.8X4	T45.8X5	T45.8X6
Padimate	T49.3X1	T49.3X2	T49.3X3	T49.3X4	T49.3X5	T49.3X6
Paint NEC	T65.6X1	T65.6X2	T65.6X3	T65.6X4	—	—
cleaner	T52.91	T52.92	T52.93	T52.94	—	—
fumes NEC	T59.891	T59.892	T59.893	T59.894	—	—
lead(fumes)	T56.0X1	T56.0X2	T56.0X3	T56.0X4	—	—
solvent NEC	T52.8X1	T52.8X2	T52.8X3	T52.8X4	—	—
stripper	T52.8X1	T52.8X2	T52.8X3	T52.8X4	—	—
Palfium	T40.2X1	T40.2X2	T40.2X3	T40.2X4	—	—
Palm kernel oil	T50.991	T50.992	T50.993	T50.994	T50.995	T50.996
Paludrine	T37.2X1	T37.2X2	T37.2X3	T37.2X4	T37.2X5	T37.2X6
PAM(pralidoxime)	T50.6X1	T50.6X2	T50.6X3	T50.6X4	T50.6X5	T50.6X6
Pamaquine (naphthoute)	T37.2X1	T37.2X2	T37.2X3	T37.2X4	T37.2X5	T37.2X6
Panadol	T39.1X1	T39.1X2	T39.1X3	T39.1X4	T39.1X5	T39.1X6
Pancreatic						
digestive secretion stimulant	T47.8X1	T47.8X2	T47.8X3	T47.8X4	T47.8X5	T47.8X6
dornase	T45.3X1	T45.3X2	T45.3X3	T45.3X4	T45.3X5	T45.3X6
Pancreatin	T47.5X1	T47.5X2	T47.5X3	T47.5X4	T47.5X5	T47.5X6
Pancrelipase	T47.5X1	T47.5X2	T47.5X3	T47.5X4	T47.5X5	T47.5X6
Pancuronium (bromide)	T48.1X1	T48.1X2	T48.1X3	T48.1X4	T48.1X5	T48.1X6
Pangamic acid	T45.2X1	T45.2X2	T45.2X3	T45.2X4	T45.2X5	T45.2X6
Panthenol	T45.2X1	T45.2X2	T45.2X3	T45.2X4	T45.2X5	T45.2X6
topical	T49.8X1	T49.8X2	T49.8X3	T49.8X4	T49.8X5	T49.8X6
Pantopon	T40.0X1	T40.0X2	T40.0X3	T40.0X4	T40.0X5	T40.0X6
Pantothenic acid	T45.2X1	T45.2X2	T45.2X3	T45.2X4	T45.2X5	T45.2X6
Panwarfin	T45.511	T45.512	T45.513	T45.514	T45.515	T45.516
Papain	T47.5X1	T47.5X2	T47.5X3	T47.5X4	T47.5X5	T47.5X6
digestant	T47.5X1	T47.5X2	T47.5X3	T47.5X4	T47.5X5	T47.5X6
Papaveretum	T40.0X1	T40.0X2	T40.0X3	T40.0X4	T40.0X5	T40.0X6
Papaverine	T44.3X1	T44.3X2	T44.3X3	T44.3X4	T44.3X5	T44.3X6
Para-acetamidophenol	T39.1X1	T39.1X2	T39.1X3	T39.1X4	T39.1X5	T39.1X6
Para-aminobenzoic acid	T49.3X1	T49.3X2	T49.3X3	T49.3X4	T49.3X5	T49.3X6
Para-aminophenol derivatives	T39.1X1	T39.1X2	T39.1X3	T39.1X4	T39.1X5	T39.1X6
Para-aminosalicylic acid	T37.1X1	T37.1X2	T37.1X3	T37.1X4	T37.1X5	T37.1X6
Paracetaldehyde	T42.6X1	T42.6X2	T42.6X3	T42.6X4	T42.6X5	T42.6X6
Paracetamol	T39.1X1	T39.1X2	T39.1X3	T39.1X4	T39.1X5	T39.1X6
Parachlorophenol (camphorated)	T49.0X1	T49.0X2	T49.0X3	T49.0X4	T49.0X5	T49.0X6

Substance	Poisoning, Accidental (unintentional)	Poisoning, Intentional self-harm	Poisoning, Assault	Poisoning, Undetermined	Adverse effect	Underdosing
Paracodin	T40.2X1	T40.2X2	T40.2X3	T40.2X4	T40.2X5	T40.2X6
Paradione	T42.2X1	T42.2X2	T42.2X3	T42.2X4	T42.2X5	T42.2X6
Paraffin(s) (wax)	T52.0X1	T52.0X2	T52.0X3	T52.0X4	—	—
liquid(medicinal)	T47.4X1	T47.4X2	T47.4X3	T47.4X4	T47.4X5	T47.4X6
nonmedicinal	T52.0X1	T52.0X2	T52.0X3	T52.0X4	—	—
Paraformaldehyde	T60.3X1	T60.3X2	T60.3X3	T60.3X4	—	—
Paraldehyde	T42.6X1	T42.6X2	T42.6X3	T42.6X4	T42.6X5	T42.6X6
Paramethadione	T42.2X1	T42.2X2	T42.2X3	T42.2X4	T42.2X5	T42.2X6
Paramethasone	T38.0X1	T38.0X2	T38.0X3	T38.0X4	T38.0X5	T38.0X6
acetate	T49.0X1	T49.0X2	T49.0X3	T49.0X4	T49.0X5	T49.0X6
Paraoxon	T60.0X1	T60.0X2	T60.0X3	T60.0X4	—	—
Paraquat	T60.3X1	T60.3X2	T60.3X3	T60.3X4	—	—
Parasympatholytic NEC	T44.3X1	T44.3X2	T44.3X3	T44.3X4	T44.3X5	T44.3X6
Parasympathomimetic drug NEC	T44.1X1	T44.1X2	T44.1X3	T44.1X4	T44.1X5	T44.1X6
Parathion	T60.0X1	T60.0X2	T60.0X3	T60.0X4	—	—
Parathormone	T50.991	T50.992	T50.993	T50.994	T50.995	T50.996
Parathyroid extract	T50.991	T50.992	T50.993	T50.994	T50.995	T50.996
Paratyphoid vaccine	T50.A91	T50.A92	T50.A93	T50.A94	T50.A95	T50.A96
Paredrine	T44.4X1	T44.4X2	T44.4X3	T44.4X4	T44.4X5	T44.4X6
Paregoric	T40.0X1	T40.0X2	T40.0X3	T40.0X4	T40.0X5	T40.0X6
Pargyline	T46.5X1	T46.5X2	T46.5X3	T46.5X4	T46.5X5	T46.5X6
Paris green	T57.0X1	T57.0X2	T57.0X3	T57.0X4	—	—
insecticide	T57.0X1	T57.0X2	T57.0X3	T57.0X4	—	—
Parnate	T43.1X1	T43.1X2	T43.1X3	T43.1X4	T43.1X5	T43.1X6
Paromomycin	T36.5X1	T36.5X2	T36.5X3	T36.5X4	T36.5X5	T36.5X6
Paroxypropione	T45.1X1	T45.1X2	T45.1X3	T45.1X4	T45.1X5	T45.1X6
Parzone	T40.2X1	T40.2X2	T40.2X3	T40.2X4	T40.2X5	T40.2X6
PAS	T37.1X1	T37.1X2	T37.1X3	T37.1X4	T37.1X5	T37.1X6
Pasiniazid	T37.1X1	T37.1X2	T37.1X3	T37.1X4	T37.1X5	T37.1X6
PBB(polybrominated biphenyls)	T65.891	T65.892	T65.893	T65.894	—	—
PCB	T65.891	T65.892	T65.893	T65.894	—	—
PCP						
meaning pentachlorophenol	T60.1X1	T60.1X2	T60.1X3	T60.1X4	—	—
fungicide	T60.3X1	T60.3X2	T60.3X3	T60.3X4	—	—
herbicide	T60.3X1	T60.3X2	T60.3X3	T60.3X4	—	—
insecticide	T60.1X1	T60.1X2	T60.1X3	T60.1X4	—	—
meaning phencyclidine	T40.991	T40.992	T40.993	T40.994	—	—
Peach kernel oil(emulsion)	T47.4X1	T47.4X2	T47.4X3	T47.4X4	T47.4X5	T47.4X6
Peanut oil(emulsion) NEC	T47.4X1	T47.4X2	T47.4X3	T47.4X4	T47.4X5	T47.4X6
topical	T49.3X1	T49.3X2	T49.3X3	T49.3X4	T49.3X5	T49.3X6
Pearly Gates(morning glory seeds)	T40.991	T40.992	T40.993	T40.994	—	—
Pecazine	T43.3X1	T43.3X2	T43.3X3	T43.3X4	T43.3X5	T43.3X6
Pectin	T47.6X1	T47.6X2	T47.6X3	T47.6X4	T47.6X5	T47.6X6
Pefloxacin	T37.8X1	T37.8X2	T37.8X3	T37.8X4	T37.8X5	T37.8X6
Pegademase, bovine	T50.Z91	T50.Z92	T50.Z93	T50.Z94	T50.Z95	T50.Z96
Pelletierine tannate	T37.4X1	T37.4X2	T37.4X3	T37.4X4	T37.4X5	T37.4X6
Pemirolast (potassium)	T48.6X1	T48.6X2	T48.6X3	T48.6X4	T48.6X5	T48.6X6

Substance	Poisoning, Accidental (unintentional)	Poisoning, Intentional self-harm	Poisoning, Assault	Poisoning, Undetermined	Adverse effect	Underdosing
Pemoline	T50.7X1	T50.7X2	T50.7X3	T50.7X4	T50.7X5	T50
Pempidine	T44.2X1	T44.2X2	T44.2X3	T44.2X4	T44.2X5	T44.
Penamecillin	T36.0X1	T36.0X2	T36.0X3	T36.0X4	T36.0X5	T36
Penbutolol	T44.7X1	T44.7X2	T44.7X3	T44.7X4	T44.7X5	T44.
Penethamate	T36.0X1	T36.0X2	T36.0X3	T36.0X4	T36.0X5	T36
Penfluridol	T43.591	T43.592	T43.593	T43.594	T43.595	T43
Penflutizide	T50.2X1	T50.2X2	T50.2X3	T50.2X4	T50.2X5	T50.
Pengitoxin	T46.0X1	T46.0X2	T46.0X3	T46.0X4	T46.0X5	T46.
Penicillamine	T50.6X1	T50.6X2	T50.6X3	T50.6X4	T50.6X5	T50.
Penicillin(any)	T36.0X1	T36.0X2	T36.0X3	T36.0X4	T36.0X5	T36.
Penicillinase	T45.3X1	T45.3X2	T45.3X3	T45.3X4	T45.3X5	T45.
Penicilloyl polylysine	T50.8X1	T50.8X2	T50.8X3	T50.8X4	T50.8X5	T50.
Penimepicycline	T36.4X1	T36.4X2	T36.4X3	T36.4X4	T36.4X5	T36.
Pentachloroethane	T53.6X1	T53.6X2	T53.6X3	T53.6X4	—	—
Pentachloronaphthalene	T53.7X1	T53.7X2	T53.7X3	T53.7X4	—	—
Pentachlorophenol (pesticide)	T60.1X1	T60.1X2	T60.1X3	T60.1X4	—	—
fungicide	T60.3X1	T60.3X2	T60.3X3	T60.3X4	—	—
herbicide	T60.3X1	T60.3X2	T60.3X3	T60.3X4	—	—
insecticide	T60.1X1	T60.1X2	T60.1X3	T60.1X4	—	—
Pentaerythritol	T46.3X1	T46.3X2	T46.3X3	T46.3X4	T46.3X5	T46.
chloral	T42.6X1	T42.6X2	T42.6X3	T42.6X4	T42.6X5	T42.
tetranitrate NEC	T46.3X1	T46.3X2	T46.3X3	T46.3X4	T46.3X5	T46.
Pentaerythrityl tetranitrate	T46.3X1	T46.3X2	T46.3X3	T46.3X4	T46.3X5	T46.
Pentagastrin	T50.8X1	T50.8X2	T50.8X3	T50.8X4	T50.8X5	T50.8
Pentalin	T53.6X1	T53.6X2	T53.6X3	T53.6X4	—	—
Pentamethonium bromide	T44.2X1	T44.2X2	T44.2X3	T44.2X4	T44.2X5	T44.2
Pentamidine	T37.3X1	T37.3X2	T37.3X3	T37.3X4	T37.3X5	T37.3
Pentanol	T51.3X1	T51.3X2	T51.3X3	T51.3X4	—	—
Pentapyrrolinium (bitartrate)	T44.2X1	T44.2X2	T44.2X3	T44.2X4	T44.2X5	T44.2
Pentaquine	T37.2X1	T37.2X2	T37.2X3	T37.2X4	T37.2X5	T37.2
Pentazocine	T40.4X1	T40.4X2	T40.4X3	T40.4X4	T40.4X5	T40.4
Pentetrazole	T50.7X1	T50.7X2	T50.7X3	T50.7X4	T50.7X5	T50.7
Penthienate bromide	T44.3X1	T44.3X2	T44.3X3	T44.3X4	T44.3X5	T44.3
Pentifylline	T46.7X1	T46.7X2	T46.7X3	T46.7X4	T46.7X5	T46.7
Pentobarbital	T42.3X1	T42.3X2	T42.3X3	T42.3X4	T42.3X5	T42.3
sodium	T42.3X1	T42.3X2	T42.3X3	T42.3X4	T42.3X5	T42.3
Pentobarbitone	T42.3X1	T42.3X2	T42.3X3	T42.3X4	T42.3X5	T42.3
Pentolonium tartrate	T44.2X1	T44.2X2	T44.2X3	T44.2X4	T44.2X5	T44.2
Pentosan polysulfate(sodium)	T39.8X1	T39.8X2	T39.8X3	T39.8X4	T39.8X5	T39.8
Pentostatin	T45.1X1	T45.1X2	T45.1X3	T45.1X4	T45.1X5	T45.1
Pentothal	T41.1X1	T41.1X2	T41.1X3	T41.1X4	T41.1X5	T41.1
Pentoxifylline	T46.7X1	T46.7X2	T46.7X3	T46.7X4	T46.7X5	T46.7
Pentoxyverine	T48.3X1	T48.3X2	T48.3X3	T48.3X4	T48.3X5	T48.3
Pentrinat	T46.3X1	T46.3X2	T46.3X3	T46.3X4	T46.3X5	T46.3
Pentylenetetrazole	T50.7X1	T50.7X2	T50.7X3	T50.7X4	T50.7X5	T50.7
Pentylsalicylamide	T37.1X1	T37.1X2	T37.1X3	T37.1X4	T37.1X5	T37.1
Pentymal	T42.3X1	T42.3X2	T42.3X3	T42.3X4	T42.3X5	T42.3
Peplomycin	T45.1X1	T45.1X2	T45.1X3	T45.1X4	T45.1X5	T45.1

Substance	Poisoning, Accidental (unintentional)	Poisoning, Intentional self-harm	Poisoning, Assault	Poisoning, Undetermined	Adverse effect	Underdosing
permint(oil)	T47.5X1	T47.5X2	T47.5X3	T47.5X4	T47.5X5	T47.5X6
sin	T47.5X1	T47.5X2	T47.5X3	T47.5X4	T47.5X5	T47.5X6
gestant	T47.5X1	T47.5X2	T47.5X3	T47.5X4	T47.5X5	T47.5X6
statin	T47.1X1	T47.1X2	T47.1X3	T47.1X4	T47.1X5	T47.1X6
avlon	T50.8X1	T50.8X2	T50.8X3	T50.8X4	T50.8X5	T50.8X6
azine	T43.3X1	T43.3X2	T43.3X3	T43.3X4	T43.3X5	T43.3X6
caine(spinal)	T41.3X1	T41.3X2	T41.3X3	T41.3X4	T41.3X5	T41.3X6
pical(surface)	T41.3X1	T41.3X2	T41.3X3	T41.3X4	T41.3X5	T41.3X6
chloroethylene	T53.3X1	T53.3X2	T53.3X3	T53.3X4	—	—
edicinal	T37.4X1	T37.4X2	T37.4X3	T37.4X4	T37.4X5	T37.4X6
apor	T53.3X1	T53.3X2	T53.3X3	T53.3X4	—	—
codan	T40.2X1	T40.2X2	T40.2X3	T40.2X4	T40.2X5	T40.2X6
cogesic—see also taminophen	T45.0X1	T45.0X2	T45.0X3	T45.0X4	T45.0X5	T45.0X6
corten	T38.0X1	T38.0X2	T38.0X3	T38.0X4	T38.0X5	T38.0X6
golide	T42.8X1	T42.8X2	T42.8X3	T42.8X4	T42.8X5	T42.8X6
gonal	T38.811	T38.812	T38.813	T38.814	T38.815	T38.816
hexilene	T46.3X1	T46.3X2	T46.3X3	T46.3X4	T46.3X5	T46.3X6
hexiline(maleate)	T46.3X1	T46.3X2	T46.3X3	T46.3X4	T46.3X5	T46.3X6
iactin	T45.0X1	T45.0X2	T45.0X3	T45.0X4	T45.0X5	T45.0X6
iciazine	T43.3X1	T43.3X2	T43.3X3	T43.3X4	T43.3X5	T43.3X6
iclor	T42.6X1	T42.6X2	T42.6X3	T42.6X4	T42.6X5	T42.6X6
indopril	T46.4X1	T46.4X2	T46.4X3	T46.4X4	T46.4X5	T46.4X6
isoxal	T39.8X1	T39.8X2	T39.8X3	T39.8X4	T39.8X5	T39.8X6
itoneal dialysis solution	T50.3X1	T50.3X2	T50.3X3	T50.3X4	T50.3X5	T50.3X6
itrate	T46.3X1	T46.3X2	T46.3X3	T46.3X4	T46.3X5	T46.3X6
lapine	T42.4X1	T42.4X2	T42.4X3	T42.4X4	T42.4X5	T42.4X6
manganate	T65.891	T65.892	T65.893	T65.894	—	—
methrin	T60.1X1	T60.1X2	T60.1X3	T60.1X4	—	—
nocton	T42.3X1	T42.3X2	T42.3X3	T42.3X4	T42.3X5	T42.3X6
noston	T42.3X1	T42.3X2	T42.3X3	T42.3X4	T42.3X5	T42.3X6
ronine	T40.2X1	T40.2X2	T40.2X3	T40.2X4	—	—
phenazine	T43.3X1	T43.3X2	T43.3X3	T43.3X4	T43.3X5	T43.3X6
tofrane	T43.011	T43.012	T43.013	T43.014	T43.015	T43.016
tussis						
mmune serum(human)	T50.Z11	T50.Z12	T50.Z13	T50.Z14	T50.Z15	T50.Z16
vaccine(with diphtheria oxoid) (with tetanus oxoid)	T50.A11	T50.A12	T50.A13	T50.A14	T50.A15	T50.A16
ruvian balsam	T49.0X1	T49.0X2	T49.0X3	T49.0X4	T49.0X5	T49.0X6
ruvoside	T46.0X1	T46.0X2	T46.0X3	T46.0X4	T46.0X5	T46.0X6
sticide(dust) (fumes) apor) NEC	T60.91	T60.92	T60.93	T60.94	—	—
arsenic	T57.0X1	T57.0X2	T57.0X3	T57.0X4	—	—
chlorinated	T60.1X1	T60.1X2	T60.1X3	T60.1X4	—	—
cyanide	T65.0X1	T65.0X2	T65.0X3	T65.0X4	—	—
kerosene	T52.0X1	T52.0X2	T52.0X3	T52.0X4	—	—
mixture(of compounds)	T60.91	T60.92	T60.93	T60.94	—	—
naphthalene	T60.2X1	T60.2X2	T60.2X3	T60.2X4	—	—
organochlorine (compounds)	T60.1X1	T60.1X2	T60.1X3	T60.1X4	—	—

Substance	Poisoning, Accidental (unintentional)	Poisoning, Intentional self-harm	Poisoning, Assault	Poisoning, Undetermined	Adverse effect	Underdosing
Pesticide(dust) (fumes) (vapor) NEC — *Continued*						
petroleum(distillate) (products) NEC	T60.8X1	T60.8X2	T60.8X3	T60.8X4	—	—
specified ingredient NEC	T60.8X1	T60.8X2	T60.8X3	T60.8X4	—	—
strychnine	T65.1X1	T65.1X2	T65.1X3	T65.1X4	—	—
thallium	T60.4X1	T60.4X2	T60.4X3	T60.4X4	—	—
Pethidine	T40.4X1	T40.4X2	T40.4X3	T40.4X4	T40.4X5	T40.4X6
Petrichloral	T42.6X1	T42.6X2	T42.6X3	T42.6X4	T42.6X5	T42.6X6
Petrol	T52.0X1	T52.0X2	T52.0X3	T52.0X4	—	—
vapor	T52.0X1	T52.0X2	T52.0X3	T52.0X4	—	—
Petrolatum	T49.3X1	T49.3X2	T49.3X3	T49.3X4	T49.3X5	T49.3X6
hydrophilic	T49.3X1	T49.3X2	T49.3X3	T49.3X4	T49.3X5	T49.3X6
liquid	T47.4X1	T47.4X2	T47.4X3	T47.4X4	T47.4X5	T47.4X6
topical	T49.3X1	T49.3X2	T49.3X3	T49.3X4	T49.3X5	T49.3X6
nonmedicinal	T52.0X1	T52.0X2	T52.0X3	T52.0X4	—	—
red veterinary	T49.3X1	T49.3X2	T49.3X3	T49.3X4	T49.3X5	T49.3X6
white	T49.3X1	T49.3X2	T49.3X3	T49.3X4	T49.3X5	T49.3X6
Petroleum(products) NEC	T52.0X1	T52.0X2	T52.0X3	T52.0X4	—	—
benzine(s)—see Ligroin						
ether—see Ligroin						
jelly—see Petrolatum						
naphtha—see Ligroin						
pesticide	T60.8X1	T60.8X2	T60.8X3	T60.8X4	—	—
solids	T52.0X1	T52.0X2	T52.0X3	T52.0X4	—	—
solvents	T52.0X1	T52.0X2	T52.0X3	T52.0X4	—	—
vapor	T52.0X1	T52.0X2	T52.0X3	T52.0X4	—	—
Peyote	T40.991	T40.992	T40.993	T40.994	—	—
Phanodorm, phanodorn	T42.3X1	T42.3X2	T42.3X3	T42.3X4	T42.3X5	T42.3X6
Phanquinone	T37.3X1	T37.3X2	T37.3X3	T37.3X4	T37.3X5	T37.3X6
Phanquone	T37.3X1	T37.3X2	T37.3X3	T37.3X4	T37.3X5	T37.3X6
Pharmaceutical						
adjunct NEC	T50.901	T50.902	T50.903	T50.904	T50.905	T50.906
excipient NEC	T50.901	T50.902	T50.903	T50.904	T50.905	T50.906
sweetener	T50.901	T50.902	T50.903	T50.904	T50.905	T50.906
viscous agent	T50.901	T50.902	T50.903	T50.904	T50.905	T50.906
Phemitone	T42.3X1	T42.3X2	T42.3X3	T42.3X4	T42.3X5	T42.3X6
Phenacaine	T41.3X1	T41.3X2	T41.3X3	T41.3X4	T41.3X5	T41.3X6
Phenacemide	T42.6X1	T42.6X2	T42.6X3	T42.6X4	T42.6X5	T42.6X6
Phenacetin	T39.1X1	T39.1X2	T39.1X3	T39.1X4	T39.1X5	T39.1X6
Phenadoxone	T40.2X1	T40.2X2	T40.2X3	T40.2X4	—	—
Phenaglycodol	T43.591	T43.592	T43.593	T43.594	T43.595	T43.596
Phenantoin	T42.0X1	T42.0X2	T42.0X3	T42.0X4	T42.0X5	T42.0X6
Phenaphthazine reagent	T50.991	T50.992	T50.993	T50.994	T50.995	T50.996
Phenazocine	T40.4X1	T40.4X2	T40.4X3	T40.4X4	T40.4X5	T40.4X6
Phenazone	T39.2X1	T39.2X2	T39.2X3	T39.2X4	T39.2X5	T39.2X6
Phenazopyridine	T39.8X1	T39.8X2	T39.8X3	T39.8X4	T39.8X5	T39.8X6
Phenbenicillin	T36.0X1	T36.0X2	T36.0X3	T36.0X4	T36.0X5	T36.0X6
Phenbutrazate	T50.5X1	T50.5X2	T50.5X3	T50.5X4	T50.5X5	T50.5X6
Phencyclidine	T40.991	T40.992	T40.993	T40.994	T40.995	T40.996
Phendimetrazine	T50.5X1	T50.5X2	T50.5X3	T50.5X4	T50.5X5	T50.5X6

Substance	Poisoning, Accidental (unintentional)	Poisoning, Intentional self-harm	Poisoning, Assault	Poisoning, Undetermined	Adverse effect	Underdosing
Phenelzine	T43.1X1	T43.1X2	T43.1X3	T43.1X4	T43.1X5	T43.1X6
Phenemal	T42.3X1	T42.3X2	T42.3X3	T42.3X4	T42.3X5	T42.3X6
Phenergan	T42.6X1	T42.6X2	T42.6X3	T42.6X4	T42.6X5	T42.6X6
Pheneticillin	T36.0X1	T36.0X2	T36.0X3	T36.0X4	T36.0X5	T36.0X6
Pheneturide	T42.6X1	T42.6X2	T42.6X3	T42.6X4	T42.6X5	T42.6X6
Phenformin	T38.3X1	T38.3X2	T38.3X3	T38.3X4	T38.3X5	T38.3X6
Phenglutarimide	T44.3X1	T44.3X2	T44.3X3	T44.3X4	T44.3X5	T44.3X6
Phenicarbazide	T39.8X1	T39.8X2	T39.8X3	T39.8X4	T39.8X5	T39.8X6
Phenindamine	T45.0X1	T45.0X2	T45.0X3	T45.0X4	T45.0X5	T45.0X6
Phenindione	T45.511	T45.512	T45.513	T45.514	T45.515	T45.516
Pheniprazine	T43.1X1	T43.1X2	T43.1X3	T43.1X4	T43.1X5	T43.1X6
Pheniramine	T45.0X1	T45.0X2	T45.0X3	T45.0X4	T45.0X5	T45.0X6
Phenisatin	T47.2X1	T47.2X2	T47.2X3	T47.2X4	T47.2X5	T47.2X6
Phenmetrazine	T50.5X1	T50.5X2	T50.5X3	T50.5X4	T50.5X5	T50.5X6
Phenobal	T42.3X1	T42.3X2	T42.3X3	T42.3X4	T42.3X5	T42.3X6
Phenobarbital	T42.3X1	T42.3X2	T42.3X3	T42.3X4	T42.3X5	T42.3X6
with						
mephenytoin	T42.3X1	T42.3X2	T42.3X3	T42.3X4	T42.3X5	T42.3X6
phenytoin	T42.3X1	T42.3X2	T42.3X3	T42.3X4	T42.3X5	T42.3X6
sodium	T42.3X1	T42.3X2	T42.3X3	T42.3X4	T42.3X5	T42.3X6
Phenobarbitone	T42.3X1	T42.3X2	T42.3X3	T42.3X4	T42.3X5	T42.3X6
Phenobutiodil	T50.8X1	T50.8X2	T50.8X3	T50.8X4	T50.8X5	T50.8X6
Phenoctide	T49.0X1	T49.0X2	T49.0X3	T49.0X4	T49.0X5	T49.0X6
Phenol	T49.0X1	T49.0X2	T49.0X3	T49.0X4	T49.0X5	T49.0X6
disinfectant	T54.0X1	T54.0X2	T54.0X3	T54.0X4	—	—
in oil injection	T46.8X1	T46.8X2	T46.8X3	T46.8X4	T46.8X5	T46.8X6
medicinal	T49.1X1	T49.1X2	T49.1X3	T49.1X4	T49.1X5	T49.1X6
nonmedicinal NEC	T54.0X1	T54.0X2	T54.0X3	T54.0X4	—	—
pesticide	T60.8X1	T60.8X2	T60.8X3	T60.8X4	—	—
red	T50.8X1	T50.8X2	T50.8X3	T50.8X4	T50.8X5	T50.8X6
Phenolic preparation	T49.1X1	T49.1X2	T49.1X3	T49.1X4	T49.1X5	T49.1X6
Phenolphthalein	T47.2X1	T47.2X2	T47.2X3	T47.2X4	T47.2X5	T47.2X6
Phenolsulfonphthalein	T50.8X1	T50.8X2	T50.8X3	T50.8X4	T50.8X5	T50.8X6
Phenomorphan	T40.2X1	T40.2X2	T40.2X3	T40.2X4	—	—
Phenonyl	T42.3X1	T42.3X2	T42.3X3	T42.3X4	T42.3X5	T42.3X6
Phenoperidine	T40.4X1	T40.4X2	T40.4X3	T40.4X4	—	—
Phenopyrazone	T46.991	T46.992	T46.993	T46.994	T46.995	T46.996
Phenoquin	T50.4X1	T50.4X2	T50.4X3	T50.4X4	T50.4X5	T50.4X6
Phenothiazine (psychotropic) NEC	T43.3X1	T43.3X2	T43.3X3	T43.3X4	T43.3X5	T43.3X6
insecticide	T60.2X1	T60.2X2	T60.2X3	T60.2X4	—	—
Phenothrin	T49.0X1	T49.0X2	T49.0X3	T49.0X4	T49.0X5	T49.0X6
Phenoxybenzamine	T46.7X1	T46.7X2	T46.7X3	T46.7X4	T46.7X5	T46.7X6
Phenoxyethanol	T49.0X1	T49.0X2	T49.0X3	T49.0X4	T49.0X5	T49.0X6
Phenoxymethyl penicillin	T36.0X1	T36.0X2	T36.0X3	T36.0X4	T36.0X5	T36.0X6
Phenprobamate	T42.8X1	T42.8X2	T42.8X3	T42.8X4	T42.8X5	T42.8X6
Phenprocoumon	T45.511	T45.512	T45.513	T45.514	T45.515	T45.516
Phensuximide	T42.2X1	T42.2X2	T42.2X3	T42.2X4	T42.2X5	T42.2X6
Phentermine	T50.5X1	T50.5X2	T50.5X3	T50.5X4	T50.5X5	T50.5X6
Phenthicillin	T36.0X1	T36.0X2	T36.0X3	T36.0X4	T36.0X5	T36.0X6
Phentolamine	T46.7X1	T46.7X2	T46.7X3	T46.7X4	T46.7X5	T46.7X6

Substance	Poisoning, Accidental (unintentional)	Poisoning, Intentional self-harm	Poisoning, Assault	Poisoning, Undetermined	Adverse effect	Underdosing
Phenyl						
butazone	T39.2X1	T39.2X2	T39.2X3	T39.2X4	T39.2X5	T39.
enediamine	T65.3X1	T65.3X2	T65.3X3	T65.3X4	—	—
hydrazine	T65.3X1	T65.3X2	T65.3X3	T65.3X4	—	—
antineoplastic	T45.1X1	T45.1X2	T45.1X3	T45.1X4	T45.1X5	T45.
mercuric compounds—see Mercury						
salicylate	T49.3X1	T49.3X2	T49.3X3	T49.3X4	T49.3X5	T49.
Phenylalanine mustard	T45.1X1	T45.1X2	T45.1X3	T45.1X4	T45.1X5	T45.
Phenylbutazone	T39.2X1	T39.2X2	T39.2X3	T39.2X4	T39.2X5	T39.2
Phenylenediamine	T65.3X1	T65.3X2	T65.3X3	T65.3X4	—	—
Phenylephrine	T44.4X1	T44.4X2	T44.4X3	T44.4X4	T44.4X5	T44.4
Phenylethylbiguanide	T38.3X1	T38.3X2	T38.3X3	T38.3X4	T38.3X5	T38.3
Phenylmercuric						
acetate	T49.0X1	T49.0X2	T49.0X3	T49.0X4	T49.0X5	T49.0
borate	T49.0X1	T49.0X2	T49.0X3	T49.0X4	T49.0X5	T49.0
nitrate	T49.0X1	T49.0X2	T49.0X3	T49.0X4	T49.0X5	T49.0
Phenylmethylbarbitone	T42.3X1	T42.3X2	T42.3X3	T42.3X4	T42.3X5	T42.3
Phenylpropanol	T47.5X1	T47.5X2	T47.5X3	T47.5X4	T47.5X5	T47.5
Phenylpropanolamine	T44.991	T44.992	T44.993	T44.994	T44.995	T44.9
Phenylsulfthion	T60.0X1	T60.0X2	T60.0X3	T60.0X4	—	—
Phenyltoloxamine	T45.0X1	T45.0X2	T45.0X3	T45.0X4	T45.0X5	T45.0
Phenyramidol, phenyramidon	T39.8X1	T39.8X2	T39.8X3	T39.8X4	T39.8X5	T39.8
Phenytoin	T42.0X1	T42.0X2	T42.0X3	T42.0X4	T42.0X5	T42.0
with Phenobarbital	T42.3X1	T42.3X2	T42.3X3	T42.3X4	T42.3X5	T42.3
pHisoHex	T49.2X1	T49.2X2	T49.2X3	T49.2X4	T49.2X5	T49.2
Pholcodine	T48.3X1	T48.3X2	T48.3X3	T48.3X4	T48.3X5	T48.3
Pholedrine	T46.991	T46.992	T46.993	T46.994	T46.995	T46.9
Phorate	T60.0X1	T60.0X2	T60.0X3	T60.0X4	—	—
Phosdrin	T60.0X1	T60.0X2	T60.0X3	T60.0X4	—	—
Phosfolan	T60.0X1	T60.0X2	T60.0X3	T60.0X4	—	—
Phosgene(gas)	T59.891	T59.892	T59.893	T59.894	—	—
Phosphamidon	T60.0X1	T60.0X2	T60.0X3	T60.0X4	—	—
Phosphate	T65.891	T65.892	T65.893	T65.894	—	—
laxative	T47.4X1	T47.4X2	T47.4X3	T47.4X4	T47.4X5	T47.4
organic	T60.0X1	T60.0X2	T60.0X3	T60.0X4	—	—
solvent	T52.91	T52.92	T52.93	T52.94	—	—
tricresyl	T65.891	T65.892	T65.893	T65.894	—	—
Phosphine	T57.1X1	T57.1X2	T57.1X3	T57.1X4	—	—
fumigant	T57.1X1	T57.1X2	T57.1X3	T57.1X4	—	—
Phospholine	T49.5X1	T49.5X2	T49.5X3	T49.5X4	T49.5X5	T49.5X
Phosphoric acid	T54.2X1	T54.2X2	T54.2X3	T54.2X4	—	—
Phosphorus(compound) NEC	T57.1X1	T57.1X2	T57.1X3	T57.1X4	—	—
pesticide	T60.0X1	T60.0X2	T60.0X3	T60.0X4	—	—
Phthalates	T65.891	T65.892	T65.893	T65.894	—	—
Phthalic anhydride	T65.891	T65.892	T65.893	T65.894	—	—
Phthalimidoglutarimide	T42.6X1	T42.6X2	T42.6X3	T42.6X4	T42.6X5	T42.6X
Phthalylsulfathiazole	T37.0X1	T37.0X2	T37.0X3	T37.0X4	T37.0X5	T37.0X
Phylloquinone	T45.7X1	T45.7X2	T45.7X3	T45.7X4	T45.7X5	T45.7X

Substance	Poisoning, Accidental (unintentional)	Poisoning, Intentional self-harm	Poisoning, Assault	Poisoning, Undetermined	Adverse effect	Underdosing
ptone	T40.3X1	T40.3X2	T40.3X3	T40.3X4	T40.3X5	T40.3X6
stigma venenosum	T62.2X1	T62.2X2	T62.2X3	T62.2X4	—	—
stigmine	T49.5X1	T49.5X2	T49.5X3	T49.5X4	T49.5X5	T49.5X6
lacca decandra	T62.2X1	T62.2X2	T62.2X3	T62.2X4	—	—
ies	T62.1X1	T62.1X2	T62.1X3	T62.1X4	—	—
menadione	T45.7X1	T45.7X2	T45.7X3	T45.7X4	T45.7X5	T45.7X6
nadione	T45.7X1	T45.7X2	T45.7X3	T45.7X4	T45.7X5	T45.7X6
erine	T48.3X1	T48.3X2	T48.3X3	T48.3X4	T48.3X5	T48.3X6
ulfate(sodium)	T47.2X1	T47.2X2	T47.2X3	T47.2X4	T47.2X5	T47.2X6
(acid)	T54.2X1	T54.2X2	T54.2X3	T54.2X4	—	—
oxin	T50.7X1	T50.7X2	T50.7X3	T50.7X4	T50.7X5	T50.7X6
profen	T49.0X1	T49.0X2	T49.0X3	T49.0X4	T49.0X5	T49.0X6
rpine	T44.1X1	T44.1X2	T44.1X3	T44.1X4	T44.1X5	T44.1X6
rpus randi) extract	T44.1X1	T44.1X2	T44.1X3	T44.1X4	T44.1X5	T44.1X6
ainide ochloride)	T46.2X1	T46.2X2	T46.2X3	T46.2X4	T46.2X5	T46.2X6
ricin	T36.7X1	T36.7X2	T36.7X3	T36.7X4	T36.7X5	T36.7X6
lone	T50.7X1	T50.7X2	T50.7X3	T50.7X4	T50.7X5	T50.7X6
ic ketone	T52.8X1	T52.8X2	T52.8X3	T52.8X4	—	—
hixene	T45.0X1	T45.0X2	T45.0X3	T45.0X4	T45.0X5	T45.0X6
odine	T40.2X1	T40.2X2	T40.2X3	T40.2X4	T40.2X5	T40.2X6
ide	T43.591	T43.592	T43.593	T43.594	T43.595	T43.596
idil	T46.5X1	T46.5X2	T46.5X3	T46.5X4	T46.5X5	T46.5X6
erium bromide	T44.3X1	T44.3X2	T44.3X3	T44.3X4	T44.3X5	T44.3X6
epam	T42.4X1	T42.4X2	T42.4X3	T42.4X4	T42.4X5	T42.4X6
lol	T44.7X1	T44.7X2	T44.7X3	T44.7X4	T44.7X5	T44.7X6
ne	T60.4X1	T60.4X2	T60.4X3	T60.4X4	—	—
il(disinfectant)	T65.891	T65.892	T65.893	T65.894	—	—
oot	T37.4X1	T37.4X2	T37.4X3	T37.4X4	T37.4X5	T37.4X6
one	T40.2X1	T40.2X2	T40.2X3	T40.2X4	—	—
nazine	T45.0X1	T45.0X2	T45.0X3	T45.0X4	T45.0X5	T45.0X6
nperone	T43.4X1	T43.4X2	T43.4X3	T43.4X4	T43.4X5	T43.4X6
etate	T48.3X1	T48.3X2	T48.3X3	T48.3X4	T48.3X5	T48.3X6
nidic acid	T37.8X1	T37.8X2	T37.8X3	T37.8X4	T37.8X5	T37.8X6
zolate bromide	T44.3X1	T44.3X2	T44.3X3	T44.3X4	T44.3X5	T44.3X6
acetazine	T43.3X1	T43.3X2	T43.3X3	T43.3X4	T43.3X5	T43.3X6
acillin	T36.0X1	T36.0X2	T36.0X3	T36.0X4	T36.0X5	T36.0X6
azine	T37.4X1	T37.4X2	T37.4X3	T37.4X4	T37.4X5	T37.4X6
one sulfate	T38.5X1	T38.5X2	T38.5X3	T38.5X4	T38.5X5	T38.5X6
cubeba	T62.2X1	T62.2X2	T62.2X3	T62.2X4	—	—
idione	T48.3X1	T48.3X2	T48.3X3	T48.3X4	T48.3X5	T48.3X6
idolate	T44.3X1	T44.3X2	T44.3X3	T44.3X4	T44.3X5	T44.3X6
ocaine	T41.3X1	T41.3X2	T41.3X3	T41.3X4	T41.3X5	T41.3X6
tration cutaneous)	T41.3X1	T41.3X2	T41.3X3	T41.3X4	T41.3X5	T41.3X6
ve block(peripheral) xus)	T41.3X1	T41.3X2	T41.3X3	T41.3X4	T41.3X5	T41.3X6
cal(surface)	T41.3X1	T41.3X2	T41.3X3	T41.3X4	T41.3X5	T41.3X6
onyl butoxide	T60.8X1	T60.8X2	T60.8X3	T60.8X4	—	—
hanate	T44.3X1	T44.3X2	T44.3X3	T44.3X4	T44.3X5	T44.3X6
roman	T45.1X1	T45.1X2	T45.1X3	T45.1X4	T45.1X5	T45.1X6

Substance	Poisoning, Accidental (unintentional)	Poisoning, Intentional self-harm	Poisoning, Assault	Poisoning, Undetermined	Adverse effect	Underdosing
Pipotiazine	T43.3X1	T43.3X2	T43.3X3	T43.3X4	T43.3X5	T43.3X6
Pipoxizine	T45.0X1	T45.0X2	T45.0X3	T45.0X4	T45.0X5	T45.0X6
Pipradrol	T43.691	T43.692	T43.693	T43.694	T43.695	T43.696
Piprinhydrinate	T45.0X1	T45.0X2	T45.0X3	T45.0X4	T45.0X5	T45.0X6
Pirarubicin	T45.1X1	T45.1X2	T45.1X3	T45.1X4	T45.1X5	T45.1X6
Pirazinamide	T37.1X1	T37.1X2	T37.1X3	T37.1X4	T37.1X5	T37.1X6
Pirbuterol	T48.6X1	T48.6X2	T48.6X3	T48.6X4	T48.6X5	T48.6X6
Pirenzepine	T47.1X1	T47.1X2	T47.1X3	T47.1X4	T47.1X5	T47.1X6
Piretanide	T50.1X1	T50.1X2	T50.1X3	T50.1X4	T50.1X5	T50.1X6
Piribedil	T42.8X1	T42.8X2	T42.8X3	T42.8X4	T42.8X5	T42.8X6
Piridoxilate	T46.3X1	T46.3X2	T46.3X3	T46.3X4	T46.3X5	T46.3X6
Piritramide	T40.4X1	T40.4X2	T40.4X3	T40.4X4	—	—
Piromidic acid	T37.8X1	T37.8X2	T37.8X3	T37.8X4	T37.8X5	T37.8X6
Piroxicam	T39.391	T39.392	T39.393	T39.394	T39.395	T39.396
beta-cyclodextrin complex	T39.8X1	T39.8X2	T39.8X3	T39.8X4	T39.8X5	T39.8X6
Pirozadil	T46.6X1	T46.6X2	T46.6X3	T46.6X4	T46.6X5	T46.6X6
Piscidia(bark) (erythrina)	T39.8X1	T39.8X2	T39.8X3	T39.8X4	T39.8X5	T39.8X6
Pitch	T65.891	T65.892	T65.893	T65.894	—	—
Pitkin's solution	T41.3X1	T41.3X2	T41.3X3	T41.3X4	T41.3X5	T41.3X6
Pitocin	T48.0X1	T48.0X2	T48.0X3	T48.0X4	T48.0X5	T48.0X6
Pitressin(tannate)	T38.891	T38.892	T38.893	T38.894	T38.895	T38.896
Pituitary extracts(posterior)	T38.891	T38.892	T38.893	T38.894	T38.895	T38.896
anterior	T38.811	T38.812	T38.813	T38.814	T38.815	T38.816
Pituitrin	T38.891	T38.892	T38.893	T38.894	T38.895	T38.896
Pivampicillin	T36.0X1	T36.0X2	T36.0X3	T36.0X4	T36.0X5	T36.0X6
Pivmecillinam	T36.0X1	T36.0X2	T36.0X3	T36.0X4	T36.0X5	T36.0X6
Placental hormone	T38.891	T38.892	T38.893	T38.894	T38.895	T38.896
Placidyl	T42.6X1	T42.6X2	T42.6X3	T42.6X4	T42.6X5	T42.6X6
Plague vaccine	T50.A91	T50.A92	T50.A93	T50.A94	T50.A95	T50.A96
Plant						
food or fertilizer NEC	T65.891	T65.892	T65.893	T65.894	—	—
containing herbicide	T60.3X1	T60.3X2	T60.3X3	T60.3X4	—	—
noxious, used as food	T62.2X1	T62.2X2	T62.2X3	T62.2X4	—	—
berries	T62.1X1	T62.1X2	T62.1X3	T62.1X4	—	—
seeds	T62.2X1	T62.2X2	T62.2X3	T62.2X4	—	—
specified type NEC	T62.2X1	T62.2X2	T62.2X3	T62.2X4	—	—
Plasma	T45.8X1	T45.8X2	T45.8X3	T45.8X4	T45.8X5	T45.8X6
expander NEC	T45.8X1	T45.8X2	T45.8X3	T45.8X4	T45.8X5	T45.8X6
protein fraction(human)	T45.8X1	T45.8X2	T45.8X3	T45.8X4	T45.8X5	T45.8X6
Plasmanate	T45.8X1	T45.8X2	T45.8X3	T45.8X4	T45.8X5	T45.8X6
Plasminogen(tissue) activator	T45.611	T45.612	T45.613	T45.614	T45.615	T45.616
Plaster dressing	T49.3X1	T49.3X2	T49.3X3	T49.3X4	T49.3X5	T49.3X6
Plastic dressing	T49.3X1	T49.3X2	T49.3X3	T49.3X4	T49.3X5	T49.3X6
Plegicil	T43.3X1	T43.3X2	T43.3X3	T43.3X4	T43.3X5	T43.3X6
Plicamycin	T45.1X1	T45.1X2	T45.1X3	T45.1X4	T45.1X5	T45.1X6
Podophyllotoxin	T49.8X1	T49.8X2	T49.8X3	T49.8X4	T49.8X5	T49.8X6
Podophyllum(resin)	T49.4X1	T49.4X2	T49.4X3	T49.4X4	T49.4X5	T49.4X6
Poison NEC	T65.91	T65.92	T65.93	T65.94	—	—
Poisonous berries	T62.1X1	T62.1X2	T62.1X3	T62.1X4	—	—

Substance	Poisoning, Accidental (unintentional)	Poisoning, Intentional self-harm	Poisoning, Assault	Poisoning, Undetermined	Adverse effect	Underdosing
Pokeweed(any part)	T62.2X1	T62.2X2	T62.2X3	T62.2X4	—	—
Poldine metilsulfate	T44.3X1	T44.3X2	T44.3X3	T44.3X4	T44.3X5	T44.3X6
Polidexide(sulfate)	T46.6X1	T46.6X2	T46.6X3	T46.6X4	T46.6X5	T46.6X6
Polidocanol	T46.8X1	T46.8X2	T46.8X3	T46.8X4	T46.8X5	T46.8X6
Poliomyelitis vaccine	T50.B91	T50.B92	T50.B93	T50.B94	T50.B95	T50.B96
Polish(car) (floor) (furniture) (metal) (porcelain) (silver)	T65.891	T65.892	T65.893	T65.894	—	
abrasive	T65.891	T65.892	T65.893	T65.894	—	—
porcelain	T65.891	T65.892	T65.893	T65.894	—	—
Poloxalkol	T47.4X1	T47.4X2	T47.4X3	T47.4X4	T47.4X5	T47.4X6
Poloxamer	T47.4X1	T47.4X2	T47.4X3	T47.4X4	T47.4X5	T47.4X6
Polyaminostyrene resins	T50.3X1	T50.3X2	T50.3X3	T50.3X4	T50.3X5	T50.3X6
Polycarbophil	T47.4X1	T47.4X2	T47.4X3	T47.4X4	T47.4X5	T47.4X6
Polychlorinated biphenyl	T65.891	T65.892	T65.893	T65.894	—	—
Polycycline	T36.4X1	T36.4X2	T36.4X3	T36.4X4	T36.4X5	T36.4X6
Polyester fumes	T59.891	T59.892	T59.893	T59.894	—	—
Polyester resin hardener	T52.91	T52.92	T52.93	T52.94	—	—
fumes	T59.891	T59.892	T59.893	T59.894	—	—
Polyestradiol phosphate	T38.5X1	T38.5X2	T38.5X3	T38.5X4	T38.5X5	T38.5X6
Polyethanolamine alkyl sulfate	T49.2X1	T49.2X2	T49.2X3	T49.2X4	T49.2X5	T49.2X6
Polyethylene adhesive	T49.3X1	T49.3X2	T49.3X3	T49.3X4	T49.3X5	T49.3X6
Polyferose	T45.4X1	T45.4X2	T45.4X3	T45.4X4	T45.4X5	T45.4X6
Polygeline	T45.8X1	T45.8X2	T45.8X3	T45.8X4	T45.8X5	T45.8X6
Polymyxin	T36.8X1	T36.8X2	T36.8X3	T36.8X4	T36.8X5	T36.8X6
B	T36.8X1	T36.8X2	T36.8X3	T36.8X4	T36.8X5	T36.8X6
ENT agent	T49.6X1	T49.6X2	T49.6X3	T49.6X4	T49.6X5	T49.6X6
ophthalmic preparation	T49.5X1	T49.5X2	T49.5X3	T49.5X4	T49.5X5	T49.5X6
topical NEC	T49.0X1	T49.0X2	T49.0X3	T49.0X4	T49.0X5	T49.0X6
E sulfate(eye preparation)	T49.5X1	T49.5X2	T49.5X3	T49.5X4	T49.5X5	T49.5X6
Polynoxylin	T49.0X1	T49.0X2	T49.0X3	T49.0X4	T49.0X5	T49.0X6
Polyoestradiol phosphate	T38.5X1	T38.5X2	T38.5X3	T38.5X4	T38.5X5	T38.5X6
Polyoxymethyleneurea	T49.0X1	T49.0X2	T49.0X3	T49.0X4	T49.0X5	T49.0X6
Polysilane	T47.8X1	T47.8X2	T47.8X3	T47.8X4	T47.8X5	T47.8X6
Polytetrafluoroethylene (inhaled)	T59.891	T59.892	T59.893	T59.894	—	—
Polythiazide	T50.2X1	T50.2X2	T50.2X3	T50.2X4	T50.2X5	T50.2X6
Polyvidone	T45.8X1	T45.8X2	T45.8X3	T45.8X4	T45.8X5	T45.8X6
Polyvinylpyrrolidone	T45.8X1	T45.8X2	T45.8X3	T45.8X4	T45.8X5	T45.8X6
Pontocaine (hydrochloride) (infiltration) (topical)	T41.3X1	T41.3X2	T41.3X3	T41.3X4	T41.3X5	T41.3X6
nerve block(peripheral) (plexus)	T41.3X1	T41.3X2	T41.3X3	T41.3X4	T41.3X5	T41.3X6
spinal	T41.3X1	T41.3X2	T41.3X3	T41.3X4	T41.3X5	T41.3X6
Porfiromycin	T45.1X1	T45.1X2	T45.1X3	T45.1X4	T45.1X5	T45.1X6
Posterior pituitary hormone NEC	T38.891	T38.892	T38.893	T38.894	T38.895	T38.896
Pot	T40.7X1	T40.7X2	T40.7X3	T40.7X4	T40.7X5	T40.7X6
Potash(caustic)	T54.3X1	T54.3X2	T54.3X3	T54.3X4	—	—
Potassic saline injection(lactated)	T50.3X1	T50.3X2	T50.3X3	T50.3X4	T50.3X5	T50.3X6

Substance	Poisoning, Accidental (unintentional)	Poisoning, Intentional self-harm	Poisoning, Assault	Poisoning, Undetermined	Adverse effect	
Potassium(salts) NEC	T50.3X1	T50.3X2	T50.3X3	T50.3X4	T50.3X5	T5
aminobenzoate	T45.8X1	T45.8X2	T45.8X3	T45.8X4	T45.8X5	T4
aminosalicylate	T37.1X1	T37.1X2	T37.1X3	T37.1X4	T37.1X5	T3
antimony 'tartrate'	T37.8X1	T37.8X2	T37.8X3	T37.8X4	T37.8X5	T3
arsenite(solution)	T57.0X1	T57.0X2	T57.0X3	T57.0X4	—	
bichromate	T56.2X1	T56.2X2	T56.2X3	T56.2X4	—	
bisulfate	T47.3X1	T47.3X2	T47.3X3	T47.3X4	T47.3X5	T4
bromide	T42.6X1	T42.6X2	T42.6X3	T42.6X4	T42.6X5	T4
canrenoate	T50.0X1	T50.0X2	T50.0X3	T50.0X4	T50.0X5	T5
carbonate	T54.3X1	T54.3X2	T54.3X3	T54.3X4	—	
chlorate NEC	T65.891	T65.892	T65.893	T65.894	—	
chloride	T50.3X1	T50.3X2	T50.3X3	T50.3X4	T50.3X5	T5
citrate	T50.991	T50.992	T50.993	T50.994	T50.995	T5
cyanide	T65.0X1	T65.0X2	T65.0X3	T65.0X4	—	
ferric hexacyano-ferrate(medicinal)	T50.6X1	T50.6X2	T50.6X3	T50.6X4	T50.6X5	T5
nonmedicinal	T65.891	T65.892	T65.893	T65.894	—	
Fluoride	T57.8X1	T57.8X2	T57.8X3	T57.8X4	—	
glucaldrate	T47.1X1	T47.1X2	T47.1X3	T47.1X4	T47.1X5	T4
hydroxide	T54.3X1	T54.3X2	T54.3X3	T54.3X4	—	
iodate	T49.0X1	T49.0X2	T49.0X3	T49.0X4	T49.0X5	T4
iodide	T48.4X1	T48.4X2	T48.4X3	T48.4X4	T48.4X5	T4
nitrate	T57.8X1	T57.8X2	T57.8X3	T57.8X4	—	
oxalate	T65.891	T65.892	T65.893	T65.894	—	
perchlorate (nonmedicinal) NEC	T65.891	T65.892	T65.893	T65.894	—	
antithyroid	T38.2X1	T38.2X2	T38.2X3	T38.2X4	T38.2X5	T3
medicinal	T38.2X1	T38.2X2	T38.2X3	T38.2X4	T38.2X5	T3
Permanganate (nonmedicinal)	T65.891	T65.892	T65.893	T65.894	—	
medicinal	T49.0X1	T49.0X2	T49.0X3	T49.0X4	T49.0X5	T4
sulfate	T47.2X1	T47.2X2	T47.2X3	T47.2X4	T47.2X5	T4
Potassium-removing resin	T50.3X1	T50.3X2	T50.3X3	T50.3X4	T50.3X5	T5
Potassium-retaining drug	T50.3X1	T50.3X2	T50.3X3	T50.3X4	T50.3X5	T5
Povidone	T45.8X1	T45.8X2	T45.8X3	T45.8X4	T45.8X5	T4
iodine	T49.0X1	T49.0X2	T49.0X3	T49.0X4	T49.0X5	T4
Practolol	T44.7X1	T44.7X2	T44.7X3	T44.7X4	T44.7X5	T4
Prajmalium bitartrate	T46.2X1	T46.2X2	T46.2X3	T46.2X4	T46.2X5	T4
Pralidoxime(iodide)	T50.6X1	T50.6X2	T50.6X3	T50.6X4	T50.6X5	T5
chloride	T50.6X1	T50.6X2	T50.6X3	T50.6X4	T50.6X5	T5
Pramiverine	T44.3X1	T44.3X2	T44.3X3	T44.3X4	T44.3X5	T4
Pramocaine	T49.1X1	T49.1X2	T49.1X3	T49.1X4	T49.1X5	T4
Pramoxine	T49.1X1	T49.1X2	T49.1X3	T49.1X4	T49.1X5	T4
Prasterone	T38.7X1	T38.7X2	T38.7X3	T38.7X4	T38.7X5	T3
Pravastatin	T46.6X1	T46.6X2	T46.6X3	T46.6X4	T46.6X5	T4
Prazepam	T42.4X1	T42.4X2	T42.4X3	T42.4X4	T42.4X5	T4
Praziquantel	T37.4X1	T37.4X2	T37.4X3	T37.4X4	T37.4X5	T3
Prazitone	T43.291	T43.292	T43.293	T43.294	T43.295	T4
Prazosin	T44.6X1	T44.6X2	T44.6X3	T44.6X4	T44.6X5	T4
Prednicarbate	T49.0X1	T49.0X2	T49.0X3	T49.0X4	T49.0X5	T4
Prednimustine	T45.1X1	T45.1X2	T45.1X3	T45.1X4	T45.1X5	T4

Substance	Poisoning, Accidental (unintentional)	Poisoning, Intentional self-harm	Poisoning, Assault	Poisoning, Undetermined	Adverse effect	Underdosing
Prednisolone	T38.0X1	T38.0X2	T38.0X3	T38.0X4	T38.0X5	T38.0X6
ENT agent	T49.6X1	T49.6X2	T49.6X3	T49.6X4	T49.6X5	T49.6X6
ophthalmic preparation	T49.5X1	T49.5X2	T49.5X3	T49.5X4	T49.5X5	T49.5X6
steaglate	T49.0X1	T49.0X2	T49.0X3	T49.0X4	T49.0X5	T49.0X6
topical NEC	T49.0X1	T49.0X2	T49.0X3	T49.0X4	T49.0X5	T49.0X6
Prednisone	T38.0X1	T38.0X2	T38.0X3	T38.0X4	T38.0X5	T38.0X6
Prednylidene	T38.0X1	T38.0X2	T38.0X3	T38.0X4	T38.0X5	T38.0X6
Pregnandiol	T38.5X1	T38.5X2	T38.5X3	T38.5X4	T38.5X5	T38.5X6
Pregneninolone	T38.5X1	T38.5X2	T38.5X3	T38.5X4	T38.5X5	T38.5X6
Preludin	T43.691	T43.692	T43.693	T43.694	T43.695	T43.696
Premarin	T38.5X1	T38.5X2	T38.5X3	T38.5X4	T38.5X5	T38.5X6
Premedication anesthetic	T41.201	T41.202	T41.203	T41.204	T41.205	T41.206
Prenalterol	T44.5X1	T44.5X2	T44.5X3	T44.5X4	T44.5X5	T44.5X6
Prenoxdiazine	T48.3X1	T48.3X2	T48.3X3	T48.3X4	T48.3X5	T48.3X6
Prenylamine	T46.3X1	T46.3X2	T46.3X3	T46.3X4	T46.3X5	T46.3X6
Preparation H	T49.8X1	T49.8X2	T49.8X3	T49.8X4	T49.8X5	T49.8X6
Preparation, local	T49.4X1	T49.4X2	T49.4X3	T49.4X4	T49.4X5	T49.4X6
Preservative (nonmedicinal)	T65.891	T65.892	T65.893	T65.894	—	—
medicinal	T50.901	T50.902	T50.903	T50.904	T50.905	T50.906
wood	T60.91	T60.92	T60.93	T60.94	—	—
Prethcamide	T50.7X1	T50.7X2	T50.7X3	T50.7X4	T50.7X5	T50.7X6
Pride of China	T62.2X1	T62.2X2	T62.2X3	T62.2X4	—	—
Pridinol	T44.3X1	T44.3X2	T44.3X3	T44.3X4	T44.3X5	T44.3X6
Prifinium bromide	T44.3X1	T44.3X2	T44.3X3	T44.3X4	T44.3X5	T44.3X6
Prilocaine	T41.3X1	T41.3X2	T41.3X3	T41.3X4	T41.3X5	T41.3X6
infiltration (subcutaneous)	T41.3X1	T41.3X2	T41.3X3	T41.3X4	T41.3X5	T41.3X6
nerve block(peripheral) (plexus)	T41.3X1	T41.3X2	T41.3X3	T41.3X4	T41.3X5	T41.3X6
regional	T41.3X1	T41.3X2	T41.3X3	T41.3X4	T41.3X5	T41.3X6
Primaquine	T37.2X1	T37.2X2	T37.2X3	T37.2X4	T37.2X5	T37.2X6
Primidone	T42.6X1	T42.6X2	T42.6X3	T42.6X4	T42.6X5	T42.6X6
Primula(veris)	T62.2X1	T62.2X2	T62.2X3	T62.2X4	—	—
Prinadol	T40.2X1	T40.2X2	T40.2X3	T40.2X4	T40.2X5	T40.2X6
Priscol, Priscoline	T44.6X1	T44.6X2	T44.6X3	T44.6X4	T44.6X5	T44.6X6
Pristinamycin	T36.3X1	T36.3X2	T36.3X3	T36.3X4	T36.3X5	T36.3X6
Privet	T62.2X1	T62.2X2	T62.2X3	T62.2X4	—	—
berries	T62.1X1	T62.1X2	T62.1X3	T62.1X4	—	—
Privine	T44.4X1	T44.4X2	T44.4X3	T44.4X4	T44.4X5	T44.4X6
Pro-Banthine	T44.3X1	T44.3X2	T44.3X3	T44.3X4	T44.3X5	T44.3X6
Probarbital	T42.3X1	T42.3X2	T42.3X3	T42.3X4	T42.3X5	T42.3X6
Probenecid	T50.4X1	T50.4X2	T50.4X3	T50.4X4	T50.4X5	T50.4X6
Probucol	T46.6X1	T46.6X2	T46.6X3	T46.6X4	T46.6X5	T46.6X6
Procainamide	T46.2X1	T46.2X2	T46.2X3	T46.2X4	T46.2X5	T46.2X6
Procaine	T41.3X1	T41.3X2	T41.3X3	T41.3X4	T41.3X5	T41.3X6
benzylpenicillin	T36.0X1	T36.0X2	T36.0X3	T36.0X4	T36.0X5	T36.0X6
nerve block(periphreal) (plexus)	T41.3X1	T41.3X2	T41.3X3	T41.3X4	T41.3X5	T41.3X6
penicillin G	T36.0X1	T36.0X2	T36.0X3	T36.0X4	T36.0X5	T36.0X6
regional	T41.3X1	T41.3X2	T41.3X3	T41.3X4	T41.3X5	T41.3X6
spinal	T41.3X1	T41.3X2	T41.3X3	T41.3X4	T41.3X5	T41.3X6
Procalmidol	T43.591	T43.592	T43.593	T43.594	T43.595	T43.596
Procarbazine	T45.1X1	T45.1X2	T45.1X3	T45.1X4	T45.1X5	T45.1X6
Procaterol	T44.5X1	T44.5X2	T44.5X3	T44.5X4	T44.5X5	T44.5X6
Prochlorperazine	T43.3X1	T43.3X2	T43.3X3	T43.3X4	T43.3X5	T43.3X6
Procyclidine	T44.3X1	T44.3X2	T44.3X3	T44.3X4	T44.3X5	T44.3X6
Producer gas	T58.8X1	T58.8X2	T58.8X3	T58.8X4	—	—
Profadol	T40.4X1	T40.4X2	T40.4X3	T40.4X4	T40.4X5	T40.4X6
Profenamine	T44.3X1	T44.3X2	T44.3X3	T44.3X4	T44.3X5	T44.3X6
Profenil	T44.3X1	T44.3X2	T44.3X3	T44.3X4	T44.3X5	T44.3X6
Proflavine	T49.0X1	T49.0X2	T49.0X3	T49.0X4	T49.0X5	T49.0X6
Progabide	T42.6X1	T42.6X2	T42.6X3	T42.6X4	T42.6X5	T42.6X6
Progesterone	T38.5X1	T38.5X2	T38.5X3	T38.5X4	T38.5X5	T38.5X6
Progestin	T38.5X1	T38.5X2	T38.5X3	T38.5X4	T38.5X5	T38.5X6
oral contraceptive	T38.4X1	T38.4X2	T38.4X3	T38.4X4	T38.4X5	T38.4X6
Progestogen NEC	T38.5X1	T38.5X2	T38.5X3	T38.5X4	T38.5X5	T38.5X6
Progestone	T38.5X1	T38.5X2	T38.5X3	T38.5X4	T38.5X5	T38.5X6
Proglumide	T47.1X1	T47.1X2	T47.1X3	T47.1X4	T47.1X5	T47.1X6
Proguanil	T37.2X1	T37.2X2	T37.2X3	T37.2X4	T37.2X5	T37.2X6
Prolactin	T38.811	T38.812	T38.813	T38.814	T38.815	T38.816
Prolintane	T43.691	T43.692	T43.693	T43.694	T43.695	T43.696
Proloid	T38.1X1	T38.1X2	T38.1X3	T38.1X4	T38.1X5	T38.1X6
Proluton	T38.5X1	T38.5X2	T38.5X3	T38.5X4	T38.5X5	T38.5X6
Promacetin	T37.1X1	T37.1X2	T37.1X3	T37.1X4	T37.1X5	T37.1X6
Promazine	T43.3X1	T43.3X2	T43.3X3	T43.3X4	T43.3X5	T43.3X6
Promedol	T40.2X1	T40.2X2	T40.2X3	T40.2X4	—	—
Promegestone	T38.5X1	T38.5X2	T38.5X3	T38.5X4	T38.5X5	T38.5X6
Promethazine (teoclate)	T43.3X1	T43.3X2	T43.3X3	T43.3X4	T43.3X5	T43.3X6
Promin	T37.1X1	T37.1X2	T37.1X3	T37.1X4	T37.1X5	T37.1X6
Pronase	T45.3X1	T45.3X2	T45.3X3	T45.3X4	T45.3X5	T45.3X6
Pronestyl (hydrochloride)	T46.2X1	T46.2X2	T46.2X3	T46.2X4	T46.2X5	T46.2X6
Pronetalol	T44.7X1	T44.7X2	T44.7X3	T44.7X4	T44.7X5	T44.7X6
Prontosil	T37.0X1	T37.0X2	T37.0X3	T37.0X4	T37.0X5	T37.0X6
Propachlor	T60.3X1	T60.3X2	T60.3X3	T60.3X4	—	—
Propafenone	T46.2X1	T46.2X2	T46.2X3	T46.2X4	T46.2X5	T46.2X6
Propallylonal	T42.3X1	T42.3X2	T42.3X3	T42.3X4	T42.3X5	T42.3X6
Propamidine	T49.0X1	T49.0X2	T49.0X3	T49.0X4	T49.0X5	T49.0X6
Propane(distributed in mobile container)	T59.891	T59.892	T59.893	T59.894	—	—
distributed through pipes	T59.891	T59.892	T59.893	T59.894	—	—
incomplete combustion	T58.11	T58.12	T58.13	T58.14	—	—
Propanidid	T41.291	T41.292	T41.293	T41.294	T41.295	T41.296
Propanil	T60.3X1	T60.3X2	T60.3X3	T60.3X4	—	—
1-Propanol	T51.3X1	T51.3X2	T51.3X3	T51.3X4	—	—
2-Propanol	T51.2X1	T51.2X2	T51.2X3	T51.2X4	—	—
Propantheline	T44.3X1	T44.3X2	T44.3X3	T44.3X4	T44.3X5	T44.3X6
bromide	T44.3X1	T44.3X2	T44.3X3	T44.3X4	T44.3X5	T44.3X6
Proparacaine	T41.3X1	T41.3X2	T41.3X3	T41.3X4	T41.3X5	T41.3X6
Propatylnitrate	T46.3X1	T46.3X2	T46.3X3	T46.3X4	T46.3X5	T46.3X6
Propicillin	T36.0X1	T36.0X2	T36.0X3	T36.0X4	T36.0X5	T36.0X6

Substance	Poisoning, Accidental (unintentional)	Poisoning, Intentional self-harm	Poisoning, Assault	Poisoning, Undetermined	Adverse effect	Underdosing
Propiolactone	T49.0X1	T49.0X2	T49.0X3	T49.0X4	T49.0X5	T49.0X6
Propiomazine	T45.0X1	T45.0X2	T45.0X3	T45.0X4	T45.0X5	T45.0X6
Propionaidehyde (medicinal)	T42.6X1	T42.6X2	T42.6X3	T42.6X4	T42.6X5	T42.6X6
Propionate (calcium) (sodium)	T49.0X1	T49.0X2	T49.0X3	T49.0X4	T49.0X5	T49.0X6
Propion gel	T49.0X1	T49.0X2	T49.0X3	T49.0X4	T49.0X5	T49.0X6
Propitocaine	T41.3X1	T41.3X2	T41.3X3	T41.3X4	T41.3X5	T41.3X6
infiltration (subcutaneous)	T41.3X1	T41.3X2	T41.3X3	T41.3X4	T41.3X5	T41.3X6
nerve block(peripheral) (plexus)	T41.3X1	T41.3X2	T41.3X3	T41.3X4	T41.3X5	T41.3X6
Propofol	T41.291	T41.292	T41.293	T41.294	T41.295	T41.296
Propoxur	T60.0X1	T60.0X2	T60.0X3	T60.0X4	—	—
Propoxycaine	T41.3X1	T41.3X2	T41.3X3	T41.3X4	T41.3X5	T41.3X6
infiltration (subcutaneous)	T41.3X1	T41.3X2	T41.3X3	T41.3X4	T41.3X5	T41.3X6
nerve block(peripheral) (plexus)	T41.3X1	T41.3X2	T41.3X3	T41.3X4	T41.3X5	T41.3X6
topical(surface)	T41.3X1	T41.3X2	T41.3X3	T41.3X4	T41.3X5	T41.3X6
Propoxyphene	T40.4X1	T40.4X2	T40.4X3	T40.4X4	T40.4X5	T40.4X6
Propranolol	T44.7X1	T44.7X2	T44.7X3	T44.7X4	T44.7X5	T44.7X6
Propyl						
alcohol	T51.3X1	T51.3X2	T51.3X3	T51.3X4	—	—
carbinol	T51.3X1	T51.3X2	T51.3X3	T51.3X4	—	—
hexadrine	T44.4X1	T44.4X2	T44.4X3	T44.4X4	T44.4X5	T44.4X6
iodone	T50.8X1	T50.8X2	T50.8X3	T50.8X4	T50.8X5	T50.8X6
thiouracil	T38.2X1	T38.2X2	T38.2X3	T38.2X4	T38.2X5	T38.2X6
Propylaminopheno-thiazine	T43.3X1	T43.3X2	T43.3X3	T43.3X4	T43.3X5	T43.3X6
Propylene	T59.891	T59.892	T59.893	T59.894	—	—
Propylhexedrine	T48.5X1	T48.5X2	T48.5X3	T48.5X4	T48.5X5	T48.5X6
Propyliodone	T50.8X1	T50.8X2	T50.8X3	T50.8X4	T50.8X5	T50.8X6
Propylparaben (ophthalmic)	T49.5X1	T49.5X2	T49.5X3	T49.5X4	T49.5X5	T49.5X6
Propylthiouracil	T38.2X1	T38.2X2	T38.2X3	T38.2X4	T38.2X5	T38.2X6
Propyphenazone	T39.2X1	T39.2X2	T39.2X3	T39.2X4	T39.2X5	T39.2X6
Proquazone	T39.391	T39.392	T39.393	T39.394	T39.395	T39.396
Proscillaridin	T46.0X1	T46.0X2	T46.0X3	T46.0X4	T46.0X5	T46.0X6
Prostacyclin	T45.521	T45.522	T45.523	T45.524	T45.525	T45.526
Prostaglandin(I2)	T45.521	T45.522	T45.523	T45.524	T45.525	T45.526
E1	T46.7X1	T46.7X2	T46.7X3	T46.7X4	T46.7X5	T46.7X6
E2	T48.0X1	T48.0X2	T48.0X3	T48.0X4	T48.0X5	T48.0X6
F2 alpha	T48.0X1	T48.0X2	T48.0X3	T48.0X4	T48.0X5	T48.0X6
Prostigmin	T44.0X1	T44.0X2	T44.0X3	T44.0X4	T44.0X5	T44.0X6
Prosultiamine	T45.2X1	T45.2X2	T45.2X3	T45.2X4	T45.2X5	T45.2X6
Protamine sulfate	T45.7X1	T45.7X2	T45.7X3	T45.7X4	T45.7X5	T45.7X6
zinc insulin	T38.3X1	T38.3X2	T38.3X3	T38.3X4	T38.3X5	T38.3X6
Protease	T47.5X1	T47.5X2	T47.5X3	T47.5X4	T47.5X5	T47.5X6
Protectant, skin NEC	T49.3X1	T49.3X2	T49.3X3	T49.3X4	T49.3X5	T49.3X6
Protein hydrolysate	T50.991	T50.992	T50.993	T50.994	T50.995	T50.996
Prothiaden—see Dothiepin hydrochloride						
Prothionamide	T37.1X1	T37.1X2	T37.1X3	T37.1X4	T37.1X5	T37.1X6
Prothipendyl	T43.591	T43.592	T43.593	T43.594	T43.595	T43.596

Substance	Poisoning, Accidental (unintentional)	Poisoning, Intentional self-harm	Poisoning, Assault	Poisoning, Undetermined	Adverse effect	Underdosing
Prothoate	T60.0X1	T60.0X2	T60.0X3	T60.0X4	—	—
Prothrombin						
activator	T45.7X1	T45.7X2	T45.7X3	T45.7X4	T45.7X5	T45.7X6
synthesis inhibitor	T45.511	T45.512	T45.513	T45.514	T45.515	T45.516
Protionamide	T37.1X1	T37.1X2	T37.1X3	T37.1X4	T37.1X5	T37.1X6
Protirelin	T38.891	T38.892	T38.893	T38.894	T38.895	T38.896
Protokylol	T48.6X1	T48.6X2	T48.6X3	T48.6X4	T48.6X5	T48.6X6
Protopam	T50.6X1	T50.6X2	T50.6X3	T50.6X4	T50.6X5	T50.6X6
Protoveratrine(s) (A) (B)	T46.5X1	T46.5X2	T46.5X3	T46.5X4	T46.5X5	T46.5X6
Protriptyline	T43.011	T43.012	T43.013	T43.014	T43.015	T43.016
Provera	T38.5X1	T38.5X2	T38.5X3	T38.5X4	T38.5X5	T38.5X6
Provitamin A	T45.2X1	T45.2X2	T45.2X3	T45.2X4	T45.2X5	T45.2X6
Proxibarbal	T42.3X1	T42.3X2	T42.3X3	T42.3X4	T42.3X5	T42.3X6
Proxymetacaine	T41.3X1	T41.3X2	T41.3X3	T41.3X4	T41.3X5	T41.3X6
Proxyphylline	T48.6X1	T48.6X2	T48.6X3	T48.6X4	T48.6X5	T48.6X6
Prozac—see Fluoxetine hydrochloride						
Prunus						
laurocerasus	T62.2X1	T62.2X2	T62.2X3	T62.2X4	—	—
virginiana	T62.2X1	T62.2X2	T62.2X3	T62.2X4	—	—
Prussian blue						
commercial	T65.891	T65.892	T65.893	T65.894	—	—
therapeutic	T50.6X1	T50.6X2	T50.6X3	T50.6X4	T50.6X5	T50.6X6
Prussic acid	T65.0X1	T65.0X2	T65.0X3	T65.0X4	—	—
vapor	T57.3X1	T57.3X2	T57.3X3	T57.3X4	—	—
Pseudoephedrine	T44.991	T44.992	T44.993	T44.994	T44.995	T44.996
Psilocin	T40.991	T40.992	T40.993	T40.994	—	—
Psilocybin	T40.991	T40.992	T40.993	T40.994	—	—
Psilocybine	T40.991	T40.992	T40.993	T40.994	—	—
Psoralene (nonmedicinal)	T65.891	T65.892	T65.893	T65.894	—	—
Psoralens(medicinal)	T50.991	T50.992	T50.993	T50.994	T50.995	T50.996
PSP(phenolsulfon-phthalein)	T50.8X1	T50.8X2	T50.8X3	T50.8X4	T50.8X5	T50.8X6
Psychodysleptic drug NEC	T40.901	T40.902	T40.903	T40.904	T40.905	T40.906
Psychostimulant	T43.601	T43.602	T43.603	T43.604	T43.605	T43.606
amphetamine	T43.621	T43.622	T43.623	T43.624	T43.625	T43.626
caffeine	T43.611	T43.612	T43.613	T43.614	T43.615	T43.616
methylphenidate	T43.631	T43.632	T43.633	T43.634	T43.635	T43.636
specified NEC	T43.691	T43.692	T43.693	T43.694	T43.695	T43.696
Psychotherapeutic drug NEC	T43.91	T43.92	T43.93	T43.94	T43.95	T43.96
antidepressants—see also Antidepressant	T43.201	T43.202	T43.203	T43.204	T43.205	T43.206
specified NEC	T43.8X1	T43.8X2	T43.8X3	T43.8X4	T43.8X5	T43.8X6
tranquilizers NEC	T43.501	T43.502	T43.503	T43.504	T43.505	T43.506
Psychotomimetic agents	T40.901	T40.902	T40.903	T40.904	T40.905	T40.906
Psychotropic drug NEC	T43.91	T43.92	T43.93	T43.94	T43.95	T43.96
specified NEC	T43.8X1	T43.8X2	T43.8X3	T43.8X4	T43.8X5	T43.8X6
Psyllium hydrophilic mucilloid	T47.4X1	T47.4X2	T47.4X3	T47.4X4	T47.4X5	T47.4X6
Pteroylglutamic acid	T45.8X1	T45.8X2	T45.8X3	T45.8X4	T45.8X5	T45.8X6

Substance	Poisoning, Accidental (unintentional)	Poisoning, Intentional self-harm	Poisoning, Assault	Poisoning, Undetermined	Adverse effect	Underdosing
eroyltriglutamate	T45.1X1	T45.1X2	T45.1X3	T45.1X4	T45.1X5	T45.1X6
TFE—see Polytetra-oroethylene						
ılp						
devitalizing paste	T49.7X1	T49.7X2	T49.7X3	T49.7X4	T49.7X5	T49.7X6
dressing	T49.7X1	T49.7X2	T49.7X3	T49.7X4	T49.7X5	T49.7X6
ılsatilla	T62.2X1	T62.2X2	T62.2X3	T62.2X4	—	—
ımpkin seed extract	T37.4X1	T37.4X2	T37.4X3	T37.4X4	T37.4X5	T37.4X6
ırex(bleach)	T54.91	T54.92	T54.93	T54.94	—	—
ırgative NEC—see also athartic	T47.4X1	T47.4X2	T47.4X3	T47.4X4	T47.4X5	T47.4X6
ırine analogue ntineoplastic)	T45.1X1	T45.1X2	T45.1X3	T45.1X4	T45.1X5	T45.1X6
ırine diuretics	T50.2X1	T50.2X2	T50.2X3	T50.2X4	T50.2X5	T50.2X6
ırinethol	T45.1X1	T45.1X2	T45.1X3	T45.1X4	T45.1X5	T45.1X6
VP	T45.8X1	T45.8X2	T45.8X3	T45.8X4	T45.8X5	T45.8X6
yrabital	T39.8X1	T39.8X2	T39.8X3	T39.8X4	T39.8X5	T39.8X6
yramidon	T39.2X1	T39.2X2	T39.2X3	T39.2X4	T39.2X5	T39.2X6
yrantel	T37.4X1	T37.4X2	T37.4X3	T37.4X4	T37.4X5	T37.4X6
yrathiazine	T45.0X1	T45.0X2	T45.0X3	T45.0X4	T45.0X5	T45.0X6
yrazinamide	T37.1X1	T37.1X2	T37.1X3	T37.1X4	T37.1X5	T37.1X6
yrazinoic acid mide)	T37.1X1	T37.1X2	T37.1X3	T37.1X4	T37.1X5	T37.1X6
yrazole erivatives)	T39.2X1	T39.2X2	T39.2X3	T39.2X4	T39.2X5	T39.2X6
yrazolone analgesic EC	T39.2X1	T39.2X2	T39.2X3	T39.2X4	T39.2X5	T39.2X6
yrethrin, pyrethrum ıonmedicinal)	T60.2X1	T60.2X2	T60.2X3	T60.2X4	—	—
yrethrum extract	T49.0X1	T49.0X2	T49.0X3	T49.0X4	T49.0X5	T49.0X6
yribenzamine	T45.0X1	T45.0X2	T45.0X3	T45.0X4	T45.0X5	T45.0X6
yridine	T52.8X1	T52.8X2	T52.8X3	T52.8X4	—	—
aldoxime methiodide	T50.6X1	T50.6X2	T50.6X3	T50.6X4	T50.6X5	T50.6X6
aldoxime methyl chloride	T50.6X1	T50.6X2	T50.6X3	T50.6X4	T50.6X5	T50.6X6
vapor	T59.891	T59.892	T59.893	T59.894	—	—
yridium	T39.8X1	T39.8X2	T39.8X3	T39.8X4	T39.8X5	T39.8X6
yridostigmine bromide	T44.0X1	T44.0X2	T44.0X3	T44.0X4	T44.0X5	T44.0X6
yridoxal phosphate	T45.2X1	T45.2X2	T45.2X3	T45.2X4	T45.2X5	T45.2X6
yridoxine	T45.2X1	T45.2X2	T45.2X3	T45.2X4	T45.2X5	T45.2X6
yrilamine	T45.0X1	T45.0X2	T45.0X3	T45.0X4	T45.0X5	T45.0X6
yrimethamine	T37.2X1	T37.2X2	T37.2X3	T37.2X4	T37.2X5	T37.2X6
with sulfadoxine	T37.2X1	T37.2X2	T37.2X3	T37.2X4	T37.2X5	T37.2X6
yrimidine antagonist	T45.1X1	T45.1X2	T45.1X3	T45.1X4	T45.1X5	T45.1X6
yriminil	T60.4X1	T60.4X2	T60.4X3	T60.4X4	—	—
yrithione zinc	T49.4X1	T49.4X2	T49.4X3	T49.4X4	T49.4X5	T49.4X6
yrithyldione	T42.6X1	T42.6X2	T42.6X3	T42.6X4	T42.6X5	T42.6X6
yrogallic acid	T49.0X1	T49.0X2	T49.0X3	T49.0X4	T49.0X5	T49.0X6
yrogallol	T49.0X1	T49.0X2	T49.0X3	T49.0X4	T49.0X5	T49.0X6
yroxylin	T49.3X1	T49.3X2	T49.3X3	T49.3X4	T49.3X5	T49.3X6
yrrobutamine	T45.0X1	T45.0X2	T45.0X3	T45.0X4	T45.0X5	T45.0X6
yrrolizidine alkaloids	T62.8X1	T62.8X2	T62.8X3	T62.8X4	—	—
yrvinium chloride	T37.4X1	T37.4X2	T37.4X3	T37.4X4	T37.4X5	T37.4X6
ZI	T38.3X1	T38.3X2	T38.3X3	T38.3X4	T38.3X5	T38.3X6

Substance	Poisoning, Accidental (unintentional)	Poisoning, Intentional self-harm	Poisoning, Assault	Poisoning, Undetermined	Adverse effect	Underdosing
Q						
Quaalude	T42.6X1	T42.6X2	T42.6X3	T42.6X4	T42.6X5	T42.6X6
Quarternary ammonium						
anti-infective	T49.0X1	T49.0X2	T49.0X3	T49.0X4	T49.0X5	T49.0X6
ganglion blocking	T44.2X1	T44.2X2	T44.2X3	T44.2X4	T44.2X5	T44.2X6
parasympatholytic	T44.3X1	T44.3X2	T44.3X3	T44.3X4	T44.3X5	T44.3X6
Quazepam	T42.4X1	T42.4X2	T42.4X3	T42.4X4	T42.4X5	T42.4X6
Quicklime	T54.3X1	T54.3X2	T54.3X3	T54.3X4	—	—
Quillaja extract	T48.4X1	T48.4X2	T48.4X3	T48.4X4	T48.4X5	T48.4X6
Quinacrine	T37.2X1	T37.2X2	T37.2X3	T37.2X4	T37.2X5	T37.2X6
Quinaglute	T46.2X1	T46.2X2	T46.2X3	T46.2X4	T46.2X5	T46.2X6
Quinalbarbital	T42.3X1	T42.3X2	T42.3X3	T42.3X4	T42.3X5	T42.3X6
Quinalbarbitone sodium	T42.3X1	T42.3X2	T42.3X3	T42.3X4	T42.3X5	T42.3X6
Quinalphos	T60.0X1	T60.0X2	T60.0X3	T60.0X4	—	—
Quinapril	T46.4X1	T46.4X2	T46.4X3	T46.4X4	T46.4X5	T46.4X6
Quinestradiol	T38.5X1	T38.5X2	T38.5X3	T38.5X4	T38.5X5	T38.5X6
Quinestradol	T38.5X1	T38.5X2	T38.5X3	T38.5X4	T38.5X5	T38.5X6
Quinestrol	T38.5X1	T38.5X2	T38.5X3	T38.5X4	T38.5X5	T38.5X6
Quinethazone	T50.2X1	T50.2X2	T50.2X3	T50.2X4	T50.2X5	T50.2X6
Quingestanol	T38.4X1	T38.4X2	T38.4X3	T38.4X4	T38.4X5	T38.4X6
Quinidine	T46.2X1	T46.2X2	T46.2X3	T46.2X4	T46.2X5	T46.2X6
Quinine	T37.2X1	T37.2X2	T37.2X3	T37.2X4	T37.2X5	T37.2X6
Quiniobine	T37.8X1	T37.8X2	T37.8X3	T37.8X4	T37.8X5	T37.8X6
Quinisocaine	T49.1X1	T49.1X2	T49.1X3	T49.1X4	T49.1X5	T49.1X6
Quinocide	T37.2X1	T37.2X2	T37.2X3	T37.2X4	T37.2X5	T37.2X6
Quinoline (derivatives) NEC	T37.8X1	T37.8X2	T37.8X3	T37.8X4	T37.8X5	T37.8X6
Quinupramine	T43.011	T43.012	T43.013	T43.014	T43.015	T43.016
Quotane	T41.3X1	T41.3X2	T41.3X3	T41.3X4	T41.3X5	T41.3X6
R						
Rabies						
immune globulin(human)	T50.Z11	T50.Z12	T50.Z13	T50.Z14	T50.Z15	T50.Z16
vaccine	T50.B91	T50.B92	T50.B93	T50.B94	T50.B95	T50.B96
Racemoramide	T40.2X1	T40.2X2	T40.2X3	T40.2X4	—	—
Racemorphan	T40.2X1	T40.2X2	T40.2X3	T40.2X4	T40.2X5	T40.2X6
Racepinefrin	T44.5X1	T44.5X2	T44.5X3	T44.5X4	T44.5X5	T44.5X6
Raclopride	T43.591	T43.592	T43.593	T43.594	T43.595	T43.596
Radiator alcohol	T51.1X1	T51.1X2	T51.1X3	T51.1X4	—	—
Radioactive drug NEC	T50.8X1	T50.8X2	T50.8X3	T50.8X4	T50.8X5	T50.8X6
Radio-opaque(drugs) (materials)	T50.8X1	T50.8X2	T50.8X3	T50.8X4	T50.8X5	T50.8X6
Ramifenazone	T39.2X1	T39.2X2	T39.2X3	T39.2X4	T39.2X5	T39.2X6
Ramipril	T46.4X1	T46.4X2	T46.4X3	T46.4X4	T46.4X5	T46.4X6
Ranitidine	T47.0X1	T47.0X2	T47.0X3	T47.0X4	T47.0X5	T47.0X6
Ranunculus	T62.2X1	T62.2X2	T62.2X3	T62.2X4	—	—
Rat poison NEC	T60.4X1	T60.4X2	T60.4X3	T60.4X4	—	—
Rattlesnake(venom)	T63.011	T63.012	T63.013	T63.014	—	—
Raubasine	T46.7X1	T46.7X2	T46.7X3	T46.7X4	T46.7X5	T46.7X6
Raudixin	T46.5X1	T46.5X2	T46.5X3	T46.5X4	T46.5X5	T46.5X6
Rautensin	T46.5X1	T46.5X2	T46.5X3	T46.5X4	T46.5X5	T46.5X6
Rautina	T46.5X1	T46.5X2	T46.5X3	T46.5X4	T46.5X5	T46.5X6
Rautotal	T46.5X1	T46.5X2	T46.5X3	T46.5X4	T46.5X5	T46.5X6

Substance	Poisoning, Accidental (unintentional)	Poisoning, Intentional self-harm	Poisoning, Assault	Poisoning, Undetermined	Adverse effect	Underdosing
Rauwiloid	T46.5X1	T46.5X2	T46.5X3	T46.5X4	T46.5X5	T46.5X6
Rauwoldin	T46.5X1	T46.5X2	T46.5X3	T46.5X4	T46.5X5	T46.5X6
Rauwolfia(alkaloids)	T46.5X1	T46.5X2	T46.5X3	T46.5X4	T46.5X5	T46.5X6
Razoxane	T45.1X1	T45.1X2	T45.1X3	T45.1X4	T45.1X5	T45.1X6
Realgar	T57.0X1	T57.0X2	T57.0X3	T57.0X4	—	—
Recombinant(R)—see specific protein						
Red blood cells, packed	T45.8X1	T45.8X2	T45.8X3	T45.8X4	T45.8X5	T45.8X6
Red squill(scilliroside)	T60.4X1	T60.4X2	T60.4X3	T60.4X4	—	—
Reducing agent, industrial NEC	T65.891	T65.892	T65.893	T65.894	—	—
Refrigerant gas(chlorofluoro-carbon)	T53.5X1	T53.5X2	T53.5X3	T53.5X4	—	—
not chlorofluoro-carbon	T59.891	T59.892	T59.893	T59.894	—	—
Regroton	T50.2X1	T50.2X2	T50.2X3	T50.2X4	T50.2X5	T50.2X6
Rehydration salts(oral)	T50.3X1	T50.3X2	T50.3X3	T50.3X4	T50.3X5	T50.3X6
Rela	T42.8X1	T42.8X2	T42.8X3	T42.8X4	T42.8X5	T42.8X6
Relaxant, muscle						
anesthetic	T48.1X1	T48.1X2	T48.1X3	T48.1X4	T48.1X5	T48.1X6
central nervous system	T42.8X1	T42.8X2	T42.8X3	T42.8X4	T42.8X5	T42.8X6
skeletal NEC	T48.1X1	T48.1X2	T48.1X3	T48.1X4	T48.1X5	T48.1X6
smooth NEC	T44.3X1	T44.3X2	T44.3X3	T44.3X4	T44.3X5	T44.3X6
Remoxipride	T43.591	T43.592	T43.593	T43.594	T43.595	T43.596
Renese	T50.2X1	T50.2X2	T50.2X3	T50.2X4	T50.2X5	T50.2X6
Renografin	T50.8X1	T50.8X2	T50.8X3	T50.8X4	T50.8X5	T50.8X6
Replacement solution	T50.3X1	T50.3X2	T50.3X3	T50.3X4	T50.3X5	T50.3X6
Reproterol	T48.6X1	T48.6X2	T48.6X3	T48.6X4	T48.6X5	T48.6X6
Rescinnamine	T46.5X1	T46.5X2	T46.5X3	T46.5X4	T46.5X5	T46.5X6
Reserpin(e)	T46.5X1	T46.5X2	T46.5X3	T46.5X4	T46.5X5	T46.5X6
Resorcin, resorcinol (nonmedicinal)	T65.891	T65.892	T65.893	T65.894	—	—
medicinal	T49.4X1	T49.4X2	T49.4X3	T49.4X4	T49.4X5	T49.4X6
Respaire	T48.4X1	T48.4X2	T48.4X3	T48.4X4	T48.4X5	T48.4X6
Respiratory drug NEC	T48.901	T48.902	T48.903	T48.904	T48.905	T48.906
antiasthmatic NEC	T48.6X1	T48.6X2	T48.6X3	T48.6X4	T48.6X5	T48.6X6
anti-common-cold NEC	T48.5X1	T48.5X2	T48.5X3	T48.5X4	T48.5X5	T48.5X6
expectorant NEC	T48.4X1	T48.4X2	T48.4X3	T48.4X4	T48.4X5	T48.4X6
stimulant	T48.901	T48.902	T48.903	T48.904	T48.905	T48.906
Retinoic acid	T49.0X1	T49.0X2	T49.0X3	T49.0X4	T49.0X5	T49.0X6
Retinol	T45.2X1	T45.2X2	T45.2X3	T45.2X4	T45.2X5	T45.2X6
Rh(D) immune globulin (human)	T50.Z11	T50.Z12	T50.Z13	T50.Z14	T50.Z15	T50.Z16
Rhodine	T39.011	T39.012	T39.013	T39.014	T39.015	T39.016
RhoGAM	T50.Z11	T50.Z12	T50.Z13	T50.Z14	T50.Z15	T50.Z16
Rhubarb						
dry extract	T47.2X1	T47.2X2	T47.2X3	T47.2X4	T47.2X5	T47.2X6
tincture, compound	T47.2X1	T47.2X2	T47.2X3	T47.2X4	T47.2X5	T47.2X6
Ribavirin	T37.5X1	T37.5X2	T37.5X3	T37.5X4	T37.5X5	T37.5X6
Riboflavin	T45.2X1	T45.2X2	T45.2X3	T45.2X4	T45.2X5	T45.2X6
Ribostamycin	T36.5X1	T36.5X2	T36.5X3	T36.5X4	T36.5X5	T36.5X6
Ricin	T62.2X1	T62.2X2	T62.2X3	T62.2X4	—	—

Substance	Poisoning, Accidental (unintentional)	Poisoning, Intentional self-harm	Poisoning, Assault	Poisoning, Undetermined	Adverse effect	Underdosing
Ricinus communis	T62.2X1	T62.2X2	T62.2X3	T62.2X4	—	—
Rickettsial vaccine NEC	T50.A91	T50.A92	T50.A93	T50.A94	T50.A95	T50.A9
Rifabutin	T36.6X1	T36.6X2	T36.6X3	T36.6X4	T36.6X5	T36.6X
Rifamide	T36.6X1	T36.6X2	T36.6X3	T36.6X4	T36.6X5	T36.6X
Rifampicin	T36.6X1	T36.6X2	T36.6X3	T36.6X4	T36.6X5	T36.6X
with isoniazid	T37.1X1	T37.1X2	T37.1X3	T37.1X4	T37.1X5	T37.1X
Rifampin	T36.6X1	T36.6X2	T36.6X3	T36.6X4	T36.6X5	T36.6X
Rifamycin	T36.6X1	T36.6X2	T36.6X3	T36.6X4	T36.6X5	T36.6X
Rifaximin	T36.6X1	T36.6X2	T36.6X3	T36.6X4	T36.6X5	T36.6X
Rimantadine	T37.5X1	T37.5X2	T37.5X3	T37.5X4	T37.5X5	T37.5X
Rimazolium metilsulfate	T39.8X1	T39.8X2	T39.8X3	T39.8X4	T39.8X5	T39.8X
Rimifon	T37.1X1	T37.1X2	T37.1X3	T37.1X4	T37.1X5	T37.1X
Rimiterol	T48.6X1	T48.6X2	T48.6X3	T48.6X4	T48.6X5	T48.6X
Ringer(lactate) solution	T50.3X1	T50.3X2	T50.3X3	T50.3X4	T50.3X5	T50.3X
Ristocetin	T36.8X1	T36.8X2	T36.8X3	T36.8X4	T36.8X5	T36.8X
Ritalin	T43.631	T43.632	T43.633	T43.634	T43.635	T43.63
Ritodrine	T44.5X1	T44.5X2	T44.5X3	T44.5X4	T44.5X5	T44.5X
Roach killer—see Insecticide						
Rociverine	T44.3X1	T44.3X2	T44.3X3	T44.3X4	T44.3X5	T44.3X
Rocky Mountain spotted fever vaccine	T50.A91	T50.A92	T50.A93	T50.A94	T50.A95	T50.A9
Rodenticide NEC	T60.4X1	T60.4X2	T60.4X3	T60.4X4	—	—
Rohypnol	T42.4X1	T42.4X2	T42.4X3	T42.4X4	T42.4X5	T42.4X
Rokitamycin	T36.3X1	T36.3X2	T36.3X3	T36.3X4	T36.3X5	T36.3X
Rolaids	T47.1X1	T47.1X2	T47.1X3	T47.1X4	T47.1X5	T47.1X
Rolitetracycline	T36.4X1	T36.4X2	T36.4X3	T36.4X4	T36.4X5	T36.4X
Romilar	T48.3X1	T48.3X2	T48.3X3	T48.3X4	T48.3X5	T48.3X
Ronifibrate	T46.6X1	T46.6X2	T46.6X3	T46.6X4	T46.6X5	T46.6X
Rosaprostol	T47.1X1	T47.1X2	T47.1X3	T47.1X4	T47.1X5	T47.1X
Rose bengal sodium(131I)	T50.8X1	T50.8X2	T50.8X3	T50.8X4	T50.8X5	T50.8X
Rose water ointment	T49.3X1	T49.3X2	T49.3X3	T49.3X4	T49.3X5	T49.3X
Rosoxacin	T37.8X1	T37.8X2	T37.8X3	T37.8X4	T37.8X5	T37.8X
Rotenone	T60.2X1	T60.2X2	T60.2X3	T60.2X4	—	—
Rotoxamine	T45.0X1	T45.0X2	T45.0X3	T45.0X4	T45.0X5	T45.0X
Rough-on-rats	T60.4X1	T60.4X2	T60.4X3	T60.4X4	—	—
Roxatidine	T47.0X1	T47.0X2	T47.0X3	T47.0X4	T47.0X5	T47.0X
Roxithromycin	T36.3X1	T36.3X2	T36.3X3	T36.3X4	T36.3X5	T36.3X
Rt-PA	T45.611	T45.612	T45.613	T45.614	T45.615	[illegible]
Rubbing alcohol	T51.2X1	T51.2X2	T51.2X3	T51.2X4	—	—
Rubefacient	T49.4X1	T49.4X2	T49.4X3	T49.4X4	T49.4X5	T49.4X
Rubella vaccine	T50.B91	T50.B92	T50.B93	T50.B94	T50.B95	T50.B9
Rubeola vaccine	T50.B91	T50.B92	T50.B93	T50.B94	T50.B95	T50.B9
Rubidium chloride Rb82	T50.8X1	T50.8X2	T50.8X3	T50.8X4	T50.8X5	T50.8X
Rubidomycin	T45.1X1	T45.1X2	T45.1X3	T45.1X4	T45.1X5	T45.1X
Rue	T62.2X1	T62.2X2	T62.2X3	T62.2X4	—	—
Rufocromomycin	T45.1X1	T45.1X2	T45.1X3	T45.1X4	T45.1X5	T45.1X
Russel's viper venin	T45.7X1	T45.7X2	T45.7X3	T45.7X4	T45.7X5	T45.7X
Ruta(graveolens)	T62.2X1	T62.2X2	T62.2X3	T62.2X4	—	—
Rutinum	T46.991	T46.992	T46.993	T46.994	T46.995	T46.99
Rutoside	T46.991	T46.992	T46.993	T46.994	T46.995	T46.99

Substance	Poisoning, Accidental (unintentional)	Poisoning, Intentional self-harm	Poisoning, Assault	Poisoning, Undetermined	Adverse effect	Underdosing
S						
abadilla(plant)	T62.2X1	T62.2X2	T62.2X3	T62.2X4	—	—
pesticide	T60.2X1	T60.2X2	T60.2X3	T60.2X4	—	—
accharated iron oxide	T45.8X1	T45.8X2	T45.8X3	T45.8X4	T45.8X5	T45.8X6
accharin	T50.901	T50.902	T50.903	T50.904	T50.905	T50.906
accharomyces boulardii	T47.6X1	T47.6X2	T47.6X3	T47.6X4	T47.6X5	T47.6X6
afflower oil	T46.6X1	T46.6X2	T46.6X3	T46.6X4	T46.6X5	T46.6X6
afrazine	T43.1X1	T43.1X2	T43.1X3	T43.1X4	T43.1X5	T43.1X6
alazosulfapyridine	T37.0X1	T37.0X2	T37.0X3	T37.0X4	T37.0X5	T37.0X6
albutamol	T48.6X1	T48.6X2	T48.6X3	T48.6X4	T48.6X5	T48.6X6
alicylamide	T39.091	T39.092	T39.093	T39.094	T39.095	T39.096
alicylate NEC	T39.091	T39.092	T39.093	T39.094	T39.095	T39.096
methyl	T49.3X1	T49.3X2	T49.3X3	T49.3X4	T49.3X5	T49.3X6
theobromine calcium	T50.2X1	T50.2X2	T50.2X3	T50.2X4	T50.2X5	T50.2X6
alicylazosulfapyridine	T37.0X1	T37.0X2	T37.0X3	T37.0X4	T37.0X5	T37.0X6
alicylhydroxamic acid	T49.0X1	T49.0X2	T49.0X3	T49.0X4	T49.0X5	T49.0X6
alicylic acid	T49.4X1	T49.4X2	T49.4X3	T49.4X4	T49.4X5	T49.4X6
with benzoic acid	T49.4X1	T49.4X2	T49.4X3	T49.4X4	T49.4X5	T49.4X6
congeners	T39.091	T39.092	T39.093	T39.094	T39.095	T39.096
derivative	T39.091	T39.092	T39.093	T39.094	T39.095	T39.096
salts	T39.091	T39.092	T39.093	T39.094	T39.095	T39.096
alinazid	T37.1X1	T37.1X2	T37.1X3	T37.1X4	T37.1X5	T37.1X6
almeterol	T48.6X1	T48.6X2	T48.6X3	T48.6X4	T48.6X5	T48.6X6
alol	T49.3X1	T49.3X2	T49.3X3	T49.3X4	T49.3X5	T49.3X6
alsalate	T39.091	T39.092	T39.093	T39.094	T39.095	T39.096
alt substitute	T50.901	T50.902	T50.903	T50.904	T50.905	T50.906
alt-replacing drug	T50.901	T50.902	T50.903	T50.904	T50.905	T50.906
alt-retaining mineralocorticoid	T50.0X1	T50.0X2	T50.0X3	T50.0X4	T50.0X5	T50.0X6
Saluretic NEC	T50.2X1	T50.2X2	T50.2X3	T50.2X4	T50.2X5	T50.2X6
Saluron	T50.2X1	T50.2X2	T50.2X3	T50.2X4	T50.2X5	T50.2X6
Salvarsan 606(neosilver) (silver)	T37.8X1	T37.8X2	T37.8X3	T37.8X4	T37.8X5	T37.8X6
Sambucus canadensis	T62.2X1	T62.2X2	T62.2X3	T62.2X4	—	—
berry	T62.1X1	T62.1X2	T62.1X3	T62.1X4	—	—
Sandril	T46.5X1	T46.5X2	T46.5X3	T46.5X4	T46.5X5	T46.5X6
Sanguinaria canadensis	T62.2X1	T62.2X2	T62.2X3	T62.2X4	—	—
Saniflush(cleaner)	T54.2X1	T54.2X2	T54.2X3	T54.2X4	—	—
Santonin	T37.4X1	T37.4X2	T37.4X3	T37.4X4	T37.4X5	T37.4X6
Santyl	T49.8X1	T49.8X2	T49.8X3	T49.8X4	T49.8X5	T49.8X6
Saralasin	T46.5X1	T46.5X2	T46.5X3	T46.5X4	T46.5X5	T46.5X6
Sarcolysin	T45.1X1	T45.1X2	T45.1X3	T45.1X4	T45.1X5	T45.1X6
Sarkomycin	T45.1X1	T45.1X2	T45.1X3	T45.1X4	T45.1X5	T45.1X6
Saroten	T43.011	T43.012	T43.013	T43.014	T43.015	T43.016
Saturnine—see Lead						
Savin(oil)	T49.4X1	T49.4X2	T49.4X3	T49.4X4	T49.4X5	T49.4X6
Scammony	T47.2X1	T47.2X2	T47.2X3	T47.2X4	T47.2X5	T47.2X6
Scarlet red	T49.8X1	T49.8X2	T49.8X3	T49.8X4	T49.8X5	T49.8X6
Scheele's green	T57.0X1	T57.0X2	T57.0X3	T57.0X4	—	—
insecticide	T57.0X1	T57.0X2	T57.0X3	T57.0X4	—	—
Schizontozide(blood) (tissue)	T37.2X1	T37.2X2	T37.2X3	T37.2X4	T37.2X5	T37.2X6
Schradan	T60.0X1	T60.0X2	T60.0X3	T60.0X4	—	—
Schweinfurth green	T57.0X1	T57.0X2	T57.0X3	T57.0X4	—	—
insecticide	T57.0X1	T57.0X2	T57.0X3	T57.0X4	—	—
Scilla, rat poison	T60.4X1	T60.4X2	T60.4X3	T60.4X4	—	—
Scillaren	T60.4X1	T60.4X2	T60.4X3	T60.4X4	—	—
Sclerosing agent	T46.8X1	T46.8X2	T46.8X3	T46.8X4	T46.8X5	T46.8X6
Scombrotoxin	T61.11	T61.12	T61.13	T61.14	—	—
Scopolamine	T44.3X1	T44.3X2	T44.3X3	T44.3X4	T44.3X5	T44.3X6
Scopolia extract	T44.3X1	T44.3X2	T44.3X3	T44.3X4	T44.3X5	T44.3X6
Scouring powder	T65.891	T65.892	T65.893	T65.894	—	—
Sea						
anemone(sting)	T63.631	T63.632	T63.633	T63.634	—	—
cucumber(sting)	T63.691	T63.692	T63.693	T63.694	—	—
snake(bite) (venom)	T63.091	T63.092	T63.093	T63.094	—	—
urchin spine(puncture)	T63.691	T63.692	T63.693	T63.694	—	—
Seafood	T61.91	T61.92	T61.93	T61.94	—	—
specified NEC	T61.8X1	T61.8X2	T61.8X3	T61.8X4	—	—
Secbutabarbital	T42.3X1	T42.3X2	T42.3X3	T42.3X4	T42.3X5	T42.3X6
Secbutabarbitone	T42.3X1	T42.3X2	T42.3X3	T42.3X4	T42.3X5	T42.3X6
Secnidazole	T37.3X1	T37.3X2	T37.3X3	T37.3X4	T37.3X5	T37.3X6
Secobarbital	T42.3X1	T42.3X2	T42.3X3	T42.3X4	T42.3X5	T42.3X6
Seconal	T42.3X1	T42.3X2	T42.3X3	T42.3X4	T42.3X5	T42.3X6
Secretin	T50.8X1	T50.8X2	T50.8X3	T50.8X4	T50.8X5	T50.8X6
Sedative NEC	T42.71	T42.72	T42.73	T42.74	T42.75	T42.76
mixed NEC	T42.6X1	T42.6X2	T42.6X3	T42.6X4	T42.6X5	T42.6X6
Sedormid	T42.6X1	T42.6X2	T42.6X3	T42.6X4	T42.6X5	T42.6X6
Seed disinfectant or dressing	T60.8X1	T60.8X2	T60.8X3	T60.8X4	—	—
Seeds(poisonous)	T62.2X1	T62.2X2	T62.2X3	T62.2X4	—	—
Selegiline	T42.8X1	T42.8X2	T42.8X3	T42.8X4	T42.8X5	T42.8X6
Selenium NEC	T56.891	T56.892	T56.893	T56.894	—	—
disulfide or sulfide	T49.4X1	T49.4X2	T49.4X3	T49.4X4	T49.4X5	T49.4X6
fumes	T59.891	T59.892	T59.893	T59.894	—	—
sulfide	T49.4X1	T49.4X2	T49.4X3	T49.4X4	T49.4X5	T49.4X6
Selenomethionine (75Se)	T50.8X1	T50.8X2	T50.8X3	T50.8X4	T50.8X5	T50.8X6
Selsun	T49.4X1	T49.4X2	T49.4X3	T49.4X4	T49.4X5	T49.4X6
Semustine	T45.1X1	T45.1X2	T45.1X3	T45.1X4	T45.1X5	T45.1X6
Senega syrup	T48.4X1	T48.4X2	T48.4X3	T48.4X4	T48.4X5	T48.4X6
Senna	T47.2X1	T47.2X2	T47.2X3	T47.2X4	T47.2X5	T47.2X6
Sennoside A+B	T47.2X1	T47.2X2	T47.2X3	T47.2X4	T47.2X5	T47.2X6
Septisol	T49.2X1	T49.2X2	T49.2X3	T49.2X4	T49.2X5	T49.2X6
Seractide	T38.811	T38.812	T38.813	T38.814	T38.815	T38.816
Serax	T42.4X1	T42.4X2	T42.4X3	T42.4X4	T42.4X5	T42.4X6
Serenesil	T42.6X1	T42.6X2	T42.6X3	T42.6X4	T42.6X5	T42.6X6
Serenium (hydrochloride)	T37.91	T37.92	T37.93	T37.94	T37.95	T37.96
Serepax—see Oxazepam						
Sermorelin	T38.891	T38.892	T38.893	T38.894	T38.895	T38.896
Sernyl	T41.1X1	T41.1X2	T41.1X3	T41.1X4	T41.1X5	T41.1X6
Serotonin	T50.991	T50.992	T50.993	T50.994	T50.995	T50.996
Serpasil	T46.5X1	T46.5X2	T46.5X3	T46.5X4	T46.5X5	T46.5X6
Serrapeptase	T45.3X1	T45.3X2	T45.3X3	T45.3X4	T45.3X5	T45.3X6

Substance	Poisoning, Accidental (unintentional)	Poisoning, Intentional self-harm	Poisoning, Assault	Poisoning, Undetermined	Adverse effect	Underdosing
Serum						
antibotulinus	T50.Z11	T50.Z12	T50.Z13	T50.Z14	T50.Z15	T50.Z16
anticytotoxic	T50.Z11	T50.Z12	T50.Z13	T50.Z14	T50.Z15	T50.Z16
antidiphtheria	T50.Z11	T50.Z12	T50.Z13	T50.Z14	T50.Z15	T50.Z16
antimeningococcus	T50.Z11	T50.Z12	T50.Z13	T50.Z14	T50.Z15	T50.Z16
anti-Rh	T50.Z11	T50.Z12	T50.Z13	T50.Z14	T50.Z15	T50.Z16
anti-snake-bite	T50.Z11	T50.Z12	T50.Z13	T50.Z14	T50.Z15	T50.Z16
antitetanic	T50.Z11	T50.Z12	T50.Z13	T50.Z14	T50.Z15	T50.Z16
antitoxic	T50.Z11	T50.Z12	T50.Z13	T50.Z14	T50.Z15	T50.Z16
complement (inhibitor)	T45.8X1	T45.8X2	T45.8X3	T45.8X4	T45.8X5	T45.8X6
convalescent	T50.Z11	T50.Z12	T50.Z13	T50.Z14	T50.Z15	T50.Z16
hemolytic complement	T45.8X1	T45.8X2	T45.8X3	T45.8X4	T45.8X5	T45.8X6
immune(human)	T50.Z11	T50.Z12	T50.Z13	T50.Z14	T50.Z15	T50.Z16
protective NEC	T50.Z11	T50.Z12	T50.Z13	T50.Z14	T50.Z15	T50.Z16
Setastine	T45.0X1	T45.0X2	T45.0X3	T45.0X4	T45.0X5	T45.0X6
Setoperone	T43.591	T43.592	T43.593	T43.594	T43.595	T43.596
Sewer gas	T59.91	T59.92	T59.93	T59.94	—	—
Shampoo	T55.0X1	T55.0X2	T55.0X3	T55.0X4	—	—
Shellfish, noxious, nonbacterial	T61.781	T61.782	T61.783	T61.784	—	—
Sildenafil	T46.7X1	T46.7X2	T46.7X3	T46.7X4	T46.7X5	T46.7X6
Silibinin	T50.991	T50.992	T50.993	T50.994	T50.995	T50.996
Silicone NEC	T65.891	T65.892	T65.893	T65.894	—	—
medicinal	T49.3X1	T49.3X2	T49.3X3	T49.3X4	T49.3X5	T49.3X6
Silvadene	T49.0X1	T49.0X2	T49.0X3	T49.0X4	T49.0X5	T49.0X6
Silver	T49.0X1	T49.0X2	T49.0X3	T49.0X4	T49.0X5	T49.0X6
anti-infectives	T49.0X1	T49.0X2	T49.0X3	T49.0X4	T49.0X5	T49.0X6
arsphenamine	T37.8X1	T37.8X2	T37.8X3	T37.8X4	T37.8X5	T37.8X6
colloidal	T49.0X1	T49.0X2	T49.0X3	T49.0X4	T49.0X5	T49.0X6
nitrate	T49.0X1	T49.0X2	T49.0X3	T49.0X4	T49.0X5	T49.0X6
ophthalmic preparation	T49.5X1	T49.5X2	T49.5X3	T49.5X4	T49.5X5	T49.5X6
toughened (keratolytic)	T49.4X1	T49.4X2	T49.4X3	T49.4X4	T49.4X5	T49.4X6
nonmedicinal(dust)	T56.891	T56.892	T56.893	T56.894	—	—
protein	T49.5X1	T49.5X2	T49.5X3	T49.5X4	T49.5X5	T49.5X6
salvarsan	T37.8X1	T37.8X2	T37.8X3	T37.8X4	T37.8X5	T37.8X6
sulfadiazine	T49.4X1	T49.4X2	T49.4X3	T49.4X4	T49.4X5	T49.4X6
Silymarin	T50.991	T50.992	T50.993	T50.994	T50.995	T50.996
Simaldrate	T47.1X1	T47.1X2	T47.1X3	T47.1X4	T47.1X5	T47.1X6
Simazine	T60.3X1	T60.3X2	T60.3X3	T60.3X4	—	—
Simethicone	T47.1X1	T47.1X2	T47.1X3	T47.1X4	T47.1X5	T47.1X6
Simfibrate	T46.6X1	T46.6X2	T46.6X3	T46.6X4	T46.6X5	T46.6X6
Simvastatin	T46.6X1	T46.6X2	T46.6X3	T46.6X4	T46.6X5	T46.6X6
Sincalide	T50.8X1	T50.8X2	T50.8X3	T50.8X4	T50.8X5	T50.8X6
Sinequan	T43.011	T43.012	T43.013	T43.014	T43.015	T43.016
Singoserp	T46.5X1	T46.5X2	T46.5X3	T46.5X4	T46.5X5	T46.5X6
Sintrom	T45.511	T45.512	T45.513	T45.514	T45.515	T45.516
Sisomicin	T36.5X1	T36.5X2	T36.5X3	T36.5X4	T36.5X5	T36.5X6
Sitosterols	T46.6X1	T46.6X2	T46.6X3	T46.6X4	T46.6X5	T46.6X6
Skeletal muscle relaxants	T48.1X1	T48.1X2	T48.1X3	T48.1X4	T48.1X5	T48.1X6
Skin						
agents(external)	T49.91	T49.92	T49.93	T49.94	T49.95	T49.96
specified NEC	T49.8X1	T49.8X2	T49.8X3	T49.8X4	T49.8X5	T49.8X6
test antigen	T50.8X1	T50.8X2	T50.8X3	T50.8X4	T50.8X5	T50.8X6
Sleep-eze	T45.0X1	T45.0X2	T45.0X3	T45.0X4	T45.0X5	T45.0X6
Sleeping draught, pill	T42.71	T42.72	T42.73	T42.74	T42.75	T42.76
Smallpox vaccine	T50.B11	T50.B12	T50.B13	T50.B14	T50.B15	T50.B16
Smelter fumes NEC	T56.91	T56.92	T56.93	T56.94	—	—
Smog	T59.1X1	T59.1X2	T59.1X3	T59.1X4	—	—
Smoke NEC	T59.811	T59.812	T59.813	T59.814	—	—
Smooth muscle relaxant	T44.3X1	T44.3X2	T44.3X3	T44.3X4	T44.3X5	T44.3X6
Snail killer NEC	T60.8X1	T60.8X2	T60.8X3	T60.8X4	—	—
Snake venom or bite	T63.001	T63.002	T63.003	T63.004	—	—
hemocoagulase	T45.7X1	T45.7X2	T45.7X3	T45.7X4	T45.7X5	T45.7X6
Snuff	T65.211	T65.212	T65.213	T65.214	—	—
Soap(powder) (product)	T55.0X1	T55.0X2	T55.0X3	T55.0X4	—	—
enema	T47.4X1	T47.4X2	T47.4X3	T47.4X4	T47.4X5	T47.4X6
medicinal, soft	T49.2X1	T49.2X2	T49.2X3	T49.2X4	T49.2X5	T49.2X6
superfatted	T49.2X1	T49.2X2	T49.2X3	T49.2X4	T49.2X5	T49.2X6
Sobrerol	T48.4X1	T48.4X2	T48.4X3	T48.4X4	T48.4X5	T48.4X6
Soda(caustic)	T54.3X1	T54.3X2	T54.3X3	T54.3X4	—	—
bicarb	T47.1X1	T47.1X2	T47.1X3	T47.1X4	T47.1X5	T47.1X6
chlorinated—see Sodium, hypochlorite						
Sodium						
acetosulfone	T37.1X1	T37.1X2	T37.1X3	T37.1X4	T37.1X5	T37.1X6
acetrizoate	T50.8X1	T50.8X2	T50.8X3	T50.8X4	T50.8X5	T50.8X6
acid phosphate	T50.3X1	T50.3X2	T50.3X3	T50.3X4	T50.3X5	T50.3X6
alginate	T47.8X1	T47.8X2	T47.8X3	T47.8X4	T47.8X5	T47.8X6
amidotrizoate	T50.8X1	T50.8X2	T50.8X3	T50.8X4	T50.8X5	T50.8X6
aminopterin	T45.1X1	T45.1X2	T45.1X3	T45.1X4	T45.1X5	T45.1X6
amylosulfate	T47.8X1	T47.8X2	T47.8X3	T47.8X4	T47.8X5	T47.8X6
amytal	T42.3X1	T42.3X2	T42.3X3	T42.3X4	T42.3X5	T42.3X6
antimony gluconate	T37.3X1	T37.3X2	T37.3X3	T37.3X4	T37.3X5	T37.3X6
arsenate	T57.0X1	T57.0X2	T57.0X3	T57.0X4	—	—
aurothiomalate	T39.4X1	T39.4X2	T39.4X3	T39.4X4	T39.4X5	T39.4X6
aurothiosulfate	T39.4X1	T39.4X2	T39.4X3	T39.4X4	T39.4X5	T39.4X6
barbiturate	T42.3X1	T42.3X2	T42.3X3	T42.3X4	T42.3X5	T42.3X6
basic phosphate	T47.4X1	T47.4X2	T47.4X3	T47.4X4	T47.4X5	T47.4X6
bicarbonate	T47.1X1	T47.1X2	T47.1X3	T47.1X4	T47.1X5	T47.1X6
bichromate	T57.8X1	T57.8X2	T57.8X3	T57.8X4	—	—
biphosphate	T50.3X1	T50.3X2	T50.3X3	T50.3X4	T50.3X5	T50.3X6
bisulfate	T65.891	T65.892	T65.893	T65.894	—	—
borate						
cleanser	T57.8X1	T57.8X2	T57.8X3	T57.8X4	—	—
eye	T49.5X1	T49.5X2	T49.5X3	T49.5X4	T49.5X5	T49.5X6
therapeutic	T49.8X1	T49.8X2	T49.8X3	T49.8X4	T49.8X5	T49.8X6
bromide	T42.6X1	T42.6X2	T42.6X3	T42.6X4	T42.6X5	T42.6X6
cacodylate (nonmedicinal) NEC	T50.8X1	T50.8X2	T50.8X3	T50.8X4	T50.8X5	T50.8X6
anti-infective	T37.8X1	T37.8X2	T37.8X3	T37.8X4	T37.8X5	T37.8X6

Substance	Poisoning, Accidental (unintentional)	Poisoning, Intentional self-harm	Poisoning, Assault	Poisoning, Undetermined	Adverse effect	Underdosing
ium — *Continued*						
herbicide	T60.3X1	T60.3X2	T60.3X3	T60.3X4	—	—
alcium edetate	T45.8X1	T45.8X2	T45.8X3	T45.8X4	T45.8X5	T45.8X6
arbonate NEC	T54.3X1	T54.3X2	T54.3X3	T54.3X4	—	—
hlorate NEC	T65.891	T65.892	T65.893	T65.894	—	—
herbicide	T54.91	T54.92	T54.93	T54.94	—	—
hloride	T50.3X1	T50.3X2	T50.3X3	T50.3X4	T50.3X5	T50.3X6
with glucose	T50.3X1	T50.3X2	T50.3X3	T50.3X4	T50.3X5	T50.3X6
hromate	T65.891	T65.892	T65.893	T65.894	—	—
trate	T50.991	T50.992	T50.993	T50.994	T50.995	T50.996
romoglicate	T48.6X1	T48.6X2	T48.6X3	T48.6X4	T48.6X5	T48.6X6
yanide	T65.0X1	T65.0X2	T65.0X3	T65.0X4	—	—
yclamate	T50.3X1	T50.3X2	T50.3X3	T50.3X4	T50.3X5	T50.3X6
ehydrocholate	T45.8X1	T45.8X2	T45.8X3	T45.8X4	T45.8X5	T45.8X6
iatrizoate	T50.8X1	T50.8X2	T50.8X3	T50.8X4	T50.8X5	T50.8X6
ibunate	T48.4X1	T48.4X2	T48.4X3	T48.4X4	T48.4X5	T48.4X6
ioctyl sulfosuccinate	T47.4X1	T47.4X2	T47.4X3	T47.4X4	T47.4X5	T47.4X6
ipantoyl ferrate	T45.8X1	T45.8X2	T45.8X3	T45.8X4	T45.8X5	T45.8X6
detate	T45.8X1	T45.8X2	T45.8X3	T45.8X4	T45.8X5	T45.8X6
thacrynate	T50.1X1	T50.1X2	T50.1X3	T50.1X4	T50.1X5	T50.1X6
eredetate	T45.8X1	T45.8X2	T45.8X3	T45.8X4	T45.8X5	T45.8X6
luoride—see Fluoride						
uoroacetate(dust) (pesticide)	T60.4X1	T60.4X2	T60.4X3	T60.4X4	—	—
ree salt	T50.3X1	T50.3X2	T50.3X3	T50.3X4	T50.3X5	T50.3X6
usidate	T36.8X1	T36.8X2	T36.8X3	T36.8X4	T36.8X5	T36.8X6
lucaldrate	T47.1X1	T47.1X2	T47.1X3	T47.1X4	T47.1X5	T47.1X6
lucosulfone	T37.1X1	T37.1X2	T37.1X3	T37.1X4	T37.1X5	T37.1X6
lutamate	T45.8X1	T45.8X2	T45.8X3	T45.8X4	T45.8X5	T45.8X6
ydrogen carbonate	T50.3X1	T50.3X2	T50.3X3	T50.3X4	T50.3X5	T50.3X6
ydroxide	T54.3X1	T54.3X2	T54.3X3	T54.3X4	—	—
ypochlorite(bleach) NEC	T54.3X1	T54.3X2	T54.3X3	T54.3X4	—	—
disinfectant	T54.3X1	T54.3X2	T54.3X3	T54.3X4	—	—
medicinal(anti-infective) (external)	T49.0X1	T49.0X2	T49.0X3	T49.0X4	T49.0X5	T49.0X6
vapor	T54.3X1	T54.3X2	T54.3X3	T54.3X4	—	—
yposulfite	T49.0X1	T49.0X2	T49.0X3	T49.0X4	T49.0X5	T49.0X6
ndigotin disulfonate	T50.8X1	T50.8X2	T50.8X3	T50.8X4	T50.8X5	T50.8X6
odide	T50.991	T50.992	T50.993	T50.994	T50.995	T50.996
I-131	T50.8X1	T50.8X2	T50.8X3	T50.8X4	T50.8X5	T50.8X6
therapeutic	T38.2X1	T38.2X2	T38.2X3	T38.2X4	T38.2X5	T38.2X6
odohippurate(131I)	T50.8X1	T50.8X2	T50.8X3	T50.8X4	T50.8X5	T50.8X6
opodate	T50.8X1	T50.8X2	T50.8X3	T50.8X4	T50.8X5	T50.8X6
othalamate	T50.8X1	T50.8X2	T50.8X3	T50.8X4	T50.8X5	T50.8X6
ron edetate	T45.4X1	T45.4X2	T45.4X3	T45.4X4	T45.4X5	T45.4X6
actate(compound solution)	T45.8X1	T45.8X2	T45.8X3	T45.8X4	T45.8X5	T45.8X6
auryl(sulfate)	T49.2X1	T49.2X2	T49.2X3	T49.2X4	T49.2X5	T49.2X6
L-triiodothyronine	T38.1X1	T38.1X2	T38.1X3	T38.1X4	T38.1X5	T38.1X6
magnesium citrate	T50.991	T50.992	T50.993	T50.994	T50.995	T50.996
mersalate	T50.2X1	T50.2X2	T50.2X3	T50.2X4	T50.2X5	T50.2X6
metasilicate	T65.891	T65.892	T65.893	T65.894	—	—

Substance	Poisoning, Accidental (unintentional)	Poisoning, Intentional self-harm	Poisoning, Assault	Poisoning, Undetermined	Adverse effect	Underdosing
Sodium — *Continued*						
metrizoate	T50.8X1	T50.8X2	T50.8X3	T50.8X4	T50.8X5	T50.8X6
monofluoroacetate (pesticide)	T60.1X1	T60.1X2	T60.1X3	T60.1X4	—	—
morrhuate	T46.8X1	T46.8X2	T46.8X3	T46.8X4	T46.8X5	T46.8X6
nafcillin	T36.0X1	T36.0X2	T36.0X3	T36.0X4	T36.0X5	T36.0X6
nitrate(oxidizing agent)	T65.891	T65.892	T65.893	T65.894	—	—
nitrite	T50.6X1	T50.6X2	T50.6X3	T50.6X4	T50.6X5	T50.6X6
nitroferricyanide	T46.5X1	T46.5X2	T46.5X3	T46.5X4	T46.5X5	T46.5X6
nitroprusside	T46.5X1	T46.5X2	T46.5X3	T46.5X4	T46.5X5	T46.5X6
oxalate	T65.891	T65.892	T65.893	T65.894	—	—
oxide/peroxide	T65.891	T65.892	T65.893	T65.894	—	—
oxybate	T41.291	T41.292	T41.293	T41.294	T41.295	T41.296
para-aminohippurate	T50.8X1	T50.8X2	T50.8X3	T50.8X4	T50.8X5	T50.8X6
perborate (nonmedicinal) NEC	T65.891	T65.892	T65.893	T65.894	—	—
medicinal	T49.0X1	T49.0X2	T49.0X3	T49.0X4	T49.0X5	T49.0X6
soap	T55.0X1	T55.0X2	T55.0X3	T55.0X4	—	—
percarbonate—see Sodium, perborate						
pertechnetate Tc99m	T50.8X1	T50.8X2	T50.8X3	T50.8X4	T50.8X5	T50.8X6
phosphate						
cellulose	T45.8X1	T45.8X2	T45.8X3	T45.8X4	T45.8X5	T45.8X6
dibasic	T47.2X1	T47.2X2	T47.2X3	T47.2X4	T47.2X5	T47.2X6
monobasic	T47.2X1	T47.2X2	T47.2X3	T47.2X4	T47.2X5	T47.2X6
phytate	T50.6X1	T50.6X2	T50.6X3	T50.6X4	T50.6X5	T50.6X6
picosulfate	T47.2X1	T47.2X2	T47.2X3	T47.2X4	T47.2X5	T47.2X6
polyhydroxyaluminium monocarbonate	T47.1X1	T47.1X2	T47.1X3	T47.1X4	T47.1X5	T47.1X6
polystyrene sulfonate	T50.3X1	T50.3X2	T50.3X3	T50.3X4	T50.3X5	T50.3X6
propionate	T49.0X1	T49.0X2	T49.0X3	T49.0X4	T49.0X5	T49.0X6
propyl hydroxybenzoate	T50.991	T50.992	T50.993	T50.994	T50.995	T50.996
psylliate	T46.8X1	T46.8X2	T46.8X3	T46.8X4	T46.8X5	T46.8X6
removing resins	T50.3X1	T50.3X2	T50.3X3	T50.3X4	T50.3X5	T50.3X6
salicylate	T39.091	T39.092	T39.093	T39.094	T39.095	T39.096
salt NEC	T50.3X1	T50.3X2	T50.3X3	T50.3X4	T50.3X5	T50.3X6
selenate	T60.2X1	T60.2X2	T60.2X3	T60.2X4	—	—
stibogluconate	T37.3X1	T37.3X2	T37.3X3	T37.3X4	T37.3X5	T37.3X6
sulfate	T47.4X1	T47.4X2	T47.4X3	T47.4X4	T47.4X5	T47.4X6
sulfoxone	T37.1X1	T37.1X2	T37.1X3	T37.1X4	T37.1X5	T37.1X6
tetradecyl sulfate	T46.8X1	T46.8X2	T46.8X3	T46.8X4	T46.8X5	T46.8X6
thiopental	T41.1X1	T41.1X2	T41.1X3	T41.1X4	T41.1X5	T41.1X6
thiosalicylate	T39.091	T39.092	T39.093	T39.094	T39.095	T39.096
thiosulfate	T50.6X1	T50.6X2	T50.6X3	T50.6X4	T50.6X5	T50.6X6
tolbutamide	T38.3X1	T38.3X2	T38.3X3	T38.3X4	T38.3X5	T38.3X6
(L)-triiodothyronine	T38.1X1	T38.1X2	T38.1X3	T38.1X4	T38.1X5	T38.1X6
tyropanoate	T50.8X1	T50.8X2	T50.8X3	T50.8X4	T50.8X5	T50.8X6
valproate	T42.6X1	T42.6X2	T42.6X3	T42.6X4	T42.6X5	T42.6X6
versenate	T50.6X1	T50.6X2	T50.6X3	T50.6X4	T50.6X5	T50.6X6
Sodium-free salt	T50.901	T50.902	T50.903	T50.904	T50.905	T50.906
Sodium-removing resin	T50.3X1	T50.3X2	T50.3X3	T50.3X4	T50.3X5	T50.3X6
Soft soap	T55.0X1	T55.0X2	T55.0X3	T55.0X4	—	—

Substance	Poisoning, Accidental (unintentional)	Poisoning, Intentional self-harm	Poisoning, Assault	Poisoning, Undetermined	Adverse effect	Underdosing
Solanine	T62.2X1	T62.2X2	T62.2X3	T62.2X4	—	—
berries	T62.1X1	T62.1X2	T62.1X3	T62.1X4	—	—
Solanum dulcamara	T62.2X1	T62.2X2	T62.2X3	T62.2X4	—	—
berries	T62.1X1	T62.1X2	T62.1X3	T62.1X4	—	—
Solapsone	T37.1X1	T37.1X2	T37.1X3	T37.1X4	T37.1X5	T37.1X6
Solar lotion	T49.3X1	T49.3X2	T49.3X3	T49.3X4	T49.3X5	T49.3X6
Solasulfone	T37.1X1	T37.1X2	T37.1X3	T37.1X4	T37.1X5	T37.1X6
Soldering fluid	T65.891	T65.892	T65.893	T65.894	—	—
Solid substance	T65.91	T65.92	T65.93	T65.94	—	—
specified NEC	T65.891	T65.892	T65.893	T65.894	—	—
Solvent, industrial NEC	T52.91	T52.92	T52.93	T52.94	—	—
naphtha	T52.0X1	T52.0X2	T52.0X3	T52.0X4	—	—
petroleum	T52.0X1	T52.0X2	T52.0X3	T52.0X4	—	—
specified NEC	T52.8X1	T52.8X2	T52.8X3	T52.8X4	—	—
Soma	T42.8X1	T42.8X2	T42.8X3	T42.8X4	T42.8X5	T42.8X6
Somatorelin	T38.891	T38.892	T38.893	T38.894	T38.895	T38.896
Somatostatin	T38.991	T38.992	T38.993	T38.994	T38.995	T38.996
Somatotropin	T38.811	T38.812	T38.813	T38.814	T38.815	T38.816
Somatrem	T38.811	T38.812	T38.813	T38.814	T38.815	T38.816
Somatropin	T38.811	T38.812	T38.813	T38.814	T38.815	T38.816
Sominex	T45.0X1	T45.0X2	T45.0X3	T45.0X4	T45.0X5	T45.0X6
Somnos	T42.6X1	T42.6X2	T42.6X3	T42.6X4	T42.6X5	T42.6X6
Somonal	T42.3X1	T42.3X2	T42.3X3	T42.3X4	T42.3X5	T42.3X6
Soneryl	T42.3X1	T42.3X2	T42.3X3	T42.3X4	T42.3X5	T42.3X6
Soothing syrup	T50.901	T50.902	T50.903	T50.904	T50.905	T50.906
Sopor	T42.6X1	T42.6X2	T42.6X3	T42.6X4	T42.6X5	T42.6X6
Soporific	T42.71	T42.72	T42.73	T42.74	T42.75	T42.76
Soporific drug	T42.71	T42.72	T42.73	T42.74	T42.75	T42.76
specified type NEC	T42.6X1	T42.6X2	T42.6X3	T42.6X4	T42.6X5	T42.6X6
Sorbide nitrate	T46.3X1	T46.3X2	T46.3X3	T46.3X4	T46.3X5	T46.3X6
Sorbitol	T47.4X1	T47.4X2	T47.4X3	T47.4X4	T47.4X5	T47.4X6
Sotalol	T44.7X1	T44.7X2	T44.7X3	T44.7X4	T44.7X5	T44.7X6
Sotradecol	T46.8X1	T46.8X2	T46.8X3	T46.8X4	T46.8X5	T46.8X6
Soysterol	T46.6X1	T46.6X2	T46.6X3	T46.6X4	T46.6X5	T46.6X6
Spacoline	T44.3X1	T44.3X2	T44.3X3	T44.3X4	T44.3X5	T44.3X6
Spanish fly	T49.8X1	T49.8X2	T49.8X3	T49.8X4	T49.8X5	T49.8X6
Sparine	T43.3X1	T43.3X2	T43.3X3	T43.3X4	T43.3X5	T43.3X6
Sparteine	T48.0X1	T48.0X2	T48.0X3	T48.0X4	T48.0X5	T48.0X6
Spasmolytic						
anticholinergics	T44.3X1	T44.3X2	T44.3X3	T44.3X4	T44.3X5	T44.3X6
autonomic	T44.3X1	T44.3X2	T44.3X3	T44.3X4	T44.3X5	T44.3X6
bronchial NEC	T48.6X1	T48.6X2	T48.6X3	T48.6X4	T48.6X5	T48.6X6
quaternary ammonium	T44.3X1	T44.3X2	T44.3X3	T44.3X4	T44.3X5	T44.3X6
skeletal muscle NEC	T48.1X1	T48.1X2	T48.1X3	T48.1X4	T48.1X5	T48.1X6
Spectinomycin	T36.5X1	T36.5X2	T36.5X3	T36.5X4	T36.5X5	T36.5X6
Speed	T43.621	T43.622	T43.623	T43.624	T43.625	T43.626
Spermicide	T49.8X1	T49.8X2	T49.8X3	T49.8X4	T49.8X5	T49.8X6
Spider(bite) (venom)	T63.391	T63.392	T63.393	T63.394	—	—
antivenin	T50.Z11	T50.Z12	T50.Z13	T50.Z14	T50.Z15	T50.Z16
Spigelia(root)	T37.4X1	T37.4X2	T37.4X3	T37.4X4	T37.4X5	T37.4X6

Substance	Poisoning, Accidental (unintentional)	Poisoning, Intentional self-harm	Poisoning, Assault	Poisoning, Undetermined	Adverse effect	Underdosing
Spindle inactivator	T50.4X1	T50.4X2	T50.4X3	T50.4X4	T50.4X5	T50.
Spiperone	T43.4X1	T43.4X2	T43.4X3	T43.4X4	T43.4X5	T43.
Spiramycin	T36.3X1	T36.3X2	T36.3X3	T36.3X4	T36.3X5	T36.
Spirapril	T46.4X1	T46.4X2	T46.4X3	T46.4X4	T46.4X5	T46.
Spirilene	T43.591	T43.592	T43.593	T43.594	T43.595	T43.
Spirit(s) (neutral) NEC	T51.0X1	T51.0X2	T51.0X3	T51.0X4	—	—
beverage	T51.0X1	T51.0X2	T51.0X3	T51.0X4	—	—
industrial	T51.0X1	T51.0X2	T51.0X3	T51.0X4	—	—
mineral	T52.0X1	T52.0X2	T52.0X3	T52.0X4	—	—
of salt—see Hydrochloric acid						
surgical	T51.0X1	T51.0X2	T51.0X3	T51.0X4	—	—
Spironolactone	T50.0X1	T50.0X2	T50.0X3	T50.0X4	T50.0X5	T50.
Spiroperidol	T43.4X1	T43.4X2	T43.4X3	T43.4X4	T43.4X5	T43.
Sponge, absorbable(gelatin)	T45.7X1	T45.7X2	T45.7X3	T45.7X4	T45.7X5	T45.
Sporostacin	T49.0X1	T49.0X2	T49.0X3	T49.0X4	T49.0X5	T49.
Spray(aerosol)	T65.91	T65.92	T65.93	T65.94	—	—
cosmetic	T65.891	T65.892	T65.893	T65.894	—	—
medicinal NEC	T50.901	T50.902	T50.903	T50.904	T50.905	T50.
pesticides—see Pesticides						
specified content—see specific substance						
Spurge flax	T62.2X1	T62.2X2	T62.2X3	T62.2X4	—	—
Spurges	T62.2X1	T62.2X2	T62.2X3	T62.2X4	—	—
Sputum viscosity-lowering drug	T48.4X1	T48.4X2	T48.4X3	T48.4X4	T48.4X5	T48.
Squill	T46.0X1	T46.0X2	T46.0X3	T46.0X4	T46.0X5	T46.
rat poison	T60.4X1	T60.4X2	T60.4X3	T60.4X4	—	—
Squirting cucumber(cathartic)	T47.2X1	T47.2X2	T47.2X3	T47.2X4	T47.2X5	T47.
Stains	T65.6X1	T65.6X2	T65.6X3	T65.6X4	—	—
Stannous fluoride	T49.7X1	T49.7X2	T49.7X3	T49.7X4	T49.7X5	T49.
Stanolone	T38.7X1	T38.7X2	T38.7X3	T38.7X4	T38.7X5	T38.
Stanozolol	T38.7X1	T38.7X2	T38.7X3	T38.7X4	T38.7X5	T38.
Staphisagria or stavesacre (pediculicide)	T49.0X1	T49.0X2	T49.0X3	T49.0X4	T49.0X5	T49.
Starch	T50.901	T50.902	T50.903	T50.904	T50.905	T50.
Stelazine	T43.3X1	T43.3X2	T43.3X3	T43.3X4	T43.3X5	T43.
Stemetil	T43.3X1	T43.3X2	T43.3X3	T43.3X4	T43.3X5	T43.
Stepronin	T48.4X1	T48.4X2	T48.4X3	T48.4X4	T48.4X5	T48.
Sterculia	T47.4X1	T47.4X2	T47.4X3	T47.4X4	T47.4X5	T47.
Sternutator gas	T59.891	T59.892	T59.893	T59.894	—	—
Steroid	T38.0X1	T38.0X2	T38.0X3	T38.0X4	T38.0X5	T38.
anabolic	T38.7X1	T38.7X2	T38.7X3	T38.7X4	T38.7X5	T38.
androgenic	T38.7X1	T38.7X2	T38.7X3	T38.7X4	T38.7X5	T38.
antineoplastic, hormone	T38.7X1	T38.7X2	T38.7X3	T38.7X4	T38.7X5	T38.
estrogen	T38.5X1	T38.5X2	T38.5X3	T38.5X4	T38.5X5	T38.
ENT agent	T49.6X1	T49.6X2	T49.6X3	T49.6X4	T49.6X5	T49.
ophthalmic preparation	T49.5X1	T49.5X2	T49.5X3	T49.5X4	T49.5X5	T49.
topical NEC	T49.0X1	T49.0X2	T49.0X3	T49.0X4	T49.0X5	T49.
Stibine	T56.891	T56.892	T56.893	T56.894	—	—
Stibogluconate	T37.3X1	T37.3X2	T37.3X3	T37.3X4	T37.3X5	T37.

Substance	Poisoning, Accidental (unintentional)	Poisoning, Intentional self-harm	Poisoning, Assault	Poisoning, Undetermined	Adverse effect	Underdosing
ophen	T37.4X1	T37.4X2	T37.4X3	T37.4X4	T37.4X5	T37.4X6
amidine (isetionate)	T37.3X1	T37.3X2	T37.3X3	T37.3X4	T37.3X5	T37.3X6
estrol	T38.5X1	T38.5X2	T38.5X3	T38.5X4	T38.5X5	T38.5X6
oestrol	T38.5X1	T38.5X2	T38.5X3	T38.5X4	T38.5X5	T38.5X6
ulant						
ntral nervous system—e also Psychostimulant	T43.601	T43.602	T43.603	T43.604	T43.605	T43.606
analeptics	T50.7X1	T50.7X2	T50.7X3	T50.7X4	T50.7X5	T50.7X6
opiate antagonist	T50.7X1	T50.7X2	T50.7X3	T50.7X4	T50.7X5	T50.7X6
psychotherapeutic NEC—see also Psychotherapeutic drug	T43.601	T43.602	T43.603	T43.604	T43.605	T43.606
specified NEC	T43.691	T43.692	T43.693	T43.694	T43.695	T43.696
spiratory	T48.901	T48.902	T48.903	T48.904	T48.905	T48.906
e-dissolving drug	T50.901	T50.902	T50.903	T50.904	T50.905	T50.906
age battery(cells) l)	T54.2X1	T54.2X2	T54.2X3	T54.2X4	—	—
aine	T41.3X1	T41.3X2	T41.3X3	T41.3X4	T41.3X5	T41.3X6
filtration ubcutaneous)	T41.3X1	T41.3X2	T41.3X3	T41.3X4	T41.3X5	T41.3X6
rve block eripheral) (plexus)	T41.3X1	T41.3X2	T41.3X3	T41.3X4	T41.3X5	T41.3X6
inal	T41.3X1	T41.3X2	T41.3X3	T41.3X4	T41.3X5	T41.3X6
pical(surface)	T41.3X1	T41.3X2	T41.3X3	T41.3X4	T41.3X5	T41.3X6
arsal	T37.8X1	T37.8X2	T37.8X3	T37.8X4	T37.8X5	T37.8X6
e gas—see Gas, stove						
il	T49.5X1	T49.5X2	T49.5X3	T49.5X4	T49.5X5	T49.5X6
monium	T48.6X1	T48.6X2	T48.6X3	T48.6X4	T48.6X5	T48.6X6
tural state	T62.2X1	T62.2X2	T62.2X3	T62.2X4	—	—
ptodornase	T45.3X1	T45.3X2	T45.3X3	T45.3X4	T45.3X5	T45.3X6
ptoduocin	T36.5X1	T36.5X2	T36.5X3	T36.5X4	T36.5X5	T36.5X6
ptokinase	T45.611	T45.612	T45.613	T45.614	T45.615	T45.616
ptomycin (derivative)	T36.5X1	T36.5X2	T36.5X3	T36.5X4	T36.5X5	T36.5X6
ptonivicin	T36.5X1	T36.5X2	T36.5X3	T36.5X4	T36.5X5	T36.5X6
ptovarycin	T36.5X1	T36.5X2	T36.5X3	T36.5X4	T36.5X5	T36.5X6
ptozocin	T45.1X1	T45.1X2	T45.1X3	T45.1X4	T45.1X5	T45.1X6
ptozotocin	T45.1X1	T45.1X2	T45.1X3	T45.1X4	T45.1X5	T45.1X6
pper(paint) (solvent)	T52.8X1	T52.8X2	T52.8X3	T52.8X4	—	—
bane	T60.1X1	T60.1X2	T60.1X3	T60.1X4	—	—
fantina	T46.0X1	T46.0X2	T46.0X3	T46.0X4	T46.0X5	T46.0X6
phanthin(g) (k)	T46.0X1	T46.0X2	T46.0X3	T46.0X4	T46.0X5	T46.0X6
phanthus	T46.0X1	T46.0X2	T46.0X3	T46.0X4	T46.0X5	T46.0X6
phantin	T46.0X1	T46.0X2	T46.0X3	T46.0X4	T46.0X5	T46.0X6
phantin-g	T46.0X1	T46.0X2	T46.0X3	T46.0X4	T46.0X5	T46.0X6
chnine (nonmedicinal) ticide) (salts)	T65.1X1	T65.1X2	T65.1X3	T65.1X4	—	—
edicinal	T48.291	T48.292	T48.293	T48.294	T48.295	T48.296
chnos(ignatii)—see chnine						
amate	T42.8X1	T42.8X2	T42.8X3	T42.8X4	T42.8X5	T42.8X6
ene	T65.891	T65.892	T65.893	T65.894	—	—
cinimide, antiepileptic nticonvulsant	T42.2X1	T42.2X2	T42.2X3	T42.2X4	T42.2X5	T42.2X6
ercuric—see Mercury						

Substance	Poisoning, Accidental (unintentional)	Poisoning, Intentional self-harm	Poisoning, Assault	Poisoning, Undetermined	Adverse effect	Underdosing
Succinylcholine	T48.1X1	T48.1X2	T48.1X3	T48.1X4	T48.1X5	T48.1X6
Succinylsulfathiazole	T37.0X1	T37.0X2	T37.0X3	T37.0X4	T37.0X5	T37.0X6
Sucralfate	T47.1X1	T47.1X2	T47.1X3	T47.1X4	T47.1X5	T47.1X6
Sucrose	T50.3X1	T50.3X2	T50.3X3	T50.3X4	T50.3X5	T50.3X6
Sufentanil	T40.4X1	T40.4X2	T40.4X3	T40.4X4	T40.4X5	T40.4X6
Sulbactam	T36.0X1	T36.0X2	T36.0X3	T36.0X4	T36.0X5	T36.0X6
Sulbenicillin	T36.0X1	T36.0X2	T36.0X3	T36.0X4	T36.0X5	T36.0X6
Sulbentine	T49.0X1	T49.0X2	T49.0X3	T49.0X4	T49.0X5	T49.0X6
Sulfacetamide	T49.0X1	T49.0X2	T49.0X3	T49.0X4	T49.0X5	T49.0X6
ophthalmic preparation	T49.5X1	T49.5X2	T49.5X3	T49.5X4	T49.5X5	T49.5X6
Sulfachlorpyridazine	T37.0X1	T37.0X2	T37.0X3	T37.0X4	T37.0X5	T37.0X6
Sulfacitine	T37.0X1	T37.0X2	T37.0X3	T37.0X4	T37.0X5	T37.0X6
Sulfadiasulfone sodium	T37.0X1	T37.0X2	T37.0X3	T37.0X4	T37.0X5	T37.0X6
Sulfadiazine	T37.0X1	T37.0X2	T37.0X3	T37.0X4	T37.0X5	T37.0X6
silver(topical)	T49.0X1	T49.0X2	T49.0X3	T49.0X4	T49.0X5	T49.0X6
Sulfadimethoxine	T37.0X1	T37.0X2	T37.0X3	T37.0X4	T37.0X5	T37.0X6
Sulfadimidine	T37.0X1	T37.0X2	T37.0X3	T37.0X4	T37.0X5	T37.0X6
Sulfadoxine	T37.0X1	T37.0X2	T37.0X3	T37.0X4	T37.0X5	T37.0X6
with pyrimethamine	T37.2X1	T37.2X2	T37.2X3	T37.2X4	T37.2X5	T37.2X6
Sulfaethidole	T37.0X1	T37.0X2	T37.0X3	T37.0X4	T37.0X5	T37.0X6
Sulfafurazole	T37.0X1	T37.0X2	T37.0X3	T37.0X4	T37.0X5	T37.0X6
Sulfaguanidine	T37.0X1	T37.0X2	T37.0X3	T37.0X4	T37.0X5	T37.0X6
Sulfalene	T37.0X1	T37.0X2	T37.0X3	T37.0X4	T37.0X5	T37.0X6
Sulfaloxate	T37.0X1	T37.0X2	T37.0X3	T37.0X4	T37.0X5	T37.0X6
Sulfaloxic acid	T37.0X1	T37.0X2	T37.0X3	T37.0X4	T37.0X5	T37.0X6
Sulfamazone	T39.2X1	T39.2X2	T39.2X3	T39.2X4	T39.2X5	T39.2X6
Sulfamerazine	T37.0X1	T37.0X2	T37.0X3	T37.0X4	T37.0X5	T37.0X6
Sulfameter	T37.0X1	T37.0X2	T37.0X3	T37.0X4	T37.0X5	T37.0X6
Sulfamethazine	T37.0X1	T37.0X2	T37.0X3	T37.0X4	T37.0X5	T37.0X6
Sulfamethizole	T37.0X1	T37.0X2	T37.0X3	T37.0X4	T37.0X5	T37.0X6
Sulfamethoxazole	T37.0X1	T37.0X2	T37.0X3	T37.0X4	T37.0X5	T37.0X6
with trimethoprim	T36.8X1	T36.8X2	T36.8X3	T36.8X4	T36.8X5	T36.8X6
Sulfamethoxydiazine	T37.0X1	T37.0X2	T37.0X3	T37.0X4	T37.0X5	T37.0X6
Sulfamethoxypyridazine	T37.0X1	T37.0X2	T37.0X3	T37.0X4	T37.0X5	T37.0X6
Sulfamethylthiazole	T37.0X1	T37.0X2	T37.0X3	T37.0X4	T37.0X5	T37.0X6
Sulfametoxydiazine	T37.0X1	T37.0X2	T37.0X3	T37.0X4	T37.0X5	T37.0X6
Sulfamidopyrine	T39.2X1	T39.2X2	T39.2X3	T39.2X4	T39.2X5	T39.2X6
Sulfamonomethoxine	T37.0X1	T37.0X2	T37.0X3	T37.0X4	T37.0X5	T37.0X6
Sulfamoxole	T37.0X1	T37.0X2	T37.0X3	T37.0X4	T37.0X5	T37.0X6
Sulfamylon	T49.0X1	T49.0X2	T49.0X3	T49.0X4	T49.0X5	T49.0X6
Sulfan blue(diagnostic dye)	T50.8X1	T50.8X2	T50.8X3	T50.8X4	T50.8X5	T50.8X6
Sulfanilamide	T37.0X1	T37.0X2	T37.0X3	T37.0X4	T37.0X5	T37.0X6
Sulfanilylguanidine	T37.0X1	T37.0X2	T37.0X3	T37.0X4	T37.0X5	T37.0X6
Sulfaperin	T37.0X1	T37.0X2	T37.0X3	T37.0X4	T37.0X5	T37.0X6
Sulfaphenazole	T37.0X1	T37.0X2	T37.0X3	T37.0X4	T37.0X5	T37.0X6
Sulfaphenylthiazole	T37.0X1	T37.0X2	T37.0X3	T37.0X4	T37.0X5	T37.0X6
Sulfaproxyline	T37.0X1	T37.0X2	T37.0X3	T37.0X4	T37.0X5	T37.0X6
Sulfapyridine	T37.0X1	T37.0X2	T37.0X3	T37.0X4	T37.0X5	T37.0X6
Sulfapyrimidine	T37.0X1	T37.0X2	T37.0X3	T37.0X4	T37.0X5	T37.0X6
Sulfarsphenamine	T37.8X1	T37.8X2	T37.8X3	T37.8X4	T37.8X5	T37.8X6
Sulfasalazine	T37.0X1	T37.0X2	T37.0X3	T37.0X4	T37.0X5	T37.0X6

Substance	Poisoning, Accidental (unintentional)	Poisoning, Intentional self-harm	Poisoning, Assault	Poisoning, Undetermined	Adverse effect	Underdosing
Sulfasuxidine	T37.0X1	T37.0X2	T37.0X3	T37.0X4	T37.0X5	T37.0X6
Sulfasymazine	T37.0X1	T37.0X2	T37.0X3	T37.0X4	T37.0X5	T37.0X6
Sulfated amylopectin	T47.8X1	T47.8X2	T47.8X3	T47.8X4	T47.8X5	T47.8X6
Sulfathiazole	T37.0X1	T37.0X2	T37.0X3	T37.0X4	T37.0X5	T37.0X6
Sulfatostearate	T49.2X1	T49.2X2	T49.2X3	T49.2X4	T49.2X5	T49.2X6
Sulfinpyrazone	T50.4X1	T50.4X2	T50.4X3	T50.4X4	T50.4X5	T50.4X6
Sulfiram	T49.0X1	T49.0X2	T49.0X3	T49.0X4	T49.0X5	T49.0X6
Sulfisomidine	T37.0X1	T37.0X2	T37.0X3	T37.0X4	T37.0X5	T37.0X6
Sulfisoxazole	T37.0X1	T37.0X2	T37.0X3	T37.0X4	T37.0X5	T37.0X6
ophthalmic preparation	T49.5X1	T49.5X2	T49.5X3	T49.5X4	T49.5X5	T49.5X6
Sulfobromophthalein (sodium)	T50.8X1	T50.8X2	T50.8X3	T50.8X4	T50.8X5	T50.8X6
Sulfobromphthalein	T50.8X1	T50.8X2	T50.8X3	T50.8X4	T50.8X5	T50.8X6
Sulfogaiacol	T48.4X1	T48.4X2	T48.4X3	T48.4X4	T48.4X5	T48.4X6
Sulfomyxin	T36.8X1	T36.8X2	T36.8X3	T36.8X4	T36.8X5	T36.8X6
Sulfonal	T42.6X1	T42.6X2	T42.6X3	T42.6X4	T42.6X5	T42.6X6
Sulfonamide NEC	T37.0X1	T37.0X2	T37.0X3	T37.0X4	T37.0X5	T37.0X6
eye	T49.5X1	T49.5X2	T49.5X3	T49.5X4	T49.5X5	T49.5X6
Sulfonazide	T37.1X1	T37.1X2	T37.1X3	T37.1X4	T37.1X5	T37.1X6
Sulfones	T37.1X1	T37.1X2	T37.1X3	T37.1X4	T37.1X5	T37.1X6
Sulfonethylmethane	T42.6X1	T42.6X2	T42.6X3	T42.6X4	T42.6X5	T42.6X6
Sulfonmethane	T42.6X1	T42.6X2	T42.6X3	T42.6X4	T42.6X5	T42.6X6
Sulfonphthal, sulfonphthol	T50.8X1	T50.8X2	T50.8X3	T50.8X4	T50.8X5	T50.8X6
Sulfonylurea derivatives, oral	T38.3X1	T38.3X2	T38.3X3	T38.3X4	T38.3X5	T38.3X6
Sulforidazine	T43.3X1	T43.3X2	T43.3X3	T43.3X4	T43.3X5	T43.3X6
Sulfoxone	T37.1X1	T37.1X2	T37.1X3	T37.1X4	T37.1X5	T37.1X6
Sulfur, sulfurated, sulfuric, sulfurous, sulfuryl(compounds NEC) (medicinal)	T49.4X1	T49.4X2	T49.4X3	T49.4X4	T49.4X5	T49.4X6
acid	T54.2X1	T54.2X2	T54.2X3	T54.2X4	—	—
dioxide(gas)	T59.1X1	T59.1X2	T59.1X3	T59.1X4	—	—
ether—see Ether(s)						
hydrogen	T59.6X1	T59.6X2	T59.6X3	T59.6X4	—	—
medicinal (keratolytic) (ointment) NEC	T49.4X1	T49.4X2	T49.4X3	T49.4X4	T49.4X5	T49.4X6
ointment	T49.0X1	T49.0X2	T49.0X3	T49.0X4	T49.0X5	T49.0X6
pesticide(vapor)	T60.91	T60.92	T60.93	T60.94	—	—
vapor NEC	T59.891	T59.892	T59.893	T59.894	—	—
Sulfuric acid	T54.2X1	T54.2X2	T54.2X3	T54.2X4	—	—
Sulglicotide	T47.1X1	T47.1X2	T47.1X3	T47.1X4	T47.1X5	T47.1X6
Sulindac	T39.391	T39.392	T39.393	T39.394	T39.395	T39.396
Sulisatin	T47.2X1	T47.2X2	T47.2X3	T47.2X4	T47.2X5	T47.2X6
Sulisobenzone	T49.3X1	T49.3X2	T49.3X3	T49.3X4	T49.3X5	T49.3X6
Sulkowitch's reagent	T50.8X1	T50.8X2	T50.8X3	T50.8X4	T50.8X5	T50.8X6
Sulmetozine	T44.3X1	T44.3X2	T44.3X3	T44.3X4	T44.3X5	T44.3X6
Suloctidil	T46.7X1	T46.7X2	T46.7X3	T46.7X4	T46.7X5	T46.7X6
Sulph-—see also Sulf-						
Sulphadiazine	T37.0X1	T37.0X2	T37.0X3	T37.0X4	T37.0X5	T37.0X6
Sulphadimethoxine	T37.0X1	T37.0X2	T37.0X3	T37.0X4	T37.0X5	T37.0X6
Sulphadimidine	T37.0X1	T37.0X2	T37.0X3	T37.0X4	T37.0X5	T37.0X6

Substance	Poisoning, Accidental (unintentional)	Poisoning, Intentional self-harm	Poisoning, Assault	Poisoning, Undetermined	Adverse effect	Underdosing
Sulphadione	T37.1X1	T37.1X2	T37.1X3	T37.1X4	T37.1X5	T37.
Sulphafurazole	T37.0X1	T37.0X2	T37.0X3	T37.0X4	T37.0X5	T37.
Sulphamethizole	T37.0X1	T37.0X2	T37.0X3	T37.0X4	T37.0X5	T37.
Sulphamethoxazole	T37.0X1	T37.0X2	T37.0X3	T37.0X4	T37.0X5	T37.
Sulphan blue	T50.8X1	T50.8X2	T50.8X3	T50.8X4	T50.8X5	T50.
Sulphaphenazole	T37.0X1	T37.0X2	T37.0X3	T37.0X4	T37.0X5	T37.
Sulphapyridine	T37.0X1	T37.0X2	T37.0X3	T37.0X4	T37.0X5	T37.
Sulphasalazine	T37.0X1	T37.0X2	T37.0X3	T37.0X4	T37.0X5	T37.
Sulphinpyrazone	T50.4X1	T50.4X2	T50.4X3	T50.4X4	T50.4X5	T50.
Sulpiride	T43.591	T43.592	T43.593	T43.594	T43.595	T43.
Sulprostone	T48.0X1	T48.0X2	T48.0X3	T48.0X4	T48.0X5	T48.
Sulpyrine	T39.2X1	T39.2X2	T39.2X3	T39.2X4	T39.2X5	T39.
Sultamicillin	T36.0X1	T36.0X2	T36.0X3	T36.0X4	T36.0X5	T36.
Sulthiame	T42.6X1	T42.6X2	T42.6X3	T42.6X4	T42.6X5	T42.
Sultiame	T42.6X1	T42.6X2	T42.6X3	T42.6X4	T42.6X5	T42.
Sultopride	T43.591	T43.592	T43.593	T43.594	T43.595	T43.
Sumatriptan	T39.8X1	T39.8X2	T39.8X3	T39.8X4	T39.8X5	T39.
Sunflower seed oil	T46.6X1	T46.6X2	T46.6X3	T46.6X4	T46.6X5	T46.
Superinone	T48.4X1	T48.4X2	T48.4X3	T48.4X4	T48.4X5	T48.
Suprofen	T39.311	T39.312	T39.313	T39.314	T39.315	T39.
Suramin(sodium)	T37.4X1	T37.4X2	T37.4X3	T37.4X4	T37.4X5	T37.
Surfacaine	T41.3X1	T41.3X2	T41.3X3	T41.3X4	T41.3X5	T41.
Surital	T41.1X1	T41.1X2	T41.1X3	T41.1X4	T41.1X5	T41.
Sutilains	T45.3X1	T45.3X2	T45.3X3	T45.3X4	T45.3X5	T45.
Suxamethonium (chloride)	T48.1X1	T48.1X2	T48.1X3	T48.1X4	T48.1X5	T48.
Suxethonium (chloride)	T48.1X1	T48.1X2	T48.1X3	T48.1X4	T48.1X5	T48.
Suxibuzone	T39.2X1	T39.2X2	T39.2X3	T39.2X4	T39.2X5	T39.
Sweet niter spirit	T46.3X1	T46.3X2	T46.3X3	T46.3X4	T46.3X5	T46.
Sweet oil(birch)	T49.3X1	T49.3X2	T49.3X3	T49.3X4	T49.3X5	T49.
Sweetener	T50.901	T50.902	T50.903	T50.904	T50.905	T50.
Sym-dichloroethyl ether	T53.6X1	T53.6X2	T53.6X3	T53.6X4	—	—
Sympatholytic NEC	T44.8X1	T44.8X2	T44.8X3	T44.8X4	T44.8X5	T44.
haloalkylamine	T44.8X1	T44.8X2	T44.8X3	T44.8X4	T44.8X5	T44.
Sympathomimetic NEC	T44.901	T44.902	T44.903	T44.904	T44.905	T44.
anti-common-cold	T48.5X1	T48.5X2	T48.5X3	T48.5X4	T48.5X5	T48.
bronchodilator	T48.6X1	T48.6X2	T48.6X3	T48.6X4	T48.6X5	T48.
specified NEC	T44.991	T44.992	T44.993	T44.994	T44.995	T44.
Synagis	T50.B91	T50.B92	T50.B93	T50.B94	T50.B95	T50.
Synalar	T49.0X1	T49.0X2	T49.0X3	T49.0X4	T49.0X5	T49.
Synthroid	T38.1X1	T38.1X2	T38.1X3	T38.1X4	T38.1X5	T38.
Syntocinon	T48.0X1	T48.0X2	T48.0X3	T48.0X4	T48.0X5	T48.
Syrosingopine	T46.5X1	T46.5X2	T46.5X3	T46.5X4	T46.5X5	T46.
Systemic drug	T45.91	T45.92	T45.93	T45.94	T45.95	T45
specified NEC	T45.8X1	T45.8X2	T45.8X3	T45.8X4	T45.8X5	T45.
2,4,5-T	T60.3X1	T60.3X2	T60.3X3	T60.3X4	—	—
T						
Tablets—see also specified substance	T50.901	T50.902	T50.903	T50.904	T50.905	T50.
Tace	T38.5X1	T38.5X2	T38.5X3	T38.5X4	T38.5X5	T38.
Tacrine	T44.0X1	T44.0X2	T44.0X3	T44.0X4	T44.0X5	T44.

Substance	Poisoning, Accidental (unintentional)	Poisoning, Intentional self-harm	Poisoning, Assault	Poisoning, Undetermined	Adverse effect	Underdosing
adalafil	T46.7X1	T46.7X2	T46.7X3	T46.7X4	T46.7X5	T46.7X6
alampicillin	T36.0X1	T36.0X2	T36.0X3	T36.0X4	T36.0X5	T36.0X6
albutal	T42.3X1	T42.3X2	T42.3X3	T42.3X4	T42.3X5	T42.3X6
alc powder	T49.3X1	T49.3X2	T49.3X3	T49.3X4	T49.3X5	T49.3X6
alcum	T49.3X1	T49.3X2	T49.3X3	T49.3X4	T49.3X5	T49.3X6
aleranol	T38.6X1	T38.6X2	T38.6X3	T38.6X4	T38.6X5	T38.6X6
amoxifen	T38.6X1	T38.6X2	T38.6X3	T38.6X4	T38.6X5	T38.6X6
amsulosin	T44.6X1	T44.6X2	T44.6X3	T44.6X4	T44.6X5	T44.6X6
andearil, tanderil	T39.2X1	T39.2X2	T39.2X3	T39.2X4	T39.2X5	T39.2X6
annic acid	T49.2X1	T49.2X2	T49.2X3	T49.2X4	T49.2X5	T49.2X6
medicinal (astringent)	T49.2X1	T49.2X2	T49.2X3	T49.2X4	T49.2X5	T49.2X6
annin—see Tannic acid						
ansy	T62.2X1	T62.2X2	T62.2X3	T62.2X4	—	—
AO	T36.3X1	T36.3X2	T36.3X3	T36.3X4	T36.3X5	T36.3X6
apazole	T38.2X1	T38.2X2	T38.2X3	T38.2X4	T38.2X5	T38.2X6
ar NEC	T52.0X1	T52.0X2	T52.0X3	T52.0X4	—	—
camphor	T60.1X1	T60.1X2	T60.1X3	T60.1X4	—	—
distillate	T49.1X1	T49.1X2	T49.1X3	T49.1X4	T49.1X5	T49.1X6
fumes	T59.891	T59.892	T59.893	T59.894	—	—
medicinal	T49.1X1	T49.1X2	T49.1X3	T49.1X4	T49.1X5	T49.1X6
ointment	T49.1X1	T49.1X2	T49.1X3	T49.1X4	T49.1X5	T49.1X6
aractan	T43.591	T43.592	T43.593	T43.594	T43.595	T43.596
arantula(venomous)	T63.321	T63.322	T63.323	T63.324	—	—
artar emetic	T37.8X1	T37.8X2	T37.8X3	T37.8X4	T37.8X5	T37.8X6
artaric acid	T65.891	T65.892	T65.893	T65.894	—	—
artrate, laxative	T47.4X1	T47.4X2	T47.4X3	T47.4X4	T47.4X5	T47.4X6
artrated antimony(anti-nfective)	T37.8X1	T37.8X2	T37.8X3	T37.8X4	T37.8X5	T37.8X6
auromustine	T45.1X1	T45.1X2	T45.1X3	T45.1X4	T45.1X5	T45.1X6
CA—see Trichloroacetic cid						
CDD	T53.7X1	T53.7X2	T53.7X3	T53.7X4	—	—
DI(vapor)	T65.0X1	T65.0X2	T65.0X3	T65.0X4	—	—
ear						
gas	T59.3X1	T59.3X2	T59.3X3	T59.3X4	—	—
solution	T49.5X1	T49.5X2	T49.5X3	T49.5X4	T49.5X5	T49.5X6
eclothiazide	T50.2X1	T50.2X2	T50.2X3	T50.2X4	T50.2X5	T50.2X6
eclozan	T37.3X1	T37.3X2	T37.3X3	T37.3X4	T37.3X5	T37.3X6
egafur	T45.1X1	T45.1X2	T45.1X3	T45.1X4	T45.1X5	T45.1X6
egretol	T42.1X1	T42.1X2	T42.1X3	T42.1X4	T42.1X5	T42.1X6
eicoplanin	T36.8X1	T36.8X2	T36.8X3	T36.8X4	T36.8X5	T36.8X6
elepaque	T50.8X1	T50.8X2	T50.8X3	T50.8X4	T50.8X5	T50.8X6
ellurium	T56.891	T56.892	T56.893	T56.894	—	—
fumes	T56.891	T56.892	T56.893	T56.894	—	—
EM	T45.1X1	T45.1X2	T45.1X3	T45.1X4	T45.1X5	T45.1X6
emazepam	T42.4X1	T42.4X2	T42.4X3	T42.4X4	T42.4X5	T42.4X6
emocillin	T36.0X1	T36.0X2	T36.0X3	T36.0X4	T36.0X5	T36.0X6
enamfetamine	T43.621	T43.622	T43.623	T43.624	T43.625	T43.626
eniposide	T45.1X1	T45.1X2	T45.1X3	T45.1X4	T45.1X5	T45.1X6
enitramine	T46.3X1	T46.3X2	T46.3X3	T46.3X4	T46.3X5	T46.3X6
Tenoglicin	T48.4X1	T48.4X2	T48.4X3	T48.4X4	T48.4X5	T48.4X6
Tenonitrozole	T37.3X1	T37.3X2	T37.3X3	T37.3X4	T37.3X5	T37.3X6

Substance	Poisoning, Accidental (unintentional)	Poisoning, Intentional self-harm	Poisoning, Assault	Poisoning, Undetermined	Adverse effect	Underdosing
Tenoxicam	T39.391	T39.392	T39.393	T39.394	T39.395	T39.396
TEPA	T45.1X1	T45.1X2	T45.1X3	T45.1X4	T45.1X5	T45.1X6
TEPP	T60.0X1	T60.0X2	T60.0X3	T60.0X4	—	—
Teprotide	T46.5X1	T46.5X2	T46.5X3	T46.5X4	T46.5X5	T46.5X6
Terazosin	T44.6X1	T44.6X2	T44.6X3	T44.6X4	T44.6X5	T44.6X6
Terbufos	T60.0X1	T60.0X2	T60.0X3	T60.0X4	—	—
Terbutaline	T48.6X1	T48.6X2	T48.6X3	T48.6X4	T48.6X5	T48.6X6
Terconazole	T49.0X1	T49.0X2	T49.0X3	T49.0X4	T49.0X5	T49.0X6
Terfenadine	T45.0X1	T45.0X2	T45.0X3	T45.0X4	T45.0X5	T45.0X6
Teriparatide (acetate)	T50.991	T50.992	T50.993	T50.994	T50.995	T50.996
Terizidone	T37.1X1	T37.1X2	T37.1X3	T37.1X4	T37.1X5	T37.1X6
Terlipressin	T38.891	T38.892	T38.893	T38.894	T38.895	T38.896
Terodiline	T46.3X1	T46.3X2	T46.3X3	T46.3X4	T46.3X5	T46.3X6
Teroxalene	T37.4X1	T37.4X2	T37.4X3	T37.4X4	T37.4X5	T37.4X6
Terpin(cis) hydrate	T48.4X1	T48.4X2	T48.4X3	T48.4X4	T48.4X5	T48.4X6
Terramycin	T36.4X1	T36.4X2	T36.4X3	T36.4X4	T36.4X5	T36.4X6
Tertatolol	T44.7X1	T44.7X2	T44.7X3	T44.7X4	T44.7X5	T44.7X6
Tessalon	T48.3X1	T48.3X2	T48.3X3	T48.3X4	T48.3X5	T48.3X6
Testolactone	T38.7X1	T38.7X2	T38.7X3	T38.7X4	T38.7X5	T38.7X6
Testosterone	T38.7X1	T38.7X2	T38.7X3	T38.7X4	T38.7X5	T38.7X6
Tetanus toxoid or vaccine	T50.A91	T50.A92	T50.A93	T50.A94	T50.A95	T50.A96
antitoxin	T50.Z11	T50.Z12	T50.Z13	T50.Z14	T50.Z15	T50.Z16
immune globulin (human)	T50.Z11	T50.Z12	T50.Z13	T50.Z14	T50.Z15	T50.Z16
toxoid	T50.A91	T50.A92	T50.A93	T50.A94	T50.A95	T50.A96
with diphtheria toxoid	T50.A21	T50.A22	T50.A23	T50.A24	T50.A25	T50.A26
with pertussis	T50.A11	T50.A12	T50.A13	T50.A14	T50.A15	T50.A16
Tetrabenazine	T43.591	T43.592	T43.593	T43.594	T43.595	T43.596
Tetracaine	T41.3X1	T41.3X2	T41.3X3	T41.3X4	T41.3X5	T41.3X6
nerve block(peripheral) (plexus)	T41.3X1	T41.3X2	T41.3X3	T41.3X4	T41.3X5	T41.3X6
regional	T41.3X1	T41.3X2	T41.3X3	T41.3X4	T41.3X5	T41.3X6
spinal	T41.3X1	T41.3X2	T41.3X3	T41.3X4	T41.3X5	T41.3X6
Tetrachlorethylene—see Tetrachloroethylene						
Tetrachlormethiazide	T50.2X1	T50.2X2	T50.2X3	T50.2X4	T50.2X5	T50.2X6
2,3,7,8-Tetrachlorodi-benzo-p-dioxin	T53.7X1	T53.7X2	T53.7X3	T53.7X4	—	—
Tetrachloroethane	T53.6X1	T53.6X2	T53.6X3	T53.6X4	—	—
vapor	T53.6X1	T53.6X2	T53.6X3	T53.6X4	—	—
paint or varnish	T53.6X1	T53.6X2	T53.6X3	T53.6X4	—	—
Tetrachloroethylene (liquid)	T53.3X1	T53.3X2	T53.3X3	T53.3X4	—	—
medicinal	T37.4X1	T37.4X2	T37.4X3	T37.4X4	T37.4X5	T37.4X6
vapor	T53.3X1	T53.3X2	T53.3X3	T53.3X4	—	—
Tetrachloromethane—see Carbon tetrachloride						
Tetracosactide	T38.811	T38.812	T38.813	T38.814	T38.815	T38.816
Tetracosactrin	T38.811	T38.812	T38.813	T38.814	T38.815	T38.816
Tetracycline	T36.4X1	T36.4X2	T36.4X3	T36.4X4	T36.4X5	T36.4X6
ophthalmic preparation	T49.5X1	T49.5X2	T49.5X3	T49.5X4	T49.5X5	T49.5X6
topical NEC	T49.0X1	T49.0X2	T49.0X3	T49.0X4	T49.0X5	T49.0X6

Substance	Poisoning, Accidental (unintentional)	Poisoning, Intentional self-harm	Poisoning, Assault	Poisoning, Undetermined	Adverse effect	Underdosing
Tetradifon	T60.8X1	T60.8X2	T60.8X3	T60.8X4	—	—
Tetradotoxin	T61.771	T61.772	T61.773	T61.774	—	—
Tetraethyl						
lead	T56.0X1	T56.0X2	T56.0X3	T56.0X4	—	—
pyrophosphate	T60.0X1	T60.0X2	T60.0X3	T60.0X4	—	—
Tetraethylammonium chloride	T44.2X1	T44.2X2	T44.2X3	T44.2X4	T44.2X5	T44.2X6
Tetraethylthiuram disulfide	T50.6X1	T50.6X2	T50.6X3	T50.6X4	T50.6X5	T50.6X6
Tetrahydroamino-acridine	T44.0X1	T44.0X2	T44.0X3	T44.0X4	T44.0X5	T44.0X6
Tetrahydrocannabinol	T40.7X1	T40.7X2	T40.7X3	T40.7X4	T40.7X5	T40.7X6
Tetrahydrofuran	T52.8X1	T52.8X2	T52.8X3	T52.8X4	—	—
Tetrahydronaphthalene	T52.8X1	T52.8X2	T52.8X3	T52.8X4	—	—
Tetrahydrozoline	T49.5X1	T49.5X2	T49.5X3	T49.5X4	T49.5X5	T49.5X6
Tetralin	T52.8X1	T52.8X2	T52.8X3	T52.8X4	—	—
Tetramethrin	T60.2X1	T60.2X2	T60.2X3	T60.2X4	—	—
Tetramethylthiuram (disulfide) NEC	T60.3X1	T60.3X2	T60.3X3	T60.3X4	—	—
medicinal	T49.0X1	T49.0X2	T49.0X3	T49.0X4	T49.0X5	T49.0X6
Tetramisole	T37.4X1	T37.4X2	T37.4X3	T37.4X4	T37.4X5	T37.4X6
Tetranicotinoyl fructose	T46.7X1	T46.7X2	T46.7X3	T46.7X4	T46.7X5	T46.7X6
Tetrazepam	T42.4X1	T42.4X2	T42.4X3	T42.4X4	T42.4X5	T42.4X6
Tetronal	T42.6X1	T42.6X2	T42.6X3	T42.6X4	T42.6X5	T42.6X6
Tetryl	T65.3X1	T65.3X2	T65.3X3	T65.3X4	—	—
Tetrylammonium chloride	T44.2X1	T44.2X2	T44.2X3	T44.2X4	T44.2X5	T44.2X6
Tetryzoline	T49.5X1	T49.5X2	T49.5X3	T49.5X4	T49.5X5	T49.5X6
Thalidomide	T45.1X1	T45.1X2	T45.1X3	T45.1X4	T45.1X5	T45.1X6
Thallium (compounds) (dust) NEC	T56.811	T56.812	T56.813	T56.814	—	—
pesticide	T60.4X1	T60.4X2	T60.4X3	T60.4X4	—	—
THC	T40.7X1	T40.7X2	T40.7X3	T40.7X4	T40.7X5	T40.7X6
Thebacon	T48.3X1	T48.3X2	T48.3X3	T48.3X4	T48.3X5	T48.3X6
Thebaine	T40.2X1	T40.2X2	T40.2X3	T40.2X4	T40.2X5	T40.2X6
Thenoic acid	T49.6X1	T49.6X2	T49.6X3	T49.6X4	T49.6X5	T49.6X6
Thenyldiamine	T45.0X1	T45.0X2	T45.0X3	T45.0X4	T45.0X5	T45.0X6
Theobromine (calcium salicylate)	T48.6X1	T48.6X2	T48.6X3	T48.6X4	T48.6X5	T48.6X6
sodium salicylate	T48.6X1	T48.6X2	T48.6X3	T48.6X4	T48.6X5	T48.6X6
Theophyllamine	T48.6X1	T48.6X2	T48.6X3	T48.6X4	T48.6X5	T48.6X6
Theophylline	T48.6X1	T48.6X2	T48.6X3	T48.6X4	T48.6X5	T48.6X6
aminobenzoic acid	T48.6X1	T48.6X2	T48.6X3	T48.6X4	T48.6X5	T48.6X6
ethylenediamine	T48.6X1	T48.6X2	T48.6X3	T48.6X4	T48.6X5	T48.6X6
piperazine p-amino-benzoate	T48.6X1	T48.6X2	T48.6X3	T48.6X4	T48.6X5	T48.6X6
Thiabendazole	T37.4X1	T37.4X2	T37.4X3	T37.4X4	T37.4X5	T37.4X6
Thialbarbital	T41.1X1	T41.1X2	T41.1X3	T41.1X4	T41.1X5	T41.1X6
Thiamazole	T38.2X1	T38.2X2	T38.2X3	T38.2X4	T38.2X5	T38.2X6
Thiambutosine	T37.1X1	T37.1X2	T37.1X3	T37.1X4	T37.1X5	T37.1X6
Thiamine	T45.2X1	T45.2X2	T45.2X3	T45.2X4	T45.2X5	T45.2X6
Thiamphenicol	T36.2X1	T36.2X2	T36.2X3	T36.2X4	T36.2X5	T36.2X6
Thiamylal	T41.1X1	T41.1X2	T41.1X3	T41.1X4	T41.1X5	T41.1X6
sodium	T41.1X1	T41.1X2	T41.1X3	T41.1X4	T41.1X5	T41.1X6

Substance	Poisoning, Accidental (unintentional)	Poisoning, Intentional self-harm	Poisoning, Assault	Poisoning, Undetermined	Adverse effect	Underdosing
Thiazesim	T43.291	T43.292	T43.293	T43.294	T43.295	T43.29
Thiazides(diuretics)	T50.2X1	T50.2X2	T50.2X3	T50.2X4	T50.2X5	T50.2X
Thiazinamium metilsulfate	T43.3X1	T43.3X2	T43.3X3	T43.3X4	T43.3X5	T43.3X
Thiethylperazine	T43.3X1	T43.3X2	T43.3X3	T43.3X4	T43.3X5	T43.3X
Thimerosal	T49.0X1	T49.0X2	T49.0X3	T49.0X4	T49.0X5	T49.0X
ophthalmic preparation	T49.5X1	T49.5X2	T49.5X3	T49.5X4	T49.5X5	T49.5X
Thioacetazone	T37.1X1	T37.1X2	T37.1X3	T37.1X4	T37.1X5	T37.1X
with isoniazid	T37.1X1	T37.1X2	T37.1X3	T37.1X4	T37.1X5	T37.1X
Thiobarbital sodium	T41.1X1	T41.1X2	T41.1X3	T41.1X4	T41.1X5	T41.1X
Thiobarbiturate anesthetic	T41.1X1	T41.1X2	T41.1X3	T41.1X4	T41.1X5	T41.1X
Thiobismol	T37.8X1	T37.8X2	T37.8X3	T37.8X4	T37.8X5	T37.8X
Thiobutabarbital sodium	T41.1X1	T41.1X2	T41.1X3	T41.1X4	T41.1X5	T41.1X
Thiocarbamate (insecticide)	T60.0X1	T60.0X2	T60.0X3	T60.0X4	—	—
Thiocarbamide	T38.2X1	T38.2X2	T38.2X3	T38.2X4	T38.2X5	T38.2X
Thiocarbarsone	T37.8X1	T37.8X2	T37.8X3	T37.8X4	T37.8X5	T37.8X
Thiocarlide	T37.1X1	T37.1X2	T37.1X3	T37.1X4	T37.1X5	T37.1X
Thioctamide	T50.991	T50.992	T50.993	T50.994	T50.995	T50.99
Thioctic acid	T50.991	T50.992	T50.993	T50.994	T50.995	T50.99
Thiofos	T60.0X1	T60.0X2	T60.0X3	T60.0X4	—	—
Thioglycolate	T49.4X1	T49.4X2	T49.4X3	T49.4X4	T49.4X5	T49.4X
Thioglycolic acid	T65.891	T65.892	T65.893	T65.894	—	—
Thioguanine	T45.1X1	T45.1X2	T45.1X3	T45.1X4	T45.1X5	T45.1X
Thiomercaptomerin	T50.2X1	T50.2X2	T50.2X3	T50.2X4	T50.2X5	T50.2X
Thiomerin	T50.2X1	T50.2X2	T50.2X3	T50.2X4	T50.2X5	T50.2X
Thiomersal	T49.0X1	T49.0X2	T49.0X3	T49.0X4	T49.0X5	T49.0X
Thionazin	T60.0X1	T60.0X2	T60.0X3	T60.0X4	—	—
Thiopental(sodium)	T41.1X1	T41.1X2	T41.1X3	T41.1X4	T41.1X5	T41.1X
Thiopentone(sodium)	T41.1X1	T41.1X2	T41.1X3	T41.1X4	T41.1X5	T41.1X
Thiopropazate	T43.3X1	T43.3X2	T43.3X3	T43.3X4	T43.3X5	T43.3X
Thioproperazine	T43.3X1	T43.3X2	T43.3X3	T43.3X4	T43.3X5	T43.3X
Thioridazine	T43.3X1	T43.3X2	T43.3X3	T43.3X4	T43.3X5	T43.3X
Thiosinamine	T49.3X1	T49.3X2	T49.3X3	T49.3X4	T49.3X5	T49.3X
Thiotepa	T45.1X1	T45.1X2	T45.1X3	T45.1X4	T45.1X5	T45.1X
Thiothixene	T43.4X1	T43.4X2	T43.4X3	T43.4X4	T43.4X5	T43.4X
Thiouracil(benzyl) (methyl) (propyl)	T38.2X1	T38.2X2	T38.2X3	T38.2X4	T38.2X5	T38.2X
Thiourea	T38.2X1	T38.2X2	T38.2X3	T38.2X4	T38.2X5	T38.2X
Thiphenamil	T44.3X1	T44.3X2	T44.3X3	T44.3X4	T44.3X5	T44.3X
Thiram	T60.3X1	T60.3X2	T60.3X3	T60.3X4	—	—
medicinal	T49.2X1	T49.2X2	T49.2X3	T49.2X4	T49.2X5	T49.2X
Thonzylamine (systemic)	T45.0X1	T45.0X2	T45.0X3	T45.0X4	T45.0X5	T45.0X
mucosal decongestant	T48.5X1	T48.5X2	T48.5X3	T48.5X4	T48.5X5	T48.5X
Thorazine	T43.3X1	T43.3X2	T43.3X3	T43.3X4	T43.3X5	T43.3X
Thorium dioxide suspension	T50.8X1	T50.8X2	T50.8X3	T50.8X4	T50.8X5	T50.8X
Thornapple	T62.2X1	T62.2X2	T62.2X3	T62.2X4	—	—
Throat drug NEC	T49.6X1	T49.6X2	T49.6X3	T49.6X4	T49.6X5	T49.6X
Thrombin	T45.7X1	T45.7X2	T45.7X3	T45.7X4	T45.7X5	T45.7X
Thrombolysin	T45.611	T45.612	T45.613	T45.614	T45.615	T45.61
Thromboplastin	T45.7X1	T45.7X2	T45.7X3	T45.7X4	T45.7X5	T45.7X

Substance	Poisoning, Accidental (unintentional)	Poisoning, Intentional self-harm	Poisoning, Assault	Poisoning, Undetermined	Adverse effect	Underdosing
urfyl nicotinate	T46.7X1	T46.7X2	T46.7X3	T46.7X4	T46.7X5	T46.7X6
ymol	T49.0X1	T49.0X2	T49.0X3	T49.0X4	T49.0X5	T49.0X6
ymopentin	T37.5X1	T37.5X2	T37.5X3	T37.5X4	T37.5X5	T37.5X6
ymoxamine	T46.7X1	T46.7X2	T46.7X3	T46.7X4	T46.7X5	T46.7X6
ymus extract	T38.891	T38.892	T38.893	T38.894	T38.895	T38.896
yreotrophic hormone	T38.811	T38.812	T38.813	T38.814	T38.815	T38.816
yroglobulin	T38.1X1	T38.1X2	T38.1X3	T38.1X4	T38.1X5	T38.1X6
yroid(hormone)	T38.1X1	T38.1X2	T38.1X3	T38.1X4	T38.1X5	T38.1X6
yrolar	T38.1X1	T38.1X2	T38.1X3	T38.1X4	T38.1X5	T38.1X6
yrotrophin	T38.811	T38.812	T38.813	T38.814	T38.815	T38.816
yrotropic hormone	T38.811	T38.812	T38.813	T38.814	T38.815	T38.816
yroxine	T38.1X1	T38.1X2	T38.1X3	T38.1X4	T38.1X5	T38.1X6
abendazole	T37.4X1	T37.4X2	T37.4X3	T37.4X4	T37.4X5	T37.4X6
amizide	T50.2X1	T50.2X2	T50.2X3	T50.2X4	T50.2X5	T50.2X6
aneptine	T43.291	T43.292	T43.293	T43.294	T43.295	T43.296
apamil	T46.1X1	T46.1X2	T46.1X3	T46.1X4	T46.1X5	T46.1X6
apride	T43.591	T43.592	T43.593	T43.594	T43.595	T43.596
aprofenic acid	T39.311	T39.312	T39.313	T39.314	T39.315	T39.316
aramide	T39.8X1	T39.8X2	T39.8X3	T39.8X4	T39.8X5	T39.8X6
carcillin	T36.0X1	T36.0X2	T36.0X3	T36.0X4	T36.0X5	T36.0X6
clatone	T49.0X1	T49.0X2	T49.0X3	T49.0X4	T49.0X5	T49.0X6
clopidine	T45.521	T45.522	T45.523	T45.524	T45.525	T45.526
crynafen	T50.1X1	T50.1X2	T50.1X3	T50.1X4	T50.1X5	T50.1X6
diacic	T50.991	T50.992	T50.993	T50.994	T50.995	T50.996
emonium	T44.3X1	T44.3X2	T44.3X3	T44.3X4	T44.3X5	T44.3X6
odide	T44.3X1	T44.3X2	T44.3X3	T44.3X4	T44.3X5	T44.3X6
enilic acid	T50.1X1	T50.1X2	T50.1X3	T50.1X4	T50.1X5	T50.1X6
fenamil	T44.3X1	T44.3X2	T44.3X3	T44.3X4	T44.3X5	T44.3X6
gan	T45.0X1	T45.0X2	T45.0X3	T45.0X4	T45.0X5	T45.0X6
gloidine	T44.3X1	T44.3X2	T44.3X3	T44.3X4	T44.3X5	T44.3X6
lactase	T47.5X1	T47.5X2	T47.5X3	T47.5X4	T47.5X5	T47.5X6
letamine	T41.291	T41.292	T41.293	T41.294	T41.295	T41.296
lidine	T40.4X1	T40.4X2	T40.4X3	T40.4X4	—	—
mepidium bromide	T44.3X1	T44.3X2	T44.3X3	T44.3X4	T44.3X5	T44.3X6
miperone	T43.4X1	T43.4X2	T43.4X3	T43.4X4	T43.4X5	T43.4X6
molol	T44.7X1	T44.7X2	T44.7X3	T44.7X4	T44.7X5	T44.7X6
n(chloride) (dust) xide) NEC	T56.6X1	T56.6X2	T56.6X3	T56.6X4	—	—
anti-infectives	T37.8X1	T37.8X2	T37.8X3	T37.8X4	T37.8X5	T37.8X6
ncture, iodine—see dine						
ndal	T43.3X1	T43.3X2	T43.3X3	T43.3X4	T43.3X5	T43.3X6
nidazole	T37.3X1	T37.3X2	T37.3X3	T37.3X4	T37.3X5	T37.3X6
noridine	T39.8X1	T39.8X2	T39.8X3	T39.8X4	T39.8X5	T39.8X6
ocarlide	T37.1X1	T37.1X2	T37.1X3	T37.1X4	T37.1X5	T37.1X6
oclomarol	T45.511	T45.512	T45.513	T45.514	T45.515	T45.516
oconazole	T49.0X1	T49.0X2	T49.0X3	T49.0X4	T49.0X5	T49.0X6
oguanine	T45.1X1	T45.1X2	T45.1X3	T45.1X4	T45.1X5	T45.1X6
opronin	T50.991	T50.992	T50.993	T50.994	T50.995	T50.996
otixene	T43.4X1	T43.4X2	T43.4X3	T43.4X4	T43.4X5	T43.4X6
oxolone	T49.4X1	T49.4X2	T49.4X3	T49.4X4	T49.4X5	T49.4X6

Substance	Poisoning, Accidental (unintentional)	Poisoning, Intentional self-harm	Poisoning, Assault	Poisoning, Undetermined	Adverse effect	Underdosing
Tipepidine	T48.3X1	T48.3X2	T48.3X3	T48.3X4	T48.3X5	T48.3X6
Tiquizium bromide	T44.3X1	T44.3X2	T44.3X3	T44.3X4	T44.3X5	T44.3X6
Tiratricol	T38.1X1	T38.1X2	T38.1X3	T38.1X4	T38.1X5	T38.1X6
Tisopurine	T50.4X1	T50.4X2	T50.4X3	T50.4X4	T50.4X5	T50.4X6
Titanium (compounds) (vapor)	T56.891	T56.892	T56.893	T56.894	—	—
dioxide	T49.3X1	T49.3X2	T49.3X3	T49.3X4	T49.3X5	T49.3X6
ointment	T49.3X1	T49.3X2	T49.3X3	T49.3X4	T49.3X5	T49.3X6
oxide	T49.3X1	T49.3X2	T49.3X3	T49.3X4	T49.3X5	T49.3X6
tetrachloride	T56.891	T56.892	T56.893	T56.894	—	—
Titanocene	T56.891	T56.892	T56.893	T56.894	—	—
Titroid	T38.1X1	T38.1X2	T38.1X3	T38.1X4	T38.1X5	T38.1X6
Tizanidine	T42.8X1	T42.8X2	T42.8X3	T42.8X4	T42.8X5	T42.8X6
TMTD	T60.3X1	T60.3X2	T60.3X3	T60.3X4	—	—
TNT(fumes)	T65.3X1	T65.3X2	T65.3X3	T65.3X4	—	—
Toadstool	T62.0X1	T62.0X2	T62.0X3	T62.0X4	—	—
Tobacco NEC	T65.291	T65.292	T65.293	T65.294	—	—
cigarettes	T65.221	T65.222	T65.223	T65.224	—	—
Indian	T62.2X1	T62.2X2	T62.2X3	T62.2X4	—	—
smoke, second-hand	T65.221	T65.222	T65.223	T65.224	—	—
Tobramycin	T36.5X1	T36.5X2	T36.5X3	T36.5X4	T36.5X5	T36.5X6
Tocainide	T46.2X1	T46.2X2	T46.2X3	T46.2X4	T46.2X5	T46.2X6
Tocoferol	T45.2X1	T45.2X2	T45.2X3	T45.2X4	T45.2X5	T45.2X6
Tocopherol	T45.2X1	T45.2X2	T45.2X3	T45.2X4	T45.2X5	T45.2X6
acetate	T45.2X1	T45.2X2	T45.2X3	T45.2X4	T45.2X5	T45.2X6
Tocosamine	T48.0X1	T48.0X2	T48.0X3	T48.0X4	T48.0X5	T48.0X6
Todralazine	T46.5X1	T46.5X2	T46.5X3	T46.5X4	T46.5X5	T46.5X6
Tofisopam	T42.4X1	T42.4X2	T42.4X3	T42.4X4	T42.4X5	T42.4X6
Tofranil	T43.011	T43.012	T43.013	T43.014	T43.015	T43.016
Toilet deodorizer	T65.891	T65.892	T65.893	T65.894	—	—
Tolamolol	T44.7X1	T44.7X2	T44.7X3	T44.7X4	T44.7X5	T44.7X6
Tolazamide	T38.3X1	T38.3X2	T38.3X3	T38.3X4	T38.3X5	T38.3X6
Tolazoline	T46.7X1	T46.7X2	T46.7X3	T46.7X4	T46.7X5	T46.7X6
Tolbutamide(sodium)	T38.3X1	T38.3X2	T38.3X3	T38.3X4	T38.3X5	T38.3X6
Tolciclate	T49.0X1	T49.0X2	T49.0X3	T49.0X4	T49.0X5	T49.0X6
Tolmetin	T39.391	T39.392	T39.393	T39.394	T39.395	T39.396
Tolnaftate	T49.0X1	T49.0X2	T49.0X3	T49.0X4	T49.0X5	T49.0X6
Tolonidine	T46.5X1	T46.5X2	T46.5X3	T46.5X4	T46.5X5	T46.5X6
Toloxatone	T42.6X1	T42.6X2	T42.6X3	T42.6X4	T42.6X5	T42.6X6
Tolperisone	T44.3X1	T44.3X2	T44.3X3	T44.3X4	T44.3X5	T44.3X6
Tolserol	T42.8X1	T42.8X2	T42.8X3	T42.8X4	T42.8X5	T42.8X6
Toluene(liquid)	T52.2X1	T52.2X2	T52.2X3	T52.2X4	—	—
diisocyanate	T65.0X1	T65.0X2	T65.0X3	T65.0X4	—	—
Toluidine	T65.891	T65.892	T65.893	T65.894	—	—
vapor	T59.891	T59.892	T59.893	T59.894	—	—
Toluol(liquid)	T52.2X1	T52.2X2	T52.2X3	T52.2X4	—	—
vapor	T52.2X1	T52.2X2	T52.2X3	T52.2X4	—	—
Toluylenediamine	T65.3X1	T65.3X2	T65.3X3	T65.3X4	—	—
Tolylene-2,4-diisocyanate	T65.0X1	T65.0X2	T65.0X3	T65.0X4	—	—
Tonic NEC	T50.901	T50.902	T50.903	T50.904	T50.905	T50.906

Substance	Poisoning, Accidental (unintentional)	Poisoning, Intentional self-harm	Poisoning, Assault	Poisoning, Undetermined	Adverse effect	Underdosing
Topical action drug NEC	T49.91	T49.92	T49.93	T49.94	T49.95	T49.96
ear, nose or throat	T49.6X1	T49.6X2	T49.6X3	T49.6X4	T49.6X5	T49.6X6
eye	T49.5X1	T49.5X2	T49.5X3	T49.5X4	T49.5X5	T49.5X6
skin	T49.91	T49.92	T49.93	T49.94	T49.95	T49.96
specified NEC	T49.8X1	T49.8X2	T49.8X3	T49.8X4	T49.8X5	T49.8X6
Toquizine	T44.3X1	T44.3X2	T44.3X3	T44.3X4	T44.3X5	T44.3X6
Toremifene	T38.6X1	T38.6X2	T38.6X3	T38.6X4	T38.6X5	T38.6X6
Tosylchloramide sodium	T49.8X1	T49.8X2	T49.8X3	T49.8X4	T49.8X5	T49.8X6
Toxaphene(dust) (spray)	T60.1X1	T60.1X2	T60.1X3	T60.1X4	—	—
Toxin, diphtheria(Schick Test)	T50.8X1	T50.8X2	T50.8X3	T50.8X4	T50.8X5	T50.8X6
Toxoid						
combined	T50.A21	T50.A22	T50.A23	T50.A24	T50.A25	T50.A26
diphtheria	T50.A91	T50.A92	T50.A93	T50.A94	T50.A95	T50.A96
tetanus	T50.A91	T50.A92	T50.A93	T50.A94	T50.A95	T50.A96
Trace element NEC	T45.8X1	T45.8X2	T45.8X3	T45.8X4	T45.8X5	T45.8X6
Tractor fuel NEC	T52.0X1	T52.0X2	T52.0X3	T52.0X4	—	—
Tragacanth	T50.991	T50.992	T50.993	T50.994	T50.995	T50.996
Tramadol	T40.4X1	T40.4X2	T40.4X3	T40.4X4	T40.4X5	T40.4X6
Tramazoline	T48.5X1	T48.5X2	T48.5X3	T48.5X4	T48.5X5	T48.5X6
Tranexamic acid	T45.621	T45.622	T45.623	T45.624	T45.625	T45.626
Tranilast	T45.0X1	T45.0X2	T45.0X3	T45.0X4	T45.0X5	T45.0X6
Tranquilizer NEC	T43.501	T43.502	T43.503	T43.504	T43.505	T43.506
with hypnotic or sedative	T42.6X1	T42.6X2	T42.6X3	T42.6X4	T42.6X5	T42.6X6
benzodiazepine NEC	T42.4X1	T42.4X2	T42.4X3	T42.4X4	T42.4X5	T42.4X6
butyrophenone NEC	T43.4X1	T43.4X2	T43.4X3	T43.4X4	T43.4X5	T43.4X6
carbamate	T43.591	T43.592	T43.593	T43.594	T43.595	T43.596
dimethylamine	T43.3X1	T43.3X2	T43.3X3	T43.3X4	T43.3X5	T43.3X6
ethylamine	T43.3X1	T43.3X2	T43.3X3	T43.3X4	T43.3X5	T43.3X6
hydroxyzine	T43.591	T43.592	T43.593	T43.594	T43.595	T43.596
major NEC	T43.501	T43.502	T43.503	T43.504	T43.505	T43.506
penothiazine NEC	T43.3X1	T43.3X2	T43.3X3	T43.3X4	T43.3X5	T43.3X6
phenothiazine-based	T43.3X1	T43.3X2	T43.3X3	T43.3X4	T43.3X5	T43.3X6
piperazine NEC	T43.3X1	T43.3X2	T43.3X3	T43.3X4	T43.3X5	T43.3X6
piperidine	T43.3X1	T43.3X2	T43.3X3	T43.3X4	T43.3X5	T43.3X6
propylamine	T43.3X1	T43.3X2	T43.3X3	T43.3X4	T43.3X5	T43.3X6
specified NEC	T43.591	T43.592	T43.593	T43.594	T43.595	T43.596
thioxanthene NEC	T43.591	T43.592	T43.593	T43.594	T43.595	T43.596
Tranxene	T42.4X1	T42.4X2	T42.4X3	T42.4X4	T42.4X5	T42.4X6
Tranylcypromine	T43.1X1	T43.1X2	T43.1X3	T43.1X4	T43.1X5	T43.1X6
Trapidil	T46.3X1	T46.3X2	T46.3X3	T46.3X4	T46.3X5	T46.3X6
Trasentine	T44.3X1	T44.3X2	T44.3X3	T44.3X4	T44.3X5	T44.3X6
Travert	T50.3X1	T50.3X2	T50.3X3	T50.3X4	T50.3X5	T50.3X6
Trazodone	T43.211	T43.212	T43.213	T43.214	T43.215	T43.216
Trecator	T37.1X1	T37.1X2	T37.1X3	T37.1X4	T37.1X5	T37.1X6
Treosulfan	T45.1X1	T45.1X2	T45.1X3	T45.1X4	T45.1X5	T45.1X6
Tretamine	T45.1X1	T45.1X2	T45.1X3	T45.1X4	T45.1X5	T45.1X6
Tretinoin	T49.0X1	T49.0X2	T49.0X3	T49.0X4	T49.0X5	T49.0X6
Tretoquinol	T48.6X1	T48.6X2	T48.6X3	T48.6X4	T48.6X5	T48.6X6

Substance	Poisoning, Accidental (unintentional)	Poisoning, Intentional self-harm	Poisoning, Assault	Poisoning, Undetermined	Adverse effect	Underdosing
Triacetin	T49.0X1	T49.0X2	T49.0X3	T49.0X4	T49.0X5	T49.0X
Triacetoxyanthracene	T49.4X1	T49.4X2	T49.4X3	T49.4X4	T49.4X5	T49.4X
Triacetyloleandomycin	T36.3X1	T36.3X2	T36.3X3	T36.3X4	T36.3X5	T36.3X
Triamcinolone	T49.0X1	T49.0X2	T49.0X3	T49.0X4	T49.0X5	T49.0X
ENT agent	T49.6X1	T49.6X2	T49.6X3	T49.6X4	T49.6X5	T49.6X
hexacetonide	T49.0X1	T49.0X2	T49.0X3	T49.0X4	T49.0X5	T49.0X
ophthalmic preparation	T49.5X1	T49.5X2	T49.5X3	T49.5X4	T49.5X5	T49.5X
topical NEC	T49.0X1	T49.0X2	T49.0X3	T49.0X4	T49.0X5	T49.0X
Triampyzine	T44.3X1	T44.3X2	T44.3X3	T44.3X4	T44.3X5	T44.3X
Triamterene	T50.2X1	T50.2X2	T50.2X3	T50.2X4	T50.2X5	T50.2X
Triazine(herbicide)	T60.3X1	T60.3X2	T60.3X3	T60.3X4	—	—
Triaziquone	T45.1X1	T45.1X2	T45.1X3	T45.1X4	T45.1X5	T45.1X
Triazolam	T42.4X1	T42.4X2	T42.4X3	T42.4X4	T42.4X5	T42.4X
Triazole(herbicide)	T60.3X1	T60.3X2	T60.3X3	T60.3X4	—	—
Tribenoside	T46.991	T46.992	T46.993	T46.994	T46.995	T46.9
Tribromacetaldehyde	T42.6X1	T42.6X2	T42.6X3	T42.6X4	T42.6X5	T42.6X
Tribromoethanol, rectal	T41.291	T41.292	T41.293	T41.294	T41.295	T41.29
Tribromomethane	T42.6X1	T42.6X2	T42.6X3	T42.6X4	T42.6X5	T42.6X
Trichlorethane	T53.2X1	T53.2X2	T53.2X3	T53.2X4	—	—
Trichlorethylene	T53.2X1	T53.2X2	T53.2X3	T53.2X4	—	—
Trichlorfon	T60.0X1	T60.0X2	T60.0X3	T60.0X4	—	—
Trichlormethiazide	T50.2X1	T50.2X2	T50.2X3	T50.2X4	T50.2X5	T50.2X
Trichlormethine	T45.1X1	T45.1X2	T45.1X3	T45.1X4	T45.1X5	T45.1X
Trichloroacetic acid, Trichloracetic acid	T54.2X1	T54.2X2	T54.2X3	T54.2X4	—	—
medicinal	T49.4X1	T49.4X2	T49.4X3	T49.4X4	T49.4X5	T49.4X
Trichloroethane	T53.2X1	T53.2X2	T53.2X3	T53.2X4	—	—
Trichloroethanol	T42.6X1	T42.6X2	T42.6X3	T42.6X4	T42.6X5	T42.6X
Trichloroethyl phosphate	T42.6X1	T42.6X2	T42.6X3	T42.6X4	T42.6X5	T42.6X
Trichloroethylene (liquid) (vapor)	T53.2X1	T53.2X2	T53.2X3	T53.2X4	—	—
anesthetic(gas)	T41.0X1	T41.0X2	T41.0X3	T41.0X4	T41.0X5	T41.0X
vapor NEC	T53.2X1	T53.2X2	T53.2X3	T53.2X4	—	—
Trichlorofluoromethane NEC	T53.5X1	T53.5X2	T53.5X3	T53.5X4	—	—
Trichloronate	T60.0X1	T60.0X2	T60.0X3	T60.0X4	—	—
2,4,5-Trichlorophen-oxyacetic acid	T60.3X1	T60.3X2	T60.3X3	T60.3X4	—	—
Trichloropropane	T53.6X1	T53.6X2	T53.6X3	T53.6X4	—	—
Trichlorotriethylamine	T45.1X1	T45.1X2	T45.1X3	T45.1X4	T45.1X5	T45.1X
Trichomonacides NEC	T37.3X1	T37.3X2	T37.3X3	T37.3X4	T37.3X5	T37.3X
Trichomycin	T36.7X1	T36.7X2	T36.7X3	T36.7X4	T36.7X5	T36.7X
Triclobisonium chloride	T49.0X1	T49.0X2	T49.0X3	T49.0X4	T49.0X5	T49.0X
Triclocarban	T49.0X1	T49.0X2	T49.0X3	T49.0X4	T49.0X5	T49.0X
Triclofos	T42.6X1	T42.6X2	T42.6X3	T42.6X4	T42.6X5	T42.6X
Triclosan	T49.0X1	T49.0X2	T49.0X3	T49.0X4	T49.0X5	T49.0X
Tricresyl phosphate	T65.891	T65.892	T65.893	T65.894	—	—
solvent	T52.91	T52.92	T52.93	T52.94	—	—
Tricyclamol chloride	T44.3X1	T44.3X2	T44.3X3	T44.3X4	T44.3X5	T44.3X
Tridesilon	T49.0X1	T49.0X2	T49.0X3	T49.0X4	T49.0X5	T49.0X
Tridihexethyl iodide	T44.3X1	T44.3X2	T44.3X3	T44.3X4	T44.3X5	T44.3X

Substance	Poisoning, Accidental (unintentional)	Poisoning, Intentional self-harm	Poisoning, Assault	Poisoning, Undetermined	Adverse effect	Underdosing
Tridione	T42.2X1	T42.2X2	T42.2X3	T42.2X4	T42.2X5	T42.2X6
Trientine	T45.8X1	T45.8X2	T45.8X3	T45.8X4	T45.8X5	T45.8X6
Triethanolamine NEC	T54.3X1	T54.3X2	T54.3X3	T54.3X4	—	—
detergent	T54.3X1	T54.3X2	T54.3X3	T54.3X4	—	—
trinitrate (biphosphate)	T46.3X1	T46.3X2	T46.3X3	T46.3X4	T46.3X5	T46.3X6
Triethanomelamine	T45.1X1	T45.1X2	T45.1X3	T45.1X4	T45.1X5	T45.1X6
Triethylenemelamine	T45.1X1	T45.1X2	T45.1X3	T45.1X4	T45.1X5	T45.1X6
Triethylenephos-phoramide	T45.1X1	T45.1X2	T45.1X3	T45.1X4	T45.1X5	T45.1X6
Triethylenethiophos-phoramide	T45.1X1	T45.1X2	T45.1X3	T45.1X4	T45.1X5	T45.1X6
Trifluoperazine	T43.3X1	T43.3X2	T43.3X3	T43.3X4	T43.3X5	T43.3X6
Trifluoroethyl vinyl ether	T41.0X1	T41.0X2	T41.0X3	T41.0X4	T41.0X5	T41.0X6
Trifluperidol	T43.4X1	T43.4X2	T43.4X3	T43.4X4	T43.4X5	T43.4X6
Triflupromazine	T43.3X1	T43.3X2	T43.3X3	T43.3X4	T43.3X5	T43.3X6
Trifluridine	T37.5X1	T37.5X2	T37.5X3	T37.5X4	T37.5X5	T37.5X6
Triflusal	T45.521	T45.522	T45.523	T45.524	T45.525	T45.526
Trihexyphenidyl	T44.3X1	T44.3X2	T44.3X3	T44.3X4	T44.3X5	T44.3X6
Triiodothyronine	T38.1X1	T38.1X2	T38.1X3	T38.1X4	T38.1X5	T38.1X6
Trilene	T41.0X1	T41.0X2	T41.0X3	T41.0X4	T41.0X5	T41.0X6
Trilostane	T38.991	T38.992	T38.993	T38.994	T38.995	T38.996
Trimebutine	T44.3X1	T44.3X2	T44.3X3	T44.3X4	T44.3X5	T44.3X6
Trimecaine	T41.3X1	T41.3X2	T41.3X3	T41.3X4	T41.3X5	T41.3X6
Trimeprazine (tartrate)	T44.3X1	T44.3X2	T44.3X3	T44.3X4	T44.3X5	T44.3X6
Trimetaphan camsilate	T44.2X1	T44.2X2	T44.2X3	T44.2X4	T44.2X5	T44.2X6
Trimetazidine	T46.7X1	T46.7X2	T46.7X3	T46.7X4	T46.7X5	T46.7X6
Trimethadione	T42.2X1	T42.2X2	T42.2X3	T42.2X4	T42.2X5	T42.2X6
Trimethaphan	T44.2X1	T44.2X2	T44.2X3	T44.2X4	T44.2X5	T44.2X6
Trimethidinium	T44.2X1	T44.2X2	T44.2X3	T44.2X4	T44.2X5	T44.2X6
Trimethobenzamide	T45.0X1	T45.0X2	T45.0X3	T45.0X4	T45.0X5	T45.0X6
Trimethoprim	T37.8X1	T37.8X2	T37.8X3	T37.8X4	T37.8X5	T37.8X6
with sulfamethoxazole	T36.8X1	T36.8X2	T36.8X3	T36.8X4	T36.8X5	T36.8X6
Trimethylcarbinol	T51.3X1	T51.3X2	T51.3X3	T51.3X4	—	—
Trimethylpsoralen	T49.3X1	T49.3X2	T49.3X3	T49.3X4	T49.3X5	T49.3X6
Trimeton	T45.0X1	T45.0X2	T45.0X3	T45.0X4	T45.0X5	T45.0X6
Trimetrexate	T45.1X1	T45.1X2	T45.1X3	T45.1X4	T45.1X5	T45.1X6
Trimipramine	T43.011	T43.012	T43.013	T43.014	T43.015	T43.016
Trimustine	T45.1X1	T45.1X2	T45.1X3	T45.1X4	T45.1X5	T45.1X6
Trinitrine	T46.3X1	T46.3X2	T46.3X3	T46.3X4	T46.3X5	T46.3X6
Trinitrobenzol	T65.3X1	T65.3X2	T65.3X3	T65.3X4	—	—
Trinitrophenol	T65.3X1	T65.3X2	T65.3X3	T65.3X4	—	—
Trinitrotoluene (fumes)	T65.3X1	T65.3X2	T65.3X3	T65.3X4	—	—
Trional	T42.6X1	T42.6X2	T42.6X3	T42.6X4	T42.6X5	T42.6X6
Triorthocresyl phosphate	T65.891	T65.892	T65.893	T65.894	—	—
Trioxide of arsenic	T57.0X1	T57.0X2	T57.0X3	T57.0X4	—	—
Trioxysalen	T49.4X1	T49.4X2	T49.4X3	T49.4X4	T49.4X5	T49.4X6
Tripamide	T50.2X1	T50.2X2	T50.2X3	T50.2X4	T50.2X5	T50.2X6
Triparanol	T46.6X1	T46.6X2	T46.6X3	T46.6X4	T46.6X5	T46.6X6
Tripelennamine	T45.0X1	T45.0X2	T45.0X3	T45.0X4	T45.0X5	T45.0X6
Triperiden	T44.3X1	T44.3X2	T44.3X3	T44.3X4	T44.3X5	T44.3X6
Triperidol	T43.4X1	T43.4X2	T43.4X3	T43.4X4	T43.4X5	T43.4X6
Triphenylphosphate	T65.891	T65.892	T65.893	T65.894	—	—
Triple						
bromides	T42.6X1	T42.6X2	T42.6X3	T42.6X4	T42.6X5	T42.6X6
carbonate	T47.1X1	T47.1X2	T47.1X3	T47.1X4	T47.1X5	T47.1X6
vaccine						
DPT	T50.A11	T50.A12	T50.A13	T50.A14	T50.A15	T50.A16
including pertussis	T50.A11	T50.A12	T50.A13	T50.A14	T50.A15	T50.A16
MMR	T50.B91	T50.B92	T50.B93	T50.B94	T50.B95	T50.B96
Triprolidine	T45.0X1	T45.0X2	T45.0X3	T45.0X4	T45.0X5	T45.0X6
Trisodium hydrogen edetate	T50.6X1	T50.6X2	T50.6X3	T50.6X4	T50.6X5	T50.6X6
Trisoralen	T49.3X1	T49.3X2	T49.3X3	T49.3X4	T49.3X5	T49.3X6
Trisulfapyrimidines	T37.0X1	T37.0X2	T37.0X3	T37.0X4	T37.0X5	T37.0X6
Trithiozine	T44.3X1	T44.3X2	T44.3X3	T44.3X4	T44.3X5	T44.3X6
Tritiozine	T44.3X1	T44.3X2	T44.3X3	T44.3X4	T44.3X5	T44.3X6
Tritoqualine	T45.0X1	T45.0X2	T45.0X3	T45.0X4	T45.0X5	T45.0X6
Trofosfamide	T45.1X1	T45.1X2	T45.1X3	T45.1X4	T45.1X5	T45.1X6
Troleandomycin	T36.3X1	T36.3X2	T36.3X3	T36.3X4	T36.3X5	T36.3X6
Trolnitrate (phosphate)	T46.3X1	T46.3X2	T46.3X3	T46.3X4	T46.3X5	T46.3X6
Tromantadine	T37.5X1	T37.5X2	T37.5X3	T37.5X4	T37.5X5	T37.5X6
Trometamol	T50.2X1	T50.2X2	T50.2X3	T50.2X4	T50.2X5	T50.2X6
Tromethamine	T50.2X1	T50.2X2	T50.2X3	T50.2X4	T50.2X5	T50.2X6
Tronothane	T41.3X1	T41.3X2	T41.3X3	T41.3X4	T41.3X5	T41.3X6
Tropacine	T44.3X1	T44.3X2	T44.3X3	T44.3X4	T44.3X5	T44.3X6
Tropatepine	T44.3X1	T44.3X2	T44.3X3	T44.3X4	T44.3X5	T44.3X6
Tropicamide	T44.3X1	T44.3X2	T44.3X3	T44.3X4	T44.3X5	T44.3X6
Trospium chloride	T44.3X1	T44.3X2	T44.3X3	T44.3X4	T44.3X5	T44.3X6
Troxerutin	T46.991	T46.992	T46.993	T46.994	T46.995	T46.996
Troxidone	T42.2X1	T42.2X2	T42.2X3	T42.2X4	T42.2X5	T42.2X6
Tryparsamide	T37.3X1	T37.3X2	T37.3X3	T37.3X4	T37.3X5	T37.3X6
Trypsin	T45.3X1	T45.3X2	T45.3X3	T45.3X4	T45.3X5	T45.3X6
Tryptizol	T43.011	T43.012	T43.013	T43.014	T43.015	T43.016
TSH	T38.811	T38.812	T38.813	T38.814	T38.815	T38.816
Tuaminoheptane	T48.5X1	T48.5X2	T48.5X3	T48.5X4	T48.5X5	T48.5X6
Tuberculin, purified protein derivative(PPD)	T50.8X1	T50.8X2	T50.8X3	T50.8X4	T50.8X5	T50.8X6
Tubocurare	T48.1X1	T48.1X2	T48.1X3	T48.1X4	T48.1X5	T48.1X6
Tubocurarine (chloride)	T48.1X1	T48.1X2	T48.1X3	T48.1X4	T48.1X5	T48.1X6
Tulobuterol	T48.6X1	T48.6X2	T48.6X3	T48.6X4	T48.6X5	T48.6X6
Turpentine(spirits of)	T52.8X1	T52.8X2	T52.8X3	T52.8X4	—	—
vapor	T52.8X1	T52.8X2	T52.8X3	T52.8X4	—	—
Tybamate	T43.591	T43.592	T43.593	T43.594	T43.595	T43.596
Tyloxapol	T48.4X1	T48.4X2	T48.4X3	T48.4X4	T48.4X5	T48.4X6
Tymazoline	T48.5X1	T48.5X2	T48.5X3	T48.5X4	T48.5X5	T48.5X6
Typhoid-paratyphoid vaccine	T50.A91	T50.A92	T50.A93	T50.A94	T50.A95	T50.A96
Typhus vaccine	T50.A91	T50.A92	T50.A93	T50.A94	T50.A95	T50.A96
Tyropanoate	T50.8X1	T50.8X2	T50.8X3	T50.8X4	T50.8X5	T50.8X6

Substance	Poisoning, Accidental (unintentional)	Poisoning, Intentional self-harm	Poisoning, Assault	Poisoning, Undetermined	Adverse effect	Underdosing
Tyrothricin	T49.6X1	T49.6X2	T49.6X3	T49.6X4	T49.6X5	T49.6X6
ENT agent	T49.6X1	T49.6X2	T49.6X3	T49.6X4	T49.6X5	T49.6X6
ophthalmic preparation	T49.5X1	T49.5X2	T49.5X3	T49.5X4	T49.5X5	T49.5X6
U						
Ufenamate	T39.391	T39.392	T39.393	T39.394	T39.395	T39.396
Ultraviolet light protectant	T49.3X1	T49.3X2	T49.3X3	T49.3X4	T49.3X5	T49.3X6
Undecenoic acid	T49.0X1	T49.0X2	T49.0X3	T49.0X4	T49.0X5	T49.0X6
Undecoylium	T49.0X1	T49.0X2	T49.0X3	T49.0X4	T49.0X5	T49.0X6
Undecylenic acid(derivatives)	T49.0X1	T49.0X2	T49.0X3	T49.0X4	T49.0X5	T49.0X6
Unna's boot	T49.3X1	T49.3X2	T49.3X3	T49.3X4	T49.3X5	T49.3X6
Unsaturated fatty acid	T46.6X1	T46.6X2	T46.6X3	T46.6X4	T46.6X5	T46.6X6
Uracil mustard	T45.1X1	T45.1X2	T45.1X3	T45.1X4	T45.1X5	T45.1X6
Uramustine	T45.1X1	T45.1X2	T45.1X3	T45.1X4	T45.1X5	T45.1X6
Urapidil	T46.5X1	T46.5X2	T46.5X3	T46.5X4	T46.5X5	T46.5X6
Urari	T48.1X1	T48.1X2	T48.1X3	T48.1X4	T48.1X5	T48.1X6
Urate oxidase	T50.4X1	T50.4X2	T50.4X3	T50.4X4	T50.4X5	T50.4X6
Urea	T47.3X1	T47.3X2	T47.3X3	T47.3X4	T47.3X5	T47.3X6
peroxide	T49.0X1	T49.0X2	T49.0X3	T49.0X4	T49.0X5	T49.0X6
stibamine	T37.4X1	T37.4X2	T37.4X3	T37.4X4	T37.4X5	T37.4X6
topical	T49.8X1	T49.8X2	T49.8X3	T49.8X4	T49.8X5	T49.8X6
Urethane	T45.1X1	T45.1X2	T45.1X3	T45.1X4	T45.1X5	T45.1X6
Urginea(maritima) (scilla)—see Squill						
Uric acid metabolism drug NEC	T50.4X1	T50.4X2	T50.4X3	T50.4X4	T50.4X5	T50.4X6
Uricosuric agent	T50.4X1	T50.4X2	T50.4X3	T50.4X4	T50.4X5	T50.4X6
Urinary anti-infective	T37.8X1	T37.8X2	T37.8X3	T37.8X4	T37.8X5	T37.8X6
Urofollitropin	T38.811	T38.812	T38.813	T38.814	T38.815	T38.816
Urokinase	T45.611	T45.612	T45.613	T45.614	T45.615	T45.616
Urokon	T50.8X1	T50.8X2	T50.8X3	T50.8X4	T50.8X5	T50.8X6
Ursodeoxycholic acid	T50.991	T50.992	T50.993	T50.994	T50.995	T50.996
Ursodiol	T50.991	T50.992	T50.993	T50.994	T50.995	T50.996
Urtica	T62.2X1	T62.2X2	T62.2X3	T62.2X4	—	—
Utility gas—see Gas, utility						
V						
Vaccine NEC	T50.Z91	T50.Z92	T50.Z93	T50.Z94	T50.Z95	T50.Z96
antineoplastic	T50.Z91	T50.Z92	T50.Z93	T50.Z94	T50.Z95	T50.Z96
bacterial NEC	T50.A91	T50.A92	T50.A93	T50.A94	T50.A95	T50.A96
with						
other bacterial component	T50.A21	T50.A22	T50.A23	T50.A24	T50.A25	T50.A26
pertussis component	T50.A11	T50.A12	T50.A13	T50.A14	T50.A15	T50.A16
viral-rickettsial component	T50.A21	T50.A22	T50.A23	T50.A24	T50.A25	T50.A26
mixed NEC	T50.A21	T50.A22	T50.A23	T50.A24	T50.A25	T50.A26
BCG	T50.A91	T50.A92	T50.A93	T50.A94	T50.A95	T50.A96
cholera	T50.A91	T50.A92	T50.A93	T50.A94	T50.A95	T50.A96
diphtheria	T50.A91	T50.A92	T50.A93	T50.A94	T50.A95	T50.A96
with tetanus	T50.A21	T50.A22	T50.A23	T50.A24	T50.A25	T50.A26
and pertussis	T50.A11	T50.A12	T50.A13	T50.A14	T50.A15	T50.A16
influenza	T50.B91	T50.B92	T50.B93	T50.B94	T50.B95	T50.B96

Substance	Poisoning, Accidental (unintentional)	Poisoning, Intentional self-harm	Poisoning, Assault	Poisoning, Undetermined	Adverse effect	Underdosing
Vaccine NEC — *Continued*						
measles	T50.B91	T50.B92	T50.B93	T50.B94	T50.B95	T50.B96
with mumps and rubella	T50.B91	T50.B92	T50.B93	T50.B94	T50.B95	T50.B96
meningococcal	T50.A91	T50.A92	T50.A93	T50.A94	T50.A95	T50.A96
mumps	T50.B91	T50.B92	T50.B93	T50.B94	T50.B95	T50.B96
paratyphoid	T50.A91	T50.A92	T50.A93	T50.A94	T50.A95	T50.A96
pertussis	T50.A11	T50.A12	T50.A13	T50.A14	T50.A15	T50.A16
with diphtheria	T50.A11	T50.A12	T50.A13	T50.A14	T50.A15	T50.A16
and tetanus	T50.A11	T50.A12	T50.A13	T50.A14	T50.A15	T50.A16
with other component	T50.A11	T50.A12	T50.A13	T50.A14	T50.A15	T50.A16
plague	T50.A91	T50.A92	T50.A93	T50.A94	T50.A95	T50.A96
poliomyelitis	T50.B91	T50.B92	T50.B93	T50.B94	T50.B95	T50.B96
poliovirus	T50.B91	T50.B92	T50.B93	T50.B94	T50.B95	T50.B96
rabies	T50.B91	T50.B92	T50.B93	T50.B94	T50.B95	T50.B96
respiratory syncytial virus	T50.B91	T50.B92	T50.B93	T50.B94	T50.B95	T50.B96
rickettsial NEC	T50.A91	T50.A92	T50.A93	T50.A94	T50.A95	T50.A96
with						
bacterial component	T50.A21	T50.A22	T50.A23	T50.A24	T50.A25	T50.A26
Rocky Mountain spotted fever	T50.A91	T50.A92	T50.A93	T50.A94	T50.A95	T50.A96
rubella	T50.B91	T50.B92	T50.B93	T50.B94	T50.B95	T50.B96
sabin oral	T50.B91	T50.B92	T50.B93	T50.B94	T50.B95	T50.B96
smallpox	T50.B11	T50.B12	T50.B13	T50.B14	T50.B15	T50.B16
TAB	T50.A91	T50.A92	T50.A93	T50.A94	T50.A95	T50.A96
tetanus	T50.A91	T50.A92	T50.A93	T50.A94	T50.A95	T50.A96
typhoid	T50.A91	T50.A92	T50.A93	T50.A94	T50.A95	T50.A96
typhus	T50.A91	T50.A92	T50.A93	T50.A94	T50.A95	T50.A96
viral NEC	T50.B91	T50.B92	T50.B93	T50.B94	T50.B95	T50.B96
yellow fever	T50.B91	T50.B92	T50.B93	T50.B94	T50.B95	T50.B96
Vaccinia immune globulin	T50.Z11	T50.Z12	T50.Z13	T50.Z14	T50.Z15	T50.Z16
Vaginal contraceptives	T49.8X1	T49.8X2	T49.8X3	T49.8X4	T49.8X5	T49.8X6
Valerian						
root	T42.6X1	T42.6X2	T42.6X3	T42.6X4	T42.6X5	T42.6X6
tincture	T42.6X1	T42.6X2	T42.6X3	T42.6X4	T42.6X5	T42.6X6
Valethamate bromide	T44.3X1	T44.3X2	T44.3X3	T44.3X4	T44.3X5	T44.3X6
Valisone	T49.0X1	T49.0X2	T49.0X3	T49.0X4	T49.0X5	T49.0X6
Valium	T42.4X1	T42.4X2	T42.4X3	T42.4X4	T42.4X5	T42.4X6
Valmid	T42.6X1	T42.6X2	T42.6X3	T42.6X4	T42.6X5	T42.6X6
Valnoctamide	T42.6X1	T42.6X2	T42.6X3	T42.6X4	T42.6X5	T42.6X6
Valproate(sodium)	T42.6X1	T42.6X2	T42.6X3	T42.6X4	T42.6X5	T42.6X6
Valproic acid	T42.6X1	T42.6X2	T42.6X3	T42.6X4	T42.6X5	T42.6X6
Valpromide	T42.6X1	T42.6X2	T42.6X3	T42.6X4	T42.6X5	T42.6X6
Vanadium	T56.891	T56.892	T56.893	T56.894	—	—
Vancomycin	T36.8X1	T36.8X2	T36.8X3	T36.8X4	T36.8X5	T36.8X6
Vapor—see also Gas	T59.91	T59.92	T59.93	T59.94	—	—
kiln(carbon monoxide)	T58.8X1	T58.8X2	T58.8X3	T58.8X4	—	—
lead—see lead						
specified source NEC	T59.891	T59.892	T59.893	T59.894	—	—
Vardenafil	T46.7X1	T46.7X2	T46.7X3	T46.7X4	T46.7X5	T46.7X6
Varicose reduction drug	T46.8X1	T46.8X2	T46.8X3	T46.8X4	T46.8X5	T46.8X6

Substance	Poisoning, Accidental (unintentional)	Poisoning, Intentional self-harm	Poisoning, Assault	Poisoning, Undetermined	Adverse effect	Underdosing
rnish	T65.4X1	T65.4X2	T65.4X3	T65.4X4	—	—
leaner	T52.91	T52.92	T52.93	T52.94	—	—
seline	T49.3X1	T49.3X2	T49.3X3	T49.3X4	T49.3X5	T49.3X6
sodilan	T46.7X1	T46.7X2	T46.7X3	T46.7X4	T46.7X5	T46.7X6
sodilator						
oronary NEC	T46.3X1	T46.3X2	T46.3X3	T46.3X4	T46.3X5	T46.3X6
eripheral NEC	T46.7X1	T46.7X2	T46.7X3	T46.7X4	T46.7X5	T46.7X6
sopressin	T38.891	T38.892	T38.893	T38.894	T38.895	T38.896
sopressor drugs	T38.891	T38.892	T38.893	T38.894	T38.895	T38.896
curonium bromide	T48.1X1	T48.1X2	T48.1X3	T48.1X4	T48.1X5	T48.1X6
getable extract, tringent	T49.2X1	T49.2X2	T49.2X3	T49.2X4	T49.2X5	T49.2X6
nlafaxine	T43.211	T43.212	T43.213	T43.214	T43.215	T43.216
nom, venomous(bite) ing)	T63.91	T63.92	T63.93	T63.94	—	—
amphibian NEC	T63.831	T63.832	T63.833	T63.834	—	—
animal NEC	T63.891	T63.892	T63.893	T63.894	—	—
ant	T63.421	T63.422	T63.423	T63.424	—	—
arthropod NEC	T63.481	T63.482	T63.483	T63.484	—	—
bee	T63.441	T63.442	T63.443	T63.444	—	—
centipede	T63.411	T63.412	T63.413	T63.414	—	—
fish	T63.591	T63.592	T63.593	T63.594	—	—
frog	T63.811	T63.812	T63.813	T63.814	—	—
hornet	T63.451	T63.452	T63.453	T63.454	—	—
insect NEC	T63.481	T63.482	T63.483	T63.484	—	—
lizard	T63.121	T63.122	T63.123	T63.124	—	—
marine						
animals	T63.691	T63.692	T63.693	T63.694	—	—
bluebottle	T63.611	T63.612	T63.613	T63.614	—	—
jellyfish NEC	T63.621	T63.622	T63.623	T63.624	—	—
Portugese Man-o-war	T63.611	T63.612	T63.613	T63.614	—	—
sea anemone	T63.631	T63.632	T63.633	T63.634	—	—
specified NEC	T63.691	T63.692	T63.693	T63.694	—	—
fish	T63.591	T63.592	T63.593	T63.594	—	—
plants	T63.711	T63.712	T63.713	T63.714	—	—
sting ray	T63.511	T63.512	T63.513	T63.514	—	—
millipede(tropical)	T63.411	T63.412	T63.413	T63.414	—	—
plant NEC	T63.791	T63.792	T63.793	T63.794	—	—
marine	T63.711	T63.712	T63.713	T63.714	—	—
reptile	T63.191	T63.192	T63.193	T63.194	—	—
gila monster	T63.111	T63.112	T63.113	T63.114	—	—
lizard NEC	T63.121	T63.122	T63.123	T63.124	—	—
scorpion	T63.2X1	T63.2X2	T63.2X3	T63.2X4	—	—
snake	T63.001	T63.002	T63.003	T63.004	—	—
African NEC	T63.081	T63.082	T63.083	T63.084	—	—
American(North) (South) NEC	T63.061	T63.062	T63.063	T63.064	—	—
Asian	T63.081	T63.082	T63.083	T63.084	—	—
Australian	T63.071	T63.072	T63.073	T63.074	—	—
cobra	T63.041	T63.042	T63.043	T63.044	—	—
coral snake	T63.021	T63.022	T63.023	T63.024	—	—
rattlesnake	T63.011	T63.012	T63.013	T63.014	—	—
Venom, venomous — *Continued*						
specified NEC	T63.091	T63.092	T63.093	T63.094	—	—
taipan	T63.031	T63.032	T63.033	T63.034	—	—
specified NEC	T63.891	T63.892	T63.893	T63.894	—	—
spider	T63.301	T63.302	T63.303	T63.304	—	—
black widow	T63.311	T63.312	T63.313	T63.314	—	—
brown recluse	T63.331	T63.332	T63.333	T63.334	—	—
specified NEC	T63.391	T63.392	T63.393	T63.394	—	—
tarantula	T63.321	T63.322	T63.323	T63.324	—	—
sting ray	T63.511	T63.512	T63.513	T63.514	—	—
toad	T63.821	T63.822	T63.823	T63.824	—	—
wasp	T63.461	T63.462	T63.463	T63.464	—	—
Venous sclerosing drug NEC	T46.8X1	T46.8X2	T46.8X3	T46.8X4	T46.8X5	T46.8X6
Ventolin—see Albuterol						
Veramon	T42.3X1	T42.3X2	T42.3X3	T42.3X4	T42.3X5	T42.3X6
Verapamil	T46.1X1	T46.1X2	T46.1X3	T46.1X4	T46.1X5	T46.1X6
Veratrine	T46.5X1	T46.5X2	T46.5X3	T46.5X4	T46.5X5	T46.5X6
Veratrum						
album	T62.2X1	T62.2X2	T62.2X3	T62.2X4	—	—
alkaloids	T46.5X1	T46.5X2	T46.5X3	T46.5X4	T46.5X5	T46.5X6
viride	T62.2X1	T62.2X2	T62.2X3	T62.2X4	—	—
Verdigris	T60.3X1	T60.3X2	T60.3X3	T60.3X4	—	—
Veronal	T42.3X1	T42.3X2	T42.3X3	T42.3X4	T42.3X5	T42.3X6
Veroxil	T37.4X1	T37.4X2	T37.4X3	T37.4X4	T37.4X5	T37.4X6
Versenate	T50.6X1	T50.6X2	T50.6X3	T50.6X4	T50.6X5	T50.6X6
Versidyne	T39.8X1	T39.8X2	T39.8X3	T39.8X4	T39.8X5	T39.8X6
Vetrabutine	T48.0X1	T48.0X2	T48.0X3	T48.0X4	T48.0X5	T48.0X6
Vidarabine	T37.5X1	T37.5X2	T37.5X3	T37.5X4	T37.5X5	T37.5X6
Vienna						
green	T57.0X1	T57.0X2	T57.0X3	T57.0X4	—	—
insecticide	T60.2X1	T60.2X2	T60.2X3	T60.2X4	—	—
red	T57.0X1	T57.0X2	T57.0X3	T57.0X4	—	—
pharmaceutical dye	T50.991	T50.992	T50.993	T50.994	T50.995	T50.996
Vigabatrin	T42.6X1	T42.6X2	T42.6X3	T42.6X4	T42.6X5	T42.6X6
Viloxazine	T43.291	T43.292	T43.293	T43.294	T43.295	T43.296
Viminol	T39.8X1	T39.8X2	T39.8X3	T39.8X4	T39.8X5	T39.8X6
Vinbarbital, vinbarbitone	T42.3X1	T42.3X2	T42.3X3	T42.3X4	T42.3X5	T42.3X6
Vinblastine	T45.1X1	T45.1X2	T45.1X3	T45.1X4	T45.1X5	T45.1X6
Vinburnine	T46.7X1	T46.7X2	T46.7X3	T46.7X4	T46.7X5	T46.7X6
Vincamine	T45.1X1	T45.1X2	T45.1X3	T45.1X4	T45.1X5	T45.1X6
Vincristine	T45.1X1	T45.1X2	T45.1X3	T45.1X4	T45.1X5	T45.1X6
Vindesine	T45.1X1	T45.1X2	T45.1X3	T45.1X4	T45.1X5	T45.1X6
Vinesthene, vinethene	T41.0X1	T41.0X2	T41.0X3	T41.0X4	T41.0X5	T41.0X6
Vinorelbine tartrate	T45.1X1	T45.1X2	T45.1X3	T45.1X4	T45.1X5	T45.1X6
Vinpocetine	T46.7X1	T46.7X2	T46.7X3	T46.7X4	T46.7X5	T46.7X6
Vinyl						
acetate	T65.891	T65.892	T65.893	T65.894	—	—
bital	T42.3X1	T42.3X2	T42.3X3	T42.3X4	T42.3X5	T42.3X6
bromide	T65.891	T65.892	T65.893	T65.894	—	—
chloride	T59.891	T59.892	T59.893	T59.894	—	—
ether	T41.0X1	T41.0X2	T41.0X3	T41.0X4	T41.0X5	T41.0X6
Vinylbital	T42.3X1	T42.3X2	T42.3X3	T42.3X4	T42.3X5	T42.3X6

Substance	Poisoning, Accidental (unintentional)	Poisoning, Intentional self-harm	Poisoning, Assault	Poisoning, Undetermined	Adverse effect	Underdosing
Vinylidene chloride	T65.891	T65.892	T65.893	T65.894	—	—
Vioform	T37.8X1	T37.8X2	T37.8X3	T37.8X4	T37.8X5	T37.8X6
topical	T49.0X1	T49.0X2	T49.0X3	T49.0X4	T49.0X5	T49.0X6
Viomycin	T36.8X1	T36.8X2	T36.8X3	T36.8X4	T36.8X5	T36.8X6
Viosterol	T45.2X1	T45.2X2	T45.2X3	T45.2X4	T45.2X5	T45.2X6
Viper(venom)	T63.091	T63.092	T63.093	T63.094	—	—
Viprynium	T37.4X1	T37.4X2	T37.4X3	T37.4X4	T37.4X5	T37.4X6
Viquidil	T46.7X1	T46.7X2	T46.7X3	T46.7X4	T46.7X5	T46.7X6
Viral vaccine NEC	T50.B91	T50.B92	T50.B93	T50.B94	T50.B95	T50.B96
Virginiamycin	T36.8X1	T36.8X2	T36.8X3	T36.8X4	T36.8X5	T36.8X6
Virugon	T37.5X1	T37.5X2	T37.5X3	T37.5X4	T37.5X5	T37.5X6
Viscous agent	T50.901	T50.902	T50.903	T50.904	T50.905	T50.906
Visine	T49.5X1	T49.5X2	T49.5X3	T49.5X4	T49.5X5	T49.5X6
Visnadine	T46.3X1	T46.3X2	T46.3X3	T46.3X4	T46.3X5	T46.3X6
Vitamin NEC	T45.2X1	T45.2X2	T45.2X3	T45.2X4	T45.2X5	T45.2X6
A	T45.2X1	T45.2X2	T45.2X3	T45.2X4	T45.2X5	T45.2X6
B NEC	T45.2X1	T45.2X2	T45.2X3	T45.2X4	T45.2X5	T45.2X6
nicotinic acid	T46.7X1	T46.7X2	T46.7X3	T46.7X4	T46.7X5	T46.7X6
B1	T45.2X1	T45.2X2	T45.2X3	T45.2X4	T45.2X5	T45.2X6
B2	T45.2X1	T45.2X2	T45.2X3	T45.2X4	T45.2X5	T45.2X6
B6	T45.2X1	T45.2X2	T45.2X3	T45.2X4	T45.2X5	T45.2X6
B12	T45.2X1	T45.2X2	T45.2X3	T45.2X4	T45.2X5	T45.2X6
B15	T45.2X1	T45.2X2	T45.2X3	T45.2X4	T45.2X5	T45.2X6
C	T45.2X1	T45.2X2	T45.2X3	T45.2X4	T45.2X5	T45.2X6
D	T45.2X1	T45.2X2	T45.2X3	T45.2X4	T45.2X5	T45.2X6
D2	T45.2X1	T45.2X2	T45.2X3	T45.2X4	T45.2X5	T45.2X6
D3	T45.2X1	T45.2X2	T45.2X3	T45.2X4	T45.2X5	T45.2X6
E	T45.2X1	T45.2X2	T45.2X3	T45.2X4	T45.2X5	T45.2X6
E acetate	T45.2X1	T45.2X2	T45.2X3	T45.2X4	T45.2X5	T45.2X6
hematopoietic	T45.8X1	T45.8X2	T45.8X3	T45.8X4	T45.8X5	T45.8X6
K NEC	T45.7X1	T45.7X2	T45.7X3	T45.7X4	T45.7X5	T45.7X6
K1	T45.7X1	T45.7X2	T45.7X3	T45.7X4	T45.7X5	T45.7X6
K2	T45.7X1	T45.7X2	T45.7X3	T45.7X4	T45.7X5	T45.7X6
PP	T45.2X1	T45.2X2	T45.2X3	T45.2X4	T45.2X5	T45.2X6
ulceroprotectant	T47.1X1	T47.1X2	T47.1X3	T47.1X4	T47.1X5	T47.1X6
Vleminckx's solution	T49.4X1	T49.4X2	T49.4X3	T49.4X4	T49.4X5	T49.4X6
Voltaren—see Diclofenac sodium						
W						
Warfarin	T45.511	T45.512	T45.513	T45.514	T45.515	T45.516
rodenticide	T60.4X1	T60.4X2	T60.4X3	T60.4X4	—	—
sodium	T60.4X1	T60.4X2	T60.4X3	T60.4X4	—	—
Wasp(sting)	T63.461	T63.462	T63.463	T63.464	—	—
Water						
balance drug	T50.3X1	T50.3X2	T50.3X3	T50.3X4	T50.3X5	T50.3X6
distilled	T50.3X1	T50.3X2	T50.3X3	T50.3X4	T50.3X5	T50.3X6
gas—see Gas, water						
incomplete combustion of—see Carbon, monoxide, fuel, utility						
hemlock	T62.2X1	T62.2X2	T62.2X3	T62.2X4	—	—
moccasin(venom)	T63.061	T63.062	T63.063	T63.064	—	—
purified	T50.3X1	T50.3X2	T50.3X3	T50.3X4	T50.3X5	T50.3X6

Substance	Poisoning, Accidental (unintentional)	Poisoning, Intentional self-harm	Poisoning, Assault	Poisoning, Undetermined	Adverse effect	Underdosing
Wax(paraffin) (petroleum)	T52.0X1	T52.0X2	T52.0X3	T52.0X4	—	—
automobile	T65.891	T65.892	T65.893	T65.894	—	—
floor	T52.0X1	T52.0X2	T52.0X3	T52.0X4	—	—
Weed killers NEC	T60.3X1	T60.3X2	T60.3X3	T60.3X4	—	—
Welldorm	T42.6X1	T42.6X2	T42.6X3	T42.6X4	T42.6X5	T42.6
White						
arsenic	T57.0X1	T57.0X2	T57.0X3	T57.0X4	—	—
hellebore	T62.2X1	T62.2X2	T62.2X3	T62.2X4	—	—
lotion(keratolytic)	T49.4X1	T49.4X2	T49.4X3	T49.4X4	T49.4X5	T49.4
spirit	T52.0X1	T52.0X2	T52.0X3	T52.0X4	—	—
Whitewash	T65.891	T65.892	T65.893	T65.894	—	—
Whole blood(human)	T45.8X1	T45.8X2	T45.8X3	T45.8X4	T45.8X5	T45.8
Wild						
black cherry	T62.2X1	T62.2X2	T62.2X3	T62.2X4	—	—
poisonous plants NEC	T62.2X1	T62.2X2	T62.2X3	T62.2X4	—	—
Window cleaning fluid	T65.891	T65.892	T65.893	T65.894	—	—
Wintergreen(oil)	T49.3X1	T49.3X2	T49.3X3	T49.3X4	T49.3X5	T49.3
Wisterine	T62.2X1	T62.2X2	T62.2X3	T62.2X4	—	—
Witch hazel	T49.2X1	T49.2X2	T49.2X3	T49.2X4	T49.2X5	T49.2
Wood alcohol or spirit	T51.1X1	T51.1X2	T51.1X3	T51.1X4	—	—
Wool fat(hydrous)	T49.3X1	T49.3X2	T49.3X3	T49.3X4	T49.3X5	T49.3
Woorali	T48.1X1	T48.1X2	T48.1X3	T48.1X4	T48.1X5	T48.1
Wormseed, American	T37.4X1	T37.4X2	T37.4X3	T37.4X4	T37.4X5	T37.4
X						
Xamoterol	T44.5X1	T44.5X2	T44.5X3	T44.5X4	T44.5X5	T44.5
Xanthine diuretics	T50.2X1	T50.2X2	T50.2X3	T50.2X4	T50.2X5	T50.2
Xanthinol nicotinate	T46.7X1	T46.7X2	T46.7X3	T46.7X4	T46.7X5	T46.7
Xanthotoxin	T49.3X1	T49.3X2	T49.3X3	T49.3X4	T49.3X5	T49.3
Xantinol nicotinate	T46.7X1	T46.7X2	T46.7X3	T46.7X4	T46.7X5	T46.7
Xantocillin	T36.0X1	T36.0X2	T36.0X3	T36.0X4	T36.0X5	T36.0
Xenon(127Xe) (133Xe)	T50.8X1	T50.8X2	T50.8X3	T50.8X4	T50.8X5	T50.8
Xenysalate	T49.4X1	T49.4X2	T49.4X3	T49.4X4	T49.4X5	T49.4
Xibornol	T37.8X1	T37.8X2	T37.8X3	T37.8X4	T37.8X5	T37.8
Xigris	T45.511	T45.512	T45.513	T45.514	T45.515	T45.5
Xipamide	T50.2X1	T50.2X2	T50.2X3	T50.2X4	T50.2X5	T50.2
Xylene(vapor)	T52.2X1	T52.2X2	T52.2X3	T52.2X4	—	—
Xylocaine (infiltration) (topical)	T41.3X1	T41.3X2	T41.3X3	T41.3X4	T41.3X5	T41.3
nerve block(peripheral) (plexus)	T41.3X1	T41.3X2	T41.3X3	T41.3X4	T41.3X5	T41.3
spinal	T41.3X1	T41.3X2	T41.3X3	T41.3X4	T41.3X5	T41.3
Xylol(vapor)	T52.2X1	T52.2X2	T52.2X3	T52.2X4	—	—
Xylometazoline	T48.5X1	T48.5X2	T48.5X3	T48.5X4	T48.5X5	T48.5
Y						
Yeast	T45.2X1	T45.2X2	T45.2X3	T45.2X4	T45.2X5	T45.2
dried	T45.2X1	T45.2X2	T45.2X3	T45.2X4	T45.2X5	T45.2
Yellow						
fever vaccine	T50.B91	T50.B92	T50.B93	T50.B94	T50.B95	T50.B
jasmine	T62.2X1	T62.2X2	T62.2X3	T62.2X4	—	—
phenolphthalein	T47.2X1	T47.2X2	T47.2X3	T47.2X4	T47.2X5	T47.2
Yew	T62.2X1	T62.2X2	T62.2X3	T62.2X4	—	—
Yohimbic acid	T40.991	T40.992	T40.993	T40.994	T40.995	T40.9

Substance	Poisoning, Accidental (unintentional)	Poisoning, Intentional self-harm	Poisoning, Assault	Poisoning, Undetermined	Adverse effect	Underdosing
Z						
ctane	T39.8X1	T39.8X2	T39.8X3	T39.8X4	T39.8X5	T39.8X6
lcitabine	T37.5X1	T37.5X2	T37.5X3	T37.5X4	T37.5X5	T37.5X6
roxolyn	T50.2X1	T50.2X2	T50.2X3	T50.2X4	T50.2X5	T50.2X6
phiran(topical)	T49.0X1	T49.0X2	T49.0X3	T49.0X4	T49.0X5	T49.0X6
phthalmic preparation	T49.5X1	T49.5X2	T49.5X3	T49.5X4	T49.5X5	T49.5X6
ranol	T38.7X1	T38.7X2	T38.7X3	T38.7X4	T38.7X5	T38.7X6
rone	T51.1X1	T51.1X2	T51.1X3	T51.1X4	—	—
dovudine	T37.5X1	T37.5X2	T37.5X3	T37.5X4	T37.5X5	T37.5X6
meldine	T43.221	T43.222	T43.223	T43.224	T43.225	T43.226
nc(compounds) (fumes) apor) NEC	T56.5X1	T56.5X2	T56.5X3	T56.5X4	—	—
anti-infectives	T49.0X1	T49.0X2	T49.0X3	T49.0X4	T49.0X5	T49.0X6
antivaricose	T46.8X1	T46.8X2	T46.8X3	T46.8X4	T46.8X5	T46.8X6
bacitracin	T49.0X1	T49.0X2	T49.0X3	T49.0X4	T49.0X5	T49.0X6
chloride (mouthwash)	T49.6X1	T49.6X2	T49.6X3	T49.6X4	T49.6X5	T49.6X6
chromate	T56.5X1	T56.5X2	T56.5X3	T56.5X4	—	—
gelatin	T49.3X1	T49.3X2	T49.3X3	T49.3X4	T49.3X5	T49.3X6
oxide	T49.3X1	T49.3X2	T49.3X3	T49.3X4	T49.3X5	T49.3X6
plaster	T49.3X1	T49.3X2	T49.3X3	T49.3X4	T49.3X5	T49.3X6
peroxide	T49.0X1	T49.0X2	T49.0X3	T49.0X4	T49.0X5	T49.0X6
pesticides	T56.5X1	T56.5X2	T56.5X3	T56.5X4	—	—
phosphide	T60.4X1	T60.4X2	T60.4X3	T60.4X4	—	—
Zinc(compounds) (fumes) (vapor) NEC — *Continued*						
pyrithionate	T49.4X1	T49.4X2	T49.4X3	T49.4X4	T49.4X5	T49.4X6
stearate	T49.3X1	T49.3X2	T49.3X3	T49.3X4	T49.3X5	T49.3X6
sulfate	T49.5X1	T49.5X2	T49.5X3	T49.5X4	T49.5X5	T49.5X6
ENT agent	T49.6X1	T49.6X2	T49.6X3	T49.6X4	T49.6X5	T49.6X6
ophthalmic solution	T49.5X1	T49.5X2	T49.5X3	T49.5X4	T49.5X5	T49.5X6
topical NEC	T49.0X1	T49.0X2	T49.0X3	T49.0X4	T49.0X5	T49.0X6
undecylenate	T49.0X1	T49.0X2	T49.0X3	T49.0X4	T49.0X5	T49.0X6
Zineb	T60.0X1	T60.0X2	T60.0X3	T60.0X4	—	—
Zinostatin	T45.1X1	T45.1X2	T45.1X3	T45.1X4	T45.1X5	T45.1X6
Zipeprol	T48.3X1	T48.3X2	T48.3X3	T48.3X4	T48.3X5	T48.3X6
Zofenopril	T46.4X1	T46.4X2	T46.4X3	T46.4X4	T46.4X5	T46.4X6
Zolpidem	T42.6X1	T42.6X2	T42.6X3	T42.6X4	T42.6X5	T42.6X6
Zomepirac	T39.391	T39.392	T39.393	T39.394	T39.395	T39.396
Zopiclone	T42.6X1	T42.6X2	T42.6X3	T42.6X4	T42.6X5	T42.6X6
Zorubicin	T45.1X1	T45.1X2	T45.1X3	T45.1X4	T45.1X5	T45.1X6
Zotepine	T43.591	T43.592	T43.593	T43.594	T43.595	T43.596
Zovant	T45.511	T45.512	T45.513	T45.514	T45.515	T45.516
Zoxazolamine	T42.8X1	T42.8X2	T42.8X3	T42.8X4	T42.8X5	T42.8X6
Zuclopenthixol	T43.4X1	T43.4X2	T43.4X3	T43.4X4	T43.4X5	T43.4X6
Zygadenus (venenosus)	T62.2X1	T62.2X2	T62.2X3	T62.2X4	—	—
Zyprexa	T43.591	T43.592	T43.593	T43.594	T43.595	T43.596

External Cause of Injuries Index

A

Accident *(continued)*
transport *(continued)*
truck occupant *(continued)*
hanger-on
collision (with)
animal (traffic) V60.7
being ridden (traffic) V66.7
nontraffic V66.2
nontraffic V60.2
animal-drawn vehicle (traffic) V66.7
nontraffic V66.2
bus (traffic) V64.7
nontraffic V64.2
car (traffic) V63.7
nontraffic V63.2
pedal cycle (traffic) V61.7
nontraffic V61.2
pickup truck (traffic) V63.7
nontraffic V63.2
railway vehicle (traffic) V65.7
nontraffic V65.2
specified vehicle NEC (traffic) V66.7
nontraffic V66.2
stationary object (traffic) V67.7
nontraffic V67.2
streetcar (traffic) V66.7
nontraffic V66.2
three wheeled motor vehicle (traffic) V62.7
nontraffic V62.2
truck (traffic) V64.7
nontraffic V64.2
two wheeled motor vehicle (traffic) V62.7
nontraffic V62.2
van (traffic) V63.7
nontraffic V63.2
noncollision accident (traffic) V68.7
nontraffic V68.2
noncollision accident (traffic) V68.9
nontraffic V68.3
while boarding or alighting V68.4
nontraffic V69.3
passenger
collision (with)
animal (traffic) V60.6
being ridden (traffic) V66.6
nontraffic V66.1
nontraffic V60.1
animal-drawn vehicle (traffic) V66.6
nontraffic V66.1
bus (traffic) V64.6
nontraffic V64.1
car (traffic) V63.6
nontraffic V63.1
motor vehicle NOS (traffic) V69.50
nontraffic V69.10
specified type NEC (traffic) V69.59
nontraffic V69.19
pedal cycle (traffic) V61.6
nontraffic V61.1
pickup truck (traffic) V63.6
nontraffic V63.1
railway vehicle (traffic) V65.6
nontraffic V65.1
specified vehicle NEC (traffic) V66.6
nontraffic V66.1

Accident *(continued)*
transport *(continued)*
truck occupant *(continued)*
passenger *(continued)*
collision *(continued)*
stationary object (traffic) V67.6
nontraffic V67.1
streetcar (traffic) V66.6
nontraffic V66.1
three wheeled motor vehicle (traffic) V62.6
nontraffic V62.1
truck (traffic) V64.6
nontraffic V64.1
two wheeled motor vehicle (traffic) V62.6
nontraffic V62.1
van (traffic) V63.6
nontraffic V63.1
noncollision accident (traffic) V68.6
nontraffic V68.1
pickup —*see* Accident, transport, pickup truck occupant
specified type NEC V69.88
military vehicle V69.81
van occupant V59.9
collision (with)
animal (traffic) V50.9
being ridden (traffic) V56.9
nontraffic V56.3
while boarding or alighting V56.4
nontraffic V50.3
while boarding or alighting V50.4
animal-drawn vehicle (traffic) V56.9
nontraffic V56.3
while boarding or alighting V56.4
bus (traffic) V54.9
nontraffic V54.3
while boarding or alighting V54.4
car (traffic) V53.9
nontraffic V53.3
while boarding or alighting V53.4
motor vehicle NOS (traffic) V59.60
nontraffic V59.20
specified type NEC (traffic) V59.69
nontraffic V59.29
pedal cycle (traffic) V51.9
nontraffic V51.3
while boarding or alighting V51.4
pickup truck (traffic) V53.9
nontraffic V53.3
while boarding or alighting V53.4
railway vehicle (traffic) V55.9
nontraffic V55.3
while boarding or alighting V55.4
specified vehicle NEC (traffic) V56.9
nontraffic V56.3
while boarding or alighting V56.4
stationary object (traffic) V57.9
nontraffic V57.3
while boarding or alighting V57.4
streetcar (traffic) V56.9
nontraffic V56.3

Accident *(continued)*
transport *(continued)*
van occupant *(continued)*
collision *(continued)*
streetcar *(continued)*
while boarding or alighting V56.4
three wheeled motor vehicle (traffic) V52.9
nontraffic V52.3
while boarding or alighting V52.4
truck (traffic) V54.9
nontraffic V54.3
while boarding or alighting V54.4
two wheeled motor vehicle (traffic) V52.9
nontraffic V52.3
while boarding or alighting V52.4
van (traffic) V53.9
nontraffic V53.3
while boarding or alighting V53.4
driver
collision (with)
animal (traffic) V50.5
being ridden (traffic) V56.5
nontraffic V56.0
nontraffic V50.0
animal-drawn vehicle (traffic) V56.5
nontraffic V56.0
bus (traffic) V54.5
nontraffic V54.0
car (traffic) V53.5
nontraffic V53.0
motor vehicle NOS (traffic) V59.40
nontraffic V59.00
specified type NEC (traffic) V59.49
nontraffic V59.09
pedal cycle (traffic) V51.5
nontraffic V51.0
pickup truck (traffic) V53.5
nontraffic V53.0
railway vehicle (traffic) V55.5
nontraffic V55.0
specified vehicle NEC (traffic) V56.5
nontraffic V56.0
stationary object (traffic) V57.5
nontraffic V57.0
streetcar (traffic) V56.5
nontraffic V56.0
three wheeled motor vehicle (traffic) V52.5
nontraffic V52.0
truck (traffic) V54.5
nontraffic V54.0
two wheeled motor vehicle (traffic) V52.5
driver
nontraffic V52.0
van (traffic) V53.5
nontraffic V53.0
noncollision accident (traffic) V58.5
nontraffic V58.0
noncollision accident (traffic) V58.9
nontraffic V58.3
while boarding or alighting V58.4
nontraffic V59.3
hanger-on

Accident *(continued)*
transport *(continued)*
van occupant *(continued)*
hanger-on *(continued)*
collision (with)
animal (traffic) V50.7
being ridden (traffic) V56.7
nontraffic V56.2
nontraffic V50.2
animal-drawn vehicle (traffic) V56.7
nontraffic V56.2
bus (traffic) V54.7
nontraffic V54.2
car (traffic) V53.7
nontraffic V53.2
pedal cycle (traffic) V51.7
nontraffic V51.2
pickup truck (traffic) V53.7
nontraffic V53.2
railway vehicle (traffic) V55.7
nontraffic V55.2
specified vehicle NEC (traffic) V56.7
nontraffic V56.2
stationary object (traffic) V57.7
nontraffic V57.2
streetcar (traffic) V56.7
nontraffic V56.2
three wheeled motor vehicle (traffic) V52.7
nontraffic V52.2
truck (traffic) V54.7
nontraffic V54.2
two wheeled motor vehic (traffic) V52.7
nontraffic V52.2
van (traffic) V53.7
nontraffic V53.2
noncollision accident (traff V58.7
nontraffic V58.2
passenger
collision (with)
animal (traffic) V50.6
being ridden (traffic) V56.6
nontraffic V56.1
nontraffic V50.1
animal-drawn vehicle (traffic) V56.6
nontraffic V56.1
bus (traffic) V54.6
nontraffic V54.1
car (traffic) V53.6
nontraffic V53.1
motor vehicle NOS (traf V59.50
nontraffic V59.10
specified type NEC (traffic) V59.59
nontraffic V59.19
pedal cycle (traffic) V51.6
nontraffic V51.1
pickup truck (traffic) V53.6
nontraffic V53.1
railway vehicle (traffic) V55.6
nontraffic V55.1
specified vehicle NEC (traffic) V56.6
nontraffic V56.1
stationary object (traffic) V57.6
nontraffic V57.1

Burn, burned, burning *(continued)*
on board watercraft *(continued)*
due to *(continued)*
accident to watercraft *(continued)*
powered craft *(continued)*
jetskis V91.03
liner V91.01
merchant ship V91.00
passenger ship V91.01
unpowered craft V91.08
canoe V91.05
inflatable V91.06
kayak V91.05
sailboat V91.04
surf-board V91.08
water skis V91.07
windsurfer V91.08
fire on board V93.09
ferry boat V93.01
fishing boat V93.02
jetskis V93.03
liner V93.01
merchant ship V93.00
passenger ship V93.01
powered craft NEC V93.03
sailboat V93.04
specified heat source NEC on board V93.19
ferry boat V93.11
fishing boat V93.12
jetskis V93.13
liner V93.11
merchant ship V93.10
passenger ship V93.11
powered craft NEC V93.13
sailboat V93.14
pipe (hot) X16
smoking X08.8
with ignition of clothing NEC X06.2
nightwear X05
powder *—see* Powder burn
radiator (hot) X16
saucepan (hot) (glass) (metal) X15.3
stated as undetermined whether accidental or intentional Y27.3
suicide (attempt) X77.3
self-inflicted X76
stated as undetermined whether accidental or intentional Y26
steam X13.1
pipe X16
stated as undetermined whether accidental or intentional Y27.8
stated as undetermined whether accidental or intentional Y27.0
suicide (attempt) X77.0
stove (hot) (kitchen) X15.0
stated as undetermined whether accidental or intentional Y27.3
suicide (attempt) X77.3
substance (hot) NEC X19
boiling X12
stated as undetermined whether accidental or intentional Y27.2
suicide (attempt) X77.2
molten (metal) X18
suicide (attempt) NEC X76
hot
household appliance X77.3
object X77.9
therapeutic misadventure
heat in local application or packing during medical or surgical procedure Y63.5
overdose of radiation Y63.2
toaster (hot) X15.1
stated as undetermined whether accidental or intentional Y27.3

Burn, burned, burning *(continued)*
toaster *(continued)*
suicide (attempt) X77.3
tool (hot) X17
torch, welding X08.8
with ignition of clothing NEC X06.2
nightwear X05
trash fire (controlled) *—see* Exposure, fire, controlled, not in building
uncontrolled *—see* Exposure, fire, uncontrolled, not in building
vapor (hot) X13.1
stated as undetermined whether accidental or intentional Y27.0
suicide (attempt) X77.0
Very pistol *—see* Discharge, firearm NEC

Butted by animal W55.82
bull W55.22
cow W55.22
goat W55.32
horse W55.12
pig W55.42
sheep W55.32

C

Caisson disease *—see* Air, pressure, change

Campfire (exposure to) (controlled) *—see also* Exposure, fire, controlled, not in building
uncontrolled *—see* Exposure, fire, uncontrolled, not in building

Capital punishment (any means) *—see* Legal, intervention

Car sickness T75.3

Casualty (not due to war) NEC X58
war *—see* War operations

Cat
bite W55.01
scratch W55.03

Cataclysm, cataclysmic (any injury) NEC *—see* Forces of nature

Catching fire *—see* Exposure, fire

Caught
between
folding object W23.0
objects (moving) (stationary and moving) W23.0
and machinery *—see* Contact, with, by type of machine
stationary W23.1
sliding door and door frame W23.0
by, in
machinery (moving parts of) *—see* Contact, with, by type of machine
washing-machine wringer W23.0
under packing crate (due to losing grip) W23.1

Cave-in caused by cataclysmic earth surface movement or eruption *—see* Landslide

Change (s) in air pressure *—see* Air, pressure, change

Choked, choking (on) (any object except food or vomitus)
food (bone) (*seed*) *—see* categories T17 and T18
vomitus T17.81-

Civil insurrection *—see* War operations

Cloudburst (any injury) X37.8

Cold, exposure to (accidental) (excessive) (extreme) (natural) (place) NEC *—see* Exposure, cold

Collapse
building W20.1
burning (uncontrolled fire) X00.2
dam or man-made structure (causing earth movement) X36.0
machinery *—see* Contact, with, by type of machine
structure W20.1
burning (uncontrolled fire) X00.2

Collision (accidental) NEC *—see also* Accident, transport V89.9
pedestrian W51
with fall W03
due to ice or snow W00.0
involving pedestrian conveyance *—see* Accident, transport, pedestrian, conveyance
and
crowd or human stampede (with fall) W52
object W22.8
with fall *—see* Fall, due to, bumping against, object
person (s) *—see* Collision, pedestrian
transport vehicle NEC V89.9
and
avalanche, fallen or not moving *—see* Accident, transport
falling or moving *—see* Landslide
landslide, fallen or not moving *—see* Accident, transport
falling or moving *—see* Landslide
due to cataclysm *—see* Forces of nature, by type
intentional, purposeful suicide (attempt) *—see* Suicide, collision

Combustion, spontaneous *—see* Ignition

Complication (delayed) of or following (medical or surgical procedure) Y84.9
with misadventure *—see* Misadventure
amputation of limb (s) Y83.5
anastomosis (arteriovenous) (blood vessel) (gastrojejunal) (tendon) (natural or artificial material) Y83.2
aspiration (of fluid) Y84.4
tissue Y84.8
biopsy Y84.8
blood
sampling Y84.7
transfusion
procedure Y84.8
bypass Y83.2
catheterization (urinary) Y84.6
cardiac Y84.0
colostomy Y83.3
cystostomy Y83.3
dialysis (kidney) Y84.1
drug *—see* Table of Drugs and Chemicals
due to misadventure *—see* Misadventure
duodenostomy Y83.3
electroshock therapy Y84.3
external stoma, creation of Y83.3
formation of external stoma Y83.3
gastrostomy Y83.3
graft Y83.2
hypothermia (medically-induced) Y84.8
implant, implantation (of)
artificial
internal device (cardiac pacemaker) (electrodes in brain) (heart valve prosthesis) (orthopedic) Y83.1
material or tissue (for anastomosis or bypass) Y83.2

Complication *(continued)*
implant, implantation *(continue*
artificial *(continued)*
material or tissue *(continue*
with creation of external stoma Y83.3
natural tissues (for anastomos bypass) Y83.2
with creation of external st Y83.3
infusion
procedure Y84.8
injection *—see* Table of Drugs a Chemicals
procedure Y84.8
insertion of gastric or duodenal s Y84.5
insulin-shock therapy Y84.3
paracentesis (abdominal) (thorac (aspirative) Y84.4
procedures other than surgical operation *—see* Complication of or following, by type of procedure
radiological procedure or therap Y84.2
removal of organ (partial) (total) NEC Y83.6
sampling
blood Y84.7
fluid NEC Y84.4
tissue Y84.8
shock therapy Y84.3
surgical operation NEC *—see al* Complication of or following, type of operation Y83.9
reconstructive NEC Y83.4
with
anastomosis, bypass or g Y83.2
formation of external sto Y83.3
specified NEC Y83.8
transfusion *—see also* Table of D and Chemicals
procedure Y84.8
transplant, transplantation (heart) (kidney) (liver) (whole organ, Y83.0
partial organ Y83.4
ureterostomy Y83.3
vaccination *—see also* Table of D and Chemicals
procedure Y84.8

Compression
divers' squeeze *—see* Air, pressu change
trachea by
food (lodged in esophagus) *—see* categories T17 and T1
vomitus (lodged in esophagus) T17.81-

Conflagration *—see* Exposure, fire uncontrolled

Constriction (external)
hair W49.01
jewelry W49.04
ring W49.04
rubber band W49.03
specified item NEC W49.09
string W49.02
thread W49.02

Contact (accidental)
with
abrasive wheel (metalworking) W31.1
alligator W58.09
bite W58.01
crushing W58.03
strike W58.02

Fall, falling *(continued)*
into *(continued)*
water *(continued)*
in *(continued)*
natural body of water *(continued)*
striking *(continued)*
bottom *(continued)*
causing drowning W16.121
side W16.132
causing drowning W16.131
specified water NEC W16.312
causing drowning W16.311
striking
bottom W16.322
causing drowning W16.321
wall W16.332
causing drowning W16.331
swimming pool W16.012
causing drowning W16.011
striking
bottom W16.022
causing drowning W16.021
wall W16.032
causing drowning W16.031
utility bucket W16.222
causing drowning W16.221
well W17.0
involving
bed W06
chair W07
furniture NEC W08
glass —*see* Fall, by type
playground equipment W09.8
jungle gym W09.2
slide W09.0
swing W09.1
roller blades —*see* Accident, transport, pedestrian, conveyance
skateboard (s) —*see* Accident, transport, pedestrian, conveyance
skates (ice) (in line) (roller) —*see* Accident, transport, pedestrian, conveyance
skis —*see* Accident, transport, pedestrian, conveyance
table W08
wheelchair, non-moving W05.0
powered —*see* Accident, transport, pedestrian, conveyance, specified type NEC
object —*see* Struck by, object, falling
off
toilet W18.11
with subsequent striking against object W18.12
on same level W18.30
due to
specified NEC W18.39
stepping on an object W18.31
out of
bed W06
building NEC W13.8
chair W07
furniture NEC W08
wheelchair, non-moving W05.0
powered —*see* Accident, transport, pedestrian, conveyance, specified type NEC
window W13.4
over
animal W01.0
cliff W15

Fall, falling *(continued)*
over *(continued)*
embankment W17.81
small object W01.0
rock W20.8
same level W18.30
from
being crushed, pushed, or stepped on by a crowd or human stampede W52
collision, pushing, shoving, by or with other person W03
slipping, stumbling, tripping W01.0
involving ice or snow W00.0
involving skates (ice) (roller), skateboard, skis —*see* Accident, transport, pedestrian, conveyance
snowslide (avalanche) —*see* Landslide
stone W20.8
structure W20.1
burning (uncontrolled fire) X00.3
through
bridge W13.1
floor W13.3
roof W13.2
wall W13.8
window W13.4
timber W20.8
tree (caused by lightning) W20.8
while being carried or supported by other person (s) W04

Fallen on by
animal (not being ridden) NEC W55.89

Felo-de-se —*see* Suicide

Fight (hand) (fists) (foot) —*see* Assault, fight

Fire (accidental) —*see* Exposure, fire

Firearm discharge
—*see* Discharge, firearm

Fireball effects from nuclear explosion in war operations —*see* War operations, nuclear weapons

Fireworks (explosion) W39

Flash burns from explosion
—*see* Explosion

Flood (any injury) (caused by) X38
collapse of man-made structure causing earth movement X36.0
tidal wave —*see* Forces of nature, tidal wave

Food (any type) in
air passages (with asphyxia, obstruction, or suffocation) —*see* categories T17 and T18
alimentary tract causing asphyxia (due to compression of trachea) —*see* categories T17 and T18

Forces of nature X39.8
avalanche X36.1
causing transport accident —*see* Accident, transport, by type of vehicle
blizzard X37.2
cataclysmic storm X37.9
with flood X38
blizzard X37.2
cloudburst X37.8
cyclone X37.1
dust storm X37.3
hurricane X37.0
specified storm NEC X37.8
storm surge X37.0
tornado X37.1

Forces of nature *(continued)*
cataclysmic storm *(continued)*
twister X37.1
typhoon X37.0
cloudburst X37.8
cold (natural) X31
cyclone X37.1
dam collapse causing earth movementX36.0
dust storm X37.3
earth movement X36.1
earthquake X34
caused by dam or structure collapse X36.0
earthquake X34
flood (caused by) X38
dam collapse X36.0
tidal wave —*see* Forces of nature, tidal wave
heat (natural) X30
hurricane X37.0
landslide X36.1
causing transport accident —*see* Accident, transport, by type of vehicle
lightning —*see subcategory* T75.0
causing fire —*see* Exposure, fire
mudslide X36.1
causing transport accident —*see* Accident, transport, by type of vehicle
radiation (natural) X39.08
radon X39.01
radon X39.01
specified force NEC X39.8
storm surge X37.0
structure collapse causing earth movement X36.0
sunlight X32
tidal wave X37.41
due to
earthquake X37.41
landslide X37.43
storm X37.42
volcanic eruption X37.41
tornado X37.1
tsunami X37.41
twister X37.1
typhoon X37.0
volcanic eruption X35

Foreign body
aspiration —*see* Index to Diseases and Injuries, Foreign body, respiratory tract
entering through skin W45.8
can lid W45.2
nail W45.0
paper W45.1
specified NEC W45.8
splinter W45.8

Forest fire (exposure to)
—*see* Exposure, fire, uncontrolled, not in building

Found injured X58
from exposure (to) —*see* Exposure
on
highway, road (way), street V89.9
railway right of way V81.9

Fracture (circumstances unknown or unspecified) X58
due to specified cause NEC X58

Freezing —*see* Exposure, cold

Frostbite X31
due to man-made conditions —*see* Exposure, cold, man-made

Frozen —*see* Exposure, cold

G

Gored by bull W55.22

Gunshot wound W34.00

H

Hailstones, injured by X39.8

Hanged herself or himself
—*see* Hanging, self-inflicted

Hanging (accidental)
—*see also* category T71
legal execution —*see* Legal, intervention, specified means N

Heat (effects of) (excessive) X30
due to
man-made conditions W92
on board watercraft V93.29
fishing boat V93.22
merchant ship V93.20
passenger ship V93.21
sailboat V93.24
specified powered craft NE V93.23
weather (conditions) X30
from
electric heating apparatus causir burning X16
nuclear explosion in war operations —*see* War operatio nuclear weapons
inappropriate in local application or packing in medical or surgica procedure Y63.5

Hemorrhage
delayed following medical or surgical treatment without menti of misadventure —*see* Index to Diseases and Injuries, Complication(s)
during medical or surgical treatmer as misadventure —*see* Index to Diseases and Injuries, Complication(s)

High
altitude (effects) —*see* Air, pressur low
level of radioactivity, effects —*see* Radiation
pressure (effects) —*see* Air, pressu high
temperature, effects —*see* Heat

Hit, hitting (accidental) by —*see* Stru by

Hitting against —*see* Striking against

Homicide (attempt) (justifiable)
—*see* Assault

Hot
place, effects —*see also* Heat
weather, effects X30

House fire (uncontrolled)
—*see* Exposure, fire, uncontrolled, building

Humidity, causing problem X39.8

Hunger X58

Hurricane (any injury) X37.0

Hypobarism, hypobaropathy
—*see* Air, pressure, low

I

Ictus
caloris —*see also* Heat
solaris X30

Jumped, jumping *(continued)*
- from *(continued)*
  - boat (into water) voluntarily, without accident *(continued)*
    - striking bottom *(continued)*
      - causing drowning W16.721
  - building —*see also* Jumped, from, high place W13.9
    - burning (uncontrolled fire) X00.5
  - high place NEC W17.89
    - suicide (attempt) X80
    - undetermined whether accidental or intentional Y30
  - structure —*see also* Jumped, from, high place W13.9
    - burning (uncontrolled fire) X00.5
- into water W16.92
  - causing drowning W16.91
  - from, off watercraft —*see* Jumped, from, boat
  - in
    - natural body W16.612
      - causing drowning W16.611
      - striking bottom W16.622
        - causing drowning W16.621
    - specified place NEC W16.812
      - causing drowning W16.811
      - striking
        - bottom W16.822
          - causing drowning W16.821
        - wall W16.832
          - causing drowning W16.831
    - swimming pool W16.512
      - causing drowning W16.511
      - striking
        - bottom W16.522
          - causing drowning W16.521
        - wall W16.532
          - causing drowning W16.531
- suicide (attempt) X71.3

K

Kicked by
- animal NEC W55.82
- person (s) (accidentally) W50.1
  - with intent to injure or kill Y04.0
  - as, or caused by, a crowd or human stampede (with fall) W52
  - assault Y04.0
  - homicide (attempt) Y04.0
  - in
    - fight Y04.0
    - legal intervention
      - injuring
        - bystander Y35.812
        - law enforcement personnel Y35.811
        - suspect Y35.813

Kicking against
- object W22.8
  - sports equipment W21.9
  - stationary wW22.09
    - sports equipment W21.89
- person —*see* Striking against, person
- sports equipment W21.9

Killed, killing (accidentally)
- NOS —*see also* Injury X58
- in action —*see* War operations
  - brawl, fight (hand) (fists) (foot) Y04.0
    - by weapon —*see also* Assault
      - cutting, piercing —*see* Assault, cutting or piercing instrument

Killed, killing *(continued)*
- in action *(continued)*
  - brawl, fight *(continued)*
    - by weapon *(continued)*
      - firearm —*see* Discharge, firearm, by type, homicide
- self
  - stated as
    - accident NOS X58
    - suicide —*see* Suicide
    - undetermined whether accidental or intentional Y33

Knocked down (accidentally) (by)
- NOS X58
- animal (not being ridden) NEC —*see also* Struck by, by type of animal
- crowd or human stampede W52
- person W51
  - in brawl, fight Y04.0
- transport vehicle NEC —*see also* Accident, transport V09.9

L

Laceration NEC —*see* Injury

Lack of
- care (helpless person) (infant) (newborn) X58
- food except as result of abandonment or neglect X58
  - due to abandonment or neglect X58
- water except as result of transport accident X58
  - due to transport accident —*see* Accident, transport, by type
  - helpless person, infant, newborn X58

Landslide (falling on transport vehicle) X36.1
- caused by collapse of man-made structure X36.0

Late effect —*see* Sequelae

Legal
- execution (any method) —*see* Legal, intervention
- intervention (by)
  - baton —*see* Legal, intervention, blunt object, baton
  - bayonet —*see* Legal, intervention, sharp object, bayonet
  - blow —*see* Legal, intervention, manhandling
  - blunt object
    - baton
      - injuring
        - bystander Y35.312
        - law enforcement personnel Y35.311
        - suspect Y35.313
    - injuring
      - bystander Y35.302
      - law enforcement personnel Y35.301
      - suspect Y35.303
    - specified NEC
      - injuring
        - bystander Y35.392
        - law enforcement personnel Y35.391
        - suspect Y35.393
    - stave
      - injuring
        - bystander Y35.392
        - law enforcement personnel Y35.391
        - suspect Y35.393
  - bomb —*see* Legal, intervention, explosive

Legal *(continued)*
- intervention *(continued)*
  - cutting or piercing instrument —*see* Legal, intervention, sharp object
  - dynamite —*see* Legal, intervention, explosive, dynamite
  - explosive (s)
    - dynamite
      - injuring
        - bystander Y35.112
        - law enforcement personnel Y35.111
        - suspect Y35.113
    - grenade
      - injuring
        - bystander Y35.192
        - law enforcement personnel Y35.191
        - suspect Y35.193
    - injuring
      - bystander Y35.102
      - law enforcement personnel Y35.101
      - suspect Y35.103
    - mortar bomb
      - injuring
        - bystander Y35.192
        - law enforcement personnel Y35.191
        - suspect Y35.193
    - shell
      - injuring
        - bystander Y35.122
        - law enforcement personnel Y35.121
        - suspect Y35.123
    - specified NEC
      - injuring
        - bystander Y35.192
        - law enforcement personnel Y35.191
        - suspect Y35.193
  - firearm (s) (discharge)
    - handgun
      - injuring
        - bystander Y35.022
        - law enforcement personnel Y35.021
        - suspect Y35.023
    - injuring
      - bystander Y35.002
      - law enforcement personnel Y35.001
      - suspect Y35.003
    - machine gun
      - injuring
        - bystander Y35.012
        - law enforcement personnel Y35.011
        - suspect Y35.013
    - rifle pellet
      - injuring
        - bystander Y35.032
        - law enforcement personnel Y35.031
        - suspect Y35.033
    - rubber bullet
      - injuring
        - bystander Y35.042
        - law enforcement personnel Y35.041
        - suspect Y35.043
    - shotgun —*see* Legal, intervention, firearm, specified NEC
    - specified NEC
      - injuring
        - bystander Y35.092
        - law enforcement personnel Y35.091
        - suspect Y35.093

Legal *(continued)*
- intervention *(continued)*
  - gas (asphyxiation) (poisoning)
    - injuring
      - bystander Y35.202
      - law enforcement personnel Y35.201
      - suspect Y35.203
    - specified NEC
      - injuring
        - bystander Y35.292
        - law enforcement person Y35.291
        - suspect Y35.293
    - tear gas
      - injuring
        - bystander Y35.212
        - law enforcement person Y35.211
        - suspect Y35.213
  - grenade —*see* Legal, interventi explosive, grenade
  - injuring
    - bystander Y35.92
    - law enforcement personnel Y35.91
    - suspect Y35.93
  - late effect (of) —*see* with 7th character S Y35
  - manhandling
    - injuring
      - bystander Y35.812
      - law enforcement personne Y35.811
      - suspect Y35.813
  - sequelae (of) —*see* with 7th character S Y35
  - sharp objects
    - bayonet
      - injuring
        - bystander Y35.412
        - law enforcement person Y35.411
        - suspect Y35.413
    - injuring
      - bystander Y35.402
      - law enforcement personne Y35.401
      - suspect Y35.403
    - specified NEC
      - injuring
        - bystander Y35.492
        - law enforcement person Y35.491
        - suspect Y35.493
  - specified means NEC
    - injuring
      - bystander Y35.892
      - law enforcement personnel Y35.891
      - suspect Y35.893
  - stabbing —*see* Legal, interventi sharp object
  - stave —*see* Legal, intervention, blunt object, stave
  - tear gas —*see* Legal, interventio gas, tear
  - gas
  - truncheon —*see* Legal, intervention, blunt object, sta

Lightning (shock) (stroke) (struck by) —*see* subcategory T75.0
- causing fire —*see* Exposure, fire

Loss of control (transport vehicle) N —*see* Accident, transport

Lost at sea NOS —*see* Drowning, du to, fall overboard

Low
- pressure (effects) —*see* Air, pressu low

Tabular List of Diseases and Injuries

ıble of Contents

structional Notations

cludes:

word 'Includes' appears immediately under certain categories to further define, or give examples of, the content of the category.

cludes Notes

ICD-10-CM has two types of excludes notes. Each note has a different definition for use but they are both similar in that they indicate that codes excluded from each other ndependent of each other.

cludes1

pe 1 Excludes note is a pure excludes. It means 'NOT CODED HERE!' An Excludes1 note indicates that the code excluded should never be used at the same time as the above the Excludes1 note. An Excludes1 is used when two conditions cannot occur together, such as a congenital form versus an acquired form of the same condition.

cludes2

pe 2 excludes note represents 'Not included here'. An Excludes2 note indicates that the condition excluded is not part of the condition it is excluded from but a patient may both conditions at the same time. When an Excludes2 note appears under a code it is acceptable to use both the code and the excluded code together.

de First/Use Additional Code notes (etiology/manifestation paired codes)

ain conditions have both an underlying etiology and multiple body system manifestations due to the underlying etiology. For such conditions the ICD-10-CM has a ng convention that requires the underlying condition be sequenced first followed by the manifestation. Wherever such a combination exists there is a 'use additional code' at the etiology code, and a 'code first' note at the manifestation code. These instructional notes indicate the proper sequencing order of the codes, etiology followed by ifestation.

ıost cases the manifestation codes will have in the code title, 'in diseases classified elsewhere.' Codes with this title are a component of the etiology/ manifestation vention. The code title indicates that it is a manifestation code. 'In diseases classified elsewhere' codes are never permitted to be used as first listed or principal diagnosis s. They must be used in conjunction with an underlying condition code and they must be listed following the underlying condition.

de Also

ode also note instructs that 2 codes may be required to fully describe a condition but the sequencing of the two codes is discretionary, depending on the severity of the litions and the reason for the encounter.

characters and placeholder X

codes less than 6 characters that require a 7th character a placeholder X should be assigned for all characters less than 6. The 7th character must always be the 7th character code

Chapter 1: Certain Infectious and Parasitic Diseases (A00-B99)

Includes: diseases generally recognized as communicable or transmissible

Use additional code to identify resistance to antimicrobial drugs (Z16-)

Excludes1: *certain localized infections - see body system-related chapters*

Excludes2: *carrier or suspected carrier of infectious disease (Z22.-)*
infectious and parasitic diseases specific to the perinatal period (P35-P39)
infectious and parasitic diseases complicating pregnancy, childbirth and the puerperium (O98.-)
influenza and other acute respiratory infections (J00-J22)

This chapter contains the following category blocks:

A00-A09	Intestinal infectious diseases
A15-A19	Tuberculosis
A20-A28	Certain zoonotic bacterial diseases
A30-A49	Other bacterial diseases
A50-A64	Infections with a predominantly sexual mode of transmission
A65-A69	Other spirochetal diseases
A70-A74	Other diseases caused by chlamydiae
A75-A79	Rickettsioses
A80-A89	Viral and prion infections of the central nervous system
A90-A99	Arthropod-borne viral fevers and viral hemorrhagic fevers
B00-B09	Viral infections characterized by skin and mucous membrane lesions
B10	Other human herpesviruses
B15-B19	Viral hepatitis
B20	Human immunodeficiency virus [HIV] disease
B25-B34	Other viral diseases
B35-B49	Mycoses
B50-B64	Protozoal diseases
B65-B83	Helminthiases
B85-B89	Pediculosis, acariasis and other infestations
B90-B94	Sequelae of infectious and parasitic diseases
B95-B97	Bacterial and viral infectious agents
B99	Other infectious diseases

C. Chapter-Specific Coding Guidelines

In addition to general coding guidelines, there are guidelines for specific diagnoses and/or conditions in the classification. Unless otherwise indicated, these guidelines apply to all health care settings. Please refer to Section II for guidelines on the selection of principal diagnosis.

1. Chapter 1: Certain Infectious and Parasitic Diseases (A00-B99)

a. Human Immunodeficiency Virus (HIV) Infections

1) Code only confirmed cases

Code only confirmed cases of HIV infection/illness. This is an exception to the hospital inpatient guideline Section II, H.

In this context, "confirmation" does not require documentation of positive serology or culture for HIV; the provider's diagnostic statement that the patient is HIV positive, or has an HIV-related illness is sufficient.

2) Selection and sequencing of HIV codes

(a) Patient admitted for HIV-related condition

If a patient is admitted for an HIV-related condition, the principal diagnosis should be B20, Human immunodeficiency virus [HIV] disease followed by additional diagnosis codes for all reported HIV-related conditions.

(b) Patient with HIV disease admitted for unrelated condition

If a patient with HIV disease is admitted for an unrelated condition (such as a traumatic injury), the code for the unrelated condition (e.g., the nature of injury code) should be the principal diagnosis. Other diagnoses would be B20 followed by additional diagnosis codes for all reported HIV-related conditions.

(c) Whether the patient is newly diagnosed

Whether the patient is newly diagnosed or has had previous admissions/encounters for HIV conditions is irrelevant to the sequencing decision.

(d) Asymptomatic human immunodeficiency virus

Z21, Asymptomatic human immunodeficiency virus [HIV] infection status, is to be applied when the patient without any documentation of symptoms is listed as being "HIV positive," "known HIV," "HIV test positive," or similar terminology. Do not use this code if the term "AIDS" is used or if the patient is treated for any HIV-related illness or is described as having any condition(s) resulting from his/her HIV positive status; use B20 in these cases.

(e) Patients with inconclusive HIV serology

Patients with inconclusive HIV serology, but no definitive diagnosis or manifestations of the illness, may be assigned code R75, Inconclusive laboratory evidence of human immunodeficiency virus [HIV].

(f) Previously diagnosed HIV-related illness

Patients with any known prior diagnosis of an HIV-related illness sh be coded to B20. Once a patient has developed an HIV-related ill the patient should always be assigned code B20 on every subseq admission/encounter. Patients previously diagnosed with any HIV il (B20) should never be assigned to R75 or Z21, Asymptomatic hu immunodeficiency virus [HIV] infection status.

(g) HIV Infection in Pregnancy, Childbirth and the Puerperium

During pregnancy, childbirth or the puerperium, a patient adm (or presenting for a health care encounter) because of an HIV-re illness should receive a principal diagnosis code of O98.7-, Hu immunodeficiency [HIV] disease complicating pregnancy, childbirth an puerperium, followed by B20 and the code(s) for the HIV-related illness

Codes from Chapter 15 always take sequencing priority.

Patients with asymptomatic HIV infection status admitted (or prese for a health care encounter) during pregnancy, childbirth, or puerperium should receive codes of O98.7- and Z21.

(h) Encounters for testing for HIV

If a patient is being seen to determine his/her HIV status, use code Z Encounter for screening for human immunodeficiency virus [HIV]. additional codes for any associated high risk behavior.

If a patient with signs or symptoms is being seen for HIV testing, the signs and symptoms. An additional counseling code Z71.7, Hu immunodeficiency virus [HIV] counseling, may be used if counseli provided during the encounter for the test.

When a patient returns to be informed of his/her HIV test results an test result is negative, use code Z71.7, Human immunodeficiency [HIV] counseling.

If the results are positive, see previous guidelines and assign code appropriate.

b. Infectious agents as the cause of diseases classified to other chapters

Certain infections are classified in chapters other than Chapter 1 and no orga is identified as part of the infection code. In these instances, it is necessa use an additional code from Chapter 1 to identify the organism. A code category B95, Streptococcus, Staphylococcus, and Enterococcus as the cau diseases classified to other chapters, B96, Other bacterial agents as the cau diseases classified to other chapters, or B97, Viral agents as the cause of dise classified to other chapters, is to be used as an additional code to identify organism. An instructional note will be found at the infection code advising an additional organism code is required.

c. Infections resistant to antibiotics

Many bacterial infections are resistant to current antibiotics. It is necessa identify all infections documented as antibiotic resistant. Assign a code category Z16, Resistance to antimicrobial drugs, following the infection only if the infection code does not identify drug resistance.

d. Sepsis, Severe Sepsis, and Septic Shock

1) Coding of Sepsis and Severe Sepsis

(a) Sepsis

For a diagnosis of sepsis, assign the appropriate code for the underl systemic infection. If the type of infection or causal organism is further specified, assign code A41.9, Sepsis, unspecified organism.

A code from subcategory R65.2, Severe sepsis, should not be assi unless severe sepsis or an associated acute organ dysfunction is docume

(i) Negative or inconclusive blood cultures and sepsis

Negative or inconclusive blood cultures do not preclude a diagnos sepsis in patients with clinical evidence of the condition, howeve provider should be queried.

(ii) Urosepsis

The term urosepsis is a nonspecific term. It is not to be consid synonymous with sepsis. It has no default code in the Alpha Index. Should a provider use this term, he/she must be querie clarification.

(iii) Sepsis with organ dysfunction

If a patient has sepsis and associated acute organ dysfunctic multiple organ dysfunction (MOD), follow the instructions for co severe sepsis.

(iv) Acute organ dysfunction that is not clearly associated with the se

If a patient has sepsis and an acute organ dysfunction, but the me record documentation indicates that the acute organ dysfunctic related to a medical condition other than the sepsis, do not assign a from subcategory R65.2, Severe sepsis. An acute organ dysfunction be associated with the sepsis in order to assign the severe sepsis co the documentation is not clear as to whether an acute organ dysfun is related to the sepsis or another medical condition, query the prov

(b) Severe sepsis

The coding of severe sepsis requires a minimum of 2 codes: first a code for the underlying systemic infection, followed by a code from subcategory R65.2, Severe sepsis. If the causal organism is not documented, assign code A41.9, Sepsis, unspecified organism, for the infection. Additional code(s) for the associated acute organ dysfunction are also required.

Due to the complex nature of severe sepsis, some cases may require querying the provider prior to assignment of the codes.

2) Septic shock

(a) Septic shock generally refers to circulatory failure associated with severe sepsis, and therefore, it represents a type of acute organ dysfunction.

For cases of septic shock, the code for the systemic infection should be sequenced first, followed by code R65.21, Severe sepsis with septic shock or code T81.12, Postprocedural septic shock. Any additional codes for the other acute organ dysfunctions should also be assigned. As noted in the sequencing instructions in the Tabular List, the code for septic shock cannot be assigned as a principal diagnosis.

3) Sequencing of severe sepsis

If severe sepsis is present on admission, and meets the definition of principal diagnosis, the underlying systemic infection should be assigned as principal diagnosis followed by the appropriate code from subcategory R65.2 as required by the sequencing rules in the Tabular List. A code from subcategory R65.2 can never be assigned as a principal diagnosis.

When severe sepsis develops during an encounter (it was not present on admission) the underlying systemic infection and the appropriate code from subcategory R65.2 should be assigned as secondary diagnoses.

Severe sepsis may be present on admission but the diagnosis may not be confirmed until sometime after admission. If the documentation is not clear whether severe sepsis was present on admission, the provider should be queried.

4) Sepsis and severe sepsis with a localized infection

If the reason for admission is both sepsis or severe sepsis and a localized infection, such as pneumonia or cellulitis, a code(s) for the underlying systemic infection should be assigned first and the code for the localized infection should be assigned as a secondary diagnosis. If the patient has severe sepsis, a code from subcategory R65.2 should also be assigned as a secondary diagnosis. If the patient is admitted with a localized infection, such as pneumonia, and sepsis/severe sepsis doesn't develop until after admission, the localized infection should be assigned first, followed by the appropriate sepsis/severe sepsis codes.

5) Sepsis due to a postprocedural infection

(a) Documentation of causal relationship

As with all postprocedural complications, code assignment is based on the provider's documentation of the relationship between the infection and the procedure.

(b) Sepsis due to a postprocedural infection

For such cases, the postprocedural infection code, such as, T80.2, Infections following infusion, transfusion, and therapeutic injection, T81.4, Infection following a procedure, T88.0, Infection following immunization, or O86.0, Infection of obstetric surgical wound, should be coded first, followed by the code for the specific infection. If the patient has severe sepsis the appropriate code from subcategory R65.2 should also be assigned with the additional code(s) for any acute organ dysfunction.

(c) Postprocedural infection and postprocedural septic shock

In cases where a postprocedural infection has occurred and has resulted in severe sepsis and postprocedural septic shock, the code for the precipitating complication such as code T81.4, Infection following a procedure, or O86.0, Infection of obstetrical surgical wound should be coded first followed by code R65.2**0**, Severe sepsis without septic shock. **A code for the systemic infection should also be assigned. If a psotprocedural infection has resulted in postprocedural septic shock, the code for the precipitating complication such as code T81.4, Infection following a procedure, or O96.0, Infection of obstetrical surgical wound should be coded first followed by code T81.12-, Postprocedural septic shock. A code for the systemic infection should also be assigned**.

6) Sepsis and severe sepsis associated with a noninfectious process (condition)

In some cases a noninfectious process (condition), such as trauma, may lead to an infection which can result in sepsis or severe sepsis. If sepsis or severe sepsis is documented as associated with a noninfectious condition, such as a burn or serious injury, and this condition meets the definition for principal diagnosis, the code for the noninfectious condition should be sequenced first, followed by the code for the resulting infection. If severe sepsis, is present a code from subcategory R65.2 should also be assigned with any associated organ dysfunction(s) codes. It is not necessary to assign a code from subcategory R65.1, Systemic inflammatory response syndrome (SIRS) of non-infectious origin, for these cases.

If the infection meets the definition of principal diagnosis it should be sequenced before the non-infectious condition. When both the associated non-infectious condition and the infection meet the definition of principal diagnosis either may be assigned as principal diagnosis.

Only one code from category R65, Symptoms and signs specifically associated with systemic inflammation and infection, should be assigned. Therefore, when a non-infectious condition leads to an infection resulting in severe sepsis, assign the appropriate code from subcategory R65.2, Severe sepsis. Do not additionally assign a code from subcategory R65.1, Systemic inflammatory response syndrome (SIRS) of non-infectious origin.

See Section I.C.18. SIRS due to non-infectious process

7) Sepsis and septic shock complicating abortion, pregnancy, childbirth, and the puerperium

See Section I.C.15. Sepsis and septic shock complicating abortion, pregnancy, childbirth and the puerperium

8) Newborn sepsis

See Section I.C.16. f. Bacterial sepsis of Newborn

e. Methicillin Resistant *Staphylococcus aureus* (MRSA) Conditions

1) Selection and sequencing of MRSA codes

(a) Combination codes for MRSA infection

When a patient is diagnosed with an infection that is due to methicillin resistant Staphylococcus aureus (MRSA), and that infection has a combination code that includes the causal organism (e.g., sepsis, pneumonia) assign the appropriate combination code for the condition (e.g., code A41.02, Sepsis due to Methicillin resistant Staphylococcus aureus or code J15.212, Pneumonia due to Methicillin resistant Staphylococcus aureus). Do not assign code B95.62, Methicillin resistant Staphylococcus aureus infection as the cause of diseases classified elsewhere, as an additional code because the combination code includes the type of infection and the MRSA organism. Do not assign a code from subcategory Z16.11, Resistance to penicillins, as an additional diagnosis.

See Section C.1. for instructions on coding and sequencing of sepsis and severe sepsis.

(b) Other codes for MRSA infection

When there is documentation of a current infection (e.g., wound infection, stitch abscess, urinary tract infection) due to MRSA, and that infection does not have a combination code that includes the causal organism, assign the appropriate code to identify the condition along with code B95.62, Methicillin resistant Staphylococcus aureus infection as the cause of diseases classified elsewhere for the MRSA infection. Do not assign a code from subcategory Z16.11, Resistance to penicillins.

(c) Methicillin susceptible Staphylococcus aureus (MSSA) and MRSA colonization

The condition or state of being colonized or carrying MSSA or MRSA is called colonization or carriage, while an individual person is described as being colonized or being a carrier. Colonization means that MSSA or MSRA is present on or in the body without necessarily causing illness. A positive MRSA colonization test might be documented by the provider as "MRSA screen positive" or "MRSA nasal swab positive".

Assign code Z22.322, Carrier or suspected carrier of Methicillin resistant Staphylococcus aureus, for patients documented as having MRSA colonization. Assign code Z22.321, Carrier or suspected carrier of Methicillin susceptible Staphylococcus aureus, for patient documented as having MSSA colonization. Colonization is not necessarily indicative of a disease process or as the cause of a specific condition the patient may have unless documented as such by the provider.

(d) MRSA colonization and infection

If a patient is documented as having both MRSA colonization and infection during a hospital admission, code Z22.322, Carrier or suspected carrier of Methicillin resistant Staphylococcus aureus, and a code for the MRSA infection may both be assigned.

Intestinal infectious diseases (A00-A09)

A00 Cholera

CC **A00.0 Cholera due to Vibrio cholerae 01, biovar cholerae**
Classical cholera
CC Exclusion see Appendix A PDX collection 0002

CC **A00.1 Cholera due to Vibrio cholerae 01, biovar eltor**
Cholera eltor
CC Exclusion see Appendix A PDX collection 0002

CC **A00.9 Cholera, unspecified**
CC Exclusion see Appendix A PDX collection 0002

A01 Typhoid and paratyphoid fevers

+ **A01.0 Typhoid fever**
Infection due to Salmonella typhi
CC **A01.00 Typhoid fever, unspecified**
CC Exclusion see Appendix A PDX collection 0003
CC **A01.01 Typhoid meningitis**
CC Exclusion see Appendix A PDX collection 0003
CC **A01.02 Typhoid fever with heart involvement**
Typhoid endocarditis
Typhoid myocarditis
CC Exclusion see Appendix A PDX collection 0003
CC **A01.03 Typhoid pneumonia**
CC Exclusion see Appendix A PDX collection 0003
CC **A01.04 Typhoid arthritis**
CC Exclusion see Appendix A PDX collection 0003
CC **A01.05 Typhoid osteomyelitis**
CC Exclusion see Appendix A PDX collection 0003
CC **A01.09 Typhoid fever with other complications**
CC Exclusion see Appendix A PDX collection 0003
CC **A01.1 Paratyphoid fever A**
CC Exclusion see Appendix A PDX collection 0003
CC **A01.2 Paratyphoid fever B**
CC Exclusion see Appendix A PDX collection 0003
CC **A01.3 Paratyphoid fever C**
CC Exclusion see Appendix A PDX collection 0003
CC **A01.4 Paratyphoid fever, unspecified**
Infection due to Salmonella paratyphi NOS
CC Exclusion see Appendix A PDX collection 0003

A02 Other salmonella infections

Includes: infection or foodborne intoxication due to any Salmonella species other than S. typhi and S. paratyphi

CC **A02.0 Salmonella enteritis**
Salmonellosis
CC Exclusion see Appendix A PDX collection 0004
MCC **A02.1 Salmonella sepsis**
MCC Exclusion see Appendix A PDX collection 0005
Review coding guideline C.1.d
+ **A02.2 Localized salmonella infections**
A02.20 Localized salmonella infection, unspecified
MCC **A02.21 Salmonella meningitis**
MCC Exclusion see Appendix A PDX collection 0006
MCC **A02.22 Salmonella pneumonia**
MCC Exclusion see Appendix A PDX collection 0007
CC **A02.23 Salmonella arthritis**
CC Exclusion see Appendix A PDX collection 0008
CC **A02.24 Salmonella osteomyelitis**
CC Exclusion see Appendix A PDX collection 0009
CC **A02.25 Salmonella pyelonephritis**
Salmonella tubulo-interstitial nephropathy
CC Exclusion see Appendix A PDX collection 0010
CC **A02.29 Salmonella with other localized infection**
CC Exclusion see Appendix A PDX collection 0010
CC **A02.8 Other specified salmonella infections**
CC Exclusion see Appendix A PDX collection 0011
CC **A02.9 Salmonella infection, unspecified**
CC Exclusion see Appendix A PDX collection 0012

A03 Shigellosis

CC **A03.0 Shigellosis due to Shigella dysenteriae**
Group A shigellosis [Shiga-Kruse dysentery]
CC Exclusion see Appendix A PDX collection 0013
A03.1 Shigellosis due to Shigella flexneri
Group B shigellosis
A03.2 Shigellosis due to Shigella boydii
Group C shigellosis
A03.3 Shigellosis due to Shigella sonnei
Group D shigellosis
A03.8 Other shigellosis
A03.9 Shigellosis, unspecified
Bacillary dysentery NOS

A04 Other bacterial intestinal infections

Excludes1: *bacterial foodborne intoxications, NEC (A05.-)*
tuberculous enteritis (A18.32)

CC **A04.0 Enteropathogenic Escherichia coli infection**
CC Exclusion see Appendix A PDX collection 0014
CC **A04.1 Enterotoxigenic Escherichia coli infection**
CC Exclusion see Appendix A PDX collection 0014
CC **A04.2 Enteroinvasive Escherichia coli infection**
CC Exclusion see Appendix A PDX collection 0014
CC **A04.3 Enterohemorrhagic Escherichia coli infection**
CC Exclusion see Appendix A PDX collection 0014
CC **A04.4 Other intestinal Escherichia coli infections**
Escherichia coli enteritis NOS
CC Exclusion see Appendix A PDX collection 0014
CC **A04.5 Campylobacter enteritis**
CC Exclusion see Appendix A PDX collection 0015
CC **A04.6 Enteritis due to Yersinia enterocolitica**
Excludes1: *extraintestinal yersiniosis (A28.2)*
CC Exclusion see Appendix A PDX collection 0015
CC **A04.7 Enterocolitis due to Clostridium difficile**
Foodborne intoxication by Clostridium difficile
Pseudomembraneous colitis
CC Exclusion see Appendix A PDX collection 0015
CC **A04.8 Other specified bacterial intestinal infections**
CC Exclusion see Appendix A PDX collection 0015
CC **A04.9 Bacterial intestinal infection, unspecified**
Bacterial enteritis NOS
CC Exclusion see Appendix A PDX collection 0016

A05 Other bacterial foodborne intoxications, not elsewhere classified

Excludes1: *Clostridium difficile foodborne intoxication and infection (A04.7)*
Escherichia coli infection (A04.0-A04.4)
listeriosis (A32.-)
salmonella foodborne intoxication and infection (A02.-)
toxic effect of noxious foodstuffs (T61-T62)

CC **A05.0 Foodborne staphylococcal intoxication**
CC Exclusion see Appendix A PDX collection 0017
CC **A05.1 Botulism food poisoning**
Botulism NOS
Classical foodborne intoxication due to Clostridium botulinum
Excludes1: *infant botulism (A48.51)*
wound botulism (A48.52)
CC Exclusion see Appendix A PDX collection 0018
CC **A05.2 Foodborne Clostridium perfringens [Clostridium welchii] intoxication**
Enteritis necroticans
Pig-bel
CC Exclusion see Appendix A PDX collection 0019
CC **A05.3 Foodborne Vibrio parahaemolyticus intoxication**
CC Exclusion see Appendix A PDX collection 0017
CC **A05.4 Foodborne Bacillus cereus intoxication**
CC Exclusion see Appendix A PDX collection 0017
CC **A05.5 Foodborne Vibrio vulnificus intoxication**
CC Exclusion see Appendix A PDX collection 0017
CC **A05.8 Other specified bacterial foodborne intoxications**
CC Exclusion see Appendix A PDX collection 0017
A05.9 Bacterial foodborne intoxication, unspecified

A06 Amebiasis

Includes: infection due to Entamoeba histolytica
Excludes1: *other protozoal intestinal diseases (A07.-)*
Excludes2: *acanthamebiasis (B60.1-)*
Naegleriasis (B60.2)

CC **A06.0 Acute amebic dysentery**
Acute amebiasis
Intestinal amebiasis NOS
CC Exclusion see Appendix A PDX collection 0020
CC **A06.1 Chronic intestinal amebiasis**
CC Exclusion see Appendix A PDX collection 0020
CC **A06.2 Amebic nondysenteric colitis**
CC Exclusion see Appendix A PDX collection 0021
CC **A06.3 Ameboma of intestine**
Ameboma NOS
CC Exclusion see Appendix A PDX collection 0022
MCC **A06.4 Amebic liver abscess**
Hepatic amebiasis
MCC Exclusion see Appendix A PDX collection 0023
MCC **A06.5 Amebic lung abscess**
Amebic abscess of lung (and liver)
MCC Exclusion see Appendix A PDX collection 0024
MCC **A06.6 Amebic brain abscess**
Amebic abscess of brain (and liver) (and lung)
MCC Exclusion see Appendix A PDX collection 0025
A06.7 Cutaneous amebiasis
+ **A06.8 Amebic infection of other sites**
CC **A06.81 Amebic cystitis**
CC Exclusion see Appendix A PDX collection 0022
CC **A06.82 Other amebic genitourinary infections**
Amebic balanitis
Amebic vesiculitis
Amebic vulvovaginitis
CC Exclusion see Appendix A PDX collection 0022
CC **A06.89 Other amebic infections**
Amebic appendicitis
Amebic splenic abscess
CC Exclusion see Appendix A PDX collection 0022
A06.9 Amebiasis, unspecified

A07 Other protozoal intestinal diseases

A07.0 Balantidiasis
Balantidial dysentery

CC **A07.1 Giardiasis [lambliasis]**
CC Exclusion see Appendix A PDX collection 0026

CC **A07.2 Cryptosporidiosis**
CC Exclusion see Appendix A PDX collection 0026

CC **A07.3 Isosporiasis**
Infection due to Isospora belli and Isospora hominis
Intestinal coccidiosis
Isosporosis
CC Exclusion see Appendix A PDX collection 0026

CC **A07.4 Cyclosporiasis**
CC Exclusion see Appendix A PDX collection 0027

CC **A07.8 Other specified protozoal intestinal diseases**
Intestinal microsporidiosis
Intestinal trichomoniasis
Sarcocystosis
Sarcosporidiosis
CC Exclusion see Appendix A PDX collection 0026

CC **A07.9 Protozoal intestinal disease, unspecified**
Flagellate diarrhea
Protozoal colitis
Protozoal diarrhea
Protozoal dysentery
CC Exclusion see Appendix A PDX collection 0026

A08 Viral and other specified intestinal infections

Excludes1: *influenza with involvement of gastrointestinal tract (J09.X3, J10.2, J11.2)*

CC **A08.0 Rotaviral enteritis**
CC Exclusion see Appendix A PDX collection 0028

\+ **A08.1 Acute gastroenteropathy due to Norwalk agent and other small round viruses**

CC **A08.11 Acute gastroenteropathy due to Norwalk agent**
Acute gastroenteropathy due to Norovirus
Acute gastroenteropathy due to Norwalk-like agent
CC Exclusion see Appendix A PDX collection 0028

CC **A08.19 Acute gastroenteropathy due to other small round viruses**
Acute gastroenteropathy due to small round virus [SRV] NOS
CC Exclusion see Appendix A PDX collection 0028

CC **A08.2 Adenoviral enteritis**
CC Exclusion see Appendix A PDX collection 0028

\+ **A08.3 Other viral enteritis**

CC **A08.31 Calicivirus enteritis**
CC Exclusion see Appendix A PDX collection 0028

CC **A08.32 Astrovirus enteritis**
CC Exclusion see Appendix A PDX collection 0028

CC **A08.39 Other viral enteritis**
Coxsackie virus enteritis
Echovirus enteritis
Enterovirus enteritis NEC
Torovirus enteritis
CC Exclusion see Appendix A PDX collection 0028

A08.4 Viral intestinal infection, unspecified
Viral enteritis NOS
Viral gastroenteritis NOS
Viral gastroenteropathy NOS

A08.8 Other specified intestinal infections

CC **A09 Infectious gastroenteritis and colitis, unspecified**

Infectious colitis NOS
Infectious enteritis NOS
Infectious gastroenteritis NOS
Excludes1: *colitis NOS (K52.9)*
diarrhea NOS (R19.7)
enteritis NOS (K52.9)
gastroenteritis NOS (K52.9)
noninfective gastroenteritis and colitis, unspecified (K52.9)
CC Exclusion see Appendix A PDX collection 0017
Valid 3-character code, no further characters required

Tuberculosis (A15-A19)

Includes: infections due to Mycobacterium tuberculosis and Mycobacterium bovis

Excludes1: *congenital tuberculosis (P37.0)*
nonspecific reaction to test for tuberculosis without active tuberculosis (R76.1-)
pneumoconiosis associated with tuberculosis, any type in A15 (J65)
positive PPD (R76.11)
positive tuberculin skin test without active tuberculosis (R76.11)
sequelae of tuberculosis (B90.-)
silicotuberculosis (J65)

A15 Respiratory tuberculosis

CC **A15.0 Tuberculosis of lung**
Tuberculous bronchiectasis
Tuberculous fibrosis of lung
Tuberculous pneumonia
Tuberculous pneumothorax
CC Exclusion see Appendix A PDX collection 0029

CC **A15.4 Tuberculosis of intrathoracic lymph nodes**
Tuberculosis of hilar lymph nodes
Tuberculosis of mediastinal lymph nodes
Tuberculosis of tracheobronchial lymph nodes
Excludes1: *tuberculosis specified as primary (A15.7)*
CC Exclusion see Appendix A PDX collection 0029

CC **A15.5 Tuberculosis of larynx, trachea and bronchus**
Tuberculosis of bronchus
Tuberculosis of glottis
Tuberculosis of larynx
Tuberculosis of trachea
CC Exclusion see Appendix A PDX collection 0029

CC **A15.6 Tuberculous pleurisy**
Tuberculosis of pleura Tuberculous empyema
Excludes1: *primary respiratory tuberculosis (A15.7)*
CC Exclusion see Appendix A PDX collection 0029

CC **A15.7 Primary respiratory tuberculosis**
CC Exclusion see Appendix A PDX collection 0030

CC **A15.8 Other respiratory tuberculosis**
Mediastinal tuberculosis
Nasopharyngeal tuberculosis
Tuberculosis of nose
Tuberculosis of sinus [any nasal]
CC Exclusion see Appendix A PDX collection 0031

CC **A15.9 Respiratory tuberculosis unspecified**
CC Exclusion see Appendix A PDX collection 0031

A17 Tuberculosis of nervous system

MCC **A17.0 Tuberculous meningitis**
Tuberculosis of meninges (cerebral)(spinal)
Tuberculous leptomeningitis
Excludes1: *tuberculous meningoencephalitis (A17.82)*
MCC Exclusion see Appendix A PDX collection 0032

MCC **A17.1 Meningeal tuberculoma**
Tuberculoma of meninges (cerebral) (spinal)
Excludes2: *tuberculoma of brain and spinal cord (A17.81)*
MCC Exclusion see Appendix A PDX collection 0032

\+ **A17.8 Other tuberculosis of nervous system**

MCC **A17.81 Tuberculoma of brain and spinal cord**
Tuberculous abscess of brain and spinal cord
MCC Exclusion see Appendix A PDX collection 0033

MCC **A17.82 Tuberculous meningoencephalitis**
Tuberculous myelitis
MCC Exclusion see Appendix A PDX collection 0033

MCC **A17.83 Tuberculous neuritis**
Tuberculous mononeuropathy
No MCC Exclusions

MCC **A17.89 Other tuberculosis of nervous system**
Tuberculous polyneuropathy
MCC Exclusion see Appendix A PDX collection 0034

CC **A17.9 Tuberculosis of nervous system, unspecified**
CC Exclusion see Appendix A PDX collection 0035

A18 Tuberculosis of other organs

\+ **A18.0 Tuberculosis of bones and joints**

CC **A18.01 Tuberculosis of spine**
Pott's disease or curvature of spine
Tuberculous arthritis
Tuberculous osteomyelitis of spine
Tuberculous spondylitis
CC Exclusion see Appendix A PDX collection 0036

CC **A18.02 Tuberculous arthritis of other joints**
Tuberculosis of hip (joint)
Tuberculosis of knee (joint)
CC Exclusion see Appendix A PDX collection 0037

CC **A18.03 Tuberculosis of other bones**
Tuberculous mastoiditis
Tuberculous osteomyelitis
CC Exclusion see Appendix A PDX collection 0038

CC **A18.09 Other musculoskeletal tuberculosis**
Tuberculous myositis
Tuberculous synovitis
Tuberculous tenosynovitis
CC Exclusion see Appendix A PDX collection 0039

+ **A18.1 Tuberculosis of genitourinary system**
- CC **A18.10 Tuberculosis of genitourinary system, unspecified**
  CC Exclusion see Appendix A PDX collection 0040
- CC **A18.11 Tuberculosis of kidney and ureter**
  CC Exclusion see Appendix A PDX collection 0041
- CC **A18.12 Tuberculosis of bladder**
  CC Exclusion see Appendix A PDX collection 0041
- CC **A18.13 Tuberculosis of other urinary organs**
  Tuberculous urethritis
  CC Exclusion see Appendix A PDX collection 0041
- ● ♂ CC **A18.14 Tuberculosis of prostate**
  CC Exclusion see Appendix A PDX collection 0042
- ♂ CC **A18.15 Tuberculosis of other male genital organs**
  CC Exclusion see Appendix A PDX collection 0042
- ♀ CC **A18.16 Tuberculosis of cervix**
  CC Exclusion see Appendix A PDX collection 0043
- ♀ CC **A18.17 Tuberculous female pelvic inflammatory disease**
  Tuberculous endometritis
  Tuberculous oophoritis and salpingitis
  CC Exclusion see Appendix A PDX collection 0043
- ♀ CC **A18.18 Tuberculosis of other female genital organs**
  Tuberculous ulceration of vulva
  CC Exclusion see Appendix A PDX collection 0043

CC **A18.2 Tuberculous peripheral lymphadenopathy**
Tuberculous adenitis
Excludes2: *tuberculosis of bronchial and mediastinal lymph nodes (A15.4)*
tuberculosis of mesenteric and retroperitoneal lymph nodes (A18.39)
tuberculous tracheobronchial adenopathy (A15.4)
CC Exclusion see Appendix A PDX collection 0044

+ **A18.3 Tuberculosis of intestines, peritoneum and mesenteric glands**
- MCC **A18.31 Tuberculous peritonitis**
  Tuberculous ascites
  MCC Exclusion see Appendix A PDX collection 0045
- CC **A18.32 Tuberculous enteritis**
  Tuberculosis of anus and rectum
  Tuberculosis of intestine (large) (small)
  CC Exclusion see Appendix A PDX collection 0045
- CC **A18.39 Retroperitoneal tuberculosis**
  Tuberculosis of mesenteric glands
  Tuberculosis of retroperitoneal (lymph glands)
  CC Exclusion see Appendix A PDX collection 0045

CC **A18.4 Tuberculosis of skin and subcutaneous tissue**
Erythema induratum, tuberculous
Lupus excedens
Lupus vulgaris NOS
Lupus vulgaris of eyelid
Scrofuloderma
Tuberculosis of external ear
Excludes2: *lupus erythematosus (L93.-)*
lupus NOS (M32.9)
systemic (M32.-)
CC Exclusion see Appendix A PDX collection 0030

+ **A18.5 Tuberculosis of eye**
Excludes2: *lupus vulgaris of eyelid (A18.4)*
- CC **A18.50 Tuberculosis of eye, unspecified**
  CC Exclusion see Appendix A PDX collection 0046
- CC **A18.51 Tuberculous episcleritis**
  CC Exclusion see Appendix A PDX collection 0046
- CC **A18.52 Tuberculous keratitis**
  Tuberculous interstitial keratitis
  Tuberculous keratoconjunctivitis (interstitial) (phlyctenular)
  CC Exclusion see Appendix A PDX collection 0046
- CC **A18.53 Tuberculous chorioretinitis**
  CC Exclusion see Appendix A PDX collection 0046
- CC **A18.54 Tuberculous iridocyclitis**
  CC Exclusion see Appendix A PDX collection 0046
- CC **A18.59 Other tuberculosis of eye**
  Tuberculous conjunctivitis
  CC Exclusion see Appendix A PDX collection 0046

CC **A18.6 Tuberculosis of (inner) (middle) ear**
Tuberculous otitis media
Excludes2: *tuberculosis of external ear (A18.4)*
tuberculous mastoiditis (A18.03)
CC Exclusion see Appendix A PDX collection 0047

CC **A18.7 Tuberculosis of adrenal glands**
Tuberculous Addison's disease
CC Exclusion see Appendix A PDX collection 0048

+ **A18.8 Tuberculosis of other specified organs**
- CC **A18.81 Tuberculosis of thyroid gland**
  CC Exclusion see Appendix A PDX collection 0049
- CC **A18.82 Tuberculosis of other endocrine glands**
  Tuberculosis of pituitary gland
  Tuberculosis of thymus gland
  CC Exclusion see Appendix A PDX collection 0035
- CC **A18.83 Tuberculosis of digestive tract organs, not elsewhere classified**
  Excludes1: *tuberculosis of intestine (A18.32)*
  CC Exclusion see Appendix A PDX collection 0045
- CC **A18.84 Tuberculosis of heart**
  Tuberculous cardiomyopathy
  Tuberculous endocarditis
  Tuberculous myocarditis
  Tuberculous pericarditis
  CC Exclusion see Appendix A PDX collection 0035
- CC **A18.85 Tuberculosis of spleen**
  CC Exclusion see Appendix A PDX collection 0050
- CC **A18.89 Tuberculosis of other sites**
  Tuberculosis of muscle
  Tuberculous cerebral arteritis
  CC Exclusion see Appendix A PDX collection 0035

A19 Miliary tuberculosis

Includes: disseminated tuberculosis
generalized tuberculosis
tuberculous polyserositis

- MCC **A19.0 Acute miliary tuberculosis of a single specified site**
  MCC Exclusion see Appendix A PDX collection 0051
- MCC **A19.1 Acute miliary tuberculosis of multiple sites**
  MCC Exclusion see Appendix A PDX collection 0051
- MCC **A19.2 Acute miliary tuberculosis, unspecified**
  MCC Exclusion see Appendix A PDX collection 0051
- MCC **A19.8 Other miliary tuberculosis**
  MCC Exclusion see Appendix A PDX collection 0051
- MCC **A19.9 Miliary tuberculosis, unspecified**
  MCC Exclusion see Appendix A PDX collection 0051

Certain zoonotic bacterial diseases (A20-A28)

A20 Plague

Includes: infection due to Yersinia pestis

- MCC **A20.0 Bubonic plague**
  MCC Exclusion see Appendix A PDX collection 0052
- MCC **A20.1 Cellulocutaneous plague**
  MCC Exclusion see Appendix A PDX collection 0052
- MCC **A20.2 Pneumonic plague**
  MCC Exclusion see Appendix A PDX collection 0053
- MCC **A20.3 Plague meningitis**
  MCC Exclusion see Appendix A PDX collection 0054
- MCC **A20.7 Septicemic plague**
  MCC Exclusion see Appendix A PDX collection 0055
  Review coding guideline C.1.d
- MCC **A20.8 Other forms of plague**
  Abortive plague
  Asymptomatic plague
  Pestis minor
  MCC Exclusion see Appendix A PDX collection 0054
- MCC **A20.9 Plague, unspecified**
  MCC Exclusion see Appendix A PDX collection 0056

A21 Tularemia

Includes: deer-fly fever
infection due to Francisella tularensis
rabbit fever

- CC **A21.0 Ulceroglandular tularemia**
  CC Exclusion see Appendix A PDX collection 0057
- CC **A21.1 Oculoglandular tularemia**
  Ophthalmic tularemia
  CC Exclusion see Appendix A PDX collection 0058
- CC **A21.2 Pulmonary tularemia**
  CC Exclusion see Appendix A PDX collection 0059
- CC **A21.3 Gastrointestinal tularemia**
  Abdominal tularemia
  CC Exclusion see Appendix A PDX collection 0060
- CC **A21.7 Generalized tularemia**
  CC Exclusion see Appendix A PDX collection 0061
  Review coding guideline C.1.d
- CC **A21.8 Other forms of tularemia**
  CC Exclusion see Appendix A PDX collection 0061
- CC **A21.9 Tularemia, unspecified**
  CC Exclusion see Appendix A PDX collection 0061

A22 Anthrax

Includes: infection due to Bacillus anthracis

CC **A22.0 Cutaneous anthrax**
Malignant carbuncle
Malignant pustule
CC Exclusion see Appendix A PDX collection 0062

MCC **A22.1 Pulmonary anthrax**
Inhalation anthrax
Ragpicker's disease
Woolsorter's disease
MCC Exclusion see Appendix A PDX collection 0063

CC **A22.2 Gastrointestinal anthrax**
CC Exclusion see Appendix A PDX collection 0064

MCC **A22.7 Anthrax sepsis**
MCC Exclusion see Appendix A PDX collection 0005
Review coding guideline C.1.d

CC **A22.8 Other forms of anthrax**
Anthrax meningitis
CC Exclusion see Appendix A PDX collection 0065

CC **A22.9 Anthrax, unspecified**
CC Exclusion see Appendix A PDX collection 0066

A23 Brucellosis

Includes: Malta fever
Mediterranean fever
undulant fever

A23.0 Brucellosis due to Brucella melitensis

A23.1 Brucellosis due to Brucella abortus

A23.2 Brucellosis due to Brucella suis

A23.3 Brucellosis due to Brucella canis

CC **A23.8 Other brucellosis**
CC Exclusion see Appendix A PDX collection 0067

CC **A23.9 Brucellosis, unspecified**
CC Exclusion see Appendix A PDX collection 0067
Review coding guideline C.1.d

A24 Glanders and melioidosis

CC **A24.0 Glanders**
Infection due to Pseudomonas mallei
Malleus
CC Exclusion see Appendix A PDX collection 0068
Review coding guideline C.1.d

CC **A24.1 Acute and fulminating melioidosis**
Melioidosis pneumonia
Melioidosis sepsis
CC Exclusion see Appendix A PDX collection 0069
Review coding guideline C.1.d

CC **A24.2 Subacute and chronic melioidosis**
CC Exclusion see Appendix A PDX collection 0069

CC **A24.3 Other melioidosis**
CC Exclusion see Appendix A PDX collection 0069

CC **A24.9 Melioidosis, unspecified**
Infection due to Pseudomonas pseudomallei NOS
Whitmore's disease
CC Exclusion see Appendix A PDX collection 0069

A25 Rat-bite fevers

CC **A25.0 Spirillosis**
Sodoku
CC Exclusion see Appendix A PDX collection 0070

CC **A25.1 Streptobacillosis**
Epidemic arthritic erythema
Haverhill fever
Streptobacillary rat-bite fever
CC Exclusion see Appendix A PDX collection 0070

CC **A25.9 Rat-bite fever, unspecified**
CC Exclusion see Appendix A PDX collection 0070

A26 Erysipeloid

A26.0 Cutaneous erysipeloid
Erythema migrans

MCC **A26.7 Erysipelothrix sepsis**
MCC Exclusion see Appendix A PDX collection 0071
Review coding guideline C.1.d

A26.8 Other forms of erysipeloid

A26.9 Erysipeloid, unspecified

A27 Leptospirosis

CC **A27.0 Leptospirosis icterohemorrhagica**
Leptospiral or spirochetal jaundice (hemorrhagic)
Weil's disease
CC Exclusion see Appendix A PDX collection 0072

\+ **A27.8 Other forms of leptospirosis**

MCC **A27.81 Aseptic meningitis in leptospirosis**
MCC Exclusion see Appendix A PDX collection 0073

CC **A27.89 Other forms of leptospirosis**
CC Exclusion see Appendix A PDX collection 0072

CC **A27.9 Leptospirosis, unspecified**
CC Exclusion see Appendix A PDX collection 0072

A28 Other zoonotic bacterial diseases, not elsewhere classified

CC **A28.0 Pasteurellosis**
CC Exclusion see Appendix A PDX collection 0074
Review coding guideline C.1.d

CC **A28.1 Cat-scratch disease**
Cat-scratch fever
CC Exclusion see Appendix A PDX collection 0075

CC **A28.2 Extraintestinal yersiniosis**
Excludes1: *enteritis due to Yersinia enterocolitica (A04.6)*
plague (A20.-)
CC Exclusion see Appendix A PDX collection 0074
Review coding guideline C.1.d

CC **A28.8 Other specified zoonotic bacterial diseases, not elsewhere classified**
CC Exclusion see Appendix A PDX collection 0074

CC **A28.9 Zoonotic bacterial disease, unspecified**
CC Exclusion see Appendix A PDX collection 0074

Other bacterial diseases (A30-A49)

A30 Leprosy [Hansen's disease]

Includes: infection due to Mycobacterium leprae
Excludes1: *sequelae of leprosy (B92)*

CC **A30.0 Indeterminate leprosy**
I leprosy
CC Exclusion see Appendix A PDX collection 0076

CC **A30.1 Tuberculoid leprosy**
TT leprosy
CC Exclusion see Appendix A PDX collection 0077

CC **A30.2 Borderline tuberculoid leprosy**
BT leprosy
CC Exclusion see Appendix A PDX collection 0078

CC **A30.3 Borderline leprosy**
BB leprosy
CC Exclusion see Appendix A PDX collection 0078

CC **A30.4 Borderline lepromatous leprosy**
BL leprosy
CC Exclusion see Appendix A PDX collection 0078

CC **A30.5 Lepromatous leprosy**
LL leprosy
CC Exclusion see Appendix A PDX collection 0079

CC **A30.8 Other forms of leprosy**
CC Exclusion see Appendix A PDX collection 0080

CC **A30.9 Leprosy, unspecified**
CC Exclusion see Appendix A PDX collection 0081

A31 Infection due to other mycobacteria

Excludes2: *leprosy (A30.-)*
tuberculosis (A15-A19)

CC **A31.0 Pulmonary mycobacterial infection**
Infection due to Mycobacterium avium
Infection due to Mycobacterium intracellulare [Battey bacillus]
Infection due to Mycobacterium kansasii
CC Exclusion see Appendix A PDX collection 0082

CC **A31.1 Cutaneous mycobacterial infection**
Buruli ulcer
Infection due to Mycobacterium marinum
Infection due to Mycobacterium ulcerans
CC Exclusion see Appendix A PDX collection 0083

CC **A31.2 Disseminated mycobacterium avium-intracellulare complex (DMAC)**
MAC sepsis
CC Exclusion see Appendix A PDX collection 0083

CC **A31.8 Other mycobacterial infections**
CC Exclusion see Appendix A PDX collection 0083

CC **A31.9 Mycobacterial infection, unspecified**
Atypical mycobacterial infection NOS
Mycobacteriosis NOS
CC Exclusion see Appendix A PDX collection 0083

A32 Listeriosis

Includes: listerial foodborne infection
Excludes1: *neonatal (disseminated) listeriosis (P37.2)*

CC **A32.0 Cutaneous listeriosis**
CC Exclusion see Appendix A PDX collection 0074

\+ **A32.1 Listerial meningitis and meningoencephalitis**

CC **A32.11 Listerial meningitis**
CC Exclusion see Appendix A PDX collection 0074

CC **A32.12 Listerial meningoencephalitis**
CC Exclusion see Appendix A PDX collection 0074

MCC **A32.7 Listerial sepsis**
MCC Exclusion see Appendix A PDX collection 0071
Review coding guideline C.1.d

\+ **A32.8 Other forms of listeriosis**
CC **A32.81 Oculoglandular listeriosis**
CC Exclusion see Appendix A PDX collection 0074
CC **A32.82 Listerial endocarditis**
CC Exclusion see Appendix A PDX collection 0074
CC **A32.89 Other forms of listeriosis**
Listerial cerebral arteritis
CC Exclusion see Appendix A PDX collection 0074

CC **A32.9 Listeriosis, unspecified**
CC Exclusion see Appendix A PDX collection 0074

MCC ● **A33 Tetanus neonatorum**
MCC Exclusion see Appendix A PDX collection 0084
Valid 3-character code, no further characters required

♀ CC ● **A34 Obstetrical tetanus**
CC Exclusion see Appendix A PDX collection 0085
Valid 3-character code, no further characters required

MCC **A35 Other tetanus**
Tetanus NOS
Excludes1: *obstetrical tetanus (A34)*
tetanus neonatorum (A33)
MCC Exclusion see Appendix A PDX collection 0086
Valid 3-character code, no further characters required

A36 Diphtheria

CC **A36.0 Pharyngeal diphtheria**
Diphtheritic membranous angina
Tonsillar diphtheria
CC Exclusion see Appendix A PDX collection 0087

CC **A36.1 Nasopharyngeal diphtheria**
CC Exclusion see Appendix A PDX collection 0087

CC **A36.2 Laryngeal diphtheria**
Diphtheritic laryngotracheitis
CC Exclusion see Appendix A PDX collection 0087

CC **A36.3 Cutaneous diphtheria**
Excludes2: *erythrasma (L08.1)*
CC Exclusion see Appendix A PDX collection 0087

\+ **A36.8 Other diphtheria**
CC **A36.81 Diphtheritic cardiomyopathy**
Diphtheritic myocarditis
CC Exclusion see Appendix A PDX collection 0088
CC **A36.82 Diphtheritic radiculomyelitis**
CC Exclusion see Appendix A PDX collection 0087
CC **A36.83 Diphtheritic polyneuritis**
CC Exclusion see Appendix A PDX collection 0087
CC **A36.84 Diphtheritic tubulo-interstitial nephropathy**
CC Exclusion see Appendix A PDX collection 0087
CC **A36.85 Diphtheritic cystitis**
CC Exclusion see Appendix A PDX collection 0087
CC **A36.86 Diphtheritic conjunctivitis**
CC Exclusion see Appendix A PDX collection 0087
CC **A36.89 Other diphtheritic complications**
Diphtheritic peritonitis
CC Exclusion see Appendix A PDX collection 0087

CC **A36.9 Diphtheria, unspecified**
CC Exclusion see Appendix A PDX collection 0087

A37 Whooping cough

\+ **A37.0 Whooping cough due to Bordetella pertussis**
CC **A37.00 Whooping cough due to Bordetella pertussis without pneumonia**
CC Exclusion see Appendix A PDX collection 0089
MCC **A37.01 Whooping cough due to Bordetella pertussis with pneumonia**
MCC Exclusion see Appendix A PDX collection 0090

\+ **A37.1 Whooping cough due to Bordetella parapertussis**
CC **A37.10 Whooping cough due to Bordetella parapertussis without pneumonia**
CC Exclusion see Appendix A PDX collection 0089
MCC **A37.11 Whooping cough due to Bordetella parapertussis with pneumonia**
MCC Exclusion see Appendix A PDX collection 0090

\+ **A37.8 Whooping cough due to other Bordetella species**
CC **A37.80 Whooping cough due to other Bordetella species without pneumonia**
CC Exclusion see Appendix A PDX collection 0089
MCC **A37.81 Whooping cough due to other Bordetella species with pneumonia**
MCC Exclusion see Appendix A PDX collection 0090

\+ **A37.9 Whooping cough, unspecified species**
CC **A37.90 Whooping cough, unspecified species without pneumonia**
CC Exclusion see Appendix A PDX collection 0089
MCC **A37.91 Whooping cough, unspecified species with pneumon**
MCC Exclusion see Appendix A PDX collection 0090

A38 Scarlet fever

Includes: scarlatina
Excludes2: *streptococcal sore throat (J02.0)*

CC **A38.0 Scarlet fever with otitis media**
CC Exclusion see Appendix A PDX collection 0091

CC **A38.1 Scarlet fever with myocarditis**
CC Exclusion see Appendix A PDX collection 0091

CC **A38.8 Scarlet fever with other complications**
CC Exclusion see Appendix A PDX collection 0091

CC **A38.9 Scarlet fever, uncomplicated**
Scarlet fever, NOS
CC Exclusion see Appendix A PDX collection 0091

A39 Meningococcal infection

MCC **A39.0 Meningococcal meningitis**
MCC Exclusion see Appendix A PDX collection 0092

MCC **A39.1 Waterhouse-Friderichsen syndrome**
Meningococcal hemorrhagic adrenalitis
Meningococcic adrenal syndrome
MCC Exclusion see Appendix A PDX collection 0093
Review coding guideline C.1.d

MCC **A39.2 Acute meningococcemia**
MCC Exclusion see Appendix A PDX collection 0094
Review coding guideline C.1.d

MCC **A39.3 Chronic meningococcemia**
MCC Exclusion see Appendix A PDX collection 0094
Review coding guideline C.1.d

MCC **A39.4 Meningococcemia, unspecified**
MCC Exclusion see Appendix A PDX collection 0094
Review coding guideline C.1.d

\+ **A39.5 Meningococcal heart disease**
MCC **A39.50 Meningococcal carditis, unspecified**
MCC Exclusion see Appendix A PDX collection 0095
MCC **A39.51 Meningococcal endocarditis**
MCC Exclusion see Appendix A PDX collection 0096
MCC **A39.52 Meningococcal myocarditis**
MCC Exclusion see Appendix A PDX collection 0097
MCC **A39.53 Meningococcal pericarditis**
MCC Exclusion see Appendix A PDX collection 0098

\+ **A39.8 Other meningococcal infections**
MCC **A39.81 Meningococcal encephalitis**
MCC Exclusion see Appendix A PDX collection 0099
CC **A39.82 Meningococcal retrobulbar neuritis**
CC Exclusion see Appendix A PDX collection 0100
CC **A39.83 Meningococcal arthritis**
CC Exclusion see Appendix A PDX collection 0101
CC **A39.84 Postmeningococcal arthritis**
CC Exclusion see Appendix A PDX collection 0101
CC **A39.89 Other meningococcal infections**
Meningococcal conjunctivitis
CC Exclusion see Appendix A PDX collection 0102

CC **A39.9 Meningococcal infection, unspecified**
Meningococcal disease NOS
CC Exclusion see Appendix A PDX collection 0102

A40 Streptococcal sepsis

Code first:
postprocedural streptococcal sepsis (T81.4)
streptococcal sepsis during labor (O75.3)
streptococcal sepsis following abortion or ectopic or molar pregnan (O03-O07, O08.0)
streptococcal sepsis following immunization (T88.0)
streptococcal sepsis following infusion, transfusion or therapeutic injection (T80.2-)
Excludes1: *neonatal (P36.0-P36.1)*
puerperal sepsis (O85)
sepsis due to Streptococcus, group D (A41.81)
Review coding guideline C.1.d

MCC **A40.0 Sepsis due to streptococcus, group A**
MCC Exclusion see Appendix A PDX collection 0071

MCC **A40.1 Sepsis due to streptococcus, group B**
MCC Exclusion see Appendix A PDX collection 0071

MCC **A40.3 Sepsis due to Streptococcus pneumoniae**
Pneumococcal sepsis
No MCC Exclusions

MCC **A40.8 Other streptococcal sepsis**
MCC Exclusion see Appendix A PDX collection 0071

MCC **A40.9 Streptococcal sepsis, unspecified**
MCC Exclusion see Appendix A PDX collection 0071

A41 Other sepsis

Code first:
postprocedural sepsis (T81.4)
sepsis during labor (O75.3)
sepsis following abortion, ectopic or molar pregnancy (O03-O07, O08.0)
sepsis following immunization (T88.0)
sepsis following infusion, transfusion or therapeutic injection (T80.2-)

Excludes1: *bacteremia NOS (R78.81)*
neonatal (P36.-)
puerperal sepsis (O85)
sepsis NOS (A41.9)
streptococcal sepsis (A40.-)

Excludes2: *sepsis (due to) (in) actinomycotic (A42.7)*
sepsis (due to) (in) anthrax (A22.7)
sepsis (due to) (in) candidal (B37.7)
sepsis (due to) (in) Erysipelothrix (A26.7)
sepsis (due to) (in) extraintestinal yersiniosis (A28.2)
sepsis (due to) (in) gonococcal (A54.86)
sepsis (due to) (in) herpesviral (B00.7)
sepsis (due to) (in) listerial (A32.7)
sepsis (due to) (in) melioidosis (A24.1)
sepsis (due to) (in) meningococcal (A39.2-A39.4)
sepsis (due to) (in) plague (A20.7)
sepsis (due to) (in) tularemia (A21.7)
toxic shock syndrome (A48.3)

Review coding guideline C.1.d

+ **A41.0 Sepsis due to Staphylococcus aureus**

MCC **A41.01 Sepsis due to Methicillin susceptible Staphylococcus aureus**
MSSA sepsis
Staphylococcus aureus sepsis NOS
MCC Exclusion see Appendix A PDX collection 0071

MCC **A41.02 Sepsis due to Methicillin resistant Staphylococcus aureus**
MCC Exclusion see Appendix A PDX collection 0071
Review coding guideline C.1.e.1.a

MCC **A41.1 Sepsis due to other specified staphylococcus**
Coagulase negative staphylococcus sepsis
MCC Exclusion see Appendix A PDX collection 0071

MCC **A41.2 Sepsis due to unspecified staphylococcus**
MCC Exclusion see Appendix A PDX collection 0071

MCC **A41.3 Sepsis due to Hemophilus influenzae**
MCC Exclusion see Appendix A PDX collection 0071

MCC **A41.4 Sepsis due to anaerobes**
Excludes1: *gas gangrene (A48.0)*
MCC Exclusion see Appendix A PDX collection 0071

+ **A41.5 Sepsis due to other Gram-negative organisms**

MCC **A41.50 Gram-negative sepsis, unspecified**
Gram-negative sepsis NOS
MCC Exclusion see Appendix A PDX collection 0071

MCC **A41.51 Sepsis due to Escherichia coli [E. coli]**
MCC Exclusion see Appendix A PDX collection 0071

MCC **A41.52 Sepsis due to Pseudomonas**
Pseudomonas aeroginosa
MCC Exclusion see Appendix A PDX collection 0071

MCC **A41.53 Sepsis due to Serratia**
MCC Exclusion see Appendix A PDX collection 0071

MCC **A41.59 Other Gram-negative sepsis**
MCC Exclusion see Appendix A PDX collection 0071

+ **A41.8 Other specified sepsis**

MCC **A41.81 Sepsis due to Enterococcus**
MCC Exclusion see Appendix A PDX collection 0071

MCC **A41.89 Other specified sepsis**
MCC Exclusion see Appendix A PDX collection 0071

MCC **A41.9 Sepsis, unspecified organism**
Septicemia NOS
MCC Exclusion see Appendix A PDX collection 0071

A42 Actinomycosis

Excludes1: *actinomycetoma (B47.1)*

CC **A42.0 Pulmonary actinomycosis**
CC Exclusion see Appendix A PDX collection 0103

CC **A42.1 Abdominal actinomycosis**
CC Exclusion see Appendix A PDX collection 0104

CC **A42.2 Cervicofacial actinomycosis**
CC Exclusion see Appendix A PDX collection 0105

MCC **A42.7 Actinomycotic sepsis**
MCC Exclusion see Appendix A PDX collection 0071
Review coding guideline C.1.d

+ **A42.8 Other forms of actinomycosis**

CC **A42.81 Actinomycotic meningitis**
CC Exclusion see Appendix A PDX collection 0106

CC **A42.82 Actinomycotic encephalitis**
CC Exclusion see Appendix A PDX collection 0106

CC **A42.89 Other forms of actinomycosis**
CC Exclusion see Appendix A PDX collection 0106

CC **A42.9 Actinomycosis, unspecified**
CC Exclusion see Appendix A PDX collection 0106

A43 Nocardiosis

CC **A43.0 Pulmonary nocardiosis**
CC Exclusion see Appendix A PDX collection 0103

CC **A43.1 Cutaneous nocardiosis**
CC Exclusion see Appendix A PDX collection 0107

CC **A43.8 Other forms of nocardiosis**
CC Exclusion see Appendix A PDX collection 0106

CC **A43.9 Nocardiosis, unspecified**
CC Exclusion see Appendix A PDX collection 0106

A44 Bartonellosis

CC **A44.0 Systemic bartonellosis**
Oroya fever
CC Exclusion see Appendix A PDX collection 0108

CC **A44.1 Cutaneous and mucocutaneous bartonellosis**
Verruga peruana
CC Exclusion see Appendix A PDX collection 0108

CC **A44.8 Other forms of bartonellosis**
CC Exclusion see Appendix A PDX collection 0108

CC **A44.9 Bartonellosis, unspecified**
CC Exclusion see Appendix A PDX collection 0108

A46 Erysipelas

Excludes1: *postpartum or puerperal erysipelas (O86.89)*
Valid 3-character code, no further characters required

A48 Other bacterial diseases, not elsewhere classified

Excludes1: *actinomycetoma (B47.1)*

MCC **A48.0 Gas gangrene**
Clostridial cellulitis
Clostridial myonecrosis
MCC Exclusion see Appendix A PDX collection 0109

MCC **A48.1 Legionnaires' disease**
MCC Exclusion see Appendix A PDX collection 0110

A48.2 Nonpneumonic Legionnaires' disease [Pontiac fever]

MCC **A48.3 Toxic shock syndrome**
Use additional code to identify the organism (B95, B96)
Excludes1: *endotoxic shock NOS (R57.8)*
sepsis NOS (A41.9)
MCC Exclusion see Appendix A PDX collection 0111

A48.4 Brazilian purpuric fever
Systemic Hemophilus aegyptius infection

+ **A48.5 Other specified botulism**
Non-foodborne intoxication due to toxins of Clostridium botulinum [C. botulinum]
Excludes1: *food poisoning due to toxins of Clostridium botulinum (A05.1)*

• CC **A48.51 Infant botulism**
CC Exclusion see Appendix A PDX collection 0018

CC **A48.52 Wound botulism**
Non-foodborne botulism NOS
Use additional code for associated wound
CC Exclusion see Appendix A PDX collection 0018

A48.8 Other specified bacterial diseases

A49 Bacterial infection of unspecified site

Excludes1: *bacterial agents as the cause of diseases classified elsewhere (B95-B96)*
chlamydial infection NOS (A74.9)
meningococcal infection NOS (A39.9)
rickettsial infection NOS (A79.9)
spirochetal infection NOS (A69.9)

+ **A49.0 Staphylococcal infection, unspecified site**

A49.01 Methicillin susceptible Staphylococcus aureus infection, unspecified site
Methicillin susceptible Staphylococcus aureus (MSSA) infection
Staphylococcus aureus infection NOS

A49.02 Methicillin resistant Staphylococcus aureus infection, unspecified site
Methicillin resistant Staphylococcus aureus (MRSA) infection

A49.1 Streptococcal infection, unspecified site
A49.2 Hemophilus influenzae infection, unspecified site
A49.3 Mycoplasma infection, unspecified site
A49.8 Other bacterial infections of unspecified site
A49.9 Bacterial infection, unspecified
Excludes1: *bacteremia NOS (R78.81)*

Infections with a predominantly sexual mode of transmission (A50-A64)

Excludes1: *human immunodeficiency virus [HIV] disease (B20)*
nonspecific and nongonococcal urethritis (N34.1)
Reiter's disease (M02.3-)

A50 Congenital syphilis

\+ **A50.0 Early congenital syphilis, symptomatic**
Any congenital syphilitic condition specified as early or manifest less than two years after birth.

CC **A50.01 Early congenital syphilitic oculopathy**
CC Exclusion see Appendix A PDX collection 0112

CC **A50.02 Early congenital syphilitic osteochondropathy**
CC Exclusion see Appendix A PDX collection 0112

CC **A50.03 Early congenital syphilitic pharyngitis**
Early congenital syphilitic laryngitis
CC Exclusion see Appendix A PDX collection 0112

CC **A50.04 Early congenital syphilitic pneumonia**
CC Exclusion see Appendix A PDX collection 0112

CC **A50.05 Early congenital syphilitic rhinitis**
CC Exclusion see Appendix A PDX collection 0112

CC **A50.06 Early cutaneous congenital syphilis**
CC Exclusion see Appendix A PDX collection 0112

CC **A50.07 Early mucocutaneous congenital syphilis**
CC Exclusion see Appendix A PDX collection 0112

CC **A50.08 Early visceral congenital syphilis**
CC Exclusion see Appendix A PDX collection 0112

CC **A50.09 Other early congenital syphilis, symptomatic**
CC Exclusion see Appendix A PDX collection 0112

A50.1 Early congenital syphilis, latent
Congenital syphilis without clinical manifestations, with positive serological reaction and negative spinal fluid test, less than two years after birth.

CC **A50.2 Early congenital syphilis, unspecified**
Congenital syphilis NOS less than two years after birth.
CC Exclusion see Appendix A PDX collection 0113

\+ **A50.3 Late congenital syphilitic oculopathy**
Excludes1: *Hutchinson's triad (A50.53)*

CC **A50.30 Late congenital syphilitic oculopathy, unspecified**
CC Exclusion see Appendix A PDX collection 0112

CC **A50.31 Late congenital syphilitic interstitial keratitis**
CC Exclusion see Appendix A PDX collection 0112

CC **A50.32 Late congenital syphilitic chorioretinitis**
CC Exclusion see Appendix A PDX collection 0112

CC **A50.39 Other late congenital syphilitic oculopathy**
CC Exclusion see Appendix A PDX collection 0112

\+ **A50.4 Late congenital neurosyphilis [juvenile neurosyphilis]**
Use additional code to identify any associated mental disorder
Excludes1: *Hutchinson's triad (A50.53)*

CC **A50.40 Late congenital neurosyphilis, unspecified**
Juvenile neurosyphilis NOS
CC Exclusion see Appendix A PDX collection 0114

MCC **A50.41 Late congenital syphilitic meningitis**
MCC Exclusion see Appendix A PDX collection 0115

MCC **A50.42 Late congenital syphilitic encephalitis**
MCC Exclusion see Appendix A PDX collection 0114

CC **A50.43 Late congenital syphilitic polyneuropathy**
CC Exclusion see Appendix A PDX collection 0114

CC **A50.44 Late congenital syphilitic optic nerve atrophy**
CC Exclusion see Appendix A PDX collection 0112

CC **A50.45 Juvenile general paresis**
Dementia paralytica juvenilis
Juvenile tabetoparetic neurosyphilis
CC Exclusion see Appendix A PDX collection 0114

CC **A50.49 Other late congenital neurosyphilis**
Juvenile tabes dorsalis
CC Exclusion see Appendix A PDX collection 0114

\+ **A50.5 Other late congenital syphilis, symptomatic**
Any congenital syphilitic condition specified as late or manifest two years or more after birth.

CC **A50.51 Clutton's joints**
CC Exclusion see Appendix A PDX collection 0112

CC **A50.52 Hutchinson's teeth**
CC Exclusion see Appendix A PDX collection 0112

CC **A50.53 Hutchinson's triad**
CC Exclusion see Appendix A PDX collection 0112

CC **A50.54 Late congenital cardiovascular syphilis**
CC Exclusion see Appendix A PDX collection 0112

CC **A50.55 Late congenital syphilitic arthropathy**
CC Exclusion see Appendix A PDX collection 0112

CC **A50.56 Late congenital syphilitic osteochondropathy**
CC Exclusion see Appendix A PDX collection 0112

CC **A50.57 Syphilitic saddle nose**
CC Exclusion see Appendix A PDX collection 0112

CC **A50.59 Other late congenital syphilis, symptomatic**
CC Exclusion see Appendix A PDX collection 0112

A50.6 Late congenital syphilis, latent
Congenital syphilis without clinical manifestations, with posi[tive] serological reaction and negative spinal fluid test, two years [or] more after birth.

A50.7 Late congenital syphilis, unspecified
Congenital syphilis NOS two years or more after birth.

A50.9 Congenital syphilis, unspecified

A51 Early syphilis

A51.0 Primary genital syphilis
Syphilitic chancre NOS

A51.1 Primary anal syphilis

A51.2 Primary syphilis of other sites

\+ **A51.3 Secondary syphilis of skin and mucous membranes**

CC **A51.31 Condyloma latum**
CC Exclusion see Appendix A PDX collection 0112

CC **A51.32 Syphilitic alopecia**
CC Exclusion see Appendix A PDX collection 0116

CC **A51.39 Other secondary syphilis of skin**
Syphilitic leukoderma
Syphilitic mucous patch
Excludes1: *late syphilitic leukoderma (A52.79)*
CC Exclusion see Appendix A PDX collection 0112

\+ **A51.4 Other secondary syphilis**

MCC **A51.41 Secondary syphilitic meningitis**
MCC Exclusion see Appendix A PDX collection 0117

♀ CC **A51.42 Secondary syphilitic female pelvic disease**
CC Exclusion see Appendix A PDX collection 0113

CC **A51.43 Secondary syphilitic oculopathy**
Secondary syphilitic chorioretinitis
Secondary syphilitic iridocyclitis, iritis
Secondary syphilitic uveitis
CC Exclusion see Appendix A PDX collection 0112

CC **A51.44 Secondary syphilitic nephritis**
CC Exclusion see Appendix A PDX collection 0113

CC **A51.45 Secondary syphilitic hepatitis**
CC Exclusion see Appendix A PDX collection 0118

CC **A51.46 Secondary syphilitic osteopathy**
CC Exclusion see Appendix A PDX collection 0119

CC **A51.49 Other secondary syphilitic conditions**
Secondary syphilitic lymphadenopathy
Secondary syphilitic myositis
No CC Exclusions

A51.5 Early syphilis, latent
Syphilis (acquired) without clinical manifestations, with posi[tive] serological reaction and negative spinal fluid test, less than [two] years after infection.

A51.9 Early syphilis, unspecified

A52 Late syphilis

\+ **A52.0 Cardiovascular and cerebrovascular syphilis**

CC **A52.00 Cardiovascular syphilis, unspecified**
CC Exclusion see Appendix A PDX collection 0114

CC **A52.01 Syphilitic aneurysm of aorta**
CC Exclusion see Appendix A PDX collection 0114

CC **A52.02 Syphilitic aortitis**
CC Exclusion see Appendix A PDX collection 0114

CC **A52.03 Syphilitic endocarditis**
Syphilitic aortic valve incompetence or stenosis
Syphilitic mitral valve stenosis
Syphilitic pulmonary valve regurgitation
CC Exclusion see Appendix A PDX collection 0114

CC **A52.04 Syphilitic cerebral arteritis**
CC Exclusion see Appendix A PDX collection 0114

CC **A52.05 Other cerebrovascular syphilis**
Syphilitic cerebral aneurysm (ruptured) (non-ruptured)
Syphilitic cerebral thrombosis
CC Exclusion see Appendix A PDX collection 0114

CC **A52.06 Other syphilitic heart involvement**
Syphilitic coronary artery disease
Syphilitic myocarditis
Syphilitic pericarditis
CC Exclusion see Appendix A PDX collection 0114

CC **A52.09 Other cardiovascular syphilis**
CC Exclusion see Appendix A PDX collection 0114

\+ **A52.1 Symptomatic neurosyphilis**

CC **A52.10 Symptomatic neurosyphilis, unspecified**
CC Exclusion see Appendix A PDX collection 0114

CC **A52.11 Tabes dorsalis**
Locomotor ataxia (progressive)
Tabetic neurosyphilis
CC Exclusion see Appendix A PDX collection 0114

CC **A52.12 Other cerebrospinal syphilis**
CC Exclusion see Appendix A PDX collection 0114

MCC **A52.13 Late syphilitic meningitis**
MCC Exclusion see Appendix A PDX collection 0115

MCC **A52.14 Late syphilitic encephalitis**
MCC Exclusion see Appendix A PDX collection 0114

CC **A52.15 Late syphilitic neuropathy**
Late syphilitic acoustic neuritis
Late syphilitic optic (nerve) atrophy
Late syphilitic polyneuropathy
Late syphilitic retrobulbar neuritis
CC Exclusion see Appendix A PDX collection 0114

CC **A52.16 Charcôt's arthropathy (tabetic)**
CC Exclusion see Appendix A PDX collection 0114

CC **A52.17 General paresis**
Dementia paralytica
CC Exclusion see Appendix A PDX collection 0114

CC **A52.19 Other symptomatic neurosyphilis**
Syphilitic parkinsonism
CC Exclusion see Appendix A PDX collection 0114

CC **A52.2 Asymptomatic neurosyphilis**
CC Exclusion see Appendix A PDX collection 0114

CC **A52.3 Neurosyphilis, unspecified**
Gumma (syphilitic)
Syphilis (late)
Syphiloma
CC Exclusion see Appendix A PDX collection 0114

+ **A52.7 Other symptomatic late syphilis**

CC **A52.71 Late syphilitic oculopathy**
Late syphilitic chorioretinitis
Late syphilitic episcleritis
CC Exclusion see Appendix A PDX collection 0120

CC **A52.72 Syphilis of lung and bronchus**
CC Exclusion see Appendix A PDX collection 0116

CC **A52.73 Symptomatic late syphilis of other respiratory organs**
CC Exclusion see Appendix A PDX collection 0116

CC **A52.74 Syphilis of liver and other viscera**
Late syphilitic peritonitis
CC Exclusion see Appendix A PDX collection 0116

CC **A52.75 Syphilis of kidney and ureter**
Syphilitic glomerular disease
CC Exclusion see Appendix A PDX collection 0116

CC **A52.76 Other genitourinary symptomatic late syphilis**
Late syphilitic female pelvic inflammatory disease
CC Exclusion see Appendix A PDX collection 0116

CC **A52.77 Syphilis of bone and joint**
CC Exclusion see Appendix A PDX collection 0116

CC **A52.78 Syphilis of other musculoskeletal tissue**
Late syphilitic bursitis
Syphilis [stage unspecified] of bursa
Syphilis [stage unspecified] of muscle
Syphilis [stage unspecified] of synovium
Syphilis [stage unspecified] of tendon
CC Exclusion see Appendix A PDX collection 0116

CC **A52.79 Other symptomatic late syphilis**
Late syphilitic leukoderma
Syphilis of adrenal gland
Syphilis of pituitary gland
Syphilis of thyroid gland
Syphilitic splenomegaly
Excludes1: *syphilitic leukoderma (secondary) (A51.39)*
CC Exclusion see Appendix A PDX collection 0116

A52.8 Late syphilis, latent
Syphilis (acquired) without clinical manifestations, with positive serological reaction and negative spinal fluid test, two years or more after infection

A52.9 Late syphilis, unspecified

A53 Other and unspecified syphilis

A53.0 Latent syphilis, unspecified as early or late
Latent syphilis NOS
Positive serological reaction for syphilis

A53.9 Syphilis, unspecified
Infection due to Treponema pallidum NOS
Syphilis (acquired) NOS
Excludes1: *syphilis NOS under two years of age (A50.2)*

A54 Gonococcal infection

+ **A54.0 Gonococcal infection of lower genitourinary tract without periurethral or accessory gland abscess**
Excludes1: *gonococcal infection with genitourinary gland abscess (A54.1)*
gonococcal infection with periurethral abscess (A54.1)

CC **A54.00 Gonococcal infection of lower genitourinary tract, unspecified**
CC Exclusion see Appendix A PDX collection 0121

CC **A54.01 Gonococcal cystitis and urethritis, unspecified**
CC Exclusion see Appendix A PDX collection 0121

♀ CC **A54.02 Gonococcal vulvovaginitis, unspecified**
CC Exclusion see Appendix A PDX collection 0121

♀ CC **A54.03 Gonococcal cervicitis, unspecified**
CC Exclusion see Appendix A PDX collection 0121

CC **A54.09 Other gonococcal infection of lower genitourinary tract**
CC Exclusion see Appendix A PDX collection 0121

CC **A54.1 Gonococcal infection of lower genitourinary tract with periurethral and accessory gland abscess**
Gonococcal Bartholin's gland abscess
CC Exclusion see Appendix A PDX collection 0121

+ **A54.2 Gonococcal pelviperitonitis and other gonococcal genitourinary infection**

CC **A54.21 Gonococcal infection of kidney and ureter**
CC Exclusion see Appendix A PDX collection 0121

♂ CC **A54.22 Gonococcal prostatitis**
CC Exclusion see Appendix A PDX collection 0121

♂ CC **A54.23 Gonococcal infection of other male genital organs**
Gonococcal epididymitis
Gonococcal orchitis
CC Exclusion see Appendix A PDX collection 0121

♀ CC **A54.24 Gonococcal female pelvic inflammatory disease**
Gonococcal pelviperitonitis
Excludes1: *gonococcal peritonitis (A54.85)*
CC Exclusion see Appendix A PDX collection 0121

CC **A54.29 Other gonococcal genitourinary infections**
CC Exclusion see Appendix A PDX collection 0121

+ **A54.3 Gonococcal infection of eye**

CC **A54.30 Gonococcal infection of eye, unspecified**
CC Exclusion see Appendix A PDX collection 0116

CC **A54.31 Gonococcal conjunctivitis**
Ophthalmia neonatorum due to gonococcus
CC Exclusion see Appendix A PDX collection 0116

CC **A54.32 Gonococcal iridocyclitis**
CC Exclusion see Appendix A PDX collection 0116

CC **A54.33 Gonococcal keratitis**
CC Exclusion see Appendix A PDX collection 0116

CC **A54.39 Other gonococcal eye infection**
Gonococcal endophthalmia
CC Exclusion see Appendix A PDX collection 0116

+ **A54.4 Gonococcal infection of musculoskeletal system**

CC **A54.40 Gonococcal infection of musculoskeletal system, unspecified**
CC Exclusion see Appendix A PDX collection 0122

CC **A54.41 Gonococcal spondylopathy**
CC Exclusion see Appendix A PDX collection 0122

CC **A54.42 Gonococcal arthritis**
Excludes2: *gonococcal infection of spine (A54.41)*
CC Exclusion see Appendix A PDX collection 0122

CC **A54.43 Gonococcal osteomyelitis**
Excludes2: *gonococcal infection of spine (A54.41)*
CC Exclusion see Appendix A PDX collection 0122

CC **A54.49 Gonococcal infection of other musculoskeletal tissue**
Gonococcal bursitis
Gonococcal myositis
Gonococcal synovitis
Gonococcal tenosynovitis
CC Exclusion see Appendix A PDX collection 0122

A54.5 Gonococcal pharyngitis

A54.6 Gonococcal infection of anus and rectum

+ **A54.8 Other gonococcal infections**

MCC **A54.81 Gonococcal meningitis**
MCC Exclusion see Appendix A PDX collection 0117

CC **A54.82 Gonococcal brain abscess**
CC Exclusion see Appendix A PDX collection 0123

CC **A54.83 Gonococcal heart infection**
Gonococcal endocarditis
Gonococcal myocarditis
Gonococcal pericarditis
CC Exclusion see Appendix A PDX collection 0124

CC **A54.84 Gonococcal pneumonia**
CC Exclusion see Appendix A PDX collection 0123

CC **A54.85 Gonococcal peritonitis**
Excludes1: *gonococcal pelviperitonitis (A54.24)*
CC Exclusion see Appendix A PDX collection 0125

MCC **A54.86 Gonococcal sepsis**
MCC Exclusion see Appendix A PDX collection 0071
Review coding guideline C.1.d

CC **A54.89 Other gonococcal infections**
Gonococcal keratoderma
Gonococcal lymphadenitis
CC Exclusion see Appendix A PDX collection 0123

CC **A54.9 Gonococcal infection, unspecified**
CC Exclusion see Appendix A PDX collection 0123

A55 Chlamydial lymphogranuloma (venereum)
Climatic or tropical bubo
Durand-Nicolas-Favre disease
Esthiomene
Lymphogranuloma inguinale
Valid 3-character code, no further characters required

A56 Other sexually transmitted chlamydial diseases
Includes: sexually transmitted diseases due to Chlamydia trachomatis
Excludes1: *neonatal chlamydial conjunctivitis (P39.1)*
neonatal chlamydial pneumonia (P23.1)
Excludes2: *chlamydial lymphogranuloma (A55)*
conditions classified to A74.-

\+ **A56.0 Chlamydial infection of lower genitourinary tract**
A56.00 Chlamydial infection of lower genitourinary tract, unspecified
A56.01 Chlamydial cystitis and urethritis
♀ **A56.02 Chlamydial vulvovaginitis**
A56.09 Other chlamydial infection of lower genitourinary tract
Chlamydial cervicitis

\+ **A56.1 Chlamydial infection of pelviperitoneum and other genitourinary organs**
♀ **A56.11 Chlamydial female pelvic inflammatory disease**
A56.19 Other chlamydial genitourinary infection
Chlamydial epididymitis
Chlamydial orchitis

A56.2 Chlamydial infection of genitourinary tract, unspecified
A56.3 Chlamydial infection of anus and rectum
A56.4 Chlamydial infection of pharynx
A56.8 Sexually transmitted chlamydial infection of other sites

A57 Chancroid
Ulcus molle
Valid 3-character code, no further characters required

A58 Granuloma inguinale
Donovanosis
Valid 3-character code, no further characters required

A59 Trichomoniasis
Excludes2: *intestinal trichomoniasis (A07.8)*

\+ **A59.0 Urogenital trichomoniasis**
A59.00 Urogenital trichomoniasis, unspecified
Fluor (vaginalis) due to Trichomonas
Leukorrhea (vaginalis) due to Trichomonas
♀ **A59.01 Trichomonal vulvovaginitis**
♂ **A59.02 Trichomonal prostatitis**
A59.03 Trichomonal cystitis and urethritis
A59.09 Other urogenital trichomoniasis
Trichomonas cervicitis

A59.8 Trichomoniasis of other sites
A59.9 Trichomoniasis, unspecified

A60 Anogenital herpesviral [herpes simplex] infections

\+ **A60.0 Herpesviral infection of genitalia and urogenital tract**
A60.00 Herpesviral infection of urogenital system, unspecified
♂ **A60.01 Herpesviral infection of penis**
♂ **A60.02 Herpesviral infection of other male genital organs**
♀ **A60.03 Herpesviral cervicitis**
♀ **A60.04 Herpesviral vulvovaginitis**
Herpesviral [herpes simplex] ulceration
Herpesviral [herpes simplex] vaginitis
Herpesviral [herpes simplex] vulvitis
A60.09 Herpesviral infection of other urogenital tract

A60.1 Herpesviral infection of perianal skin and rectum
A60.9 Anogenital herpesviral infection, unspecified

A63 Other predominantly sexually transmitted diseases, not elsewhere classified
Excludes2: *molluscum contagiosum (B08.1)*
papilloma of cervix (D26.0)

A63.0 Anogenital (venereal) warts
Anogenital warts due to (human) papillomavirus [HPV]
Condyloma acuminatum
A63.8 Other specified predominantly sexually transmitted diseases

A64 Unspecified sexually transmitted disease
Valid 3-character code, no further characters required

Other spirochetal diseases (A65-A69)

Excludes2: *leptospirosis (A27.-)*
syphilis (A50-A53)

A65 Nonvenereal syphilis
Bejel
Endemic syphilis
Njovera
Valid 3-character code, no further characters required

A66 Yaws
Includes: bouba
frambesia (tropica)
pian

A66.0 Initial lesions of yaws
Chancre of yaws
Frambesia, initial or primary
Initial frambesial ulcer
Mother yaw
A66.1 Multiple papillomata and wet crab yaws
Frambesioma
Pianoma
Plantar or palmar papilloma of yaws
A66.2 Other early skin lesions of yaws
Cutaneous yaws, less than five years after infection
Early yaws (cutaneous)(macular)(maculopapular)(micropapular)(papular)
Frambeside of early yaws
A66.3 Hyperkeratosis of yaws
Ghoul hand
Hyperkeratosis, palmar or plantar (early) (late) due to yaws
Worm-eaten soles
A66.4 Gummata and ulcers of yaws
Gummatous frambeside
Nodular late yaws (ulcerated)
A66.5 Gangosa
Rhinopharyngitis mutilans
A66.6 Bone and joint lesions of yaws
Yaws ganglion
Yaws goundou
Yaws gumma, bone
Yaws gummatous osteitis or periostitis
Yaws hydrarthrosis
Yaws osteitis
Yaws periostitis (hypertrophic)
A66.7 Other manifestations of yaws
Juxta-articular nodules of yaws
Mucosal yaws
A66.8 Latent yaws
Yaws without clinical manifestations, with positive serology
A66.9 Yaws, unspecified

A67 Pinta [carate]

A67.0 Primary lesions of pinta
Chancre (primary) of pinta
Papule (primary) of pinta
A67.1 Intermediate lesions of pinta
Erythematous plaques of pinta
Hyperchromic lesions of pinta
Hyperkeratosis of pinta
Pintids
A67.2 Late lesions of pinta
Achromic skin lesions of pinta
Cicatricial skin lesions of pinta
Dyschromic skin lesions of pinta
A67.3 Mixed lesions of pinta
Achromic with hyperchromic skin lesions of pinta [carate]
A67.9 Pinta, unspecified

A68 **Relapsing fevers**

Includes: recurrent fever
Excludes2: *Lyme disease (A69.2-)*

CC **A68.0 Louse-borne relapsing fever**
Relapsing fever due to Borrelia recurrentis
CC Exclusion see Appendix A PDX collection 0108

CC **A68.1 Tick-borne relapsing fever**
Relapsing fever due to any Borrelia species other than Borrelia recurrentis
CC Exclusion see Appendix A PDX collection 0108

CC **A68.9 Relapsing fever, unspecified**
CC Exclusion see Appendix A PDX collection 0108

A69 **Other spirochetal infections**

A69.0 Necrotizing ulcerative stomatitis
Cancrum oris
Fusospirochetal gangrene
Noma
Stomatitis gangrenosa

CC **A69.1 Other Vincent's infections**
Fusospirochetal pharyngitis
Necrotizing ulcerative (acute) gingivitis
Necrotizing ulcerative (acute) gingivostomatitis
Spirochetal stomatitis
Trench mouth
Vincent's angina
Vincent's gingivitis
CC Exclusion see Appendix A PDX collection 0126

\+ **A69.2 Lyme disease**
Erythema chronicum migrans due to Borrelia burgdorferi

CC **A69.20 Lyme disease, unspecified**
CC Exclusion see Appendix A PDX collection 0108

CC **A69.21 Meningitis due to Lyme disease**
CC Exclusion see Appendix A PDX collection 0108

CC **A69.22 Other neurologic disorders in Lyme disease**
Cranial neuritis
Meningoencephalitis
Polyneuropathy
CC Exclusion see Appendix A PDX collection 0108

CC **A69.23 Arthritis due to Lyme disease**
CC Exclusion see Appendix A PDX collection 0108

CC **A69.29 Other conditions associated with Lyme disease**
Myopericarditis due to Lyme disease
CC Exclusion see Appendix A PDX collection 0108

A69.8 Other specified spirochetal infections
A69.9 Spirochetal infection, unspecified

ther diseases caused by chlamydiae (A70-A74)

cludes1: *sexually transmitted chlamydial diseases (A55-A56)*

: A70 **Chlamydia psittaci infections**
Ornithosis
Parrot fever
Psittacosis
CC Exclusion see Appendix A PDX collection 0127
Valid 3-character code, no further characters required

A71 **Trachoma**

Excludes1: *sequelae of trachoma (B94.0)*

A71.0 Initial stage of trachoma
Trachoma dubium

A71.1 Active stage of trachoma
Granular conjunctivitis (trachomatous)
Trachomatous follicular conjunctivitis
Trachomatous pannus

A71.9 Trachoma, unspecified

A74 **Other diseases caused by chlamydiae**

Excludes1: *neonatal chlamydial conjunctivitis (P39.1)*
neonatal chlamydial pneumonia (P23.1)
Reiter's disease (M02.3-)
sexually transmitted chlamydial diseases (A55-A56)
Excludes2: *chlamydial pneumonia (J16.0)*

A74.0 Chlamydial conjunctivitis
Paratrachoma

\+ **A74.8 Other chlamydial diseases**
A74.81 Chlamydial peritonitis
A74.89 Other chlamydial diseases

A74.9 Chlamydial infection, unspecified
Chlamydiosis NOS

Rickettsioses (A75-A79)

A75 **Typhus fever**

Excludes1: *rickettsiosis due to Ehrlichia sennetsu (A79.81)*

CC **A75.0 Epidemic louse-borne typhus fever due to Rickettsia prowazekii**
Classical typhus (fever)
Epidemic (louse-borne) typhus
CC Exclusion see Appendix A PDX collection 0108

CC **A75.1 Recrudescent typhus [Brill's disease]**
Brill-Zinsser disease
CC Exclusion see Appendix A PDX collection 0108

CC **A75.2 Typhus fever due to Rickettsia typhi**
Murine (flea-borne) typhus
CC Exclusion see Appendix A PDX collection 0108

CC **A75.3 Typhus fever due to Rickettsia tsutsugamushi**
Scrub (mite-borne) typhus
Tsutsugamushi fever
CC Exclusion see Appendix A PDX collection 0108

CC **A75.9 Typhus fever, unspecified**
Typhus (fever) NOS
CC Exclusion see Appendix A PDX collection 0128

A77 **Spotted fever [tick-borne rickettsioses]**

CC **A77.0 Spotted fever due to Rickettsia rickettsii**
Rocky Mountain spotted fever
Sao Paulo fever
CC Exclusion see Appendix A PDX collection 0108

CC **A77.1 Spotted fever due to Rickettsia conorii**
African tick typhus
Boutonneuse fever
India tick typhus
Kenya tick typhus
Marseilles fever
Mediterranean tick fever
CC Exclusion see Appendix A PDX collection 0108

CC **A77.2 Spotted fever due to Rickettsia siberica**
North Asian tick fever
Siberian tick typhus
CC Exclusion see Appendix A PDX collection 0108

CC **A77.3 Spotted fever due to Rickettsia australis**
Queensland tick typhus
CC Exclusion see Appendix A PDX collection 0108

\+ **A77.4 Ehrlichiosis**
Excludes1: *Rickettsiosis due to Ehrlichia sennetsu (A79.81)*

CC **A77.40 Ehrlichiosis, unspecified**
CC Exclusion see Appendix A PDX collection 0108

CC **A77.41 Ehrlichiosis chafeensis [E. chafeensis]**
CC Exclusion see Appendix A PDX collection 0108

CC **A77.49 Other ehrlichiosis**
CC Exclusion see Appendix A PDX collection 0108

CC **A77.8 Other spotted fevers**
CC Exclusion see Appendix A PDX collection 0108

CC **A77.9 Spotted fever, unspecified**
Tick-borne typhus NOS
CC Exclusion see Appendix A PDX collection 0108

CC A78 **Q fever**
Infection due to Coxiella burnetii
Nine Mile fever
Quadrilateral fever
CC Exclusion see Appendix A PDX collection 0108
Valid 3-character code, no further characters required

A79 **Other rickettsioses**

CC **A79.0 Trench fever**
Quintan fever
Wolhynian fever
CC Exclusion see Appendix A PDX collection 0108

CC **A79.1 Rickettsialpox due to Rickettsia akari**
Kew Garden fever
Vesicular rickettsiosis
CC Exclusion see Appendix A PDX collection 0129

A79.8 Other specified rickettsioses

CC **A79.81 Rickettsiosis due to Ehrlichia sennetsu**
Excludes1: *rickettsiosis due to Ehrlichia sennetsu (A79.81)*
CC Exclusion see Appendix A PDX collection 0129

CC **A79.89 Other specified rickettsioses**
CC Exclusion see Appendix A PDX collection 0129

CC **A79.9 Rickettsiosis, unspecified**
Rickettsial infection NOS
CC Exclusion see Appendix A PDX collection 0129

Viral and prion infections of the central nervous system (A80-A89)

Excludes1: *postpolio syndrome (G14)*
sequelae of poliomyelitis (B91)
sequelae of viral encephalitis (B94.1)

A80 Acute poliomyelitis

MCC **A80.0 Acute paralytic poliomyelitis, vaccine-associated**
MCC Exclusion see Appendix A PDX collection 0130

MCC **A80.1 Acute paralytic poliomyelitis, wild virus, imported**
MCC Exclusion see Appendix A PDX collection 0130

MCC **A80.2 Acute paralytic poliomyelitis, wild virus, indigenous**
MCC Exclusion see Appendix A PDX collection 0130

\+ **A80.3 Acute paralytic poliomyelitis, other and unspecified**

MCC **A80.30 Acute paralytic poliomyelitis, unspecified**
MCC Exclusion see Appendix A PDX collection 0130

MCC **A80.39 Other acute paralytic poliomyelitis**
MCC Exclusion see Appendix A PDX collection 0130

A80.4 Acute nonparalytic poliomyelitis

A80.9 Acute poliomyelitis, unspecified

A81 Atypical virus infections of central nervous system

Includes: diseases of the central nervous system caused by prions
Use additional code to identify:
dementia with behavioral disturbance (F02.81)
dementia without behavioral disturbance (F02.80)

\+ **A81.0 Creutzfeldt-Jakob disease**

CC **A81.00 Creutzfeldt-Jakob disease, unspecified**
Jakob-Creutzfeldt disease, unspecified
CC Exclusion see Appendix A PDX collection 0131

CC **A81.01 Variant Creutzfeldt-Jakob disease**
CJD
CC Exclusion see Appendix A PDX collection 0131

CC **A81.09 Other Creutzfeldt-Jakob disease**
CJD
Familial Creutzfeldt-Jakob disease
Iatrogenic Creutzfeldt-Jakob disease
Sporadic Creutzfeldt-Jakob disease
Subacute spongiform encephalopathy (with dementia)
CC Exclusion see Appendix A PDX collection 0131

CC **A81.1 Subacute sclerosing panencephalitis**
Dawson's inclusion body encephalitis
Van Bogaert's sclerosing leukoencephalopathy
CC Exclusion see Appendix A PDX collection 0132

CC **A81.2 Progressive multifocal leukoencephalopathy**
Multifocal leukoencephalopathy NOS
CC Exclusion see Appendix A PDX collection 0133

\+ **A81.8 Other atypical virus infections of central nervous system**

CC **A81.81 Kuru**
CC Exclusion see Appendix A PDX collection 0134

CC **A81.82 Gerstmann-Sträussler-Scheinker syndrome**
GSS syndrome
CC Exclusion see Appendix A PDX collection 0135

CC **A81.83 Fatal familial insomnia**
FFI
CC Exclusion see Appendix A PDX collection 0135

CC **A81.89 Other atypical virus infections of central nervous system**
CC Exclusion see Appendix A PDX collection 0135

CC **A81.9 Atypical virus infection of central nervous system, unspecified**
Prion diseases of the central nervous system NOS
CC Exclusion see Appendix A PDX collection 0134

A82 Rabies

CC **A82.0 Sylvatic rabies**
CC Exclusion see Appendix A PDX collection 0136

CC **A82.1 Urban rabies**
CC Exclusion see Appendix A PDX collection 0136

CC **A82.9 Rabies, unspecified**
CC Exclusion see Appendix A PDX collection 0136

A83 Mosquito-borne viral encephalitis

Includes: mosquito-borne viral meningoencephalitis
Excludes2: *Venezuelan equine encephalitis (A92.2)*
West Nile fever (A92.3-)
West Nile virus (A92.3-)

MCC **A83.0 Japanese encephalitis**
MCC Exclusion see Appendix A PDX collection 0137

MCC **A83.1 Western equine encephalitis**
MCC Exclusion see Appendix A PDX collection 0137

MCC **A83.2 Eastern equine encephalitis**
MCC Exclusion see Appendix A PDX collection 0137

MCC **A83.3 St Louis encephalitis**
MCC Exclusion see Appendix A PDX collection 0137

MCC **A83.4 Australian encephalitis**
Kunjin virus disease
MCC Exclusion see Appendix A PDX collection 0137

MCC **A83.5 California encephalitis**
California meningoencephalitis
La Crosse encephalitis
MCC Exclusion see Appendix A PDX collection 0137

MCC **A83.6 Rocio virus disease**
MCC Exclusion see Appendix A PDX collection 0137

MCC **A83.8 Other mosquito-borne viral encephalitis**
MCC Exclusion see Appendix A PDX collection 0137

MCC **A83.9 Mosquito-borne viral encephalitis, unspecified**
MCC Exclusion see Appendix A PDX collection 0137

A84 Tick-borne viral encephalitis

Includes: tick-borne viral meningoencephalitis

MCC **A84.0 Far Eastern tick-borne encephalitis [Russian spring-summer encephalitis]**
MCC Exclusion see Appendix A PDX collection 0137

MCC **A84.1 Central European tick-borne encephalitis**
MCC Exclusion see Appendix A PDX collection 0137

MCC **A84.8 Other tick-borne viral encephalitis**
Louping ill
Powassan virus disease
MCC Exclusion see Appendix A PDX collection 0137

MCC **A84.9 Tick-borne viral encephalitis, unspecified**
MCC Exclusion see Appendix A PDX collection 0137

A85 Other viral encephalitis, not elsewhere classified

Includes: specified viral encephalomyelitis NEC
specified viral meningoencephalitis NEC
Excludes1: *benign myalgic encephalomyelitis (G93.3)*
encephalitis due to cytomegalovirus (B25.8)
encephalitis due to herpesvirus NEC (B10.0-)
encephalitis due to herpesvirus [herpes simplex] (B00.4)
encephalitis due to measles virus (B05.0)
encephalitis due to mumps virus (B26.2)
encephalitis due to poliomyelitis virus (A80.-)
encephalitis due to zoster (B02.0)
lymphocytic choriomeningitis (A87.2)

CC **A85.0 Enteroviral encephalitis**
Enteroviral encephalomyelitis
CC Exclusion see Appendix A PDX collection 0138

CC **A85.1 Adenoviral encephalitis**
Adenoviral meningoencephalitis
CC Exclusion see Appendix A PDX collection 0138

MCC **A85.2 Arthropod-borne viral encephalitis, unspecified**
Excludes1: *West nile virus with encephalitis (A92.31)*
MCC Exclusion see Appendix A PDX collection 0137

CC **A85.8 Other specified viral encephalitis**
Encephalitis lethargica
Von Economo-Cruchet disease
CC Exclusion see Appendix A PDX collection 0138

CC A86 Unspecified viral encephalitis

Viral encephalomyelitis NOS
Viral meningoencephalitis NOS
CC Exclusion see Appendix A PDX collection 0139
Valid 3-character code, no further characters required

A87 Viral meningitis

Excludes1: *meningitis due to herpesvirus [herpes simplex] (B00.3)*
meningitis due to herpesvirus [herpes simplex] (B00.3)
meningitis due to measles virus (B05.1)
meningitis due to mumps virus (B26.1)
meningitis due to poliomyelitis virus (A80.-)
meningitis due to zoster (B02.1)

CC **A87.0 Enteroviral meningitis**
Coxsackievirus meningitis
Echovirus meningitis
CC Exclusion see Appendix A PDX collection 0140

CC **A87.1 Adenoviral meningitis**
CC Exclusion see Appendix A PDX collection 0140

CC **A87.2 Lymphocytic choriomeningitis**
Lymphocytic meningoencephalitis
CC Exclusion see Appendix A PDX collection 0141

CC **A87.8 Other viral meningitis**
CC Exclusion see Appendix A PDX collection 0140

CC **A87.9 Viral meningitis, unspecified**
CC Exclusion see Appendix A PDX collection 0140

A88 Other viral infections of central nervous system, not elsewhere classified

Excludes1: *viral encephalitis NOS (A86)*
viral meningitis NOS (A87.9)

CC **A88.0 Enteroviral exanthematous fever [Boston exanthem]**
CC Exclusion see Appendix A PDX collection 0137

A88.1 Epidemic vertigo

CC **A88.8 Other specified viral infections of central nervous system**
CC Exclusion see Appendix A PDX collection 0138

CC **A89 Unspecified viral infection of central nervous system**
CC Exclusion see Appendix A PDX collection 0139
Valid 3-character code, no further characters required

Arthropod-borne viral fevers and viral hemorrhagic fevers (A90-A99)

CC **A90 Dengue fever [classical dengue]**

Excludes1: *dengue hemorrhagic fever (A91)*
CC Exclusion see Appendix A PDX collection 0142
Valid 3-character code, no further characters required

CC **A91 Dengue hemorrhagic fever**
CC Exclusion see Appendix A PDX collection 0143
Valid 3-character code, no further characters required

A92 Other mosquito-borne viral fevers

Excludes1: *Ross River disease (B33.1)*

CC **A92.0 Chikungunya virus disease**
Chikungunya (hemorrhagic) fever
CC Exclusion see Appendix A PDX collection 0143

CC **A92.1 O'nyong-nyong fever**
CC Exclusion see Appendix A PDX collection 0144

CC **A92.2 Venezuelan equine fever**
Venezuelan equine encephalitis
Venezuelan equine encephalomyelitis virus disease
CC Exclusion see Appendix A PDX collection 0144

\+ **A92.3 West Nile virus infection**
West Nile fever

MCC **A92.30 West Nile virus infection, unspecified**
West Nile fever NOS
West Nile fever without complications
West Nile virus NOS
MCC Exclusion see Appendix A PDX collection 0145

MCC **A92.31 West Nile virus infection with encephalitis**
West Nile encephalitis
West Nile encephalomyelitis
MCC Exclusion see Appendix A PDX collection 0145

MCC **A92.32 West Nile virus infection with other neurologic manifestation**
Use additional code to specify the neurologic manifestation
MCC Exclusion see Appendix A PDX collection 0145

MCC **A92.39 West Nile virus infection with other complications**
Use additional code to specify the other conditions
MCC Exclusion see Appendix A PDX collection 0145

CC **A92.4 Rift Valley fever**
CC Exclusion see Appendix A PDX collection 0144

CC **A92.8 Other specified mosquito-borne viral fevers**
CC Exclusion see Appendix A PDX collection 0144

CC **A92.9 Mosquito-borne viral fever, unspecified**
CC Exclusion see Appendix A PDX collection 0143

A93 Other arthropod-borne viral fevers, not elsewhere classified

CC **A93.0 Oropouche virus disease**
Oropouche fever
CC Exclusion see Appendix A PDX collection 0144

CC **A93.1 Sandfly fever**
Pappataci fever
Phlebotomus fever
CC Exclusion see Appendix A PDX collection 0143

CC **A93.2 Colorado tick fever**
CC Exclusion see Appendix A PDX collection 0143

CC **A93.8 Other specified arthropod-borne viral fevers**
Piry virus disease
Vesicular stomatitis virus disease [Indiana fever]
CC Exclusion see Appendix A PDX collection 0143

CC **A94 Unspecified arthropod-borne viral fever**
Arboviral fever NOS
Arbovirus infection NOS
CC Exclusion see Appendix A PDX collection 0143
Valid 3-character code, no further characters required

A95 Yellow fever

CC **A95.0 Sylvatic yellow fever**
Jungle yellow fever
CC Exclusion see Appendix A PDX collection 0146

CC **A95.1 Urban yellow fever**
CC Exclusion see Appendix A PDX collection 0146

CC **A95.9 Yellow fever, unspecified**
CC Exclusion see Appendix A PDX collection 0146

A96 Arenaviral hemorrhagic fever

CC **A96.0 Junin hemorrhagic fever**
Argentinian hemorrhagic fever
CC Exclusion see Appendix A PDX collection 0147

CC **A96.1 Machupo hemorrhagic fever**
Bolivian hemorrhagic fever
CC Exclusion see Appendix A PDX collection 0147

A96.2 Lassa fever

CC **A96.8 Other arenaviral hemorrhagic fevers**
CC Exclusion see Appendix A PDX collection 0147

CC **A96.9 Arenaviral hemorrhagic fever, unspecified**
CC Exclusion see Appendix A PDX collection 0147

A98 Other viral hemorrhagic fevers, not elsewhere classified

Excludes1: *chikungunya hemorrhagic fever (A92.0)*
dengue hemorrhagic fever (A91)

CC **A98.0 Crimean-Congo hemorrhagic fever**
Central Asian hemorrhagic fever
CC Exclusion see Appendix A PDX collection 0143

CC **A98.1 Omsk hemorrhagic fever**
CC Exclusion see Appendix A PDX collection 0143

CC **A98.2 Kyasanur Forest disease**
CC Exclusion see Appendix A PDX collection 0143

A98.3 Marburg virus disease

A98.4 Ebola virus disease

CC **A98.5 Hemorrhagic fever with renal syndrome**
Epidemic hemorrhagic fever
Korean hemorrhagic fever
Russian hemorrhagic fever
Hantaan virus disease
Hantavirus disease with renal manifestations
Nephropathia epidemica
Songo fever
Excludes1: *hantavirus (cardio)-pulmonary syndrome (B33.4)*
CC Exclusion see Appendix A PDX collection 0148

CC **A98.8 Other specified viral hemorrhagic fevers**
CC Exclusion see Appendix A PDX collection 0143

CC **A99 Unspecified viral hemorrhagic fever**
CC Exclusion see Appendix A PDX collection 0143
Valid 3-character code, no further characters

Viral infections characterized by skin and mucous membrane lesions (B00-B09)

B00 Herpesviral [herpes simplex] infections

Excludes1: *congenital herpesviral infections (P35.2)*
Excludes2: *anogenital herpesviral infection (A60.-)*
gammaherpesviral mononucleosis (B27.0-)
herpangina (B08.5)

B00.0 Eczema herpeticum
Kaposi's varicelliform eruption

B00.1 Herpesviral vesicular dermatitis
Herpes simplex facialis
Herpes simplex labialis
Herpes simplex otitis externa
Vesicular dermatitis of ear
Vesicular dermatitis of lip

CC **B00.2 Herpesviral gingivostomatitis and pharyngotonsillitis**
Herpesviral pharyngitis
CC Exclusion see Appendix A PDX collection 0149

MCC **B00.3 Herpesviral meningitis**
MCC Exclusion see Appendix A PDX collection 0150

MCC **B00.4 Herpesviral encephalitis**
Herpesviral meningoencephalitis
Simian B disease
Excludes1: *herpesviral encephalitis due to herpesvirus 6 and 7 (B10.01, B10.09)*
non-simplex herpesviral encephalitis (B10.0-)
MCC Exclusion see Appendix A PDX collection 0151

\+ **B00.5 Herpesviral ocular disease**

CC **B00.50 Herpesviral ocular disease, unspecified**
CC Exclusion see Appendix A PDX collection 0152

CC **B00.51 Herpesviral iridocyclitis**
Herpesviral iritis
Herpesviral uveitis, anterior
CC Exclusion see Appendix A PDX collection 0152

CC **B00.52 Herpesviral keratitis**
Herpesviral keratoconjunctivitis
CC Exclusion see Appendix A PDX collection 0152

CC **B00.53 Herpesviral conjunctivitis**
CC Exclusion see Appendix A PDX collection 0152

CC **B00.59 Other herpesviral disease of eye**
Herpesviral dermatitis of eyelid
CC Exclusion see Appendix A PDX collection 0152

MCC **B00.7 Disseminated herpesviral disease**
Herpesviral sepsis
MCC Exclusion see Appendix A PDX collection 0153
Review coding guideline C.1.d

+ **B00.8 Other forms of herpesviral infections**

CC **B00.81 Herpesviral hepatitis**
CC Exclusion see Appendix A PDX collection 0154

MCC **B00.82 Herpes simplex myelitis**
MCC Exclusion see Appendix A PDX collection 0155

CC **B00.89 Other herpesviral infection**
Herpesviral whitlow
CC Exclusion see Appendix A PDX collection 0156

B00.9 Herpesviral infection, unspecified
Herpes simplex infection NOS

B01 Varicella [chickenpox]

CC **B01.0 Varicella meningitis**
CC Exclusion see Appendix A PDX collection 0157

+ **B01.1 Varicella encephalitis, myelitis and encephalomyelitis**
Postchickenpox encephalitis, myelitis and encephalomyelitis

MCC **B01.11 Varicella encephalitis and encephalomyelitis**
Postchickenpox encephalitis and encephalomyelitis
MCC Exclusion see Appendix A PDX collection 0158

MCC **B01.12 Varicella myelitis**
Postchickenpox myelitis
MCC Exclusion see Appendix A PDX collection 0159

MCC **B01.2 Varicella pneumonia**
MCC Exclusion see Appendix A PDX collection 0160

+ **B01.8 Varicella with other complications**

CC **B01.81 Varicella keratitis**
CC Exclusion see Appendix A PDX collection 0157

CC **B01.89 Other varicella complications**
CC Exclusion see Appendix A PDX collection 0157

CC **B01.9 Varicella without complication**
Varicella NOS
CC Exclusion see Appendix A PDX collection 0157

B02 Zoster [herpes zoster]

Includes: shingles
zona

CC **B02.0 Zoster encephalitis**
Zoster meningoencephalitis
CC Exclusion see Appendix A PDX collection 0161

MCC **B02.1 Zoster meningitis**
MCC Exclusion see Appendix A PDX collection 0162

+ **B02.2 Zoster with other nervous system involvement**

CC **B02.21 Postherpetic geniculate ganglionitis**
CC Exclusion see Appendix A PDX collection 0161

CC **B02.22 Postherpetic trigeminal neuralgia**
CC Exclusion see Appendix A PDX collection 0161

CC **B02.23 Postherpetic polyneuropathy**
CC Exclusion see Appendix A PDX collection 0161

MCC **B02.24 Postherpetic myelitis**
Herpes zoster myelitis
MCC Exclusion see Appendix A PDX collection 0163

CC **B02.29 Other postherpetic nervous system involvement**
Postherpetic radiculopathy
CC Exclusion see Appendix A PDX collection 0161

+ **B02.3 Zoster ocular disease**

CC **B02.30 Zoster ocular disease, unspecified**
CC Exclusion see Appendix A PDX collection 0164

CC **B02.31 Zoster conjunctivitis**
CC Exclusion see Appendix A PDX collection 0164

CC **B02.32 Zoster iridocyclitis**
CC Exclusion see Appendix A PDX collection 0164

CC **B02.33 Zoster keratitis**
Herpes zoster keratoconjunctivitis
CC Exclusion see Appendix A PDX collection 0164

CC **B02.34 Zoster scleritis**
CC Exclusion see Appendix A PDX collection 0164

CC **B02.39 Other herpes zoster eye disease**
Zoster blepharitis
CC Exclusion see Appendix A PDX collection 0164

CC **B02.7 Disseminated zoster**
CC Exclusion see Appendix A PDX collection 0165

CC **B02.8 Zoster with other complications**
Herpes zoster otitis externa
CC Exclusion see Appendix A PDX collection 0165

B02.9 Zoster without complications
Zoster NOS

CC **B03 Smallpox**

NOTE In 1980 the 33rd World Health Assembly declared that smallpox had been eradicated.
The classification is maintained for surveillance purposes.

CC Exclusion see Appendix A PDX collection 0166
Valid 3-character code, no further characters required

CC **B04 Monkeypox**

CC Exclusion see Appendix A PDX collection 0167
Valid 3-character code, no further characters required

B05 Measles

Includes: morbilli
Excludes1: *subacute sclerosing panencephalitis (A81.1)*

MCC **B05.0 Measles complicated by encephalitis**
Postmeasles encephalitis
MCC Exclusion see Appendix A PDX collection 0168

CC **B05.1 Measles complicated by meningitis**
Postmeasles meningitis
CC Exclusion see Appendix A PDX collection 0169

MCC **B05.2 Measles complicated by pneumonia**
Postmeasles pneumonia
MCC Exclusion see Appendix A PDX collection 0170

B05.3 Measles complicated by otitis media
Postmeasles otitis media

CC **B05.4 Measles with intestinal complications**
CC Exclusion see Appendix A PDX collection 0169

+ **B05.8 Measles with other complications**

CC **B05.81 Measles keratitis and keratoconjunctivitis**
CC Exclusion see Appendix A PDX collection 0171

CC **B05.89 Other measles complications**
CC Exclusion see Appendix A PDX collection 0169

B05.9 Measles without complication
Measles NOS

B06 Rubella [German measles]

Excludes1: *congenital rubella (P35.0)*

+ **B06.0 Rubella with neurological complications**

CC **B06.00 Rubella with neurological complication, unspecified**
CC Exclusion see Appendix A PDX collection 0172

MCC **B06.01 Rubella encephalitis**
Rubella meningoencephalitis
MCC Exclusion see Appendix A PDX collection 0172

CC **B06.02 Rubella meningitis**
CC Exclusion see Appendix A PDX collection 0172

CC **B06.09 Other neurological complications of rubella**
CC Exclusion see Appendix A PDX collection 0172

+ **B06.8 Rubella with other complications**

CC **B06.81 Rubella pneumonia**
CC Exclusion see Appendix A PDX collection 0172

CC **B06.82 Rubella arthritis**
CC Exclusion see Appendix A PDX collection 0173

CC **B06.89 Other rubella complications**
CC Exclusion see Appendix A PDX collection 0172

B06.9 Rubella without complication
Rubella NOS

B07 Viral warts

Includes: verruca simplex
verruca vulgaris
viral warts due to human papillomavirus
Excludes2: *anogenital (venereal) warts (A63.0)*
papilloma of bladder (D41.4)
papilloma of cervix (D26.0)
papilloma larynx (D14.1)

B07.0 Plantar wart
Verruca plantaris

B07.8 Other viral warts
Common wart
Flat wart
Verruca plana

B07.9 Viral wart, unspecified

B08 Other viral infections characterized by skin and mucous membrane lesions, not elsewhere classified

Excludes1: *vesicular stomatitis virus disease (A93.8)*

B08.0 Other orthopoxvirus infections

Excludes2: *monkeypox (B04)*

\+ **B08.01 Cowpox and vaccinia not from vaccine**

B08.010 Cowpox

B08.011 Vaccinia not from vaccine

Excludes1: *vaccinia (from vaccination) (generalized) (T88.1)*

B08.02 Orf virus disease

Contagious pustular dermatitis
Ecthyma contagiosum

B08.03 Pseudocowpox [milker's node]

B08.04 Paravaccinia, unspecified

B08.09 Other orthopoxvirus infections

Orthopoxvirus infection NOS

B08.1 Molluscum contagiosum

\+ **B08.2 Exanthema subitum [sixth disease]**

Roseola infantum

• **B08.20 Exanthema subitum [sixth disease], unspecified**

Roseola infantum, unspecified

• **B08.21 Exanthema subitum [sixth disease] due to human herpesvirus 6**

Roseola infantum due to human herpesvirus 6

• **B08.22 Exanthema subitum [sixth disease] due to human herpesvirus 7**

Roseola infantum due to human herpesvirus 7

CC **B08.3 Erythema infectiosum [fifth disease]**

CC Exclusion see Appendix A PDX collection 0174

B08.4 Enteroviral vesicular stomatitis with exanthem

Hand, foot and mouth disease

B08.5 Enteroviral vesicular pharyngitis

Herpangina

\+ **B08.6 Parapoxvirus infections**

B08.60 Parapoxvirus infection, unspecified

B08.61 Bovine stomatitis

B08.62 Sealpox

B08.69 Other parapoxvirus infections

\+ **B08.7 Yatapoxvirus infections**

B08.70 Yatapoxvirus infection, unspecified

CC **B08.71 Tanapox virus disease**

CC Exclusion see Appendix A PDX collection 0167

B08.72 Yaba pox virus disease

Yaba monkey tumor disease

B08.79 Other yatapoxvirus infections

B08.8 Other specified viral infections characterized by skin and mucous membrane lesions

Enteroviral lymphonodular pharyngitis
Foot-and-mouth disease
Poxvirus NEC

B09 Unspecified viral infection characterized by skin and mucous membrane lesions

Viral enanthema NOS
Viral exanthema NOS
Valid 3-character code, no further characters required

Other human herpesviruses (B10)

B10 Other human herpesviruses

Excludes2: *cytomegalovirus (B25.9)*
Epstein-Barr virus (B27.0-)
herpes NOS (B00.9)
herpes simplex (B00.-)
herpes zoster (B02.-)
human herpesvirus NOS (B00.-)
human herpesvirus 1 and 2 (B00.-)
human herpesvirus 3 (B01.-, B02.-)
human herpesvirus 4 (B27.0-)
human herpesvirus 5 (B25.-)
varicella (B01.-)
zoster (B02.-)

\+ **B10.0 Other human herpesvirus encephalitis**

Excludes2: *herpes encephalitis NOS (B00.4)*
herpes simplex encephalitis (B00.4)
human herpesvirus encephalitis (B00.4)
simian B herpes virus encephalitis (B00.4)

MCC **B10.01 Human herpesvirus 6 encephalitis**

MCC Exclusion see Appendix A PDX collection 0151

MCC **B10.09 Other human herpesvirus encephalitis**

Human herpesvirus 7 encephalitis
MCC Exclusion see Appendix A PDX collection 0151

\+ **B10.8 Other human herpesvirus infection**

B10.81 Human herpesvirus 6 infection

B10.82 Human herpesvirus 7 infection

B10.89 Other human herpesvirus infection

Human herpesvirus 8 infection
Kaposi's sarcoma-associated herpesvirus infection

Viral hepatitis (B15-B19)

Excludes1: *sequelae of viral hepatitis (B94.2)*

Excludes2: *cytomegaloviral hepatitis (B25.1)*
herpesviral [herpes simplex] hepatitis (B00.81)

B15 Acute hepatitis A

MCC **B15.0 Hepatitis A with hepatic coma**

MCC Exclusion see Appendix A PDX collection 0175

CC **B15.9 Hepatitis A without hepatic coma**

Hepatitis A (acute)(viral) NOS
CC Exclusion see Appendix A PDX collection 0175

B16 Acute hepatitis B

MCC **B16.0 Acute hepatitis B with delta-agent with hepatic coma**

MCC Exclusion see Appendix A PDX collection 0175

CC **B16.1 Acute hepatitis B with delta-agent without hepatic coma**

CC Exclusion see Appendix A PDX collection 0175

MCC **B16.2 Acute hepatitis B without delta-agent with hepatic coma**

MCC Exclusion see Appendix A PDX collection 0175

CC **B16.9 Acute hepatitis B without delta-agent and without hepatic coma**

Hepatitis B (acute) (viral) NOS
CC Exclusion see Appendix A PDX collection 0175

B17 Other acute viral hepatitis

CC **B17.0 Acute delta-(super) infection of hepatitis B carrier**

CC Exclusion see Appendix A PDX collection 0175

\+ **B17.1 Acute hepatitis C**

CC **B17.10 Acute hepatitis C without hepatic coma**

Acute hepatitis C NOS
CC Exclusion see Appendix A PDX collection 0175

MCC **B17.11 Acute hepatitis C with hepatic coma**

MCC Exclusion see Appendix A PDX collection 0175

CC **B17.2 Acute hepatitis E**

CC Exclusion see Appendix A PDX collection 0175

CC **B17.8 Other specified acute viral hepatitis**

Hepatitis non-A non-B (acute) (viral) NEC
CC Exclusion see Appendix A PDX collection 0175

CC **B17.9 Acute viral hepatitis, unspecified**

Acute hepatitis NOS
CC Exclusion see Appendix A PDX collection 0175

B18 Chronic viral hepatitis

CC **B18.0 Chronic viral hepatitis B with delta-agent**

CC Exclusion see Appendix A PDX collection 0175

CC **B18.1 Chronic viral hepatitis B without delta-agent**

Chronic (viral) hepatitis B
CC Exclusion see Appendix A PDX collection 0175

B18.2 Chronic viral hepatitis C

CC **B18.8 Other chronic viral hepatitis**

CC Exclusion see Appendix A PDX collection 0175

CC **B18.9 Chronic viral hepatitis, unspecified**

CC Exclusion see Appendix A PDX collection 0175

B19 Unspecified viral hepatitis

MCC **B19.0 Unspecified viral hepatitis with hepatic coma**

MCC Exclusion see Appendix A PDX collection 0175

\+ **B19.1 Unspecified viral hepatitis B**

CC **B19.10 Unspecified viral hepatitis B without hepatic coma**

Unspecified viral hepatitis B NOS
CC Exclusion see Appendix A PDX collection 0175

MCC **B19.11 Unspecified viral hepatitis B with hepatic coma**

MCC Exclusion see Appendix A PDX collection 0175

\+ **B19.2 Unspecified viral hepatitis C**

B19.20 Unspecified viral hepatitis C without hepatic coma

Viral hepatitis C NOS

MCC **B19.21 Unspecified viral hepatitis C with hepatic coma**

MCC Exclusion see Appendix A PDX collection 0175

CC **B19.9 Unspecified viral hepatitis without hepatic coma**

Viral hepatitis NOS
CC Exclusion see Appendix A PDX collection 0175

Human immunodeficiency virus [HIV] disease (B20)

MCC **B20 Human immunodeficiency virus [HIV] disease**

Includes: acquired immune deficiency syndrome [AIDS]
AIDS-related complex [ARC]
HIV infection, symptomatic

Code first Human immunodeficiency virus [HIV] disease complicating pregnancy, childbirth and the puerperium, if applicable (O98.7-)

Use additional code(s) to identify all manifestations of HIV infection

Excludes1: *asymptomatic human immunodeficiency virus [HIV] infection status (Z21)*
exposure to HIV virus (Z20.6)
inconclusive serologic evidence of HIV (R75)

MCC Exclusion see Appendix A PDX collection 0176
Review coding guideline C.1.a
Valid 3-character code, no further characters required

Other viral diseases (B25-B34)

B25 Cytomegaloviral disease

Excludes1: *congenital cytomegalovirus infection (P35.1)*
cytomegaloviral mononucleosis (B27.1-)

MCC **B25.0 Cytomegaloviral pneumonitis**
MCC Exclusion see Appendix A PDX collection 0110

CC **B25.1 Cytomegaloviral hepatitis**
No CC Exclusions

MCC **B25.2 Cytomegaloviral pancreatitis**
MCC Exclusion see Appendix A PDX collection 0177

CC **B25.8 Other cytomegaloviral diseases**
Cytomegaloviral encephalitis
CC Exclusion see Appendix A PDX collection 0178

CC **B25.9 Cytomegaloviral disease, unspecified**
CC Exclusion see Appendix A PDX collection 0178

B26 Mumps

Includes: epidemic parotitis
infectious parotitis

♂ CC **B26.0 Mumps orchitis**
CC Exclusion see Appendix A PDX collection 0179

MCC **B26.1 Mumps meningitis**
MCC Exclusion see Appendix A PDX collection 0180

MCC **B26.2 Mumps encephalitis**
MCC Exclusion see Appendix A PDX collection 0181

CC **B26.3 Mumps pancreatitis**
CC Exclusion see Appendix A PDX collection 0182

\+ **B26.8 Mumps with other complications**

CC **B26.81 Mumps hepatitis**
CC Exclusion see Appendix A PDX collection 0183

CC **B26.82 Mumps myocarditis**
CC Exclusion see Appendix A PDX collection 0184

CC **B26.83 Mumps nephritis**
CC Exclusion see Appendix A PDX collection 0184

CC **B26.84 Mumps polyneuropathy**
CC Exclusion see Appendix A PDX collection 0185

CC **B26.85 Mumps arthritis**
CC Exclusion see Appendix A PDX collection 0184

CC **B26.89 Other mumps complications**
CC Exclusion see Appendix A PDX collection 0184

B26.9 Mumps without complication
Mumps NOS
Mumps parotitis NOS

B27 Infectious mononucleosis

Includes: glandular fever
monocytic angina
Pfeiffer's disease

\+ **B27.0 Gammaherpesviral mononucleosis**
Mononucleosis due to Epstein-Barr virus

B27.00 Gammaherpesviral mononucleosis without complication
B27.01 Gammaherpesviral mononucleosis with polyneuropathy
B27.02 Gammaherpesviral mononucleosis with meningitis
B27.09 Gammaherpesviral mononucleosis with other complications
Hepatomegaly in gammaherpesviral mononucleosis

\+ **B27.1 Cytomegaloviral mononucleosis**

B27.10 Cytomegaloviral mononucleosis without complications
B27.11 Cytomegaloviral mononucleosis with polyneuropathy
B27.12 Cytomegaloviral mononucleosis with meningitis
B27.19 Cytomegaloviral mononucleosis with other complication
Hepatomegaly in cytomegaloviral mononucleosis

\+ **B27.8 Other infectious mononucleosis**

B27.80 Other infectious mononucleosis without complicatio
B27.81 Other infectious mononucleosis with polyneuropathy
B27.82 Other infectious mononucleosis with meningitis
B27.89 Other infectious mononucleosis with other complication
Hepatomegaly in other infectious mononucleosis

\+ **B27.9 Infectious mononucleosis, unspecified**

B27.90 Infectious mononucleosis, unspecified without complication
B27.91 Infectious mononucleosis, unspecified with polyneuropathy
B27.92 Infectious mononucleosis, unspecified with meningit
B27.99 Infectious mononucleosis, unspecified with other complication
Hepatomegaly in unspecified infectious mononucleosi

B30 Viral conjunctivitis

Excludes1: *herpesviral [herpes simplex] ocular disease (B00.5)*
ocular zoster (B02.3)

B30.0 Keratoconjunctivitis due to adenovirus
Epidemic keratoconjunctivitis
Shipyard eye

B30.1 Conjunctivitis due to adenovirus
Acute adenoviral follicular conjunctivitis
Swimming-pool conjunctivitis

B30.2 Viral pharyngoconjunctivitis

B30.3 Acute epidemic hemorrhagic conjunctivitis (enteroviral)
Conjunctivitis due to coxsackievirus 24
Conjunctivitis due to enterovirus 70
Hemorrhagic conjunctivitis (acute)(epidemic)

B30.8 Other viral conjunctivitis
Newcastle conjunctivitis

B30.9 Viral conjunctivitis, unspecified

B33 Other viral diseases, not elsewhere classified

B33.0 Epidemic myalgia
Bornholm disease

CC **B33.1 Ross River disease**
Epidemic polyarthritis and exanthema
Ross River fever
CC Exclusion see Appendix A PDX collection 0144

\+ **B33.2 Viral carditis**
Coxsackie (virus) carditis

CC **B33.20 Viral carditis, unspecified**
CC Exclusion see Appendix A PDX collection 0186

CC **B33.21 Viral endocarditis**
CC Exclusion see Appendix A PDX collection 0187

CC **B33.22 Viral myocarditis**
CC Exclusion see Appendix A PDX collection 0186

CC **B33.23 Viral pericarditis**
CC Exclusion see Appendix A PDX collection 0188

B33.24 Viral cardiomyopathy

B33.3 Retrovirus infections, not elsewhere classified
Retrovirus infection NOS

CC **B33.4 Hantavirus (cardio)-pulmonary syndrome [HPS] [HCPS]**
Hantavirus disease with pulmonary manifestations
Sin nombre virus disease
Use additional code to identify any associated acute kidney failure (N17.9)

Excludes1: *hantavirus disease with renal manifestations (A98.*
hemorrhagic fever with renal manifestations (A98.

CC Exclusion see Appendix A PDX collection 0189

B33.8 Other specified viral diseases

Excludes1: *anogenital human papillomavirus infection (A63.0)*
viral warts due to human papillomavirus infection (B07)

B34 Viral infection of unspecified site

Excludes1: *anogenital human papillomavirus infection (A63.0)*
cytomegaloviral disease NOS (B25.9)
herpesvirus [herpes simplex] infection NOS (B00.9)
retrovirus infection NOS (B33.3)
viral agents as the cause of diseases classified elsewhere (B97.-)
viral warts due to human papillomavirus infection (B07)

B34.0 Adenovirus infection, unspecified

B34.1 Enterovirus infection, unspecified
Coxsackievirus infection NOS
Echovirus infection NOS

B34.2 Coronavirus infection, unspecified

Excludes1: *pneumonia due to SARS-associated coronavirus (J12.81)*

CC **B34.3 Parvovirus infection, unspecified**
CC Exclusion see Appendix A PDX collection 0174
B34.4 Papovavirus infection, unspecified
B34.8 Other viral infections of unspecified site
B34.9 Viral infection, unspecified
Viremia NOS

ycoses (B35-B49)

cludes2: *hypersensitivity pneumonitis due to organic dust (J67.-)*
mycosis fungoides (C84.0-)

B35 Dermatophytosis

Includes: favus
infections due to species of Epidermophyton, Micro-sporum and Trichophyton
tinea, any type except those in B36.-

B35.0 Tinea barbae and tinea capitis
Beard ringworm
Kerion
Scalp ringworm
Sycosis, mycotic

B35.1 Tinea unguium
Dermatophytic onychia
Dermatophytosis of nail
Onychomycosis
Ringworm of nails

B35.2 Tinea manuum
Dermatophytosis of hand
Hand ringworm

B35.3 Tinea pedis
Athlete's foot
Dermatophytosis of foot
Foot ringworm

B35.4 Tinea corporis
Ringworm of the body

B35.5 Tinea imbricata
Tokelau

B35.6 Tinea cruris
Dhobi itch
Groin ringworm
Jock itch

B35.8 Other dermatophytoses
Disseminated dermatophytosis
Granulomatous dermatophytosis

B35.9 Dermatophytosis, unspecified
Ringworm NOS

B36 Other superficial mycoses

B36.0 Pityriasis versicolor
Tinea flava
Tinea versicolor

B36.1 Tinea nigra
Keratomycosis nigricans palmaris
Microsporosis nigra
Pityriasis nigra

B36.2 White piedra
Tinea blanca

B36.3 Black piedra
B36.8 Other specified superficial mycoses
B36.9 Superficial mycosis, unspecified

B37 Candidiasis

Includes: candidosis
moniliasis

Excludes1: *neonatal candidiasis (P37.5)*

CC **B37.0 Candidal stomatitis**
Oral thrush
CC Exclusion see Appendix A PDX collection 0190

MCC **B37.1 Pulmonary candidiasis**
Candidal bronchitis
Candidal pneumonia
MCC Exclusion see Appendix A PDX collection 0190

B37.2 Candidiasis of skin and nail
Candidal onychia
Candidal paronychia
Excludes2: *diaper dermatitis (L22)*

♀ **B37.3 Candidiasis of vulva and vagina**
Candidal vulvovaginitis
Monilial vulvovaginitis
Vaginal thrush

\+ **B37.4 Candidiasis of other urogenital sites**

CC **B37.41 Candidal cystitis and urethritis**
CC Exclusion see Appendix A PDX collection 0191
HAC see Appendix B for HAC conditional logic

B37.42 Candidal balanitis

CC **B37.49 Other urogenital candidiasis**
Candidal pyelonephritis
CC Exclusion see Appendix A PDX collection 0191
HAC see Appendix B for HAC conditional logic

MCC **B37.5 Candidal meningitis**
MCC Exclusion see Appendix A PDX collection 0192

MCC **B37.6 Candidal endocarditis**
MCC Exclusion see Appendix A PDX collection 0190

MCC **B37.7 Candidal sepsis**
Disseminated candidiasis
Systemic candidiasis
MCC Exclusion see Appendix A PDX collection 0193
Review coding guideline C.1.d

\+ **B37.8 Candidiasis of other sites**

CC **B37.81 Candidal esophagitis**
CC Exclusion see Appendix A PDX collection 0190

CC **B37.82 Candidal enteritis**
Candidal proctitis
CC Exclusion see Appendix A PDX collection 0190

CC **B37.83 Candidal cheilitis**
CC Exclusion see Appendix A PDX collection 0190

CC **B37.84 Candidal otitis externa**
CC Exclusion see Appendix A PDX collection 0190

CC **B37.89 Other sites of candidiasis**
Candidal osteomyelitis
CC Exclusion see Appendix A PDX collection 0194

B37.9 Candidiasis, unspecified
Thrush NOS

B38 Coccidioidomycosis

CC **B38.0 Acute pulmonary coccidioidomycosis**
CC Exclusion see Appendix A PDX collection 0195

CC **B38.1 Chronic pulmonary coccidioidomycosis**
CC Exclusion see Appendix A PDX collection 0196

CC **B38.2 Pulmonary coccidioidomycosis, unspecified**
CC Exclusion see Appendix A PDX collection 0196

CC **B38.3 Cutaneous coccidioidomycosis**
CC Exclusion see Appendix A PDX collection 0197

MCC **B38.4 Coccidioidomycosis meningitis**
MCC Exclusion see Appendix A PDX collection 0198

CC **B38.7 Disseminated coccidioidomycosis**
Generalized coccidioidomycosis
CC Exclusion see Appendix A PDX collection 0199

\+ **B38.8 Other forms of coccidioidomycosis**

♂ CC **B38.81 Prostatic coccidioidomycosis**
CC Exclusion see Appendix A PDX collection 0197

CC **B38.89 Other forms of coccidioidomycosis**
CC Exclusion see Appendix A PDX collection 0199

CC **B38.9 Coccidioidomycosis, unspecified**
CC Exclusion see Appendix A PDX collection 0199

B39 Histoplasmosis

Code first associated AIDS (B20)

Use additional code for any associated manifestations, such as:
endocarditis (I39)
meningitis (G02)
pericarditis (I32)
retinitits (H32)

MCC **B39.0 Acute pulmonary histoplasmosis capsulati**
MCC Exclusion see Appendix A PDX collection 0200

MCC **B39.1 Chronic pulmonary histoplasmosis capsulati**
MCC Exclusion see Appendix A PDX collection 0200

MCC **B39.2 Pulmonary histoplasmosis capsulati, unspecified**
MCC Exclusion see Appendix A PDX collection 0200

CC **B39.3 Disseminated histoplasmosis capsulati**
Generalized histoplasmosis capsulati
CC Exclusion see Appendix A PDX collection 0201

B39.4 Histoplasmosis capsulati, unspecified
American histoplasmosis

B39.5 Histoplasmosis duboisii
African histoplasmosis

B39.9 Histoplasmosis, unspecified

B40 Blastomycosis

Excludes1: *Brazilian blastomycosis (B41.-)*
keloidal blastomycosis (B48.0)

CC **B40.0 Acute pulmonary blastomycosis**
CC Exclusion see Appendix A PDX collection 0202

CC **B40.1 Chronic pulmonary blastomycosis**
CC Exclusion see Appendix A PDX collection 0202

CC **B40.2 Pulmonary blastomycosis, unspecified**
CC Exclusion see Appendix A PDX collection 0202

CC **B40.3 Cutaneous blastomycosis**
CC Exclusion see Appendix A PDX collection 0202

CC **B40.7 Disseminated blastomycosis**
Generalized blastomycosis
CC Exclusion see Appendix A PDX collection 0202

\+ **B40.8 Other forms of blastomycosis**

CC **B40.81 Blastomycotic meningoencephalitis**
Meningomyelitis due to blastomycosis
CC Exclusion see Appendix A PDX collection 0202

CC **B40.89 Other forms of blastomycosis**
CC Exclusion see Appendix A PDX collection 0202

CC **B40.9 Blastomycosis, unspecified**
CC Exclusion see Appendix A PDX collection 0202

B41 Paracoccidioidomycosis

Includes: Brazilian blastomycosis
Lutz' disease

CC **B41.0 Pulmonary paracoccidioidomycosis**
CC Exclusion see Appendix A PDX collection 0203

CC **B41.7 Disseminated paracoccidioidomycosis**
Generalized paracoccidioidomycosis
CC Exclusion see Appendix A PDX collection 0203

CC **B41.8 Other forms of paracoccidioidomycosis**
CC Exclusion see Appendix A PDX collection 0203

CC **B41.9 Paracoccidioidomycosis, unspecified**
CC Exclusion see Appendix A PDX collection 0203

B42 Sporotrichosis

B42.0 Pulmonary sporotrichosis

B42.1 Lymphocutaneous sporotrichosis

B42.7 Disseminated sporotrichosis
Generalized sporotrichosis

\+ **B42.8 Other forms of sporotrichosis**

B42.81 Cerebral sporotrichosis
Meningitis due to sporotrichosis

B42.82 Sporotrichosis arthritis

B42.89 Other forms of sporotrichosis

B42.9 Sporotrichosis, unspecified

B43 Chromomycosis and pheomycotic abscess

B43.0 Cutaneous chromomycosis
Dermatitis verrucosa

B43.1 Pheomycotic brain abscess
Cerebral chromomycosis

B43.2 Subcutaneous pheomycotic abscess and cyst

B43.8 Other forms of chromomycosis

B43.9 Chromomycosis, unspecified

B44 Aspergillosis

Includes: aspergilloma

MCC **B44.0 Invasive pulmonary aspergillosis**
MCC Exclusion see Appendix A PDX collection 0110

CC **B44.1 Other pulmonary aspergillosis**
CC Exclusion see Appendix A PDX collection 0204

CC **B44.2 Tonsillar aspergillosis**
CC Exclusion see Appendix A PDX collection 0204

CC **B44.7 Disseminated aspergillosis**
Generalized aspergillosis
CC Exclusion see Appendix A PDX collection 0204

\+ **B44.8 Other forms of aspergillosis**

CC **B44.81 Allergic bronchopulmonary aspergillosis**
CC Exclusion see Appendix A PDX collection 0205

CC **B44.89 Other forms of aspergillosis**
CC Exclusion see Appendix A PDX collection 0204

CC **B44.9 Aspergillosis, unspecified**
CC Exclusion see Appendix A PDX collection 0204

B45 Cryptococcosis

CC **B45.0 Pulmonary cryptococcosis**
CC Exclusion see Appendix A PDX collection 0206

MCC **B45.1 Cerebral cryptococcosis**
Cryptococcal meningitis
Cryptococcosis meningocerebralis
MCC Exclusion see Appendix A PDX collection 0207

CC **B45.2 Cutaneous cryptococcosis**
CC Exclusion see Appendix A PDX collection 0206

CC **B45.3 Osseous cryptococcosis**
CC Exclusion see Appendix A PDX collection 0206

CC **B45.7 Disseminated cryptococcosis**
Generalized cryptococcosis
CC Exclusion see Appendix A PDX collection 0206

CC **B45.8 Other forms of cryptococcosis**
CC Exclusion see Appendix A PDX collection 0206

CC **B45.9 Cryptococcosis, unspecified**
CC Exclusion see Appendix A PDX collection 0206

B46 Zygomycosis

MCC **B46.0 Pulmonary mucormycosis**
MCC Exclusion see Appendix A PDX collection 0208

MCC **B46.1 Rhinocerebral mucormycosis**
MCC Exclusion see Appendix A PDX collection 0208

MCC **B46.2 Gastrointestinal mucormycosis**
MCC Exclusion see Appendix A PDX collection 0208

MCC **B46.3 Cutaneous mucormycosis**
Subcutaneous mucormycosis
MCC Exclusion see Appendix A PDX collection 0208

MCC **B46.4 Disseminated mucormycosis**
Generalized mucormycosis
MCC Exclusion see Appendix A PDX collection 0208

MCC **B46.5 Mucormycosis, unspecified**
MCC Exclusion see Appendix A PDX collection 0208

MCC **B46.8 Other zygomycoses**
Entomophthoromycosis
MCC Exclusion see Appendix A PDX collection 0208

MCC **B46.9 Zygomycosis, unspecified**
Phycomycosis NOS
MCC Exclusion see Appendix A PDX collection 0208

B47 Mycetoma

CC **B47.0 Eumycetoma**
Madura foot, mycotic
Maduromycosis
CC Exclusion see Appendix A PDX collection 0209

CC **B47.1 Actinomycetoma**
CC Exclusion see Appendix A PDX collection 0106

CC **B47.9 Mycetoma, unspecified**
Madura foot NOS
CC Exclusion see Appendix A PDX collection 0210

B48 Other mycoses, not elsewhere classified

B48.0 Lobomycosis
Keloidal blastomycosis
Lobo's disease

B48.1 Rhinosporidiosis

CC **B48.2 Allescheriasis**
Infection due to Pseudallescheria boydii
Excludes1: *eumycetoma (B47.0)*
CC Exclusion see Appendix A PDX collection 0211

CC **B48.3 Geotrichosis**
Geotrichum stomatitis
CC Exclusion see Appendix A PDX collection 0212

CC **B48.4 Penicillosis**
CC Exclusion see Appendix A PDX collection 0204

CC **B48.8 Other specified mycoses**
Adiaspiromycosis
Infection of tissue and organs by Alternaria
Infection of tissue and organs by Drechslera
Infection of tissue and organs by Fusarium
Infection of tissue and organs by saprophytic fungi NEC
CC Exclusion see Appendix A PDX collection 0213
AHA CC: 2Q, 2014, 13

CC **B49 Unspecified mycosis**

Fungemia NOS
CC Exclusion see Appendix A PDX collection 0212
Valid 3-character code, no further characters required

Protozoal diseases (B50-B64)

Excludes1: *amebiasis (A06.-)*
other protozoal intestinal diseases (A07.-)

B50 Plasmodium falciparum malaria

Includes: mixed infections of Plasmodium falciparum with any other Plasmodium species

CC **B50.0 Plasmodium falciparum malaria with cerebral complications**
Cerebral malaria NOS
CC Exclusion see Appendix A PDX collection 0214

CC **B50.8 Other severe and complicated Plasmodium falciparum malaria**
Severe or complicated Plasmodium falciparum malaria NOS
CC Exclusion see Appendix A PDX collection 0214

MCC **B50.9 Plasmodium falciparum malaria, unspecified**
MCC Exclusion see Appendix A PDX collection 0214

B51 Plasmodium vivax malaria

Includes: mixed infections of Plasmodium vivax with other Plasmodium species, except Plasmodium falciparum
Excludes1: *plasmodium vivav with Plasmodium falciparum (B50.-)*

CC **B51.0 Plasmodium vivax malaria with rupture of spleen**
CC Exclusion see Appendix A PDX collection 0214

CC **B51.8 Plasmodium vivax malaria with other complications**
CC Exclusion see Appendix A PDX collection 0214

CC **B51.9 Plasmodium vivax malaria without complication**
Plasmodium vivax malaria NOS
CC Exclusion see Appendix A PDX collection 0215

B52 Plasmodium malariae malaria

Includes: mixed infections of Plasmodium malariae with other Plasmodium species, except Plasmodium falciparum and Plasmodium vivax
Excludes1: *Plasmodium falciparum (B50.-)*
Plasmodium vivax (B51.-)

CC **B52.0 Plasmodium malariae malaria with nephropathy**
CC Exclusion see Appendix A PDX collection 0216

CC **B52.8 Plasmodium malariae malaria with other complications**
CC Exclusion see Appendix A PDX collection 0214

CC **B52.9 Plasmodium malariae malaria without complication**
Plasmodium malariae malaria NOS
CC Exclusion see Appendix A PDX collection 0214

B53 Other specified malaria

CC **B53.0 Plasmodium ovale malaria**
Excludes1: *Plasmodium ovale with Plasmodium falciparum (B50.-)*
Plasmodium ovale with Plasmodium malariae (B52.-)
Plasmodium ovale with Plasmodium vivax (B51.-)
CC Exclusion see Appendix A PDX collection 0214

CC **B53.1 Malaria due to simian plasmodia**
Excludes1: *Malaria due to simian plasmodia with Plasmodium falciparum (B50.-)*
Malaria due to simian plasmodia with Plasmodium malariae (B52.-)
Malaria due to simian plasmodia with Plasmodium ovale (B53.0)
Malaria due to simian plasmodia with Plasmodium vivax (B51.-)
CC Exclusion see Appendix A PDX collection 0214

CC **B53.8 Other malaria, not elsewhere classified**
CC Exclusion see Appendix A PDX collection 0214

C B54 Unspecified malaria
CC Exclusion see Appendix A PDX collection 0217
Valid 3-character code, no further characters required

B55 Leishmaniasis

CC **B55.0 Visceral leishmaniasis**
Kala-azar
Post-kala-azar dermal leishmaniasis
CC Exclusion see Appendix A PDX collection 0218

CC **B55.1 Cutaneous leishmaniasis**
CC Exclusion see Appendix A PDX collection 0218

CC **B55.2 Mucocutaneous leishmaniasis**
CC Exclusion see Appendix A PDX collection 0218

CC **B55.9 Leishmaniasis, unspecified**
CC Exclusion see Appendix A PDX collection 0218

B56 African trypanosomiasis

CC **B56.0 Gambiense trypanosomiasis**
Infection due to Trypanosoma brucei gambiense
West African sleeping sickness
CC Exclusion see Appendix A PDX collection 0218

CC **B56.1 Rhodesiense trypanosomiasis**
East African sleeping sickness
Infection due to Trypanosoma brucei rhodesiense
CC Exclusion see Appendix A PDX collection 0218

CC **B56.9 African trypanosomiasis, unspecified**
Sleeping sickness NOS
CC Exclusion see Appendix A PDX collection 0218

B57 Chagas' disease

Includes: American trypanosomiasis
infection due to Trypanosoma cruzi

CC **B57.0 Acute Chagas' disease with heart involvement**
Acute Chagas' disease with myocarditis
CC Exclusion see Appendix A PDX collection 0219

CC **B57.1 Acute Chagas' disease without heart involvement**
Acute Chagas' disease NOS
CC Exclusion see Appendix A PDX collection 0218

CC **B57.2 Chagas' disease (chronic) with heart involvement**
American trypanosomiasis NOS
Chagas' disease (chronic) NOS
Chagas' disease (chronic) with myocarditis
Trypanosomiasis NOS
CC Exclusion see Appendix A PDX collection 0219

\+ **B57.3 Chagas' disease (chronic) with digestive system involvement**

CC **B57.30 Chagas' disease with digestive system involvement, unspecified**
CC Exclusion see Appendix A PDX collection 0218

CC **B57.31 Megaesophagus in Chagas' disease**
CC Exclusion see Appendix A PDX collection 0218

CC **B57.32 Megacolon in Chagas' disease**
CC Exclusion see Appendix A PDX collection 0218

CC **B57.39 Other digestive system involvement in Chagas' disease**
CC Exclusion see Appendix A PDX collection 0218

\+ **B57.4 Chagas' disease (chronic) with nervous system involvement**

CC **B57.40 Chagas' disease with nervous system involvement, unspecified**
CC Exclusion see Appendix A PDX collection 0218

CC **B57.41 Meningitis in Chagas' disease**
CC Exclusion see Appendix A PDX collection 0218

CC **B57.42 Meningoencephalitis in Chagas' disease**
CC Exclusion see Appendix A PDX collection 0218

CC **B57.49 Other nervous system involvement in Chagas' disease**
CC Exclusion see Appendix A PDX collection 0218

CC **B57.5 Chagas' disease (chronic) with other organ involvement**
CC Exclusion see Appendix A PDX collection 0218

B58 Toxoplasmosis

Includes: infection due to Toxoplasma gondii
Excludes1: *congenital toxoplasmosis (P37.1)*

\+ **B58.0 Toxoplasma oculopathy**

CC **B58.00 Toxoplasma oculopathy, unspecified**
CC Exclusion see Appendix A PDX collection 0220

CC **B58.01 Toxoplasma chorioretinitis**
CC Exclusion see Appendix A PDX collection 0221

CC **B58.09 Other toxoplasma oculopathy**
Toxoplasma uveitis
CC Exclusion see Appendix A PDX collection 0222

CC **B58.1 Toxoplasma hepatitis**
CC Exclusion see Appendix A PDX collection 0223

MCC **B58.2 Toxoplasma meningoencephalitis**
MCC Exclusion see Appendix A PDX collection 0224

MCC **B58.3 Pulmonary toxoplasmosis**
MCC Exclusion see Appendix A PDX collection 0225

\+ **B58.8 Toxoplasmosis with other organ involvement**

MCC **B58.81 Toxoplasma myocarditis**
MCC Exclusion see Appendix A PDX collection 0226

CC **B58.82 Toxoplasma myositis**
CC Exclusion see Appendix A PDX collection 0220

CC **B58.83 Toxoplasma tubulo-interstitial nephropathy**
Toxoplasma pyelonephritis
CC Exclusion see Appendix A PDX collection 0220

CC **B58.89 Toxoplasmosis with other organ involvement**
CC Exclusion see Appendix A PDX collection 0220

CC **B58.9 Toxoplasmosis, unspecified**
CC Exclusion see Appendix A PDX collection 0227

MCC B59 Pneumocystosis

Pneumonia due to Pneumocystis carinii
Pneumonia due to Pneumocystis jiroveci
MCC Exclusion see Appendix A PDX collection 0228
Valid 3-character code, no further characters required

B60 Other protozoal diseases, not elsewhere classified

Excludes1: *cryptosporidiosis (A07.2)*
intestinal microsporidiosis (A07.8)
isosporiasis (A07.3)

CC **B60.0 Babesiosis**
Piroplasmosis
CC Exclusion see Appendix A PDX collection 0218

\+ **B60.1 Acanthamebiasis**

CC **B60.10 Acanthamebiasis, unspecified**
CC Exclusion see Appendix A PDX collection 0229

B60.11 Meningoencephalitis due to Acanthamoeba (culbertsoni)

B60.12 Conjunctivitis due to Acanthamoeba

B60.13 Keratoconjunctivitis due to Acanthamoeba

CC **B60.19 Other acanthamebic disease**
CC Exclusion see Appendix A PDX collection 0229

CC **B60.2 Naegleriasis**
Primary amebic meningoencephalitis
CC Exclusion see Appendix A PDX collection 0229
B60.8 Other specified protozoal diseases
Microsporidiosis

B64 Unspecified protozoal disease
Valid 3-character code, no further characters required

Helminthiases (B65-B83)

B65 Schistosomiasis [bilharziasis]
Includes: snail fever
CC **B65.0 Schistosomiasis due to Schistosoma haematobium [urinary schistosomiasis]**
CC Exclusion see Appendix A PDX collection 0230
CC **B65.1 Schistosomiasis due to Schistosoma mansoni [intestinal schistosomiasis]**
CC Exclusion see Appendix A PDX collection 0230
CC **B65.2 Schistosomiasis due to Schistosoma japonicum**
Asiatic schistosomiasis
CC Exclusion see Appendix A PDX collection 0230
CC **B65.3 Cercarial dermatitis**
Swimmer's itch
CC Exclusion see Appendix A PDX collection 0230
CC **B65.8 Other schistosomiasis**
Infection due to Schistosoma intercalatum
Infection due to Schistosoma mattheei
Infection due to Schistosoma mekongi
CC Exclusion see Appendix A PDX collection 0230
CC **B65.9 Schistosomiasis, unspecified**
CC Exclusion see Appendix A PDX collection 0230

B66 Other fluke infections
CC **B66.0 Opisthorchiasis**
Infection due to cat liver fluke
Infection due to Opisthorchis (felineus)(viverrini)
CC Exclusion see Appendix A PDX collection 0231
CC **B66.1 Clonorchiasis**
Chinese liver fluke disease
Infection due to Clonorchis sinensis
Oriental liver fluke disease
CC Exclusion see Appendix A PDX collection 0231
CC **B66.2 Dicroceliasis**
Infection due to Dicrocoelium dendriticum
Lancet fluke infection
CC Exclusion see Appendix A PDX collection 0231
CC **B66.3 Fascioliasis**
Infection due to Fasciola gigantica
Infection due to Fasciola hepatica
Infection due to Fasciola indica
Sheep liver fluke disease
CC Exclusion see Appendix A PDX collection 0231
CC **B66.4 Paragonimiasis**
Infection due to Paragonimus species
Lung fluke disease
Pulmonary distomiasis
CC Exclusion see Appendix A PDX collection 0231
CC **B66.5 Fasciolopsiasis**
Infection due to Fasciolopsis buski
Intestinal distomiasis
CC Exclusion see Appendix A PDX collection 0231
CC **B66.8 Other specified fluke infections**
Echinostomiasis
Heterophyiasis
Metagonimiasis
Nanophyetiasis
Watsoniasis
CC Exclusion see Appendix A PDX collection 0231
B66.9 Fluke infection, unspecified

B67 Echinococcosis
Includes: hydatidosis
CC **B67.0 Echinococcus granulosus infection of liver**
CC Exclusion see Appendix A PDX collection 0232
CC **B67.1 Echinococcus granulosus infection of lung**
CC Exclusion see Appendix A PDX collection 0233
CC **B67.2 Echinococcus granulosus infection of bone**
CC Exclusion see Appendix A PDX collection 0234
\+ **B67.3 Echinococcus granulosus infection, other and multiple sites**
CC **B67.31 Echinococcus granulosus infection, thyroid gland**
CC Exclusion see Appendix A PDX collection 0235
CC **B67.32 Echinococcus granulosus infection, multiple sites**
CC Exclusion see Appendix A PDX collection 0234
CC **B67.39 Echinococcus granulosus infection, other sites**
CC Exclusion see Appendix A PDX collection 0234
CC **B67.4 Echinococcus granulosus infection, unspecified**
Dog tapeworm (infection)
CC Exclusion see Appendix A PDX collection 0236
CC **B67.5 Echinococcus multilocularis infection of liver**
CC Exclusion see Appendix A PDX collection 0237
\+ **B67.6 Echinococcus multilocularis infection, other and multiple sites**
CC **B67.61 Echinococcus multilocularis infection, multiple sites**
CC Exclusion see Appendix A PDX collection 0238
CC **B67.69 Echinococcus multilocularis infection, other sites**
CC Exclusion see Appendix A PDX collection 0238
CC **B67.7 Echinococcus multilocularis infection, unspecified**
CC Exclusion see Appendix A PDX collection 0239
CC **B67.8 Echinococcosis, unspecified, of liver**
CC Exclusion see Appendix A PDX collection 0240
\+ **B67.9 Echinococcosis, other and unspecified**
CC **B67.90 Echinococcosis, unspecified**
Echinococcosis NOS
CC Exclusion see Appendix A PDX collection 0240
CC **B67.99 Other echinococcosis**
CC Exclusion see Appendix A PDX collection 0240

B68 Taeniasis
Excludes1: *cysticercosis (B69.-)*
CC **B68.0 Taenia solium taeniasis**
Pork tapeworm (infection)
CC Exclusion see Appendix A PDX collection 0241
CC **B68.1 Taenia saginata taeniasis**
Beef tapeworm (infection)
Infection due to adult tapeworm Taenia saginata
CC Exclusion see Appendix A PDX collection 0242
CC **B68.9 Taeniasis, unspecified**
CC Exclusion see Appendix A PDX collection 0242

B69 Cysticercosis
Includes: cysticerciasis infection due to larval form of Taenia solium
CC **B69.0 Cysticercosis of central nervous system**
CC Exclusion see Appendix A PDX collection 0242
CC **B69.1 Cysticercosis of eye**
CC Exclusion see Appendix A PDX collection 0242
\+ **B69.8 Cysticercosis of other sites**
CC **B69.81 Myositis in cysticercosis**
CC Exclusion see Appendix A PDX collection 0242
CC **B69.89 Cysticercosis of other sites**
CC Exclusion see Appendix A PDX collection 0242
CC **B69.9 Cysticercosis, unspecified**
CC Exclusion see Appendix A PDX collection 0242

B70 Diphyllobothriasis and sparganosis
CC **B70.0 Diphyllobothriasis**
Diphyllobothrium (adult) (latum) (pacificum) infection
Fish tapeworm (infection)
Excludes2: *larval diphyllobothriasis (B70.1)*
CC Exclusion see Appendix A PDX collection 0242
CC **B70.1 Sparganosis**
Infection due to Sparganum (mansoni) (proliferum)
Infection due to Spirometra larva
Larval diphyllobothriasis
Spirometrosis
CC Exclusion see Appendix A PDX collection 0242

B71 Other cestode infections
CC **B71.0 Hymenolepiasis**
Dwarf tapeworm infection
Rat tapeworm (infection)
CC Exclusion see Appendix A PDX collection 0242
CC **B71.1 Dipylidiasis**
CC Exclusion see Appendix A PDX collection 0242
CC **B71.8 Other specified cestode infections**
Coenurosis
CC Exclusion see Appendix A PDX collection 0242
B71.9 Cestode infection, unspecified
Tapeworm (infection) NOS

CC **B72 Dracunculiasis**
Includes: guinea worm infection
infection due to Dracunculus medinensis
CC Exclusion see Appendix A PDX collection 0243
Valid 3-character code, no further characters required

B73 Onchocerciasis

Includes: onchocerca volvulus infection
onchocercosis
river blindness

+ **B73.0 Onchocerciasis with eye disease**

CC **B73.00 Onchocerciasis with eye involvement, unspecified**
CC Exclusion see Appendix A PDX collection 0243

CC **B73.01 Onchocerciasis with endophthalmitis**
CC Exclusion see Appendix A PDX collection 0243

CC **B73.02 Onchocerciasis with glaucoma**
CC Exclusion see Appendix A PDX collection 0243

CC **B73.09 Onchocerciasis with other eye involvement**
Infestation of eyelid due to onchocerciasis
CC Exclusion see Appendix A PDX collection 0243

CC **B73.1 Onchocerciasis without eye disease**
CC Exclusion see Appendix A PDX collection 0243

B74 Filariasis

Excludes2: *onchocerciasis (B73)*
tropical (pulmonary) eosinophilia NOS (J82)

CC **B74.0 Filariasis due to Wuchereria bancrofti**
Bancroftian elephantiasis
Bancroftian filariasis
CC Exclusion see Appendix A PDX collection 0243

CC **B74.1 Filariasis due to Brugia malayi**
CC Exclusion see Appendix A PDX collection 0243

CC **B74.2 Filariasis due to Brugia timori**
CC Exclusion see Appendix A PDX collection 0243

CC **B74.3 Loiasis**
Calabar swelling
Eyeworm disease of Africa
Loa loa infection
CC Exclusion see Appendix A PDX collection 0243

CC **B74.4 Mansonelliasis**
Infection due to Mansonella ozzardi
Infection due to Mansonella perstans
Infection due to Mansonella streptocerca
CC Exclusion see Appendix A PDX collection 0243

CC **B74.8 Other filariases**
Dirofilariasis
CC Exclusion see Appendix A PDX collection 0243

CC **B74.9 Filariasis, unspecified**
CC Exclusion see Appendix A PDX collection 0243

B75 Trichinellosis

Includes: infection due to Trichinella species
trichiniasis
CC Exclusion see Appendix A PDX collection 0244
Valid 3-character code, no further characters required

B76 Hookworm diseases

Includes: uncinariasis

CC **B76.0 Ancylostomiasis**
Infection due to Ancylostoma species
CC Exclusion see Appendix A PDX collection 0245

CC **B76.1 Necatoriasis**
Infection due to Necator americanus
CC Exclusion see Appendix A PDX collection 0245

CC **B76.8 Other hookworm diseases**
CC Exclusion see Appendix A PDX collection 0245

CC **B76.9 Hookworm disease, unspecified**
Cutaneous larva migrans NOS
CC Exclusion see Appendix A PDX collection 0245

B77 Ascariasis

Includes: ascaridiasis
roundworm infection

CC **B77.0 Ascariasis with intestinal complications**
CC Exclusion see Appendix A PDX collection 0246

+ **B77.8 Ascariasis with other complications**

MCC **B77.81 Ascariasis pneumonia**
MCC Exclusion see Appendix A PDX collection 0247

CC **B77.89 Ascariasis with other complications**
CC Exclusion see Appendix A PDX collection 0246

CC **B77.9 Ascariasis, unspecified**
CC Exclusion see Appendix A PDX collection 0246

B78 Strongyloidiasis

Excludes1: *trichostrongyliasis (B81.2)*

CC **B78.0 Intestinal strongyloidiasis**
CC Exclusion see Appendix A PDX collection 0246

B78.1 Cutaneous strongyloidiasis

CC **B78.7 Disseminated strongyloidiasis**
CC Exclusion see Appendix A PDX collection 0246

CC **B78.9 Strongyloidiasis, unspecified**
CC Exclusion see Appendix A PDX collection 0246

CC **B79 Trichuriasis**

Includes: trichocephaliasis
whipworm (disease)(infection)
CC Exclusion see Appendix A PDX collection 0246
Valid 3-character code, no further characters required

CC **B80 Enterobiasis**

Includes: oxyuriasis
pinworm infection
threadworm infection
CC Exclusion see Appendix A PDX collection 0246
Valid 3-character code, no further characters required

B81 Other intestinal helminthiases, not elsewhere classified

Excludes1: *angiostrongyliasis due to Parastrongylus cantonensis (B83.2)*

CC **B81.0 Anisakiasis**
Infection due to Anisakis larva
CC Exclusion see Appendix A PDX collection 0246

CC **B81.1 Intestinal capillariasis**
Capillariasis NOS
Infection due to Capillaria philippinensis
Excludes2: *hepatic capillariasis (B83.8)*
CC Exclusion see Appendix A PDX collection 0246

CC **B81.2 Trichostrongyliasis**
CC Exclusion see Appendix A PDX collection 0246

CC **B81.3 Intestinal angiostrongyliasis**
Angiostrongyliasis due to Parastrongylus costaricensis
CC Exclusion see Appendix A PDX collection 0248

CC **B81.4 Mixed intestinal helminthiases**
Infection due to intestinal helminths classified to more than one of the categories B65.0-B81.3 and B81.8
Mixed helminthiasis NOS
CC Exclusion see Appendix A PDX collection 0248

CC **B81.8 Other specified intestinal helminthiases**
Infection due to Oesophagostomum species [esophagostomiasis]
Infection due to Ternidens diminutus [ternidensiasis]
CC Exclusion see Appendix A PDX collection 0248

B82 Unspecified intestinal parasitism

CC **B82.0 Intestinal helminthiasis, unspecified**
CC Exclusion see Appendix A PDX collection 0248

B82.9 Intestinal parasitism, unspecified

B83 Other helminthiases

Excludes1: *capillariasis NOS (B81.1)*
Excludes2: *intestinal capillariasis (B81.1)*

B83.0 Visceral larva migrans
Toxocariasis

B83.1 Gnathostomiasis
Wandering swelling

B83.2 Angiostrongyliasis due to Parastrongylus cantonensis
Eosinophilic meningoencephalitis due to Parastrongylus cantonensis
Excludes2: *intestinal angiostrongyliasis (B81.3)*

B83.3 Syngamiasis
Syngamosis

B83.4 Internal hirudiniasis
Excludes2: *external hirudiniasis (B88.3)*

B83.8 Other specified helminthiases
Acanthocephaliasis
Gongylonemiasis
Hepatic capillariasis
Metastrongyliasis
Thelaziasis

B83.9 Helminthiasis, unspecified
Worms NOS
Excludes1: *intestinal helminthiasis NOS (B82.0)*

Pediculosis, acariasis and other infestations (B85-B89)

B85 Pediculosis and phthiriasis

B85.0 Pediculosis due to Pediculus humanus capitis
Head-louse infestation

B85.1 Pediculosis due to Pediculus humanus corporis
Body-louse infestation

B85.2 Pediculosis, unspecified

B85.3 Phthiriasis
Infestation by crab-louse
Infestation by Phthirus pubis

B85.4 Mixed pediculosis and phthiriasis
Infestation classifiable to more than one of the categories B85.0-B85.3

B86 Scabies
Sarcoptic itch
Valid 3-character code, no further characters required

B87 Myiasis
Includes: infestation by larva of flies
B87.0 Cutaneous myiasis
Creeping myiasis
B87.1 Wound myiasis
Traumatic myiasis
B87.2 Ocular myiasis
B87.3 Nasopharyngeal myiasis
Laryngeal myiasis
B87.4 Aural myiasis
+ **B87.8 Myiasis of other sites**
B87.81 Genitourinary myiasis
B87.82 Intestinal myiasis
B87.89 Myiasis of other sites
B87.9 Myiasis, unspecified

B88 Other infestations
B88.0 Other acariasis
Acarine dermatitis
Dermatitis due to Demodex species
Dermatitis due to Dermanyssus gallinae
Dermatitis due to Liponyssoides sanguineus
Trombiculosis
Excludes2: *scabies (B86)*
B88.1 Tungiasis [sandflea infestation]
B88.2 Other arthropod infestations
Scarabiasis
B88.3 External hirudiniasis
Leech infestation NOS
Excludes2: *internal hirudiniasis (B83.4)*
B88.8 Other specified infestations
Ichthyoparasitism due to Vandellia cirrhosa
Linguatulosis
Porocephaliasis
B88.9 Infestation, unspecified
Infestation (skin) NOS
Infestation by mites NOS
Skin parasites NOS

B89 Unspecified parasitic disease
Valid 3-character code, no further characters required

Sequelae of infectious and parasitic diseases (B90-B94)

NOTE Categories B90-B94 are to be used to indicate conditions in categories A00-B89 as the cause of sequelae, which are themselves classified elsewhere. The 'sequelae' include conditions specified as such; they also include residuals of diseases classifiable to the above categories if there is evidence that the disease itself is no longer present. Codes from these categories are not to be used for chronic infections. Code chronic current infections to active infectious disease as appropriate.

Code first condition resulting from (sequela) the infectious or parasitic disease

B90 Sequelae of tuberculosis
B90.0 Sequelae of central nervous system tuberculosis
B90.1 Sequelae of genitourinary tuberculosis
B90.2 Sequelae of tuberculosis of bones and joints
B90.8 Sequelae of tuberculosis of other organs
Excludes2: *sequelae of respiratory tuberculosis (B90.9)*
B90.9 Sequelae of respiratory and unspecified tuberculosis
Sequelae of tuberculosis NOS

B91 Sequelae of poliomyelitis
Excludes1: *postpolio syndrome (G14)*
Valid 3-character code, no further characters required

B92 Sequelae of leprosy
Valid 3-character code, no further characters required

B94 Sequelae of other and unspecified infectious and parasitic diseases
B94.0 Sequelae of trachoma
B94.1 Sequelae of viral encephalitis
B94.2 Sequelae of viral hepatitis
B94.8 Sequelae of other specified infectious and parasitic diseases
B94.9 Sequelae of unspecified infectious and parasitic disease

Bacterial and viral infectious agents (B95-B97)

NOTE These categories are provided for use as supplementary or additional cod[e] to identify the infectious agent(s) in diseases classified elsewhere.

B95 Streptococcus, Staphylococcus, and Enterococcus as the cause of diseases classified elsewhere
Review coding guideline C.1.b
B95.0 Streptococcus, group A, as the cause of diseases classified elsewhere
B95.1 Streptococcus, group B, as the cause of diseases classified elsewhere
B95.2 Enterococcus as the cause of diseases classified elsewhere
B95.3 Streptococcus pneumoniae as the cause of diseases classified elsewhere
B95.4 Other streptococcus as the cause of diseases classified elsewhe[re]
B95.5 Unspecified streptococcus as the cause of diseases classified elsewhere
+ **B95.6 Staphylococcus aureus as the cause of diseases classified elsewhere**
B95.61 Methicillin susceptible Staphylococcus aureus infection as the cause of diseases classified elsewher[e]
Methicillin susceptible Staphylococcus aureus (MSS[A]) infection as the cause of diseases classified elsewhe[re]
Staphylococcus aureus infection NOS as the cause of diseases classified elsewhere
B95.62 Methicillin resistant Staphylococcus aureus infectio[n] as the cause of diseases classified elsewhere
Methicillin resistant staphylococcus aureus (MRSA) infection as the cause of diseases classified elsewhe[re]
Review coding guidelines C.1.e.1.a and C.1.e.1.b
B95.7 Other staphylococcus as the cause of diseases classified elsewhere
B95.8 Unspecified staphylococcus as the cause of diseases classified elsewhere

B96 Other bacterial agents as the cause of diseases classified elsewhere
Review coding guideline C.1.b
B96.0 Mycoplasma pneumoniae [M. pneumoniae] as the cause of diseases classified elsewhere
Pleuro-pneumonia-like-organism [PPLO]
B96.1 Klebsiella pneumoniae [K. pneumoniae] as the cause of diseas[es] classified elsewhere
+ **B96.2 Escherichia coli [E. coli] as the cause of diseases classified elsewhere**
B96.20 Unspecified Escherichia coli [E. coli] as the cause of diseases classified elsewhere
Escherichia coli [E. coli] NOS
B96.21 Shiga toxin-producing Escherichia coli [E. coli] (STEC) O157 as the cause of diseases classified elsewhere
E. coli O157:H- (nonmotile) with confirmation of Shi[ga] toxin
E. coli O157 with confirmation of Shiga toxin when H antigen is unknown, or is not H7
O157:H7 Escherichia coli [E.coli] with or without confirmation of Shiga toxin-production
Shiga toxin-producing Escherichia coli [E.coli] O157:H7 with or without confirmation of Shiga tox[in] production
STEC O157:H7 with or without confirmation of Shig[a] toxin-production
B96.22 Other specified Shiga toxin-producing Escherichia coli [E. coli] (STEC) as the cause of diseases classifie[d] elsewhere
Non-O157 Shiga toxin-producing Escherichia coli [E.coli]
Non-O157 Shiga toxin-producing Escherichia coli [E.coli] with known O group
B96.23 Unspecified Shiga toxin-producing Escherichia coli [E. coli] (STEC) as the cause of diseases classified elsewhere
Shiga toxin-producing Escherichia coli [E. coli] with unspecified O group
STEC NOS
B96.29 Other Escherichia coli [E. coli] as the cause of diseas[es] classified elsewhere
Non-Shiga toxin-producing E. coli
B96.3 Hemophilus influenzae [H. influenzae] as the cause of diseases classified elsewhere
B96.4 Proteus (mirabilis) (morganii) as the cause of diseases classifie[d] elsewhere

B96.5 **Pseudomonas (aeruginosa) (mallei) (pseudomallei) as the cause of diseases classified elsewhere**

B96.6 **Bacteroides fragilis [B. fragilis] as the cause of diseases classified elsewhere**

B96.7 **Clostridium perfringens [C. perfringens] as the cause of diseases classified elsewhere**

\+ **B96.8** **Other specified bacterial agents as the cause of diseases classified elsewhere**

B96.81 **Helicobacter pylori [H. pylori] as the cause of diseases classified elsewhere**

B96.82 **Vibrio vulnificus as the cause of diseases classified elsewhere**

B96.89 **Other specified bacterial agents as the cause of diseases classified elsewhere**

B97 **Viral agents as the cause of diseases classified elsewhere**

Review coding guideline C.1.b

B97.0 **Adenovirus as the cause of diseases classified elsewhere**

\+ **B97.1** **Enterovirus as the cause of diseases classified elsewhere**

B97.10 **Unspecified enterovirus as the cause of diseases classified elsewhere**

B97.11 **Coxsackievirus as the cause of diseases classified elsewhere**

B97.12 **Echovirus as the cause of diseases classified elsewhere**

B97.19 **Other enterovirus as the cause of diseases classified elsewhere**

\+ **B97.2** **Coronavirus as the cause of diseases classified elsewhere**

CC **B97.21** **SARS-associated coronavirus as the cause of diseases classified elsewhere**

Excludes1: *pneumonia due to SARS-associated coronavirus (J12.81)*

CC Exclusion see Appendix A PDX collection 0249

B97.29 **Other coronavirus as the cause of diseases classified elsewhere**

\+ **B97.3** **Retrovirus as the cause of diseases classified elsewhere**

Excludes1: *Human immunodeficiency virus [HIV] disease (B20)*

B97.30 **Unspecified retrovirus as the cause of diseases classified elsewhere**

B97.31 **Lentivirus as the cause of diseases classified elsewhere**

B97.32 **Oncovirus as the cause of diseases classified elsewhere**

CC **B97.33** **Human T-cell lymphotrophic virus, type I [HTLV-I] as the cause of diseases classified elsewhere**

CC Exclusion see Appendix A PDX collection 0250

CC **B97.34** **Human T-cell lymphotrophic virus, type II [HTLV-II] as the cause of diseases classified elsewhere**

CC Exclusion see Appendix A PDX collection 0251

CC **B97.35** **Human immunodeficiency virus, type 2 [HIV 2] as the cause of diseases classified elsewhere**

CC Exclusion see Appendix A PDX collection 0252

B97.39 **Other retrovirus as the cause of diseases classified elsewhere**

B97.4 **Respiratory syncytial virus as the cause of diseases classified elsewhere**

B97.5 **Reovirus as the cause of diseases classified elsewhere**

B97.6 **Parvovirus as the cause of diseases classified elsewhere**

B97.7 **Papillomavirus as the cause of diseases classified elsewhere**

\+ **B97.8** **Other viral agents as the cause of diseases classified elsewhere**

B97.81 **Human metapneumovirus as the cause of diseases classified elsewhere**

B97.89 **Other viral agents as the cause of diseases classified elsewhere**

Other infectious diseases (B99)

B99 **Other and unspecified infectious diseases**

B99.8 **Other infectious disease**

B99.9 **Unspecified infectious disease**

Chapter 2: Neoplasms (C00-D49)

NOTE **Functional activity**

All neoplasms are classified in this chapter, whether they are functionally active or not. An additional code from Chapter 4 may be used, to identify functional activity associated with any neoplasm.

Morphology [Histology]

Chapter 2 classifies neoplasms primarily by site (topography), with broad groupings for behavior, malignant, in situ, benign, etc. The Table of Neoplasms should be used to identify the correct topography code. In a few cases, such as for malignant melanoma and certain neuroendocrine tumors, the morphology (histologic type) is included in the category and codes.

Primary malignant neoplasms overlapping site boundaries

A primary malignant neoplasm that overlaps two or more contiguous (next to each other) sites should be classified to the subcategory/ code .8 ('overlapping lesion'), unless the combination is specifically indexed elsewhere. For multiple neoplasms of the same site that are not contiguous, such as tumors in different quadrants of the same breast, codes for each site should be assigned.

Malignant neoplasm of ectopic tissue

Malignant neoplasms of ectopic tissue are to be coded to the site mentioned, e.g., ectopic pancreatic malignant neoplasms are coded to pancreas, unspecified (C25.9).

This chapter contains the following category blocks:

C00-C14	Malignant neoplasms of lip, oral cavity and pharynx
C15-C26	Malignant neoplasms of digestive organs
C30-C39	Malignant neoplasms of respiratory and intrathoracic organs
C40-C41	Malignant neoplasms of bone and articular cartilage
C43-C44	Melanoma and other malignant neoplasms of skin
C45-C49	Malignant neoplasms of mesothelial and soft tissue
C50	Malignant neoplasms of breast
C51-C58	Malignant neoplasms of female genital organs
C60-C63	Malignant neoplasms of male genital organs
C64-C68	Malignant neoplasms of urinary tract
C69-C72	Malignant neoplasms of eye, brain and other parts of central nervous system
C73-C75	Malignant neoplasms of thyroid and other endocrine glands
C7A	Malignant neuroendocrine tumors
C7B	Secondary neuroendocrine tumors
C76-C80	Malignant neoplasms of ill-defined, other secondary and unspecified sites
C81-C96	Malignant neoplasms of lymphoid, hematopoietic and related tissue
D00-D09	In situ neoplasms
D10-D36	Benign neoplasms, except benign neuroendocrine tumors
D3A	Benign neuroendocrine tumors
D37-D48	Neoplasms of uncertain behavior, polycythemia vera and myelodysplastic syndromes
D49	Neoplasms of unspecified behavior

C. Chapter-Specific Coding Guidelines

In addition to general coding guidelines, there are guidelines for specific diagnoses and/or conditions in the classification. Unless otherwise indicated, these guidelines apply to all health care settings. Please refer to Section II for guidelines on the selection of principal diagnosis.

2. Chapter 2: Neoplasms (C00-D49)

General guidelines

Chapter 2 of the ICD-10-CM contains the codes for most benign and all malignant neoplasms. Certain benign neoplasms, such as prostatic adenomas, may be found in the specific body system chapters. To properly code a neoplasm it is necessary to determine from the record if the neoplasm is benign, in-situ, malignant, or of uncertain histologic behavior. If malignant, any secondary (metastatic) sites should also be determined.

Primary malignant neoplasms overlapping site boundaries

A primary malignant neoplasm that overlaps two or more contiguous (next to each other) sites should be classified to the subcategory/code .8 ('overlapping lesion'), unless the combination is specifically indexed elsewhere. For multiple neoplasms of the same site that are not contiguous such as tumors in different quadrants of the same breast, codes for each site should be assigned.

Malignant neoplasm of ectopic tissue

Malignant neoplasms of ectopic tissue are to be coded to the site of origin mentioned, e.g., ectopic pancreatic malignant neoplasms involving the stomach are coded to pancreas, unspecified (C25.9).

The neoplasm table in the Alphabetic Index should be referenced first. However, if the histological term is documented, that term should be referenced first, rather than going immediately to the Neoplasm Table, in order to determine wh[...] column in the Neoplasm Table is appropriate. For example, if the documentat[...] indicates "adenoma," refer to the term in the Alphabetic Index to review [...] entries under this term and the instructional note to "see also neoplasm, by s[...] benign." The table provides the proper code based on the type of neoplasm a[...] the site. It is important to select the proper column in the table that correspo[...] to the type of neoplasm. The Tabular List should then be referenced to verify t[...] the correct code has been selected from the table and that a more specific s[...] code does not exist.

See Section I.C.21. Factors influencing health status and contact w[...] health services, Status, for information regarding Z15.0, codes for gen[...] susceptibility to cancer.

a. Treatment directed at the malignancy

If the treatment is directed at the malignancy, designate the malignancy as [...] principal diagnosis.

The only exception to this guideline is if a patient admission/encounter is sol[...] for the administration of chemotherapy, immunotherapy or radiation thera[...] assign the appropriate Z51.-- code as the first-listed or principal diagno[...] and the diagnosis or problem for which the service is being performed a[...] secondary diagnosis.

b. Treatment of secondary site

When a patient is admitted because of a primary neoplasm with metastasis a[...] treatment is directed toward the secondary site only, the secondary neopla[...] is designated as the principal diagnosis even though the primary maligna[...] is still present.

c. Coding and sequencing of complications

Coding and sequencing of complications associated with the malignancies [...] with the therapy thereof are subject to the following guidelines:

1) Anemia associated with malignancy

When admission/encounter is for management of an anemia associated w[...] the malignancy, and the treatment is only for anemia, the appropriate co[...] for the malignancy is sequenced as the principal or first-listed diagno[...] followed by the appropriate code for the anemia (such as code D63[...] Anemia in neoplastic disease).

2) Anemia associated with chemotherapy, immunotherapy and radiati[...] therapy

When the admission/encounter is for management of an anem[...] associated with an adverse effect of the administration of chemothera[...] or immunotherapy and the only treatment is for the anemia, the anem[...] code is sequenced first followed by the appropriate codes for the neopla[...] and the adverse effect (T45.1X5, Adverse effect of antineoplastic a[...] immunosuppressive drugs).

When the admission/encounter is for management of an anemia associat[...] with an adverse effect of radiotherapy, the anemia code should [...] sequenced first, followed by the appropriate neoplasm code and code Y84[...] Radiological procedure and radiotherapy as the cause of abnormal reacti[...] of the patient, or of later complication, without mention of misadventure [...] the time of the procedure.

3) Management of dehydration due to the malignancy

When the admission/encounter is for management of dehydration due [...] the malignancy and only the dehydration is being treated (intraveno[...] rehydration), the dehydration is sequenced first, followed by the code(s) [...] the malignancy.

4) Treatment of a complication resulting from a surgical procedure

When the admission/encounter is for treatment of a complication resulti[...] from a surgical procedure, designate the complication as the principal [...] first-listed diagnosis if treatment is directed at resolving the complication.

d. Primary malignancy previously excised

When a primary malignancy has been previously excised or eradicated from [...] site and there is no further treatment directed to that site and there is no eviden[...] of any existing primary malignancy, a code from category Z85, Perso[...] history of malignant neoplasm, should be used to indicate the former site [...] the malignancy. Any mention of extension, invasion, or metastasis to anot[...] site is coded as a secondary malignant neoplasm to that site. The secondary s[...] may be the principal or first-listed with the Z85 code used as a secondary co[...]

e. Admissions/Encounters involving chemotherapy, immunotherapy a[...] radiation therapy

1) Episode of care involves surgical removal of neoplasm

When an episode of care involves the surgical removal of a neoplas[...] primary or secondary site, followed by adjunct chemotherapy or radiati[...] treatment during the same episode of care, the code for the neoplasm shou[...] be assigned as principal or first-listed diagnosis.

2) Patient admission/encounter solely for administration of chemotherapy, immunotherapy and radiation therapy

If a patient admission/encounter is solely for the administration of chemotherapy, immunotherapy or radiation therapy assign code Z51.0, Encounter for antineoplastic radiation therapy, or Z51.11, Encounter for antineoplastic chemotherapy, or Z51.12, Encounter for antineoplastic immunotherapy as the first-listed or principal diagnosis. If a patient receives more than one of these therapies during the same admission more than one of these codes may be assigned, in any sequence.

The malignancy for which the therapy is being administered should be assigned as a secondary diagnosis.

3) Patient admitted for radiation therapy, chemotherapy or immunotherapy and develops complications

When a patient is admitted for the purpose of radiotherapy, immunotherapy or chemotherapy and develops complications such as uncontrolled nausea and vomiting or dehydration, the principal or first-listed diagnosis is Z51.0, Encounter for antineoplastic radiation therapy, or Z51.11, Encounter for antineoplastic chemotherapy, or Z51.12, Encounter for antineoplastic immunotherapy followed by any codes for the complications.

f. Admission/encounter to determine extent of malignancy

When the reason for admission/encounter is to determine the extent of the malignancy, or for a procedure such as paracentesis or thoracentesis, the primary malignancy or appropriate metastatic site is designated as the principal or first-listed diagnosis, even though chemotherapy or radiotherapy is administered.

g. Symptoms, signs, and abnormal findings listed in Chapter 18 associated with neoplasms

Symptoms, signs, and ill-defined conditions listed in Chapter 18 characteristic of, or associated with, an existing primary or secondary site malignancy cannot be used to replace the malignancy as principal or first-listed diagnosis, regardless of the number of admissions or encounters for treatment and care of the neoplasm.

See section I.C.21. Factors influencing health status and contact with health services, Encounter for prophylactic organ removal.

h. Admission/encounter for pain control/management

See Section I.C.6. for information on coding admission/encounter for pain control/management.

i. Malignancy in two or more noncontiguous sites

A patient may have more than one malignant tumor in the same organ. These tumors may represent different primaries or metastatic disease, depending on the site. Should the documentation be unclear, the provider should be queried as to the status of each tumor so that the correct codes can be assigned.

j. Disseminated malignant neoplasm, unspecified

Code C80.0, Disseminated malignant neoplasm, unspecified, is for use only in those cases where the patient has advanced metastatic disease and no known primary or secondary sites are specified. It should not be used in place of assigning codes for the primary site and all known secondary sites.

k. Malignant neoplasm without specification of site

Code C80.1, Malignant (primary) neoplasm, unspecified, equates to Cancer, unspecified. This code should only be used when no determination can be made as to the primary site of a malignancy. This code should rarely be used in the inpatient setting.

l. Sequencing of neoplasm codes

1) Encounter for treatment of primary malignancy

If the reason for the encounter is for treatment of a primary malignancy, assign the malignancy as the principal/first-listed diagnosis. The primary site is to be sequenced first, followed by any metastatic sites.

2) Encounter for treatment of secondary malignancy

When an encounter is for a primary malignancy with metastasis and treatment is directed toward the metastatic (secondary) site(s) only, the metastatic site(s) is designated as the principal/first-listed diagnosis. The primary malignancy is coded as an additional code.

3) Malignant neoplasm in a pregnant patient

When a pregnant woman has a malignant neoplasm, a code from subcategory O9A.1-, Malignant neoplasm complicating pregnancy, childbirth, and the puerperium, should be sequenced first, followed by the appropriate code from Chapter 2 to indicate the type of neoplasm.

4) Encounter for complication associated with a neoplasm

When an encounter is for management of a complication associated with a neoplasm, such as dehydration, and the treatment is only for the complication, the complication is coded first, followed by the appropriate code(s) for the neoplasm.

The exception to this guideline is anemia. When the admission/encounter is for management of an anemia associated with the malignancy, and the treatment is only for anemia, the appropriate code for the malignancy is sequenced as the principal or first-listed diagnosis followed by code D63.0, Anemia in neoplastic disease.

5) Complication from surgical procedure for treatment of a neoplasm

When an encounter is for treatment of a complication resulting from a surgical procedure performed for the treatment of the neoplasm, designate the complication as the principal/first- listed diagnosis. See guideline regarding the coding of a current malignancy versus personal history to determine if the code for the neoplasm should also be assigned.

6) Pathologic fracture due to a neoplasm

When an encounter is for a pathological fracture due to a neoplasm, and the focus of treatment is the fracture, a code from subcategory M84.5, Pathological fracture in neoplastic disease, should be sequenced first, followed by the code for the neoplasm.

If the focus of treatment is the neoplasm with an associated pathological fracture, the neoplasm code should be sequenced first, followed by a code from M84.5 for the pathological fracture.

m. Current malignancy versus personal history of malignancy

When a primary malignancy has been excised but further treatment, such as an additional surgery for the malignancy, radiation therapy or chemotherapy is directed to that site, the primary malignancy code should be used until treatment is completed.

When a primary malignancy has been previously excised or eradicated from its site, there is no further treatment (of the malignancy) directed to that site, and there is no evidence of any existing primary malignancy, a code from category Z85, Personal history of malignant neoplasm, should be used to indicate the former site of the malignancy.

See Section I.C.21. Factors influencing health status and contact with health services, History (of)

n. Leukemia, Multiple Myeloma, and Malignant Plasma Cell Neoplasms in remission versus personal history

The categories for leukemia, and category C90, Multiple myeloma and malignant plasma cell neoplasms, have codes indicating whether or not the leukemia has achieved remission. There are also codes Z85.6, Personal history of leukemia, and Z85.79, Personal history of other malignant neoplasms of lymphoid, hematopoietic and related tissues. If the documentation is unclear, as to whether the leukemia has achieved remission, the provider should be queried.

See Section I.C.21. Factors influencing health status and contact with health services, History (of)

o. Aftercare following surgery for neoplasm

See Section I.C.21. Factors influencing health status and contact with health services, Aftercare

p. Follow-up care for completed treatment of a malignancy

See Section I.C.21. Factors influencing health status and contact with health services, Follow-up

q. Prophylactic organ removal for prevention of malignancy

See Section I.C. 21, Factors influencing health status and contact with health services, Prophylactic organ removal

r. Malignant neoplasm associated with transplanted organ

A malignant neoplasm of a transplanted organ should be coded as a transplant complication. Assign first the appropriate code from category T86.-, Complications of transplanted organs and tissue, followed by code C80.2, Malignant neoplasm associated with transplanted organ. Use an additional code for the specific malignancy.

Malignant neoplasms (C00-C96)

Malignant neoplasms, stated or presumed to be primary (of specified sites), and certain specified histologies, except neuroendocrine, and of lymphoid, hematopoietic and related tissue (C00-C75)

Malignant neoplasms of lip, oral cavity and pharynx (C00-C14)

C00 Malignant neoplasm of lip

Use additional code to identify:
alcohol abuse and dependence (F10.-)
history of tobacco use (Z87.891)
tobacco dependence (F17.-)
tobacco use (Z72.0)

Excludes1: *malignant melanoma of lip (C43.0)*
Merkel cell carcinoma of lip (C4A.0)
other and unspecified malignant neoplasm of skin of lip (C44.0-)

C00.0 Malignant neoplasm of external upper lip
Malignant neoplasm of lipstick area of upper lip
Malignant neoplasm of upper lip NOS
Malignant neoplasm of vermilion border of upper lip

C00.1 Malignant neoplasm of external lower lip
Malignant neoplasm of lower lip NOS
Malignant neoplasm of lipstick area of lower lip
Malignant neoplasm of vermilion border of lower lip

C00.2 Malignant neoplasm of external lip, unspecified
Malignant neoplasm of vermilion border of lip NOS

C00.3 Malignant neoplasm of upper lip, inner aspect
Malignant neoplasm of buccal aspect of upper lip
Malignant neoplasm of frenulum of upper lip
Malignant neoplasm of mucosa of upper lip
Malignant neoplasm of oral aspect of upper lip

C00.4 Malignant neoplasm of lower lip, inner aspect
Malignant neoplasm of buccal aspect of lower lip
Malignant neoplasm of frenulum of lower lip
Malignant neoplasm of mucosa of lower lip
Malignant neoplasm of oral aspect of lower lip

C00.5 Malignant neoplasm of lip, unspecified, inner aspect
Malignant neoplasm of buccal aspect of lip, unspecified
Malignant neoplasm of frenulum of lip, unspecified
Malignant neoplasm of mucosa of lip, unspecified
Malignant neoplasm of oral aspect of lip, unspecified

C00.6 Malignant neoplasm of commissure of lip, unspecified

C00.8 Malignant neoplasm of overlapping sites of lip

C00.9 Malignant neoplasm of lip, unspecified

C01 Malignant neoplasm of base of tongue

Malignant neoplasm of dorsal surface of base of tongue
Malignant neoplasm of fixed part of tongue NOS
Malignant neoplasm of posterior third of tongue
Use additional code to identify:
alcohol abuse and dependence (F10.-)
history of tobacco use (Z87.891)
tobacco dependence (F17.-)
tobacco use (Z72.0)

Valid 3-character code, no further characters required

C02 Malignant neoplasm of other and unspecified parts of tongue

Use additional code to identify:
alcohol abuse and dependence (F10.-)
history of tobacco use (Z87.891)
tobacco dependence (F17.-)
tobacco use (Z72.0)

C02.0 Malignant neoplasm of dorsal surface of tongue
Malignant neoplasm of anterior two-thirds of tongue, dorsal surface
Excludes2: *malignant neoplasm of dorsal surface of base of tongue (C01)*

C02.1 Malignant neoplasm of border of tongue
Malignant neoplasm of tip of tongue

C02.2 Malignant neoplasm of ventral surface of tongue
Malignant neoplasm of anterior two-thirds of tongue, ventral surface
Malignant neoplasm of frenulum linguae

C02.3 Malignant neoplasm of anterior two-thirds of tongue, part unspecified
Malignant neoplasm of middle third of tongue NOS
Malignant neoplasm of mobile part of tongue NOS

C02.4 Malignant neoplasm of lingual tonsil
Excludes2: *malignant neoplasm of tonsil NOS (C09.9)*

C02.8 Malignant neoplasm of overlapping sites of tongue
Malignant neoplasm of two or more contiguous sites of tongue

C02.9 Malignant neoplasm of tongue, unspecified

C03 Malignant neoplasm of gum

Includes: malignant neoplasm of alveolar (ridge) mucosa
malignant neoplasm of gingiva

Use additional code to identify:
alcohol abuse and dependence (F10.-)
history of tobacco use (Z87.891)
tobacco dependence (F17.-)
tobacco use (Z72.0)

Excludes2: *malignant odontogenic neoplasms (C41.0-C41.1)*

C03.0 Malignant neoplasm of upper gum

C03.1 Malignant neoplasm of lower gum

C03.9 Malignant neoplasm of gum, unspecified

C04 Malignant neoplasm of floor of mouth

Use additional code to identify:
alcohol abuse and dependence (F10.-)
history of tobacco use (Z87.891)
tobacco dependence (F17.-)
tobacco use (Z72.0)

C04.0 Malignant neoplasm of anterior floor of mouth
Malignant neoplasm of anterior to the premolar-canine junction

C04.1 Malignant neoplasm of lateral floor of mouth

C04.8 Malignant neoplasm of overlapping sites of floor of mouth

C04.9 Malignant neoplasm of floor of mouth, unspecified

C05 Malignant neoplasm of palate

Use additional code to identify:
alcohol abuse and dependence (F10.-)
history of tobacco use (Z87.891)
tobacco dependence (F17.-)
tobacco use (Z72.0)

Excludes1: *Kaposi's sarcoma of palate (C46.2)*

C05.0 Malignant neoplasm of hard palate

C05.1 Malignant neoplasm of soft palate
Excludes2: *malignant neoplasm of nasopharyngeal surface of soft palate (C11.3)*

C05.2 Malignant neoplasm of uvula

C05.8 Malignant neoplasm of overlapping sites of palate

C05.9 Malignant neoplasm of palate, unspecified
Malignant neoplasm of roof of mouth

C06 Malignant neoplasm of other and unspecified parts of mouth

Use additional code to identify:
alcohol abuse and dependence (F10.-)
history of tobacco use (Z87.891)
tobacco dependence (F17.-)
tobacco use (Z72.0)

C06.0 Malignant neoplasm of cheek mucosa
Malignant neoplasm of buccal mucosa NOS
Malignant neoplasm of internal cheek

C06.1 Malignant neoplasm of vestibule of mouth
Malignant neoplasm of buccal sulcus (upper) (lower)
Malignant neoplasm of labial sulcus (upper) (lower)

C06.2 Malignant neoplasm of retromolar area

\+ **C06.8 Malignant neoplasm of overlapping sites of other and unspecified parts of mouth**

C06.80 Malignant neoplasm of overlapping sites of unspecified parts of mouth

C06.89 Malignant neoplasm of overlapping sites of other parts of mouth
'book leaf' neoplasm [ventral surface of tongue and floor of mouth]

C06.9 Malignant neoplasm of mouth, unspecified
Malignant neoplasm of minor salivary gland, unspecified site
Malignant neoplasm of oral cavity NOS

C07 Malignant neoplasm of parotid gland

Use additional code to identify:
alcohol abuse and dependence (F10.-)
exposure to environmental tobacco smoke (Z77.22)
exposure to tobacco smoke in the perinatal period (P96.81)
history of tobacco use (Z87.891)
occupational exposure to environmental tobacco smoke (Z57.31)
tobacco dependence (F17.-)
tobacco use (Z72.0)

Valid 3-character code, no further characters required

C08 Malignant neoplasm of other and unspecified major salivary glands

Includes: malignant neoplasm of salivary ducts
Use additional code to identify:
alcohol abuse and dependence (F10.-)
exposure to environmental tobacco smoke (Z77.22)
exposure to tobacco smoke in the perinatal period (P96.81)
history of tobacco use (Z87.891)
occupational exposure to environmental tobacco smoke (Z57.31)
tobacco dependence (F17.-)
tobacco use (Z72.0)
Excludes1: *malignant neoplasms of specified minor salivary glands which are classified according to their anatomical location*
Excludes2: *malignant neoplasms of minor salivary glands NOS (C06.9)*
malignant neoplasm of parotid gland (C07)

C08.0 Malignant neoplasm of submandibular gland
Malignant neoplasm of submaxillary gland
C08.1 Malignant neoplasm of sublingual gland
C08.9 Malignant neoplasm of major salivary gland, unspecified
Malignant neoplasm of salivary gland (major) NOS

C09 Malignant neoplasm of tonsil

Use additional code to identify:
alcohol abuse and dependence (F10.-)
exposure to environmental tobacco smoke (Z77.22)
exposure to tobacco smoke in the perinatal period (P96.81)
history of tobacco use (Z87.891)
occupational exposure to environmental tobacco smoke (Z57.31)
tobacco dependence (F17.-)
tobacco use (Z72.0)
Excludes2: *malignant neoplasm of lingual tonsil (C02.4)*
malignant neoplasm of pharyngeal tonsil (C11.1)

C09.0 Malignant neoplasm of tonsillar fossa
C09.1 Malignant neoplasm of tonsillar pillar (anterior) (posterior)
C09.8 Malignant neoplasm of overlapping sites of tonsil
C09.9 Malignant neoplasm of tonsil, unspecified
Malignant neoplasm of tonsil NOS
Malignant neoplasm of faucial tonsils
Malignant neoplasm of palatine tonsils

C10 Malignant neoplasm of oropharynx

Use additional code to identify:
alcohol abuse and dependence (F10.-)
exposure to environmental tobacco smoke (Z77.22)
exposure to tobacco smoke in the perinatal period (P96.81)
history of tobacco use (Z87.891)
occupational exposure to environmental tobacco smoke (Z57.31)
tobacco dependence (F17.-)
tobacco use (Z72.0)
Excludes2: *malignant neoplasm of tonsil (C09.-)*

C10.0 Malignant neoplasm of vallecula
C10.1 Malignant neoplasm of anterior surface of epiglottis
Malignant neoplasm of epiglottis, free border [margin]
Malignant neoplasm of glossoepiglottic fold(s)
Excludes2: *malignant neoplasm of epiglottis (suprahyoid portion) NOS (C32.1)*
C10.2 Malignant neoplasm of lateral wall of oropharynx
C10.3 Malignant neoplasm of posterior wall of oropharynx
C10.4 Malignant neoplasm of branchial cleft
Malignant neoplasm of branchial cyst [site of neoplasm]
C10.8 Malignant neoplasm of overlapping sites of oropharynx
Malignant neoplasm of junctional region of oropharynx
C10.9 Malignant neoplasm of oropharynx, unspecified

C11 Malignant neoplasm of nasopharynx

Use additional code to identify:
exposure to environmental tobacco smoke (Z77.22)
exposure to tobacco smoke in the perinatal period (P96.81)
history of tobacco use (Z87.891)
occupational exposure to environmental tobacco smoke (Z57.31)
tobacco dependence (F17.-)
tobacco use (Z72.0)

C11.0 Malignant neoplasm of superior wall of nasopharynx
Malignant neoplasm of roof of nasopharynx
C11.1 Malignant neoplasm of posterior wall of nasopharynx
Malignant neoplasm of adenoid
Malignant neoplasm of pharyngeal tonsil
C11.2 Malignant neoplasm of lateral wall of nasopharynx
Malignant neoplasm of fossa of Rosenmüller
Malignant neoplasm of opening of auditory tube
Malignant neoplasm of pharyngeal recess
C11.3 Malignant neoplasm of anterior wall of nasopharynx
Malignant neoplasm of floor of nasopharynx
Malignant neoplasm of nasopharyngeal (anterior) (posterior) surface of soft palate
Malignant neoplasm of posterior margin of nasal choana
Malignant neoplasm of posterior margin of nasal septum
C11.8 Malignant neoplasm of overlapping sites of nasopharynx
C11.9 Malignant neoplasm of nasopharynx, unspecified
Malignant neoplasm of nasopharyngeal wall NOS

C12 Malignant neoplasm of pyriform sinus

Malignant neoplasm of pyriform fossa
Use additional code to identify:
exposure to environmental tobacco smoke (Z77.22)
exposure to tobacco smoke in the perinatal period (P96.81)
history of tobacco use (Z87.891)
occupational exposure to environmental tobacco smoke (Z57.31)
tobacco dependence (F17.-)
tobacco use (Z72.0)
Valid 3-character code, no further characters required

C13 Malignant neoplasm of hypopharynx

Use additional code to identify:
exposure to environmental tobacco smoke (Z77.22)
exposure to tobacco smoke in the perinatal period (P96.81)
history of tobacco use (Z87.891)
occupational exposure to environmental tobacco smoke (Z57.31)
tobacco dependence (F17.-)
tobacco use (Z72.0)
Excludes2: *malignant neoplasm of pyriform sinus (C12)*

C13.0 Malignant neoplasm of postcricoid region
C13.1 Malignant neoplasm of aryepiglottic fold, hypopharyngeal aspect
Malignant neoplasm of aryepiglottic fold NOS
Malignant neoplasm of interarytenoid fold NOS
Malignant neoplasm of aryepiglottic fold, marginal zone
Malignant neoplasm of interarytenoid fold, marginal zone
Excludes2: *malignant neoplasm of aryepiglottic fold or interarytenoid fold, laryngeal aspect (C32.1)*
C13.2 Malignant neoplasm of posterior wall of hypopharynx
C13.8 Malignant neoplasm of overlapping sites of hypopharynx
C13.9 Malignant neoplasm of hypopharynx, unspecified
Malignant neoplasm of hypopharyngeal wall NOS

C14 Malignant neoplasm of other and ill-defined sites in the lip, oral cavity and pharynx

Use additional code to identify:
alcohol abuse and dependence (F10.-)
exposure to environmental tobacco smoke (Z77.22)
exposure to tobacco smoke in the perinatal period (P96.81)
history of tobacco use (Z87.891)
occupational exposure to environmental tobacco smoke (Z57.31)
tobacco dependence (F17.-)
tobacco use (Z72.0)
Excludes1: *malignant neoplasm of oral cavity NOS (C06.9)*

C14.0 Malignant neoplasm of pharynx, unspecified
C14.2 Malignant neoplasm of Waldeyer's ring
C14.8 Malignant neoplasm of overlapping sites of lip, oral cavity and pharynx
Primary malignant neoplasm of two or more contiguous sites of lip, oral cavity and pharynx
Excludes1: *'book leaf' neoplasm [ventral surface of tongue and floor of mouth] (C06.89)*

Malignant neoplasms of digestive organs (C15-C26)

Excludes1: *Kaposi's sarcoma of gastrointestinal sites (C46.4)*

C15 Malignant neoplasm of esophagus

Use additional code to identify:
alcohol abuse and dependence (F10.-)

CC **C15.3 Malignant neoplasm of upper third of esophagus**
CC Exclusion see Appendix A PDX collection 0253
CC **C15.4 Malignant neoplasm of middle third of esophagus**
CC Exclusion see Appendix A PDX collection 0253
CC **C15.5 Malignant neoplasm of lower third of esophagus**
Excludes1: *malignant neoplasm of cardio-esophageal junction (C16.0)*
CC Exclusion see Appendix A PDX collection 0253
CC **C15.8 Malignant neoplasm of overlapping sites of esophagus**
CC Exclusion see Appendix A PDX collection 0253
CC **C15.9 Malignant neoplasm of esophagus, unspecified**
CC Exclusion see Appendix A PDX collection 0253

C16 Malignant neoplasm of stomach
Use additional code to identify:
alcohol abuse and dependence (F10.-)
Excludes2: *malignant carcinoid tumor of the stomach (C7A.092)*

CC **C16.0 Malignant neoplasm of cardia**
Malignant neoplasm of cardiac orifice
Malignant neoplasm of cardio-esophageal junction
Malignant neoplasm of esophagus and stomach
Malignant neoplasm of gastro-esophageal junction
CC Exclusion see Appendix A PDX collection 0254

CC **C16.1 Malignant neoplasm of fundus of stomach**
CC Exclusion see Appendix A PDX collection 0254

CC **C16.2 Malignant neoplasm of body of stomach**
CC Exclusion see Appendix A PDX collection 0254

CC **C16.3 Malignant neoplasm of pyloric antrum**
Malignant neoplasm of gastric antrum
CC Exclusion see Appendix A PDX collection 0254

CC **C16.4 Malignant neoplasm of pylorus**
Malignant neoplasm of prepylorus
Malignant neoplasm of pyloric canal
CC Exclusion see Appendix A PDX collection 0254

CC **C16.5 Malignant neoplasm of lesser curvature of stomach, unspecified**
Malignant neoplasm of lesser curvature of stomach, not classifiable to C16.1-C16.4
CC Exclusion see Appendix A PDX collection 0254

CC **C16.6 Malignant neoplasm of greater curvature of stomach, unspecified**
Malignant neoplasm of greater curvature of stomach, not classifiable to C16.0-C16.4
CC Exclusion see Appendix A PDX collection 0254

CC **C16.8 Malignant neoplasm of overlapping sites of stomach**
CC Exclusion see Appendix A PDX collection 0254

CC **C16.9 Malignant neoplasm of stomach, unspecified**
Gastric cancer NOS
CC Exclusion see Appendix A PDX collection 0254

C17 Malignant neoplasm of small intestine
Excludes1: *malignant carcinoid tumors of the small intestine (C7A.01)*

CC **C17.0 Malignant neoplasm of duodenum**
CC Exclusion see Appendix A PDX collection 0255

CC **C17.1 Malignant neoplasm of jejunum**
CC Exclusion see Appendix A PDX collection 0256

CC **C17.2 Malignant neoplasm of ileum**
Excludes1: *malignant neoplasm of ileocecal valve (C18.0)*
CC Exclusion see Appendix A PDX collection 0257

CC **C17.3 Meckel's diverticulum, malignant**
Excludes1: *Meckel's diverticulum, congenital (Q43.0)*
CC Exclusion see Appendix A PDX collection 0258

CC **C17.8 Malignant neoplasm of overlapping sites of small intestine**
CC Exclusion see Appendix A PDX collection 0259

CC **C17.9 Malignant neoplasm of small intestine, unspecified**
CC Exclusion see Appendix A PDX collection 0259

C18 Malignant neoplasm of colon
Excludes1: *malignant carcinoid tumors of the colon (C7A.02-)*

CC **C18.0 Malignant neoplasm of cecum**
Malignant neoplasm of ileocecal valve
CC Exclusion see Appendix A PDX collection 0260

CC **C18.1 Malignant neoplasm of appendix**
CC Exclusion see Appendix A PDX collection 0261

CC **C18.2 Malignant neoplasm of ascending colon**
CC Exclusion see Appendix A PDX collection 0262

CC **C18.3 Malignant neoplasm of hepatic flexure**
CC Exclusion see Appendix A PDX collection 0263

CC **C18.4 Malignant neoplasm of transverse colon**
CC Exclusion see Appendix A PDX collection 0264

CC **C18.5 Malignant neoplasm of splenic flexure**
CC Exclusion see Appendix A PDX collection 0265

CC **C18.6 Malignant neoplasm of descending colon**
CC Exclusion see Appendix A PDX collection 0266

CC **C18.7 Malignant neoplasm of sigmoid colon**
Malignant neoplasm of sigmoid (flexure)
Excludes1: *malignant neoplasm of rectosigmoid junction (C19)*
CC Exclusion see Appendix A PDX collection 0267

CC **C18.8 Malignant neoplasm of overlapping sites of colon**
CC Exclusion see Appendix A PDX collection 0268

CC **C18.9 Malignant neoplasm of colon, unspecified**
Malignant neoplasm of large intestine NOS
CC Exclusion see Appendix A PDX collection 0268

CC **C19 Malignant neoplasm of rectosigmoid junction**
Malignant neoplasm of colon with rectum
Malignant neoplasm of rectosigmoid (colon)
Excludes1: *malignant carcinoid tumors of the colon (C7A.02-)*
CC Exclusion see Appendix A PDX collection 0269
Valid 3-character code, no further characters required

CC **C20 Malignant neoplasm of rectum**
Malignant neoplasm of rectal ampulla
Excludes1: *malignant carcinoid tumor of the rectum (C7A.026)*
CC Exclusion see Appendix A PDX collection 0270
Valid 3-character code, no further characters required

C21 Malignant neoplasm of anus and anal canal
Excludes2: *malignant carcinoid tumors of the colon (C7A.02-)*
malignant melanoma of anal margin (C43.51)
malignant melanoma of anal skin (C43.51)
malignant melanoma of perianal skin (C43.51)
other and unspecified malignant neoplasm of anal margin (C44.500, C44.510, C44.520, C44.590)
other and unspecified malignant neoplasm of anal skin (C44.500, C44.510, C44.520, C44.590)
other and unspecified malignant neoplasm of perianal skin (C44.500, C44.510, C44.520, C44.590)

CC **C21.0 Malignant neoplasm of anus, unspecified**
CC Exclusion see Appendix A PDX collection 0271

CC **C21.1 Malignant neoplasm of anal canal**
Malignant neoplasm of anal sphincter
CC Exclusion see Appendix A PDX collection 0271

CC **C21.2 Malignant neoplasm of cloacogenic zone**
CC Exclusion see Appendix A PDX collection 0272

CC **C21.8 Malignant neoplasm of overlapping sites of rectum, anus and anal canal**
Malignant neoplasm of anorectal junction
Malignant neoplasm of anorectum
Primary malignant neoplasm of two or more contiguous sites of rectum, anus and anal canal
CC Exclusion see Appendix A PDX collection 0272

C22 Malignant neoplasm of liver and intrahepatic bile ducts
Excludes1: *malignant neoplasm of biliary tract NOS (C24.9)*
secondary malignant neoplasm of liver and intrahepatic bile duct (C78.7)
Use additional code to identify:
alcohol abuse and dependence (F10.-)
hepatitis B (B16.-, B18.0-B18.1)
hepatitis C (B17.1-, B18.2)

CC **C22.0 Liver cell carcinoma**
Hepatocellular carcinoma
Hepatoma
CC Exclusion see Appendix A PDX collection 0273

CC **C22.1 Intrahepatic bile duct carcinoma**
Cholangiocarcinoma
Excludes1: *malignant neoplasm of hepatic duct (C24.0)*
CC Exclusion see Appendix A PDX collection 0273

CC **C22.2 Hepatoblastoma**
CC Exclusion see Appendix A PDX collection 0273

CC **C22.3 Angiosarcoma of liver**
Kupffer cell sarcoma
CC Exclusion see Appendix A PDX collection 0273

CC **C22.4 Other sarcomas of liver**
CC Exclusion see Appendix A PDX collection 0273

CC **C22.7 Other specified carcinomas of liver**
CC Exclusion see Appendix A PDX collection 0273

CC **C22.8 Malignant neoplasm of liver, primary, unspecified as to type**
CC Exclusion see Appendix A PDX collection 0273

CC **C22.9 Malignant neoplasm of liver, not specified as primary or secondary**
CC Exclusion see Appendix A PDX collection 0273

CC **C23 Malignant neoplasm of gallbladder**
CC Exclusion see Appendix A PDX collection 0274
Valid 3-character code, no further characters required

C24 Malignant neoplasm of other and unspecified parts of biliary tract
Excludes1: *malignant neoplasm of intrahepatic bile duct (C22.1)*

CC **C24.0 Malignant neoplasm of extrahepatic bile duct**
Malignant neoplasm of biliary duct or passage NOS
Malignant neoplasm of common bile duct
Malignant neoplasm of cystic duct
Malignant neoplasm of hepatic duct
CC Exclusion see Appendix A PDX collection 0275

CC **C24.1 Malignant neoplasm of ampulla of Vater**
CC Exclusion see Appendix A PDX collection 0276

CC **C24.8 Malignant neoplasm of overlapping sites of biliary tract**
Malignant neoplasm involving both intrahepatic and extrahepatic bile ducts
Primary malignant neoplasm of two or more contiguous sites of biliary tract
CC Exclusion see Appendix A PDX collection 0277

CC **C24.9 Malignant neoplasm of biliary tract, unspecified**
CC Exclusion see Appendix A PDX collection 0277

C25 Malignant neoplasm of pancreas
Use additional code to identify:
alcohol abuse and dependence (F10.-)

CC **C25.0 Malignant neoplasm of head of pancreas**
CC Exclusion see Appendix A PDX collection 0278

CC **C25.1 Malignant neoplasm of body of pancreas**
CC Exclusion see Appendix A PDX collection 0278

CC **C25.2 Malignant neoplasm of tail of pancreas**
CC Exclusion see Appendix A PDX collection 0278

CC **C25.3 Malignant neoplasm of pancreatic duct**
CC Exclusion see Appendix A PDX collection 0278

CC **C25.4 Malignant neoplasm of endocrine pancreas**
Malignant neoplasm of islets of Langerhans
Use additional code to identify any functional activity.
CC Exclusion see Appendix A PDX collection 0278

CC **C25.7 Malignant neoplasm of other parts of pancreas**
Malignant neoplasm of neck of pancreas
CC Exclusion see Appendix A PDX collection 0278

CC **C25.8 Malignant neoplasm of overlapping sites of pancreas**
CC Exclusion see Appendix A PDX collection 0278

CC **C25.9 Malignant neoplasm of pancreas, unspecified**
CC Exclusion see Appendix A PDX collection 0278

C26 Malignant neoplasm of other and ill-defined digestive organs
Excludes1: *malignant neoplasm of peritoneum and retroperitoneum (C48.-)*

C26.0 Malignant neoplasm of intestinal tract, part unspecified
Malignant neoplasm of intestine NOS

C26.1 Malignant neoplasm of spleen
Excludes1: *Hodgkin lymphoma (C81.-)*
non-Hodgkin lymphoma (C82-C85)

C26.9 Malignant neoplasm of ill-defined sites within the digestive system
Malignant neoplasm of alimentary canal or tract NOS
Malignant neoplasm of gastrointestinal tract NOS
Excludes1: *malignant neoplasm of abdominal NOS (C76.2)*
malignant neoplasm of intra-abdominal NOS (C76.2)

alignant neoplasms of respiratory and intrathoracic organs :30-C39)

cludes: malignant neoplasm of middle ear
cludes1: *mesothelioma (C45.-)*

C30 Malignant neoplasm of nasal cavity and middle ear

C30.0 Malignant neoplasm of nasal cavity
Malignant neoplasm of cartilage of nose
Malignant neoplasm of nasal concha
Malignant neoplasm of internal nose
Malignant neoplasm of septum of nose
Malignant neoplasm of vestibule of nose
Excludes1: *malignant neoplasm of nasal bone (C41.0)*
malignant neoplasm of nose NOS (C76.0)
malignant neoplasm of olfactory bulb (C72.2-)
malignant neoplasm of posterior margin of nasal septum and choana (C11.3)
malignant melanoma of skin of nose (C43.31)
malignant neoplasm of turbinates (C41.0)
other and unspecified malignant neoplasm of skin of nose C44.301, C44.311, C44.321, C44.391)

C30.1 Malignant neoplasm of middle ear
Malignant neoplasm of antrum tympanicum
Malignant neoplasm of auditory tube
Malignant neoplasm of eustachian tube
Malignant neoplasm of inner ear
Malignant neoplasm of mastoid air cells
Malignant neoplasm of tympanic cavity
Excludes1: *malignant neoplasm of auricular canal (external) (C43.2-,C44.2-)*
malignant neoplasm of bone of ear (meatus) (C41.0)
malignant neoplasm of cartilage of ear (C49.0)
malignant melanoma of skin of (external) ear (C43.2-)
other and unspecified malignant neoplasm of skin of (external) ear (C44.2-)

C31 Malignant neoplasm of accessory sinuses

C31.0 Malignant neoplasm of maxillary sinus
Malignant neoplasm of antrum (Highmore) (maxillary)

C31.1 Malignant neoplasm of ethmoidal sinus

C31.2 Malignant neoplasm of frontal sinus

C31.3 Malignant neoplasm of sphenoid sinus

C31.8 Malignant neoplasm of overlapping sites of accessory sinuses

C31.9 Malignant neoplasm of accessory sinus, unspecified

C32 Malignant neoplasm of larynx
Use additional code to identify:
alcohol abuse and dependence (F10.-)
exposure to environmental tobacco smoke (Z77.22)
exposure to tobacco smoke in the perinatal period (P96.81)
history of tobacco use (Z87.891)
occupational exposure to environmental tobacco smoke (Z57.31)
tobacco dependence (F17.-)
tobacco use (Z72.0)

C32.0 Malignant neoplasm of glottis
Malignant neoplasm of intrinsic larynx
Malignant neoplasm of laryngeal commissure (anterior) (posterior)
Malignant neoplasm of vocal cord (true) NOS

C32.1 Malignant neoplasm of supraglottis
Malignant neoplasm of aryepiglottic fold or interarytenoid fold, laryngeal aspect
Malignant neoplasm of epiglottis (suprahyoid portion) NOS
Malignant neoplasm of extrinsic larynx
Malignant neoplasm of false vocal cord
Malignant neoplasm of posterior (laryngeal) surface of epiglottis
Malignant neoplasm of ventricular bands
Excludes2: *malignant neoplasm of anterior surface of epiglottis (C10.1)*
malignant neoplasm of aryepiglottic fold or interarytenoid fold, hypopharyngeal aspect (C13.1)
malignant neoplasm of aryepiglottic fold or interarytenoid fold, marginal zone (C13.1)
malignant neoplasm of aryepiglottic fold or interarytenoid fold NOS (C13.1)

C32.2 Malignant neoplasm of subglottis

C32.3 Malignant neoplasm of laryngeal cartilage

C32.8 Malignant neoplasm of overlapping sites of larynx

C32.9 Malignant neoplasm of larynx, unspecified

CC **C33 Malignant neoplasm of trachea**
Use additional code to identify:
exposure to environmental tobacco smoke (Z77.22)
exposure to tobacco smoke in the perinatal period (P96.81)
history of tobacco use (Z87.891)
occupational exposure to environmental tobacco smoke (Z57.31)
tobacco dependence (F17.-)
tobacco use (Z72.0)
CC Exclusion see Appendix A PDX collection 0279
Valid 3-character code, no further characters required

Lungs

C34 Malignant neoplasm of bronchus and lung

Use additional code to identify:
exposure to environmental tobacco smoke (Z77.22)
exposure to tobacco smoke in the perinatal period (P96.81)
history of tobacco use (Z87.891)
occupational exposure to environmental tobacco smoke (Z57.31)
tobacco dependence (F17.-)
tobacco use (Z72.0)

Excludes1: *Kaposi's sarcoma of lung (C46.5-)*
malignant carcinoid tumor of the bronchus and lung (C7A.090)

\+ **C34.0 Malignant neoplasm of main bronchus**
Malignant neoplasm of carina
Malignant neoplasm of hilus (of lung)

CC **C34.00 Malignant neoplasm of unspecified main bronchus**
CC Exclusion see Appendix A PDX collection 0280

CC **C34.01 Malignant neoplasm of right main bronchus**
CC Exclusion see Appendix A PDX collection 0280

CC **C34.02 Malignant neoplasm of left main bronchus**
CC Exclusion see Appendix A PDX collection 0280

\+ **C34.1 Malignant neoplasm of upper lobe, bronchus or lung**

CC **C34.10 Malignant neoplasm of upper lobe, unspecified bronchus or lung**
CC Exclusion see Appendix A PDX collection 0281

CC **C34.11 Malignant neoplasm of upper lobe, right bronchus or lung**
CC Exclusion see Appendix A PDX collection 0281

CC **C34.12 Malignant neoplasm of upper lobe, left bronchus or lung**
CC Exclusion see Appendix A PDX collection 0281

CC **C34.2 Malignant neoplasm of middle lobe, bronchus or lung**
CC Exclusion see Appendix A PDX collection 0282

\+ **C34.3 Malignant neoplasm of lower lobe, bronchus or lung**

CC **C34.30 Malignant neoplasm of lower lobe, unspecified bronchus or lung**
CC Exclusion see Appendix A PDX collection 0283

CC **C34.31 Malignant neoplasm of lower lobe, right bronchus or lung**
CC Exclusion see Appendix A PDX collection 0283

CC **C34.32 Malignant neoplasm of lower lobe, left bronchus or lung**
CC Exclusion see Appendix A PDX collection 0283

\+ **C34.8 Malignant neoplasm of overlapping sites of bronchus and lung**

CC **C34.80 Malignant neoplasm of overlapping sites of unspecified bronchus and lung**
CC Exclusion see Appendix A PDX collection 0284

CC **C34.81 Malignant neoplasm of overlapping sites of right bronchus and lung**
CC Exclusion see Appendix A PDX collection 0284

CC **C34.82 Malignant neoplasm of overlapping sites of left bronchus and lung**
CC Exclusion see Appendix A PDX collection 0284

\+ **C34.9 Malignant neoplasm of unspecified part of bronchus or lung**

CC **C34.90 Malignant neoplasm of unspecified part of unspecifi bronchus or lung**
Lung cancer NOS
CC Exclusion see Appendix A PDX collection 0284
AHA CC: 2Q, 2014, 10

CC **C34.91 Malignant neoplasm of unspecified part of right bronchus or lung**
CC Exclusion see Appendix A PDX collection 0284

CC **C34.92 Malignant neoplasm of unspecified part of left bronchus or lung**
CC Exclusion see Appendix A PDX collection 0284

CC **C37 Malignant neoplasm of thymus**

Excludes1: *malignant carcinoid tumor of the thymus (C7A.091)*
CC Exclusion see Appendix A PDX collection 0285
Valid 3-character code, no further characters required

C38 Malignant neoplasm of heart, mediastinum and pleura

Excludes1: *mesothelioma (C45.-)*

CC **C38.0 Malignant neoplasm of heart**
Malignant neoplasm of pericardium
Excludes1: *malignant neoplasm of great vessels (C49.3)*
CC Exclusion see Appendix A PDX collection 0286

CC **C38.1 Malignant neoplasm of anterior mediastinum**
CC Exclusion see Appendix A PDX collection 0287

CC **C38.2 Malignant neoplasm of posterior mediastinum**
CC Exclusion see Appendix A PDX collection 0287

CC **C38.3 Malignant neoplasm of mediastinum, part unspecified**
CC Exclusion see Appendix A PDX collection 0287

CC **C38.4 Malignant neoplasm of pleura**
CC Exclusion see Appendix A PDX collection 0288

CC **C38.8 Malignant neoplasm of overlapping sites of heart, mediastinu and pleura**
CC Exclusion see Appendix A PDX collection 0287

C39 Malignant neoplasm of other and ill-defined sites in the respiratory system and intrathoracic organs

Use additional code to identify:
exposure to environmental tobacco smoke (Z77.22)
exposure to tobacco smoke in the perinatal period (P96.81)
history of tobacco use (Z87.891)
occupational exposure to environmental tobacco smoke (Z57.31)
tobacco dependence (F17.-)
tobacco use (Z72.0)

Excludes1: *intrathoracic malignant neoplasm NOS (C76.1)*
thoracic malignant neoplasm NOS (C76.1)

C39.0 Malignant neoplasm of upper respiratory tract, part unspecifi

C39.9 Malignant neoplasm of lower respiratory tract, part unspecifi
Malignant neoplasm of respiratory tract NOS

CC **C49.3 Malignant neoplasm of connective and soft tissue of thorax**
Malignant neoplasm of axilla
Malignant neoplasm of diaphragm
Malignant neoplasm of great vessels
Excludes1: *malignant neoplasm of breast (C50.-)*
malignant neoplasm of heart (C38.0)
malignant neoplasm of mediastinum (C38.1-C38.3)
malignant neoplasm of thymus (C37)
CC Exclusion see Appendix A PDX collection 0307

CC **C49.4 Malignant neoplasm of connective and soft tissue of abdomen**
Malignant neoplasm of abdominal wall
Malignant neoplasm of hypochondrium
CC Exclusion see Appendix A PDX collection 0307

CC **C49.5 Malignant neoplasm of connective and soft tissue of pelvis**
Malignant neoplasm of buttock
Malignant neoplasm of groin
Malignant neoplasm of perineum
CC Exclusion see Appendix A PDX collection 0307

CC **C49.6 Malignant neoplasm of connective and soft tissue of trunk, unspecified**
Malignant neoplasm of back NOS
CC Exclusion see Appendix A PDX collection 0307

CC **C49.8 Malignant neoplasm of overlapping sites of connective and soft tissue**
Primary malignant neoplasm of two or more contiguous sites of connective and soft tissue
CC Exclusion see Appendix A PDX collection 0307

CC **C49.9 Malignant neoplasm of connective and soft tissue, unspecified**
CC Exclusion see Appendix A PDX collection 0307

alignant neoplasms of breast (C50)

C50 Malignant neoplasm of breast

Includes: connective tissue of breast
Paget's disease of breast
Paget's disease of nipple

Use additional code to identify estrogen receptor status (Z17.0, Z17.1)

Excludes1: *skin of breast (C44.501, C44.511, C44.521, C44.591)*

+ **C50.0 Malignant neoplasm of nipple and areola**
  + **C50.01 Malignant neoplasm of nipple and areola, female**
    - ♀ **C50.011 Malignant neoplasm of nipple and areola, right female breast**
    - ♀ **C50.012 Malignant neoplasm of nipple and areola, left female breast**
    - ♀ **C50.019 Malignant neoplasm of nipple and areola, unspecified female breast**
  + **C50.02 Malignant neoplasm of nipple and areola, male**
    - ♂ **C50.021 Malignant neoplasm of nipple and areola, right male breast**
    - ♂ **C50.022 Malignant neoplasm of nipple and areola, left male breast**
    - ♂ **C50.029 Malignant neoplasm of nipple and areola, unspecified male breast**
+ **C50.1 Malignant neoplasm of central portion of breast**
  + **C50.11 Malignant neoplasm of central portion of breast, female**
    - ♀ **C50.111 Malignant neoplasm of central portion of right female breast**
    - ♀ **C50.112 Malignant neoplasm of central portion of left female breast**
    - ♀ **C50.119 Malignant neoplasm of central portion of unspecified female breast**
  + **C50.12 Malignant neoplasm of central portion of breast, male**
    - ♂ **C50.121 Malignant neoplasm of central portion of right male breast**
    - ♂ **C50.122 Malignant neoplasm of central portion of left male breast**
    - ♂ **C50.129 Malignant neoplasm of central portion of unspecified male breast**
+ **C50.2 Malignant neoplasm of upper-inner quadrant of breast**
  + **C50.21 Malignant neoplasm of upper-inner quadrant of breast, female**
    - ♀ **C50.211 Malignant neoplasm of upper-inner quadrant of right female breast**
    - ♀ **C50.212 Malignant neoplasm of upper-inner quadrant of left female breast**
    - ♀ **C50.219 Malignant neoplasm of upper-inner quadrant of unspecified female breast**
  + **C50.22 Malignant neoplasm of upper-inner quadrant of breast, male**
    - ♂ **C50.221 Malignant neoplasm of upper-inner quadrant of right male breast**
    - ♂ **C50.222 Malignant neoplasm of upper-inner quadrant of left male breast**
    - ♂ **C50.229 Malignant neoplasm of upper-inner quadrant of unspecified male breast**
+ **C50.3 Malignant neoplasm of lower-inner quadrant of breast**
  + **C50.31 Malignant neoplasm of lower-inner quadrant of breast, female**
    - ♀ **C50.311 Malignant neoplasm of lower-inner quadrant of right female breast**
    - ♀ **C50.312 Malignant neoplasm of lower-inner quadrant of left female breast**
    - ♀ **C50.319 Malignant neoplasm of lower-inner quadrant of unspecified female breast**
  + **C50.32 Malignant neoplasm of lower-inner quadrant of breast, male**
    - ♂ **C50.321 Malignant neoplasm of lower-inner quadrant of right male breast**
    - ♂ **C50.322 Malignant neoplasm of lower-inner quadrant of left male breast**
    - ♂ **C50.329 Malignant neoplasm of lower-inner quadrant of unspecified male breast**
+ **C50.4 Malignant neoplasm of upper-outer quadrant of breast**
  + **C50.41 Malignant neoplasm of upper-outer quadrant of breast, female**
    - ♀ **C50.411 Malignant neoplasm of upper-outer quadrant of right female breast**
    - ♀ **C50.412 Malignant neoplasm of upper-outer quadrant of left female breast**
    - ♀ **C50.419 Malignant neoplasm of upper-outer quadrant of unspecified female breast**
  + **C50.42 Malignant neoplasm of upper-outer quadrant of breast, male**
    - ♂ **C50.421 Malignant neoplasm of upper-outer quadrant of right male breast**
    - ♂ **C50.422 Malignant neoplasm of upper-outer quadrant of left male breast**
    - ♂ **C50.429 Malignant neoplasm of upper-outer quadrant of unspecified male breast**
+ **C50.5 Malignant neoplasm of lower-outer quadrant of breast**
  + **C50.51 Malignant neoplasm of lower-outer quadrant of breast, female**
    - ♀ **C50.511 Malignant neoplasm of lower-outer quadrant of right female breast**
    - ♀ **C50.512 Malignant neoplasm of lower-outer quadrant of left female breast**
    - ♀ **C50.519 Malignant neoplasm of lower-outer quadrant of unspecified female breast**
  + **C50.52 Malignant neoplasm of lower-outer quadrant of breast, male**
    - ♂ **C50.521 Malignant neoplasm of lower-outer quadrant of right male breast**
    - ♂ **C50.522 Malignant neoplasm of lower-outer quadrant of left male breast**
    - ♂ **C50.529 Malignant neoplasm of lower-outer quadrant of unspecified male breast**
+ **C50.6 Malignant neoplasm of axillary tail of breast**
  + **C50.61 Malignant neoplasm of axillary tail of breast, female**
    - ♀ **C50.611 Malignant neoplasm of axillary tail of right female breast**
    - ♀ **C50.612 Malignant neoplasm of axillary tail of left female breast**
    - ♀ **C50.619 Malignant neoplasm of axillary tail of unspecified female breast**
  + **C50.62 Malignant neoplasm of axillary tail of breast, male**
    - ♂ **C50.621 Malignant neoplasm of axillary tail of right male breast**
    - ♂ **C50.622 Malignant neoplasm of axillary tail of left male breast**
    - ♂ **C50.629 Malignant neoplasm of axillary tail of unspecified male breast**
+ **C50.8 Malignant neoplasm of overlapping sites of breast**
  + **C50.81 Malignant neoplasm of overlapping sites of breast, female**
    - ♀ **C50.811 Malignant neoplasm of overlapping sites of right female breast**
    - ♀ **C50.812 Malignant neoplasm of overlapping sites of left female breast**
    - ♀ **C50.819 Malignant neoplasm of overlapping sites of unspecified female breast**

+ **C50.82 Malignant neoplasm of overlapping sites of breast, male**
- ♂ **C50.821 Malignant neoplasm of overlapping sites of right male breast**
- ♂ **C50.822 Malignant neoplasm of overlapping sites of left male breast**
- ♂ **C50.829 Malignant neoplasm of overlapping sites of unspecified male breast**

+ **C50.9 Malignant neoplasm of breast of unspecified site**
+ **C50.91 Malignant neoplasm of breast of unspecified site, female**
- ♀ **C50.911 Malignant neoplasm of unspecified site of right female breast**
- ♀ **C50.912 Malignant neoplasm of unspecified site of left female breast**
- ♀ **C50.919 Malignant neoplasm of unspecified site of unspecified female breast**

+ **C50.92 Malignant neoplasm of breast of unspecified site, male**
- ♂ **C50.921 Malignant neoplasm of unspecified site of right male breast**
- ♂ **C50.922 Malignant neoplasm of unspecified site of left male breast**
- ♂ **C50.929 Malignant neoplasm of unspecified site of unspecified male breast**

Malignant neoplasms of female genital organs (C51-C58)

Includes: malignant neoplasm of skin of female genital organs

C51 Malignant neoplasm of vulva

Excludes1: *carcinoma in situ of vulva (D07.1)*

♀ **C51.0 Malignant neoplasm of labium majus**
Malignant neoplasm of Bartholin's [greater vestibular] gland
♀ **C51.1 Malignant neoplasm of labium minus**
♀ **C51.2 Malignant neoplasm of clitoris**
♀ **C51.8 Malignant neoplasm of overlapping sites of vulva**
♀ **C51.9 Malignant neoplasm of vulva, unspecified**
Malignant neoplasm of external female genitalia NOS
Malignant neoplasm of pudendum

♀ **C52 Malignant neoplasm of vagina**

Excludes1: *carcinoma in situ of vagina (D07.2)*
Valid 3-character code, no further characters required

C53 Malignant neoplasm of cervix uteri

Excludes1: *carcinoma in situ of cervix uteri (D06.-)*

♀ **C53.0 Malignant neoplasm of endocervix**
♀ **C53.1 Malignant neoplasm of exocervix**
♀ **C53.8 Malignant neoplasm of overlapping sites of cervix uteri**
♀ **C53.9 Malignant neoplasm of cervix uteri, unspecified**

C54 Malignant neoplasm of corpus uteri

♀ **C54.0 Malignant neoplasm of isthmus uteri**
Malignant neoplasm of lower uterine segment
♀ **C54.1 Malignant neoplasm of endometrium**
♀ **C54.2 Malignant neoplasm of myometrium**
♀ **C54.3 Malignant neoplasm of fundus uteri**
♀ **C54.8 Malignant neoplasm of overlapping sites of corpus uteri**
♀ **C54.9 Malignant neoplasm of corpus uteri, unspecified**

♀ **C55 Malignant neoplasm of uterus, part unspecified**

Valid 3-character code, no further characters required

C56 Malignant neoplasm of ovary

Use additional code to identify any functional activity

CC ♀ **C56.1 Malignant neoplasm of right ovary**
CC Exclusion see Appendix A PDX collection 0309
CC ♀ **C56.2 Malignant neoplasm of left ovary**
CC Exclusion see Appendix A PDX collection 0309
CC ♀ **C56.9 Malignant neoplasm of unspecified ovary**
CC Exclusion see Appendix A PDX collection 0309

C57 Malignant neoplasm of other and unspecified female genital organs

+ **C57.0 Malignant neoplasm of fallopian tube**
Malignant neoplasm of oviduct
Malignant neoplasm of uterine tube
- ♀ **C57.00 Malignant neoplasm of unspecified fallopian tube**
- ♀ **C57.01 Malignant neoplasm of right fallopian tube**
- ♀ **C57.02 Malignant neoplasm of left fallopian tube**

+ **C57.1 Malignant neoplasm of broad ligament**
- ♀ **C57.10 Malignant neoplasm of unspecified broad ligament**
- ♀ **C57.11 Malignant neoplasm of right broad ligament**
- ♀ **C57.12 Malignant neoplasm of left broad ligament**

+ **C57.2 Malignant neoplasm of round ligament**
- ♀ **C57.20 Malignant neoplasm of unspecified round ligament**
- ♀ **C57.21 Malignant neoplasm of right round ligament**
- ♀ **C57.22 Malignant neoplasm of left round ligament**

♀ **C57.3 Malignant neoplasm of parametrium**
Malignant neoplasm of uterine ligament NOS
♀ **C57.4 Malignant neoplasm of uterine adnexa, unspecified**
♀ **C57.7 Malignant neoplasm of other specified female genital organs**
Malignant neoplasm of wolffian body or duct
♀ **C57.8 Malignant neoplasm of overlapping sites of female genital organs**
Primary malignant neoplasm of two or more contiguous sites of the female genital organs whose point of origin cannot be determined
Primary tubo-ovarian malignant neoplasm whose point of origin cannot be determined
Primary utero-ovarian malignant neoplasm whose point of origin cannot be determined
♀ **C57.9 Malignant neoplasm of female genital organ, unspecified**
Malignant neoplasm of female genitourinary tract NOS

♀ **C58 Malignant neoplasm of placenta**

Includes: choriocarcinoma NOS
chorionepithelioma NOS
Excludes1: *chorioadenoma (destruens) (D39.2)*
hydatidiform mole NOS (O01.9)
invasive hydatidiform mole (D39.2)
male choriocarcinoma NOS (C62.9-)
malignant hydatidiform mole (D39.2)
Valid 3-character code, no further characters required

Malignant neoplasms of male genital organs (C60-C63)

Includes: malignant neoplasm of skin of male genital organs

C60 Malignant neoplasm of penis

♂ **C60.0 Malignant neoplasm of prepuce**
Malignant neoplasm of foreskin
♂ **C60.1 Malignant neoplasm of glans penis**
♂ **C60.2 Malignant neoplasm of body of penis**
Malignant neoplasm of corpus cavernosum
♂ **C60.8 Malignant neoplasm of overlapping sites of penis**
♂ **C60.9 Malignant neoplasm of penis, unspecified**
Malignant neoplasm of skin of penis NOS

♂ **C61 Malignant neoplasm of prostate**

Excludes1: *malignant neoplasm of seminal vesicle (C63.7)*
Valid 3-character code, no further characters required

C62 Malignant neoplasm of testis

Use additional code to identify any functional activity

+ **C62.0 Malignant neoplasm of undescended testis**
Malignant neoplasm of ectopic testis
Malignant neoplasm of retained testis
- ♂ **C62.00 Malignant neoplasm of unspecified undescended testis**
- ♂ **C62.01 Malignant neoplasm of undescended right testis**
- ♂ **C62.02 Malignant neoplasm of undescended left testis**

+ **C62.1 Malignant neoplasm of descended testis**
Malignant neoplasm of scrotal testis
- ♂ **C62.10 Malignant neoplasm of unspecified descended testis**
- ♂ **C62.11 Malignant neoplasm of descended right testis**
- ♂ **C62.12 Malignant neoplasm of descended left testis**

+ **C62.9 Malignant neoplasm of testis, unspecified whether descended or undescended**
- ♂ **C62.90 Malignant neoplasm of unspecified testis, unspecified whether descended or undescended**
  Malignant neoplasm of testis NOS
- ♂ **C62.91 Malignant neoplasm of right testis, unspecified whether descended or undescended**
- ♂ **C62.92 Malignant neoplasm of left testis, unspecified whether descended or undescended**

C63 Malignant neoplasm of other and unspecified male genital organs

+ **C63.0 Malignant neoplasm of epididymis**
- ♂ **C63.00 Malignant neoplasm of unspecified epididymis**
- ♂ **C63.01 Malignant neoplasm of right epididymis**
- ♂ **C63.02 Malignant neoplasm of left epididymis**

+ **C63.1 Malignant neoplasm of spermatic cord**
- ♂ **C63.10 Malignant neoplasm of unspecified spermatic cord**
- ♂ **C63.11 Malignant neoplasm of right spermatic cord**
- ♂ **C63.12 Malignant neoplasm of left spermatic cord**

♂ **C63.2 Malignant neoplasm of scrotum**
Malignant neoplasm of skin of scrotum

♂ **C63.7 Malignant neoplasm of other specified male genital organs**
Malignant neoplasm of seminal vesicle
Malignant neoplasm of tunica vaginalis

♂ **C63.8 Malignant neoplasm of overlapping sites of male genital organs**
Primary malignant neoplasm of two or more contiguous sites of male genital organs whose point of origin cannot be determined

♂ **C63.9 Malignant neoplasm of male genital organ, unspecified**
Malignant neoplasm of male genitourinary tract NOS

Malignant neoplasms of urinary tract (C64-C68)

C64 Malignant neoplasm of kidney, except renal pelvis

Excludes1: *malignant carcinoid tumor of the kidney (C7A.093)*
malignant neoplasm of renal calyces (C65.-)
malignant neoplasm of renal pelvis (C65.-)

CC **C64.1 Malignant neoplasm of right kidney, except renal pelvis**
CC Exclusion see Appendix A PDX collection 0310

CC **C64.2 Malignant neoplasm of left kidney, except renal pelvis**
CC Exclusion see Appendix A PDX collection 0310

CC **C64.9 Malignant neoplasm of unspecified kidney, except renal pelvis**
CC Exclusion see Appendix A PDX collection 0310

C65 Malignant neoplasm of renal pelvis

Includes: malignant neoplasm of pelviureteric junction
malignant neoplasm of renal calyces

CC **C65.1 Malignant neoplasm of right renal pelvis**
CC Exclusion see Appendix A PDX collection 0310

CC **C65.2 Malignant neoplasm of left renal pelvis**
CC Exclusion see Appendix A PDX collection 0310

CC **C65.9 Malignant neoplasm of unspecified renal pelvis**
CC Exclusion see Appendix A PDX collection 0310

C66 Malignant neoplasm of ureter

Excludes1: *malignant neoplasm of ureteric orifice of bladder (C67.6)*

CC **C66.1 Malignant neoplasm of right ureter**
CC Exclusion see Appendix A PDX collection 0311

CC **C66.2 Malignant neoplasm of left ureter**
CC Exclusion see Appendix A PDX collection 0311

CC **C66.9 Malignant neoplasm of unspecified ureter**
CC Exclusion see Appendix A PDX collection 0311

C67 Malignant neoplasm of bladder

C67.0 Malignant neoplasm of trigone of bladder
C67.1 Malignant neoplasm of dome of bladder
C67.2 Malignant neoplasm of lateral wall of bladder
C67.3 Malignant neoplasm of anterior wall of bladder
C67.4 Malignant neoplasm of posterior wall of bladder
C67.5 Malignant neoplasm of bladder neck
Malignant neoplasm of internal urethral orifice
C67.6 Malignant neoplasm of ureteric orifice
C67.7 Malignant neoplasm of urachus
C67.8 Malignant neoplasm of overlapping sites of bladder
C67.9 Malignant neoplasm of bladder, unspecified

C68 Malignant neoplasm of other and unspecified urinary organs

Excludes1: *malignant neoplasm of female genitourinary tract NOS (C57.9)*
malignant neoplasm of male genitourinary tract NOS (C63.9)

CC **C68.0 Malignant neoplasm of urethra**
Excludes1: *malignant neoplasm of urethral orifice of bladder (C67.5)*
CC Exclusion see Appendix A PDX collection 0312

CC **C68.1 Malignant neoplasm of paraurethral glands**
CC Exclusion see Appendix A PDX collection 0312

CC **C68.8 Malignant neoplasm of overlapping sites of urinary organs**
Primary malignant neoplasm of two or more contiguous sites of urinary organs whose point of origin cannot be determined
CC Exclusion see Appendix A PDX collection 0313

CC **C68.9 Malignant neoplasm of urinary organ, unspecified**
Malignant neoplasm of urinary system NOS
CC Exclusion see Appendix A PDX collection 0313

Malignant neoplasms of eye, brain and other parts of central nervous system (C69-C72)

C69 Malignant neoplasm of eye and adnexa

Excludes1: *malignant neoplasm of connective tissue of eyelid (C49.0)*
malignant neoplasm of eyelid (skin) (C43.1-, C44.1-)
malignant neoplasm of optic nerve (C72.3-)

+ **C69.0 Malignant neoplasm of conjunctiva**
C69.00 Malignant neoplasm of unspecified conjunctiva
C69.01 Malignant neoplasm of right conjunctiva
C69.02 Malignant neoplasm of left conjunctiva

+ **C69.1 Malignant neoplasm of cornea**
C69.10 Malignant neoplasm of unspecified cornea
C69.11 Malignant neoplasm of right cornea
C69.12 Malignant neoplasm of left cornea

+ **C69.2 Malignant neoplasm of retina**
Excludes1: *dark area on retina (D49.81)*
neoplasm of unspecified behavior of retina and choroid (D49.81)
retinal freckle (D49.81)
C69.20 Malignant neoplasm of unspecified retina
C69.21 Malignant neoplasm of right retina
C69.22 Malignant neoplasm of left retina

+ **C69.3 Malignant neoplasm of choroid**
C69.30 Malignant neoplasm of unspecified choroid
C69.31 Malignant neoplasm of right choroid
C69.32 Malignant neoplasm of left choroid

+ **C69.4 Malignant neoplasm of ciliary body**
C69.40 Malignant neoplasm of unspecified ciliary body
C69.41 Malignant neoplasm of right ciliary body
C69.42 Malignant neoplasm of left ciliary body

+ **C69.5 Malignant neoplasm of lacrimal gland and duct**
Malignant neoplasm of lacrimal sac
Malignant neoplasm of nasolacrimal duct
C69.50 Malignant neoplasm of unspecified lacrimal gland and duct
C69.51 Malignant neoplasm of right lacrimal gland and duct
C69.52 Malignant neoplasm of left lacrimal gland and duct

+ **C69.6 Malignant neoplasm of orbit**
Malignant neoplasm of connective tissue of orbit
Malignant neoplasm of extraocular muscle
Malignant neoplasm of peripheral nerves of orbit
Malignant neoplasm of retrobulbar tissue
Malignant neoplasm of retro-ocular tissue
Excludes1: *malignant neoplasm of orbital bone (C41.0)*
C69.60 Malignant neoplasm of unspecified orbit
C69.61 Malignant neoplasm of right orbit
C69.62 Malignant neoplasm of left orbit

+ **C69.8 Malignant neoplasm of overlapping sites of eye and adnexa**
C69.80 Malignant neoplasm of overlapping sites of unspecified eye and adnexa
C69.81 Malignant neoplasm of overlapping sites of right eye and adnexa
C69.82 Malignant neoplasm of overlapping sites of left eye and adnexa

+ **C69.9 Malignant neoplasm of unspecified site of eye**
Malignant neoplasm of eyeball
C69.90 Malignant neoplasm of unspecified site of unspecified eye
C69.91 Malignant neoplasm of unspecified site of right eye
C69.92 Malignant neoplasm of unspecified site of left eye

C70 Malignant neoplasm of meninges

CC **C70.0 Malignant neoplasm of cerebral meninges**
CC Exclusion see Appendix A PDX collection 0314

CC **C70.1 Malignant neoplasm of spinal meninges**
CC Exclusion see Appendix A PDX collection 0315

CC **C70.9 Malignant neoplasm of meninges, unspecified**
CC Exclusion see Appendix A PDX collection 0314

C71 Malignant neoplasm of brain

Excludes1: *malignant neoplasm of cranial nerves (C72.2-C72.5)*
retrobulbar malignant neoplasm (C69.6-)

CC **C71.0 Malignant neoplasm of cerebrum, except lobes and ventricles**
Malignant neoplasm of supratentorial NOS
CC Exclusion see Appendix A PDX collection 0316

CC **C71.1 Malignant neoplasm of frontal lobe**
CC Exclusion see Appendix A PDX collection 0316

CC **C71.2 Malignant neoplasm of temporal lobe**
CC Exclusion see Appendix A PDX collection 0316

CC **C71.3 Malignant neoplasm of parietal lobe**
CC Exclusion see Appendix A PDX collection 0316

CC **C71.4 Malignant neoplasm of occipital lobe**
CC Exclusion see Appendix A PDX collection 0316

CC **C71.5 Malignant neoplasm of cerebral ventricle**
Excludes1: *malignant neoplasm of fourth cerebral ventricle (C71.7)*
CC Exclusion see Appendix A PDX collection 0316

CC **C71.6 Malignant neoplasm of cerebellum**
CC Exclusion see Appendix A PDX collection 0316

CC **C71.7 Malignant neoplasm of brain stem**
Malignant neoplasm of fourth cerebral ventricle
Infratentorial malignant neoplasm NOS
CC Exclusion see Appendix A PDX collection 0316

CC **C71.8 Malignant neoplasm of overlapping sites of brain**
CC Exclusion see Appendix A PDX collection 0316

CC **C71.9 Malignant neoplasm of brain, unspecified**
CC Exclusion see Appendix A PDX collection 0316

C72 Malignant neoplasm of spinal cord, cranial nerves and other parts of central nervous system

Excludes1: *malignant neoplasm of meninges (C70.-)*
malignant neoplasm of peripheral nerves and autonomic nervous system (C47.-)

CC **C72.0 Malignant neoplasm of spinal cord**
CC Exclusion see Appendix A PDX collection 0317

CC **C72.1 Malignant neoplasm of cauda equina**
CC Exclusion see Appendix A PDX collection 0317

\+ **C72.2 Malignant neoplasm of olfactory nerve**
Malignant neoplasm of olfactory bulb

CC **C72.20 Malignant neoplasm of unspecified olfactory nerve**
CC Exclusion see Appendix A PDX collection 0318

CC **C72.21 Malignant neoplasm of right olfactory nerve**
CC Exclusion see Appendix A PDX collection 0318

CC **C72.22 Malignant neoplasm of left olfactory nerve**
CC Exclusion see Appendix A PDX collection 0318

\+ **C72.3 Malignant neoplasm of optic nerve**

CC **C72.30 Malignant neoplasm of unspecified optic nerve**
CC Exclusion see Appendix A PDX collection 0318

CC **C72.31 Malignant neoplasm of right optic nerve**
CC Exclusion see Appendix A PDX collection 0318

CC **C72.32 Malignant neoplasm of left optic nerve**
CC Exclusion see Appendix A PDX collection 0318

\+ **C72.4 Malignant neoplasm of acoustic nerve**

CC **C72.40 Malignant neoplasm of unspecified acoustic nerve**
CC Exclusion see Appendix A PDX collection 0318

CC **C72.41 Malignant neoplasm of right acoustic nerve**
CC Exclusion see Appendix A PDX collection 0318

CC **C72.42 Malignant neoplasm of left acoustic nerve**
CC Exclusion see Appendix A PDX collection 0318

\+ **C72.5 Malignant neoplasm of other and unspecified cranial nerves**

CC **C72.50 Malignant neoplasm of unspecified cranial nerve**
Malignant neoplasm of cranial nerve NOS
CC Exclusion see Appendix A PDX collection 0318

CC **C72.59 Malignant neoplasm of other cranial nerves**
CC Exclusion see Appendix A PDX collection 0318

CC **C72.9 Malignant neoplasm of central nervous system, unspecified**
Malignant neoplasm of unspecified site of central nervous system
Malignant neoplasm of nervous system NOS
CC Exclusion see Appendix A PDX collection 0319

Malignant neoplasms of thyroid and other endocrine glands (C73-C75)

C73 Malignant neoplasm of thyroid gland
Use additional code to identify any functional activity
Valid 3-character code, no further characters required

C74 Malignant neoplasm of adrenal gland

\+ **C74.0 Malignant neoplasm of cortex of adrenal gland**

CC **C74.00 Malignant neoplasm of cortex of unspecified adrenal gland**
CC Exclusion see Appendix A PDX collection 0320

CC **C74.01 Malignant neoplasm of cortex of right adrenal gland**
CC Exclusion see Appendix A PDX collection 0320

CC **C74.02 Malignant neoplasm of cortex of left adrenal gland**
CC Exclusion see Appendix A PDX collection 0320

\+ **C74.1 Malignant neoplasm of medulla of adrenal gland**

CC **C74.10 Malignant neoplasm of medulla of unspecified adrenal gland**
CC Exclusion see Appendix A PDX collection 0320

CC **C74.11 Malignant neoplasm of medulla of right adrenal gland**
CC Exclusion see Appendix A PDX collection 0320

CC **C74.12 Malignant neoplasm of medulla of left adrenal gland**
CC Exclusion see Appendix A PDX collection 0320

\+ **C74.9 Malignant neoplasm of unspecified part of adrenal gland**

CC **C74.90 Malignant neoplasm of unspecified part of unspecified adrenal gland**
CC Exclusion see Appendix A PDX collection 0320

CC **C74.91 Malignant neoplasm of unspecified part of right adrenal gland**
CC Exclusion see Appendix A PDX collection 0320

CC **C74.92 Malignant neoplasm of unspecified part of left adrenal gland**
CC Exclusion see Appendix A PDX collection 0320

C75 Malignant neoplasm of other endocrine glands and related structu

Excludes1: *malignant carcinoid tumors (C7A.0-)*
malignant neoplasm of adrenal gland (C74.-)
malignant neoplasm of endocrine pancreas (C25.4)
malignant neoplasm of islets of Langerhans (C25.4)
malignant neoplasm of ovary (C56.-)
malignant neoplasm of testis (C62.-)
malignant neoplasm of thymus (C37)
malignant neoplasm of thyroid gland (C73)
malignant neuroendocrine tumors (C7A.-)

CC **C75.0 Malignant neoplasm of parathyroid gland**
CC Exclusion see Appendix A PDX collection 0321

CC **C75.1 Malignant neoplasm of pituitary gland**
CC Exclusion see Appendix A PDX collection 0322

CC **C75.2 Malignant neoplasm of craniopharyngeal duct**
CC Exclusion see Appendix A PDX collection 0322

CC **C75.3 Malignant neoplasm of pineal gland**
CC Exclusion see Appendix A PDX collection 0323

CC **C75.4 Malignant neoplasm of carotid body**
CC Exclusion see Appendix A PDX collection 0324

CC **C75.5 Malignant neoplasm of aortic body and other paraganglia**
CC Exclusion see Appendix A PDX collection 0325

CC **C75.8 Malignant neoplasm with pluriglandular involvement, unspecified**
CC Exclusion see Appendix A PDX collection 0326

CC **C75.9 Malignant neoplasm of endocrine gland, unspecified**
CC Exclusion see Appendix A PDX collection 0326

Malignant neuroendocrine tumors (C7A)

C7A Malignant neuroendocrine tumors

Code also any associated multiple endocrine neoplasia [MEN] syndro (E31.2-)

Use additional code to identify any associated endocrine syndrome, such as:
carcinoid syndrome (E34.0)

Excludes2: *malignant pancreatic islet cell tumors (C25.4)*
Merkel cell carcinoma (C4A.-)

\+ **C7A.0 Malignant carcinoid tumors**

CC **C7A.00 Malignant carcinoid tumor of unspecified site**
CC Exclusion see Appendix A PDX collection 0346

\+ **C7A.01 Malignant carcinoid tumors of the small intestine**

CC **C7A.010 Malignant carcinoid tumor of the duodenu**
CC Exclusion see Appendix A PDX collection 0347

CC **C7A.011 Malignant carcinoid tumor ofthe jejunum**
CC Exclusion see Appendix A PDX collection 0348

CC **C7A.012 Malignant carcinoid tumor of the ileum**
CC Exclusion see Appendix A PDX collection 0349

CC **C7A.019 Malignant carcinoid tumor of the small intestine, unspecified portion**
CC Exclusion see Appendix A PDX collection 0350

\+ **C7A.02 Malignant carcinoid tumors of the appendix, large intestine, and rectum**

CC **C7A.020 Malignant carcinoid tumor of the appendi**
CC Exclusion see Appendix A PDX collection 0351

CC **C7A.021 Malignant carcinoid tumor of the cecum**
CC Exclusion see Appendix A PDX collection 0352

CC **C7A.022 Malignant carcinoid tumor of the ascendin colon**
CC Exclusion see Appendix A PDX collection 0353

CC **C7A.023 Malignant carcinoid tumor of the transver colon**
CC Exclusion see Appendix A PDX collection 0354

CC **C7A.024 Malignant carcinoid tumor of the descendi colon**
CC Exclusion see Appendix A PDX collection 0355

CC **C7A.025 Malignant carcinoid tumor of the sigmoid colon**
CC Exclusion see Appendix A PDX collection 0356

Lymphatic System

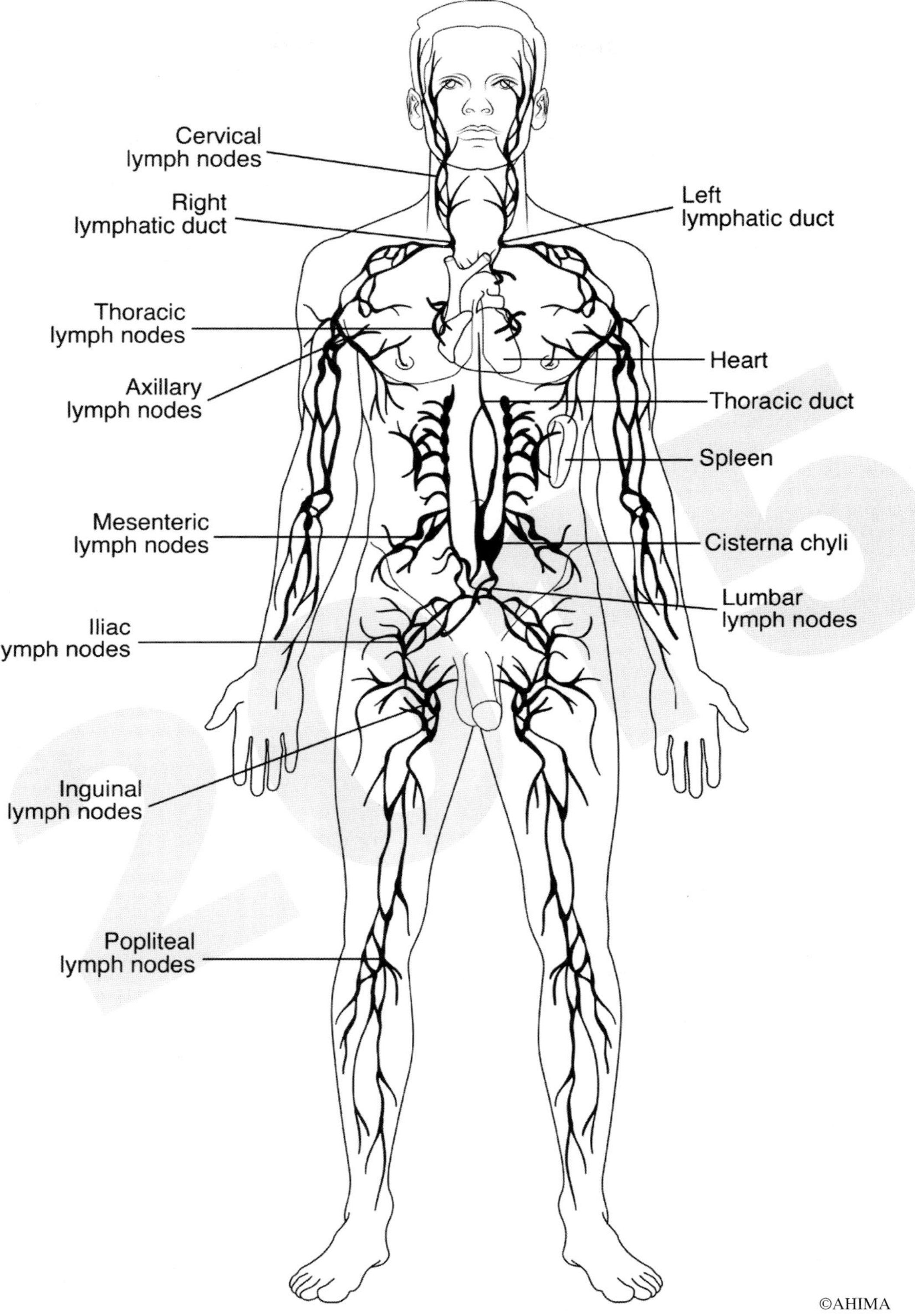
Cervical lymph nodes
Right lymphatic duct
Thoracic lymph nodes
Axillary lymph nodes
Mesenteric lymph nodes
Iliac lymph nodes
Inguinal lymph nodes
Popliteal lymph nodes
Left lymphatic duct
Heart
Thoracic duct
Spleen
Cisterna chyli
Lumbar lymph nodes

CC **C7A.026 Malignant carcinoid tumor of the rectum**
CC Exclusion see Appendix A PDX collection 0357

CC **C7A.029 Malignant carcinoid tumor of the large intestine, unspecified portion**
Malignant carcinoid tumor of the colon NOS
CC Exclusion see Appendix A PDX collection 0358

+ **C7A.09 Malignant carcinoid tumors of other sites**

CC **C7A.090 Malignant carcinoid tumor of the bronchus and lung**
CC Exclusion see Appendix A PDX collection 0359

CC **C7A.091 Malignant carcinoid tumor of the thymus**
CC Exclusion see Appendix A PDX collection 0360

CC **C7A.092 Malignant carcinoid tumor of the stomach**
CC Exclusion see Appendix A PDX collection 0361

CC **C7A.093 Malignant carcinoid tumor of the kidney**
CC Exclusion see Appendix A PDX collection 0362

CC **C7A.094 Malignant carcinoid tumor of the foregut NOS**
CC Exclusion see Appendix A PDX collection 0361

CC **C7A.095 Malignant carcinoid tumor of the midgut NOS**
CC Exclusion see Appendix A PDX collection 0361

CC **C7A.096 Malignant carcinoid tumor of the hindgut NOS**
CC Exclusion see Appendix A PDX collection 0361

CC **C7A.098 Malignant carcinoid tumors of other sites**
CC Exclusion see Appendix A PDX collection 0346

CC **C7A.1 Malignant poorly differentiated neuroendocrine tumors**
Malignant poorly differentiated neuroendocrine tumor NOS
Malignant poorly differentiated neuroendocrine carcinoma, any site
High grade neuroendocrine carcinoma, any site
CC Exclusion see Appendix A PDX collection 0346

CC **C7A.8 Other malignant neuroendocrine tumors**
CC Exclusion see Appendix A PDX collection 0346

Secondary neuroendocrine tumors (C7B)

C7B Secondary neuroendocrine tumors

Use additional code to identify any functional activity

+ **C7B.0 Secondary carcinoid tumors**

C7B.00 Secondary carcinoid tumors, unspecified site

CC **C7B.01 Secondary carcinoid tumors of distant lymph nodes**
CC Exclusion see Appendix A PDX collection 0363

CC **C7B.02 Secondary carcinoid tumors of liver**
CC Exclusion see Appendix A PDX collection 0364

CC **C7B.03 Secondary carcinoid tumors of bone**
CC Exclusion see Appendix A PDX collection 0365

CC **C7B.04 Secondary carcinoid tumors of peritoneum**
Mesentary metastasis of carcinoid tumor
CC Exclusion see Appendix A PDX collection 0366

CC **C7B.09 Secondary carcinoid tumors of other sites**
CC Exclusion see Appendix A PDX collection 0367

C7B.1 Secondary Merkel cell carcinoma
Merkel cell carcinoma nodal presentation
Merkel cell carcinoma visceral metastatic presentation

CC **C7B.8 Other secondary neuroendocrine tumors**
CC Exclusion see Appendix A PDX collection 0367

Malignant neoplasms of ill-defined, other secondary and unspecified sites (C76-C80)

Review coding guidelines C.2.b and C.2.l.2

C76 Malignant neoplasm of other and ill-defined sites

Excludes1: *malignant neoplasm of female genitourinary tract NOS (C57.9)*
malignant neoplasm of male genitourinary tract NOS (C63.9)
malignant neoplasm of lymphoid, hematopoietic and related tissue (C81-C96)
malignant neoplasm of skin (C44.-)
malignant neoplasm of unspecified site NOS (C80.1)

C76.0 Malignant neoplasm of head, face and neck
Malignant neoplasm of cheek NOS
Malignant neoplasm of nose NOS

C76.1 Malignant neoplasm of thorax
Intrathoracic malignant neoplasm NOS
Malignant neoplasm of axilla NOS
Thoracic malignant neoplasm NOS

C76.2 Malignant neoplasm of abdomen

C76.3 Malignant neoplasm of pelvis
Malignant neoplasm of groin NOS
Malignant neoplasm of sites overlapping systems within the pelvis
Rectovaginal (septum) malignant neoplasm
Rectovesical (septum) malignant neoplasm

+ **C76.4 Malignant neoplasm of upper limb**

C76.40 Malignant neoplasm of unspecified upper limb

C76.41 Malignant neoplasm of right upper limb

C76.42 Malignant neoplasm of left upper limb

+ **C76.5 Malignant neoplasm of lower limb**

C76.50 Malignant neoplasm of unspecified lower limb

C76.51 Malignant neoplasm of right lower limb

C76.52 Malignant neoplasm of left lower limb

C76.8 Malignant neoplasm of other specified ill-defined sites
Malignant neoplasm of overlapping ill-defined sites

+ **C77 Secondary and unspecified malignant neoplasm of lymph nodes**

Excludes1: *malignant neoplasm of lymph nodes, specified as primary (C81-C86, C88, C96.-)*
mesentary metastasis of carcinoid tumor (C7B.04)
secondary carcinoid tumors of distant lymph nodes (C7B.0

CC **C77.0 Secondary and unspecified malignant neoplasm of lymph nod of head, face and neck**
Secondary and unspecified malignant neoplasm of supraclavicu lymph nodes
CC Exclusion see Appendix A PDX collection 0303

CC **C77.1 Secondary and unspecified malignant neoplasm of intrathora lymph nodes**
CC Exclusion see Appendix A PDX collection 0303

CC **C77.2 Secondary and unspecified malignant neoplasm of intra-abdominal lymph nodes**
CC Exclusion see Appendix A PDX collection 0303

CC **C77.3 Secondary and unspecified malignant neoplasm of axilla and upper limb lymph nodes**
Secondary and unspecified malignant neoplasm of pectoral lym nodes
CC Exclusion see Appendix A PDX collection 0303

CC **C77.4 Secondary and unspecified malignant neoplasm of inguinal an lower limb lymph nodes**
CC Exclusion see Appendix A PDX collection 0303

CC **C77.5 Secondary and unspecified malignant neoplasm of intrapelvic lymph nodes**
CC Exclusion see Appendix A PDX collection 0303

CC **C77.8 Secondary and unspecified malignant neoplasm of lymph nod of multiple regions**
CC Exclusion see Appendix A PDX collection 0303

CC **C77.9 Secondary and unspecified malignant neoplasm of lymph nod unspecified**
CC Exclusion see Appendix A PDX collection 0303

C78 Secondary malignant neoplasm of respiratory and digestive organs

Excludes1: *lymph node metastases (C77.0)*
secondary carcinoid tumors of liver (C7B.02)
secondary carcinoid tumors of peritoneum (C7B.04)

+ **C78.0 Secondary malignant neoplasm of lung**

CC **C78.00 Secondary malignant neoplasm of unspecified lung**
CC Exclusion see Appendix A PDX collection 0327

CC **C78.01 Secondary malignant neoplasm of right lung**
CC Exclusion see Appendix A PDX collection 0327

CC **C78.02 Secondary malignant neoplasm of left lung**
CC Exclusion see Appendix A PDX collection 0327

CC **C78.1 Secondary malignant neoplasm of mediastinum**
CC Exclusion see Appendix A PDX collection 0328

CC **C78.2 Secondary malignant neoplasm of pleura**
CC Exclusion see Appendix A PDX collection 0329

+ **C78.3 Secondary malignant neoplasm of other and unspecified respiratory organs**

CC **C78.30 Secondary malignant neoplasm of unspecified respiratory organ**
CC Exclusion see Appendix A PDX collection 0330

CC **C78.39 Secondary malignant neoplasm of other respiratory organs**
CC Exclusion see Appendix A PDX collection 0330

CC **C78.4 Secondary malignant neoplasm of small intestine**
CC Exclusion see Appendix A PDX collection 0331

CC **C78.5 Secondary malignant neoplasm of large intestine and rectum**
CC Exclusion see Appendix A PDX collection 0332

CC **C78.6 Secondary malignant neoplasm of retroperitoneum and peritoneum**
CC Exclusion see Appendix A PDX collection 0333

CC **C78.7 Secondary malignant neoplasm of liver and intrahepatic bile duct**
CC Exclusion see Appendix A PDX collection 0334

\+ **C78.8 Secondary malignant neoplasm of other and unspecified digestive organs**

CC **C78.80 Secondary malignant neoplasm of unspecified digestive organ**
CC Exclusion see Appendix A PDX collection 0335

CC **C78.89 Secondary malignant neoplasm of other digestive organs**
CC Exclusion see Appendix A PDX collection 0335

C79 Secondary malignant neoplasm of other and unspecified sites

Excludes1: *lymph node metastases (C77.0)*
secondary carcinoid tumors (C7B.-)
secondary neuroendocrine tumors (C7B.-)

\+ **C79.0 Secondary malignant neoplasm of kidney and renal pelvis**

CC **C79.00 Secondary malignant neoplasm of unspecified kidney and renal pelvis**
CC Exclusion see Appendix A PDX collection 0336

CC **C79.01 Secondary malignant neoplasm of right kidney and renal pelvis**
CC Exclusion see Appendix A PDX collection 0336

CC **C79.02 Secondary malignant neoplasm of left kidney and renal pelvis**
CC Exclusion see Appendix A PDX collection 0336

\+ **C79.1 Secondary malignant neoplasm of bladder and other and unspecified urinary organs**

CC **C79.10 Secondary malignant neoplasm of unspecified urinary organs**
CC Exclusion see Appendix A PDX collection 0336

CC **C79.11 Secondary malignant neoplasm of bladder**
CC Exclusion see Appendix A PDX collection 0336

CC **C79.19 Secondary malignant neoplasm of other urinary organs**
CC Exclusion see Appendix A PDX collection 0336

CC **C79.2 Secondary malignant neoplasm of skin**
Excludes1: *secondary Merkel cell carcinoma (C7B.1)*
CC Exclusion see Appendix A PDX collection 0337

\+ **C79.3 Secondary malignant neoplasm of brain and cerebral meninges**

CC **C79.31 Secondary malignant neoplasm of brain**
CC Exclusion see Appendix A PDX collection 0338

CC **C79.32 Secondary malignant neoplasm of cerebral meninges**
CC Exclusion see Appendix A PDX collection 0339

\+ **C79.4 Secondary malignant neoplasm of other and unspecified parts of nervous system**

CC **C79.40 Secondary malignant neoplasm of unspecified part of nervous system**
CC Exclusion see Appendix A PDX collection 0339

CC **C79.49 Secondary malignant neoplasm of other parts of nervous system**
CC Exclusion see Appendix A PDX collection 0339

\+ **C79.5 Secondary malignant neoplasm of bone and bone marrow**
Excludes1: *secondary carcinoid tumors of bone (C7B.03)*

CC **C79.51 Secondary malignant neoplasm of bone**
CC Exclusion see Appendix A PDX collection 0340

CC **C79.52 Secondary malignant neoplasm of bone marrow**
CC Exclusion see Appendix A PDX collection 0340

\+ **C79.6 Secondary malignant neoplasm of ovary**

CC ♀ **C79.60 Secondary malignant neoplasm of unspecified ovary**
CC Exclusion see Appendix A PDX collection 0341

CC ♀ **C79.61 Secondary malignant neoplasm of right ovary**
CC Exclusion see Appendix A PDX collection 0341

CC ♀ **C79.62 Secondary malignant neoplasm of left ovary**
CC Exclusion see Appendix A PDX collection 0341

\+ **C79.7 Secondary malignant neoplasm of adrenal gland**

CC **C79.70 Secondary malignant neoplasm of unspecified adrenal gland**
CC Exclusion see Appendix A PDX collection 0342

CC **C79.71 Secondary malignant neoplasm of right adrenal gland**
CC Exclusion see Appendix A PDX collection 0342

CC **C79.72 Secondary malignant neoplasm of left adrenal gland**
CC Exclusion see Appendix A PDX collection 0342

\+ **C79.8 Secondary malignant neoplasm of other specified sites**

CC **C79.81 Secondary malignant neoplasm of breast**
CC Exclusion see Appendix A PDX collection 0343

CC **C79.82 Secondary malignant neoplasm of genital organs**
CC Exclusion see Appendix A PDX collection 0344

CC **C79.89 Secondary malignant neoplasm of other specified sites**
CC Exclusion see Appendix A PDX collection 0345

CC **C79.9 Secondary malignant neoplasm of unspecified site**
Metastatic cancer NOS
Metastatic disease NOS
Excludes1: *carcinomatosis NOS (C80.0)*
generalized cancer NOS (C80.0)
malignant (primary) neoplasm of unspecified site (C80.1)
CC Exclusion see Appendix A PDX collection 0345

C80 Malignant neoplasm without specification of site

Excludes1: *malignant carcinoid tumor of unspecified site (C7A.00)*
malignant neoplasm of specified multiple sites- code to each site

CC **C80.0 Disseminated malignant neoplasm, unspecified**
Carcinomatosis NOS
Generalized cancer, unspecified site (primary) (secondary)
Generalized malignancy, unspecified site (primary) (secondary)
CC Exclusion see Appendix A PDX collection 0345
Review coding guideline C.2.j

C80.1 Malignant (primary) neoplasm, unspecified
Cancer NOS
Cancer unspecified site (primary)
Carcinoma unspecified site (primary)
Malignancy unspecified site (primary)
Excludes1: *secondary malignant neoplasm of unspecified site (C79.9)*
Review coding guideline C.2.k

CC **C80.2 Malignant neoplasm associated with transplanted organ**
Code first complication of transplanted organ (T86.-)

Use additional code to identify the specific malignancy
CC Exclusion see Appendix A PDX collection 0345
Review coding guideline C.2.r

Malignant neoplasms of lymphoid, hematopoietic and related tissue (C81-C96)

Excludes2: *Kaposi's sarcoma of lymph nodes (C46.3)*
secondary and unspecified neoplasm of lymph nodes (C77.-)
secondary neoplasm of bone marrow (C79.52)
secondary neoplasm of spleen (C78.89)

C81 Hodgkin lymphoma

Excludes1: *personal history of Hodgkin lymphoma (Z85.71)*

\+ **C81.0 Nodular lymphocyte predominant Hodgkin lymphoma**

CC **C81.00 Nodular lymphocyte predominant Hodgkin lymphoma, unspecified site**
CC Exclusion see Appendix A PDX collection 0368

CC **C81.01 Nodular lymphocyte predominant Hodgkin lymphoma, lymph nodes of head, face, and neck**
CC Exclusion see Appendix A PDX collection 0369

CC **C81.02 Nodular lymphocyte predominant Hodgkin lymphoma, intrathoracic lymph nodes**
CC Exclusion see Appendix A PDX collection 0370

CC **C81.03 Nodular lymphocyte predominant Hodgkin lymphoma, intra-abdominal lymph nodes**
CC Exclusion see Appendix A PDX collection 0371

CC **C81.04 Nodular lymphocyte predominant Hodgkin lymphoma, lymph nodes of axilla and upper limb**
CC Exclusion see Appendix A PDX collection 0372

CC **C81.05 Nodular lymphocyte predominant Hodgkin lymphoma, lymph nodes of inguinal region and lower limb**
CC Exclusion see Appendix A PDX collection 0373

CC **C81.06 Nodular lymphocyte predominant Hodgkin lymphoma, intrapelvic lymph nodes**
CC Exclusion see Appendix A PDX collection 0374

CC **C81.07 Nodular lymphocyte predominant Hodgkin lymphoma, spleen**
CC Exclusion see Appendix A PDX collection 0375

CC **C81.08 Nodular lymphocyte predominant Hodgkin lymphoma, lymph nodes of multiple sites**
CC Exclusion see Appendix A PDX collection 0368

CC **C81.09 Nodular lymphocyte predominant Hodgkin lymphoma, extranodal and solid organ sites**
CC Exclusion see Appendix A PDX collection 0368

\+ **C81.1 Nodular sclerosis classical Hodgkin lymphoma**

CC **C81.10 Nodular sclerosis classical Hodgkin lymphoma, unspecified site**
CC Exclusion see Appendix A PDX collection 0376

CC **C81.11 Nodular sclerosis classical Hodgkin lymphoma, lymph nodes of head, face, and neck**
CC Exclusion see Appendix A PDX collection 0377

CC **C81.12 Nodular sclerosis classical Hodgkin lymphoma, intrathoracic lymph nodes**
CC Exclusion see Appendix A PDX collection 0378

CC **C81.13 Nodular sclerosis classical Hodgkin lymphoma, intra-abdominal lymph nodes**
CC Exclusion see Appendix A PDX collection 0379
CC **C81.14 Nodular sclerosis classical Hodgkin lymphoma, lymph nodes of axilla and upper limb**
CC Exclusion see Appendix A PDX collection 0380
CC **C81.15 Nodular sclerosis classical Hodgkin lymphoma, lymph nodes of inguinal region and lower limb**
CC Exclusion see Appendix A PDX collection 0381
CC **C81.16 Nodular sclerosis classical Hodgkin lymphoma, intrapelvic lymph nodes**
CC Exclusion see Appendix A PDX collection 0382
CC **C81.17 Nodular sclerosis classical Hodgkin lymphoma, spleen**
CC Exclusion see Appendix A PDX collection 0383
CC **C81.18 Nodular sclerosis classical Hodgkin lymphoma, lymph nodes of multiple sites**
CC Exclusion see Appendix A PDX collection 0376
CC **C81.19 Nodular sclerosis classical Hodgkin lymphoma, extranodal and solid organ sites**
CC Exclusion see Appendix A PDX collection 0376

\+ **C81.2 Mixed cellularity classical Hodgkin lymphoma**
CC **C81.20 Mixed cellularity classical Hodgkin lymphoma, unspecified site**
CC Exclusion see Appendix A PDX collection 0384
CC **C81.21 Mixed cellularity classical Hodgkin lymphoma, lymph nodes of head, face, and neck**
CC Exclusion see Appendix A PDX collection 0385
CC **C81.22 Mixed cellularity classical Hodgkin lymphoma, intrathoracic lymph nodes**
CC Exclusion see Appendix A PDX collection 0386
CC **C81.23 Mixed cellularity classical Hodgkin lymphoma, intra-abdominal lymph nodes**
CC Exclusion see Appendix A PDX collection 0387
CC **C81.24 Mixed cellularity classical Hodgkin lymphoma, lymph nodes of axilla and upper limb**
CC Exclusion see Appendix A PDX collection 0388
CC **C81.25 Mixed cellularity classical Hodgkin lymphoma, lymph nodes of inguinal region and lower limb**
CC Exclusion see Appendix A PDX collection 0389
CC **C81.26 Mixed cellularity classical Hodgkin lymphoma, intrapelvic lymph nodes**
CC Exclusion see Appendix A PDX collection 0390
CC **C81.27 Mixed cellularity classical Hodgkin lymphoma, spleen**
CC Exclusion see Appendix A PDX collection 0391
CC **C81.28 Mixed cellularity classical Hodgkin lymphoma, lymph nodes of multiple sites**
CC Exclusion see Appendix A PDX collection 0384
CC **C81.29 Mixed cellularity classical Hodgkin lymphoma, extranodal and solid organ sites**
CC Exclusion see Appendix A PDX collection 0384

\+ **C81.3 Lymphocyte depleted classical Hodgkin lymphoma**
CC **C81.30 Lymphocyte depleted classical Hodgkin lymphoma, unspecified site**
CC Exclusion see Appendix A PDX collection 0392
CC **C81.31 Lymphocyte depleted classical Hodgkin lymphoma, lymph nodes of head, face, and neck**
CC Exclusion see Appendix A PDX collection 0393
CC **C81.32 Lymphocyte depleted classical Hodgkin lymphoma, intrathoracic lymph nodes**
CC Exclusion see Appendix A PDX collection 0394
CC **C81.33 Lymphocyte depleted classical Hodgkin lymphoma, intra-abdominal lymph nodes**
CC Exclusion see Appendix A PDX collection 0395
CC **C81.34 Lymphocyte depleted classical Hodgkin lymphoma, lymph nodes of axilla and upper limb**
CC Exclusion see Appendix A PDX collection 0396
CC **C81.35 Lymphocyte depleted classical Hodgkin lymphoma, lymph nodes of inguinal region and lower limb**
CC Exclusion see Appendix A PDX collection 0397
CC **C81.36 Lymphocyte depleted classical Hodgkin lymphoma, intrapelvic lymph nodes**
CC Exclusion see Appendix A PDX collection 0398
CC **C81.37 Lymphocyte depleted classical Hodgkin lymphoma, spleen**
CC Exclusion see Appendix A PDX collection 0399
CC **C81.38 Lymphocyte depleted classical Hodgkin lymphoma, lymph nodes of multiple sites**
CC Exclusion see Appendix A PDX collection 0400
CC **C81.39 Lymphocyte depleted classical Hodgkin lymphoma, extranodal and solid organ sites**
CC Exclusion see Appendix A PDX collection 0392

\+ **C81.4 Lymphocyte-rich classical Hodgkin lymphoma**
Excludes1: *nodular lymphocyte predominant Hodgkin lymphoma (C81.0-)*
CC **C81.40 Lymphocyte-rich classical Hodgkin lymphoma, unspecified site**
CC Exclusion see Appendix A PDX collection 0368
CC **C81.41 Lymphocyte-rich classical Hodgkin lymphoma, lym[ph] nodes of head, face, and neck**
CC Exclusion see Appendix A PDX collection 0369
CC **C81.42 Lymphocyte-rich classical Hodgkin lymphoma, intrathoracic lymph nodes**
CC Exclusion see Appendix A PDX collection 0370
CC **C81.43 Lymphocyte-rich classical Hodgkin lymphoma, int[ra-]abdominal lymph nodes**
CC Exclusion see Appendix A PDX collection 0371
CC **C81.44 Lymphocyte-rich classical Hodgkin lymphoma, lym[ph] nodes of axilla and upper limb**
CC Exclusion see Appendix A PDX collection 0372
CC **C81.45 Lymphocyte-rich classical Hodgkin lymphoma, lym[ph] nodes of inguinal region and lower limb**
CC Exclusion see Appendix A PDX collection 0373
CC **C81.46 Lymphocyte-rich classical Hodgkin lymphoma, intrapelvic lymph nodes**
CC Exclusion see Appendix A PDX collection 0374
CC **C81.47 Lymphocyte-rich classical Hodgkin lymphoma, spl[een]**
CC Exclusion see Appendix A PDX collection 0375
CC **C81.48 Lymphocyte-rich classical Hodgkin lymphoma, lym[ph] nodes of multiple sites**
CC Exclusion see Appendix A PDX collection 0368
CC **C81.49 Lymphocyte-rich classical Hodgkin lymphoma, extranodal and solid organ sites**
CC Exclusion see Appendix A PDX collection 0368

\+ **C81.7 Other classical Hodgkin lymphoma**
Classical Hodgkin lymphoma NOS
CC **C81.70 Other classical Hodgkin lymphoma, unspecified si[te]**
CC Exclusion see Appendix A PDX collection 0401
CC **C81.71 Other classical Hodgkin lymphoma, lymph nodes o[f] head, face, and neck**
CC Exclusion see Appendix A PDX collection 0402
CC **C81.72 Other classical Hodgkin lymphoma, intrathoracic lymph nodes**
CC Exclusion see Appendix A PDX collection 0403
CC **C81.73 Other classical Hodgkin lymphoma, intra-abdomin[al] lymph nodes**
CC Exclusion see Appendix A PDX collection 0404
CC **C81.74 Other classical Hodgkin lymphoma, lymph nodes o[f] axilla and upper limb**
CC Exclusion see Appendix A PDX collection 0405
CC **C81.75 Other classical Hodgkin lymphoma, lymph nodes o[f] inguinal region and lower limb**
CC Exclusion see Appendix A PDX collection 0406
CC **C81.76 Other classical Hodgkin lymphoma, intrapelvic lym[ph] nodes**
CC Exclusion see Appendix A PDX collection 0407
CC **C81.77 Other classical Hodgkin lymphoma, spleen**
CC Exclusion see Appendix A PDX collection 0408
CC **C81.78 Other classical Hodgkin lymphoma, lymph nodes o[f] multiple sites**
CC Exclusion see Appendix A PDX collection 0401
CC **C81.79 Other classical Hodgkin lymphoma, extranodal an[d] solid organ sites**
CC Exclusion see Appendix A PDX collection 0401

\+ **C81.9 Hodgkin lymphoma, unspecified**
CC **C81.90 Hodgkin lymphoma, unspecified, unspecified site**
CC Exclusion see Appendix A PDX collection 0409
CC **C81.91 Hodgkin lymphoma, unspecified, lymph nodes of head, face, and neck**
CC Exclusion see Appendix A PDX collection 0410
CC **C81.92 Hodgkin lymphoma, unspecified, intrathoracic lym[ph] nodes**
CC Exclusion see Appendix A PDX collection 0411
CC **C81.93 Hodgkin lymphoma, unspecified, intra-abdominal lymph nodes**
CC Exclusion see Appendix A PDX collection 0412
CC **C81.94 Hodgkin lymphoma, unspecified, lymph nodes of axilla and upper limb**
CC Exclusion see Appendix A PDX collection 0413
CC **C81.95 Hodgkin lymphoma, unspecified, lymph nodes of inguinal region and lower limb**
CC Exclusion see Appendix A PDX collection 0414
CC **C81.96 Hodgkin lymphoma, unspecified, intrapelvic lymph nodes**
CC Exclusion see Appendix A PDX collection 0415
CC **C81.97 Hodgkin lymphoma, unspecified, spleen**
CC Exclusion see Appendix A PDX collection 0416

CC **C81.98 Hodgkin lymphoma, unspecified, lymph nodes of multiple sites**
CC Exclusion see Appendix A PDX collection 0409

CC **C81.99 Hodgkin lymphoma, unspecified, extranodal and solid organ sites**
No CC Exclusions

C82 Follicular lymphoma

Includes: follicular lymphoma with or without diffuse areas
Excludes1: *mature T/NK-cell lymphomas (C84.-)*
personal history of non-Hodgkin lymphoma (Z85.72)

\+ **C82.0 Follicular lymphoma grade I**

CC **C82.00 Follicular lymphoma grade I, unspecified site**
CC Exclusion see Appendix A PDX collection 0417

CC **C82.01 Follicular lymphoma grade I, lymph nodes of head, face, and neck**
CC Exclusion see Appendix A PDX collection 0418

CC **C82.02 Follicular lymphoma grade I, intrathoracic lymph nodes**
CC Exclusion see Appendix A PDX collection 0419

CC **C82.03 Follicular lymphoma grade I, intra-abdominal lymph nodes**
CC Exclusion see Appendix A PDX collection 0420

CC **C82.04 Follicular lymphoma grade I, lymph nodes of axilla and upper limb**
CC Exclusion see Appendix A PDX collection 0421

CC **C82.05 Follicular lymphoma grade I, lymph nodes of inguinal region and lower limb**
CC Exclusion see Appendix A PDX collection 0422

CC **C82.06 Follicular lymphoma grade I, intrapelvic lymph nodes**
CC Exclusion see Appendix A PDX collection 0423

CC **C82.07 Follicular lymphoma grade I, spleen**
CC Exclusion see Appendix A PDX collection 0424

CC **C82.08 Follicular lymphoma grade I, lymph nodes of multiple sites**
CC Exclusion see Appendix A PDX collection 0425

CC **C82.09 Follicular lymphoma grade I, extranodal and solid organ sites**
CC Exclusion see Appendix A PDX collection 0417

\+ **C82.1 Follicular lymphoma grade II**

CC **C82.10 Follicular lymphoma grade II, unspecified site**
CC Exclusion see Appendix A PDX collection 0417

CC **C82.11 Follicular lymphoma grade II, lymph nodes of head, face, and neck**
CC Exclusion see Appendix A PDX collection 0418

CC **C82.12 Follicular lymphoma grade II, intrathoracic lymph nodes**
CC Exclusion see Appendix A PDX collection 0419

CC **C82.13 Follicular lymphoma grade II, intra-abdominal lymph nodes**
CC Exclusion see Appendix A PDX collection 0420

CC **C82.14 Follicular lymphoma grade II, lymph nodes of axilla and upper limb**
CC Exclusion see Appendix A PDX collection 0421

CC **C82.15 Follicular lymphoma grade II, lymph nodes of inguinal region and lower limb**
CC Exclusion see Appendix A PDX collection 0422

CC **C82.16 Follicular lymphoma grade II, intrapelvic lymph nodes**
CC Exclusion see Appendix A PDX collection 0423

CC **C82.17 Follicular lymphoma grade II, spleen**
CC Exclusion see Appendix A PDX collection 0424

CC **C82.18 Follicular lymphoma grade II, lymph nodes of multiple sites**
CC Exclusion see Appendix A PDX collection 0425

CC **C82.19 Follicular lymphoma grade II, extranodal and solid organ sites**
CC Exclusion see Appendix A PDX collection 0417

\+ **C82.2 Follicular lymphoma grade III, unspecified**

CC **C82.20 Follicular lymphoma grade III, unspecified, unspecified site**
CC Exclusion see Appendix A PDX collection 0417

CC **C82.21 Follicular lymphoma grade III, unspecified, lymph nodes of head, face, and neck**
CC Exclusion see Appendix A PDX collection 0418

CC **C82.22 Follicular lymphoma grade III, unspecified, intrathoracic lymph nodes**
CC Exclusion see Appendix A PDX collection 0419

CC **C82.23 Follicular lymphoma grade III, unspecified, intra-abdominal lymph nodes**
CC Exclusion see Appendix A PDX collection 0420

CC **C82.24 Follicular lymphoma grade III, unspecified, lymph nodes of axilla and upper limb**
CC Exclusion see Appendix A PDX collection 0421

CC **C82.25 Follicular lymphoma grade III, unspecified, lymph nodes of inguinal region and lower limb**
CC Exclusion see Appendix A PDX collection 0422

CC **C82.26 Follicular lymphoma grade III, unspecified, intrapelvic lymph nodes**
CC Exclusion see Appendix A PDX collection 0423

CC **C82.27 Follicular lymphoma grade III, unspecified, spleen**
CC Exclusion see Appendix A PDX collection 0424

CC **C82.28 Follicular lymphoma grade III, unspecified, lymph nodes of multiple sites**
CC Exclusion see Appendix A PDX collection 0425

CC **C82.29 Follicular lymphoma grade III, unspecified, extranodal and solid organ sites**
CC Exclusion see Appendix A PDX collection 0417

\+ **C82.3 Follicular lymphoma grade IIIa**

CC **C82.30 Follicular lymphoma grade IIIa, unspecified site**
CC Exclusion see Appendix A PDX collection 0417

CC **C82.31 Follicular lymphoma grade IIIa, lymph nodes of head, face, and neck**
CC Exclusion see Appendix A PDX collection 0418

CC **C82.32 Follicular lymphoma grade IIIa, intrathoracic lymph nodes**
CC Exclusion see Appendix A PDX collection 0419

CC **C82.33 Follicular lymphoma grade IIIa, intra-abdominal lymph nodes**
CC Exclusion see Appendix A PDX collection 0420

CC **C82.34 Follicular lymphoma grade IIIa, lymph nodes of axilla and upper limb**
CC Exclusion see Appendix A PDX collection 0421

CC **C82.35 Follicular lymphoma grade IIIa, lymph nodes of inguinal region and lower limb**
CC Exclusion see Appendix A PDX collection 0422

CC **C82.36 Follicular lymphoma grade IIIa, intrapelvic lymph nodes**
CC Exclusion see Appendix A PDX collection 0423

CC **C82.37 Follicular lymphoma grade IIIa, spleen**
CC Exclusion see Appendix A PDX collection 0424

CC **C82.38 Follicular lymphoma grade IIIa, lymph nodes of multiple sites**
CC Exclusion see Appendix A PDX collection 0425

CC **C82.39 Follicular lymphoma grade IIIa, extranodal and solid organ sites**
CC Exclusion see Appendix A PDX collection 0417

\+ **C82.4 Follicular lymphoma grade IIIb**

CC **C82.40 Follicular lymphoma grade IIIb, unspecified site**
CC Exclusion see Appendix A PDX collection 0417

CC **C82.41 Follicular lymphoma grade IIIb, lymph nodes of head, face, and neck**
CC Exclusion see Appendix A PDX collection 0418

CC **C82.42 Follicular lymphoma grade IIIb, intrathoracic lymph nodes**
CC Exclusion see Appendix A PDX collection 0419

CC **C82.43 Follicular lymphoma grade IIIb, intra-abdominal lymph nodes**
CC Exclusion see Appendix A PDX collection 0420

CC **C82.44 Follicular lymphoma grade IIIb, lymph nodes of axilla and upper limb**
CC Exclusion see Appendix A PDX collection 0421

CC **C82.45 Follicular lymphoma grade IIIb, lymph nodes of inguinal region and lower limb**
CC Exclusion see Appendix A PDX collection 0422

CC **C82.46 Follicular lymphoma grade IIIb, intrapelvic lymph nodes**
CC Exclusion see Appendix A PDX collection 0423

CC **C82.47 Follicular lymphoma grade IIIb, spleen**
CC Exclusion see Appendix A PDX collection 0424

CC **C82.48 Follicular lymphoma grade IIIb, lymph nodes of multiple sites**
CC Exclusion see Appendix A PDX collection 0425

CC **C82.49 Follicular lymphoma grade IIIb, extranodal and solid organ sites**
CC Exclusion see Appendix A PDX collection 0417

\+ **C82.5 Diffuse follicle center lymphoma**

CC **C82.50 Diffuse follicle center lymphoma, unspecified site**
CC Exclusion see Appendix A PDX collection 0426

CC **C82.51 Diffuse follicle center lymphoma, lymph nodes of head, face, and neck**
CC Exclusion see Appendix A PDX collection 0427

CC **C82.52 Diffuse follicle center lymphoma, intrathoracic lymph nodes**
CC Exclusion see Appendix A PDX collection 0428

CC **C82.53 Diffuse follicle center lymphoma, intra-abdominal lymph nodes**
CC Exclusion see Appendix A PDX collection 0429

CC **C82.54 Diffuse follicle center lymphoma, lymph nodes of axilla and upper limb**
CC Exclusion see Appendix A PDX collection 0430

CC **C82.55 Diffuse follicle center lymphoma, lymph nodes of inguinal region and lower limb**
CC Exclusion see Appendix A PDX collection 0431

CC **C82.56 Diffuse follicle center lymphoma, intrapelvic lymph nodes**
CC Exclusion see Appendix A PDX collection 0432

CC **C82.57 Diffuse follicle center lymphoma, spleen**
CC Exclusion see Appendix A PDX collection 0433

CC **C82.58 Diffuse follicle center lymphoma, lymph nodes of multiple sites**
CC Exclusion see Appendix A PDX collection 0434

CC **C82.59 Diffuse follicle center lymphoma, extranodal and solid organ sites**
CC Exclusion see Appendix A PDX collection 0426

\+ **C82.6** Cutaneous follicle center lymphoma

CC **C82.60 Cutaneous follicle center lymphoma, unspecified site**
CC Exclusion see Appendix A PDX collection 0417

CC **C82.61 Cutaneous follicle center lymphoma, lymph nodes of head, face, and neck**
CC Exclusion see Appendix A PDX collection 0418

CC **C82.62 Cutaneous follicle center lymphoma, intrathoracic lymph nodes**
CC Exclusion see Appendix A PDX collection 0419

CC **C82.63 Cutaneous follicle center lymphoma, intra-abdominal lymph nodes**
CC Exclusion see Appendix A PDX collection 0420

CC **C82.64 Cutaneous follicle center lymphoma, lymph nodes of axilla and upper limb**
CC Exclusion see Appendix A PDX collection 0421

CC **C82.65 Cutaneous follicle center lymphoma, lymph nodes of inguinal region and lower limb**
CC Exclusion see Appendix A PDX collection 0422

CC **C82.66 Cutaneous follicle center lymphoma, intrapelvic lymph nodes**
CC Exclusion see Appendix A PDX collection 0423

CC **C82.67 Cutaneous follicle center lymphoma, spleen**
CC Exclusion see Appendix A PDX collection 0424

CC **C82.68 Cutaneous follicle center lymphoma, lymph nodes of multiple sites**
CC Exclusion see Appendix A PDX collection 0425

CC **C82.69 Cutaneous follicle center lymphoma, extranodal and solid organ sites**
CC Exclusion see Appendix A PDX collection 0417

\+ **C82.8** Other types of follicular lymphoma

CC **C82.80 Other types of follicular lymphoma, unspecified site**
CC Exclusion see Appendix A PDX collection 0417

CC **C82.81 Other types of follicular lymphoma, lymph nodes of head, face, and neck**
CC Exclusion see Appendix A PDX collection 0418

CC **C82.82 Other types of follicular lymphoma, intrathoracic lymph nodes**
CC Exclusion see Appendix A PDX collection 0419

CC **C82.83 Other types of follicular lymphoma, intra-abdominal lymph nodes**
CC Exclusion see Appendix A PDX collection 0420

CC **C82.84 Other types of follicular lymphoma, lymph nodes of axilla and upper limb**
CC Exclusion see Appendix A PDX collection 0421

CC **C82.85 Other types of follicular lymphoma, lymph nodes of inguinal region and lower limb**
CC Exclusion see Appendix A PDX collection 0422

CC **C82.86 Other types of follicular lymphoma, intrapelvic lymph nodes**
CC Exclusion see Appendix A PDX collection 0423

CC **C82.87 Other types of follicular lymphoma, spleen**
CC Exclusion see Appendix A PDX collection 0424

CC **C82.88 Other types of follicular lymphoma, lymph nodes of multiple sites**
CC Exclusion see Appendix A PDX collection 0425

CC **C82.89 Other types of follicular lymphoma, extranodal and solid organ sites**
CC Exclusion see Appendix A PDX collection 0417

\+ **C82.9** Follicular lymphoma, unspecified

CC **C82.90 Follicular lymphoma, unspecified, unspecified site**
CC Exclusion see Appendix A PDX collection 0417

CC **C82.91 Follicular lymphoma, unspecified, lymph nodes of head, face, and neck**
CC Exclusion see Appendix A PDX collection 0418

CC **C82.92 Follicular lymphoma, unspecified, intrathoracic lymph nodes**
CC Exclusion see Appendix A PDX collection 0419

CC **C82.93 Follicular lymphoma, unspecified, intra-abdominal lymph nodes**
CC Exclusion see Appendix A PDX collection 0420

CC **C82.94 Follicular lymphoma, unspecified, lymph nodes of axilla and upper limb**
CC Exclusion see Appendix A PDX collection 0421

CC **C82.95 Follicular lymphoma, unspecified, lymph nodes of inguinal region and lower limb**
CC Exclusion see Appendix A PDX collection 0422

CC **C82.96 Follicular lymphoma, unspecified, intrapelvic lymp nodes**
CC Exclusion see Appendix A PDX collection 0423

CC **C82.97 Follicular lymphoma, unspecified, spleen**
CC Exclusion see Appendix A PDX collection 0424

CC **C82.98 Follicular lymphoma, unspecified, lymph nodes of multiple sites**
CC Exclusion see Appendix A PDX collection 0425

CC **C82.99 Follicular lymphoma, unspecified, extranodal and solid organ sites**
CC Exclusion see Appendix A PDX collection 0417

C83 Non-follicular lymphoma

Excludes1: *personal history of non-Hodgkin lymphoma (Z85.72)*

\+ **C83.0 Small cell B-cell lymphoma**
Lymphoplasmacytic lymphoma
Nodal marginal zone lymphoma
Non-leukemic variant of B-CLL
Splenic marginal zone lymphoma
Excludes1: *chronic lymphocytic leukemia (C91.1)*
mature T/NK-cell lymphomas (C84.-)
Waldenström macroglobulinemia (C88.0)

CC **C83.00 Small cell B-cell lymphoma, unspecified site**
CC Exclusion see Appendix A PDX collection 0435

CC **C83.01 Small cell B-cell lymphoma, lymph nodes of head, face, and neck**
CC Exclusion see Appendix A PDX collection 0436

CC **C83.02 Small cell B-cell lymphoma, intrathoracic lymph nodes**
CC Exclusion see Appendix A PDX collection 0437

CC **C83.03 Small cell B-cell lymphoma, intra-abdominal lymph nodes**
CC Exclusion see Appendix A PDX collection 0438

CC **C83.04 Small cell B-cell lymphoma, lymph nodes of axilla a upper limb**
CC Exclusion see Appendix A PDX collection 0439

CC **C83.05 Small cell B-cell lymphoma, lymph nodes of inguina region and lower limb**
CC Exclusion see Appendix A PDX collection 0440

CC **C83.06 Small cell B-cell lymphoma, intrapelvic lymph node**
CC Exclusion see Appendix A PDX collection 0441

CC **C83.07 Small cell B-cell lymphoma, spleen**
CC Exclusion see Appendix A PDX collection 0442

CC **C83.08 Small cell B-cell lymphoma, lymph nodes of multipl sites**
CC Exclusion see Appendix A PDX collection 0435

CC **C83.09 Small cell B-cell lymphoma, extranodal and solid organ sites**
CC Exclusion see Appendix A PDX collection 0435

\+ **C83.1 Mantle cell lymphoma**
Centrocytic lymphoma
Malignant lymphomatous polyposis

CC **C83.10 Mantle cell lymphoma, unspecified site**
CC Exclusion see Appendix A PDX collection 0426

CC **C83.11 Mantle cell lymphoma, lymph nodes of head, face, a neck**
CC Exclusion see Appendix A PDX collection 0427

CC **C83.12 Mantle cell lymphoma, intrathoracic lymph nodes**
CC Exclusion see Appendix A PDX collection 0428

CC **C83.13 Mantle cell lymphoma, intra-abdominal lymph node**
CC Exclusion see Appendix A PDX collection 0429

CC **C83.14 Mantle cell lymphoma, lymph nodes of axilla and upper limb**
CC Exclusion see Appendix A PDX collection 0430

CC **C83.15 Mantle cell lymphoma, lymph nodes of inguinal regi and lower limb**
CC Exclusion see Appendix A PDX collection 0431

CC **C83.16 Mantle cell lymphoma, intrapelvic lymph nodes**
CC Exclusion see Appendix A PDX collection 0432

CC **C83.17 Mantle cell lymphoma, spleen**
CC Exclusion see Appendix A PDX collection 0433

CC **C83.18 Mantle cell lymphoma, lymph nodes of multiple sites**
CC Exclusion see Appendix A PDX collection 0434

CC **C83.19 Mantle cell lymphoma, extranodal and solid organ sites**
CC Exclusion see Appendix A PDX collection 0426

\+ **C83.3 Diffuse large B-cell lymphoma**
Anaplastic diffuse large B-cell lymphoma
CD30-positive diffuse large B-cell lymphoma
Centroblastic diffuse large B-cell lymphoma
Diffuse large B-cell lymphoma, subtype not specified
Immunoblastic diffuse large B-cell lymphoma
Plasmablastic diffuse large B-cell lymphoma
Diffuse large B-cell lymphoma, subtype not specified
T-cell rich diffuse large B-cell lymphoma
Excludes1: *mediastinal (thymic) large B-cell lymphoma (C85.2-)*
mature T/NK-cell lymphomas (C84.-)

CC **C83.30 Diffuse large B-cell lymphoma, unspecified site**
CC Exclusion see Appendix A PDX collection 0443

CC **C83.31 Diffuse large B-cell lymphoma, lymph nodes of head, face, and neck**
CC Exclusion see Appendix A PDX collection 0444

CC **C83.32 Diffuse large B-cell lymphoma, intrathoracic lymph nodes**
CC Exclusion see Appendix A PDX collection 0445

CC **C83.33 Diffuse large B-cell lymphoma, intra-abdominal lymph nodes**
CC Exclusion see Appendix A PDX collection 0446

CC **C83.34 Diffuse large B-cell lymphoma, lymph nodes of axilla and upper limb**
CC Exclusion see Appendix A PDX collection 0447

CC **C83.35 Diffuse large B-cell lymphoma, lymph nodes of inguinal region and lower limb**
CC Exclusion see Appendix A PDX collection 0448

CC **C83.36 Diffuse large B-cell lymphoma, intrapelvic lymph nodes**
CC Exclusion see Appendix A PDX collection 0449

CC **C83.37 Diffuse large B-cell lymphoma, spleen**
CC Exclusion see Appendix A PDX collection 0450

CC **C83.38 Diffuse large B-cell lymphoma, lymph nodes of multiple sites**
CC Exclusion see Appendix A PDX collection 0443

CC **C83.39 Diffuse large B-cell lymphoma, extranodal and solid organ sites**
CC Exclusion see Appendix A PDX collection 0443

\+ **C83.5 Lymphoblastic (diffuse) lymphoma**
B-precursor lymphoma
Lymphoblastic B-cell lymphoma
Lymphoblastic lymphoma NOS
Lymphoblastic T-cell lymphoma
T-precursor lymphoma

CC **C83.50 Lymphoblastic (diffuse) lymphoma, unspecified site**
CC Exclusion see Appendix A PDX collection 0451

CC **C83.51 Lymphoblastic (diffuse) lymphoma, lymph nodes of head, face, and neck**
CC Exclusion see Appendix A PDX collection 0452

CC **C83.52 Lymphoblastic (diffuse) lymphoma, intrathoracic lymph nodes**
CC Exclusion see Appendix A PDX collection 0453

CC **C83.53 Lymphoblastic (diffuse) lymphoma, intra-abdominal lymph nodes**
CC Exclusion see Appendix A PDX collection 0454

CC **C83.54 Lymphoblastic (diffuse) lymphoma, lymph nodes of axilla and upper limb**
CC Exclusion see Appendix A PDX collection 0455

CC **C83.55 Lymphoblastic (diffuse) lymphoma, lymph nodes of inguinal region and lower limb**
CC Exclusion see Appendix A PDX collection 0456

CC **C83.56 Lymphoblastic (diffuse) lymphoma, intrapelvic lymph nodes**
CC Exclusion see Appendix A PDX collection 0457

CC **C83.57 Lymphoblastic (diffuse) lymphoma, spleen**
CC Exclusion see Appendix A PDX collection 0458

CC **C83.58 Lymphoblastic (diffuse) lymphoma, lymph nodes of multiple sites**
CC Exclusion see Appendix A PDX collection 0451

CC **C83.59 Lymphoblastic (diffuse) lymphoma, extranodal and solid organ sites**
CC Exclusion see Appendix A PDX collection 0451

\+ **C83.7 Burkitt lymphoma**
Atypical Burkitt lymphoma
Burkitt-like lymphoma
Excludes1: *mature B-cell leukemia Burkitt type (C91.A-)*

CC **C83.70 Burkitt lymphoma, unspecified site**
CC Exclusion see Appendix A PDX collection 0459

CC **C83.71 Burkitt lymphoma, lymph nodes of head, face, and neck**
CC Exclusion see Appendix A PDX collection 0460

CC **C83.72 Burkitt lymphoma, intrathoracic lymph nodes**
CC Exclusion see Appendix A PDX collection 0461

CC **C83.73 Burkitt lymphoma, intra-abdominal lymph nodes**
CC Exclusion see Appendix A PDX collection 0462

CC **C83.74 Burkitt lymphoma, lymph nodes of axilla and upper limb**
CC Exclusion see Appendix A PDX collection 0463

CC **C83.75 Burkitt lymphoma, lymph nodes of inguinal region and lower limb**
CC Exclusion see Appendix A PDX collection 0464

CC **C83.76 Burkitt lymphoma, intrapelvic lymph nodes**
CC Exclusion see Appendix A PDX collection 0465

CC **C83.77 Burkitt lymphoma, spleen**
CC Exclusion see Appendix A PDX collection 0466

CC **C83.78 Burkitt lymphoma, lymph nodes of multiple sites**
CC Exclusion see Appendix A PDX collection 0459

CC **C83.79 Burkitt lymphoma, extranodal and solid organ sites**
CC Exclusion see Appendix A PDX collection 0459

\+ **C83.8 Other non-follicular lymphoma**
Intravascular large B-cell lymphoma
Lymphoid granulomatosis
Primary effusion B-cell lymphoma
Excludes1: *mediastinal (thymic) large B-cell lymphoma (C85.2-)*
T-cell rich B-cell lymphoma (C83.3-)

CC **C83.80 Other non-follicular lymphoma, unspecified site**
CC Exclusion see Appendix A PDX collection 0435

CC **C83.81 Other non-follicular lymphoma, lymph nodes of head, face, and neck**
CC Exclusion see Appendix A PDX collection 0436

CC **C83.82 Other non-follicular lymphoma, intrathoracic lymph nodes**
CC Exclusion see Appendix A PDX collection 0437

CC **C83.83 Other non-follicular lymphoma, intra-abdominal lymph nodes**
CC Exclusion see Appendix A PDX collection 0438

CC **C83.84 Other non-follicular lymphoma, lymph nodes of axilla and upper limb**
CC Exclusion see Appendix A PDX collection 0439

CC **C83.85 Other non-follicular lymphoma, lymph nodes of inguinal region and lower limb**
CC Exclusion see Appendix A PDX collection 0440

CC **C83.86 Other non-follicular lymphoma, intrapelvic lymph nodes**
CC Exclusion see Appendix A PDX collection 0441

CC **C83.87 Other non-follicular lymphoma, spleen**
CC Exclusion see Appendix A PDX collection 0442

CC **C83.88 Other non-follicular lymphoma, lymph nodes of multiple sites**
CC Exclusion see Appendix A PDX collection 0435

CC **C83.89 Other non-follicular lymphoma, extranodal and solid organ sites**
CC Exclusion see Appendix A PDX collection 0435

\+ **C83.9 Non-follicular (diffuse) lymphoma, unspecified**

CC **C83.90 Non-follicular (diffuse) lymphoma, unspecified, unspecified site**
CC Exclusion see Appendix A PDX collection 0435

CC **C83.91 Non-follicular (diffuse) lymphoma, unspecified, lymph nodes of head, face, and neck**
CC Exclusion see Appendix A PDX collection 0436

CC **C83.92 Non-follicular (diffuse) lymphoma, unspecified, intrathoracic lymph nodes**
CC Exclusion see Appendix A PDX collection 0437

CC **C83.93 Non-follicular (diffuse) lymphoma, unspecified, intra-abdominal lymph nodes**
CC Exclusion see Appendix A PDX collection 0438

CC **C83.94 Non-follicular (diffuse) lymphoma, unspecified, lymph nodes of axilla and upper limb**
CC Exclusion see Appendix A PDX collection 0439

CC **C83.95 Non-follicular (diffuse) lymphoma, unspecified, lymph nodes of inguinal region and lower limb**
CC Exclusion see Appendix A PDX collection 0440

CC **C83.96 Non-follicular (diffuse) lymphoma, unspecified, intrapelvic lymph nodes**
CC Exclusion see Appendix A PDX collection 0441

CC **C83.97 Non-follicular (diffuse) lymphoma, unspecified, spleen**
CC Exclusion see Appendix A PDX collection 0442

CC **C83.98 Non-follicular (diffuse) lymphoma, unspecified, lymph nodes of multiple sites**
CC Exclusion see Appendix A PDX collection 0435

CC **C83.99 Non-follicular (diffuse) lymphoma, unspecified, extranodal and solid organ sites**
CC Exclusion see Appendix A PDX collection 0435

C84 Mature T/NK-cell lymphomas

Excludes1: *personal history of non-Hodgkin lymphoma (Z85.72)*

\+ **C84.0 Mycosis fungoides**

Excludes1: *peripheral T-cell lymphoma, not classified (C84.4-)*

CC **C84.00 Mycosis fungoides, unspecified site**
CC Exclusion see Appendix A PDX collection 0467

CC **C84.01 Mycosis fungoides, lymph nodes of head, face, and neck**
CC Exclusion see Appendix A PDX collection 0468

CC **C84.02 Mycosis fungoides, intrathoracic lymph nodes**
CC Exclusion see Appendix A PDX collection 0469

CC **C84.03 Mycosis fungoides, intra-abdominal lymph nodes**
CC Exclusion see Appendix A PDX collection 0470

CC **C84.04 Mycosis fungoides, lymph nodes of axilla and upper limb**
CC Exclusion see Appendix A PDX collection 0471

CC **C84.05 Mycosis fungoides, lymph nodes of inguinal region and lower limb**
CC Exclusion see Appendix A PDX collection 0472

CC **C84.06 Mycosis fungoides, intrapelvic lymph nodes**
CC Exclusion see Appendix A PDX collection 0473

CC **C84.07 Mycosis fungoides, spleen**
CC Exclusion see Appendix A PDX collection 0474

CC **C84.08 Mycosis fungoides, lymph nodes of multiple sites**
CC Exclusion see Appendix A PDX collection 0475

CC **C84.09 Mycosis fungoides, extranodal and solid organ sites**
CC Exclusion see Appendix A PDX collection 0467

\+ **C84.1 Sézary disease**

CC **C84.10 Sézary disease, unspecified site**
CC Exclusion see Appendix A PDX collection 0476

CC **C84.11 Sézary disease, lymph nodes of head, face, and neck**
CC Exclusion see Appendix A PDX collection 0477

CC **C84.12 Sézary disease, intrathoracic lymph nodes**
CC Exclusion see Appendix A PDX collection 0478

CC **C84.13 Sézary disease, intra-abdominal lymph nodes**
CC Exclusion see Appendix A PDX collection 0479

CC **C84.14 Sézary disease, lymph nodes of axilla and upper limb**
CC Exclusion see Appendix A PDX collection 0480

CC **C84.15 Sézary disease, lymph nodes of inguinal region and lower limb**
CC Exclusion see Appendix A PDX collection 0481

CC **C84.16 Sézary disease, intrapelvic lymph nodes**
CC Exclusion see Appendix A PDX collection 0482

CC **C84.17 Sézary disease, spleen**
CC Exclusion see Appendix A PDX collection 0483

CC **C84.18 Sézary disease, lymph nodes of multiple sites**
CC Exclusion see Appendix A PDX collection 0484

CC **C84.19 Sézary disease, extranodal and solid organ sites**
CC Exclusion see Appendix A PDX collection 0476

\+ **C84.4 Peripheral T-cell lymphoma, not classified**
Lennert's lymphoma
Lymphoepithelioid lymphoma
Mature T-cell lymphoma, not elsewhere classified

CC **C84.40 Peripheral T-cell lymphoma, not classified, unspecified site**
CC Exclusion see Appendix A PDX collection 0426

CC **C84.41 Peripheral T-cell lymphoma, not classified, lymph nodes of head, face, and neck**
CC Exclusion see Appendix A PDX collection 0427

CC **C84.42 Peripheral T-cell lymphoma, not classified, intrathoracic lymph nodes**
CC Exclusion see Appendix A PDX collection 0428

CC **C84.43 Peripheral T-cell lymphoma, not classified, intra-abdominal lymph nodes**
CC Exclusion see Appendix A PDX collection 0429

CC **C84.44 Peripheral T-cell lymphoma, not classified, lymph nodes of axilla and upper limb**
CC Exclusion see Appendix A PDX collection 0430

CC **C84.45 Peripheral T-cell lymphoma, not classified, lymph nodes of inguinal region and lower limb**
CC Exclusion see Appendix A PDX collection 0431

CC **C84.46 Peripheral T-cell lymphoma, not classified, intrapelvic lymph nodes**
CC Exclusion see Appendix A PDX collection 0432

CC **C84.47 Peripheral T-cell lymphoma, not classified, spleen**
CC Exclusion see Appendix A PDX collection 0433

CC **C84.48 Peripheral T-cell lymphoma, not classified, lymph nodes of multiple sites**
CC Exclusion see Appendix A PDX collection 0434

CC **C84.49 Peripheral T-cell lymphoma, not classified, extranodal and solid organ sites**
CC Exclusion see Appendix A PDX collection 0426

\+ **C84.6 Anaplastic large cell lymphoma, ALK-positive**
Anaplastic large cell lymphoma, CD30-positive

CC **C84.60 Anaplastic large cell lymphoma, ALK-positive, unspecified site**
CC Exclusion see Appendix A PDX collection 0426

CC **C84.61 Anaplastic large cell lymphoma, ALK-positive, lym[ph] nodes of head, face, and neck**
CC Exclusion see Appendix A PDX collection 0427

CC **C84.62 Anaplastic large cell lymphoma, ALK-positive, intrathoracic lymph nodes**
CC Exclusion see Appendix A PDX collection 0428

CC **C84.63 Anaplastic large cell lymphoma, ALK-positive, intr[a-] abdominal lymph nodes**
CC Exclusion see Appendix A PDX collection 0429

CC **C84.64 Anaplastic large cell lymphoma, ALK-positive, lym[ph] nodes of axilla and upper limb**
CC Exclusion see Appendix A PDX collection 0430

CC **C84.65 Anaplastic large cell lymphoma, ALK-positive, lym[ph] nodes of inguinal region and lower limb**
CC Exclusion see Appendix A PDX collection 0431

CC **C84.66 Anaplastic large cell lymphoma, ALK-positive, intrapelvic lymph nodes**
CC Exclusion see Appendix A PDX collection 0432

CC **C84.67 Anaplastic large cell lymphoma, ALK-positive, sple[en]**
CC Exclusion see Appendix A PDX collection 0433

CC **C84.68 Anaplastic large cell lymphoma, ALK-positive, lym[ph] nodes of multiple sites**
CC Exclusion see Appendix A PDX collection 0434

CC **C84.69 Anaplastic large cell lymphoma, ALK-positive, extranodal and solid organ sites**
CC Exclusion see Appendix A PDX collection 0426

\+ **C84.7 Anaplastic large cell lymphoma, ALK-negative**

Excludes1: *primary cutaneous CD30-positive T-cell proliferations (C86.6-)*

CC **C84.70 Anaplastic large cell lymphoma, ALK-negative, unspecified site**
CC Exclusion see Appendix A PDX collection 0426

CC **C84.71 Anaplastic large cell lymphoma, ALK-negative, lym[ph] nodes of head, face, and neck**
CC Exclusion see Appendix A PDX collection 0427

CC **C84.72 Anaplastic large cell lymphoma, ALK-negative, intrathoracic lymph nodes**
CC Exclusion see Appendix A PDX collection 0428

CC **C84.73 Anaplastic large cell lymphoma, ALK-negative, intr[a-] abdominal lymph nodes**
CC Exclusion see Appendix A PDX collection 0429

CC **C84.74 Anaplastic large cell lymphoma, ALK-negative, lym[ph] nodes of axilla and upper limb**
CC Exclusion see Appendix A PDX collection 0430

CC **C84.75 Anaplastic large cell lymphoma, ALK-negative, lym[ph] nodes of inguinal region and lower limb**
CC Exclusion see Appendix A PDX collection 0431

CC **C84.76 Anaplastic large cell lymphoma, ALK-negative, intrapelvic lymph nodes**
CC Exclusion see Appendix A PDX collection 0432

CC **C84.77 Anaplastic large cell lymphoma, ALK-negative, sple[en]**
CC Exclusion see Appendix A PDX collection 0433

CC **C84.78 Anaplastic large cell lymphoma, ALK-negative, lym[ph] nodes of multiple sites**
CC Exclusion see Appendix A PDX collection 0434

CC **C84.79 Anaplastic large cell lymphoma, ALK-negative, extranodal and solid organ sites**
CC Exclusion see Appendix A PDX collection 0426

\+ **C84.A Cutaneous T-cell lymphoma, unspecified**

CC **C84.A0 Cutaneous T-cell lymphoma, unspecified, unspecified site**
CC Exclusion see Appendix A PDX collection 0426

CC **C84.A1 Cutaneous T-cell lymphoma, unspecified lymph nod[es] of head, face, and neck**
CC Exclusion see Appendix A PDX collection 0427

CC **C84.A2 Cutaneous T-cell lymphoma, unspecified, intrathora[cic] lymph nodes**
CC Exclusion see Appendix A PDX collection 0428

CC **C84.A3 Cutaneous T-cell lymphoma, unspecified, intra-abdominal lymph nodes**
CC Exclusion see Appendix A PDX collection 0429

CC **C84.A4 Cutaneous T-cell lymphoma, unspecified, lymph nod[es] of axilla and upper limb**
CC Exclusion see Appendix A PDX collection 0430

CC **C84.A5 Cutaneous T-cell lymphoma, unspecified, lymph nod[es] of inguinal region and lower limb**
CC Exclusion see Appendix A PDX collection 0431

CC **C84.A6 Cutaneous T-cell lymphoma, unspecified, intrapelvi[c] lymph nodes**
CC Exclusion see Appendix A PDX collection 0432

CC **C84.A7 Cutaneous T-cell lymphoma, unspecified, spleen**
CC Exclusion see Appendix A PDX collection 0433

CC **C84.A8 Cutaneous T-cell lymphoma, unspecified, lymph nodes of multiple sites**
CC Exclusion see Appendix A PDX collection 0434

CC **C84.A9 Cutaneous T-cell lymphoma, unspecified, extranodal and solid organ sites**
CC Exclusion see Appendix A PDX collection 0426

\+ **C84.Z Other mature T/NK-cell lymphomas**
NOTE If T-cell lineage or involvement is mentioned in conjunction with a specific lymphoma, code to the more specific description.
Excludes1: *angioimmunoblastic T-cell lymphoma (C86.5)*
blastic NK-cell lymphoma (C86.4)
enteropathy-type T-cell lymphoma (C86.2)
extranodal NK-cell lymphoma, nasal type (C86.0)
hepatosplenic T-cell lymphoma (C86.1)
primary cutaneous CD30-positive T-cell proliferations (C86.6)
subcutaneous panniculitis-like T-cell lymphoma (C86.3)
T-cell leukemia (C91.1-)

CC **C84.Z0 Other mature T/NK-cell lymphomas, unspecified site**
CC Exclusion see Appendix A PDX collection 0426

CC **C84.Z1 Other mature T/NK-cell lymphomas, lymph nodes of head, face, and neck**
CC Exclusion see Appendix A PDX collection 0427

CC **C84.Z2 Other mature T/NK-cell lymphomas, intrathoracic lymph nodes**
CC Exclusion see Appendix A PDX collection 0428

CC **C84.Z3 Other mature T/NK-cell lymphomas, intra-abdominal lymph nodes**
CC Exclusion see Appendix A PDX collection 0429

CC **C84.Z4 Other mature T/NK-cell lymphomas, lymph nodes of axilla and upper limb**
CC Exclusion see Appendix A PDX collection 0430

CC **C84.Z5 Other mature T/NK-cell lymphomas, lymph nodes of inguinal region and lower limb**
CC Exclusion see Appendix A PDX collection 0431

CC **C84.Z6 Other mature T/NK-cell lymphomas, intrapelvic lymph nodes**
CC Exclusion see Appendix A PDX collection 0432

CC **C84.Z7 Other mature T/NK-cell lymphomas, spleen**
CC Exclusion see Appendix A PDX collection 0433

CC **C84.Z8 Other mature T/NK-cell lymphomas, lymph nodes of multiple sites**
CC Exclusion see Appendix A PDX collection 0434

CC **C84.Z9 Other mature T/NK-cell lymphomas, extranodal and solid organ sites**
CC Exclusion see Appendix A PDX collection 0426

\+ **C84.9 Mature T/NK-cell lymphomas, unspecified**
NK/T cell lymphoma NOS
Excludes1: *mature T-cell lymphoma, not elsewhere classified (C84.4-)*

CC **C84.90 Mature T/NK-cell lymphomas, unspecified, unspecified site**
CC Exclusion see Appendix A PDX collection 0426

CC **C84.91 Mature T/NK-cell lymphomas, unspecified, lymph nodes of head, face, and neck**
CC Exclusion see Appendix A PDX collection 0427

CC **C84.92 Mature T/NK-cell lymphomas, unspecified, intrathoracic lymph nodes**
CC Exclusion see Appendix A PDX collection 0428

CC **C84.93 Mature T/NK-cell lymphomas, unspecified, intra-abdominal lymph nodes**
CC Exclusion see Appendix A PDX collection 0429

CC **C84.94 Mature T/NK-cell lymphomas, unspecified, lymph nodes of axilla and upper limb**
CC Exclusion see Appendix A PDX collection 0430

CC **C84.95 Mature T/NK-cell lymphomas, unspecified, lymph nodes of inguinal region and lower limb**
CC Exclusion see Appendix A PDX collection 0431

CC **C84.96 Mature T/NK-cell lymphomas, unspecified, intrapelvic lymph nodes**
CC Exclusion see Appendix A PDX collection 0432

CC **C84.97 Mature T/NK-cell lymphomas, unspecified, spleen**
CC Exclusion see Appendix A PDX collection 0433

CC **C84.98 Mature T/NK-cell lymphomas, unspecified, lymph nodes of multiple sites**
CC Exclusion see Appendix A PDX collection 0434

CC **C84.99 Mature T/NK-cell lymphomas, unspecified, extranodal and solid organ sites**
CC Exclusion see Appendix A PDX collection 0426

C85 Other specified and unspecified types of non-Hodgkin lymphoma

Excludes1: *other specified types of T/NK-cell lymphoma (C86.-)*
personal history of non-Hodgkin lymphoma (Z85.72)

\+ **C85.1 Unspecified B-cell lymphoma**
NOTE If B-cell lineage or involvement is mentioned in conjunction with a specific lymphoma, code to the more specific description.

CC **C85.10 Unspecified B-cell lymphoma, unspecified site**
CC Exclusion see Appendix A PDX collection 0426

CC **C85.11 Unspecified B-cell lymphoma, lymph nodes of head, face, and neck**
CC Exclusion see Appendix A PDX collection 0427

CC **C85.12 Unspecified B-cell lymphoma, intrathoracic lymph nodes**
CC Exclusion see Appendix A PDX collection 0428

CC **C85.13 Unspecified B-cell lymphoma, intra-abdominal lymph nodes**
CC Exclusion see Appendix A PDX collection 0429

CC **C85.14 Unspecified B-cell lymphoma, lymph nodes of axilla and upper limb**
CC Exclusion see Appendix A PDX collection 0430

CC **C85.15 Unspecified B-cell lymphoma, lymph nodes of inguinal region and lower limb**
CC Exclusion see Appendix A PDX collection 0431

CC **C85.16 Unspecified B-cell lymphoma, intrapelvic lymph nodes**
CC Exclusion see Appendix A PDX collection 0432

CC **C85.17 Unspecified B-cell lymphoma, spleen**
CC Exclusion see Appendix A PDX collection 0433

CC **C85.18 Unspecified B-cell lymphoma, lymph nodes of multiple sites**
CC Exclusion see Appendix A PDX collection 0434

CC **C85.19 Unspecified B-cell lymphoma, extranodal and solid organ sites**
CC Exclusion see Appendix A PDX collection 0426

\+ **C85.2 Mediastinal (thymic) large B-cell lymphoma**

CC **C85.20 Mediastinal (thymic) large B-cell lymphoma, unspecified site**
CC Exclusion see Appendix A PDX collection 0426

CC **C85.21 Mediastinal (thymic) large B-cell lymphoma, lymph nodes of head, face, and neck**
CC Exclusion see Appendix A PDX collection 0427

CC **C85.22 Mediastinal (thymic) large B-cell lymphoma, intrathoracic lymph nodes**
CC Exclusion see Appendix A PDX collection 0428

CC **C85.23 Mediastinal (thymic) large B-cell lymphoma, intra-abdominal lymph nodes**
CC Exclusion see Appendix A PDX collection 0429

CC **C85.24 Mediastinal (thymic) large B-cell lymphoma, lymph nodes of axilla and upper limb**
CC Exclusion see Appendix A PDX collection 0430

CC **C85.25 Mediastinal (thymic) large B-cell lymphoma, lymph nodes of inguinal region and lower limb**
CC Exclusion see Appendix A PDX collection 0431

CC **C85.26 Mediastinal (thymic) large B-cell lymphoma, intrapelvic lymph nodes**
CC Exclusion see Appendix A PDX collection 0432

CC **C85.27 Mediastinal (thymic) large B-cell lymphoma, spleen**
CC Exclusion see Appendix A PDX collection 0433

CC **C85.28 Mediastinal (thymic) large B-cell lymphoma, lymph nodes of multiple sites**
CC Exclusion see Appendix A PDX collection 0434

CC **C85.29 Mediastinal (thymic) large B-cell lymphoma, extranodal and solid organ sites**
CC Exclusion see Appendix A PDX collection 0426

\+ **C85.8 Other specified types of non-Hodgkin lymphoma**

CC **C85.80 Other specified types of non-Hodgkin lymphoma, unspecified site**
CC Exclusion see Appendix A PDX collection 0426

CC **C85.81 Other specified types of non-Hodgkin lymphoma, lymph nodes of head, face, and neck**
CC Exclusion see Appendix A PDX collection 0427

CC **C85.82 Other specified types of non-Hodgkin lymphoma, intrathoracic lymph nodes**
CC Exclusion see Appendix A PDX collection 0428

CC **C85.83 Other specified types of non-Hodgkin lymphoma, intra-abdominal lymph nodes**
CC Exclusion see Appendix A PDX collection 0429

CC **C85.84 Other specified types of non-Hodgkin lymphoma, lymph nodes of axilla and upper limb**
CC Exclusion see Appendix A PDX collection 0430

CC **C85.85 Other specified types of non-Hodgkin lymphoma, lymph nodes of inguinal region and lower limb**
CC Exclusion see Appendix A PDX collection 0431

CC **C85.86 Other specified types of non-Hodgkin lymphoma, intrapelvic lymph nodes**
CC Exclusion see Appendix A PDX collection 0432
CC **C85.87 Other specified types of non-Hodgkin lymphoma, spleen**
CC Exclusion see Appendix A PDX collection 0433
CC **C85.88 Other specified types of non-Hodgkin lymphoma, lymph nodes of multiple sites**
CC Exclusion see Appendix A PDX collection 0434
CC **C85.89 Other specified types of non-Hodgkin lymphoma, extranodal and solid organ sites**
CC Exclusion see Appendix A PDX collection 0426
+ **C85.9 Non-Hodgkin lymphoma, unspecified**
Lymphoma NOS
Malignant lymphoma NOS
Non-Hodgkin lymphoma NOS
CC **C85.90 Non-Hodgkin lymphoma, unspecified, unspecified site**
CC Exclusion see Appendix A PDX collection 0426
CC **C85.91 Non-Hodgkin lymphoma, unspecified, lymph nodes of head, face, and neck**
CC Exclusion see Appendix A PDX collection 0427
CC **C85.92 Non-Hodgkin lymphoma, unspecified, intrathoracic lymph nodes**
CC Exclusion see Appendix A PDX collection 0428
CC **C85.93 Non-Hodgkin lymphoma, unspecified, intra-abdominal lymph nodes**
CC Exclusion see Appendix A PDX collection 0429
CC **C85.94 Non-Hodgkin lymphoma, unspecified, lymph nodes of axilla and upper limb**
CC Exclusion see Appendix A PDX collection 0430
CC **C85.95 Non-Hodgkin lymphoma, unspecified, lymph nodes of inguinal region and lower limb**
CC Exclusion see Appendix A PDX collection 0431
CC **C85.96 Non-Hodgkin lymphoma, unspecified, intrapelvic lymph nodes**
CC Exclusion see Appendix A PDX collection 0432
CC **C85.97 Non-Hodgkin lymphoma, unspecified, spleen**
CC Exclusion see Appendix A PDX collection 0433
CC **C85.98 Non-Hodgkin lymphoma, unspecified, lymph nodes of multiple sites**
CC Exclusion see Appendix A PDX collection 0434
CC **C85.99 Non-Hodgkin lymphoma, unspecified, extranodal and solid organ sites**
CC Exclusion see Appendix A PDX collection 0426

C86 Other specified types of T/NK-cell lymphoma

Excludes1: *anaplastic large cell lymphoma, ALK negative (C84.7-)*
anaplastic large cell lymphoma, ALK positive (C84.6-)
mature T/NK-cell lymphomas (C84.-)
other specified types of non-Hodgkin lymphoma (C85.8-)

CC **C86.0 Extranodal NK/T-cell lymphoma, nasal type**
CC Exclusion see Appendix A PDX collection 0427
CC **C86.1 Hepatosplenic T-cell lymphoma**
Alpha-beta and gamma delta types
CC Exclusion see Appendix A PDX collection 0433
CC **C86.2 Enteropathy-type (intestinal) T-cell lymphoma**
Enteropathy associated T-cell lymphoma
CC Exclusion see Appendix A PDX collection 0429
CC **C86.3 Subcutaneous panniculitis-like T-cell lymphoma**
CC Exclusion see Appendix A PDX collection 0429
CC **C86.4 Blastic NK-cell lymphoma**
CC Exclusion see Appendix A PDX collection 0426
CC **C86.5 Angioimmunoblastic T-cell lymphoma**
Angioimmunoblastic lymphadenopathy with dysproteinemia (AILD)
CC Exclusion see Appendix A PDX collection 0435
CC **C86.6 Primary cutaneous CD30-positive T-cell proliferations**
Lymphomatoid papulosis
Primary cutaneous anaplastic large cell lymphoma
Primary cutaneous CD30-positive large T-cell lymphoma
CC Exclusion see Appendix A PDX collection 0435

C88 Malignant immunoproliferative diseases and certain other B-cell lymphomas

Excludes1: *B-cell lymphoma, unspecified (C85.1-)*
personal history of other malignant neoplasms of lymphoid, hematopoietic and related tissues (Z85.79)

C88.0 Waldenström macroglobulinemia
Lymphoplasmacytic lymphoma with IgM-production
Macroglobulinemia (idiopathic) (primary)
Excludes1: *small cell B-cell lymphoma (C83.0)*

CC **C88.2 Heavy chain disease**
Franklin disease
Gamma heavy chain disease
Mu heavy chain disease
CC Exclusion see Appendix A PDX collection 0485
CC **C88.3 Immunoproliferative small intestinal disease**
Alpha heavy chain disease
Mediterranean lymphoma
CC Exclusion see Appendix A PDX collection 0485
CC **C88.4 Extranodal marginal zone B-cell lymphoma of mucosa-associated lymphoid tissue [MALT-lymphoma]**
Lymphoma of skin-associated lymphoid tissue [SALT-lymphoma]
Lymphoma of bronchial-associated lymphoid tissue [BALT-lymphoma]
Excludes1: *high malignant (diffuse large B-cell) lymphoma (C83.3-)*
CC Exclusion see Appendix A PDX collection 0426
CC **C88.8 Other malignant immunoproliferative diseases**
CC Exclusion see Appendix A PDX collection 0486
CC **C88.9 Malignant immunoproliferative disease, unspecified**
Immunoproliferative disease NOS
CC Exclusion see Appendix A PDX collection 0485

C90 Multiple myeloma and malignant plasma cell neoplasms

Excludes1: *personal history of other malignant neoplasms of lympho[id,] hematopoietic and related tissues (Z85.79)*

+ **C90.0 Multiple myeloma**
Kahler's disease
Medullary plasmacytoma
Myelomatosis
Plasma cell myeloma
Excludes1: *solitary myeloma (C90.3-)*
solitary plasmactyoma (C90.3-)
CC **C90.00 Multiple myeloma not having achieved remission**
Multiple myeloma with failed remission
Multiple myeloma NOS
CC Exclusion see Appendix A PDX collection 0485
CC **C90.01 Multiple myeloma in remission**
CC Exclusion see Appendix A PDX collection 0485
CC **C90.02 Multiple myeloma in relapse**
CC Exclusion see Appendix A PDX collection 0485
+ **C90.1 Plasma cell leukemia**
Plasmacytic leukemia
CC **C90.10 Plasma cell leukemia not having achieved remission**
Plasma cell leukemia with failed remission
Plasma cell leukemia NOS
CC Exclusion see Appendix A PDX collection 0485
CC **C90.11 Plasma cell leukemia in remission**
CC Exclusion see Appendix A PDX collection 0485
CC **C90.12 Plasma cell leukemia in relapse**
CC Exclusion see Appendix A PDX collection 0485
+ **C90.2 Extramedullary plasmacytoma**
CC **C90.20 Extramedullary plasmacytoma not having achieved remission**
Extramedullary plasmacytoma with failed remission
Extramedullary plasmacytoma NOS
CC Exclusion see Appendix A PDX collection 0485
CC **C90.21 Extramedullary plasmacytoma in remission**
CC Exclusion see Appendix A PDX collection 0485
CC **C90.22 Extramedullary plasmacytoma in relapse**
CC Exclusion see Appendix A PDX collection 0485
+ **C90.3 Solitary plasmacytoma**
Localized malignant plasma cell tumor NOS
Plasmacytoma NOS
Solitary myeloma
CC **C90.30 Solitary plasmacytoma not having achieved remissi[on]**
Solitary plasmacytoma with failed remission
Solitary plasmacytoma NOS
CC Exclusion see Appendix A PDX collection 0485
CC **C90.31 Solitary plasmacytoma in remission**
CC Exclusion see Appendix A PDX collection 0485
CC **C90.32 Solitary plasmacytoma in relapse**
CC Exclusion see Appendix A PDX collection 0485

C91 Lymphoid leukemia

Excludes1: *personal history of leukemia (Z85.6)*

+ **C91.0 Acute lymphoblastic leukemia [ALL]**
NOTE Code C91.0 should only be used for T-cell and B-cell precursor leukemia
CC **C91.00 Acute lymphoblastic leukemia not having achieved remission**
Acute lymphoblastic leukemia with failed remission
Acute lymphoblastic leukemia NOS
CC Exclusion see Appendix A PDX collection 0485

CC **C91.01 Acute lymphoblastic leukemia, in remission**
CC Exclusion see Appendix A PDX collection 0485

CC **C91.02 Acute lymphoblastic leukemia, in relapse**
CC Exclusion see Appendix A PDX collection 0485

+ **C91.1 Chronic lymphocytic leukemia of B-cell type**
Lymphoplasmacytic leukemia
Richter syndrome
Excludes1: *lymphoplasmacytic lymphoma (C83.0-)*

CC **C91.10 Chronic lymphocytic leukemia of B-cell type not having achieved remission**
Chronic lymphocytic leukemia of B-cell type with failed remission
Chronic lymphocytic leukemia of B-cell type NOS
CC Exclusion see Appendix A PDX collection 0485

CC **C91.11 Chronic lymphocytic leukemia of B-cell type in remission**
CC Exclusion see Appendix A PDX collection 0485

CC **C91.12 Chronic lymphocytic leukemia of B-cell type in relapse**
CC Exclusion see Appendix A PDX collection 0485

+ **C91.3 Prolymphocytic leukemia of B-cell type**

CC **C91.30 Prolymphocytic leukemia of B-cell type not having achieved remission**
Prolymphocytic leukemia of B-cell type with failed remission
Prolymphocytic leukemia of B-cell type NOS
CC Exclusion see Appendix A PDX collection 0485

CC **C91.31 Prolymphocytic leukemia of B-cell type, in remission**
CC Exclusion see Appendix A PDX collection 0485

CC **C91.32 Prolymphocytic leukemia of B-cell type, in relapse**
CC Exclusion see Appendix A PDX collection 0485

+ **C91.4 Hairy cell leukemia**
Leukemic reticuloendotheliosis

CC **C91.40 Hairy cell leukemia not having achieved remission**
Hairy cell leukemia with failed remission
Hairy cell leukemia NOS
CC Exclusion see Appendix A PDX collection 0487

CC **C91.41 Hairy cell leukemia, in remission**
CC Exclusion see Appendix A PDX collection 0487

CC **C91.42 Hairy cell leukemia, in relapse**
CC Exclusion see Appendix A PDX collection 0487

+ **C91.5 Adult T-cell lymphoma/leukemia (HTLV-1-associated)**
Acute variant of adult T-cell lymphoma/leukemia (HTLV-1-associated)
Chronic variant of adult T-cell lymphoma/leukemia (HTLV-1-associated)
Lymphomatoid variant of adult T-cell lymphoma/leukemia (HTLV-1-associated)
Smouldering variant of adult T-cell lymphoma/leukemia (HTLV-1-associated)

• CC **C91.50 Adult T-cell lymphoma/leukemia (HTLV-1-associated) not having achieved remission**
Adult T-cell lymphoma/leukemia (HTLV-1-associated) with failed remission
Adult T-cell lymphoma/leukemia (HTLV-1-associated) NOS
CC Exclusion see Appendix A PDX collection 0485

• CC **C91.51 Adult T-cell lymphoma/leukemia (HTLV-1-associated), in remission**
CC Exclusion see Appendix A PDX collection 0485

• CC **C91.52 Adult T-cell lymphoma/leukemia (HTLV-1-associated), in relapse**
CC Exclusion see Appendix A PDX collection 0485

+ **C91.6 Prolymphocytic leukemia of T-cell type**

CC **C91.60 Prolymphocytic leukemia of T-cell type not having achieved remission**
Prolymphocytic leukemia of T-cell type with failed remission
Prolymphocytic leukemia of T-cell type NOS
CC Exclusion see Appendix A PDX collection 0485

CC **C91.61 Prolymphocytic leukemia of T-cell type, in remission**
CC Exclusion see Appendix A PDX collection 0485

CC **C91.62 Prolymphocytic leukemia of T-cell type, in relapse**
CC Exclusion see Appendix A PDX collection 0485

+ **C91.A Mature B-cell leukemia Burkitt-type**
Excludes1: *Burkitt lymphoma (C83.7-)*

CC **C91.A0 Mature B-cell leukemia Burkitt-type not having achieved remission**
Mature B-cell leukemia Burkitt-type with failed remission
Mature B-cell leukemia Burkitt-type NOS
CC Exclusion see Appendix A PDX collection 0485

CC **C91.A1 Mature B-cell leukemia Burkitt-type, in remission**
CC Exclusion see Appendix A PDX collection 0485

CC **C91.A2 Mature B-cell leukemia Burkitt-type, in relapse**
CC Exclusion see Appendix A PDX collection 0485

+ **C91.Z Other lymphoid leukemia**
T-cell large granular lymphocytic leukemia (associated with rheumatoid arthritis)

CC **C91.Z0 Other lymphoid leukemia not having achieved remission**
Other lymphoid leukemia with failed remission
Other lymphoid leukemia NOS
CC Exclusion see Appendix A PDX collection 0485

CC **C91.Z1 Other lymphoid leukemia, in remission**
CC Exclusion see Appendix A PDX collection 0485

CC **C91.Z2 Other lymphoid leukemia, in relapse**
CC Exclusion see Appendix A PDX collection 0485

+ **C91.9 Lymphoid leukemia, unspecified**

CC **C91.90 Lymphoid leukemia, unspecified not having achieved remission**
Lymphoid leukemia with failed remission
Lymphoid leukemia NOS
CC Exclusion see Appendix A PDX collection 0485

CC **C91.91 Lymphoid leukemia, unspecified, in remission**
CC Exclusion see Appendix A PDX collection 0485

CC **C91.92 Lymphoid leukemia, unspecified, in relapse**
CC Exclusion see Appendix A PDX collection 0485

C92 Myeloid leukemia

Includes: granulocytic leukemia
myelogenous leukemia
Excludes1: *personal history of leukemia (Z85.6)*

+ **C92.0 Acute myeloblastic leukemia**
Acute myeloblastic leukemia, minimal differentiation
Acute myeloblastic leukemia (with maturation)
Acute myeloblastic leukemia 1/ETO
Acute myeloblastic leukemia M0
Acute myeloblastic leukemia M1
Acute myeloblastic leukemia M2
Acute myeloblastic leukemia with t(8;21)
Acute myeloblastic leukemia (without a FAB classification) NOS
Refractory anemia with excess blasts in transformation [RAEB T]
Excludes1: *acute exacerbation of chronic myeloid leukemia (C92.10)*
refractory anemia with excess of blasts not in transformation (D46.2-)

CC **C92.00 Acute myeloblastic leukemia, not having achieved remission**
Acute myeloblastic leukemia with failed remission
Acute myeloblastic leukemia NOS
CC Exclusion see Appendix A PDX collection 0485

CC **C92.01 Acute myeloblastic leukemia, in remission**
CC Exclusion see Appendix A PDX collection 0485

CC **C92.02 Acute myeloblastic leukemia, in relapse**
CC Exclusion see Appendix A PDX collection 0485

+ **C92.1 Chronic myeloid leukemia, BCR/ABL-positive**
Chronic myelogenous leukemia, Philadelphia chromosome (Ph1) positive
Chronic myelogenous leukemia, t(9;22) (q34;q11)
Chronic myelogenous leukemia with crisis of blast cells
Excludes1: *atypical chronic myeloid leukemia BCR/ABL-negative (C92.2-)*
chronic myelomonocytic leukemia (C93.1-)
chronic myeloproliferative disease (D47.1)

CC **C92.10 Chronic myeloid leukemia, BCR/ABL-positive, not having achieved remission**
Chronic myeloid leukemia, BCR/ABL-positive with failed remission
Chronic myeloid leukemia, BCR/ABL-positive NOS
CC Exclusion see Appendix A PDX collection 0485

CC **C92.11 Chronic myeloid leukemia, BCR/ABL-positive, in remission**
CC Exclusion see Appendix A PDX collection 0485

CC **C92.12 Chronic myeloid leukemia, BCR/ABL-positive, in relapse**
CC Exclusion see Appendix A PDX collection 0485

+ **C92.2 Atypical chronic myeloid leukemia, BCR/ABL-negative**

CC **C92.20 Atypical chronic myeloid leukemia, BCR/ABL-negative, not having achieved remission**
Atypical chronic myeloid leukemia, BCR/ABL-negative with failed remission
Atypical chronic myeloid leukemia, BCR/ABL-negative NOS
CC Exclusion see Appendix A PDX collection 0485

CC **C92.21 Atypical chronic myeloid leukemia, BCR/ABL-negative, in remission**
CC Exclusion see Appendix A PDX collection 0485

CC **C92.22 Atypical chronic myeloid leukemia, BCR/ABL-negative, in relapse**
CC Exclusion see Appendix A PDX collection 0485

+ **C92.3 Myeloid sarcoma**
A malignant tumor of immature myeloid cells
Chloroma
Granulocytic sarcoma

CC **C92.30 Myeloid sarcoma, not having achieved remission**
Myeloid sarcoma with failed remission
Myeloid sarcoma NOS
CC Exclusion see Appendix A PDX collection 0485

CC **C92.31 Myeloid sarcoma, in remission**
CC Exclusion see Appendix A PDX collection 0485

CC **C92.32 Myeloid sarcoma, in relapse**
CC Exclusion see Appendix A PDX collection 0485

+ **C92.4 Acute promyelocytic leukemia**
AML M3
AML Me with t(15;17) and variants

CC **C92.40 Acute promyelocytic leukemia, not having achieved remission**
Acute promyelocytic leukemia with failed remission
Acute promyelocytic leukemia NOS
CC Exclusion see Appendix A PDX collection 0485

CC **C92.41 Acute promyelocytic leukemia, in remission**
CC Exclusion see Appendix A PDX collection 0485

CC **C92.42 Acute promyelocytic leukemia, in relapse**
CC Exclusion see Appendix A PDX collection 0485

+ **C92.5 Acute myelomonocytic leukemia**
AML M4
AML M4 Eo with inv(16) or t(16;16)

CC **C92.50 Acute myelomonocytic leukemia, not having achieved remission**
Acute myelomonocytic leukemia with failed remission
Acute myelomonocytic leukemia NOS
CC Exclusion see Appendix A PDX collection 0485

CC **C92.51 Acute myelomonocytic leukemia, in remission**
CC Exclusion see Appendix A PDX collection 0485

CC **C92.52 Acute myelomonocytic leukemia, in relapse**
CC Exclusion see Appendix A PDX collection 0485

+ **C92.6 Acute myeloid leukemia with 11q23-abnormality**
Acute myeloid leukemia with variation of MLL-gene

CC **C92.60 Acute myeloid leukemia with 11q23-abnormality not having achieved remission**
Acute myeloid leukemia with 11q23-abnormality with failed remission
Acute myeloid leukemia with 11q23-abnormality NOS
CC Exclusion see Appendix A PDX collection 0485

CC **C92.61 Acute myeloid leukemia with 11q23-abnormality in remission**
CC Exclusion see Appendix A PDX collection 0485

CC **C92.62 Acute myeloid leukemia with 11q23-abnormality in relapse**
CC Exclusion see Appendix A PDX collection 0485

+ **C92.A Acute myeloid leukemia with multilineage dysplasia**
Acute myeloid leukemia with dysplasia of remaining hematopoesis and/or myelodysplastic disease in its history

CC **C92.A0 Acute myeloid leukemia with multilineage dysplasia, not having achieved remission**
Acute myeloid leukemia with multilineage dysplasia with failed remission
Acute myeloid leukemia with multilineage dysplasia NOS
CC Exclusion see Appendix A PDX collection 0485

CC **C92.A1 Acute myeloid leukemia with multilineage dysplasia, in remission**
CC Exclusion see Appendix A PDX collection 0485

CC **C92.A2 Acute myeloid leukemia with multilineage dysplasia, in relapse**
CC Exclusion see Appendix A PDX collection 0485

+ **C92.Z Other myeloid leukemia**

CC **C92.Z0 Other myeloid leukemia not having achieved remission**
Myeloid leukemia NEC with failed remission
Myeloid leukemia NEC
CC Exclusion see Appendix A PDX collection 0485

CC **C92.Z1 Other myeloid leukemia, in remission**
CC Exclusion see Appendix A PDX collection 0485

CC **C92.Z2 Other myeloid leukemia, in relapse**
CC Exclusion see Appendix A PDX collection 0485

+ **C92.9 Myeloid leukemia, unspecified**

CC **C92.90 Myeloid leukemia, unspecified, not having achieved remission**
Myeloid leukemia, unspecified with failed remission
Myeloid leukemia, unspecified NOS
CC Exclusion see Appendix A PDX collection 0485

CC **C92.91 Myeloid leukemia, unspecified in remission**
CC Exclusion see Appendix A PDX collection 0485

CC **C92.92 Myeloid leukemia, unspecified in relapse**
CC Exclusion see Appendix A PDX collection 0485

C93 Monocytic leukemia

Includes: monocytoid leukemia
Excludes1: *personal history of leukemia (Z85.6)*

+ **C93.0 Acute monoblastic/monocytic leukemia**
AML M5
AML M5a
AML M5b

CC **C93.00 Acute monoblastic/monocytic leukemia, not having achieved remission**
Acute monoblastic/monocytic leukemia with failed remission
Acute monoblastic/monocytic leukemia NOS
CC Exclusion see Appendix A PDX collection 0485

CC **C93.01 Acute monoblastic/monocytic leukemia, in remissi**
CC Exclusion see Appendix A PDX collection 0485

CC **C93.02 Acute monoblastic/monocytic leukemia, in relapse**
CC Exclusion see Appendix A PDX collection 0485

+ **C93.1 Chronic myelomonocytic leukemia**
Chronic monocytic leukemia
CMML-1
CMML-2
CMML with eosinophilia

CC **C93.10 Chronic myelomonocytic leukemia not having achieved remission**
Chronic myelomonocytic leukemia with failed remis
Chronic myelomonocytic leukemia NOS
CC Exclusion see Appendix A PDX collection 0485

CC **C93.11 Chronic myelomonocytic leukemia, in remission**
CC Exclusion see Appendix A PDX collection 0485

CC **C93.12 Chronic myelomonocytic leukemia, in relapse**
CC Exclusion see Appendix A PDX collection 0485

+ **C93.3 Juvenile myelomonocytic leukemia**

• CC **C93.30 Juvenile myelomonocytic leukemia, not having achieved remission**
Juvenile myelomonocytic leukemia with failed remis
Juvenile myelomonocytic leukemia NOS
CC Exclusion see Appendix A PDX collection 0485

• CC **C93.31 Juvenile myelomonocytic leukemia, in remission**
CC Exclusion see Appendix A PDX collection 0485

• CC **C93.32 Juvenile myelomonocytic leukemia, in relapse**
CC Exclusion see Appendix A PDX collection 0485

+ **C93.Z Other monocytic leukemia**

CC **C93.Z0 Other monocytic leukemia, not having achieved remission**
Other monocytic leukemia NOS
CC Exclusion see Appendix A PDX collection 0485

CC **C93.Z1 Other monocytic leukemia, in remission**
CC Exclusion see Appendix A PDX collection 0485

CC **C93.Z2 Other monocytic leukemia, in relapse**
CC Exclusion see Appendix A PDX collection 0485

+ **C93.9 Monocytic leukemia, unspecified**

CC **C93.90 Monocytic leukemia, unspecified, not having achie remission**
Monocytic leukemia, unspecified with failed remissi
Monocytic leukemia, unspecified NOS
CC Exclusion see Appendix A PDX collection 0485

CC **C93.91 Monocytic leukemia, unspecified in remission**
CC Exclusion see Appendix A PDX collection 0485

CC **C93.92 Monocytic leukemia, unspecified in relapse**
CC Exclusion see Appendix A PDX collection 0485

C94 Other leukemias of specified cell type

Excludes1: *leukemic reticuloendotheliosis (C91.4-)*
myelodysplastic syndromes (D46.-)
personal history of leukemia (Z85.6)
plasma cell leukemia (C90.1-)

+ **C94.0 Acute erythroid leukemia**
Acute myeloid leukemia M6(a)(b)
Erythroleukemia

CC **C94.00 Acute erythroid leukemia, not having achieved remission**
Acute erythroid leukemia with failed remission
Acute erythroid leukemia NOS
CC Exclusion see Appendix A PDX collection 0485

CC **C94.01 Acute erythroid leukemia, in remission**
CC Exclusion see Appendix A PDX collection 0485

CC **C94.02 Acute erythroid leukemia, in relapse**
CC Exclusion see Appendix A PDX collection 0485

\+ **C94.2 Acute megakaryoblastic leukemia**
Acute myeloid leukemia M7
Acute megakaryocytic leukemia

CC **C94.20 Acute megakaryoblastic leukemia not having achieved remission**
Acute megakaryoblastic leukemia with failied remission
Acute megakaryoblastic leukemia NOS
CC Exclusion see Appendix A PDX collection 0485

CC **C94.21 Acute megakaryoblastic leukemia, in remission**
CC Exclusion see Appendix A PDX collection 0485

CC **C94.22 Acute megakaryoblastic leukemia, in relapse**
CC Exclusion see Appendix A PDX collection 0485

\+ **C94.3 Mast cell leukemia**

CC **C94.30 Mast cell leukemia not having achieved remission**
Mast cell leukemia with failed remission
Mast cell leukemia NOS
CC Exclusion see Appendix A PDX collection 0485

CC **C94.31 Mast cell leukemia, in remission**
CC Exclusion see Appendix A PDX collection 0485

CC **C94.32 Mast cell leukemia, in relapse**
CC Exclusion see Appendix A PDX collection 0485

\+ **C94.4 Acute panmyelosis with myelofibrosis**
Acute myelofibrosis
Excludes1: *myelofibrosis NOS (D75.81)*
secondary myelofibrosis NOS (D75.81)

CC **C94.40 Acute panmyelosis with myelofibrosis not having achieved remission**
Acute myelofibrosis NOS
Acute panmyelosis with myelofibrosis with failed remission
Acute panmyelosis NOS
CC Exclusion see Appendix A PDX collection 0488

CC **C94.41 Acute panmyelosis with myelofibrosis, in remission**
CC Exclusion see Appendix A PDX collection 0488

CC **C94.42 Acute panmyelosis with myelofibrosis, in relapse**
CC Exclusion see Appendix A PDX collection 0488

CC **C94.6 Myelodysplastic disease, not classified**
Myeloproliferative disease, not classified
CC Exclusion see Appendix A PDX collection 0488

\+ **C94.8 Other specified leukemias**
Aggressive NK-cell leukemia
Acute basophilic leukemia

CC **C94.80 Other specified leukemias not having achieved remission**
Other specified leukemia with failed remission
Other specified leukemias NOS
CC Exclusion see Appendix A PDX collection 0485

CC **C94.81 Other specified leukemias, in remission**
CC Exclusion see Appendix A PDX collection 0485

CC **C94.82 Other specified leukemias, in relapse**
CC Exclusion see Appendix A PDX collection 0485

C95 Leukemia of unspecified cell type

Excludes1: *personal history of leukemia (Z85.6)*

\+ **C95.0 Acute leukemia of unspecified cell type**
Acute bilineal leukemia
Acute mixed lineage leukemia
Biphenotypic acute leukemia
Stem cell leukemia of unclear lineage
Excludes1: *acute exacerbation of unspecified chronic leukemia (C95.10)*

CC **C95.00 Acute leukemia of unspecified cell type not having achieved remission**
Acute leukemia of unspecified cell type with failed remission
Acute leukemia NOS
CC Exclusion see Appendix A PDX collection 0485

CC **C95.01 Acute leukemia of unspecified cell type, in remission**
CC Exclusion see Appendix A PDX collection 0485

CC **C95.02 Acute leukemia of unspecified cell type, in relapse**
CC Exclusion see Appendix A PDX collection 0485

\+ **C95.1 Chronic leukemia of unspecified cell type**

CC **C95.10 Chronic leukemia of unspecified cell type not having achieved remission**
Chronic leukemia of unspecified cell type with failed remission
Chronic leukemia NOS
CC Exclusion see Appendix A PDX collection 0485

CC **C95.11 Chronic leukemia of unspecified cell type, in remission**
CC Exclusion see Appendix A PDX collection 0485

CC **C95.12 Chronic leukemia of unspecified cell type, in relapse**
CC Exclusion see Appendix A PDX collection 0485

\+ **C95.9 Leukemia, unspecified**

CC **C95.90 Leukemia, unspecified not having achieved remission**
Leukemia, unspecified with failed remission
Leukemia NOS
CC Exclusion see Appendix A PDX collection 0485

CC **C95.91 Leukemia, unspecified, in remission**
CC Exclusion see Appendix A PDX collection 0485

CC **C95.92 Leukemia, unspecified, in relapse**
CC Exclusion see Appendix A PDX collection 0485

C96 Other and unspecified malignant neoplasms of lymphoid, hematopoietic and related tissue

Excludes1: *personal history of other malignant neoplasms of lymphoid, hematopoietic and related tissues (Z85.79)*

CC **C96.0 Multifocal and multisystemic (disseminated) Langerhans-cell histiocytosis**
Histiocytosis X, multisystemic
Letterer-Siwe disease
Excludes1: *adult pulmonary Langerhans cell histiocytosis (J84.82)*
multifocal and unisystemic Langerhans-cell histiocytosis (C96.5)
unifocal Langerhans-cell histiocytosis (C96.6)
CC Exclusion see Appendix A PDX collection 0489

CC **C96.2 Malignant mast cell tumor**
Aggressive systemic mastocytosis
Mast cell sarcoma
Excludes1: *indolent mastocytosis (D47.0)*
mast cell leukemia (C94.30)
mastocytosis (congenital) (cutaneous) (Q82.2)
CC Exclusion see Appendix A PDX collection 0490

CC **C96.4 Sarcoma of dendritic cells (accessory cells)**
Follicular dendritic cell sarcoma
Interdigitating dendritic cell sarcoma
Langerhans cell sarcoma
CC Exclusion see Appendix A PDX collection 0491

CC **C96.5 Multifocal and unisystemic Langerhans-cell histiocytosis**
Hand-Schüller-Christian disease
Histiocytosis X, multifocal
Excludes1: *multifocal and multisystemic (disseminated) Langerhans-cell histiocytosis (C96.0)*
unifocal Langerhans-cell histiocytosis (C96.6)
CC Exclusion see Appendix A PDX collection 0492

CC **C96.6 Unifocal Langerhans-cell histiocytosis**
Eosinophilic granuloma
Histiocytosis X, unifocal
Histiocytosis X NOS
Langerhans-cell histiocytosis NOS
Excludes1: *multifocal and multisysemic (disseminated) Langerhans-cell histiocytosis (C96.0)*
multifocal and unisystemic Langerhans-cell histiocytosis (C96.5)
CC Exclusion see Appendix A PDX collection 0492

CC **C96.A Histiocytic sarcoma**
Malignant histiocytosis
CC Exclusion see Appendix A PDX collection 0493

CC **C96.Z Other specified malignant neoplasms of lymphoid, hematopoietic and related tissue**
CC Exclusion see Appendix A PDX collection 0491

CC **C96.9 Malignant neoplasm of lymphoid, hematopoietic and related tissue, unspecified**
CC Exclusion see Appendix A PDX collection 0491

In situ neoplasms (D00-D09)

Includes: Bowen's disease
erythroplasia
grade III intraepithelial neoplasia
Queyrat's erythroplasia

D00 Carcinoma in situ of oral cavity, esophagus and stomach

Excludes1: melanoma in situ (D03.-)

+ **D00.0 Carcinoma in situ of lip, oral cavity and pharynx**
Use additional code to identify:
exposure to environmental tobacco smoke (Z77.22)
exposure to tobacco smoke in the perinatal period (P96.81)
history of tobacco use (Z87.891)
occupational exposure to environmental tobacco smoke (Z57.31)
tobacco dependence (F17.-)
tobacco use (Z72.0)
Excludes1: carcinoma in situ of aryepiglottic fold or interarytenoid fold, laryngeal aspect (D02.0)
carcinoma in situ of epiglottis NOS (D02.0)
carcinoma in situ of epiglottis suprahyoid portion (D02.0)
carcinoma in situ of skin of lip (D03.0, D04.0)
D00.00 Carcinoma in situ of oral cavity, unspecified site
D00.01 Carcinoma in situ of labial mucosa and vermilion border
D00.02 Carcinoma in situ of buccal mucosa
D00.03 Carcinoma in situ of gingiva and edentulous alveolar ridge
D00.04 Carcinoma in situ of soft palate
D00.05 Carcinoma in situ of hard palate
D00.06 Carcinoma in situ of floor of mouth
D00.07 Carcinoma in situ of tongue
D00.08 Carcinoma in situ of pharynx
Carcinoma in situ of aryepiglottic fold NOS
Carcinoma in situ of hypopharyngeal aspect of aryepiglottic fold
Carcinoma in situ of marginal zone of aryepiglottic fold

D00.1 Carcinoma in situ of esophagus
D00.2 Carcinoma in situ of stomach

D01 Carcinoma in situ of other and unspecified digestive organs

Excludes1: melanoma in situ (D03.-)

D01.0 Carcinoma in situ of colon
Excludes1: carcinoma in situ of rectosigmoid junction (D01.1)
D01.1 Carcinoma in situ of rectosigmoid junction
D01.2 Carcinoma in situ of rectum
D01.3 Carcinoma in situ of anus and anal canal
Excludes1: carcinoma in situ of anal margin (D04.5)
carcinoma in situ of anal skin (D04.5)
carcinoma in situ of perianal skin (D04.5)
+ **D01.4 Carcinoma in situ of other and unspecified parts of intestine**
Excludes1: carcinoma in situ of ampulla of Vater (D01.5)
D01.40 Carcinoma in situ of unspecified part of intestine
D01.49 Carcinoma in situ of other parts of intestine
D01.5 Carcinoma in situ of liver, gallbladder and bile ducts
Carcinoma in situ of ampulla of Vater
D01.7 Carcinoma in situ of other specified digestive organs
Carcinoma in situ of pancreas
D01.9 Carcinoma in situ of digestive organ, unspecified

D02 Carcinoma in situ of middle ear and respiratory system

Use additional code to identify:
exposure to environmental tobacco smoke (Z77.22)
exposure to tobacco smoke in the perinatal period (P96.81)
history of tobacco use (Z87.891)
occupational exposure to environmental tobacco smoke (Z57.31)
tobacco dependence (F17.-)
tobacco use (Z72.0)
Excludes1: melanoma in situ (D03.-)

D02.0 Carcinoma in situ of larynx
Carcinoma in situ of aryepiglottic fold or interarytenoid fold, laryngeal aspect
Carcinoma in situ of epiglottis (suprahyoid portion)
Excludes1: carcinoma in situ of aryepiglottic fold or interarytenoid fold NOS (D00.08)
carcinoma in situ of hypopharyngeal aspect (D00.08)
carcinoma in situ of marginal zone (D00.08)
D02.1 Carcinoma in situ of trachea
+ **D02.2 Carcinoma in situ of bronchus and lung**
D02.20 Carcinoma in situ of unspecified bronchus and lung
D02.21 Carcinoma in situ of right bronchus and lung
D02.22 Carcinoma in situ of left bronchus and lung
D02.3 Carcinoma in situ of other parts of respiratory system
Carcinoma in situ of accessory sinuses
Carcinoma in situ of middle ear
Carcinoma in situ of nasal cavities
Excludes1: carcinoma in situ of ear (external) (skin) (D04.2-)
carcinoma in situ of nose NOS D09.8
carcinoma in situ of skin of nose (D04.3)
D02.4 Carcinoma in situ of respiratory system, unspecified

D03 Melanoma in situ

D03.0 Melanoma in situ of lip
+ **D03.1 Melanoma in situ of eyelid, including canthus**
D03.10 Melanoma in situ of unspecified eyelid, including canthus
D03.11 Melanoma in situ of right eyelid, including canthus
D03.12 Melanoma in situ of left eyelid, including canthus
+ **D03.2 Melanoma in situ of ear and external auricular canal**
D03.20 Melanoma in situ of unspecified ear and external auricular canal
D03.21 Melanoma in situ of right ear and external auricular canal
D03.22 Melanoma in situ of left ear and external auricular canal
+ **D03.3 Melanoma in situ of other and unspecified parts of face**
D03.30 Melanoma in situ of unspecified part of face
D03.39 Melanoma in situ of other parts of face
D03.4 Melanoma in situ of scalp and neck
+ **D03.5 Melanoma in situ of trunk**
D03.51 Melanoma in situ of anal skin
Melanoma in situ of anal margin
Melanoma in situ of perianal skin
D03.52 Melanoma in situ of breast (skin) (soft tissue)
D03.59 Melanoma in situ of other part of trunk
+ **D03.6 Melanoma in situ of upper limb, including shoulder**
D03.60 Melanoma in situ of unspecified upper limb, including shoulder
D03.61 Melanoma in situ of right upper limb, including shoulder
D03.62 Melanoma in situ of left upper limb, including shoulder
+ **D03.7 Melanoma in situ of lower limb, including hip**
D03.70 Melanoma in situ of unspecified lower limb, including hip
D03.71 Melanoma in situ of right lower limb, including hip
D03.72 Melanoma in situ of left lower limb, including hip
D03.8 Melanoma in situ of other sites
Melanoma in situ of scrotum
Excludes1: carcinoma in situ of scrotum (D07.61)
D03.9 Melanoma in situ, unspecified

D04 Carcinoma in situ of skin

Excludes1: erythroplasia of Queyrat (penis) NOS (D07.4)
melanoma in situ (D03.-)

D04.0 Carcinoma in situ of skin of lip
Excludes1: carcinoma in situ of vermilion border of lip (D00.0
+ **D04.1 Carcinoma in situ of skin of eyelid, including canthus**
D04.10 Carcinoma in situ of skin of unspecified eyelid, including canthus
D04.11 Carcinoma in situ of skin of right eyelid, including canthus
D04.12 Carcinoma in situ of skin of left eyelid, including canthus
+ **D04.2 Carcinoma in situ of skin of ear and external auricular canal**
D04.20 Carcinoma in situ of skin of unspecified ear and external auricular canal
D04.21 Carcinoma in situ of skin of right ear and external auricular canal
D04.22 Carcinoma in situ of skin of left ear and external auricular canal
+ **D04.3 Carcinoma in situ of skin of other and unspecified parts of face**
D04.30 Carcinoma in situ of skin of unspecified part of face
D04.39 Carcinoma in situ of skin of other parts of face
D04.4 Carcinoma in situ of skin of scalp and neck

D04.5 Carcinoma in situ of skin of trunk
Carcinoma in situ of anal margin
Carcinoma in situ of anal skin
Carcinoma in situ of perianal skin
Carcinoma in situ of skin of breast
Excludes1: *carcinoma in situ of anus NOS (D01.3)*
carcinoma in situ of scrotum (D07.61)
carcinoma in situ of skin of genital organs (D07.-)

\+ **D04.6 Carcinoma in situ of skin of upper limb, including shoulder**
D04.60 Carcinoma in situ of skin of unspecified upper limb, including shoulder
D04.61 Carcinoma in situ of skin of right upper limb, including shoulder
D04.62 Carcinoma in situ of skin of left upper limb, including shoulder

\+ **D04.7 Carcinoma in situ of skin of lower limb, including hip**
D04.70 Carcinoma in situ of skin of unspecified lower limb, including hip
D04.71 Carcinoma in situ of skin of right lower limb, including hip
D04.72 Carcinoma in situ of skin of left lower limb, including hip

D04.8 Carcinoma in situ of skin of other sites
D04.9 Carcinoma in situ of skin, unspecified

D05 Carcinoma in situ of breast

Excludes1: *carcinoma in situ of skin of breast (D04.5)*
melanoma in situ of breast (skin) (D03.5)
Paget's disease of breast or nipple (C50.-)

\+ **D05.0 Lobular carcinoma in situ of breast**
D05.00 Lobular carcinoma in situ of unspecified breast
D05.01 Lobular carcinoma in situ of right breast
D05.02 Lobular carcinoma in situ of left breast

\+ **D05.1 Intraductal carcinoma in situ of breast**
D05.10 Intraductal carcinoma in situ of unspecified breast
D05.11 Intraductal carcinoma in situ of right breast
D05.12 Intraductal carcinoma in situ of left breast

\+ **D05.8 Other specified type of carcinoma in situ of breast**
D05.80 Other specified type of carcinoma in situ of unspecified breast
D05.81 Other specified type of carcinoma in situ of right breast
D05.82 Other specified type of carcinoma in situ of left breast

\+ **D05.9 Unspecified type of carcinoma in situ of breast**
D05.90 Unspecified type of carcinoma in situ of unspecified breast
D05.91 Unspecified type of carcinoma in situ of right breast
D05.92 Unspecified type of carcinoma in situ of left breast

D06 Carcinoma in situ of cervix uteri

Includes: cervical adenocarcinoma in situ
cervical intraepithelial glandular neoplasia
cervical intraepithelial neoplasia III [CIN III]
severe dysplasia of cervix uteri

Excludes1: *cervical intraepithelial neoplasia II [CIN II] (N87.1)*
cytologic evidence of malignancy of cervix without histologic confirmation (R87.614)
high grade squamous intraepithelial lesion (HGSIL) of cervix (R87.613)
melanoma in situ of cervix (D03.5)
moderate cervical dysplasia (N87.1)

♀ **D06.0 Carcinoma in situ of endocervix**
♀ **D06.1 Carcinoma in situ of exocervix**
♀ **D06.7 Carcinoma in situ of other parts of cervix**
♀ **D06.9 Carcinoma in situ of cervix, unspecified**

D07 Carcinoma in situ of other and unspecified genital organs

Excludes1: *melanoma in situ of trunk (D03.5)*

♀ **D07.0 Carcinoma in situ of endometrium**
♀ **D07.1 Carcinoma in situ of vulva**
Severe dysplasia of vulva
Vulvar intraepithelial neoplasia III [VIN III]
Excludes1: *moderate dysplasia of vulva (N90.1)*
vulvar intraepithelial neoplasia II [VIN II] (N90.1)

♀ **D07.2 Carcinoma in situ of vagina**
Severe dysplasia of vagina
Vaginal intraepithelial neoplasia III [VAIN III]
Excludes1: *moderate dysplasia of vagina (N89.1)*
vaginal intraepithelial neoplasia II [VIN II] (N89.1)

\+ **D07.3 Carcinoma in situ of other and unspecified female genital organs**
♀ **D07.30 Carcinoma in situ of unspecified female genital organs**
♀ **D07.39 Carcinoma in situ of other female genital organs**

♂ **D07.4 Carcinoma in situ of penis**
Erythroplasia of Queyrat NOS

♂ **D07.5 Carcinoma in situ of prostate**
Prostatic intraepithelial neoplasia III (PIN III)
Severe dysplasia of prostate
Excludes1: *dysplasia (mild) (moderate) of prostate (N42.3)*

\+ **D07.6 Carcinoma in situ of other and unspecified male genital organs**
♂ **D07.60 Carcinoma in situ of unspecified male genital organs**
♂ **D07.61 Carcinoma in situ of scrotum**
♂ **D07.69 Carcinoma in situ of other male genital organs**

D09 Carcinoma in situ of other and unspecified sites

Excludes1: *melanoma in situ (D03.-)*

D09.0 Carcinoma in situ of bladder

\+ **D09.1 Carcinoma in situ of other and unspecified urinary organs**
D09.10 Carcinoma in situ of unspecified urinary organ
D09.19 Carcinoma in situ of other urinary organs

\+ **D09.2 Carcinoma in situ of eye**
Excludes1: *carcinoma in situ of skin of eyelid (D04.1-)*
D09.20 Carcinoma in situ of unspecified eye
D09.21 Carcinoma in situ of right eye
D09.22 Carcinoma in situ of left eye

D09.3 Carcinoma in situ of thyroid and other endocrine glands
Excludes1: *carcinoma in situ of endocrine pancreas (D01.7)*
carcinoma in situ of ovary (D07.39)
carcinoma in situ of testis (D07.69)

D09.8 Carcinoma in situ of other specified sites
D09.9 Carcinoma in situ, unspecified

Benign neoplasms, except benign neuroendocrine tumors (D10-D36)

D10 Benign neoplasm of mouth and pharynx

D10.0 Benign neoplasm of lip
Benign neoplasm of lip (frenulum) (inner aspect) (mucosa) (vermilion border)
Excludes1: *benign neoplasm of skin of lip (D22.0, D23.0)*

D10.1 Benign neoplasm of tongue
Benign neoplasm of lingual tonsil

D10.2 Benign neoplasm of floor of mouth

\+ **D10.3 Other and unspecified parts of mouth**
D10.30 Benign neoplasm of unspecified part of mouth
D10.39 Benign neoplasm of other parts of mouth
Benign neoplasm of minor salivary gland NOS
Excludes1: *benign odontogenic neoplasms (D16.4-D16.5)*
benign neoplasm of mucosa of lip (D10.0)
benign neoplasm of nasopharyngeal surface of soft palate (D10.6)

D10.4 Benign neoplasm of tonsil
Benign neoplasm of tonsil (faucial) (palatine)
Excludes1: *benign neoplasm of lingual tonsil (D10.1)*
benign neoplasm of pharyngeal tonsil (D10.6)
benign neoplasm of tonsillar fossa (D10.5)
benign neoplasm of tonsillar pillars (D10.5)

D10.5 Benign neoplasm of other parts of oropharynx
Benign neoplasm of epiglottis, anterior aspect
Benign neoplasm of tonsillar fossa
Benign neoplasm of tonsillar pillars
Benign neoplasm of vallecula
Excludes1: *benign neoplasm of epiglottis NOS (D14.1)*
benign neoplasm of epiglottis, suprahyoid portion (D14.1)

D10.6 Benign neoplasm of nasopharynx
Benign neoplasm of pharyngeal tonsil
Benign neoplasm of posterior margin of septum and choanae

D10.7 Benign neoplasm of hypopharynx
D10.9 Benign neoplasm of pharynx, unspecified

D11 Benign neoplasm of major salivary glands

Excludes1: *benign neoplasms of specified minor salivary glands which are classified according to their anatomical location*
benign neoplasms of minor salivary glands NOS (D10.39)

D11.0 Benign neoplasm of parotid gland
D11.7 Benign neoplasm of other major salivary glands
Benign neoplasm of sublingual salivary gland
Benign neoplasm of submandibular salivary gland
D11.9 Benign neoplasm of major salivary gland, unspecified

D12 Benign neoplasm of colon, rectum, anus and anal canal

Excludes1: *benign carcinoid tumors of the large intestine, and rectum (D3A.02-)*

D12.0 Benign neoplasm of cecum
Benign neoplasm of ileocecal valve

D12.1 Benign neoplasm of appendix
Excludes1: *benign carcinoid tumor of the appendix (D3A.020)*

D12.2 Benign neoplasm of ascending colon

D12.3 Benign neoplasm of transverse colon
Benign neoplasm of hepatic flexure
Benign neoplasm of splenic flexure

D12.4 Benign neoplasm of descending colon

D12.5 Benign neoplasm of sigmoid colon

D12.6 Benign neoplasm of colon, unspecified
Adenomatosis of colon
Benign neoplasm of large intestine NOS
Polyposis (hereditary) of colon
Excludes1: *inflammatory polyp of colon (K51.4-)*
polyp of colon NOS (K63.5)

D12.7 Benign neoplasm of rectosigmoid junction

D12.8 Benign neoplasm of rectum
Excludes1: *benign carcinoid tumor of the rectum (D3A.026)*

D12.9 Benign neoplasm of anus and anal canal
Benign neoplasm of anus NOS
Excludes1: *benign neoplasm of anal margin (D22.5, D23.5)*
benign neoplasm of anal skin (D22.5, D23.5)
benign neoplasm of perianal skin (D22.5, D23.5)

D13 Benign neoplasm of other and ill-defined parts of digestive system

Excludes1: *benign stromal tumors of digestive system (D21.4)*

D13.0 Benign neoplasm of esophagus

D13.1 Benign neoplasm of stomach
Excludes1: *benign carcinoid tumor of the stomach (D3A.092)*

D13.2 Benign neoplasm of duodenum
Excludes1: *benign carcinoid tumor of the duodenum (D3A.010)*

\+ **D13.3 Benign neoplasm of other and unspecified parts of small intestine**
Excludes1: *benign carcinoid tumors of the small intestine(D3A.01-)*
benign neoplasm of ileocecal valve (D12.0)

D13.30 Benign neoplasm of unspecified part of small intestine

D13.39 Benign neoplasm of other parts of small intestine

D13.4 Benign neoplasm of liver
Benign neoplasm of intrahepatic bile ducts

D13.5 Benign neoplasm of extrahepatic bile ducts

D13.6 Benign neoplasm of pancreas
Excludes1: *benign neoplasm of endocrine pancreas (D13.7)*

D13.7 Benign neoplasm of endocrine pancreas
Islet cell tumor
Benign neoplasm of islets of Langerhans
Use additional code to identify any functional activity.

D13.9 Benign neoplasm of ill-defined sites within the digestive system
Benign neoplasm of digestive system NOS
Benign neoplasm of intestine NOS
Benign neoplasm of spleen

D14 Benign neoplasm of middle ear and respiratory system

D14.0 Benign neoplasm of middle ear, nasal cavity and accessory sinuses
Benign neoplasm of cartilage of nose
Excludes1: *benign neoplasm of auricular canal (external) (D22.2-, D23.2-)*
benign neoplasm of bone of ear (D16.4)
benign neoplasm of bone of nose (D16.4)
benign neoplasm of cartilage of ear (D21.0)
benign neoplasm of ear (external)(skin) (D22.2-, D23.2-)
benign neoplasm of nose NOS (D36.7)
benign neoplasm of skin of nose (D22.39, D23.39)
benign neoplasm of olfactory bulb (D33.3)
benign neoplasm of posterior margin of septum and choanae (D10.6)
polyp of accessory sinus (J33.8)
polyp of ear (middle) (H74.4)
polyp of nasal (cavity) (J33.-)

D14.1 Benign neoplasm of larynx
Adenomatous polyp of larynx
Benign neoplasm of epiglottis (suprahyoid portion)
Excludes1: *benign neoplasm of epiglottis, anterior aspect (D10.5)*
polyp (nonadenomatous) of vocal cord or larynx (J38.1)

D14.2 Benign neoplasm of trachea

\+ **D14.3 Benign neoplasm of bronchus and lung**
Excludes1: *benign carcinoid tumor of the bronchus and lung (D3A.090)*

D14.30 Benign neoplasm of unspecified bronchus and lung

D14.31 Benign neoplasm of right bronchus and lung

D14.32 Benign neoplasm of left bronchus and lung

D14.4 Benign neoplasm of respiratory system, unspecified

D15 Benign neoplasm of other and unspecified intrathoracic organs

Excludes1: *benign neoplasm of mesothelial tissue (D19.-)*

D15.0 Benign neoplasm of thymus
Excludes1: *benign carcinoid tumor of the thymus (D3A.091)*

D15.1 Benign neoplasm of heart
Excludes1: *benign neoplasm of great vessels (D21.3)*

D15.2 Benign neoplasm of mediastinum

D15.7 Benign neoplasm of other specified intrathoracic organs

D15.9 Benign neoplasm of intrathoracic organ, unspecified

D16 Benign neoplasm of bone and articular cartilage

Excludes1: *benign neoplasm of connective tissue of ear (D21.0)*
benign neoplasm of connective tissue of eyelid (D21.0)
benign neoplasm of connective tissue of larynx (D14.1)
benign neoplasm of connective tissue of nose (D14.0)
benign neoplasm of synovia (D21.-)

\+ **D16.0 Benign neoplasm of scapula and long bones of upper limb**

D16.00 Benign neoplasm of scapula and long bones of unspecified upper limb

D16.01 Benign neoplasm of scapula and long bones of right upper limb

D16.02 Benign neoplasm of scapula and long bones of left upper limb

\+ **D16.1 Benign neoplasm of short bones of upper limb**

D16.10 Benign neoplasm of short bones of unspecified upper limb

D16.11 Benign neoplasm of short bones of right upper limb

D16.12 Benign neoplasm of short bones of left upper limb

\+ **D16.2 Benign neoplasm of long bones of lower limb**

D16.20 Benign neoplasm of long bones of unspecified lower limb

D16.21 Benign neoplasm of long bones of right lower limb

D16.22 Benign neoplasm of long bones of left lower limb

\+ **D16.3 Benign neoplasm of short bones of lower limb**

D16.30 Benign neoplasm of short bones of unspecified lower limb

D16.31 Benign neoplasm of short bones of right lower limb

D16.32 Benign neoplasm of short bones of left lower limb

D16.4 Benign neoplasm of bones of skull and face
Benign neoplasm of maxilla (superior)
Benign neoplasm of orbital bone
Keratocyst of maxilla
Keratocystic odontogenic tumor of maxilla
Excludes1: *benign neoplasm of lower jaw bone (D16.5)*

D16.5 Benign neoplasm of lower jaw bone
Keratocyst of mandible
Keratocystic odontogenic tumor of mandible

D16.6 Benign neoplasm of vertebral column
Excludes1: *benign neoplasm of sacrum and coccyx (D16.8)*

D16.7 Benign neoplasm of ribs, sternum and clavicle

D16.8 Benign neoplasm of pelvic bones, sacrum and coccyx

D16.9 Benign neoplasm of bone and articular cartilage, unspecified

D17 Benign lipomatous neoplasm

D17.0 Benign lipomatous neoplasm of skin and subcutaneous tissue of head, face and neck

D17.1 Benign lipomatous neoplasm of skin and subcutaneous tissue of trunk

\+ **D17.2 Benign lipomatous neoplasm of skin and subcutaneous tissue of limb**

D17.20 Benign lipomatous neoplasm of skin and subcutaneous tissue of unspecified limb

D17.21 Benign lipomatous neoplasm of skin and subcutaneous tissue of right arm

D17.22 Benign lipomatous neoplasm of skin and subcutaneous tissue of left arm

D17.23 Benign lipomatous neoplasm of skin and subcutaneous tissue of right leg
D17.24 Benign lipomatous neoplasm of skin and subcutaneous tissue of left leg
+ **D17.3 Benign lipomatous neoplasm of skin and subcutaneous tissue of other and unspecified sites**
D17.30 Benign lipomatous neoplasm of skin and subcutaneous tissue of unspecified sites
D17.39 Benign lipomatous neoplasm of skin and subcutaneous tissue of other sites
D17.4 Benign lipomatous neoplasm of intrathoracic organs
D17.5 Benign lipomatous neoplasm of intra-abdominal organs
Excludes1: *benign lipomatous neoplasm of peritoneum and retroperitoneum (D17.79)*
♂ **D17.6 Benign lipomatous neoplasm of spermatic cord**
+ **D17.7 Benign lipomatous neoplasm of other sites**
D17.71 Benign lipomatous neoplasm of kidney
D17.72 Benign lipomatous neoplasm of other genitourinary organ
D17.79 Benign lipomatous neoplasm of other sites
Benign lipomatous neoplasm of peritoneum
Benign lipomatous neoplasm of retroperitoneum
D17.9 Benign lipomatous neoplasm, unspecified
Lipoma NOS

D18 Hemangioma and lymphangioma, any site
Excludes1: *benign neoplasm of glomus jugulare (D35.6)*
blue or pigmented nevus (D22.-)
nevus NOS (D22.-)
vascular nevus (Q82.5)
+ **D18.0 Hemangioma**
Angioma NOS
Cavernous nevus
D18.00 Hemangioma unspecified site
D18.01 Hemangioma of skin and subcutaneous tissue
D18.02 Hemangioma of intracranial structures
D18.03 Hemangioma of intra-abdominal structures
D18.09 Hemangioma of other sites
D18.1 Lymphangioma, any site

D19 Benign neoplasm of mesothelial tissue
D19.0 Benign neoplasm of mesothelial tissue of pleura
D19.1 Benign neoplasm of mesothelial tissue of peritoneum
D19.7 Benign neoplasm of mesothelial tissue of other sites
D19.9 Benign neoplasm of mesothelial tissue, unspecified
Benign mesothelioma NOS

D20 Benign neoplasm of soft tissue of retroperitoneum and peritoneum
Excludes1: *benign lipomatous neoplasm of peritoneum and retroperitoneum (D17.79)*
benign neoplasm of mesothelial tissue (D19.-)
D20.0 Benign neoplasm of soft tissue of retroperitoneum
D20.1 Benign neoplasm of soft tissue of peritoneum

D21 Other benign neoplasms of connective and other soft tissue
Includes: benign neoplasm of blood vessel
benign neoplasm of bursa
benign neoplasm of cartilage
benign neoplasm of fascia
benign neoplasm of fat
benign neoplasm of ligament, except uterine
benign neoplasm of lymphatic channel
benign neoplasm of muscle
benign neoplasm of synovia
benign neoplasm of tendon (sheath)
benign stromal tumors
Excludes1: *benign neoplasm of articular cartilage (D16.-)*
benign neoplasm of cartilage of larynx (D14.1)
benign neoplasm of cartilage of nose (D14.0)
benign neoplasm of connective tissue of breast (D24.-)
benign neoplasm of peripheral nerves and autonomic nervous system (D36.1-)
benign neoplasm of peritoneum (D20.1)
benign neoplasm of retroperitoneum (D20.0)
benign neoplasm of uterine ligament, any (D28.2)
benign neoplasm of vascular tissue (D18.-)
hemangioma (D18.0-)
lipomatous neoplasm (D17.-)
lymphangioma (D18.1)
uterine leiomyoma (D25.-)

D21.0 Benign neoplasm of connective and other soft tissue of head, face and neck
Benign neoplasm of connective tissue of ear
Benign neoplasm of connective tissue of eyelid
Excludes1: *benign neoplasm of connective tissue of orbit (D31.6-)*
+ **D21.1 Benign neoplasm of connective and other soft tissue of upper limb, including shoulder**
D21.10 Benign neoplasm of connective and other soft tissue of unspecified upper limb, including shoulder
D21.11 Benign neoplasm of connective and other soft tissue of right upper limb, including shoulder
D21.12 Benign neoplasm of connective and other soft tissue of left upper limb, including shoulder
+ **D21.2 Benign neoplasm of connective and other soft tissue of lower limb, including hip**
D21.20 Benign neoplasm of connective and other soft tissue of unspecified lower limb, including hip
D21.21 Benign neoplasm of connective and other soft tissue of right lower limb, including hip
D21.22 Benign neoplasm of connective and other soft tissue of left lower limb, including hip
D21.3 Benign neoplasm of connective and other soft tissue of thorax
Benign neoplasm of axilla
Benign neoplasm of diaphragm
Benign neoplasm of great vessels
Excludes1: *benign neoplasm of heart (D15.1)*
benign neoplasm of mediastinum (D15.2)
benign neoplasm of thymus (D15.0)
D21.4 Benign neoplasm of connective and other soft tissue of abdomen
Benign stromal tumors of abdomen
D21.5 Benign neoplasm of connective and other soft tissue of pelvis
Excludes1: *benign neoplasm of any uterine ligament (D28.2)*
uterine leiomyoma (D25.-)
D21.6 Benign neoplasm of connective and other soft tissue of trunk, unspecified
Benign neoplasm of back NOS
D21.9 Benign neoplasm of connective and other soft tissue, unspecified

D22 Melanocytic nevi
Includes: atypical nevus
blue hairy pigmented nevus
nevus NOS
D22.0 Melanocytic nevi of lip
+ **D22.1 Melanocytic nevi of eyelid, including canthus**
D22.10 Melanocytic nevi of unspecified eyelid, including canthus
D22.11 Melanocytic nevi of right eyelid, including canthus
D22.12 Melanocytic nevi of left eyelid, including canthus
+ **D22.2 Melanocytic nevi of ear and external auricular canal**
D22.20 Melanocytic nevi of unspecified ear and external auricular canal
D22.21 Melanocytic nevi of right ear and external auricular canal
D22.22 Melanocytic nevi of left ear and external auricular canal
+ **D22.3 Melanocytic nevi of other and unspecified parts of face**
D22.30 Melanocytic nevi of unspecified part of face
D22.39 Melanocytic nevi of other parts of face
D22.4 Melanocytic nevi of scalp and neck
D22.5 Melanocytic nevi of trunk
Melanocytic nevi of anal margin
Melanocytic nevi of anal skin
Melanocytic nevi of perianal skin
Melanocytic nevi of skin of breast
+ **D22.6 Melanocytic nevi of upper limb, including shoulder**
D22.60 Melanocytic nevi of unspecified upper limb, including shoulder
D22.61 Melanocytic nevi of right upper limb, including shoulder
D22.62 Melanocytic nevi of left upper limb, including shoulder
+ **D22.7 Melanocytic nevi of lower limb, including hip**
D22.70 Melanocytic nevi of unspecified lower limb, including hip
D22.71 Melanocytic nevi of right lower limb, including hip
D22.72 Melanocytic nevi of left lower limb, including hip
D22.9 Melanocytic nevi, unspecified

D23 Other benign neoplasms of skin

Includes: benign neoplasm of hair follicles
benign neoplasm of sebaceous glands
benign neoplasm of sweat glands

Excludes1: *benign lipomatous neoplasms of skin (D17.0-D17.3)*
melanocytic nevi (D22.-)

D23.0 Other benign neoplasm of skin of lip
Excludes1: *benign neoplasm of vermilion border of lip (D10.0)*

\+ **D23.1 Other benign neoplasm of skin of eyelid, including canthus**
D23.10 Other benign neoplasm of skin of unspecified eyelid, including canthus
D23.11 Other benign neoplasm of skin of right eyelid, including canthus
D23.12 Other benign neoplasm of skin of left eyelid, including canthus

\+ **D23.2 Other benign neoplasm of skin of ear and external auricular canal**
D23.20 Other benign neoplasm of skin of unspecified ear and external auricular canal
D23.21 Other benign neoplasm of skin of right ear and external auricular canal
D23.22 Other benign neoplasm of skin of left ear and external auricular canal

\+ **D23.3 Other benign neoplasm of skin of other and unspecified parts of face**
D23.30 Other benign neoplasm of skin of unspecified part of face
D23.39 Other benign neoplasm of skin of other parts of face

D23.4 Other benign neoplasm of skin of scalp and neck

D23.5 Other benign neoplasm of skin of trunk
Other benign neoplasm of anal margin
Other benign neoplasm of anal skin
Other benign neoplasm of perianal skin
Other benign neoplasm of skin of breast
Excludes1: *benign neoplasm of anus NOS (D12.9)*

\+ **D23.6 Other benign neoplasm of skin of upper limb, including shoulder**
D23.60 Other benign neoplasm of skin of unspecified upper limb, including shoulder
D23.61 Other benign neoplasm of skin of right upper limb, including shoulder
D23.62 Other benign neoplasm of skin of left upper limb, including shoulder

\+ **D23.7 Other benign neoplasm of skin of lower limb, including hip**
D23.70 Other benign neoplasm of skin of unspecified lower limb, including hip
D23.71 Other benign neoplasm of skin of right lower limb, including hip
D23.72 Other benign neoplasm of skin of left lower limb, including hip

D23.9 Other benign neoplasm of skin, unspecified

D24 Benign neoplasm of breast

Includes: benign neoplasm of connective tissue of breast
benign neoplasm of soft parts of breast
fibroadenoma of breast

Excludes2: *adenofibrosis of breast (N60.2)*
benign cyst of breast (N60.-)
benign mammary dysplasia (N60.-)
benign neoplasm of skin of breast (D22.5, D23.5)
fibrocystic disease of breast (N60.-)

D24.1 Benign neoplasm of right breast
D24.2 Benign neoplasm of left breast
D24.9 Benign neoplasm of unspecified breast

D25 Leiomyoma of uterus

Includes: uterine fibroid
uterine fibromyoma
uterine myoma

♀ **D25.0 Submucous leiomyoma of uterus**
♀ **D25.1 Intramural leiomyoma of uterus**
Interstitial leiomyoma of uterus
♀ **D25.2 Subserosal leiomyoma of uterus**
Subperitoneal leiomyoma of uterus
♀ **D25.9 Leiomyoma of uterus, unspecified**

D26 Other benign neoplasms of uterus

♀ **D26.0 Other benign neoplasm of cervix uteri**
♀ **D26.1 Other benign neoplasm of corpus uteri**
♀ **D26.7 Other benign neoplasm of other parts of uterus**
♀ **D26.9 Other benign neoplasm of uterus, unspecified**

D27 Benign neoplasm of ovary

Use additional code to identify any functional activity.

Excludes2: *corpus albicans cyst (N83.2)*
corpus luteum cyst (N83.1)
endometrial cyst (N80.1)
follicular (atretic) cyst (N83.0)
graafian follicle cyst (N83.0)
ovarian cyst NEC (N83.2)
ovarian retention cyst (N83.2)

♀ **D27.0 Benign neoplasm of right ovary**
♀ **D27.1 Benign neoplasm of left ovary**
♀ **D27.9 Benign neoplasm of unspecified ovary**

D28 Benign neoplasm of other and unspecified female genital organs

Includes: adenomatous polyp
benign neoplasm of skin of female genital organs
benign teratoma

Excludes1: *epoophoron cyst (Q50.5)*
fimbrial cyst (Q50.4)
Gartner's duct cyst (Q52.4)
parovarian cyst (Q50.5)

♀ **D28.0 Benign neoplasm of vulva**
♀ **D28.1 Benign neoplasm of vagina**
♀ **D28.2 Benign neoplasm of uterine tubes and ligaments**
Benign neoplasm of fallopian tube
Benign neoplasm of uterine ligament (broad) (round)
♀ **D28.7 Benign neoplasm of other specified female genital organs**
♀ **D28.9 Benign neoplasm of female genital organ, unspecified**

D29 Benign neoplasm of male genital organs

Includes: benign neoplasm of skin of male genital organs

♂ **D29.0 Benign neoplasm of penis**
♂ **D29.1 Benign neoplasm of prostate**
Excludes1: *enlarged prostate (N40.-)*

\+ **D29.2 Benign neoplasm of testis**
Use additional code to identify any functional activity.
♂ **D29.20 Benign neoplasm of unspecified testis**
♂ **D29.21 Benign neoplasm of right testis**
♂ **D29.22 Benign neoplasm of left testis**

\+ **D29.3 Benign neoplasm of epididymis**
♂ **D29.30 Benign neoplasm of unspecified epididymis**
♂ **D29.31 Benign neoplasm of right epididymis**
♂ **D29.32 Benign neoplasm of left epididymis**

♂ **D29.4 Benign neoplasm of scrotum**
Benign neoplasm of skin of scrotum
♂ **D29.8 Benign neoplasm of other specified male genital organs**
Benign neoplasm of seminal vesicle
Benign neoplasm of spermatic cord
Benign neoplasm of tunica vaginalis
♂ **D29.9 Benign neoplasm of male genital organ, unspecified**

D30 Benign neoplasm of urinary organs

\+ **D30.0 Benign neoplasm of kidney**
Excludes1: *benign carcinoid tumor of the kidney (D3A.093)*
benign neoplasm of renal calyces (D30.1-)
benign neoplasm of renal pelvis (D30.1-)
D30.00 Benign neoplasm of unspecified kidney
D30.01 Benign neoplasm of right kidney
D30.02 Benign neoplasm of left kidney

\+ **D30.1 Benign neoplasm of renal pelvis**
D30.10 Benign neoplasm of unspecified renal pelvis
D30.11 Benign neoplasm of right renal pelvis
D30.12 Benign neoplasm of left renal pelvis

\+ **D30.2 Benign neoplasm of ureter**
Excludes1: *benign neoplasm of ureteric orifice of bladder (D30.3)*
D30.20 Benign neoplasm of unspecified ureter
D30.21 Benign neoplasm of right ureter
D30.22 Benign neoplasm of left ureter

D30.3 Benign neoplasm of bladder
Benign neoplasm of ureteric orifice of bladder
Benign neoplasm of urethral orifice of bladder

D30.4 Benign neoplasm of urethra
Excludes1: *benign neoplasm of urethral orifice of bladder (D30.3)*

D30.8 Benign neoplasm of other specified urinary organs
Benign neoplasm of paraurethral glands

D30.9 Benign neoplasm of urinary organ, unspecified
Benign neoplasm of urinary system NOS

D31 Benign neoplasm of eye and adnexa

Excludes1: *benign neoplasm of connective tissue of eyelid (D21.0)*
benign neoplasm of optic nerve (D33.3)
benign neoplasm of skin of eyelid (D22.1-, D23.1-)

+ **D31.0 Benign neoplasm of conjunctiva**
  - **D31.00 Benign neoplasm of unspecified conjunctiva**
  - **D31.01 Benign neoplasm of right conjunctiva**
  - **D31.02 Benign neoplasm of left conjunctiva**
+ **D31.1 Benign neoplasm of cornea**
  - **D31.10 Benign neoplasm of unspecified cornea**
  - **D31.11 Benign neoplasm of right cornea**
  - **D31.12 Benign neoplasm of left cornea**
+ **D31.2 Benign neoplasm of retina**

  Excludes1: *dark area on retina (D49.81)*
  hemangioma of retina (D49.81)
  neoplasm of unspecified behavior of retina and choroid (D49.81)
  retinal freckle (D49.81)
  - **D31.20 Benign neoplasm of unspecified retina**
  - **D31.21 Benign neoplasm of right retina**
  - **D31.22 Benign neoplasm of left retina**
+ **D31.3 Benign neoplasm of choroid**
  - **D31.30 Benign neoplasm of unspecified choroid**
  - **D31.31 Benign neoplasm of right choroid**
  - **D31.32 Benign neoplasm of left choroid**
+ **D31.4 Benign neoplasm of ciliary body**
  - **D31.40 Benign neoplasm of unspecified ciliary body**
  - **D31.41 Benign neoplasm of right ciliary body**
  - **D31.42 Benign neoplasm of left ciliary body**
+ **D31.5 Benign neoplasm of lacrimal gland and duct**

  Benign neoplasm of lacrimal sac
  Benign neoplasm of nasolacrimal duct
  - **D31.50 Benign neoplasm of unspecified lacrimal gland and duct**
  - **D31.51 Benign neoplasm of right lacrimal gland and duct**
  - **D31.52 Benign neoplasm of left lacrimal gland and duct**
+ **D31.6 Benign neoplasm of unspecified site of orbit**

  Benign neoplasm of connective tissue of orbit
  Benign neoplasm of extraocular muscle
  Benign neoplasm of peripheral nerves of orbit
  Benign neoplasm of retrobulbar tissue
  Benign neoplasm of retro-ocular tissue
  Excludes1: *benign neoplasm of orbital bone (D16.4)*
  - **D31.60 Benign neoplasm of unspecified site of unspecified orbit**
  - **D31.61 Benign neoplasm of unspecified site of right orbit**
  - **D31.62 Benign neoplasm of unspecified site of left orbit**
+ **D31.9 Benign neoplasm of unspecified part of eye**

  Benign neoplasm of eyeball
  - **D31.90 Benign neoplasm of unspecified part of unspecified eye**
  - **D31.91 Benign neoplasm of unspecified part of right eye**
  - **D31.92 Benign neoplasm of unspecified part of left eye**

D32 Benign neoplasm of meninges

- **D32.0 Benign neoplasm of cerebral meninges**
- **D32.1 Benign neoplasm of spinal meninges**
- **D32.9 Benign neoplasm of meninges, unspecified**

  Meningioma NOS

D33 Benign neoplasm of brain and other parts of central nervous system

Excludes1: *angioma (D18.0-)*
benign neoplasm of meninges (D32.-)
benign neoplasm of peripheral nerves and autonomic nervous system (D36.1-)
hemangioma (D18.0-)
neurofibromatosis (Q85.0-)
retro-ocular benign neoplasm (D31.6-)

- **D33.0 Benign neoplasm of brain, supratentorial**

  Benign neoplasm of cerebral ventricle
  Benign neoplasm of cerebrum
  Benign neoplasm of frontal lobe
  Benign neoplasm of occipital lobe
  Benign neoplasm of parietal lobe
  Benign neoplasm of temporal lobe
  Excludes1: *benign neoplasm of fourth ventricle (D33.1)*
- **D33.1 Benign neoplasm of brain, infratentorial**

  Benign neoplasm of brain stem
  Benign neoplasm of cerebellum
  Benign neoplasm of fourth ventricle
- **D33.2 Benign neoplasm of brain, unspecified**
- **D33.3 Benign neoplasm of cranial nerves**

  Benign neoplasm of olfactory bulb
- **D33.4 Benign neoplasm of spinal cord**
- **D33.7 Benign neoplasm of other specified parts of central nervous system**
- **D33.9 Benign neoplasm of central nervous system, unspecified**

  Benign neoplasm of nervous system (central) NOS

D34 Benign neoplasm of thyroid gland

Use additional code to identify any functional activity
Valid 3-character code, no further characters required

D35 Benign neoplasm of other and unspecified endocrine glands

Use additional code to identify any functional activity
Excludes1: *benign neoplasm of endocrine pancreas (D13.7)*
benign neoplasm of ovary (D27.-)
benign neoplasm of testis (D29.2.-)
benign neoplasm of thymus (D15.0)

+ **D35.0 Benign neoplasm of adrenal gland**
  - **D35.00 Benign neoplasm of unspecified adrenal gland**
  - **D35.01 Benign neoplasm of right adrenal gland**
  - **D35.02 Benign neoplasm of left adrenal gland**
- **D35.1 Benign neoplasm of parathyroid gland**
- **D35.2 Benign neoplasm of pituitary gland**
- **D35.3 Benign neoplasm of craniopharyngeal duct**
- **D35.4 Benign neoplasm of pineal gland**
- **D35.5 Benign neoplasm of carotid body**
- **D35.6 Benign neoplasm of aortic body and other paraganglia**

  Benign tumor of glomus jugulare
- **D35.7 Benign neoplasm of other specified endocrine glands**
- **D35.9 Benign neoplasm of endocrine gland, unspecified**

  Benign neoplasm of unspecified endocrine gland

D36 Benign neoplasm of other and unspecified sites

- **D36.0 Benign neoplasm of lymph nodes**

  Excludes1: *lymphangioma (D18.1)*
+ **D36.1 Benign neoplasm of peripheral nerves and autonomic nervous system**

  Excludes1: *benign neoplasm of peripheral nerves of orbit (D31.6-)*
  neurofibromatosis (Q85.0-)
  - **D36.10 Benign neoplasm of peripheral nerves and autonomic nervous system, unspecified**
  - **D36.11 Benign neoplasm of peripheral nerves and autonomic nervous system of face, head, and neck**
  - **D36.12 Benign neoplasm of peripheral nerves and autonomic nervous system, upper limb, including shoulder**
  - **D36.13 Benign neoplasm of peripheral nerves and autonomic nervous system of lower limb, including hip**
  - **D36.14 Benign neoplasm of peripheral nerves and autonomic nervous system of thorax**
  - **D36.15 Benign neoplasm of peripheral nerves and autonomic nervous system of abdomen**
  - **D36.16 Benign neoplasm of peripheral nerves and autonomic nervous system of pelvis**
  - **D36.17 Benign neoplasm of peripheral nerves and autonomic nervous system of trunk, unspecified**
- **D36.7 Benign neoplasm of other specified sites**

  Benign neoplasm of nose NOS
- **D36.9 Benign neoplasm, unspecified site**

Benign neuroendocrine tumors (D3A)

D3A Benign neuroendocrine tumors

Code also any associated multiple endocrine neoplasia [MEN] syndromes (E31.2-)

Use additional code to identify any associated endocrine syndrome, such as:
carcinoid syndrome (E34.0)

Excludes2: *benign pancreatic islet cell tumors (D13.7)*

+ **D3A.0 Benign carcinoid tumors**
  - **D3A.00 Benign carcinoid tumor of unspecified site**

    Carcinoid tumor NOS
  + **D3A.01 Benign carcinoid tumors of the small intestine**
    - **D3A.010 Benign carcinoid tumor of the duodenum**
    - **D3A.011 Benign carcinoid tumor of the jejunum**
    - **D3A.012 Benign carcinoid tumor of the ileum**
    - **D3A.019 Benign carcinoid tumor of the small intestine, unspecified portion**

+ **D3A.02 Benign carcinoid tumors of the appendix, large intestine, and rectum**
D3A.020 Benign carcinoid tumor of the appendix
D3A.021 Benign carcinoid tumor of the cecum
D3A.022 Benign carcinoid tumor of the ascending colon
D3A.023 Benign carcinoid tumor of the transverse colon
D3A.024 Benign carcinoid tumor of the descending colon
D3A.025 Benign carcinoid tumor of the sigmoid colon
D3A.026 Benign carcinoid tumor of the rectum
D3A.029 Benign carcinoid tumor of the large intestine, unspecified portion
Benign carcinoid tumor of the colon NOS
+ **D3A.09 Benign carcinoid tumors of other sites**
D3A.090 Benign carcinoid tumor of the bronchus and lung
D3A.091 Benign carcinoid tumor of the thymus
D3A.092 Benign carcinoid tumor of the stomach
D3A.093 Benign carcinoid tumor of the kidney
D3A.094 Benign carcinoid tumor of the foregut NOS
D3A.095 Benign carcinoid tumor of the midgut NOS
D3A.096 Benign carcinoid tumor of the hindgut NOS
D3A.098 Benign carcinoid tumors of other sites
D3A.8 Other benign neuroendocrine tumors
Neuroendocrine tumor NOS

Neoplasms of uncertain behavior, polycythemia vera and myelodysplastic syndromes (D37-D48)

NOTE Categories D37-D44, and D48 classify by site neoplasms of uncertain behavior, i.e., histologic confirmation whether the neoplasm is malignant or benign cannot be made.

Excludes1: *neoplasms of unspecified behavior (D49.-)*

D37 Neoplasm of uncertain behavior of oral cavity and digestive organs
Excludes1: *stromal tumors of uncertain behavior of digestive system (D48.1)*
+ **D37.0 Neoplasm of uncertain behavior of lip, oral cavity and pharynx**
Excludes1: *neoplasm of uncertain behavior of aryepiglottic fold or interarytenoid fold, laryngeal aspect (D38.0)*
neoplasm of uncertain behavior of epiglottis NOS (D38.0)
neoplasm of uncertain behavior of skin of lip (D48.5)
neoplasm of uncertain behavior of suprahyoid portion of epiglottis (D38.0)
D37.01 Neoplasm of uncertain behavior of lip
Neoplasm of uncertain behavior of vermilion border of lip
D37.02 Neoplasm of uncertain behavior of tongue
+ **D37.03 Neoplasm of uncertain behavior of the major salivary glands**
D37.030 Neoplasm of uncertain behavior of the parotid salivary glands
D37.031 Neoplasm of uncertain behavior of the sublingual salivary glands
D37.032 Neoplasm of uncertain behavior of the submandibular salivary glands
D37.039 Neoplasm of uncertain behavior of the major salivary glands, unspecified
D37.04 Neoplasm of uncertain behavior of the minor salivary glands
Neoplasm of uncertain behavior of submucosal salivary glands of lip
Neoplasm of uncertain behavior of submucosal salivary glands of cheek
Neoplasm of uncertain behavior of submucosal salivary glands of hard palate
Neoplasm of uncertain behavior of submucosal salivary glands of soft palate
D37.05 Neoplasm of uncertain behavior of pharynx
Neoplasm of uncertain behavior of aryepiglottic fold of pharynx NOS
Neoplasm of uncertain behavior of hypopharyngeal aspect of aryepiglottic fold of pharynx
Neoplasm of uncertain behavior of marginal zone of aryepiglottic fold of pharynx
D37.09 Neoplasm of uncertain behavior of other specified sites of the oral cavity
D37.1 Neoplasm of uncertain behavior of stomach
D37.2 Neoplasm of uncertain behavior of small intestine
D37.3 Neoplasm of uncertain behavior of appendix
D37.4 Neoplasm of uncertain behavior of colon
D37.5 Neoplasm of uncertain behavior of rectum
Neoplasm of uncertain behavior of rectosigmoid junction
D37.6 Neoplasm of uncertain behavior of liver, gallbladder and bile ducts
Neoplasm of uncertain behavior of ampulla of Vater
D37.8 Neoplasm of uncertain behavior of other specified digestive organs
Neoplasm of uncertain behavior of anal canal
Neoplasm of uncertain behavior of anal sphincter
Neoplasm of uncertain behavior of anus NOS
Neoplasm of uncertain behavior of esophagus
Neoplasm of uncertain behavior of intestine NOS
Neoplasm of uncertain behavior of pancreas
Excludes1: *neoplasm of uncertain behavior of anal margin (D48.5)*
neoplasm of uncertain behavior of anal skin (D48
neoplasm of uncertain behavior of perianal skin (D48.5)
D37.9 Neoplasm of uncertain behavior of digestive organ, unspecifie

D38 Neoplasm of uncertain behavior of middle ear and respiratory and intrathoracic organs
Excludes1: *neoplasm of uncertain behavior of heart (D48.7)*
D38.0 Neoplasm of uncertain behavior of larynx
Neoplasm of uncertain behavior of aryepiglottic fold or interarytenoid fold, laryngeal aspect
Neoplasm of uncertain behavior of epiglottis (suprahyoid portio
Excludes1: *neoplasm of uncertain behavior of aryepiglottic fo or interarytenoid fold NOS (D37.05)*
neoplasm of uncertain behavior of hypopharynge aspect of aryepiglottic fold (D37.05)
neoplasm of uncertain behavior of marginal zone aryepiglottic fold (D37.05)
D38.1 Neoplasm of uncertain behavior of trachea, bronchus and lun
D38.2 Neoplasm of uncertain behavior of pleura
D38.3 Neoplasm of uncertain behavior of mediastinum
D38.4 Neoplasm of uncertain behavior of thymus
D38.5 Neoplasm of uncertain behavior of other respiratory organs
Neoplasm of uncertain behavior of accessory sinuses
Neoplasm of uncertain behavior of cartilage of nose
Neoplasm of uncertain behavior of middle ear
Neoplasm of uncertain behavior of nasal cavities
Excludes1: *neoplasm of uncertain behavior of ear (external) (skin) (D48.5)*
neoplasm of uncertain behavior of nose NOS (D48.7)
neoplasm of uncertain behavior of skin of nose (D48.5)
D38.6 Neoplasm of uncertain behavior of respiratory organ, unspecified

D39 Neoplasm of uncertain behavior of female genital organs
♀ **D39.0 Neoplasm of uncertain behavior of uterus**
+ **D39.1 Neoplasm of uncertain behavior of ovary**
Use additional code to identify any functional activity.
♀ **D39.10 Neoplasm of uncertain behavior of unspecified ovary**
♀ **D39.11 Neoplasm of uncertain behavior of right ovary**
♀ **D39.12 Neoplasm of uncertain behavior of left ovary**
♀ **D39.2 Neoplasm of uncertain behavior of placenta**
Chorioadenoma destruens
Invasive hydatidiform mole
Malignant hydatidiform mole
Excludes1: *hydatidiform mole NOS (O01.9)*
♀ **D39.8 Neoplasm of uncertain behavior of other specified female genit organs**
Neoplasm of uncertain behavior of skin of female genital organs
♀ **D39.9 Neoplasm of uncertain behavior of female genital organ, unspecified**

D40 Neoplasm of uncertain behavior of male genital organs
♂ **D40.0 Neoplasm of uncertain behavior of prostate**
+ **D40.1 Neoplasm of uncertain behavior of testis**
♂ **D40.10 Neoplasm of uncertain behavior of unspecified testis**
♂ **D40.11 Neoplasm of uncertain behavior of right testis**
♂ **D40.12 Neoplasm of uncertain behavior of left testis**
♂ **D40.8 Neoplasm of uncertain behavior of other specified male genital organs**
Neoplasm of uncertain behavior of skin of male genital organs
♂ **D40.9 Neoplasm of uncertain behavior of male genital organ, unspecified**

D41 Neoplasm of uncertain behavior of urinary organs

+ **D41.0 Neoplasm of uncertain behavior of kidney**
Excludes1: *neoplasm of uncertain behavior of renal pelvis (D41.1-)*
D41.00 Neoplasm of uncertain behavior of unspecified kidney
D41.01 Neoplasm of uncertain behavior of right kidney
D41.02 Neoplasm of uncertain behavior of left kidney

+ **D41.1 Neoplasm of uncertain behavior of renal pelvis**
D41.10 Neoplasm of uncertain behavior of unspecified renal pelvis
D41.11 Neoplasm of uncertain behavior of right renal pelvis
D41.12 Neoplasm of uncertain behavior of left renal pelvis

+ **D41.2 Neoplasm of uncertain behavior of ureter**
D41.20 Neoplasm of uncertain behavior of unspecified ureter
D41.21 Neoplasm of uncertain behavior of right ureter
D41.22 Neoplasm of uncertain behavior of left ureter

D41.3 Neoplasm of uncertain behavior of urethra
D41.4 Neoplasm of uncertain behavior of bladder
D41.8 Neoplasm of uncertain behavior of other specified urinary organs
D41.9 Neoplasm of uncertain behavior of unspecified urinary organ

D42 Neoplasm of uncertain behavior of meninges

D42.0 Neoplasm of uncertain behavior of cerebral meninges
D42.1 Neoplasm of uncertain behavior of spinal meninges
D42.9 Neoplasm of uncertain behavior of meninges, unspecified

D43 Neoplasm of uncertain behavior of brain and central nervous system

Excludes1: *neoplasm of uncertain behavior of peripheral nerves and autonomic nervous system (D48.2)*

D43.0 Neoplasm of uncertain behavior of brain, supratentorial
Neoplasm of uncertain behavior of cerebral ventricle
Neoplasm of uncertain behavior of cerebrum
Neoplasm of uncertain behavior of frontal lobe
Neoplasm of uncertain behavior of occipital lobe
Neoplasm of uncertain behavior of parietal lobe
Neoplasm of uncertain behavior of temporal lobe
Excludes1: *neoplasm of uncertain behavior of fourth ventricle (D43.1)*

D43.1 Neoplasm of uncertain behavior of brain, infratentorial
Neoplasm of uncertain behavior of brain stem
Neoplasm of uncertain behavior of cerebellum
Neoplasm of uncertain behavior of fourth ventricle

D43.2 Neoplasm of uncertain behavior of brain, unspecified
D43.3 Neoplasm of uncertain behavior of cranial nerves
D43.4 Neoplasm of uncertain behavior of spinal cord
D43.8 Neoplasm of uncertain behavior of other specified parts of central nervous system
D43.9 Neoplasm of uncertain behavior of central nervous system, unspecified
Neoplasm of uncertain behavior of nervous system (central) NOS

D44 Neoplasm of uncertain behavior of endocrine glands

Excludes1: *multiple endocrine adenomatosis (E31.2-)*
multiple endocrine neoplasia (E31.2-)
neoplasm of uncertain behavior of endocrine pancreas (D37.8)
neoplasm of uncertain behavior of ovary (D39.1-)
neoplasm of uncertain behavior of testis (D40.1-)
neoplasm of uncertain behavior of thymus (D38.4)

D44.0 Neoplasm of uncertain behavior of thyroid gland

+ **D44.1 Neoplasm of uncertain behavior of adrenal gland**
Use additional code to identify any functional activity.
D44.10 Neoplasm of uncertain behavior of unspecified adrenal gland
D44.11 Neoplasm of uncertain behavior of right adrenal gland
D44.12 Neoplasm of uncertain behavior of left adrenal gland

D44.2 Neoplasm of uncertain behavior of parathyroid gland
D44.3 Neoplasm of uncertain behavior of pituitary gland
Use additional code to identify any functional activity.
D44.4 Neoplasm of uncertain behavior of craniopharyngeal duct
D44.5 Neoplasm of uncertain behavior of pineal gland
D44.6 Neoplasm of uncertain behavior of carotid body
D44.7 Neoplasm of uncertain behavior of aortic body and other paraganglia
D44.9 Neoplasm of uncertain behavior of unspecified endocrine gland

D45 Polycythemia vera

Excludes1: *familial polycythemia (D75.0)*
secondary polycythemia (D75.1)
Valid 3-character code, no further characters required

D46 Myelodysplastic syndromes

Use additional code for adverse effect, if applicable, to identify drug (T36-T50 with fifth or sixth character 5)
Excludes2: *drug-induced aplastic anemia (D61.1)*

D46.0 Refractory anemia without ring sideroblasts, so stated
Refractory anemia without sideroblasts, without excess of blasts
D46.1 Refractory anemia with ring sideroblasts
RARS

+ **D46.2 Refractory anemia with excess of blasts**
D46.20 Refractory anemia with excess of blasts, unspecified
RAEB NOS
D46.21 Refractory anemia with excess of blasts 1
RAEB 1
CC **D46.22 Refractory anemia with excess of blasts 2**
RAEB 2
CC Exclusion see Appendix A PDX collection 0488

D46.A Refractory cytopenia with multilineage dysplasia
D46.B Refractory cytopenia with multilineage dysplasia and ring sideroblasts
RCMD RS
CC **D46.C Myelodysplastic syndrome with isolated del(5q) chromosomal abnormality**
Myelodysplastic syndrome with 5q deletion
5q minus syndrome NOS
CC Exclusion see Appendix A PDX collection 0488
D46.4 Refractory anemia, unspecified
D46.Z Other myelodysplastic syndromes
Excludes1: *chronic myelomonocytic leukemia (C93.1-)*
D46.9 Myelodysplastic syndrome, unspecified
Myelodysplasia NOS

D47 Other neoplasms of uncertain behavior of lymphoid, hematopoietic and related tissue

CC **D47.0 Histiocytic and mast cell tumors of uncertain behavior**
Indolent systemic mastocytosis
Mast cell tumor NOS
Mastocytoma NOS
Excludes1: *malignant mast cell tumor (C96.2)*
mastocytosis (congenital) (cutaneous) (Q82.2)
CC Exclusion see Appendix A PDX collection 0494

CC **D47.1 Chronic myeloproliferative disease**
Chronic neutrophilic leukemia
Myeloproliferative disease, unspecified
Excludes1: *atypical chronic myeloid leukemia BCR/ABL-negative (C92.2-)*
chronic myeloid leukemia BCR/ABL-positive (C92.1-)
myelofibrosis NOS (D75.81)
myelophthisic anemia (D61.82)
myelophthisis (D61.82)
secondary myelofibrosis NOS (D75.81)
CC Exclusion see Appendix A PDX collection 0488

D47.2 Monoclonal gammopathy
Monoclonal gammopathy of undetermined significance [MGUS]
D47.3 Essential (hemorrhagic) thrombocythemia
Essential thrombocytosis
Idiopathic hemorrhagic thrombocythemia
D47.4 Osteomyelofibrosis
Chronic idiopathic myelofibrosis
Myelofibrosis (idiopathic) (with myeloid metaplasia)
Myelosclerosis (megakaryocytic) with myeloid metaplasia
Secondary myelofibrosis in myeloproliferative disease
Excludes1: *acute myelofibrosis (C94.4-)*

+ **D47.Z Other specified neoplasms of uncertain behavior of lymphoid, hematopoietic and related tissue**
CC **D47.Z1 Post-transplant lymphoproliferative disorder (PTLD)**
Code first complications of transplanted organs and tissue (T86.-)
CC Exclusion see Appendix A PDX collection 0495
CC **D47.Z9 Other specified neoplasms of uncertain behavior of lymphoid, hematopoietic and related tissue**
Histiocytic tumors of uncertain behavior
CC Exclusion see Appendix A PDX collection 0488

CC **D47.9 Neoplasm of uncertain behavior of lymphoid, hematopoietic and related tissue, unspecified**
Lymphoproliferative disease NOS
CC Exclusion see Appendix A PDX collection 0488

D48 Neoplasm of uncertain behavior of other and unspecified sites

Excludes1: *neurofibromatosis (nonmalignant) (Q85.0-)*

D48.0 Neoplasm of uncertain behavior of bone and articular cartilage

Excludes1: *neoplasm of uncertain behavior of cartilage of ear (D48.1)*
neoplasm of uncertain behavior of cartilage of larynx (D38.0)
neoplasm of uncertain behavior of cartilage of nose (D38.5)
neoplasm of uncertain behavior of connective tissue of eyelid (D48.1)
neoplasm of uncertain behavior of synovia (D48.1)

D48.1 Neoplasm of uncertain behavior of connective and other soft tissue

Neoplasm of uncertain behavior of connective tissue of ear
Neoplasm of uncertain behavior of connective tissue of eyelid
Stromal tumors of uncertain behavior of digestive system

Excludes1: *neoplasm of uncertain behavior of articular cartilage (D48.0)*
neoplasm of uncertain behavior of cartilage of larynx (D38.0)
neoplasm of uncertain behavior of cartilage of nose (D38.5)
neoplasm of uncertain behavior of connective tissue of breast (D48.6-)

D48.2 Neoplasm of uncertain behavior of peripheral nerves and autonomic nervous system

Excludes1: *neoplasm of uncertain behavior of peripheral nerves of orbit (D48.7)*

D48.3 Neoplasm of uncertain behavior of retroperitoneum

D48.4 Neoplasm of uncertain behavior of peritoneum

D48.5 Neoplasm of uncertain behavior of skin

Neoplasm of uncertain behavior of anal margin
Neoplasm of uncertain behavior of anal skin
Neoplasm of uncertain behavior of perianal skin
Neoplasm of uncertain behavior of skin of breast

Excludes1: *neoplasm of uncertain behavior of anus NOS (D37.8)*
neoplasm of uncertain behavior of skin of genital organs (D39.8, D40.8)
neoplasm of uncertain behavior of vermilion border of lip (D37.0)

+ D48.6 Neoplasm of uncertain behavior of breast

Neoplasm of uncertain behavior of connective tissue of breast
Cystosarcoma phyllodes

Excludes1: *neoplasm of uncertain behavior of skin of breast (D48.5)*

D48.60 Neoplasm of uncertain behavior of unspecified breast

D48.61 Neoplasm of uncertain behavior of right breast

D48.62 Neoplasm of uncertain behavior of left breast

D48.7 Neoplasm of uncertain behavior of other specified sites

Neoplasm of uncertain behavior of eye
Neoplasm of uncertain behavior of heart
Neoplasm of uncertain behavior of peripheral nerves of orbit

Excludes1: *neoplasm of uncertain behavior of connective tissue (D48.1)*
neoplasm of uncertain behavior of skin of eyelid (D48.5)

D48.9 Neoplasm of uncertain behavior, unspecified

Neoplasms of unspecified behavior (D49)

D49 Neoplasms of unspecified behavior

NOTE Category D49 classifies by site neoplasms ofunspecified morphology and behavior. The term'mass', unless otherwise stated, is not to be regarded as a neoplastic growth.

Includes: 'growth' NOS
neoplasm NOS
new growth NOS
tumor NOS

Excludes1: *neoplasms of uncertain behavior (D37-D44, D48)*

D49.0 Neoplasm of unspecified behavior of digestive system

Excludes1: *neoplasm of unspecified behavior of margin of anus (D49.2)*
neoplasm of unspecified behavior of perianal skin (D49.2)
neoplasm of unspecified behavior of skin of anus (D49.2)

D49.1 Neoplasm of unspecified behavior of respiratory system

D49.2 Neoplasm of unspecified behavior of bone, soft tissue, and ski

Excludes1: *neoplasm of unspecified behavior of anal canal (D49.0)*
neoplasm of unspecified behavior of anus NOS (D49.0)
neoplasm of unspecified behavior of bone marrow (D49.89)
neoplasm of unspecified behavior of cartilage of larynx (D49.1)
neoplasm of unspecified behavior of cartilage of nose (D49.1)
neoplasm of unspecified behavior of connective tissue of breast (D49.3)
neoplasm of unspecified behavior of skin of genit organs (D49.5)
neoplasm of unspecified behavior of vermilion border of lip (D49.0)

D49.3 Neoplasm of unspecified behavior of breast

Excludes1: *neoplasm of unspecified behavior of skin of breas (D49.2)*

D49.4 Neoplasm of unspecified behavior of bladder

D49.5 Neoplasm of unspecified behavior of other genitourinary orga

D49.6 Neoplasm of unspecified behavior of brain

Excludes1: *neoplasm of unspecified behavior of cerebral meninges (D49.7)*
neoplasm of unspecified behavior of cranial nerve (D49.7)

D49.7 Neoplasm of unspecified behavior of endocrine glands and ot parts of nervous system

Excludes1: *neoplasm of unspecified behavior of peripheral, sympathetic, and parasympathetic nerves and ganglia (D49.2)*

+ D49.8 Neoplasm of unspecified behavior of other specified sites

Excludes1: *neoplasm of unspecified behavior of eyelid (skin) (D49.2)*
neoplasm of unspecified behavior of eyelid cartila (D49.2)
neoplasm of unspecified behavior of great vessels (D49.2)
neoplasm of unspecified behavior of optic nerve (D49.7)

D49.81 Neoplasm of unspecified behavior of retina and choroid

Dark area on retina
Retinal freckle

D49.89 Neoplasm of unspecified behavior of other specified sites

D49.9 Neoplasm of unspecified behavior of unspecified site

apter 3: Diseases of the Blood and Blood-Forming gans and Certain Disorders Involving the Immune echanism (D50-D89)

ludes2: *autoimmune disease (systemic) NOS (M35.9)*
certain conditions originating in the perinatal period (P00-P96)
complications of pregnancy, childbirth and the puerperium (O00-O9A)
congenital malformations, deformations and chromosomal abnormalities (Q00-Q99)
endocrine, nutritional and metabolic diseases (E00-E88)
human immunodeficiency virus [HIV] disease (B20)
injury, poisoning and certain other consequences of external causes (S00-T88)
neoplasms (C00-D49)
symptoms, signs and abnormal clinical and laboratory findings, not elsewhere classified (R00-R94)

s chapter contains the following category blocks:
D50-D53 Nutritional anemias
D55-D59 Hemolytic anemias
D60-D64 Aplastic and other anemias and other bone marrow failure syndromes
D65-D69 Coagulation defects, purpura and other hemorrhagic conditions
D70-D77 Other disorders of blood and blood-forming organs
D78 Intraoperative and postprocedural complications of the spleen
D80-D89 Certain disorders involving the immune mechanism

hapter-Specific Coding Guidelines

ddition to general coding guidelines, there are guidelines for specific diagnoses or conditions in the classification. Unless otherwise indicated, these guidelines ly to all health care settings. Please refer to Section II for guidelines on the ction of principal diagnosis.

Chapter 3: Diseases of the Blood and Blood-Forming Organs and Certain Disorders Involving the Immune Mechanism (D50-D89)

Reserved for future guideline expansion

tritional anemias (D50-D53)

D50 Iron deficiency anemia
Includes: asiderotic anemia
hypochromic anemia
D50.0 Iron deficiency anemia secondary to blood loss (chronic)
Posthemorrhagic anemia (chronic)
Excludes1: *acute posthemorrhagic anemia (D62)*
congenital anemia from fetal blood loss (P61.3)
D50.1 Sideropenic dysphagia
Kelly-Paterson syndrome
Plummer-Vinson syndrome
D50.8 Other iron deficiency anemias
Iron deficiency anemia due to inadequate dietary iron intake
D50.9 Iron deficiency anemia, unspecified

D51 Vitamin B12 deficiency anemia
Excludes1: *vitamin B12 deficiency (E53.8)*
D51.0 Vitamin B12 deficiency anemia due to intrinsic factor deficiency
Addison anemia
Biermer anemia
Pernicious (congenital) anemia
Congenital intrinsic factor deficiency
D51.1 Vitamin B12 deficiency anemia due to selective vitamin B12 malabsorption with proteinuria
Imerslund (Gräsbeck) syndrome
Megaloblastic hereditary anemia
D51.2 Transcobalamin II deficiency
D51.3 Other dietary vitamin B12 deficiency anemia
Vegan anemia
D51.8 Other vitamin B12 deficiency anemias
D51.9 Vitamin B12 deficiency anemia, unspecified

D52 Folate deficiency anemia
Excludes1: *folate deficiency without anemia (E53.8)*
D52.0 Dietary folate deficiency anemia
Nutritional megaloblastic anemia
D52.1 Drug-induced folate deficiency anemia
Use additional code for adverse effect, if applicable, to identify drug (T36-T50 with fifth or sixth character 5)
D52.8 Other folate deficiency anemias
D52.9 Folate deficiency anemia, unspecified
Folic acid deficiency anemia NOS

D53 Other nutritional anemias
Includes: megaloblastic anemia unresponsive to vitamin B12 or folate therapy
D53.0 Protein deficiency anemia
Amino-acid deficiency anemia
Orotaciduric anemia
Excludes1: *Lesch-Nyhan syndrome (E79.1)*
D53.1 Other megaloblastic anemias, not elsewhere classified
Megaloblastic anemia NOS
Excludes1: *Di Guglielmo's disease (C94.0)*
D53.2 Scorbutic anemia
Excludes1: *scurvy (E54)*
D53.8 Other specified nutritional anemias
Anemia associated with deficiency of copper
Anemia associated with deficiency of molybdenum
Anemia associated with deficiency of zinc
Excludes1: *nutritional deficiencies without anemia, such as:*
copper deficiency NOS (E61.0)
molybdenum deficiency NOS (E61.5)
zinc deficiency NOS (E60)
D53.9 Nutritional anemia, unspecified
Simple chronic anemia
Excludes1: *anemia NOS (D64.9)*

Hemolytic anemias (D55-D59)

D55 Anemia due to enzyme disorders
Excludes1: *drug-induced enzyme deficiency anemia (D59.2)*
D55.0 Anemia due to glucose-6-phosphate dehydrogenase [G6PD] deficiency
Favism
G6PD deficiency anemia
D55.1 Anemia due to other disorders of glutathione metabolism
Anemia (due to) enzyme deficiencies, except G6PD, related to the hexose monophosphate [HMP] shunt pathway
Anemia (due to) hemolytic nonspherocytic (hereditary), type I
D55.2 Anemia due to disorders of glycolytic enzymes
Hemolytic nonspherocytic (hereditary) anemia, type II
Hexokinase deficiency anemia
Pyruvate kinase [PK] deficiency anemia
Triose-phosphate isomerase deficiency anemia
Excludes1: *disorders of glycolysis not associated with anemia (E74.8)*
D55.3 Anemia due to disorders of nucleotide metabolism
D55.8 Other anemias due to enzyme disorders
D55.9 Anemia due to enzyme disorder, unspecified

D56 Thalassemia
Excludes1: *sickle-cell thalassemia (D57.4-)*
D56.0 Alpha thalassemia
Alpha thalassemia major
Hemoglobin H Constant Spring
Hemoglobin H disease
Hydrops fetalis due to alpha thalassemia
Severe alpha thalassemia
Triple gene defect alpha thalassemia
Use additional code, if applicable, for hydrops fetalis due to alpha thalassemia (P56.99)
Excludes1: *alpha thalassemia trait or minor (D56.3)*
asymptomatic alpha thalassemia (D56.3)
hydrops fetalis due to isoimmunization (P56.0)
hydrops fetalis not due to immune hemolysis (P83.2)
D56.1 Beta thalassemia
Beta thalassemia major
Cooley's anemia
Homozygous beta thalassemia
Severe beta thalassemia
Thalassemia intermedia
Thalassemia major
Excludes1: *beta thalassemia minor (D56.3)*
beta thalassemia trait (D56.3)
delta-beta thalassemia (D56.2)
hemoglobin E-beta thalassemia (D56.5)
sickle-cell beta thalassemia (D57.4-)
D56.2 Delta-beta thalassemia
Homozygous delta-beta thalassemia
Excludes1: *delta-beta thalassemia minor (D56.3)*
delta-beta thalassemia trait (D56.3)

D56.3 Thalassemia minor
Alpha thalassemia minor
Alpha thalassemia silent carrier
Alpha thalassemia trait
Beta thalassemia minor
Beta thalassemia trait
Delta-beta thalassemia minor
Delta-beta thalassemia trait
Thalassemia trait NOS
Excludes1: *alpha thalassemia (D56.0)*
beta thalassemia (D56.1)
delta-beta thalassemia (D56.2)
hemoglobin E-beta thalassemia (D56.5)
sickle-cell trait (D57.3)

D56.4 Hereditary persistence of fetal hemoglobin [HPFH]

D56.5 Hemoglobin E-beta thalassemia
Excludes1: *beta thalassemia (D56.1)*
beta thalassemia minor (D56.3)
beta thalassemia trait (D56.3)
delta-beta thalassemia (D56.2)
delta-beta thalassemia trait (D56.3)
hemoglobin E disease (D58.2)
other hemoglobinopathies (D58.2)
sickle-cell beta thalassemia (D57.4-)

D56.8 Other thalassemias
Dominant thalassemia
Hemoglobin C thalassemia
Mixed thalassemia
Thalassemia with other hemoglobinopathy
Excludes1: *hemoglobin C disease (D58.2)*
hemoglobin E disease (D58.2)
other hemoglobinopathies (D58.2)
sickle-cell anemia (D57.-)
sickle-cell thalassemia (D57.4)

D56.9 Thalassemia, unspecified
Mediterranean anemia (with other hemoglobinopathy)

D57 Sickle-cell disorders
Use additional code for any associated fever (R50.81)
Excludes1: *other hemoglobinopathies (D58.-)*

+ **D57.0 Hb-SS disease with crisis**
Sickle-cell disease NOS with crisis
Hb-SS disease with vasoocclusive pain

MCC **D57.00 Hb-SS disease with crisis, unspecified**
MCC Exclusion see Appendix A PDX collection 0496

MCC **D57.01 Hb-SS disease with acute chest syndrome**
MCC Exclusion see Appendix A PDX collection 0496

MCC **D57.02 Hb-SS disease with splenic sequestration**
MCC Exclusion see Appendix A PDX collection 0496

D57.1 Sickle-cell disease without crisis
Hb-SS disease without crisis
Sickle-cell anemia NOS
Sickle-cell disease NOS
Sickle-cell disorder NOS

+ **D57.2 Sickle-cell/Hb-C disease**
Hb-SC disease
Hb-S/Hb-C disease

D57.20 Sickle-cell/Hb-C disease without crisis

D57.21 Sickle-cell/Hb-C disease with crisis

MCC **D57.211 Sickle-cell/Hb-C disease with acute chest syndrome**
MCC Exclusion see Appendix A PDX collection 0496

MCC **D57.212 Sickle-cell/Hb-C disease with splenic sequestration**
MCC Exclusion see Appendix A PDX collection 0496

MCC **D57.219 Sickle-cell/Hb-C disease with crisis, unspecified**
Sickle-cell/Hb-C disease with crisis NOS
MCC Exclusion see Appendix A PDX collection 0496

D57.3 Sickle-cell trait
Hb-S trait
Heterozygous hemoglobin S

+ **D57.4 Sickle-cell thalassemia**
Sickle-cell beta thalassemia
Thalassemia Hb-S disease

D57.40 Sickle-cell thalassemia without crisis
Microdrepanocytosis
Sickle-cell thalassemia NOS

+ **D57.41 Sickle-cell thalassemia with crisis**
Sickle-cell thalassemia with vasoocclusive pain

MCC **D57.411 Sickle-cell thalassemia with acute chest syndrome**
MCC Exclusion see Appendix A PDX collectio 0496

MCC **D57.412 Sickle-cell thalassemia with splenic sequestration**
MCC Exclusion see Appendix A PDX collectio 0496

MCC **D57.419 Sickle-cell thalassemia with crisis, unspecified**
Sickle-cell thalassemia with crisis NOS
MCC Exclusion see Appendix A PDX collectio 0496

+ **D57.8 Other sickle-cell disorders**
Hb-SD disease
Hb-SE disease

D57.80 Other sickle-cell disorders without crisis

+ **D57.81 Other sickle-cell disorders with crisis**

MCC **D57.811 Other sickle-cell disorders with acute che syndrome**
MCC Exclusion see Appendix A PDX collectio 0496

MCC **D57.812 Other sickle-cell disorders with splenic sequestration**
MCC Exclusion see Appendix A PDX collectio 0496

MCC **D57.819 Other sickle-cell disorders with crisis, unspecified**
Other sickle-cell disorders with crisis NOS
MCC Exclusion see Appendix A PDX collectio 0496

D58 Other hereditary hemolytic anemias
Excludes1: *hemolytic anemia of the newborn (P55.-)*

D58.0 Hereditary spherocytosis
Acholuric (familial) jaundice
Congenital (spherocytic) hemolytic icterus
Minkowski-Chauffard syndrome

D58.1 Hereditary elliptocytosis
Elliptocytosis (congenital)
Ovalocytosis (congenital) (hereditary)

D58.2 Other hemoglobinopathies
Abnormal hemoglobin NOS
Congenital Heinz body anemia
Hb-C disease
Hb-D disease
Hb-E disease
Hemoglobinopathy NOS
Unstable hemoglobin hemolytic disease
Excludes1: *familial polycythemia (D75.0)*
Hb-M disease (D74.0)
hemoglobin E-beta thalassemia (D56.5)
hereditary persistence of fetal hemoglobin [HPF (D56.4)
high-altitude polycythemia (D75.1)
methemoglobinemia (D74.-)
other hemoglobinopathies with thalassemia (D56

CC **D58.8 Other specified hereditary hemolytic anemias**
Stomatocytosis
CC Exclusion see Appendix A PDX collection 0497

CC **D58.9 Hereditary hemolytic anemia, unspecified**
CC Exclusion see Appendix A PDX collection 0497

D59 Acquired hemolytic anemia

CC **D59.0 Drug-induced autoimmune hemolytic anemia**
Use additional code for adverse effect, if applicable, to identif drug (T36-T50 with fifth or sixth character 5)
CC Exclusion see Appendix A PDX collection 0496

CC **D59.1 Other autoimmune hemolytic anemias**
Autoimmune hemolytic disease (cold type) (warm type)
Chronic cold hemagglutinin disease
Cold agglutinin disease
Cold agglutinin hemoglobinuria
Cold type (secondary) (symptomatic) hemolytic anemia
Warm type (secondary) (symptomatic) hemolytic anemia
Excludes1: *Evans syndrome (D69.41)*
hemolytic disease of newborn (P55.-)
paroxysmal cold hemoglobinuria (D59.6)
CC Exclusion see Appendix A PDX collection 0496

CC **D59.2 Drug-induced nonautoimmune hemolytic anemia**
Drug-induced enzyme deficiency anemia
Use additional code for adverse effect, if applicable, to identif drug (T36-T50 with fifth or sixth character 5)
CC Exclusion see Appendix A PDX collection 0496

MCC **D59.3 Hemolytic-uremic syndrome**
Use additional code to identify associated:
E. coli infection (B96.2-)
Pneumococcal pneumonia (J13)
Shigella dysenteriae (A03.9)
MCC Exclusion see Appendix A PDX collection 0496

CC **D59.4 Other nonautoimmune hemolytic anemias**
Mechanical hemolytic anemia
Microangiopathic hemolytic anemia
Toxic hemolytic anemia
CC Exclusion see Appendix A PDX collection 0496

D59.5 Paroxysmal nocturnal hemoglobinuria [Marchiafava-Micheli]
Excludes1: *hemoglobinuria NOS (R82.3)*

D59.6 Hemoglobinuria due to hemolysis from other external causes
Hemoglobinuria from exertion
March hemoglobinuria
Paroxysmal cold hemoglobinuria
Use additional code (Chapter 20) to identify external cause
Excludes1: *hemoglobinuria NOS (R82.3)*

D59.8 Other acquired hemolytic anemias

CC **D59.9 Acquired hemolytic anemia, unspecified**
Idiopathic hemolytic anemia, chronic
CC Exclusion see Appendix A PDX collection 0496

Aplastic and other anemias and other bone marrow failure syndromes (D60-D64)

D60 Acquired pure red cell aplasia [erythroblastopenia]
Includes: red cell aplasia (acquired) (adult) (with thymoma)
Excludes1: *congenital red cell aplasia (D61.01)*

MCC **D60.0 Chronic acquired pure red cell aplasia**
MCC Exclusion see Appendix A PDX collection 0496

MCC **D60.1 Transient acquired pure red cell aplasia**
MCC Exclusion see Appendix A PDX collection 0496

MCC **D60.8 Other acquired pure red cell aplasias**
MCC Exclusion see Appendix A PDX collection 0496

MCC **D60.9 Acquired pure red cell aplasia, unspecified**
MCC Exclusion see Appendix A PDX collection 0496

D61 Other aplastic anemias and other bone marrow failure syndromes
Excludes1: *neutropenia (D70.-)*

\+ **D61.0 Constitutional aplastic anemia**

CC **D61.01 Constitutional (pure) red blood cell aplasia**
Blackfan-Diamond syndrome
Congenital (pure) red cell aplasia
Familial hypoplastic anemia
Primary (pure) red cell aplasia
Red cell (pure) aplasia of infants
Excludes1: *acquired red cell aplasia (D60.9)*
CC Exclusion see Appendix A PDX collection 0498

CC **D61.09 Other constitutional aplastic anemia**
Fanconi's anemia
Pancytopenia with malformations
CC Exclusion see Appendix A PDX collection 0499

MCC **D61.1 Drug-induced aplastic anemia**
Use additional code for adverse effect, if applicable, to identify drug (T36-T50 with fifth or sixth character 5)
MCC Exclusion see Appendix A PDX collection 0496

MCC **D61.2 Aplastic anemia due to other external agents**
Code first, if applicable, toxic effects of substances chiefly nonmedicinal as to source (T51-T65)
MCC Exclusion see Appendix A PDX collection 0496

MCC **D61.3 Idiopathic aplastic anemia**
MCC Exclusion see Appendix A PDX collection 0496

\+ **D61.8 Other specified aplastic anemias and other bone marrow failure syndromes**

\+ **D61.81 Pancytopenia**
Excludes1: *pancytopenia (due to) (with) aplastic anemia (D61.9)*
pancytopenia (due to) (with) bone marrow infiltration (D61.82)
pancytopenia (due to) (with) congenital (pure) red cell aplasia (D61.01)
pancytopenia (due to) (with) hairy cell leukemia (C91.4-)
pancytopenia (due to) (with) human immunodeficiency virus disease (B20.-)
pancytopenia (due to) (with) leukoerythroblastic anemia (D61.82)
pancytopenia (due to) (with) myelodysplastic syndromes (D46.-)
pancytopenia (due to) (with) myeloproliferative disease (D47.1)

MCC **D61.810 Antineoplastic chemotherapy induced pancytopenia**
Excludes2: *aplastic anemia due to antineoplastic chemotherapy (D61.1)*
MCC Exclusion see Appendix A PDX collection 0500

MCC **D61.811 Other drug-induced pancytopenia**
Excludes2: *aplastic anemia due to drugs (D61.1)*
MCC Exclusion see Appendix A PDX collection 0500

CC **D61.818 Other pancytopenia**
CC Exclusion see Appendix A PDX collection 0500

CC **D61.82 Myelophthisis**
Leukoerythroblastic anemia
Myelophthisic anemia
Panmyelophthisis
Code also the underlying disorder, such as:
malignant neoplasm of breast (C50.-)
tuberculosis (A15.-)
Excludes1: *idiopathic myelofibrosis (D47.1)*
myelofibrosis NOS (D75.81)
myelofibrosis with myeloid metaplasia (D47.4)
primary myelofibrosis (D47.1)
secondary myelofibrosis (D75.81)
CC Exclusion see Appendix A PDX collection 0500

MCC **D61.89 Other specified aplastic anemias and other bone marrow failure syndromes**
MCC Exclusion see Appendix A PDX collection 0496

CC **D61.9 Aplastic anemia, unspecified**
Hypoplastic anemia NOS
Medullary hypoplasia
CC Exclusion see Appendix A PDX collection 0496

CC **D62 Acute posthemorrhagic anemia**
Excludes1: *anemia due to chronic blood loss (D50.0)*
blood loss anemia NOS (D50.0)
congenital anemia from fetal blood loss (P61.3)
CC Exclusion see Appendix A PDX collection 0501
Valid 3-character code, no further characters required

D63 Anemia in chronic diseases classified elsewhere

D63.0 Anemia in neoplastic disease
Code first neoplasm (C00-D49)
Excludes1: *anemia due to antineoplastic chemotherapy (D64.81)*
aplastic anemia due to antineoplastic chemotherapy (D61.1)
Review coding guidelines C.2.c.1, C.2.c.2 and C.2.l.4

D63.1 Anemia in chronic kidney disease
Erythropoietin resistant anemia (EPO resistant anemia)
Code first underlying chronic kidney disease (CKD) (N18.-)

D63.8 Anemia in other chronic diseases classified elsewhere
Code first underlying disease, such as:
diphyllobothriasis (B70.0)
hookworm disease (B76.0-B76.9)
hypothyroidism (E00.0-E03.9)
malaria (B50.0-B54)
symptomatic late syphilis (A52.79)
tuberculosis (A18.89)

D64 Other anemias
Excludes1: *refractory anemia (D46.-)*
refractory anemia with excess blasts in transformation [RAEB T] (C92.0-)

D64.0 Hereditary sideroblastic anemia
Sex-linked hypochromic sideroblastic anemia

D64.1 Secondary sideroblastic anemia due to disease
Code first underlying disease

D64.2 Secondary sideroblastic anemia due to drugs and toxins
Code first poisoning due to drug or toxin, if applicable (T36-T65 with fifth or sixth character 1-4 or 6)

Use additional code for adverse effect, if applicable, to identify drug (T36-T50 with fifth or sixth character 5)

D64.3 Other sideroblastic anemias
Sideroblastic anemia NOS
Pyridoxine-responsive sideroblastic anemia NEC

D64.4 Congenital dyserythropoietic anemia
Dyshematopoietic anemia (congenital)
Excludes1: *Blackfan-Diamond syndrome (D61.01)*
Di Guglielmo's disease (C94.0)

+ **D64.8 Other specified anemias**

D64.81 Anemia due to antineoplastic chemotherapy
Antineoplastic chemotherapy induced anemia
Excludes1: *anemia in neoplastic disease (D63.0)*
aplastic anemia due to antineoplastic chemotherapy (D61.1)

D64.89 Other specified anemias
Infantile pseudoleukemia

D64.9 Anemia, unspecified

Coagulation defects, purpura and other hemorrhagic conditions (D65-D69)

MCC **D65 Disseminated intravascular coagulation [defibrination syndrome]**
Afibrinogenemia, acquired
Consumption coagulopathy
Diffuse or disseminated intravascular coagulation [DIC]
Fibrinolytic hemorrhage, acquired
Fibrinolytic purpura
Purpura fulminans
Excludes1: *disseminated intravascular coagulation (complicating):*
abortion or ectopic or molar pregnancy (O00-O07, O08.1)
in newborn (P60)
pregnancy, childbirth and the puerperium (O45.0, O46.0, O67.0, O72.3)
MCC Exclusion see Appendix A PDX collection 0502
Valid 3-character code, no further characters required

MCC **D66 Hereditary factor VIII deficiency**
Classical hemophilia
Deficiency factor VIII (with functional defect)
Hemophilia NOS
Hemophilia A
Excludes1: *factor VIII deficiency with vascular defect (D68.0)*
MCC Exclusion see Appendix A PDX collection 0502
Valid 3-character code, no further characters required

MCC **D67 Hereditary factor IX deficiency**
Christmas disease
Factor IX deficiency (with functional defect)
Hemophilia B
Plasma thromboplastin component [PTC] deficiency
MCC Exclusion see Appendix A PDX collection 0502
Valid 3-character code, no further characters required

D68 Other coagulation defects
Excludes1: *abnormal coagulation profile (R79.1)*
coagulation defects complicating abortion or ectopic or molar pregnancy (O00-O07, O08.1)
coagulation defects complicating pregnancy, childbirth and the puerperium (O45.0, O46.0, O67.0, O72.3)

CC **D68.0 Von Willebrand's disease**
Angiohemophilia
Factor VIII deficiency with vascular defect
Vascular hemophilia
Excludes1: *capillary fragility (hereditary) (D69.8)*
factor VIII deficiency NOS (D66)
factor VIII deficiency with functional defect (D66)
CC Exclusion see Appendix A PDX collection 0502

CC **D68.1 Hereditary factor XI deficiency**
Hemophilia C
Plasma thromboplastin antecedent [PTA] deficiency
Rosenthal's disease
CC Exclusion see Appendix A PDX collection 0502

CC **D68.2 Hereditary deficiency of other clotting factors**
AC globulin deficiency
Congenital afibrinogenemia
Deficiency of factor I [fibrinogen]
Deficiency of factor II [prothrombin]
Deficiency of factor V [labile]
Deficiency of factor VII [stable]
Deficiency of factor X [Stuart-Prower]
Deficiency of factor XII [Hageman]
Deficiency of factor XIII [fibrin stabilizing]
Dysfibrinogenemia (congenital)
Hypoproconvertinemia
Owren's disease
Proaccelerin deficiency
CC Exclusion see Appendix A PDX collection 0502

+ **D68.3 Hemorrhagic disorder due to circulating anticoagulants**

+ **D68.31 Hemorrhagic disorder due to intrinsic circulating anticoagulants, antibodies, or inhibitors**

CC **D68.311 Acquired hemophilia**
Autoimmune hemophilia
Autoimmune inhibitors to clotting factors
Secondary hemophilia
CC Exclusion see Appendix A PDX collection 0503

CC **D68.312 Antiphospholipid antibody with hemorrhagic disorder**
Lupus anticoagulant (LAC) with hemorrh[agic] disorder
Systemic lupus erythematosus [SLE] inhi[bitor] with hemorrhagic disorder
Excludes1: *antiphospholipid antibody, finding without diagnosis (R76.0)*
antiphospholipid antibody syndrome (D68.61)
antiphospholipid antibody wi[th] hypercoagulable state (D6[8.61])
lupus anticoagulant (LAC) fi[nding] without diagnosis (R76.0)
lupus anticoagulant (LAC) w[ith] hypercoagulable state (D6[8.62])
systemic lupus erythematosus [SLE] inhibitor finding wit[hout] diagnosis (R76.0)
systemic lupus erythematosus [SLE] inhibitor with hypercoagulable state (D6[8.69])
CC Exclusion see Appendix A PDX collection 0504

CC **D68.318 Other hemorrhagic disorder due to intri[nsic] circulating anticoagulants, antibodies, or inhibitors**
Antithromboplastinemia
Antithromboplastinogenemia
Hemorrhagic disorder due to intrinsic incr[ease] in antithrombin
Hemorrhagic disorder due to intrinsic inc[rease] in anti-VIIIa
Hemorrhagic disorder due to intrinsic inc[rease] in anti-IXa
Hemorrhagic disorder due to intrinsic inc[rease] in anti-XIa
CC Exclusion see Appendix A PDX collection 0503

CC **D68.32 Hemorrhagic disorder due to extrinsic circulating anticoagulants**
Drug-induced hemorrhagic disorder
Hemorrhagic disorder due to increase in anti-IIa
Hemorrhagic disorder due to increase in anti-Xa
Hyperheparinemia
Use additional code for adverse effect, if applicable, [to] identify drug (T45.515, T45.525)
CC Exclusion see Appendix A PDX collection 0502

CC **D68.4 Acquired coagulation factor deficiency**
Deficiency of coagulation factor due to liver disease
Deficiency of coagulation factor due to vitamin K deficiency
Excludes1: *vitamin K deficiency of newborn (P53)*
CC Exclusion see Appendix A PDX collection 0502

+ **D68.5 Primary thrombophilia**
Primary hypercoagulable states
Excludes1: *antiphospholipid syndrome (D68.61)*
lupus anticoagulant (D68.62)
secondary activated protein C resistance (D68.6[9])
secondary antiphospholipid antibody syndrome (D68.69)
secondary lupus anticoagulant with hypercoagu[lable] state (D68.69)
secondary systemic lupus erythematosus [SLE] inhibitor with hypercoagulable state (D68.69)
systemic lupus erythematosus [SLE] inhibitor fi[nding] without diagnosis (R76.0)
systemic lupus erythematosus [SLE] inhibitor wi[th] hemorrhagic disorder (D68.312)
thrombotic thrombocytopenic purpura (M31.1)

CC **D68.51 Activated protein C resistance**
Factor V Leiden mutation
CC Exclusion see Appendix A PDX collection 0505

CC **D68.52 Prothrombin gene mutation**
CC Exclusion see Appendix A PDX collection 0505

CC **D68.59 Other primary thrombophilia**
Antithrombin III deficiency
Hypercoagulable state NOS
Primary hypercoagulable state NEC
Primary thrombophilia NEC
Protein C deficiency
Protein S deficiency
Thrombophilia NOS
CC Exclusion see Appendix A PDX collection 0505

+ **D68.6 Other thrombophilia**
Other hypercoagulable states
Excludes1: *diffuse or disseminated intravascular coagulation [DIC] (D65)*
heparin induced thrombocytopenia (HIT) (D75.82)
hyperhomocysteinemia (E72.11)

CC **D68.61 Antiphospholipid syndrome**
Anticardiolipin syndrome
Antiphospholipid antibody syndrome
Excludes1: *anti-phospholipid antibody, finding without diagnosis (R76.0)*
anti-phospholipid antibody with hemorrhagic disorder (D68.312)
lupus anticoagulant syndrome (D68.62)
CC Exclusion see Appendix A PDX collection 0505

CC **D68.62 Lupus anticoagulant syndrome**
Lupus anticoagulant
Presence of systemic lupus erythematosus [SLE] inhibitor
Excludes1: *anticardiolipin syndrome (D68.61)*
antiphospholipid syndrome (D68.61)
lupus anticoagulant (LAC) finding without diagnosis (R79.0)
lupus anticoagulant (LAC) with hemorrhagic disorder (D68.312)
CC Exclusion see Appendix A PDX collection 0505

CC **D68.69 Other thrombophilia**
Hypercoagulable states NEC
Secondary hypercoagulable state NOS
CC Exclusion see Appendix A PDX collection 0505

CC **D68.8 Other specified coagulation defects**
Excludes1: *hemorrhagic disease of newborn (P53)*
CC Exclusion see Appendix A PDX collection 0502

CC **D68.9 Coagulation defect, unspecified**
CC Exclusion see Appendix A PDX collection 0502

D69 Purpura and other hemorrhagic conditions
Excludes1: *benign hypergammaglobulinemic purpura (D89.0)*
cryoglobulinemic purpura (D89.1)
essential (hemorrhagic) thrombocythemia (D47.3)
hemorrhagic thrombocythemia (D47.3)
purpura fulminans (D65)
thrombotic thrombocytopenic purpura (M31.1)
Waldenström hypergammaglobulinemic purpura (D89.0)

CC **D69.0 Allergic purpura**
Allergic vasculitis
Nonthrombocytopenic hemorrhagic purpura
Nonthrombocytopenic idiopathic purpura
Purpura anaphylactoid
Purpura Henoch(-Schönlein)
Purpura rheumatica
Vascular purpura
Excludes1: *thrombocytopenic hemorrhagic purpura (D69.3)*
CC Exclusion see Appendix A PDX collection 0502

D69.1 Qualitative platelet defects
Bernard-Soulier [giant platelet] syndrome
Glanzmann's disease
Grey platelet syndrome
Thromboasthenia (hemorrhagic) (hereditary)
Thrombocytopathy
Excludes1: *von Willebrand's disease (D68.0)*

D69.2 Other nonthrombocytopenic purpura
Purpura NOS
Purpura simplex
Senile purpura

CC **D69.3 Immune thrombocytopenic purpura**
Hemorrhagic (thrombocytopenic) purpura
Idiopathic thrombocytopenic purpura
Tidal platelet dysgenesis
CC Exclusion see Appendix A PDX collection 0502

+ **D69.4 Other primary thrombocytopenia**
Excludes1: *transient neonatal thrombocytopenia (P61.0)*
Wiskott-Aldrich syndrome (D82.0)

CC **D69.41 Evans syndrome**
CC Exclusion see Appendix A PDX collection 0502

CC **D69.42 Congenital and hereditary thrombocytopenia purpura**
Congenital thrombocytopenia
Hereditary thrombocytopenia
Code first congential or hereditary disorder, such as:
thrombocytopenia with absent radius (TAR syndrome) (Q87.2)
CC Exclusion see Appendix A PDX collection 0502

D69.49 Other primary thrombocytopenia
Megakaryocytic hypoplasia
Primary thrombocytopenia NOS

+ **D69.5 Secondary thrombocytopenia**
Excludes1: *heparin induced thrombocytopenia (HIT) (D75.82)*
transient thrombocytopenia of newborn (P61.0)

D69.51 Posttransfusion purpura
Posttransfusion purpura from whole blood (fresh) or blood products PTP

D69.59 Other secondary thrombocytopenia

D69.6 Thrombocytopenia, unspecified

D69.8 Other specified hemorrhagic conditions
Capillary fragility (hereditary)
Vascular pseudohemophilia

D69.9 Hemorrhagic condition, unspecified

Other disorders of blood and blood-forming organs (D70-D77)

D70 Neutropenia
Includes: agranulocytosis
decreased absolute neurophile count (ANC)
Use additional code for any associated:
fever (R50.81)
mucositis (J34.81, K12.3-, K92.81, N76.81)
Excludes1: *neutropenic splenomegaly (D73.81)*
transient neonatal neutropenia (P61.5)

D70.0 Congenital agranulocytosis
Congenital neutropenia
Infantile genetic agranulocytosis
Kostmann's disease

D70.1 Agranulocytosis secondary to cancer chemotherapy
Use additional code for adverse effect, if applicable, to identify drug (T45.1X5)
Code also underlying neoplasm

D70.2 Other drug-induced agranulocytosis
Use additional code for adverse effect, if applicable, to identify drug (T36-T50 with fifth or sixth character 5)

D70.3 Neutropenia due to infection

D70.4 Cyclic neutropenia
Cyclic hematopoiesis
Periodic neutropenia

D70.8 Other neutropenia

D70.9 Neutropenia, unspecified

D71 Functional disorders of polymorphonuclear neutrophils
Cell membrane receptor complex [CR3] defect
Chronic (childhood) granulomatous disease
Congenital dysphagocytosis
Progressive septic granulomatosis
Valid 3-character code, no further characters required

D72 Other disorders of white blood cells
Excludes1: *basophilia (D72.824)*
immunity disorders (D80-D89)
neutropenia (D70)
preleukemia (syndrome) (D46.9)

D72.0 Genetic anomalies of leukocytes
Alder (granulation) (granulocyte) anomaly
Alder syndrome
Hereditary leukocytic hypersegmentation
Hereditary leukocytic hyposegmentation
Hereditary leukomelanopathy
May-Hegglin (granulation) (granulocyte) anomaly
May-Hegglin syndrome
Pelger-Huët (granulation) (granulocyte) anomaly
Pelger-Huët syndrome
Excludes1: *Chédiak (-Steinbrinck)-Higashi syndrome (E70.330)*

D72.1 Eosinophilia
Allergic eosinophilia
Hereditary eosinophilia
Excludes1: *Löffler's syndrome (J82)*
pulmonary eosinophilia (J82)

\+ **D72.8 Other specified disorders of white blood cells**
Excludes1: *leukemia (C91-C95)*

\+ **D72.81 Decreased white blood cell count**
Excludes1: *neutropenia (D70.-)*

D72.810 Lymphocytopenia
Decreased lymphocytes

D72.818 Other decreased white blood cell count
Basophilic leukopenia
Eosinophilic leukopenia
Monocytopenia
Other decreased leukocytes
Plasmacytopenia

D72.819 Decreased white blood cell count, unspecified
Decreased leukocytes, unspecified
Leukocytopenia, unspecified
Leukopenia
Excludes1: *malignant leukopenia (D70.9)*

\+ **D72.82 Elevated white blood cell count**
Excludes1: *eosinophilia (D72.1)*

D72.820 Lymphocytosis (symptomatic)
Elevated lymphocytes

D72.821 Monocytosis (symptomatic)
Excludes1: *infectious mononucleosis (B27.-)*

D72.822 Plasmacytosis

D72.823 Leukemoid reaction
Basophilic leukemoid reaction
Leukemoid reaction NOS
Lymphocytic leukemoid reaction
Monocytic leukemoid reaction
Myelocytic leukemoid reaction
Neutrophilic leukemoid reaction

D72.824 Basophilia

D72.825 Bandemia
Bandemia without diagnosis of specific infection
Excludes1: *confirmed infection - code to infection*
leukemia (C91.-, C92.-, C93.-, C94.-, C95.-)

D72.828 Other elevated white blood cell count

D72.829 Elevated white blood cell count, unspecified
Elevated leukocytes, unspecified
Leukocytosis, unspecified

D72.89 Other specified disorders of white blood cells
Abnormality of white blood cells NEC

D72.9 Disorder of white blood cells, unspecified
Abnormal leukocyte differential NOS

D73 Diseases of spleen

D73.0 Hyposplenism
Atrophy of spleen
Excludes1: *asplenia (congenital) (Q89.01)*
postsurgical absence of spleen (Z90.81)

D73.1 Hypersplenism
Excludes1: *neutropenic splenomegaly (D73.81)*
primary splenic neutropenia (D73.81)
splenitis, splenomegaly in late syphilis (A52.79)
splenitis, splenomegaly in tuberculosis (A18.85)
splenomegaly NOS (R16.1)
splenomegaly congenital (Q89.0)

D73.2 Chronic congestive splenomegaly

D73.3 Abscess of spleen

D73.4 Cyst of spleen

D73.5 Infarction of spleen
Splenic rupture, nontraumatic
Torsion of spleen
Excludes1: *rupture of spleen due to Plasmodium vivax malaria (B51.0)*
traumatic rupture of spleen (S36.03-)

\+ **D73.8 Other diseases of spleen**

D73.81 Neutropenic splenomegaly
Werner-Schultz disease

D73.89 Other diseases of spleen
Fibrosis of spleen NOS
Perisplenitis
Splenitis NOS

D73.9 Disease of spleen, unspecified

D74 Methemoglobinemia

CC **D74.0 Congenital methemoglobinemia**
Congenital NADH-methemoglobin reductase deficiency
Hemoglobin-M [Hb-M] disease
Methemoglobinemia, hereditary
CC Exclusion see Appendix A PDX collection 0506

CC **D74.8 Other methemoglobinemias**
Acquired methemoglobinemia (with sulfhemoglobinemia)
Toxic methemoglobinemia
CC Exclusion see Appendix A PDX collection 0506

CC **D74.9 Methemoglobinemia, unspecified**
CC Exclusion see Appendix A PDX collection 0506

D75 Other and unspecified diseases of blood and blood-forming organs

Excludes2: *acute lymphadenitis (L04.-)*
chronic lymphadenitis (I88.1)
enlarged lymph nodes (R59.-)
hypergammaglobulinemia NOS (D89.2)
lymphadenitis NOS (I88.9)
mesenteric lymphadenitis (acute) (chronic) (I88.0)

D75.0 Familial erythrocytosis
Benign polycythemia
Familial polycythemia
Excludes1: *hereditary ovalocytosis (D58.1)*

D75.1 Secondary polycythemia
Acquired polycythemia
Emotional polycythemia
Erythrocytosis NOS
Hypoxemic polycythemia
Nephrogenous polycythemia
Polycythemia due to erythropoietin
Polycythemia due to fall in plasma volume
Polycythemia due to high altitude
Polycythemia due to stress
Polycythemia NOS
Relative polycythemia
Excludes1: *polycythemia neonatorum (P61.1)*
polycythemia vera (D45)

\+ **D75.8 Other specified diseases of blood and blood-forming organs**

CC **D75.81 Myelofibrosis**
Myelofibrosis NOS
Secondary myelofibrosis NOS
Code first the underlying disorder, such as:
malignant neoplasm of breast (C50.-)

Use additional code, if applicable, for associated therapy-related myelodysplastic syndrome (D46.-)

Use additional code for adverse effect, if applicable, to identify drug (T45.1X5)

Excludes1: *acute myelofibrosis (C94.4-)*
idiopathic myelofibrosis (D47.1)
leukoerythroblastic anemia (D61.82)
myelofibrosis with myeloid metaplasia (D47.4)
myelophthisic anemia (D61.82)
myelophthisis (D61.82)
primary myelofibrosis (D47.1)
CC Exclusion see Appendix A PDX collection 0488

D75.82 Heparin induced thrombocytopenia (HIT)

D75.89 Other specified diseases of blood and blood-forming organs

D75.9 Disease of blood and blood-forming organs, unspecified

D76 Other specified diseases with participation of lymphoreticular and reticulohistiocytic tissue

Excludes1: *(Abt-) Letterer-Siwe disease (C96.0)*
eosinophilic granuloma (C96.6)
Hand-Schüller-Christian disease (C96.5)
histiocytic sarcoma (C96.A)
histiocytosis X, multifocal (C96.5)
histiocytosis X, unifocal (C96.6)
malignant histiocytosis (C96.A)
Langerhans-cell histiocytosis, multifocal (C96.5)
Langerhans-cell histiocytosis NOS (C96.6)
Langerhans-cell histiocytosis, unifocal (C96.6)
leukemic reticuloendotheliosis or reticulosis (C91.4-)
lipomelanotic reticuloendotheliosis or reticulosis (I89.8)

CC **D76.1 Hemophagocytic lymphohistiocytosis**
Familial hemophagocytic reticulosis
Histiocytoses of mononuclear phagocytes
CC Exclusion see Appendix A PDX collection 0507

CC **D76.2 Hemophagocytic syndrome, infection-associated**
Use additional code to identify infectious agent or disease.
CC Exclusion see Appendix A PDX collection 0507

CC **D76.3 Other histiocytosis syndromes**
Reticulohistiocytoma (giant-cell)
Sinus histiocytosis with massive lymphadenopathy
Xanthogranuloma
CC Exclusion see Appendix A PDX collection 0507

D77 Other disorders of blood and blood-forming organs in diseases classified elsewhere
Code first underlying disease, such as:
amyloidosis (E85.-)
congenital early syphilis (A50.0)
echinococcosis (B67.0-B67.9)
malaria (B50.0-B54)
schistosomiasis [bilharziasis] (B65.0-B65.9)
vitamin C deficiency (E54)
Excludes1: *rupture of spleen due to Plasmodium vivax malaria (B51.0)*
splenitis, splenomegaly in late syphilis (A52.79)
splenitis, splenomegaly in tuberculosis (A18.85)
Valid 3-character code, no further characters required

raoperative and postprocedural complications of the een (D78)

D78 Intraoperative and postprocedural complications of the spleen

+ **D78.0 Intraoperative hemorrhage and hematoma of the spleen complicating a procedure**
Excludes1: *intraoperative hemorrhage and hematoma of the spleen due to accidental puncture or laceration during a procedure (D78.1-)*

CC **D78.01 Intraoperative hemorrhage and hematoma of the spleen complicating a procedure on the spleen**
CC Exclusion see Appendix A PDX collection 0508

CC **D78.02 Intraoperative hemorrhage and hematoma of the spleen complicating other procedure**
CC Exclusion see Appendix A PDX collection 0508

+ **D78.1 Accidental puncture and laceration of the spleen during a procedure**

CC **D78.11 Accidental puncture and laceration of the spleen during a procedure on the spleen**
CC Exclusion see Appendix A PDX collection 0509

CC **D78.12 Accidental puncture and laceration of the spleen during other procedure**
CC Exclusion see Appendix A PDX collection 0509

+ **D78.2 Postprocedural hemorrhage and hematoma of the spleen following a procedure**

CC **D78.21 Postprocedural hemorrhage and hematoma of the spleen following a procedure on the spleen**
CC Exclusion see Appendix A PDX collection 0508

CC **D78.22 Postprocedural hemorrhage and hematoma of the spleen following other procedure**
CC Exclusion see Appendix A PDX collection 0508

+ **D78.8 Other intraoperative and postprocedural complications of the spleen**
Use additional code, if applicable, to further specify disorder

CC **D78.81 Other intraoperative complications of the spleen**
CC Exclusion see Appendix A PDX collection 0510

CC **D78.89 Other postprocedural complications of the spleen**
CC Exclusion see Appendix A PDX collection 0510

rtain disorders involving the immune mechanism (D80-D89)

udes: defects in the complement system
immunodeficiency disorders, except human immunodeficiency virus [HIV] disease sarcoidosis

ludes1: *autoimmune disease (systemic) NOS (M35.9)*
functional disorders of polymorphonuclear neutrophils (D71)
human immunodeficiency virus [HIV] disease (B20)

D80 Immunodeficiency with predominantly antibody defects

CC **D80.0 Hereditary hypogammaglobulinemia**
Autosomal recessive agammaglobulinemia (Swiss type)
X-linked agammaglobulinemia [Bruton] (with growth hormone deficiency)
CC Exclusion see Appendix A PDX collection 0511

CC **D80.1 Nonfamilial hypogammaglobulinemia**
Agammaglobulinemia with immunoglobulin-bearing B-lymphocytes
Common variable agammaglobulinemia [CVAgamma]
Hypogammaglobulinemia NOS
CC Exclusion see Appendix A PDX collection 0512

CC **D80.2 Selective deficiency of immunoglobulin A [IgA]**
CC Exclusion see Appendix A PDX collection 0512

CC **D80.3 Selective deficiency of immunoglobulin G [IgG] subclasses**
CC Exclusion see Appendix A PDX collection 0511

CC **D80.4 Selective deficiency of immunoglobulin M [IgM]**
CC Exclusion see Appendix A PDX collection 0511

CC **D80.5 Immunodeficiency with increased immunoglobulin M [IgM]**
CC Exclusion see Appendix A PDX collection 0511

CC **D80.6 Antibody deficiency with near-normal immunoglobulins or with hyperimmunoglobulinemia**
CC Exclusion see Appendix A PDX collection 0511

• CC **D80.7 Transient hypogammaglobulinemia of infancy**
CC Exclusion see Appendix A PDX collection 0511

CC **D80.8 Other immunodeficiencies with predominantly antibody defects**
Kappa light chain deficiency
CC Exclusion see Appendix A PDX collection 0511

CC **D80.9 Immunodeficiency with predominantly antibody defects, unspecified**
CC Exclusion see Appendix A PDX collection 0511

D81 Combined immunodeficiencies
Excludes1: *autosomal recessive agammaglobulinemia (Swiss type) (D80.0)*

CC **D81.0 Severe combined immunodeficiency [SCID] with reticular dysgenesis**
CC Exclusion see Appendix A PDX collection 0511

CC **D81.1 Severe combined immunodeficiency [SCID] with low T- and B-cell numbers**
CC Exclusion see Appendix A PDX collection 0511

CC **D81.2 Severe combined immunodeficiency [SCID] with low or normal B-cell numbers**
CC Exclusion see Appendix A PDX collection 0511

CC **D81.3 Adenosine deaminase [ADA] deficiency**
CC Exclusion see Appendix A PDX collection 0513

CC **D81.4 Nezelof's syndrome**
CC Exclusion see Appendix A PDX collection 0511

CC **D81.5 Purine nucleoside phosphorylase [PNP] deficiency**
CC Exclusion see Appendix A PDX collection 0513

CC **D81.6 Major histocompatibility complex class I deficiency**
Bare lymphocyte syndrome
CC Exclusion see Appendix A PDX collection 0511

CC **D81.7 Major histocompatibility complex class II deficiency**
CC Exclusion see Appendix A PDX collection 0511

+ **D81.8 Other combined immunodeficiencies**

+ **D81.81 Biotin-dependent carboxylase deficiency**
Multiple carboxylase deficiency
Excludes1: *biotin-dependent carboxylase deficiency due to dietary deficiency of biotin (E53.8)*

D81.810 Biotinidase deficiency

D81.818 Other biotin-dependent carboxylase deficiency
Holocarboxylase synthetase deficiency
Other multiple carboxylase deficiency

D81.819 Biotin-dependent carboxylase deficiency, unspecified
Multiple carboxylase deficiency, unspecified

CC **D81.89 Other combined immunodeficiencies**
CC Exclusion see Appendix A PDX collection 0511

CC **D81.9 Combined immunodeficiency, unspecified**
Severe combined immunodeficiency disorder [SCID] NOS
CC Exclusion see Appendix A PDX collection 0511

D82 Immunodeficiency associated with other major defects
Excludes1: *ataxia telangiectasia [Louis-Bar] (G11.3)*

CC **D82.0 Wiskott-Aldrich syndrome**
Immunodeficiency with thrombocytopenia and eczema
CC Exclusion see Appendix A PDX collection 0511

CC **D82.1 Di George's syndrome**
Pharyngeal pouch syndrome
Thymic alymphoplasia
Thymic aplasia or hypoplasia with immunodeficiency
CC Exclusion see Appendix A PDX collection 0511

D82.2 Immunodeficiency with short-limbed stature

D82.3 Immunodeficiency following hereditary defective response to Epstein-Barr virus
X-linked lymphoproliferative disease

D82.4 Hyperimmunoglobulin E [IgE] syndrome

D82.8 Immunodeficiency associated with other specified major defects

D82.9 Immunodeficiency associated with major defect, unspecified

D83 Common variable immunodeficiency

CC **D83.0 Common variable immunodeficiency with predominant abnormalities of B-cell numbers and function**
CC Exclusion see Appendix A PDX collection 0511

CC **D83.1 Common variable immunodeficiency with predominant immunoregulatory T-cell disorders**
CC Exclusion see Appendix A PDX collection 0511

CC **D83.2 Common variable immunodeficiency with autoantibodies to B- or T-cells**
CC Exclusion see Appendix A PDX collection 0511

CC **D83.8 Other common variable immunodeficiencies**
CC Exclusion see Appendix A PDX collection 0511

CC **D83.9 Common variable immunodeficiency, unspecified**
CC Exclusion see Appendix A PDX collection 0511

D84 Other immunodeficiencies

D84.0 Lymphocyte function antigen-1 [LFA-1] defect

D84.1 Defects in the complement system
C1 esterase inhibitor [C1-INH] deficiency

CC **D84.8 Other specified immunodeficiencies**
CC Exclusion see Appendix A PDX collection 0511

CC **D84.9 Immunodeficiency, unspecified**
CC Exclusion see Appendix A PDX collection 0511

D86 Sarcoidosis

D86.0 Sarcoidosis of lung
D86.1 Sarcoidosis of lymph nodes
D86.2 Sarcoidosis of lung with sarcoidosis of lymph nodes
D86.3 Sarcoidosis of skin
+ **D86.8 Sarcoidosis of other sites**
D86.81 Sarcoid meningitis
D86.82 Multiple cranial nerve palsies in sarcoidosis
D86.83 Sarcoid iridocyclitis
D86.84 Sarcoid pyelonephritis
Tubulo-interstitial nephropathy in sarcoidosis
D86.85 Sarcoid myocarditis
D86.86 Sarcoid arthropathy
Polyarthritis in sarcoidosis
D86.87 Sarcoid myositis
D86.89 Sarcoidosis of other sites
Hepatic granuloma
Uveoparotid fever [Heerfordt]
D86.9 Sarcoidosis, unspecified

D89 Other disorders involving the immune mechanism, not elsewhere classified

Excludes1: *hyperglobulinemia NOS (R77.1)*
monoclonal gammopathy (of undetermined significance) (D47.2)

Excludes2: *transplant failure and rejection (T86.-)*

D89.0 Polyclonal hypergammaglobulinemia
Benign hypergammaglobulinemic purpura
Polyclonal gammopathy NOS

D89.1 Cryoglobulinemia
Cryoglobulinemic purpura
Cryoglobulinemic vasculitis
Essential cryoglobulinemia
Idiopathic cryoglobulinemia
Mixed cryoglobulinemia
Primary cryoglobulinemia
Secondary cryoglobulinemia

D89.2 Hypergammaglobulinemia, unspecified

D89.3 Immune reconstitution syndrome
Immune reconstitution inflammatory syndrome [IRIS]
Use additional code for adverse effect, if applicable, to identif drug (T36-T50 with fifth or sixth character 5)

+ **D89.8 Other specified disorders involving the immune mechanism, elsewhere classified**

+ **D89.81 Graft-versus-host disease**
Code first underlying cause, such as:
complications of transplanted organs and tissues (T86.-)
complications of blood transfusion (T80.89)

Use additional code to identify associated manifestations, such as:
desquamative dermatitis (L30.8)
diarrhea (R19.7)
elevated bilirubin (R17)
hair loss (L65.9)

CC **D89.810 Acute graft-versus-host disease**
CC Exclusion see Appendix A PDX collection 0514

CC **D89.811 Chronic graft-versus-host disease**
CC Exclusion see Appendix A PDX collection 0514

CC **D89.812 Acute on chronic graft-versus-host diseas**
CC Exclusion see Appendix A PDX collection 0514

CC **D89.813 Graft-versus-host disease, unspecified**
CC Exclusion see Appendix A PDX collection 0514

D89.82 Autoimmune lymphoproliferative syndrome [ALPS

D89.89 Other specified disorders involving the immune mechanism, not elsewhere classified
Excludes1: *human immunodeficiency virus disease (B20)*

D89.9 Disorder involving the immune mechanism, unspecified
Immune disease NOS

apter 4: Endocrine, Nutritional and Metabolic
ease (E00-E89)

E All neoplasms, whether functionally active or not, are classified in Chapter 2. Appropriate codes in this chapter (i.e. E05.8, E07.0, E16-E31, E34.-) may be used as additional codes to indicate either functional activity by neoplasms and ectopic endocrine tissue or hyperfunction and hypofunction of endocrine glands associated with neoplasms and other conditions classified elsewhere.

udes1: *transitory endocrine and metabolic disorders specific to newborn (P70-P74)*

chapter contains the following category blocks:

00-E07 Disorders of thyroid gland
08-E13 Diabetes mellitus
15-E16 Other disorders of glucose regulation and pancreatic internal secretion
20-E35 Disorders of other endocrine glands
36 Intraoperative complications of endocrine system
40-E46 Malnutrition
50-E64 Other nutritional deficiencies
65-E68 Overweight, obesity and other hyperalimentation
70-E88 Metabolic disorders
89 Postprocedural endocrine and metabolic complications and disorders, not elsewhere classified

hapter-Specific Coding Guidelines

ldition to general coding guidelines, there are guidelines for specific diagnoses or conditions in the classification. Unless otherwise indicated, these guidelines y to all health care settings. Please refer to Section II for guidelines on the ction of principal diagnosis.

hapter 4: Endocrine, Nutritional and Metabolic Diseases (E00-E89)

Diabetes mellitus

The diabetes mellitus codes are combination codes that include the type of diabetes mellitus, the body system affected, and the complications affecting that body system. As many codes within a particular category as are necessary to describe all of the complications of the disease may be used. They should be sequenced based on the reason for a particular encounter. Assign as many codes from categories E08 – E13 as needed to identify all of the associated conditions that the patient has.

1) Type of diabetes

The age of a patient is not the sole determining factor, though most type 1 diabetics develop the condition before reaching puberty. For this reason type 1 diabetes mellitus is also referred to as juvenile diabetes.

2) Type of diabetes mellitus not documented

If the type of diabetes mellitus is not documented in the medical record the default is E11.-, Type 2 diabetes mellitus.

3) Diabetes mellitus and the use of insulin

If the documentation in a medical record does not indicate the type of diabetes but does indicate that the patient uses insulin, code E11, Type 2 diabetes mellitus, should be assigned. Code Z79.4, Long-term (current) use of insulin, should also be assigned to indicate that the patient uses insulin. Code Z79.4 should not be assigned if insulin is given temporarily to bring a type 2 patient's blood sugar under control during an encounter.

4) Diabetes mellitus in pregnancy and gestational diabetes

See Section I.C.15. Diabetes mellitus in pregnancy.

See Section I.C.15. Gestational (pregnancy induced) diabetes

5) Complications due to insulin pump malfunction

(a) Underdose of insulin due to insulin pump failure

An underdose of insulin due to an insulin pump failure should be assigned to a code from subcategory T85.6, Mechanical complication of other specified internal and external prosthetic devices, implants and grafts, that specifies the type of pump malfunction, as the principal or first-listed code, followed by code T38.3x6-, Underdosing of insulin and oral hypoglycemic [antidiabetic] drugs. Additional codes for the type of diabetes mellitus and any associated complications due to the underdosing should also be assigned.

(b) Overdose of insulin due to insulin pump failure

The principal or first-listed code for an encounter due to an insulin pump malfunction resulting in an overdose of insulin, should also be T85.6-, Mechanical complication of other specified internal and external prosthetic devices, implants and grafts, followed by code T38.3x1-, Poisoning by insulin and oral hypoglycemic [antidiabetic] drugs, accidental (unintentional).

6) Secondary diabetes mellitus

Codes under categories E08, Diabetes mellitus due to underlying condition, E09, Drug or chemical induced diabetes mellitus, and E13, Other specified diabetes mellitus, identify complications/manifestations associated with secondary diabetes mellitus. Secondary diabetes is always caused by another condition or event (e.g., cystic fibrosis, malignant neoplasm of pancreas, pancreatectomy, adverse effect of drug, or poisoning).

(a) Secondary diabetes mellitus and the use of insulin

For patients who routinely use insulin, code Z79.4, Long-term (current) use of insulin, should also be assigned. Code Z79.4 should not be assigned if insulin is given temporarily to bring a patient's blood sugar under control during an encounter.

(b) Assigning and sequencing secondary diabetes codes and its causes

The sequencing of the secondary diabetes codes in relationship to codes for the cause of the diabetes is based on the Tabular List instructions for categories E08, E09 and E13.

(i) Secondary diabetes mellitus due to pancreatectomy

For postpancreatectomy diabetes mellitus (lack of insulin due to the surgical removal of all or part of the pancreas), assign code E89.1, Postprocedural hypoinsulinemia. Assign a code from category E13 and a code from subcategory Z90.41-, Acquired absence of pancreas, as additional codes.

(ii) Secondary diabetes due to drugs

Secondary diabetes may be caused by an adverse effect of correctly administered medications, poisoning or sequela of poisoning.

See section I.C.19.e for coding of adverse effects and poisoning, and section I.C.20 for external cause code reporting.

Disorders of thyroid gland (E00-E07)

E00 Congenital iodine-deficiency syndrome

Use additional code (F70-F79) to identify associated intellectual disabilities.

Excludes1: *subclinical iodine-deficiency hypothyroidism (E02)*

E00.0 Congenital iodine-deficiency syndrome, neurological type
Endemic cretinism, neurological type

E00.1 Congenital iodine-deficiency syndrome, myxedematous type
Endemic hypothyroid cretinism
Endemic cretinism, myxedematous type

E00.2 Congenital iodine-deficiency syndrome, mixed type
Endemic cretinism, mixed type

E00.9 Congenital iodine-deficiency syndrome, unspecified
Congenital iodine-deficiency hypothyroidism NOS
Endemic cretinism NOS

E01 Iodine-deficiency related thyroid disorders and allied conditions

Excludes1: *congenital iodine-deficiency syndrome (E00.-)*
subclinical iodine-deficiency hypothyroidism (E02)

E01.0 Iodine-deficiency related diffuse (endemic) goiter

E01.1 Iodine-deficiency related multinodular (endemic) goiter
Iodine-deficiency related nodular goiter

E01.2 Iodine-deficiency related (endemic) goiter, unspecified
Endemic goiter NOS

E01.8 Other iodine-deficiency related thyroid disorders and allied conditions
Acquired iodine-deficiency hypothyroidism NOS

E02 Subclinical iodine-deficiency hypothyroidism

Valid 3-character code, no further characters required

E03 Other hypothyroidism

Excludes1: *iodine-deficiency related hypothyroidism (E00-E02)*
postprocedural hypothyroidism (E89.0)

E03.0 Congenital hypothyroidism with diffuse goiter
Congenital parenchymatous goiter (nontoxic)
Congenital goiter (nontoxic) NOS
Excludes1: *transitory congenital goiter with normal function (P72.0)*

E03.1 Congenital hypothyroidism without goiter
Aplasia of thyroid (with myxedema)
Congenital atrophy of thyroid
Congenital hypothyroidism NOS

E03.2 Hypothyroidism due to medicaments and other exogenous substances
Code first poisoning due to drug or toxin, if applicable (T36-T65 with fifth or sixth character 1-4 or 6)

Use additional code for adverse effect, if applicable, to identify drug (T36-T50 with fifth or sixth character 5)

E03.3 Postinfectious hypothyroidism

Endocrine System

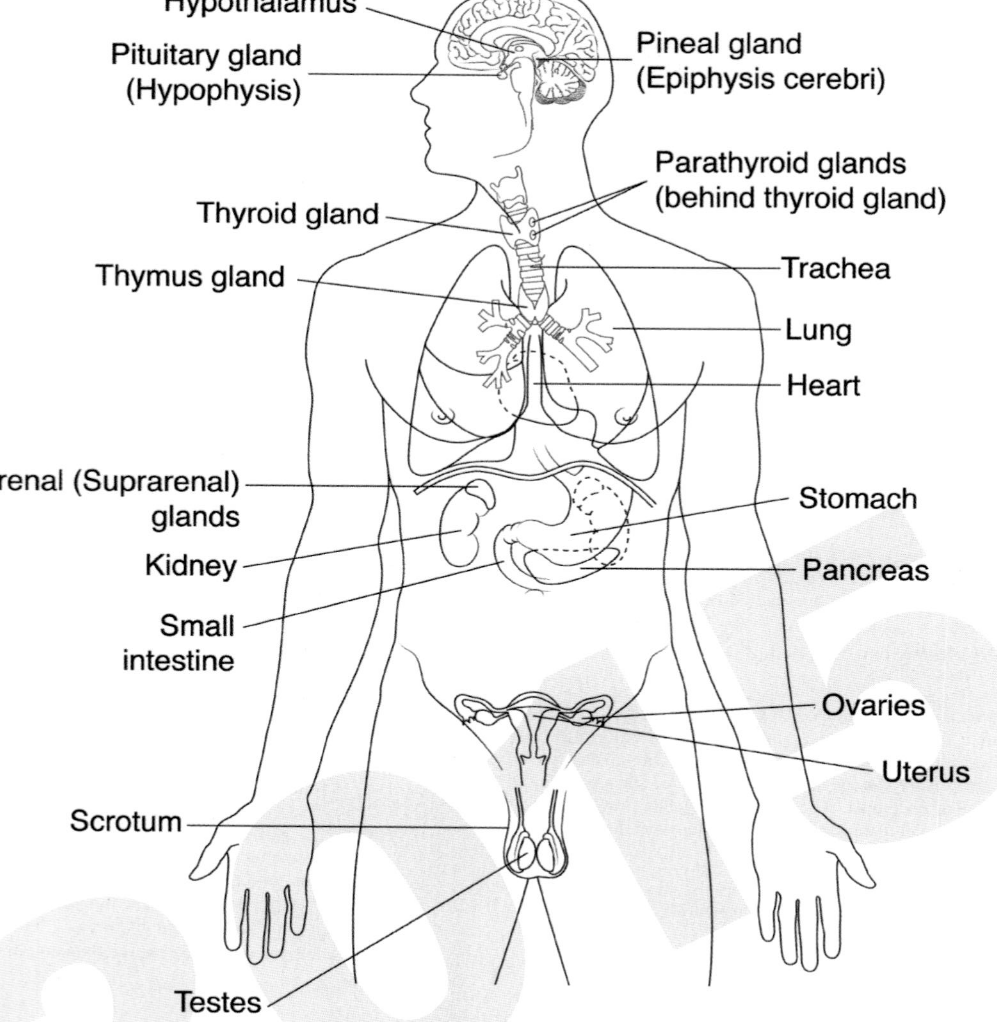

E03.4 **Atrophy of thyroid (acquired)**
Excludes1: congenital atrophy of thyroid (E03.1)

MCC E03.5 **Myxedema coma**
MCC Exclusion see Appendix A PDX collection 0515

E03.8 **Other specified hypothyroidism**

E03.9 **Hypothyroidism, unspecified**
Myxedema NOS

E04 Other nontoxic goiter

Excludes1: congenital goiter (NOS) (diffuse) (parenchymatous) (E03.0)
iodine-deficiency related goiter (E00-E02)

E04.0 **Nontoxic diffuse goiter**
Diffuse (colloid) nontoxic goiter
Simple nontoxic goiter

E04.1 **Nontoxic single thyroid nodule**
Colloid nodule (cystic) (thyroid)
Nontoxic uninodular goiter
Thyroid (cystic) nodule NOS

E04.2 **Nontoxic multinodular goiter**
Cystic goiter NOS
Multinodular (cystic) goiter NOS

E04.8 **Other specified nontoxic goiter**

E04.9 **Nontoxic goiter, unspecified**
Goiter NOS
Nodular goiter (nontoxic) NOS

E05 Thyrotoxicosis [hyperthyroidism]

Excludes1: chronic thyroiditis with transient thyrotoxicosis (E06.2)
neonatal thyrotoxicosis (P72.1)

\+ E05.0 **Thyrotoxicosis with diffuse goiter**
Exophthalmic or toxic goiter NOS
Graves' disease
Toxic diffuse goiter

E05.00 **Thyrotoxicosis with diffuse goiter without thyrotoxic crisis or storm**

MCC E05.01 **Thyrotoxicosis with diffuse goiter with thyrotoxic crisis or storm**
MCC Exclusion see Appendix A PDX collection 0516

\+ E05.1 **Thyrotoxicosis with toxic single thyroid nodule**
Thyrotoxicosis with toxic uninodular goiter

E05.10 **Thyrotoxicosis with toxic single thyroid nodule without thyrotoxic crisis or storm**

MCC E05.11 **Thyrotoxicosis with toxic single thyroid nodule with thyrotoxic crisis or storm**
MCC Exclusion see Appendix A PDX collection 0516

\+ E05.2 **Thyrotoxicosis with toxic multinodular goiter**
Toxic nodular goiter NOS

E05.20 **Thyrotoxicosis with toxic multinodular goiter without thyrotoxic crisis or storm**

MCC E05.21 **Thyrotoxicosis with toxic multinodular goiter with thyrotoxic crisis or storm**
MCC Exclusion see Appendix A PDX collection 0516

+ **E05.3 Thyrotoxicosis from ectopic thyroid tissue**
E05.30 Thyrotoxicosis from ectopic thyroid tissue without thyrotoxic crisis or storm
MCC **E05.31 Thyrotoxicosis from ectopic thyroid tissue with thyrotoxic crisis or storm**
MCC Exclusion see Appendix A PDX collection 0516
+ **E05.4 Thyrotoxicosis factitia**
E05.40 Thyrotoxicosis factitia without thyrotoxic crisis or storm
MCC **E05.41 Thyrotoxicosis factitia with thyrotoxic crisis or storm**
MCC Exclusion see Appendix A PDX collection 0516
+ **E05.8 Other thyrotoxicosis**
Overproduction of thyroid-stimulating hormone
E05.80 Other thyrotoxicosis without thyrotoxic crisis or storm
MCC **E05.81 Other thyrotoxicosis with thyrotoxic crisis or storm**
MCC Exclusion see Appendix A PDX collection 0516
+ **E05.9 Thyrotoxicosis, unspecified**
Hyperthyroidism NOS
E05.90 Thyrotoxicosis, unspecified without thyrotoxic crisis or storm
MCC **E05.91 Thyrotoxicosis, unspecified with thyrotoxic crisis or storm**
MCC Exclusion see Appendix A PDX collection 0516

E06 Thyroiditis
Excludes1: *postpartum thyroiditis (O90.5)*
CC **E06.0 Acute thyroiditis**
Abscess of thyroid
Pyogenic thyroiditis
Suppurative thyroiditis
Use additional code (B95-B97) to identify infectious agent.
CC Exclusion see Appendix A PDX collection 0517
E06.1 Subacute thyroiditis
de Quervain thyroiditis
Giant-cell thyroiditis
Granulomatous thyroiditis
Nonsuppurative thyroiditis
Viral thyroiditis
Excludes1: *autoimmune thyroiditis (E06.3)*
E06.2 Chronic thyroiditis with transient thyrotoxicosis
Excludes1: *autoimmune thyroiditis (E06.3)*
E06.3 Autoimmune thyroiditis
Hashimoto's thyroiditis
Hashitoxicosis (transient)
Lymphadenoid goiter
Lymphocytic thyroiditis
Struma lymphomatosa
E06.4 Drug-induced thyroiditis
Use additional code for adverse effect, if applicable, to identify drug (T36-T50 with fifth or sixth character 5)
E06.5 Other chronic thyroiditis
Chronic fibrous thyroiditis
Chronic thyroiditis NOS
Ligneous thyroiditis
Riedel thyroiditis
E06.9 Thyroiditis, unspecified

E07 Other disorders of thyroid
E07.0 Hypersecretion of calcitonin
C-cell hyperplasia of thyroid
Hypersecretion of thyrocalcitonin
E07.1 Dyshormogenetic goiter
Familial dyshormogenetic goiter
Pendred's syndrome
Excludes1: *transitory congenital goiter with normal function (P72.0)*
+ **E07.8 Other specified disorders of thyroid**
E07.81 Sick-euthyroid syndrome
Euthyroid sick-syndrome
E07.89 Other specified disorders of thyroid
Abnormality of thyroid-binding globulin
Hemorrhage of thyroid
Infarction of thyroid
E07.9 Disorder of thyroid, unspecified

Diabetes mellitus (E08-E13)

Review coding guideline C.4.a

E08 Diabetes mellitus due to underlying condition
Code first the underlying condition, such as:
congenital rubella (P35.0)
Cushing's syndrome (E24.-)
cystic fibrosis (E84.-)
malignant neoplasm (C00-C96)
malnutrition (E40-E46)
pancreatitis and other diseases of the pancreas (K85-K86.-)

Use additional code to identify any insulin use (Z79.4)
Excludes1: *drug or chemical induced diabetes mellitus (E09.-)*
gestational diabetes (O24.4-)
neonatal diabetes mellitus (P70.2)
postpancreatectomy diabetes mellitus (E13.-)
postprocedural diabetes mellitus (E13.-)
secondary diabetes mellitus NEC (E13.-)
type 1 diabetes mellitus (E10.-)
type 2 diabetes mellitus (E11.-)
Review coding guideline C.4.a.6.a
+ **E08.0 Diabetes mellitus due to underlying condition with hyperosmolarity**
MCC **E08.00 Diabetes mellitus due to underlying condition with hyperosmolarity without nonketotic hyperglycemic-hyperosmolar coma (NKHHC)**
MCC Exclusion see Appendix A PDX collection 0518
HAC see Appendix B for HAC conditional logic
MCC **E08.01 Diabetes mellitus due to underlying condition with hyperosmolarity with coma**
MCC Exclusion see Appendix A PDX collection 0518
HAC see Appendix B for HAC conditional logic
+ **E08.1 Diabetes mellitus due to underlying condition with ketoacidosis**
MCC **E08.10 Diabetes mellitus due to underlying condition with ketoacidosis without coma**
MCC Exclusion see Appendix A PDX collection 0518
HAC see Appendix B for HAC conditional logic
MCC **E08.11 Diabetes mellitus due to underlying condition with ketoacidosis with coma**
MCC Exclusion see Appendix A PDX collection 0518
+ **E08.2 Diabetes mellitus due to underlying condition with kidney complications**
E08.21 Diabetes mellitus due to underlying condition with diabetic nephropathy
Diabetes mellitus due to underlying condition with intercapillary glomerulosclerosis
Diabetes mellitus due to underlying condition with intracapillary glomerulonephrosis
Diabetes mellitus due to underlying condition with Kimmelstiel-Wilson disease
E08.22 Diabetes mellitus due to underlying condition with diabetic chronic kidney disease
Use additional code to identify stage of chronic kidney disease (N18.1-N18.6)
E08.29 Diabetes mellitus due to underlying condition with other diabetic kidney complication
Renal tubular degeneration in diabetes mellitus due to underlying condition
+ **E08.3 Diabetes mellitus due to underlying condition with ophthalmic complications**
+ **E08.31 Diabetes mellitus due to underlying condition with unspecified diabetic retinopathy**
E08.311 Diabetes mellitus due to underlying condition with unspecified diabetic retinopathy with macular edema
E08.319 Diabetes mellitus due to underlying condition with unspecified diabetic retinopathy without macular edema
+ **E08.32 Diabetes mellitus due to underlying condition with mild nonproliferative diabetic retinopathy**
Diabetes mellitus due to underlying condition with nonproliferative diabetic retinopathy NOS
E08.321 Diabetes mellitus due to underlying condition with mild nonproliferative diabetic retinopathy with macular edema
E08.329 Diabetes mellitus due to underlying condition with mild nonproliferative diabetic retinopathy without macular edema

+ **E08.33 Diabetes mellitus due to underlying condition with moderate nonproliferative diabetic retinopathy**
  - **E08.331 Diabetes mellitus due to underlying condition with moderate nonproliferative diabetic retinopathy with macular edema**
  - **E08.339 Diabetes mellitus due to underlying condition with moderate nonproliferative diabetic retinopathy without macular edema**

+ **E08.34 Diabetes mellitus due to underlying condition with severe nonproliferative diabetic retinopathy**
  - **E08.341 Diabetes mellitus due to underlying condition with severe nonproliferative diabetic retinopathy with macular edema**
  - **E08.349 Diabetes mellitus due to underlying condition with severe nonproliferative diabetic retinopathy without macular edema**

+ **E08.35 Diabetes mellitus due to underlying condition with proliferative diabetic retinopathy**
  - **E08.351 Diabetes mellitus due to underlying condition with proliferative diabetic retinopathy with macular edema**
  - **E08.359 Diabetes mellitus due to underlying condition with proliferative diabetic retinopathy without macular edema**

E08.36 Diabetes mellitus due to underlying condition with diabetic cataract

E08.39 Diabetes mellitus due to underlying condition with other diabetic ophthalmic complication

Use additional code to identify manifestation, such as: diabetic glaucoma (H40-H42)

+ **E08.4 Diabetes mellitus due to underlying condition with neurological complications**
  - **E08.40 Diabetes mellitus due to underlying condition with diabetic neuropathy, unspecified**
  - **E08.41 Diabetes mellitus due to underlying condition with diabetic mononeuropathy**
  - **E08.42 Diabetes mellitus due to underlying condition with diabetic polyneuropathy**
    Diabetes mellitus due to underlying condition with diabetic neuralgia
  - **E08.43 Diabetes mellitus due to underlying condition with diabetic autonomic (poly)neuropathy**
    Diabetes mellitus due to underlying condition with diabetic gastroparesis
    AHA CC: 3Q, 2013, 114-115
  - **E08.44 Diabetes mellitus due to underlying condition with diabetic amyotrophy**
  - **E08.49 Diabetes mellitus due to underlying condition with other diabetic neurological complication**

+ **E08.5 Diabetes mellitus due to underlying condition with circulatory complications**
  - **E08.51 Diabetes mellitus due to underlying condition with diabetic peripheral angiopathy without gangrene**
  - CC **E08.52 Diabetes mellitus due to underlying condition with diabetic peripheral angiopathy with gangrene**
    Diabetes mellitus due to underlying condition with diabetic gangrene
    CC Exclusion see Appendix A PDX collection 0519
  - **E08.59 Diabetes mellitus due to underlying condition with other circulatory complications**

+ **E08.6 Diabetes mellitus due to underlying condition with other specified complications**
  - + **E08.61 Diabetes mellitus due to underlying condition with diabetic arthropathy**
    - **E08.610 Diabetes mellitus due to underlying condition with diabetic neuropathic arthropathy**
      Diabetes mellitus due to underlying condition with Charcôt's joints
    - **E08.618 Diabetes mellitus due to underlying condition with other diabetic arthropathy**
  - + **E08.62 Diabetes mellitus due to underlying condition with skin complications**
    - **E08.620 Diabetes mellitus due to underlying condition with diabetic dermatitis**
      Diabetes mellitus due to underlying condition with diabetic necrobiosis lipoidica
    - **E08.621 Diabetes mellitus due to underlying condition with foot ulcer**
      Use additional code to identify site of ulcer (L97.4-, L97.5-)
    - **E08.622 Diabetes mellitus due to underlying condition with other skin ulcer**
      Use additional code to identify site of ulcer (L97.1-L97.9, L98.41-L98.49)
    - **E08.628 Diabetes mellitus due to underlying condition with other skin complications**
  - + **E08.63 Diabetes mellitus due to underlying condition with oral complications**
    - **E08.630 Diabetes mellitus due to underlying condition with periodontal disease**
    - **E08.638 Diabetes mellitus due to underlying condition with other oral complications**
  - + **E08.64 Diabetes mellitus due to underlying condition with hypoglycemia**
    - MCC **E08.641 Diabetes mellitus due to underlying condition with hypoglycemia with coma**
      MCC Exclusion see Appendix A PDX collection 0518
    - **E08.649 Diabetes mellitus due to underlying condition with hypoglycemia without coma**
  - **E08.65 Diabetes mellitus due to underlying condition with hyperglycemia**
  - **E08.69 Diabetes mellitus due to underlying condition with other specified complication**
    Use additional code to identify complication

E08.8 Diabetes mellitus due to underlying condition with unspecified complications

E08.9 Diabetes mellitus due to underlying condition without complications

E09 Drug or chemical induced diabetes mellitus

Code first poisoning due to drug or toxin, if applicable (T36-T65 with fifth or sixth character 1-4 or 6)

Use additional code for adverse effect, if applicable, to identify drug (T36-T50 with fifth or sixth character 5)

Use additional code to identify any insulin use (Z79.4)

Excludes1: *diabetes mellitus due to underlying condition (E08.-)*
gestational diabetes (O24.4-)
neonatal diabetes mellitus (P70.2)
postpancreatectomy diabetes mellitus (E13.-)
postprocedural diabetes mellitus (E13.-)
secondary diabetes mellitus NEC (E13.-)
type 1 diabetes mellitus (E10.-)
type 2 diabetes mellitus (E11.-)

Review coding guideline C.4.a.6.a

+ **E09.0 Drug or chemical induced diabetes mellitus with hyperosmolarity**
  - MCC **E09.00 Drug or chemical induced diabetes mellitus with hyperosmolarity without nonketotic hyperglycemic-hyperosmolar coma (NKHHC)**
    MCC Exclusion see Appendix A PDX collection 0518
    HAC see Appendix B for HAC conditional logic
  - MCC **E09.01 Drug or chemical induced diabetes mellitus with hyperosmolarity with coma**
    MCC Exclusion see Appendix A PDX collection 0518
    HAC see Appendix B for HAC conditional logic

+ **E09.1 Drug or chemical induced diabetes mellitus with ketoacidosis**
  - MCC **E09.10 Drug or chemical induced diabetes mellitus with ketoacidosis without coma**
    MCC Exclusion see Appendix A PDX collection 0518
    HAC see Appendix B for HAC conditional logic
  - MCC **E09.11 Drug or chemical induced diabetes mellitus with ketoacidosis with coma**
    MCC Exclusion see Appendix A PDX collection 0518

+ **E09.2 Drug or chemical induced diabetes mellitus with kidney complications**
  - **E09.21 Drug or chemical induced diabetes mellitus with diabetic nephropathy**
    Drug or chemical induced diabetes mellitus with intercapillary glomerulosclerosis
    Drug or chemical induced diabetes mellitus with intracapillary glomerulonephrosis
    Drug or chemical induced diabetes mellitus with Kimmelstiel-Wilson disease
  - **E09.22 Drug or chemical induced diabetes mellitus with diabetic chronic kidney disease**
    Use additional code to identify stage of chronic kidney disease (N18.1-N18.6)

E09.29 Drug or chemical induced diabetes mellitus with other diabetic kidney complication
Drug or chemical induced diabetes mellitus with renal tubular degeneration

+ **E09.3 Drug or chemical induced diabetes mellitus with ophthalmic complications**

+ **E09.31 Drug or chemical induced diabetes mellitus with unspecified diabetic retinopathy**

E09.311 Drug or chemical induced diabetes mellitus with unspecified diabetic retinopathy with macular edema

E09.319 Drug or chemical induced diabetes mellitus with unspecified diabetic retinopathy without macular edema

+ **E09.32 Drug or chemical induced diabetes mellitus with mild nonproliferative diabetic retinopathy**
Drug or chemical induced diabetes mellitus with nonproliferative diabetic retinopathy NOS

E09.321 Drug or chemical induced diabetes mellitus with mild nonproliferative diabetic retinopathy with macular edema

E09.329 Drug or chemical induced diabetes mellitus with mild nonproliferative diabetic retinopathy without macular edema

+ **E09.33 Drug or chemical induced diabetes mellitus with moderate nonproliferative diabetic retinopathy**

E09.331 Drug or chemical induced diabetes mellitus with moderate nonproliferative diabetic retinopathy with macular edema

E09.339 Drug or chemical induced diabetes mellitus with moderate nonproliferative diabetic retinopathy without macular edema

+ **E09.34 Drug or chemical induced diabetes mellitus with severe nonproliferative diabetic retinopathy**

E09.341 Drug or chemical induced diabetes mellitus with severe nonproliferative diabetic retinopathy with macular edema

E09.349 Drug or chemical induced diabetes mellitus with severe nonproliferative diabetic retinopathy without macular edema

+ **E09.35 Drug or chemical induced diabetes mellitus with proliferative diabetic retinopathy**

E09.351 Drug or chemical induced diabetes mellitus with proliferative diabetic retinopathy with macular edema

E09.359 Drug or chemical induced diabetes mellitus with proliferative diabetic retinopathy without macular edema

E09.36 Drug or chemical induced diabetes mellitus with diabetic cataract

E09.39 Drug or chemical induced diabetes mellitus with other diabetic ophthalmic complication
Use additional code to identify manifestation, such as:
diabetic glaucoma (H40-H42)

+ **E09.4 Drug or chemical induced diabetes mellitus with neurological complications**

E09.40 Drug or chemical induced diabetes mellitus with neurological complications with diabetic neuropathy, unspecified

E09.41 Drug or chemical induced diabetes mellitus with neurological complications with diabetic mononeuropathy

E09.42 Drug or chemical induced diabetes mellitus with neurological complications with diabetic polyneuropathy
Drug or chemical induced diabetes mellitus with diabetic neuralgia

E09.43 Drug or chemical induced diabetes mellitus with neurological complications with diabetic autonomic (poly)neuropathy
Drug or chemical induced diabetes mellitus with diabetic gastroparesis
AHA CC: 3Q, 2013, 114-115

E09.44 Drug or chemical induced diabetes mellitus with neurological complications with diabetic amyotrophy

E09.49 Drug or chemical induced diabetes mellitus with neurological complications with other diabetic neurological complication

+ **E09.5 Drug or chemical induced diabetes mellitus with circulatory complications**

E09.51 Drug or chemical induced diabetes mellitus with diabetic peripheral angiopathy without gangrene

CC **E09.52 Drug or chemical induced diabetes mellitus with diabetic peripheral angiopathy with gangrene**
Drug or chemical induced diabetes mellitus with diabetic gangrene
CC Exclusion see Appendix A PDX collection 0519

E09.59 Drug or chemical induced diabetes mellitus with other circulatory complications

+ **E09.6 Drug or chemical induced diabetes mellitus with other specified complications**

+ **E09.61 Drug or chemical induced diabetes mellitus with diabetic arthropathy**

E09.610 Drug or chemical induced diabetes mellitus with diabetic neuropathic arthropathy
Drug or chemical induced diabetes mellitus with Charcôt's joints

E09.618 Drug or chemical induced diabetes mellitus with other diabetic arthropathy

+ **E09.62 Drug or chemical induced diabetes mellitus with skin complications**

E09.620 Drug or chemical induced diabetes mellitus with diabetic dermatitis
Drug or chemical induced diabetes mellitus with diabetic necrobiosis lipoidica

E09.621 Drug or chemical induced diabetes mellitus with foot ulcer
Use additional code to identify site of ulcer (L97.4-, L97.5-)

E09.622 Drug or chemical induced diabetes mellitus with other skin ulcer
Use additional code to identify site of ulcer (L97.1-L97.9, L98.41-L98.49)

E09.628 Drug or chemical induced diabetes mellitus with other skin complications

+ **E09.63 Drug or chemical induced diabetes mellitus with oral complications**

E09.630 Drug or chemical induced diabetes mellitus with periodontal disease

E09.638 Drug or chemical induced diabetes mellitus with other oral complications

+ **E09.64 Drug or chemical induced diabetes mellitus with hypoglycemia**

MCC **E09.641 Drug or chemical induced diabetes mellitus with hypoglycemia with coma**
MCC Exclusion see Appendix A PDX collection 0518

E09.649 Drug or chemical induced diabetes mellitus with hypoglycemia without coma

E09.65 Drug or chemical induced diabetes mellitus with hyperglycemia

E09.69 Drug or chemical induced diabetes mellitus with other specified complication
Use additional code to identify complication

E09.8 Drug or chemical induced diabetes mellitus with unspecified complications

E09.9 Drug or chemical induced diabetes mellitus without complications

E10 Type 1 diabetes mellitus

Includes: brittle diabetes (mellitus)
diabetes (mellitus) due to autoimmune process
diabetes (mellitus) due to immune mediated pancreatic islet beta-cell destruction
idiopathic diabetes (mellitus)
juvenile onset diabetes (mellitus)
ketosis-prone diabetes (mellitus)

Excludes1: *diabetes mellitus due to underlying condition (E08.-)*
drug or chemical induced diabetes mellitus (E09.-)
gestational diabetes (O24.4-)
hyperglycemia NOS (R73.9)
neonatal diabetes mellitus (P70.2)
postpancreatectomy diabetes mellitus (E13.-)
postprocedural diabetes mellitus (E13.-)
secondary diabetes mellitus NEC (E13.-)
type 2 diabetes mellitus (E11.-)

+ **E10.1 Type 1 diabetes mellitus with ketoacidosis**

MCC **E10.10 Type 1 diabetes mellitus with ketoacidosis without coma**
MCC Exclusion see Appendix A PDX collection 0520
HAC see Appendix B for HAC conditional logic
AHA CC: 3Q, 2013, 20

MCC **E10.11 Type 1 diabetes mellitus with ketoacidosis with coma**
MCC Exclusion see Appendix A PDX collection 0520

+ E10.2 Type 1 diabetes mellitus with kidney complications
E10.21 Type 1 diabetes mellitus with diabetic nephropathy
Type 1 diabetes mellitus with intercapillary glomerulosclerosis
Type 1 diabetes mellitus with intracapillary glomerulonephrosis
Type 1 diabetes mellitus with Kimmelstiel-Wilson disease
E10.22 Type 1 diabetes mellitus with diabetic chronic kidney disease
Use additional code to identify stage of chronic kidney disease (N18.1-N18.6)
E10.29 Type 1 diabetes mellitus with other diabetic kidney complication
Type 1 diabetes mellitus with renal tubular degeneration
+ E10.3 Type 1 diabetes mellitus with ophthalmic complications
+ E10.31 Type 1 diabetes mellitus with unspecified diabetic retinopathy
E10.311 Type 1 diabetes mellitus with unspecified diabetic retinopathy with macular edema
E10.319 Type 1 diabetes mellitus with unspecified diabetic retinopathy without macular edema
+ E10.32 Type 1 diabetes mellitus with mild nonproliferative diabetic retinopathy
Type 1 diabetes mellitus with nonproliferative diabetic retinopathy NOS
E10.321 Type 1 diabetes mellitus with mild nonproliferative diabetic retinopathy with macular edema
E10.329 Type 1 diabetes mellitus with mild nonproliferative diabetic retinopathy without macular edema
+ E10.33 Type 1 diabetes mellitus with moderate nonproliferative diabetic retinopathy
E10.331 Type 1 diabetes mellitus with moderate nonproliferative diabetic retinopathy with macular edema
E10.339 Type 1 diabetes mellitus with moderate nonproliferative diabetic retinopathy without macular edema
+ E10.34 Type 1 diabetes mellitus with severe nonproliferative diabetic retinopathy
E10.341 Type 1 diabetes mellitus with severe nonproliferative diabetic retinopathy with macular edema
E10.349 Type 1 diabetes mellitus with severe nonproliferative diabetic retinopathy without macular edema
+ E10.35 Type 1 diabetes mellitus with proliferative diabetic retinopathy
E10.351 Type 1 diabetes mellitus with proliferative diabetic retinopathy with macular edema
E10.359 Type 1 diabetes mellitus with proliferative diabetic retinopathy without macular edema
E10.36 Type 1 diabetes mellitus with diabetic cataract
E10.39 Type 1 diabetes mellitus with other diabetic ophthalmic complication
Use additional code to identify manifestation, such as: diabetic glaucoma (H40-H42)
+ E10.4 Type 1 diabetes mellitus with neurological complications
E10.40 Type 1 diabetes mellitus with diabetic neuropathy, unspecified
E10.41 Type 1 diabetes mellitus with diabetic mononeuropathy
E10.42 Type 1 diabetes mellitus with diabetic polyneuropathy
Type 1 diabetes mellitus with diabetic neuralgia
E10.43 Type 1 diabetes mellitus with diabetic autonomic (poly)neuropathy
Type 1 diabetes mellitus with diabetic gastroparesis
AHA CC: 3Q, 2013, 114-115
E10.44 Type 1 diabetes mellitus with diabetic amyotrophy
E10.49 Type 1 diabetes mellitus with other diabetic neurological complication
+ E10.5 Type 1 diabetes mellitus with circulatory complications
E10.51 Type 1 diabetes mellitus with diabetic peripheral angiopathy without gangrene
CC **E10.52 Type 1 diabetes mellitus with diabetic peripheral angiopathy with gangrene**
Type 1 diabetes mellitus with diabetic gangrene
CC Exclusion see Appendix A PDX collection 0519
E10.59 Type 1 diabetes mellitus with other circulatory complications

+ E10.6 Type 1 diabetes mellitus with other specified complications
+ E10.61 Type 1 diabetes mellitus with diabetic arthropathy
E10.610 Type 1 diabetes mellitus with diabetic neuropathic arthropathy
Type 1 diabetes mellitus with Charcôt's joi
E10.618 Type 1 diabetes mellitus with other diabet arthropathy
+ E10.62 Type 1 diabetes mellitus with skin complications
E10.620 Type 1 diabetes mellitus with diabetic dermatitis
Type 1 diabetes mellitus with diabetic necrobiosis lipoidica
E10.621 Type 1 diabetes mellitus with foot ulcer
Use additional code to identify site of ulcer (L97.4-, L97.5-)
E10.622 Type 1 diabetes mellitus with other skin ulcer
Use additional code to identify site of ulcer (L97.1-L97.9, L98.41-L98.49)
E10.628 Type 1 diabetes mellitus with other skin complications
+ E10.63 Type 1 diabetes mellitus with oral complications
E10.630 Type 1 diabetes mellitus with periodontal disease
E10.638 Type 1 diabetes mellitus with other oral complications
+ E10.64 Type 1 diabetes mellitus with hypoglycemia
MCC **E10.641 Type 1 diabetes mellitus with hypoglycemi with coma**
MCC Exclusion see Appendix A PDX collectio 0520
E10.649 Type 1 diabetes mellitus with hypoglycemi without coma
E10.65 Type 1 diabetes mellitus with hyperglycemia
E10.69 Type 1 diabetes mellitus with other specified complication
Use additional code to identify complication
E10.8 Type 1 diabetes mellitus with unspecified complications
E10.9 Type 1 diabetes mellitus without complications

E11 Type 2 diabetes mellitus

Includes: diabetes (mellitus) due to insulin secretory defect
diabetes NOS
insulin resistant diabetes (mellitus)
Use additional code to identify any insulin use (Z79.4)
Excludes1: *diabetes mellitus due to underlying condition (E08.-)*
drug or chemical induced diabetes mellitus (E09.-)
gestational diabetes (O24.4-)
neonatal diabetes mellitus (P70.2)
postpancreatectomy diabetes mellitus (E13.-)
postprocedural diabetes mellitus (E13.-)
secondary diabetes mellitus NEC (E13.-)
type 1 diabetes mellitus (E10.-)
Review coding guidelines C.4.a.2 and C.4.a.3
+ E11.0 Type 2 diabetes mellitus with hyperosmolarity
MCC **E11.00 Type 2 diabetes mellitus with hyperosmolarity with nonketotic hyperglycemic-hyperosmolar coma (NKHHC)**
MCC Exclusion see Appendix A PDX collection 0518
HAC see Appendix B for HAC conditional logic
MCC **E11.01 Type 2 diabetes mellitus with hyperosmolarity with coma**
MCC Exclusion see Appendix A PDX collection 0518
HAC see Appendix B for HAC conditional logic
+ E11.2 Type 2 diabetes mellitus with kidney complications
E11.21 Type 2 diabetes mellitus with diabetic nephropathy
Type 2 diabetes mellitus with intercapillary glomerulosclerosis
Type 2 diabetes mellitus with intracapillary glomerulonephrosis
Type 2 diabetes mellitus with Kimmelstiel-Wilson disease
E11.22 Type 2 diabetes mellitus with diabetic chronic kidne disease
Use additional code to identify stage of chronic kidney disease (N18.1-N18.6)
E11.29 Type 2 diabetes mellitus with other diabetic kidney complication
Type 2 diabetes mellitus with renal tubular degeneratio
+ E11.3 Type 2 diabetes mellitus with ophthalmic complications
+ E11.31 Type 2 diabetes mellitus with unspecified diabetic retinopathy

E11.311 Type 2 diabetes mellitus with unspecified diabetic retinopathy with macular edema

E11.319 Type 2 diabetes mellitus with unspecified diabetic retinopathy without macular edema

AHA CC: 3Q, 2013, 20

+ **E11.32 Type 2 diabetes mellitus with mild nonproliferative diabetic retinopathy**

Type 2 diabetes mellitus with nonproliferative diabetic retinopathy NOS

E11.321 Type 2 diabetes mellitus with mild nonproliferative diabetic retinopathy with macular edema

E11.329 Type 2 diabetes mellitus with mild nonproliferative diabetic retinopathy without macular edema

+ **E11.33 Type 2 diabetes mellitus with moderate nonproliferative diabetic retinopathy**

E11.331 Type 2 diabetes mellitus with moderate nonproliferative diabetic retinopathy with macular edema

E11.339 Type 2 diabetes mellitus with moderate nonproliferative diabetic retinopathy without macular edema

+ **E11.34 Type 2 diabetes mellitus with severe nonproliferative diabetic retinopathy**

E11.341 Type 2 diabetes mellitus with severe nonproliferative diabetic retinopathy with macular edema

E11.349 Type 2 diabetes mellitus with severe nonproliferative diabetic retinopathy without macular edema

+ **E11.35 Type 2 diabetes mellitus with proliferative diabetic retinopathy**

E11.351 Type 2 diabetes mellitus with proliferative diabetic retinopathy with macular edema

E11.359 Type 2 diabetes mellitus with proliferative diabetic retinopathy without macular edema

E11.36 Type 2 diabetes mellitus with diabetic cataract

E11.39 Type 2 diabetes mellitus with other diabetic ophthalmic complication

Use additional code to identify manifestation, such as: diabetic glaucoma (H40-H42)

+ **E11.4 Type 2 diabetes mellitus with neurological complications**

E11.40 Type 2 diabetes mellitus with diabetic neuropathy, unspecified

AHA CC: 4Q, 2013, 129

E11.41 Type 2 diabetes mellitus with diabetic mononeuropathy

E11.42 Type 2 diabetes mellitus with diabetic polyneuropathy

Type 2 diabetes mellitus with diabetic neuralgia

E11.43 Type 2 diabetes mellitus with diabetic autonomic (poly)neuropathy

AHA CC: 4Q, 2013, 114-115

Type 2 diabetes mellitus with diabetic gastroparesis

E11.44 Type 2 diabetes mellitus with diabetic amyotrophy

E11.49 Type 2 diabetes mellitus with other diabetic neurological complication

+ **E11.5 Type 2 diabetes mellitus with circulatory complications**

E11.51 Type 2 diabetes mellitus with diabetic peripheral angiopathy without gangrene

CC **E11.52 Type 2 diabetes mellitus with diabetic peripheral angiopathy with gangrene**

Type 2 diabetes mellitus with diabetic gangrene

CC Exclusion see Appendix A PDX collection 0519

E11.59 Type 2 diabetes mellitus with other circulatory complications

+ **E11.6 Type 2 diabetes mellitus with other specified complications**

+ **E11.61 Type 2 diabetes mellitus with diabetic arthropathy**

E11.610 Type 2 diabetes mellitus with diabetic neuropathic arthropathy

Type 2 diabetes mellitus with Charcôt's joints

E11.618 Type 2 diabetes mellitus with other diabetic arthropathy

+ **E11.62 Type 2 diabetes mellitus with skin complications**

E11.620 Type 2 diabetes mellitus with diabetic dermatitis

Type 2 diabetes mellitus with diabetic necrobiosis lipoidica

E11.621 Type 2 diabetes mellitus with foot ulcer

Use additional code to identify site of ulcer (L97.4-, L97.5-)

E11.622 Type 2 diabetes mellitus with other skin ulcer

Use additional code to identify site of ulcer (L97.1-L97.9, L98.41-L98.49)

E11.628 Type 2 diabetes mellitus with other skin complications

+ **E11.63 Type 2 diabetes mellitus with oral complications**

E11.630 Type 2 diabetes mellitus with periodontal disease

E11.638 Type 2 diabetes mellitus with other oral complications

+ **E11.64 Type 2 diabetes mellitus with hypoglycemia**

MCC **E11.641 Type 2 diabetes mellitus with hypoglycemia with coma**

MCC Exclusion see Appendix A PDX collection 0518

E11.649 Type 2 diabetes mellitus with hypoglycemia without coma

E11.65 Type 2 diabetes mellitus with hyperglycemia

AHA CC: 3Q, 2013, 20

E11.69 Type 2 diabetes mellitus with other specified complication

Use additional code to identify complication

E11.8 Type 2 diabetes mellitus with unspecified complications

E11.9 Type 2 diabetes mellitus without complications

AHA CC: 4Q, 2013, 128

E13 Other specified diabetes mellitus

Includes: diabetes mellitus due to genetic defects of beta-cell function
diabetes mellitus due to genetic defects in insulin action
postpancreatectomy diabetes mellitus postprocedural
diabetes mellitus secondary diabetes mellitus NEC

Use additional code to identify any insulin use (Z79.4)

Excludes1: *diabetes (mellitus) due to autoimmune process (E10.-)*
diabetes (mellitus) due to immune mediated pancreatic islet beta-cell destruction (E10.-)
diabetes mellitus due to underlying condition (E08.-)
drug or chemical induced diabetes mellitus (E09.-)
gestational diabetes (O24.4-)
neonatal diabetes mellitus (P70.2)
type 2 diabetes mellitus (E11.-)

Review coding guidelines C.4.a.6.a and C.4.a.6.b.i

+ **E13.0 Other specified diabetes mellitus with hyperosmolarity**

MCC **E13.00 Other specified diabetes mellitus with hyperosmolarity without nonketotic hyperglycemic-hyperosmolar coma (NKHHC)**

MCC Exclusion see Appendix A PDX collection 0518

HAC see Appendix B for HAC conditional logic

MCC **E13.01 Other specified diabetes mellitus with hyperosmolarity with coma**

MCC Exclusion see Appendix A PDX collection 0518

HAC see Appendix B for HAC conditional logic

+ **E13.1 Other specified diabetes mellitus with ketoacidosis**

MCC **E13.10 Other specified diabetes mellitus with ketoacidosis without coma**

MCC Exclusion see Appendix A PDX collection 0518

HAC see Appendix B for HAC conditional logic

AHA CC: 1Q, 2013, 26-27

MCC **E13.11 Other specified diabetes mellitus with ketoacidosis with coma**

MCC Exclusion see Appendix A PDX collection 0518

+ **E13.2 Other specified diabetes mellitus with kidney complications**

E13.21 Other specified diabetes mellitus with diabetic nephropathy

Other specified diabetes mellitus with intercapillary glomerulosclerosis

Other specified diabetes mellitus with intracapillary glomerulonephrosis

Other specified diabetes mellitus with Kimmelstiel-Wilson disease

E13.22 Other specified diabetes mellitus with diabetic chronic kidney disease

Use additional code to identify stage of chronic kidney disease (N18.1-N18.6)

E13.29 Other specified diabetes mellitus with other diabetic kidney complication

Other specified diabetes mellitus with renal tubular degeneration

+ **E13.3 Other specified diabetes mellitus with ophthalmic complications**

+ **E13.31 Other specified diabetes mellitus with unspecified diabetic retinopathy**

E13.311 Other specified diabetes mellitus with unspecified diabetic retinopathy with macular edema

E13.319 Other specified diabetes mellitus with unspecified diabetic retinopathy without macular edema

+ **E13.32 Other specified diabetes mellitus with mild nonproliferative diabetic retinopathy**
Other specified diabetes mellitus with nonproliferative diabetic retinopathy NOS

E13.321 Other specified diabetes mellitus with mild nonproliferative diabetic retinopathy with macular edema

E13.329 Other specified diabetes mellitus with mild nonproliferative diabetic retinopathy without macular edema

+ **E13.33 Other specified diabetes mellitus with moderate nonproliferative diabetic retinopathy**

E13.331 Other specified diabetes mellitus with moderate nonproliferative diabetic retinopathy with macular edema

E13.339 Other specified diabetes mellitus with moderate nonproliferative diabetic retinopathy without macular edema

+ **E13.34 Other specified diabetes mellitus with severe nonproliferative diabetic retinopathy**

E13.341 Other specified diabetes mellitus with severe nonproliferative diabetic retinopathy with macular edema

E13.349 Other specified diabetes mellitus with severe nonproliferative diabetic retinopathy without macular edema

+ **E13.35 Other specified diabetes mellitus with proliferative diabetic retinopathy**

E13.351 Other specified diabetes mellitus with proliferative diabetic retinopathy with macular edema

E13.359 Other specified diabetes mellitus with proliferative diabetic retinopathy without macular edema

E13.36 Other specified diabetes mellitus with diabetic cataract

E13.39 Other specified diabetes mellitus with other diabetic ophthalmic complication
Use additional code to identify manifestation, such as:
diabetic glaucoma (H40-H42)

+ **E13.4 Other specified diabetes mellitus with neurological complications**

E13.40 Other specified diabetes mellitus with diabetic neuropathy, unspecified
AHA CC: 4Q, 2013, 129

E13.41 Other specified diabetes mellitus with diabetic mononeuropathy

E13.42 Other specified diabetes mellitus with diabetic polyneuropathy
Other specified diabetes mellitus with diabetic neuralgia

E13.43 Other specified diabetes mellitus with diabetic autonomic (poly)neuropathy
Other specified diabetes mellitus with diabetic gastroparesis
AHA CC: 4Q, 2013, 114-115

E13.44 Other specified diabetes mellitus with diabetic amyotrophy

E13.49 Other specified diabetes mellitus with other diabetic neurological complication

+ **E13.5 Other specified diabetes mellitus with circulatory complications**

E13.51 Other specified diabetes mellitus with diabetic peripheral angiopathy without gangrene

CC **E13.52 Other specified diabetes mellitus with diabetic peripheral angiopathy with gangrene**
Other specified diabetes mellitus with diabetic gangrene
CC Exclusion see Appendix A PDX collection 0519

E13.59 Other specified diabetes mellitus with other circulatory complications

+ **E13.6 Other specified diabetes mellitus with other specified complications**

+ **E13.61 Other specified diabetes mellitus with diabetic arthropathy**

E13.610 Other specified diabetes mellitus with diabetic neuropathic arthropathy
Other specified diabetes mellitus with Charcôt's joints

E13.618 Other specified diabetes mellitus with othe[r] diabetic arthropathy

+ **E13.62 Other specified diabetes mellitus with skin complications**

E13.620 Other specified diabetes mellitus with diabetic dermatitis
Other specified diabetes mellitus with diabe[tic] necrobiosis lipoidica

E13.621 Other specified diabetes mellitus with foot ulcer
Use additional code to identify site of ulcer (L97.4-, L97.5-)

E13.622 Other specified diabetes mellitus with othe[r] skin ulcer
Use additional code to identify site of ulcer (L97.1-L97.9, L98.41-L98.49)

E13.628 Other specified diabetes mellitus with othe[r] skin complications

+ **E13.63 Other specified diabetes mellitus with oral complications**

E13.630 Other specified diabetes mellitus with periodontal disease

E13.638 Other specified diabetes mellitus with other oral complications

+ **E13.64 Other specified diabetes mellitus with hypoglycemia**

MCC **E13.641 Other specified diabetes mellitus with hypoglycemia with coma**
MCC Exclusion see Appendix A PDX collection 0518

E13.649 Other specified diabetes mellitus with hypoglycemia without coma

E13.65 Other specified diabetes mellitus with hyperglycemia

E13.69 Other specified diabetes mellitus with other specified complication
Use additional code to identify complication

E13.8 Other specified diabetes mellitus with unspecified complication

E13.9 Other specified diabetes mellitus without complications

Other disorders of glucose regulation and pancreatic internal secretion (E15-E16)

CC **E15 Nondiabetic hypoglycemic coma**

Includes: drug-induced insulin coma in nondiabetic
hyperinsulinism with hypoglycemic coma
hypoglycemic coma NOS

CC Exclusion see Appendix A PDX collection 0520

HAC see Appendix B for HAC conditional logic

Valid 3-character code, no further characters required

E16 Other disorders of pancreatic internal secretion

E16.0 Drug-induced hypoglycemia without coma
Use additional code for adverse effect, if applicable, to identify drug (T36-T50 with fifth or sixth character 5)

E16.1 Other hypoglycemia
Functional hyperinsulinism
Functional nonhyperinsulinemic hypoglycemia
Hyperinsulinism NOS
Hyperplasia of pancreatic islet beta cells NOS
Excludes1: *hypoglycemia in infant of diabetic mother (P70.1)*
neonatal hypoglycemia (P70.4)

E16.2 Hypoglycemia, unspecified

E16.3 Increased secretion of glucagon
Hyperplasia of pancreatic endocrine cells with glucagon excess

E16.4 Increased secretion of gastrin
Hypergastrinemia
Hyperplasia of pancreatic endocrine cells with gastrin excess
Zollinger-Ellison syndrome

E16.8 Other specified disorders of pancreatic internal secretion
Increased secretion from endocrine pancreas of growth hormone-releasing hormone
Increased secretion from endocrine pancreas of pancreatic polypeptide
Increased secretion from endocrine pancreas of somatostatin
Increased secretion from endocrine pancreas of vasoactive-intestinal polypeptide

E16.9 Disorder of pancreatic internal secretion, unspecified
Islet-cell hyperplasia NOS
Pancreatic endocrine cell hyperplasia NOS

sorders of other endocrine glands (E20-E35)

Excludes1: *galactorrhea (N64.3)*
gynecomastia (N62)

E20 Hypoparathyroidism

Excludes1: *Di George's syndrome (D82.1)*
postprocedural hypoparathyroidism (E89.2)
tetany NOS (R29.0)
transitory neonatal hypoparathyroidism (P71.4)

E20.0 Idiopathic hypoparathyroidism
E20.1 Pseudohypoparathyroidism
E20.8 Other hypoparathyroidism
E20.9 Hypoparathyroidism, unspecified
Parathyroid tetany

E21 Hyperparathyroidism and other disorders of parathyroid gland

Excludes1: *adult osteomalacia (M83.-)*
ectopic hyperparathyroidism (E34.2)
familial hypocalciuric hypercalcemia (E83.52)
hungry bone syndrome (E83.81)
infantile and juvenile osteomalacia (E55.0)

E21.0 Primary hyperparathyroidism
Hyperplasia of parathyroid
Osteitis fibrosa cystica generalisata [von Recklinghausen's disease of bone]

E21.1 Secondary hyperparathyroidism, not elsewhere classified
Excludes1: *secondary hyperparathyroidism of renal origin (N25.81)*

E21.2 Other hyperparathyroidism
Tertiary hyperparathyroidism
Excludes1: *familial hypocalciuric hypercalcemia (E83.52)*

E21.3 Hyperparathyroidism, unspecified
E21.4 Other specified disorders of parathyroid gland
E21.5 Disorder of parathyroid gland, unspecified

E22 Hyperfunction of pituitary gland

Excludes1: *Cushing's syndrome (E24.-)*
Nelson's syndrome (E24.1)
overproduction of ACTH not associated with Cushing's disease (E27.0)
overproduction of pituitary ACTH (E24.0)
overproduction of thyroid-stimulating hormone (E05.8-)

E22.0 Acromegaly and pituitary gigantism
Overproduction of growth hormone
Excludes1: *constitutional gigantism (E34.4)*
constitutional tall stature (E34.4)
increased secretion from endocrine pancreas of growth hormone-releasing hormone (E16.8)

CC **E22.1 Hyperprolactinemia**
Use additional code for adverse effect, if applicable, to identify drug (T36-T50 with fifth or sixth character 5)
CC Exclusion see Appendix A PDX collection 0521

CC **E22.2 Syndrome of inappropriate secretion of antidiuretic hormone**
CC Exclusion see Appendix A PDX collection 0522

CC **E22.8 Other hyperfunction of pituitary gland**
Central precocious puberty
CC Exclusion see Appendix A PDX collection 0521

CC **E22.9 Hyperfunction of pituitary gland, unspecified**
CC Exclusion see Appendix A PDX collection 0521

E23 Hypofunction and other disorders of the pituitary gland

Includes: the listed conditions whether the disorder is in the pituitary or the hypothalamus
Excludes1: *postprocedural hypopituitarism (E89.3)*

CC **E23.0 Hypopituitarism**
Fertile eunuch syndrome
Hypogonadotropic hypogonadism
Idiopathic growth hormone deficiency
Isolated deficiency of gonadotropin
Isolated deficiency of growth hormone
Isolated deficiency of pituitary hormone
Kallmann's syndrome
Lorain-Levi short stature
Necrosis of pituitary gland (postpartum)
Panhypopituitarism
Pituitary cachexia
Pituitary insufficiency NOS
Pituitary short stature
Sheehan's syndrome
Simmonds' disease
CC Exclusion see Appendix A PDX collection 0523

E23.1 Drug-induced hypopituitarism
Use additional code for adverse effect, if applicable, to identify drug (T36-T50 with fifth or sixth character 5)

CC **E23.2 Diabetes insipidus**
Excludes1: *nephrogenic diabetes insipidus (N25.1)*
CC Exclusion see Appendix A PDX collection 0524

E23.3 Hypothalamic dysfunction, not elsewhere classified
Excludes1: *Prader-Willi syndrome (Q87.1)*
Russell-Silver syndrome (Q87.1)

E23.6 Other disorders of pituitary gland
Abscess of pituitary
Adiposogenital dystrophy

E23.7 Disorder of pituitary gland, unspecified

E24 Cushing's syndrome

Excludes1: *congenital adrenal hyperplasia (E25.0)*

CC **E24.0 Pituitary-dependent Cushing's disease**
Overproduction of pituitary ACTH
Pituitary-dependent hypercorticalism
CC Exclusion see Appendix A PDX collection 0525

E24.1 Nelson's syndrome

CC **E24.2 Drug-induced Cushing's syndrome**
Use additional code for adverse effect, if applicable, to identify drug (T36-T50 with fifth or sixth character 5)
CC Exclusion see Appendix A PDX collection 0525

CC **E24.3 Ectopic ACTH syndrome**
CC Exclusion see Appendix A PDX collection 0525

CC **E24.4 Alcohol-induced pseudo-Cushing's syndrome**
CC Exclusion see Appendix A PDX collection 0525

CC **E24.8 Other Cushing's syndrome**
CC Exclusion see Appendix A PDX collection 0525

CC **E24.9 Cushing's syndrome, unspecified**
CC Exclusion see Appendix A PDX collection 0525

E25 Adrenogenital disorders

Includes: adrenogenital syndromes, virilizing or feminizing, whether acquired or due to adrenal hyperplasia consequent on inborn enzyme defects in hormone synthesis
Female adrenal pseudohermaphroditism
Female heterosexual precocious pseudopuberty
Male isosexual precocious pseudopuberty
Male macrogenitosomia praecox
Male sexual precocity with adrenal hyperplasia
Male virilization (female)

Excludes1: *indeterminate sex and pseudohermaphroditism (Q56)*
chromosomal abnormalities (Q90-Q99)

E25.0 Congenital adrenogenital disorders associated with enzyme deficiency
Congenital adrenal hyperplasia
21-Hydroxylase deficiency
Salt-losing congenital adrenal hyperplasia

E25.8 Other adrenogenital disorders
Idiopathic adrenogenital disorder
Use additional code for adverse effect, if applicable, to identify drug (T36-T50 with fifth or sixth character 5)

E25.9 Adrenogenital disorder, unspecified
Adrenogenital syndrome NOS

E26 Hyperaldosteronism

\+ **E26.0 Primary hyperaldosteronism**
E26.01 Conn's syndrome
Code also adrenal adenoma (D35.0-)
E26.02 Glucocorticoid-remediable aldosteronism
Familial aldosteronism type I
E26.09 Other primary hyperaldosteronism
Primary aldosteronism due to adrenal hyperplasia (bilateral)

E26.1 Secondary hyperaldosteronism

\+ **E26.8 Other hyperaldosteronism**
E26.81 Bartter's syndrome
E26.89 Other hyperaldosteronism

E26.9 Hyperaldosteronism, unspecified
Aldosteronism NOS
Hyperaldosteronism NOS

E27 Other disorders of adrenal gland

CC **E27.0 Other adrenocortical overactivity**
Overproduction of ACTH, not associated with Cushing's disease
Premature adrenarche
Excludes1: *Cushing's syndrome (E24.-)*
CC Exclusion see Appendix A PDX collection 0526

CC **E27.1 Primary adrenocortical insufficiency**
Addison's disease
Autoimmune adrenalitis
Excludes1: *Addison only phenotype adrenoleukodystrophy (E71.528)*
amyloidosis (E85.-)
tuberculous Addison's disease (A18.7)
Waterhouse-Friderichsen syndrome (A39.1)
CC Exclusion see Appendix A PDX collection 0526

CC **E27.2 Addisonian crisis**
Adrenal crisis
Adrenocortical crisis
CC Exclusion see Appendix A PDX collection 0526

CC **E27.3 Drug-induced adrenocortical insufficiency**
Use additional code for adverse effect, if applicable, to identify drug (T36-T50 with fifth or sixth character 5)
CC Exclusion see Appendix A PDX collection 0526

\+ **E27.4 Other and unspecified adrenocortical insufficiency**
Excludes1: *adrenoleukodystrophy [Addison-Schilder] (E71.528)*
Waterhouse-Friderichsen syndrome (A39.1)

CC **E27.40 Unspecified adrenocortical insufficiency**
Adrenocortical insufficiency NOS
Hypoaldosteronism
CC Exclusion see Appendix A PDX collection 0526

CC **E27.49 Other adrenocortical insufficiency**
Adrenal hemorrhage
Adrenal infarction
CC Exclusion see Appendix A PDX collection 0526

CC **E27.5 Adrenomedullary hyperfunction**
Adrenomedullary hyperplasia
Catecholamine hypersecretion
CC Exclusion see Appendix A PDX collection 0526

E27.8 Other specified disorders of adrenal gland
Abnormality of cortisol-binding globulin

E27.9 Disorder of adrenal gland, unspecified

E28 Ovarian dysfunction

Excludes1: *isolated gonadotropin deficiency (E23.0)*
postprocedural ovarian failure (E89.4-)

♀ **E28.0 Estrogen excess**
Use additional code for adverse effect, if applicable, to identify drug (T36-T50 with fifth or sixth character 5)

♀ **E28.1 Androgen excess**
Hypersecretion of ovarian androgens
Use additional code for adverse effect, if applicable, to identify drug (T36-T50 with fifth or sixth character 5)

♀ **E28.2 Polycystic ovarian syndrome**
Sclerocystic ovary syndrome
Stein-Leventhal syndrome

\+ **E28.3 Primary ovarian failure**
Excludes1: *pure gonadal dysgenesis (Q99.1)*
Turner's syndrome (Q96.-)

\+ **E28.31 Premature menopause**

• ♀ **E28.310 Symptomatic premature menopause**
Symptoms such as flushing, sleeplessness, headache, lack of concentration, associated with premature menopause

• ♀ **E28.319 Asymptomatic premature menopause**
Premature menopause NOS

♀ **E28.39 Other primary ovarian failure**
Decreased estrogen
Resistant ovary syndrome

♀ **E28.8 Other ovarian dysfunction**
Ovarian hyperfunction NOS
Excludes1: *postprocedural ovarian failure (E89.4-)*

♀ **E28.9 Ovarian dysfunction, unspecified**

E29 Testicular dysfunction

Excludes1: *androgen insensitivity syndrome (E34.5-)*
azoospermia or oligospermia NOS (N46.0-N46.1)
isolated gonadotropin deficiency (E23.0)
Klinefelter's syndrome (Q98.0-Q98.2, Q98.4)

♂ **E29.0 Testicular hyperfunction**
Hypersecretion of testicular hormones

♂ **E29.1 Testicular hypofunction**
Defective biosynthesis of testicular androgen NOS
5-delta-Reductase deficiency (with male pseudohermaphroditism)
Testicular hypogonadism NOS
Use additional code for adverse effect, if applicable, to identify drug (T36-T50 with fifth or sixth character 5)
Excludes1: *postprocedural testicular hypofunction (E89.5)*

♂ **E29.8 Other testicular dysfunction**

♂ **E29.9 Testicular dysfunction, unspecified**

E30 Disorders of puberty, not elsewhere classified

E30.0 Delayed puberty
Constitutional delay of puberty
Delayed sexual development

• **E30.1 Precocious puberty**
Precocious menstruation
Excludes1: *Albright (-McCune) (-Sternberg) syndrome (Q78.1*
central precocious puberty (E22.8)
congenital adrenal hyperplasia (E25.0)
female heterosexual precocious pseudopuberty (E25.-)
male isosexual precocious pseudopuberty (E25.-)

• **E30.8 Other disorders of puberty**
Premature thelarche

E30.9 Disorder of puberty, unspecified

E31 Polyglandular dysfunction

Excludes1: *ataxia telangiectasia [Louis-Bar] (G11.3)*
dystrophia myotonica [Steinert] (G71.11)
pseudohypoparathyroidism (E20.1)

E31.0 Autoimmune polyglandular failure
Schmidt's syndrome

E31.1 Polyglandular hyperfunction
Excludes1: *multiple endocrine adenomatosis (E31.2-)*
multiple endocrine neoplasia (E31.2-)

\+ **E31.2 Multiple endocrine neoplasia [MEN] syndromes**
Multiple endocrine adenomatosis
Code also any associated malignancies and other conditions associated with the syndromes

E31.20 Multiple endocrine neoplasia [MEN] syndrome, unspecified
Multiple endocrine adenomatosis NOS
Multiple endocrine neoplasia [MEN] syndrome NOS

E31.21 Multiple endocrine neoplasia [MEN] type I
Wermer's syndrome

E31.22 Multiple endocrine neoplasia [MEN] type IIA
Sipple's syndrome

E31.23 Multiple endocrine neoplasia [MEN] type IIB

E31.8 Other polyglandular dysfunction

E31.9 Polyglandular dysfunction, unspecified

E32 Diseases of thymus

Excludes1: *aplasia or hypoplasia of thymus with immunodeficiency (D82.1)*
myasthenia gravis (G70.0)

E32.0 Persistent hyperplasia of thymus
Hypertrophy of thymus

CC **E32.1 Abscess of thymus**
CC Exclusion see Appendix A PDX collection 0527

E32.8 Other diseases of thymus
Excludes1: *aplasia or hypoplasia with immunodeficiency (D82.1)*
thymoma (D15.0)

E32.9 Disease of thymus, unspecified

E34 Other endocrine disorders

Excludes1: *pseudohypoparathyroidism (E20.1)*

CC **E34.0 Carcinoid syndrome**
NOTE May be used as an additional code to identify function activity associated with a carcinoid tumor.
CC Exclusion see Appendix A PDX collection 0528

E34.1 Other hypersecretion of intestinal hormones

E34.2 Ectopic hormone secretion, not elsewhere classified
Excludes1: *ectopic ACTH syndrome (E24.3)*

E34.3 Short stature due to endocrine disorder
Constitutional short stature
Laron-type short stature
Excludes1: *achondroplastic short stature (Q77.4)*
hypochondroplastic short stature (Q77.4)
nutritional short stature (E45)
pituitary short stature (E23.0)
progeria (E34.8)
renal short stature (N25.0)
Russell-Silver syndrome (Q87.1)
short-limbed stature with immunodeficiency (D82.
short stature in specific dysmorphic syndromes - code to syndrome - see Alphabetical Index
short stature NOS (R62.52)

E34.4 Constitutional tall stature
Constitutional gigantism

\+ **E34.5 Androgen insensitivity syndrome**
E34.50 Androgen insensitivity syndrome, unspecified
Androgen insensitivity NOS
E34.51 Complete androgen insensitivity syndrome
Complete androgen insensitivity
de Quervain syndrome
Goldberg-Maxwell syndrome
E34.52 Partial androgen insensitivity syndrome
Partial androgen insensitivity
Reifenstein syndrome
E34.8 Other specified endocrine disorders
Pineal gland dysfunction
Progeria
Excludes2: *pseudohypoparathyroidism (E20.1)*
E34.9 Endocrine disorder, unspecified
Endocrine disturbance NOS
Hormone disturbance NOS

E35 Disorders of endocrine glands in diseases classified elsewhere

Code first underlying disease, such as:
late congenital syphilis of thymus gland [Dubois disease] (A50.5)

Use additional code, if applicable, to identify:
sequelae of tuberculosis of other organs (B90.8)
Excludes1: *Echinococcus granulosus infection of thyroid gland (B67.3)*
meningococcal hemorrhagic adrenalitis (A39.1)
syphilis of endocrine gland (A52.79)
tuberculosis of adrenal gland, except calcification (A18.7)
tuberculosis of endocrine gland NEC (A18.82)
tuberculosis of thyroid gland (A18.81)
Waterhouse-Friderichsen syndrome (A39.1)
Valid 3-character code, no further characters required

ıtraoperative complications of endocrine system (E36)

E36 Intraoperative complications of endocrine system

Excludes2: *postprocedural endocrine and metabolic complications and disorders, not elsewhere classified (E89.-)*

\+ **E36.0 Intraoperative hemorrhage and hematoma of an endocrine system organ or structure complicating a procedure**
Excludes1: *intraoperative hemorrhage and hematoma of an endocrine system organ or structure due to accidental puncture or laceration during a procedure (E36.1-)*
CC **E36.01 Intraoperative hemorrhage and hematoma of an endocrine system organ or structure complicating an endocrine system procedure**
CC Exclusion see Appendix A PDX collection 0529
CC **E36.02 Intraoperative hemorrhage and hematoma of an endocrine system organ or structure complicating other procedure**
CC Exclusion see Appendix A PDX collection 0529
\+ **E36.1 Accidental puncture and laceration of an endocrine system organ or structure during a procedure**
CC **E36.11 Accidental puncture and laceration of an endocrine system organ or structure during an endocrine system procedure**
CC Exclusion see Appendix A PDX collection 0509
CC **E36.12 Accidental puncture and laceration of an endocrine system organ or structure during other procedure**
CC Exclusion see Appendix A PDX collection 0509
E36.8 Other intraoperative complications of endocrine system
Use additional code, if applicable, to further specify disorder

ıalnutrition (E40-E46)

ccludes1: *intestinal malabsorption (K90.-)*
sequelae of protein-calorie malnutrition (E64.0)
ccludes2: *nutritional anemias (D50-D53)*
starvation (T73.0)

C E40 Kwashiorkor

Severe malnutrition with nutritional edema with dyspigmentation of skin and hair
Excludes1: *marasmic kwashiorkor (E42)*
MCC Exclusion see Appendix A PDX collection 0530
Valid 3-character code, no further characters required

C E41 Nutritional marasmus

Severe malnutrition with marasmus
Excludes1: *marasmic kwashiorkor (E42)*
MCC Exclusion see Appendix A PDX collection 0530
Valid 3-character code, no further characters required

MCC **E42 Marasmic kwashiorkor**

Intermediate form severe protein-calorie malnutrition
Severe protein-calorie malnutrition with signs of both kwashiorkor and marasmus
MCC Exclusion see Appendix A PDX collection 0530
Valid 3-character code, no further characters required

MCC **E43 Unspecified severe protein-calorie malnutrition**

Starvation edema
MCC Exclusion see Appendix A PDX collection 0530
Valid 3-character code, no further characters required

E44 Protein-calorie malnutrition of moderate and mild degree

CC **E44.0 Moderate protein-calorie malnutrition**
CC Exclusion see Appendix A PDX collection 0530
CC **E44.1 Mild protein-calorie malnutrition**
CC Exclusion see Appendix A PDX collection 0530

CC **E45 Retarded development following protein-calorie malnutrition**

Nutritional short stature
Nutritional stunting
Physical retardation due to malnutrition
CC Exclusion see Appendix A PDX collection 0530
Valid 3-character code, no further characters required

CC **E46 Unspecified protein-calorie malnutrition**

Malnutrition NOS
Protein-calorie imbalance NOS
Excludes1: *nutritional deficiency NOS (E63.9)*
CC Exclusion see Appendix A PDX collection 0530
Valid 3-character code, no further characters required

Other nutritional deficiencies (E50-E64)

Excludes2: *nutritional anemias (D50-D53)*

E50 Vitamin A deficiency

Excludes1: *sequelae of vitamin A deficiency (E64.1)*
E50.0 Vitamin A deficiency with conjunctival xerosis
E50.1 Vitamin A deficiency with Bitot's spot and conjunctival xerosis
Bitot's spot in the young child
E50.2 Vitamin A deficiency with corneal xerosis
E50.3 Vitamin A deficiency with corneal ulceration and xerosis
E50.4 Vitamin A deficiency with keratomalacia
E50.5 Vitamin A deficiency with night blindness
E50.6 Vitamin A deficiency with xerophthalmic scars of cornea
E50.7 Other ocular manifestations of vitamin A deficiency
Xerophthalmia NOS
E50.8 Other manifestations of vitamin A deficiency
Follicular keratosis
Xeroderma
E50.9 Vitamin A deficiency, unspecified
Hypovitaminosis A NOS

E51 Thiamine deficiency

Excludes1: *sequelae of thiamine deficiency (E64.8)*
\+ **E51.1 Beriberi**
CC **E51.11 Dry beriberi**
Beriberi NOS
Beriberi with polyneuropathy
CC Exclusion see Appendix A PDX collection 0531
CC **E51.12 Wet beriberi**
Beriberi with cardiovascular manifestations
Cardiovascular beriberi
Shoshin disease
CC Exclusion see Appendix A PDX collection 0531
CC **E51.2 Wernicke's encephalopathy**
CC Exclusion see Appendix A PDX collection 0531
CC **E51.8 Other manifestations of thiamine deficiency**
CC Exclusion see Appendix A PDX collection 0531
CC **E51.9 Thiamine deficiency, unspecified**
CC Exclusion see Appendix A PDX collection 0531

E52 Niacin deficiency [pellagra]

Niacin (-tryptophan) deficiency
Nicotinamide deficiency
Pellagra (alcoholic)
Excludes1: *sequelae of niacin deficiency (E64.8)*
Valid 3-character code, no further characters required

E53 Deficiency of other B group vitamins

Excludes1: *sequelae of vitamin B deficiency (E64.8)*

CC **E53.0 Riboflavin deficiency**
Ariboflavinosis
Vitamin B2 deficiency
CC Exclusion see Appendix A PDX collection 0531

E53.1 Pyridoxine deficiency
Vitamin B6 deficiency
Excludes1: *pyridoxine-responsive sideroblastic anemia (D64.3)*

E53.8 Deficiency of other specified B group vitamins
Biotin deficiency
Cyanocobalamin deficiency
Folate deficiency
Folic acid deficiency
Pantothenic acid deficiency
Vitamin B12 deficiency
Excludes1: *folate deficiency anemia (D52.-)*
vitamin B12 deficiency anemia (D51.-)

E53.9 Vitamin B deficiency, unspecified

E54 Ascorbic acid deficiency

Deficiency of vitamin C
Scurvy
Excludes1: *scorbutic anemia (D53.2)*
sequelae of vitamin C deficiency (E64.2)
Valid 3-character code, no further characters required

E55 Vitamin D deficiency

Excludes1: *adult osteomalacia (M83.-)*
osteoporosis (M80.-)
sequelae of rickets (E64.3)

CC **E55.0 Rickets, active**
Infantile osteomalacia
Juvenile osteomalacia
Excludes1: *celiac rickets (K90.0)*
Crohn's rickets (K50.-)
hereditary vitamin D-dependent rickets (E83.32)
inactive rickets (E64.3)
renal rickets (N25.0)
sequelae of rickets (E64.3)
vitamin D-resistant rickets (E83.31)
CC Exclusion see Appendix A PDX collection 0532

E55.9 Vitamin D deficiency, unspecified
Avitaminosis D

E56 Other vitamin deficiencies

Excludes1: *sequelae of other vitamin deficiencies (E64.8)*

E56.0 Deficiency of vitamin E

E56.1 Deficiency of vitamin K
Excludes1: *deficiency of coagulation factor due to vitamin K deficiency (D68.4)*
vitamin K deficiency of newborn (P53)

E56.8 Deficiency of other vitamins

E56.9 Vitamin deficiency, unspecified

E58 Dietary calcium deficiency

Excludes1: *disorders of calcium metabolism (E83.5-)*
sequelae of calcium deficiency (E64.8)
Valid 3-character code, no further characters required

E59 Dietary selenium deficiency

Keshan disease
Excludes1: *sequelae of selenium deficiency (E64.8)*
Valid 3-character code, no further characters required

E60 Dietary zinc deficiency

Valid 3-character code, no further characters required

E61 Deficiency of other nutrient elements

Use additional code for adverse effect, if applicable, to identify drug (T36-T50 with fifth or sixth character 5)
Excludes1: *disorders of mineral metabolism (E83.-)*
iodine deficiency related thyroid disorders (E00-E02)
sequelae of malnutrition and other nutritional deficiencies (E64.-)

E61.0 Copper deficiency

E61.1 Iron deficiency
Excludes1: *iron deficiency anemia (D50.-)*

E61.2 Magnesium deficiency

E61.3 Manganese deficiency

E61.4 Chromium deficiency

E61.5 Molybdenum deficiency

E61.6 Vanadium deficiency

E61.7 Deficiency of multiple nutrient elements

E61.8 Deficiency of other specified nutrient elements

E61.9 Deficiency of nutrient element, unspecified

E63 Other nutritional deficiencies

Excludes1: *dehydration (E86.0)*
failure to thrive, adult (R62.7)
failure to thrive, child (R62.51)
feeding problems in newborn (P92.-)
sequelae of malnutrition and other nutritional deficiencies (E64.-)

E63.0 Essential fatty acid [EFA] deficiency

E63.1 Imbalance of constituents of food intake

E63.8 Other specified nutritional deficiencies

E63.9 Nutritional deficiency, unspecified

E64 Sequelae of malnutrition and other nutritional deficiencies

NOTE This category is to be used to indicate conditions in categories E43, E44, E46, E50-E63 as the cause of sequelae, which are themselves classified elsewhere. The 'sequelae' include conditions specified as such; they also include the late effects o diseases classifiable to the above categories if the disease itself is no longer present

Code first condition resulting from (sequela) of malnutrition and other nutritional deficiencies

CC **E64.0 Sequelae of protein-calorie malnutrition**
Excludes2: *retarded development following protein-calorie malnutrition (E45)*
CC Exclusion see Appendix A PDX collection 0530

E64.1 Sequelae of vitamin A deficiency

E64.2 Sequelae of vitamin C deficiency

E64.3 Sequelae of rickets

E64.8 Sequelae of other nutritional deficiencies

E64.9 Sequelae of unspecified nutritional deficiency

Overweight, obesity and other hyperalimentation (E65-E68)

E65 Localized adiposity

Fat pad
Valid 3-character code, no further characters required

E66 Overweight and obesity

Code first obesity complicating pregnancy, childbirth and the puerperium if applicable (O99.21-)

Use additional code to identify body mass index (BMI), if known (Z68.-)
Excludes1: *adiposogenital dystrophy (E23.6)*
lipomatosis NOS (E88.2)
lipomatosis dolorosa [Dercum] (E88.2)
Prader-Willi syndrome (Q87.1)

\+ **E66.0 Obesity due to excess calories**

E66.01 Morbid (severe) obesity due to excess calories
Excludes1: *morbid (severe) obesity with alveolar hypoventilation (E66.2)*
HAC see Appendix B for HAC conditional logic

E66.09 Other obesity due to excess calories

E66.1 Drug-induced obesity
Use additional code for adverse effect, if applicable, to identify drug (T36-T50 with fifth or sixth character 5)

CC **E66.2 Morbid (severe) obesity with alveolar hypoventilation**
Pickwickian syndrome
CC Exclusion see Appendix A PDX collection 0533

E66.3 Overweight

E66.8 Other obesity

E66.9 Obesity, unspecified
Obesity NOS
AHA CC: 4Q, 2013, 129

E67 Other hyperalimentation

Excludes1: *hyperalimentation NOS (R63.2)*
sequelae of hyperalimentation (E68)

E67.0 Hypervitaminosis A

E67.1 Hypercarotinemia

E67.2 Megavitamin-B6 syndrome

E67.3 Hypervitaminosis D

E67.8 Other specified hyperalimentation

E68 Sequelae of hyperalimentation

Code first condition resulting from (sequela) of hyperalimentation
Valid 3-character code, no further characters required

etabolic disorders (E70-E88)

xcludes1: *androgen insensitivity syndrome (E34.5-)*
congenital adrenal hyperplasia (E25.0)
Ehlers-Danlos syndrome (Q79.6)
hemolytic anemias attributable to enzyme disorders (D55.-)
Marfan's syndrome (Q87.4)
5-alpha-reductase deficiency (E29.1)

E70 Disorders of aromatic amino-acid metabolism

CC **E70.0 Classical phenylketonuria**
CC Exclusion see Appendix A PDX collection 0534

CC **E70.1 Other hyperphenylalaninemias**
CC Exclusion see Appendix A PDX collection 0534

\+ **E70.2 Disorders of tyrosine metabolism**
Excludes1: *transitory tyrosinemia of newborn (P74.5)*

CC **E70.20 Disorder of tyrosine metabolism, unspecified**
CC Exclusion see Appendix A PDX collection 0534

CC **E70.21 Tyrosinemia**
Hypertyrosinemia
CC Exclusion see Appendix A PDX collection 0534

CC **E70.29 Other disorders of tyrosine metabolism**
Alkaptonuria
Ochronosis
CC Exclusion see Appendix A PDX collection 0534

\+ **E70.3 Albinism**

CC **E70.30 Albinism, unspecified**
CC Exclusion see Appendix A PDX collection 0534

\+ **E70.31 Ocular albinism**

CC **E70.310 X-linked ocular albinism**
CC Exclusion see Appendix A PDX collection 0534

CC **E70.311 Autosomal recessive ocular albinism**
CC Exclusion see Appendix A PDX collection 0534

CC **E70.318 Other ocular albinism**
CC Exclusion see Appendix A PDX collection 0534

CC **E70.319 Ocular albinism, unspecified**
CC Exclusion see Appendix A PDX collection 0534

\+ **E70.32 Oculocutaneous albinism**
Excludes1: *Chediak-Higashi syndrome (E70.330)*
Hermansky-Pudlak syndrome (E70.331)

CC **E70.320 Tyrosinase negative oculocutaneous albinism**
Albinism I
Oculocutaneous albinism ty-neg
CC Exclusion see Appendix A PDX collection 0534

CC **E70.321 Tyrosinase positive oculocutaneous albinism**
Albinism II
Oculocutaneous albinism ty-pos
CC Exclusion see Appendix A PDX collection 0534

CC **E70.328 Other oculocutaneous albinism**
Cross syndrome
CC Exclusion see Appendix A PDX collection 0534

CC **E70.329 Oculocutaneous albinism, unspecified**
CC Exclusion see Appendix A PDX collection 0534

\+ **E70.33 Albinism with hematologic abnormality**

CC **E70.330 Chediak-Higashi syndrome**
CC Exclusion see Appendix A PDX collection 0534

CC **E70.331 Hermansky-Pudlak syndrome**
CC Exclusion see Appendix A PDX collection 0534

CC **E70.338 Other albinism with hematologic abnormality**
CC Exclusion see Appendix A PDX collection 0534

CC **E70.339 Albinism with hematologic abnormality, unspecified**
CC Exclusion see Appendix A PDX collection 0534

CC **E70.39 Other specified albinism**
Piebaldism
CC Exclusion see Appendix A PDX collection 0534

\+ **E70.4 Disorders of histidine metabolism**

CC **E70.40 Disorders of histidine metabolism, unspecified**
CC Exclusion see Appendix A PDX collection 0534

CC **E70.41 Histidinemia**
CC Exclusion see Appendix A PDX collection 0534

CC **E70.49 Other disorders of histidine metabolism**
CC Exclusion see Appendix A PDX collection 0534

CC **E70.5 Disorders of tryptophan metabolism**
CC Exclusion see Appendix A PDX collection 0534

CC **E70.8 Other disorders of aromatic amino-acid metabolism**
CC Exclusion see Appendix A PDX collection 0534

CC **E70.9 Disorder of aromatic amino-acid metabolism, unspecified**
CC Exclusion see Appendix A PDX collection 0534

E71 Disorders of branched-chain amino-acid metabolism and fatty-acid metabolism

CC **E71.0 Maple-syrup-urine disease**
CC Exclusion see Appendix A PDX collection 0534

\+ **E71.1 Other disorders of branched-chain amino-acid metabolism**

\+ **E71.11 Branched-chain organic acidurias**

CC **E71.110 Isovaleric acidemia**
CC Exclusion see Appendix A PDX collection 0534

CC **E71.111 3-methylglutaconic aciduria**
CC Exclusion see Appendix A PDX collection 0534

CC **E71.118 Other branched-chain organic acidurias**
CC Exclusion see Appendix A PDX collection 0534

\+ **E71.12 Disorders of propionate metabolism**

CC **E71.120 Methylmalonic acidemia**
CC Exclusion see Appendix A PDX collection 0534

CC **E71.121 Propionic acidemia**
CC Exclusion see Appendix A PDX collection 0534

CC **E71.128 Other disorders of propionate metabolism**
CC Exclusion see Appendix A PDX collection 0534

CC **E71.19 Other disorders of branched-chain amino-acid metabolism**
Hyperleucine-isoleucinemia
Hypervalinemia
CC Exclusion see Appendix A PDX collection 0534

CC **E71.2 Disorder of branched-chain amino-acid metabolism, unspecified**
CC Exclusion see Appendix A PDX collection 0534

\+ **E71.3 Disorders of fatty-acid metabolism**
Excludes1: *peroxisomal disorders (E71.5)*
Refsum's disease (G60.1)
Schilder's disease (G37.0)
Excludes2: *carnitine deficiency due to inborn error of metabolism (E71.42)*

E71.30 Disorder of fatty-acid metabolism, unspecified

\+ **E71.31 Disorders of fatty-acid oxidation**

CC **E71.310 Long chain/very long chain acyl CoA dehydrogenase deficiency**
LCAD
VLCAD
CC Exclusion see Appendix A PDX collection 0535

CC **E71.311 Medium chain acyl CoA dehydrogenase deficiency**
MCAD
CC Exclusion see Appendix A PDX collection 0535

CC **E71.312 Short chain acyl CoA dehydrogenase deficiency**
SCAD
CC Exclusion see Appendix A PDX collection 0535

CC **E71.313 Glutaric aciduria type II**
Glutaric aciduria type II A
Glutaric aciduria type II B
Glutaric aciduria type II C
Excludes1: *glutaric aciduria (type 1) NOS (E72.3)*
CC Exclusion see Appendix A PDX collection 0535

CC **E71.314 Muscle carnitine palmitoyltransferase deficiency**
CC Exclusion see Appendix A PDX collection 0535

CC **E71.318 Other disorders of fatty-acid oxidation**
CC Exclusion see Appendix A PDX collection 0535

CC **E71.32 Disorders of ketone metabolism**
CC Exclusion see Appendix A PDX collection 0535

CC **E71.39 Other disorders of fatty-acid metabolism**
CC Exclusion see Appendix A PDX collection 0492

+ **E71.4 Disorders of carnitine metabolism**
Excludes1: Muscle carnitine palmitoyltransferase deficiency (E71.314)
E71.40 Disorder of carnitine metabolism, unspecified
E71.41 Primary carnitine deficiency
E71.42 Carnitine deficiency due to inborn errors of metabolism
Code also associated inborn error or metabolism
E71.43 Iatrogenic carnitine deficiency
Carnitine deficiency due to hemodialysis
Carnitine deficiency due to Valproic acid therapy
+ **E71.44 Other secondary carnitine deficiency**
E71.440 Ruvalcaba-Myhre-Smith syndrome
E71.448 Other secondary carnitine deficiency
+ **E71.5 Peroxisomal disorders**
Excludes1: Schilder's disease (G37.0)
CC **E71.50 Peroxisomal disorder, unspecified**
CC Exclusion see Appendix A PDX collection 0536
+ **E71.51 Disorders of peroxisome biogenesis**
Group 1 peroxisomal disorders
Excludes1: Refsum's disease (G60.1)
CC **E71.510 Zellweger syndrome**
CC Exclusion see Appendix A PDX collection 0536
• CC **E71.511 Neonatal adrenoleukodystrophy**
Excludes1: X-linked adrenoleukodystrophy (E71.42-)
CC Exclusion see Appendix A PDX collection 0536
CC **E71.518 Other disorders of peroxisome biogenesis**
CC Exclusion see Appendix A PDX collection 0536
+ **E71.52 X-linked adrenoleukodystrophy**
CC **E71.520 Childhood cerebral X-linked adrenoleukodystrophy**
CC Exclusion see Appendix A PDX collection 0536
CC **E71.521 Adolescent X-linked adrenoleukodystrophy**
CC Exclusion see Appendix A PDX collection 0536
CC **E71.522 Adrenomyeloneuropathy**
CC Exclusion see Appendix A PDX collection 0536
CC **E71.528 Other X-linked adrenoleukodystrophy**
Addison only phenotype adrenoleukodystrophy
Addison-Schilder adrenoleukodystrophy
CC Exclusion see Appendix A PDX collection 0536
CC **E71.529 X-linked adrenoleukodystrophy, unspecified type**
CC Exclusion see Appendix A PDX collection 0536
CC **E71.53 Other group 2 peroxisomal disorders**
CC Exclusion see Appendix A PDX collection 0536
+ **E71.54 Other peroxisomal disorders**
CC **E71.540 Rhizomelic chondrodysplasia punctata**
Excludes1: chondrodysplasia punctata NOS (Q77.3)
CC Exclusion see Appendix A PDX collection 0536
CC **E71.541 Zellweger-like syndrome**
CC Exclusion see Appendix A PDX collection 0536
CC **E71.542 Other group 3 peroxisomal disorders**
CC Exclusion see Appendix A PDX collection 0536
CC **E71.548 Other peroxisomal disorders**
CC Exclusion see Appendix A PDX collection 0536

E72 Other disorders of amino-acid metabolism

Excludes1: disorders of:
aromatic amino-acid metabolism (E70.-)
branched-chain amino-acid metabolism (E71.0-E71.2)
fatty-acid metabolism (E71.3)
purine and pyrimidine metabolism (E79.-)
gout (M1A.-, M10.-)

+ **E72.0 Disorders of amino-acid transport**
Excludes1: disorders of tryptophan metabolism (E70.5)
CC **E72.00 Disorders of amino-acid transport, unspecified**
CC Exclusion see Appendix A PDX collection 0534
CC **E72.01 Cystinuria**
CC Exclusion see Appendix A PDX collection 0534
CC **E72.02 Hartnup's disease**
CC Exclusion see Appendix A PDX collection 0534
CC **E72.03 Lowe's syndrome**
Use additional code for associated glaucoma (H42)
No CC Exclusions
CC **E72.04 Cystinosis**
Fanconi (-de Toni) (-Debré) syndrome with cystinosis
Excludes1: Fanconi (-de Toni) (-Debré) syndrome without cystinosis (E72.09)
CC Exclusion see Appendix A PDX collection 0534
CC **E72.09 Other disorders of amino-acid transport**
Fanconi (-de Toni) (-Debré) syndrome, unspecified
CC Exclusion see Appendix A PDX collection 0534
+ **E72.1 Disorders of sulfur-bearing amino-acid metabolism**
Excludes1: cystinosis (E72.04)
cystinuria (E72.01)
transcobalamin II deficiency (D51.2)
CC **E72.10 Disorders of sulfur-bearing amino-acid metabolism, unspecified**
CC Exclusion see Appendix A PDX collection 0534
CC **E72.11 Homocystinuria**
Cystathionine synthase deficiency
CC Exclusion see Appendix A PDX collection 0534
CC **E72.12 Methylenetetrahydrofolate reductase deficiency**
CC Exclusion see Appendix A PDX collection 0534
CC **E72.19 Other disorders of sulfur-bearing amino-acid metabolism**
Cystathioninuria
Methioninemia
Sulfite oxidase deficiency
CC Exclusion see Appendix A PDX collection 0534
+ **E72.2 Disorders of urea cycle metabolism**
Excludes1: disorders of ornithine metabolism (E72.4)
CC **E72.20 Disorder of urea cycle metabolism, unspecified**
Hyperammonemia
Excludes1: hyperammonemia-hyperornithinemia-homocitrullinemia syndrome E72.4
transient hyperammonemia of newborn (P74.6)
CC Exclusion see Appendix A PDX collection 0534
CC **E72.21 Argininemia**
CC Exclusion see Appendix A PDX collection 0534
CC **E72.22 Arginosuccinic aciduria**
CC Exclusion see Appendix A PDX collection 0534
CC **E72.23 Citrullinemia**
CC Exclusion see Appendix A PDX collection 0534
CC **E72.29 Other disorders of urea cycle metabolism**
CC Exclusion see Appendix A PDX collection 0534
CC **E72.3 Disorders of lysine and hydroxylysine metabolism**
Glutaric aciduria NOS
Glutaric aciduria (type I)
Hydroxylysinemia
Hyperlysinemia
Excludes1: glutaric aciduria type II (E71.313)
Refsum's disease (G60.1)
Zellweger syndrome (E71.510)
CC Exclusion see Appendix A PDX collection 0534
CC **E72.4 Disorders of ornithine metabolism**
Hyperammonemia-Hyperornithinemia-Homocitrullinemia syndrome
Ornithinemia (types I, II)
Ornithine transcarbamylase deficiency
Excludes1: hereditary choroidal dystrophy (H31.2-)
CC Exclusion see Appendix A PDX collection 0534
+ **E72.5 Disorders of glycine metabolism**
CC **E72.50 Disorder of glycine metabolism, unspecified**
CC Exclusion see Appendix A PDX collection 0534
CC **E72.51 Non-ketotic hyperglycinemia**
CC Exclusion see Appendix A PDX collection 0534
CC **E72.52 Trimethylaminuria**
CC Exclusion see Appendix A PDX collection 0534
CC **E72.53 Hyperoxaluria**
Oxalosis
Oxaluria
CC Exclusion see Appendix A PDX collection 0534
CC **E72.59 Other disorders of glycine metabolism**
D-glycericacidemia
Hyperhydroxyprolinemia
Hyperprolinemia (types I, II)
Sarcosinemia
CC Exclusion see Appendix A PDX collection 0534
CC **E72.8 Other specified disorders of amino-acid metabolism**
Disorders of beta-amino-acid metabolism
Disorders of gamma-glutamyl cycle
CC Exclusion see Appendix A PDX collection 0534
CC **E72.9 Disorder of amino-acid metabolism, unspecified**
CC Exclusion see Appendix A PDX collection 0534

E73 Lactose intolerance

E73.0 Congenital lactase deficiency
E73.1 Secondary lactase deficiency
E73.8 Other lactose intolerance
E73.9 Lactose intolerance, unspecified

E74 Other disorders of carbohydrate metabolism

Excludes1: *diabetes mellitus (E08-E13)*
NOS (E16.2)
increased secretion of glucagon (E16.3)
mucopolysaccharidosis (E76.0-E76.3)

\+ **E74.0 Glycogen storage disease**
CC **E74.00 Glycogen storage disease, unspecified**
CC Exclusion see Appendix A PDX collection 0534
CC **E74.01 von Gierke disease**
Type I glycogen storage disease
CC Exclusion see Appendix A PDX collection 0534
CC **E74.02 Pompe disease**
Cardiac glycogenosis
Type II glycogen storage disease
CC Exclusion see Appendix A PDX collection 0534
CC **E74.03 Cori disease**
Forbes disease
Type III glycogen storage disease
CC Exclusion see Appendix A PDX collection 0534
CC **E74.04 McArdle disease**
Type V glycogen storage disease
CC Exclusion see Appendix A PDX collection 0534
CC **E74.09 Other glycogen storage disease**
Andersen disease
Hers disease
Tauri disease
Glycogen storage disease, types 0, IV, VI-XI
Liver phosphorylase deficiency
Muscle phosphofructokinase deficiency
CC Exclusion see Appendix A PDX collection 0534

\+ **E74.1 Disorders of fructose metabolism**
Excludes1: *muscle phosphofructokinase deficiency (E74.09)*
E74.10 Disorder of fructose metabolism, unspecified
E74.11 Essential fructosuria
Fructokinase deficiency
E74.12 Hereditary fructose intolerance
Fructosemia
E74.19 Other disorders of fructose metabolism
Fructose-1, 6-diphosphatase deficiency

\+ **E74.2 Disorders of galactose metabolism**
CC **E74.20 Disorders of galactose metabolism, unspecified**
CC Exclusion see Appendix A PDX collection 0534
CC **E74.21 Galactosemia**
CC Exclusion see Appendix A PDX collection 0534
CC **E74.29 Other disorders of galactose metabolism**
Galactokinase deficiency
CC Exclusion see Appendix A PDX collection 0534

\+ **E74.3 Other disorders of intestinal carbohydrate absorption**
Excludes2: *lactose intolerance (E73.-)*
E74.31 Sucrase-isomaltase deficiency
E74.39 Other disorders of intestinal carbohydrate absorption
Disorder of intestinal carbohydrate absorption NOS
Glucose-galactose malabsorption
Sucrase deficiency

CC **E74.4 Disorders of pyruvate metabolism and gluconeogenesis**
Deficiency of phosphoenolpyruvate carboxykinase
Deficiency of pyruvate carboxylase
Deficiency of pyruvate dehydrogenase
Excludes1: *disorders of pyruvate metabolism and gluconeogenesis with anemia (D55.-)*
Leigh's syndrome (G31.82)
CC Exclusion see Appendix A PDX collection 0534

CC **E74.8 Other specified disorders of carbohydrate metabolism**
Essential pentosuria
Renal glycosuria
CC Exclusion see Appendix A PDX collection 0534

E74.9 Disorder of carbohydrate metabolism, unspecified

E75 Disorders of sphingolipid metabolism and other lipid storage disorders

Excludes1: *mucolipidosis, types I-III (E77.0-E77.1)*
Refsum's disease (G60.1)

\+ **E75.0 GM2 gangliosidosis**
CC **E75.00 GM2 gangliosidosis, unspecified**
CC Exclusion see Appendix A PDX collection 0537
CC **E75.01 Sandhoff disease**
CC Exclusion see Appendix A PDX collection 0537
CC **E75.02 Tay-Sachs disease**
CC Exclusion see Appendix A PDX collection 0537
CC **E75.09 Other GM2 gangliosidosis**
Adult GM2 gangliosidosis
Juvenile GM2 gangliosidosis
CC Exclusion see Appendix A PDX collection 0537

\+ **E75.1 Other and unspecified gangliosidosis**
CC **E75.10 Unspecified gangliosidosis**
Gangliosidosis NOS
CC Exclusion see Appendix A PDX collection 0537
CC **E75.11 Mucolipidosis IV**
CC Exclusion see Appendix A PDX collection 0537
CC **E75.19 Other gangliosidosis**
GM1 gangliosidosis
GM3 gangliosidosis
CC Exclusion see Appendix A PDX collection 0537

\+ **E75.2 Other sphingolipidosis**
Excludes1: *adrenoleukodystrophy [Addison-Schilder] (E71.528)*
E75.21 Fabry (-Anderson) disease
E75.22 Gaucher disease
CC **E75.23 Krabbe disease**
CC Exclusion see Appendix A PDX collection 0538
\+ **E75.24 Niemann-Pick disease**
E75.240 Niemann-Pick disease type A
E75.241 Niemann-Pick disease type B
E75.242 Niemann-Pick disease type C
E75.243 Niemann-Pick disease type D
E75.248 Other Niemann-Pick disease
E75.249 Niemann-Pick disease, unspecified
CC **E75.25 Metachromatic leukodystrophy**
CC Exclusion see Appendix A PDX collection 0538
CC **E75.29 Other sphingolipidosis**
Farber's syndrome
Sulfatase deficiency
Sulfatide lipidosis
CC Exclusion see Appendix A PDX collection 0538

E75.3 Sphingolipidosis, unspecified

CC **E75.4 Neuronal ceroid lipofuscinosis**
Batten disease
Bielschowsky-Jansky disease
Kufs disease
Spielmeyer-Vogt disease
CC Exclusion see Appendix A PDX collection 0537

E75.5 Other lipid storage disorders
Cerebrotendinous cholesterosis [van Bogaert-Scherer-Epstein]
Wolman's disease

E75.6 Lipid storage disorder, unspecified

E76 Disorders of glycosaminoglycan metabolism

\+ **E76.0 Mucopolysaccharidosis, type I**
CC **E76.01 Hurler's syndrome**
CC Exclusion see Appendix A PDX collection 0539
CC **E76.02 Hurler-Scheie syndrome**
CC Exclusion see Appendix A PDX collection 0539
CC **E76.03 Scheie's syndrome**
CC Exclusion see Appendix A PDX collection 0539

CC **E76.1 Mucopolysaccharidosis, type II**
Hunter's syndrome
CC Exclusion see Appendix A PDX collection 0539

\+ **E76.2 Other mucopolysaccharidoses**
\+ **E76.21 Morquio mucopolysaccharidoses**
CC **E76.210 Morquio A mucopolysaccharidoses**
Classic Morquio syndrome
Morquio syndrome A
Mucopolysaccharidosis, type IVA
CC Exclusion see Appendix A PDX collection 0539
CC **E76.211 Morquio B mucopolysaccharidoses**
Morquio-like mucopolysaccharidoses
Morquio-like syndrome
Morquio syndrome B
Mucopolysaccharidosis, type IVB
CC Exclusion see Appendix A PDX collection 0539
CC **E76.219 Morquio mucopolysaccharidoses, unspecified**
Morquio syndrome
Mucopolysaccharidosis, type IV
CC Exclusion see Appendix A PDX collection 0539

CC **E76.22 Sanfilippo mucopolysaccharidoses**
Mucopolysaccharidosis, type III (A) (B) (C) (D)
Sanfilippo A syndrome
Sanfilippo B syndrome
Sanfilippo C syndrome
Sanfilippo D syndrome
CC Exclusion see Appendix A PDX collection 0539

CC **E76.29 Other mucopolysaccharidoses**
beta-Glucuronidase deficiency
Maroteaux-Lamy (mild) (severe) syndrome
Mucopolysaccharidosis, types VI, VII
CC Exclusion see Appendix A PDX collection 0539

CC **E76.3 Mucopolysaccharidosis, unspecified**
CC Exclusion see Appendix A PDX collection 0539

CC **E76.8 Other disorders of glucosaminoglycan metabolism**
CC Exclusion see Appendix A PDX collection 0539

CC **E76.9 Glucosaminoglycan metabolism disorder, unspecified**
CC Exclusion see Appendix A PDX collection 0539

E77 Disorders of glycoprotein metabolism

E77.0 Defects in post-translational modification of lysosomal enzymes
Mucolipidosis II [I-cell disease]
Mucolipidosis III [pseudo-Hurler polydystrophy]

E77.1 Defects in glycoprotein degradation
Aspartylglucosaminuria
Fucosidosis
Mannosidosis
Sialidosis [mucolipidosis I]

E77.8 Other disorders of glycoprotein metabolism

E77.9 Disorder of glycoprotein metabolism, unspecified

E78 Disorders of lipoprotein metabolism and other lipidemias

Excludes1: *sphingolipidosis (E75.0-E75.3)*

E78.0 Pure hypercholesterolemia
Familial hypercholesterolemia
Fredrickson's hyperlipoproteinemia, type IIa
Hyperbetalipoproteinemia
Hyperlipidemia, Group A
Low-density-lipoprotein-type [LDL] hyperlipoproteinemia

E78.1 Pure hyperglyceridemia
Elevated fasting triglycerides
Endogenous hyperglyceridemia
Fredrickson's hyperlipoproteinemia, type IV
Hyperlipidemia, group B
Hyperprebetalipoproteinemia
Very-low-density-lipoprotein-type [VLDL] hyperlipoproteinemia

E78.2 Mixed hyperlipidemia
Broad- or floating-betalipoproteinemia
Combined hyperlipidemia NOS
Elevated cholesterol with elevated triglycerides NEC
Fredrickson's hyperlipoproteinemia, type IIb or III
Hyperbetalipoproteinemia with prebetalipoproteinemia
Hypercholesteremia with endogenous hyperglyceridemia
Hyperlipidemia, group C
Tubo-eruptive xanthoma
Xanthoma tuberosum
Excludes1: *cerebrotendinous cholesterosis [van Bogaert-Scherer-Epstein] (E75.5)*
familial combined hyperlipidemia (E78.4)

E78.3 Hyperchylomicronemia
Chylomicron retention disease
Fredrickson's hyperlipoproteinemia, type I or V
Hyperlipidemia, group D
Mixed hyperglyceridemia

E78.4 Other hyperlipidemia
Familial combined hyperlipidemia

E78.5 Hyperlipidemia, unspecified

E78.6 Lipoprotein deficiency
Abetalipoproteinemia
Depressed HDL cholesterol
High-density lipoprotein deficiency
Hypoalphalipoproteinemia
Hypobetalipoproteinemia (familial)
Lecithin cholesterol acyltransferase deficiency
Tangier disease

+ **E78.7 Disorders of bile acid and cholesterol metabolism**
Excludes1: *Niemann-Pick disease type C (E75.242)*

E78.70 Disorder of bile acid and cholesterol metabolism, unspecified

CC **E78.71 Barth syndrome**
CC Exclusion see Appendix A PDX collection 0540

CC **E78.72 Smith-Lemli-Opitz syndrome**
CC Exclusion see Appendix A PDX collection 0540

E78.79 Other disorders of bile acid and cholesterol metabolism

+ **E78.8 Other disorders of lipoprotein metabolism**

E78.81 Lipoid dermatoarthritis

E78.89 Other lipoprotein metabolism disorders

E78.9 Disorder of lipoprotein metabolism, unspecified

E79 Disorders of purine and pyrimidine metabolism

Excludes1: *Ataxia-telangiectasia (Q87.1)*
Bloom's syndrome (Q82.8)
Cockayne's syndrome (Q87.1)
calculus of kidney (N20.0)
combined immunodeficiency disorders (D81.-)
Fanconi's anemia (D61.09)
gout (M1A.-, M10.-)
orotaciduric anemia (D53.0)
progeria (E34.8)
Werner's syndrome (E34.8)
xeroderma pigmentosum (Q82.1)

E79.0 Hyperuricemia without signs of inflammatory arthritis and tophaceous disease
Asymptomatic hyperuricemia

CC **E79.1 Lesch-Nyhan syndrome**
HGPRT deficiency
CC Exclusion see Appendix A PDX collection 0513

CC **E79.2 Myoadenylate deaminase deficiency**
CC Exclusion see Appendix A PDX collection 0513

CC **E79.8 Other disorders of purine and pyrimidine metabolism**
Hereditary xanthinuria
CC Exclusion see Appendix A PDX collection 0513

CC **E79.9 Disorder of purine and pyrimidine metabolism, unspecified**
CC Exclusion see Appendix A PDX collection 0513

E80 Disorders of porphyrin and bilirubin metabolism

Includes: defects of catalase and peroxidase

CC **E80.0 Hereditary erythropoietic porphyria**
Congenital erythropoietic porphyria
Erythropoietic protoporphyria
CC Exclusion see Appendix A PDX collection 0513

CC **E80.1 Porphyria cutanea tarda**
CC Exclusion see Appendix A PDX collection 0513

+ **E80.2 Other and unspecified porphyria**

CC **E80.20 Unspecified porphyria**
Porphyria NOS
CC Exclusion see Appendix A PDX collection 0513

CC **E80.21 Acute intermittent (hepatic) porphyria**
CC Exclusion see Appendix A PDX collection 0513

CC **E80.29 Other porphyria**
Hereditary coproporphyria
CC Exclusion see Appendix A PDX collection 0513

CC **E80.3 Defects of catalase and peroxidase**
Acatalasia [Takahara]
CC Exclusion see Appendix A PDX collection 0492

E80.4 Gilbert syndrome

E80.5 Crigler-Najjar syndrome

E80.6 Other disorders of bilirubin metabolism
Dubin-Johnson syndrome
Rotor's syndrome

E80.7 Disorder of bilirubin metabolism, unspecified

E83 Disorders of mineral metabolism

Excludes1: *dietary mineral deficiency (E58-E61)*
parathyroid disorders (E20-E21)
vitamin D deficiency (E55.-)

+ **E83.0 Disorders of copper metabolism**

E83.00 Disorder of copper metabolism, unspecified

E83.01 Wilson's disease
Code also associated Kayser Fleischer ring (H18.04-)

E83.09 Other disorders of copper metabolism
Menkes' (kinky hair) (steely hair) disease

+ **E83.1 Disorders of iron metabolism**
Excludes1: *iron deficiency anemia (D50.-)*
sideroblastic anemia (D64.0-D64.3)

E83.10 Disorder of iron metabolism, unspecified

+ **E83.11 Hemochromatosis**

E83.110 Hereditary hemochromatosis
Bronzed diabetes
Pigmentary cirrhosis (of liver)
Primary (hereditary) hemochromatosis

E83.111 Hemochromatosis due to repeated red blood cell transfusions
Iron overload due to repeated red blood cell transfusions
Transfusion (red blood cell) associated hemochromatosis
E83.118 Other hemochromatosis
E83.119 Hemochromatosis, unspecified
E83.19 Other disorders of iron metabolism
Use additional code, if applicable, for idiopathic pulmonary hemosiderosis (J84.03)
E83.2 Disorders of zinc metabolism
Acrodermatitis enteropathica
\+ **E83.3 Disorders of phosphorus metabolism and phosphatases**
Excludes1: *adult osteomalacia (M83.-)*
osteoporosis (M80.-)
E83.30 Disorder of phosphorus metabolism, unspecified
E83.31 Familial hypophosphatemia
Vitamin D-resistant osteomalacia
Vitamin D-resistant rickets
Excludes1: *vitamin D-deficiency rickets (E55.0)*
E83.32 Hereditary vitamin D-dependent rickets (type 1) (type 2)
25-hydroxyvitamin D 1-alpha-hydroxylase deficiency
Pseudovitamin D deficiency
Vitamin D receptor defect
E83.39 Other disorders of phosphorus metabolism
Acid phosphatase deficiency
Hypophosphatasia
\+ **E83.4 Disorders of magnesium metabolism**
E83.40 Disorders of magnesium metabolism, unspecified
E83.41 Hypermagnesemia
E83.42 Hypomagnesemia
E83.49 Other disorders of magnesium metabolism
\+ **E83.5 Disorders of calcium metabolism**
Excludes1: *chondrocalcinosis (M11.1-M11.2)*
hungry bone syndrome (E83.81)
hyperparathyroidism (E21.0-E21.3)
E83.50 Unspecified disorder of calcium metabolism
E83.51 Hypocalcemia
E83.52 Hypercalcemia
Familial hypocalciuric hypercalcemia
E83.59 Other disorders of calcium metabolism
Idiopathic hypercalciuria
\+ **E83.8 Other disorders of mineral metabolism**
E83.81 Hungry bone syndrome
E83.89 Other disorders of mineral metabolism
E83.9 Disorder of mineral metabolism, unspecified

E84 Cystic fibrosis

Includes: mucoviscidosis
MCC **E84.0 Cystic fibrosis with pulmonary manifestations**
Use additional code to identify any infectious organism present, such as:
Pseudomonas (B96.5)
MCC Exclusion see Appendix A PDX collection 0541
\+ **E84.1 Cystic fibrosis with intestinal manifestations**
• MCC **E84.11 Meconium ileus in cystic fibrosis**
Excludes1: *meconium ileus not due to cystic fibrosis (P76.0)*
MCC Exclusion see Appendix A PDX collection 0541
CC **E84.19 Cystic fibrosis with other intestinal manifestations**
Distal intestinal obstruction syndrome
CC Exclusion see Appendix A PDX collection 0541
CC **E84.8 Cystic fibrosis with other manifestations**
CC Exclusion see Appendix A PDX collection 0541
CC **E84.9 Cystic fibrosis, unspecified**
CC Exclusion see Appendix A PDX collection 0541

E85 Amyloidosis

Excludes1: *Alzheimer's disease (G30.0-)*
CC **E85.0 Non-neuropathic heredofamilial amyloidosis**
Familial Mediterranean fever
Hereditary amyloid nephropathy
CC Exclusion see Appendix A PDX collection 0542
CC **E85.1 Neuropathic heredofamilial amyloidosis**
Amyloid polyneuropathy (Portuguese)
CC Exclusion see Appendix A PDX collection 0542
AHA CC: 4Q, 2012, 99-101
CC **E85.2 Heredofamilial amyloidosis, unspecified**
CC Exclusion see Appendix A PDX collection 0542
CC **E85.3 Secondary systemic amyloidosis**
Hemodialysis-associated amyloidosis
CC Exclusion see Appendix A PDX collection 0542
CC **E85.4 Organ-limited amyloidosis**
Localized amyloidosis
CC Exclusion see Appendix A PDX collection 0542
CC **E85.8 Other amyloidosis**
CC Exclusion see Appendix A PDX collection 0542
CC **E85.9 Amyloidosis, unspecified**
CC Exclusion see Appendix A PDX collection 0542

E86 Volume depletion

Excludes1: *dehydration of newborn (P74.1)*
hypovolemic shock NOS (R57.1)
postprocedural hypovolemic shock (T81.19)
traumatic hypovolemic shock (T79.4)
E86.0 Dehydration
Review coding guidelines C.2.c.3
AHA CC: 1Q, 2014, 7
E86.1 Hypovolemia
Depletion of volume of plasma
E86.9 Volume depletion, unspecified

E87 Other disorders of fluid, electrolyte and acid-base balance

Excludes1: *diabetes insipidus (E23.2)*
electrolyte imbalance associated with hyperemesis gravidarum (O21.1)
electrolyte imbalance following ectopic or molar pregnancy (O08.5)
familial periodic paralysis (G72.3)
CC **E87.0 Hyperosmolality and hypernatremia**
Sodium [Na] excess
Sodium [Na] overload
CC Exclusion see Appendix A PDX collection 0543
AHA CC: 1Q, 2014, 7
CC **E87.1 Hypo-osmolality and hyponatremia**
Sodium [Na] deficiency
Excludes1: *syndrome of inappropriate secretion of antidiuretic hormone (E22.2)*
CC Exclusion see Appendix A PDX collection 0543
AHA CC: 1Q, 2014, 7
CC **E87.2 Acidosis**
Acidosis NOS
Lactic acidosis
Metabolic acidosis
Respiratory acidosis
Excludes1: *diabetic acidosis - see categories E08-E10, E13 with ketoacidosis*
CC Exclusion see Appendix A PDX collection 0543
CC **E87.3 Alkalosis**
Alkalosis NOS
Metabolic alkalosis
Respiratory alkalosis
CC Exclusion see Appendix A PDX collection 0543
CC **E87.4 Mixed disorder of acid-base balance**
CC Exclusion see Appendix A PDX collection 0543
E87.5 Hyperkalemia
Potassium [K] excess
Potassium [K] overload
E87.6 Hypokalemia
Potassium [K] deficiency
\+ **E87.7 Fluid overload**
Excludes1: *edema NOS (R60.9)*
fluid retention (R60.9)
E87.70 Fluid overload, unspecified
E87.71 Transfusion associated circulatory overload
Fluid overload due to transfusion (blood) (blood components)
TACO
E87.79 Other fluid overload
E87.8 Other disorders of electrolyte and fluid balance, not elsewhere classified
Electrolyte imbalance NOS
Hyperchloremia
Hypochloremia

E88 Other and unspecified metabolic disorders

Use additional codes for associated conditions
Excludes1: *histiocytosis X (chronic) (C96.6)*
\+ **E88.0 Disorders of plasma-protein metabolism, not elsewhere classified**
Excludes1: *disorder of lipoprotein metabolism (E78.-)*
monoclonal gammopathy (of undetermined significance) (D47.2)
polyclonal hypergammaglobulinemia (D89.0)
Waldenström macroglobulinemia (C88.0)
E88.01 Alpha-1-antitrypsin deficiency
AAT deficiency

E88.09 Other disorders of plasma-protein metabolism, not elsewhere classified
Bisalbuminemia

E88.1 Lipodystrophy, not elsewhere classified
Lipodystrophy NOS
Excludes1: *Whipple's disease (K90.81)*

E88.2 Lipomatosis, not elsewhere classified
Lipomatosis NOS
Lipomatosis (Check) dolorosa [Dercum]

MCC **E88.3 Tumor lysis syndrome**
Tumor lysis syndrome (spontaneous)
Tumor lysis syndrome following antineoplastic drug chemotherapy
Use additional code for adverse effect, if applicable, to identify drug (T45.1X5)
MCC Exclusion see Appendix A PDX collection 0544

\+ **E88.4 Mitochondrial metabolism disorders**
Excludes1: disorders of pyruvate metabolism (E74.4)
Kearns-Sayre syndrome (H49.81)
Leber's disease (H47.22)
Leigh's encephalopathy (G31.82)
Mitochondrial myopathy, NEC (G71.3)
Reye's syndrome (G93.7)

CC **E88.40 Mitochondrial metabolism disorder, unspecified**
CC Exclusion see Appendix A PDX collection 0545

CC **E88.41 MELAS syndrome**
Mitochondrial myopathy, encephalopathy, lactic acidosis and stroke-like episodes
CC Exclusion see Appendix A PDX collection 0545

CC **E88.42 MERRF syndrome**
Myoclonic epilepsy associated with ragged-red fibers
Code also myoclonic epilepsy (G40.3-)
CC Exclusion see Appendix A PDX collection 0545

CC **E88.49 Other mitochondrial metabolism disorders**
CC Exclusion see Appendix A PDX collection 0545

\+ **E88.8 Other specified metabolic disorders**

E88.81 Metabolic syndrome
Dysmetabolic syndrome X
Use additional codes for associated manifestations, such as:
obesity (E66.-)

E88.89 Other specified metabolic disorders
Launois-Bensaude adenolipomatosis
Excludes1: *adult pulmonary Langerhans cell histiocytosis (J84.82)*

E88.9 Metabolic disorder, unspecified

Postprocedural endocrine and metabolic complications and disorders, not elsewhere classified (E89)

E89 Postprocedural endocrine and metabolic complications and disorders, not elsewhere classified

Excludes2: *intraoperative complications of endocrine system organ or structure (E36.0-, E36.1-, E36.8)*

E89.0 Postprocedural hypothyroidism
Postirradiation hypothyroidism
Postsurgical hypothyroidism

CC **E89.1 Postprocedural hypoinsulinemia**
Postpancreatectomy hyperglycemia
Postsurgical hypoinsulinemia
Use additional code, if applicable, to identify:
acquired absence of pancreas (Z90.41-)
diabetes mellitus (postpancreatectomy) (postprocedural) (E13.-)
insulin use (Z79.4)
Excludes1: *transient postprocedural hyperglycemia (R73.9)*
transient postprocedural hypoglycemia (E16.2)
CC Exclusion see Appendix A PDX collection 0520
Review coding guideline C.4.a.6.b.i

E89.2 Postprocedural hypoparathyroidism
Parathyroprival tetany

E89.3 Postprocedural hypopituitarism
Postirradiation hypopituitarism

\+ **E89.4 Postprocedural ovarian failure**

♀ **E89.40 Asymptomatic postprocedural ovarian failure**
Postprocedural ovarian failure NOS

♀ **E89.41 Symptomatic postprocedural ovarian failure**
Symptoms such as flushing, sleeplessness, headache, lack of concentration, associated with postprocedural menopause

♂ **E89.5 Postprocedural testicular hypofunction**

CC **E89.6 Postprocedural adrenocortical (-medullary) hypofunction**
CC Exclusion see Appendix A PDX collection 0526

\+ **E89.8 Other postprocedural endocrine and metabolic complications and disorders**

\+ **E89.81 Postprocedural hemorrhage and hematoma of an endocrine system organ or structure following a procedure**

CC **E89.810 Postprocedural hemorrhage and hematoma of an endocrine system organ or structure following an endocrine system procedure**
CC Exclusion see Appendix A PDX collection 0546

CC **E89.811 Postprocedural hemorrhage and hematoma of an endocrine system organ or structure following other procedure**
CC Exclusion see Appendix A PDX collection 0546

CC **E89.89 Other postprocedural endocrine and metabolic complications and disorders**
Use additional code, if applicable, to further specify disorder
CC Exclusion see Appendix A PDX collection 0546

hapter 5: Mental, Behavioral and eurodevelopmental Disorders (F01-F99)

:ludes: disorders of psychological development

:cludes2: *symptoms, signs and abnormal clinical laboratory findings, not elsewhere classified (R00-R99)*

is chapter contains the following category blocks:

F01-F09 Mental disorders due to known physiological conditions
F10-F19 Mental and behavioral disorders due to psychoactive substance use
F20-F29 Schizophrenia, schizotypal, delusional, and other non-mood psychotic disorders
F30-F39 Mood [affective] disorders
F40-F48 Anxiety, dissociative, stress-related, somatoform and other nonpsychotic mental disorders
F50-F59 Behavioral syndromes associated with physiological disturbances and physical factors
F60-F69 Disorders of adult personality and behavior
F70-F79 Intellectual disabilities
F80-F89 Pervasive and specific developmental disorders
F90-F98 Behavioral and emotional disorders with onset usually occurring in childhood and adolescence
F99 Unspecified mental disorder

Chapter-Specific Coding Guidelines

addition to general coding guidelines, there are guidelines for specific diagnoses l/or conditions in the classification. Unless otherwise indicated, these guidelines ɔly to all health care settings. Please refer to Section II for guidelines on the ection of principal diagnosis.

Chapter 5: Mental, Behavioral and Neurodevelopmental Disorders (F01-F99)

ı. Pain disorders related to psychological factors

Assign code F45.41, for pain that is exclusively related to psychological disorders. As indicated by the Excludes 1 note under category G89, a code from category G89 should not be assigned with code F45.41

Code F45.42, Pain disorders with related psychological factors, should be used with a code from category G89, Pain, not elsewhere classified, if there is documentation of a psychological component for a patient with acute or chronic pain.

See Section I.C.6. Pain

b. Mental and behavioral disorders due to psychoactive substance use

1) In Remission

Selection of codes for "in remission" for categories F10-F19, Mental and behavioral disorders due to psychoactive substance use (categories F10-F19 with -.21) requires the provider's clinical judgment. The appropriate codes for "in remission" are assigned only on the basis of provider documentation (as defined in the Official Guidelines for Coding and Reporting).

2) Psychoactive Substance Use, Abuse And Dependence

When the provider documentation refers to use, abuse and dependence of the same substance (e.g. alcohol, opioid, cannabis, etc.), only one code should be assigned to identify the pattern of use based on the following hierarchy:

- If both use and abuse are documented, assign only the code for abuse
- If both abuse and dependence are documented, assign only the code for dependence
- If use, abuse and dependence are all documented, assign only the code for dependence
- If both use and dependence are documented, assign only the code for dependence.

3) Psychoactive Substance Use

As with all other diagnoses, the codes for psychoactive substance use (F10.9-, F11.9-, F12.9-, F13.9-, F14.9-, F15.9-, F16.9-) should only be assigned based on provider documentation and when they meet the definition of a reportable diagnosis (see Section III, Reporting Additional Diagnoses). The codes are to be used only when the psychoactive substance use is associated with a mental or behavioral disorder, and such a relationship is documented by the provider.

Mental disorders due to known physiological conditions (F01-F09)

NOTE This block comprises a range of mental disorders grouped together on the basis of their having in common a demonstrable etiology in cerebral disease, brain injury, or other insult leading to cerebral dysfunction. The dysfunction may be primary, as in diseases, injuries, and insults that affect the brain directly and selectively; or secondary, as in systemic diseases and disorders that attack the brain only as one of the multiple organs or systems of the body that are involved.

F01 Vascular dementia

Vascular dementia as a result of infarction of the brain due to vascular disease, including hypertensive cerebrovascular disease.

Includes: arteriosclerotic dementia

Code first the underlying physiological condition or sequelae of cerebrovascular disease.

+ F01.5 Vascular dementia

• F01.50 Vascular dementia without behavioral disturbance

• CC F01.51 Vascular dementia with behavioral disturbance

Vascular dementia with aggressive behavior
Vascular dementia with combative behavior
Vascular dementia with violent behavior
Use additional code, if applicable, to identify wandering in vascular dementia (Z91.83)

CC Exclusion see Appendix A PDX collection 0547

F02 Dementia in other diseases classified elsewhere

Code first the underlying physiological condition, such as:
Alzheimer's (G30.-)
cerebral lipidosis (E75.4)
Creutzfeldt-Jakob disease (A81.0-)
dementia with Lewy bodies (G31.83)
epilepsy and recurrent seizures (G40.-)
frontotemporal dementia (G31.09)
hepatolenticular degeneration (E83.0)
human immunodeficiency virus [HIV] disease (B20)
hypercalcemia (E83.52)
hypothyroidism, acquired (E00-E03.-)
intoxications (T36-T65)
Jakob-Creutzfeldt disease (A81.0-)
multiple sclerosis (G35)
neurosyphilis (A52.17)
niacin deficiency [pellagra] (E52)
Parkinson's disease (G20)
Pick's disease (G31.01)
polyarteritis nodosa (M30.0)
systemic lupus erythematosus (M32.-)
trypanosomiasis (B56.-, B57.-)
vitamin B deficiency (E53.8)

Excludes1: *dementia with Parkinsonism (G31.83)*

Excludes2: *dementia in alcohol and psychoactive substance disorders (F10-F19, with .17, .27, .97)*
vascular dementia (F01.5-)

+ F02.8 Dementia in other diseases classified elsewhere

F02.80 Dementia in other diseases classified elsewhere without behavioral disturbance

Dementia in other diseases classified elsewhere NOS

CC F02.81 Dementia in other diseases classified elsewhere with behavioral disturbance

Dementia in other diseases classified elsewhere with aggressive behavior
Dementia in other diseases classified elsewhere with combative behavior
Dementia in other diseases classified elsewhere with violent behavior
Use additional code, if applicable, to identify wandering in dementia in conditions classified elsewhere (Z91.83)

CC Exclusion see Appendix A PDX collection 0548

F03 Unspecified dementia

Presenile dementia NOS
Presenile psychosis NOS
Primary degenerative dementia NOS
Senile dementia NOS
Senile dementia depressed or paranoid type
Senile psychosis NOS

Excludes1: *senility NOS (R41.81)*

Excludes2: *mild memory disturbance due to known physiological condition (F06.8)*
senile dementia with delirium or acute confusional state (F05)

+ **F03.9 Unspecified dementia**

• **F03.90 Unspecified dementia without behavioral disturbance**
Dementia NOS
AHA CC: 4Q, 2012, 92-93

• CC **F03.91 Unspecified dementia with behavioral disturbance**
Unspecified dementia with aggressive behavior
Unspecified dementia with combative behavior
Unspecified dementia with violent behavior
Use additional code, if applicable, to identify wandering in unspecified dementia (Z91.83)
CC Exclusion see Appendix A PDX collection 0548

F04 Amnestic disorder due to known physiological condition

Korsakov's psychosis or syndrome, nonalcoholic
Code first the underlying physiological condition
Excludes1: *amnesia NOS (R41.3)*
anterograde amnesia (R41.1)
dissociative amnesia (F44.0)
retrograde amnesia (R41.2)
Excludes2: *alcohol-induced or unspecified Korsakov's syndrome (F10.26, F10.96)*
Korsakov's syndrome induced by other psychoactive substances (F13.26, F13.96, F19.16, F19.26, F19.96)
Valid 3-character code, no further characters required

CC **F05 Delirium due to known physiological condition**

Acute or subacute brain syndrome
Acute or subacute confusional state (nonalcoholic)
Acute or subacute infective psychosis
Acute or subacute organic reaction
Acute or subacute psycho-organic syndrome
Delirium of mixed etiology
Delirium superimposed on dementia
Sundowning
Code first the underlying physiological condition
Excludes1: *delirium NOS (R41.0)*
Excludes2: *delirium tremens alcohol-induced or unspecified (F10.231, F10.921)*
CC Exclusion see Appendix A PDX collection 0549
Valid 3-character code, no further characters required

F06 Other mental disorders due to known physiological condition

Includes: mental disorders due to endocrine disorder
mental disorders due to exogenous hormone
mental disorders due to exogenous toxic substance
mental disorders due to primary cerebral disease
mental disorders due to somatic illness
mental disorders due to systemic disease affecting the brain
Code first the underlying physiological condition
Excludes1: *unspecified dementia (F03)*
Excludes2: *delirium due to known physiological condition (F05)*
dementia as classified in F01-F02
other mental disorders associated with alcohol and other psychoactive substances (F10-F19)

CC **F06.0 Psychotic disorder with hallucinations due to known physiological condition**
Organic hallucinatory state (nonalcoholic)
Excludes2: *hallucinations and perceptual disturbance induced by alcohol and other psychoactive substances (F10-F19 with .151, .251, .951)*
schizophrenia (F20.-)
CC Exclusion see Appendix A PDX collection 0550

F06.1 Catatonic disorder due to known physiological condition
Excludes1: *catatonic stupor (R40.1)*
stupor NOS (R40.1)
Excludes2: *catatonic schizophrenia (F20.2)*
dissociative stupor (F44.2)

CC **F06.2 Psychotic disorder with delusions due to known physiological condition**
Paranoid and paranoid-hallucinatory organic states
Schizophrenia-like psychosis in epilepsy
Excludes2: *alcohol and drug-induced psychotic disorder (F10-F19 with .150, .250, .950)*
brief psychotic disorder (F23)
delusional disorder (F22)
schizophrenia (F20.-)
CC Exclusion see Appendix A PDX collection 0550

+ **F06.3 Mood disorder due to known physiological condition**
Excludes2: *mood disorders due to alcohol and other psychoactive substances (F10-F19 with .14, .24, .94)*
mood disorders, not due to known physiological condition or unspecified (F30-F39)

F06.30 Mood disorder due to known physiological condition, unspecified

F06.31 Mood disorder due to known physiological condition with depressive features

F06.32 Mood disorder due to known physiological condition with major depressive-like episode

F06.33 Mood disorder due to known physiological condition with manic features

F06.34 Mood disorder due to known physiological condition with mixed features

F06.4 Anxiety disorder due to known physiological condition
Excludes2: *anxiety disorders due to alcohol and other psychoactive substances (F10-F19 with .180, .280, .980)*
anxiety disorders, not due to known physiological condition or unspecified (F40.-, F41.-)

F06.8 Other specified mental disorders due to known physiological condition
Epileptic psychosis NOS
Organic dissociative disorder
Organic emotionally labile [asthenic] disorder

F07 Personality and behavioral disorders due to known physiological condition

Code first the underlying physiological condition

F07.0 Personality change due to known physiological condition
Frontal lobe syndrome
Limbic epilepsy personality syndrome
Lobotomy syndrome
Organic personality disorder
Organic pseudopsychopathic personality
Organic pseudoretarded personality
Postleucotomy syndrome
Code first underlying physiological condition
Excludes1: *mild cognitive impairment (G31.84)*
postconcussional syndrome (F07.81)
postencephalitic syndrome (F07.89)
signs and symptoms involving emotional state (R45.-)
Excludes2: *specific personality disorder (F60.-)*

+ **F07.8 Other personality and behavioral disorders due to known physiological condition**

F07.81 Postconcussional syndrome
Postcontusional syndrome (encephalopathy)
Post-traumatic brain syndrome, nonpsychotic
Use additional code to identify associated post-traumatic headache, if applicable (G44.3-)
Excludes1: *current concussion (brain) (S06.0-)*
postencephalitic syndrome (F07.89)

F07.89 Other personality and behavioral disorders due to known physiological condition
Postencephalitic syndrome
Right hemispheric organic affective disorder

F07.9 Unspecified personality and behavioral disorder due to known physiological condition
Organic psychosyndrome

F09 Unspecified mental disorder due to known physiological condition

Mental disorder NOS due to known physiological condition
Organic brain syndrome NOS
Organic mental disorder NOS
Organic psychosis NOS
Symptomatic psychosis NOS
Code first the underlying physiological condition
Excludes1: *psychosis NOS (F29)*
Valid 3-character code, no further characters required

ental and behavioral disorders due to psychoactive substance e (F10-F19)

Review coding guideline C.5.b

F10 Alcohol related disorders

Use additional code for blood alcohol level, if applicable (Y90.-)

+ F10.1 Alcohol abuse

Excludes1: *alcohol dependence (F10.2-)*
alcohol use, unspecified (F10.9-)

F10.10 Alcohol abuse, uncomplicated

+ F10.12 Alcohol abuse with intoxication

F10.120 Alcohol abuse with intoxication, uncomplicated

CC **F10.121 Alcohol abuse with intoxication delirium**
CC Exclusion see Appendix A PDX collection 0550

F10.129 Alcohol abuse with intoxication, unspecified

CC **F10.14 Alcohol abuse with alcohol-induced mood disorder**
CC Exclusion see Appendix A PDX collection 0550

+ F10.15 Alcohol abuse with alcohol-induced psychotic disorder

F10.150 Alcohol abuse with alcohol-induced psychotic disorder with delusions

CC **F10.151 Alcohol abuse with alcohol-induced psychotic disorder with hallucinations**
CC Exclusion see Appendix A PDX collection 0550

CC **F10.159 Alcohol abuse with alcohol-induced psychotic disorder, unspecified**
CC Exclusion see Appendix A PDX collection 0550

+ F10.18 Alcohol abuse with other alcohol-induced disorders

CC **F10.180 Alcohol abuse with alcohol-induced anxiety disorder**
CC Exclusion see Appendix A PDX collection 0550

CC **F10.181 Alcohol abuse with alcohol-induced sexual dysfunction**
CC Exclusion see Appendix A PDX collection 0550

F10.182 Alcohol abuse with alcohol-induced sleep disorder

CC **F10.188 Alcohol abuse with other alcohol-induced disorder**
CC Exclusion see Appendix A PDX collection 0550

CC **F10.19 Alcohol abuse with unspecified alcohol-induced disorder**
CC Exclusion see Appendix A PDX collection 0550

+ F10.2 Alcohol dependence

Excludes1: *alcohol abuse (F10.1-)*
alcohol use, unspecified (F10.9-)

Excludes2: *toxic effect of alcohol (T51.0-)*

F10.20 Alcohol dependence, uncomplicated

F10.21 Alcohol dependence, in remission

+ F10.22 Alcohol dependence with intoxication

Acute drunkenness (in alcoholism)

Excludes1: *alcohol dependence with withdrawal (F10.23-)*

F10.220 Alcohol dependence with intoxication, uncomplicated

CC **F10.221 Alcohol dependence with intoxication delirium**
CC Exclusion see Appendix A PDX collection 0550

F10.229 Alcohol dependence with intoxication, unspecified

+ F10.23 Alcohol dependence with withdrawal

Excludes1: *Alcohol dependence with intoxication (F10.22-)*

CC **F10.230 Alcohol dependence with withdrawal, uncomplicated**
CC Exclusion see Appendix A PDX collection 0550

CC **F10.231 Alcohol dependence with withdrawal delirium**
CC Exclusion see Appendix A PDX collection 0550

CC **F10.232 Alcohol dependence with withdrawal with perceptual disturbance**
CC Exclusion see Appendix A PDX collection 0550

CC **F10.239 Alcohol dependence with withdrawal, unspecified**
CC Exclusion see Appendix A PDX collection 0550

CC **F10.24 Alcohol dependence with alcohol-induced mood disorder**
CC Exclusion see Appendix A PDX collection 0550

+ F10.25 Alcohol dependence with alcohol-induced psychotic disorder

F10.250 Alcohol dependence with alcohol-induced psychotic disorder with delusions

CC **F10.251 Alcohol dependence with alcohol-induced psychotic disorder with hallucinations**
CC Exclusion see Appendix A PDX collection 0550

CC **F10.259 Alcohol dependence with alcohol-induced psychotic disorder, unspecified**
CC Exclusion see Appendix A PDX collection 0550

F10.26 Alcohol dependence with alcohol-induced persisting amnestic disorder

CC **F10.27 Alcohol dependence with alcohol-induced persisting dementia**
CC Exclusion see Appendix A PDX collection 0550

+ F10.28 Alcohol dependence with other alcohol-induced disorders

CC **F10.280 Alcohol dependence with alcohol-induced anxiety disorder**
CC Exclusion see Appendix A PDX collection 0550

CC **F10.281 Alcohol dependence with alcohol-induced sexual dysfunction**
CC Exclusion see Appendix A PDX collection 0550

F10.282 Alcohol dependence with alcohol-induced sleep disorder

CC **F10.288 Alcohol dependence with other alcohol-induced disorder**
CC Exclusion see Appendix A PDX collection 0550

CC **F10.29 Alcohol dependence with unspecified alcohol-induced disorder**
CC Exclusion see Appendix A PDX collection 0550

+ F10.9 Alcohol use, unspecified

Excludes1: *alcohol abuse (F10.1-)*
alcohol dependence (F10.2-)

+ F10.92 Alcohol use, unspecified with intoxication

F10.920 Alcohol use, unspecified with intoxication, uncomplicated

CC **F10.921 Alcohol use, unspecified with intoxication delirium**
CC Exclusion see Appendix A PDX collection 0550

F10.929 Alcohol use, unspecified with intoxication, unspecified

CC **F10.94 Alcohol use, unspecified with alcohol-induced mood disorder**
CC Exclusion see Appendix A PDX collection 0550

+ F10.95 Alcohol use, unspecified with alcohol-induced psychotic disorder

F10.950 Alcohol use, unspecified with alcohol-induced psychotic disorder with delusions

CC **F10.951 Alcohol use, unspecified with alcohol-induced psychotic disorder with hallucinations**
CC Exclusion see Appendix A PDX collection 0550

CC **F10.959 Alcohol use, unspecified with alcohol-induced psychotic disorder, unspecified**
CC Exclusion see Appendix A PDX collection 0550

F10.96 Alcohol use, unspecified with alcohol-induced persisting amnestic disorder

F10.97 Alcohol use, unspecified with alcohol-induced persisting dementia

+ F10.98 Alcohol use, unspecified with other alcohol-induced disorders

CC **F10.980 Alcohol use, unspecified with alcohol-induced anxiety disorder**
CC Exclusion see Appendix A PDX collection 0550

CC **F10.981 Alcohol use, unspecified with alcohol-induced sexual dysfunction**
CC Exclusion see Appendix A PDX collection 0550

F10.982 **Alcohol use, unspecified with alcohol-induced sleep disorder**

CC F10.988 **Alcohol use, unspecified with other alcohol-induced disorder**
CC Exclusion see Appendix A PDX collection 0550

CC F10.99 **Alcohol use, unspecified with unspecified alcohol-induced disorder**
CC Exclusion see Appendix A PDX collection 0550

F11 Opioid related disorders

+ F11.1 **Opioid abuse**
Excludes1: *opioid dependence (F11.2-)*
opioid use, unspecified (F11.9-)

F11.10 **Opioid abuse, uncomplicated**

+ F11.12 **Opioid abuse with intoxication**

F11.120 **Opioid abuse with intoxication, uncomplicated**

CC F11.121 **Opioid abuse with intoxication delirium**
CC Exclusion see Appendix A PDX collection 0550

F11.122 **Opioid abuse with intoxication with perceptual disturbance**

F11.129 **Opioid abuse with intoxication, unspecified**

F11.14 **Opioid abuse with opioid-induced mood disorder**

+ F11.15 **Opioid abuse with opioid-induced psychotic disorder**

CC F11.150 **Opioid abuse with opioid-induced psychotic disorder with delusions**
CC Exclusion see Appendix A PDX collection 0550

CC F11.151 **Opioid abuse with opioid-induced psychotic disorder with hallucinations**
CC Exclusion see Appendix A PDX collection 0550

F11.159 **Opioid abuse with opioid-induced psychotic disorder, unspecified**

+ F11.18 **Opioid abuse with other opioid-induced disorder**

F11.181 **Opioid abuse with opioid-induced sexual dysfunction**

F11.182 **Opioid abuse with opioid-induced sleep disorder**

F11.188 **Opioid abuse with other opioid-induced disorder**

F11.19 **Opioid abuse with unspecified opioid-induced disorder**

+ F11.2 **Opioid dependence**
Excludes1: *opioid abuse (F11.1-)*
opioid use, unspecified (F11.9-)
Excludes2: *opioid poisoning (T40.0-T40.2-)*

CC F11.20 **Opioid dependence, uncomplicated**
No CC Exclusions

F11.21 **Opioid dependence, in remission**

+ F11.22 **Opioid dependence with intoxication**
Excludes1: *opioid dependence with withdrawal (F11.23)*

F11.220 **Opioid dependence with intoxication, uncomplicated**

CC F11.221 **Opioid dependence with intoxication delirium**
CC Exclusion see Appendix A PDX collection 0550

CC F11.222 **Opioid dependence with intoxication with perceptual disturbance**
No CC Exclusions

F11.229 **Opioid dependence with intoxication, unspecified**

CC F11.23 **Opioid dependence with withdrawal**
Excludes1: *opioid dependence with intoxication (F11.22-)*
CC Exclusion see Appendix A PDX collection 0550

F11.24 **Opioid dependence with opioid-induced mood disorder**

+ F11.25 **Opioid dependence with opioid-induced psychotic disorder**

CC F11.250 **Opioid dependence with opioid-induced psychotic disorder with delusions**
CC Exclusion see Appendix A PDX collection 0550

CC F11.251 **Opioid dependence with opioid-induced psychotic disorder with hallucinations**
CC Exclusion see Appendix A PDX collection 0550

CC F11.259 **Opioid dependence with opioid-induced psychotic disorder, unspecified**
No CC Exclusions

+ F11.28 **Opioid dependence with other opioid-induced disorder**

CC F11.281 **Opioid dependence with opioid-induced sexual dysfunction**
No CC Exclusions

CC F11.282 **Opioid dependence with opioid-induced sleep disorder**
No CC Exclusions

CC F11.288 **Opioid dependence with other opioid-induced disorder**
No CC Exclusions

F11.29 **Opioid dependence with unspecified opioid-induced disorder**

+ F11.9 **Opioid use, unspecified**
Excludes1: *opioid abuse (F11.1-)*
opioid dependence (F11.2-)

F11.90 **Opioid use, unspecified, uncomplicated**

+ F11.92 **Opioid use, unspecified with intoxication**
Excludes1: *opioid use, unspecified with withdrawal (F11.93)*

F11.920 **Opioid use, unspecified with intoxication, uncomplicated**

CC F11.921 **Opioid use, unspecified with intoxication delirium**
CC Exclusion see Appendix A PDX collection 0550

F11.922 **Opioid use, unspecified with intoxication with perceptual disturbance**

F11.929 **Opioid use, unspecified with intoxication, unspecified**

CC F11.93 **Opioid use, unspecified with withdrawal**
Excludes1: *opioid use, unspecified with intoxication (F11.92-)*
CC Exclusion see Appendix A PDX collection 0550

F11.94 **Opioid use, unspecified with opioid-induced mood disorder**

+ F11.95 **Opioid use, unspecified with opioid-induced psychotic disorder**

CC F11.950 **Opioid use, unspecified with opioid-induced psychotic disorder with delusions**
CC Exclusion see Appendix A PDX collection 0550

CC F11.951 **Opioid use, unspecified with opioid-induced psychotic disorder with hallucinations**
CC Exclusion see Appendix A PDX collection 0550

F11.959 **Opioid use, unspecified with opioid-induced psychotic disorder, unspecified**

+ F11.98 **Opioid use, unspecified with other specified opioid-induced disorder**

F11.981 **Opioid use, unspecified with opioid-induced sexual dysfunction**

F11.982 **Opioid use, unspecified with opioid-induced sleep disorder**

F11.988 **Opioid use, unspecified with other opioid-induced disorder**

F11.99 **Opioid use, unspecified with unspecified opioid-induced disorder**

F12 Cannabis related disorders

Includes: marijuana

+ F12.1 **Cannabis abuse**
Excludes1: *cannabis dependence (F12.2-)*
cannabis use, unspecified (F12.9-)

F12.10 **Cannabis abuse, uncomplicated**

+ F12.12 **Cannabis abuse with intoxication**

F12.120 **Cannabis abuse with intoxication, uncomplicated**

CC F12.121 **Cannabis abuse with intoxication delirium**
CC Exclusion see Appendix A PDX collection 0550

F12.122 **Cannabis abuse with intoxication with perceptual disturbance**

F12.129 **Cannabis abuse with intoxication, unspecified**

+ F12.15 **Cannabis abuse with psychotic disorder**

CC F12.150 **Cannabis abuse with psychotic disorder with delusions**
CC Exclusion see Appendix A PDX collection 0550

CC **F12.151 Cannabis abuse with psychotic disorder with hallucinations**
CC Exclusion see Appendix A PDX collection 0550

F12.159 Cannabis abuse with psychotic disorder, unspecified

+ **F12.18 Cannabis abuse with other cannabis-induced disorder**

F12.180 Cannabis abuse with cannabis-induced anxiety disorder

F12.188 Cannabis abuse with other cannabis-induced disorder

F12.19 Cannabis abuse with unspecified cannabis-induced disorder

+ **F12.2 Cannabis dependence**

Excludes1: *cannabis abuse (F12.1-)*
cannabis use, unspecified (F12.9-)

Excludes2: *cannabis poisoning (T40.7-)*

F12.20 Cannabis dependence, uncomplicated

F12.21 Cannabis dependence, in remission

+ **F12.22 Cannabis dependence with intoxication**

F12.220 Cannabis dependence with intoxication, uncomplicated

CC **F12.221 Cannabis dependence with intoxication delirium**
CC Exclusion see Appendix A PDX collection 0550

F12.222 Cannabis dependence with intoxication with perceptual disturbance

F12.229 Cannabis dependence with intoxication, unspecified

+ **F12.25 Cannabis dependence with psychotic disorder**

CC **F12.250 Cannabis dependence with psychotic disorder with delusions**
CC Exclusion see Appendix A PDX collection 0550

CC **F12.251 Cannabis dependence with psychotic disorder with hallucinations**
CC Exclusion see Appendix A PDX collection 0550

F12.259 Cannabis dependence with psychotic disorder, unspecified

+ **F12.28 Cannabis dependence with other cannabis-induced disorder**

F12.280 Cannabis dependence with cannabis-induced anxiety disorder

F12.288 Cannabis dependence with other cannabis-induced disorder

F12.29 Cannabis dependence with unspecified cannabis-induced disorder

+ **F12.9 Cannabis use, unspecified**

Excludes1: *cannabis abuse (F12.1-)*
cannabis dependence (F12.2-)

F12.90 Cannabis use, unspecified, uncomplicated

+ **F12.92 Cannabis use, unspecified with intoxication**

F12.920 Cannabis use, unspecified with intoxication, uncomplicated

CC **F12.921 Cannabis use, unspecified with intoxication delirium**
CC Exclusion see Appendix A PDX collection 0550

F12.922 Cannabis use, unspecified with intoxication with perceptual disturbance

F12.929 Cannabis use, unspecified with intoxication, unspecified

+ **F12.95 Cannabis use, unspecified with psychotic disorder**

CC **F12.950 Cannabis use, unspecified with psychotic disorder with delusions**
CC Exclusion see Appendix A PDX collection 0550

CC **F12.951 Cannabis use, unspecified with psychotic disorder with hallucinations**
CC Exclusion see Appendix A PDX collection 0550

F12.959 Cannabis use, unspecified with psychotic disorder, unspecified

+ **F12.98 Cannabis use, unspecified with other cannabis-induced disorder**

F12.980 Cannabis use, unspecified with anxiety disorder

F12.988 Cannabis use, unspecified with other cannabis-induced disorder

F12.99 Cannabis use, unspecified with unspecified cannabis-induced disorder

F13 Sedative, hypnotic, or anxiolytic related disorders

+ **F13.1 Sedative, hypnotic or anxiolytic-related abuse**

Excludes1: *sedative, hypnotic or anxiolytic-related dependence (F13.2-)*
sedative, hypnotic, or anxiolytic use, unspecified (F13.9-)

F13.10 Sedative, hypnotic or anxiolytic abuse, uncomplicated

+ **F13.12 Sedative, hypnotic or anxiolytic abuse with intoxication**

F13.120 Sedative, hypnotic or anxiolytic abuse with intoxication, uncomplicated

CC **F13.121 Sedative, hypnotic or anxiolytic abuse with intoxication delirium**
CC Exclusion see Appendix A PDX collection 0550

F13.129 Sedative, hypnotic or anxiolytic abuse with intoxication, unspecified

F13.14 Sedative, hypnotic or anxiolytic abuse with sedative, hypnotic or anxiolytic-induced mood disorder

+ **F13.15 Sedative, hypnotic or anxiolytic abuse with sedative, hypnotic or anxiolytic-induced psychotic disorder**

CC **F13.150 Sedative, hypnotic or anxiolytic abuse with sedative, hypnotic or anxiolytic-induced psychotic disorder with delusions**
CC Exclusion see Appendix A PDX collection 0550

CC **F13.151 Sedative, hypnotic or anxiolytic abuse with sedative, hypnotic or anxiolytic-induced psychotic disorder with hallucinations**
CC Exclusion see Appendix A PDX collection 0550

F13.159 Sedative, hypnotic or anxiolytic abuse with sedative, hypnotic or anxiolytic-induced psychotic disorder, unspecified

+ **F13.18 Sedative, hypnotic or anxiolytic abuse with other sedative, hypnotic or anxiolytic-induced disorders**

F13.180 Sedative, hypnotic or anxiolytic abuse with sedative, hypnotic or anxiolytic-induced anxiety disorder

F13.181 Sedative, hypnotic or anxiolytic abuse with sedative, hypnotic or anxiolytic-induced sexual dysfunction

F13.182 Sedative, hypnotic or anxiolytic abuse with sedative, hypnotic or anxiolytic-induced sleep disorder

F13.188 Sedative, hypnotic or anxiolytic abuse with other sedative, hypnotic or anxiolytic-induced disorder

F13.19 Sedative, hypnotic or anxiolytic abuse with unspecified sedative, hypnotic or anxiolytic-induced disorder

+ **F13.2 Sedative, hypnotic or anxiolytic-related dependence**

Excludes1: *sedative, hypnotic or anxiolytic-related abuse (F13.1-)*
sedative, hypnotic, or anxiolytic use, unspecified (F13.9-)

Excludes2: *sedative, hypnotic, or anxiolytic poisoning (T42.-)*

CC **F13.20 Sedative, hypnotic or anxiolytic dependence, uncomplicated**
No CC Exclusions

F13.21 Sedative, hypnotic or anxiolytic dependence, in remission

+ **F13.22 Sedative, hypnotic or anxiolytic dependence with intoxication**

Excludes1: *sedative, hypnotic or anxiolytic dependence with withdrawal (F13.23-)*

F13.220 Sedative, hypnotic or anxiolytic dependence with intoxication, uncomplicated

CC **F13.221 Sedative, hypnotic or anxiolytic dependence with intoxication delirium**
CC Exclusion see Appendix A PDX collection 0550

F13.229 Sedative, hypnotic or anxiolytic dependence with intoxication, unspecified

+ **F13.23 Sedative, hypnotic or anxiolytic dependence with withdrawal**

Excludes1: *sedative, hypnotic or anxiolytic dependence with intoxication (F13.22-)*

CC **F13.230 Sedative, hypnotic or anxiolytic dependence with withdrawal, uncomplicated**
CC Exclusion see Appendix A PDX collection 0550

CC **F13.231 Sedative, hypnotic or anxiolytic dependence with withdrawal delirium**
CC Exclusion see Appendix A PDX collection 0550

CC **F13.232 Sedative, hypnotic or anxiolytic dependence with withdrawal with perceptual disturbance**
CC Exclusion see Appendix A PDX collection 0550

CC **F13.239 Sedative, hypnotic or anxiolytic dependence with withdrawal, unspecified**
CC Exclusion see Appendix A PDX collection 0550

F13.24 Sedative, hypnotic or anxiolytic dependence with sedative, hypnotic or anxiolytic-induced mood disorder

+ **F13.25 Sedative, hypnotic or anxiolytic dependence with sedative, hypnotic or anxiolytic-induced psychotic disorder**

CC **F13.250 Sedative, hypnotic or anxiolytic dependence with sedative, hypnotic or anxiolytic-induced psychotic disorder with delusions**
CC Exclusion see Appendix A PDX collection 0550

CC **F13.251 Sedative, hypnotic or anxiolytic dependence with sedative, hypnotic or anxiolytic-induced psychotic disorder with hallucinations**
CC Exclusion see Appendix A PDX collection 0550

CC **F13.259 Sedative, hypnotic or anxiolytic dependence with sedative, hypnotic or anxiolytic-induced psychotic disorder, unspecified**
No CC Exclusions

CC **F13.26 Sedative, hypnotic or anxiolytic dependence with sedative, hypnotic or anxiolytic-induced persisting amnestic disorder**
No CC Exclusions

CC **F13.27 Sedative, hypnotic or anxiolytic dependence with sedative, hypnotic or anxiolytic-induced persisting dementia**
CC Exclusion see Appendix A PDX collection 0550

+ **F13.28 Sedative, hypnotic or anxiolytic dependence with other sedative, hypnotic or anxiolytic-induced disorders**

CC **F13.280 Sedative, hypnotic or anxiolytic dependence with sedative, hypnotic or anxiolytic-induced anxiety disorder**
No CC Exclusions

CC **F13.281 Sedative, hypnotic or anxiolytic dependence with sedative, hypnotic or anxiolytic-induced sexual dysfunction**
No CC Exclusions

CC **F13.282 Sedative, hypnotic or anxiolytic dependence with sedative, hypnotic or anxiolytic-induced sleep disorder**
No CC Exclusions

CC **F13.288 Sedative, hypnotic or anxiolytic dependence with other sedative, hypnotic or anxiolytic-induced disorder**
No CC Exclusions

F13.29 Sedative, hypnotic or anxiolytic dependence with unspecified sedative, hypnotic or anxiolytic-induced disorder

+ **F13.9 Sedative, hypnotic or anxiolytic-related use, unspecified**
Excludes1: *sedative, hypnotic or anxiolytic-related abuse (F13.1-)*
sedative, hypnotic or anxiolytic-related dependence (F13.2-)

F13.90 Sedative, hypnotic, or anxiolytic use, unspecified, uncomplicated

+ **F13.92 Sedative, hypnotic or anxiolytic use, unspecified with intoxication**
Excludes1: *sedative, hypnotic or anxiolytic use, unspecified with withdrawal (F13.93-)*

F13.920 Sedative, hypnotic or anxiolytic use, unspecified with intoxication, uncomplicated

CC **F13.921 Sedative, hypnotic or anxiolytic use, unspecified with intoxication delirium**
CC Exclusion see Appendix A PDX collection 0550

F13.929 Sedative, hypnotic or anxiolytic use, unspecified with intoxication, unspecified

+ **F13.93 Sedative, hypnotic or anxiolytic use, unspecified wi[th] withdrawal**
Excludes1: *sedative, hypnotic or anxiolytic use, unspecified with intoxication (F13.92*

CC **F13.930 Sedative, hypnotic or anxiolytic use, unspecified with withdrawal, uncomplica[ted]**
CC Exclusion see Appendix A PDX collection 0550

CC **F13.931 Sedative, hypnotic or anxiolytic use, unspecified with withdrawal delirium**
CC Exclusion see Appendix A PDX collection 0550

CC **F13.932 Sedative, hypnotic or anxiolytic use, unspecified with withdrawal with percep[tual] disturbances**
CC Exclusion see Appendix A PDX collection 0550

CC **F13.939 Sedative, hypnotic or anxiolytic use, unspecified with withdrawal, unspecified**
CC Exclusion see Appendix A PDX collection 0550

F13.94 Sedative, hypnotic or anxiolytic use, unspecified with sedative, hypnotic or anxiolytic-induced mood disorder

+ **F13.95 Sedative, hypnotic or anxiolytic use, unspecified with sedative, hypnotic or anxiolytic-induced psychotic disorder**

CC **F13.950 Sedative, hypnotic or anxiolytic use, unspecified with sedative, hypnotic or anxiolytic-induced psychotic disorder wi[th] delusions**
CC Exclusion see Appendix A PDX collection 0550

CC **F13.951 Sedative, hypnotic or anxiolytic use, unspecified with sedative, hypnotic or anxiolytic-induced psychotic disorder wi[th] hallucinations**
CC Exclusion see Appendix A PDX collection 0550

F13.959 Sedative, hypnotic or anxiolytic use, unspecified with sedative, hypnotic or anxiolytic-induced psychotic disorder, unspecified

F13.96 Sedative, hypnotic or anxiolytic use, unspecified wi[th] sedative, hypnotic or anxiolytic-induced persisting amnestic disorder

CC **F13.97 Sedative, hypnotic or anxiolytic use, unspecified wi[th] sedative, hypnotic or anxiolytic-induced persisting dementia**
CC Exclusion see Appendix A PDX collection 0550

+ **F13.98 Sedative, hypnotic or anxiolytic use, unspecified with other sedative, hypnotic or anxiolytic-induced disorders**

F13.980 Sedative, hypnotic or anxiolytic use, unspecified with sedative, hypnotic or anxiolytic-induced anxiety disorder

F13.981 Sedative, hypnotic or anxiolytic use, unspecified with sedative, hypnotic or anxiolytic-induced sexual dysfunction

F13.982 Sedative, hypnotic or anxiolytic use, unspecified with sedative, hypnotic or anxiolytic-induced sleep disorder

F13.988 Sedative, hypnotic or anxiolytic use, unspecified with other sedative, hypnotic [or] anxiolytic-induced disorder

F13.99 Sedative, hypnotic or anxiolytic use, unspecified wi[th] unspecified sedative, hypnotic or anxiolytic-induced disorder

F14 Cocaine related disorders

Excludes2: *other stimulant-related disorders (F15.-)*

+ **F14.1 Cocaine abuse**
Excludes1: *cocaine dependence (F14.2-)*
cocaine use, unspecified (F14.9-)

F14.10 Cocaine abuse, uncomplicated

+ **F14.12 Cocaine abuse with intoxication**

F14.120 Cocaine abuse with intoxication, uncomplicated

CC **F14.121 Cocaine abuse with intoxication with delirium**
CC Exclusion see Appendix A PDX collection 0550

F14.122 **Cocaine abuse with intoxication with perceptual disturbance**
F14.129 **Cocaine abuse with intoxication, unspecified**
F14.14 **Cocaine abuse with cocaine-induced mood disorder**
+ **F14.15** **Cocaine abuse with cocaine-induced psychotic disorder**
CC **F14.150** **Cocaine abuse with cocaine-induced psychotic disorder with delusions**
CC Exclusion see Appendix A PDX collection 0550
CC **F14.151** **Cocaine abuse with cocaine-induced psychotic disorder with hallucinations**
CC Exclusion see Appendix A PDX collection 0550
F14.159 **Cocaine abuse with cocaine-induced psychotic disorder, unspecified**
+ **F14.18** **Cocaine abuse with other cocaine-induced disorder**
F14.180 **Cocaine abuse with cocaine-induced anxiety disorder**
F14.181 **Cocaine abuse with cocaine-induced sexual dysfunction**
F14.182 **Cocaine abuse with cocaine-induced sleep disorder**
F14.188 **Cocaine abuse with other cocaine-induced disorder**
F14.19 **Cocaine abuse with unspecified cocaine-induced disorder**
+ **F14.2** **Cocaine dependence**
Excludes1: *cocaine abuse (F14.1-)*
cocaine use, unspecified (F14.9-)
Excludes2: *cocaine poisoning (T40.5-)*
CC **F14.20** **Cocaine dependence, uncomplicated**
No CC Exclusions
F14.21 **Cocaine dependence, in remission**
+ **F14.22** **Cocaine dependence with intoxication**
Excludes1: *cocaine dependence with withdrawal (F14.23)*
F14.220 **Cocaine dependence with intoxication, uncomplicated**
CC **F14.221** **Cocaine dependence with intoxication delirium**
CC Exclusion see Appendix A PDX collection 0550
CC **F14.222** **Cocaine dependence with intoxication with perceptual disturbance**
No CC Exclusions
CC **F14.229** **Cocaine dependence with intoxication, unspecified**
No CC Exclusions
CC **F14.23** **Cocaine dependence with withdrawal**
Excludes1: *cocaine dependence with intoxication (F14.22-)*
CC Exclusion see Appendix A PDX collection 0550
F14.24 **Cocaine dependence with cocaine-induced mood disorder**
+ **F14.25** **Cocaine dependence with cocaine-induced psychotic disorder**
CC **F14.250** **Cocaine dependence with cocaine-induced psychotic disorder with delusions**
CC Exclusion see Appendix A PDX collection 0550
CC **F14.251** **Cocaine dependence with cocaine-induced psychotic disorder with hallucinations**
CC Exclusion see Appendix A PDX collection 0550
CC **F14.259** **Cocaine dependence with cocaine-induced psychotic disorder, unspecified**
No CC Exclusions
+ **F14.28** **Cocaine dependence with other cocaine-induced disorder**
CC **F14.280** **Cocaine dependence with cocaine-induced anxiety disorder**
No CC Exclusions
CC **F14.281** **Cocaine dependence with cocaine-induced sexual dysfunction**
No CC Exclusions
CC **F14.282** **Cocaine dependence with cocaine-induced sleep disorder**
No CC Exclusions
CC **F14.288** **Cocaine dependence with other cocaine-induced disorder**
No CC Exclusions
F14.29 **Cocaine dependence with unspecified cocaine-induced disorder**

+ **F14.9** **Cocaine use, unspecified**
Excludes1: *cocaine abuse (F14.1-)*
cocaine dependence (F14.2-)
F14.90 **Cocaine use, unspecified, uncomplicated**
+ **F14.92** **Cocaine use, unspecified with intoxication**
F14.920 **Cocaine use, unspecified with intoxication, uncomplicated**
CC **F14.921** **Cocaine use, unspecified with intoxication delirium**
CC Exclusion see Appendix A PDX collection 0550
F14.922 **Cocaine use, unspecified with intoxication with perceptual disturbance**
F14.929 **Cocaine use, unspecified with intoxication, unspecified**
F14.94 **Cocaine use, unspecified with cocaine-induced mood disorder**
+ **F14.95** **Cocaine use, unspecified with cocaine-induced psychotic disorder**
CC **F14.950** **Cocaine use, unspecified with cocaine-induced psychotic disorder with delusions**
CC Exclusion see Appendix A PDX collection 0550
CC **F14.951** **Cocaine use, unspecified with cocaine-induced psychotic disorder with hallucinations**
CC Exclusion see Appendix A PDX collection 0550
F14.959 **Cocaine use, unspecified with cocaine-induced psychotic disorder, unspecified**
+ **F14.98** **Cocaine use, unspecified with other specified cocaine-induced disorder**
F14.980 **Cocaine use, unspecified with cocaine-induced anxiety disorder**
F14.981 **Cocaine use, unspecified with cocaine-induced sexual dysfunction**
F14.982 **Cocaine use, unspecified with cocaine-induced sleep disorder**
F14.988 **Cocaine use, unspecified with other cocaine-induced disorder**
F14.99 **Cocaine use, unspecified with unspecified cocaine-induced disorder**

F15 Other stimulant related disorders

Includes: amphetamine-related disorders
caffeine
Excludes2: *cocaine-related disorders (F14.-)*
+ **F15.1** **Other stimulant abuse**
Excludes1: *other stimulant dependence (F15.2-)*
other stimulant use, unspecified (F15.9-)
F15.10 **Other stimulant abuse, uncomplicated**
+ **F15.12** **Other stimulant abuse with intoxication**
F15.120 **Other stimulant abuse with intoxication, uncomplicated**
CC **F15.121** **Other stimulant abuse with intoxication delirium**
CC Exclusion see Appendix A PDX collection 0550
F15.122 **Other stimulant abuse with intoxication with perceptual disturbance**
F15.129 **Other stimulant abuse with intoxication, unspecified**
F15.14 **Other stimulant abuse with stimulant-induced mood disorder**
+ **F15.15** **Other stimulant abuse with stimulant-induced psychotic disorder**
CC **F15.150** **Other stimulant abuse with stimulant-induced psychotic disorder with delusions**
CC Exclusion see Appendix A PDX collection 0550
CC **F15.151** **Other stimulant abuse with stimulant-induced psychotic disorder with hallucinations**
CC Exclusion see Appendix A PDX collection 0550
F15.159 **Other stimulant abuse with stimulant-induced psychotic disorder, unspecified**
+ **F15.18** **Other stimulant abuse with other stimulant-induced disorder**
F15.180 **Other stimulant abuse with stimulant-induced anxiety disorder**
F15.181 **Other stimulant abuse with stimulant-induced sexual dysfunction**

F15.182 Other stimulant abuse with stimulant-induced sleep disorder
F15.188 Other stimulant abuse with other stimulant-induced disorder
F15.19 Other stimulant abuse with unspecified stimulant-induced disorder
+ F15.2 Other stimulant dependence
Excludes1: *other stimulant abuse (F15.1-)*
other stimulant use, unspecified (F15.9-)
CC **F15.20 Other stimulant dependence, uncomplicated**
No CC Exclusions
F15.21 Other stimulant dependence, in remission
+ F15.22 Other stimulant dependence with intoxication
Excludes1: *other stimulant dependence with withdrawal (F15.23)*
F15.220 Other stimulant dependence with intoxication, uncomplicated
CC **F15.221 Other stimulant dependence with intoxication delirium**
CC Exclusion see Appendix A PDX collection 0550
CC **F15.222 Other stimulant dependence with intoxication with perceptual disturbance**
No CC Exclusions
F15.229 Other stimulant dependence with intoxication, unspecified
CC **F15.23 Other stimulant dependence with withdrawal**
Excludes1: *other stimulant dependence with intoxication (F15.22-)*
CC Exclusion see Appendix A PDX collection 0550
F15.24 Other stimulant dependence with stimulant-induced mood disorder
+ F15.25 Other stimulant dependence with stimulant-induced psychotic disorder
CC **F15.250 Other stimulant dependence with stimulant-induced psychotic disorder with delusions**
CC Exclusion see Appendix A PDX collection 0550
CC **F15.251 Other stimulant dependence with stimulant-induced psychotic disorder with hallucinations**
CC Exclusion see Appendix A PDX collection 0550
CC **F15.259 Other stimulant dependence with stimulant-induced psychotic disorder, unspecified**
No CC Exclusions
+ F15.28 Other stimulant dependence with other stimulant-induced disorder
CC **F15.280 Other stimulant dependence with stimulant-induced anxiety disorder**
No CC Exclusions
CC **F15.281 Other stimulant dependence with stimulant-induced sexual dysfunction**
No CC Exclusions
CC **F15.282 Other stimulant dependence with stimulant-induced sleep disorder**
No CC Exclusions
CC **F15.288 Other stimulant dependence with other stimulant-induced disorder**
No CC Exclusions
F15.29 Other stimulant dependence with unspecified stimulant-induced disorder
+ F15.9 Other stimulant use, unspecified
Excludes1: *other stimulant abuse (F15.1-)*
other stimulant dependence (F15.2-)
F15.90 Other stimulant use, unspecified, uncomplicated
+ F15.92 Other stimulant use, unspecified with intoxication
Excludes1: *other stimulant use, unspecified with withdrawal (F15.93)*
F15.920 Other stimulant use, unspecified with intoxication, uncomplicated
CC **F15.921 Other stimulant use, unspecified with intoxication delirium**
CC Exclusion see Appendix A PDX collection 0550
F15.922 Other stimulant use, unspecified with intoxication with perceptual disturbance
F15.929 Other stimulant use, unspecified with intoxication, unspecified
CC **F15.93 Other stimulant use, unspecified with withdrawal**
Excludes1: *other stimulant use, unspecified with intoxication (F15.92-)*
CC Exclusion see Appendix A PDX collection 0550

F15.94 Other stimulant use, unspecified with stimulant-induced mood disorder
+ F15.95 Other stimulant use, unspecified with stimulant-induced psychotic disorder
CC **F15.950 Other stimulant use, unspecified with stimulant-induced psychotic disorder wit[h] delusions**
CC Exclusion see Appendix A PDX collection 0550
CC **F15.951 Other stimulant use, unspecified with stimulant-induced psychotic disorder wit[h] hallucinations**
CC Exclusion see Appendix A PDX collection 0550
F15.959 Other stimulant use, unspecified with stimulant-induced psychotic disorder, unspecified
+ F15.98 Other stimulant use, unspecified with other stimula[nt-] induced disorder
F15.980 Other stimulant use, unspecified with stimulant-induced anxiety disorder
F15.981 Other stimulant use, unspecified with stimulant-induced sexual dysfunction
F15.982 Other stimulant use, unspecified with stimulant-induced sleep disorder
F15.988 Other stimulant use, unspecified with oth[er] stimulant-induced disorder
F15.99 Other stimulant use, unspecified with unspecified stimulant-induced disorder

F16 Hallucinogen related disorders

Includes: ecstasy
PCP
phencyclidine

+ F16.1 Hallucinogen abuse
Excludes1: *hallucinogen dependence (F16.2-)*
hallucinogen use, unspecified (F16.9-)
F16.10 Hallucinogen abuse, uncomplicated
+ F16.12 Hallucinogen abuse with intoxication
F16.120 Hallucinogen abuse with intoxication, uncomplicated
CC **F16.121 Hallucinogen abuse with intoxication wit[h] delirium**
CC Exclusion see Appendix A PDX collection 0550
F16.122 Hallucinogen abuse with intoxication wit[h] perceptual disturbance
F16.129 Hallucinogen abuse with intoxication, unspecified
F16.14 Hallucinogen abuse with hallucinogen-induced mo[od] disorder
+ F16.15 Hallucinogen abuse with hallucinogen-induced psychotic disorder
CC **F16.150 Hallucinogen abuse with hallucinogen-induced psychotic disorder with delusions**
CC Exclusion see Appendix A PDX collection 0550
CC **F16.151 Hallucinogen abuse with hallucinogen-induced psychotic disorder with hallucinations**
CC Exclusion see Appendix A PDX collection 0550
F16.159 Hallucinogen abuse with hallucinogen-induced psychotic disorder, unspecified
+ F16.18 Hallucinogen abuse with other hallucinogen-induce[d] disorder
F16.180 Hallucinogen abuse with hallucinogen-induced anxiety disorder
F16.183 Hallucinogen abuse with hallucinogen persisting perception disorder (flashbacks)
F16.188 Hallucinogen abuse with other hallucinog[en-] induced disorder
F16.19 Hallucinogen abuse with unspecified hallucinogen-induced disorder
+ F16.2 Hallucinogen dependence
Excludes1: *hallucinogen abuse (F16.1-)*
hallucinogen use, unspecified (F16.9-)
CC **F16.20 Hallucinogen dependence, uncomplicated**
No CC Exclusions
F16.21 Hallucinogen dependence, in remission

+ **F16.22 Hallucinogen dependence with intoxication**
F16.220 Hallucinogen dependence with intoxication, uncomplicated
CC **F16.221 Hallucinogen dependence with intoxication with delirium**
CC Exclusion see Appendix A PDX collection 0550
F16.229 Hallucinogen dependence with intoxication, unspecified
F16.24 Hallucinogen dependence with hallucinogen-induced mood disorder
+ **F16.25 Hallucinogen dependence with hallucinogen-induced psychotic disorder**
CC **F16.250 Hallucinogen dependence with hallucinogen-induced psychotic disorder with delusions**
CC Exclusion see Appendix A PDX collection 0550
CC **F16.251 Hallucinogen dependence with hallucinogen-induced psychotic disorder with hallucinations**
CC Exclusion see Appendix A PDX collection 0550
CC **F16.259 Hallucinogen dependence with hallucinogen-induced psychotic disorder, unspecified**
No CC Exclusions
+ **F16.28 Hallucinogen dependence with other hallucinogen-induced disorder**
CC **F16.280 Hallucinogen dependence with hallucinogen-induced anxiety disorder**
No CC Exclusions
CC **F16.283 Hallucinogen dependence with hallucinogen persisting perception disorder (flashbacks)**
No CC Exclusions
CC **F16.288 Hallucinogen dependence with other hallucinogen-induced disorder**
No CC Exclusions
F16.29 Hallucinogen dependence with unspecified hallucinogen-induced disorder
+ **F16.9 Hallucinogen use, unspecified**
Excludes1: *hallucinogen abuse (F16.1-)*
hallucinogen dependence (F16.2-)
F16.90 Hallucinogen use, unspecified, uncomplicated
+ **F16.92 Hallucinogen use, unspecified with intoxication**
F16.920 Hallucinogen use, unspecified with intoxication, uncomplicated
CC **F16.921 Hallucinogen use, unspecified with intoxication with delirium**
CC Exclusion see Appendix A PDX collection 0550
F16.929 Hallucinogen use, unspecified with intoxication, unspecified
F16.94 Hallucinogen use, unspecified with hallucinogen-induced mood disorder
+ **F16.95 Hallucinogen use, unspecified with hallucinogen-induced psychotic disorder**
CC **F16.950 Hallucinogen use, unspecified with hallucinogen-induced psychotic disorder with delusions**
CC Exclusion see Appendix A PDX collection 0550
CC **F16.951 Hallucinogen use, unspecified with hallucinogen-induced psychotic disorder with hallucinations**
CC Exclusion see Appendix A PDX collection 0550
F16.959 Hallucinogen use, unspecified with hallucinogen-induced psychotic disorder, unspecified
+ **F16.98 Hallucinogen use, unspecified with other specified hallucinogen-induced disorder**
F16.980 Hallucinogen use, unspecified with hallucinogen-induced anxiety disorder
F16.983 Hallucinogen use, unspecified with hallucinogen persisting perception disorder (flashbacks)
F16.988 Hallucinogen use, unspecified with other hallucinogen-induced disorder
F16.99 Hallucinogen use, unspecified with unspecified hallucinogen-induced disorder

F17 Nicotine dependence
Excludes1: *history of tobacco dependence (Z87.891)*
tobacco use NOS (Z72.0)
Excludes2: *tobacco use (smoking) during pregnancy, childbirth and the puerperium (O99.33-)*
toxic effect of nicotine (T65.2-)
Review coding guideline C.15.1.2
+ **F17.2 Nicotine dependence**
+ **F17.20 Nicotine dependence, unspecified**
F17.200 Nicotine dependence, unspecified, uncomplicated
AHA CC: 4Q, 2013, 108
F17.201 Nicotine dependence, unspecified, in remission
CC **F17.203 Nicotine dependence unspecified, with withdrawal**
CC Exclusion see Appendix A PDX collection 0550
F17.208 Nicotine dependence, unspecified, with other nicotine-induced disorders
F17.209 Nicotine dependence, unspecified, with unspecified nicotine-induced disorders
+ **F17.21 Nicotine dependence, cigarettes**
F17.210 Nicotine dependence, cigarettes, uncomplicated
AHA CC: 4Q, 2013, 109
F17.211 Nicotine dependence, cigarettes, in remission
CC **F17.213 Nicotine dependence, cigarettes, with withdrawal**
CC Exclusion see Appendix A PDX collection 0550
F17.218 Nicotine dependence, cigarettes, with other nicotine-induced disorders
F17.219 Nicotine dependence, cigarettes, with unspecified nicotine-induced disorders
+ **F17.22 Nicotine dependence, chewing tobacco**
F17.220 Nicotine dependence, chewing tobacco, uncomplicated
F17.221 Nicotine dependence, chewing tobacco, in remission
CC **F17.223 Nicotine dependence, chewing tobacco, with withdrawal**
CC Exclusion see Appendix A PDX collection 0550
F17.228 Nicotine dependence, chewing tobacco, with other nicotine-induced disorders
F17.229 Nicotine dependence, chewing tobacco, with unspecified nicotine-induced disorders
+ **F17.29 Nicotine dependence, other tobacco product**
F17.290 Nicotine dependence, other tobacco product, uncomplicated
F17.291 Nicotine dependence, other tobacco product, in remission
CC **F17.293 Nicotine dependence, other tobacco product, with withdrawal**
CC Exclusion see Appendix A PDX collection 0550
F17.298 Nicotine dependence, other tobacco product, with other nicotine-induced disorders
F17.299 Nicotine dependence, other tobacco product, with unspecified nicotine-induced disorders

F18 Inhalant related disorders
Includes: volatile solvents
+ **F18.1 Inhalant abuse**
Excludes1: *inhalant dependence (F18.2-)*
inhalant use, unspecified (F18.9-)
F18.10 Inhalant abuse, uncomplicated
+ **F18.12 Inhalant abuse with intoxication**
F18.120 Inhalant abuse with intoxication, uncomplicated
CC **F18.121 Inhalant abuse with intoxication delirium**
CC Exclusion see Appendix A PDX collection 0550
F18.129 Inhalant abuse with intoxication, unspecified
F18.14 Inhalant abuse with inhalant-induced mood disorder
+ **F18.15 Inhalant abuse with inhalant-induced psychotic disorder**
CC **F18.150 Inhalant abuse with inhalant-induced psychotic disorder with delusions**
CC Exclusion see Appendix A PDX collection 0550

CC **F18.151 Inhalant abuse with inhalant-induced psychotic disorder with hallucinations**
CC Exclusion see Appendix A PDX collection 0550

F18.159 Inhalant abuse with inhalant-induced psychotic disorder, unspecified

CC **F18.17 Inhalant abuse with inhalant-induced dementia**
CC Exclusion see Appendix A PDX collection 0550

\+ **F18.18 Inhalant abuse with other inhalant-induced disorders**

F18.180 Inhalant abuse with inhalant-induced anxiety disorder

F18.188 Inhalant abuse with other inhalant-induced disorder

F18.19 Inhalant abuse with unspecified inhalant-induced disorder

\+ **F18.2 Inhalant dependence**

Excludes1: *inhalant abuse (F18.1-)*
inhalant use, unspecified (F18.9-)

CC **F18.20 Inhalant dependence, uncomplicated**
No CC Exclusions

F18.21 Inhalant dependence, in remission

\+ **F18.22 Inhalant dependence with intoxication**

F18.220 Inhalant dependence with intoxication, uncomplicated

CC **F18.221 Inhalant dependence with intoxication delirium**
CC Exclusion see Appendix A PDX collection 0550

F18.229 Inhalant dependence with intoxication, unspecified

F18.24 Inhalant dependence with inhalant-induced mood disorder

\+ **F18.25 Inhalant dependence with inhalant-induced psychotic disorder**

CC **F18.250 Inhalant dependence with inhalant-induced psychotic disorder with delusions**
CC Exclusion see Appendix A PDX collection 0550

CC **F18.251 Inhalant dependence with inhalant-induced psychotic disorder with hallucinations**
CC Exclusion see Appendix A PDX collection 0550

CC **F18.259 Inhalant dependence with inhalant-induced psychotic disorder, unspecified**
No CC Exclusions

CC **F18.27 Inhalant dependence with inhalant-induced dementia**
CC Exclusion see Appendix A PDX collection 0550

\+ **F18.28 Inhalant dependence with other inhalant-induced disorders**

CC **F18.280 Inhalant dependence with inhalant-induced anxiety disorder**
No CC Exclusions

CC **F18.288 Inhalant dependence with other inhalant-induced disorder**
No CC Exclusions

F18.29 Inhalant dependence with unspecified inhalant-induced disorder

\+ **F18.9 Inhalant use, unspecified**

Excludes1: *inhalant abuse (F18.1-)*
inhalant dependence (F18.2-)

F18.90 Inhalant use, unspecified, uncomplicated

\+ **F18.92 Inhalant use, unspecified with intoxication**

F18.920 Inhalant use, unspecified with intoxication, uncomplicated

CC **F18.921 Inhalant use, unspecified with intoxication with delirium**
CC Exclusion see Appendix A PDX collection 0550

F18.929 Inhalant use, unspecified with intoxication, unspecified

F18.94 Inhalant use, unspecified with inhalant-induced mood disorder

\+ **F18.95 Inhalant use, unspecified with inhalant-induced psychotic disorder**

CC **F18.950 Inhalant use, unspecified with inhalant-induced psychotic disorder with delusions**
CC Exclusion see Appendix A PDX collection 0550

CC **F18.951 Inhalant use, unspecified with inhalant-induced psychoticdisorder with hallucinations**
CC Exclusion see Appendix A PDX collection 0550

F18.959 Inhalant use, unspecified with inhalant-induced psychotic disorder, unspecified

CC **F18.97 Inhalant use, unspecified with inhalant-induced persisting dementia**
CC Exclusion see Appendix A PDX collection 0550

\+ **F18.98 Inhalant use, unspecified with other inhalant-induc[ed] disorders**

F18.980 Inhalant use, unspecified with inhalant-induced anxiety disorder

F18.988 Inhalant use, unspecified with other inhalant-induced disorder

F18.99 Inhalant use, unspecified with unspecified inhalant-induced disorder

F19 Other psychoactive substance related disorders

Includes: polysubstance drug use (indiscriminate drug use)

\+ **F19.1 Other psychoactive substance abuse**

Excludes1: *other psychoactive substance dependence (F19.2-)*
other psychoactive substance use, unspecified (F19.9-)

F19.10 Other psychoactive substance abuse, uncomplicate[d]

\+ **F19.12 Other psychoactive substance abuse with intoxicati[on]**

F19.120 Other psychoactive substance abuse with intoxication, uncomplicated

CC **F19.121 Other psychoactive substance abuse with intoxication delirium**
CC Exclusion see Appendix A PDX collection 0550

F19.122 Other psychoactive substance abuse with intoxication with perceptual disturbances

F19.129 Other psychoactive substance abuse with intoxication, unspecified

F19.14 Other psychoactive substance abuse with psychoac[tive] substance-induced mood disorder

\+ **F19.15 Other psychoactive substance abuse with psychoac[tive] substance-induced psychotic disorder**

CC **F19.150 Other psychoactive substance abuse with psychoactive substance-induced psychotic disorder with delusions**
CC Exclusion see Appendix A PDX collection 0550

CC **F19.151 Other psychoactive substance abuse with psychoactive substance-induced psychotic disorder with hallucinations**
CC Exclusion see Appendix A PDX collection 0550

F19.159 Other psychoactive substance abuse with psychoactive substance-induced psychotic disorder, unspecified

F19.16 Other psychoactive substance abuse with psychoac[tive] substance-induced persisting amnestic disorder

CC **F19.17 Other psychoactive substance abuse with psychoac[tive] substance-induced persisting dementia**
CC Exclusion see Appendix A PDX collection 0550

\+ **F19.18 Other psychoactive substance abuse with other psychoactive substance-induced disorders**

F19.180 Other psychoactive substance abuse with psychoactive substance-induced anxiety disorder

F19.181 Other psychoactive substance abuse with psychoactive substance-induced sexual dysfunction

F19.182 Other psychoactive substance abuse with psychoactive substance-induced sleep disorder

F19.188 Other psychoactive substance abuse with other psychoactive substance-induced disorder

F19.19 Other psychoactive substance abuse with unspecified psychoactive substance-induced disorder

\+ **F19.2 Other psychoactive substance dependence**

Excludes1: *other psychoactive substance abuse (F19.1-)*
other psychoactive substance use, unspecified (F19.9-)

CC **F19.20 Other psychoactive substance dependence, uncomplicated**
No CC Exclusions

F19.21 Other psychoactive substance dependence, in remission

+ **F19.22 Other psychoactive substance dependence with intoxication**
  Excludes1: *other psychoactive substance dependence with withdrawal (F19.23-)*
  F19.220 Other psychoactive substance dependence with intoxication, uncomplicated
  CC **F19.221 Other psychoactive substance dependence with intoxication delirium**
  CC Exclusion see Appendix A PDX collection 0550
  CC **F19.222 Other psychoactive substance dependence with intoxication with perceptual disturbance**
  No CC Exclusions
  F19.229 Other psychoactive substance dependence with intoxication, unspecified

+ **F19.23 Other psychoactive substance dependence with withdrawal**
  Excludes1: *other psychoactive substance dependence with intoxication (F19.22-)*
  CC **F19.230 Other psychoactive substance dependence with withdrawal, uncomplicated**
  CC Exclusion see Appendix A PDX collection 0550
  CC **F19.231 Other psychoactive substance dependence with withdrawal delirium**
  CC Exclusion see Appendix A PDX collection 0550
  CC **F19.232 Other psychoactive substance dependence with withdrawal with perceptual disturbance**
  CC Exclusion see Appendix A PDX collection 0550
  CC **F19.239 Other psychoactive substance dependence with withdrawal, unspecified**
  CC Exclusion see Appendix A PDX collection 0550

F19.24 Other psychoactive substance dependence with psychoactive substance-induced mood disorder

+ **F19.25 Other psychoactive substance dependence with psychoactive substance-induced psychotic disorder**
  CC **F19.250 Other psychoactive substance dependence with psychoactive substance-induced psychotic disorder with delusions**
  CC Exclusion see Appendix A PDX collection 0550
  CC **F19.251 Other psychoactive substance dependence with psychoactive substance-induced psychotic disorder with hallucinations**
  CC Exclusion see Appendix A PDX collection 0550
  CC **F19.259 Other psychoactive substance dependence with psychoactive substance-induced psychotic disorder, unspecified**
  No CC Exclusions

CC **F19.26 Other psychoactive substance dependence with psychoactive substance-induced persisting amnestic disorder**
No CC Exclusions

CC **F19.27 Other psychoactive substance dependence with psychoactive substance-induced persisting dementia**
CC Exclusion see Appendix A PDX collection 0550

+ **F19.28 Other psychoactive substance dependence with other psychoactive substance-induced disorders**
  CC **F19.280 Other psychoactive substance dependence with psychoactive substance-induced anxiety disorder**
  No CC Exclusions
  CC **F19.281 Other psychoactive substance dependence with psychoactive substance-induced sexual dysfunction**
  No CC Exclusions
  CC **F19.282 Other psychoactive substance dependence with psychoactive substance-induced sleep disorder**
  No CC Exclusions
  CC **F19.288 Other psychoactive substance dependence with other psychoactive substance-induced disorder**
  No CC Exclusions

F19.29 Other psychoactive substance dependence with unspecified psychoactive substance-induced disorder

+ **F19.9 Other psychoactive substance use, unspecified**
  Excludes1: *other psychoactive substance abuse (F19.1-)*
  other psychoactive substance dependence (F19.2-)

F19.90 Other psychoactive substance use, unspecified, uncomplicated

+ **F19.92 Other psychoactive substance use, unspecified with intoxication**
  Excludes1: *other psychoactive substance use, unspecified with withdrawal (F19.93)*
  F19.920 Other psychoactive substance use, unspecified with intoxication, uncomplicated
  CC **F19.921 Other psychoactive substance use, unspecified with intoxication with delirium**
  CC Exclusion see Appendix A PDX collection 0550
  F19.922 Other psychoactive substance use, unspecified with intoxication with perceptual disturbance
  F19.929 Other psychoactive substance use, unspecified with intoxication, unspecified

+ **F19.93 Other psychoactive substance use, unspecified with withdrawal**
  Excludes1: *other psychoactive substance use, unspecified with intoxication (F19.92-)*
  CC **F19.930 Other psychoactive substance use, unspecified with withdrawal, uncomplicated**
  CC Exclusion see Appendix A PDX collection 0550
  CC **F19.931 Other psychoactive substance use, unspecified with withdrawal delirium**
  CC Exclusion see Appendix A PDX collection 0550
  CC **F19.932 Other psychoactive substance use, unspecified with withdrawal with perceptual disturbance**
  CC Exclusion see Appendix A PDX collection 0550
  CC **F19.939 Other psychoactive substance use, unspecified with withdrawal, unspecified**
  CC Exclusion see Appendix A PDX collection 0550

F19.94 Other psychoactive substance use, unspecified with psychoactive substance-induced mood disorder

+ **F19.95 Other psychoactive substance use, unspecified with psychoactive substance-induced psychotic disorder**
  CC **F19.950 Other psychoactive substance use, unspecified with psychoactive substance-induced psychotic disorder with delusions**
  CC Exclusion see Appendix A PDX collection 0550
  CC **F19.951 Other psychoactive substance use, unspecified with psychoactive substance-induced psychotic disorder with hallucinations**
  CC Exclusion see Appendix A PDX collection 0550
  F19.959 Other psychoactive substance use, unspecified with psychoactive substance-induced psychotic disorder, unspecified

F19.96 Other psychoactive substance use, unspecified with psychoactive substance-induced persisting amnestic disorder

CC **F19.97 Other psychoactive substance use, unspecified with psychoactive substance-induced persisting dementia**
CC Exclusion see Appendix A PDX collection 0550

+ **F19.98 Other psychoactive substance use, unspecified with other psychoactive substance-induced disorders**
  F19.980 Other psychoactive substance use, unspecified with psychoactive substance-induced anxiety disorder
  F19.981 Other psychoactive substance use, unspecified with psychoactive substance-induced sexual dysfunction
  F19.982 Other psychoactive substance use, unspecified with psychoactive substance-induced sleep disorder
  F19.988 Other psychoactive substance use, unspecified with other psychoactive substance-induced disorder

F19.99 Other psychoactive substance use, unspecified with unspecified psychoactive substance-induced disorder

Schizophrenia, schizotypal, delusional, and other non-mood psychotic disorders (F20-F29)

F20 Schizophrenia

Excludes1: *brief psychotic disorder (F23)*
cyclic schizophrenia (F25.0)
mood [affective] disorders with psychotic symptoms (F30.2, F31.2, F31.5, F31.64, F32.3, F33.3)
schizoaffective disorder (F25.-)
schizophrenic reaction NOS (F23)

Excludes2: *schizophrenic reaction in:*
alcoholism (F10.15-, F10.25-, F10.95-)
brain disease (F06.2)
epilepsy (F06.2)
psychoactive drug use (F11-F19 with .15. .25, .95)
schizotypal disorder (F21)

CC **F20.0 Paranoid schizophrenia**
Paraphrenic schizophrenia
Excludes1: *involutional paranoid state (F22)*
paranoia (F22)
CC Exclusion see Appendix A PDX collection 0551

CC **F20.1 Disorganized schizophrenia**
Hebephrenic schizophrenia
Hebephrenia
CC Exclusion see Appendix A PDX collection 0551

CC **F20.2 Catatonic schizophrenia**
Schizophrenic catalepsy
Schizophrenic catatonia
Schizophrenic flexibilitas cerea
Excludes1: *catatonic stupor (R40.1)*
CC Exclusion see Appendix A PDX collection 0551

F20.3 Undifferentiated schizophrenia
Atypical schizophrenia
Excludes1: *acute schizophrenia-like psychotic disorder (F23)*
Excludes2: *post-schizophrenic depression (F32.8)*

CC **F20.5 Residual schizophrenia**
Restzustand (schizophrenic)
Schizophrenic residual state
CC Exclusion see Appendix A PDX collection 0551

\+ **F20.8 Other schizophrenia**

CC **F20.81 Schizophreniform disorder**
Schizophreniform psychosis NOS
CC Exclusion see Appendix A PDX collection 0551

CC **F20.89 Other schizophrenia**
Cenesthopathic schizophrenia
Simple schizophrenia
CC Exclusion see Appendix A PDX collection 0551

F20.9 Schizophrenia, unspecified

F21 Schizotypal disorder

Borderline schizophrenia
Latent schizophrenia
Latent schizophrenic reaction
Prepsychotic schizophrenia
Prodromal schizophrenia
Pseudoneurotic schizophrenia
Pseudopsychopathic schizophrenia
Schizotypal personality disorder
Excludes2: *Asperger's syndrome (F84.5)*
schizoid personality disorder (F60.1)
Valid 3-character code, no further characters required

F22 Delusional disorders

Delusional dysmorphophobia
Involutional paranoid state
Paranoia
Paranoia querulans
Paranoid psychosis
Paranoid state
Paraphrenia (late)
Sensitiver Beziehungswahn
Excludes1: *mood [affective] disorders with psychotic symptoms (F30.2, F31.2, F31.5, F31.64, F32.3, F33.3)*
paranoid schizophrenia (F20.0)
Excludes2: *paranoid personality disorder (F60.0)*
paranoid psychosis, psychogenic (F23)
paranoid reaction (F23)
Valid 3-character code, no further characters required

CC **F23 Brief psychotic disorder**

Paranoid reaction
Psychogenic paranoid psychosis
Excludes2: *mood [affective] disorders with psychotic symptoms (F30.2, F31.2, F31.5, F31.64, F32.3, F33.3)*
No CC Exclusions
Valid 3-character code, no further characters required

F24 Shared psychotic disorder

Folie à deux
Induced paranoid disorder
Induced psychotic disorder
Valid 3-character code, no further characters required

F25 Schizoaffective disorders

Excludes1: *mood [affective] disorders with psychotic symptoms (F30.2, F31.2, F31.5, F31.64, F32.3, F33.3)*
schizophrenia (F20.-)

F25.0 Schizoaffective disorder, bipolar type
Cyclic schizophrenia
Schizoaffective disorder, manic type
Schizoaffective disorder, mixed type
Schizoaffective psychosis, bipolar type
Schizophreniform psychosis, manic type

F25.1 Schizoaffective disorder, depressive type
Schizoaffective psychosis, depressive type
Schizophreniform psychosis, depressive type

F25.8 Other schizoaffective disorders

F25.9 Schizoaffective disorder, unspecified
Schizoaffective psychosis NOS

F28 Other psychotic disorder not due to a substance or known physiological condition

Chronic hallucinatory psychosis
Valid 3-character code, no further characters required

F29 Unspecified psychosis not due to a substance or known physiological condition

Psychosis NOS
Excludes1: *mental disorder NOS (F99)*
unspecified mental disorder due to known physiological condition (F09)
Valid 3-character code, no further characters required

Mood [affective] disorders (F30-F39)

F30 Manic episode

Includes: bipolar disorder, single manic episode
mixed affective episode
Excludes1: *bipolar disorder (F31.-)*
major depressive disorder, single episode (F32.-)
major depressive disorder, recurrent (F33.-)

\+ **F30.1 Manic episode without psychotic symptoms**

CC **F30.10 Manic episode without psychotic symptoms, unspecified**
CC Exclusion see Appendix A PDX collection 0551

CC **F30.11 Manic episode without psychotic symptoms, mild**
CC Exclusion see Appendix A PDX collection 0551

CC **F30.12 Manic episode without psychotic symptoms, moder**
CC Exclusion see Appendix A PDX collection 0551

CC **F30.13 Manic episode, severe, without psychotic symptoms**
CC Exclusion see Appendix A PDX collection 0552

CC **F30.2 Manic episode, severe with psychotic symptoms**
Manic stupor
Mania with mood-congruent psychotic symptoms
Mania with mood-incongruent psychotic symptoms
CC Exclusion see Appendix A PDX collection 0551

F30.3 Manic episode in partial remission

F30.4 Manic episode in full remission

F30.8 Other manic episodes
Hypomania

CC **F30.9 Manic episode, unspecified**
Mania NOS
CC Exclusion see Appendix A PDX collection 0551

F31 Bipolar disorder

Includes: manic-depressive illness
manic-depressive psychosis
manic-depressive reaction

Excludes1: *bipolar disorder, single manic episode (F30.-)*
major depressive disorder, single episode (F32.-)
major depressive disorder, recurrent (F33.-)

Excludes2: *cyclothymia (F34.0)*

CC **F31.0 Bipolar disorder, current episode hypomanic**
CC Exclusion see Appendix A PDX collection 0551

\+ **F31.1 Bipolar disorder, current episode manic without psychotic features**

CC **F31.10 Bipolar disorder, current episode manic without psychotic features, unspecified**
CC Exclusion see Appendix A PDX collection 0551

CC **F31.11 Bipolar disorder, current episode manic without psychotic features, mild**
CC Exclusion see Appendix A PDX collection 0551

CC **F31.12 Bipolar disorder, current episode manic without psychotic features, moderate**
CC Exclusion see Appendix A PDX collection 0551

CC **F31.13 Bipolar disorder, current episode manic without psychotic features, severe**
CC Exclusion see Appendix A PDX collection 0553

CC **F31.2 Bipolar disorder, current episode manic severe with psychotic features**
Bipolar disorder, current episode manic with mood-congruent psychotic symptoms
Bipolar disorder, current episode manic with mood-incongruent psychotic symptoms
CC Exclusion see Appendix A PDX collection 0551

\+ **F31.3 Bipolar disorder, current episode depressed, mild or moderate severity**

CC **F31.30 Bipolar disorder, current episode depressed, mild or moderate severity, unspecified**
CC Exclusion see Appendix A PDX collection 0551

CC **F31.31 Bipolar disorder, current episode depressed, mild**
CC Exclusion see Appendix A PDX collection 0551

CC **F31.32 Bipolar disorder, current episode depressed, moderate**
CC Exclusion see Appendix A PDX collection 0551

CC **F31.4 Bipolar disorder, current episode depressed, severe, without psychotic features**
CC Exclusion see Appendix A PDX collection 0554

CC **F31.5 Bipolar disorder, current episode depressed, severe, with psychotic features**
Bipolar disorder, current episode depressed with mood-incongruent psychotic symptoms
Bipolar disorder, current episode depressed with mood-congruent psychotic symptoms
CC Exclusion see Appendix A PDX collection 0551

\+ **F31.6 Bipolar disorder, current episode mixed**

CC **F31.60 Bipolar disorder, current episode mixed, unspecified**
CC Exclusion see Appendix A PDX collection 0551

CC **F31.61 Bipolar disorder, current episode mixed, mild**
CC Exclusion see Appendix A PDX collection 0551

CC **F31.62 Bipolar disorder, current episode mixed, moderate**
CC Exclusion see Appendix A PDX collection 0551

CC **F31.63 Bipolar disorder, current episode mixed, severe, without psychotic features**
CC Exclusion see Appendix A PDX collection 0554

CC **F31.64 Bipolar disorder, current episode mixed, severe, with psychotic features**
Bipolar disorder, current episode mixed with mood-congruent psychotic symptoms
Bipolar disorder, current episode mixed with mood-incongruent psychotic symptoms
CC Exclusion see Appendix A PDX collection 0551

\+ **F31.7 Bipolar disorder, currently in remission**

F31.70 Bipolar disorder, currently in remission, most recent episode unspecified

F31.71 Bipolar disorder, in partial remission, most recent episode hypomanic

F31.72 Bipolar disorder, in full remission, most recent episode hypomanic

F31.73 Bipolar disorder, in partial remission, most recent episode manic

F31.74 Bipolar disorder, in full remission, most recent episode manic

F31.75 Bipolar disorder, in partial remission, most recent episode depressed

F31.76 Bipolar disorder, in full remission, most recent episode depressed

F31.77 Bipolar disorder, in partial remission, most recent episode mixed

F31.78 Bipolar disorder, in full remission, most recent episode mixed

\+ **F31.8 Other bipolar disorders**

CC **F31.81 Bipolar II disorder**
CC Exclusion see Appendix A PDX collection 0551

CC **F31.89 Other bipolar disorder**
Recurrent manic episodes NOS
CC Exclusion see Appendix A PDX collection 0551

F31.9 Bipolar disorder, unspecified

F32 Major depressive disorder, single episode

Includes: single episode of agitated depression
single episode of depressive reaction
single episode of major depression
single episode of psychogenic depression
single episode of reactive depression
single episode of vital depression

Excludes1: *bipolar disorder (F31.-)*
manic episode (F30.-)
recurrent depressive disorder (F33.-)

Excludes2: *adjustment disorder (F43.2)*

CC **F32.0 Major depressive disorder, single episode, mild**
CC Exclusion see Appendix A PDX collection 0555

CC **F32.1 Major depressive disorder, single episode, moderate**
CC Exclusion see Appendix A PDX collection 0555

CC **F32.2 Major depressive disorder, single episode, severe without psychotic features**
CC Exclusion see Appendix A PDX collection 0555

CC **F32.3 Major depressive disorder, single episode, severe with psychotic features**
Single episode of major depression with mood-congruent psychotic symptoms
Single episode of major depression with mood-incongruent psychotic symptoms
Single episode of major depression with psychotic symptoms
Single episode of psychogenic depressive psychosis
Single episode of psychotic depression
Single episode of reactive depressive psychosis
CC Exclusion see Appendix A PDX collection 0555

F32.4 Major depressive disorder, single episode, in partial remission

F32.5 Major depressive disorder, single episode, in full remission

F32.8 Other depressive episodes
Atypical depression
Post-schizophrenic depression
Single episode of 'masked' depression NOS

F32.9 Major depressive disorder, single episode, unspecified
Depression NOS
Depressive disorder NOS
Major depression NOS
AHA CC: 4Q, 2013, 107-108

F33 Major depressive disorder, recurrent

Includes: recurrent episodes of depressive reaction
recurrent episodes of endogenous depression
recurrent episodes of major depression
recurrent episodes of psychogenic depression
recurrent episodes of reactive depression
recurrent episodes of seasonal depressive disorder
recurrent episodes of vital depression

Excludes1: *bipolar disorder (F31.-)*
manic episode (F30.-)

CC **F33.0 Major depressive disorder, recurrent, mild**
CC Exclusion see Appendix A PDX collection 0555

CC **F33.1 Major depressive disorder, recurrent, moderate**
CC Exclusion see Appendix A PDX collection 0555

CC **F33.2 Major depressive disorder, recurrent severe without psychotic features**
CC Exclusion see Appendix A PDX collection 0555

CC **F33.3 Major depressive disorder, recurrent, severe with psychotic symptoms**
Endogenous depression with psychotic symptoms
Recurrent severe episodes of major depression with mood-congruent psychotic symptoms
Recurrent severe episodes of major depression with mood-incongruent psychotic symptoms
Recurrent severe episodes of major depression with psychotic symptoms
Recurrent severe episodes of psychogenic depressive psychosis
Recurrent severe episodes of psychotic depression
Recurrent severe episodes of reactive depressive psychosis
CC Exclusion see Appendix A PDX collection 0551

+ F33.4 **Major depressive disorder, recurrent, in remission**
CC F33.40 **Major depressive disorder, recurrent, in remission, unspecified**
CC Exclusion see Appendix A PDX collection 0555
F33.41 **Major depressive disorder, recurrent, in partial remission**
F33.42 **Major depressive disorder, recurrent, in full remission**
CC F33.8 **Other recurrent depressive disorders**
Recurrent brief depressive episodes
CC Exclusion see Appendix A PDX collection 0551
CC F33.9 **Major depressive disorder, recurrent, unspecified**
Monopolar depression NOS
CC Exclusion see Appendix A PDX collection 0555

F34 **Persistent mood [affective] disorders**
F34.0 **Cyclothymic disorder**
Affective personality disorder
Cycloid personality
Cyclothymia
Cyclothymic personality
F34.1 **Dysthymic disorder**
Depressive neurosis
Depressive personality disorder
Dysthymia
Neurotic depression
Persistent anxiety depression
Excludes2: *anxiety depression (mild or not persistent) (F41.8)*
CC F34.8 **Other persistent mood [affective] disorders**
CC Exclusion see Appendix A PDX collection 0551
CC F34.9 **Persistent mood [affective] disorder, unspecified**
CC Exclusion see Appendix A PDX collection 0551

F39 **Unspecified mood [affective] disorder**
Affective psychosis NOS
Valid 3-character code, no further characters required

Anxiety, dissociative, stress-related, somatoform and other nonpsychotic mental disorders (F40-F48)

F40 **Phobic anxiety disorders**
+ F40.0 **Agoraphobia**
F40.00 **Agoraphobia, unspecified**
F40.01 **Agoraphobia with panic disorder**
Panic disorder with agoraphobia
Excludes1: *panic disorder without agoraphobia (F41.0)*
F40.02 **Agoraphobia without panic disorder**
+ F40.1 **Social phobias**
Anthropophobia
Social anxiety disorder of childhood
Social neurosis
F40.10 **Social phobia, unspecified**
F40.11 **Social phobia, generalized**
+ F40.2 **Specific (isolated) phobias**
Excludes2: *dysmorphophobia (nondelusional) (F45.22)*
nosophobia (F45.22)
+ F40.21 **Animal type phobia**
F40.210 **Arachnophobia**
Fear of spiders
F40.218 **Other animal type phobia**
+ F40.22 **Natural environment type phobia**
F40.220 **Fear of thunderstorms**
F40.228 **Other natural environment type phobia**
+ F40.23 **Blood, injection, injury type phobia**
F40.230 **Fear of blood**
F40.231 **Fear of injections and transfusions**
F40.232 **Fear of other medical care**
F40.233 **Fear of injury**
+ F40.24 **Situational type phobia**
F40.240 **Claustrophobia**
F40.241 **Acrophobia**
F40.242 **Fear of bridges**
F40.243 **Fear of flying**
F40.248 **Other situational type phobia**
+ F40.29 **Other specified phobia**
F40.290 **Androphobia**
Fear of men
F40.291 **Gynephobia**
Fear of women
F40.298 **Other specified phobia**
F40.8 **Other phobic anxiety disorders**
Phobic anxiety disorder of childhood
F40.9 **Phobic anxiety disorder, unspecified**
Phobia NOS
Phobic state NOS

F41 **Other anxiety disorders**
Excludes2: *anxiety in:*
acute stress reaction (F43.0)
transient adjustment reaction (F43.2)
neurasthenia (F48.8)
psychophysiologic disorders (F45.-)
separation anxiety (F93.0)
F41.0 **Panic disorder [episodic paroxysmal anxiety] without agoraphobia**
Panic attack
Panic state
Excludes1: *panic disorder with agoraphobia (F40.01)*
F41.1 **Generalized anxiety disorder**
Anxiety neurosis
Anxiety reaction
Anxiety state
Overanxious disorder
Excludes2: *neurasthenia (F48.8)*
F41.3 **Other mixed anxiety disorders**
F41.8 **Other specified anxiety disorders**
Anxiety depression (mild or not persistent)
Anxiety hysteria
Mixed anxiety and depressive disorder
F41.9 **Anxiety disorder, unspecified**
Anxiety NOS

F42 **Obsessive-compulsive disorder**
Anancastic neurosis
Obsessive-compulsive neurosis
Excludes2: *obsessive-compulsive personality (disorder) (F60.5)*
obsessive-compulsive symptoms occurring in depression (F32-F33)
obsessive-compulsive symptoms occurring in schizophren (F20.-)
Valid 3-character code, no further characters required

F43 **Reaction to severe stress, and adjustment disorders**
F43.0 **Acute stress reaction**
Acute crisis reaction
Acute reaction to stress
Combat and operational stress reaction
Combat fatigue
Crisis state
Psychic shock
+ F43.1 **Post-traumatic stress disorder (PTSD)**
Traumatic neurosis
F43.10 **Post-traumatic stress disorder, unspecified**
F43.11 **Post-traumatic stress disorder, acute**
F43.12 **Post-traumatic stress disorder, chronic**
+ F43.2 **Adjustment disorders**
Culture shock
Grief reaction
Hospitalism in children
Excludes2: *separation anxiety disorder of childhood (F93.0)*
F43.20 **Adjustment disorder, unspecified**
F43.21 **Adjustment disorder with depressed mood**
AHA CC: 1Q, 2014, 25
F43.22 **Adjustment disorder with anxiety**
F43.23 **Adjustment disorder with mixed anxiety and depressed mood**
F43.24 **Adjustment disorder with disturbance of conduct**
F43.25 **Adjustment disorder with mixed disturbance of emotions and conduct**
F43.29 **Adjustment disorder with other symptoms**
F43.8 **Other reactions to severe stress**
F43.9 **Reaction to severe stress, unspecified**

F44 **Dissociative and conversion disorders**
Includes: conversion hysteria
conversion reaction
hysteria
hysterical psychosis
Excludes2: *malingering [conscious simulation] (Z76.5)*

F44.0 Dissociative amnesia
Excludes1: *amnesia NOS (R41.3)*
anterograde amnesia (R41.1)
retrograde amnesia (R41.2)
Excludes2: *alcohol-or other psychoactive substance-induced amnestic disorder (F10, F13, F19 with .26, .96)*
amnestic disorder due to known physiological condition (F04)
postictal amnesia in epilepsy (G40.-)

F44.1 Dissociative fugue
Excludes2: *postictal fugue in epilepsy (G40.-)*

F44.2 Dissociative stupor
Excludes1: *catatonic stupor (R40.1)*
stupor NOS (R40.1)
Excludes2: *catatonic disorder due to known physiological condition (F06.1)*
depressive stupor (F32, F33)
manic stupor (F30, F31)

F44.4 Conversion disorder with motor symptom or deficit
Dissociative motor disorders
Psychogenic aphonia
Psychogenic dysphonia

F44.5 Conversion disorder with seizures or convulsions
Dissociative convulsions

F44.6 Conversion disorder with sensory symptom or deficit
Dissociative anesthesia and sensory loss
Psychogenic deafness

F44.7 Conversion disorder with mixed symptom presentation

+ **F44.8 Other dissociative and conversion disorders**

F44.81 Dissociative identity disorder
Multiple personality disorder

F44.89 Other dissociative and conversion disorders
Ganser's syndrome
Psychogenic confusion
Psychogenic twilight state
Trance and possession disorders

F44.9 Dissociative and conversion disorder, unspecified
Dissociative disorder NOS

F45 Somatoform disorders

Excludes2: *dissociative and conversion disorders (F44.-)*
factitious disorders (F68.1-)
hair-plucking (F63.3)
lalling (F80.0)
lisping (F80.0)
malingering [conscious simulation] (Z76.5)
nail-biting (F98.8)
psychological or behavioral factors associated with disorders or diseases classified elsewhere (F54)
sexual dysfunction, not due to a substance or known physiological condition (F52.-)
thumb-sucking (F98.8)
tic disorders (in childhood and adolescence) (F95.-)
Tourette's syndrome (F95.2)
trichotillomania (F63.3)

F45.0 Somatization disorder
Briquet's disorder
Multiple psychosomatic disorder

F45.1 Undifferentiated somatoform disorder
Undifferentiated psychosomatic disorder

+ **F45.2 Hypochondriacal disorders**
Excludes2: *delusional dysmorphophobia (F22)*
fixed delusions about bodily functions or shape (F22)

F45.20 Hypochondriacal disorder, unspecified

F45.21 Hypochondriasis
Hypochondriacal neurosis

F45.22 Body dysmorphic disorder
Dysmorphophobia (nondelusional)
Nosophobia

F45.29 Other hypochondriacal disorders

+ **F45.4 Pain disorders related to psychological factors**
Excludes1: *pain NOS (R52)*

F45.41 Pain disorder exclusively related to psychological factors
Somatoform pain disorder (persistent)
Review coding guideline C.5.a

F45.42 Pain disorder with related psychological factors
Code also associated acute or chronic pain (G89.-)
Review coding guideline C.5.a

F45.8 Other somatoform disorders
Psychogenic dysmenorrhea
Psychogenic dysphagia, including 'globus hystericus'
Psychogenic pruritus
Psychogenic torticollis
Somatoform autonomic dysfunction
Teeth grinding
Excludes1: *sleep related teeth grinding (G47.63)*

F45.9 Somatoform disorder, unspecified
Psychosomatic disorder NOS

F48 Other nonpsychotic mental disorders

F48.1 Depersonalization-derealization syndrome

F48.2 Pseudobulbar affect
Involuntary emotional expression disorder
Code first underlying cause, if known, such as:
amyotrophic lateral sclerosis (G12.21)
multiple sclerosis (G35)
sequelae of cerebrovascular disease (I69.-)
sequelae of traumatic intracranial injury (S06.-)

F48.8 Other specified nonpsychotic mental disorders
Dhat syndrome
Neurasthenia
Occupational neurosis, including writer's cramp
Psychasthenia
Psychasthenic neurosis
Psychogenic syncope

F48.9 Nonpsychotic mental disorder, unspecified
Neurosis NOS

Behavioral syndromes associated with physiological disturbances and physical factors (F50-F59)

F50 Eating disorders

Excludes1: *anorexia NOS (R63.0)*
feeding difficulties (R63.3)
polyphagia (R63.2)
Excludes2: *feeding disorder in infancy or childhood (F98.2-)*

+ **F50.0 Anorexia nervosa**
Excludes1: *loss of appetite (R63.0)*
psychogenic loss of appetite (F50.8)

CC **F50.00 Anorexia nervosa, unspecified**
CC Exclusion see Appendix A PDX collection 0556

CC **F50.01 Anorexia nervosa, restricting type**
CC Exclusion see Appendix A PDX collection 0556

CC **F50.02 Anorexia nervosa, binge eating/purging type**
Excludes1: *bulimia nervosa (F50.2)*
CC Exclusion see Appendix A PDX collection 0556

CC **F50.2 Bulimia nervosa**
Bulimia NOS
Hyperorexia nervosa
Excludes1: *anorexia nervosa, binge eating/purging type (F50.02)*
CC Exclusion see Appendix A PDX collection 0557

F50.8 Other eating disorders
Pica in adults
Psychogenic loss of appetite
Excludes2: *pica of infancy and childhood (F98.3)*

F50.9 Eating disorder, unspecified
Atypical anorexia nervosa
Atypical bulimia nervosa

F51 Sleep disorders not due to a substance or known physiological condition

Excludes2: *organic sleep disorders (G47.-)*

+ **F51.0 Insomnia not due to a substance or known physiological condition**
Excludes2: *alcohol related insomnia (F10.182, F10.282, F10.982)*
drug-related insomnia (F11.182, F11.282, F11.982, F13.182, F13.282, F13.982, F14.182, F14.282, F14.982, F15.182, F15.282, F15.982, F19.182, F19.282, F19.982)
insomnia NOS (G47.0-)
insomnia due to known physiological condition (G47.0-)
organic insomnia (G47.0-)
sleep deprivation (Z72.820)

F51.01 Primary insomnia
Idiopathic insomnia

F51.02 Adjustment insomnia

F51.03 Paradoxical insomnia

F51.04 Psychophysiologic insomnia
F51.05 Insomnia due to other mental disorder
Code also associated mental disorder
F51.09 Other insomnia not due to a substance or known physiological condition
+ **F51.1 Hypersomnia not due to a substance or known physiological condition**
Excludes2: *alcohol related hypersomnia (F10.182, F10.282, F10.982)*
drug-related hypersomnia (F11.182, F11.282, F11.982, F13.182, F13.282, F13.982, F14.182, F14.282, F14.982, F15.182, F15.282, F15.982, F19.182, F19.282, F19.982)
hypersomnia NOS (G47.10)
hypersomnia due to known physiological condition (G47.10)
idiopathic hypersomnia (G47.11, G47.12)
narcolepsy (G47.4-)
F51.11 Primary hypersomnia
F51.12 Insufficient sleep syndrome
Excludes1: *sleep deprivation (Z72.820)*
F51.13 Hypersomnia due to other mental disorder
Code also associated mental disorder
F51.19 Other hypersomnia not due to a substance or known physiological condition
F51.3 Sleepwalking [somnambulism]
F51.4 Sleep terrors [night terrors]
F51.5 Nightmare disorder
Dream anxiety disorder
F51.8 Other sleep disorders not due to a substance or known physiological condition
F51.9 Sleep disorder not due to a substance or known physiological condition, unspecified
Emotional sleep disorder NOS

F52 Sexual dysfunction not due to a substance or known physiological condition
Excludes2: *Dhat syndrome (F48.8)*
F52.0 Hypoactive sexual desire disorder
Anhedonia (sexual)
Lack or loss of sexual desire
Excludes1: *decreased libido (R68.82)*
F52.1 Sexual aversion disorder
Sexual aversion and lack of sexual enjoyment
+ **F52.2 Sexual arousal disorders**
Failure of genital response
♂ **F52.21 Male erectile disorder**
Psychogenic impotence
Excludes1: *impotence of organic origin (N52.-)*
impotence NOS (N52.-)
♀ **F52.22 Female sexual arousal disorder**
Frigidity
+ **F52.3 Orgasmic disorder**
Inhibited orgasm
Psychogenic anorgasmy
♀ **F52.31 Female orgasmic disorder**
♂ **F52.32 Male orgasmic disorder**
♂ **F52.4 Premature ejaculation**
♀ **F52.5 Vaginismus not due to a substance or known physiological condition**
Psychogenic vaginismus
Excludes2: *vaginismus (due to a known physiological condition) (N94.2)*
♀ **F52.6 Dyspareunia not due to a substance or known physiological condition**
Psychogenic dyspareunia
Excludes2: *dyspareunia (due to a known physiological condition) (N94.1)*
F52.8 Other sexual dysfunction not due to a substance or known physiological condition
Excessive sexual drive
Nymphomania
Satyriasis
F52.9 Unspecified sexual dysfunction not due to a substance or known physiological condition
Sexual dysfunction NOS

♀ **F53 Puerperal psychosis**
Postpartum depression
Excludes1: *mood disorders with psychotic features (F30.2, F31.2, F3 F31.64, F32.3, F33.3)*
postpartum dysphoria (O90.6)
psychosis in schizophrenia, schizotypal, delusional, and other psychotic disorders (F20-F29)
Valid 3-character code, no further characters required

F54 Psychological and behavioral factors associated with disorders or diseases classified elsewhere
Psychological factors affecting physical conditions
Code first the associated physical disorder, such as:
asthma (J45.-)
dermatitis (L23-L25)
gastric ulcer (K25.-)
mucous colitis (K58.-)
ulcerative colitis (K51.-)
urticaria (L50.-)
Excludes2: *tension-type headache (G44.2)*
Valid 3-character code, no further characters required

F55 Abuse of non-psychoactive substances
Excludes2: *abuse of psychoactive substances (F10-F19)*
F55.0 Abuse of antacids
F55.1 Abuse of herbal or folk remedies
F55.2 Abuse of laxatives
F55.3 Abuse of steroids or hormones
F55.4 Abuse of vitamins
F55.8 Abuse of other non-psychoactive substances

F59 Unspecified behavioral syndromes associated with physiological disturbances and physical factors
Psychogenic physiological dysfunction NOS
Valid 3-character code, no further characters required

Disorders of adult personality and behavior (F60-F69)

F60 Specific personality disorders
F60.0 Paranoid personality disorder
Expansive paranoid personality (disorder)
Fanatic personality (disorder)
Querulant personality (disorder)
Paranoid personality (disorder)
Sensitive paranoid personality (disorder)
Excludes2: *paranoia (F22)*
paranoia querulans (F22)
paranoid psychosis (F22)
paranoid schizophrenia (F20.0)
paranoid state (F22)
F60.1 Schizoid personality disorder
Excludes2: *Asperger's syndrome (F84.5)*
delusional disorder (F22)
schizoid disorder of childhood (F84.5)
schizophrenia (F20.-)
schizotypal disorder (F21)
F60.2 Antisocial personality disorder
Amoral personality (disorder)
Asocial personality (disorder)
Dissocial personality disorder
Psychopathic personality (disorder)
Sociopathic personality (disorder)
Excludes1: *conduct disorders (F91.-)*
Excludes2: *borderline personality disorder (F60.3)*
F60.3 Borderline personality disorder
Aggressive personality (disorder)
Emotionally unstable personality disorder
Explosive personality (disorder)
Excludes2: *antisocial personality disorder (F60.2)*
F60.4 Histrionic personality disorder
Hysterical personality (disorder)
Psychoinfantile personality (disorder)
F60.5 Obsessive-compulsive personality disorder
Anankastic personality (disorder)
Compulsive personality (disorder)
Obsessional personality (disorder)
Excludes2: *obsessive-compulsive disorder (F42)*
F60.6 Avoidant personality disorder
Anxious personality disorder
F60.7 Dependent personality disorder
Asthenic personality (disorder)
Inadequate personality (disorder)
Passive personality (disorder)

+ **F60.8 Other specific personality disorders**
  - **F60.81 Narcissistic personality disorder**
  - **F60.89 Other specific personality disorders**
    - Eccentric personality disorder
    - 'Haltlose' type personality disorder
    - Immature personality disorder
    - Passive-aggressive personality disorder
    - Psychoneurotic personality disorder
    - Self-defeating personality disorder

F60.9 Personality disorder, unspecified
- Character disorder NOS
- Character neurosis NOS
- Pathological personality NOS

F63 Impulse disorders

Excludes2: *habitual excessive use of alcohol or psychoactive substances (F10-F19)*
impulse disorders involving sexual behavior (F65.-)

F63.0 Pathological gambling
- Compulsive gambling
- **Excludes1:** *gambling and betting NOS (Z72.6)*
- **Excludes2:** *excessive gambling by manic patients (F30, F31)*
  gambling in antisocial personality disorder (F60.2)

F63.1 Pyromania
- Pathological fire-setting
- **Excludes2:** *fire-setting (by) (in):*
  adult with antisocial personality disorder (F60.2)
  alcohol or psychoactive substance intoxication (F10-F19)
  conduct disorders (F91.-)
  mental disorders due to known physiological condition (F01-F09)
  schizophrenia (F20.-)

F63.2 Kleptomania
- Pathological stealing
- **Excludes1:** *shoplifting as the reason for observation for suspected mental disorder (Z03.8)*
- **Excludes2:** *depressive disorder with stealing (F31-F33)*
  stealing due to underlying mental condition-code to mental condition
  stealing in mental disorders due to known physiological condition (F01-F09)

F63.3 Trichotillomania
- Hair plucking
- **Excludes2:** *other stereotyped movement disorder(F98.4)*

+ **F63.8 Other impulse disorders**
  - **F63.81 Intermittent explosive disorder**
  - **F63.89 Other impulse disorders**

F63.9 Impulse disorder, unspecified
- Impulse control disorder NOS

F64 Gender identity disorders

F64.1 Gender identity disorder in adolescence and adulthood
- Dual role transvestism
- Transsexualism
- Use additional code to identify sex reassignment status (Z87.890)
- **Excludes1:** *gender identity disorder in childhood (F64.2)*
- **Excludes2:** *fetishistic transvestism (F65.1)*

• **F64.2 Gender identity disorder of childhood**
- **Excludes1:** *gender identity disorder in adolescence and adulthood (F64.1)*
- **Excludes2:** *sexual maturation disorder (F66)*

F64.8 Other gender identity disorders

F64.9 Gender identity disorder, unspecified
- Gender-role disorder NOS

F65 Paraphilias

F65.0 Fetishism

F65.1 Transvestic fetishism
- Fetishistic transvestism

F65.2 Exhibitionism

F65.3 Voyeurism

F65.4 Pedophilia

+ **F65.5 Sadomasochism**
  - **F65.50 Sadomasochism, unspecified**
  - **F65.51 Sexual masochism**
  - **F65.52 Sexual sadism**

+ **F65.8 Other paraphilias**
  - **F65.81 Frotteurism**
  - **F65.89 Other paraphilias**
    - Necrophilia

F65.9 Paraphilia, unspecified
- Sexual deviation NOS

F66 Other sexual disorders
- Sexual maturation disorder
- Sexual relationship disorder
- Valid 3-character code, no further characters required

F68 Other disorders of adult personality and behavior

+ **F68.1 Factitious disorder**
  - Compensation neurosis
  - Elaboration of physical symptoms for psychological reasons
  - Hospital hopper syndrome
  - Münchausen's syndrome
  - Peregrinating patient
  - **Excludes2:** *factitial dermatitis (L98.1)*
    person feigning illness (with obvious motivation) (Z76.5)
  - CC **F68.10 Factitious disorder, unspecified**
  - **F68.11 Factitious disorder with predominantly psychological signs and symptoms**
    - CC Exclusion see Appendix A PDX collection 0550
  - CC **F68.12 Factitious disorder with predominantly physical signs and symptoms**
    - CC Exclusion see Appendix A PDX collection 0551
  - **F68.13 Factitious disorder with combined psychological and physical signs and symptoms**

F68.8 Other specified disorders of adult personality and behavior

• **F69 Unspecified disorder of adult personality and behavior**
- Valid 3-character code, no further characters required

Intellectual Disabilities (F70-F79)

Code first any associated physical or developmental disorders

Excludes1: *borderline intellectual functioning, IQ above 70 to 84 (R41.83)*

F70 Mild intellectual disabilities
- IQ level 50-55 to approximately 70
- Mild mental subnormality
- Valid 3-character code, no further characters required

F71 Moderate intellectual disabilities
- IQ level 35-40 to 50-55
- Moderate mental subnormality
- Valid 3-character code, no further characters required

CC **F72 Severe intellectual disabilities**
- IQ 20-25 to 35-40
- Severe mental subnormality
- CC Exclusion see Appendix A PDX collection 0558
- Valid 3-character code, no further characters required

CC **F73 Profound intellectual disabilities**
- IQ level below 20-25
- Profound mental subnormality
- CC Exclusion see Appendix A PDX collection 0558
- Valid 3-character code, no further characters required

F78 Other intellectual disabilities
- Valid 3-character code, no further characters required

F79 Unspecified intellectual disabilities
- Mental deficiency NOS
- Mental subnormality NOS
- Valid 3-character code, no further characters required

Pervasive and specific developmental disorders (F80-F89)

F80 Specific developmental disorders of speech and language

F80.0 Phonological disorder
- Dyslalia
- Functional speech articulation disorder
- Lalling
- Lisping
- Phonological developmental disorder
- Speech articulation developmental disorder
- **Excludes1:** *speech articulation impairment due to aphasia NOS (R47.01)*
  speech articulation impairment due to apraxia (R48.2)
- **Excludes2:** *speech articulation impairment due to hearing loss (F80.4)*
  speech articulation impairment due to intellectual disabilities (F70-F79)
  speech articulation impairment with expressive language developmental disorder (F80.1)
  speech articulation impairment with mixed receptive expressive language developmental disorder (F80.2)

F80.1 Expressive language disorder
Developmental dysphasia or aphasia, expressive type
Excludes1: *mixed receptive-expressive language disorder (F80.2)*
dysphasia and aphasia NOS (R47.-)
Excludes2: *acquired aphasia with epilepsy [Landau-Kleffner] (G40.80-)*
selective mutism (F94.0)
intellectual disabilities (F70-F79)
pervasive developmental disorders (F84.-)

F80.2 Mixed receptive-expressive language disorder
Developmental dysphasia or aphasia, receptive type
Developmental Wernicke's aphasia
Excludes1: *central auditory processing disorder (H93.25)*
dysphasia or aphasia NOS (R47.-)
expressive language disorder (F80.1)
expressive type dysphasia or aphasia (F80.1)
word deafness (H93.25)
Excludes2: *acquired aphasia with epilepsy [Landau-Kleffner] (G40.80-)*
pervasive developmental disorders (F84.-)
selective mutism (F94.0)
intellectual disabilities (F70-F79)

F80.4 Speech and language development delay due to hearing loss
Code also type of hearing loss (H90.-, H91.-)

\+ **F80.8 Other developmental disorders of speech and language**

F80.81 Childhood onset fluency disorder
Cluttering NOS
Stuttering NOS
Excludes1: *adult onset fluency disorder (F98.5)*
fluency disorder in conditions classified elsewhere (R47.82)
fluency disorder (stuttering) following cerebrovascular disease (I69. with final characters -23)

F80.89 Other developmental disorders of speech and language

F80.9 Developmental disorder of speech and language, unspecified
Communication disorder NOS
Language disorder NOS

F81 Specific developmental disorders of scholastic skills

F81.0 Specific reading disorder
'Backward reading'
Developmental dyslexia
Specific reading retardation
Excludes1: *alexia NOS (R48.0)*
dyslexia NOS (R48.0)

F81.2 Mathematics disorder
Developmental acalculia
Developmental arithmetical disorder
Developmental Gerstmann's syndrome
Excludes1: *acalculia NOS (R48.8)*
Excludes2: *arithmetical difficulties associated with a reading disorder (F81.0)*
arithmetical difficulties associated with a spelling disorder (F81.81)
arithmetical difficulties due to inadequate teaching (Z55.8)

\+ **F81.8 Other developmental disorders of scholastic skills**

F81.81 Disorder of written expression
Specific spelling disorder

F81.89 Other developmental disorders of scholastic skills

F81.9 Developmental disorder of scholastic skills, unspecified
Knowledge acquisition disability NOS
Learning disability NOS
Learning disorder NOS

F82 Specific developmental disorder of motor function
Clumsy child syndrome
Developmental coordination disorder
Developmental dyspraxia
Excludes1: *abnormalities of gait and mobility (R26.-)*
lack of coordination (R27.-)
Excludes2: *lack of coordination secondary to intellectual disabilities (F70-F79)*
Valid 3-character code, no further characters required

F84 Pervasive developmental disorders
Use additional code to identify any associated medical condition and intellectual disabilities.

CC **F84.0 Autistic disorder**
Infantile autism
Infantile psychosis
Kanner's syndrome
Excludes1: *Asperger's syndrome (F84.5)*
CC Exclusion see Appendix A PDX collection 0551

CC **F84.2 Rett's syndrome**
Excludes1: *Asperger's syndrome (F84.5)*
Autistic disorder (F84.0)
Other childhood disintegrative disorder (F84.3)
CC Exclusion see Appendix A PDX collection 0537

• CC **F84.3 Other childhood disintegrative disorder**
Dementia infantilis
Disintegrative psychosis
Heller's syndrome
Symbiotic psychosis
Use additional code to identify any associated neurological condition.
Excludes1: *Asperger's syndrome (F84.5)*
Autistic disorder (F84.0)
Rett's syndrome (F84.2)
CC Exclusion see Appendix A PDX collection 0551

CC **F84.5 Asperger's syndrome**
Asperger's disorder
Autistic psychopathy
Schizoid disorder of childhood
CC Exclusion see Appendix A PDX collection 0551

CC **F84.8 Other pervasive developmental disorders**
Overactive disorder associated with intellectual disabilities an stereotyped movements
CC Exclusion see Appendix A PDX collection 0551

CC **F84.9 Pervasive developmental disorder, unspecified**
Atypical autism
CC Exclusion see Appendix A PDX collection 0551

F88 Other disorders of psychological development
Developmental agnosia
Valid 3-character code, no further characters required

F89 Unspecified disorder of psychological development
Developmental disorder NOS
Valid 3-character code, no further characters required

Behavioral and emotional disorders with onset usually occurring in childhood and adolescence (F90-F98)

NOTE Codes within categories F90-F98 may be used regardless of the age of a patient. These disorders generally have onset within the childhood or adolescent years, but may continue throughout life or not be diagnosed until adulthood

F90 Attention-deficit hyperactivity disorders
Includes: attention deficit disorder with hyperactivity
attention deficit syndrome with hyperactivity
Excludes2: *anxiety disorders (F40.-, F41.-)*
mood [affective] disorders (F30-F39)
pervasive developmental disorders (F84.-)
schizophrenia (F20.-)

F90.0 Attention-deficit hyperactivity disorder, predominantly inattentive type

F90.1 Attention-deficit hyperactivity disorder, predominantly hyperactive type

F90.2 Attention-deficit hyperactivity disorder, combined type

F90.8 Attention-deficit hyperactivity disorder, other type

F90.9 Attention-deficit hyperactivity disorder, unspecified type
Attention-deficit hyperactivity disorder of childhood or adolescence NOS
Attention-deficit hyperactivity disorder NOS

F91 Conduct disorders
Excludes1: *antisocial behavior (Z72.81-)*
antisocial personality disorder (F60.2)
Excludes2: *conduct problems associated with attention-deficit hyperactivity disorder (F90.-)*
mood [affective] disorders (F30-F39)
pervasive developmental disorders (F84.-)
schizophrenia (F20.-)

F91.0 Conduct disorder confined to family context

F91.1 Conduct disorder, childhood-onset type
Unsocialized conduct disorder
Conduct disorder, solitary aggressive type
Unsocialized aggressive disorder

F91.2 Conduct disorder, adolescent-onset type
Socialized conduct disorder
Conduct disorder, group type

F91.3 Oppositional defiant disorder

F91.8 Other conduct disorders

F91.9 Conduct disorder, unspecified
Behavioral disorder NOS
Conduct disorder NOS
Disruptive behavior disorder NOS

F93 Emotional disorders with onset specific to childhood

• **F93.0 Separation anxiety disorder of childhood**
Excludes2: *mood [affective] disorders (F30-F39)*
nonpsychotic mental disorders (F40-F48)
phobic anxiety disorder of childhood (F40.8)
social phobia (F40.1)

• **F93.8 Other childhood emotional disorders**
Identity disorder
Excludes2: *gender identity disorder of childhood (F64.2)*

• **F93.9 Childhood emotional disorder, unspecified**

F94 Disorders of social functioning with onset specific to childhood and adolescence

F94.0 Selective mutism
Elective mutism
Excludes2: *pervasive developmental disorders (F84.-)*
schizophrenia (F20.-)
specific developmental disorders of speech and language (F80.-)
transient mutism as part of separation anxiety in young children (F93.0)

• **F94.1 Reactive attachment disorder of childhood**
Use additional code to identify any associated failure to thrive or growth retardation
Excludes1: *disinhibited attachment disorder of childhood (F94.2)*
normal variation in pattern of selective attachment
Excludes2: *Asperger's syndrome (F84.5)*
maltreatment syndromes (T74.-)
sexual or physical abuse in childhood, resulting in psychosocial problems (Z62.81-)

• **F94.2 Disinhibited attachment disorder of childhood**
Affectionless psychopathy
Institutional syndrome
Excludes1: *reactive attachment disorder of childhood (F94.1)*
Excludes2: *Asperger's syndrome (F84.5)*
attention-deficit hyperactivity disorders (F90.-)
hospitalism in children (F43.2-)

• **F94.8 Other childhood disorders of social functioning**

• **F94.9 Childhood disorder of social functioning, unspecified**

F95 Tic disorder

F95.0 Transient tic disorder

F95.1 Chronic motor or vocal tic disorder

F95.2 Tourette's disorder
Combined vocal and multiple motor tic disorder [de la Tourette]
Tourette's syndrome

F95.8 Other tic disorders

F95.9 Tic disorder, unspecified
Tic NOS

F98 Other behavioral and emotional disorders with onset usually occurring in childhood and adolescence
Excludes2: *breath-holding spells (R06.89)*
gender identity disorder of childhood (F64.2)
Kleine-Levin syndrome (G47.13)
obsessive-compulsive disorder (F42)
sleep disorders not due to a substance or known physiological condition (F51.-)

F98.0 Enuresis not due to a substance or known physiological condition
Enuresis (primary) (secondary) of nonorganic origin
Functional enuresis
Psychogenic enuresis
Urinary incontinence of nonorganic origin
Excludes1: *enuresis NOS (R32)*

F98.1 Encopresis not due to a substance or known physiological condition
Functional encopresis
Incontinence of feces of nonorganic origin
Psychogenic encopresis
Use additional code to identify the cause of any coexisting constipation.
Excludes1: *encopresis NOS (R15.-)*

\+ **F98.2 Other feeding disorders of infancy and childhood**
Excludes1: *feeding difficulties (R63.3)*
Excludes2: *anorexia nervosa and other eating disorders (F50.-)*
feeding problems of newborn (P92.-)
pica of infancy or childhood (F98.3)

• **F98.21 Rumination disorder of infancy**

• **F98.29 Other feeding disorders of infancy and early childhood**

• **F98.3 Pica of infancy and childhood**

F98.4 Stereotyped movement disorders
Stereotype/habit disorder
Excludes1: *abnormal involuntary movements (R25.-)*
Excludes2: *compulsions in obsessive-compulsive disorder (F42)*
hair plucking (F63.3)
movement disorders of organic origin (G20-G25)
8nail-biting (F98.8)
nose-picking (F98.8)
stereotypies that are part of a broader psychiatric condition (F01-F95)
thumb-sucking (F98.8)
tic disorders (F95.-)
trichotillomania (F63.3)

F98.5 Adult onset fluency disorder
Excludes1: *childhood onset fluency disorder (F80.81)*
dysphasia (R47.02)
fluency disorder in conditions classified elsewhere (R47.82)
fluency disorder (stuttering) following cerebrovascular disease (I69. with final characters -23)
tic disorders (F95.-)

• **F98.8 Other specified behavioral and emotional disorders with onset usually occurring in childhood and adolescence**
Excessive masturbation
Nail-biting
Nose-picking
Thumb-sucking

• **F98.9 Unspecified behavioral and emotional disorders with onset usually occurring in childhood and adolescence**

Unspecified mental disorder (F99)

F99 Mental disorder, not otherwise specified
Mental illness NOS
Excludes1: *unspecified mental disorder due to known physiological condition (F09)*
Valid 3-character code, no further characters required

Chapter 6: Diseases of the Nervous System (G00-G99)

Excludes2: *certain conditions originating in the perinatal period (P04-P96)*
certain infectious and parasitic diseases (A00-B99)
complications of pregnancy, childbirth and the puerperium (O00-O9A)
congenital malformations, deformations, and chromosomal abnormalities (Q00-Q99)
endocrine, nutritional and metabolic diseases (E00-E88)
injury, poisoning and certain other consequences of external causes (S00-T88)
neoplasms (C00-D49)
symptoms, signs and abnormal clinical and laboratory findings, not elsewhere classified (R00-R94)

This chapter contains the following category blocks:

G00-G09	Inflammatory diseases of the central nervous system
G10-G14	Systemic atrophies primarily affecting the central nervous system
G20-G26	Extrapyramidal and movement disorders
G30-G32	Other degenerative diseases of the nervous system
G35-G37	Demyelinating diseases of the central nervous system
G40-G47	Episodic and paroxysmal disorders
G50-G59	Nerve, nerve root and plexus disorders
G60-G65	Polyneuropathies and other disorders of the peripheral nervous system
G70-G73	Diseases of myoneural junction and muscle
G80-G83	Cerebral palsy and other paralytic syndromes
G89-G99	Other disorders of the nervous system

C. Chapter-Specific Coding Guidelines

In addition to general coding guidelines, there are guidelines for specific diagnoses and/or conditions in the classification. Unless otherwise indicated, these guidelines apply to all health care settings. Please refer to Section II for guidelines on the selection of principal diagnosis.

6. Chapter 6: Diseases of the Nervous System (G00-G99)

a. Dominant/nondominant side

Codes from category G81, Hemiplegia and hemiparesis, and subcategories, G83.1, Monoplegia of lower limb, G83.2, Monoplegia of upper limb, and G83.3, Monoplegia, unspecified, identify whether the dominant or nondominant side is affected. Should the affected side be documented, but not specified as dominant or nondominant, and the classification system does not indicate a default, code selection is as follows:

- For ambidextrous patients, the default should be dominant.
- If the left side is affected, the default is non-dominant.
- If the right side is affected, the default is dominant.

b. Pain-Category G89

1) General coding information

Codes in category G89, Pain, not elsewhere classified, may be used in conjunction with codes from other categories and chapters to provide more detail about acute or chronic pain and neoplasm-related pain, unless otherwise indicated below.

If the pain is not specified as acute or chronic, post- thoracotomy, post procedural, or neoplasm-related, do not assign codes from category G89.

A code from category G89 should not be assigned if the underlying (definitive) diagnosis is known, unless the reason for the encounter is pain control/management and not management of the underlying condition.

When an admission or encounter is for a procedure aimed at treating the underlying condition (e.g., spinal fusion, kyphoplasty), a code for the underlying condition (e.g., vertebral fracture, spinal stenosis) should be assigned as the principal diagnosis. No code from category G89 should be assigned.

(a) Category G89 Codes as Principal or First-Listed Diagnosis

Category G89 codes are acceptable as principal diagnosis or the first-listed code:

- When pain control or pain management is the reason for the admission/encounter (e.g., a patient with displaced intervertebral disc, nerve impingement and severe back pain presents for injection of steroid into the spinal canal). The underlying cause of the pain should be reported as an additional diagnosis, if known.
- When a patient is admitted for the insertion of a neurostimulator for pain control, assign the appropriate pain code as the principal or first-listed diagnosis. When an admission or encounter is for a procedure aimed at treating the underlying condition and a neurostimulator is inserted for pain control during the same admission/encounter, a code for the underlying condition should be assigned as the principal diagnosis and the appropriate pain code should be assigned as a secondary diagnosis.

(b) Use of Category G89 Codes in Conjunction with Site Specific Codes

(i) Assigning Category G89 and Site-Specific Pain Codes

Codes from category G89 may be used in conjunction with c that identify the site of pain (including codes from chapter 18) category G89 code provides additional information. For examp the code describes the site of the pain, but does not fully des whether the pain is acute or chronic, then both codes shoul assigned.

(ii) Sequencing of Category G89 Codes with Site- Specific Pain C

The sequencing of category G89 codes with site-specific pain c (including chapter 18 codes), is dependent on the circumstanc the encounter/admission as follows:

- If the encounter is for pain control or pain management, a the code from category G89 followed by the code identi the specific site of pain (e.g., encounter for pain manageme acute neck pain from trauma is assigned code G89.11, Acute due to trauma, followed by code M54.2, Cervicalgia, to ide the site of pain).
- If the encounter is for any other reason except pain contr pain management, and a related definitive diagnosis has not established (confirmed) by the provider, assign the code fo specific site of pain first, followed by the appropriate code category G89.

2) Pain due to devices, implants and grafts

See Section I.C.19. Pain due to medical devices

3) Postoperative Pain

The provider's documentation should be used to guide the codin postoperative pain, as well *as Section III. Reporting Additional Diag and Section IV. Diagnostic Coding* and *Reporting in the Outpatient Sett*

The default for post-thoracotomy and other postoperative pain not spe as acute or chronic is the code for the acute form.

Routine or expected postoperative pain immediately after surgery shoul be coded.

(a) Postoperative pain not associated with specific postoper complication

Postoperative pain not associated with a specific postope complication is assigned to the appropriate postoperative pain co category G89.

(b) Postoperative pain associated with specific postoperative complic

Postoperative pain associated with a specific postoperative complic (such as painful wire sutures) is assigned to the appropriate co found in Chapter 19, Injury, poisoning, and certain other consequ of external causes. If appropriate, use additional code(s) from cate G89 to identify acute or chronic pain (G89.18 or G89.28).

4) Chronic pain

Chronic pain is classified to subcategory G89.2. There is no time defining when pain becomes chronic pain. The provider's document should be used to guide use of these codes.

5) Neoplasm Related Pain

Code G89.3 is assigned to pain documented as being related, assoc or due to cancer, primary or secondary malignancy, or tumor. This co assigned regardless of whether the pain is acute or chronic.

This code may be assigned as the principal or first- listed code whe stated reason for the admission/encounter is documented as pain control management. The underlying neoplasm should be reported as an addit diagnosis.

When the reason for the admission/encounter is management of the neop and the pain associated with the neoplasm is also documented, code C may be assigned as an additional diagnosis. It is not necessary to assig additional code for the site of the pain.

See Section I.C.2 for instructions on the sequencing of neoplasms fo other stated reasons for the admission/encounter (except for pain co pain management).

6) Chronic pain syndrome

Central pain syndrome (G89.0) and chronic pain syndrome (G89.4 different than the term "chronic pain," and therefore codes should on used when the provider has specifically documented this condition.

See Section I.C.5. Pain disorders related to psychological factors

[In]flammatory diseases of the central nervous system (G00-G09)

G00 Bacterial meningitis, not elsewhere classified

Includes: bacterial arachnoiditis
bacterial leptomeningitis
bacterial meningitis
bacterial pachymeningitis

Excludes1: *bacterial:*
meningoencephalitis (G04.2)
meningomyelitis (G04.2)

MCC **G00.0 Hemophilus meningitis**
Meningitis due to Hemophilus influenzae
MCC Exclusion see Appendix A PDX collection 0207

MCC **G00.1 Pneumococcal meningitis**
MCC Exclusion see Appendix A PDX collection 0207

MCC **G00.2 Streptococcal meningitis**
Use additional code to further identify organism (B95.0-B95.5)
MCC Exclusion see Appendix A PDX collection 0207

MCC **G00.3 Staphylococcal meningitis**
Use additional code to further identify organism (B95.61-B95.8)
MCC Exclusion see Appendix A PDX collection 0207

MCC **G00.8 Other bacterial meningitis**
Meningitis due to Escherichia coli
Meningitis due to Friedländer's bacillus
Meningitis due to Klebsiella
Use additional code to further identify organism (B96.-)
MCC Exclusion see Appendix A PDX collection 0207

MCC **G00.9 Bacterial meningitis, unspecified**
Meningitis due to gram-negative bacteria, unspecified
Purulent meningitis NOS
Pyogenic meningitis NOS
Suppurative meningitis NOS
MCC Exclusion see Appendix A PDX collection 0207

G01 Meningitis in bacterial diseases classified elsewhere

Code first underlying disease

Excludes1: *meningitis (in):*
gonococcal (A54.81)
leptospirosis (A27.81)
listeriosis (A32.11)
Lyme disease (A69.21)
meningococcal (A39.0)
neurosyphilis (A52.13)
tuberculosis (A17.0)
meningoencephalitis and meningomyelitis in bacterial diseases classified elsewhere (G05)

MCC Exclusion see Appendix A PDX collection 0207
Valid 3-character code, no further characters required

G02 Meningitis in other infectious and parasitic diseases classified elsewhere

Code first underlying disease, such as:
African trypanosomiasis (B56.-)
poliovirus infection (A80.-)

Excludes1: *candidal meningitis (B37.5)*
coccidioidomycosis meningitis (B38.4)
cryptococcal meningitis (B45.1)
herpesviral [herpes simplex] meningitis (B00.3)
infectious mononucleosis complicated by meningitis (B27.- with fourth character 2)
measles complicated by meningitis (B05.1)
meningoencephalitis and meningomyelitis in other infectious and parasitic diseases classified elsewhere (G05)
mumps meningitis (B26.1)
rubella meningitis (B06.02)
varicella [chickenpox] meningitis (B01.0)
zoster meningitis (B02.1)

MCC Exclusion see Appendix A PDX collection 0559
Valid 3-character code, no further characters required

G03 Meningitis due to other and unspecified causes

Includes: arachnoiditis NOS
leptomeningitis NOS
meningitis NOS
pachymeningitis NOS

Excludes1: *meningoencephalitis (G04.-)*
meningomyelitis (G04.-)

MCC **G03.0 Nonpyogenic meningitis**
Aseptic meningitis
Nonbacterial meningitis
MCC Exclusion see Appendix A PDX collection 0207

CC **G03.1 Chronic meningitis**
CC Exclusion see Appendix A PDX collection 0207

CC **G03.2 Benign recurrent meningitis [Mollaret]**
CC Exclusion see Appendix A PDX collection 0140

MCC **G03.8 Meningitis due to other specified causes**
MCC Exclusion see Appendix A PDX collection 0207

MCC **G03.9 Meningitis, unspecified**
Arachnoiditis (spinal) NOS
MCC Exclusion see Appendix A PDX collection 0207

G04 Encephalitis, myelitis and encephalomyelitis

Includes: acute ascending myelitis
meningoencephalitis
meningomyelitis

Excludes1: *encephalopathy NOS (G93.40)*

Excludes2: *acute transverse myelitis (G37.3-)*
alcoholic encephalopathy (G31.2)
benign myalgic encephalomyelitis (G93.3)
multiple sclerosis (G35)
subacute necrotizing myelitis (G37.4)
toxic encephalitis (G92)
toxic encephalopathy (G92)

\+ **G04.0 Acute disseminated encephalitis and encephalomyelitis (ADEM)**

Excludes1: *acute necrotizing hemorrhagic encephalopathy (G04.3-)*
other noninfectious acute disseminated encephalomyelitis (noninfectious ADEM) (G04.81)

MCC **G04.00 Acute disseminated encephalitis and encephalomyelitis, unspecified**
MCC Exclusion see Appendix A PDX collection 0560

MCC **G04.01 Postinfectious acute disseminated encephalitis and encephalomyelitis (postinfectious ADEM)**
Excludes1: *post chickenpox encephalitis (B01.1)*
post measles encephalitis (B05.0)
post measles myelitis (B05.1)
MCC Exclusion see Appendix A PDX collection 0560

MCC **G04.02 Postimmunization acute disseminated encephalitis, myelitis and encephalomyelitis**
Encephalitis, post immunization
Encephalomyelitis, post immunization
Use additional code to identify the vaccine (T50.A-, T50.B-, T50.Z-)
No MCC Exclusions

CC **G04.1 Tropical spastic paraplegia**
CC Exclusion see Appendix A PDX collection 0561

MCC **G04.2 Bacterial meningoencephalitis and meningomyelitis, not elsewhere classified**
MCC Exclusion see Appendix A PDX collection 0207

\+ **G04.3 Acute necrotizing hemorrhagic encephalopathy**

Excludes1: *acute disseminated encephalitis and encephalomyelitis (G04.0-)*

MCC **G04.30 Acute necrotizing hemorrhagic encephalopathy, unspecified**
No MCC Exclusions

MCC **G04.31 Postinfectious acute necrotizing hemorrhagic encephalopathy**
MCC Exclusion see Appendix A PDX collection 0560

MCC **G04.32 Postimmunization acute necrotizing hemorrhagic encephalopathy**
Use additional code to identify the vaccine (T50.A-, T50.B-, T50.Z-)
No MCC Exclusions

MCC **G04.39 Other acute necrotizing hemorrhagic encephalopathy**
Code also underlying etiology, if applicable
No MCC Exclusions

\+ **G04.8 Other encephalitis, myelitis and encephalomyelitis**
Code also any associated seizure (G40.-, R56.9)

MCC **G04.81 Other encephalitis and encephalomyelitis**
Noninfectious acute disseminated encephalomyelitis (noninfectious ADEM)
MCC Exclusion see Appendix A PDX collection 0560

MCC **G04.89 Other myelitis**
MCC Exclusion see Appendix A PDX collection 0560

\+ **G04.9 Encephalitis, myelitis and encephalomyelitis, unspecified**

MCC **G04.90 Encephalitis and encephalomyelitis, unspecified**
Ventriculitis (cerebral) NOS
MCC Exclusion see Appendix A PDX collection 0562

MCC **G04.91 Myelitis, unspecified**
MCC Exclusion see Appendix A PDX collection 0562

G05 Encephalitis, myelitis and encephalomyelitis in diseases classified elsewhere

Code first underlying disease, such as:
human immunodeficiency virus [HIV] disease (B20)
poliovirus (A80.-)
suppurative otitis media (H66.01-H66.4)
trichinellosis (B75)

Excludes1: *adenoviral encephalitis, myelitis and encephalomyelitis (A85.1)*
congenital toxoplasmosis encephalitis, myelitis and encephalomyelitis (P37.1)
cytomegaloviral encephalitis, myelitis and encephalomyelitis (B25.8)
encephalitis, myelitis and encephalomyelitis (in) measles (B05.0)
encephalitis, myelitis and encephalomyelitis (in) systemic lupus erythematosus (M32.19)
enteroviral encephalitis, myelitis and encephalomyelitis (A85.0)
eosinophilic meningoencephalitis (B83.2)
herpesviral [herpes simplex] encephalitis, myelitis and encephalomyelitis (B00.4)
listerial encephalitis, myelitis and encephalomyelitis (A32.12)
meningococcal encephalitis, myelitis and encephalomyelitis (A39.81)
mumps encephalitis, myelitis and encephalomyelitis (B26.2)
postchickenpox encephalitis, myelitis and encephalomyelitis (B01.1-)
rubella encephalitis, myelitis and encephalomyelitis (B06.01)
toxoplasmosis encephalitis, myelitis and encephalomyelitis (B58.2)
zoster encephalitis, myelitis and encephalomyelitis (B02.0)

MCC **G05.3 Encephalitis and encephalomyelitis in diseases classified elsewhere**
Meningoencephalitis in diseases classified elsewhere
MCC Exclusion see Appendix A PDX collection 0560

MCC **G05.4 Myelitis in diseases classified elsewhere**
Meningomyelitis in diseases classified elsewhere
MCC Exclusion see Appendix A PDX collection 0560

G06 Intracranial and intraspinal abscess and granuloma

Use additional code (B95-B97) to identify infectious agent.

MCC **G06.0 Intracranial abscess and granuloma**
Brain [any part] abscess (embolic)
Cerebellar abscess (embolic)
Cerebral abscess (embolic)
Intracranial epidural abscess or granuloma
Intracranial extradural abscess or granuloma
Intracranial subdural abscess or granuloma
Otogenic abscess (embolic)
Excludes1: *tuberculous intracranial abscess and granuloma (A17.81)*
MCC Exclusion see Appendix A PDX collection 0563

MCC **G06.1 Intraspinal abscess and granuloma**
Abscess (embolic) of spinal cord [any part]
Intraspinal epidural abscess or granuloma
Intraspinal extradural abscess or granuloma
Intraspinal subdural abscess or granuloma
Excludes1: *tuberculous intraspinal abscess and granuloma (A17.81)*
MCC Exclusion see Appendix A PDX collection 0564

MCC **G06.2 Extradural and subdural abscess, unspecified**
MCC Exclusion see Appendix A PDX collection 0565

MCC **G07 Intracranial and intraspinal abscess and granuloma in diseases classified elsewhere**

Code first underlying disease such as:
schistosomiasis granuloma of brain (B65.-)
Excludes1: *abscess of brain:*
amebic (A06.6)
chromomycotic (B43.1)
gonococcal (A54.82)
tuberculous (A17.81)
tuberculoma of meninges (A17.1)
MCC Exclusion see Appendix A PDX collection 0565
Valid 3-character code, no further characters required

MCC **G08 Intracranial and intraspinal phlebitis and thrombophlebitis**

Septic embolism of intracranial or intraspinal venous sinuses and veins
Septic endophlebitis of intracranial or intraspinal venous sinuses and veins
Septic phlebitis of intracranial or intraspinal venous sinuses and veins
Septic thrombophlebitis of intracranial or intraspinal venous sinuses and veins
Septic thrombosis of intracranial or intraspinal venous sinuses and veins
Excludes1: *intracranial phlebitis and thrombophlebitis complicating:*
abortion, ectopic or molar pregnancy (O00-O07, O08.7)
pregnancy, childbirth and the puerperium (O22.5, O87.
nonpyogenic intracranial phlebitis and thrombophlebitis (I67.6)
Excludes2: *intracranial phlebitis and thrombophlebitis complicating nonpyogenic intraspinal phlebitis and thrombophlebitis (G95.1)*
MCC Exclusion see Appendix A PDX collection 0565
Valid 3-character code, no further characters required

G09 Sequelae of inflammatory diseases of central nervous system

NOTE Category G09 is to be used to indicate conditions whose primary classification is to G00-G08 as the cause of sequelae themselves classifiable elsewhere. The 'sequelae' include conditions specified as residuals.

Code first condition resulting from (sequela) of inflammatory diseases central nervous system
Valid 3-character code, no further characters required

Systemic atrophies primarily affecting the central nervous system (G10-G14)

CC **G10 Huntington's disease**
Huntington's chorea
Huntington's dementia
CC Exclusion see Appendix A PDX collection 0566
Valid 3-character code, no further characters required

G11 Hereditary ataxia

Excludes2: *cerebral palsy (G80.-)*
hereditary and idiopathic neuropathy (G60.-)
metabolic disorders (E70-E88)

CC **G11.0 Congenital nonprogressive ataxia**
CC Exclusion see Appendix A PDX collection 0567

CC **G11.1 Early-onset cerebellar ataxia**
Early-onset cerebellar ataxia with essential tremor
Early-onset cerebellar ataxia with myoclonus [Hunt's ataxia]
Early-onset cerebellar ataxia with retained tendon reflexes
Friedreich's ataxia (autosomal recessive)
X-linked recessive spinocerebellar ataxia
CC Exclusion see Appendix A PDX collection 0567

• CC **G11.2 Late-onset cerebellar ataxia**
CC Exclusion see Appendix A PDX collection 0567

CC **G11.3 Cerebellar ataxia with defective DNA repair**
Ataxia telangiectasia [Louis-Bar]
Excludes2: *Cockayne's syndrome (Q87.1)*
other disorders of purine and pyrimidine metabo (E79.-)
xeroderma pigmentosum (Q82.1)
CC Exclusion see Appendix A PDX collection 0567

CC **G11.4 Hereditary spastic paraplegia**
CC Exclusion see Appendix A PDX collection 0568

CC **G11.8 Other hereditary ataxias**
CC Exclusion see Appendix A PDX collection 0567

CC **G11.9 Hereditary ataxia, unspecified**
Hereditary cerebellar ataxia NOS
Hereditary cerebellar degeneration
Hereditary cerebellar disease
Hereditary cerebellar syndrome
CC Exclusion see Appendix A PDX collection 0569

G12 Spinal muscular atrophy and related syndromes

CC **G12.0 Infantile spinal muscular atrophy, type I [Werdnig-Hoffmar**
CC Exclusion see Appendix A PDX collection 0570

CC **G12.1 Other inherited spinal muscular atrophy**
Adult form spinal muscular atrophy
Childhood form, type II spinal muscular atrophy
Distal spinal muscular atrophy
Juvenile form, type III spinal muscular atrophy [Kugelberg-Welander]
Progressive bulbar palsy of childhood [Fazio-Londe]
Scapuloperoneal form spinal muscular atrophy
CC Exclusion see Appendix A PDX collection 0570

+ **G12.2 Motor neuron disease**
CC **G12.20 Motor neuron disease, unspecified**
CC Exclusion see Appendix A PDX collection 0570
• CC **G12.21 Amyotrophic lateral sclerosis**
Progressive spinal muscle atrophy
CC Exclusion see Appendix A PDX collection 0570
CC **G12.22 Progressive bulbar palsy**
CC Exclusion see Appendix A PDX collection 0570
CC **G12.29 Other motor neuron disease**
Familial motor neuron disease
Primary lateral sclerosis
CC Exclusion see Appendix A PDX collection 0570
CC **G12.8 Other spinal muscular atrophies and related syndromes**
CC Exclusion see Appendix A PDX collection 0570
CC **G12.9 Spinal muscular atrophy, unspecified**
CC Exclusion see Appendix A PDX collection 0570

G13 Systemic atrophies primarily affecting central nervous system in diseases classified elsewhere

G13.0 Paraneoplastic neuromyopathy and neuropathy
Carcinomatous neuromyopathy
Sensorial paraneoplastic neuropathy [Denny Brown]
Code first underlying neoplasm (C00-D49)
G13.1 Other systemic atrophy primarily affecting central nervous system in neoplastic disease
Paraneoplastic limbic encephalopathy
Code first underlying neoplasm (C00-D49)
G13.2 Systemic atrophy primarily affecting the central nervous system in myxedema
Code first underlying disease, such as:
hypothyroidism (E03.-)
myxedematous congenital iodine deficiency (E00.1)
G13.8 Systemic atrophy primarily affecting central nervous system in other diseases classified elsewhere
Code first underlying disease

G14 Postpolio syndrome

Includes: postpolio myelitic syndrome
Excludes1: *sequelae of poliomyelitis (B91)*
Valid 3-character code, no further characters required

Extrapyramidal and movement disorders (G20-G26)

G20 Parkinson's disease

Hemiparkinsonism
Idiopathic Parkinsonism or Parkinson's disease
Paralysis agitans
Parkinsonism or Parkinson's disease NOS
Primary Parkinsonism or Parkinson's disease
Excludes1: *dementia with Parkinsonism (G31.83)*
Valid 3-character code, no further characters required

G21 Secondary parkinsonism

Excludes1: *dementia with Parkinsonism (G31.83)*
Huntington's disease (G10)
Shy-Drager syndrome (G90.3)
syphilitic Parkinsonism (A52.19)

MCC **G21.0 Malignant neuroleptic syndrome**
Use additional code for adverse effect, if applicable, to identify drug (T43.3X5, T43.4X5, T43.505, T43.595)
Excludes1: *neuroleptic induced parkinsonism (G21.11)*
MCC Exclusion see Appendix A PDX collection 0571
+ **G21.1 Other drug-induced secondary parkinsonism**
CC **G21.11 Neuroleptic induced parkinsonism**
Use additional code for adverse effect, if applicable, to identify drug (T43.3X5, T43.4X5, T43.505, T43.595)
Excludes1: *malignant neuroleptic syndrome (G21.0)*
CC Exclusion see Appendix A PDX collection 0572
CC **G21.19 Other drug induced secondary parkinsonism**
Use additional code for adverse effect, if applicable, to identify drug (T36-T50 with fifth or sixth character 5)
CC Exclusion see Appendix A PDX collection 0572
CC **G21.2 Secondary parkinsonism due to other external agents**
Code first (T51-T65) to identify external agent
CC Exclusion see Appendix A PDX collection 0572
CC **G21.3 Postencephalitic parkinsonism**
CC Exclusion see Appendix A PDX collection 0572
G21.4 Vascular parkinsonism
CC **G21.8 Other secondary parkinsonism**
CC Exclusion see Appendix A PDX collection 0572
CC **G21.9 Secondary parkinsonism, unspecified**
CC Exclusion see Appendix A PDX collection 0572

G23 Other degenerative diseases of basal ganglia

Excludes2: *multi-system degeneration of the autonomic nervous system (G90.3)*

CC **G23.0 Hallervorden-Spatz disease**
Pigmentary pallidal degeneration
CC Exclusion see Appendix A PDX collection 0573
CC **G23.1 Progressive supranuclear ophthalmoplegia [Steele-Richardson-Olszewski]**
Progressive supranuclear palsy
CC Exclusion see Appendix A PDX collection 0573
CC **G23.2 Striatonigral degeneration**
CC Exclusion see Appendix A PDX collection 0573
CC **G23.8 Other specified degenerative diseases of basal ganglia**
Calcification of basal ganglia
CC Exclusion see Appendix A PDX collection 0573
CC **G23.9 Degenerative disease of basal ganglia, unspecified**
CC Exclusion see Appendix A PDX collection 0573

G24 Dystonia

Includes: dyskinesia
Excludes2: *athetoid cerebral palsy (G80.3)*

+ **G24.0 Drug induced dystonia**
Use additional code code for adverse effect, if applicable, to identify drug (T36-T50 with fifth or sixth character 5)
G24.01 Drug induced subacute dyskinesia
Drug induced blepharospasm
Drug induced orofacial dyskinesia
Neuroleptic induced tardive dyskinesia
Tardive dyskinesia
CC **G24.02 Drug induced acute dystonia**
Acute dystonic reaction to drugs
Neuroleptic induced acute dystonia
CC Exclusion see Appendix A PDX collection 0574
CC **G24.09 Other drug induced dystonia**
CC Exclusion see Appendix A PDX collection 0574
G24.1 Genetic torsion dystonia
Dystonia deformans progressiva
Dystonia musculorum deformans
Familial torsion dystonia
Idiopathic familial dystonia
Idiopathic (torsion) dystonia NOS
(Schwalbe-) Ziehen-Oppenheim disease
CC **G24.2 Idiopathic nonfamilial dystonia**
CC Exclusion see Appendix A PDX collection 0574
G24.3 Spasmodic torticollis
Excludes1: *congenital torticollis (Q68.0)*
hysterical torticollis (F44.4)
ocular torticollis (R29.891)
psychogenic torticollis (F45.8)
torticollis NOS (M43.6)
traumatic recurrent torticollis (S13.4)
G24.4 Idiopathic orofacial dystonia
Orofacial dyskinesia
Excludes1: *drug induced orofacial dyskinesia (G24.01)*
G24.5 Blepharospasm
Excludes1: *drug induced blepharospasm (G24.01)*
CC **G24.8 Other dystonia**
Acquired torsion dystonia NOS
CC Exclusion see Appendix A PDX collection 0574
G24.9 Dystonia, unspecified
Dyskinesia NOS

G25 Other extrapyramidal and movement disorders

Excludes2: *sleep related movement disorders (G47.6-)*

G25.0 Essential tremor
Familial tremor
Excludes1: *tremor NOS (R25.1)*
G25.1 Drug-induced tremor
Use additional code for adverse effect, if applicable, to identify drug (T36-T50 with fifth or sixth character 5)
G25.2 Other specified forms of tremor
Intention tremor
G25.3 Myoclonus
Drug-induced myoclonus
Palatal myoclonus
Use additional code for adverse effect, if applicable, to identify drug (T36-T50 with fifth or sixth character 5)
Excludes1: *facial myokymia (G51.4)*
myoclonic epilepsy (G40.-)
G25.4 Drug-induced chorea
Use additional code for adverse effect, if applicable, to identify drug (T36-T50 with fifth or sixth character 5)

G25.5 Other chorea
Chorea NOS
Excludes1: *chorea NOS with heart involvement (I02.0)*
Huntington's chorea (G10)
rheumatic chorea (I02.-)
Sydenham's chorea (I02.-)

+ **G25.6 Drug induced tics and other tics of organic origin**
G25.61 Drug induced tics
Use additional code for adverse effect, if applicable, to identify drug (T36-T50 with fifth or sixth character 5)
G25.69 Other tics of organic origin
Excludes1: *habit spasm (F95.9)*
tic NOS (F95.9)
Tourette's syndrome (F95.2)

+ **G25.7 Other and unspecified drug induced movement disorders**
Use additional code for adverse effect, if applicable, to identify drug (T36-T50 with fifth or sixth character 5)
G25.70 Drug induced movement disorder, unspecified
G25.71 Drug induced akathisia
Drug induced acathisia
Neuroleptic induced acute akathisia
G25.79 Other drug induced movement disorders

+ **G25.8 Other specified extrapyramidal and movement disorders**
G25.81 Restless legs syndrome
CC **G25.82 Stiff-man syndrome**
CC Exclusion see Appendix A PDX collection 0575
G25.83 Benign shuddering attacks
G25.89 Other specified extrapyramidal and movement disorders

CC **G25.9 Extrapyramidal and movement disorder, unspecified**
CC Exclusion see Appendix A PDX collection 0575

G26 Extrapyramidal and movement disorders in diseases classified elsewhere
Code first underlying disease
Valid 3-character code, no further characters required

Other degenerative diseases of the nervous system (G30-G32)

G30 Alzheimer's disease
Includes: Alzheimer's dementia senile and presenile forms
Use additional code to identify:
delirium, if applicable (F05)
dementia with behavioral disturbance (F02.81)
dementia without behavioral disturbance (F02.80)
Excludes1: *senile degeneration of brain NEC (G31.1)*
senile dementia NOS (F03)
senility NOS (R41.81)
G30.0 Alzheimer's disease with early onset
• **G30.1 Alzheimer's disease with late onset**
G30.8 Other Alzheimer's disease
G30.9 Alzheimer's disease, unspecified
AHA CC: 4Q, 2012, 95-96

G31 Other degenerative diseases of nervous system, not elsewhere classified
Use additional code to identify:
dementia with behavioral disturbance (F02.81)
dementia without behavioral disturbance (F02.80)
Excludes2: *Reye's syndrome (G93.7)*

+ **G31.0 Frontotemporal dementia**
G31.01 Pick's disease
Primary progressive aphasia
Progressive isolated aphasia
G31.09 Other frontotemporal dementia
Frontal dementia

G31.1 Senile degeneration of brain, not elsewhere classified
Excludes1: *Alzheimer's disease (G30.-)*
senility NOS (R41.81)

G31.2 Degeneration of nervous system due to alcohol
Alcoholic cerebellar ataxia
Alcoholic cerebellar degeneration
Alcoholic cerebral degeneration
Alcoholic encephalopathy
Dysfunction of the autonomic nervous system due to alcohol
Code also associated alcoholism (F10.-)

+ **G31.8 Other specified degenerative diseases of nervous system**
CC **G31.81 Alpers disease**
Grey-matter degeneration
CC Exclusion see Appendix A PDX collection 0537
CC **G31.82 Leigh's disease**
Subacute necrotizing encephalopathy
CC Exclusion see Appendix A PDX collection 0537
G31.83 Dementia with Lewy bodies
Dementia with Parkinsonism
Lewy body dementia
Lewy body disease
G31.84 Mild cognitive impairment, so stated
Excludes1: *age related cognitive decline (R41.81)*
altered mental status (R41.82)
cerebral degeneration (G31.9)
change in mental status (R41.82)
cognitive deficits following (sequelae of) cerebral hemorrhage or infarction (I69.[illegible] I69.11, I69.21, I69.31, I69.81, I69.91)
cognitive impairment due to intracranial head injury (S06.-)
dementia (F01.-, F02.-, F03)
mild memory disturbance (F06.8)
neurologic neglect syndrome (R41.4)
personality change, nonpsychotic (F68.8)
G31.85 Corticobasal degeneration
G31.89 Other specified degenerative diseases of nervous system

G31.9 Degenerative disease of nervous system, unspecified

G32 Other degenerative disorders of nervous system in diseases classified elsewhere

CC **G32.0 Subacute combined degeneration of spinal cord in diseases classified elsewhere**
Dana-Putnam syndrome
Sclerosis of spinal cord (combined) (dorsolateral) (posterolater[illegible]
Code first underlying disease, such as:
anemia (D51.9)
dietary (D51.3)
pernicious (D51.0)
vitamin B12 deficiency (E53.8)
Excludes1: *syphilitic combined degeneration of spinal cord (A52.11)*
CC Exclusion see Appendix A PDX collection 0576

+ **G32.8 Other specified degenerative disorders of nervous system in diseases classified elsewhere**
Code first underlying disease, such as:
amyloidosis cerebral degeneration (E85.-)
cerebral degeneration (due to) hypothyroidism (E00.0-E03.9[illegible]
cerebral degeneration (due to) neoplasm (C00-D49)
cerebral degeneration (due to) vitamin B deficiency, except thiamine (E52-E53.-)
non-celiac gluten ataxia (M35.9)
Excludes1: *superior hemorrhagic polioencephalitis [Wernicke's encephalopathy] (E51.2)*
CC **G32.81 Cerebellar ataxia in diseases classified elsewhere**
Code first underlying disease, such as:
celiac disease (with gluten ataxia) (K90.0)
cerebellar ataxia (in) neoplastic disease (paraneoplastic cerebellar degeneration) (C00-D[illegible]
non-celiac gluten ataxia (M35.9)
Excludes1: *systemic atrophy primarily affecting the central nervous system in alcoholic cerebellar ataxia (G31.2)*
systemic atrophy primarily affecting the central nervous system in myxedema (G13.2)
CC Exclusion see Appendix A PDX collection 0567
G32.89 Other specified degenerative disorders of nervous system in diseases classified elsewhere
Degenerative encephalopathy in diseases classified elsewhere

Demyelinating diseases of the central nervous system (G35-G[illegible]

G35 Multiple sclerosis
Disseminated multiple sclerosis
Generalized multiple sclerosis
Multiple sclerosis NOS
Multiple sclerosis of brain stem
Multiple sclerosis of cord
Valid 3-character code, no further characters required

G36 Other acute disseminated demyelination
Excludes1: *postinfectious encephalitis and encephalomyelitis NOS (G04.01)*

CC **G36.0 Neuromyelitis optica [Devic]**
Demyelination in optic neuritis
Excludes1: *optic neuritis NOS (H46)*
CC Exclusion see Appendix A PDX collection 0577

CC **G36.1 Acute and subacute hemorrhagic leukoencephalitis [Hurst]**
CC Exclusion see Appendix A PDX collection 0578

CC **G36.8 Other specified acute disseminated demyelination**
CC Exclusion see Appendix A PDX collection 0578

CC **G36.9 Acute disseminated demyelination, unspecified**
CC Exclusion see Appendix A PDX collection 0578

G37 Other demyelinating diseases of central nervous system

CC **G37.0 Diffuse sclerosis of central nervous system**
Periaxial encephalitis
Schilder's disease
Excludes1: *X linked adrenoleukodystrophy (E71.52-)*
CC Exclusion see Appendix A PDX collection 0579

CC **G37.1 Central demyelination of corpus callosum**
CC Exclusion see Appendix A PDX collection 0578

CC **G37.2 Central pontine myelinolysis**
CC Exclusion see Appendix A PDX collection 0578

CC **G37.3 Acute transverse myelitis in demyelinating disease of central nervous system**
Acute transverse myelitis NOS
Acute transverse myelopathy
Excludes1: *multiple sclerosis (G35)*
neuromyelitis optica [Devic] (G36.0)
CC Exclusion see Appendix A PDX collection 0580

MCC **G37.4 Subacute necrotizing myelitis of central nervous system**
MCC Exclusion see Appendix A PDX collection 0562

CC **G37.5 Concentric sclerosis [Balo] of central nervous system**
CC Exclusion see Appendix A PDX collection 0579

CC **G37.8 Other specified demyelinating diseases of central nervous system**
CC Exclusion see Appendix A PDX collection 0578

CC **G37.9 Demyelinating disease of central nervous system, unspecified**
CC Exclusion see Appendix A PDX collection 0578

sodic and paroxysmal disorders (G40-G47)

G40 Epilepsy and recurrent seizures

NOTE the following terms are to be considered equivalent to intractable: pharmacoresistant (pharmacologically resistant), treatment resistant, refractory (medically) and poorly controlled

Excludes1: *conversion disorder with seizures (F44.5)*
convulsions NOS (R56.9)
hippocampal sclerosis (G93.81)
mesial temporal sclerosis (G93.81)
post traumatic seizures (R56.1)
seizure (convulsive) NOS (R56.9)
seizure of newborn (P90)
temporal sclerosis (G93.81)
Todd's paralysis (G83.8)

\+ **G40.0 Localization-related (focal) (partial) idiopathic epilepsy and epileptic syndromes with seizures of localized onset**
Benign childhood epilepsy with centrotemporal EEG spikes
Childhood epilepsy with occipital EEG paroxysms
Excludes1: *adult onset localization-related epilepsy (G40.1-, G40.2-)*

\+ **G40.00 Localization-related (focal) (partial) idiopathic epilepsy and epileptic syndromes with seizures of localized onset, not intractable**
Localization-related (focal) (partial) idiopathic epilepsy and epileptic syndromes with seizures of localized onset without intractability

CC **G40.001 Localization-related (focal) (partial) idiopathic epilepsy and epileptic syndromes with seizures of localized onset, not intractable, with status epilepticus**
CC Exclusion see Appendix A PDX collection 0581

CC **G40.009 Localization-related (focal) (partial) idiopathic epilepsy and epileptic syndromes with seizures of localized onset, not intractable, without status epilepticus**
Localization-related (focal) (partial) idiopathic epilepsy and epileptic syndromes with seizures of localized onset NOS
CC Exclusion see Appendix A PDX collection 0581

\+ **G40.01 Localization-related (focal) (partial) idiopathic epilepsy and epileptic syndromes with seizures of localized onset, intractable**

CC **G40.011 Localization-related (focal) (partial) idiopathic epilepsy and epileptic syndromes with seizures of localized onset, intractable, with status epilepticus**
CC Exclusion see Appendix A PDX collection 0582

CC **G40.019 Localization-related (focal) (partial) idiopathic epilepsy and epileptic syndromes with seizures of localized onset, intractable, without status epilepticus**
CC Exclusion see Appendix A PDX collection 0582

\+ **G40.1 Localization-related (focal) (partial) symptomatic epilepsy and epileptic syndromes with simple partial seizures**
Attacks without alteration of consciousness
Epilepsia partialis continua [Kozhevnikof]
Simple partial seizures developing into secondarily generalized seizures

\+ **G40.10 Localization-related (focal) (partial) symptomatic epilepsy and epileptic syndromes with simple partial seizures, not intractable**
Localization-related (focal) (partial) symptomatic epilepsy and epileptic syndromes with simple partial seizures without intractability

CC **G40.101 Localization-related (focal) (partial) symptomatic epilepsy and epileptic syndromes with simple partial seizures, not intractable, with status epilepticus**
CC Exclusion see Appendix A PDX collection 0581

CC **G40.109 Localization-related (focal) (partial) symptomatic epilepsy and epileptic syndromes with simple partial seizures, not intractable, without status epilepticus**
Localization-related (focal) (partial) symptomatic epilepsy and epileptic syndromes with simple partial seizures NOS
CC Exclusion see Appendix A PDX collection 0581

\+ **G40.11 Localization-related (focal) (partial) symptomatic epilepsy and epileptic syndromes with simple partial seizures, intractable**

CC **G40.111 Localization-related (focal) (partial) symptomatic epilepsy and epileptic syndromes with simple partial seizures, intractable, with status epilepticus**
CC Exclusion see Appendix A PDX collection 0582

CC **G40.119 Localization-related (focal) (partial) symptomatic epilepsy and epileptic syndromes with simple partial seizures, intractable, without status epilepticus**
CC Exclusion see Appendix A PDX collection 0582

\+ **G40.2 Localization-related (focal) (partial) symptomatic epilepsy and epileptic syndromes with complex partial seizures**
Attacks with alteration of consciousness, often with automatisms
Complex partial seizures developing into secondarily generalized seizures

\+ **G40.20 Localization-related (focal) (partial) symptomatic epilepsy and epileptic syndromes with complex partial seizures, not intractable**
Localization-related (focal) (partial) symptomatic epilepsy and epileptic syndromes with complex partial seizures without intractability

CC **G40.201 Localization-related (focal) (partial) symptomatic epilepsy and epileptic syndromes with complex partial seizures, not intractable, with status epilepticus**
CC Exclusion see Appendix A PDX collection 0581

CC **G40.209 Localization-related (focal) (partial) symptomatic epilepsy and epileptic syndromes with complex partial seizures, not intractable, without status epilepticus**
Localization-related (focal) (partial) symptomatic epilepsy and epileptic syndromes with complex partial seizures NOS
CC Exclusion see Appendix A PDX collection 0581

\+ **G40.21 Localization-related (focal) (partial) symptomatic epilepsy and epileptic syndromes with complex partial seizures, intractable**

CC **G40.211 Localization-related (focal) (partial) symptomatic epilepsy and epileptic syndromes with complex partial seizures, intractable, with status epilepticus**
CC Exclusion see Appendix A PDX collection 0582

CC **G40.219 Localization-related (focal) (partial) symptomatic epilepsy and epileptic syndromes with complex partial seizures, intractable, without status epilepticus**
CC Exclusion see Appendix A PDX collection 0582

\+ **G40.3 Generalized idiopathic epilepsy and epileptic syndromes**
Code also MERRF syndrome, if applicable (E88.42)

\+ **G40.30 Generalized idiopathic epilepsy and epileptic syndromes, not intractable**
Generalized idiopathic epilepsy and epileptic syndromes without intractability

MCC **G40.301 Generalized idiopathic epilepsy and epileptic syndromes, not intractable, with status epilepticus**
MCC Exclusion see Appendix A PDX collection 0583

G40.309 Generalized idiopathic epilepsy and epileptic syndromes, not intractable, without status epilepticus
Generalized idiopathic epilepsy and epileptic syndromes NOS

\+ **G40.31 Generalized idiopathic epilepsy and epileptic syndromes, intractable**

MCC **G40.311 Generalized idiopathic epilepsy and epileptic syndromes, intractable, with status epilepticus**
MCC Exclusion see Appendix A PDX collection 0583

MCC **G40.319 Generalized idiopathic epilepsy and epileptic syndromes, intractable, without status epilepticus**
MCC Exclusion see Appendix A PDX collection 0583

\+ **G40.A Absence epileptic syndrome**
Childhood absence epilepsy [pyknolepsy]
Juvenile absence epilepsy
Absence epileptic syndrome, NOS

\+ **G40.A0 Absence epileptic syndrome, not intractable**

G40.A01 Absence epileptic syndrome, not intractable, with status epilepticus

G40.A09 Absence epileptic syndrome, not intractable, without status epilepticus

\+ **G40.A1 Absence epileptic syndrome, intractable**

CC **G40.A11 Absence epileptic syndrome, intractable, with status epilepticus**
CC Exclusion see Appendix A PDX collection 0582

CC **G40.A19 Absence epileptic syndrome, intractable, without status epilepticus**
CC Exclusion see Appendix A PDX collection 0582

\+ **G40.B Juvenile myoclonic epilepsy [impulsive petit mal]**

\+ **G40.B0 Juvenile myoclonic epilepsy, not intractable**

CC **G40.B01 Juvenile myoclonic epilepsy, not intractable, with status epilepticus**
CC Exclusion see Appendix A PDX collection 0582

CC **G40.B09 Juvenile myoclonic epilepsy, not intractable, without status epilepticus**
CC Exclusion see Appendix A PDX collection 0582

\+ **G40.B1 Juvenile myoclonic epilepsy, intractable**

CC **G40.B11 Juvenile myoclonic epilepsy, intractable, with status epilepticus**
CC Exclusion see Appendix A PDX collection 0582

CC **G40.B19 Juvenile myoclonic epilepsy, intractable, without status epilepticus**
CC Exclusion see Appendix A PDX collection 0582

\+ **G40.4 Other generalized epilepsy and epileptic syndromes**
Epilepsy with grand mal seizures on awakening
Epilepsy with myoclonic absences
Epilepsy with myoclonic-astatic seizures
Grand mal seizure NOS
Nonspecific atonic epileptic seizures
Nonspecific clonic epileptic seizures
Nonspecific myoclonic epileptic seizures
Nonspecific tonic epileptic seizures
Nonspecific tonic-clonic epileptic seizures
Symptomatic early myoclonic encephalopathy

\+ **G40.40 Other generalized epilepsy and epileptic syndromes not intractable**
Other generalized epilepsy and epileptic syndromes without intractability
Other generalized epilepsy and epileptic syndromes NOS

G40.401 Other generalized epilepsy and epileptic syndromes, not intractable, with status epilepticus

G40.409 Other generalized epilepsy and epileptic syndromes, not intractable, without statu[s] epilepticus

\+ **G40.41 Other generalized epilepsy and epileptic syndrome[s] intractable**

CC **G40.411 Other generalized epilepsy and epileptic syndromes, intractable, with status epilepticus**
CC Exclusion see Appendix A PDX collection 0582

CC **G40.419 Other generalized epilepsy and epileptic syndromes, intractable, without status epilepticus**
CC Exclusion see Appendix A PDX collection 0582

\+ **G40.5 Epileptic seizures related to external causes**
Epileptic seizures related to alcohol
Epileptic seizures related to drugs
Epileptic seizures related to hormonal changes
Epileptic seizures related to sleep deprivation
Epileptic seizures related to stress
Use additional code for adverse effect, if applicable, to identi[fy] drug (T36-T50 with fifth or sixth character 5)
Code also if applicable, associated epilepsy and recurrent seiz[ures] (G40.-)

\+ **G40.50 Epileptic seizures related to external causes, not intractable**

CC **G40.501 Epileptic seizures related to external cau[ses,] not intractable, with status epilepticus**
CC Exclusion see Appendix A PDX collection 0582

CC **G40.509 Epileptic seizures related to external cau[ses,] not intractable, without status epileptic[us]**
Epileptic seizures related to external caus[es] NOS
CC Exclusion see Appendix A PDX collection 0582

\+ **G40.8 Other epilepsy and recurrent seizures**
Epilepsies and epileptic syndromes undetermined as to wheth[er] they are focal or generalized
Landau-Kleffner syndrome

\+ **G40.80 Other epilepsy**

CC **G40.801 Other epilepsy, not intractable, with stat[us] epilepticus**
Other epilepsy without intractability with status epilepticus
CC Exclusion see Appendix A PDX collection 0582

CC **G40.802 Other epilepsy, not intractable, without status epilepticus**
Other epilepsy NOS
Other epilepsy without intractability with[out] status epilepticus
CC Exclusion see Appendix A PDX collection 0582

CC **G40.803 Other epilepsy, intractable, with status epilepticus**
CC Exclusion see Appendix A PDX collection 0582

CC **G40.804 Other epilepsy, intractable, without stat[us] epilepticus**
CC Exclusion see Appendix A PDX collection 0582

\+ **G40.81 Lennox-Gastaut syndrome**

CC **G40.811 Lennox-Gastaut syndrome, not intracta[ble,] with status epilepticus**
CC Exclusion see Appendix A PDX collection 0582

CC **G40.812 Lennox-Gastaut syndrome, not intractable, without status epilepticus**
CC Exclusion see Appendix A PDX collection 0582

CC **G40.813 Lennox-Gastaut syndrome, intractable, with status epilepticus**
CC Exclusion see Appendix A PDX collection 0582

CC **G40.814 Lennox-Gastaut syndrome, intractable, without status epilepticus**
CC Exclusion see Appendix A PDX collection 0582

+ **G40.82 Epileptic spasms**
Infantile spasms
Salaam attacks
West's syndrome

CC **G40.821 Epileptic spasms, not intractable, with status epilepticus**
CC Exclusion see Appendix A PDX collection 0582

CC **G40.822 Epileptic spasms, not intractable, without status epilepticus**
CC Exclusion see Appendix A PDX collection 0582

CC **G40.823 Epileptic spasms, intractable, with status epilepticus**
CC Exclusion see Appendix A PDX collection 0582

CC **G40.824 Epileptic spasms, intractable, without status epilepticus**
CC Exclusion see Appendix A PDX collection 0582

CC **G40.89 Other seizures**
Excludes1: *post traumatic seizures (R56.1)*
recurrent seizures NOS (G40.909)
seizure NOS (R56.9)
CC Exclusion see Appendix A PDX collection 0582

+ **G40.9 Epilepsy, unspecified**

+ **G40.90 Epilepsy, unspecified, not intractable**
Epilepsy, unspecified, without intractability

G40.901 Epilepsy, unspecified, not intractable, with status epilepticus

G40.909 Epilepsy, unspecified, not intractable, without status epilepticus
Epilepsy NOS
Epileptic convulsions NOS
Epileptic fits NOS
Epileptic seizures NOS
Recurrent seizures NOS
Seizure disorder NOS

+ **G40.91 Epilepsy, unspecified, intractable**
Intractable seizure disorder NOS

CC **G40.911 Epilepsy, unspecified, intractable, with status epilepticus**
CC Exclusion see Appendix A PDX collection 0582

CC **G40.919 Epilepsy, unspecified, intractable, without status epilepticus**
CC Exclusion see Appendix A PDX collection 0582

G43 Migraine

NOTE the following terms are to be considered equivalent to intractable: pharmacoresistant (pharmacologically resistant), treatment resistant, refractory (medically) and poorly controlled

Use additional code for adverse effect, if applicable, to identify drug (T36-T50 with fifth or sixth character 5)

Excludes1: *headache NOS (R51)*
lower half migraine (G44.00)

Excludes2: *headache syndromes (G44.-)*

+ **G43.0 Migraine without aura**
Common migraine
Excludes1: *chronic migraine without aura (G43.7-)*

+ **G43.00 Migraine without aura, not intractable**
Migraine without aura without mention of refractory migraine

G43.001 Migraine without aura, not intractable, with status migrainosus

G43.009 Migraine without aura, not intractable, without status migrainosus
Migraine without aura NOS

+ **G43.01 Migraine without aura, intractable**
Migraine without aura with refractory migraine

G43.011 Migraine without aura, intractable, with status migrainosus

G43.019 Migraine without aura, intractable, without status migrainosus

+ **G43.1 Migraine with aura**
Basilar migraine
Classical migraine
Migraine equivalents
Migraine preceded or accompanied by transient focal neurological phenomena
Migraine triggered seizures
Migraine with acute-onset aura
Migraine with aura without headache (migraine equivalents)
Migraine with prolonged aura
Migraine with typical aura
Retinal migraine
Code also any associated seizure (G40.-, R56.9)
Excludes1: *persistent migraine aura (G43.5-, G43.6-)*

+ **G43.10 Migraine with aura, not intractable**
Migraine with aura without mention of refractory migraine

G43.101 Migraine with aura, not intractable, with status migrainosus

G43.109 Migraine with aura, not intractable, without status migrainosus
Migraine with aura NOS

+ **G43.11 Migraine with aura, intractable**
Migraine with aura with refractory migraine

G43.111 Migraine with aura, intractable, with status migrainosus

G43.119 Migraine with aura, intractable, without status migrainosus

+ **G43.4 Hemiplegic migraine**
Familial migraine
Sporadic migraine

+ **G43.40 Hemiplegic migraine, not intractable**
Hemiplegic migraine without refractory migraine

G43.401 Hemiplegic migraine, not intractable, with status migrainosus

G43.409 Hemiplegic migraine, not intractable, without status migrainosus
Hemiplegic migraine NOS

+ **G43.41 Hemiplegic migraine, intractable**
Hemiplegic migraine with refractory migraine

G43.411 Hemiplegic migraine, intractable, with status migrainosus

G43.419 Hemiplegic migraine, intractable, without status migrainosus

+ **G43.5 Persistent migraine aura without cerebral infarction**

+ **G43.50 Persistent migraine aura without cerebral infarction, not intractable**
Persistent migraine aura without cerebral infarction, without refractory migraine

G43.501 Persistent migraine aura without cerebral infarction, not intractable, with status migrainosus

G43.509 Persistent migraine aura without cerebral infarction, not intractable, without status migrainosus
Persistent migraine aura NOS

+ **G43.51 Persistent migraine aura without cerebral infarction, intractable**
Persistent migraine aura without cerebral infarction, with refractory migraine

G43.511 Persistent migraine aura without cerebral infarction, intractable, with status migrainosus

G43.519 Persistent migraine aura without cerebral infarction, intractable, without status migrainosus

+ **G43.6 Persistent migraine aura with cerebral infarction**
Code also the type of cerebral infarction (I63.-)

+ **G43.60 Persistent migraine aura with cerebral infarction, not intractable**
Persistent migraine aura with cerebral infarction, without refractory migraine

CC **G43.601 Persistent migraine aura with cerebral infarction, not intractable, with status migrainosus**
CC Exclusion see Appendix A PDX collection 0584

CC **G43.609 Persistent migraine aura with cerebral infarction, not intractable, without status migrainosus**
CC Exclusion see Appendix A PDX collection 0585

+ **G43.61 Persistent migraine aura with cerebral infarction, intractable**
Persistent migraine aura with cerebral infarction, with refractory migraine

CC **G43.611 Persistent migraine aura with cerebral infarction, intractable, with status migrainosus**
CC Exclusion see Appendix A PDX collection 0584

CC **G43.619 Persistent migraine aura with cerebral infarction, intractable, without status migrainosus**
CC Exclusion see Appendix A PDX collection 0584

+ **G43.7 Chronic migraine without aura**
Transformed migraine
Excludes1: *migraine without aura (G43.0-)*

+ **G43.70 Chronic migraine without aura, not intractable**
Chronic migraine without aura, without refractory migraine

G43.701 Chronic migraine without aura, not intractable, with status migrainosus

G43.709 Chronic migraine without aura, not intractable, without status migrainosus
Chronic migraine without aura NOS

+ **G43.71 Chronic migraine without aura, intractable**
Chronic migraine without aura, with refractory migraine

G43.711 Chronic migraine without aura, intractable, with status migrainosus

G43.719 Chronic migraine without aura, intractable, without status migrainosus

+ **G43.A Cyclical vomiting**

G43.A0 Cyclical vomiting, not intractable
Cyclical vomiting, without refractory migraine

G43.A1 Cyclical vomiting, intractable
Cyclical vomiting, with refractory migraine

+ **G43.B Ophthalmoplegic migraine**

G43.B0 Ophthalmoplegic migraine, not intractable
Ophthalmoplegic migraine, without refractory migraine

G43.B1 Ophthalmoplegic migraine, intractable
Ophthalmoplegic migraine, with refractory migraine

+ **G43.C Periodic headache syndromes in child or adult**

G43.C0 Periodic headache syndromes in child or adult, not intractable
Periodic headache syndromes in child or adult, without refractory migraine

G43.C1 Periodic headache syndromes in child or adult, intractable
Periodic headache syndromes in child or adult, with refractory migraine

+ **G43.D Abdominal migraine**

G43.D0 Abdominal migraine, not intractable
Abdominal migraine, without refractory migraine

G43.D1 Abdominal migraine, intractable
Abdominal migraine, with refractory migraine

+ **G43.8 Other migraine**

+ **G43.80 Other migraine, not intractable**
Other migraine, without refractory migraine

G43.801 Other migraine, not intractable, with status migrainosus

G43.809 Other migraine, not intractable, without status migrainosus

+ **G43.81 Other migraine, intractable**
Other migraine, with refractory migraine

G43.811 Other migraine, intractable, with status migrainosus

G43.819 Other migraine, intractable, without status migrainosus

+ **G43.82 Menstrual migraine, not intractable**
Menstrual headache, not intractable
Menstrual migraine, without refractory migraine
Menstrually related migraine, not intractable
Pre-menstrual headache, not intractable
Pre-menstrual migraine, not intractable
Pure menstrual migraine, not intractable
Code also associated premenstrual tension syndrome (N94.3)

♀ **G43.821 Menstrual migraine, not intractable, with status migrainosus**

♀ **G43.829 Menstrual migraine, not intractable, witho[ut] status migrainosus**
Menstrual migraine NOS

+ **G43.83 Menstrual migraine, intractable**
Menstrual headache, intractable
Menstrual migraine, with refractory migraine
Menstrually related migraine, intractable
Pre-menstrual headache, intractable
Pre-menstrual migraine, intractable
Pure menstrual migraine, intractable
Code also associated premenstrual tension syndrome (N94.3)

♀ **G43.831 Menstrual migraine, intractable, with stat[us] migrainosus**

♀ **G43.839 Menstrual migraine, intractable, without status migrainosus**

+ **G43.9 Migraine, unspecified**

+ **G43.90 Migraine, unspecified, not intractable**
Migraine, unspecified, without refractory migraine

G43.901 Migraine, unspecified, not intractable, wit[h] status migrainosus
Status migrainosus NOS

G43.909 Migraine, unspecified, not intractable, without status migrainosus
Migraine NOS

+ **G43.91 Migraine, unspecified, intractable**
Migraine, unspecified, with refractory migraine

G43.911 Migraine, unspecified, intractable, with status migrainosus

G43.919 Migraine, unspecified, intractable, without status migrainosus

G44 Other headache syndromes

Excludes1: *headache NOS (R51)*
Excludes2: *atypical facial pain (G50.1)*
headache due to lumbar puncture (G97.1)
migraines (G43.-)
trigeminal neuralgia (G50.0)

+ **G44.0 Cluster headaches and other trigeminal autonomic cephalgias (TAC)**

+ **G44.00 Cluster headache syndrome, unspecified**
Ciliary neuralgia
Cluster headache NOS
Histamine cephalgia
Lower half migraine
Migrainous neuralgia

G44.001 Cluster headache syndrome, unspecified, intractable

G44.009 Cluster headache syndrome, unspecified, n[ot] intractable
Cluster headache syndrome NOS

+ **G44.01 Episodic cluster headache**

G44.011 Episodic cluster headache, intractable

G44.019 Episodic cluster headache, not intractable
Episodic cluster headache NOS

+ **G44.02 Chronic cluster headache**

G44.021 Chronic cluster headache, intractable

G44.029 Chronic cluster headache, not intractable
Chronic cluster headache NOS

+ **G44.03 Episodic paroxysmal hemicrania**
Paroxysmal hemicrania NOS

G44.031 Episodic paroxysmal hemicrania, intractable

G44.039 Episodic paroxysmal hemicrania, not intractable
Episodic paroxysmal hemicrania NOS

+ **G44.04 Chronic paroxysmal hemicrania**

G44.041 Chronic paroxysmal hemicrania, intractable

G44.049 Chronic paroxysmal hemicrania, not intractable
Chronic paroxysmal hemicrania NOS

+ **G44.05 Short lasting unilateral neuralgiform headache with conjunctival injection and tearing (SUNCT)**

G44.051 Short lasting unilateral neuralgiform headache with conjunctival injection and tearing (SUNCT), intractable

G44.059 Short lasting unilateral neuralgiform headache with conjunctival injection and tearing (SUNCT), not intractable
Short lasting unilateral neuralgiform headache with conjunctival injection and tearing (SUNCT) NOS

+ **G44.09 Other trigeminal autonomic cephalgias (TAC)**
G44.091 Other trigeminal autonomic cephalgias (TAC), intractable
G44.099 Other trigeminal autonomic cephalgias (TAC), not intractable

G44.1 Vascular headache, not elsewhere classified
Excludes2: *cluster headache (G44.0)*
complicated headache syndromes (G44.5-)
drug-induced headache (G44.4-)
migraine (G43.-)
other specified headache syndromes (G44.8-)
post-traumatic headache (G44.3-)
tension-type headache (G44.2-)

+ **G44.2 Tension-type headache**
+ **G44.20 Tension-type headache, unspecified**
G44.201 Tension-type headache, unspecified, intractable
G44.209 Tension-type headache, unspecified, not intractable
Tension headache NOS
+ **G44.21 Episodic tension-type headache**
G44.211 Episodic tension-type headache, intractable
G44.219 Episodic tension-type headache, not intractable
Episodic tension-type headache NOS
+ **G44.22 Chronic tension-type headache**
G44.221 Chronic tension-type headache, intractable
G44.229 Chronic tension-type headache, not intractable
Chronic tension-type headache NOS

+ **G44.3 Post-traumatic headache**
+ **G44.30 Post-traumatic headache, unspecified**
G44.301 Post-traumatic headache, unspecified, intractable
G44.309 Post-traumatic headache, unspecified, not intractable
Post-traumatic headache NOS
+ **G44.31 Acute post-traumatic headache**
G44.311 Acute post-traumatic headache, intractable
G44.319 Acute post-traumatic headache, not intractable
Acute post-traumatic headache NOS
+ **G44.32 Chronic post-traumatic headache**
G44.321 Chronic post-traumatic headache, intractable
G44.329 Chronic post-traumatic headache, not intractable
Chronic post-traumatic headache NOS

+ **G44.4 Drug-induced headache, not elsewhere classified**
Medication overuse headache
Use additional code for adverse effect, if applicable, to identify drug (T36-T50 with fifth or sixth character 5)
G44.40 Drug-induced headache, not elsewhere classified, not intractable
G44.41 Drug-induced headache, not elsewhere classified, intractable

+ **G44.5 Complicated headache syndromes**
G44.51 Hemicrania continua
G44.52 New daily persistent headache (NDPH)
G44.53 Primary thunderclap headache
G44.59 Other complicated headache syndrome

+ **G44.8 Other specified headache syndromes**
G44.81 Hypnic headache
G44.82 Headache associated with sexual activity
Orgasmic headache
Preorgasmic headache
G44.83 Primary cough headache
G44.84 Primary exertional headache
G44.85 Primary stabbing headache
G44.89 Other headache syndrome

G45 Transient cerebral ischemic attacks and related syndromes

Excludes1: *neonatal cerebral ischemia (P91.0)*
transient retinal artery occlusion (H34.0-)

CC **G45.0 Vertebro-basilar artery syndrome**
CC Exclusion see Appendix A PDX collection 0586
CC **G45.1 Carotid artery syndrome (hemispheric)**
CC Exclusion see Appendix A PDX collection 0586
CC **G45.2 Multiple and bilateral precerebral artery syndromes**
CC Exclusion see Appendix A PDX collection 0586
CC **G45.3 Amaurosis fugax**
CC Exclusion see Appendix A PDX collection 0587
G45.4 Transient global amnesia
Excludes1: *amnesia NOS (R41.3)*
CC **G45.8 Other transient cerebral ischemic attacks and related syndromes**
CC Exclusion see Appendix A PDX collection 0586
CC **G45.9 Transient cerebral ischemic attack, unspecified**
Spasm of cerebral artery
TIA
Transient cerebral ischemia NOS
CC Exclusion see Appendix A PDX collection 0586

G46 Vascular syndromes of brain in cerebrovascular diseases

Code first underlying cerebrovascular disease (I60-I69)

CC **G46.0 Middle cerebral artery syndrome**
CC Exclusion see Appendix A PDX collection 0586
CC **G46.1 Anterior cerebral artery syndrome**
CC Exclusion see Appendix A PDX collection 0586
CC **G46.2 Posterior cerebral artery syndrome**
CC Exclusion see Appendix A PDX collection 0586
G46.3 Brain stem stroke syndrome
Benedikt syndrome
Claude syndrome
Foville syndrome
Millard-Gubler syndrome
Wallenberg syndrome
Weber syndrome
G46.4 Cerebellar stroke syndrome
G46.5 Pure motor lacunar syndrome
G46.6 Pure sensory lacunar syndrome
G46.7 Other lacunar syndromes
G46.8 Other vascular syndromes of brain in cerebrovascular diseases

G47 Sleep disorders

Excludes2: *nightmares (F51.5)*
nonorganic sleep disorders (F51.-)
sleep terrors (F51.4)
sleepwalking (F51.3)

+ **G47.0 Insomnia**
Excludes2: *alcohol related insomnia (F10.182, F10.282, F10.982)*
drug-related insomnia (F11.182, F11.282, F11.982, F13.182, F13.282, F13.982, F14.182, F14.282, F14.982, F15.182, F15.282, F15.982, F19.182, F19.282, F19.982)
idiopathic insomnia (F51.01)
insomnia due to a mental disorder (F51.05)
insomnia not due to a substance or known physiological condition (F51.0-)
nonorganic insomnia (F51.0-)
primary insomnia (F51.01)
sleep apnea (G47.3-)
G47.00 Insomnia, unspecified
Insomnia NOS
G47.01 Insomnia due to medical condition
Code also associated medical condition
G47.09 Other insomnia

+ **G47.1 Hypersomnia**
Excludes2: *alcohol-related hypersomnia (F10.182, F10.282, F10.982)*
drug-related hypersomnia (F11.182, F11.282, F11.982, F13.182, F13.282, F13.982, F14.182, F14.282, F14.982, F15.182, F15.282, F15.982, F19.182, F19.282, F19.982)
hypersomnia due to a mental disorder (F51.13)
hypersomnia not due to a substance or known physiological condition (F51.1-)
primary hypersomnia (F51.11)
sleep apnea (G47.3-)
G47.10 Hypersomnia, unspecified
Hypersomnia NOS
G47.11 Idiopathic hypersomnia with long sleep time
Idiopathic hypersomnia NOS
G47.12 Idiopathic hypersomnia without long sleep time
G47.13 Recurrent hypersomnia
Kleine-Levin syndrome
Menstrual related hypersomnia

Brain

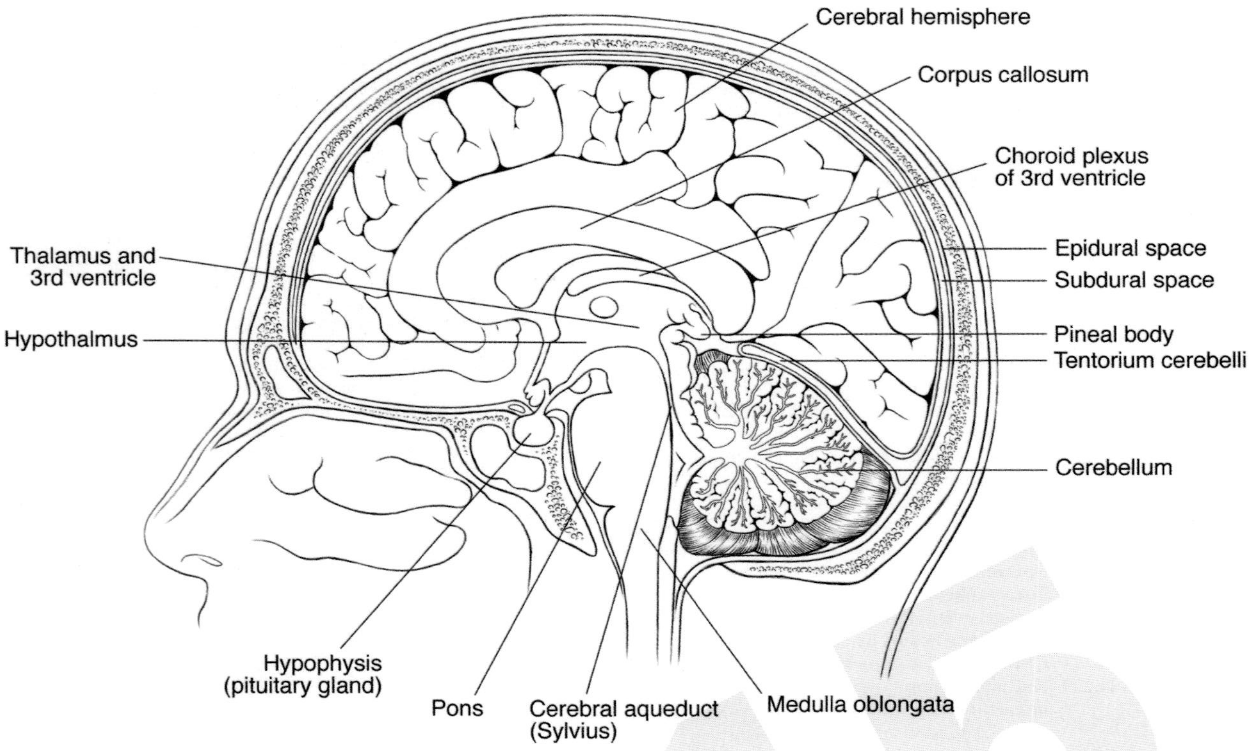

Cerebral hemisphere
Corpus callosum
Choroid plexus of 3rd ventricle
Thalamus and 3rd ventricle
Epidural space
Subdural space
Hypothalmus
Pineal body
Tentorium cerebelli
Cerebellum
Hypophysis (pituitary gland)
Pons
Cerebral aqueduct (Sylvius)
Medulla oblongata

Cranial Nerves

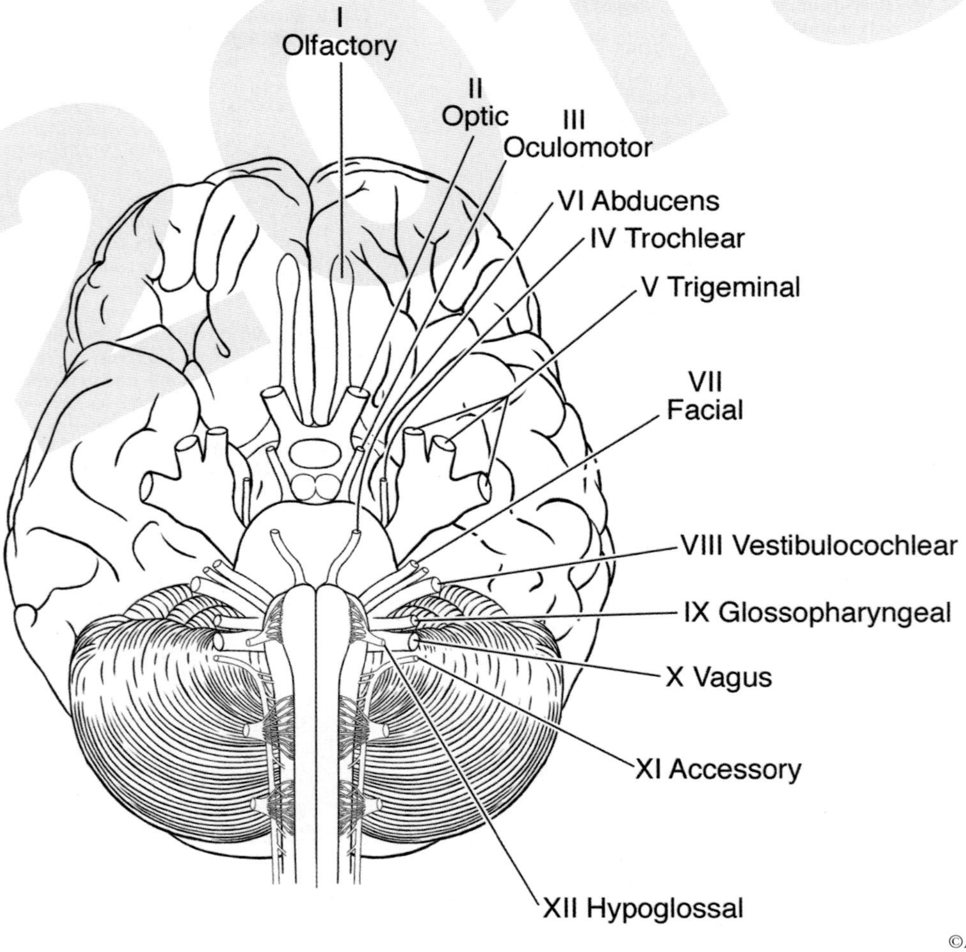

I Olfactory
II Optic
III Oculomotor
VI Abducens
IV Trochlear
V Trigeminal
VII Facial
VIII Vestibulocochlear
IX Glossopharyngeal
X Vagus
XI Accessory
XII Hypoglossal

Peripheral Nervous System

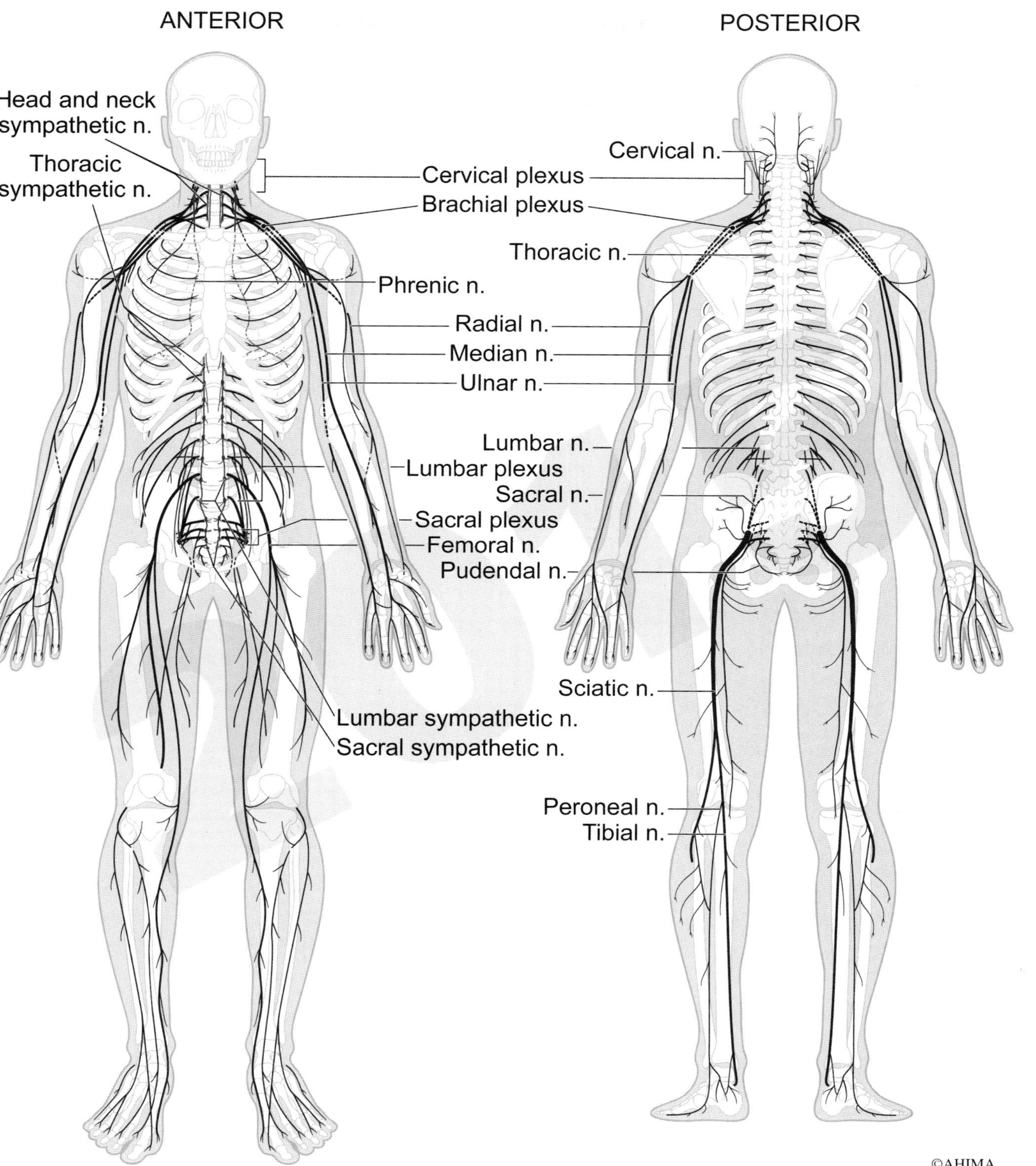
ANTERIOR
POSTERIOR
Head and neck sympathetic n.
Thoracic sympathetic n.
Cervical plexus
Brachial plexus
Phrenic n.
Radial n.
Median n.
Ulnar n.
Lumbar plexus
Sacral plexus
Femoral n.
Lumbar sympathetic n.
Sacral sympathetic n.
Cervical n.
Thoracic n.
Lumbar n.
Sacral n.
Pudendal n.
Sciatic n.
Peroneal n.
Tibial n.

G47.14 Hypersomnia due to medical condition
Code also associated medical condition
G47.19 Other hypersomnia
+ **G47.2 Circadian rhythm sleep disorders**
Disorders of the sleep wake schedule
Inversion of nyctohemeral rhythm
Inversion of sleep rhythm
G47.20 Circadian rhythm sleep disorder, unspecified type
Sleep wake schedule disorder NOS
G47.21 Circadian rhythm sleep disorder, delayed sleep phase type
Delayed sleep phase syndrome
G47.22 Circadian rhythm sleep disorder, advanced sleep phase type
G47.23 Circadian rhythm sleep disorder, irregular sleep wake type
Irregular sleep-wake pattern
G47.24 Circadian rhythm sleep disorder, free running type
G47.25 Circadian rhythm sleep disorder, jet lag type
G47.26 Circadian rhythm sleep disorder, shift work type
G47.27 Circadian rhythm sleep disorder in conditions classified elsewhere
Code first underlying condition
G47.29 Other circadian rhythm sleep disorder
+ **G47.3 Sleep apnea**
Code also any associated underlying condition
Excludes1: *apnea NOS (R06.81)*
Cheyne-Stokes breathing (R06.3)
pickwickian syndrome (E66.2)
sleep apnea of newborn (P28.3)
G47.30 Sleep apnea, unspecified
Sleep apnea NOS
G47.31 Primary central sleep apnea
G47.32 High altitude periodic breathing
G47.33 Obstructive sleep apnea (adult) (pediatric)
Excludes1: *obstructive sleep apnea of newborn (P28.3)*
G47.34 Idiopathic sleep related nonobstructive alveolar hypoventilation
Sleep related hypoxia
G47.35 Congenital central alveolar hypoventilation syndrome
G47.36 Sleep related hypoventilation in conditions classified elsewhere
Sleep related hypoxemia in conditions classified elsewhere
Code first underlying condition
G47.37 Central sleep apnea in conditions classified elsewhere
Code first underlying condition
G47.39 Other sleep apnea
+ **G47.4 Narcolepsy and cataplexy**
+ **G47.41 Narcolepsy**
G47.411 Narcolepsy with cataplexy
G47.419 Narcolepsy without cataplexy
Narcolepsy NOS
+ **G47.42 Narcolepsy in conditions classified elsewhere**
Code first underlying condition
G47.421 Narcolepsy in conditions classified elsewhere with cataplexy
G47.429 Narcolepsy in conditions classified elsewhere without cataplexy
+ **G47.5 Parasomnia**
Excludes1: *alcohol induced parasomnia (F10.182, F10.282, F10.982)*
drug induced parasomnia (F11.182, F11.282, F11.982, F13.182, F13.282, F13.982, F14.182, F14.282, F14.982, F15.182, F15.282, F15.982, F19.182, F19.282, F19.982)
parasomnia not due to a substance or known physiological condition (F51.8)
G47.50 Parasomnia, unspecified
Parasomnia NOS
G47.51 Confusional arousals
G47.52 REM sleep behavior disorder
G47.53 Recurrent isolated sleep paralysis
G47.54 Parasomnia in conditions classified elsewhere
Code first underlying condition
G47.59 Other parasomnia
+ **G47.6 Sleep related movement disorders**
Excludes2: *restless legs syndrome (G25.81)*
G47.61 Periodic limb movement disorder
Periodic limb movement disorder
G47.62 Sleep related leg cramps
G47.63 Sleep related bruxism
Excludes1: *psychogenic bruxism (F45.8)*
G47.69 Other sleep related movement disorders
G47.8 Other sleep disorders
G47.9 Sleep disorder, unspecified
Sleep disorder NOS

Nerve, nerve root and plexus disorders (G50-G59)

Excludes1: *current traumatic nerve, nerve root and plexus disorders - see Injury, nerve by body region*
neuralgia NOS (M79.2)
neuritis NOS (M79.2)
peripheral neuritis in pregnancy (O26.82-)
radiculitis NOS (M54.1-)

G50 Disorders of trigeminal nerve
Includes: disorders of 5th cranial nerve
G50.0 Trigeminal neuralgia
Syndrome of paroxysmal facial pain
Tic douloureux
G50.1 Atypical facial pain
G50.8 Other disorders of trigeminal nerve
G50.9 Disorder of trigeminal nerve, unspecified

G51 Facial nerve disorders
Includes: disorders of 7th cranial nerve
G51.0 Bell's palsy
Facial palsy
G51.1 Geniculate ganglionitis
Excludes1: *postherpetic geniculate ganglionitis (B02.21)*
G51.2 Melkersson's syndrome
Melkersson-Rosenthal syndrome
G51.3 Clonic hemifacial spasm
G51.4 Facial myokymia
G51.8 Other disorders of facial nerve
G51.9 Disorder of facial nerve, unspecified

G52 Disorders of other cranial nerves
Excludes2: *disorders of acoustic [8th] nerve (H93.3)*
disorders of optic [2nd] nerve (H46, H47.0)
paralytic strabismus due to nerve palsy (H49.0-H49.2)
G52.0 Disorders of olfactory nerve
Disorders of 1st cranial nerve
G52.1 Disorders of glossopharyngeal nerve
Disorder of 9th cranial nerve
Glossopharyngeal neuralgia
G52.2 Disorders of vagus nerve
Disorders of pneumogastric [10th] nerve
G52.3 Disorders of hypoglossal nerve
Disorders of 12th cranial nerve
G52.7 Disorders of multiple cranial nerves
Polyneuritis cranialis
G52.8 Disorders of other specified cranial nerves
G52.9 Cranial nerve disorder, unspecified

G53 Cranial nerve disorders in diseases classified elsewhere
Code first underlying disease, such as:
neoplasm (C00-D49)
Excludes1: *multiple cranial nerve palsy in sarcoidosis (D86.82)*
multiple cranial nerve palsy in syphilis (A52.15)
postherpetic geniculate ganglionitis (B02.21)
postherpetic trigeminal neuralgia (B02.22)
Valid 3-character code, no further characters required

G54 Nerve root and plexus disorders
Excludes1: *current traumatic nerve root and plexus disorders - see nerve injury by body region*
intervertebral disc disorders (M50-M51)
neuralgia or neuritis NOS (M79.2)
neuritis or radiculitis brachial NOS (M54.13)
neuritis or radiculitis lumbar NOS (M54.16)
neuritis or radiculitis lumbosacral NOS (M54.17)
neuritis or radiculitis thoracic NOS (M54.14)
radiculitis NOS (M54.10)
radiculopathy NOS (M54.10)
spondylosis (M47.-)
G54.0 Brachial plexus disorders
Thoracic outlet syndrome
G54.1 Lumbosacral plexus disorders
G54.2 Cervical root disorders, not elsewhere classified
G54.3 Thoracic root disorders, not elsewhere classified
G54.4 Lumbosacral root disorders, not elsewhere classified

G54.5 Neuralgic amyotrophy
Parsonage-Aldren-Turner syndrome
Shoulder-girdle neuritis
Excludes1: *neuralgic amyotrophy in diabetes mellitus (E08-E13 with .44)*
G54.6 Phantom limb syndrome with pain
G54.7 Phantom limb syndrome without pain
Phantom limb syndrome NOS
G54.8 Other nerve root and plexus disorders
G54.9 Nerve root and plexus disorder, unspecified

G55 Nerve root and plexus compressions in diseases classified elsewhere
Code first underlying disease, such as:
neoplasm (C00-D49)
Excludes1: *nerve root compression (due to) (in) ankylosing spondylitis (M45.-)*
nerve root compression (due to) (in) ankylosing spondylitis (M45.-)
nerve root compression (due to) (in) dorsopathies (M53.-, M54.-)
nerve root compression (due to) (in) intervertebral disc disorders (M50.1.-, M51.1.-)
nerve root compression (due to) (in) spondylopathies (M46.-, M48.-)
Valid 3-character code, no further characters required

G56 Mononeuropathies of upper limb
Excludes1: *current traumatic nerve disorder - see nerve injury by body region*
+ G56.0 Carpal tunnel syndrome
G56.00 Carpal tunnel syndrome, unspecified upper limb
G56.01 Carpal tunnel syndrome, right upper limb
G56.02 Carpal tunnel syndrome, left upper limb
+ G56.1 Other lesions of median nerve
G56.10 Other lesions of median nerve, unspecified upper limb
G56.11 Other lesions of median nerve, right upper limb
G56.12 Other lesions of median nerve, left upper limb
+ G56.2 Lesion of ulnar nerve
Tardy ulnar nerve palsy
G56.20 Lesion of ulnar nerve, unspecified upper limb
G56.21 Lesion of ulnar nerve, right upper limb
G56.22 Lesion of ulnar nerve, left upper limb
+ G56.3 Lesion of radial nerve
G56.30 Lesion of radial nerve, unspecified upper limb
G56.31 Lesion of radial nerve, right upper limb
G56.32 Lesion of radial nerve, left upper limb
+ G56.4 Causalgia of upper limb
Complex regional pain syndrome II of upper limb
Excludes1: *complex regional pain syndrome I of lower limb (G90.52-)*
complex regional pain syndrome I of upper limb (G90.51-)
complex regional pain syndrome II of lower limb (G57.7-)
reflex sympathetic dystrophy of lower limb (G90.52-)
reflex sympathetic dystrophy of upper limb (G90.51-)
G56.40 Causalgia of unspecified upper limb
G56.41 Causalgia of right upper limb
G56.42 Causalgia of left upper limb
+ G56.8 Other specified mononeuropathies of upper limb
Interdigital neuroma of upper limb
G56.80 Other specified mononeuropathies of unspecified upper limb
G56.81 Other specified mononeuropathies of right upper limb
G56.82 Other specified mononeuropathies of left upper limb
+ G56.9 Unspecified mononeuropathy of upper limb
G56.90 Unspecified mononeuropathy of unspecified upper limb
G56.91 Unspecified mononeuropathy of right upper limb
G56.92 Unspecified mononeuropathy of left upper limb

G57 Mononeuropathies of lower limb
Excludes1: *current traumatic nerve disorder - see nerve injury by body region*
+ G57.0 Lesion of sciatic nerve
Excludes1: *sciatica NOS (M54.3-)*
Excludes2: *sciatica attributed to intervertebral disc disorder (M51.1.-)*
G57.00 Lesion of sciatic nerve, unspecified lower limb
G57.01 Lesion of sciatic nerve, right lower limb
G57.02 Lesion of sciatic nerve, left lower limb
+ G57.1 Meralgia paresthetica
Lateral cutaneous nerve of thigh syndrome
G57.10 Meralgia paresthetica, unspecified lower limb
G57.11 Meralgia paresthetica, right lower limb
G57.12 Meralgia paresthetica, left lower limb
+ G57.2 Lesion of femoral nerve
G57.20 Lesion of femoral nerve, unspecified lower limb
G57.21 Lesion of femoral nerve, right lower limb
G57.22 Lesion of femoral nerve, left lower limb
+ G57.3 Lesion of lateral popliteal nerve
Peroneal nerve palsy
G57.30 Lesion of lateral popliteal nerve, unspecified lower limb
G57.31 Lesion of lateral popliteal nerve, right lower limb
G57.32 Lesion of lateral popliteal nerve, left lower limb
+ G57.4 Lesion of medial popliteal nerve
G57.40 Lesion of medial popliteal nerve, unspecified lower limb
G57.41 Lesion of medial popliteal nerve, right lower limb
G57.42 Lesion of medial popliteal nerve, left lower limb
+ G57.5 Tarsal tunnel syndrome
G57.50 Tarsal tunnel syndrome, unspecified lower limb
G57.51 Tarsal tunnel syndrome, right lower limb
G57.52 Tarsal tunnel syndrome, left lower limb
+ G57.6 Lesion of plantar nerve
Morton's metatarsalgia
G57.60 Lesion of plantar nerve, unspecified lower limb
G57.61 Lesion of plantar nerve, right lower limb
G57.62 Lesion of plantar nerve, left lower limb
+ G57.7 Causalgia of lower limb
Complex regional pain syndrome II of lower limb
Excludes1: *complex regional pain syndrome I of lower limb (G90.52-)*
complex regional pain syndrome I of upper limb (G90.51-)
complex regional pain syndrome II of upper limb (G56.4-)
reflex sympathetic dystrophy of lower limb (G90.52-)
reflex sympathetic dystrophy of upper limb (G90.51-)
G57.70 Causalgia of unspecified lower limb
G57.71 Causalgia of right lower limb
G57.72 Causalgia of left lower limb
+ G57.8 Other specified mononeuropathies of lower limb
Interdigital neuroma of lower limb
G57.80 Other specified mononeuropathies of unspecified lower limb
G57.81 Other specified mononeuropathies of right lower limb
G57.82 Other specified mononeuropathies of left lower limb
+ G57.9 Unspecified mononeuropathy of lower limb
G57.90 Unspecified mononeuropathy of unspecified lower limb
G57.91 Unspecified mononeuropathy of right lower limb
G57.92 Unspecified mononeuropathy of left lower limb

G58 Other mononeuropathies
G58.0 Intercostal neuropathy
G58.7 Mononeuritis multiplex
G58.8 Other specified mononeuropathies
G58.9 Mononeuropathy, unspecified

G59 Mononeuropathy in diseases classified elsewhere
Code first underlying disease
Excludes1: *diabetic mononeuropathy (E08-E13 with .41)*
syphilitic nerve paralysis (A52.19)
syphilitic neuritis (A52.15)
tuberculous mononeuropathy (A17.83)
Valid 3-character code, no further characters required

Polyneuropathies and other disorders of the peripheral nervous system (G60-G65)

Excludes1: *neuralgia NOS (M79.2)*
neuritis NOS (M79.2)
peripheral neuritis in pregnancy (O26.82-)
radiculitis NOS (M54.10)

G60 Hereditary and idiopathic neuropathy
G60.0 Hereditary motor and sensory neuropathy
Charcot-Marie-Tooth disease
Déjérine-Sottas disease
Hereditary motor and sensory neuropathy, types I-IV
Hypertrophic neuropathy of infancy
Peroneal muscular atrophy (axonal type) (hypertrophic type)
Roussy-Levy syndrome

CC **G60.1 Refsum's disease**
Infantile Refsum disease
CC Exclusion see Appendix A PDX collection 0588
G60.2 Neuropathy in association with hereditary ataxia
G60.3 Idiopathic progressive neuropathy
G60.8 Other hereditary and idiopathic neuropathies
Dominantly inherited sensory neuropathy
Morvan's disease
Nelaton's syndrome
Recessively inherited sensory neuropathy
G60.9 Hereditary and idiopathic neuropathy, unspecified

G61 Inflammatory polyneuropathy

CC **G61.0 Guillain-Barre syndrome**
Acute (post-)infective polyneuritis
Miller Fisher Syndrome
CC Exclusion see Appendix A PDX collection 0092
AHA CC: 2Q, 2014, 4
G61.1 Serum neuropathy
Use additional code for adverse effect, if applicable, to identify serum (T50.-)
G61.8 Other inflammatory polyneuropathies
CC **G61.81 Chronic inflammatory demyelinating polyneuritis**
CC Exclusion see Appendix A PDX collection 0589
G61.89 Other inflammatory polyneuropathies
G61.9 Inflammatory polyneuropathy, unspecified

G62 Other and unspecified polyneuropathies

G62.0 Drug-induced polyneuropathy
Use additional code for adverse effect, if applicable, to identify drug (T36-T50 with fifth or sixth character 5)
G62.1 Alcoholic polyneuropathy
G62.2 Polyneuropathy due to other toxic agents
Code first (T51-T65) to identify toxic agent
\+ **G62.8 Other specified polyneuropathies**
CC **G62.81 Critical illness polyneuropathy**
Acute motor neuropathy
CC Exclusion see Appendix A PDX collection 0590
G62.82 Radiation-induced polyneuropathy
Use additional external cause code (W88-W90, X39.0-) to identify cause
G62.89 Other specified polyneuropathies
G62.9 Polyneuropathy, unspecified
Neuropathy NOS

G63 Polyneuropathy in diseases classified elsewhere

Code first underlying disease, such as:
amyloidosis (E85.-)
endocrine disease, except diabetes (E00-E07, E15-E16, E20-E34)
metabolic diseases (E70-E88)
neoplasm (C00-D49)
nutritional deficiency (E40-E64)
Excludes1: *polyneuropathy (in):*
diabetes mellitus (E08-E13 with .42)
diphtheria (A36.83)
infectious mononucleosis (B27.0-B27.9 with 1)
Lyme disease (A69.22)
mumps (B26.84)
postherpetic (B02.23)
rheumatoid arthritis (M05.33)
scleroderma (M34.83)
systemic lupus erythematosus (M32.19)
AHA CC: 4Q, 2012, 99-101
Valid 3-character code, no further characters required

G64 Other disorders of peripheral nervous system

Disorder of peripheral nervous system NOS
Valid 3-character code, no further characters required

G65 Sequelae of inflammatory and toxic polyneuropathies

Code first condition resulting from (sequela) of inflammatory and toxic polyneuropathies
G65.0 Sequelae of Guillain-Barré syndrome
G65.1 Sequelae of other inflammatory polyneuropathy
G65.2 Sequelae of toxic polyneuropathy

Diseases of myoneural junction and muscle (G70-G73)

G70 Myasthenia gravis and other myoneural disorders

Excludes1: *botulism (A05.1, A48.51-A48.52)*
transient neonatal myasthenia gravis (P94.0)
\+ **G70.0 Myasthenia gravis**
G70.00 Myasthenia gravis without (acute) exacerbation
Myasthenia gravis NOS
MCC **G70.01 Myasthenia gravis with (acute) exacerbation**
Myasthenia gravis in crisis
MCC Exclusion see Appendix A PDX collection 0591
G70.1 Toxic myoneural disorders
Code first (T51-T65) to identify toxic agent
G70.2 Congenital and developmental myasthenia
\+ **G70.8 Other specified myoneural disorders**
CC **G70.80 Lambert-Eaton syndrome, unspecified**
Lambert-Eaton syndrome NOS
CC Exclusion see Appendix A PDX collection 0591
CC **G70.81 Lambert-Eaton syndrome in disease classified elsewhere**
Code first underlying disease
Excludes1: *Lambert-Eaton syndrome in neoplastic disease (G73.1)*
CC Exclusion see Appendix A PDX collection 0591
G70.89 Other specified myoneural disorders
G70.9 Myoneural disorder, unspecified

G71 Primary disorders of muscles

Excludes2: *arthrogryposis multiplex congenita (Q74.3)*
metabolic disorders (E70-E88)
myositis (M60.-)
CC **G71.0 Muscular dystrophy**
Autosomal recessive, childhood type, muscular dystrophy resembling Duchenne or Becker muscular dystrophy
Benign [Becker] muscular dystrophy
Benign scapuloperoneal muscular dystrophy with early contractures [Emery-Dreifuss]
Congenital muscular dystrophy NOS
Congenital muscular dystrophy with specific morphological abnormalities of the muscle fiber
Distal muscular dystrophy
Facioscapulohumeral muscular dystrophy
Limb-girdle muscular dystrophy
Ocular muscular dystrophy
Oculopharyngeal muscular dystrophy
Scapuloperoneal muscular dystrophy
Severe [Duchenne] muscular dystrophy
CC Exclusion see Appendix A PDX collection 0592
\+ **G71.1 Myotonic disorders**
G71.11 Myotonic muscular dystrophy
Dystrophia myotonica [Steinert]
Myotonia atrophica
Myotonic dystrophy
Proximal myotonic myopathy (PROMM)
Steinert disease
G71.12 Myotonia congenita
Acetazolamide responsive myotonia congenita
Dominant myotonia congenita [Thomsen disease]
Myotonia levior
Recessive myotonia congenita [Becker disease]
G71.13 Myotonic chondrodystrophy
Chondrodystrophic myotonia
Congenital myotonic chondrodystrophy
Schwartz-Jampel disease
G71.14 Drug induced myotonia
Use additional code for adverse effect, if applicable, to identify drug (T36-T50 with fifth or sixth character
G71.19 Other specified myotonic disorders
Myotonia fluctuans
Myotonia permanens
Neuromyotonia [Isaacs]
Paramyotonia congenita (of von Eulenburg)
Pseudomyotonia
Symptomatic myotonia
CC **G71.2 Congenital myopathies**
Central core disease
Fiber-type disproportion
Minicore disease
Multicore disease
Myotubular (centronuclear) myopathy
Nemaline myopathy
Excludes1: *arthrogryposis multiplex congenita (Q74.3)*
CC Exclusion see Appendix A PDX collection 0592
G71.3 Mitochondrial myopathy, not elsewhere classified
Excludes1: *Kearns-Sayre syndrome (H49.81)*
Leber's disease (H47.21)
Leigh's encephalopathy (G31.82)
mitochondrial metabolism disorders (E88.4.-)
Reye's syndrome (G93.7)

CC **G71.8 Other primary disorders of muscles**
G71.9 Primary disorder of muscle, unspecified
Hereditary myopathy NOS

G72 Other and unspecified myopathies

Excludes1: *arthrogryposis multiplex congenita (Q74.3)*
dermatopolymyositis (M33.-)
ischemic infarction of muscle (M62.2-)
myositis (M60.-)
polymyositis (M33.2.-)

CC **G72.0 Drug-induced myopathy**
Use additional code for adverse effect, if applicable, to identify drug (T36-T50 with fifth or sixth character 5)
CC Exclusion see Appendix A PDX collection 0593

CC **G72.1 Alcoholic myopathy**
Use additional code to identify alcoholism (F10.-)
CC Exclusion see Appendix A PDX collection 0593

CC **G72.2 Myopathy due to other toxic agents**
Code first (T51-T65) to identify toxic agent
CC Exclusion see Appendix A PDX collection 0593

G72.3 Periodic paralysis
Familial periodic paralysis
Hyperkalemic periodic paralysis (familial)
Hypokalemic periodic paralysis (familial)
Myotonic periodic paralysis (familial)
Normokalemic paralysis (familial)
Potassium sensitive periodic paralysis
Excludes1: *paramyotonia congenita (of von Eulenburg) (G71.19)*

\+ **G72.4 Inflammatory and immune myopathies, not elsewhere classified**
G72.41 Inclusion body myositis [IBM]
G72.49 Other inflammatory and immune myopathies, not elsewhere classified
Inflammatory myopathy NOS

\+ **G72.8 Other specified myopathies**
CC **G72.81 Critical illness myopathy**
Acute necrotizing myopathy
Acute quadriplegic myopathy
Intensive care (ICU) myopathy
Myopathy of critical illness
CC Exclusion see Appendix A PDX collection 0594
G72.89 Other specified myopathies

G72.9 Myopathy, unspecified

G73 Disorders of myoneural junction and muscle in diseases classified elsewhere

CC **G73.1 Lambert-Eaton syndrome in neoplastic disease**
Code first underlying neoplasm (C00-D49)
Excludes1: *Lambert-Eaton syndrome not associated with neoplasm (G70.80-G70.81)*
CC Exclusion see Appendix A PDX collection 0591

CC **G73.3 Myasthenic syndromes in other diseases classified elsewhere**
Code first underlying disease, such as:
neoplasm (C00-D49)
thyrotoxicosis (E05.-)
CC Exclusion see Appendix A PDX collection 0591

G73.7 Myopathy in diseases classified elsewhere
Code first underlying disease, such as:
hyperparathyroidism (E21.0, E21.3)
hypoparathyroidism (E20.-)
glycogen storage disease (E74.0)
lipid storage disorders (E75.-)
Excludes1: *myopathy in:*
rheumatoid arthritis (M05.32)
sarcoidosis (D86.87)
scleroderma (M34.82)
sicca syndrome [Sjögren] (M35.03)
systemic lupus erythematosus (M32.19)

erebral palsy and other paralytic syndromes (G80-G83)

G80 Cerebral palsy

Excludes1: *hereditary spastic paraplegia (G11.4)*

MCC **G80.0 Spastic quadriplegic cerebral palsy**
Congenital spastic paralysis (cerebral)
MCC Exclusion see Appendix A PDX collection 0595

CC **G80.1 Spastic diplegic cerebral palsy**
Spastic cerebral palsy NOS
CC Exclusion see Appendix A PDX collection 0596

CC **G80.2 Spastic hemiplegic cerebral palsy**
CC Exclusion see Appendix A PDX collection 0597

CC **G80.3 Athetoid cerebral palsy**
Double athetosis (syndrome)
Dyskinetic cerebral palsy
Dystonic cerebral palsy
Vogt disease
CC Exclusion see Appendix A PDX collection 0598

G80.4 Ataxic cerebral palsy

G80.8 Other cerebral palsy
Mixed cerebral palsy syndromes

G80.9 Cerebral palsy, unspecified
Cerebral palsy NOS

G81 Hemiplegia and hemiparesis

NOTE This category is to be used only when hemiplegia (complete) (incomplete) is reported without further specification, or is stated to be old or longstanding but of unspecified cause. The category is also for use in multiple coding to identify these types of hemiplegia resulting from any cause.

Excludes1: *congenital cerebral palsy (G80.-)*
hemiplegia and hemiparesis due to sequela of cerebrovascular disease (I69.05-, I69.15-, I69.25-, I69.35-, I69.85-, I69.95-)

Review coding guideline C.6.a

\+ **G81.0 Flaccid hemiplegia**
CC **G81.00 Flaccid hemiplegia affecting unspecified side**
CC Exclusion see Appendix A PDX collection 0561
CC **G81.01 Flaccid hemiplegia affecting right dominant side**
CC Exclusion see Appendix A PDX collection 0561
CC **G81.02 Flaccid hemiplegia affecting left dominant side**
CC Exclusion see Appendix A PDX collection 0561
CC **G81.03 Flaccid hemiplegia affecting right nondominant side**
CC Exclusion see Appendix A PDX collection 0561
CC **G81.04 Flaccid hemiplegia affecting left nondominant side**
CC Exclusion see Appendix A PDX collection 0561

\+ **G81.1 Spastic hemiplegia**
CC **G81.10 Spastic hemiplegia affecting unspecified side**
CC Exclusion see Appendix A PDX collection 0561
CC **G81.11 Spastic hemiplegia affecting right dominant side**
CC Exclusion see Appendix A PDX collection 0561
CC **G81.12 Spastic hemiplegia affecting left dominant side**
CC Exclusion see Appendix A PDX collection 0561
CC **G81.13 Spastic hemiplegia affecting right nondominant side**
CC Exclusion see Appendix A PDX collection 0561
CC **G81.14 Spastic hemiplegia affecting left nondominant side**
CC Exclusion see Appendix A PDX collection 0561

\+ **G81.9 Hemiplegia, unspecified**
CC **G81.90 Hemiplegia, unspecified affecting unspecified side**
CC Exclusion see Appendix A PDX collection 0561
CC **G81.91 Hemiplegia, unspecified affecting right dominant side**
CC Exclusion see Appendix A PDX collection 0561
CC **G81.92 Hemiplegia, unspecified affecting left dominant side**
CC Exclusion see Appendix A PDX collection 0561
CC **G81.93 Hemiplegia, unspecified affecting right nondominant side**
CC Exclusion see Appendix A PDX collection 0561
CC **G81.94 Hemiplegia, unspecified affecting left nondominant side**
CC Exclusion see Appendix A PDX collection 0561

G82 Paraplegia (paraparesis) and quadriplegia (quadriparesis)

NOTE This category is to be used only when the listed conditions are reported without further specification, or are stated to be old or longstanding but of unspecified cause. The category is also for use in multiple coding to identify these conditions resulting from any cause

Excludes1: *congenital cerebral palsy (G80.-)*
functional quadriplegia (R53.2)
hysterical paralysis (F44.4)

\+ **G82.2 Paraplegia**
Paralysis of both lower limbs NOS
Paraparesis (lower) NOS
Paraplegia (lower) NOS
CC **G82.20 Paraplegia, unspecified**
CC Exclusion see Appendix A PDX collection 0561
CC **G82.21 Paraplegia, complete**
CC Exclusion see Appendix A PDX collection 0561
CC **G82.22 Paraplegia, incomplete**
CC Exclusion see Appendix A PDX collection 0561

\+ **G82.5 Quadriplegia**
MCC **G82.50 Quadriplegia, unspecified**
MCC Exclusion see Appendix A PDX collection 0595
MCC **G82.51 Quadriplegia, C1-C4 complete**
MCC Exclusion see Appendix A PDX collection 0595
MCC **G82.52 Quadriplegia, C1-C4 incomplete**
MCC Exclusion see Appendix A PDX collection 0595

MCC **G82.53 Quadriplegia, C5-C7 complete**
MCC Exclusion see Appendix A PDX collection 0595
MCC **G82.54 Quadriplegia, C5-C7 incomplete**
MCC Exclusion see Appendix A PDX collection 0595

G83 Other paralytic syndromes

NOTE This category is to be used only when the listed conditions are reported without further specification, or are stated to be old or longstanding but of unspecified cause. The category is also for use in multiple coding to identify these conditions resulting from any cause.

Includes: paralysis (complete) (incomplete), except as in G80-G82

CC **G83.0 Diplegia of upper limbs**
Diplegia (upper)
Paralysis of both upper limbs
CC Exclusion see Appendix A PDX collection 0599

\+ **G83.1 Monoplegia of lower limb**
Paralysis of lower limb
Excludes1: *monoplegia of lower limbs due to sequela of cerebrovasculardisease(I69.04-,I69.14-,I69.24-, I69.34-, I69.84-, I69.94-)*
Review coding guideline C.6.a
G83.10 Monoplegia of lower limb affecting unspecified side
G83.11 Monoplegia of lower limb affecting right dominant side
G83.12 Monoplegia of lower limb affecting left dominant side
G83.13 Monoplegia of lower limb affecting right nondominant side
G83.14 Monoplegia of lower limb affecting left nondominant side

\+ **G83.2 Monoplegia of upper limb**
Paralysis of upper limb
Excludes1: *monoplegia of upper limbs due to sequela of cerebrovasculardisease(I69.03-,I69.13-,I69.23-, I69.33-, I69.83-, I69.93-)*
Review coding guideline C.6.a
G83.20 Monoplegia of upper limb affecting unspecified side
G83.21 Monoplegia of upper limb affecting right dominant side
G83.22 Monoplegia of upper limb affecting left dominant side
G83.23 Monoplegia of upper limb affecting right nondominant side
G83.24 Monoplegia of upper limb affecting left nondominant side

\+ **G83.3 Monoplegia, unspecified**
Review coding guideline C.6.a
G83.30 Monoplegia, unspecified affecting unspecified side
G83.31 Monoplegia, unspecified affecting right dominant side
G83.32 Monoplegia, unspecified affecting left dominant side
G83.33 Monoplegia, unspecified affecting right nondominant side
G83.34 Monoplegia, unspecified affecting left nondominant side

CC **G83.4 Cauda equina syndrome**
Neurogenic bladder due to cauda equina syndrome
Excludes1: *cord bladder NOS (G95.89)*
neurogenic bladder NOS (N31.9)
CC Exclusion see Appendix A PDX collection 0600

MCC **G83.5 Locked-in state**
MCC Exclusion see Appendix A PDX collection 0601

\+ **G83.8 Other specified paralytic syndromes**
Excludes1: *paralytic syndromes due to current spinal cord injury-code to spinal cord injury (S14, S24, S34)*
G83.81 Brown-Séquard syndrome
G83.82 Anterior cord syndrome
G83.83 Posterior cord syndrome
G83.84 Todd's paralysis (postepileptic)
G83.89 Other specified paralytic syndromes

G83.9 Paralytic syndrome, unspecified

Other disorders of the nervous system (G89-G99)

G89 Pain, not elsewhere classified

Code also related psychological factors associated with pain (F45.42)
Excludes1: *generalized pain NOS (R52)*
pain disorders exclusively related to psychological factors (F45.41)
pain NOS (R52)
Excludes2: *atypical face pain (G50.1)*
headache syndromes (G44.-)
localized pain, unspecified type - code to pain by site, such as:
abdomen pain (R10.-)
back pain (M54.9)
breast pain (N64.4)
chest pain (R07.1-R07.9)
ear pain (H92.0-)
eye pain (H57.1)
headache (R51)
joint pain (M25.5-)
limb pain (M79.6-)
lumbar region pain (M54.5)
painful urination (R30.9)
pelvic and perineal pain (R10.2)
shoulder pain (M25.51-)
spine pain (M54.-)
throat pain (R07.0)
tongue pain (K14.6)
tooth pain (K08.8)
renal colic (N23)
migraines (G43.-)
myalgia (M79.1)
pain from prosthetic devices, implants, and grafts (T82.8 T83.84, T84.84, T85.84)
phantom limb syndrome with pain (G54.6)
vulvar vestibulitis (N94.810)
vulvodynia (N94.81-)
Review coding guideline C.5.a
Review coding guidelines C.6.b.1 and C.6.b.3
Review coding guideline C.19.g.2

G89.0 Central pain syndrome
Déjérine-Roussy syndrome
Myelopathic pain syndrome
Thalamic pain syndrome (hyperesthetic)
Review coding guideline C.6.b.6

\+ **G89.1 Acute pain, not elsewhere classified**
G89.11 Acute pain due to trauma
G89.12 Acute post-thoracotomy pain
Post-thoracotomy pain NOS
G89.18 Other acute postprocedural pain
Postoperative pain NOS
Postprocedural pain NOS

\+ **G89.2 Chronic pain, not elsewhere classified**
Excludes1: *causalgia, lower limb (G57.7-)*
causalgia, upper limb (G56.4-)
central pain syndrome (G89.0)
chronic pain syndrome (G89.4)
complex regional pain syndrome II, lower limb (G57.7-)
complex regional pain syndrome II, upper limb (G56.4-)
neoplasm related chronic pain (G89.3)
reflex sympathetic dystrophy (G90.5-)
Review coding guideline C.6.b.4
G89.21 Chronic pain due to trauma
G89.22 Chronic post-thoracotomy pain
G89.28 Other chronic postprocedural pain
Other chronic postoperative pain
G89.29 Other chronic pain

G89.3 Neoplasm related pain (acute) (chronic)
Cancer associated pain
Pain due to malignancy (primary) (secondary)
Tumor associated pain
Review coding guideline C.6.b.5

G89.4 Chronic pain syndrome
Chronic pain associated with significant psychosocial dysfunction
Review coding guideline C.6.b.6

G90 Disorders of autonomic nervous system

Excludes1: *dysfunction of the autonomic nervous system due to alcohol (G31.2)*

\+ **G90.0 Idiopathic peripheral autonomic neuropathy**

G90.01 Carotid sinus syncope

Carotid sinus syndrome

G90.09 Other idiopathic peripheral autonomic neuropathy

Idiopathic peripheral autonomic neuropathy NOS

G90.1 Familial dysautonomia [Riley-Day]

G90.2 Horner's syndrome

Bernard(-Horner) syndrome

Cervical sympathetic dystrophy or paralysis

CC **G90.3 Multi-system degeneration of the autonomic nervous system**

Neurogenic orthostatic hypotension [Shy-Drager]

Excludes1: *orthostatic hypotension NOS (I95.1)*

CC Exclusion see Appendix A PDX collection 0573

G90.4 Autonomic dysreflexia

Use additional code to identify the cause, such as:

fecal impaction (K56.41)

pressure ulcer (pressure area) (L89.-)

urinary tract infection (N39.0)

\+ **G90.5 Complex regional pain syndrome I (CRPS I)**

Reflex sympathetic dystrophy

Excludes1: *causalgia of lower limb (G57.7-)*
causalgia of upper limb (G56.4-)
complex regional pain syndrome II of lower limb (G57.7-)
complex regional pain syndrome II of upper limb (G56.4-)

CC **G90.50 Complex regional pain syndrome I, unspecified**

CC Exclusion see Appendix A PDX collection 0602

\+ **G90.51 Complex regional pain syndrome I of upper limb**

CC **G90.511 Complex regional pain syndrome I of right upper limb**

CC Exclusion see Appendix A PDX collection 0603

CC **G90.512 Complex regional pain syndrome I of left upper limb**

CC Exclusion see Appendix A PDX collection 0603

CC **G90.513 Complex regional pain syndrome I of upper limb, bilateral**

CC Exclusion see Appendix A PDX collection 0603

CC **G90.519 Complex regional pain syndrome I of unspecified upper limb**

CC Exclusion see Appendix A PDX collection 0603

\+ **G90.52 Complex regional pain syndrome I of lower limb**

CC **G90.521 Complex regional pain syndrome I of right lower limb**

CC Exclusion see Appendix A PDX collection 0603

CC **G90.522 Complex regional pain syndrome I of left lower limb**

CC Exclusion see Appendix A PDX collection 0603

CC **G90.523 Complex regional pain syndrome I of lower limb, bilateral**

CC Exclusion see Appendix A PDX collection 0603

CC **G90.529 Complex regional pain syndrome I of unspecified lower limb**

CC Exclusion see Appendix A PDX collection 0603

CC **G90.59 Complex regional pain syndrome I of other specified site**

CC Exclusion see Appendix A PDX collection 0603

G90.8 Other disorders of autonomic nervous system

G90.9 Disorder of the autonomic nervous system, unspecified

G91 Hydrocephalus

Includes: acquired hydrocephalus

Excludes1: *Arnold-Chiari syndrome with hydrocephalus (Q07.-)*
congenital hydrocephalus (Q03.-)
spina bifida with hydrocephalus (Q05.-)

CC **G91.0 Communicating hydrocephalus**

Secondary normal pressure hydrocephalus

CC Exclusion see Appendix A PDX collection 0604

CC **G91.1 Obstructive hydrocephalus**

CC Exclusion see Appendix A PDX collection 0605

CC **G91.2 (Idiopathic) normal pressure hydrocephalus**

Normal pressure hydrocephalus NOS

CC Exclusion see Appendix A PDX collection 0604

CC **G91.3 Post-traumatic hydrocephalus, unspecified**

CC Exclusion see Appendix A PDX collection 0605

G91.4 Hydrocephalus in diseases classified elsewhere

Code first underlying condition, such as:

congenital syphilis (A50.4-)

neoplasm (C00-D49)

Excludes1: *hydrocephalus due to congenital toxoplasmosis (P37.1)*

CC **G91.8 Other hydrocephalus**

CC Exclusion see Appendix A PDX collection 0605

CC **G91.9 Hydrocephalus, unspecified**

CC Exclusion see Appendix A PDX collection 0605

MCC **G92 Toxic encephalopathy**

Toxic encephalitis

Toxic metabolic encephalopathy

Code first (T51-T65) to identify toxic agent

MCC Exclusion see Appendix A PDX collection 0606

Valid 3-character code, no further characters required

G93 Other disorders of brain

G93.0 Cerebral cysts

Arachnoid cyst

Porencephalic cyst, acquired

Excludes1: *acquired periventricular cysts of newborn (P91.1)*
congenital cerebral cysts (Q04.6)

CC **G93.1 Anoxic brain damage, not elsewhere classified**

Excludes1: *cerebral anoxia due to anesthesia during labor and delivery (O74.3)*
cerebral anoxia due to anesthesia during the puerperium (O89.2)
neonatal anoxia (P84)

CC Exclusion see Appendix A PDX collection 0607

G93.2 Benign intracranial hypertension

Excludes1: *hypertensive encephalopathy (I67.4)*

G93.3 Postviral fatigue syndrome

Benign myalgic encephalomyelitis

Excludes1: *chronic fatigue syndrome NOS (R53.82)*

\+ **G93.4 Other and unspecified encephalopathy**

Excludes1: alcoholic encephalopathy (G31.2)
encephalopathy in diseases classified elsewhere (G94)
hypertensive encephalopathy (I67.4)
toxic (metabolic) encephalopathy (G92)

MCC **G93.40 Encephalopathy, unspecified**

MCC Exclusion see Appendix A PDX collection 0608

MCC **G93.41 Metabolic encephalopathy**

Septic encephalopathy

MCC Exclusion see Appendix A PDX collection 0609

MCC **G93.49 Other encephalopathy**

Encephalopathy NEC

MCC Exclusion see Appendix A PDX collection 0610

MCC **G93.5 Compression of brain**

Arnold-Chiari type 1 compression of brain

Compression of brain (stem)

Herniation of brain (stem)

Excludes1: *diffuse traumatic compression of brain (S06.2-)*
focal traumatic compression of brain (S06.3-)

MCC Exclusion see Appendix A PDX collection 0611

MCC **G93.6 Cerebral edema**

Excludes1: *cerebral edema due to birth injury (P11.0)*
traumatic cerebral edema (S06.1-)

MCC Exclusion see Appendix A PDX collection 0612

• MCC **G93.7 Reye's syndrome**

Code first (T39.0-), if salicylates-induced

MCC Exclusion see Appendix A PDX collection 0613

\+ **G93.8 Other specified disorders of brain**

G93.81 Temporal sclerosis

Hippocampal sclerosis

Mesial temporal sclerosis

MCC **G93.82 Brain death**

MCC Exclusion see Appendix A PDX collection 0515

G93.89 Other specified disorders of brain

Postradiation encephalopathy

G93.9 Disorder of brain, unspecified

G94 Other disorders of brain in diseases classified elsewhere

Code first underlying disease

Excludes1: *encephalopathy in congenital syphilis (A50.49)*
encephalopathy in influenza (J09.X9, J10.81, J11.81)
encephalopathy in syphilis (A52.19)
hydrocephalus in diseases classified elsewhere (G91.4)

Valid 3-character code, no further characters required

G95 Other and unspecified diseases of spinal cord

Excludes2: *myelitis (G04.-)*

CC **G95.0 Syringomyelia and syringobulbia**
CC Exclusion see Appendix A PDX collection 0614

+ **G95.1 Vascular myelopathies**
Excludes2: *intraspinal phlebitis and thrombophlebitis, except non-pyogenic (G08)*

MCC **G95.11 Acute infarction of spinal cord (embolic) (nonembolic)**
Anoxia of spinal cord
Arterial thrombosis of spinal cord
MCC Exclusion see Appendix A PDX collection 0603

MCC **G95.19 Other vascular myelopathies**
Edema of spinal cord
Hematomyelia
Nonpyogenic intraspinal phlebitis and thrombophlebitis
Subacute necrotic myelopathy
MCC Exclusion see Appendix A PDX collection 0603

+ **G95.2 Other and unspecified cord compression**

CC **G95.20 Unspecified cord compression**
CC Exclusion see Appendix A PDX collection 0615

CC **G95.29 Other cord compression**
CC Exclusion see Appendix A PDX collection 0615

+ **G95.8 Other specified diseases of spinal cord**
Excludes1: *neurogenic bladder NOS (N31.9)*
neurogenic bladder due to cauda equina syndrome (G83.4)
neuromuscular dysfunction of bladder without spinal cord lesion (N31.-)

CC **G95.81 Conus medullaris syndrome**
CC Exclusion see Appendix A PDX collection 0603

CC **G95.89 Other specified diseases of spinal cord**
Cord bladder NOS
Drug-induced myelopathy
Radiation-induced myelopathy
Excludes1: *myelopathy NOS (G95.9)*
CC Exclusion see Appendix A PDX collection 0603

CC **G95.9 Disease of spinal cord, unspecified**
Myelopathy NOS
CC Exclusion see Appendix A PDX collection 0615

G96 Other disorders of central nervous system

CC **G96.0 Cerebrospinal fluid leak**
Excludes1: *cerebrospinal fluid leak from spinal puncture (G97.0)*
CC Exclusion see Appendix A PDX collection 0616

+ **G96.1 Disorders of meninges, not elsewhere classified**

CC **G96.11 Dural tear**
Excludes1: *accidental puncture or laceration of dura during a procedure (G97.41)*
CC Exclusion see Appendix A PDX collection 0509

G96.12 Meningeal adhesions (cerebral) (spinal)

G96.19 Other disorders of meninges, not elsewhere classified

G96.8 Other specified disorders of central nervous system

G96.9 Disorder of central nervous system, unspecified

G97 Intraoperative and postprocedural complications and disorders of nervous system, not elsewhere classified

Excludes2: *intraoperative and postprocedural cerebrovascular infarction (I97.81-, I97.82-)*

CC **G97.0 Cerebrospinal fluid leak from spinal puncture**
CC Exclusion see Appendix A PDX collection 0617

G97.1 Other reaction to spinal and lumbar puncture
Headache due to lumbar puncture

CC **G97.2 Intracranial hypotension following ventricular shunting**
CC Exclusion see Appendix A PDX collection 0617

+ **G97.3 Intraoperative hemorrhage and hematoma of a nervous system organ or structure complicating a procedure**
Excludes1: *intraoperative hemorrhage and hematoma of a nervous system organ or structure due to accidental puncture and laceration during a procedure (G97.4-)*

CC **G97.31 Intraoperative hemorrhage and hematoma of a nervous system organ or structure complicating a nervous system procedure**
CC Exclusion see Appendix A PDX collection 0618

CC **G97.32 Intraoperative hemorrhage and hematoma of a nervous system organ or structure complicating other procedure**
CC Exclusion see Appendix A PDX collection 0618

+ **G97.4 Accidental puncture and laceration of a nervous system orga or structure during a procedure**

CC **G97.41 Accidental puncture or laceration of dura during a procedure**
Incidental (inadvertent) durotomy
CC Exclusion see Appendix A PDX collection 0509

CC **G97.48 Accidental puncture and laceration of other nervou system organ or structure during a nervous system procedure**
CC Exclusion see Appendix A PDX collection 0509

CC **G97.49 Accidental puncture and laceration of other nervou system organ or structure during other procedure**
CC Exclusion see Appendix A PDX collection 0509

+ **G97.5 Postprocedural hemorrhage and hematoma of a nervous syst organ or structure following a procedure**

CC **G97.51 Postprocedural hemorrhage and hematoma of a nervous system organ or structure following a nerv system procedure**
CC Exclusion see Appendix A PDX collection 0619

CC **G97.52 Postprocedural hemorrhage and hematoma of a nervous system organ or structure following other procedure**
CC Exclusion see Appendix A PDX collection 0619

+ **G97.8 Other intraoperative and postprocedural complications and disorders of nervous system**
Use additional code to further specify disorder

CC **G97.81 Other intraoperative complications of nervous syste**
CC Exclusion see Appendix A PDX collection 0617

CC **G97.82 Other postprocedural complications and disorders nervous system**
CC Exclusion see Appendix A PDX collection 0617

G98 Other disorders of nervous system not elsewhere classified

Includes: nervous system disorder NOS

G98.0 Neurogenic arthritis, not elsewhere classified
Nonsyphilitic neurogenic arthropathy NEC
Nonsyphilitic neurogenic spondylopathy NEC
Excludes1: *spondylopathy (in):*
syringomyelia and syringobulbia (G95.0)
tabes dorsalis (A52.11)

G98.8 Other disorders of nervous system
Nervous system disorder NOS

G99 Other disorders of nervous system in diseases classified elsewhere

CC **G99.0 Autonomic neuropathy in diseases classified elsewhere**
Code first underlying disease, such as:
amyloidosis (E85.-)
gout (M1A.-, M10.-)
hyperthyroidism (E05.-)
Excludes1: *diabetic autonomic neuropathy (E08-E13 with .43*
CC Exclusion see Appendix A PDX collection 0620

CC **G99.2 Myelopathy in diseases classified elsewhere**
Code first underlying disease, such as:
neoplasm (C00-D49)
Excludes1: *myelopathy in:*
intervertebral disease (M50.0-, M51.0-)
spondylosis (M47.0-, M47.1-)
CC Exclusion see Appendix A PDX collection 0603

G99.8 Other specified disorders of nervous system in diseases classifi elsewhere
Code first underlying disorder, such as:
amyloidosis (E85.-)
avitaminosis (E56.9)
Excludes1: *nervous system involvement in:*
cysticercosis (B69.0)
rubella (B06.0-)
syphilis (A52.1-)

hapter 7: Diseases of the Eye and Adnexa (00-H59)

TE Use an external cause code following the code for the eye condition, if applicable, to identify the cause of the eye condition

cludes2: *certain conditions originating in the perinatal period (P04-P96)*
certain infectious and parasitic diseases (A00-B99)
complications of pregnancy, childbirth and the puerperium (O00-O9A)
congenital malformations, deformations, and chromosomal abnormalities (Q00-Q99)
diabetes mellitus related eye conditions (E09.3-, E10.3-, E11.3-, E13.3-)
endocrine, nutritional and metabolic diseases (E00-E88)
injury (trauma) of eye and orbit (S05.-)
injury, poisoning and certain other consequences of external causes (S00-T88)
neoplasms (C00-D49)
symptoms, signs and abnormal clinical and laboratory findings, not elsewhere classified (R00-R94)
syphilis related eye disorders (A50.01, A50.3-, A51.43, A52.71)

is chapter contains the following category blocks:

H00-H05	Disorders of eyelid, lacrimal system and orbit
H10-H11	Disorders of conjunctiva
H15-H22	Disorders of sclera, cornea, iris and ciliary body
H25-H28	Disorders of lens
H30-H36	Disorders of choroid and retina
H40-H42	Glaucoma
H43-H44	Disorders of vitreous body and globe
H46-H47	Disorders of optic nerve and visual pathways
H49-H52	Disorders of ocular muscles, binocular movement, accommodation and refraction
H53-H54	Visual disturbances and blindness
H55-H57	Other disorders of eye and adnexa
H59	Intraoperative and postprocedural complications and disorders of eye and adnexa, not elsewhere classified

Chapter-Specific Coding Guidelines

addition to general coding guidelines, there are guidelines for specific diagnoses d/or conditions in the classification. Unless otherwise indicated, these guidelines ply to all health care settings. Please refer to Section II for guidelines on the ection of principal diagnosis.

Chapter 7: Diseases of the Eye and Adnexa (H00-H59)

a. Glaucoma

1) Assigning Glaucoma Codes

Assign as many codes from category H40, Glaucoma, as needed to identify the type of glaucoma, the affected eye, and the glaucoma stage.

2) Bilateral glaucoma with same type and stage

When a patient has bilateral glaucoma and both eyes are documented as being the same type and stage, and there is a code for bilateral glaucoma, report only the code for the type of glaucoma, bilateral, with the seventh character for the stage.

When a patient has bilateral glaucoma and both eyes are documented as being the same type and stage, and the classification does not provide a code for bilateral glaucoma (i.e. subcategories H40.10, H40.11 and H40.20) report only one code for the type of glaucoma with the appropriate seventh character for the stage.

3) Bilateral glaucoma stage with different types or stages

When a patient has bilateral glaucoma and each eye is documented as having a different type or stage, and the classification distinguishes laterality, assign the appropriatecode for each eye rather than the code for bilateral glaucoma.

When a patient has bilateral glaucoma and each eye is documented as having a different type, and the classification does not distinguish laterality (i.e. subcategories H40.10, H40.11 and H40.20), assign one code for each type of glaucoma with the appropriate seventh character for the stage.

When a patient has bilateral glaucoma and each eye is documented as having the same type, but different stage, and the classification does not distinguish laterality (i.e. subcategories H40.10, H40.11 and H40.20), assign a code for the type of glaucoma for each eye with the seventh character for the specific glaucoma stage documented for each eye.

4) Patient admitted with glaucoma and stage evolves during the admission

If a patient is admitted with glaucoma and the stage progresses during the admission, assign the code for highest stage documented.

5) Indeterminate stage glaucoma

Assignment of the seventh character "4" for "indeterminate stage" should be based on the clinical documentation. The seventh character "4" is used for glaucomas whose stage cannot be clinically determined. This seventh character should not be confused with the seventh character "0", unspecified, which should be assigned when there is no documentation regarding the stage of the glaucoma.

Disorders of eyelid, lacrimal system and orbit (H00-H05)

Excludes2: *open wound of eyelid (S01.1-)*
superficial injury of eyelid (S00.1-, S00.2-)

H00 Hordeolum and chalazion

\+ **H00.0 Hordeolum (externum) (internum) of eyelid**

\+ **H00.01 Hordeolum externum**
Hordeolum NOS
Stye
H00.011 Hordeolum externum right upper eyelid
H00.012 Hordeolum externum right lower eyelid
H00.013 Hordeolum externum right eye, unspecified eyelid
H00.014 Hordeolum externum left upper eyelid
H00.015 Hordeolum externum left lower eyelid
H00.016 Hordeolum externum left eye, unspecified eyelid
H00.019 Hordeolum externum unspecified eye, unspecified eyelid

\+ **H00.02 Hordeolum internum**
Infection of meibomian gland
H00.021 Hordeolum internum right upper eyelid
H00.022 Hordeolum internum right lower eyelid
H00.023 Hordeolum internum right eye, unspecified eyelid
H00.024 Hordeolum internum left upper eyelid
H00.025 Hordeolum internum left lower eyelid
H00.026 Hordeolum internum left eye, unspecified eyelid
H00.029 Hordeolum internum unspecified eye, unspecified eyelid

\+ **H00.03 Abscess of eyelid**
Furuncle of eyelid
H00.031 Abscess of right upper eyelid
H00.032 Abscess of right lower eyelid
H00.033 Abscess of eyelid right eye, unspecified eyelid
H00.034 Abscess of left upper eyelid
H00.035 Abscess of left lower eyelid
H00.036 Abscess of eyelid left eye, unspecified eyelid
H00.039 Abscess of eyelid unspecified eye, unspecified eyelid

\+ **H00.1 Chalazion**
Meibomian (gland) cyst
Excludes2: *infected meibomian gland (H00.02-)*
H00.11 Chalazion right upper eyelid
H00.12 Chalazion right lower eyelid
H00.13 Chalazion right eye, unspecified eyelid
H00.14 Chalazion left upper eyelid
H00.15 Chalazion left lower eyelid
H00.16 Chalazion left eye, unspecified eyelid
H00.19 Chalazion unspecified eye, unspecified eyelid

H01 Other inflammation of eyelid

\+ **H01.0 Blepharitis**
Excludes1: *blepharoconjunctivitis (H10.5-)*

\+ **H01.00 Unspecified blepharitis**
H01.001 Unspecified blepharitis right upper eyelid
H01.002 Unspecified blepharitis right lower eyelid
H01.003 Unspecified blepharitis right eye, unspecified eyelid
H01.004 Unspecified blepharitis left upper eyelid
H01.005 Unspecified blepharitis left lower eyelid
H01.006 Unspecified blepharitis left eye, unspecified eyelid
H01.009 Unspecified blepharitis unspecified eye, unspecified eyelid

\+ **H01.01 Ulcerative blepharitis**
H01.011 Ulcerative blepharitis right upper eyelid
H01.012 Ulcerative blepharitis right lower eyelid
H01.013 Ulcerative blepharitis right eye, unspecified eyelid
H01.014 Ulcerative blepharitis left upper eyelid
H01.015 Ulcerative blepharitis left lower eyelid
H01.016 Ulcerative blepharitis left eye, unspecified eyelid
H01.019 Ulcerative blepharitis unspecified eye, unspecified eyelid

Eye

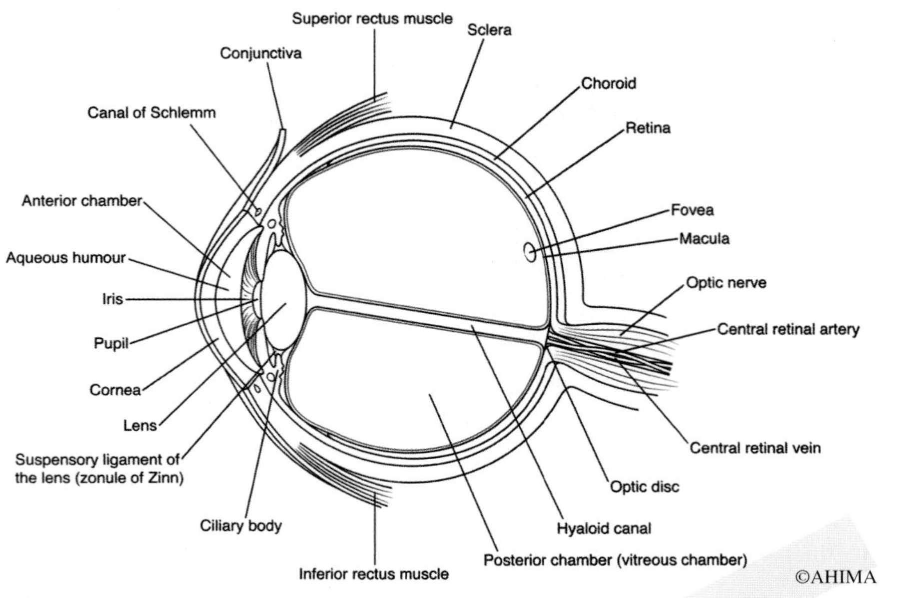
Superior rectus muscle
Sclera
Conjunctiva
Choroid
Canal of Schlemm
Retina
Anterior chamber
Fovea
Macula
Aqueous humour
Optic nerve
Iris
Central retinal artery
Pupil
Cornea
Lens
Central retinal vein
Suspensory ligament of the lens (zonule of Zinn)
Optic disc
Ciliary body
Hyaloid canal
Posterior chamber (vitreous chamber)
Inferior rectus muscle
©AHIMA

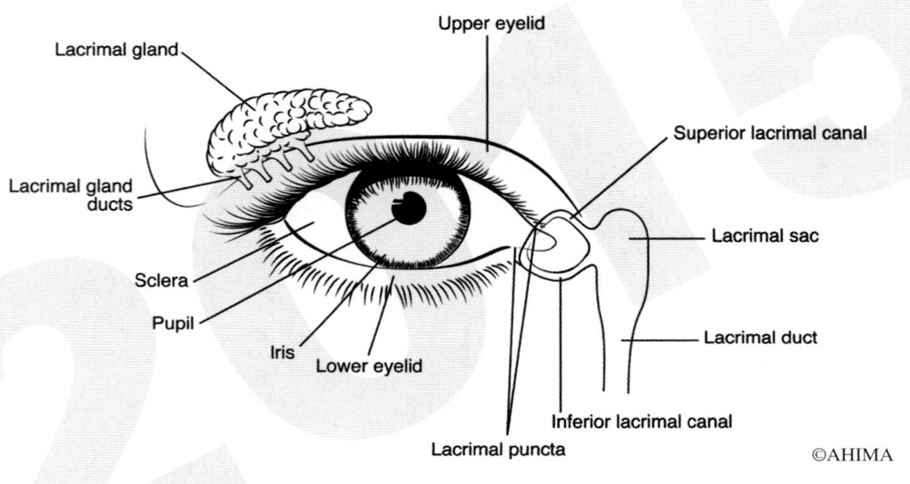
Upper eyelid
Lacrimal gland
Superior lacrimal canal
Lacrimal gland ducts
Lacrimal sac
Sclera
Pupil
Iris
Lower eyelid
Lacrimal duct
Inferior lacrimal canal
Lacrimal puncta
©AHIMA

Muscles of the Eye

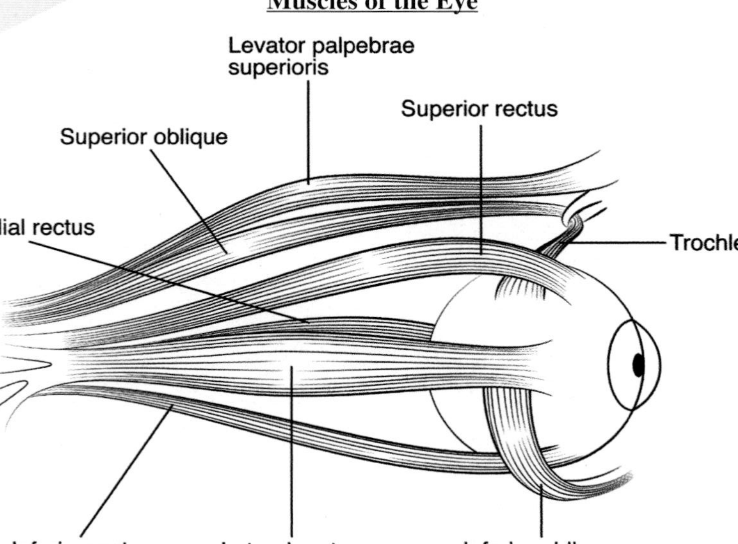
Levator palpebrae superioris
Superior rectus
Superior oblique
Medial rectus
Trochlea
Inferior rectus
Lateral rectus
Inferior oblique
©AHIMA

\+ **H01.02 Squamous blepharitis**
- **H01.021 Squamous blepharitis right upper eyelid**
- **H01.022 Squamous blepharitis right lower eyelid**
- **H01.023 Squamous blepharitis right eye, unspecified eyelid**
- **H01.024 Squamous blepharitis left upper eyelid**
- **H01.025 Squamous blepharitis left lower eyelid**
- **H01.026 Squamous blepharitis left eye, unspecified eyelid**
- **H01.029 Squamous blepharitis unspecified eye, unspecified eyelid**

\+ **H01.1 Noninfectious dermatoses of eyelid**

\+ **H01.11 Allergic dermatitis of eyelid**

Contact dermatitis of eyelid
- **H01.111 Allergic dermatitis of right upper eyelid**
- **H01.112 Allergic dermatitis of right lower eyelid**
- **H01.113 Allergic dermatitis of right eye, unspecified eyelid**
- **H01.114 Allergic dermatitis of left upper eyelid**
- **H01.115 Allergic dermatitis of left lower eyelid**
- **H01.116 Allergic dermatitis of left eye, unspecified eyelid**
- **H01.119 Allergic dermatitis of unspecified eye, unspecified eyelid**

\+ **H01.12 Discoid lupus erythematosus of eyelid**
- **H01.121 Discoid lupus erythematosus of right upper eyelid**
- **H01.122 Discoid lupus erythematosus of right lower eyelid**
- **H01.123 Discoid lupus erythematosus of right eye, unspecified eyelid**
- **H01.124 Discoid lupus erythematosus of left upper eyelid**
- **H01.125 Discoid lupus erythematosus of left lower eyelid**
- **H01.126 Discoid lupus erythematosus of left eye, unspecified eyelid**
- **H01.129 Discoid lupus erythematosus of unspecified eye, unspecified eyelid**

\+ **H01.13 Eczematous dermatitis of eyelid**
- **H01.131 Eczematous dermatitis of right upper eyelid**
- **H01.132 Eczematous dermatitis of right lower eyelid**
- **H01.133 Eczematous dermatitis of right eye, unspecified eyelid**
- **H01.134 Eczematous dermatitis of left upper eyelid**
- **H01.135 Eczematous dermatitis of left lower eyelid**
- **H01.136 Eczematous dermatitis of left eye, unspecified eyelid**
- **H01.139 Eczematous dermatitis of unspecified eye, unspecified eyelid**

\+ **H01.14 Xeroderma of eyelid**
- **H01.141 Xeroderma of right upper eyelid**
- **H01.142 Xeroderma of right lower eyelid**
- **H01.143 Xeroderma of right eye, unspecified eyelid**
- **H01.144 Xeroderma of left upper eyelid**
- **H01.145 Xeroderma of left lower eyelid**
- **H01.146 Xeroderma of left eye, unspecified eyelid**
- **H01.149 Xeroderma of unspecified eye, unspecified eyelid**

H01.8 Other specified inflammations of eyelid

H01.9 Unspecified inflammation of eyelid

Inflammation of eyelid NOS

H02 Other disorders of eyelid

Excludes1: *congenital malformations of eyelid (Q10.0-Q10.3)*

\+ **H02.0 Entropion and trichiasis of eyelid**

\+ **H02.00 Unspecified entropion of eyelid**
- **H02.001 Unspecified entropion of right upper eyelid**
- **H02.002 Unspecified entropion of right lower eyelid**
- **H02.003 Unspecified entropion of right eye, unspecified eyelid**
- **H02.004 Unspecified entropion of left upper eyelid**
- **H02.005 Unspecified entropion of left lower eyelid**
- **H02.006 Unspecified entropion of left eye, unspecified eyelid**
- **H02.009 Unspecified entropion of unspecified eye, unspecified eyelid**

\+ **H02.01 Cicatricial entropion of eyelid**
- **H02.011 Cicatricial entropion of right upper eyelid**
- **H02.012 Cicatricial entropion of right lower eyelid**
- **H02.013 Cicatricial entropion of right eye, unspecified eyelid**
- **H02.014 Cicatricial entropion of left upper eyelid**
- **H02.015 Cicatricial entropion of left lower eyelid**
- **H02.016 Cicatricial entropion of left eye, unspecified eyelid**
- **H02.019 Cicatricial entropion of unspecified eye, unspecified eyelid**

\+ **H02.02 Mechanical entropion of eyelid**
- **H02.021 Mechanical entropion of right upper eyelid**
- **H02.022 Mechanical entropion of right lower eyelid**
- **H02.023 Mechanical entropion of right eye, unspecified eyelid**
- **H02.024 Mechanical entropion of left upper eyelid**
- **H02.025 Mechanical entropion of left lower eyelid**
- **H02.026 Mechanical entropion of left eye, unspecified eyelid**
- **H02.029 Mechanical entropion of unspecified eye, unspecified eyelid**

\+ **H02.03 Senile entropion of eyelid**
- • **H02.031 Senile entropion of right upper eyelid**
- • **H02.032 Senile entropion of right lower eyelid**
- • **H02.033 Senile entropion of right eye, unspecified eyelid**
- • **H02.034 Senile entropion of left upper eyelid**
- • **H02.035 Senile entropion of left lower eyelid**
- • **H02.036 Senile entropion of left eye, unspecified eyelid**
- • **H02.039 Senile entropion of unspecified eye, unspecified eyelid**

\+ **H02.04 Spastic entropion of eyelid**
- **H02.041 Spastic entropion of right upper eyelid**
- **H02.042 Spastic entropion of right lower eyelid**
- **H02.043 Spastic entropion of right eye, unspecified eyelid**
- **H02.044 Spastic entropion of left upper eyelid**
- **H02.045 Spastic entropion of left lower eyelid**
- **H02.046 Spastic entropion of left eye, unspecified eyelid**
- **H02.049 Spastic entropion of unspecified eye, unspecified eyelid**

\+ **H02.05 Trichiasis without entropian**
- **H02.051 Trichiasis without entropian right upper eyelid**
- **H02.052 Trichiasis without entropian right lower eyelid**
- **H02.053 Trichiasis without entropian right eye, unspecified eyelid**
- **H02.054 Trichiasis without entropian left upper eyelid**
- **H02.055 Trichiasis without entropian left lower eyelid**
- **H02.056 Trichiasis without entropian left eye, unspecified eyelid**
- **H02.059 Trichiasis without entropian unspecified eye, unspecified eyelid**

\+ **H02.1 Ectropion of eyelid**

\+ **H02.10 Unspecified ectropion of eyelid**
- **H02.101 Unspecified ectropion of right upper eyelid**
- **H02.102 Unspecified ectropion of right lower eyelid**
- **H02.103 Unspecified ectropion of right eye, unspecified eyelid**
- **H02.104 Unspecified ectropion of left upper eyelid**
- **H02.105 Unspecified ectropion of left lower eyelid**
- **H02.106 Unspecified ectropion of left eye, unspecified eyelid**
- **H02.109 Unspecified ectropion of unspecified eye, unspecified eyelid**

\+ **H02.11 Cicatricial ectropion of eyelid**
- **H02.111 Cicatricial ectropion of right upper eyelid**
- **H02.112 Cicatricial ectropion of right lower eyelid**
- **H02.113 Cicatricial ectropion of right eye, unspecified eyelid**
- **H02.114 Cicatricial ectropion of left upper eyelid**
- **H02.115 Cicatricial ectropion of left lower eyelid**
- **H02.116 Cicatricial ectropion of left eye, unspecified eyelid**
- **H02.119 Cicatricial ectropion of unspecified eye, unspecified eyelid**

\+ **H02.12 Mechanical ectropion of eyelid**
- **H02.121 Mechanical ectropion of right upper eyelid**
- **H02.122 Mechanical ectropion of right lower eyelid**
- **H02.123 Mechanical ectropion of right eye, unspecified eyelid**
- **H02.124 Mechanical ectropion of left upper eyelid**

H02.125 **Mechanical ectropion of left lower eyelid**
H02.126 **Mechanical ectropion of left eye, unspecified eyelid**
H02.129 **Mechanical ectropion of unspecified eye, unspecified eyelid**
+ **H02.13** Senile ectropion of eyelid
• **H02.131** **Senile ectropion of right upper eyelid**
• **H02.132** **Senile ectropion of right lower eyelid**
• **H02.133** **Senile ectropion of right eye, unspecified eyelid**
• **H02.134** **Senile ectropion of left upper eyelid**
• **H02.135** **Senile ectropion of left lower eyelid**
• **H02.136** **Senile ectropion of left eye, unspecified eyelid**
• **H02.139** **Senile ectropion of unspecified eye, unspecified eyelid**
+ **H02.14** Spastic ectropion of eyelid
H02.141 **Spastic ectropion of right upper eyelid**
H02.142 **Spastic ectropion of right lower eyelid**
H02.143 **Spastic ectropion of right eye, unspecified eyelid**
H02.144 **Spastic ectropion of left upper eyelid**
H02.145 **Spastic ectropion of left lower eyelid**
H02.146 **Spastic ectropion of left eye, unspecified eyelid**
H02.149 **Spastic ectropion of unspecified eye, unspecified eyelid**
+ **H02.2** Lagophthalmos
+ **H02.20** Unspecified lagophthalmos
H02.201 **Unspecified lagophthalmos right upper eyelid**
H02.202 **Unspecified lagophthalmos right lower eyelid**
H02.203 **Unspecified lagophthalmos right eye, unspecified eyelid**
H02.204 **Unspecified lagophthalmos left upper eyelid**
H02.205 **Unspecified lagophthalmos left lower eyelid**
H02.206 **Unspecified lagophthalmos left eye, unspecified eyelid**
H02.209 **Unspecified lagophthalmos unspecified eye, unspecified eyelid**
+ **H02.21** Cicatricial lagophthalmos
H02.211 **Cicatricial lagophthalmos right upper eyelid**
H02.212 **Cicatricial lagophthalmos right lower eyelid**
H02.213 **Cicatricial lagophthalmos right eye, unspecified eyelid**
H02.214 **Cicatricial lagophthalmos left upper eyelid**
H02.215 **Cicatricial lagophthalmos left lower eyelid**
H02.216 **Cicatricial lagophthalmos left eye, unspecified eyelid**
H02.219 **Cicatricial lagophthalmos unspecified eye, unspecified eyelid**
+ **H02.22** Mechanical lagophthalmos
H02.221 **Mechanical lagophthalmos right upper eyelid**
H02.222 **Mechanical lagophthalmos right lower eyelid**
H02.223 **Mechanical lagophthalmos right eye, unspecified eyelid**
H02.224 **Mechanical lagophthalmos left upper eyelid**
H02.225 **Mechanical lagophthalmos left lower eyelid**
H02.226 **Mechanical lagophthalmos left eye, unspecified eyelid**
H02.229 **Mechanical lagophthalmos unspecified eye, unspecified eyelid**
+ **H02.23** Paralytic lagophthalmos
H02.231 **Paralytic lagophthalmos right upper eyelid**
H02.232 **Paralytic lagophthalmos right lower eyelid**
H02.233 **Paralytic lagophthalmos right eye, unspecified eyelid**
H02.234 **Paralytic lagophthalmos left upper eyelid**
H02.235 **Paralytic lagophthalmos left lower eyelid**
H02.236 **Paralytic lagophthalmos left eye, unspecified eyelid**
H02.239 **Paralytic lagophthalmos unspecified eye, unspecified eyelid**
+ **H02.3** Blepharochalasis
Pseudoptosis
H02.30 **Blepharochalasis unspecified eye, unspecified eyelid**
H02.31 **Blepharochalasis right upper eyelid**
H02.32 **Blepharochalasis right lower eyelid**
H02.33 **Blepharochalasis right eye, unspecified eyelid**
H02.34 **Blepharochalasis left upper eyelid**
H02.35 **Blepharochalasis left lower eyelid**
H02.36 **Blepharochalasis left eye, unspecified eyelid**

+ **H02.4** Ptosis of eyelid
+ **H02.40** Unspecified ptosis of eyelid
H02.401 **Unspecified ptosis of right eyelid**
H02.402 **Unspecified ptosis of left eyelid**
H02.403 **Unspecified ptosis of bilateral eyelids**
H02.409 **Unspecified ptosis of unspecified eyelid**
+ **H02.41** Mechanical ptosis of eyelid
H02.411 **Mechanical ptosis of right eyelid**
H02.412 **Mechanical ptosis of left eyelid**
H02.413 **Mechanical ptosis of bilateral eyelids**
H02.419 **Mechanical ptosis of unspecified eyelid**
+ **H02.42** Myogenic ptosis of eyelid
H02.421 **Myogenic ptosis of right eyelid**
H02.422 **Myogenic ptosis of left eyelid**
H02.423 **Myogenic ptosis of bilateral eyelids**
H02.429 **Myogenic ptosis of unspecified eyelid**
+ **H02.43** Paralytic ptosis of eyelid
Neurogenic ptosis of eyelid
H02.431 **Paralytic ptosis of right eyelid**
H02.432 **Paralytic ptosis of left eyelid**
H02.433 **Paralytic ptosis of bilateral eyelids**
H02.439 **Paralytic ptosis unspecified eyelid**
+ **H02.5** Other disorders affecting eyelid function
Excludes2: *blepharospasm (G24.5)*
organic tic (G25.69)
psychogenic tic (F95.-)
+ **H02.51** Abnormal innervation syndrome
H02.511 **Abnormal innervation syndrome right u eyelid**
H02.512 **Abnormal innervation syndrome right lo eyelid**
H02.513 **Abnormal innervation syndrome right eye, unspecified eyelid**
H02.514 **Abnormal innervation syndrome left up eyelid**
H02.515 **Abnormal innervation syndrome left low eyelid**
H02.516 **Abnormal innervation syndrome left eye, unspecified eyelid**
H02.519 **Abnormal innervation syndrome unspeci eye, unspecified eyelid**
+ **H02.52** Blepharophimosis
Ankyloblepharon
H02.521 **Blepharophimosis right upper eyelid**
H02.522 **Blepharophimosis right lower eyelid**
H02.523 **Blepharophimosis right eye, unspecified eyelid**
H02.524 **Blepharophimosis left upper eyelid**
H02.525 **Blepharophimosis left lower eyelid**
H02.526 **Blepharophimosis left eye, unspecified eyelid**
H02.529 **Blepharophimosis unspecified eye, unspecified lid**
+ **H02.53** Eyelid retraction
Eyelid lag
H02.531 **Eyelid retraction right upper eyelid**
H02.532 **Eyelid retraction right lower eyelid**
H02.533 **Eyelid retraction right eye, unspecified eyelid**
H02.534 **Eyelid retraction left upper eyelid**
H02.535 **Eyelid retraction left lower eyelid**
H02.536 **Eyelid retraction left eye, unspecified eyelid**
H02.539 **Eyelid retraction unspecified eye, unspecified lid**
H02.59 **Other disorders affecting eyelid function**
Deficient blink reflex
Sensory disorders
+ **H02.6** Xanthelasma of eyelid
H02.60 **Xanthelasma of unspecified eye, unspecified eyelid**
H02.61 **Xanthelasma of right upper eyelid**
H02.62 **Xanthelasma of right lower eyelid**
H02.63 **Xanthelasma of right eye, unspecified eyelid**
H02.64 **Xanthelasma of left upper eyelid**
H02.65 **Xanthelasma of left lower eyelid**
H02.66 **Xanthelasma of left eye, unspecified eyelid**
+ **H02.7** Other and unspecified degenerative disorders of eyelid and periocular area
H02.70 **Unspecified degenerative disorders of eyelid and periocular area**

+ **H02.71 Chloasma of eyelid and periocular area**
Dyspigmentation of eyelid
Hyperpigmentation of eyelid
H02.711 Chloasma of right upper eyelid and periocular area
H02.712 Chloasma of right lower eyelid and periocular area
H02.713 Chloasma of right eye, unspecified eyelid and periocular area
H02.714 Chloasma of left upper eyelid and periocular area
H02.715 Chloasma of left lower eyelid and periocular area
H02.716 Chloasma of left eye, unspecified eyelid and periocular area
H02.719 Chloasma of unspecified eye, unspecified eyelid and periocular area

+ **H02.72 Madarosis of eyelid and periocular area**
Hypotrichosis of eyelid
H02.721 Madarosis of right upper eyelid and periocular area
H02.722 Madarosis of right lower eyelid and periocular area
H02.723 Madarosis of right eye, unspecified eyelid and periocular area
H02.724 Madarosis of left upper eyelid and periocular area
H02.725 Madarosis of left lower eyelid and periocular area
H02.726 Madarosis of left eye, unspecified eyelid and periocular area
H02.729 Madarosis of unspecified eye, unspecified eyelid and periocular area

+ **H02.73 Vitiligo of eyelid and periocular area**
Hypopigmentation of eyelid
H02.731 Vitiligo of right upper eyelid and periocular area
H02.732 Vitiligo of right lower eyelid and periocular area
H02.733 Vitiligo of right eye, unspecified eyelid and periocular area
H02.734 Vitiligo of left upper eyelid and periocular area
H02.735 Vitiligo of left lower eyelid and periocular area
H02.736 Vitiligo of left eye, unspecified eyelid and periocular area
H02.739 Vitiligo of unspecified eye, unspecified eyelid and periocular area

H02.79 Other degenerative disorders of eyelid and periocular area

+ **H02.8 Other specified disorders of eyelid**

+ **H02.81 Retained foreign body in eyelid**
Use additional code to identify the type of retained foreign body (Z18.-)
Excludes1: *laceration of eyelid with foreign body (S01.12-)*
retained intraocular foreign body (H44.6-, H44.7-)
superficial foreign body of eyelid and periocular area (S00.25-)
H02.811 Retained foreign body in right upper eyelid
H02.812 Retained foreign body in right lower eyelid
H02.813 Retained foreign body in right eye, unspecified eyelid
H02.814 Retained foreign body in left upper eyelid
H02.815 Retained foreign body in left lower eyelid
H02.816 Retained foreign body in left eye, unspecified eyelid
H02.819 Retained foreign body in unspecified eye, unspecified eyelid

+ **H02.82 Cysts of eyelid**
Sebaceous cyst of eyelid
H02.821 Cysts of right upper eyelid
H02.822 Cysts of right lower eyelid
H02.823 Cysts of right eye, unspecified eyelid
H02.824 Cysts of left upper eyelid
H02.825 Cysts of left lower eyelid
H02.826 Cysts of left eye, unspecified eyelid
H02.829 Cysts of unspecified eye, unspecified eyelid

+ **H02.83 Dermatochalasis of eyelid**
H02.831 Dermatochalasis of right upper eyelid
H02.832 Dermatochalasis of right lower eyelid
H02.833 Dermatochalasis of right eye, unspecified eyelid
H02.834 Dermatochalasis of left upper eyelid
H02.835 Dermatochalasis of left lower eyelid
H02.836 Dermatochalasis of left eye, unspecified eyelid
H02.839 Dermatochalasis of unspecified eye, unspecified eyelid

+ **H02.84 Edema of eyelid**
Hyperemia of eyelid
H02.841 Edema of right upper eyelid
H02.842 Edema of right lower eyelid
H02.843 Edema of right eye, unspecified eyelid
H02.844 Edema of left upper eyelid
H02.845 Edema of left lower eyelid
H02.846 Edema of left eye, unspecified eyelid
H02.849 Edema of unspecified eye, unspecified eyelid

+ **H02.85 Elephantiasis of eyelid**
H02.851 Elephantiasis of right upper eyelid
H02.852 Elephantiasis of right lower eyelid
H02.853 Elephantiasis of right eye, unspecified eyelid
H02.854 Elephantiasis of left upper eyelid
H02.855 Elephantiasis of left lower eyelid
H02.856 Elephantiasis of left eye, unspecified eyelid
H02.859 Elephantiasis of unspecified eye, unspecified eyelid

+ **H02.86 Hypertrichosis of eyelid**
H02.861 Hypertrichosis of right upper eyelid
H02.862 Hypertrichosis of right lower eyelid
H02.863 Hypertrichosis of right eye, unspecified eyelid
H02.864 Hypertrichosis of left upper eyelid
H02.865 Hypertrichosis of left lower eyelid
H02.866 Hypertrichosis of left eye, unspecified eyelid
H02.869 Hypertrichosis of unspecified eye, unspecified eyelid

+ **H02.87 Vascular anomalies of eyelid**
H02.871 Vascular anomalies of right upper eyelid
H02.872 Vascular anomalies of right lower eyelid
H02.873 Vascular anomalies of right eye, unspecified eyelid
H02.874 Vascular anomalies of left upper eyelid
H02.875 Vascular anomalies of left lower eyelid
H02.876 Vascular anomalies of left eye, unspecified eyelid
H02.879 Vascular anomalies of unspecified eye, unspecified eyelid

H02.89 Other specified disorders of eyelid
Hemorrhage of eyelid

H02.9 Unspecified disorder of eyelid
Disorder of eyelid NOS

H04 Disorders of lacrimal system
Excludes1: *congenital malformations of lacrimal system (Q10.4-Q10.6)*

+ **H04.0 Dacryoadenitis**

+ **H04.00 Unspecified dacryoadenitis**
H04.001 Unspecified dacryoadenitis, right lacrimal gland
H04.002 Unspecified dacryoadenitis, left lacrimal gland
H04.003 Unspecified dacryoadenitis, bilateral lacrimal glands
H04.009 Unspecified dacryoadenitis, unspecified lacrimal gland

+ **H04.01 Acute dacryoadenitis**
H04.011 Acute dacryoadenitis, right lacrimal gland
H04.012 Acute dacryoadenitis, left lacrimal gland
H04.013 Acute dacryoadenitis, bilateral lacrimal glands
H04.019 Acute dacryoadenitis, unspecified lacrimal gland

+ **H04.02 Chronic dacryoadenitis**
H04.021 Chronic dacryoadenitis, right lacrimal gland
H04.022 Chronic dacryoadenitis, left lacrimal gland
H04.023 Chronic dacryoadenitis, bilateral lacrimal gland
H04.029 Chronic dacryoadenitis, unspecified lacrimal gland

+ **H04.03** **Chronic enlargement of lacrimal gland**
 H04.031 **Chronic enlargement of right lacrimal gland**
 H04.032 **Chronic enlargement of left lacrimal gland**
 H04.033 **Chronic enlargement of bilateral lacrimal glands**
 H04.039 **Chronic enlargement of unspecified lacrimal gland**

+ **H04.1** **Other disorders of lacrimal gland**
+ **H04.11** **Dacryops**
 H04.111 **Dacryops of right lacrimal gland**
 H04.112 **Dacryops of left lacrimal gland**
 H04.113 **Dacryops of bilateral lacrimal glands**
 H04.119 **Dacryops of unspecified lacrimal gland**
+ **H04.12** **Dry eye syndrome**
 Tear film insufficiency, NOS
 H04.121 **Dry eye syndrome of right lacrimal gland**
 H04.122 **Dry eye syndrome of left lacrimal gland**
 H04.123 **Dry eye syndrome of bilateral lacrimal glands**
 H04.129 **Dry eye syndrome of unspecified lacrimal gland**
+ **H04.13** **Lacrimal cyst**
 Lacrimal cystic degeneration
 H04.131 **Lacrimal cyst, right lacrimal gland**
 H04.132 **Lacrimal cyst, left lacrimal gland**
 H04.133 **Lacrimal cyst, bilateral lacrimal glands**
 H04.139 **Lacrimal cyst, unspecified lacrimal gland**
+ **H04.14** **Primary lacrimal gland atrophy**
 H04.141 **Primary lacrimal gland atrophy, right lacrimal gland**
 H04.142 **Primary lacrimal gland atrophy, left lacrimal gland**
 H04.143 **Primary lacrimal gland atrophy, bilateral lacrimal glands**
 H04.149 **Primary lacrimal gland atrophy, unspecified lacrimal gland**
+ **H04.15** **Secondary lacrimal gland atrophy**
 H04.151 **Secondary lacrimal gland atrophy, right lacrimal gland**
 H04.152 **Secondary lacrimal gland atrophy, left lacrimal gland**
 H04.153 **Secondary lacrimal gland atrophy, bilateral lacrimal glands**
 H04.159 **Secondary lacrimal gland atrophy, unspecified lacrimal gland**
+ **H04.16** **Lacrimal gland dislocation**
 H04.161 **Lacrimal gland dislocation, right lacrimal gland**
 H04.162 **Lacrimal gland dislocation, left lacrimal gland**
 H04.163 **Lacrimal gland dislocation, bilateral lacrimal glands**
 H04.169 **Lacrimal gland dislocation, unspecified lacrimal gland**
 H04.19 **Other specified disorders of lacrimal gland**

+ **H04.2** **Epiphora**
+ **H04.20** **Unspecified epiphora**
 H04.201 **Unspecified epiphora, right lacrimal gland**
 H04.202 **Unspecified epiphora, left lacrimal gland**
 H04.203 **Unspecified epiphora, bilateral lacrimal glands**
 H04.209 **Unspecified epiphora, unspecified lacrimal gland**
+ **H04.21** **Epiphora due to excess lacrimation**
 H04.211 **Epiphora due to excess lacrimation, right lacrimal gland**
 H04.212 **Epiphora due to excess lacrimation, left lacrimal gland**
 H04.213 **Epiphora due to excess lacrimation, bilateral lacrimal glands**
 H04.219 **Epiphora due to excess lacrimation, unspecified lacrimal gland**
+ **H04.22** **Epiphora due to insufficient drainage**
 H04.221 **Epiphora due to insufficient drainage, right lacrimal gland**
 H04.222 **Epiphora due to insufficient drainage, left lacrimal gland**
 H04.223 **Epiphora due to insufficient drainage, bilateral lacrimal glands**
 H04.229 **Epiphora due to insufficient drainage, unspecified lacrimal gland**

+ **H04.3** **Acute and unspecified inflammation of lacrimal passages**
 Excludes1: *neonatal dacryocystitis (P39.1)*
+ **H04.30** **Unspecified dacryocystitis**
 H04.301 **Unspecified dacryocystitis of right lacrima passage**
 H04.302 **Unspecified dacryocystitis of left lacrimal passage**
 H04.303 **Unspecified dacryocystitis of bilateral lacrimal passages**
 H04.309 **Unspecified dacryocystitis of unspecified lacrimal passage**
+ **H04.31** **Phlegmonous dacryocystitis**
 H04.311 **Phlegmonous dacryocystitis of right lacrin passage**
 H04.312 **Phlegmonous dacryocystitis of left lacrima passage**
 H04.313 **Phlegmonous dacryocystitis of bilateral lacrimal passages**
 H04.319 **Phlegmonous dacryocystitis of unspecified lacrimal passage**
+ **H04.32** **Acute dacryocystitis**
 Acute dacryopericystitis
 H04.321 **Acute dacryocystitis of right lacrimal passage**
 H04.322 **Acute dacryocystitis of left lacrimal passa**
 H04.323 **Acute dacryocystitis of bilateral lacrimal passages**
 H04.329 **Acute dacryocystitis of unspecified lacrima passage**
+ **H04.33** **Acute lacrimal canaliculitis**
 H04.331 **Acute lacrimal canaliculitis of right lacrin passage**
 H04.332 **Acute lacrimal canaliculitis of left lacrima passage**
 H04.333 **Acute lacrimal canaliculitis of bilateral lacrimal passages**
 H04.339 **Acute lacrimal canaliculitis of unspecified lacrimal passage**

+ **H04.4** **Chronic inflammation of lacrimal passages**
+ **H04.41** **Chronic dacryocystitis**
 H04.411 **Chronic dacryocystitis of right lacrimal passage**
 H04.412 **Chronic dacryocystitis of left lacrimal passage**
 H04.413 **Chronic dacryocystitis of bilateral lacrima passages**
 H04.419 **Chronic dacryocystitis of unspecified lacrimal passage**
+ **H04.42** **Chronic lacrimal canaliculitis**
 H04.421 **Chronic lacrimal canaliculitis of right lacrimal passage**
 H04.422 **Chronic lacrimal canaliculitis of left lacrin passage**
 H04.423 **Chronic lacrimal canaliculitis of bilateral lacrimal passages**
 H04.429 **Chronic lacrimal canaliculitis of unspecifie lacrimal passage**
+ **H04.43** **Chronic lacrimal mucocele**
 H04.431 **Chronic lacrimal mucocele of right lacrim passage**
 H04.432 **Chronic lacrimal mucocele of left lacrimal passage**
 H04.433 **Chronic lacrimal mucocele of bilateral lacrimal passages**
 H04.439 **Chronic lacrimal mucocele of unspecified lacrimal passage**

+ **H04.5** **Stenosis and insufficiency of lacrimal passages**
+ **H04.51** **Dacryolith**
 H04.511 **Dacryolith of right lacrimal passage**
 H04.512 **Dacryolith of left lacrimal passage**
 H04.513 **Dacryolith of bilateral lacrimal passages**
 H04.519 **Dacryolith of unspecified lacrimal passage**
+ **H04.52** **Eversion of lacrimal punctum**
 H04.521 **Eversion of right lacrimal punctum**
 H04.522 **Eversion of left lacrimal punctum**
 H04.523 **Eversion of bilateral lacrimal punctum**
 H04.529 **Eversion of unspecified lacrimal punctum**

+ **H04.53 Neonatal obstruction of nasolacrimal duct**
  Excludes1: *congenital stenosis and stricture of lacrimal duct (Q10.5)*
  - • **H04.531 Neonatal obstruction of right nasolacrimal duct**
  - • **H04.532 Neonatal obstruction of left nasolacrimal duct**
  - • **H04.533 Neonatal obstruction of bilateral nasolacrimal duct**
  - • **H04.539 Neonatal obstruction of unspecified nasolacrimal duct**

+ **H04.54 Stenosis of lacrimal canaliculi**
  - **H04.541 Stenosis of right lacrimal canaliculi**
  - **H04.542 Stenosis of left lacrimal canaliculi**
  - **H04.543 Stenosis of bilateral lacrimal canaliculi**
  - **H04.549 Stenosis of unspecified lacrimal canaliculi**

+ **H04.55 Acquired stenosis of nasolacrimal duct**
  - **H04.551 Acquired stenosis of right nasolacrimal duct**
  - **H04.552 Acquired stenosis of left nasolacrimal duct**
  - **H04.553 Acquired stenosis of bilateral nasolacrimal duct**
  - **H04.559 Acquired stenosis of unspecified nasolacrimal duct**

+ **H04.56 Stenosis of lacrimal punctum**
  - **H04.561 Stenosis of right lacrimal punctum**
  - **H04.562 Stenosis of left lacrimal punctum**
  - **H04.563 Stenosis of bilateral lacrimal punctum**
  - **H04.569 Stenosis of unspecified lacrimal punctum**

+ **H04.57 Stenosis of lacrimal sac**
  - **H04.571 Stenosis of right lacrimal sac**
  - **H04.572 Stenosis of left lacrimal sac**
  - **H04.573 Stenosis of bilateral lacrimal sac**
  - **H04.579 Stenosis of unspecified lacrimal sac**

+ **H04.6 Other changes of lacrimal passages**
  + **H04.61 Lacrimal fistula**
    - **H04.611 Lacrimal fistula right lacrimal passage**
    - **H04.612 Lacrimal fistula left lacrimal passage**
    - **H04.613 Lacrimal fistula bilateral lacrimal passages**
    - **H04.619 Lacrimal fistula unspecified lacrimal passage**
  - **H04.69 Other changes of lacrimal passages**

+ **H04.8 Other disorders of lacrimal system**
  + **H04.81 Granuloma of lacrimal passages**
    - **H04.811 Granuloma of right lacrimal passage**
    - **H04.812 Granuloma of left lacrimal passage**
    - **H04.813 Granuloma of bilateral lacrimal passages**
    - **H04.819 Granuloma of unspecified lacrimal passage**
  - **H04.89 Other disorders of lacrimal system**

H04.9 Disorder of lacrimal system, unspecified

H05 Disorders of orbit

Excludes1: *congenital malformation of orbit (Q10.7)*

+ **H05.0 Acute inflammation of orbit**
  - **H05.00 Unspecified acute inflammation of orbit**
  + **H05.01 Cellulitis of orbit**
    Abscess of orbit
    - CC **H05.011 Cellulitis of right orbit**
      CC Exclusion see Appendix A PDX collection 0621
    - CC **H05.012 Cellulitis of left orbit**
      CC Exclusion see Appendix A PDX collection 0621
    - CC **H05.013 Cellulitis of bilateral orbits**
      CC Exclusion see Appendix A PDX collection 0621
    - CC **H05.019 Cellulitis of unspecified orbit**
      CC Exclusion see Appendix A PDX collection 0621
  + **H05.02 Osteomyelitis of orbit**
    - CC **H05.021 Osteomyelitis of right orbit**
      CC Exclusion see Appendix A PDX collection 0622
    - CC **H05.022 Osteomyelitis of left orbit**
      CC Exclusion see Appendix A PDX collection 0622
    - CC **H05.023 Osteomyelitis of bilateral orbits**
      CC Exclusion see Appendix A PDX collection 0622
    - CC **H05.029 Osteomyelitis of unspecified orbit**
      CC Exclusion see Appendix A PDX collection 0622
  + **H05.03 Periostitis of orbit**
    - CC **H05.031 Periostitis of right orbit**
      CC Exclusion see Appendix A PDX collection 0623
    - CC **H05.032 Periostitis of left orbit**
      CC Exclusion see Appendix A PDX collection 0623
    - CC **H05.033 Periostitis of bilateral orbits**
      CC Exclusion see Appendix A PDX collection 0623
    - CC **H05.039 Periostitis of unspecified orbit**
      CC Exclusion see Appendix A PDX collection 0623
  + **H05.04 Tenonitis of orbit**
    - **H05.041 Tenonitis of right orbit**
    - **H05.042 Tenonitis of left orbit**
    - **H05.043 Tenonitis of bilateral orbits**
    - **H05.049 Tenonitis of unspecified orbit**

+ **H05.1 Chronic inflammatory disorders of orbit**
  - **H05.10 Unspecified chronic inflammatory disorders of orbit**
  + **H05.11 Granuloma of orbit**
    Pseudotumor (inflammatory) of orbit
    - **H05.111 Granuloma of right orbit**
    - **H05.112 Granuloma of left orbit**
    - **H05.113 Granuloma of bilateral orbits**
    - **H05.119 Granuloma of unspecified orbit**
  + **H05.12 Orbital myositis**
    - **H05.121 Orbital myositis, right orbit**
    - **H05.122 Orbital myositis, left orbit**
    - **H05.123 Orbital myositis, bilateral**
    - **H05.129 Orbital myositis, unspecified orbit**

+ **H05.2 Exophthalmic conditions**
  - **H05.20 Unspecified exophthalmos**
  + **H05.21 Displacement (lateral) of globe**
    - **H05.211 Displacement (lateral) of globe, right eye**
    - **H05.212 Displacement (lateral) of globe, left eye**
    - **H05.213 Displacement (lateral) of globe, bilateral**
    - **H05.219 Displacement (lateral) of globe, unspecified eye**
  + **H05.22 Edema of orbit**
    Orbital congestion
    - **H05.221 Edema of right orbit**
    - **H05.222 Edema of left orbit**
    - **H05.223 Edema of bilateral orbit**
    - **H05.229 Edema of unspecified orbit**
  + **H05.23 Hemorrhage of orbit**
    - **H05.231 Hemorrhage of right orbit**
    - **H05.232 Hemorrhage of left orbit**
    - **H05.233 Hemorrhage of bilateral orbit**
    - **H05.239 Hemorrhage of unspecified orbit**
  + **H05.24 Constant exophthalmos**
    - **H05.241 Constant exophthalmos, right eye**
    - **H05.242 Constant exophthalmos, left eye**
    - **H05.243 Constant exophthalmos, bilateral**
    - **H05.249 Constant exophthalmos, unspecified eye**
  + **H05.25 Intermittent exophthalmos**
    - **H05.251 Intermittent exophthalmos, right eye**
    - **H05.252 Intermittent exophthalmos, left eye**
    - **H05.253 Intermittent exophthalmos, bilateral**
    - **H05.259 Intermittent exophthalmos, unspecified eye**
  + **H05.26 Pulsating exophthalmos**
    - **H05.261 Pulsating exophthalmos, right eye**
    - **H05.262 Pulsating exophthalmos, left eye**
    - **H05.263 Pulsating exophthalmos, bilateral**
    - **H05.269 Pulsating exophthalmos, unspecified eye**

+ **H05.3 Deformity of orbit**
  Excludes1: *congenital deformity of orbit (Q10.7)*
  hypertelorism (Q75.2)
  - **H05.30 Unspecified deformity of orbit**
  + **H05.31 Atrophy of orbit**
    - **H05.311 Atrophy of right orbit**
    - **H05.312 Atrophy of left orbit**
    - **H05.313 Atrophy of bilateral orbit**
    - **H05.319 Atrophy of unspecified orbit**
  + **H05.32 Deformity of orbit due to bone disease**
    Code also associated bone disease
    - **H05.321 Deformity of right orbit due to bone disease**
    - **H05.322 Deformity of left orbit due to bone disease**
    - **H05.323 Deformity of bilateral orbits due to bone disease**
    - **H05.329 Deformity of unspecified orbit due to bone disease**

+ **H05.33 Deformity of orbit due to trauma or surgery**
  - **H05.331 Deformity of right orbit due to trauma or surgery**
  - **H05.332 Deformity of left orbit due to trauma or surgery**
  - **H05.333 Deformity of bilateral orbits due to trauma or surgery**
  - **H05.339 Deformity of unspecified orbit due to trauma or surgery**

+ **H05.34 Enlargement of orbit**
  - **H05.341 Enlargement of right orbit**
  - **H05.342 Enlargement of left orbit**
  - **H05.343 Enlargement of bilateral orbits**
  - **H05.349 Enlargement of unspecified orbit**

+ **H05.35 Exostosis of orbit**
  - **H05.351 Exostosis of right orbit**
  - **H05.352 Exostosis of left orbit**
  - **H05.353 Exostosis of bilateral orbits**
  - **H05.359 Exostosis of unspecified orbit**

+ **H05.4 Enophthalmos**

+ **H05.40 Unspecified enophthalmos**
  - **H05.401 Unspecified enophthalmos, right eye**
  - **H05.402 Unspecified enophthalmos, left eye**
  - **H05.403 Unspecified enophthalmos, bilateral**
  - **H05.409 Unspecified enophthalmos, unspecified eye**

+ **H05.41 Enophthalmos due to atrophy of orbital tissue**
  - **H05.411 Enophthalmos due to atrophy of orbital tissue, right eye**
  - **H05.412 Enophthalmos due to atrophy of orbital tissue, left eye**
  - **H05.413 Enophthalmos due to atrophy of orbital tissue, bilateral**
  - **H05.419 Enophthalmos due to atrophy of orbital tissue, unspecified eye**

+ **H05.42 Enophthalmos due to trauma or surgery**
  - **H05.421 Enophthalmos due to trauma or surgery, right eye**
  - **H05.422 Enophthalmos due to trauma or surgery, left eye**
  - **H05.423 Enophthalmos due to trauma or surgery, bilateral**
  - **H05.429 Enophthalmos due to trauma or surgery, unspecified eye**

+ **H05.5 Retained (old) foreign body following penetrating wound of orbit**

  Retrobulbar foreign body

  Use additional code to identify the type of retained foreign body (Z18.-)

  Excludes1: *current penetrating wound of orbit (S05.4-)*

  Excludes2: *retained foreign body of eyelid (H02.81-)*
  retained intraocular foreign body (H44.6-, H44.7-)

  - **H05.50 Retained (old) foreign body following penetrating wound of unspecified orbit**
  - **H05.51 Retained (old) foreign body following penetrating wound of right orbit**
  - **H05.52 Retained (old) foreign body following penetrating wound of left orbit**
  - **H05.53 Retained (old) foreign body following penetrating wound of bilateral orbits**

+ **H05.8 Other disorders of orbit**

+ **H05.81 Cyst of orbit**

  Encephalocele of orbit
  - **H05.811 Cyst of right orbit**
  - **H05.812 Cyst of left orbit**
  - **H05.813 Cyst of bilateral orbits**
  - **H05.819 Cyst of unspecified orbit**

+ **H05.82 Myopathy of extraocular muscles**
  - **H05.821 Myopathy of extraocular muscles, right orbit**
  - **H05.822 Myopathy of extraocular muscles, left orbit**
  - **H05.823 Myopathy of extraocular muscles, bilateral**
  - **H05.829 Myopathy of extraocular muscles, unspecified orbit**

H05.89 Other disorders of orbit

H05.9 Unspecified disorder of orbit

Disorders of conjunctiva (H10-H11)

H10 Conjunctivitis

Excludes1: *keratoconjunctivitis (H16.2-)*

+ **H10.0 Mucopurulent conjunctivitis**

+ **H10.01 Acute follicular conjunctivitis**
  - **H10.011 Acute follicular conjunctivitis, right eye**
  - **H10.012 Acute follicular conjunctivitis, left eye**
  - **H10.013 Acute follicular conjunctivitis, bilateral**
  - **H10.019 Acute follicular conjunctivitis, unspecified eye**

+ **H10.02 Other mucopurulent conjunctivitis**
  - **H10.021 Other mucopurulent conjunctivitis, right e**
  - **H10.022 Other mucopurulent conjunctivitis, left ey**
  - **H10.023 Other mucopurulent conjunctivitis, bilater**
  - **H10.029 Other mucopurulent conjunctivitis, unspecified eye**

+ **H10.1 Acute atopic conjunctivitis**

  Acute papillary conjunctivitis
  - **H10.10 Acute atopic conjunctivitis, unspecified eye**
  - **H10.11 Acute atopic conjunctivitis, right eye**
  - **H10.12 Acute atopic conjunctivitis, left eye**
  - **H10.13 Acute atopic conjunctivitis, bilateral**

+ **H10.2 Other acute conjunctivitis**

+ **H10.21 Acute toxic conjunctivitis**

  Acute chemical conjunctivitis

  Code first (T51-T65) to identify chemical and intent

  Excludes1: *burn and corrosion of eye and adnexa (T26.-)*
  - **H10.211 Acute toxic conjunctivitis, right eye**
  - **H10.212 Acute toxic conjunctivitis, left eye**
  - **H10.213 Acute toxic conjunctivitis, bilateral**
  - **H10.219 Acute toxic conjunctivitis, unspecified eye**

+ **H10.22 Pseudomembranous conjunctivitis**
  - **H10.221 Pseudomembranous conjunctivitis, right ey**
  - **H10.222 Pseudomembranous conjunctivitis, left eye**
  - **H10.223 Pseudomembranous conjunctivitis, bilatera**
  - **H10.229 Pseudomembranous conjunctivitis, unspecified eye**

+ **H10.23 Serous conjunctivitis, except viral**

  Excludes1: *viral conjunctivitis (B30.-)*
  - **H10.231 Serous conjunctivitis, except viral, right ey**
  - **H10.232 Serous conjunctivitis, except viral, left eye**
  - **H10.233 Serous conjunctivitis, except viral, bilatera**
  - **H10.239 Serous conjunctivitis, except viral, unspecified eye**

+ **H10.3 Unspecified acute conjunctivitis**

  Excludes1: *ophthalmia neonatorum NOS (P39.1)*
  - **H10.30 Unspecified acute conjunctivitis, unspecified eye**
  - **H10.31 Unspecified acute conjunctivitis, right eye**
  - **H10.32 Unspecified acute conjunctivitis, left eye**
  - **H10.33 Unspecified acute conjunctivitis, bilateral**

+ **H10.4 Chronic conjunctivitis**

+ **H10.40 Unspecified chronic conjunctivitis**
  - **H10.401 Unspecified chronic conjunctivitis, right ey**
  - **H10.402 Unspecified chronic conjunctivitis, left eye**
  - **H10.403 Unspecified chronic conjunctivitis, bilatera**
  - **H10.409 Unspecified chronic conjunctivitis, unspecified eye**

+ **H10.41 Chronic giant papillary conjunctivitis**
  - **H10.411 Chronic giant papillary conjunctivitis, right eye**
  - **H10.412 Chronic giant papillary conjunctivitis, left eye**
  - **H10.413 Chronic giant papillary conjunctivitis, bilateral**
  - **H10.419 Chronic giant papillary conjunctivitis, unspecified eye**

+ **H10.42 Simple chronic conjunctivitis**
  - **H10.421 Simple chronic conjunctivitis, right eye**
  - **H10.422 Simple chronic conjunctivitis, left eye**
  - **H10.423 Simple chronic conjunctivitis, bilateral**
  - **H10.429 Simple chronic conjunctivitis, unspecified eye**

+ **H10.43 Chronic follicular conjunctivitis**
  - **H10.431 Chronic follicular conjunctivitis, right eye**
  - **H10.432 Chronic follicular conjunctivitis, left eye**
  - **H10.433 Chronic follicular conjunctivitis, bilateral**
  - **H10.439 Chronic follicular conjunctivitis, unspecifie eye**

H10.44 **Vernal conjunctivitis**
Excludes1: *vernal keratoconjunctivitis with limbar and corneal involvement (H16.26-)*
H10.45 **Other chronic allergic conjunctivitis**
+ **H10.5** **Blepharoconjunctivitis**
+ **H10.50** **Unspecified blepharoconjunctivitis**
H10.501 **Unspecified blepharoconjunctivitis, right eye**
H10.502 **Unspecified blepharoconjunctivitis, left eye**
H10.503 **Unspecified blepharoconjunctivitis, bilateral**
H10.509 **Unspecified blepharoconjunctivitis, unspecified eye**
+ **H10.51** **Ligneous conjunctivitis**
H10.511 **Ligneous conjunctivitis, right eye**
H10.512 **Ligneous conjunctivitis, left eye**
H10.513 **Ligneous conjunctivitis, bilateral**
H10.519 **Ligneous conjunctivitis, unspecified eye**
+ **H10.52** **Angular blepharoconjunctivitis**
H10.521 **Angular blepharoconjunctivitis, right eye**
H10.522 **Angular blepharoconjunctivitis, left eye**
H10.523 **Angular blepharoconjunctivitis, bilateral**
H10.529 **Angular blepharoconjunctivitis, unspecified eye**
+ **H10.53** **Contact blepharoconjunctivitis**
H10.531 **Contact blepharoconjunctivitis, right eye**
H10.532 **Contact blepharoconjunctivitis, left eye**
H10.533 **Contact blepharoconjunctivitis, bilateral**
H10.539 **Contact blepharoconjunctivitis, unspecified eye**
+ **H10.8** **Other conjunctivitis**
+ **H10.81** **Pingueculitis**
Excludes1: *pinguecula (H11.15-)*
H10.811 **Pingueculitis, right eye**
H10.812 **Pingueculitis, left eye**
H10.813 **Pingueculitis, bilateral**
H10.819 **Pingueculitis, unspecified eye**
H10.89 **Other conjunctivitis**
H10.9 **Unspecified conjunctivitis**

H11 Other disorders of conjunctiva

Excludes1: *keratoconjunctivitis (H16.2-)*
+ **H11.0** **Pterygium of eye**
Excludes1: *pseudopterygium (H11.81-)*
+ **H11.00** **Unspecified pterygium of eye**
H11.001 **Unspecified pterygium of right eye**
H11.002 **Unspecified pterygium of left eye**
H11.003 **Unspecified pterygium of eye, bilateral**
H11.009 **Unspecified pterygium of unspecified eye**
+ **H11.01** **Amyloid pterygium**
H11.011 **Amyloid pterygium of right eye**
H11.012 **Amyloid pterygium of left eye**
H11.013 **Amyloid pterygium of eye, bilateral**
H11.019 **Amyloid pterygium of unspecified eye**
+ **H11.02** **Central pterygium of eye**
H11.021 **Central pterygium of right eye**
H11.022 **Central pterygium of left eye**
H11.023 **Central pterygium of eye, bilateral**
H11.029 **Central pterygium of unspecified eye**
+ **H11.03** **Double pterygium of eye**
H11.031 **Double pterygium of right eye**
H11.032 **Double pterygium of left eye**
H11.033 **Double pterygium of eye, bilateral**
H11.039 **Double pterygium of unspecified eye**
+ **H11.04** **Peripheral pterygium of eye, stationary**
H11.041 **Peripheral pterygium, stationary, right eye**
H11.042 **Peripheral pterygium, stationary, left eye**
H11.043 **Peripheral pterygium, stationary, bilateral**
H11.049 **Peripheral pterygium, stationary, unspecified eye**
+ **H11.05** **Peripheral pterygium of eye, progressive**
H11.051 **Peripheral pterygium, progressive, right eye**
H11.052 **Peripheral pterygium, progressive, left eye**
H11.053 **Peripheral pterygium, progressive, bilateral**
H11.059 **Peripheral pterygium, progressive, unspecified eye**
+ **H11.06** **Recurrent pterygium of eye**
H11.061 **Recurrent pterygium of right eye**
H11.062 **Recurrent pterygium of left eye**
H11.063 **Recurrent pterygium of eye, bilateral**
H11.069 **Recurrent pterygium of unspecified eye**

+ **H11.1** **Conjunctival degenerations and deposits**
Excludes2: *pseudopterygium (H11.81)*
H11.10 **Unspecified conjunctival degenerations**
+ **H11.11** **Conjunctival deposits**
H11.111 **Conjunctival deposits, right eye**
H11.112 **Conjunctival deposits, left eye**
H11.113 **Conjunctival deposits, bilateral**
H11.119 **Conjunctival deposits, unspecified eye**
+ **H11.12** **Conjunctival concretions**
H11.121 **Conjunctival concretions, right eye**
H11.122 **Conjunctival concretions, left eye**
H11.123 **Conjunctival concretions, bilateral**
H11.129 **Conjunctival concretions, unspecified eye**
+ **H11.13** **Conjunctival pigmentations**
Conjunctival argyrosis [argyria]
H11.131 **Conjunctival pigmentations, right eye**
H11.132 **Conjunctival pigmentations, left eye**
H11.133 **Conjunctival pigmentations, bilateral**
H11.139 **Conjunctival pigmentations, unspecified eye**
+ **H11.14** **Conjunctival xerosis, unspecified**
Excludes1: *xerosis of conjunctiva due to vitamin A deficiency (E50.0, E50.1)*
H11.141 **Conjunctival xerosis, unspecified, right eye**
H11.142 **Conjunctival xerosis, unspecified, left eye**
H11.143 **Conjunctival xerosis, unspecified, bilateral**
H11.149 **Conjunctival xerosis, unspecified, unspecified eye**
+ **H11.15** **Pinguecula**
Excludes1: pingueculitis (H10.81-)
H11.151 **Pinguecula, right eye**
H11.152 **Pinguecula, left eye**
H11.153 **Pinguecula, bilateral**
H11.159 **Pinguecula, unspecified eye**
+ **H11.2** **Conjunctival scars**
+ **H11.21** **Conjunctival adhesions and strands (localized)**
H11.211 **Conjunctival adhesions and strands (localized), right eye**
H11.212 **Conjunctival adhesions and strands (localized), left eye**
H11.213 **Conjunctival adhesions and strands (localized), bilateral**
H11.219 **Conjunctival adhesions and strands (localized), unspecified eye**
+ **H11.22** **Conjunctival granuloma**
H11.221 **Conjunctival granuloma, right eye**
H11.222 **Conjunctival granuloma, left eye**
H11.223 **Conjunctival granuloma, bilateral**
H11.229 **Conjunctival granuloma, unspecified**
+ **H11.23** **Symblepharon**
H11.231 **Symblepharon, right eye**
H11.232 **Symblepharon, left eye**
H11.233 **Symblepharon, bilateral**
H11.239 **Symblepharon, unspecified eye**
+ **H11.24** **Scarring of conjunctiva**
H11.241 **Scarring of conjunctiva, right eye**
H11.242 **Scarring of conjunctiva, left eye**
H11.243 **Scarring of conjunctiva, bilateral**
H11.249 **Scarring of conjunctiva, unspecified eye**
+ **H11.3** **Conjunctival hemorrhage**
Subconjunctival hemorrhage
H11.30 **Conjunctival hemorrhage, unspecified eye**
H11.31 **Conjunctival hemorrhage, right eye**
H11.32 **Conjunctival hemorrhage, left eye**
H11.33 **Conjunctival hemorrhage, bilateral**
+ **H11.4** **Other conjunctival vascular disorders and cysts**
+ **H11.41** **Vascular abnormalities of conjunctiva**
Conjunctival aneurysm
H11.411 **Vascular abnormalities of conjunctiva, right eye**
H11.412 **Vascular abnormalities of conjunctiva, left eye**
H11.413 **Vascular abnormalities of conjunctiva, bilateral**
H11.419 **Vascular abnormalities of conjunctiva, unspecified eye**
+ **H11.42** **Conjunctival edema**
H11.421 **Conjunctival edema, right eye**
H11.422 **Conjunctival edema, left eye**
H11.423 **Conjunctival edema, bilateral**
H11.429 **Conjunctival edema, unspecified eye**

+ **H11.43 Conjunctival hyperemia**
  - **H11.431 Conjunctival hyperemia, right eye**
  - **H11.432 Conjunctival hyperemia, left eye**
  - **H11.433 Conjunctival hyperemia, bilateral**
  - **H11.439 Conjunctival hyperemia, unspecified eye**

+ **H11.44 Conjunctival cysts**
  - **H11.441 Conjunctival cysts, right eye**
  - **H11.442 Conjunctival cysts, left eye**
  - **H11.443 Conjunctival cysts, bilateral**
  - **H11.449 Conjunctival cysts, unspecified eye**

+ **H11.8 Other specified disorders of conjunctiva**

+ **H11.81 Pseudopterygium of conjunctiva**
  - **H11.811 Pseudopterygium of conjunctiva, right eye**
  - **H11.812 Pseudopterygium of conjunctiva, left eye**
  - **H11.813 Pseudopterygium of conjunctiva, bilateral**
  - **H11.819 Pseudopterygium of conjunctiva, unspecified eye**

+ **H11.82 Conjunctivochalasis**
  - **H11.821 Conjunctivochalasis, right eye**
  - **H11.822 Conjunctivochalasis, left eye**
  - **H11.823 Conjunctivochalasis, bilateral**
  - **H11.829 Conjunctivochalasis, unspecified eye**

H11.89 Other specified disorders of conjunctiva

H11.9 Unspecified disorder of conjunctiva

Disorders of sclera, cornea, iris and ciliary body (H15-H22)

+ **H15 Disorders of sclera**

+ **H15.0 Scleritis**

+ **H15.00 Unspecified scleritis**
  - **H15.001 Unspecified scleritis, right eye**
  - **H15.002 Unspecified scleritis, left eye**
  - **H15.003 Unspecified scleritis, bilateral**
  - **H15.009 Unspecified scleritis, unspecified eye**

+ **H15.01 Anterior scleritis**
  - **H15.011 Anterior scleritis, right eye**
  - **H15.012 Anterior scleritis, left eye**
  - **H15.013 Anterior scleritis, bilateral**
  - **H15.019 Anterior scleritis, unspecified eye**

+ **H15.02 Brawny scleritis**
  - **H15.021 Brawny scleritis, right eye**
  - **H15.022 Brawny scleritis, left eye**
  - **H15.023 Brawny scleritis, bilateral**
  - **H15.029 Brawny scleritis, unspecified eye**

+ **H15.03 Posterior scleritis**

  Sclerotenonitis
  - **H15.031 Posterior scleritis, right eye**
  - **H15.032 Posterior scleritis, left eye**
  - **H15.033 Posterior scleritis, bilateral**
  - **H15.039 Posterior scleritis, unspecified eye**

+ **H15.04 Scleritis with corneal involvement**
  - **H15.041 Scleritis with corneal involvement, right eye**
  - **H15.042 Scleritis with corneal involvement, left eye**
  - **H15.043 Scleritis with corneal involvement, bilateral**
  - **H15.049 Scleritis with corneal involvement, unspecified eye**

+ **H15.05 Scleromalacia perforans**
  - **H15.051 Scleromalacia perforans, right eye**
  - **H15.052 Scleromalacia perforans, left eye**
  - **H15.053 Scleromalacia perforans, bilateral**
  - **H15.059 Scleromalacia perforans, unspecified eye**

+ **H15.09 Other scleritis**

  Scleral abscess
  - **H15.091 Other scleritis, right eye**
  - **H15.092 Other scleritis, left eye**
  - **H15.093 Other scleritis, bilateral**
  - **H15.099 Other scleritis, unspecified eye**

+ **H15.1 Episcleritis**

+ **H15.10 Unspecified episcleritis**
  - **H15.101 Unspecified episcleritis, right eye**
  - **H15.102 Unspecified episcleritis, left eye**
  - **H15.103 Unspecified episcleritis, bilateral**
  - **H15.109 Unspecified episcleritis, unspecified eye**

+ **H15.11 Episcleritis periodica fugax**
  - **H15.111 Episcleritis periodica fugax, right eye**
  - **H15.112 Episcleritis periodica fugax, left eye**
  - **H15.113 Episcleritis periodica fugax, bilateral**
  - **H15.119 Episcleritis periodica fugax, unspecified eye**

+ **H15.12 Nodular episcleritis**
  - **H15.121 Nodular episcleritis, right eye**
  - **H15.122 Nodular episcleritis, left eye**
  - **H15.123 Nodular episcleritis, bilateral**
  - **H15.129 Nodular episcleritis, unspecified eye**

+ **H15.8 Other disorders of sclera**

  Excludes2: *blue sclera (Q13.5)*
  degenerative myopia (H44.2-)

+ **H15.81 Equatorial staphyloma**
  - **H15.811 Equatorial staphyloma, right eye**
  - **H15.812 Equatorial staphyloma, left eye**
  - **H15.813 Equatorial staphyloma, bilateral**
  - **H15.819 Equatorial staphyloma, unspecified eye**

+ **H15.82 Localized anterior staphyloma**
  - **H15.821 Localized anterior staphyloma, right eye**
  - **H15.822 Localized anterior staphyloma, left eye**
  - **H15.823 Localized anterior staphyloma, bilateral**
  - **H15.829 Localized anterior staphyloma, unspecified eye**

+ **H15.83 Staphyloma posticum**
  - **H15.831 Staphyloma posticum, right eye**
  - **H15.832 Staphyloma posticum, left eye**
  - **H15.833 Staphyloma posticum, bilateral**
  - **H15.839 Staphyloma posticum, unspecified eye**

+ **H15.84 Scleral ectasia**
  - **H15.841 Scleral ectasia, right eye**
  - **H15.842 Scleral ectasia, left eye**
  - **H15.843 Scleral ectasia, bilateral**
  - **H15.849 Scleral ectasia, unspecified eye**

+ **H15.85 Ring staphyloma**
  - **H15.851 Ring staphyloma, right eye**
  - **H15.852 Ring staphyloma, left eye**
  - **H15.853 Ring staphyloma, bilateral**
  - **H15.859 Ring staphyloma, unspecified eye**

H15.89 Other disorders of sclera

H15.9 Unspecified disorder of sclera

H16 Keratitis

+ **H16.0 Corneal ulcer**

+ **H16.00 Unspecified corneal ulcer**
  - **H16.001 Unspecified corneal ulcer, right eye**
  - **H16.002 Unspecified corneal ulcer, left eye**
  - **H16.003 Unspecified corneal ulcer, bilateral**
  - **H16.009 Unspecified corneal ulcer, unspecified eye**

+ **H16.01 Central corneal ulcer**
  - **H16.011 Central corneal ulcer, right eye**
  - **H16.012 Central corneal ulcer, left eye**
  - **H16.013 Central corneal ulcer, bilateral**
  - **H16.019 Central corneal ulcer, unspecified eye**

+ **H16.02 Ring corneal ulcer**
  - **H16.021 Ring corneal ulcer, right eye**
  - **H16.022 Ring corneal ulcer, left eye**
  - **H16.023 Ring corneal ulcer, bilateral**
  - **H16.029 Ring corneal ulcer, unspecified eye**

+ **H16.03 Corneal ulcer with hypopyon**
  - **H16.031 Corneal ulcer with hypopyon, right eye**
  - **H16.032 Corneal ulcer with hypopyon, left eye**
  - **H16.033 Corneal ulcer with hypopyon, bilateral**
  - **H16.039 Corneal ulcer with hypopyon, unspecified eye**

+ **H16.04 Marginal corneal ulcer**
  - **H16.041 Marginal corneal ulcer, right eye**
  - **H16.042 Marginal corneal ulcer, left eye**
  - **H16.043 Marginal corneal ulcer, bilateral**
  - **H16.049 Marginal corneal ulcer, unspecified eye**

+ **H16.05 Mooren's corneal ulcer**
  - **H16.051 Mooren's corneal ulcer, right eye**
  - **H16.052 Mooren's corneal ulcer, left eye**
  - **H16.053 Mooren's corneal ulcer, bilateral**
  - **H16.059 Mooren's corneal ulcer, unspecified eye**

+ **H16.06 Mycotic corneal ulcer**
  - **H16.061 Mycotic corneal ulcer, right eye**
  - **H16.062 Mycotic corneal ulcer, left eye**
  - **H16.063 Mycotic corneal ulcer, bilateral**
  - **H16.069 Mycotic corneal ulcer, unspecified eye**

+ **H16.07 Perforated corneal ulcer**
  - **H16.071 Perforated corneal ulcer, right eye**
  - **H16.072 Perforated corneal ulcer, left eye**
  - **H16.073 Perforated corneal ulcer, bilateral**
  - **H16.079 Perforated corneal ulcer, unspecified eye**

+ **H16.1 Other and unspecified superficial keratitis without conjunctivitis**

+ **H16.10 Unspecified superficial keratitis**
  - **H16.101 Unspecified superficial keratitis, right eye**
  - **H16.102 Unspecified superficial keratitis, left eye**

H16.103 **Unspecified superficial keratitis, bilateral**
H16.109 **Unspecified superficial keratitis, unspecified eye**

+ H16.11 Macular keratitis
Areolar keratitis
Nummular keratitis
Stellate keratitis
Striate keratitis
H16.111 **Macular keratitis, right eye**
H16.112 **Macular keratitis, left eye**
H16.113 **Macular keratitis, bilateral**
H16.119 **Macular keratitis, unspecified eye**

+ H16.12 Filamentary keratitis
H16.121 **Filamentary keratitis, right eye**
H16.122 **Filamentary keratitis, left eye**
H16.123 **Filamentary keratitis, bilateral**
H16.129 **Filamentary keratitis, unspecified eye**

+ H16.13 Photokeratitis
Snow blindness
Welders keratitis
H16.131 **Photokeratitis, right eye**
H16.132 **Photokeratitis, left eye**
H16.133 **Photokeratitis, bilateral**
H16.139 **Photokeratitis, unspecified eye**

+ H16.14 Punctate keratitis
H16.141 **Punctate keratitis, right eye**
H16.142 **Punctate keratitis, left eye**
H16.143 **Punctate keratitis, bilateral**
H16.149 **Punctate keratitis, unspecified eye**

+ H16.2 Keratoconjunctivitis

+ H16.20 Unspecified keratoconjunctivitis
Superficial keratitis with conjunctivitis NOS
H16.201 **Unspecified keratoconjunctivitis, right eye**
H16.202 **Unspecified keratoconjunctivitis, left eye**
H16.203 **Unspecified keratoconjunctivitis, bilateral**
H16.209 **Unspecified keratoconjunctivitis, unspecified eye**

+ H16.21 Exposure keratoconjunctivitis
H16.211 **Exposure keratoconjunctivitis, right eye**
H16.212 **Exposure keratoconjunctivitis, left eye**
H16.213 **Exposure keratoconjunctivitis, bilateral**
H16.219 **Exposure keratoconjunctivitis, unspecified eye**

+ H16.22 Keratoconjunctivitis sicca, not specified as Sjögren's
Excludes1: *Sjögren's syndrome (M35.01)*
H16.221 **Keratoconjunctivitis sicca, not specified as Sjögren's, right eye**
H16.222 **Keratoconjunctivitis sicca, not specified as Sjögren's, left eye**
H16.223 **Keratoconjunctivitis sicca, not specified as Sjögren's, bilateral**
H16.229 **Keratoconjunctivitis sicca, not specified as Sjögren's, unspecified eye**

+ H16.23 Neurotrophic keratoconjunctivitis
H16.231 **Neurotrophic keratoconjunctivitis, right eye**
H16.232 **Neurotrophic keratoconjunctivitis, left eye**
H16.233 **Neurotrophic keratoconjunctivitis, bilateral**
H16.239 **Neurotrophic keratoconjunctivitis, unspecified eye**

+ H16.24 Ophthalmia nodosa
H16.241 **Ophthalmia nodosa, right eye**
H16.242 **Ophthalmia nodosa, left eye**
H16.243 **Ophthalmia nodosa, bilateral**
H16.249 **Ophthalmia nodosa, unspecified eye**

+ H16.25 Phlyctenular keratoconjunctivitis
H16.251 **Phlyctenular keratoconjunctivitis, right eye**
H16.252 **Phlyctenular keratoconjunctivitis, left eye**
H16.253 **Phlyctenular keratoconjunctivitis, bilateral**
H16.259 **Phlyctenular keratoconjunctivitis, unspecified eye**

+ H16.26 Vernal keratoconjunctivitis, with limbar and corneal involvement
Excludes1: *vernal conjunctivitis without limbar and corneal involvement (H10.44)*
H16.261 **Vernal keratoconjunctivitis, with limbar and corneal involvement, right eye**
H16.262 **Vernal keratoconjunctivitis, with limbar and corneal involvement, left eye**
H16.263 **Vernal keratoconjunctivitis, with limbar and corneal involvement, bilateral**
H16.269 **Vernal keratoconjunctivitis, with limbar and corneal involvement, unspecified eye**

+ H16.29 Other keratoconjunctivitis
H16.291 **Other keratoconjunctivitis, right eye**
H16.292 **Other keratoconjunctivitis, left eye**
H16.293 **Other keratoconjunctivitis, bilateral**
H16.299 **Other keratoconjunctivitis, unspecified eye**

+ H16.3 Interstitial and deep keratitis

+ H16.30 Unspecified interstitial keratitis
H16.301 **Unspecified interstitial keratitis, right eye**
H16.302 **Unspecified interstitial keratitis, left eye**
H16.303 **Unspecified interstitial keratitis, bilateral**
H16.309 **Unspecified interstitial keratitis, unspecified eye**

+ H16.31 Corneal abscess
H16.311 **Corneal abscess, right eye**
H16.312 **Corneal abscess, left eye**
H16.313 **Corneal abscess, bilateral**
H16.319 **Corneal abscess, unspecified eye**

+ H16.32 Diffuse interstitial keratitis
Cogan's syndrome
H16.321 **Diffuse interstitial keratitis, right eye**
H16.322 **Diffuse interstitial keratitis, left eye**
H16.323 **Diffuse interstitial keratitis, bilateral**
H16.329 **Diffuse interstitial keratitis, unspecified eye**

+ H16.33 Sclerosing keratitis
H16.331 **Sclerosing keratitis, right eye**
H16.332 **Sclerosing keratitis, left eye**
H16.333 **Sclerosing keratitis, bilateral**
H16.339 **Sclerosing keratitis, unspecified eye**

+ H16.39 Other interstitial and deep keratitis
H16.391 **Other interstitial and deep keratitis, right eye**
H16.392 **Other interstitial and deep keratitis, left eye**
H16.393 **Other interstitial and deep keratitis, bilateral**
H16.399 **Other interstitial and deep keratitis, unspecified eye**

+ H16.4 Corneal neovascularization

+ H16.40 Unspecified corneal neovascularization
H16.401 **Unspecified corneal neovascularization, right eye**
H16.402 **Unspecified corneal neovascularization, left eye**
H16.403 **Unspecified corneal neovascularization, bilateral**
H16.409 **Unspecified corneal neovascularization, unspecified eye**

+ H16.41 Ghost vessels (corneal)
H16.411 **Ghost vessels (corneal), right eye**
H16.412 **Ghost vessels (corneal), left eye**
H16.413 **Ghost vessels (corneal), bilateral**
H16.419 **Ghost vessels (corneal), unspecified eye**

+ H16.42 Pannus (corneal)
H16.421 **Pannus (corneal), right eye**
H16.422 **Pannus (corneal), left eye**
H16.423 **Pannus (corneal), bilateral**
H16.429 **Pannus (corneal), unspecified eye**

+ H16.43 Localized vascularization of cornea
H16.431 **Localized vascularization of cornea, right eye**
H16.432 **Localized vascularization of cornea, left eye**
H16.433 **Localized vascularization of cornea, bilateral**
H16.439 **Localized vascularization of cornea, unspecified eye**

+ H16.44 Deep vascularization of cornea
H16.441 **Deep vascularization of cornea, right eye**
H16.442 **Deep vascularization of cornea, left eye**
H16.443 **Deep vascularization of cornea, bilateral**
H16.449 **Deep vascularization of cornea, unspecified eye**

H16.8 **Other keratitis**
H16.9 **Unspecified keratitis**

H17 Corneal scars and opacities

+ H17.0 Adherent leukoma
H17.00 **Adherent leukoma, unspecified eye**
H17.01 **Adherent leukoma, right eye**
H17.02 **Adherent leukoma, left eye**
H17.03 **Adherent leukoma, bilateral**

+ H17.1 Central corneal opacity
H17.10 **Central corneal opacity, unspecified eye**
H17.11 **Central corneal opacity, right eye**

H17.12 **Central corneal opacity, left eye**
H17.13 **Central corneal opacity, bilateral**
\+ **H17.8** **Other corneal scars and opacities**
\+ **H17.81** **Minor opacity of cornea**
Corneal nebula
H17.811 **Minor opacity of cornea, right eye**
H17.812 **Minor opacity of cornea, left eye**
H17.813 **Minor opacity of cornea, bilateral**
H17.819 **Minor opacity of cornea, unspecified eye**
\+ **H17.82** **Peripheral opacity of cornea**
H17.821 **Peripheral opacity of cornea, right eye**
H17.822 **Peripheral opacity of cornea, left eye**
H17.823 **Peripheral opacity of cornea, bilateral**
H17.829 **Peripheral opacity of cornea, unspecified eye**
H17.89 **Other corneal scars and opacities**
H17.9 **Unspecified corneal scar and opacity**

H18 **Other disorders of cornea**

\+ **H18.0** **Corneal pigmentations and deposits**
\+ **H18.00** **Unspecified corneal deposit**
H18.001 **Unspecified corneal deposit, right eye**
H18.002 **Unspecified corneal deposit, left eye**
H18.003 **Unspecified corneal deposit, bilateral**
H18.009 **Unspecified corneal deposit, unspecified eye**
\+ **H18.01** **Anterior corneal pigmentations**
Staehli's line
H18.011 **Anterior corneal pigmentations, right eye**
H18.012 **Anterior corneal pigmentations, left eye**
H18.013 **Anterior corneal pigmentations, bilateral**
H18.019 **Anterior corneal pigmentations, unspecified eye**
\+ **H18.02** **Argentous corneal deposits**
H18.021 **Argentous corneal deposits, right eye**
H18.022 **Argentous corneal deposits, left eye**
H18.023 **Argentous corneal deposits, bilateral**
H18.029 **Argentous corneal deposits, unspecified eye**
\+ **H18.03** **Corneal deposits in metabolic disorders**
Code also associated metabolic disorder
H18.031 **Corneal deposits in metabolic disorders, right eye**
H18.032 **Corneal deposits in metabolic disorders, left eye**
H18.033 **Corneal deposits in metabolic disorders, bilateral**
H18.039 **Corneal deposits in metabolic disorders, unspecified eye**
\+ **H18.04** **Kayser-Fleischer ring**
Code also associated Wilson's disease (E83.01)
H18.041 **Kayser-Fleischer ring, right eye**
H18.042 **Kayser-Fleischer ring, left eye**
H18.043 **Kayser-Fleischer ring, bilateral**
H18.049 **Kayser-Fleischer ring, unspecified eye**
\+ **H18.05** **Posterior corneal pigmentations**
Krukenberg's spindle
H18.051 **Posterior corneal pigmentations, right eye**
H18.052 **Posterior corneal pigmentations, left eye**
H18.053 **Posterior corneal pigmentations, bilateral**
H18.059 **Posterior corneal pigmentations, unspecified eye**
\+ **H18.06** **Stromal corneal pigmentations**
Hematocornea
H18.061 **Stromal corneal pigmentations, right eye**
H18.062 **Stromal corneal pigmentations, left eye**
H18.063 **Stromal corneal pigmentations, bilateral**
H18.069 **Stromal corneal pigmentations, unspecified eye**
\+ **H18.1** **Bullous keratopathy**
H18.10 **Bullous keratopathy, unspecified eye**
H18.11 **Bullous keratopathy, right eye**
H18.12 **Bullous keratopathy, left eye**
H18.13 **Bullous keratopathy, bilateral**
\+ **H18.2** **Other and unspecified corneal edema**
H18.20 **Unspecified corneal edema**
\+ **H18.21** **Corneal edema secondary to contact lens**
Excludes2: *other corneal disorders due to contact lens (H18.82-)*
H18.211 **Corneal edema secondary to contact lens, right eye**
H18.212 **Corneal edema secondary to contact lens, left eye**
H18.213 **Corneal edema secondary to contact lens, bilateral**
H18.219 **Corneal edema secondary to contact lens, unspecified eye**
\+ **H18.22** **Idiopathic corneal edema**
H18.221 **Idiopathic corneal edema, right eye**
H18.222 **Idiopathic corneal edema, left eye**
H18.223 **Idiopathic corneal edema, bilateral**
H18.229 **Idiopathic corneal edema, unspecified eye**
\+ **H18.23** **Secondary corneal edema**
H18.231 **Secondary corneal edema, right eye**
H18.232 **Secondary corneal edema, left eye**
H18.233 **Secondary corneal edema, bilateral**
H18.239 **Secondary corneal edema, unspecified eye**
\+ **H18.3** **Changes of corneal membranes**
H18.30 **Unspecified corneal membrane change**
\+ **H18.31** **Folds and rupture in Bowman's membrane**
H18.311 **Folds and rupture in Bowman's membrane, right eye**
H18.312 **Folds and rupture in Bowman's membrane, left eye**
H18.313 **Folds and rupture in Bowman's membrane, bilateral**
H18.319 **Folds and rupture in Bowman's membrane, unspecified eye**
\+ **H18.32** **Folds in Descemet's membrane**
H18.321 **Folds in Descemet's membrane, right eye**
H18.322 **Folds in Descemet's membrane, left eye**
H18.323 **Folds in Descemet's membrane, bilateral**
H18.329 **Folds in Descemet's membrane, unspecified eye**
\+ **H18.33** **Rupture in Descemet's membrane**
H18.331 **Rupture in Descemet's membrane, right eye**
H18.332 **Rupture in Descemet's membrane, left eye**
H18.333 **Rupture in Descemet's membrane, bilateral**
H18.339 **Rupture in Descemet's membrane, unspecified eye**
\+ **H18.4** **Corneal degeneration**
Excludes1: *Mooren's ulcer (H16.0-)*
recurrent erosion of cornea (H18.83-)
H18.40 **Unspecified corneal degeneration**
\+ **H18.41** **Arcus senilis**
Senile corneal changes
H18.411 **Arcus senilis, right eye**
H18.412 **Arcus senilis, left eye**
H18.413 **Arcus senilis, bilateral**
H18.419 **Arcus senilis, unspecified eye**
\+ **H18.42** **Band keratopathy**
H18.421 **Band keratopathy, right eye**
H18.422 **Band keratopathy, left eye**
H18.423 **Band keratopathy, bilateral**
H18.429 **Band keratopathy, unspecified eye**
H18.43 **Other calcerous corneal degeneration**
\+ **H18.44** **Keratomalacia**
Excludes1: *keratomalacia due to vitamin A deficiency (E50.4)*
H18.441 **Keratomalacia, right eye**
H18.442 **Keratomalacia, left eye**
H18.443 **Keratomalacia, bilateral**
H18.449 **Keratomalacia, unspecified eye**
\+ **H18.45** **Nodular corneal degeneration**
H18.451 **Nodular corneal degeneration, right eye**
H18.452 **Nodular corneal degeneration, left eye**
H18.453 **Nodular corneal degeneration, bilateral**
H18.459 **Nodular corneal degeneration, unspecified eye**
\+ **H18.46** **Peripheral corneal degeneration**
H18.461 **Peripheral corneal degeneration, right eye**
H18.462 **Peripheral corneal degeneration, left eye**
H18.463 **Peripheral corneal degeneration, bilateral**
H18.469 **Peripheral corneal degeneration, unspecified eye**
H18.49 **Other corneal degeneration**
\+ **H18.5** **Hereditary corneal dystrophies**
H18.50 **Unspecified hereditary corneal dystrophies**
H18.51 **Endothelial corneal dystrophy**
Fuchs' dystrophy
H18.52 **Epithelial (juvenile) corneal dystrophy**
H18.53 **Granular corneal dystrophy**
H18.54 **Lattice corneal dystrophy**
H18.55 **Macular corneal dystrophy**
H18.59 **Other hereditary corneal dystrophies**

+ **H18.6 Keratoconus**
  + **H18.60 Keratoconus, unspecified**
    - **H18.601 Keratoconus, unspecified, right eye**
    - **H18.602 Keratoconus, unspecified, left eye**
    - **H18.603 Keratoconus, unspecified, bilateral**
    - **H18.609 Keratoconus, unspecified, unspecified eye**
  + **H18.61 Keratoconus, stable**
    - **H18.611 Keratoconus, stable, right eye**
    - **H18.612 Keratoconus, stable, left eye**
    - **H18.613 Keratoconus, stable, bilateral**
    - **H18.619 Keratoconus, stable, unspecified eye**
  + **H18.62 Keratoconus, unstable**
    Acute hydrops
    - **H18.621 Keratoconus, unstable, right eye**
    - **H18.622 Keratoconus, unstable, left eye**
    - **H18.623 Keratoconus, unstable, bilateral**
    - **H18.629 Keratoconus, unstable, unspecified eye**

+ **H18.7 Other and unspecified corneal deformities**
  Excludes1: *congenital malformations of cornea (Q13.3-Q13.4)*
  H18.70 Unspecified corneal deformity
  + **H18.71 Corneal ectasia**
    - **H18.711 Corneal ectasia, right eye**
    - **H18.712 Corneal ectasia, left eye**
    - **H18.713 Corneal ectasia, bilateral**
    - **H18.719 Corneal ectasia, unspecified eye**
  + **H18.72 Corneal staphyloma**
    - **H18.721 Corneal staphyloma, right eye**
    - **H18.722 Corneal staphyloma, left eye**
    - **H18.723 Corneal staphyloma, bilateral**
    - **H18.729 Corneal staphyloma, unspecified eye**
  + **H18.73 Descemetocele**
    - **H18.731 Descemetocele, right eye**
    - **H18.732 Descemetocele, left eye**
    - **H18.733 Descemetocele, bilateral**
    - **H18.739 Descemetocele, unspecified eye**
  + **H18.79 Other corneal deformities**
    - **H18.791 Other corneal deformities, right eye**
    - **H18.792 Other corneal deformities, left eye**
    - **H18.793 Other corneal deformities, bilateral**
    - **H18.799 Other corneal deformities, unspecified eye**

+ **H18.8 Other specified disorders of cornea**
  + **H18.81 Anesthesia and hypoesthesia of cornea**
    - **H18.811 Anesthesia and hypoesthesia of cornea, right eye**
    - **H18.812 Anesthesia and hypoesthesia of cornea, left eye**
    - **H18.813 Anesthesia and hypoesthesia of cornea, bilateral**
    - **H18.819 Anesthesia and hypoesthesia of cornea, unspecified eye**
  + **H18.82 Corneal disorder due to contact lens**
    Excludes2: *corneal edema due to contact lens (H18.21-)*
    - **H18.821 Corneal disorder due to contact lens, right eye**
    - **H18.822 Corneal disorder due to contact lens, left eye**
    - **H18.823 Corneal disorder due to contact lens, bilateral**
    - **H18.829 Corneal disorder due to contact lens, unspecified eye**
  + **H18.83 Recurrent erosion of cornea**
    - **H18.831 Recurrent erosion of cornea, right eye**
    - **H18.832 Recurrent erosion of cornea, left eye**
    - **H18.833 Recurrent erosion of cornea, bilateral**
    - **H18.839 Recurrent erosion of cornea, unspecified eye**
  + **H18.89 Other specified disorders of cornea**
    - **H18.891 Other specified disorders of cornea, right eye**
    - **H18.892 Other specified disorders of cornea, left eye**
    - **H18.893 Other specified disorders of cornea, bilateral**
    - **H18.899 Other specified disorders of cornea, unspecified eye**

H18.9 Unspecified disorder of cornea

H20 Iridocyclitis

+ **H20.0 Acute and subacute iridocyclitis**
  Acute anterior uveitis
  Acute cyclitis
  Acute iritis
  Subacute anterior uveitis
  Subacute cyclitis
  Subacute iritis
  Excludes1: *iridocyclitis, iritis, uveitis (due to) (in) diabetes mellitus (E08-E13 with .39)*
  iridocyclitis, iritis, uveitis (due to) (in) diphtheria (A36.89)
  iridocyclitis, iritis, uveitis (due to) (in) gonococcal (A54.32)
  iridocyclitis, iritis, uveitis (due to) (in) herpes (simplex) (B00.51)
  iridocyclitis, iritis, uveitis (due to) (in) herpes zoster (B02.32)
  iridocyclitis, iritis, uveitis (due to) (in) late congenital syphilis (A50.39)
  iridocyclitis, iritis, uveitis (due to) (in) late syphilis (A52.71)
  iridocyclitis, iritis, uveitis (due to) (in) sarcoidosis (D86.83)
  iridocyclitis, iritis, uveitis (due to) (in) syphilis (A51.43)
  iridocyclitis, iritis, uveitis (due to) (in) toxoplasmosis (B58.09)
  iridocyclitis, iritis, uveitis (due to) (in) tuberculosis (A18.54)
  CC **H20.00 Unspecified acute and subacute iridocyclitis**
    CC Exclusion see Appendix A PDX collection 0624
  + **H20.01 Primary iridocyclitis**
    - CC **H20.011 Primary iridocyclitis, right eye**
      CC Exclusion see Appendix A PDX collection 0624
    - CC **H20.012 Primary iridocyclitis, left eye**
      CC Exclusion see Appendix A PDX collection 0624
    - CC **H20.013 Primary iridocyclitis, bilateral**
      CC Exclusion see Appendix A PDX collection 0624
    - CC **H20.019 Primary iridocyclitis, unspecified eye**
      CC Exclusion see Appendix A PDX collection 0624
  + **H20.02 Recurrent acute iridocyclitis**
    - CC **H20.021 Recurrent acute iridocyclitis, right eye**
      CC Exclusion see Appendix A PDX collection 0624
    - CC **H20.022 Recurrent acute iridocyclitis, left eye**
      CC Exclusion see Appendix A PDX collection 0624
    - CC **H20.023 Recurrent acute iridocyclitis, bilateral**
      CC Exclusion see Appendix A PDX collection 0624
    - CC **H20.029 Recurrent acute iridocyclitis, unspecified eye**
      CC Exclusion see Appendix A PDX collection 0624
  + **H20.03 Secondary infectious iridocyclitis**
    - CC **H20.031 Secondary infectious iridocyclitis, right eye**
      CC Exclusion see Appendix A PDX collection 0624
    - CC **H20.032 Secondary infectious iridocyclitis, left eye**
      CC Exclusion see Appendix A PDX collection 0624
    - CC **H20.033 Secondary infectious iridocyclitis, bilateral**
      CC Exclusion see Appendix A PDX collection 0624
    - CC **H20.039 Secondary infectious iridocyclitis, unspecified eye**
      CC Exclusion see Appendix A PDX collection 0624
  + **H20.04 Secondary noninfectious iridocyclitis**
    - **H20.041 Secondary noninfectious iridocyclitis, right eye**
    - **H20.042 Secondary noninfectious iridocyclitis, left eye**
    - **H20.043 Secondary noninfectious iridocyclitis, bilateral**
    - **H20.049 Secondary noninfectious iridocyclitis, unspecified eye**
  + **H20.05 Hypopyon**
    - **H20.051 Hypopyon, right eye**
    - **H20.052 Hypopyon, left eye**
    - **H20.053 Hypopyon, bilateral**
    - **H20.059 Hypopyon, unspecified eye**

+ **H20.1 Chronic iridocyclitis**
Use additional code for any associated cataract (H26.21-)
Excludes2: *posterior cyclitis (H30.2-)*
H20.10 Chronic iridocyclitis, unspecified eye
H20.11 Chronic iridocyclitis, right eye
H20.12 Chronic iridocyclitis, left eye
H20.13 Chronic iridocyclitis, bilateral

+ **H20.2 Lens-induced iridocyclitis**
H20.20 Lens-induced iridocyclitis, unspecified eye
H20.21 Lens-induced iridocyclitis, right eye
H20.22 Lens-induced iridocyclitis, left eye
H20.23 Lens-induced iridocyclitis, bilateral

+ **H20.8 Other iridocyclitis**
Excludes2: *glaucomatocyclitis crises (H40.4-)*
posterior cyclitis (H30.2-)
sympathetic uveitis (H44.13-)
+ **H20.81 Fuchs' heterochromic cyclitis**
H20.811 Fuchs' heterochromic cyclitis, right eye
H20.812 Fuchs' heterochromic cyclitis, left eye
H20.813 Fuchs' heterochromic cyclitis, bilateral
H20.819 Fuchs' heterochromic cyclitis, unspecified eye
+ **H20.82 Vogt-Koyanagi syndrome**
H20.821 Vogt-Koyanagi syndrome, right eye
H20.822 Vogt-Koyanagi syndrome, left eye
H20.823 Vogt-Koyanagi syndrome, bilateral
H20.829 Vogt-Koyanagi syndrome, unspecified eye

CC **H20.9 Unspecified iridocyclitis**
Uveitis NOS
CC Exclusion see Appendix A PDX collection 0624

H21 Other disorders of iris and ciliary body
Excludes2: *sympathetic uveitis (H44.1-)*

+ **H21.0 Hyphema**
Excludes1: *traumatic hyphema (S05.1-)*
H21.00 Hyphema, unspecified eye
H21.01 Hyphema, right eye
H21.02 Hyphema, left eye
H21.03 Hyphema, bilateral

+ **H21.1 Other vascular disorders of iris and ciliary body**
Neovascularization of iris or ciliary body
Rubeosis iridis
Rubeosis of iris
+ **H21.1X Other vascular disorders of iris and ciliary body**
H21.1X1 Other vascular disorders of iris and ciliary body, right eye
H21.1X2 Other vascular disorders of iris and ciliary body, left eye
H21.1X3 Other vascular disorders of iris and ciliary body, bilateral
H21.1X9 Other vascular disorders of iris and ciliary body, unspecified eye

+ **H21.2 Degeneration of iris and ciliary body**
+ **H21.21 Degeneration of chamber angle**
H21.211 Degeneration of chamber angle, right eye
H21.212 Degeneration of chamber angle, left eye
H21.213 Degeneration of chamber angle, bilateral
H21.219 Degeneration of chamber angle, unspecified eye
+ **H21.22 Degeneration of ciliary body**
H21.221 Degeneration of ciliary body, right eye
H21.222 Degeneration of ciliary body, left eye
H21.223 Degeneration of ciliary body, bilateral
H21.229 Degeneration of ciliary body, unspecified eye
+ **H21.23 Degeneration of iris (pigmentary)**
Translucency of iris
H21.231 Degeneration of iris (pigmentary), right eye
H21.232 Degeneration of iris (pigmentary), left eye
H21.233 Degeneration of iris (pigmentary), bilateral
H21.239 Degeneration of iris (pigmentary), unspecified eye
+ **H21.24 Degeneration of pupillary margin**
H21.241 Degeneration of pupillary margin, right eye
H21.242 Degeneration of pupillary margin, left eye
H21.243 Degeneration of pupillary margin, bilateral
H21.249 Degeneration of pupillary margin, unspecified eye
+ **H21.25 Iridoschisis**
H21.251 Iridoschisis, right eye
H21.252 Iridoschisis, left eye
H21.253 Iridoschisis, bilateral
H21.259 Iridoschisis, unspecified eye
+ **H21.26 Iris atrophy (essential) (progressive)**
H21.261 Iris atrophy (essential) (progressive), right eye
H21.262 Iris atrophy (essential) (progressive), left eye
H21.263 Iris atrophy (essential) (progressive), bilateral
H21.269 Iris atrophy (essential) (progressive), unspecified eye
+ **H21.27 Miotic pupillary cyst**
H21.271 Miotic pupillary cyst, right eye
H21.272 Miotic pupillary cyst, left eye
H21.273 Miotic pupillary cyst, bilateral
H21.279 Miotic pupillary cyst, unspecified eye
H21.29 Other iris atrophy

+ **H21.3 Cyst of iris, ciliary body and anterior chamber**
Excludes2: *miotic pupillary cyst (H21.27-)*
+ **H21.30 Idiopathic cysts of iris, ciliary body or anterior chamber**
Cyst of iris, ciliary body or anterior chamber NOS
H21.301 Idiopathic cysts of iris, ciliary body or anterior chamber, right eye
H21.302 Idiopathic cysts of iris, ciliary body or anterior chamber, left eye
H21.303 Idiopathic cysts of iris, ciliary body or anterior chamber, bilateral
H21.309 Idiopathic cysts of iris, ciliary body or anterior chamber, unspecified eye
+ **H21.31 Exudative cysts of iris or anterior chamber**
H21.311 Exudative cysts of iris or anterior chamber, right eye
H21.312 Exudative cysts of iris or anterior chamber, left eye
H21.313 Exudative cysts of iris or anterior chamber, bilateral
H21.319 Exudative cysts of iris or anterior chamber, unspecified eye
+ **H21.32 Implantation cysts of iris, ciliary body or anterior chamber**
H21.321 Implantation cysts of iris, ciliary body or anterior chamber, right eye
H21.322 Implantation cysts of iris, ciliary body or anterior chamber, left eye
H21.323 Implantation cysts of iris, ciliary body or anterior chamber, bilateral
H21.329 Implantation cysts of iris, ciliary body or anterior chamber, unspecified eye
+ **H21.33 Parasitic cyst of iris, ciliary body or anterior chamber**
CC **H21.331 Parasitic cyst of iris, ciliary body or anterior chamber, right eye**
CC Exclusion see Appendix A PDX collection 0625
CC **H21.332 Parasitic cyst of iris, ciliary body or anterior chamber, left eye**
CC Exclusion see Appendix A PDX collection 0625
CC **H21.333 Parasitic cyst of iris, ciliary body or anterior chamber, bilateral**
CC Exclusion see Appendix A PDX collection 0625
CC **H21.339 Parasitic cyst of iris, ciliary body or anterior chamber, unspecified eye**
CC Exclusion see Appendix A PDX collection 0625
+ **H21.34 Primary cyst of pars plana**
H21.341 Primary cyst of pars plana, right eye
H21.342 Primary cyst of pars plana, left eye
H21.343 Primary cyst of pars plana, bilateral
H21.349 Primary cyst of pars plana, unspecified eye
+ **H21.35 Exudative cyst of pars plana**
H21.351 Exudative cyst of pars plana, right eye
H21.352 Exudative cyst of pars plana, left eye
H21.353 Exudative cyst of pars plana, bilateral
H21.359 Exudative cyst of pars plana, unspecified eye

+ **H21.4 Pupillary membranes**
  Iris bombé
  Pupillary occlusion
  Pupillary seclusion
  Excludes1: *congenital pupillary membranes (Q13.8)*
  H21.40 Pupillary membranes, unspecified eye
  H21.41 Pupillary membranes, right eye
  H21.42 Pupillary membranes, left eye
  H21.43 Pupillary membranes, bilateral

+ **H21.5 Other and unspecified adhesions and disruptions of iris and ciliary body**
  Excludes1: *corectopia (Q13.2)*
  + **H21.50 Unspecified adhesions of iris**
    Synechia (iris) NOS
    H21.501 Unspecified adhesions of iris, right eye
    H21.502 Unspecified adhesions of iris, left eye
    H21.503 Unspecified adhesions of iris, bilateral
    H21.509 Unspecified adhesions of iris and ciliary body, unspecified eye
  + **H21.51 Anterior synechiae (iris)**
    H21.511 Anterior synechiae (iris), right eye
    H21.512 Anterior synechiae (iris), left eye
    H21.513 Anterior synechiae (iris), bilateral
    H21.519 Anterior synechiae (iris), unspecified eye
  + **H21.52 Goniosynechiae**
    H21.521 Goniosynechiae, right eye
    H21.522 Goniosynechiae, left eye
    H21.523 Goniosynechiae, bilateral
    H21.529 Goniosynechiae, unspecified eye
  + **H21.53 Iridodialysis**
    H21.531 Iridodialysis, right eye
    H21.532 Iridodialysis, left eye
    H21.533 Iridodialysis, bilateral
    H21.539 Iridodialysis, unspecified eye
  + **H21.54 Posterior synechiae (iris)**
    H21.541 Posterior synechiae (iris), right eye
    H21.542 Posterior synechiae (iris), left eye
    H21.543 Posterior synechiae (iris), bilateral
    H21.549 Posterior synechiae (iris), unspecified eye
  + **H21.55 Recession of chamber angle**
    H21.551 Recession of chamber angle, right eye
    H21.552 Recession of chamber angle, left eye
    H21.553 Recession of chamber angle, bilateral
    H21.559 Recession of chamber angle, unspecified eye
  + **H21.56 Pupillary abnormalities**
    Deformed pupil
    Ectopic pupil
    Rupture of sphincter, pupil
    Excludes1: *congenital deformity of pupil (Q13.2-)*
    H21.561 Pupillary abnormality, right eye
    H21.562 Pupillary abnormality, left eye
    H21.563 Pupillary abnormality, bilateral
    H21.569 Pupillary abnormality, unspecified eye

+ **H21.8 Other specified disorders of iris and ciliary body**
  H21.81 Floppy iris syndrome
    Intraoperative floppy iris syndrome (IFIS)
    Use additional code for adverse effect, if applicable, to identify drug (T36-T50 with fifth or sixth character 5)
  H21.82 Plateau iris syndrome (post-iridectomy) (postprocedural)
  H21.89 Other specified disorders of iris and ciliary body

H21.9 Unspecified disorder of iris and ciliary body

H22 Disorders of iris and ciliary body in diseases classified elsewhere

Code first underlying disease, such as:
  gout (M1A.-, M10.-)
  leprosy (A30.-)
  parasitic disease (B89)

Valid 3-character code, no further characters required

isorders of lens (H25-H28)

H25 Age-related cataract

Senile cataract
Excludes2: capsular glaucoma with pseudoexfoliation of lens (H40.1-)

+ **H25.0 Age-related incipient cataract**
  + **H25.01 Cortical age-related cataract**
    • **H25.011 Cortical age-related cataract, right eye**
    • **H25.012 Cortical age-related cataract, left eye**
    • **H25.013 Cortical age-related cataract, bilateral**
    • **H25.019 Cortical age-related cataract, unspecified eye**
  + **H25.03 Anterior subcapsular polar age-related cataract**
    • **H25.031 Anterior subcapsular polar age-related cataract, right eye**
    • **H25.032 Anterior subcapsular polar age-related cataract, left eye**
    • **H25.033 Anterior subcapsular polar age-related cataract, bilateral**
    • **H25.039 Anterior subcapsular polar age-related cataract, unspecified eye**
  + **H25.04 Posterior subcapsular polar age-related cataract**
    • **H25.041 Posterior subcapsular polar age-related cataract, right eye**
    • **H25.042 Posterior subcapsular polar age-related cataract, left eye**
    • **H25.043 Posterior subcapsular polar age-related cataract, bilateral**
    • **H25.049 Posterior subcapsular polar age-related cataract, unspecified eye**
  + **H25.09 Other age-related incipient cataract**
    Coronary age-related cataract
    Punctate age-related cataract
    Water clefts
    • **H25.091 Other age-related incipient cataract, right eye**
    • **H25.092 Other age-related incipient cataract, left eye**
    • **H25.093 Other age-related incipient cataract, bilateral**
    • **H25.099 Other age-related incipient cataract, unspecified eye**

+ **H25.1 Age-related nuclear cataract**
  Cataracta brunescens
  Nuclear sclerosis cataract
  • **H25.10 Age-related nuclear cataract, unspecified eye**
  • **H25.11 Age-related nuclear cataract, right eye**
  • **H25.12 Age-related nuclear cataract, left eye**
  • **H25.13 Age-related nuclear cataract, bilateral**

+ **H25.2 Age-related cataract, morgagnian type**
  Age-related hypermature cataract
  • **H25.20 Age-related cataract, morgagnian type, unspecified eye**
  • **H25.21 Age-related cataract, morgagnian type, right eye**
  • **H25.22 Age-related cataract, morgagnian type, left eye**
  • **H25.23 Age-related cataract, morgagnian type, bilateral**

+ **H25.8 Other age-related cataract**
  + **H25.81 Combined forms of age-related cataract**
    • **H25.811 Combined forms of age-related cataract, right eye**
    • **H25.812 Combined forms of age-related cataract, left eye**
    • **H25.813 Combined forms of age-related cataract, bilateral**
    • **H25.819 Combined forms of age-related cataract, unspecified eye**
  • **H25.89 Other age-related cataract**

• **H25.9 Unspecified age-related cataract**

H26 Other cataract

Excludes1: *congenital cataract (Q12.0)*

+ **H26.0 Infantile and juvenile cataract**
  + **H26.00 Unspecified infantile and juvenile cataract**
    • **H26.001 Unspecified infantile and juvenile cataract, right eye**
    • **H26.002 Unspecified infantile and juvenile cataract, left eye**
    • **H26.003 Unspecified infantile and juvenile cataract, bilateral**
    • **H26.009 Unspecified infantile and juvenile cataract, unspecified eye**
  + **H26.01 Infantile and juvenile cortical, lamellar, or zonular cataract**
    • **H26.011 Infantile and juvenile cortical, lamellar, or zonular cataract, right eye**
    • **H26.012 Infantile and juvenile cortical, lamellar, or zonular cataract, left eye**
    • **H26.013 Infantile and juvenile cortical, lamellar, or zonular cataract, bilateral**
    • **H26.019 Infantile and juvenile cortical, lamellar, or zonular cataract, unspecified eye**
  + **H26.03 Infantile and juvenile nuclear cataract**
    • **H26.031 Infantile and juvenile nuclear cataract, right eye**
    • **H26.032 Infantile and juvenile nuclear cataract, left eye**

- • **H26.033 Infantile and juvenile nuclear cataract, bilateral**
- • **H26.039 Infantile and juvenile nuclear cataract, unspecified eye**
- \+ **H26.04 Anterior subcapsular polar infantile and juvenile cataract**
  - • **H26.041 Anterior subcapsular polar infantile and juvenile cataract, right eye**
  - • **H26.042 Anterior subcapsular polar infantile and juvenile cataract, left eye**
  - • **H26.043 Anterior subcapsular polar infantile and juvenile cataract, bilateral**
  - • **H26.049 Anterior subcapsular polar infantile and juvenile cataract, unspecified eye**
- \+ **H26.05 Posterior subcapsular polar infantile and juvenile cataract**
  - • **H26.051 Posterior subcapsular polar infantile and juvenile cataract, right eye**
  - • **H26.052 Posterior subcapsular polar infantile and juvenile cataract, left eye**
  - • **H26.053 Posterior subcapsular polar infantile and juvenile cataract, bilateral**
  - • **H26.059 Posterior subcapsular polar infantile and juvenile cataract, unspecified eye**
- \+ **H26.06 Combined forms of infantile and juvenile cataract**
  - • **H26.061 Combined forms of infantile and juvenile cataract, right eye**
  - • **H26.062 Combined forms of infantile and juvenile cataract, left eye**
  - • **H26.063 Combined forms of infantile and juvenile cataract, bilateral**
  - • **H26.069 Combined forms of infantile and juvenile cataract, unspecified eye**
- • **H26.09 Other infantile and juvenile cataract**

\+ **H26.1 Traumatic cataract**

Use additional code (Chapter 20) to identify external cause

- \+ **H26.10 Unspecified traumatic cataract**
  - **H26.101 Unspecified traumatic cataract, right eye**
  - **H26.102 Unspecified traumatic cataract, left eye**
  - **H26.103 Unspecified traumatic cataract, bilateral**
  - **H26.109 Unspecified traumatic cataract, unspecified eye**
- \+ **H26.11 Localized traumatic opacities**
  - **H26.111 Localized traumatic opacities, right eye**
  - **H26.112 Localized traumatic opacities, left eye**
  - **H26.113 Localized traumatic opacities, bilateral**
  - **H26.119 Localized traumatic opacities, unspecified eye**
- \+ **H26.12 Partially resolved traumatic cataract**
  - **H26.121 Partially resolved traumatic cataract, right eye**
  - **H26.122 Partially resolved traumatic cataract, left eye**
  - **H26.123 Partially resolved traumatic cataract, bilateral**
  - **H26.129 Partially resolved traumatic cataract, unspecified eye**
- \+ **H26.13 Total traumatic cataract**
  - **H26.131 Total traumatic cataract, right eye**
  - **H26.132 Total traumatic cataract, left eye**
  - **H26.133 Total traumatic cataract, bilateral**
  - **H26.139 Total traumatic cataract, unspecified eye**

\+ **H26.2 Complicated cataract**

- **H26.20 Unspecified complicated cataract**
  Cataracta complicata NOS
- \+ **H26.21 Cataract with neovascularization**
  Code also associated condition, such as:
  chronic iridocyclitis (H20.1-)
  - **H26.211 Cataract with neovascularization, right eye**
  - **H26.212 Cataract with neovascularization, left eye**
  - **H26.213 Cataract with neovascularization, bilateral**
  - **H26.219 Cataract with neovascularization, unspecified eye**
- \+ **H26.22 Cataract secondary to ocular disorders (degenerative) (inflammatory)**
  Code also associated ocular disorder
  - **H26.221 Cataract secondary to ocular disorders (degenerative) (inflammatory), right eye**
  - **H26.222 Cataract secondary to ocular disorders (degenerative) (inflammatory), left eye**
  - **H26.223 Cataract secondary to ocular disorders (degenerative) (inflammatory), bilateral**
  - **H26.229 Cataract secondary to ocular disorders (degenerative) (inflammatory), unspecified eye**
- \+ **H26.23 Glaucomatous flecks (subcapsular)**
  Code first underlying glaucoma (H40-H42)
  - **H26.231 Glaucomatous flecks (subcapsular), right e[ye]**
  - **H26.232 Glaucomatous flecks (subcapsular), left ey[e]**
  - **H26.233 Glaucomatous flecks (subcapsular), bilater[al]**
  - **H26.239 Glaucomatous flecks (subcapsular), unspecified eye**

\+ **H26.3 Drug-induced cataract**

Toxic cataract

Use additional code for adverse effect, if applicable, to identify dr[ug] (T36-T50 with fifth or sixth character 5)

- **H26.30 Drug-induced cataract, unspecified eye**
- **H26.31 Drug-induced cataract, right eye**
- **H26.32 Drug-induced cataract, left eye**
- **H26.33 Drug-induced cataract, bilateral**

\+ **H26.4 Secondary cataract**

- **H26.40 Unspecified secondary cataract**
- \+ **H26.41 Soemmering's ring**
  - **H26.411 Soemmering's ring, right eye**
  - **H26.412 Soemmering's ring, left eye**
  - **H26.413 Soemmering's ring, bilateral**
  - **H26.419 Soemmering's ring, unspecified eye**
- \+ **H26.49 Other secondary cataract**
  - **H26.491 Other secondary cataract, right eye**
  - **H26.492 Other secondary cataract, left eye**
  - **H26.493 Other secondary cataract, bilateral**
  - **H26.499 Other secondary cataract, unspecified eye**

H26.8 Other specified cataract

H26.9 Unspecified cataract

H27 Other disorders of lens

Excludes1: *congenital lens malformations (Q12.-)*
mechanical complications of intraocular lens implant (T85.2)
pseudophakia (Z96.1)

\+ **H27.0 Aphakia**

Acquired absence of lens
Acquired aphakia
Aphakia due to trauma

Excludes1: *cataract extraction status (Z98.4-)*
congenital absence of lens (Q12.3)
congenital aphakia (Q12.3)

- **H27.00 Aphakia, unspecified eye**
- **H27.01 Aphakia, right eye**
- **H27.02 Aphakia, left eye**
- **H27.03 Aphakia, bilateral**

\+ **H27.1 Dislocation of lens**

- **H27.10 Unspecified dislocation of lens**
- \+ **H27.11 Subluxation of lens**
  - **H27.111 Subluxation of lens, right eye**
  - **H27.112 Subluxation of lens, left eye**
  - **H27.113 Subluxation of lens, bilateral**
  - **H27.119 Subluxation of lens, unspecified eye**
- \+ **H27.12 Anterior dislocation of lens**
  - **H27.121 Anterior dislocation of lens, right eye**
  - **H27.122 Anterior dislocation of lens, left eye**
  - **H27.123 Anterior dislocation of lens, bilateral**
  - **H27.129 Anterior dislocation of lens, unspecified eye**
- \+ **H27.13 Posterior dislocation of lens**
  - **H27.131 Posterior dislocation of lens, right eye**
  - **H27.132 Posterior dislocation of lens, left eye**
  - **H27.133 Posterior dislocation of lens, bilateral**
  - **H27.139 Posterior dislocation of lens, unspecified ey[e]**

H27.8 Other specified disorders of lens

H27.9 Unspecified disorder of lens

H28 Cataract in diseases classified elsewhere

Code first underlying disease, such as:
hypoparathyroidism (E20.-)
myotonia (G71.1-)
myxedema (E03.-)
protein-calorie malnutrition (E40-E46)

Excludes1: *cataract in diabetes mellitus (E08.36, E09.36, E10.36, E11.36, E13.36)*

Valid 3-character code, no further characters required

sorders of choroid and retina (H30-H36)

H30 Chorioretinal inflammation

+ **H30.0 Focal chorioretinal inflammation**
  Focal chorioretinitis
  Focal choroiditis
  Focal retinitis
  Focal retinochoroiditis
  + **H30.00 Unspecified focal chorioretinal inflammation**
    Focal chorioretinitis NOS
    Focal choroiditis NOS
    Focal retinitis NOS
    Focal retinochoroiditis NOS
    H30.001 Unspecified focal chorioretinal inflammation, right eye
    H30.002 Unspecified focal chorioretinal inflammation, left eye
    H30.003 Unspecified focal chorioretinal inflammation, bilateral
    H30.009 Unspecified focal chorioretinal inflammation, unspecified eye
  + **H30.01 Focal chorioretinal inflammation, juxtapapillary**
    H30.011 Focal chorioretinal inflammation, juxtapapillary, right eye
    H30.012 Focal chorioretinal inflammation, juxtapapillary, left eye
    H30.013 Focal chorioretinal inflammation, juxtapapillary, bilateral
    H30.019 Focal chorioretinal inflammation, juxtapapillary, unspecified eye
  + **H30.02 Focal chorioretinal inflammation of posterior pole**
    H30.021 Focal chorioretinal inflammation of posterior pole, right eye
    H30.022 Focal chorioretinal inflammation of posterior pole, left eye
    H30.023 Focal chorioretinal inflammation of posterior pole, bilateral
    H30.029 Focal chorioretinal inflammation of posterior pole, unspecified eye
  + **H30.03 Focal chorioretinal inflammation, peripheral**
    H30.031 Focal chorioretinal inflammation, peripheral, right eye
    H30.032 Focal chorioretinal inflammation, peripheral, left eye
    H30.033 Focal chorioretinal inflammation, peripheral, bilateral
    H30.039 Focal chorioretinal inflammation, peripheral, unspecified eye
  + **H30.04 Focal chorioretinal inflammation, macular or paramacular**
    H30.041 Focal chorioretinal inflammation, macular or paramacular, right eye
    H30.042 Focal chorioretinal inflammation, macular or paramacular, left eye
    H30.043 Focal chorioretinal inflammation, macular or paramacular, bilateral
    H30.049 Focal chorioretinal inflammation, macular or paramacular, unspecified eye

+ **H30.1 Disseminated chorioretinal inflammation**
  Disseminated chorioretinitis
  Disseminated choroiditis
  Disseminated retinitis
  Disseminated retinochoroiditis
  Excludes2: *exudative retinopathy (H35.02-)*
  + **H30.10 Unspecified disseminated chorioretinal inflammation**
    Disseminated chorioretinitis NOS
    Disseminated choroiditis NOS
    Disseminated retinitis NOS
    Disseminated retinochoroiditis NOS
    CC **H30.101 Unspecified disseminated chorioretinal inflammation, right eye**
      CC Exclusion see Appendix A PDX collection 0626
    CC **H30.102 Unspecified disseminated chorioretinal inflammation, left eye**
      CC Exclusion see Appendix A PDX collection 0626
    CC **H30.103 Unspecified disseminated chorioretinal inflammation, bilateral**
      CC Exclusion see Appendix A PDX collection 0626
    CC **H30.109 Unspecified disseminated chorioretinal inflammation, unspecified eye**
      CC Exclusion see Appendix A PDX collection 0626
  + **H30.11 Disseminated chorioretinal inflammation of posterior pole**
    CC **H30.111 Disseminated chorioretinal inflammation of posterior pole, right eye**
      CC Exclusion see Appendix A PDX collection 0626
    CC **H30.112 Disseminated chorioretinal inflammation of posterior pole, left eye**
      CC Exclusion see Appendix A PDX collection 0626
    CC **H30.113 Disseminated chorioretinal inflammation of posterior pole, bilateral**
      CC Exclusion see Appendix A PDX collection 0626
    CC **H30.119 Disseminated chorioretinal inflammation of posterior pole, unspecified eye**
      CC Exclusion see Appendix A PDX collection 0626
  + **H30.12 Disseminated chorioretinal inflammation, peripheral**
    CC **H30.121 Disseminated chorioretinal inflammation, peripheral right eye**
      CC Exclusion see Appendix A PDX collection 0626
    CC **H30.122 Disseminated chorioretinal inflammation, peripheral, left eye**
      CC Exclusion see Appendix A PDX collection 0626
    CC **H30.123 Disseminated chorioretinal inflammation, peripheral, bilateral**
      CC Exclusion see Appendix A PDX collection 0626
    CC **H30.129 Disseminated chorioretinal inflammation, peripheral, unspecified eye**
      CC Exclusion see Appendix A PDX collection 0626
  + **H30.13 Disseminated chorioretinal inflammation, generalized**
    CC **H30.131 Disseminated chorioretinal inflammation, generalized, right eye**
      CC Exclusion see Appendix A PDX collection 0626
    CC **H30.132 Disseminated chorioretinal inflammation, generalized, left eye**
      CC Exclusion see Appendix A PDX collection 0626
    CC **H30.133 Disseminated chorioretinal inflammation, generalized, bilateral**
      CC Exclusion see Appendix A PDX collection 0626
    CC **H30.139 Disseminated chorioretinal inflammation, generalized, unspecified eye**
      CC Exclusion see Appendix A PDX collection 0626
  + **H30.14 Acute posterior multifocal placoid pigment epitheliopathy**
    CC **H30.141 Acute posterior multifocal placoid pigment epitheliopathy, right eye**
      CC Exclusion see Appendix A PDX collection 0626
    CC **H30.142 Acute posterior multifocal placoid pigment epitheliopathy, left eye**
      CC Exclusion see Appendix A PDX collection 0626
    CC **H30.143 Acute posterior multifocal placoid pigment epitheliopathy, bilateral**
      CC Exclusion see Appendix A PDX collection 0626
    CC **H30.149 Acute posterior multifocal placoid pigment epitheliopathy, unspecified eye**
      CC Exclusion see Appendix A PDX collection 0626

+ **H30.2 Posterior cyclitis**
  Pars planitis
  H30.20 Posterior cyclitis, unspecified eye
  H30.21 Posterior cyclitis, right eye
  H30.22 Posterior cyclitis, left eye
  H30.23 Posterior cyclitis, bilateral

+ **H30.8 Other chorioretinal inflammations**
  + **H30.81 Harada's disease**
    H30.811 Harada's disease, right eye
    H30.812 Harada's disease, left eye
    H30.813 Harada's disease, bilateral
    H30.819 Harada's disease, unspecified eye

+ H30.89 Other chorioretinal inflammations
CC H30.891 Other chorioretinal inflammations, right eye
CC Exclusion see Appendix A PDX collection 0626
CC H30.892 Other chorioretinal inflammations, left eye
CC Exclusion see Appendix A PDX collection 0626
CC H30.893 Other chorioretinal inflammations, bilateral
CC Exclusion see Appendix A PDX collection 0626
CC H30.899 Other chorioretinal inflammations, unspecified eye
CC Exclusion see Appendix A PDX collection 0626
+ H30.9 Unspecified chorioretinal inflammation
Chorioretinitis NOS
Choroiditis NOS
Neuroretinitis NOS
Retinitis NOS
Retinochoroiditis NOS
CC H30.90 Unspecified chorioretinal inflammation, unspecified eye
CC Exclusion see Appendix A PDX collection 0626
CC H30.91 Unspecified chorioretinal inflammation, right eye
CC Exclusion see Appendix A PDX collection 0626
CC H30.92 Unspecified chorioretinal inflammation, left eye
CC Exclusion see Appendix A PDX collection 0626
CC H30.93 Unspecified chorioretinal inflammation, bilateral
CC Exclusion see Appendix A PDX collection 0626

H31 Other disorders of choroid
+ H31.0 Chorioretinal scars
Excludes2: *postsurgical chorioretinal scars (H59.81-)*
+ H31.00 Unspecified chorioretinal scars
H31.001 Unspecified chorioretinal scars, righ eye
H31.002 Unspecified chorioretinal scars, left eye
H31.003 Unspecified chorioretinal scars, bilateral
H31.009 Unspecified chorioretinal scars, unspecified eye
+ H31.01 Macula scars of posterior pole (postinflammatory) (post-traumatic)
Excludes1: *postprocedural choriorentinal scar (H59.81-)*
H31.011 Macula scars of posterior pole (postinflammatory) (post-traumatic), right eye
H31.012 Macula scars of posterior pole (postinflammatory) (post-traumatic), left eye
H31.013 Macula scars of posterior pole (postinflammatory) (post-traumatic), bilateral
H31.019 Macula scars of posterior pole (postinflammatory) (post-traumatic), unspecified eye
+ H31.02 Solar retinopathy
H31.021 Solar retinopathy, right eye
H31.022 Solar retinopathy, left eye
H31.023 Solar retinopathy, bilateral
H31.029 Solar retinopathy, unspecified eye
+ H31.09 Other chorioretinal scars
H31.091 Other chorioretinal scars, right eye
H31.092 Other chorioretinal scars, left eye
H31.093 Other chorioretinal scars, bilateral
H31.099 Other chorioretinal scars, unspecified eye
+ H31.1 Choroidal degeneration
Excludes2: *angioid streaks of macula (H35.33)*
+ H31.10 Unspecified choroidal degeneration
Choroidal sclerosis NOS
H31.101 Choroidal degeneration, unspecified, right eye
H31.102 Choroidal degeneration, unspecified, left eye
H31.103 Choroidal degeneration, unspecified, bilateral
H31.109 Choroidal degeneration, unspecified, unspecified eye
+ H31.11 Age-related choroidal atrophy
• H31.111 Age-related choroidal atrophy, right eye
• H31.112 Age-related choroidal atrophy, left eye
• H31.113 Age-related choroidal atrophy, bilateral
• H31.119 Age-related choroidal atrophy, unspecified eye
+ H31.12 Diffuse secondary atrophy of choroid
H31.121 Diffuse secondary atrophy of choroid, right eye
H31.122 Diffuse secondary atrophy of choroid, left eye
H31.123 Diffuse secondary atrophy of choroid, bilateral
H31.129 Diffuse secondary atrophy of choroid, unspecified eye
+ H31.2 Hereditary choroidal dystrophy
Excludes2: *hyperornithinemia (E72.4)*
ornithinemia (E72.4)
H31.20 Hereditary choroidal dystrophy, unspecified
H31.21 Choroideremia
H31.22 Choroidal dystrophy (central areolar) (generalized) (peripapillary)
H31.23 Gyrate atrophy, choroid
H31.29 Other hereditary choroidal dystrophy
+ H31.3 Choroidal hemorrhage and rupture
+ H31.30 Unspecified choroidal hemorrhage
H31.301 Unspecified choroidal hemorrhage, right e
H31.302 Unspecified choroidal hemorrhage, left eye
H31.303 Unspecified choroidal hemorrhage, bilater
H31.309 Unspecified choroidal hemorrhage, unspecified eye
+ H31.31 Expulsive choroidal hemorrhage
H31.311 Expulsive choroidal hemorrhage, right eye
H31.312 Expulsive choroidal hemorrhage, left eye
H31.313 Expulsive choroidal hemorrhage, bilateral
H31.319 Expulsive choroidal hemorrhage, unspecifi eye
+ H31.32 Choroidal rupture
CC H31.321 Choroidal rupture, right eye
CC Exclusion see Appendix A PDX collection 0627
CC H31.322 Choroidal rupture, left eye
CC Exclusion see Appendix A PDX collection 0627
CC H31.323 Choroidal rupture, bilateral
CC Exclusion see Appendix A PDX collection 0627
CC H31.329 Choroidal rupture, unspecified eye
CC Exclusion see Appendix A PDX collection 0627
+ H31.4 Choroidal detachment
+ H31.40 Unspecified choroidal detachment
CC H31.401 Unspecified choroidal detachment, right ey
CC Exclusion see Appendix A PDX collection 0627
CC H31.402 Unspecified choroidal detachment, left eye
CC Exclusion see Appendix A PDX collection 0627
CC H31.403 Unspecified choroidal detachment, bilatera
CC Exclusion see Appendix A PDX collection 0627
CC H31.409 Unspecified choroidal detachment, unspecified eye
CC Exclusion see Appendix A PDX collection 0627
+ H31.41 Hemorrhagic choroidal detachment
CC H31.411 Hemorrhagic choroidal detachment, right eye
CC Exclusion see Appendix A PDX collection 0627
CC H31.412 Hemorrhagic choroidal detachment, left ey
CC Exclusion see Appendix A PDX collection 0627
CC H31.413 Hemorrhagic choroidal detachment, bilateral
CC Exclusion see Appendix A PDX collection 06
CC H31.419 Hemorrhagic choroidal detachment, unspecified eye
CC Exclusion see Appendix A PDX collection 0627
+ H31.42 Serous choroidal detachment
CC H31.421 Serous choroidal detachment, right eye
CC Exclusion see Appendix A PDX collection 0627
CC H31.422 Serous choroidal detachment, left eye
CC Exclusion see Appendix A PDX collection 0627
CC H31.423 Serous choroidal detachment, bilateral
CC Exclusion see Appendix A PDX collection 0627
CC H31.429 Serous choroidal detachment, unspecified e
CC Exclusion see Appendix A PDX collection 06
H31.8 Other specified disorders of choroid
H31.9 Unspecified disorder of choroid

H32 Chorioretinal disorders in diseases classified elsewhere
Code first underlying disease, such as:
congenital toxoplasmosis (P37.1)
histoplasmosis (B39.-)
leprosy (A30.-)
Excludes1: *chorioretinitis (in):*
toxoplasmosis (acquired) (B58.01)
tuberculosis (A18.53)
Valid 3-character code, no further characters required

H33 Retinal detachments and breaks
Excludes1: *detachment of retinal pigment epithelium (H35.72-, H35.73-)*

\+ **H33.0 Retinal detachment with retinal break**
Rhegmatogenous retinal detachment
Excludes1: *serous retinal detachment (without retinal break) (H33.2-)*

\+ **H33.00 Unspecified retinal detachment with retinal break**
H33.001 Unspecified retinal detachment with retinal break, right eye
H33.002 Unspecified retinal detachment with retinal break, left eye
H33.003 Unspecified retinal detachment with retinal break, bilateral
H33.009 Unspecified retinal detachment with retinal break, unspecified eye

\+ **H33.01 Retinal detachment with single break**
H33.011 Retinal detachment with single break, right eye
H33.012 Retinal detachment with single break, left eye
H33.013 Retinal detachment with single break, bilateral
H33.019 Retinal detachment with single break, unspecified eye

\+ **H33.02 Retinal detachment with multiple breaks**
H33.021 Retinal detachment with multiple breaks, right eye
H33.022 Retinal detachment with multiple breaks, left eye
H33.023 Retinal detachment with multiple breaks, bilateral
H33.029 Retinal detachment with multiple breaks, unspecified eye

\+ **H33.03 Retinal detachment with giant retinal tear**
H33.031 Retinal detachment with giant retinal tear, right eye
H33.032 Retinal detachment with giant retinal tear, left eye
H33.033 Retinal detachment with giant retinal tear, bilateral
H33.039 Retinal detachment with giant retinal tear, unspecified eye

\+ **H33.04 Retinal detachment with retinal dialysis**
H33.041 Retinal detachment with retinal dialysis, right eye
H33.042 Retinal detachment with retinal dialysis, left eye
H33.043 Retinal detachment with retinal dialysis, bilateral
H33.049 Retinal detachment with retinal dialysis, unspecified eye

\+ **H33.05 Total retinal detachment**
H33.051 Total retinal detachment, right eye
H33.052 Total retinal detachment, left eye
H33.053 Total retinal detachment, bilateral
H33.059 Total retinal detachment, unspecified eye

\+ **H33.1 Retinoschisis and retinal cysts**
Excludes1: *congenital retinoschisis (Q14.1)*
microcystoid degeneration of retina (H35.42-)

\+ **H33.10 Unspecified retinoschisis**
H33.101 Unspecified retinoschisis, right eye
H33.102 Unspecified retinoschisis, left eye
H33.103 Unspecified retinoschisis, bilateral
H33.109 Unspecified retinoschisis, unspecified eye

\+ **H33.11 Cyst of ora serrata**
H33.111 Cyst of ora serrata, right eye
H33.112 Cyst of ora serrata, left eye
H33.113 Cyst of ora serrata, bilateral
H33.119 Cyst of ora serrata, unspecified eye

\+ **H33.12 Parasitic cyst of retina**
CC **H33.121 Parasitic cyst of retina, right eye**
CC Exclusion see Appendix A PDX collection 0625
CC **H33.122 Parasitic cyst of retina, left eye**
CC Exclusion see Appendix A PDX collection 0625
CC **H33.123 Parasitic cyst of retina, bilateral**
CC Exclusion see Appendix A PDX collection 0625
CC **H33.129 Parasitic cyst of retina, unspecified eye**
CC Exclusion see Appendix A PDX collection 0625

\+ **H33.19 Other retinoschisis and retinal cysts**
Pseudocyst of retina
H33.191 Other retinoschisis and retinal cysts, right eye
H33.192 Other retinoschisis and retinal cysts, left eye
H33.193 Other retinoschisis and retinal cysts, bilateral
H33.199 Other retinoschisis and retinal cysts, unspecified eye

\+ **H33.2 Serous retinal detachment**
Retinal detachment NOS
Retinal detachment without retinal break
Excludes1: *central serous chorioretinopathy (H35.71-)*
CC **H33.20 Serous retinal detachment, unspecified eye**
CC Exclusion see Appendix A PDX collection 0628
CC **H33.21 Serous retinal detachment, right eye**
CC Exclusion see Appendix A PDX collection 0628
CC **H33.22 Serous retinal detachment, left eye**
CC Exclusion see Appendix A PDX collection 0628
CC **H33.23 Serous retinal detachment, bilateral**
CC Exclusion see Appendix A PDX collection 0628

\+ **H33.3 Retinal breaks without detachment**
Excludes1: *chorioretinal scars after surgery for detachment (H59.81-)*
peripheral retinal degeneration without break (H35.4-)

\+ **H33.30 Unspecified retinal break**
H33.301 Unspecified retinal break, right eye
H33.302 Unspecified retinal break, left eye
H33.303 Unspecified retinal break, bilateral
H33.309 Unspecified retinal break, unspecified eye

\+ **H33.31 Horseshoe tear of retina without detachment**
Operculum of retina without detachment
H33.311 Horseshoe tear of retina without detachment, right eye
H33.312 Horseshoe tear of retina without detachment, left eye
H33.313 Horseshoe tear of retina without detachment, bilateral
H33.319 Horseshoe tear of retina without detachment, unspecified eye

\+ **H33.32 Round hole of retina without detachment**
H33.321 Round hole, right eye
H33.322 Round hole, left eye
H33.323 Round hole, bilateral
H33.329 Round hole, unspecified eye

\+ **H33.33 Multiple defects of retina without detachment**
H33.331 Multiple defects of retina without detachment, right eye
H33.332 Multiple defects of retina without detachment, left eye
H33.333 Multiple defects of retina without detachment, bilateral
H33.339 Multiple defects of retina without detachment, unspecified eye

\+ **H33.4 Traction detachment of retina**
Proliferative vitreo-retinopathy with retinal detachment
CC **H33.40 Traction detachment of retina, unspecified eye**
CC Exclusion see Appendix A PDX collection 0628
CC **H33.41 Traction detachment of retina, right eye**
CC Exclusion see Appendix A PDX collection 0628
CC **H33.42 Traction detachment of retina, left eye**
CC Exclusion see Appendix A PDX collection 0628
CC **H33.43 Traction detachment of retina, bilateral**
CC Exclusion see Appendix A PDX collection 0628

CC **H33.8 Other retinal detachments**
CC Exclusion see Appendix A PDX collection 0628

H34 Retinal vascular occlusions

Excludes1: *amaurosis fugax (G45.3)*

+ **H34.0 Transient retinal artery occlusion**
  - CC **H34.00 Transient retinal artery occlusion, unspecified eye**
    CC Exclusion see Appendix A PDX collection 0587
  - CC **H34.01 Transient retinal artery occlusion, right eye**
    CC Exclusion see Appendix A PDX collection 0587
  - CC **H34.02 Transient retinal artery occlusion, left eye**
    CC Exclusion see Appendix A PDX collection 0587
  - CC **H34.03 Transient retinal artery occlusion, bilateral**
    CC Exclusion see Appendix A PDX collection 0587

+ **H34.1 Central retinal artery occlusion**
  - CC **H34.10 Central retinal artery occlusion, unspecified eye**
    CC Exclusion see Appendix A PDX collection 0587
  - CC **H34.11 Central retinal artery occlusion, right eye**
    CC Exclusion see Appendix A PDX collection 0587
  - CC **H34.12 Central retinal artery occlusion, left eye**
    CC Exclusion see Appendix A PDX collection 0587
  - CC **H34.13 Central retinal artery occlusion, bilateral**
    CC Exclusion see Appendix A PDX collection 0587

+ **H34.2 Other retinal artery occlusions**
  + **H34.21 Partial retinal artery occlusion**
    Hollenhorst's plaque
    Retinal microembolism
    - CC **H34.211 Partial retinal artery occlusion, right eye**
      CC Exclusion see Appendix A PDX collection 0587
    - CC **H34.212 Partial retinal artery occlusion, left eye**
      CC Exclusion see Appendix A PDX collection 0587
    - CC **H34.213 Partial retinal artery occlusion, bilateral**
      CC Exclusion see Appendix A PDX collection 0587
    - CC **H34.219 Partial retinal artery occlusion, unspecified eye**
      CC Exclusion see Appendix A PDX collection 0587
  + **H34.23 Retinal artery branch occlusion**
    - CC **H34.231 Retinal artery branch occlusion, right eye**
      CC Exclusion see Appendix A PDX collection 0587
    - CC **H34.232 Retinal artery branch occlusion, left eye**
      CC Exclusion see Appendix A PDX collection 0587
    - CC **H34.233 Retinal artery branch occlusion, bilateral**
      CC Exclusion see Appendix A PDX collection 0587
    - CC **H34.239 Retinal artery branch occlusion, unspecified eye**
      CC Exclusion see Appendix A PDX collection 0587

+ **H34.8 Other retinal vascular occlusions**
  + **H34.81 Central retinal vein occlusion**
    - CC **H34.811 Central retinal vein occlusion, right eye**
      CC Exclusion see Appendix A PDX collection 0587
    - CC **H34.812 Central retinal vein occlusion, left eye**
      CC Exclusion see Appendix A PDX collection 0587
    - CC **H34.813 Central retinal vein occlusion, bilateral**
      CC Exclusion see Appendix A PDX collection 0587
    - CC **H34.819 Central retinal vein occlusion, unspecified eye**
      CC Exclusion see Appendix A PDX collection 0587
  + **H34.82 Venous engorgement**
    Incipient retinal vein occlusion
    Partial retinal vein occlusion
    - **H34.821 Venous engorgement, right eye**
    - **H34.822 Venous engorgement, left eye**
    - **H34.823 Venous engorgement, bilateral**
    - **H34.829 Venous engorgement, unspecified eye**
  + **H34.83 Tributary (branch) retinal vein occlusion**
    - **H34.831 Tributary (branch) retinal vein occlusion, right eye**
    - **H34.832 Tributary (branch) retinal vein occlusion, left eye**
    - **H34.833 Tributary (branch) retinal vein occlusion, bilateral**
    - **H34.839 Tributary (branch) retinal vein occlusion, unspecified eye**

CC **H34.9 Unspecified retinal vascular occlusion**
  CC Exclusion see Appendix A PDX collection 0587

H35 Other retinal disorders

Excludes2: *diabetic retinal disorders (E08.311-E08.359, E09.311-E09.359, E10.311-E10.359, E11.311-E11.359, E13.311-E13.359)*

+ **H35.0 Background retinopathy and retinal vascular changes**
  Review coding guideline C.9.a.5
  Code also any associated hypertension (I10)
  - **H35.00 Unspecified background retinopathy**
  + **H35.01 Changes in retinal vascular appearance**
    Retinal vascular sheathing
    - **H35.011 Changes in retinal vascular appearance, right eye**
    - **H35.012 Changes in retinal vascular appearance, left eye**
    - **H35.013 Changes in retinal vascular appearance, bilateral**
    - **H35.019 Changes in retinal vascular appearance, unspecified eye**
  + **H35.02 Exudative retinopathy**
    Coats retinopathy
    - **H35.021 Exudative retinopathy, right eye**
    - **H35.022 Exudative retinopathy, left eye**
    - **H35.023 Exudative retinopathy, bilateral**
    - **H35.029 Exudative retinopathy, unspecified eye**
  + **H35.03 Hypertensive retinopathy**
    - **H35.031 Hypertensive retinopathy, right eye**
    - **H35.032 Hypertensive retinopathy, left eye**
    - **H35.033 Hypertensive retinopathy, bilateral**
    - **H35.039 Hypertensive retinopathy, unspecified eye**
  + **H35.04 Retinal micro-aneurysms, unspecified**
    - **H35.041 Retinal micro-aneurysms, unspecified, right eye**
    - **H35.042 Retinal micro-aneurysms, unspecified, left eye**
    - **H35.043 Retinal micro-aneurysms, unspecified, bilateral**
    - **H35.049 Retinal micro-aneurysms, unspecified, unspecified eye**
  + **H35.05 Retinal neovascularization, unspecified**
    - **H35.051 Retinal neovascularization, unspecified, right eye**
    - **H35.052 Retinal neovascularization, unspecified, left eye**
    - **H35.053 Retinal neovascularization, unspecified, bilateral**
    - **H35.059 Retinal neovascularization, unspecified, unspecified eye**
  + **H35.06 Retinal vasculitis**
    Eales disease
    Retinal perivasculitis
    - **H35.061 Retinal vasculitis, right eye**
    - **H35.062 Retinal vasculitis, left eye**
    - **H35.063 Retinal vasculitis, bilateral**
    - **H35.069 Retinal vasculitis, unspecified eye**
  + **H35.07 Retinal telangiectasis**
    - **H35.071 Retinal telangiectasis, right eye**
    - **H35.072 Retinal telangiectasis, left eye**
    - **H35.073 Retinal telangiectasis, bilateral**
    - **H35.079 Retinal telangiectasis, unspecified eye**
  - **H35.09 Other intraretinal microvascular abnormalities**
    Retinal varices

+ **H35.1 Retinopathy of prematurity**
  + **H35.10 Retinopathy of prematurity, unspecified**
    Retinopathy of prematurity NOS
    - **H35.101 Retinopathy of prematurity, unspecified, right eye**
    - **H35.102 Retinopathy of prematurity, unspecified, left eye**
    - **H35.103 Retinopathy of prematurity, unspecified, bilateral**
    - **H35.109 Retinopathy of prematurity, unspecified, unspecified eye**
  + **H35.11 Retinopathy of prematurity, stage 0**
    - **H35.111 Retinopathy of prematurity, stage 0, right eye**
    - **H35.112 Retinopathy of prematurity, stage 0, left eye**
    - **H35.113 Retinopathy of prematurity, stage 0, bilateral**
    - **H35.119 Retinopathy of prematurity, stage 0, unspecified eye**

+ **H35.12 Retinopathy of prematurity, stage 1**
  - **H35.121 Retinopathy of prematurity, stage 1, right eye**
  - **H35.122 Retinopathy of prematurity, stage 1, left eye**
  - **H35.123 Retinopathy of prematurity, stage 1, bilateral**
  - **H35.129 Retinopathy of prematurity, stage 1, unspecified eye**

+ **H35.13 Retinopathy of prematurity, stage 2**
  - **H35.131 Retinopathy of prematurity, stage 2, right eye**
  - **H35.132 Retinopathy of prematurity, stage 2, left eye**
  - **H35.133 Retinopathy of prematurity, stage 2, bilateral**
  - **H35.139 Retinopathy of prematurity, stage 2, unspecified eye**

+ **H35.14 Retinopathy of prematurity, stage 3**
  - **H35.141 Retinopathy of prematurity, stage 3, right eye**
  - **H35.142 Retinopathy of prematurity, stage 3, left eye**
  - **H35.143 Retinopathy of prematurity, stage 3, bilateral**
  - **H35.149 Retinopathy of prematurity, stage 3, unspecified eye**

+ **H35.15 Retinopathy of prematurity, stage 4**
  - **H35.151 Retinopathy of prematurity, stage 4, right eye**
  - **H35.152 Retinopathy of prematurity, stage 4, left eye**
  - **H35.153 Retinopathy of prematurity, stage 4, bilateral**
  - **H35.159 Retinopathy of prematurity, stage 4, unspecified eye**

+ **H35.16 Retinopathy of prematurity, stage 5**
  - **H35.161 Retinopathy of prematurity, stage 5, right eye**
  - **H35.162 Retinopathy of prematurity, stage 5, left eye**
  - **H35.163 Retinopathy of prematurity, stage 5, bilateral**
  - **H35.169 Retinopathy of prematurity, stage 5, unspecified eye**

+ **H35.17 Retrolental fibroplasia**
  - **H35.171 Retrolental fibroplasia, right eye**
  - **H35.172 Retrolental fibroplasia, left eye**
  - **H35.173 Retrolental fibroplasia, bilateral**
  - **H35.179 Retrolental fibroplasia, unspecified eye**

+ **H35.2 Other non-diabetic proliferative retinopathy**
  Proliferative vitreo-retinopathy
  Excludes1: *proliferative vitreo-retinopathy with retinal detachment (H33.4-)*
  - **H35.20 Other non-diabetic proliferative retinopathy, unspecified eye**
  - **H35.21 Other non-diabetic proliferative retinopathy, right eye**
  - **H35.22 Other non-diabetic proliferative retinopathy, left eye**
  - **H35.23 Other non-diabetic proliferative retinopathy, bilateral**

+ **H35.3 Degeneration of macula and posterior pole**
  - • **H35.30 Unspecified macular degeneration**
    Age-related macular degeneration
  - • **H35.31 Nonexudative age-related macular degeneration**
    Atrophic age-related macular degeneration
  - • **H35.32 Exudative age-related macular degeneration**
  - **H35.33 Angioid streaks of macula**
  - + **H35.34 Macular cyst, hole, or pseudohole**
    - **H35.341 Macular cyst, hole, or pseudohole, right eye**
    - **H35.342 Macular cyst, hole, or pseudohole, left eye**
    - **H35.343 Macular cyst, hole, or pseudohole, bilateral**
    - **H35.349 Macular cyst, hole, or pseudohole, unspecified eye**
  - + **H35.35 Cystoid macular degeneration**
    Excludes1: cystoid macular edema following cataract surgery (H59.03-)
    - **H35.351 Cystoid macular degeneration, right eye**
    - **H35.352 Cystoid macular degeneration, left eye**
    - **H35.353 Cystoid macular degeneration, bilateral**
    - **H35.359 Cystoid macular degeneration, unspecified eye**
  - + **H35.36 Drusen (degenerative) of macula**
    - **H35.361 Drusen (degenerative) of macula, right eye**
    - **H35.362 Drusen (degenerative) of macula, left eye**
    - **H35.363 Drusen (degenerative) of macula, bilateral**
    - **H35.369 Drusen (degenerative) of macula, unspecified eye**
  - + **H35.37 Puckering of macula**
    - **H35.371 Puckering of macula, right eye**
    - **H35.372 Puckering of macula, left eye**
    - **H35.373 Puckering of macula, bilateral**
    - **H35.379 Puckering of macula, unspecified eye**
  - + **H35.38 Toxic maculopathy**
    Code first poisoning due to drug or toxin, if applicable (T36-T65 with fifth or sixth character 1-4 or 6)
    Use additional code for adverse effect, if applicable, to identify drug (T36-T50 with fifth or sixth character 5)
    - **H35.381 Toxic maculopathy, right eye**
    - **H35.382 Toxic maculopathy, left eye**
    - **H35.383 Toxic maculopathy, bilateral**
    - **H35.389 Toxic maculopathy, unspecified eye**

+ **H35.4 Peripheral retinal degeneration**
  Excludes1: *hereditary retinal degeneration (dystrophy) (H35.5-)*
  peripheral retinal degeneration with retinal break (H33.3-)
  - **H35.40 Unspecified peripheral retinal degeneration**
  - + **H35.41 Lattice degeneration of retina**
    Palisade degeneration of retina
    - **H35.411 Lattice degeneration of retina, right eye**
    - **H35.412 Lattice degeneration of retina, left eye**
    - **H35.413 Lattice degeneration of retina, bilateral**
    - **H35.419 Lattice degeneration of retina, unspecified eye**
  - + **H35.42 Microcystoid degeneration of retina**
    - **H35.421 Microcystoid degeneration of retina, right eye**
    - **H35.422 Microcystoid degeneration of retina, left eye**
    - **H35.423 Microcystoid degeneration of retina, bilateral**
    - **H35.429 Microcystoid degeneration of retina, unspecified eye**
  - + **H35.43 Paving stone degeneration of retina**
    - **H35.431 Paving stone degeneration of retina, right eye**
    - **H35.432 Paving stone degeneration of retina, left eye**
    - **H35.433 Paving stone degeneration of retina, bilateral**
    - **H35.439 Paving stone degeneration of retina, unspecified eye**
  - + **H35.44 Age-related reticular degeneration of retina**
    - • **H35.441 Age-related reticular degeneration of retina, right eye**
    - • **H35.442 Age-related reticular degeneration of retina, left eye**
    - • **H35.443 Age-related reticular degeneration of retina, bilateral**
    - • **H35.449 Age-related reticular degeneration of retina, unspecified eye**
  - + **H35.45 Secondary pigmentary degeneration**
    - **H35.451 Secondary pigmentary degeneration, right eye**
    - **H35.452 Secondary pigmentary degeneration, left eye**
    - **H35.453 Secondary pigmentary degeneration, bilateral**
    - **H35.459 Secondary pigmentary degeneration, unspecified eye**
  - + **H35.46 Secondary vitreoretinal degeneration**
    - **H35.461 Secondary vitreoretinal degeneration, right eye**
    - **H35.462 Secondary vitreoretinal degeneration, left eye**
    - **H35.463 Secondary vitreoretinal degeneration, bilateral**
    - **H35.469 Secondary vitreoretinal degeneration, unspecified eye**

+ **H35.5 Hereditary retinal dystrophy**
  Excludes1: *dystrophies primarily involving Bruch's membrane (H31.1-)*
  - **H35.50 Unspecified hereditary retinal dystrophy**
  - **H35.51 Vitreoretinal dystrophy**
  - **H35.52 Pigmentary retinal dystrophy**
    Albipunctate retinal dystrophy
    Retinitis pigmentosa
    Tapetoretinal dystrophy
  - **H35.53 Other dystrophies primarily involving the sensory retina**
    Stargardt's disease
  - **H35.54 Dystrophies primarily involving the retinal pigment epithelium**
    Vitelliform retinal dystrophy

+ **H35.6 Retinal hemorrhage**
H35.60 Retinal hemorrhage, unspecified eye
H35.61 Retinal hemorrhage, right eye
H35.62 Retinal hemorrhage, left eye
H35.63 Retinal hemorrhage, bilateral

+ **H35.7 Separation of retinal layers**
Excludes1: *retinal detachment (serous) (H33.2-)*
rhegmatogenous retinal detachment (H33.0-)
CC **H35.70 Unspecified separation of retinal layers**
CC Exclusion see Appendix A PDX collection 0628
+ **H35.71 Central serous chorioretinopathy**
H35.711 Central serous chorioretinopathy, right eye
H35.712 Central serous chorioretinopathy, left eye
H35.713 Central serous chorioretinopathy, bilateral
H35.719 Central serous chorioretinopathy, unspecified eye
+ **H35.72 Serous detachment of retinal pigment epithelium**
CC **H35.721 Serous detachment of retinal pigment epithelium, right eye**
CC Exclusion see Appendix A PDX collection 0628
CC **H35.722 Serous detachment of retinal pigment epithelium, left eye**
CC Exclusion see Appendix A PDX collection 0628
CC **H35.723 Serous detachment of retinal pigment epithelium, bilateral**
CC Exclusion see Appendix A PDX collection 0628
CC **H35.729 Serous detachment of retinal pigment epithelium, unspecified eye**
CC Exclusion see Appendix A PDX collection 0628
+ **H35.73 Hemorrhagic detachment of retinal pigment epithelium**
CC **H35.731 Hemorrhagic detachment of retinal pigment epithelium, right eye**
CC Exclusion see Appendix A PDX collection 0628
CC **H35.732 Hemorrhagic detachment of retinal pigment epithelium, left eye**
CC Exclusion see Appendix A PDX collection 0628
CC **H35.733 Hemorrhagic detachment of retinal pigment epithelium, bilateral**
CC Exclusion see Appendix A PDX collection 0628
CC **H35.739 Hemorrhagic detachment of retinal pigment epithelium, unspecified eye**
CC Exclusion see Appendix A PDX collection 0628

+ **H35.8 Other specified retinal disorders**
Excludes2: *retinal hemorrhage (H35.6-)*
H35.81 Retinal edema
Retinal cotton wool spots
CC **H35.82 Retinal ischemia**
CC Exclusion see Appendix A PDX collection 0629
H35.89 Other specified retinal disorders

H35.9 Unspecified retinal disorder

H36 Retinal disorders in diseases classified elsewhere

Code first underlying disease, such as:
lipid storage disorders (E75.-)
sickle-cell disorders (D57.-)
Excludes1: *arteriosclerotic retinopathy (H35.0-)*
diabetic retinopathy (E08.3-, E09.3-, E10.3-, E11.3-, E13.3-)
Valid 3-character code, no further characters required

Glaucoma (H40-H42)

H40 Glaucoma

Excludes1: *absolute glaucoma (H44.51-)*
congenital glaucoma (Q15.0)
traumatic glaucoma due to birth injury (P15.3)
Review coding guideline C.7.a

+ **H40.0 Glaucoma suspect**
+ **H40.00 Preglaucoma, unspecified**
H40.001 Preglaucoma, unspecified, right eye
H40.002 Preglaucoma, unspecified, left eye
H40.003 Preglaucoma, unspecified, bilateral
H40.009 Preglaucoma, unspecified, unspecified eye
+ **H40.01 Open angle with borderline findings, low risk**
Open angle, low risk
H40.011 Open angle with borderline findings, low risk, right eye
H40.012 Open angle with borderline findings, low risk, left eye
H40.013 Open angle with borderline findings, low risk, bilateral
H40.019 Open angle with borderline findings, low risk, unspecified eye
+ **H40.02 Open angle with borderline findings, high risk**
Open angle, high risk
H40.021 Open angle with borderline findings, high risk, right eye
H40.022 Open angle with borderline findings, high risk, left eye
H40.023 Open angle with borderline findings, high risk, bilateral
H40.029 Open angle with borderline findings, high risk, unspecified eye
+ **H40.03 Anatomical narrow angle**
Primary angle closure suspect
H40.031 Anatomical narrow angle, right eye
H40.032 Anatomical narrow angle, left eye
H40.033 Anatomical narrow angle, bilateral
H40.039 Anatomical narrow angle, unspecified eye
+ **H40.04 Steroid responder**
H40.041 Steroid responder, right eye
H40.042 Steroid responder, left eye
H40.043 Steroid responder, bilateral
H40.049 Steroid responder, unspecified eye
+ **H40.05 Ocular hypertension**
H40.051 Ocular hypertension, right eye
H40.052 Ocular hypertension, left eye
H40.053 Ocular hypertension, bilateral
H40.059 Ocular hypertension, unspecified eye
+ **H40.06 Primary angle closure without glaucoma damage**
H40.061 Primary angle closure without glaucoma damage, right eye
H40.062 Primary angle closure without glaucoma damage, left eye
H40.063 Primary angle closure without glaucoma damage, bilateral
H40.069 Primary angle closure without glaucoma damage, unspecified eye

+ **H40.1 Open-angle glaucoma**
X+7th **H40.10 Unspecified open-angle glaucoma**

One of the following 7th characters is to be assigned to code H40.10 to designate the stage of glaucoma
0 stage unspecified
1 mild stage
2 moderate stage
3 severe stage
4 indeterminate stage

X+7th **H40.11 Primary open-angle glaucoma**
Chronic simple glaucoma

One of the following 7th characters is to be assigned to code H40.11 to designate the stage of glaucoma
0 stage unspecified
1 mild stage
2 moderate stage
3 severe stage
4 indeterminate stage

+ **H40.12 Low-tension glaucoma**

One of the following 7th characters is to be assigned to each code in subcategory H40.12 to designate the stage of glaucoma
0 stage unspecified
1 mild stage
2 moderate stage
3 severe stage
4 indeterminate stage

+7th **H40.121 Low-tension glaucoma, right eye**
+7th **H40.122 Low-tension glaucoma, left eye**
+7th **H40.123 Low-tension glaucoma, bilateral**
+7th **H40.129 Low-tension glaucoma, unspecified eye**

+ **H40.13 Pigmentary glaucoma**

One of the following 7th characters is to be assigned to each code in subcategory H40.13 to designate the stage of glaucoma
0 stage unspecified
1 mild stage
2 moderate stage
3 severe stage
4 indeterminate stage

+7th **H40.131 Pigmentary glaucoma, right eye**
+7th **H40.132 Pigmentary glaucoma, left eye**
+7th **H40.133 Pigmentary glaucoma, bilateral**
+7th **H40.139 Pigmentary glaucoma, unspecified eye**

+ **H40.14 Capsular glaucoma with pseudoexfoliation of lens**

One of the following 7th characters is to be assigned to each code in subcategory H40.14 to designate the stage of glaucoma
0 stage unspecified
1 mild stage
2 moderate stage
3 severe stage
4 indeterminate stage

+7th **H40.141 Capsular glaucoma with pseudoexfoliation of lens, right eye**
+7th **H40.142 Capsular glaucoma with pseudoexfoliation of lens, left eye**
+7th **H40.143 Capsular glaucoma with pseudoexfoliation of lens, bilateral**
+7th **H40.149 Capsular glaucoma with pseudoexfoliation of lens, unspecified eye**

+ **H40.15 Residual stage of open-angle glaucoma**
H40.151 Residual stage of open-angle glaucoma, right eye
H40.152 Residual stage of open-angle glaucoma, left eye
H40.153 Residual stage of open-angle glaucoma, bilateral
H40.159 Residual stage of open-angle glaucoma, unspecified eye

+ **H40.2 Primary angle-closure glaucoma**
Excludes1: *aqueous misdirection (H40.83-)*
malignant glaucoma (H40.83-)

X+7th **H40.20 Unspecified primary angle-closure glaucoma**

One of the following 7th characters is to be assigned to code H40.20 to designate the stage of glaucoma
0 stage unspecified
1 mild stage
2 moderate stage
3 severe stage
4 indeterminate stage

+ **H40.21 Acute angle-closure glaucoma**
Acute angle-closure glaucoma attack
Acute angle-closure glaucoma crisis

CC **H40.211 Acute angle-closure glaucoma, right eye**
CC Exclusion see Appendix A PDX collection 0630
CC **H40.212 Acute angle-closure glaucoma, left eye**
CC Exclusion see Appendix A PDX collection 0630
CC **H40.213 Acute angle-closure glaucoma, bilateral**
CC Exclusion see Appendix A PDX collection 0630
CC **H40.219 Acute angle-closure glaucoma, unspecified eye**
CC Exclusion see Appendix A PDX collection 0630

+ **H40.22 Chronic angle-closure glaucoma**
Chronic primary angle closure glaucoma

One of the following 7th characters is to be assigned to each code in subcategory H40.22 to designate the stage of glaucoma
0 stage unspecified
1 mild stage
2 moderate stage
3 severe stage
4 indeterminate stage

+7th **H40.221 Chronic angle-closure glaucoma, right eye**
+7th **H40.222 Chronic angle-closure glaucoma, left eye**
+7th **H40.223 Chronic angle-closure glaucoma, bilateral**
+7th **H40.229 Chronic angle-closure glaucoma, unspecified eye**

+ **H40.23 Intermittent angle-closure glaucoma**
H40.231 Intermittent angle-closure glaucoma, right eye
H40.232 Intermittent angle-closure glaucoma, left eye
H40.233 Intermittent angle-closure glaucoma, bilateral
H40.239 Intermittent angle-closure glaucoma, unspecified eye

+ **H40.24 Residual stage of angle-closure glaucoma**
H40.241 Residual stage of angle-closure glaucoma, right eye
H40.242 Residual stage of angle-closure glaucoma, left eye
H40.243 Residual stage of angle-closure glaucoma, bilateral
H40.249 Residual stage of angle-closure glaucoma, unspecified eye

+ **H40.3 Glaucoma secondary to eye trauma**
Code also underlying condition

One of the following 7th characters is to be assigned to each code in subcategory H40.3 to designate the stage of glaucoma
0 stage unspecified
1 mild stage
2 moderate stage
3 severe stage
4 indeterminate stage

X+7th **H40.30 Glaucoma secondary to eye trauma, unspecified eye**
X+7th **H40.31 Glaucoma secondary to eye trauma, right eye**
X+7th **H40.32 Glaucoma secondary to eye trauma, left eye**
X+7th **H40.33 Glaucoma secondary to eye trauma, bilateral**

+ **H40.4 Glaucoma secondary to eye inflammation**
Code also underlying condition

One of the following 7th characters is to be assigned to each code in subcategory H40.4 to designate the stage of glaucoma
0 stage unspecified
1 mild stage
2 moderate stage
3 severe stage
4 indeterminate stage

X+7th **H40.40 Glaucoma secondary to eye inflammation, unspecified eye**
X+7th **H40.41 Glaucoma secondary to eye inflammation, right eye**
X+7th **H40.42 Glaucoma secondary to eye inflammation, left eye**
X+7th **H40.43 Glaucoma secondary to eye inflammation, bilateral**

+ **H40.5 Glaucoma secondary to other eye disorders**
Code also underlying eye disorder

One of the following 7th characters is to be assigned to each code in subcategory H40.5 to designate the stage of glaucoma
0 stage unspecified
1 mild stage
2 moderate stage
3 severe stage
4 indeterminate stage

X+7th **H40.50 Glaucoma secondary to other eye disorders, unspecified eye**
X+7th **H40.51 Glaucoma secondary to other eye disorders, right eye**
X+7th **H40.52 Glaucoma secondary to other eye disorders, left eye**
X+7th **H40.53 Glaucoma secondary to other eye disorders, bilateral**

+ **H40.6 Glaucoma secondary to drugs**
Use additional code for adverse effect, if applicable, to identify drug (T36-T50 with fifth or sixth character 5)

One of the following 7th characters is to be assigned to each code in subcategory H40.6 to designate the stage of glaucoma
0 stage unspecified
1 mild stage
2 moderate stage
3 severe stage
4 indeterminate stage

X+7th **H40.60 Glaucoma secondary to drugs, unspecified eye**
X+7th **H40.61 Glaucoma secondary to drugs, right eye**
X+7th **H40.62 Glaucoma secondary to drugs, left eye**
X+7th **H40.63 Glaucoma secondary to drugs, bilateral**

+ **H40.8 Other glaucoma**
+ **H40.81 Glaucoma with increased episcleral venous pressure**
  - **H40.811 Glaucoma with increased episcleral venous pressure, right eye**
  - **H40.812 Glaucoma with increased episcleral venous pressure, left eye**
  - **H40.813 Glaucoma with increased episcleral venous pressure, bilateral**
  - **H40.819 Glaucoma with increased episcleral venous pressure, unspecified eye**
+ **H40.82 Hypersecretion glaucoma**
  - **H40.821 Hypersecretion glaucoma, right eye**
  - **H40.822 Hypersecretion glaucoma, left eye**
  - **H40.823 Hypersecretion glaucoma, bilateral**
  - **H40.829 Hypersecretion glaucoma, unspecified eye**
+ **H40.83 Aqueous misdirection**
  Malignant glaucoma
  - **H40.831 Aqueous misdirection, right eye**
  - **H40.832 Aqueous misdirection, left eye**
  - **H40.833 Aqueous misdirection, bilateral**
  - **H40.839 Aqueous misdirection, unspecified eye**

H40.89 Other specified glaucoma

H40.9 Unspecified glaucoma

H42 Glaucoma in diseases classified elsewhere

Code first underlying condition, such as:
amyloidosis (E85.-)
aniridia (Q13.1)
Lowe's syndrome (E72.03)
Reiger's anomaly (Q13.81)
specified metabolic disorder (E70-E88)

Excludes1: *glaucoma (in):*
diabetes mellitus (E08.39, E09.39, E10.39, E11.39, E13.39)
onchocerciasis (B73.02)
syphilis (A52.71)
tuberculous (A18.59)

Valid 3-character code, no further characters required

Disorders of vitreous body and globe (H43-H44)

H43 Disorders of vitreous body

+ **H43.0 Vitreous prolapse**

Excludes1: *vitreous syndrome following cataract surgery (H59.0-)*
traumatic vitreous prolapse (S05.2-)

- **H43.00 Vitreous prolapse, unspecified eye**
- **H43.01 Vitreous prolapse, right eye**
- **H43.02 Vitreous prolapse, left eye**
- **H43.03 Vitreous prolapse, bilateral**

+ **H43.1 Vitreous hemorrhage**
- **H43.10 Vitreous hemorrhage, unspecified eye**
- **H43.11 Vitreous hemorrhage, right eye**
- **H43.12 Vitreous hemorrhage, left eye**
- **H43.13 Vitreous hemorrhage, bilateral**

+ **H43.2 Crystalline deposits in vitreous body**
- **H43.20 Crystalline deposits in vitreous body, unspecified eye**
- **H43.21 Crystalline deposits in vitreous body, right eye**
- **H43.22 Crystalline deposits in vitreous body, left eye**
- **H43.23 Crystalline deposits in vitreous body, bilateral**

+ **H43.3 Other vitreous opacities**
+ **H43.31 Vitreous membranes and strands**
  - **H43.311 Vitreous membranes and strands, right eye**
  - **H43.312 Vitreous membranes and strands, left eye**
  - **H43.313 Vitreous membranes and strands, bilateral**
  - **H43.319 Vitreous membranes and strands, unspecified eye**
+ **H43.39 Other vitreous opacities**
  Vitreous floaters
  - **H43.391 Other vitreous opacities, right eye**
  - **H43.392 Other vitreous opacities, left eye**
  - **H43.393 Other vitreous opacities, bilateral**
  - **H43.399 Other vitreous opacities, unspecified eye**

+ **H43.8 Other disorders of vitreous body**

Excludes1: *proliferative vitreo-retinopathy with retinal detachment (H33.4-)*

Excludes2: *vitreous abscess (H44.02-)*

+ **H43.81 Vitreous degeneration**
  Vitreous detachment
  - **H43.811 Vitreous degeneration, right eye**
  - **H43.812 Vitreous degeneration, left eye**
  - **H43.813 Vitreous degeneration, bilateral**
  - **H43.819 Vitreous degeneration, unspecified eye**
+ **H43.82 Vitreomacular adhesion**
  Vitreomacular traction
  - • **H43.821 Vitreomacular adhesion, right eye**
  - • **H43.822 Vitreomacular adhesion, left eye**
  - • **H43.823 Vitreomacular adhesion, bilateral**
  - • **H43.829 Vitreomacular adhesion, unspecified eye**

H43.89 Other disorders of vitreous body

H43.9 Unspecified disorder of vitreous body

H44 Disorders of globe

Includes: disorders affecting multiple structures of eye

+ **H44.0 Purulent endophthalmitis**

Use additional code to identify organism

Excludes1: *bleb associated endophthalmitis (H59.4-)*

+ **H44.00 Unspecified purulent endophthalmitis**
  - CC **H44.001 Unspecified purulent endophthalmitis, right eye**
    CC Exclusion see Appendix A PDX collection 0625
  - CC **H44.002 Unspecified purulent endophthalmitis, left eye**
    CC Exclusion see Appendix A PDX collection 0625
  - CC **H44.003 Unspecified purulent endophthalmitis, bilateral**
    CC Exclusion see Appendix A PDX collection 0625
  - CC **H44.009 Unspecified purulent endophthalmitis, unspecified eye**
    CC Exclusion see Appendix A PDX collection 0625
+ **H44.01 Panophthalmitis (acute)**
  - CC **H44.011 Panophthalmitis (acute), right eye**
    CC Exclusion see Appendix A PDX collection 0625
  - CC **H44.012 Panophthalmitis (acute), left eye**
    CC Exclusion see Appendix A PDX collection 0625
  - CC **H44.013 Panophthalmitis (acute), bilateral**
    CC Exclusion see Appendix A PDX collection 0625
  - CC **H44.019 Panophthalmitis (acute), unspecified eye**
    CC Exclusion see Appendix A PDX collection 0625
+ **H44.02 Vitreous abscess (chronic)**
  - CC **H44.021 Vitreous abscess (chronic), right eye**
    CC Exclusion see Appendix A PDX collection 0631
  - CC **H44.022 Vitreous abscess (chronic), left eye**
    CC Exclusion see Appendix A PDX collection 0631
  - CC **H44.023 Vitreous abscess (chronic), bilateral**
    CC Exclusion see Appendix A PDX collection 0631
  - CC **H44.029 Vitreous abscess (chronic), unspecified eye**
    CC Exclusion see Appendix A PDX collection 0631

+ **H44.1 Other endophthalmitis**

Excludes1: *bleb associated endophthalmitis (H59.4-)*

Excludes2: *ophthalmia nodosa (H16.2-)*

+ **H44.11 Panuveitis**
  - CC **H44.111 Panuveitis, right eye**
    CC Exclusion see Appendix A PDX collection 0632
  - CC **H44.112 Panuveitis, left eye**
    CC Exclusion see Appendix A PDX collection 0632
  - CC **H44.113 Panuveitis, bilateral**
    CC Exclusion see Appendix A PDX collection 0632
  - CC **H44.119 Panuveitis, unspecified eye**
    CC Exclusion see Appendix A PDX collection 0632
+ **H44.12 Parasitic endophthalmitis, unspecified**
  - CC **H44.121 Parasitic endophthalmitis, unspecified, right eye**
    CC Exclusion see Appendix A PDX collection 0625
  - CC **H44.122 Parasitic endophthalmitis, unspecified, left eye**
    CC Exclusion see Appendix A PDX collection 0625

CC **H44.123** **Parasitic endophthalmitis, unspecified, bilateral**
CC Exclusion see Appendix A PDX collection 0625

CC **H44.129** **Parasitic endophthalmitis, unspecified, unspecified eye**
CC Exclusion see Appendix A PDX collection 0625

+ **H44.13** **Sympathetic uveitis**

CC **H44.131** **Sympathetic uveitis, right eye**
CC Exclusion see Appendix A PDX collection 0632

CC **H44.132** **Sympathetic uveitis, left eye**
CC Exclusion see Appendix A PDX collection 0632

CC **H44.133** **Sympathetic uveitis, bilateral**
CC Exclusion see Appendix A PDX collection 0632

CC **H44.139** **Sympathetic uveitis, unspecified eye**
CC Exclusion see Appendix A PDX collection 0632

CC **H44.19** **Other endophthalmitis**
CC Exclusion see Appendix A PDX collection 0625

+ **H44.2** **Degenerative myopia**
Malignant myopia
H44.20 **Degenerative myopia, unspecified eye**
H44.21 **Degenerative myopia, right eye**
H44.22 **Degenerative myopia, left eye**
H44.23 **Degenerative myopia, bilateral**

+ **H44.3** **Other and unspecified degenerative disorders of globe**
H44.30 **Unspecified degenerative disorder of globe**

+ **H44.31** **Chalcosis**
H44.311 **Chalcosis, right eye**
H44.312 **Chalcosis, left eye**
H44.313 **Chalcosis, bilateral**
H44.319 **Chalcosis, unspecified eye**

+ **H44.32** **Siderosis of eye**
H44.321 **Siderosis of eye, right eye**
H44.322 **Siderosis of eye, left eye**
H44.323 **Siderosis of eye, bilateral**
H44.329 **Siderosis of eye, unspecified eye**

+ **H44.39** **Other degenerative disorders of globe**
H44.391 **Other degenerative disorders of globe, right eye**
H44.392 **Other degenerative disorders of globe, left eye**
H44.393 **Other degenerative disorders of globe, bilateral**
H44.399 **Other degenerative disorders of globe, unspecified eye**

+ **H44.4** **Hypotony of eye**
H44.40 **Unspecified hypotony of eye**

+ **H44.41** **Flat anterior chamber hypotony of eye**
H44.411 **Flat anterior chamber hypotony of right eye**
H44.412 **Flat anterior chamber hypotony of left eye**
H44.413 **Flat anterior chamber hypotony of eye, bilateral**
H44.419 **Flat anterior chamber hypotony of unspecified eye**

+ **H44.42** **Hypotony of eye due to ocular fistula**
H44.421 **Hypotony of right eye due to ocular fistula**
H44.422 **Hypotony of left eye due to ocular fistula**
H44.423 **Hypotony of eye due to ocular fistula, bilateral**
H44.429 **Hypotony of unspecified eye due to ocular fistula**

+ **H44.43** **Hypotony of eye due to other ocular disorders**
H44.431 **Hypotony of eye due to other ocular disorders, right eye**
H44.432 **Hypotony of eye due to other ocular disorders, left eye**
H44.433 **Hypotony of eye due to other ocular disorders, bilateral**
H44.439 **Hypotony of eye due to other ocular disorders, unspecified eye**

+ **H44.44** **Primary hypotony of eye**
H44.441 **Primary hypotony of right eye**
H44.442 **Primary hypotony of left eye**
H44.443 **Primary hypotony of eye, bilateral**
H44.449 **Primary hypotony of unspecified eye**

+ **H44.5** **Degenerated conditions of globe**
H44.50 **Unspecified degenerated conditions of globe**

+ **H44.51** **Absolute glaucoma**
H44.511 **Absolute glaucoma, right eye**
H44.512 **Absolute glaucoma, left eye**
H44.513 **Absolute glaucoma, bilateral**
H44.519 **Absolute glaucoma, unspecified eye**

+ **H44.52** **Atrophy of globe**
Phthisis bulbi
H44.521 **Atrophy of globe, right eye**
H44.522 **Atrophy of globe, left eye**
H44.523 **Atrophy of globe, bilateral**
H44.529 **Atrophy of globe, unspecified eye**

+ **H44.53** **Leucocoria**
H44.531 **Leucocoria, right eye**
H44.532 **Leucocoria, left eye**
H44.533 **Leucocoria, bilateral**
H44.539 **Leucocoria, unspecified eye**

+ **H44.6** **Retained (old) intraocular foreign body, magnetic**
Use additional code to identify magnetic foreign body (Z18.11)
Excludes1: *current intraocular foreign body (S05.-)*
Excludes2: *retained foreign body in eyelid (H02.81-)*
retained (old) foreign body following penetrating wound of orbit (H05.5-)
retained (old) intraocular foreign body, nonmagnetic (H44.7-)

+ **H44.60** **Unspecified retained (old) intraocular foreign body, magnetic**
H44.601 **Unspecified retained (old) intraocular foreign body, magnetic, right eye**
H44.602 **Unspecified retained (old) intraocular foreign body, magnetic, left eye**
H44.603 **Unspecified retained (old) intraocular foreign body, magnetic, bilateral**
H44.609 **Unspecified retained (old) intraocular foreign body, magnetic, unspecified eye**

+ **H44.61** **Retained (old) magnetic foreign body in anterior chamber**
H44.611 **Retained (old) magnetic foreign body in anterior chamber, right eye**
H44.612 **Retained (old) magnetic foreign body in anterior chamber, left eye**
H44.613 **Retained (old) magnetic foreign body in anterior chamber, bilateral**
H44.619 **Retained (old) magnetic foreign body in anterior chamber, unspecified eye**

+ **H44.62** **Retained (old) magnetic foreign body in iris or ciliary body**
H44.621 **Retained (old) magnetic foreign body in iris or ciliary body, right eye**
H44.622 **Retained (old) magnetic foreign body in iris or ciliary body, left eye**
H44.623 **Retained (old) magnetic foreign body in iris or ciliary body, bilateral**
H44.629 **Retained (old) magnetic foreign body in iris or ciliary body, unspecified eye**

+ **H44.63** **Retained (old) magnetic foreign body in lens**
H44.631 **Retained (old) magnetic foreign body in lens, right eye**
H44.632 **Retained (old) magnetic foreign body in lens, left eye**
H44.633 **Retained (old) magnetic foreign body in lens, bilateral**
H44.639 **Retained (old) magnetic foreign body in lens, unspecified eye**

+ **H44.64** **Retained (old) magnetic foreign body in posterior wall of globe**
H44.641 **Retained (old) magnetic foreign body in posterior wall of globe, right eye**
H44.642 **Retained (old) magnetic foreign body in posterior wall of globe, left eye**
H44.643 **Retained (old) magnetic foreign body in posterior wall of globe, bilateral**
H44.649 **Retained (old) magnetic foreign body in posterior wall of globe, unspecified eye**

+ **H44.65** **Retained (old) magnetic foreign body in vitreous body**
H44.651 **Retained (old) magnetic foreign body in vitreous body, right eye**
H44.652 **Retained (old) magnetic foreign body in vitreous body, left eye**

H44.653 Retained (old) magnetic foreign body in vitreous body, bilateral
H44.659 Retained (old) magnetic foreign body in vitreous body, unspecified eye
+ H44.69 Retained (old) intraocular foreign body, magnetic, in other or multiple sites
H44.691 Retained (old) intraocular foreign body, magnetic, in other or multiple sites, right eye
H44.692 Retained (old) intraocular foreign body, magnetic, in other or multiple sites, left eye
H44.693 Retained (old) intraocular foreign body, magnetic, in other or multiple sites, bilateral
H44.699 Retained (old) intraocular foreign body, magnetic, in other or multiple sites, unspecified eye
+ H44.7 Retained (old) intraocular foreign body, nonmagnetic
Use additional code to identify nonmagnetic foreign body (Z18.01-Z18.10, Z18.12, Z18.2-Z18.9)
Excludes1: *current intraocular foreign body (S05.-)*
Excludes2: *retained foreign body in eyelid (H02.81-)*
retained (old) foreign body following penetrating wound of orbit (H05.5-)
retained (old) intraocular foreign body, magnetic (H44.6-)
+ H44.70 Unspecified retained (old) intraocular foreign body, nonmagnetic
H44.701 Unspecified retained (old) intraocular foreign body, nonmagnetic, right eye
H44.702 Unspecified retained (old) intraocular foreign body, nonmagnetic, left eye
H44.703 Unspecified retained (old) intraocular foreign body, nonmagnetic, bilateral
H44.709 Unspecified retained (old) intraocular foreign body, nonmagnetic, unspecified eye
Retained (old) intraocular foreign body NOS
+ H44.71 Retained (nonmagnetic) (old) foreign body in anterior chamber
H44.711 Retained (nonmagnetic) (old) foreign body in anterior chamber, right eye
H44.712 Retained (nonmagnetic) (old) foreign body in anterior chamber, left eye
H44.713 Retained (nonmagnetic) (old) foreign body in anterior chamber, bilateral
H44.719 Retained (nonmagnetic) (old) foreign body in anterior chamber, unspecified eye
+ H44.72 Retained (nonmagnetic) (old) foreign body in iris or ciliary body
H44.721 Retained (nonmagnetic) (old) foreign body in iris or ciliary body, right eye
H44.722 Retained (nonmagnetic) (old) foreign body in iris or ciliary body, left eye
H44.723 Retained (nonmagnetic) (old) foreign body in iris or ciliary body, bilateral
H44.729 Retained (nonmagnetic) (old) foreign body in iris or ciliary body, unspecified eye
+ H44.73 Retained (nonmagnetic) (old) foreign body in lens
H44.731 Retained (nonmagnetic) (old) foreign body in lens, right eye
H44.732 Retained (nonmagnetic) (old) foreign body in lens, left eye
H44.733 Retained (nonmagnetic) (old) foreign body in lens, bilateral
H44.739 Retained (nonmagnetic) (old) foreign body in lens, unspecified eye
+ H44.74 Retained (nonmagnetic) (old) foreign body in posterior wall of globe
H44.741 Retained (nonmagnetic) (old) foreign body in posterior wall of globe, right eye
H44.742 Retained (nonmagnetic) (old) foreign body in posterior wall of globe, left eye
H44.743 Retained (nonmagnetic) (old) foreign body in posterior wall of globe, bilateral
H44.749 Retained (nonmagnetic) (old) foreign body in posterior wall of globe, unspecified eye
+ H44.75 Retained (nonmagnetic) (old) foreign body in vitreous body
H44.751 Retained (nonmagnetic) (old) foreign body in vitreous body, right eye
H44.752 Retained (nonmagnetic) (old) foreign body in vitreous body, left eye
H44.753 Retained (nonmagnetic) (old) foreign body in vitreous body, bilateral
H44.759 Retained (nonmagnetic) (old) foreign body in vitreous body, unspecified eye
+ H44.79 Retained (old) intraocular foreign body, nonmagnetic in other or multiple sites
H44.791 Retained (old) intraocular foreign body, nonmagnetic, in other or multiple sites, right eye
H44.792 Retained (old) intraocular foreign body, nonmagnetic, in other or multiple sites, left eye
H44.793 Retained (old) intraocular foreign body, nonmagnetic, in other or multiple sites, bilateral
H44.799 Retained (old) intraocular foreign body, nonmagnetic, in other or multiple sites, unspecified eye
+ H44.8 Other disorders of globe
+ H44.81 Hemophthalmos
H44.811 Hemophthalmos, right eye
H44.812 Hemophthalmos, left eye
H44.813 Hemophthalmos, bilateral
H44.819 Hemophthalmos, unspecified eye
+ H44.82 Luxation of globe
H44.821 Luxation of globe, right eye
H44.822 Luxation of globe, left eye
H44.823 Luxation of globe, bilateral
H44.829 Luxation of globe, unspecified eye
H44.89 Other disorders of globe
H44.9 Unspecified disorder of globe

Disorders of optic nerve and visual pathways (H46-H47)

H46 Optic neuritis
Excludes2: *ischemic optic neuropathy (H47.01-)*
neuromyelitis optica [Devic] (G36.0)
+ H46.0 Optic papillitis
CC H46.00 Optic papillitis, unspecified eye
CC Exclusion see Appendix A PDX collection 0633
CC H46.01 Optic papillitis, right eye
CC Exclusion see Appendix A PDX collection 0633
CC H46.02 Optic papillitis, left eye
CC Exclusion see Appendix A PDX collection 0633
CC H46.03 Optic papillitis, bilateral
CC Exclusion see Appendix A PDX collection 0633
+ H46.1 Retrobulbar neuritis
Retrobulbar neuritis NOS
Excludes1: *syphilitic retrobulbar neuritis (A52.15)*
CC H46.10 Retrobulbar neuritis, unspecified eye
CC Exclusion see Appendix A PDX collection 0633
CC H46.11 Retrobulbar neuritis, right eye
CC Exclusion see Appendix A PDX collection 0633
CC H46.12 Retrobulbar neuritis, left eye
CC Exclusion see Appendix A PDX collection 0633
CC H46.13 Retrobulbar neuritis, bilateral
CC Exclusion see Appendix A PDX collection 0633
H46.2 Nutritional optic neuropathy
H46.3 Toxic optic neuropathy
Code first (T51-T65) to identify cause
CC H46.8 Other optic neuritis
CC Exclusion see Appendix A PDX collection 0633
CC H46.9 Unspecified optic neuritis
CC Exclusion see Appendix A PDX collection 0633

H47 Other disorders of optic [2nd] nerve and visual pathways
+ H47.0 Disorders of optic nerve, not elsewhere classified
+ H47.01 Ischemic optic neuropathy
H47.011 Ischemic optic neuropathy, right eye
H47.012 Ischemic optic neuropathy, left eye
H47.013 Ischemic optic neuropathy, bilateral
H47.019 Ischemic optic neuropathy, unspecified eye
+ H47.02 Hemorrhage in optic nerve sheath
H47.021 Hemorrhage in optic nerve sheath, right eye
H47.022 Hemorrhage in optic nerve sheath, left eye
H47.023 Hemorrhage in optic nerve sheath, bilateral
H47.029 Hemorrhage in optic nerve sheath, unspecified eye
+ H47.03 Optic nerve hypoplasia
H47.031 Optic nerve hypoplasia, right eye
H47.032 Optic nerve hypoplasia, left eye
H47.033 Optic nerve hypoplasia, bilateral
H47.039 Optic nerve hypoplasia, unspecified eye

+ **H47.09 Other disorders of optic nerve, not elsewhere classified**
Compression of optic nerve
H47.091 Other disorders of optic nerve, not elsewhere classified, right eye
H47.092 Other disorders of optic nerve, not elsewhere classified, left eye
H47.093 Other disorders of optic nerve, not elsewhere classified, bilateral
H47.099 Other disorders of optic nerve, not elsewhere classified, unspecified eye

+ **H47.1 Papilledema**
CC **H47.10 Unspecified papilledema**
CC Exclusion see Appendix A PDX collection 0634
CC **H47.11 Papilledema associated with increased intracranial pressure**
CC Exclusion see Appendix A PDX collection 0634
H47.12 Papilledema associated with decreased ocular pressure
H47.13 Papilledema associated with retinal disorder
+ **H47.14 Foster-Kennedy syndrome**
H47.141 Foster-Kennedy syndrome, right eye
H47.142 Foster-Kennedy syndrome, left eye
H47.143 Foster-Kennedy syndrome, bilateral
H47.149 Foster-Kennedy syndrome, unspecified eye

+ **H47.2 Optic atrophy**
H47.20 Unspecified optic atrophy
+ **H47.21 Primary optic atrophy**
H47.211 Primary optic atrophy, right eye
H47.212 Primary optic atrophy, left eye
H47.213 Primary optic atrophy, bilateral
H47.219 Primary optic atrophy, unspecified eye
H47.22 Hereditary optic atrophy
Leber's optic atrophy
+ **H47.23 Glaucomatous optic atrophy**
H47.231 Glaucomatous optic atrophy, right eye
H47.232 Glaucomatous optic atrophy, left eye
H47.233 Glaucomatous optic atrophy, bilateral
H47.239 Glaucomatous optic atrophy, unspecified eye
+ **H47.29 Other optic atrophy**
Temporal pallor of optic disc
H47.291 Other optic atrophy, right eye
H47.292 Other optic atrophy, left eye
H47.293 Other optic atrophy, bilateral
H47.299 Other optic atrophy, unspecified eye

+ **H47.3 Other disorders of optic disc**
+ **H47.31 Coloboma of optic disc**
H47.311 Coloboma of optic disc, right eye
H47.312 Coloboma of optic disc, left eye
H47.313 Coloboma of optic disc, bilateral
H47.319 Coloboma of optic disc, unspecified eye
+ **H47.32 Drusen of optic disc**
H47.321 Drusen of optic disc, right eye
H47.322 Drusen of optic disc, left eye
H47.323 Drusen of optic disc, bilateral
H47.329 Drusen of optic disc, unspecified eye
+ **H47.33 Pseudopapilledema of optic disc**
H47.331 Pseudopapilledema of optic disc, right eye
H47.332 Pseudopapilledema of optic disc, left eye
H47.333 Pseudopapilledema of optic disc, bilateral
H47.339 Pseudopapilledema of optic disc, unspecified eye
+ **H47.39 Other disorders of optic disc**
H47.391 Other disorders of optic disc, right eye
H47.392 Other disorders of optic disc, left eye
H47.393 Other disorders of optic disc, bilateral
H47.399 Other disorders of optic disc, unspecified eye

+ **H47.4 Disorders of optic chiasm**
Code also underlying condition
CC **H47.41 Disorders of optic chiasm in (due to) inflammatory disorders**
CC Exclusion see Appendix A PDX collection 0635
CC **H47.42 Disorders of optic chiasm in (due to) neoplasm**
CC Exclusion see Appendix A PDX collection 0635
CC **H47.43 Disorders of optic chiasm in (due to) vascular disorders**
CC Exclusion see Appendix A PDX collection 0635
CC **H47.49 Disorders of optic chiasm in (due to) other disorders**
CC Exclusion see Appendix A PDX collection 0635

+ **H47.5 Disorders of other visual pathways**
Disorders of optic tracts, geniculate nuclei and optic radiations
Code also underlying condition
+ **H47.51 Disorders of visual pathways in (due to) inflammatory disorders**
CC **H47.511 Disorders of visual pathways in (due to) inflammatory disorders, right side**
CC Exclusion see Appendix A PDX collection 0635
CC **H47.512 Disorders of visual pathways in (due to) inflammatory disorders, left side**
CC Exclusion see Appendix A PDX collection 0635
CC **H47.519 Disorders of visual pathways in (due to) inflammatory disorders, unspecified side**
CC Exclusion see Appendix A PDX collection 0635
+ **H47.52 Disorders of visual pathways in (due to) neoplasm**
CC **H47.521 Disorders of visual pathways in (due to) neoplasm, right side**
CC Exclusion see Appendix A PDX collection 0635
CC **H47.522 Disorders of visual pathways in (due to) neoplasm, left side**
CC Exclusion see Appendix A PDX collection 0635
CC **H47.529 Disorders of visual pathways in (due to) neoplasm, unspecified side**
CC Exclusion see Appendix A PDX collection 0635
+ **H47.53 Disorders of visual pathways in (due to) vascular disorders**
CC **H47.531 Disorders of visual pathways in (due to) vascular disorders, right side**
CC Exclusion see Appendix A PDX collection 0635
CC **H47.532 Disorders of visual pathways in (due to) vascular disorders, left side**
CC Exclusion see Appendix A PDX collection 0635
CC **H47.539 Disorders of visual pathways in (due to) vascular disorders, unspecified side**
CC Exclusion see Appendix A PDX collection 0635

+ **H47.6 Disorders of visual cortex**
Code also underlying condition
Excludes1: *injury to visual cortex S04.04*
+ **H47.61 Cortical blindness**
H47.611 Cortical blindness, right side of brain
H47.612 Cortical blindness, left side of brain
H47.619 Cortical blindness, unspecified side of brain
+ **H47.62 Disorders of visual cortex in (due to) inflammatory disorders**
CC **H47.621 Disorders of visual cortex in (due to) inflammatory disorders, right side of brain**
CC Exclusion see Appendix A PDX collection 0636
CC **H47.622 Disorders of visual cortex in (due to) inflammatory disorders, left side of brain**
CC Exclusion see Appendix A PDX collection 0636
CC **H47.629 Disorders of visual cortex in (due to) inflammatory disorders, unspecified side of brain**
CC Exclusion see Appendix A PDX collection 0636
+ **H47.63 Disorders of visual cortex in (due to) neoplasm**
CC **H47.631 Disorders of visual cortex in (due to) neoplasm, right side of brain**
CC Exclusion see Appendix A PDX collection 0636
CC **H47.632 Disorders of visual cortex in (due to) neoplasm, left side of brain**
CC Exclusion see Appendix A PDX collection 0636
CC **H47.639 Disorders of visual cortex in (due to) neoplasm, unspecified side of brain**
CC Exclusion see Appendix A PDX collection 0636
+ **H47.64 Disorders of visual cortex in (due to) vascular disorders**
CC **H47.641 Disorders of visual cortex in (due to) vascular disorders, right side of brain**
CC Exclusion see Appendix A PDX collection 0636

CC **H47.642 Disorders of visual cortex in (due to) vascular disorders, left side of brain**
CC Exclusion see Appendix A PDX collection 0636

CC **H47.649 Disorders of visual cortex in (due to) vascular disorders, unspecified side of brain**
CC Exclusion see Appendix A PDX collection 0636

H47.9 Unspecified disorder of visual pathways

Disorders of ocular muscles, binocular movement, accommodation and refraction (H49-H52)

Excludes2: *nystagmus and other irregular eye movements (H55)*

H49 Paralytic strabismus

Excludes2: *internal ophthalmoplegia (H52.51-)*
internuclear ophthalmoplegia (H51.2-)
progressive supranuclear ophthalmoplegia (G23.1)

+ **H49.0 Third [oculomotor] nerve palsy**
  - **H49.00 Third [oculomotor] nerve palsy, unspecified eye**
  - **H49.01 Third [oculomotor] nerve palsy, right eye**
  - **H49.02 Third [oculomotor] nerve palsy, left eye**
  - **H49.03 Third [oculomotor] nerve palsy, bilateral**

+ **H49.1 Fourth [trochlear] nerve palsy**
  - **H49.10 Fourth [trochlear] nerve palsy, unspecified eye**
  - **H49.11 Fourth [trochlear] nerve palsy, right eye**
  - **H49.12 Fourth [trochlear] nerve palsy, left eye**
  - **H49.13 Fourth [trochlear] nerve palsy, bilateral**

+ **H49.2 Sixth [abducent] nerve palsy**
  - **H49.20 Sixth [abducent] nerve palsy, unspecified eye**
  - **H49.21 Sixth [abducent] nerve palsy, right eye**
  - **H49.22 Sixth [abducent] nerve palsy, left eye**
  - **H49.23 Sixth [abducent] nerve palsy, bilateral**

+ **H49.3 Total (external) ophthalmoplegia**
  - **H49.30 Total (external) ophthalmoplegia, unspecified eye**
  - **H49.31 Total (external) ophthalmoplegia, right eye**
  - **H49.32 Total (external) ophthalmoplegia, left eye**
  - **H49.33 Total (external) ophthalmoplegia, bilateral**

+ **H49.4 Progressive external ophthalmoplegia**
  Excludes1: *Kearns-Sayre syndrome (H49.81-)*
  - **H49.40 Progressive external ophthalmoplegia, unspecified eye**
  - **H49.41 Progressive external ophthalmoplegia, right eye**
  - **H49.42 Progressive external ophthalmoplegia, left eye**
  - **H49.43 Progressive external ophthalmoplegia, bilateral**

+ **H49.8 Other paralytic strabismus**
  + **H49.81 Kearns-Sayre syndrome**
    Progressive external ophthalmoplegia with pigmentary retinopathy
    Use additional code for other manifestation, such as: heart block (I45.9)
    - CC **H49.811 Kearns-Sayre syndrome, right eye** **CC Exclusion see Appendix A PDX collection 0545**
    - CC **H49.812 Kearns-Sayre syndrome, left eye** **CC Exclusion see Appendix A PDX collection 0545**
    - CC **H49.813 Kearns-Sayre syndrome, bilateral** **CC Exclusion see Appendix A PDX collection 0545**
    - CC **H49.819 Kearns-Sayre syndrome, unspecified eye** **CC Exclusion see Appendix A PDX collection 0545**
  + **H49.88 Other paralytic strabismus**
    External ophthalmoplegia NOS
    - **H49.881 Other paralytic strabismus, right eye**
    - **H49.882 Other paralytic strabismus, left eye**
    - **H49.883 Other paralytic strabismus, bilateral**
    - **H49.889 Other paralytic strabismus, unspecified eye**

H49.9 Unspecified paralytic strabismus

H50 Other strabismus

+ **H50.0 Esotropia**
  Convergent concomitant strabismus
  Excludes1: *intermittent esotropia (H50.31-, H50.32)*
  - **H50.00 Unspecified esotropia**
  + **H50.01 Monocular esotropia**
    - **H50.011 Monocular esotropia, right eye**
    - **H50.012 Monocular esotropia, left eye**
  + **H50.02 Monocular esotropia with A pattern**
    - **H50.021 Monocular esotropia with A pattern, right eye**
    - **H50.022 Monocular esotropia with A pattern, left eye**
  + **H50.03 Monocular esotropia with V pattern**
    - **H50.031 Monocular esotropia with V pattern, right eye**
    - **H50.032 Monocular esotropia with V pattern, left eye**
  + **H50.04 Monocular esotropia with other noncomitancies**
    - **H50.041 Monocular esotropia with other noncomitancies, right eye**
    - **H50.042 Monocular esotropia with other noncomitancies, left eye**
  - **H50.05 Alternating esotropia**
  - **H50.06 Alternating esotropia with A pattern**
  - **H50.07 Alternating esotropia with V pattern**
  - **H50.08 Alternating esotropia with other noncomitancies**

+ **H50.1 Exotropia**
  Divergent concomitant strabismus
  Excludes1: *intermittent exotropia (H50.33-, H50.34)*
  - **H50.10 Unspecified exotropia**
  + **H50.11 Monocular exotropia**
    - **H50.111 Monocular exotropia, right eye**
    - **H50.112 Monocular exotropia, left eye**
  + **H50.12 Monocular exotropia with A pattern**
    - **H50.121 Monocular exotropia with A pattern, right eye**
    - **H50.122 Monocular exotropia with A pattern, left eye**
  + **H50.13 Monocular exotropia with V pattern**
    - **H50.131 Monocular exotropia with V pattern, right eye**
    - **H50.132 Monocular exotropia with V pattern, left eye**
  + **H50.14 Monocular exotropia with other noncomitancies**
    - **H50.141 Monocular exotropia with other noncomitancies, right eye**
    - **H50.142 Monocular exotropia with other noncomitancies, left eye**
  - **H50.15 Alternating exotropia**
  - **H50.16 Alternating exotropia with A pattern**
  - **H50.17 Alternating exotropia with V pattern**
  - **H50.18 Alternating exotropia with other noncomitancies**

+ **H50.2 Vertical strabismus**
  Hypertropia
  - **H50.21 Vertical strabismus, right eye**
  - **H50.22 Vertical strabismus, left eye**

+ **H50.3 Intermittent heterotropia**
  - **H50.30 Unspecified intermittent heterotropia**
  + **H50.31 Intermittent monocular esotropia**
    - **H50.311 Intermittent monocular esotropia, right eye**
    - **H50.312 Intermittent monocular esotropia, left eye**
  - **H50.32 Intermittent alternating esotropia**
  + **H50.33 Intermittent monocular exotropia**
    - **H50.331 Intermittent monocular exotropia, right eye**
    - **H50.332 Intermittent monocular exotropia, left eye**
  - **H50.34 Intermittent alternating exotropia**

+ **H50.4 Other and unspecified heterotropia**
  - **H50.40 Unspecified heterotropia**
  + **H50.41 Cyclotropia**
    - **H50.411 Cyclotropia, right eye**
    - **H50.412 Cyclotropia, left eye**
  - **H50.42 Monofixation syndrome**
  - **H50.43 Accommodative component in esotropia**

+ **H50.5 Heterophoria**
  - **H50.50 Unspecified heterophoria**
  - **H50.51 Esophoria**
  - **H50.52 Exophoria**
  - **H50.53 Vertical heterophoria**
  - **H50.54 Cyclophoria**
  - **H50.55 Alternating heterophoria**

+ **H50.6 Mechanical strabismus**
  - **H50.60 Mechanical strabismus, unspecified**
  + **H50.61 Brown's sheath syndrome**
    - **H50.611 Brown's sheath syndrome, right eye**
    - **H50.612 Brown's sheath syndrome, left eye**
  - **H50.69 Other mechanical strabismus**
    Strabismus due to adhesions
    Traumatic limitation of duction of eye muscle

+ **H50.8 Other specified strabismus**
  + **H50.81 Duane's syndrome**
    - **H50.811 Duane's syndrome, right eye**
    - **H50.812 Duane's syndrome, left eye**
  - **H50.89 Other specified strabismus**

H50.9 Unspecified strabismus

H51 Other disorders of binocular movement
H51.0 Palsy (spasm) of conjugate gaze
+ H51.1 Convergence insufficiency and excess
H51.11 Convergence insufficiency
H51.12 Convergence excess
+ H51.2 Internuclear ophthalmoplegia
H51.20 Internuclear ophthalmoplegia, unspecified eye
H51.21 Internuclear ophthalmoplegia, right eye
H51.22 Internuclear ophthalmoplegia, left eye
H51.23 Internuclear ophthalmoplegia, bilateral
H51.8 Other specified disorders of binocular movement
H51.9 Unspecified disorder of binocular movement

H52 Disorders of refraction and accommodation
+ H52.0 Hypermetropia
H52.00 Hypermetropia, unspecified eye
H52.01 Hypermetropia, right eye
H52.02 Hypermetropia, left eye
H52.03 Hypermetropia, bilateral
+ H52.1 Myopia
Excludes1: *degenerative myopia (H44.2-)*
H52.10 Myopia, unspecified eye
H52.11 Myopia, right eye
H52.12 Myopia, left eye
H52.13 Myopia, bilateral
+ H52.2 Astigmatism
+ H52.20 Unspecified astigmatism
H52.201 Unspecified astigmatism, right eye
H52.202 Unspecified astigmatism, left eye
H52.203 Unspecified astigmatism, bilateral
H52.209 Unspecified astigmatism, unspecified eye
+ H52.21 Irregular astigmatism
H52.211 Irregular astigmatism, right eye
H52.212 Irregular astigmatism, left eye
H52.213 Irregular astigmatism, bilateral
H52.219 Irregular astigmatism, unspecified eye
+ H52.22 Regular astigmatism
H52.221 Regular astigmatism, right eye
H52.222 Regular astigmatism, left eye
H52.223 Regular astigmatism, bilateral
H52.229 Regular astigmatism, unspecified eye
+ H52.3 Anisometropia and aniseikonia
H52.31 Anisometropia
H52.32 Aniseikonia
H52.4 Presbyopia
+ H52.5 Disorders of accommodation
+ H52.51 Internal ophthalmoplegia (complete) (total)
H52.511 Internal ophthalmoplegia (complete) (total), right eye
H52.512 Internal ophthalmoplegia (complete) (total), left eye
H52.513 Internal ophthalmoplegia (complete) (total), bilateral
H52.519 Internal ophthalmoplegia (complete) (total), unspecified eye
+ H52.52 Paresis of accommodation
H52.521 Paresis of accommodation, right eye
H52.522 Paresis of accommodation, left eye
H52.523 Paresis of accommodation, bilateral
H52.529 Paresis of accommodation, unspecified eye
+ H52.53 Spasm of accommodation
H52.531 Spasm of accommodation, right eye
H52.532 Spasm of accommodation, left eye
H52.533 Spasm of accommodation, bilateral
H52.539 Spasm of accommodation, unspecified eye
H52.6 Other disorders of refraction
H52.7 Unspecified disorder of refraction

Visual disturbances and blindness (H53-H54)

H53 Visual disturbances
+ H53.0 Amblyopia ex anopsia
Excludes1: *amblyopia due to vitamin A deficiency (E50.5)*
+ H53.00 Unspecified amblyopia
H53.001 Unspecified amblyopia, right eye
H53.002 Unspecified amblyopia, left eye
H53.003 Unspecified amblyopia, bilateral
H53.009 Unspecified amblyopia, unspecified eye
+ H53.01 Deprivation amblyopia
H53.011 Deprivation amblyopia, right eye
H53.012 Deprivation amblyopia, left eye
H53.013 Deprivation amblyopia, bilateral
H53.019 Deprivation amblyopia, unspecified eye
+ H53.02 Refractive amblyopia
H53.021 Refractive amblyopia, right eye
H53.022 Refractive amblyopia, left eye
H53.023 Refractive amblyopia, bilateral
H53.029 Refractive amblyopia, unspecified eye
+ H53.03 Strabismic amblyopia
Excludes1: *strabismus (H50.-)*
H53.031 Strabismic amblyopia, right eye
H53.032 Strabismic amblyopia, left eye
H53.033 Strabismic amblyopia, bilateral
H53.039 Strabismic amblyopia, unspecified eye
+ H53.1 Subjective visual disturbances
Excludes1: *subjective visual disturbances due to vitamin A deficiency (E50.5)*
visual hallucinations (R44.1)
H53.10 Unspecified subjective visual disturbances
H53.11 Day blindness
Hemeralopia
+ H53.12 Transient visual loss
Scintillating scotoma
Excludes1: *amaurosis fugax (G45.3-)*
transient retinal artery occlusion (H34.0-)
CC H53.121 Transient visual loss, right eye
CC Exclusion see Appendix A PDX collection 0637
CC H53.122 Transient visual loss, left eye
CC Exclusion see Appendix A PDX collection 0637
CC H53.123 Transient visual loss, bilateral
CC Exclusion see Appendix A PDX collection 0637
CC H53.129 Transient visual loss, unspecified eye
CC Exclusion see Appendix A PDX collection 0637
+ H53.13 Sudden visual loss
CC H53.131 Sudden visual loss, right eye
CC Exclusion see Appendix A PDX collection 0637
CC H53.132 Sudden visual loss, left eye
CC Exclusion see Appendix A PDX collection 0637
CC H53.133 Sudden visual loss, bilateral
CC Exclusion see Appendix A PDX collection 0637
CC H53.139 Sudden visual loss, unspecified eye
CC Exclusion see Appendix A PDX collection 0637
+ H53.14 Visual discomfort
Asthenopia
Photophobia
H53.141 Visual discomfort, right eye
H53.142 Visual discomfort, left eye
H53.143 Visual discomfort, bilateral
H53.149 Visual discomfort, unspecified
H53.15 Visual distortions of shape and size
Metamorphopsia
H53.16 Psychophysical visual disturbances
H53.19 Other subjective visual disturbances
Visual halos
H53.2 Diplopia
Double vision
+ H53.3 Other and unspecified disorders of binocular vision
H53.30 Unspecified disorder of binocular vision
H53.31 Abnormal retinal correspondence
H53.32 Fusion with defective stereopsis
H53.33 Simultaneous visual perception without fusion
H53.34 Suppression of binocular vision
+ H53.4 Visual field defects
H53.40 Unspecified visual field defects
+ H53.41 Scotoma involving central area
Central scotoma
H53.411 Scotoma involving central area, right eye
H53.412 Scotoma involving central area, left eye
H53.413 Scotoma involving central area, bilateral
H53.419 Scotoma involving central area, unspecified eye
+ H53.42 Scotoma of blind spot area
Enlarged blind spot
H53.421 Scotoma of blind spot area, right eye
H53.422 Scotoma of blind spot area, left eye

H53.423 Scotoma of blind spot area, bilateral
H53.429 Scotoma of blind spot area, unspecified eye
+ **H53.43 Sector or arcuate defects**
Arcuate scotoma
Bjerrum scotoma
H53.431 Sector or arcuate defects, right eye
H53.432 Sector or arcuate defects, left eye
H53.433 Sector or arcuate defects, bilateral
H53.439 Sector or arcuate defects, unspecified eye
+ **H53.45 Other localized visual field defect**
Peripheral visual field defect
Ring scotoma NOS
Scotoma NOS
H53.451 Other localized visual field defect, right eye
H53.452 Other localized visual field defect, left eye
H53.453 Other localized visual field defect, bilateral
H53.459 Other localized visual field defect, unspecified eye
+ **H53.46 Homonymous bilateral field defects**
Homonymous hemianopsia
Quadrant anopia
Quadrant anopsia
H53.461 Homonymous bilateral field defects, right side
H53.462 Homonymous bilateral field defects, left side
H53.469 Homonymous bilateral field defects, unspecified side
Homonymous bilateral field defects NOS
H53.47 Heteronymous bilateral field defects
Heteronymous hemianop(s)ia
+ **H53.48 Generalized contraction of visual field**
H53.481 Generalized contraction of visual field, right eye
H53.482 Generalized contraction of visual field, left eye
H53.483 Generalized contraction of visual field, bilateral
H53.489 Generalized contraction of visual field, unspecified eye
+ **H53.5 Color vision deficiencies**
Color blindness
Excludes2: *day blindness (H53.11)*
H53.50 Unspecified color vision deficiencies
Color blindness NOS
H53.51 Achromatopsia
H53.52 Acquired color vision deficiency
H53.53 Deuteranomaly
Deuteranopia
H53.54 Protanomaly
Protanopia
H53.55 Tritanomaly
Tritanopia
H53.59 Other color vision deficiencies
+ **H53.6 Night blindness**
Excludes1: *night blindness due to vitamin A deficiency (E50.5)*
H53.60 Unspecified night blindness
H53.61 Abnormal dark adaptation curve
H53.62 Acquired night blindness
H53.63 Congenital night blindness
H53.69 Other night blindness
+ **H53.7 Vision sensitivity deficiencies**
H53.71 Glare sensitivity
H53.72 Impaired contrast sensitivity
H53.8 Other visual disturbances
H53.9 Unspecified visual disturbance

H54 Blindness and low vision

NOTE For definition of visual impairment categories see table below
Code first any associated underlying cause of the blindness
Excludes1: *amaurosis fugax (G45.3)*
H54.0 Blindness, both eyes
Visual impairment categories 3, 4, 5 in both eyes.
+ **H54.1 Blindness, one eye, low vision other eye**
Visual impairment categories 3, 4, 5 in one eye, with categories 1 or 2 in the other eye.
H54.10 Blindness, one eye, low vision other eye, unspecified eyes
H54.11 Blindness, right eye, low vision left eye
H54.12 Blindness, left eye, low vision right eye
H54.2 Low vision, both eyes
Visual impairment categories 1 or 2 in both eyes.
H54.3 Unqualified visual loss, both eyes
Visual impairment category 9 in both eyes.
+ **H54.4 Blindness, one eye**
Visual impairment categories 3, 4, 5 in one eye [normal vision other eye]
H54.40 Blindness, one eye, unspecified eye
H54.41 Blindness, right eye, normal vision left eye
H54.42 Blindness, left eye, normal vision right eye
+ **H54.5 Low vision, one eye**
Visual impairment categories 1 or 2 in one eye [normal vision in other eye].
H54.50 Low vision, one eye, unspecified eye
H54.51 Low vision, right eye, normal vision left eye
H54.52 Low vision, left eye, normal vision right eye
+ **H54.6 Unqualified visual loss, one eye**
Visual impairment category 9 in one eye [normal vision in other eye].
H54.60 Unqualified visual loss, one eye, unspecified
H54.61 Unqualified visual loss, right eye, normal vision left eye
H54.62 Unqualified visual loss, left eye, normal vision right eye
H54.7 Unspecified visual loss
Visual impairment category 9 NOS
H54.8 Legal blindness, as defined in USA
Blindness NOS according to USA definition
Excludes1: *legal blindness with specification of impairment le (H54.0-H54.7)*

NOTE The table below gives a classification of severity of visual impairment recommended by a WHO Study Group on the Prevention of Blindness, Geneva, 6-10 November 1972.
The term 'low vision' in category H54 comprises categories 1 and 2 of the table, the term 'blindness' categories 3, 4 and 5, and the term 'unqualified visual loss' category 9.
If the extent of the visual field is taken into account, patients with a field no greater than 10 but greater than 5 around central fixation should be place in category 3 and patients with a field no greater than 5 around central fixation should be placed in category even if the central acuity is not impaired.

Category of visual impairment	Visual acuity with best possible correction	
	Maximum less than:	Minimum equal to or better than:
	6/18	6/60
3/10(0.3)	1/10(0.1)	
20/70	20/200	
	6/60	3/60
1/10(0.1)	1/20(0.05)	
20/200	20/400	
	3/60	1/60(finger countin at one meter)
1/20(0.05)	1/50(0.02)	
20/400	5/300(20/1200)	
	1/60(finger counting at one meter)	Light perception
1/50(0.02)		
5/300		
	No light perception	
	Undetermined or unspecified	

er disorders of eye and adnexa (H55-H57)

H55 Nystagmus and other irregular eye movements

+ **H55.0** Nystagmus
  - **H55.00** Unspecified nystagmus
  - **H55.01** Congenital nystagmus
  - **H55.02** Latent nystagmus
  - **H55.03** Visual deprivation nystagmus
  - **H55.04** Dissociated nystagmus
  - **H55.09** Other forms of nystagmus

+ **H55.8** Other irregular eye movements
  - **H55.81** Saccadic eye movements
  - **H55.89** Other irregular eye movements

H57 Other disorders of eye and adnexa

+ **H57.0** Anomalies of pupillary function
  - **H57.00** Unspecified anomaly of pupillary function
  - **H57.01** Argyll Robertson pupil, atypical
    - ***Excludes1:*** *syphilitic Argyll Robertson pupil (A52.19)*
  - **H57.02** Anisocoria
  - **H57.03** Miosis
  - **H57.04** Mydriasis
  - + **H57.05** Tonic pupil
    - **H57.051** Tonic pupil, right eye
    - **H57.052** Tonic pupil, left eye
    - **H57.053** Tonic pupil, bilateral
    - **H57.059** Tonic pupil, unspecified eye
  - **H57.09** Other anomalies of pupillary function

+ **H57.1** Ocular pain
  - **H57.10** Ocular pain, unspecified eye
  - **H57.11** Ocular pain, right eye
  - **H57.12** Ocular pain, left eye
  - **H57.13** Ocular pain, bilateral

H57.8 Other specified disorders of eye and adnexa

H57.9 Unspecified disorder of eye and adnexa

aoperative and postprocedural complications and disorders ye and adnexa, not elsewhere classified (H59)

H59 Intraoperative and postprocedural complications and disorders of eye and adnexa, not elsewhere classified

Excludes1: *mechanical complication of intraocular lens (T85.2)*
mechanical complication of other ocular prosthetic devices, implants and grafts (T85.3)
pseudophakia (Z96.1)
secondary cataracts (H26.4-)

+ **H59.0** Disorders of the eye following cataract surgery
  - + **H59.01** Keratopathy (bullous aphakic) following cataract surgery
    - Vitreal corneal syndrome
    - Vitreous (touch) syndrome
    - CC **H59.011** Keratopathy (bullous aphakic) following cataract surgery, right eye
      - CC Exclusion see Appendix A PDX collection 0638
    - CC **H59.012** Keratopathy (bullous aphakic) following cataract surgery, left eye
      - CC Exclusion see Appendix A PDX collection 0638
    - CC **H59.013** Keratopathy (bullous aphakic) following cataract surgery, bilateral
      - CC Exclusion see Appendix A PDX collection 0638
    - CC **H59.019** Keratopathy (bullous aphakic) following cataract surgery, unspecified eye
      - CC Exclusion see Appendix A PDX collection 0638
  - + **H59.02** Cataract (lens) fragments in eye following cataract surgery
    - **H59.021** Cataract (lens) fragments in eye following cataract surgery, right eye
    - **H59.022** Cataract (lens) fragments in eye following cataract surgery, left eye
    - **H59.023** Cataract (lens) fragments in eye following cataract surgery, bilateral
    - **H59.029** Cataract (lens) fragments in eye following cataract surgery, unspecified eye
  - + **H59.03** Cystoid macular edema following cataract surgery
    - CC **H59.031** Cystoid macular edema following cataract surgery, right eye
      - CC Exclusion see Appendix A PDX collection 0638
    - CC **H59.032** Cystoid macular edema following cataract surgery, left eye
      - CC Exclusion see Appendix A PDX collection 0638
    - CC **H59.033** Cystoid macular edema following cataract surgery, bilateral
      - CC Exclusion see Appendix A PDX collection 0638
    - CC **H59.039** Cystoid macular edema following cataract surgery, unspecified eye
      - CC Exclusion see Appendix A PDX collection 0638
  - + **H59.09** Other disorders of the eye following cataract surgery
    - CC **H59.091** Other disorders of the right eye following cataract surgery
      - CC Exclusion see Appendix A PDX collection 0638
    - CC **H59.092** Other disorders of the left eye following cataract surgery
      - CC Exclusion see Appendix A PDX collection 0638
    - CC **H59.093** Other disorders of the eye following cataract surgery, bilateral
      - CC Exclusion see Appendix A PDX collection 0638
    - CC **H59.099** Other disorders of unspecified eye following cataract surgery
      - CC Exclusion see Appendix A PDX collection 0638

+ **H59.1** Intraoperative hemorrhage and hematoma of eye and adnexa complicating a procedure
  - ***Excludes1:*** *intraoperative hemorrhage and hematoma of eye and adnexa due to accidental puncture or laceration during a procedure (H59.2-)*
  - + **H59.11** Intraoperative hemorrhage and hematoma of eye and adnexa complicating an ophthalmic procedure
    - CC **H59.111** Intraoperative hemorrhage and hematoma of right eye and adnexa complicating an ophthalmic procedure
      - CC Exclusion see Appendix A PDX collection 0639
    - CC **H59.112** Intraoperative hemorrhage and hematoma of left eye and adnexa complicating an ophthalmic procedure
      - CC Exclusion see Appendix A PDX collection 0639
    - CC **H59.113** Intraoperative hemorrhage and hematoma of eye and adnexa complicating an ophthalmic procedure, bilateral
      - CC Exclusion see Appendix A PDX collection 0639
    - CC **H59.119** Intraoperative hemorrhage and hematoma of unspecified eye and adnexa complicating an ophthalmic procedure
      - CC Exclusion see Appendix A PDX collection 0639
  - + **H59.12** Intraoperative hemorrhage and hematoma of eye and adnexa complicating other procedure
    - CC **H59.121** Intraoperative hemorrhage and hematoma of right eye and adnexa complicating other procedure
      - CC Exclusion see Appendix A PDX collection 0639
    - CC **H59.122** Intraoperative hemorrhage and hematoma of left eye and adnexa complicating other procedure
      - CC Exclusion see Appendix A PDX collection 0639
    - CC **H59.123** Intraoperative hemorrhage and hematoma of eye and adnexa complicating other procedure, bilateral
      - CC Exclusion see Appendix A PDX collection 0639
    - CC **H59.129** Intraoperative hemorrhage and hematoma of unspecified eye and adnexa complicating other procedure
      - CC Exclusion see Appendix A PDX collection 0639

+ **H59.2 Accidental puncture and laceration of eye and adnexa during a procedure**

+ **H59.21 Accidental puncture and laceration of eye and adnexa during an ophthalmic procedure**

CC **H59.211 Accidental puncture and laceration of right eye and adnexa during an ophthalmic procedure**
CC Exclusion see Appendix A PDX collection 0509

CC **H59.212 Accidental puncture and laceration of left eye and adnexa during an ophthalmic procedure**
CC Exclusion see Appendix A PDX collection 0509

CC **H59.213 Accidental puncture and laceration of eye and adnexa during an ophthalmic procedure, bilateral**
CC Exclusion see Appendix A PDX collection 0509

CC **H59.219 Accidental puncture and laceration of unspecified eye and adnexa during an ophthalmic procedure**
CC Exclusion see Appendix A PDX collection 0509

+ **H59.22 Accidental puncture and laceration of eye and adnexa during other procedure**

CC **H59.221 Accidental puncture and laceration of right eye and adnexa during other procedure**
CC Exclusion see Appendix A PDX collection 0509

CC **H59.222 Accidental puncture and laceration of left eye and adnexa during other procedure**
CC Exclusion see Appendix A PDX collection 0509

CC **H59.223 Accidental puncture and laceration of eye and adnexa during other procedure, bilateral**
CC Exclusion see Appendix A PDX collection 0509

CC **H59.229 Accidental puncture and laceration of unspecified eye and adnexa during other procedure**
CC Exclusion see Appendix A PDX collection 0509

+ **H59.3 Postprocedural hemorrhage and hematoma of eye and adnexa following a procedure**

+ **H59.31 Postprocedural hemorrhage and hematoma of eye and adnexa following an ophthalmic procedure**

CC **H59.311 Postprocedural hemorrhage and hematoma of right eye and adnexa following an ophthalmic procedure**
CC Exclusion see Appendix A PDX collection 0639

CC **H59.312 Postprocedural hemorrhage and hematoma of left eye and adnexa following an ophthalmic procedure**
CC Exclusion see Appendix A PDX collection 0639

CC **H59.313 Postprocedural hemorrhage and hematoma of eye and adnexa following an ophthalmic procedure, bilateral**
CC Exclusion see Appendix A PDX collection 0639

CC **H59.319 Postprocedural hemorrhage and hematoma of unspecified eye and adnexa following an ophthalmic procedure**
CC Exclusion see Appendix A PDX collection 0639

+ **H59.32 Postprocedural hemorrhage and hematoma of eye adnexa following other procedure**

CC **H59.321 Postprocedural hemorrhage and hemato of right eye and adnexa following other procedure**
CC Exclusion see Appendix A PDX collection 0639

CC **H59.322 Postprocedural hemorrhage and hemato of left eye and adnexa following other procedure**
CC Exclusion see Appendix A PDX collection 0639

CC **H59.323 Postprocedural hemorrhage and hemato of eye and adnexa following other proced bilateral**
CC Exclusion see Appendix A PDX collection 0639

CC **H59.329 Postprocedural hemorrhage and hemato of unspecified eye and adnexa following other procedure**
CC Exclusion see Appendix A PDX collection 0639

+ **H59.4 Inflammation (infection) of postprocedural bleb**
Postprocedural blebitis
Excludes1: *filtering (vitreous) bleb after glaucoma surgery status (Z98.83)*

H59.40 Inflammation (infection) of postprocedural bleb, unspecified

H59.41 Inflammation (infection) of postprocedural bleb, stage 1

H59.42 Inflammation (infection) of postprocedural bleb, stage 2

H59.43 Inflammation (infection) of postprocedural bleb, stage 3
Bleb endophthalmitis

+ **H59.8 Other intraoperative and postprocedural complications and disorders of eye and adnexa, not elsewhere classified**

+ **H59.81 Chorioretinal scars after surgery for detachment**

CC **H59.811 Chorioretinal scars after surgery for detachment, right eye**
CC Exclusion see Appendix A PDX collection 0638

CC **H59.812 Chorioretinal scars after surgery for detachment, left eye**
CC Exclusion see Appendix A PDX collection 0638

CC **H59.813 Chorioretinal scars after surgery for detachment, bilateral**
CC Exclusion see Appendix A PDX collection 0638

CC **H59.819 Chorioretinal scars after surgery for detachment, unspecified eye**
CC Exclusion see Appendix A PDX collection 0638

CC **H59.88 Other intraoperative complications of eye and adne not elsewhere classified**
CC Exclusion see Appendix A PDX collection 0638

CC **H59.89 Other postprocedural complications and disorders o eye and adnexa, not elsewhere classified**
CC Exclusion see Appendix A PDX collection 0638
One of the following 7th characters is to be assigned t code H40.10 to designate the stage of glaucoma

...apter 8: Diseases of the Ear and Mastoid Process (...0-H95)

E Use an external cause code following the code for the ear condition, if applicable, to identify the cause of the ear condition

...des2: *certain conditions originating in the perinatal period (P04-P96)*
certain infectious and parasitic diseases (A00-B99)
complications of pregnancy, childbirth and the puerperium (O00-O9A)
congenital malformations, deformations and chromosomal abnormalities (Q00-Q99)
endocrine, nutritional and metabolic diseases (E00-E88)
injury, poisoning and certain other consequences of external causes (S00-T88)
neoplasms (C00-D49)
symptoms, signs and abnormal clinical and laboratory findings, not elsewhere classified (R00-R94)

This chapter contains the following category blocks:

H60-H62	Diseases of external ear
H65-H75	Diseases of middle ear and mastoid
H80-H83	Diseases of inner ear
H90-H94	Other disorders of ear
H95	Intraoperative and postprocedural complications and disorders of ear and mastoid process, not elsewhere classified

C. Chapter-Specific Coding Guidelines

In addition to general coding guidelines, there are guidelines for specific diagnoses and/or conditions in the classification. Unless otherwise indicated, these guidelines apply to all health care settings. Please refer to Section II for guidelines on the selection of principal diagnosis.

8. Chapter 8: Diseases of the Ear and Mastoid Process (H60-H95)

Reserved for future guideline expansion

Ear

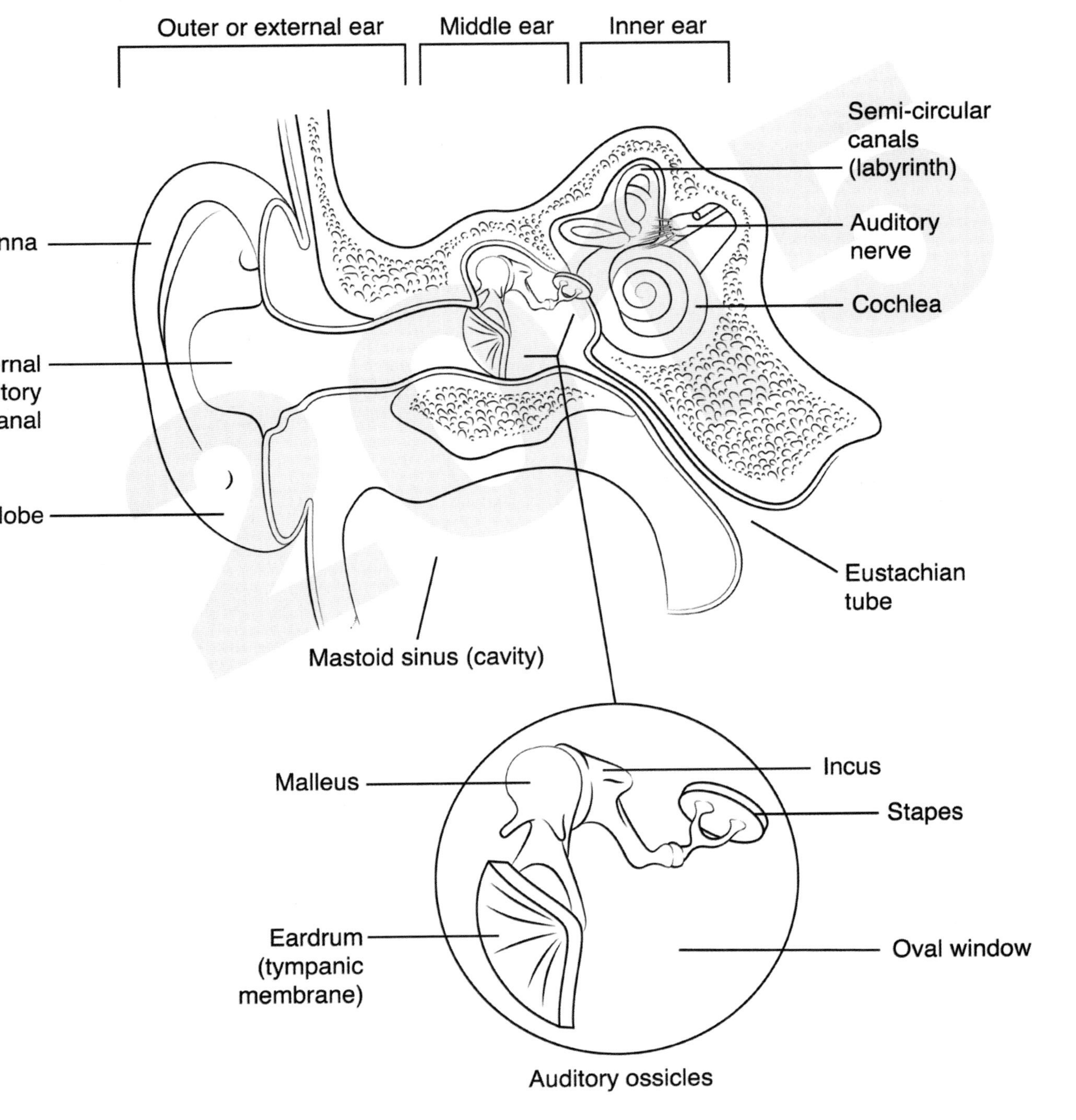

Diseases of external ear (H60-H62)

H60 Otitis externa

+ H60.0 Abscess of external ear
Boil of external ear
Carbuncle of auricle or external auditory canal
Furuncle of external ear
H60.00 Abscess of external ear, unspecified ear
H60.01 Abscess of right external ear
H60.02 Abscess of left external ear
H60.03 Abscess of external ear, bilateral

+ H60.1 Cellulitis of external ear
Cellulitis of auricle
Cellulitis of external auditory canal
H60.10 Cellulitis of external ear, unspecified ear
H60.11 Cellulitis of right external ear
H60.12 Cellulitis of left external ear
H60.13 Cellulitis of external ear, bilateral

+ H60.2 Malignant otitis externa
CC **H60.20 Malignant otitis externa, unspecified ear**
CC Exclusion see Appendix A PDX collection 0640
CC **H60.21 Malignant otitis externa, right ear**
CC Exclusion see Appendix A PDX collection 0640
CC **H60.22 Malignant otitis externa, left ear**
CC Exclusion see Appendix A PDX collection 0640
CC **H60.23 Malignant otitis externa, bilateral**
CC Exclusion see Appendix A PDX collection 0640

+ H60.3 Other infective otitis externa
+ H60.31 Diffuse otitis externa
H60.311 Diffuse otitis externa, right ear
H60.312 Diffuse otitis externa, left ear
H60.313 Diffuse otitis externa, bilateral
H60.319 Diffuse otitis externa, unspecified ear
+ H60.32 Hemorrhagic otitis externa
H60.321 Hemorrhagic otitis externa, right ear
H60.322 Hemorrhagic otitis externa, left ear
H60.323 Hemorrhagic otitis externa, bilateral
H60.329 Hemorrhagic otitis externa, unspecified ear
+ H60.33 Swimmer's ear
H60.331 Swimmer's ear, right ear
H60.332 Swimmer's ear, left ear
H60.333 Swimmer's ear, bilateral
H60.339 Swimmer's ear, unspecified ear
+ H60.39 Other infective otitis externa
H60.391 Other infective otitis externa, right ear
H60.392 Other infective otitis externa, left ear
H60.393 Other infective otitis externa, bilateral
H60.399 Other infective otitis externa, unspecified ear

+ H60.4 Cholesteatoma of external ear
Keratosis obturans of external ear (canal)
Excludes2: *cholesteatoma of middle ear (H71.-)*
recurrent cholesteatoma of postmastoidectomy cavity (H95.0-)
H60.40 Cholesteatoma of external ear, unspecified ear
H60.41 Cholesteatoma of right external ear
H60.42 Cholesteatoma of left external ear
H60.43 Cholesteatoma of external ear, bilateral

+ H60.5 Acute noninfective otitis externa
+ H60.50 Unspecified acute noninfective otitis externa
Acute otitis externa NOS
H60.501 Unspecified acute noninfective otitis externa, right ear
H60.502 Unspecified acute noninfective otitis externa, left ear
H60.503 Unspecified acute noninfective otitis externa, bilateral
H60.509 Unspecified acute noninfective otitis externa, unspecified ear
+ H60.51 Acute actinic otitis externa
H60.511 Acute actinic otitis externa, right ear
H60.512 Acute actinic otitis externa, left ear
H60.513 Acute actinic otitis externa, bilateral
H60.519 Acute actinic otitis externa, unspecified ear
+ H60.52 Acute chemical otitis externa
H60.521 Acute chemical otitis externa, right ear
H60.522 Acute chemical otitis externa, left ear
H60.523 Acute chemical otitis externa, bilateral
H60.529 Acute chemical otitis externa, unspecified ear
+ H60.53 Acute contact otitis externa
H60.531 Acute contact otitis externa, right ear
H60.532 Acute contact otitis externa, left ear
H60.533 Acute contact otitis externa, bilateral
H60.539 Acute contact otitis externa, unspecified
+ H60.54 Acute eczematoid otitis externa
H60.541 Acute eczematoid otitis externa, right ea
H60.542 Acute eczematoid otitis externa, left ear
H60.543 Acute eczematoid otitis externa, bilateral
H60.549 Acute eczematoid otitis externa, unspeci ear
+ H60.55 Acute reactive otitis externa
H60.551 Acute reactive otitis externa, right ear
H60.552 Acute reactive otitis externa, left ear
H60.553 Acute reactive otitis externa, bilateral
H60.559 Acute reactive otitis externa, unspecified
+ H60.59 Other noninfective acute otitis externa
H60.591 Other noninfective acute otitis externa, r ear
H60.592 Other noninfective acute otitis externa, le ear
H60.593 Other noninfective acute otitis externa, bilateral
H60.599 Other noninfective acute otitis externa, unspecified ear

+ H60.6 Unspecified chronic otitis externa
H60.60 Unspecified chronic otitis externa, unspecified ear
H60.61 Unspecified chronic otitis externa, right ear
H60.62 Unspecified chronic otitis externa, left ear
H60.63 Unspecified chronic otitis externa, bilateral

+ H60.8 Other otitis externa
+ H60.8X Other otitis externa
H60.8X1 Other otitis externa, right ear
H60.8X2 Other otitis externa, left ear
H60.8X3 Other otitis externa, bilateral
H60.8X9 Other otitis externa, unspecified ear

+ H60.9 Unspecified otitis externa
H60.90 Unspecified otitis externa, unspecified ear
H60.91 Unspecified otitis externa, right ear
H60.92 Unspecified otitis externa, left ear
H60.93 Unspecified otitis externa, bilateral

H61 Other disorders of external ear

+ H61.0 Chondritis and perichondritis of external ear
Chondrodermatitis nodularis chronica helicis
Perichondritis of auricle
Perichondritis of pinna
+ H61.00 Unspecified perichondritis of external ear
H61.001 Unspecified perichondritis of right extern ear
H61.002 Unspecified perichondritis of left external ear
H61.003 Unspecified perichondritis of external ear bilateral
H61.009 Unspecified perichondritis of external ear unspecified ear
+ H61.01 Acute perichondritis of external ear
H61.011 Acute perichondritis of right external ear
H61.012 Acute perichondritis of left external ear
H61.013 Acute perichondritis of external ear, bilateral
H61.019 Acute perichondritis of external ear, unspecified ear
+ H61.02 Chronic perichondritis of external ear
H61.021 Chronic perichondritis of right external e
H61.022 Chronic perichondritis of left external ear
H61.023 Chronic perichondritis of external ear, bilateral
H61.029 Chronic perichondritis of external ear, unspecified ear
+ H61.03 Chondritis of external ear
Chondritis of auricle
Chondritis of pinna
H61.031 Chondritis of right external ear
H61.032 Chondritis of left external ear
H61.033 Chondritis of external ear, bilateral
H61.039 Chondritis of external ear, unspecified ear

+ **H61.1 Noninfective disorders of pinna**
Excludes2: *cauliflower ear (M95.1-)*
gouty tophi of ear (M1A.-)
+ **H61.10 Unspecified noninfective disorders of pinna**
Disorder of pinna NOS
H61.101 Unspecified noninfective disorders of pinna, right ear
H61.102 Unspecified noninfective disorders of pinna, left ear
H61.103 Unspecified noninfective disorders of pinna, bilateral
H61.109 Unspecified noninfective disorders of pinna, unspecified ear
+ **H61.11 Acquired deformity of pinna**
Acquired deformity of auricle
Excludes2: *cauliflower ear (M95.1-)*
H61.111 Acquired deformity of pinna, right ear
H61.112 Acquired deformity of pinna, left ear
H61.113 Acquired deformity of pinna, bilateral
H61.119 Acquired deformity of pinna, unspecified ear
+ **H61.12 Hematoma of pinna**
Hematoma of auricle
H61.121 Hematoma of pinna, right ear
H61.122 Hematoma of pinna, left ear
H61.123 Hematoma of pinna, bilateral
H61.129 Hematoma of pinna, unspecified ear
+ **H61.19 Other noninfective disorders of pinna**
H61.191 Noninfective disorders of pinna, right ear
H61.192 Noninfective disorders of pinna, left ear
H61.193 Noninfective disorders of pinna, bilateral
H61.199 Noninfective disorders of pinna, unspecified ear
+ **H61.2 Impacted cerumen**
Wax in ear
H61.20 Impacted cerumen, unspecified ear
H61.21 Impacted cerumen, right ear
H61.22 Impacted cerumen, left ear
H61.23 Impacted cerumen, bilateral
+ **H61.3 Acquired stenosis of external ear canal**
Collapse of external ear canal
Excludes1: *postprocedural stenosis of external ear canal (H95.81-)*
+ **H61.30 Acquired stenosis of external ear canal, unspecified**
H61.301 Acquired stenosis of right external ear canal, unspecified
H61.302 Acquired stenosis of left external ear canal, unspecified
H61.303 Acquired stenosis of external ear canal, unspecified, bilateral
H61.309 Acquired stenosis of external ear canal, unspecified, unspecified ear
+ **H61.31 Acquired stenosis of external ear canal secondary to trauma**
H61.311 Acquired stenosis of right external ear canal secondary to trauma
H61.312 Acquired stenosis of left external ear canal secondary to trauma
H61.313 Acquired stenosis of external ear canal secondary to trauma, bilateral
H61.319 Acquired stenosis of external ear canal secondary to trauma, unspecified ear
+ **H61.32 Acquired stenosis of external ear canal secondary to inflammation and infection**
H61.321 Acquired stenosis of right external ear canal secondary to inflammation and infection
H61.322 Acquired stenosis of left external ear canal secondary to inflammation and infection
H61.323 Acquired stenosis of external ear canal secondary to inflammation and infection, bilateral
H61.329 Acquired stenosis of external ear canal secondary to inflammation and infection, unspecified ear
+ **H61.39 Other acquired stenosis of external ear canal**
H61.391 Other acquired stenosis of right external ear canal
H61.392 Other acquired stenosis of left external ear canal
H61.393 Other acquired stenosis of external ear canal, bilateral
H61.399 Other acquired stenosis of external ear canal, unspecified ear
+ **H61.8 Other specified disorders of external ear**
+ **H61.81 Exostosis of external canal**
H61.811 Exostosis of right external canal
H61.812 Exostosis of left external canal
H61.813 Exostosis of external canal, bilateral
H61.819 Exostosis of external canal, unspecified ear
+ **H61.89 Other specified disorders of external ear**
H61.891 Other specified disorders of right external ear
H61.892 Other specified disorders of left external ear
H61.893 Other specified disorders of external ear, bilateral
H61.899 Other specified disorders of external ear, unspecified ear
+ **H61.9 Disorder of external ear, unspecified**
H61.90 Disorder of external ear, unspecified, unspecified ear
H61.91 Disorder of right external ear, unspecified
H61.92 Disorder of left external ear, unspecified
H61.93 Disorder of external ear, unspecified, bilateral

H62 Disorders of external ear in diseases classified elsewhere
+ **H62.4 Otitis externa in other diseases classified elsewhere**
Code first underlying disease, such as:
erysipelas (A46)
impetigo (L01.0)
Excludes1: *otitis externa (in):*
candidiasis (B37.84)
herpes viral [herpes simplex] (B00.1)
herpes zoster (B02.8)
H62.40 Otitis externa in other diseases classified elsewhere, unspecified ear
H62.41 Otitis externa in other diseases classified elsewhere, right ear
H62.42 Otitis externa in other diseases classified elsewhere, left ear
H62.43 Otitis externa in other diseases classified elsewhere, bilateral
+ **H62.8 Other disorders of external ear in diseases classified elsewhere**
Code first underlying disease, such as:
gout (M1A.-, M10.-)
+ **H62.8X Other disorders of external ear in diseases classified elsewhere**
H62.8X1 Other disorders of right external ear in diseases classified elsewhere
H62.8X2 Other disorders of left external ear in diseases classified elsewhere
H62.8X3 Other disorders of external ear in diseases classified elsewhere, bilateral
H62.8X9 Other disorders of external ear in diseases classified elsewhere, unspecified ear

Diseases of middle ear and mastoid (H65-H75)

H65 Nonsuppurative otitis media
Includes: nonsuppurative otitis media with myringitis
Use additional code for any associated perforated tympanic membrane (H72.-)

Use additional code to identify:
exposure to environmental tobacco smoke (Z77.22)
exposure to tobacco smoke in the perinatal period (P96.81)
history of tobacco use (Z87.891)
occupational exposure to environmental tobacco smoke (Z57.31)
tobacco dependence (F17.-)
tobacco use (Z72.0)
+ **H65.0 Acute serous otitis media**
Acute and subacute secretory otitis
H65.00 Acute serous otitis media, unspecified ear
H65.01 Acute serous otitis media, right ear
H65.02 Acute serous otitis media, left ear
H65.03 Acute serous otitis media, bilateral
H65.04 Acute serous otitis media, recurrent, right ear
H65.05 Acute serous otitis media, recurrent, left ear
H65.06 Acute serous otitis media, recurrent, bilateral
H65.07 Acute serous otitis media, recurrent, unspecified ear
+ **H65.1 Other acute nonsuppurative otitis media**
Excludes1: *otitic barotrauma (T70.0)*
otitis media (acute) NOS (H66.9)
+ **H65.11 Acute and subacute allergic otitis media (mucoid) (sanguinous) (serous)**
H65.111 Acute and subacute allergic otitis media (mucoid) (sanguinous) (serous), right ear

H65.112 Acute and subacute allergic otitis media (mucoid) (sanguinous) (serous), left ear
H65.113 Acute and subacute allergic otitis media (mucoid) (sanguinous) (serous), bilateral
H65.114 Acute and subacute allergic otitis media (mucoid) (sanguinous) (serous), recurrent, right ear
H65.115 Acute and subacute allergic otitis media (mucoid) (sanguinous) (serous), recurrent, left ear
H65.116 Acute and subacute allergic otitis media (mucoid) (sanguinous) (serous), recurrent, bilateral
H65.117 Acute and subacute allergic otitis media (mucoid) (sanguinous) (serous), recurrent, unspecified ear
H65.119 Acute and subacute allergic otitis media (mucoid) (sanguinous) (serous), unspecified ear

+ **H65.19 Other acute nonsuppurative otitis media**
Acute and subacute mucoid otitis media
Acute and subacute nonsuppurative otitis media NOS
Acute and subacute sanguinous otitis media
Acute and subacute seromucinous otitis media
H65.191 Other acute nonsuppurative otitis media, right ear
H65.192 Other acute nonsuppurative otitis media, left ear
H65.193 Other acute nonsuppurative otitis media, bilateral
H65.194 Other acute nonsuppurative otitis media, recurrent, right ear
H65.195 Other acute nonsuppurative otitis media, recurrent, left ear
H65.196 Other acute nonsuppurative otitis media, recurrent, bilateral
H65.197 Other acute nonsuppurative otitis media recurrent, unspecified ear
H65.199 Other acute nonsuppurative otitis media, unspecified ear

+ **H65.2 Chronic serous otitis media**
Chronic tubotympanal catarrh
H65.20 Chronic serous otitis media, unspecified ear
H65.21 Chronic serous otitis media, right ear
H65.22 Chronic serous otitis media, left ear
H65.23 Chronic serous otitis media, bilateral

+ **H65.3 Chronic mucoid otitis media**
Chronic mucinous otitis media
Chronic secretory otitis media
Chronic transudative otitis media
Glue ear
Excludes1: *adhesive middle ear disease (H74.1)*
H65.30 Chronic mucoid otitis media, unspecified ear
H65.31 Chronic mucoid otitis media, right ear
H65.32 Chronic mucoid otitis media, left ear
H65.33 Chronic mucoid otitis media, bilateral

+ **H65.4 Other chronic nonsuppurative otitis media**
+ **H65.41 Chronic allergic otitis media**
H65.411 Chronic allergic otitis media, right ear
H65.412 Chronic allergic otitis media, left ear
H65.413 Chronic allergic otitis media, bilateral
H65.419 Chronic allergic otitis media, unspecified ear
+ **H65.49 Other chronic nonsuppurative otitis media**
Chronic exudative otitis media
Chronic nonsuppurative otitis media NOS
Chronic otitis media with effusion (nonpurulent)
Chronic seromucinous otitis media
H65.491 Other chronic nonsuppurative otitis media, right ear
H65.492 Other chronic nonsuppurative otitis media, left ear
H65.493 Other chronic nonsuppurative otitis media, bilateral
H65.499 Other chronic nonsuppurative otitis media, unspecified ear

+ **H65.9 Unspecified nonsuppurative otitis media**
Allergic otitis media NOS
Catarrhal otitis media NOS
Exudative otitis media NOS
Mucoid otitis media NOS
Otitis media with effusion (nonpurulent) NOS
Secretory otitis media NOS
Seromucinous otitis media NOS
Serous otitis media NOS
Transudative otitis media NOS
H65.90 Unspecified nonsuppurative otitis media, unspecified ear
H65.91 Unspecified nonsuppurative otitis media, right ear
H65.92 Unspecified nonsuppurative otitis media, left ear
H65.93 Unspecified nonsuppurative otitis media, bilateral

H66 Suppurative and unspecified otitis media

Includes: suppurative and unspecified otitis media with myringitis
Use additional code to identify:
exposure to environmental tobacco smoke (Z77.22)
exposure to tobacco smoke in the perinatal period (P96.81)
history of tobacco use (Z87.891)
occupational exposure to environmental tobacco smoke (Z57.31)
tobacco dependence (F17.-)
tobacco use (Z72.0)

+ **H66.0 Acute suppurative otitis media**
+ **H66.00 Acute suppurative otitis media without spontaneous rupture of ear drum**
H66.001 Acute suppurative otitis media without spontaneous rupture of ear drum, right ea
H66.002 Acute suppurative otitis media without spontaneous rupture of ear drum, left ear
H66.003 Acute suppurative otitis media without spontaneous rupture of ear drum, bilatera
H66.004 Acute suppurative otitis media without spontaneous rupture of ear drum, recurre right ear
H66.005 Acute suppurative otitis media without spontaneous rupture of ear drum, recurre left ear
H66.006 Acute suppurative otitis media without spontaneous rupture of ear drum, recurre bilateral
H66.007 Acute suppurative otitis media without spontaneous rupture of ear drum, recurre unspecified ear
H66.009 Acute suppurative otitis media without spontaneous rupture of ear drum, unspecified ear
+ **H66.01 Acute suppurative otitis media with spontaneous rupture of ear drum**
H66.011 Acute suppurative otitis media with spontaneous rupture of ear drum, right ea
H66.012 Acute suppurative otitis media with spontaneous rupture of ear drum, left ear
H66.013 Acute suppurative otitis media with spontaneous rupture of ear drum, bilatera
H66.014 Acute suppurative otitis media with spontaneous rupture of ear drum, recurre right ear
H66.015 Acute suppurative otitis media with spontaneous rupture of ear drum, recurre left ear
H66.016 Acute suppurative otitis media with spontaneous rupture of ear drum, recurre bilateral
H66.017 Acute suppurative otitis media with spontaneous rupture of ear drum, recurre unspecified ear
H66.019 Acute suppurative otitis media with spontaneous rupture of ear drum, unspecified ear

+ **H66.1 Chronic tubotympanic suppurative otitis media**
Benign chronic suppurative otitis media
Chronic tubotympanic disease
Use additional code for any associated perforated tympanic membrane (H72.-)
H66.10 Chronic tubotympanic suppurative otitis media, unspecified
H66.11 Chronic tubotympanic suppurative otitis media, righ ear

H66.12 Chronic tubotympanic suppurative otitis media, left ear
H66.13 Chronic tubotympanic suppurative otitis media, bilateral

+ H66.2 Chronic atticoantral suppurative otitis media
Chronic atticoantral disease
Use additional code for any associated perforated tympanic membrane (H72.-)
H66.20 Chronic atticoantral suppurative otitis media, unspecified ear
H66.21 Chronic atticoantral suppurative otitis media, right ear
H66.22 Chronic atticoantral suppurative otitis media, left ear
H66.23 Chronic atticoantral suppurative otitis media, bilateral

+ H66.3 Other chronic suppurative otitis media
Chronic suppurative otitis media NOS
Use additional code for any associated perforated tympanic membrane (H72.-)
Excludes1: *tuberculous otitis media (A18.6)*
+ H66.3X Other chronic suppurative otitis media
H66.3X1 Other chronic suppurative otitis media, right ear
H66.3X2 Other chronic suppurative otitis media, left ear
H66.3X3 Other chronic suppurative otitis media, bilateral
H66.3X9 Other chronic suppurative otitis media, unspecified ear

+ H66.4 Suppurative otitis media, unspecified
Purulent otitis media NOS
Use additional code for any associated perforated tympanic membrane (H72.-)
H66.40 Suppurative otitis media, unspecified, unspecified ear
H66.41 Suppurative otitis media, unspecified, right ear
H66.42 Suppurative otitis media, unspecified, left ear
H66.43 Suppurative otitis media, unspecified, bilateral

+ H66.9 Otitis media, unspecified
Otitis media NOS
Acute otitis media NOS
Chronic otitis media NOS
Use additional code for any associated perforated tympanic membrane (H72.-)
H66.90 Otitis media, unspecified, unspecified ear
H66.91 Otitis media, unspecified, right ear
H66.92 Otitis media, unspecified, left ear
H66.93 Otitis media, unspecified, bilateral

H67 Otitis media in diseases classified elsewhere
Code first underlying disease, such as:
viral disease NEC (B00-B34)

Use additional code for any associated perforated tympanic membrane (H72.-)
Excludes1: *otitis media in:*
influenza (J09.X9, J10.83, J11.83)
measles (B05.3)
scarlet fever (A38.0)
tuberculosis (A18.6)
H67.1 Otitis media in diseases classified elsewhere, right ear
H67.2 Otitis media in diseases classified elsewhere, left ear
H67.3 Otitis media in diseases classified elsewhere, bilateral
H67.9 Otitis media in diseases classified elsewhere, unspecified ear

H68 Eustachian salpingitis and obstruction

+ H68.0 Eustachian salpingitis
+ H68.00 Unspecified Eustachian salpingitis
H68.001 Unspecified Eustachian salpingitis, right ear
H68.002 Unspecified Eustachian salpingitis, left ear
H68.003 Unspecified Eustachian salpingitis, bilateral
H68.009 Unspecified Eustachian salpingitis, unspecified ear
+ H68.01 Acute Eustachian salpingitis
H68.011 Acute Eustachian salpingitis, right ear
H68.012 Acute Eustachian salpingitis, left ear
H68.013 Acute Eustachian salpingitis, bilateral
H68.019 Acute Eustachian salpingitis, unspecified ear
+ H68.02 Chronic Eustachian salpingitis
H68.021 Chronic Eustachian salpingitis, right ear
H68.022 Chronic Eustachian salpingitis, left ear
H68.023 Chronic Eustachian salpingitis, bilateral
H68.029 Chronic Eustachian salpingitis, unspecified ear

+ H68.1 Obstruction of Eustachian tube
Stenosis of Eustachian tube
Stricture of Eustachian tube
+ H68.10 Unspecified obstruction of Eustachian tube
H68.101 Unspecified obstruction of Eustachian tube, right ear
H68.102 Unspecified obstruction of Eustachian tube, left ear
H68.103 Unspecified obstruction of Eustachian tube, bilateral
H68.109 Unspecified obstruction of Eustachian tube, unspecified ear
+ H68.11 Osseous obstruction of Eustachian tube
H68.111 Osseous obstruction of Eustachian tube, right ear
H68.112 Osseous obstruction of Eustachian tube, left ear
H68.113 Osseous obstruction of Eustachian tube, bilateral
H68.119 Osseous obstruction of Eustachian tube, unspecified ear
+ H68.12 Intrinsic cartilagenous obstruction of Eustachian tube
H68.121 Intrinsic cartilagenous obstruction of Eustachian tube, right ear
H68.122 Intrinsic cartilagenous obstruction of Eustachian tube, left ear
H68.123 Intrinsic cartilagenous obstruction of Eustachian tube, bilateral
H68.129 Intrinsic cartilagenous obstruction of Eustachian tube, unspecified ear
+ H68.13 Extrinsic cartilagenous obstruction of Eustachian tube
Compression of Eustachian tube
H68.131 Extrinsic cartilagenous obstruction of Eustachian tube, right ear
H68.132 Extrinsic cartilagenous obstruction of Eustachian tube, left ear
H68.133 Extrinsic cartilagenous obstruction of Eustachian tube, bilateral
H68.139 Extrinsic cartilagenous obstruction of Eustachian tube, unspecified ear

H69 Other and unspecified disorders of Eustachian tube

+ H69.0 Patulous Eustachian tube
H69.00 Patulous Eustachian tube, unspecified ear
H69.01 Patulous Eustachian tube, right ear
H69.02 Patulous Eustachian tube, left ear
H69.03 Patulous Eustachian tube, bilateral
+ H69.8 Other specified disorders of Eustachian tube
H69.80 Other specified disorders of Eustachian tube, unspecified ear
H69.81 Other specified disorders of Eustachian tube, right ear
H69.82 Other specified disorders of Eustachian tube, left ear
H69.83 Other specified disorders of Eustachian tube, bilateral
+ H69.9 Unspecified Eustachian tube disorder
H69.90 Unspecified Eustachian tube disorder, unspecified ear
H69.91 Unspecified Eustachian tube disorder, right ear
H69.92 Unspecified Eustachian tube disorder, left ear
H69.93 Unspecified Eustachian tube disorder, bilateral

H70 Mastoiditis and related conditions

+ H70.0 Acute mastoiditis
Abscess of mastoid
Empyema of mastoid
+ H70.00 Acute mastoiditis without complications
CC **H70.001 Acute mastoiditis without complications, right ear**
CC Exclusion see Appendix A PDX collection 0641
CC **H70.002 Acute mastoiditis without complications, left ear**
CC Exclusion see Appendix A PDX collection 0641
CC **H70.003 Acute mastoiditis without complications, bilateral**
CC Exclusion see Appendix A PDX collection 0641
CC **H70.009 Acute mastoiditis without complications, unspecified ear**
CC Exclusion see Appendix A PDX collection 0641
+ H70.01 Subperiosteal abscess of mastoid
CC **H70.011 Subperiosteal abscess of mastoid, right ear**
CC Exclusion see Appendix A PDX collection 0641

CC **H70.012 Subperiosteal abscess of mastoid, left ear**
CC Exclusion see Appendix A PDX collection 0641

CC **H70.013 Subperiosteal abscess of mastoid, bilateral**
CC Exclusion see Appendix A PDX collection 0641

CC **H70.019 Subperiosteal abscess of mastoid, unspecified ear**
CC Exclusion see Appendix A PDX collection 0641

\+ **H70.09 Acute mastoiditis with other complications**

CC **H70.091 Acute mastoiditis with other complications, right ear**
CC Exclusion see Appendix A PDX collection 0641

CC **H70.092 Acute mastoiditis with other complications, left ear**
CC Exclusion see Appendix A PDX collection 0641

CC **H70.093 Acute mastoiditis with other complications, bilateral**
CC Exclusion see Appendix A PDX collection 0641

CC **H70.099 Acute mastoiditis with other complications, unspecified ear**
CC Exclusion see Appendix A PDX collection 0641

\+ **H70.1 Chronic mastoiditis**
Caries of mastoid
Fistula of mastoid
Excludes1: *tuberculous mastoiditis (A18.03)*
H70.10 Chronic mastoiditis, unspecified ear
H70.11 Chronic mastoiditis, right ear
H70.12 Chronic mastoiditis, left ear
H70.13 Chronic mastoiditis, bilateral

\+ **H70.2 Petrositis**
Inflammation of petrous bone

\+ **H70.20 Unspecified petrositis**
H70.201 Unspecified petrositis, right ear
H70.202 Unspecified petrositis, left ear
H70.203 Unspecified petrositis, bilateral
H70.209 Unspecified petrositis, unspecified ear

\+ **H70.21 Acute petrositis**
H70.211 Acute petrositis, right ear
H70.212 Acute petrositis, left ear
H70.213 Acute petrositis, bilateral
H70.219 Acute petrositis, unspecified ear

\+ **H70.22 Chronic petrositis**
H70.221 Chronic petrositis, right ear
H70.222 Chronic petrositis, left ear
H70.223 Chronic petrositis, bilateral
H70.229 Chronic petrositis, unspecified ear

\+ **H70.8 Other mastoiditis and related conditions**
Excludes1: *preauricular sinus and cyst (Q18.1)*
sinus, fistula, and cyst of branchial cleft (Q18.0)

\+ **H70.81 Postauricular fistula**
H70.811 Postauricular fistula, right ear
H70.812 Postauricular fistula, left ear
H70.813 Postauricular fistula, bilateral
H70.819 Postauricular fistula, unspecified ear

\+ **H70.89 Other mastoiditis and related conditions**
H70.891 Other mastoiditis and related conditions, right ear
H70.892 Other mastoiditis and related conditions, left ear
H70.893 Other mastoiditis and related conditions, bilateral
H70.899 Other mastoiditis and related conditions, unspecified ear

\+ **H70.9 Unspecified mastoiditis**
H70.90 Unspecified mastoiditis, unspecified ear
H70.91 Unspecified mastoiditis, right ear
H70.92 Unspecified mastoiditis, left ear
H70.93 Unspecified mastoiditis, bilateral

H71 Cholesteatoma of middle ear

Excludes2: *cholesteatoma of external ear (H60.4-)*
recurrent cholesteatoma of postmastoidectomy cavity (H95.0-)

\+ **H71.0 Cholesteatoma of attic**
H71.00 Cholesteatoma of attic, unspecified ear
H71.01 Cholesteatoma of attic, right ear
H71.02 Cholesteatoma of attic, left ear
H71.03 Cholesteatoma of attic, bilateral

\+ **H71.1 Cholesteatoma of tympanum**
H71.10 Cholesteatoma of tympanum, unspecified ear
H71.11 Cholesteatoma of tympanum, right ear
H71.12 Cholesteatoma of tympanum, left ear
H71.13 Cholesteatoma of tympanum, bilateral

\+ **H71.2 Cholesteatoma of mastoid**
H71.20 Cholesteatoma of mastoid, unspecified ear
H71.21 Cholesteatoma of mastoid, right ear
H71.22 Cholesteatoma of mastoid, left ear
H71.23 Cholesteatoma of mastoid, bilateral

\+ **H71.3 Diffuse cholesteatosis**
H71.30 Diffuse cholesteatosis, unspecified ear
H71.31 Diffuse cholesteatosis, right ear
H71.32 Diffuse cholesteatosis, left ear
H71.33 Diffuse cholesteatosis, bilateral

\+ **H71.9 Unspecified cholesteatoma**
H71.90 Unspecified cholesteatoma, unspecified ear
H71.91 Unspecified cholesteatoma, right ear
H71.92 Unspecified cholesteatoma, left ear
H71.93 Unspecified cholesteatoma, bilateral

H72 Perforation of tympanic membrane

Includes: persistent post-traumatic perforation of ear drum
postinflammatory perforation of ear drum
Code first any associated otitis media (H65.-, H66.1-, H66.2-, H66.3-, H66.4-, H66.9-, H67.-)
Excludes1: *acute suppurative otitis media with rupture of the tympanic membrane (H66.01-)*
traumatic rupture of ear drum (S09.2-)

\+ **H72.0 Central perforation of tympanic membrane**
H72.00 Central perforation of tympanic membrane, unspecified ear
H72.01 Central perforation of tympanic membrane, right ear
H72.02 Central perforation of tympanic membrane, left ear
H72.03 Central perforation of tympanic membrane, bilateral

\+ **H72.1 Attic perforation of tympanic membrane**
Perforation of pars flaccida
H72.10 Attic perforation of tympanic membrane, unspecified ear
H72.11 Attic perforation of tympanic membrane, right ear
H72.12 Attic perforation of tympanic membrane, left ear
H72.13 Attic perforation of tympanic membrane, bilateral

\+ **H72.2 Other marginal perforations of tympanic membrane**

\+ **H72.2X Other marginal perforations of tympanic membrane**
H72.2X1 Other marginal perforations of tympanic membrane, right ear
H72.2X2 Other marginal perforations of tympanic membrane, left ear
H72.2X3 Other marginal perforations of tympanic membrane, bilateral
H72.2X9 Other marginal perforations of tympanic membrane, unspecified ear

\+ **H72.8 Other perforations of tympanic membrane**

\+ **H72.81 Multiple perforations of tympanic membrane**
H72.811 Multiple perforations of tympanic membrane, right ear
H72.812 Multiple perforations of tympanic membrane, left ear
H72.813 Multiple perforations of tympanic membrane, bilateral
H72.819 Multiple perforations of tympanic membrane, unspecified ear

\+ **H72.82 Total perforations of tympanic membrane**
H72.821 Total perforations of tympanic membrane, right ear
H72.822 Total perforations of tympanic membrane, left ear
H72.823 Total perforations of tympanic membrane, bilateral
H72.829 Total perforations of tympanic membrane, unspecified ear

\+ **H72.9 Unspecified perforation of tympanic membrane**
H72.90 Unspecified perforation of tympanic membrane, unspecified ear
H72.91 Unspecified perforation of tympanic membrane, right ear
H72.92 Unspecified perforation of tympanic membrane, left ear
H72.93 Unspecified perforation of tympanic membrane, bilateral

H73 Other disorders of tympanic membrane

+ **H73.0 Acute myringitis**
  Excludes1: acute myringitis with otitis media (H65, H66)
  + **H73.00 Unspecified acute myringitis**
    Acute tympanitis NOS
    H73.001 Acute myringitis, right ear
    H73.002 Acute myringitis, left ear
    H73.003 Acute myringitis, bilateral
    H73.009 Acute myringitis, unspecified ear
  + **H73.01 Bullous myringitis**
    H73.011 Bullous myringitis, right ear
    H73.012 Bullous myringitis, left ear
    H73.013 Bullous myringitis, bilateral
    H73.019 Bullous myringitis, unspecified ear
  + **H73.09 Other acute myringitis**
    H73.091 Other acute myringitis, right ear
    H73.092 Other acute myringitis, left ear
    H73.093 Other acute myringitis, bilateral
    H73.099 Other acute myringitis, unspecified ear

+ **H73.1 Chronic myringitis**
  Chronic tympanitis
  Excludes1: chronic myringitis with otitis media (H65, H66)
  H73.10 Chronic myringitis, unspecified ear
  H73.11 Chronic myringitis, right ear
  H73.12 Chronic myringitis, left ear
  H73.13 Chronic myringitis, bilateral

+ **H73.2 Unspecified myringitis**
  H73.20 Unspecified myringitis, unspecified ear
  H73.21 Unspecified myringitis, right ear
  H73.22 Unspecified myringitis, left ear
  H73.23 Unspecified myringitis, bilateral

+ **H73.8 Other specified disorders of tympanic membrane**
  + **H73.81 Atrophic flaccid tympanic membrane**
    H73.811 Atrophic flaccid tympanic membrane, right ear
    H73.812 Atrophic flaccid tympanic membrane, left ear
    H73.813 Atrophic flaccid tympanic membrane, bilateral
    H73.819 Atrophic flaccid tympanic membrane, unspecified ear
  + **H73.82 Atrophic nonflaccid tympanic membrane**
    H73.821 Atrophic nonflaccid tympanic membrane, right ear
    H73.822 Atrophic nonflaccid tympanic membrane, left ear
    H73.823 Atrophic nonflaccid tympanic membrane, bilateral
    H73.829 Atrophic nonflaccid tympanic membrane, unspecified ear
  + **H73.89 Other specified disorders of tympanic membrane**
    H73.891 Other specified disorders of tympanic membrane, right ear
    H73.892 Other specified disorders of tympanic membrane, left ear
    H73.893 Other specified disorders of tympanic membrane, bilateral
    H73.899 Other specified disorders of tympanic membrane, unspecified ear

+ **H73.9 Unspecified disorder of tympanic membrane**
  H73.90 Unspecified disorder of tympanic membrane, unspecified ear
  H73.91 Unspecified disorder of tympanic membrane, right ear
  H73.92 Unspecified disorder of tympanic membrane, left ear
  H73.93 Unspecified disorder of tympanic membrane, bilateral

H74 Other disorders of middle ear mastoid

Excludes2: mastoiditis (H70.-)

+ **H74.0 Tympanosclerosis**
  H74.01 Tympanosclerosis, right ear
  H74.02 Tympanosclerosis, left ear
  H74.03 Tympanosclerosis, bilateral
  H74.09 Tympanosclerosis, unspecified ear

+ **H74.1 Adhesive middle ear disease**
  Adhesive otitis
  Excludes1: glue ear (H65.3-)
  H74.11 Adhesive right middle ear disease
  H74.12 Adhesive left middle ear disease
  H74.13 Adhesive middle ear disease, bilateral
  H74.19 Adhesive middle ear disease, unspecified ear

+ **H74.2 Discontinuity and dislocation of ear ossicles**
  H74.20 Discontinuity and dislocation of ear ossicles, unspecified ear
  H74.21 Discontinuity and dislocation of right ear ossicles
  H74.22 Discontinuity and dislocation of left ear ossicles
  H74.23 Discontinuity and dislocation of ear ossicles, bilateral

+ **H74.3 Other acquired abnormalities of ear ossicles**
  + **H74.31 Ankylosis of ear ossicles**
    H74.311 Ankylosis of ear ossicles, right ear
    H74.312 Ankylosis of ear ossicles, left ear
    H74.313 Ankylosis of ear ossicles, bilateral
    H74.319 Ankylosis of ear ossicles, unspecified ear
  + **H74.32 Partial loss of ear ossicles**
    H74.321 Partial loss of ear ossicles, right ear
    H74.322 Partial loss of ear ossicles, left ear
    H74.323 Partial loss of ear ossicles, bilateral
    H74.329 Partial loss of ear ossicles, unspecified ear
  + **H74.39 Other acquired abnormalities of ear ossicles**
    H74.391 Other acquired abnormalities of right ear ossicles
    H74.392 Other acquired abnormalities of left ear ossicles
    H74.393 Other acquired abnormalities of ear ossicles, bilateral
    H74.399 Other acquired abnormalities of ear ossicles, unspecified ear

+ **H74.4 Polyp of middle ear**
  H74.40 Polyp of middle ear, unspecified ear
  H74.41 Polyp of right middle ear
  H74.42 Polyp of left middle ear
  H74.43 Polyp of middle ear, bilateral

+ **H74.8 Other specified disorders of middle ear and mastoid**
  + **H74.8X Other specified disorders of middle ear and mastoid**
    H74.8X1 Other specified disorders of right middle ear and mastoid
    H74.8X2 Other specified disorders of left middle ear and mastoid
    H74.8X3 Other specified disorders of middle ear and mastoid, bilateral
    H74.8X9 Other specified disorders of middle ear and mastoid, unspecified ear

+ **H74.9 Unspecified disorder of middle ear and mastoid**
  H74.90 Unspecified disorder of middle ear and mastoid, unspecified ear
  H74.91 Unspecified disorder of right middle ear and mastoid
  H74.92 Unspecified disorder of left middle ear and mastoid
  H74.93 Unspecified disorder of middle ear and mastoid, bilateral

H75 Other disorders of middle ear and mastoid in diseases classified elsewhere

Code first underlying disease

+ **H75.0 Mastoiditis in infectious and parasitic diseases classified elsewhere**
  Excludes1: mastoiditis (in):
  syphilis (A52.77)
  tuberculosis (A18.03)
  H75.00 Mastoiditis in infectious and parasitic diseases classified elsewhere, unspecified ear
  H75.01 Mastoiditis in infectious and parasitic diseases classified elsewhere, right ear
  H75.02 Mastoiditis in infectious and parasitic diseases classified elsewhere, left ear
  H75.03 Mastoiditis in infectious and parasitic diseases classified elsewhere, bilateral

+ **H75.8 Other specified disorders of middle ear and mastoid in diseases classified elsewhere**
  H75.80 Other specified disorders of middle ear and mastoid in diseases classified elsewhere, unspecified ear
  H75.81 Other specified disorders of right middle ear and mastoid in diseases classified elsewhere
  H75.82 Other specified disorders of left middle ear and mastoid in diseases classified elsewhere
  H75.83 Other specified disorders of middle ear and mastoid in diseases classified elsewhere, bilateral

Diseases of inner ear (H80-H83)

H80 Otosclerosis

Includes: Otospongiosis

+ **H80.0 Otosclerosis involving oval window, nonobliterative**
  H80.00 Otosclerosis involving oval window, nonobliterative, unspecified ear

H80.01 Otosclerosis involving oval window, nonobliterative, right ear
H80.02 Otosclerosis involving oval window, nonobliterative, left ear
H80.03 Otosclerosis involving oval window, nonobliterative, bilateral
+ H80.1 Otosclerosis involving oval window, obliterative
H80.10 Otosclerosis involving oval window, obliterative, unspecified ear
H80.11 Otosclerosis involving oval window, obliterative, right ear
H80.12 Otosclerosis involving oval window, obliterative, left ear
H80.13 Otosclerosis involving oval window, obliterative, bilateral
+ H80.2 Cochlear otosclerosis
Otosclerosis involving otic capsule
Otosclerosis involving round window
H80.20 Cochlear otosclerosis, unspecified ear
H80.21 Cochlear otosclerosis, right ear
H80.22 Cochlear otosclerosis, left ear
H80.23 Cochlear otosclerosis, bilateral
+ H80.8 Other otosclerosis
H80.80 Other otosclerosis, unspecified ear
H80.81 Other otosclerosis, right ear
H80.82 Other otosclerosis, left ear
H80.83 Other otosclerosis, bilateral
H80.9 Unspecified otosclerosis
H80.90 Unspecified otosclerosis, unspecified ear
H80.91 Unspecified otosclerosis, right ear
H80.92 Unspecified otosclerosis, left ear
H80.93 Unspecified otosclerosis, bilateral

H81 Disorders of vestibular function
Excludes1: *epidemic vertigo (A88.1)*
vertigo NOS (R42)
+ H81.0 Ménière's disease
Labyrinthine hydrops
Ménière's syndrome or vertigo
H81.01 Ménière's disease, right ear
H81.02 Ménière's disease, left ear
H81.03 Ménière's disease, bilateral
H81.09 Ménière's disease, unspecified ear
+ H81.1 Benign paroxysmal vertigo
H81.10 Benign paroxysmal vertigo, unspecified ear
H81.11 Benign paroxysmal vertigo, right ear
H81.12 Benign paroxysmal vertigo, left ear
H81.13 Benign paroxysmal vertigo, bilateral
+ H81.2 Vestibular neuronitis
H81.20 Vestibular neuronitis, unspecified ear
H81.21 Vestibular neuronitis, right ear
H81.22 Vestibular neuronitis, left ear
H81.23 Vestibular neuronitis, bilateral
+ H81.3 Other peripheral vertigo
+ H81.31 Aural vertigo
H81.311 Aural vertigo, right ear
H81.312 Aural vertigo, left ear
H81.313 Aural vertigo, bilateral
H81.319 Aural vertigo, unspecified ear
+ H81.39 Other peripheral vertigo
Lermoyez' syndrome
Otogenic vertigo
Peripheral vertigo NOS
H81.391 Other peripheral vertigo, right ear
H81.392 Other peripheral vertigo, left ear
H81.393 Other peripheral vertigo, bilateral
H81.399 Other peripheral vertigo, unspecified ear
+ H81.4 Vertigo of central origin
Central positional nystagmus
H81.41 Vertigo of central origin, right ear
H81.42 Vertigo of central origin, left ear
H81.43 Vertigo of central origin, bilateral
H81.49 Vertigo of central origin, unspecified ear
+ H81.8 Other disorders of vestibular function
+ H81.8X Other disorders of vestibular function
H81.8X1 Other disorders of vestibular function, right ear
H81.8X2 Other disorders of vestibular function, left ear
H81.8X3 Other disorders of vestibular function, bilateral
H81.8X9 Other disorders of vestibular function, unspecified ear
+ H81.9 Unspecified disorder of vestibular function
Vertiginous syndrome NOS
H81.90 Unspecified disorder of vestibular function, unspecified ear
H81.91 Unspecified disorder of vestibular function, right
H81.92 Unspecified disorder of vestibular function, left ea
H81.93 Unspecified disorder of vestibular function, bilate

H82 Vertiginous syndromes in diseases classified elsewhere
Code first underlying disease
Excludes1: *epidemic vertigo (A88.1)*
H82.1 Vertiginous syndromes in diseases classified elsewhere, righ
H82.2 Vertiginous syndromes in diseases classified elsewhere, left e
H82.3 Vertiginous syndromes in diseases classified elsewhere, bila
H82.9 Vertiginous syndromes in diseases classified elsewhere, unspecified ear

H83 Other diseases of inner ear
+ H83.0 Labyrinthitis
H83.01 Labyrinthitis, right ear
H83.02 Labyrinthitis, left ear
H83.03 Labyrinthitis, bilateral
H83.09 Labyrinthitis, unspecified ear
+ H83.1 Labyrinthine fistula
H83.11 Labyrinthine fistula, right ear
H83.12 Labyrinthine fistula, left ear
H83.13 Labyrinthine fistula, bilateral
H83.19 Labyrinthine fistula, unspecified ear
+ H83.2 Labyrinthine dysfunction
Labyrinthine hypersensitivity
Labyrinthine hypofunction
Labyrinthine loss of function
+ H83.2X Labyrinthine dysfunction
H83.2X1 Labyrinthine dysfunction, right ear
H83.2X2 Labyrinthine dysfunction, left ear
H83.2X3 Labyrinthine dysfunction, bilateral
H83.2X9 Labyrinthine dysfunction, unspecified ea
+ H83.3 Noise effects on inner ear
Acoustic trauma of inner ear
Noise-induced hearing loss of inner ear
+ H83.3X Noise effects on inner ear
H83.3X1 Noise effects on right inner ear
H83.3X2 Noise effects on left inner ear
H83.3X3 Noise effects on inner ear, bilateral
H83.3X9 Noise effects on inner ear, unspecified ea
+ H83.8 Other specified diseases of inner ear
+ H83.8X Other specified diseases of inner ear
H83.8X1 Other specified diseases of right inner ea
H83.8X2 Other specified diseases of left inner ear
H83.8X3 Other specified diseases of inner ear, bilateral
H83.8X9 Other specified diseases of inner ear, unspecified ear
+ H83.9 Unspecified disease of inner ear
H83.90 Unspecified disease of inner ear, unspecified ear
H83.91 Unspecified disease of right inner ear
H83.92 Unspecified disease of left inner ear
H83.93 Unspecified disease of inner ear, bilateral

Other disorders of ear (H90-H94)

H90 Conductive and sensorineural hearing loss
Excludes1: *deaf nonspeaking NEC (H91.3)*
deafness NOS (H91.9-)
hearing loss NOS (H91.9-)
noise-induced hearing loss (H83.3-)
ototoxic hearing loss (H91.0-)
sudden (idiopathic) hearing loss (H91.2-)
H90.0 Conductive hearing loss, bilateral
+ H90.1 Conductive hearing loss, unilateral with unrestricted hearing the contralateral side
H90.11 Conductive hearing loss, unilateral, right ear, with unrestricted hearing on the contralateral side
H90.12 Conductive hearing loss, unilateral, left ear, with unrestricted hearing on the contralateral side
H90.2 Conductive hearing loss, unspecified
Conductive deafness NOS
H90.3 Sensorineural hearing loss, bilateral
+ H90.4 Sensorineural hearing loss, unilateral with unrestricted heari on the contralateral side

H90.41 Sensorineural hearing loss, unilateral, right ear, with unrestricted hearing on the contralateral side
H90.42 Sensorineural hearing loss, unilateral, left ear, with unrestricted hearing on the contralateral side

H90.5 Unspecified sensorineural hearing loss
Central hearing loss NOS
Congenital deafness NOS
Neural hearing loss NOS
Perceptive hearing loss NOS
Sensorineural deafness NOS
Sensory hearing loss NOS
Excludes1: *abnormal auditory perception (H93.2-)*
psychogenic deafness (F44.6)

H90.6 Mixed conductive and sensorineural hearing loss, bilateral
\+ **H90.7 Mixed conductive and sensorineural hearing loss, unilateral with unrestricted hearing on the contralateral side**
H90.71 Mixed conductive and sensorineural hearing loss, unilateral, right ear, with unrestricted hearing on the contralateral side
H90.72 Mixed conductive and sensorineural hearing loss, unilateral, left ear, with unrestricted hearing on the contralateral side
H90.8 Mixed conductive and sensorineural hearing loss, unspecified

H91 Other and unspecified hearing loss
Excludes1: *abnormal auditory perception (H93.2-)*
hearing loss as classified in H90.-
impacted cerumen (H61.2-)
noise-induced hearing loss (H83.3-)
psychogenic deafness (F44.6)
transient ischemic deafness (H93.01-)

\+ **H91.0 Ototoxic hearing loss**
Code first poisoning due to drug or toxin, if applicable (T36-T65 with fifth or sixth character 1-4 or 6)
Use additional code for adverse effect, if applicable, to identify drug (T36-T50 with fifth or sixth character 5)
H91.01 Ototoxic hearing loss, right ear
H91.02 Ototoxic hearing loss, left ear
H91.03 Ototoxic hearing loss, bilateral
H91.09 Ototoxic hearing loss, unspecified ear
\+ **H91.1 Presbycusis**
Presbyacusia
H91.10 Presbycusis, unspecified ear
H91.11 Presbycusis, right ear
H91.12 Presbycusis, left ear
H91.13 Presbycusis, bilateral
\+ **H91.2 Sudden idiopathic hearing loss**
Sudden hearing loss NOS
H91.20 Sudden idiopathic hearing loss, unspecified ear
H91.21 Sudden idiopathic hearing loss, right ear
H91.22 Sudden idiopathic hearing loss, left ear
H91.23 Sudden idiopathic hearing loss, bilateral
H91.3 Deaf nonspeaking, not elsewhere classified
\+ **H91.8 Other specified hearing loss**
\+ **H91.8X Other specified hearing loss**
H91.8X1 Other specified hearing loss, right ear
H91.8X2 Other specified hearing loss, left ear
H91.8X3 Other specified hearing loss, bilateral
H91.8X9 Other specified hearing loss, unspecified ear
\+ **H91.9 Unspecified hearing loss**
Deafness NOS
High frequency deafness
Low frequency deafness
H91.90 Unspecified hearing loss, unspecified ear
H91.91 Unspecified hearing loss, right ear
H91.92 Unspecified hearing loss, left ear
H91.93 Unspecified hearing loss, bilateral

H92 Otalgia and effusion of ear
\+ **H92.0 Otalgia**
H92.01 Otalgia, right ear
H92.02 Otalgia, left ear
H92.03 Otalgia, bilateral
H92.09 Otalgia, unspecified ear
\+ **H92.1 Otorrhea**
Excludes1: *leakage of cerebrospinal fluid through ear (G96.0)*
H92.10 Otorrhea, unspecified ear
H92.11 Otorrhea, right ear
H92.12 Otorrhea, left ear
H92.13 Otorrhea, bilateral
\+ **H92.2 Otorrhagia**
Excludes1: *traumatic otorrhagia - code to injury*
H92.20 Otorrhagia, unspecified ear
H92.21 Otorrhagia, right ear
H92.22 Otorrhagia, left ear
H92.23 Otorrhagia, bilateral

H93 Other disorders of ear, not elsewhere classified
\+ **H93.0 Degenerative and vascular disorders of ear**
Excludes1: *presbycusis (H91.1)*
\+ **H93.01 Transient ischemic deafness**
H93.011 Transient ischemic deafness, right ear
H93.012 Transient ischemic deafness, left ear
H93.013 Transient ischemic deafness, bilateral
H93.019 Transient ischemic deafness, unspecified ear
\+ **H93.09 Unspecified degenerative and vascular disorders of ear**
H93.091 Unspecified degenerative and vascular disorders of right ear
H93.092 Unspecified degenerative and vascular disorders of left ear
H93.093 Unspecified degenerative and vascular disorders of ear, bilateral
H93.099 Unspecified degenerative and vascular disorders of unspecified ear
\+ **H93.1 Tinnitus**
H93.11 Tinnitus, right ear
H93.12 Tinnitus, left ear
H93.13 Tinnitus, bilateral
H93.19 Tinnitus, unspecified ear
\+ **H93.2 Other abnormal auditory perceptions**
Excludes2: *auditory hallucinations (R44.0)*
\+ **H93.21 Auditory recruitment**
H93.211 Auditory recruitment, right ear
H93.212 Auditory recruitment, left ear
H93.213 Auditory recruitment, bilateral
H93.219 Auditory recruitment, unspecified ear
\+ **H93.22 Diplacusis**
H93.221 Diplacusis, right ear
H93.222 Diplacusis, left ear
H93.223 Diplacusis, bilateral
H93.229 Diplacusis, unspecified ear
\+ **H93.23 Hyperacusis**
H93.231 Hyperacusis, right ear
H93.232 Hyperacusis, left ear
H93.233 Hyperacusis, bilateral
H93.239 Hyperacusis, unspecified ear
\+ **H93.24 Temporary auditory threshold shift**
H93.241 Temporary auditory threshold shift, right ear
H93.242 Temporary auditory threshold shift, left ear
H93.243 Temporary auditory threshold shift, bilateral
H93.249 Temporary auditory threshold shift, unspecified ear
H93.25 Central auditory processing disorder
Congenital auditory imperception
Word deafness
Excludes1: *mixed receptive-expressive language disorder (F80.2)*
\+ **H93.29 Other abnormal auditory perceptions**
H93.291 Other abnormal auditory perceptions, right ear
H93.292 Other abnormal auditory perceptions, left ear
H93.293 Other abnormal auditory perceptions, bilateral
H93.299 Other abnormal auditory perceptions, unspecified ear
\+ **H93.3 Disorders of acoustic nerve**
Disorder of 8th cranial nerve
Excludes1: *acoustic neuroma (D33.3)*
syphilitic acoustic neuritis (A52.15)
\+ **H93.3X Disorders of acoustic nerve**
H93.3X1 Disorders of right acoustic nerve
H93.3X2 Disorders of left acoustic nerve
H93.3X3 Disorders of bilateral acoustic nerves
H93.3X9 Disorders of unspecified acoustic nerve
\+ **H93.8 Other specified disorders of ear**
\+ **H93.8X Other specified disorders of ear**
H93.8X1 Other specified disorders of right ear
H93.8X2 Other specified disorders of left ear
H93.8X3 Other specified disorders of ear, bilateral
H93.8X9 Other specified disorders of ear, unspecified ear

+ H93.9 Unspecified disorder of ear
- **H93.90 Unspecified disorder of ear, unspecified ear**
- **H93.91 Unspecified disorder of right ear**
- **H93.92 Unspecified disorder of left ear**
- **H93.93 Unspecified disorder of ear, bilateral**

H94 Other disorders of ear in diseases classified elsewhere

+ H94.0 Acoustic neuritis in infectious and parasitic diseases classified elsewhere
Code first underlying disease, such as:
parasitic disease (B65-B89)
Excludes1: *acoustic neuritis (in):*
herpes zoster (B02.29)
syphilis (A52.15)
- **H94.00 Acoustic neuritis in infectious and parasitic diseases classified elsewhere, unspecified ear**
- **H94.01 Acoustic neuritis in infectious and parasitic diseases classified elsewhere, right ear**
- **H94.02 Acoustic neuritis in infectious and parasitic diseases classified elsewhere, left ear**
- **H94.03 Acoustic neuritis in infectious and parasitic diseases classified elsewhere, bilateral**

+ H94.8 Other specified disorders of ear in diseases classified elsewhere
Code first underlying disease, such as:
congenital syphilis (A50.0)
Excludes1: *aural myiasis (B87.4)*
syphilitic labyrinthitis (A52.79)
- **H94.80 Other specified disorders of ear in diseases classified elsewhere, unspecified ear**
- **H94.81 Other specified disorders of right ear in diseases classified elsewhere**
- **H94.82 Other specified disorders of left ear in diseases classified elsewhere**
- **H94.83 Other specified disorders of ear in diseases classified elsewhere, bilateral**

Intraoperative and postprocedural complications and disorders of ear and mastoid process, not elsewhere classified (H95)

H95 Intraoperative and postprocedural complications and disorders of ear and mastoid process, not elsewhere classified

+ H95.0 Recurrent cholesteatoma of postmastoidectomy cavity
- **H95.00 Recurrent cholesteatoma of postmastoidectomy cavity, unspecified ear**
- **H95.01 Recurrent cholesteatoma of postmastoidectomy cavity, right ear**
- **H95.02 Recurrent cholesteatoma of postmastoidectomy cavity, left ear**
- **H95.03 Recurrent cholesteatoma of postmastoidectomy cavity, bilateral ears**

+ H95.1 Other disorders of ear and mastoid process following mastoidectomy

+ H95.11 Chronic inflammation of postmastoidectomy cavity
- **H95.111 Chronic inflammation of postmastoidectomy cavity, right ear**
- **H95.112 Chronic inflammation of postmastoidectomy cavity, left ear**
- **H95.113 Chronic inflammation of postmastoidectomy cavity, bilateral ears**
- **H95.119 Chronic inflammation of postmastoidectomy cavity, unspecified ear**

+ H95.12 Granulation of postmastoidectomy cavity
- **H95.121 Granulation of postmastoidectomy cavity, right ear**
- **H95.122 Granulation of postmastoidectomy cavity, left ear**
- **H95.123 Granulation of postmastoidectomy cavity, bilateral ears**
- **H95.129 Granulation of postmastoidectomy cavity, unspecified ear**

+ H95.13 Mucosal cyst of postmastoidectomy cavity
- **H95.131 Mucosal cyst of postmastoidectomy cavity, right ear**
- **H95.132 Mucosal cyst of postmastoidectomy cavity, left ear**
- **H95.133 Mucosal cyst of postmastoidectomy cavit[y,] bilateral ears**
- **H95.139 Mucosal cyst of postmastoidectomy cavit[y,] unspecified ear**

+ H95.19 Other disorders following mastoidectomy
- **H95.191 Other disorders following mastoidectomy[,] right ear**
- **H95.192 Other disorders following mastoidectomy[,] left ear**
- **H95.193 Other disorders following mastoidectomy[,] bilateral ears**
- **H95.199 Other disorders following mastoidectomy[,] unspecified ear**

+ H95.2 Intraoperative hemorrhage and hematoma of ear and masto[id] process complicating a procedure
Excludes1: *intraoperative hemorrhage and hematoma of ear and mastoid process due to accidental puncture o[r] laceration during a procedure (H95.3-)*

CC **H95.21 Intraoperative hemorrhage and hematoma of ear a[nd] mastoid process complicating a procedure on the e[ar] and mastoid process**
CC Exclusion see Appendix A PDX collection 0642

CC **H95.22 Intraoperative hemorrhage and hematoma of ear a[nd] mastoid process complicating other procedure**
CC Exclusion see Appendix A PDX collection 0642

+ H95.3 Accidental puncture and laceration of ear and mastoid proce[ss] during a procedure

CC **H95.31 Accidental puncture and laceration of the ear and mastoid process during a procedure on the ear and mastoid process**
CC Exclusion see Appendix A PDX collection 0509

CC **H95.32 Accidental puncture and laceration of the ear and mastoid process during other procedure**
CC Exclusion see Appendix A PDX collection 0509

+ H95.4 Postprocedural hemorrhage and hematoma of ear and masto[id] process following a procedure

CC **H95.41 Postprocedural hemorrhage and hematoma of ear a[nd] mastoid process following a procedure on the ear a[nd] mastoid process**
CC Exclusion see Appendix A PDX collection 0642

CC **H95.42 Postprocedural hemorrhage and hematoma of ear a[nd] mastoid process following other procedure**
CC Exclusion see Appendix A PDX collection 0642

+ H95.8 Other intraoperative and postprocedural complications and disorders of the ear and mastoid process, not elsewhere classified
Excludes2: *postprocedural complications and disorders following mastoidectomy (H95.0-, H95.1-)*

+ H95.81 Postprocedural stenosis of external ear canal

CC **H95.811 Postprocedural stenosis of right external e[ar] canal**
CC Exclusion see Appendix A PDX collection 0643

CC **H95.812 Postprocedural stenosis of left external ea[r] canal**
CC Exclusion see Appendix A PDX collection 0643

CC **H95.813 Postprocedural stenosis of external ear canal, bilateral**
CC Exclusion see Appendix A PDX collection 0643

CC **H95.819 Postprocedural stenosis of unspecified external ear canal**
CC Exclusion see Appendix A PDX collection 0643

CC **H95.88 Other intraoperative complications and disorders of the ear and mastoid process, not elsewhere classified**
Use additional code, if applicable, to further specify disorder
CC Exclusion see Appendix A PDX collection 0643

CC **H95.89 Other postprocedural complications and disorders of the ear and mastoid process, not elsewhere classified**
Use additional code, if applicable, to further specify disorder
CC Exclusion see Appendix A PDX collection 0643

des2: *certain conditions originating in the perinatal period (P04-P96)*
certain infectious and parasitic diseases (A00-B99)
complications of pregnancy, childbirth and the puerperium (O00-O9A)
congenital malformations, deformations, and chromosomal abnormalities (Q00-Q99)
endocrine, nutritional and metabolic diseases (E00-E88)
injury, poisoning and certain other consequences of external causes (S00-T88)
neoplasms (C00-D49)
symptoms, signs and abnormal clinical and laboratory findings, not elsewhere classified (R00-R94)
systemic connective tissue disorders (M30-M36)
transient cerebral ischemic attacks and related syndromes (G45.-)

chapter contains the following category blocks:

)0-I02 Acute rheumatic fever
)5-I09 Chronic rheumatic heart diseases
10-I15 Hypertensive diseases
20-I25 Ischemic heart diseases
26-I28 Pulmonary heart disease and diseases of pulmonary circulation
30-I52 Other forms of heart disease
50-I69 Cerebrovascular diseases
70-I79 Diseases of arteries, arterioles and capillaries
80-I89 Diseases of veins, lymphatic vessels and lymph nodes, not elsewhere classified
95-I99 Other and unspecified disorders of the circulatory system

:hapter-Specific Coding Guidelines

ldition to general coding guidelines, there are guidelines for specific diagnoses or conditions in the classification. Unless otherwise indicated, these guidelines y to all health care settings. Please refer to Section II for guidelines on the :tion of principal diagnosis.

:hapter 9: Diseases of the Circulatory System (I00-I99)

. Hypertension

1) Hypertension with Heart Disease

Heart conditions classified to I50.- or I51.4-I51.9, are assigned to, a code from category I11, Hypertensive heart disease, when a causal relationship is stated (due to hypertension) or implied (hypertensive). Use an additional code from category I50, Heart failure, to identify the type of heart failure in those patients with heart failure.

The same heart conditions (I50.-, I51.4-I51.9) with hypertension, but without a stated causal relationship, are coded separately. Sequence according to the circumstances of the admission/encounter.

2) Hypertensive Chronic Kidney Disease

Assign codes from category I12, Hypertensive chronic kidney disease, when both hypertension and a condition classifiable to category N18, Chronic kidney disease (CKD), are present. Unlike hypertension with heart disease, ICD-10-CM presumes a cause-and-effect relationship and classifies chronic kidney disease with hypertension as hypertensive chronic kidney disease.

The appropriate code from category N18 should be used as a secondary code with a code from category I12 to identify the stage of chronic kidney disease.

See Section I.C.14. Chronic kidney disease.

If a patient has hypertensive chronic kidney disease and acute renal failure, an additional code for the acute renal failure is required.

3) Hypertensive Heart and Chronic Kidney Disease

Assign codes from combination category I13, Hypertensive heart and chronic kidney disease, when both hypertensive kidney disease and hypertensive heart disease are stated in the diagnosis. Assume a relationship between the hypertension and the chronic kidney disease, whether or not the condition is so designated. If heart failure is present, assign an additional code from category I50 to identify the type of heart failure.

The appropriate code from category N18, Chronic kidney disease, should be used as a secondary code with a code from category I13 to identify the stage of chronic kidney disease.

See Section I.C.14. Chronic kidney disease.

The codes in category I13, Hypertensive heart and chronic kidney disease, are combination codes that include hypertension, heart disease and chronic kidney disease. The Includes note at I13 specifies that the conditions included at I11 and I12 are included together in I13. If a patient has hypertension, heart disease and chronic kidney disease then a code from I13 should be used, not individual codes for hypertension, heart disease and chronic kidney disease, or codes from I11 or I12.

For patients with both acute renal failure and chronic kidney disease an additional code for acute renal failure is required.

4) Hypertensive Cerebrovascular Disease

For hypertensive cerebrovascular disease, first assign the appropriate code from categories I60-I69, followed by the appropriate hypertension code.

5) Hypertensive Retinopathy

Subcategory H35.0, Background retinopathy and retinal vascular changes, should be used with a code from category I10 – I15, Hypertensive disease to include the systemic hypertension. The sequencing is based on the reason for the encounter.

6) Hypertension, Secondary

Secondary hypertension is due to an underlying condition. Two codes are required: one to identify the underlying etiology and one from category I15 to identify the hypertension. Sequencing of codes is determined by the reason for admission/encounter.

7) Hypertension, Transient

Assign code R03.0, Elevated blood pressure reading without diagnosis of hypertension, unless patient has an established diagnosis of hypertension. Assign code O13.-, Gestational [pregnancy-induced] hypertension without significant proteinuria, or O14.-, Pre-eclampsia, for transient hypertension of pregnancy.

8) Hypertension, Controlled

This diagnostic statement usually refers to an existing state of hypertension under control by therapy. Assign the appropriate code from categories I10-I15, Hypertensive diseases.

9) Hypertension, Uncontrolled

Uncontrolled hypertension may refer to untreated hypertension or hypertension not responding to current therapeutic regimen. In either case, assign the appropriate code from categories I10-I15, Hypertensive diseases.

b. Atherosclerotic Coronary Artery Disease and Angina

ICD-10-CM has combination codes for atherosclerotic heart disease with angina pectoris. The subcategories for these codes are I25.11, Atherosclerotic heart disease of native coronary artery with angina pectoris and I25.7, Atherosclerosis of coronary artery bypass graft(s) and coronary artery of transplanted heart with angina pectoris.

When using one of these combination codes it is not necessary to use an additional code for angina pectoris. A causal relationship can be assumed in a patient with both atherosclerosis and angina pectoris, unless the documentation indicates the angina is due to something other than the atherosclerosis.

If a patient with coronary artery disease is admitted due to an acute myocardial infarction (AMI), the AMI should be sequenced before the coronary artery disease.

See Section I.C.9. Acute myocardial infarction (AMI)

c. Intraoperative and Postprocedural Cerebrovascular Accident

Medical record documentation should clearly specify the cause- and-effect relationship between the medical intervention and the cerebrovascular accident in order to assign a code for intraoperative or postprocedural cerebrovascular accident.

Proper code assignment depends on whether it was an infarction or hemorrhage and whether it occurred intraoperatively or postoperatively. If it was a cerebral hemorrhage, code assignment depends on the type of procedure performed.

d. Sequelae of Cerebrovascular Disease

1) Category I69, Sequelae of Cerebrovascular disease

Category I69 is used to indicate conditions classifiable to categories I60-I67 as the causes of sequela (neurologic deficits), themselves classified elsewhere. These "late effects" include neurologic deficits that persist after initial onset of conditions classifiable to categories I60-I67. The neurologic deficits caused by cerebrovascular disease may be present from the onset or may arise at any time after the onset of the condition classifiable to categories I60-I67.

Codes from category I69, Sequelae of cerebrovascular disease, that specify hemiplegia, hemiparesis and monoplegia identify whether the dominant or nondominant side is affected. Should the affected side be documented, but not specified as dominant or nondominant, and the classification system does not indicate a default, code selection is as follows:

- For ambidextrous patients, the default should be dominant.
- If the left side is affected, the default is non-dominant.
- If the right side is affected, the default is dominant.

2) Codes from category I69 with codes from I60-I67

Codes from category I69 may be assigned on a health care record with codes from I60-I67, if the patient has a current cerebrovascular disease and deficits from an old cerebrovascular disease.

3) Codes from category I69 and Personal history of transient ischemic attack (TIA) and cerebral infarction (Z86.73)

Codes from category I69 should not be assigned if the patient does not have neurologic deficits.

See Section I.C.21. 4. History (of) for use of personal history codes

1) **ST elevation myocardial infarction (STEMI) and non ST elevation myocardial infarction (NSTEMI)**

The ICD-10-CM codes for acute myocardial infarction (AMI) identify the site, such as anterolateral wall or true posterior wall. Subcategories I21.0-I21.2 and code I21.3 are used for ST elevation myocardial infarction (STEMI). Code I21.4, Non-ST elevation (NSTEMI) myocardial infarction, is used for non ST elevation myocardial infarction (NSTEMI) and nontransmural MIs.

If NSTEMI evolves to STEMI, assign the STEMI code. If STEMI converts to NSTEMI due to thrombolytic therapy, it is still coded as STEMI.

For encounters occurring while the myocardial infarction is equal to, or less than, four weeks old, including transfers to another acute setting or a postacute setting, and the patient requires continued care for the myocardial infarction, codes from category I21 may continue to be reported. For encounters after the 4 week time frame and the patient is still receiving care related to the myocardial infarction, the appropriate aftercare code should be assigned, rather than a code from category I21. For old or healed myocardial infarctions not requiring further care, code I25.2, Old myocardial infarction, may be assigned.

2) **Acute myocardial infarction, unspecified**

Code I21.3, ST elevation (STEMI) myocardial infarction of unspecifie is the default for unspecified acute myocardial infarction. If only STE transmural MI without the site is documented, assign code I21.3.

3) **AMI documented as nontransmural or subendocardial but site provid**

If an AMI is documented as nontransmural or subendocardial, but the provided, it is still coded as a subendocardial AMI.

See Section I.C.21.3 for information on coding status post administrat tPA in a different facility within the last 24 hours.

4) **Subsequent acute myocardial infarction**

A code from category I22, Subsequent ST elevation (STEMI) and no elevation (NSTEMI) myocardial infarction, is to be used when a patient has suffered an AMI has a new AMI within the 4 week time frame of the i AMI. A code from category I22 must be used in conjunction with a from category I21. The sequencing of the I22 and I21 codes depends o circumstances of the encounter.

Arteries

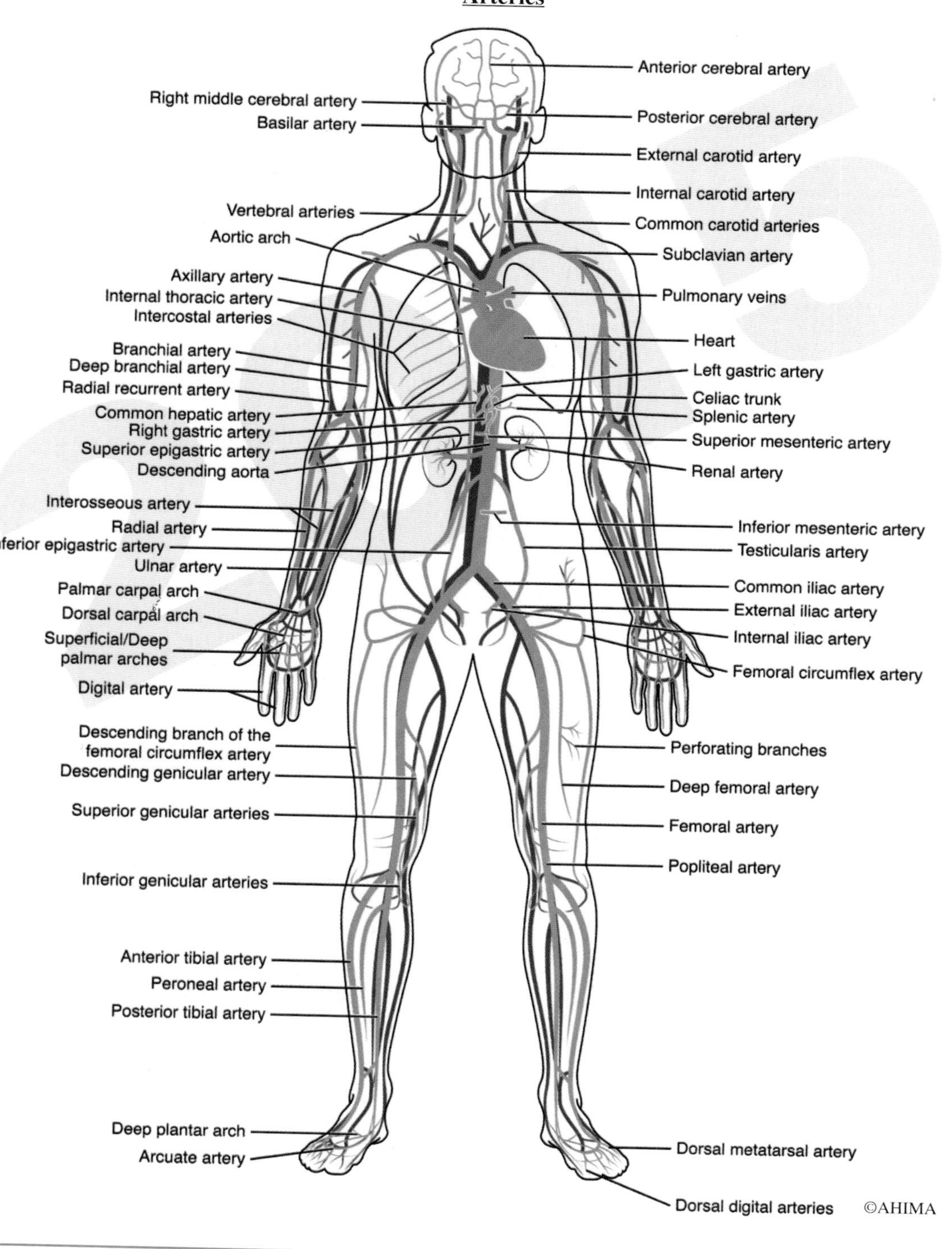

Veins

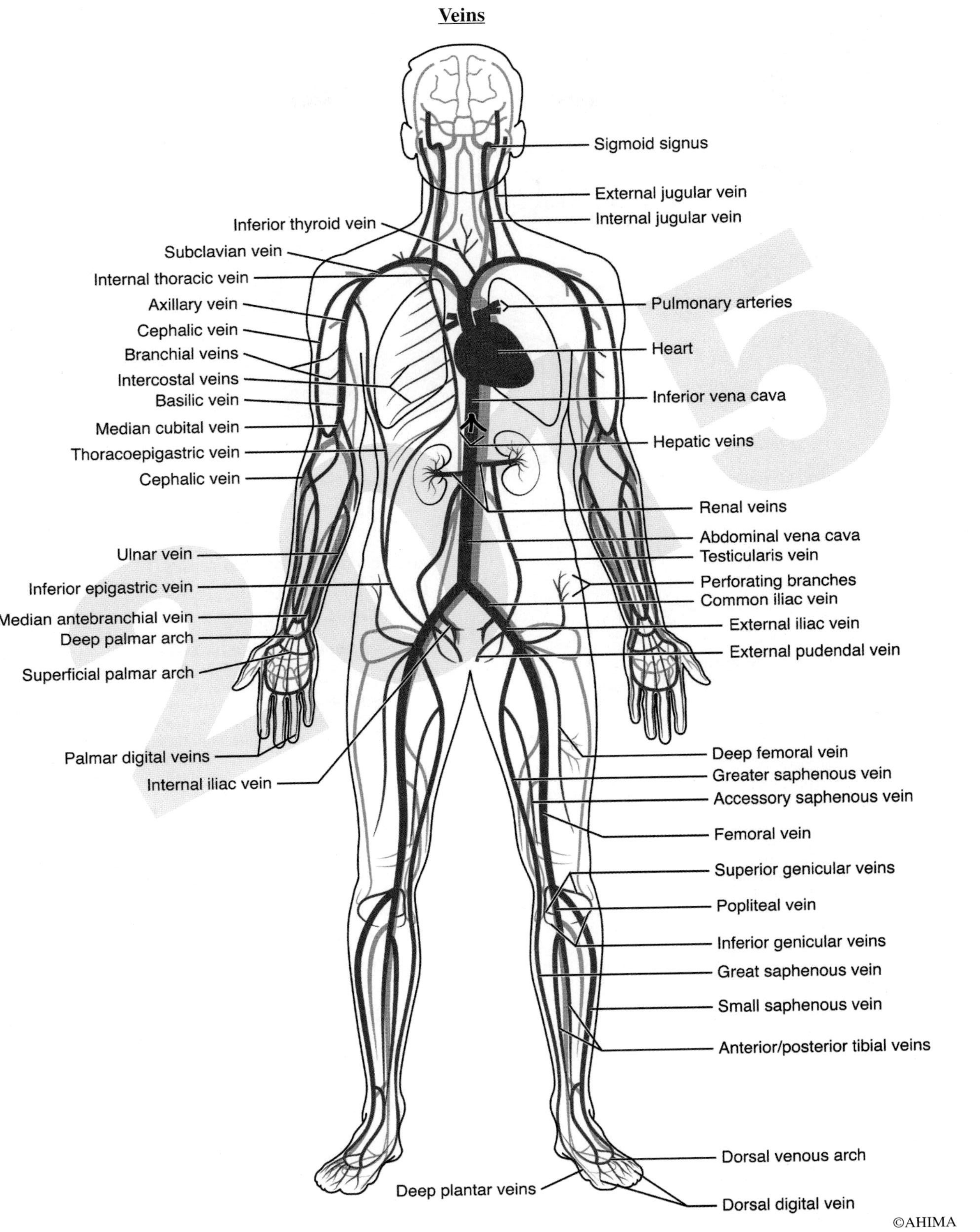

Sigmoid signus
External jugular vein
Internal jugular vein
Inferior thyroid vein
Subclavian vein
Internal thoracic vein
Axillary vein
Cephalic vein
Branchial veins
Intercostal veins
Basilic vein
Median cubital vein
Thoracoepigastric vein
Cephalic vein
Pulmonary arteries
Heart
Inferior vena cava
Hepatic veins
Renal veins
Abdominal vena cava
Testicularis vein
Perforating branches
Common iliac vein
External iliac vein
External pudendal vein
Ulnar vein
Inferior epigastric vein
Median antebranchial vein
Deep palmar arch
Superficial palmar arch
Palmar digital veins
Internal iliac vein
Deep femoral vein
Greater saphenous vein
Accessory saphenous vein
Femoral vein
Superior genicular veins
Popliteal vein
Inferior genicular veins
Great saphenous vein
Small saphenous vein
Anterior/posterior tibial veins
Dorsal venous arch
Deep plantar veins
Dorsal digital vein

Heart

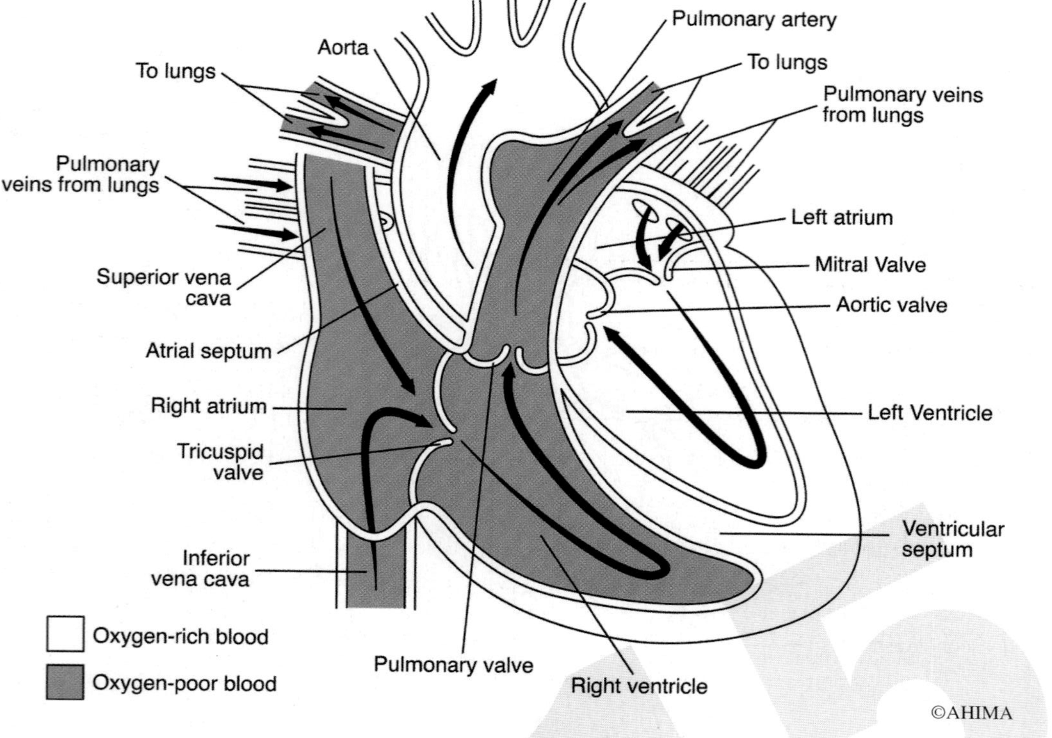

Acute rheumatic fever (I00-I02)

I00 Rheumatic fever without heart involvement

Includes: arthritis, rheumatic, acute or subacute
Excludes1: *rheumatic fever with heart involvement (I01.0-I01.9)*
Valid 3-character code, no further characters required

I01 Rheumatic fever with heart involvement

Excludes1: *chronic diseases of rheumatic origin (I05-I09) unless rheumatic fever is also present or there is evidence of reactivation or activity of the rheumatic process.*

CC **I01.0 Acute rheumatic pericarditis**
Any condition in I00 with pericarditis
Rheumatic pericarditis (acute)
Excludes1: *acute pericarditis not specified as rheumatic (I30.-)*
CC Exclusion see Appendix A PDX collection 0188

CC **I01.1 Acute rheumatic endocarditis**
Any condition in I00 with endocarditis or valvulitis
Acute rheumatic valvulitis
CC Exclusion see Appendix A PDX collection 0644

CC **I01.2 Acute rheumatic myocarditis**
Any condition in I00 with myocarditis
CC Exclusion see Appendix A PDX collection 0186

CC **I01.8 Other acute rheumatic heart disease**
Any condition in I00 with other or multiple types of heart involvement
Acute rheumatic pancarditis
CC Exclusion see Appendix A PDX collection 0645

CC **I01.9 Acute rheumatic heart disease, unspecified**
Any condition in I00 with unspecified type of heart involvement
Rheumatic carditis, acute
Rheumatic heart disease, active or acute
CC Exclusion see Appendix A PDX collection 0646

I02 Rheumatic chorea

Includes: Sydenham's chorea
Excludes1: *chorea NOS (G25.5)*
Huntington's chorea (G10)

CC **I02.0 Rheumatic chorea with heart involvement**
Chorea NOS with heart involvement
Rheumatic chorea with heart involvement of any type classifiable under I01.-
CC Exclusion see Appendix A PDX collection 0645

CC **I02.9 Rheumatic chorea without heart involvement**
Rheumatic chorea NOS
CC Exclusion see Appendix A PDX collection 0646

Chronic rheumatic heart diseases (I05-I09)

I05 Rheumatic mitral valve diseases

Includes: conditions classifiable to both I05.0 and I05.2-I05.9, whet[h]er specified as rheumatic or not
Excludes1: *mitral valve disease specified as nonrheumatic (I34.-)*
mitral valve disease with aortic and/or tricuspid valve involvement (I08.-)

I05.0 Rheumatic mitral stenosis
Mitral (valve) obstruction (rheumatic)

I05.1 Rheumatic mitral insufficiency
Rheumatic mitral incompetence
Rheumatic mitral regurgitation
Excludes1: *mitral insufficiency not specified as rheumatic (I34.0)*

I05.2 Rheumatic mitral stenosis with insufficiency
Rheumatic mitral stenosis with incompetence or regurgitation

I05.8 Other rheumatic mitral valve diseases
Rheumatic mitral (valve) failure

I05.9 Rheumatic mitral valve disease, unspecified
Rheumatic mitral (valve) disorder (chronic) NOS

I06 Rheumatic aortic valve diseases

Excludes1: *aortic valve disease not specified as rheumatic (I35.-)*
aortic valve disease with mitral and/or tricuspid valve involvement (I08.-)

I06.0 Rheumatic aortic stenosis
Rheumatic aortic (valve) obstruction

I06.1 Rheumatic aortic insufficiency
Rheumatic aortic incompetence
Rheumatic aortic regurgitation

I06.2 Rheumatic aortic stenosis with insufficiency
Rheumatic aortic stenosis with incompetence or regurgitation

I06.8 Other rheumatic aortic valve diseases

I06.9 Rheumatic aortic valve disease, unspecified
Rheumatic aortic (valve) disease NOS

I07 Rheumatic tricuspid valve diseases

Includes: rheumatic tricuspid valve diseases specified as rheumatic o[r] unspecified
Excludes1: *tricuspid valve disease specified as nonrheumatic (I36.-)*
tricuspid valve disease with aortic and/or mitral valve involvement (I08.-)

I07.0 Rheumatic tricuspid stenosis
Tricuspid (valve) stenosis (rheumatic)

I07.1 Rheumatic tricuspid insufficiency
Tricuspid (valve) insufficiency (rheumatic)
I07.2 Rheumatic tricuspid stenosis and insufficiency
I07.8 Other rheumatic tricuspid valve diseases
I07.9 Rheumatic tricuspid valve disease, unspecified
Rheumatic tricuspid valve disorder NOS

I08 Multiple valve diseases
Includes: multiple valve diseases specified as rheumatic or unspecified
Excludes1: *endocarditis, valve unspecified (I38)*
multiple valve disease specified a nonrheumatic (I34.-, I35.-, I36.-, I37.-, I38.-, Q22.-, Q23.-, Q24.8-)
rheumatic valve disease NOS (I09.1)
I08.0 Rheumatic disorders of both mitral and aortic valves
Involvement of both mitral and aortic valves specified as rheumatic or unspecified
I08.1 Rheumatic disorders of both mitral and tricuspid valves
I08.2 Rheumatic disorders of both aortic and tricuspid valves
I08.3 Combined rheumatic disorders of mitral, aortic and tricuspid valves
I08.8 Other rheumatic multiple valve diseases
I08.9 Rheumatic multiple valve disease, unspecified

I09 Other rheumatic heart diseases
CC **I09.0 Rheumatic myocarditis**
Excludes1: *myocarditis not specified as rheumatic (I51.4)*
CC Exclusion see Appendix A PDX collection 0647
I09.1 Rheumatic diseases of endocardium, valve unspecified
Rheumatic endocarditis (chronic)
Rheumatic valvulitis (chronic)
Excludes1: *endocarditis, valve unspecified (I38)*
CC **I09.2 Chronic rheumatic pericarditis**
Adherent pericardium, rheumatic
Chronic rheumatic mediastinopericarditis
Chronic rheumatic myopericarditis
Excludes1: *chronic pericarditis not specified as rheumatic (I31.-)*
CC Exclusion see Appendix A PDX collection 0188
+ **I09.8 Other specified rheumatic heart diseases**
CC **I09.81 Rheumatic heart failure**
Use additional code to identify type of heart failure (I50.-)
CC Exclusion see Appendix A PDX collection 0648
I09.89 Other specified rheumatic heart diseases
Rheumatic disease of pulmonary valve
I09.9 Rheumatic heart disease, unspecified
Rheumatic carditis
Excludes1: *rheumatoid carditis (M05.31)*

pertensive diseases (I10-I15)

additional code to identify:
posure to environmental tobacco smoke (Z77.22)
story of tobacco use (Z87.891)
cupational exposure to environmental tobacco smoke (Z57.31)
bacco dependence (F17.-)
bacco use (Z72.0)

udes1: *hypertensive disease complicating pregnancy, childbirth and the puerperium (O10-O11, O13-O16)*
neonatal hypertension (P29.2)
primary pulmonary hypertension (I27.0)
w coding guidelines C.9.a.5, C.9.a.8 and C.9.a.9

I10 Essential (primary) hypertension
Includes: high blood pressure
hypertension (arterial) (benign) (essential) (malignant) (primary) (systemic)
Excludes1: *hypertensive disease complicating pregnancy, childbirth and the puerperium (O10-O11, O13-O16)*
Excludes2: *essential (primary) hypertension involving vessels of brain (I60-I69)*
essential (primary) hypertension involving vessels of eye (H35.0-)
Valid 3-character code, no further characters required
AHA CC: 4Q, 2013, 128

I11 Hypertensive heart disease
Includes: any condition in I51.4-I51.9 due to hypertension
Review coding guidelines C.9.a.1 and C.9.a.3
I11.0 Hypertensive heart disease with heart failure
Hypertensive heart failure
Use additional code to identify type of heart failure (I50.-)
I11.9 Hypertensive heart disease without heart failure
Hypertensive heart disease NOS

I12 Hypertensive chronic kidney disease
Includes: any condition in N18 and N26 - due to hypertension
arteriosclerosis of kidney
arteriosclerotic nephritis (chronic) (interstitial)
hypertensive nephropathy
nephrosclerosis
Excludes1: *hypertension due to kidney disease (I15.0, I15.1)*
renovascular hypertension (I15.0)
secondary hypertension (I15.-)
Excludes2: *acute kidney failure (N17.-)*
Review coding guidelines C.9.a.2 and C.9.a.3
CC **I12.0 Hypertensive chronic kidney disease with stage 5 chronic kidney disease or end stage renal disease**
Use additional code to identify the stage of chronic kidney disease (N18.5, N18.6)
CC Exclusion see Appendix A PDX collection 0649
I12.9 Hypertensive chronic kidney disease with stage 1 through stage 4 chronic kidney disease, or unspecified chronic kidney disease
Hypertensive chronic kidney disease NOS
Hypertensive renal disease NOS
Use additional code to identify the stage of chronic kidney disease (N18.1-N18.4, N18.9)

I13 Hypertensive heart and chronic kidney disease
Includes: any condition in I11.- with any condition in I12.-
cardiorenal disease
cardiovascular renal disease
Review coding guideline C.9.a.3
CC **I13.0 Hypertensive heart and chronic kidney disease with heart failure and stage 1 through stage 4 chronic kidney disease, or unspecified chronic kidney disease**
Use additional code to identify type of heart failure (I50.-)
Use additional code to identify stage of chronic kidney disease (N18.1-N18.4, N18.9)
CC Exclusion see Appendix A PDX collection 0650
+ **I13.1 Hypertensive heart and chronic kidney disease without heart failure**
I13.10 Hypertensive heart and chronic kidney disease without heart failure, with stage 1 through stage 4 chronic kidney disease, or unspecified chronic kidney disease
Hypertensive heart disease and hypertensive chronic kidney disease NOS
Use additional code to identify the stage of chronic kidney disease (N18.1-N18.4, N18.9)
CC **I13.11 Hypertensive heart and chronic kidney disease without heart failure, with stage 5 chronic kidney disease, or end stage renal disease**
Use additional code to identify the stage of chronic kidney disease (N18.5, N18.6)
CC Exclusion see Appendix A PDX collection 0650
CC **I13.2 Hypertensive heart and chronic kidney disease with heart failure and with stage 5 chronic kidney disease, or end stage renal disease**
Use additional code to identify type of heart failure (I50.-)
Use additional code to identify the stage of chronic kidney disease (N18.5, N18.6)
CC Exclusion see Appendix A PDX collection 0650

I15 Secondary hypertension
Code also underlying condition
Excludes1: *postprocedural hypertension (I97.3)*
Excludes2: *secondary hypertension involving vessels of brain (I60-I69)*
secondary hypertension involving vessels of eye (H35.0-)
Review coding guideline C.9.a.6
I15.0 Renovascular hypertension
I15.1 Hypertension secondary to other renal disorders
I15.2 Hypertension secondary to endocrine disorders
I15.8 Other secondary hypertension
I15.9 Secondary hypertension, unspecified

Ischemic heart diseases (I20-I25)

Use additional code to identify presence of hypertension (I10-I15)

I20 Angina pectoris

Use additional code to identify:
exposure to environmental tobacco smoke (Z77.22)
history of tobacco use (Z87.891)
occupational exposure to environmental tobacco smoke (Z57.31)
tobacco dependence (F17.-)
tobacco use (Z72.0)

Excludes1: *angina pectoris with atherosclerotic heart disease of native coronary arteries (I25.1-)*
atherosclerosis of coronary artery bypass graft(s) and coronary artery of transplanted heart with angina pectoris (I25.7-)
postinfarction angina (I23.7)

CC **I20.0 Unstable angina**
Accelerated angina
Crescendo angina
De novo effort angina
Intermediate coronary syndrome
Preinfarction syndrome
Worsening effort angina
CC Exclusion see Appendix A PDX collection 0651

CC **I20.1 Angina pectoris with documented spasm**
Angiospastic angina
Prinzmetal angina
Spasm-induced angina
Variant angina
CC Exclusion see Appendix A PDX collection 0652

I20.8 Other forms of angina pectoris
Angina equivalent
Angina of effort
Coronary slow flow syndrome
Stenocardia
Use additional code(s) for symptoms associated with angina equivalent

I20.9 Angina pectoris, unspecified
Angina NOS
Anginal syndrome
Cardiac angina
Ischemic chest pain

I21 ST elevation (STEMI) and non-ST elevation (NSTEMI) myocardial infarction

Includes: cardiac infarction
coronary (artery) embolism
coronary (artery) occlusion
coronary (artery) rupture
coronary (artery) thrombosis
infarction of heart, myocardium, or ventricle
myocardial infarction specified as acute or with a stated duration of 4 weeks (28 days) or less from onset

Use additional code, if applicable, to identify:
exposure to environmental tobacco smoke (Z77.22)
history of tobacco use (Z87.891)
occupational exposure to environmental tobacco smoke (Z57.31)
status post administration of tPA (rtPA) in a different facility within the last 24 hours prior to admission to current facility (Z92.82)
tobacco dependence (F17.-)
tobacco use (Z72.0)

Excludes2: *old myocardial infarction (I25.2)*
postmyocardial infarction syndrome (I24.1)
subsequent myocardial infarction (I22.-)
AHA CC: 1Q, 2013, 25

+ **I21.0 ST elevation (STEMI) myocardial infarction of anterior wall**
Review coding guideline C.9.e.1

MCC **I21.01 ST elevation (STEMI) myocardial infarction involving left main coronary artery**
MCC Exclusion see Appendix A PDX collection 0653

MCC **I21.02 ST elevation (STEMI) myocardial infarction involving left anterior descending coronary artery**
ST elevation (STEMI) myocardial infarction involving diagonal coronary artery
MCC Exclusion see Appendix A PDX collection 0653
AHA CC: 1Q, 2013, 25-26

MCC **I21.09 ST elevation (STEMI) myocardial infarction involvi[ng] other coronary artery of anterior wall**
Acute transmural myocardial infarction of anterior wall
Anteroapical transmural (Q wave) infarction (acute)
Anterolateral transmural (Q wave) infarction (acute)
Anteroseptal transmural (Q wave) infarction (acute)
Transmural (Q wave) infarction (acute) (of) anterior (wall) NOS
MCC Exclusion see Appendix A PDX collection 0653
AHA CC: 4Q, 2012, 102-104

+ **I21.1 ST elevation (STEMI) myocardial infarction of inferior wall**
Review coding guideline C.9.e.1

MCC **I21.11 ST elevation (STEMI) myocardial infarction involvi[ng] right coronary artery**
Inferoposterior transmural (Q wave) infarction (acute[)]
MCC Exclusion see Appendix A PDX collection 0653

MCC **I21.19 ST elevation (STEMI) myocardial infarction involvi[ng] other coronary artery of inferior wall**
Acute transmural myocardial infarction of inferior wa[ll]
Inferolateral transmural (Q wave) infarction (acute)
Transmural (Q wave) infarction (acute) (of) diaphragmatic wall
Transmural (Q wave) infarction (acute) (of) inferior (wall) NOS

Excludes2: *ST elevation (STEMI) myocardial infarc[tion] involving left circumflex coronary arter[y] (I21.21)*

MCC Exclusion see Appendix A PDX collection 0653
AHA CC: 4Q, 2012, 97

+ **I21.2 ST elevation (STEMI) myocardial infarction of other sites**
Review coding guideline C.9.e.1

MCC **I21.21 ST elevation (STEMI) myocardial infarction involv[ing] left circumflex coronary artery**
ST elevation (STEMI) myocardial infarction involvin[g] oblique marginal coronary artery
MCC Exclusion see Appendix A PDX collection 0653

MCC **I21.29 ST elevation (STEMI) myocardial infarction involv[ing] other sites**
Acute transmural myocardial infarction of other sites
Apical-lateral transmural (Q wave) infarction (acute)
Basal-lateral transmural (Q wave) infarction (acute)
High lateral transmural (Q wave) infarction (acute)
Lateral (wall) NOS transmural (Q wave) infarction (acute)
Posterior (true) transmural (Q wave) infarction (acute[)]
Posterobasal transmural (Q wave) infarction (acute)
Posterolateral transmural (Q wave) infarction (acute)
Posteroseptal transmural (Q wave) infarction (acute)
Septal transmural (Q wave) infarction (acute) NOS
MCC Exclusion see Appendix A PDX collection 0653

MCC **I21.3 ST elevation (STEMI) myocardial infarction of unspecified si[te]**
Acute transmural myocardial infarction of unspecified site
Myocardial infarction (acute) NOS
Transmural (Q wave) myocardial infarction NOS
MCC Exclusion see Appendix A PDX collection 0653
Review coding guidelines C.9.e.1 and C.9.e.2

MCC **I21.4 Non-ST elevation (NSTEMI) myocardial infarction**
Acute subendocardial myocardial infarction
Non-Q wave myocardial infarction NOS
Nontransmural myocardial infarction NOS
MCC Exclusion see Appendix A PDX collection 0653
Review coding guideline C.9.e.1

I22 **Subsequent ST elevation (STEMI) and non-ST elevation (NSTEMI) myocardial infarction**

Includes: acute myocardial infarction occurring within four weeks (28 days) of a previous acute myocardial infarction, regardless of site
cardiac infarction
coronary (artery) embolism
coronary (artery) occlusion
coronary (artery) rupture
coronary (artery) thrombosis
infarction of heart, myocardium, or ventricle
recurrent myocardial infarction
reinfarction of myocardium
rupture of heart, myocardium, or ventricle

Use additional code, if applicable, to identify:
exposure to environmental tobacco smoke (Z77.22)
history of tobacco use (Z87.891)
occupational exposure to environmental tobacco smoke (Z57.31)
status post administration of tPA (rtPA) in a different facility within the last 24 hours prior to admission to current facility (Z92.82)
tobacco dependence (F17.-)
tobacco use (Z72.0)

Review coding guideline C.9.e.4
AHA CC: 1Q, 2013, 25

CC **I22.0 Subsequent ST elevation (STEMI) myocardial infarction of anterior wall**
Subsequent acute transmural myocardial infarction of anterior wall
Subsequent transmural (Q wave) infarction (acute)(of) anterior (wall) NOS
Subsequent anteroapical transmural (Q wave) infarction (acute)
Subsequent anterolateral transmural (Q wave) infarction (acute)
Subsequent anteroseptal transmural (Q wave) infarction (acute)
MCC Exclusion see Appendix A PDX collection 0653

CC **I22.1 Subsequent ST elevation (STEMI) myocardial infarction of inferior wall**
Subsequent acute transmural myocardial infarction of inferior wall
Subsequent transmural (Q wave) infarction (acute)(of) diaphragmatic wall
Subsequent transmural (Q wave) infarction (acute)(of) inferior (wall) NOS
Subsequent inferolateral transmural (Q wave) infarction (acute)
Subsequent inferoposterior transmural (Q wave) infarction (acute)
MCC Exclusion see Appendix A PDX collection 0653
AHA CC: 4Q, 2012, 102-104

CC **I22.2 Subsequent non-ST elevation (NSTEMI) myocardial infarction**
Subsequent acute subendocardial myocardial infarction
Subsequent non-Q wave myocardial infarction NOS
Subsequent nontransmural myocardial infarction NOS
MCC Exclusion see Appendix A PDX collection 0653

CC **I22.8 Subsequent ST elevation (STEMI) myocardial infarction of other sites**
Subsequent acute transmural myocardial infarction of other sites
Subsequent apical-lateral transmural (Q wave) myocardial infarction (acute)
Subsequent basal-lateral transmural (Q wave) myocardial infarction (acute)
Subsequent high lateral transmural (Q wave) myocardial infarction (acute)
Subsequent transmural (Q wave) myocardial infarction (acute) (of) lateral (wall) NOS
Subsequent posterior (true)transmural (Q wave) myocardial infarction (acute)
Subsequent posterobasal transmural (Q wave) myocardial infarction (acute)
Subsequent posterolateral transmural (Q wave) myocardial infarction (acute)
Subsequent posteroseptal transmural (Q wave) myocardial infarction (acute)
Subsequent septal NOS transmural (Q wave) myocardial infarction (acute)
MCC Exclusion see Appendix A PDX collection 0653

CC **I22.9 Subsequent ST elevation (STEMI) myocardial infarction of unspecified site**
Subsequent acute myocardial infarction of unspecified site
Subsequent myocardial infarction (acute) NOS
MCC Exclusion see Appendix A PDX collection 0653

I23 **Certain current complications following ST elevation (STEMI) and non-ST elevation (NSTEMI) myocardial infarction (within the 28 day period)**

• CC **I23.0 Hemopericardium as current complication following acute myocardial infarction**
Excludes1: *hemopericardium not specified as current complication following acute myocardial infarction (I31.2)*
CC Exclusion see Appendix A PDX collection 0654

• CC **I23.1 Atrial septal defect as current complication following acute myocardial infarction**
Excludes1: *acquired atrial septal defect not specified as current complication following acute myocardial infarction (I51.0)*
CC Exclusion see Appendix A PDX collection 0654

• CC **I23.2 Ventricular septal defect as current complication following acute myocardial infarction**
Excludes1: *acquired ventricular septal defect not specified as current complication following acute myocardial infarction (I51.0)*
CC Exclusion see Appendix A PDX collection 0654

• CC **I23.3 Rupture of cardiac wall without hemopericardium as current complication following acute myocardial infarction**
CC Exclusion see Appendix A PDX collection 0654

MCC **I23.4 Rupture of chordae tendineae as current complication following acute myocardial infarction**
Excludes1: *rupture of chordae tendineae not specified as current complication following acute myocardial infarction (I51.1)*
MCC Exclusion see Appendix A PDX collection 0655

MCC **I23.5 Rupture of papillary muscle as current complication following acute myocardial infarction**
Excludes1: *rupture of papillary muscle not specified as current complication following acute myocardial infarction (I51.2)*
MCC Exclusion see Appendix A PDX collection 0656

• CC **I23.6 Thrombosis of atrium, auricular appendage, and ventricle as current complications following acute myocardial infarction**
Excludes1: *thrombosis of atrium, auricular appendage, and ventricle not specified as current complication following acute myocardial infarction (I51.3)*
CC Exclusion see Appendix A PDX collection 0654

• CC **I23.7 Postinfarction angina**
CC Exclusion see Appendix A PDX collection 0654

• CC **I23.8 Other current complications following acute myocardial infarction**
CC Exclusion see Appendix A PDX collection 0654

I24 **Other acute ischemic heart diseases**
Excludes1: *angina pectoris (I20.-)*
transient myocardial ischemia in newborn (P29.4)

CC **I24.0 Acute coronary thrombosis not resulting in myocardial infarction**
Acute coronary (artery) (vein) embolism not resulting in myocardial infarction
Acute coronary (artery) (vein) occlusion not resulting in myocardial infarction
Acute coronary (artery) (vein) thromboembolism not resulting in myocardial infarction
Excludes1: *atherosclerotic heart disease (I25.1-)*
CC Exclusion see Appendix A PDX collection 0657

CC **I24.1 Dressler's syndrome**
Postmyocardial infarction syndrome
Excludes1: *postinfarction angina (I23.7)*
CC Exclusion see Appendix A PDX collection 0658

CC **I24.8 Other forms of acute ischemic heart disease**
CC Exclusion see Appendix A PDX collection 0657

CC **I24.9 Acute ischemic heart disease, unspecified**
Excludes1: *ischemic heart disease (chronic) NOS (I25.9)*
CC Exclusion see Appendix A PDX collection 0657

Great Vessels of the Heart

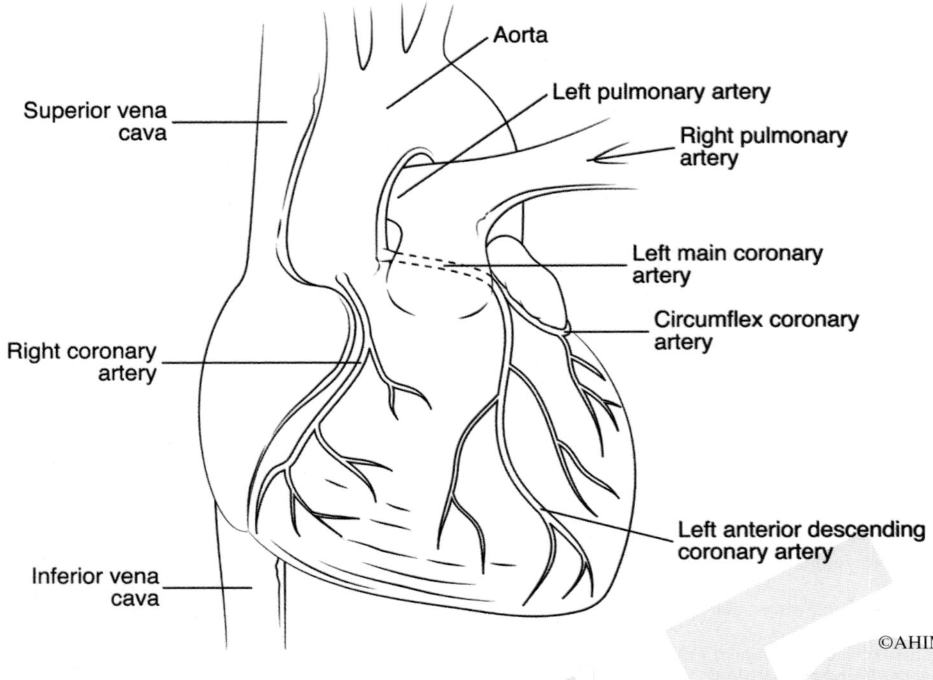

Aorta
Superior vena cava
Left pulmonary artery
Right pulmonary artery
Left main coronary artery
Circumflex coronary artery
Right coronary artery
Left anterior descending coronary artery
Inferior vena cava

I25 Chronic ischemic heart disease

Use additional code to identify:
- chronic total occlusion of coronary artery (I25.82)
- exposure to environmental tobacco smoke (Z77.22)
- history of tobacco use (Z87.891)
- occupational exposure to environmental tobacco smoke (Z57.31)
- tobacco dependence (F17.-)
- tobacco use (Z72.0)

\+ **I25.1 Atherosclerotic heart disease of native coronary artery**
Atherosclerotic cardiovascular disease
Coronary (artery) atheroma
Coronary (artery) atherosclerosis
Coronary (artery) disease
Coronary (artery) sclerosis
Use additional code, if applicable, to identify:
coronary atherosclerosis due to calcified coronary lesion (I25.84)
coronary atherosclerosis due to lipid rich plaque (I25.83)
Excludes2: *atheroembolism (I75.-)*
atherosclerosis of coronary artery bypass graft(s) and transplanted heart (I25.7-)

• **I25.10 Atherosclerotic heart disease of native coronary artery without angina pectoris**
Atherosclerotic heart disease NOS
AHA CC: 4Q, 2012, 92-92; 4Q, 2013, 128

\+ **I25.11 Atherosclerotic heart disease of native coronary artery with angina pectoris**
Review coding guideline C.9.b

• CC **I25.110 Atherosclerotic heart disease of native coronary artery with unstable angina pectoris**
Excludes1: *unstable angina without atherosclerotic heart disease (I20.0)*
CC Exclusion see Appendix A PDX collection 0651

• **I25.111 Atherosclerotic heart disease of native coronary artery with angina pectoris with documented spasm**
Excludes1: *angina pectoris with documented spasm without atherosclerotic heart disease (I20.1)*

• **I25.118 Atherosclerotic heart disease of native coronary artery with other forms of angina pectoris**
Excludes1: *other forms of angina pectoris without atherosclerotic heart disease (I20.8)*

• **I25.119 Atherosclerotic heart disease of native coronary artery with unspecified angina pectoris**
Atherosclerotic heart disease with angina NOS
Atherosclerotic heart disease with ischem[ic] chest pain
Excludes1: *unspecified angina pectoris without atherosclerotic he[art] disease (I20.9)*

I25.2 Old myocardial infarction
Healed myocardial infarction
Past myocardial infarction diagnosed by ECG or other investigation, but currently presenting no symptoms

CC **I25.3 Aneurysm of heart**
Mural aneurysm
Ventricular aneurysm
CC Exclusion see Appendix A PDX collection 0659

\+ **I25.4 Coronary artery aneurysm and dissection**

I25.41 Coronary artery aneurysm
Coronary arteriovenous fistula, acquired
Excludes1: *congenital coronary (artery) aneurysm (Q24.5)*

MCC **I25.42 Coronary artery dissection**
MCC Exclusion see Appendix A PDX collection 0660

I25.5 Ischemic cardiomyopathy
Excludes2: *coronary atherosclerosis (I25.1-, I25.7-)*

I25.6 Silent myocardial ischemia

\+ **I25.7 Atherosclerosis of coronary artery bypass graft(s) and coro[nary] artery of transplanted heart with angina pectoris**
Use additional code, if applicable, to identify:
coronary atherosclerosis due to calcified coronary lesion (I25.84)
coronary atherosclerosis due to lipid rich plaque (I25.83)
Excludes1: *atherosclerosis of bypass graft(s) of transplante[d] heart without angina pectoris (I25.812)*
atherosclerosis of coronary artery bypass graft(without angina pectoris (I25.810)
atherosclerosis of native coronary artery of transplanted heart without angina pectoris (I25.811)
embolism or thrombus of coronary artery bypas[s] graft(s) (T82.8-)
Review coding guideline C.9.b

\+ **I25.70 Atherosclerosis of coronary artery bypass graft(s) unspecified, with angina pectoris**

• CC **I25.700 Atherosclerosis of coronary artery bypass graft(s), unspecified, with unstable angina pectoris**
Excludes1: *unstable angina pectoris without atherosclerosis of coronary artery bypass graft (I20.0)*
CC Exclusion see Appendix A PDX collection 0651

• **I25.701 Atherosclerosis of coronary artery bypass graft(s), unspecified, with angina pectoris with documented spasm**
Excludes1: *angina pectoris with documented spasm without atherosclerosis of coronary artery bypass graft (I20.1)*

• **I25.708 Atherosclerosis of coronary artery bypass graft(s), unspecified, with other forms of angina pectoris**
Excludes1: *other forms of angina pectoris without atherosclerosis of coronary artery bypass graft (I20.8)*

• **I25.709 Atherosclerosis of coronary artery bypass graft(s), unspecified, with unspecified angina pectoris**
Excludes1: *unspecified angina pectoris without atherosclerosis of coronary artery bypass graft (I20.9)*

+ **I25.71 Atherosclerosis of autologous vein coronary artery bypass graft(s) with angina pectoris**

• CC **I25.710 Atherosclerosis of autologous vein coronary artery bypass graft(s) with unstable angina pectoris**
Excludes1: *unstable angina without atherosclerosis of autologous vein coronary artery bypass graft(s) (I20.0)*
CC Exclusion see Appendix A PDX collection 0661

• CC **I25.711 Atherosclerosis of autologous vein coronary artery bypass graft(s) with angina pectoris with documented spasm**
Excludes1: *angina pectoris with documented spasm without atherosclerosis of autologous vein coronary artery bypass graft(s) (I20.1)*
CC Exclusion see Appendix A PDX collection 0662

• CC **I25.718 Atherosclerosis of autologous vein coronary artery bypass graft(s) with other forms of angina pectoris**
Excludes1: *other forms of angina pectoris without atherosclerosis of autologous vein coronary artery bypass graft(s) (I20.8)*
CC Exclusion see Appendix A PDX collection 0662

• CC **I25.719 Atherosclerosis of autologous vein coronary artery bypass graft(s) with unspecified angina pectoris**
Excludes1: *unspecified angina pectoris without atherosclerosis of autologous vein coronary artery bypass graft(s) (I20.9)*
CC Exclusion see Appendix A PDX collection 0662

+ **I25.72 Atherosclerosis of autologous artery coronary artery bypass graft(s) with angina pectoris**
Atherosclerosis of internal mammary artery graft with angina pectoris

• CC **I25.720 Atherosclerosis of autologous artery coronary artery bypass graft(s) with unstable angina pectoris**
Excludes1: *unstable angina without atherosclerosis of autologous artery coronary artery bypass graft(s) (I20.0)*
CC Exclusion see Appendix A PDX collection 0661

• CC **I25.721 Atherosclerosis of autologous artery coronary artery bypass graft(s) with angina pectoris with documented spasm**
Excludes1: *angina pectoris with documented spasm without atherosclerosis of autologous artery coronary artery bypass graft(s) (I20.1)*
CC Exclusion see Appendix A PDX collection 0662

• CC **I25.728 Atherosclerosis of autologous artery coronary artery bypass graft(s) with other forms of angina pectoris**
Excludes1: *other forms of angina pectoris without atherosclerosis of autologous artery coronary artery bypass graft(s) (I20.8)*
CC Exclusion see Appendix A PDX collection 0662

• CC **I25.729 Atherosclerosis of autologous artery coronary artery bypass graft(s) with unspecified angina pectoris**
Excludes1: *unspecified angina pectoris without atherosclerosis of autologous artery coronary artery bypass graft(s) (I20.9)*
CC Exclusion see Appendix A PDX collection 0662

+ **I25.73 Atherosclerosis of nonautologous biological coronary artery bypass graft(s) with angina pectoris**

• CC **I25.730 Atherosclerosis of nonautologous biological coronary artery bypass graft(s) with unstable angina pectoris**
Excludes1: *unstable angina without atherosclerosis of nonautologous biological coronaryarterybypassgraft(s) (I20.0)*
CC Exclusion see Appendix A PDX collection 0661

• CC **I25.731 Atherosclerosis of nonautologous biological coronary artery bypass graft(s) with angina pectoris with documented spasm**
Excludes1: *angina pectoris with documented spasm without atherosclerosis of nonautologous biological coronaryarterybypassgraft(s) (I20.1)*
CC Exclusion see Appendix A PDX collection 0662

• CC **I25.738 Atherosclerosis of nonautologous biological coronary artery bypass graft(s) with other forms of angina pectoris**
Excludes1: *other forms of angina pectoris without atherosclerosis of nonautologous biological coronaryarterybypassgraft(s) (I20.8)*
CC Exclusion see Appendix A PDX collection 0662

• CC **I25.739 Atherosclerosis of nonautologous biological coronary artery bypass graft(s) with unspecified angina pectoris**
Excludes1: *unspecified angina pectoris without atherosclerosis of nonautologous biological coronaryarterybypassgraft(s) (I20.9)*
CC Exclusion see Appendix A PDX collection 0662

+ **I25.75 Atherosclerosis of native coronary artery of transplanted heart with angina pectoris**
Excludes1: *atherosclerosis of native coronary artery of transplanted heart without angina pectoris (I25.811)*

CC **I25.750 Atherosclerosis of native coronary artery of transplanted heart with unstable angina**
CC Exclusion see Appendix A PDX collection 0663

CC **I25.751 Atherosclerosis of native coronary artery of transplanted heart with angina pectoris with documented spasm**
CC Exclusion see Appendix A PDX collection 0664

CC **I25.758 Atherosclerosis of native coronary artery of transplanted heart with other forms of angina pectoris**
CC Exclusion see Appendix A PDX collection 0664

CC **I25.759 Atherosclerosis of native coronary artery of transplanted heart with unspecified angina pectoris**
CC Exclusion see Appendix A PDX collection 0664

+ **I25.76 Atherosclerosis of bypass graft of coronary artery of transplanted heart with angina pectoris**
Excludes1: *atherosclerosis of bypass graft of coronary artery of transplanted heart without angina pectoris (I25.812)*

• CC **I25.760 Atherosclerosis of bypass graft of coronary artery of transplanted heart with unstable angina**
CC Exclusion see Appendix A PDX collection 0665

• CC **I25.761 Atherosclerosis of bypass graft of coronary artery of transplanted heart with angina pectoris with documented spasm**
CC Exclusion see Appendix A PDX collection 0666

• CC **I25.768 Atherosclerosis of bypass graft of coronary artery of transplanted heart with other forms of angina pectoris**
CC Exclusion see Appendix A PDX collection 0666

• CC **I25.769 Atherosclerosis of bypass graft of coronary artery of transplanted heart with unspecified angina pectoris**
CC Exclusion see Appendix A PDX collection 0666

+ **I25.79 Atherosclerosis of other coronary artery bypass graft(s) with angina pectoris**

• CC **I25.790 Atherosclerosis of other coronary artery bypass graft(s) with unstable angina pectoris**
Excludes1: *unstable angina without atherosclerosis of other coronaryarterybypassgraft(s) (I20.0)*
CC Exclusion see Appendix A PDX collection 0651

• CC **I25.791 Atherosclerosis of other coronary artery bypass graft(s) with angina pectoris with documented spasm**
Excludes1: *angina pectoris with documented spasm without atherosclerosis ofothercoronaryarterybypass graft(s) (I20.1)*
No CC Exclusions

• CC **I25.798 Atherosclerosis of other coronary artery bypass graft(s) with other forms of angina pectoris**
Excludes1: *other forms of angina pectoris without atherosclerosis of other coronary artery bypass graft(s) (I20.8)*
No CC Exclusions

• CC **I25.799 Atherosclerosis of other coronary artery bypass graft(s) with unspecified angina pectoris**
Excludes1: *unspecified angina pectoris without atherosclerosis of other coronary artery bypass graft(s) (I20.9)*
No CC Exclusions

+ **I25.8 Other forms of chronic ischemic heart disease**

+ **I25.81 Atherosclerosis of other coronary vessels without angina pectoris**
Use additional code, if applicable, to identify:
coronary atherosclerosis due to calcified coronary lesion (I25.84)
coronary atherosclerosis due to lipid rich plaque (I25.83)
Excludes1: *atherosclerotic heart disease of native coronary artery without angina pectoris (I25.10)*

• CC **I25.810 Atherosclerosis of coronary artery bypass graft(s) without angina pectoris**
Atherosclerosis of coronary artery bypass graft NOS
Excludes1: *atherosclerosis of coronary byp graft(s) with angina pectoris (I25.70-I25.73-, I25.79-)*
No CC Exclusions

CC **I25.811 Atherosclerosis of native coronary artery of transplanted heart without angina pectoris**
Atherosclerosis of native coronary artery of transplanted heart NOS
Excludes1: *atherosclerosis of native coronaryarteryoftransplante heart with angina pectoris (I25.75-)*
CC Exclusion see Appendix A PDX collection 0

• CC **I25.812 Atherosclerosis of bypass graft of coronar artery of transplanted heart without angin pectoris**
Atherosclerosis of bypass graft of transplan heart NOS
Excludes1: *atherosclerosis of bypass graft transplantedheartwithangin pectoris (I25.76)*
CC Exclusion see Appendix A PDX collection 0

I25.82 Chronic total occlusion of coronary artery
Complete occlusion of coronary artery
Total occlusion of coronary artery
Code first coronary atherosclerosis (I25.1-, I25.7-, I25.81-)
Excludes1: *acute coronary occulsion with myocardia infarction (I21.-, I22.-)*
acute coronary occulsion without myocardial infarction (I24.0)

• **I25.83 Coronary atherosclerosis due to lipid rich plaque**
Code first coronary atherosclerosis (I25.1-, I25.7-, I25.81-)

I25.84 Coronary atherosclerosis due to calcified coronary lesion
Coronary atherosclerosis due to severely calcified coronary lesion
Code first coronary atherosclerosis (I25.1-, I25.7-, I25.8

I25.89 Other forms of chronic ischemic heart disease

I25.9 Chronic ischemic heart disease, unspecified
Ischemic heart disease (chronic) NOS

Pulmonary heart disease and diseases of pulmonary circulatio (I26-I28)

I26 Pulmonary embolism

Includes: pulmonary (acute) (artery)(vein) infarction
pulmonary (acute) (artery)(vein) thromboembolism
pulmonary (acute) (artery)(vein) thrombosis

Excludes2: *chronic pulmonary embolism (I27.82)*
personal history of pulmonary embolism (Z86.711)
pulmonary embolism due to trauma (T79.0, T79.1)
pulmonary embolism due to complications of surgical and medical care (T80.0, T81.7-, T82.8-)
pulmonary embolism complicating abortion, ectopic or molar pregnancy (O00-O07, O08.2)
pulmonary embolism complicating pregnancy, childbirth ar the puerperium (O88.-)
septic (non-pulmonary) arterial embolism (I76)

+ **I26.0 Pulmonary embolism with acute cor pulmonale**

MCC **I26.01 Septic pulmonary embolism with acute cor pulmona**
Code first underlying infection

MCC **I26.02 Saddle embolus of pulmonary artery with acute cor pulmonale**
MCC Exclusion see Appendix A PDX collection 0667
HAC *see Appendix B for HAC conditional logic*

MCC **I26.09 Other pulmonary embolism with acute cor pulmonal**
Acute cor pulmonale NOS
MCC Exclusion see Appendix A PDX collection 0667
HAC *see Appendix B for HAC conditional logic*

+ **I26.9 Pulmonary embolism without acute cor pulmonale**

MCC **I26.90 Septic pulmonary embolism without acute cor pulmonale**
Code first underlying infection
MCC Exclusion see Appendix A PDX collection 0668

MCC **I26.92 Saddle embolus of pulmonary artery without acute cor pulmonale**
MCC Exclusion see Appendix A PDX collection 0669
HAC *see Appendix B for HAC conditional logic*

MCC **I26.99 Other pulmonary embolism without acute cor pulmonale**
Acute pulmonary embolism NOS
Pulmonary embolism NOS
MCC Exclusion see Appendix A PDX collection 0670
HAC *see Appendix B for HAC conditional logic*

I27 Other pulmonary heart diseases

CC **I27.0 Primary pulmonary hypertension**
Excludes1: *pulmonary hypertension NOS (I27.2)*
secondary pulmonary hypertension (I27.2)
CC Exclusion see Appendix A PDX collection 0671

CC **I27.1 Kyphoscoliotic heart disease**
CC Exclusion see Appendix A PDX collection 0533

I27.2 Other secondary pulmonary hypertension
Pulmonary hypertension NOS
Code also associated underlying condition

\+ **I27.8 Other specified pulmonary heart diseases**

I27.81 Cor pulmonale (chronic)
Cor pulmonale NOS
Excludes1: *acute cor pulmonale (I26.0-)*

CC **I27.82 Chronic pulmonary embolism**
Use additional code, if applicable, for associated long-term (current) use of anticoagulants (Z79.01)
Excludes1: *personal history of pulmonary embolism (Z86.711)*
CC Exclusion see Appendix A PDX collection 0669

I27.89 Other specified pulmonary heart diseases
Eisenmenger's complex
Eisenmenger's syndrome
Excludes1: *Eisenmenger's defect (Q21.8)*

I27.9 Pulmonary heart disease, unspecified
Chronic cardiopulmonary disease

I28 Other diseases of pulmonary vessels

CC **I28.0 Arteriovenous fistula of pulmonary vessels**
Excludes1: *congenital arteriovenous fistula (Q25.72)*
CC Exclusion see Appendix A PDX collection 0672

CC **I28.1 Aneurysm of pulmonary artery**
Excludes1: *congenital aneurysm (Q25.79)*
congenital arteriovenous aneurysm (Q25.72)
CC Exclusion see Appendix A PDX collection 0672

I28.8 Other diseases of pulmonary vessels
Pulmonary arteritis
Pulmonary endarteritis
Rupture of pulmonary vessels
Stenosis of pulmonary vessels
Stricture of pulmonary vessels

I28.9 Disease of pulmonary vessels, unspecified

er forms of heart disease (I30-I52)

30 Acute pericarditis

Includes: acute mediastinopericarditis
acute myopericarditis
acute pericardial effusion
acute pleuropericarditis
acute pneumopericarditis
Excludes1: *Dressler's syndrome (I24.1)*
rheumatic pericarditis (acute) (I01.0)

CC **I30.0 Acute nonspecific idiopathic pericarditis**
CC Exclusion see Appendix A PDX collection 0673

CC **I30.1 Infective pericarditis**
Pneumococcal pericarditis
Pneumopyopericardium
Purulent pericarditis
Pyopericarditis
Pyopericardium
Pyopneumopericardium
Staphylococcal pericarditis
Streptococcal pericarditis
Suppurative pericarditis
Viral pericarditis
Use additional code (B95-B97) to identify infectious agent
CC Exclusion see Appendix A PDX collection 0673

CC **I30.8 Other forms of acute pericarditis**
CC Exclusion see Appendix A PDX collection 0673

CC **I30.9 Acute pericarditis, unspecified**
CC Exclusion see Appendix A PDX collection 0673

I31 Other diseases of pericardium

Excludes1: *diseases of pericardium specified as rheumatic (I09.2)*
postcardiotomy syndrome (I97.0)
traumatic injury to pericardium (S26.-)

CC **I31.0 Chronic adhesive pericarditis**
Accretio cordis
Adherent pericardium
Adhesive mediastinopericarditis
CC Exclusion see Appendix A PDX collection 0674

CC **I31.1 Chronic constrictive pericarditis**
Concretio cordis
Pericardial calcification
CC Exclusion see Appendix A PDX collection 0674

CC **I31.2 Hemopericardium, not elsewhere classified**
Excludes1: *hemopericardium as current complication following acute myocardial infarction (I23.0)*
CC Exclusion see Appendix A PDX collection 0674

CC **I31.3 Pericardial effusion (noninflammatory)**
Chylopericardium
Excludes1: *acute pericardial effusion (I30.9)*
CC Exclusion see Appendix A PDX collection 0188

CC **I31.4 Cardiac tamponade**
Code first underlying cause
CC Exclusion see Appendix A PDX collection 0188

CC **I31.8 Other specified diseases of pericardium**
Epicardial plaques
Focal pericardial adhesions
CC Exclusion see Appendix A PDX collection 0188

CC **I31.9 Disease of pericardium, unspecified**
Pericarditis (chronic) NOS
CC Exclusion see Appendix A PDX collection 0188

CC I32 Pericarditis in diseases classified elsewhere

Code first underlying disease
Excludes1: *pericarditis (in):*
coxsackie (virus) (B33.23)
gonococcal (A54.83)
meningococcal (A39.53)
rheumatoid (arthritis) (M05.31)
syphilitic (A52.06)
systemic lupus erythematosus (M32.12)
tuberculosis (A18.84)
CC Exclusion see Appendix A PDX collection 0673
Valid 3-character code, no further characters required

I33 Acute and subacute endocarditis

Excludes1: *acute rheumatic endocarditis (I01.1)*
endocarditis NOS (I38)

MCC **I33.0 Acute and subacute infective endocarditis**
Bacterial endocarditis (acute) (subacute)
Infective endocarditis (acute) (subacute) NOS
Endocarditis lenta (acute) (subacute)
Malignant endocarditis (acute) (subacute)
Purulent endocarditis (acute) (subacute)
Septic endocarditis (acute) (subacute)
Ulcerative endocarditis (acute) (subacute)
Vegetative endocarditis (acute) (subacute)
Use additional code (B95-B97) to identify infectious agent
MCC Exclusion see Appendix A PDX collection 0675

MCC **I33.9 Acute and subacute endocarditis, unspecified**
Acute endocarditis NOS
Acute myoendocarditis NOS
Acute periendocarditis NOS
Subacute endocarditis NOS
Subacute myoendocarditis NOS
Subacute periendocarditis NOS
MCC Exclusion see Appendix A PDX collection 0675

I34 Nonrheumatic mitral valve disorders

Excludes1: *mitral valve disease (I05.9)*
mitral valve failure (I05.8)
mitral valve stenosis (I05.0)
mitral valve disorder of unspecified cause with diseases of aortic and/or tricuspid valve(s) (I08.-)
mitral valve disorder of unspecified cause with mitral stenosis or obstruction (I05.0)
mitral valve disorder specified as congenital (Q23.2, Q23.3)
mitral valve disorder specified as rheumatic (I05.-)

I34.0 Nonrheumatic mitral (valve) insufficiency
Nonrheumatic mitral (valve) incompetence NOS
Nonrheumatic mitral (valve) regurgitation NOS

I34.1 Nonrheumatic mitral (valve) prolapse
Floppy nonrheumatic mitral valve syndrome
Excludes1: *Marfan's syndrome (Q87.4-)*

I34.2 Nonrheumatic mitral (valve) stenosis
I34.8 Other nonrheumatic mitral valve disorders
I34.9 Nonrheumatic mitral valve disorder, unspecified

I35 Nonrheumatic aortic valve disorders

Excludes1: *aortic valve disorder of unspecified cause but with diseases of mitral and/or tricuspid valve(s) (I08.-)*
aortic valve disorder specified as congenital (Q23.0, Q23.1)
aortic valve disorder specified as rheumatic (I06.-)
hypertrophic subaortic stenosis (I42.1)

I35.0 Nonrheumatic aortic (valve) stenosis
I35.1 Nonrheumatic aortic (valve) insufficiency
Nonrheumatic aortic (valve) incompetence NOS
Nonrheumatic aortic (valve) regurgitation NOS
I35.2 Nonrheumatic aortic (valve) stenosis with insufficiency
I35.8 Other nonrheumatic aortic valve disorders
I35.9 Nonrheumatic aortic valve disorder, unspecified

I36 Nonrheumatic tricuspid valve disorders

Excludes1: *tricuspid valve disorders of unspecified cause (I07.-)*
tricuspid valve disorders specified as congenital (Q22.4, Q22.8, Q22.9)
tricuspid valve disorders specified as rheumatic (I07.-)
tricuspid valve disorders with aortic and/or mitral valve involvement (I08.-)

I36.0 Nonrheumatic tricuspid (valve) stenosis
I36.1 Nonrheumatic tricuspid (valve) insufficiency
Nonrheumatic tricuspid (valve) incompetence
Nonrheumatic tricuspid (valve) regurgitation
I36.2 Nonrheumatic tricuspid (valve) stenosis with insufficiency
I36.8 Other nonrheumatic tricuspid valve disorders
I36.9 Nonrheumatic tricuspid valve disorder, unspecified

I37 Nonrheumatic pulmonary valve disorders

Excludes1: *pulmonary valve disorder specified as congenital (Q22.1, Q22.2, Q22.3)*
pulmonary valve disorder specified as rheumatic (I09.89)

I37.0 Nonrheumatic pulmonary valve stenosis
I37.1 Nonrheumatic pulmonary valve insufficiency
Nonrheumatic pulmonary valve incompetence
Nonrheumatic pulmonary valve regurgitation
I37.2 Nonrheumatic pulmonary valve stenosis with insufficiency
I37.8 Other nonrheumatic pulmonary valve disorders
I37.9 Nonrheumatic pulmonary valve disorder, unspecified

CC **I38 Endocarditis, valve unspecified**

Includes: endocarditis (chronic) NOS
valvular incompetence NOS
valvular insufficiency NOS
valvular regurgitation NOS
valvular stenosis NOS
valvulitis (chronic) NOS

Excludes1: *congenital insufficiency of cardiac valve NOS (Q24.8)*
congenital stenosis of cardiac valve NOS (Q24.8)
endocardial fibroelastosis (I42.4)
endocarditis specified as rheumatic (I09.1)

CC Exclusion see Appendix A PDX collection 0676
Valid 3-character code, no further characters required

CC **I39 Endocarditis and heart valve disorders in diseases classified elsewhere**

Code first underlying disease, such as:
Q fever (A78)

Excludes1: *endocardial involvement in:*
candidiasis (B37.6)
gonococcal infection (A54.83)
Libman-Sacks disease (M32.11)
listerosis (A32.82)
meningococcal infection (A39.51)
rheumatoid arthritis (M05.31)
syphilis (A52.03)
tuberculosis (A18.84)
typhoid fever (A01.02)

CC Exclusion see Appendix A PDX collection 0676
Valid 3-character code, no further characters required

I40 Acute myocarditis

Includes: subacute myocarditis
Excludes1: *acute rheumatic myocarditis (I01.2)*

MCC **I40.0 Infective myocarditis**
Septic myocarditis
Use additional code (B95-B97) to identify infectious agent
MCC Exclusion see Appendix A PDX collection 0677

MCC **I40.1 Isolated myocarditis**
Fiedler's myocarditis
Giant cell myocarditis
Idiopathic myocarditis
MCC Exclusion see Appendix A PDX collection 0677

MCC **I40.8 Other acute myocarditis**
MCC Exclusion see Appendix A PDX collection 0677

MCC **I40.9 Acute myocarditis, unspecified**
MCC Exclusion see Appendix A PDX collection 0677

MCC **I41 Myocarditis in diseases classified elsewhere**

Code first underlying disease, such as:
typhus (A75.0-A75.9)

Excludes1: *myocarditis (in):*
Chagas' disease (chronic) (B57.2)
acute (B57.0)
coxsackie (virus) infection (B33.22)
diphtheritic (A36.81)
gonococcal (A54.83)
influenzal (J09.X9, J10.82, J11.82)
meningococcal (A39.52)
mumps (B26.82)
rheumatoid arthritis (M05.31)
sarcoid (D86.85)
syphilis (A52.06)
toxoplasmosis (B58.81)
tuberculous (A18.84)

MCC Exclusion see Appendix A PDX collection 0677
Valid 3-character code, no further characters required

I42 Cardiomyopathy

Includes: myocardiopathy
Code first pre-existing cardiomyopathy complicating pregnancy and puerperium (O99.4)
Excludes1: *ischemic cardiomyopathy (I25.5)*
peripartum cardiomyopathy (O90.3)
Excludes2: *ventricular hypertrophy (I51.7)*

CC **I42.0 Dilated cardiomyopathy**
Congestive cardiomyopathy
CC Exclusion see Appendix A PDX collection 0678

CC **I42.1 Obstructive hypertrophic cardiomyopathy**
Hypertrophic subaortic stenosis (idiopathic)
CC Exclusion see Appendix A PDX collection 0678

CC **I42.2 Other hypertrophic cardiomyopathy**
Nonobstructive hypertrophic cardiomyopathy
CC Exclusion see Appendix A PDX collection 0678

CC **I42.3 Endomyocardial (eosinophilic) disease**
Endomyocardial (tropical) fibrosis
Löffler's endocarditis
CC Exclusion see Appendix A PDX collection 0678

CC **I42.4 Endocardial fibroelastosis**
Congenital cardiomyopathy
Elastomyofibrosis
CC Exclusion see Appendix A PDX collection 0678

CC **I42.5 Other restrictive cardiomyopathy**
Constrictive cardiomyopathy NOS
CC Exclusion see Appendix A PDX collection 0678

CC **I42.6 Alcoholic cardiomyopathy**
Code also presence of alcoholism (F10.-)
CC Exclusion see Appendix A PDX collection 0678

CC **I42.7 Cardiomyopathy due to drug and external agent**
Code first poisoning due to drug or toxin, if applicable (T36-T6 with fifth or sixth character 1-4 or 6)

Use additional code for adverse effect, if appv licable, to identi drug (T36-T50 with fifth or sixth character 5)
CC Exclusion see Appendix A PDX collection 0678

CC **I42.8 Other cardiomyopathies**
CC Exclusion see Appendix A PDX collection 0678

CC **I42.9 Cardiomyopathy, unspecified**
Cardiomyopathy (primary) (secondary) NOS
CC Exclusion see Appendix A PDX collection 0678

CC **I43 Cardiomyopathy in diseases classified elsewhere**

Code first underlying disease, such as:
amyloidosis (E85.-)
glycogen storage disease (E74.0)
gout (M10.0-)
thyrotoxicosis (E05.0-E05.9-)

Excludes1: *cardiomyopathy (in):*
coxsackie (virus) (B33.24)
diphtheria (A36.81)
sarcoidosis (D86.85)
tuberculosis (A18.84)

CC Exclusion see Appendix A PDX collection 0678
Valid 3-character code, no further characters required

I44 Atrioventricular and left bundle-branch block

I44.0 Atrioventricular block, first degree
I44.1 Atrioventricular block, second degree
Atrioventricular block, type I and II
Möbitz block block, type I and II
Second degree block, type I and II
Wenckebach's block
CC **I44.2 Atrioventricular block, complete**
Complete heart block NOS
Third degree block
CC Exclusion see Appendix A PDX collection 0679
+ **I44.3 Other and unspecified atrioventricular block**
Atrioventricular block NOS
I44.30 Unspecified atrioventricular block
I44.39 Other atrioventricular block
I44.4 Left anterior fascicular block
I44.5 Left posterior fascicular block
+ **I44.6 Other and unspecified fascicular block**
I44.60 Unspecified fascicular block
Left bundle-branch hemiblock NOS
I44.69 Other fascicular block
I44.7 Left bundle-branch block, unspecified

I45 Other conduction disorders

I45.0 Right fascicular block
+ **I45.1 Other and unspecified right bundle-branch block**
I45.10 Unspecified right bundle-branch block
Right bundle-branch block NOS
I45.19 Other right bundle-branch block
CC **I45.2 Bifascicular block**
CC Exclusion see Appendix A PDX collection 0679
CC **I45.3 Trifascicular block**
CC Exclusion see Appendix A PDX collection 0679
I45.4 Nonspecific intraventricular block
Bundle-branch block NOS
I45.5 Other specified heart block
Sinoatrial block
Sinoauricular block
Excludes1: *heart block NOS (I45.9)*
I45.6 Pre-excitation syndrome
Accelerated atrioventricular conduction
Accessory atrioventricular conduction
Anomalous atrioventricular excitation
Lown-Ganong-Levine syndrome
Pre-excitation atrioventricular conduction
Wolff-Parkinson-White syndrome
+ **I45.8 Other specified conduction disorders**
I45.81 Long QT syndrome
CC **I45.89 Other specified conduction disorders**
Atrioventricular [AV] dissociation
Interference dissociation
Isorhythmic dissociation
Nonparoxysmal AV nodal tachycardia
CC Exclusion see Appendix A PDX collection 0679
AHA CC: 2Q, 2013, 31-32
I45.9 Conduction disorder, unspecified
Heart block NOS
Stokes-Adams syndrome

I46 Cardiac arrest

Excludes1: *cardiogenic shock (R57.0)*
MCC **I46.2 Cardiac arrest due to underlying cardiac condition**
Code first underlying cardiac condition
MCC Exclusion see Appendix A PDX collection 0680
MCC **I46.8 Cardiac arrest due to other underlying condition**
Code first underlying condition
MCC Exclusion see Appendix A PDX collection 0680
MCC **I46.9 Cardiac arrest, cause unspecified**
MCC Exclusion see Appendix A PDX collection 0680

I47 Paroxysmal tachycardia

Code first tachycardia complicating:
abortion or ectopic or molar pregnancy (O00-O07, O08.8)
obstetric surgery and procedures (O75.4)
Excludes1: *tachycardia NOS (R00.0)*
sinoauricular tachycardia NOS (R00.0)
sinus [sinusal] tachycardia NOS (R00.0)
CC **I47.0 Re-entry ventricular arrhythmia**
CC Exclusion see Appendix A PDX collection 0679
CC **I47.1 Supraventricular tachycardia**
Atrial (paroxysmal) tachycardia
Atrioventricular [AV] (paroxysmal) tachycardia
Atrioventricular re-entrant (nodal) tachycardia [AVNRT] [AVRT]
Junctional (paroxysmal) tachycardia
Nodal (paroxysmal) tachycardia
CC Exclusion see Appendix A PDX collection 0679
CC **I47.2 Ventricular tachycardia**
CC Exclusion see Appendix A PDX collection 0679
AHA CC: 3Q, 2013, 23-24
I47.9 Paroxysmal tachycardia, unspecified
Bouveret (-Hoffman) syndrome

I48 Atrial fibrillation and flutter

I48.0 Paroxysmal atrial fibrillation
CC **I48.1 Persistent atrial fibrillation**
CC Exclusion see Appendix A PDX collection 0679
I48.2 Chronic atrial fibrillation
Permanent atrial fibrillation
AHA CC: 4Q, 2013, 128
CC **I48.3 Typical atrial flutter**
Type I atrial flutter
CC Exclusion see Appendix A PDX collection 0679
CC **I48.4 Atypical atrial flutter**
Type II atrial flutter
CC Exclusion see Appendix A PDX collection 0679
+ **I48.9 Unspecified atrial fibrillation and atrial flutter**
I48.91 Unspecified atrial fibrillation
CC **I48.92 Unspecified atrial flutter**
CC Exclusion see Appendix A PDX collection 0679

I49 Other cardiac arrhythmias

Code first cardiac arrhythmia complicating:
abortion or ectopic or molar pregnancy (O00-O07, O08.8)
obstetric surgery and procedures (O75.4)
Excludes1: *bradycardia NOS (R00.1)*
sinoatrial bradycardia (R00.1)
sinus bradycardia (R00.1)
vagal bradycardia (R00.1)
neonatal dysrhythmia (P29.1-)
+ **I49.0 Ventricular fibrillation and flutter**
MCC **I49.01 Ventricular fibrillation**
MCC Exclusion see Appendix A PDX collection 0679
MCC **I49.02 Ventricular flutter**
MCC Exclusion see Appendix A PDX collection 0679
I49.1 Atrial premature depolarization
Atrial premature beats
CC **I49.2 Junctional premature depolarization**
CC Exclusion see Appendix A PDX collection 0679
I49.3 Ventricular premature depolarization
+ **I49.4 Other and unspecified premature depolarization**
I49.40 Unspecified premature depolarization
Premature beats NOS
I49.49 Other premature depolarization
Ectopic beats
Extrasystoles
Extrasystolic arrhythmias
Premature contractions
I49.5 Sick sinus syndrome
Tachycardia-bradycardia syndrome
I49.8 Other specified cardiac arrhythmias
Coronary sinus rhythm disorder
Ectopic rhythm disorder
Nodal rhythm disorder
I49.9 Cardiac arrhythmia, unspecified
Arrhythmia (cardiac) NOS

I50 Heart failure

Code first heart failure complicating abortion or ectopic or molar pregnancy (O00-O07, O08.8)
heart failure following surgery (I97.13-)
heart failure due to hypertension (I11.0)
heart failure due to hypertension with chronic kidney disease (I13.-)
obstetric surgery and procedures (O75.4)
rheumatic heart failure (I09.81)
Excludes1: *cardiac arrest (I46.-)*
neonatal cardiac failure (P29.0)
Review coding guidelines C.9.a.1 and C.9.a.3

CC **I50.1 Left ventricular failure**
Cardiac asthma
Edema of lung with heart disease NOS
Edema of lung with heart failure
Left heart failure
Pulmonary edema with heart disease NOS
Pulmonary edema with heart failure
Excludes1: *edema of lung without heart disease or heart failure (J81.-)*
pulmonary edema without heart disease or failure (J81.-)
CC Exclusion see Appendix A PDX collection 0681

\+ **I50.2 Systolic (congestive) heart failure**
Excludes1: *combined systolic (congestive) and diastolic (congestive) heart failure (I50.4-)*

CC **I50.20 Unspecified systolic (congestive) heart failure**
CC Exclusion see Appendix A PDX collection 0682

MCC **I50.21 Acute systolic (congestive) heart failure**
MCC Exclusion see Appendix A PDX collection 0682

CC **I50.22 Chronic systolic (congestive) heart failure**
CC Exclusion see Appendix A PDX collection 0682

MCC **I50.23 Acute on chronic systolic (congestive) heart failure**
MCC Exclusion see Appendix A PDX collection 0682
AHA CC: 2Q, 2013, 33

\+ **I50.3 Diastolic (congestive) heart failure**
Excludes1: *combined systolic (congestive) and diastolic (congestive) heart failure (I50.4-)*

CC **I50.30 Unspecified diastolic (congestive) heart failure**
CC Exclusion see Appendix A PDX collection 0682

MCC **I50.31 Acute diastolic (congestive) heart failure**
MCC Exclusion see Appendix A PDX collection 0682

CC **I50.32 Chronic diastolic (congestive) heart failure**
CC Exclusion see Appendix A PDX collection 0682

MCC **I50.33 Acute on chronic diastolic (congestive) heart failure**
MCC Exclusion see Appendix A PDX collection 0682

\+ **I50.4 Combined systolic (congestive) and diastolic (congestive) heart failure**

CC **I50.40 Unspecified combined systolic (congestive) and diastolic (congestive) heart failure**
CC Exclusion see Appendix A PDX collection 0682

MCC **I50.41 Acute combined systolic (congestive) and diastolic (congestive) heart failure**
MCC Exclusion see Appendix A PDX collection 0682

CC **I50.42 Chronic combined systolic (congestive) and diastolic (congestive) heart failure**
CC Exclusion see Appendix A PDX collection 0682

MCC **I50.43 Acute on chronic combined systolic (congestive) and diastolic (congestive) heart failure**
MCC Exclusion see Appendix A PDX collection 0682

I50.9 Heart failure, unspecified
Biventricular (heart) failure NOS
Cardiac, heart or myocardial failure NOS
Congestive heart disease
Congestive heart failure NOS
Right ventricular failure (secondary to left heart failure)
Excludes1: *fluid overload (E87.70)*
AHA CC: 4Q, 2012, 92-93

I51 Complications and ill-defined descriptions of heart disease
Excludes1: *any condition in I51.4-I51.9 due to hypertension (I11.-)*
any condition in I51.4-I51.9 due to hypertension and chronic kidney disease (I13.-)
heart disease specified as rheumatic (I00-I09)

• CC **I51.0 Cardiac septal defect, acquired**
Acquired septal atrial defect (old)
Acquired septal auricular defect (old)
Acquired septal ventricular defect (old)
Excludes1: *cardiac septal defect as current complication following acute myocardial infarction (I23.1, I23.2)*
CC Exclusion see Appendix A PDX collection 0654

MCC **I51.1 Rupture of chordae tendineae, not elsewhere classified**
Excludes1: *rupture of chordae tendineae as current complication following acute myocardial infarction (I23.4)*
MCC Exclusion see Appendix A PDX collection 0655

MCC **I51.2 Rupture of papillary muscle, not elsewhere classified**
Excludes1: *rupture of papillary muscle as current complication following acute myocardial infarction (I23.5)*
MCC Exclusion see Appendix A PDX collection 0656

• **I51.3 Intracardiac thrombosis, not elsewhere classified**
Apical thrombosis (old)
Atrial thrombosis (old)
Auricular thrombosis (old)
Mural thrombosis (old)
Ventricular thrombosis (old)
Excludes1: *intracardiac thrombosis as current complication following acute myocardial infarction (I23.6)*
AHA CC: 1Q, 2013, 24

I51.4 Myocarditis, unspecified
Chronic (interstitial) myocarditis
Myocardial fibrosis
Myocarditis NOS
Excludes1: *acute or subacute myocarditis (I40.-)*
Review coding guideline C.9.a.1

I51.5 Myocardial degeneration
Fatty degeneration of heart or myocardium
Myocardial disease
Senile degeneration of heart or myocardium
Review coding guideline C.9.a.1

I51.7 Cardiomegaly
Cardiac dilatation
Cardiac hypertrophy
Ventricular dilatation
Review coding guideline C.9.a.1

\+ **I51.8 Other ill-defined heart diseases**
Review coding guideline C.9.a.1

CC **I51.81 Takotsubo syndrome**
Reversible left ventricular dysfunction following sud
emotional stress
Stress induced cardiomyopathy
Takotsubo cardiomyopathy
Transient left ventricular apical ballooning syndrome
CC Exclusion see Appendix A PDX collection 0683

I51.89 Other ill-defined heart diseases
Carditis (acute)(chronic)
Pancarditis (acute)(chronic)

I51.9 Heart disease, unspecified
Review coding guideline C.9.a.1

I52 Other heart disorders in diseases classified elsewhere
Code first underlying disease, such as:
congenital syphilis (A50.5)
mucopolysaccharidosis (E76.3)
schistosomiasis (B65.0-B65.9)
Excludes1: *heart disease (in):*
gonococcal infection (A54.83)
meningococcal infection (A39.50)
rheumatoid arthritis (M05.31)
syphilis (A52.06)
Valid 3-character code, no further characters required

Cerebrovascular diseases (I60-I69)

Use additional code to identify presence of:
alcohol abuse and dependence (F10.-)
exposure to environmental tobacco smoke (Z77.22)
history of tobacco use (Z87.891)
hypertension (I10-I15)
occupational exposure to environmental tobacco smoke (Z57.31)
tobacco dependence (F17.-)
tobacco use (Z72.0)

Excludes1: *transient cerebral ischemic attacks and related syndromes (G45.-)*
traumatic intracranial hemorrhage (S06.-)

Review coding guidelines C.9.a.4 and C.9.d

I60 Nontraumatic subarachnoid hemorrhage
Includes: ruptured cerebral aneurysm
Excludes1: *sequelae of subarachnoid hemorrhage (I69.0-)*
syphilitic ruptured cerebral aneurysm (A52.05)

\+ **I60.0 Nontraumatic subarachnoid hemorrhage from carotid sipho and bifurcation**

MCC **I60.00 Nontraumatic subarachnoid hemorrhage from unspecified carotid siphon and bifurcation**
MCC Exclusion see Appendix A PDX collection 0684

MCC **I60.01 Nontraumatic subarachnoid hemorrhage from rig carotid siphon and bifurcation**
MCC Exclusion see Appendix A PDX collection 0684

MCC **I60.02 Nontraumatic subarachnoid hemorrhage from lef carotid siphon and bifurcation**
MCC Exclusion see Appendix A PDX collection 0684

+ **I60.1 Nontraumatic subarachnoid hemorrhage from middle cerebral artery**
 MCC **I60.10 Nontraumatic subarachnoid hemorrhage from unspecified middle cerebral artery**
 MCC Exclusion see Appendix A PDX collection 0684
 MCC **I60.11 Nontraumatic subarachnoid hemorrhage from right middle cerebral artery**
 MCC Exclusion see Appendix A PDX collection 0684
 MCC **I60.12 Nontraumatic subarachnoid hemorrhage from left middle cerebral artery**
 MCC Exclusion see Appendix A PDX collection 0684

+ **I60.2 Nontraumatic subarachnoid hemorrhage from anterior communicating artery**
 MCC **I60.20 Nontraumatic subarachnoid hemorrhage from unspecified anterior communicating artery**
 MCC Exclusion see Appendix A PDX collection 0684
 MCC **I60.21 Nontraumatic subarachnoid hemorrhage from right anterior communicating artery**
 MCC Exclusion see Appendix A PDX collection 0684
 MCC **I60.22 Nontraumatic subarachnoid hemorrhage from left anterior communicating artery**
 MCC Exclusion see Appendix A PDX collection 0684

+ **I60.3 Nontraumatic subarachnoid hemorrhage from posterior communicating artery**
 MCC **I60.30 Nontraumatic subarachnoid hemorrhage from unspecified posterior communicating artery**
 MCC Exclusion see Appendix A PDX collection 0684
 MCC **I60.31 Nontraumatic subarachnoid hemorrhage from right posterior communicating artery**
 MCC Exclusion see Appendix A PDX collection 0684
 MCC **I60.32 Nontraumatic subarachnoid hemorrhage from left posterior communicating artery**
 MCC Exclusion see Appendix A PDX collection 0684

MCC **I60.4 Nontraumatic subarachnoid hemorrhage from basilar artery**
 MCC Exclusion see Appendix A PDX collection 0684

+ **I60.5 Nontraumatic subarachnoid hemorrhage from vertebral artery**
 MCC **I60.50 Nontraumatic subarachnoid hemorrhage from unspecified vertebral artery**
 MCC Exclusion see Appendix A PDX collection 0684
 MCC **I60.51 Nontraumatic subarachnoid hemorrhage from right vertebral artery**
 MCC Exclusion see Appendix A PDX collection 0684
 MCC **I60.52 Nontraumatic subarachnoid hemorrhage from left vertebral artery**
 MCC Exclusion see Appendix A PDX collection 0684

MCC **I60.6 Nontraumatic subarachnoid hemorrhage from other intracranial arteries**
 MCC Exclusion see Appendix A PDX collection 0684

MCC **I60.7 Nontraumatic subarachnoid hemorrhage from unspecified intracranial artery**
 Ruptured (congenital) berry aneurysm
 Ruptured (congenital) cerebral aneurysm
 Subarachnoid hemorrhage (nontraumatic) from cerebral artery NOS
 Subarachnoid hemorrhage (nontraumatic) from communicating artery NOS
 Excludes1: *berry aneurysm, nonruptured (I67.1)*
 MCC Exclusion see Appendix A PDX collection 0684

MCC **I60.8 Other nontraumatic subarachnoid hemorrhage**
 Meningeal hemorrhage
 Rupture of cerebral arteriovenous malformation
 MCC Exclusion see Appendix A PDX collection 0684

MCC **I60.9 Nontraumatic subarachnoid hemorrhage, unspecified**
 MCC Exclusion see Appendix A PDX collection 0684

I61 Nontraumatic intracerebral hemorrhage

Excludes1: *sequelae of intracerebral hemorrhage (I69.1-)*

MCC **I61.0 Nontraumatic intracerebral hemorrhage in hemisphere, subcortical**
 Deep intracerebral hemorrhage (nontraumatic)
 MCC Exclusion see Appendix A PDX collection 0684

MCC **I61.1 Nontraumatic intracerebral hemorrhage in hemisphere, cortical**
 Cerebral lobe hemorrhage (nontraumatic)
 Superficial intracerebral hemorrhage (nontraumatic)
 MCC Exclusion see Appendix A PDX collection 0684

MCC **I61.2 Nontraumatic intracerebral hemorrhage in hemisphere, unspecified**
 MCC Exclusion see Appendix A PDX collection 0684

MCC **I61.3 Nontraumatic intracerebral hemorrhage in brain stem**
 MCC Exclusion see Appendix A PDX collection 0684

MCC **I61.4 Nontraumatic intracerebral hemorrhage in cerebellum**
 MCC Exclusion see Appendix A PDX collection 0684

MCC **I61.5 Nontraumatic intracerebral hemorrhage, intraventricular**
 MCC Exclusion see Appendix A PDX collection 0684

MCC **I61.6 Nontraumatic intracerebral hemorrhage, multiple localized**
 MCC Exclusion see Appendix A PDX collection 0684

MCC **I61.8 Other nontraumatic intracerebral hemorrhage**
 MCC Exclusion see Appendix A PDX collection 0684

MCC **I61.9 Nontraumatic intracerebral hemorrhage, unspecified**
 MCC Exclusion see Appendix A PDX collection 0684

I62 Other and unspecified nontraumatic intracranial hemorrhage

Excludes1: *sequelae of intracranial hemorrhage (I69.2)*

+ **I62.0 Nontraumatic subdural hemorrhage**
 MCC **I62.00 Nontraumatic subdural hemorrhage, unspecified**
 MCC Exclusion see Appendix A PDX collection 0684
 MCC **I62.01 Nontraumatic acute subdural hemorrhage**
 MCC Exclusion see Appendix A PDX collection 0684
 MCC **I62.02 Nontraumatic subacute subdural hemorrhage**
 MCC Exclusion see Appendix A PDX collection 0684
 MCC **I62.03 Nontraumatic chronic subdural hemorrhage**
 MCC Exclusion see Appendix A PDX collection 0684

MCC **I62.1 Nontraumatic extradural hemorrhage**
 Nontraumatic epidural hemorrhage
 MCC Exclusion see Appendix A PDX collection 0684

CC **I62.9 Nontraumatic intracranial hemorrhage, unspecified**
 CC Exclusion see Appendix A PDX collection 0684

I63 Cerebral infarction

Includes: occlusion and stenosis of cerebral and precerebral arteries, resulting in cerebral infarction

Use additional code, if applicable, to identify status post administration of tPA (rtPA) in a different facility within the last 24 hours prior to admission to current facility (Z92.82)

Excludes1: *sequelae of cerebral infarction (I69.3-)*

+ **I63.0 Cerebral infarction due to thrombosis of precerebral arteries**
 MCC **I63.00 Cerebral infarction due to thrombosis of unspecified precerebral artery**
 MCC Exclusion see Appendix A PDX collection 0685
 + **I63.01 Cerebral infarction due to thrombosis of vertebral artery**
 MCC **I63.011 Cerebral infarction due to thrombosis of right vertebral artery**
 MCC Exclusion see Appendix A PDX collection 0686
 MCC **I63.012 Cerebral infarction due to thrombosis of left vertebral artery**
 MCC Exclusion see Appendix A PDX collection 0686
 MCC **I63.019 Cerebral infarction due to thrombosis of unspecified vertebral artery**
 MCC Exclusion see Appendix A PDX collection 0686
 MCC **I63.02 Cerebral infarction due to thrombosis of basilar artery**
 MCC Exclusion see Appendix A PDX collection 0685
 + **I63.03 Cerebral infarction due to thrombosis of carotid artery**
 MCC **I63.031 Cerebral infarction due to thrombosis of right carotid artery**
 MCC Exclusion see Appendix A PDX collection 0687
 MCC **I63.032 Cerebral infarction due to thrombosis of left carotid artery**
 MCC Exclusion see Appendix A PDX collection 0687
 MCC **I63.039 Cerebral infarction due to thrombosis of unspecified carotid artery**
 MCC Exclusion see Appendix A PDX collection 0687
 MCC **I63.09 Cerebral infarction due to thrombosis of other precerebral artery**
 MCC Exclusion see Appendix A PDX collection 0685

+ **I63.1 Cerebral infarction due to embolism of precerebral arteries**
 MCC **I63.10 Cerebral infarction due to embolism of unspecified precerebral artery**
 MCC Exclusion see Appendix A PDX collection 0685
 + **I63.11 Cerebral infarction due to embolism of vertebral artery**
 MCC **I63.111 Cerebral infarction due to embolism of right vertebral artery**
 MCC Exclusion see Appendix A PDX collection 0686
 MCC **I63.112 Cerebral infarction due to embolism of left vertebral artery**
 MCC Exclusion see Appendix A PDX collection 0686
 MCC **I63.119 Cerebral infarction due to embolism of unspecified vertebral artery**
 MCC Exclusion see Appendix A PDX collection 0686

MCC **I63.12** **Cerebral infarction due to embolism of basilar artery**
MCC Exclusion see Appendix A PDX collection 0685

+ **I63.13** **Cerebral infarction due to embolism of carotid artery**

MCC **I63.131** **Cerebral infarction due to embolism of right carotid artery**
MCC Exclusion see Appendix A PDX collection 0687

MCC **I63.132** **Cerebral infarction due to embolism of left carotid artery**
MCC Exclusion see Appendix A PDX collection 0687

MCC **I63.139** **Cerebral infarction due to embolism of unspecified carotid artery**
MCC Exclusion see Appendix A PDX collection 0687

MCC **I63.19** **Cerebral infarction due to embolism of other precerebral artery**
MCC Exclusion see Appendix A PDX collection 0685

+ **I63.2** **Cerebral infarction due to unspecified occlusion or stenosis of precerebral arteries**

MCC **I63.20** **Cerebral infarction due to unspecified occlusion or stenosis of unspecified precerebral arteries**
MCC Exclusion see Appendix A PDX collection 0685

+ **I63.21** **Cerebral infarction due to unspecified occlusion or stenosis of vertebral arteries**

MCC **I63.211** **Cerebral infarction due to unspecified occlusion or stenosis of right vertebral arteries**
MCC Exclusion see Appendix A PDX collection 0686

MCC **I63.212** **Cerebral infarction due to unspecified occlusion or stenosis of left vertebral arteries**
MCC Exclusion see Appendix A PDX collection 0686

MCC **I63.219** **Cerebral infarction due to unspecified occlusion or stenosis of unspecified vertebral arteries**
MCC Exclusion see Appendix A PDX collection 0686

MCC **I63.22** **Cerebral infarction due to unspecified occlusion or stenosis of basilar arteries**
MCC Exclusion see Appendix A PDX collection 0685

+ **I63.23** **Cerebral infarction due to unspecified occlusion or stenosis of carotid arteries**

MCC **I63.231** **Cerebral infarction due to unspecified occlusion or stenosis of right carotid arteries**
MCC Exclusion see Appendix A PDX collection 0687

MCC **I63.232** **Cerebral infarction due to unspecified occlusion or stenosis of left carotid arteries**
MCC Exclusion see Appendix A PDX collection 0687

MCC **I63.239** **Cerebral infarction due to unspecified occlusion or stenosis of unspecified carotid arteries**
MCC Exclusion see Appendix A PDX collection 0687

MCC **I63.29** **Cerebral infarction due to unspecified occlusion or stenosis of other precerebral arteries**
MCC Exclusion see Appendix A PDX collection 0685

+ **I63.3** **Cerebral infarction due to thrombosis of cerebral arteries**

MCC **I63.30** **Cerebral infarction due to thrombosis of unspecified cerebral artery**
MCC Exclusion see Appendix A PDX collection 0688

+ **I63.31** **Cerebral infarction due to thrombosis of middle cerebral artery**

MCC **I63.311** **Cerebral infarction due to thrombosis of right middle cerebral artery**
MCC Exclusion see Appendix A PDX collection 0688

MCC **I63.312** **Cerebral infarction due to thrombosis of left middle cerebral artery**
MCC Exclusion see Appendix A PDX collection 0688

MCC **I63.319** **Cerebral infarction due to thrombosis of unspecified middle cerebral artery**
MCC Exclusion see Appendix A PDX collection 0688

+ **I63.32** **Cerebral infarction due to thrombosis of anterior cerebral artery**

MCC **I63.321** **Cerebral infarction due to thrombosis of right anterior cerebral artery**
MCC Exclusion see Appendix A PDX collection 0688

MCC **I63.322** **Cerebral infarction due to thrombosis of le[ft] anterior cerebral artery**
MCC Exclusion see Appendix A PDX collection 0688

MCC **I63.329** **Cerebral infarction due to thrombosis of unspecified anterior cerebral artery**
MCC Exclusion see Appendix A PDX collection 0688

+ **I63.33** **Cerebral infarction due to thrombosis of posterior cerebral artery**

MCC **I63.331** **Cerebral infarction due to thrombosis of right posterior cerebral artery**
MCC Exclusion see Appendix A PDX collection 0688

MCC **I63.332** **Cerebral infarction due to thrombosis of le[ft] posterior cerebral artery**
MCC Exclusion see Appendix A PDX collection 0688

MCC **I63.339** **Cerebral infarction due to thrombosis of unspecified posterior cerebral artery**
MCC Exclusion see Appendix A PDX collection 0688

+ **I63.34** **Cerebral infarction due to thrombosis of cerebellar artery**

MCC **I63.341** **Cerebral infarction due to thrombosis of right cerebellar artery**
MCC Exclusion see Appendix A PDX collection 0688

MCC **I63.342** **Cerebral infarction due to thrombosis of le[ft] cerebellar artery**
MCC Exclusion see Appendix A PDX collection 0688

MCC **I63.349** **Cerebral infarction due to thrombosis of unspecified cerebellar artery**
MCC Exclusion see Appendix A PDX collection 0688

MCC **I63.39** **Cerebral infarction due to thrombosis of other cerebral artery**
MCC Exclusion see Appendix A PDX collection 0688

+ **I63.4** **Cerebral infarction due to embolism of cerebral arteries**

MCC **I63.40** **Cerebral infarction due to embolism of unspecified cerebral artery**
MCC Exclusion see Appendix A PDX collection 0688

+ **I63.41** **Cerebral infarction due to embolism of middle cerebral artery**

MCC **I63.411** **Cerebral infarction due to embolism of rig[ht] middle cerebral artery**
MCC Exclusion see Appendix A PDX collection 0688

MCC **I63.412** **Cerebral infarction due to embolism of left middle cerebral artery**
MCC Exclusion see Appendix A PDX collection 0688

MCC **I63.419** **Cerebral infarction due to embolism of unspecified middle cerebral artery**
MCC Exclusion see Appendix A PDX collection 0688

+ **I63.42** **Cerebral infarction due to embolism of anterior cerebral artery**

MCC **I63.421** **Cerebral infarction due to embolism of righ[t] anterior cerebral artery**
MCC Exclusion see Appendix A PDX collection 0688

MCC **I63.422** **Cerebral infarction due to embolism of left anterior cerebral artery**
MCC Exclusion see Appendix A PDX collection 0688

MCC **I63.429** **Cerebral infarction due to embolism of unspecified anterior cerebral artery**
MCC Exclusion see Appendix A PDX collection 0688

+ **I63.43** **Cerebral infarction due to embolism of posterior cerebral artery**

MCC **I63.431** **Cerebral infarction due to embolism of righ[t] posterior cerebral artery**
MCC Exclusion see Appendix A PDX collection 0688

MCC **I63.432** **Cerebral infarction due to embolism of left posterior cerebral artery**
MCC Exclusion see Appendix A PDX collection 0688

MCC **I63.439** **Cerebral infarction due to embolism of unspecified posterior cerebral artery**
MCC Exclusion see Appendix A PDX collection 0688

+ **I63.44** **Cerebral infarction due to embolism of cerebellar artery**

MCC **I63.441** **Cerebral infarction due to embolism of right cerebellar artery**
MCC Exclusion see Appendix A PDX collection 0688

MCC **I63.442** **Cerebral infarction due to embolism of left cerebellar artery**
MCC Exclusion see Appendix A PDX collection 0688

MCC **I63.449** **Cerebral infarction due to embolism of unspecified cerebellar artery**
MCC Exclusion see Appendix A PDX collection 0688

MCC **I63.49** **Cerebral infarction due to embolism of other cerebral artery**
MCC Exclusion see Appendix A PDX collection 0688

+ **I63.5** **Cerebral infarction due to unspecified occlusion or stenosis of cerebral arteries**

MCC **I63.50** **Cerebral infarction due to unspecified occlusion or stenosis of unspecified cerebral artery**
MCC Exclusion see Appendix A PDX collection 0688

+ **I63.51** **Cerebral infarction due to unspecified occlusion or stenosis of middle cerebral artery**

MCC **I63.511** **Cerebral infarction due to unspecified occlusion or stenosis of right middle cerebral artery**
MCC Exclusion see Appendix A PDX collection 0688

MCC **I63.512** **Cerebral infarction due to unspecified occlusion or stenosis of left middle cerebral artery**
MCC Exclusion see Appendix A PDX collection 0688

MCC **I63.519** **Cerebral infarction due to unspecified occlusion or stenosis of unspecified middle cerebral artery**
MCC Exclusion see Appendix A PDX collection 0688

+ **I63.52** **Cerebral infarction due to unspecified occlusion or stenosis of anterior cerebral artery**

MCC **I63.521** **Cerebral infarction due to unspecified occlusion or stenosis of right anterior cerebral artery**
MCC Exclusion see Appendix A PDX collection 0688

MCC **I63.522** **Cerebral infarction due to unspecified occlusion or stenosis of left anterior cerebral artery**
MCC Exclusion see Appendix A PDX collection 0688

MCC **I63.529** **Cerebral infarction due to unspecified occlusion or stenosis of unspecified anterior cerebral artery**
MCC Exclusion see Appendix A PDX collection 0688

+ **I63.53** **Cerebral infarction due to unspecified occlusion or stenosis of posterior cerebral artery**

MCC **I63.531** **Cerebral infarction due to unspecified occlusion or stenosis of right posterior cerebral artery**
MCC Exclusion see Appendix A PDX collection 0688

MCC **I63.532** **Cerebral infarction due to unspecified occlusion or stenosis of left posterior cerebral artery**
MCC Exclusion see Appendix A PDX collection 0688

MCC **I63.539** **Cerebral infarction due to unspecified occlusion or stenosis of unspecified posterior cerebral artery**
MCC Exclusion see Appendix A PDX collection 0688

+ **I63.54** **Cerebral infarction due to unspecified occlusion or stenosis of cerebellar artery**

MCC **I63.541** **Cerebral infarction due to unspecified occlusion or stenosis of right cerebellar artery**
MCC Exclusion see Appendix A PDX collection 0688

MCC **I63.542** **Cerebral infarction due to unspecified occlusion or stenosis of left cerebellar artery**
MCC Exclusion see Appendix A PDX collection 0688

MCC **I63.549** **Cerebral infarction due to unspecified occlusion or stenosis of unspecified cerebellar artery**
MCC Exclusion see Appendix A PDX collection 0688

MCC **I63.59** **Cerebral infarction due to unspecified occlusion or stenosis of other cerebral artery**
MCC Exclusion see Appendix A PDX collection 0688

MCC **I63.6** **Cerebral infarction due to cerebral venous thrombosis, nonpyogenic**
MCC Exclusion see Appendix A PDX collection 0688

MCC **I63.8** **Other cerebral infarction**
MCC Exclusion see Appendix A PDX collection 0688

MCC **I63.9** **Cerebral infarction, unspecified**
Stroke NOS
MCC Exclusion see Appendix A PDX collection 0688

I65 **Occlusion and stenosis of precerebral arteries, not resulting in cerebral infarction**

Includes: embolism of precerebral artery
narrowing of precerebral artery
obstruction (complete) (partial) of precerebral artery
thrombosis of precerebral artery

Excludes1: *insufficiency, NOS, of precerebral artery (G45.-)*
insufficiency of precerebral arteries causing cerebral infarction (I63.0-I63.2)

+ **I65.0** **Occlusion and stenosis of vertebral artery**
I65.01 **Occlusion and stenosis of right vertebral artery**
I65.02 **Occlusion and stenosis of left vertebral artery**
I65.03 **Occlusion and stenosis of bilateral vertebral arteries**
I65.09 **Occlusion and stenosis of unspecified vertebral artery**

I65.1 **Occlusion and stenosis of basilar artery**

+ **I65.2** **Occlusion and stenosis of carotid artery**
I65.21 **Occlusion and stenosis of right carotid artery**
I65.22 **Occlusion and stenosis of left carotid artery**
I65.23 **Occlusion and stenosis of bilateral carotid arteries**
I65.29 **Occlusion and stenosis of unspecified carotid artery**

I65.8 **Occlusion and stenosis of other precerebral arteries**

I65.9 **Occlusion and stenosis of unspecified precerebral artery**
Occlusion and stenosis of precerebral artery NOS

I66 **Occlusion and stenosis of cerebral arteries, not resulting in cerebral infarction**

Includes: embolism of cerebral artery
narrowing of cerebral artery
obstruction (complete) (partial) of cerebral artery
thrombosis of cerebral artery

Excludes1: *Occlusion and stenosis of cerebral artery causing cerebral infarction (I63.3-I63.5)*

+ **I66.0** **Occlusion and stenosis of middle cerebral artery**
I66.01 **Occlusion and stenosis of right middle cerebral artery**
I66.02 **Occlusion and stenosis of left middle cerebral artery**
I66.03 **Occlusion and stenosis of bilateral middle cerebral arteries**
I66.09 **Occlusion and stenosis of unspecified middle cerebral artery**

+ **I66.1** **Occlusion and stenosis of anterior cerebral artery**
I66.11 **Occlusion and stenosis of right anterior cerebral artery**
I66.12 **Occlusion and stenosis of left anterior cerebral artery**
I66.13 **Occlusion and stenosis of bilateral anterior cerebral arteries**
I66.19 **Occlusion and stenosis of unspecified anterior cerebral artery**

+ **I66.2** **Occlusion and stenosis of posterior cerebral artery**
I66.21 **Occlusion and stenosis of right posterior cerebral artery**
I66.22 **Occlusion and stenosis of left posterior cerebral artery**
I66.23 **Occlusion and stenosis of bilateral posterior cerebral arteries**
I66.29 **Occlusion and stenosis of unspecified posterior cerebral artery**

I66.3 Occlusion and stenosis of cerebellar arteries
I66.8 Occlusion and stenosis of other cerebral arteries
Occlusion and stenosis of perforating arteries
I66.9 Occlusion and stenosis of unspecified cerebral artery

I67 Other cerebrovascular diseases
Excludes1: *sequelae of the listed conditions (I69.8)*

MCC **I67.0 Dissection of cerebral arteries, nonruptured**
Excludes1: *ruptured cerebral arteries (I60.7)*
MCC Exclusion see Appendix A PDX collection 0689

I67.1 Cerebral aneurysm, nonruptured
Cerebral aneurysm NOS
Cerebral arteriovenous fistula, acquired
Internal carotid artery aneurysm, intracranial portion
Internal carotid artery aneurysm, NOS
Excludes1: *congenital cerebral aneurysm, nonruptured (Q28.-)*
ruptured cerebral aneurysm (I60.7)

• **I67.2 Cerebral atherosclerosis**
Atheroma of cerebral and precerebral arteries

CC **I67.3 Progressive vascular leukoencephalopathy**
Binswanger's disease
CC Exclusion see Appendix A PDX collection 0133

CC **I67.4 Hypertensive encephalopathy**
CC Exclusion see Appendix A PDX collection 0690

CC **I67.5 Moyamoya disease**
CC Exclusion see Appendix A PDX collection 0691

CC **I67.6 Nonpyogenic thrombosis of intracranial venous system**
Nonpyogenic thrombosis of cerebral vein
Nonpyogenic thrombosis of intracranial venous sinus
Excludes1: *nonpyogenic thrombosis of intracranial venous system causing infarction (I63.6)*
CC Exclusion see Appendix A PDX collection 0692

CC **I67.7 Cerebral arteritis, not elsewhere classified**
Granulomatous angiitis of the nervous system
Excludes1: *allergic granulomatous angiitis (M30.1)*
CC Exclusion see Appendix A PDX collection 0693

\+ **I67.8 Other specified cerebrovascular diseases**

CC **I67.81 Acute cerebrovascular insufficiency**
Acute cerebrovascular insufficiency unspecified as to location or reversibility
CC Exclusion see Appendix A PDX collection 0694

CC **I67.82 Cerebral ischemia**
Chronic cerebral ischemia
CC Exclusion see Appendix A PDX collection 0694

MCC **I67.83 Posterior reversible encephalopathy syndrome**
PRES
MCC Exclusion see Appendix A PDX collection 0610

\+ **I67.84 Cerebral vasospasm and vasoconstriction**

CC **I67.841 Reversible cerebrovascular vasoconstriction syndrome**
Call-Fleming syndrome
Code first underlying condition, if applicable, such as eclampsia (O15.00-O15.9)
CC Exclusion see Appendix A PDX collection 0586

CC **I67.848 Other cerebrovascular vasospasm and vasoconstriction**
CC Exclusion see Appendix A PDX collection 0586

CC **I67.89 Other cerebrovascular disease**
CC Exclusion see Appendix A PDX collection 0694

I67.9 Cerebrovascular disease, unspecified

I68 Cerebrovascular disorders in diseases classified elsewhere

I68.0 Cerebral amyloid angiopathy
Code first underlying amyloidosis (E85.-)

CC **I68.2 Cerebral arteritis in other diseases classified elsewhere**
Code first underlying disease
Excludes1: *cerebral arteritis (in):*
listerosis (A32.89)
systemic lupus erythematosus (M32.19)
syphilis (A52.04)
tuberculosis (A18.89)
CC Exclusion see Appendix A PDX collection 0693

I68.8 Other cerebrovascular disorders in diseases classified elsewhere
Code first underlying disease
Excludes1: *syphilitic cerebral aneurysm (A52.05)*

I69 Sequelae of cerebrovascular disease

NOTE Category I69 is to be used to indicate conditions in I60-I67 as the cause of sequelae. The 'sequelae' include conditions specified as such or as residuals which may occu any time after the onset of the causal condition

Excludes1: *personal history of cerebral infarction without residual deficit (Z86.73)*
personal history of prolonged reversible ischemic neurolo deficit (PRIND) (Z86.73)
personal history of reversible ischemic neurologcial defic (RIND) (Z86.73)
sequelae of traumatic intracranial injury (S06.-)
transient ischemic attack (TIA) (G45.9)

Review coding guideline C.9.d

\+ **I69.0 Sequelae of nontraumatic subarachnoid hemorrhage**

I69.00 Unspecified sequelae of nontraumatic subarachnoi hemorrhage

I69.01 Cognitive deficits following nontraumatic subarachnoid hemorrhage

\+ **I69.02 Speech and language deficits following nontraumat subarachnoid hemorrhage**

I69.020 Aphasia following nontraumatic subarachnoid hemorrhage

I69.021 Dysphasia following nontraumatic subarachnoid hemorrhage

I69.022 Dysarthria following nontraumatic subarachnoid hemorrhage

I69.023 Fluency disorder following nontraumatic subarachnoid hemorrhage
Stuttering following nontraumatic subarachnoid hemorrhage

I69.028 Other speech and language deficits follow nontraumatic subarachnoid hemorrhage

\+ **I69.03 Monoplegia of upper limb following nontraumatic subarachnoid hemorrhage**

I69.031 Monoplegia of upper limb following nontraumatic subarachnoid hemorrhage affecting right dominant side

I69.032 Monoplegia of upper limb following nontraumatic subarachnoid hemorrhage affecting left dominant side

I69.033 Monoplegia of upper limb following nontraumatic subarachnoid hemorrhage affecting right non-dominan side

I69.034 Monoplegia of upper limb following nontraumatic subarachnoid hemorrhage affecting left non-dominant s

I69.039 Monoplegia of upper limb following nontraumatic subarachnoid hemorrhage affecting unspecified side

\+ **I69.04 Monoplegia of lower limb following nontraumatic subarachnoid hemorrhage**

I69.041 Monoplegia of lower limb following nontraumatic subarachnoid hemorrhage affecting right dominant side

I69.042 Monoplegia of lower limb following nontraumatic subarachnoid hemorrhage affecting left dominant side

I69.043 Monoplegia of lower limb following nontraumatic subarachnoid hemorrhage affecting right non-dominan side

I69.044 Monoplegia of lower limb following nontraumatic subarachnoid hemorrhage affecting left non-dominant s

I69.049 Monoplegia of lower limb following nontraumatic subarachnoid hemorrhage affecting unspecified side

\+ **I69.05 Hemiplegia and hemiparesis following nontraumat subarachnoid hemorrhage**

CC **I69.051 Hemiplegia and hemiparesis following nontraumatic subarachnoid hemorrhage affecting right dominant side**
CC Exclusion see Appendix A PDX collection 0695

CC **I69.052 Hemiplegia and hemiparesis following nontraumatic subarachnoid hemorrhage affecting left dominant side**
CC Exclusion see Appendix A PDX collection 0695

CC **I69.053 Hemiplegia and hemiparesis following nontraumatic subarachnoid hemorrhage affecting right non-dominant side**
CC Exclusion see Appendix A PDX collection 0696

CC **I69.054 Hemiplegia and hemiparesis following nontraumatic subarachnoid hemorrhage affecting left non-dominant side**
CC Exclusion see Appendix A PDX collection 0696

CC **I69.059 Hemiplegia and hemiparesis following nontraumatic subarachnoid hemorrhage affecting unspecified side**
CC Exclusion see Appendix A PDX collection 0697

\+ **I69.06 Other paralytic syndrome following nontraumatic subarachnoid hemorrhage**
Use additional code to identify type of paralytic syndrome, such as:
locked-in state (G83.5)
quadriplegia (G82.5-)
Excludes1: *hemiplegia/hemiparesis following nontraumatic subarachnoid hemorrhage (I69.05-)*
monoplegia of lower limb following nontraumatic subarachnoid hemorrhage (I69.04-)
monoplegia of upper limb following nontraumatic subarachnoid hemorrhage (I69.03-)

I69.061 Other paralytic syndrome following nontraumatic subarachnoid hemorrhage affecting right dominant side

I69.062 Other paralytic syndrome following nontraumatic subarachnoid hemorrhage affecting left dominant side

I69.063 Other paralytic syndrome following nontraumatic subarachnoid hemorrhage affecting right non-dominant side

I69.064 Other paralytic syndrome following nontraumatic subarachnoid hemorrhage affecting left non-dominant side

I69.065 Other paralytic syndrome following nontraumatic subarachnoid hemorrhage, bilateral

I69.069 Other paralytic syndrome following nontraumatic subarachnoid hemorrhage affecting unspecified side

\+ **I69.09 Other sequelae of nontraumatic subarachnoid hemorrhage**

I69.090 Apraxia following nontraumatic subarachnoid hemorrhage

I69.091 Dysphagia following nontraumatic subarachnoid hemorrhage
Use additional code to identify the type of dysphagia, if known (R13.1-)

I69.092 Facial weakness following nontraumatic subarachnoid hemorrhage
Facial droop following nontraumatic subarachnoid hemorrhage

I69.093 Ataxia following nontraumatic subarachnoid hemorrhage

I69.098 Other sequelae following nontraumatic subarachnoid hemorrhage
Alterations of sensation following nontraumatic subarachnoid hemorrhage
Disturbance of vision following nontraumatic subarachnoid hemorrhage
Use additional code to identify the sequelae

\+ **I69.1 Sequelae of nontraumatic intracerebral hemorrhage**

I69.10 Unspecified sequelae of nontraumatic intracerebral hemorrhage

I69.11 Cognitive deficits following nontraumatic intracerebral hemorrhage

\+ **I69.12 Speech and language deficits following nontraumatic intracerebral hemorrhage**

I69.120 Aphasia following nontraumatic intracerebral hemorrhage

I69.121 Dysphasia following nontraumatic intracerebral hemorrhage

I69.122 Dysarthria following nontraumatic intracerebral hemorrhage

I69.123 Fluency disorder following nontraumatic intracerebral hemorrhage
Stuttering following nontraumatic subarachnoid hemorrhage

I69.128 Other speech and language deficits following nontraumatic intracerebral hemorrhage

\+ **I69.13 Monoplegia of upper limb following nontraumatic intracerebral hemorrhage**

I69.131 Monoplegia of upper limb following nontraumatic intracerebral hemorrhage affecting right dominant side

I69.132 Monoplegia of upper limb following nontraumatic intracerebral hemorrhage affecting left dominant side

I69.133 Monoplegia of upper limb following nontraumatic intracerebral hemorrhage affecting right non-dominant side

I69.134 Monoplegia of upper limb following nontraumatic intracerebral hemorrhage affecting left non-dominant side

I69.139 Monoplegia of upper limb following nontraumatic intracerebral hemorrhage affecting unspecified side

\+ **I69.14 Monoplegia of lower limb following nontraumatic intracerebral hemorrhage**

I69.141 Monoplegia of lower limb following nontraumatic intracerebral hemorrhage affecting right dominant side

I69.142 Monoplegia of lower limb following nontraumatic intracerebral hemorrhage affecting left dominant side

I69.143 Monoplegia of lower limb following nontraumatic intracerebral hemorrhage affecting right non-dominant side

I69.144 Monoplegia of lower limb following nontraumatic intracerebral hemorrhage affecting left non-dominant side

I69.149 Monoplegia of lower limb following nontraumatic intracerebral hemorrhage affecting unspecified side

\+ **I69.15 Hemiplegia and hemiparesis following nontraumatic intracerebral hemorrhage**

CC **I69.151 Hemiplegia and hemiparesis following nontraumatic intracerebral hemorrhage affecting right dominant side**
CC Exclusion see Appendix A PDX collection 0695

CC **I69.152 Hemiplegia and hemiparesis following nontraumatic intracerebral hemorrhage affecting left dominant side**
CC Exclusion see Appendix A PDX collection 0695

CC **I69.153 Hemiplegia and hemiparesis following nontraumatic intracerebral hemorrhage affecting right non-dominant side**
CC Exclusion see Appendix A PDX collection 0696

CC **I69.154 Hemiplegia and hemiparesis following nontraumatic intracerebral hemorrhage affecting left non-dominant side**
CC Exclusion see Appendix A PDX collection 0696

CC **I69.159 Hemiplegia and hemiparesis following nontraumatic intracerebral hemorrhage affecting unspecified side**
CC Exclusion see Appendix A PDX collection 0697

+ **I69.16 Other paralytic syndrome following nontraumatic intracerebral hemorrhage**
Use additional code to identify type of paralytic syndrome, such as:
locked-in state (G83.5)
quadriplegia (G82.5-)
Excludes1: *hemiplegia/hemiparesis following nontraumatic intracerebral hemorrhage (I69.15-)*
monoplegia of lower limb following nontraumatic intracerebral hemorrhage (I69.14-)
monoplegia of upper limb following nontraumatic intracerebral hemorrhage (I69.13-)
I69.161 Other paralytic syndrome following nontraumatic intracerebral hemorrhage affecting right dominant side
I69.162 Other paralytic syndrome following nontraumatic intracerebral hemorrhage affecting left dominant side
I69.163 Other paralytic syndrome following nontraumatic intracerebral hemorrhage affecting right non-dominant side
I69.164 Other paralytic syndrome following nontraumatic intracerebral hemorrhage affecting left non-dominant side
I69.165 Other paralytic syndrome following nontraumatic intracerebral hemorrhage, bilateral
I69.169 Other paralytic syndrome following nontraumatic intracerebral hemorrhage affecting unspecified side

+ **I69.19 Other sequelae of nontraumatic intracerebral hemorrhage**
I69.190 Apraxia following nontraumatic intracerebral hemorrhage
I69.191 Dysphagia following nontraumatic intracerebral hemorrhage
Use additional code to identify the type of dysphagia, if known (R13.1-)
I69.192 Facial weakness following nontraumatic intracerebral hemorrhage
Facial droop following nontraumatic intracerebral hemorrhage
I69.193 Ataxia following nontraumatic intracerebral hemorrhage
I69.198 Other sequelae of nontraumatic intracerebral hemorrhage
Alteration of sensations following nontraumatic intracerebral hemorrhage
Disturbance of vision following nontraumatic intracerebral hemorrhage
Use additional code to identify the sequelae

+ **I69.2 Sequelae of other nontraumatic intracranial hemorrhage**
I69.20 Unspecified sequelae of other nontraumatic intracranial hemorrhage
I69.21 Cognitive deficits following other nontraumatic intracranial hemorrhage

+ **I69.22 Speech and language deficits following other nontraumatic intracranial hemorrhage**
I69.220 Aphasia following other nontraumatic intracranial hemorrhage
I69.221 Dysphasia following other nontraumatic intracranial hemorrhage
I69.222 Dysarthria following other nontraumatic intracranial hemorrhage
I69.223 Fluency disorder following other nontraumatic intracranial hemorrhage
Stuttering following nontraumatic subarachnoid hemorrhage
I69.228 Other speech and language deficits following other nontraumatic intracranial hemorrhage

+ **I69.23 Monoplegia of upper limb following other nontraumatic intracranial hemorrhage**
I69.231 Monoplegia of upper limb following other nontraumatic intracranial hemorrhage affecting right dominant side
I69.232 Monoplegia of upper limb following other nontraumatic intracranial hemorrhage affecting left dominant side
I69.233 Monoplegia of upper limb following other nontraumatic intracranial hemorrhage affecting right non-dominant side
I69.234 Monoplegia of upper limb following other nontraumatic intracranial hemorrhage affecting left non-dominant side
I69.239 Monoplegia of upper limb following other nontraumatic intracranial hemorrhage affecting unspecified side

+ **I69.24 Monoplegia of lower limb following other nontraumatic intracranial hemorrhage**
I69.241 Monoplegia of lower limb following other nontraumatic intracranial hemorrhage affecting right dominant side
I69.242 Monoplegia of lower limb following other nontraumatic intracranial hemorrhage affecting left dominant side
I69.243 Monoplegia of lower limb following other nontraumatic intracranial hemorrhage affecting right non-dominant side
I69.244 Monoplegia of lower limb following other nontraumatic intracranial hemorrhage affecting left non-dominant si
I69.249 Monoplegia of lower limb following other nontraumatic intracranial hemorrhage affecting unspecified side

+ **I69.25 Hemiplegia and hemiparesis following other nontraumatic intracranial hemorrhage**
CC **I69.251 Hemiplegia and hemiparesis following othe nontraumatic intracranial hemorrhage affecting right dominant side**
CC Exclusion see Appendix A PDX collection 06
CC **I69.252 Hemiplegia and hemiparesis following othe nontraumatic intracranial hemorrhage affecting left dominant side**
CC Exclusion see Appendix A PDX collection 06
CC **I69.253 Hemiplegia and hemiparesis following other nontraumatic intracranial hemorrhage affecting right non-dominant side**
CC Exclusion see Appendix A PDX collection 06
CC **I69.254 Hemiplegia and hemiparesis following other nontraumatic intracranial hemorrhage affecting left non-dominant si**
CC Exclusion see Appendix A PDX collection 06
CC **I69.259 Hemiplegia and hemiparesis following othe nontraumatic intracranial hemorrhage affecting unspecified side**
CC Exclusion see Appendix A PDX collection 06

+ **I69.26 Other paralytic syndrome following other nontraumatic intracranial hemorrhage**
Use additional code to identify type of paralytic syndrome, such as:
locked-in state (G83.5)
quadriplegia (G82.5-)
Excludes1: *hemiplegia/hemiparesis following other nontraumatic intracranial hemorrhage (I69.25-)*
monoplegia of lower limb following other nontraumatic intracranial hemorrhage (I69.24-)
monoplegia of upper limb following other nontraumatic intracranial hemorrhage (I69.23-)
I69.261 Other paralytic syndrome following other nontraumatic intracranial hemorrhage affecting right dominant side
I69.262 Other paralytic syndrome following other nontraumatic intracranial hemorrhage affecting left dominant side
I69.263 Other paralytic syndrome following other nontraumatic intracranial hemorrhage affecting right non-dominant side
I69.264 Other paralytic syndrome following other nontraumatic intracranial hemorrhage affecting left non-dominant sid
I69.265 Other paralytic syndrome following other nontraumatic intracranial hemorrhage, bilateral

I69.269 Other paralytic syndrome following other nontraumatic intracranial hemorrhage affecting unspecified side

+ I69.29 Other sequelae of other nontraumatic intracranial hemorrhage

I69.290 Apraxia following other nontraumatic intracranial hemorrhage

I69.291 Dysphagia following other nontraumatic intracranial hemorrhage
Use additional code to identify the type of dysphagia, if known (R13.1-)

I69.292 Facial weakness following other nontraumatic intracranial hemorrhage
Facial droop following other nontraumatic intracranial hemorrhage

I69.293 Ataxia following other nontraumatic intracranial hemorrhage

I69.298 Other sequelae of other nontraumatic intracranial hemorrhage
Alteration of sensation following other nontraumatic intracranial hemorrhage
Disturbance of vision following other nontraumatic intracranial hemorrhage
Use additional code to identify the sequelae

+ I69.3 Sequelae of cerebral infarction
Sequelae of stroke NOS
AHA CC: 4Q, 2012, 95; 4Q, 2013, 127-128

I69.30 Unspecified sequelae of cerebral infarction

I69.31 Cognitive deficits following cerebral infarction

+ I69.32 Speech and language deficits following cerebral infarction

I69.320 Aphasia following cerebral infarction
AHA CC: 4Q, 2013, 128

I69.321 Dysphasia following cerebral infarction
AHA CC: 4Q, 2012, 91

I69.322 Dysarthria following cerebral infarction

I69.323 Fluency disorder following cerebral infarction
Stuttering following nontraumatic subarachnoid hemorrhage

I69.328 Other speech and language deficits following cerebral infarction

+ I69.33 Monoplegia of upper limb following cerebral infarction

I69.331 Monoplegia of upper limb following cerebral infarction affecting right dominant side

I69.332 Monoplegia of upper limb following cerebral infarction affecting left dominant side

I69.333 Monoplegia of upper limb following cerebral infarction affecting right non-dominant side

I69.334 Monoplegia of upper limb following cerebral infarction affecting left non-dominant side

I69.339 Monoplegia of upper limb following cerebral infarction affecting unspecified side

+ I69.34 Monoplegia of lower limb following cerebral infarction

I69.341 Monoplegia of lower limb following cerebral infarction affecting right dominant side

I69.342 Monoplegia of lower limb following cerebral infarction affecting left dominant side

I69.343 Monoplegia of lower limb following cerebral infarction affecting right non-dominant side

I69.344 Monoplegia of lower limb following cerebral infarction affecting left non-dominant side

I69.349 Monoplegia of lower limb following cerebral infarction affecting unspecified side

+ I69.35 Hemiplegia and hemiparesis following cerebral infarction

CC **I69.351 Hemiplegia and hemiparesis following cerebral infarction affecting right dominant side**
CC Exclusion see Appendix A PDX collection 0695
AHA CC: 4Q, 2013, 128

CC **I69.352 Hemiplegia and hemiparesis following cerebral infarction affecting left dominant side**
CC Exclusion see Appendix A PDX collection 0695

CC **I69.353 Hemiplegia and hemiparesis following cerebral infarction affecting right non-dominant side**
CC Exclusion see Appendix A PDX collection 0696

CC **I69.354 Hemiplegia and hemiparesis following cerebral infarction affecting left non-dominant side**
CC Exclusion see Appendix A PDX collection 0696
AHA CC: 4Q, 2012, 91

CC **I69.359 Hemiplegia and hemiparesis following cerebral infarction affecting unspecified side**
CC Exclusion see Appendix A PDX collection 0697

+ I69.36 Other paralytic syndrome following cerebral infarction
Use additional code to identify type of paralytic syndrome, such as:
locked-in state (G83.5)
quadriplegia (G82.5-)
Excludes1: *hemiplegia/hemiparesis following cerebral infarction (I69.35-)*
monoplegia of lower limb following cerebral infarction (I69.34-)
monoplegia of upper limb following cerebral infarction (I69.33-)

I69.361 Other paralytic syndrome following cerebral infarction affecting right dominant side

I69.362 Other paralytic syndrome following cerebral infarction affecting left dominant side

I69.363 Other paralytic syndrome following cerebral infarction affecting right non-dominant side

I69.364 Other paralytic syndrome following cerebral infarction affecting left non-dominant side

I69.365 Other paralytic syndrome following cerebral infarction, bilateral

I69.369 Other paralytic syndrome following cerebral infarction affecting unspecified side

+ I69.39 Other sequelae of cerebral infarction

I69.390 Apraxia following cerebral infarction

I69.391 Dysphagia following cerebral infarction
Use additional code to identify the type of dysphagia, if known (R13.1-)

I69.392 Facial weakness following cerebral infarction
Facial droop following cerebral infarction

I69.393 Ataxia following cerebral infarction

I69.398 Other sequelae of cerebral infarction
Alteration of sensation following cerebral infarction
Disturbance of vision following cerebral infarction
Use additional code to identify the sequelae

+ I69.8 Sequelae of other cerebrovascular diseases
Excludes1: *sequelae of traumatic intracranial injury (S06.-)*

I69.80 Unspecified sequelae of other cerebrovascular disease

I69.81 Cognitive deficits following other cerebrovascular disease

+ I69.82 Speech and language deficits following other cerebrovascular disease

I69.820 Aphasia following other cerebrovascular disease

I69.821 Dysphasia following other cerebrovascular disease

I69.822 Dysarthria following other cerebrovascular disease

I69.823 Fluency disorder following other cerebrovascular disease
Stuttering following nontraumatic subarachnoid hemorrhage

I69.828 Other speech and language deficits following other cerebrovascular disease

+ I69.83 Monoplegia of upper limb following other cerebrovascular disease

I69.831 Monoplegia of upper limb following other cerebrovascular disease affecting right dominant side

I69.832 Monoplegia of upper limb following other cerebrovascular disease affecting left dominant side

I69.833 Monoplegia of upper limb following other cerebrovascular disease affecting right non-dominant side

I69.834 Monoplegia of upper limb following other cerebrovascular disease affecting left non-dominant side

I69.839 Monoplegia of upper limb following other cerebrovascular disease affecting unspecified side

+ I69.84 Monoplegia of lower limb following other cerebrovascular disease

I69.841 Monoplegia of lower limb following other cerebrovascular disease affecting right dominant side

I69.842 Monoplegia of lower limb following other cerebrovascular disease affecting left dominant side

I69.843 Monoplegia of lower limb following other cerebrovascular disease affecting right non-dominant side

I69.844 Monoplegia of lower limb following other cerebrovascular disease affecting left non-dominant side

I69.849 Monoplegia of lower limb following other cerebrovascular disease affecting unspecified side

+ I69.85 Hemiplegia and hemiparesis following other cerebrovascular disease

CC **I69.851 Hemiplegia and hemiparesis following other cerebrovascular disease affecting right dominant side**
CC Exclusion see Appendix A PDX collection 0695

CC **I69.852 Hemiplegia and hemiparesis following other cerebrovascular disease affecting left dominant side**
CC Exclusion see Appendix A PDX collection 0695

CC **I69.853 Hemiplegia and hemiparesis following other cerebrovascular disease affecting right non-dominant side**
CC Exclusion see Appendix A PDX collection 0696

CC **I69.854 Hemiplegia and hemiparesis following other cerebrovascular disease affecting left non-dominant side**
CC Exclusion see Appendix A PDX collection 0696

CC **I69.859 Hemiplegia and hemiparesis following other cerebrovascular disease affecting unspecified side**
CC Exclusion see Appendix A PDX collection 0697

+ I69.86 Other paralytic syndrome following other cerebrovascular disease

Use additional code to identify type of paralytic syndrome, such as:
locked-in state (G83.5)
quadriplegia (G82.5-)

Excludes1: *hemiplegia/hemiparesis following other cerebrovascular disease (I69.85-)*
monoplegia of lower limb following other cerebrovascular disease (I69.84-)
monoplegia of upper limb following other cerebrovascular disease (I69.83-)

I69.861 Other paralytic syndrome following other cerebrovascular disease affecting right dominant side

I69.862 Other paralytic syndrome following other cerebrovascular disease affecting left dominant side

I69.863 Other paralytic syndrome following other cerebrovascular disease affecting right non-dominant side

I69.864 Other paralytic syndrome following other cerebrovascular disease affecting left non-dominant side

I69.865 Other paralytic syndrome following other cerebrovascular disease, bilateral

I69.869 Other paralytic syndrome following other cerebrovascular disease affecting unspecified side

+ I69.89 Other sequelae of other cerebrovascular disease

I69.890 Apraxia following other cerebrovascular disease

I69.891 Dysphagia following other cerebrovascular disease

Use additional code to identify the type of dysphagia, if known (R13.1-)

I69.892 Facial weakness following other cerebrovascular disease

Facial droop following other cerebrovascular disease

I69.893 Ataxia following other cerebrovascular disease

I69.898 Other sequelae of other cerebrovascular disease

Alteration of sensation following other cerebrovascular disease
Disturbance of vision following other cerebrovascular disease
Use additional code to identify the sequelae

+ I69.9 Sequelae of unspecified cerebrovascular diseases

Excludes1: *sequelae of stroke (I69.3)*
sequelae of traumatic intracranial injury (S06.-)

I69.90 Unspecified sequelae of unspecified cerebrovascular disease

I69.91 Cognitive deficits following unspecified cerebrovascular disease

+ I69.92 Speech and language deficits following unspecified cerebrovascular disease

I69.920 Aphasia following unspecified cerebrovascular disease

I69.921 Dysphasia following unspecified cerebrovascular disease

I69.922 Dysarthria following unspecified cerebrovascular disease

I69.923 Fluency disorder following unspecified cerebrovascular disease

Stuttering following nontraumatic subarachnoid hemorrhage

I69.928 Other speech and language deficits follow[ing] unspecified cerebrovascular disease

+ I69.93 Monoplegia of upper limb following unspecified cerebrovascular disease

I69.931 Monoplegia of upper limb following unspecified cerebrovascular disease affec[ting] right dominant side

I69.932 Monoplegia of upper limb following unspecified cerebrovascular disease affec[ting] left dominant side

I69.933 Monoplegia of upper limb following unspecified cerebrovascular disease affec[ting] right non-dominant side

I69.934 Monoplegia of upper limb following unspecified cerebrovascular disease affec[ting] left non-dominant side

I69.939 Monoplegia of upper limb following unspecified cerebrovascular disease affec[ting] unspecified side

+ I69.94 Monoplegia of lower limb following unspecified cerebrovascular disease

I69.941 Monoplegia of lower limb following unspecified cerebrovascular disease affec[ting] right dominant side

I69.942 Monoplegia of lower limb following unspecified cerebrovascular disease affec[ting] left dominant side

I69.943 Monoplegia of lower limb following unspecified cerebrovascular disease affec[ting] right non-dominant side

I69.944 Monoplegia of lower limb following unspecified cerebrovascular disease affec[ting] left non-dominant side

I69.949 Monoplegia of lower limb following unspecified cerebrovascular disease affec[ting] unspecified side

+ I69.95 Hemiplegia and hemiparesis following unspecified cerebrovascular disease

CC **I69.951 Hemiplegia and hemiparesis following unspecified cerebrovascular disease affec[ting] right dominant side**
CC Exclusion see Appendix A PDX collection

CC **I69.952 Hemiplegia and hemiparesis following unspecified cerebrovascular disease affec[ting] left dominant side**
CC Exclusion see Appendix A PDX collection

CC **I69.953 Hemiplegia and hemiparesis following unspecified cerebrovascular disease affec[ting] right non-dominant side**
CC Exclusion see Appendix A PDX collection

CC **I69.954 Hemiplegia and hemiparesis following unspecified cerebrovascular disease affecting left non-dominant side**
CC Exclusion see Appendix A PDX collection 0696

CC **I69.959 Hemiplegia and hemiparesis following unspecified cerebrovascular disease affecting unspecified side**
CC Exclusion see Appendix A PDX collection 0697

+ **I69.96 Other paralytic syndrome following unspecified cerebrovascular disease**
Use additional code to identify type of paralytic syndrome, such as:
locked-in state (G83.5)
quadriplegia (G82.5-)
Excludes1: *hemiplegia/hemiparesis following unspecified cerebrovascular disease (I69.95-)*
monoplegia of lower limb following unspecified cerebrovascular disease (I69.94-)
monoplegia of upper limb following unspecified cerebrovascular disease (I69.93-)

I69.961 Other paralytic syndrome following unspecified cerebrovascular disease affecting right dominant side

I69.962 Other paralytic syndrome following unspecified cerebrovascular disease affecting left dominant side

I69.963 Other paralytic syndrome following unspecified cerebrovascular disease affecting right non-dominant side

I69.964 Other paralytic syndrome following unspecified cerebrovascular disease affecting left non-dominant side

I69.965 Other paralytic syndrome following unspecified cerebrovascular disease, bilateral

I69.969 Other paralytic syndrome following unspecified cerebrovascular disease affecting unspecified side

+ **I69.99 Other sequelae of unspecified cerebrovascular disease**

I69.990 Apraxia following unspecified cerebrovascular disease

I69.991 Dysphagia following unspecified cerebrovascular disease
Use additional code to identify the type of dysphagia, if known (R13.1-)

I69.992 Facial weakness following unspecified cerebrovascular disease
Facial droop following unspecified cerebrovascular disease

I69.993 Ataxia following unspecified cerebrovascular disease

I69.998 Other sequelae following unspecified cerebrovascular disease
Alteration in sensation following unspecified cerebrovascular disease
Disturbance of vision following unspecified cerebrovascular disease
Use additional code to identify the sequelae

Diseases of arteries, arterioles and capillaries (I70-I79)

I70 Atherosclerosis

Includes: arteriolosclerosis
arterial degeneration
arteriosclerosis
arteriosclerotic vascular disease
arteriovascular degeneration
atheroma
endarteritis deformans or obliterans
senile arteritis
senile endarteritis
vascular degeneration

Use additional code to identify:
exposure to environmental tobacco smoke (Z77.22)
history of tobacco use (Z87.891)
occupational exposure to environmental tobacco smoke (Z57.31)
tobacco dependence (F17.-)
tobacco use (Z72.0)

Excludes2: *arteriosclerotic cardiovascular disease (I25.1-)*
arteriosclerotic heart disease (I25.1-)
atheroembolism (I75.-)
cerebral atherosclerosis (I67.2)
coronary atherosclerosis (I25.1-)
mesenteric atherosclerosis (K55.1)
precerebral atherosclerosis (I67.2)
primary pulmonary atherosclerosis (I27.0)

• **I70.0 Atherosclerosis of aorta**

• **I70.1 Atherosclerosis of renal artery**
Goldblatt's kidney
Excludes2: *atherosclerosis of renal arterioles (I12.-)*

+ **I70.2 Atherosclerosis of native arteries of the extremities**
Mönckeberg's (medial) sclerosis
Use additional code, if applicable, to identify chronic total occlusion of artery of extremity (I70.92)
Excludes2: *atherosclerosis of bypass graft of extremities (I70.30-I70.79)*

+ **I70.20 Unspecified atherosclerosis of native arteries of extremities**

• **I70.201 Unspecified atherosclerosis of native arteries of extremities, right leg**

• **I70.202 Unspecified atherosclerosis of native arteries of extremities, left leg**

• **I70.203 Unspecified atherosclerosis of native arteries of extremities, bilateral legs**

• **I70.208 Unspecified atherosclerosis of native arteries of extremities, other extremity**

• **I70.209 Unspecified atherosclerosis of native arteries of extremities, unspecified extremity**

+ **I70.21 Atherosclerosis of native arteries of extremities with intermittent claudication**

• **I70.211 Atherosclerosis of native arteries of extremities with intermittent claudication, right leg**

• **I70.212 Atherosclerosis of native arteries of extremities with intermittent claudication, left leg**

• **I70.213 Atherosclerosis of native arteries of extremities with intermittent claudication, bilateral legs**

• **I70.218 Atherosclerosis of native arteries of extremities with intermittent claudication, other extremity**

• **I70.219 Atherosclerosis of native arteries of extremities with intermittent claudication, unspecified extremity**

+ **I70.22 Atherosclerosis of native arteries of extremities with rest pain**
Includes: any condition classifiable to I70.21-

• **I70.221 Atherosclerosis of native arteries of extremities with rest pain, right leg**

• **I70.222 Atherosclerosis of native arteries of extremities with rest pain, left leg**

• **I70.223 Atherosclerosis of native arteries of extremities with rest pain, bilateral legs**

• **I70.228 Atherosclerosis of native arteries of extremities with rest pain, other extremity**

• **I70.229 Atherosclerosis of native arteries of extremities with rest pain, unspecified extremity**

+ **I70.23 Atherosclerosis of native arteries of right leg with ulceration**
Includes: any condition classifiable to I70.211 and I70.221
Use additional code to identify severity of ulcer (L97.-)
- • **I70.231 Atherosclerosis of native arteries of right leg with ulceration of thigh**
- • **I70.232 Atherosclerosis of native arteries of right leg with ulceration of calf**
- • **I70.233 Atherosclerosis of native arteries of right leg with ulceration of ankle**
- • **I70.234 Atherosclerosis of native arteries of right leg with ulceration of heel and midfoot**
  Atherosclerosis of native arteries of right leg with ulceration of plantar surface of midfoot
- • **I70.235 Atherosclerosis of native arteries of right leg with ulceration of other part of foot**
  Atherosclerosis of native arteries of right leg extremities with ulceration of toe
- • **I70.238 Atherosclerosis of native arteries of right leg with ulceration of other part of lower right leg**
- • **I70.239 Atherosclerosis of native arteries of right leg with ulceration of unspecified site**

+ **I70.24 Atherosclerosis of native arteries of left leg with ulceration**
Includes: any condition classifiable to I70.212 and I70.222
Use additional code to identify severity of ulcer (L97.-)
- • **I70.241 Atherosclerosis of native arteries of left leg with ulceration of thigh**
- • **I70.242 Atherosclerosis of native arteries of left leg with ulceration of calf**
- • **I70.243 Atherosclerosis of native arteries of left leg with ulceration of ankle**
- • **I70.244 Atherosclerosis of native arteries of left leg with ulceration of heel and midfoot**
  Atherosclerosis of native arteries of left leg with ulceration of plantar surface of midfoot
- • **I70.245 Atherosclerosis of native arteries of left leg with ulceration of other part of foot**
  Atherosclerosis of native arteries of left leg extremities with ulceration of toe
- • **I70.248 Atherosclerosis of native arteries of left leg with ulceration of other part of lower left leg**
- • **I70.249 Atherosclerosis of native arteries of left leg with ulceration of unspecified site**

• **I70.25 Atherosclerosis of native arteries of other extremities with ulceration**
Includes: any condition classifiable to I70.218 and I70.228
Use additional code to identify the severity of the ulcer (L98.49-)

+ **I70.26 Atherosclerosis of native arteries of extremities with gangrene**
Includes: any condition classifiable to I70.21-, I70.22-, I70.23-, I70.24-, and I70.25-
Use additional code to identify the severity of any ulcer (L97.-, L98.49-), if applicable
- • CC **I70.261 Atherosclerosis of native arteries of extremities with gangrene, right leg**
  CC Exclusion see Appendix A PDX collection 0519
- • CC **I70.262 Atherosclerosis of native arteries of extremities with gangrene, left leg**
  CC Exclusion see Appendix A PDX collection 0519
- • CC **I70.263 Atherosclerosis of native arteries of extremities with gangrene, bilateral legs**
  CC Exclusion see Appendix A PDX collection 0519
- • CC **I70.268 Atherosclerosis of native arteries of extremities with gangrene, other extremity**
  CC Exclusion see Appendix A PDX collection 0519
- • CC **I70.269 Atherosclerosis of native arteries of extremities with gangrene, unspecified extremity**
  CC Exclusion see Appendix A PDX collection 0519

+ **I70.29 Other atherosclerosis of native arteries of extremities**
- • **I70.291 Other atherosclerosis of native arteries of extremities, right leg**
- • **I70.292 Other atherosclerosis of native arteries of extremities, left leg**
- • **I70.293 Other atherosclerosis of native arteries of extremities, bilateral legs**
- • **I70.298 Other atherosclerosis of native arteries of extremities, other extremity**
- • **I70.299 Other atherosclerosis of native arteries of extremities, unspecified extremity**

+ **I70.3 Atherosclerosis of unspecified type of bypass graft(s) of the extremities**
Use additional code, if applicable, to identify chronic total occlusion of artery of extremity (I70.92)
Excludes1: *embolism or thrombus of bypass graft(s) of extremities (T82.8-)*

+ **I70.30 Unspecified atherosclerosis of unspecified type of bypass graft(s) of the extremities**
- • **I70.301 Unspecified atherosclerosis of unspecified type of bypass graft(s) of the extremities, right leg**
- • **I70.302 Unspecified atherosclerosis of unspecified type of bypass graft(s) of the extremities, left leg**
- • **I70.303 Unspecified atherosclerosis of unspecified type of bypass graft(s) of the extremities, bilateral legs**
- • **I70.308 Unspecified atherosclerosis of unspecified type of bypass graft(s) of the extremities, other extremity**
- • **I70.309 Unspecified atherosclerosis of unspecified type of bypass graft(s) of the extremities, unspecified extremity**

+ **I70.31 Atherosclerosis of unspecified type of bypass graft(s of the extremities with intermittent claudication**
- • **I70.311 Atherosclerosis of unspecified type of bypa graft(s) of the extremities with intermitten claudication, right leg**
- • **I70.312 Atherosclerosis of unspecified type of bypa graft(s) of the extremities with intermitten claudication, left leg**
- • **I70.313 Atherosclerosis of unspecified type of bypa graft(s) of the extremities with intermitten claudication, bilateral legs**
- • **I70.318 Atherosclerosis of unspecified type of bypa graft(s) of the extremities with intermittent claudication, other extremity**
- • **I70.319 Atherosclerosis of unspecified type of bypa graft(s) of the extremities with intermitten claudication, unspecified extremity**

+ **I70.32 Atherosclerosis of unspecified type of bypass graft(s of the extremities with rest pain**
Includes: any condition classifiable to I70.31-
- • **I70.321 Atherosclerosis of unspecified type of bypa graft(s) of the extremities with rest pain, right leg**
- • **I70.322 Atherosclerosis of unspecified type of bypa graft(s) of the extremities with rest pain, le leg**
- • **I70.323 Atherosclerosis of unspecified type of bypa graft(s) of the extremities with rest pain, bilateral legs**
- • **I70.328 Atherosclerosis of unspecified type of bypa graft(s) of the extremities with rest pain, other extremity**
- • **I70.329 Atherosclerosis of unspecified type of bypa graft(s) of the extremities with rest pain, unspecified extremity**

+ **I70.33 Atherosclerosis of unspecified type of bypass graft(s) of the right leg with ulceration**
Includes: any condition classifiable to I70.311 and I70.321
Use additional code to identify severity of ulcer (L97.-
- • CC **I70.331 Atherosclerosis of unspecified type of bypa graft(s) of the right leg with ulceration of thigh**
  CC Exclusion see Appendix A PDX collection 06
- • CC **I70.332 Atherosclerosis of unspecified type of bypa graft(s) of the right leg with ulceration of calf**
  CC Exclusion see Appendix A PDX collection 06

• CC **I70.333 Atherosclerosis of unspecified type of bypass graft(s) of the right leg with ulceration of ankle**
CC Exclusion see Appendix A PDX collection 0698

• CC **I70.334 Atherosclerosis of unspecified type of bypass graft(s) of the right leg with ulceration of heel and midfoot**
Atherosclerosis of unspecified type of bypass graft(s) of right leg with ulceration of plantar surface of midfoot
CC Exclusion see Appendix A PDX collection 0698

• **I70.335 Atherosclerosis of unspecified type of bypass graft(s) of the right leg with ulceration of other part of foot**
Atherosclerosis of unspecified type of bypass graft(s) of the right leg with ulceration of toe

• CC **I70.338 Atherosclerosis of unspecified type of bypass graft(s) of the right leg with ulceration of other part of lower leg**
CC Exclusion see Appendix A PDX collection 0698

• CC **I70.339 Atherosclerosis of unspecified type of bypass graft(s) of the right leg with ulceration of unspecified site**
CC Exclusion see Appendix A PDX collection 0698

+ **I70.34 Atherosclerosis of unspecified type of bypass graft(s) of the left leg with ulceration**
Includes: any condition classifiable to I70.312 and I70.322
Use additional code to identify severity of ulcer (L97.-)

• CC **I70.341 Atherosclerosis of unspecified type of bypass graft(s) of the left leg with ulceration of thigh**
CC Exclusion see Appendix A PDX collection 0698

• CC **I70.342 Atherosclerosis of unspecified type of bypass graft(s) of the left leg with ulceration of calf**
CC Exclusion see Appendix A PDX collection 0698

• CC **I70.343 Atherosclerosis of unspecified type of bypass graft(s) of the left leg with ulceration of ankle**
CC Exclusion see Appendix A PDX collection 0698

• CC **I70.344 Atherosclerosis of unspecified type of bypass graft(s) of the left leg with ulceration of heel and midfoot**
Atherosclerosis of unspecified type of bypass graft(s) of left leg with ulceration of plantar surface of midfoot
CC Exclusion see Appendix A PDX collection 0698

• **I70.345 Atherosclerosis of unspecified type of bypass graft(s) of the left leg with ulceration of other part of foot**
Atherosclerosis of unspecified type of bypass graft(s) of the left leg with ulceration of toe

• CC **I70.348 Atherosclerosis of unspecified type of bypass graft(s) of the left leg with ulceration of other part of lower leg**
CC Exclusion see Appendix A PDX collection 0698

• CC **I70.349 Atherosclerosis of unspecified type of bypass graft(s) of the left leg with ulceration of unspecified site**
CC Exclusion see Appendix A PDX collection 0698

• **I70.35 Atherosclerosis of unspecified type of bypass graft(s) of other extremity with ulceration**
Includes: any condition classifiable to I70.318 and I70.328
Use additional code to identify severity of ulcer (L98.49-)

+ **I70.36 Atherosclerosis of unspecified type of bypass graft(s) of the extremities with gangrene**
Includes: any condition classifiable to I70.31-, I70.32-, I70.33-, I70.34-, I70.35
Use additional code to identify the severity of any ulcer (L97.-, L98.49-), if applicable

• CC **I70.361 Atherosclerosis of unspecified type of bypass graft(s) of the extremities with gangrene, right leg**
CC Exclusion see Appendix A PDX collection 0519

• CC **I70.362 Atherosclerosis of unspecified type of bypass graft(s) of the extremities with gangrene, left leg**
CC Exclusion see Appendix A PDX collection 0519

• CC **I70.363 Atherosclerosis of unspecified type of bypass graft(s) of the extremities with gangrene, bilateral legs**
CC Exclusion see Appendix A PDX collection 0519

• CC **I70.368 Atherosclerosis of unspecified type of bypass graft(s) of the extremities with gangrene, other extremity**
CC Exclusion see Appendix A PDX collection 0519

• CC **I70.369 Atherosclerosis of unspecified type of bypass graft(s) of the extremities with gangrene, unspecified extremity**
CC Exclusion see Appendix A PDX collection 0519

+ **I70.39 Other atherosclerosis of unspecified type of bypass graft(s) of the extremities**

• **I70.391 Other atherosclerosis of unspecified type of bypass graft(s) of the extremities, right leg**

• **I70.392 Other atherosclerosis of unspecified type of bypass graft(s) of the extremities, left leg**

• **I70.393 Other atherosclerosis of unspecified type of bypass graft(s) of the extremities, bilateral legs**

• **I70.398 Other atherosclerosis of unspecified type of bypass graft(s) of the extremities, other extremity**

• **I70.399 Other atherosclerosis of unspecified type of bypass graft(s) of the extremities, unspecified extremity**

+ **I70.4 Atherosclerosis of autologous vein bypass graft(s) of the extremities**
Use additional code, if applicable, to identify chronic total occlusion of artery of extremity (I70.92)

+ **I70.40 Unspecified atherosclerosis of autologous vein bypass graft(s) of the extremities**

• **I70.401 Unspecified atherosclerosis of autologous vein bypass graft(s) of the extremities, right leg**

• **I70.402 Unspecified atherosclerosis of autologous vein bypass graft(s) of the extremities, left leg**

• **I70.403 Unspecified atherosclerosis of autologous vein bypass graft(s) of the extremities, bilateral legs**

• **I70.408 Unspecified atherosclerosis of autologous vein bypass graft(s) of the extremities, other extremity**

• **I70.409 Unspecified atherosclerosis of autologous vein bypass graft(s) of the extremities, unspecified extremity**

+ **I70.41 Atherosclerosis of autologous vein bypass graft(s) of the extremities with intermittent claudication**

• **I70.411 Atherosclerosis of autologous vein bypass graft(s) of the extremities with intermittent claudication, right leg**

• **I70.412 Atherosclerosis of autologous vein bypass graft(s) of the extremities with intermittent claudication, left leg**

• **I70.413 Atherosclerosis of autologous vein bypass graft(s) of the extremities with intermittent claudication, bilateral legs**

• **I70.418 Atherosclerosis of autologous vein bypass graft(s) of the extremities with intermittent claudication, other extremity**

• **I70.419 Atherosclerosis of autologous vein bypass graft(s) of the extremities with intermittent claudication, unspecified extremity**

+ **I70.42 Atherosclerosis of autologous vein bypass graft(s) of the extremities with rest pain**
Includes: any condition classifiable to I70.41-

• **I70.421 Atherosclerosis of autologous vein bypass graft(s) of the extremities with rest pain, right leg**

• **I70.422 Atherosclerosis of autologous vein bypass graft(s) of the extremities with rest pain, left leg**

• **I70.423 Atherosclerosis of autologous vein bypass graft(s) of the extremities with rest pain, bilateral legs**

• **I70.428 Atherosclerosis of autologous vein bypass graft(s) of the extremities with rest pain, other extremity**

• **I70.429 Atherosclerosis of autologous vein bypass graft(s) of the extremities with rest pain, unspecified extremity**

+ **I70.43 Atherosclerosis of autologous vein bypass graft(s) of the right leg with ulceration**

Includes: any condition classifiable to I70.411 and I70.421

Use additional code to identify severity of ulcer (L97.-)

• CC **I70.431 Atherosclerosis of autologous vein bypass graft(s) of the right leg with ulceration of thigh**

CC Exclusion see Appendix A PDX collection 0698

• CC **I70.432 Atherosclerosis of autologous vein bypass graft(s) of the right leg with ulceration of calf**

CC Exclusion see Appendix A PDX collection 0698

• CC **I70.433 Atherosclerosis of autologous vein bypass graft(s) of the right leg with ulceration of ankle**

CC Exclusion see Appendix A PDX collection 0698

• CC **I70.434 Atherosclerosis of autologous vein bypass graft(s) of the right leg with ulceration of heel and midfoot**

CC Exclusion see Appendix A PDX collection 0698

Atherosclerosis of autologous vein bypass graft(s) of right leg with ulceration of plantar surface of midfoot

• **I70.435 Atherosclerosis of autologous vein bypass graft(s) of the right leg with ulceration of other part of foot**

Atherosclerosis of autologous vein bypass graft(s) of right leg with ulceration of toe

• CC **I70.438 Atherosclerosis of autologous vein bypass graft(s) of the right leg with ulceration of other part of lower leg**

CC Exclusion see Appendix A PDX collection 0698

• CC **I70.439 Atherosclerosis of autologous vein bypass graft(s) of the right leg with ulceration of unspecified site**

CC Exclusion see Appendix A PDX collection 0698

+ **I70.44 Atherosclerosis of autologous vein bypass graft(s) of the left leg with ulceration**

Includes: any condition classifiable to I70.412 and I70.422

Use additional code to identify severity of ulcer (L97.-)

• CC **I70.441 Atherosclerosis of autologous vein bypass graft(s) of the left leg with ulceration of thigh**

CC Exclusion see Appendix A PDX collection 0698

• CC **I70.442 Atherosclerosis of autologous vein bypass graft(s) of the left leg with ulceration of calf**

CC Exclusion see Appendix A PDX collection 0698

• CC **I70.443 Atherosclerosis of autologous vein bypass graft(s) of the left leg with ulceration of ankle**

CC Exclusion see Appendix A PDX collection 0698

• CC **I70.444 Atherosclerosis of autologous vein bypass graft(s) of the left leg with ulceration of heel and midfoot**

Atherosclerosis of autologous vein bypass graft(s) of left leg with ulceration of plantar surface of midfoot

CC Exclusion see Appendix A PDX collection 0698

• **I70.445 Atherosclerosis of autologous vein bypass graft(s) of the left leg with ulceration of other part of foot**

Atherosclerosis of autologous vein bypass graft(s) of left leg with ulceration of toe

• CC **I70.448 Atherosclerosis of autologous vein bypass graft(s) of the left leg with ulceration of other part of lower leg**

CC Exclusion see Appendix A PDX collection 0698

• CC **I70.449 Atherosclerosis of autologous vein bypass graft(s) of the left leg with ulceration of unspecified site**

CC Exclusion see Appendix A PDX collection 0698

• **I70.45 Atherosclerosis of autologous vein bypass graft(s) other extremity with ulceration**

Includes: any condition classifiable to I70.418, I70. and I70.438

Use additional code to identify severity of ulcer (L98

+ **I70.46 Atherosclerosis of autologous vein bypass graft(s) the extremities with gangrene**

Includes: any condition classifiable to I70.41-, I70. and I70.43-, I70.44-, I70.45

Use additional code to identify the severity of any ul (L97.-, L98.49-), if applicable

• CC **I70.461 Atherosclerosis of autologous vein bypass graft(s) of the extremities with gangrene, right leg**

CC Exclusion see Appendix A PDX collection

• CC **I70.462 Atherosclerosis of autologous vein bypass graft(s) of the extremities with gangrene, left leg**

CC Exclusion see Appendix A PDX collection

• CC **I70.463 Atherosclerosis of autologous vein bypass graft(s) of the extremities with gangrene, bilateral legs**

CC Exclusion see Appendix A PDX collection

• CC **I70.468 Atherosclerosis of autologous vein bypass graft(s) of the extremities with gangrene, other extremity**

CC Exclusion see Appendix A PDX collection

• CC **I70.469 Atherosclerosis of autologous vein bypass graft(s) of the extremities with gangrene, unspecified extremity**

CC Exclusion see Appendix A PDX collection

+ **I70.49 Other atherosclerosis of autologous vein bypass graft(s) of the extremities**

• **I70.491 Other atherosclerosis of autologous vein bypass graft(s) of the extremities, right le**

• **I70.492 Other atherosclerosis of autologous vein bypass graft(s) of the extremities, left leg**

• **I70.493 Other atherosclerosis of autologous vein bypass graft(s) of the extremities, bilater legs**

• **I70.498 Other atherosclerosis of autologous vein bypass graft(s) of the extremities, other extremity**

• **I70.499 Other atherosclerosis of autologous vein bypass graft(s) of the extremities, unspec extremity**

+ **I70.5 Atherosclerosis of nonautologous biological bypass graft(s) o the extremities**

Use additional code, if applicable, to identify chronic total occlusion of artery of extremity (I70.92)

+ **I70.50 Unspecified atherosclerosis of nonautologous biological bypass graft(s) of the extremities**

• **I70.501 Unspecified atherosclerosis of nonautolog biological bypass graft(s) of the extremit right leg**

• **I70.502 Unspecified atherosclerosis of nonautolog biological bypass graft(s) of the extremit left leg**

• **I70.503 Unspecified atherosclerosis of nonautolog biological bypass graft(s) of the extremit bilateral legs**

• **I70.508 Unspecified atherosclerosis of nonautolog biological bypass graft(s) of the extremit other extremity**

• **I70.509 Unspecified atherosclerosis of nonautolog biological bypass graft(s) of the extremit unspecified extremity**

+ **I70.51 Atherosclerosis of nonautologous biological bypass graft(s) of the extremities intermittent claudicatio**

• **I70.511 Atherosclerosis of nonautologous biologi bypass graft(s) of the extremities with intermittent claudication, right leg**

• **I70.512 Atherosclerosis of nonautologous biologi bypass graft(s) of the extremities with intermittent claudication, left leg**

• **I70.513 Atherosclerosis of nonautologous biologi bypass graft(s) of the extremities with intermittent claudication, bilateral legs**

• **I70.518 Atherosclerosis of nonautologous biologi bypass graft(s) of the extremities with intermittent claudication, other extremit**

• **I70.519 Atherosclerosis of nonautologous biological bypass graft(s) of the extremities with intermittent claudication, unspecified extremity**

+ **I70.52 Atherosclerosis of nonautologous biological bypass graft(s) of the extremities with rest pain**
Includes: any condition classifiable to I70.51-

• **I70.521 Atherosclerosis of nonautologous biological bypass graft(s) of the extremities with rest pain, right leg**

• **I70.522 Atherosclerosis of nonautologous biological bypass graft(s) of the extremities with rest pain, left leg**

• **I70.523 Atherosclerosis of nonautologous biological bypass graft(s) of the extremities with rest pain, bilateral legs**

• **I70.528 Atherosclerosis of nonautologous biological bypass graft(s) of the extremities with rest pain, other extremity**

• **I70.529 Atherosclerosis of nonautologous biological bypass graft(s) of the extremities with rest pain, unspecified extremity**

+ **I70.53 Atherosclerosis of nonautologous biological bypass graft(s) of the right leg with ulceration**
Includes: *any condition classifiable to I70.511 and I70.521*
Use additional code to identify severity of ulcer (L97.-)

• CC **I70.531 Atherosclerosis of nonautologous biological bypass graft(s) of the right leg with ulceration of thigh**
CC Exclusion see Appendix A PDX collection 0698

• CC **I70.532 Atherosclerosis of nonautologous biological bypass graft(s) of the right leg with ulceration of calf**
CC Exclusion see Appendix A PDX collection 0698

• CC **I70.533 Atherosclerosis of nonautologous biological bypass graft(s) of the right leg with ulceration of ankle**
CC Exclusion see Appendix A PDX collection 0698

• CC **I70.534 Atherosclerosis of nonautologous biological bypass graft(s) of the right leg with ulceration of heel and midfoot**
Atherosclerosis of nonautologous biological bypass graft(s) of right leg with ulceration of plantar surface of midfoot
CC Exclusion see Appendix A PDX collection 0698

• **I70.535 Atherosclerosis of nonautologous biological bypass graft(s) of the right leg with ulceration of other part of foot**
Atherosclerosis of nonautologous biological bypass graft(s) of the right leg with ulceration of toe

• CC **I70.538 Atherosclerosis of nonautologous biological bypass graft(s) of the right leg with ulceration of other part of lower leg**
CC Exclusion see Appendix A PDX collection 0698

• CC **I70.539 Atherosclerosis of nonautologous biological bypass graft(s) of the right leg with ulceration of unspecified site**
CC Exclusion see Appendix A PDX collection 0698

+ **I70.54 Atherosclerosis of nonautologous biological bypass graft(s) of the left leg with ulceration**
Includes: any condition classifiable to I70.512 and I70.522
Use additional code to identify severity of ulcer (L97.-)

• CC **I70.541 Atherosclerosis of nonautologous biological bypass graft(s) of the left leg with ulceration of thigh**
CC Exclusion see Appendix A PDX collection 0698

• CC **I70.542 Atherosclerosis of nonautologous biological bypass graft(s) of the left leg with ulceration of calf**
CC Exclusion see Appendix A PDX collection 0698

• CC **I70.543 Atherosclerosis of nonautologous biological bypass graft(s) of the left leg with ulceration of ankle**
CC Exclusion see Appendix A PDX collection 0698

• CC **I70.544 Atherosclerosis of nonautologous biological bypass graft(s) of the left leg with ulceration of heel and midfoot**
Atherosclerosis of nonautologous biological bypass graft(s) of left leg with ulceration of plantar surface of midfoot
CC Exclusion see Appendix A PDX collection 0698

• **I70.545 Atherosclerosis of nonautologous biological bypass graft(s) of the left leg with ulceration of other part of foot**
Atherosclerosis of nonautologous biological bypass graft(s) of the left leg with ulceration of toe

• CC **I70.548 Atherosclerosis of nonautologous biological bypass graft(s) of the left leg with ulceration of other part of lower leg**
CC Exclusion see Appendix A PDX collection 0698

• CC **I70.549 Atherosclerosis of nonautologous biological bypass graft(s) of the left leg with ulceration of unspecified site**
CC Exclusion see Appendix A PDX collection 0698

• **I70.55 Atherosclerosis of nonautologous biological bypass graft(s) of other extremity with ulceration**
Includes: any condition classifiable to I70.518, I70.528, and I70.538
Use additional code to identify severity of ulcer (L98.49)

+ **I70.56 Atherosclerosis of nonautologous biological bypass graft(s) of the extremities with gangrene**
Includes: any condition classifiable to I70.51-, I70.52-, and I70.53-, I70.54-, I70.55
Use additional code to identify the severity of any ulcer (L97.-, L98.49-), if applicable

• CC **I70.561 Atherosclerosis of nonautologous biological bypass graft(s) of the extremities with gangrene, right leg**
CC Exclusion see Appendix A PDX collection 0519

• CC **I70.562 Atherosclerosis of nonautologous biological bypass graft(s) of the extremities with gangrene, left leg**
CC Exclusion see Appendix A PDX collection 0519

• CC **I70.563 Atherosclerosis of nonautologous biological bypass graft(s) of the extremities with gangrene, bilateral legs**
CC Exclusion see Appendix A PDX collection 0519

• CC **I70.568 Atherosclerosis of nonautologous biological bypass graft(s) of the extremities with gangrene, other extremity**
CC Exclusion see Appendix A PDX collection 0519

• CC **I70.569 Atherosclerosis of nonautologous biological bypass graft(s) of the extremities with gangrene, unspecified extremity**
CC Exclusion see Appendix A PDX collection 0519

+ **I70.59 Other atherosclerosis of nonautologous biological bypass graft(s) of the extremities**

• **I70.591 Other atherosclerosis of nonautologous biological bypass graft(s) of the extremities, right leg**

• **I70.592 Other atherosclerosis of nonautologous biological bypass graft(s) of the extremities, left leg**

• **I70.593 Other atherosclerosis of nonautologous biological bypass graft(s) of the extremities, bilateral legs**

• **I70.598 Other atherosclerosis of nonautologous biological bypass graft(s) of the extremities, other extremity**

• **I70.599 Other atherosclerosis of nonautologous biological bypass graft(s) of the extremities, unspecified extremity**

+ **I70.6 Atherosclerosis of nonbiological bypass graft(s) of the extremities**
Use additional code, if applicable, to identify chronic total occlusion of artery of extremity (I70.92)

+ **I70.60 Unspecified atherosclerosis of nonbiological bypass graft(s) of the extremities**

• **I70.601 Unspecified atherosclerosis of nonbiological bypass graft(s) of the extremities, right leg**

• **I70.602 Unspecified atherosclerosis of nonbiological bypass graft(s) of the extremities, left leg**

• **I70.603 Unspecified atherosclerosis of nonbiological bypass graft(s) of the extremities, bilateral legs**

• **I70.608 Unspecified atherosclerosis of nonbiological bypass graft(s) of the extremities, other extremity**

• **I70.609 Unspecified atherosclerosis of nonbiological bypass graft(s) of the extremities, unspecified extremity**

+ **I70.61 Atherosclerosis of nonbiological bypass graft(s) of the extremities with intermittent claudication**

• **I70.611 Atherosclerosis of nonbiological bypass graft(s) of the extremities with intermittent claudication, right leg**

• **I70.612 Atherosclerosis of nonbiological bypass graft(s) of the extremities with intermittent claudication, left leg**

• **I70.613 Atherosclerosis of nonbiological bypass graft(s) of the extremities with intermittent claudication, bilateral legs**

• **I70.618 Atherosclerosis of nonbiological bypass graft(s) of the extremities with intermittent claudication, other extremity**

• **I70.619 Atherosclerosis of nonbiological bypass graft(s) of the extremities with intermittent claudication, unspecified extremity**

+ **I70.62 Atherosclerosis of nonbiological bypass graft(s) of the extremities with rest pain**

Includes: any condition classifiable to I70.61-

• **I70.621 Atherosclerosis of nonbiological bypass graft(s) of the extremities with rest pain, right leg**

• **I70.622 Atherosclerosis of nonbiological bypass graft(s) of the extremities with rest pain, left leg**

• **I70.623 Atherosclerosis of nonbiological bypass graft(s) of the extremities with rest pain, bilateral legs**

• **I70.628 Atherosclerosis of nonbiological bypass graft(s) of the extremities with rest pain, other extremity**

• **I70.629 Atherosclerosis of nonbiological bypass graft(s) of the extremities with rest pain, unspecified extremity**

+ **I70.63 Atherosclerosis of nonbiological bypass graft(s) of the right leg with ulceration**

Includes: any condition classifiable to I70.611 and I70.621

Use additional code to identify severity of ulcer (L97.-)

• CC **I70.631 Atherosclerosis of nonbiological bypass graft(s) of the right leg with ulceration of thigh**

CC Exclusion see Appendix A PDX collection 0698

• CC **I70.632 Atherosclerosis of nonbiological bypass graft(s) of the right leg with ulceration of calf**

CC Exclusion see Appendix A PDX collection 0698

• CC **I70.633 Atherosclerosis of nonbiological bypass graft(s) of the right leg with ulceration of ankle**

CC Exclusion see Appendix A PDX collection 0698

• CC **I70.634 Atherosclerosis of nonbiological bypass graft(s) of the right leg with ulceration of heel and midfoot**

Atherosclerosis of nonbiological bypass graft(s) of right leg with ulceration of plantar surface of midfoot

CC Exclusion see Appendix A PDX collection 0698

• **I70.635 Atherosclerosis of nonbiological bypass graft(s) of the right leg with ulceration of other part of foot**

Atherosclerosis of nonbiological bypass graft(s) of the right leg with ulceration of toe

• CC **I70.638 Atherosclerosis of nonbiological bypass graft(s) of the right leg with ulceration of other part of lower leg**

CC Exclusion see Appendix A PDX collection 0698

• CC **I70.639 Atherosclerosis of nonbiological bypass graft(s) of the right leg with ulceration of unspecified site**

CC Exclusion see Appendix A PDX collection 0698

+ **I70.64 Atherosclerosis of nonbiological bypass graft(s) of t[he] left leg with ulceration**

Includes: any condition classifiable to I70.612 and I70.622

Use additional code to identify severity of ulcer (L97.

• CC **I70.641 Atherosclerosis of nonbiological bypass graft(s) of the left leg with ulceration of th**

CC Exclusion see Appendix A PDX collection 0

• CC **I70.642 Atherosclerosis of nonbiological bypass graft(s) of the left leg with ulceration of ca**

CC Exclusion see Appendix A PDX collection 0

• CC **I70.643 Atherosclerosis of nonbiological bypass graft(s) of the left leg with ulceration of ankle**

CC Exclusion see Appendix A PDX collection 0

• CC **I70.644 Atherosclerosis of nonbiological bypass graft(s) of the left leg with ulceration of he and midfoot**

Atherosclerosis of nonbiological bypass graft(s) of left leg with ulceration of plan surface of midfoot

CC Exclusion see Appendix A PDX collection 0

• **I70.645 Atherosclerosis of nonbiological bypass graft(s) of the left leg with ulceration of other part of foot**

Atherosclerosis of nonbiological bypass graft(s) of the left leg with ulceration of

• CC **I70.648 Atherosclerosis of nonbiological bypass graft(s) of the left leg with ulceration of other part of lower leg**

CC Exclusion see Appendix A PDX collection 0

• CC **I70.649 Atherosclerosis of nonbiological bypass graft(s) of the left leg with ulceration of unspecified site**

CC Exclusion see Appendix A PDX collection 0

• **I70.65 Atherosclerosis of nonbiological bypass graft(s) of other extremity with ulceration**

Includes: any condition classifiable to I70.618 and I70.628

Use additional code to identify severity of ulcer (L98.

+ **I70.66 Atherosclerosis of nonbiological bypass graft(s) of t extremities with gangrene**

Includes: any condition classifiable to I70.61-, I70.6 I70.63-, I70.64-, I70.65

Use additional code to identify the severity of any ulc (L97.-, L98.49-), if applicable

• CC **I70.661 Atherosclerosis of nonbiological bypass graft(s) of the extremities with gangrene, right leg**

CC Exclusion see Appendix A PDX collection 0

• CC **I70.662 Atherosclerosis of nonbiological bypass graft(s) of the extremities with gangrene, left leg**

CC Exclusion see Appendix A PDX collection 0

• CC **I70.663 Atherosclerosis of nonbiological bypass graft(s) of the extremities with gangrene, bilateral legs**

CC Exclusion see Appendix A PDX collection 0

• CC **I70.668 Atherosclerosis of nonbiological bypass graft(s) of the extremities with gangrene, other extremity**

CC Exclusion see Appendix A PDX collection 0

• CC **I70.669 Atherosclerosis of nonbiological bypass graft(s) of the extremities with gangrene, unspecified extremity**

CC Exclusion see Appendix A PDX collection 0

+ **I70.69 Other atherosclerosis of nonbiological bypass graft(of the extremities**

• **I70.691 Other atherosclerosis of nonbiological bypass graft(s) of the extremities, right leg**

• **I70.692 Other atherosclerosis of nonbiological bypass graft(s) of the extremities, left leg**

• **I70.693 Other atherosclerosis of nonbiological bypass graft(s) of the extremities, bilateral legs**

• **I70.698 Other atherosclerosis of nonbiological bypass graft(s) of the extremities, other extremity**

• **I70.699 Other atherosclerosis of nonbiological bypass graft(s) of the extremities, unspeci extremity**

+ **I70.7 Atherosclerosis of other type of bypass graft(s) of the extremities**
  Use additional code, if applicable, to identify chronic total occlusion of artery of extremity (I70.92)
  + **I70.70 Unspecified atherosclerosis of other type of bypass graft(s) of the extremities**
    - • **I70.701 Unspecified atherosclerosis of other type of bypass graft(s) of the extremities, right leg**
    - • **I70.702 Unspecified atherosclerosis of other type of bypass graft(s) of the extremities, left leg**
    - • **I70.703 Unspecified atherosclerosis of other type of bypass graft(s) of the extremities, bilateral legs**
    - • **I70.708 Unspecified atherosclerosis of other type of bypass graft(s) of the extremities, other extremity**
    - • **I70.709 Unspecified atherosclerosis of other type of bypass graft(s) of the extremities, unspecified extremity**
  + **I70.71 Atherosclerosis of other type of bypass graft(s) of the extremities with intermittent claudication**
    - • **I70.711 Atherosclerosis of other type of bypass graft(s) of the extremities with intermittent claudication, right leg**
    - • **I70.712 Atherosclerosis of other type of bypass graft(s) of the extremities with intermittent claudication, left leg**
    - • **I70.713 Atherosclerosis of other type of bypass graft(s) of the extremities with intermittent claudication, bilateral legs**
    - • **I70.718 Atherosclerosis of other type of bypass graft(s) of the extremities with intermittent claudication, other extremity**
    - • **I70.719 Atherosclerosis of other type of bypass graft(s) of the extremities with intermittent claudication, unspecified extremity**
  + **I70.72 Atherosclerosis of other type of bypass graft(s) of the extremities with rest pain**
    Includes: any condition classifiable to I70.71-
    - • **I70.721 Atherosclerosis of other type of bypass graft(s) of the extremities with rest pain, right leg**
    - • **I70.722 Atherosclerosis of other type of bypass graft(s) of the extremities with rest pain, left leg**
    - • **I70.723 Atherosclerosis of other type of bypass graft(s) of the extremities with rest pain, bilateral legs**
    - • **I70.728 Atherosclerosis of other type of bypass graft(s) of the extremities with rest pain, other extremity**
    - • **I70.729 Atherosclerosis of other type of bypass graft(s) of the extremities with rest pain, unspecified extremity**
  + **I70.73 Atherosclerosis of other type of bypass graft(s) of the right leg with ulceration**
    Includes: any condition classifiable to I70.711 and I70.721
    Use additional code to identify severity of ulcer (L97.-)
    - • CC **I70.731 Atherosclerosis of other type of bypass graft(s) of the right leg with ulceration of thigh**
      CC Exclusion see Appendix A PDX collection 0698
    - • CC **I70.732 Atherosclerosis of other type of bypass graft(s) of the right leg with ulceration of calf**
      CC Exclusion see Appendix A PDX collection 0698
    - • CC **I70.733 Atherosclerosis of other type of bypass graft(s) of the right leg with ulceration of ankle**
      CC Exclusion see Appendix A PDX collection 0698
    - • CC **I70.734 Atherosclerosis of other type of bypass graft(s) of the right leg with ulceration of heel and midfoot**
      Atherosclerosis of other type of bypass graft(s) of right leg with ulceration of plantar surface of midfoot
      CC Exclusion see Appendix A PDX collection 0698
    - • **I70.735 Atherosclerosis of other type of bypass graft(s) of the right leg with ulceration of other part of foot**
      Atherosclerosis of other type of bypass graft(s) of right leg with ulceration of toe
    - • CC **I70.738 Atherosclerosis of other type of bypass graft(s) of the right leg with ulceration of other part of lower leg**
      CC Exclusion see Appendix A PDX collection 0698
    - • CC **I70.739 Atherosclerosis of other type of bypass graft(s) of the right leg with ulceration of unspecified site**
      CC Exclusion see Appendix A PDX collection 0698
  + **I70.74 Atherosclerosis of other type of bypass graft(s) of the left leg with ulceration**
    Includes: any condition classifiable to I70.712 and I70.722
    Use additional code to identify severity of ulcer (L97.-
    - • CC **I70.741 Atherosclerosis of other type of bypass graft(s) of the left leg with ulceration of thigh**
      CC Exclusion see Appendix A PDX collection 0698
    - • CC **I70.742 Atherosclerosis of other type of bypass graft(s) of the left leg with ulceration of calf**
      CC Exclusion see Appendix A PDX collection 0698
    - • CC **I70.743 Atherosclerosis of other type of bypass graft(s) of the left leg with ulceration of ankle**
      CC Exclusion see Appendix A PDX collection 0698
    - • CC **I70.744 Atherosclerosis of other type of bypass graft(s) of the left leg with ulceration of heel and midfoot**
      Atherosclerosis of other type of bypass graft(s) of left leg with ulceration of plantar surface of midfoot
      CC Exclusion see Appendix A PDX collection 0698
    - • **I70.745 Atherosclerosis of other type of bypass graft(s) of the left leg with ulceration of other part of foot**
      Atherosclerosis of other type of bypass graft(s) of left leg with ulceration of toe
    - • CC **I70.748 Atherosclerosis of other type of bypass graft(s) of the left leg with ulceration of other part of lower leg**
      CC Exclusion see Appendix A PDX collection 0698
    - • CC **I70.749 Atherosclerosis of other type of bypass graft(s) of the left leg with ulceration of unspecified site**
      CC Exclusion see Appendix A PDX collection 0698
  - • **I70.75 Atherosclerosis of other type of bypass graft(s) of other extremity with ulceration**
    Includes: any condition classifiable to I70.718 and I70.728
    Use additional code to identify severity of ulcer (L98.49)
  + **I70.76 Atherosclerosis of other type of bypass graft(s) of the extremities with gangrene**
    Includes: any condition classifiable to I70.71-, I70.72-, I70.73-, I70.74-, I70.75
    Use additional code to identify the severity of any ulcer (L97.-, L98.49-), if applicable
    - • CC **I70.761 Atherosclerosis of other type of bypass graft(s) of the extremities with gangrene, right leg**
      CC Exclusion see Appendix A PDX collection 0519
    - • CC **I70.762 Atherosclerosis of other type of bypass graft(s) of the extremities with gangrene, left leg**
      CC Exclusion see Appendix A PDX collection 0519
    - • CC **I70.763 Atherosclerosis of other type of bypass graft(s) of the extremities with gangrene, bilateral legs**
      CC Exclusion see Appendix A PDX collection 0519
    - • CC **I70.768 Atherosclerosis of other type of bypass graft(s) of the extremities with gangrene, other extremity**
      CC Exclusion see Appendix A PDX collection 0519
    - • CC **I70.769 Atherosclerosis of other type of bypass graft(s) of the extremities with gangrene, unspecified extremity**
      CC Exclusion see Appendix A PDX collection 0519

+ **I70.79 Other atherosclerosis of other type of bypass graft(s) of the extremities**
• **I70.791 Other atherosclerosis of other type of bypass graft(s) of the extremities, right leg**
• **I70.792 Other atherosclerosis of other type of bypass graft(s) of the extremities, left leg**
• **I70.793 Other atherosclerosis of other type of bypass graft(s) of the extremities, bilateral legs**
• **I70.798 Other atherosclerosis of other type of bypass graft(s) of the extremities, other extremity**
• **I70.799 Other atherosclerosis of other type of bypass graft(s) of the extremities, unspecified extremity**
• **I70.8 Atherosclerosis of other arteries**
+ **I70.9 Other and unspecified atherosclerosis**
• **I70.90 Unspecified atherosclerosis**
• **I70.91 Generalized atherosclerosis**
• CC **I70.92 Chronic total occlusion of artery of the extremities**
Complete occlusion of artery of the extremities
Total occlusion of artery of the extremities
Code first atherosclerosis of arteries of the extremities (I70.2-, I70.3-, I70.4-, I70.5-, I70.6-, I70.7-)
CC Exclusion see Appendix A PDX collection 0699

I71 Aortic aneurysm and dissection

Excludes1: *aortic ectasia (I77.81-)*
syphilitic aortic aneurysm (A52.01)
traumatic aortic aneurysm (S25.09, S35.09)

+ **I71.0 Dissection of aorta**
MCC **I71.00 Dissection of unspecified site of aorta**
MCC Exclusion see Appendix A PDX collection 0700
MCC **I71.01 Dissection of thoracic aorta**
MCC Exclusion see Appendix A PDX collection 0700
MCC **I71.02 Dissection of abdominal aorta**
MCC Exclusion see Appendix A PDX collection 0700
MCC **I71.03 Dissection of thoracoabdominal aorta**
MCC Exclusion see Appendix A PDX collection 0700
MCC **I71.1 Thoracic aortic aneurysm, ruptured**
MCC Exclusion see Appendix A PDX collection 0700
I71.2 Thoracic aortic aneurysm, without rupture
MCC **I71.3 Abdominal aortic aneurysm, ruptured**
MCC Exclusion see Appendix A PDX collection 0700
I71.4 Abdominal aortic aneurysm, without rupture
MCC **I71.5 Thoracoabdominal aortic aneurysm, ruptured**
MCC Exclusion see Appendix A PDX collection 0700
I71.6 Thoracoabdominal aortic aneurysm, without rupture
MCC **I71.8 Aortic aneurysm of unspecified site, ruptured**
Rupture of aorta NOS
MCC Exclusion see Appendix A PDX collection 0700
I71.9 Aortic aneurysm of unspecified site, without rupture
Aneurysm of aorta
Dilatation of aorta
Hyaline necrosis of aorta

I72 Other aneurysm

Includes: aneurysm (cirsoid) (false) (ruptured)
Excludes2: *acquired aneurysm (I77.0)*
aneurysm (of) aorta (I71.-)
aneurysm (of) arteriovenous NOS (Q27.3-)
carotid artery dissection (I77.71)
cerebral (nonruptured) aneurysm (I67.1)
coronary aneurysm (I25.4)
coronary artery dissection (I25.42)
dissection of artery NEC (I77.79)
heart aneurysm (I25.3)
iliac artery dissection (I77.72)
pulmonary artery aneurysm (I28.1)
renal artery dissection (I77.73)
retinal aneurysm (H35.0)
ruptured cerebral aneurysm (I60.7)
varicose aneurysm (I77.0)
vertebral artery dissection (I77.74)

I72.0 Aneurysm of carotid artery
Aneurysm of common carotid artery
Aneurysm of external carotid artery
Aneurysm of internal carotid artery, extracranial portion
Excludes1: *aneurysm of internal carotid artery, intracranial portion (I67.1)*
aneurysm of internal carotid artery NOS (I67.1)
I72.1 Aneurysm of artery of upper extremity
I72.2 Aneurysm of renal artery
I72.3 Aneurysm of iliac artery
I72.4 Aneurysm of artery of lower extremity
I72.8 Aneurysm of other specified arteries
I72.9 Aneurysm of unspecified site

I73 Other peripheral vascular diseases

Excludes2: *chilblains (T69.1)*
frostbite (T33-T34)
immersion hand or foot (T69.0-)
spasm of cerebral artery (G45.9)

+ **I73.0 Raynaud's syndrome**
Raynaud's disease
Raynaud's phenomenon (secondary)
I73.00 Raynaud's syndrome without gangrene
CC **I73.01 Raynaud's syndrome with gangrene**
CC Exclusion see Appendix A PDX collection 0519
I73.1 Thromboangiitis obliterans [Buerger's disease]
+ **I73.8 Other specified peripheral vascular diseases**
Excludes1: *diabetic (peripheral) angiopathy (E08-E13 with .51-.52)*
I73.81 Erythromelalgia
I73.89 Other specified peripheral vascular diseases
Acrocyanosis
Erythrocyanosis
Simple acroparesthesia [Schultze's type]
Vasomotor acroparesthesia [Nothnagel's type]
I73.9 Peripheral vascular disease, unspecified
Intermittent claudication
Peripheral angiopathy NOS
Spasm of artery
Excludes1: *atherosclerosis of the extremities (I70.2--I70.7-)*

I74 Arterial embolism and thrombosis

Includes: embolic infarction
embolic occlusion
thrombotic infarction
thrombotic occlusion

Code first embolism and thrombosis complicating abortion or ectopic o molar pregnancy (O00-O07, O08.2)
embolism and thrombosis complicating pregnancy, childbirth and the puerperium (O88.-)

Excludes2: *atheroembolism (I75.-)*
basilar embolism and thrombosis (I63.0-I63.2, I65.1)
carotid embolism and thrombosis (I63.0-I63.2, I65.2)
cerebral embolism and thrombosis (I63.3-I63.5, I66.-)
coronary embolism and thrombosis (I21-I25)
mesenteric embolism and thrombosis (K55.0)
ophthalmic embolism and thrombosis (H34.-)
precerebral embolism and thrombosis NOS (I63.0-I63.2, I65.9)
pulmonary embolism and thrombosis (I26.-)
renal embolism and thrombosis (N28.0)
retinal embolism and thrombosis (H34.-)
septic embolism and thrombosis (I76)
vertebral embolism and thrombosis (I63.0-I63.2, I65.0)

+ **I74.0 Embolism and thrombosis of abdominal aorta**
MCC **I74.01 Saddle embolus of abdominal aorta**
MCC Exclusion see Appendix A PDX collection 0669
CC **I74.09 Other arterial embolism and thrombosis of abdomina aorta**
Aortic bifurcation syndrome
Aortoiliac obstruction
Leriche's syndrome
CC Exclusion see Appendix A PDX collection 0669
+ **I74.1 Embolism and thrombosis of other and unspecified parts of aorta**
CC **I74.10 Embolism and thrombosis of unspecified parts of aorta**
CC Exclusion see Appendix A PDX collection 0669
CC **I74.11 Embolism and thrombosis of thoracic aorta**
CC Exclusion see Appendix A PDX collection 0701
CC **I74.19 Embolism and thrombosis of other parts of aorta**
CC Exclusion see Appendix A PDX collection 0669
CC **I74.2 Embolism and thrombosis of arteries of the upper extremities**
CC Exclusion see Appendix A PDX collection 0702
CC **I74.3 Embolism and thrombosis of arteries of the lower extremities**
CC Exclusion see Appendix A PDX collection 0703
CC **I74.4 Embolism and thrombosis of arteries of extremities, unspecified**
Peripheral arterial embolism NOS
CC Exclusion see Appendix A PDX collection 0703

CC **I74.5 Embolism and thrombosis of iliac artery**
CC Exclusion see Appendix A PDX collection 0704

CC **I74.8 Embolism and thrombosis of other arteries**
CC Exclusion see Appendix A PDX collection 0705

CC **I74.9 Embolism and thrombosis of unspecified artery**
CC Exclusion see Appendix A PDX collection 0705

I75 Atheroembolism

Includes: atherothrombotic microembolism
cholesterol embolism

\+ **I75.0 Atheroembolism of extremities**

\+ **I75.01 Atheroembolism of upper extremity**

CC **I75.011 Atheroembolism of right upper extremity**
CC Exclusion see Appendix A PDX collection 0706

CC **I75.012 Atheroembolism of left upper extremity**
CC Exclusion see Appendix A PDX collection 0706

CC **I75.013 Atheroembolism of bilateral upper extremities**
CC Exclusion see Appendix A PDX collection 0706

CC **I75.019 Atheroembolism of unspecified upper extremity**
CC Exclusion see Appendix A PDX collection 0706

\+ **I75.02 Atheroembolism of lower extremity**

CC **I75.021 Atheroembolism of right lower extremity**
CC Exclusion see Appendix A PDX collection 0707

CC **I75.022 Atheroembolism of left lower extremity**
CC Exclusion see Appendix A PDX collection 0707

CC **I75.023 Atheroembolism of bilateral lower extremities**
CC Exclusion see Appendix A PDX collection 0707

CC **I75.029 Atheroembolism of unspecified lower extremity**
CC Exclusion see Appendix A PDX collection 0707

\+ **I75.8 Atheroembolism of other sites**

CC **I75.81 Atheroembolism of kidney**
Use additional code for any associated acute kidney failure and chronic kidney disease (N17.-, N18.-)
CC Exclusion see Appendix A PDX collection 0708

CC **I75.89 Atheroembolism of other site**
CC Exclusion see Appendix A PDX collection 0709

I76 Septic arterial embolism

Code first underlying infection, such as:
infective endocarditis (I33.0)
lung abscess (J85.-)

Use additional code to identify the site of the embolism (I74.-)
Excludes2: *septic pulmonary embolism (I26.01, I26.90)*
CC Exclusion see Appendix A PDX collection 0705
Valid 3-character code, no further characters required

I77 Other disorders of arteries and arterioles

Excludes2: *collagen (vascular) diseases (M30-M36)*
hypersensitivity angiitis (M31.0)
pulmonary artery (I28.-)

I77.0 Arteriovenous fistula, acquired
Aneurysmal varix
Arteriovenous aneurysm, acquired
Excludes1: *arteriovenous aneurysm NOS (Q27.3-)*
presence of arteriovenous shunt (fistula) for dialysis (Z99.2)
traumatic - see injury of blood vessel by body region
Excludes2: *cerebral (I67.1)*
coronary (I25.4)

I77.1 Stricture of artery
Narrowing of artery

CC **I77.2 Rupture of artery**
Erosion of artery
Fistula of artery
Ulcer of artery
Excludes1: *traumatic rupture of artery - see injury of blood vessel by body region*
CC Exclusion see Appendix A PDX collection 0710

I77.3 Arterial fibromuscular dysplasia
Fibromuscular hyperplasia (of) carotid artery
Fibromuscular hyperplasia (of) renal artery

CC **I77.4 Celiac artery compression syndrome**
CC Exclusion see Appendix A PDX collection 0711

CC **I77.5 Necrosis of artery**
CC Exclusion see Appendix A PDX collection 0712

I77.6 Arteritis, unspecified
Aortitis NOS
Endarteritis NOS
Excludes1: *arteritis or endarteritis:*
aortic arch (M31.4)
cerebral NEC (I67.7)
coronary (I25.89)
deformans (I70.-)
giant cell (M31.5, M31.6)
obliterans (I70.-)
senile (I70.-)

\+ **I77.7 Other arterial dissection**
Excludes2: *dissection of aorta (I71.0-)*
dissection of coronary artery (I25.42)

MCC **I77.71 Dissection of carotid artery**
MCC Exclusion see Appendix A PDX collection 0689

MCC **I77.72 Dissection of iliac artery**
MCC Exclusion see Appendix A PDX collection 0689

MCC **I77.73 Dissection of renal artery**
MCC Exclusion see Appendix A PDX collection 0689

MCC **I77.74 Dissection of vertebral artery**
MCC Exclusion see Appendix A PDX collection 0689

MCC **I77.79 Dissection of other artery**
MCC Exclusion see Appendix A PDX collection 0689

\+ **I77.8 Other specified disorders of arteries and arterioles**

\+ **I77.81 Aortic ectasia**
Ectasis aorta
Excludes1: *aortic aneurysm and dissection (I71.0-)*
I77.810 Thoracic aortic ectasia
I77.811 Abdominal aortic ectasia
I77.812 Thoracoabdominal aortic ectasia
I77.819 Aortic ectasia, unspecified site

I77.89 Other specified disorders of arteries and arterioles

I77.9 Disorder of arteries and arterioles, unspecified

I78 Diseases of capillaries

I78.0 Hereditary hemorrhagic telangiectasia
Rendu-Osler-Weber disease

I78.1 Nevus, non-neoplastic
Araneus nevus
Senile nevus
Spider nevus
Stellar nevus
Excludes1: *nevus NOS (D22.-)*
vascular NOS (Q82.5)
Excludes2: *blue nevus (D22.-)*
flammeus nevus (Q82.5)
hairy nevus (D22.-)
melanocytic nevus (D22.-)
pigmented nevus (D22.-)
portwine nevus (Q82.5)
sanguineous nevus (Q82.5)
strawberry nevus (Q82.5)
verrucous nevus (Q82.5)

I78.8 Other diseases of capillaries

I78.9 Disease of capillaries, unspecified

I79 Disorders of arteries, arterioles and capillaries in diseases classified elsewhere

I79.0 Aneurysm of aorta in diseases classified elsewhere
Code first underlying disease
Excludes1: *syphilitic aneurysm (A52.01)*

I79.1 Aortitis in diseases classified elsewhere
Code first underlying disease
Excludes1: *syphilitic aortitis (A52.02)*

I79.8 Other disorders of arteries, arterioles and capillaries in diseases classified elsewhere
Code first underlying disease, such as:
amyloidosis (E85.-)
Excludes1: *diabetic (peripheral) angiopathy (E08-E13 with .51-.52)*
syphilitic endarteritis (A52.09)
tuberculous endarteritis (A18.89)

Diseases of veins, lymphatic vessels and lymph nodes, not elsewhere classified (I80-I89)

I80 Phlebitis and thrombophlebitis

Includes: endophlebitis
inflammation, vein
periphlebitis
suppurative phlebitis

Code first phlebitis and thrombophlebitis complicating abortion, ectopic or molar pregnancy (O00-O07, O08.7)
phlebitis and thrombophlebitis complicating pregnancy, childbirth and the puerperium (O22.-, O87.-)

Excludes1: *venous embolism and thrombosis of lower extremities (I82.4-, I82.5-, I82.81-)*

+ **I80.0 Phlebitis and thrombophlebitis of superficial vessels of lower extremities**
Phlebitis and thrombophlebitis of femoropopliteal vein
I80.00 Phlebitis and thrombophlebitis of superficial vessels of unspecified lower extremity
I80.01 Phlebitis and thrombophlebitis of superficial vessels of right lower extremity
I80.02 Phlebitis and thrombophlebitis of superficial vessels of left lower extremity
I80.03 Phlebitis and thrombophlebitis of superficial vessels of lower extremities, bilateral

+ **I80.1 Phlebitis and thrombophlebitis of femoral vein**
CC **I80.10 Phlebitis and thrombophlebitis of unspecified femoral vein**
CC Exclusion see Appendix A PDX collection 0713
CC **I80.11 Phlebitis and thrombophlebitis of right femoral vein**
CC Exclusion see Appendix A PDX collection 0713
CC **I80.12 Phlebitis and thrombophlebitis of left femoral vein**
CC Exclusion see Appendix A PDX collection 0713
CC **I80.13 Phlebitis and thrombophlebitis of femoral vein, bilateral**
CC Exclusion see Appendix A PDX collection 0713

+ **I80.2 Phlebitis and thrombophlebitis of other and unspecified deep vessels of lower extremities**
+ **I80.20 Phlebitis and thrombophlebitis of unspecified deep vessels of lower extremities**
CC **I80.201 Phlebitis and thrombophlebitis of unspecified deep vessels of right lower extremity**
CC Exclusion see Appendix A PDX collection 0713
CC **I80.202 Phlebitis and thrombophlebitis of unspecified deep vessels of left lower extremity**
CC Exclusion see Appendix A PDX collection 0713
CC **I80.203 Phlebitis and thrombophlebitis of unspecified deep vessels of lower extremities, bilateral**
CC Exclusion see Appendix A PDX collection 0713
CC **I80.209 Phlebitis and thrombophlebitis of unspecified deep vessels of unspecified lower extremity**
CC Exclusion see Appendix A PDX collection 0713
+ **I80.21 Phlebitis and thrombophlebitis of iliac vein**
CC **I80.211 Phlebitis and thrombophlebitis of right iliac vein**
CC Exclusion see Appendix A PDX collection 0713
CC **I80.212 Phlebitis and thrombophlebitis of left iliac vein**
CC Exclusion see Appendix A PDX collection 0713
CC **I80.213 Phlebitis and thrombophlebitis of iliac vein, bilateral**
CC Exclusion see Appendix A PDX collection 0713
CC **I80.219 Phlebitis and thrombophlebitis of unspecified iliac vein**
CC Exclusion see Appendix A PDX collection 0713
+ **I80.22 Phlebitis and thrombophlebitis of popliteal vein**
CC **I80.221 Phlebitis and thrombophlebitis of right popliteal vein**
CC Exclusion see Appendix A PDX collection 0713
CC **I80.222 Phlebitis and thrombophlebitis of left popliteal vein**
CC Exclusion see Appendix A PDX collection 0713
CC **I80.223 Phlebitis and thrombophlebitis of popliteal vein, bilateral**
CC Exclusion see Appendix A PDX collection 0713
CC **I80.229 Phlebitis and thrombophlebitis of unspecified popliteal vein**
CC Exclusion see Appendix A PDX collection 0713
+ **I80.23 Phlebitis and thrombophlebitis of tibial vein**
CC **I80.231 Phlebitis and thrombophlebitis of right ti[bial] vein**
CC Exclusion see Appendix A PDX collection
CC **I80.232 Phlebitis and thrombophlebitis of left tib[ial] vein**
CC Exclusion see Appendix A PDX collection
CC **I80.233 Phlebitis and thrombophlebitis of tibial v[ein], bilateral**
CC Exclusion see Appendix A PDX collection
CC **I80.239 Phlebitis and thrombophlebitis of unspecified tibial vein**
CC Exclusion see Appendix A PDX collection
+ **I80.29 Phlebitis and thrombophlebitis of other deep vesse[ls of] lower extremities**
CC **I80.291 Phlebitis and thrombophlebitis of other d[eep] vessels of right lower extremity**
CC Exclusion see Appendix A PDX collection
CC **I80.292 Phlebitis and thrombophlebitis of other d[eep] vessels of left lower extremity**
CC Exclusion see Appendix A PDX collection
CC **I80.293 Phlebitis and thrombophlebitis of other d[eep] vessels of lower extremity, bilateral**
CC Exclusion see Appendix A PDX collection
CC **I80.299 Phlebitis and thrombophlebitis of other d[eep] vessels of unspecified lower extremity**
CC Exclusion see Appendix A PDX collection

I80.3 Phlebitis and thrombophlebitis of lower extremities, unspeci[fied]
I80.8 Phlebitis and thrombophlebitis of other sites
I80.9 Phlebitis and thrombophlebitis of unspecified site

MCC **I81 Portal vein thrombosis**
Portal (vein) obstruction
Excludes2: *hepatic vein thrombosis (I82.0)*
phlebitis of portal vein (K75.1)
MCC Exclusion see Appendix A PDX collection 0714
Valid 3-character code, no further characters required

I82 Other venous embolism and thrombosis
Code first venous embolism and thrombosis complicating:
abortion, ectopic or molar pregnancy (O00-O07, O08.7)
pregnancy, childbirth and the puerperium (O22.-, O87.-)
Excludes2: *venous embolism and thrombosis (of):*
cerebral (I63.6, I67.6)
coronary (I21-I25)
intracranial and intraspinal, septic or NOS (G08)
intracranial, nonpyogenic (I67.6)
intraspinal, nonpyogenic (G95.1)
mesenteric (K55.0)
portal (I81)
pulmonary (I26.-)

MCC **I82.0 Budd-Chiari syndrome**
Hepatic vein thrombosis
MCC Exclusion see Appendix A PDX collection 0715
CC **I82.1 Thrombophlebitis migrans**
CC Exclusion see Appendix A PDX collection 0716
+ **I82.2 Embolism and thrombosis of vena cava and other thoracic ve[ins]**
+ **I82.21 Embolism and thrombosis of superior vena cava**
CC **I82.210 Acute embolism and thrombosis of super[ior] vena cava**
Embolism and thrombosis of superior vena cava NOS
CC Exclusion see Appendix A PDX collection
CC **I82.211 Chronic embolism and thrombosis of superior vena cava**
CC Exclusion see Appendix A PDX collection
+ **I82.22 Embolism and thrombosis of inferior vena cava**
MCC **I82.220 Acute embolism and thrombosis of inferi[or] vena cava**
Embolism and thrombosis of inferior vena cava NOS
MCC Exclusion see Appendix A PDX collection 0718
MCC **I82.221 Chronic embolism and thrombosis of inferior vena cava**
MCC Exclusion see Appendix A PDX collection 0718

+ I82.29 Embolism and thrombosis of other thoracic veins
Embolism and thrombosis of brachiocephalic (innominate) vein
CC I82.290 Acute embolism and thrombosis of other thoracic veins
CC Exclusion see Appendix A PDX collection 0717
CC I82.291 Chronic embolism and thrombosis of other thoracic veins
CC Exclusion see Appendix A PDX collection 0717

CC I82.3 Embolism and thrombosis of renal vein
CC Exclusion see Appendix A PDX collection 0719

+ I82.4 Acute embolism and thrombosis of deep veins of lower extremity

+ I82.40 Acute embolism and thrombosis of unspecified deep veins of lower extremity
Deep vein thrombosis NOS
DVT NOS
Excludes1: *acute embolism and thrombosis of unspecified deep veins of distal lower extremity (I82.4Z-)*
acute embolism and thrombosis of unspecified deep veins of proximal lower extremity (I82.4Y-)

CC I82.401 Acute embolism and thrombosis of unspecified deep veins of right lower extremity
CC Exclusion see Appendix A PDX collection 0717
HAC see Appendix B for HAC conditional logic
CC I82.402 Acute embolism and thrombosis of unspecified deep veins of left lower extremity
CC Exclusion see Appendix A PDX collection 0717
HAC see Appendix B for HAC conditional logic
CC I82.403 Acute embolism and thrombosis of unspecified deep veins of lower extremity, bilateral
CC Exclusion see Appendix A PDX collection 0717
HAC see Appendix B for HAC conditional logic
CC I82.409 Acute embolism and thrombosis of unspecified deep veins of unspecified lower extremity
CC Exclusion see Appendix A PDX collection 0717
HAC see Appendix B for HAC conditional logic

+ I82.41 Acute embolism and thrombosis of femoral vein
CC I82.411 Acute embolism and thrombosis of right femoral vein
CC Exclusion see Appendix A PDX collection 0717
HAC see Appendix B for HAC conditional logic
CC I82.412 Acute embolism and thrombosis of left femoral vein
CC Exclusion see Appendix A PDX collection 0717
HAC see Appendix B for HAC conditional logic
CC I82.413 Acute embolism and thrombosis of femoral vein, bilateral
CC Exclusion see Appendix A PDX collection 0717
HAC see Appendix B for HAC conditional logic
CC I82.419 Acute embolism and thrombosis of unspecified femoral vein
CC Exclusion see Appendix A PDX collection 0717
HAC see Appendix B for HAC conditional logic

+ I82.42 Acute embolism and thrombosis of iliac vein
CC I82.421 Acute embolism and thrombosis of right iliac vein
CC Exclusion see Appendix A PDX collection 0717
HAC see Appendix B for HAC conditional logic
CC I82.422 Acute embolism and thrombosis of left iliac vein
CC Exclusion see Appendix A PDX collection 0717
HAC see Appendix B for HAC conditional logic
CC I82.423 Acute embolism and thrombosis of iliac vein, bilateral
CC Exclusion see Appendix A PDX collection 0717
HAC see Appendix B for HAC conditional logic
CC I82.429 Acute embolism and thrombosis of unspecified iliac vein
CC Exclusion see Appendix A PDX collection 0717
HAC see Appendix B for HAC conditional logic

+ I82.43 Acute embolism and thrombosis of popliteal vein
CC I82.431 Acute embolism and thrombosis of right popliteal vein
CC Exclusion see Appendix A PDX collection 0717
HAC see Appendix B for HAC conditional logic
CC I82.432 Acute embolism and thrombosis of left popliteal vein
CC Exclusion see Appendix A PDX collection 0717
HAC see Appendix B for HAC conditional logic
CC I82.433 Acute embolism and thrombosis of popliteal vein, bilateral
CC Exclusion see Appendix A PDX collection 0717
HAC see Appendix B for HAC conditional logic
CC I82.439 Acute embolism and thrombosis of unspecified popliteal vein
CC Exclusion see Appendix A PDX collection 0717
HAC see Appendix B for HAC conditional logic

+ I82.44 Acute embolism and thrombosis of tibial vein
CC I82.441 Acute embolism and thrombosis of right tibial vein
CC Exclusion see Appendix A PDX collection 0717
HAC see Appendix B for HAC conditional logic
CC I82.442 Acute embolism and thrombosis of left tibial vein
CC Exclusion see Appendix A PDX collection 0717
HAC see Appendix B for HAC conditional logic
CC I82.443 Acute embolism and thrombosis of tibial vein, bilateral
CC Exclusion see Appendix A PDX collection 0717
HAC see Appendix B for HAC conditional logic
CC I82.449 Acute embolism and thrombosis of unspecified tibial vein
CC Exclusion see Appendix A PDX collection 0717
HAC see Appendix B for HAC conditional logic

+ I82.49 Acute embolism and thrombosis of other specified deep vein of lower extremity
CC I82.491 Acute embolism and thrombosis of other specified deep vein of right lower extremity
CC Exclusion see Appendix A PDX collection 0717
HAC see Appendix B for HAC conditional logic
CC I82.492 Acute embolism and thrombosis of other specified deep vein of left lower extremity
CC Exclusion see Appendix A PDX collection 0717
HAC see Appendix B for HAC conditional logic
CC I82.493 Acute embolism and thrombosis of other specified deep vein of lower extremity, bilateral
CC Exclusion see Appendix A PDX collection 0717
HAC see Appendix B for HAC conditional logic
CC I82.499 Acute embolism and thrombosis of other specified deep vein of unspecified lower extremity
CC Exclusion see Appendix A PDX collection 0717
HAC see Appendix B for HAC conditional logic

+ I82.4Y Acute embolism and thrombosis of unspecified deep veins of proximal lower extremity
Acute embolism and thrombosis of deep vein of thigh NOS
Acute embolism and thrombosis of deep vein of upper leg NOS
CC I82.4Y1 Acute embolism and thrombosis of unspecified deep veins of right proximal lower extremity
CC Exclusion see Appendix A PDX collection 0717
HAC see Appendix B for HAC conditional logic
CC I82.4Y2 Acute embolism and thrombosis of unspecified deep veins of left proximal lower extremity
CC Exclusion see Appendix A PDX collection 0717
HAC see Appendix B for HAC conditional logic
CC I82.4Y3 Acute embolism and thrombosis of unspecified deep veins of proximal lower extremity, bilateral
CC Exclusion see Appendix A PDX collection 0717
HAC see Appendix B for HAC conditional logic
CC I82.4Y9 Acute embolism and thrombosis of unspecified deep veins of unspecified proximal lower extremity
CC Exclusion see Appendix A PDX collection 0717
HAC see Appendix B for HAC conditional logic

+ I82.4Z Acute embolism and thrombosis of unspecified deep veins of distal lower extremity
Acute embolism and thrombosis of deep vein of calf NOS
Acute embolism and thrombosis of deep vein of lower leg NOS
CC I82.4Z1 Acute embolism and thrombosis of unspecified deep veins of right distal lower extremity
CC Exclusion see Appendix A PDX collection 0717
HAC see Appendix B for HAC conditional logic

CC **I82.4Z2 Acute embolism and thrombosis of unspecified deep veins of left distal lower extremity**
CC Exclusion see Appendix A PDX collection 0717
HAC see Appendix B for HAC conditional logic

CC **I82.4Z3 Acute embolism and thrombosis of unspecified deep veins of distal lower extremity, bilateral**
CC Exclusion see Appendix A PDX collection 0717
HAC see Appendix B for HAC conditional logic

CC **I82.4Z9 Acute embolism and thrombosis of unspecified deep veins of unspecified distal lower extremity**
CC Exclusion see Appendix A PDX collection 0717
HAC see Appendix B for HAC conditional logic

+ **I82.5 Chronic embolism and thrombosis of deep veins of lower extremity**
Use additional code, if applicable, for associated long-term (current) use of anticoagulants (Z79.01)
Excludes1: *personal history of venous embolism and thrombosis (Z86.718)*

+ **I82.50 Chronic embolism and thrombosis of unspecified deep veins of lower extremity**
Excludes1: *chronic embolism and thrombosis of unspecified deep veins of distal lower extremity (I82.5Z-)*
chronic embolism and thrombosis of unspecified deep veins of proximal lower extremity (I82.5Y-)

CC **I82.501 Chronic embolism and thrombosis of unspecified deep veins of right lower extremity**
CC Exclusion see Appendix A PDX collection 0717

CC **I82.502 Chronic embolism and thrombosis of unspecified deep veins of left lower extremity**
CC Exclusion see Appendix A PDX collection 0717

CC **I82.503 Chronic embolism and thrombosis of unspecified deep veins of lower extremity, bilateral**
CC Exclusion see Appendix A PDX collection 0717

CC **I82.509 Chronic embolism and thrombosis of unspecified deep veins of unspecified lower extremity**
CC Exclusion see Appendix A PDX collection 0717

+ **I82.51 Chronic embolism and thrombosis of femoral vein**

CC **I82.511 Chronic embolism and thrombosis of right femoral vein**
CC Exclusion see Appendix A PDX collection 0717

CC **I82.512 Chronic embolism and thrombosis of left femoral vein**
CC Exclusion see Appendix A PDX collection 0717

CC **I82.513 Chronic embolism and thrombosis of femoral vein, bilateral**
CC Exclusion see Appendix A PDX collection 0717

CC **I82.519 Chronic embolism and thrombosis of unspecified femoral vein**
CC Exclusion see Appendix A PDX collection 0717

+ **I82.52 Chronic embolism and thrombosis of iliac vein**

CC **I82.521 Chronic embolism and thrombosis of right iliac vein**
CC Exclusion see Appendix A PDX collection 0717

CC **I82.522 Chronic embolism and thrombosis of left iliac vein**
CC Exclusion see Appendix A PDX collection 0717

CC **I82.523 Chronic embolism and thrombosis of iliac vein, bilateral**
CC Exclusion see Appendix A PDX collection 0717

CC **I82.529 Chronic embolism and thrombosis of unspecified iliac vein**
CC Exclusion see Appendix A PDX collection 0717

+ **I82.53 Chronic embolism and thrombosis of popliteal vein**

CC **I82.531 Chronic embolism and thrombosis of right popliteal vein**
CC Exclusion see Appendix A PDX collection 0717

CC **I82.532 Chronic embolism and thrombosis of left popliteal vein**
CC Exclusion see Appendix A PDX collection 0717

CC **I82.533 Chronic embolism and thrombosis of popliteal vein, bilateral**
CC Exclusion see Appendix A PDX collection 0717

CC **I82.539 Chronic embolism and thrombosis of unspecified popliteal vein**
CC Exclusion see Appendix A PDX collection 0717

+ **I82.54 Chronic embolism and thrombosis of tibial vein**

CC **I82.541 Chronic embolism and thrombosis of righ[t] tibial vein**
CC Exclusion see Appendix A PDX collection 0

CC **I82.542 Chronic embolism and thrombosis of left tibial vein**
CC Exclusion see Appendix A PDX collection 0

CC **I82.543 Chronic embolism and thrombosis of tibia[l] vein, bilateral**
CC Exclusion see Appendix A PDX collection 0

CC **I82.549 Chronic embolism and thrombosis of unspecified tibial vein**
CC Exclusion see Appendix A PDX collection 0

+ **I82.59 Chronic embolism and thrombosis of other specified deep vein of lower extremity**

CC **I82.591 Chronic embolism and thrombosis of othe[r] specified deep vein of right lower extremit[y]**
CC Exclusion see Appendix A PDX collection 0

CC **I82.592 Chronic embolism and thrombosis of othe[r] specified deep vein of left lower extremity**
CC Exclusion see Appendix A PDX collection 0

CC **I82.593 Chronic embolism and thrombosis of othe[r] specified deep vein of lower extremity, bilateral**
CC Exclusion see Appendix A PDX collection 07

CC **I82.599 Chronic embolism and thrombosis of othe[r] specified deep vein of unspecified lower extremity**
CC Exclusion see Appendix A PDX collection 07

+ **I82.5Y Chronic embolism and thrombosis of unspecified de[ep] veins of proximal lower extremity**
Chronic embolism and thrombosis of deep veins of thi[gh] NOS
Chronic embolism and thrombosis of deep veins of upper leg NOS

CC **I82.5Y1 Chronic embolism and thrombosis of unspecified deep veins of right proximal lower extremity**
CC Exclusion see Appendix A PDX collection 07

CC **I82.5Y2 Chronic embolism and thrombosis of unspecified deep veins of left proximal low[er] extremity**
CC Exclusion see Appendix A PDX collection 07

CC **I82.5Y3 Chronic embolism and thrombosis of unspecified deep veins of proximal lower extremity, bilateral**
CC Exclusion see Appendix A PDX collection 07

CC **I82.5Y9 Chronic embolism and thrombosis of unspecified deep veins of unspecified proximal lower extremity**
CC Exclusion see Appendix A PDX collection 07

+ **I82.5Z Chronic embolism and thrombosis of unspecified dee[p] veins of distal lower extremity**
Chronic embolism and thrombosis of deep veins of ca[lf] NOS
Chronic embolism and thrombosis of deep veins of lower leg NOS

CC **I82.5Z1 Chronic embolism and thrombosis of unspecified deep veins of right distal lower extremity**
CC Exclusion see Appendix A PDX collection 07

CC **I82.5Z2 Chronic embolism and thrombosis of unspecified deep veins of left distal lower extremity**
CC Exclusion see Appendix A PDX collection 07

CC **I82.5Z3 Chronic embolism and thrombosis of unspecified deep veins of distal lower extremity, bilateral**
CC Exclusion see Appendix A PDX collection 07

CC **I82.5Z9 Chronic embolism and thrombosis of unspecified deep veins of unspecified distal lower extremity**
CC Exclusion see Appendix A PDX collection 07

+ **I82.6 Acute embolism and thrombosis of veins of upper extremity**

+ **I82.60 Acute embolism and thrombosis of unspecified veins of upper extremity**

CC **I82.601 Acute embolism and thrombosis of unspecified veins of right upper extremity**
CC Exclusion see Appendix A PDX collection 07

CC **I82.602 Acute embolism and thrombosis of unspecified veins of left upper extremity**
CC Exclusion see Appendix A PDX collection 07

CC **I82.603 Acute embolism and thrombosis of unspecified veins of upper extremity, bilateral**
CC Exclusion see Appendix A PDX collection 0717

CC **I82.609 Acute embolism and thrombosis of unspecified veins of unspecified upper extremity**
CC Exclusion see Appendix A PDX collection 0717

+ **I82.61 Acute embolism and thrombosis of superficial veins of upper extremity**
Acute embolism and thrombosis of antecubital vein
Acute embolism and thrombosis of basilic vein
Acute embolism and thrombosis of cephalic vein

CC **I82.611 Acute embolism and thrombosis of superficial veins of right upper extremity**
CC Exclusion see Appendix A PDX collection 0717

CC **I82.612 Acute embolism and thrombosis of superficial veins of left upper extremity**
CC Exclusion see Appendix A PDX collection 0717

CC **I82.613 Acute embolism and thrombosis of superficial veins of upper extremity, bilateral**
CC Exclusion see Appendix A PDX collection 0717

CC **I82.619 Acute embolism and thrombosis of superficial veins of unspecified upper extremity**
CC Exclusion see Appendix A PDX collection 0717

+ **I82.62 Acute embolism and thrombosis of deep veins of upper extremity**
Acute embolism and thrombosis of brachial vein
Acute embolism and thrombosis of radial vein
Acute embolism and thrombosis of ulnar vein

CC **I82.621 Acute embolism and thrombosis of deep veins of right upper extremity**
CC Exclusion see Appendix A PDX collection 0717

CC **I82.622 Acute embolism and thrombosis of deep veins of left upper extremity**
CC Exclusion see Appendix A PDX collection 0717

CC **I82.623 Acute embolism and thrombosis of deep veins of upper extremity, bilateral**
CC Exclusion see Appendix A PDX collection 0717

CC **I82.629 Acute embolism and thrombosis of deep veins of unspecified upper extremity**
CC Exclusion see Appendix A PDX collection 0717

+ **I82.7 Chronic embolism and thrombosis of veins of upper extremity**
Use additional code, if applicable, for associated long-term (current) use of anticoagulants (Z79.01)
Excludes1: *personal history of venous embolism and thrombosis (Z86.718)*

+ **I82.70 Chronic embolism and thrombosis of unspecified veins of upper extremity**

CC **I82.701 Chronic embolism and thrombosis of unspecified veins of right upper extremity**
CC Exclusion see Appendix A PDX collection 0717

CC **I82.702 Chronic embolism and thrombosis of unspecified veins of left upper extremity**
CC Exclusion see Appendix A PDX collection 0717

CC **I82.703 Chronic embolism and thrombosis of unspecified veins of upper extremity, bilateral**
CC Exclusion see Appendix A PDX collection 0717

CC **I82.709 Chronic embolism and thrombosis of unspecified veins of unspecified upper extremity**
CC Exclusion see Appendix A PDX collection 0717

+ **I82.71 Chronic embolism and thrombosis of superficial veins of upper extremity**
Chronic embolism and thrombosis of antecubital vein
Chronic embolism and thrombosis of basilic vein
Chronic embolism and thrombosis of cephalic vein

CC **I82.711 Chronic embolism and thrombosis of superficial veins of right upper extremity**
CC Exclusion see Appendix A PDX collection 0717

CC **I82.712 Chronic embolism and thrombosis of superficial veins of left upper extremity**
CC Exclusion see Appendix A PDX collection 0717

CC **I82.713 Chronic embolism and thrombosis of superficial veins of upper extremity, bilateral**
CC Exclusion see Appendix A PDX collection 0717

CC **I82.719 Chronic embolism and thrombosis of superficial veins of unspecified upper extremity**
CC Exclusion see Appendix A PDX collection 0717

+ **I82.72 Chronic embolism and thrombosis of deep veins of upper extremity**
Chronic embolism and thrombosis of brachial vein
Chronic embolism and thrombosis of radial vein
Chronic embolism and thrombosis of ulnar vein

CC **I82.721 Chronic embolism and thrombosis of deep veins of right upper extremity**
CC Exclusion see Appendix A PDX collection 0717

CC **I82.722 Chronic embolism and thrombosis of deep veins of left upper extremity**
CC Exclusion see Appendix A PDX collection 0717

CC **I82.723 Chronic embolism and thrombosis of deep veins of upper extremity, bilateral**
CC Exclusion see Appendix A PDX collection 0717

CC **I82.729 Chronic embolism and thrombosis of deep veins of unspecified upper extremity**
CC Exclusion see Appendix A PDX collection 0717

+ **I82.A Embolism and thrombosis of axillary vein**

+ **I82.A1 Acute embolism and thrombosis of axillary vein**

CC **I82.A11 Acute embolism and thrombosis of right axillary vein**
CC Exclusion see Appendix A PDX collection 0717

CC **I82.A12 Acute embolism and thrombosis of left axillary vein**
CC Exclusion see Appendix A PDX collection 0717

CC **I82.A13 Acute embolism and thrombosis of axillary vein, bilateral**
CC Exclusion see Appendix A PDX collection 0717

CC **I82.A19 Acute embolism and thrombosis of unspecified axillary vein**
CC Exclusion see Appendix A PDX collection 0717

+ **I82.A2 Chronic embolism and thrombosis of axillary vein**

CC **I82.A21 Chronic embolism and thrombosis of right axillary vein**
CC Exclusion see Appendix A PDX collection 0717

CC **I82.A22 Chronic embolism and thrombosis of left axillary vein**
CC Exclusion see Appendix A PDX collection 0717

CC **I82.A23 Chronic embolism and thrombosis of axillary vein, bilateral**
CC Exclusion see Appendix A PDX collection 0717

CC **I82.A29 Chronic embolism and thrombosis of unspecified axillary vein**
CC Exclusion see Appendix A PDX collection 0717

+ **I82.B Embolism and thrombosis of subclavian vein**

+ **I82.B1 Acute embolism and thrombosis of subclavian≈vein**

CC **I82.B11 Acute embolism and thrombosis of right subclavian vein**
CC Exclusion see Appendix A PDX collection 0717

CC **I82.B12 Acute embolism and thrombosis of left subclavian vein**
CC Exclusion see Appendix A PDX collection 0717

CC **I82.B13 Acute embolism and thrombosis of subclavian vein, bilateral**
CC Exclusion see Appendix A PDX collection 0717

CC **I82.B19 Acute embolism and thrombosis of unspecified subclavian vein**
CC Exclusion see Appendix A PDX collection 0717

+ **I82.B2 Chronic embolism and thrombosis of subclavian vein**

CC **I82.B21 Chronic embolism and thrombosis of right subclavian vein**
CC Exclusion see Appendix A PDX collection 0717

CC **I82.B22 Chronic embolism and thrombosis of left subclavian vein**
CC Exclusion see Appendix A PDX collection 0717

CC **I82.B23 Chronic embolism and thrombosis of subclavian vein, bilateral**
CC Exclusion see Appendix A PDX collection 0717

CC **I82.B29 Chronic embolism and thrombosis of unspecified subclavian vein**
CC Exclusion see Appendix A PDX collection 0717

+ **I82.C Embolism and thrombosis of internal jugular vein**

+ **I82.C1 Acute embolism and thrombosis of internal jugular vein**

CC **I82.C11 Acute embolism and thrombosis of right internal jugular vein**
CC Exclusion see Appendix A PDX collection 0717

CC **I82.C12 Acute embolism and thrombosis of left internal jugular vein**
CC Exclusion see Appendix A PDX collection 0717

CC **I82.C13 Acute embolism and thrombosis of internal jugular vein, bilateral**
CC Exclusion see Appendix A PDX collection 0717

CC **I82.C19 Acute embolism and thrombosis of unspecified internal jugular vein**
CC Exclusion see Appendix A PDX collection 0717

+ **I82.C2 Chronic embolism and thrombosis of internal jugular vein**

CC **I82.C21 Chronic embolism and thrombosis of right internal jugular vein**
CC Exclusion see Appendix A PDX collection 0717

CC **I82.C22 Chronic embolism and thrombosis of left internal jugular vein**
CC Exclusion see Appendix A PDX collection 0717

CC **I82.C23 Chronic embolism and thrombosis of internal jugular vein, bilateral**
CC Exclusion see Appendix A PDX collection 0717

CC **I82.C29 Chronic embolism and thrombosis of unspecified internal jugular vein**
CC Exclusion see Appendix A PDX collection 0717

+ **I82.8 Embolism and thrombosis of other specified veins**
Use additional code, if applicable, for associated long-term (current) use of anticoagulants (Z79.01)

+ **I82.81 Embolism and thrombosis of superficial veins of lower extremities**
Embolism and thrombosis of saphenous vein (greater) (lesser)

CC **I82.811 Embolism and thrombosis of superficial veins of right lower extremities**
CC Exclusion see Appendix A PDX collection 0717

CC **I82.812 Embolism and thrombosis of superficial veins of left lower extremities**
CC Exclusion see Appendix A PDX collection 0717

CC **I82.813 Embolism and thrombosis of superficial veins of lower extremities, bilateral**
CC Exclusion see Appendix A PDX collection 0717

CC **I82.819 Embolism and thrombosis of superficial veins of unspecified lower extremities**
CC Exclusion see Appendix A PDX collection 0717

+ **I82.89 Embolism and thrombosis of other specified veins**

CC **I82.890 Acute embolism and thrombosis of other specified veins**
CC Exclusion see Appendix A PDX collection 0717

CC **I82.891 Chronic embolism and thrombosis of other specified veins**
CC Exclusion see Appendix A PDX collection 0717

+ **I82.9 Embolism and thrombosis of unspecified vein**

CC **I82.90 Acute embolism and thrombosis of unspecified vein**
Embolism of vein NOS
Thrombosis (vein) NOS
CC Exclusion see Appendix A PDX collection 0717

CC **I82.91 Chronic embolism and thrombosis of unspecified vein**
CC Exclusion see Appendix A PDX collection 0717

I83 Varicose veins of lower extremities

Excludes1: *varicose veins complicating pregnancy (O22.0-)*
varicose veins complicating the puerperium (O87.4)

+ **I83.0 Varicose veins of lower extremities with ulcer**
Use additional code to identify severity of ulcer (L97.-)

+ **I83.00 Varicose veins of unspecified lower extremity with ulcer**

• **I83.001 Varicose veins of unspecified lower extremity with ulcer of thigh**

• **I83.002 Varicose veins of unspecified lower extremity with ulcer of calf**

• **I83.003 Varicose veins of unspecified lower extremity with ulcer of ankle**

• **I83.004 Varicose veins of unspecified lower extremity with ulcer of heel and midfoot**
Varicose veins of unspecified lower extremity with ulcer of plantar surface of midfoot

• **I83.005 Varicose veins of unspecified lower extremity with ulcer other part of foot**
Varicose veins of unspecified lower extremity with ulcer of toe

• **I83.008 Varicose veins of unspecified lower extremity with ulcer other part of lower leg**

• **I83.009 Varicose veins of unspecified lower extremity with ulcer of unspecified site**

+ **I83.01 Varicose veins of right lower extremity with ulcer**

• **I83.011 Varicose veins of right lower extremity with ulcer of thigh**

• **I83.012 Varicose veins of right lower extremity with ulcer of calf**

• **I83.013 Varicose veins of right lower extremity wi ulcer of ankle**

• **I83.014 Varicose veins of right lower extremity wi ulcer of heel and midfoot**
Varicose veins of right lower extremity wit ulcer of plantar surface of midfoot

• **I83.015 Varicose veins of right lower extremity wi ulcer other part of foot**
Varicose veins of right lower extremity wit ulcer of toe

• **I83.018 Varicose veins of right lower extremity wi ulcer other part of lower leg**

• **I83.019 Varicose veins of right lower extremity wi ulcer of unspecified site**

+ **I83.02 Varicose veins of left lower extremity with ulcer**

• **I83.021 Varicose veins of left lower extremity with ulcer of thigh**

• **I83.022 Varicose veins of left lower extremity with ulcer of calf**

• **I83.023 Varicose veins of left lower extremity with ulcer of ankle**

• **I83.024 Varicose veins of left lower extremity with ulcer of heel and midfoot**
Varicose veins of left lower extremity with ulcer of plantar surface of midfoot

• **I83.025 Varicose veins of left lower extremity with ulcer other part of foot**
Varicose veins of left lower extremity with ulcer of toe

• **I83.028 Varicose veins of left lower extremity with ulcer other part of lower leg**

• **I83.029 Varicose veins of left lower extremity with ulcer of unspecified site**

+ **I83.1 Varicose veins of lower extremities with inflammation**
Stasis dermatitis

• **I83.10 Varicose veins of unspecified lower extremity with inflammation**

• **I83.11 Varicose veins of right lower extremity with inflammation**

• **I83.12 Varicose veins of left lower extremity with inflammation**

+ **I83.2 Varicose veins of lower extremities with both ulcer and inflammation**
Use additional code to identify severity of ulcer (L97.-)

+ **I83.20 Varicose veins of unspecified lower extremity with both ulcer and inflammation**

• CC **I83.201 Varicose veins of unspecified lower extrem with both ulcer of thigh and inflammation**
CC Exclusion see Appendix A PDX collection 0

• CC **I83.202 Varicose veins of unspecified lower extrem with both ulcer of calf and inflammation**
CC Exclusion see Appendix A PDX collection 0

• CC **I83.203 Varicose veins of unspecified lower extrem with both ulcer of ankle and inflammation**
CC Exclusion see Appendix A PDX collection 0

• CC **I83.204 Varicose veins of unspecified lower extrem with both ulcer of heel and midfoot and inflammation**
Varicose veins of unspecified lower extremi with both ulcer of plantar surface of midfoot and inflammation
CC Exclusion see Appendix A PDX collection 0

• CC **I83.205 Varicose veins of unspecified lower extrem with both ulcer other part of foot and inflammation**
Varicose veins of unspecified lower extremi with both ulcer of toe and inflammation
CC Exclusion see Appendix A PDX collection 0

• CC **I83.208 Varicose veins of unspecified lower extrem with both ulcer of other part of lower extremity and inflammation**
CC Exclusion see Appendix A PDX collection 0

• CC **I83.209 Varicose veins of unspecified lower extrem with both ulcer of unspecified site and inflammation**
CC Exclusion see Appendix A PDX collection 0

+ **I83.21 Varicose veins of right lower extremity with both ul and inflammation**

• CC **I83.211 Varicose veins of right lower extremity wi both ulcer of thigh and inflammation**
CC Exclusion see Appendix A PDX collection 0

• CC **I83.212 Varicose veins of right lower extremity with both ulcer of calf and inflammation**
CC Exclusion see Appendix A PDX collection 0720

• CC **I83.213 Varicose veins of right lower extremity with both ulcer of ankle and inflammation**
CC Exclusion see Appendix A PDX collection 0720

• CC **I83.214 Varicose veins of right lower extremity with both ulcer of heel and midfoot and inflammation**
Varicose veins of right lower extremity with both ulcer of plantar surface of midfoot and inflammation
CC Exclusion see Appendix A PDX collection 0720

• CC **I83.215 Varicose veins of right lower extremity with both ulcer other part of foot and inflammation**
Varicose veins of right lower extremity with both ulcer of toe and inflammation
CC Exclusion see Appendix A PDX collection 0720

• CC **I83.218 Varicose veins of right lower extremity with both ulcer of other part of lower extremity and inflammation**
CC Exclusion see Appendix A PDX collection 0720

• CC **I83.219 Varicose veins of right lower extremity with both ulcer of unspecified site and inflammation**
CC Exclusion see Appendix A PDX collection 0720

\+ **I83.22 Varicose veins of left lower extremity with both ulcer and inflammation**

• CC **I83.221 Varicose veins of left lower extremity with both ulcer of thigh and inflammation**
CC Exclusion see Appendix A PDX collection 0720

• CC **I83.222 Varicose veins of left lower extremity with both ulcer of calf and inflammation**
CC Exclusion see Appendix A PDX collection 0720

• CC **I83.223 Varicose veins of left lower extremity with both ulcer of ankle and inflammation**
CC Exclusion see Appendix A PDX collection 0720

• CC **I83.224 Varicose veins of left lower extremity with both ulcer of heel and midfoot and inflammation**
Varicose veins of left lower extremity with both ulcer of plantar surface of midfoot and inflammation
CC Exclusion see Appendix A PDX collection 0720

• CC **I83.225 Varicose veins of left lower extremity with both ulcer other part of foot and inflammation**
Varicose veins of left lower extremity with both ulcer of toe and inflammation
CC Exclusion see Appendix A PDX collection 0720

• CC **I83.228 Varicose veins of left lower extremity with both ulcer of other part of lower extremity and inflammation**
CC Exclusion see Appendix A PDX collection 0720

• CC **I83.229 Varicose veins of left lower extremity with both ulcer of unspecified site and inflammation**
CC Exclusion see Appendix A PDX collection 0720

\+ **I83.8 Varicose veins of lower extremities with other complications**

\+ **I83.81 Varicose veins of lower extremities with pain**

• **I83.811 Varicose veins of right lower extremities with pain**

• **I83.812 Varicose veins of left lower extremities with pain**

• **I83.813 Varicose veins of bilateral lower extremities with pain**

• **I83.819 Varicose veins of unspecified lower extremities with pain**

\+ **I83.89 Varicose veins of lower extremities with other complications**
Varicose veins of lower extremities with edema
Varicose veins of lower extremities with swelling

• **I83.891 Varicose veins of right lower extremities with other complications**

• **I83.892 Varicose veins of left lower extremities with other complications**

• **I83.893 Varicose veins of bilateral lower extremities with other complications**

• **I83.899 Varicose veins of unspecified lower extremities with other complications**

\+ **I83.9 Asymptomatic varicose veins of lower extremities**
Phlebectasia of lower extremities
Varicose veins of lower extremities
Varix of lower extremities

• **I83.90 Asymptomatic varicose veins of unspecified lower extremity**
Varicose veins NOS

• **I83.91 Asymptomatic varicose veins of right lower extremity**

• **I83.92 Asymptomatic varicose veins of left lower extremity**

• **I83.93 Asymptomatic varicose veins of bilateral lower extremities**

I85 Esophageal varices

Use additional code to identify:
alcohol abuse and dependence (F10.-)

\+ **I85.0 Esophageal varices**
Idiopathic esophageal varices
Primary esophageal varices

CC **I85.00 Esophageal varices without bleeding**
Esophageal varices NOS
CC Exclusion see Appendix A PDX collection 0721

MCC **I85.01 Esophageal varices with bleeding**
MCC Exclusion see Appendix A PDX collection 0722

\+ **I85.1 Secondary esophageal varices**
Esophageal varices secondary to alcoholic liver disease
Esophageal varices secondary to cirrhosis of liver
Esophageal varices secondary to schistosomiasis
Esophageal varices secondary to toxic liver disease
Code first underlying disease

CC **I85.10 Secondary esophageal varices without bleeding**
CC Exclusion see Appendix A PDX collection 0723

MCC **I85.11 Secondary esophageal varices with bleeding**
MCC Exclusion see Appendix A PDX collection 0724

I86 Varicose veins of other sites

Excludes1: *varicose veins of unspecified site (I83.9-)*
Excludes2: *retinal varices (H35.0-)*

I86.0 Sublingual varices

♂ **I86.1 Scrotal varices**
Varicocele

I86.2 Pelvic varices

♀ **I86.3 Vulval varices**
Excludes1: *vulval varices complicating childbirth and the puerperium (O87.8)*
vulval varices complicating pregnancy (O22.1-)

I86.4 Gastric varices

• **I86.8 Varicose veins of other specified sites**
Varicose ulcer of nasal septum

I87 Other disorders of veins

\+ **I87.0 Postthrombotic syndrome**
Chronic venous hypertension due to deep vein thrombosis
Postphlebitic syndrome
Excludes1: *chronic venous hypertension without deep vein thrombosis (I87.3-)*

\+ **I87.00 Postthrombotic syndrome without complications**
Asymptomatic Postthrombotic syndrome

I87.001 Postthrombotic syndrome without complications of right lower extremity

I87.002 Postthrombotic syndrome without complications of left lower extremity

I87.003 Postthrombotic syndrome without complications of bilateral lower extremity

I87.009 Postthrombotic syndrome without complications of unspecified extremity
Postthrombotic syndrome NOS

\+ **I87.01 Postthrombotic syndrome with ulcer**
Use additional code to specify site and severity of ulcer (L97.-)

CC **I87.011 Postthrombotic syndrome with ulcer of right lower extremity**
CC Exclusion see Appendix A PDX collection 0725

CC **I87.012 Postthrombotic syndrome with ulcer of left lower extremity**
CC Exclusion see Appendix A PDX collection 0725

CC **I87.013 Postthrombotic syndrome with ulcer of bilateral lower extremity**
CC Exclusion see Appendix A PDX collection 0725

CC **I87.019 Postthrombotic syndrome with ulcer of unspecified lower extremity**
CC Exclusion see Appendix A PDX collection 0725

\+ **I87.02 Postthrombotic syndrome with inflammation**

I87.021 Postthrombotic syndrome with inflammation of right lower extremity

I87.022 Postthrombotic syndrome with inflammation of left lower extremity
I87.023 Postthrombotic syndrome with inflammation of bilateral lower extremity
I87.029 Postthrombotic syndrome with inflammation of unspecified lower extremity

+ I87.03 Postthrombotic syndrome with ulcer and inflammation
Use additional code to specify site and severity of ulcer (L97.-)
CC **I87.031 Postthrombotic syndrome with ulcer and inflammation of right lower extremity**
CC Exclusion see Appendix A PDX collection 0725
CC **I87.032 Postthrombotic syndrome with ulcer and inflammation of left lower extremity**
CC Exclusion see Appendix A PDX collection 0725
CC **I87.033 Postthrombotic syndrome with ulcer and inflammation of bilateral lower extremity**
CC Exclusion see Appendix A PDX collection 0725
CC **I87.039 Postthrombotic syndrome with ulcer and inflammation of unspecified lower extremity**
CC Exclusion see Appendix A PDX collection 0725

+ I87.09 Postthrombotic syndrome with other complications
I87.091 Postthrombotic syndrome with other complications of right lower extremity
I87.092 Postthrombotic syndrome with other complications of left lower extremity
I87.093 Postthrombotic syndrome with other complications of bilateral lower extremity
I87.099 Postthrombotic syndrome with other complications of unspecified lower extremity

CC **I87.1 Compression of vein**
Stricture of vein
Vena cava syndrome (inferior) (superior)
Excludes2: *compression of pulmonary vein (I28.8)*
CC Exclusion see Appendix A PDX collection 0726

I87.2 Venous insufficiency (chronic) (peripheral)

+ I87.3 Chronic venous hypertension (idiopathic)
Stasis edema
Excludes1: *chronic venous hypertension due to deep vein thrombosis (I87.0-)*
varicose veins of lower extremities (I83.-)

+ I87.30 Chronic venous hypertension (idiopathic) without complications
Asymptomatic chronic venous hypertension (idiopathic)
I87.301 Chronic venous hypertension (idiopathic) without complications of right lower extremity
I87.302 Chronic venous hypertension (idiopathic) without complications of left lower extremity
I87.303 Chronic venous hypertension (idiopathic) without complications of bilateral lower extremity
I87.309 Chronic venous hypertension (idiopathic) without complications of unspecified lower extremity
Chronic venous hypertension NOS

+ I87.31 Chronic venous hypertension (idiopathic) with ulcer
Use additional code to specify site and severity of ulcer (L97.-)
CC **I87.311 Chronic venous hypertension (idiopathic) with ulcer of right lower extremity**
CC Exclusion see Appendix A PDX collection 0727
CC **I87.312 Chronic venous hypertension (idiopathic) with ulcer of left lower extremity**
CC Exclusion see Appendix A PDX collection 0727
CC **I87.313 Chronic venous hypertension (idiopathic) with ulcer of bilateral lower extremity**
CC Exclusion see Appendix A PDX collection 0727
CC **I87.319 Chronic venous hypertension (idiopathic) with ulcer of unspecified lower extremity**
CC Exclusion see Appendix A PDX collection 0727

+ I87.32 Chronic venous hypertension (idiopathic) with inflammation
I87.321 Chronic venous hypertension (idiopathic) with inflammation of right lower extremity
I87.322 Chronic venous hypertension (idiopathic) with inflammation of left lower extremity
I87.323 Chronic venous hypertension (idiopathic) with inflammation of bilateral lower extremity
I87.329 Chronic venous hypertension (idiopathic) with inflammation of unspecified lower extremity

+ I87.33 Chronic venous hypertension (idiopathic) with ulcer and inflammation
Use additional code to specify site and severity of ulcer (L97.-)
CC **I87.331 Chronic venous hypertension (idiopathic) with ulcer and inflammation of right lower extremity**
CC Exclusion see Appendix A PDX collection 0727
CC **I87.332 Chronic venous hypertension (idiopathic) with ulcer and inflammation of left lower extremity**
CC Exclusion see Appendix A PDX collection 0727
CC **I87.333 Chronic venous hypertension (idiopathic) with ulcer and inflammation of bilateral lower extremity**
CC Exclusion see Appendix A PDX collection 0727
CC **I87.339 Chronic venous hypertension (idiopathic) with ulcer and inflammation of unspecified lower extremity**
CC Exclusion see Appendix A PDX collection 0727

+ I87.39 Chronic venous hypertension (idiopathic) with other complications
I87.391 Chronic venous hypertension (idiopathic) with other complications of right lower extremity
I87.392 Chronic venous hypertension (idiopathic) with other complications of left lower extremity
I87.393 Chronic venous hypertension (idiopathic) with other complications of bilateral lower extremity
I87.399 Chronic venous hypertension (idiopathic) with other complications of unspecified lower extremity

I87.8 Other specified disorders of veins
Phlebosclerosis
Venofibrosis

I87.9 Disorder of vein, unspecified

I88 Nonspecific lymphadenitis

Excludes1: *acute lymphadenitis, except mesenteric (L04.-)*
enlarged lymph nodes NOS (R59.-)
human immunodeficiency virus [HIV] disease resulting in generalized lymphadenopathy (B20)

I88.0 Nonspecific mesenteric lymphadenitis
Mesenteric lymphadenitis (acute)(chronic)

I88.1 Chronic lymphadenitis, except mesenteric
Adenitis
Lymphadenitis

I88.8 Other nonspecific lymphadenitis

I88.9 Nonspecific lymphadenitis, unspecified
Lymphadenitis NOS

I89 Other noninfective disorders of lymphatic vessels and lymph nodes

Excludes1: *chylocele, tunica vaginalis (nonfilarial) NOS (N50.8)*
enlarged lymph nodes NOS (R59.-)
filarial chylocele (B74.-)
hereditary lymphedema (Q82.0)

I89.0 Lymphedema, not elsewhere classified
Elephantiasis (nonfilarial) NOS
Lymphangiectasis
Obliteration, lymphatic vessel
Praecox lymphedema
Secondary lymphedema
Excludes1: *postmastectomy lymphedema (I97.2)*

I89.1 Lymphangitis
Chronic lymphangitis
Lymphangitis NOS
Subacute lymphangitis
Excludes1: *acute lymphangitis (L03.-)*

I89.8 Other specified noninfective disorders of lymphatic vessels and lymph nodes
Chylocele (nonfilarial)
Chylous ascites
Chylous cyst
Lipomelanotic reticulosis
Lymph node or vessel fistula
Lymph node or vessel infarction
Lymph node or vessel rupture

I89.9 Noninfective disorder of lymphatic vessels and lymph nodes, unspecified
Disease of lymphatic vessels NOS

ther and unspecified disorders of the circulatory system 95-I99)

I95 Hypotension
Excludes1: *cardiovascular collapse (R57.9)*
maternal hypotension syndrome (O26.5-)
nonspecific low blood pressure reading NOS (R03.1)

I95.0 Idiopathic hypotension

I95.1 Orthostatic hypotension
Hypotension, postural
Excludes1: *neurogenic orthostatic hypotension [Shy-Drager] (G90.3)*
orthostatic hypotension due to drugs (I95.2)

I95.2 Hypotension due to drugs
Orthostatic hypotension due to drugs
Use additional code for adverse effect, if applicable, to identify drug (T36-T50 with fifth or sixth character 5)

I95.3 Hypotension of hemodialysis
Intra-dialytic hypotension

I95.8 Other hypotension
I95.81 Postprocedural hypotension
I95.89 Other hypotension
Chronic hypotension

I95.9 Hypotension, unspecified

C **I96 Gangrene, not elsewhere classified**
Gangrenous cellulitis
Excludes1: *gangrene in atherosclerosis of native arteries of the extremities (I70.26)*
gangrene in diabetes mellitus (E08-E13)
gangrene in hernia (K40.1, K40.4, K41.1, K41.4, K42.1, K43.1-, K44.1, K45.1, K46.1)
gangrene in other peripheral vascular diseases (I73.-)
gangrene of certain specified sites - see Alphabetical Index
gas gangrene (A48.0)
pyoderma gangrenosum (L88)
CC Exclusion see Appendix A PDX collection 0519
Valid 3-character code, no further characters required

I97 Intraoperative and postprocedural complications and disorders of circulatory system, not elsewhere classified
Excludes2: *postprocedural shock (T81.1-)*

I97.0 Postcardiotomy syndrome

\+ **I97.1 Other postprocedural cardiac functional disturbances**
Excludes2: *acute pulmonary insufficiency following thoracic surgery (J95.1)*
intraoperative cardiac functional disturbances (I97.7-)

\+ **I97.11 Postprocedural cardiac insufficiency**
CC **I97.110 Postprocedural cardiac insufficiency following cardiac surgery**
CC Exclusion see Appendix A PDX collection 0728
CC **I97.111 Postprocedural cardiac insufficiency following other surgery**
CC Exclusion see Appendix A PDX collection 0728

\+ **I97.12 Postprocedural cardiac arrest**
CC **I97.120 Postprocedural cardiac arrest following cardiac surgery**
CC Exclusion see Appendix A PDX collection 0728
CC **I97.121 Postprocedural cardiac arrest following other surgery**
CC Exclusion see Appendix A PDX collection 0728

\+ **I97.13 Postprocedural heart failure**
Use additional code to identify the heart failure (I50.-)
CC **I97.130 Postprocedural heart failure following cardiac surgery**
CC Exclusion see Appendix A PDX collection 0728
CC **I97.131 Postprocedural heart failure following other surgery**
CC Exclusion see Appendix A PDX collection 0728

\+ **I97.19 Other postprocedural cardiac functional disturbances**
Use additional code, if applicable, to further specify disorder
CC **I97.190 Other postprocedural cardiac functional disturbances following cardiac surgery**
CC Exclusion see Appendix A PDX collection 0728
CC **I97.191 Other postprocedural cardiac functional disturbances following other surgery**
CC Exclusion see Appendix A PDX collection 0728

• **I97.2 Postmastectomy lymphedema syndrome**
Elephantiasis due to mastectomy
Obliteration of lymphatic vessels

I97.3 Postprocedural hypertension

\+ **I97.4 Intraoperative hemorrhage and hematoma of a circulatory system organ or structure complicating a procedure**
Excludes1: *intraoperative hemorrhage and hematoma of a circulatory system organ or structure due to accidental puncture and laceration during a procedure (I97.5-)*
Excludes2: *intraoperative cerebrovascular hemorrhage complicating a procedure (G97.3-)*

\+ **I97.41 Intraoperative hemorrhage and hematoma of a circulatory system organ or structure complicating a circulatory system procedure**
CC **I97.410 Intraoperative hemorrhage and hematoma of a circulatory system organ or structure complicating a cardiac catheterization**
CC Exclusion see Appendix A PDX collection 0729
CC **I97.411 Intraoperative hemorrhage and hematoma of a circulatory system organ or structure complicating a cardiac bypass**
CC Exclusion see Appendix A PDX collection 0729
CC **I97.418 Intraoperative hemorrhage and hematoma of a circulatory system organ or structure complicating other circulatory system procedure**
CC Exclusion see Appendix A PDX collection 0729

CC **I97.42 Intraoperative hemorrhage and hematoma of a circulatory system organ or structure complicating other procedure**
CC Exclusion see Appendix A PDX collection 0729

\+ **I97.5 Accidental puncture and laceration of a circulatory system organ or structure during a procedure**
Excludes2: *accidental puncture and laceration of brain during a procedure (G97.4-)*

CC **I97.51 Accidental puncture and laceration of a circulatory system organ or structure during a circulatory system procedure**
CC Exclusion see Appendix A PDX collection 0509
CC **I97.52 Accidental puncture and laceration of a circulatory system organ or structure during other procedure**
CC Exclusion see Appendix A PDX collection 0509

\+ **I97.6 Postprocedural hemorrhage and hematoma of a circulatory system organ or structure following a procedure**
Excludes2: *postprocedural cerebrovascular hemorrhage complicating a procedure (G97.5-)*

\+ **I97.61 Postprocedural hemorrhage and hematoma of a circulatory system organ or structure following a circulatory system procedure**
CC **I97.610 Postprocedural hemorrhage and hematoma of a circulatory system organ or structure following a cardiac catheterization**
CC Exclusion see Appendix A PDX collection 0729
CC **I97.611 Postprocedural hemorrhage and hematoma of a circulatory system organ or structure following cardiac bypass**
CC Exclusion see Appendix A PDX collection 0729
CC **I97.618 Postprocedural hemorrhage and hematoma of a circulatory system organ or structure following other circulatory system procedure**
CC Exclusion see Appendix A PDX collection 0729

CC **I97.62 Postprocedural hemorrhage and hematoma of a circulatory system organ or structure following other procedure**
CC Exclusion see Appendix A PDX collection 0729

\+ **I97.7 Intraoperative cardiac functional disturbances**
Excludes2: *acute pulmonary insufficiency following thoracic surgery (J95.1)*
postprocedural cardiac functional disturbances (I97.1-)

+ I97.71 Intraoperative cardiac arrest

CC **I97.710 Intraoperative cardiac arrest during cardiac surgery**
CC Exclusion see Appendix A PDX collection 0728

CC **I97.711 Intraoperative cardiac arrest during other surgery**
CC Exclusion see Appendix A PDX collection 0728

+ I97.79 Other intraoperative cardiac functional disturbances
Use additional code, if applicable, to further specify disorder

CC **I97.790 Other intraoperative cardiac functional disturbances during cardiac surgery**
CC Exclusion see Appendix A PDX collection 0728

CC **I97.791 Other intraoperative cardiac functional disturbances during other surgery**
CC Exclusion see Appendix A PDX collection 0728

+ I97.8 Other intraoperative and postprocedural complications and disorders of the circulatory system, not elsewhere classified
Use additional code, if applicable, to further specify disorder

+ I97.81 Intraoperative cerebrovascular infarction

CC **I97.810 Intraoperative cerebrovascular infarction during cardiac surgery**
CC Exclusion see Appendix A PDX collection 0617

CC **I97.811 Intraoperative cerebrovascular infarction during other surgery**
CC Exclusion see Appendix A PDX collection 0

+ I97.82 Postprocedural cerebrovascular infarction

CC **I97.820 Postprocedural cerebrovascular infarction during cardiac surgery**
CC Exclusion see Appendix A PDX collection 0

CC **I97.821 Postprocedural cerebrovascular infarction during other surgery**
CC Exclusion see Appendix A PDX collection 0

CC **I97.88 Other intraoperative complications of the circulator system, not elsewhere classified**
CC Exclusion see Appendix A PDX collection 07

CC **I97.89 Other postprocedural complications and disorders o the circulatory system, not elsewhere classified**
CC Exclusion see Appendix A PDX collection 07

I99 Other and unspecified disorders of circulatory system

I99.8 Other disorder of circulatory system

I99.9 Unspecified disorder of circulatory system

hapter 10: Diseases of the Respiratory System (00-J99)

OTE When a respiratory condition is described as occurring in more than one site and is not specifically indexed, it should be classified to the lower anatomic site (e.g. tracheobronchitis to bronchitis in J40).

se additional code, where applicable, to identify:
exposure to environmental tobacco smoke (Z77.22)
exposure to tobacco smoke in the perinatal period (P96.81)
history of tobacco use (Z87.891)
occupational exposure to environmental tobacco smoke (Z57.31)
tobacco dependence (F17.-)
tobacco use (Z72.0)

xcludes2: *certain conditions originating in the perinatal period (P04-P96)*
certain infectious and parasitic diseases (A00-B99)
complications of pregnancy, childbirth and the puerperium (O00-O9A)
congenital malformations, deformations and chromosomal abnormalities (Q00-Q99)
endocrine, nutritional and metabolic diseases (E00-E88)
injury, poisoning and certain other consequences of external causes (S00-T88)
neoplasms (C00-D49)
smoke inhalation (T59.81-)
symptoms, signs and abnormal clinical and laboratory findings, not elsewhere classified (R00-R94)

his chapter contains the following category blocks:

J00-J06	Acute upper respiratory infections
J09-J18	Influenza and pneumonia
J20-J22	Other acute lower respiratory infections
J30-J39	Other diseases of upper respiratory tract
J40-J47	Chronic lower respiratory diseases
J60-J70	Lung diseases due to external agents
J80-J84	Other respiratory diseases principally affecting the interstitium
J85-J86	Suppurative and necrotic conditions of the lower respiratory tract
J90-J94	Other diseases of the pleura
J95	Intraoperative and postprocedural complications and disorders of respiratory system, not elsewhere classified
J96-J99	Other diseases of the respiratory system

. Chapter-Specific Coding Guidelines

n addition to general coding guidelines, there are guidelines for specific diagnoses nd/or conditions in the classification. Unless otherwise indicated, these guidelines pply to all health care settings. Please refer to Section II for guidelines on the election of principal diagnosis.

0. Chapter 10: Diseases of the Respiratory System (J00-J99)

a. Chronic Obstructive Pulmonary Disease [COPD] and Asthma

1) Acute exacerbation of chronic obstructive bronchitis and asthma

The codes in categories J44 and J45 distinguish between uncomplicated cases and those in acute exacerbation. An acute exacerbation is a worsening or a decompensation of a chronic condition. An acute exacerbation is not equivalent to an infection superimposed on a chronic condition, though an exacerbation may be triggered by an infection.

b. Acute Respiratory Failure

1) Acute respiratory failure as principal diagnosis

A code from subcategory J96.0, Acute respiratory failure, or subcategory J96.2, Acute and chronic respiratory failure, may be assigned as a principal diagnosis when it is the condition established after study to be chiefly responsible for occasioning the admission to the hospital, and the selection is supported by the Alphabetic Index and Tabular List. However, chapter-specific coding guidelines (such as obstetrics, poisoning, HIV, newborn) that provide sequencing direction take precedence.

2) Acute respiratory failure as secondary diagnosis

Respiratory failure may be listed as a secondary diagnosis if it occurs after admission, or if it is present on admission, but does not meet the definition of principal diagnosis.

3) Sequencing of acute respiratory failure and another acute condition

When a patient is admitted with respiratory failure and another acute condition, (e.g., myocardial infarction, cerebrovascular accident, aspiration pneumonia), the principal diagnosis will not be the same in every situation. This applies whether the other acute condition is a respiratory or nonrespiratory condition. Selection of the principal diagnosis will be dependent on the circumstances of admission. If both the respiratory failure and the other acute condition are equally responsible for occasioning the admission to the hospital, and there are no chapter-specific sequencing rules, the guideline regarding two or more diagnoses that equally meet the definition for principal diagnosis (Section II, C.) may be applied in these situations.

If the documentation is not clear as to whether acute respiratory failure and another condition are equally responsible for occasioning the admission, query the provider for clarification.

c. Influenza due to certain identified influenza viruses

Code only confirmed cases of influenza due to certain identified influenza viruses (category J09), and due to other identified influenza virus (category J10). This is an exception to the hospital inpatient guideline Section II, H. (Uncertain Diagnosis).

In this context, "confirmation" does not require documentation of positive laboratory testing specific for avian or other novel influenza A or other identified influenza virus. However, coding should be based on the provider's diagnostic statement that the patient has avian influenza, or other novel influenza A, for category J09, or has another particular identified strain of influenza, such as H1N1 or H3N2, but not identified as novel or variant, for category J10.

If the provider records "suspected" or "possible" or "probable" avian influenza, or novel influenza, or other identified influenza, then the appropriate influenza code from category J11, Influenza due to unidentified influenza virus, should be assigned. A code from category J09, Influenza due to certain identified influenza viruses, should not be assigned nor should a code from category J10, Influenza due to other identified influenza virus.

d. Ventilator associated Pneumonia

1) Documentation of Ventilator associated Pneumonia

As with all procedural or postprocedural complications, code assignment is based on the provider's documentation of the relationship between the condition and the procedure.

Code J95.851, Ventilator associated pneumonia, should be assigned only when the provider has documented ventilator associated pneumonia (VAP). An additional code to identify the organism (e.g., Pseudomonas aeruginosa, code B96.5) should also be assigned. Do not assign an additional code from categories J12-J18 to identify the type of pneumonia.

Code J95.851 should not be assigned for cases where the patient has pneumonia and is on a mechanical ventilator and the provider has not specifically stated that the pneumonia is ventilator-associated pneumonia. If the documentation is unclear as to whether the patient has a pneumonia that is a complication attributable to the mechanical ventilator, query the provider.

2) Ventilator associated Pneumonia Develops after Admission

A patient may be admitted with one type of pneumonia (e.g., code J13, Pneumonia due to Streptococcus pneumonia) and subsequently develop VAP. In this instance, the principal diagnosis would be the appropriate code from categories J12- J18 for the pneumonia diagnosed at the time of admission. Code J95.851, Ventilator associated pneumonia, would be assigned as an additional diagnosis when the provider has also documented the presence of ventilator associated pneumonia.

Acute upper respiratory infections (J00-J06)

Excludes1: *chronic obstructive pulmonary disease with acute lower respiratory infection (J44.0)*
influenza virus with other respiratory manifestations (J09.X2, J10.1, J11.1)

J00 Acute nasopharyngitis [common cold]

Acute rhinitis
Coryza (acute)
Infective nasopharyngitis NOS
Infective rhinitis
Nasal catarrh, acute
Nasopharyngitis NOS

Excludes1: *acute pharyngitis (J02.-)*
acute sore throat NOS (J02.9)
pharyngitis NOS (J02.9)
rhinitis NOS (J31.0)
sore throat NOS (J02.9)

Excludes2: *allergic rhinitis (J30.1-J30.9)*
chronic pharyngitis (J31.2)
chronic rhinitis (J31.0)
chronic sore throat (J31.2)
nasopharyngitis, chronic (J31.1)
vasomotor rhinitis (J30.0)

Valid 3-character code, no further characters required

Nose and Sinus

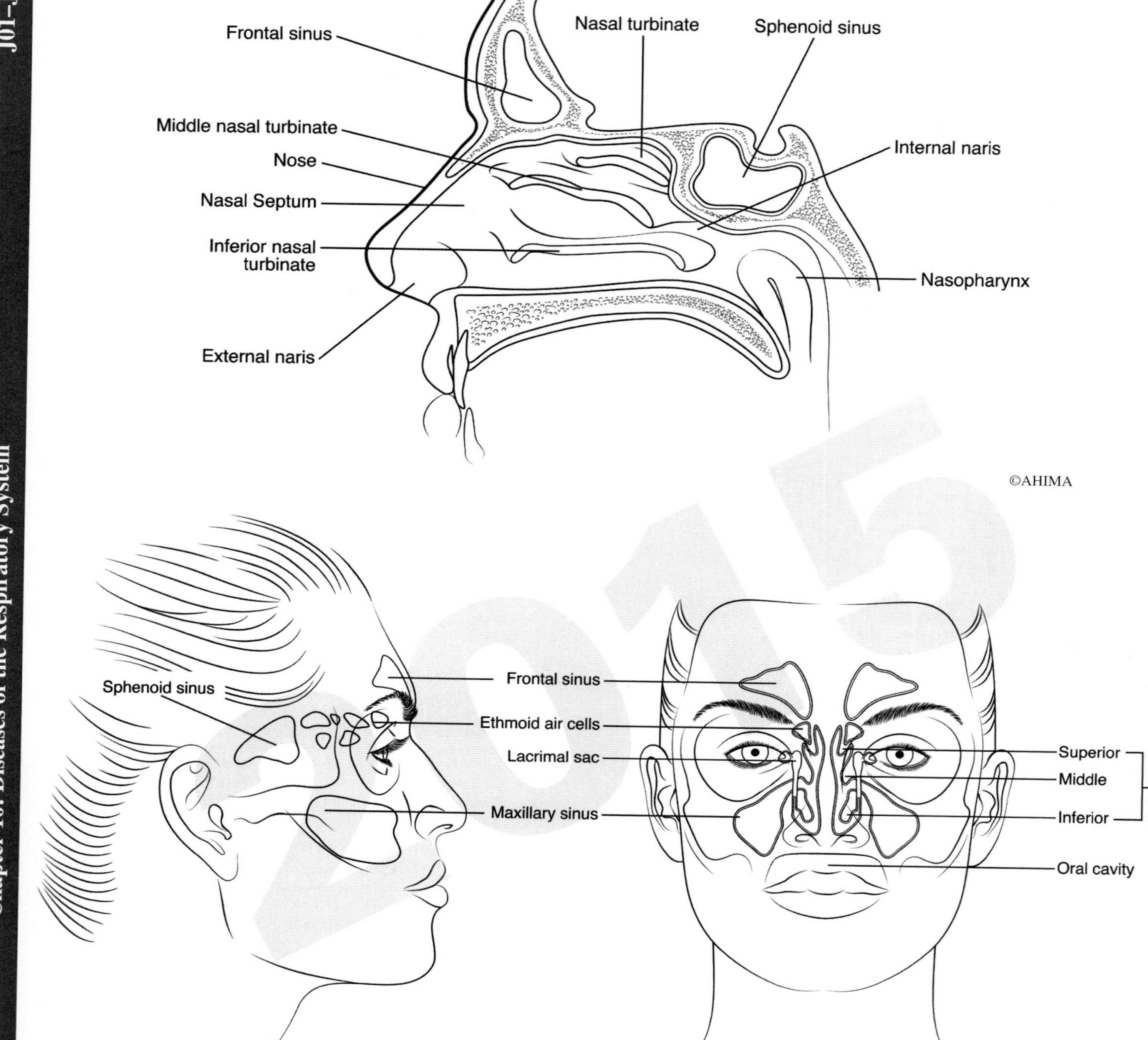

J01 Acute sinusitis

Includes: acute abscess of sinus
acute empyema of sinus
acute infection of sinus
acute inflammation of sinus
acute suppuration of sinus

Use additional code (B95-B97) to identify infectious agent.

Excludes1: *sinusitis NOS (J32.9)*

Excludes2: *chronic sinusitis (J32.0-J32.8)*

+ **J01.0 Acute maxillary sinusitis**
  Acute antritis
  J01.00 Acute maxillary sinusitis, unspecified
  J01.01 Acute recurrent maxillary sinusitis
+ **J01.1 Acute frontal sinusitis**
  J01.10 Acute frontal sinusitis, unspecified
  J01.11 Acute recurrent frontal sinusitis
+ **J01.2 Acute ethmoidal sinusitis**
  J01.20 Acute ethmoidal sinusitis, unspecified
  J01.21 Acute recurrent ethmoidal sinusitis
+ **J01.3 Acute sphenoidal sinusitis**
  J01.30 Acute sphenoidal sinusitis, unspecified
  J01.31 Acute recurrent sphenoidal sinusitis
+ **J01.4 Acute pansinusitis**
  J01.40 Acute pansinusitis, unspecified
  J01.41 Acute recurrent pansinusitis
+ **J01.8 Other acute sinusitis**
  J01.80 Other acute sinusitis
  Acute sinusitis involving more than one sinus but not pansinusitis
  J01.81 Other acute recurrent sinusitis
  Acute recurrent sinusitis involving more than one sinus but not pansinusitis

+ **J01.9 Acute sinusitis, unspecified**
J01.90 Acute sinusitis, unspecified
J01.91 Acute recurrent sinusitis, unspecified

J02 Acute pharyngitis
Includes: acute sore throat
Excludes1: *acute laryngopharyngitis (J06.0)*
peritonsillar abscess (J36)
pharyngeal abscess (J39.1)
retropharyngeal abscess (J39.0)
Excludes2: *chronic pharyngitis (J31.2)*

J02.0 Streptococcal pharyngitis
Septic pharyngitis
Streptococcal sore throat
Excludes2: *scarlet fever (A38.-)*

J02.8 Acute pharyngitis due to other specified organisms
Use additional code (B95-B97) to identify infectious agent
Excludes1: *acute pharyngitis due to coxsackie virus (B08.5)*
acute pharyngitis due to gonococcus (A54.5)
acute pharyngitis due to herpes [simplex] virus (B00.2)
acute pharyngitis due to infectious mononucleosis (B27.-)
enteroviral vesicular pharyngitis (B08.5)

J02.9 Acute pharyngitis, unspecified
Gangrenous pharyngitis (acute)
Infective pharyngitis (acute) NOS
Pharyngitis (acute) NOS
Sore throat (acute) NOS
Suppurative pharyngitis (acute)
Ulcerative pharyngitis (acute)

J03 Acute tonsillitis
Excludes1: *acute sore throat (J02.-)*
hypertrophy of tonsils (J35.1)
peritonsillar abscess (J36)
sore throat NOS (J02.9)
streptococcal sore throat (J02.0)
Excludes2: *chronic tonsillitis (J35.0)*

+ **J03.0 Streptococcal tonsillitis**
J03.00 Acute streptococcal tonsillitis, unspecified
J03.01 Acute recurrent streptococcal tonsillitis

+ **J03.8 Acute tonsillitis due to other specified organisms**
Use additional code (B95-B97) to identify infectious agent.
Excludes1: *diphtheritic tonsillitis (A36.0)*
herpesviral pharyngotonsillitis (B00.2)
streptococcal tonsillitis (J03.0)
tuberculous tonsillitis (A15.8)
Vincent's tonsillitis (A69.1)
J03.80 Acute tonsillitis due to other specified organisms
J03.81 Acute recurrent tonsillitis due to other specified organisms

J03.9 Acute tonsillitis, unspecified
Follicular tonsillitis (acute)
Gangrenous tonsillitis (acute)
Infective tonsillitis (acute)
Tonsillitis (acute) NOS
Ulcerative tonsillitis (acute)
J03.90 Acute tonsillitis, unspecified
J03.91 Acute recurrent tonsillitis, unspecified

J04 Acute laryngitis and tracheitis
Use additional code (B95-B97) to identify infectious agent.
Excludes1: *acute obstructive laryngitis [croup] and epiglottitis (J05.-)*
Excludes2: *laryngismus (stridulus) (J38.5)*

J04.0 Acute laryngitis
Edematous laryngitis (acute)
Laryngitis (acute) NOS
Subglottic laryngitis (acute)
Suppurative laryngitis (acute)
Ulcerative laryngitis (acute)
Excludes1: *acute obstructive laryngitis (J05.0)*
Excludes2: *chronic laryngitis (J37.0)*

+ **J04.1 Acute tracheitis**
Acute viral tracheitis
Catarrhal tracheitis (acute)
Tracheitis (acute) NOS
Excludes2: *chronic tracheitis (J42)*
J04.10 Acute tracheitis without obstruction
MCC **J04.11 Acute tracheitis with obstruction**
MCC Exclusion see Appendix A PDX collection 0730

J04.2 Acute laryngotracheitis
Laryngotracheitis NOS
Tracheitis (acute) with laryngitis (acute)
Excludes1: *acute obstructive laryngotracheitis (J05.0)*
Excludes2: *chronic laryngotracheitis (J37.1)*

+ **J04.3 Supraglottitis, unspecified**
J04.30 Supraglottitis, unspecified, without obstruction
MCC **J04.31 Supraglottitis, unspecified, with obstruction**
MCC Exclusion see Appendix A PDX collection 0731

J05 Acute obstructive laryngitis [croup] and epiglottitis
Use additional code (B95-B97) to identify infectious agent.

J05.0 Acute obstructive laryngitis [croup]
Obstructive laryngitis (acute) NOS
Obstructive laryngotracheitis NOS

+ **J05.1 Acute epiglottitis**
Excludes2: *epiglottitis, chronic (J37.0)*
CC **J05.10 Acute epiglottitis without obstruction**
Epiglottitis NOS
CC Exclusion see Appendix A PDX collection 0732
MCC **J05.11 Acute epiglottitis with obstruction**
MCC Exclusion see Appendix A PDX collection 0730

J06 Acute upper respiratory infections of multiple and unspecified sites
Excludes1: *acute respiratory infection NOS (J22)*
streptococcal pharyngitis (J02.0)
J06.0 Acute laryngopharyngitis
J06.9 Acute upper respiratory infection, unspecified
Upper respiratory disease, acute
Upper respiratory infection NOS

Influenza and pneumonia (J09-J18)

Excludes2: *allergic or eosinophilic pneumonia (J82)*
aspiration pneumonia NOS (J69.0)
meconium pneumonia (P24.01)
neonatal aspiration pneumonia (P24.-)
pneumonia due to solids and liquids (J69-)
congenital pneumonia (P23.9)
lipid pneumonia (J69.1)
rheumatic pneumonia (I00)
ventilator associated pneumonia (J95.851)

J09 Influenza due to certain identified influenza viruses
Excludes1: *influenza due to other identified influenza virus (J10.-)*
influenza due to unidentified influenza virus (J11.-)
seasonal influenza due to other identified influenza virus (J10.-)
seasonal influenza due to unidentified influenza virus (J11.-)
Review coding guideline C.10.c

+ **J09.X Influenza due to identified novel influenza A virus**
Avian influenza
Bird influenza
Influenza A/H5N1
Influenza of other animal origin, not bird or swine
Swine influenza virus (viruses that normally cause infections in pigs)

MCC **J09.X1 Influenza due to identified novel influenza A virus with pneumonia**
Code also if applicable, associated:
lung abscess (J85.1)
other specified type of pneumonia
MCC Exclusion see Appendix A PDX collection 0110

J09.X2 Influenza due to identified novel influenza A virus with other respiratory manifestations
Influenza due to identified novel influenza A virus NOS
Influenza due to identified novel influenza A virus with laryngitis
Influenza due to identified novel influenza A virus with pharyngitis
Influenza due to identified novel influenza A virus with upper respiratory symptoms
Use additional code, if applicable, for associated:
pleural effusion (J91.8)
sinusitis (J01.-)

J09.X3 Influenza due to identified novel influenza A virus with gastrointestinal manifestations
Influenza due to identified novel influenza A virus gastroenteritis
Excludes1: *'intestinal flu' [viral gastroenteritis] (A08.-)*

Lungs

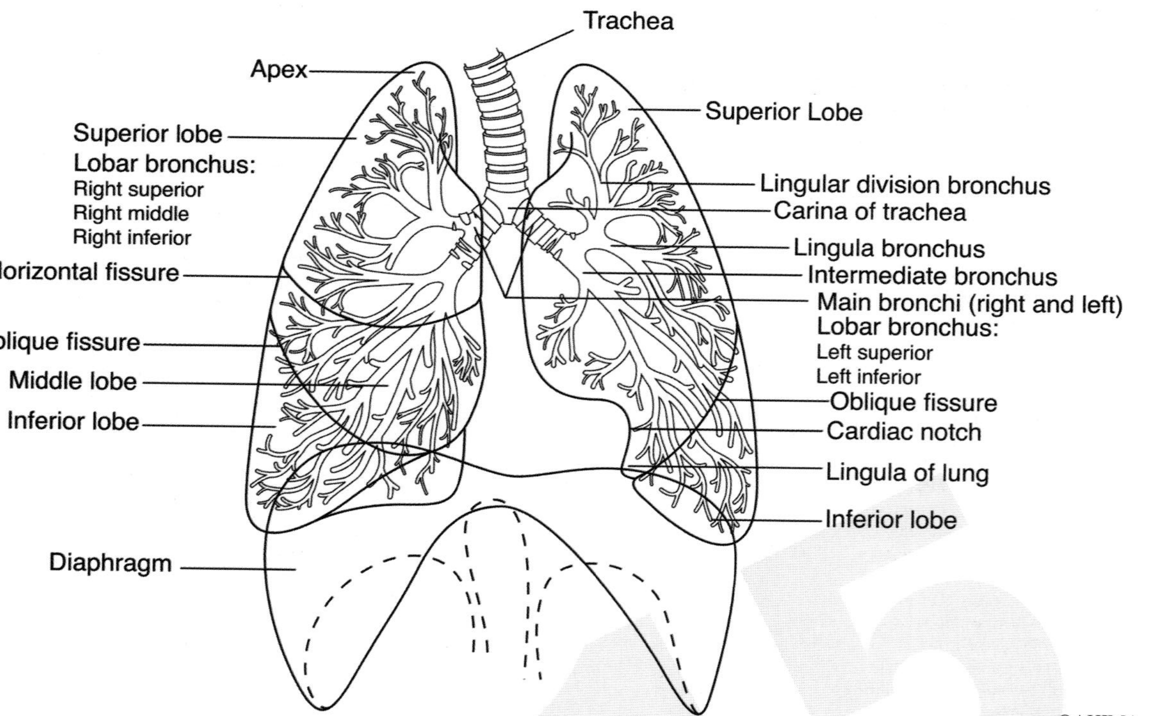

J09.X9 Influenza due to identified novel influenza A virus with other manifestations
Influenza due to identified novel influenza A virus with encephalopathy
Influenza due to identified novel influenza A virus with myocarditis
Influenza due to identified novel influenza A virus with otitis media
Use additional code to identify manifestation

J10 Influenza due to other identified influenza virus
Excludes1: *influenza due to avian influenza virus (J09.X-)*
influenza due to swine flu (J09.X-)
influenza due to unidentifed influenza virus (J11.-)
Review coding guideline C.10.c

+ **J10.0 Influenza due to other identified influenza virus with pneumonia**
Code also associated lung abscess, if applicable (J85.1)

MCC **J10.00 Influenza due to other identified influenza virus with unspecified type of pneumonia**
MCC Exclusion see Appendix A PDX collection 0110

MCC **J10.01 Influenza due to other identified influenza virus with the same other identified influenza virus pneumonia**
MCC Exclusion see Appendix A PDX collection 0110

MCC **J10.08 Influenza due to other identified influenza virus with other specified pneumonia**
Code also other specified type of pneumonia
MCC Exclusion see Appendix A PDX collection 0733

J10.1 Influenza due to other identified influenza virus with other respiratory manifestations
Influenza due to other identified influenza virus NOS
Influenza due to other identified influenza virus with laryngitis
Influenza due to other identified influenza virus with pharyngitis
Influenza due to other identified influenza virus with upper respiratory symptoms
Use additional code for associated pleural effusion, if applicable (J91.8)

Use additional code for associated sinusitis, if applicable (J01.-)

J10.2 Influenza due to other identified influenza virus with gastrointestinal manifestations
Influenza due to other identified influenza virus gastroenteritis
Excludes1: *'intestinal flu' [viral gastroenteritis] (A08.-)*

+ **J10.8 Influenza due to other identified influenza virus with other manifestations**

J10.81 Influenza due to other identified influenza virus with encephalopathy

J10.82 Influenza due to other identified influenza virus with myocarditis

J10.83 Influenza due to other identified influenza virus with otitis media
Use additional code for any associated perforated tympanic membrane (H72.-)

J10.89 Influenza due to other identified influenza virus with other manifestations
Use additional codes to identify the manifestations

J11 Influenza due to unidentified influenza virus

+ **J11.0 Influenza due to unidentified influenza virus with pneumonia**
Code also associated lung abscess, if applicable (J85.1)

MCC **J11.00 Influenza due to unidentified influenza virus with unspecified type of pneumonia**
Influenza with pneumonia NOS
MCC Exclusion see Appendix A PDX collection 0110

MCC **J11.08 Influenza due to unidentified influenza virus with specified pneumonia**
Code also other specified type of pneumonia
MCC Exclusion see Appendix A PDX collection 0110

J11.1 Influenza due to unidentified influenza virus with other respiratory manifestations
Influenza NOS
Influenzal laryngitis NOS
Influenzal pharyngitis NOS
Influenza with upper respiratory symptoms NOS
Use additional code for associated pleural effusion, if applicable (J91.8)

Use additional code for associated sinusitis, if applicable (J01.-)

J11.2 Influenza due to unidentified influenza virus with gastrointestinal manifestations
Influenza gastroenteritis NOS
Excludes1: 'intestinal flu' [viral gastroenteritis] (A08.-)

+ **J11.8 Influenza due to unidentified influenza virus with other manifestations**

J11.81 Influenza due to unidentified influenza virus with encephalopathy
Influenzal encephalopathy NOS

J11.82 Influenza due to unidentified influenza virus with myocarditis
Influenzal myocarditis NOS
J11.83 Influenza due to unidentified influenza virus with otitis media
Influenzal otitis media NOS
Use additional code for any associated perforated tympanic membrane (H72.-)
J11.89 Influenza due to unidentified influenza virus with other manifestations
Use additional codes to identify the manifestations

J12 Viral pneumonia, not elsewhere classified
Includes: bronchopneumonia due to viruses other than influenza viruses
Code first associated influenza, if applicable (J09.X1, J10.0-, J11.0-)

Code also associated abscess, if applicable (J85.1)
Excludes1: *aspiration pneumonia due to anesthesia during labor and delivery (O74.0)*
aspiration pneumonia due to anesthesia during pregnancy (O29)
aspiration pneumonia due to anesthesia during puerperium (O89.0)
aspiration pneumonia due to solids and liquids (J69.-)
aspiration pneumonia NOS (J69.0)
congenital pneumonia (P23.0)
congenital rubella pneumonitis (P35.0)
interstitial pneumonia NOS (J84.9)
lipid pneumonia (J69.1)
neonatal aspiration pneumonia (P24.-)

MCC **J12.0 Adenoviral pneumonia**
MCC Exclusion see Appendix A PDX collection 0734
MCC **J12.1 Respiratory syncytial virus pneumonia**
MCC Exclusion see Appendix A PDX collection 0734
MCC **J12.2 Parainfluenza virus pneumonia**
MCC Exclusion see Appendix A PDX collection 0734
MCC **J12.3 Human metapneumovirus pneumonia**
MCC Exclusion see Appendix A PDX collection 0734
\+ **J12.8 Other viral pneumonia**
MCC **J12.81 Pneumonia due to SARS-associated coronavirus**
Severe acute respiratory syndrome NOS
MCC Exclusion see Appendix A PDX collection 0735
MCC **J12.89 Other viral pneumonia**
MCC Exclusion see Appendix A PDX collection 0734
MCC **J12.9 Viral pneumonia, unspecified**
MCC Exclusion see Appendix A PDX collection 0734

CC **J13 Pneumonia due to Streptococcus pneumoniae**
Bronchopneumonia due to S. pneumoniae
Code first associated influenza, if applicable (J09.X1, J10.0-, J11.0-)

Code also associated abscess, if applicable (J85.1)
Excludes1: *congenital pneumonia due to S. pneumoniae (P23.6)*
lobar pneumonia, unspecified organism (J18.1)
pneumonia due to other streptococci (J15.3-J15.4)
MCC Exclusion see Appendix A PDX collection 0110
Valid 3-character code, no further characters required

CC **J14 Pneumonia due to Hemophilus influenzae**
Bronchopneumonia due to H. influenzae
Code first associated influenza, if applicable (J09.X1, J10.0-, J11.0-)

Code also associated abscess, if applicable (J85.1)
Excludes1: *congenital pneumonia due to H. influenzae (P23.6)*
MCC Exclusion see Appendix A PDX collection 0110
Valid 3-character code, no further characters required

J15 Bacterial pneumonia, not elsewhere classified
Includes: bronchopneumonia due to bacteria other than S. pneumoniae and H. influenzae
Code first associated influenza, if applicable (J09.X1, J10.0-, J11.0-)

Code also associated abscess, if applicable (J85.1)
Excludes1: *chlamydial pneumonia (J16.0)*
congenital pneumonia (P23.-)
Legionnaires' disease (A48.1)
spirochetal pneumonia (A69.8)

MCC **J15.0 Pneumonia due to Klebsiella pneumoniae**
MCC Exclusion see Appendix A PDX collection 0110
MCC **J15.1 Pneumonia due to Pseudomonas**
MCC Exclusion see Appendix A PDX collection 0110
\+ **J15.2 Pneumonia due to staphylococcus**
MCC **J15.20 Pneumonia due to staphylococcus, unspecified**
MCC Exclusion see Appendix A PDX collection 0110
\+ **J15.21 Pneumonia due to staphylococcus aureus**
MCC **J15.211 Pneumonia due to Methicillin susceptible Staphylococcus aureus**
MSSA pneumonia
Pneumonia due to Staphylococcus aureus NOS
MCC Exclusion see Appendix A PDX collection 0110
MCC **J15.212 Pneumonia due to Methicillin resistant Staphylococcus aureus**
MCC Exclusion see Appendix A PDX collection 0110
Review coding guideline C.1.e.1.a
MCC **J15.29 Pneumonia due to other staphylococcus**
MCC Exclusion see Appendix A PDX collection 0110
MCC **J15.3 Pneumonia due to streptococcus, group B**
MCC Exclusion see Appendix A PDX collection 0110
MCC **J15.4 Pneumonia due to other streptococci**
Excludes1: *pneumonia due to streptococcus, group B (J15.3)*
pneumonia due to Streptococcus pneumoniae (J13)
MCC Exclusion see Appendix A PDX collection 0110
MCC **J15.5 Pneumonia due to Escherichia coli**
MCC Exclusion see Appendix A PDX collection 0110
MCC **J15.6 Pneumonia due to other aerobic Gram-negative bacteria**
Pneumonia due to Serratia marcescens
MCC Exclusion see Appendix A PDX collection 0110
MCC **J15.7 Pneumonia due to Mycoplasma pneumoniae**
MCC **J15.8 Pneumonia due to other specified bacteria**
MCC Exclusion see Appendix A PDX collection 0110
MCC **J15.9 Unspecified bacterial pneumonia**
Pneumonia due to gram-positive bacteria
MCC Exclusion see Appendix A PDX collection 0110

J16 Pneumonia due to other infectious organisms, not elsewhere classified
Code first associated influenza, if applicable (J09.X1, J10.0-, J11.0-)

Code also associated abscess, if applicable (J85.1)
Excludes1: *congenital pneumonia (P23.-)*
ornithosis (A70)
pneumocystosis (B59)
pneumonia NOS (J18.9)

MCC **J16.0 Chlamydial pneumonia**
MCC Exclusion see Appendix A PDX collection 0110
MCC **J16.8 Pneumonia due to other specified infectious organisms**
MCC Exclusion see Appendix A PDX collection 0110

MCC **J17 Pneumonia in diseases classified elsewhere**
Code first underlying disease, such as:
Q fever (A78)
rheumatic fever (I00)
schistosomiasis (B65.0-B65.9)
Excludes1: *candidial pneumonia (B37.1)*
chlamydial pneumonia (J16.0)
gonorrheal pneumonia (A54.84)
histoplasmosis pneumonia (B39.0-B39.2)
measles pneumonia (B05.2)
nocardiosis pneumonia (A43.0)
pneumocystosis (B59)
pneumonia due to Pneumocystis carinii (B59)
pneumonia due to Pneumocystis jiroveci (B59)
pneumonia in actinomycosis (A42.0)
pneumonia in anthrax (A22.1)
pneumonia in ascariasis (B77.81)
pneumonia in aspergillosis (B44.0-B44.1)
pneumonia in coccidioidomycosis (B38.0-B38.2)
pneumonia in cytomegalovirus disease(B25.0)
pneumonia in toxoplasmosis (B58.3)
rubella pneumonia (B06.81)
salmonella pneumonia (A02.22)
spirochetal infection NEC with pneumonia (A69.8)
tularemia pneumonia (A21.2)
typhoid fever with pneumonia (A01.03)
varicella pneumonia (B01.2)
whooping cough with pneumonia (A37 with fifth-character 1)
MCC Exclusion see Appendix A PDX collection 0110
Valid 3-character code, no further characters required

J18 Pneumonia, unspecified organism

Code first associated influenza, if applicable (J09.X1, J10.0-, J11.0-)
Excludes1: *abscess of lung with pneumonia (J85.1)*
aspiration pneumonia due to anesthesia during labor and delivery (O74.0)
aspiration pneumonia due to anesthesia during pregnancy (O29)
aspiration pneumonia due to anesthesia during puerperium (O89.0)
aspiration pneumonia due to solids and liquids (J69.-)
aspiration pneumonia NOS (J69.0)
congenital pneumonia (P23.0)
drug-induced interstitial lung disorder (J70.2-J70.4)
interstitial pneumonia NOS (J84.9)
lipid pneumonia (J69.1)
neonatal aspiration pneumonia (P24.-)
pneumonitis due to external agents (J67-J70)
pneumonitis due to fumes and vapors (J68.0)
usual interstitial pneumonia (J84.17)

MCC **J18.0 Bronchopneumonia, unspecified organism**
Excludes1: *hypostatic bronchopneumonia (J18.2)*
lipid pneumonia (J69.1)
Excludes2: *acute bronchiolitis (J21.-)*
chronic bronchiolitis (J44.9)
MCC Exclusion see Appendix A PDX collection 0110

MCC **J18.1 Lobar pneumonia, unspecified organism**
MCC Exclusion see Appendix A PDX collection 0110

CC **J18.2 Hypostatic pneumonia, unspecified organism**
Hypostatic bronchopneumonia
Passive pneumonia
CC Exclusion see Appendix A PDX collection 0736

MCC **J18.8 Other pneumonia, unspecified organism**
MCC Exclusion see Appendix A PDX collection 0110

MCC **J18.9 Pneumonia, unspecified organism**
MCC Exclusion see Appendix A PDX collection 0110
AHA CC: 4Q, 2012, 94

Other acute lower respiratory infections (J20-J22)

Excludes2: *chronic obstructive pulmonary disease with acute lower respiratory infection (J44.0)*

J20 Acute bronchitis

Includes: acute and subacute bronchitis (with) bronchospasm
acute and subacute bronchitis (with) tracheitis
acute and subacute bronchitis (with) tracheobronchitis, acute
acute and subacute fibrinous bronchitis
acute and subacute membranous bronchitis
acute and subacute purulent bronchitis
acute and subacute septic bronchitis
Excludes1: *bronchitis NOS (J40)*
tracheobronchitis NOS (J40)
Excludes2: *acute bronchitis with bronchiectasis (J47.0)*
acute bronchitis with chronic obstructive asthma (J44.0)
acute bronchitis with chronic obstructive pulmonary disease (J44.0)
allergic bronchitis NOS (J45.909-)
bronchitis due to chemicals, fumes and vapors (J68.0)
chronic bronchitis NOS (J42)
chronic mucopurulent bronchitis (J41.1)
chronic obstructive bronchitis (J44.-)
chronic obstructive tracheobronchitis (J44.-)
chronic simple bronchitis (J41.0)
chronic tracheobronchitis (J42)

J20.0 Acute bronchitis due to Mycoplasma pneumoniae
J20.1 Acute bronchitis due to Hemophilus influenzae
J20.2 Acute bronchitis due to streptococcus
J20.3 Acute bronchitis due to coxsackievirus
J20.4 Acute bronchitis due to parainfluenza virus
J20.5 Acute bronchitis due to respiratory syncytial virus
J20.6 Acute bronchitis due to rhinovirus
J20.7 Acute bronchitis due to echovirus
J20.8 Acute bronchitis due to other specified organisms
J20.9 Acute bronchitis, unspecified

J21 Acute bronchiolitis

Includes: *acute bronchiolitis with bronchospasm*
Excludes2: *respiratory bronchiolitis interstitial lung disease (J84.115)*

CC **J21.0 Acute bronchiolitis due to respiratory syncytial virus**
CC Exclusion see Appendix A PDX collection 0737

CC **J21.1 Acute bronchiolitis due to human metapneumovirus**
CC Exclusion see Appendix A PDX collection 0738

CC **J21.8 Acute bronchiolitis due to other specified organisms**
CC Exclusion see Appendix A PDX collection 0738

CC **J21.9 Acute bronchiolitis, unspecified**
Bronchiolitis (acute)
Excludes1: *chronic bronchiolitis (J44.-)*
CC Exclusion see Appendix A PDX collection 0738

J22 Unspecified acute lower respiratory infection

Acute (lower) respiratory (tract) infection NOS
Excludes1: *upper respiratory infection (acute) (J06.9)*
Valid 3-character code, no further characters required

Other diseases of upper respiratory tract (J30-J39)

J30 Vasomotor and allergic rhinitis

Includes: spasmodic rhinorrhea
Excludes1: *allergic rhinitis with asthma (bronchial) (J45.909)*
rhinitis NOS (J31.0)

J30.0 Vasomotor rhinitis
J30.1 Allergic rhinitis due to pollen
Allergy NOS due to pollen
Hay fever
Pollinosis
J30.2 Other seasonal allergic rhinitis
J30.5 Allergic rhinitis due to food
\+ **J30.8 Other allergic rhinitis**
J30.81 Allergic rhinitis due to animal (cat) (dog) hair and dander
J30.89 Other allergic rhinitis
Perennial allergic rhinitis
J30.9 Allergic rhinitis, unspecified

J31 Chronic rhinitis, nasopharyngitis and pharyngitis

Use additional code to identify:
exposure to environmental tobacco smoke (Z77.22)
exposure to tobacco smoke in the perinatal period (P96.81)
history of tobacco use (Z87.891)
occupational exposure to environmental tobacco smoke (Z57.31)
tobacco dependence (F17.-)
tobacco use (Z72.0)

J31.0 Chronic rhinitis
Atrophic rhinitis (chronic)
Granulomatous rhinitis (chronic)
Hypertrophic rhinitis (chronic)
Obstructive rhinitis (chronic)
Ozena
Purulent rhinitis (chronic)
Rhinitis (chronic) NOS
Ulcerative rhinitis (chronic)
Excludes1: *allergic rhinitis (J30.1-J30.9)*
vasomotor rhinitis (J30.0)

J31.1 Chronic nasopharyngitis
Excludes2: *acute nasopharyngitis (J00)*

J31.2 Chronic pharyngitis
Chronic sore throat
Atrophic pharyngitis (chronic)
Granular pharyngitis (chronic)
Hypertrophic pharyngitis (chronic)
Excludes2: *acute pharyngitis (J02.9)*

J32 Chronic sinusitis

Includes: sinus abscess
sinus empyema
sinus infection
sinus suppuration
Use additional code to identify:
exposure to environmental tobacco smoke (Z77.22)
exposure to tobacco smoke in the perinatal period (P96.81)
history of tobacco use (Z87.891)
infectious agent (B95-B97)
occupational exposure to environmental tobacco smoke (Z57.31)
tobacco dependence (F17.-)
tobacco use (Z72.0)
Excludes2: *acute sinusitis (J01.-)*

J32.0 Chronic maxillary sinusitis
Antritis (chronic)
Maxillary sinusitis NOS
J32.1 Chronic frontal sinusitis
Frontal sinusitis NOS
J32.2 Chronic ethmoidal sinusitis
Ethmoidal sinusitis NOS
Excludes1: *Woakes' ethmoiditis (J33.1)*

J32.3 Chronic sphenoidal sinusitis
Sphenoidal sinusitis NOS
J32.4 Chronic pansinusitis
Pansinusitis NOS
J32.8 Other chronic sinusitis
Sinusitis (chronic) involving more than one sinus but not pansinusitis
J32.9 Chronic sinusitis, unspecified
Sinusitis (chronic) NOS

J33 Nasal polyp
Use additional code to identify:
exposure to environmental tobacco smoke (Z77.22)
exposure to tobacco smoke in the perinatal period (P96.81)
history of tobacco use (Z87.891)
occupational exposure to environmental tobacco smoke (Z57.31)
tobacco dependence (F17.-)
tobacco use (Z72.0)
Excludes1: *adenomatous polyps (D14.0)*
J33.0 Polyp of nasal cavity
Choanal polyp
Nasopharyngeal polyp
J33.1 Polypoid sinus degeneration
Woakes' syndrome or ethmoiditis
J33.8 Other polyp of sinus
Accessory polyp of sinus
Ethmoidal polyp of sinus
Maxillary polyp of sinus
Sphenoidal polyp of sinus
J33.9 Nasal polyp, unspecified

J34 Other and unspecified disorders of nose and nasal sinuses
Excludes2: *varicose ulcer of nasal septum (I86.8)*
J34.0 Abscess, furuncle and carbuncle of nose
Cellulitis of nose
Necrosis of nose
Ulceration of nose
J34.1 Cyst and mucocele of nose and nasal sinus
J34.2 Deviated nasal septum
Deflection or deviation of septum (nasal) (acquired)
Excludes1: *congenital deviated nasal septum (Q67.4)*
J34.3 Hypertrophy of nasal turbinates
+ **J34.8 Other specified disorders of nose and nasal sinuses**
J34.81 Nasal mucositis (ulcerative)
Code also type of associated therapy, such as:
antineoplastic and immunosuppressive drugs (T45.1X-)
radiological procedure and radiotherapy (Y84.2)
Excludes2: *gastrointestinal mucositis (ulcerative) (K92.81)*
mucositis (ulcerative) of vagina and vulva (N76.81)
oral mucositis (ulcerative) (K12.3-)
J34.89 Other specified disorders of nose and nasal sinuses
Perforation of nasal septum NOS
Rhinolith
J34.9 Unspecified disorder of nose and nasal sinuses

J35 Chronic diseases of tonsils and adenoids
Use additional code to identify:
exposure to environmental tobacco smoke (Z77.22)
exposure to tobacco smoke in the perinatal period (P96.81)
history of tobacco use (Z87.891)
occupational exposure to environmental tobacco smoke (Z57.31)
tobacco dependence (F17.-)
tobacco use (Z72.0)
+ **J35.0 Chronic tonsillitis and adenoiditis**
Excludes2: *acute tonsillitis (J03.-)*
J35.01 Chronic tonsillitis
J35.02 Chronic adenoiditis
J35.03 Chronic tonsillitis and adenoiditis
J35.1 Hypertrophy of tonsils
Enlargement of tonsils
Excludes1: *hypertrophy of tonsils with tonsillitis (J35.0-)*
J35.2 Hypertrophy of adenoids
Enlargement of adenoids
Excludes1: *hypertrophy of adenoids with adenoiditis (J35.0-)*
J35.3 Hypertrophy of tonsils with hypertrophy of adenoids
Excludes1: *hypertrophy of tonsils and adenoids with tonsillitis and adenoiditis (J35.03)*
J35.8 Other chronic diseases of tonsils and adenoids
Adenoid vegetations
Amygdalolith
Calculus, tonsil
Cicatrix of tonsil (and adenoid)
Tonsillar tag
Ulcer of tonsil
J35.9 Chronic disease of tonsils and adenoids, unspecified
Disease (chronic) of tonsils and adenoids NOS

CC **J36 Peritonsillar abscess**
Includes: abscess of tonsil
peritonsillar cellulitis
quinsy
Use additional code (B95-B97) to identify infectious agent.
Excludes1: *acute tonsillitis (J03.-)*
chronic tonsillitis (J35.0)
retropharyngeal abscess (J39.0)
tonsillitis NOS (J03.9-)
CC Exclusion see Appendix A PDX collection 0739
Valid 3-character code, no further characters required

J37 Chronic laryngitis and laryngotracheitis
Use additional code to identify:
exposure to environmental tobacco smoke (Z77.22)
exposure to tobacco smoke in the perinatal period (P96.81)
history of tobacco use (Z87.891)
infectious agent (B95-B97)
occupational exposure to environmental tobacco smoke (Z57.31)
tobacco dependence (F17.-)
tobacco use (Z72.0)
J37.0 Chronic laryngitis
Catarrhal laryngitis
Hypertrophic laryngitis
Sicca laryngitis
Excludes2: *acute laryngitis (J04.0)*
obstructive (acute) laryngitis (J05.0)
J37.1 Chronic laryngotracheitis
Laryngitis, chronic, with tracheitis (chronic)
Tracheitis, chronic, with laryngitis
Excludes1: *chronic tracheitis (J42)*
Excludes2: *acute laryngotracheitis (J04.2)*
acute tracheitis (J04.1)

J38 Diseases of vocal cords and larynx, not elsewhere classified
Use additional code to identify:
exposure to environmental tobacco smoke (Z77.22)
exposure to tobacco smoke in the perinatal period (P96.81)
history of tobacco use (Z87.891)
occupational exposure to environmental tobacco smoke (Z57.31)
tobacco dependence (F17.-)
tobacco use (Z72.0)
Excludes1: *congenital laryngeal stridor (P28.89)*
obstructive laryngitis (acute) (J05.0)
postprocedural subglottic stenosis (J95.5)
stridor (R06.1)
ulcerative laryngitis (J04.0)
+ **J38.0 Paralysis of vocal cords and larynx**
Laryngoplegia
Paralysis of glottis
J38.00 Paralysis of vocal cords and larynx, unspecified
J38.01 Paralysis of vocal cords and larynx, unilateral
J38.02 Paralysis of vocal cords and larynx, bilateral
J38.1 Polyp of vocal cord and larynx
Excludes1: *adenomatous polyps (D14.1)*
J38.2 Nodules of vocal cords
Chorditis (fibrinous)(nodosa)(tuberosa)
Singer's nodes
Teacher's nodes
J38.3 Other diseases of vocal cords
Abscess of vocal cords
Cellulitis of vocal cords
Granuloma of vocal cords
Leukokeratosis of vocal cords
Leukoplakia of vocal cords
J38.4 Edema of larynx
Edema (of) glottis
Subglottic edema
Supraglottic edema
Excludes1: *acute obstructive laryngitis [croup] (J05.0)*
edematous laryngitis (J04.0)
J38.5 Laryngeal spasm
Laryngismus (stridulus)

J38.6 Stenosis of larynx
J38.7 Other diseases of larynx
Abscess of larynx
Cellulitis of larynx
Disease of larynx NOS
Necrosis of larynx
Pachyderma of larynx
Perichondritis of larynx
Ulcer of larynx

J39 Other diseases of upper respiratory tract
Excludes1: *acute respiratory infection NOS (J22)*
acute upper respiratory infection (J06.9)
upper respiratory inflammation due to chemicals, gases, fumes or vapors (J68.2)

CC **J39.0 Retropharyngeal and parapharyngeal abscess**
Peripharyngeal abscess
Excludes1: *peritonsillar abscess (J36)*
CC Exclusion see Appendix A PDX collection 0740

CC **J39.1 Other abscess of pharynx**
Cellulitis of pharynx
Nasopharyngeal abscess
CC Exclusion see Appendix A PDX collection 0740

J39.2 Other diseases of pharynx
Cyst of pharynx
Edema of pharynx
Excludes2: *chronic pharyngitis (J31.2)*
ulcerative pharyngitis (J02.9)

J39.3 Upper respiratory tract hypersensitivity reaction, site unspecified
Excludes1: *hypersensitivity reaction of upper respiratory tract, such as:*
extrinsic allergic alveolitis (J67.9)
pneumoconiosis (J60-J67.9)

J39.8 Other specified diseases of upper respiratory tract
J39.9 Disease of upper respiratory tract, unspecified

Chronic lower respiratory diseases (J40-J47)

Excludes1: *bronchitis due to chemicals, gases, fumes and vapors (J68.0)*
Excludes2: *cystic fibrosis (E84.-)*

J40 Bronchitis, not specified as acute or chronic
Bronchitis NOS
Bronchitis with tracheitis NOS
Catarrhal bronchitis
Tracheobronchitis NOS
Use additional code to identify:
exposure to environmental tobacco smoke (Z77.22)
exposure to tobacco smoke in the perinatal period (P96.81)
history of tobacco use (Z87.891)
occupational exposure to environmental tobacco smoke (Z57.31)
tobacco dependence (F17.-)
tobacco use (Z72.0)
Excludes1: *allergic bronchitis NOS (J45.909-)*
asthmatic bronchitis NOS (J45.9-)
acute bronchitis (J20.-)
bronchitis due to chemicals, gases, fumes and vapors (J68.0)
Valid 3-character code, no further characters required

J41 Simple and mucopurulent chronic bronchitis
Use additional code to identify:
exposure to environmental tobacco smoke (Z77.22)
exposure to tobacco smoke in the perinatal period (P96.81)
history of tobacco use (Z87.891)
occupational exposure to environmental tobacco smoke (Z57.31)
tobacco dependence (F17.-)
tobacco use (Z72.0)
Excludes1: *chronic bronchitis NOS (J42)*
chronic obstructive bronchitis (J44.-)

J41.0 Simple chronic bronchitis
J41.1 Mucopurulent chronic bronchitis
J41.8 Mixed simple and mucopurulent chronic bronchitis

J42 Unspecified chronic bronchitis
Chronic bronchitis NOS
Chronic tracheitis
Chronic tracheobronchitis
Use additional code to identify:
exposure to environmental tobacco smoke (Z77.22)
exposure to tobacco smoke in the perinatal period (P96.81)
history of tobacco use (Z87.891)
occupational exposure to environmental tobacco smoke (Z57.31)
tobacco dependence (F17.-)
tobacco use (Z72.0)
Excludes1: *chronic asthmatic bronchitis (J44.-)*
chronic bronchitis with airways obstruction (J44.-)
chronic emphysematous bronchitis (J44.-)
chronic obstructive pulmonary disease NOS (J44.9)
simple and mucopurulent chronic bronchitis (J41.-)
Valid 3-character code, no further characters required

J43 Emphysema
Use additional code to identify:
exposure to environmental tobacco smoke (Z77.22)
history of tobacco use (Z87.891)
occupational exposure to environmental tobacco smoke (Z57.31)
tobacco dependence (F17.-)
tobacco use (Z72.0)
Excludes1: *compensatory emphysema (J98.3)*
emphysema due to inhalation of chemicals, gases, fumes or vapors (J68.4)
emphysema with chronic (obstructive) bronchitis (J44.-)
emphysematous (obstructive) bronchitis (J44.-)
interstitial emphysema (J98.2)
mediastinal emphysema (J98.2)
neonatal interstitial emphysema (P25.0)
surgical (subcutaneous) emphysema (T81.82)
traumatic subcutaneous emphysema (T79.7)

J43.0 Unilateral pulmonary emphysema [MacLeod's syndrome]
Swyer-James syndrome
Unilateral emphysema
Unilateral hyperlucent lung
Unilateral pulmonary artery functional hypoplasia
Unilateral transparency of lung

J43.1 Panlobular emphysema
Panacinar emphysema

J43.2 Centrilobular emphysema
J43.8 Other emphysema
J43.9 Emphysema, unspecified
Bullous emphysema (lung)(pulmonary)
Emphysema (lung)(pulmonary) NOS
Emphysematous bleb
Vesicular emphysema (lung)(pulmonary)

J44 Other chronic obstructive pulmonary disease
Includes: asthma with chronic obstructive pulmonary disease
chronic asthmatic (obstructive) bronchitis
chronic bronchitis with airways obstruction
chronic bronchitis with emphysema
chronic emphysematous bronchitis
chronic obstructive asthma
chronic obstructive bronchitis
chronic obstructive tracheobronchitis
Code also type of asthma, if applicable (J45.-)

Use additional code to identify:
exposure to environmental tobacco smoke (Z77.22)
history of tobacco use (Z87.891)
occupational exposure to environmental tobacco smoke (Z57.31)
tobacco dependence (F17.-)
tobacco use (Z72.0)
Excludes1: *bronchiectasis (J47.-)*
chronic bronchitis NOS (J42)
chronic simple and mucopurulent bronchitis (J41.-)
chronic tracheitis (J42)
chronic tracheobronchitis (J42)
emphysema without chronic bronchitis (J43.-)
lung diseases due to external agents (J60-J70)
Review coding guideline C.10.a.1

CC **J44.0 Chronic obstructive pulmonary disease with acute lower respiratory infection**
Use additional code to identify the infection
CC Exclusion see Appendix A PDX collection 0741

CC **J44.1 Chronic obstructive pulmonary disease with (acute) exacerbation**
Decompensated COPD
Decompensated COPD with (acute) exacerbation
Excludes2: *chronic obstructive pulmonary disease [COPD] with acute bronchitis (J44.0)*
CC Exclusion see Appendix A PDX collection 0741

J44.9 Chronic obstructive pulmonary disease, unspecified
Chronic obstructive airway disease NOS
Chronic obstructive lung disease NOS
AHA CC: 4Q, 2013, 109, 129

J45 Asthma

Includes: allergic (predominantly) asthma
allergic bronchitis NOS
allergic rhinitis with asthma
atopic asthma
extrinsic allergic asthma
hay fever with asthma
idiosyncratic asthma
intrinsic nonallergic asthma
nonallergic asthma

Use additional code to identify:
exposure to environmental tobacco smoke (Z77.22)
exposure to tobacco smoke in the perinatal period (P96.81)
history of tobacco use (Z87.891)
occupational exposure to environmental tobacco smoke (Z57.31)
tobacco dependence (F17.-)
tobacco use (Z72.0)

Excludes1: *detergent asthma (J69.8)*
eosinophilic asthma (J82)
lung diseases due to external agents (J60-J70)
miner's asthma (J60)
wheezing NOS (R06.2)
wood asthma (J67.8)

Excludes2: *asthma with chronic obstructive pulmonary disease (J44.9)*
chronic asthmatic (obstructive) bronchitis (J44.9)
chronic obstructive asthma (J44.9)

Review coding guideline C.10.a.1

\+ **J45.2 Mild intermittent asthma**
J45.20 Mild intermittent asthma, uncomplicated
Mild intermittent asthma NOS
CC **J45.21 Mild intermittent asthma with (acute) exacerbation**
CC Exclusion see Appendix A PDX collection 0742
CC **J45.22 Mild intermittent asthma with status asthmaticus**
CC Exclusion see Appendix A PDX collection 0742

\+ **J45.3 Mild persistent asthma**
J45.30 Mild persistent asthma, uncomplicated
Mild persistent asthma NOS
CC **J45.31 Mild persistent asthma with (acute) exacerbation**
CC Exclusion see Appendix A PDX collection 0742
CC **J45.32 Mild persistent asthma with status asthmaticus**
CC Exclusion see Appendix A PDX collection 0742

\+ **J45.4 Moderate persistent asthma**
J45.40 Moderate persistent asthma, uncomplicated
Moderate persistent asthma NOS
CC **J45.41 Moderate persistent asthma with (acute) exacerbation**
CC Exclusion see Appendix A PDX collection 0742
CC **J45.42 Moderate persistent asthma with status asthmaticus**
CC Exclusion see Appendix A PDX collection 0742

\+ **J45.5 Severe persistent asthma**
J45.50 Severe persistent asthma, uncomplicated
Severe persistent asthma NOS
CC **J45.51 Severe persistent asthma with (acute) exacerbation**
CC Exclusion see Appendix A PDX collection 0742
CC **J45.52 Severe persistent asthma with status asthmaticus**
CC Exclusion see Appendix A PDX collection 0742

\+ **J45.9 Other and unspecified asthma**
\+ **J45.90 Unspecified asthma**
Asthmatic bronchitis NOS
Childhood asthma NOS
Late onset asthma
CC **J45.901 Unspecified asthma with (acute) exacerbation**
CC Exclusion see Appendix A PDX collection 0742
CC **J45.902 Unspecified asthma with status asthmaticus**
CC Exclusion see Appendix A PDX collection 0742
J45.909 Unspecified asthma, uncomplicated
Asthma NOS

\+ **J45.99 Other asthma**
J45.990 Exercise induced bronchospasm
J45.991 Cough variant asthma
J45.998 Other asthma

J47 Bronchiectasis

Includes: bronchiolectasis

Use additional code to identify:
exposure to environmental tobacco smoke (Z77.22)
exposure to tobacco smoke in the perinatal period (P96.81)
history of tobacco use (Z87.891)
occupational exposure to environmental tobacco smoke (Z57.31)
tobacco dependence (F17.-)
tobacco use (Z72.0)

Excludes1: *congenital bronchiectasis (Q33.4)*
tuberculous bronchiectasis (current disease) (A15.0)

CC **J47.0 Bronchiectasis with acute lower respiratory infection**
Bronchiectasis with acute bronchitis
CC Exclusion see Appendix A PDX collection 0743
CC **J47.1 Bronchiectasis with (acute) exacerbation**
CC Exclusion see Appendix A PDX collection 0743
J47.9 Bronchiectasis, uncomplicated
Bronchiectasis NOS

Lung diseases due to external agents (J60-J70)

Excludes2: *asthma (J45.-)*
malignant neoplasm of bronchus and lung (C34.-)

• **J60 Coalworker's pneumoconiosis**

Anthracosilicosis
Anthracosis
Black lung disease
Coalworker's lung
Excludes1: *coalworker pneumoconiosis with tuberculosis, any type in A15 (J65)*
Valid 3-character code, no further characters required

• **J61 Pneumoconiosis due to asbestos and other mineral fibers**

Asbestosis
Excludes1: *pleural plaque with asbestosis (J92.0)*
pneumoconiosis with tuberculosis, any type in A15 (J65)
Valid 3-character code, no further characters required

J62 Pneumoconiosis due to dust containing silica

Includes: silicotic fibrosis (massive) of lung
Excludes1: *pneumoconiosis with tuberculosis, any type in A15 (J65)*
J62.0 Pneumoconiosis due to talc dust
J62.8 Pneumoconiosis due to other dust containing silica
Silicosis NOS

J63 Pneumoconiosis due to other inorganic dusts

Excludes1: *pneumoconiosis with tuberculosis, any type in A15 (J65)*
J63.0 Aluminosis (of lung)
J63.1 Bauxite fibrosis (of lung)
J63.2 Berylliosis
J63.3 Graphite fibrosis (of lung)
J63.4 Siderosis
J63.5 Stannosis
J63.6 Pneumoconiosis due to other specified inorganic dusts

J64 Unspecified pneumoconiosis

Excludes1: *pneumonoconiosis with tuberculosis, any type in A15 (J65)*
Valid 3-character code, no further characters required

J65 Pneumoconiosis associated with tuberculosis

Any condition in J60-J64 with tuberculosis, any type in A15
Silicotuberculosis
Valid 3-character code, no further characters required

J66 Airway disease due to specific organic dust

Excludes2: *allergic alveolitis (J67.-)*
asbestosis (J61)
bagassosis (J67.1)
farmer's lung (J67.0)
hypersensitivity pneumonitis due to organic dust (J67.-)
reactive airways dysfunction syndrome (J68.3)

J66.0 Byssinosis
Airway disease due to cotton dust
J66.1 Flax-dressers' disease
J66.2 Cannabinosis
J66.8 Airway disease due to other specific organic dusts

J67 Hypersensitivity pneumonitis due to organic dust

Includes: allergic alveolitis and pneumonitis due to inhaled organic dust and particles of fungal, actinomycetic or other origin

Excludes1: *pneumonitis due to inhalation of chemicals, gases, fumes or vapors (J68.0)*

J67.0 Farmer's lung
Harvester's lung
Haymaker's lung
Moldy hay disease

J67.1 Bagassosis
Bagasse disease
Bagasse pneumonitis

J67.2 Bird fancier's lung
Budgerigar fancier's disease or lung
Pigeon fancier's disease or lung

J67.3 Suberosis
Corkhandler's disease or lung
Corkworker's disease or lung

J67.4 Maltworker's lung
Alveolitis due to Aspergillus clavatus

J67.5 Mushroom-worker's lung

J67.6 Maple-bark-stripper's lung
Alveolitis due to Cryptostroma corticale
Cryptostromosis

CC **J67.7 Air conditioner and humidifier lung**
Allergic alveolitis due to fungal, thermophilic actinomycetes and other organisms growing in ventilation [air conditioning] systems
CC Exclusion see Appendix A PDX collection 0110

CC **J67.8 Hypersensitivity pneumonitis due to other organic dusts**
Cheese-washer's lung
Coffee-worker's lung
Fish-meal worker's lung
Furrier's lung
Sequoiosis
CC Exclusion see Appendix A PDX collection 0110

CC **J67.9 Hypersensitivity pneumonitis due to unspecified organic dust**
Allergic alveolitis (extrinsic) NOS
Hypersensitivity pneumonitis NOS
CC Exclusion see Appendix A PDX collection 0110

J68 Respiratory conditions due to inhalation of chemicals, gases, fumes and vapors

Code first (T51-T65) to identify cause

Use additional code to identify associated respiratory conditions, such as: acute respiratory failure (J96.0-)

CC **J68.0 Bronchitis and pneumonitis due to chemicals, gases, fumes and vapors**
Chemical bronchitis (acute)
CC Exclusion see Appendix A PDX collection 0110

MCC **J68.1 Pulmonary edema due to chemicals, gases, fumes and vapors**
Chemical pulmonary edema (acute) (chronic)
Excludes1: *pulmonary edema (acute) (chronic) NOS (J81.-)*
MCC Exclusion see Appendix A PDX collection 0110

J68.2 Upper respiratory inflammation due to chemicals, gases, fumes and vapors, not elsewhere classified

J68.3 Other acute and subacute respiratory conditions due to chemicals, gases, fumes and vapors
Reactive airways dysfunction syndrome

J68.4 Chronic respiratory conditions due to chemicals, gases, fumes and vapors
Emphysema (diffuse) (chronic) due to inhalation of chemicals, gases, fumes and vapors
Obliterative bronchiolitis (chronic) (subacute) due to inhalation of chemicals, gases, fumes and vapors
Pulmonary fibrosis (chronic) due to inhalation of chemicals, gases, fumes and vapors
Excludes1: *chronic pulmonary edema due to chemicals, gases, fumes and vapors (J68.1)*

J68.8 Other respiratory conditions due to chemicals, gases, fumes and vapors

J68.9 Unspecified respiratory condition due to chemicals, gases, fumes and vapors

J69 Pneumonitis due to solids and liquids

Excludes1: *neonatal aspiration syndromes (P24.-)*
postprocedural pneumonitis (J95.4)

MCC **J69.0 Pneumonitis due to inhalation of food and vomit**
Aspiration pneumonia NOS
Aspiration pneumonia (due to) food (regurgitated)
Aspiration pneumonia (due to) gastric secretions
Aspiration pneumonia (due to) milk
Aspiration pneumonia (due to) vomit
Code also any associated foreign body in respiratory tract (T17.-)
Excludes1: *chemical pneumonitis due to anesthesia (J95.4)*
obstetric aspiration pneumonitis (O74.0)
MCC Exclusion see Appendix A PDX collection 0110

MCC **J69.1 Pneumonitis due to inhalation of oils and essences**
Exogenous lipoid pneumonia
Lipid pneumonia NOS
Code first (T51-T65) to identify substance
Excludes1: *endogenous lipoid pneumonia (J84.89)*
MCC Exclusion see Appendix A PDX collection 0110

MCC **J69.8 Pneumonitis due to inhalation of other solids and liquids**
Pneumonitis due to aspiration of blood
Pneumonitis due to aspiration of detergent
Code first (T51-T65) to identify substance
MCC Exclusion see Appendix A PDX collection 0110

J70 Respiratory conditions due to other external agents

CC **J70.0 Acute pulmonary manifestations due to radiation**
Radiation pneumonitis
Use additional code (W88-W90, X39.0-) to identify the external ca
CC Exclusion see Appendix A PDX collection 0110

CC **J70.1 Chronic and other pulmonary manifestations due to radiatio**
Fibrosis of lung following radiation
Use additional code (W88-W90, X39.0-) to identify the external cau
CC Exclusion see Appendix A PDX collection 0110

J70.2 Acute drug-induced interstitial lung disorders
Use additional code for adverse effect, if applicable, to identify drug (T36-T50 with fifth or sixth character 5)
Excludes1: *interstitial pneumonia NOS (J84.9)*
lymphoid interstitial pneumonia (J84.2)

J70.3 Chronic drug-induced interstitial lung disorders
Use additional code for adverse effect, if applicable, to identify drug (T36-T50 with fifth or sixth character 5)
Excludes1: *interstitial pneumonia NOS (J84.9)*
lymphoid interstitial pneumonia (J84.2)

J70.4 Drug-induced interstitial lung disorders, unspecified
Use additional code for adverse effect, if applicable, to identify drug (T36-T50 with fifth or sixth character 5)
Excludes1: *interstitial pneumonia NOS (J84.9)*
lymphoid interstitial pneumonia (J84.2)

J70.5 Respiratory conditions due to smoke inhalation
Smoke inhalation NOS
Excludes1: *smoke inhalation due to chemicals, gases, fumes ar vapors (J68.9)*

J70.8 Respiratory conditions due to other specified external agents
Code first (T51-T65) to identify the external agent

J70.9 Respiratory conditions due to unspecified external agent
Code first (T51-T65) to identify the external agent

Other respiratory diseases principally affecting the interstitium (J80-J84)

CC **J80 Acute respiratory distress syndrome**

Acute respiratory distress syndrome in adult or child
Adult hyaline membrane disease
Excludes1: *respiratory distress syndrome in newborn (perinatal) (P22.*
CC Exclusion see Appendix A PDX collection 0744
Valid 3-character code, no further characters required

J81 Pulmonary edema

Use additional code to identify:
exposure to environmental tobacco smoke (Z77.22)
history of tobacco use (Z87.891)
occupational exposure to environmental tobacco smoke (Z57.31)
tobacco dependence (F17.-)
tobacco use (Z72.0)

Excludes1: *chemical (acute) pulmonary edema (J68.1)*
hypostatic pneumonia (J18.2)
passive pneumonia (J18.2)
pulmonary edema due to external agents (J60-J70)
pulmonary edema with heart disease NOS (I50.1)
pulmonary edema with heart failure (I50.1)

MCC **J81.0 Acute pulmonary edema**
Acute edema of lung
MCC Exclusion see Appendix A PDX collection 0745

CC **J81.1 Chronic pulmonary edema**
Pulmonary congestion (chronic) (passive)
Pulmonary edema NOS
CC Exclusion see Appendix A PDX collection 0736

J82 Pulmonary eosinophilia, not elsewhere classified
Allergic pneumonia
Eosinophilic asthma
Eosinophilic pneumonia
Löffler's pneumonia
Tropical (pulmonary) eosinophilia NOS
Excludes1: *pulmonary eosinophilia due to aspergillosis (B44.-)*
pulmonary eosinophilia due to drugs (J70.2-J70.4)
pulmonary eosinophilia due to specified parasitic infection (B50-B83)
pulmonary eosinophilia due to systemic connective tissue disorders (M30-M36)
pulmonary infiltrate NOS (R91.8)
CC Exclusion see Appendix A PDX collection 0746
Valid 3-character code, no further characters required

J84 Other interstitial pulmonary diseases
Excludes1: *drug-induced interstitial lung disorders (J70.2-J70.4)*
interstitial emphysema (J98.2)
lung diseases due to external agents (J60-J70)

\+ **J84.0 Alveolar and parieto-alveolar conditions**

CC **J84.01 Alveolar proteinosis**
CC Exclusion see Appendix A PDX collection 0747

CC **J84.02 Pulmonary alveolar microlithiasis**
CC Exclusion see Appendix A PDX collection 0747

CC **J84.03 Idiopathic pulmonary hemosiderosis**
Essential brown induration of lung
Code first underlying disease, such as:
disorders of iron metabolism (E83.1-)
Excludes1: *acute idiopathic pulmonary hemorrhage in infants [AIPHI] (R04.81)*
CC Exclusion see Appendix A PDX collection 0747

CC **J84.09 Other alveolar and parieto-alveolar conditions**
CC Exclusion see Appendix A PDX collection 0747

\+ **J84.1 Other interstitial pulmonary diseases with fibrosis**
Excludes1: *pulmonary fibrosis (chronic) due to inhalation of chemicals, gases, fumes or vapors (J68.4)*
pulmonary fibrosis (chronic) following radiation (J70.1)

J84.10 Pulmonary fibrosis, unspecified
Capillary fibrosis of lung
Cirrhosis of lung (chronic) NOS
Fibrosis of lung (atrophic) (chronic) (confluent) (massive) (perialveolar) (peribronchial) NOS
Induration of lung (chronic) NOS
Postinflammatory pulmonary fibrosis

\+ **J84.11 Idiopathic interstitial pneumonia**
Excludes1: *lymphoid interstitial pneumonia (J84.2)*
pneumocystis pneumonia (B59)

J84.111 Idiopathic interstitial pneumonia, not otherwise specified

J84.112 Idiopathic pulmonary fibrosis
Cryptogenic fibrosing alveolitis
Idiopathic fibrosing alveolitis

J84.113 Idiopathic non-specific interstitial pneumonitis
Excludes1: *non-specific interstitial pneumonia NOS, or due to known underlying cause (J84.89)*

CC **J84.114 Acute interstitial pneumonitis**
Hamman-Rich syndrome
Excludes1: *pneumocystis pneumonia (B59)*
CC Exclusion see Appendix A PDX collection 0747

J84.115 Respiratory bronchiolitis interstitial lung disease

CC **J84.116 Cryptogenic organizing pneumonia**
Excludes1: *organizing pneumonia NOS, or due to known underlying cause (J84.89)*
CC Exclusion see Appendix A PDX collection 0747

CC **J84.117 Desquamative interstitial pneumonia**
CC Exclusion see Appendix A PDX collection 0747

J84.17 Other interstitial pulmonary diseases with fibrosis in diseases classified elsewhere
Interstitial pneumonia (nonspecific) (usual) due to collagen vascular disease
Interstitial pneumonia (nonspecific) (usual) in diseases classified elsewhere
Organizing pneumonia due to collagen vascular disease
Organizing pneumonia in diseases classified elsewhere
Code first underlying disease, such as:
progressive systemic sclerosis (M34.0)
rheumatoid arthritis (M05.00-M06.9)
systemic lupus erythematosis (M32.0-M32.9)

CC **J84.2 Lymphoid interstitial pneumonia**
Lymphoid interstitial pneumonitis
CC Exclusion see Appendix A PDX collection 0747

\+ **J84.8 Other specified interstitial pulmonary diseases**
Excludes1: *exogenous lipoid pneumonia (J69.1)*
unspecified lipoid pneumonia (J69.1)

♀ MCC **J84.81 Lymphangioleiomyomatosis**
Lymphangiomyomatosis
MCC Exclusion see Appendix A PDX collection 0747

• CC **J84.82 Adult pulmonary Langerhans cell histiocytosis**
Adult PLCH
CC Exclusion see Appendix A PDX collection 0747

MCC **J84.83 Surfactant mutations of the lung**
MCC Exclusion see Appendix A PDX collection 0748

\+ **J84.84 Other interstitial lung diseases of childhood**

MCC **J84.841 Neuroendocrine cell hyperplasia of infancy**
MCC Exclusion see Appendix A PDX collection 0748

MCC **J84.842 Pulmonary interstitial glycogenosis**
MCC Exclusion see Appendix A PDX collection 0748

MCC **J84.843 Alveolar capillary dysplasia with vein misalignment**
MCC Exclusion see Appendix A PDX collection 0748

MCC **J84.848 Other interstitial lung diseases of childhood**
MCC Exclusion see Appendix A PDX collection 0748

J84.89 Other specified interstitial pulmonary diseases
Endogenous lipoid pneumonia
Interstitial pneumonitis
Non-specific interstitial pneumonitis NOS
Organizing pneumonia due to known underlying cause
Organizing pneumonia NOS
Code first if applicable:
poisoning due to drug or toxin (T51-T65 with fifth or sixth character to indicate intent), for toxic pneumonopathy
underlying cause of pneumonopathy, if known

Use additional code, for adverse effect, to identify drug (T36-T50 with fifth or sixth character 5), if drug-induced
Excludes1: *cryptogenic organizing pneumonia (J84.116)*
idiopathic non-specific interstitial pneumonitis (J84.113)
lipoid pneumonia, exogenous or unspecified (J69.1)
lymphoid interstitial pneumonia (J84.2)

CC **J84.9 Interstitial pulmonary disease, unspecified**
Interstitial pneumonia NOS
CC Exclusion see Appendix A PDX collection 0747

Suppurative and necrotic conditions of the lower respiratory tract (J85-J86)

J85 Abscess of lung and mediastinum
Use additional code (B95-B97) to identify infectious agent.

MCC **J85.0 Gangrene and necrosis of lung**
MCC Exclusion see Appendix A PDX collection 0749

MCC **J85.1 Abscess of lung with pneumonia**
Code also the type of pneumonia
MCC Exclusion see Appendix A PDX collection 0749

MCC **J85.2 Abscess of lung without pneumonia**
Abscess of lung NOS
MCC Exclusion see Appendix A PDX collection 0749

MCC **J85.3 Abscess of mediastinum**
MCC Exclusion see Appendix A PDX collection 0750

J86 Pyothorax

Use additional code (B95-B97) to identify infectious agent.
Excludes1: *abscess of lung (J85.-)*
pyothorax due to tuberculosis (A15.6)

MCC **J86.0 Pyothorax with fistula**
Bronchocutaneous fistula
Bronchopleural fistula
Hepatopleural fistula
Mediastinal fistula
Pleural fistula
Thoracic fistula
Any condition classifiable to J86.9 with fistula
MCC Exclusion see Appendix A PDX collection 0751

MCC **J86.9 Pyothorax without fistula**
Abscess of pleura
Abscess of thorax
Empyema (chest) (lung) (pleura)
Fibrinopurulent pleurisy
Purulent pleurisy
Pyopneumothorax
Septic pleurisy
Seropurulent pleurisy
Suppurative pleurisy
MCC Exclusion see Appendix A PDX collection 0751

Other diseases of the pleura (J90-J94)

CC **J90 Pleural effusion, not elsewhere classified**

Encysted pleurisy
Pleural effusion NOS
Pleurisy with effusion (exudative) (serous)
Excludes1: *chylous (pleural) effusion (J94.0)*
malignant pleural effusion (J91.0)
pleurisy NOS (R09.1)
tuberculous pleural effusion (A15.6)
CC Exclusion see Appendix A PDX collection 0752
Valid 3-character code, no further characters required

J91 Pleural effusion in conditions classified elsewhere

Excludes2: *pleural effusion in heart failure (I50.-)*
pleural effusion in systemic lupus erythematosus (M32.13)

CC **J91.0 Malignant pleural effusion**
Code first underlying neoplasm
CC Exclusion see Appendix A PDX collection 0753

CC **J91.8 Pleural effusion in other conditions classified elsewhere**
Code first underlying disease, such as:
filariasis (B74.0-B74.9)
influenza (J09.X2, J10.1, J11.1)
CC Exclusion see Appendix A PDX collection 0752

J92 Pleural plaque

Includes: pleural thickening
J92.0 Pleural plaque with presence of asbestos
J92.9 Pleural plaque without asbestos
Pleural plaque NOS

J93 Pneumothorax and air leak

Excludes1: *congenital or perinatal pneumothorax (P25.1)*
postprocedural air leak (J95.812)
postprocedural pneumothorax (J95.811)
traumatic pneumothorax (S27.0)
tuberculous (current disease) pneumothorax (A15.-)
pyopneumothorax (J86.-)

MCC **J93.0 Spontaneous tension pneumothorax**
MCC Exclusion see Appendix A PDX collection 0754

+ **J93.1 Other spontaneous pneumothorax**

CC **J93.11 Primary spontaneous pneumothorax**
CC Exclusion see Appendix A PDX collection 0754

CC **J93.12 Secondary spontaneous pneumothorax**
Code first underlying condition, such as:
catamenial pneumothorax due to endometriosis (N80.8)
cystic fibrosis (E84.-)
eosinophilic pneumonia (J82)
lymphangioleiomyomatosis (J84.81)
malignant neoplasm of bronchus and lung (C34.-)
Marfan's syndrome (Q87.4)
pneumonia due to Pneumocystis carinii (B59)
secondary malignant neoplasm of lung (C78.0-)
spontaneous rupture of the esophagus (K22.3)
CC Exclusion see Appendix A PDX collection 0754

+ **J93.8 Other pneumothorax and air leak**

CC **J93.81 Chronic pneumothorax**
CC Exclusion see Appendix A PDX collection 0754

CC **J93.82 Other air leak**
Persistent air leak
CC Exclusion see Appendix A PDX collection 0754

CC **J93.83 Other pneumothorax**
Acute pneumothorax
Spontaneous pneumothorax NOS
CC Exclusion see Appendix A PDX collection 0754

CC **J93.9 Pneumothorax, unspecified**
Pneumothorax NOS
CC Exclusion see Appendix A PDX collection 0754

J94 Other pleural conditions

Excludes1: *pleurisy NOS (R09.1)*
traumatic hemopneumothorax (S27.2)
traumatic hemothorax (S27.1)
tuberculous pleural conditions (current disease) (A15.-)

CC **J94.0 Chylous effusion**
Chyliform effusion
CC Exclusion see Appendix A PDX collection 0752

J94.1 Fibrothorax

CC **J94.2 Hemothorax**
Hemopneumothorax
CC Exclusion see Appendix A PDX collection 0752

CC **J94.8 Other specified pleural conditions**
Hydropneumothorax
Hydrothorax
No CC Exclusions

J94.9 Pleural condition, unspecified

Intraoperative and postprocedural complications and disorders of respiratory system, not elsewhere classified (J95)

J95 Intraoperative and postprocedural complications and disorders of respiratory system, not elsewhere classified

Excludes2: *aspiration pneumonia (J69.-)*
emphysema (subcutaneous) resulting from a procedure (T81.82)
hypostatic pneumonia (J18.2)
pulmonary manifestations due to radiation (J70.0-J70.1)

+ **J95.0 Tracheostomy complications**

CC **J95.00 Unspecified tracheostomy complication**
CC Exclusion see Appendix A PDX collection 0755

CC **J95.01 Hemorrhage from tracheostomy stoma**
CC Exclusion see Appendix A PDX collection 0755

CC **J95.02 Infection of tracheostomy stoma**
Use additional code to identify type of infection, such as:
cellulitis of neck (L03.8)
sepsis (A40, A41.-)
CC Exclusion see Appendix A PDX collection 0755

CC **J95.03 Malfunction of tracheostomy stoma**
Mechanical complication of tracheostomy stoma
Obstruction of tracheostomy airway
Tracheal stenosis due to tracheostomy
CC Exclusion see Appendix A PDX collection 0755

CC **J95.04 Tracheo-esophageal fistula following tracheostomy**
CC Exclusion see Appendix A PDX collection 0755

CC **J95.09 Other tracheostomy complication**
CC Exclusion see Appendix A PDX collection 0755

MCC **J95.1 Acute pulmonary insufficiency following thoracic surgery**
Excludes2: *Functional disturbances following cardiac surgery (I97.0, I97.1-)*
MCC Exclusion see Appendix A PDX collection 0756

MCC **J95.2 Acute pulmonary insufficiency following nonthoracic surgery**
Excludes2: *Functional disturbances following cardiac surgery (I97.0, I97.1-)*
MCC Exclusion see Appendix A PDX collection 0756

MCC **J95.3 Chronic pulmonary insufficiency following surgery**
Excludes2: *Functional disturbances following cardiac surgery (I97.0, I97.1-)*
MCC Exclusion see Appendix A PDX collection 0756

CC **J95.4 Chemical pneumonitis due to anesthesia**
Mendelson's syndrome
Postprocedural aspiration pneumonia
Use additional code for adverse effect, if applicable, to identify drug (T41.- with fifth or sixth character 5)
Excludes1: *aspiration pneumonitis due to anesthesia complicating labor and delivery (O74.0)*
aspiration pneumonitis due to anesthesia complicating pregnancy (O29)
aspiration pneumonitis due to anesthesia complicating the puerperium (O89.01)
CC Exclusion see Appendix A PDX collection 0757

CC **J95.5 Postprocedural subglottic stenosis**
CC Exclusion see Appendix A PDX collection 0757

\+ **J95.6 Intraoperative hemorrhage and hematoma of a respiratory system organ or structure complicating a procedure**
Excludes1: *intraoperative hemorrhage and hematoma of a respiratory system organ or structure due to accidental puncture and laceration during procedure (J95.7-)*

CC **J95.61 Intraoperative hemorrhage and hematoma of a respiratory system organ or structure complicating a respiratory system procedure**
CC Exclusion see Appendix A PDX collection 0758

CC **J95.62 Intraoperative hemorrhage and hematoma of a respiratory system organ or structure complicating other procedure**
CC Exclusion see Appendix A PDX collection 0758

\+ **J95.7 Accidental puncture and laceration of a respiratory system organ or structure during a procedure**
Excludes2: *postprocedural pneumothorax (J95.811)*

CC **J95.71 Accidental puncture and laceration of a respiratory system organ or structure during a respiratory system procedure**
CC Exclusion see Appendix A PDX collection 0509

CC **J95.72 Accidental puncture and laceration of a respiratory system organ or structure during other procedure**
CC Exclusion see Appendix A PDX collection 0509

\+ **J95.8 Other intraoperative and postprocedural complications and disorders of respiratory system, not elsewhere classified**

\+ **J95.81 Postprocedural pneumothorax and air leak**

CC **J95.811 Postprocedural pneumothorax**
CC Exclusion see Appendix A PDX collection 0754
HAC see Appendix B for HAC conditional logic

CC **J95.812 Postprocedural air leak**
CC Exclusion see Appendix A PDX collection 0754

\+ **J95.82 Postprocedural respiratory failure**
Excludes1: *Respiratory failure in other conditions (J96.-)*

MCC **J95.821 Acute postprocedural respiratory failure**
Postprocedural respiratory failure NOS
MCC Exclusion see Appendix A PDX collection 0756

MCC **J95.822 Acute and chronic postprocedural respiratory failure**
MCC Exclusion see Appendix A PDX collection 0756

\+ **J95.83 Postprocedural hemorrhage and hematoma of a respiratory system organ or structure following a procedure**

CC **J95.830 Postprocedural hemorrhage and hematoma of a respiratory system organ or structure following a respiratory system procedure**
CC Exclusion see Appendix A PDX collection 0758

CC **J95.831 Postprocedural hemorrhage and hematoma of a respiratory system organ or structure following other procedure**
CC Exclusion see Appendix A PDX collection 0758

CC **J95.84 Transfusion-related acute lung injury (TRALI)**
CC Exclusion see Appendix A PDX collection 0757

\+ **J95.85 Complication of respirator [ventilator]**

CC **J95.850 Mechanical complication of respirator**
Excludes1: *encounter for respirator [ventilator]dependenceduring power failure (Z99.12)*
CC Exclusion see Appendix A PDX collection 0759

CC **J95.851 Ventilator associated pneumonia**
Ventilator associated pneumonitis
Use additional code to identify the organism, if known (B95.-, B96.-, B97.-)
Excludes1: *ventilator lung in newborn (P27.8)*
CC Exclusion see Appendix A PDX collection 0757
Review coding guideline C.10.d.1

CC **J95.859 Other complication of respirator [ventilator]**
CC Exclusion see Appendix A PDX collection 0757

CC **J95.88 Other intraoperative complications of respiratory system, not elsewhere classified**
CC Exclusion see Appendix A PDX collection 0757

CC **J95.89 Other postprocedural complications and disorders of respiratory system, not elsewhere classified**
Use additional code to identify disorder, such as:
aspiration pneumonia (J69.-)
bacterial or viral pneumonia (J12-J18)
Excludes2: *acute pulmonary insufficiency following thoracic surgery (J95.1)*
postprocedural subglottic stenosis (J95.5)
CC Exclusion see Appendix A PDX collection 0757

Other diseases of the respiratory system (J96-J99)

J96 Respiratory failure, not elsewhere classified
Excludes1: *acute respiratory distress syndrome (J80)*
cardiorespiratory failure (R09.2)
newborn respiratory distress syndrome (P22.0)
postprocedural respiratory failure (J95.82-)
respiratory arrest (R09.2)
respiratory arrest of newborn (P28.81)
respiratory failure of newborn (P28.5)

\+ **J96.0 Acute respiratory failure**
Review coding guideline C.10.b

MCC **J96.00 Acute respiratory failure, unspecified whether with hypoxia or hypercapnia**
MCC Exclusion see Appendix A PDX collection 0744
AHA CC: 4Q, 2013, 121

MCC **J96.01 Acute respiratory failure with hypoxia**
MCC Exclusion see Appendix A PDX collection 0744

MCC **J96.02 Acute respiratory failure with hypercapnia**
MCC Exclusion see Appendix A PDX collection 0744

\+ **J96.1 Chronic respiratory failure**

CC **J96.10 Chronic respiratory failure, unspecified whether with hypoxia or hypercapnia**
CC Exclusion see Appendix A PDX collection 0744

CC **J96.11 Chronic respiratory failure with hypoxia**
CC Exclusion see Appendix A PDX collection 0744
AHA CC: 4Q, 2013, 129

CC **J96.12 Chronic respiratory failure with hypercapnia**
CC Exclusion see Appendix A PDX collection 0744

\+ **J96.2 Acute and chronic respiratory failure**
Acute on chronic respiratory failure
Review coding guideline C.10.b

MCC **J96.20 Acute and chronic respiratory failure, unspecified whether with hypoxia or hypercapnia**
MCC Exclusion see Appendix A PDX collection 0744

MCC **J96.21 Acute and chronic respiratory failure with hypoxia**
MCC Exclusion see Appendix A PDX collection 0744

MCC **J96.22 Acute and chronic respiratory failure with hypercapnia**
MCC Exclusion see Appendix A PDX collection 0744

\+ **J96.9 Respiratory failure, unspecified**

MCC **J96.90 Respiratory failure, unspecified, unspecified whether with hypoxia or hypercapnia**
MCC Exclusion see Appendix A PDX collection 0744

MCC **J96.91 Respiratory failure, unspecified with hypoxia**
MCC Exclusion see Appendix A PDX collection 0744

MCC **J96.92 Respiratory failure, unspecified with hypercapnia**
MCC Exclusion see Appendix A PDX collection 0744

J98 Other respiratory disorders
Use additional code to identify:
exposure to environmental tobacco smoke (Z77.22)
exposure to tobacco smoke in the perinatal period (P96.81)
history of tobacco use (Z87.891)
occupational exposure to environmental tobacco smoke (Z57.31)
tobacco dependence (F17.-)
tobacco use (Z72.0)
Excludes1: *newborn apnea (P28.4)*
newborn sleep apnea (P28.3)
Excludes2: *apnea NOS (R06.81)*
sleep apnea (G47.3-)

\+ **J98.0 Diseases of bronchus, not elsewhere classified**

J98.01 Acute bronchospasm
Excludes1: *acute bronchiolitis with bronchospasm (J21.-)*
acute bronchitis with bronchospasm (J20.-)
asthma (J45.-)
exercise induced bronchospasm (J45.990)

J98.09 Other diseases of bronchus, not elsewhere classified
Broncholithiasis
Calcification of bronchus
Stenosis of bronchus
Tracheobronchial collapse
Tracheobronchial dyskinesia
Ulcer of bronchus

\+ **J98.1 Pulmonary collapse**
Excludes1: *therapeutic collapse of lung status (Z98.3)*

CC **J98.11 Atelectasis**
Excludes1: *newborn atelectasis tuberculous atelectasis (current disease) (A15)*
CC Exclusion see Appendix A PDX collection 0760

CC **J98.19 Other pulmonary collapse**
CC Exclusion see Appendix A PDX collection 0760

J98.2 Interstitial emphysema
Mediastinal emphysema
Excludes1: *emphysema NOS (J43.9)*
emphysema in newborn (P25.0)
surgical emphysema (subcutaneous) (T81.82)
traumatic subcutaneous emphysema (T79.7)

J98.3 Compensatory emphysema

J98.4 Other disorders of lung
Calcification of lung
Cystic lung disease (acquired)
Lung disease NOS
Pulmolithiasis
Excludes1: *acute interstitial pneumonitis (J84.114)*
pulmonary insufficiency following surgery (J95.1-J95.2)

MCC **J98.5 Diseases of mediastinum, not elsewhere classified**
Fibrosis of mediastinum
Hernia of mediastinum
Retraction of mediastinum
Mediastinitis
Excludes2: *abscess of mediastinum (J85.3)*
No MCC Exclusions
HAC see Appendix B for HAC conditional logic

J98.6 Disorders of diaphragm
Diaphragmatitis
Paralysis of diaphragm
Relaxation of diaphragm
Excludes1: *congenital malformation of diaphragm NEC (Q7*
congenital diaphragmatic hernia (Q79.0)
Excludes2: *diaphragmatic hernia (K44.-)*

J98.8 Other specified respiratory disorders

J98.9 Respiratory disorder, unspecified
Respiratory disease (chronic) NOS

J99 Respiratory disorders in diseases classified elsewhere

Code first underlying disease, such as:
amyloidosis (E85.-)
ankylosing spondylitis (M45)
congenital syphilis (A50.5)
cryoglobulinemia (D89.1)
early congenital syphilis (A50.0)
schistosomiasis (B65.0-B65.9)
Excludes1: *respiratory disorders in:*
amebiasis (A06.5)
blastomycosis (B40.0-B40.2)
candidiasis (B37.1)
coccidioidomycosis (B38.0-B38.2)
cystic fibrosis with pulmonary manifestations (E84.0)
dermatomyositis (M33.01, M33.11)
histoplasmosis (B39.0-B39.2)
late syphilis (A52.72, A52.73)
polymyositis (M33.21)
sicca syndrome (M35.02)
systemic lupus erythematosus (M32.13)
systemic sclerosis (M34.81)
Wegener's granulomatosis (M31.30-M31.31)
Valid 3-character code, no further characters required

apter 11: Diseases of the Digestive System (00-K95)

cludes2: *certain conditions originating in the perinatal period (P04-P96)*
certain infectious and parasitic diseases (A00-B99)
complications of pregnancy, childbirth and the puerperium (O00-O9A)
congenital malformations, deformations and chromosomal abnormalities (Q00-Q99)
endocrine, nutritional and metabolic diseases (E00-E88)
injury, poisoning and certain other consequences of external causes (S00-T88)
neoplasms (C00-D49)
symptoms, signs and abnormal clinical and laboratory findings, not elsewhere classified (R00-R94)

is chapter contains the following category blocks:

K00-K14 Diseases of oral cavity and salivary glands
K20-K31 Diseases of esophagus, stomach and duodenum
K35-K38 Diseases of appendix
K40-K46 Hernia
K50-K52 Noninfective enteritis and colitis
K55-K64 Other diseases of intestines
K65-K68 Diseases of peritoneum and retroperitoneum
K70-K77 Diseases of liver
K80-K87 Disorders of gallbladder, biliary tract and pancreas
K90-K95 Other diseases of the digestive system

Chapter-Specific Coding Guidelines

addition to general coding guidelines, there are guidelines for specific diagnoses d/or conditions in the classification. Unless otherwise indicated, these guidelines ply to all health care settings. Please refer to Section II for guidelines on the lection of principal diagnosis.

. Chapter 11: Diseases of the Digestive System (K00-K95)

Reserved for future guideline expansion

iseases of oral cavity and salivary glands (K00-K14)

K00 Disorders of tooth development and eruption

Excludes2: *embedded and impacted teeth (K01.-)*

K00.0 Anodontia
Hypodontia
Oligodontia
Excludes1: *acquired absence of teeth (K08.1-)*

K00.1 Supernumerary teeth
Distomolar
Fourth molar
Mesiodens
Paramolar
Supplementary teeth
Excludes2: *supernumerary roots (K00.2)*

K00.2 Abnormalities of size and form of teeth
Concrescence of teeth
Fusion of teeth
Gemination of teeth
Dens evaginatus
Dens in dente
Dens invaginatus
Enamel pearls
Macrodontia
Microdontia
Peg-shaped [conical] teeth
Supernumerary roots
Taurodontism
Tuberculum paramolare
Excludes1: *abnormalities of teeth due to congenital syphilis (A50.5)*
tuberculum Carabelli, which is regarded as a normal variation and should not be coded

K00.3 Mottled teeth
Dental fluorosis
Mottling of enamel
Nonfluoride enamel opacities
Excludes2: *deposits [accretions] on teeth (K03.6)*

K00.4 Disturbances in tooth formation
Aplasia and hypoplasia of cementum
Dilaceration of tooth
Enamel hypoplasia (neonatal) (postnatal) (prenatal)
Regional odontodysplasia
Turner's tooth
Excludes1: *Hutchinson's teeth and mulberry molars in congenital syphilis (A50.5)*
Excludes2: *mottled teeth (K00.3)*

K00.5 Hereditary disturbances in tooth structure, not elsewhere classified
Amelogenesis imperfecta
Dentinogenesis imperfecta
Odontogenesis imperfecta
Dentinal dysplasia
Shell teeth

Oral Cavity

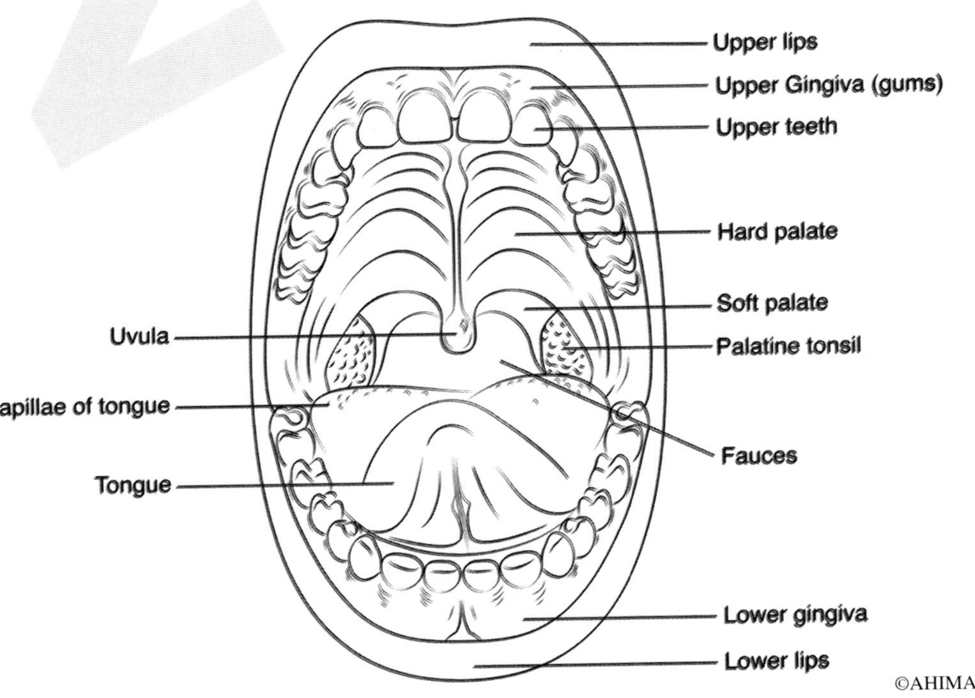

Glands of the Oral Cavity

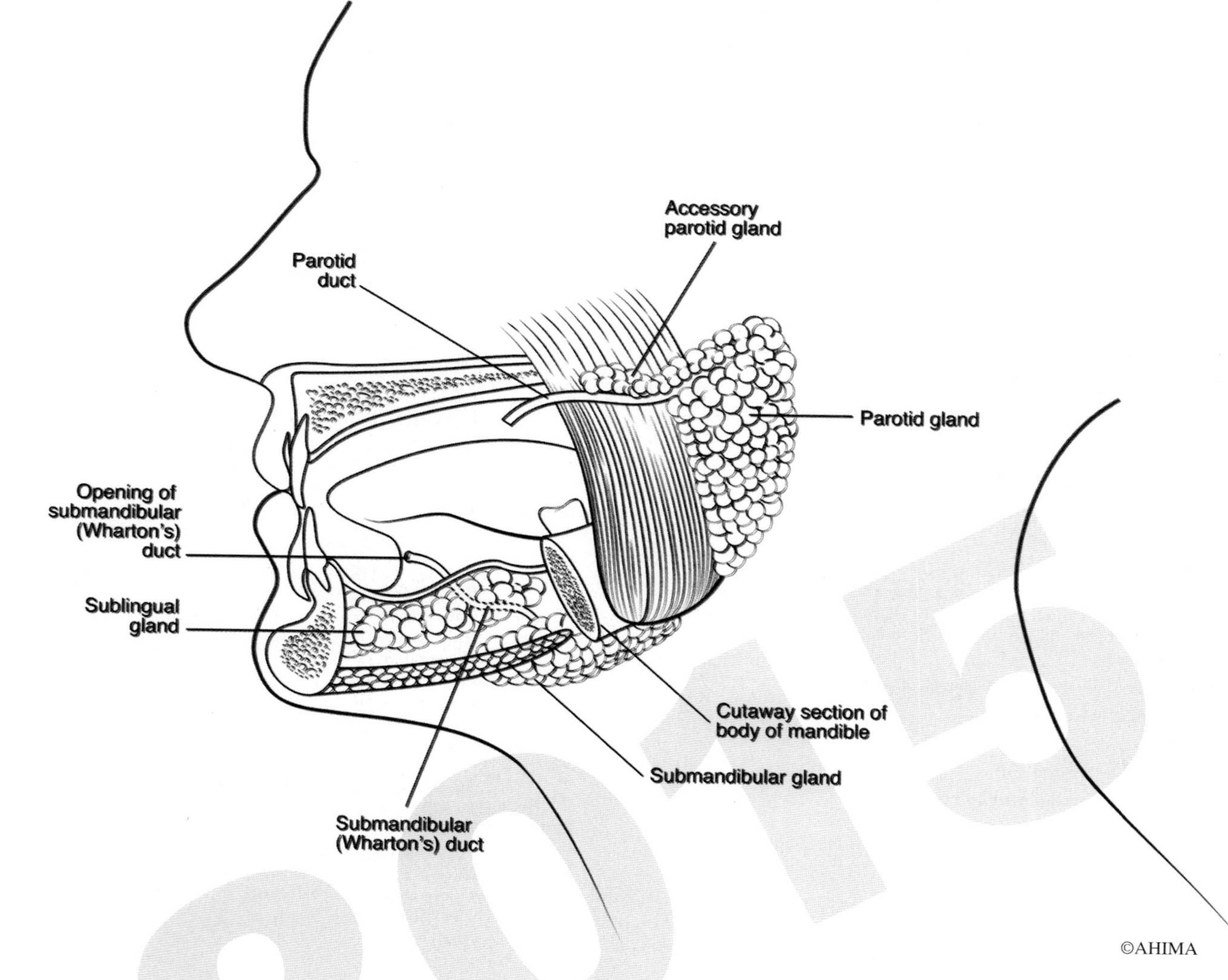

K00.6 Disturbances in tooth eruption
Dentia praecox
Natal tooth
Neonatal tooth
Premature eruption of tooth
Premature shedding of primary [deciduous] tooth
Prenatal teeth
Retained [persistent] primary tooth
Excludes2: *embedded and impacted teeth (K01.-)*

K00.7 Teething syndrome

K00.8 Other disorders of tooth development
Color changes during tooth formation
Intrinsic staining of teeth NOS
Excludes2: *posteruptive color changes (K03.7)*

K00.9 Disorder of tooth development, unspecified
Disorder of odontogenesis NOS

K01 Embedded and impacted teeth

Excludes1: *abnormal position of fully erupted teeth (M26.3-)*

K01.0 Embedded teeth

K01.1 Impacted teeth

K02 Dental caries

Includes: dental cavities
tooth decay

K02.3 Arrested dental caries
Arrested coronal and root caries

+ **K02.5 Dental caries on pit and fissure surface**
Dental caries on chewing surface of tooth

K02.51 Dental caries on pit and fissure surface limited to enamel
White spot lesions [initial caries] on pit and fissure surface of tooth

K02.52 Dental caries on pit and fissure surface penetrating into dentin

K02.53 Dental caries on pit and fissure surface penetrating into pulp

+ **K02.6 Dental caries on smooth surface**

K02.61 Dental caries on smooth surface limited to enamel
White spot lesions [initial caries] on smooth surface of tooth

K02.62 Dental caries on smooth surface penetrating into dentin

K02.63 Dental caries on smooth surface penetrating into pulp

K02.7 Dental root caries

K02.9 Dental caries, unspecified

K03 Other diseases of hard tissues of teeth

Excludes2: *bruxism (F45.8)*
dental caries (K02.-)
teeth-grinding NOS (F45.8)

K03.0 Excessive attrition of teeth
Approximal wear of teeth
Occlusal wear of teeth

K03.1 Abrasion of teeth
Dentifrice abrasion of teeth
Habitual abrasion of teeth
Occupational abrasion of teeth
Ritual abrasion of teeth
Traditional abrasion of teeth
Wedge defect NOS

K03.2 Erosion of teeth
Erosion of teeth due to diet
Erosion of teeth due to drugs and medicaments
Erosion of teeth due to persistent vomiting
Erosion of teeth NOS
Idiopathic erosion of teeth
Occupational erosion of teeth

K03.3 Pathological resorption of teeth
Internal granuloma of pulp
Resorption of teeth (external)

K03.4 Hypercementosis
Cementation hyperplasia

K03.5 Ankylosis of teeth

K03.6 Deposits [accretions] on teeth
Betel deposits [accretions] on teeth
Black deposits [accretions] on teeth
Extrinsic staining of teeth NOS
Green deposits [accretions] on teeth
Materia alba deposits [accretions] on teeth
Orange deposits [accretions] on teeth
Staining of teeth NOS
Subgingival dental calculus
Supragingival dental calculus
Tobacco deposits [accretions] on teeth

K03.7 Posteruptive color changes of dental hard tissues
Excludes2: *deposits [accretions] on teeth (K03.6)*

\+ **K03.8 Other specified diseases of hard tissues of teeth**

K03.81 Cracked tooth
Excludes1: *asymptomatic craze lines in enamel - omit code*
broken or fractured tooth due to trauma (S02.5)

K03.89 Other specified diseases of hard tissues of teeth

K03.9 Disease of hard tissues of teeth, unspecified

K04 Diseases of pulp and periapical tissues

CC **K04.0 Pulpitis**
Acute pulpitis
Chronic (hyperplastic) (ulcerative) pulpitis
Irreversible pulpitis
Reversible pulpitis
CC Exclusion see Appendix A PDX collection 0761

K04.1 Necrosis of pulp
Pulpal gangrene

K04.2 Pulp degeneration
Denticles
Pulpal calcifications
Pulpal stones

K04.3 Abnormal hard tissue formation in pulp
Secondary or irregular dentine

CC **K04.4 Acute apical periodontitis of pulpal origin**
Acute apical periodontitis NOS
Excludes1: *acute periodontitis (K05.2-)*
CC Exclusion see Appendix A PDX collection 0761

K04.5 Chronic apical periodontitis
Apical or periapical granuloma
Apical periodontitis NOS
Excludes1: *chronic periodontitis (K05.3-)*

K04.6 Periapical abscess with sinus
Dental abscess with sinus
Dentoalveolar abscess with sinus

K04.7 Periapical abscess without sinus
Dental abscess without sinus
Dentoalveolar abscess without sinus
Periapical abscess without sinus

K04.8 Radicular cyst
Apical (periodontal) cyst
Periapical cyst
Residual radicular cyst
Excludes2: *lateral periodontal cyst (K09.0)*

\+ **K04.9 Other and unspecified diseases of pulp and periapical tissues**

K04.90 Unspecified diseases of pulp and periapical tissues

K04.99 Other diseases of pulp and periapical tissues

K05 Gingivitis and periodontal diseases

Use additional code to identify:
alcohol abuse and dependence (F10.-)
exposure to environmental tobacco smoke (Z77.22)
exposure to tobacco smoke in the perinatal period (P96.81)
history of tobacco use (Z87.891)
occupational exposure to environmental tobacco smoke (Z57.31)
tobacco dependence (F17.-)
tobacco use (Z72.0)

\+ **K05.0 Acute gingivitis**
Excludes1: *acute necrotizing ulcerative gingivitis (A69.1)*
herpesviral [herpes simplex] gingivostomatitis (B00.2)

K05.00 Acute gingivitis, plaque induced
Acute gingivitis NOS

K05.01 Acute gingivitis, non-plaque induced

\+ **K05.1 Chronic gingivitis**
Desquamative gingivitis (chronic)
Gingivitis (chronic) NOS
Hyperplastic gingivitis (chronic)
Simple marginal gingivitis (chronic)
Ulcerative gingivitis (chronic)

K05.10 Chronic gingivitis, plaque induced
Chronic gingivitis NOS
Gingivitis NOS

K05.11 Chronic gingivitis, non-plaque induced

\+ **K05.2 Aggressive periodontitis**
Acute pericoronitis
Excludes1: *acute apical periodontitis (K04.4)*
periapical abscess (K04.7)
periapical abscess with sinus (K04.6)

K05.20 Aggressive periodontitis, unspecified

K05.21 Aggressive periodontitis, localized
Periodontal abscess

K05.22 Aggressive periodontitis, generalized

\+ **K05.3 Chronic periodontitis**
Chronic pericoronitis
Complex periodontitis
Periodontitis NOS
Simplex periodontitis
Excludes1: *chronic apical periodontitis (K04.5)*

K05.30 Chronic periodontitis, unspecified

K05.31 Chronic periodontitis, localized

K05.32 Chronic periodontitis, generalized

K05.4 Periodontosis
Juvenile periodontosis

K05.5 Other periodontal diseases
Excludes2: *leukoplakia of gingiva (K13.21)*

K05.6 Periodontal disease, unspecified

K06 Other disorders of gingiva and edentulous alveolar ridge

Excludes2: *acute gingivitis (K05.0)*
atrophy of edentulous alveolar ridge (K08.2)
chronic gingivitis (K05.1)
gingivitis NOS (K05.1)

K06.0 Gingival recession
Gingival recession (generalized) (localized) (postinfective) (postprocedural)

K06.1 Gingival enlargement
Gingival fibromatosis

K06.2 Gingival and edentulous alveolar ridge lesions associated with trauma
Irritative hyperplasia of edentulous ridge [denture hyperplasia]
Use additional code (Chapter 20) to identify external cause or denture status (Z97.2)

K06.8 Other specified disorders of gingiva and edentulous alveolar ridge
Fibrous epulis
Flabby alveolar ridge
Giant cell epulis
Peripheral giant cell granuloma of gingiva
Pyogenic granuloma of gingiva
Excludes2: *gingival cyst (K09.0)*

K06.9 Disorder of gingiva and edentulous alveolar ridge, unspecified

K08 Other disorders of teeth and supporting structures

Excludes2: *dentofacial anomalies [including malocclusion] (M26.-)*
disorders of jaw (M27.-)

K08.0 Exfoliation of teeth due to systemic causes
Code also underlying systemic condition

+ K08.1 Complete loss of teeth
Acquired loss of teeth, complete
Excludes1: *congenital absence of teeth (K00.0)*
exfoliation of teeth due to systemic causes (K08.0)
partial loss of teeth (K08.4-)

+ K08.10 Complete loss of teeth, unspecified cause
K08.101 Complete loss of teeth, unspecified cause, class I
K08.102 Complete loss of teeth, unspecified cause, class II
K08.103 Complete loss of teeth, unspecified cause, class III
K08.104 Complete loss of teeth, unspecified cause, class IV
K08.109 Complete loss of teeth, unspecified cause, unspecified class
Edentulism NOS

+ K08.11 Complete loss of teeth due to trauma
K08.111 Complete loss of teeth due to trauma, class I
K08.112 Complete loss of teeth due to trauma, class II
K08.113 Complete loss of teeth due to trauma, class III
K08.114 Complete loss of teeth due to trauma, class IV
K08.119 Complete loss of teeth due to trauma, unspecified class

+ K08.12 Complete loss of teeth due to periodontal diseases
K08.121 Complete loss of teeth due to periodontal diseases, class I
K08.122 Complete loss of teeth due to periodontal diseases, class II
K08.123 Complete loss of teeth due to periodontal diseases, class III
K08.124 Complete loss of teeth due to periodontal diseases, class IV
K08.129 Complete loss of teeth due to periodontal diseases, unspecified class

+ K08.13 Complete loss of teeth due to caries
K08.131 Complete loss of teeth due to caries, class I
K08.132 Complete loss of teeth due to caries, class II
K08.133 Complete loss of teeth due to caries, class III
K08.134 Complete loss of teeth due to caries, class IV
K08.139 Complete loss of teeth due to caries, unspecified class

+ K08.19 Complete loss of teeth due to other specified cause
K08.191 Complete loss of teeth due to other specified cause, class I
K08.192 Complete loss of teeth due to other specified cause, class II
K08.193 Complete loss of teeth due to other specified cause, class III
K08.194 Complete loss of teeth due to other specified cause, class IV
K08.199 Complete loss of teeth due to other specified cause, unspecified class

+ K08.2 Atrophy of edentulous alveolar ridge
K08.20 Unspecified atrophy of edentulous alveolar ridge
Atrophy of the mandible NOS
Atrophy of the maxilla NOS
K08.21 Minimal atrophy of the mandible
Minimal atrophy of the edentulous mandible
K08.22 Moderate atrophy of the mandible
Moderate atrophy of the edentulous mandible
K08.23 Severe atrophy of the mandible
Severe atrophy of the edentulous mandible
K08.24 Minimal atrophy of maxilla
Minimal atrophy of the edentulous maxilla
K08.25 Moderate atrophy of the maxilla
Moderate atrophy of the edentulous maxilla
K08.26 Severe atrophy of the maxilla
Severe atrophy of the edentulous maxilla

K08.3 Retained dental root

+ K08.4 Partial loss of teeth
Acquired loss of teeth, partial
Excludes1: *complete loss of teeth (K08.1-)*
congenital absence of teeth (K00.0)
Excludes2: *exfoliation of teeth due to systemic causes (K08.*

+ K08.40 Partial loss of teeth, unspecified cause
K08.401 Partial loss of teeth, unspecified cause, cl
K08.402 Partial loss of teeth, unspecified cause, class II
K08.403 Partial loss of teeth, unspecified cause, class III
K08.404 Partial loss of teeth, unspecified cause, class IV
K08.409 Partial loss of teeth, unspecified cause, unspecified class
Tooth extraction status NOS

+ K08.41 Partial loss of teeth due to trauma
K08.411 Partial loss of teeth due to trauma, class I
K08.412 Partial loss of teeth due to trauma, class
K08.413 Partial loss of teeth due to trauma, class
K08.414 Partial loss of teeth due to trauma, class
K08.419 Partial loss of teeth due to trauma, unspecified class

+ K08.42 Partial loss of teeth due to periodontal diseases
K08.421 Partial loss of teeth due to periodontal diseases, class I
K08.422 Partial loss of teeth due to periodontal diseases, class II
K08.423 Partial loss of teeth due to periodontal diseases, class III
K08.424 Partial loss of teeth due to periodontal diseases, class IV
K08.429 Partial loss of teeth due to periodontal diseases, unspecified class

+ K08.43 Partial loss of teeth due to caries
K08.431 Partial loss of teeth due to caries, class I
K08.432 Partial loss of teeth due to caries, class II
K08.433 Partial loss of teeth due to caries, class III
K08.434 Partial loss of teeth due to caries, class IV
K08.439 Partial loss of teeth due to caries, unspeci class

+ K08.49 Partial loss of teeth due to other specified cause
K08.491 Partial loss of teeth due to other specified cause, class I
K08.492 Partial loss of teeth due to other specified cause, class II
K08.493 Partial loss of teeth due to other specified cause, class III
K08.494 Partial loss of teeth due to other specified cause, class IV
K08.499 Partial loss of teeth due to other specified cause, unspecified class

+ K08.5 Unsatisfactory restoration of tooth
Defective bridge, crown, filling
Defective dental restoration
Excludes1: *dental restoration status (Z98.811)*
Excludes2: *endosseous dental implant failure (M27.6-)*
unsatisfactory endodontic treatment (M27.5-)

K08.50 Unsatisfactory restoration of tooth, unspecified
Defective dental restoration NOS
K08.51 Open restoration margins of tooth
Dental restoration failure of marginal integrity
Open margin on tooth restoration
Poor gingival margin to tooth restoration
K08.52 Unrepairable overhanging of dental restorative materials
Overhanging of tooth restoration

+ K08.53 Fractured dental restorative material
Excludes1: *cracked tooth (K03.81)*
traumatic fracture of tooth (S02.5)
K08.530 Fractured dental restorative material without loss of material
K08.531 Fractured dental restorative material with loss of material
K08.539 Fractured dental restorative material, unspecified

K08.54 Contour of existing restoration of tooth biologically incompatible with oral health
Dental restoration failure of periodontal anatomical integrity
Unacceptable contours of existing restoration of tooth
Unacceptable morphology of existing restoration of tooth

K08.55 Allergy to existing dental restorative material
Use additional code to identify the specific type of allergy

K08.56 Poor aesthetic of existing restoration of tooth
Dental restoration aesthetically inadequate or displeasing

K08.59 Other unsatisfactory restoration of tooth
Other defective dental restoration

K08.8 Other specified disorders of teeth and supporting structures
Enlargement of alveolar ridge NOS
Irregular alveolar process
Toothache NOS

K08.9 Disorder of teeth and supporting structures, unspecified

K09 Cysts of oral region, not elsewhere classified

Includes: lesions showing histological features both of aneurysmal cyst and of another fibro-osseous lesion
Excludes2: *cysts of jaw (M27.0-, M27.4-)*
radicular cyst (K04.8)

K09.0 Developmental odontogenic cysts
Dentigerous cyst
Eruption cyst
Follicular cyst
Gingival cyst
Lateral periodontal cyst
Primordial cyst
Excludes2: *keratocysts (D16.4, D16.5)*
odontogenic keratocystic tumors (D16.4, D16.5)

K09.1 Developmental (nonodontogenic) cysts of oral region
Cyst (of) incisive canal
Cyst (of) palatine of papilla
Globulomaxillary cyst
Median palatal cyst
Nasoalveolar cyst
Nasolabial cyst
Nasopalatine duct cyst

K09.8 Other cysts of oral region, not elsewhere classified
Dermoid cyst
Epidermoid cyst
Lymphoepithelial cyst
Epstein's pearl

K09.9 Cyst of oral region, unspecified

K11 Diseases of salivary glands

Use additional code to identify:
alcohol abuse and dependence (F10.-)
exposure to environmental tobacco smoke (Z77.22)
exposure to tobacco smoke in the perinatal period (P96.81)
history of tobacco use (Z87.891)
occupational exposure to environmental tobacco smoke (Z57.31)
tobacco dependence (F17.-)
tobacco use (Z72.0)

K11.0 Atrophy of salivary gland

K11.1 Hypertrophy of salivary gland

\+ **K11.2 Sialoadenitis**
Parotitis
Excludes1: *epidemic parotitis (B26.-)*
mumps (B26.-)
uveoparotid fever [Heerfordt] (D86.89)

K11.20 Sialoadenitis, unspecified

K11.21 Acute sialoadenitis
Excludes1: *acute recurrent sialoadenitis (K11.22)*

K11.22 Acute recurrent sialoadenitis

K11.23 Chronic sialoadenitis

CC **K11.3 Abscess of salivary gland**
CC Exclusion see Appendix A PDX collection 0762

CC **K11.4 Fistula of salivary gland**
Excludes1: *congenital fistula of salivary gland (Q38.4)*
CC Exclusion see Appendix A PDX collection 0762

K11.5 Sialolithiasis
Calculus of salivary gland or duct
Stone of salivary gland or duct

K11.6 Mucocele of salivary gland
Mucous extravasation cyst of salivary gland
Mucous retention cyst of salivary gland
Ranula

K11.7 Disturbances of salivary secretion
Hypoptyalism
Ptyalism
Xerostomia
Excludes2: *dry mouth NOS (R68.2)*

K11.8 Other diseases of salivary glands
Benign lymphoepithelial lesion of salivary gland
Mikulicz' disease
Necrotizing sialometaplasia
Sialectasia
Stenosis of salivary duct
Stricture of salivary duct
Excludes1: *sicca syndrome [Sjögren] (M35.0-)*

K11.9 Disease of salivary gland, unspecified
Sialoadenopathy NOS

K12 Stomatitis and related lesions

Use additional code to identify:
alcohol abuse and dependence (F10.-)
exposure to environmental tobacco smoke (Z77.22)
exposure to tobacco smoke in the perinatal period (P96.81)
history of tobacco use (Z87.891)
occupational exposure to environmental tobacco smoke (Z57.31)
tobacco dependence (F17.-)
tobacco use (Z72.0)
Excludes1: *cancrum oris (A69.0)*
cheilitis (K13.0)
gangrenous stomatitis (A69.0)
herpesviral [herpes simplex] gingivostomatitis (B00.2)
noma (A69.0)

K12.0 Recurrent oral aphthae
Aphthous stomatitis (major) (minor)
Bednar's aphthae
Periadenitis mucosa necrotica recurrens
Recurrent aphthous ulcer
Stomatitis herpetiformis

K12.1 Other forms of stomatitis
Stomatitis NOS
Denture stomatitis
Ulcerative stomatitis
Vesicular stomatitis
Excludes1: *acute necrotizing ulcerative stomatitis (A69.1)*
Vincent's stomatitis (A69.1)

CC **K12.2 Cellulitis and abscess of mouth**
Cellulitis of mouth (floor)
Submandibular abscess
Excludes2: *abscess of salivary gland (K11.3)*
abscess of tongue (K14.0)
periapical abscess (K04.6-K04.7)
periodontal abscess (K05.21)
peritonsillar abscess (J36)
CC Exclusion see Appendix A PDX collection 0763

\+ **K12.3 Oral mucositis (ulcerative)**
Mucositis (oral) (oropharyneal)
Excludes2: *gastrointestinal mucositis (ulcerative) (K92.81)*
mucositis (ulcerative) of vagina and vulva (N76.81)
nasal mucositis (ulcerative) (J34.81)

K12.30 Oral mucositis (ulcerative), unspecified

K12.31 Oral mucositis (ulcerative) due to antineoplastic therapy
Use additional code for adverse effect, if applicable, to identify antineoplastic and immunosuppressive drugs (T45.1X5)

Use additional code for other antineoplastic therapy, such as: radiological procedure and radiotherapy (Y84.2)

K12.32 Oral mucositis (ulcerative) due to other drugs
Use additional code for adverse effect, if applicable, to identify drug (T36-T50 with fifth or sixth character 5)

K12.33 Oral mucositis (ulcerative) due to radiation
Use additional external cause code (W88-W90, X39.0-) to identify cause

K12.39 Other oral mucositis (ulcerative)
Viral oral mucositis (ulcerative)

K13 Other diseases of lip and oral mucosa

Includes: epithelial disturbances of tongue
Use additional code to identify:
alcohol abuse and dependence (F10.-)
exposure to environmental tobacco smoke (Z77.22)
exposure to tobacco smoke in the perinatal period (P96.81)
history of tobacco use (Z87.891)
occupational exposure to environmental tobacco smoke (Z57.31)
tobacco dependence (F17.-)
tobacco use (Z72.0)
Excludes2: *certain disorders of gingiva and edentulous alveolar ridge (K05-K06)*
cysts of oral region (K09.-)
diseases of tongue (K14.-)
stomatitis and related lesions (K12.-)

K13.0 Diseases of lips
Abscess of lips
Angular cheilitis
Cellulitis of lips
Cheilitis NOS
Cheilodynia
Cheilosis
Exfoliative cheilitis
Fistula of lips
Glandular cheilitis
Hypertrophy of lips
Perlèche NEC
Excludes1: *ariboflavinosis (E53.0)*
cheilitis due to radiation-related disorders (L55-L59)
congenital fistula of lips (Q38.0)
congenital hypertrophy of lips (Q18.6)
Perlèche due to candidiasis (B37.83)
Perlèche due to riboflavin deficiency (E53.0)

K13.1 Cheek and lip biting

+ **K13.2 Leukoplakia and other disturbances of oral epithelium, including tongue**
Excludes1: *carcinoma in situ of oral epithelium (D00.0-)*
hairy leukoplakia (K13.3)

K13.21 Leukoplakia of oral mucosa, including tongue
Leukokeratosis of oral mucosa
Leukoplakia of gingiva, lips, tongue
Excludes1: *hairy leukoplakia (K13.3)*
leukokeratosis nicotina palati (K13.24)

K13.22 Minimal keratinized residual ridge mucosa
Minimal keratinization of alveolar ridge mucosa

K13.23 Excessive keratinized residual ridge mucosa
Excessive keratinization of alveolar ridge mucosa

K13.24 Leukokeratosis nicotina palati
Smoker's palate

K13.29 Other disturbances of oral epithelium, including tongue
Erythroplakia of mouth or tongue
Focal epithelial hyperplasia of mouth or tongue
Leukoedema of mouth or tongue
Other oral epithelium disturbances

K13.3 Hairy leukoplakia

K13.4 Granuloma and granuloma-like lesions of oral mucosa
Eosinophilic granuloma
Granuloma pyogenicum
Verrucous xanthoma

K13.5 Oral submucous fibrosis
Submucous fibrosis of tongue

K13.6 Irritative hyperplasia of oral mucosa
Excludes2: *irritative hyperplasia of edentulous ridge [denture hyperplasia] (K06.2)*

+ **K13.7 Other and unspecified lesions of oral mucosa**

K13.70 Unspecified lesions of oral mucosa

K13.79 Other lesions of oral mucosa
Focal oral mucinosis

K14 Diseases of tongue

Use additional code to identify:
alcohol abuse and dependence (F10.-)
exposure to environmental tobacco smoke (Z77.22)
history of tobacco use (Z87.891)
occupational exposure to environmental tobacco smoke (Z57.31)
tobacco dependence (F17.-)
tobacco use (Z72.0)
Excludes2: *erythroplakia (K13.29)*
focal epithelial hyperplasia (K13.29)
leukedema of tongue (K13.29)
leukoplakia of tongue (K13.21)
hairy leukoplakia (K13.3)
macroglossia (congenital) (Q38.2)
submucous fibrosis of tongue (K13.5)

K14.0 Glossitis
Abscess of tongue
Ulceration (traumatic) of tongue
Excludes1: *atrophic glossitis (K14.4)*

K14.1 Geographic tongue
Benign migratory glossitis
Glossitis areata exfoliativa

K14.2 Median rhomboid glossitis

K14.3 Hypertrophy of tongue papillae
Black hairy tongue
Coated tongue
Hypertrophy of foliate papillae
Lingua villosa nigra

K14.4 Atrophy of tongue papillae
Atrophic glossitis

K14.5 Plicated tongue
Fissured tongue
Furrowed tongue
Scrotal tongue
Excludes1: *fissured tongue, congenital (Q38.3)*

K14.6 Glossodynia
Glossopyrosis
Painful tongue

K14.8 Other diseases of tongue
Atrophy of tongue
Crenated tongue
Enlargement of tongue
Glossocele
Glossoptosis
Hypertrophy of tongue

K14.9 Disease of tongue, unspecified
Glossopathy NOS

Diseases of esophagus, stomach and duodenum (K20-K31)

Excludes2: *hiatus hernia (K44.-)*

K20 Esophagitis

Use additional code to identify:
alcohol abuse and dependence (F10.-)
Excludes1: *erosion of esophagus (K22.1-)*
esophagitis with gastro-esophageal reflux disease (K21.0)
reflux esophagitis (K21.0)
ulcerative esophagitis (K22.1-)
Excludes2: *eosinophilic gastritis or gastroenteritis (K52.81)*

K20.0 Eosinophilic esophagitis

K20.8 Other esophagitis
Abscess of esophagus

K20.9 Esophagitis, unspecified Esophagitis NOS

K21 Gastro-esophageal reflux disease

Excludes1: *newborn esophageal reflux (P78.83)*

K21.0 Gastro-esophageal reflux disease with esophagitis
Reflux esophagitis

K21.9 Gastro-esophageal reflux disease without esophagitis
Esophageal reflux NOS

K22 Other diseases of esophagus

Excludes2: *esophageal varices (I85.-)*

K22.0 Achalasia of cardia
Achalasia NOS
Cardiospasm
Excludes1: *congenital cardiospasm (Q39.5)*

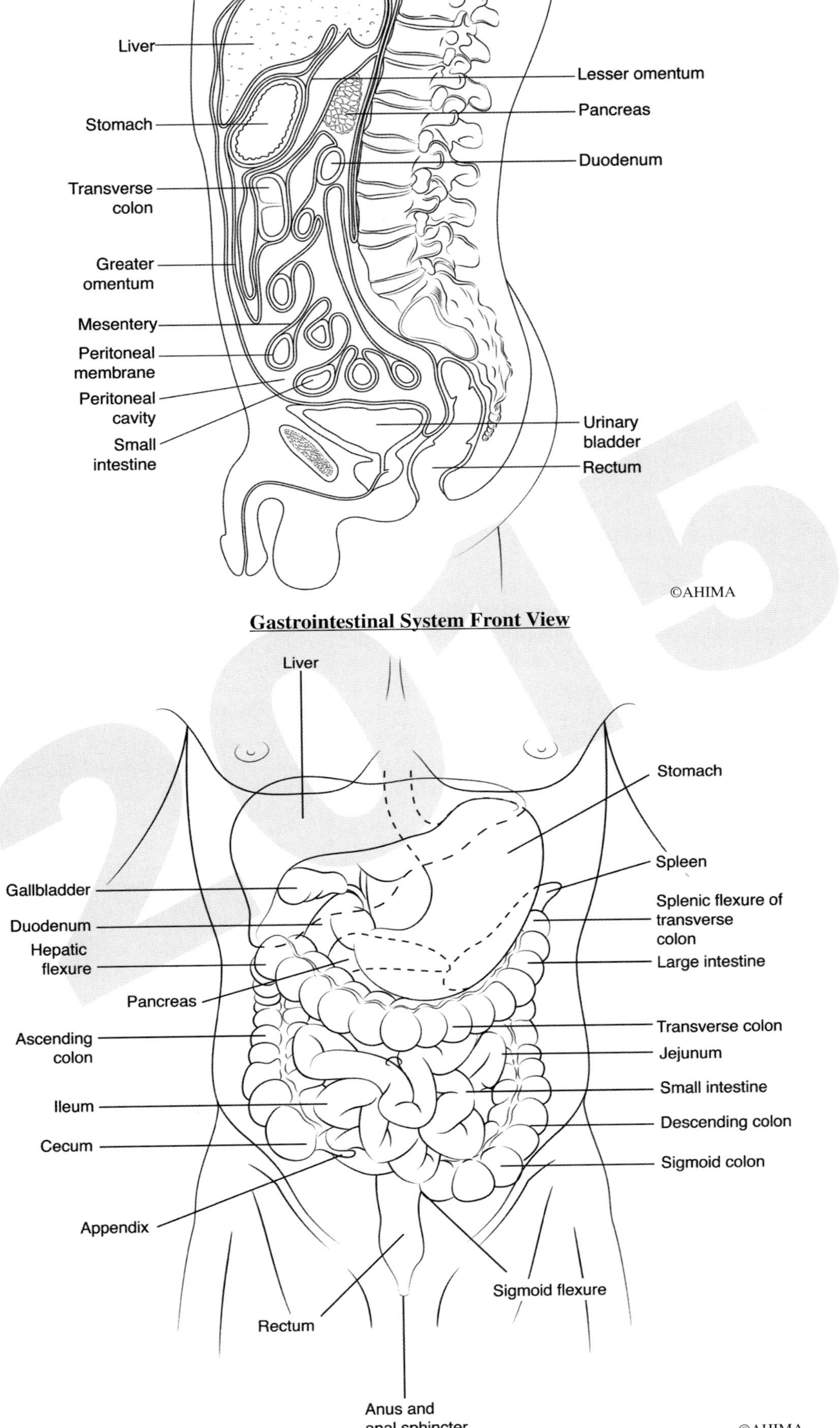
Gastrointestinal System Side View
Liver
Stomach
Transverse colon
Greater omentum
Mesentery
Peritoneal membrane
Peritoneal cavity
Small intestine
Lesser omentum
Pancreas
Duodenum
Urinary bladder
Rectum
©AHIMA
Gastrointestinal System Front View
Liver
Gallbladder
Duodenum
Hepatic flexure
Pancreas
Ascending colon
Ileum
Cecum
Appendix
Rectum
Anus and anal sphincter
Stomach
Spleen
Splenic flexure of transverse colon
Large intestine
Transverse colon
Jejunum
Small intestine
Descending colon
Sigmoid colon
Sigmoid flexure
©AHIMA

Upper Gastrointestinal System

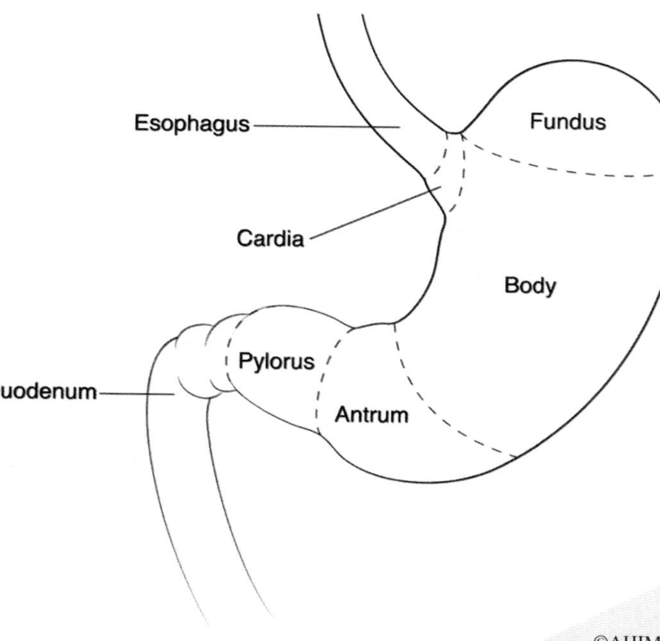

©AHIMA

+ **K22.1 Ulcer of esophagus**
Barrett's ulcer
Erosion of esophagus
Fungal ulcer of esophagus
Peptic ulcer of esophagus
Ulcer of esophagus due to ingestion of chemicals
Ulcer of esophagus due to ingestion of drugs and medicaments
Ulcerative esophagitis
Code first poisoning due to drug or toxin, if applicable (T36-T65 with fifth or sixth character 1-4 or 6)

Use additional code for adverse effect, if applicable, to identify drug (T36-T50 with fifth or sixth character 5)
Excludes1: *Barrett's esophagus (K22.7-)*

CC **K22.10 Ulcer of esophagus without bleeding**
Ulcer of esophagus NOS
CC Exclusion see Appendix A PDX collection 0764

MCC **K22.11 Ulcer of esophagus with bleeding**
Excludes2: *bleeding esophageal varices (I85.01, I85.11)*
MCC Exclusion see Appendix A PDX collection 0765

K22.2 Esophageal obstruction
Compression of esophagus
Constriction of esophagus
Stenosis of esophagus
Stricture of esophagus
Excludes1: *congenital stenosis or stricture of esophagus (Q39.3)*

MCC **K22.3 Perforation of esophagus**
Rupture of esophagus
Excludes1: *traumatic perforation of (thoracic) esophagus (S27.8-)*
MCC Exclusion see Appendix A PDX collection 0766

K22.4 Dyskinesia of esophagus
Corkscrew esophagus
Diffuse esophageal spasm
Spasm of esophagus
Excludes1: *cardiospasm (K22.0)*

K22.5 Diverticulum of esophagus, acquired
Esophageal pouch, acquired
Excludes1: *diverticulum of esophagus (congenital) (Q39.6)*

MCC **K22.6 Gastro-esophageal laceration-hemorrhage syndrome**
Mallory-Weiss syndrome
MCC Exclusion see Appendix A PDX collection 0767

+ **K22.7 Barrett's esophagus**
Barrett's disease
Barrett's syndrome
Excludes1: *Barrett's ulcer (K22.1)*
malignant neoplasm of esophagus (C15.-)

K22.70 Barrett's esophagus without dysplasia
Barrett's esophagus NOS

+ **K22.71 Barrett's esophagus with dysplasia**

K22.710 Barrett's esophagus with low grade dysplasia

K22.711 Barrett's esophagus with high grade dysplasia

K22.719 Barrett's esophagus with dysplasia, unspecified

K22.8 Other specified diseases of esophagus
Hemorrhage of esophagus NOS
Excludes2: *esophageal varices (I85.-)*
Paterson-Kelly syndrome (D50.1)

K22.9 Disease of esophagus, unspecified

K23 Disorders of esophagus in diseases classified elsewhere
Code first underlying disease, such as:
congenital syphilis (A50.5)
Excludes1: *late syphilis (A52.79)*
megaesophagus due to Chagas' disease (B57.31)
tuberculosis (A18.83)

Valid 3-character code, no further characters required

K25 Gastric ulcer
Includes: erosion (acute) of stomach
pylorus ulcer (peptic)
stomach ulcer (peptic)
Use additional code to identify:
alcohol abuse and dependence (F10.-)
Excludes1: *acute gastritis (K29.0-)*
peptic ulcer NOS (K27.-)

MCC **K25.0 Acute gastric ulcer with hemorrhage**
MCC Exclusion see Appendix A PDX collection 0765

MCC **K25.1 Acute gastric ulcer with perforation**
MCC Exclusion see Appendix A PDX collection 0765

MCC **K25.2 Acute gastric ulcer with both hemorrhage and perforation**
MCC Exclusion see Appendix A PDX collection 0765

CC **K25.3 Acute gastric ulcer without hemorrhage or perforation**
CC Exclusion see Appendix A PDX collection 0765

MCC **K25.4 Chronic or unspecified gastric ulcer with hemorrhage**
MCC Exclusion see Appendix A PDX collection 0765

MCC **K25.5 Chronic or unspecified gastric ulcer with perforation**
MCC Exclusion see Appendix A PDX collection 0765

MCC **K25.6 Chronic or unspecified gastric ulcer with both hemorrhage and perforation**
MCC Exclusion see Appendix A PDX collection 0765

K25.7 Chronic gastric ulcer without hemorrhage or perforation

K25.9 Gastric ulcer, unspecified as acute or chronic, without hemorrhage or perforation

K26 Duodenal ulcer

Includes: erosion (acute) of duodenum
duodenum ulcer (peptic)
postpyloric ulcer (peptic)

Use additional code to identify:
alcohol abuse and dependence (F10.-)

Excludes1: *peptic ulcer NOS (K27.-)*

MCC **K26.0 Acute duodenal ulcer with hemorrhage**
MCC Exclusion see Appendix A PDX collection 0768

K26.1 Acute duodenal ulcer with perforation
MCC Exclusion see Appendix A PDX collection 0768

K26.2 Acute duodenal ulcer with both hemorrhage and perforation
MCC Exclusion see Appendix A PDX collection 0768

CC **K26.3 Acute duodenal ulcer without hemorrhage or perforation**
CC Exclusion see Appendix A PDX collection 0769

MCC **K26.4 Chronic or unspecified duodenal ulcer with hemorrhage**
MCC Exclusion see Appendix A PDX collection 0768

MCC **K26.5 Chronic or unspecified duodenal ulcer with perforation**
MCC Exclusion see Appendix A PDX collection 0768

MCC **K26.6 Chronic or unspecified duodenal ulcer with both hemorrhage and perforation**
MCC Exclusion see Appendix A PDX collection 0768

K26.7 Chronic duodenal ulcer without hemorrhage or perforation

K26.9 Duodenal ulcer, unspecified as acute or chronic, without hemorrhage or perforation

K27 Peptic ulcer, site unspecified

Includes: gastroduodenal ulcer NOS
peptic ulcer NOS

Use additional code to identify:
alcohol abuse and dependence (F10.-)

Excludes1: *peptic ulcer of newborn (P78.82)*

MCC **K27.0 Acute peptic ulcer, site unspecified, with hemorrhage**
MCC Exclusion see Appendix A PDX collection 0768

MCC **K27.1 Acute peptic ulcer, site unspecified, with perforation**
MCC Exclusion see Appendix A PDX collection 0768

K27.2 Acute peptic ulcer, site unspecified, with both hemorrhage and perforation
MCC Exclusion see Appendix A PDX collection 0768

CC **K27.3 Acute peptic ulcer, site unspecified, without hemorrhage or perforation**
CC Exclusion see Appendix A PDX collection 0768

MCC **K27.4 Chronic or unspecified peptic ulcer, site unspecified, with hemorrhage**
MCC Exclusion see Appendix A PDX collection 0768

MCC **K27.5 Chronic or unspecified peptic ulcer, site unspecified, with perforation**
MCC Exclusion see Appendix A PDX collection 0768

MCC **K27.6 Chronic or unspecified peptic ulcer, site unspecified, with both hemorrhage and perforation**
MCC Exclusion see Appendix A PDX collection 0768

K27.7 Chronic peptic ulcer, site unspecified, without hemorrhage or perforation

K27.9 Peptic ulcer, site unspecified, unspecified as acute or chronic, without hemorrhage or perforation

K28 Gastrojejunal ulcer

Includes: anastomotic ulcer (peptic) or erosion
gastrocolic ulcer (peptic) or erosion
gastrointestinal ulcer (peptic) or erosion
gastrojejunal ulcer (peptic) or erosion
jejunal ulcer (peptic) or erosion
marginal ulcer (peptic) or erosion
stomal ulcer (peptic) or erosion

Use additional code to identify:
alcohol abuse and dependence (F10.-)

Excludes1: *primary ulcer of small intestine (K63.3)*

MCC **K28.0 Acute gastrojejunal ulcer with hemorrhage**
MCC Exclusion see Appendix A PDX collection 0765

MCC **K28.1 Acute gastrojejunal ulcer with perforation**
MCC Exclusion see Appendix A PDX collection 0765

MCC **K28.2 Acute gastrojejunal ulcer with both hemorrhage and perforation**
MCC Exclusion see Appendix A PDX collection 0765

CC **K28.3 Acute gastrojejunal ulcer without hemorrhage or perforation**
CC Exclusion see Appendix A PDX collection 0765

MCC **K28.4 Chronic or unspecified gastrojejunal ulcer with hemorrhage**
MCC Exclusion see Appendix A PDX collection 0765

MCC **K28.5 Chronic or unspecified gastrojejunal ulcer with perforation**
MCC Exclusion see Appendix A PDX collection 0765

MCC **K28.6 Chronic or unspecified gastrojejunal ulcer with both hemorrhage and perforation**
MCC Exclusion see Appendix A PDX collection 0765

K28.7 Chronic gastrojejunal ulcer without hemorrhage or perforation

K28.9 Gastrojejunal ulcer, unspecified as acute or chronic, without hemorrhage or perforation

K29 Gastritis and duodenitis

Excludes1: *eosinophilic gastritis or gastroenteritis (K52.81)*
Zollinger-Ellison syndrome (E16.4)

\+ **K29.0 Acute gastritis**

Use additional code to identify:
alcohol abuse and dependence (F10.-)

Excludes1: *erosion (acute) of stomach (K25.-)*

K29.00 Acute gastritis without bleeding

MCC **K29.01 Acute gastritis with bleeding**
MCC Exclusion see Appendix A PDX collection 0770

\+ **K29.2 Alcoholic gastritis**

Use additional code to identify:
alcohol abuse and dependence (F10.-)

K29.20 Alcoholic gastritis without bleeding

MCC **K29.21 Alcoholic gastritis with bleeding**
MCC Exclusion see Appendix A PDX collection 0770

\+ **K29.3 Chronic superficial gastritis**

K29.30 Chronic superficial gastritis without bleeding

MCC **K29.31 Chronic superficial gastritis with bleeding**
MCC Exclusion see Appendix A PDX collection 0770

\+ **K29.4 Chronic atrophic gastritis**

Gastric atrophy

K29.40 Chronic atrophic gastritis without bleeding

MCC **K29.41 Chronic atrophic gastritis with bleeding**
MCC Exclusion see Appendix A PDX collection 0770

\+ **K29.5 Unspecified chronic gastritis**

Chronic antral gastritis
Chronic fundal gastritis

K29.50 Unspecified chronic gastritis without bleeding

MCC **K29.51 Unspecified chronic gastritis with bleeding**
MCC Exclusion see Appendix A PDX collection 0770

\+ **K29.6 Other gastritis**

Giant hypertrophic gastritis
Granulomatous gastritis
Ménétrier's disease

K29.60 Other gastritis without bleeding

MCC **K29.61 Other gastritis with bleeding**
MCC Exclusion see Appendix A PDX collection 0770

\+ **K29.7 Gastritis, unspecified**

K29.70 Gastritis, unspecified, without bleeding

MCC **K29.71 Gastritis, unspecified, with bleeding**
MCC Exclusion see Appendix A PDX collection 0770

\+ **K29.8 Duodenitis**

K29.80 Duodenitis without bleeding

MCC **K29.81 Duodenitis with bleeding**
MCC Exclusion see Appendix A PDX collection 0770

\+ **K29.9 Gastroduodenitis, unspecified**

K29.90 Gastroduodenitis, unspecified, without bleeding

MCC **K29.91 Gastroduodenitis, unspecified, with bleeding**
MCC Exclusion see Appendix A PDX collection 0770

K30 Functional dyspepsia

Indigestion

Excludes1: *dyspepsia NOS (R10.13)*
heartburn (R12)
nervous dyspepsia (F45.8)
neurotic dyspepsia (F45.8)
psychogenic dyspepsia (F45.8)

Valid 3-character code, no further characters required

K31 Other diseases of stomach and duodenum

Includes: functional disorders of stomach

Excludes2: *diabetic gastroparesis (E08.43, E09.43, E10.43, E11.43, E13.43)*
diverticulum of duodenum (K57.00-K57.13)

CC **K31.0 Acute dilatation of stomach**
Acute distention of stomach
CC Exclusion see Appendix A PDX collection 0771

• CC **K31.1 Adult hypertrophic pyloric stenosis**
Pyloric stenosis NOS

Excludes1: *congenital or infantile pyloric stenosis (Q40.0)*

CC Exclusion see Appendix A PDX collection 0772

K31.2 Hourglass stricture and stenosis of stomach

Excludes1: *congenital hourglass stomach (Q40.2)*
hourglass contraction of stomach (K31.89)

K31.3 Pylorospasm, not elsewhere classified

Excludes1: *congenital or infantile pylorospasm (Q40.0)*
neurotic pylorospasm (F45.8)
psychogenic pylorospasm (F45.8)

K31.4 Gastric diverticulum

Excludes1: *congenital diverticulum of stomach (Q40.2)*

CC **K31.5 Obstruction of duodenum**
Constriction of duodenum
Duodenal ileus (chronic)
Stenosis of duodenum
Stricture of duodenum
Volvulus of duodenum
Excludes1: *congenital stenosis of duodenum (Q41.0)*
CC Exclusion see Appendix A PDX collection 0773

CC **K31.6 Fistula of stomach and duodenum**
Gastrocolic fistula
Gastrojejunocolic fistula
CC Exclusion see Appendix A PDX collection 0774

K31.7 Polyp of stomach and duodenum
Excludes1: *adenomatous polyp of stomach (D13.1)*

+ K31.8 Other specified diseases of stomach and duodenum

+ K31.81 Angiodysplasia of stomach and duodenum

MCC **K31.811 Angiodysplasia of stomach and duodenum with bleeding**
MCC Exclusion see Appendix A PDX collection 0770

K31.819 Angiodysplasia of stomach and duodenum without bleeding
Angiodysplasia of stomach and duodenum NOS

MCC **K31.82 Dieulafoy lesion (hemorrhagic) of stomach and duodenum**
Excludes2: *Dieulafoy lesion of intestine (K63.81)*
MCC Exclusion see Appendix A PDX collection 0775

K31.83 Achlorhydria

K31.84 Gastroparesis
Gastroparalysis
Code first underlying disease, if known, such as:
anorexia nervosa (F50.0-)
diabetes mellitus (E08.43, E09.43, E10.43, E11.43, E13.43)
scleroderma (M34.-)
AHA CC: 4Q, 2013, 114-115

K31.89 Other diseases of stomach and duodenum

K31.9 Disease of stomach and duodenum, unspecified

Diseases of appendix (K35-K38)

K35 Acute appendicitis

MCC **K35.2 Acute appendicitis with generalized peritonitis**
Appendicitis (acute) with generalized (diffuse) peritonitis following rupture or perforation of appendix
Perforated appendix NOS
Ruptured appendix NOS
MCC Exclusion see Appendix A PDX collection 0776

MCC **K35.3 Acute appendicitis with localized peritonitis**
Acute appendicitis with or without perforation or rupture NOS
Acute appendicitis with or without perforation or rupture with localized peritonitis
Acute appendicitis with peritoneal abscess
MCC Exclusion see Appendix A PDX collection 0776

+ K35.8 Other and unspecified acute appendicitis

CC **K35.80 Unspecified acute appendicitis**
Acute appendicitis NOS
Acute appendicitis without (localized) (generalized) peritonitis
CC Exclusion see Appendix A PDX collection 0776

CC **K35.89 Other acute appendicitis**
CC Exclusion see Appendix A PDX collection 0776

K36 Other appendicitis
Chronic appendicitis
Recurrent appendicitis
Valid 3-character code, no further characters required

K37 Unspecified appendicitis
Excludes1: *-unspecified appendicitis with peritonitis (K35.2-K35.3)*
Valid 3-character code, no further characters required

K38 Other diseases of appendix

K38.0 Hyperplasia of appendix

K38.1 Appendicular concretions
Fecalith of appendix
Stercolith of appendix

K38.2 Diverticulum of appendix

K38.3 Fistula of appendix

K38.8 Other specified diseases of appendix
Intussusception of appendix

K38.9 Disease of appendix, unspecified

Hernia (K40-K46)

NOTE Hernia with both gangrene and obstruction is classified to hernia with gangrene.

Includes: acquired hernia
congenital [except diaphragmatic or hiatus] hernia
recurrent hernia

K40 Inguinal hernia

Includes: bubonocele
direct inguinal hernia
double inguinal hernia
indirect inguinal hernia
inguinal hernia NOS
oblique inguinal hernia
scrotal hernia

+ K40.0 Bilateral inguinal hernia, with obstruction, without gangrene
Inguinal hernia (bilateral) causing obstruction without gangrene
Incarcerated inguinal hernia (bilateral) without gangrene
Irreducible inguinal hernia (bilateral) without gangrene
Strangulated inguinal hernia (bilateral) without gangrene

CC **K40.00 Bilateral inguinal hernia, with obstruction, without gangrene, not specified as recurrent**
Bilateral inguinal hernia, with obstruction, without gangrene NOS
CC Exclusion see Appendix A PDX collection 0777

CC **K40.01 Bilateral inguinal hernia, with obstruction, without gangrene, recurrent**
CC Exclusion see Appendix A PDX collection 0777

+ K40.1 Bilateral inguinal hernia, with gangrene

MCC **K40.10 Bilateral inguinal hernia, with gangrene, not specified as recurrent**
Bilateral inguinal hernia, with gangrene NOS
MCC Exclusion see Appendix A PDX collection 0777

MCC **K40.11 Bilateral inguinal hernia, with gangrene, recurrent**
MCC Exclusion see Appendix A PDX collection 0777

+ K40.2 Bilateral inguinal hernia, without obstruction or gangrene

K40.20 Bilateral inguinal hernia, without obstruction or gangrene, not specified as recurrent
Bilateral inguinal hernia NOS

K40.21 Bilateral inguinal hernia, without obstruction or gangrene, recurrent

+ K40.3 Unilateral inguinal hernia, with obstruction, without gangrene
Inguinal hernia (unilateral) causing obstruction without gangrene
Incarcerated inguinal hernia (unilateral) without gangrene
Irreducible inguinal hernia (unilateral) without gangrene
Strangulated inguinal hernia (unilateral) without gangrene

CC **K40.30 Unilateral inguinal hernia, with obstruction, without gangrene, not specified as recurrent**
Inguinal hernia, with obstruction NOS
Unilateral inguinal hernia, with obstruction, without gangrene NOS
CC Exclusion see Appendix A PDX collection 0777

CC **K40.31 Unilateral inguinal hernia, with obstruction, without gangrene, recurrent**
CC Exclusion see Appendix A PDX collection 0777

+ K40.4 Unilateral inguinal hernia, with gangrene

MCC **K40.40 Unilateral inguinal hernia, with gangrene, not specified as recurrent**
Inguinal hernia with gangrene NOS
Unilateral inguinal hernia with gangrene NOS
MCC Exclusion see Appendix A PDX collection 0777

MCC **K40.41 Unilateral inguinal hernia, with gangrene, recurrent**
MCC Exclusion see Appendix A PDX collection 0777

+ K40.9 Unilateral inguinal hernia, without obstruction or gangrene

K40.90 Unilateral inguinal hernia, without obstruction or gangrene, not specified as recurrent
Inguinal hernia NOS
Unilateral inguinal hernia NOS

K40.91 Unilateral inguinal hernia, without obstruction or gangrene, recurrent

K41 Femoral hernia

+ K41.0 Bilateral femoral hernia, with obstruction, without gangrene
Femoral hernia (bilateral) causing obstruction, without gangrene
Incarcerated femoral hernia (bilateral), without gangrene
Irreducible femoral hernia (bilateral), without gangrene
Strangulated femoral hernia (bilateral), without gangrene

CC **K41.00 Bilateral femoral hernia, with obstruction, without gangrene, not specified as recurrent**
Bilateral femoral hernia, with obstruction, without gangrene NOS
CC Exclusion see Appendix A PDX collection 0778

CC **K41.01 Bilateral femoral hernia, with obstruction, without gangrene, recurrent**
CC Exclusion see Appendix A PDX collection 0778

\+ **K41.1 Bilateral femoral hernia, with gangrene**

MCC **K41.10 Bilateral femoral hernia, with gangrene, not specified as recurrent**
Bilateral femoral hernia, with gangrene NOS
MCC Exclusion see Appendix A PDX collection 0779

MCC **K41.11 Bilateral femoral hernia, with gangrene, recurrent**
MCC Exclusion see Appendix A PDX collection 0779

\+ **K41.2 Bilateral femoral hernia, without obstruction or gangrene**

K41.20 Bilateral femoral hernia, without obstruction or gangrene, not specified as recurrent
Bilateral femoral hernia NOS

K41.21 Bilateral femoral hernia, without obstruction or gangrene, recurrent

\+ **K41.3 Unilateral femoral hernia, with obstruction, without gangrene**
Femoral hernia (unilateral) causing obstruction, without gangrene
Incarcerated femoral hernia (unilateral), without gangrene
Irreducible femoral hernia (unilateral), without gangrene
Strangulated femoral hernia (unilateral), without gangrene

CC **K41.30 Unilateral femoral hernia, with obstruction, without gangrene, not specified as recurrent**
Femoral hernia, with obstruction NOS
Unilateral femoral hernia, with obstruction NOS
CC Exclusion see Appendix A PDX collection 0778

CC **K41.31 Unilateral femoral hernia, with obstruction, without gangrene, recurrent**
CC Exclusion see Appendix A PDX collection 0778

\+ **K41.4 Unilateral femoral hernia, with gangrene**

MCC **K41.40 Unilateral femoral hernia, with gangrene, not specified as recurrent**
Femoral hernia, with gangrene NOS
Unilateral femoral hernia, with gangrene NOS
MCC Exclusion see Appendix A PDX collection 0779

MCC **K41.41 Unilateral femoral hernia, with gangrene, recurrent**
MCC Exclusion see Appendix A PDX collection 0779

\+ **K41.9 Unilateral femoral hernia, without obstruction or gangrene**

K41.90 Unilateral femoral hernia, without obstruction or gangrene, not specified as recurrent
Femoral hernia NOS
Unilateral femoral hernia NOS

K41.91 Unilateral femoral hernia, without obstruction or gangrene, recurrent

K42 Umbilical hernia

Includes: paraumbilical hernia
Excludes1: *omphalocele (Q79.2)*

CC **K42.0 Umbilical hernia with obstruction, without gangrene**
Umbilical hernia causing obstruction, without gangrene
Incarcerated umbilical hernia, without gangrene
Irreducible umbilical hernia, without gangrene
Strangulated umbilical hernia, without gangrene
CC Exclusion see Appendix A PDX collection 0780

MCC **K42.1 Umbilical hernia with gangrene**
Gangrenous umbilical hernia
MCC Exclusion see Appendix A PDX collection 0781

K42.9 Umbilical hernia without obstruction or gangrene
Umbilical hernia NOS

K43 Ventral hernia

CC **K43.0 Incisional hernia with obstruction, without gangrene**
Incisional hernia causing obstruction, without gangrene
Incarcerated incisional hernia, without gangrene
Irreducible incisional hernia, without gangrene
Strangulated incisional hernia, without gangrene
CC Exclusion see Appendix A PDX collection 0780

MCC **K43.1 Incisional hernia with gangrene**
Gangrenous incisional hernia
MCC Exclusion see Appendix A PDX collection 0781

K43.2 Incisional hernia without obstruction or gangrene
Incisional hernia NOS

CC **K43.3 Parastomal hernia with obstruction, without gangrene**
Incarcerated parastomal hernia, without gangrene
Irreducible parastomal hernia, without gangrene
Parastomal hernia causing obstruction, without gangrene
Strangulated parastomal hernia, without gangrene
CC Exclusion see Appendix A PDX collection 0780

MCC **K43.4 Parastomal hernia with gangrene**
Gangrenous parastomal hernia
MCC Exclusion see Appendix A PDX collection 0781

K43.5 Parastomal hernia without obstruction or gangrene
Parastomal hernia NOS

CC **K43.6 Other and unspecified ventral hernia with obstruction, without gangrene**
Epigastric hernia causing obstruction, without gangrene
Hypogastric hernia causing obstruction, without gangrene
Incarcerated epigastric hernia without gangrene
Incarcerated hypogastric hernia without gangrene
Incarcerated midline hernia without gangrene
Incarcerated spigelian hernia without gangrene
Incarcerated subxiphoid hernia without gangrene
Irreducible epigastric hernia without gangrene
Irreducible hypogastric hernia without gangrene
Irreducible midline hernia without gangrene
Irreducible spigelian hernia without gangrene
Irreducible subxiphoid hernia without gangrene
Midline hernia causing obstruction, without gangrene
Spigelian hernia causing obstruction, without gangrene
Strangulated epigastric hernia without gangrene
Strangulated hypogastric hernia without gangrene
Strangulated midline hernia without gangrene
Strangulated spigelian hernia without gangrene
Strangulated subxiphoid hernia without gangrene
Subxiphoid hernia causing obstruction, without gangrene
CC Exclusion see Appendix A PDX collection 0780

MCC **K43.7 Other and unspecified ventral hernia with gangrene**
Any condition listed under K43.6 specified as gangrenous
MCC Exclusion see Appendix A PDX collection 0781

K43.9 Ventral hernia without obstruction or gangrene
Epigastric hernia
Ventral hernia NOS

K44 Diaphragmatic hernia

Includes: hiatus hernia (esophageal) (sliding)
paraesophageal hernia
Excludes1: *congenital diaphragmatic hernia (Q79.0)*
congenital hiatus hernia (Q40.1)

CC **K44.0 Diaphragmatic hernia with obstruction, without gangrene**
Diaphragmatic hernia causing obstruction
Incarcerated diaphragmatic hernia
Irreducible diaphragmatic hernia
Strangulated diaphragmatic hernia
CC Exclusion see Appendix A PDX collection 0782

MCC **K44.1 Diaphragmatic hernia with gangrene**
Gangrenous diaphragmatic hernia
MCC Exclusion see Appendix A PDX collection 0782

K44.9 Diaphragmatic hernia without obstruction or gangrene
Diaphragmatic hernia NOS

K45 Other abdominal hernia

Includes: abdominal hernia, specified site NEC
lumbar hernia
obturator hernia
pudendal hernia
retroperitoneal hernia
sciatic hernia

CC **K45.0 Other specified abdominal hernia with obstruction, without gangrene**
Other specified abdominal hernia causing obstruction
Other specified incarcerated abdominal hernia
Other specified irreducible abdominal hernia
Other specified strangulated abdominal hernia
CC Exclusion see Appendix A PDX collection 0783

MCC **K45.1 Other specified abdominal hernia with gangrene**
Any condition listed under K45 specified as gangrenous
MCC Exclusion see Appendix A PDX collection 0784

K45.8 Other specified abdominal hernia without obstruction or gangrene

K46 Unspecified abdominal hernia

Includes: enterocele
epiplocele
hernia NOS
interstitial hernia
intestinal hernia
intra-abdominal hernia
Excludes1: *vaginal enterocele (N81.5)*

CC **K46.0 Unspecified abdominal hernia with obstruction, without gangrene**
Unspecified abdominal hernia causing obstruction
Unspecified incarcerated abdominal hernia
Unspecified irreducible abdominal hernia
Unspecified strangulated abdominal hernia
CC Exclusion see Appendix A PDX collection 0783

MCC **K46.1 Unspecified abdominal hernia with gangrene**
Any condition listed under K46 specified as gangrenous
MCC Exclusion see Appendix A PDX collection 0784

K46.9 Unspecified abdominal hernia without obstruction or gangrene
Abdominal hernia NOS

Noninfective enteritis and colitis (K50-K52)

Includes: noninfective inflammatory bowel disease
Excludes1: *irritable bowel syndrome (K58.-)*
megacolon (K59.3)

K50 **Crohn's disease [regional enteritis]**
Includes: granulomatous enteritis
Use additional code to identify manifestations, such as:
pyoderma gangrenosum (L88)
Excludes1: *ulcerative colitis (K51.-)*

\+ **K50.0 Crohn's disease of small intestine**
Crohn's disease [regional enteritis] of duodenum
Crohn's disease [regional enteritis] of ileum
Crohn's disease [regional enteritis] of jejunum
Regional ileitis
Terminal ileitis
Excludes1: *Crohn's disease of both small and large intestine (K50.8-)*

CC **K50.00 Crohn's disease of small intestine without complications**
CC Exclusion see Appendix A PDX collection 0785

\+ **K50.01 Crohn's disease of small intestine with complications**

CC **K50.011 Crohn's disease of small intestine with rectal bleeding**
CC Exclusion see Appendix A PDX collection 0785

CC **K50.012 Crohn's disease of small intestine with intestinal obstruction**
CC Exclusion see Appendix A PDX collection 0785

CC **K50.013 Crohn's disease of small intestine with fistula**
CC Exclusion see Appendix A PDX collection 0785

CC **K50.014 Crohn's disease of small intestine with abscess**
CC Exclusion see Appendix A PDX collection 0785
AHA CC: 4Q, 2012, 104

CC **K50.018 Crohn's disease of small intestine with other complication**
CC Exclusion see Appendix A PDX collection 0785

CC **K50.019 Crohn's disease of small intestine with unspecified complications**
CC Exclusion see Appendix A PDX collection 0785

\+ **K50.1 Crohn's disease of large intestine**
Crohn's disease [regional enteritis] of colon
Crohn's disease [regional enteritis] of large bowel
Crohn's disease [regional enteritis] of rectum
Granulomatous colitis
Regional colitis
Excludes1: *Crohn's disease of both small and large intestine (K50.8)*

CC **K50.10 Crohn's disease of large intestine without complications**
CC Exclusion see Appendix A PDX collection 0785

\+ **K50.11 Crohn's disease of large intestine with complications**

CC **K50.111 Crohn's disease of large intestine with rectal bleeding**
CC Exclusion see Appendix A PDX collection 0785

CC **K50.112 Crohn's disease of large intestine with intestinal obstruction**
CC Exclusion see Appendix A PDX collection 0785

CC **K50.113 Crohn's disease of large intestine with fistula**
CC Exclusion see Appendix A PDX collection 0785

CC **K50.114 Crohn's disease of large intestine with abscess**
CC Exclusion see Appendix A PDX collection 0785
AHA CC: 4Q, 2012, 104

CC **K50.118 Crohn's disease of large intestine with other complication**
CC Exclusion see Appendix A PDX collection 0785

CC **K50.119 Crohn's disease of large intestine with unspecified complications**
CC Exclusion see Appendix A PDX collection 0785

\+ **K50.8 Crohn's disease of both small and large intestine**

CC **K50.80 Crohn's disease of both small and large intestine without complications**
CC Exclusion see Appendix A PDX collection 0785

\+ **K50.81 Crohn's disease of both small and large intestine wi complications**

CC **K50.811 Crohn's disease of both small and large intestine with rectal bleeding**
CC Exclusion see Appendix A PDX collection (

CC **K50.812 Crohn's disease of both small and large intestine with intestinal obstruction**
CC Exclusion see Appendix A PDX collection 0

CC **K50.813 Crohn's disease of both small and large intestine with fistula**
CC Exclusion see Appendix A PDX collection 0

CC **K50.814 Crohn's disease of both small and large intestine with abscess**
CC Exclusion see Appendix A PDX collection 0

CC **K50.818 Crohn's disease of both small and large intestine with other complication**
CC Exclusion see Appendix A PDX collection 0

CC **K50.819 Crohn's disease of both small and large intestine with unspecified complications**
CC Exclusion see Appendix A PDX collection 0

\+ **K50.9 Crohn's disease, unspecified**

CC **K50.90 Crohn's disease, unspecified, without complications**
Crohn's disease NOS
Regional enteritis NOS
CC Exclusion see Appendix A PDX collection 0786

\+ **K50.91 Crohn's disease, unspecified, with complications**

CC **K50.911 Crohn's disease, unspecified, with rectal bleeding**
CC Exclusion see Appendix A PDX collection 07

CC **K50.912 Crohn's disease, unspecified, with intestina obstruction**
CC Exclusion see Appendix A PDX collection 07

CC **K50.913 Crohn's disease, unspecified, with fistula**
CC Exclusion see Appendix A PDX collection 07

CC **K50.914 Crohn's disease, unspecified, with abscess**
CC Exclusion see Appendix A PDX collection 07

CC **K50.918 Crohn's disease, unspecified, with other complication**
CC Exclusion see Appendix A PDX collection 07

CC **K50.919 Crohn's disease, unspecified, with unspecified complications**
CC Exclusion see Appendix A PDX collection 07

K51 **Ulcerative colitis**
Use additional code to identify manifestations, such as:
pyoderma gangrenosum (L88)
Excludes1: *Crohn's disease [regional enteritis] (K50.-)*

\+ **K51.0 Ulcerative (chronic) pancolitis**
Backwash ileitis

CC **K51.00 Ulcerative (chronic) pancolitis without complications**
Ulcerative (chronic) pancolitis NOS
CC Exclusion see Appendix A PDX collection 0785

\+ **K51.01 Ulcerative (chronic) pancolitis with complications**

CC **K51.011 Ulcerative (chronic) pancolitis with rectal bleeding**
CC Exclusion see Appendix A PDX collection 07

CC **K51.012 Ulcerative (chronic) pancolitis with intestin obstruction**
CC Exclusion see Appendix A PDX collection 07

CC **K51.013 Ulcerative (chronic) pancolitis with fistula**
CC Exclusion see Appendix A PDX collection 07

CC **K51.014 Ulcerative (chronic) pancolitis with abscess**
CC Exclusion see Appendix A PDX collection 07

CC **K51.018 Ulcerative (chronic) pancolitis with other complication**
CC Exclusion see Appendix A PDX collection 07

CC **K51.019 Ulcerative (chronic) pancolitis with unspecified complications**
CC Exclusion see Appendix A PDX collection 07

\+ **K51.2 Ulcerative (chronic) proctitis**

CC **K51.20 Ulcerative (chronic) proctitis without complications**
Ulcerative (chronic) proctitis NOS
CC Exclusion see Appendix A PDX collection 0785

\+ **K51.21 Ulcerative (chronic) proctitis with complications**

CC **K51.211 Ulcerative (chronic) proctitis with rectal bleeding**
CC Exclusion see Appendix A PDX collection 078

CC **K51.212 Ulcerative (chronic) proctitis with intestinal obstruction**
CC Exclusion see Appendix A PDX collection 078

CC **K51.213 Ulcerative (chronic) proctitis with fistula**
CC Exclusion see Appendix A PDX collection 078

CC **K51.214 Ulcerative (chronic) proctitis with abscess**
CC Exclusion see Appendix A PDX collection 078

CC **K51.218 Ulcerative (chronic) proctitis with other complication**
CC Exclusion see Appendix A PDX collection 0785

CC **K51.219 Ulcerative (chronic) proctitis with unspecified complications**
CC Exclusion see Appendix A PDX collection 0785

+ **K51.3 Ulcerative (chronic) rectosigmoiditis**

CC **K51.30 Ulcerative (chronic) rectosigmoiditis without complications**
Ulcerative (chronic) rectosigmoiditis NOS
CC Exclusion see Appendix A PDX collection 0785

+ **K51.31 Ulcerative (chronic) rectosigmoiditis with complications**

CC **K51.311 Ulcerative (chronic) rectosigmoiditis with rectal bleeding**
CC Exclusion see Appendix A PDX collection 0785

CC **K51.312 Ulcerative (chronic) rectosigmoiditis with intestinal obstruction**
CC Exclusion see Appendix A PDX collection 0785

CC **K51.313 Ulcerative (chronic) rectosigmoiditis with fistula**
CC Exclusion see Appendix A PDX collection 0785

CC **K51.314 Ulcerative (chronic) rectosigmoiditis with abscess**
CC Exclusion see Appendix A PDX collection 0785

CC **K51.318 Ulcerative (chronic) rectosigmoiditis with other complication**
CC Exclusion see Appendix A PDX collection 0785

CC **K51.319 Ulcerative (chronic) rectosigmoiditis with unspecified complications**
CC Exclusion see Appendix A PDX collection 0785

+ **K51.4 Inflammatory polyps of colon**
Excludes1: *adenomatous polyp of colon (D12.6)*
polyposis of colon (D12.6)
polyps of colon NOS (K63.5)

CC **K51.40 Inflammatory polyps of colon without complications**
Inflammatory polyps of colon NOS
CC Exclusion see Appendix A PDX collection 0785

+ **K51.41 Inflammatory polyps of colon with complications**

CC **K51.411 Inflammatory polyps of colon with rectal bleeding**
CC Exclusion see Appendix A PDX collection 0785

CC **K51.412 Inflammatory polyps of colon with intestinal obstruction**
CC Exclusion see Appendix A PDX collection 0785

CC **K51.413 Inflammatory polyps of colon with fistula**
CC Exclusion see Appendix A PDX collection 0785

CC **K51.414 Inflammatory polyps of colon with abscess**
CC Exclusion see Appendix A PDX collection 0785

CC **K51.418 Inflammatory polyps of colon with other complication**
CC Exclusion see Appendix A PDX collection 0785

CC **K51.419 Inflammatory polyps of colon with unspecified complications**
CC Exclusion see Appendix A PDX collection 0785

+ **K51.5 Left sided colitis**
Left hemicolitis

CC **K51.50 Left sided colitis without complications**
Left sided colitis NOS
CC Exclusion see Appendix A PDX collection 0785

+ **K51.51 Left sided colitis with complications**

CC **K51.511 Left sided colitis with rectal bleeding**
CC Exclusion see Appendix A PDX collection 0785

CC **K51.512 Left sided colitis with intestinal obstruction**
CC Exclusion see Appendix A PDX collection 0785

CC **K51.513 Left sided colitis with fistula**
CC Exclusion see Appendix A PDX collection 0785

CC **K51.514 Left sided colitis with abscess**
CC Exclusion see Appendix A PDX collection 0785

CC **K51.518 Left sided colitis with other complication**
CC Exclusion see Appendix A PDX collection 0785

CC **K51.519 Left sided colitis with unspecified complications**
CC Exclusion see Appendix A PDX collection 0785

+ **K51.8 Other ulcerative colitis**

CC **K51.80 Other ulcerative colitis without complications**
CC Exclusion see Appendix A PDX collection 0785

+ **K51.81 Other ulcerative colitis with complications**

CC **K51.811 Other ulcerative colitis with rectal bleeding**
CC Exclusion see Appendix A PDX collection 0785

CC **K51.812 Other ulcerative colitis with intestinal obstruction**
CC Exclusion see Appendix A PDX collection 0785

CC **K51.813 Other ulcerative colitis with fistula**
CC Exclusion see Appendix A PDX collection 0785

CC **K51.814 Other ulcerative colitis with abscess**
CC Exclusion see Appendix A PDX collection 0785

CC **K51.818 Other ulcerative colitis with other complication**
CC Exclusion see Appendix A PDX collection 0785

CC **K51.819 Other ulcerative colitis with unspecified complications**
CC Exclusion see Appendix A PDX collection 0785

+ **K51.9 Ulcerative colitis, unspecified**

CC **K51.90 Ulcerative colitis, unspecified, without complications**
CC Exclusion see Appendix A PDX collection 0787

+ **K51.91 Ulcerative colitis, unspecified, with complications**

CC **K51.911 Ulcerative colitis, unspecified with rectal bleeding**
CC Exclusion see Appendix A PDX collection 0787

CC **K51.912 Ulcerative colitis, unspecified with intestinal obstruction**
CC Exclusion see Appendix A PDX collection 0787

CC **K51.913 Ulcerative colitis, unspecified with fistula**
CC Exclusion see Appendix A PDX collection 0787

CC **K51.914 Ulcerative colitis, unspecified with abscess**
CC Exclusion see Appendix A PDX collection 0787

CC **K51.918 Ulcerative colitis, unspecified with other complication**
CC Exclusion see Appendix A PDX collection 0787

CC **K51.919 Ulcerative colitis, unspecified with unspecified complications**
CC Exclusion see Appendix A PDX collection 0787

K52 Other and unspecified noninfective gastroenteritis and colitis

CC **K52.0 Gastroenteritis and colitis due to radiation**
CC Exclusion see Appendix A PDX collection 0788

CC **K52.1 Toxic gastroenteritis and colitis**
CC Exclusion see Appendix A PDX collection 0789
Drug-induced gastroenteritis and colitis
Code first (T51-T65) to identify toxic agent
Use additional code for adverse effect, if applicable, to identify drug (T36-T50 with fifth or sixth character 5)

K52.2 Allergic and dietetic gastroenteritis and colitis
Food hypersensitivity gastroenteritis or colitis
Use additional code to identify type of food allergy (Z91.01-, Z91.02-)

+ **K52.8 Other specified noninfective gastroenteritis and colitis**

K52.81 Eosinophilic gastritis or gastroenteritis
Eosinophilic enteritis
Excludes1: *eosinophilic esophagitis (K20.0)*

K52.82 Eosinophilic colitis

K52.89 Other specified noninfective gastroenteritis and colitis
Collagenous colitis
Lymphocytic colitis
Microscopic colitis (collagenous or lymphocytic)

K52.9 Noninfective gastroenteritis and colitis, unspecified
Colitis NOS
Enteritis NOS
Gastroenteritis NOS
Ileitis NOS
Jejunitis NOS
Sigmoiditis NOS
Excludes1: *diarrhea NOS (R19.7)*
functional diarrhea (K59.1)
infectious gastroenteritis and colitis NOS (A09)
neonatal diarrhea (noninfective) (P78.3)
psychogenic diarrhea (F45.8)

Other diseases of intestines (K55-K64)

K55 Vascular disorders of intestine
Excludes1: *necrotizing enterocolitis of newborn (P77.-)*

MCC **K55.0 Acute vascular disorders of intestine**
Acute fulminant ischemic colitis
Acute intestinal infarction
Acute small intestine ischemia
Infarction of appendices epiploicae
Mesenteric (artery) (vein) embolism
Mesenteric (artery) (vein) infarction
Mesenteric (artery) (vein) thrombosis
Necrosis of intestine
Subacute ischemic colitis
MCC Exclusion see Appendix A PDX collection 0790

CC **K55.1 Chronic vascular disorders of intestine**
Chronic ischemic colitis
Chronic ischemic enteritis
Chronic ischemic enterocolitis
Ischemic stricture of intestine
Mesenteric atherosclerosis
Mesenteric vascular insufficiency
CC Exclusion see Appendix A PDX collection 0791

\+ **K55.2 Angiodysplasia of colon**
K55.20 Angiodysplasia of colon without hemorrhage
MCC **K55.21 Angiodysplasia of colon with hemorrhage**
MCC Exclusion see Appendix A PDX collection 0770

CC **K55.8 Other vascular disorders of intestine**
CC Exclusion see Appendix A PDX collection 0791

CC **K55.9 Vascular disorder of intestine, unspecified**
Ischemic colitis
Ischemic enteritis
Ischemic enterocolitis
CC Exclusion see Appendix A PDX collection 0791

K56 Paralytic ileus and intestinal obstruction without hernia

Excludes1: *congenital stricture or stenosis of intestine (Q41-Q42)*
cystic fibrosis with meconium ileus (E84.11)
ischemic stricture of intestine (K55.1)
meconium ileus NOS (P76.0)
neonatal intestinal obstructions classifiable to P76.-
obstruction of duodenum (K31.5)
postprocedural intestinal obstruction (K91.3)
stenosis of anus or rectum (K62.4)
intestinal obstruction with hernia (K40-K46)

CC **K56.0 Paralytic ileus**
Paralysis of bowel
Paralysis of colon
Paralysis of intestine
Excludes1: *gallstone ileus (K56.3)*
ileus NOS (K56.7)
obstructive ileus NOS (K56.69)
CC Exclusion see Appendix A PDX collection 0792

CC **K56.1 Intussusception**
Intussusception or invagination of bowel
Intussusception or invagination of colon
Intussusception or invagination of intestine
Intussusception or invagination of rectum
Excludes2: *intussusception of appendix (K38.8)*
CC Exclusion see Appendix A PDX collection 0792

MCC **K56.2 Volvulus**
Strangulation of colon or intestine
Torsion of colon or intestine
Twist of colon or intestine
Excludes2: *volvulus of duodenum (K31.5)*
MCC Exclusion see Appendix A PDX collection 0792

K56.3 Gallstone ileus
Obstruction of intestine by gallstone
CC Exclusion see Appendix A PDX collection 0792

\+ **K56.4 Other impaction of intestine**
K56.41 Fecal impaction
Excludes1: *constipation (K59.0-)*
incomplete defecation (R15.0)
CC **K56.49 Other impaction of intestine**
CC Exclusion see Appendix A PDX collection 0792

CC **K56.5 Intestinal adhesions [bands] with obstruction (postprocedural) (postinfection)**
Abdominal hernia due to adhesions with obstruction
Peritoneal adhesions [bands] with intestinal obstruction (postprocedural) (postinfection)
CC Exclusion see Appendix A PDX collection 0792

\+ **K56.6 Other and unspecified intestinal obstruction**
CC **K56.60 Unspecified intestinal obstruction**
Intestinal obstruction NOS
Excludes1: *intestinal obstruction due to specified condition-code to condition*
CC Exclusion see Appendix A PDX collection 0792
CC **K56.69 Other intestinal obstruction**
Enterostenosis NOS
Obstructive ileus NOS
Occlusion of colon or intestine NOS
Stenosis of colon or intestine NOS
Stricture of colon or intestine NOS
Excludes1: *intestinal obstruction due to specified condition-code to condition*
CC Exclusion see Appendix A PDX collection 0792

CC **K56.7 Ileus, unspecified**
Excludes1: *obstructive ileus (K56.69)*
CC Exclusion see Appendix A PDX collection 0792

K57 Diverticular disease of intestine

Excludes1: *congenital diverticulum of intestine (Q43.8)*
Meckel's diverticulum (Q43.0)
Excludes2: *diverticulum of appendix (K38.2)*

\+ **K57.0 Diverticulitis of small intestine with perforation and abscess**
Diverticulitis of small intestine with peritonitis
Excludes1: *diverticulitis of both small and large intestine w perforation and abscess (K57.4-)*
CC **K57.00 Diverticulitis of small intestine with perforation ar abscess without bleeding**
CC Exclusion see Appendix A PDX collection 0793
MCC **K57.01 Diverticulitis of small intestine with perforation ar abscess with bleeding**
MCC Exclusion see Appendix A PDX collection 0770

\+ **K57.1 Diverticular disease of small intestine without perforation or abscess**
Excludes1: *diverticular disease of both small and large intes without perforation or abscess (K57.5-)*
K57.10 Diverticulosis of small intestine without perforatio abscess without bleeding
Diverticular disease of small intestine NOS
MCC **K57.11 Diverticulosis of small intestine without perforatio abscess with bleeding**
MCC Exclusion see Appendix A PDX collection 0770
CC **K57.12 Diverticulitis of small intestine without perforation abscess without bleeding**
CC Exclusion see Appendix A PDX collection 0793
MCC **K57.13 Diverticulitis of small intestine without perforation abscess with bleeding**
MCC Exclusion see Appendix A PDX collection 0770

\+ **K57.2 Diverticulitis of large intestine with perforation and abscess**
Diverticulitis of colon with peritonitis
Excludes1: *diverticulitis of both small and large intestine wit perforation and abscess (K57.4-)*
CC **K57.20 Diverticulitis of large intestine with perforation an abscess without bleeding**
CC Exclusion see Appendix A PDX collection 0794
MCC **K57.21 Diverticulitis of large intestine with perforation and abscess with bleeding**
MCC Exclusion see Appendix A PDX collection 0770

\+ **K57.3 Diverticular disease of large intestine without perforation or abscess**
Excludes1: *diverticular disease of both small and large intest without perforation or abscess (K57.5-)*
K57.30 Diverticulosis of large intestine without perforation abscess without bleeding
Diverticular disease of colon NOS
MCC **K57.31 Diverticulosis of large intestine without perforation abscess with bleeding**
MCC Exclusion see Appendix A PDX collection 0770
CC **K57.32 Diverticulitis of large intestine without perforation abscess without bleeding**
CC Exclusion see Appendix A PDX collection 0794
MCC **K57.33 Diverticulitis of large intestine without perforation abscess with bleeding**
MCC Exclusion see Appendix A PDX collection 0770

\+ **K57.4 Diverticulitis of both small and large intestine with perforatio and abscess**
Diverticulitis of both small and large intestine with peritonitis
CC **K57.40 Diverticulitis of both small and large intestine with perforation and abscess without bleeding**
CC Exclusion see Appendix A PDX collection 0794
MCC **K57.41 Diverticulitis of both small and large intestine with perforation and abscess with bleeding**
MCC Exclusion see Appendix A PDX collection 0770

\+ **K57.5 Diverticular disease of both small and large intestine without perforation or abscess**
K57.50 Diverticulosis of both small and large intestine witho perforation or abscess without bleeding
Diverticular disease of both small and large intestine NOS
MCC **K57.51 Diverticulosis of both small and large intestine witho perforation or abscess with bleeding**
MCC Exclusion see Appendix A PDX collection 0770
CC **K57.52 Diverticulitis of both small and large intestine witho perforation or abscess without bleeding**
CC Exclusion see Appendix A PDX collection 0794
MCC **K57.53 Diverticulitis of both small and large intestine withou perforation or abscess with bleeding**
MCC Exclusion see Appendix A PDX collection 0770

\+ **K57.8 Diverticulitis of intestine, part unspecified, with perforation and abscess**
Diverticulitis of intestine NOS with peritonitis
CC **K57.80 Diverticulitis of intestine, part unspecified, with perforation and abscess without bleeding**
CC Exclusion see Appendix A PDX collection 0794
MCC **K57.81 Diverticulitis of intestine, part unspecified, with perforation and abscess with bleeding**
MCC Exclusion see Appendix A PDX collection 0770
\+ **K57.9 Diverticular disease of intestine, part unspecified, without perforation or abscess**
K57.90 Diverticulosis of intestine, part unspecified, without perforation or abscess without bleeding
Diverticular disease of intestine NOS
MCC **K57.91 Diverticulosis of intestine, part unspecified, without perforation or abscess with bleeding**
MCC Exclusion see Appendix A PDX collection 0770
CC **K57.92 Diverticulitis of intestine, part unspecified, without perforation or abscess without bleeding**
CC Exclusion see Appendix A PDX collection 0794
MCC **K57.93 Diverticulitis of intestine, part unspecified, without perforation or abscess with bleeding**
MCC Exclusion see Appendix A PDX collection 0770

K58 Irritable bowel syndrome

Includes: irritable colon
spastic colon
K58.0 Irritable bowel syndrome with diarrhea
K58.9 Irritable bowel syndrome without diarrhea
Irritable bowel syndrome NOS

K59 Other functional intestinal disorders

Excludes1: *change in bowel habit NOS (R19.4)*
intestinal malabsorption (K90.-)
psychogenic intestinal disorders (F45.8)
Excludes2: *functional disorders of stomach (K31.-)*
\+ **K59.0 Constipation**
Excludes1: *fecal impaction (K56.41)*
incomplete defecation (R15.0)
K59.00 Constipation, unspecified
K59.01 Slow transit constipation
K59.02 Outlet dysfunction constipation
K59.09 Other constipation
K59.1 Functional diarrhea
Excludes1: *diarrhea NOS (R19.7)*
irritable bowel syndrome with diarrhea (K58.0)
CC **K59.2 Neurogenic bowel, not elsewhere classified**
CC Exclusion see Appendix A PDX collection 0795
CC **K59.3 Megacolon, not elsewhere classified**
Dilatation of colon
Toxic megacolon
Code first (T51-T65) to identify toxic agent
Excludes1: *congenital megacolon (aganglionic) (Q43.1)*
megacolon (due to) (in) Chagas' disease (B57.32)
megacolon (due to) (in) Clostridium difficile (A04.7)
megacolon (due to) (in) Hirschsprung's disease (Q43.1)
CC Exclusion see Appendix A PDX collection 0795
K59.4 Anal spasm
Proctalgia fugax
K59.8 Other specified functional intestinal disorders
Atony of colon
Pseudo-obstruction (acute) (chronic) of intestine
K59.9 Functional intestinal disorder, unspecified

K60 Fissure and fistula of anal and rectal regions

Excludes1: *fissure and fistula of anal and rectal regions with abscess or cellulitis (K61.-)*
Excludes2: *anal sphincter tear (healed) (nontraumatic) (old) (K62.81)*
K60.0 Acute anal fissure
K60.1 Chronic anal fissure
K60.2 Anal fissure, unspecified
K60.3 Anal fistula
K60.4 Rectal fistula
Fistula of rectum to skin
Excludes1: *rectovaginal fistula (N82.3)*
vesicorectal fistual (N32.1)
K60.5 Anorectal fistula

K61 Abscess of anal and rectal regions

Includes: abscess of anal and rectal regions
cellulitis of anal and rectal regions
CC **K61.0 Anal abscess**
Perianal abscess
Excludes1: *intrasphincteric abscess (K61.4)*
CC Exclusion see Appendix A PDX collection 0796
CC **K61.1 Rectal abscess**
Perirectal abscess
Excludes1: *ischiorectal abscess (K61.3)*
CC Exclusion see Appendix A PDX collection 0796
CC **K61.2 Anorectal abscess**
CC Exclusion see Appendix A PDX collection 0796
CC **K61.3 Ischiorectal abscess**
Abscess of ischiorectal fossa
CC Exclusion see Appendix A PDX collection 0796
CC **K61.4 Intrasphincteric abscess**
CC Exclusion see Appendix A PDX collection 0796

K62 Other diseases of anus and rectum

Includes: anal canal
Excludes2: *colostomy and enterostomy malfunction (K94.0-, K94.1-)*
fecal incontinence (R15.-)
hemorrhoids (K64.-)
K62.0 Anal polyp
K62.1 Rectal polyp
Excludes1: *adenomatous polyp (D12.8)*
K62.2 Anal prolapse
Prolapse of anal canal
K62.3 Rectal prolapse
Prolapse of rectal mucosa
K62.4 Stenosis of anus and rectum
Stricture of anus (sphincter)
CC **K62.5 Hemorrhage of anus and rectum**
Excludes1: *gastrointestinal bleeding NOS (K92.2)*
melena (K92.1)
neonatal rectal hemorrhage (P54.2)
CC Exclusion see Appendix A PDX collection 0770
CC **K62.6 Ulcer of anus and rectum**
Solitary ulcer of anus and rectum
Stercoral ulcer of anus and rectum
Excludes1: *fissure and fistula of anus and rectum (K60.-)*
ulcerative colitis (K51.-)
CC Exclusion see Appendix A PDX collection 0797
K62.7 Radiation proctitis
Use additional code to identify the type of radiation (W90.-)
\+ **K62.8 Other specified diseases of anus and rectum**
Excludes2: *ulcerative proctitis (K51.2)*
K62.81 Anal sphincter tear (healed) (nontraumatic) (old)
Tear of anus, nontraumatic
Use additional code for any associated fecal incontinence (R15.-)
Excludes2: *anal fissure (K60.-)*
anal sphincter tear (healed) (old) complicating delivery (O34.7-)
traumatic tear of anal sphincter (S31.831)
K62.82 Dysplasia of anus
Anal intraepithelial neoplasia I and II (AIN I and II) (histologically confirmed)
Dysplasia of anus NOS
Mild and moderate dysplasia of anus (histologically confirmed)
Excludes1: *abnormal results from anal cytologic examination without histologic confirmation (R85.61-)*
anal intraepithelial neoplasia III (D01.3)
carcinoma in situ of anus (D01.3)
HGSIL of anus (R85.613)
severe dysplasia of anus (D01.3)
K62.89 Other specified diseases of anus and rectum
Proctitis NOS
Use additional code for any associated fecal incontinence (R15.-)
K62.9 Disease of anus and rectum, unspecified

K63 Other diseases of intestine

CC **K63.0 Abscess of intestine**
Excludes1: *abscess of intestine with Crohn's disease (K50.014, K50.114, K50.814, K50.914,)*
abscess of intestine with diverticular disease (K57.0, K57.2, K57.4, K57.8)
abscess of intestine with ulcerative colitis (K51.014, K51.214, K51.314, K51.414, K51.514, K51.814, K51.914)
Excludes2: *abscess of anal and rectal regions (K61.-)*
abscess of appendix (K35.3)
CC Exclusion see Appendix A PDX collection 0798

MCC **K63.1 Perforation of intestine (nontraumatic)**
Perforation (nontraumatic) of rectum
Excludes1: *perforation (nontraumatic) of duodenum (K26.-)*
perforation (nontraumatic) of intestine with diverticular disease (K57.0, K57.2, K57.4, K57.8)
Excludes2: *perforation (nontraumatic) of appendix (K35.2, K35.3)*
MCC Exclusion see Appendix A PDX collection 0799

CC **K63.2 Fistula of intestine**
Excludes1: *fistula of duodenum (K31.6)*
fistula of intestine with Crohn's disease (K50.013, K50.113, K50.813, K50.913,)
fistula of intestine with ulcerative colitis (K51.013, K51.213, K51.313, K51.413, K51.513, K51.813, K51.913)
Excludes2: *fistula of anal and rectal regions (K60.-)*
fistula of appendix (K38.3)
intestinal-genital fistula, female (N82.2-N82.4)
vesicointestinal fistula (N32.1)
CC Exclusion see Appendix A PDX collection 0800

CC **K63.3 Ulcer of intestine**
Primary ulcer of small intestine
Excludes1: *duodenal ulcer (K26.-)*
gastrointestinal ulcer (K28.-)
gastrojejunal ulcer (K28.-)
jejunal ulcer (K28.-)
peptic ulcer, site unspecified (K27.-)
ulcer of intestine with perforation (K63.1)
ulcer of anus or rectum (K62.6)
ulcerative colitis (K51.-)
CC Exclusion see Appendix A PDX collection 0801

CC **K63.4 Enteroptosis**
CC Exclusion see Appendix A PDX collection 0803

K63.5 Polyp of colon
Excludes1: *adenomatous polyp of colon (D12.6)*
inflammatory polyp of colon (K51.4-)
polyposis of colon (D12.6)

\+ **K63.8 Other specified diseases of intestine**

MCC **K63.81 Dieulafoy lesion of intestine**
Excludes2: *Dieulafoy lesion of stomach and duodenum (K31.82)*
MCC Exclusion see Appendix A PDX collection 0802

K63.89 Other specified diseases of intestine

K63.9 Disease of intestine, unspecified

K64 Hemorrhoids and perianal venous thrombosis

Includes: piles
Excludes1: *hemorrhoids complicating childbirth and the puerperium (O87.2)*
hemorrhoids complicating pregnancy (O22.4)

K64.0 First degree hemorrhoids
Grade/stage I hemorrhoids
Hemorrhoids (bleeding) without prolapse outside of anal canal

K64.1 Second degree hemorrhoids
Grade/stage II hemorrhoids
Hemorrhoids (bleeding) that prolapse with straining, but retract spontaneously

K64.2 Third degree hemorrhoids
Grade/stage III hemorrhoids
Hemorrhoids (bleeding) that prolapse with straining and require manual replacement back inside anal canal

K64.3 Fourth degree hemorrhoids
Grade/stage IV hemorrhoids
Hemorrhoids (bleeding) with prolapsed tissue that cannot be manually replaced

K64.4 Residual hemorrhoidal skin tags
External hemorrhoids, NOS
Skin tags of anus

K64.5 Perianal venous thrombosis
External hemorrhoids with thrombosis
Perianal hematoma
Thrombosed hemorrhoids NOS

K64.8 Other hemorrhoids
Internal hemorrhoids, without mention of degree
Prolapsed hemorrhoids, degree not specified

K64.9 Unspecified hemorrhoids
Hemorrhoids (bleeding) NOS
Hemorrhoids (bleeding) without mention of degree

Diseases of peritoneum and retroperitoneum (K65-K68)

K65 Peritonitis

Use additional code (B95-B97), to identify infectious agent
Excludes1: *acute appendicitis with generalized peritonitis (K35.2)*
aseptic peritonitis (T81.6)
benign paroxysmal peritonitis (E85.0)
chemical peritonitis (T81.6)
diverticulitis of both small and large intestine with perito[illegible] (K57.4-)
diverticulitis of colon with peritonitis (K57.2-)
diverticulitis of intestine, NOS, with peritonitis (K57.8-)
diverticulitis of small intestine with peritonitis (K57.0-)
gonococcal peritonitis (A54.85)
neonatal peritonitis (P78.0-P78.1)
pelvic peritonitis, female (N73.3-N73.5)
periodic familial peritonitis (E85.0)
peritonitis due to talc or other foreign substance (T81.6)
peritonitis in chlamydia (A74.81)
peritonitis in diphtheria (A36.89)
peritonitis in syphilis (late) (A52.74)
peritonitis in tuberculosis (A18.31)
peritonitis with or following abortion or ectopic or molar pregnancy (O00-O07, O08.0)
peritonitis with or following appendicitis (K35.-)
peritonitis with or following diverticular disease of intestine (K57.-)
puerperal peritonitis (O85)
retroperitoneal infections (K68.-)

MCC **K65.0 Generalized (acute) peritonitis**
Pelvic peritonitis (acute), male
Subphrenic peritonitis (acute)
Suppurative peritonitis (acute)
MCC Exclusion see Appendix A PDX collection 0803

MCC **K65.1 Peritoneal abscess**
Abdominopelvic abscess
Abscess (of) omentum
Abscess (of) peritoneum
Mesenteric abscess
Retrocecal abscess
Subdiaphragmatic abscess
Subhepatic abscess
Subphrenic abscess
MCC Exclusion see Appendix A PDX collection 0803

MCC **K65.2 Spontaneous bacterial peritonitis**
Excludes1: *bacterial peritonitis NOS (K65.9)*
MCC Exclusion see Appendix A PDX collection 0803

MCC **K65.3 Choleperitonitis**
Peritonitis due to bile
MCC Exclusion see Appendix A PDX collection 0803

CC **K65.4 Sclerosing mesenteritis**
Fat necrosis of peritoneum
(Idiopathic) sclerosing mesenteric fibrosis
Mesenteric lipodystrophy
Mesenteric panniculitis
Retractile mesenteritis
CC Exclusion see Appendix A PDX collection 0803

MCC **K65.8 Other peritonitis**
Chronic proliferative peritonitis
Peritonitis due to urine
MCC Exclusion see Appendix A PDX collection 0803

MCC **K65.9 Peritonitis, unspecified**
Bacterial peritonitis NOS
MCC Exclusion see Appendix A PDX collection 0803
AHA CC: 2Q, 2013, 31

K66 Other disorders of peritoneum

Excludes2: *ascites (R18.-)*
peritoneal effusion (chronic) (R18.8)

K66.0 Peritoneal adhesions (postprocedural) (postinfection)
Adhesions (of) abdominal (wall)
Adhesions (of) diaphragm
Adhesions (of) intestine
Adhesions (of) male pelvis
Adhesions (of) omentum
Adhesions (of) stomach
Adhesive bands
Mesenteric adhesions
Excludes1: *female pelvic adhesions [bands] (N73.6)*
peritoneal adhesions with intestinal obstruction (K56.5)

MCC **K66.1 Hemoperitoneum**
Excludes1: *traumatic hemoperitoneum (S36.8-)*
MCC Exclusion see Appendix A PDX collection 0804

K66.8 Other specified disorders of peritoneum

K66.9 Disorder of peritoneum, unspecified

K67 Disorders of peritoneum in infectious diseases classified elsewhere

Code first underlying disease, such as :
congenital syphilis (A50.0)
helminthiasis (B65.0-B83.9)

Excludes1: *peritonitis in chlamydia (A74.81)*
peritonitis in diphtheria (A36.89)
peritonitis in gonococcal (A54.85)
peritonitis in syphilis (late) (A52.74)
peritonitis in tuberculosis (A18.31)

MCC Exclusion see Appendix A PDX collection 0803
Valid 3-character code, no further characters required

K68 Disorders of retroperitoneum

\+ **K68.1 Retroperitoneal abscess**

CC **K68.11 Postprocedural retroperitoneal abscess**
CC Exclusion see Appendix A PDX collection 0805
HAC see Appendix B for HAC conditional logic

MCC **K68.12 Psoas muscle abscess**
MCC Exclusion see Appendix A PDX collection 0806

MCC **K68.19 Other retroperitoneal abscess**
MCC Exclusion see Appendix A PDX collection 0803

MCC **K68.9 Other disorders of retroperitoneum**
MCC Exclusion see Appendix A PDX collection 0803

Diseases of liver (K70-K77)

Excludes1: *jaundice NOS (R17)*

Excludes2: *hemochromatosis (E83.11-)*
Reye's syndrome (G93.7)
viral hepatitis (B15-B19)
Wilson's disease (E83.0)

K70 Alcoholic liver disease

Use additional code to identify:
alcohol abuse and dependence (F10.-)

• **K70.0 Alcoholic fatty liver**

\+ **K70.1 Alcoholic hepatitis**

• **K70.10 Alcoholic hepatitis without ascites**

• **K70.11 Alcoholic hepatitis with ascites**

• **K70.2 Alcoholic fibrosis and sclerosis of liver**

\+ **K70.3 Alcoholic cirrhosis of liver**
Alcoholic cirrhosis NOS

• **K70.30 Alcoholic cirrhosis of liver without ascites**

• **K70.31 Alcoholic cirrhosis of liver with ascites**

\+ **K70.4 Alcoholic hepatic failure**
Acute alcoholic hepatic failure
Alcoholic hepatic failure NOS
Chronic alcoholic hepatic failure
Subacute alcoholic hepatic failure

• **K70.40 Alcoholic hepatic failure without coma**

• MCC **K70.41 Alcoholic hepatic failure with coma**
MCC Exclusion see Appendix A PDX collection 0807

• **K70.9 Alcoholic liver disease, unspecified**

K71 Toxic liver disease

Includes: drug-induced idiosyncratic (unpredictable) liver disease
drug-induced toxic (predictable) liver disease

Code first poisoning due to drug or toxin, if applicable (T36-T65 with fifth or sixth character 1-4 or 6)

Use additional code for adverse effect, if applicable, to identify drug (T36-T50 with fifth or sixth character 5)

Excludes2: *alcoholic liver disease (K70.-)*
Budd-Chiari syndrome (I82.0)

K71.0 Toxic liver disease with cholestasis
Cholestasis with hepatocyte injury
'Pure' cholestasis

\+ **K71.1 Toxic liver disease with hepatic necrosis**
Hepatic failure (acute) (chronic) due to drugs

K71.10 Toxic liver disease with hepatic necrosis, without coma

MCC **K71.11 Toxic liver disease with hepatic necrosis, with coma**
MCC Exclusion see Appendix A PDX collection 0807

K71.2 Toxic liver disease with acute hepatitis

K71.3 Toxic liver disease with chronic persistent hepatitis

K71.4 Toxic liver disease with chronic lobular hepatitis

Hepatobiliary System and Pancreas

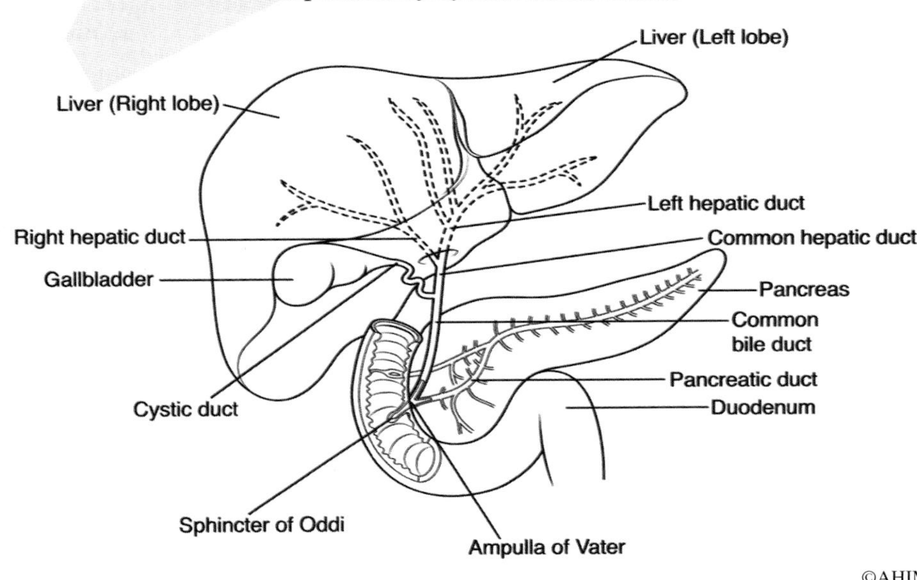

+ **K71.5 Toxic liver disease with chronic active hepatitis**
Toxic liver disease with lupoid hepatitis
K71.50 Toxic liver disease with chronic active hepatitis without ascites
K71.51 Toxic liver disease with chronic active hepatitis with ascites
K71.6 Toxic liver disease with hepatitis, not elsewhere classified
K71.7 Toxic liver disease with fibrosis and cirrhosis of liver
K71.8 Toxic liver disease with other disorders of liver
Toxic liver disease with focal nodular hyperplasia
Toxic liver disease with hepatic granulomas
Toxic liver disease with peliosis hepatis
Toxic liver disease with veno-occlusive disease of liver
K71.9 Toxic liver disease, unspecified

K72 Hepatic failure, not elsewhere classified

Includes: acute hepatitis NEC, with hepatic failure
fulminant hepatitis NEC, with hepatic failure
hepatic encephalopathy NOS
liver (cell) necrosis with hepatic failure
malignant hepatitis NEC, with hepatic failure
yellow liver atrophy or dystrophy
Excludes1: *alcoholic hepatic failure (K70.4)*
hepatic failure with toxic liver disease (K71.1-)
icterus of newborn (P55-P59)
postprocedural hepatic failure (K91.82)
viral hepatitis with hepatic coma (B15-B19)
Excludes2: *hepatic failure complicating abortion or ectopic or molar pregnancy (O00-O07, O08.8)*
hepatic failure complicating pregnancy, childbirth and the puerperium (O26.6-)
+ **K72.0 Acute and subacute hepatic failure**
AHA CC: 2Q, 2014, 13
MCC **K72.00 Acute and subacute hepatic failure without coma**
MCC Exclusion see Appendix A PDX collection 0808
MCC **K72.01 Acute and subacute hepatic failure with coma**
MCC Exclusion see Appendix A PDX collection 0808
+ **K72.1 Chronic hepatic failure**
K72.10 Chronic hepatic failure without coma
MCC **K72.11 Chronic hepatic failure with coma**
MCC Exclusion see Appendix A PDX collection 0807
+ **K72.9 Hepatic failure, unspecified**
K72.90 Hepatic failure, unspecified without coma
K72.91 Hepatic failure, unspecified with coma
Hepatic coma NOS
MCC Exclusion see Appendix A PDX collection 0807

K73 Chronic hepatitis, not elsewhere classified

Excludes1: *alcoholic hepatitis (chronic) (K70.1-)*
drug-induced hepatitis (chronic) (K71.-)
granulomatous hepatitis (chronic) NEC (K75.3)
reactive, nonspecific hepatitis (chronic) (K75.2)
viral hepatitis (chronic) (B15-B19)
K73.0 Chronic persistent hepatitis, not elsewhere classified
K73.1 Chronic lobular hepatitis, not elsewhere classified
K73.2 Chronic active hepatitis, not elsewhere classified
K73.8 Other chronic hepatitis, not elsewhere classified
K73.9 Chronic hepatitis, unspecified

K74 Fibrosis and cirrhosis of liver

Code also, if applicable, viral hepatitis (acute) (chronic) (B15-B19)
Excludes1: *alcoholic cirrhosis (of liver) (K70.3)*
alcoholic fibrosis of liver (K70.2)
cardiac sclerosis of liver (K76.1)
cirrhosis (of liver) with toxic liver disease (K71.7)
congenital cirrhosis (of liver) (P78.81)
pigmentary cirrhosis (of liver) (E83.110)
K74.0 Hepatic fibrosis
K74.1 Hepatic sclerosis
K74.2 Hepatic fibrosis with hepatic sclerosis
K74.3 Primary biliary cirrhosis
Chronic nonsuppurative destructive cholangitis
K74.4 Secondary biliary cirrhosis
K74.5 Biliary cirrhosis, unspecified
+ **K74.6 Other and unspecified cirrhosis of liver**
K74.60 Unspecified cirrhosis of liver
Cirrhosis (of liver) NOS
K74.69 Other cirrhosis of liver
Cryptogenic cirrhosis (of liver)
Macronodular cirrhosis (of liver)
Micronodular cirrhosis (of liver)
Mixed type cirrhosis (of liver)
Portal cirrhosis (of liver)
Postnecrotic cirrhosis (of liver)

K75 Other inflammatory liver diseases

Excludes2: *toxic liver disease (K71.-)*
MCC **K75.0 Abscess of liver**
Cholangitic hepatic abscess
Hematogenic hepatic abscess
Hepatic abscess NOS
Lymphogenic hepatic abscess
Pylephlebitic hepatic abscess
Excludes1: *amebic liver abscess (A06.4)*
cholangitis without liver abscess (K83.0)
pylephlebitis without liver abscess (K75.1)
MCC Exclusion see Appendix A PDX collection 0809
MCC **K75.1 Phlebitis of portal vein**
Pylephlebitis
Excludes1: *pylephlebitic liver abscess (K75.0)*
MCC Exclusion see Appendix A PDX collection 0809
K75.2 Nonspecific reactive hepatitis
Excludes1: *acute or subacute hepatitis (K72.0-)*
chronic hepatitis NEC (K73.-)
viral hepatitis (B15-B19)
K75.3 Granulomatous hepatitis, not elsewhere classified
Excludes1: *acute or subacute hepatitis (K72.0-)*
chronic hepatitis NEC (K73.-)
viral hepatitis (B15-B19)
K75.4 Autoimmune hepatitis
Lupoid hepatitis NEC
+ **K75.8 Other specified inflammatory liver diseases**
K75.81 Nonalcoholic steatohepatitis (NASH)
K75.89 Other specified inflammatory liver diseases
K75.9 Inflammatory liver disease, unspecified
Hepatitis NOS
Excludes1: *acute or subacute hepatitis (K72.0-)*
chronic hepatitis NEC (K73.-)
viral hepatitis (B15-B19)

K76 Other diseases of liver

Excludes2: *alcoholic liver disease (K70.-)*
amyloid degeneration of liver (E85.-)
cystic disease of liver (congenital) (Q44.6)
hepatic vein thrombosis (I82.0)
hepatomegaly NOS (R16.0)
pigmentary cirrhosis (of liver) (E83.110)
portal vein thrombosis (I81)
toxic liver disease (K71.-)
K76.0 Fatty (change of) liver, not elsewhere classified
Nonalcoholic fatty liver disease (NAFLD)
Excludes1: *nonalcoholic steatohepatitis (NASH) (K75.81)*
K76.1 Chronic passive congestion of liver
Cardiac cirrhosis
Cardiac sclerosis
MCC **K76.2 Central hemorrhagic necrosis of liver**
Excludes1: *liver necrosis with hepatic failure (K72.-)*
MCC Exclusion see Appendix A PDX collection 0808
MCC **K76.3 Infarction of liver**
MCC Exclusion see Appendix A PDX collection 0808
K76.4 Peliosis hepatis
Hepatic angiomatosis
K76.5 Hepatic veno-occlusive disease
Excludes1: *Budd-Chiari syndrome (I82.0)*
CC **K76.6 Portal hypertension**
Use additional code for any associated complications, such as:
portal hypertensive gastropathy (K31.89)
CC Exclusion see Appendix A PDX collection 0810
MCC **K76.7 Hepatorenal syndrome**
Excludes1: *hepatorenal syndrome following labor and delivery (O90.4)*
postprocedural hepatorenal syndrome (K91.82)
MCC Exclusion see Appendix A PDX collection 0811
+ **K76.8 Other specified diseases of liver**
K76.81 Hepatopulmonary syndrome
Code first underlying liver disease, such as:
alcoholic cirrhosis of liver (K70.3-)
cirrhosis of liver without mention of alcohol (K74.6
K76.89 Other specified diseases of liver
Cyst (simple) of liver
Focal nodular hyperplasia of liver
Hepatoptosis
K76.9 Liver disease, unspecified

K77 Liver disorders in diseases classified elsewhere
Code first underlying disease, such as:
amyloidosis (E85.-)
congenital syphilis (A50.0, A50.5)
congenital toxoplasmosis (P37.1)
schistosomiasis (B65.0-B65.9)
Excludes1: *alcoholic hepatitis (K70.1-)*
alcoholic liver disease (K70.-)
cytomegaloviral hepatitis (B25.1)
herpesviral [herpes simplex] hepatitis (B00.81)
infectious mononucleosis with liver disease (B27.0-B27.9 with .9)
mumps hepatitis (B26.81)
sarcoidosis with liver disease (D86.89)
secondary syphilis with liver disease (A51.45)
syphilis (late) with liver disease (A52.74)
toxoplasmosis (acquired) hepatitis (B58.1)
tuberculosis with liver disease (A18.83)
No CC Exclusions
Valid 3-character code, no further characters required

orders of gallbladder, biliary tract and pancreas (K80-K87)

K80 Cholelithiasis
Excludes1: *retained cholelithiasis following cholecystectomy (K91.86)*

\+ **K80.0 Calculus of gallbladder with acute cholecystitis**
Any condition listed in K80.2 with acute cholecystitis
CC **K80.00 Calculus of gallbladder with acute cholecystitis without obstruction**
CC Exclusion see Appendix A PDX collection 0812
CC **K80.01 Calculus of gallbladder with acute cholecystitis with obstruction**
CC Exclusion see Appendix A PDX collection 0813

\+ **K80.1 Calculus of gallbladder with other cholecystitis**
CC **K80.10 Calculus of gallbladder with chronic cholecystitis without obstruction**
Cholelithiasis with cholecystitis NOS
CC Exclusion see Appendix A PDX collection 0813
CC **K80.11 Calculus of gallbladder with chronic cholecystitis with obstruction**
CC Exclusion see Appendix A PDX collection 0813
CC **K80.12 Calculus of gallbladder with acute and chronic cholecystitis without obstruction**
CC Exclusion see Appendix A PDX collection 0812
CC **K80.13 Calculus of gallbladder with acute and chronic cholecystitis with obstruction**
CC Exclusion see Appendix A PDX collection 0813
CC **K80.18 Calculus of gallbladder with other cholecystitis without obstruction**
CC Exclusion see Appendix A PDX collection 0813
CC **K80.19 Calculus of gallbladder with other cholecystitis with obstruction**
CC Exclusion see Appendix A PDX collection 0813

\+ **K80.2 Calculus of gallbladder without cholecystitis**
Cholecystolithiasis without cholecystitis
Cholelithiasis (without cholecystitis)
Colic (recurrent) of gallbladder (without cholecystitis)
Gallstone (impacted) of cystic duct (without cholecystitis)
Gallstone (impacted) of gallbladder (without cholecystitis)
K80.20 Calculus of gallbladder without cholecystitis without obstruction
CC **K80.21 Calculus of gallbladder without cholecystitis with obstruction**
CC Exclusion see Appendix A PDX collection 0813

\+ **K80.3 Calculus of bile duct with cholangitis**
Any condition listed in K80.5 with cholangitis
CC **K80.30 Calculus of bile duct with cholangitis, unspecified, without obstruction**
CC Exclusion see Appendix A PDX collection 0814
CC **K80.31 Calculus of bile duct with cholangitis, unspecified, with obstruction**
CC Exclusion see Appendix A PDX collection 0815
CC **K80.32 Calculus of bile duct with acute cholangitis without obstruction**
CC Exclusion see Appendix A PDX collection 0814
CC **K80.33 Calculus of bile duct with acute cholangitis with obstruction**
CC Exclusion see Appendix A PDX collection 0815
CC **K80.34 Calculus of bile duct with chronic cholangitis without obstruction**
CC Exclusion see Appendix A PDX collection 0814
CC **K80.35 Calculus of bile duct with chronic cholangitis with obstruction**
CC Exclusion see Appendix A PDX collection 0815
CC **K80.36 Calculus of bile duct with acute and chronic cholangitis without obstruction**
CC Exclusion see Appendix A PDX collection 0814
CC **K80.37 Calculus of bile duct with acute and chronic cholangitis with obstruction**
CC Exclusion see Appendix A PDX collection 0815

\+ **K80.4 Calculus of bile duct with cholecystitis**
Any condition listed in K80.5 with cholecystitis (with cholangitis)
CC **K80.40 Calculus of bile duct with cholecystitis, unspecified, without obstruction**
CC Exclusion see Appendix A PDX collection 0815
CC **K80.41 Calculus of bile duct with cholecystitis, unspecified, with obstruction**
CC Exclusion see Appendix A PDX collection 0815
CC **K80.42 Calculus of bile duct with acute cholecystitis without obstruction**
CC Exclusion see Appendix A PDX collection 0815
CC **K80.43 Calculus of bile duct with acute cholecystitis with obstruction**
CC Exclusion see Appendix A PDX collection 0815
CC **K80.44 Calculus of bile duct with chronic cholecystitis without obstruction**
CC Exclusion see Appendix A PDX collection 0815
CC **K80.45 Calculus of bile duct with chronic cholecystitis with obstruction**
CC Exclusion see Appendix A PDX collection 0815
CC **K80.46 Calculus of bile duct with acute and chronic cholecystitis without obstruction**
CC Exclusion see Appendix A PDX collection 0815
CC **K80.47 Calculus of bile duct with acute and chronic cholecystitis with obstruction**
CC Exclusion see Appendix A PDX collection 0815

\+ **K80.5 Calculus of bile duct without cholangitis or cholecystitis**
Choledocholithiasis (without cholangitis or cholecystitis)
Gallstone (impacted) of bile duct NOS (without cholangitis or cholecystitis)
Gallstone (impacted) of common duct (without cholangitis or cholecystitis)
Gallstone (impacted) of hepatic duct (without cholangitis or cholecystitis)
Hepatic cholelithiasis (without cholangitis or cholecystitis)
Hepatic colic (recurrent) (without cholangitis or cholecystitis)
K80.50 Calculus of bile duct without cholangitis or cholecystitis without obstruction
CC **K80.51 Calculus of bile duct without cholangitis or cholecystitis with obstruction**
CC Exclusion see Appendix A PDX collection 0815

\+ **K80.6 Calculus of gallbladder and bile duct with cholecystitis**
CC **K80.60 Calculus of gallbladder and bile duct with cholecystitis, unspecified, without obstruction**
CC Exclusion see Appendix A PDX collection 0815
CC **K80.61 Calculus of gallbladder and bile duct with cholecystitis, unspecified, with obstruction**
CC Exclusion see Appendix A PDX collection 0815
CC **K80.62 Calculus of gallbladder and bile duct with acute cholecystitis without obstruction**
CC Exclusion see Appendix A PDX collection 0816
CC **K80.63 Calculus of gallbladder and bile duct with acute cholecystitis with obstruction**
CC Exclusion see Appendix A PDX collection 0816
CC **K80.64 Calculus of gallbladder and bile duct with chronic cholecystitis without obstruction**
CC Exclusion see Appendix A PDX collection 0815
CC **K80.65 Calculus of gallbladder and bile duct with chronic cholecystitis with obstruction**
CC Exclusion see Appendix A PDX collection 0815
CC **K80.66 Calculus of gallbladder and bile duct with acute and chronic cholecystitis without obstruction**
CC Exclusion see Appendix A PDX collection 0817
MCC **K80.67 Calculus of gallbladder and bile duct with acute and chronic cholecystitis with obstruction**
MCC Exclusion see Appendix A PDX collection 0817

\+ **K80.7 Calculus of gallbladder and bile duct without cholecystitis**
K80.70 Calculus of gallbladder and bile duct without cholecystitis without obstruction
CC **K80.71 Calculus of gallbladder and bile duct without cholecystitis with obstruction**
CC Exclusion see Appendix A PDX collection 0815

\+ **K80.8 Other cholelithiasis**
K80.80 Other cholelithiasis without obstruction
CC **K80.81 Other cholelithiasis with obstruction**
CC Exclusion see Appendix A PDX collection 0815

K81 Cholecystitis

Excludes1: *cholecystitis with cholelithiasis (K80.-)*
K81.0 Acute cholecystitis
Abscess of gallbladder
Angiocholecystitis
Emphysematous (acute) cholecystitis
Empyema of gallbladder
Gangrene of gallbladder
Gangrenous cholecystitis
Suppurative cholecystitis
K81.1 Chronic cholecystitis
CC **K81.2 Acute cholecystitis with chronic cholecystitis**
CC Exclusion see Appendix A PDX collection 0819
K81.9 Cholecystitis, unspecified

K82 Other diseases of gallbladder

Excludes1: *nonvisualization of gallbladder (R93.2)*
postcholecystectomy syndrome (K91.5)
CC **K82.0 Obstruction of gallbladder**
Occlusion of cystic duct or gallbladder without cholelithiasis
Stenosis of cystic duct or gallbladder without cholelithiasis
Stricture of cystic duct or gallbladder without cholelithiasis
Excludes1: *obstruction of gallbladder with cholelithiasis (K80.-)*
CC Exclusion see Appendix A PDX collection 0820
CC **K82.1 Hydrops of gallbladder**
Mucocele of gallbladder
CC Exclusion see Appendix A PDX collection 0820
MCC **K82.2 Perforation of gallbladder**
Rupture of cystic duct or gallbladder
MCC Exclusion see Appendix A PDX collection 0820
CC **K82.3 Fistula of gallbladder**
Cholecystocolic fistula
Cholecystoduodenal fistula
CC Exclusion see Appendix A PDX collection 0820
K82.4 Cholesterolosis of gallbladder
Strawberry gallbladder
Excludes1: *cholesterolosis of gallbladder with cholecystitis (K81.-)*
cholesterolosis of gallbladder with cholelithiasis (K80.-)
K82.8 Other specified diseases of gallbladder
Adhesions of cystic duct or gallbladder
Atrophy of cystic duct or gallbladder
Cyst of cystic duct or gallbladder
Dyskinesia of cystic duct or gallbladder
Hypertrophy of cystic duct or gallbladder
Nonfunctioning of cystic duct or gallbladder
Ulcer of cystic duct or gallbladder
K82.9 Disease of gallbladder, unspecified

K83 Other diseases of biliary tract

Excludes1: *postcholecystectomy syndrome (K91.5)*
Excludes2: *conditions involving the gallbladder (K81-K82)*
conditions involving the cystic duct (K81-K82)
CC **K83.0 Cholangitis**
Ascending cholangitis
Cholangitis NOS
Primary cholangitis
Recurrent cholangitis
Sclerosing cholangitis
Secondary cholangitis
Stenosing cholangitis
Suppurative cholangitis
Excludes1: *cholangitic liver abscess (K75.0)*
cholangitis with choledocholithiasis (K80.3-, K80.4-)
chronic nonsuppurative destructive cholangitis (K74.3)
CC Exclusion see Appendix A PDX collection 0814
MCC **K83.1 Obstruction of bile duct**
Occlusion of bile duct without cholelithiasis
Stenosis of bile duct without cholelithiasis
Stricture of bile duct without cholelithiasis
Excludes1: *congenital obstruction of bile duct (Q44.3)*
obstruction of bile duct with cholelithiasis (K80.-)
MCC Exclusion see Appendix A PDX collection 0821
MCC **K83.2 Perforation of bile duct**
Rupture of bile duct
MCC Exclusion see Appendix A PDX collection 0822
CC **K83.3 Fistula of bile duct**
Choledochoduodenal fistula
CC Exclusion see Appendix A PDX collection 0822
K83.4 Spasm of sphincter of Oddi
K83.5 Biliary cyst
K83.8 Other specified diseases of biliary tract
Adhesions of biliary tract
Atrophy of biliary tract
Hypertrophy of biliary tract
Ulcer of biliary tract
K83.9 Disease of biliary tract, unspecified

K85 Acute pancreatitis

Includes: abscess of pancreas
acute necrosis of pancreas
acute (recurrent) pancreatitis
gangrene of (gangrenous) pancreas
hemorrhagic pancreatitis
infective necrosis of pancreas
subacute pancreatitis
suppurative pancreatitis
MCC **K85.0 Idiopathic acute pancreatitis**
MCC Exclusion see Appendix A PDX collection 0177
MCC **K85.1 Biliary acute pancreatitis**
Gallstone pancreatitis
MCC Exclusion see Appendix A PDX collection 0177
MCC **K85.2 Alcohol induced acute pancreatitis**
Excludes2: *alcohol induced chronic pancreatitis (K86.0)*
MCC Exclusion see Appendix A PDX collection 0177
MCC **K85.3 Drug induced acute pancreatitis**
Use additional code for adverse effect, if applicable, to identify drug (T36-T50 with fifth or sixth character 5)

Use additional code to identify drug abuse and dependence (F11.-F17.-)
MCC Exclusion see Appendix A PDX collection 0177
MCC **K85.8 Other acute pancreatitis**
MCC Exclusion see Appendix A PDX collection 0177
MCC **K85.9 Acute pancreatitis, unspecified**
Pancreatitis NOS
MCC Exclusion see Appendix A PDX collection 0177

K86 Other diseases of pancreas

Excludes2: *fibrocystic disease of pancreas (E84.-)*
islet cell tumor (of pancreas) (D13.7)
pancreatic steatorrhea (K90.3)
CC **K86.0 Alcohol-induced chronic pancreatitis**
Use additional code to identify:
alcohol abuse and dependence (F10.-)
Excludes2: *alcohol induced acute pancreatitis (K85.2)*
CC Exclusion see Appendix A PDX collection 0823
CC **K86.1 Other chronic pancreatitis**
Chronic pancreatitis NOS
Infectious chronic pancreatitis
Recurrent chronic pancreatitis
Relapsing chronic pancreatitis
CC Exclusion see Appendix A PDX collection 0823
CC **K86.2 Cyst of pancreas**
CC Exclusion see Appendix A PDX collection 0824
CC **K86.3 Pseudocyst of pancreas**
CC Exclusion see Appendix A PDX collection 0824
K86.8 Other specified diseases of pancreas
Aseptic pancreatic necrosis
Atrophy of pancreas
Calculus of pancreas
Cirrhosis of pancreas
Fibrosis of pancreas
Pancreatic fat necrosis
Pancreatic infantilism
Pancreatic necrosis NOS
K86.9 Disease of pancreas, unspecified

K87 Disorders of gallbladder, biliary tract and pancreas in diseases classified elsewhere

Code first underlying disease
Excludes1: *cytomegaloviral pancreatitis(B25.2)*
mumps pancreatitis (B26.3)
syphilitic gallbladder (A52.74)
syphilitic pancreas (A52.74)
tuberculosis of gallbladder (A18.83)
tuberculosis of pancreas (A18.83)
Valid 3-character code, no further characters required

her diseases of the digestive system (K90-K95)

K90 Intestinal malabsorption

Excludes1: *intestinal malabsorption following gastrointestinal surgery (K91.2)*

K90.0 Celiac disease
Gluten-sensitive enteropathy
Idiopathic steatorrhea
Nontropical sprue
Use additional code for associated disorders including:
dermatitis herpetiformis (L13.0)
gluten ataxia (G32.81)

CC **K90.1 Tropical sprue**
Sprue NOS
Tropical steatorrhea
CC Exclusion see Appendix A PDX collection 0825

CC **K90.2 Blind loop syndrome, not elsewhere classified**
Blind loop syndrome NOS
Excludes1: *congenital blind loop syndrome (Q43.8)*
postsurgical blind loop syndrome (K91.2)
CC Exclusion see Appendix A PDX collection 0825

CC **K90.3 Pancreatic steatorrhea**
CC Exclusion see Appendix A PDX collection 0825

CC **K90.4 Malabsorption due to intolerance, not elsewhere classified**
Malabsorption due to intolerance to carbohydrate
Malabsorption due to intolerance to fat
Malabsorption due to intolerance to protein
Malabsorption due to intolerance to starch
Excludes2: *gluten-sensitive enteropathy (K90.0)*
lactose intolerance (E73.-)
CC Exclusion see Appendix A PDX collection 0825

\+ **K90.8 Other intestinal malabsorption**

CC **K90.81 Whipple's disease**
CC Exclusion see Appendix A PDX collection 0826

CC **K90.89 Other intestinal malabsorption**
CC Exclusion see Appendix A PDX collection 0825

CC **K90.9 Intestinal malabsorption, unspecified**
CC Exclusion see Appendix A PDX collection 0825

K91 Intraoperative and postprocedural complications and disorders of digestive system, not elsewhere classified

Excludes2: *complications of artificial opening of digestive system (K94.-)*
complications of bariatric procedures (K95.-)
gastrojejunal ulcer (K28.-)
postprocedural (radiation) retroperitoneal abscess (K68.11)
radiation colitis (K52.0)
radiation gastroenteritis (K52.0)
radiation proctitis (K62.7)

K91.0 Vomiting following gastrointestinal surgery

K91.1 Postgastric surgery syndromes
Dumping syndrome
Postgastrectomy syndrome
Postvagotomy syndrome

CC **K91.2 Postsurgical malabsorption, not elsewhere classified**
Postsurgical blind loop syndrome
Excludes1: *malabsorption osteomalacia in adults (M83.2)*
malabsorption osteoporosis, postsurgical (M80.8-, M81.8)
CC Exclusion see Appendix A PDX collection 0827

CC **K91.3 Postprocedural intestinal obstruction**
CC Exclusion see Appendix A PDX collection 0828

K91.5 Postcholecystectomy syndrome

\+ **K91.6 Intraoperative hemorrhage and hematoma of a digestive system organ or structure complicating a procedure**
Excludes1: *intraoperative hemorrhage and hematoma of a digestive system organ or structure due to accidental puncture and laceration during a procedure (K91.7-)*

CC **K91.61 Intraoperative hemorrhage and hematoma of a digestive system organ or structure complicating a digestive sytem procedure**
CC Exclusion see Appendix A PDX collection 0829

CC **K91.62 Intraoperative hemorrhage and hematoma of a digestive system organ or structure complicating other procedure**
CC Exclusion see Appendix A PDX collection 0829

\+ **K91.7 Accidental puncture and laceration of a digestive system organ or structure during a procedure**

CC **K91.71 Accidental puncture and laceration of a digestive system organ or structure during a digestive system procedure**
CC Exclusion see Appendix A PDX collection 0509

CC **K91.72 Accidental puncture and laceration of a digestive system organ or structure during other procedure**
CC Exclusion see Appendix A PDX collection 0509

\+ **K91.8 Other intraoperative and postprocedural complications and disorders of digestive system**

CC **K91.81 Other intraoperative complications of digestive system**
CC Exclusion see Appendix A PDX collection 0828

CC **K91.82 Postprocedural hepatic failure**
CC Exclusion see Appendix A PDX collection 0828

CC **K91.83 Postprocedural hepatorenal syndrome**
CC Exclusion see Appendix A PDX collection 0828

\+ **K91.84 Postprocedural hemorrhage and hematoma of a digestive system organ or structure following a procedure**

CC **K91.840 Postprocedural hemorrhage and hematoma of a digestive system organ or structure following a digestive system procedure**
CC Exclusion see Appendix A PDX collection 0829

CC **K91.841 Postprocedural hemorrhage and hematoma of a digestive system organ or structure following other procedure**
CC Exclusion see Appendix A PDX collection 0829

\+ **K91.85 Complications of intestinal pouch**

CC **K91.850 Pouchitis**
Inflammation of internal ileoanal pouch
CC Exclusion see Appendix A PDX collection 0828

CC **K91.858 Other complications of intestinal pouch**
CC Exclusion see Appendix A PDX collection 0828

CC **K91.86 Retained cholelithiasis following cholecystectomy**
CC Exclusion see Appendix A PDX collection 0828

CC **K91.89 Other postprocedural complications and disorders of digestive system**
Use additional code, if applicable, to further specify disorder
Excludes2: *postprocedural retroperitoneal abscess (K68.11)*
CC Exclusion see Appendix A PDX collection 0828

K92 Other diseases of digestive system

Excludes1: *neonatal gastrointestinal hemorrhage (P54.0-P54.3)*

CC **K92.0 Hematemesis**
CC Exclusion see Appendix A PDX collection 0770

CC **K92.1 Melena**
Excludes1: *occult blood in feces (R19.5)*
CC Exclusion see Appendix A PDX collection 0770

CC **K92.2 Gastrointestinal hemorrhage, unspecified**
Gastric hemorrhage NOS
Intestinal hemorrhage NOS
Excludes1: *acute hemorrhagic gastritis (K29.01)*
hemorrhage of anus and rectum (K62.5)
angiodysplasia of stomach with hemorrhage (K31.811)
diverticular disease with hemorrhage (K57.-)
gastritis and duodenitis with hemorrhage (K29.-)
peptic ulcer with hemorrhage (K25-K28)
CC Exclusion see Appendix A PDX collection 0770

\+ **K92.8 Other specified diseases of the digestive system**

CC **K92.81 Gastrointestinal mucositis (ulcerative)**
Code also type of associated therapy, such as:
antineoplastic and immunosuppressive drugs (T45.1X-)
radiological procedure and radiotherapy (Y84.2)
Excludes2: *mucositis (ulcerative) of vagina and vulva (N76.81)*
nasal mucositis (ulcerative) (J34.81)
oral mucositis (ulcerative) (K12.3-)
CC Exclusion see Appendix A PDX collection 0765

K92.89 Other specified diseases of the digestive system

K92.9 Disease of digestive system, unspecified

K94 Complications of artificial openings of the digestive system

\+ **K94.0 Colostomy complications**

K94.00 Colostomy complication, unspecified

CC **K94.01 Colostomy hemorrhage**
CC Exclusion see Appendix A PDX collection 0830

CC **K94.02 Colostomy infection**
Use additional code to specify type of infection, such as:
cellulitis of abdominal wall (L03.311)
sepsis (A40.-, A41.-)
CC Exclusion see Appendix A PDX collection 0830

CC **K94.03 Colostomy malfunction**
Mechanical complication of colostomy
CC Exclusion see Appendix A PDX collection 0831

K94.09 Other complications of colostomy
CC Exclusion see Appendix A PDX collection 0830

\+ **K94.1 Enterostomy complications**

K94.10 Enterostomy complication, unspecified

CC **K94.11 Enterostomy hemorrhage**
CC Exclusion see Appendix A PDX collection 0830

CC **K94.12 Enterostomy infection**
Use additional code to specify type of infection, such as:
cellulitis of abdominal wall (L03.311)
sepsis (A40.-, A41.-)
CC Exclusion see Appendix A PDX collection 0830

CC **K94.13 Enterostomy malfunction**
Mechanical complication of enterostomy
CC Exclusion see Appendix A PDX collection 0831

CC **K94.19 Other complications of enterostomy**
CC Exclusion see Appendix A PDX collection 0830

\+ **K94.2 Gastrostomy complications**

K94.20 Gastrostomy complication, unspecified

K94.21 Gastrostomy hemorrhage

CC **K94.22 Gastrostomy infection**
Use additional code to specify type of infection, such as:
cellulitis of abdominal wall (L03.311)
sepsis (A40.-, A41.-)
CC Exclusion see Appendix A PDX collection 0828

CC **K94.23 Gastrostomy malfunction**
Mechanical complication of gastrostomy
CC Exclusion see Appendix A PDX collection 0828

K94.29 Other complications of gastrostomy

\+ **K94.3 Esophagostomy complications**

CC **K94.30 Esophagostomy complications, unspecified**
CC Exclusion see Appendix A PDX collection 0828

CC **K94.31 Esophagostomy hemorrhage**
CC Exclusion see Appendix A PDX collection 0828

CC **K94.32 Esophagostomy infection**
Use additional code to identify the infection
CC Exclusion see Appendix A PDX collection 0828

CC **K94.33 Esophagostomy malfunction**
Mechanical complication of esophagostomy
CC Exclusion see Appendix A PDX collection 0828

CC **K94.39 Other complications of esophagostomy**
CC Exclusion see Appendix A PDX collection 0828

\+ K95 Complications of bariatric procedures

\+ **K95.0 Complications of gastric band procedure**

CC **K95.01 Infection due to gastric band procedure**
Use additional code to specify type of infection or organism, such as:
bacterial and viral infectious agents (B95.-, B96.
cellulitis of abdominal wall (L03.311)
sepsis (A40.-, A41.-)
CC Exclusion see Appendix A PDX collection 0828
HAC see Appendix B for HAC conditional logic

CC **K95.09 Other complications of gastric band procedure**
Use additional code, if applicable, to further specify complication
CC Exclusion see Appendix A PDX collection 0828

\+ **K95.8 Complications of other bariatric procedure**
Excludes1: *complications of gastric band surgery (K95.0-)*

CC **K95.81 Infection due to other bariatric procedure**
Use additional code to specify type of infection or organism, such as:
bacterial and viral infectious agents (B95.-, B96.-)
cellulitis of abdominal wall (L03.311)
sepsis (A40.-, A41.-)
CC Exclusion see Appendix A PDX collection 0828
HAC see Appendix B for HAC conditional logic

CC **K95.89 Other complications of other bariatric procedure**
Use additional code, if applicable, to further specify complication
CC Exclusion see Appendix A PDX collection 0828

hapter 12: Diseases of the Skin and Subcutaneous ssue (L00-L99)

:ludes2: certain conditions originating in the perinatal period (P04-P96)
certain infectious and parasitic diseases (A00-B99)
complications of pregnancy, childbirth and the puerperium (O00-O9A)
congenital malformations, deformations, and chromosomal abnormalities (Q00-Q99)
endocrine, nutritional and metabolic diseases (E00-E88)
lipomelanotic reticulosis (I89.8)
neoplasms (C00-D49)
symptoms, signs and abnormal clinical and laboratory findings, not elsewhere classified (R00-R94)
systemic connective tissue disorders (M30-M36)
viral warts (B07.-)

s chapter contains the following category blocks:

L00-L08	Infections of the skin and subcutaneous tissue
L10-L14	Bullous disorders
L20-L30	Dermatitis and eczema
L40-L45	Papulosquamous disorders
L49-L54	Urticaria and erythema
L55-L59	Radiation-related disorders of the skin and subcutaneous tissue
L60-L75	Disorders of skin appendages
L76	Intraoperative and postprocedural complications of skin and subcutaneous tissue
L80-L99	Other disorders of the skin and subcutaneous tissue

Chapter-Specific Coding Guidelines

ıddition to general coding guidelines, there are guidelines for specific diagnoses /or conditions in the classification. Unless otherwise indicated, these guidelines ly to all health care settings. Please refer to Section II for guidelines on the ction of principal diagnosis.

Chapter 12: Diseases of the Skin and Subcutaneous Tissue (L00-L99)

a. Pressure ulcer stage codes

1) Pressure ulcer stages

Codes from category L89, Pressure ulcer, are combination codes that identify the site of the pressure ulcer as well as the stage of the ulcer.

The ICD-10-CM classifies pressure ulcer stages based on severity, which is designated by stages 1-4, unspecified stage and unstageable.

Assign as many codes from category L89 as needed to identify all the pressure ulcers the patient has, if applicable.

2) Unstageable pressure ulcers

Assignment of the code for unstageable pressure ulcer (L89.--0) should be based on the clinical documentation. These codes are used for pressure ulcers whose stage cannot be clinically determined (e.g., the ulcer is covered by eschar or has been treated with a skin or muscle graft) and pressure ulcers that are documented as deep tissue injury but not documented as due to trauma. This code should not be confused with the codes for unspecified stage (L89.--9). When there is no documentation regarding the stage of the pressure ulcer, assign the appropriate code for unspecified stage (L89.--9).

3) Documented pressure ulcer stage

Assignment of the pressure ulcer stage code should be guided by clinical documentation of the stage or documentation of the terms found in the Alphabetic Index. For clinical terms describing the stage that are not found in the Alphabetic Index, and there is no documentation of the stage, the provider should be queried.

4) Patients admitted with pressure ulcers documented as healed

No code is assigned if the documentation states that the pressure ulcer is completely healed.

5) Patients admitted with pressure ulcers documented as healing

Pressure ulcers described as healing should be assigned the appropriate pressure ulcer stage code based on the documentation in the medical record. If the documentation does not provide information about the stage of the healing pressure ulcer, assign the appropriate code for unspecified stage.

If the documentation is unclear as to whether the patient has a current (new) pressure ulcer or if the patient is being treated for a healing pressure ulcer, query the provider.

6) Patient admitted with pressure ulcer evolving into another stage during the admission

If a patient is admitted with a pressure ulcer at one stage and it progresses to a higher stage, assign the code for the highest stage reported for that site.

Skin and Subcutaneous Tissue

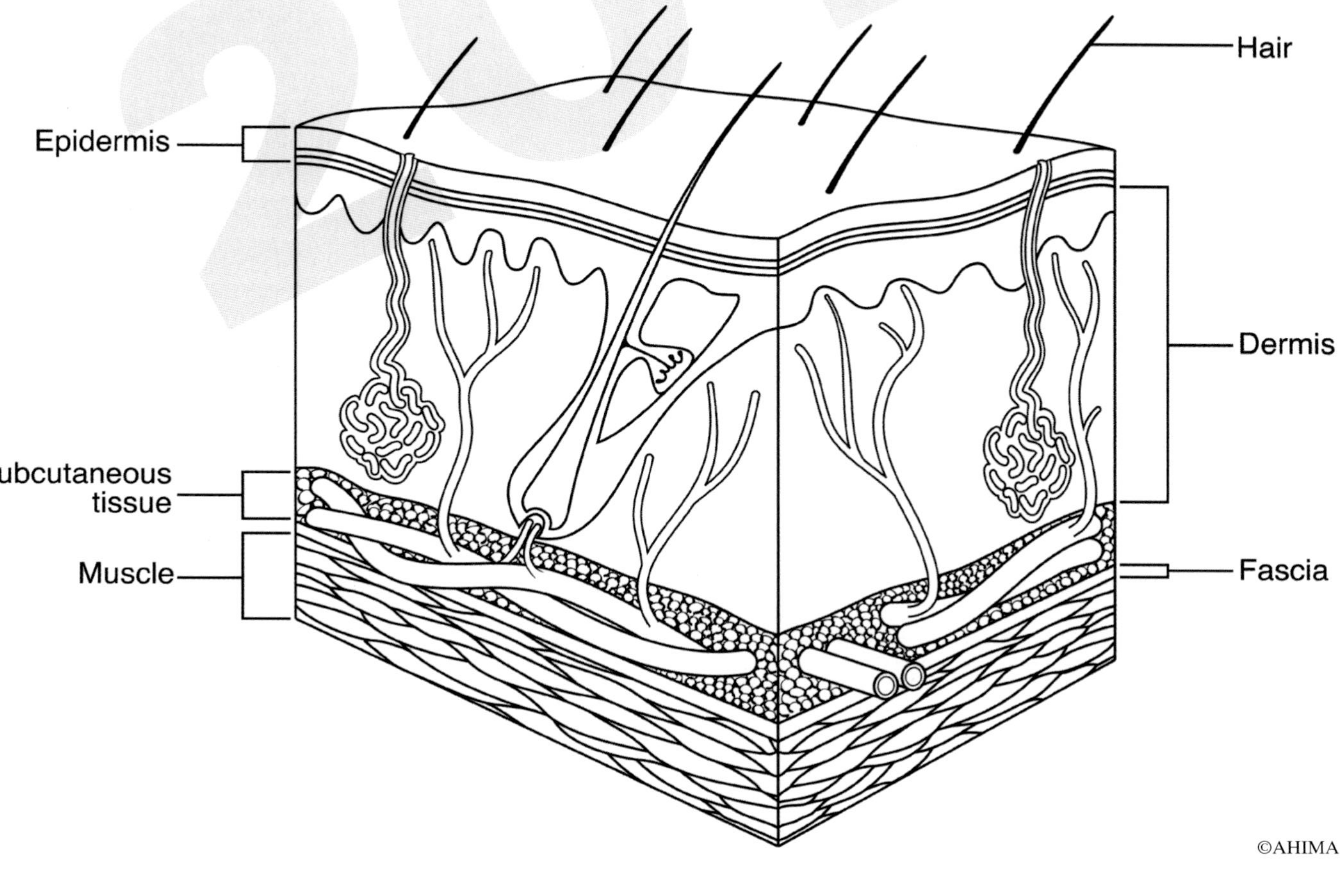

Infections of the skin and subcutaneous tissue (L00-L08)

Use additional code (B95-B97) to identify infectious agent.

Excludes2: *hordeolum (H00.0)*
infective dermatitis (L30.3)
local infections of skin classified in Chapter 1
lupus panniculitis (L93.2)
panniculitis NOS (M79.3)
panniculitis of neck and back (M54.0-)
Perlèche NOS (K13.0)
Perlèche due to candidiasis (B37.0)
Perlèche due to riboflavin deficiency (E53.0)
pyogenic granuloma (L98.0)
relapsing panniculitis [Weber-Christian] (M35.6)
viral warts (B07.-)
zoster (B02.-)

L00 Staphylococcal scalded skin syndrome
Ritter's disease
Use additional code to identify percentage of skin exfoliation (L49.-)
Excludes1: *bullous impetigo (L01.03)*
pemphigus neonatorum (L01.03)
toxic epidermal necrolysis [Lyell] (L51.2)
Valid 3-character code, no further characters required

L01 Impetigo
Excludes1: *impetigo herpetiformis (L40.1)*
\+ **L01.0 Impetigo**
Impetigo contagiosa
Impetigo vulgaris
L01.00 Impetigo, unspecified
Impetigo NOS
L01.01 Non-bullous impetigo
L01.02 Bockhart's impetigo
Impetigo follicularis
Perifolliculitis NOS
Superficial pustular perifolliculitis
L01.03 Bullous impetigo
Impetigo neonatorum
Pemphigus neonatorum
L01.09 Other impetigo
Ulcerative impetigo
L01.1 Impetiginization of other dermatoses

L02 Cutaneous abscess, furuncle and carbuncle
Use additional code to identify organism (B95-B96)
Excludes2: *abscess of anus and rectal regions (K61.-)*
abscess of female genital organs (external) (N76.4)
abscess of male genital organs (external) (N48.2, N49.-)
\+ **L02.0 Cutaneous abscess, furuncle and carbuncle of face**
Excludes2: *abscess of ear, external (H60.0)*
abscess of eyelid (H00.0)
abscess of head [any part, except face] (L02.8)
abscess of lacrimal gland (H04.0)
abscess of lacrimal passages (H04.3)
abscess of mouth (K12.2)
abscess of nose (J34.0)
abscess of orbit (H05.0)
submandibular abscess (K12.2)
CC **L02.01 Cutaneous abscess of face**
No CC Exclusions
L02.02 Furuncle of face
Boil of face
Folliculitis of face
L02.03 Carbuncle of face
\+ **L02.1 Cutaneous abscess, furuncle and carbuncle of neck**
CC **L02.11 Cutaneous abscess of neck**
CC Exclusion see Appendix A PDX collection 0832
L02.12 Furuncle of neck
Boil of neck
Folliculitis of neck
L02.13 Carbuncle of neck
\+ **L02.2 Cutaneous abscess, furuncle and carbuncle of trunk**
Excludes1: *non-newborn omphalitis (L08.82)*
omphalitis of newborn (P38.-)
Excludes2: *abscess of breast (N61)*
abscess of buttocks (L02.3)
abscess of female external genital organs (N76.4)
abscess of male external genital organs (N48.2, N49.-)
abscess of hip (L02.4)
CC **L02.21 Cutaneous abscess of trunk**
CC **L02.211 Cutaneous abscess of abdominal wall**
CC Exclusion see Appendix A PDX collection 0833
CC **L02.212 Cutaneous abscess of back [any part, exce buttock]**
CC Exclusion see Appendix A PDX collection 0
CC **L02.213 Cutaneous abscess of chest wall**
CC Exclusion see Appendix A PDX collection 0
CC **L02.214 Cutaneous abscess of groin**
CC Exclusion see Appendix A PDX collection 0
CC **L02.215 Cutaneous abscess of perineum**
CC Exclusion see Appendix A PDX collection 0
CC **L02.216 Cutaneous abscess of umbilicus**
CC Exclusion see Appendix A PDX collection 0
CC **L02.219 Cutaneous abscess of trunk, unspecified**
CC Exclusion see Appendix A PDX collection 0
\+ **L02.22 Furuncle of trunk**
Boil of trunk
Folliculitis of trunk
L02.221 Furuncle of abdominal wall
L02.222 Furuncle of back [any part, except buttock
L02.223 Furuncle of chest wall
L02.224 Furuncle of groin
L02.225 Furuncle of perineum
L02.226 Furuncle of umbilicus
L02.229 Furuncle of trunk, unspecified
\+ **L02.23 Carbuncle of trunk**
L02.231 Carbuncle of abdominal wall
L02.232 Carbuncle of back [any part, except butto
L02.233 Carbuncle of chest wall
L02.234 Carbuncle of groin
L02.235 Carbuncle of perineum
L02.236 Carbuncle of umbilicus
L02.239 Carbuncle of trunk, unspecified
\+ **L02.3 Cutaneous abscess, furuncle and carbuncle of buttock**
Excludes1: *pilonidal cyst with abscess (L05.01)*
CC **L02.31 Cutaneous abscess of buttock**
Cutaneous abscess of gluteal region
CC Exclusion see Appendix A PDX collection 0834
L02.32 Furuncle of buttock
Boil of buttock
Folliculitis of buttock
Furuncle of gluteal region
L02.33 Carbuncle of buttock
Carbuncle of gluteal region
\+ **L02.4 Cutaneous abscess, furuncle and carbuncle of limb**
Excludes2: *Cutaneous abscess, furuncle and carbuncle of groi (L02.214, L02.224, L02.234)*
Cutaneous abscess, furuncle and carbuncle of han (L02.5-)
Cutaneous abscess, furuncle and carbuncle of foot (L02.6-)
\+ **L02.41 Cutaneous abscess of limb**
CC **L02.411 Cutaneous abscess of right axilla**
CC Exclusion see Appendix A PDX collection 08
CC **L02.412 Cutaneous abscess of left axilla**
CC Exclusion see Appendix A PDX collection 08
CC **L02.413 Cutaneous abscess of right upper limb**
CC Exclusion see Appendix A PDX collection 08
CC **L02.414 Cutaneous abscess of left upper limb**
CC Exclusion see Appendix A PDX collection 08
CC **L02.415 Cutaneous abscess of right lower limb**
CC Exclusion see Appendix A PDX collection 08
CC **L02.416 Cutaneous abscess of left lower limb**
CC Exclusion see Appendix A PDX collection 08
CC **L02.419 Cutaneous abscess of limb, unspecified**
CC Exclusion see Appendix A PDX collection 08
\+ **L02.42 Furuncle of limb**
Boil of limb
Folliculitis of limb
L02.421 Furuncle of right axilla
L02.422 Furuncle of left axilla
L02.423 Furuncle of right upper limb
L02.424 Furuncle of left upper limb
L02.425 Furuncle of right lower limb
L02.426 Furuncle of left lower limb
L02.429 Furuncle of limb, unspecified
\+ **L02.43 Carbuncle of limb**
L02.431 Carbuncle of right axilla
L02.432 Carbuncle of left axilla
L02.433 Carbuncle of right upper limb
L02.434 Carbuncle of left upper limb
L02.435 Carbuncle of right lower limb
L02.436 Carbuncle of left lower limb
L02.439 Carbuncle of limb, unspecified

\+ **L02.5 Cutaneous abscess, furuncle and carbuncle of hand**
  \+ **L02.51 Cutaneous abscess of hand**
    CC **L02.511 Cutaneous abscess of right hand**
      CC Exclusion see Appendix A PDX collection 0837
    CC **L02.512 Cutaneous abscess of left hand**
      CC Exclusion see Appendix A PDX collection 0837
    CC **L02.519 Cutaneous abscess of unspecified hand**
      CC Exclusion see Appendix A PDX collection 0837
  \+ **L02.52 Furuncle hand**
    Boil of hand
    Folliculitis of hand
    L02.521 Furuncle right hand
    L02.522 Furuncle left hand
    L02.529 Furuncle unspecified hand
  \+ **L02.53 Carbuncle of hand**
    L02.531 Carbuncle of right hand
    L02.532 Carbuncle of left hand
    L02.539 Carbuncle of unspecified hand

\+ **L02.6 Cutaneous abscess, furuncle and carbuncle of foot**
  \+ **L02.61 Cutaneous abscess of foot**
    CC **L02.611 Cutaneous abscess of right foot**
      CC Exclusion see Appendix A PDX collection 0838
    CC **L02.612 Cutaneous abscess of left foot**
      CC Exclusion see Appendix A PDX collection 0838
    CC **L02.619 Cutaneous abscess of unspecified foot**
      CC Exclusion see Appendix A PDX collection 0838
  \+ **L02.62 Furuncle of foot**
    Boil of foot
    Folliculitis of foot
    L02.621 Furuncle of right foot
    L02.622 Furuncle of left foot
    L02.629 Furuncle of unspecified foot
  \+ **L02.63 Carbuncle of foot**
    L02.631 Carbuncle of right foot
    L02.632 Carbuncle of left foot
    L02.639 Carbuncle of unspecified foot

\+ **L02.8 Cutaneous abscess, furuncle and carbuncle of other sites**
  \+ **L02.81 Cutaneous abscess of other sites**
    CC **L02.811 Cutaneous abscess of head [any part, except face]**
      CC Exclusion see Appendix A PDX collection 0839
    CC **L02.818 Cutaneous abscess of other sites**
      CC Exclusion see Appendix A PDX collection 0839
  \+ **L02.82 Furuncle of other sites**
    Boil of other sites
    Folliculitis of other sites
    L02.821 Furuncle of head [any part, except face]
    L02.828 Furuncle of other sites
  \+ **L02.83 Carbuncle of other sites**
    L02.831 Carbuncle of head [any part, except face]
    L02.838 Carbuncle of other sites

\+ **L02.9 Cutaneous abscess, furuncle and carbuncle, unspecified**
  CC **L02.91 Cutaneous abscess, unspecified**
    CC Exclusion see Appendix A PDX collection 0839
  L02.92 Furuncle, unspecified
    Boil NOS
    Furunculosis NOS
  L02.93 Carbuncle, unspecified

L03 Cellulitis and acute lymphangitis

Excludes2: *cellulitis of anal and rectal region (K61.-)*
cellulitis of external auditory canal (H60.1)
cellulitis of eyelid (H00.0)
cellulitis of female external genital organs (N76.4)
cellulitis of lacrimal apparatus (H04.3)
cellulitis of male external genital organs (N48.2, N49.-)
cellulitis of mouth (K12.2)
cellulitis of nose (J34.0)
eosinophilic cellulitis [Wells] (L98.3)
febrile neutrophilic dermatosis [Sweet] (L98.2)
lymphangitis (chronic) (subacute) (I89.1)

\+ **L03.0 Cellulitis and acute lymphangitis of finger and toe**
  Infection of nail
  Onychia
  Paronychia
  Perionychia
  \+ **L03.01 Cellulitis of finger**
    Felon
    Whitlow
    Excludes1: herpetic whitlow (B00.89)
    L03.011 Cellulitis of right finger
    L03.012 Cellulitis of left finger
    L03.019 Cellulitis of unspecified finger
  \+ **L03.02 Acute lymphangitis of finger**
    Hangnail with lymphangitis of finger
    L03.021 Acute lymphangitis of right finger
    L03.022 Acute lymphangitis of left finger
    L03.029 Acute lymphangitis of unspecified finger
  \+ **L03.03 Cellulitis of toe**
    L03.031 Cellulitis of right toe
    L03.032 Cellulitis of left toe
    L03.039 Cellulitis of unspecified toe
  \+ **L03.04 Acute lymphangitis of toe**
    Hangnail with lymphangitis of toe
    L03.041 Acute lymphangitis of right toe
    L03.042 Acute lymphangitis of left toe
    L03.049 Acute lymphangitis of unspecified toe

\+ **L03.1 Cellulitis and acute lymphangitis of other parts of limb**
  \+ **L03.11 Cellulitis of other parts of limb**
    Excludes2: *cellulitis of fingers (L03.01-)*
    cellulitis of toes (L03.03-)
    groin (L03.314)
    CC **L03.111 Cellulitis of right axilla**
      CC Exclusion see Appendix A PDX collection 0835
    CC **L03.112 Cellulitis of left axilla**
      CC Exclusion see Appendix A PDX collection 0835
    CC **L03.113 Cellulitis of right upper limb**
      CC Exclusion see Appendix A PDX collection 0835
    CC **L03.114 Cellulitis of left upper limb**
      CC Exclusion see Appendix A PDX collection 0835
    CC **L03.115 Cellulitis of right lower limb**
      CC Exclusion see Appendix A PDX collection 0836
    CC **L03.116 Cellulitis of left lower limb**
      CC Exclusion see Appendix A PDX collection 0836
    CC **L03.119 Cellulitis of unspecified part of limb**
      CC Exclusion see Appendix A PDX collection 0836
  \+ **L03.12 Acute lymphangitis of other parts of limb**
    Excludes2: *acute lymphangitis of fingers (L03.2-)*
    acute lymphangitis of toes (L03.04-)
    acute lymphangitis of groin (L03.324)
    CC **L03.121 Acute lymphangitis of right axilla**
      CC Exclusion see Appendix A PDX collection 0835
    CC **L03.122 Acute lymphangitis of left axilla**
      CC Exclusion see Appendix A PDX collection 0835
    CC **L03.123 Acute lymphangitis of right upper limb**
      CC Exclusion see Appendix A PDX collection 0835
    CC **L03.124 Acute lymphangitis of left upper limb**
      CC Exclusion see Appendix A PDX collection 0835
    CC **L03.125 Acute lymphangitis of right lower limb**
      CC Exclusion see Appendix A PDX collection 0836
    CC **L03.126 Acute lymphangitis of left lower limb**
      CC Exclusion see Appendix A PDX collection 0836
    CC **L03.129 Acute lymphangitis of unspecified part of limb**
      CC Exclusion see Appendix A PDX collection 0836

\+ **L03.2 Cellulitis and acute lymphangitis of face and neck**
  \+ **L03.21 Cellulitis and acute lymphangitis of face**
    CC **L03.211 Cellulitis of face**
      Excludes2: *cellulitis of ear (H60.1-)*
      cellulitis of eyelid (H00.0-)
      cellulitis of head (L03.81)
      cellulitis of lacrimal apparatus (H04.3)
      cellulitis of lip (K13.0)
      cellulitis of mouth (K12.2)
      cellulitis of nose (internal) (J34.0)
      cellulitis of orbit (H05.0)
      cellulitis of scalp (L03.81)
      CC Exclusion see Appendix A PDX collection 0840
      AHA CC: 4Q, 2013, 123
    CC **L03.212 Acute lymphangitis of face**
      No CC Exclusions
  \+ **L03.22 Cellulitis and acute lymphangitis of neck**
    CC **L03.221 Cellulitis of neck**
      CC Exclusion see Appendix A PDX collection 0832
    CC **L03.222 Acute lymphangitis of neck**
      CC Exclusion see Appendix A PDX collection 0832

+ **L03.3 Cellulitis and acute lymphangitis of trunk**
+ **L03.31 Cellulitis of trunk**
Excludes2: *cellulitis of anal and rectal regions (K61.-)*
cellulitis of breast NOS (N61)
cellulitis of female external genital organs (N76.4)
cellulitis of male external genital organs (N48.2, N49.-)
omphalitis of newborn (P38.-)
puerperal cellulitis of breast (O91.2)

CC **L03.311 Cellulitis of abdominal wall**
Excludes2: *cellulitis of umbilicus (L03.316)*
cellulitis of groin (L03.314)
CC Exclusion see Appendix A PDX collection 0833

CC **L03.312 Cellulitis of back [any part except buttock]**
CC Exclusion see Appendix A PDX collection 0833

CC **L03.313 Cellulitis of chest wall**
CC Exclusion see Appendix A PDX collection 0833

CC **L03.314 Cellulitis of groin**
CC Exclusion see Appendix A PDX collection 0833

CC **L03.315 Cellulitis of perineum**
CC Exclusion see Appendix A PDX collection 0833

CC **L03.316 Cellulitis of umbilicus**
CC Exclusion see Appendix A PDX collection 0833

CC **L03.317 Cellulitis of buttock**
CC Exclusion see Appendix A PDX collection 0834

CC **L03.319 Cellulitis of trunk, unspecified**
CC Exclusion see Appendix A PDX collection 0833

+ **L03.32 Acute lymphangitis of trunk**

CC **L03.321 Acute lymphangitis of abdominal wall**
CC Exclusion see Appendix A PDX collection 0833

CC **L03.322 Acute lymphangitis of back [any part except buttock]**
CC Exclusion see Appendix A PDX collection 0833

CC **L03.323 Acute lymphangitis of chest wall**
CC Exclusion see Appendix A PDX collection 0833

CC **L03.324 Acute lymphangitis of groin**
CC Exclusion see Appendix A PDX collection 0833

CC **L03.325 Acute lymphangitis of perineum**
CC Exclusion see Appendix A PDX collection 0833

CC **L03.326 Acute lymphangitis of umbilicus**
CC Exclusion see Appendix A PDX collection 0833

CC **L03.327 Acute lymphangitis of buttock**
CC Exclusion see Appendix A PDX collection 0834

CC **L03.329 Acute lymphangitis of trunk, unspecified**
CC Exclusion see Appendix A PDX collection 0833

+ **L03.8 Cellulitis and acute lymphangitis of other sites**
+ **L03.81 Cellulitis of other sites**

CC **L03.811 Cellulitis of head [any part, except face]**
Cellulitis of scalp
Excludes2: *cellulitis of face (L03.211)*
CC Exclusion see Appendix A PDX collection 0839

CC **L03.818 Cellulitis of other sites**
CC Exclusion see Appendix A PDX collection 0839

+ **L03.89 Acute lymphangitis of other sites**

CC **L03.891 Acute lymphangitis of head [any part, except face]**
CC Exclusion see Appendix A PDX collection 0839

CC **L03.898 Acute lymphangitis of other sites**
CC Exclusion see Appendix A PDX collection 0839

+ **L03.9 Cellulitis and acute lymphangitis, unspecified**

CC **L03.90 Cellulitis, unspecified**
CC Exclusion see Appendix A PDX collection 0839

CC **L03.91 Acute lymphangitis, unspecified**
Excludes1: *lymphangitis NOS (I89.1)*
CC Exclusion see Appendix A PDX collection 0839

L04 Acute lymphadenitis

Includes: abscess (acute) of lymph nodes, except mesenteric
acute lymphadenitis, except mesenteric
Excludes1: *chronic or subacute lymphadenitis, except mesenteric (I88.1)*
enlarged lymph nodes (R59.-)
human immunodeficiency virus [HIV] disease resulting in generalized lymphadenopathy (B20)
lymphadenitis NOS (I88.9)
nonspecific mesenteric lymphadenitis (I88.0)

L04.0 Acute lymphadenitis of face, head and neck
L04.1 Acute lymphadenitis of trunk
L04.2 Acute lymphadenitis of upper limb
Acute lymphadenitis of axilla
Acute lymphadenitis of shoulder

L04.3 Acute lymphadenitis of lower limb
Acute lymphadenitis of hip
Excludes2: *acute lymphadenitis of groin (L04.1)*
L04.8 Acute lymphadenitis of other sites
L04.9 Acute lymphadenitis, unspecified

L05 Pilonidal cyst and sinus

+ **L05.0 Pilonidal cyst and sinus with abscess**

CC **L05.01 Pilonidal cyst with abscess**
Parasacral dimple with abscess
Pilonidal abscess
Pilonidal dimple with abscess
Postanal dimple with abscess
CC Exclusion see Appendix A PDX collection 0841

CC **L05.02 Pilonidal sinus with abscess**
Coccygeal fistula with abscess
Coccygeal sinus with abscess
Pilonidal fistula with abscess
CC Exclusion see Appendix A PDX collection 0841

+ **L05.9 Pilonidal cyst and sinus without abscess**
L05.91 Pilonidal cyst without abscess
Parasacral dimple
Pilonidal dimple
Postanal dimple
Pilonidal cyst NOS
L05.92 Pilonidal sinus without abscess
Coccygeal fistula
Coccygeal sinus without abscess
Pilonidal fistula

L08 Other local infections of skin and subcutaneous tissue

L08.0 Pyoderma
Dermatitis gangrenosa
Purulent dermatitis
Septic dermatitis
Suppurative dermatitis
Excludes1: *pyoderma gangrenosum (L88)*
pyoderma vegetans (L08.81)

CC **L08.1 Erythrasma**
CC Exclusion see Appendix A PDX collection 0107

+ **L08.8 Other specified local infections of the skin and subcutaneous tissue**
L08.81 Pyoderma vegetans
Excludes1: *pyoderma gangrenosum (L88)*
pyoderma NOS (L08.0)
L08.82 Omphalitis not of newborn
Excludes1: *omphalitis of newborn (P38.-)*
L08.89 Other specified local infections of the skin and subcutaneous tissue
L08.9 Local infection of the skin and subcutaneous tissue, unspecifi

Bullous disorders (L10-L14)

Excludes1: *benign familial pemphigus [Hailey-Hailey] (Q82.8)*
staphylococcal scalded skin syndrome (L00)
toxic epidermal necrolysis [Lyell] (L51.2)

L10 Pemphigus

Excludes1: *pemphigus neonatorum (L01.03)*

CC **L10.0 Pemphigus vulgaris**
CC Exclusion see Appendix A PDX collection 0842

CC **L10.1 Pemphigus vegetans**
CC Exclusion see Appendix A PDX collection 0842

CC **L10.2 Pemphigus foliaceous**
CC Exclusion see Appendix A PDX collection 0842

CC **L10.3 Brazilian pemphigus [fogo selvagem]**
CC Exclusion see Appendix A PDX collection 0842

CC **L10.4 Pemphigus erythematosus**
Senear-Usher syndrome
CC Exclusion see Appendix A PDX collection 0842

CC **L10.5 Drug-induced pemphigus**
Use additional code for adverse effect, if applicable, to identif drug (T36-T50 with fifth or sixth character 5)
CC Exclusion see Appendix A PDX collection 0842

+ **L10.8 Other pemphigus**

CC **L10.81 Paraneoplastic pemphigus**
CC Exclusion see Appendix A PDX collection 0842

CC **L10.89 Other pemphigus**
CC Exclusion see Appendix A PDX collection 0842

CC **L10.9 Pemphigus, unspecified**
CC Exclusion see Appendix A PDX collection 0842

L11 Other acantholytic disorders

L11.0 Acquired keratosis follicularis
Excludes1: *keratosis follicularis (congenital) [Darier-White] (Q82.8)*

L11.1 Transient acantholytic dermatosis [Grover]

L11.8 Other specified acantholytic disorders

L11.9 Acantholytic disorder, unspecified

L12 Pemphigoid

Excludes1: *herpes gestationis (O26.4-)*
impetigo herpetiformis (L40.1)

CC **L12.0 Bullous pemphigoid**
CC Exclusion see Appendix A PDX collection 0842

L12.1 Cicatricial pemphigoid
Benign mucous membrane pemphigoid

• **L12.2 Chronic bullous disease of childhood**
Juvenile dermatitis herpetiformis

\+ **L12.3 Acquired epidermolysis bullosa**
Excludes1: *epidermolysis bullosa (congenital) (Q81.-)*

CC **L12.30 Acquired epidermolysis bullosa, unspecified**
CC Exclusion see Appendix A PDX collection 0843

CC **L12.31 Epidermolysis bullosa due to drug**
Use additional code for adverse effect, if applicable, to identify drug (T36-T50 with fifth or sixth character 5)
CC Exclusion see Appendix A PDX collection 0843

CC **L12.35 Other acquired epidermolysis bullosa**
CC Exclusion see Appendix A PDX collection 0843

CC **L12.8 Other pemphigoid**
CC Exclusion see Appendix A PDX collection 0842

CC **L12.9 Pemphigoid, unspecified**
CC Exclusion see Appendix A PDX collection 0842

L13 Other bullous disorders

L13.0 Dermatitis herpetiformis
Duhring's disease
Hydroa herpetiformis
Excludes1: *juvenile dermatitis herpetiformis (L12.2)*
senile dermatitis herpetiformis (L12.0)

L13.1 Subcorneal pustular dermatitis
Sneddon-Wilkinson disease

L13.8 Other specified bullous disorders

L13.9 Bullous disorder, unspecified

L14 Bullous disorders in diseases classified elsewhere
Code first underlying disease

ermatitis and eczema (L20-L30)

OTE In this block the terms dermatitis and eczema are used synonymously and interchangeably.

cludes2: *chronic (childhood) granulomatous disease (D71)*
dermatitis gangrenosa (L08.0)
dermatitis herpetiformis (L13.0)
dry skin dermatitis (L85.3)
factitial dermatitis (L98.1)
perioral dermatitis (L71.0)
radiation-related disorders of the skin and subcutaneous tissue (L55-L59)
stasis dermatitis (I83.1-I83.2)

L20 Atopic dermatitis

L20.0 Besnier's prurigo

\+ **L20.8 Other atopic dermatitis**
Excludes2: *circumscribed neurodermatitis (L28.0)*

L20.81 Atopic neurodermatitis
Diffuse neurodermatitis

L20.82 Flexural eczema

• **L20.83 Infantile (acute) (chronic) eczema**

L20.84 Intrinsic (allergic) eczema

L20.89 Other atopic dermatitis

L20.9 Atopic dermatitis, unspecified

L21 Seborrheic dermatitis

Excludes2: *infective dermatitis (L30.3)*
seborrheic keratosis (L82.-)

• **L21.0 Seborrhea capitis**
Cradle cap

• **L21.1 Seborrheic infantile dermatitis**

L21.8 Other seborrheic dermatitis

L21.9 Seborrheic dermatitis, unspecified
Seborrhea NOS

L22 Diaper dermatitis
Diaper erythema
Diaper rash
Psoriasiform diaper rash
Valid 3-character code, no further characters required

L23 Allergic contact dermatitis

Excludes1: *allergy NOS (T78.40)*
contact dermatitis NOS (L25.9)
dermatitis NOS (L30.9)
Excludes2: *dermatitis due to substances taken internally (L27.-)*
dermatitis of eyelid (H01.1-)
diaper dermatitis (L22)
eczema of external ear (H60.5-)
irritant contact dermatitis (L24.-)
perioral dermatitis (L71.0)
radiation-related disorders of the skin and subcutaneous tissue (L55-L59)

L23.0 Allergic contact dermatitis due to metals
Allergic contact dermatitis due to chromium
Allergic contact dermatitis due to nickel

L23.1 Allergic contact dermatitis due to adhesives

L23.2 Allergic contact dermatitis due to cosmetics

L23.3 Allergic contact dermatitis due to drugs in contact with skin
Use additional code for adverse effect, if applicable, to identify drug (T36-T50 with fifth or sixth character 5)
Excludes2: *dermatitis due to ingested drugs and medicaments (L27.0-L27.1)*

L23.4 Allergic contact dermatitis due to dyes

L23.5 Allergic contact dermatitis due to other chemical products
Allergic contact dermatitis due to cement
Allergic contact dermatitis due to insecticide
Allergic contact dermatitis due to plastic
Allergic contact dermatitis due to rubber

L23.6 Allergic contact dermatitis due to food in contact with the skin
Excludes2: *dermatitis due to ingested food (L27.2)*

L23.7 Allergic contact dermatitis due to plants, except food
Excludes2: *allergy NOS due to pollen (J30.1)*

\+ **L23.8 Allergic contact dermatitis due to other agents**

L23.81 Allergic contact dermatitis due to animal (cat) (dog) dander
Allergic contact dermatitis due to animal (cat) (dog) hair

L23.89 Allergic contact dermatitis due to other agents

L23.9 Allergic contact dermatitis, unspecified cause
Allergic contact eczema NOS

L24 Irritant contact dermatitis

Excludes1: *allergy NOS (T78.40)*
contact dermatitis NOS (L25.9)
dermatitis NOS (L30.9)
Excludes2: *allergic contact dermatitis (L23.-)*
dermatitis due to substances taken internally (L27.-)
dermatitis of eyelid (H01.1-)
diaper dermatitis (L22)
eczema of external ear (H60.5-)
perioral dermatitis (L71.0)
radiation-related disorders of the skin and subcutaneous tissue (L55-L59)

L24.0 Irritant contact dermatitis due to detergents

L24.1 Irritant contact dermatitis due to oils and greases

L24.2 Irritant contact dermatitis due to solvents
Irritant contact dermatitis due to chlorocompound
Irritant contact dermatitis due to cyclohexane
Irritant contact dermatitis due to ester
Irritant contact dermatitis due to glycol
Irritant contact dermatitis due to hydrocarbon
Irritant contact dermatitis due to ketone

L24.3 Irritant contact dermatitis due to cosmetics

L24.4 Irritant contact dermatitis due to drugs in contact with skin
Use additional code for adverse effect, if applicable, to identify drug (T36-T50 with fifth or sixth character 5)

L24.5 Irritant contact dermatitis due to other chemical products
Irritant contact dermatitis due to cement
Irritant contact dermatitis due to insecticide
Irritant contact dermatitis due to plastic
Irritant contact dermatitis due to rubber

L24.6 Irritant contact dermatitis due to food in contact with skin
Excludes2: *dermatitis due to ingested food (L27.2)*

L24.7 Irritant contact dermatitis due to plants, except food
Excludes2: *allergy NOS to pollen (J30.1)*

\+ **L24.8 Irritant contact dermatitis due to other agents**
L24.81 Irritant contact dermatitis due to metals
Irritant contact dermatitis due to chromium
Irritant contact dermatitis due to nickel
L24.89 Irritant contact dermatitis due to other agents
Irritant contact dermatitis due to dyes
L24.9 Irritant contact dermatitis, unspecified cause
Irritant contact eczema NOS

L25 Unspecified contact dermatitis

Excludes1: *allergic contact dermatitis (L23.-)*
allergy NOS (T78.40)
dermatitis NOS (L30.9)
irritant contact dermatitis (L24.-)
Excludes2: *dermatitis due to ingested substances (L27.-)*
dermatitis of eyelid (H01.1-)
eczema of external ear (H60.5-)
perioral dermatitis (L71.0)
radiation-related disorders of the skin and subcutaneous tissue (L55-L59)
L25.0 Unspecified contact dermatitis due to cosmetics
L25.1 Unspecified contact dermatitis due to drugs in contact with skin
Use additional code for adverse effect, if applicable, to identify drug (T36-T50 with fifth or sixth character 5)
Excludes2: *dermatitis due to ingested drugs and medicaments (L27.0-L27.1)*
L25.2 Unspecified contact dermatitis due to dyes
L25.3 Unspecified contact dermatitis due to other chemical products
Unspecified contact dermatitis due to cement
Unspecified contact dermatitis due to insecticide
L25.4 Unspecified contact dermatitis due to food in contact with skin
Excludes2: *dermatitis due to ingested food (L27.2)*
L25.5 Unspecified contact dermatitis due to plants, except food
Excludes1: *nettle rash (L50.9)*
Excludes2: *allergy NOS due to pollen (J30.1)*
L25.8 Unspecified contact dermatitis due to other agents
L25.9 Unspecified contact dermatitis, unspecified cause
Contact dermatitis (occupational) NOS
Contact eczema (occupational) NOS

L26 Exfoliative dermatitis

Hebra's pityriasis
Excludes1: *Ritter's disease (L00)*
Valid 3-character code, no further characters required

L27 Dermatitis due to substances taken internally

Excludes1: *allergy NOS (T78.40)*
Excludes2: *adverse food reaction, except dermatitis (T78.0-T78.1)*
contact dermatitis (L23-L25)
drug photoallergic response (L56.1)
drug phototoxic response (L56.0)
urticaria (L50.-)
L27.0 Generalized skin eruption due to drugs and medicaments taken internally
Use additional code for adverse effect, if applicable, to identify drug (T36-T50 with fifth or sixth character 5)
L27.1 Localized skin eruption due to drugs and medicaments taken internally
Use additional code for adverse effect, if applicable, to identify drug (T36-T50 with fifth or sixth character 5)
L27.2 Dermatitis due to ingested food
Excludes2: *dermatitis due to food in contact with skin (L23.6, L24.6, L25.4)*
L27.8 Dermatitis due to other substances taken internally
L27.9 Dermatitis due to unspecified substance taken internally

L28 Lichen simplex chronicus and prurigo

L28.0 Lichen simplex chronicus
Circumscribed neurodermatitis
Lichen NOS
L28.1 Prurigo nodularis
L28.2 Other prurigo
Prurigo NOS
Prurigo Hebra
Prurigo mitis
Urticaria papulosa

L29 Pruritus

Excludes1: *neurotic excoriation (L98.1)*
psychogenic pruritus (F45.8)
L29.0 Pruritus ani
♂ **L29.1 Pruritus scroti**
♀ **L29.2 Pruritus vulvae**
L29.3 Anogenital pruritus, unspecified
L29.8 Other pruritus
L29.9 Pruritus, unspecified
Itch NOS

L30 Other and unspecified dermatitis

Excludes2: *contact dermatitis (L23-L25)*
dry skin dermatitis (L85.3)
small plaque parapsoriasis (L41.3)
stasis dermatitis (I83.1-.2)
L30.0 Nummular dermatitis
L30.1 Dyshidrosis [pompholyx]
L30.2 Cutaneous autosensitization
Candidid [levurid]
Dermatophytid
Eczematid
L30.3 Infective dermatitis
Infectious eczematoid dermatitis
L30.4 Erythema intertrigo
L30.5 Pityriasis alba
L30.8 Other specified dermatitis
L30.9 Dermatitis, unspecified
Eczema NOS

Papulosquamous disorders (L40-L45)

L40 Psoriasis

L40.0 Psoriasis vulgaris
Nummular psoriasis
Plaque psoriasis
L40.1 Generalized pustular psoriasis
Impetigo herpetiformis
Von Zumbusch's disease
L40.2 Acrodermatitis continua
L40.3 Pustulosis palmaris et plantaris
L40.4 Guttate psoriasis
\+ **L40.5 Arthropathic psoriasis**
L40.50 Arthropathic psoriasis, unspecified
L40.51 Distal interphalangeal psoriatic arthropathy
L40.52 Psoriatic arthritis mutilans
L40.53 Psoriatic spondylitis
L40.54 Psoriatic juvenile arthropathy
L40.59 Other psoriatic arthropathy
L40.8 Other psoriasis
Flexural psoriasis
L40.9 Psoriasis, unspecified

L41 Parapsoriasis

Excludes1: *poikiloderma vasculare atrophicans (L94.5)*
L41.0 Pityriasis lichenoides et varioliformis acuta
Mucha-Habermann disease
L41.1 Pityriasis lichenoides chronica
L41.3 Small plaque parapsoriasis
L41.4 Large plaque parapsoriasis
L41.5 Retiform parapsoriasis
L41.8 Other parapsoriasis
L41.9 Parapsoriasis, unspecified

L42 Pityriasis rosea

Valid 3-character code, no further characters required

L43 Lichen planus

Excludes1: *lichen planopilaris (L66.1)*
L43.0 Hypertrophic lichen planus
L43.1 Bullous lichen planus
L43.2 Lichenoid drug reaction
Use additional code for adverse effect, if applicable, to identify drug (T36-T50 with fifth or sixth character 5)
L43.3 Subacute (active) lichen planus
Lichen planus tropicus
L43.8 Other lichen planus
L43.9 Lichen planus, unspecified

L44 Other papulosquamous disorders

L44.0 Pityriasis rubra pilaris
L44.1 Lichen nitidus
L44.2 Lichen striatus
L44.3 Lichen ruber moniliformis
● **L44.4 Infantile papular acrodermatitis [Gianotti-Crosti]**
L44.8 Other specified papulosquamous disorders
L44.9 Papulosquamous disorder, unspecified

L45 Papulosquamous disorders in diseases classified elsewhere

Code first underlying disease.
Valid 3-character code, no further characters required

ticaria and erythema (L49-L54)

ludes1: *Lyme disease (A69.2-)*
rosacea (L71.-)

L49 Exfoliation due to erythematous conditions according to extent of body surface involved

Code first erythematous condition causing exfoliation, such as:
Ritter's disease (L00)
(Staphylococcal) scalded skin syndrom (L00)
Stevens-Johnson syndrome (L51.1)
Stevens-Johnson syndrome-toxic epidermal necrolysis overlap syndrome (L51.3)
Toxic epidermal necrolysis (L51.2)

L49.0 Exfoliation due to erythematous condition involving less than 10 percent of body surface
Exfoliation due to erythematous condition NOS

L49.1 Exfoliation due to erythematous condition involving 10-19 percent of body surface

L49.2 Exfoliation due to erythematous condition involving 20-29 percent of body surface

CC **L49.3 Exfoliation due to erythematous condition involving 30-39 percent of body surface**
CC Exclusion see Appendix A PDX collection 0844

CC **L49.4 Exfoliation due to erythematous condition involving 40-49 percent of body surface**
CC Exclusion see Appendix A PDX collection 0845

CC **L49.5 Exfoliation due to erythematous condition involving 50-59 percent of body surface**
CC Exclusion see Appendix A PDX collection 0846

CC **L49.6 Exfoliation due to erythematous condition involving 60-69 percent of body surface**
CC Exclusion see Appendix A PDX collection 0847

CC **L49.7 Exfoliation due to erythematous condition involving 70-79 percent of body surface**
CC Exclusion see Appendix A PDX collection 0848

CC **L49.8 Exfoliation due to erythematous condition involving 80-89 percent of body surface**
CC Exclusion see Appendix A PDX collection 0849

CC **L49.9 Exfoliation due to erythematous condition involving 90 or more percent of body surface**
CC Exclusion see Appendix A PDX collection 0850

L50 Urticaria

Excludes1: *allergic contact dermatitis (L23.-)*
angioneurotic edema (T78.3)
giant urticaria (T78.3)
hereditary angio-edema (D84.1)
Quincke's edema (T78.3)
serum urticaria (T80.6-)
solar urticaria (L56.3)
urticaria neonatorum (P83.8)
urticaria papulosa (L28.2)
urticaria pigmentosa (Q82.2)

L50.0 Allergic urticaria
L50.1 Idiopathic urticaria
L50.2 Urticaria due to cold and heat
L50.3 Dermatographic urticaria
L50.4 Vibratory urticaria
L50.5 Cholinergic urticaria
L50.6 Contact urticaria
L50.8 Other urticaria
Chronic urticaria
Recurrent periodic urticaria
L50.9 Urticaria, unspecified

L51 Erythema multiforme

Use additional code for adverse effect, if applicable, to identify drug (T36-T50 with fifth or sixth character 5)

Use additional code to identify associated manifestations, such as:
arthropathy associated with dermatological disorders (M14.8-)
conjunctival edema (H11.42)
conjunctivitis (H10.22-)
corneal scars and opacities (H17.-)
corneal ulcer (H16.0-)
edema of eyelid (H02.84)
inflammation of eyelid (H01.8)
keratoconjunctivitis sicca (H16.22-)
mechanical lagophthalmos (H02.22-)
stomatitis (K12.-)
symblepharon (H11.23-)

Use additional code to identify percentage of skin exfoliation (L49.-)
Excludes1: *staphylococcal scalded skin syndrome (L00)*
Ritter's disease (L00)

L51.0 Nonbullous erythema multiforme

CC **L51.1 Stevens-Johnson syndrome**
CC Exclusion see Appendix A PDX collection 0843

CC **L51.2 Toxic epidermal necrolysis [Lyell]**
CC Exclusion see Appendix A PDX collection 0843

CC **L51.3 Stevens-Johnson syndrome-toxic epidermal necrolysis overlap syndrome**
SJS-TEN overlap syndrome
CC Exclusion see Appendix A PDX collection 0843

L51.8 Other erythema multiforme
L51.9 Erythema multiforme, unspecified
Erythema iris
Erythema multiforme major NOS
Erythema multiforme minor NOS
Herpes iris

L52 Erythema nodosum

Excludes1: *tuberculous erythema nodosum (A18.4)*
Valid 3-character code, no further characters required

L53 Other erythematous conditions

Excludes1: *erythema ab igne (L59.0)*
erythema due to external agents in contact with skin (L23-L25)
erythema intertrigo (L30.4)

CC **L53.0 Toxic erythema**
Code first poisoning due to drug or toxin, if applicable (T36-T65 with fifth or sixth character 1-4 or 6)

Use additional code for adverse effect, if applicable, to identify drug (T36-T50 with fifth or sixth character 5)
Excludes1: *neonatal erythema toxicum (P83.1)*
CC Exclusion see Appendix A PDX collection 0851

CC **L53.1 Erythema annulare centrifugum**
CC Exclusion see Appendix A PDX collection 0851

CC **L53.2 Erythema marginatum**
CC Exclusion see Appendix A PDX collection 0851

CC **L53.3 Other chronic figurate erythema**
CC Exclusion see Appendix A PDX collection 0851

L53.8 Other specified erythematous conditions
L53.9 Erythematous condition, unspecified
Erythema NOS
Erythroderma NOS

L54 Erythema in diseases classified elsewhere

Code first underlying disease.
Valid 3-character code, no further characters required

Radiation-related disorders of the skin and subcutaneous tissue (L55-L59)

L55 Sunburn

L55.0 Sunburn of first degree
L55.1 Sunburn of second degree
L55.2 Sunburn of third degree
L55.9 Sunburn, unspecified

L56 Other acute skin changes due to ultraviolet radiation

Use additional code to identify the source of the ultraviolet radiation (W89, X32)

L56.0 Drug phototoxic response
Use additional code for adverse effect, if applicable, to identify drug (T36-T50 with fifth or sixth character 5)

L56.1 Drug photoallergic response
Use additional code for adverse effect, if applicable, to identify drug (T36-T50 with fifth or sixth character 5)
L56.2 Photocontact dermatitis [berloque dermatitis]
L56.3 Solar urticaria
L56.4 Polymorphous light eruption
L56.5 Disseminated superficial actinic porokeratosis (DSAP)
L56.8 Other specified acute skin changes due to ultraviolet radiation
L56.9 Acute skin change due to ultraviolet radiation, unspecified

L57 Skin changes due to chronic exposure to nonionizing radiation
Use additional code to identify the source of the ultraviolet radiation (W89, X32)
L57.0 Actinic keratosis
Keratosis NOS
Senile keratosis
Solar keratosis
L57.1 Actinic reticuloid
L57.2 Cutis rhomboidalis nuchae
L57.3 Poikiloderma of Civatte
L57.4 Cutis laxa senilis
Elastosis senilis
L57.5 Actinic granuloma
L57.8 Other skin changes due to chronic exposure to nonionizing radiation
Farmer's skin
Sailor's skin
Solar dermatitis
L57.9 Skin changes due to chronic exposure to nonionizing radiation, unspecified

L58 Radiodermatitis
Use additional code to identify the source of the radiation (W88, W90)
L58.0 Acute radiodermatitis
L58.1 Chronic radiodermatitis
L58.9 Radiodermatitis, unspecified

L59 Other disorders of skin and subcutaneous tissue related to radiation
L59.0 Erythema ab igne [dermatitis ab igne]
L59.8 Other specified disorders of the skin and subcutaneous tissue related to radiation
L59.9 Disorder of the skin and subcutaneous tissue related to radiation, unspecified

Disorders of skin appendages (L60-L75)

Excludes1: *congenital malformations of integument (Q84.-)*

L60 Nail disorders
Excludes2: *clubbing of nails (R68.3)*
onychia and paronychia (L03.0-)
L60.0 Ingrowing nail
L60.1 Onycholysis
L60.2 Onychogryphosis
L60.3 Nail dystrophy
L60.4 Beau's lines
L60.5 Yellow nail syndrome
L60.8 Other nail disorders
L60.9 Nail disorder, unspecified

L62 Nail disorders in diseases classified elsewhere
Code first underlying disease, such as:
pachydermoperiostosis (M89.4-)
Valid 3-character code, no further characters required

L63 Alopecia areata
L63.0 Alopecia (capitis) totalis
L63.1 Alopecia universalis
L63.2 Ophiasis
L63.8 Other alopecia areata
L63.9 Alopecia areata, unspecified

L64 Androgenic alopecia
Includes: male-pattern baldness
L64.0 Drug-induced androgenic alopecia
Use additional code for adverse effect, if applicable, to identify drug (T36-T50 with fifth or sixth character 5)
L64.8 Other androgenic alopecia
L64.9 Androgenic alopecia, unspecified

L65 Other nonscarring hair loss
Use additional code for adverse effect, if applicable, to identify drug (T36-T50 with fifth or sixth character 5)
Excludes1: *trichotillomania (F63.3)*
L65.0 Telogen effluvium
L65.1 Anagen effluvium
L65.2 Alopecia mucinosa
L65.8 Other specified nonscarring hair loss
L65.9 Nonscarring hair loss, unspecified
Alopecia NOS

L66 Cicatricial alopecia [scarring hair loss]
L66.0 Pseudopelade
L66.1 Lichen planopilaris
Follicular lichen planus
L66.2 Folliculitis decalvans
L66.3 Perifolliculitis capitis abscedens
L66.4 Folliculitis ulerythematosa reticulata
L66.8 Other cicatricial alopecia
L66.9 Cicatricial alopecia, unspecified

L67 Hair color and hair shaft abnormalities
Excludes1: *monilethrix (Q84.1)*
pili annulati (Q84.1)
telogen effluvium (L65.0)
L67.0 Trichorrhexis nodosa
L67.1 Variations in hair color
Canities
Greyness, hair (premature)
Heterochromia of hair
Poliosis circumscripta, acquired
Poliosis NOS
L67.8 Other hair color and hair shaft abnormalities
Fragilitas crinium
L67.9 Hair color and hair shaft abnormality, unspecified

L68 Hypertrichosis
Includes: excess hair
Excludes1: *congenital hypertrichosis (Q84.2)*
persistent lanugo (Q84.2)
L68.0 Hirsutism
L68.1 Acquired hypertrichosis lanuginosa
L68.2 Localized hypertrichosis
L68.3 Polytrichia
L68.8 Other hypertrichosis
L68.9 Hypertrichosis, unspecified

L70 Acne
Excludes2: *acne keloid (L73.0)*
L70.0 Acne vulgaris
L70.1 Acne conglobata
L70.2 Acne varioliformis
Acne necrotica miliaris
L70.3 Acne tropica
• **L70.4 Infantile acne**
L70.5 Acné excoriée des jeunes filles
Picker's acne
L70.8 Other acne
L70.9 Acne, unspecified

L71 Rosacea
Use additional code for adverse effect, if applicable, to identify drug (T36-T50 with fifth or sixth character 5)
L71.0 Perioral dermatitis
L71.1 Rhinophyma
L71.8 Other rosacea
L71.9 Rosacea, unspecified

L72 Follicular cysts of skin and subcutaneous tissue
L72.0 Epidermal cyst
\+ **L72.1 Pilar and trichodermal cyst**
L72.11 Pilar cyst
L72.12 Trichodermal cyst
Trichilemmal (proliferating) cyst
L72.2 Steatocystoma multiplex
L72.3 Sebaceous cyst
Excludes2: *pilar cyst (L72.11)*
trichilemmal (proliferating) cyst (L72.12)
L72.8 Other follicular cysts of the skin and subcutaneous tissue
L72.9 Follicular cyst of the skin and subcutaneous tissue, unspecified

L73 Other follicular disorders

L73.0 Acne keloid
L73.1 Pseudofolliculitis barbae
L73.2 Hidradenitis suppurativa
L73.8 Other specified follicular disorders
Sycosis barbae
L73.9 Follicular disorder, unspecified

L74 Eccrine sweat disorders

Excludes2: *generalized hyperhidrosis (R61)*
L74.0 Miliaria rubra
L74.1 Miliaria crystallina
L74.2 Miliaria profunda
Miliaria tropicalis
L74.3 Miliaria, unspecified
L74.4 Anhidrosis
Hypohidrosis
+ **L74.5 Focal hyperhidrosis**
+ **L74.51 Primary focal hyperhidrosis**
L74.510 Primary focal hyperhidrosis, axilla
L74.511 Primary focal hyperhidrosis, face
L74.512 Primary focal hyperhidrosis, palms
L74.513 Primary focal hyperhidrosis, soles
L74.519 Primary focal hyperhidrosis, unspecified
L74.52 Secondary focal hyperhidrosis
Frey's syndrome
L74.8 Other eccrine sweat disorders
L74.9 Eccrine sweat disorder, unspecified
Sweat gland disorder NOS

L75 Apocrine sweat disorders

Excludes1: *dyshidrosis (L30.1)*
hidradenitis suppurativa (L73.2)
L75.0 Bromhidrosis
L75.1 Chromhidrosis
L75.2 Apocrine miliaria
Fox-Fordyce disease
L75.8 Other apocrine sweat disorders
L75.9 Apocrine sweat disorder, unspecified

ntraoperative and postprocedural complications of skin and ubcutaneous tissue (L76)

L76 Intraoperative and postprocedural complications of skin and subcutaneous tissue

+ **L76.0 Intraoperative hemorrhage and hematoma of skin and subcutaneous tissue complicating a procedure**
Excludes1: *intraoperative hemorrhage and hematoma of skin and subcutaneous tissue due to accidental puncture and laceration during a procedure (L76.1-)*
CC **L76.01 Intraoperative hemorrhage and hematoma of skin and subcutaneous tissue complicating a dermatologic procedure**
CC Exclusion see Appendix A PDX collection 0852
CC **L76.02 Intraoperative hemorrhage and hematoma of skin and subcutaneous tissue complicating other procedure**
CC Exclusion see Appendix A PDX collection 0852
+ **L76.1 Accidental puncture and laceration of skin and subcutaneous tissue during a procedure**
CC **L76.11 Accidental puncture and laceration of skin and subcutaneous tissue during a dermatologic procedure**
CC Exclusion see Appendix A PDX collection 0509
CC **L76.12 Accidental puncture and laceration of skin and subcutaneous tissue during other procedure**
CC Exclusion see Appendix A PDX collection 0509
+ **L76.2 Postprocedural hemorrhage and hematoma of skin and subcutaneous tissue following a procedure**
CC **L76.21 Postprocedural hemorrhage and hematoma of skin and subcutaneous tissue following a dermatologic procedure**
CC Exclusion see Appendix A PDX collection 0852
CC **L76.22 Postprocedural hemorrhage and hematoma of skin and subcutaneous tissue following other procedure**
CC Exclusion see Appendix A PDX collection 0852
+ **L76.8 Other intraoperative and postprocedural complications of skin and subcutaneous tissue**
Use additional code, if applicable, to further specify disorder
L76.81 Other intraoperative complications of skin and subcutaneous tissue
L76.82 Other postprocedural complications of skin and subcutaneous tissue

Other disorders of the skin and subcutaneous tissue (L80-L99)

L80 Vitiligo

Excludes2: *vitiligo of eyelids (H02.73-)*
vitiligo of vulva (N90.89)
Valid 3-character code, no further characters required

L81 Other disorders of pigmentation

Excludes1: *birthmark NOS (Q82.5)*
Peutz-Jeghers syndrome (Q85.8)
Excludes2: *nevus - see Alphabetical Index*
L81.0 Postinflammatory hyperpigmentation
L81.1 Chloasma
L81.2 Freckles
L81.3 Café au lait spots
L81.4 Other melanin hyperpigmentation
Lentigo
L81.5 Leukoderma, not elsewhere classified
L81.6 Other disorders of diminished melanin formation
L81.7 Pigmented purpuric dermatosis
Angioma serpiginosum
L81.8 Other specified disorders of pigmentation
Iron pigmentation
Tattoo pigmentation
L81.9 Disorder of pigmentation, unspecified

L82 Seborrheic keratosis

Includes: dermatosis papulosa nigra
Leser-Trélat disease
Excludes2: *seborrheic dermatitis (L21.-)*
L82.0 Inflamed seborrheic keratosis
L82.1 Other seborrheic keratosis
Seborrheic keratosis NOS

L83 Acanthosis nigricans

Confluent and reticulated papillomatosis
Valid 3-character code, no further characters required

L84 Corns and callosities

Callus
Clavus
Valid 3-character code, no further characters required

L85 Other epidermal thickening

Excludes2: *hypertrophic disorders of the skin (L91.-)*
L85.0 Acquired ichthyosis
Excludes1: *congenital ichthyosis (Q80.-)*
L85.1 Acquired keratosis [keratoderma] palmaris et plantaris
Excludes1: *inherited keratosis palmaris et plantaris (Q82.8)*
L85.2 Keratosis punctata (palmaris et plantaris)
L85.3 Xerosis cutis
Dry skin dermatitis
L85.8 Other specified epidermal thickening
Cutaneous horn
L85.9 Epidermal thickening, unspecified

L86 Keratoderma in diseases classified elsewhere

Code first underlying disease, such as:
Reiter's disease (M02.3-)
Excludes1: *gonococcal keratoderma (A54.89)*
gonococcal keratosis (A54.89)
keratoderma due to vitamin A deficiency (E50.8)
keratosis due to vitamin A deficiency (E50.8)
xeroderma due to vitamin A deficiency (E50.8)
Valid 3-character code, no further characters required

L87 Transepidermal elimination disorders

Excludes1: *granuloma annulare (perforating) (L92.0)*
L87.0 Keratosis follicularis et parafollicularis in cutem penetrans
Kyrle disease
Hyperkeratosis follicularis penetrans
L87.1 Reactive perforating collagenosis
L87.2 Elastosis perforans serpiginosa
L87.8 Other transepidermal elimination disorders
L87.9 Transepidermal elimination disorder, unspecified

CC **L88 Pyoderma gangrenosum**

Phagedenic pyoderma
Excludes1: *dermatitis gangrenosa (L08.0)*
CC Exclusion see Appendix A PDX collection 0853
Valid 3-character code, no further characters required

L89 Pressure ulcer

Includes: bed sore
decubitus ulcer
plaster ulcer
pressure area
pressure sore

Code first any associated gangrene (I96)

Excludes2: *decubitus (trophic) ulcer of cervix (uteri) (N86)*
diabetic ulcers (E08.621, E08.622, E09.621, E09.622, E10.621, E10.622, E11.621, E11.622, E13.621, E13.622)
non-pressure chronic ulcer of skin (L97.-)
skin infections (L00-L08)
varicose ulcer (I83.0, I83.2)

Review coding guideline C.12.a

+ **L89.0 Pressure ulcer of elbow**

+ **L89.00 Pressure ulcer of unspecified elbow**

L89.000 Pressure ulcer of unspecified elbow, unstageable

L89.001 Pressure ulcer of unspecified elbow, stage 1
Healing pressure ulcer of unspecified elbow, stage 1
Pressure pre-ulcer skin changes limited to persistent focal edema, unspecified elbow

L89.002 Pressure ulcer of unspecified elbow, stage 2
Healing pressure ulcer of unspecified elbow, stage 2
Pressure ulcer with abrasion, blister, partial thickness skin loss involving epidermis and/or dermis, unspecified elbow

MCC **L89.003 Pressure ulcer of unspecified elbow, stage 3**
Healing pressure ulcer of unspecified elbow, stage 3
Pressure ulcer with full thickness skin loss involving damage or necrosis of subcutaneous tissue, unspecified elbow
MCC Exclusion see Appendix A PDX collection 0854
HAC see Appendix B for HAC conditional logic

MCC **L89.004 Pressure ulcer of unspecified elbow, stage 4**
Healing pressure ulcer of unspecified elbow, stage 4
Pressure ulcer with necrosis of soft tissues through to underlying muscle, tendon, or bone, unspecified elbow
MCC Exclusion see Appendix A PDX collection 0854
HAC see Appendix B for HAC conditional logic

L89.009 Pressure ulcer of unspecified elbow, unspecified stage
Healing pressure ulcer of elbow NOS
Healing pressure ulcer of unspecified elbow, unspecified stage

+ **L89.01 Pressure ulcer of right elbow**

L89.010 Pressure ulcer of right elbow, unstageable

L89.011 Pressure ulcer of right elbow, stage 1
Healing pressure ulcer of right elbow, stage 1
Pressure pre-ulcer skin changes limited to persistent focal edema, right elbow

L89.012 Pressure ulcer of right elbow, stage 2
Healing pressure ulcer of right elbow, stage 2
Pressure ulcer with abrasion, blister, partial thickness skin loss involving epidermis and/or dermis, right elbow

MCC **L89.013 Pressure ulcer of right elbow, stage 3**
Healing pressure ulcer of right elbow, stage 3
Pressure ulcer with full thickness skin loss involving damage or necrosis of subcutaneous tissue, right elbow
MCC Exclusion see Appendix A PDX collection 0854
HAC see Appendix B for HAC conditional logic

MCC **L89.014 Pressure ulcer of right elbow, stage 4**
Healing pressure ulcer of right elbow, stage 4
Pressure ulcer with necrosis of soft tissues through to underlying muscle, tendon, or bone, right elbow
MCC Exclusion see Appendix A PDX collection 0854
HAC see Appendix B for HAC conditional logic

L89.019 Pressure ulcer of right elbow, unspecified stage
Healing pressure right of elbow NOS
Healing pressure ulcer of unspecified elbow unspecified stage

+ **L89.02 Pressure ulcer of left elbow**

L89.020 Pressure ulcer of left elbow, unstageable

L89.021 Pressure ulcer of left elbow, stage 1
Healing pressure ulcer of left elbow, stage 1
Pressure pre-ulcer skin changes limited to persistent focal edema, left elbow

L89.022 Pressure ulcer of left elbow, stage 2
Healing pressure ulcer of left elbow, stage 2
Pressure ulcer with abrasion, blister, partial thickness skin loss involving epidermis an or dermis, left elbow

MCC **L89.023 Pressure ulcer of left elbow, stage 3**
Healing pressure ulcer of left elbow, stage 3
Pressure ulcer with full thickness skin loss involving damage or necrosis of subcutaneous tissue, left elbow
MCC Exclusion see Appendix A PDX collection 0854
HAC see Appendix B for HAC conditional logic

MCC **L89.024 Pressure ulcer of left elbow, stage 4**
Healing pressure ulcer of left elbow, stage 4
Pressure ulcer with necrosis of soft tissues through to underlying muscle, tendon, or bone, left elbow
MCC Exclusion see Appendix A PDX collection 0854
HAC see Appendix B for HAC conditional logic

L89.029 Pressure ulcer of left elbow, unspecified sta
Healing pressure ulcer of left of elbow NOS
Healing pressure ulcer of unspecified elbow, unspecified stage

+ **L89.1 Pressure ulcer of back**

+ **L89.10 Pressure ulcer of unspecified part of back**

L89.100 Pressure ulcer of unspecified part of back, unstageable

L89.101 Pressure ulcer of unspecified part of back, stage 1
Healing pressure ulcer of unspecified part of back, stage 1
Pressure pre-ulcer skin changes limited to persistent focal edema, unspecified part of back

L89.102 Pressure ulcer of unspecified part of back, stage 2
Healing pressure ulcer of unspecified part of back, stage 2
Pressure ulcer with abrasion, blister, partial thickness skin loss involving epidermis an or dermis, unspecified part of back

MCC **L89.103 Pressure ulcer of unspecified part of back, stage 3**
Healing pressure ulcer of unspecified part of back, stage 3
Pressure ulcer with full thickness skin loss involving damage or necrosis of subcutaneous tissue, unspecified part of back
MCC Exclusion see Appendix A PDX collection 0854
HAC see Appendix B for HAC conditional logic

MCC **L89.104 Pressure ulcer of unspecified part of back, stage 4**
Healing pressure ulcer of unspecified part of back, stage 4
Pressure ulcer with necrosis of soft tissues through to underlying muscle, tendon, or bone, unspecified part of back
MCC Exclusion see Appendix A PDX collection 0854
HAC see Appendix B for HAC conditional logic

L89.109 Pressure ulcer of unspecified part of back, unspecified stage
Healing pressure ulcer of unspecified part of back NOS
Healing pressure ulcer of unspecified part of back, unspecified stage

+ **L89.11 Pressure ulcer of right upper back**
Pressure ulcer of right shoulder blade

L89.110 Pressure ulcer of right upper back, unstageable

L89.111 Pressure ulcer of right upper back, stage 1
Healing pressure ulcer of right upper back, stage 1
Pressure pre-ulcer skin changes limited to persistent focal edema, right upper back

L89.112 Pressure ulcer of right upper back, stage 2
Healing pressure ulcer of right upper back, stage 2
Pressure ulcer with abrasion, blister, partial thickness skin loss involving epidermis and/or dermis, right upper back

MCC **L89.113 Pressure ulcer of right upper back, stage 3**
Healing pressure ulcer of right upper back, stage 3
Pressure ulcer with full thickness skin loss involving damage or necrosis of subcutaneous tissue, right upper back
MCC Exclusion see Appendix A PDX collection 0854
HAC see Appendix B for HAC conditional logic

MCC **L89.114 Pressure ulcer of right upper back, stage 4**
Healing pressure ulcer of right upper back, stage 4
Pressure ulcer with necrosis of soft tissues through to underlying muscle, tendon, or bone, right upper back
MCC Exclusion see Appendix A PDX collection 0854
HAC see Appendix B for HAC conditional logic

L89.119 Pressure ulcer of right upper back, unspecified stage
Healing pressure ulcer of right upper back NOS
Healing pressure ulcer of right upper back, unspecified stage

+ **L89.12 Pressure ulcer of left upper back**
Pressure ulcer of left shoulder blade

L89.120 Pressure ulcer of left upper back, unstageable

L89.121 Pressure ulcer of left upper back, stage 1
Healing pressure ulcer of left upper back, stage 1
Pressure pre-ulcer skin changes limited to persistent focal edema, left upper back

L89.122 Pressure ulcer of left upper back, stage 2
Healing pressure ulcer of left upper back, stage 2
Pressure ulcer with abrasion, blister, partial thickness skin loss involving epidermis and/or dermis, left upper back

MCC **L89.123 Pressure ulcer of left upper back, stage 3**
Healing pressure ulcer of left upper back, stage 3
Pressure ulcer with full thickness skin loss involving damage or necrosis of subcutaneous tissue, left upper back
MCC Exclusion see Appendix A PDX collection 0854
HAC see Appendix B for HAC conditional logic

MCC **L89.124 Pressure ulcer of left upper back, stage 4**
Healing pressure ulcer of left upper back, stage 4
Pressure ulcer with necrosis of soft tissues through to underlying muscle, tendon, or bone, left upper back
MCC Exclusion see Appendix A PDX collection 0854
HAC see Appendix B for HAC conditional logic

L89.129 Pressure ulcer of left upper back, unspecified stage
Healing pressure ulcer of left upper back NOS
Healing pressure ulcer of left upper back, unspecified stage

+ **L89.13 Pressure ulcer of right lower back**

L89.130 Pressure ulcer of right lower back, unstageable

L89.131 Pressure ulcer of right lower back, stage 1
Healing pressure ulcer of right lower back, stage 1
Pressure pre-ulcer skin changes limited to persistent focal edema, right lower back

L89.132 Pressure ulcer of right lower back, stage 2
Healing pressure ulcer of right lower back, stage 2
Pressure ulcer with abrasion, blister, partial thickness skin loss involving epidermis and/or dermis, right lower back

MCC **L89.133 Pressure ulcer of right lower back, stage 3**
Healing pressure ulcer of right lower back, stage 3
Pressure ulcer with full thickness skin loss involving damage or necrosis of subcutaneous tissue, right lower back
MCC Exclusion see Appendix A PDX collection 0854
HAC see Appendix B for HAC conditional logic

MCC **L89.134 Pressure ulcer of right lower back, stage 4**
Healing pressure ulcer of right lower back, stage 4
Pressure ulcer with necrosis of soft tissues through to underlying muscle, tendon, or bone, right lower back
MCC Exclusion see Appendix A PDX collection 0854
HAC see Appendix B for HAC conditional logic

L89.139 Pressure ulcer of right lower back, unspecified stage
Healing pressure ulcer of right lower back NOS
Healing pressure ulcer of right lower back, unspecified stage

+ **L89.14 Pressure ulcer of left lower back**

L89.140 Pressure ulcer of left lower back, unstageable

L89.141 Pressure ulcer of left lower back, stage 1
Healing pressure ulcer of left lower back, stage 1
Pressure pre-ulcer skin changes limited to persistent focal edema, left lower back

L89.142 Pressure ulcer of left lower back, stage 2
Healing pressure ulcer of left lower back, stage 2
Pressure ulcer with abrasion, blister, partial thickness skin loss involving epidermis and/or dermis, left lower back

MCC **L89.143 Pressure ulcer of left lower back, stage 3**
Healing pressure ulcer of left lower back, stage 3
Pressure ulcer with full thickness skin loss involving damage or necrosis of subcutaneous tissue, left lower back
MCC Exclusion see Appendix A PDX collection 0854
HAC see Appendix B for HAC conditional logic

MCC **L89.144 Pressure ulcer of left lower back, stage 4**
Healing pressure ulcer of left lower back, stage 4
Pressure ulcer with necrosis of soft tissues through to underlying muscle, tendon, or bone, left lower back
MCC Exclusion see Appendix A PDX collection 0854
HAC see Appendix B for HAC conditional logic

L89.149 Pressure ulcer of left lower back, unspecified stage
Healing pressure ulcer of left lower back NOS
Healing pressure ulcer of left lower back, unspecified stage

+ **L89.15 Pressure ulcer of sacral region**
Pressure ulcer of coccyx
Pressure ulcer of tailbone

L89.150 Pressure ulcer of sacral region, unstageable

L89.151 Pressure ulcer of sacral region, stage 1
Healing pressure ulcer of sacral region, stage 1
Pressure pre-ulcer skin changes limited to persistent focal edema, sacral region

L89.152 Pressure ulcer of sacral region, stage 2
Healing pressure ulcer of sacral region, stage 2
Pressure ulcer with abrasion, blister, partial thickness skin loss involving epidermis and/or dermis, sacral region

MCC **L89.153 Pressure ulcer of sacral region, stage 3**
Healing pressure ulcer of sacral region, stage 3
Pressure ulcer with full thickness skin loss involving damage or necrosis of subcutaneous tissue, sacral region
MCC Exclusion see Appendix A PDX collection 0854
HAC see Appendix B for HAC conditional logic

MCC **L89.154 Pressure ulcer of sacral region, stage 4**
Healing pressure ulcer of sacral region, stage 4
Pressure ulcer with necrosis of soft tissues through to underlying muscle, tendon, or bone, sacral region
MCC Exclusion see Appendix A PDX collection 0854
HAC see Appendix B for HAC conditional logic

L89.159 Pressure ulcer of sacral region, unspecified stage
Healing pressure ulcer of sacral region NOS
Healing pressure ulcer of sacral region, unspecified stage

+ **L89.2 Pressure ulcer of hip**

+ **L89.20 Pressure ulcer of unspecified hip**

L89.200 Pressure ulcer of unspecified hip, unstageable

L89.201 Pressure ulcer of unspecified hip, stage 1
Healing pressure ulcer of unspecified hip back, stage 1
Pressure pre-ulcer skin changes limited to persistent focal edema, unspecified hip

L89.202 Pressure ulcer of unspecified hip, stage 2
Healing pressure ulcer of unspecified hip, stage 2
Pressure ulcer with abrasion, blister, partial thickness skin loss involving epidermis and/or dermis, unspecified hip

MCC **L89.203 Pressure ulcer of unspecified hip, stage 3**
Healing pressure ulcer of unspecified hip, stage 3
Pressure ulcer with full thickness skin loss involving damage or necrosis of subcutaneous tissue, unspecified hip
MCC Exclusion see Appendix A PDX collection 0854
HAC see Appendix B for HAC conditional logic

MCC **L89.204 Pressure ulcer of unspecified hip, stage 4**
Healing pressure ulcer of unspecified hip, stage 4
Pressure ulcer with necrosis of soft tissues through to underlying muscle, tendon, or bone, unspecified hip
MCC Exclusion see Appendix A PDX collection 0854
HAC see Appendix B for HAC conditional logic

L89.209 Pressure ulcer of unspecified hip, unspecified stage
Healing pressure ulcer of unspecified hip NOS
Healing pressure ulcer of unspecified hip, unspecified stage

+ **L89.21 Pressure ulcer of right hip**

L89.210 Pressure ulcer of right hip, unstageable

L89.211 Pressure ulcer of right hip, stage 1
Healing pressure ulcer of right hip back, stage 1
Pressure pre-ulcer skin changes limited to persistent focal edema, right hip

L89.212 Pressure ulcer of right hip, stage 2
Healing pressure ulcer of right hip, stage 2
Pressure ulcer with abrasion, blister, partial thickness skin loss involving epidermis and/or dermis, right hip

MCC **L89.213 Pressure ulcer of right hip, stage 3**
Healing pressure ulcer of right hip, stage 3
Pressure ulcer with full thickness skin loss involving damage or necrosis of subcutaneous tissue, right hip
MCC Exclusion see Appendix A PDX collection 0854
HAC see Appendix B for HAC conditional logic

MCC **L89.214 Pressure ulcer of right hip, stage 4**
Healing pressure ulcer of right hip, stage 4
Pressure ulcer with necrosis of soft tissues through to underlying muscle, tendon, or bone, right hip
MCC Exclusion see Appendix A PDX collectio
0854
HAC see Appendix B for HAC conditional logi

L89.219 Pressure ulcer of right hip, unspecified sta
Healing pressure ulcer of right hip NOS
Healing pressure ulcer of right hip, unspecified stage

+ **L89.22 Pressure ulcer of left hip**

L89.220 Pressure ulcer of left hip, unstageable

L89.221 Pressure ulcer of left hip, stage 1
Healing pressure ulcer of left hip back, stag
Pressure pre-ulcer skin changes limited to persistent focal edema, left hip

L89.222 Pressure ulcer of left hip, stage 2
Healing pressure ulcer of left hip, stage 2
Pressure ulcer with abrasion, blister, partial thickness skin loss involving epidermis a or dermis, left hip

MCC **L89.223 Pressure ulcer of left hip, stage 3**
Healing pressure ulcer of left hip, stage 3
Pressure ulcer with full thickness skin loss involving damage or necrosis of subcutaneous tissue, left hip
MCC Exclusion see Appendix A PDX collection 0854
HAC see Appendix B for HAC conditional logic

MCC **L89.224 Pressure ulcer of left hip, stage 4**
Healing pressure ulcer of left hip, stage 4
Pressure ulcer with necrosis of soft tissues through to underlying muscle, tendon, or bone, left hip
MCC Exclusion see Appendix A PDX collection 0854
HAC see Appendix B for HAC conditional logic

L89.229 Pressure ulcer of left hip, unspecified stage
Healing pressure ulcer of left hip NOS
Healing pressure ulcer of left hip, unspecifie stage

+ **L89.3 Pressure ulcer of buttock**

+ **L89.30 Pressure ulcer of unspecified buttock**

L89.300 Pressure ulcer of unspecified buttock, unstageable

L89.301 Pressure ulcer of unspecified buttock, stage
Healing pressure ulcer of unspecified buttoc stage 1
Pressure pre-ulcer skin changes limited to persistent focal edema, unspecified buttoc

L89.302 Pressure ulcer of unspecified buttock, stage
Healing pressure ulcer of unspecified buttock stage 2
Pressure ulcer with abrasion, blister, partial thickness skin loss involving epidermis an or dermis, unspecified buttock

MCC **L89.303 Pressure ulcer of unspecified buttock, stage**
Healing pressure ulcer of unspecified buttock stage 3
Pressure ulcer with full thickness skin loss involving damage or necrosis of subcutaneous tissue, unspecified buttock
MCC Exclusion see Appendix A PDX collection 0854
HAC see Appendix B for HAC conditional logic

MCC **L89.304 Pressure ulcer of unspecified buttock, stage**
Healing pressure ulcer of unspecified buttock stage 4
Pressure ulcer with necrosis of soft tissues through to underlying muscle, tendon, or bone, unspecified buttock
MCC Exclusion see Appendix A PDX collection 0854
HAC see Appendix B for HAC conditional logic

L89.309 Pressure ulcer of unspecified buttock, unspecified stage
Healing pressure ulcer of unspecified buttock NOS
Healing pressure ulcer of unspecified buttock unspecified stage

+ **L89.31 Pressure ulcer of right buttock**

L89.310 Pressure ulcer of right buttock, unstageable

L89.311 Pressure ulcer of right buttock, stage 1
Healing pressure ulcer of right buttock, stage 1
Pressure pre-ulcer skin changes limited to persistent focal edema, right buttock

L89.312 Pressure ulcer of right buttock, stage 2
Healing pressure ulcer of right buttock, stage 2
Pressure ulcer with abrasion, blister, partial thickness skin loss involving epidermis and/or dermis, right buttock

MCC **L89.313 Pressure ulcer of right buttock, stage 3**
Healing pressure ulcer of right buttock, stage 3
Pressure ulcer with full thickness skin loss involving damage or necrosis of subcutaneous tissue, right buttock
MCC Exclusion see Appendix A PDX collection 0854
HAC see Appendix B for HAC conditional logic

MCC **L89.314 Pressure ulcer of right buttock, stage 4**
Healing pressure ulcer of right buttock, stage 4
Pressure ulcer with necrosis of soft tissues through to underlying muscle, tendon, or bone, right buttock
MCC Exclusion see Appendix A PDX collection 0854
HAC see Appendix B for HAC conditional logic

L89.319 Pressure ulcer of right buttock, unspecified stage
Healing pressure ulcer of right buttock NOS
Healing pressure ulcer of right buttock, unspecified stage

+ **L89.32 Pressure ulcer of left buttock**

L89.320 Pressure ulcer of left buttock, unstageable

L89.321 Pressure ulcer of left buttock, stage 1
Healing pressure ulcer of left buttock, stage 1
Pressure pre-ulcer skin changes limited to persistent focal edema, left buttock

L89.322 Pressure ulcer of left buttock, stage 2
Healing pressure ulcer of left buttock, stage 2
Pressure ulcer with abrasion, blister, partial thickness skin loss involving epidermis and/or dermis, left buttock

MCC **L89.323 Pressure ulcer of left buttock, stage 3**
Healing pressure ulcer of left buttock, stage 3
Pressure ulcer with full thickness skin loss involving damage or necrosis of subcutaneous tissue, left buttock
MCC Exclusion see Appendix A PDX collection 0854
HAC see Appendix B for HAC conditional logic

MCC **L89.324 Pressure ulcer of left buttock, stage 4**
Healing pressure ulcer of left buttock, stage 4
Pressure ulcer with necrosis of soft tissues through to underlying muscle, tendon, or bone, left buttock
MCC Exclusion see Appendix A PDX collection 0854
HAC see Appendix B for HAC conditional logic

L89.329 Pressure ulcer of left buttock, unspecified stage
Healing pressure ulcer of left buttock NOS
Healing pressure ulcer of left buttock, unspecified stage

+ **L89.4 Pressure ulcer of contiguous site of back, buttock and hip**

L89.40 Pressure ulcer of contiguous site of back, buttock and hip, unspecified stage
Healing pressure ulcer of contiguous site of back, buttock and hip NOS
Healing pressure ulcer of contiguous site of back, buttock and hip, unspecified stage

L89.41 Pressure ulcer of contiguous site of back, buttock and hip, stage 1
Healing pressure ulcer of contiguous site of back, buttock and hip, stage 1
Pressure pre-ulcer skin changes limited to persistent focal edema, contiguous site of back, buttock and hip

L89.42 Pressure ulcer of contiguous site of back, buttock and hip, stage 2
Healing pressure ulcer of contiguous site of back, buttock and hip, stage 2
Pressure ulcer with abrasion, blister, partial thickness skin loss involving epidermis and/or dermis, contiguous site of back, buttock and hip

MCC **L89.43 Pressure ulcer of contiguous site of back, buttock and hip, stage 3**
Healing pressure ulcer of contiguous site of back, buttock and hip, stage 3
Pressure ulcer with full thickness skin loss involving damage or necrosis of subcutaneous tissue, contiguous site of back, buttock and hip
MCC Exclusion see Appendix A PDX collection 0854
HAC see Appendix B for HAC conditional logic

MCC **L89.44 Pressure ulcer of contiguous site of back, buttock and hip, stage 4**
Healing pressure ulcer of contiguous site of back, buttock and hip, stage 4
Pressure ulcer with necrosis of soft tissues through to underlying muscle, tendon, or bone, contiguous site of back, buttock and hip
MCC Exclusion see Appendix A PDX collection 0854
HAC see Appendix B for HAC conditional logic

L89.45 Pressure ulcer of contiguous site of back, buttock and hip, unstageable

+ **L89.5 Pressure ulcer of ankle**

+ **L89.50 Pressure ulcer of unspecified ankle**

L89.500 Pressure ulcer of unspecified ankle, unstageable

L89.501 Pressure ulcer of unspecified ankle, stage 1
Healing pressure ulcer of unspecified ankle, stage 1
Pressure pre-ulcer skin changes limited to persistent focal edema, unspecified ankle

L89.502 Pressure ulcer of unspecified ankle, stage 2
Healing pressure ulcer of unspecified ankle, stage 2
Pressure ulcer with abrasion, blister, partial thickness skin loss involving epidermis and/or dermis, unspecified ankle

MCC **L89.503 Pressure ulcer of unspecified ankle, stage 3**
Healing pressure ulcer of unspecified ankle, stage 3
Pressure ulcer with full thickness skin loss involving damage or necrosis of subcutaneous tissue, unspecified ankle
MCC Exclusion see Appendix A PDX collection 0854
HAC see Appendix B for HAC conditional logic

MCC **L89.504 Pressure ulcer of unspecified ankle, stage 4**
Healing pressure ulcer of unspecified ankle, stage 4
Pressure ulcer with necrosis of soft tissues through to underlying muscle, tendon, or bone, unspecified ankle
MCC Exclusion see Appendix A PDX collection 0854
HAC see Appendix B for HAC conditional logic

L89.509 Pressure ulcer of unspecified ankle, unspecified stage
Healing pressure ulcer of unspecified ankle NOS
Healing pressure ulcer of unspecified ankle, unspecified stage

+ **L89.51 Pressure ulcer of right ankle**

L89.510 Pressure ulcer of right ankle, unstageable

L89.511 Pressure ulcer of right ankle, stage 1
Healing pressure ulcer of right ankle, stage 1
Pressure pre-ulcer skin changes limited to persistent focal edema, right ankle

L89.512 Pressure ulcer of right ankle, stage 2
Healing pressure ulcer of right ankle, stage 2
Pressure ulcer with abrasion, blister, partial thickness skin loss involving epidermis and/or dermis, right ankle

MCC **L89.513 Pressure ulcer of right ankle, stage 3**
Healing pressure ulcer of right ankle, stage 3
Pressure ulcer with full thickness skin loss involving damage or necrosis of subcutaneous tissue, right ankle
MCC Exclusion see Appendix A PDX collection 0854
HAC see Appendix B for HAC conditional logic

MCC **L89.514 Pressure ulcer of right ankle, stage 4**
Healing pressure ulcer of right ankle, stage 4
Pressure ulcer with necrosis of soft tissues through to underlying muscle, tendon, or bone, right ankle
MCC Exclusion see Appendix A PDX collection 0854
HAC see Appendix B for HAC conditional logic

L89.519 Pressure ulcer of right ankle, unspecified stage
Healing pressure ulcer of right ankle NOS
Healing pressure ulcer of right ankle, unspecified stage

\+ **L89.52 Pressure ulcer of left ankle**

L89.520 Pressure ulcer of left ankle, unstageable

L89.521 Pressure ulcer of left ankle, stage 1
Healing pressure ulcer of left ankle, stage 1
Pressure pre-ulcer skin changes limited to persistnt focal edema, left ankle

L89.522 Pressure ulcer of left ankle, stage 2
Healing pressure ulcer of left ankle, stage 2
Pressure ulcer with abrasion, blister, partial thickness skin loss involving epidermis and/or dermis, left ankle

MCC **L89.523 Pressure ulcer of left ankle, stage 3**
Healing pressure ulcer of left ankle, stage 3
Pressure ulcer with full thickness skin loss involving damage or necrosis of subcutaneous tissue, left ankle
MCC Exclusion see Appendix A PDX collection 0854
HAC see Appendix B for HAC conditional logic

MCC **L89.524 Pressure ulcer of left ankle, stage 4**
Healing pressure ulcer of left ankle, stage 4
Pressure ulcer with necrosis of soft tissues through to underlying muscle, tendon, or bone, left ankle
MCC Exclusion see Appendix A PDX collection 0854
HAC see Appendix B for HAC conditional logic

L89.529 Pressure ulcer of left ankle, unspecified stage
Healing pressure ulcer of left ankle NOS
Healing pressure ulcer of left ankle, unspecified stage

\+ **L89.6 Pressure ulcer of heel**

\+ **L89.60 Pressure ulcer of unspecified heel**

L89.600 Pressure ulcer of unspecified heel, unstageable

L89.601 Pressure ulcer of unspecified heel, stage 1
Healing pressure ulcer of unspecified heel, stage 1
Pressure pre-ulcer skin changes limited to persistent focal edema, unspecified heel

L89.602 Pressure ulcer of unspecified heel, stage 2
Healing pressure ulcer of unspecified heel, stage 2
Pressure ulcer with abrasion, blister, partial thickness skin loss involving epidermis and/or dermis, unspecified heel

MCC **L89.603 Pressure ulcer of unspecified heel, stage 3**
Healing pressure ulcer of unspecified heel, stage 3
Pressure ulcer with full thickness skin loss involving damage or necrosis of subcutaneous tissue, unspecified heel
MCC Exclusion see Appendix A PDX collection 0854
HAC see Appendix B for HAC conditional logic

MCC **L89.604 Pressure ulcer of unspecified heel, stage 4**
Healing pressure ulcer of unspecified heel, stage 4
Pressure ulcer with necrosis of soft tissues through to underlying muscle, tendon, or bone, unspecified heel
MCC Exclusion see Appendix A PDX collection 0854
HAC see Appendix B for HAC conditional logic

L89.609 Pressure ulcer of unspecified heel, unspecified stage
Healing pressure ulcer of unspecified heel NOS
Healing pressure ulcer of unspecified heel, unspecified stage

\+ **L89.61 Pressure ulcer of right heel**

L89.610 Pressure ulcer of right heel, unstageable

L89.611 Pressure ulcer of right heel, stage 1
Healing pressure ulcer of right heel, stage 1
Pressure pre-ulcer skin changes limited to persistent focal edema, right heel

L89.612 Pressure ulcer of right heel, stage 2
Healing pressure ulcer of right heel, stage 2
Pressure ulcer with abrasion, blister, partial thickness skin loss involving epidermis a[nd/] or dermis, right heel

MCC **L89.613 Pressure ulcer of right heel, stage 3**
Healing pressure ulcer of right heel, stage 3
Pressure ulcer with full thickness skin loss involving damage or necrosis of subcutaneous tissue, right heel
MCC Exclusion see Appendix A PDX collection 0854
HAC see Appendix B for HAC conditional logic

MCC **L89.614 Pressure ulcer of right heel, stage 4**
Healing pressure ulcer of right heel, stage 4
Pressure ulcer with necrosis of soft tissues through to underlying muscle, tendon, or bone, right heel
MCC Exclusion see Appendix A PDX collection 0854
HAC see Appendix B for HAC conditional logic

L89.619 Pressure ulcer of right heel, unspecified st[age]
Healing pressure ulcer of right heel NOS
Healing pressure ulcer of unspecified heel, right stage

\+ **L89.62 Pressure ulcer of left heel**

L89.620 Pressure ulcer of left heel, unstageable

L89.621 Pressure ulcer of left heel, stage 1
Healing pressure ulcer of left heel, stage 1
Pressure pre-ulcer skin changes limited to persistent focal edema, left heel

L89.622 Pressure ulcer of left heel, stage 2
Healing pressure ulcer of left heel, stage 2
Pressure ulcer with abrasion, blister, partial thickness skin loss involving epidermis a[nd/] or dermis, left heel

MCC **L89.623 Pressure ulcer of left heel, stage 3**
Healing pressure ulcer of left heel, stage 3
Pressure ulcer with full thickness skin loss involving damage or necrosis of subcutaneous tissue, left heel
MCC Exclusion see Appendix A PDX collection 0854
HAC see Appendix B for HAC conditional logic

MCC **L89.624 Pressure ulcer of left heel, stage 4**
Healing pressure ulcer of left heel, stage 4
Pressure ulcer with necrosis of soft tissues through to underlying muscle, tendon, or bone, left heel
MCC Exclusion see Appendix A PDX collection 0854
HAC see Appendix B for HAC conditional logic

L89.629 Pressure ulcer of left heel, unspecified stag[e]
Healing pressure ulcer of left heel NOS
Healing pressure ulcer of left heel, unspecif[ied] stage

\+ **L89.8 Pressure ulcer of other site**

\+ **L89.81 Pressure ulcer of head**
Pressure ulcer of face

L89.810 Pressure ulcer of head, unstageable

L89.811 Pressure ulcer of head, stage 1
Healing pressure ulcer of head, stage 1
Pressure pre-ulcer skin changes limited to persistent focal edema, head

L89.812 Pressure ulcer of head, stage 2
Healing pressure ulcer of head, stage 2
Pressure ulcer with abrasion, blister, partial thickness skin loss involving epidermis and/or dermis, head

MCC **L89.813 Pressure ulcer of head, stage 3**
Healing pressure ulcer of head, stage 3
Pressure ulcer with full thickness skin loss involving damage or necrosis of subcutaneous tissue, head
MCC Exclusion see Appendix A PDX collection 0854
HAC see Appendix B for HAC conditional logic

MCC **L89.814 Pressure ulcer of head, stage 4**
Healing pressure ulcer of head, stage 4
Pressure ulcer with necrosis of soft tissues through to underlying muscle, tendon, or bone, head
MCC Exclusion see Appendix A PDX collection 0854
HAC see Appendix B for HAC conditional logic

L89.819 Pressure ulcer of head, unspecified stage
Healing pressure ulcer of head NOS
Healing pressure ulcer of head, unspecified stage

\+ **L89.89 Pressure ulcer of other site**

L89.890 Pressure ulcer of other site, unstageable

L89.891 Pressure ulcer of other site, stage 1
Healing pressure ulcer of other site, stage 1
Pressure pre-ulcer skin changes limited to persistent focal edema, other site

L89.892 Pressure ulcer of other site, stage 2
Healing pressure ulcer of other site, stage 2
Pressure ulcer with abrasion, blister, partial thickness skin loss involving epidermis and/or dermis, other site

MCC **L89.893 Pressure ulcer of other site, stage 3**
Healing pressure ulcer of other site, stage 3
Pressure ulcer with full thickness skin loss involving damage or necrosis of subcutaneous tissue, other site
MCC Exclusion see Appendix A PDX collection 0854
HAC see Appendix B for HAC conditional logic

MCC **L89.894 Pressure ulcer of other site, stage 4**
Healing pressure ulcer of other site, stage 4
Pressure ulcer with necrosis of soft tissues through to underlying muscle, tendon, or bone, other site
MCC Exclusion see Appendix A PDX collection 0854
HAC see Appendix B for HAC conditional logic

L89.899 Pressure ulcer of other site, unspecified stage
Healing pressure ulcer of other site NOS
Healing pressure ulcer of other site, unspecified stage

\+ **L89.9 Pressure ulcer of unspecified site**

L89.90 Pressure ulcer of unspecified site, unspecified stage
Healing pressure ulcer of unspecified site NOS
Healing pressure ulcer of unspecified site, unspecified stage

L89.91 Pressure ulcer of unspecified site, stage 1
Healing pressure ulcer of unspecified site, stage 1
Pressure pre-ulcer skin changes limited to persistent focal edema, unspecified site

L89.92 Pressure ulcer of unspecified site, stage 2
Healing pressure ulcer of unspecified site, stage 2
Pressure ulcer with abrasion, blister, partial thickness skin loss involving epidermis and/or dermis, unspecified site

MCC **L89.93 Pressure ulcer of unspecified site, stage 3**
Healing pressure ulcer of unspecified site, stage 3
Pressure ulcer with full thickness skin loss involving damage or necrosis of subcutaneous tissue, unspecified site
MCC Exclusion see Appendix A PDX collection 0854
HAC see Appendix B for HAC conditional logic

MCC **L89.94 Pressure ulcer of unspecified site, stage 4**
Healing pressure ulcer of unspecified site, stage 4
Pressure ulcer with necrosis of soft tissues through to underlying muscle, tendon, or bone, unspecified site
MCC Exclusion see Appendix A PDX collection 0854
HAC see Appendix B for HAC conditional logic

L89.95 Pressure ulcer of unspecified site, unstageable

L90 Atrophic disorders of skin

L90.0 Lichen sclerosus et atrophicus
Excludes2: *lichen sclerosus of external female genital organs (N90.4)*
lichen sclerosus of external male genital organs (N48.0)

L90.1 Anetoderma of Schweninger-Buzzi

L90.2 Anetoderma of Jadassohn-Pellizzari

L90.3 Atrophoderma of Pasini and Pierini

L90.4 Acrodermatitis chronica atrophicans

L90.5 Scar conditions and fibrosis of skin
Adherent scar (skin)
Cicatrix
Disfigurement of skin due to scar
Fibrosis of skin NOS
Scar NOS
Excludes2: *hypertrophic scar (L91.0)*
keloid scar (L91.0)

L90.6 Striae atrophicae

L90.8 Other atrophic disorders of skin

L90.9 Atrophic disorder of skin, unspecified

L91 Hypertrophic disorders of skin

L91.0 Hypertrophic scar
Keloid
Keloid scar
Excludes2: *acne keloid (L73.0)*
scar NOS (L90.5)

L91.8 Other hypertrophic disorders of the skin

L91.9 Hypertrophic disorder of the skin, unspecified

L92 Granulomatous disorders of skin and subcutaneous tissue

Excludes2: *actinic granuloma (L57.5)*

L92.0 Granuloma annulare
Perforating granuloma annulare

L92.1 Necrobiosis lipoidica, not elsewhere classified
Excludes1: *necrobiosis lipoidica associated with diabetes mellitus (E08-E13 with .620)*

L92.2 Granuloma faciale [eosinophilic granuloma of skin]

L92.3 Foreign body granuloma of the skin and subcutaneous tissue
Use additional code to identify the type of retained foreign body (Z18.-)

L92.8 Other granulomatous disorders of the skin and subcutaneous tissue

L92.9 Granulomatous disorder of the skin and subcutaneous tissue, unspecified

L93 Lupus erythematosus

Use additional code for adverse effect, if applicable, to identify drug (T36-T50 with fifth or sixth character 5)
Excludes1: *lupus exedens (A18.4)*
lupus vulgaris (A18.4)
scleroderma (M34.-)
systemic lupus erythematosus (M32.-)

L93.0 Discoid lupus erythematosus
Lupus erythematosus NOS

L93.1 Subacute cutaneous lupus erythematosus

L93.2 Other local lupus erythematosus
Lupus erythematosus profundus
Lupus panniculitis

L94 Other localized connective tissue disorders

Excludes1: *systemic connective tissue disorders (M30-M36)*

L94.0 Localized scleroderma [morphea]
Circumscribed scleroderma

L94.1 Linear scleroderma
En coup de sabre lesion

L94.2 Calcinosis cutis

L94.3 Sclerodactyly

L94.4 Gottron's papules

L94.5 Poikiloderma vasculare atrophicans

L94.6 Ainhum

L94.8 Other specified localized connective tissue disorders

L94.9 Localized connective tissue disorder, unspecified

L95 Vasculitis limited to skin, not elsewhere classified

Excludes1: *angioma serpiginosum (L81.7)*
Henoch(-Schönlein) purpura (D69.0)
hypersensitivity angiitis (M31.0)
lupus panniculitis (L93.2)
panniculitis NOS (M79.3)
panniculitis of neck and back (M54.0-)
polyarteritis nodosa (M30.0)
relapsing panniculitis (M35.6)
rheumatoid vasculitis (M05.2)
serum sickness (T80.6-)
urticaria (L50.-)
Wegener's granulomatosis (M31.3-)

L95.0 Livedoid vasculitis
Atrophie blanche (en plaque)

L95.1 Erythema elevatum diutinum

L95.8 Other vasculitis limited to the skin

L95.9 Vasculitis limited to the skin, unspecified

L97 Non-pressure chronic ulcer of lower limb, not elsewhere classified

Includes: chronic ulcer of skin of lower limb NOS
non-healing ulcer of skin
non-infected sinus of skin
trophic ulcer NOS
tropical ulcer NOS
ulcer of skin of lower limb NOS

Code first any associated underlying condition, such as:
any associated gangrene (I96)
atherosclerosis of the lower extremities (I70.23-, I70.24-, I70.33-, I70.34-, I70.43-, I70.44-, I70.53-, I70.54-, I70.63-, I70.64-, I70.73-, I70.74-)
chronic venous hypertension (I87.31-, I87.33-)
diabetic ulcers (E08.621, E08.622, E09.621, E09.622, E10.621, E10.622, E11.621, E11.622, E13.621, E13.622)
postphlebitic syndrome (I87.01-, I87.03-)
postthrombotic syndrome (I87.01-, I87.03-)
varicose ulcer (I83.0-, I83.2-)

Excludes2: *pressure ulcer (pressure area) (L89.-)*
skin infections (L00-L08)
specific infections classified to A00-B99

+ **L97.1 Non-pressure chronic ulcer of thigh**

+ **L97.10 Non-pressure chronic ulcer of unspecified thigh**

CC **L97.101 Non-pressure chronic ulcer of unspecified thigh limited to breakdown of skin**
CC Exclusion see Appendix A PDX collection 0698

CC **L97.102 Non-pressure chronic ulcer of unspecified thigh with fat layer exposed**
CC Exclusion see Appendix A PDX collection 0698

CC **L97.103 Non-pressure chronic ulcer of unspecified thigh with necrosis of muscle**
CC Exclusion see Appendix A PDX collection 0698

CC **L97.104 Non-pressure chronic ulcer of unspecified thigh with necrosis of bone**
CC Exclusion see Appendix A PDX collection 0698

CC **L97.109 Non-pressure chronic ulcer of unspecified thigh with unspecified severity**
CC Exclusion see Appendix A PDX collection 0698

+ **L97.11 Non-pressure chronic ulcer of right thigh**

CC **L97.111 Non-pressure chronic ulcer of right thigh limited to breakdown of skin**
CC Exclusion see Appendix A PDX collection 0698

CC **L97.112 Non-pressure chronic ulcer of right thigh with fat layer exposed**
CC Exclusion see Appendix A PDX collection 0698

CC **L97.113 Non-pressure chronic ulcer of right thigh with necrosis of muscle**
CC Exclusion see Appendix A PDX collection 0698

CC **L97.114 Non-pressure chronic ulcer of right thigh with necrosis of bone**
CC Exclusion see Appendix A PDX collection 0698

CC **L97.119 Non-pressure chronic ulcer of right thigh with unspecified severity**
CC Exclusion see Appendix A PDX collection 0698

+ **L97.12 Non-pressure chronic ulcer of left thigh**

CC **L97.121 Non-pressure chronic ulcer of left thigh limited to breakdown of skin**
CC Exclusion see Appendix A PDX collection 0698

CC **L97.122 Non-pressure chronic ulcer of left thigh with fat layer exposed**
CC Exclusion see Appendix A PDX collection 0698

CC **L97.123 Non-pressure chronic ulcer of left thigh with necrosis of muscle**
CC Exclusion see Appendix A PDX collection 0698

CC **L97.124 Non-pressure chronic ulcer of left thigh wi necrosis of bone**
CC Exclusion see Appendix A PDX collection 06

CC **L97.129 Non-pressure chronic ulcer of left thigh wi unspecified severity**
CC Exclusion see Appendix A PDX collection 06

+ **L97.2 Non-pressure chronic ulcer of calf**

+ **L97.20 Non-pressure chronic ulcer of unspecified calf**

CC **L97.201 Non-pressure chronic ulcer of unspecified calf limited to breakdown of skin**
CC Exclusion see Appendix A PDX collection 06

CC **L97.202 Non-pressure chronic ulcer of unspecified calf with fat layer exposed**
CC Exclusion see Appendix A PDX collection 06

CC **L97.203 Non-pressure chronic ulcer of unspecified calf with necrosis of muscle**
CC Exclusion see Appendix A PDX collection 06

CC **L97.204 Non-pressure chronic ulcer of unspecified calf with necrosis of bone**
CC Exclusion see Appendix A PDX collection 06

CC **L97.209 Non-pressure chronic ulcer of unspecified calf with unspecified severity**
CC Exclusion see Appendix A PDX collection 06

+ **L97.21 Non-pressure chronic ulcer of right calf**

CC **L97.211 Non-pressure chronic ulcer of right calf limited to breakdown of skin**
CC Exclusion see Appendix A PDX collection 06

CC **L97.212 Non-pressure chronic ulcer of right calf wi fat layer exposed**
CC Exclusion see Appendix A PDX collection 06

CC **L97.213 Non-pressure chronic ulcer of right calf wi necrosis of muscle**
CC Exclusion see Appendix A PDX collection 06

CC **L97.214 Non-pressure chronic ulcer of right calf wi necrosis of bone**
CC Exclusion see Appendix A PDX collection 06

CC **L97.219 Non-pressure chronic ulcer of right calf wi unspecified severity**
CC Exclusion see Appendix A PDX collection 06

+ **L97.22 Non-pressure chronic ulcer of left calf**

CC **L97.221 Non-pressure chronic ulcer of left calf limited to breakdown of skin**
CC Exclusion see Appendix A PDX collection 06

CC **L97.222 Non-pressure chronic ulcer of left calf with fat layer exposed**
CC Exclusion see Appendix A PDX collection 06

CC **L97.223 Non-pressure chronic ulcer of left calf with necrosis of muscle**
CC Exclusion see Appendix A PDX collection 06

CC **L97.224 Non-pressure chronic ulcer of left calf with necrosis of bone**
CC Exclusion see Appendix A PDX collection 06

CC **L97.229 Non-pressure chronic ulcer of left calf with unspecified severity**
CC Exclusion see Appendix A PDX collection 06

+ **L97.3 Non-pressure chronic ulcer of ankle**

+ **L97.30 Non-pressure chronic ulcer of unspecified ankle**

CC **L97.301 Non-pressure chronic ulcer of unspecified ankle limited to breakdown of skin**
CC Exclusion see Appendix A PDX collection 06

CC **L97.302 Non-pressure chronic ulcer of unspecified ankle with fat layer exposed**
CC Exclusion see Appendix A PDX collection 06

CC **L97.303 Non-pressure chronic ulcer of unspecified ankle with necrosis of muscle**
CC Exclusion see Appendix A PDX collection 06

CC **L97.304 Non-pressure chronic ulcer of unspecified ankle with necrosis of bone**
CC Exclusion see Appendix A PDX collection 06

CC **L97.309 Non-pressure chronic ulcer of unspecified ankle with unspecified severity**
CC Exclusion see Appendix A PDX collection 06

+ **L97.31 Non-pressure chronic ulcer of right ankle**

CC **L97.311 Non-pressure chronic ulcer of right ankle limited to breakdown of skin**
CC Exclusion see Appendix A PDX collection 06

CC **L97.312 Non-pressure chronic ulcer of right ankle with fat layer exposed**
CC Exclusion see Appendix A PDX collection 06

CC **L97.313 Non-pressure chronic ulcer of right ankle with necrosis of muscle**
CC Exclusion see Appendix A PDX collection 06

CC **L97.314 Non-pressure chronic ulcer of right ankle with necrosis of bone**
CC Exclusion see Appendix A PDX collection 06

CC **L97.319 Non-pressure chronic ulcer of right ankle with unspecified severity**
CC Exclusion see Appendix A PDX collection 0698

\+ **L97.32 Non-pressure chronic ulcer of left ankle**

CC **L97.321 Non-pressure chronic ulcer of left ankle limited to breakdown of skin**
CC Exclusion see Appendix A PDX collection 0698

CC **L97.322 Non-pressure chronic ulcer of left ankle with fat layer exposed**
CC Exclusion see Appendix A PDX collection 0698

CC **L97.323 Non-pressure chronic ulcer of left ankle with necrosis of muscle**
CC Exclusion see Appendix A PDX collection 0698

CC **L97.324 Non-pressure chronic ulcer of left ankle with necrosis of bone**
CC Exclusion see Appendix A PDX collection 0698

CC **L97.329 Non-pressure chronic ulcer of left ankle with unspecified severity**
CC Exclusion see Appendix A PDX collection 0698

\+ **L97.4 Non-pressure chronic ulcer of heel and midfoot**
Non-pressure chronic ulcer of plantar surface of midfoot

\+ **L97.40 Non-pressure chronic ulcer of unspecified heel and midfoot**

CC **L97.401 Non-pressure chronic ulcer of unspecified heel and midfoot limited to breakdown of skin**
CC Exclusion see Appendix A PDX collection 0698

CC **L97.402 Non-pressure chronic ulcer of unspecified heel and midfoot with fat layer exposed**
CC Exclusion see Appendix A PDX collection 0698

CC **L97.403 Non-pressure chronic ulcer of unspecified heel and midfoot with necrosis of muscle**
CC Exclusion see Appendix A PDX collection 0698

CC **L97.404 Non-pressure chronic ulcer of unspecified heel and midfoot with necrosis of bone**
CC Exclusion see Appendix A PDX collection 0698

CC **L97.409 Non-pressure chronic ulcer of unspecified heel and midfoot with unspecified severity**
CC Exclusion see Appendix A PDX collection 0698

\+ **L97.41 Non-pressure chronic ulcer of right heel and midfoot**

CC **L97.411 Non-pressure chronic ulcer of right heel and midfoot limited to breakdown of skin**
CC Exclusion see Appendix A PDX collection 0698

CC **L97.412 Non-pressure chronic ulcer of right heel and midfoot with fat layer exposed**
CC Exclusion see Appendix A PDX collection 0698

CC **L97.413 Non-pressure chronic ulcer of right heel and midfoot with necrosis of muscle**
CC Exclusion see Appendix A PDX collection 0698

CC **L97.414 Non-pressure chronic ulcer of right heel and midfoot with necrosis of bone**
CC Exclusion see Appendix A PDX collection 0698

CC **L97.419 Non-pressure chronic ulcer of right heel and midfoot with unspecified severity**
CC Exclusion see Appendix A PDX collection 0698

\+ **L97.42 Non-pressure chronic ulcer of left heel and midfoot**

CC **L97.421 Non-pressure chronic ulcer of left heel and midfoot limited to breakdown of skin**
CC Exclusion see Appendix A PDX collection 0698

CC **L97.422 Non-pressure chronic ulcer of left heel and midfoot with fat layer exposed**
CC Exclusion see Appendix A PDX collection 0698

CC **L97.423 Non-pressure chronic ulcer of left heel and midfoot with necrosis of muscle**
CC Exclusion see Appendix A PDX collection 0698

CC **L97.424 Non-pressure chronic ulcer of left heel and midfoot with necrosis of bone**
CC Exclusion see Appendix A PDX collection 0698

CC **L97.429 Non-pressure chronic ulcer of left heel and midfoot with unspecified severity**
CC Exclusion see Appendix A PDX collection 0698

\+ **L97.5 Non-pressure chronic ulcer of other part of foot**
Non-pressure chronic ulcer of toe

\+ **L97.50 Non-pressure chronic ulcer of other part of unspecified foot**

L97.501 Non-pressure chronic ulcer of other part of unspecified foot limited to breakdown of skin

L97.502 Non-pressure chronic ulcer of other part of unspecified foot with fat layer exposed

L97.503 Non-pressure chronic ulcer of other part of unspecified foot with necrosis of muscle

L97.504 Non-pressure chronic ulcer of other part of unspecified foot with necrosis of bone

L97.509 Non-pressure chronic ulcer of other part of unspecified foot with unspecified severity

\+ **L97.51 Non-pressure chronic ulcer of other part of right foot**

L97.511 Non-pressure chronic ulcer of other part of right foot limited to breakdown of skin

L97.512 Non-pressure chronic ulcer of other part of right foot with fat layer exposed

L97.513 Non-pressure chronic ulcer of other part of right foot with necrosis of muscle

L97.514 Non-pressure chronic ulcer of other part of right foot with necrosis of bone

L97.519 Non-pressure chronic ulcer of other part of right foot with unspecified severity

\+ **L97.52 Non-pressure chronic ulcer of other part of left foot**

L97.521 Non-pressure chronic ulcer of other part of left foot limited to breakdown of skin

L97.522 Non-pressure chronic ulcer of other part of left foot with fat layer exposed

L97.523 Non-pressure chronic ulcer of other part of left foot with necrosis of muscle

L97.524 Non-pressure chronic ulcer of other part of left foot with necrosis of bone

L97.529 Non-pressure chronic ulcer of other part of left foot with unspecified severity

\+ **L97.8 Non-pressure chronic ulcer of other part of lower leg**

\+ **L97.80 Non-pressure chronic ulcer of other part of unspecified lower leg**

CC **L97.801 Non-pressure chronic ulcer of other part of unspecified lower leg limited to breakdown of skin**
CC Exclusion see Appendix A PDX collection 0698

CC **L97.802 Non-pressure chronic ulcer of other part of unspecified lower leg with fat layer exposed**
CC Exclusion see Appendix A PDX collection 0698

CC **L97.803 Non-pressure chronic ulcer of other part of unspecified lower leg with necrosis of muscle**
CC Exclusion see Appendix A PDX collection 0698

CC **L97.804 Non-pressure chronic ulcer of other part of unspecified lower leg with necrosis of bone**
CC Exclusion see Appendix A PDX collection 0698

CC **L97.809 Non-pressure chronic ulcer of other part of unspecified lower leg with unspecified severity**
CC Exclusion see Appendix A PDX collection 0698

\+ **L97.81 Non-pressure chronic ulcer of other part of right lower leg**

CC **L97.811 Non-pressure chronic ulcer of other part of right lower leg limited to breakdown of skin**
CC Exclusion see Appendix A PDX collection 0698

CC **L97.812 Non-pressure chronic ulcer of other part of right lower leg with fat layer exposed**
CC Exclusion see Appendix A PDX collection 0698

CC **L97.813 Non-pressure chronic ulcer of other part of right lower leg with necrosis of muscle**
CC Exclusion see Appendix A PDX collection 0698

CC **L97.814 Non-pressure chronic ulcer of other part of right lower leg with necrosis of bone**
CC Exclusion see Appendix A PDX collection 0698

CC **L97.819 Non-pressure chronic ulcer of other part of right lower leg with unspecified severity**
CC Exclusion see Appendix A PDX collection 0698

\+ **L97.82 Non-pressure chronic ulcer of other part of left lower leg**

CC **L97.821 Non-pressure chronic ulcer of other part of left lower leg limited to breakdown of skin**
CC Exclusion see Appendix A PDX collection 0698

CC **L97.822 Non-pressure chronic ulcer of other part of left lower leg with fat layer exposed**
CC Exclusion see Appendix A PDX collection 0698

CC **L97.823 Non-pressure chronic ulcer of other part of left lower leg with necrosis of muscle**
CC Exclusion see Appendix A PDX collection 0698

CC **L97.824 Non-pressure chronic ulcer of other part of left lower leg with necrosis of bone**
CC Exclusion see Appendix A PDX collection 0698

CC **L97.829 Non-pressure chronic ulcer of other part of left lower leg with unspecified severity**
CC Exclusion see Appendix A PDX collection 0698

\+ **L97.9 Non-pressure chronic ulcer of unspecified part of lower leg**

\+ **L97.90 Non-pressure chronic ulcer of unspecified part of unspecified lower leg**

CC **L97.901 Non-pressure chronic ulcer of unspecified part of unspecified lower leg limited to breakdown of skin**
CC Exclusion see Appendix A PDX collection 0698

CC **L97.902 Non-pressure chronic ulcer of unspecified part of unspecified lower leg with fat layer exposed**
CC Exclusion see Appendix A PDX collection 0698

CC **L97.903 Non-pressure chronic ulcer of unspecified part of unspecified lower leg with necrosis of muscle**
CC Exclusion see Appendix A PDX collection 0698

CC **L97.904 Non-pressure chronic ulcer of unspecified part of unspecified lower leg with necrosis of bone**
CC Exclusion see Appendix A PDX collection 0698

CC **L97.909 Non-pressure chronic ulcer of unspecified part of unspecified lower leg with unspecified severity**
CC Exclusion see Appendix A PDX collection 0698

\+ **L97.91 Non-pressure chronic ulcer of unspecified part of right lower leg**

CC **L97.911 Non-pressure chronic ulcer of unspecified part of right lower leg limited to breakdown of skin**
CC Exclusion see Appendix A PDX collection 0698

CC **L97.912 Non-pressure chronic ulcer of unspecified part of right lower leg with fat layer exposed**
CC Exclusion see Appendix A PDX collection 0698

CC **L97.913 Non-pressure chronic ulcer of unspecified part of right lower leg with necrosis of muscle**
CC Exclusion see Appendix A PDX collection 0698

CC **L97.914 Non-pressure chronic ulcer of unspecified part of right lower leg with necrosis of bone**
CC Exclusion see Appendix A PDX collection 0698

CC **L97.919 Non-pressure chronic ulcer of unspecified part of right lower leg with unspecified severity**
CC Exclusion see Appendix A PDX collection 0698

\+ **L97.92 Non-pressure chronic ulcer of unspecified part of left lower leg**

CC **L97.921 Non-pressure chronic ulcer of unspecified part of left lower leg limited to breakdown of skin**
CC Exclusion see Appendix A PDX collection 0698

CC **L97.922 Non-pressure chronic ulcer of unspecified part of left lower leg with fat layer exposed**
CC Exclusion see Appendix A PDX collection 0698

CC **L97.923 Non-pressure chronic ulcer of unspecified part of left lower leg with necrosis of muscle**
CC Exclusion see Appendix A PDX collection 0698

CC **L97.924 Non-pressure chronic ulcer of unspecified part of left lower leg with necrosis of bone**
CC Exclusion see Appendix A PDX collection 0698

CC **L97.929 Non-pressure chronic ulcer of unspecified part of left lower leg with unspecified severity**
CC Exclusion see Appendix A PDX collection 0698

L98 Other disorders of skin and subcutaneous tissue, not elsewhere classified

L98.0 Pyogenic granuloma
Excludes2: *pyogenic granuloma of gingiva (K06.8)*
pyogenic granuloma of maxillary alveolar ridge (K04.5)
pyogenic granuloma of oral mucosa (K13.4)

L98.1 Factitial dermatitis
Neurotic excoriation

L98.2 Febrile neutrophilic dermatosis [Sweet]

CC **L98.3 Eosinophilic cellulitis [Wells]**
CC Exclusion see Appendix A PDX collection 0839

\+ **L98.4 Non-pressure chronic ulcer of skin, not elsewhere classified**
Chronic ulcer of skin NOS
Tropical ulcer NOS
Ulcer of skin NOS
Excludes2: *pressure ulcer (pressure area) (L89.-)*
gangrene (I96)
skin infections (L00-L08)
specific infections classified to A00-B99
ulcer of lower limb NEC (L97.-)
varicose ulcer (I83.0-I82.2)

\+ **L98.41 Non-pressure chronic ulcer of buttock**
L98.411 Non-pressure chronic ulcer of buttock limited to breakdown of skin
L98.412 Non-pressure chronic ulcer of buttock with fat layer exposed
L98.413 Non-pressure chronic ulcer of buttock with necrosis of muscle
L98.414 Non-pressure chronic ulcer of buttock with necrosis of bone
L98.419 Non-pressure chronic ulcer of buttock with unspecified severity

\+ **L98.42 Non-pressure chronic ulcer of back**
L98.421 Non-pressure chronic ulcer of back limited to breakdown of skin
L98.422 Non-pressure chronic ulcer of back with fat layer exposed
L98.423 Non-pressure chronic ulcer of back with necrosis of muscle
L98.424 Non-pressure chronic ulcer of back with necrosis of bone
L98.429 Non-pressure chronic ulcer of back with unspecified severity

\+ **L98.49 Non-pressure chronic ulcer of skin of other sites**
Non-pressure chronic ulcer of skin NOS
L98.491 Non-pressure chronic ulcer of skin of other sites limited to breakdown of skin
L98.492 Non-pressure chronic ulcer of skin of other sites with fat layer exposed
L98.493 Non-pressure chronic ulcer of skin of other sites with necrosis of muscle
L98.494 Non-pressure chronic ulcer of skin of other sites with necrosis of bone
L98.499 Non-pressure chronic ulcer of skin of other sites with unspecified severity

L98.5 Mucinosis of the skin
Focal mucinosis
Lichen myxedematosus
Reticular erythematous mucinosis
Excludes1: *focal oral mucinosis (K13.79)*
myxedema (E03.9)

L98.6 Other infiltrative disorders of the skin and subcutaneous tissue
Excludes1: *hyalinosis cutis et mucosae (E78.89)*

L98.8 Other specified disorders of the skin and subcutaneous tissue

L98.9 Disorder of the skin and subcutaneous tissue, unspecified
AHA CC: 2Q, 2013, 32-33

L99 Other disorders of skin and subcutaneous tissue in diseases classified elsewhere

Code first underlying disease, such as:
amyloidosis (E85.-)
Excludes1: *skin disorders in diabetes (E08-E13 with .62)*
skin disorders in gonorrhea (A54.89)
skin disorders in syphilis (A51.31, A52.79)

Valid 3-character code, no further characters required

Intervertebral Joint

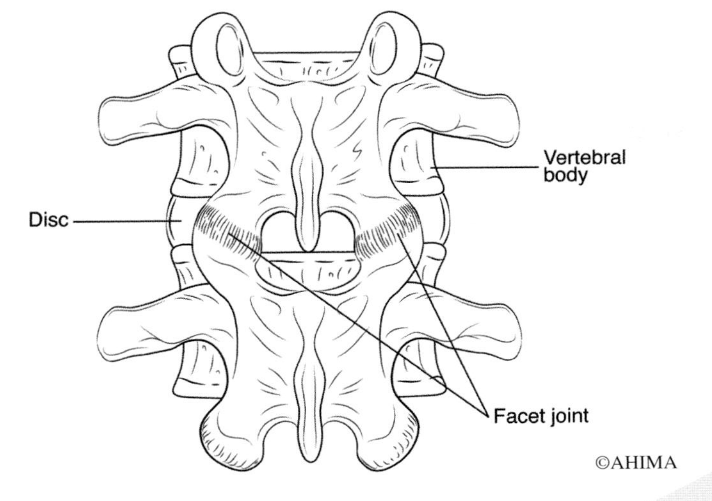

Shoulder Joint

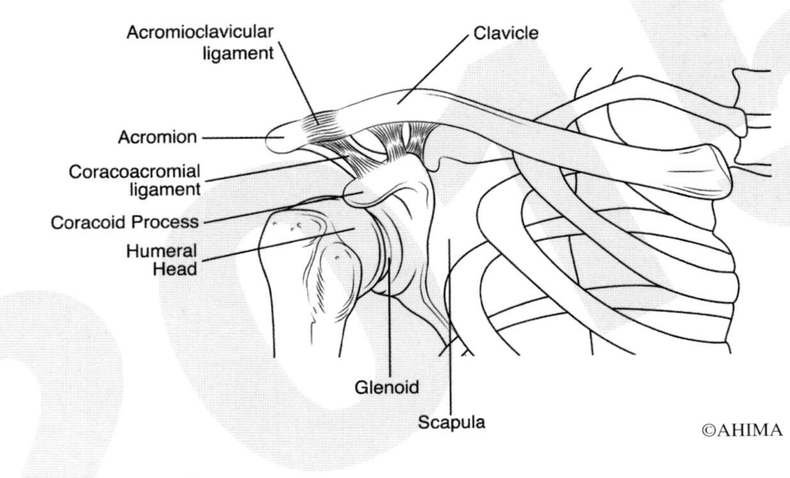

Elbow

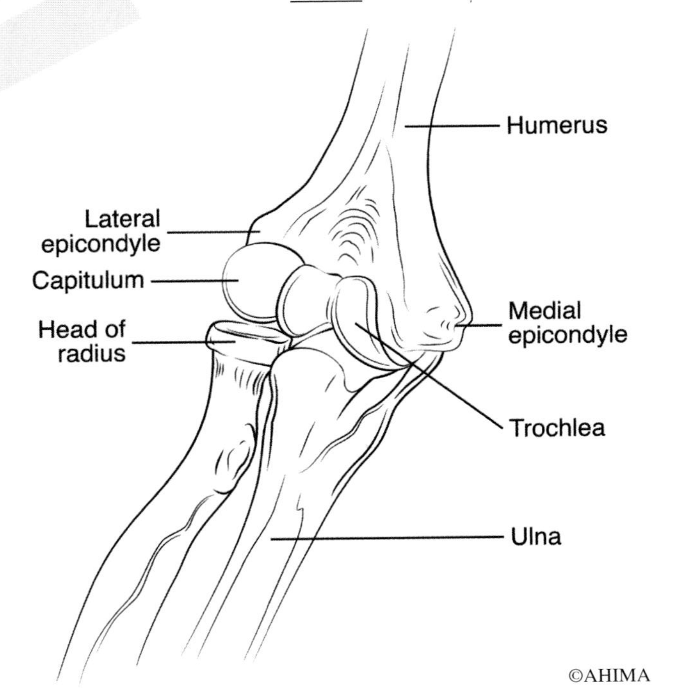

Wrist

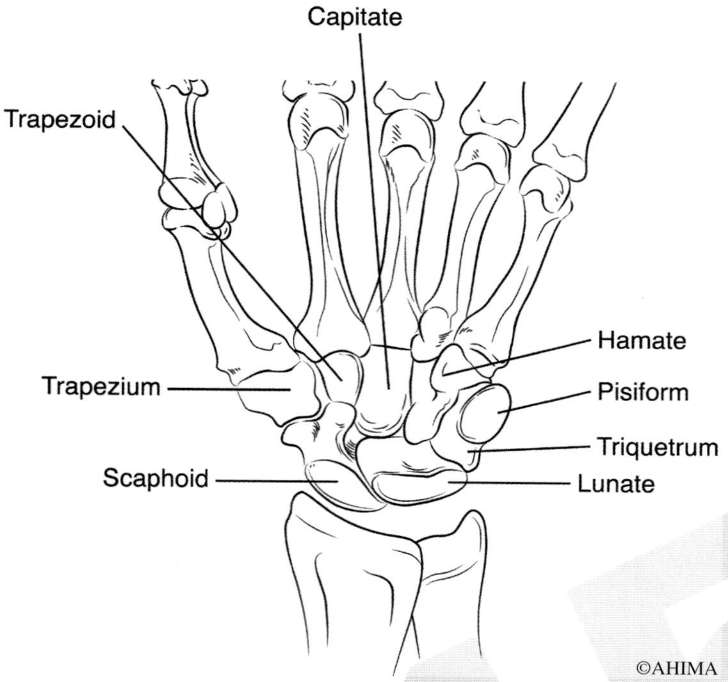

Hip Joint

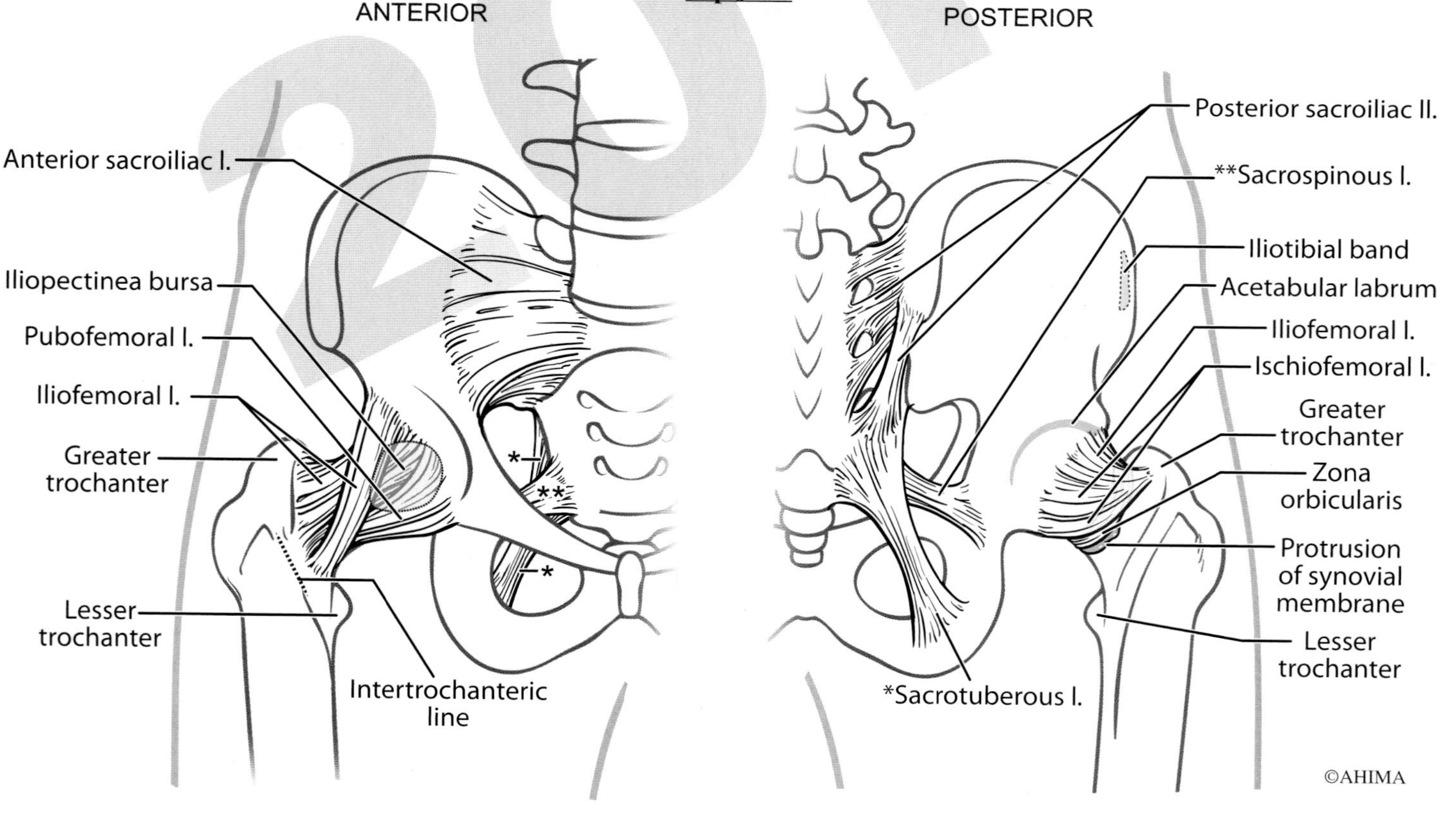

Knee Joint

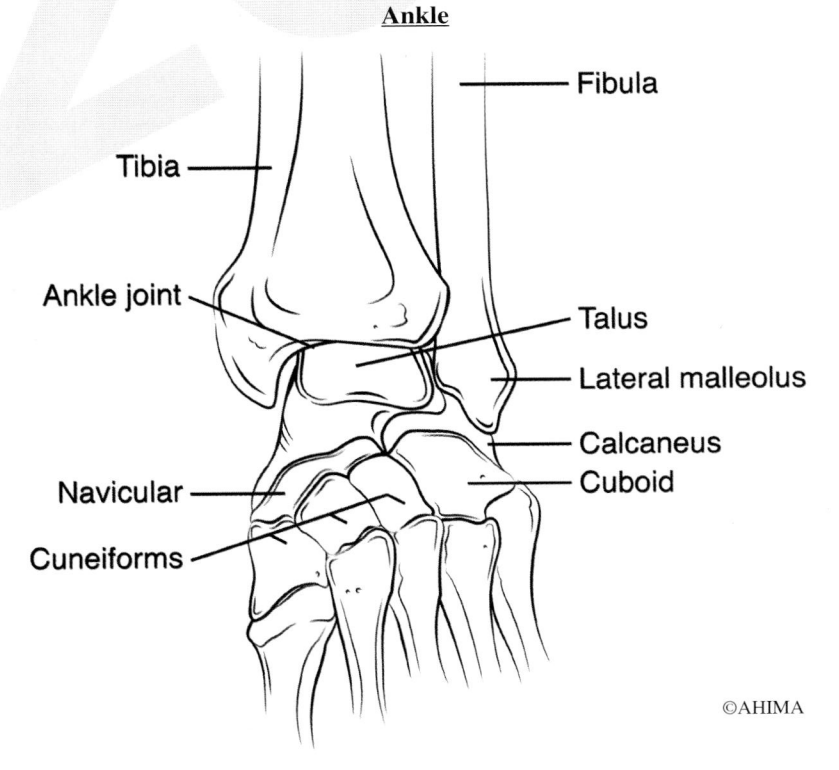

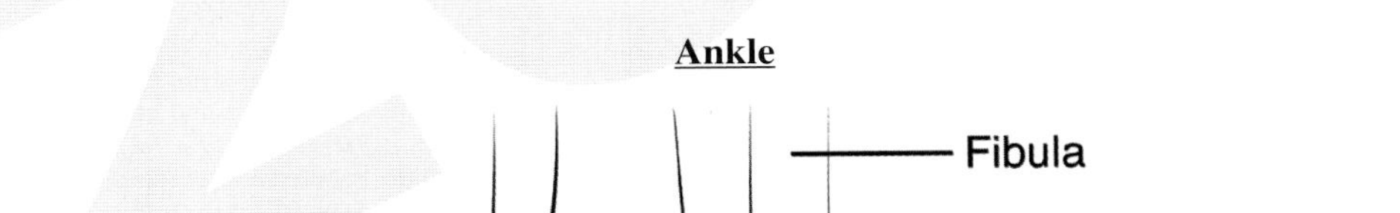
ANTERIOR
Femur
Patella
Lat. condyle of femur
Ant. cruciate l.
Fibular collateral l.
Lat. meniscus
at. condyle of tibia
Head of fibula
Post. cruciate l.
Med. condyle of femur
Tibial collateral l.
Med. meniscus
Med. condyle of tibia
Transverse l. of knee
Tibial tuberosity
Tibia
POSTERIOR
Femur
Post. meniscofemoral l.
Ant. cruciate l.
Lat. condyle of femur
Fibular collateral l.
Popliteus tendon
Lat. meniscus
Head of fibula
Post. cruciate l.
Tibia

Ankle

Fibula
Tibia
Ankle joint
Talus
Lateral malleolus
Calcaneus
Cuboid
Navicular
Cuneiforms

Chatper 13: Diseases of the Musculoskeletal System and Connective Tissue (M00-M99)

NOTE Use an external cause code following the code for the musculoskeletal condition, if applicable, to identify the cause of the musculoskeletal condition

Excludes2: *arthropathic psoriasis (L40.5-)*
certain conditions originating in the perinatal period (P04-P96)
certain infectious and parasitic diseases (A00-B99)
compartment syndrome (traumatic) (T79.A-)
complications of pregnancy, childbirth and the puerperium (O00-O9A)
congenital malformations, deformations, and chromosomal abnormalities (Q00-Q99)
endocrine, nutritional and metabolic diseases (E00-E88)
injury, poisoning and certain other consequences of external causes (S00-T88)
neoplasms (C00-D49)
symptoms, signs and abnormal clinical and laboratory findings, not elsewhere classified (R00-R94)

This chapter contains the following category blocks:

M00-M02 Infectious arthropathies
M05-M14 Inflammatory polyarthropathies
M15-M19 Osteoarthritis
M20-M25 Other joint disorders
M26-M27 Dentofacial anomalies [including malocclusion] and other disorders of jaw
M30-M36 Systemic connective tissue disorders
M40-M43 Deforming dorsopathies
M45-M49 Spondylopathies
M50-M54 Other dorsopathies
M60-M63 Disorders of muscles
M65-M67 Disorders of synovium and tendon
M70-M79 Other soft tissue disorders
M80-M85 Disorders of bone density and structure
M86-M90 Other osteopathies
M91-M94 Chondropathies
M95 Other disorders of the musculoskeletal system and connective tissue
M96 Intraoperative and postprocedural complications and disorders of musculoskeletal system, not elsewhere classified
M99 Biomechanical lesions, not elsewhere classified

C. Chapter-Specific Coding Guidelines

In addition to general coding guidelines, there are guidelines for specific diagnoses and/or conditions in the classification. Unless otherwise indicated, these guidelines apply to all health care settings. Please refer to Section II for guidelines on the selection of principal diagnosis.

13. Chapter 13: Diseases of the Musculoskeletal System and Connective Tissue (M00-M99)

a. Site and laterality

Most of the codes within Chapter 13 have site and laterality designations. The site represents the bone, joint or the muscle involved. For some conditions where more than one bone, joint or muscle is usually involved, such as osteoarthritis, there is a "multiple sites" code available. For categories where no multiple site code is provided and more than one bone, joint or muscle is involved, multiple codes should be used to indicate the different sites involved.

1) Bone versus joint

For certain conditions, the bone may be affected at the upper or lower end, (e.g., avascular necrosis of bone, M87, Osteoporosis, M80, M81). Though the portion of the bone affected may be at the joint, the site designation will be the bone, not the joint.

b. Acute traumatic versus chronic or recurrent musculoskeletal conditions

Many musculoskeletal conditions are a result of previous injury or trauma to a site, or are recurrent conditions. Bone, joint or muscle conditions that are the result of a healed injury are usually found in chapter 13. Recurrent bone, joint or muscle conditions are also usually found in chapter 13. Any current, acute injury should be coded to the appropriate injury code from chapter 19. Chronic or recurrent conditions should generally be coded with a code from chapter 13. If it is difficult to determine from the documentation in the record which code is best to describe a condition, query the provider.

c. Coding of Pathologic Fractures

7th character A is for use as long as the patient is receiving active treatment for the fracture. Examples of active treatment are: surgical treatment, emergency department encounter, evaluation and **continuing** treatment by **the same of a different** physician. **While the patient may be seen by a new or different provider over the course of treatment for a pathological fracture, assignment of the 7th character is based on whether the patient is undergoing active treatment and not whether the provider is seeing the patient for the f time.** 7th character, D is to be used for encounters after the patient has comple active treatment. The other 7th characters, listed under each subcategory in Tabular List, are to be used for subsequent encounters for treatment of proble associated with the healing, such as malunions, nonunions, and sequelae.

Care for complications of surgical treatment for fracture repairs during the heal or recovery phase should be coded with the appropriate complication codes.

See Section I.C.19. Coding of traumatic fractures.

d. Osteoporosis

Osteoporosis is a systemic condition, meaning that all bones of the musculoskel system are affected. Therefore, site is not a component of the codes un category M81, Osteoporosis without current pathological fracture. The site co under category M80, Osteoporosis with current pathological fracture, identify site of the fracture, not the osteoporosis.

1) Osteoporosis without pathological fracture

Category M81, Osteoporosis without current pathological fracture, is for for patients with osteoporosis who do not currently have a pathologic fract due to the osteoporosis, even if they have had a fracture in the past. For patie with a history of osteoporosis fractures, status code Z87.310, Personal hist of (healed) osteoporosis fracture, should follow the code from M81.

2) Osteoporosis with current pathological fracture

Category M80, Osteoporosis with current pathological fracture, is for patie who have a current pathologic fracture at the time of an encounter. The co under M80 identify the site of the fracture. A code from category M not a traumatic fracture code, should be used for any patient with kno osteoporosis who suffers a fracture, even if the patient had a minor fall trauma, if that fall or trauma would not usually break a normal, healthy bor

ARTHROPATHIES (M00-M25)

Includes: Disorders affecting predominantly peripheral (limb) joints

Infectious arthropathies (M00-M02)

NOTE This block comprises arthropathies due to microbiological agents. Distinction is made between the following types of etiological relationshi
a) direct infection of joint, where organisms invade synovial tissue and microbial antigen is present in the joint;
b) indirect infection, which may be of two types: a reactive arthropathy, where microbial infection of the body is established but neither organism nor antigens can be identified in the joint, and a postinfective arthropathy, where microbial antigen is present but recovery of an organism is inconstant and evidence of local multiplication is lacking.

M00 Pyogenic arthritis

+ **M00.0 Staphylococcal arthritis and polyarthritis**
  Use additional code (B95.61-B95.8) to identify bacterial agent
  Excludes2: *infection and inflammatory reaction due to interna joint prosthesis (T84.5-)*
  - CC **M00.00 Staphylococcal arthritis, unspecified joint**
    CC Exclusion see Appendix A PDX collection 0855
  - + **M00.01 Staphylococcal arthritis, shoulder**
    - **M00.011 Staphylococcal arthritis, right shoulder**
    - **M00.012 Staphylococcal arthritis, left shoulder**
    - CC **M00.019 Staphylococcal arthritis, unspecified shoulder**
      CC Exclusion see Appendix A PDX collection 08
  - + **M00.02 Staphylococcal arthritis, elbow**
    - **M00.021 Staphylococcal arthritis, right elbow**
    - **M00.022 Staphylococcal arthritis, left elbow**
    - CC **M00.029 Staphylococcal arthritis, unspecified elbow**
      CC Exclusion see Appendix A PDX collection 08
  - + **M00.03 Staphylococcal arthritis, wrist**
    Staphylococcal arthritis of carpal bones
    - **M00.031 Staphylococcal arthritis, right wrist**
    - **M00.032 Staphylococcal arthritis, left wrist**
    - CC **M00.039 Staphylococcal arthritis, unspecified wrist**
      CC Exclusion see Appendix A PDX collection 08
  - + **M00.04 Staphylococcal arthritis, hand**
    Staphylococcal arthritis of metacarpus and phalanges
    - **M00.041 Staphylococcal arthritis, right hand**
    - **M00.042 Staphylococcal arthritis, left hand**
    - CC **M00.049 Staphylococcal arthritis, unspecified hand**
      CC Exclusion see Appendix A PDX collection 08
  - + **M00.05 Staphylococcal arthritis, hip**
    - **M00.051 Staphylococcal arthritis, right hip**

M00.052 Staphylococcal arthritis, left hip
CC **M00.059 Staphylococcal arthritis, unspecified hip**
CC Exclusion see Appendix A PDX collection 0860
\+ **M00.06 Staphylococcal arthritis, knee**
M00.061 Staphylococcal arthritis, right knee
M00.062 Staphylococcal arthritis, left knee
CC **M00.069 Staphylococcal arthritis, unspecified knee**
CC Exclusion see Appendix A PDX collection 0861
\+ **M00.07 Staphylococcal arthritis, ankle and foot**
Staphylococcal arthritis, tarsus, metatarsus and phalanges
M00.071 Staphylococcal arthritis, right ankle and foot
M00.072 Staphylococcal arthritis, left ankle and foot
CC **M00.079 Staphylococcal arthritis, unspecified ankle and foot**
CC Exclusion see Appendix A PDX collection 0862
CC **M00.08 Staphylococcal arthritis, vertebrae**
CC Exclusion see Appendix A PDX collection 0855
CC **M00.09 Staphylococcal polyarthritis**
CC Exclusion see Appendix A PDX collection 0855
\+ **M00.1 Pneumococcal arthritis and polyarthritis**
CC **M00.10 Pneumococcal arthritis, unspecified joint**
CC Exclusion see Appendix A PDX collection 0855
\+ **M00.11 Pneumococcal arthritis, shoulder**
CC **M00.111 Pneumococcal arthritis, right shoulder**
CC Exclusion see Appendix A PDX collection 0856
CC **M00.112 Pneumococcal arthritis, left shoulder**
CC Exclusion see Appendix A PDX collection 0856
CC **M00.119 Pneumococcal arthritis, unspecified shoulder**
CC Exclusion see Appendix A PDX collection 0856
\+ **M00.12 Pneumococcal arthritis, elbow**
CC **M00.121 Pneumococcal arthritis, right elbow**
CC Exclusion see Appendix A PDX collection 0857
CC **M00.122 Pneumococcal arthritis, left elbow**
CC Exclusion see Appendix A PDX collection 0857
CC **M00.129 Pneumococcal arthritis, unspecified elbow**
CC Exclusion see Appendix A PDX collection 0857
\+ **M00.13 Pneumococcal arthritis, wrist**
Pneumococcal arthritis of carpal bones
CC **M00.131 Pneumococcal arthritis, right wrist**
CC Exclusion see Appendix A PDX collection 0858
CC **M00.132 Pneumococcal arthritis, left wrist**
CC Exclusion see Appendix A PDX collection 0858
CC **M00.139 Pneumococcal arthritis, unspecified wrist**
CC Exclusion see Appendix A PDX collection 0858
\+ **M00.14 Pneumococcal arthritis, hand**
Pneumococcal arthritis of metacarpus and phalanges
CC **M00.141 Pneumococcal arthritis, right hand**
CC Exclusion see Appendix A PDX collection 0859
CC **M00.142 Pneumococcal arthritis, left hand**
CC Exclusion see Appendix A PDX collection 0859
CC **M00.149 Pneumococcal arthritis, unspecified hand**
CC Exclusion see Appendix A PDX collection 0859
\+ **M00.15 Pneumococcal arthritis, hip**
CC **M00.151 Pneumococcal arthritis, right hip**
CC Exclusion see Appendix A PDX collection 0860
CC **M00.152 Pneumococcal arthritis, left hip**
CC Exclusion see Appendix A PDX collection 0860
CC **M00.159 Pneumococcal arthritis, unspecified hip**
CC Exclusion see Appendix A PDX collection 0860
\+ **M00.16 Pneumococcal arthritis, knee**
CC **M00.161 Pneumococcal arthritis, right knee**
CC Exclusion see Appendix A PDX collection 0861
CC **M00.162 Pneumococcal arthritis, left knee**
CC Exclusion see Appendix A PDX collection 0861
CC **M00.169 Pneumococcal arthritis, unspecified knee**
CC Exclusion see Appendix A PDX collection 0861
\+ **M00.17 Pneumococcal arthritis, ankle and foot**
Pneumococcal arthritis, tarsus, metatarsus and phalanges
CC **M00.171 Pneumococcal arthritis, right ankle and foot**
CC Exclusion see Appendix A PDX collection 0862
CC **M00.172 Pneumococcal arthritis, left ankle and foot**
CC Exclusion see Appendix A PDX collection 0862
CC **M00.179 Pneumococcal arthritis, unspecified ankle and foot**
CC Exclusion see Appendix A PDX collection 0862
CC **M00.18 Pneumococcal arthritis, vertebrae**
CC Exclusion see Appendix A PDX collection 0855
CC **M00.19 Pneumococcal polyarthritis**
CC Exclusion see Appendix A PDX collection 0855

\+ **M00.2 Other streptococcal arthritis and polyarthritis**
Use additional code (B95.0-B95.2, B95.4-B95.5) to identify bacterial agent
CC **M00.20 Other streptococcal arthritis, unspecified joint**
CC Exclusion see Appendix A PDX collection 0855
\+ **M00.21 Other streptococcal arthritis, shoulder**
CC **M00.211 Other streptococcal arthritis, right shoulder**
CC Exclusion see Appendix A PDX collection 0856
CC **M00.212 Other streptococcal arthritis, left shoulder**
CC Exclusion see Appendix A PDX collection 0856
CC **M00.219 Other streptococcal arthritis, unspecified shoulder**
CC Exclusion see Appendix A PDX collection 0856
\+ **M00.22 Other streptococcal arthritis, elbow**
CC **M00.221 Other streptococcal arthritis, right elbow**
CC Exclusion see Appendix A PDX collection 0857
CC **M00.222 Other streptococcal arthritis, left elbow**
CC Exclusion see Appendix A PDX collection 0857
CC **M00.229 Other streptococcal arthritis, unspecified elbow**
CC Exclusion see Appendix A PDX collection 0857
\+ **M00.23 Other streptococcal arthritis, wrist**
Other streptococcal arthritis of carpal bones
CC **M00.231 Other streptococcal arthritis, right wrist**
CC Exclusion see Appendix A PDX collection 0858
CC **M00.232 Other streptococcal arthritis, left wrist**
CC Exclusion see Appendix A PDX collection 0858
CC **M00.239 Other streptococcal arthritis, unspecified wrist**
CC Exclusion see Appendix A PDX collection 0858
\+ **M00.24 Other streptococcal arthritis, hand**
Other streptococcal arthritis metacarpus and phalanges
CC **M00.241 Other streptococcal arthritis, right hand**
CC Exclusion see Appendix A PDX collection 0859
CC **M00.242 Other streptococcal arthritis, left hand**
CC Exclusion see Appendix A PDX collection 0859
CC **M00.249 Other streptococcal arthritis, unspecified hand**
CC Exclusion see Appendix A PDX collection 0859
\+ **M00.25 Other streptococcal arthritis, hip**
CC **M00.251 Other streptococcal arthritis, right hip**
CC Exclusion see Appendix A PDX collection 0860
CC **M00.252 Other streptococcal arthritis, left hip**
CC Exclusion see Appendix A PDX collection 0860
CC **M00.259 Other streptococcal arthritis, unspecified hip**
CC Exclusion see Appendix A PDX collection 0860
\+ **M00.26 Other streptococcal arthritis, knee**
CC **M00.261 Other streptococcal arthritis, right knee**
CC Exclusion see Appendix A PDX collection 0861
CC **M00.262 Other streptococcal arthritis, left knee**
CC Exclusion see Appendix A PDX collection 0861
CC **M00.269 Other streptococcal arthritis, unspecified knee**
CC Exclusion see Appendix A PDX collection 0861
\+ **M00.27 Other streptococcal arthritis, ankle and foot**
Other streptococcal arthritis, tarsus, metatarsus and phalanges
CC **M00.271 Other streptococcal arthritis, right ankle and foot**
CC Exclusion see Appendix A PDX collection 0862
CC **M00.272 Other streptococcal arthritis, left ankle and foot**
CC Exclusion see Appendix A PDX collection 0862
CC **M00.279 Other streptococcal arthritis, unspecified ankle and foot**
CC Exclusion see Appendix A PDX collection 0862
CC **M00.28 Other streptococcal arthritis, vertebrae**
CC Exclusion see Appendix A PDX collection 0855
CC **M00.29 Other streptococcal polyarthritis**
CC Exclusion see Appendix A PDX collection 0855
\+ **M00.8 Arthritis and polyarthritis due to other bacteria**
Use additional code (B96) to identify bacteria
CC **M00.80 Arthritis due to other bacteria, unspecified joint**
CC Exclusion see Appendix A PDX collection 0855
\+ **M00.81 Arthritis due to other bacteria, shoulder**
CC **M00.811 Arthritis due to other bacteria, right shoulder**
CC Exclusion see Appendix A PDX collection 0856
CC **M00.812 Arthritis due to other bacteria, left shoulder**
CC Exclusion see Appendix A PDX collection 0856
CC **M00.819 Arthritis due to other bacteria, unspecified shoulder**
CC Exclusion see Appendix A PDX collection 0856

+ **M00.82 Arthritis due to other bacteria, elbow**
  - CC **M00.821 Arthritis due to other bacteria, right elbow**
    CC Exclusion see Appendix A PDX collection 0857
  - CC **M00.822 Arthritis due to other bacteria, left elbow**
    CC Exclusion see Appendix A PDX collection 0857
  - CC **M00.829 Arthritis due to other bacteria, unspecified elbow**
    CC Exclusion see Appendix A PDX collection 0857

+ **M00.83 Arthritis due to other bacteria, wrist**
  Arthritis due to other bacteria, carpal bones
  - CC **M00.831 Arthritis due to other bacteria, right wrist**
    CC Exclusion see Appendix A PDX collection 0858
  - CC **M00.832 Arthritis due to other bacteria, left wrist**
    CC Exclusion see Appendix A PDX collection 0858
  - CC **M00.839 Arthritis due to other bacteria, unspecified wrist**
    CC Exclusion see Appendix A PDX collection 0858

+ **M00.84 Arthritis due to other bacteria, hand**
  Arthritis due to other bacteria, metacarpus and phalanges
  - CC **M00.841 Arthritis due to other bacteria, right hand**
    CC Exclusion see Appendix A PDX collection 0859
  - CC **M00.842 Arthritis due to other bacteria, left hand**
    CC Exclusion see Appendix A PDX collection 0859
  - CC **M00.849 Arthritis due to other bacteria, unspecified hand**
    CC Exclusion see Appendix A PDX collection 0859

+ **M00.85 Arthritis due to other bacteria, hip**
  - CC **M00.851 Arthritis due to other bacteria, right hip**
    CC Exclusion see Appendix A PDX collection 0860
  - CC **M00.852 Arthritis due to other bacteria, left hip**
    CC Exclusion see Appendix A PDX collection 0860
  - CC **M00.859 Arthritis due to other bacteria, unspecified hip**
    CC Exclusion see Appendix A PDX collection 0860

+ **M00.86 Arthritis due to other bacteria, knee**
  - CC **M00.861 Arthritis due to other bacteria, right knee**
    CC Exclusion see Appendix A PDX collection 0861
  - CC **M00.862 Arthritis due to other bacteria, left knee**
    CC Exclusion see Appendix A PDX collection 0861
  - CC **M00.869 Arthritis due to other bacteria, unspecified knee**
    CC Exclusion see Appendix A PDX collection 0861

+ **M00.87 Arthritis due to other bacteria, ankle and foot**
  Arthritis due to other bacteria, tarsus, metatarsus, and phalanges
  - CC **M00.871 Arthritis due to other bacteria, right ankle and foot**
    CC Exclusion see Appendix A PDX collection 0862
  - CC **M00.872 Arthritis due to other bacteria, left ankle and foot**
    CC Exclusion see Appendix A PDX collection 0862
  - CC **M00.879 Arthritis due to other bacteria, unspecified ankle and foot**
    CC Exclusion see Appendix A PDX collection 0862

CC **M00.88 Arthritis due to other bacteria, vertebrae**
CC Exclusion see Appendix A PDX collection 0855

CC **M00.89 Polyarthritis due to other bacteria**
CC Exclusion see Appendix A PDX collection 0855

CC **M00.9 Pyogenic arthritis, unspecified**
Infective arthritis NOS
CC Exclusion see Appendix A PDX collection 0855

M01 Direct infections of joint in infectious and parasitic diseases classified elsewhere

Code first underlying disease, such as:
leprosy [Hansen's disease] (A30.-)
mycoses (B35-B49)
O'nyong-nyong fever (A92.1)
paratyphoid fever (A01.1-A01.4)

Excludes1: *arthropathy in Lyme disease (A69.23)*
gonococcal arthritis (A54.42)
meningococcal arthritis (A39.83)
mumps arthritis (B26.85)
postinfective arthropathy (M02.-)
postmeningococcal arthritis (39.84)
reactive arthritis (M02.3)
rubella arthritis (B06.82)
sarcoidosis arthritis (D86.86)
tuberculosis arthritis (A18.01-A18.02)
typhoid fever arthritis (A01.04)

+ **M01.X Direct infection of joint in infectious and parasitic diseases classified elsewhere**

CC **M01.X0 Direct infection of unspecified joint in infectious and parasitic diseases classified elsewhere**
CC Exclusion see Appendix A PDX collection 0863

+ **M01.X1 Direct infection of shoulder joint in infectious and parasitic diseases classified elsewhere**
  - CC **M01.X11 Direct infection of right shoulder in infectious and parasitic diseases classified elsewhere**
    CC Exclusion see Appendix A PDX collection 08
  - CC **M01.X12 Direct infection of left shoulder in infectiou and parasitic diseases classified elsewhere**
    CC Exclusion see Appendix A PDX collection 08
  - CC **M01.X19 Direct infection of unspecified shoulder in infectious and parasitic diseases classified elsewhere**
    CC Exclusion see Appendix A PDX collection 08

+ **M01.X2 Direct infection of elbow in infectious and parasitic diseases classified elsewhere**
  - CC **M01.X21 Direct infection of right elbow in infectious and parasitic diseases classified elsewhere**
    CC Exclusion see Appendix A PDX collection 08
  - CC **M01.X22 Direct infection of left elbow in infectious and parasitic diseases classified elsewhere**
    CC Exclusion see Appendix A PDX collection 08
  - CC **M01.X29 Direct infection of unspecified elbow in infectious and parasitic diseases classified elsewhere**
    CC Exclusion see Appendix A PDX collection 08

+ **M01.X3 Direct infection of wrist in infectious and parasitic diseases classified elsewhere**
  Direct infection of carpal bones in infectious and parasitic diseases classified elsewhere
  - CC **M01.X31 Direct infection of right wrist in infectious and parasitic diseases classified elsewhere**
    CC Exclusion see Appendix A PDX collection 08
  - CC **M01.X32 Direct infection of left wrist in infectious an parasitic diseases classified elsewhere**
    CC Exclusion see Appendix A PDX collection 08
  - CC **M01.X39 Direct infection of unspecified wrist in infectious and parasitic diseases classified elsewhere**
    CC Exclusion see Appendix A PDX collection 08

+ **M01.X4 Direct infection of hand in infectious and parasitic diseases classified elsewhere**
  Direct infection of metacarpus and phalanges in infectious and parasitic diseases classified elsewhere
  - CC **M01.X41 Direct infection of right hand in infectious and parasitic diseases classified elsewhere**
    CC Exclusion see Appendix A PDX collection 08
  - CC **M01.X42 Direct infection of left hand in infectious an parasitic diseases classified elsewhere**
    CC Exclusion see Appendix A PDX collection 08
  - CC **M01.X49 Direct infection of unspecified hand in infectious and parasitic diseases classified elsewhere**
    CC Exclusion see Appendix A PDX collection 08

+ **M01.X5 Direct infection of hip in infectious and parasitic diseases classified elsewhere**
  - CC **M01.X51 Direct infection of right hip in infectious an parasitic diseases classified elsewhere**
    CC Exclusion see Appendix A PDX collection 08
  - CC **M01.X52 Direct infection of left hip in infectious and parasitic diseases classified elsewhere**
    CC Exclusion see Appendix A PDX collection 08
  - CC **M01.X59 Direct infection of unspecified hip in infectious and parasitic diseases classified elsewhere**
    CC Exclusion see Appendix A PDX collection 08

+ **M01.X6 Direct infection of knee in infectious and parasitic diseases classified elsewhere**
  - CC **M01.X61 Direct infection of right knee in infectious and parasitic diseases classified elsewhere**
    CC Exclusion see Appendix A PDX collection 08
  - CC **M01.X62 Direct infection of left knee in infectious an parasitic diseases classified elsewhere**
    CC Exclusion see Appendix A PDX collection 08
  - CC **M01.X69 Direct infection of unspecified knee in infectious and parasitic diseases classified elsewhere**
    CC Exclusion see Appendix A PDX collection 08

+ **M01.X7 Direct infection of ankle and foot in infectious and parasitic diseases classified elsewhere**
  Direct infection of tarsus, metatarsus and phalanges in infectious and parasitic diseases classified elsewhere

CC **M01.X71 Direct infection of right ankle and foot in infectious and parasitic diseases classified elsewhere**
CC Exclusion see Appendix A PDX collection 0863

CC **M01.X72 Direct infection of left ankle and foot in infectious and parasitic diseases classified elsewhere**
CC Exclusion see Appendix A PDX collection 0863

CC **M01.X79 Direct infection of unspecified ankle and foot in infectious and parasitic diseases classified elsewhere**
CC Exclusion see Appendix A PDX collection 0863

CC **M01.X8 Direct infection of vertebrae in infectious and parasitic diseases classified elsewhere**
CC Exclusion see Appendix A PDX collection 0863

CC **M01.X9 Direct infection of multiple joints in infectious and parasitic diseases classified elsewhere**
CC Exclusion see Appendix A PDX collection 0863

M02 Postinfective and reactive arthropathies

Code first underlying disease, such as:
congenital syphilis [Clutton's joints] (A50.5)
enteritis due to Yersinia enterocolitica (A04.6)
infective endocarditis (I33.0)
viral hepatitis (B15-B19)

Excludes1: *Behçet's disease (M35.2)*
direct infections of joint in infectious and parasitic diseases classified elsewhere (M01.-)
postmeningcoccal arthritis (A39.84)
mumps arthritis (B26.85)
rubella arthritis (B06.82)
syphilis arthritis (late) (A52.77)
rheumatic fever (I00)
tabetic arthropathy [Charcôt's] (A52.16)

\+ **M02.0 Arthropathy following intestinal bypass**
M02.00 Arthropathy following intestinal bypass, unspecified site
\+ **M02.01 Arthropathy following intestinal bypass, shoulder**
M02.011 Arthropathy following intestinal bypass, right shoulder
M02.012 Arthropathy following intestinal bypass, left shoulder
M02.019 Arthropathy following intestinal bypass, unspecified shoulder
\+ **M02.02 Arthropathy following intestinal bypass, elbow**
M02.021 Arthropathy following intestinal bypass, right elbow
M02.022 Arthropathy following intestinal bypass, left elbow
M02.029 Arthropathy following intestinal bypass, unspecified elbow
\+ **M02.03 Arthropathy following intestinal bypass, wrist**
Arthropathy following intestinal bypass, carpal bones
M02.031 Arthropathy following intestinal bypass, right wrist
M02.032 Arthropathy following intestinal bypass, left wrist
M02.039 Arthropathy following intestinal bypass, unspecified wrist
\+ **M02.04 Arthropathy following intestinal bypass, hand**
Arthropathy following intestinal bypass, metacarpals and phalanges
M02.041 Arthropathy following intestinal bypass, right hand
M02.042 Arthropathy following intestinal bypass, left hand
M02.049 Arthropathy following intestinal bypass, unspecified hand
\+ **M02.05 Arthropathy following intestinal bypass, hip**
M02.051 Arthropathy following intestinal bypass, right hip
M02.052 Arthropathy following intestinal bypass, left hip
M02.059 Arthropathy following intestinal bypass, unspecified hip
\+ **M02.06 Arthropathy following intestinal bypass, knee**
M02.061 Arthropathy following intestinal bypass, right knee
M02.062 Arthropathy following intestinal bypass, left knee
M02.069 Arthropathy following intestinal bypass, unspecified knee
\+ **M02.07 Arthropathy following intestinal bypass, ankle and foot**
Arthropathy following intestinal bypass, tarsus, metatarsus and phalanges
M02.071 Arthropathy following intestinal bypass, right ankle and foot
M02.072 Arthropathy following intestinal bypass, left ankle and foot
M02.079 Arthropathy following intestinal bypass, unspecified ankle and foot
M02.08 Arthropathy following intestinal bypass, vertebrae
M02.09 Arthropathy following intestinal bypass, multiple sites

\+ **M02.1 Postdysenteric arthropathy**
CC **M02.10 Postdysenteric arthropathy, unspecified site**
CC Exclusion see Appendix A PDX collection 0863
\+ **M02.11 Postdysenteric arthropathy, shoulder**
CC **M02.111 Postdysenteric arthropathy, right shoulder**
CC Exclusion see Appendix A PDX collection 0863
CC **M02.112 Postdysenteric arthropathy, left shoulder**
CC Exclusion see Appendix A PDX collection 0863
CC **M02.119 Postdysenteric arthropathy, unspecified shoulder**
CC Exclusion see Appendix A PDX collection 0863
\+ **M02.12 Postdysenteric arthropathy, elbow**
CC **M02.121 Postdysenteric arthropathy, right elbow**
CC Exclusion see Appendix A PDX collection 0863
CC **M02.122 Postdysenteric arthropathy, left elbow**
CC Exclusion see Appendix A PDX collection 0863
CC **M02.129 Postdysenteric arthropathy, unspecified elbow**
CC Exclusion see Appendix A PDX collection 0863
\+ **M02.13 Postdysenteric arthropathy, wrist**
Postdysenteric arthropathy, carpal bones
CC **M02.131 Postdysenteric arthropathy, right wrist**
CC Exclusion see Appendix A PDX collection 0863
CC **M02.132 Postdysenteric arthropathy, left wrist**
CC Exclusion see Appendix A PDX collection 0863
CC **M02.139 Postdysenteric arthropathy, unspecified wrist**
CC Exclusion see Appendix A PDX collection 0863
\+ **M02.14 Postdysenteric arthropathy, hand**
Postdysenteric arthropathy, metacarpus and phalanges
CC **M02.141 Postdysenteric arthropathy, right hand**
CC Exclusion see Appendix A PDX collection 0863
CC **M02.142 Postdysenteric arthropathy, left hand**
CC Exclusion see Appendix A PDX collection 0863
CC **M02.149 Postdysenteric arthropathy, unspecified hand**
CC Exclusion see Appendix A PDX collection 0863
\+ **M02.15 Postdysenteric arthropathy, hip**
CC **M02.151 Postdysenteric arthropathy, right hip**
CC Exclusion see Appendix A PDX collection 0863
CC **M02.152 Postdysenteric arthropathy, left hip**
CC Exclusion see Appendix A PDX collection 0863
CC **M02.159 Postdysenteric arthropathy, unspecified hip**
CC Exclusion see Appendix A PDX collection 0863
\+ **M02.16 Postdysenteric arthropathy, knee**
CC **M02.161 Postdysenteric arthropathy, right knee**
CC Exclusion see Appendix A PDX collection 0865
CC **M02.162 Postdysenteric arthropathy, left knee**
CC Exclusion see Appendix A PDX collection 0865
CC **M02.169 Postdysenteric arthropathy, unspecified knee**
CC Exclusion see Appendix A PDX collection 0865
\+ **M02.17 Postdysenteric arthropathy, ankle and foot**
Postdysenteric arthropathy, tarsus, metatarsus and phalanges
CC **M02.171 Postdysenteric arthropathy, right ankle and foot**
CC Exclusion see Appendix A PDX collection 0863
CC **M02.172 Postdysenteric arthropathy, left ankle and foot**
CC Exclusion see Appendix A PDX collection 0863
CC **M02.179 Postdysenteric arthropathy, unspecified ankle and foot**
CC Exclusion see Appendix A PDX collection 0863
CC **M02.18 Postdysenteric arthropathy, vertebrae**
CC Exclusion see Appendix A PDX collection 0866
CC **M02.19 Postdysenteric arthropathy, multiple sites**
CC Exclusion see Appendix A PDX collection 0863

\+ **M02.2 Postimmunization arthropathy**
M02.20 Postimmunization arthropathy, unspecified site
\+ **M02.21 Postimmunization arthropathy, shoulder**
M02.211 Postimmunization arthropathy, right shoulder
M02.212 Postimmunization arthropathy, left shoulder
M02.219 Postimmunization arthropathy, unspecified shoulder

+ **M02.22 Postimmunization arthropathy, elbow**
  - **M02.221 Postimmunization arthropathy, right elbow**
  - **M02.222 Postimmunization arthropathy, left elbow**
  - **M02.229 Postimmunization arthropathy, unspecified elbow**

+ **M02.23 Postimmunization arthropathy, wrist**
  Postimmunization arthropathy, carpal bones
  - **M02.231 Postimmunization arthropathy, right wrist**
  - **M02.232 Postimmunization arthropathy, left wrist**
  - **M02.239 Postimmunization arthropathy, unspecified wrist**

+ **M02.24 Postimmunization arthropathy, hand**
  Postimmunization arthropathy, metacarpus and phalanges
  - **M02.241 Postimmunization arthropathy, right hand**
  - **M02.242 Postimmunization arthropathy, left hand**
  - **M02.249 Postimmunization arthropathy, unspecified hand**

+ **M02.25 Postimmunization arthropathy, hip**
  - **M02.251 Postimmunization arthropathy, right hip**
  - **M02.252 Postimmunization arthropathy, left hip**
  - **M02.259 Postimmunization arthropathy, unspecified hip**

+ **M02.26 Postimmunization arthropathy, knee**
  - **M02.261 Postimmunization arthropathy, right knee**
  - **M02.262 Postimmunization arthropathy, left knee**
  - **M02.269 Postimmunization arthropathy, unspecified knee**

+ **M02.27 Postimmunization arthropathy, ankle and foot**
  Postimmunization arthropathy, tarsus, metatarsus and phalanges
  - **M02.271 Postimmunization arthropathy, right ankle and foot**
  - **M02.272 Postimmunization arthropathy, left ankle and foot**
  - **M02.279 Postimmunization arthropathy, unspecified ankle and foot**

M02.28 Postimmunization arthropathy, vertebrae

M02.29 Postimmunization arthropathy, multiple sites

+ **M02.3 Reiter's disease**
  Reactive arthritis

CC **M02.30 Reiter's disease, unspecified site**
  CC Exclusion see Appendix A PDX collection 0863

+ **M02.31 Reiter's disease, shoulder**
  - CC **M02.311 Reiter's disease, right shoulder**
    CC Exclusion see Appendix A PDX collection 0863
  - CC **M02.312 Reiter's disease, left shoulder**
    CC Exclusion see Appendix A PDX collection 0863
  - CC **M02.319 Reiter's disease, unspecified shoulder**
    CC Exclusion see Appendix A PDX collection 0863

+ **M02.32 Reiter's disease, elbow**
  - CC **M02.321 Reiter's disease, right elbow**
    CC Exclusion see Appendix A PDX collection 0863
  - CC **M02.322 Reiter's disease, left elbow**
    CC Exclusion see Appendix A PDX collection 0863
  - CC **M02.329 Reiter's disease, unspecified elbow**
    CC Exclusion see Appendix A PDX collection 0863

+ **M02.33 Reiter's disease, wrist**
  Reiter's disease, carpal bones
  - CC **M02.331 Reiter's disease, right wrist**
    CC Exclusion see Appendix A PDX collection 0863
  - CC **M02.332 Reiter's disease, left wrist**
    CC Exclusion see Appendix A PDX collection 0863
  - CC **M02.339 Reiter's disease, unspecified wrist**
    CC Exclusion see Appendix A PDX collection 0863

+ **M02.34 Reiter's disease, hand**
  Reiter's disease, metacarpus and phalanges
  - CC **M02.341 Reiter's disease, right hand**
    CC Exclusion see Appendix A PDX collection 0863
  - CC **M02.342 Reiter's disease, left hand**
    CC Exclusion see Appendix A PDX collection 0863
  - CC **M02.349 Reiter's disease, unspecified hand**
    CC Exclusion see Appendix A PDX collection 0863

+ **M02.35 Reiter's disease, hip**
  - CC **M02.351 Reiter's disease, right hip**
    CC Exclusion see Appendix A PDX collection 0863
  - CC **M02.352 Reiter's disease, left hip**
    CC Exclusion see Appendix A PDX collection 0863
  - CC **M02.359 Reiter's disease, unspecified hip**
    CC Exclusion see Appendix A PDX collection 0863

+ **M02.36 Reiter's disease, knee**
  - CC **M02.361 Reiter's disease, right knee**
    CC Exclusion see Appendix A PDX collection 0
  - CC **M02.362 Reiter's disease, left knee**
    CC Exclusion see Appendix A PDX collection 0
  - CC **M02.369 Reiter's disease, unspecified knee**
    CC Exclusion see Appendix A PDX collection 0

+ **M02.37 Reiter's disease, ankle and foot**
  Reiter's disease, tarsus, metatarsus and phalanges
  - CC **M02.371 Reiter's disease, right ankle and foot**
    CC Exclusion see Appendix A PDX collection 0
  - CC **M02.372 Reiter's disease, left ankle and foot**
    CC Exclusion see Appendix A PDX collection 0
  - CC **M02.379 Reiter's disease, unspecified ankle and foo**
    CC Exclusion see Appendix A PDX collection 0

CC **M02.38 Reiter's disease, vertebrae**
  CC Exclusion see Appendix A PDX collection 0863

CC **M02.39 Reiter's disease, multiple sites**
  CC Exclusion see Appendix A PDX collection 0863

+ **M02.8 Other reactive arthropathies**

CC **M02.80 Other reactive arthropathies, unspecified site**
  CC Exclusion see Appendix A PDX collection 0863

+ **M02.81 Other reactive arthropathies, shoulder**
  - CC **M02.811 Other reactive arthropathies, right should**
    CC Exclusion see Appendix A PDX collection 0
  - CC **M02.812 Other reactive arthropathies, left shoulder**
    CC Exclusion see Appendix A PDX collection 0
  - CC **M02.819 Other reactive arthropathies, unspecified shoulder**
    CC Exclusion see Appendix A PDX collection 0

+ **M02.82 Other reactive arthropathies, elbow**
  - CC **M02.821 Other reactive arthropathies, right elbow**
    CC Exclusion see Appendix A PDX collection 0
  - CC **M02.822 Other reactive arthropathies, left elbow**
    CC Exclusion see Appendix A PDX collection 0
  - CC **M02.829 Other reactive arthropathies, unspecified elbow**
    CC Exclusion see Appendix A PDX collection 0

+ **M02.83 Other reactive arthropathies, wrist**
  Other reactive arthropathies, carpal bones
  - CC **M02.831 Other reactive arthropathies, right wrist**
    CC Exclusion see Appendix A PDX collection 0
  - CC **M02.832 Other reactive arthropathies, left wrist**
    CC Exclusion see Appendix A PDX collection 0
  - CC **M02.839 Other reactive arthropathies, unspecified wrist**
    CC Exclusion see Appendix A PDX collection 0

+ **M02.84 Other reactive arthropathies, hand**
  Other reactive arthropathies, metacarpus and phalange
  - CC **M02.841 Other reactive arthropathies, right hand**
    CC Exclusion see Appendix A PDX collection 0
  - CC **M02.842 Other reactive arthropathies, left hand**
    CC Exclusion see Appendix A PDX collection 0
  - CC **M02.849 Other reactive arthropathies, unspecified hand**
    CC Exclusion see Appendix A PDX collection 0

+ **M02.85 Other reactive arthropathies, hip**
  - CC **M02.851 Other reactive arthropathies, right hip**
    CC Exclusion see Appendix A PDX collection 0
  - CC **M02.852 Other reactive arthropathies, left hip**
    CC Exclusion see Appendix A PDX collection 0
  - CC **M02.859 Other reactive arthropathies, unspecified h**
    CC Exclusion see Appendix A PDX collection 0

+ **M02.86 Other reactive arthropathies, knee**
  - CC **M02.861 Other reactive arthropathies, right knee**
    CC Exclusion see Appendix A PDX collection 0
  - CC **M02.862 Other reactive arthropathies, left knee**
    CC Exclusion see Appendix A PDX collection 0
  - CC **M02.869 Other reactive arthropathies, unspecified knee**
    CC Exclusion see Appendix A PDX collection 0

+ **M02.87 Other reactive arthropathies, ankle and foot**
  Other reactive arthropathies, tarsus, metatarsus and phalanges
  - CC **M02.871 Other reactive arthropathies, right ankle and foot**
    CC Exclusion see Appendix A PDX collection 0
  - CC **M02.872 Other reactive arthropathies, left ankle and foot**
    CC Exclusion see Appendix A PDX collection 0
  - CC **M02.879 Other reactive arthropathies, unspecified ankle and foot**
    CC Exclusion see Appendix A PDX collection 0

CC **M02.88 Other reactive arthropathies, vertebrae**
CC Exclusion see Appendix A PDX collection 0863

CC **M02.89 Other reactive arthropathies, multiple sites**
CC Exclusion see Appendix A PDX collection 0863

M02.9 Reactive arthropathy, unspecified

flammatory polyarthropathies (M05-M14)

M05 Rheumatoid arthritis with rheumatoid factor

Excludes1: *rheumatic fever (I00)*
juvenile rheumatoid arthritis (M08.-)
rheumatoid arthritis of spine (M45.-)

+ **M05.0 Felty's syndrome**
  Rheumatoid arthritis with splenoadenomegaly and leukopenia
  M05.00 Felty's syndrome, unspecified site
  + **M05.01 Felty's syndrome, shoulder**
    M05.011 Felty's syndrome, right shoulder
    M05.012 Felty's syndrome, left shoulder
    M05.019 Felty's syndrome, unspecified shoulder
  + **M05.02 Felty's syndrome, elbow**
    M05.021 Felty's syndrome, right elbow
    M05.022 Felty's syndrome, left elbow
    M05.029 Felty's syndrome, unspecified elbow
  + **M05.03 Felty's syndrome, wrist**
    Felty's syndrome, carpal bones
    M05.031 Felty's syndrome, right wrist
    M05.032 Felty's syndrome, left wrist
    M05.039 Felty's syndrome, unspecified wrist
  + **M05.04 Felty's syndrome, hand**
    Felty's syndrome, metacarpus and phalanges
    M05.041 Felty's syndrome, right hand
    M05.042 Felty's syndrome, left hand
    M05.049 Felty's syndrome, unspecified hand
  + **M05.05 Felty's syndrome, hip**
    M05.051 Felty's syndrome, right hip
    M05.052 Felty's syndrome, left hip
    M05.059 Felty's syndrome, unspecified hip
  + **M05.06 Felty's syndrome, knee**
    M05.061 Felty's syndrome, right knee
    M05.062 Felty's syndrome, left knee
    M05.069 Felty's syndrome, unspecified knee
  + **M05.07 Felty's syndrome, ankle and foot**
    Felty's syndrome, tarsus, metatarsus and phalanges
    M05.071 Felty's syndrome, right ankle and foot
    M05.072 Felty's syndrome, left ankle and foot
    M05.079 Felty's syndrome, unspecified ankle and foot
  M05.09 Felty's syndrome, multiple sites

+ **M05.1 Rheumatoid lung disease with rheumatoid arthritis**
  M05.10 Rheumatoid lung disease with rheumatoid arthritis of unspecified site
  + **M05.11 Rheumatoid lung disease with rheumatoid arthritis of shoulder**
    M05.111 Rheumatoid lung disease with rheumatoid arthritis of right shoulder
    M05.112 Rheumatoid lung disease with rheumatoid arthritis of left shoulder
    M05.119 Rheumatoid lung disease with rheumatoid arthritis of unspecified shoulder
  + **M05.12 Rheumatoid lung disease with rheumatoid arthritis of elbow**
    M05.121 Rheumatoid lung disease with rheumatoid arthritis of right elbow
    M05.122 Rheumatoid lung disease with rheumatoid arthritis of left elbow
    M05.129 Rheumatoid lung disease with rheumatoid arthritis of unspecified elbow
  + **M05.13 Rheumatoid lung disease with rheumatoid arthritis of wrist**
    Rheumatoid lung disease with rheumatoid arthritis, carpal bones
    M05.131 Rheumatoid lung disease with rheumatoid arthritis of right wrist
    M05.132 Rheumatoid lung disease with rheumatoid arthritis of left wrist
    M05.139 Rheumatoid lung disease with rheumatoid arthritis of unspecified wrist
  + **M05.14 Rheumatoid lung disease with rheumatoid arthritis of hand**
    Rheumatoid lung disease with rheumatoid arthritis, metacarpus and phalanges
    M05.141 Rheumatoid lung disease with rheumatoid arthritis of right hand
    M05.142 Rheumatoid lung disease with rheumatoid arthritis of left hand
    M05.149 Rheumatoid lung disease with rheumatoid arthritis of unspecified hand
  + **M05.15 Rheumatoid lung disease with rheumatoid arthritis of hip**
    M05.151 Rheumatoid lung disease with rheumatoid arthritis of right hip
    M05.152 Rheumatoid lung disease with rheumatoid arthritis of left hip
    M05.159 Rheumatoid lung disease with rheumatoid arthritis of unspecified hip
  + **M05.16 Rheumatoid lung disease with rheumatoid arthritis of knee**
    M05.161 Rheumatoid lung disease with rheumatoid arthritis of right knee
    M05.162 Rheumatoid lung disease with rheumatoid arthritis of left knee
    M05.169 Rheumatoid lung disease with rheumatoid arthritis of unspecified knee
  + **M05.17 Rheumatoid lung disease with rheumatoid arthritis of ankle and foot**
    Rheumatoid lung disease with rheumatoid arthritis, tarsus, metatarsus and phalanges
    M05.171 Rheumatoid lung disease with rheumatoid arthritis of right ankle and foot
    M05.172 Rheumatoid lung disease with rheumatoid arthritis of left ankle and foot
    M05.179 Rheumatoid lung disease with rheumatoid arthritis of unspecified ankle and foot
  M05.19 Rheumatoid lung disease with rheumatoid arthritis of multiple sites

+ **M05.2 Rheumatoid vasculitis with rheumatoid arthritis**
  M05.20 Rheumatoid vasculitis with rheumatoid arthritis of unspecified site
  + **M05.21 Rheumatoid vasculitis with rheumatoid arthritis of shoulder**
    M05.211 Rheumatoid vasculitis with rheumatoid arthritis of right shoulder
    M05.212 Rheumatoid vasculitis with rheumatoid arthritis of left shoulder
    M05.219 Rheumatoid vasculitis with rheumatoid arthritis of unspecified shoulder
  + **M05.22 Rheumatoid vasculitis with rheumatoid arthritis of elbow**
    M05.221 Rheumatoid vasculitis with rheumatoid arthritis of right elbow
    M05.222 Rheumatoid vasculitis with rheumatoid arthritis of left elbow
    M05.229 Rheumatoid vasculitis with rheumatoid arthritis of unspecified elbow
  + **M05.23 Rheumatoid vasculitis with rheumatoid arthritis of wrist**
    Rheumatoid vasculitis with rheumatoid arthritis, carpal bones
    M05.231 Rheumatoid vasculitis with rheumatoid arthritis of right wrist
    M05.232 Rheumatoid vasculitis with rheumatoid arthritis of left wrist
    M05.239 Rheumatoid vasculitis with rheumatoid arthritis of unspecified wrist
  + **M05.24 Rheumatoid vasculitis with rheumatoid arthritis of hand**
    Rheumatoid vasculitis with rheumatoid arthritis, metacarpus and phalanges
    M05.241 Rheumatoid vasculitis with rheumatoid arthritis of right hand
    M05.242 Rheumatoid vasculitis with rheumatoid arthritis of left hand
    M05.249 Rheumatoid vasculitis with rheumatoid arthritis of unspecified hand
  + **M05.25 Rheumatoid vasculitis with rheumatoid arthritis of hip**
    M05.251 Rheumatoid vasculitis with rheumatoid arthritis of right hip
    M05.252 Rheumatoid vasculitis with rheumatoid arthritis of left hip
    M05.259 Rheumatoid vasculitis with rheumatoid arthritis of unspecified hip

+ **M05.26 Rheumatoid vasculitis with rheumatoid arthritis of knee**
  - **M05.261 Rheumatoid vasculitis with rheumatoid arthritis of right knee**
  - **M05.262 Rheumatoid vasculitis with rheumatoid arthritis of left knee**
  - **M05.269 Rheumatoid vasculitis with rheumatoid arthritis of unspecified knee**

+ **M05.27 Rheumatoid vasculitis with rheumatoid arthritis of ankle and foot**
  Rheumatoid vasculitis with rheumatoid arthritis, tarsus, metatarsus and phalanges
  - **M05.271 Rheumatoid vasculitis with rheumatoid arthritis of right ankle and foot**
  - **M05.272 Rheumatoid vasculitis with rheumatoid arthritis of left ankle and foot**
  - **M05.279 Rheumatoid vasculitis with rheumatoid arthritis of unspecified ankle and foot**

M05.29 Rheumatoid vasculitis with rheumatoid arthritis of multiple sites

+ **M05.3 Rheumatoid heart disease with rheumatoid arthritis**
  Rheumatoid carditis
  Rheumatoid endocarditis
  Rheumatoid myocarditis
  Rheumatoid pericarditis

M05.30 Rheumatoid heart disease with rheumatoid arthritis of unspecified site

+ **M05.31 Rheumatoid heart disease with rheumatoid arthritis of shoulder**
  - **M05.311 Rheumatoid heart disease with rheumatoid arthritis of right shoulder**
  - **M05.312 Rheumatoid heart disease with rheumatoid arthritis of left shoulder**
  - **M05.319 Rheumatoid heart disease with rheumatoid arthritis of unspecified shoulder**

+ **M05.32 Rheumatoid heart disease with rheumatoid arthritis of elbow**
  - **M05.321 Rheumatoid heart disease with rheumatoid arthritis of right elbow**
  - **M05.322 Rheumatoid heart disease with rheumatoid arthritis of left elbow**
  - **M05.329 Rheumatoid heart disease with rheumatoid arthritis of unspecified elbow**

+ **M05.33 Rheumatoid heart disease with rheumatoid arthritis of wrist**
  Rheumatoid heart disease with rheumatoid arthritis, carpal bones
  - **M05.331 Rheumatoid heart disease with rheumatoid arthritis of right wrist**
  - **M05.332 Rheumatoid heart disease with rheumatoid arthritis of left wrist**
  - **M05.339 Rheumatoid heart disease with rheumatoid arthritis of unspecified wrist**

+ **M05.34 Rheumatoid heart disease with rheumatoid arthritis of hand**
  Rheumatoid heart disease with rheumatoid arthritis, metacarpus and phalanges
  - **M05.341 Rheumatoid heart disease with rheumatoid arthritis of right hand**
  - **M05.342 Rheumatoid heart disease with rheumatoid arthritis of left hand**
  - **M05.349 Rheumatoid heart disease with rheumatoid arthritis of unspecified hand**

+ **M05.35 Rheumatoid heart disease with rheumatoid arthritis of hip**
  - **M05.351 Rheumatoid heart disease with rheumatoid arthritis of right hip**
  - **M05.352 Rheumatoid heart disease with rheumatoid arthritis of left hip**
  - **M05.359 Rheumatoid heart disease with rheumatoid arthritis of unspecified hip**

+ **M05.36 Rheumatoid heart disease with rheumatoid arthritis of knee**
  - **M05.361 Rheumatoid heart disease with rheumatoid arthritis of right knee**
  - **M05.362 Rheumatoid heart disease with rheumatoid arthritis of left knee**
  - **M05.369 Rheumatoid heart disease with rheumatoid arthritis of unspecified knee**

+ **M05.37 Rheumatoid heart disease with rheumatoid arthriti of ankle and foot**
  Rheumatoid heart disease with rheumatoid arthritis, tarsus, metatarsus and phalanges
  - **M05.371 Rheumatoid heart disease with rheumatoi arthritis of right ankle and foot**
  - **M05.372 Rheumatoid heart disease with rheumatoi arthritis of left ankle and foot**
  - **M05.379 Rheumatoid heart disease with rheumatoi arthritis of unspecified ankle and foot**

M05.39 Rheumatoid heart disease with rheumatoid arthriti of multiple sites

+ **M05.4 Rheumatoid myopathy with rheumatoid arthritis**

CC **M05.40 Rheumatoid myopathy with rheumatoid arthritis of unspecified site**
  CC Exclusion see Appendix A PDX collection 0867

+ **M05.41 Rheumatoid myopathy with rheumatoid arthritis of shoulder**
  - CC **M05.411 Rheumatoid myopathy with rheumatoid arthritis of right shoulder**
    CC Exclusion see Appendix A PDX collection 0
  - CC **M05.412 Rheumatoid myopathy with rheumatoid arthritis of left shoulder**
    CC Exclusion see Appendix A PDX collection 0
  - CC **M05.419 Rheumatoid myopathy with rheumatoid arthritis of unspecified shoulder**
    CC Exclusion see Appendix A PDX collection 0

+ **M05.42 Rheumatoid myopathy with rheumatoid arthritis of elbow**
  - CC **M05.421 Rheumatoid myopathy with rheumatoid arthritis of right elbow**
    CC Exclusion see Appendix A PDX collection 0
  - CC **M05.422 Rheumatoid myopathy with rheumatoid arthritis of left elbow**
    CC Exclusion see Appendix A PDX collection 0
  - CC **M05.429 Rheumatoid myopathy with rheumatoid arthritis of unspecified elbow**
    CC Exclusion see Appendix A PDX collection 0

+ **M05.43 Rheumatoid myopathy with rheumatoid arthritis of wrist**
  Rheumatoid myopathy with rheumatoid arthritis, carp bones
  - CC **M05.431 Rheumatoid myopathy with rheumatoid arthritis of right wrist**
    CC Exclusion see Appendix A PDX collection 08
  - CC **M05.432 Rheumatoid myopathy with rheumatoid arthritis of left wrist**
    CC Exclusion see Appendix A PDX collection 08
  - CC **M05.439 Rheumatoid myopathy with rheumatoid arthritis of unspecified wrist**
    CC Exclusion see Appendix A PDX collection 08

+ **M05.44 Rheumatoid myopathy with rheumatoid arthritis of hand**
  Rheumatoid myopathy with rheumatoid arthritis, metacarpus and phalanges
  - CC **M05.441 Rheumatoid myopathy with rheumatoid arthritis of right hand**
    CC Exclusion see Appendix A PDX collection 08
  - CC **M05.442 Rheumatoid myopathy with rheumatoid arthritis of left hand**
    CC Exclusion see Appendix A PDX collection 08
  - CC **M05.449 Rheumatoid myopathy with rheumatoid arthritis of unspecified hand**
    CC Exclusion see Appendix A PDX collection 08

+ **M05.45 Rheumatoid myopathy with rheumatoid arthritis of h**
  - CC **M05.451 Rheumatoid myopathy with rheumatoid arthritis of right hip**
    CC Exclusion see Appendix A PDX collection 08
  - CC **M05.452 Rheumatoid myopathy with rheumatoid arthritis of left hip**
    CC Exclusion see Appendix A PDX collection 08
  - CC **M05.459 Rheumatoid myopathy with rheumatoid arthritis of unspecified hip**
    CC Exclusion see Appendix A PDX collection 08

+ **M05.46 Rheumatoid myopathy with rheumatoid arthritis of knee**
  - CC **M05.461 Rheumatoid myopathy with rheumatoid arthritis of right knee**
    CC Exclusion see Appendix A PDX collection 08
  - CC **M05.462 Rheumatoid myopathy with rheumatoid arthritis of left knee**
    CC Exclusion see Appendix A PDX collection 08

CC **M05.469 Rheumatoid myopathy with rheumatoid arthritis of unspecified knee**
CC Exclusion see Appendix A PDX collection 0867

+ **M05.47 Rheumatoid myopathy with rheumatoid arthritis of ankle and foot**
Rheumatoid myopathy with rheumatoid arthritis, tarsus, metatarsus and phalanges

CC **M05.471 Rheumatoid myopathy with rheumatoid arthritis of right ankle and foot**
CC Exclusion see Appendix A PDX collection 0867

CC **M05.472 Rheumatoid myopathy with rheumatoid arthritis of left ankle and foot**
CC Exclusion see Appendix A PDX collection 0867

CC **M05.479 Rheumatoid myopathy with rheumatoid arthritis of unspecified ankle and foot**
CC Exclusion see Appendix A PDX collection 0867

CC **M05.49 Rheumatoid myopathy with rheumatoid arthritis of multiple sites**
CC Exclusion see Appendix A PDX collection 0867

+ **M05.5 Rheumatoid polyneuropathy with rheumatoid arthritis**

M05.50 Rheumatoid polyneuropathy with rheumatoid arthritis of unspecified site

+ **M05.51 Rheumatoid polyneuropathy with rheumatoid arthritis of shoulder**

M05.511 Rheumatoid polyneuropathy with rheumatoid arthritis of right shoulder

M05.512 Rheumatoid polyneuropathy with rheumatoid arthritis of left shoulder

M05.519 Rheumatoid polyneuropathy with rheumatoid arthritis of unspecified shoulder

+ **M05.52 Rheumatoid polyneuropathy with rheumatoid arthritis of elbow**

M05.521 Rheumatoid polyneuropathy with rheumatoid arthritis of right elbow

M05.522 Rheumatoid polyneuropathy with rheumatoid arthritis of left elbow

M05.529 Rheumatoid polyneuropathy with rheumatoid arthritis of unspecified elbow

+ **M05.53 Rheumatoid polyneuropathy with rheumatoid arthritis of wrist**
Rheumatoid polyneuropathy with rheumatoid arthritis, carpal bones

M05.531 Rheumatoid polyneuropathy with rheumatoid arthritis of right wrist

M05.532 Rheumatoid polyneuropathy with rheumatoid arthritis of left wrist

M05.539 Rheumatoid polyneuropathy with rheumatoid arthritis of unspecified wrist

+ **M05.54 Rheumatoid polyneuropathy with rheumatoid arthritis of hand**
Rheumatoid polyneuropathy with rheumatoid arthritis, metacarpus and phalanges

M05.541 Rheumatoid polyneuropathy with rheumatoid arthritis of right hand

M05.542 Rheumatoid polyneuropathy with rheumatoid arthritis of left hand

M05.549 Rheumatoid polyneuropathy with rheumatoid arthritis of unspecified hand

+ **M05.55 Rheumatoid polyneuropathy with rheumatoid arthritis of hip**

M05.551 Rheumatoid polyneuropathy with rheumatoid arthritis of right hip

M05.552 Rheumatoid polyneuropathy with rheumatoid arthritis of left hip

M05.559 Rheumatoid polyneuropathy with rheumatoid arthritis of unspecified hip

+ **M05.56 Rheumatoid polyneuropathy with rheumatoid arthritis of knee**

M05.561 Rheumatoid polyneuropathy with rheumatoid arthritis of right knee

M05.562 Rheumatoid polyneuropathy with rheumatoid arthritis of left knee

M05.569 Rheumatoid polyneuropathy with rheumatoid arthritis of unspecified knee

+ **M05.57 Rheumatoid polyneuropathy with rheumatoid arthritis of ankle and foot**
Rheumatoid polyneuropathy with rheumatoid arthritis, tarsus, metatarsus and phalanges

M05.571 Rheumatoid polyneuropathy with rheumatoid arthritis of right ankle and foot

M05.572 Rheumatoid polyneuropathy with rheumatoid arthritis of left ankle and foot

M05.579 Rheumatoid polyneuropathy with rheumatoid arthritis of unspecified ankle and foot

M05.59 Rheumatoid polyneuropathy with rheumatoid arthritis of multiple sites

+ **M05.6 Rheumatoid arthritis with involvement of other organs and systems**

M05.60 Rheumatoid arthritis of unspecified site with involvement of other organs and systems

+ **M05.61 Rheumatoid arthritis of shoulder with involvement of other organs and systems**

M05.611 Rheumatoid arthritis of right shoulder with involvement of other organs and systems

M05.612 Rheumatoid arthritis of left shoulder with involvement of other organs and systems

M05.619 Rheumatoid arthritis of unspecified shoulder with involvement of other organs and systems

+ **M05.62 Rheumatoid arthritis of elbow with involvement of other organs and systems**

M05.621 Rheumatoid arthritis of right elbow with involvement of other organs and systems

M05.622 Rheumatoid arthritis of left elbow with involvement of other organs and systems

M05.629 Rheumatoid arthritis of unspecified elbow with involvement of other organs and systems

+ **M05.63 Rheumatoid arthritis of wrist with involvement of other organs and systems**
Rheumatoid arthritis of carpal bones with involvement of other organs and systems

M05.631 Rheumatoid arthritis of right wrist with involvement of other organs and systems

M05.632 Rheumatoid arthritis of left wrist with involvement of other organs and systems

M05.639 Rheumatoid arthritis of unspecified wrist with involvement of other organs and systems

+ **M05.64 Rheumatoid arthritis of hand with involvement of other organs and systems**
Rheumatoid arthritis of metacarpus and phalanges with involvement of other organs and systems

M05.641 Rheumatoid arthritis of right hand with involvement of other organs and systems

M05.642 Rheumatoid arthritis of left hand with involvement of other organs and systems

M05.649 Rheumatoid arthritis of unspecified hand with involvement of other organs and systems

+ **M05.65 Rheumatoid arthritis of hip with involvement of other organs and systems**

M05.651 Rheumatoid arthritis of right hip with involvement of other organs and systems

M05.652 Rheumatoid arthritis of left hip with involvement of other organs and systems

M05.659 Rheumatoid arthritis of unspecified hip with involvement of other organs and systems

+ **M05.66 Rheumatoid arthritis of knee with involvement of other organs and systems**

M05.661 Rheumatoid arthritis of right knee with involvement of other organs and systems

M05.662 Rheumatoid arthritis of left knee with involvement of other organs and systems

M05.669 Rheumatoid arthritis of unspecified knee with involvement of other organs and systems

+ **M05.67 Rheumatoid arthritis of ankle and foot with involvement of other organs and systems**
Rheumatoid arthritis of tarsus, metatarsus and phalanges with involvement of other organs and systems

M05.671 Rheumatoid arthritis of right ankle and foot with involvement of other organs and systems

M05.672 Rheumatoid arthritis of left ankle and foot with involvement of other organs and systems

M05.679 Rheumatoid arthritis of unspecified ankle and foot with involvement of other organs and systems

M05.69 Rheumatoid arthritis of multiple sites with involvement of other organs and systems

+ M05.7 Rheumatoid arthritis with rheumatoid factor without organ or systems involvement

M05.70 Rheumatoid arthritis with rheumatoid factor of unspecified site without organ or systems involvement

+ M05.71 Rheumatoid arthritis with rheumatoid factor of shoulder without organ or systems involvement

M05.711 Rheumatoid arthritis with rheumatoid factor of right shoulder without organ or systems involvement

M05.712 Rheumatoid arthritis with rheumatoid factor of left shoulder without organ or systems involvement

M05.719 Rheumatoid arthritis with rheumatoid factor of unspecified shoulder without organ or systems involvement

+ M05.72 Rheumatoid arthritis with rheumatoid factor of elbow without organ or systems involvement

M05.721 Rheumatoid arthritis with rheumatoid factor of right elbow without organ or systems involvement

M05.722 Rheumatoid arthritis with rheumatoid factor of left elbow without organ or systems involvement

M05.729 Rheumatoid arthritis with rheumatoid factor of unspecified elbow without organ or systems involvement

+ M05.73 Rheumatoid arthritis with rheumatoid factor of wrist without organ or systems involvement

M05.731 Rheumatoid arthritis with rheumatoid factor of right wrist without organ or systems involvement

M05.732 Rheumatoid arthritis with rheumatoid factor of left wrist without organ or systems involvement

M05.739 Rheumatoid arthritis with rheumatoid factor of unspecified wrist without organ or systems involvement

+ M05.74 Rheumatoid arthritis with rheumatoid factor of hand without organ or systems involvement

M05.741 Rheumatoid arthritis with rheumatoid factor of right hand without organ or systems involvement

M05.742 Rheumatoid arthritis with rheumatoid factor of left hand without organ or systems involvement

M05.749 Rheumatoid arthritis with rheumatoid factor of unspecified hand without organ or systems involvement

+ M05.75 Rheumatoid arthritis with rheumatoid factor of hip without organ or systems involvement

M05.751 Rheumatoid arthritis with rheumatoid factor of right hip without organ or systems involvement

M05.752 Rheumatoid arthritis with rheumatoid factor of left hip without organ or systems involvement

M05.759 Rheumatoid arthritis with rheumatoid factor of unspecified hip without organ or systems involvement

+ M05.76 Rheumatoid arthritis with rheumatoid factor of knee without organ or systems involvement

M05.761 Rheumatoid arthritis with rheumatoid factor of right knee without organ or systems involvement

M05.762 Rheumatoid arthritis with rheumatoid factor of left knee without organ or systems involvement

M05.769 Rheumatoid arthritis with rheumatoid factor of unspecified knee without organ or systems involvement

+ M05.77 Rheumatoid arthritis with rheumatoid factor of ankle and foot without organ or systems involvement

M05.771 Rheumatoid arthritis with rheumatoid factor of right ankle and foot without organ or systems involvement

M05.772 Rheumatoid arthritis with rheumatoid factor of left ankle and foot without organ systems involvement

M05.779 Rheumatoid arthritis with rheumatoid factor of unspecified ankle and foot witho organ or systems involvement

M05.79 Rheumatoid arthritis with rheumatoid factor of multiple sites without organ or systems involvement

+ M05.8 Other rheumatoid arthritis with rheumatoid factor

M05.80 Other rheumatoid arthritis with rheumatoid factor unspecified site

+ M05.81 Other rheumatoid arthritis with rheumatoid factor shoulder

M05.811 Other rheumatoid arthritis with rheumat factor of right shoulder

M05.812 Other rheumatoid arthritis with rheumat factor of left shoulder

M05.819 Other rheumatoid arthritis with rheumat factor of unspecified shoulder

+ M05.82 Other rheumatoid arthritis with rheumatoid factor elbow

M05.821 Other rheumatoid arthritis with rheumat factor of right elbow

M05.822 Other rheumatoid arthritis with rheumat factor of left elbow

M05.829 Other rheumatoid arthritis with rheumat factor of unspecified elbow

+ M05.83 Other rheumatoid arthritis with rheumatoid factor wrist

M05.831 Other rheumatoid arthritis with rheumat factor of right wrist

M05.832 Other rheumatoid arthritis with rheumat factor of left wrist

M05.839 Other rheumatoid arthritis with rheumat factor of unspecified wrist

+ M05.84 Other rheumatoid arthritis with rheumatoid factor hand

M05.841 Other rheumatoid arthritis with rheumat factor of right hand

M05.842 Other rheumatoid arthritis with rheumat factor of left hand

M05.849 Other rheumatoid arthritis with rheumat factor of unspecified hand

+ M05.85 Other rheumatoid arthritis with rheumatoid factor hip

M05.851 Other rheumatoid arthritis with rheumato factor of right hip

M05.852 Other rheumatoid arthritis with rheumato factor of left hip

M05.859 Other rheumatoid arthritis with rheumato factor of unspecified hip

+ M05.86 Other rheumatoid arthritis with rheumatoid factor knee

M05.861 Other rheumatoid arthritis with rheumato factor of right knee

M05.862 Other rheumatoid arthritis with rheumato factor of left knee

M05.869 Other rheumatoid arthritis with rheumato factor of unspecified knee

+ M05.87 Other rheumatoid arthritis with rheumatoid factor ankle and foot

M05.871 Other rheumatoid arthritis with rheumato factor of right ankle and foot

M05.872 Other rheumatoid arthritis with rheumato factor of left ankle and foot

M05.879 Other rheumatoid arthritis with rheumato factor of unspecified ankle and foot

M05.89 Other rheumatoid arthritis with rheumatoid factor o multiple sites

M05.9 Rheumatoid arthritis with rheumatoid factor, unspecified

M06 Other rheumatoid arthritis

+ M06.0 Rheumatoid arthritis without rheumatoid factor

M06.00 Rheumatoid arthritis without rheumatoid factor, unspecified site

+ M06.01 Rheumatoid arthritis without rheumatoid factor, shoulder

M06.011 Rheumatoid arthritis without rheumatoid factor, right shoulder

M06.012 Rheumatoid arthritis without rheumatoid factor, left shoulder

M06.019 Rheumatoid arthritis without rheumatoid factor, unspecified shoulder

+ M06.02 Rheumatoid arthritis without rheumatoid factor, elbow
- **M06.021 Rheumatoid arthritis without rheumatoid factor, right elbow**
- **M06.022 Rheumatoid arthritis without rheumatoid factor, left elbow**
- **M06.029 Rheumatoid arthritis without rheumatoid factor, unspecified elbow**

+ M06.03 Rheumatoid arthritis without rheumatoid factor, wrist
- **M06.031 Rheumatoid arthritis without rheumatoid factor, right wrist**
- **M06.032 Rheumatoid arthritis without rheumatoid factor, left wrist**
- **M06.039 Rheumatoid arthritis without rheumatoid factor, unspecified wrist**

+ M06.04 Rheumatoid arthritis without rheumatoid factor, hand
- **M06.041 Rheumatoid arthritis without rheumatoid factor, right hand**
- **M06.042 Rheumatoid arthritis without rheumatoid factor, left hand**
- **M06.049 Rheumatoid arthritis without rheumatoid factor, unspecified hand**

+ M06.05 Rheumatoid arthritis without rheumatoid factor, hip
- **M06.051 Rheumatoid arthritis without rheumatoid factor, right hip**
- **M06.052 Rheumatoid arthritis without rheumatoid factor, left hip**
- **M06.059 Rheumatoid arthritis without rheumatoid factor, unspecified hip**

+ M06.06 Rheumatoid arthritis without rheumatoid factor, knee
- **M06.061 Rheumatoid arthritis without rheumatoid factor, right knee**
- **M06.062 Rheumatoid arthritis without rheumatoid factor, left knee**
- **M06.069 Rheumatoid arthritis without rheumatoid factor, unspecified knee**

+ M06.07 Rheumatoid arthritis without rheumatoid factor, ankle and foot
- **M06.071 Rheumatoid arthritis without rheumatoid factor, right ankle and foot**
- **M06.072 Rheumatoid arthritis without rheumatoid factor, left ankle and foot**
- **M06.079 Rheumatoid arthritis without rheumatoid factor, unspecified ankle and foot**

M06.08 Rheumatoid arthritis without rheumatoid factor, vertebrae

M06.09 Rheumatoid arthritis without rheumatoid factor, multiple sites

• M06.1 Adult-onset Still's disease
Excludes1: *Still's disease NOS (M08.2-)*

+ M06.2 Rheumatoid bursitis
- **M06.20 Rheumatoid bursitis, unspecified site**

+ M06.21 Rheumatoid bursitis, shoulder
- **M06.211 Rheumatoid bursitis, right shoulder**
- **M06.212 Rheumatoid bursitis, left shoulder**
- **M06.219 Rheumatoid bursitis, unspecified shoulder**

+ M06.22 Rheumatoid bursitis, elbow
- **M06.221 Rheumatoid bursitis, right elbow**
- **M06.222 Rheumatoid bursitis, left elbow**
- **M06.229 Rheumatoid bursitis, unspecified elbow**

+ M06.23 Rheumatoid bursitis, wrist
- **M06.231 Rheumatoid bursitis, right wrist**
- **M06.232 Rheumatoid bursitis, left wrist**
- **M06.239 Rheumatoid bursitis, unspecified wrist**

+ M06.24 Rheumatoid bursitis, hand
- **M06.241 Rheumatoid bursitis, right hand**
- **M06.242 Rheumatoid bursitis, left hand**
- **M06.249 Rheumatoid bursitis, unspecified hand**

+ M06.25 Rheumatoid bursitis, hip
- **M06.251 Rheumatoid bursitis, right hip**
- **M06.252 Rheumatoid bursitis, left hip**
- **M06.259 Rheumatoid bursitis, unspecified hip**

+ M06.26 Rheumatoid bursitis, knee
- **M06.261 Rheumatoid bursitis, right knee**
- **M06.262 Rheumatoid bursitis, left knee**
- **M06.269 Rheumatoid bursitis, unspecified knee**

+ M06.27 Rheumatoid bursitis, ankle and foot
- **M06.271 Rheumatoid bursitis, right ankle and foot**
- **M06.272 Rheumatoid bursitis, left ankle and foot**
- **M06.279 Rheumatoid bursitis, unspecified ankle and foot**

M06.28 Rheumatoid bursitis, vertebrae

M06.29 Rheumatoid bursitis, multiple sites

+ M06.3 Rheumatoid nodule
- **M06.30 Rheumatoid nodule, unspecified site**

+ M06.31 Rheumatoid nodule, shoulder
- **M06.311 Rheumatoid nodule, right shoulder**
- **M06.312 Rheumatoid nodule, left shoulder**
- **M06.319 Rheumatoid nodule, unspecified shoulder**

+ M06.32 Rheumatoid nodule, elbow
- **M06.321 Rheumatoid nodule, right elbow**
- **M06.322 Rheumatoid nodule, left elbow**
- **M06.329 Rheumatoid nodule, unspecified elbow**

+ M06.33 Rheumatoid nodule, wrist
- **M06.331 Rheumatoid nodule, right wrist**
- **M06.332 Rheumatoid nodule, left wrist**
- **M06.339 Rheumatoid nodule, unspecified wrist**

+ M06.34 Rheumatoid nodule, hand
- **M06.341 Rheumatoid nodule, right hand**
- **M06.342 Rheumatoid nodule, left hand**
- **M06.349 Rheumatoid nodule, unspecified hand**

+ M06.35 Rheumatoid nodule, hip
- **M06.351 Rheumatoid nodule, right hip**
- **M06.352 Rheumatoid nodule, left hip**
- **M06.359 Rheumatoid nodule, unspecified hip**

+ M06.36 Rheumatoid nodule, knee
- **M06.361 Rheumatoid nodule, right knee**
- **M06.362 Rheumatoid nodule, left knee**
- **M06.369 Rheumatoid nodule, unspecified knee**

+ M06.37 Rheumatoid nodule, ankle and foot
- **M06.371 Rheumatoid nodule, right ankle and foot**
- **M06.372 Rheumatoid nodule, left ankle and foot**
- **M06.379 Rheumatoid nodule, unspecified ankle and foot**

M06.38 Rheumatoid nodule, vertebrae

M06.39 Rheumatoid nodule, multiple sites

M06.4 Inflammatory polyarthropathy
Excludes1: *polyarthritis NOS (M13.0)*

+ M06.8 Other specified rheumatoid arthritis
- **M06.80 Other specified rheumatoid arthritis, unspecified site**

+ M06.81 Other specified rheumatoid arthritis, shoulder
- **M06.811 Other specified rheumatoid arthritis, right shoulder**
- **M06.812 Other specified rheumatoid arthritis, left shoulder**
- **M06.819 Other specified rheumatoid arthritis, unspecified shoulder**

+ M06.82 Other specified rheumatoid arthritis, elbow
- **M06.821 Other specified rheumatoid arthritis, right elbow**
- **M06.822 Other specified rheumatoid arthritis, left elbow**
- **M06.829 Other specified rheumatoid arthritis, unspecified elbow**

+ M06.83 Other specified rheumatoid arthritis, wrist
- **M06.831 Other specified rheumatoid arthritis, right wrist**
- **M06.832 Other specified rheumatoid arthritis, left wrist**
- **M06.839 Other specified rheumatoid arthritis, unspecified wrist**

+ M06.84 Other specified rheumatoid arthritis, hand
- **M06.841 Other specified rheumatoid arthritis, right hand**
- **M06.842 Other specified rheumatoid arthritis, left hand**
- **M06.849 Other specified rheumatoid arthritis, unspecified hand**

+ M06.85 Other specified rheumatoid arthritis, hip
- **M06.851 Other specified rheumatoid arthritis, right hip**
- **M06.852 Other specified rheumatoid arthritis, left hip**
- **M06.859 Other specified rheumatoid arthritis, unspecified hip**

+ M06.86 Other specified rheumatoid arthritis, knee
- **M06.861 Other specified rheumatoid arthritis, right knee**
- **M06.862 Other specified rheumatoid arthritis, left knee**
- **M06.869 Other specified rheumatoid arthritis, unspecified knee**

+ **M06.87 Other specified rheumatoid arthritis, ankle and foot**
  - **M06.871 Other specified rheumatoid arthritis, right ankle and foot**
  - **M06.872 Other specified rheumatoid arthritis, left ankle and foot**
  - **M06.879 Other specified rheumatoid arthritis, unspecified ankle and foot**

M06.88 Other specified rheumatoid arthritis, vertebrae
M06.89 Other specified rheumatoid arthritis, multiple sites
M06.9 Rheumatoid arthritis, unspecified

M07 Enteropathic arthropathies

Code also associated enteropathy, such as:
regional enteritis [Crohn's disease] (K50.-)
ulcerative colitis (K51.-)

Excludes1: *psoriatic arthropathies (L40.5-)*

+ **M07.6 Enteropathic arthropathies**
  - **M07.60 Enteropathic arthropathies, unspecified site**
  - + **M07.61 Enteropathic arthropathies, shoulder**
    - **M07.611 Enteropathic arthropathies, right shoulder**
    - **M07.612 Enteropathic arthropathies, left shoulder**
    - **M07.619 Enteropathic arthropathies, unspecified shoulder**
  - + **M07.62 Enteropathic arthropathies, elbow**
    - **M07.621 Enteropathic arthropathies, right elbow**
    - **M07.622 Enteropathic arthropathies, left elbow**
    - **M07.629 Enteropathic arthropathies, unspecified elbow**
  - + **M07.63 Enteropathic arthropathies, wrist**
    - **M07.631 Enteropathic arthropathies, right wrist**
    - **M07.632 Enteropathic arthropathies, left wrist**
    - **M07.639 Enteropathic arthropathies, unspecified wrist**
  - + **M07.64 Enteropathic arthropathies, hand**
    - **M07.641 Enteropathic arthropathies, right hand**
    - **M07.642 Enteropathic arthropathies, lefthand**
    - **M07.649 Enteropathic arthropathies, unspecified hand**
  - + **M07.65 Enteropathic arthropathies, hip**
    - **M07.651 Enteropathic arthropathies, right hip**
    - **M07.652 Enteropathic arthropathies, left hip**
    - **M07.659 Enteropathic arthropathies, unspecified hip**
  - + **M07.66 Enteropathic arthropathies, knee**
    - **M07.661 Enteropathic arthropathies, right knee**
    - **M07.662 Enteropathic arthropathies, left knee**
    - **M07.669 Enteropathic arthropathies, unspecified knee**
  - + **M07.67 Enteropathic arthropathies, ankle and foot**
    - **M07.671 Enteropathic arthropathies, right ankle and foot**
    - **M07.672 Enteropathic arthropathies, left ankle and foot**
    - **M07.679 Enteropathic arthropathies, unspecified ankle and foot**
  - **M07.68 Enteropathic arthropathies, vertebrae**
  - **M07.69 Enteropathic arthropathies, multiple sites**

M08 Juvenile arthritis

Code also any associated underlying condition, such as:
regional enteritis [Crohn's disease] (K50.-)
ulcerative colitis (K51.-)

Excludes1: *arthropathy in Whipple's disease (M14.8)*
Felty's syndrome (M05.0)
juvenile dermatomyositis (M33.0-)
psoriatic juvenile arthropathy (L40.54)

+ **M08.0 Unspecified juvenile rheumatoid arthritis**
  Juvenile rheumatoid arthritis with or without rheumatoid factor
  - **M08.00 Unspecified juvenile rheumatoid arthritis of unspecified site**
  - + **M08.01 Unspecified juvenile rheumatoid arthritis, shoulder**
    - **M08.011 Unspecified juvenile rheumatoid arthritis, right shoulder**
    - **M08.012 Unspecified juvenile rheumatoid arthritis, left shoulder**
    - **M08.019 Unspecified juvenile rheumatoid arthritis, unspecified shoulder**
  - + **M08.02 Unspecified juvenile rheumatoid arthritis of elbow**
    - **M08.021 Unspecified juvenile rheumatoid arthritis, right elbow**
    - **M08.022 Unspecified juvenile rheumatoid arthritis, left elbow**
    - **M08.029 Unspecified juvenile rheumatoid arthritis, unspecified elbow**
  - + **M08.03 Unspecified juvenile rheumatoid arthritis, wrist**
    - **M08.031 Unspecified juvenile rheumatoid arthritis, right wrist**
    - **M08.032 Unspecified juvenile rheumatoid arthritis, left wrist**
    - **M08.039 Unspecified juvenile rheumatoid arthritis, unspecified wrist**
  - + **M08.04 Unspecified juvenile rheumatoid arthritis, hand**
    - **M08.041 Unspecified juvenile rheumatoid arthritis, right hand**
    - **M08.042 Unspecified juvenile rheumatoid arthritis, left hand**
    - **M08.049 Unspecified juvenile rheumatoid arthritis, unspecified hand**
  - + **M08.05 Unspecified juvenile rheumatoid arthritis, hip**
    - **M08.051 Unspecified juvenile rheumatoid arthritis, right hip**
    - **M08.052 Unspecified juvenile rheumatoid arthritis, left hip**
    - **M08.059 Unspecified juvenile rheumatoid arthritis, unspecified hip**
  - + **M08.06 Unspecified juvenile rheumatoid arthritis, knee**
    - **M08.061 Unspecified juvenile rheumatoid arthritis, right knee**
    - **M08.062 Unspecified juvenile rheumatoid arthritis, left knee**
    - **M08.069 Unspecified juvenile rheumatoid arthritis, unspecified knee**
  - + **M08.07 Unspecified juvenile rheumatoid arthritis, ankle an foot**
    - **M08.071 Unspecified juvenile rheumatoid arthritis, right ankle and foot**
    - **M08.072 Unspecified juvenile rheumatoid arthritis, left ankle and foot**
    - **M08.079 Unspecified juvenile rheumatoid arthritis, unspecified ankle and foot**
  - **M08.08 Unspecified juvenile rheumatoid arthritis, vertebrae**
  - **M08.09 Unspecified juvenile rheumatoid arthritis, multiple sites**

M08.1 Juvenile ankylosing spondylitis
Excludes1: *ankylosing spondylitis in adults (M45.0-)*

+ **M08.2 Juvenile rheumatoid arthritis with systemic onset**
  Still's disease NOS
  Excludes1: *adult-onset Still's disease (M06.1-)*
  - **M08.20 Juvenile rheumatoid arthritis with systemic onset, unspecified site**
  - + **M08.21 Juvenile rheumatoid arthritis with systemic onset, shoulder**
    - **M08.211 Juvenile rheumatoid arthritis with systemi onset, right shoulder**
    - **M08.212 Juvenile rheumatoid arthritis with systemi onset, left shoulder**
    - **M08.219 Juvenile rheumatoid arthritis with systemi onset, unspecified shoulder**
  - + **M08.22 Juvenile rheumatoid arthritis with systemic onset, elbow**
    - **M08.221 Juvenile rheumatoid arthritis with systemi onset, right elbow**
    - **M08.222 Juvenile rheumatoid arthritis with systemi onset, left elbow**
    - **M08.229 Juvenile rheumatoid arthritis with systemi onset, unspecified elbow**
  - + **M08.23 Juvenile rheumatoid arthritis with systemic onset, wrist**
    - **M08.231 Juvenile rheumatoid arthritis with systemi onset, right wrist**
    - **M08.232 Juvenile rheumatoid arthritis with systemi onset, left wrist**
    - **M08.239 Juvenile rheumatoid arthritis with systemi onset, unspecified wrist**
  - + **M08.24 Juvenile rheumatoid arthritis with systemic onset, hand**
    - **M08.241 Juvenile rheumatoid arthritis with systemi onset, right hand**
    - **M08.242 Juvenile rheumatoid arthritis with systemi onset, left hand**
    - **M08.249 Juvenile rheumatoid arthritis with systemi onset, unspecified hand**
  - + **M08.25 Juvenile rheumatoid arthritis with systemic onset, hi**
    - **M08.251 Juvenile rheumatoid arthritis with systemi onset, right hip**

M08.252 **Juvenile rheumatoid arthritis with systemic onset, left hip**
M08.259 **Juvenile rheumatoid arthritis with systemic onset, unspecified hip**
\+ **M08.26** **Juvenile rheumatoid arthritis with systemic onset, knee**
M08.261 **Juvenile rheumatoid arthritis with systemic onset, right knee**
M08.262 **Juvenile rheumatoid arthritis with systemic onset, left knee**
M08.269 **Juvenile rheumatoid arthritis with systemic onset, unspecified knee**
\+ **M08.27** **Juvenile rheumatoid arthritis with systemic onset, ankle and foot**
M08.271 **Juvenile rheumatoid arthritis with systemic onset, right ankle and foot**
M08.272 **Juvenile rheumatoid arthritis with systemic onset, left ankle and foot**
M08.279 **Juvenile rheumatoid arthritis with systemic onset, unspecified ankle and foot**
M08.28 **Juvenile rheumatoid arthritis with systemic onset, vertebrae**
M08.29 **Juvenile rheumatoid arthritis with systemic onset, multiple sites**
M08.3 **Juvenile rheumatoid polyarthritis (seronegative)**
\+ **M08.4** **Pauciarticular juvenile rheumatoid arthritis**
M08.40 **Pauciarticular juvenile rheumatoid arthritis, unspecified site**
\+ **M08.41** **Pauciarticular juvenile rheumatoid arthritis, shoulder**
M08.411 **Pauciarticular juvenile rheumatoid arthritis, right shoulder**
M08.412 **Pauciarticular juvenile rheumatoid arthritis, left shoulder**
M08.419 **Pauciarticular juvenile rheumatoid arthritis, unspecified shoulder**
\+ **M08.42** **Pauciarticular juvenile rheumatoid arthritis, elbow**
M08.421 **Pauciarticular juvenile rheumatoid arthritis, right elbow**
M08.422 **Pauciarticular juvenile rheumatoid arthritis, left elbow**
M08.429 **Pauciarticular juvenile rheumatoid arthritis, unspecified elbow**
\+ **M08.43** **Pauciarticular juvenile rheumatoid arthritis, wrist**
M08.431 **Pauciarticular juvenile rheumatoid arthritis, right wrist**
M08.432 **Pauciarticular juvenile rheumatoid arthritis, left wrist**
M08.439 **Pauciarticular juvenile rheumatoid arthritis, unspecified wrist**
\+ **M08.44** **Pauciarticular juvenile rheumatoid arthritis, hand**
M08.441 **Pauciarticular juvenile rheumatoid arthritis, right hand**
M08.442 **Pauciarticular juvenile rheumatoid arthritis, left hand**
M08.449 **Pauciarticular juvenile rheumatoid arthritis, unspecified hand**
\+ **M08.45** **Pauciarticular juvenile rheumatoid arthritis, hip**
M08.451 **Pauciarticular juvenile rheumatoid arthritis, right hip**
M08.452 **Pauciarticular juvenile rheumatoid arthritis, left hip**
M08.459 **Pauciarticular juvenile rheumatoid arthritis, unspecified hip**
\+ **M08.46** **Pauciarticular juvenile rheumatoid arthritis, knee**
M08.461 **Pauciarticular juvenile rheumatoid arthritis, right knee**
M08.462 **Pauciarticular juvenile rheumatoid arthritis, left knee**
M08.469 **Pauciarticular juvenile rheumatoid arthritis, unspecified knee**
\+ **M08.47** **Pauciarticular juvenile rheumatoid arthritis, ankle and foot**
M08.471 **Pauciarticular juvenile rheumatoid arthritis, right ankle and foot**
M08.472 **Pauciarticular juvenile rheumatoid arthritis, left ankle and foot**
M08.479 **Pauciarticular juvenile rheumatoid arthritis, unspecified ankle and foot**
M08.48 **Pauciarticular juvenile rheumatoid arthritis, vertebrae**

\+ **M08.8** **Other juvenile arthritis**
M08.80 **Other juvenile arthritis, unspecified site**
\+ **M08.81** **Other juvenile arthritis, shoulder**
M08.811 **Other juvenile arthritis, right shoulder**
M08.812 **Other juvenile arthritis, left shoulder**
M08.819 **Other juvenile arthritis, unspecified shoulder**
\+ **M08.82** **Other juvenile arthritis, elbow**
M08.821 **Other juvenile arthritis, right elbow**
M08.822 **Other juvenile arthritis, left elbow**
M08.829 **Other juvenile arthritis, unspecified elbow**
\+ **M08.83** **Other juvenile arthritis, wrist**
M08.831 **Other juvenile arthritis, right wrist**
M08.832 **Other juvenile arthritis, left wrist**
M08.839 **Other juvenile arthritis, unspecified wrist**
\+ **M08.84** **Other juvenile arthritis, hand**
M08.841 **Other juvenile arthritis, right hand**
M08.842 **Other juvenile arthritis, left hand**
M08.849 **Other juvenile arthritis, unspecified hand**
\+ **M08.85** **Other juvenile arthritis, hip**
M08.851 **Other juvenile arthritis, right hip**
M08.852 **Other juvenile arthritis, left hip**
M08.859 **Other juvenile arthritis, unspecified hip**
\+ **M08.86** **Other juvenile arthritis, knee**
M08.861 **Other juvenile arthritis, right knee**
M08.862 **Other juvenile arthritis, left knee**
M08.869 **Other juvenile arthritis, unspecified knee**
\+ **M08.87** **Other juvenile arthritis, ankle and foot**
M08.871 **Other juvenile arthritis, right ankle and foot**
M08.872 **Other juvenile arthritis, left ankle and foot**
M08.879 **Other juvenile arthritis, unspecified ankle and foot**
M08.88 **Other juvenile arthritis, other specified site**
Other juvenile arthritis, vertebrae
M08.89 **Other juvenile arthritis, multiple sites**
\+ **M08.9** **Juvenile arthritis, unspecified**
Excludes1: *juvenile rheumatoid arthritis, unspecified (M08.0-)*
M08.90 **Juvenile arthritis, unspecified, unspecified site**
\+ **M08.91** **Juvenile arthritis, unspecified, shoulder**
M08.911 **Juvenile arthritis, unspecified, right shoulder**
M08.912 **Juvenile arthritis, unspecified, left shoulder**
M08.919 **Juvenile arthritis, unspecified, unspecified shoulder**
\+ **M08.92** **Juvenile arthritis, unspecified, elbow**
M08.921 **Juvenile arthritis, unspecified, right elbow**
M08.922 **Juvenile arthritis, unspecified, left elbow**
M08.929 **Juvenile arthritis, unspecified, unspecified elbow**
\+ **M08.93** **Juvenile arthritis, unspecified, wrist**
M08.931 **Juvenile arthritis, unspecified, right wrist**
M08.932 **Juvenile arthritis, unspecified, left wrist**
M08.939 **Juvenile arthritis, unspecified, unspecified wrist**
\+ **M08.94** **Juvenile arthritis, unspecified, hand**
M08.941 **Juvenile arthritis, unspecified, right hand**
M08.942 **Juvenile arthritis, unspecified, left hand**
M08.949 **Juvenile arthritis, unspecified, unspecified hand**
\+ **M08.95** **Juvenile arthritis, unspecified, hip**
M08.951 **Juvenile arthritis, unspecified, right hip**
M08.952 **Juvenile arthritis, unspecified, left hip**
M08.959 **Juvenile arthritis, unspecified, unspecified hip**
\+ **M08.96** **Juvenile arthritis, unspecified, knee**
M08.961 **Juvenile arthritis, unspecified, right knee**
M08.962 **Juvenile arthritis, unspecified, left knee**
M08.969 **Juvenile arthritis, unspecified, unspecified knee**
\+ **M08.97** **Juvenile arthritis, unspecified, ankle and foot**
M08.971 **Juvenile arthritis, unspecified, right ankle and foot**
M08.972 **Juvenile arthritis, unspecified, left ankle and foot**
M08.979 **Juvenile arthritis, unspecified, unspecified ankle and foot**
M08.98 **Juvenile arthritis, unspecified, vertebrae**
M08.99 **Juvenile arthritis, unspecified, multiple sites**

M1A Chronic gout

Use additional code to identify:
Autonomic neuropathy in diseases classified elsewhere (G99.0)
Calculus of urinary tract in diseases classified elsewhere (N22)
Cardiomyopathy in diseases classified elsewhere (I43)
Disorders of external ear in diseases classified elsewhere (H61.1-, H62.8-)
Disorders of iris and ciliary body in diseases classified elsewhere (H22)
Glomerular disorders in diseases classified elsewhere (N08)

Excludes1: *acute gout (M10.-)*
gout NOS (M10.-)

The appropriate 7th character is to be added to each code from category M1A
0 without tophus (tophi)
1 with tophus (tophi)

\+ **M1A.0 Idiopathic chronic gout**
Chronic gouty bursitis
Primary chronic gout
X+7th **M1A.00 Idiopathic chronic gout, unspecified site**
\+ **M1A.01 Idiopathic chronic gout, shoulder**
+7th **M1A.011 Idiopathic chronic gout, right shoulder**
+7th **M1A.012 Idiopathic chronic gout, left shoulder**
+7th **M1A.019 Idiopathic chronic gout, unspecified shoulder**
\+ **M1A.02 Idiopathic chronic gout, elbow**
+7th **M1A.021 Idiopathic chronic gout, right elbow**
+7th **M1A.022 Idiopathic chronic gout, left elbow**
+7th **M1A.029 Idiopathic chronic gout, unspecified elbow**
\+ **M1A.03 Idiopathic chronic gout, wrist**
+7th **M1A.031 Idiopathic chronic gout, right wrist**
+7th **M1A.032 Idiopathic chronic gout, left wrist**
+7th **M1A.039 Idiopathic chronic gout, unspecified wrist**
\+ **M1A.04 Idiopathic chronic gout, hand**
+7th **M1A.041 Idiopathic chronic gout, right hand**
+7th **M1A.042 Idiopathic chronic gout, left hand**
+7th **M1A.049 Idiopathic chronic gout, unspecified hand**
\+ **M1A.05 Idiopathic chronic gout, hip**
+7th **M1A.051 Idiopathic chronic gout, right hip**
+7th **M1A.052 Idiopathic chronic gout, left hip**
+7th **M1A.059 Idiopathic chronic gout, unspecified hip**
\+ **M1A.06 Idiopathic chronic gout, knee**
+7th **M1A.061 Idiopathic chronic gout, right knee**
+7th **M1A.062 Idiopathic chronic gout, left knee**
+7th **M1A.069 Idiopathic chronic gout, unspecified knee**
\+ **M1A.07 Idiopathic chronic gout, ankle and foot**
+7th **M1A.071 Idiopathic chronic gout, right ankle and foot**
+7th **M1A.072 Idiopathic chronic gout, left ankle and foot**
+7th **M1A.079 Idiopathic chronic gout, unspecified ankle and foot**
X+7th **M1A.08 Idiopathic chronic gout, vertebrae**
M1A.09 Idiopathic chronic gout, multiple sites
\+ **M1A.1 Lead-induced chronic gout**
Code first toxic effects of lead and its compounds (T56.0-)
X+7th **M1A.10 Lead-induced chronic gout, unspecified site**
\+ **M1A.11 Lead-induced chronic gout, shoulder**
+7th **M1A.111 Lead-induced chronic gout, right shoulder**
+7th **M1A.112 Lead-induced chronic gout, left shoulder**
+7th **M1A.119 Lead-induced chronic gout, unspecified shoulder**
\+ **M1A.12 Lead-induced chronic gout, elbow**
+7th **M1A.121 Lead-induced chronic gout, right elbow**
+7th **M1A.122 Lead-induced chronic gout, left elbow**
+7th **M1A.129 Lead-induced chronic gout, unspecified elbow**
\+ **M1A.13 Lead-induced chronic gout, wrist**
+7th **M1A.131 Lead-induced chronic gout, right wrist**
+7th **M1A.132 Lead-induced chronic gout, left wrist**
+7th **M1A.139 Lead-induced chronic gout, unspecified wrist**
\+ **M1A.14 Lead-induced chronic gout, hand**
+7th **M1A.141 Lead-induced chronic gout, right hand**
+7th **M1A.142 Lead-induced chronic gout, left hand**
+7th **M1A.149 Lead-induced chronic gout, unspecified hand**
\+ **M1A.15 Lead-induced chronic gout, hip**
+7th **M1A.151 Lead-induced chronic gout, right hip**
+7th **M1A.152 Lead-induced chronic gout, left hip**
+7th **M1A.159 Lead-induced chronic gout, unspecified hip**
\+ **M1A.16 Lead-induced chronic gout, knee**
+7th **M1A.161 Lead-induced chronic gout, right knee**
+7th **M1A.162 Lead-induced chronic gout, left knee**
+7th **M1A.169 Lead-induced chronic gout, unspecified knee**
\+ **M1A.17 Lead-induced chronic gout, ankle and foot**
+7th **M1A.171 Lead-induced chronic gout, right ankle and foot**
+7th **M1A.172 Lead-induced chronic gout, left ankle and foot**
+7th **M1A.179 Lead-induced chronic gout, unspecified ankle and foot**
X+7th **M1A.18 Lead-induced chronic gout, vertebrae**
X+7th **M1A.19 Lead-induced chronic gout, multiple sites**
\+ **M1A.2 Drug-induced chronic gout**
Use additional code for adverse effect, if applicable, to identify drug (T36-T50 with fifth or sixth character 5)
X+7th **M1A.20 Drug-induced chronic gout, unspecified site**
\+ **M1A.21 Drug-induced chronic gout, shoulder**
+7th **M1A.211 Drug-induced chronic gout, right shoulde**
+7th **M1A.212 Drug-induced chronic gout, left shoulder**
+7th **M1A.219 Drug-induced chronic gout, unspecified shoulder**
\+ **M1A.22 Drug-induced chronic gout, elbow**
+7th **M1A.221 Drug-induced chronic gout, right elbow**
+7th **M1A.222 Drug-induced chronic gout, left elbow**
+7th **M1A.229 Drug-induced chronic gout, unspecified elbow**
\+ **M1A.23 Drug-induced chronic gout, wrist**
+7th **M1A.231 Drug-induced chronic gout, right wrist**
+7th **M1A.232 Drug-induced chronic gout, left wrist**
+7th **M1A.239 Drug-induced chronic gout, unspecified wrist**
\+ **M1A.24 Drug-induced chronic gout, hand**
+7th **M1A.241 Drug-induced chronic gout, right hand**
+7th **M1A.242 Drug-induced chronic gout, left hand**
+7th **M1A.249 Drug-induced chronic gout, unspecified hand**
\+ **M1A.25 Drug-induced chronic gout, hip**
+7th **M1A.251 Drug-induced chronic gout, right hip**
+7th **M1A.252 Drug-induced chronic gout, left hip**
+7th **M1A.259 Drug-induced chronic gout, unspecified hi**
\+ **M1A.26 Drug-induced chronic gout, knee**
+7th **M1A.261 Drug-induced chronic gout, right knee**
+7th **M1A.262 Drug-induced chronic gout, left knee**
+7th **M1A.269 Drug-induced chronic gout, unspecified k**
\+ **M1A.27 Drug-induced chronic gout, ankle and foot**
+7th **M1A.271 Drug-induced chronic gout, right ankle and foot**
+7th **M1A.272 Drug-induced chronic gout, left ankle and foot**
+7th **M1A.279 Drug-induced chronic gout, unspecified ankle and foot**
X+7th **M1A.28 Drug-induced chronic gout, vertebrae**
X+7th **M1A.29 Drug-induced chronic gout, multiple sites**
\+ **M1A.3 Chronic gout due to renal impairment**
Code first associated renal disease
X+7th **M1A.30 Chronic gout due to renal impairment, unspecified s**
\+ **M1A.31 Chronic gout due to renal impairment, shoulder**
+7th **M1A.311 Chronic gout due to renal impairment, rig shoulder**
+7th **M1A.312 Chronic gout due to renal impairment, left shoulder**
+7th **M1A.319 Chronic gout due to renal impairment, unspecified shoulder**
\+ **M1A.32 Chronic gout due to renal impairment, elbow**
+7th **M1A.321 Chronic gout due to renal impairment, rig elbow**
+7th **M1A.322 Chronic gout due to renal impairment, left elbow**
+7th **M1A.329 Chronic gout due to renal impairment, unspecified elbow**
\+ **M1A.33 Chronic gout due to renal impairment, wrist**
+7th **M1A.331 Chronic gout due to renal impairment, rig wrist**
+7th **M1A.332 Chronic gout due to renal impairment, left wrist**
+7th **M1A.339 Chronic gout due to renal impairment, unspecified wrist**
\+ **M1A.34 Chronic gout due to renal impairment, hand**
+7th **M1A.341 Chronic gout due to renal impairment, rig hand**
+7th **M1A.342 Chronic gout due to renal impairment, left hand**
+7th **M1A.349 Chronic gout due to renal impairment, unspecified hand**

+ **M1A.35 Chronic gout due to renal impairment, hip**
  - +7th **M1A.351 Chronic gout due to renal impairment, right hip**
  - +7th **M1A.352 Chronic gout due to renal impairment, left hip**
  - +7th **M1A.359 Chronic gout due to renal impairment, unspecified hip**

+ **M1A.36 Chronic gout due to renal impairment, knee**
  - +7th **M1A.361 Chronic gout due to renal impairment, right knee**
  - +7th **M1A.362 Chronic gout due to renal impairment, left knee**
  - +7th **M1A.369 Chronic gout due to renal impairment, unspecified knee**

+ **M1A.37 Chronic gout due to renal impairment, ankle and foot**
  - +7th **M1A.371 Chronic gout due to renal impairment, right ankle and foot**
  - +7th **M1A.372 Chronic gout due to renal impairment, left ankle and foot**
  - +7th **M1A.379 Chronic gout due to renal impairment, unspecified ankle and foot**

X+7th **M1A.38 Chronic gout due to renal impairment, vertebrae**

X+7th **M1A.39 Chronic gout due to renal impairment, multiple sites**

+ **M1A.4 Other secondary chronic gout**

  Code first associated condition

X+7th **M1A.40 Other secondary chronic gout, unspecified site**

+ **M1A.41 Other secondary chronic gout, shoulder**
  - +7th **M1A.411 Other secondary chronic gout, right shoulder**
  - +7th **M1A.412 Other secondary chronic gout, left shoulder**
  - +7th **M1A.419 Other secondary chronic gout, unspecified shoulder**

+ **M1A.42 Other secondary chronic gout, elbow**
  - +7th **M1A.421 Other secondary chronic gout, right elbow**
  - +7th **M1A.422 Other secondary chronic gout, left elbow**
  - +7th **M1A.429 Other secondary chronic gout, unspecified elbow**

+ **M1A.43 Other secondary chronic gout, wrist**
  - +7th **M1A.431 Other secondary chronic gout, right wrist**
  - +7th **M1A.432 Other secondary chronic gout, left wrist**
  - +7th **M1A.439 Other secondary chronic gout, unspecified wrist**

+ **M1A.44 Other secondary chronic gout, hand**
  - +7th **M1A.441 Other secondary chronic gout, right hand**
  - +7th **M1A.442 Other secondary chronic gout, left hand**
  - +7th **M1A.449 Other secondary chronic gout, unspecified hand**

+ **M1A.45 Other secondary chronic gout, hip**
  - +7th **M1A.451 Other secondary chronic gout, right hip**
  - +7th **M1A.452 Other secondary chronic gout, left hip**
  - +7th **M1A.459 Other secondary chronic gout, unspecified hip**

+ **M1A.46 Other secondary chronic gout, knee**
  - +7th **M1A.461 Other secondary chronic gout, right knee**
  - +7th **M1A.462 Other secondary chronic gout, left knee**
  - +7th **M1A.469 Other secondary chronic gout, unspecified knee**

+ **M1A.47 Other secondary chronic gout, ankle and foot**
  - +7th **M1A.471 Other secondary chronic gout, right ankle and foot**
  - +7th **M1A.472 Other secondary chronic gout, left ankle and foot**
  - +7th **M1A.479 Other secondary chronic gout, unspecified ankle and foot**

X+7th **M1A.48 Other secondary chronic gout, vertebrae**

X+7th **M1A.49 Other secondary chronic gout, multiple sites**

X+7th **M1A.9 Chronic gout, unspecified**

M10 Gout

Acute gout
Gout attack
Gout flare
Gout NOS
Podagra

Use additional code to identify:
Autonomic neuropathy in diseases classified elsewhere (G99.0)
Calculus of urinary tract in diseases classified elsewhere (N22)
Cardiomyopathy in diseases classified elsewhere (I43)
Disorders of external ear in diseases classified elsewhere (H61.1-, H62.8-)
Disorders of iris and ciliary body in diseases classified elsewhere (H22)
Glomerular disorders in diseases classified elsewhere (N08)

Excludes1: *chronic gout (M1A.-)*

+ **M10.0 Idiopathic gout**

  Gouty bursitis
  Primary gout

M10.00 Idiopathic gout, unspecified site

+ **M10.01 Idiopathic gout, shoulder**
  - **M10.011 Idiopathic gout, right shoulder**
  - **M10.012 Idiopathic gout, left shoulder**
  - **M10.019 Idiopathic gout, unspecified shoulder**

+ **M10.02 Idiopathic gout, elbow**
  - **M10.021 Idiopathic gout, right elbow**
  - **M10.022 Idiopathic gout, left elbow**
  - **M10.029 Idiopathic gout, unspecified elbow**

+ **M10.03 Idiopathic gout, wrist**
  - **M10.031 Idiopathic gout, right wrist**
  - **M10.032 Idiopathic gout, left wrist**
  - **M10.039 Idiopathic gout, unspecified wrist**

+ **M10.04 Idiopathic gout, hand**
  - **M10.041 Idiopathic gout, right hand**
  - **M10.042 Idiopathic gout, left hand**
  - **M10.049 Idiopathic gout, unspecified hand**

+ **M10.05 Idiopathic gout, hip**
  - **M10.051 Idiopathic gout, right hip**
  - **M10.052 Idiopathic gout, left hip**
  - **M10.059 Idiopathic gout, unspecified hip**

+ **M10.06 Idiopathic gout, knee**
  - **M10.061 Idiopathic gout, right knee**
  - **M10.062 Idiopathic gout, left knee**
  - **M10.069 Idiopathic gout, unspecified knee**

+ **M10.07 Idiopathic gout, ankle and foot**
  - **M10.071 Idiopathic gout, right ankle and foot**
  - **M10.072 Idiopathic gout, left ankle and foot**
  - **M10.079 Idiopathic gout, unspecified ankle and foot**

M10.08 Idiopathic gout, vertebrae

M10.09 Idiopathic gout, multiple sites

+ **M10.1 Lead-induced gout**

  Code first toxic effects of lead and its compounds (T56.0-)

M10.10 Lead-induced gout, unspecified site

+ **M10.11 Lead-induced gout, shoulder**
  - **M10.111 Lead-induced gout, right shoulder**
  - **M10.112 Lead-induced gout, left shoulder**
  - **M10.119 Lead-induced gout, unspecified shoulder**

+ **M10.12 Lead-induced gout, elbow**
  - **M10.121 Lead-induced gout, right elbow**
  - **M10.122 Lead-induced gout, left elbow**
  - **M10.129 Lead-induced gout, unspecified elbow**

+ **M10.13 Lead-induced gout, wrist**
  - **M10.131 Lead-induced gout, right wrist**
  - **M10.132 Lead-induced gout, left wrist**
  - **M10.139 Lead-induced gout, unspecified wrist**

+ **M10.14 Lead-induced gout, hand**
  - **M10.141 Lead-induced gout, right hand**
  - **M10.142 Lead-induced gout, left hand**
  - **M10.149 Lead-induced gout, unspecified hand**

+ **M10.15 Lead-induced gout, hip**
  - **M10.151 Lead-induced gout, right hip**
  - **M10.152 Lead-induced gout, left hip**
  - **M10.159 Lead-induced gout, unspecified hip**

+ **M10.16 Lead-induced gout, knee**
  - **M10.161 Lead-induced gout, right knee**
  - **M10.162 Lead-induced gout, left knee**
  - **M10.169 Lead-induced gout, unspecified knee**

+ **M10.17 Lead-induced gout, ankle and foot**
  - **M10.171 Lead-induced gout, right ankle and foot**
  - **M10.172 Lead-induced gout, left ankle and foot**
  - **M10.179 Lead-induced gout, unspecified ankle and foot**

M10.18 **Lead-induced gout, vertebrae**
M10.19 **Lead-induced gout, multiple sites**
+ **M10.2** **Drug-induced gout**
Use additional code for adverse effect, if applicable, to identify drug (T36-T50 with fifth or sixth character 5)
M10.20 **Drug-induced gout, unspecified site**
+ **M10.21** **Drug-induced gout, shoulder**
M10.211 **Drug-induced gout, right shoulder**
M10.212 **Drug-induced gout, left shoulder**
M10.219 **Drug-induced gout, unspecified shoulder**
+ **M10.22** **Drug-induced gout, elbow**
M10.221 **Drug-induced gout, right elbow**
M10.222 **Drug-induced gout, left elbow**
M10.229 **Drug-induced gout, unspecified elbow**
+ **M10.23** **Drug-induced gout, wrist**
M10.231 **Drug-induced gout, right wrist**
M10.232 **Drug-induced gout, left wrist**
M10.239 **Drug-induced gout, unspecified wrist**
+ **M10.24** **Drug-induced gout, hand**
M10.241 **Drug-induced gout, right hand**
M10.242 **Drug-induced gout, left hand**
M10.249 **Drug-induced gout, unspecified hand**
+ **M10.25** **Drug-induced gout, hip**
M10.251 **Drug-induced gout, right hip**
M10.252 **Drug-induced gout, left hip**
M10.259 **Drug-induced gout, unspecified hip**
+ **M10.26** **Drug-induced gout, knee**
M10.261 **Drug-induced gout, right knee**
M10.262 **Drug-induced gout, left knee**
M10.269 **Drug-induced gout, unspecified knee**
+ **M10.27** **Drug-induced gout, ankle and foot**
M10.271 **Drug-induced gout, right ankle and foot**
M10.272 **Drug-induced gout, left ankle and foot**
M10.279 **Drug-induced gout, unspecified ankle and foot**
M10.28 **Drug-induced gout, vertebrae**
M10.29 **Drug-induced gout, multiple sites**
+ **M10.3** **Gout due to renal impairment**
Code first associated renal disease
M10.30 **Gout due to renal impairment, unspecified site**
+ **M10.31** **Gout due to renal impairment, shoulder**
M10.311 **Gout due to renal impairment, right shoulder**
M10.312 **Gout due to renal impairment, left shoulder**
M10.319 **Gout due to renal impairment, unspecified shoulder**
+ **M10.32** **Gout due to renal impairment, elbow**
M10.321 **Gout due to renal impairment, right elbow**
M10.322 **Gout due to renal impairment, left elbow**
M10.329 **Gout due to renal impairment, unspecified elbow**
+ **M10.33** **Gout due to renal impairment, wrist**
M10.331 **Gout due to renal impairment, right wrist**
M10.332 **Gout due to renal impairment, left wrist**
M10.339 **Gout due to renal impairment, unspecified wrist**
+ **M10.34** **Gout due to renal impairment, hand**
M10.341 **Gout due to renal impairment, right hand**
M10.342 **Gout due to renal impairment, left hand**
M10.349 **Gout due to renal impairment, unspecified hand**
+ **M10.35** **Gout due to renal impairment, hip**
M10.351 **Gout due to renal impairment, right hip**
M10.352 **Gout due to renal impairment, left hip**
M10.359 **Gout due to renal impairment, unspecified hip**
+ **M10.36** **Gout due to renal impairment, knee**
M10.361 **Gout due to renal impairment, right knee**
M10.362 **Gout due to renal impairment, left knee**
M10.369 **Gout due to renal impairment, unspecified knee**
+ **M10.37** **Gout due to renal impairment, ankle and foot**
M10.371 **Gout due to renal impairment, right ankle and foot**
M10.372 **Gout due to renal impairment, left ankle and foot**
M10.379 **Gout due to renal impairment, unspecified ankle and foot**
M10.38 **Gout due to renal impairment, vertebrae**
M10.39 **Gout due to renal impairment, multiple sites**
+ **M10.4** **Other secondary gout**
Code first associated condition
M10.40 **Other secondary gout, unspecified site**
+ **M10.41** **Other secondary gout, shoulder**
M10.411 **Other secondary gout, right shoulder**
M10.412 **Other secondary gout, left shoulder**
M10.419 **Other secondary gout, unspecified should**
+ **M10.42** **Other secondary gout, elbow**
M10.421 **Other secondary gout, right elbow**
M10.422 **Other secondary gout, left elbow**
M10.429 **Other secondary gout, unspecified elbow**
+ **M10.43** **Other secondary gout, wrist**
M10.431 **Other secondary gout, right wrist**
M10.432 **Other secondary gout, left wrist**
M10.439 **Other secondary gout, unspecified wrist**
+ **M10.44** **Other secondary gout, hand**
M10.441 **Other secondary gout, right hand**
M10.442 **Other secondary gout, left hand**
M10.449 **Other secondary gout, unspecified hand**
+ **M10.45** **Other secondary gout, hip**
M10.451 **Other secondary gout, right hip**
M10.452 **Other secondary gout, left hip**
M10.459 **Other secondary gout, unspecified hip**
+ **M10.46** **Other secondary gout, knee**
M10.461 **Other secondary gout, right knee**
M10.462 **Other secondary gout, left knee**
M10.469 **Other secondary gout, unspecified knee**
+ **M10.47** **Other secondary gout, ankle and foot**
M10.471 **Other secondary gout, right ankle and foo**
M10.472 **Other secondary gout, left ankle and foot**
M10.479 **Other secondary gout, unspecified ankle and foot**
M10.48 **Other secondary gout, vertebrae**
M10.49 **Other secondary gout, multiple sites**
M10.9 **Gout, unspecified**
Gout NOS

M11 Other crystal arthropathies

+ **M11.0** **Hydroxyapatite deposition disease**
M11.00 **Hydroxyapatite deposition disease, unspecified site**
+ **M11.01** **Hydroxyapatite deposition disease, shoulder**
M11.011 **Hydroxyapatite deposition disease, right shoulder**
M11.012 **Hydroxyapatite deposition disease, left shoulder**
M11.019 **Hydroxyapatite deposition disease, unspecified shoulder**
+ **M11.02** **Hydroxyapatite deposition disease, elbow**
M11.021 **Hydroxyapatite deposition disease, right elbow**
M11.022 **Hydroxyapatite deposition disease, left elb**
M11.029 **Hydroxyapatite deposition disease, unspecified elbow**
+ **M11.03** **Hydroxyapatite deposition disease, wrist**
M11.031 **Hydroxyapatite deposition disease, right wrist**
M11.032 **Hydroxyapatite deposition disease, left wr**
M11.039 **Hydroxyapatite deposition disease, unspecified wrist**
+ **M11.04** **Hydroxyapatite deposition disease, hand**
M11.041 **Hydroxyapatite deposition disease, right hand**
M11.042 **Hydroxyapatite deposition disease, left ha**
M11.049 **Hydroxyapatite deposition disease, unspecified hand**
+ **M11.05** **Hydroxyapatite deposition disease, hip**
M11.051 **Hydroxyapatite deposition disease, right h**
M11.052 **Hydroxyapatite deposition disease, left hip**
M11.059 **Hydroxyapatite deposition disease, unspecified hip**
+ **M11.06** **Hydroxyapatite deposition disease, knee**
M11.061 **Hydroxyapatite deposition disease, right kr**
M11.062 **Hydroxyapatite deposition disease, left kn**
M11.069 **Hydroxyapatite deposition disease, unspecified knee**
+ **M11.07** **Hydroxyapatite deposition disease, ankle and foot**
M11.071 **Hydroxyapatite deposition disease, right ankle and foot**
M11.072 **Hydroxyapatite deposition disease, left an and foot**
M11.079 **Hydroxyapatite deposition disease, unspecified ankle and foot**

M11.08 **Hydroxyapatite deposition disease, vertebrae**
M11.09 **Hydroxyapatite deposition disease, multiple sites**
+ **M11.1** **Familial chondrocalcinosis**
M11.10 **Familial chondrocalcinosis, unspecified site**
+ **M11.11** **Familial chondrocalcinosis, shoulder**
M11.111 **Familial chondrocalcinosis, right shoulder**
M11.112 **Familial chondrocalcinosis, left shoulder**
M11.119 **Familial chondrocalcinosis, unspecified shoulder**
+ **M11.12** **Familial chondrocalcinosis, elbow**
M11.121 **Familial chondrocalcinosis, right elbow**
M11.122 **Familial chondrocalcinosis, left elbow**
M11.129 **Familial chondrocalcinosis, unspecified elbow**
+ **M11.13** **Familial chondrocalcinosis, wrist**
M11.131 **Familial chondrocalcinosis, right wrist**
M11.132 **Familial chondrocalcinosis, left wrist**
M11.139 **Familial chondrocalcinosis, unspecified wrist**
+ **M11.14** **Familial chondrocalcinosis, hand**
M11.141 **Familial chondrocalcinosis, right hand**
M11.142 **Familial chondrocalcinosis, left hand**
M11.149 **Familial chondrocalcinosis, unspecified hand**
+ **M11.15** **Familial chondrocalcinosis, hip**
M11.151 **Familial chondrocalcinosis, right hip**
M11.152 **Familial chondrocalcinosis, left hip**
M11.159 **Familial chondrocalcinosis, unspecified hip**
+ **M11.16** **Familial chondrocalcinosis, knee**
M11.161 **Familial chondrocalcinosis, right knee**
M11.162 **Familial chondrocalcinosis, left knee**
M11.169 **Familial chondrocalcinosis, unspecified knee**
+ **M11.17** **Familial chondrocalcinosis, ankle and foot**
M11.171 **Familial chondrocalcinosis, right ankle and foot**
M11.172 **Familial chondrocalcinosis, left ankle and foot**
M11.179 **Familial chondrocalcinosis, unspecified ankle and foot**
M11.18 **Familial chondrocalcinosis, vertebrae**
M11.19 **Familial chondrocalcinosis, multiple sites**
+ **M11.2** **Other chondrocalcinosis**
Chondrocalcinosis NOS
M11.20 **Other chondrocalcinosis, unspecified site**
+ **M11.21** **Other chondrocalcinosis, shoulder**
M11.211 **Other chondrocalcinosis, right shoulder**
M11.212 **Other chondrocalcinosis, left shoulder**
M11.219 **Other chondrocalcinosis, unspecified shoulder**
+ **M11.22** **Other chondrocalcinosis, elbow**
M11.221 **Other chondrocalcinosis, right elbow**
M11.222 **Other chondrocalcinosis, left elbow**
M11.229 **Other chondrocalcinosis, unspecified elbow**
+ **M11.23** **Other chondrocalcinosis, wrist**
M11.231 **Other chondrocalcinosis, right wrist**
M11.232 **Other chondrocalcinosis, left wrist**
M11.239 **Other chondrocalcinosis, unspecified wrist**
+ **M11.24** **Other chondrocalcinosis, hand**
M11.241 **Other chondrocalcinosis, right hand**
M11.242 **Other chondrocalcinosis, left hand**
M11.249 **Other chondrocalcinosis, unspecified hand**
+ **M11.25** **Other chondrocalcinosis, hip**
M11.251 **Other chondrocalcinosis, right hip**
M11.252 **Other chondrocalcinosis, left hip**
M11.259 **Other chondrocalcinosis, unspecified hip**
+ **M11.26** **Other chondrocalcinosis, knee**
M11.261 **Other chondrocalcinosis, right knee**
M11.262 **Other chondrocalcinosis, left knee**
M11.269 **Other chondrocalcinosis, unspecified knee**
+ **M11.27** **Other chondrocalcinosis, ankle and foot**
M11.271 **Other chondrocalcinosis, right ankle and foot**
M11.272 **Other chondrocalcinosis, left ankle and foot**
M11.279 **Other chondrocalcinosis, unspecified ankle and foot**
M11.28 **Other chondrocalcinosis, vertebrae**
M11.29 **Other chondrocalcinosis, multiple sites**
+ **M11.8** **Other specified crystal arthropathies**
M11.80 **Other specified crystal arthropathies, unspecified site**
+ **M11.81** **Other specified crystal arthropathies, shoulder**
M11.811 **Other specified crystal arthropathies, right shoulder**
M11.812 **Other specified crystal arthropathies, left shoulder**
M11.819 **Other specified crystal arthropathies, unspecified shoulder**
+ **M11.82** **Other specified crystal arthropathies, elbow**
M11.821 **Other specified crystal arthropathies, right elbow**
M11.822 **Other specified crystal arthropathies, left elbow**
M11.829 **Other specified crystal arthropathies, unspecified elbow**
+ **M11.83** **Other specified crystal arthropathies, wrist**
M11.831 **Other specified crystal arthropathies, right wrist**
M11.832 **Other specified crystal arthropathies, left wrist**
M11.839 **Other specified crystal arthropathies, unspecified wrist**
+ **M11.84** **Other specified crystal arthropathies, hand**
M11.841 **Other specified crystal arthropathies, right hand**
M11.842 **Other specified crystal arthropathies, left hand**
M11.849 **Other specified crystal arthropathies, unspecified hand**
+ **M11.85** **Other specified crystal arthropathies, hip**
M11.851 **Other specified crystal arthropathies, right hip**
M11.852 **Other specified crystal arthropathies, left hip**
M11.859 **Other specified crystal arthropathies, unspecified hip**
+ **M11.86** **Other specified crystal arthropathies, knee**
M11.861 **Other specified crystal arthropathies, right knee**
M11.862 **Other specified crystal arthropathies, left knee**
M11.869 **Other specified crystal arthropathies, unspecified knee**
+ **M11.87** **Other specified crystal arthropathies, ankle and foot**
M11.871 **Other specified crystal arthropathies, right ankle and foot**
M11.872 **Other specified crystal arthropathies, left ankle and foot**
M11.879 **Other specified crystal arthropathies, unspecified ankle and foot**
M11.88 **Other specified crystal arthropathies, vertebrae**
M11.89 **Other specified crystal arthropathies, multiple sites**
M11.9 **Crystal arthropathy, unspecified**

M12 Other and unspecified arthropathy

Excludes1: *arthrosis (M15-M19)*
cricoarytenoid arthropathy (J38.7)

+ **M12.0** **Chronic postrheumatic arthropathy [Jaccoud]**
M12.00 **Chronic postrheumatic arthropathy [Jaccoud], unspecified site**
+ **M12.01** **Chronic postrheumatic arthropathy [Jaccoud], shoulder**
M12.011 **Chronic postrheumatic arthropathy [Jaccoud], right shoulder**
M12.012 **Chronic postrheumatic arthropathy [Jaccoud], left shoulder**
M12.019 **Chronic postrheumatic arthropathy [Jaccoud], unspecified shoulder**
+ **M12.02** **Chronic postrheumatic arthropathy [Jaccoud], elbow**
M12.021 **Chronic postrheumatic arthropathy [Jaccoud], right elbow**
M12.022 **Chronic postrheumatic arthropathy [Jaccoud], left elbow**
M12.029 **Chronic postrheumatic arthropathy [Jaccoud], unspecified elbow**
+ **M12.03** **Chronic postrheumatic arthropathy [Jaccoud], wrist**
M12.031 **Chronic postrheumatic arthropathy [Jaccoud], right wrist**
M12.032 **Chronic postrheumatic arthropathy [Jaccoud], left wrist**
M12.039 **Chronic postrheumatic arthropathy [Jaccoud], unspecified wrist**
+ **M12.04** **Chronic postrheumatic arthropathy [Jaccoud], hand**
M12.041 **Chronic postrheumatic arthropathy [Jaccoud], right hand**

M12.042 Chronic postrheumatic arthropathy [Jaccoud], left hand
M12.049 Chronic postrheumatic arthropathy [Jaccoud], unspecified hand
+ M12.05 Chronic postrheumatic arthropathy [Jaccoud], hip
M12.051 Chronic postrheumatic arthropathy [Jaccoud], right hip
M12.052 Chronic postrheumatic arthropathy [Jaccoud], left hip
M12.059 Chronic postrheumatic arthropathy [Jaccoud], unspecified hip
+ M12.06 Chronic postrheumatic arthropathy [Jaccoud], knee
M12.061 Chronic postrheumatic arthropathy [Jaccoud], right knee
M12.062 Chronic postrheumatic arthropathy [Jaccoud], left knee
M12.069 Chronic postrheumatic arthropathy [Jaccoud], unspecified knee
+ M12.07 Chronic postrheumatic arthropathy [Jaccoud], ankle and foot
M12.071 Chronic postrheumatic arthropathy [Jaccoud], right ankle and foot
M12.072 Chronic postrheumatic arthropathy [Jaccoud], left ankle and foot
M12.079 Chronic postrheumatic arthropathy [Jaccoud], unspecified ankle and foot
M12.08 Chronic postrheumatic arthropathy [Jaccoud], other specified site
Chronic postrheumatic arthropathy [Jaccoud], vertebrae
M12.09 Chronic postrheumatic arthropathy [Jaccoud], multiple sites
+ M12.1 Kaschin-Beck disease
Osteochondroarthrosis deformans endemica
M12.10 Kaschin-Beck disease, unspecified site
+ M12.11 Kaschin-Beck disease, shoulder
M12.111 Kaschin-Beck disease, right shoulder
M12.112 Kaschin-Beck disease, left shoulder
M12.119 Kaschin-Beck disease, unspecified shoulder
+ M12.12 Kaschin-Beck disease, elbow
M12.121 Kaschin-Beck disease, right elbow
M12.122 Kaschin-Beck disease, left elbow
M12.129 Kaschin-Beck disease, unspecified elbow
+ M12.13 Kaschin-Beck disease, wrist
M12.131 Kaschin-Beck disease, right wrist
M12.132 Kaschin-Beck disease, left wrist
M12.139 Kaschin-Beck disease, unspecified wrist
+ M12.14 Kaschin-Beck disease, hand
M12.141 Kaschin-Beck disease, right hand
M12.142 Kaschin-Beck disease, left hand
M12.149 Kaschin-Beck disease, unspecified hand
+ M12.15 Kaschin-Beck disease, hip
M12.151 Kaschin-Beck disease, right hip
M12.152 Kaschin-Beck disease, left hip
M12.159 Kaschin-Beck disease, unspecified hip
+ M12.16 Kaschin-Beck disease, knee
M12.161 Kaschin-Beck disease, right knee
M12.162 Kaschin-Beck disease, left knee
M12.169 Kaschin-Beck disease, unspecified knee
+ M12.17 Kaschin-Beck disease, ankle and foot
M12.171 Kaschin-Beck disease, right ankle and foot
M12.172 Kaschin-Beck disease, left ankle and foot
M12.179 Kaschin-Beck disease, unspecified ankle and foot
M12.18 Kaschin-Beck disease, vertebrae
M12.19 Kaschin-Beck disease, multiple sites
+ M12.2 Villonodular synovitis (pigmented)
M12.20 Villonodular synovitis (pigmented), unspecified site
+ M12.21 Villonodular synovitis (pigmented), shoulder
M12.211 Villonodular synovitis (pigmented), right shoulder
M12.212 Villonodular synovitis (pigmented), left shoulder
M12.219 Villonodular synovitis (pigmented), unspecified shoulder
+ M12.22 Villonodular synovitis (pigmented), elbow
M12.221 Villonodular synovitis (pigmented), right elbow
M12.222 Villonodular synovitis (pigmented), left elbow
M12.229 Villonodular synovitis (pigmented), unspecified elbow
+ M12.23 Villonodular synovitis (pigmented), wrist
M12.231 Villonodular synovitis (pigmented), right w
M12.232 Villonodular synovitis (pigmented), left w
M12.239 Villonodular synovitis (pigmented), unspecified wrist
+ M12.24 Villonodular synovitis (pigmented), hand
M12.241 Villonodular synovitis (pigmented), right hand
M12.242 Villonodular synovitis (pigmented), left ha
M12.249 Villonodular synovitis (pigmented), unspecified hand
+ M12.25 Villonodular synovitis (pigmented), hip
M12.251 Villonodular synovitis (pigmented), right
M12.252 Villonodular synovitis (pigmented), left hi
M12.259 Villonodular synovitis (pigmented), unspecified hip
+ M12.26 Villonodular synovitis (pigmented), knee
M12.261 Villonodular synovitis (pigmented), right k
M12.262 Villonodular synovitis (pigmented), left kn
M12.269 Villonodular synovitis (pigmented), unspecified knee
+ M12.27 Villonodular synovitis (pigmented), ankle and foot
M12.271 Villonodular synovitis (pigmented), right ankle and foot
M12.272 Villonodular synovitis (pigmented), left ankle and foot
M12.279 Villonodular synovitis (pigmented), unspecified ankle and foot
M12.28 Villonodular synovitis (pigmented), other specified s
Villonodular synovitis (pigmented), vertebrae
M12.29 Villonodular synovitis (pigmented), multiple sites
+ M12.3 Palindromic rheumatism
M12.30 Palindromic rheumatism, unspecified site
+ M12.31 Palindromic rheumatism, shoulder
M12.311 Palindromic rheumatism, right shoulder
M12.312 Palindromic rheumatism, left shoulder
M12.319 Palindromic rheumatism, unspecified shoulder
+ M12.32 Palindromic rheumatism, elbow
M12.321 Palindromic rheumatism, right elbow
M12.322 Palindromic rheumatism, left elbow
M12.329 Palindromic rheumatism, unspecified elbo
+ M12.33 Palindromic rheumatism, wrist
M12.331 Palindromic rheumatism, right wrist
M12.332 Palindromic rheumatism, left wrist
M12.339 Palindromic rheumatism, unspecified wris
+ M12.34 Palindromic rheumatism, hand
M12.341 Palindromic rheumatism, right hand
M12.342 Palindromic rheumatism, left hand
M12.349 Palindromic rheumatism, unspecified han
+ M12.35 Palindromic rheumatism, hip
M12.351 Palindromic rheumatism, right hip
M12.352 Palindromic rheumatism, left hip
M12.359 Palindromic rheumatism, unspecified hip
+ M12.36 Palindromic rheumatism, knee
M12.361 Palindromic rheumatism, right knee
M12.362 Palindromic rheumatism, left knee
M12.369 Palindromic rheumatism, unspecified knee
+ M12.37 Palindromic rheumatism, ankle and foot
M12.371 Palindromic rheumatism, right ankle and foot
M12.372 Palindromic rheumatism, left ankle and fo
M12.379 Palindromic rheumatism, unspecified ank and foot
M12.38 Palindromic rheumatism, other specified site
Palindromic rheumatism, vertebrae
M12.39 Palindromic rheumatism, multiple sites
+ M12.4 Intermittent hydrarthrosis
M12.40 Intermittent hydrarthrosis, unspecified site
+ M12.41 Intermittent hydrarthrosis, shoulder
M12.411 Intermittent hydrarthrosis, right shoulder
M12.412 Intermittent hydrarthrosis, left shoulder
M12.419 Intermittent hydrarthrosis, unspecified shoulder
+ M12.42 Intermittent hydrarthrosis, elbow
M12.421 Intermittent hydrarthrosis, right elbow
M12.422 Intermittent hydrarthrosis, left elbow
M12.429 Intermittent hydrarthrosis, unspecified elbow

+ **M12.43 Intermittent hydrarthrosis, wrist**
M12.431 Intermittent hydrarthrosis, right wrist
M12.432 Intermittent hydrarthrosis, left wrist
M12.439 Intermittent hydrarthrosis, unspecified wrist
+ **M12.44 Intermittent hydrarthrosis, hand**
M12.441 Intermittent hydrarthrosis, right hand
M12.442 Intermittent hydrarthrosis, left hand
M12.449 Intermittent hydrarthrosis, unspecified hand
+ **M12.45 Intermittent hydrarthrosis, hip**
M12.451 Intermittent hydrarthrosis, right hip
M12.452 Intermittent hydrarthrosis, left hip
M12.459 Intermittent hydrarthrosis, unspecified hip
+ **M12.46 Intermittent hydrarthrosis, knee**
M12.461 Intermittent hydrarthrosis, right knee
M12.462 Intermittent hydrarthrosis, left knee
M12.469 Intermittent hydrarthrosis, unspecified knee
+ **M12.47 Intermittent hydrarthrosis, ankle and foot**
M12.471 Intermittent hydrarthrosis, right ankle and foot
M12.472 Intermittent hydrarthrosis, left ankle and foot
M12.479 Intermittent hydrarthrosis, unspecified ankle and foot
M12.48 Intermittent hydrarthrosis, other site
M12.49 Intermittent hydrarthrosis, multiple sites
+ **M12.5 Traumatic arthropathy**
Excludes1: *current injury-see Alphabetic Index*
post-traumatic osteoarthritis of first carpometacarpal joint (M18.2-M18.3)
post-traumatic osteoarthritis of hip (M16.4-M16.5)
post-traumatic osteoarthritis of knee (M17.2-M17.3)
post-traumatic osteoarthritis NOS (M19.1-)
post-traumatic osteoarthritis of other single joints (M19.1-)
M12.50 Traumatic arthropathy, unspecified site
+ **M12.51 Traumatic arthropathy, shoulder**
M12.511 Traumatic arthropathy, right shoulder
M12.512 Traumatic arthropathy, left shoulder
M12.519 Traumatic arthropathy, unspecified shoulder
+ **M12.52 Traumatic arthropathy, elbow**
M12.521 Traumatic arthropathy, right elbow
M12.522 Traumatic arthropathy, left elbow
M12.529 Traumatic arthropathy, unspecified elbow
+ **M12.53 Traumatic arthropathy, wrist**
M12.531 Traumatic arthropathy, right wrist
M12.532 Traumatic arthropathy, left wrist
M12.539 Traumatic arthropathy, unspecified wrist
+ **M12.54 Traumatic arthropathy, hand**
M12.541 Traumatic arthropathy, right hand
M12.542 Traumatic arthropathy, left hand
M12.549 Traumatic arthropathy, unspecified hand
+ **M12.55 Traumatic arthropathy, hip**
M12.551 Traumatic arthropathy, right hip
M12.552 Traumatic arthropathy, left hip
M12.559 Traumatic arthropathy, unspecified hip
+ **M12.56 Traumatic arthropathy, knee**
M12.561 Traumatic arthropathy, right knee
M12.562 Traumatic arthropathy, left knee
M12.569 Traumatic arthropathy, unspecified knee
+ **M12.57 Traumatic arthropathy, ankle and foot**
M12.571 Traumatic arthropathy, right ankle and foot
M12.572 Traumatic arthropathy, left ankle and foot
M12.579 Traumatic arthropathy, unspecified ankle and foot
M12.58 Traumatic arthropathy, other specified site
Traumatic arthropathy, vertebrae
M12.59 Traumatic arthropathy, multiple sites
+ **M12.8 Other specific arthropathies, not elsewhere classified**
Transient arthropathy
M12.80 Other specific arthropathies, not elsewhere classified, unspecified site
+ **M12.81 Other specific arthropathies, not elsewhere classified, shoulder**
M12.811 Other specific arthropathies, not elsewhere classified, right shoulder
M12.812 Other specific arthropathies, not elsewhere classified, left shoulder
M12.819 Other specific arthropathies, not elsewhere classified, unspecified shoulder
+ **M12.82 Other specific arthropathies, not elsewhere classified, elbow**
M12.821 Other specific arthropathies, not elsewhere classified, right elbow
M12.822 Other specific arthropathies, not elsewhere classified, left elbow
M12.829 Other specific arthropathies, not elsewhere classified, unspecified elbow
+ **M12.83 Other specific arthropathies, not elsewhere classified, wrist**
M12.831 Other specific arthropathies, not elsewhere classified, right wrist
M12.832 Other specific arthropathies, not elsewhere classified, left wrist
M12.839 Other specific arthropathies, not elsewhere classified, unspecified wrist
+ **M12.84 Other specific arthropathies, not elsewhere classified, hand**
M12.841 Other specific arthropathies, not elsewhere classified, right hand
M12.842 Other specific arthropathies, not elsewhere classified, left hand
M12.849 Other specific arthropathies, not elsewhere classified, unspecified hand
+ **M12.85 Other specific arthropathies, not elsewhere classified, hip**
M12.851 Other specific arthropathies, not elsewhere classified, right hip
M12.852 Other specific arthropathies, not elsewhere classified, left hip
M12.859 Other specific arthropathies, not elsewhere classified, unspecified hip
+ **M12.86 Other specific arthropathies, not elsewhere classified, knee**
M12.861 Other specific arthropathies, not elsewhere classified, right knee
M12.862 Other specific arthropathies, not elsewhere classified, left knee
M12.869 Other specific arthropathies, not elsewhere classified, unspecified knee
+ **M12.87 Other specific arthropathies, not elsewhere classified, ankle and foot**
M12.871 Other specific arthropathies, not elsewhere classified, right ankle and foot
M12.872 Other specific arthropathies, not elsewhere classified, left ankle and foot
M12.879 Other specific arthropathies, not elsewhere classified, unspecified ankle and foot
M12.88 Other specific arthropathies, not elsewhere classified, other specified site
Other specific arthropathies, not elsewhere classified, vertebrae
M12.89 Other specific arthropathies, not elsewhere classified, multiple sites
M12.9 Arthropathy, unspecified

M13 Other arthritis

Excludes1: *arthrosis (M15-M19)*
osteoarthritis (M15-M19)
M13.0 Polyarthritis, unspecified
+ **M13.1 Monoarthritis, not elsewhere classified**
M13.10 Monoarthritis, not elsewhere classified, unspecified site
+ **M13.11 Monoarthritis, not elsewhere classified, shoulder**
M13.111 Monoarthritis, not elsewhere classified, right shoulder
M13.112 Monoarthritis, not elsewhere classified, left shoulder
M13.119 Monoarthritis, not elsewhere classified, unspecified shoulder
+ **M13.12 Monoarthritis, not elsewhere classified, elbow**
M13.121 Monoarthritis, not elsewhere classified, right elbow
M13.122 Monoarthritis, not elsewhere classified, left elbow
M13.129 Monoarthritis, not elsewhere classified, unspecified elbow

+ **M13.13 Monoarthritis, not elsewhere classified, wrist**
M13.131 Monoarthritis, not elsewhere classified, right wrist
M13.132 Monoarthritis, not elsewhere classified, left wrist
M13.139 Monoarthritis, not elsewhere classified, unspecified wrist
+ **M13.14 Monoarthritis, not elsewhere classified, hand**
M13.141 Monoarthritis, not elsewhere classified, right hand
M13.142 Monoarthritis, not elsewhere classified, left hand
M13.149 Monoarthritis, not elsewhere classified, unspecified hand
+ **M13.15 Monoarthritis, not elsewhere classified, hip**
M13.151 Monoarthritis, not elsewhere classified, right hip
M13.152 Monoarthritis, not elsewhere classified, left hip
M13.159 Monoarthritis, not elsewhere classified, unspecified hip
+ **M13.16 Monoarthritis, not elsewhere classified, knee**
M13.161 Monoarthritis, not elsewhere classified, right knee
M13.162 Monoarthritis, not elsewhere classified, left knee
M13.169 Monoarthritis, not elsewhere classified, unspecified knee
+ **M13.17 Monoarthritis, not elsewhere classified, ankle and foot**
M13.171 Monoarthritis, not elsewhere classified, right ankle and foot
M13.172 Monoarthritis, not elsewhere classified, left ankle and foot
M13.179 Monoarthritis, not elsewhere classified, unspecified ankle and foot
+ **M13.8 Other specified arthritis**
Allergic arthritis
Excludes1: *osteoarthritis (M15-M19)*
M13.80 Other specified arthritis, unspecified site
+ **M13.81 Other specified arthritis, shoulder**
M13.811 Other specified arthritis, right shoulder
M13.812 Other specified arthritis, left shoulder
M13.819 Other specified arthritis, unspecified shoulder
+ **M13.82 Other specified arthritis, elbow**
M13.821 Other specified arthritis, right elbow
M13.822 Other specified arthritis, left elbow
M13.829 Other specified arthritis, unspecified elbow
+ **M13.83 Other specified arthritis, wrist**
M13.831 Other specified arthritis, right wrist
M13.832 Other specified arthritis, left wrist
M13.839 Other specified arthritis, unspecified wrist
+ **M13.84 Other specified arthritis, hand**
M13.841 Other specified arthritis, right hand
M13.842 Other specified arthritis, left hand
M13.849 Other specified arthritis, unspecified hand
+ **M13.85 Other specified arthritis, hip**
M13.851 Other specified arthritis, right hip
M13.852 Other specified arthritis, left hip
M13.859 Other specified arthritis, unspecified hip
+ **M13.86 Other specified arthritis, knee**
M13.861 Other specified arthritis, right knee
M13.862 Other specified arthritis, left knee
M13.869 Other specified arthritis, unspecified knee
+ **M13.87 Other specified arthritis, ankle and foot**
M13.871 Other specified arthritis, right ankle and foot
M13.872 Other specified arthritis, left ankle and foot
M13.879 Other specified arthritis, unspecified ankle and foot
M13.88 Other specified arthritis, other site
M13.89 Other specified arthritis, multiple sites

M14 Arthropathies in other diseases classified elsewhere
Excludes1: *arthropathy in:*
diabetes mellitus (E08-E13 with .61-)
hematological disorders (M36.2-M36.3)
hypersensitivity reactions (M36.4)
neoplastic disease (M36.1)
neurosyphillis (A52.16)
sarcoidosis (D86.86)
enteropathic arthropathies (M07.-)
juvenile psoriatic arthropathy (L40.54)
lipoid dermatoarthritis (E78.81)
+ **M14.6 Charcôt's joint**
Neuropathic arthropathy
Excludes1: *Charcôt's joint in diabetes mellitus (E08-E13 wit .610)*
Charcôt's joint in tabes dorsalis (A52.16)
M14.60 Charcôt's joint, unspecified site
+ **M14.61 Charcôt's joint, shoulder**
M14.611 Charcôt's joint, right shoulder
M14.612 Charcôt's joint, left shoulder
M14.619 Charcôt's joint, unspecified shoulder
+ **M14.62 Charcôt's joint, elbow**
M14.621 Charcôt's joint, right elbow
M14.622 Charcôt's joint, left elbow
M14.629 Charcôt's joint, unspecified elbow
+ **M14.63 Charcôt's joint, wrist**
M14.631 Charcôt's joint, right wrist
M14.632 Charcôt's joint, left wrist
M14.639 Charcôt's joint, unspecified wrist
+ **M14.64 Charcôt's joint, hand**
M14.641 Charcôt's joint, right hand
M14.642 Charcôt's joint, left hand
M14.649 Charcôt's joint, unspecified hand
+ **M14.65 Charcôt's joint, hip**
M14.651 Charcôt's joint, right hip
M14.652 Charcôt's joint, left hip
M14.659 Charcôt's joint, unspecified hip
+ **M14.66 Charcôt's joint, knee**
M14.661 Charcôt's joint, right knee
M14.662 Charcôt's joint, left knee
M14.669 Charcôt's joint, unspecified knee
+ **M14.67 Charcôt's joint, ankle and foot**
M14.671 Charcôt's joint, right ankle and foot
M14.672 Charcôt's joint, left ankle and foot
M14.679 Charcôt's joint, unspecified ankle and foot
M14.68 Charcôt's joint, vertebrae
M14.69 Charcôt's joint, multiple sites
+ **M14.8 Arthropathies in other specified diseases classified elsewhere**
Code first underlying disease, such as:
amyloidosis (E85.-)
erythema multiforme (L51.-)
erythema nodosum (L52)
hemochromatosis (E83.11-)
hyperparathyroidism (E21.-)
hypothyroidism (E00-E03)
sickle-cell disorders (D57.-)
thyrotoxicosis [hyperthyroidism] (E05.-)
Whipple's disease (K90.81)
M14.80 Arthropathies in other specified diseases classified elsewhere, unspecified site
+ **M14.81 Arthropathies in other specified diseases classified elsewhere, shoulder**
M14.811 Arthropathies in other specified diseases classified elsewhere, right shoulder
M14.812 Arthropathies in other specified diseases classified elsewhere, left shoulder
M14.819 Arthropathies in other specified diseases classified elsewhere, unspecified shoulder
+ **M14.82 Arthropathies in other specified diseases classified elsewhere, elbow**
M14.821 Arthropathies in other specified diseases classified elsewhere, right elbow
M14.822 Arthropathies in other specified diseases classified elsewhere, left elbow
M14.829 Arthropathies in other specified diseases classified elsewhere, unspecified elbow
+ **M14.83 Arthropathies in other specified diseases classified elsewhere, wrist**
M14.831 Arthropathies in other specified diseases classified elsewhere, right wrist

M14.832 **Arthropathies in other specified diseases classified elsewhere, left wrist**
M14.839 **Arthropathies in other specified diseases classified elsewhere, unspecified wrist**
+ **M14.84** **Arthropathies in other specified diseases classified elsewhere, hand**
M14.841 **Arthropathies in other specified diseases classified elsewhere, right hand**
M14.842 **Arthropathies in other specified diseases classified elsewhere, left hand**
M14.849 **Arthropathies in other specified diseases classified elsewhere, unspecified hand**
+ **M14.85** **Arthropathies in other specified diseases classified elsewhere, hip**
M14.851 **Arthropathies in other specified diseases classified elsewhere, right hip**
M14.852 **Arthropathies in other specified diseases classified elsewhere, left hip**
M14.859 **Arthropathies in other specified diseases classified elsewhere, unspecified hip**
+ **M14.86** **Arthropathies in other specified diseases classified elsewhere, knee**
M14.861 **Arthropathies in other specified diseases classified elsewhere, right knee**
M14.862 **Arthropathies in other specified diseases classified elsewhere, left knee**
M14.869 **Arthropathies in other specified diseases classified elsewhere, unspecified knee**
+ **M14.87** **Arthropathies in other specified diseases classified elsewhere, ankle and foot**
M14.871 **Arthropathies in other specified diseases classified elsewhere, right ankle and foot**
M14.872 **Arthropathies in other specified diseases classified elsewhere, left ankle and foot**
M14.879 **Arthropathies in other specified diseases classified elsewhere, unspecified ankle and foot**
M14.88 **Arthropathies in other specified diseases classified elsewhere, vertebrae**
M14.89 **Arthropathies in other specified diseases classified elsewhere, multiple sites**

steoarthritis (M15-M19)

cludes2: *osteoarthritis of spine (M47.-)*

M15 Polyosteoarthritis

Includes: arthritis of multiple sites
Excludes1: *bilateral involvement of single joint (M16-M19)*

M15.0 **Primary generalized (osteo)arthritis**
M15.1 **Heberden's nodes (with arthropathy)**
Interphalangeal distal osteoarthritis
M15.2 **Bouchard's nodes (with arthropathy)**
Juxtaphalangeal distal osteoarthritis
M15.3 **Secondary multiple arthritis**
Post-traumatic polyosteoarthritis
M15.4 **Erosive (osteo)arthritis**
M15.8 **Other polyosteoarthritis**
M15.9 **Polyosteoarthritis, unspecified**
Generalized osteoarthritis NOS

M16 Osteoarthritis of hip

M16.0 **Bilateral primary osteoarthritis of hip**
+ **M16.1** **Unilateral primary osteoarthritis of hip**
Primary osteoarthritis of hip NOS
M16.10 **Unilateral primary osteoarthritis, unspecified hip**
M16.11 **Unilateral primary osteoarthritis, right hip**
M16.12 **Unilateral primary osteoarthritis, left hip**
M16.2 **Bilateral osteoarthritis resulting from hip dysplasia**
+ **M16.3** **Unilateral osteoarthritis resulting from hip dysplasia**
Dysplastic osteoarthritis of hip NOS
M16.30 **Unilateral osteoarthritis resulting from hip dysplasia, unspecified hip**
M16.31 **Unilateral osteoarthritis resulting from hip dysplasia, right hip**
M16.32 **Unilateral osteoarthritis resulting from hip dysplasia, left hip**
M16.4 **Bilateral post-traumatic osteoarthritis of hip**
+ **M16.5** **Unilateral post-traumatic osteoarthritis of hip**
Post-traumatic osteoarthritis of hip NOS
M16.50 **Unilateral post-traumatic osteoarthritis, unspecified hip**
M16.51 **Unilateral post-traumatic osteoarthritis, right hip**
M16.52 **Unilateral post-traumatic osteoarthritis, left hip**
M16.6 **Other bilateral secondary osteoarthritis of hip**
M16.7 **Other unilateral secondary osteoarthritis of hip**
Secondary osteoarthritis of hip NOS
M16.9 **Osteoarthritis of hip, unspecified**

M17 Osteoarthritis of knee

M17.0 **Bilateral primary osteoarthritis of knee**
+ **M17.1** **Unilateral primary osteoarthritis of knee**
Primary osteoarthritis of knee NOS
M17.10 **Unilateral primary osteoarthritis, unspecified knee**
M17.11 **Unilateral primary osteoarthritis, right knee**
M17.12 **Unilateral primary osteoarthritis, left knee**
M17.2 **Bilateral post-traumatic osteoarthritis of knee**
+ **M17.3** **Unilateral post-traumatic osteoarthritis of knee**
Post-traumatic osteoarthritis of knee NOS
M17.30 **Unilateral post-traumatic osteoarthritis, unspecified knee**
M17.31 **Unilateral post-traumatic osteoarthritis, right knee**
M17.32 **Unilateral post-traumatic osteoarthritis, left knee**
M17.4 **Other bilateral secondary osteoarthritis of knee**
M17.5 **Other unilateral secondary osteoarthritis of knee**
Secondary osteoarthritis of knee NOS
M17.9 **Osteoarthritis of knee, unspecified**

M18 Osteoarthritis of first carpometacarpal joint

M18.0 **Bilateral primary osteoarthritis of first carpometacarpal joints**
+ **M18.1** **Unilateravl primary osteoarthritis of first carpometacarpal joint**
Primary osteoarthritis of first carpometacarpal joint NOS
M18.10 **Unilateral primary osteoarthritis of first carpometacarpal joint, unspecified hand**
M18.11 **Unilateral primary osteoarthritis of first carpometacarpal joint, right hand**
M18.12 **Unilateral primary osteoarthritis of first carpometacarpal joint, left hand**
M18.2 **Bilateral post-traumatic osteoarthritis of first carpometacarpal joints**
+ **M18.3** **Unilateral post-traumatic osteoarthritis of first carpometacarpal joint**
Post-traumatic osteoarthritis of first carpometacarpal joint NOS
M18.30 **Unilateral post-traumatic osteoarthritis of first carpometacarpal joint, unspecified hand**
M18.31 **Unilateral post-traumatic osteoarthritis of first carpometacarpal joint, right hand**
M18.32 **Unilateral post-traumatic osteoarthritis of first carpometacarpal joint, left hand**
M18.4 **Other bilateral secondary osteoarthritis of first carpometacarpal joints**
+ **M18.5** **Other unilateral secondary osteoarthritis of first carpometacarpal joint**
Secondary osteoarthritis of first carpometacarpal joint NOS
M18.50 **Other unilateral secondary osteoarthritis of first carpometacarpal joint, unspecified hand**
M18.51 **Other unilateral secondary osteoarthritis of first carpometacarpal joint, right hand**
M18.52 **Other unilateral secondary osteoarthritis of first carpometacarpal joint, left hand**
M18.9 **Osteoarthritis of first carpometacarpal joint, unspecified**

M19 Other and unspecified osteoarthritis

Excludes1: *polyarthritis (M15.-)*
Excludes2: *arthrosis of spine (M47.-)*
hallux rigidus (M20.2)
osteoarthritis of spine (M47.-)

+ **M19.0** **Primary osteoarthritis of other joints**
+ **M19.01** **Primary osteoarthritis, shoulder**
M19.011 **Primary osteoarthritis, right shoulder**
M19.012 **Primary osteoarthritis, left shoulder**
M19.019 **Primary osteoarthritis, unspecified shoulder**
+ **M19.02** **Primary osteoarthritis, elbow**
M19.021 **Primary osteoarthritis, right elbow**
M19.022 **Primary osteoarthritis, left elbow**
M19.029 **Primary osteoarthritis, unspecified elbow**
+ **M19.03** **Primary osteoarthritis, wrist**
M19.031 **Primary osteoarthritis, right wrist**
M19.032 **Primary osteoarthritis, left wrist**
M19.039 **Primary osteoarthritis, unspecified wrist**
+ **M19.04** **Primary osteoarthritis, hand**
Excludes2: *primary osteoarthritis of first carpometacarpaljoint(M18.0-,M18.1-)*
M19.041 **Primary osteoarthritis, right hand**
M19.042 **Primary osteoarthritis, left hand**
M19.049 **Primary osteoarthritis, unspecified hand**

+ **M19.07 Primary osteoarthritis ankle and foot**
M19.071 Primary osteoarthritis, right ankle and foot
M19.072 Primary osteoarthritis, left ankle and foot
M19.079 Primary osteoarthritis, unspecified ankle and foot

+ **M19.1 Post-traumatic osteoarthritis of other joints**
+ **M19.11 Post-traumatic osteoarthritis, shoulder**
M19.111 Post-traumatic osteoarthritis, right shoulder
M19.112 Post-traumatic osteoarthritis, left shoulder
M19.119 Post-traumatic osteoarthritis, unspecified shoulder
+ **M19.12 Post-traumatic osteoarthritis, elbow**
M19.121 Post-traumatic osteoarthritis, right elbow
M19.122 Post-traumatic osteoarthritis, left elbow
M19.129 Post-traumatic osteoarthritis, unspecified elbow
+ **M19.13 Post-traumatic osteoarthritis, wrist**
M19.131 Post-traumatic osteoarthritis, right wrist
M19.132 Post-traumatic osteoarthritis, left wrist
M19.139 Post-traumatic osteoarthritis, unspecified wrist
+ **M19.14 Post-traumatic osteoarthritis, hand**
Excludes2: *post-traumatic osteoarthritis of first carpometacarpal joint (M18.2-, M18.3-)*
M19.141 Post-traumatic osteoarthritis, right hand
M19.142 Post-traumatic osteoarthritis, left hand
M19.149 Post-traumatic osteoarthritis, unspecified hand
+ **M19.17 Post-traumatic osteoarthritis, ankle and foot**
M19.171 Post-traumatic osteoarthritis, right ankle and foot
M19.172 Post-traumatic osteoarthritis, left ankle and foot
M19.179 Post-traumatic osteoarthritis, unspecified ankle and foot

+ **M19.2 Secondary osteoarthritis of other joints**
+ **M19.21 Secondary osteoarthritis, shoulder**
M19.211 Secondary osteoarthritis, right shoulder
M19.212 Secondary osteoarthritis, left shoulder
M19.219 Secondary osteoarthritis, unspecified shoulder
+ **M19.22 Secondary osteoarthritis, elbow**
M19.221 Secondary osteoarthritis, right elbow
M19.222 Secondary osteoarthritis, left elbow
M19.229 Secondary osteoarthritis, unspecified elbow
+ **M19.23 Secondary osteoarthritis, wrist**
M19.231 Secondary osteoarthritis, right wrist
M19.232 Secondary osteoarthritis, left wrist
M19.239 Secondary osteoarthritis, unspecified wrist
+ **M19.24 Secondary osteoarthritis, hand**
M19.241 Secondary osteoarthritis, right hand
M19.242 Secondary osteoarthritis, left hand
M19.249 Secondary osteoarthritis, unspecified hand
+ **M19.27 Secondary osteoarthritis, ankle and foot**
M19.271 Secondary osteoarthritis, right ankle and foot
M19.272 Secondary osteoarthritis, left ankle and foot
M19.279 Secondary osteoarthritis, unspecified ankle and foot

+ **M19.9 Osteoarthritis, unspecified site**
M19.90 Unspecified osteoarthritis, unspecified site
Arthrosis NOS
Arthritis NOS
Osteoarthritis NOS
M19.91 Primary osteoarthritis, unspecified site
Primary osteoarthritis NOS
M19.92 Post-traumatic osteoarthritis, unspecified site
Post-traumatic osteoarthritis NOS
M19.93 Secondary osteoarthritis, unspecified site
Secondary osteoarthritis NOS

Other joint disorders (M20-M25)

Excludes2: *joints of the spine (M40-M54)*

M20 Acquired deformities of fingers and toes

Excludes1: *acquired absence of fingers and toes (Z89.-)*
congenital absence of fingers and toes (Q71.3-, Q72.3-)
congenital deformities and malformations of fingers and t (Q66.-, Q68-Q70, Q74.-)

+ **M20.0 Deformity of finger(s)**
Excludes1: *clubbing of fingers (R68.3)*
palmar fascial fibromatosis [Dupuytren] (M72.0)
trigger finger (M65.3)
+ **M20.00 Unspecified deformity of finger(s)**
M20.001 Unspecified deformity of right finger(s)
M20.002 Unspecified deformity of left finger(s)
M20.009 Unspecified deformity of unspecified finger(s)
+ **M20.01 Mallet finger**
M20.011 Mallet finger of right finger(s)
M20.012 Mallet finger of left finger(s)
M20.019 Mallet finger of unspecified finger(s)
+ **M20.02 Boutonnière deformity**
M20.021 Boutonnière deformity of right finger(s)
M20.022 Boutonnière deformity of left finger(s)
M20.029 Boutonnière deformity of unspecified finger(s)
+ **M20.03 Swan-neck deformity**
M20.031 Swan-neck deformity of right finger(s)
M20.032 Swan-neck deformity of left finger(s)
M20.039 Swan-neck deformity of unspecified finger
+ **M20.09 Other deformity of finger(s)**
M20.091 Other deformity of right finger(s)
M20.092 Other deformity of left finger(s)
M20.099 Other deformity of finger(s), unspecified finger(s)

+ **M20.1 Hallux valgus (acquired)**
Bunion
M20.10 Hallux valgus (acquired), unspecified foot
M20.11 Hallux valgus (acquired), right foot
M20.12 Hallux valgus (acquired), left foot

+ **M20.2 Hallux rigidus**
M20.20 Hallux rigidus, unspecified foot
M20.21 Hallux rigidus, right foot
M20.22 Hallux rigidus, left foot

+ **M20.3 Hallux varus (acquired)**
M20.30 Hallux varus (acquired), unspecified foot
M20.31 Hallux varus (acquired), right foot
M20.32 Hallux varus (acquired), left foot

+ **M20.4 Other hammer toe(s) (acquired)**
M20.40 Other hammer toe(s) (acquired), unspecified foot
M20.41 Other hammer toe(s) (acquired), right foot
M20.42 Other hammer toe(s) (acquired), left foot

+ **M20.5 Other deformities of toe(s) (acquired)**
+ **M20.5X Other deformities of toe(s) (acquired)**
M20.5X1 Other deformities of toe(s) (acquired), right foot
M20.5X2 Other deformities of toe(s) (acquired), left foot
M20.5X9 Other deformities of toe(s) (acquired), unspecified foot

+ **M20.6 Acquired deformities of toe(s), unspecified**
M20.60 Acquired deformities of toe(s), unspecified, unspecifi foot
M20.61 Acquired deformities of toe(s), unspecified, right foo
M20.62 Acquired deformities of toe(s), unspecified, left foot

M21 Other acquired deformities of limbs

Excludes1: *acquired absence of limb (Z89.-)*
congenital absence of limbs (Q71-Q73)
congenital deformities and malformations of limbs (Q65-Q66, Q68-Q74)
Excludes2: *acquired deformities of fingers or toes (M20.-)*
coxa plana (M91.2)

+ **M21.0 Valgus deformity, not elsewhere classified**
Excludes1: *metatarsus valgus (Q66.6)*
talipes calcaneovalgus (Q66.4)
M21.00 Valgus deformity, not elsewhere classified, unspecified site
+ **M21.02 Valgus deformity, not elsewhere classified, elbow**
Cubitus valgus
M21.021 Valgus deformity, not elsewhere classified, right elbow

M21.022 **Valgus deformity, not elsewhere classified, left elbow**
M21.029 **Valgus deformity, not elsewhere classified, unspecified elbow**
+ **M21.05** **Valgus deformity, not elsewhere classified, hip**
M21.051 **Valgus deformity, not elsewhere classified, right hip**
M21.052 **Valgus deformity, not elsewhere classified, left hip**
M21.059 **Valgus deformity, not elsewhere classified, unspecified hip**
+ **M21.06** **Valgus deformity, not elsewhere classified, knee**
Genu valgum
Knock knee
M21.061 **Valgus deformity, not elsewhere classified, right knee**
M21.062 **Valgus deformity, not elsewhere classified, left knee**
M21.069 **Valgus deformity, not elsewhere classified, unspecified knee**
+ **M21.07** **Valgus deformity, not elsewhere classified, ankle**
M21.071 **Valgus deformity, not elsewhere classified, right ankle**
M21.072 **Valgus deformity, not elsewhere classified, left ankle**
M21.079 **Valgus deformity, not elsewhere classified, unspecified ankle**
+ **M21.1** **Varus deformity, not elsewhere classified**
Excludes1: *metatarsus varus (Q66.2)*
tibia vara (M92.5)
M21.10 **Varus deformity, not elsewhere classified, unspecified site**
+ **M21.12** **Varus deformity, not elsewhere classified, elbow**
Cubitus varus, elbow
M21.121 **Varus deformity, not elsewhere classified, right elbow**
M21.122 **Varus deformity, not elsewhere classified, left elbow**
M21.129 **Varus deformity, not elsewhere classified, unspecified elbow**
+ **M21.15** **Varus deformity, not elsewhere classified, hip**
M21.151 **Varus deformity, not elsewhere classified, right hip**
M21.152 **Varus deformity, not elsewhere classified, left hip**
M21.159 **Varus deformity, not elsewhere classified, unspecified**
+ **M21.16** **Varus deformity, not elsewhere classified, knee**
Bow leg
Genu varum
M21.161 **Varus deformity, not elsewhere classified, right knee**
M21.162 **Varus deformity, not elsewhere classified, left knee**
M21.169 **Varus deformity, not elsewhere classified, unspecified knee**
+ **M21.17** **Varus deformity, not elsewhere classified, ankle**
M21.171 **Varus deformity, not elsewhere classified, right ankle**
M21.172 **Varus deformity, not elsewhere classified, left ankle**
M21.179 **Varus deformity, not elsewhere classified, unspecified ankle**
+ **M21.2** **Flexion deformity**
M21.20 **Flexion deformity, unspecified site**
+ **M21.21** **Flexion deformity, shoulder**
M21.211 **Flexion deformity, right shoulder**
M21.212 **Flexion deformity, left shoulder**
M21.219 **Flexion deformity, unspecified shoulder**
+ **M21.22** **Flexion deformity, elbow**
M21.221 **Flexion deformity, right elbow**
M21.222 **Flexion deformity, left elbow**
M21.229 **Flexion deformity, unspecified elbow**
+ **M21.23** **Flexion deformity, wrist**
M21.231 **Flexion deformity, right wrist**
M21.232 **Flexion deformity, left wrist**
M21.239 **Flexion deformity, unspecified wrist**
+ **M21.24** **Flexion deformity, finger joints**
M21.241 **Flexion deformity, right finger joints**
M21.242 **Flexion deformity, left finger joints**
M21.249 **Flexion deformity, unspecified finger joints**
+ **M21.25** **Flexion deformity, hip**
M21.251 **Flexion deformity, right hip**
M21.252 **Flexion deformity, left hip**
M21.259 **Flexion deformity, unspecified hip**
+ **M21.26** **Flexion deformity, knee**
M21.261 **Flexion deformity, right knee**
M21.262 **Flexion deformity, left knee**
M21.269 **Flexion deformity, unspecified knee**
+ **M21.27** **Flexion deformity, ankle and toes**
M21.271 **Flexion deformity, right ankle and toes**
M21.272 **Flexion deformity, left ankle and toes**
M21.279 **Flexion deformity, unspecified ankle and toes**
+ **M21.3** **Wrist or foot drop (acquired)**
+ **M21.33** **Wrist drop (acquired)**
M21.331 **Wrist drop, right wrist**
M21.332 **Wrist drop, left wrist**
M21.339 **Wrist drop, unspecified wrist**
+ **M21.37** **Foot drop (acquired)**
M21.371 **Foot drop, right foot**
M21.372 **Foot drop, left foot**
M21.379 **Foot drop, unspecified foot**
+ **M21.4** **Flat foot [pes planus] (acquired)**
Excludes1: *congenital pes planus (Q66.5-)*
M21.40 **Flat foot [pes planus] (acquired), unspecified foot**
M21.41 **Flat foot [pes planus] (acquired), right foot**
M21.42 **Flat foot [pes planus] (acquired), left foot**
+ **M21.5** **Acquired clawhand, clubhand, clawfoot and clubfoot**
Excludes1: *clubfoot, not specified as acquired (Q66.89)*
+ **M21.51** **Acquired clawhand**
M21.511 **Acquired clawhand, right hand**
M21.512 **Acquired clawhand, left hand**
M21.519 **Acquired clawhand, unspecified hand**
+ **M21.52** **Acquired clubhand**
M21.521 **Acquired clubhand, right hand**
M21.522 **Acquired clubhand, left hand**
M21.529 **Acquired clubhand, unspecified hand**
+ **M21.53** **Acquired clawfoot**
M21.531 **Acquired clawfoot, right foot**
M21.532 **Acquired clawfoot, left foot**
M21.539 **Acquired clawfoot, unspecified foot**
+ **M21.54** **Acquired clubfoot**
M21.541 **Acquired clubfoot, right foot**
M21.542 **Acquired clubfoot, left foot**
M21.549 **Acquired clubfoot, unspecified foot**
+ **M21.6** **Other acquired deformities of foot**
Excludes2: *deformities of toe (acquired) (M20.1-M20.6)*
+ **M21.6X** **Other acquired deformities of foot**
M21.6X1 **Other acquired deformities of right foot**
M21.6X2 **Other acquired deformities of left foot**
M21.6X9 **Other acquired deformities of unspecified foot**
+ **M21.7** **Unequal limb length (acquired)**
NOTE The site used should correspond to the shorter limb
M21.70 **Unequal limb length (acquired), unspecified site**
+ **M21.72** **Unequal limb length (acquired), humerus**
M21.721 **Unequal limb length (acquired), right humerus**
M21.722 **Unequal limb length (acquired), left humerus**
M21.729 **Unequal limb length (acquired), unspecified humerus**
+ **M21.73** **Unequal limb length (acquired), ulna and radius**
M21.731 **Unequal limb length (acquired), right ulna**
M21.732 **Unequal limb length (acquired), left ulna**
M21.733 **Unequal limb length (acquired), right radius**
M21.734 **Unequal limb length (acquired), left radius**
M21.739 **Unequal limb length (acquired), unspecified ulna and radius**
+ **M21.75** **Unequal limb length (acquired), femur**
M21.751 **Unequal limb length (acquired), right femur**
M21.752 **Unequal limb length (acquired), left femur**
M21.759 **Unequal limb length (acquired), unspecified femur**
+ **M21.76** **Unequal limb length (acquired), tibia and fibula**
M21.761 **Unequal limb length (acquired), right tibia**
M21.762 **Unequal limb length (acquired), left tibia**
M21.763 **Unequal limb length (acquired), right fibula**
M21.764 **Unequal limb length (acquired), left fibula**
M21.769 **Unequal limb length (acquired), unspecified tibia and fibula**

\+ **M21.8 Other specified acquired deformities of limbs**
Excludes2: *coxa plana (M91.2)*
M21.80 Other specified acquired deformities of unspecified limb
\+ **M21.82 Other specified acquired deformities of upper arm**
M21.821 Other specified acquired deformities of right upper arm
M21.822 Other specified acquired deformities of left upper arm
M21.829 Other specified acquired deformities of unspecified upper arm
\+ **M21.83 Other specified acquired deformities of forearm**
M21.831 Other specified acquired deformities of right forearm
M21.832 Other specified acquired deformities of left forearm
M21.839 Other specified acquired deformities of unspecified forearm
\+ **M21.85 Other specified acquired deformities of thigh**
M21.851 Other specified acquired deformities of right thigh
M21.852 Other specified acquired deformities of left thigh
M21.859 Other specified acquired deformities of unspecified thigh
\+ **M21.86 Other specified acquired deformities of lower leg**
M21.861 Other specified acquired deformities of right lower leg
M21.862 Other specified acquired deformities of left lower leg
M21.869 Other specified acquired deformities of unspecified lower leg
\+ **M21.9 Unspecified acquired deformity of limb and hand**
M21.90 Unspecified acquired deformity of unspecified limb
\+ **M21.92 Unspecified acquired deformity of upper arm**
M21.921 Unspecified acquired deformity of right upper arm
M21.922 Unspecified acquired deformity of left upper arm
M21.929 Unspecified acquired deformity of unspecified upper arm
\+ **M21.93 Unspecified acquired deformity of forearm**
M21.931 Unspecified acquired deformity of right forearm
M21.932 Unspecified acquired deformity of left forearm
M21.939 Unspecified acquired deformity of unspecified forearm
\+ **M21.94 Unspecified acquired deformity of hand**
M21.941 Unspecified acquired deformity of hand, right hand
M21.942 Unspecified acquired deformity of hand, left hand
M21.949 Unspecified acquired deformity of hand, unspecified hand
\+ **M21.95 Unspecified acquired deformity of thigh**
M21.951 Unspecified acquired deformity of right thigh
M21.952 Unspecified acquired deformity of left thigh
M21.959 Unspecified acquired deformity of unspecified thigh
\+ **M21.96 Unspecified acquired deformity of lower leg**
M21.961 Unspecified acquired deformity of right lower leg
M21.962 Unspecified acquired deformity of left lower leg
M21.969 Unspecified acquired deformity of unspecified lower leg

M22 Disorder of patella

Excludes1: *traumatic dislocation of patella (S83.0-)*
\+ **M22.0 Recurrent dislocation of patella**
M22.00 Recurrent dislocation of patella, unspecified knee
M22.01 Recurrent dislocation of patella, right knee
M22.02 Recurrent dislocation of patella, left knee
\+ **M22.1 Recurrent subluxation of patella**
Incomplete dislocation of patella
M22.10 Recurrent subluxation of patella, unspecified knee
M22.11 Recurrent subluxation of patella, right knee
M22.12 Recurrent subluxation of patella, left knee
\+ **M22.2 Patellofemoral disorders**
\+ **M22.2X Patellofemoral disorders**
M22.2X1 Patellofemoral disorders, right knee
M22.2X2 Patellofemoral disorders, left knee
M22.2X9 Patellofemoral disorders, unspecified kne
\+ **M22.3 Other derangements of patella**
\+ **M22.3X Other derangements of patella**
M22.3X1 Other derangements of patella, right kne
M22.3X2 Other derangements of patella, left knee
M22.3X9 Other derangements of patella, unspecified knee
\+ **M22.4 Chondromalacia patellae**
M22.40 Chondromalacia patellae, unspecified knee
M22.41 Chondromalacia patellae, right knee
M22.42 Chondromalacia patellae, left knee
\+ **M22.8 Other disorders of patella**
\+ **M22.8X Other disorders of patella**
M22.8X1 Other disorders of patella, right knee
M22.8X2 Other disorders of patella, left knee
M22.8X9 Other disorders of patella, unspecified kn
\+ **M22.9 Unspecified disorder of patella**
M22.90 Unspecified disorder of patella, unspecified knee
M22.91 Unspecified disorder of patella, right knee
M22.92 Unspecified disorder of patella, left knee

M23 Internal derangement of knee

Excludes1: *ankylosis (M24.66)*
current injury - see injury of knee and lower leg (S80-S89
deformity of knee (M21.-)
osteochondritis dissecans (M93.2)
recurrent dislocation or subluxation of joints (M24.4)
recurrent dislocation or subluxation of patella (M22.0-M2
\+ **M23.0 Cystic meniscus**
\+ **M23.00 Cystic meniscus, unspecified meniscus**
Cystic meniscus, unspecified lateral meniscus
Cystic meniscus, unspecified medial meniscus
M23.000 Cystic meniscus, unspecified lateral meniscus, right knee
M23.001 Cystic meniscus, unspecified lateral meniscus, left knee
M23.002 Cystic meniscus, unspecified lateral meniscus, unspecified knee
M23.003 Cystic meniscus, unspecified medial meniscus, right knee
M23.004 Cystic meniscus, unspecified medial meniscus, left knee
M23.005 Cystic meniscus, unspecified medial meniscus, unspecified knee
M23.006 Cystic meniscus, unspecified meniscus, right knee
M23.007 Cystic meniscus, unspecified meniscus, left knee
M23.009 Cystic meniscus, unspecified meniscus, unspecified knee
\+ **M23.01 Cystic meniscus, anterior horn of medial meniscus**
M23.011 Cystic meniscus, anterior horn of medial meniscus, right knee
M23.012 Cystic meniscus, anterior horn of medial meniscus, left knee
M23.019 Cystic meniscus, anterior horn of medial meniscus, unspecified knee
\+ **M23.02 Cystic meniscus, posterior horn of medial meniscus**
M23.021 Cystic meniscus, posterior horn of medial meniscus, right knee
M23.022 Cystic meniscus, posterior horn of medial meniscus, left knee
M23.029 Cystic meniscus, posterior horn of medial meniscus, unspecified knee
\+ **M23.03 Cystic meniscus, other medial meniscus**
M23.031 Cystic meniscus, other medial meniscus, right knee
M23.032 Cystic meniscus, other medial meniscus, left knee
M23.039 Cystic meniscus, other medial meniscus, unspecified knee
\+ **M23.04 Cystic meniscus, anterior horn of lateral meniscus**
M23.041 Cystic meniscus, anterior horn of lateral meniscus, right knee
M23.042 Cystic meniscus, anterior horn of lateral meniscus, left knee
M23.049 Cystic meniscus, anterior horn of lateral meniscus, unspecified knee

+ **M23.05 Cystic meniscus, posterior horn of lateral meniscus**
  - **M23.051 Cystic meniscus, posterior horn of lateral meniscus, right knee**
  - **M23.052 Cystic meniscus, posterior horn of lateral meniscus, left knee**
  - **M23.059 Cystic meniscus, posterior horn of lateral meniscus, unspecified knee**

+ **M23.06 Cystic meniscus, other lateral meniscus**
  - **M23.061 Cystic meniscus, other lateral meniscus, right knee**
  - **M23.062 Cystic meniscus, other lateral meniscus, left knee**
  - **M23.069 Cystic meniscus, other lateral meniscus, unspecified knee**

+ **M23.2 Derangement of meniscus due to old tear or injury**

  Old bucket-handle tear

+ **M23.20 Derangement of unspecified meniscus due to old tear or injury**

  Derangement of unspecified lateral meniscus due to old tear or injury

  Derangement of unspecified medial meniscus due to old tear or injury
  - **M23.200 Derangement of unspecified lateral meniscus due to old tear or injury, right knee**
  - **M23.201 Derangement of unspecified lateral meniscus due to old tear or injury, left knee**
  - **M23.202 Derangement of unspecified lateral meniscus due to old tear or injury, unspecified knee**
  - **M23.203 Derangement of unspecified medial meniscus due to old tear or injury, right knee**
  - **M23.204 Derangement of unspecified medial meniscus due to old tear or injury, left knee**
  - **M23.205 Derangement of unspecified medial meniscus due to old tear or injury, unspecified knee**
  - **M23.206 Derangement of unspecified meniscus due to old tear or injury, right knee**
  - **M23.207 Derangement of unspecified meniscus due to old tear or injury, left knee**
  - **M23.209 Derangement of unspecified meniscus due to old tear or injury, unspecified knee**

+ **M23.21 Derangement of anterior horn of medial meniscus due to old tear or injury**
  - **M23.211 Derangement of anterior horn of medial meniscus due to old tear or injury, right knee**
  - **M23.212 Derangement of anterior horn of medial meniscus due to old tear or injury, left knee**
  - **M23.219 Derangement of anterior horn of medial meniscus due to old tear or injury, unspecified knee**

+ **M23.22 Derangement of posterior horn of medial meniscus due to old tear or injury**
  - **M23.221 Derangement of posterior horn of medial meniscus due to old tear or injury, right knee**
  - **M23.222 Derangement of posterior horn of medial meniscus due to old tear or injury, left knee**
  - **M23.229 Derangement of posterior horn of medial meniscus due to old tear or injury, unspecified knee**

+ **M23.23 Derangement of other medial meniscus due to old tear or injury**
  - **M23.231 Derangement of other medial meniscus due to old tear or injury, right knee**
  - **M23.232 Derangement of other medial meniscus due to old tear or injury, left knee**
  - **M23.239 Derangement of other medial meniscus due to old tear or injury, unspecified knee**

+ **M23.24 Derangement of anterior horn of lateral meniscus due to old tear or injury**
  - **M23.241 Derangement of anterior horn of lateral meniscus due to old tear or injury, right knee**
  - **M23.242 Derangement of anterior horn of lateral meniscus due to old tear or injury, left knee**
  - **M23.249 Derangement of anterior horn of lateral meniscus due to old tear or injury, unspecified knee**

+ **M23.25 Derangement of posterior horn of lateral meniscus due to old tear or injury**
  - **M23.251 Derangement of posterior horn of lateral meniscus due to old tear or injury, right knee**
  - **M23.252 Derangement of posterior horn of lateral meniscus due to old tear or injury, left knee**
  - **M23.259 Derangement of posterior horn of lateral meniscus due to old tear or injury, unspecified knee**

+ **M23.26 Derangement of other lateral meniscus due to old tear or injury**
  - **M23.261 Derangement of other lateral meniscus due to old tear or injury, right knee**
  - **M23.262 Derangement of other lateral meniscus due to old tear or injury, left knee**
  - **M23.269 Derangement of other lateral meniscus due to old tear or injury, unspecified knee**

+ **M23.3 Other meniscus derangements**

  Degenerate meniscus

  Detached meniscus

  Retained meniscus

+ **M23.30 Other meniscus derangements, unspecified meniscus**

  Other meniscus derangements, unspecified lateral meniscus

  Other meniscus derangements, unspecified medial meniscus
  - **M23.300 Other meniscus derangements, unspecified lateral meniscus, right knee**
  - **M23.301 Other meniscus derangements, unspecified lateral meniscus, left knee**
  - **M23.302 Other meniscus derangements, unspecified lateral meniscus, unspecified knee**
  - **M23.303 Other meniscus derangements, unspecified medial meniscus, right knee**
  - **M23.304 Other meniscus derangements, unspecified medial meniscus, left knee**
  - **M23.305 Other meniscus derangements, unspecified medial meniscus, unspecified knee**
  - **M23.306 Other meniscus derangements, unspecified meniscus, right knee**
  - **M23.307 Other meniscus derangements, unspecified meniscus, left knee**
  - **M23.309 Other meniscus derangements, unspecified meniscus, unspecified knee**

+ **M23.31 Other meniscus derangements, anterior horn of medial meniscus**
  - **M23.311 Other meniscus derangements, anterior horn of medial meniscus, right knee**
  - **M23.312 Other meniscus derangements, anterior horn of medial meniscus, left knee**
  - **M23.319 Other meniscus derangements, anterior horn of medial meniscus, unspecified knee**

+ **M23.32 Other meniscus derangements, posterior horn of medial meniscus**
  - **M23.321 Other meniscus derangements, posterior horn of medial meniscus, right knee**
  - **M23.322 Other meniscus derangements, posterior horn of medial meniscus, left knee**
  - **M23.329 Other meniscus derangements, posterior horn of medial meniscus, unspecified knee**

+ **M23.33 Other meniscus derangements, other medial meniscus**
  - **M23.331 Other meniscus derangements, other medial meniscus, right knee**
  - **M23.332 Other meniscus derangements, other medial meniscus, left knee**
  - **M23.339 Other meniscus derangements, other medial meniscus, unspecified knee**

+ **M23.34 Other meniscus derangements, anterior horn of lateral meniscus**
  - **M23.341 Other meniscus derangements, anterior horn of lateral meniscus, right knee**
  - **M23.342 Other meniscus derangements, anterior horn of lateral meniscus, left knee**
  - **M23.349 Other meniscus derangements, anterior horn of lateral meniscus, unspecified knee**

+ **M23.35 Other meniscus derangements, posterior horn of lateral meniscus**
  - **M23.351 Other meniscus derangements, posterior horn of lateral meniscus, right knee**

M23.352 Other meniscus derangements, posterior horn of lateral meniscus, left knee
M23.359 Other meniscus derangements, posterior horn of lateral meniscus, unspecified knee
+ M23.36 Other meniscus derangements, other lateral meniscus
M23.361 Other meniscus derangements, other lateral meniscus, right knee
M23.362 Other meniscus derangements, other lateral meniscus, left knee
M23.369 Other meniscus derangements, other lateral meniscus, unspecified knee
+ M23.4 Loose body in knee
M23.40 Loose body in knee, unspecified knee
M23.41 Loose body in knee, right knee
M23.42 Loose body in knee, left knee
+ M23.5 Chronic instability of knee
M23.50 Chronic instability of knee, unspecified knee
M23.51 Chronic instability of knee, right knee
M23.52 Chronic instability of knee, left knee
+ M23.6 Other spontaneous disruption of ligament(s) of knee
+ M23.60 Other spontaneous disruption of unspecified ligament of knee
M23.601 Other spontaneous disruption of unspecified ligament of right knee
M23.602 Other spontaneous disruption of unspecified ligament of left knee
M23.609 Other spontaneous disruption of unspecified ligament of unspecified knee
+ M23.61 Other spontaneous disruption of anterior cruciate ligament of knee
M23.611 Other spontaneous disruption of anterior cruciate ligament of right knee
M23.612 Other spontaneous disruption of anterior cruciate ligament of left knee
M23.619 Other spontaneous disruption of anterior cruciate ligament of unspecified knee
+ M23.62 Other spontaneous disruption of posterior cruciate ligament of knee
M23.621 Other spontaneous disruption of posterior cruciate ligament of right knee
M23.622 Other spontaneous disruption of posterior cruciate ligament of left knee
M23.629 Other spontaneous disruption of posterior cruciate ligament of unspecified knee
+ M23.63 Other spontaneous disruption of medial collateral ligament of knee
M23.631 Other spontaneous disruption of medial collateral ligament of right knee
M23.632 Other spontaneous disruption of medial collateral ligament of left knee
M23.639 Other spontaneous disruption of medial collateral ligament of unspecified knee
+ M23.64 Other spontaneous disruption of lateral collateral ligament of knee
M23.641 Other spontaneous disruption of lateral collateral ligament of right knee
M23.642 Other spontaneous disruption of lateral collateral ligament of left knee
M23.649 Other spontaneous disruption of lateral collateral ligament of unspecified knee
+ M23.67 Other spontaneous disruption of capsular ligament of knee
M23.671 Other spontaneous disruption of capsular ligament of right knee
M23.672 Other spontaneous disruption of capsular ligament of left knee
M23.679 Other spontaneous disruption of capsular ligament of unspecified knee
+ M23.8 Other internal derangements of knee
Laxity of ligament of knee
Snapping knee
+ M23.8X Other internal derangements of knee
M23.8X1 Other internal derangements of right knee
M23.8X2 Other internal derangements of left knee
M23.8X9 Other internal derangements of unspecified knee
+ M23.9 Unspecified internal derangement of knee
M23.90 Unspecified internal derangement of unspecified knee
M23.91 Unspecified internal derangement of right knee
M23.92 Unspecified internal derangement of left knee

M24 Other specific joint derangements
Excludes1: *current injury - see injury of joint by body region*
Excludes2: *ganglion (M67.4)*
snapping knee (M23.8-)
temporomandibular joint disorders (M26.6-)
+ M24.0 Loose body in joint
Excludes2: *loose body in knee (M23.4)*
M24.00 Loose body in unspecified joint
+ M24.01 Loose body in shoulder
M24.011 Loose body in right shoulder
M24.012 Loose body in left shoulder
M24.019 Loose body in unspecified shoulder
+ M24.02 Loose body in elbow
M24.021 Loose body in right elbow
M24.022 Loose body in left elbow
M24.029 Loose body in unspecified elbow
+ M24.03 Loose body in wrist
M24.031 Loose body in right wrist
M24.032 Loose body in left wrist
M24.039 Loose body in unspecified wrist
+ M24.04 Loose body in finger joints
M24.041 Loose body in right finger joint(s)
M24.042 Loose body in left finger joint(s)
M24.049 Loose body in unspecified finger joint(s)
+ M24.05 Loose body in hip
M24.051 Loose body in right hip
M24.052 Loose body in left hip
M24.059 Loose body in unspecified hip
+ M24.07 Loose body in ankle and toe joints
M24.071 Loose body in right ankle
M24.072 Loose body in left ankle
M24.073 Loose body in unspecified ankle
M24.074 Loose body in right toe joint(s)
M24.075 Loose body in left toe joint(s)
M24.076 Loose body in unspecified toe joints
M24.08 Loose body, other site
+ M24.1 Other articular cartilage disorders
Excludes2: *chondrocalcinosis (M11.1, M11.2-)*
internal derangement of knee (M23.-)
metastatic calcification (E83.5)
ochronosis (E70.2)
M24.10 Other articular cartilage disorders, unspecified site
+ M24.11 Other articular cartilage disorders, shoulder
M24.111 Other articular cartilage disorders, right shoulder
M24.112 Other articular cartilage disorders, left shoulder
M24.119 Other articular cartilage disorders, unspecified shoulder
+ M24.12 Other articular cartilage disorders, elbow
M24.121 Other articular cartilage disorders, right elbow
M24.122 Other articular cartilage disorders, left elbow
M24.129 Other articular cartilage disorders, unspecified elbow
+ M24.13 Other articular cartilage disorders, wrist
M24.131 Other articular cartilage disorders, right wrist
M24.132 Other articular cartilage disorders, left wri
M24.139 Other articular cartilage disorders, unspecified wrist
+ M24.14 Other articular cartilage disorders, hand
M24.141 Other articular cartilage disorders, right hand
M24.142 Other articular cartilage disorders, left ha
M24.149 Other articular cartilage disorders, unspecified hand
+ M24.15 Other articular cartilage disorders, hip
M24.151 Other articular cartilage disorders, right h
M24.152 Other articular cartilage disorders, left hip
M24.159 Other articular cartilage disorders, unspecified hip
+ M24.17 Other articular cartilage disorders, ankle and foot
M24.171 Other articular cartilage disorders, right ankle
M24.172 Other articular cartilage disorders, left ankle
M24.173 Other articular cartilage disorders, unspecified ankle

M24.174 Other articular cartilage disorders, right foot
M24.175 Other articular cartilage disorders, left foot
M24.176 Other articular cartilage disorders, unspecified foot

+ M24.2 Disorder of ligament
Instability secondary to old ligament injury
Ligamentous laxity NOS
Excludes1: *familial ligamentous laxity (M35.7)*
Excludes2: *internal derangement of knee (M23.5-M23.89)*
M24.20 Disorder of ligament, unspecified site
+ M24.21 Disorder of ligament, shoulder
M24.211 Disorder of ligament, right shoulder
M24.212 Disorder of ligament, left shoulder
M24.219 Disorder of ligament, unspecified shoulder
+ M24.22 Disorder of ligament, elbow
M24.221 Disorder of ligament, right elbow
M24.222 Disorder of ligament, left elbow
M24.229 Disorder of ligament, unspecified elbow
+ M24.23 Disorder of ligament, wrist
M24.231 Disorder of ligament, right wrist
M24.232 Disorder of ligament, left wrist
M24.239 Disorder of ligament, unspecified wrist
+ M24.24 Disorder of ligament, hand
M24.241 Disorder of ligament, right hand
M24.242 Disorder of ligament, left hand
M24.249 Disorder of ligament, unspecified hand
+ M24.25 Disorder of ligament, hip
M24.251 Disorder of ligament, right hip
M24.252 Disorder of ligament, left hip
M24.259 Disorder of ligament, unspecified hip
+ M24.27 Disorder of ligament, ankle and foot
M24.271 Disorder of ligament, right ankle
M24.272 Disorder of ligament, left ankle
M24.273 Disorder of ligament, unspecified ankle
M24.274 Disorder of ligament, right foot
M24.275 Disorder of ligament, left foot
M24.276 Disorder of ligament, unspecifiedfoot
M24.28 Disorder of ligament, vertebrae

+ M24.3 Pathological dislocation of joint, not elsewhere classified
Excludes1: *congenital dislocation or displacement of joint- see congenital malformations and deformations of the musculoskeletal system (Q65-Q79)*
current injury - see injury of joints and ligaments by body region
recurrent dislocation of joint (M24.4-)
M24.30 Pathological dislocation of unspecified joint, not elsewhere classified
+ M24.31 Pathological dislocation of shoulder, not elsewhere classified
M24.311 Pathological dislocation of right shoulder, not elsewhere classified
M24.312 Pathological dislocation of left shoulder, not elsewhere classified
M24.319 Pathological dislocation of unspecified shoulder, not elsewhere classified
+ M24.32 Pathological dislocation of elbow, not elsewhere classified
M24.321 Pathological dislocation of right elbow, not elsewhere classified
M24.322 Pathological dislocation of left elbow, not elsewhere classified
M24.329 Pathological dislocation of unspecified elbow, not elsewhere classified
+ M24.33 Pathological dislocation of wrist, not elsewhere classified
M24.331 Pathological dislocation of right wrist, not elsewhere classified
M24.332 Pathological dislocation of left wrist, not elsewhere classified
M24.339 Pathological dislocation of unspecified wrist, not elsewhere classified
+ M24.34 Pathological dislocation of hand, not elsewhere classified
M24.341 Pathological dislocation of right hand, not elsewhere classified
M24.342 Pathological dislocation of left hand, not elsewhere classified
M24.349 Pathological dislocation of unspecified hand, not elsewhere classified
+ M24.35 Pathological dislocation of hip, not elsewhere classified
M24.351 Pathological dislocation of right hip, not elsewhere classified
M24.352 Pathological dislocation of left hip, not elsewhere classified
M24.359 Pathological dislocation of unspecified hip, not elsewhere classified
+ M24.36 Pathological dislocation of knee, not elsewhere classified
M24.361 Pathological dislocation of right knee, not elsewhere classified
M24.362 Pathological dislocation of left knee, not elsewhere classified
M24.369 Pathological dislocation of unspecified knee, not elsewhere classified
+ M24.37 Pathological dislocation of ankle and foot, not elsewhere classified
M24.371 Pathological dislocation of right ankle, not elsewhere classified
M24.372 Pathological dislocation of left ankle, not elsewhere classified
M24.373 Pathological dislocation of unspecified ankle, not elsewhere classified
M24.374 Pathological dislocation of right foot, not elsewhere classified
M24.375 Pathological dislocation of left foot, not elsewhere classified
M24.376 Pathological dislocation of unspecified foot, not elsewhere classified

+ M24.4 Recurrent dislocation of joint
Recurrent subluxation of joint
Excludes2: *recurrent dislocation of patella (M22.0-M22.1)*
recurrent vertebral dislocation (M43.3-, M43.4, M43.5-)
M24.40 Recurrent dislocation, unspecified joint
+ M24.41 Recurrent dislocation, shoulder
M24.411 Recurrent dislocation, right shoulder
M24.412 Recurrent dislocation, left shoulder
M24.419 Recurrent dislocation, unspecified shoulder
+ M24.42 Recurrent dislocation, elbow
M24.421 Recurrent dislocation, right elbow
M24.422 Recurrent dislocation, left elbow
M24.429 Recurrent dislocation, unspecified elbow
+ M24.43 Recurrent dislocation, wrist
M24.431 Recurrent dislocation, right wrist
M24.432 Recurrent dislocation, left wrist
M24.439 Recurrent dislocation, unspecified wrist
+ M24.44 Recurrent dislocation, hand and finger(s)
M24.441 Recurrent dislocation, right hand
M24.442 Recurrent dislocation, left hand
M24.443 Recurrent dislocation, unspecified hand
M24.444 Recurrent dislocation, right finger
M24.445 Recurrent dislocation, left finger
M24.446 Recurrent dislocation, unspecified finger
+ M24.45 Recurrent dislocation, hip
M24.451 Recurrent dislocation, right hip
M24.452 Recurrent dislocation, left hip
M24.459 Recurrent dislocation, unspecified hip
+ M24.46 Recurrent dislocation, knee
M24.461 Recurrent dislocation, right knee
M24.462 Recurrent dislocation, left knee
M24.469 Recurrent dislocation, unspecified knee
+ M24.47 Recurrent dislocation, ankle, foot and toes
M24.471 Recurrent dislocation, right ankle
M24.472 Recurrent dislocation, left ankle
M24.473 Recurrent dislocation, unspecified ankle
M24.474 Recurrent dislocation, right foot
M24.475 Recurrent dislocation, left foot
M24.476 Recurrent dislocation, unspecified foot
M24.477 Recurrent dislocation, right toe(s)
M24.478 Recurrent dislocation, left toe(s)
M24.479 Recurrent dislocation, unspecified toe(s)

+ M24.5 Contracture of joint
Excludes1: *contracture of muscle without contracture of joint (M62.4-)*
contracture of tendon (sheath) without contracture of joint (M62.4-)
Dupuytren's contracture (M72.0)
Excludes2: *acquired deformities of limbs (M20-M21)*
M24.50 Contracture, unspecified joint
+ M24.51 Contracture, shoulder
M24.511 Contracture, right shoulder
M24.512 Contracture, left shoulder
M24.519 Contracture, unspecified shoulder

+ **M24.52 Contracture, elbow**
- **M24.521 Contracture, right elbow**
- **M24.522 Contracture, left elbow**
- **M24.529 Contracture, unspecified elbow**

+ **M24.53 Contracture, wrist**
- **M24.531 Contracture, right wrist**
- **M24.532 Contracture, left wrist**
- **M24.539 Contracture, unspecified wrist**

+ **M24.54 Contracture, hand**
- **M24.541 Contracture, right hand**
- **M24.542 Contracture, left hand**
- **M24.549 Contracture, unspecified hand**

+ **M24.55 Contracture, hip**
- **M24.551 Contracture, right hip**
- **M24.552 Contracture, left hip**
- **M24.559 Contracture, unspecified hip**

+ **M24.56 Contracture, knee**
- **M24.561 Contracture, right knee**
- **M24.562 Contracture, left knee**
- **M24.569 Contracture, unspecified knee**

+ **M24.57 Contracture, ankle and foot**
- **M24.571 Contracture, right ankle**
- **M24.572 Contracture, left ankle**
- **M24.573 Contracture, unspecified ankle**
- **M24.574 Contracture, right foot**
- **M24.575 Contracture, left foot**
- **M24.576 Contracture, unspecified foot**

+ **M24.6 Ankylosis of joint**

Excludes1: *stiffness of joint without ankylosis (M25.6-)*

Excludes2: *spine (M43.2-)*

M24.60 Ankylosis, unspecified joint

+ **M24.61 Ankylosis, shoulder**
- **M24.611 Ankylosis, right shoulder**
- **M24.612 Ankylosis, left shoulder**
- **M24.619 Ankylosis, unspecified shoulder**

+ **M24.62 Ankylosis, elbow**
- **M24.621 Ankylosis, right elbow**
- **M24.622 Ankylosis, left elbow**
- **M24.629 Ankylosis, unspecified elbow**

+ **M24.63 Ankylosis, wrist**
- **M24.631 Ankylosis, right wrist**
- **M24.632 Ankylosis, left wrist**
- **M24.639 Ankylosis, unspecified wrist**

+ **M24.64 Ankylosis, hand**
- **M24.641 Ankylosis, right hand**
- **M24.642 Ankylosis, left hand**
- **M24.649 Ankylosis, unspecified hand**

+ **M24.65 Ankylosis, hip**
- **M24.651 Ankylosis, right hip**
- **M24.652 Ankylosis, left hip**
- **M24.659 Ankylosis, unspecified hip**

+ **M24.66 Ankylosis, knee**
- **M24.661 Ankylosis, right knee**
- **M24.662 Ankylosis, left knee**
- **M24.669 Ankylosis, unspecified knee**

+ **M24.67 Ankylosis, ankle and foot**
- **M24.671 Ankylosis, right ankle**
- **M24.672 Ankylosis, left ankle**
- **M24.673 Ankylosis, unspecified ankle**
- **M24.674 Ankylosis, right foot**
- **M24.675 Ankylosis, left foot**
- **M24.676 Ankylosis, unspecified foot**

M24.7 Protrusio acetabuli

+ **M24.8 Other specific joint derangements, not elsewhere classified**

Excludes2: *iliotibial band syndrome (M76.3)*

M24.80 Other specific joint derangements of unspecified joint, not elsewhere classified

+ **M24.81 Other specific joint derangements of shoulder, not elsewhere classified**
- **M24.811 Other specific joint derangements of right shoulder, not elsewhere classified**
- **M24.812 Other specific joint derangements of left shoulder, not elsewhere classified**
- **M24.819 Other specific joint derangements of unspecified shoulder, not elsewhere classified**

+ **M24.82 Other specific joint derangements of elbow, not elsewhere classified**
- **M24.821 Other specific joint derangements of right elbow, not elsewhere classified**
- **M24.822 Other specific joint derangements of left elbow, not elsewhere classified**
- **M24.829 Other specific joint derangements of unspecified elbow, not elsewhere classifie**

+ **M24.83 Other specific joint derangements of wrist, not elsewhere classified**
- **M24.831 Other specific joint derangements of righ wrist, not elsewhere classified**
- **M24.832 Other specific joint derangements of left wrist, not elsewhere classified**
- **M24.839 Other specific joint derangements of unspecified wrist, not elsewhere classified**

+ **M24.84 Other specific joint derangements of hand, not elsewhere classified**
- **M24.841 Other specific joint derangements of righ hand, not elsewhere classified**
- **M24.842 Other specific joint derangements of left hand, not elsewhere classified**
- **M24.849 Other specific joint derangements of unspecified hand, not elsewhere classified**

+ **M24.85 Other specific joint derangements of hip, not elsewhere classified**

Irritable hip
- **M24.851 Other specific joint derangements of righ hip, not elsewhere classified**
- **M24.852 Other specific joint derangements of left not elsewhere classified**
- **M24.859 Other specific joint derangements of unspecified hip, not elsewhere classified**

+ **M24.87 Other specific joint derangements of ankle and foo not elsewhere classified**
- **M24.871 Other specific joint derangements of righ ankle, not elsewhere classified**
- **M24.872 Other specific joint derangements of left ankle, not elsewhere classified**
- **M24.873 Other specific joint derangements of unspecified ankle, not elsewhere classified**
- **M24.874 Other specific joint derangements of righ foot, not elsewhere classified**
- **M24.875 Other specific joint derangements left foo not elsewhere classified**
- **M24.876 Other specific joint derangements of unspecified foot, not elsewhere classified**

M24.9 Joint derangement, unspecified

M25 Other joint disorder, not elsewhere classified

Excludes2: *abnormality of gait and mobility (R26.-)*
acquired deformities of limb (M20-M21)
calcification of bursa (M71.4-)
calcification of shoulder (joint) (M75.3)
calcification of tendon (M65.2-)
difficulty in walking (R26.2)
temporomandibular joint disorder (M26.6-)

+ **M25.0 Hemarthrosis**

Excludes1: *current injury - see injury of joint by body region*
hemophilic arthropathy (M36.2)

CC **M25.00 Hemarthrosis, unspecified joint**
CC Exclusion see Appendix A PDX collection 0868

+ **M25.01 Hemarthrosis, shoulder**
- CC **M25.011 Hemarthrosis, right shoulder**
  CC Exclusion see Appendix A PDX collection 0
- CC **M25.012 Hemarthrosis, left shoulder**
  CC Exclusion see Appendix A PDX collection 0
- CC **M25.019 Hemarthrosis, unspecified shoulder**
  CC Exclusion see Appendix A PDX collection 0

+ **M25.02 Hemarthrosis, elbow**
- CC **M25.021 Hemarthrosis, right elbow**
  CC Exclusion see Appendix A PDX collection 0
- CC **M25.022 Hemarthrosis, left elbow**
  CC Exclusion see Appendix A PDX collection 0
- CC **M25.029 Hemarthrosis, unspecified elbow**
  CC Exclusion see Appendix A PDX collection 0

+ **M25.03 Hemarthrosis, wrist**
- CC **M25.031 Hemarthrosis, right wrist**
  CC Exclusion see Appendix A PDX collection 0
- CC **M25.032 Hemarthrosis, left wrist**
  CC Exclusion see Appendix A PDX collection 0
- CC **M25.039 Hemarthrosis, unspecified wrist**
  CC Exclusion see Appendix A PDX collection 0

+ **M25.04 Hemarthrosis, hand**
- CC **M25.041 Hemarthrosis, right hand**
  CC Exclusion see Appendix A PDX collection 0

CC **M25.042 Hemarthrosis, left hand**
CC Exclusion see Appendix A PDX collection 0872
CC **M25.049 Hemarthrosis, unspecified hand**
CC Exclusion see Appendix A PDX collection 0872
\+ **M25.05 Hemarthrosis, hip**
CC **M25.051 Hemarthrosis, right hip**
CC Exclusion see Appendix A PDX collection 0868
CC **M25.052 Hemarthrosis, left hip**
CC Exclusion see Appendix A PDX collection 0868
CC **M25.059 Hemarthrosis, unspecified hip**
CC Exclusion see Appendix A PDX collection 0868
\+ **M25.06 Hemarthrosis, knee**
CC **M25.061 Hemarthrosis, right knee**
CC Exclusion see Appendix A PDX collection 0873
CC **M25.062 Hemarthrosis, left knee**
CC Exclusion see Appendix A PDX collection 0873
CC **M25.069 Hemarthrosis, unspecified knee**
CC Exclusion see Appendix A PDX collection 0873
\+ **M25.07 Hemarthrosis, ankle and foot**
CC **M25.071 Hemarthrosis, right ankle**
CC Exclusion see Appendix A PDX collection 0873
CC **M25.072 Hemarthrosis, left ankle**
CC Exclusion see Appendix A PDX collection 0873
CC **M25.073 Hemarthrosis, unspecified ankle**
CC Exclusion see Appendix A PDX collection 0873
CC **M25.074 Hemarthrosis, right foot**
CC Exclusion see Appendix A PDX collection 0873
CC **M25.075 Hemarthrosis, left foot**
CC Exclusion see Appendix A PDX collection 0873
CC **M25.076 Hemarthrosis, unspecified foot**
CC Exclusion see Appendix A PDX collection 0873
CC **M25.08 Hemarthrosis, other specified site**
Hemarthrosis, vertebrae
CC Exclusion see Appendix A PDX collection 0868
\+ **M25.1 Fistula of joint**
M25.10 Fistula, unspecified joint
\+ **M25.11 Fistula, shoulder**
M25.111 Fistula, right shoulder
M25.112 Fistula, left shoulder
M25.119 Fistula, unspecified shoulder
\+ **M25.12 Fistula, elbow**
M25.121 Fistula, right elbow
M25.122 Fistula, left elbow
M25.129 Fistula, unspecified elbow
\+ **M25.13 Fistula, wrist**
M25.131 Fistula, right wrist
M25.132 Fistula, left wrist
M25.139 Fistula, unspecified wrist
\+ **M25.14 Fistula, hand**
M25.141 Fistula, right hand
M25.142 Fistula, left hand
M25.149 Fistula, unspecified hand
\+ **M25.15 Fistula, hip**
M25.151 Fistula, right hip
M25.152 Fistula, left hip
M25.159 Fistula, unspecified hip
\+ **M25.16 Fistula, knee**
M25.161 Fistula, right knee
M25.162 Fistula, left knee
M25.169 Fistula, unspecified knee
\+ **M25.17 Fistula, ankle and foot**
M25.171 Fistula, right ankle
M25.172 Fistula, left ankle
M25.173 Fistula, unspecified ankle
M25.174 Fistula, right foot
M25.175 Fistula, left foot
M25.176 Fistula, unspecified foot
M25.18 Fistula, other specified site
Fistula, vertebrae
\+ **M25.2 Flail joint**
M25.20 Flail joint, unspecified joint
\+ **M25.21 Flail joint, shoulder**
M25.211 Flail joint, right shoulder
M25.212 Flail joint, left shoulder
M25.219 Flail joint, unspecified shoulder
\+ **M25.22 Flail joint, elbow**
M25.221 Flail joint, right elbow
M25.222 Flail joint, left elbow
M25.229 Flail joint, unspecified elbow
\+ **M25.23 Flail joint, wrist**
M25.231 Flail joint, right wrist
M25.232 Flail joint, left wrist
M25.239 Flail joint, unspecified wrist
\+ **M25.24 Flail joint, hand**
M25.241 Flail joint, right hand
M25.242 Flail joint, left hand
M25.249 Flail joint, unspecified hand
\+ **M25.25 Flail joint, hip**
M25.251 Flail joint, right hip
M25.252 Flail joint, left hip
M25.259 Flail joint, unspecified hip
\+ **M25.26 Flail joint, knee**
M25.261 Flail joint, right knee
M25.262 Flail joint, left knee
M25.269 Flail joint, unspecified knee
\+ **M25.27 Flail joint, ankle and foot**
M25.271 Flail joint, right ankle and foot
M25.272 Flail joint, left ankle and foot
M25.279 Flail joint, unspecified ankle and foot
M25.28 Flail joint, other site
\+ **M25.3 Other instability of joint**
Excludes1: *instability of joint secondary to old ligament injury (M24.2-)*
instability of joint secondary to removal of joint prosthesis (M96.8-)
Excludes2: *spinal instabilities (M53.2-)*
M25.30 Other instability, unspecified joint
\+ **M25.31 Other instability, shoulder**
M25.311 Other instability, right shoulder
M25.312 Other instability, left shoulder
M25.319 Other instability, unspecified shoulder
\+ **M25.32 Other instability, elbow**
M25.321 Other instability, right elbow
M25.322 Other instability, left elbow
M25.329 Other instability, unspecified elbow
\+ **M25.33 Other instability, wrist**
M25.331 Other instability, right wrist
M25.332 Other instability, left wrist
M25.339 Other instability, unspecified wrist
\+ **M25.34 Other instability, hand**
M25.341 Other instability, right hand
M25.342 Other instability, left hand
M25.349 Other instability, unspecified hand
\+ **M25.35 Other instability, hip**
M25.351 Other instability, right hip
M25.352 Other instability, left hip
M25.359 Other instability, unspecified hip
\+ **M25.36 Other instability, knee**
M25.361 Other instability, right knee
M25.362 Other instability, left knee
M25.369 Other instability, unspecified knee
\+ **M25.37 Other instability, ankle and foot**
M25.371 Other instability, right ankle
M25.372 Other instability, left ankle
M25.373 Other instability, unspecified ankle
M25.374 Other instability, right foot
M25.375 Other instability, left foot
M25.376 Other instability, unspecified foot
\+ **M25.4 Effusion of joint**
Excludes1: *hydrarthrosis in yaws (A66.6)*
intermittent hydrarthrosis (M12.4-)
other infective (teno)synovitis (M65.1-)
M25.40 Effusion, unspecified joint
\+ **M25.41 Effusion, shoulder**
M25.411 Effusion, right shoulder
M25.412 Effusion, left shoulder
M25.419 Effusion, unspecified shoulder
\+ **M25.42 Effusion, elbow**
M25.421 Effusion, right elbow
M25.422 Effusion, left elbow
M25.429 Effusion, unspecified elbow
\+ **M25.43 Effusion, wrist**
M25.431 Effusion, right wrist
M25.432 Effusion, left wrist
M25.439 Effusion, unspecified wrist
\+ **M25.44 Effusion, hand**
M25.441 Effusion, right hand
M25.442 Effusion, left hand
M25.449 Effusion, unspecified hand

+ M25.45 Effusion, hip
M25.451 Effusion, right hip
M25.452 Effusion, left hip
M25.459 Effusion, unspecified hip
+ M25.46 Effusion, knee
M25.461 Effusion, right knee
M25.462 Effusion, left knee
M25.469 Effusion, unspecified knee
+ M25.47 Effusion, ankle and foot
M25.471 Effusion, right ankle
M25.472 Effusion, left ankle
M25.473 Effusion, unspecified ankle
M25.474 Effusion, right foot
M25.475 Effusion, left foot
M25.476 Effusion, unspecified foot
M25.48 Effusion, other site
+ M25.5 Pain in joint
Excludes2: *pain in hand (M79.64-)*
pain in fingers (M79.64-)
pain in foot (M79.67-)
pain in limb (M79.6-)
pain in toes (M79.67-)
M25.50 Pain in unspecified joint
+ M25.51 Pain in shoulder
M25.511 Pain in right shoulder
M25.512 Pain in left shoulder
M25.519 Pain in unspecified shoulder
+ M25.52 Pain in elbow
M25.521 Pain in right elbow
M25.522 Pain in left elbow
M25.529 Pain in unspecified elbow
+ M25.53 Pain in wrist
M25.531 Pain in right wrist
M25.532 Pain in left wrist
M25.539 Pain in unspecified wrist
+ M25.55 Pain in hip
M25.551 Pain in right hip
M25.552 Pain in left hip
M25.559 Pain in unspecified hip
+ M25.56 Pain in knee
M25.561 Pain in right knee
M25.562 Pain in left knee
M25.569 Pain in unspecified knee
+ M25.57 Pain in ankle and joints of foot
M25.571 Pain in right ankle and joints of right foot
M25.572 Pain in left ankle and joints of left foot
M25.579 Pain in unspecified ankle and joints of unspecified foot
+ M25.6 Stiffness of joint, not elsewhere classified
Excludes1: *ankylosis of joint (M24.6-)*
contracture of joint (M24.5-)
M25.60 Stiffness of unspecified joint, not elsewhere classified
+ M25.61 Stiffness of shoulder, not elsewhere classified
M25.611 Stiffness of right shoulder, not elsewhere classified
M25.612 Stiffness of left shoulder, not elsewhere classified
M25.619 Stiffness of unspecified shoulder, not elsewhere classified
+ M25.62 Stiffness of elbow, not elsewhere classified
M25.621 Stiffness of right elbow, not elsewhere classified
M25.622 Stiffness of left elbow, not elsewhere classified
M25.629 Stiffness of unspecified elbow, not elsewhere classified
+ M25.63 Stiffness of wrist, not elsewhere classified
M25.631 Stiffness of right wrist, not elsewhere classified
M25.632 Stiffness of left wrist, not elsewhere classified
M25.639 Stiffness of unspecified wrist, not elsewhere classified
+ M25.64 Stiffness of hand, not elsewhere classified
M25.641 Stiffness of right hand, not elsewhere classified
M25.642 Stiffness of left hand, not elsewhere classified
M25.649 Stiffness of unspecified hand, not elsewhere classified
+ M25.65 Stiffness of hip, not elsewhere classified
M25.651 Stiffness of right hip, not elsewhere classi
M25.652 Stiffness of left hip, not elsewhere classifi
M25.659 Stiffness of unspecified hip, not elsewhere classified
+ M25.66 Stiffness of knee, not elsewhere classified
M25.661 Stiffness of right knee, not elsewhere classified
M25.662 Stiffness of left knee, not elsewhere classi
M25.669 Stiffness of unspecified knee, not elsewhe classified
+ M25.67 Stiffness of ankle and foot, not elsewhere classified
M25.671 Stiffness of right ankle, not elsewhere classified
M25.672 Stiffness of left ankle, not elsewhere classi
M25.673 Stiffness of unspecified ankle, not elsewh classified
M25.674 Stiffness of right foot, not elsewhere classi
M25.675 Stiffness of left foot, not elsewhere classifi
M25.676 Stiffness of unspecified foot, not elsewher classified
+ M25.7 Osteophyte
M25.70 Osteophyte, unspecified joint
+ M25.71 Osteophyte, shoulder
M25.711 Osteophyte, right shoulder
M25.712 Osteophyte, left shoulder
M25.719 Osteophyte, unspecified shoulder
+ M25.72 Osteophyte, elbow
M25.721 Osteophyte, right elbow
M25.722 Osteophyte, left elbow
M25.729 Osteophyte, unspecified elbow
+ M25.73 Osteophyte, wrist
M25.731 Osteophyte, right wrist
M25.732 Osteophyte, left wrist
M25.739 Osteophyte, unspecified wrist
+ M25.74 Osteophyte, hand
M25.741 Osteophyte, right hand
M25.742 Osteophyte, left hand
M25.749 Osteophyte, unspecified hand
+ M25.75 Osteophyte, hip
M25.751 Osteophyte, right hip
M25.752 Osteophyte, left hip
M25.759 Osteophyte, unspecified hip
+ M25.76 Osteophyte, knee
M25.761 Osteophyte, right knee
M25.762 Osteophyte, left knee
M25.769 Osteophyte, unspecified knee
+ M25.77 Osteophyte, ankle and foot
M25.771 Osteophyte, right ankle
M25.772 Osteophyte, left ankle
M25.773 Osteophyte, unspecified ankle
M25.774 Osteophyte, right foot
M25.775 Osteophyte, left foot
M25.776 Osteophyte, unspecified foot
M25.78 Osteophyte, vertebrae
+ M25.8 Other specified joint disorders
M25.80 Other specified joint disorders, unspecified joint
+ M25.81 Other specified joint disorders, shoulder
M25.811 Other specified joint disorders, right shoulder
M25.812 Other specified joint disorders, left shoul
M25.819 Other specified joint disorders, unspecifie shoulder
+ M25.82 Other specified joint disorders, elbow
M25.821 Other specified joint disorders, right elbo
M25.822 Other specified joint disorders, left elbow
M25.829 Other specified joint disorders, unspecified elbow
+ M25.83 Other specified joint disorders, wrist
M25.831 Other specified joint disorders, right wris
M25.832 Other specified joint disorders, left wrist
M25.839 Other specified joint disorders, unspecified wrist
+ M25.84 Other specified joint disorders, hand
M25.841 Other specified joint disorders, right hanc
M25.842 Other specified joint disorders, left hand
M25.849 Other specified joint disorders, unspecified hand

+ **M25.85 Other specified joint disorders, hip**
  - **M25.851 Other specified joint disorders, right hip**
  - **M25.852 Other specified joint disorders, left hip**
  - **M25.859 Other specified joint disorders, unspecified hip**

+ **M25.86 Other specified joint disorders, knee**
  - **M25.861 Other specified joint disorders, right knee**
  - **M25.862 Other specified joint disorders, left knee**
  - **M25.869 Other specified joint disorders, unspecified knee**

+ **M25.87 Other specified joint disorders, ankle and foot**
  - **M25.871 Other specified joint disorders, right ankle and foot**
  - **M25.872 Other specified joint disorders, left ankle and foot**
  - **M25.879 Other specified joint disorders, unspecified ankle and foot**

M25.9 Joint disorder, unspecified

ntofacial anomalies [including malocclusion] and other orders of jaw (M26-M27)

cludes1: *hemifacial atrophy or hypertrophy (Q67.4)*
unilateral condylar hyperplasia or hypoplasia (M27.8)

M26 Dentofacial anomalies [including malocclusion]

+ **M26.0 Major anomalies of jaw size**
  Excludes1: *acromegaly (E22.0)*
  Robin's syndrome (Q87.0)
  - **M26.00 Unspecified anomaly of jaw size**
  - **M26.01 Maxillary hyperplasia**
  - **M26.02 Maxillary hypoplasia**
  - **M26.03 Mandibular hyperplasia**
  - **M26.04 Mandibular hypoplasia**
  - **M26.05 Macrogenia**
  - **M26.06 Microgenia**
  - **M26.07 Excessive tuberosity of jaw**
    Entire maxillary tuberosity
  - **M26.09 Other specified anomalies of jaw size**

+ **M26.1 Anomalies of jaw-cranial base relationship**
  - **M26.10 Unspecified anomaly of jaw-cranial base relationship**
  - **M26.11 Maxillary asymmetry**
  - **M26.12 Other jaw asymmetry**
  - **M26.19 Other specified anomalies of jaw-cranial base relationship**

+ **M26.2 Anomalies of dental arch relationship**
  - **M26.20 Unspecified anomaly of dental arch relationship**
  - + **M26.21 Malocclusion, Angle's class**
    - **M26.211 Malocclusion, Angle's class I**
      Neutro-occlusion
    - **M26.212 Malocclusion, Angle's class II**
      Disto-occlusion Division I
      Disto-occlusion Division II
    - **M26.213 Malocclusion, Angle's class III**
      Mesio-occlusion
    - **M26.219 Malocclusion, Angle's class, unspecified**
  - + **M26.22 Open occlusal relationship**
    - **M26.220 Open anterior occlusal relationship**
      Anterior openbite
    - **M26.221 Open posterior occlusal relationship**
      Posterior openbite
  - **M26.23 Excessive horizontal overlap**
    Excessive horizontal overjet
  - **M26.24 Reverse articulation**
    Crossbite (anterior) (posterior)
  - **M26.25 Anomalies of interarch distance**
  - **M26.29 Other anomalies of dental arch relationship**
    Midline deviation of dental arch
    Overbite (excessive) deep
    Overbite (excessive) horizontal
    Overbite (excessive) vertical
    Posterior lingual occlusion of mandibular teeth

+ **M26.3 Anomalies of tooth position of fully erupted tooth or teeth**
  Excludes2: *embedded and impacted teeth (K01.-)*
  - **M26.30 Unspecified anomaly of tooth position of fully erupted tooth or teeth**
    Abnormal spacing of fully erupted tooth or teeth NOS
    Displacement of fully erupted tooth or teeth NOS
    Transposition of fully erupted tooth or teeth NOS
  - **M26.31 Crowding of fully erupted teeth**
  - **M26.32 Excessive spacing of fully erupted teeth**
    Diastema of fully erupted tooth or teeth NOS
  - **M26.33 Horizontal displacement of fully erupted tooth or teeth**
    Tipped tooth or teeth
    Tipping of fully erupted tooth
  - **M26.34 Vertical displacement of fully erupted tooth or teeth**
    Extruded tooth
    Infraeruption of tooth or teeth
    Supraeruption of tooth or teeth
  - **M26.35 Rotation of fully erupted tooth or teeth**
  - **M26.36 Insufficient interocclusal distance of fully erupted teeth (ridge)**
    Lack of adequate intermaxillary vertical dimension of fully erupted teeth
  - **M26.37 Excessive interocclusal distance of fully erupted teeth**
    Excessive intermaxillary vertical dimension of fully erupted teeth
    Loss of occlusal vertical dimension of fully erupted teeth
  - **M26.39 Other anomalies of tooth position of fully erupted tooth or teeth**

M26.4 Malocclusion, unspecified

+ **M26.5 Dentofacial functional abnormalities**
  Excludes1: *bruxism (F45.8)*
  teeth-grinding NOS (F45.8)
  - **M26.50 Dentofacial functional abnormalities, unspecified**
  - **M26.51 Abnormal jaw closure**
  - **M26.52 Limited mandibular range of motion**
  - **M26.53 Deviation in opening and closing of the mandible**
  - **M26.54 Insufficient anterior guidance**
    Insufficient anterior occlusal guidance
  - **M26.55 Centric occlusion maximum intercuspation discrepancy**
    Excludes1: *centric occlusion NOS (M26.59)*
  - **M26.56 Non-working side interference**
    Balancing side interference
  - **M26.57 Lack of posterior occlusal support**
  - **M26.59 Other dentofacial functional abnormalities**
    Centric occlusion (of teeth) NOS
    Malocclusion due to abnormal swallowing
    Malocclusion due to mouth breathing
    Malocclusion due to tongue, lip or finger habits

+ **M26.6 Temporomandibular joint disorders**
  Excludes2: *current temporomandibular joint dislocation (S03.0)*
  current temporomandibular joint sprain (S03.4)
  - **M26.60 Temporomandibular joint disorder, unspecified**
  - **M26.61 Adhesions and ankylosis of temporomandibular joint**
  - **M26.62 Arthralgia of temporomandibular joint**
  - **M26.63 Articular disc disorder of temporomandibular joint**
  - **M26.69 Other specified disorders of temporomandibular joint**

+ **M26.7 Dental alveolar anomalies**
  - **M26.70 Unspecified alveolar anomaly**
  - **M26.71 Alveolar maxillary hyperplasia**
  - **M26.72 Alveolar mandibular hyperplasia**
  - **M26.73 Alveolar maxillary hypoplasia**
  - **M26.74 Alveolar mandibular hypoplasia**
  - **M26.79 Other specified alveolar anomalies**

+ **M26.8 Other dentofacial anomalies**
  - **M26.81 Anterior soft tissue impingement**
    Anterior soft tissue impingement on teeth
  - **M26.82 Posterior soft tissue impingement**
    Posterior soft tissue impingement on teeth
  - **M26.89 Other dentofacial anomalies**

M26.9 Dentofacial anomaly, unspecified

M27 Other diseases of jaws

M27.0 Developmental disorders of jaws
Latent bone cyst of jaw
Stafne's cyst
Torus mandibularis
Torus palatinus

M27.1 Giant cell granuloma, central
Giant cell granuloma NOS
Excludes1: *peripheral giant cell granuloma (K06.8)*

M27.2 Inflammatory conditions of jaws
Osteitis of jaw(s)
Osteomyelitis (neonatal) jaw(s)
Osteoradionecrosis jaw(s)
Periostitis jaw(s)
Sequestrum of jaw bone
Use additional code (W88-W90, X39.0) to identify radiation, if radiation-induced
Excludes2: *osteonecrosis of jaw due to drug (M87.180)*

M27.3 Alveolitis of jaws
Alveolar osteitis
Dry socket

+ M27.4 Other and unspecified cysts of jaw
Excludes1: *cysts of oral region (K09.-)*
latent bone cyst of jaw (M27.0)
Stafne's cyst (M27.0)

M27.40 Unspecified cyst of jaw
Cyst of jaw NOS

M27.49 Other cysts of jaw
Aneurysmal cyst of jaw
Hemorrhagic cyst of jaw
Traumatic cyst of jaw

+ M27.5 Periradicular pathology associated with previous endodontic treatment

M27.51 Perforation of root canal space due to endodontic treatment

M27.52 Endodontic overfill

M27.53 Endodontic underfill

M27.59 Other periradicular pathology associated with previous endodontic treatment

+ M27.6 Endosseous dental implant failure

M27.61 Osseointegration failure of dental implant
Hemorrhagic complications of dental implant placement
Iatrogenic osseointegration failure of dental implant
Osseointegration failure of dental implant due to complications of systemic disease
Osseointegration failure of dental implant due to poor bone quality
Pre-integration failure of dental implant NOS
Pre-osseointegration failure of dental implant

M27.62 Post-osseointegration biological failure of dental implant
Failure of dental implant due to lack of attached gingiva
Failure of dental implant due to occlusal trauma (caused by poor prosthetic design)
Failure of dental implant due to parafunctional habits
Failure of dental implant due to periodontal infection (peri-implantitis)
Failure of dental implant due to poor oral hygiene
Iatrogenic post-osseointegration failure of dental implant
Post-osseointegration failure of dental implant due to complications of systemic disease

M27.63 Post-osseointegration mechanical failure of dental implant
Failure of dental prosthesis causing loss of dental implant
Fracture of dental implant
Excludes2: *cracked tooth (K03.81)*
fractured dental restorative material with loss of material (K08.531)
fractured dental restorative material without loss of material (K08.530)
fractured tooth (S02.5)

M27.69 Other endosseous dental implant failure
Dental implant failure NOS

M27.8 Other specified diseases of jaws
Cherubism
Exostosis
Fibrous dysplasia
Unilateral condylar hyperplasia
Unilateral condylar hypoplasia
Excludes1: *jaw pain (R68.84)*

M27.9 Disease of jaws, unspecified

Systemic connective tissue disorders (M30-M36)

Includes: autoimmune disease NOS
collagen (vascular) disease NOS
systemic autoimmune disease
systemic collagen (vascular) disease

Excludes1: *autoimmune disease, single organ or single cell-type -code to relevant condition category*

M30 Polyarteritis nodosa and related conditions

Excludes1: *microscopic polyarteritis (M31.7)*

CC **M30.0 Polyarteritis nodosa**
CC Exclusion see Appendix A PDX collection 0874

CC **M30.1 Polyarteritis with lung involvement [Churg-Strauss]**
Allergic granulomatous angiitis
CC Exclusion see Appendix A PDX collection 0874

CC **M30.2 Juvenile polyarteritis**
CC Exclusion see Appendix A PDX collection 0874

CC **M30.3 Mucocutaneous lymph node syndrome [Kawasaki]**
CC Exclusion see Appendix A PDX collection 0875

CC **M30.8 Other conditions related to polyarteritis nodosa**
Polyangiitis overlap syndrome
CC Exclusion see Appendix A PDX collection 0874

M31 Other necrotizing vasculopathies

CC **M31.0 Hypersensitivity angiitis**
Goodpasture's syndrome
CC Exclusion see Appendix A PDX collection 0874

MCC **M31.1 Thrombotic microangiopathy**
Thrombotic thrombocytopenic purpura
MCC Exclusion see Appendix A PDX collection 0874

CC **M31.2 Lethal midline granuloma**
CC Exclusion see Appendix A PDX collection 0874

+ M31.3 Wegener's granulomatosis
Necrotizing respiratory granulomatosis

CC **M31.30 Wegener's granulomatosis without renal involveme**
Wegener's granulomatosis NOS
CC Exclusion see Appendix A PDX collection 0874

CC **M31.31 Wegener's granulomatosis with renal involvement**
CC Exclusion see Appendix A PDX collection 0874

CC **M31.4 Aortic arch syndrome [Takayasu]**
CC Exclusion see Appendix A PDX collection 0874

M31.5 Giant cell arteritis with polymyalgia rheumatica

M31.6 Other giant cell arteritis

CC **M31.7 Microscopic polyangiitis**
Microscopic polyarteritis
Excludes1: *polyarteritis nodosa (M30.0)*
CC Exclusion see Appendix A PDX collection 0874

CC **M31.8 Other specified necrotizing vasculopathies**
Hypocomplementemic vasculitis
Septic vasculitis
CC Exclusion see Appendix A PDX collection 0712

CC **M31.9 Necrotizing vasculopathy, unspecified**
CC Exclusion see Appendix A PDX collection 0712

M32 Systemic lupus erythematosus (SLE)

Excludes1: *lupus erythematosus (discoid) (NOS) (L93.0)*

M32.0 Drug-induced systemic lupus erythematosus
Use additional code for adverse effect, if applicable, to identify drug (T36-T50 with fifth or sixth character 5)

+ M32.1 Systemic lupus erythematosus with organ or system involvem

M32.10 Systemic lupus erythematosus, organ or system involvement unspecified

CC **M32.11 Endocarditis in systemic lupus erythematosus**
Libman-Sacks disease
CC Exclusion see Appendix A PDX collection 0676

CC **M32.12 Pericarditis in systemic lupus erythematosus**
Lupus pericarditis
CC Exclusion see Appendix A PDX collection 0673

M32.13 Lung involvement in systemic lupus erythematosus
Pleural effusion due to systemic lupus erythematosus

M32.14 Glomerular disease in systemic lupus erythematosu
Lupus renal disease NOS
AHA CC: 4Q, 2013, 125

M32.15 Tubulo-interstitial nephropathy in systemic lupus erythematosus

M32.19 Other organ or system involvement in systemic lupu erythematosus

M32.8 Other forms of systemic lupus erythematosus

M32.9 Systemic lupus erythematosus, unspecified
SLE NOS
Systemic lupus erythematosus NOS
Systemic lupus erythematosus without organ involvement

M33 Dermatopolymyositis

+ M33.0 Juvenile dermatopolymyositis

CC **M33.00 Juvenile dermatopolymyositis, organ involvement unspecified**
CC Exclusion see Appendix A PDX collection 0876

CC **M33.01 Juvenile dermatopolymyositis with respiratory involvement**
CC Exclusion see Appendix A PDX collection 0876

CC **M33.02 Juvenile dermatopolymyositis with myopathy**
CC Exclusion see Appendix A PDX collection 0877

CC **M33.09 Juvenile dermatopolymyositis with other organ involvement**
CC Exclusion see Appendix A PDX collection 0876

+ M33.1 Other dermatopolymyositis

CC **M33.10 Other dermatopolymyositis, organ involvement unspecified**
CC Exclusion see Appendix A PDX collection 0876

CC **M33.11 Other dermatopolymyositis with respiratory involvement**
CC Exclusion see Appendix A PDX collection 0876
CC **M33.12 Other dermatopolymyositis with myopathy**
CC Exclusion see Appendix A PDX collection 0877
CC **M33.19 Other dermatopolymyositis with other organ involvement**
CC Exclusion see Appendix A PDX collection 0876
+ **M33.2 Polymyositis**
CC **M33.20 Polymyositis, organ involvement unspecified**
CC Exclusion see Appendix A PDX collection 0878
CC **M33.21 Polymyositis with respiratory involvement**
CC Exclusion see Appendix A PDX collection 0878
CC **M33.22 Polymyositis with myopathy**
CC Exclusion see Appendix A PDX collection 0879
CC **M33.29 Polymyositis with other organ involvement**
CC Exclusion see Appendix A PDX collection 0878
+ **M33.9 Dermatopolymyositis, unspecified**
CC **M33.90 Dermatopolymyositis, unspecified, organ involvement unspecified**
CC Exclusion see Appendix A PDX collection 0876
CC **M33.91 Dermatopolymyositis, unspecified with respiratory involvement**
CC Exclusion see Appendix A PDX collection 0876
CC **M33.92 Dermatopolymyositis, unspecified with myopathy**
CC Exclusion see Appendix A PDX collection 0877
CC **M33.99 Dermatopolymyositis, unspecified with other organ involvement**
CC Exclusion see Appendix A PDX collection 0876

M34 Systemic sclerosis [scleroderma]
Excludes1: *circumscribed scleroderma (L94.0)*
neonatal scleroderma (P83.8)
M34.0 Progressive systemic sclerosis
M34.1 CR(E)ST syndrome
Combination of calcinosis, Raynaud's phenomenon, esophageal dysfunction, sclerodactyly, telangiectasia
M34.2 Systemic sclerosis induced by drug and chemical
Code first poisoning due to drug or toxin, if applicable (T36-T65 with fifth or sixth character 1-4 or 6)
Use additional code for adverse effect, if applicable, to identify drug (T36-T50 with fifth or sixth character 5)
+ **M34.8 Other forms of systemic sclerosis**
CC **M34.81 Systemic sclerosis with lung involvement**
No CC Exclusions
CC **M34.82 Systemic sclerosis with myopathy**
CC Exclusion see Appendix A PDX collection 0867
M34.83 Systemic sclerosis with polyneuropathy
M34.89 Other systemic sclerosis
M34.9 Systemic sclerosis, unspecified

M35 Other systemic involvement of connective tissue
Excludes1: *reactive perforating collagenosis (L87.1)*
+ **M35.0 Sicca syndrome [Sjögren]**
M35.00 Sicca syndrome, unspecified
M35.01 Sicca syndrome with keratoconjunctivitis
M35.02 Sicca syndrome with lung involvement
CC **M35.03 Sicca syndrome with myopathy**
CC Exclusion see Appendix A PDX collection 0867
M35.04 Sicca syndrome with tubulo-interstitial nephropathy
Renal tubular acidosis in sicca syndrome
M35.09 Sicca syndrome with other organ involvement
CC **M35.1 Other overlap syndromes**
Mixed connective tissue disease
Excludes1: *polyangiitis overlap syndrome (M30.8)*
CC Exclusion see Appendix A PDX collection 0880
CC **M35.2 Behçet's disease**
CC Exclusion see Appendix A PDX collection 0863
M35.3 Polymyalgia rheumatica
Excludes1: *polymyalgia rheumatica with giant cell arteritis (M31.5)*
M35.4 Diffuse (eosinophilic) fasciitis
CC **M35.5 Multifocal fibrosclerosis**
CC Exclusion see Appendix A PDX collection 0880
M35.6 Relapsing panniculitis [Weber-Christian]
Excludes1: *lupus panniculitis (L93.2)*
panniculitis NOS (M79.3-)
M35.7 Hypermobility syndrome
Familial ligamentous laxity
Excludes1: *Ehlers-Danlos syndrome (Q79.6)*
ligamentous laxity, NOS (M24.2-)
CC **M35.8 Other specified systemic involvement of connective tissue**
CC Exclusion see Appendix A PDX collection 0880
M35.9 Systemic involvement of connective tissue, unspecified
Autoimmune disease (systemic) NOS
Collagen (vascular) disease NOS

M36 Systemic disorders of connective tissue in diseases classified elsewhere
Excludes2: *arthropathies in diseases classified elsewhere (M14.-)*
CC **M36.0 Dermato(poly)myositis in neoplastic disease**
Code first underlying neoplasm (C00-D49)
CC Exclusion see Appendix A PDX collection 0876
M36.1 Arthropathy in neoplastic disease
Code first underlying neoplasm, such as:
leukemia (C91-C95)
malignant histiocytosis (C96.A)
multiple myeloma (C90.0)
M36.2 Hemophilic arthropathy
Hemarthrosis in hemophilic arthropathy
Code first underlying disease, such as:
factor VIII deficiency (D66)
with vascular defect (D68.0)
factor IX deficiency (D67)
hemophilia (classical) (D66)
hemophilia B (D67)
hemophilia C (D68.1)
M36.3 Arthropathy in other blood disorders
M36.4 Arthropathy in hypersensitivity reactions classified elsewhere
Code first underlying disease, such as:
Henoch (-Schönlein) purpura (D69.0)
serum sickness (T80.6-)
M36.8 Systemic disorders of connective tissue in other diseases classified elsewhere
Code first underlying disease, such as:
alkaptonuria (E70.2)
hypogammaglobulinemia (D80.-)
ochronosis (E70.2)

DORSOPATHIES (M40-M54)

Deforming dorsopathies (M40-M43)

M40 Kyphosis and lordosis
Excludes1: *congenital kyphosis and lordosis (Q76.4)*
kyphoscoliosis (M41.-)
postprocedural kyphosis and lordosis (M96.-)
+ **M40.0 Postural kyphosis**
Excludes1: *osteochondrosis of spine (M42.-)*
M40.00 Postural kyphosis, site unspecified
M40.03 Postural kyphosis, cervicothoracic region
M40.04 Postural kyphosis, thoracic region
M40.05 Postural kyphosis, thoracolumbar region
+ **M40.1 Other secondary kyphosis**
M40.10 Other secondary kyphosis, site unspecified
M40.12 Other secondary kyphosis, cervical region
M40.13 Other secondary kyphosis, cervicothoracic region
M40.14 Other secondary kyphosis, thoracic region
M40.15 Other secondary kyphosis, thoracolumbar region
+ **M40.2 Other and unspecified kyphosis**
+ **M40.20 Unspecified kyphosis**
M40.202 Unspecified kyphosis, cervical region
M40.203 Unspecified kyphosis, cervicothoracic region
M40.204 Unspecified kyphosis, thoracic region
M40.205 Unspecified kyphosis, thoracolumbar region
M40.209 Unspecified kyphosis, site unspecified
+ **M40.29 Other kyphosis**
M40.292 Other kyphosis, cervical region
M40.293 Other kyphosis, cervicothoracic region
M40.294 Other kyphosis, thoracic region
M40.295 Other kyphosis, thoracolumbar region
M40.299 Other kyphosis, site unspecified
+ **M40.3 Flatback syndrome**
M40.30 Flatback syndrome, site unspecified
M40.35 Flatback syndrome, thoracolumbar region
M40.36 Flatback syndrome, lumbar region
M40.37 Flatback syndrome, lumbosacral region
+ **M40.4 Postural lordosis**
Acquired lordosis
M40.40 Postural lordosis, site unspecified
M40.45 Postural lordosis, thoracolumbar region
M40.46 Postural lordosis, lumbar region
M40.47 Postural lordosis, lumbosacral region

+ **M40.5 Lordosis, unspecified**
M40.50 Lordosis, unspecified, site unspecified
M40.55 Lordosis, unspecified, thoracolumbar region
M40.56 Lordosis, unspecified, lumbar region
M40.57 Lordosis, unspecified, lumbosacral region

M41 Scoliosis

Includes: kyphoscoliosis
Excludes1: *congenital scoliosis NOS (Q67.5)*
congenital scoliosis due to bony malformation (Q76.3)
postural congenital scoliosis (Q67.5)
kyphoscoliotic heart disease (I27.1)
postprocedural scoliosis (M96.-)

+ **M41.0 Infantile idiopathic scoliosis**
M41.00 Infantile idiopathic scoliosis, site unspecified
M41.02 Infantile idiopathic scoliosis, cervical region
M41.03 Infantile idiopathic scoliosis, cervicothoracic region
M41.04 Infantile idiopathic scoliosis, thoracic region
M41.05 Infantile idiopathic scoliosis, thoracolumbar region
M41.06 Infantile idiopathic scoliosis, lumbar region
M41.07 Infantile idiopathic scoliosis, lumbosacral region
M41.08 Infantile idiopathic scoliosis, sacral and sacrococcygeal region

+ **M41.1 Juvenile and adolescent idiopathic scoliosis**
+ **M41.11 Juvenile idiopathic scoliosis**
M41.112 Juvenile idiopathic scoliosis, cervical region
M41.113 Juvenile idiopathic scoliosis, cervicothoracic region
M41.114 Juvenile idiopathic scoliosis, thoracic region
M41.115 Juvenile idiopathic scoliosis, thoracolumbar region
M41.116 Juvenile idiopathic scoliosis, lumbar region
M41.117 Juvenile idiopathic scoliosis, lumbosacral region
M41.119 Juvenile idiopathic scoliosis, site unspecified
+ **M41.12 Adolescent scoliosis**
M41.122 Adolescent idiopathic scoliosis, cervical region
M41.123 Adolescent idiopathic scoliosis, cervicothoracic region
M41.124 Adolescent idiopathic scoliosis, thoracic region
M41.125 Adolescent idiopathic scoliosis, thoracolumbar region
M41.126 Adolescent idiopathic scoliosis, lumbar region
M41.127 Adolescent idiopathic scoliosis, lumbosacral region
M41.129 Adolescent idiopathic scoliosis, site unspecified

+ **M41.2 Other idiopathic scoliosis**
M41.20 Other idiopathic scoliosis, site unspecified
M41.22 Other idiopathic scoliosis, cervical region
M41.23 Other idiopathic scoliosis, cervicothoracic region
M41.24 Other idiopathic scoliosis, thoracic region
M41.25 Other idiopathic scoliosis, thoracolumbar region
M41.26 Other idiopathic scoliosis, lumbar region
M41.27 Other idiopathic scoliosis, lumbosacral region

+ **M41.3 Thoracogenic scoliosis**
M41.30 Thoracogenic scoliosis, site unspecified
M41.34 Thoracogenic scoliosis, thoracic region
M41.35 Thoracogenic scoliosis, thoracolumbar region

+ **M41.4 Neuromuscular scoliosis**
Scoliosis secondary to cerebral palsy, Friedreich's ataxia, poliomyelitis and other neuromuscular disorders
Code also underlying condition
M41.40 Neuromuscular scoliosis, site unspecified
M41.41 Neuromuscular scoliosis, occipito-atlanto-axial region
M41.42 Neuromuscular scoliosis, cervical region
M41.43 Neuromuscular scoliosis, cervicothoracic region
M41.44 Neuromuscular scoliosis, thoracic region
M41.45 Neuromuscular scoliosis, thoracolumbar region
M41.46 Neuromuscular scoliosis, lumbar region
M41.47 Neuromuscular scoliosis, lumbosacral region

+ **M41.5 Other secondary scoliosis**
M41.50 Other secondary scoliosis, site unspecified
M41.52 Other secondary scoliosis, cervical region
M41.53 Other secondary scoliosis, cervicothoracic region
M41.54 Other secondary scoliosis, thoracic region
M41.55 Other secondary scoliosis, thoracolumbar region
M41.56 Other secondary scoliosis, lumbar region
M41.57 Other secondary scoliosis, lumbosacral region

+ **M41.8 Other forms of scoliosis**
M41.80 Other forms of scoliosis, site unspecified
M41.82 Other forms of scoliosis, cervical region
M41.83 Other forms of scoliosis, cervicothoracic region
M41.84 Other forms of scoliosis, thoracic region
M41.85 Other forms of scoliosis, thoracolumbar region
M41.86 Other forms of scoliosis, lumbar region
M41.87 Other forms of scoliosis, lumbosacral region

M41.9 Scoliosis, unspecified

M42 Spinal osteochondrosis

+ **M42.0 Juvenile osteochondrosis of spine**
Calvé's disease
Scheuermann's disease
Excludes1: *postural kyphosis (M40.0)*
M42.00 Juvenile osteochondrosis of spine, site unspecified
M42.01 Juvenile osteochondrosis of spine, occipito-atlanto-axial region
M42.02 Juvenile osteochondrosis of spine, cervical region
M42.03 Juvenile osteochondrosis of spine, cervicothoracic region
M42.04 Juvenile osteochondrosis of spine, thoracic region
M42.05 Juvenile osteochondrosis of spine, thoracolumbar re[illegible]
M42.06 Juvenile osteochondrosis of spine, lumbar region
M42.07 Juvenile osteochondrosis of spine, lumbosacral reg[illegible]
M42.08 Juvenile osteochondrosis of spine, sacral and sacrococcygeal region
M42.09 Juvenile osteochondrosis of spine, multiple sites in spine

+ **M42.1 Adult osteochondrosis of spine**
• **M42.10 Adult osteochondrosis of spine, site unspecified**
• **M42.11 Adult osteochondrosis of spine, occipito-atlanto-ax[illegible] region**
• **M42.12 Adult osteochondrosis of spine, cervical region**
• **M42.13 Adult osteochondrosis of spine, cervicothoracic reg[illegible]**
• **M42.14 Adult osteochondrosis of spine, thoracic region**
• **M42.15 Adult osteochondrosis of spine, thoracolumbar reg[illegible]**
• **M42.16 Adult osteochondrosis of spine, lumbar region**
• **M42.17 Adult osteochondrosis of spine, lumbosacral region**
• **M42.18 Adult osteochondrosis of spine, sacral and sacrococcygeal region**
• **M42.19 Adult osteochondrosis of spine, multiple sites in sp[illegible]**

M42.9 Spinal osteochondrosis, unspecified

M43 Other deforming dorsopathies

Excludes1: *congenital spondylolysis and spondylolisthesis (Q76.2)*
hemivertebra (Q76.3-Q76.4)
Klippel-Feil syndrome (Q76.1)
lumbarization and sacralization (Q76.4)
platyspondylisis (Q76.4)
spina bifida occulta (Q76.0)
spinal curvature in osteoporosis (M80.-)
spinal curvature in Paget's disease of bone [osteitis deformans] (M88.-)

+ **M43.0 Spondylolysis**
Excludes1: *congenital spondylolysis (Q76.2)*
spondylolisthesis (M43.1)
M43.00 Spondylolysis, site unspecified
M43.01 Spondylolysis, occipito-atlanto-axial region
M43.02 Spondylolysis, cervical region
M43.03 Spondylolysis, cervicothoracic region
M43.04 Spondylolysis, thoracic region
M43.05 Spondylolysis, thoracolumbar region
M43.06 Spondylolysis, lumbar region
M43.07 Spondylolysis, lumbosacral region
M43.08 Spondylolysis, sacral and sacrococcygeal region
M43.09 Spondylolysis, multiple sites in spine

+ **M43.1 Spondylolisthesis**
Excludes1: *acute traumatic of lumbosacral region (S33.1)*
acute traumatic of sites other than lumbosacral- code to Fracture, vertebra, by region
congenital spondylolisthesis (Q76.2)
M43.10 Spondylolisthesis, site unspecified
M43.11 Spondylolisthesis, occipito-atlanto-axial region
M43.12 Spondylolisthesis, cervical region
M43.13 Spondylolisthesis, cervicothoracic region
M43.14 Spondylolisthesis, thoracic region
M43.15 Spondylolisthesis, thoracolumbar region
M43.16 Spondylolisthesis, lumbar region
M43.17 Spondylolisthesis, lumbosacral region
M43.18 Spondylolisthesis, sacral and sacrococcygeal region
M43.19 Spondylolisthesis, multiple sites in spine

+ **M43.2 Fusion of spine**
  Ankylosis of spinal joint
  Excludes1: *ankylosing spondylitis (M45.0-)*
  congenital fusion of spine (Q76.4)
  Excludes2: *arthrodesis status (Z98.1)*
  pseudoarthrosis after fusion or arthrodesis (M96.0)
  M43.20 Fusion of spine, site unspecified
  M43.21 Fusion of spine, occipito-atlanto-axial region
  M43.22 Fusion of spine, cervical region
  M43.23 Fusion of spine, cervicothoracic region
  M43.24 Fusion of spine, thoracic region
  M43.25 Fusion of spine, thoracolumbar region
  M43.26 Fusion of spine, lumbar region
  M43.27 Fusion of spine, lumbosacral region
  M43.28 Fusion of spine, sacral and sacrococcygeal region

M43.3 Recurrent atlantoaxial dislocation with myelopathy

M43.4 Other recurrent atlantoaxial dislocation

+ **M43.5 Other recurrent vertebral dislocation**
  Excludes1: *biomechanical lesions NEC (M99.-)*
  + **M43.5X Other recurrent vertebral dislocation**
    M43.5X2 Other recurrent vertebral dislocation, cervical region
    M43.5X3 Other recurrent vertebral dislocation, cervicothoracic region
    M43.5X4 Other recurrent vertebral dislocation, thoracic region
    M43.5X5 Other recurrent vertebral dislocation, thoracolumbar region
    M43.5X6 Other recurrent vertebral dislocation, lumbar region
    M43.5X7 Other recurrent vertebral dislocation, lumbosacral region
    M43.5X8 Other recurrent vertebral dislocation, sacral and sacrococcygeal region
    M43.5X9 Other recurrent vertebral dislocation, site unspecified

M43.6 Torticollis
  Excludes1: *congenital (sternomastoid) torticollis (Q68.0)*
  current injury - see Injury, of spine, by body region
  ocular torticollis (R29.891)
  psychogenic torticollis (F45.8)
  spasmodic torticollis (G24.3)
  torticollis due to birth injury (P15.2)

+ **M43.8 Other specified deforming dorsopathies**
  Excludes2: *kyphosis and lordosis (M40.-)*
  scoliosis (M41.-)
  + **M43.8X Other specified deforming dorsopathies**
    M43.8X1 Other specified deforming dorsopathies, occipito-atlanto-axial region
    M43.8X2 Other specified deforming dorsopathies, cervical region
    M43.8X3 Other specified deforming dorsopathies, cervicothoracic region
    M43.8X4 Other specified deforming dorsopathies, thoracic region
    M43.8X5 Other specified deforming dorsopathies, thoracolumbar region
    M43.8X6 Other specified deforming dorsopathies, lumbar region
    M43.8X7 Other specified deforming dorsopathies, lumbosacral region
    M43.8X8 Other specified deforming dorsopathies, sacral and sacrococcygeal region
    M43.8X9 Other specified deforming dorsopathies, site unspecified

M43.9 Deforming dorsopathy, unspecified
  Curvature of spine NOS

ondylopathies (M45-M49)

M45 Ankylosing spondylitis
  Rheumatoid arthritis of spine
  Excludes1: *arthropathy in Reiter's disease (M02.3-)*
  juvenile (ankylosing) spondylitis (M08.1)
  Excludes2: *Behçet's disease (M35.2)*
  M45.0 Ankylosing spondylitis of multiple sites in spine
  M45.1 Ankylosing spondylitis of occipito-atlanto-axial region
  M45.2 Ankylosing spondylitis of cervical region
  M45.3 Ankylosing spondylitis of cervicothoracic region
  M45.4 Ankylosing spondylitis of thoracic region
  M45.5 Ankylosing spondylitis of thoracolumbar region
  M45.6 Ankylosing spondylitis lumbar region
  M45.7 Ankylosing spondylitis of lumbosacral region
  M45.8 Ankylosing spondylitis sacral and sacrococcygeal region
  M45.9 Ankylosing spondylitis of unspecified sites in spine

M46 Other inflammatory spondylopathies

+ **M46.0 Spinal enthesopathy**
  Disorder of ligamentous or muscular attachments of spine
  M46.00 Spinal enthesopathy, site unspecified
  M46.01 Spinal enthesopathy, occipito-atlanto-axial region
  M46.02 Spinal enthesopathy, cervical region
  M46.03 Spinal enthesopathy, cervicothoracic region
  M46.04 Spinal enthesopathy, thoracic region
  M46.05 Spinal enthesopathy, thoracolumbar region
  M46.06 Spinal enthesopathy, lumbar region
  M46.07 Spinal enthesopathy, lumbosacral region
  M46.08 Spinal enthesopathy, sacral and sacrococcygeal region
  M46.09 Spinal enthesopathy, multiple sites in spine

M46.1 Sacroiliitis, not elsewhere classified

+ **M46.2 Osteomyelitis of vertebra**
  CC **M46.20 Osteomyelitis of vertebra, site unspecified**
  CC Exclusion see Appendix A PDX collection 0881
  CC **M46.21 Osteomyelitis of vertebra, occipito-atlanto-axial region**
  CC Exclusion see Appendix A PDX collection 0881
  CC **M46.22 Osteomyelitis of vertebra, cervical region**
  CC Exclusion see Appendix A PDX collection 0881
  CC **M46.23 Osteomyelitis of vertebra, cervicothoracic region**
  CC Exclusion see Appendix A PDX collection 0881
  CC **M46.24 Osteomyelitis of vertebra, thoracic region**
  CC Exclusion see Appendix A PDX collection 0881
  CC **M46.25 Osteomyelitis of vertebra, thoracolumbar region**
  CC Exclusion see Appendix A PDX collection 0881
  CC **M46.26 Osteomyelitis of vertebra, lumbar region**
  CC Exclusion see Appendix A PDX collection 0881
  CC **M46.27 Osteomyelitis of vertebra, lumbosacral region**
  CC Exclusion see Appendix A PDX collection 0881
  CC **M46.28 Osteomyelitis of vertebra, sacral and sacrococcygeal region**
  CC Exclusion see Appendix A PDX collection 0881

+ **M46.3 Infection of intervertebral disc (pyogenic)**
  Use additional code (B95-B97) to identify infectious agent.
  CC **M46.30 Infection of intervertebral disc (pyogenic), site unspecified**
  CC Exclusion see Appendix A PDX collection 0882
  CC **M46.31 Infection of intervertebral disc (pyogenic), occipito-atlanto-axial region**
  CC Exclusion see Appendix A PDX collection 0882
  CC **M46.32 Infection of intervertebral disc (pyogenic), cervical region**
  CC Exclusion see Appendix A PDX collection 0882
  CC **M46.33 Infection of intervertebral disc (pyogenic), cervicothoracic region**
  CC Exclusion see Appendix A PDX collection 0882
  CC **M46.34 Infection of intervertebral disc (pyogenic), thoracic region**
  CC Exclusion see Appendix A PDX collection 0882
  CC **M46.35 Infection of intervertebral disc (pyogenic), thoracolumbar region**
  CC Exclusion see Appendix A PDX collection 0882
  CC **M46.36 Infection of intervertebral disc (pyogenic), lumbar region**
  CC Exclusion see Appendix A PDX collection 0882
  CC **M46.37 Infection of intervertebral disc (pyogenic), lumbosacral region**
  CC Exclusion see Appendix A PDX collection 0882
  CC **M46.38 Infection of intervertebral disc (pyogenic), sacral and sacrococcygeal region**
  CC Exclusion see Appendix A PDX collection 0882
  CC **M46.39 Infection of intervertebral disc (pyogenic), multiple sites in spine**
  CC Exclusion see Appendix A PDX collection 0882

+ **M46.4 Discitis, unspecified**
  M46.40 Discitis, unspecified, site unspecified
  M46.41 Discitis, unspecified, occipito-atlanto-axial region
  M46.42 Discitis, unspecified, cervical region
  M46.43 Discitis, unspecified, cervicothoracic region
  M46.44 Discitis, unspecified, thoracic region
  M46.45 Discitis, unspecified, thoracolumbar region
  M46.46 Discitis, unspecified, lumbar region
  M46.47 Discitis, unspecified, lumbosacral region
  M46.48 Discitis, unspecified, sacral and sacrococcygeal region
  M46.49 Discitis, unspecified, multiple sites in spine

+ **M46.5 Other infective spondylopathies**
  - **M46.50 Other infective spondylopathies, site unspecified**
  - **M46.51 Other infective spondylopathies, occipito-atlanto-axial region**
  - **M46.52 Other infective spondylopathies, cervical region**
  - **M46.53 Other infective spondylopathies, cervicothoracic region**
  - **M46.54 Other infective spondylopathies, thoracic region**
  - **M46.55 Other infective spondylopathies, thoracolumbar region**
  - **M46.56 Other infective spondylopathies, lumbar region**
  - **M46.57 Other infective spondylopathies, lumbosacral region**
  - **M46.58 Other infective spondylopathies, sacral and sacrococcygeal region**
  - **M46.59 Other infective spondylopathies, multiple sites in spine**

+ **M46.8 Other specified inflammatory spondylopathies**
  - **M46.80 Other specified inflammatory spondylopathies, site unspecified**
  - **M46.81 Other specified inflammatory spondylopathies, occipito-atlanto-axial region**
  - **M46.82 Other specified inflammatory spondylopathies, cervical region**
  - **M46.83 Other specified inflammatory spondylopathies, cervicothoracic region**
  - **M46.84 Other specified inflammatory spondylopathies, thoracic region**
  - **M46.85 Other specified inflammatory spondylopathies, thoracolumbar region**
  - **M46.86 Other specified inflammatory spondylopathies, lumbar region**
  - **M46.87 Other specified inflammatory spondylopathies, lumbosacral region**
  - **M46.88 Other specified inflammatory spondylopathies, sacral and sacrococcygeal region**
  - **M46.89 Other specified inflammatory spondylopathies, multiple sites in spine**

+ **M46.9 Unspecified inflammatory spondylopathy**
  - **M46.90 Unspecified inflammatory spondylopathy, site unspecified**
  - **M46.91 Unspecified inflammatory spondylopathy, occipito-atlanto-axial region**
  - **M46.92 Unspecified inflammatory spondylopathy, cervical region**
  - **M46.93 Unspecified inflammatory spondylopathy, cervicothoracic region**
  - **M46.94 Unspecified inflammatory spondylopathy, thoracic region**
  - **M46.95 Unspecified inflammatory spondylopathy, thoracolumbar region**
  - **M46.96 Unspecified inflammatory spondylopathy, lumbar region**
  - **M46.97 Unspecified inflammatory spondylopathy, lumbosacral region**
  - **M46.98 Unspecified inflammatory spondylopathy, sacral and sacrococcygeal region**
  - **M46.99 Unspecified inflammatory spondylopathy, multiple sites in spine**

M47 Spondylosis

Includes: arthrosis or osteoarthritis of spine
degeneration of facet joints

+ **M47.0 Anterior spinal and vertebral artery compression syndromes**
  + **M47.01 Anterior spinal artery compression syndromes**
    - CC **M47.011 Anterior spinal artery compression syndromes, occipito-atlanto-axial region**
      CC Exclusion see Appendix A PDX collection 0883
    - CC **M47.012 Anterior spinal artery compression syndromes, cervical region**
      CC Exclusion see Appendix A PDX collection 0883
    - CC **M47.013 Anterior spinal artery compression syndromes, cervicothoracic region**
      CC Exclusion see Appendix A PDX collection 0883
    - CC **M47.014 Anterior spinal artery compression syndromes, thoracic region**
      CC Exclusion see Appendix A PDX collection 0883
    - CC **M47.015 Anterior spinal artery compression syndromes, thoracolumbar region**
      CC Exclusion see Appendix A PDX collection
    - CC **M47.016 Anterior spinal artery compression syndromes, lumbar region**
      CC Exclusion see Appendix A PDX collection
    - CC **M47.019 Anterior spinal artery compression syndromes, site unspecified**
      CC Exclusion see Appendix A PDX collection
  + **M47.02 Vertebral artery compression syndromes**
    - CC **M47.021 Vertebral artery compression syndromes, occipito-atlanto-axial region**
      CC Exclusion see Appendix A PDX collection
    - CC **M47.022 Vertebral artery compression syndromes, cervical region**
      CC Exclusion see Appendix A PDX collection
    - CC **M47.029 Vertebral artery compression syndromes, site unspecified**
      CC Exclusion see Appendix A PDX collection

+ **M47.1 Other spondylosis with myelopathy**
  Spondylogenic compression of spinal cord
  Excludes1: *vertebral subluxation (M43.3-M43.59)*
  - CC **M47.10 Other spondylosis with myelopathy, site unspecified**
    CC Exclusion see Appendix A PDX collection 0884
  - CC **M47.11 Other spondylosis with myelopathy, occipito-atlanto-axial region**
    CC Exclusion see Appendix A PDX collection 0883
  - CC **M47.12 Other spondylosis with myelopathy, cervical region**
    CC Exclusion see Appendix A PDX collection 0883
  - CC **M47.13 Other spondylosis with myelopathy, cervicothoracic region**
    CC Exclusion see Appendix A PDX collection 0883
  - CC **M47.14 Other spondylosis with myelopathy, thoracic region**
    CC Exclusion see Appendix A PDX collection 0885
  - CC **M47.15 Other spondylosis with myelopathy, thoracolumbar region**
    CC Exclusion see Appendix A PDX collection 0885
  - CC **M47.16 Other spondylosis with myelopathy, lumbar region**
    CC Exclusion see Appendix A PDX collection 0886

+ **M47.2 Other spondylosis with radiculopathy**
  - **M47.20 Other spondylosis with radiculopathy, site unspecified**
  - **M47.21 Other spondylosis with radiculopathy, occipito-atlanto-axial region**
  - **M47.22 Other spondylosis with radiculopathy, cervical region**
  - **M47.23 Other spondylosis with radiculopathy, cervicothoracic region**
  - **M47.24 Other spondylosis with radiculopathy, thoracic region**
  - **M47.25 Other spondylosis with radiculopathy, thoracolumbar region**
  - **M47.26 Other spondylosis with radiculopathy, lumbar region**
  - **M47.27 Other spondylosis with radiculopathy, lumbosacral region**
  - **M47.28 Other spondylosis with radiculopathy, sacral and sacrococcygeal region**

+ **M47.8 Other spondylosis**
  + **M47.81 Spondylosis without myelopathy or radiculopathy**
    - **M47.811 Spondylosis without myelopathy or radiculopathy, occipito-atlanto-axial region**
    - **M47.812 Spondylosis without myelopathy or radiculopathy, cervical region**
    - **M47.813 Spondylosis without myelopathy or radiculopathy, cervicothoracic region**
    - **M47.814 Spondylosis without myelopathy or radiculopathy, thoracic region**
    - **M47.815 Spondylosis without myelopathy or radiculopathy, thoracolumbar region**
    - **M47.816 Spondylosis without myelopathy or radiculopathy, lumbar region**
    - **M47.817 Spondylosis without myelopathy or radiculopathy, lumbosacral region**
    - **M47.818 Spondylosis without myelopathy or radiculopathy, sacral and sacrococcygeal region**
    - **M47.819 Spondylosis without myelopathy or radiculopathy, site unspecified**

\+ **M47.89 Other spondylosis**
M47.891 Other spondylosis, occipito-atlanto-axial region
M47.892 Other spondylosis, cervical region
M47.893 Other spondylosis, cervicothoracic region
M47.894 Other spondylosis, thoracic region
M47.895 Other spondylosis, thoracolumbar region
M47.896 Other spondylosis, lumbar region
M47.897 Other spondylosis, lumbosacral region
M47.898 Other spondylosis, sacral and sacrococcygeal region
M47.899 Other spondylosis, site unspecified
M47.9 Spondylosis, unspecified

M48 Other spondylopathies

\+ **M48.0 Spinal stenosis**
Caudal stenosis
M48.00 Spinal stenosis, site unspecified
M48.01 Spinal stenosis, occipito-atlanto-axial region
M48.02 Spinal stenosis, cervical region
M48.03 Spinal stenosis, cervicothoracic region
M48.04 Spinal stenosis, thoracic region
M48.05 Spinal stenosis, thoracolumbar region
M48.06 Spinal stenosis, lumbar region
M48.07 Spinal stenosis, lumbosacral region
M48.08 Spinal stenosis, sacral and sacrococcygeal region

\+ **M48.1 Ankylosing hyperostosis [Forestier]**
Diffuse idiopathic skeletal hyperostosis [DISH]
M48.10 Ankylosing hyperostosis [Forestier], site unspecified
M48.11 Ankylosing hyperostosis [Forestier], occipito-atlanto-axial region
M48.12 Ankylosing hyperostosis [Forestier], cervical region
M48.13 Ankylosing hyperostosis [Forestier], cervicothoracic region
M48.14 Ankylosing hyperostosis [Forestier], thoracic region
M48.15 Ankylosing hyperostosis [Forestier], thoracolumbar region
M48.16 Ankylosing hyperostosis [Forestier], lumbar region
M48.17 Ankylosing hyperostosis [Forestier], lumbosacral region
M48.18 Ankylosing hyperostosis [Forestier], sacral and sacrococcygeal region
M48.19 Ankylosing hyperostosis [Forestier], multiple sites in spine

\+ **M48.2 Kissing spine**
M48.20 Kissing spine, site unspecified
M48.21 Kissing spine, occipito-atlanto-axial region
M48.22 Kissing spine, cervical region
M48.23 Kissing spine, cervicothoracic region
M48.24 Kissing spine, thoracic region
M48.25 Kissing spine, thoracolumbar region
M48.26 Kissing spine, lumbar region
M48.27 Kissing spine, lumbosacral region

\+ **M48.3 Traumatic spondylopathy**
CC **M48.30 Traumatic spondylopathy, site unspecified**
CC Exclusion see Appendix A PDX collection 0887
CC **M48.31 Traumatic spondylopathy, occipito-atlanto-axial region**
CC Exclusion see Appendix A PDX collection 0887
CC **M48.32 Traumatic spondylopathy, cervical region**
CC Exclusion see Appendix A PDX collection 0887
CC **M48.33 Traumatic spondylopathy, cervicothoracic region**
CC Exclusion see Appendix A PDX collection 0887
CC **M48.34 Traumatic spondylopathy, thoracic region**
CC Exclusion see Appendix A PDX collection 0887
CC **M48.35 Traumatic spondylopathy, thoracolumbar region**
CC Exclusion see Appendix A PDX collection 0887
CC **M48.36 Traumatic spondylopathy, lumbar region**
CC Exclusion see Appendix A PDX collection 0887
CC **M48.37 Traumatic spondylopathy, lumbosacral region**
CC Exclusion see Appendix A PDX collection 0887
CC **M48.38 Traumatic spondylopathy, sacral and sacrococcygeal region**
CC Exclusion see Appendix A PDX collection 0887

\+ **M48.4 Fatigue fracture of vertebra**
Stress fracture of vertebra
Excludes1: *pathological fracture NOS (M84.4-)*
pathological fracture of vertebra due to neoplasm (M84.58)
pathological fracture of vertebra due to other diagnosis (M84.68)
pathological fracture of vertebra due to osteoporosis (M80.-)
traumatic fracture of vertebrae (S12.0-S12.3-, S22.0-, S32.0-)

The appropriate 7th character is to be added to each code from subcategory M48.4:
A initial encounter for fracture
D subsequent encounter for fracture with routine healing
G subsequent encounter for fracture with delayed healing
S sequela of fracture

X+7th **M48.40 Fatigue fracture of vertebra, site unspecified**
X+7th **M48.41 Fatigue fracture of vertebra, occipito-atlanto-axial region**
X+7th **M48.42 Fatigue fracture of vertebra, cervical region**
X+7th **M48.43 Fatigue fracture of vertebra, cervicothoracic region**
X+7th **M48.44 Fatigue fracture of vertebra, thoracic region**
X+7th **M48.45 Fatigue fracture of vertebra, thoracolumbar region**
X+7th **M48.46 Fatigue fracture of vertebra, lumbar region**
X+7th **M48.47 Fatigue fracture of vertebra, lumbosacral region**
X+7th **M48.48 Fatigue fracture of vertebra, sacral and sacrococcygeal region**

\+ **M48.5 Collapsed vertebra, not elsewhere classified**
Collapsed vertebra NOS
Wedging of vertebra NOS
Excludes1: *current injury - see Injury of spine, by body region*
fatigue fracture of vertebra (M48.4)
pathological fracture of vertebra due to neoplasm (M84.58)
pathological fracture of vertebra due to other diagnosis (M84.68)
pathological fracture of vertebra due to osteoporosis (M80.-)
pathological fracture NOS (M84.4-)
stress fracture of vertebra (M48.4-)
traumatic fracture of vertebra (S12.-, S22.-, S32.-)

The appropriate 7th character is to be added to each code from subcategory M48.5:
A initial encounter for fracture
D subsequent encounter for fracture with routine healing
G subsequent encounter for fracture with delayed healing
S sequela of fracture

CC X+7th **M48.50 Collapsed vertebra, not elsewhere classified, site unspecified**
CC Exclusion 7th character A see Appendix A PDX collection 0888
CC X+7th **M48.51 Collapsed vertebra, not elsewhere classified, occipito-atlanto-axial region**
CC Exclusion 7th character A see Appendix A PDX collection 0888
CC X+7th **M48.52 Collapsed vertebra, not elsewhere classified, cervical region**
CC Exclusion 7th character A see Appendix A PDX collection 0888
CC X+7th **M48.53 Collapsed vertebra, not elsewhere classified, cervicothoracic region**
CC Exclusion 7th character A see Appendix A PDX collection 0888
CC X+7th **M48.54 Collapsed vertebra, not elsewhere classified, thoracic region**
CC Exclusion 7th character A see Appendix A PDX collection 0888
CC X+7th **M48.55 Collapsed vertebra, not elsewhere classified, thoracolumbar region**
CC Exclusion 7th character A see Appendix A PDX collection 0888
CC X+7th **M48.56 Collapsed vertebra, not elsewhere classified, lumbar region**
CC Exclusion 7th character A see Appendix A PDX collection 0888
CC X+7th **M48.57 Collapsed vertebra, not elsewhere classified, lumbosacral region**
CC Exclusion 7th character A see Appendix A PDX collection 0888

CC X+7th **M48.58 Collapsed vertebra, not elsewhere classified, sacral and sacrococcygeal region**
CC Exclusion 7th character A see Appendix A PDX collection 0888

+ **M48.8 Other specified spondylopathies**
Ossification of posterior longitudinal ligament
+ **M48.8X Other specified spondylopathies**
M48.8X1 Other specified spondylopathies, occipito-atlanto-axial region
M48.8X2 Other specified spondylopathies, cervical region
M48.8X3 Other specified spondylopathies, cervicothoracic region
M48.8X4 Other specified spondylopathies, thoracic region
M48.8X5 Other specified spondylopathies, thoracolumbar region
M48.8X6 Other specified spondylopathies, lumbar region
M48.8X7 Other specified spondylopathies, lumbosacral region
M48.8X8 Other specified spondylopathies, sacral and sacrococcygeal region
M48.8X9 Other specified spondylopathies, site unspecified

M48.9 Spondylopathy, unspecified

M49 Spondylopathies in diseases classified elsewhere

Includes: curvature of spine in diseases classified elsewhere
deformity of spine in diseases classified elsewhere
kyphosis in diseases classified elsewhere
scoliosis in diseases classified elsewhere
spondylopathy in diseases classified elsewhere

Code first *underlying disease, such as:*
brucellosis (A23.-)
Charcot-Marie-Tooth disease (G60.0)
enterobacterial infections (A01-A04)
osteitis fibrosa cystica (E21.0)

Excludes1: *curvature of spine in tuberculosis [Pott's] (A18.01)*
enteropathic arthropathies (M07.-)
gonococcal spondylitis (A54.41)
neuropathic [tabes dorsalis] spondylitis (A52.11)
neuropathic spondylopathy in syringomyelia (G95.0)
neuropathic spondylopathy in tabes dorsalis (A52.11)
nonsyphilitic neuropathic spondylopathy NEC (G98.0)
spondylitis in syphilis (acquired) (A52.77)
tuberculous spondylitis (A18.01)
typhoid fever spondylitis (A01.05)

+ **M49.8 Spondylopathy in diseases classified elsewhere**
M49.80 Spondylopathy in diseases classified elsewhere, site unspecified
M49.81 Spondylopathy in diseases classified elsewhere, occipito-atlanto-axial region
M49.82 Spondylopathy in diseases classified elsewhere, cervical region
M49.83 Spondylopathy in diseases classified elsewhere, cervicothoracic region
M49.84 Spondylopathy in diseases classified elsewhere, thoracic region
M49.85 Spondylopathy in diseases classified elsewhere, thoracolumbar region
M49.86 Spondylopathy in diseases classified elsewhere, lumbar region
M49.87 Spondylopathy in diseases classified elsewhere, lumbosacral region
M49.88 Spondylopathy in diseases classified elsewhere, sacral and sacrococcygeal region
M49.89 Spondylopathy in diseases classified elsewhere, multiple sites in spine

Other dorsopathies (M50-M54)

Excludes1: *current injury - see injury of spine by body region*
discitis NOS (M46.4-)

M50 Cervical disc disorders

NOTE code to the most superior level of disorder
Includes: cervicothoracic disc disorders with cervicalgia
cervicothoracic disc disorders

+ **M50.0 Cervical disc disorder with myelopathy**
CC **M50.00 Cervical disc disorder with myelopathy, unspecified cervical region**
CC Exclusion see Appendix A PDX collection 0889
CC **M50.01 Cervical disc disorder with myelopathy, high cervical region**
C2-C3 disc disorder with myelopathy
C3-C4 disc disorder with myelopathy
CC Exclusion see Appendix A PDX collection 0889
CC **M50.02 Cervical disc disorder with myelopathy, mid-cervical region**
C4-C5 disc disorder with myelopathy
C5-C6 disc disorder with myelopathy
C6-C7 disc disorder with myelopathy
CC Exclusion see Appendix A PDX collection 0889
CC **M50.03 Cervical disc disorder with myelopathy, cervicothoracic region**
C7-T1 disc disorder with myelopathy
CC Exclusion see Appendix A PDX collection 0889

+ **M50.1 Cervical disc disorder with radiculopathy**
Excludes2: *brachial radiculitis NOS (M54.13)*
M50.10 Cervical disc disorder with radiculopathy, unspecified cervical region
M50.11 Cervical disc disorder with radiculopathy, high cervical region
C2-C3 disc disorder with radiculopathy
C3 radiculopathy due to disc disorder
C3-C4 disc disorder with radiculopathy
C4 radiculopathy due to disc disorder
M50.12 Cervical disc disorder with radiculopathy, mid-cervical region
C4-C5 disc disorder with radiculopathy
C5 radiculopathy due to disc disorder
C5-C6 disc disorder with radiculopathy
C6 radiculopathy due to disc disorder
C6-C7 disc disorder with radiculopathy
C7 radiculopathy due to disc disorder
M50.13 Cervical disc disorder with radiculopathy, cervicothoracic region
C7-T1 disc disorder with radiculopathy
C8 radiculopathy due to disc disorder

+ **M50.2 Other cervical disc displacement**
M50.20 Other cervical disc displacement, unspecified cervical region
M50.21 Other cervical disc displacement, high cervical region
Other C2-C3 cervical disc displacement
Other C3-C4 cervical disc displacement
M50.22 Other cervical disc displacement, mid-cervical region
Other C4-C5 cervical disc displacement
Other C5-C6 cervical disc displacement
Other C6-C7 cervical disc displacement
M50.23 Other cervical disc displacement, cervicothoracic region
Other C7-T1 cervical disc displacement

+ **M50.3 Other cervical disc degeneration**
M50.30 Other cervical disc degeneration, unspecified cervical region
M50.31 Other cervical disc degeneration, high cervical region
Other C2-C3 cervical disc degeneration
Other C3-C4 cervical disc degeneration
M50.32 Other cervical disc degeneration, mid-cervical region
Other C4-C5 cervical disc degeneration
Other C5-C6 cervical disc degeneration
Other C6-C7 cervical disc degeneration
M50.33 Other cervical disc degeneration, cervicothoracic region
Other C7-T1 cervical disc degeneration

+ **M50.8 Other cervical disc disorders**
M50.80 Other cervical disc disorders, unspecified cervical region
M50.81 Other cervical disc disorders, high cervical region
Other C2-C3 cervical disc disorders
Other C3-C4 cervical disc disorders
M50.82 Other cervical disc disorders, mid-cervical region
Other C4-C5 cervical disc disorders
Other C5-C6 cervical disc disorders
Other C6-C7 cervical disc disorders
M50.83 Other cervical disc disorders, cervicothoracic region
Other C7-T1 cervical disc disorders

+ **M50.9 Cervical disc disorder, unspecified**
M50.90 Cervical disc disorder, unspecified, unspecified cervical region
M50.91 Cervical disc disorder, unspecified, high cervical region
Other C2-C3 cervical disc disorder, unspecified
Other C3-C4 cervical disc disorder, unspecified

M50.92 Cervical disc disorder, unspecified, mid-cervical region
Other C4-C5 cervical disc disorder, unspecified
Other C5-C6 cervical disc disorder, unspecified
Other C6-C7 cervical disc disorder, unspecified

M50.93 Cervical disc disorder, unspecified, cervicothoracic region
Other C7-T1 cervical disc disorder, unspecified

M51 Thoracic, thoracolumbar, and lumbosacral intervertebral disc disorders

Excludes2: *cervical and cervicothoracic disc disorders (M50.-)*
sacral and sacrococcygeal disorders (M53.3)

\+ **M51.0 Thoracic, thoracolumbar and lumbosacral intervertebral disc disorders with myelopathy**

CC **M51.04 Intervertebral disc disorders with myelopathy, thoracic region**
CC Exclusion see Appendix A PDX collection 0890

CC **M51.05 Intervertebral disc disorders with myelopathy, thoracolumbar region**
CC Exclusion see Appendix A PDX collection 0890

CC **M51.06 Intervertebral disc disorders with myelopathy, lumbar region**
CC Exclusion see Appendix A PDX collection 0891

\+ **M51.1 Thoracic, thoracolumbar and lumbosacral intervertebral disc disorders with radiculopathy**
Sciatica due to intervertebral disc disorder
Excludes1: *lumbar radiculitis NOS (M54.16)*
sciatica NOS (M54.3)

M51.14 Intervertebral disc disorders with radiculopathy, thoracic region
M51.15 Intervertebral disc disorders with radiculopathy, thoracolumbar region
M51.16 Intervertebral disc disorders with radiculopathy, lumbar region
M51.17 Intervertebral disc disorders with radiculopathy, lumbosacral region

\+ **M51.2 Other thoracic, thoracolumbar and lumbosacral intervertebral disc displacement**
Lumbago due to displacement of intervertebral disc

M51.24 Other intervertebral disc displacement, thoracic region
M51.25 Other intervertebral disc displacement, thoracolumbar region
M51.26 Other intervertebral disc displacement, lumbar region
M51.27 Other intervertebral disc displacement, lumbosacral region

\+ **M51.3 Other thoracic, thoracolumbar and lumbosacral intervertebral disc degeneration**

M51.34 Other intervertebral disc degeneration, thoracic region
M51.35 Other intervertebral disc degeneration, thoracolumbar region
M51.36 Other intervertebral disc degeneration, lumbar region
M51.37 Other intervertebral disc degeneration, lumbosacral region

\+ **M51.4 Schmorl's nodes**

M51.44 Schmorl's nodes, thoracic region
M51.45 Schmorl's nodes, thoracolumbar region
M51.46 Schmorl's nodes, lumbar region
M51.47 Schmorl's nodes, lumbosacral region

\+ **M51.8 Other thoracic, thoracolumbar and lumbosacral intervertebral disc disorders**

M51.84 Other intervertebral disc disorders, thoracic region
M51.85 Other intervertebral disc disorders, thoracolumbar region
M51.86 Other intervertebral disc disorders, lumbar region
M51.87 Other intervertebral disc disorders, lumbosacral region

M51.9 Unspecified thoracic, thoracolumbar and lumbosacral intervertebral disc disorder

M53 Other and unspecified dorsopathies, not elsewhere classified

M53.0 Cervicocranial syndrome
Posterior cervical sympathetic syndrome

M53.1 Cervicobrachial syndrome
Excludes2: *cervical disc disorder (M50.-)*
thoracic outlet syndrome (G54.0)

\+ **M53.2 Spinal instabilities**

M53.2X Spinal instabilities

M53.2X1 Spinal instabilities, occipito-atlanto-axial region
M53.2X2 Spinal instabilities, cervical region
M53.2X3 Spinal instabilities, cervicothoracic region
M53.2X4 Spinal instabilities, thoracic region
M53.2X5 Spinal instabilities, thoracolumbar region
M53.2X6 Spinal instabilities, lumbar region
M53.2X7 Spinal instabilities, lumbosacral region
M53.2X8 Spinal instabilities, sacral and sacrococcygeal region
M53.2X9 Spinal instabilities, site unspecified

M53.3 Sacrococcygeal disorders, not elsewhere classified
Coccygodynia

\+ **M53.8 Other specified dorsopathies**

M53.80 Other specified dorsopathies, site unspecified
M53.81 Other specified dorsopathies, occipito-atlanto-axial region
M53.82 Other specified dorsopathies, cervical region
M53.83 Other specified dorsopathies, cervicothoracic region
M53.84 Other specified dorsopathies, thoracic region
M53.85 Other specified dorsopathies, thoracolumbar region
M53.86 Other specified dorsopathies, lumbar region
M53.87 Other specified dorsopathies, lumbosacral region
M53.88 Other specified dorsopathies, sacral and sacrococcygeal region

M53.9 Dorsopathy, unspecified

M54 Dorsalgia

Excludes1: *psychogenic dorsalgia (F45.41)*

\+ **M54.0 Panniculitis affecting regions of neck and back**
Excludes1: *lupus panniculitis (L93.2)*
panniculitis NOS (M79.3)
relapsing [Weber-Christian] panniculitis (M35.6)

M54.00 Panniculitis affecting regions of neck and back, site unspecified
M54.01 Panniculitis affecting regions of neck and back, occipito-atlanto-axial region
M54.02 Panniculitis affecting regions of neck and back, cervical region
M54.03 Panniculitis affecting regions of neck and back, cervicothoracic region
M54.04 Panniculitis affecting regions of neck and back, thoracic region
M54.05 Panniculitis affecting regions of neck and back, thoracolumbar region
M54.06 Panniculitis affecting regions of neck and back, lumbar region
M54.07 Panniculitis affecting regions of neck and back, lumbosacral region
M54.08 Panniculitis affecting regions of neck and back, sacral and sacrococcygeal region
M54.09 Panniculitis affecting regions, neck and back, multiple sites in spine

\+ **M54.1 Radiculopathy**
Brachial neuritis or radiculitis NOS
Lumbar neuritis or radiculitis NOS
Lumbosacral neuritis or radiculitis NOS
Thoracic neuritis or radiculitis NOS
Radiculitis NOS
Excludes1: *neuralgia and neuritis NOS (M79.2)*
radiculopathy with cervical disc disorder (M50.1)
radiculopathy with lumbar and other intervertebral disc disorder (M51.1-)
radiculopathy with spondylosis (M47.2-)

M54.10 Radiculopathy, site unspecified
M54.11 Radiculopathy, occipito-atlanto-axial region
M54.12 Radiculopathy, cervical region
M54.13 Radiculopathy, cervicothoracic region
M54.14 Radiculopathy, thoracic region
M54.15 Radiculopathy, thoracolumbar region
M54.16 Radiculopathy, lumbar region
M54.17 Radiculopathy, lumbosacral region
M54.18 Radiculopathy, sacral and sacrococcygeal region

M54.2 Cervicalgia
Excludes1: *cervicalgia due to intervertebral cervical disc disorder (M50.-)*

\+ **M54.3 Sciatica**
Excludes1: *lesion of sciatic nerve (G57.0)*
sciatica due to intervertebral disc disorder (M51.1-)
sciatica with lumbago (M54.4-)

M54.30 Sciatica, unspecified side
M54.31 Sciatica, right side
M54.32 Sciatica, left side

+ **M54.4 Lumbago with sciatica**
Excludes1: *lumbago with sciatica due to intervertebral disc disorder (M51.1-)*
M54.40 Lumbago with sciatica, unspecified side
M54.41 Lumbago with sciatica, right side
M54.42 Lumbago with sciatica, left side
M54.5 Low back pain
Loin pain
Lumbago NOS
Excludes1: *low back strain (S39.012)*
lumbago due to intervertebral disc displacement (M51.2-)
lumbago with sciatica (M54.4-)
M54.6 Pain in thoracic spine
Excludes1: *pain in thoracic spine due to intervertebral disc disorder (M51.-)*
+ **M54.8 Other dorsalgia**
Excludes1: *dorsalgia in thoracic region (M54.6)*
low back pain (M54.5)
M54.81 Occipital neuralgia
M54.89 Other dorsalgia
M54.9 Dorsalgia, unspecified
Backache NOS
Back pain NOS

SOFT TISSUE DISORDERS (M60-M79)

Disorders of muscles (M60-M63)

Excludes1: *dermatopolymyositis (M33.-)*
muscular dystrophies and myopathies (G71-G72)
myopathy in amyloidosis (E85.-)
myopathy in polyarteritis nodosa (M30.0)
myopathy in rheumatoid arthritis (M05.32)
myopathy in scleroderma (M34.-)
myopathy in Sjögren's syndrome (M35.03)
myopathy in systemic lupus erythematosus (M32.-)

M60 Myositis
Excludes2: *inclusion body myositis [IBM] (G72.41)*
+ **M60.0 Infective myositis**
Tropical pyomyositis
Use additional code (B95-B97) to identify infectious agent
+ **M60.00 Infective myositis, unspecified site**
CC **M60.000 Infective myositis, unspecified right arm**
Infective myositis, right upper limb NOS
CC Exclusion see Appendix A PDX collection 0806
CC **M60.001 Infective myositis, unspecified left arm**
Infective myositis, left upper limb NOS
CC Exclusion see Appendix A PDX collection 0806
CC **M60.002 Infective myositis, unspecified arm**
Infective myositis, upper limb NOS
CC Exclusion see Appendix A PDX collection 0806
CC **M60.003 Infective myositis, unspecified right leg**
Infective myositis, right lower limb NOS
CC Exclusion see Appendix A PDX collection 0806
CC **M60.004 Infective myositis, unspecified left leg**
Infective myositis, left lower limb NOS
CC Exclusion see Appendix A PDX collection 0806
CC **M60.005 Infective myositis, unspecified leg**
Infective myositis, lower limb NOS
CC Exclusion see Appendix A PDX collection 0806
CC **M60.009 Infective myositis, unspecified site**
CC Exclusion see Appendix A PDX collection 0806
+ **M60.01 Infective myositis, shoulder**
CC **M60.011 Infective myositis, right shoulder**
CC Exclusion see Appendix A PDX collection 0806
CC **M60.012 Infective myositis, left shoulder**
CC Exclusion see Appendix A PDX collection 0806
CC **M60.019 Infective myositis, unspecified shoulder**
CC Exclusion see Appendix A PDX collection 0806
+ **M60.02 Infective myositis, upper arm**
CC **M60.021 Infective myositis, right upper arm**
CC Exclusion see Appendix A PDX collection 0806
CC **M60.022 Infective myositis, left upper arm**
CC Exclusion see Appendix A PDX collection 0806
CC **M60.029 Infective myositis, unspecified upper arm**
CC Exclusion see Appendix A PDX collection 0806
+ **M60.03 Infective myositis, forearm**
CC **M60.031 Infective myositis, right forearm**
CC Exclusion see Appendix A PDX collection 0806
CC **M60.032 Infective myositis, left forearm**
CC Exclusion see Appendix A PDX collection 0806
CC **M60.039 Infective myositis, unspecified forearm**
CC Exclusion see Appendix A PDX collection 0806

+ **M60.04 Infective myositis, hand and fingers**
CC **M60.041 Infective myositis, right hand**
CC Exclusion see Appendix A PDX collection
CC **M60.042 Infective myositis, left hand**
CC Exclusion see Appendix A PDX collection
CC **M60.043 Infective myositis, unspecified hand**
CC Exclusion see Appendix A PDX collection
CC **M60.044 Infective myositis, right finger(s)**
CC Exclusion see Appendix A PDX collection
CC **M60.045 Infective myositis, left finger(s)**
CC Exclusion see Appendix A PDX collection
CC **M60.046 Infective myositis, unspecified finger(s)**
CC Exclusion see Appendix A PDX collection
+ **M60.05 Infective myositis, thigh**
CC **M60.051 Infective myositis, right thigh**
CC Exclusion see Appendix A PDX collection
CC **M60.052 Infective myositis, left thigh**
CC Exclusion see Appendix A PDX collection
CC **M60.059 Infective myositis, unspecified thigh**
CC Exclusion see Appendix A PDX collection
+ **M60.06 Infective myositis, lower leg**
CC **M60.061 Infective myositis, right lower leg**
CC Exclusion see Appendix A PDX collection
CC **M60.062 Infective myositis, left lower leg**
CC Exclusion see Appendix A PDX collection
CC **M60.069 Infective myositis, unspecified lower leg**
CC Exclusion see Appendix A PDX collection
+ **M60.07 Infective myositis, ankle, foot and toes**
CC **M60.070 Infective myositis, right ankle**
CC Exclusion see Appendix A PDX collection
CC **M60.071 Infective myositis, left ankle**
CC Exclusion see Appendix A PDX collection
CC **M60.072 Infective myositis, unspecified ankle**
CC Exclusion see Appendix A PDX collection
CC **M60.073 Infective myositis, right foot**
CC Exclusion see Appendix A PDX collection
CC **M60.074 Infective myositis, left foot**
CC Exclusion see Appendix A PDX collection
CC **M60.075 Infective myositis, unspecified foot**
CC Exclusion see Appendix A PDX collection
CC **M60.076 Infective myositis, right toe(s)**
CC Exclusion see Appendix A PDX collection
CC **M60.077 Infective myositis, left toe(s)**
CC Exclusion see Appendix A PDX collection
CC **M60.078 Infective myositis, unspecified toe(s)**
CC Exclusion see Appendix A PDX collection
CC **M60.08 Infective myositis, other site**
CC Exclusion see Appendix A PDX collection 0806
CC **M60.09 Infective myositis, multiple sites**
CC Exclusion see Appendix A PDX collection 0806
+ **M60.1 Interstitial myositis**
M60.10 Interstitial myositis of unspecified site
+ **M60.11 Interstitial myositis, shoulder**
M60.111 Interstitial myositis, right shoulder
M60.112 Interstitial myositis, left shoulder
M60.119 Interstitial myositis, unspecified shoulde
+ **M60.12 Interstitial myositis, upper arm**
M60.121 Interstitial myositis, right upper arm
M60.122 Interstitial myositis, left upper arm
M60.129 Interstitial myositis, unspecified upper a
+ **M60.13 Interstitial myositis, forearm**
M60.131 Interstitial myositis, right forearm
M60.132 Interstitial myositis, left forearm
M60.139 Interstitial myositis, unspecified forearm
+ **M60.14 Interstitial myositis, hand**
M60.141 Interstitial myositis, right hand
M60.142 Interstitial myositis, left hand
M60.149 Interstitial myositis, unspecifiedhand
+ **M60.15 Interstitial myositis, thigh**
M60.151 Interstitial myositis, right thigh
M60.152 Interstitial myositis, left thigh
M60.159 Interstitial myositis, unspecifiedthigh
+ **M60.16 Interstitial myositis, lower leg**
M60.161 Interstitial myositis, right lower leg
M60.162 Interstitial myositis, left lower leg
M60.169 Interstitial myositis, unspecified lower le
+ **M60.17 Interstitial myositis, ankle and foot**
M60.171 Interstitial myositis, right ankle and foot
M60.172 Interstitial myositis, left ankle and foot
M60.179 Interstitial myositis, unspecified ankle and foot
M60.18 Interstitial myositis, other site
M60.19 Interstitial myositis, multiple sites

+ **M60.2 Foreign body granuloma of soft tissue, not elsewhere classified**
Use additional code to identify the type of retained foreign body (Z18.-)
Excludes1: *foreign body granuloma of skin and subcutaneous tissue (L92.3)*
M60.20 Foreign body granuloma of soft tissue, not elsewhere classified, unspecified site
+ **M60.21 Foreign body granuloma of soft tissue, not elsewhere classified, shoulder**
M60.211 Foreign body granuloma of soft tissue, not elsewhere classified, right shoulder
M60.212 Foreign body granuloma of soft tissue, not elsewhere classified, left shoulder
M60.219 Foreign body granuloma of soft tissue, not elsewhere classified, unspecified shoulder
+ **M60.22 Foreign body granuloma of soft tissue, not elsewhere classified, upper arm**
M60.221 Foreign body granuloma of soft tissue, not elsewhere classified, right upper arm
M60.222 Foreign body granuloma of soft tissue, not elsewhere classified, left upper arm
M60.229 Foreign body granuloma of soft tissue, not elsewhere classified, unspecified upper arm
+ **M60.23 Foreign body granuloma of soft tissue, not elsewhere classified, forearm**
M60.231 Foreign body granuloma of soft tissue, not elsewhere classified, right forearm
M60.232 Foreign body granuloma of soft tissue, not elsewhere classified, left forearm
M60.239 Foreign body granuloma of soft tissue, not elsewhere classified, unspecified forearm
+ **M60.24 Foreign body granuloma of soft tissue, not elsewhere classified, hand**
M60.241 Foreign body granuloma of soft tissue, not elsewhere classified, right hand
M60.242 Foreign body granuloma of soft tissue, not elsewhere classified, left hand
M60.249 Foreign body granuloma of soft tissue, not elsewhere classified, unspecified hand
+ **M60.25 Foreign body granuloma of soft tissue, not elsewhere classified, thigh**
M60.251 Foreign body granuloma of soft tissue, not elsewhere classified, right thigh
M60.252 Foreign body granuloma of soft tissue, not elsewhere classified, left thigh
M60.259 Foreign body granuloma of soft tissue, not elsewhere classified, unspecified thigh
+ **M60.26 Foreign body granuloma of soft tissue, not elsewhere classified, lower leg**
M60.261 Foreign body granuloma of soft tissue, not elsewhere classified, right lower leg
M60.262 Foreign body granuloma of soft tissue, not elsewhere classified, left lower leg
M60.269 Foreign body granuloma of soft tissue, not elsewhere classified, unspecified lower leg
+ **M60.27 Foreign body granuloma of soft tissue, not elsewhere classified, ankle and foot**
M60.271 Foreign body granuloma of soft tissue, not elsewhere classified, right ankle and foot
M60.272 Foreign body granuloma of soft tissue, not elsewhere classified, left ankle and foot
M60.279 Foreign body granuloma of soft tissue, not elsewhere classified, unspecified ankle and foot
M60.28 Foreign body granuloma of soft tissue, not elsewhere classified, other site
+ **M60.8 Other myositis**
M60.80 Other myositis, unspecified site
+ **M60.81 Other myositis shoulder**
M60.811 Other myositis, right shoulder
M60.812 Other myositis, left shoulder
M60.819 Other myositis, unspecified shoulder
+ **M60.82 Other myositis, upper arm**
M60.821 Other myositis, right upper arm
M60.822 Other myositis, left upper arm
M60.829 Other myositis, unspecified upper arm
+ **M60.83 Other myositis, forearm**
M60.831 Other myositis, right forearm
M60.832 Other myositis, left forearm
M60.839 Other myositis, unspecified forearm
+ **M60.84 Other myositis, hand**
M60.841 Other myositis, right hand
M60.842 Other myositis, left hand
M60.849 Other myositis, unspecified hand
+ **M60.85 Other myositis, thigh**
M60.851 Other myositis, right thigh
M60.852 Other myositis, left thigh
M60.859 Other myositis, unspecified thigh
+ **M60.86 Other myositis, lower leg**
M60.861 Other myositis, right lower leg
M60.862 Other myositis, left lower leg
M60.869 Other myositis, unspecified lower leg
+ **M60.87 Other myositis, ankle and foot**
M60.871 Other myositis, right ankle and foot
M60.872 Other myositis, left ankle and foot
M60.879 Other myositis, unspecified ankle and foot
M60.88 Other myositis, other site
M60.89 Other myositis, multiple sites
M60.9 Myositis, unspecified

M61 Calcification and ossification of muscle

+ **M61.0 Myositis ossificans traumatica**
M61.00 Myositis ossificans traumatica, unspecified site
+ **M61.01 Myositis ossificans traumatica, shoulder**
M61.011 Myositis ossificans traumatica, right shoulder
M61.012 Myositis ossificans traumatica, left shoulder
M61.019 Myositis ossificans traumatica, unspecified shoulder
+ **M61.02 Myositis ossificans traumatica, upper arm**
M61.021 Myositis ossificans traumatica, right upper arm
M61.022 Myositis ossificans traumatica, left upper arm
M61.029 Myositis ossificans traumatica, unspecified upper arm
+ **M61.03 Myositis ossificans traumatica, forearm**
M61.031 Myositis ossificans traumatica, right forearm
M61.032 Myositis ossificans traumatica, left forearm
M61.039 Myositis ossificans traumatica, unspecified forearm
+ **M61.04 Myositis ossificans traumatica, hand**
M61.041 Myositis ossificans traumatica, right hand
M61.042 Myositis ossificans traumatica, left hand
M61.049 Myositis ossificans traumatica, unspecified hand
+ **M61.05 Myositis ossificans traumatica, thigh**
M61.051 Myositis ossificans traumatica, right thigh
M61.052 Myositis ossificans traumatica, left thigh
M61.059 Myositis ossificans traumatica, unspecified thigh
+ **M61.06 Myositis ossificans traumatica, lower leg**
M61.061 Myositis ossificans traumatica, right lower leg
M61.062 Myositis ossificans traumatica, left lower leg
M61.069 Myositis ossificans traumatica, unspecified lower leg
+ **M61.07 Myositis ossificans traumatica, ankle and foot**
M61.071 Myositis ossificans traumatica, right ankle and foot
M61.072 Myositis ossificans traumatica, left ankle and foot
M61.079 Myositis ossificans traumatica, unspecified ankle and foot
M61.08 Myositis ossificans traumatica, other site
M61.09 Myositis ossificans traumatica, multiple sites
+ **M61.1 Myositis ossificans progressiva**
Fibrodysplasia ossificans progressiva
M61.10 Myositis ossificans progressiva, unspecified site
+ **M61.11 Myositis ossificans progressiva, shoulder**
M61.111 Myositis ossificans progressiva, right shoulder
M61.112 Myositis ossificans progressiva, left shoulder
M61.119 Myositis ossificans progressiva, unspecified shoulder
+ **M61.12 Myositis ossificans progressiva, upper arm**
M61.121 Myositis ossificans progressiva, right upper arm
M61.122 Myositis ossificans progressiva, left upper arm
M61.129 Myositis ossificans progressiva, unspecified arm

+ **M61.13** Myositis ossificans progressiva, forearm
M61.131 Myositis ossificans progressiva, right forearm
M61.132 Myositis ossificans progressiva, left forearm
M61.139 Myositis ossificans progressiva, unspecified forearm
+ **M61.14** Myositis ossificans progressiva, hand and finger(s)
M61.141 Myositis ossificans progressiva, right hand
M61.142 Myositis ossificans progressiva, left hand
M61.143 Myositis ossificans progressiva, unspecified hand
M61.144 Myositis ossificans progressiva, right finger(s)
M61.145 Myositis ossificans progressiva, left finger(s)
M61.146 Myositis ossificans progressiva, unspecified finger(s)
+ **M61.15** Myositis ossificans progressiva, thigh
M61.151 Myositis ossificans progressiva, right thigh
M61.152 Myositis ossificans progressiva, left thigh
M61.159 Myositis ossificans progressiva, unspecified thigh
+ **M61.16** Myositis ossificans progressiva, lower leg
M61.161 Myositis ossificans progressiva, right lower leg
M61.162 Myositis ossificans progressiva, left lower leg
M61.169 Myositis ossificans progressiva, unspecified lower leg
+ **M61.17** Myositis ossificans progressiva, ankle, foot and toe(s)
M61.171 Myositis ossificans progressiva, right ankle
M61.172 Myositis ossificans progressiva, left ankle
M61.173 Myositis ossificans progressiva, unspecified ankle
M61.174 Myositis ossificans progressiva, right foot
M61.175 Myositis ossificans progressiva, left foot
M61.176 Myositis ossificans progressiva, unspecified foot
M61.177 Myositis ossificans progressiva, right toe(s)
M61.178 Myositis ossificans progressiva, left toe(s)
M61.179 Myositis ossificans progressiva, unspecified toe(s)
M61.18 Myositis ossificans progressiva, other site
M61.19 Myositis ossificans progressiva, multiple sites
+ **M61.2** Paralytic calcification and ossification of muscle
Myositis ossificans associated with quadriplegia or paraplegia
M61.20 Paralytic calcification and ossification of muscle, unspecified site
+ **M61.21** Paralytic calcification and ossification of muscle, shoulder
M61.211 Paralytic calcification and ossification of muscle, right shoulder
M61.212 Paralytic calcification and ossification of muscle, left shoulder
M61.219 Paralytic calcification and ossification of muscle, unspecified shoulder
+ **M61.22** Paralytic calcification and ossification of muscle, upper arm
M61.221 Paralytic calcification and ossification of muscle, right upper arm
M61.222 Paralytic calcification and ossification of muscle, left upper arm
M61.229 Paralytic calcification and ossification of muscle, unspecified upper arm
+ **M61.23** Paralytic calcification and ossification of muscle, forearm
M61.231 Paralytic calcification and ossification of muscle, right forearm
M61.232 Paralytic calcification and ossification of muscle, left forearm
M61.239 Paralytic calcification and ossification of muscle, unspecified forearm
+ **M61.24** Paralytic calcification and ossification of muscle, hand
M61.241 Paralytic calcification and ossification of muscle, right hand
M61.242 Paralytic calcification and ossification of muscle, left hand
M61.249 Paralytic calcification and ossification of muscle, unspecified hand
+ **M61.25** Paralytic calcification and ossification of muscle, thigh
M61.251 Paralytic calcification and ossification of muscle, right thigh
M61.252 Paralytic calcification and ossification of muscle, left thigh
M61.259 Paralytic calcification and ossification of muscle, unspecified thigh
+ **M61.26** Paralytic calcification and ossification of muscle, lo[wer] leg
M61.261 Paralytic calcification and ossification of muscle, right lower leg
M61.262 Paralytic calcification and ossification of muscle, left lower leg
M61.269 Paralytic calcification and ossification of muscle, unspecified lower leg
+ **M61.27** Paralytic calcification and ossification of muscle, an[kle] and foot
M61.271 Paralytic calcification and ossification of muscle, right ankle and foot
M61.272 Paralytic calcification and ossification of muscle, left ankle and foot
M61.279 Paralytic calcification and ossification of muscle, unspecified ankle and foot
M61.28 Paralytic calcification and ossification of muscle, ot[her] site
M61.29 Paralytic calcification and ossification of muscle, multiple sites
+ **M61.3** Calcification and ossification of muscles associated with burn[s]
Myositis ossificans associated with burns
M61.30 Calcification and ossification of muscles associated with burns, unspecified site
+ **M61.31** Calcification and ossification of muscles associated with burns, shoulder
M61.311 Calcification and ossification of muscles associated with burns, right shoulder
M61.312 Calcification and ossification of muscles associated with burns, left shoulder
M61.319 Calcification and ossification of muscles associated with burns, unspecified should[er]
+ **M61.32** Calcification and ossification of muscles associated with burns, upper arm
M61.321 Calcification and ossification of muscles associated with burns, right upper arm
M61.322 Calcification and ossification of muscles associated with burns, left upper arm
M61.329 Calcification and ossification of muscles associated with burns, unspecified upper arm
+ **M61.33** Calcification and ossification of muscles associated with burns, forearm
M61.331 Calcification and ossification of muscles associated with burns, right forearm
M61.332 Calcification and ossification of muscles associated with burns, left forearm
M61.339 Calcification and ossification of muscles associated with burns, unspecified forear[m]
+ **M61.34** Calcification and ossification of muscles associated with burns, hand
M61.341 Calcification and ossification of muscles associated with burns, right hand
M61.342 Calcification and ossification of muscles associated with burns, left hand
M61.349 Calcification and ossification of muscles associated with burns, unspecified hand
+ **M61.35** Calcification and ossification of muscles associated with burns, thigh
M61.351 Calcification and ossification of muscles associated with burns, right thigh
M61.352 Calcification and ossification of muscles associated with burns, left thigh
M61.359 Calcification and ossification of muscles associated with burns, unspecified thigh
+ **M61.36** Calcification and ossification of muscles associated with burns, lower leg
M61.361 Calcification and ossification of muscles associated with burns, right lower leg
M61.362 Calcification and ossification of muscles associated with burns, left lower leg
M61.369 Calcification and ossification of muscles associated with burns, unspecified lower l[eg]
+ **M61.37** Calcification and ossification of muscles associated with burns, ankle and foot
M61.371 Calcification and ossification of muscles associated with burns, right ankle and foo[t]

M61.372 **Calcification and ossification of muscles associated with burns, left ankle and foot**
M61.379 **Calcification and ossification of muscles associated with burns, unspecified ankle and foot**
M61.38 **Calcification and ossification of muscles associated with burns, other site**
M61.39 **Calcification and ossification of muscles associated with burns, multiple sites**
+ **M61.4** **Other calcification of muscle**
Excludes1: *calcific tendinitis NOS (M65.2-)*
calcific tendinitis of shoulder (M75.3)
M61.40 **Other calcification of muscle, unspecified site**
+ **M61.41** **Other calcification of muscle, shoulder**
M61.411 **Other calcification of muscle, right shoulder**
M61.412 **Other calcification of muscle, left shoulder**
M61.419 **Other calcification of muscle, unspecified shoulder**
+ **M61.42** **Other calcification of muscle, upper arm**
M61.421 **Other calcification of muscle, right upper arm**
M61.422 **Other calcification of muscle, left upper arm**
M61.429 **Other calcification of muscle, unspecified upper arm**
+ **M61.43** **Other calcification of muscle, forearm**
M61.431 **Other calcification of muscle, right forearm**
M61.432 **Other calcification of muscle, left forearm**
M61.439 **Other calcification of muscle, unspecified forearm**
+ **M61.44** **Other calcification of muscle, hand**
M61.441 **Other calcification of muscle, right hand**
M61.442 **Other calcification of muscle, left hand**
M61.449 **Other calcification of muscle, unspecified hand**
+ **M61.45** **Other calcification of muscle, thigh**
M61.451 **Other calcification of muscle, right thigh**
M61.452 **Other calcification of muscle, left thigh**
M61.459 **Other calcification of muscle, unspecified thigh**
+ **M61.46** **Other calcification of muscle, lower leg**
M61.461 **Other calcification of muscle, right lower leg**
M61.462 **Other calcification of muscle, left lower leg**
M61.469 **Other calcification of muscle, unspecified lower leg**
+ **M61.47** **Other calcification of muscle, ankle and foot**
M61.471 **Other calcification of muscle, right ankle and foot**
M61.472 **Other calcification of muscle, left ankle and foot**
M61.479 **Other calcification of muscle, unspecified ankle and foot**
M61.48 **Other calcification of muscle, other site**
M61.49 **Other calcification of muscle, multiple sites**
+ **M61.5** **Other ossification of muscle**
M61.50 **Other ossification of muscle, unspecified site**
+ **M61.51** **Other ossification of muscle, shoulder**
M61.511 **Other ossification of muscle, right shoulder**
M61.512 **Other ossification of muscle, left shoulder**
M61.519 **Other ossification of muscle, unspecified shoulder**
+ **M61.52** **Other ossification of muscle, upper arm**
M61.521 **Other ossification of muscle, right upper arm**
M61.522 **Other ossification of muscle, left upper arm**
M61.529 **Other ossification of muscle, unspecified upper arm**
+ **M61.53** **Other ossification of muscle, forearm**
M61.531 **Other ossification of muscle, right forearm**
M61.532 **Other ossification of muscle, left forearm**
M61.539 **Other ossification of muscle, unspecified forearm**
+ **M61.54** **Other ossification of muscle, hand**
M61.541 **Other ossification of muscle, right hand**
M61.542 **Other ossification of muscle, left hand**
M61.549 **Other ossification of muscle, unspecified hand**
+ **M61.55** **Other ossification of muscle, thigh**
M61.551 **Other ossification of muscle, right thigh**
M61.552 **Other ossification of muscle, left thigh**
M61.559 **Other ossification of muscle, unspecified thigh**
+ **M61.56** **Other ossification of muscle, lower leg**
M61.561 **Other ossification of muscle, right lower leg**
M61.562 **Other ossification of muscle, left lower leg**
M61.569 **Other ossification of muscle, unspecified lower leg**
+ **M61.57** **Other ossification of muscle, ankle and foot**
M61.571 **Other ossification of muscle, right ankle and foot**
M61.572 **Other ossification of muscle, left ankle and foot**
M61.579 **Other ossification of muscle, unspecified ankle and foot**
M61.58 **Other ossification of muscle, other site**
M61.59 **Other ossification of muscle, multiple sites**
M61.9 **Calcification and ossification of muscle, unspecified**

M62 Other disorders of muscle

Excludes1: *alcoholic myopathy (G72.1)*
cramp and spasm (R25.2)
drug-induced myopathy (G72.0)
myalgia (M79.1)
stiff-man syndrome (G25.82)
Excludes2: *nontraumatic hematoma of muscle (M79.81)*
+ **M62.0** **Separation of muscle (nontraumatic)**
Diastasis of muscle
Excludes1: *diastasis recti complicating pregnancy, labor and delivery (O71.8)*
traumatic separation of muscle- see strain of muscle by body region
M62.00 **Separation of muscle (nontraumatic), unspecified site**
+ **M62.01** **Separation of muscle (nontraumatic), shoulder**
M62.011 **Separation of muscle (nontraumatic), right shoulder**
M62.012 **Separation of muscle (nontraumatic), left shoulder**
M62.019 **Separation of muscle (nontraumatic), unspecified shoulder**
+ **M62.02** **Separation of muscle (nontraumatic), upper arm**
M62.021 **Separation of muscle (nontraumatic), right upper arm**
M62.022 **Separation of muscle (nontraumatic), left upper arm**
M62.029 **Separation of muscle (nontraumatic), unspecified upper arm**
+ **M62.03** **Separation of muscle (nontraumatic), forearm**
M62.031 **Separation of muscle (nontraumatic), right forearm**
M62.032 **Separation of muscle (nontraumatic), left forearm**
M62.039 **Separation of muscle (nontraumatic), unspecified forearm**
+ **M62.04** **Separation of muscle (nontraumatic), hand**
M62.041 **Separation of muscle (nontraumatic), right hand**
M62.042 **Separation of muscle (nontraumatic), left hand**
M62.049 **Separation of muscle (nontraumatic), unspecified hand**
+ **M62.05** **Separation of muscle (nontraumatic), thigh**
M62.051 **Separation of muscle (nontraumatic), right thigh**
M62.052 **Separation of muscle (nontraumatic), left thigh**
M62.059 **Separation of muscle (nontraumatic), unspecified thigh**
+ **M62.06** **Separation of muscle (nontraumatic), lower leg**
M62.061 **Separation of muscle (nontraumatic), right lower leg**
M62.062 **Separation of muscle (nontraumatic), left lower leg**
M62.069 **Separation of muscle (nontraumatic), unspecified lower leg**
+ **M62.07** **Separation of muscle (nontraumatic), ankle and foot**
M62.071 **Separation of muscle (nontraumatic), right ankle and foot**
M62.072 **Separation of muscle (nontraumatic), left ankle and foot**
M62.079 **Separation of muscle (nontraumatic), unspecified ankle and foot**
M62.08 **Separation of muscle (nontraumatic), other site**

\+ **M62.1 Other rupture of muscle (nontraumatic)**
Excludes1: *traumatic rupture of muscle - see strain of muscle by body region*
Excludes2: *rupture of tendon (M66.-)*
M62.10 Other rupture of muscle (nontraumatic), unspecified site
\+ **M62.11 Other rupture of muscle (nontraumatic), shoulder**
M62.111 Other rupture of muscle (nontraumatic), right shoulder
M62.112 Other rupture of muscle (nontraumatic), left shoulder
M62.119 Other rupture of muscle (nontraumatic), unspecified shoulder
\+ **M62.12 Other rupture of muscle (nontraumatic), upper arm**
M62.121 Other rupture of muscle (nontraumatic), right upper arm
M62.122 Other rupture of muscle (nontraumatic), left upper arm
M62.129 Other rupture of muscle (nontraumatic), unspecified upper arm
\+ **M62.13 Other rupture of muscle (nontraumatic), forearm**
M62.131 Other rupture of muscle (nontraumatic), right forearm
M62.132 Other rupture of muscle (nontraumatic), left forearm
M62.139 Other rupture of muscle (nontraumatic), unspecified forearm
\+ **M62.14 Other rupture of muscle (nontraumatic), hand**
M62.141 Other rupture of muscle (nontraumatic), right hand
M62.142 Other rupture of muscle (nontraumatic), left hand
M62.149 Other rupture of muscle (nontraumatic), unspecified hand
\+ **M62.15 Other rupture of muscle (nontraumatic), thigh**
M62.151 Other rupture of muscle (nontraumatic), right thigh
M62.152 Other rupture of muscle (nontraumatic), left thigh
M62.159 Other rupture of muscle (nontraumatic), unspecified thigh
\+ **M62.16 Other rupture of muscle (nontraumatic), lower leg**
M62.161 Other rupture of muscle (nontraumatic), right lower leg
M62.162 Other rupture of muscle (nontraumatic), left lower leg
M62.169 Other rupture of muscle (nontraumatic), unspecified lower leg
\+ **M62.17 Other rupture of muscle (nontraumatic), ankle and foot**
M62.171 Other rupture of muscle (nontraumatic), right ankle and foot
M62.172 Other rupture of muscle (nontraumatic), left ankle and foot
M62.179 Other rupture of muscle (nontraumatic), unspecified ankle and foot
M62.18 Other rupture of muscle (nontraumatic), other site
\+ **M62.2 Nontraumatic ischemic infarction of muscle**
Excludes1: *compartment syndrome (traumatic) (T79.A-)*
nontraumatic compartment syndrome (M79.A-)
traumatic ischemia of muscle (T79.6)
rhabdomyolysis (M62.82)
Volkmann's ischemic contracture (T79.6)
M62.20 Nontraumatic ischemic infarction of muscle, unspecified site
\+ **M62.21 Nontraumatic ischemic infarction of muscle, shoulder**
M62.211 Nontraumatic ischemic infarction of muscle, right shoulder
M62.212 Nontraumatic ischemic infarction of muscle, left shoulder
M62.219 Nontraumatic ischemic infarction of muscle, unspecified shoulder
\+ **M62.22 Nontraumatic ischemic infarction of muscle, upper arm**
M62.221 Nontraumatic ischemic infarction of muscle, right upper arm
M62.222 Nontraumatic ischemic infarction of muscle, left upper arm
M62.229 Nontraumatic ischemic infarction of muscle, unspecified upper arm
\+ **M62.23 Nontraumatic ischemic infarction of muscle, forear**
M62.231 Nontraumatic ischemic infarction of mus right forearm
M62.232 Nontraumatic ischemic infarction of mus left forearm
M62.239 Nontraumatic ischemic infarction of mus unspecified forearm
\+ **M62.24 Nontraumatic ischemic infarction of muscle, hand**
M62.241 Nontraumatic ischemic infarction of mus right hand
M62.242 Nontraumatic ischemic infarction of mus left hand
M62.249 Nontraumatic ischemic infarction of mus unspecified hand
\+ **M62.25 Nontraumatic ischemic infarction of muscle, thigh**
M62.251 Nontraumatic ischemic infarction of mus right thigh
M62.252 Nontraumatic ischemic infarction of mus left thigh
M62.259 Nontraumatic ischemic infarction of mus unspecified thigh
\+ **M62.26 Nontraumatic ischemic infarction of muscle, lower**
M62.261 Nontraumatic ischemic infarction of mus right lower leg
M62.262 Nontraumatic ischemic infarction of mus left lower leg
M62.269 Nontraumatic ischemic infarction of mus unspecified lower leg
\+ **M62.27 Nontraumatic ischemic infarction of muscle, ankle and foot**
M62.271 Nontraumatic ischemic infarction of mus right ankle and foot
M62.272 Nontraumatic ischemic infarction of mus left ankle and foot
M62.279 Nontraumatic ischemic infarction of mus unspecified ankle and foot
M62.28 Nontraumatic ischemic infarction of muscle, other
M62.3 Immobility syndrome (paraplegic)
\+ **M62.4 Contracture of muscle**
Contracture of tendon (sheath)
Excludes1: *contracture of joint (M24.5-)*
M62.40 Contracture of muscle, unspecified site
\+ **M62.41 Contracture of muscle, shoulder**
M62.411 Contracture of muscle, right shoulder
M62.412 Contracture of muscle, left shoulder
M62.419 Contracture of muscle, unspecified should
\+ **M62.42 Contracture of muscle, upper arm**
M62.421 Contracture of muscle, right upper arm
M62.422 Contracture of muscle, left upper arm
M62.429 Contracture of muscle, unspecified upper arm
\+ **M62.43 Contracture of muscle, forearm**
M62.431 Contracture of muscle, right forearm
M62.432 Contracture of muscle, left forearm
M62.439 Contracture of muscle, unspecified forear
\+ **M62.44 Contracture of muscle, hand**
M62.441 Contracture of muscle, right hand
M62.442 Contracture of muscle, left hand
M62.449 Contracture of muscle, unspecified hand
\+ **M62.45 Contracture of muscle, thigh**
M62.451 Contracture of muscle, right thigh
M62.452 Contracture of muscle, left thigh
M62.459 Contracture of muscle, unspecified thigh
\+ **M62.46 Contracture of muscle, lower leg**
M62.461 Contracture of muscle, right lower leg
M62.462 Contracture of muscle, left lower leg
M62.469 Contracture of muscle, unspecified lower
\+ **M62.47 Contracture of muscle, ankle and foot**
M62.471 Contracture of muscle, right ankle and fo
M62.472 Contracture of muscle, left ankle and foot
M62.479 Contracture of muscle, unspecified ankle and foot
M62.48 Contracture of muscle, other site
M62.49 Contracture of muscle, multiple sites

+ **M62.5 Muscle wasting and atrophy, not elsewhere classified**
  Disuse atrophy NEC
  Excludes1: *neuralgic amyotrophy (G54.5)*
  progressive muscular atrophy (G12.29)
  Excludes2: *pelvic muscle wasting (N81.84)*
  M62.50 Muscle wasting and atrophy, not elsewhere classified, unspecified site
  + **M62.51 Muscle wasting and atrophy, not elsewhere classified, shoulder**
    M62.511 Muscle wasting and atrophy, not elsewhere classified, right shoulder
    M62.512 Muscle wasting and atrophy, not elsewhere classified, left shoulder
    M62.519 Muscle wasting and atrophy, not elsewhere classified, unspecified shoulder
  + **M62.52 Muscle wasting and atrophy, not elsewhere classified, upper arm**
    M62.521 Muscle wasting and atrophy, not elsewhere classified, right upper arm
    M62.522 Muscle wasting and atrophy, not elsewhere classified, left upper arm
    M62.529 Muscle wasting and atrophy, not elsewhere classified, unspecified upper arm
  + **M62.53 Muscle wasting and atrophy, not elsewhere classified, forearm**
    M62.531 Muscle wasting and atrophy, not elsewhere classified, right forearm
    M62.532 Muscle wasting and atrophy, not elsewhere classified, left forearm
    M62.539 Muscle wasting and atrophy, not elsewhere classified, unspecified forearm
  + **M62.54 Muscle wasting and atrophy, not elsewhere classified, hand**
    M62.541 Muscle wasting and atrophy, not elsewhere classified, right hand
    M62.542 Muscle wasting and atrophy, not elsewhere classified, left hand
    M62.549 Muscle wasting and atrophy, not elsewhere classified, unspecified hand
  + **M62.55 Muscle wasting and atrophy, not elsewhere classified, thigh**
    M62.551 Muscle wasting and atrophy, not elsewhere classified, right thigh
    M62.552 Muscle wasting and atrophy, not elsewhere classified, left thigh
    M62.559 Muscle wasting and atrophy, not elsewhere classified, unspecified thigh
  + **M62.56 Muscle wasting and atrophy, not elsewhere classified, lower leg**
    M62.561 Muscle wasting and atrophy, not elsewhere classified, right lower leg
    M62.562 Muscle wasting and atrophy, not elsewhere classified, left lower leg
    M62.569 Muscle wasting and atrophy, not elsewhere classified, unspecified lower leg
  + **M62.57 Muscle wasting and atrophy, not elsewhere classified, ankle and foot**
    M62.571 Muscle wasting and atrophy, not elsewhere classified, right ankle and foot
    M62.572 Muscle wasting and atrophy, not elsewhere classified, left ankle and foot
    M62.579 Muscle wasting and atrophy, not elsewhere classified, unspecified ankle and foot
  M62.58 Muscle wasting and atrophy, not elsewhere classified, other site
  M62.59 Muscle wasting and atrophy, not elsewhere classified, multiple sites

+ **M62.8 Other specified disorders of muscle**
  Excludes2: *nontraumatic hematoma of muscle (M79.81)*
  M62.81 Muscle weakness (generalized)
  CC **M62.82 Rhabdomyolysis**
  Excludes1: *traumatic rhabdomyolysis (T79.6)*
  CC Exclusion see Appendix A PDX collection 0892
  + **M62.83 Muscle spasm**
    M62.830 Muscle spasm of back
    M62.831 Muscle spasm of calf
    Charley-horse
    M62.838 Other muscle spasm
  M62.89 Other specified disorders of muscle
  Muscle (sheath) hernia

M62.9 Disorder of muscle, unspecified

M63 Disorders of muscle in diseases classified elsewhere
Code first underlying disease, such as:
leprosy (A30.-)
neoplasm (C49.-, C79.89, D21.-, D48.1)
schistosomiasis (B65.-)
trichinellosis (B75)
Excludes1: *myopathy in cysticercosis (B69.81)*
myopathy in endocrine diseases (G73.7)
myopathy in metabolic diseases (G73.7)
myopathy in sarcoidosis (D86.87)
myopathy in secondary syphilis (A51.49)
myopathy in syphilis (late) (A52.78)
myopathy in toxoplasmosis (B58.82)
myopathy in tuberculosis (A18.09)

+ **M63.8 Disorders of muscle in diseases classified elsewhere**
  M63.80 Disorders of muscle in diseases classified elsewhere, unspecified site
  + **M63.81 Disorders of muscle in diseases classified elsewhere, shoulder**
    M63.811 Disorders of muscle in diseases classified elsewhere, right shoulder
    M63.812 Disorders of muscle in diseases classified elsewhere, left shoulder
    M63.819 Disorders of muscle in diseases classified elsewhere, unspecified shoulder
  + **M63.82 Disorders of muscle in diseases classified elsewhere, upper arm**
    M63.821 Disorders of muscle in diseases classified elsewhere, right upper arm
    M63.822 Disorders of muscle in diseases classified elsewhere, left upper arm
    M63.829 Disorders of muscle in diseases classified elsewhere, unspecified upper arm
  + **M63.83 Disorders of muscle in diseases classified elsewhere, forearm**
    M63.831 Disorders of muscle in diseases classified elsewhere, right forearm
    M63.832 Disorders of muscle in diseases classified elsewhere, left forearm
    M63.839 Disorders of muscle in diseases classified elsewhere, unspecified forearm
  + **M63.84 Disorders of muscle in diseases classified elsewhere, hand**
    M63.841 Disorders of muscle in diseases classified elsewhere, right hand
    M63.842 Disorders of muscle in diseases classified elsewhere, left hand
    M63.849 Disorders of muscle in diseases classified elsewhere, unspecified hand
  + **M63.85 Disorders of muscle in diseases classified elsewhere, thigh**
    M63.851 Disorders of muscle in diseases classified elsewhere, right thigh
    M63.852 Disorders of muscle in diseases classified elsewhere, left thigh
    M63.859 Disorders of muscle in diseases classified elsewhere, unspecified thigh
  + **M63.86 Disorders of muscle in diseases classified elsewhere, lower leg**
    M63.861 Disorders of muscle in diseases classified elsewhere, right lower leg
    M63.862 Disorders of muscle in diseases classified elsewhere, left lower leg
    M63.869 Disorders of muscle in diseases classified elsewhere, unspecified lower leg
  + **M63.87 Disorders of muscle in diseases classified elsewhere, ankle and foot**
    M63.871 Disorders of muscle in diseases classified elsewhere, right ankle and foot
    M63.872 Disorders of muscle in diseases classified elsewhere, left ankle and foot
    M63.879 Disorders of muscle in diseases classified elsewhere, unspecified ankle and foot
  M63.88 Disorders of muscle in diseases classified elsewhere, other site
  M63.89 Disorders of muscle in diseases classified elsewhere, multiple sites

Disorders of synovium and tendon (M65-M67)

M65 Synovitis and tenosynovitis

Excludes1: *chronic crepitant synovitis of hand and wrist (M70.0-)*
current injury - see injury of ligament or tendon by body region
soft tissue disorders related to use, overuse and pressure (M70.-)

\+ **M65.0 Abscess of tendon sheath**
Use additional code (B95-B96) to identify bacterial agent.
M65.00 Abscess of tendon sheath, unspecified site
\+ **M65.01 Abscess of tendon sheath, shoulder**
M65.011 Abscess of tendon sheath, right shoulder
M65.012 Abscess of tendon sheath, left shoulder
M65.019 Abscess of tendon sheath, unspecified shoulder
\+ **M65.02 Abscess of tendon sheath, upper arm**
M65.021 Abscess of tendon sheath, right upper arm
M65.022 Abscess of tendon sheath, left upper arm
M65.029 Abscess of tendon sheath, unspecified upper arm
\+ **M65.03 Abscess of tendon sheath, forearm**
M65.031 Abscess of tendon sheath, right forearm
M65.032 Abscess of tendon sheath, left forearm
M65.039 Abscess of tendon sheath, unspecified forearm
\+ **M65.04 Abscess of tendon sheath, hand**
M65.041 Abscess of tendon sheath, right hand
M65.042 Abscess of tendon sheath, left hand
M65.049 Abscess of tendon sheath, unspecified hand
\+ **M65.05 Abscess of tendon sheath, thigh**
M65.051 Abscess of tendon sheath, right thigh
M65.052 Abscess of tendon sheath, left thigh
M65.059 Abscess of tendon sheath, unspecified thigh
\+ **M65.06 Abscess of tendon sheath, lower leg**
M65.061 Abscess of tendon sheath, right lower leg
M65.062 Abscess of tendon sheath, left lower leg
M65.069 Abscess of tendon sheath, unspecified lower leg
\+ **M65.07 Abscess of tendon sheath, ankle and foot**
M65.071 Abscess of tendon sheath, right ankle and foot
M65.072 Abscess of tendon sheath, left ankle and foot
M65.079 Abscess of tendon sheath, unspecified ankle and foot
M65.08 Abscess of tendon sheath, other site
\+ **M65.1 Other infective (teno)synovitis**
M65.10 Other infective (teno)synovitis, unspecified site
\+ **M65.11 Other infective (teno)synovitis, shoulder**
M65.111 Other infective (teno)synovitis, right shoulder
M65.112 Other infective (teno)synovitis, left shoulder
M65.119 Other infective (teno)synovitis, unspecified shoulder
\+ **M65.12 Other infective (teno)synovitis, elbow**
M65.121 Other infective (teno)synovitis, right elbow
M65.122 Other infective (teno)synovitis, left elbow
M65.129 Other infective (teno)synovitis, unspecified elbow
\+ **M65.13 Other infective (teno)synovitis, wrist**
M65.131 Other infective (teno)synovitis, right wrist
M65.132 Other infective (teno)synovitis, left wrist
M65.139 Other infective (teno)synovitis, unspecified wrist
\+ **M65.14 Other infective (teno)synovitis, hand**
M65.141 Other infective (teno)synovitis, right hand
M65.142 Other infective (teno)synovitis, left hand
M65.149 Other infective (teno)synovitis, unspecified hand
\+ **M65.15 Other infective (teno)synovitis, hip**
M65.151 Other infective (teno)synovitis, right hip
M65.152 Other infective (teno)synovitis, left hip
M65.159 Other infective (teno)synovitis, unspecified hip
\+ **M65.16 Other infective (teno)synovitis, knee**
M65.161 Other infective (teno)synovitis, right knee
M65.162 Other infective (teno)synovitis, left knee
M65.169 Other infective (teno)synovitis, unspecified knee
\+ **M65.17 Other infective (teno)synovitis, ankle and foot**
M65.171 Other infective (teno)synovitis, right ankle and foot
M65.172 Other infective (teno)synovitis, left ankle and foot
M65.179 Other infective (teno)synovitis, unspecified ankle and foot
M65.18 Other infective (teno)synovitis, other site
M65.19 Other infective (teno)synovitis, multiple sites
\+ **M65.2 Calcific tendinitis**
Excludes1: *tendinitis as classified in M75-M77*
calcified tendinitis of shoulder (M75.3)
M65.20 Calcific tendinitis, unspecified site
\+ **M65.22 Calcific tendinitis, upper arm**
M65.221 Calcific tendinitis, right upper arm
M65.222 Calcific tendinitis, left upper arm
M65.229 Calcific tendinitis, unspecified upper arm
\+ **M65.23 Calcific tendinitis, forearm**
M65.231 Calcific tendinitis, right forearm
M65.232 Calcific tendinitis, left forearm
M65.239 Calcific tendinitis, unspecified forearm
\+ **M65.24 Calcific tendinitis, hand**
M65.241 Calcific tendinitis, right hand
M65.242 Calcific tendinitis, left hand
M65.249 Calcific tendinitis, unspecified hand
\+ **M65.25 Calcific tendinitis, thigh**
M65.251 Calcific tendinitis, right thigh
M65.252 Calcific tendinitis, left thigh
M65.259 Calcific tendinitis, unspecified thigh
\+ **M65.26 Calcific tendinitis, lower leg**
M65.261 Calcific tendinitis, right lower leg
M65.262 Calcific tendinitis, left lower leg
M65.269 Calcific tendinitis, unspecified lower leg
\+ **M65.27 Calcific tendinitis, ankle and foot**
M65.271 Calcific tendinitis, right ankle and foot
M65.272 Calcific tendinitis, left ankle and foot
M65.279 Calcific tendinitis, unspecified ankle and foot
M65.28 Calcific tendinitis, other site
M65.29 Calcific tendinitis, multiple sites
\+ **M65.3 Trigger finger**
Nodular tendinous disease
M65.30 Trigger finger, unspecified finger
\+ **M65.31 Trigger thumb**
M65.311 Trigger thumb, right thumb
M65.312 Trigger thumb, left thumb
M65.319 Trigger thumb, unspecified thumb
\+ **M65.32 Trigger finger, index finger**
M65.321 Trigger finger, right index finger
M65.322 Trigger finger, left index finger
M65.329 Trigger finger, unspecified index finger
\+ **M65.33 Trigger finger, middle finger**
M65.331 Trigger finger, right middle finger
M65.332 Trigger finger, left middle finger
M65.339 Trigger finger, unspecified middle finger
\+ **M65.34 Trigger finger, ring finger**
M65.341 Trigger finger, right ring finger
M65.342 Trigger finger, left ring finger
M65.349 Trigger finger, unspecified ring finger
\+ **M65.35 Trigger finger, little finger**
M65.351 Trigger finger, right little finger
M65.352 Trigger finger, left little finger
M65.359 Trigger finger, unspecified little finger
M65.4 Radial styloid tenosynovitis [de Quervain]
\+ **M65.8 Other synovitis and tenosynovitis**
M65.80 Other synovitis and tenosynovitis, unspecified site
\+ **M65.81 Other synovitis and tenosynovitis, shoulder**
M65.811 Other synovitis and tenosynovitis, right shoulder
M65.812 Other synovitis and tenosynovitis, left shoulder
M65.819 Other synovitis and tenosynovitis, unspecified shoulder
\+ **M65.82 Other synovitis and tenosynovitis, upper arm**
M65.821 Other synovitis and tenosynovitis, right upper arm
M65.822 Other synovitis and tenosynovitis, left upper arm
M65.829 Other synovitis and tenosynovitis, unspecified upper arm
\+ **M65.83 Other synovitis and tenosynovitis, forearm**
M65.831 Other synovitis and tenosynovitis, right forearm
M65.832 Other synovitis and tenosynovitis, left forearm
M65.839 Other synovitis and tenosynovitis, unspecified forearm

+ M67.32 Transient synovitis, elbow
M67.321 Transient synovitis, right elbow
M67.322 Transient synovitis, left elbow
M67.329 Transient synovitis, unspecified elbow
+ M67.33 Transient synovitis, wrist
M67.331 Transient synovitis, right wrist
M67.332 Transient synovitis, left wrist
M67.339 Transient synovitis, unspecified wrist
+ M67.34 Transient synovitis, hand
M67.341 Transient synovitis, right hand
M67.342 Transient synovitis, left hand
M67.349 Transient synovitis, unspecified hand
+ M67.35 Transient synovitis, hip
M67.351 Transient synovitis, right hip
M67.352 Transient synovitis, left hip
M67.359 Transient synovitis, unspecified hip
+ M67.36 Transient synovitis, knee
M67.361 Transient synovitis, right knee
M67.362 Transient synovitis, left knee
M67.369 Transient synovitis, unspecified knee
+ M67.37 Transient synovitis, ankle and foot
M67.371 Transient synovitis, right ankle and foot
M67.372 Transient synovitis, left ankle and foot
M67.379 Transient synovitis, unspecified ankle and foot
M67.38 Transient synovitis, other site
M67.39 Transient synovitis, multiple sites
+ M67.4 Ganglion
Ganglion of joint or tendon (sheath)
Excludes1: *ganglion in yaws (A66.6)*
Excludes2: *cyst of bursa (M71.2-M71.3)*
cyst of synovium (M71.2-M71.3)
M67.40 Ganglion, unspecified site
+ M67.41 Ganglion, shoulder
M67.411 Ganglion, right shoulder
M67.412 Ganglion, left shoulder
M67.419 Ganglion, unspecified shoulder
+ M67.42 Ganglion, elbow
M67.421 Ganglion, right elbow
M67.422 Ganglion, left elbow
M67.429 Ganglion, unspecified elbow
+ M67.43 Ganglion, wrist
M67.431 Ganglion, right wrist
M67.432 Ganglion, left wrist
M67.439 Ganglion, unspecified wrist
+ M67.44 Ganglion, hand
M67.441 Ganglion, right hand
M67.442 Ganglion, left hand
M67.449 Ganglion, unspecified hand
+ M67.45 Ganglion, hip
M67.451 Ganglion, right hip
M67.452 Ganglion, left hip
M67.459 Ganglion, unspecified hip
+ M67.46 Ganglion, knee
M67.461 Ganglion, right knee
M67.462 Ganglion, left knee
M67.469 Ganglion, unspecified knee
+ M67.47 Ganglion, ankle and foot
M67.471 Ganglion, right ankle and foot
M67.472 Ganglion, left ankle and foot
M67.479 Ganglion, unspecified ankle and foot
M67.48 Ganglion, other site
M67.49 Ganglion, multiple sites
+ M67.5 Plica syndrome
Plica knee
M67.50 Plica syndrome, unspecified knee
M67.51 Plica syndrome, right knee
M67.52 Plica syndrome, left knee
+ M67.8 Other specified disorders of synovium and tendon
M67.80 Other specified disorders of synovium and tendon, unspecified site
+ M67.81 Other specified disorders of synovium and tendon, shoulder
M67.811 Other specified disorders of synovium, right shoulder
M67.812 Other specified disorders of synovium, left shoulder
M67.813 Other specified disorders of tendon, right shoulder
M67.814 Other specified disorders of tendon, left shoulder
M67.819 Other specified disorders of synovium and tendon, unspecified shoulder
+ M67.82 Other specified disorders of synovium and tendon, elbow
M67.821 Other specified disorders of synovium, right elbow
M67.822 Other specified disorders of synovium, left elbow
M67.823 Other specified disorders of tendon, right elbow
M67.824 Other specified disorders of tendon, left elbow
M67.829 Other specified disorders of synovium and tendon, unspecified elbow
+ M67.83 Other specified disorders of synovium and tendon, wrist
M67.831 Other specified disorders of synovium, right wrist
M67.832 Other specified disorders of synovium, left wrist
M67.833 Other specified disorders of tendon, right wrist
M67.834 Other specified disorders of tendon, left wrist
M67.839 Other specified disorders of synovium and tendon, unspecified forearm
+ M67.84 Other specified disorders of synovium and tendon, hand
M67.841 Other specified disorders of synovium, right hand
M67.842 Other specified disorders of synovium, left hand
M67.843 Other specified disorders of tendon, right hand
M67.844 Other specified disorders of tendon, left hand
M67.849 Other specified disorders of synovium and tendon, unspecified hand
+ M67.85 Other specified disorders of synovium and tendon, hip
M67.851 Other specified disorders of synovium, right hip
M67.852 Other specified disorders of synovium, left hip
M67.853 Other specified disorders of tendon, right hip
M67.854 Other specified disorders of tendon, left hip
M67.859 Other specified disorders of synovium and tendon, unspecified hip
+ M67.86 Other specified disorders of synovium and tendon, knee
M67.861 Other specified disorders of synovium, right knee
M67.862 Other specified disorders of synovium, left knee
M67.863 Other specified disorders of tendon, right knee
M67.864 Other specified disorders of tendon, left knee
M67.869 Other specified disorders of synovium and tendon, unspecified knee
+ M67.87 Other specified disorders of synovium and tendon, ankle and foot
M67.871 Other specified disorders of synovium, right ankle and foot
M67.872 Other specified disorders of synovium, left ankle and foot
M67.873 Other specified disorders of tendon, right ankle and foot
M67.874 Other specified disorders of tendon, left ankle and foot
M67.879 Other specified disorders of synovium and tendon, unspecified ankle and foot
M67.88 Other specified disorders of synovium and tendon, other site
M67.89 Other specified disorders of synovium and tendon, multiple sites
+ M67.9 Unspecified disorder of synovium and tendon
M67.90 Unspecified disorder of synovium and tendon, unspecified site
+ M67.91 Unspecified disorder of synovium and tendon, shoulder

M67.911 Unspecified disorder of synovium and tendon, right shoulder
M67.912 Unspecified disorder of synovium and tendon, left shoulder
M67.919 Unspecified disorder of synovium and tendon, unspecified shoulder
+ M67.92 Unspecified disorder of synovium and tendon, upper arm
M67.921 Unspecified disorder of synovium and tendon, right upper arm
M67.922 Unspecified disorder of synovium and tendon, left upper arm
M67.929 Unspecified disorder of synovium and tendon, unspecified upper arm
+ M67.93 Unspecified disorder of synovium and tendon, forearm
M67.931 Unspecified disorder of synovium and tendon, right forearm
M67.932 Unspecified disorder of synovium and tendon, left forearm
M67.939 Unspecified disorder of synovium and tendon, unspecified forearm
+ M67.94 Unspecified disorder of synovium and tendon, hand
M67.941 Unspecified disorder of synovium and tendon, right hand
M67.942 Unspecified disorder of synovium and tendon, left hand
M67.949 Unspecified disorder of synovium and tendon, unspecified hand
+ M67.95 Unspecified disorder of synovium and tendon, thigh
M67.951 Unspecified disorder of synovium and tendon, right thigh
M67.952 Unspecified disorder of synovium and tendon, left thigh
M67.959 Unspecified disorder of synovium and tendon, unspecified thigh
+ M67.96 Unspecified disorder of synovium and tendon, lower leg
M67.961 Unspecified disorder of synovium and tendon, right lower leg
M67.962 Unspecified disorder of synovium and tendon, left lower leg
M67.969 Unspecified disorder of synovium and tendon, unspecified lower leg
+ M67.97 Unspecified disorder of synovium and tendon, ankle and foot
M67.971 Unspecified disorder of synovium and tendon, right ankle and foot
M67.972 Unspecified disorder of synovium and tendon, left ankle and foot
M67.979 Unspecified disorder of synovium and tendon, unspecified ankle and foot
M67.98 Unspecified disorder of synovium and tendon, other site
M67.99 Unspecified disorder of synovium and tendon, multiple sites

Other soft tissue disorders (M70-M79)

M70 Soft tissue disorders related to use, overuse and pressure

Includes: soft tissue disorders of occupational origin
Use additional external cause code to identify activity causing disorder (Y93.-)
Excludes1: *bursitis NOS (M71.9-)*
Excludes2: *bursitis of shoulder (M75.5)*
enthesopathies (M76-M77)
pressure ulcer (pressure area) (L89.-)

+ M70.0 Crepitant synovitis (acute) (chronic) of hand and wrist
+ M70.03 Crepitant synovitis (acute) (chronic), wrist
M70.031 Crepitant synovitis (acute) (chronic), right wrist
M70.032 Crepitant synovitis (acute) (chronic), left wrist
M70.039 Crepitant synovitis (acute) (chronic), unspecified wrist
+ M70.04 Crepitant synovitis (acute) (chronic), hand
M70.041 Crepitant synovitis (acute) (chronic), right hand
M70.042 Crepitant synovitis (acute) (chronic), left hand
M70.049 Crepitant synovitis (acute) (chronic), unspecified hand

+ M70.1 Bursitis of hand
M70.10 Bursitis, unspecified hand
M70.11 Bursitis, right hand
M70.12 Bursitis, left hand
+ M70.2 Olecranon bursitis
M70.20 Olecranon bursitis, unspecified elbow
M70.21 Olecranon bursitis, right elbow
M70.22 Olecranon bursitis, left elbow
+ M70.3 Other bursitis of elbow
M70.30 Other bursitis of elbow, unspecified elbow
M70.31 Other bursitis of elbow, right elbow
M70.32 Other bursitis of elbow, left elbow
+ M70.4 Prepatellar bursitis
M70.40 Prepatellar bursitis, unspecified knee
M70.41 Prepatellar bursitis, right knee
M70.42 Prepatellar bursitis, left knee
+ M70.5 Other bursitis of knee
M70.50 Other bursitis of knee, unspecified knee
M70.51 Other bursitis of knee, right knee
M70.52 Other bursitis of knee, left knee
+ M70.6 Trochanteric bursitis
Trochanteric tendinitis
M70.60 Trochanteric bursitis, unspecified hip
M70.61 Trochanteric bursitis, right hip
M70.62 Trochanteric bursitis, left hip
+ M70.7 Other bursitis of hip
Ischial bursitis
M70.70 Other bursitis of hip, unspecified hip
M70.71 Other bursitis of hip, right hip
M70.72 Other bursitis of hip, left hip
+ M70.8 Other soft tissue disorders related to use, overuse and pressu
M70.80 Other soft tissue disorders related to use, overuse a pressure of unspecified site
+ M70.81 Other soft tissue disorders related to use, overuse a pressure of shoulder
M70.811 Other soft tissue disorders related to use, overuse and pressure, right shoulder
M70.812 Other soft tissue disorders related to use, overuse and pressure, left shoulder
M70.819 Other soft tissue disorders related to use, overuse and pressure, unspecified should
+ M70.82 Other soft tissue disorders related to use, overuse a pressure of upper arm
M70.821 Other soft tissue disorders related to use, overuse and pressure, right upper arm
M70.822 Other soft tissue disorders related to use, overuse and pressure, left upper arm
M70.829 Other soft tissue disorders related to use, overuse and pressure, unspecified upper arms
+ M70.83 Other soft tissue disorders related to use, overuse a pressure of forearm
M70.831 Other soft tissue disorders related to use, overuse and pressure, right forearm
M70.832 Other soft tissue disorders related to use, overuse and pressure, left forearm
M70.839 Other soft tissue disorders related to use, overuse and pressure, unspecified forearr
+ M70.84 Other soft tissue disorders related to use, overuse a pressure of hand
M70.841 Other soft tissue disorders related to use, overuse and pressure, right hand
M70.842 Other soft tissue disorders related to use, overuse and pressure, left hand
M70.849 Other soft tissue disorders related to use, overuse and pressure, unspecified hand
+ M70.85 Other soft tissue disorders related to use, overuse a pressure of thigh
M70.851 Other soft tissue disorders related to use, overuse and pressure, right thigh
M70.852 Other soft tissue disorders related to use, overuse and pressure, left thigh
M70.859 Other soft tissue disorders related to use, overuse and pressure, unspecified thigh
+ M70.86 Other soft tissue disorders related to use, overuse a pressure lower leg
M70.861 Other soft tissue disorders related to use, overuse and pressure, right lower leg
M70.862 Other soft tissue disorders related to use, overuse and pressure, left lower leg
M70.869 Other soft tissue disorders related to use, overuse and pressure, unspecified leg

+ **M70.87** **Other soft tissue disorders related to use, overuse and pressure of ankle and foot**
  - **M70.871** **Other soft tissue disorders related to use, overuse and pressure, right ankle and foot**
  - **M70.872** **Other soft tissue disorders related to use, overuse and pressure, left ankle and foot**
  - **M70.879** **Other soft tissue disorders related to use, overuse and pressure, unspecified ankle and foot**

M70.88 **Other soft tissue disorders related to use, overuse and pressure other site**

M70.89 **Other soft tissue disorders related to use, overuse and pressure multiple sites**

+ **M70.9** **Unspecified soft tissue disorder related to use, overuse and pressure**
  - **M70.90** **Unspecified soft tissue disorder related to use, overuse and pressure of unspecified site**
  - + **M70.91** **Unspecified soft tissue disorder related to use, overuse and pressure of shoulder**
    - **M70.911** **Unspecified soft tissue disorder related to use, overuse and pressure, right shoulder**
    - **M70.912** **Unspecified soft tissue disorder related to use, overuse and pressure, left shoulder**
    - **M70.919** **Unspecified soft tissue disorder related to use, overuse and pressure, unspecified shoulder**
  - + **M70.92** **Unspecified soft tissue disorder related to use, overuse and pressure of upper arm**
    - **M70.921** **Unspecified soft tissue disorder related to use, overuse and pressure, right upper arm**
    - **M70.922** **Unspecified soft tissue disorder related to use, overuse and pressure, left upper arm**
    - **M70.929** **Unspecified soft tissue disorder related to use, overuse and pressure, unspecified upper arm**
  - + **M70.93** **Unspecified soft tissue disorder related to use, overuse and pressure of forearm**
    - **M70.931** **Unspecified soft tissue disorder related to use, overuse and pressure, right forearm**
    - **M70.932** **Unspecified soft tissue disorder related to use, overuse and pressure, left forearm**
    - **M70.939** **Unspecified soft tissue disorder related to use, overuse and pressure, unspecified forearm**
  - + **M70.94** **Unspecified soft tissue disorder related to use, overuse and pressure of hand**
    - **M70.941** **Unspecified soft tissue disorder related to use, overuse and pressure, right hand**
    - **M70.942** **Unspecified soft tissue disorder related to use, overuse and pressure, left hand**
    - **M70.949** **Unspecified soft tissue disorder related to use, overuse and pressure, unspecified hand**
  - + **M70.95** **Unspecified soft tissue disorder related to use, overuse and pressure of thigh**
    - **M70.951** **Unspecified soft tissue disorder related to use, overuse and pressure, right thigh**
    - **M70.952** **Unspecified soft tissue disorder related to use, overuse and pressure, left thigh**
    - **M70.959** **Unspecified soft tissue disorder related to use, overuse and pressure, unspecified thigh**
  - + **M70.96** **Unspecified soft tissue disorder related to use, overuse and pressure lower leg**
    - **M70.961** **Unspecified soft tissue disorder related to use, overuse and pressure, right lower leg**
    - **M70.962** **Unspecified soft tissue disorder related to use, overuse and pressure, left lower leg**
    - **M70.969** **Unspecified soft tissue disorder related to use, overuse and pressure, unspecified lower leg**
  - + **M70.97** **Unspecified soft tissue disorder related to use, overuse and pressure of ankle and foot**
    - **M70.971** **Unspecified soft tissue disorder related to use, overuse and pressure, right ankle and foot**
    - **M70.972** **Unspecified soft tissue disorder related to use, overuse and pressure, left ankle and foot**
    - **M70.979** **Unspecified soft tissue disorder related to use, overuse and pressure, unspecified ankle and foot**
  - **M70.98** **Unspecified soft tissue disorder related to use, overuse and pressure other**
  - **M70.99** **Unspecified soft tissue disorder related to use, overuse and pressure multiple sites**

M71 Other bursopathies

Excludes1: *bunion (M20.1)*
bursitis related to use, overuse or pressure (M70.-)
enthesopathies (M76-M77)

+ **M71.0** **Abscess of bursa**
  Use additional code (B95.-, B96.-) to identify causative organism
  - **M71.00** **Abscess of bursa, unspecified site**
  - + **M71.01** **Abscess of bursa, shoulder**
    - **M71.011** **Abscess of bursa, right shoulder**
    - **M71.012** **Abscess of bursa, left shoulder**
    - **M71.019** **Abscess of bursa, unspecified shoulder**
  - + **M71.02** **Abscess of bursa, elbow**
    - **M71.021** **Abscess of bursa, right elbow**
    - **M71.022** **Abscess of bursa, left elbow**
    - **M71.029** **Abscess of bursa, unspecified elbow**
  - + **M71.03** **Abscess of bursa, wrist**
    - **M71.031** **Abscess of bursa, right wrist**
    - **M71.032** **Abscess of bursa, left wrist**
    - **M71.039** **Abscess of bursa, unspecified wrist**
  - + **M71.04** **Abscess of bursa, hand**
    - **M71.041** **Abscess of bursa, right hand**
    - **M71.042** **Abscess of bursa, left hand**
    - **M71.049** **Abscess of bursa, unspecified hand**
  - + **M71.05** **Abscess of bursa, hip**
    - **M71.051** **Abscess of bursa, right hip**
    - **M71.052** **Abscess of bursa, left hip**
    - **M71.059** **Abscess of bursa, unspecified hip**
  - + **M71.06** **Abscess of bursa, knee**
    - **M71.061** **Abscess of bursa, right knee**
    - **M71.062** **Abscess of bursa, left knee**
    - **M71.069** **Abscess of bursa, unspecified knee**
  - + **M71.07** **Abscess of bursa, ankle and foot**
    - **M71.071** **Abscess of bursa, right ankle and foot**
    - **M71.072** **Abscess of bursa, left ankle and foot**
    - **M71.079** **Abscess of bursa, unspecified ankle and foot**
  - **M71.08** **Abscess of bursa, other site**
  - **M71.09** **Abscess of bursa, multiple sites**

+ **M71.1** **Other infective bursitis**
  Use additional code (B95.-, B96.-) to identify causative organism
  - **M71.10** **Other infective bursitis, unspecified site**
  - + **M71.11** **Other infective bursitis, shoulder**
    - **M71.111** **Other infective bursitis, right shoulder**
    - **M71.112** **Other infective bursitis, left shoulder**
    - **M71.119** **Other infective bursitis, unspecified shoulder**
  - + **M71.12** **Other infective bursitis, elbow**
    - **M71.121** **Other infective bursitis, right elbow**
    - **M71.122** **Other infective bursitis, left elbow**
    - **M71.129** **Other infective bursitis, unspecified elbow**
  - + **M71.13** **Other infective bursitis, wrist**
    - **M71.131** **Other infective bursitis, right wrist**
    - **M71.132** **Other infective bursitis, left wrist**
    - **M71.139** **Other infective bursitis, unspecified wrist**
  - + **M71.14** **Other infective bursitis, hand**
    - **M71.141** **Other infective bursitis, right hand**
    - **M71.142** **Other infective bursitis, left hand**
    - **M71.149** **Other infective bursitis, unspecified hand**
  - + **M71.15** **Other infective bursitis, hip**
    - **M71.151** **Other infective bursitis, right hip**
    - **M71.152** **Other infective bursitis, left hip**
    - **M71.159** **Other infective bursitis, unspecified hip**
  - + **M71.16** **Other infective bursitis, knee**
    - **M71.161** **Other infective bursitis, right knee**
    - **M71.162** **Other infective bursitis, left knee**
    - **M71.169** **Other infective bursitis, unspecified knee**
  - + **M71.17** **Other infective bursitis, ankle and foot**
    - **M71.171** **Other infective bursitis, right ankle and foot**
    - **M71.172** **Other infective bursitis, left ankle and foot**
    - **M71.179** **Other infective bursitis, unspecified ankle and foot**
  - **M71.18** **Other infective bursitis, other site**
  - **M71.19** **Other infective bursitis, multiple sites**

+ **M71.2** **Synovial cyst of popliteal space [Baker]**
  Excludes1: *synovial cyst of popliteal space with rupture (M66.0)*
  - **M71.20** **Synovial cyst of popliteal space [Baker], unspecified knee**
  - **M71.21** **Synovial cyst of popliteal space [Baker], right knee**
  - **M71.22** **Synovial cyst of popliteal space [Baker], left knee**

+ **M71.3 Other bursal cyst**
  Synovial cyst NOS
  Excludes1: *synovial cyst with rupture (M66.1-)*
  M71.30 Other bursal cyst, unspecified site
  + **M71.31 Other bursal cyst, shoulder**
    M71.311 Other bursal cyst, right shoulder
    M71.312 Other bursal cyst, left shoulder
    M71.319 Other bursal cyst, unspecified shoulder
  + **M71.32 Other bursal cyst, elbow**
    M71.321 Other bursal cyst, right elbow
    M71.322 Other bursal cyst, left elbow
    M71.329 Other bursal cyst, unspecified elbow
  + **M71.33 Other bursal cyst, wrist**
    M71.331 Other bursal cyst, right wrist
    M71.332 Other bursal cyst, left wrist
    M71.339 Other bursal cyst, unspecified wrist
  + **M71.34 Other bursal cyst, hand**
    M71.341 Other bursal cyst, right hand
    M71.342 Other bursal cyst, left hand
    M71.349 Other bursal cyst, unspecified hand
  + **M71.35 Other bursal cyst, hip**
    M71.351 Other bursal cyst, right hip
    M71.352 Other bursal cyst, left hip
    M71.359 Other bursal cyst, unspecified hip
  + **M71.37 Other bursal cyst, ankle and foot**
    M71.371 Other bursal cyst, right ankle and foot
    M71.372 Other bursal cyst, left ankle and foot
    M71.379 Other bursal cyst, unspecified ankle and foot
  M71.38 Other bursal cyst, other site
  M71.39 Other bursal cyst, multiple sites

+ **M71.4 Calcium deposit in bursa**
  Excludes2: *calcium deposit in bursa of shoulder (M75.3)*
  M71.40 Calcium deposit in bursa, unspecified site
  + **M71.42 Calcium deposit in bursa, elbow**
    M71.421 Calcium deposit in bursa, right elbow
    M71.422 Calcium deposit in bursa, left elbow
    M71.429 Calcium deposit in bursa, unspecified elbow
  + **M71.43 Calcium deposit in bursa, wrist**
    M71.431 Calcium deposit in bursa, right wrist
    M71.432 Calcium deposit in bursa, left wrist
    M71.439 Calcium deposit in bursa, unspecified wrist
  + **M71.44 Calcium deposit in bursa, hand**
    M71.441 Calcium deposit in bursa, right hand
    M71.442 Calcium deposit in bursa, left hand
    M71.449 Calcium deposit in bursa, unspecified hand
  + **M71.45 Calcium deposit in bursa, hip**
    M71.451 Calcium deposit in bursa, right hip
    M71.452 Calcium deposit in bursa, left hip
    M71.459 Calcium deposit in bursa, unspecified hip
  + **M71.46 Calcium deposit in bursa, knee**
    M71.461 Calcium deposit in bursa, right knee
    M71.462 Calcium deposit in bursa, left knee
    M71.469 Calcium deposit in bursa, unspecified knee
  + **M71.47 Calcium deposit in bursa, ankle and foot**
    M71.471 Calcium deposit in bursa, right ankle and foot
    M71.472 Calcium deposit in bursa, left ankle and foot
    M71.479 Calcium deposit in bursa, unspecified ankle and foot
  M71.48 Calcium deposit in bursa, other site
  M71.49 Calcium deposit in bursa, multiple sites

+ **M71.5 Other bursitis, not elsewhere classified**
  Excludes1: *bursitis NOS (M71.9-)*
  Excludes2: *bursitis of shoulder (M75.5)*
  bursitis of tibial collateral [Pellegrini-Stieda] (M76.4)
  M71.50 Other bursitis, not elsewhere classified, unspecified site
  + **M71.52 Other bursitis, not elsewhere classified, elbow**
    M71.521 Other bursitis, not elsewhere classified, right elbow
    M71.522 Other bursitis, not elsewhere classified, left elbow
    M71.529 Other bursitis, not elsewhere classified, unspecified elbow
  + **M71.53 Other bursitis, not elsewhere classified, wrist**
    M71.531 Other bursitis, not elsewhere classified, right wrist
    M71.532 Other bursitis, not elsewhere classified, left wrist
    M71.539 Other bursitis, not elsewhere classified, unspecified wrist
  + **M71.54 Other bursitis, not elsewhere classified, hand**
    M71.541 Other bursitis, not elsewhere classified, ri hand
    M71.542 Other bursitis, not elsewhere classified, le hand
    M71.549 Other bursitis, not elsewhere classified, unspecified hand
  + **M71.55 Other bursitis, not elsewhere classified, hip**
    M71.551 Other bursitis, not elsewhere classified, ri hip
    M71.552 Other bursitis, not elsewhere classified, le hip
    M71.559 Other bursitis, not elsewhere classified, unspecified hip
  + **M71.56 Other bursitis, not elsewhere classified, knee**
    M71.561 Other bursitis, not elsewhere classified, ri knee
    M71.562 Other bursitis, not elsewhere classified, le knee
    M71.569 Other bursitis, not elsewhere classified, unspecified knee
  + **M71.57 Other bursitis, not elsewhere classified, ankle and f**
    M71.571 Other bursitis, not elsewhere classified, ri ankle and foot
    M71.572 Other bursitis, not elsewhere classified, le ankle and foot
    M71.579 Other bursitis, not elsewhere classified, unspecified ankle and foot
  M71.58 Other bursitis, not elsewhere classified, other site

+ **M71.8 Other specified bursopathies**
  M71.80 Other specified bursopathies, unspecified site
  + **M71.81 Other specified bursopathies, shoulder**
    M71.811 Other specified bursopathies, right should
    M71.812 Other specified bursopathies, left shoulde
    M71.819 Other specified bursopathies, unspecified shoulder
  + **M71.82 Other specified bursopathies, elbow**
    M71.821 Other specified bursopathies, right elbow
    M71.822 Other specified bursopathies, left elbow
    M71.829 Other specified bursopathies, unspecified elbow
  + **M71.83 Other specified bursopathies, wrist**
    M71.831 Other specified bursopathies, right wrist
    M71.832 Other specified bursopathies, left wrist
    M71.839 Other specified bursopathies, unspecified wrist
  + **M71.84 Other specified bursopathies, hand**
    M71.841 Other specified bursopathies, right hand
    M71.842 Other specified bursopathies, left hand
    M71.849 Other specified bursopathies, unspecified hand
  + **M71.85 Other specified bursopathies, hip**
    M71.851 Other specified bursopathies, right hip
    M71.852 Other specified bursopathies, left hip
    M71.859 Other specified bursopathies, unspecified
  + **M71.86 Other specified bursopathies, knee**
    M71.861 Other specified bursopathies, right knee
    M71.862 Other specified bursopathies, left knee
    M71.869 Other specified bursopathies, unspecified knee
  + **M71.87 Other specified bursopathies, ankle and foot**
    M71.871 Other specified bursopathies, right ankle and foot
    M71.872 Other specified bursopathies, left ankle ar foot
    M71.879 Other specified bursopathies, unspecified ankle and foot
  M71.88 Other specified bursopathies, other site
  M71.89 Other specified bursopathies, multiple sites

M71.9 Bursopathy, unspecified
  Bursitis NOS

M72 Fibroblastic disorders

Excludes2: *retroperitoneal fibromatosis (D48.3)*

• **M72.0 Palmar fascial fibromatosis [Dupuytren]**
M72.1 Knuckle pads
M72.2 Plantar fascial fibromatosis
  Plantar fasciitis
M72.4 Pseudosarcomatous fibromatosis
  Nodular fasciitis

MCC **M72.6 Necrotizing fasciitis**
Use additional code (B95.-, B96.-) to identify causative organism
MCC Exclusion see Appendix A PDX collection 0806

M72.8 Other fibroblastic disorders
Abscess of fascia
Fasciitis NEC
Other infective fasciitis
Use additional code to (B95.-, B96.-) identify causative organism
Excludes1: *diffuse (eosinophilic) fasciitis (M35.4)*
necrotizing fasciitis (M72.6)
nodular fasciitis (M72.4)
perirenal fasciitis NOS (N13.5)
perirenal fasciitis with infection (N13.6)
plantar fasciitis (M72.2)

M72.9 Fibroblastic disorder, unspecified
Fasciitis NOS
Fibromatosis NOS

M75 Shoulder lesions

Excludes2: *shoulder-hand syndrome (M89.0-)*

+ **M75.0 Adhesive capsulitis of shoulder**
Frozen shoulder
Periarthritis of shoulder
M75.00 Adhesive capsulitis of unspecified shoulder
M75.01 Adhesive capsulitis of right shoulder
M75.02 Adhesive capsulitis of left shoulder

+ **M75.1 Rotator cuff tear or rupture, not specified as traumatic**
Rotator cuff syndrome
Supraspinatus tear or rupture, not specified as traumatic
Supraspinatus syndrome
Excludes1: *tear of rotator cuff, traumatic (S46.01-)*
+ **M75.10 Unspecified rotator cuff tear or rupture, not specified as traumatic**
M75.100 Unspecified rotator cuff tear or rupture of unspecified shoulder, not specified as traumatic
M75.101 Unspecified rotator cuff tear or rupture of right shoulder, not specified as traumatic
M75.102 Unspecified rotator cuff tear or rupture of left shoulder, not specified as traumatic
+ **M75.11 Incomplete rotator cuff tear or rupture not specified as traumatic**
M75.110 Incomplete rotator cuff tear or rupture of unspecified shoulder, not specified as traumatic
M75.111 Incomplete rotator cuff tear or rupture of right shoulder, not specified as traumatic
M75.112 Incomplete rotator cuff tear or rupture of left shoulder, not specified as traumatic
+ **M75.12 Complete rotator cuff tear or rupture not specified as traumatic**
M75.120 Complete rotator cuff tear or rupture of unspecified shoulder, not specified as traumatic
M75.121 Complete rotator cuff tear or rupture of right shoulder, not specified as traumatic
M75.122 Complete rotator cuff tear or rupture of left shoulder, not specified as traumatic

+ **M75.2 Bicipital tendinitis**
M75.20 Bicipital tendinitis, unspecified shoulder
M75.21 Bicipital tendinitis, right shoulder
M75.22 Bicipital tendinitis, left shoulder

+ **M75.3 Calcific tendinitis of shoulder**
Calcified bursa of shoulder
M75.30 Calcific tendinitis of unspecified shoulder
M75.31 Calcific tendinitis of right shoulder
M75.32 Calcific tendinitis of left shoulder

+ **M75.4 Impingement syndrome of shoulder**
M75.40 Impingement syndrome of unspecified shoulder
M75.41 Impingement syndrome of right shoulder
M75.42 Impingement syndrome of left shoulder

+ **M75.5 Bursitis of shoulder**
M75.50 Bursitis of unspecified shoulder
M75.51 Bursitis of right shoulder
M75.52 Bursitis of left shoulder

+ **M75.8 Other shoulder lesions**
M75.80 Other shoulder lesions, unspecified shoulder
M75.81 Other shoulder lesions, right shoulder
M75.82 Other shoulder lesions, left shoulder

+ **M75.9 Shoulder lesion, unspecified**
M75.90 Shoulder lesion, unspecified, unspecified shoulder
M75.91 Shoulder lesion, unspecified, right shoulder
M75.92 Shoulder lesion, unspecified, left shoulder

M76 Enthesopathies, lower limb, excluding foot

Excludes2: *bursitis due to use, overuse and pressure (M70.-)*
enthesopathies of ankle and foot (M77.5-)

+ **M76.0 Gluteal tendinitis**
M76.00 Gluteal tendinitis, unspecified hip
M76.01 Gluteal tendinitis, right hip
M76.02 Gluteal tendinitis, left hip

+ **M76.1 Psoas tendinitis**
M76.10 Psoas tendinitis, unspecified hip
M76.11 Psoas tendinitis, right hip
M76.12 Psoas tendinitis, left hip

+ **M76.2 Iliac crest spur**
M76.20 Iliac crest spur, unspecified hip
M76.21 Iliac crest spur, right hip
M76.22 Iliac crest spur, left hip

+ **M76.3 Iliotibial band syndrome**
M76.30 Iliotibial band syndrome, unspecified leg
M76.31 Iliotibial band syndrome, right leg
M76.32 Iliotibial band syndrome, left leg

+ **M76.4 Tibial collateral bursitis [Pellegrini-Stieda]**
M76.40 Tibial collateral bursitis [Pellegrini-Stieda], unspecified leg
M76.41 Tibial collateral bursitis [Pellegrini-Stieda], right leg
M76.42 Tibial collateral bursitis [Pellegrini-Stieda], left leg

+ **M76.5 Patellar tendinitis**
M76.50 Patellar tendinitis, unspecified knee
M76.51 Patellar tendinitis, right knee
M76.52 Patellar tendinitis, left knee

+ **M76.6 Achilles tendinitis**
Achilles bursitis
M76.60 Achilles tendinitis, unspecified leg
M76.61 Achilles tendinitis, right leg
M76.62 Achilles tendinitis, left leg

+ **M76.7 Peroneal tendinitis**
M76.70 Peroneal tendinitis, unspecified leg
M76.71 Peroneal tendinitis, right leg
M76.72 Peroneal tendinitis, left leg

+ **M76.8 Other specified enthesopathies of lower limb, excluding foot**
+ **M76.81 Anterior tibial syndrome**
M76.811 Anterior tibial syndrome, right leg
M76.812 Anterior tibial syndrome, left leg
M76.819 Anterior tibial syndrome, unspecified leg
+ **M76.82 Posterior tibial tendinitis**
M76.821 Posterior tibial tendinitis, right leg
M76.822 Posterior tibial tendinitis, left leg
M76.829 Posterior tibial tendinitis, unspecified leg
+ **M76.89 Other specified enthesopathies of lower limb, excluding foot**
M76.891 Other specified enthesopathies of right lower limb, excluding foot
M76.892 Other specified enthesopathies of left lower limb, excluding foot
M76.899 Other specified enthesopathies of unspecified lower limb, excluding foot

M76.9 Unspecified enthesopathy, lower limb, excluding foot

M77 Other enthesopathies

Excludes1: *bursitis NOS (M71.9-)*
Excludes2: *bursitis due to use, overuse and pressure (M70.-)*
osteophyte (M25.7)
spinal enthesopathy (M46.0-)

+ **M77.0 Medial epicondylitis**
M77.00 Medial epicondylitis, unspecified elbow
M77.01 Medial epicondylitis, right elbow
M77.02 Medial epicondylitis, left elbow

+ **M77.1 Lateral epicondylitis**
Tennis elbow
M77.10 Lateral epicondylitis, unspecified elbow
M77.11 Lateral epicondylitis, right elbow
M77.12 Lateral epicondylitis, left elbow

+ **M77.2 Periarthritis of wrist**
M77.20 Periarthritis, unspecified wrist
M77.21 Periarthritis, right wrist
M77.22 Periarthritis, left wrist

+ **M77.3 Calcaneal spur**
M77.30 Calcaneal spur, unspecified foot
M77.31 Calcaneal spur, right foot
M77.32 Calcaneal spur, left foot
+ **M77.4 Metatarsalgia**
Excludes1: *Morton's metatarsalgia (G57.6)*
M77.40 Metatarsalgia, unspecified foot
M77.41 Metatarsalgia, right foot
M77.42 Metatarsalgia, left foot
+ **M77.5 Other enthesopathy of foot**
M77.50 Other enthesopathy of unspecified foot
M77.51 Other enthesopathy of right foot
M77.52 Other enthesopathy of left foot
M77.8 Other enthesopathies, not elsewhere classified
M77.9 Enthesopathy, unspecified
Bone spur NOS
Capsulitis NOS
Periarthritis NOS
Tendinitis NOS

M79 Other and unspecified soft tissue disorders, not elsewhere classified
Excludes1: *psychogenic rheumatism (F45.8)*
soft tissue pain, psychogenic (F45.41)
M79.0 Rheumatism, unspecified
Excludes1: *fibromyalgia (M79.7)*
palindromic rheumatism (M12.3-)
M79.1 Myalgia
Myofascial pain syndrome
Excludes1: *fibromyalgia (M79.7)*
myositis (M60.-)
M79.2 Neuralgia and neuritis, unspecified
Excludes1: *brachial radiculitis NOS (M54.1)*
lumbosacral radiculitis NOS (M54.1)
mononeuropathies (G56-G58)
radiculitis NOS (M54.1)
sciatica (M54.3-M54.4)
M79.3 Panniculitis, unspecified
Excludes1: *lupus panniculitis (L93.2)*
neck and back panniculitis (M54.0-)
relapsing [Weber-Christian] panniculitis (M35.6)
M79.4 Hypertrophy of (infrapatellar) fat pad
M79.5 Residual foreign body in soft tissue
Excludes1: *foreign body granuloma of skin and subcutaneous tissue (L92.3)*
foreign body granuloma of soft tissue (M60.2-)
+ **M79.6 Pain in limb, hand, foot, fingers and toes**
Excludes2: *pain in joint (M25.5-)*
+ **M79.60 Pain in limb, unspecified**
M79.601 Pain in right arm
Pain in right upper limb NOS
M79.602 Pain in left arm
Pain in left upper limb NOS
M79.603 Pain in arm, unspecified
Pain in upper limb NOS
M79.604 Pain in right leg
Pain in right lower limb NOS
M79.605 Pain in left leg
Pain in left lower limb NOS
M79.606 Pain in leg, unspecified
Pain in lower limb NOS
M79.609 Pain in unspecified limb
Pain in limb NOS
+ **M79.62 Pain in upper arm**
Pain in axillary region
M79.621 Pain in right upper arm
M79.622 Pain in left upper arm
M79.629 Pain in unspecified upper arm
+ **M79.63 Pain in forearm**
M79.631 Pain in right forearm
M79.632 Pain in left forearm
M79.639 Pain in unspecified forearm
+ **M79.64 Pain in hand and fingers**
M79.641 Pain in right hand
M79.642 Pain in left hand
M79.643 Pain in unspecified hand
M79.644 Pain in right finger(s)
M79.645 Pain in left finger(s)
M79.646 Pain in unspecified finger(s)
+ **M79.65 Pain in thigh**
M79.651 Pain in right thigh
M79.652 Pain in left thigh
M79.659 Pain in unspecified thigh
+ **M79.66 Pain in lower leg**
M79.661 Pain in right lower leg
M79.662 Pain in left lower leg
M79.669 Pain in unspecified lower leg
+ **M79.67 Pain in foot and toes**
M79.671 Pain in right foot
M79.672 Pain in left foot
M79.673 Pain in unspecified foot
M79.674 Pain in right toe(s)
M79.675 Pain in left toe(s)
M79.676 Pain in unspecified toe(s)
M79.7 Fibromyalgia
Fibromyositis
Fibrositis
Myofibrositis
+ **M79.A Nontraumatic compartment syndrome**
Code first if applicable, associated postprocedural complication
Excludes1: *compartment syndrome NOS (T79.A-)*
fibromyalgia (M79.7)
nontraumatic ischemic infarction of muscle (M62..
traumatic compartment syndrome (T79.A-)
+ **M79.A1 Nontraumatic compartment syndrome of upper extremity**
Nontraumatic compartment syndrome of shoulder, arm, forearm, wrist, hand, and fingers
CC **M79.A11 Nontraumatic compartment syndrome of right upper extremity**
CC Exclusion see Appendix A PDX collection 0
CC **M79.A12 Nontraumatic compartment syndrome of upper extremity**
CC Exclusion see Appendix A PDX collection 0
CC **M79.A19 Nontraumatic compartment syndrome of unspecified upper extremity**
CC Exclusion see Appendix A PDX collection 0
+ **M79.A2 Nontraumatic compartment syndrome of lower extremity**
Nontraumatic compartment syndrome of hip, buttock, thigh, leg, foot, and toes
CC **M79.A21 Nontraumatic compartment syndrome of right lower extremity**
CC Exclusion see Appendix A PDX collection 0
CC **M79.A22 Nontraumatic compartment syndrome of lower extremity**
CC Exclusion see Appendix A PDX collection 0
CC **M79.A29 Nontraumatic compartment syndrome of unspecified lower extremity**
CC Exclusion see Appendix A PDX collection 0
CC **M79.A3 Nontraumatic compartment syndrome of abdomen**
CC Exclusion see Appendix A PDX collection 0895
CC **M79.A9 Nontraumatic compartment syndrome of other sites**
CC Exclusion see Appendix A PDX collection 0896
+ **M79.8 Other specified soft tissue disorders**
M79.81 Nontraumatic hematoma of soft tissue
Nontraumatic hematoma of muscle
Nontraumatic seroma of muscle and soft tissue
M79.89 Other specified soft tissue disorders
Polyalgia
M79.9 Soft tissue disorder, unspecified

OSTEOPATHIES AND CHONDROPATHIES (M80-M94)

sorders of bone density and structure (M80-M85)

M80 Osteoporosis with current pathological fracture

Includes: osteoporosis with current fragility fracture

Use additional code to identify major osseous defect, if applicable (M89.7-)

Excludes1: *collapsed vertebra NOS (M48.5)*
pathological fracture NOS (M84.4)
wedging of vertebra NOS (M48.5)

Excludes2: *personal history of (healed) osteoporosis fracture (Z87.310)*

The appropriate 7th character is to be added to each code from category M80:
- A initial encounter for fracture
- D subsequent encounter for fracture with routine healing
- G subsequent encounter for fracture with delayed healing
- K subsequent encounter for fracture with nonunion
- P subsequent encounter for fracture with malunion
- S sequela

Review coding guideline C.13.c
Review coding guideline C.19.c.1

+ **M80.0 Age-related osteoporosis with current pathological fracture**
Involutional osteoporosis with current pathological fracture
Osteoporosis NOS with current pathological fracture
Postmenopausal osteoporosis with current pathological fracture
Senile osteoporosis with current pathological fracture

• CC X+7th **M80.00 Age-related osteoporosis with current pathological fracture, unspecified site**
CC Exclusion 7th character A see Appendix A PDX collection 0888
CC Exclusion 7th characters K & P see Appendix A PDX collection 0897

+ **M80.01 Age-related osteoporosis with current pathological fracture, shoulder**

• CC +7th **M80.011 Age-related osteoporosis with current pathological fracture, right shoulder**
CC Exclusion 7th character A see Appendix A PDX collection 0888
CC Exclusion 7th characters K & P see Appendix A PDX collection 0897

• CC +7th **M80.012 Age-related osteoporosis with current pathological fracture, left shoulder**
CC Exclusion 7th character A see Appendix A PDX collection 0888
CC Exclusion 7th characters K & P see Appendix A PDX collection 0897

• CC +7th **M80.019 Age-related osteoporosis with current pathological fracture, unspecified shoulder**
CC Exclusion 7th character A see Appendix A PDX collection 0888
CC Exclusion 7th characters K & P see Appendix A PDX collection 0897

+ **M80.02 Age-related osteoporosis with current pathological fracture, humerus**

• CC +7th **M80.021 Age-related osteoporosis with current pathological fracture, right humerus**
CC Exclusion 7th character A see Appendix A PDX collection 0888
CC Exclusion 7th characters K & P see Appendix A PDX collection 0897

• CC +7th **M80.022 Age-related osteoporosis with current pathological fracture, left humerus**
CC Exclusion 7th character A see Appendix A PDX collection 0888
CC Exclusion 7th characters K & P see Appendix A PDX collection 0897

• CC +7th **M80.029 Age-related osteoporosis with current pathological fracture, unspecified humerus**
CC Exclusion 7th character A see Appendix A PDX collection 0888
CC Exclusion 7th characters K & P see Appendix A PDX collection 0897

+ **M80.03 Age-related osteoporosis with current pathological fracture, forearm**
Age-related osteoporosis with current pathological fracture of wrist

• CC +7th **M80.031 Age-related osteoporosis with current pathological fracture, right forearm**
CC Exclusion 7th character A see Appendix A PDX collection 0888
CC Exclusion 7th characters K & P see Appendix A PDX collection 0897

• CC +7th **M80.032 Age-related osteoporosis with current pathological fracture, left forearm**
CC Exclusion 7th character A see Appendix A PDX collection 0888
CC Exclusion 7th characters K & P see Appendix A PDX collection 0897

• CC +7th **M80.039 Age-related osteoporosis with current pathological fracture, unspecified forearm**
CC Exclusion 7th character A see Appendix A PDX collection 0888
CC Exclusion 7th characters K & P see Appendix A PDX collection 0897

+ **M80.04 Age-related osteoporosis with current pathological fracture, hand**

• CC +7th **M80.041 Age-related osteoporosis with current pathological fracture, right hand**
CC Exclusion 7th character A see Appendix A PDX collection 0888
CC Exclusion 7th characters K & P see Appendix A PDX collection 0897

• CC +7th **M80.042 Age-related osteoporosis with current pathological fracture, left hand**
CC Exclusion 7th character A see Appendix A PDX collection 0888
CC Exclusion 7th characters K & P see Appendix A PDX collection 0897

• CC +7th **M80.049 Age-related osteoporosis with current pathological fracture, unspecified hand**
CC Exclusion 7th character A see Appendix A PDX collection 0888
CC Exclusion 7th characters K & P see Appendix A PDX collection 0897

+ **M80.05 Age-related osteoporosis with current pathological fracture, femur**
Age-related osteoporosis with current pathological fracture of hip

• CC +7th **M80.051 Age-related osteoporosis with current pathological fracture, right femur**
CC Exclusion 7th character A see Appendix A PDX collection 0888
CC Exclusion 7th characters K & P see Appendix A PDX collection 0897

• CC +7th **M80.052 Age-related osteoporosis with current pathological fracture, left femur**
CC Exclusion 7th character A see Appendix A PDX collection 0888
CC Exclusion 7th characters K & P see Appendix A PDX collection 0897

• CC +7th **M80.059 Age-related osteoporosis with current pathological fracture, unspecified femur**
CC Exclusion 7th character A see Appendix A PDX collection 0888
CC Exclusion 7th characters K & P see Appendix A PDX collection 0897

+ **M80.06 Age-related osteoporosis with current pathological fracture, lower leg**

• CC +7th **M80.061 Age-related osteoporosis with current pathological fracture, right lower leg**
CC Exclusion 7th character A see Appendix A PDX collection 0888
CC Exclusion 7th characters K & P see Appendix A PDX collection 0897

• CC +7th **M80.062 Age-related osteoporosis with current pathological fracture, left lower leg**
CC Exclusion 7th character A see Appendix A PDX collection 0888
CC Exclusion 7th characters K & P see Appendix A PDX collection 0897

• CC +7th **M80.069 Age-related osteoporosis with current pathological fracture, unspecified lower leg**
CC Exclusion 7th character A see Appendix A PDX collection 0888
CC Exclusion 7th characters K & P see Appendix A PDX collection 0897

+ **M80.07 Age-related osteoporosis with current pathological fracture, ankle and foot**

• CC +7th **M80.071 Age-related osteoporosis with current pathological fracture, right ankle and foot**
CC Exclusion 7th character A see Appendix A PDX collection 0888
CC Exclusion 7th characters K & P see Appendix A PDX collection 0897

• CC +7th **M80.072 Age-related osteoporosis with current pathological fracture, left ankle and foot**
CC Exclusion 7th character A see Appendix A PDX collection 0888
CC Exclusion 7th characters K & P see Appendix A PDX collection 0897

• CC +7th **M80.079 Age-related osteoporosis with current pathological fracture, unspecified ankle and foot**
CC Exclusion 7th character A see Appendix A PDX collection 0888
CC Exclusion 7th characters K & P see Appendix A PDX collection 0897

• CC +7th **M80.08 Age-related osteoporosis with current pathological fracture, vertebra(e)**
CC Exclusion 7th character A see Appendix A PDX collection 0888
CC Exclusion 7th characters K & P see Appendix A PDX collection 0897

+ **M80.8 Other osteoporosis with current pathological fracture**
Drug-induced osteoporosis with current pathological fracture
Idiopathic osteoporosis with current pathological fracture
Osteoporosis of disuse with current pathological fracture
Postoophorectomy osteoporosis with current pathological fracture
Postsurgical malabsorption osteoporosis with current pathological fracture
Post-traumatic osteoporosis with current pathological fracture
Use additional code for adverse effect, if applicable, to identify drug (T36-T50 with fifth or sixth character 5)

CC X+7th **M80.80 Other osteoporosis with current pathological fracture, unspecified site**
CC Exclusion 7th character A see Appendix A PDX collection 0888
CC Exclusion 7th characters K & P see Appendix A PDX collection 0897

+ **M80.81 Other osteoporosis with pathological fracture, shoulder**

CC +7th **M80.811 Other osteoporosis with current pathological fracture, right shoulder**
CC Exclusion 7th character A see Appendix A PDX collection 0888
CC Exclusion 7th characters K & P see Appendix A PDX collection 0897

CC +7th **M80.812 Other osteoporosis with current pathological fracture, left shoulder**
CC Exclusion 7th character A see Appendix A PDX collection 0888
CC Exclusion 7th characters K & P see Appendix A PDX collection 0897

CC +7th **M80.819 Other osteoporosis with current pathological fracture, unspecified shoulder**
CC Exclusion 7th character A see Appendix A PDX collection 0888
CC Exclusion 7th characters K & P see Appendix A PDX collection 0897

+ **M80.82 Other osteoporosis with current pathological fracture, humerus**

CC +7th **M80.821 Other osteoporosis with current pathological fracture, right humerus**
CC Exclusion 7th character A see Appendix A PDX collection 0888
CC Exclusion 7th characters K & P see Appendix A PDX collection 0897

CC +7th **M80.822 Other osteoporosis with current pathological fracture, left humerus**
CC Exclusion 7th character A see Appendix A PDX collection 0888
CC Exclusion 7th characters K & P see Appendix A PDX collection 0897

CC +7th **M80.829 Other osteoporosis with current pathological fracture, unspecified humerus**
CC Exclusion 7th character A see Appendix A PDX collection 0888
CC Exclusion 7th characters K & P see Appendix A PDX collection 0897

+ **M80.83 Other osteoporosis with current pathological fracture, forearm**
Other osteoporosis with current pathological fracture of wrist

CC +7th **M80.831 Other osteoporosis with current pathological fracture, right forearm**
CC Exclusion 7th character A see Appendix A PDX collection 0888
CC Exclusion 7th characters K & P see Appendix A PDX collection 0897

CC +7th **M80.832 Other osteoporosis with current pathological fracture, left forearm**
CC Exclusion 7th character A see Appendix A PDX collection 0888
CC Exclusion 7th characters K & P see Appendix A PDX collection 0897

CC +7th **M80.839 Other osteoporosis with current pathologi fracture, unspecified forearm**
CC Exclusion 7th character A see Appendix A PDX collection 0888
CC Exclusion 7th characters K & P see Append A PDX collection 0897

+ **M80.84 Other osteoporosis with current pathological fractu hand**

CC +7th **M80.841 Other osteoporosis with current pathologi fracture, right hand**
CC Exclusion 7th character A see Appendix A PDX collection 0888
CC Exclusion 7th characters K & P see Append A PDX collection 0897

CC +7th **M80.842 Other osteoporosis with current pathologi fracture, left hand**
CC Exclusion 7th character A see Appendix A PDX collection 0888
CC Exclusion 7th characters K & P see Append A PDX collection 0897

CC +7th **M80.849 Other osteoporosis with current pathologi fracture, unspecified hand**
CC Exclusion 7th character A see Appendix A PDX collection 0888
CC Exclusion 7th characters K & P see Append A PDX collection 0897

+ **M80.85 Other osteoporosis with current pathological fractu femur**
Other osteoporosis with current pathological fracture of hip

CC +7th **M80.851 Other osteoporosis with current pathologi fracture, right femur**
CC Exclusion 7th character A see Appendix A PDX collection 0888
CC Exclusion 7th characters K & P see Appen A PDX collection 0897

CC +7th **M80.852 Other osteoporosis with current pathologi fracture, left femur**
CC Exclusion 7th character A see Appendix A PDX collection 0888
CC Exclusion 7th characters K & P see Appen A PDX collection 0897

CC +7th **M80.859 Other osteoporosis with current pathologi fracture, unspecified femur**
CC Exclusion 7th character A see Appendix A PDX collection 0888
CC Exclusion 7th characters K & P see Appen A PDX collection 0897

+ **M80.86 Other osteoporosis with current pathological fractu lower leg**

CC +7th **M80.861 Other osteoporosis with current pathologi fracture, right lower leg**
CC Exclusion 7th character A see Appendix A PDX collection 0888
CC Exclusion 7th characters K & P see Appen A PDX collection 0897

CC +7th **M80.862 Other osteoporosis with current pathologi fracture, left lower leg**
CC Exclusion 7th character A see Appendix A PDX collection 0888
CC Exclusion 7th characters K & P see Append A PDX collection 0897

CC +7th **M80.869 Other osteoporosis with current pathologi fracture, unspecified lower leg**
CC Exclusion 7th character A see Appendix A PDX collection 0888
CC Exclusion 7th characters K & P see Appen A PDX collection 0897

+ **M80.87 Other osteoporosis with current pathological fractu ankle and foot**

CC +7th **M80.871 Other osteoporosis with current pathologi fracture, right ankle and foot**
CC Exclusion 7th character A see Appendix A PDX collection 0888
CC Exclusion 7th characters K & P see Appen A PDX collection 0897

CC +7th **M80.872 Other osteoporosis with current pathologi fracture, left ankle and foot**
CC Exclusion 7th character A see Appendix A PDX collection 0888
CC Exclusion 7th characters K & P see Appen A PDX collection 0897

CC +7th **M80.879 Other osteoporosis with current pathologi fracture, unspecified ankle and foot**
CC Exclusion 7th character A see Appendix A PDX collection 0888
CC Exclusion 7th characters K & P see Append A PDX collection 0897

CC X+7th **M80.88 Other osteoporosis with current pathological fracture, vertebra(e)**
CC Exclusion 7th character A see Appendix A PDX collection 0888
CC Exclusion 7th characters K & P see Appendix A PDX collection 0897

M81 Osteoporosis without current pathological fracture
Use additional code to identify:
major osseous defect, if applicable (M89.7-)
personal history of (healed) osteoporosis fracture, if applicable (Z87.310)
Excludes1: *osteoporosis with current pathological fracture (M80.-)*
Sudeck's atrophy (M89.0)
Review coding guideline C.13.d

- **M81.0 Age-related osteoporosis without current pathological fracture**
  Involutional osteoporosis without current pathological fracture
  Osteoporosis NOS
  Postmenopausal osteoporosis without current pathological fracture
  Senile osteoporosis without current pathological fracture

M81.6 Localized osteoporosis [Lequesne]
Excludes1: *Sudeck's atrophy (M89.0)*

M81.8 Other osteoporosis without current pathological fracture
Drug-induced osteoporosis without current pathological fracture
Idiopathic osteoporosis without current pathological fracture
Osteoporosis of disuse without current pathological fracture
Postoophorectomy osteoporosis without current pathological fracture
Postsurgical malabsorption osteoporosis without current pathological fracture
Post-traumatic osteoporosis without current pathological fracture
Use additional code for adverse effect, if applicable, to identify drug (T36-T50 with fifth or sixth character 5)

M83 Adult osteomalacia
Excludes1: *infantile and juvenile osteomalacia (E55.0)*
renal osteodystrophy (N25.0)
rickets (active) (E55.0)
rickets (active) sequelae (E64.3)
vitamin D-resistant osteomalacia (E83.3)
vitamin D-resistant rickets (active) (E83.3)

- ♀ **M83.0 Puerperal osteomalacia**
- **M83.1 Senile osteomalacia**
- **M83.2 Adult osteomalacia due to malabsorption**
  Postsurgical malabsorption osteomalacia in adults
- **M83.3 Adult osteomalacia due to malnutrition**

M83.4 Aluminum bone disease
- **M83.5 Other drug-induced osteomalacia in adults**
  Use additional code for adverse effect, if applicable, to identify drug (T36-T50 with fifth or sixth character 5)
- **M83.8 Other adult osteomalacia**
- **M83.9 Adult osteomalacia, unspecified**

M84 Disorder of continuity of bone
Excludes2: *traumatic fracture of bone-see fracture, by site*

\+ **M84.3 Stress fracture**
Fatigue fracture
March fracture
Stress fracture NOS
Stress reaction
external cause code(s) to identify the cause of the stress fracture
Excludes1: *pathological fracture NOS (M84.4.-)*
pathological fracture due to osteoporosis (M80.-)
traumatic fracture (S12.-, S22.-, S32.-, S42.-, S52.-, S62.-, S72.-, S82.-, S92.-)
Excludes2: *personal history of (healed) stress (fatigue) fracture (Z87.312)*
stress fracture of vertebra (M48.4-)

The appropriate 7th character is to be added to each code from subcategory M84.3:
A initial encounter for fracture
D subsequent encounter for fracture with routine healing
G subsequent encounter for fracture with delayed healing
K subsequent encounter for fracture with nonunion
P subsequent encounter for fracture with malunion
S sequela

CC X+7th **M84.30 Stress fracture, unspecified site**
CC Exclusion 7th characters K & P see Appendix A PDX collection 0897

\+ **M84.31 Stress fracture, shoulder**

CC +7th **M84.311 Stress fracture, right shoulder**
CC Exclusion 7th characters K & P see Appendix A PDX collection 0897

CC +7th **M84.312 Stress fracture, left shoulder**
CC Exclusion 7th characters K & P see Appendix A PDX collection 0897

CC +7th **M84.319 Stress fracture, unspecified shoulder**
CC Exclusion 7th characters K & P see Appendix A PDX collection 0897

\+ **M84.32 Stress fracture, humerus**

CC +7th **M84.321 Stress fracture, right humerus**
CC Exclusion 7th characters K & P see Appendix A PDX collection 0897

CC +7th **M84.322 Stress fracture, left humerus**
CC Exclusion 7th characters K & P see Appendix A PDX collection 0897

CC +7th **M84.329 Stress fracture, unspecified humerus**
CC Exclusion 7th characters K & P see Appendix A PDX collection 0897

\+ **M84.33 Stress fracture, ulna and radius**

CC +7th **M84.331 Stress fracture, right ulna**
CC Exclusion 7th characters K & P see Appendix A PDX collection 0897

CC +7th **M84.332 Stress fracture, left ulna**
CC Exclusion 7th characters K & P see Appendix A PDX collection 0897

CC +7th **M84.333 Stress fracture, right radius**
CC Exclusion 7th characters K & P see Appendix A PDX collection 0897

CC +7th **M84.334 Stress fracture, left radius**
CC Exclusion 7th characters K & P see Appendix A PDX collection 0897

CC +7th **M84.339 Stress fracture, unspecified ulna and radius**
CC Exclusion 7th characters K & P see Appendix A PDX collection 0897

\+ **M84.34 Stress fracture, hand and fingers**

CC +7th **M84.341 Stress fracture, right hand**
CC Exclusion 7th characters K & P see Appendix A PDX collection 0897

CC +7th **M84.342 Stress fracture, left hand**
CC Exclusion 7th characters K & P see Appendix A PDX collection 0897

CC +7th **M84.343 Stress fracture, unspecified hand**
CC Exclusion 7th characters K & P see Appendix A PDX collection 0897

CC +7th **M84.344 Stress fracture, right finger(s)**
CC Exclusion 7th characters K & P see Appendix A PDX collection 0897

CC +7th **M84.345 Stress fracture, left finger(s)**
CC Exclusion 7th characters K & P see Appendix A PDX collection 0897

CC +7th **M84.346 Stress fracture, unspecified finger(s)**
CC Exclusion 7th characters K & P see Appendix A PDX collection 0897

\+ **M84.35 Stress fracture, pelvis and femur**
Stress fracture, hip

CC +7th **M84.350 Stress fracture, pelvis**
CC Exclusion 7th characters K & P see Appendix A PDX collection 0897

CC +7th **M84.351 Stress fracture, right femur**
CC Exclusion 7th characters K & P see Appendix A PDX collection 0897

CC +7th **M84.352 Stress fracture, left femur**
CC Exclusion 7th characters K & P see Appendix A PDX collection 0897

CC +7th **M84.353 Stress fracture, unspecified femur**
CC Exclusion 7th characters K & P see Appendix A PDX collection 0897

CC +7th **M84.359 Stress fracture, hip, unspecified**
CC Exclusion 7th characters K & P see Appendix A PDX collection 0897

\+ **M84.36 Stress fracture, tibia and fibula**

CC +7th **M84.361 Stress fracture, right tibia**
CC Exclusion 7th characters K & P see Appendix A PDX collection 0897

CC +7th **M84.362 Stress fracture, left tibia**
CC Exclusion 7th characters K & P see Appendix A PDX collection 0897

CC +7th **M84.363 Stress fracture, right fibula**
CC Exclusion 7th characters K & P see Appendix A PDX collection 0897

CC +7th **M84.364 Stress fracture, left fibula**
CC Exclusion 7th characters K & P see Appendix A PDX collection 0897

CC +7th **M84.369 Stress fracture, unspecified tibia and fibula**
CC Exclusion 7th characters K & P see Appendix A PDX collection 0897

+ M84.37 Stress fracture, ankle, foot and toes

CC +7th **M84.371 Stress fracture, right ankle**
CC Exclusion 7th characters K & P see Appendix A PDX collection 0897

CC +7th **M84.372 Stress fracture, left ankle**
CC Exclusion 7th characters K & P see Appendix A PDX collection 0897

CC +7th **M84.373 Stress fracture, unspecified ankle**
CC Exclusion 7th characters K & P see Appendix A PDX collection 0897

CC +7th **M84.374 Stress fracture, right foot**
CC Exclusion 7th characters K & P see Appendix A PDX collection 0897

CC +7th **M84.375 Stress fracture, left foot**
CC Exclusion 7th characters K & P see Appendix A PDX collection 0897

CC +7th **M84.376 Stress fracture, unspecified foot**
CC Exclusion 7th characters K & P see Appendix A PDX collection 0897

CC +7th **M84.377 Stress fracture, right toe(s)**
CC Exclusion 7th characters K & P see Appendix A PDX collection 0897

CC +7th **M84.378 Stress fracture, left toe(s)**
CC Exclusion 7th characters K & P see Appendix A PDX collection 0897

CC +7th **M84.379 Stress fracture, unspecified toe(s)**
CC Exclusion 7th characters K & P see Appendix A PDX collection 0897

CC X+7th **M84.38 Stress fracture, other site**
Excludes2: *stress fracture of vertebra (M48.4-)*
CC Exclusion 7th characters K & P see Appendix A PDX collection 0897

+ M84.4 Pathological fracture, not elsewhere classified
Chronic fracture
Pathological fracture NOS
Excludes1: *collapsed vertebra NEC (M48.5)*
pathological fracture in neoplastic disease (M84.5-)
pathological fracture in osteoporosis (M80.-)
pathological fracture in other disease (M84.6-)
stress fracture (M84.3-)
traumatic fracture (S12.-, S22.-, S32.-, S42.-, S52.-, S62.-, S72.-, S82.-, S92.-)
Excludes2: *personal history of (healed) pathological fracture (Z87.311)*

The appropriate 7th character is to be added to each code from subcategory M84.4:
A initial encounter for fracture
D subsequent encounter for fracture with routine healing
G subsequent encounter for fracture with delayed healing
K subsequent encounter for fracture with nonunion
P subsequent encounter for fracture with malunion
S sequela

CC X+7th **M84.40 Pathological fracture, unspecified site**
CC Exclusion 7th character A see Appendix A PDX collection 0888
CC Exclusion 7th characters K & P see Appendix A PDX collection 0897

+ M84.41 Pathological fracture, shoulder

CC +7th **M84.411 Pathological fracture, right shoulder**
CC Exclusion 7th character A see Appendix A PDX collection 0888
CC Exclusion 7th characters K & P see Appendix A PDX collection 0897

CC +7th **M84.412 Pathological fracture, left shoulder**
CC Exclusion 7th character A see Appendix A PDX collection 0888
CC Exclusion 7th characters K & P see Appendix A PDX collection 0897

CC +7th **M84.419 Pathological fracture, unspecified shoulder**
CC Exclusion 7th character A see Appendix A PDX collection 0888
CC Exclusion 7th characters K & P see Appendix A PDX collection 0897

+ M84.42 Pathological fracture, humerus

CC +7th **M84.421 Pathological fracture, right humerus**
CC Exclusion 7th character A see Appendix A PDX collection 0888
CC Exclusion 7th characters K & P see Appendix A PDX collection 0897

CC +7th **M84.422 Pathological fracture, left humerus**
CC Exclusion 7th character A see Appendix A PDX collection 0888
CC Exclusion 7th characters K & P see Appendix A PDX collection 0897

CC +7th **M84.429 Pathological fracture, unspecified humeru**
CC Exclusion 7th character A see Appendix A PDX collection 0888
CC Exclusion 7th characters K & P see Appenc A PDX collection 0897

+ M84.43 Pathological fracture, ulna and radius

CC +7th **M84.431 Pathological fracture, right ulna**
CC Exclusion 7th character A see Appendix A PDX collection 0888
CC Exclusion 7th characters K & P see Append A PDX collection 0897

CC +7th **M84.432 Pathological fracture, left ulna**
CC Exclusion 7th character A see Appendix A PDX collection 0888
CC Exclusion 7th characters K & P see Append A PDX collection 0897

CC +7th **M84.433 Pathological fracture, right radius**
CC Exclusion 7th character A see Appendix A PDX collection 0888
CC Exclusion 7th characters K & P see Append A PDX collection 0897

CC +7th **M84.434 Pathological fracture, left radius**
CC Exclusion 7th character A see Appendix A PDX collection 0888
CC Exclusion 7th characters K & P see Append A PDX collection 0897

CC +7th **M84.439 Pathological fracture, unspecified ulna and radius**
CC Exclusion 7th character A see Appendix A PDX collection 0888
CC Exclusion 7th characters K & P see Append A PDX collection 0897

+ M84.44 Pathological fracture, hand and fingers

CC +7th **M84.441 Pathological fracture, right hand**
CC Exclusion 7th character A see Appendix A PDX collection 0888
CC Exclusion 7th characters K & P see Appendi A PDX collection 0897

CC +7th **M84.442 Pathological fracture, left hand**
CC Exclusion 7th character A see Appendix A PDX collection 0888
CC Exclusion 7th characters K & P see Appendi A PDX collection 0897

CC +7th **M84.443 Pathological fracture, unspecified hand**
CC Exclusion 7th character A see Appendix A PDX collection 0888
CC Exclusion 7th characters K & P see Appendi A PDX collection 0897

CC +7th **M84.444 Pathological fracture, right finger(s)**
CC Exclusion 7th character A see Appendix A PDX collection 0888
CC Exclusion 7th characters K & P see Appendi A PDX collection 0897

CC +7th **M84.445 Pathological fracture, left finger(s)**
CC Exclusion 7th character A see Appendix A PDX collection 0888
CC Exclusion 7th characters K & P see Appendi A PDX collection 0897

CC +7th **M84.446 Pathological fracture, unspecified finger(s)**
CC Exclusion 7th character A see Appendix A PDX collection 0888
CC Exclusion 7th characters K & P see Appendix A PDX collection 0897

+ M84.45 Pathological fracture, femur and pelvis

CC +7th **M84.451 Pathological fracture, right femur**
CC Exclusion 7th character A see Appendix A PDX collection 0888
CC Exclusion 7th characters K & P see Appendix A PDX collection 0897

CC +7th **M84.452 Pathological fracture, left femur**
CC Exclusion 7th character A see Appendix A PDX collection 0888
CC Exclusion 7th characters K & P see Appendix A PDX collection 0897

CC +7th **M84.453 Pathological fracture, unspecified femur**
CC Exclusion 7th character A see Appendix A PDX collection 0888
CC Exclusion 7th characters K & P see Appendix A PDX collection 0897

CC +7th **M84.454 Pathological fracture, pelvis**
CC Exclusion 7th character A see Appendix A PDX collection 0888
CC Exclusion 7th characters K & P see Appendix A PDX collection 0897

CC +7th **M84.459 Pathological fracture, hip, unspecified**
CC Exclusion 7th character A see Appendix A PDX collection 0888
CC Exclusion 7th characters K & P see Appendix A PDX collection 0897

+ **M84.46 Pathological fracture, tibia and fibula**

CC +7th **M84.461 Pathological fracture, right tibia**
CC Exclusion 7th character A see Appendix A PDX collection 0888
CC Exclusion 7th characters K & P see Appendix A PDX collection 0897

CC +7th **M84.462 Pathological fracture, left tibia**
CC Exclusion 7th character A see Appendix A PDX collection 0888
CC Exclusion 7th characters K & P see Appendix A PDX collection 0897

CC +7th **M84.463 Pathological fracture, right fibula**
CC Exclusion 7th character A see Appendix A PDX collection 0888
CC Exclusion 7th characters K & P see Appendix A PDX collection 0897

CC +7th **M84.464 Pathological fracture, left fibula**
CC Exclusion 7th character A see Appendix A PDX collection 0888
CC Exclusion 7th characters K & P see Appendix A PDX collection 0897

CC +7th **M84.469 Pathological fracture, unspecified tibia and fibula**
CC Exclusion 7th character A see Appendix A PDX collection 0888
CC Exclusion 7th characters K & P see Appendix A PDX collection 0897

+ **M84.47 Pathological fracture, ankle, foot and toes**

CC +7th **M84.471 Pathological fracture, right ankle**
CC Exclusion 7th character A see Appendix A PDX collection 0888
CC Exclusion 7th characters K & P see Appendix A PDX collection 0897

CC +7th **M84.472 Pathological fracture, left ankle**
CC Exclusion 7th character A see Appendix A PDX collection 0888
CC Exclusion 7th characters K & P see Appendix A PDX collection 0897

CC +7th **M84.473 Pathological fracture, unspecified ankle**
CC Exclusion 7th character A see Appendix A PDX collection 0888
CC Exclusion 7th characters K & P see Appendix A PDX collection 0897

CC +7th **M84.474 Pathological fracture, right foot**
CC Exclusion 7th character A see Appendix A PDX collection 0888
CC Exclusion 7th characters K & P see Appendix A PDX collection 0897

CC +7th **M84.475 Pathological fracture, left foot**
CC Exclusion 7th character A see Appendix A PDX collection 0888
CC Exclusion 7th characters K & P see Appendix A PDX collection 0897

CC +7th **M84.476 Pathological fracture, unspecified foot**
CC Exclusion 7th character A see Appendix A PDX collection 0888
CC Exclusion 7th characters K & P see Appendix A PDX collection 0897

CC +7th **M84.477 Pathological fracture, right toe(s)**
CC Exclusion 7th character A see Appendix A PDX collection 0888
CC Exclusion 7th characters K & P see Appendix A PDX collection 0897

CC +7th **M84.478 Pathological fracture, left toe(s)**
CC Exclusion 7th character A see Appendix A PDX collection 0888
CC Exclusion 7th characters K & P see Appendix A PDX collection 0897

CC +7th **M84.479 Pathological fracture, unspecified toe(s)**
CC Exclusion 7th character A see Appendix A PDX collection 0888
CC Exclusion 7th characters K & P see Appendix A PDX collection 0897

CC X+7th **M84.48 Pathological fracture, other site**
CC Exclusion 7th character A see Appendix A PDX collection 0888
CC Exclusion 7th characters K & P see Appendix A PDX collection 0897

+ **M84.5 Pathological fracture in neoplastic disease**
Code also underlying neoplasm

The appropriate 7th character is to be added to each code from subcategory M84.5:
A initial encounter for fracture
D subsequent encounter for fracture with routine healing
G subsequent encounter for fracture with delayed healing
K subsequent encounter for fracture with nonunion
P subsequent encounter for fracture with malunion
S sequela

Review coding guideline C.2.l.6

CC X+7th **M84.50 Pathological fracture in neoplastic disease, unspecified site**
CC Exclusion 7th character A see Appendix A PDX collection 0888
CC Exclusion 7th characters K & P see Appendix A PDX collection 0897

+ **M84.51 Pathological fracture in neoplastic disease, shoulder**

CC +7th **M84.511 Pathological fracture in neoplastic disease, right shoulder**
CC Exclusion 7th character A see Appendix A PDX collection 0888
CC Exclusion 7th characters K & P see Appendix A PDX collection 0897

CC +7th **M84.512 Pathological fracture in neoplastic disease, left shoulder**
CC Exclusion 7th character A see Appendix A PDX collection 0888
CC Exclusion 7th characters K & P see Appendix A PDX collection 0897

CC +7th **M84.519 Pathological fracture in neoplastic disease, unspecified shoulder**
CC Exclusion 7th character A see Appendix A PDX collection 0888
CC Exclusion 7th characters K & P see Appendix A PDX collection 0897

+ **M84.52 Pathological fracture in neoplastic disease, humerus**

CC +7th **M84.521 Pathological fracture in neoplastic disease, right humerus**
CC Exclusion 7th character A see Appendix A PDX collection 0888
CC Exclusion 7th characters K & P see Appendix A PDX collection 0897

CC +7th **M84.522 Pathological fracture in neoplastic disease, left humerus**
CC Exclusion 7th character A see Appendix A PDX collection 0888
CC Exclusion 7th characters K & P see Appendix A PDX collection 0897

CC +7th **M84.529 Pathological fracture in neoplastic disease, unspecified humerus**
CC Exclusion 7th character A see Appendix A PDX collection 0888
CC Exclusion 7th characters K & P see Appendix A PDX collection 0897

+ **M84.53 Pathological fracture in neoplastic disease, ulna and radius**

CC +7th **M84.531 Pathological fracture in neoplastic disease, right ulna**
CC Exclusion 7th character A see Appendix A PDX collection 0888
CC Exclusion 7th characters K & P see Appendix A PDX collection 0897

CC +7th **M84.532 Pathological fracture in neoplastic disease, left ulna**
CC Exclusion 7th character A see Appendix A PDX collection 0888
CC Exclusion 7th characters K & P see Appendix A PDX collection 0897

CC +7th **M84.533 Pathological fracture in neoplastic disease, right radius**
CC Exclusion 7th character A see Appendix A PDX collection 0888
CC Exclusion 7th characters K & P see Appendix A PDX collection 0897

CC +7th **M84.534 Pathological fracture in neoplastic disease, left radius**
CC Exclusion 7th character A see Appendix A PDX collection 0888
CC Exclusion 7th characters K & P see Appendix A PDX collection 0897

CC +7th **M84.539 Pathological fracture in neoplastic disease, unspecified ulna and radius**
CC Exclusion 7th character A see Appendix A PDX collection 0888
CC Exclusion 7th characters K & P see Appendix A PDX collection 0897

+ **M84.54 Pathological fracture in neoplastic disease, hand**
  CC +7th **M84.541 Pathological fracture in neoplastic disease, right hand**
    CC Exclusion 7th character A see Appendix A PDX collection 0888
    CC Exclusion 7th characters K & P see Appendix A PDX collection 0897
  CC +7th **M84.542 Pathological fracture in neoplastic disease, left hand**
    CC Exclusion 7th character A see Appendix A PDX collection 0888
    CC Exclusion 7th characters K & P see Appendix A PDX collection 0897
  CC +7th **M84.549 Pathological fracture in neoplastic disease, unspecified hand**
    CC Exclusion 7th character A see Appendix A PDX collection 0888
    CC Exclusion 7th characters K & P see Appendix A PDX collection 0897

+ **M84.55 Pathological fracture in neoplastic disease, pelvis and femur**
  CC +7th **M84.550 Pathological fracture in neoplastic disease, pelvis**
    CC Exclusion 7th character A see Appendix A PDX collection 0888
    CC Exclusion 7th characters K & P see Appendix A PDX collection 0897
  CC +7th **M84.551 Pathological fracture in neoplastic disease, right femur**
    CC Exclusion 7th character A see Appendix A PDX collection 0888
    CC Exclusion 7th characters K & P see Appendix A PDX collection 0897
  CC +7th **M84.552 Pathological fracture in neoplastic disease, left femur**
    CC Exclusion 7th character A see Appendix A PDX collection 0888
    CC Exclusion 7th characters K & P see Appendix A PDX collection 0897
  CC +7th **M84.553 Pathological fracture in neoplastic disease, unspecified femur**
    CC Exclusion 7th character A see Appendix A PDX collection 0888
    CC Exclusion 7th characters K & P see Appendix A PDX collection 0897
  CC +7th **M84.559 Pathological fracture in neoplastic disease, hip, unspecified**
    CC Exclusion 7th character A see Appendix A PDX collection 0888
    CC Exclusion 7th characters K & P see Appendix A PDX collection 0897

+ **M84.56 Pathological fracture in neoplastic disease, tibia and fibula**
  CC +7th **M84.561 Pathological fracture in neoplastic disease, right tibia**
    CC Exclusion 7th character A see Appendix A PDX collection 0888
    CC Exclusion 7th characters K & P see Appendix A PDX collection 0897
  CC +7th **M84.562 Pathological fracture in neoplastic disease, left tibia**
    CC Exclusion 7th character A see Appendix A PDX collection 0888
    CC Exclusion 7th characters K & P see Appendix A PDX collection 0897
  CC +7th **M84.563 Pathological fracture in neoplastic disease, right fibula**
    CC Exclusion 7th character A see Appendix A PDX collection 0888
    CC Exclusion 7th characters K & P see Appendix A PDX collection 0897
  CC +7th **M84.564 Pathological fracture in neoplastic disease, left fibula**
    CC Exclusion 7th character A see Appendix A PDX collection 0888
    CC Exclusion 7th characters K & P see Appendix A PDX collection 0897
  CC +7th **M84.569 Pathological fracture in neoplastic disease, unspecified tibia and fibula**
    CC Exclusion 7th character A see Appendix A PDX collection 0888
    CC Exclusion 7th characters K & P see Appendix A PDX collection 0897

+ **M84.57 Pathological fracture in neoplastic disease, ankle an[d] foot**
  CC +7th **M84.571 Pathological fracture in neoplastic disease, right ankle**
    CC Exclusion 7th character A see Appendix A PDX collection 0888
    CC Exclusion 7th characters K & P see Append[ix] A PDX collection 0897
  CC +7th **M84.572 Pathological fracture in neoplastic disease, left ankle**
    CC Exclusion 7th character A see Appendix A PDX collection 0888
    CC Exclusion 7th characters K & P see Append[ix] A PDX collection 0897
  CC +7th **M84.573 Pathological fracture in neoplastic disease, unspecified ankle**
    CC Exclusion 7th character A see Appendix A PDX collection 0888
    CC Exclusion 7th characters K & P see Append[ix] A PDX collection 0897
  CC +7th **M84.574 Pathological fracture in neoplastic disease, right foot**
    CC Exclusion 7th character A see Appendix A PDX collection 0888
    CC Exclusion 7th characters K & P see Append[ix] A PDX collection 0897
  CC +7th **M84.575 Pathological fracture in neoplastic disease, left foot**
    CC Exclusion 7th character A see Appendix A PDX collection 0888
    CC Exclusion 7th characters K & P see Append[ix] A PDX collection 0897
  CC +7th **M84.576 Pathological fracture in neoplastic disease, unspecified foot**
    CC Exclusion 7th character A see Appendix A PDX collection 0888
    CC Exclusion 7th characters K & P see Append[ix] A PDX collection 0897

CC X+7th **M84.58 Pathological fracture in neoplastic disease, other specified site**
  M84.58 Pathological fracture in neoplastic disease, other specified site
    Pathological fracture in neoplastic disease, vertebrae
  CC Exclusion 7th character A see Appendix A PDX collecti[on] 0888
  CC Exclusion 7th characters K & P see Appendix A PDX collection 0897

+ **M84.6 Pathological fracture in other disease**
  Code also underlying condition
  Excludes1: *pathological fracture in osteoporosis (M80.-)*

The appropriate 7th character is to be added to each code from subcategory M84.6:
A initial encounter for fracture
D subsequent encounter for fracture with routine healing
G subsequent encounter for fracture with delayed healing
K subsequent encounter for fracture with nonunion
P subsequent encounter for fracture with malunion
S sequela

CC X+7th **M84.60 Pathological fracture in other disease, unspecified si[te]**
  CC Exclusion 7th character A see Appendix A PDX collecti[on] 0888
  CC Exclusion 7th characters K & P see Appendix A PDX collection 0897

+ **M84.61 Pathological fracture in other disease, shoulder**
  CC +7th **M84.611 Pathological fracture in other disease, righ[t] shoulder**
    CC Exclusion 7th character A see Appendix A PDX collection 0888
    CC Exclusion 7th characters K & P see Appendi[x] A PDX collection 0897
  CC +7th **M84.612 Pathological fracture in other disease, left shoulder**
    CC Exclusion 7th character A see Appendix A PDX collection 0888
    CC Exclusion 7th characters K & P see Appendi[x] A PDX collection 0897
  CC +7th **M84.619 Pathological fracture in other disease, unspecified shoulder**
    CC Exclusion 7th character A see Appendix A PDX collection 0888
    CC Exclusion 7th characters K & P see Appendi[x] A PDX collection 0897

\+ **M84.62 Pathological fracture in other disease, humerus**

CC +7th **M84.621 Pathological fracture in other disease, right humerus**
CC Exclusion 7th character A see Appendix A PDX collection 0888
CC Exclusion 7th characters K & P see Appendix A PDX collection 0897

CC +7th **M84.622 Pathological fracture in other disease, left humerus**
CC Exclusion 7th character A see Appendix A PDX collection 0888
CC Exclusion 7th characters K & P see Appendix A PDX collection 0897

CC +7th **M84.629 Pathological fracture in other disease, unspecified humerus**
CC Exclusion 7th character A see Appendix A PDX collection 0888
CC Exclusion 7th characters K & P see Appendix A PDX collection 0897

\+ **M84.63 Pathological fracture in other disease, ulna and radius**

CC +7th **M84.631 Pathological fracture in other disease, right ulna**
CC Exclusion 7th character A see Appendix A PDX collection 0888
CC Exclusion 7th characters K & P see Appendix A PDX collection 0897

CC +7th **M84.632 Pathological fracture in other disease, left ulna**
CC Exclusion 7th character A see Appendix A PDX collection 0888
CC Exclusion 7th characters K & P see Appendix A PDX collection 0897

CC +7th **M84.633 Pathological fracture in other disease, right radius**
CC Exclusion 7th character A see Appendix A PDX collection 0888
CC Exclusion 7th characters K & P see Appendix A PDX collection 0897

CC +7th **M84.634 Pathological fracture in other disease, left radius**
CC Exclusion 7th character A see Appendix A PDX collection 0888
CC Exclusion 7th characters K & P see Appendix A PDX collection 0897

CC +7th **M84.639 Pathological fracture in other disease, unspecified ulna and radius**
CC Exclusion 7th character A see Appendix A PDX collection 0888
CC Exclusion 7th characters K & P see Appendix A PDX collection 0897

\+ **M84.64 Pathological fracture in other disease, hand**

CC +7th **M84.641 Pathological fracture in other disease, right hand**
CC Exclusion 7th character A see Appendix A PDX collection 0888
CC Exclusion 7th characters K & P see Appendix A PDX collection 0897

CC +7th **M84.642 Pathological fracture in other disease, left hand**
CC Exclusion 7th character A see Appendix A PDX collection 0888
CC Exclusion 7th characters K & P see Appendix A PDX collection 0897

CC +7th **M84.649 Pathological fracture in other disease, unspecified hand**
CC Exclusion 7th character A see Appendix A PDX collection 0888
CC Exclusion 7th characters K & P see Appendix A PDX collection 0897

\+ **M84.65 Pathological fracture in other disease, pelvis and femur**

M84.650 Pathological fracture in other disease, pelvis

CC +7th **M84.651 Pathological fracture in other disease, right femur**
CC Exclusion 7th character A see Appendix A PDX collection 0888
CC Exclusion 7th characters K & P see Appendix A PDX collection 0897

CC +7th **M84.652 Pathological fracture in other disease, left femur**
CC Exclusion 7th character A see Appendix A PDX collection 0888
CC Exclusion 7th characters K & P see Appendix A PDX collection 0897

CC +7th **M84.653 Pathological fracture in other disease, unspecified femur**
CC Exclusion 7th character A see Appendix A PDX collection 0888
CC Exclusion 7th characters K & P see Appendix A PDX collection 0897

CC +7th **M84.659 Pathological fracture in other disease, hip, unspecified**
CC Exclusion 7th character A see Appendix A PDX collection 0888
CC Exclusion 7th characters K & P see Appendix A PDX collection 0897

\+ **M84.66 Pathological fracture in other disease, tibia and fibula**

CC +7th **M84.661 Pathological fracture in other disease, right tibia**
CC Exclusion 7th character A see Appendix A PDX collection 0888
CC Exclusion 7th characters K & P see Appendix A PDX collection 0897

CC +7th **M84.662 Pathological fracture in other disease, left tibia**
CC Exclusion 7th character A see Appendix A PDX collection 0888
CC Exclusion 7th characters K & P see Appendix A PDX collection 0897

CC +7th **M84.663 Pathological fracture in other disease, right fibula**
CC Exclusion 7th character A see Appendix A PDX collection 0888
CC Exclusion 7th characters K & P see Appendix A PDX collection 0897

CC +7th **M84.664 Pathological fracture in other disease, left fibula**
CC Exclusion 7th character A see Appendix A PDX collection 0888
CC Exclusion 7th characters K & P see Appendix A PDX collection 0897

CC +7th **M84.669 Pathological fracture in other disease, unspecified tibia and fibula**
CC Exclusion 7th character A see Appendix A PDX collection 0888
CC Exclusion 7th characters K & P see Appendix A PDX collection 0897

\+ **M84.67 Pathological fracture in other disease, ankle and foot**

CC +7th **M84.671 Pathological fracture in other disease, right ankle**
CC Exclusion 7th character A see Appendix A PDX collection 0888
CC Exclusion 7th characters K & P see Appendix A PDX collection 0897

CC +7th **M84.672 Pathological fracture in other disease, left ankle**
CC Exclusion 7th character A see Appendix A PDX collection 0888
CC Exclusion 7th characters K & P see Appendix A PDX collection 0897

CC +7th **M84.673 Pathological fracture in other disease, unspecified ankle**
CC Exclusion 7th character A see Appendix A PDX collection 0888
CC Exclusion 7th characters K & P see Appendix A PDX collection 0897

CC +7th **M84.674 Pathological fracture in other disease, right foot**
CC Exclusion 7th character A see Appendix A PDX collection 0888
CC Exclusion 7th characters K & P see Appendix A PDX collection 0897

CC +7th **M84.675 Pathological fracture in other disease, left foot**
CC Exclusion 7th character A see Appendix A PDX collection 0888
CC Exclusion 7th characters K & P see Appendix A PDX collection 0897

CC +7th **M84.676 Pathological fracture in other disease, unspecified foot**
CC Exclusion 7th character A see Appendix A PDX collection 0888
CC Exclusion 7th characters K & P see Appendix A PDX collection 0897

CC X+7th **M84.68 Pathological fracture in other disease, other site**
CC Exclusion 7th character A see Appendix A PDX collection 0888
CC Exclusion 7th characters K & P see Appendix A PDX collection 0897

\+ **M84.8 Other disorders of continuity of bone**
M84.80 Other disorders of continuity of bone, unspecified site
\+ **M84.81 Other disorders of continuity of bone, shoulder**
M84.811 Other disorders of continuity of bone, right shoulder
M84.812 Other disorders of continuity of bone, left shoulder
M84.819 Other disorders of continuity of bone, unspecified shoulder
\+ **M84.82 Other disorders of continuity of bone, humerus**
M84.821 Other disorders of continuity of bone, right humerus
M84.822 Other disorders of continuity of bone, left humerus
M84.829 Other disorders of continuity of bone, unspecified humerus
\+ **M84.83 Other disorders of continuity of bone, ulna and radius**
M84.831 Other disorders of continuity of bone, right ulna
M84.832 Other disorders of continuity of bone, left ulna
M84.833 Other disorders of continuity of bone, right radius
M84.834 Other disorders of continuity of bone, left radius
M84.839 Other disorders of continuity of bone, unspecified ulna and radius
\+ **M84.84 Other disorders of continuity of bone, hand**
M84.841 Other disorders of continuity of bone, right hand
M84.842 Other disorders of continuity of bone, left hand
M84.849 Other disorders of continuity of bone, unspecified hand
\+ **M84.85 Other disorders of continuity of bone, pelvic region and thigh**
M84.851 Other disorders of continuity of bone, right pelvic region and thigh
M84.852 Other disorders of continuity of bone, left pelvic region and thigh
M84.859 Other disorders of continuity of bone, unspecified pelvic region and thigh
\+ **M84.86 Other disorders of continuity of bone, tibia and fibula**
M84.861 Other disorders of continuity of bone, right tibia
M84.862 Other disorders of continuity of bone, left tibia
M84.863 Other disorders of continuity of bone, right fibula
M84.864 Other disorders of continuity of bone, left fibula
M84.869 Other disorders of continuity of bone, unspecified tibia and fibula
\+ **M84.87 Other disorders of continuity of bone, ankle and foot**
M84.871 Other disorders of continuity of bone, right ankle and foot
M84.872 Other disorders of continuity of bone, left ankle and foot
M84.879 Other disorders of continuity of bone, unspecified ankle and foot
M84.88 Other disorders of continuity of bone, other site
M84.9 Disorder of continuity of bone, unspecified

M85 Other disorders of bone density and structure

Excludes1: *osteogenesis imperfecta (Q78.0)*
osteopetrosis (Q78.2)
osteopoikilosis (Q78.8)
polyostotic fibrous dysplasia (Q78.1)

\+ **M85.0 Fibrous dysplasia (monostotic)**
Excludes2: *fibrous dysplasia of jaw (M27.8)*
M85.00 Fibrous dysplasia (monostotic), unspecified site
\+ **M85.01 Fibrous dysplasia (monostotic), shoulder**
M85.011 Fibrous dysplasia (monostotic), right shoulder
M85.012 Fibrous dysplasia (monostotic), left shoulder
M85.019 Fibrous dysplasia (monostotic), unspecified shoulder
\+ **M85.02 Fibrous dysplasia (monostotic), upper arm**
M85.021 Fibrous dysplasia (monostotic), right upper arm
M85.022 Fibrous dysplasia (monostotic), left upper arm
M85.029 Fibrous dysplasia (monostotic), unspecifie upper arm
\+ **M85.03 Fibrous dysplasia (monostotic), forearm**
M85.031 Fibrous dysplasia (monostotic), right forearm
M85.032 Fibrous dysplasia (monostotic), left forear
M85.039 Fibrous dysplasia (monostotic), unspecifie forearm
\+ **M85.04 Fibrous dysplasia (monostotic), hand**
M85.041 Fibrous dysplasia (monostotic), right hand
M85.042 Fibrous dysplasia (monostotic), left hand
M85.049 Fibrous dysplasia (monostotic), unspecified hand
\+ **M85.05 Fibrous dysplasia (monostotic), thigh**
M85.051 Fibrous dysplasia (monostotic), right thig
M85.052 Fibrous dysplasia (monostotic), left thigh
M85.059 Fibrous dysplasia (monostotic), unspecifie thigh
\+ **M85.06 Fibrous dysplasia (monostotic), lower leg**
M85.061 Fibrous dysplasia (monostotic), right lower leg
M85.062 Fibrous dysplasia (monostotic), left lower
M85.069 Fibrous dysplasia (monostotic), unspecified lower leg
\+ **M85.07 Fibrous dysplasia (monostotic), ankle and foot**
M85.071 Fibrous dysplasia (monostotic), right ankl and foot
M85.072 Fibrous dysplasia (monostotic), left ankle and foot
M85.079 Fibrous dysplasia (monostotic), unspecifie ankle and foot
M85.08 Fibrous dysplasia (monostotic), other site
M85.09 Fibrous dysplasia (monostotic), multiple sites
\+ **M85.1 Skeletal fluorosis**
M85.10 Skeletal fluorosis, unspecified site
\+ **M85.11 Skeletal fluorosis, shoulder**
M85.111 Skeletal fluorosis, right shoulder
M85.112 Skeletal fluorosis, left shoulder
M85.119 Skeletal fluorosis, unspecified shoulder
\+ **M85.12 Skeletal fluorosis, upper arm**
M85.121 Skeletal fluorosis, right upper arm
M85.122 Skeletal fluorosis, left upper arm
M85.129 Skeletal fluorosis, unspecified upper arm
\+ **M85.13 Skeletal fluorosis, forearm**
M85.131 Skeletal fluorosis, right forearm
M85.132 Skeletal fluorosis, left forearm
M85.139 Skeletal fluorosis, unspecified forearm
\+ **M85.14 Skeletal fluorosis, hand**
M85.141 Skeletal fluorosis, right hand
M85.142 Skeletal fluorosis, left hand
M85.149 Skeletal fluorosis, unspecified hand
\+ **M85.15 Skeletal fluorosis, thigh**
M85.151 Skeletal fluorosis, right thigh
M85.152 Skeletal fluorosis, left thigh
M85.159 Skeletal fluorosis, unspecified thigh
\+ **M85.16 Skeletal fluorosis, lower leg**
M85.161 Skeletal fluorosis, right lower leg
M85.162 Skeletal fluorosis, left lower leg
M85.169 Skeletal fluorosis, unspecified lower leg
\+ **M85.17 Skeletal fluorosis, ankle and foot**
M85.171 Skeletal fluorosis, right ankle and foot
M85.172 Skeletal fluorosis, left ankle and foot
M85.179 Skeletal fluorosis, unspecified ankle and fo
M85.18 Skeletal fluorosis, other site
M85.19 Skeletal fluorosis, multiple sites
M85.2 Hyperostosis of skull
\+ **M85.3 Osteitis condensans**
M85.30 Osteitis condensans, unspecified site
\+ **M85.31 Osteitis condensans, shoulder**
M85.311 Osteitis condensans, right shoulder
M85.312 Osteitis condensans, left shoulder
M85.319 Osteitis condensans, unspecified shoulder
\+ **M85.32 Osteitis condensans, upper arm**
M85.321 Osteitis condensans, right upper arm
M85.322 Osteitis condensans, left upper arm
M85.329 Osteitis condensans, unspecified upper arn
\+ **M85.33 Osteitis condensans, forearm**
M85.331 Osteitis condensans, right forearm
M85.332 Osteitis condensans, left forearm
M85.339 Osteitis condensans, unspecified forearm

+ **M85.34 Osteitis condensans, hand**
  - **M85.341 Osteitis condensans, right hand**
  - **M85.342 Osteitis condensans, left hand**
  - **M85.349 Osteitis condensans, unspecified hand**
+ **M85.35 Osteitis condensans, thigh**
  - **M85.351 Osteitis condensans, right thigh**
  - **M85.352 Osteitis condensans, left thigh**
  - **M85.359 Osteitis condensans, unspecified thigh**
+ **M85.36 Osteitis condensans, lower leg**
  - **M85.361 Osteitis condensans, right lower leg**
  - **M85.362 Osteitis condensans, left lower leg**
  - **M85.369 Osteitis condensans, unspecified lower leg**
+ **M85.37 Osteitis condensans, ankle and foot**
  - **M85.371 Osteitis condensans, right ankle and foot**
  - **M85.372 Osteitis condensans, left ankle and foot**
  - **M85.379 Osteitis condensans, unspecified ankle and foot**

M85.38 Osteitis condensans, other site
M85.39 Osteitis condensans, multiple sites

+ **M85.4 Solitary bone cyst**
  Excludes2: *solitary cyst of jaw (M27.4)*
  M85.40 Solitary bone cyst, unspecified site
+ **M85.41 Solitary bone cyst, shoulder**
  - **M85.411 Solitary bone cyst, right shoulder**
  - **M85.412 Solitary bone cyst, left shoulder**
  - **M85.419 Solitary bone cyst, unspecified shoulder**
+ **M85.42 Solitary bone cyst, humerus**
  - **M85.421 Solitary bone cyst, right humerus**
  - **M85.422 Solitary bone cyst, left humerus**
  - **M85.429 Solitary bone cyst, unspecified humerus**
+ **M85.43 Solitary bone cyst, ulna and radius**
  - **M85.431 Solitary bone cyst, right ulna and radius**
  - **M85.432 Solitary bone cyst, left ulna and radius**
  - **M85.439 Solitary bone cyst, unspecified ulna and radius**
+ **M85.44 Solitary bone cyst, hand**
  - **M85.441 Solitary bone cyst, right hand**
  - **M85.442 Solitary bone cyst, left hand**
  - **M85.449 Solitary bone cyst, unspecified hand**
+ **M85.45 Solitary bone cyst, pelvis**
  - **M85.451 Solitary bone cyst, right pelvis**
  - **M85.452 Solitary bone cyst, left pelvis**
  - **M85.459 Solitary bone cyst, unspecified pelvis**
+ **M85.46 Solitary bone cyst, tibia and fibula**
  - **M85.461 Solitary bone cyst, right tibia and fibula**
  - **M85.462 Solitary bone cyst, left tibia and fibula**
  - **M85.469 Solitary bone cyst, unspecified tibia and fibula**
+ **M85.47 Solitary bone cyst, ankle and foot**
  - **M85.471 Solitary bone cyst, right ankle and foot**
  - **M85.472 Solitary bone cyst, left ankle and foot**
  - **M85.479 Solitary bone cyst, unspecified ankle and foot**

M85.48 Solitary bone cyst, other site

+ **M85.5 Aneurysmal bone cyst**
  Excludes2: *aneurysmal cyst of jaw (M27.4)*
  M85.50 Aneurysmal bone cyst, unspecified site
+ **M85.51 Aneurysmal bone cyst, shoulder**
  - **M85.511 Aneurysmal bone cyst, right shoulder**
  - **M85.512 Aneurysmal bone cyst, left shoulder**
  - **M85.519 Aneurysmal bone cyst, unspecified shoulder**
+ **M85.52 Aneurysmal bone cyst, upper arm**
  - **M85.521 Aneurysmal bone cyst, right upper arm**
  - **M85.522 Aneurysmal bone cyst, left upper arm**
  - **M85.529 Aneurysmal bone cyst, unspecified upper arm**
+ **M85.53 Aneurysmal bone cyst, forearm**
  - **M85.531 Aneurysmal bone cyst, right forearm**
  - **M85.532 Aneurysmal bone cyst, left forearm**
  - **M85.539 Aneurysmal bone cyst, unspecified forearm**
+ **M85.54 Aneurysmal bone cyst, hand**
  - **M85.541 Aneurysmal bone cyst, right hand**
  - **M85.542 Aneurysmal bone cyst, left hand**
  - **M85.549 Aneurysmal bone cyst, unspecified hand**
+ **M85.55 Aneurysmal bone cyst, thigh**
  - **M85.551 Aneurysmal bone cyst, right thigh**
  - **M85.552 Aneurysmal bone cyst, left thigh**
  - **M85.559 Aneurysmal bone cyst, unspecified thigh**
+ **M85.56 Aneurysmal bone cyst, lower leg**
  - **M85.561 Aneurysmal bone cyst, right lower leg**
  - **M85.562 Aneurysmal bone cyst, left lower leg**
  - **M85.569 Aneurysmal bone cyst, unspecified lower leg**
+ **M85.57 Aneurysmal bone cyst, ankle and foot**
  - **M85.571 Aneurysmal bone cyst, right ankle and foot**
  - **M85.572 Aneurysmal bone cyst, left ankle and foot**
  - **M85.579 Aneurysmal bone cyst, unspecified ankle and foot**

M85.58 Aneurysmal bone cyst, other site
M85.59 Aneurysmal bone cyst, multiple sites

+ **M85.6 Other cyst of bone**
  Excludes1: *cyst of jaw NEC (M27.4)*
  osteitis fibrosa cystica generalisata [von Recklinghausen's disease of bone] (E21.0)
  M85.60 Other cyst of bone, unspecified site
+ **M85.61 Other cyst of bone, shoulder**
  - **M85.611 Other cyst of bone, right shoulder**
  - **M85.612 Other cyst of bone, left shoulder**
  - **M85.619 Other cyst of bone, unspecified shoulder**
+ **M85.62 Other cyst of bone, upper arm**
  - **M85.621 Other cyst of bone, right upper arm**
  - **M85.622 Other cyst of bone, left upper arm**
  - **M85.629 Other cyst of bone, unspecified upper arm**
+ **M85.63 Other cyst of bone, forearm**
  - **M85.631 Other cyst of bone, right forearm**
  - **M85.632 Other cyst of bone, left forearm**
  - **M85.639 Other cyst of bone, unspecified forearm**
+ **M85.64 Other cyst of bone, hand**
  - **M85.641 Other cyst of bone, right hand**
  - **M85.642 Other cyst of bone, left hand**
  - **M85.649 Other cyst of bone, unspecified hand**
+ **M85.65 Other cyst of bone, thigh**
  - **M85.651 Other cyst of bone, right thigh**
  - **M85.652 Other cyst of bone, left thigh**
  - **M85.659 Other cyst of bone, unspecified thigh**
+ **M85.66 Other cyst of bone, lower leg**
  - **M85.661 Other cyst of bone, right lower leg**
  - **M85.662 Other cyst of bone, left lower leg**
  - **M85.669 Other cyst of bone, unspecified lower leg**
+ **M85.67 Other cyst of bone, ankle and foot**
  - **M85.671 Other cyst of bone, right ankle and foot**
  - **M85.672 Other cyst of bone, left ankle and foot**
  - **M85.679 Other cyst of bone, unspecified ankle and foot**

M85.68 Other cyst of bone, other site
M85.69 Other cyst of bone, multiple sites

+ **M85.8 Other specified disorders of bone density and structure**
  Hyperostosis of bones, except skull
  Osteosclerosis, acquired
  Excludes1: *diffuse idiopathic skeletal hyperostosis [DISH] (M48.1)*
  osteosclerosis congenita (Q77.4)
  osteosclerosis fragilitas (generalista) (Q78.2)
  osteosclerosis myelofibrosis (D75.81)
  M85.80 Other specified disorders of bone density and structure, unspecified site
+ **M85.81 Other specified disorders of bone density and structure, shoulder**
  - **M85.811 Other specified disorders of bone density and structure, right shoulder**
  - **M85.812 Other specified disorders of bone density and structure, left shoulder**
  - **M85.819 Other specified disorders of bone density and structure, unspecified shoulder**
+ **M85.82 Other specified disorders of bone density and structure, upper arm**
  - **M85.821 Other specified disorders of bone density and structure, right upper arm**
  - **M85.822 Other specified disorders of bone density and structure, left upper arm**
  - **M85.829 Other specified disorders of bone density and structure, unspecified upper arm**
+ **M85.83 Other specified disorders of bone density and structure, forearm**
  - **M85.831 Other specified disorders of bone density and structure, right forearm**
  - **M85.832 Other specified disorders of bone density and structure, left forearm**
  - **M85.839 Other specified disorders of bone density and structure, unspecified forearm**
+ **M85.84 Other specified disorders of bone density and structure, hand**
  - **M85.841 Other specified disorders of bone density and structure, right hand**

M85.842 **Other specified disorders of bone density and structure, left hand**
M85.849 **Other specified disorders of bone density and structure, unspecified hand**
\+ M85.85 **Other specified disorders of bone density and structure, thigh**
M85.851 **Other specified disorders of bone density and structure, right thigh**
M85.852 **Other specified disorders of bone density and structure, left thigh**
M85.859 **Other specified disorders of bone density and structure, unspecified thigh**
\+ M85.86 **Other specified disorders of bone density and structure, lower leg**
M85.861 **Other specified disorders of bone density and structure, right lower leg**
M85.862 **Other specified disorders of bone density and structure, left lower leg**
M85.869 **Other specified disorders of bone density and structure, unspecified lower leg**
\+ M85.87 **Other specified disorders of bone density and structure, ankle and foot**
M85.871 **Other specified disorders of bone density and structure, right ankle and foot**
M85.872 **Other specified disorders of bone density and structure, left ankle and foot**
M85.879 **Other specified disorders of bone density and structure, unspecified ankle and foot**
M85.88 **Other specified disorders of bone density and structure, other site**
M85.89 **Other specified disorders of bone density and structure, multiple sites**
M85.9 **Disorder of bone density and structure, unspecified**

Other osteopathies (M86-M90)

Excludes1: *postprocedural osteopathies (M96.-)*

M86 Osteomyelitis

Use additional code (B95-B97) to identify infectious agent

Use additional code to identify major osseous defect, if applicable (M89.7-)

Excludes1: *osteomyelitis due to:*
echinococcus (B67.2)
gonococcus (A54.43)
salmonella (A02.24)

Excludes2: *ostemyelitis of:*
orbit (H05.0-)
petrous bone (H70.2-)
vertebra (M46.2-)

\+ M86.0 **Acute hematogenous osteomyelitis**
CC M86.00 **Acute hematogenous osteomyelitis, unspecified site**
CC Exclusion see Appendix A PDX collection 0898
\+ M86.01 **Acute hematogenous osteomyelitis, shoulder**
CC M86.011 **Acute hematogenous osteomyelitis, right shoulder**
CC Exclusion see Appendix A PDX collection 0899
CC M86.012 **Acute hematogenous osteomyelitis, left shoulder**
CC Exclusion see Appendix A PDX collection 0899
CC M86.019 **Acute hematogenous osteomyelitis, unspecified shoulder**
CC Exclusion see Appendix A PDX collection 0899
\+ M86.02 **Acute hematogenous osteomyelitis, humerus**
CC M86.021 **Acute hematogenous osteomyelitis, right humerus**
CC Exclusion see Appendix A PDX collection 0900
CC M86.022 **Acute hematogenous osteomyelitis, left humerus**
CC Exclusion see Appendix A PDX collection 0900
CC M86.029 **Acute hematogenous osteomyelitis, unspecified humerus**
CC Exclusion see Appendix A PDX collection 0900
\+ M86.03 **Acute hematogenous osteomyelitis, radius and ulna**
CC M86.031 **Acute hematogenous osteomyelitis, right radius and ulna**
CC Exclusion see Appendix A PDX collection 0901
CC M86.032 **Acute hematogenous osteomyelitis, left radius and ulna**
CC Exclusion see Appendix A PDX collection 0901
CC M86.039 **Acute hematogenous osteomyelitis, unspecified radius and ulna**
CC Exclusion see Appendix A PDX collection 0901

\+ M86.04 **Acute hematogenous osteomyelitis, hand**
CC M86.041 **Acute hematogenous osteomyelitis, right hand**
CC Exclusion see Appendix A PDX collection 0
CC M86.042 **Acute hematogenous osteomyelitis, left ha**
CC Exclusion see Appendix A PDX collection 0
CC M86.049 **Acute hematogenous osteomyelitis, unspecified hand**
CC Exclusion see Appendix A PDX collection 0
\+ M86.05 **Acute hematogenous osteomyelitis, femur**
CC M86.051 **Acute hematogenous osteomyelitis, right femur**
CC Exclusion see Appendix A PDX collection 0
CC M86.052 **Acute hematogenous osteomyelitis, left femur**
CC Exclusion see Appendix A PDX collection 0
CC M86.059 **Acute hematogenous osteomyelitis, unspecified femur**
CC Exclusion see Appendix A PDX collection 0
\+ M86.06 **Acute hematogenous osteomyelitis, tibia and fibula**
CC M86.061 **Acute hematogenous osteomyelitis, right tibia and fibula**
CC Exclusion see Appendix A PDX collection 0
CC M86.062 **Acute hematogenous osteomyelitis, left tib and fibula**
CC Exclusion see Appendix A PDX collection 0
CC M86.069 **Acute hematogenous osteomyelitis, unspecified tibia and fibula**
CC Exclusion see Appendix A PDX collection 0
\+ M86.07 **Acute hematogenous osteomyelitis, ankle and foot**
CC M86.071 **Acute hematogenous osteomyelitis, right ankle and foot**
CC Exclusion see Appendix A PDX collection 0
CC M86.072 **Acute hematogenous osteomyelitis, left an and foot**
CC Exclusion see Appendix A PDX collection 0
CC M86.079 **Acute hematogenous osteomyelitis, unspecified ankle and foot**
CC Exclusion see Appendix A PDX collection 0
CC M86.08 **Acute hematogenous osteomyelitis, other sites**
CC Exclusion see Appendix A PDX collection 0882
CC M86.09 **Acute hematogenous osteomyelitis, multiple sites**
CC Exclusion see Appendix A PDX collection 0898
\+ M86.1 **Other acute osteomyelitis**
CC M86.10 **Other acute osteomyelitis, unspecified site**
CC Exclusion see Appendix A PDX collection 0898
\+ M86.11 **Other acute osteomyelitis, shoulder**
CC M86.111 **Other acute osteomyelitis, right shoulder**
CC Exclusion see Appendix A PDX collection 0
CC M86.112 **Other acute osteomyelitis, left shoulder**
CC Exclusion see Appendix A PDX collection 0
CC M86.119 **Other acute osteomyelitis, unspecified shoulder**
CC Exclusion see Appendix A PDX collection 0
\+ M86.12 **Other acute osteomyelitis, humerus**
CC M86.121 **Other acute osteomyelitis, right humerus**
CC Exclusion see Appendix A PDX collection 0
CC M86.122 **Other acute osteomyelitis, left humerus**
CC Exclusion see Appendix A PDX collection 0
CC M86.129 **Other acute osteomyelitis, unspecified humerus**
CC Exclusion see Appendix A PDX collection 0
\+ M86.13 **Other acute osteomyelitis, radius and ulna**
CC M86.131 **Other acute osteomyelitis, right radius and ulna**
CC Exclusion see Appendix A PDX collection 0
CC M86.132 **Other acute osteomyelitis, left radius and ulna**
CC Exclusion see Appendix A PDX collection 0
CC M86.139 **Other acute osteomyelitis, unspecified radi and ulna**
CC Exclusion see Appendix A PDX collection 0
\+ M86.14 **Other acute osteomyelitis, hand**
CC M86.141 **Other acute osteomyelitis, righthand**
CC Exclusion see Appendix A PDX collection 0
CC M86.142 **Other acute osteomyelitis, left hand**
CC Exclusion see Appendix A PDX collection 0
CC M86.149 **Other acute osteomyelitis, unspecified han**
CC Exclusion see Appendix A PDX collection 0
\+ M86.15 **Other acute osteomyelitis, femur**
CC M86.151 **Other acute osteomyelitis, right femur**
CC Exclusion see Appendix A PDX collection 0
CC M86.152 **Other acute osteomyelitis, left femur**
CC Exclusion see Appendix A PDX collection 0

CC **M86.159** Other acute osteomyelitis, unspecified femur
CC Exclusion see Appendix A PDX collection 0903
+ **M86.16** Other acute osteomyelitis, tibia and fibula
CC **M86.161** Other acute osteomyelitis, right tibia and fibula
CC Exclusion see Appendix A PDX collection 0904
CC **M86.162** Other acute osteomyelitis, left tibia and fibula
CC Exclusion see Appendix A PDX collection 0904
CC **M86.169** Other acute osteomyelitis, unspecified tibia and fibula
CC Exclusion see Appendix A PDX collection 0904
+ **M86.17** Other acute osteomyelitis, ankle and foot
CC **M86.171** Other acute osteomyelitis, right ankle and foot
CC Exclusion see Appendix A PDX collection 0905
CC **M86.172** Other acute osteomyelitis, left ankle and foot
CC Exclusion see Appendix A PDX collection 0905
CC **M86.179** Other acute osteomyelitis, unspecified ankle and foot
CC Exclusion see Appendix A PDX collection 0905
CC **M86.18** Other acute osteomyelitis, other site
CC Exclusion see Appendix A PDX collection 0882
CC **M86.19** Other acute osteomyelitis, multiple sites
CC Exclusion see Appendix A PDX collection 0898
+ **M86.2** Subacute osteomyelitis
CC **M86.20** Subacute osteomyelitis, unspecified site
CC Exclusion see Appendix A PDX collection 0898
+ **M86.21** Subacute osteomyelitis, shoulder
CC **M86.211** Subacute osteomyelitis, right shoulder
CC Exclusion see Appendix A PDX collection 0899
CC **M86.212** Subacute osteomyelitis, left shoulder
CC Exclusion see Appendix A PDX collection 0899
CC **M86.219** Subacute osteomyelitis, unspecified shoulder
CC Exclusion see Appendix A PDX collection 0899
+ **M86.22** Subacute osteomyelitis, humerus
CC **M86.221** Subacute osteomyelitis, right humerus
CC Exclusion see Appendix A PDX collection 0900
CC **M86.222** Subacute osteomyelitis, left humerus
CC Exclusion see Appendix A PDX collection 0900
CC **M86.229** Subacute osteomyelitis, unspecified humerus
CC Exclusion see Appendix A PDX collection 0900
+ **M86.23** Subacute osteomyelitis, radius and ulna
CC **M86.231** Subacute osteomyelitis, right radius and ulna
CC Exclusion see Appendix A PDX collection 0901
CC **M86.232** Subacute osteomyelitis, left radius and ulna
CC Exclusion see Appendix A PDX collection 0901
CC **M86.239** Subacute osteomyelitis, unspecified radius and ulna
CC Exclusion see Appendix A PDX collection 0901
+ **M86.24** Subacute osteomyelitis, hand
CC **M86.241** Subacute osteomyelitis, right hand
CC Exclusion see Appendix A PDX collection 0902
CC **M86.242** Subacute osteomyelitis, left hand
CC Exclusion see Appendix A PDX collection 0902
CC **M86.249** Subacute osteomyelitis, unspecified hand
CC Exclusion see Appendix A PDX collection 0902
+ **M86.25** Subacute osteomyelitis, femur
CC **M86.251** Subacute osteomyelitis, right femur
CC Exclusion see Appendix A PDX collection 0903
CC **M86.252** Subacute osteomyelitis, left femur
CC Exclusion see Appendix A PDX collection 0903
CC **M86.259** Subacute osteomyelitis, unspecified femur
CC Exclusion see Appendix A PDX collection 0903
+ **M86.26** Subacute osteomyelitis, tibia and fibula
CC **M86.261** Subacute osteomyelitis, right tibia and fibula
CC Exclusion see Appendix A PDX collection 0904
CC **M86.262** Subacute osteomyelitis, left tibia and fibula
CC Exclusion see Appendix A PDX collection 0904
CC **M86.269** Subacute osteomyelitis, unspecified tibia and fibula
CC Exclusion see Appendix A PDX collection 0904
+ **M86.27** Subacute osteomyelitis, ankle and foot
CC **M86.271** Subacute osteomyelitis, right ankle and foot
CC Exclusion see Appendix A PDX collection 0905
CC **M86.272** Subacute osteomyelitis, left ankle and foot
CC Exclusion see Appendix A PDX collection 0905
CC **M86.279** Subacute osteomyelitis, unspecified ankle and foot
CC Exclusion see Appendix A PDX collection 0905
CC **M86.28** Subacute osteomyelitis, other site
CC Exclusion see Appendix A PDX collection 0882
CC **M86.29** Subacute osteomyelitis, multiple sites
CC Exclusion see Appendix A PDX collection 0898

+ **M86.3** Chronic multifocal osteomyelitis
CC **M86.30** Chronic multifocal osteomyelitis, unspecified site
CC Exclusion see Appendix A PDX collection 0906
+ **M86.31** Chronic multifocal osteomyelitis, shoulder
CC **M86.311** Chronic multifocal osteomyelitis, right shoulder
CC Exclusion see Appendix A PDX collection 0881
CC **M86.312** Chronic multifocal osteomyelitis, left shoulder
CC Exclusion see Appendix A PDX collection 0881
CC **M86.319** Chronic multifocal osteomyelitis, unspecified shoulder
CC Exclusion see Appendix A PDX collection 0881
+ **M86.32** Chronic multifocal osteomyelitis, humerus
CC **M86.321** Chronic multifocal osteomyelitis, right humerus
CC Exclusion see Appendix A PDX collection 0881
CC **M86.322** Chronic multifocal osteomyelitis, left humerus
CC Exclusion see Appendix A PDX collection 0881
CC **M86.329** Chronic multifocal osteomyelitis, unspecified humerus
CC Exclusion see Appendix A PDX collection 0881
+ **M86.33** Chronic multifocal osteomyelitis, radius and ulna
CC **M86.331** Chronic multifocal osteomyelitis, right radius and ulna
CC Exclusion see Appendix A PDX collection 0881
CC **M86.332** Chronic multifocal osteomyelitis, left radius and ulna
CC Exclusion see Appendix A PDX collection 0881
CC **M86.339** Chronic multifocal osteomyelitis, unspecified radius and ulna
CC Exclusion see Appendix A PDX collection 0881
+ **M86.34** Chronic multifocal osteomyelitis, hand
CC **M86.341** Chronic multifocal osteomyelitis, right hand
CC Exclusion see Appendix A PDX collection 0881
CC **M86.342** Chronic multifocal osteomyelitis, left hand
CC Exclusion see Appendix A PDX collection 0881
CC **M86.349** Chronic multifocal osteomyelitis, unspecified hand
CC Exclusion see Appendix A PDX collection 0881
+ **M86.35** Chronic multifocal osteomyelitis, femur
CC **M86.351** Chronic multifocal osteomyelitis, right femur
CC Exclusion see Appendix A PDX collection 0881
CC **M86.352** Chronic multifocal osteomyelitis, left femur
CC Exclusion see Appendix A PDX collection 0881
CC **M86.359** Chronic multifocal osteomyelitis, unspecified femur
CC Exclusion see Appendix A PDX collection 0881
+ **M86.36** Chronic multifocal osteomyelitis, tibia and fibula
CC **M86.361** Chronic multifocal osteomyelitis, right tibia and fibula
CC Exclusion see Appendix A PDX collection 0881
CC **M86.362** Chronic multifocal osteomyelitis, left tibia and fibula
CC Exclusion see Appendix A PDX collection 0881
CC **M86.369** Chronic multifocal osteomyelitis, unspecified tibia and fibula
CC Exclusion see Appendix A PDX collection 0881
+ **M86.37** Chronic multifocal osteomyelitis, ankle and foot
CC **M86.371** Chronic multifocal osteomyelitis, right ankle and foot
CC Exclusion see Appendix A PDX collection 0881
CC **M86.372** Chronic multifocal osteomyelitis, left ankle and foot
CC Exclusion see Appendix A PDX collection 0881
CC **M86.379** Chronic multifocal osteomyelitis, unspecified ankle and foot
CC Exclusion see Appendix A PDX collection 0881
CC **M86.38** Chronic multifocal osteomyelitis, other site
CC Exclusion see Appendix A PDX collection 0881
CC **M86.39** Chronic multifocal osteomyelitis, multiple sites
CC Exclusion see Appendix A PDX collection 0881
+ **M86.4** Chronic osteomyelitis with draining sinus
CC **M86.40** Chronic osteomyelitis with draining sinus, unspecified site
CC Exclusion see Appendix A PDX collection 0906
+ **M86.41** Chronic osteomyelitis with draining sinus, shoulder
CC **M86.411** Chronic osteomyelitis with draining sinus, right shoulder
CC Exclusion see Appendix A PDX collection 0881
CC **M86.412** Chronic osteomyelitis with draining sinus, left shoulder
CC Exclusion see Appendix A PDX collection 0881

CC **M86.419** **Chronic osteomyelitis with draining sinus, unspecified shoulder**
CC Exclusion see Appendix A PDX collection 0881

\+ **M86.42** **Chronic osteomyelitis with draining sinus, humerus**
CC **M86.421** **Chronic osteomyelitis with draining sinus, right humerus**
CC Exclusion see Appendix A PDX collection 0881
CC **M86.422** **Chronic osteomyelitis with draining sinus, left humerus**
CC Exclusion see Appendix A PDX collection 0881
CC **M86.429** **Chronic osteomyelitis with draining sinus, unspecified humerus**
CC Exclusion see Appendix A PDX collection 0881

\+ **M86.43** **Chronic osteomyelitis with draining sinus, radius and ulna**
CC **M86.431** **Chronic osteomyelitis with draining sinus, right radius and ulna**
CC Exclusion see Appendix A PDX collection 0881
CC **M86.432** **Chronic osteomyelitis with draining sinus, left radius and ulna**
CC Exclusion see Appendix A PDX collection 0881
CC **M86.439** **Chronic osteomyelitis with draining sinus, unspecified radius and ulna**
CC Exclusion see Appendix A PDX collection 0881

\+ **M86.44** **Chronic osteomyelitis with draining sinus, hand**
CC **M86.441** **Chronic osteomyelitis with draining sinus, right hand**
CC Exclusion see Appendix A PDX collection 0881
CC **M86.442** **Chronic osteomyelitis with draining sinus, left hand**
CC Exclusion see Appendix A PDX collection 0881
CC **M86.449** **Chronic osteomyelitis with draining sinus, unspecified hand**
CC Exclusion see Appendix A PDX collection 0881

\+ **M86.45** **Chronic osteomyelitis with draining sinus, femur**
CC **M86.451** **Chronic osteomyelitis with draining sinus, right femur**
CC Exclusion see Appendix A PDX collection 0881
CC **M86.452** **Chronic osteomyelitis with draining sinus, left femur**
CC Exclusion see Appendix A PDX collection 0881
CC **M86.459** **Chronic osteomyelitis with draining sinus, unspecified femur**
CC Exclusion see Appendix A PDX collection 0881

\+ **M86.46** **Chronic osteomyelitis with draining sinus, tibia and fibula**
CC **M86.461** **Chronic osteomyelitis with draining sinus, right tibia and fibula**
CC Exclusion see Appendix A PDX collection 0881
CC **M86.462** **Chronic osteomyelitis with draining sinus, left tibia and fibula**
CC Exclusion see Appendix A PDX collection 0881
CC **M86.469** **Chronic osteomyelitis with draining sinus, unspecified tibia and fibula**
CC Exclusion see Appendix A PDX collection 0881

\+ **M86.47** **Chronic osteomyelitis with draining sinus, ankle and foot**
CC **M86.471** **Chronic osteomyelitis with draining sinus, right ankle and foot**
CC Exclusion see Appendix A PDX collection 0881
CC **M86.472** **Chronic osteomyelitis with draining sinus, left ankle and foot**
CC Exclusion see Appendix A PDX collection 0881
CC **M86.479** **Chronic osteomyelitis with draining sinus, unspecified ankle and foot**
CC Exclusion see Appendix A PDX collection 0881

CC **M86.48** **Chronic osteomyelitis with draining sinus, other site**
CC Exclusion see Appendix A PDX collection 0881
CC **M86.49** **Chronic osteomyelitis with draining sinus, multiple sites**
CC Exclusion see Appendix A PDX collection 0881

\+ **M86.5** **Other chronic hematogenous osteomyelitis**
CC **M86.50** **Other chronic hematogenous osteomyelitis, unspecified site**
CC Exclusion see Appendix A PDX collection 0906

\+ **M86.51** **Other chronic hematogenous osteomyelitis, shoulder**
CC **M86.511** **Other chronic hematogenous osteomyelitis, right shoulder**
CC Exclusion see Appendix A PDX collection 0881
CC **M86.512** **Other chronic hematogenous osteomyelitis, left shoulder**
CC Exclusion see Appendix A PDX collection 0881
CC **M86.519** **Other chronic hematogenous osteomyelitis unspecified shoulder**
CC Exclusion see Appendix A PDX collection 0

\+ **M86.52** **Other chronic hematogenous osteomyelitis, humeru**
CC **M86.521** **Other chronic hematogenous osteomyelitis right humerus**
CC Exclusion see Appendix A PDX collection 0
CC **M86.522** **Other chronic hematogenous osteomyelitis left humerus**
CC Exclusion see Appendix A PDX collection 0
CC **M86.529** **Other chronic hematogenous osteomyelitis unspecified humerus**
CC Exclusion see Appendix A PDX collection 0

\+ **M86.53** **Other chronic hematogenous osteomyelitis, radius a ulna**
CC **M86.531** **Other chronic hematogenous osteomyelitis right radius and ulna**
CC Exclusion see Appendix A PDX collection 0
CC **M86.532** **Other chronic hematogenous osteomyelitis left radius and ulna**
CC Exclusion see Appendix A PDX collection 0
CC **M86.539** **Other chronic hematogenous osteomyelitis unspecified radius and ulna**
CC Exclusion see Appendix A PDX collection 0

\+ **M86.54** **Other chronic hematogenous osteomyelitis, hand**
CC **M86.541** **Other chronic hematogenous osteomyelitis right hand**
CC Exclusion see Appendix A PDX collection 0
CC **M86.542** **Other chronic hematogenous osteomyelitis left hand**
CC Exclusion see Appendix A PDX collection 0
CC **M86.549** **Other chronic hematogenous osteomyelitis unspecified hand**
CC Exclusion see Appendix A PDX collection 0

\+ **M86.55** **Other chronic hematogenous osteomyelitis, femur**
CC **M86.551** **Other chronic hematogenous osteomyelitis right femur**
CC Exclusion see Appendix A PDX collection 0
CC **M86.552** **Other chronic hematogenous osteomyelitis left femur**
CC Exclusion see Appendix A PDX collection 0
CC **M86.559** **Other chronic hematogenous osteomyelitis unspecified femur**
CC Exclusion see Appendix A PDX collection 0

\+ **M86.56** **Other chronic hematogenous osteomyelitis, tibia an fibula**
CC **M86.561** **Other chronic hematogenous osteomyelitis right tibia and fibula**
CC Exclusion see Appendix A PDX collection 0
CC **M86.562** **Other chronic hematogenous osteomyelitis left tibia and fibula**
CC Exclusion see Appendix A PDX collection 0
CC **M86.569** **Other chronic hematogenous osteomyelitis unspecified tibia and fibula**
CC Exclusion see Appendix A PDX collection 0

\+ **M86.57** **Other chronic hematogenous osteomyelitis, ankle an foot**
CC **M86.571** **Other chronic hematogenous osteomyelitis right ankle and foot**
CC Exclusion see Appendix A PDX collection 0
CC **M86.572** **Other chronic hematogenous osteomyelitis left ankle and foot**
CC Exclusion see Appendix A PDX collection 0
CC **M86.579** **Other chronic hematogenous osteomyelitis unspecified ankle and foot**
CC Exclusion see Appendix A PDX collection 0

CC **M86.58** **Other chronic hematogenous osteomyelitis, other sit**
CC Exclusion see Appendix A PDX collection 0881
CC **M86.59** **Other chronic hematogenous osteomyelitis, multiple sites**
CC Exclusion see Appendix A PDX collection 0881

\+ **M86.6** **Other chronic osteomyelitis**
CC **M86.60** **Other chronic osteomyelitis, unspecified site**
CC Exclusion see Appendix A PDX collection 0906

\+ **M86.61** **Other chronic osteomyelitis, shoulder**
CC **M86.611** **Other chronic osteomyelitis, right shoulde**
CC Exclusion see Appendix A PDX collection 0
CC **M86.612** **Other chronic osteomyelitis, left shoulder**
CC Exclusion see Appendix A PDX collection 0
CC **M86.619** **Other chronic osteomyelitis, unspecified shoulder**
CC Exclusion see Appendix A PDX collection 0

+ **M86.62 Other chronic osteomyelitis, humerus**
CC **M86.621 Other chronic osteomyelitis, right humerus**
CC Exclusion see Appendix A PDX collection 0881
CC **M86.622 Other chronic osteomyelitis, left humerus**
CC Exclusion see Appendix A PDX collection 0881
CC **M86.629 Other chronic osteomyelitis, unspecified humerus**
CC Exclusion see Appendix A PDX collection 0881
+ **M86.63 Other chronic osteomyelitis, radius and ulna**
CC **M86.631 Other chronic osteomyelitis, right radius and ulna**
CC Exclusion see Appendix A PDX collection 0881
CC **M86.632 Other chronic osteomyelitis, left radius and ulna**
CC Exclusion see Appendix A PDX collection 0881
CC **M86.639 Other chronic osteomyelitis, unspecified radius and ulna**
CC Exclusion see Appendix A PDX collection 0881
+ **M86.64 Other chronic osteomyelitis, hand**
CC **M86.641 Other chronic osteomyelitis, right hand**
CC Exclusion see Appendix A PDX collection 0881
CC **M86.642 Other chronic osteomyelitis, left hand**
CC Exclusion see Appendix A PDX collection 0881
CC **M86.649 Other chronic osteomyelitis, unspecified hand**
CC Exclusion see Appendix A PDX collection 0881
+ **M86.65 Other chronic osteomyelitis, thigh**
CC **M86.651 Other chronic osteomyelitis, right thigh**
CC Exclusion see Appendix A PDX collection 0881
CC **M86.652 Other chronic osteomyelitis, left thigh**
CC Exclusion see Appendix A PDX collection 0881
CC **M86.659 Other chronic osteomyelitis, unspecified thigh**
CC Exclusion see Appendix A PDX collection 0881
+ **M86.66 Other chronic osteomyelitis, tibia and fibula**
CC **M86.661 Other chronic osteomyelitis, right tibia and fibula**
CC Exclusion see Appendix A PDX collection 0881
CC **M86.662 Other chronic osteomyelitis, left tibia and fibula**
CC Exclusion see Appendix A PDX collection 0881
CC **M86.669 Other chronic osteomyelitis, unspecified tibia and fibula**
CC Exclusion see Appendix A PDX collection 0881
+ **M86.67 Other chronic osteomyelitis, ankle and foot**
CC **M86.671 Other chronic osteomyelitis, right ankle and foot**
CC Exclusion see Appendix A PDX collection 0881
CC **M86.672 Other chronic osteomyelitis, left ankle and foot**
CC Exclusion see Appendix A PDX collection 0881
CC **M86.679 Other chronic osteomyelitis, unspecified ankle and foot**
CC Exclusion see Appendix A PDX collection 0881
CC **M86.68 Other chronic osteomyelitis, other site**
CC Exclusion see Appendix A PDX collection 0881
CC **M86.69 Other chronic osteomyelitis, multiple sites**
CC Exclusion see Appendix A PDX collection 0881
+ **M86.8 Other osteomyelitis**
Brodie's abscess
+ **M86.8X Other osteomyelitis**
CC **M86.8X0 Other osteomyelitis, multiple sites**
CC Exclusion see Appendix A PDX collection 0881
CC **M86.8X1 Other osteomyelitis, shoulder**
CC Exclusion see Appendix A PDX collection 0881
CC **M86.8X2 Other osteomyelitis, upper arm**
CC Exclusion see Appendix A PDX collection 0881
CC **M86.8X3 Other osteomyelitis, forearm**
CC Exclusion see Appendix A PDX collection 0881
CC **M86.8X4 Other osteomyelitis, hand**
CC Exclusion see Appendix A PDX collection 0881
CC **M86.8X5 Other osteomyelitis, thigh**
CC Exclusion see Appendix A PDX collection 0881
CC **M86.8X6 Other osteomyelitis, lower leg**
CC Exclusion see Appendix A PDX collection 0881
CC **M86.8X7 Other osteomyelitis, ankle and foot**
CC Exclusion see Appendix A PDX collection 0881
CC **M86.8X8 Other osteomyelitis, other site**
CC Exclusion see Appendix A PDX collection 0881
CC **M86.8X9 Other osteomyelitis, unspecified sites**
CC Exclusion see Appendix A PDX collection 0906
CC **M86.9 Osteomyelitis, unspecified**
Infection of bone NOS
Periostitis without osteomyelitis
CC Exclusion see Appendix A PDX collection 0906

M87 Osteonecrosis

Includes: avascular necrosis of bone
Use additional code to identify major osseous defect, if applicable (M89.7-)
Excludes1: *juvenile osteonecrosis (M91-M92)*
osteochondropathies (M90-M93)

+ **M87.0 Idiopathic aseptic necrosis of bone**
CC **M87.00 Idiopathic aseptic necrosis of unspecifiedbone**
CC Exclusion see Appendix A PDX collection 0907
+ **M87.01 Idiopathic aseptic necrosis of shoulder**
Idiopathic aseptic necrosis of clavicle and scapula
CC **M87.011 Idiopathic aseptic necrosis of right shoulder**
CC Exclusion see Appendix A PDX collection 0908
CC **M87.012 Idiopathic aseptic necrosis of left shoulder**
CC Exclusion see Appendix A PDX collection 0908
CC **M87.019 Idiopathic aseptic necrosis of unspecified shoulder**
CC Exclusion see Appendix A PDX collection 0908
+ **M87.02 Idiopathic aseptic necrosis of humerus**
CC **M87.021 Idiopathic aseptic necrosis of right humerus**
CC Exclusion see Appendix A PDX collection 0908
CC **M87.022 Idiopathic aseptic necrosis of left humerus**
CC Exclusion see Appendix A PDX collection 0908
CC **M87.029 Idiopathic aseptic necrosis of unspecified humerus**
CC Exclusion see Appendix A PDX collection 0908
+ **M87.03 Idiopathic aseptic necrosis of radius, ulna and carpus**
CC **M87.031 Idiopathic aseptic necrosis of right radius**
CC Exclusion see Appendix A PDX collection 0907
CC **M87.032 Idiopathic aseptic necrosis of left radius**
CC Exclusion see Appendix A PDX collection 0907
CC **M87.033 Idiopathic aseptic necrosis of unspecified radius**
CC Exclusion see Appendix A PDX collection 0907
CC **M87.034 Idiopathic aseptic necrosis of right ulna**
CC Exclusion see Appendix A PDX collection 0907
CC **M87.035 Idiopathic aseptic necrosis of left ulna**
CC Exclusion see Appendix A PDX collection 0907
CC **M87.036 Idiopathic aseptic necrosis of unspecified ulna**
CC Exclusion see Appendix A PDX collection 0907
CC **M87.037 Idiopathic aseptic necrosis of right carpus**
CC Exclusion see Appendix A PDX collection 0907
CC **M87.038 Idiopathic aseptic necrosis of left carpus**
CC Exclusion see Appendix A PDX collection 0907
CC **M87.039 Idiopathic aseptic necrosis of unspecified carpus**
CC Exclusion see Appendix A PDX collection 0907
+ **M87.04 Idiopathic aseptic necrosis of hand and fingers**
Idiopathic aseptic necrosis of metacarpals and phalanges of hands
CC **M87.041 Idiopathic aseptic necrosis of right hand**
CC Exclusion see Appendix A PDX collection 0907
CC **M87.042 Idiopathic aseptic necrosis of left hand**
CC Exclusion see Appendix A PDX collection 0907
CC **M87.043 Idiopathic aseptic necrosis of unspecified hand**
CC Exclusion see Appendix A PDX collection 0907
CC **M87.044 Idiopathic aseptic necrosis of right finger(s)**
CC Exclusion see Appendix A PDX collection 0907
CC **M87.045 Idiopathic aseptic necrosis of left finger(s)**
CC Exclusion see Appendix A PDX collection 0907
CC **M87.046 Idiopathic aseptic necrosis of unspecified finger(s)**
CC Exclusion see Appendix A PDX collection 0907
+ **M87.05 Idiopathic aseptic necrosis of pelvis and femur**
CC **M87.050 Idiopathic aseptic necrosis of pelvis**
CC Exclusion see Appendix A PDX collection 0907
CC **M87.051 Idiopathic aseptic necrosis of right femur**
CC Exclusion see Appendix A PDX collection 0909
CC **M87.052 Idiopathic aseptic necrosis of left femur**
CC Exclusion see Appendix A PDX collection 0909
CC **M87.059 Idiopathic aseptic necrosis of unspecified femur**
Idiopathic aseptic necrosis of hip NOS
CC Exclusion see Appendix A PDX collection 0909
+ **M87.06 Idiopathic aseptic necrosis of tibia and fibula**
CC **M87.061 Idiopathic aseptic necrosis of right tibia**
CC Exclusion see Appendix A PDX collection 0907
CC **M87.062 Idiopathic aseptic necrosis of left tibia**
CC Exclusion see Appendix A PDX collection 0907
CC **M87.063 Idiopathic aseptic necrosis of unspecified tibia**
CC Exclusion see Appendix A PDX collection 0907

CC **M87.064 Idiopathic aseptic necrosis of right fibula**
CC Exclusion see Appendix A PDX collection 0907

CC **M87.065 Idiopathic aseptic necrosis of left fibula**
CC Exclusion see Appendix A PDX collection 0907

CC **M87.066 Idiopathic aseptic necrosis of unspecified fibula**
CC Exclusion see Appendix A PDX collection 0907

+ **M87.07 Idiopathic aseptic necrosis of ankle, foot and toes**
Idiopathic aseptic necrosis of metatarsus, tarsus, and phalanges of toes

CC **M87.071 Idiopathic aseptic necrosis of right ankle**
CC Exclusion see Appendix A PDX collection 0907

CC **M87.072 Idiopathic aseptic necrosis of left ankle**
CC Exclusion see Appendix A PDX collection 0907

CC **M87.073 Idiopathic aseptic necrosis of unspecified ankle**
CC Exclusion see Appendix A PDX collection 0907

CC **M87.074 Idiopathic aseptic necrosis of right foot**
CC Exclusion see Appendix A PDX collection 0910

CC **M87.075 Idiopathic aseptic necrosis of left foot**
CC Exclusion see Appendix A PDX collection 0910

CC **M87.076 Idiopathic aseptic necrosis of unspecified foot**
CC Exclusion see Appendix A PDX collection 0910

CC **M87.077 Idiopathic aseptic necrosis of right toe(s)**
CC Exclusion see Appendix A PDX collection 0907

CC **M87.078 Idiopathic aseptic necrosis of left toe(s)**
CC Exclusion see Appendix A PDX collection 0907

CC **M87.079 Idiopathic aseptic necrosis of unspecified toe(s)**
CC Exclusion see Appendix A PDX collection 0907

CC **M87.08 Idiopathic aseptic necrosis of bone, other site**
CC Exclusion see Appendix A PDX collection 0907

CC **M87.09 Idiopathic aseptic necrosis of bone, multiple sites**
CC Exclusion see Appendix A PDX collection 0907

+ **M87.1 Osteonecrosis due to drugs**
Use additional code for adverse effect, if applicable, to identify drug (T36-T50 with fifth or sixth character 5)

CC **M87.10 Osteonecrosis due to drugs, unspecified bone**
CC Exclusion see Appendix A PDX collection 0907

+ **M87.11 Osteonecrosis due to drugs, shoulder**

CC **M87.111 Osteonecrosis due to drugs, right shoulder**
CC Exclusion see Appendix A PDX collection 0907

CC **M87.112 Osteonecrosis due to drugs, left shoulder**
CC Exclusion see Appendix A PDX collection 0907

CC **M87.119 Osteonecrosis due to drugs, unspecified shoulder**
CC Exclusion see Appendix A PDX collection 0907

+ **M87.12 Osteonecrosis due to drugs, humerus**

CC **M87.121 Osteonecrosis due to drugs, right humerus**
CC Exclusion see Appendix A PDX collection 0908

CC **M87.122 Osteonecrosis due to drugs, left humerus**
CC Exclusion see Appendix A PDX collection 0908

CC **M87.129 Osteonecrosis due to drugs, unspecified humerus**
CC Exclusion see Appendix A PDX collection 0908

+ **M87.13 Osteonecrosis due to drugs of radius, ulna and carpus**

CC **M87.131 Osteonecrosis due to drugs of right radius**
CC Exclusion see Appendix A PDX collection 0907

CC **M87.132 Osteonecrosis due to drugs of left radius**
CC Exclusion see Appendix A PDX collection 0907

CC **M87.133 Osteonecrosis due to drugs of unspecified radius**
CC Exclusion see Appendix A PDX collection 0907

CC **M87.134 Osteonecrosis due to drugs of right ulna**
CC Exclusion see Appendix A PDX collection 0907

CC **M87.135 Osteonecrosis due to drugs of left ulna**
CC Exclusion see Appendix A PDX collection 0907

CC **M87.136 Osteonecrosis due to drugs of unspecified ulna**
CC Exclusion see Appendix A PDX collection 0907

CC **M87.137 Osteonecrosis due to drugs of right carpus**
CC Exclusion see Appendix A PDX collection 0907

CC **M87.138 Osteonecrosis due to drugs of left carpus**
CC Exclusion see Appendix A PDX collection 0907

CC **M87.139 Osteonecrosis due to drugs of unspecified carpus**
CC Exclusion see Appendix A PDX collection 0907

+ **M87.14 Osteonecrosis due to drugs, hand and fingers**

CC **M87.141 Osteonecrosis due to drugs, right hand**
CC Exclusion see Appendix A PDX collection 0907

CC **M87.142 Osteonecrosis due to drugs, left hand**
CC Exclusion see Appendix A PDX collection 0907

CC **M87.143 Osteonecrosis due to drugs, unspecified ha**
CC Exclusion see Appendix A PDX collection 09

CC **M87.144 Osteonecrosis due to drugs, right finger(s)**
CC Exclusion see Appendix A PDX collection 09

CC **M87.145 Osteonecrosis due to drugs, left finger(s)**
CC Exclusion see Appendix A PDX collection 09

CC **M87.146 Osteonecrosis due to drugs, unspecified finger(s)**
CC Exclusion see Appendix A PDX collection 09

+ **M87.15 Osteonecrosis due to drugs, pelvis and femur**

CC **M87.150 Osteonecrosis due to drugs, pelvis**
CC Exclusion see Appendix A PDX collection 09

CC **M87.151 Osteonecrosis due to drugs, right femur**
CC Exclusion see Appendix A PDX collection 09

CC **M87.152 Osteonecrosis due to drugs, left femur**
CC Exclusion see Appendix A PDX collection 09

CC **M87.159 Osteonecrosis due to drugs, unspecified femur**
CC Exclusion see Appendix A PDX collection 09

+ **M87.16 Osteonecrosis due to drugs, tibia and fibula**

CC **M87.161 Osteonecrosis due to drugs, right tibia**
CC Exclusion see Appendix A PDX collection 09

CC **M87.162 Osteonecrosis due to drugs, left tibia**
CC Exclusion see Appendix A PDX collection 09

CC **M87.163 Osteonecrosis due to drugs, unspecified tib**
CC Exclusion see Appendix A PDX collection 09

CC **M87.164 Osteonecrosis due to drugs, right fibula**
CC Exclusion see Appendix A PDX collection 09

CC **M87.165 Osteonecrosis due to drugs, left fibula**
CC Exclusion see Appendix A PDX collection 09

CC **M87.166 Osteonecrosis due to drugs, unspecified fibula**
CC Exclusion see Appendix A PDX collection 09

+ **M87.17 Osteonecrosis due to drugs, ankle, foot and toes**

CC **M87.171 Osteonecrosis due to drugs, right ankle**
CC Exclusion see Appendix A PDX collection 09

CC **M87.172 Osteonecrosis due to drugs, left ankle**
CC Exclusion see Appendix A PDX collection 09

CC **M87.173 Osteonecrosis due to drugs, unspecified ankle**
CC Exclusion see Appendix A PDX collection 09

CC **M87.174 Osteonecrosis due to drugs, right foot**
CC Exclusion see Appendix A PDX collection 09

CC **M87.175 Osteonecrosis due to drugs, left foot**
CC Exclusion see Appendix A PDX collection 09

CC **M87.176 Osteonecrosis due to drugs, unspecified foo**
CC Exclusion see Appendix A PDX collection 09

CC **M87.177 Osteonecrosis due to drugs, right toe(s)**
CC Exclusion see Appendix A PDX collection 09

CC **M87.178 Osteonecrosis due to drugs, left toe(s)**
CC Exclusion see Appendix A PDX collection 09

CC **M87.179 Osteonecrosis due to drugs, unspecified toe(s)**
CC Exclusion see Appendix A PDX collection 09

+ **M87.18 Osteonecrosis due to drugs, other site**

CC **M87.180 Osteonecrosis due to drugs, jaw**
CC Exclusion see Appendix A PDX collection 09

CC **M87.188 Osteonecrosis due to drugs, other site**
CC Exclusion see Appendix A PDX collection 09

CC **M87.19 Osteonecrosis due to drugs, multiple sites**
CC Exclusion see Appendix A PDX collection 0907

+ **M87.2 Osteonecrosis due to previous trauma**

CC **M87.20 Osteonecrosis due to previous trauma, unspecified bone**
CC Exclusion see Appendix A PDX collection 0907

+ **M87.21 Osteonecrosis due to previous trauma, shoulder**

CC **M87.211 Osteonecrosis due to previous trauma, righ shoulder**
CC Exclusion see Appendix A PDX collection 09

CC **M87.212 Osteonecrosis due to previous trauma, left shoulder**
CC Exclusion see Appendix A PDX collection 09

CC **M87.219 Osteonecrosis due to previous trauma, unspecified shoulder**
CC Exclusion see Appendix A PDX collection 09

+ **M87.22 Osteonecrosis due to previous trauma, humerus**

CC **M87.221 Osteonecrosis due to previous trauma, righ humerus**
CC Exclusion see Appendix A PDX collection 09

CC **M87.222 Osteonecrosis due to previous trauma, left humerus**
CC Exclusion see Appendix A PDX collection 09

CC **M87.229 Osteonecrosis due to previous trauma, unspecified humerus**
CC Exclusion see Appendix A PDX collection 09

+ **M87.23 Osteonecrosis due to previous trauma of radius, ulna and carpus**
- CC **M87.231 Osteonecrosis due to previous trauma of right radius**
  CC Exclusion see Appendix A PDX collection 0907
- CC **M87.232 Osteonecrosis due to previous trauma of left radius**
  CC Exclusion see Appendix A PDX collection 0907
- CC **M87.233 Osteonecrosis due to previous trauma of unspecified radius**
  CC Exclusion see Appendix A PDX collection 0907
- CC **M87.234 Osteonecrosis due to previous trauma of right ulna**
  CC Exclusion see Appendix A PDX collection 0907
- CC **M87.235 Osteonecrosis due to previous trauma of left ulna**
  CC Exclusion see Appendix A PDX collection 0907
- CC **M87.236 Osteonecrosis due to previous trauma of unspecified ulna**
  CC Exclusion see Appendix A PDX collection 0907
- CC **M87.237 Osteonecrosis due to previous trauma of right carpus**
  CC Exclusion see Appendix A PDX collection 0907
- CC **M87.238 Osteonecrosis due to previous trauma of left carpus**
  CC Exclusion see Appendix A PDX collection 0907
- CC **M87.239 Osteonecrosis due to previous trauma of unspecified carpus**
  CC Exclusion see Appendix A PDX collection 0907

+ **M87.24 Osteonecrosis due to previous trauma, hand and fingers**
- CC **M87.241 Osteonecrosis due to previous trauma, right hand**
  CC Exclusion see Appendix A PDX collection 0907
- CC **M87.242 Osteonecrosis due to previous trauma, left hand**
  CC Exclusion see Appendix A PDX collection 0907
- CC **M87.243 Osteonecrosis due to previous trauma, unspecified hand**
  CC Exclusion see Appendix A PDX collection 0907
- CC **M87.244 Osteonecrosis due to previous trauma, right finger(s)**
  CC Exclusion see Appendix A PDX collection 0907
- CC **M87.245 Osteonecrosis due to previous trauma, left finger(s)**
  CC Exclusion see Appendix A PDX collection 0907
- CC **M87.246 Osteonecrosis due to previous trauma, unspecified finger(s)**
  CC Exclusion see Appendix A PDX collection 0907

+ **M87.25 Osteonecrosis due to previous trauma, pelvis and femur**
- CC **M87.250 Osteonecrosis due to previous trauma, pelvis**
  CC Exclusion see Appendix A PDX collection 0907
- CC **M87.251 Osteonecrosis due to previous trauma, right femur**
  CC Exclusion see Appendix A PDX collection 0909
- CC **M87.252 Osteonecrosis due to previous trauma, left femur**
  CC Exclusion see Appendix A PDX collection 0909
- CC **M87.256 Osteonecrosis due to previous trauma, unspecified femur**
  CC Exclusion see Appendix A PDX collection 0909

+ **M87.26 Osteonecrosis due to previous trauma, tibia and fibula**
- CC **M87.261 Osteonecrosis due to previous trauma, right tibia**
  CC Exclusion see Appendix A PDX collection 0907
- CC **M87.262 Osteonecrosis due to previous trauma, left tibia**
  CC Exclusion see Appendix A PDX collection 0907
- CC **M87.263 Osteonecrosis due to previous trauma, unspecified tibia**
  CC Exclusion see Appendix A PDX collection 0907
- CC **M87.264 Osteonecrosis due to previous trauma, right fibula**
  CC Exclusion see Appendix A PDX collection 0907
- CC **M87.265 Osteonecrosis due to previous trauma, left fibula**
  CC Exclusion see Appendix A PDX collection 0907
- CC **M87.266 Osteonecrosis due to previous trauma, unspecified fibula**
  CC Exclusion see Appendix A PDX collection 0907

+ **M87.27 Osteonecrosis due to previous trauma, ankle, foot and toes**
- CC **M87.271 Osteonecrosis due to previous trauma, right ankle**
  CC Exclusion see Appendix A PDX collection 0907
- CC **M87.272 Osteonecrosis due to previous trauma, left ankle**
  CC Exclusion see Appendix A PDX collection 0907
- CC **M87.273 Osteonecrosis due to previous trauma, unspecified ankle**
  CC Exclusion see Appendix A PDX collection 0907
- CC **M87.274 Osteonecrosis due to previous trauma, right foot**
  CC Exclusion see Appendix A PDX collection 0910
- CC **M87.275 Osteonecrosis due to previous trauma, left foot**
  CC Exclusion see Appendix A PDX collection 0910
- CC **M87.276 Osteonecrosis due to previous trauma, unspecified foot**
  CC Exclusion see Appendix A PDX collection 0910
- CC **M87.277 Osteonecrosis due to previous trauma, right toe(s)**
  CC Exclusion see Appendix A PDX collection 0907
- CC **M87.278 Osteonecrosis due to previous trauma, left toe(s)**
  CC Exclusion see Appendix A PDX collection 0907
- CC **M87.279 Osteonecrosis due to previous trauma, unspecified toe(s)**
  CC Exclusion see Appendix A PDX collection 0907

CC **M87.28 Osteonecrosis due to previous trauma, other site**
CC Exclusion see Appendix A PDX collection 0907

CC **M87.29 Osteonecrosis due to previous trauma, multiple sites**
CC Exclusion see Appendix A PDX collection 0907

+ **M87.3 Other secondary osteonecrosis**

CC **M87.30 Other secondary osteonecrosis, unspecified bone**
CC Exclusion see Appendix A PDX collection 0907

+ **M87.31 Other secondary osteonecrosis, shoulder**
- CC **M87.311 Other secondary osteonecrosis, right shoulder**
  CC Exclusion see Appendix A PDX collection 0907
- CC **M87.312 Other secondary osteonecrosis, left shoulder**
  CC Exclusion see Appendix A PDX collection 0907
- CC **M87.319 Other secondary osteonecrosis, unspecified shoulder**
  CC Exclusion see Appendix A PDX collection 0907

+ **M87.32 Other secondary osteonecrosis, humerus**
- CC **M87.321 Other secondary osteonecrosis, right humerus**
  CC Exclusion see Appendix A PDX collection 0908
- CC **M87.322 Other secondary osteonecrosis, left humerus**
  CC Exclusion see Appendix A PDX collection 0908
- CC **M87.329 Other secondary osteonecrosis, unspecified humerus**
  CC Exclusion see Appendix A PDX collection 0908

+ **M87.33 Other secondary osteonecrosis of radius, ulna and carpus**
- CC **M87.331 Other secondary osteonecrosis of right radius**
  CC Exclusion see Appendix A PDX collection 0907
- CC **M87.332 Other secondary osteonecrosis of left radius**
  CC Exclusion see Appendix A PDX collection 0907
- CC **M87.333 Other secondary osteonecrosis of unspecified radius**
  CC Exclusion see Appendix A PDX collection 0907
- CC **M87.334 Other secondary osteonecrosis of right ulna**
  CC Exclusion see Appendix A PDX collection 0907
- CC **M87.335 Other secondary osteonecrosis of left ulna**
  CC Exclusion see Appendix A PDX collection 0907
- CC **M87.336 Other secondary osteonecrosis of unspecified ulna**
  CC Exclusion see Appendix A PDX collection 0907
- CC **M87.337 Other secondary osteonecrosis of right carpus**
  CC Exclusion see Appendix A PDX collection 0907
- CC **M87.338 Other secondary osteonecrosis of left carpus**
  CC Exclusion see Appendix A PDX collection 0907
- CC **M87.339 Other secondary osteonecrosis of unspecified carpus**
  CC Exclusion see Appendix A PDX collection 0907

+ **M87.34 Other secondary osteonecrosis, hand and fingers**
- CC **M87.341 Other secondary osteonecrosis, right hand**
  CC Exclusion see Appendix A PDX collection 0907
- CC **M87.342 Other secondary osteonecrosis, left hand**
  CC Exclusion see Appendix A PDX collection 0907

CC M87.343 Other secondary osteonecrosis, unspecified hand
CC Exclusion see Appendix A PDX collection 0907
CC M87.344 Other secondary osteonecrosis, right finger(s)
CC Exclusion see Appendix A PDX collection 0907
CC M87.345 Other secondary osteonecrosis, left finger(s)
CC Exclusion see Appendix A PDX collection 0907
CC M87.346 Other secondary osteonecrosis, unspecified finger(s)
CC Exclusion see Appendix A PDX collection 0907
+ M87.35 Other secondary osteonecrosis, pelvis and femur
CC M87.350 Other secondary osteonecrosis, pelvis
CC Exclusion see Appendix A PDX collection 0909
CC M87.351 Other secondary osteonecrosis, right femur
CC Exclusion see Appendix A PDX collection 0909
CC M87.352 Other secondary osteonecrosis, left femur
CC Exclusion see Appendix A PDX collection 0909
CC M87.353 Other secondary osteonecrosis, unspecified femur
CC Exclusion see Appendix A PDX collection 0909
+ M87.36 Other secondary osteonecrosis, tibia and fibula
CC M87.361 Other secondary osteonecrosis, right tibia
CC Exclusion see Appendix A PDX collection 0907
CC M87.362 Other secondary osteonecrosis, left tibia
CC Exclusion see Appendix A PDX collection 0907
CC M87.363 Other secondary osteonecrosis, unspecified tibia
CC Exclusion see Appendix A PDX collection 0907
CC M87.364 Other secondary osteonecrosis, right fibula
CC Exclusion see Appendix A PDX collection 0907
CC M87.365 Other secondary osteonecrosis, left fibula
CC Exclusion see Appendix A PDX collection 0907
CC M87.366 Other secondary osteonecrosis, unspecified fibula
CC Exclusion see Appendix A PDX collection 0907
+ M87.37 Other secondary osteonecrosis, ankle and foot
CC M87.371 Other secondary osteonecrosis, right ankle
CC Exclusion see Appendix A PDX collection 0907
CC M87.372 Other secondary osteonecrosis, left ankle
CC Exclusion see Appendix A PDX collection 0907
CC M87.373 Other secondary osteonecrosis, unspecified ankle
CC Exclusion see Appendix A PDX collection 0907
CC M87.374 Other secondary osteonecrosis, right foot
CC Exclusion see Appendix A PDX collection 0910
CC M87.375 Other secondary osteonecrosis, left foot
CC Exclusion see Appendix A PDX collection 0910
CC M87.376 Other secondary osteonecrosis, unspecified foot
CC Exclusion see Appendix A PDX collection 0910
CC M87.377 Other secondary osteonecrosis, right toe(s)
CC Exclusion see Appendix A PDX collection 0907
CC M87.378 Other secondary osteonecrosis, left toe(s)
CC Exclusion see Appendix A PDX collection 0907
CC M87.379 Other secondary osteonecrosis, unspecified toe(s)
CC Exclusion see Appendix A PDX collection 0907
CC M87.38 Other secondary osteonecrosis, other site
CC Exclusion see Appendix A PDX collection 0907
CC M87.39 Other secondary osteonecrosis, multiple sites
CC Exclusion see Appendix A PDX collection 0907
+ M87.8 Other osteonecrosis
CC M87.80 Other osteonecrosis, unspecified bone
CC Exclusion see Appendix A PDX collection 0907
+ M87.81 Other osteonecrosis, shoulder
CC M87.811 Other osteonecrosis, right shoulder
CC Exclusion see Appendix A PDX collection 0907
CC M87.812 Other osteonecrosis, left shoulder
CC Exclusion see Appendix A PDX collection 0907
CC M87.819 Other osteonecrosis, unspecified shoulder
CC Exclusion see Appendix A PDX collection 0907
+ M87.82 Other osteonecrosis, humerus
CC M87.821 Other osteonecrosis, right humerus
CC Exclusion see Appendix A PDX collection 0908
CC M87.822 Other osteonecrosis, left humerus
CC Exclusion see Appendix A PDX collection 0908
CC M87.829 Other osteonecrosis, unspecified humerus
CC Exclusion see Appendix A PDX collection 0908
+ M87.83 Other osteonecrosis of radius, ulna and carpus
CC M87.831 Other osteonecrosis of right radius
CC Exclusion see Appendix A PDX collection 0907
CC M87.832 Other osteonecrosis of left radius
CC Exclusion see Appendix A PDX collection 0907
CC M87.833 Other osteonecrosis of unspecified radius
CC Exclusion see Appendix A PDX collection 0907
CC M87.834 Other osteonecrosis of right ulna
CC Exclusion see Appendix A PDX collection 0
CC M87.835 Other osteonecrosis of left ulna
CC Exclusion see Appendix A PDX collection 0
CC M87.836 Other osteonecrosis of unspecified ulna
CC Exclusion see Appendix A PDX collection 0
CC M87.837 Other osteonecrosis of right carpus
CC Exclusion see Appendix A PDX collection 0
CC M87.838 Other osteonecrosis of left carpus
CC Exclusion see Appendix A PDX collection 0
CC M87.839 Other osteonecrosis of unspecified carpus
CC Exclusion see Appendix A PDX collection 0
+ M87.84 Other osteonecrosis, hand and fingers
CC M87.841 Other osteonecrosis, right hand
CC Exclusion see Appendix A PDX collection 09
CC M87.842 Other osteonecrosis, left hand
CC Exclusion see Appendix A PDX collection 09
CC M87.843 Other osteonecrosis, unspecified hand
CC Exclusion see Appendix A PDX collection 09
CC M87.844 Other osteonecrosis, right finger(s)
CC Exclusion see Appendix A PDX collection 09
CC M87.845 Other osteonecrosis, left finger(s)
CC Exclusion see Appendix A PDX collection 09
CC M87.849 Other osteonecrosis, unspecified finger(s)
CC Exclusion see Appendix A PDX collection 09
+ M87.85 Other osteonecrosis, pelvis and femur
CC M87.850 Other osteonecrosis, pelvis
CC Exclusion see Appendix A PDX collection 09
CC M87.851 Other osteonecrosis, right femur
CC Exclusion see Appendix A PDX collection 09
CC M87.852 Other osteonecrosis, left femur
CC Exclusion see Appendix A PDX collection 09
CC M87.859 Other osteonecrosis, unspecified femur
CC Exclusion see Appendix A PDX collection 09
+ M87.86 Other osteonecrosis, tibia and fibula
CC M87.861 Other osteonecrosis, right tibia
CC Exclusion see Appendix A PDX collection 09
CC M87.862 Other osteonecrosis, left tibia
CC Exclusion see Appendix A PDX collection 09
CC M87.863 Other osteonecrosis, unspecified tibia
CC Exclusion see Appendix A PDX collection 09
CC M87.864 Other osteonecrosis, right fibula
CC Exclusion see Appendix A PDX collection 09
CC M87.865 Other osteonecrosis, left fibula
CC Exclusion see Appendix A PDX collection 09
CC M87.869 Other osteonecrosis, unspecified fibula
CC Exclusion see Appendix A PDX collection 09
+ M87.87 Other osteonecrosis, ankle, foot and toes
CC M87.871 Other osteonecrosis, right ankle
CC Exclusion see Appendix A PDX collection 09
CC M87.872 Other osteonecrosis, left ankle
CC Exclusion see Appendix A PDX collection 09
CC M87.873 Other osteonecrosis, unspecified ankle
CC Exclusion see Appendix A PDX collection 09
CC M87.874 Other osteonecrosis, right foot
CC Exclusion see Appendix A PDX collection 09
CC M87.875 Other osteonecrosis, left foot
CC Exclusion see Appendix A PDX collection 09
CC M87.876 Other osteonecrosis, unspecified foot
CC Exclusion see Appendix A PDX collection 09
CC M87.877 Other osteonecrosis, right toe(s)
CC Exclusion see Appendix A PDX collection 090
CC M87.878 Other osteonecrosis, left toe(s)
CC Exclusion see Appendix A PDX collection 090
CC M87.879 Other osteonecrosis, unspecified toe(s)
CC Exclusion see Appendix A PDX collection 090
CC M87.88 Other osteonecrosis, other site
CC Exclusion see Appendix A PDX collection 0907
CC M87.89 Other osteonecrosis, multiple sites
CC Exclusion see Appendix A PDX collection 0907
CC M87.9 Osteonecrosis, unspecified
Necrosis of bone NOS
CC Exclusion see Appendix A PDX collection 0907

M88 Osteitis deformans [Paget's disease of bone]

Excludes1: *osteitis deformans in neoplastic disease (M90.6)*
M88.0 Osteitis deformans of skull
M88.1 Osteitis deformans of vertebrae
+ M88.8 Osteitis deformans of other bones
+ M88.81 Osteitis deformans of shoulder
M88.811 Osteitis deformans of right shoulder
M88.812 Osteitis deformans of left shoulder
M88.819 Osteitis deformans of unspecified shoulder

+ **M88.82 Osteitis deformans of upper arm**
M88.821 Osteitis deformans of right upper arm
M88.822 Osteitis deformans of left upper arm
M88.829 Osteitis deformans of unspecified upper arm
+ **M88.83 Osteitis deformans of forearm**
M88.831 Osteitis deformans of right forearm
M88.832 Osteitis deformans of left forearm
M88.839 Osteitis deformans of unspecified forearm
+ **M88.84 Osteitis deformans of hand**
M88.841 Osteitis deformans of right hand
M88.842 Osteitis deformans of left hand
M88.849 Osteitis deformans of unspecified hand
+ **M88.85 Osteitis deformans of thigh**
M88.851 Osteitis deformans of right thigh
M88.852 Osteitis deformans of left thigh
M88.859 Osteitis deformans of unspecified thigh
+ **M88.86 Osteitis deformans of lower leg**
M88.861 Osteitis deformans of right lower leg
M88.862 Osteitis deformans of left lower leg
M88.869 Osteitis deformans of unspecified lower leg
+ **M88.87 Osteitis deformans of ankle and foot**
M88.871 Osteitis deformans of right ankle and foot
M88.872 Osteitis deformans of left ankle and foot
M88.879 Osteitis deformans of unspecified ankle and foot
M88.88 Osteitis deformans of other bones
Excludes2: *osteitis deformans of skull (M88.0)*
osteitis deformans of vertebrae (M88.1)
M88.89 Osteitis deformans of multiple sites
M88.9 Osteitis deformans of unspecified bone

M89 Other disorders of bone

+ **M89.0 Algoneurodystrophy**
Shoulder-hand syndrome
Sudeck's atrophy
Excludes1: *causalgia, lower limb (G57.7-)*
causalgia, upper limb (G56.4-)
complex regional pain syndrome II, lower limb (G57.7-)
complex regional pain syndrome II, upper limb (G56.4-)
reflex sympathetic dystrophy (G90.5-)
M89.00 Algoneurodystrophy, unspecified site
+ **M89.01 Algoneurodystrophy, shoulder**
M89.011 Algoneurodystrophy, right shoulder
M89.012 Algoneurodystrophy, left shoulder
M89.019 Algoneurodystrophy, unspecified shoulder
+ **M89.02 Algoneurodystrophy, upper arm**
M89.021 Algoneurodystrophy, right upper arm
M89.022 Algoneurodystrophy, left upper arm
M89.029 Algoneurodystrophy, unspecified upper arm
+ **M89.03 Algoneurodystrophy, forearm**
M89.031 Algoneurodystrophy, right forearm
M89.032 Algoneurodystrophy, left forearm
M89.039 Algoneurodystrophy, unspecified forearm
+ **M89.04 Algoneurodystrophy, hand**
M89.041 Algoneurodystrophy, right≈hand
M89.042 Algoneurodystrophy, left hand
M89.049 Algoneurodystrophy, unspecified hand
+ **M89.05 Algoneurodystrophy, thigh**
M89.051 Algoneurodystrophy, right thigh
M89.052 Algoneurodystrophy, left thigh
M89.059 Algoneurodystrophy, unspecified thigh
+ **M89.06 Algoneurodystrophy, lower leg**
M89.061 Algoneurodystrophy, right lower leg
M89.062 Algoneurodystrophy, left lower leg
M89.069 Algoneurodystrophy, unspecified lower leg
+ **M89.07 Algoneurodystrophy, ankle and foot**
M89.071 Algoneurodystrophy, right ankle and foot
M89.072 Algoneurodystrophy, left ankle and foot
M89.079 Algoneurodystrophy, unspecified ankle and foot
M89.08 Algoneurodystrophy, other site
M89.09 Algoneurodystrophy, multiple sites
+ **M89.1 Physeal arrest**
Arrest of growth plate
Epiphyseal arrest
Growth plate arrest
+ **M89.12 Physeal arrest, humerus**
M89.121 Complete physeal arrest, right proximal humerus
M89.122 Complete physeal arrest, left proximal humerus
M89.123 Partial physeal arrest, right proximal humerus
M89.124 Partial physeal arrest, left proximal humerus
M89.125 Complete physeal arrest, right distal humerus
M89.126 Complete physeal arrest, left distal humerus
M89.127 Partial physeal arrest, right distal humerus
M89.128 Partial physeal arrest, left distal humerus
M89.129 Physeal arrest, humerus, unspecified
+ **M89.13 Physeal arrest, forearm**
M89.131 Complete physeal arrest, right distal radius
M89.132 Complete physeal arrest, left distal radius
M89.133 Partial physeal arrest, right distal radius
M89.134 Partial physeal arrest, left distal radius
M89.138 Other physeal arrest of forearm
M89.139 Physeal arrest, forearm, unspecified
+ **M89.15 Physeal arrest, femur**
M89.151 Complete physeal arrest, right proximal femur
M89.152 Complete physeal arrest, left proximal femur
M89.153 Partial physeal arrest, right proximal femur
M89.154 Partial physeal arrest, left proximal femur
M89.155 Complete physeal arrest, right distal femur
M89.156 Complete physeal arrest, left distal femur
M89.157 Partial physeal arrest, right distal femur
M89.158 Partial physeal arrest, left distal femur
M89.159 Physeal arrest, femur, unspecified
+ **M89.16 Physeal arrest, lower leg**
M89.160 Complete physeal arrest, right proximal tibia
M89.161 Complete physeal arrest, left proximal tibia
M89.162 Partial physeal arrest, right proximal tibia
M89.163 Partial physeal arrest, left proximal tibia
M89.164 Complete physeal arrest, right distal tibia
M89.165 Complete physeal arrest, left distal tibia
M89.166 Partial physeal arrest, right distal tibia
M89.167 Partial physeal arrest, left distal tibia
M89.168 Other physeal arrest of lower leg
M89.169 Physeal arrest, lower leg, unspecified
M89.18 Physeal arrest, other site
+ **M89.2 Other disorders of bone development and growth**
M89.20 Other disorders of bone development and growth, unspecified site
+ **M89.21 Other disorders of bone development and growth, shoulder**
M89.211 Other disorders of bone development and growth, right shoulder
M89.212 Other disorders of bone development and growth, left shoulder
M89.219 Other disorders of bone development and growth, unspecified shoulder
+ **M89.22 Other disorders of bone development and growth, humerus**
M89.221 Other disorders of bone development and growth, right humerus
M89.222 Other disorders of bone development and growth, left humerus
M89.229 Other disorders of bone development and growth, unspecified humerus
+ **M89.23 Other disorders of bone development and growth, ulna and radius**
M89.231 Other disorders of bone development and growth, right ulna
M89.232 Other disorders of bone development and growth, left ulna
M89.233 Other disorders of bone development and growth, right radius
M89.234 Other disorders of bone development and growth, left radius
M89.239 Other disorders of bone development and growth, unspecified ulna and radius
+ **M89.24 Other disorders of bone development and growth, hand**
M89.241 Other disorders of bone development and growth, right hand
M89.242 Other disorders of bone development and growth, left hand
M89.249 Other disorders of bone development and growth, unspecified hand

+ M89.25 Other disorders of bone development and growth, femur
- **M89.251 Other disorders of bone development and growth, right femur**
- **M89.252 Other disorders of bone development and growth, left femur**
- **M89.259 Other disorders of bone development and growth, unspecified femur**

+ M89.26 Other disorders of bone development and growth, tibia and fibula
- **M89.261 Other disorders of bone development and growth, right tibia**
- **M89.262 Other disorders of bone development and growth, left tibia**
- **M89.263 Other disorders of bone development and growth, right fibula**
- **M89.264 Other disorders of bone development and growth, left fibula**
- **M89.269 Other disorders of bone development and growth, unspecified lower leg**

+ M89.27 Other disorders of bone development and growth, ankle and foot
- **M89.271 Other disorders of bone development and growth, right ankle and foot**
- **M89.272 Other disorders of bone development and growth, left ankle and foot**
- **M89.279 Other disorders of bone development and growth, unspecified ankle and foot**

M89.28 Other disorders of bone development and growth, other site

M89.29 Other disorders of bone development and growth, multiple sites

+ M89.3 Hypertrophy of bone

M89.30 Hypertrophy of bone, unspecified site

+ M89.31 Hypertrophy of bone, shoulder
- **M89.311 Hypertrophy of bone, right shoulder**
- **M89.312 Hypertrophy of bone, left shoulder**
- **M89.319 Hypertrophy of bone, unspecified shoulder**

+ M89.32 Hypertrophy of bone, humerus
- **M89.321 Hypertrophy of bone, right humerus**
- **M89.322 Hypertrophy of bone, left humerus**
- **M89.329 Hypertrophy of bone, unspecified humerus**

+ M89.33 Hypertrophy of bone, ulna and radius
- **M89.331 Hypertrophy of bone, right ulna**
- **M89.332 Hypertrophy of bone, left ulna**
- **M89.333 Hypertrophy of bone, right radius**
- **M89.334 Hypertrophy of bone, left radius**
- **M89.339 Hypertrophy of bone, unspecified ulna and radius**

+ M89.34 Hypertrophy of bone, hand
- **M89.341 Hypertrophy of bone, right hand**
- **M89.342 Hypertrophy of bone, left hand**
- **M89.349 Hypertrophy of bone, unspecified hand**

+ M89.35 Hypertrophy of bone, femur
- **M89.351 Hypertrophy of bone, right femur**
- **M89.352 Hypertrophy of bone, left femur**
- **M89.359 Hypertrophy of bone, unspecified femur**

+ M89.36 Hypertrophy of bone, tibia and fibula
- **M89.361 Hypertrophy of bone, right tibia**
- **M89.362 Hypertrophy of bone, left tibia**
- **M89.363 Hypertrophy of bone, right fibula**
- **M89.364 Hypertrophy of bone, left fibula**
- **M89.369 Hypertrophy of bone, unspecified tibia and fibula**

+ M89.37 Hypertrophy of bone, ankle and foot
- **M89.371 Hypertrophy of bone, right ankle and foot**
- **M89.372 Hypertrophy of bone, left ankle and foot**
- **M89.379 Hypertrophy of bone, unspecified ankle and foot**

M89.38 Hypertrophy of bone, other site

M89.39 Hypertrophy of bone, multiple sites

+ M89.4 Other hypertrophic osteoarthropathy

Marie-Bamberger disease
Pachydermoperiostosis

M89.40 Other hypertrophic osteoarthropathy, unspecified site

+ M89.41 Other hypertrophic osteoarthropathy, shoulder
- **M89.411 Other hypertrophic osteoarthropathy, right shoulder**
- **M89.412 Other hypertrophic osteoarthropathy, left shoulder**
- **M89.419 Other hypertrophic osteoarthropathy, unspecified shoulder**

+ M89.42 Other hypertrophic osteoarthropathy, upper arm
- **M89.421 Other hypertrophic osteoarthropathy, righ upper arm**
- **M89.422 Other hypertrophic osteoarthropathy, left upper arm**
- **M89.429 Other hypertrophic osteoarthropathy, unspecified upper arm**

+ M89.43 Other hypertrophic osteoarthropathy, forearm
- **M89.431 Other hypertrophic osteoarthropathy, righ forearm**
- **M89.432 Other hypertrophic osteoarthropathy, left forearm**
- **M89.439 Other hypertrophic osteoarthropathy, unspecified forearm**

+ M89.44 Other hypertrophic osteoarthropathy, hand
- **M89.441 Other hypertrophic osteoarthropathy, right hand**
- **M89.442 Other hypertrophic osteoarthropathy, left hand**
- **M89.449 Other hypertrophic osteoarthropathy, unspecified hand**

+ M89.45 Other hypertrophic osteoarthropathy, thigh
- **M89.451 Other hypertrophic osteoarthropathy, right thigh**
- **M89.452 Other hypertrophic osteoarthropathy, left thigh**
- **M89.459 Other hypertrophic osteoarthropathy, unspecified thigh**

+ M89.46 Other hypertrophic osteoarthropathy, lower leg
- **M89.461 Other hypertrophic osteoarthropathy, right lower leg**
- **M89.462 Other hypertrophic osteoarthropathy, left lower leg**
- **M89.469 Other hypertrophic osteoarthropathy, unspecified lower leg**

+ M89.47 Other hypertrophic osteoarthropathy, ankle and foot
- **M89.471 Other hypertrophic osteoarthropathy, right ankle and foot**
- **M89.472 Other hypertrophic osteoarthropathy, left ankle and foot**
- **M89.479 Other hypertrophic osteoarthropathy, unspecified ankle and foot**

M89.48 Other hypertrophic osteoarthropathy, other site

M89.49 Other hypertrophic osteoarthropathy, multiple sites

+ M89.5 Osteolysis

Use additional code to identify major osseous defect, if applicabl (M89.7-)

Excludes2: *periprosthetic osteolysis of internal prosthetic joint (T84.05-)*

M89.50 Osteolysis, unspecified site

+ M89.51 Osteolysis, shoulder
- **M89.511 Osteolysis, right shoulder**
- **M89.512 Osteolysis, left shoulder**
- **M89.519 Osteolysis, unspecified shoulder**

+ M89.52 Osteolysis, upper arm
- **M89.521 Osteolysis, right upper arm**
- **M89.522 Osteolysis, left upper arm**
- **M89.529 Osteolysis, unspecified upper arm**

+ M89.53 Osteolysis, forearm
- **M89.531 Osteolysis, right forearm**
- **M89.532 Osteolysis, left forearm**
- **M89.539 Osteolysis, unspecified forearm**

+ M89.54 Osteolysis, hand
- **M89.541 Osteolysis, right hand**
- **M89.542 Osteolysis, left hand**
- **M89.549 Osteolysis, unspecified hand**

+ M89.55 Osteolysis, thigh
- **M89.551 Osteolysis, right thigh**
- **M89.552 Osteolysis, left thigh**
- **M89.559 Osteolysis, unspecified thigh**

+ M89.56 Osteolysis, lower leg
- **M89.561 Osteolysis, right lower leg**
- **M89.562 Osteolysis, left lower leg**
- **M89.569 Osteolysis, unspecified lower leg**

+ M89.57 Osteolysis, ankle and foot
- **M89.571 Osteolysis, right ankle and foot**
- **M89.572 Osteolysis, left ankle and foot**
- **M89.579 Osteolysis, unspecified ankle and foot**

M89.58 Osteolysis, other site

M89.59 Osteolysis, multiple sites

\+ **M89.6 Osteopathy after poliomyelitis**
Use additional code (B91) to identify previous poliomyelitis
Excludes1: *postpolio syndrome (G14)*
M89.60 Osteopathy after poliomyelitis, unspecified site
\+ **M89.61 Osteopathy after poliomyelitis, shoulder**
M89.611 Osteopathy after poliomyelitis, right shoulder
M89.612 Osteopathy after poliomyelitis, left shoulder
M89.619 Osteopathy after poliomyelitis, unspecified shoulder
\+ **M89.62 Osteopathy after poliomyelitis, upper arm**
M89.621 Osteopathy after poliomyelitis, right upper arm
M89.622 Osteopathy after poliomyelitis, left upper arm
M89.629 Osteopathy after poliomyelitis, unspecified upper arm
\+ **M89.63 Osteopathy after poliomyelitis, forearm**
M89.631 Osteopathy after poliomyelitis, right forearm
M89.632 Osteopathy after poliomyelitis, left forearm
M89.639 Osteopathy after poliomyelitis, unspecified forearm
\+ **M89.64 Osteopathy after poliomyelitis, hand**
M89.641 Osteopathy after poliomyelitis, right hand
M89.642 Osteopathy after poliomyelitis, left hand
M89.649 Osteopathy after poliomyelitis, unspecified hand
\+ **M89.65 Osteopathy after poliomyelitis, thigh**
M89.651 Osteopathy after poliomyelitis, right thigh
M89.652 Osteopathy after poliomyelitis, left thigh
M89.659 Osteopathy after poliomyelitis, unspecified thigh
\+ **M89.66 Osteopathy after poliomyelitis, lower leg**
M89.661 Osteopathy after poliomyelitis, right lower leg
M89.662 Osteopathy after poliomyelitis, left lower leg
M89.669 Osteopathy after poliomyelitis, unspecified lower leg
\+ **M89.67 Osteopathy after poliomyelitis, ankle and foot**
M89.671 Osteopathy after poliomyelitis, right ankle and foot
M89.672 Osteopathy after poliomyelitis, left ankle and foot
M89.679 Osteopathy after poliomyelitis, unspecified ankle and foot
M89.68 Osteopathy after poliomyelitis, other site
M89.69 Osteopathy after poliomyelitis, multiple sites
\+ **M89.7 Major osseous defect**
Code first underlying disease, if known, such as:
aseptic necrosis of bone (M87.-)
malignant neoplasm of bone (C40.-)
osteolysis (M89.5)
osteomyelitis (M86.-)
osteonecrosis (M87.-)
osteoporosis (M80.-, M81.-)
periprosthetic osteolysis (T84.05-)
M89.70 Major osseous defect, unspecified site
\+ **M89.71 Major osseous defect, shoulder region**
Major osseous defect clavicle or scapula
M89.711 Major osseous defect, right shoulder region
M89.712 Major osseous defect, left shoulder region
M89.719 Major osseous defect, unspecified shoulder region
\+ **M89.72 Major osseous defect, humerus**
M89.721 Major osseous defect, right humerus
M89.722 Major osseous defect, left humerus
M89.729 Major osseous defect, unspecified humerus
\+ **M89.73 Major osseous defect, forearm**
Major osseous defect of radius and ulna
M89.731 Major osseous defect, right forearm
M89.732 Major osseous defect, left forearm
M89.739 Major osseous defect, unspecified forearm
\+ **M89.74 Major osseous defect, hand**
Major osseous defect of carpus, fingers, metacarpus
M89.741 Major osseous defect, right hand
M89.742 Major osseous defect, left hand
M89.749 Major osseous defect, unspecified hand
\+ **M89.75 Major osseous defect, pelvic region and thigh**
Major osseous defect of femur and pelvis
M89.751 Major osseous defect, right pelvic region and thigh
M89.752 Major osseous defect, left pelvic region and thigh
M89.759 Major osseous defect, unspecified pelvic region and thigh
\+ **M89.76 Major osseous defect, lower leg**
Major osseous defect of fibula and tibia
M89.761 Major osseous defect, right lower leg
M89.762 Major osseous defect, left lower leg
M89.769 Major osseous defect, unspecified lower leg
\+ **M89.77 Major osseous defect, ankle and foot**
Major osseous defect of metatarsus, tarsus, toes
M89.771 Major osseous defect, right ankle and foot
M89.772 Major osseous defect, left ankle and foot
M89.779 Major osseous defect, unspecified ankle and foot
M89.78 Major osseous defect, other site
M89.79 Major osseous defect, multiple sites
\+ **M89.8 Other specified disorders of bone**
Infantile cortical hyperostoses
Post-traumatic subperiosteal ossification
\+ **M89.8X Other specified disorders of bone**
M89.8X0 Other specified disorders of bone, multiple sites
M89.8X1 Other specified disorders of bone, shoulder
M89.8X2 Other specified disorders of bone, upper arm
M89.8X3 Other specified disorders of bone, forearm
M89.8X4 Other specified disorders of bone, hand
M89.8X5 Other specified disorders of bone, thigh
M89.8X6 Other specified disorders of bone, lower leg
M89.8X7 Other specified disorders of bone, ankle and foot
M89.8X8 Other specified disorders of bone, other site
M89.8X9 Other specified disorders of bone, unspecified site
M89.9 Disorder of bone, unspecified

M90 Osteopathies in diseases classified elsewhere
Excludes1: *osteochondritis, osteomyelitis, and osteopathy (in):*
cryptococcosis (B45.3)
diabetes mellitus (E08-E13 with .61-)
gonococcal (A54.43)
neurogenic syphilis (A52.11)
renal osteodystrophy (N25.0)
salmonellosis (A02.24)
secondary syphilis (A51.46)
syphilis (late) (A52.77)
\+ **M90.5 Osteonecrosis in diseases classified elsewhere**
Code first underlying disease, such as:
caisson disease (T70.3)
hemoglobinopathy (D50-D64)
CC **M90.50 Osteonecrosis in diseases classified elsewhere, unspecified site**
CC Exclusion see Appendix A PDX collection 0907
\+ **M90.51 Osteonecrosis in diseases classified elsewhere, shoulder**
CC **M90.511 Osteonecrosis in diseasesclassified elsewhere, rightshoulder**
CC Exclusion see Appendix A PDX collection 0908
CC **M90.512 Osteonecrosis in diseases classified elsewhere, left shoulder**
CC Exclusion see Appendix A PDX collection 0908
CC **M90.519 Osteonecrosis in diseases classified elsewhere, unspecified shoulder**
CC Exclusion see Appendix A PDX collection 0908
\+ **M90.52 Osteonecrosis in diseases classified elsewhere, upper arm**
CC **M90.521 Osteonecrosis in diseases classified elsewhere, right upper arm**
CC Exclusion see Appendix A PDX collection 0907
CC **M90.522 Osteonecrosis in diseases classified elsewhere, left upper arm**
CC Exclusion see Appendix A PDX collection 0907
CC **M90.529 Osteonecrosis in diseases classified elsewhere, unspecified upper arm**
CC Exclusion see Appendix A PDX collection 0907
\+ **M90.53 Osteonecrosis in diseases classified elsewhere, forearm**
CC **M90.531 Osteonecrosis in diseases classified elsewhere, right forearm**
CC Exclusion see Appendix A PDX collection 0907
CC **M90.532 Osteonecrosis in diseases classified elsewhere, left forearm**
CC Exclusion see Appendix A PDX collection 0907
CC **M90.539 Osteonecrosis in diseases classified elsewhere, unspecified forearm**
CC Exclusion see Appendix A PDX collection 0907

+ **M90.54** **Osteonecrosis in diseases classified elsewhere, hand**
- CC **M90.541** **Osteonecrosis in diseases classified elsewhere, right hand**
  - CC Exclusion see Appendix A PDX collection 0907
- CC **M90.542** **Osteonecrosis in diseases classified elsewhere, left hand**
  - CC Exclusion see Appendix A PDX collection 0907
- CC **M90.549** **Osteonecrosis in diseases classified elsewhere, unspecified hand**
  - CC Exclusion see Appendix A PDX collection 0907

+ **M90.55** **Osteonecrosis in diseases classified elsewhere, thigh**
- CC **M90.551** **Osteonecrosis in diseases classified elsewhere, right thigh**
  - CC Exclusion see Appendix A PDX collection 0909
- CC **M90.552** **Osteonecrosis in diseases classified elsewhere, left thigh**
  - CC Exclusion see Appendix A PDX collection 0909
- CC **M90.559** **Osteonecrosis in diseases classified elsewhere, unspecified thigh**
  - CC Exclusion see Appendix A PDX collection 0909

+ **M90.56** **Osteonecrosis in diseases classified elsewhere, lower leg**
- CC **M90.561** **Osteonecrosis in diseases classified elsewhere, right lower leg**
  - CC Exclusion see Appendix A PDX collection 0907
- CC **M90.562** **Osteonecrosis in diseases classified elsewhere, left lower leg**
  - CC Exclusion see Appendix A PDX collection 0907
- CC **M90.569** **Osteonecrosis in diseases classified elsewhere, unspecified lower leg**
  - CC Exclusion see Appendix A PDX collection 0907

+ **M90.57** **Osteonecrosis in diseases classified elsewhere, ankle and foot**
- CC **M90.571** **Osteonecrosis in diseases classified elsewhere, right ankle and foot**
  - CC Exclusion see Appendix A PDX collection 0907
- CC **M90.572** **Osteonecrosis in diseases classified elsewhere, left ankle and foot**
  - CC Exclusion see Appendix A PDX collection 0907
- CC **M90.579** **Osteonecrosis in diseases classified elsewhere, unspecified ankle and foot**
  - CC Exclusion see Appendix A PDX collection 0907

CC **M90.58** **Osteonecrosis in diseases classified elsewhere, other site**
- CC Exclusion see Appendix A PDX collection 0907

CC **M90.59** **Osteonecrosis in diseases classified elsewhere, multiple sites**
- CC Exclusion see Appendix A PDX collection 0907

+ **M90.6** **Osteitis deformans in neoplastic diseases**

Osteitis deformans in malignant neoplasm of bone
Code first the neoplasm (C40.-, C41.-)
Excludes1: *osteitis deformans [Paget's disease of bone] (M88.-)*

M90.60 **Osteitis deformans in neoplastic diseases, unspecified site**

+ **M90.61** **Osteitis deformans in neoplastic diseases, shoulder**
- **M90.611** **Osteitis deformans in neoplastic diseases, right shoulder**
- **M90.612** **Osteitis deformans in neoplastic diseases, left shoulder**
- **M90.619** **Osteitis deformans in neoplastic diseases, unspecified shoulder**

+ **M90.62** **Osteitis deformans in neoplastic diseases, upper arm**
- **M90.621** **Osteitis deformans in neoplastic diseases, right upper arm**
- **M90.622** **Osteitis deformans in neoplastic diseases, left upper arm**
- **M90.629** **Osteitis deformans in neoplastic diseases, unspecified upper arm**

+ **M90.63** **Osteitis deformans in neoplastic diseases, forearm**
- **M90.631** **Osteitis deformans in neoplastic diseases, right forearm**
- **M90.632** **Osteitis deformans in neoplastic diseases, left forearm**
- **M90.639** **Osteitis deformans in neoplastic diseases, unspecified forearm**

+ **M90.64** **Osteitis deformans in neoplastic diseases, hand**
- **M90.641** **Osteitis deformans in neoplastic diseases, right hand**
- **M90.642** **Osteitis deformans in neoplastic diseases, left hand**
- **M90.649** **Osteitis deformans in neoplastic diseases, unspecified hand**

+ **M90.65** **Osteitis deformans in neoplastic diseases, thigh**
- **M90.651** **Osteitis deformans in neoplastic diseases, right thigh**
- **M90.652** **Osteitis deformans in neoplastic diseases, thigh**
- **M90.659** **Osteitis deformans in neoplastic diseases, unspecified thigh**

+ **M90.66** **Osteitis deformans in neoplastic diseases, lower leg**
- **M90.661** **Osteitis deformans in neoplastic diseases, right lower leg**
- **M90.662** **Osteitis deformans in neoplastic diseases, l lower leg**
- **M90.669** **Osteitis deformans in neoplastic diseases, unspecified lower leg**

+ **M90.67** **Osteitis deformans in neoplastic diseases, ankle and foot**
- **M90.671** **Osteitis deformans in neoplastic diseases, right ankle and foot**
- **M90.672** **Osteitis deformans in neoplastic diseases, l ankle and foot**
- **M90.679** **Osteitis deformans in neoplastic diseases, unspecified ankle and foot**

M90.68 **Osteitis deformans in neoplastic diseases, other site**

M90.69 **Osteitis deformans in neoplastic diseases, multiple sites**

+ **M90.8** **Osteopathy in diseases classified elsewhere**

Code first underlying disease, such as:
- rickets (E55.0)
- vitamin-D-resistant rickets (E83.3)

M90.80 **Osteopathy in diseases classified elsewhere, unspecifi site**

+ **M90.81** **Osteopathy in diseases classified elsewhere, shoulder**
- **M90.811** **Osteopathy in diseases classified elsewhere, right shoulder**
- **M90.812** **Osteopathy in diseases classified elsewhere, left shoulder**
- **M90.819** **Osteopathy in diseases classified elsewhere, unspecified shoulder**

+ **M90.82** **Osteopathy in diseases classified elsewhere, upper ar**
- **M90.821** **Osteopathy in diseases classified elsewhere, right upper arm**
- **M90.822** **Osteopathy in diseases classified elsewhere, left upper arm**
- **M90.829** **Osteopathy in diseases classified elsewhere, unspecified upper arm**

+ **M90.83** **Osteopathy in diseases classified elsewhere, forearm**
- **M90.831** **Osteopathy in diseases classified elsewhere, right forearm**
- **M90.832** **Osteopathy in diseases classified elsewhere, left forearm**
- **M90.839** **Osteopathy in diseases classified elsewhere, unspecified forearm**

+ **M90.84** **Osteopathy in diseases classified elsewhere, hand**
- **M90.841** **Osteopathy in diseases classified elsewhere, right hand**
- **M90.842** **Osteopathy in diseases classified elsewhere, left hand**
- **M90.849** **Osteopathy in diseases classified elsewhere, unspecified hand**

+ **M90.85** **Osteopathy in diseases classified elsewhere, thigh**
- **M90.851** **Osteopathy in diseases classified elsewhere, right thigh**
- **M90.852** **Osteopathy in diseases classified elsewhere, left thigh**
- **M90.859** **Osteopathy in diseases classified elsewhere, unspecified thigh**

+ **M90.86** **Osteopathy in diseases classified elsewhere, lower leg**
- **M90.861** **Osteopathy in diseases classified elsewhere, right lower leg**
- **M90.862** **Osteopathy in diseases classified elsewhere, left lower leg**
- **M90.869** **Osteopathy in diseases classified elsewhere, unspecified lower leg**

+ **M90.87** **Osteopathy in diseases classified elsewhere, ankle and foot**
- **M90.871** **Osteopathy in diseases classified elsewhere, right ankle and foot**
- **M90.872** **Osteopathy in diseases classified elsewhere, left ankle and foot**
- **M90.879** **Osteopathy in diseases classified elsewhere, unspecified ankle and foot**

M90.88 **Osteopathy in diseases classified elsewhere, other site**
M90.89 **Osteopathy in diseases classified elsewhere, multiple sites**

ondropathies (M91-M94)

cludes1: *postprocedural chondropathies (M96.-)*

M91 Juvenile osteochondrosis of hip and pelvis

Excludes1: *slipped upper femoral epiphysis (nontraumatic) (M93.0)*

M91.0 Juvenile osteochondrosis of pelvis
Osteochondrosis (juvenile) of acetabulum
Osteochondrosis (juvenile) of iliac crest [Buchanan]
Osteochondrosis (juvenile) of ischiopubic synchondrosis [van Neck]
Osteochondrosis (juvenile) of symphysis pubis [Pierson]

\+ **M91.1 Juvenile osteochondrosis of head of femur [Legg-Calvé-Perthes]**
M91.10 Juvenile osteochondrosis of head of femur [Legg-Calvé-Perthes], unspecified leg
M91.11 Juvenile osteochondrosis of head of femur [Legg-Calvé-Perthes], right leg
M91.12 Juvenile osteochondrosis of head of femur [Legg-Calvé-Perthes], left leg

\+ **M91.2 Coxa plana**
Hip deformity due to previous juvenile osteochondrosis
M91.20 Coxa plana, unspecified hip
M91.21 Coxa plana, right hip
M91.22 Coxa plana, left hip

\+ **M91.3 Pseudocoxalgia**
M91.30 Pseudocoxalgia, unspecified hip
M91.31 Pseudocoxalgia, right hip
M91.32 Pseudocoxalgia, left hip

\+ **M91.4 Coxa magna**
M91.40 Coxa magna, unspecified hip
M91.41 Coxa magna, right hip
M91.42 Coxa magna, left hip

\+ **M91.8 Other juvenile osteochondrosis of hip and pelvis**
Juvenile osteochondrosis after reduction of congenital dislocation of hip
M91.80 Other juvenile osteochondrosis of hip and pelvis, unspecified leg
M91.81 Other juvenile osteochondrosis of hip and pelvis, right leg
M91.82 Other juvenile osteochondrosis of hip and pelvis, left leg

\+ **M91.9 Juvenile osteochondrosis of hip and pelvis, unspecified**
M91.90 Juvenile osteochondrosis of hip and pelvis, unspecified, unspecified leg
M91.91 Juvenile osteochondrosis of hip and pelvis, unspecified, right leg
M91.92 Juvenile osteochondrosis of hip and pelvis, unspecified, left leg

M92 Other juvenile osteochondrosis

\+ **M92.0 Juvenile osteochondrosis of humerus**
Osteochondrosis (juvenile) of capitulum of humerus [Panner]
Osteochondrosis (juvenile) of head of humerus [Haas]
M92.00 Juvenile osteochondrosis of humerus, unspecified arm
M92.01 Juvenile osteochondrosis of humerus, right arm
M92.02 Juvenile osteochondrosis of humerus, left arm

\+ **M92.1 Juvenile osteochondrosis of radius and ulna**
Osteochondrosis (juvenile) of lower ulna [Burns]
Osteochondrosis (juvenile) of radial head [Brailsford]
M92.10 Juvenile osteochondrosis of radius and ulna, unspecified arm
M92.11 Juvenile osteochondrosis of radius and ulna, right arm
M92.12 Juvenile osteochondrosis of radius and ulna, left arm

\+ **M92.2 Juvenile osteochondrosis, hand**
\+ **M92.20 Unspecified juvenile osteochondrosis, hand**
M92.201 Unspecified juvenile osteochondrosis, right hand
M92.202 Unspecified juvenile osteochondrosis, left hand
M92.209 Unspecified juvenile osteochondrosis, unspecified hand
\+ **M92.21 Osteochondrosis (juvenile) of carpal lunate [Kienböck]**
M92.211 Osteochondrosis (juvenile) of carpal lunate [Kienböck], right hand
M92.212 Osteochondrosis (juvenile) of carpal lunate [Kienböck], left hand
M92.219 Osteochondrosis (juvenile) of carpal lunate [Kienböck], unspecified hand
\+ **M92.22 Osteochondrosis (juvenile) of metacarpal heads [Mauclaire]**
M92.221 Osteochondrosis (juvenile) of metacarpal heads [Mauclaire], right hand
M92.222 Osteochondrosis (juvenile) of metacarpal heads [Mauclaire], left hand
M92.229 Osteochondrosis (juvenile) of metacarpal heads [Mauclaire], unspecified hand
\+ **M92.29 Other juvenile osteochondrosis, hand**
M92.291 Other juvenile osteochondrosis, right hand
M92.292 Other juvenile osteochondrosis, left hand
M92.299 Other juvenile osteochondrosis, unspecified hand

\+ **M92.3 Other juvenile osteochondrosis, upper limb**
M92.30 Other juvenile osteochondrosis, unspecified upper limb
M92.31 Other juvenile osteochondrosis, right upper limb
M92.32 Other juvenile osteochondrosis, left upper limb

\+ **M92.4 Juvenile osteochondrosis of patella**
Osteochondrosis (juvenile) of primary patellar center [Köhler]
Osteochondrosis (juvenile) of secondary patellar centre [Sinding Larsen]
M92.40 Juvenile osteochondrosis of patella, unspecified knee
M92.41 Juvenile osteochondrosis of patella, right knee
M92.42 Juvenile osteochondrosis of patella, left knee

\+ **M92.5 Juvenile osteochondrosis of tibia and fibula**
Osteochondrosis (juvenile) of proximal tibia [Blount]
Osteochondrosis (juvenile) of tibial tubercle [Osgood-Schlatter]
Tibia vara
M92.50 Juvenile osteochondrosis of tibia and fibula, unspecified leg
M92.51 Juvenile osteochondrosis of tibia and fibula, right leg
M92.52 Juvenile osteochondrosis of tibia and fibula, left leg

\+ **M92.6 Juvenile osteochondrosis of tarsus**
Osteochondrosis (juvenile) of calcaneum [Sever]
Osteochondrosis (juvenile) of os tibiale externum [Haglund]
Osteochondrosis (juvenile) of talus [Diaz]
Osteochondrosis (juvenile) of tarsal navicular [Köhler]
M92.60 Juvenile osteochondrosis of tarsus, unspecified ankle
M92.61 Juvenile osteochondrosis of tarsus, right ankle
M92.62 Juvenile osteochondrosis of tarsus, left ankle

\+ **M92.7 Juvenile osteochondrosis of metatarsus**
Osteochondrosis (juvenile) of fifth metatarsus [Iselin]
Osteochondrosis (juvenile) of second metatarsus [Freiberg]
M92.70 Juvenile osteochondrosis of metatarsus, unspecified foot
M92.71 Juvenile osteochondrosis of metatarsus, right foot
M92.72 Juvenile osteochondrosis of metatarsus, left foot

M92.8 Other specified juvenile osteochondrosis
Calcaneal apophysitis

M92.9 Juvenile osteochondrosis, unspecified
Juvenile apophysitis NOS
Juvenile epiphysitis NOS
Juvenile osteochondritis NOS
Juvenile osteochondrosis NOS

M93 Other osteochondropathies

Excludes2: *osteochondrosis of spine (M42.-)*

\+ **M93.0 Slipped upper femoral epiphysis (nontraumatic)**
Use additional code for associated chondrolysis (M94.3)
\+ **M93.00 Unspecified slipped upper femoral epiphysis (nontraumatic)**
M93.001 Unspecified slipped upper femoral epiphysis (nontraumatic), right hip
M93.002 Unspecified slipped upper femoral epiphysis (nontraumatic), left hip
M93.003 Unspecified slipped upper femoral epiphysis (nontraumatic), unspecified hip
\+ **M93.01 Acute slipped upper femoral epiphysis (nontraumatic)**
M93.011 Acute slipped upper femoral epiphysis (nontraumatic), right hip
M93.012 Acute slipped upper femoral epiphysis (nontraumatic), left hip
M93.013 Acute slipped upper femoral epiphysis (nontraumatic), unspecified hip
\+ **M93.02 Chronic slipped upper femoral epiphysis (nontraumatic)**
M93.021 Chronic slipped upper femoral epiphysis (nontraumatic), right hip
M93.022 Chronic slipped upper femoral epiphysis (nontraumatic), left hip
M93.023 Chronic slipped upper femoral epiphysis (nontraumatic), unspecified hip

+ **M93.03 Acute on chronic slipped upper femoral epiphysis (nontraumatic)**
M93.031 Acute on chronic slipped upper femoral epiphysis (nontraumatic), right hip
M93.032 Acute on chronic slipped upper femoral epiphysis (nontraumatic), left hip
M93.033 Acute on chronic slipped upper femoral epiphysis (nontraumatic), unspecified hip
• **M93.1 Kienböck's disease of adults**
Adult osteochondrosis of carpal lunates
+ **M93.2 Osteochondritis dissecans**
M93.20 Osteochondritis dissecans of unspecified site
+ **M93.21 Osteochondritis dissecans of shoulder**
M93.211 Osteochondritis dissecans, right shoulder
M93.212 Osteochondritis dissecans, left shoulder
M93.219 Osteochondritis dissecans, unspecified shoulder
+ **M93.22 Osteochondritis dissecans of elbow**
M93.221 Osteochondritis dissecans, right elbow
M93.222 Osteochondritis dissecans, left elbow
M93.229 Osteochondritis dissecans, unspecified elbow
+ **M93.23 Osteochondritis dissecans of wrist**
M93.231 Osteochondritis dissecans, right wrist
M93.232 Osteochondritis dissecans, left wrist
M93.239 Osteochondritis dissecans, unspecified wrist
+ **M93.24 Osteochondritis dissecans of joints of hand**
M93.241 Osteochondritis dissecans, joints of right hand
M93.242 Osteochondritis dissecans, joints of left hand
M93.249 Osteochondritis dissecans, joints of unspecified hand
+ **M93.25 Osteochondritis dissecans of hip**
M93.251 Osteochondritis dissecans, right hip
M93.252 Osteochondritis dissecans, left hip
M93.259 Osteochondritis dissecans, unspecified hip
+ **M93.26 Osteochondritis dissecans knee**
M93.261 Osteochondritis dissecans, right knee
M93.262 Osteochondritis dissecans, left knee
M93.269 Osteochondritis dissecans, unspecified knee
+ **M93.27 Osteochondritis dissecans of ankle and joints of foot**
M93.271 Osteochondritis dissecans, right ankle and joints of right foot
M93.272 Osteochondritis dissecans, left ankle and joints of left foot
M93.279 Osteochondritis dissecans, unspecified ankle and joints of foot
M93.28 Osteochondritis dissecans other site
M93.29 Osteochondritis dissecans multiple sites
+ **M93.8 Other specified osteochondropathies**
M93.80 Other specified osteochondropathies of unspecified site
+ **M93.81 Other specified osteochondropathies of shoulder**
M93.811 Other specified osteochondropathies, right shoulder
M93.812 Other specified osteochondropathies, left shoulder
M93.819 Other specified osteochondropathies, unspecified shoulder
+ **M93.82 Other specified osteochondropathies of upper arm**
M93.821 Other specified osteochondropathies, right upper arm
M93.822 Other specified osteochondropathies, left upper arm
M93.829 Other specified osteochondropathies, unspecified upper arm
+ **M93.83 Other specified osteochondropathies of forearm**
M93.831 Other specified osteochondropathies, right forearm
M93.832 Other specified osteochondropathies, left forearm
M93.839 Other specified osteochondropathies, unspecified forearm
+ **M93.84 Other specified osteochondropathies of hand**
M93.841 Other specified osteochondropathies, right hand
M93.842 Other specified osteochondropathies, left hand
M93.849 Other specified osteochondropathies, unspecified hand
+ **M93.85 Other specified osteochondropathies of thigh**
M93.851 Other specified osteochondropathies, right thigh
M93.852 Other specified osteochondropathies, left thigh
M93.859 Other specified osteochondropathies, unspecified thigh
+ **M93.86 Other specified osteochondropathies lower leg**
M93.861 Other specified osteochondropathies, righ lower leg
M93.862 Other specified osteochondropathies, left lower leg
M93.869 Other specified osteochondropathies, unspecified lower leg
+ **M93.87 Other specified osteochondropathies of ankle and fo**
M93.871 Other specified osteochondropathies, righ ankle and foot
M93.872 Other specified osteochondropathies, left ankle and foot
M93.879 Other specified osteochondropathies, unspecified ankle and foot
M93.88 Other specified osteochondropathies other
M93.89 Other specified osteochondropathies multiple sites
+ **M93.9 Osteochondropathy, unspecified**
Apophysitis NOS
Epiphysitis NOS
Osteochondritis NOS
Osteochondrosis NOS
M93.90 Osteochondropathy, unspecified of unspecified site
+ **M93.91 Osteochondropathy, unspecified of shoulder**
M93.911 Osteochondropathy, unspecified, right shoulder
M93.912 Osteochondropathy, unspecified, left shoulder
M93.919 Osteochondropathy, unspecified, unspecifi shoulder
+ **M93.92 Osteochondropathy, unspecified of upper arm**
M93.921 Osteochondropathy, unspecified, right upp arm
M93.922 Osteochondropathy, unspecified, left uppe arm
M93.929 Osteochondropathy, unspecified, unspecifi upper arm
+ **M93.93 Osteochondropathy, unspecified of forearm**
M93.931 Osteochondropathy, unspecified, right forearm
M93.932 Osteochondropathy, unspecified, left forea
M93.939 Osteochondropathy, unspecified, unspecifi forearm
+ **M93.94 Osteochondropathy, unspecified of hand**
M93.941 Osteochondropathy, unspecified, right han
M93.942 Osteochondropathy, unspecified, left hand
M93.949 Osteochondropathy, unspecified, unspecifi hand
+ **M93.95 Osteochondropathy, unspecified of thigh**
M93.951 Osteochondropathy, unspecified, right thig
M93.952 Osteochondropathy, unspecified, left thigh
M93.959 Osteochondropathy, unspecified, unspecifie thigh
+ **M93.96 Osteochondropathy, unspecified lower leg**
M93.961 Osteochondropathy, unspecified, right lowe leg
M93.962 Osteochondropathy, unspecified, left lower leg
M93.969 Osteochondropathy, unspecified, unspecifie lower leg
+ **M93.97 Osteochondropathy, unspecified of ankle and foot**
M93.971 Osteochondropathy, unspecified, right ank and foot
M93.972 Osteochondropathy, unspecified, left ankle and foot
M93.979 Osteochondropathy, unspecified, unspecifie ankle and foot
M93.98 Osteochondropathy, unspecified other
M93.99 Osteochondropathy, unspecified multiple sites

M94 Other disorders of cartilage

M94.0 Chondrocostal junction syndrome [Tietze]
Costochondritis
M94.1 Relapsing polychondritis
+ **M94.2 Chondromalacia**
Excludes1: *chondromalacia patellae (M22.4)*
M94.20 Chondromalacia, unspecified site
+ **M94.21 Chondromalacia, shoulder**
M94.211 Chondromalacia, right shoulder

M94.212 Chondromalacia, left shoulder
M94.219 Chondromalacia, unspecified shoulder
+ M94.22 Chondromalacia, elbow
M94.221 Chondromalacia, right elbow
M94.222 Chondromalacia, left elbow
M94.229 Chondromalacia, unspecified elbow
+ M94.23 Chondromalacia, wrist
M94.231 Chondromalacia, right wrist
M94.232 Chondromalacia, left wrist
M94.239 Chondromalacia, unspecified wrist
+ M94.24 Chondromalacia, joints of hand
M94.241 Chondromalacia, joints of right hand
M94.242 Chondromalacia, joints of left hand
M94.249 Chondromalacia, joints of unspecified hand
+ M94.25 Chondromalacia, hip
M94.251 Chondromalacia, right hip
M94.252 Chondromalacia, left hip
M94.259 Chondromalacia, unspecified hip
+ M94.26 Chondromalacia, knee
M94.261 Chondromalacia, right knee
M94.262 Chondromalacia, left knee
M94.269 Chondromalacia, unspecified knee
+ M94.27 Chondromalacia, ankle and joints of foot
M94.271 Chondromalacia, right ankle and joints of right foot
M94.272 Chondromalacia, left ankle and joints of left foot
M94.279 Chondromalacia, unspecified ankle and joints of foot
M94.28 Chondromalacia, other site
M94.29 Chondromalacia, multiple sites
+ M94.3 Chondrolysis
Code first any associated slipped upper femoral epiphysis (nontraumatic) (M93.0-)
+ M94.35 Chondrolysis, hip
M94.351 Chondrolysis, right hip
M94.352 Chondrolysis, left hip
M94.359 Chondrolysis, unspecified hip
+ M94.8 Other specified disorders of cartilage
+ M94.8X Other specified disorders of cartilage
M94.8X0 Other specified disorders of cartilage, multiple sites
M94.8X1 Other specified disorders of cartilage, shoulder
M94.8X2 Other specified disorders of cartilage, upper arm
M94.8X3 Other specified disorders of cartilage, forearm
M94.8X4 Other specified disorders of cartilage, hand
M94.8X5 Other specified disorders of cartilage, thigh
M94.8X6 Other specified disorders of cartilage, lower leg
M94.8X7 Other specified disorders of cartilage, ankle and foot
M94.8X8 Other specified disorders of cartilage, other site
M94.8X9 Other specified disorders of cartilage, unspecified sites
M94.9 Disorder of cartilage, unspecified

Other disorders of the musculoskeletal system and connective tissue (M95)

M95 Other acquired deformities of musculoskeletal system and connective tissue

Excludes2: *acquired absence of limbs and organs (Z89-Z90)*
acquired deformities of limbs (M20-M21)
congenital malformations and deformations of the musculoskeletal system (Q65-Q79)
deforming dorsopathies (M40-M43)
dentofacial anomalies [including malocclusion] (M26.-)
postprocedural musculoskeletal disorders (M96.-)

M95.0 Acquired deformity of nose
Excludes2: *deviated nasal septum (J34.2)*
+ M95.1 Cauliflower ear
Excludes2: *other acquired deformities of ear (H61.1)*
M95.10 Cauliflower ear, unspecified ear
M95.11 Cauliflower ear, right ear
M95.12 Cauliflower ear, left ear
M95.2 Other acquired deformity of head
M95.3 Acquired deformity of neck
M95.4 Acquired deformity of chest and rib
M95.5 Acquired deformity of pelvis
Excludes1: *maternal care for known or suspected disproportion (O33.-)*
M95.8 Other specified acquired deformities of musculoskeletal system
M95.9 Acquired deformity of musculoskeletal system, unspecified

Intraoperative and postprocedural complications and disorders of musculoskeletal system, not elsewhere classified (M96)

M96 Intraoperative and postprocedural complications and disorders of musculoskeletal system, not elsewhere classified

Excludes2: *arthropathy following intestinal bypass (M02.0-)*
complications of internal orthopedic prosthetic devices, implants and grafts (T84.-)
disorders associated with osteoporosis (M80)
presence of functional implants and other devices (Z96-Z97)

CC M96.0 Pseudarthrosis after fusion or arthrodesis
There are no CC exclusions for this code
M96.1 Postlaminectomy syndrome, not elsewhere classified
M96.2 Postradiation kyphosis
M96.3 Postlaminectomy kyphosis
M96.4 Postsurgical lordosis
M96.5 Postradiation scoliosis
+ M96.6 Fracture of bone following insertion of orthopedic implant, joint prosthesis, or bone plate
Intraoperative fracture of bone during insertion of orthopedic implant, joint prosthesis, or bone plate
Excludes2: *complication of internal orthopedic devices, implants or grafts (T84.-)*
+ M96.62 Fracture of humerus following insertion of orthopedic implant, joint prosthesis, or bone plate
CC M96.621 Fracture of humerus following insertion of orthopedic implant, joint prosthesis, or bone plate, right arm
CC Exclusion see Appendix A PDX collection 0911
CC M96.622 Fracture of humerus following insertion of orthopedic implant, joint prosthesis, or bone plate, left arm
CC Exclusion see Appendix A PDX collection 0911
CC M96.629 Fracture of humerus following insertion of orthopedic implant, joint prosthesis, or bone plate, unspecified arm
CC Exclusion see Appendix A PDX collection 0911
+ M96.63 Fracture of radius or ulna following insertion of orthopedic implant, joint prosthesis, or bone plate
CC M96.631 Fracture of radius or ulna following insertion of orthopedic implant, joint prosthesis, or bone plate, right arm
CC Exclusion see Appendix A PDX collection 0911
CC M96.632 Fracture of radius or ulna following insertion of orthopedic implant, joint prosthesis, or bone plate, left arm
CC Exclusion see Appendix A PDX collection 0911
CC M96.639 Fracture of radius or ulna following insertion of orthopedic implant, joint prosthesis, or bone plate, unspecified arm
CC Exclusion see Appendix A PDX collection 0911
CC M96.65 Fracture of pelvis following insertion of orthopedic implant, joint prosthesis, or bone plate
CC Exclusion see Appendix A PDX collection 0911
+ M96.66 Fracture of femur following insertion of orthopedic implant, joint prosthesis, or bone plate
CC M96.661 Fracture of femur following insertion of orthopedic implant, joint prosthesis, or bone plate, right leg
CC Exclusion see Appendix A PDX collection 0911
CC M96.662 Fracture of femur following insertion of orthopedic implant, joint prosthesis, or bone plate, left leg
CC Exclusion see Appendix A PDX collection 0911
CC M96.669 Fracture of femur following insertion of orthopedic implant, joint prosthesis, or bone plate, unspecified leg
CC Exclusion see Appendix A PDX collection 0911
+ M96.67 Fracture of tibia or fibula following insertion of orthopedic implant, joint prosthesis, or bone plate
CC M96.671 Fracture of tibia or fibula following insertion of orthopedic implant, joint prosthesis, or bone plate, right leg
CC Exclusion see Appendix A PDX collection 0911

CC **M96.672** **Fracture of tibia or fibula following insertion of orthopedic implant, joint prosthesis, or bone plate, left leg**
CC Exclusion see Appendix A PDX collection 0911

CC **M96.679** **Fracture of tibia or fibula following insertion of orthopedic implant, joint prosthesis, or bone plate, unspecified leg**
CC Exclusion see Appendix A PDX collection 0911

CC **M96.69** **Fracture of other bone following insertion of orthopedic implant, joint prosthesis, or bone plate**
CC Exclusion see Appendix A PDX collection 0911

\+ **M96.8** **Other intraoperative and postprocedural complications and disorders of musculoskeletal system, not elsewhere classified**

\+ **M96.81** **Intraoperative hemorrhage and hematoma of a musculoskeletal structure complicating a procedure**
Excludes1: *intraoperative hemorrhage and hematoma of a musculoskeletal structure due to accidental puncture and laceration during a procedure (M96.82)*

CC **M96.810** **Intraoperative hemorrhage and hematoma of a musculoskeletal structure complicating a musculoskeletal system procedure**
CC Exclusion see Appendix A PDX collection 0912

CC **M96.811** **Intraoperative hemorrhage and hematoma of a musculoskeletal structure complicating other procedure**
CC Exclusion see Appendix A PDX collection 0912

\+ **M96.82** **Accidental puncture and laceration of a musculoskeletal structure during a procedure**

CC **M96.820** **Accidental puncture and laceration of a musculoskeletal structure during a musculoskeletal system procedure**
CC Exclusion see Appendix A PDX collection 0509

CC **M96.821** **Accidental puncture and laceration of a musculoskeletal structure during other procedure**
CC Exclusion see Appendix A PDX collection 0509

\+ **M96.83** **Postprocedural hemorrhage and hematoma of a musculoskeletal structure following a procedure**

CC **M96.830** **Postprocedural hemorrhage and hematoma of a musculoskeletal structure following a musculoskeletal system procedure**
CC Exclusion see Appendix A PDX collection 0912

CC **M96.831** **Postprocedural hemorrhage and hematoma of a musculoskeletal structure following other procedure**
CC Exclusion see Appendix A PDX collection 0912

\+ CC **M96.89** **Other intraoperative and postprocedural complications and disorders of the musculoskeletal system**
Instability of joint secondary to removal of joint prosthesis
Use additional code, if applicable, to further specify disorder
CC Exclusion see Appendix A PDX collection 0643

Biomechanical lesions, not elsewhere classified (M99)

M99 Biomechanical lesions, not elsewhere classified

NOTE This category should not be used if the condition can be classified elsewhere.

\+ **M99.0** **Segmental and somatic dysfunction**
M99.00 **Segmental and somatic dysfunction of head region**
M99.01 **Segmental and somatic dysfunction of cervical region**
M99.02 **Segmental and somatic dysfunction of thoracic region**
M99.03 **Segmental and somatic dysfunction of lumbar region**
M99.04 **Segmental and somatic dysfunction of sacral region**
M99.05 **Segmental and somatic dysfunction of pelvic region**
M99.06 **Segmental and somatic dysfunction of lower extremity**
M99.07 **Segmental and somatic dysfunction of upper extremity**
M99.08 **Segmental and somatic dysfunction of rib cage**
M99.09 **Segmental and somatic dysfunction of abdomen and other regions**

\+ **M99.1** **Subluxation complex (vertebral)**
CC **M99.10** **Subluxation complex (vertebral) of head region**
CC Exclusion see Appendix A PDX collection 0913
HAC see Appendix B for HAC conditional logic
CC **M99.11** **Subluxation complex (vertebral) of cervical region**
CC Exclusion see Appendix A PDX collection 0913
HAC see Appendix B for HAC conditional logic
M99.12 **Subluxation complex (vertebral) of thoracic region**
M99.13 **Subluxation complex (vertebral) of lumbar region**
M99.14 **Subluxation complex (vertebral) of sacral region**
M99.15 **Subluxation complex (vertebral) of pelvic region**
M99.16 **Subluxation complex (vertebral) of lower extremity**
M99.17 **Subluxation complex (vertebral) of upper extremity**
CC **M99.18** **Subluxation complex (vertebral) of rib cage**
CC Exclusion see Appendix A PDX collection 0914
HAC see Appendix B for HAC conditional logic
M99.19 **Subluxation complex (vertebral) of abdomen and other regions**

\+ **M99.2** **Subluxation stenosis of neural canal**
M99.20 **Subluxation stenosis of neural canal of head region**
M99.21 **Subluxation stenosis of neural canal of cervical region**
M99.22 **Subluxation stenosis of neural canal of thoracic region**
M99.23 **Subluxation stenosis of neural canal of lumbar region**
M99.24 **Subluxation stenosis of neural canal of sacral region**
M99.25 **Subluxation stenosis of neural canal of pelvic region**
M99.26 **Subluxation stenosis of neural canal of lower extremity**
M99.27 **Subluxation stenosis of neural canal of upper extremity**
M99.28 **Subluxation stenosis of neural canal of rib cage**
M99.29 **Subluxation stenosis of neural canal of abdomen and other regions**

\+ **M99.3** **Osseous stenosis of neural canal**
M99.30 **Osseous stenosis of neural canal of head region**
M99.31 **Osseous stenosis of neural canal of cervical region**
M99.32 **Osseous stenosis of neural canal of thoracic region**
M99.33 **Osseous stenosis of neural canal of lumbar region**
M99.34 **Osseous stenosis of neural canal of sacral region**
M99.35 **Osseous stenosis of neural canal of pelvic region**
M99.36 **Osseous stenosis of neural canal of lower extremity**
M99.37 **Osseous stenosis of neural canal of upper extremity**
M99.38 **Osseous stenosis of neural canal of rib cage**
M99.39 **Osseous stenosis of neural canal of abdomen and other regions**

\+ **M99.4** **Connective tissue stenosis of neural canal**
M99.40 **Connective tissue stenosis of neural canal of head region**
M99.41 **Connective tissue stenosis of neural canal of cervical region**
M99.42 **Connective tissue stenosis of neural canal of thoracic region**
M99.43 **Connective tissue stenosis of neural canal of lumbar region**
M99.44 **Connective tissue stenosis of neural canal of sacral region**
M99.45 **Connective tissue stenosis of neural canal of pelvic region**
M99.46 **Connective tissue stenosis of neural canal of lower extremity**
M99.47 **Connective tissue stenosis of neural canal of upper extremity**
M99.48 **Connective tissue stenosis of neural canal of rib cage**
M99.49 **Connective tissue stenosis of neural canal of abdomen and other regions**

\+ **M99.5** **Intervertebral disc stenosis of neural canal**
M99.50 **Intervertebral disc stenosis of neural canal of head region**
M99.51 **Intervertebral disc stenosis of neural canal of cervical region**
M99.52 **Intervertebral disc stenosis of neural canal of thoracic region**
M99.53 **Intervertebral disc stenosis of neural canal of lumbar region**
M99.54 **Intervertebral disc stenosis of neural canal of sacral region**
M99.55 **Intervertebral disc stenosis of neural canal of pelvic region**
M99.56 **Intervertebral disc stenosis of neural canal of lower extremity**
M99.57 **Intervertebral disc stenosis of neural canal of upper extremity**
M99.58 **Intervertebral disc stenosis of neural canal of rib cage**
M99.59 **Intervertebral disc stenosis of neural canal of abdomen and other regions**

\+ **M99.6** **Osseous and subluxation stenosis of intervertebral foramina**
M99.60 **Osseous and subluxation stenosis of intervertebral foramina of head region**
M99.61 **Osseous and subluxation stenosis of intervertebral foramina of cervical region**
M99.62 **Osseous and subluxation stenosis of intervertebral foramina of thoracic region**

M99.63 Osseous and subluxation stenosis of intervertebral foramina of lumbar region
M99.64 Osseous and subluxation stenosis of intervertebral foramina of sacral region
M99.65 Osseous and subluxation stenosis of intervertebral foramina of pelvic region
M99.66 Osseous and subluxation stenosis of intervertebral foramina of lower extremity
M99.67 Osseous and subluxation stenosis of intervertebral foramina of upper extremity
M99.68 Osseous and subluxation stenosis of intervertebral foramina of rib cage
M99.69 Osseous and subluxation stenosis of intervertebral foramina of abdomen and other regions

+ **M99.7** Connective tissue and disc stenosis of intervertebral foramina
M99.70 Connective tissue and disc stenosis of intervertebral foramina of head region
M99.71 Connective tissue and disc stenosis of intervertebral foramina of cervical region
M99.72 Connective tissue and disc stenosis of intervertebral foramina of thoracic region
M99.73 Connective tissue and disc stenosis of intervertebral foramina of lumbar region
M99.74 Connective tissue and disc stenosis of intervertebral foramina of sacral region
M99.75 Connective tissue and disc stenosis of intervertebral foramina of pelvic region
M99.76 Connective tissue and disc stenosis of intervertebral foramina of lower extremity
M99.77 Connective tissue and disc stenosis of intervertebral foramina of upper extremity
M99.78 Connective tissue and disc stenosis of intervertebral foramina of rib cage
M99.79 Connective tissue and disc stenosis of intervertebral foramina of abdomen and other regions

+ **M99.8** Other biomechanical lesions
M99.80 Other biomechanical lesions of head region
M99.81 Other biomechanical lesions of cervical region
M99.82 Other biomechanical lesions of thoracic region
M99.83 Other biomechanical lesions of lumbar region
M99.84 Other biomechanical lesions of sacral region
M99.85 Other biomechanical lesions of pelvic region
M99.86 Other biomechanical lesions of lower extremity
M99.87 Other biomechanical lesions of upper extremity
M99.88 Other biomechanical lesions of rib cage
M99.89 Other biomechanical lesions of abdomen and other regions

M99.9 Biomechanical lesion, unspecified

Chapter 14: Diseases of the Genitourinary System (N00-N99)

Excludes2: *certain conditions originating in the perinatal period (P04-P96)*
certain infectious and parasitic diseases (A00-B99)
complications of pregnancy, childbirth and the puerperium (O00-O9A)
congenital malformations, deformations and chromosomal abnormalities (Q00-Q99)
endocrine, nutritional and metabolic diseases (E00-E88)
injury, poisoning and certain other consequences of external causes (S00-T88)
neoplasms (C00-D49)
symptoms, signs and abnormal clinical and laboratory findings, not elsewhere classified (R00-R94)

This chapter contains the following category blocks:

N00-N08	Glomerular diseases
N10-N16	Renal tubulo-interstitial diseases
N17-N19	Acute kidney failure and chronic kidney disease
N20-N23	Urolithiasis
N25-N29	Other disorders of kidney and ureter
N30-N39	Other diseases of the urinary system
N40-N53	Diseases of male genital organs
N60-N65	Disorders of breast
N70-N77	Inflammatory diseases of female pelvic organs
N80-N98	Noninflammatory disorders of female genital tract
N99	Intraoperative and postprocedural complications and disorders of genitourinary system, not elsewhere classified

C. Chapter-Specific Coding Guidelines

In addition to general coding guidelines, there are guidelines for specific diagnoses and/or conditions in the classification. Unless otherwise indicated, these guidelines apply to all health care settings. Please refer to Section II for guidelines on selection of principal diagnosis.

14. Chapter 14: Diseases of the Genitourinary System (N00-N99)

a. Chronic kidney disease

1) Stages of chronic kidney disease (CKD)

The ICD-10-CM classifies CKD based on severity. The severity of CK[D] designated by stages 1-5. Stage 2, code N18.2, equates to mild CKD; stag[e] code N18.3, equates to moderate CKD; and stage 4, code N18.4, equates severe CKD. Code N18.6, End stage renal disease (ESRD), is assigned w[h] the provider has documented end-stage-renal disease (ESRD).

If both a stage of CKD and ESRD are documented, assign code N18.6 onl[y]

2) Chronic kidney disease and kidney transplant status

Patients who have undergone kidney transplant may still have some fo[rm] of chronic kidney disease (CKD) because the kidney transplant may [not] fully restore kidney function. Therefore, the presence of CKD alone d[oes] not constitute a transplant complication. Assign the appropriate N18 co[de] for the patient's stage of CKD and code Z94.0, Kidney transplant stat[us]. If a transplant complication such as failure or rejection or other transpl[ant] complication is documented, see section I.C.19.g for information on codi[ng] complications of a kidney transplant. If the documentation is unclear as whether the patient has a complication of the transplant, query the provid[er].

3) Chronic kidney disease with other conditions

Patients with CKD may also suffer from other serious conditions, m[ost] commonly diabetes mellitus and hypertension. The sequencing of the CK[D] code in relationship to codes for other contributing conditions is based on t[he] conventions in the Tabular List.

See I.C.9. Hypertensive chronic kidney disease.

See I.C.19. Chronic kidney disease and kidney transplant complications.

Urinary System

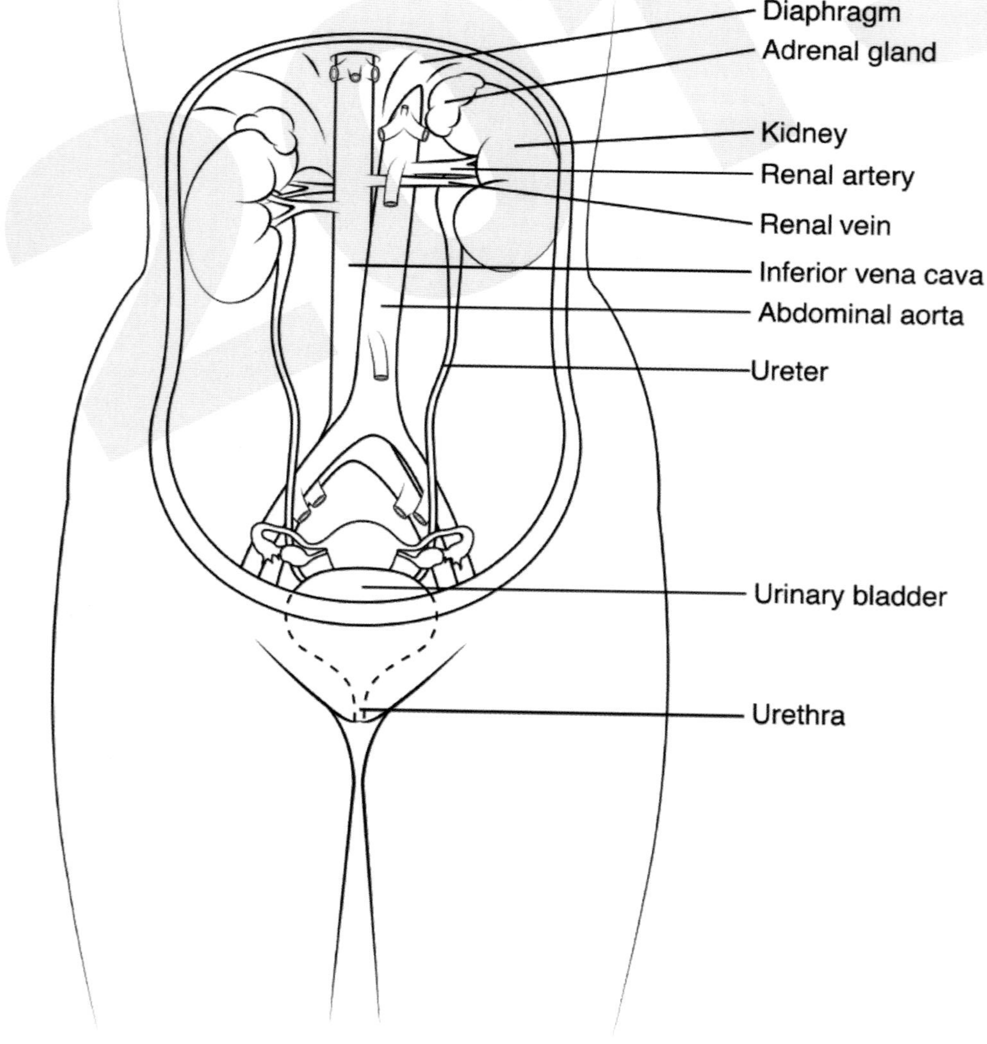

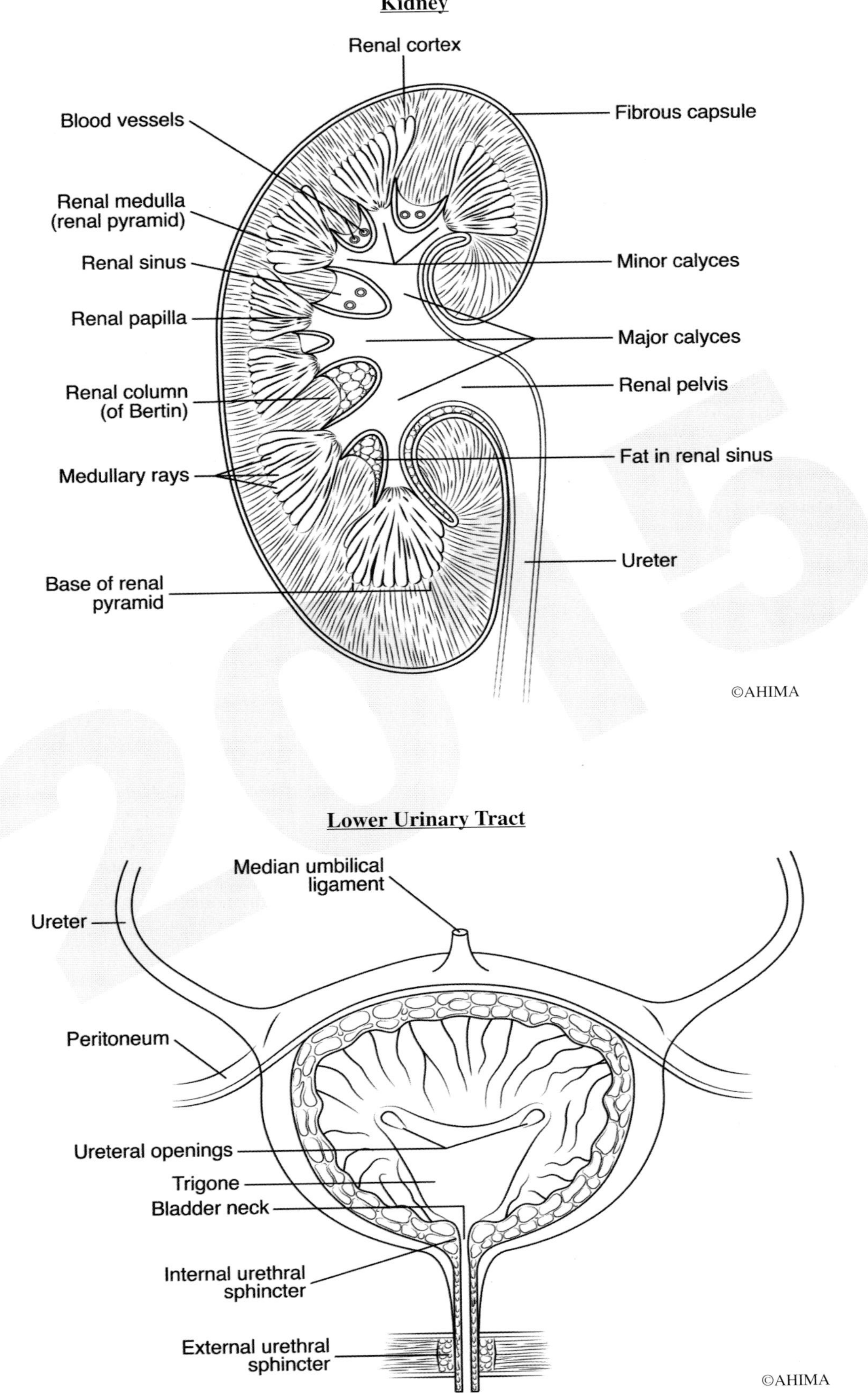
Kidney
Renal cortex
Fibrous capsule
Blood vessels
Renal medulla (renal pyramid)
Minor calyces
Renal sinus
Renal papilla
Major calyces
Renal pelvis
Renal column (of Bertin)
Fat in renal sinus
Medullary rays
Ureter
Base of renal pyramid
©AHIMA
Lower Urinary Tract
Median umbilical ligament
Ureter
Peritoneum
Ureteral openings
Trigone
Bladder neck
Internal urethral sphincter
External urethral sphincter
©AHIMA

Glomerular diseases (N00-N08)

Code also any associated kidney failure (N17-N19).

Excludes1: *hypertensive chronic kidney disease (I12.-)*

N00 Acute nephritic syndrome

Includes: acute glomerular disease
acute glomerulonephritis
acute nephritis

Excludes1: *acute tubulo-interstitial nephritis (N10)*
nephritic syndrome NOS (N05.-)

MCC **N00.0 Acute nephritic syndrome with minor glomerular abnormality**
Acute nephritic syndrome with minimal change lesion
MCC Exclusion see Appendix A PDX collection 0915

MCC **N00.1 Acute nephritic syndrome with focal and segmental glomerular lesions**
Acute nephritic syndrome with focal and segmental hyalinosis
Acute nephritic syndrome with focal and segmental sclerosis
Acute nephritic syndrome with focal glomerulonephritis
MCC Exclusion see Appendix A PDX collection 0915

MCC **N00.2 Acute nephritic syndrome with diffuse membranous glomerulonephritis**
MCC Exclusion see Appendix A PDX collection 0915

MCC **N00.3 Acute nephritic syndrome with diffuse mesangial proliferative glomerulonephritis**
MCC Exclusion see Appendix A PDX collection 0915

MCC **N00.4 Acute nephritic syndrome with diffuse endocapillary proliferative glomerulonephritis**
MCC Exclusion see Appendix A PDX collection 0915

MCC **N00.5 Acute nephritic syndrome with diffuse mesangiocapillary glomerulonephritis**
Acute nephritic syndrome with membranoproliferative glomerulonephritis, types 1 and 3, or NOS
MCC Exclusion see Appendix A PDX collection 0915

MCC **N00.6 Acute nephritic syndrome with dense deposit disease**
Acute nephritic syndrome with membranoproliferative glomerulonephritis, type 2
MCC Exclusion see Appendix A PDX collection 0915

MCC **N00.7 Acute nephritic syndrome with diffuse crescentic glomerulonephritis**
Acute nephritic syndrome with extracapillary glomerulonephritis
MCC Exclusion see Appendix A PDX collection 0915

MCC **N00.8 Acute nephritic syndrome with other morphologic changes**
Acute nephritic syndrome with proliferative glomerulonephritis NOS
MCC Exclusion see Appendix A PDX collection 0916

MCC **N00.9 Acute nephritic syndrome with unspecified morphologic changes**
MCC Exclusion see Appendix A PDX collection 0915

N01 Rapidly progressive nephritic syndrome

Includes: rapidly progressive glomerular disease
rapidly progressive glomerulonephritis
rapidly progressive nephritis

Excludes1: *nephritic syndrome NOS (N05.-)*

MCC **N01.0 Rapidly progressive nephritic syndrome with minor glomerular abnormality**
Rapidly progressive nephritic syndrome with minimal change lesion
MCC Exclusion see Appendix A PDX collection 0915

MCC **N01.1 Rapidly progressive nephritic syndrome with focal and segmental glomerular lesions**
Rapidly progressive nephritic syndrome with focal and segmental hyalinosis
Rapidly progressive nephritic syndrome with focal and segmental sclerosis
Rapidly progressive nephritic syndrome with focal glomerulonephritis
MCC Exclusion see Appendix A PDX collection 0915

MCC **N01.2 Rapidly progressive nephritic syndrome with diffuse membranous glomerulonephritis**
MCC Exclusion see Appendix A PDX collection 0915

MCC **N01.3 Rapidly progressive nephritic syndrome with diffuse mesangial proliferative glomerulonephritis**
MCC Exclusion see Appendix A PDX collection 0915

MCC **N01.4 Rapidly progressive nephritic syndrome with diffuse endocapillary proliferative glomerulonephritis**
MCC Exclusion see Appendix A PDX collection 0915

MCC **N01.5 Rapidly progressive nephritic syndrome with diffuse mesangiocapillary glomerulonephritis**
Rapidly progressive nephritic syndrome with membranoproliferative glomerulonephritis, types 1 and 3, or NOS
MCC Exclusion see Appendix A PDX collection 0915

MCC **N01.6 Rapidly progressive nephritic syndrome with dense deposit disease**
Rapidly progressive nephritic syndrome with membranoproliferative glomerulonephritis, type 2
MCC Exclusion see Appendix A PDX collection 0915

MCC **N01.7 Rapidly progressive nephritic syndrome with diffuse crescentic glomerulonephritis**
Rapidly progressive nephritic syndrome with extracapillary glomerulonephritis
MCC Exclusion see Appendix A PDX collection 0915

MCC **N01.8 Rapidly progressive nephritic syndrome with other morphologic changes**
Rapidly progressive nephritic syndrome with proliferative glomerulonephritis NOS
MCC Exclusion see Appendix A PDX collection 0915

MCC **N01.9 Rapidly progressive nephritic syndrome with unspecified morphologic changes**
MCC Exclusion see Appendix A PDX collection 0915

N02 Recurrent and persistent hematuria

Excludes1: *acute cystitis with hematuria (N30.01)*
hematuria NOS (R31.9)
hematuria not associated with specified morphologic lesions (R31.-)

CC **N02.0 Recurrent and persistent hematuria with minor glomerular abnormality**
Recurrent and persistent hematuria with minimal change lesion
CC Exclusion see Appendix A PDX collection 0917

CC **N02.1 Recurrent and persistent hematuria with focal and segmental glomerular lesions**
Recurrent and persistent hematuria with focal and segmental hyalinosis
Recurrent and persistent hematuria with focal and segmental sclerosis
Recurrent and persistent hematuria with focal glomerulonephritis
CC Exclusion see Appendix A PDX collection 0917

CC **N02.2 Recurrent and persistent hematuria with diffuse membranous glomerulonephritis**
CC Exclusion see Appendix A PDX collection 0917

CC **N02.3 Recurrent and persistent hematuria with diffuse mesangial proliferative glomerulonephritis**
CC Exclusion see Appendix A PDX collection 0917

CC **N02.4 Recurrent and persistent hematuria with diffuse endocapillary proliferative glomerulonephritis**
CC Exclusion see Appendix A PDX collection 0917

CC **N02.5 Recurrent and persistent hematuria with diffuse mesangiocapillary glomerulonephritis**
Recurrent and persistent hematuria with membranoproliferative glomerulonephritis, types 1 and 3, or NOS
CC Exclusion see Appendix A PDX collection 0917

CC **N02.6 Recurrent and persistent hematuria with dense deposit disease**
Recurrent and persistent hematuria with membranoproliferative glomerulonephritis, type 2
CC Exclusion see Appendix A PDX collection 0917

CC **N02.7 Recurrent and persistent hematuria with diffuse crescentic glomerulonephritis**
Recurrent and persistent hematuria with extracapillary glomerulonephritis
CC Exclusion see Appendix A PDX collection 0917

CC **N02.8 Recurrent and persistent hematuria with other morphologic changes**
Recurrent and persistent hematuria with proliferative glomerulonephritis NOS
CC Exclusion see Appendix A PDX collection 0915

CC **N02.9 Recurrent and persistent hematuria with unspecified morphologic changes**
CC Exclusion see Appendix A PDX collection 0915

N03 Chronic nephritic syndrome

Includes: chronic glomerular disease
chronic glomerulonephritis
chronic nephritis

Excludes1: *chronic tubulo-interstitial nephritis (N11.-)*
diffuse sclerosing glomerulonephritis (N05.8-)
nephritic syndrome NOS (N05.-)

CC **N03.0 Chronic nephritic syndrome with minor glomerular abnormality**
Chronic nephritic syndrome with minimal change lesion
CC Exclusion see Appendix A PDX collection 0918

CC **N03.1 Chronic nephritic syndrome with focal and segmental glomerular lesions**
Chronic nephritic syndrome with focal and segmental hyalinosis
Chronic nephritic syndrome with focal and segmental sclerosis
Chronic nephritic syndrome with focal glomerulonephritis
CC Exclusion see Appendix A PDX collection 0918

CC **N03.2 Chronic nephritic syndrome with diffuse membranous glomerulonephritis**
CC Exclusion see Appendix A PDX collection 0918

CC **N03.3 Chronic nephritic syndrome with diffuse mesangial proliferative glomerulonephritis**
CC Exclusion see Appendix A PDX collection 0918

CC **N03.4 Chronic nephritic syndrome with diffuse endocapillary proliferative glomerulonephritis**
CC Exclusion see Appendix A PDX collection 0918

CC **N03.5 Chronic nephritic syndrome with diffuse mesangiocapillary glomerulonephritis**
Chronic nephritic syndrome with membranoproliferative glomerulonephritis, types 1 and 3, or NOS
CC Exclusion see Appendix A PDX collection 0918

CC **N03.6 Chronic nephritic syndrome with dense deposit disease**
Chronic nephritic syndrome with membranoproliferative glomerulonephritis, type 2
CC Exclusion see Appendix A PDX collection 0918

CC **N03.7 Chronic nephritic syndrome with diffuse crescentic glomerulonephritis**
Chronic nephritic syndrome with extracapillary glomerulonephritis
CC Exclusion see Appendix A PDX collection 0918

CC **N03.8 Chronic nephritic syndrome with other morphologic changes**
Chronic nephritic syndrome with proliferative glomerulonephritis NOS
CC Exclusion see Appendix A PDX collection 0918

CC **N03.9 Chronic nephritic syndrome with unspecified morphologic changes**
CC Exclusion see Appendix A PDX collection 0918

N04 Nephrotic syndrome

Includes: congenital nephrotic syndrome
lipoid nephrosis

CC **N04.0 Nephrotic syndrome with minor glomerular abnormality**
Nephrotic syndrome with minimal change lesion
CC Exclusion see Appendix A PDX collection 0917

CC **N04.1 Nephrotic syndrome with focal and segmental glomerular lesions**
Nephrotic syndrome with focal and segmental hyalinosis
Nephrotic syndrome with focal and segmental sclerosis
Nephrotic syndrome with focal glomerulonephritis
CC Exclusion see Appendix A PDX collection 0917

CC **N04.2 Nephrotic syndrome with diffuse membranous glomerulonephritis**
CC Exclusion see Appendix A PDX collection 0917

CC **N04.3 Nephrotic syndrome with diffuse mesangial proliferative glomerulonephritis**
CC Exclusion see Appendix A PDX collection 0917

CC **N04.4 Nephrotic syndrome with diffuse endocapillary proliferative glomerulonephritis**
CC Exclusion see Appendix A PDX collection 0917

CC **N04.5 Nephrotic syndrome with diffuse mesangiocapillary glomerulonephritis**
Nephrotic syndrome with membranoproliferative glomerulonephritis, types 1 and 3, or NOS
CC Exclusion see Appendix A PDX collection 0917

CC **N04.6 Nephrotic syndrome with dense deposit disease**
Nephrotic syndrome with membranoproliferative glomerulonephritis, type 2
CC Exclusion see Appendix A PDX collection 0917

CC **N04.7 Nephrotic syndrome with diffuse crescentic glomerulonephritis**
Nephrotic syndrome with extracapillary glomerulonephritis
CC Exclusion see Appendix A PDX collection 0915

CC **N04.8 Nephrotic syndrome with other morphologic changes**
Nephrotic syndrome with proliferative glomerulonephritis NOS
CC Exclusion see Appendix A PDX collection 0915

CC **N04.9 Nephrotic syndrome with unspecified morphologic changes**
CC Exclusion see Appendix A PDX collection 0915

N05 Unspecified nephritic syndrome

Includes: glomerular disease NOS
glomerulonephritis NOS
nephritis NOS
nephropathy NOS and renal disease NOS with morphological lesion specified in .0-.8

Excludes1: *nephropathy NOS with no stated morphological lesion (N28.9)*
renal disease NOS with no stated morphological lesion (N28.9)
tubulo-interstitial nephritis NOS (N12)

N05.0 Unspecified nephritic syndrome with minor glomerular abnormality
Unspecified nephritic syndrome with minimal change lesion

N05.1 Unspecified nephritic syndrome with focal and segmental glomerular lesions
Unspecified nephritic syndrome with focal and segmental hyalinosis
Unspecified nephritic syndrome with focal and segmental sclerosis
Unspecified nephritic syndrome with focal glomerulonephritis

CC **N05.2 Unspecified nephritic syndrome with diffuse membranous glomerulonephritis**
CC Exclusion see Appendix A PDX collection 0918

CC **N05.3 Unspecified nephritic syndrome with diffuse mesangial proliferative glomerulonephritis**
CC Exclusion see Appendix A PDX collection 0918

CC **N05.4 Unspecified nephritic syndrome with diffuse endocapillary proliferative glomerulonephritis**
CC Exclusion see Appendix A PDX collection 0918

CC **N05.5 Unspecified nephritic syndrome with diffuse mesangiocapillary glomerulonephritis**
Unspecified nephritic syndrome with membranoproliferative glomerulonephritis, types 1 and 3, or NOS
CC Exclusion see Appendix A PDX collection 0918

N05.6 Unspecified nephritic syndrome with dense deposit disease
Unspecified nephritic syndrome with membranoproliferative glomerulonephritis, type 2

N05.7 Unspecified nephritic syndrome with diffuse crescentic glomerulonephritis
Unspecified nephritic syndrome with extracapillary glomerulonephritis

N05.8 Unspecified nephritic syndrome with other morphologic changes
Unspecified nephritic syndrome with proliferative glomerulonephritis NOS

N05.9 Unspecified nephritic syndrome with unspecified morphologic changes

N06 Isolated proteinuria with specified morphological lesion

Excludes1: *Proteinuria not associated with specific morphologic lesions (R80.0)*

N06.0 Isolated proteinuria with minor glomerular abnormality
Isolated proteinuria with minimal change lesion

N06.1 Isolated proteinuria with focal and segmental glomerular lesions
Isolated proteinuria with focal and segmental hyalinosis
Isolated proteinuria with focal and segmental sclerosis
Isolated proteinuria with focal glomerulonephritis

CC **N06.2 Isolated proteinuria with diffuse membranous glomerulonephritis**
CC Exclusion see Appendix A PDX collection 0918

CC **N06.3 Isolated proteinuria with diffuse mesangial proliferative glomerulonephritis**
CC Exclusion see Appendix A PDX collection 0918

CC **N06.4 Isolated proteinuria with diffuse endocapillary proliferative glomerulonephritis**
CC Exclusion see Appendix A PDX collection 0918

CC **N06.5 Isolated proteinuria with diffuse mesangiocapillary glomerulonephritis**
Isolated proteinuria with membranoproliferative glomerulonephritis, types 1 and 3, or NOS
CC Exclusion see Appendix A PDX collection 0918

N06.6 Isolated proteinuria with dense deposit disease
Isolated proteinuria with membranoproliferative glomerulonephritis, type 2

N06.7 Isolated proteinuria with diffuse crescentic glomerulonephritis
Isolated proteinuria with extracapillary glomerulonephritis

N06.8 Isolated proteinuria with other morphologic lesion
Isolated proteinuria with proliferative glomerulonephritis NOS

N06.9 Isolated proteinuria with unspecified morphologic lesion

N07 Hereditary nephropathy, not elsewhere classified

Excludes2: *Alport's syndrome (Q87.81-)*
hereditary amyloid nephropathy (E85.-)
nail patella syndrome (Q87.2)
non-neuropathic heredofamilial amyloidosis (E85.-)

N07.0 Hereditary nephropathy, not elsewhere classified with minor glomerular abnormality
Hereditary nephropathy, not elsewhere classified with minimal change lesion

N07.1 Hereditary nephropathy, not elsewhere classified with focal and segmental glomerular lesions
Hereditary nephropathy, not elsewhere classified with focal and segmental hyalinosis
Hereditary nephropathy, not elsewhere classified with focal and segmental sclerosis
Hereditary nephropathy, not elsewhere classified with focal glomerulonephritis

CC **N07.2 Hereditary nephropathy, not elsewhere classified with diffuse membranous glomerulonephritis**
CC Exclusion see Appendix A PDX collection 0918

CC **N07.3 Hereditary nephropathy, not elsewhere classified with diffuse mesangial proliferative glomerulonephritis**
CC Exclusion see Appendix A PDX collection 0918

CC **N07.4 Hereditary nephropathy, not elsewhere classified with diffuse endocapillary proliferative glomerulonephritis**
CC Exclusion see Appendix A PDX collection 0918

CC **N07.5 Hereditary nephropathy, not elsewhere classified with diffuse mesangiocapillary glomerulonephritis**
Hereditary nephropathy, not elsewhere classified with membranoproliferative glomerulonephritis, types 1 and 3, or NOS
CC Exclusion see Appendix A PDX collection 0918

N07.6 Hereditary nephropathy, not elsewhere classified with dense deposit disease
Hereditary nephropathy, not elsewhere classified with membranoproliferative glomerulonephritis, type 2

N07.7 Hereditary nephropathy, not elsewhere classified with diffuse crescentic glomerulonephritis
Hereditary nephropathy, not elsewhere classified with extracapillary glomerulonephritis

N07.8 Hereditary nephropathy, not elsewhere classified with other morphologic lesions
Hereditary nephropathy, not elsewhere classified with proliferative glomerulonephritis NOS

N07.9 Hereditary nephropathy, not elsewhere classified with unspecified morphologic lesions

N08 Glomerular disorders in diseases classified elsewhere

Glomerulonephritis
Nephritis
Nephropathy
Code first underlying disease, such as:
amyloidosis (E85.-)
congenital syphilis (A50.5)
cryoglobulinemia (D89.1)
disseminated intravascular coagulation (D65)
gout (M1A.-, M10.-)
microscopic polyangiitis (M31.7)
multiple myeloma (C90.0-)
sepsis (A40.0-A41.9)
sickle-cell disease (D57.0-D57.8)

Excludes1: *glomerulonephritis, nephritis and nephropathy (in):*
antiglomerular basement membrane disease (M31.0)
diabetes (E08-E13 with .21)
gonococcal (A54.21)
Goodpasture's syndrome (M31.0)
hemolytic-uremic syndrome (D59.3)
lupus (M32.14)
mumps (B26.83)
syphilis (A52.75)
systemic lupus erythematosus (M32.14)
Wegener's granulomatosis (M31.31)
pyelonephritis in diseases classified elsewhere (N16)
renal tubulo-interstitial disorders classified elsewhere (N16)

Valid 3-character code, no further characters required

Renal tubulo-interstitial diseases (N10-N16)

Includes: pyelonephritis

Excludes1: *pyeloureteritis cystica (N28.85)*

CC **N10 Acute tubulo-interstitial nephritis**

Acute infectious interstitial nephritis
Acute pyelitis
Acute pyelonephritis
Hemoglobin nephrosis
Myoglobin nephrosis
Use additional code (B95-B97), to identify infectious agent.
CC Exclusion see Appendix A PDX collection 0919
HAC see Appendix B for HAC conditional logic
Valid 3-character code, no further characters required

N11 Chronic tubulo-interstitial nephritis

Includes: chronic infectious interstitial nephritis
chronic pyelitis
chronic pyelonephritis

Use additional code (B95-B97), to identify infectious agent.

N11.0 Nonobstructive reflux-associated chronic pyelonephritis
Pyelonephritis (chronic) associated with (vesicoureteral) reflux
Excludes1: *vesicoureteral reflux NOS (N13.70)*

CC **N11.1 Chronic obstructive pyelonephritis**
Pyelonephritis (chronic) associated with anomaly of pelviureteric junction
Pyelonephritis (chronic) associated with anomaly of pyeloureteric junction
Pyelonephritis (chronic) associated with crossing of vessel
Pyelonephritis (chronic) associated with kinking of ureter
Pyelonephritis (chronic) associated with obstruction of ureter
Pyelonephritis (chronic) associated with stricture of pelviureteric junction
Pyelonephritis (chronic) associated with stricture of ureter
Excludes1: *calculous pyelonephritis (N20.9)*
obstructive uropathy (N13.-)
CC Exclusion see Appendix A PDX collection 0920

CC **N11.8 Other chronic tubulo-interstitial nephritis**
Nonobstructive chronic pyelonephritis NOS
CC Exclusion see Appendix A PDX collection 0921

CC **N11.9 Chronic tubulo-interstitial nephritis, unspecified**
Chronic interstitial nephritis NOS
Chronic pyelitis NOS
Chronic pyelonephritis NOS
CC Exclusion see Appendix A PDX collection 0922
HAC see Appendix B for HAC conditional logic

N12 Tubulo-interstitial nephritis, not specified as acute or chronic
Interstitial nephritis NOS
Pyelitis NOS
Pyelonephritis NOS
Excludes1: *calculous pyelonephritis (N20.9)*
CC Exclusion see Appendix A PDX collection 0922
HAC see Appendix B for HAC conditional logic
Valid 3-character code, no further characters required

N13 Obstructive and reflux uropathy
Excludes2: *calculus of kidney and ureter without hydronephrosis (N20.-)*
congenital obstructive defects of renal pelvis and ureter (Q62.0-Q62.3)
hydronephrosis with ureteropelvic junction obstruction (Q62.1)
obstructive pyelonephritis (N11.1)

CC **N13.1 Hydronephrosis with ureteral stricture, not elsewhere classified**
Excludes1: *Hydronephrosis with ureteral stricture with infection (N13.6)*
CC Exclusion see Appendix A PDX collection 0922

N13.2 Hydronephrosis with renal and ureteral calculous obstruction
Excludes1: *Hydronephrosis with renal and ureteral calculous obstruction with infection (N13.6)*
CC Exclusion see Appendix A PDX collection 0922

\+ **N13.3 Other and unspecified hydronephrosis**
Excludes1: *hydronephrosis with infection (N13.6)*
CC **N13.30 Unspecified hydronephrosis**
CC Exclusion see Appendix A PDX collection 0922
CC **N13.39 Other hydronephrosis**
CC Exclusion see Appendix A PDX collection 0922

CC **N13.4 Hydroureter**
Excludes1: *congenital hydroureter (Q62.3-)*
hydroureter with infection (N13.6)
vesicoureteral-reflux with hydroureter (N13.73-)
CC Exclusion see Appendix A PDX collection 0923

N13.5 Crossing vessel and stricture of ureter without hydronephrosis
Kinking and stricture of ureter without hydronephrosis
Excludes1: *Crossing vessel and stricture of ureter without hydronephrosis with infection (N13.6)*

CC **N13.6 Pyonephrosis**
Conditions in N13.1-N13.5 with infection
Obstructive uropathy with infection
CC Exclusion see Appendix A PDX collection 0922
Use additional code (B95-B97), to identify infectious agent.
HAC see Appendix B for HAC conditional logic

\+ **N13.7 Vesicoureteral-reflux**
Excludes1: *reflux-associated pyelonephritis (N11.0)*
N13.70 Vesicoureteral-reflux, unspecified
Vesicoureteral-reflux NOS
N13.71 Vesicoureteral-reflux without reflux nephropathy
\+ **N13.72 Vesicoureteral-reflux with reflux nephropathy without hydroureter**
N13.721 Vesicoureteral-reflux with reflux nephropathy without hydroureter, unilateral
N13.722 Vesicoureteral-reflux with reflux nephropathy without hydroureter, bilateral
N13.729 Vesicoureteral-reflux with reflux nephropathy without hydroureter, unspecified
\+ **N13.73 Vesicoureteral-reflux with reflux nephropathy with hydroureter**
N13.731 Vesicoureteral-reflux with reflux nephropathy with hydroureter, unilateral
N13.732 Vesicoureteral-reflux with reflux nephropathy with hydroureter, bilateral
N13.739 Vesicoureteral-reflux with reflux nephropathy with hydroureter, unspecified

CC **N13.8 Other obstructive and reflux uropathy**
Urinary tract obstruction due to specified cause
Code first, if applicable, any causal condition, such as:
enlarged prostate (N40.1)
CC Exclusion see Appendix A PDX collection 0920

N13.9 Obstructive and reflux uropathy, unspecified
Urinary tract obstruction NOS

N14 Drug- and heavy-metal-induced tubulo-interstitial and tubular conditions
Code first poisoning due to drug or toxin, if applicable (T36-T65 with fifth or sixth character 1-4 or 6)

Use additional code for adverse effect, if applicable, to identify drug (T36-T50 with fifth or sixth character 5)
N14.0 Analgesic nephropathy
N14.1 Nephropathy induced by other drugs, medicaments and biological substances
N14.2 Nephropathy induced by unspecified drug, medicament or biological substance
N14.3 Nephropathy induced by heavy metals
N14.4 Toxic nephropathy, not elsewhere classified

N15 Other renal tubulo-interstitial diseases
N15.0 Balkan nephropathy
Balkan endemic nephropathy
MCC **N15.1 Renal and perinephric abscess**
MCC Exclusion see Appendix A PDX collection 0919
HAC see Appendix B for HAC conditional logic
N15.8 Other specified renal tubulo-interstitial diseases
N15.9 Renal tubulo-interstitial disease, unspecified
Infection of kidney NOS
Excludes1: *urinary tract infection NOS (N39.0)*

N16 Renal tubulo-interstitial disorders in diseases classified elsewhere
Pyelonephritis
Tubulo-interstitial nephritis
Code first underlying disease, such as:
brucellosis (A23.0-A23.9)
cryoglobulinemia (D89.1)
glycogen storage disease (E74.0)
leukemia (C91-C95)
lymphoma (C81.0-C85.9, C96.0-C96.9)
multiple myeloma (C90.0-)
sepsis (A40.0-A41.9)
Wilson's disease (E83.0)
Excludes1: *diphtheritic pyelonephritis and tubulo-interstitial nephritis (A36.84)*
pyelonephritis and tubulo-interstitial nephritis in candidiasis (B37.49)
pyelonephritis and tubulo-interstitial nephritis in cystinosis (E72.04)
pyelonephritis and tubulo-interstitial nephritis in salmonella infection (A02.25)
pyelonephritis and tubulo-interstitial nephritis in sarcoidosis (D86.84)
pyelonephritis and tubulo-interstitial nephritis in sicca syndrome [Sjogren's] (M35.04)
pyelonephritis and tubulo-interstitial nephritis in systemic lupus erythematosus (M32.15)
pyelonephritis and tubulo-interstitial nephritis in toxoplasmosis (B58.83)
renal tubular degeneration in diabetes (E08-E13 with .29)
syphilitic pyelonephritis and tubulo-interstitial nephritis (A52.75)
Valid 3-character code, no further characters required

Acute kidney failure and chronic kidney disease (N17-N19)

Excludes2: *congenital renal failure (P96.0)*
drug- and heavy-metal-induced tubulo-interstitial and tubular conditions (N14.-)
extrarenal uremia (R39.2)
hemolytic-uremic syndrome (D59.3)
hepatorenal syndrome (K76.7)
postpartum hepatorenal syndrome (O90.4)
posttraumatic renal failure (T79.5)
prerenal uremia (R39.2)
renal failure complicating abortion or ectopic or molar pregnancy (O00-O07, O08.4)
renal failure following labor and delivery (O90.4)
renal failure postprocedural (N99.0)

N17 Acute kidney failure
Code also associated underlying condition
Excludes1: *posttraumatic renal failure (T79.5)*
MCC **N17.0 Acute kidney failure with tubular necrosis**
Acute tubular necrosis
Renal tubular necrosis
Tubular necrosis NOS
MCC Exclusion see Appendix A PDX collection 0924

MCC **N17.1 Acute kidney failure with acute cortical necrosis**
Acute cortical necrosis
Cortical necrosis NOS
Renal cortical necrosis
MCC Exclusion see Appendix A PDX collection 0924

N17.2 Acute kidney failure with medullary necrosis
Medullary [papillary] necrosis NOS
Acute medullary [papillary] necrosis
Renal medullary [papillary] necrosis
MCC Exclusion see Appendix A PDX collection 0924

CC **N17.8 Other acute kidney failure**
CC Exclusion see Appendix A PDX collection 0925

CC **N17.9 Acute kidney failure, unspecified**
Acute kidney injury (nontraumatic)
Excludes2: *traumatic kidney injury (S37.0-)*
CC Exclusion see Appendix A PDX collection 0924

N18 Chronic kidney disease (CKD)

Code first any associated:
diabetic chronic kidney disease (E08.22, E09.22, E10.22, E11.22, E13.22)
hypertensive chronic kidney disease (I12.-, I13.-)

Use additional code to identify kidney transplant status, if applicable, (Z94.0)
Review coding guidelines C.9.a.2 and C.9.a.3
Review coding guidelines C.14.a.1 and C.14.a.2

N18.1 Chronic kidney disease, stage 1
N18.2 Chronic kidney disease, stage 2 (mild)
N18.3 Chronic kidney disease, stage 3 (moderate)
CC **N18.4 Chronic kidney disease, stage 4 (severe)**
CC Exclusion see Appendix A PDX collection 0926
CC **N18.5 Chronic kidney disease, stage 5**
Excludes1: *chronic kidney disease, stage 5 requiring chronic dialysis (N18.6)*
CC Exclusion see Appendix A PDX collection 0926

MCC **N18.6 End stage renal disease**
Chronic kidney disease requiring chronic dialysis
Use additional code to identify dialysis status (Z99.2)
MCC Exclusion see Appendix A PDX collection 0927
AHA CC: 4Q, 2013, 125

N18.9 Chronic kidney disease, unspecified
Chronic renal disease
Chronic renal failure NOS
Chronic renal insufficiency
Chronic uremia

N19 Unspecified kidney failure
Uremia NOS
Excludes1: *acute kidney failure (N17.-)*
chronic kidney disease (N18.-)
chronic uremia (N18.9)
extrarenal uremia (R39.2)
prerenal uremia (R39.2)
renal insufficiency (acute) (N28.9)
uremia of newborn (P96.0)
Valid 3-character code, no further characters required

Urolithiasis (N20-N23)

N20 Calculus of kidney and ureter
Calculous pyelonephritis
Excludes1: *nephrocalcinosis (E83.5)*
that with hydronephrosis (N13.2)

N20.0 Calculus of kidney
Nephrolithiasis NOS
Renal calculus
Renal stone
Staghorn calculus
Stone in kidney

CC **N20.1 Calculus of ureter**
Ureteric stone
CC Exclusion see Appendix A PDX collection 0928

CC **N20.2 Calculus of kidney with calculus of ureter**
CC Exclusion see Appendix A PDX collection 0928

N20.9 Urinary calculus, unspecified

N21 Calculus of lower urinary tract
Includes: calculus of lower urinary tract with cystitis and urethritis

N21.0 Calculus in bladder
Calculus in diverticulum of bladder
Urinary bladder stone
Excludes2: *staghorn calculus (N20.0)*

N21.1 Calculus in urethra
Excludes2: *calculus of prostate (N42.0)*
N21.8 Other lower urinary tract calculus
N21.9 Calculus of lower urinary tract, unspecified
Excludes1: *calculus of urinary tract NOS (N20.9)*

N22 Calculus of urinary tract in diseases classified elsewhere
Code first underlying disease, such as:
gout (M1A.-, M10.-)
schistosomiasis (B65.0-B65.9)
Valid 3-character code, no further characters required

N23 Unspecified renal colic
Valid 3-character code, no further characters required

Other disorders of kidney and ureter (N25-N29)

Excludes2: *disorders of kidney and ureter with urolithiasis (N20-N23)*

N25 Disorders resulting from impaired renal tubular function
Excludes1: *metabolic disorders classifiable to E70-E88*

N25.0 Renal osteodystrophy
Azotemic osteodystrophy
Phosphate-losing tubular disorders
Renal rickets
Renal short stature

CC **N25.1 Nephrogenic diabetes insipidus**
Excludes1: *diabetes insipidus NOS (E23.2)*
CC Exclusion see Appendix A PDX collection 0929

+ **N25.8 Other disorders resulting from impaired renal tubular function**
CC **N25.81 Secondary hyperparathyroidism of renal origin**
Excludes1: *secondary hyperparathyroidism, non-renal (E21.1)*
CC Exclusion see Appendix A PDX collection 0930
N25.89 Other disorders resulting from impaired renal tubular function
Hypokalemic nephropathy
Lightwood-Albright syndrome
Renal tubular acidosis NOS

N25.9 Disorder resulting from impaired renal tubular function, unspecified

N26 Unspecified contracted kidney
Excludes1: *contracted kidney due to hypertension (I12.-)*
diffuse sclerosing glomerulonephritis (N05.8.-)
hypertensive nephrosclerosis (arteriolar) (arteriosclerotic) (I12.-)
small kidney of unknown cause (N27.-)

N26.1 Atrophy of kidney (terminal)
N26.2 Page kidney
N26.9 Renal sclerosis, unspecified

N27 Small kidney of unknown cause
Includes: oligonephronia
N27.0 Small kidney, unilateral
N27.1 Small kidney, bilateral
N27.9 Small kidney, unspecified

N28 Other disorders of kidney and ureter, not elsewhere classified

CC **N28.0 Ischemia and infarction of kidney**
Renal artery embolism
Renal artery obstruction
Renal artery occlusion
Renal artery thrombosis
Renal infarct
Excludes1: *atherosclerosis of renal artery (extrarenal part) (I70.1)*
congenital stenosis of renal artery (Q27.1)
Goldblatt's kidney (I70.1)
CC Exclusion see Appendix A PDX collection 0931

N28.1 Cyst of kidney, acquired
Cyst (multiple)(solitary) of kidney, acquired
Excludes1: *cystic kidney disease (congenital) (Q61.-)*

+ **N28.8 Other specified disorders of kidney and ureter**
Excludes1: *hydroureter (N13.4)*
ureteric stricture with hydronephrosis (N13.1)
ureteric stricture without hydronephrosis (N13.5)

N28.81 Hypertrophy of kidney
N28.82 Megaloureter
N28.83 Nephroptosis
CC **N28.84 Pyelitis cystica**
CC Exclusion see Appendix A PDX collection 0922
HAC see Appendix B for HAC conditional logic

CC **N28.85 Pyeloureteritis cystica**
CC Exclusion see Appendix A PDX collection 0922
HAC see Appendix B for HAC conditional logic

CC **N28.86 Ureteritis cystica**
CC Exclusion see Appendix A PDX collection 0922
HAC see Appendix B for HAC conditional logic

N28.89 Other specified disorders of kidney and ureter

N28.9 Disorder of kidney and ureter, unspecified
Nephropathy NOS
Renal disease (acute) NOS
Renal insufficiency (acute)
Excludes1: *chronic renal insufficiency (N18.9)*
unspecified nephritic syndrome (N05.-)

N29 Other disorders of kidney and ureter in diseases classified elsewhere
Code first underlying disease, such as:
amyloidosis (E85.-)
nephrocalcinosis (E83.5)
schistosomiasis (B65.0-B65.9)
Excludes1: *disorders of kidney and ureter in:*
cystinosis (E72.0)
gonorrhea (A54.21)
syphilis (A52.75)
tuberculosis (A18.11)
Valid 3-character code, no further characters required

ther diseases of the urinary system (N30-N39)

cludes1: *urinary infection (complicating):*
abortion or ectopic or molar pregnancy (O00-O07, O08.8)
pregnancy, childbirth and the puerperium (O23.-, O75.3, O86.2-)

N30 Cystitis
Use additional code to identify infectious agent (B95-B97)
Excludes1: *prostatocystitis (N41.3)*

\+ **N30.0 Acute cystitis**
Excludes1: *irradiation cystitis (N30.4-)*
trigonitis (N30.3-)

CC **N30.00 Acute cystitis without hematuria**
CC Exclusion see Appendix A PDX collection 0932
HAC see Appendix B for HAC conditional logic

CC **N30.01 Acute cystitis with hematuria**
CC Exclusion see Appendix A PDX collection 0932
HAC see Appendix B for HAC conditional logic

\+ **N30.1 Interstitial cystitis (chronic)**
N30.10 Interstitial cystitis (chronic) without hematuria
N30.11 Interstitial cystitis (chronic) with hematuria

\+ **N30.2 Other chronic cystitis**
N30.20 Other chronic cystitis without hematuria
N30.21 Other chronic cystitis with hematuria

\+ **N30.3 Trigonitis**
Urethrotrigonitis
N30.30 Trigonitis without hematuria
N30.31 Trigonitis with hematuria

\+ **N30.4 Irradiation cystitis**
CC **N30.40 Irradiation cystitis without hematuria**
CC Exclusion see Appendix A PDX collection 0932
CC **N30.41 Irradiation cystitis with hematuria**
CC Exclusion see Appendix A PDX collection 0932

\+ **N30.8 Other cystitis**
Abscess of bladder
N30.80 Other cystitis without hematuria
N30.81 Other cystitis with hematuria

\+ **N30.9 Cystitis, unspecified**
N30.90 Cystitis, unspecified without hematuria
N30.91 Cystitis, unspecified with hematuria

N31 Neuromuscular dysfunction of bladder, not elsewhere classified
Use additional code to identify any associated urinary incontinence (N39.3-N39.4-)
Excludes1: *cord bladder NOS (G95.89)*
neurogenic bladder due to cauda equina syndrome (G83.4)
neuromuscular dysfunction due to spinal cord lesion (G95.89)

N31.0 Uninhibited neuropathic bladder, not elsewhere classified
N31.1 Reflex neuropathic bladder, not elsewhere classified
N31.2 Flaccid neuropathic bladder, not elsewhere classified
Atonic (motor) (sensory) neuropathic bladder
Autonomous neuropathic bladder
Nonreflex neuropathic bladder
N31.8 Other neuromuscular dysfunction of bladder
N31.9 Neuromuscular dysfunction of bladder, unspecified
Neurogenic bladder dysfunction NOS

N32 Other disorders of bladder
Excludes2: *calculus of bladder (N21.0)*
cystocele (N81.1-)
hernia or prolapse of bladder, female (N81.1-)

N32.0 Bladder-neck obstruction
Bladder-neck stenosis (acquired)
Excludes1: *congenital bladder-neck obstruction (Q64.3-)*

CC **N32.1 Vesicointestinal fistula**
Vesicorectal fistula
CC Exclusion see Appendix A PDX collection 0933

CC **N32.2 Vesical fistula, not elsewhere classified**
Excludes1: *fistula between bladder and female genital tract (N82.0-N82.1)*
CC Exclusion see Appendix A PDX collection 0933

N32.3 Diverticulum of bladder
Excludes1: *congenital diverticulum of bladder (Q64.6)*
diverticulitis of bladder (N30.8-)

\+ **N32.8 Other specified disorders of bladder**
N32.81 Overactive bladder
Detrusor muscle hyperactivity
Excludes1: *frequent urination due to specified bladder condition- code to condition*
N32.89 Other specified disorders of bladder
Bladder hemorrhage
Bladder hypertrophy
Calcified bladder
Contracted bladder

N32.9 Bladder disorder, unspecified

N33 Bladder disorders in diseases classified elsewhere
Code first underlying disease, such as:
schistosomiasis (B65.0-B65.9)
Excludes1: *bladder disorder in syphilis (A52.76)*
bladder disorder in tuberculosis (A18.12)
candidal cystitis (B37.41)
chlamydial cystitis (A56.01)
cystitis in gonorrhea (A54.01)
cystitis in neurogenic bladder (N31.-)
diphtheritic cystitis (A36.85)
syphilitic cystitis (A52.76)
trichomonal cystitis (A59.03)
Valid 3-character code, no further characters required

N34 Urethritis and urethral syndrome
Use additional code (B95-B97), to identify infectious agent.
Excludes2: *Reiter's disease (M02.3-)*
urethritis in diseases with a predominantly sexual mode of transmission (A50-A64)
urethrotrigonitis (N30.3-)

CC **N34.0 Urethral abscess**
Abscess (of) Cowper's gland
Abscess (of) Littré's gland
Abscess (of) urethral (gland)
Periurethral abscess
Excludes1: *urethral caruncle (N36.2)*
CC Exclusion see Appendix A PDX collection 0934
HAC see Appendix B for HAC conditional logic

N34.1 Nonspecific urethritis
Nongonococcal urethritis
Nonvenereal urethritis

N34.2 Other urethritis
Meatitis, urethral
Postmenopausal urethritis
Ulcer of urethra (meatus)
Urethritis NOS

N34.3 Urethral syndrome, unspecified

N35 Urethral stricture
Excludes1: *congenital urethral stricture (Q64.3-)*
postprocedural urethral stricture (N99.1-)

\+ **N35.0 Post-traumatic urethral stricture**
Urethral stricture due to injury
Excludes1: *postprocedural urethral stricture (N99.1-)*

\+ **N35.01 Post-traumatic urethral stricture, male**
♂ **N35.010 Post-traumatic urethral stricture, male, meatal**
N35.011 Post-traumatic bulbous urethral stricture
N35.012 Post-traumatic membranous urethral stricture
N35.013 Post-traumatic anterior urethral stricture
♂ **N35.014 Post-traumatic urethral stricture, male, unspecified**

+ **N35.02 Post-traumatic urethral stricture, female**
♀ **N35.021 Urethral stricture due to childbirth**
♀ **N35.028 Other post-traumatic urethral stricture, female**
+ **N35.1 Postinfective urethral stricture, not elsewhere classified**
Excludes1: *urethral stricture associated with schistosomiasis (B65.-, N29)*
gonococcal urethral stricture (A54.01)
syphilitic urethral stricture (A52.76)
+ **N35.11 Postinfective urethral stricture, not elsewhere classified, male**
♂ **N35.111 Postinfective urethral stricture, not elsewhere classified, male, meatal**
N35.112 Postinfective bulbous urethral stricture, not elsewhere classified
N35.113 Postinfective membranous urethral stricture, not elsewhere classified
N35.114 Postinfective anterior urethral stricture, not elsewhere classified
♂ **N35.119 Postinfective urethral stricture, not elsewhere classified, male, unspecified**
♀ **N35.12 Postinfective urethral stricture, not elsewhere classified, female**
N35.8 Other urethral stricture
Excludes1: *postprocedural urethral stricture (N99.1-)*
N35.9 Urethral stricture, unspecified

N36 Other disorders of urethra

CC **N36.0 Urethral fistula**
Urethroperineal fistula
Urethrorectal fistula
Urinary fistula NOS
Excludes1: *urethroscrotal fistula (N50.8)*
urethrovaginal fistula (N82.1)
urethrovesicovaginal fistula (N82.1)
CC Exclusion see Appendix A PDX collection 0935
N36.1 Urethral diverticulum
N36.2 Urethral caruncle
+ **N36.4 Urethral functional and muscular disorders**
Use additional code to identify associated urinary stress incontinence (N39.3)
N36.41 Hypermobility of urethra
N36.42 Intrinsic sphincter deficiency (ISD)
N36.43 Combined hypermobility of urethra and intrinsic sphincter deficiency
N36.44 Muscular disorders of urethra
Bladder sphincter dyssynergy
N36.5 Urethral false passage
N36.8 Other specified disorders of urethra
N36.9 Urethral disorder, unspecified

N37 Urethral disorders in diseases classified elsewhere
Code first underlying disease
Excludes1: *urethritis (in):*
candidal infection (B37.41)
chlamydial (A56.01)
gonorrhea (A54.01)
syphilis (A52.76)
trichomonal infection (A59.03)
tuberculosis (A18.13)

N39 Other disorders of urinary system
Excludes2: *hematuria NOS (R31.-)*
recurrent or persistent hematuria (N02.-)
recurrent or persistent hematuria with specified morphological lesion (N02.-)
proteinuria NOS (R80.-)

CC **N39.0 Urinary tract infection, site not specified**
Use additional code (B95-B97), to identify infectious agent.
Excludes1: *candidiasis of urinary tract (B37.4-)*
neonatal urinary tract infection (P39.3)
urinary tract infection of specified site, such as:
cystitis (N30.-)
urethritis (N34.-)
CC Exclusion see Appendix A PDX collection 0936
HAC see Appendix B for HAC conditional logic
AHA CC: 4Q, 2012, 94
N39.3 Stress incontinence (female) (male)
Code also any associated overactive bladder (N32.81)
Excludes1: *mixed incontinence (N39.46)*
+ **N39.4 Other specified urinary incontinence**
Code also any associated overactive bladder (N32.81)
Excludes1: *enuresis NOS (R32)*
functional urinary incontinence (R39.81)
urinary incontinence associated with cognitive impairment (R39.81)
urinary incontinence NOS (R32)
urinary incontinence of nonorganic origin (F98.0)
N39.41 Urge incontinence
Excludes1: *mixed incontinence (N39.46)*
N39.42 Incontinence without sensory awareness
N39.43 Post-void dribbling
N39.44 Nocturnal enuresis
N39.45 Continuous leakage
N39.46 Mixed incontinence
Urge and stress incontinence
+ **N39.49 Other specified urinary incontinence**
N39.490 Overflow incontinence
N39.498 Other specified urinary incontinence
Reflex incontinence
Total incontinence
N39.8 Other specified disorders of urinary system
N39.9 Disorder of urinary system, unspecified

Diseases of male genital organs (N40-N53)

N40 Enlarged prostate
Includes: adenofibromatous hypertrophy of prostate
benign hypertrophy of the prostate
benign prostatic hyperplasia
benign prostatic hypertrophy
BPH
nodular prostate
polyp of prostate
Excludes1: *benign neoplasms of prostate (adenoma, benign) (fibroadenoma) (fibroma) (myoma) (D29.1)*
Excludes2: *malignant neoplasm of prostate (C61)*
• ♂ **N40.0 Enlarged prostate without lower urinary tract symptoms**
Enlarged prostate without LUTS
Enlarged prostate NOS
• ♂ **N40.1 Enlarged prostate with lower urinary tract symptoms**
Enlarged prostate with LUTS
Use additional code for associated symptoms, when specified:
incomplete bladder emptying (R39.14)
nocturia (R35.1)
straining on urination (R39.16)
urinary frequency (R35.0)
urinary hesitancy (R39.11)
urinary incontinence (N39.4-)
urinary obstruction (N13.8)
urinary retention (R33.8)
urinary urgency (R39.15)
weak urinary stream (R39.12)
• ♂ **N40.2 Nodular prostate without lower urinary tract symptoms**
Nodular prostate without LUTS
• ♂ **N40.3 Nodular prostate with lower urinary tract symptoms**
Use additional code for associated symptoms, when specified:
incomplete bladder emptying (R39.14)
nocturia (R35.1)
straining on urination (R39.16)
urinary frequency (R35.0)
urinary hesitancy (R39.11)
urinary incontinence (N39.4-)
urinary obstruction (N13.8)
urinary retention (R33.8)
urinary urgency (R39.15)
weak urinary stream (R39.12)

N41 Inflammatory diseases of prostate
Use additional code (B95-B97), to identify infectious agent.
• ♂ CC **N41.0 Acute prostatitis**
CC Exclusion see Appendix A PDX collection 0937
• ♂ **N41.1 Chronic prostatitis**
• ♂ CC **N41.2 Abscess of prostate**
CC Exclusion see Appendix A PDX collection 0937
• ♂ **N41.3 Prostatocystitis**
• ♂ **N41.4 Granulomatous prostatitis**
• ♂ **N41.8 Other inflammatory diseases of prostate**
• ♂ **N41.9 Inflammatory disease of prostate, unspecified**
Prostatitis NOS

Male Reproductive System

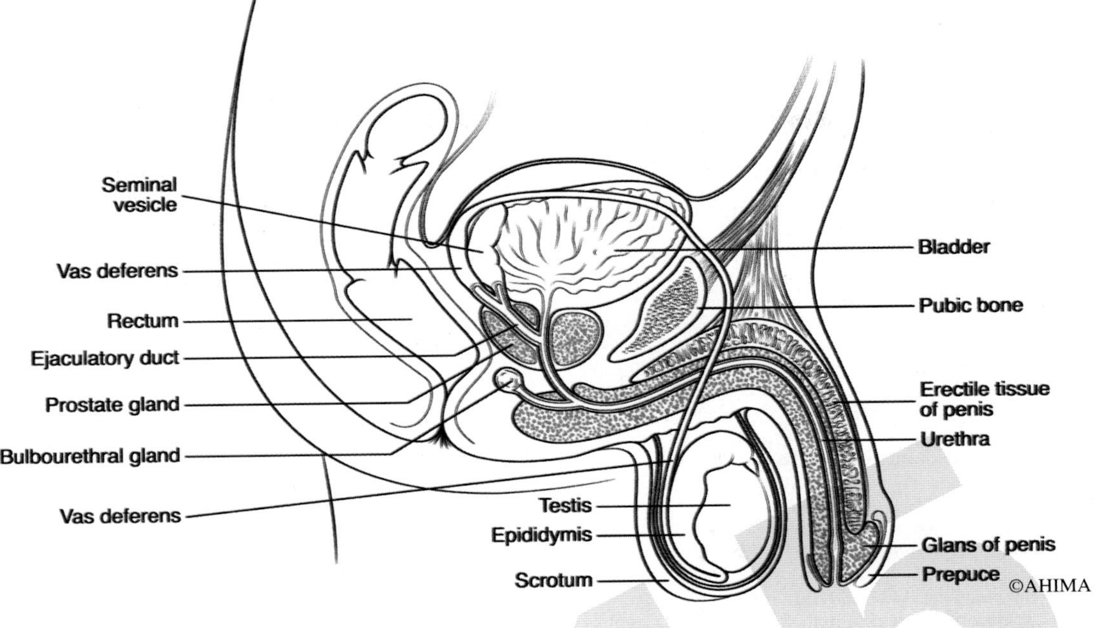

Seminal vesicle
Vas deferens
Rectum
Ejaculatory duct
Prostate gland
Bulbourethral gland
Vas deferens
Testis
Epididymis
Scrotum
Bladder
Pubic bone
Erectile tissue of penis
Urethra
Glans of penis
Prepuce
©AHIMA

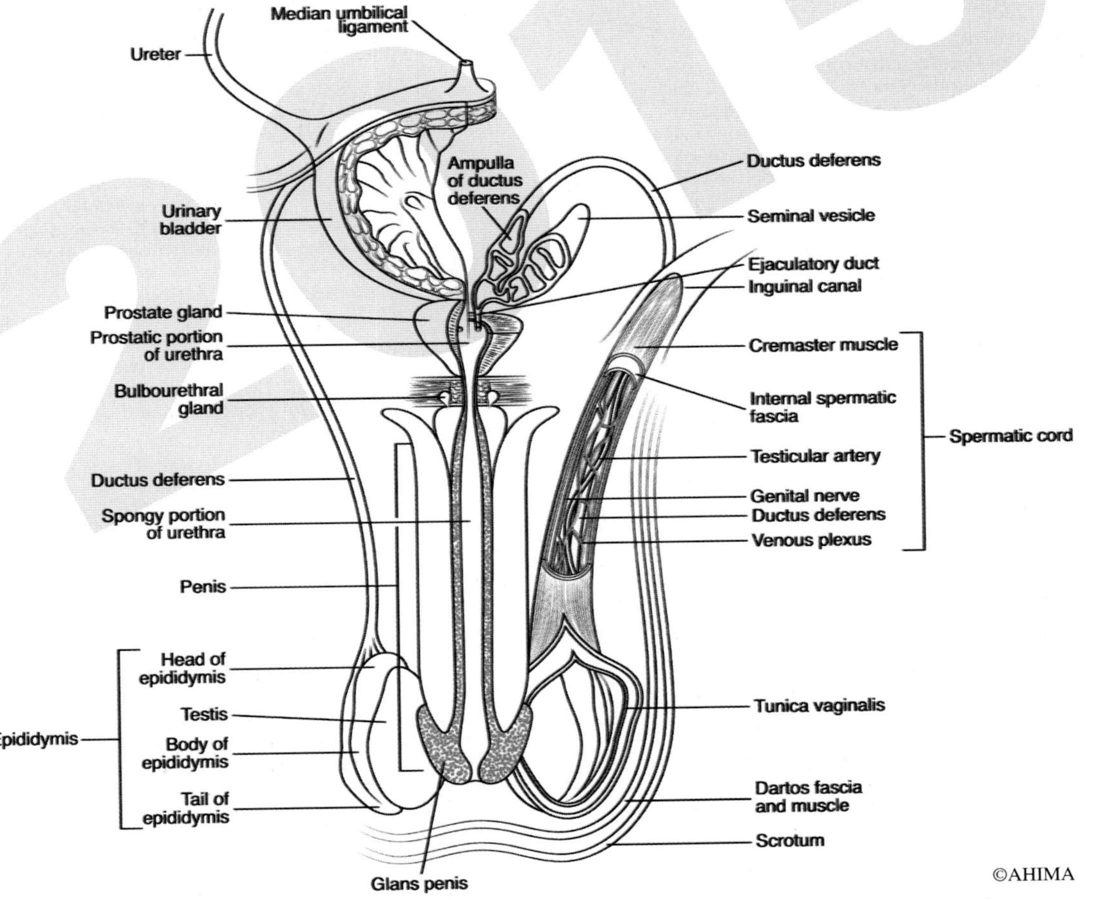

Median umbilical ligament
Ureter
Urinary bladder
Ampulla of ductus deferens
Prostate gland
Prostatic portion of urethra
Bulbourethral gland
Ductus deferens
Spongy portion of urethra
Penis
Epididymis
Head of epididymis
Testis
Body of epididymis
Tail of epididymis
Glans penis
Ductus deferens
Seminal vesicle
Ejaculatory duct
Inguinal canal
Cremaster muscle
Internal spermatic fascia
Testicular artery
Genital nerve
Ductus deferens
Venous plexus
Spermatic cord
Tunica vaginalis
Dartos fascia and muscle
Scrotum
©AHIMA

N42 Other and unspecified disorders of prostate

● ♂ **N42.0 Calculus of prostate**
Prostatic stone

● ♂ **N42.1 Congestion and hemorrhage of prostate**
Excludes1: *enlarged prostate (N40.-)*
hematuria (R31.-)
hyperplasia of prostate (N40.-)
inflammatory diseases of prostate (N41.-)

♂ **N42.3 Dysplasia of prostate**
Prostatic intraepithelial neoplasia I (PIN I)
Prostatic intraepithelial neoplasia II (PIN II)
Excludes1: *prostatic intraepithelial neoplasia III (PIN III) (D07.5)*

+ **N42.8 Other specified disorders of prostate**
● ♂ **N42.81 Prostatodynia syndrome**
Painful prostate syndrome
● ♂ **N42.82 Prostatosis syndrome**
● ♂ **N42.83 Cyst of prostate**
● ♂ **N42.89 Other specified disorders of prostate**

● ♂ **N42.9 Disorder of prostate, unspecified**

N43 Hydrocele and spermatocele

Includes: hydrocele of spermatic cord, testis or tunica vaginalis
Excludes1: *congenital hydrocele (P83.5)*

♂ **N43.0 Encysted hydrocele**

CC ♂ **N43.1 Infected hydrocele**
CC Exclusion see Appendix A PDX collection 0938
Use additional code (B95-B97), to identify infectious agent

♂ **N43.2 Other hydrocele**

♂ **N43.3 Hydrocele, unspecified**

+ **N43.4 Spermatocele of epididymis**
Spermatic cyst
♂ **N43.40 Spermatocele of epididymis, unspecified**
♂ **N43.41 Spermatocele of epididymis, single**
♂ **N43.42 Spermatocele of epididymis, multiple**

N44 Noninflammatory disorders of testis

+ **N44.0 Torsion of testis**
CC ♂ **N44.00 Torsion of testis, unspecified**
CC Exclusion see Appendix A PDX collection 0939
CC ♂ **N44.01 Extravaginal torsion of spermatic cord**
CC Exclusion see Appendix A PDX collection 0939
CC ♂ **N44.02 Intravaginal torsion of spermatic cord**
Torsion of spermatic cord NOS
CC Exclusion see Appendix A PDX collection 0939
CC ♂ **N44.03 Torsion of appendix testis**
CC Exclusion see Appendix A PDX collection 0939
CC ♂ **N44.04 Torsion of appendix epididymis**
CC Exclusion see Appendix A PDX collection 0939

♂ **N44.1 Cyst of tunica albuginea testis**

♂ **N44.2 Benign cyst of testis**

♂ **N44.8 Other noninflammatory disorders of the testis**

N45 Orchitis and epididymitis

Use additional code (B95-B97), to identify infectious agent.

♂ **N45.1 Epididymitis**

♂ **N45.2 Orchitis**

♂ **N45.3 Epididymo-orchitis**

CC ♂ **N45.4 Abscess of epididymis or testis**
CC Exclusion see Appendix A PDX collection 0940

N46 Male infertility

Excludes1: *vasectomy status (Z98.52)*

+ **N46.0 Azoospermia**
Absolute male infertility
Male infertility due to germinal (cell) aplasia
Male infertility due to spermatogenic arrest (complete)
● ♂ **N46.01 Organic azoospermia**
Azoospermia NOS
+ **N46.02 Azoospermia due to extratesticular causes**
Code also associated cause
● ♂ **N46.021 Azoospermia due to drug therapy**
● ♂ **N46.022 Azoospermia due to infection**
● ♂ **N46.023 Azoospermia due to obstruction of efferent ducts**
● ♂ **N46.024 Azoospermia due to radiation**
● ♂ **N46.025 Azoospermia due to systemic disease**
● ♂ **N46.029 Azoospermia due to other extratesticular causes**

+ **N46.1 Oligospermia**
Male infertility due to germinal cell desquamation
Male infertility due to hypospermatogenesis
Male infertility due to incomplete spermatogenic arrest
● ♂ **N46.11 Organic oligospermia**
Oligospermia NOS
+ **N46.12 Oligospermia due to extratesticular causes**
Code also associated cause
● ♂ **N46.121 Oligospermia due to drug therapy**
● ♂ **N46.122 Oligospermia due to infection**
● ♂ **N46.123 Oligospermia due to obstruction of efferent ducts**
● ♂ **N46.124 Oligospermia due to radiation**
● ♂ **N46.125 Oligospermia due to systemic disease**
● ♂ **N46.129 Oligospermia due to other extratesticular causes**

● ♂ CC **N46.8 Other male infertility**

● ♂ CC **N46.9 Male infertility, unspecified**

N47 Disorders of prepuce

● ♂ **N47.0 Adherent prepuce, newborn**

♂ **N47.1 Phimosis**

♂ **N47.2 Paraphimosis**

♂ **N47.3 Deficient foreskin**

♂ **N47.4 Benign cyst of prepuce**

♂ **N47.5 Adhesions of prepuce and glans penis**

♂ **N47.6 Balanoposthitis**
Use additional code (B95-B97), to identify infectious agent.
Excludes1: *balanitis (N48.1)*

♂ **N47.7 Other inflammatory diseases of prepuce**
Use additional code (B95-B97), to identify infectious agent.

♂ **N47.8 Other disorders of prepuce**

N48 Other disorders of penis

♂ **N48.0 Leukoplakia of penis**
Balanitis xerotica obliterans
Kraurosis of penis
Lichen sclerosus of external male genital organs
Excludes1: *carcinoma in situ of penis (D07.4)*

♂ **N48.1 Balanitis**
Use additional code (B95-B97), to identify infectious agent
Excludes1: *amebic balanitis (A06.8)*
balanitis xerotica obliterans (N48.0)
candidal balanitis (B37.42)
gonococcal balanitis (A54.23)
herpesviral [herpes simplex] balanitis (A60.01)

+ **N48.2 Other inflammatory disorders of penis**
Use additional code (B95-B97), to identify infectious agent.
Excludes1: *balanitis (N48.1)*
balanitis xerotica obliterans (N48.0)
balanoposthitis (N47.6)
♂ **N48.21 Abscess of corpus cavernosum and penis**
♂ **N48.22 Cellulitis of corpus cavernosum and penis**
♂ **N48.29 Other inflammatory disorders of penis**

+ **N48.3 Priapism**
Painful erection
Code first underlying cause
CC ♂ **N48.30 Priapism, unspecified**
CC Exclusion see Appendix A PDX collection 0941
CC ♂ **N48.31 Priapism due to trauma**
CC Exclusion see Appendix A PDX collection 0941
CC ♂ **N48.32 Priapism due to disease classified elsewhere**
CC Exclusion see Appendix A PDX collection 0941
CC ♂ **N48.33 Priapism, drug-induced**
CC Exclusion see Appendix A PDX collection 0941
CC ♂ **N48.39 Other priapism**
CC Exclusion see Appendix A PDX collection 0941

♂ **N48.5 Ulcer of penis**

♂ **N48.6 Induration penis plastica**
Peyronie's disease
Plastic induration of penis

+ **N48.8 Other specified disorders of penis**
♂ **N48.81 Thrombosis of superficial vein of penis**
♂ **N48.82 Acquired torsion of penis**
Acquired torsion of penis NOS
Excludes1: *congenital torsion of penis (Q55.63)*
♂ **N48.83 Acquired buried penis**
Excludes1: *congenital hidden penis (Q55.64)*
♂ **N48.89 Other specified disorders of penis**

♂ **N48.9 Disorder of penis, unspecified**

N49 Inflammatory disorders of male genital organs, not elsewhere classified

Use additional code (B95-B97), to identify infectious agent

\+ ***Excludes1:*** *inflammation of penis (N48.1, N48.2-)*
orchitis and epididymitis (N45.-)

♂ **N49.0 Inflammatory disorders of seminal vesicle**
Vesiculitis NOS

♂ **N49.1 Inflammatory disorders of spermatic cord, tunica vaginalis and vas deferens**
Vasitis

♂ **N49.2 Inflammatory disorders of scrotum**

♂ **N49.3 Fournier gangrene**

♂ **N49.8 Inflammatory disorders of other specified male genital organs**
Inflammation of multiple sites in male genital organs

♂ **N49.9 Inflammatory disorder of unspecified male genital organ**
Abscess of unspecified male genital organ
Boil of unspecified male genital organ
Carbuncle of unspecified male genital organ
Cellulitis of unspecified male genital organ

N50 Other and unspecified disorders of male genital organs

Excludes2: *torsion of testis (N44.0-)*

♂ **N50.0 Atrophy of testis**

♂ **N50.1 Vascular disorders of male genital organs**
Hematocele, NOS, of male genital organs
Hemorrhage of male genital organs
Thrombosis of male genital organs

♂ **N50.3 Cyst of epididymis**

♂ **N50.8 Other specified disorders of male genital organs**
Atrophy of scrotum, seminal vesicle, spermatic cord, tunica vaginalis and vas deferens
Edema of scrotum, seminal vesicle, spermatic cord, testis, tunica vaginalis and vas deferens
Hypertrophy of scrotum, seminal vesicle, spermatic cord, testis, tunica vaginalis and vas deferens
Ulcer of scrotum, seminal vesicle, spermatic cord, testis, tunica vaginalis and vas deferens
Chylocele, tunica vaginalis (nonfilarial) NOS
Urethroscrotal fistula
Stricture of spermatic cord, tunica vaginalis, and vas deferens

♂ **N50.9 Disorder of male genital organs, unspecified**

♂ **N51 Disorders of male genital organs in diseases classified elsewhere**

Code first underlying disease, such as:
filariasis (B74.0-B74.9)

Excludes1: *amebic balanitis (A06.8)*
candidal balanitis (B37.42)
gonococcal balanitis (A54.23)
gonococcal prostatitis (A54.22)
herpesviral [herpes simplex] balanitis (A60.01)
trichomonal prostatitis (A59.02)
tuberculous prostatitis (A18.14)

Valid 3-character code, no further characters required

N52 Male erectile dysfunction

Excludes1: *psychogenic impotence (F52.21)*

\+ **N52.0 Vasculogenic erectile dysfunction**

• ♂ CC **N52.01 Erectile dysfunction due to arterial insufficiency**

• ♂ CC **N52.02 Corporo-venous occlusive erectile dysfunction**

• ♂ CC **N52.03 Combined arterial insufficiency and corporo-venous occlusive erectile dysfunction**

• ♂ CC **N52.1 Erectile dysfunction due to diseases classified elsewhere**
Code first underlying disease

• ♂ CC **N52.2 Drug-induced erectile dysfunction**

\+ **N52.3 Post-surgical erectile dysfunction**

• ♂ CC **N52.31 Erectile dysfunction following radical prostatectomy**

• ♂ CC **N52.32 Erectile dysfunction following radical cystectomy**

• ♂ CC **N52.33 Erectile dysfunction following urethral surgery**

• ♂ CC **N52.34 Erectile dysfunction following simple prostatectomy**

• ♂ CC **N52.39 Other post-surgical erectile dysfunction**

• ♂ CC **N52.8 Other male erectile dysfunction**

• ♂ CC **N52.9 Male erectile dysfunction, unspecified**
Impotence NOS

N53 Other male sexual dysfunction

Excludes1: *psychogenic sexual dysfunction (F52.-)*

\+ **N53.1 Ejaculatory dysfunction**
Excludes1: *premature ejaculation (F52.4)*

♂ **N53.11 Retarded ejaculation**

♂ **N53.12 Painful ejaculation**

♂ **N53.13 Anejaculatory orgasm**

♂ **N53.14 Retrograde ejaculation**

♂ **N53.19 Other ejaculatory dysfunction**
Ejaculatory dysfunction NOS

♂ **N53.8 Other male sexual dysfunction**

♂ **N53.9 Unspecified male sexual dysfunction**

Disorders of breast (N60-N65)

Excludes1: *disorders of breast associated with childbirth (O91-O92)*

N60 Benign mammary dysplasia

Includes: fibrocystic mastopathy

\+ **N60.0 Solitary cyst of breast**
Cyst of breast

N60.01 Solitary cyst of right breast

N60.02 Solitary cyst of left breast

N60.09 Solitary cyst of unspecified breast

\+ **N60.1 Diffuse cystic mastopathy**
Cystic breast
Fibrocystic disease of breast
Excludes1: *diffuse cystic mastopathy with epithelial proliferation (N60.3-)*

• CC **N60.11 Diffuse cystic mastopathy of right breast**

• CC **N60.12 Diffuse cystic mastopathy of left breast**

• CC **N60.19 Diffuse cystic mastopathy of unspecified breast**

\+ **N60.2 Fibroadenosis of breast**
Adenofibrosis of breast
Excludes2: *fibroadenoma of breast (D24.-)*

N60.21 Fibroadenosis of right breast

N60.22 Fibroadenosis of left breast

N60.29 Fibroadenosis of unspecified breast

\+ **N60.3 Fibrosclerosis of breast**
Cystic mastopathy with epithelial proliferation

N60.31 Fibrosclerosis of right breast

N60.32 Fibrosclerosis of left breast

N60.39 Fibrosclerosis of unspecified breast

\+ **N60.4 Mammary duct ectasia**

N60.41 Mammary duct ectasia of right breast

N60.42 Mammary duct ectasia of left breast

N60.49 Mammary duct ectasia of unspecified breast

\+ **N60.8 Other benign mammary dysplasias**

N60.81 Other benign mammary dysplasias of right breast

N60.82 Other benign mammary dysplasias of left breast

N60.89 Other benign mammary dysplasias of unspecified breast

\+ **N60.9 Unspecified benign mammary dysplasia**

N60.91 Unspecified benign mammary dysplasia of right breast

N60.92 Unspecified benign mammary dysplasia of left breast

N60.99 Unspecified benign mammary dysplasia of unspecified breast

N61 Inflammatory disorders of breast

Abscess (acute) (chronic) (nonpuerperal) of areola
Abscess (acute) (chronic) (nonpuerperal) of breast
Carbuncle of breast
Infective mastitis (acute) (subacute) (nonpuerperal)
Mastitis (acute) (subacute) (nonpuerperal) NOS

Excludes1: *inflammatory carcinoma of breast (C50.9)*
inflammatory disorder of breast associated with childbirth (O91.-)
neonatal infective mastitis (P39.0)
thrombophlebitis of breast [Mondor's disease] (I80.8)

Valid 3-character code, no further characters required

N62 Hypertrophy of breast

Gynecomastia
Hypertrophy of breast NOS
Massive pubertal hypertrophy of breast

Excludes1: *breast engorgement of newborn (P83.4)*
disproportion of reconstructed breast (N65.1)

Valid 3-character code, no further characters required

N63 Unspecified lump in breast

Nodule(s) NOS in breast

Valid 3-character code, no further characters required

N64 Other disorders of breast

Excludes2: *mechanical complication of breast prosthesis and implant (T85.4-)*

N64.0 Fissure and fistula of nipple

N64.1 Fat necrosis of breast
Fat necrosis (segmental) of breast
Code first breast necrosis due to breast graft (T85.89)

N64.2 Atrophy of breast

Breast

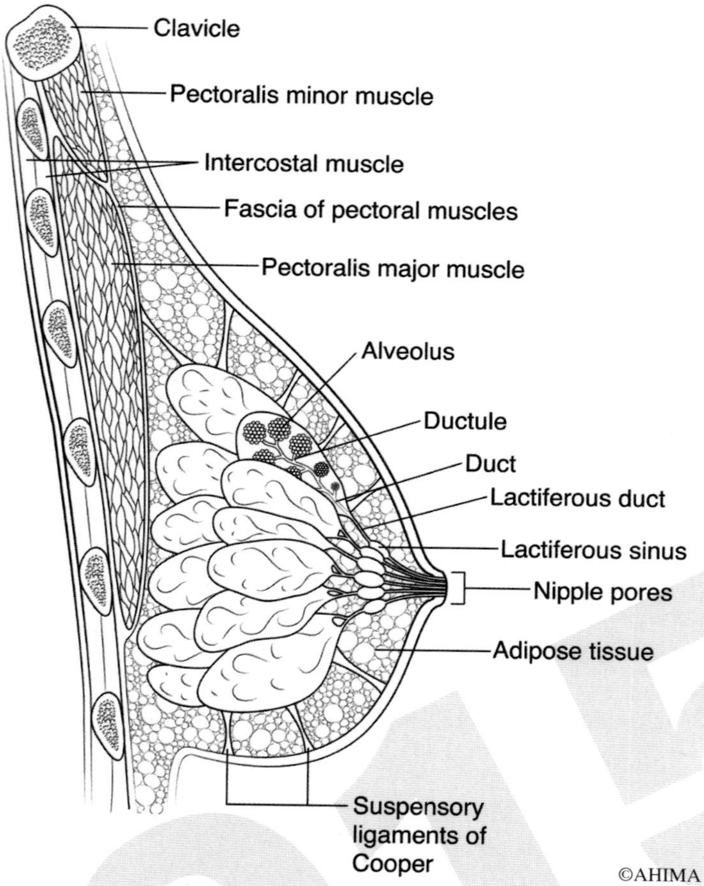

Clavicle
Pectoralis minor muscle
Intercostal muscle
Fascia of pectoral muscles
Pectoralis major muscle
Alveolus
Ductule
Duct
Lactiferous duct
Lactiferous sinus
Nipple pores
Adipose tissue
Suspensory ligaments of Cooper

N64.3 Galactorrhea not associated with childbirth
N64.4 Mastodynia
\+ **N64.5 Other signs and symptoms in breast**
Excludes2: *abnormal findings on diagnostic imaging of breast (R92.-)*
N64.51 Induration of breast
N64.52 Nipple discharge
Excludes1: *abnormal findings in nipple discharge (R89.-)*
N64.53 Retraction of nipple
N64.59 Other signs and symptoms in breast
\+ **N64.8 Other specified disorders of breast**
• CC **N64.81 Ptosis of breast**
Excludes1: *ptosis of native breast in relation to reconstructed breast (N65.1)*
• CC **N64.82 Hypoplasia of breast**
Micromastia
Excludes1: *congenital absence of breast (Q83.0)*
hypoplasia of native breast in relation to reconstructed breast (N65.1)
N64.89 Other specified disorders of breast
Galactocele
Subinvolution of breast (postlactational)
N64.9 Disorder of breast, unspecified

N65 Deformity and disproportion of reconstructed breast

• CC **N65.0 Deformity of reconstructed breast**
Contour irregularity in reconstructed breast
Excess tissue in reconstructed breast
Misshapen reconstructed breast
• CC **N65.1 Disproportion of reconstructed breast**
Breast asymmetry between native breast and reconstructed breast
Disproportion between native breast and reconstructed breast

Inflammatory diseases of female pelvic organs (N70-N77)

Excludes1: *inflammatory diseases of female pelvic organs complicating:*
abortion or ectopic or molar pregnancy (O00-O07, O08.0)
pregnancy, childbirth and the puerperium (O23.-, O75.3, O85, O86

N70 Salpingitis and oophoritis

Includes: abscess (of) fallopian tube
abscess (of) ovary
pyosalpinx
salpingo-oophoritis
tubo-ovarian abscess
tubo-ovarian inflammatory disease
Use additional code (B95-B97), to identify infectious agent
Excludes1: *gonococcal infection (A54.24)*
tuberculous infection (A18.17)
\+ **N70.0 Acute salpingitis and oophoritis**
♀ CC **N70.01 Acute salpingitis**
CC Exclusion see Appendix A PDX collection 0942
♀ CC **N70.02 Acute oophoritis**
CC Exclusion see Appendix A PDX collection 0942
♀ CC **N70.03 Acute salpingitis and oophoritis**
CC Exclusion see Appendix A PDX collection 0942
\+ **N70.1 Chronic salpingitis and oophoritis**
Hydrosalpinx
♀ **N70.11 Chronic salpingitis**
♀ **N70.12 Chronic oophoritis**
♀ **N70.13 Chronic salpingitis and oophoritis**
\+ **N70.9 Salpingitis and oophoritis, unspecified**
♀ **N70.91 Salpingitis, unspecified**
♀ **N70.92 Oophoritis, unspecified**
♀ **N70.93 Salpingitis and oophoritis, unspecified**

Female Reproductive System

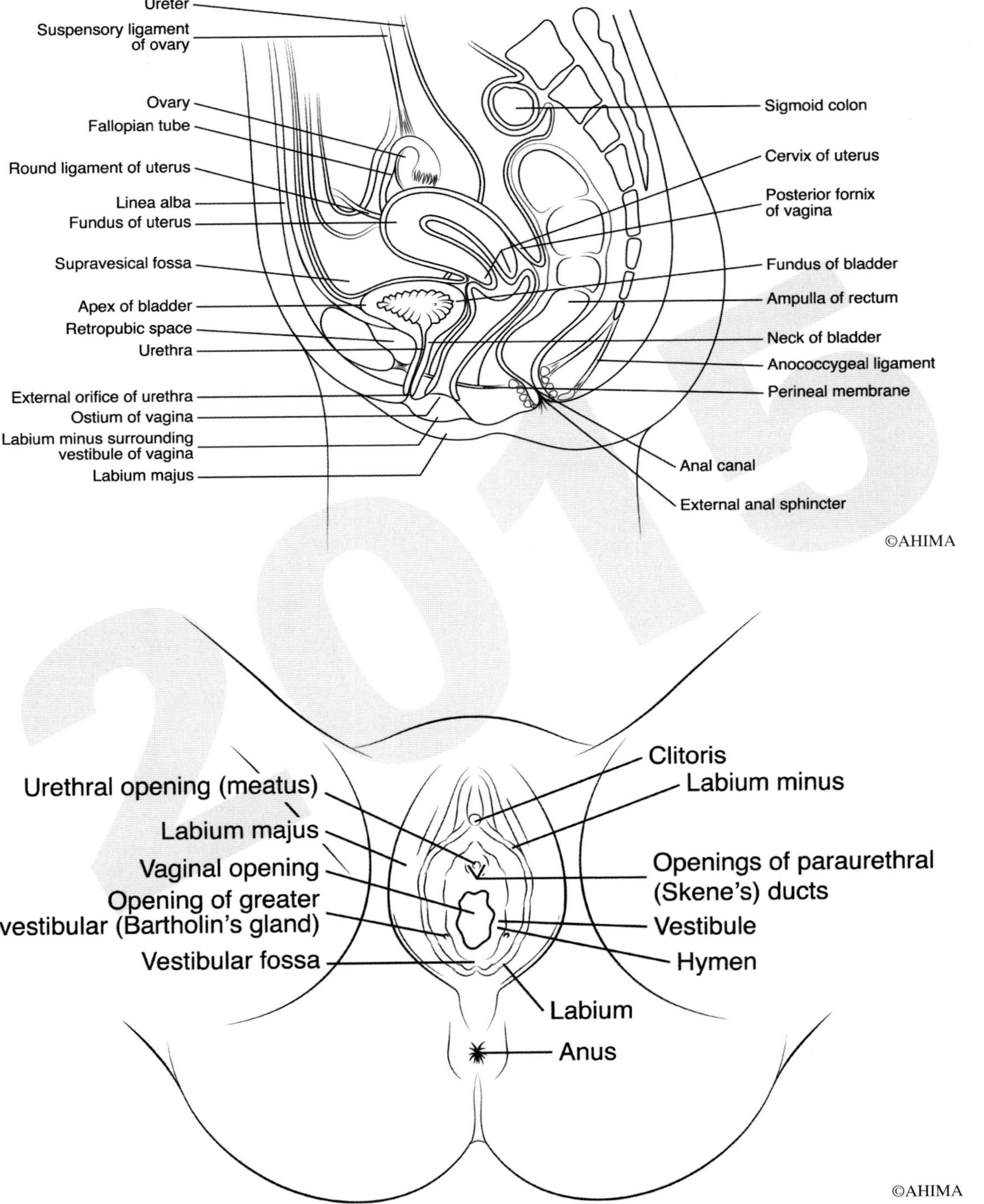

N71 **Inflammatory disease of uterus, except cervix**
Includes: endo (myo) metritis
metritis
myometritis
pyometra
uterine abscess
Use additional code (B95-B97), to identify infectious agent
Excludes1: *hyperplastic endometritis (N85.0-)*
infection of uterus following delivery (O85, O86.-)
♀ CC **N71.0 Acute inflammatory disease of uterus**
CC Exclusion see Appendix A PDX collection 0943
♀ **N71.1 Chronic inflammatory disease of uterus**
♀ **N71.9 Inflammatory disease of uterus, unspecified**

♀ N72 **Inflammatory disease of cervix uteri**
Includes: cervicitis (with or without erosion or ectropion)
endocervicitis (with or without erosion or ectropion)
exocervicitis (with or without erosion or ectropion)
Use additional code (B95-B97), to identify infectious agent
Excludes1: *erosion and ectropion of cervix without cervicitis (N86)*
Valid 3-character code, no further characters required

N73 **Other female pelvic inflammatory diseases**
Use additional code (B95-B97), to identify infectious agent.
♀ CC **N73.0 Acute parametritis and pelvic cellulitis**
Abscess of broad ligament
Abscess of parametrium
Pelvic cellulitis, female
CC Exclusion see Appendix A PDX collection 0942
♀ **N73.1 Chronic parametritis and pelvic cellulitis**
Any condition in N73.0 specified as chronic
Excludes1: *tuberculous parametritis and pelvic cellultis (A18.17)*
♀ **N73.2 Unspecified parametritis and pelvic cellulitis**
Any condition in N73.0 unspecified whether acute or chronic
♀ MCC **N73.3 Female acute pelvic peritonitis**
MCC Exclusion see Appendix A PDX collection 0942
♀ CC **N73.4 Female chronic pelvic peritonitis**
Excludes1: *tuberculous pelvic (female) peritonitis (A18.17)*
CC Exclusion see Appendix A PDX collection 0942
♀ **N73.5 Female pelvic peritonitis, unspecified**
♀ **N73.6 Female pelvic peritoneal adhesions (postinfective)**
Excludes2: *postprocedural pelvic peritoneal adhesions (N99.4)*
AHA CC: 1Q, 2014, 6
♀ **N73.8 Other specified female pelvic inflammatory diseases**
♀ **N73.9 Female pelvic inflammatory disease, unspecified**
Female pelvic infection or inflammation NOS

♀ N74 **Female pelvic inflammatory disorders in diseases classified elsewhere**
Code first underlying disease
Excludes1: *chlamydial cervicitis (A56.02)*
chlamydial pelvic inflammatory disease (A56.11)
gonococcal cervicitis (A54.03)
gonococcal pelvic inflammatory disease (A54.24)
herpesviral [herpes simplex] cervicitis (A60.03)
herpesviral [herpes simplex] pelvic inflammatory disease (A60.09)
syphilitic cervicitis (A52.76
syphilitic pelvic inflammatory disease (A52.76)
trichomonal cervicitis (A59.09)
tuberculous cervicitis (A18.16)
tuberculous pelvic inflammatory disease (A18.17)
Valid 3-character code, no further characters required

N75 **Diseases of Bartholin's gland**
♀ **N75.0 Cyst of Bartholin's gland**
♀ CC **N75.1 Abscess of Bartholin's gland**
♀ **N75.8 Other diseases of Bartholin's gland**
Bartholinitis
CC Exclusion see Appendix A PDX collection 0944
♀ **N75.9 Disease of Bartholin's gland, unspecified**

N76 **Other inflammation of vagina and vulva**
Use additional code (B95-B97), to identify infectious agent
Excludes2: *senile (atrophic) vaginitis (N95.2)*
vulvar vestibulitis (N94.810)
♀ **N76.0 Acute vaginitis**
Acute vulvovaginitis
Vaginitis NOS
Vulvovaginitis NOS
♀ **N76.1 Subacute and chronic vaginitis**
Chronic vulvovaginitis
Subacute vulvovaginitis
♀ **N76.2 Acute vulvitis**
Vulvitis NOS
♀ **N76.3 Subacute and chronic vulvitis**
♀ CC **N76.4 Abscess of vulva**
Furuncle of vulva
CC Exclusion see Appendix A PDX collection 0944
♀ **N76.5 Ulceration of vagina**
♀ **N76.6 Ulceration of vulva**
\+ **N76.8 Other specified inflammation of vagina and vulva**
♀ CC **N76.81 Mucositis (ulcerative) of vagina and vulva**
Code also type of associated therapy, such as:
antineoplastic and immunosuppressive drugs (T45.1X-)
radiological procedure and radiotherapy (Y84.2)
Excludes2: *gastrointestinal mucositis (ulcerative) (K92.81)*
nasal mucositis (ulcerative) (J34.81)
oral mucositis (ulcerative) (K12.3-)
CC Exclusion see Appendix A PDX collection 0945
♀ **N76.89 Other specified inflammation of vagina and vulva**

N77 **Vulvovaginal ulceration and inflammation in diseases classified elsewhere**
♀ **N77.0 Ulceration of vulva in diseases classified elsewhere**
Code first underlying disease, such as:
Behçet's disease (M35.2)
Excludes1: *ulceration of vulva in gonococcal infection (A54.0*
ulceration of vulva in herpesviral [herpes simplex infection (A60.04)
ulceration of vulva in syphilis (A51.0)
ulceration of vulva in tuberculosis (A18.18)
♀ **N77.1 Vaginitis, vulvitis and vulvovaginitis in diseases classified elsewhere**
Code first underlying disease, such as:
pinworm (B80)
Excludes1: *candidal vulvovaginitis (B37.3)*
chlamydial vulvovaginitis (A56.02)
gonococcal vulvovaginitis (A54.02)
herpesviral [herpes simplex] vulvovaginitis (A60.0
trichomonal vulvovaginitis (A59.01)
tuberculous vulvovaginitis (A18.18)
vulvovaginitis in early syphilis (A51.0)
vulvovaginitis in late syphilis (A52.76)

Noninflammatory disorders of female genital tract (N80-N98)

N80 **Endometriosis**
♀ **N80.0 Endometriosis of uterus**
Adenomyosis
Excludes1: *stromal endometriosis (D39.0)*
♀ **N80.1 Endometriosis of ovary**
♀ **N80.2 Endometriosis of fallopian tube**
♀ **N80.3 Endometriosis of pelvic peritoneum**
♀ **N80.4 Endometriosis of rectovaginal septum and vagina**
♀ **N80.5 Endometriosis of intestine**
♀ **N80.6 Endometriosis in cutaneous scar**
♀ **N80.8 Other endometriosis**
♀ **N80.9 Endometriosis, unspecified**

N81 **Female genital prolapse**
Excludes1: *genital prolapse complicating pregnancy, labor or delivery (O34.5-)*
prolapse and hernia of ovary and fallopian tube (N83.4)
prolapse of vaginal vault after hysterectomy (N99.3)
♀ **N81.0 Urethrocele**
Excludes1: *urethrocele with cystocele (N81.1-)*
urethrocele with prolapse of uterus (N81.2-N81.4)
\+ **N81.1 Cystocele**
Cystocele with urethrocele
Cystourethrocele
Excludes1: *cystocele with prolapse of uterus (N81.2-N81.4)*
♀ **N81.10 Cystocele, unspecified**
Prolapse of (anterior) vaginal wall NOS
♀ **N81.11 Cystocele, midline**
♀ **N81.12 Cystocele, lateral**
Paravaginal cystocele

♀ **N81.2 Incomplete uterovaginal prolapse**
First degree uterine prolapse
Prolapse of cervix NOS
Second degree uterine prolapse
Excludes1: *cervical stump prolaspe (N81.85)*

♀ **N81.3 Complete uterovaginal prolapse**
Procidentia (uteri) NOS
Third degree uterine prolapse

♀ **N81.4 Uterovaginal prolapse, unspecified**
Prolapse of uterus NOS

♀ **N81.5 Vaginal enterocele**
Excludes1: *enterocele with prolapse of uterus (N81.2-N81.4)*

♀ **N81.6 Rectocele**
Prolapse of posterior vaginal wall
Use additional code for any associated fecal incontinence, if applicable (R15.-)
Excludes2: *perineocele (N81.81)*
rectal prolapse (K62.3)
rectocele with prolapse of uterus (N81.2-N81.4)

\+ **N81.8 Other female genital prolapse**
♀ **N81.81 Perineocele**
♀ **N81.82 Incompetence or weakening of pubocervical tissue**
♀ **N81.83 Incompetence or weakening of rectovaginal tissue**
♀ **N81.84 Pelvic muscle wasting**
Disuse atrophy of pelvic muscles and anal sphincter
♀ **N81.85 Cervical stump prolapse**
♀ **N81.89 Other female genital prolapse**
Deficient perineum
Old laceration of muscles of pelvic floor

♀ **N81.9 Female genital prolapse, unspecified**

N82 Fistulae involving female genital tract
Excludes1: *vesicointestinal fistulae (N32.1)*

♀ CC **N82.0 Vesicovaginal fistula**
CC Exclusion see Appendix A PDX collection 0946

♀ CC **N82.1 Other female urinary-genital tract fistulae**
Cervicovesical fistula
Ureterovaginal fistula
Urethrovaginal fistula
Uteroureteric fistula
Uterovesical fistula
CC Exclusion see Appendix A PDX collection 0946

♀ CC **N82.2 Fistula of vagina to small intestine**
CC Exclusion see Appendix A PDX collection 0946

♀ CC **N82.3 Fistula of vagina to large intestine**
Rectovaginal fistula
CC Exclusion see Appendix A PDX collection 0946

♀ CC **N82.4 Other female intestinal-genital tract fistulae**
Intestinouterine fistula
CC Exclusion see Appendix A PDX collection 0946

♀ CC **N82.5 Female genital tract-skin fistulae**
Uterus to abdominal wall fistula
Vaginoperineal fistula
CC Exclusion see Appendix A PDX collection 0946

♀ CC **N82.8 Other female genital tract fistulae**
CC Exclusion see Appendix A PDX collection 0946

♀ CC **N82.9 Female genital tract fistula, unspecified**
CC Exclusion see Appendix A PDX collection 0946

N83 Noninflammatory disorders of ovary, fallopian tube and broad ligament
Excludes2: *hydrosalpinx (N70.1-)*

♀ **N83.0 Follicular cyst of ovary**
Cyst of graafian follicle
Hemorrhagic follicular cyst (of ovary)

♀ **N83.1 Corpus luteum cyst**
Hemorrhagic corpus luteum cyst

\+ **N83.2 Other and unspecified ovarian cysts**
Excludes1: *developmental ovarian cyst (Q50.1)*
neoplastic ovarian cyst (D27.-)
polycystic ovarian syndrome (E28.2)
Stein-Leventhal syndrome (E28.2)
♀ **N83.20 Unspecified ovarian cysts**
♀ **N83.29 Other ovarian cysts**
Retention cyst of ovary
Simple cyst of ovary

\+ **N83.3 Acquired atrophy of ovary and fallopian tube**
♀ **N83.31 Acquired atrophy of ovary**
♀ **N83.32 Acquired atrophy of fallopian tube**
♀ **N83.33 Acquired atrophy of ovary and fallopian tube**

♀ **N83.4 Prolapse and hernia of ovary and fallopian tube**

\+ **N83.5 Torsion of ovary, ovarian pedicle and fallopian tube**
Torsion of accessory tube
♀ CC **N83.51 Torsion of ovary and ovarian pedicle**
CC Exclusion see Appendix A PDX collection 0947
♀ CC **N83.52 Torsion of fallopian tube**
Torsion of hydatid of Morgagni
CC Exclusion see Appendix A PDX collection 0947
♀ CC **N83.53 Torsion of ovary, ovarian pedicle and fallopian tube**
CC Exclusion see Appendix A PDX collection 0947

♀ **N83.6 Hematosalpinx**
Excludes1: *hematosalpinx (with) (in):*
hematocolpos (N89.7)
hematometra (N85.7)
tubal pregnancy (O00.1)

♀ **N83.7 Hematoma of broad ligament**

♀ **N83.8 Other noninflammatory disorders of ovary, fallopian tube and broad ligament**
Broad ligament laceration syndrome [Allen-Masters]

♀ **N83.9 Noninflammatory disorder of ovary, fallopian tube and broad ligament, unspecified**

N84 Polyp of female genital tract
Excludes1: *adenomatous polyp (D28.-)*
placental polyp (O90.89)

♀ **N84.0 Polyp of corpus uteri**
Polyp of endometrium
Polyp of uterus NOS
Excludes1: *polypoid endometrial hyperplasia (N85.0-)*

♀ **N84.1 Polyp of cervix uteri**
Mucous polyp of cervix

♀ **N84.2 Polyp of vagina**

♀ **N84.3 Polyp of vulva**
Polyp of labia

♀ **N84.8 Polyp of other parts of female genital tract**

♀ **N84.9 Polyp of female genital tract, unspecified**

N85 Other noninflammatory disorders of uterus, except cervix
Excludes1: *endometriosis (N80.-)*
inflammatory diseases of uterus (N71.-)
noninflammatory disorders of cervix, except malposition (N86-N88)
polyp of corpus uteri (N84.0)
uterine prolapse (N81.-)

\+ **N85.0 Endometrial hyperplasia**
♀ **N85.00 Endometrial hyperplasia, unspecified**
Hyperplasia (adenomatous) (cystic) (glandular) of endometrium
Hyperplastic endometritis
♀ **N85.01 Benign endometrial hyperplasia**
Endometrial hyperplasia (complex) (simple) without atypia
♀ **N85.02 Endometrial intraepithelial neoplasia [EIN]**
Endometrial hyperplasia with atypia
Excludes1: *malignant neoplasm of endometrium (with endometrial intraepithelial neoplasia [EIN]) (C54.1)*

♀ **N85.2 Hypertrophy of uterus**
Bulky or enlarged uterus
Excludes1: *puerperal hypertrophy of uterus (O90.89)*

♀ **N85.3 Subinvolution of uterus**
Excludes1: *puerperal subinvolution of uterus (O90.89)*

♀ **N85.4 Malposition of uterus**
Anteversion of uterus
Retroflexion of uterus
Retroversion of uterus
Excludes1: *malposition of uterus complicating pregnancy, labor or delivery (O34.5-, O65.5)*

♀ **N85.5 Inversion of uterus**
Excludes1: *current obstetric trauma (O71.2)*
postpartum inversion of uterus (O71.2)

♀ **N85.6 Intrauterine synechiae**

♀ **N85.7 Hematometra**
Hematosalpinx with hematometra
Excludes1: *hematometra with hematocolpos (N89.7)*

♀ **N85.8 Other specified noninflammatory disorders of uterus**
Atrophy of uterus, acquired
Fibrosis of uterus NOS

♀ **N85.9 Noninflammatory disorder of uterus, unspecified**
Disorder of uterus NOS

♀ N86 Erosion and ectropion of cervix uteri

Decubitus (trophic) ulcer of cervix
Eversion of cervix
Excludes1: *erosion and ectropion of cervix with cervicitis (N72)*
Valid 3-character code, no further characters required

N87 Dysplasia of cervix uteri

Excludes1: *abnormal results from cervical cytologic examination without histologic confirmation (R87.61-)*
carcinoma in situ of cervix uteri (D06.-)
cervical intraepithelial neoplasia III [CIN III] (D06.-)
HGSIL of cervix (R87.613)
severe dysplasia of cervix uteri (D06.-)

♀ **N87.0 Mild cervical dysplasia**
Cervical intraepithelial neoplasia I [CIN I]

♀ **N87.1 Moderate cervical dysplasia**
Cervical intraepithelial neoplasia II [CIN II]

♀ **N87.9 Dysplasia of cervix uteri, unspecified**
Anaplasia of cervix
Cervical atypism
Cervical dysplasia NOS

N88 Other noninflammatory disorders of cervix uteri

Excludes2: *inflammatory disease of cervix (N72)*
polyp of cervix (N84.1)

♀ **N88.0 Leukoplakia of cervix uteri**

♀ **N88.1 Old laceration of cervix uteri**
Adhesions of cervix
Excludes1: *current obstetric trauma (O71.3)*

♀ **N88.2 Stricture and stenosis of cervix uteri**
Excludes1: *stricture and stenosis of cervix uteri complicating labor (O65.5)*

♀ **N88.3 Incompetence of cervix uteri**
Investigation and management of (suspected) cervical incompetence in a nonpregnant woman
Excludes1: *cervical incompetence complicating pregnancy (O34.3-)*

♀ **N88.4 Hypertrophic elongation of cervix uteri**

♀ **N88.8 Other specified noninflammatory disorders of cervix uteri**
Excludes1: *current obstetric trauma (O71.3)*

♀ **N88.9 Noninflammatory disorder of cervix uteri, unspecified**

N89 Other noninflammatory disorders of vagina

Excludes1: *abnormal results from vaginal cytologic examination without histologic confirmation (R87.62-)*
carcinoma in situ of vagina (D07.2)
HGSIL of vagina (R87.623)
inflammation of vagina (N76.-)
senile (atrophic) vaginitis (N95.2)
severe dysplasia of vagina (D07.2)
trichomonal leukorrhea (A59.00)
vaginal intraepithelial neoplasia [VAIN], grade III (D07.2)

♀ **N89.0 Mild vaginal dysplasia**
Vaginal intraepithelial neoplasia [VAIN], grade I

♀ **N89.1 Moderate vaginal dysplasia**
Vaginal intraepithelial neoplasia [VAIN], grade II

♀ **N89.3 Dysplasia of vagina, unspecified**

♀ **N89.4 Leukoplakia of vagina**

♀ **N89.5 Stricture and atresia of vagina**
Vaginal adhesions
Vaginal stenosis
Excludes1: *congenital atresia or stricture (Q52.4)*
postprocedural adhesions of vagina (N99.2)

♀ **N89.6 Tight hymenal ring**
Rigid hymen
Tight introitus
Excludes1: *imperforate hymen (Q52.3)*

♀ **N89.7 Hematocolpos**
Hematocolpos with hematometra or hematosalpinx

♀ **N89.8 Other specified noninflammatory disorders of vagina**
Leukorrhea NOS
Old vaginal laceration
Pessary ulcer of vagina
Excludes1: *current obstetric trauma (O70.-, O71.4, O71.7-O71.8)*
old laceration involving muscles of pelvic floor (N81.8)

♀ **N89.9 Noninflammatory disorder of vagina, unspecified**

N90 Other noninflammatory disorders of vulva and perineum

Excludes1: *anogenital (venereal) warts (A63.0)*
carcinoma in situ of vulva (D07.1)
condyloma acuminatum (A63.0)
current obstetric trauma (O70.-, O71.7-O71.8)
inflammation of vulva (N76.-)
severe dysplasia of vulva (D07.1)
vulvar intraepithelial neoplasm III [VIN III] (D07.1)

♀ **N90.0 Mild vulvar dysplasia**
Vulvar intraepithelial neoplasia [VIN], grade I

♀ **N90.1 Moderate vulvar dysplasia**
Vulvar intraepithelial neoplasia [VIN], grade II

♀ **N90.3 Dysplasia of vulva, unspecified**

♀ **N90.4 Leukoplakia of vulva**
Dystrophy of vulva
Kraurosis of vulva
Lichen sclerosus of external female genital organs

♀ **N90.5 Atrophy of vulva**
Stenosis of vulva

♀ **N90.6 Hypertrophy of vulva**
Hypertrophy of labia

♀ **N90.7 Vulvar cyst**

+ **N90.8 Other specified noninflammatory disorders of vulva and perineum**

+ **N90.81 Female genital mutilation status**
Female genital cutting status

♀ **N90.810 Female genital mutilation status, unspecified**
Female genital cutting status, unspecified
Female genital mutilation status NOS

♀ **N90.811 Female genital mutilation Type I status**
Clitorectomy status
Female genital cutting Type I status

♀ **N90.812 Female genital mutilation Type II status**
Clitorectomy with excision of labia minora status
Female genital cutting Type II status

♀ **N90.813 Female genital mutilation Type III status**
Female genital cutting Type III status
Infibulation status

♀ **N90.818 Other female genital mutilation status**
Female genital cutting Type IV status
Female genital mutilation Type IV status
Other female genital cutting status

♀ **N90.89 Other specified noninflammatory disorders of vulva and perineum**
Adhesions of vulva
Hypertrophy of clitoris

♀ **N90.9 Noninflammatory disorder of vulva and perineum, unspecified**

N91 Absent, scanty and rare menstruation

Excludes1: *ovarian dysfunction (E28.-)*

♀ **N91.0 Primary amenorrhea**

♀ **N91.1 Secondary amenorrhea**

♀ **N91.2 Amenorrhea, unspecified**

♀ **N91.3 Primary oligomenorrhea**

♀ **N91.4 Secondary oligomenorrhea**

♀ **N91.5 Oligomenorrhea, unspecified**
Hypomenorrhea NOS

N92 Excessive, frequent and irregular menstruation

Excludes1: *postmenopausal bleeding (N95.0)*
precocious puberty (menstruation) (E30.1)

♀ **N92.0 Excessive and frequent menstruation with regular cycle**
Heavy periods NOS
Menorrhagia NOS
Polymenorrhea

♀ **N92.1 Excessive and frequent menstruation with irregular cycle**
Irregular intermenstrual bleeding
Irregular, shortened intervals between menstrual bleeding
Menometrorrhagia
Metrorrhagia

• ♀ **N92.2 Excessive menstruation at puberty**
Excessive bleeding associated with onset of menstrual periods
Pubertal menorrhagia
Puberty bleeding

♀ **N92.3 Ovulation bleeding**
Regular intermenstrual bleeding

♀ **N92.4 Excessive bleeding in the premenopausal period**
Climacteric menorrhagia or metrorrhagia
Menopausal menorrhagia or metrorrhagia
Preclimacteric menorrhagia or metrorrhagia
Premenopausal menorrhagia or metrorrhagia

♀ **N92.5 Other specified irregular menstruation**
♀ **N92.6 Irregular menstruation, unspecified**
Irregular bleeding NOS
Irregular periods NOS
Excludes1: *irregular menstruation with:*
lengthened intervals or scanty bleeding (N91.3-N91.5)
shortened intervals or excessive bleeding (N92.1)

N93 Other abnormal uterine and vaginal bleeding
Excludes1: *neonatal vaginal hemorrhage (P54.6)*
precocious puberty (menstruation) (E30.1)
pseudomenses (P54.6)
♀ **N93.0 Postcoital and contact bleeding**
♀ **N93.8 Other specified abnormal uterine and vaginal bleeding**
Dysfunctional or functional uterine or vaginal bleeding NOS
♀ **N93.9 Abnormal uterine and vaginal bleeding,unspecified**

N94 Pain and other conditions associated with female genital organs and menstrual cycle
♀ **N94.0 Mittelschmerz**
♀ **N94.1 Dyspareunia**
Excludes1: *psychogenic dyspareunia (F52.6)*
♀ **N94.2 Vaginismus**
Excludes1: *psychogenic vaginismus (F52.5)*
♀ **N94.3 Premenstrual tension syndrome**
Premenstrual dysphoric disorder
Code also associated menstrual migraine (G43.82-, G43.83-)
♀ **N94.4 Primary dysmenorrhea**
♀ **N94.5 Secondary dysmenorrhea**
♀ **N94.6 Dysmenorrhea, unspecified**
Excludes1: *psychogenic dysmenorrhea (F45.8)*
+ **N94.8 Other specified conditions associated with female genital organs and menstrual cycle**
+ **N94.81 Vulvodynia**
♀ **N94.810 Vulvar vestibulitis**
♀ **N94.818 Other vulvodynia**
♀ **N94.819 Vulvodynia, unspecified**
Vulvodynia NOS
♀ **N94.89 Other specified conditions associated with female genital organs and menstrual cycle**
♀ **N94.9 Unspecified condition associated with female genital organs and menstrual cycle**

N95 Menopausal and other perimenopausal disorders
Menopausal and other perimenopausal disorders due to naturally occurring (age-related) menopause and perimenopause
Excludes1: *excessive bleeding in the premenopausal period (N92.4)*
menopausal and perimenopausal disorders due to artificial or premature menopause (E89.4-, E28.31-)
premature menopause (E28.31-)
Excludes2: *postmenopausal osteoporosis (M81.0-)*
postmenopausal osteoporosis with current pathological fracture (M80.0-)
postmenopausal urethritis (N34.2)
♀ **N95.0 Postmenopausal bleeding**
♀ **N95.1 Menopausal and female climacteric states**
Symptoms such as flushing, sleeplessness, headache, lack of concentration, associated with natural (age-related) menopause
Use additional code for associated symptoms
Excludes1: *asymptomatic menopausal state (Z78.0)*
symptoms associated with artificial menopause (E89.41)
symptoms associated with premature menopause (E28.310)
♀ **N95.2 Postmenopausal atrophic vaginitis**
Senile (atrophic) vaginitis
♀ **N95.8 Other specified menopausal and perimenopausal disorders**
♀ **N95.9 Unspecified menopausal and perimenopausal disorder**

♀ **N96 Recurrent pregnancy loss**
Investigation or care in a nonpregnant woman with history of recurrent pregnancy loss
Excludes1: *recurrent pregancy loss with current pregnancy (O26.2-)*
Valid 3-character code, no further characters required

N97 Female infertility
Includes: inability to achieve a pregnancy
sterility, female NOS
Excludes1: *female infertility associated with:*
hypopituitarism (E23.0)
Stein-Leventhal syndrome (E28.2)
Excludes2: *incompetence of cervix uteri (N88.3)*
♀ **N97.0 Female infertility associated with anovulation**
♀ **N97.1 Female infertility of tubal origin**
Female infertility associated with congenital anomaly of tube
Female infertility due to tubal block
Female infertility due to tubal occlusion
Female infertility due to tubal stenosis
♀ **N97.2 Female infertility of uterine origin**
Female infertility associated with congenital anomaly of uterus
Female infertility due to nonimplantation of ovum
♀ **N97.8 Female infertility of other origin**
♀ **N97.9 Female infertility, unspecified**

N98 Complications associated with artificial fertilization
♀ CC **N98.0 Infection associated with artificial insemination**
CC Exclusion see Appendix A PDX collection 0948
♀ CC **N98.1 Hyperstimulation of ovaries**
Hyperstimulation of ovaries NOS
Hyperstimulation of ovaries associated with induced ovulation
CC Exclusion see Appendix A PDX collection 0643
♀ CC **N98.2 Complications of attempted introduction of fertilized ovum following in vitro fertilization**
CC Exclusion see Appendix A PDX collection 0643
♀ CC **N98.3 Complications of attempted introduction of embryo in embryo transfer**
CC Exclusion see Appendix A PDX collection 0643
♀ CC **N98.8 Other complications associated with artificial fertilization**
CC Exclusion see Appendix A PDX collection 0643
♀ **N98.9 Complication associated with artificial fertilization, unspecified**
CC Exclusion see Appendix A PDX collection 0643

Intraoperative and postprocedural complications and disorders of genitourinary system, not elsewhere classified (N99)

N99 Intraoperative and postprocedural complications and disorders of genitourinary system, not elsewhere classified
Excludes2: *irradiation cystitis (N30.4-)*
postoophorectomy osteoporosis with current pathological fracture (M80.8-)
postoophorectomy osteoporosis without current pathological fracture (M81.8-)
N99.0 Postprocedural (acute) (chronic) kidney failure
Use additional code to type of kidney disease
+ **N99.1 Postprocedural urethral stricture**
Postcatheterization urethral stricture
+ **N99.11 Postprocedural urethral stricture, male**
♂ **N99.110 Postprocedural urethral stricture, male, meatal**
N99.111 Postprocedural bulbous urethral stricture
N99.112 Postprocedural membranous urethral stricture
N99.113 Postprocedural anterior urethral stricture
♂ **N99.114 Postprocedural urethral stricture, male, unspecified**
♀ **N99.12 Postprocedural urethral stricture, female**
♀ **N99.2 Postprocedural adhesions of vagina**
♀ **N99.3 Prolapse of vaginal vault after hysterectomy**
N99.4 Postprocedural pelvic peritoneal adhesions
Excludes2: *pelvic peritoneal adhesions NOS (N73.6)*
postinfective pelvic peritoneal adhesions (N73.6)

+ N99.5 Complications of stoma of urinary tract

Excludes2: *mechanical complication of urinary (indwelling) catheter (T83.0-)*

+ N99.51 Complication of cystostomy

N99.510 Cystostomy hemorrhage
CC Exclusion see Appendix A PDX collection 0949

CC N99.511 Cystostomy infection
CC Exclusion see Appendix A PDX collection 0950

CC N99.512 Cystostomy malfunction
CC Exclusion see Appendix A PDX collection 0951

CC N99.518 Other cystostomy complication
CC Exclusion see Appendix A PDX collection 0949

+ N99.52 Complication of other external stoma of urinary tract

N99.520 Hemorrhage of other external stoma of urinary tract

N99.521 Infection of other external stoma of urinary tract

N99.522 Malfunction of other external stoma of urinary tract

N99.528 Other complication of other external stoma of urinary tract

+ N99.53 Complication of other stoma of urinary tract

N99.530 Hemorrhage of other stoma of urinary tract

N99.531 Infection of other stoma of urinary tract

N99.532 Malfunction of other stoma of urinary tract

N99.538 Other complication of other stoma of urinary tract

+ N99.6 Intraoperative hemorrhage and hematoma of a genitourinary system organ or structure complicating a procedure

Excludes1: *intraoperative hemorrhage and hematoma of a genitourinary system organ or structure due to accidental puncture or laceration during a procedure (N99.7-)*

N99.61 Intraoperative hemorrhage and hematoma of a genitourinary system organ or structure complicating a genitourinary system procedure
CC Exclusion see Appendix A PDX collection 0952

CC N99.62 Intraoperative hemorrhage and hematoma of a genitourinary system organ or structure complicating other procedure
CC Exclusion see Appendix A PDX collection 0952

+ N99.7 Accidental puncture and laceration of a genitourinary system organ or structure during a procedure

CC N99.71 Accidental puncture and laceration of a genitourinary system organ or structure during a genitourinary system procedure
CC Exclusion see Appendix A PDX collection 0509

CC N99.72 Accidental puncture and laceration of a genitourinary system organ or structure during other procedure
CC Exclusion see Appendix A PDX collection 0509

+ N99.8 Other intraoperative and postprocedural complications and disorders of genitourinary system

N99.81 Other intraoperative complications of genitourinary system

+ N99.82 Postprocedural hemorrhage and hematoma of a genitourinary system organ or structure following a procedure

CC N99.820 Postprocedural hemorrhage and hematoma of a genitourinary system organ or structure following a genitourinary system procedure
CC Exclusion see Appendix A PDX collection 0952

CC N99.821 Postprocedural hemorrhage and hematoma of a genitourinary system organ or structure following other procedure
CC Exclusion see Appendix A PDX collection 0952

♀ N99.83 Residual ovary syndrome

N99.89 Other postprocedural complications and disorders of genitourinary system

ıapter 15: Pregnancy, Childbirth and the erperium (O00-O9A)

TE Codes from this chapter are for use only on maternal records, never on newborn records
Codes from this chapter are for use for conditions related to or aggravated by the pregnancy, childbirth, or by the puerperium (maternal causes or obstetric causes)

TE Trimesters are counted from the first day of the last menstrual period. They are defined as follows:
1st trimester- less than 14 weeks 0 days
2nd trimester- 14 weeks 0 days to less than 28 weeks 0 days
3rd trimester- 28 weeks 0 days until delivery

additional code from category Z3A, Weeks of gestation, to identify the specific k of the pregnancy

ludes1: *supervision of normal pregnancy (Z34.-)*

ludes2: *mental and behavioral disorders associated with the puerperium (F53)*
obstetrical tetanus (A34)
postpartum necrosis of pituitary gland (E23.0)
puerperal osteomalacia (M83.0)

s chapter contains the following category blocks:

O00-O08 Pregnancy with abortive outcome
O09 Supervision of high risk pregnancy
O10-O16 Edema, proteinuria and hypertensive disorders in pregnancy, childbirth and the puerperium
O20-O29 Other maternal disorders predominantly related to pregnancy
O30-O48 Maternal care related to the fetus and amniotic cavity and possible delivery problems
O60-O77 Complications of labor and delivery
O80-O82 Encounter for delivery
O85-O92 Complications predominantly related to the puerperium
O94-O9A Other obstetric conditions, not elsewhere classified

Chapter-Specific Coding Guidelines

ddition to general coding guidelines, there are guidelines for specific diagnoses /or conditions in the classification. Unless otherwise indicated, these guidelines ly to all health care settings. Please refer to Section II for guidelines on the ction of principal diagnosis.

Chapter 15: Pregnancy, Childbirth and the Puerperium (O00-O9A)

a. General Rules for Obstetric Cases

1) Codes from chapter 15 and sequencing priority

Obstetric cases require codes from chapter 15, codes in the range O00-O9A, Pregnancy, Childbirth, and the Puerperium. Chapter 15 codes have sequencing priority over codes from other chapters. Additional codes from other chapters may be used in conjunction with chapter 15 codes to further specify conditions. Should the provider document that the pregnancy is incidental to the encounter, then code Z33.1, Pregnant state, incidental, should be used in place of any chapter 15 codes. It is the provider's responsibility to state that the condition being treated is not affecting the pregnancy.

2) Chapter 15 codes used only on the maternal record

Chapter 15 codes are to be used only on the maternal record, never on the record of the newborn.

3) Final character for trimester

The majority of codes in Chapter 15 have a final character indicating the trimester of pregnancy. The timeframes for the trimesters are indicated at the beginning of the chapter. If trimester is not a component of a code it is because the condition always occurs in a specific trimester, or the concept of trimester of pregnancy is not applicable. Certain codes have characters for only certain trimesters because the condition does not occur in all trimesters, but it may occur in more than just one.

Assignment of the final character for trimester should be based on the provider's documentation of the trimester (or number of weeks) for the current admission/encounter. This applies to the assignment of trimester for pre-existing conditions as well as those that develop during or are due to the pregnancy. The provider's documentation of the number of weeks may be used to assign the appropriate code identifying the trimester.

Whenever delivery occurs during the current admission, and there is an "in childbirth" option for the obstetric complication being coded, the "in childbirth" code should be assigned.

4) Selection of trimester for inpatient admissions that encompass more than one trimester

In instances when a patient is admitted to a hospital for complications of pregnancy during one trimester and remains in the hospital into a subsequent trimester, the trimester character for the antepartum complication code should be assigned on the basis of the trimester when the complication developed, not the trimester of the discharge. If the condition developed prior to the current admission/encounter or represents a pre-existing condition, the trimester character for the trimester at the time of the admission/encounter should be assigned.

5) Unspecified trimester

Each category that includes codes for trimester has a code for "unspecified trimester." The "unspecified trimester" code should rarely be used, such as when the documentation in the record is insufficient to determine the trimester and it is not possible to obtain clarification.

6) 7th character for Fetus Identification

Where applicable, a 7th character is to be assigned for certain categories (O31, O32, O33.3 - O33.6, O35, O36, O40, O41, O60.1, O60.2, O64, and O69) to identify the fetus for which the complication code applies.

Assign 7th character "0":

- For single gestations
- When the documentation in the record is insufficient to determine the fetus affected and it is not possible to obtain clarification.
- When it is not possible to clinically determine which fetus is affected.

b. Selection of OB Principal or First-listed Diagnosis

1) Routine outpatient prenatal visits

For routine outpatient prenatal visits when no complications are present, a code from category Z34, Encounter for supervision of normal pregnancy, should be used as the first-listed diagnosis. These codes should not be used in conjunction with chapter 15 codes.

2) Prenatal outpatient visits for high-risk patients

For routine prenatal outpatient visits for patients with high-risk pregnancies, a code from category O09, Supervision of high-risk pregnancy, should be used as the first-listed diagnosis. Secondary chapter 15 codes may be used in conjunction with these codes if appropriate.

3) Episodes when no delivery occurs

In episodes when no delivery occurs, the principal diagnosis should correspond to the principal complication of the pregnancy which necessitated the encounter. Should more than one complication exist, all of which are treated or monitored, any of the complications codes may be sequenced first.

4) When a delivery occurs

When a delivery occurs, the principal diagnosis should correspond to the main circumstances or complication of the delivery. In cases of cesarean delivery, the selection of the principal diagnosis should be the condition established after study that was responsible for the patient's admission. If the patient was admitted with a condition that resulted in the performance of a cesarean procedure, that condition should be selected as the principal diagnosis. If the reason for the admission/encounter was unrelated to the condition resulting in the cesarean delivery, the condition related to the reason for the admission/encounter should be selected as the principal diagnosis.

5) Outcome of delivery

A code from category Z37, Outcome of delivery, should be included on every maternal record when a delivery has occurred. These codes are not to be used on subsequent records or on the newborn record.

c. Pre-existing conditions versus conditions due to the pregnancy

Certain categories in Chapter 15 distinguish between conditions of the mother that existed prior to pregnancy (pre-existing) and those that are a direct result of pregnancy. When assigning codes from Chapter 15, it is important to assess if a condition was pre-existing prior to pregnancy or developed during or due to the pregnancy in order to assign the correct code.

Categories that do not distinguish between pre-existing and pregnancy- related conditions may be used for either. It is acceptable to use codes specifically for the puerperium with codes complicating pregnancy and childbirth if a condition arises postpartum during the delivery encounter.

d. Pre-existing hypertension in pregnancy

Category O10, Pre-existing hypertension complicating pregnancy, childbirth and the puerperium, includes codes for hypertensive heart and hypertensive chronic kidney disease. When assigning one of the O10 codes that includes hypertensive heart disease or hypertensive chronic kidney disease, it is necessary to add a secondary code from the appropriate hypertension category to specify the type of heart failure or chronic kidney disease.

See Section I.C.9. Hypertension.

e. Fetal Conditions Affecting the Management of the Mother

1) Codes from categories O35 and O36

Codes from categories O35, Maternal care for known or suspected fetal abnormality and damage, and O36, Maternal care for other fetal problems, are assigned only when the fetal condition is actually responsible for modifying the management of the mother, i.e., by requiring diagnostic studies, additional observation, special care, or termination of pregnancy. The fact that the fetal condition exists does not justify assigning a code from this series to the mother's record.

2) In utero surgery

In cases when surgery is performed on the fetus, a diagnosis code from category O35, Maternal care for known or suspected fetal abnormality and damage, should be assigned identifying the fetal condition. Assign the appropriate procedure code for the procedure performed.

No code from Chapter 16, the perinatal codes, should be used on the mother's record to identify fetal conditions. Surgery performed in utero on a fetus is still to be coded as an obstetric encounter.

f. HIV Infection in Pregnancy, Childbirth and the Puerperium

During pregnancy, childbirth or the puerperium, a patient admitted because of an HIV-related illness should receive a principal diagnosis from subcategory O98.7-, Human immunodeficiency [HIV] disease complicating pregnancy, childbirth and the puerperium, followed by the code(s) for the HIV-related illness(es).

Patients with asymptomatic HIV infection status admitted during pregnancy, childbirth, or the puerperium should receive codes of O98.7- and Z21, Asymptomatic human immunodeficiency virus [HIV] infection status.

g. Diabetes mellitus in pregnancy

Diabetes mellitus is a significant complicating factor in pregnancy. Pregnant women who are diabetic should be assigned a code from category O24, Diabetes mellitus in pregnancy, childbirth, and the puerperium, first, followed by the appropriate diabetes code(s) (E08- E13) from Chapter 4.

h. Long term use of insulin

Code Z79.4, Long-term (current) use of insulin, should also be assigned if the diabetes mellitus is being treated with insulin.

i. Gestational (pregnancy induced) diabetes

Gestational (pregnancy induced) diabetes can occur during the second and third trimester of pregnancy in women who were not diabetic prior to pregnancy. Gestational diabetes can cause complications in the pregnancy similar to those of pre-existing diabetes mellitus. It also puts the woman at greater risk of developing diabetes after the pregnancy. Codes for gestational diabetes are in subcategory O24.4, Gestational diabetes mellitus. No other code from category O24, Diabetes mellitus in pregnancy, childbirth, and the puerperium, should be used with a code from O24.4

The codes under subcategory O24.4 include diet controlled and insulin controlled. If a patient with gestational diabetes is treated with both diet and insulin, only the code for insulin-controlled is required.

Code Z79.4, Long-term (current) use of insulin, should not be assigned with codes from subcategory O24.4.

An abnormal glucose tolerance in pregnancy is assigned a code from subcategory O99.81, Abnormal glucose complicating pregnancy, childbirth, and the puerperium.

j. Sepsis and septic shock complicating abortion, pregnancy, childbirth and the puerperium

When assigning a chapter 15 code for sepsis complicating abortion, pregnancy, childbirth, and the puerperium, a code for the specific type of infection should be assigned as an additional diagnosis. If severe sepsis is present, a code from subcategory R65.2, Severe sepsis, and code(s) for associated organ dysfunction(s) should also be assigned as additional diagnoses.

k. Puerperal sepsis

Code O85, Puerperal sepsis, should be assigned with a secondary code to identify the causal organism (e.g., for a bacterial infection, assign a code from category B95-B96, Bacterial infections in conditions classified elsewhere). A code from category A40, Streptococcal sepsis, or A41, Other sepsis, should not be used for puerperal sepsis. If applicable, use additional codes to identify severe sepsis (R65.2-) and any associated acute organ dysfunction.

l. Alcohol and tobacco use during pregnancy, childbirth and the puerperium

1) Alcohol use during pregnancy, childbirth and the puerperium

Codes under subcategory O99.31, Alcohol use complicating pregnancy, childbirth, and the puerperium, should be assigned for any pregnancy case when a mother uses alcohol during the pregnancy or postpartum. A secondary code from category F10, Alcohol related disorders, should also be assigned to identify manifestations of the alcohol use.

2) Tobacco use during pregnancy, childbirth and the puerperium

Codes under subcategory O99.33, Smoking (tobacco) complicating pregnancy, childbirth, and the puerperium, should be assigned for any pregnancy case when a mother uses any type of tobacco product during the pregnancy or postpartum.

A secondary code from category F17, Nicotine dependence, should also be assigned to identify the type of nicotine dependence.

m. Poisoning, toxic effects, adverse effects and underdosing in a preg patient

A code from subcategory O9A.2, Injury, poisoning and certain c consequences of external causes complicating pregnancy, childbirth, and puerperium, should be sequenced first, followed by the appropriate in poisoning, toxic effect, adverse effect or underdosing code, and then additional code(s) that specifies the condition caused by the poisoning, t effect, adverse effect or underdosing.

See Section I.C.19. Adverse effects, poisoning, underdosing and toxic effec

n. Normal Delivery, Code O80

1) Encounter for full term uncomplicated delivery

Code O80 should be assigned when a woman is admitted for a term normal delivery and delivers a single, healthy infant without complications antepartum, during the delivery, or postpartum during delivery episode. Code O80 is always a principal diagnosis. It is nc be used if any other code from chapter 15 is needed to describe a cur complication of the antenatal, delivery, or perinatal period. Additional c from other chapters may be used with code O80 if they are not related t are in any way complicating the pregnancy.

2) Uncomplicated delivery with resolved antepartum complication

Code O80 may be used if the patient had a complication at some p during the pregnancy, but the complication is not present at the time of admission for delivery.

3) Outcome of delivery for O80

Z37.0, Single live birth, is the only outcome of delivery code appropriate use with O80.

o. The Peripartum and Postpartum Periods

1) Peripartum and Postpartum periods

The postpartum period begins immediately after delivery and continues six weeks following delivery. The peripartum period is defined as the month of pregnancy to five months postpartum.

2) Peripartum and postpartum complication

A postpartum complication is any complication occurring within the week period.

3) Pregnancy-related complications after 6 week period

Chapter 15 codes may also be used to describe pregnancy-rel complications after the peripartum or postpartum period if the prov documents that a condition is pregnancy related.

4) Admission for routine postpartum care following delivery out hospital

When the mother delivers outside the hospital prior to admission an admitted for routine postpartum care and no complications are noted, c Z39.0, Encounter for care and examination of mother immediately a delivery, should be assigned as the principal diagnosis.

5) Pregnancy associated cardiomyopathy

Pregnancy associated cardiomyopathy, code O90.3, is unique in tha may be diagnosed in the third trimester of pregnancy but may continu progress months after delivery. For this reason, it is referred to as peripar cardiomyopathy. Code O90.3 is only for use when the cardiomyopa develops as a result of pregnancy in a woman who did not have pre-exis heart disease.

p. Code O94, Sequelae of complication of pregnancy, childbirth, and puerperium

1) Code O94

Code O94, Sequelae of complication of pregnancy, childbirth, and puerperium, is for use in those cases when an initial complication c pregnancy develops a sequelae requiring care or treatment at a future date.

2) After the initial postpartum period

This code may be used at any time after the initial postpartum period.

3) Sequencing of Code O94

This code, like all sequela codes, is to be sequenced following the c describing the sequelae of the complication.

q. *Termination of Pregnancy and Spontaneous abortions*

1) Abortion with Liveborn Fetus

When an attempted termination of pregnancy results in a liveborn fe assign code Z33.2, Encounter for elective termination of pregnancy an code from category Z37, Outcome of Delivery.

2) Retained Products of Conception following an abortion

Subsequent encounters for retained products of conception followin spontaneous abortion or elective termination of pregnancy are assigned appropriate code from category O03, Spontaneous abortion, or codes O0

Failed attempted termination of pregnancy without complication and Z33.2, Encounter for elective termination of pregnancy. This advice is appropriate even when the patient was discharged previously with a discharge diagnosis of complete abortion.

3) Complications leading to abortion

Codes from Chapter 15 may be used as additional codes to identify any documented complications of the pregnancy in conjunction with codes in categories in O07 and O08.

r. Abuse in a pregnant patient

For suspected or confirmed cases of abuse of a pregnant patient, a code(s) from subcategories O9A.3, Physical abuse complicating pregnancy, childbirth, and the puerperium, O9A.4, Sexual abuse complicating pregnancy, childbirth, and the puerperium, and O9A.5, Psychological abuse complicating pregnancy, childbirth, and the puerperium, should be sequenced first, followed by the appropriate codes (if applicable) to identify any associated current injury due to physical abuse, sexual abuse, and the perpetrator of abuse.

See Section I.C.19. Adult and child abuse, neglect and other maltreatment.

egnancy with abortive outcome (O00-O08)

cludes1: *continuing pregnancy in multiple gestation after abortion of one fetus or more (O31.1-, O31.3-)*

O00 Ectopic pregnancy

Includes: ruptured ectopic pregnancy
Use additional code from category O08 to identify any associated complication

• ♀ CC **O00.0 Abdominal pregnancy**
Excludes1: *maternal care for viable fetus in abdominal pregnancy (O36.7-)*
CC Exclusion see Appendix A PDX collection 0953

• ♀ CC **O00.1 Tubal pregnancy**
Fallopian pregnancy
Rupture of (fallopian) tube due to pregnancy
Tubal abortion
CC Exclusion see Appendix A PDX collection 0953

• ♀ CC **O00.2 Ovarian pregnancy**
CC Exclusion see Appendix A PDX collection 0953

• ♀ CC **O00.8 Other ectopic pregnancy**
Cervical pregnancy
Cornual pregnancy
Intraligamentous pregnancy
Mural pregnancy
CC Exclusion see Appendix A PDX collection 0953

• ♀ CC **O00.9 Ectopic pregnancy, unspecified**
CC Exclusion see Appendix A PDX collection 0953

O01 Hydatidiform mole

Use additional code from category O08 to identify any associated complication.
Excludes1: *chorioadenoma (destruens) (D39.2)*
malignant hydatidiform mole (D39.2)

• ♀ **O01.0 Classical hydatidiform mole**
Complete hydatidiform mole

• ♀ **O01.1 Incomplete and partial hydatidiform mole**

• ♀ **O01.9 Hydatidiform mole, unspecified**
Trophoblastic disease NOS
Vesicular mole NOS

O02 Other abnormal products of conception

Use additional code from category O08 to identify any associated complication.
Excludes1: *papyraceous fetus (O31.0-)*

• ♀ **O02.0 Blighted ovum and nonhydatidiform mole**
Carneous mole
Fleshy mole
Intrauterine mole NOS
Molar pregnancy NEC
Pathological ovum

• ♀ **O02.1 Missed abortion**
Early fetal death, before completion of 20 weeks of gestation, with retention of dead fetus
Excludes1: *failed induced abortion (O07.-)*
fetal death (intrauterine) (late) (O36.4)
missed abortion with blighted ovum (O02.0)
missed abortion with hydatidiform mole (O01.-)
missed abortion with nonhydatidiform (O02.0)
missed abortion with other abnormal products of conception (O02.8-)
missed delivery (O36.4)
stillbirth (P95)

\+ **O02.8 Other specified abnormal products of conception**
Excludes1: *abnormal products of conception with blighted ovum (O02.0)*
abnormal products of conception with hydatidiform mole (O01.-)
abnormal products of conception with nonhydatidiform mole (O02.0)

• ♀ **O02.81 Inappropriate change in quantitative human chorionic gonadotropin (hCG) in early pregnancy**
Biochemical pregnancy
Chemical pregnancy
Inappropriate level of quantitative human chorionic gonadotropin (hCG) for gestational age in early pregnancy

• ♀ **O02.89 Other abnormal products of conception**

• ♀ **O02.9 Abnormal product of conception, unspecified**

O03 Spontaneous abortion

NOTE Incomplete abortion includes retained products of conception following spontaneous abortion
Includes: miscarriage
Review coding guideline C.15.q.2

• ♀ CC **O03.0 Genital tract and pelvic infection following incomplete spontaneous abortion**
Endometritis following incomplete spontaneous abortion
Oophoritis following incomplete spontaneous abortion
Parametritis following incomplete spontaneous abortion
Pelvic peritonitis following incomplete spontaneous abortion
Salpingitis following incomplete spontaneous abortion
Salpingo-oophoritis following incomplete spontaneous abortion
Excludes1: *sepsis following incomplete spontaneous abortion (O03.37)*
urinary tract infection following incomplete spontaneous abortion (O03.38)
CC Exclusion see Appendix A PDX collection 0954

• ♀ **O03.1 Delayed or excessive hemorrhage following incomplete spontaneous abortion**
Afibrinogenemia following incomplete spontaneous abortion
Defibrination syndrome following incomplete spontaneous abortion
Hemolysis following incomplete spontaneous abortion
Intravascular coagulation following incomplete spontaneous abortion

• ♀ MCC **O03.2 Embolism following incomplete spontaneous abortion**
Air embolism following incomplete spontaneous abortion
Amniotic fluid embolism following incomplete spontaneous abortion
Blood-clot embolism following incomplete spontaneous abortion
Embolism NOS following incomplete spontaneous abortion
Fat embolism following incomplete spontaneous abortion
Pulmonary embolism following incomplete spontaneous abortion
Pyemic embolism following incomplete spontaneous abortion
Septic or septicopyemic embolism following incomplete spontaneous abortion
Soap embolism following incomplete spontaneous abortion
MCC Exclusion see Appendix A PDX collection 0954
Review coding guideline C.15.j

\+ **O03.3 Other and unspecified complications following incomplete spontaneous abortion**

• ♀ CC **O03.30 Unspecified complication following incomplete spontaneous abortion**
CC Exclusion see Appendix A PDX collection 0954

• ♀ MCC **O03.31 Shock following incomplete spontaneous abortion**
Circulatory collapse following incomplete spontaneous abortion
Shock (postprocedural) following incomplete spontaneous abortion
Excludes1: *shock due to infection following incomplete spontaneous abortion (O03.37)*
MCC Exclusion see Appendix A PDX collection 0954

• ♀ MCC **O03.32 Renal failure following incomplete spontaneous abortion**
Kidney failure (acute) following incomplete spontaneous abortion
Oliguria following incomplete spontaneous abortion
Renal shutdown following incomplete spontaneous abortion
Renal tubular necrosis following incomplete spontaneous abortion
Uremia following incomplete spontaneous abortion
MCC Exclusion see Appendix A PDX collection 0954

● ♀ CC **O03.33 Metabolic disorder following incomplete spontaneous abortion**
CC Exclusion see Appendix A PDX collection 0954

● ♀ CC **O03.34 Damage to pelvic organs following incomplete spontaneous abortion**
Laceration, perforation, tear or chemical damage of bladder following incomplete spontaneous abortion
Laceration, perforation, tear or chemical damage of bowel following incomplete spontaneous abortion
Laceration, perforation, tear or chemical damage of broad ligament following incomplete spontaneous abortion
Laceration, perforation, tear or chemical damage of cervix following incomplete spontaneous abortion
Laceration, perforation, tear or chemical damage of periurethral tissue following incomplete spontaneous abortion
Laceration, perforation, tear or chemical damage of uterus following incomplete spontaneous abortion
Laceration, perforation, tear or chemical damage of vagina following incomplete spontaneous abortion
CC Exclusion see Appendix A PDX collection 0954

● ♀ CC **O03.35 Other venous complications following incomplete spontaneous abortion**
CC Exclusion see Appendix A PDX collection 0954

● ♀ CC **O03.36 Cardiac arrest following incomplete spontaneous abortion**
CC Exclusion see Appendix A PDX collection 0954

● ♀ CC **O03.37 Sepsis following incomplete spontaneous abortion**
Use additional code to identify infectious agent (B95-B97)

Use additional code to identify severe sepsis, if applicable (R65.2-)
Excludes1: *septic or septicopyemic embolism following incomplete spontaneous abortion (O03.2)*
CC Exclusion see Appendix A PDX collection 0954
Review coding guideline C.15.j

● ♀ CC **O03.38 Urinary tract infection following incomplete spontaneous abortion**
Cystitis following incomplete spontaneous abortion
CC Exclusion see Appendix A PDX collection 0954

● ♀ CC **O03.39 Incomplete spontaneous abortion with other complications**
CC Exclusion see Appendix A PDX collection 0954

● ♀ **O03.4 Incomplete spontaneous abortion without complication**

● ♀ CC **O03.5 Genital tract and pelvic infection following complete or unspecified spontaneous abortion**
Endometritis following complete or unspecified spontaneous abortion
Oophoritis following complete or unspecified spontaneous abortion
Parametritis following complete or unspecified spontaneous abortion
Pelvic peritonitis following complete or unspecified spontaneous abortion
Salpingitis following complete or unspecified spontaneous abortion
Salpingo-oophoritis following complete or unspecified spontaneous abortion
Excludes1: *sepsis following complete or unspecified spontaneous abortion (O03.87)*
urinary tract infection following complete or unspecified spontaneous abortion (O03.88)
CC Exclusion see Appendix A PDX collection 0954

● ♀ **O03.6 Delayed or excessive hemorrhage following complete or unspecified spontaneous abortion**
Afibrinogenemia following complete or unspecified spontaneous abortion
Defibrination syndrome following complete or unspecified spontaneous abortion
Hemolysis following complete or unspecified spontaneous abortion
Intravascular coagulation following complete or unspecified spontaneous abortion

● ♀ CC **O03.7 Embolism following complete or unspecified spontaneous abortion**
Air embolism following complete or unspecified spontaneous abortion
Amniotic fluid embolism following complete or unspecified spontaneous abortion
Blood-clot embolism following complete or unspecified spontaneous abortion
Embolism NOS following complete or unspecified spontaneous abortion
Fat embolism following complete or unspecified spontaneous abortion
Pulmonary embolism following complete or unspecified spontaneous abortion
Pyemic embolism following complete or unspecified spontaneous abortion
Septic or septicopyemic embolism following complete or unspecified spontaneous abortion
Soap embolism following complete or unspecified spontaneous abortion
CC Exclusion see Appendix A PDX collection 0954

\+ **O03.8 Other and unspecified complications following complete or unspecified spontaneous abortion**

● ♀ CC **O03.80 Unspecified complication following complete or unspecified spontaneous abortion**
CC Exclusion see Appendix A PDX collection 0954

● ♀ MCC **O03.81 Shock following complete or unspecified spontaneous abortion**
Circulatory collapse following complete or unspecified spontaneous abortion
Shock (postprocedural) following complete or unspecified spontaneous abortion
Excludes1: *shock due to infection following complete or unspecified spontaneous abortion (O03.87)*
MCC Exclusion see Appendix A PDX collection 0954

● ♀ MCC **O03.82 Renal failure following complete or unspecified spontaneous abortion**
Kidney failure (acute) following complete or unspecified spontaneous abortion
Oliguria following complete or unspecified spontaneous abortion
Renal shutdown following complete or unspecified spontaneous abortion
Renal tubular necrosis following complete or unspecified spontaneous abortion
Uremia following complete or unspecified spontaneous abortion
MCC Exclusion see Appendix A PDX collection 0954

● ♀ CC **O03.83 Metabolic disorder following complete or unspecified spontaneous abortion**
CC Exclusion see Appendix A PDX collection 0954

● ♀ CC **O03.84 Damage to pelvic organs following complete or unspecified spontaneous abortion**
Laceration, perforation, tear or chemical damage of bladder following complete or unspecified spontaneous abortion
Laceration, perforation, tear or chemical damage of bowel following complete or unspecified spontaneous abortion
Laceration, perforation, tear or chemical damage of broad ligament following complete or unspecified spontaneous abortion
Laceration, perforation, tear or chemical damage of cervix following complete or unspecified spontaneous abortion
Laceration, perforation, tear or chemical damage of periurethral tissue following complete or unspecified spontaneous abortion
Laceration, perforation, tear or chemical damage of uterus following complete or unspecified spontaneous abortion
Laceration, perforation, tear or chemical damage of vagina following complete or unspecified spontaneous abortion
CC Exclusion see Appendix A PDX collection 0954

● ♀ CC **O03.85 Other venous complications following complete or unspecified spontaneous abortion**
CC Exclusion see Appendix A PDX collection 0954

● ♀ CC **O03.86 Cardiac arrest following complete or unspecified spontaneous abortion**

• ♀ CC **O03.87 Sepsis following complete or unspecified spontaneous abortion**
Use additional code to identify infectious agent (B95-B97)
Use additional code to identify severe sepsis, if applicable (R65.2-)
Excludes1: *septic or septicopyemic embolism following complete or unspecified spontaneous abortion (O03.7)*
CC Exclusion see Appendix A PDX collection 0954
Review coding guideline C.15.j

• ♀ CC **O03.88 Urinary tract infection following complete or unspecified spontaneous abortion**
Cystitis following complete or unspecified spontaneous abortion
CC Exclusion see Appendix A PDX collection 0954

• ♀ CC **O03.89 Complete or unspecified spontaneous abortion with other complications**
CC Exclusion see Appendix A PDX collection 0954

• ♀ **O03.9 Complete or unspecified spontaneous abortion without complication**
Miscarriage NOS
Spontaneous abortion NOS

O04 Complications following (induced) termination of pregnancy

Includes: complications following (induced) termination of pregnancy
Excludes1: *encounter for elective termination of pregnancy, uncomplicated (Z33.2)*
failed attempted termination of pregnancy (O07.-)

♀ CC **O04.5 Genital tract and pelvic infection following (induced) termination of pregnancy**
Endometritis following (induced) termination of pregnancy
Oophoritis following (induced) termination of pregnancy
Parametritis following (induced) termination of pregnancy
Pelvic peritonitis following (induced) termination of pregnancy
Salpingitis following (induced) termination of pregnancy
Salpingo-oophoritis following (induced) termination of pregnancy
Excludes1: *sepsis following (induced) termination of pregnancy (O04.87)*
urinary tract infection following (induced) termination of pregnancy (O04.88)
CC Exclusion see Appendix A PDX collection 0954

• ♀ **O04.6 Delayed or excessive hemorrhage following (induced) termination of pregnancy**
Afibrinogenemia following (induced) termination of pregnancy
Defibrination syndrome following (induced) termination of pregnancy
Hemolysis following (induced) termination of pregnancy
Intravascular coagulation following (induced) termination of pregnancy

MCC **O04.7 Embolism following (induced) termination of pregnancy**
Air embolism following (induced) termination of pregnancy
Amniotic fluid embolism following (induced) termination of pregnancy
Blood-clot embolism following (induced) termination of pregnancy
Embolism NOS following (induced) termination of pregnancy
Fat embolism following (induced) termination of pregnancy
Pulmonary embolism following (induced) termination of pregnancy
Pyemic embolism following (induced) termination of pregnancy
Septic or septicopyemic embolism following (induced) termination of pregnancy
Soap embolism following (induced) termination of pregnancy
MCC Exclusion see Appendix A PDX collection 0954

\+ **O04.8 (Induced) termination of pregnancy with other and unspecified complications**

• ♀ CC **O04.80 (Induced) termination of pregnancy with unspecified complications**
CC Exclusion see Appendix A PDX collection 0954

• ♀ MCC **O04.81 Shock following (induced) termination of pregnancy**
Circulatory collapse following (induced) termination of pregnancy
Shock (postprocedural) following (induced) termination of pregnancy
Excludes1: *shock due to infection following (induced) termination of pregnancy (O04.87)*
MCC Exclusion see Appendix A PDX collection 0954

• ♀ MCC **O04.82 Renal failure following (induced) termination of pregnancy**
Kidney failure (acute) following (induced) termination of pregnancy
Oliguria following (induced) termination of pregnancy
Renal shutdown following (induced) termination of pregnancy
Renal tubular necrosis following (induced) termination of pregnancy
Uremia following (induced) termination of pregnancy
MCC Exclusion see Appendix A PDX collection 0954

• ♀ CC **O04.83 Metabolic disorder following (induced) termination of pregnancy**
CC Exclusion see Appendix A PDX collection 0954

• ♀ CC **O04.84 Damage to pelvic organs following (induced) termination of pregnancy**
Laceration, perforation, tear or chemical damage of bladder following (induced) termination of pregnancy
Laceration, perforation, tear or chemical damage of bowel following (induced) termination of pregnancy
Laceration, perforation, tear or chemical damage of broad ligament following (induced) termination of pregnancy
Laceration, perforation, tear or chemical damage of cervix following (induced) termination of pregnancy
Laceration, perforation, tear or chemical damage of periurethral tissue following (induced) termination of pregnancy
Laceration, perforation, tear or chemical damage of uterus following (induced) termination of pregnancy
Laceration, perforation, tear or chemical damage of vagina following (induced) termination of pregnancy
CC Exclusion see Appendix A PDX collection 0954

• ♀ CC **O04.85 Other venous complications following (induced) termination of pregnancy**
CC Exclusion see Appendix A PDX collection 0954

• ♀ CC **O04.86 Cardiac arrest following (induced) termination of pregnancy**
CC Exclusion see Appendix A PDX collection 0954

• ♀ CC **O04.87 Sepsis following (induced) termination of pregnancy**
Use additional code to identify infectious agent (B95-B97)
Use additional code to identify severe sepsis, if applicable (R65.2-)
Excludes1: *septic or septicopyemic embolism following (induced) termination of pregnancy (O04.7)*
CC Exclusion see Appendix A PDX collection 0954
Review coding guideline C.15.j

• ♀ CC **O04.88 Urinary tract infection following (induced) termination of pregnancy**
Cystitis following (induced) termination of pregnancy
CC Exclusion see Appendix A PDX collection 0954

• ♀ CC **O04.89 (Induced) termination of pregnancy with other complications**
CC Exclusion see Appendix A PDX collection 0954

O07 Failed attempted termination of pregnancy

Includes: failure of attempted induction of termination of pregnancy
incomplete elective abortion
Excludes1: *incomplete spontaneous abortion (O03.0-)*

• ♀ CC **O07.0 Genital tract and pelvic infection following failed attempted termination of pregnancy**
Endometritis following failed attempted termination of pregnancy
Oophoritis following failed attempted termination of pregnancy
Parametritis following failed attempted termination of pregnancy
Pelvic peritonitis following failed attempted termination of pregnancy
Salpingitis following failed attempted termination of pregnancy
Salpingo-oophoritis following failed attempted termination of pregnancy
Excludes1: *sepsis following failed attempted termination of pregnancy (O07.37)*
urinary tract infection following failed attempted termination of pregnancy (O07.38)
CC Exclusion see Appendix A PDX collection 0956

• ♀ CC **O07.1 Delayed or excessive hemorrhage following failed attempted termination of pregnancy**
Afibrinogenemia following failed attempted termination of pregnancy
Defibrination syndrome following failed attempted termination of pregnancy
Hemolysis following failed attempted termination of pregnancy
Intravascular coagulation following failed attempted termination of pregnancy
CC Exclusion see Appendix A PDX collection 0957

• ♀ MCC **O07.2 Embolism following failed attempted termination of pregnancy**
Air embolism following failed attempted termination of pregnancy
Amniotic fluid embolism following failed attempted termination of pregnancy
Blood-clot embolism following failed attempted termination of pregnancy
Embolism NOS following failed attempted termination of pregnancy
Fat embolism following failed attempted termination of pregnancy
Pulmonary embolism following failed attempted termination of pregnancy
Pyemic embolism following failed attempted termination of pregnancy
Septic or septicopyemic embolism following failed attempted termination of pregnancy
Soap embolism following failed attempted termination of pregnancy
MCC Exclusion see Appendix A PDX collection 0958

+ **O07.3 Failed attempted termination of pregnancy with other and unspecified complications**

• ♀ CC **O07.30 Failed attempted termination of pregnancy with unspecified complications**
CC Exclusion see Appendix A PDX collection 0954

• ♀ MCC **O07.31 Shock following failed attempted termination of pregnancy**
Circulatory collapse following failed attempted termination of pregnancy
Shock (postprocedural) following failed attempted termination of pregnancy
Excludes1: *shock due to infection following failed attempted termination of pregnancy (O07.37)*
MCC Exclusion see Appendix A PDX collection 0959

• ♀ MCC **O07.32 Renal failure following failed attempted termination of pregnancy**
Kidney failure (acute) following failed attempted termination of pregnancy
Oliguria following failed attempted termination of pregnancy
Renal shutdown following failed attempted termination of pregnancy
Renal tubular necrosis following failed attempted termination of pregnancy
Uremia following failed attempted termination of pregnancy
MCC Exclusion see Appendix A PDX collection 0960

• ♀ CC **O07.33 Metabolic disorder following failed attempted termination of pregnancy**
CC Exclusion see Appendix A PDX collection 0954

• ♀ CC **O07.34 Damage to pelvic organs following failed attempted termination of pregnancy**
Laceration, perforation, tear or chemical damage of bladder following failed attempted termination of pregnancy
Laceration, perforation, tear or chemical damage of bowel following failed attempted termination of pregnancy
Laceration, perforation, tear or chemical damage of broad ligament following failed attempted termination of pregnancy
Laceration, perforation, tear or chemical damage of cervix following failed attempted termination of pregnancy
Laceration, perforation, tear or chemical damage of periurethral tissue following failed attempted termination of pregnancy
Laceration, perforation, tear or chemical damage of uterus following failed attempted termination of pregnancy
Laceration, perforation, tear or chemical damage of vagina following failed attempted termination of pregnancy
CC Exclusion see Appendix A PDX collection 0961

• ♀ CC **O07.35 Other venous complications following failed attem termination of pregnancy**
CC Exclusion see Appendix A PDX collection 0954

• ♀ CC **O07.36 Cardiac arrest following failed attempted termina of pregnancy**
CC Exclusion see Appendix A PDX collection 0954

• ♀ CC **O07.37 Sepsis following failed attempted termination of pregnancy**
Use additional code (B95-B97), to identify infectiou agent

Use additional code (R65.2-) to identify severe sepsis, applicable
Excludes1: *septic or septicopyemic embolism follo failed attempted termination of pregnancy (O07.2)*
CC Exclusion see Appendix A PDX collection 0956
Review coding guideline C.15.j

• ♀ CC **O07.38 Urinary tract infection following failed attempted termination of pregnancy**
Cystitis following failed attempted termination of pregnancy
CC Exclusion see Appendix A PDX collection 0954

• ♀ CC **O07.39 Failed attempted termination of pregnancy with o complications**
CC Exclusion see Appendix A PDX collection 0954

• ♀ CC **O07.4 Failed attempted termination of pregnancy without complication**
Review coding guideline C.15.q.2

O08 Complications following ectopic and molar pregnancy

This category is for use with categories O00-O02 to identify any associated complications

• ♀ CC **O08.0 Genital tract and pelvic infection following ectopic and mol pregnancy**
Endometritis following ectopic and molar pregnancy
Oophoritis following ectopic and molar pregnancy
Parametritis following ectopic and molar pregnancy
Pelvic peritonitis following ectopic and molar pregnancy
Salpingitis following ectopic and molar pregnancy
Salpingo-oophoritis following ectopic and molar pregnancy
Excludes1: *sepsis following ectopic and molar pregnancy (O08.82)*
urinary tract infection (O08.83)
CC Exclusion see Appendix A PDX collection 0085

• ♀ CC **O08.1 Delayed or excessive hemorrhage following ectopic and mol pregnancy**
Afibrinogenemia following ectopic and molar pregnancy
Defibrination syndrome following ectopic and molar pregnar
Hemolysis following ectopic and molar pregnancy
Intravascular coagulation following ectopic and molar pregnan
Excludes1: *delayed or excessive hemorrhage due to incomp abortion (O03.1)*
CC Exclusion see Appendix A PDX collection 0962

• ♀ MCC **O08.2 Embolism following ectopic and molar pregnancy**
Air embolism following ectopic and molar pregnancy
Amniotic fluid embolism following ectopic and molar pregn
Blood-clot embolism following ectopic and molar pregnancy
Embolism NOS following ectopic and molar pregnancy
Fat embolism following ectopic and molar pregnancy
Pulmonary embolism following ectopic and molar pregnancy
Pyemic embolism following ectopic and molar pregnancy
Septic or septicopyemic embolism following ectopic and mc pregnancy
Soap embolism following ectopic and molar pregnancy
MCC Exclusion see Appendix A PDX collection 0963

• ♀ MCC **O08.3 Shock following ectopic and molar pregnancy**
Circulatory collapse following ectopic and molar pregnancy
Shock (postprocedural) following ectopic and molar pregnar
Excludes1: *shock due to infection following ectopic and mo pregnancy (O08.82)*
MCC Exclusion see Appendix A PDX collection 0963

• ♀ MCC **O08.4 Renal failure following ectopic and molar pregnancy**
Kidney failure (acute) following ectopic and molar pregnancy
Oliguria following ectopic and molar pregnancy
Renal shutdown following ectopic and molar pregnancy
Renal tubular necrosis following ectopic and molar pregnancy
Uremia following ectopic and molar pregnancy
MCC Exclusion see Appendix A PDX collection 0963

• ♀ CC **O08.5 Metabolic disorders following an ectopic and molar pregna**
CC Exclusion see Appendix A PDX collection 0963

• ♀ CC **O08.6 Damage to pelvic organs and tissues following an ectopic and molar pregnancy**
Laceration, perforation, tear or chemical damage of bladder following an ectopic and molar pregnancy
Laceration, perforation, tear or chemical damage of bowel following an ectopic and molar pregnancy
Laceration, perforation, tear or chemical damage of broad ligament following an ectopic and molar pregnancy
Laceration, perforation, tear or chemical damage of cervix following an ectopic and molar pregnancy
Laceration, perforation, tear or chemical damage of periurethral tissue following an ectopic and molar pregnancy
Laceration, perforation, tear or chemical damage of uterus following an ectopic and molar pregnancy
Laceration, perforation, tear or chemical damage of vagina following an ectopic and molar pregnancy
CC Exclusion see Appendix A PDX collection 0963

• ♀ CC **O08.7 Other venous complications following an ectopic and molar pregnancy**
CC Exclusion see Appendix A PDX collection 0963

+ **O08.8 Other complications following an ectopic and molar pregnancy**
• ♀ CC **O08.81 Cardiac arrest following an ectopic and molar pregnancy**
CC Exclusion see Appendix A PDX collection 0963
• ♀ CC **O08.82 Sepsis following ectopic and molar pregnancy**
Use additional code (B95-B97), to identify infectious agent

Use additional code (R65.2-) to identify severe sepsis, if applicable
Excludes1: *septic or septicopyemic embolism following ectopic and molar pregnancy (O08.2)*
CC Exclusion see Appendix A PDX collection 0085
Review coding guideline C.15.j
• ♀ CC **O08.83 Urinary tract infection following an ectopic and molar pregnancy**
Cystitis following an ectopic and molar pregnancy
CC Exclusion see Appendix A PDX collection 0963
• ♀ CC **O08.89 Other complications following an ectopic and molar pregnancy**
CC Exclusion see Appendix A PDX collection 0963

• ♀ CC **O08.9 Unspecified complication following an ectopic and molar pregnancy**
CC Exclusion see Appendix A PDX collection 0963

upervision of high risk pregnancy (O09)

O09 Supervision of high risk pregnancy
Review coding guideline C.15.b.2

+ **O09.0 Supervision of pregnancy with history of infertility**
• ♀ **O09.00 Supervision of pregnancy with history of infertility, unspecified trimester**
• ♀ **O09.01 Supervision of pregnancy with history of infertility, first trimester**
• ♀ **O09.02 Supervision of pregnancy with history of infertility, second trimester**
• ♀ **O09.03 Supervision of pregnancy with history of infertility, third trimester**

+ **O09.1 Supervision of pregnancy with history of ectopic or molar pregnancy**
• ♀ **O09.10 Supervision of pregnancy with history of ectopic or molar pregnancy, unspecified trimester**
• ♀ **O09.11 Supervision of pregnancy with history of ectopic or molar pregnancy, first trimester**
• ♀ **O09.12 Supervision of pregnancy with history of ectopic or molar pregnancy, second trimester**
• ♀ **O09.13 Supervision of pregnancy with history of ectopic or molar pregnancy, third trimester**

+ **O09.2 Supervision of pregnancy with other poor reproductive or obstetric history**
Excludes2: *pregnancy care for patient with history of recurrent pregnancy loss (O26.2-)*
+ **O09.21 Supervision of pregnancy with history of pre-term labor**
• ♀ **O09.211 Supervision of pregnancy with history of pre-term labor, first trimester**
• ♀ **O09.212 Supervision of pregnancy with history of pre-term labor, second trimester**
• ♀ **O09.213 Supervision of pregnancy with history of pre-term labor, third trimester**
• ♀ **O09.219 Supervision of pregnancy with history of pre-term labor, unspecified trimester**
+ **O09.29 Supervision of pregnancy with other poor reproductive or obstetric history**
Supervision of pregnancy with history of neonatal death
Supervision of pregnancy with history of stillbirth
• ♀ **O09.291 Supervision of pregnancy with other poor reproductive or obstetric history, first trimester**
• ♀ **O09.292 Supervision of pregnancy with other poor reproductive or obstetric history, second trimester**
• ♀ **O09.293 Supervision of pregnancy with other poor reproductive or obstetric history, third trimester**
• ♀ **O09.299 Supervision of pregnancy with other poor reproductive or obstetric history, unspecified trimester**

+ **O09.3 Supervision of pregnancy with insufficient antenatal care**
Supervision of concealed pregnancy
Supervision of hidden pregnancy
• ♀ **O09.30 Supervision of pregnancy with insufficient antenatal care, unspecified trimester**
• ♀ **O09.31 Supervision of pregnancy with insufficient antenatal care, first trimester**
• ♀ **O09.32 Supervision of pregnancy with insufficient antenatal care, second trimester**
• ♀ **O09.33 Supervision of pregnancy with insufficient antenatal care, third trimester**

+ **O09.4 Supervision of pregnancy with grand multiparity**
• ♀ **O09.40 Supervision of pregnancy with grand multiparity, unspecified trimester**
• ♀ **O09.41 Supervision of pregnancy with grand multiparity, first trimester**
• ♀ **O09.42 Supervision of pregnancy with grand multiparity, second trimester**
• ♀ **O09.43 Supervision of pregnancy with grand multiparity, third trimester**

+ **O09.5 Supervision of elderly primigravida and multigravida**
Pregnancy for a female 35 years and older at expected date of delivery
+ **O09.51 Supervision of elderly primigravida**
• ♀ **O09.511 Supervision of elderly primigravida, first trimester**
• ♀ **O09.512 Supervision of elderly primigravida, second trimester**
• ♀ **O09.513 Supervision of elderly primigravida, third trimester**
• ♀ **O09.519 Supervision of elderly primigravida, unspecified trimester**
+ **O09.52 Supervision of elderly multigravida**
• ♀ **O09.521 Supervision of elderly multigravida, first trimester**
• ♀ **O09.522 Supervision of elderly multigravida, second trimester**
• ♀ **O09.523 Supervision of elderly multigravida, third trimester**
• ♀ **O09.529 Supervision of elderly multigravida, unspecified trimester**

+ **O09.6 Supervision of young primigravida and multigravida**
Supervision of pregnancy for a female less than 16 years old at expected date of delivery
+ **O09.61 Supervision of young primigravida**
• ♀ **O09.611 Supervision of young primigravida, first trimester**
• ♀ **O09.612 Supervision of young primigravida, second trimester**
• ♀ **O09.613 Supervision of young primigravida, third trimester**
• ♀ **O09.619 Supervision of young primigravida, unspecified trimester**
+ **O09.62 Supervision of young multigravida**
• ♀ **O09.621 Supervision of young multigravida, first trimester**
• ♀ **O09.622 Supervision of young multigravida, second trimester**
• ♀ **O09.623 Supervision of young multigravida, third trimester**
• ♀ **O09.629 Supervision of young multigravida, unspecified trimester**

+ **O09.7 Supervision of high risk pregnancy due to social problems**
- • ♀ **O09.70 Supervision of high risk pregnancy due to social problems, unspecified trimester**
- • ♀ **O09.71 Supervision of high risk pregnancy due to social problems, first trimester**
- • ♀ **O09.72 Supervision of high risk pregnancy due to social problems, second trimester**
- • ♀ **O09.73 Supervision of high risk pregnancy due to social problems, third trimester**

+ **O09.8 Supervision of other high risk pregnancies**
+ **O09.81 Supervision of pregnancy resulting from assisted reproductive technology**
  Supervision of pregnancy resulting from in-vitro fertilization
- • ♀ **O09.811 Supervision of pregnancy resulting from assisted reproductive technology, first trimester**
- • ♀ **O09.812 Supervision of pregnancy resulting from assisted reproductive technology, second trimester**
- • ♀ **O09.813 Supervision of pregnancy resulting from assisted reproductive technology, third trimester**
- • ♀ **O09.819 Supervision of pregnancy resulting from assisted reproductive technology, unspecified trimester**

+ **O09.82 Supervision of pregnancy with history of in utero procedure during previous pregnancy**
- • ♀ **O09.821 Supervision of pregnancy with history of in utero procedure during previous pregnancy, first trimester**
- • ♀ **O09.822 Supervision of pregnancy with history of in utero procedure during previous pregnancy, second trimester**
- • ♀ **O09.823 Supervision of pregnancy with history of in utero procedure during previous pregnancy, third trimester**
- • ♀ **O09.829 Supervision of pregnancy with history of in utero procedure during previous pregnancy, unspecified trimester**
  Excludes1: *supervision of pregnancy affected by in utero procedure during current pregnancy (O35.7)*

+ **O09.89 Supervision of other high risk pregnancies**
- • ♀ **O09.891 Supervision of other high risk pregnancies, first trimester**
- • ♀ **O09.892 Supervision of other high risk pregnancies, second trimester**
- • ♀ **O09.893 Supervision of other high risk pregnancies, third trimester**
- • ♀ **O09.899 Supervision of other high risk pregnancies, unspecified trimester**

+ **O09.9 Supervision of high risk pregnancy, unspecified**
- • ♀ **O09.90 Supervision of high risk pregnancy, unspecified, unspecified trimester**
- • ♀ **O09.91 Supervision of high risk pregnancy, unspecified, first trimester**
- • ♀ **O09.92 Supervision of high risk pregnancy, unspecified, second trimester**
- • ♀ **O09.93 Supervision of high risk pregnancy, unspecified, third trimester**

Edema, proteinuria and hypertensive disorders in pregnancy, childbirth and the puerperium (O10-O16)

O10 Pre-existing hypertension complicating pregnancy, childbirth and the puerperium

Includes: pre-existing hypertension with pre-existing proteinuria complicating pregnancy, childbirth and the puerperium

Excludes2: *pre-existing hypertension with superimposed pre-eclampsia complicating pregnancy, childbirth and the puerperium (O11.-)*

Review coding guideline C.15.d

+ **O10.0 Pre-existing essential hypertension complicating pregnancy, childbirth and the puerperium**
  Any condition in I10 specified as a reason for obstetric care during pregnancy, childbirth or the puerperium
+ **O10.01 Pre-existing essential hypertension complicating pregnancy,**
- • ♀ CC **O10.011 Pre-existing essential hypertension complicating pregnancy, first trimester**
  CC Exclusion see Appendix A PDX collection 0964
- • ♀ CC **O10.012 Pre-existing essential hypertension complicating pregnancy, second trimester**
  CC Exclusion see Appendix A PDX collection 0964
- • ♀ CC **O10.013 Pre-existing essential hypertension complicating pregnancy, third trimester**
  CC Exclusion see Appendix A PDX collection 0964
- • ♀ **O10.019 Pre-existing essential hypertension complicating pregnancy, unspecified trimester**
- • ♀ CC **O10.02 Pre-existing essential hypertension complicating childbirth**
  CC Exclusion see Appendix A PDX collection 0964
- • ♀ **O10.03 Pre-existing essential hypertension complicating the puerperium**

+ **O10.1 Pre-existing hypertensive heart disease complicating pregnanc[y], childbirth and the puerperium**
  Any condition in I11 specified as a reason for obstetric care duri[ng] pregnancy, childbirth or the puerperium
  Use additional code from I11 to identify the type of hypertensi[ve] heart disease
+ **O10.11 Pre-existing hypertensive heart disease complicating pregnancy**
- • ♀ **O10.111 Pre-existing hypertensive heart disease complicating pregnancy, first trimester**
- • ♀ **O10.112 Pre-existing hypertensive heart disease complicating pregnancy, second trimester**
- • ♀ **O10.113 Pre-existing hypertensive heart disease complicating pregnancy, third trimester**
- • ♀ **O10.119 Pre-existing hypertensive heart disease complicating pregnancy, unspecified trimester**
- • ♀ **O10.12 Pre-existing hypertensive heart disease complicating childbirth**
- • ♀ **O10.13 Pre-existing hypertensive heart disease complicating the puerperium**

+ **O10.2 Pre-existing hypertensive chronic kidney disease complicating pregnancy, childbirth and the puerperium**
  Any condition in I12 specified as a reason for obstetric care during pregnancy, childbirth or the puerperium
  Use additional code from I12 to identify the type of hypertensi[ve] chronic kidney disease
+ **O10.21 Pre-existing hypertensive chronic kidney disease complicating pregnancy**
- • ♀ **O10.211 Pre-existing hypertensive chronic kidney disease complicating pregnancy, first trimester**
- • ♀ **O10.212 Pre-existing hypertensive chronic kidney disease complicating pregnancy, second trimester**
- • ♀ **O10.213 Pre-existing hypertensive chronic kidney disease complicating pregnancy, third trimester**
- • ♀ **O10.219 Pre-existing hypertensive chronic kidney disease complicating pregnancy, unspecifi[ed] trimester**
- • ♀ **O10.22 Pre-existing hypertensive chronic kidney disease complicating childbirth**
- • ♀ **O10.23 Pre-existing hypertensive chronic kidney disease complicating the puerperium**

+ **O10.3 Pre-existing hypertensive heart and chronic kidney disease complicating pregnancy, childbirth and the puerperium**
  Any condition in I13 specified as a reason for obstetric care during pregnancy, childbirth or the puerperium
  Use additional code from I13 to identify the type of hypertensi[ve] heart and chronic kidney disease
+ **O10.31 Pre-existing hypertensive heart and chronic kidney disease complicating pregnancy**
- • ♀ **O10.311 Pre-existing hypertensive heart and chron[ic] kidney disease complicating pregnancy, fi[rst] trimester**

• ♀ **O10.312 Pre-existing hypertensive heart and chronic kidney disease complicating pregnancy, second trimester**

• ♀ **O10.313 Pre-existing hypertensive heart and chronic kidney disease complicating pregnancy, third trimester**

• ♀ **O10.319 Pre-existing hypertensive heart and chronic kidney disease complicating pregnancy, unspecified trimester**

• ♀ **O10.32 Pre-existing hypertensive heart and chronic kidney disease complicating childbirth**

• ♀ **O10.33 Pre-existing hypertensive heart and chronic kidney disease complicating the puerperium**

+ **O10.4 Pre-existing secondary hypertension complicating pregnancy, childbirth and the puerperium**

Any condition in I15 specified as a reason for obstetric care during pregnancy, childbirth or the puerperium

Use additional code from I15 to identify the type of secondary hypertension

+ **O10.41 Pre-existing secondary hypertension complicating pregnancy**

• ♀ CC **O10.411 Pre-existing secondary hypertension complicating pregnancy, first trimester**
CC Exclusion see Appendix A PDX collection 0964

• ♀ CC **O10.412 Pre-existing secondary hypertension complicating pregnancy, second trimester**
CC Exclusion see Appendix A PDX collection 0964

• ♀ CC **O10.413 Pre-existing secondary hypertension complicating pregnancy, third trimester**
CC Exclusion see Appendix A PDX collection 0964

• ♀ **O10.419 Pre-existing secondary hypertension complicating pregnancy, unspecified trimester**

• ♀ MCC **O10.42 Pre-existing secondary hypertension complicating childbirth**
MCC Exclusion see Appendix A PDX collection 0964

• ♀ CC **O10.43 Pre-existing secondary hypertension complicating the puerperium**
CC Exclusion see Appendix A PDX collection 0964

+ **O10.9 Unspecified pre-existing hypertension complicating pregnancy, childbirth and the puerperium**

+ **O10.91 Unspecified pre-existing hypertension complicating pregnancy**

• ♀ CC **O10.911 Unspecified pre-existing hypertension complicating pregnancy, first trimester**
CC Exclusion see Appendix A PDX collection 0964

• ♀ CC **O10.912 Unspecified pre-existing hypertension complicating pregnancy, second trimester**
CC Exclusion see Appendix A PDX collection 0964

• ♀ CC **O10.913 Unspecified pre-existing hypertension complicating pregnancy, third trimester**
CC Exclusion see Appendix A PDX collection 0964

• ♀ **O10.919 Unspecified pre-existing hypertension complicating pregnancy, unspecified trimester**

• ♀ CC **O10.92 Unspecified pre-existing hypertension complicating childbirth**
CC Exclusion see Appendix A PDX collection 0964

• ♀ **O10.93 Unspecified pre-existing hypertension complicating the puerperium**

O11 Pre-existing hypertension with pre-eclampsia

Includes: conditions in O10 complicated by pre-eclampsia
pre-eclampsia superimposed pre-existing hypertension

Use additional code from O10 to identify the type of hypertension

♀ MCC **O11.1 Pre-existing hypertension with pre-eclampsia, first trimester**
MCC Exclusion see Appendix A PDX collection 0964

♀ MCC **O11.2 Pre-existing hypertension with pre-eclampsia, second trimester**
MCC Exclusion see Appendix A PDX collection 0964

♀ MCC **O11.3 Pre-existing hypertension with pre-eclampsia, third trimester**
MCC Exclusion see Appendix A PDX collection 0964

• ♀ **O11.9 Pre-existing hypertension with pre-eclampsia, unspecified trimester**

O12 Gestational [pregnancy-induced] edema and proteinuria without hypertension

+ **O12.0 Gestational edema**

• ♀ **O12.00 Gestational edema, unspecified trimester**

• ♀ **O12.01 Gestational edema, first trimester**

• ♀ **O12.02 Gestational edema, second trimester**

• ♀ **O12.03 Gestational edema, third trimester**

+ **O12.1 Gestational proteinuria**

• ♀ **O12.10 Gestational proteinuria, unspecified trimester**

• ♀ CC **O12.11 Gestational proteinuria, first trimester**
CC Exclusion see Appendix A PDX collection 0965

• ♀ CC **O12.12 Gestational proteinuria, second trimester**
CC Exclusion see Appendix A PDX collection 0965

• ♀ CC **O12.13 Gestational proteinuria, third trimester**
CC Exclusion see Appendix A PDX collection 0965

+ **O12.2 Gestational edema with proteinuria**

• ♀ **O12.20 Gestational edema with proteinuria, unspecified trimester**

• ♀ CC **O12.21 Gestational edema with proteinuria, first trimester**
CC Exclusion see Appendix A PDX collection 0965

• ♀ CC **O12.22 Gestational edema with proteinuria, second trimester**
CC Exclusion see Appendix A PDX collection 0965

• ♀ CC **O12.23 Gestational edema with proteinuria, third trimester**
CC Exclusion see Appendix A PDX collection 0965

O13 Gestational [pregnancy-induced] hypertension without significant proteinuria

Includes: gestational hypertension NOS

Review coding guideline C.9.a.7

• ♀ **O13.1 Gestational [pregnancy-induced] hypertension without significant proteinuria, first trimester**

• ♀ **O13.2 Gestational [pregnancy-induced] hypertension without significant proteinuria, second trimester**

• ♀ **O13.3 Gestational [pregnancy-induced] hypertension without significant proteinuria, third trimester**

• ♀ **O13.9 Gestational [pregnancy-induced] hypertension without significant proteinuria, unspecified trimester**

O14 Pre-eclampsia

Excludes1: *pre-existing hypertension with pre-eclampsia (O11)*

Review coding guideline C.9.a.7

+ **O14.0 Mild to moderate pre-eclampsia**

• ♀ **O14.00 Mild to moderate pre-eclampsia, unspecified trimester**

• ♀ CC **O14.02 Mild to moderate pre-eclampsia, second trimester**
CC Exclusion see Appendix A PDX collection 0964

• ♀ CC **O14.03 Mild to moderate pre-eclampsia, third trimester**
CC Exclusion see Appendix A PDX collection 0964

+ **O14.1 Severe pre-eclampsia**

Excludes1: *HELLP syndrome (O14.2-)*

• ♀ **O14.10 Severe pre-eclampsia, unspecified trimester**

• ♀ MCC **O14.12 Severe pre-eclampsia, second trimester**
MCC Exclusion see Appendix A PDX collection 0964

• ♀ MCC **O14.13 Severe pre-eclampsia, third trimester**
MCC Exclusion see Appendix A PDX collection 0964

+ **O14.2 HELLP syndrome**

Severe pre-eclampsia with hemolysis, elevated liver enzymes and low platelet count (HELLP)

• ♀ **O14.20 HELLP syndrome (HELLP), unspecified trimester**

• ♀ MCC **O14.22 HELLP syndrome (HELLP), second trimester**
MCC Exclusion see Appendix A PDX collection 0964

• ♀ MCC **O14.23 HELLP syndrome (HELLP), third trimester**
MCC Exclusion see Appendix A PDX collection 0964

+ **O14.9 Unspecified pre-eclampsia**

• ♀ **O14.90 Unspecified pre-eclampsia, unspecified trimester**

• ♀ CC **O14.92 Unspecified pre-eclampsia, second trimester**
CC Exclusion see Appendix A PDX collection 0964

• ♀ CC **O14.93 Unspecified pre-eclampsia, third trimester**
CC Exclusion see Appendix A PDX collection 0964

O15 Eclampsia

Includes: convulsions following conditions in O10-O14 and O16

+ **O15.0 Eclampsia in pregnancy**

• ♀ **O15.00 Eclampsia in pregnancy, unspecified trimester**

• ♀ MCC **O15.02 Eclampsia in pregnancy, second trimester**
MCC Exclusion see Appendix A PDX collection 0964

• ♀ MCC **O15.03 Eclampsia in pregnancy, third trimester**
MCC Exclusion see Appendix A PDX collection 0964

• ♀ MCC **O15.1 Eclampsia in labor**
MCC Exclusion see Appendix A PDX collection 0964

• ♀ MCC **O15.2 Eclampsia in the puerperium**
MCC Exclusion see Appendix A PDX collection 0964

• ♀ **O15.9 Eclampsia, unspecified as to time period**
Eclampsia NOS

O16 Unspecified maternal hypertension

• ♀ CC **O16.1 Unspecified maternal hypertension, first trimester**
CC Exclusion see Appendix A PDX collection 0964

• ♀ CC **O16.2 Unspecified maternal hypertension, second trimester**
CC Exclusion see Appendix A PDX collection 0964

• ♀ CC **O16.3 Unspecified maternal hypertension, third trimester**
CC Exclusion see Appendix A PDX collection 0964

• ♀ **O16.9 Unspecified maternal hypertension, unspecified trimester**

Other maternal disorders predominantly related to pregnancy (O20-O29)

Excludes2: *maternal care related to the fetus and amniotic cavity and possible delivery problems (O30-O48)*
maternal diseases classifiable elsewhere but complicating pregnancy, labor and delivery, and the puerperium (O98-O99)

O20 Hemorrhage in early pregnancy

Includes: hemorrhage before completion of 20 weeks gestation
Excludes1: *pregnancy with abortive outcome (O00-O08)*

• ♀ CC **O20.0 Threatened abortion**
Hemorrhage specified as due to threatened abortion
CC Exclusion see Appendix A PDX collection 0966

• ♀ **O20.8 Other hemorrhage in early pregnancy**

• ♀ CC **O20.9 Hemorrhage in early pregnancy, unspecified**
CC Exclusion see Appendix A PDX collection 0966

O21 Excessive vomiting in pregnancy

• ♀ **O21.0 Mild hyperemesis gravidarum**
Hyperemesis gravidarum, mild or unspecified, starting before the end of the 20th week of gestation

• ♀ **O21.1 Hyperemesis gravidarum with metabolic disturbance**
Hyperemesis gravidarum, starting before the end of the 20th week of gestation, with metabolic disturbance such as carbohydrate depletion
Hyperemesis gravidarum, starting before the end of the 20th week of gestation, with metabolic disturbance such as dehydration
Hyperemesis gravidarum, starting before the end of the 20th week of gestation, with metabolic disturbance such as electrolyte imbalance

• ♀ **O21.2 Late vomiting of pregnancy**
Excessive vomiting starting after 20 completed weeks of gestation

• ♀ **O21.8 Other vomiting complicating pregnancy**
Vomiting due to diseases classified elsewhere, complicating pregnancy
Use additional code, to identify cause.

• ♀ **O21.9 Vomiting of pregnancy, unspecified**

O22 Venous complications and hemorrhoids in pregnancy

Excludes1: *venous complications of:*
abortion NOS (O03.9)
ectopic or molar pregnancy (O08.7)
failed attempted abortion (O07.35)
induced abortion (O04.85)
spontaneous abortion (O03.89)

Excludes2: *obstetric pulmonary embolism (O88.-)*
venous complications and hemorrhoids of childbirth and the puerperium (O87.-)

+ **O22.0 Varicose veins of lower extremity in pregnancy**
Varicose veins NOS in pregnancy

• ♀ **O22.00 Varicose veins of lower extremity in pregnancy, unspecified trimester**

• ♀ **O22.01 Varicose veins of lower extremity in pregnancy, first trimester**

• ♀ **O22.02 Varicose veins of lower extremity in pregnancy, second trimester**

• ♀ **O22.03 Varicose veins of lower extremity in pregnancy, third trimester**

+ **O22.1 Genital varices in pregnancy**
Perineal varices in pregnancy
Vaginal varices in pregnancy
Vulval varices in pregnancy

• ♀ **O22.10 Genital varices in pregnancy, unspecified trimester**

• ♀ **O22.11 Genital varices in pregnancy, first trimester**

• ♀ **O22.12 Genital varices in pregnancy, second trimester**

• ♀ **O22.13 Genital varices in pregnancy, third trimester**

+ **O22.2 Superficial thrombophlebitis in pregnancy**
Phlebitis in pregnancy NOS
Thrombophlebitis of legs in pregnancy
Thrombosis in pregnancy NOS
Use additional code to identify the superficial thrombophlebitis (I80.0-)

• ♀ CC **O22.20 Superficial thrombophlebitis in pregnancy, unspeci trimester**
CC Exclusion see Appendix A PDX collection 0967

• ♀ CC **O22.21 Superficial thrombophlebitis in pregnancy, first trimester**
CC Exclusion see Appendix A PDX collection 0967

• ♀ CC **O22.22 Superficial thrombophlebitis in pregnancy, second trimester**
CC Exclusion see Appendix A PDX collection 0967

• ♀ CC **O22.23 Superficial thrombophlebitis in pregnancy, third trimester**
CC Exclusion see Appendix A PDX collection 0967

+ **O22.3 Deep phlebothrombosis in pregnancy**
Deep vein thrombosis, antepartum
Use additional code to identify the deep vein thrombosis (I82.4-, I82.5-, I82.62-. I82.72-)

Use additional code, if applicable, for associated long-term (current) use of anticoagulants (Z79.01)

• ♀ CC **O22.30 Deep phlebothrombosis in pregnancy, unspecified trimester**
CC Exclusion see Appendix A PDX collection 0967

• ♀ MCC **O22.31 Deep phlebothrombosis in pregnancy, first trimeste**
MCC Exclusion see Appendix A PDX collection 0967

• ♀ MCC **O22.32 Deep phlebothrombosis in pregnancy, second trime**
MCC Exclusion see Appendix A PDX collection 0967

• ♀ MCC **O22.33 Deep phlebothrombosis in pregnancy, third trimester**
MCC Exclusion see Appendix A PDX collection 0967

+ **O22.4 Hemorrhoids in pregnancy**

• ♀ CC **O22.40 Hemorrhoids in pregnancy, unspecified trimester**
CC Exclusion see Appendix A PDX collection 0967

• ♀ CC **O22.41 Hemorrhoids in pregnancy, first trimester**
CC Exclusion see Appendix A PDX collection 0967

• ♀ CC **O22.42 Hemorrhoids in pregnancy, second trimester**
CC Exclusion see Appendix A PDX collection 0967

• ♀ CC **O22.43 Hemorrhoids in pregnancy, third trimester**
CC Exclusion see Appendix A PDX collection 0967

+ **O22.5 Cerebral venous thrombosis in pregnancy**
Cerebrovenous sinus thrombosis in pregnancy

• ♀ CC **O22.50 Cerebral venous thrombosis in pregnancy, unspeci trimester**
CC Exclusion see Appendix A PDX collection 0967

• ♀ CC **O22.51 Cerebral venous thrombosis in pregnancy, first trimester**
CC Exclusion see Appendix A PDX collection 0967

• ♀ CC **O22.52 Cerebral venous thrombosis in pregnancy, second trimester**
CC Exclusion see Appendix A PDX collection 0967

• ♀ CC **O22.53 Cerebral venous thrombosis in pregnancy, third trimester**
CC Exclusion see Appendix A PDX collection 0967

+ **O22.8 Other venous complications in pregnancy**

+ **O22.8X Other venous complications in pregnancy**

• ♀ CC **O22.8X1 Other venous complications in pregnancy first trimester**
CC Exclusion see Appendix A PDX collection 0967

• ♀ CC **O22.8X2 Other venous complications in pregnancy second trimester**
CC Exclusion see Appendix A PDX collection 0967

• ♀ CC **O22.8X3 Other venous complications in pregnancy third trimester**
CC Exclusion see Appendix A PDX collection 0967

• ♀ CC **O22.8X9 Other venous complications in pregnancy, unspecified trimester**
CC Exclusion see Appendix A PDX collection 0967

+ **O22.9 Venous complication in pregnancy, unspecified**
Gestational phlebitis NOS
Gestational phlebopathy NOS
Gestational thrombosis NOS

• ♀ CC **O22.90 Venous complication in pregnancy, unspecified, unspecified trimester**
CC Exclusion see Appendix A PDX collection 0967

• ♀ **O22.91 Venous complication in pregnancy, unspecified, firs trimester**

• ♀ **O22.92 Venous complication in pregnancy, unspecified, sec trimester**

• ♀ **O22.93 Venous complication in pregnancy, unspecified, thi trimester**

O23 Infections of genitourinary tract in pregnancy

Use additional code to identify organism (B95.-, B96.-)

Excludes2: *gonococcal infections complicating pregnancy, childbirth and the puerperium (O98.2)*
infections with a predominantly sexual mode of transmission NOS complicating pregnancy, childbirth and the puerperium (O98.3)
syphilis complicating pregnancy, childbirth and the puerperium (O98.1)
tuberculosis of genitourinary system complicating pregnancy, childbirth and the puerperium (O98.0)
venereal disease NOS complicating pregnancy, childbirth and the puerperium (O98.3)

+ **O23.0 Infections of kidney in pregnancy**
Pyelonephritis in pregnancy
- • ♀ **O23.00 Infections of kidney in pregnancy, unspecified trimester**
- • ♀ CC **O23.01 Infections of kidney in pregnancy, first trimester**
CC Exclusion see Appendix A PDX collection 0968
- • ♀ CC **O23.02 Infections of kidney in pregnancy, second trimester**
CC Exclusion see Appendix A PDX collection 0968
- • ♀ CC **O23.03 Infections of kidney in pregnancy, third trimester**
CC Exclusion see Appendix A PDX collection 0968

+ **O23.1 Infections of bladder in pregnancy**
- • ♀ **O23.10 Infections of bladder in pregnancy, unspecified trimester**
- • ♀ CC **O23.11 Infections of bladder in pregnancy, first trimester**
CC Exclusion see Appendix A PDX collection 0968
- • ♀ CC **O23.12 Infections of bladder in pregnancy, second trimester**
CC Exclusion see Appendix A PDX collection 0968
- • ♀ CC **O23.13 Infections of bladder in pregnancy, third trimester**
CC Exclusion see Appendix A PDX collection 0968

+ **O23.2 Infections of urethra in pregnancy**
- • ♀ **O23.20 Infections of urethra in pregnancy, unspecified trimester**
- • ♀ CC **O23.21 Infections of urethra in pregnancy, first trimester**
CC Exclusion see Appendix A PDX collection 0968
- • ♀ CC **O23.22 Infections of urethra in pregnancy, second trimester**
CC Exclusion see Appendix A PDX collection 0968
- • ♀ CC **O23.23 Infections of urethra in pregnancy, third trimester**
CC Exclusion see Appendix A PDX collection 0968

+ **O23.3 Infections of other parts of urinary tract in pregnancy**
- • ♀ **O23.30 Infections of other parts of urinary tract in pregnancy, unspecified trimester**
- • ♀ CC **O23.31 Infections of other parts of urinary tract in pregnancy, first trimester**
CC Exclusion see Appendix A PDX collection 0968
- • ♀ CC **O23.32 Infections of other parts of urinary tract in pregnancy, second trimester**
CC Exclusion see Appendix A PDX collection 0968
- • ♀ CC **O23.33 Infections of other parts of urinary tract in pregnancy, third trimester**
CC Exclusion see Appendix A PDX collection 0968

+ **O23.4 Unspecified infection of urinary tract in pregnancy**
- • ♀ **O23.40 Unspecified infection of urinary tract in pregnancy, unspecified trimester**
- • ♀ CC **O23.41 Unspecified infection of urinary tract in pregnancy, first trimester**
CC Exclusion see Appendix A PDX collection 0968
- • ♀ CC **O23.42 Unspecified infection of urinary tract in pregnancy, second trimester**
CC Exclusion see Appendix A PDX collection 0968
- • ♀ CC **O23.43 Unspecified infection of urinary tract in pregnancy, third trimester**
CC Exclusion see Appendix A PDX collection 0968

+ **O23.5 Infections of the genital tract in pregnancy**

+ **O23.51 Infection of cervix in pregnancy**
- • ♀ CC **O23.511 Infections of cervix in pregnancy, first trimester**
CC Exclusion see Appendix A PDX collection 0968
- • ♀ CC **O23.512 Infections of cervix in pregnancy, second trimester**
CC Exclusion see Appendix A PDX collection 0968
- • ♀ CC **O23.513 Infections of cervix in pregnancy, third trimester**
CC Exclusion see Appendix A PDX collection 0968
- • ♀ **O23.519 Infections of cervix in pregnancy, unspecified trimester**

+ **O23.52 Salpingo-oophoritis in pregnancy**
Oophoritis in pregnancy
Salpingitis in pregnancy
- • ♀ CC **O23.521 Salpingo-oophoritis in pregnancy, first trimester**
CC Exclusion see Appendix A PDX collection 0968
- • ♀ CC **O23.522 Salpingo-oophoritis in pregnancy, second trimester**
CC Exclusion see Appendix A PDX collection 0968
- • ♀ CC **O23.523 Salpingo-oophoritis in pregnancy, third trimester**
CC Exclusion see Appendix A PDX collection 0968
- • ♀ **O23.529 Salpingo-oophoritis in pregnancy, unspecified trimester**

+ **O23.59 Infection of other part of genital tract in pregnancy**
- • ♀ CC **O23.591 Infection of other part of genital tract in pregnancy, first trimester**
CC Exclusion see Appendix A PDX collection 0968
- • ♀ CC **O23.592 Infection of other part of genital tract in pregnancy, second trimester**
CC Exclusion see Appendix A PDX collection 0968
- • ♀ CC **O23.593 Infection of other part of genital tract in pregnancy, third trimester**
CC Exclusion see Appendix A PDX collection 0968
- • ♀ **O23.599 Infection of other part of genital tract in pregnancy, unspecified trimester**

+ **O23.9 Unspecified genitourinary tract infection in pregnancy**
Genitourinary tract infection in pregnancy NOS
- • ♀ **O23.90 Unspecified genitourinary tract infection in pregnancy, unspecified trimester**
- • ♀ CC **O23.91 Unspecified genitourinary tract infection in pregnancy, first trimester**
CC Exclusion see Appendix A PDX collection 0968
- • ♀ CC **O23.92 Unspecified genitourinary tract infection in pregnancy, second trimester**
CC Exclusion see Appendix A PDX collection 0968
- • ♀ CC **O23.93 Unspecified genitourinary tract infection in pregnancy, third trimester**
CC Exclusion see Appendix A PDX collection 0968

O24 Diabetes mellitus in pregnancy, childbirth, and the puerperium

Review coding guideline C.15.g

+ **O24.0 Pre-existing diabetes mellitus, type 1, in pregnancy, childbirth and the puerperium**
Juvenile onset diabetes mellitus, in pregnancy, childbirth and the puerperium
Ketosis-prone diabetes mellitus in pregnancy, childbirth and the puerperium
Use additional code from category E10 to further identify any manifestations

+ **O24.01 Pre-existing diabetes mellitus, type 1, in pregnancy**
- • ♀ CC **O24.011 Pre-existing diabetes mellitus, type 1, in pregnancy, first trimester**
CC Exclusion see Appendix A PDX collection 0969
- • ♀ CC **O24.012 Pre-existing diabetes mellitus, type 1, in pregnancy, second trimester**
CC Exclusion see Appendix A PDX collection 0969
- • ♀ CC **O24.013 Pre-existing diabetes mellitus, type 1, in pregnancy, third trimester**
CC Exclusion see Appendix A PDX collection 0969
- • ♀ CC **O24.019 Pre-existing diabetes mellitus, type 1, in pregnancy, unspecified trimester**
CC Exclusion see Appendix A PDX collection 0969

- • ♀ MCC **O24.02 Pre-existing diabetes mellitus, type 1, in childbirth**
MCC Exclusion see Appendix A PDX collection 0969
- • ♀ CC **O24.03 Pre-existing diabetes mellitus, type 1, in the puerperium**
CC Exclusion see Appendix A PDX collection 0969

+ **O24.1 Pre-existing diabetes mellitus, type 2, in pregnancy, childbirth and the puerperium**
Insulin-resistant diabetes mellitus in pregnancy, childbirth and the puerperium
Use additional code (for):
from category E11 to further identify any manifestations
long-term (current) use of insulin (Z79.4)

+ **O24.11 Pre-existing diabetes mellitus, type 2, in pregnancy**
  - ● ♀ CC **O24.111 Pre-existing diabetes mellitus, type 2, in pregnancy, first trimester**
    CC Exclusion see Appendix A PDX collection 0969
  - ● ♀ CC **O24.112 Pre-existing diabetes mellitus, type 2, in pregnancy, second trimester**
    CC Exclusion see Appendix A PDX collection 0969
  - ● ♀ CC **O24.113 Pre-existing diabetes mellitus, type 2, in pregnancy, third trimester**
    CC Exclusion see Appendix A PDX collection 0969
  - ● ♀ CC **O24.119 Pre-existing diabetes mellitus, type 2, in pregnancy, unspecified trimester**
    CC Exclusion see Appendix A PDX collection 0969

● ♀ MCC **O24.12 Pre-existing diabetes mellitus, type 2, in childbirth**
MCC Exclusion see Appendix A PDX collection 0969

● ♀ CC **O24.13 Pre-existing diabetes mellitus, type 2, in the puerperium**
CC Exclusion see Appendix A PDX collection 0969

+ **O24.3 Unspecified pre-existing diabetes mellitus in pregnancy, childbirth and the puerperium**
  Use additional code (for):
  from category E11 to further identify any manifestation
  long-term (current) use of insulin (Z79.4)

+ **O24.31 Unspecified pre-existing diabetes mellitus in pregnancy**
  - ● ♀ CC **O24.311 Unspecified pre-existing diabetes mellitus in pregnancy, first trimester**
    CC Exclusion see Appendix A PDX collection 0969
  - ● ♀ CC **O24.312 Unspecified pre-existing diabetes mellitus in pregnancy, second trimester**
    CC Exclusion see Appendix A PDX collection 0969
  - ● ♀ CC **O24.313 Unspecified pre-existing diabetes mellitus in pregnancy, third trimester**
    CC Exclusion see Appendix A PDX collection 0969
  - ● ♀ CC **O24.319 Unspecified pre-existing diabetes mellitus in pregnancy, unspecified trimester**
    CC Exclusion see Appendix A PDX collection 0969

● ♀ MCC **O24.32 Unspecified pre-existing diabetes mellitus in childbirth**
MCC Exclusion see Appendix A PDX collection 0969

● ♀ CC **O24.33 Unspecified pre-existing diabetes mellitus in the puerperium**
CC Exclusion see Appendix A PDX collection 0969

+ **O24.4 Gestational diabetes mellitus**
  Diabetes mellitus arising in pregnancy
  Gestational diabetes mellitus NOS
  Review coding guideline C.15.i

+ **O24.41 Gestational diabetes mellitus in pregnancy**
  - ● ♀ **O24.410 Gestational diabetes mellitus in pregnancy, diet controlled**
  - ● ♀ **O24.414 Gestational diabetes mellitus in pregnancy, insulin controlled**
  - ● ♀ **O24.419 Gestational diabetes mellitus in pregnancy, unspecified control**

+ **O24.42 Gestational diabetes mellitus in childbirth**
  - ● ♀ **O24.420 Gestational diabetes mellitus in childbirth, diet controlled**
  - ● ♀ **O24.424 Gestational diabetes mellitus in childbirth, insulin controlled**
  - ● ♀ **O24.429 Gestational diabetes mellitus in childbirth, unspecified control**

+ **O24.43 Gestational diabetes mellitus in the puerperium**
  - ● ♀ **O24.430 Gestational diabetes mellitus in the puerperium, diet controlled**
  - ● ♀ **O24.434 Gestational diabetes mellitus in the puerperium, insulin controlled**
  - ● ♀ **O24.439 Gestational diabetes mellitus in the puerperium, unspecified control**

+ **O24.8 Other pre-existing diabetes mellitus in pregnancy, childbirth, and the puerperium**
  Use additional code (for):
  from categories E08, E09 and E13 to further identify any manifestation
  long-term (current) use of insulin (Z79.4)

+ **O24.81 Other pre-existing diabetes mellitus in pregnancy**
  - ● ♀ CC **O24.811 Other pre-existing diabetes mellitus in pregnancy, first trimester**
    CC Exclusion see Appendix A PDX collection 0969
  - ● ♀ CC **O24.812 Other pre-existing diabetes mellitus in pregnancy, second trimester**
    CC Exclusion see Appendix A PDX collection 0969
  - ● ♀ CC **O24.813 Other pre-existing diabetes mellitus in pregnancy, third trimester**
    CC Exclusion see Appendix A PDX collection 0969
  - ● ♀ CC **O24.819 Other pre-existing diabetes mellitus in pregnancy, unspecified trimester**
    CC Exclusion see Appendix A PDX collection 0969

● ♀ MCC **O24.82 Other pre-existing diabetes mellitus in childbirth**
MCC Exclusion see Appendix A PDX collection 0969

● ♀ CC **O24.83 Other pre-existing diabetes mellitus in the puerperi**
CC Exclusion see Appendix A PDX collection 0969

+ **O24.9 Unspecified diabetes mellitus in pregnancy, childbirth and th puerperium**
  Use additional code for long-term (current) use of insulin (Z79

+ **O24.91 Unspecified diabetes mellitus in pregnancy**
  - ● ♀ CC **O24.911 Unspecified diabetes mellitus in pregnanc first trimester**
    CC Exclusion see Appendix A PDX collection 0969
  - ● ♀ CC **O24.912 Unspecified diabetes mellitus in pregnanc second trimester**
    CC Exclusion see Appendix A PDX collection 0969
  - ● ♀ CC **O24.913 Unspecified diabetes mellitus in pregnanc third trimester**
    CC Exclusion see Appendix A PDX collection 0969
  - ● ♀ CC **O24.919 Unspecified diabetes mellitus in pregnanc unspecified trimester**
    CC Exclusion see Appendix A PDX collection 0969

● ♀ **O24.92 Unspecified diabetes mellitus in childbirth**

● ♀ CC **O24.93 Unspecified diabetes mellitus in the puerperium**
CC Exclusion see Appendix A PDX collection 0969

O25 Malnutrition in pregnancy, childbirth and the puerperium

+ **O25.1 Malnutrition in pregnancy**
  - ● ♀ **O25.10 Malnutrition in pregnancy, unspecified trimester**
  - ● ♀ **O25.11 Malnutrition in pregnancy, first trimester**
  - ● ♀ **O25.12 Malnutrition in pregnancy, second trimester**
  - ● ♀ **O25.13 Malnutrition in pregnancy, third trimester**

● ♀ **O25.2 Malnutrition in childbirth**

● ♀ **O25.3 Malnutrition in the puerperium**

O26 Maternal care for other conditions predominantly related to pregnancy

+ **O26.0 Excessive weight gain in pregnancy**
  Excludes2: *gestational edema (O12.0, O12.2)*
  - ● ♀ **O26.00 Excessive weight gain in pregnancy, unspecified trimester**
  - ● ♀ **O26.01 Excessive weight gain in pregnancy, first trimester**
  - ● ♀ **O26.02 Excessive weight gain in pregnancy, second trimest**
  - ● ♀ **O26.03 Excessive weight gain in pregnancy, third trimester**

+ **O26.1 Low weight gain in pregnancy**
  - ● ♀ **O26.10 Low weight gain in pregnancy, unspecified trimeste**
  - ● ♀ **O26.11 Low weight gain in pregnancy, first trimester**
  - ● ♀ **O26.12 Low weight gain in pregnancy, second trimester**
  - ● ♀ **O26.13 Low weight gain in pregnancy, third trimester**

+ **O26.2 Pregnancy care for patient with recurrent pregnancy loss**
  - ● ♀ **O26.20 Pregnancy care for patient with recurrent pregnan loss, unspecified trimester**
  - ● ♀ **O26.21 Pregnancy care for patient with recurrent pregnan loss, first trimester**
  - ● ♀ **O26.22 Pregnancy care for patient with recurrent pregnan loss, second trimester**
  - ● ♀ **O26.23 Pregnancy care for patient with recurrent pregnan loss, third trimester**

+ **O26.3 Retained intrauterine contraceptive device in pregnancy**
  - ● ♀ **O26.30 Retained intrauterine contraceptive device in pregnancy, unspecified trimester**
  - ● ♀ **O26.31 Retained intrauterine contraceptive device in pregnancy, first trimester**

• ♀ **O26.32 Retained intrauterine contraceptive device in pregnancy, second trimester**
• ♀ **O26.33 Retained intrauterine contraceptive device in pregnancy, third trimester**

\+ **O26.4 Herpes gestationis**
• ♀ **O26.40 Herpes gestationis, unspecified trimester**
• ♀ **O26.41 Herpes gestationis, first trimester**
• ♀ **O26.42 Herpes gestationis, second trimester**
• ♀ **O26.43 Herpes gestationis, third trimester**

\+ **O26.5 Maternal hypotension syndrome**
Supine hypotensive syndrome
• ♀ **O26.50 Maternal hypotension syndrome, unspecified trimester**
• ♀ **O26.51 Maternal hypotension syndrome, first trimester**
• ♀ **O26.52 Maternal hypotension syndrome, second trimester**
• ♀ **O26.53 Maternal hypotension syndrome, third trimester**

\+ **O26.6 Liver and biliary tract disorders in pregnancy, childbirth and the puerperium**
Use additional code to identify the specific disorder
Excludes2: *hepatorenal syndrome following labor and delivery (O90.4)*

\+ **O26.61 Liver and biliary tract disorders in pregnancy**
• ♀ CC **O26.611 Liver and biliary tract disorders in pregnancy, first trimester**
CC Exclusion see Appendix A PDX collection 0972
• ♀ CC **O26.612 Liver and biliary tract disorders in pregnancy, second trimester**
CC Exclusion see Appendix A PDX collection 0972
• ♀ CC **O26.613 Liver and biliary tract disorders in pregnancy, third trimester**
CC Exclusion see Appendix A PDX collection 0972
• ♀ **O26.619 Liver and biliary tract disorders in pregnancy, unspecified trimester**
• ♀ CC **O26.62 Liver and biliary tract disorders in childbirth**
CC Exclusion see Appendix A PDX collection 0972
• ♀ **O26.63 Liver and biliary tract disorders in the puerperium**

\+ **O26.7 Subluxation of symphysis (pubis) in pregnancy, childbirth and the puerperium**
Excludes1: *traumatic separation of symphysis (pubis) during childbirth (O71.6)*

\+ **O26.71 Subluxation of symphysis (pubis) in pregnancy**
• ♀ **O26.711 Subluxation of symphysis (pubis) in pregnancy, first trimester**
• ♀ **O26.712 Subluxation of symphysis (pubis) in pregnancy, second trimester**
• ♀ **O26.713 Subluxation of symphysis (pubis) in pregnancy, third trimester**
• ♀ **O26.719 Subluxation of symphysis (pubis) in pregnancy, unspecified trimester**
• ♀ **O26.72 Subluxation of symphysis (pubis) in childbirth**
• ♀ **O26.73 Subluxation of symphysis (pubis) in the puerperium**

\+ **O26.8 Other specified pregnancy related conditions**

\+ **O26.81 Pregnancy related exhaustion and fatigue**
• ♀ **O26.811 Pregnancy related exhaustion and fatigue, first trimester**
• ♀ **O26.812 Pregnancy related exhaustion and fatigue, second trimester**
• ♀ **O26.813 Pregnancy related exhaustion and fatigue, third trimester**
• ♀ **O26.819 Pregnancy related exhaustion and fatigue, unspecified trimester**

\+ **O26.82 Pregnancy related peripheral neuritis**
• ♀ **O26.821 Pregnancy related peripheral neuritis, first trimester**
• ♀ **O26.822 Pregnancy related peripheral neuritis, second trimester**
• ♀ **O26.823 Pregnancy related peripheral neuritis, third trimester**
• ♀ **O26.829 Pregnancy related peripheral neuritis, unspecified trimester**

\+ **O26.83 Pregnancy related renal disease**
Use additional code to identify the specific disorder
• ♀ CC **O26.831 Pregnancy related renal disease, first trimester**
CC Exclusion see Appendix A PDX collection 0965
• ♀ CC **O26.832 Pregnancy related renal disease, second trimester**
CC Exclusion see Appendix A PDX collection 0965
• ♀ CC **O26.833 Pregnancy related renal disease, third trimester**
CC Exclusion see Appendix A PDX collection 0965
• ♀ **O26.839 Pregnancy related renal disease, unspecified trimester**

\+ **O26.84 Uterine size-date discrepancy complicating pregnancy**
Excludes1: *encounter for suspected problem with fetal growth ruled out (Z03.74)*
• ♀ **O26.841 Uterine size-date discrepancy, first trimester**
• ♀ **O26.842 Uterine size-date discrepancy, second trimester**
• ♀ **O26.843 Uterine size-date discrepancy, third trimester**
• ♀ **O26.849 Uterine size-date discrepancy, unspecified trimester**

\+ **O26.85 Spotting complicating pregnancy**
• ♀ **O26.851 Spotting complicating pregnancy, first trimester**
• ♀ **O26.852 Spotting complicating pregnancy, second trimester**
• ♀ **O26.853 Spotting complicating pregnancy, third trimester**
• ♀ **O26.859 Spotting complicating pregnancy, unspecified trimester**
• ♀ **O26.86 Pruritic urticarial papules and plaques of pregnancy (PUPPP)**
Polymorphic eruption of pregnancy

\+ **O26.87 Cervical shortening**
Excludes1: *encounter for suspected cervical shortening ruled out (Z03.75)*
• ♀ CC **O26.872 Cervical shortening, second trimester**
CC Exclusion see Appendix A PDX collection 0973
• ♀ CC **O26.873 Cervical shortening, third trimester**
CC Exclusion see Appendix A PDX collection 0973
• ♀ CC **O26.879 Cervical shortening, unspecified trimester**
CC Exclusion see Appendix A PDX collection 0973

\+ **O26.89 Other specified pregnancy related conditions**
• ♀ **O26.891 Other specified pregnancy related conditions, first trimester**
• ♀ **O26.892 Other specified pregnancy related conditions, second trimester**
• ♀ **O26.893 Other specified pregnancy related conditions, third trimester**
• ♀ **O26.899 Other specified pregnancy related conditions, unspecified trimester**

\+ **O26.9 Pregnancy related conditions, unspecified**
• ♀ **O26.90 Pregnancy related conditions, unspecified, unspecified trimester**
• ♀ **O26.91 Pregnancy related conditions, unspecified, first trimester**
• ♀ **O26.92 Pregnancy related conditions, unspecified, second trimester**
• ♀ **O26.93 Pregnancy related conditions, unspecified, third trimester**

O28 Abnormal findings on antenatal screening of mother
Excludes1: *diagnostic findings classified elsewhere - see Alphabetical Index*
• ♀ **O28.0 Abnormal hematological finding on antenatal screening of mother**
• ♀ **O28.1 Abnormal biochemical finding on antenatal screening of mother**
• ♀ **O28.2 Abnormal cytological finding on antenatal screening of mother**
• ♀ **O28.3 Abnormal ultrasonic finding on antenatal screening of mother**
• ♀ **O28.4 Abnormal radiological finding on antenatal screening of mother**
• ♀ **O28.5 Abnormal chromosomal and genetic finding on antenatal screening of mother**
• ♀ **O28.8 Other abnormal findings on antenatal screening of mother**
• ♀ **O28.9 Unspecified abnormal findings on antenatal screening of mother**

O29 Complications of anesthesia during pregnancy
Includes: maternal complications arising from the administration of a general, regional or local anesthetic, analgesic or other sedation during pregnancy
Use additional code, if necessary, to identify the complication
Excludes2: *complications of anesthesia during labor and delivery (O74.-)*
complications of anesthesia during the puerperium (O89.-)

+ O29.0 Pulmonary complications of anesthesia during pregnancy
+ O29.01 Aspiration pneumonitis due to anesthesia during pregnancy
Inhalation of stomach contents or secretions NOS due to anesthesia during pregnancy
Mendelson's syndrome due to anesthesia during pregnancy
• ♀ O29.011 Aspiration pneumonitis due to anesthesia during pregnancy, first trimester
• ♀ O29.012 Aspiration pneumonitis due to anesthesia during pregnancy, second trimester
• ♀ O29.013 Aspiration pneumonitis due to anesthesia during pregnancy, third trimester
• ♀ O29.019 Aspiration pneumonitis due to anesthesia during pregnancy, unspecified trimester
+ O29.02 Pressure collapse of lung due to anesthesia during pregnancy
• ♀ O29.021 Pressure collapse of lung due to anesthesia during pregnancy, first trimester
• ♀ O29.022 Pressure collapse of lung due to anesthesia during pregnancy, second trimester
• ♀ O29.023 Pressure collapse of lung due to anesthesia during pregnancy, third trimester
• ♀ O29.029 Pressure collapse of lung due to anesthesia during pregnancy, unspecified trimester
+ O29.09 Other pulmonary complications of anesthesia during pregnancy
• ♀ O29.091 Other pulmonary complications of anesthesia during pregnancy, first trimester
• ♀ O29.092 Other pulmonary complications of anesthesia during pregnancy, second trimester
• ♀ O29.093 Other pulmonary complications of anesthesia during pregnancy, third trimester
• ♀ O29.099 Other pulmonary complications of anesthesia during pregnancy, unspecified trimester
+ O29.1 Cardiac complications of anesthesia during pregnancy
+ O29.11 Cardiac arrest due to anesthesia during pregnancy
• ♀ O29.111 Cardiac arrest due to anesthesia during pregnancy, first trimester
• ♀ O29.112 Cardiac arrest due to anesthesia during pregnancy, second trimester
• ♀ O29.113 Cardiac arrest due to anesthesia during pregnancy, third trimester
• ♀ O29.119 Cardiac arrest due to anesthesia during pregnancy, unspecified trimester
+ O29.12 Cardiac failure due to anesthesia during pregnancy
• ♀ O29.121 Cardiac failure due to anesthesia during pregnancy, first trimester
• ♀ O29.122 Cardiac failure due to anesthesia during pregnancy, second trimester
• ♀ O29.123 Cardiac failure due to anesthesia during pregnancy, third trimester
• ♀ O29.129 Cardiac failure due to anesthesia during pregnancy, unspecified trimester
+ O29.19 Other cardiac complications of anesthesia during pregnancy
• ♀ O29.191 Other cardiac complications of anesthesia during pregnancy, first trimester
• ♀ O29.192 Other cardiac complications of anesthesia during pregnancy, second trimester
• ♀ O29.193 Other cardiac complications of anesthesia during pregnancy, third trimester
• ♀ O29.199 Other cardiac complications of anesthesia during pregnancy, unspecified trimester
+ O29.2 Central nervous system complications of anesthesia during pregnancy
+ O29.21 Cerebral anoxia due to anesthesia during pregnancy
• ♀ O29.211 Cerebral anoxia due to anesthesia during pregnancy, first trimester
• ♀ O29.212 Cerebral anoxia due to anesthesia during pregnancy, second trimester
• ♀ O29.213 Cerebral anoxia due to anesthesia during pregnancy, third trimester
• ♀ O29.219 Cerebral anoxia due to anesthesia during pregnancy, unspecified trimester
+ O29.29 Other central nervous system complications of anesthesia during pregnancy
• ♀ O29.291 Other central nervous system complications of anesthesia during pregnancy, first trimester
• ♀ O29.292 Other central nervous system complication of anesthesia during pregnancy, second trimester
• ♀ O29.293 Other central nervous system complications anesthesia during pregnancy, third trimeste
• ♀ O29.299 Other central nervous system complicatior of anesthesia during pregnancy, unspecifie trimester
+ O29.3 Toxic reaction to local anesthesia during pregnancy
+ O29.3X Toxic reaction to local anesthesia during pregnancy
• ♀ O29.3X1 Toxic reaction to local anesthesia during pregnancy, first trimester
• ♀ O29.3X2 Toxic reaction to local anesthesia during pregnancy, second trimester
• ♀ O29.3X3 Toxic reaction to local anesthesia during pregnancy, third trimester
• ♀ O29.3X9 Toxic reaction to local anesthesia during pregnancy, unspecified trimester
+ O29.4 Spinal and epidural anesthesia induced headache during pregnancy
• ♀ O29.40 Spinal and epidural anesthesia induced headache during pregnancy, unspecified trimester
• ♀ O29.41 Spinal and epidural anesthesia induced headache during pregnancy, first trimester
• ♀ O29.42 Spinal and epidural anesthesia induced headache during pregnancy, second trimester
• ♀ O29.43 Spinal and epidural anesthesia induced headache during pregnancy, third trimester
+ O29.5 Other complications of spinal and epidural anesthesia during pregnancy
+ O29.5X Other complications of spinal and epidural anesthes during pregnancy
• ♀ O29.5X1 Other complications of spinal and epidura anesthesia during pregnancy, first trimeste
• ♀ O29.5X2 Other complications of spinal and epidural anesthesia during pregnancy, second trimes
• ♀ O29.5X3 Other complications of spinal and epidura anesthesia during pregnancy, third trimes
• ♀ O29.5X9 Other complications of spinal and epidural anesthesia during pregnancy, unspecified trimester
+ O29.6 Failed or difficult intubation for anesthesia during pregnancy
• ♀ O29.60 Failed or difficult intubation for anesthesia during pregnancy, unspecified trimester
• ♀ O29.61 Failed or difficult intubation for anesthesia during pregnancy, first trimester
• ♀ O29.62 Failed or difficult intubation for anesthesia during pregnancy, second trimester
• ♀ O29.63 Failed or difficult intubation for anesthesia during pregnancy, third trimester
+ O29.8 Other complications of anesthesia during pregnancy
+ O29.8X Other complications of anesthesia during pregnancy
• ♀ O29.8X1 Other complications of anesthesia during pregnancy, first trimester
• ♀ O29.8X2 Other complications of anesthesia during pregnancy, second trimester
• ♀ O29.8X3 Other complications of anesthesia during pregnancy, third trimester
• ♀ O29.8X9 Other complications of anesthesia during pregnancy, unspecified trimester
+ O29.9 Unspecified complication of anesthesia during pregnancy
• ♀ O29.90 Unspecified complication of anesthesia during pregnancy, unspecified trimester
• ♀ O29.91 Unspecified complication of anesthesia during pregnancy, first trimester
• ♀ O29.92 Unspecified complication of anesthesia during pregnancy, second trimester
• ♀ O29.93 Unspecified complication of anesthesia during pregnancy, third trimester

Maternal care related to the fetus and amniotic cavity and possible delivery problems (O30-O48)

O30 Multiple gestation

Code also any complications specific to multiple gestation

+ O30.0 Twin pregnancy
+ O30.00 Twin pregnancy, unspecified number of placenta an unspecified number of amniotic sacs
• ♀ O30.001 Twin pregnancy, unspecified number of placenta and unspecified number of amni sacs, first trimester

- • ♀ **O30.002** **Twin pregnancy, unspecified number of placenta and unspecified number of amniotic sacs, second trimester**
- • ♀ **O30.003** **Twin pregnancy, unspecified number of placenta and unspecified number of amniotic sacs, third trimester**
- • ♀ **O30.009** **Twin pregnancy, unspecified number of placenta and unspecified number of amniotic sacs, unspecified trimester**

+ **O30.01 Twin pregnancy, monochorionic/monoamniotic**
  Twin pregnancy, one placenta, one amniotic sac
  Excludes1: *conjoined twins (O30.02-)*
- • ♀ **O30.011** **Twin pregnancy, monochorionic/monoamniotic, first trimester**
- • ♀ **O30.012** **Twin pregnancy, monochorionic/monoamniotic, second trimester**
- • ♀ **O30.013** **Twin pregnancy, monochorionic/monoamniotic, third trimester**
- • ♀ **O30.019** **Twin pregnancy, monochorionic/monoamniotic, unspecified trimester**

+ **O30.02 Conjoined twin pregnancy**
- • ♀ **O30.021 Conjoined twin pregnancy, first trimester**
- • ♀ **O30.022 Conjoined twin pregnancy, second trimester**
- • ♀ **O30.023 Conjoined twin pregnancy, third trimester**
- • ♀ **O30.029 Conjoined twin pregnancy, unspecified trimester**

+ **O30.03 Twin pregnancy, monochorionic/diamniotic**
  Twin pregnancy, one placenta, two amniotic sacs
- • ♀ **O30.031** **Twin pregnancy, monochorionic/diamniotic, first trimester**
- • ♀ **O30.032** **Twin pregnancy, monochorionic/diamniotic, second trimester**
- • ♀ **O30.033** **Twin pregnancy, monochorionic/diamniotic, third trimester**
- • ♀ **O30.039** **Twin pregnancy, monochorionic/diamniotic, unspecified trimester**

+ **O30.04 Twin pregnancy, dichorionic/diamniotic**
  Twin pregnancy, two placentae, two amniotic sacs
- • ♀ **O30.041** **Twin pregnancy, dichorionic/diamniotic, first trimester**
- • ♀ **O30.042** **Twin pregnancy, dichorionic/diamniotic, second trimester**
- • ♀ **O30.043** **Twin pregnancy, dichorionic/diamniotic, third trimester**
- • ♀ **O30.049** **Twin pregnancy, dichorionic/diamniotic, unspecified trimester**

+ **O30.09 Twin pregnancy, unable to determine number of placenta and number of amniotic sacs**
- • ♀ **O30.091** **Twin pregnancy, unable to determine number of placenta and number of amniotic sacs, first trimester**
- • ♀ **O30.092** **Twin pregnancy, unable to determine number of placenta and number of amniotic sacs, second trimester**
- • ♀ **O30.093** **Twin pregnancy, unable to determine number of placenta and number of amniotic sacs, third trimester**
- • ♀ **O30.099** **Twin pregnancy, unable to determine number of placenta and number of amniotic sacs, unspecified trimester**

+ **O30.1 Triplet pregnancy**

+ **O30.10 Triplet pregnancy, unspecified number of placenta and unspecified number of amniotic sacs**
- • ♀ CC **O30.101** **Triplet pregnancy, unspecified number of placenta and unspecified number of amniotic sacs, first trimester**
  CC Exclusion see Appendix A PDX collection 0976
- • ♀ CC **O30.102** **Triplet pregnancy, unspecified number of placenta and unspecified number of amniotic sacs, second trimester**
  CC Exclusion see Appendix A PDX collection 0976
- • ♀ CC **O30.103** **Triplet pregnancy, unspecified number of placenta and unspecified number of amniotic sacs, third trimester**
  CC Exclusion see Appendix A PDX collection 0976
- • ♀ **O30.109** **Triplet pregnancy, unspecified number of placenta and unspecified number of amniotic sacs, unspecified trimester**

+ **O30.11 Triplet pregnancy with two or more monochorionic fetuses**
- • ♀ CC **O30.111** **Triplet pregnancy with two or more monochorionic fetuses, first trimester**
  CC Exclusion see Appendix A PDX collection 0976
- • ♀ CC **O30.112** **Triplet pregnancy with two or more monochorionic fetuses, second trimester**
  CC Exclusion see Appendix A PDX collection 0976
- • ♀ CC **O30.113** **Triplet pregnancy with two or more monochorionic fetuses, third trimester**
  CC Exclusion see Appendix A PDX collection 0976
- • ♀ **O30.119** **Triplet pregnancy with two or more monochorionic fetuses, unspecified trimester**

+ **O30.12 Triplet pregnancy with two or more monoamniotic fetuses**
- • ♀ CC **O30.121** **Triplet pregnancy with two or more monoamniotic fetuses, first trimester**
  CC Exclusion see Appendix A PDX collection 0976
- • ♀ CC **O30.122** **Triplet pregnancy with two or more monoamniotic fetuses, second trimester**
  CC Exclusion see Appendix A PDX collection 0976
- • ♀ CC **O30.123** **Triplet pregnancy with two or more monoamniotic fetuses, third trimester**
  CC Exclusion see Appendix A PDX collection 0976
- • ♀ **O30.129** **Triplet pregnancy with two or more monoamniotic fetuses, unspecified trimester**

+ **O30.19 Triplet pregnancy, unable to determine number of placenta and number of amniotic sacs**
- • ♀ CC **O30.191** **Triplet pregnancy, unable to determine number of placenta and number of amniotic sacs, first trimester**
  CC Exclusion see Appendix A PDX collection 0976
- • ♀ CC **O30.192** **Triplet pregnancy, unable to determine number of placenta and number of amniotic sacs, second trimester**
  CC Exclusion see Appendix A PDX collection 0976
- • ♀ CC **O30.193** **Triplet pregnancy, unable to determine number of placenta and number of amniotic sacs, third trimester**
  CC Exclusion see Appendix A PDX collection 0976
- • ♀ **O30.199** **Triplet pregnancy, unable to determine number of placenta and number of amniotic sacs, unspecified trimester**

+ **O30.2 Quadruplet pregnancy**

+ **O30.20 Quadruplet pregnancy, unspecified number of placenta and unspecified number of amniotic sacs**
- • ♀ CC **O30.201** **Quadruplet pregnancy, unspecified number of placenta and unspecified number of amniotic sacs, first trimester**
  CC Exclusion see Appendix A PDX collection 0976
- • ♀ CC **O30.202** **Quadruplet pregnancy, unspecified number of placenta and unspecified number of amniotic sacs, second trimester**
  CC Exclusion see Appendix A PDX collection 0976
- • ♀ CC **O30.203** **Quadruplet pregnancy, unspecified number of placenta and unspecified number of amniotic sacs, third trimester**
  CC Exclusion see Appendix A PDX collection 0976
- • ♀ **O30.209** **Quadruplet pregnancy, unspecified number of placenta and unspecified number of amniotic sacs, unspecified trimester**

+ **O30.21 Quadruplet pregnancy with two or more monochorionic fetuses**
- • ♀ CC **O30.211** **Quadruplet pregnancy with two or more monochorionic fetuses, first trimester**
  CC Exclusion see Appendix A PDX collection 0976

• ♀ CC **O30.212 Quadruplet pregnancy with two or more monochorionic fetuses, second trimester**
CC Exclusion see Appendix A PDX collection 0976

• ♀ CC **O30.213 Quadruplet pregnancy with two or more monochorionic fetuses, third trimester**
CC Exclusion see Appendix A PDX collection 0976

• ♀ **O30.219 Quadruplet pregnancy with two or more monochorionic fetuses, unspecified trimester**

\+ **O30.22 Quadruplet pregnancy with two or more monoamniotic fetuses**

• ♀ CC **O30.221 Quadruplet pregnancy with two or more monoamniotic fetuses, first trimester**
CC Exclusion see Appendix A PDX collection 0976

• ♀ CC **O30.222 Quadruplet pregnancy with two or more monoamniotic fetuses, second trimester**
CC Exclusion see Appendix A PDX collection 0976

• ♀ CC **O30.223 Quadruplet pregnancy with two or more monoamniotic fetuses, third trimester**
CC Exclusion see Appendix A PDX collection 0976

• ♀ **O30.229 Quadruplet pregnancy with two or more monoamniotic fetuses, unspecified trimester**

\+ **O30.29 Quadruplet pregnancy, unable to determine number of placenta and number of amniotic sacs**

• ♀ CC **O30.291 Quadruplet pregnancy, unable to determine number of placenta and number of amniotic sacs, first trimester**
CC Exclusion see Appendix A PDX collection 0976

• ♀ CC **O30.292 Quadruplet pregnancy, unable to determine number of placenta and number of amniotic sacs, second trimester**
CC Exclusion see Appendix A PDX collection 0976

• ♀ CC **O30.293 Quadruplet pregnancy, unable to determine number of placenta and number of amniotic sacs, third trimester**
CC Exclusion see Appendix A PDX collection 0976

• ♀ **O30.299 Quadruplet pregnancy, unable to determine number of placenta and number of amniotic sacs, unspecified trimester**

\+ **O30.8 Other specified multiple gestation**
Multiple gestation pregnancy greater then quadruplets

\+ **O30.80 Other specified multiple gestation, unspecified number of placenta and unspecified number of amniotic sacs**

• ♀ CC **O30.801 Other specified multiple gestation, unspecified number of placenta and unspecified number of amniotic sacs, first trimester**
CC Exclusion see Appendix A PDX collection 0976

• ♀ CC **O30.802 Other specified multiple gestation, unspecified number of placenta and unspecified number of amniotic sacs, second trimester**
CC Exclusion see Appendix A PDX collection 0976

• ♀ CC **O30.803 Other specified multiple gestation, unspecified number of placenta and unspecified number of amniotic sacs, third trimester**
CC Exclusion see Appendix A PDX collection 0976

• ♀ **O30.809 Other specified multiple gestation, unspecified number of placenta and unspecified number of amniotic sacs, unspecified trimester**

\+ **O30.81 Other specified multiple gestation with two or more monochorionic fetuses**

• ♀ CC **O30.811 Other specified multiple gestation with two or more monochorionic fetuses, first trimester**
CC Exclusion see Appendix A PDX collection 0976

• ♀ CC **O30.812 Other specified multiple gestation with two or more monochorionic fetuses, second trimester**
CC Exclusion see Appendix A PDX collection 0976

• ♀ CC **O30.813 Other specified multiple gestation with two or more monochorionic fetuses, thir[d] trimester**
CC Exclusion see Appendix A PDX collection 0976

• ♀ **O30.819 Other specified multiple gestation with t[wo] or more monochorionic fetuses, unspecifi[ed] trimester**

\+ **O30.82 Other specified multiple gestation with two or mor[e] monoamniotic fetuses**

• ♀ CC **O30.821 Other specified multiple gestation with two or more monoamniotic fetuses, first trimester**
CC Exclusion see Appendix A PDX collection 0976

• ♀ CC **O30.822 Other specified multiple gestation with two or more monoamniotic fetuses, secon[d] trimester**
CC Exclusion see Appendix A PDX collection 0976

• ♀ CC **O30.823 Other specified multiple gestation with two or more monoamniotic fetuses, third trimester**
CC Exclusion see Appendix A PDX collection 0976

• ♀ **O30.829 Other specified multiple gestation with t[wo] or more monoamniotic fetuses, unspecifi[ed] trimester**

\+ **O30.89 Other specified multiple gestation, unable to determine number of placenta and number of amniotic sacs**

• ♀ CC **O30.891 Other specified multiple gestation, unab[le to] determine number of placenta and num[ber] of amniotic sacs, first trimester**
CC Exclusion see Appendix A PDX collection 0976

• ♀ CC **O30.892 Other specified multiple gestation, unab[le to] determine number of placenta and num[ber] of amniotic sacs, second trimester**
CC Exclusion see Appendix A PDX collection 0976

• ♀ CC **O30.893 Other specified multiple gestation, unab[le to] determine number of placenta and num[ber] of amniotic sacs, third trimester**
CC Exclusion see Appendix A PDX collection 0976

• ♀ **O30.899 Other specified multiple gestation, unab[le to] determine number of placenta and num[ber] of amniotic sacs, unspecified trimester**

\+ **O30.9 Multiple gestation, unspecified**
Multiple pregnancy NOS

• ♀ **O30.90 Multiple gestation, unspecified, unspecified trimes[ter]**
• ♀ **O30.91 Multiple gestation, unspecified, first trimester**
• ♀ **O30.92 Multiple gestation, unspecified, second trimester**
• ♀ **O30.93 Multiple gestation, unspecified, third trimester**

O31 Complications specific to multiple gestation

Excludes2: *delayed delivery of second twin, triplet, etc. (O63.2)*
malpresentation of one fetus or more (O32.9)
placental transfusion syndromes (O43.0-)

One of the following 7th characters is to be assigned to each code un[der] category O31. 7th character 0 is for single gestations and multiple gestations where the fetus is unspecified. 7th characters 1 through 9 a[re] for cases of multiple gestations to identify the fetus for which the cod[e] applies. The appropriate code from category O30, Multiple gestation, must also be assigned when assigning a code from category O31 that a 7th character of 1 through 9.

0 - not applicable or unspecified
1 - fetus 1
2 - fetus 2
3 - fetus 3
4 - fetus 4
5 - fetus 5
9 - other fetus

\+ **O31.0 Papyraceous fetus**
Fetus compressus

• ♀ X+7th **O31.00 Papyraceous fetus, unspecified trimester**
• ♀ X+7th **O31.01 Papyraceous fetus, first trimester**
• ♀ X+7th **O31.02 Papyraceous fetus, second trimester**
• ♀ X+7th **O31.03 Papyraceous fetus, third trimester**

+ O31.1 Continuing pregnancy after spontaneous abortion of one fetus or more

• ♀ X+7th **O31.10 Continuing pregnancy after spontaneous abortion of one fetus or more, unspecified trimester**

• ♀ X+7th **O31.11 Continuing pregnancy after spontaneous abortion of one fetus or more, first trimester**

• ♀ X+7th **O31.12 Continuing pregnancy after spontaneous abortion of one fetus or more, second trimester**

• ♀ X+7th **O31.13 Continuing pregnancy after spontaneous abortion of one fetus or more, third trimester**

+ O31.2 Continuing pregnancy after intrauterine death of one fetus or more

• ♀ X+7th **O31.20 Continuing pregnancy after intrauterine death of one fetus or more, unspecified trimester**

• ♀ X+7th **O31.21 Continuing pregnancy after intrauterine death of one fetus or more, first trimester**

• ♀ X+7th **O31.22 Continuing pregnancy after intrauterine death of one fetus or more, second trimester**

• ♀ X+7th **O31.23 Continuing pregnancy after intrauterine death of one fetus or more, third trimester**

+ O31.3 Continuing pregnancy after elective fetal reduction of one fetus or more

Continuing pregnancy after selective termination of one fetus or more

• ♀ X+7th **O31.30 Continuing pregnancy after elective fetal reduction of one fetus or more, unspecified trimester**

• ♀ X+7th **O31.31 Continuing pregnancy after elective fetal reduction of one fetus or more, first trimester**

• ♀ X+7th **O31.32 Continuing pregnancy after elective fetal reduction of one fetus or more, second trimester**

• ♀ X+7th **O31.33 Continuing pregnancy after elective fetal reduction of one fetus or more, third trimester**

+ O31.8 Other complications specific to multiple gestation

+ O31.8X Other complications specific to multiple gestation

• ♀ CC +7th **O31.8X1 Other complications specific to multiple gestation, first trimester**

CC Exclusion for all 7th characters see Appendix A PDX collection 0976

• ♀ +7th **O31.8X2 Other complications specific to multiple gestation, second trimester**

• ♀ +7th **O31.8X3 Other complications specific to multiple gestation, third trimester**

• ♀ +7th **O31.8X9 Other complications specific to multiple gestation, unspecified trimester**

O32 **Maternal care for malpresentation of fetus**

Includes: the listed conditions as a reason for observation, hospitalization or other obstetric care of the mother, or for cesarean delivery before onset of labor

Excludes1: *malpresentation of fetus with obstructed labor (O64.-)*

One of the following 7th characters is to be assigned to each code under category O32. 7th character 0 is for single gestations and multiple gestations where the fetus is unspecified. 7th characters 1 through 9 are for cases of multiple gestations to identify the fetus for which the code applies. The appropriate code from category O30, Multiple gestation, must also be assigned when assigning a code from category O32 that has a 7th character of 1 through 9.

0 - not applicable or unspecified
1 - fetus 1
2 - fetus 2
3 - fetus 3
4 - fetus 4
5 - fetus 5
9 - other fetus

• ♀ X+7th **O32.0 Maternal care for unstable lie**

• ♀ X+7th **O32.1 Maternal care for breech presentation**

Maternal care for buttocks presentation
Maternal care for complete breech
Maternal care for frank breech

Excludes1: *footling presentation (O32.8)*
incomplete breech (O32.8)

• ♀ X+7th **O32.2 Maternal care for transverse and oblique lie**

Maternal care for oblique presentation
Maternal care for transverse presentation

• ♀ X+7th **O32.3 Maternal care for face, brow and chin presentation**

• ♀ X+7th **O32.4 Maternal care for high head at term**

Maternal care for failure of head to enter pelvic brim

• ♀ X+7th **O32.6 Maternal care for compound presentation**

• ♀ X+7th **O32.8 Maternal care for other malpresentation of fetus**

Maternal care for footling presentation
Maternal care for incomplete breech

• ♀ X+7th **O32.9 Maternal care for malpresentation of fetus, unspecified**

O33 **Maternal care for disproportion**

Includes: the listed conditions as a reason for observation, hospitalization or other obstetric care of the mother, or for cesarean delivery before onset of labor

Excludes1: *disproportion with obstructed labor (O65-O66)*

• ♀ CC **O33.0 Maternal care for disproportion due to deformity of maternal pelvic bones**

Maternal care for disproportion due to pelvic deformity causing disproportion NOS

CC Exclusion see Appendix A PDX collection 0977

• ♀ **O33.1 Maternal care for disproportion due to generally contracted pelvis**

Maternal care for disproportion due to contracted pelvis NOS causing disproportion

• ♀ **O33.2 Maternal care for disproportion due to inlet contraction of pelvis**

Maternal care for disproportion due to inlet contraction (pelvis) causing disproportion

• ♀ +7th **O33.3 Maternal care for disproportion due to outlet contraction of pelvis**

Maternal care for disproportion due to mid-cavity contraction (pelvis)
Maternal care for disproportion due to outlet contraction (pelvis)

One of the following 7th characters is to be assigned to code O33.3. 7th character 0 is for single gestations and multiple gestations where the fetus is unspecified. 7th characters 1 through 9 are for cases of multiple gestations to identify the fetus for which the code applies. The appropriate code from category O30, Multiple gestation, must also be assigned when assigning code O33.3 with a 7th character of 1 through 9.

0 - not applicable or unspecified
1 - fetus 1
2 - fetus 2
3 - fetus 3
4 - fetus 4
5 - fetus 5
9 - other fetus

• ♀ X+7th **O33.4 Maternal care for disproportion of mixed maternal and fetal origin**

One of the following 7th characters is to be assigned to code O33.4. 7th character 0 is for single gestations and multiple gestations where the fetus is unspecified. 7th characters 1 through 9 are for cases of multiple gestations to identify the fetus for which the code applies. The appropriate code from category O30, Multiple gestation, must also be assigned when assigning code O33.4 with a 7th character of 1 through 9.

0 - not applicable or unspecified
1 - fetus 1
2 - fetus 2
3 - fetus 3
4 - fetus 4
5 - fetus 5
9 - other fetus

• ♀ X+7th **O33.5 Maternal care for disproportion due to unusually large fetus**

Maternal care for disproportion due to disproportion of fetal origin with normally formed fetus
Maternal care for disproportion due to fetal disproportion NOS

One of the following 7th characters is to be assigned to code O33.5. 7th character 0 is for single gestations and multiple gestations where the fetus is unspecified. 7th characters 1 through 9 are for cases of multiple gestations to identify the fetus for which the code applies. The appropriate code from category O30, Multiple gestation, must also be assigned when assigning code O33.5 with a 7th character of 1 through 9.

0 - not applicable or unspecified
1 - fetus 1
2 - fetus 2
3 - fetus 3
4 - fetus 4
5 - fetus 5
9 - other fetus

• ♀ X+7th **O33.6 Maternal care for disproportion due to hydrocephalic fetus**

One of the following 7th characters is to be assigned to code O33.6. 7th character 0 is for single gestations and multiple gestations where the fetus is unspecified. 7th characters 1 through 9 are for cases of multiple gestations to identify the fetus for which the code applies. The appropriate code from category O30, Multiple gestation, must also be assigned when assigning code O33.6 with a 7th character of 1 through 9.
0 - not applicable or unspecified
1 - fetus 1
2 - fetus 2
3 - fetus 3
4 - fetus 4
5 - fetus 5
9 - other fetus

• ♀ **O33.7 Maternal care for disproportion due to other fetal deformities**
Maternal care for disproportion due to fetal ascites
Maternal care for disproportion due to fetal hydrops
Maternal care for disproportion due to fetal meningomyelocele
Maternal care for disproportion due to fetal sacral teratoma
Maternal care for disproportion due to fetal tumor
Excludes1: *obstructed labor due to other fetal deformities (O66.3)*

• ♀ **O33.8 Maternal care for disproportion of other origin**

• ♀ **O33.9 Maternal care for disproportion, unspecified**
Maternal care for disproportion due to cephalopelvic disproportion NOS
Maternal care for disproportion due to fetopelvic disproportion NOS

O34 Maternal care for abnormality of pelvic organs

Includes: the listed conditions as a reason for hospitalization or other obstetric care of the mother, or for cesarean delivery before onset of labor

Code first any associated obstructed labor (O65.5)

Use additional code for specific condition

+ **O34.0 Maternal care for congenital malformation of uterus**
• ♀ **O34.00 Maternal care for unspecified congenital malformation of uterus, unspecified trimester**
• ♀ **O34.01 Maternal care for unspecified congenital malformation of uterus, first trimester**
• ♀ **O34.02 Maternal care for unspecified congenital malformation of uterus, second trimester**
• ♀ **O34.03 Maternal care for unspecified congenital malformation of uterus, third trimester**

+ **O34.1 Maternal care for benign tumor of corpus uteri**
Excludes2: *maternal care for benign tumor of cervix (O34.4-)*
maternal care for malignant neoplasm of uterus (O9A.1-)
• ♀ **O34.10 Maternal care for benign tumor of corpus uteri, unspecified trimester**
• ♀ **O34.11 Maternal care for benign tumor of corpus uteri, first trimester**
• ♀ **O34.12 Maternal care for benign tumor of corpus uteri, second trimester**
• ♀ **O34.13 Maternal care for benign tumor of corpus uteri, third trimester**

+ **O34.2 Maternal care due to uterine scar from previous surgery**
• ♀ **O34.21 Maternal care for scar from previous cesarean delivery**
• ♀ **O34.29 Maternal care due to uterine scar from other previous surgery**

+ **O34.3 Maternal care for cervical incompetence**
Maternal care for cerclage with or without cervical incompetence
Maternal care for Shirodkar suture with or without cervical incompetence
• ♀ **O34.30 Maternal care for cervical incompetence, unspecified trimester**
• ♀ MCC **O34.31 Maternal care for cervical incompetence, first trimester**
MCC Exclusion see Appendix A PDX collection 0973
• ♀ MCC **O34.32 Maternal care for cervical incompetence, second trimester**
MCC Exclusion see Appendix A PDX collection 0973
• ♀ MCC **O34.33 Maternal care for cervical incompetence, third trimester**
MCC Exclusion see Appendix A PDX collection 0973

+ **O34.4 Maternal care for other abnormalities of cervix**
• ♀ **O34.40 Maternal care for other abnormalities of cervix, unspecified trimester**
• ♀ **O34.41 Maternal care for other abnormalities of cervix, first trimester**
• ♀ **O34.42 Maternal care for other abnormalities of cervix, second trimester**
• ♀ **O34.43 Maternal care for other abnormalities of cervix, third trimester**

+ **O34.5 Maternal care for other abnormalities of gravid uterus**
+ **O34.51 Maternal care for incarceration of gravid uterus**
• ♀ **O34.511 Maternal care for incarceration of gravid uterus, first trimester**
• ♀ **O34.512 Maternal care for incarceration of gravid uterus, second trimester**
• ♀ **O34.513 Maternal care for incarceration of gravid uterus, third trimester**
• ♀ **O34.519 Maternal care for incarceration of gravid uterus, unspecified trimester**
+ **O34.52 Maternal care for prolapse of gravid uterus**
• ♀ **O34.521 Maternal care for prolapse of gravid uterus, first trimester**
• ♀ **O34.522 Maternal care for prolapse of gravid uterus, second trimester**
• ♀ **O34.523 Maternal care for prolapse of gravid uterus, third trimester**
• ♀ **O34.529 Maternal care for prolapse of gravid uterus, unspecified trimester**
+ **O34.53 Maternal care for retroversion of gravid uterus**
• ♀ **O34.531 Maternal care for retroversion of gravid uterus, first trimester**
• ♀ **O34.532 Maternal care for retroversion of gravid uterus, second trimester**
• ♀ **O34.533 Maternal care for retroversion of gravid uterus, third trimester**
• ♀ **O34.539 Maternal care for retroversion of gravid uterus, unspecified trimester**
+ **O34.59 Maternal care for other abnormalities of gravid uterus**
• ♀ **O34.591 Maternal care for other abnormalities of gravid uterus, first trimester**
• ♀ **O34.592 Maternal care for other abnormalities of gravid uterus, second trimester**
• ♀ **O34.593 Maternal care for other abnormalities of gravid uterus, third trimester**
• ♀ **O34.599 Maternal care for other abnormalities of gravid uterus, unspecified trimester**

O34.6 Maternal care for abnormality of vagina
Excludes2: *maternal care for vaginal varices in pregnancy (O22.1-)*
• ♀ **O34.60 Maternal care for abnormality of vagina, unspecified trimester**
• ♀ **O34.61 Maternal care for abnormality of vagina, first trimester**
• ♀ **O34.62 Maternal care for abnormality of vagina, second trimester**
• ♀ **O34.63 Maternal care for abnormality of vagina, third trimester**

+ **O34.7 Maternal care for abnormality of vulva and perineum**
Excludes2: *maternal care for perineal and vulval varices in pregnancy (O22.1-)*
• ♀ **O34.70 Maternal care for abnormality of vulva and perineum, unspecified trimester**
• ♀ **O34.71 Maternal care for abnormality of vulva and perineum, first trimester**
• ♀ **O34.72 Maternal care for abnormality of vulva and perineum, second trimester**
• ♀ **O34.73 Maternal care for abnormality of vulva and perineum, third trimester**

+ **O34.8 Maternal care for other abnormalities of pelvic organs**
• ♀ **O34.80 Maternal care for other abnormalities of pelvic organs, unspecified trimester**
• ♀ **O34.81 Maternal care for other abnormalities of pelvic organs, first trimester**
• ♀ **O34.82 Maternal care for other abnormalities of pelvic organs, second trimester**
• ♀ **O34.83 Maternal care for other abnormalities of pelvic organs, third trimester**

+ **O34.9 Maternal care for abnormality of pelvic organ, unspecified**
• ♀ **O34.90 Maternal care for abnormality of pelvic organ, unspecified, unspecified trimester**
• ♀ **O34.91 Maternal care for abnormality of pelvic organ, unspecified, first trimester**

• ♀ **O34.92 Maternal care for abnormality of pelvic organ, unspecified, second trimester**

• ♀ **O34.93 Maternal care for abnormality of pelvic organ, unspecified, third trimester**

O35 Maternal care for known or suspected fetal abnormality and damage

Includes: the listed conditions in the fetus as a reason for hospitalization or other obstetric care to the mother, or for termination of pregnancy

Code also any associated maternal condition

Excludes1: *encounter for suspected maternal and fetal conditions ruled out (Z03.7-)*

One of the following 7th characters is to be assigned to each code under category O35. 7th character 0 is for single gestations and multiple gestations where the fetus is unspecified. 7th characters 1 through 9 are for cases of multiple gestations to identify the fetus for which the code applies. The appropriate code from category O30, Multiple gestation, must also be assigned when assigning a code from category O35 that has a 7th character of 1 through 9.

0 - not applicable or unspecified
1 - fetus 1
2 - fetus 2
3 - fetus 3
4 - fetus 4
5 - fetus 5
9 - other fetus

Review coding guideline C.15.e

♀ X+7th **O35.0 Maternal care for (suspected) central nervous system malformation in fetus**
Maternal care for fetal anencephaly
Maternal care for fetal hydrocephalus
Maternal care for fetal spina bifida
Excludes2: *chromosomal abnormality in fetus (O35.1)*

♀ X+7th **O35.1 Maternal care for (suspected) chromosomal abnormality in fetus**

• ♀ **O35.2 Maternal care for (suspected) hereditary disease in fetus**
Excludes2: *chromosomal abnormality in fetus (O35.1)*

♀ X+7th **O35.3 Maternal care for (suspected) damage to fetus from viral disease in mother**
Maternal care for damage to fetus from maternal cytomegalovirus infection
Maternal care for damage to fetus from maternal rubella

♀ X+7th **O35.4 Maternal care for (suspected) damage to fetus from alcohol**

♀ X+7th **O35.5 Maternal care for (suspected) damage to fetus by drugs**
Maternal care for damage to fetus from drug addiction

♀ X+7th **O35.6 Maternal care for (suspected) damage to fetus by radiation**

♀ X+7th **O35.7 Maternal care for (suspected) damage to fetus by other medical procedures**
Maternal care for damage to fetus by amniocentesis
Maternal care for damage to fetus by biopsy procedures
Maternal care for damage to fetus by hematological investigation
Maternal care for damage to fetus by intrauterine contraceptive device
Maternal care for damage to fetus by intrauterine surgery

• ♀ X+7th **O35.8 Maternal care for other (suspected) fetal abnormality and damage**
Maternal care for damage to fetus from maternal listeriosis
Maternal care for damage to fetus from maternal toxoplasmosis

• ♀ X+7th **O35.9 Maternal care for (suspected) fetal abnormality and damage, unspecified**

O36 Maternal care for other fetal problems

Includes: the listed conditions in the fetus as a reason for hospitalization or other obstetric care of the mother, or for termination of pregnancy

Excludes1: *encounter for suspected maternal and fetal conditions ruled out (Z03.7-)*
placental transfusion syndromes (O43.0-)

Excludes2: *labor and delivery complicated by fetal stress (O77.-)*

One of the following 7th characters is to be assigned to each code under category O36. 7th character 0 is for single gestations and multiple gestations where the fetus is unspecified. 7th characters 1 through 9 are for cases of multiple gestations to identify the fetus for which the code applies. The appropriate code from category O30, Multiple gestation, must also be assigned when assigning a code from category O36 that has a 7th character of 1 through 9.

0 - not applicable or unspecified
1 - fetus 1
2 - fetus 2
3 - fetus 3
4 - fetus 4
5 - fetus 5
9 - other fetus

Review coding guideline C.15.e

\+ **O36.0 Maternal care for rhesus isoimmunization**
Maternal care for Rh incompatibility (with hydrops fetalis)

\+ **O36.01 Maternal care for anti-D [Rh] antibodies**

• ♀ CC +7th **O36.011 Maternal care for anti-D [Rh] antibodies, first trimester**
CC Exclusion for all 7th characters see Appendix A PDX collection 0978

• ♀ CC +7th **O36.012 Maternal care for anti-D [Rh] antibodies, second trimester**
CC Exclusion for all 7th characters see Appendix A PDX collection 0978

• ♀ CC +7th **O36.013 Maternal care for anti-D [Rh] antibodies, third trimester**
CC Exclusion for all 7th characters see Appendix A PDX collection 0978

• ♀ +7th **O36.019 Maternal care for anti-D [Rh] antibodies, unspecified trimester**

\+ **O36.09 Maternal care for other rhesus isoimmunization**

• ♀ CC +7th **O36.091 Maternal care for other rhesus isoimmunization, first trimester**
CC Exclusion for all 7th characters see Appendix A PDX collection 0978

• ♀ CC +7th **O36.092 Maternal care for other rhesus isoimmunization, second trimester**
CC Exclusion for all 7th characters see Appendix A PDX collection 0978

• ♀ CC +7th **O36.093 Maternal care for other rhesus isoimmunization, third trimester**
CC Exclusion for all 7th characters see Appendix A PDX collection 0978

• ♀ +7th **O36.099 Maternal care for other rhesus isoimmunization, unspecified trimester**

\+ **O36.1 Maternal care for other isoimmunization**
Maternal care for ABO isoimmunization

\+ **O36.11 Maternal care for Anti-A sensitization**
Maternal care for isoimmunization NOS (with hydrops fetalis)

• ♀ +7th **O36.111 Maternal care for Anti-A sensitization, first trimester**

• ♀ +7th **O36.112 Maternal care for Anti-A sensitization, second trimester**

• ♀ +7th **O36.113 Maternal care for Anti-A sensitization, third trimester**

• ♀ +7th **O36.119 Maternal care for Anti-A sensitization, unspecified trimester**

\+ **O36.19 Maternal care for other isoimmunization**
Maternal care for Anti-B sensitization

• ♀ +7th **O36.191 Maternal care for other isoimmunization, first trimester**

• ♀ +7th **O36.192 Maternal care for other isoimmunization, second trimester**

• ♀ +7th **O36.193 Maternal care for other isoimmunization, third trimester**

• ♀ +7th **O36.199 Maternal care for other isoimmunization, unspecified trimester**

+ **O36.2 Maternal care for hydrops fetalis**
Maternal care for hydrops fetalis NOS
Maternal care for hydrops fetalis not associated with isoimmunization
Excludes1: *hydrops fetalis associated with ABO isoimmunization (O36.1-)*
hydrops fetalis associated with rhesus isoimmunization (O36.0-)

- ● ♀ X+7th **O36.20 Maternal care for hydrops fetalis, unspecified trimester**
- ● ♀ X+7th **O36.21 Maternal care for hydrops fetalis, first trimester**
- ● ♀ X+7th **O36.22 Maternal care for hydrops fetalis, second trimester**
- ● ♀ X+7th **O36.23 Maternal care for hydrops fetalis, third trimester**

● ♀ CC X+7th **O36.4 Maternal care for intrauterine death**
Maternal care for intrauterine fetal death NOS
Maternal care for intrauterine fetal death after completion of 20 weeks of gestation
Maternal care for late fetal death
Maternal care for missed delivery
Excludes1: *missed abortion (O02.1)stillbirth (P95)*
CC Exclusion for all 7th characters see Appendix A PDX collection 0979

+ **O36.5 Maternal care for known or suspected poor fetal growth**
+ **O36.51 Maternal care for known or suspected placental insufficiency**
- ● ♀ +7th **O36.511 Maternal care for known or suspected placental insufficiency, first trimester**
- ● ♀ +7th **O36.512 Maternal care for known or suspected placental insufficiency, second trimester**
- ● ♀ +7th **O36.513 Maternal care for known or suspected placental insufficiency, third trimester**
- ● ♀ +7th **O36.519 Maternal care for known or suspected placental insufficiency, unspecified trimester**

+ **O36.59 Maternal care for other known or suspected poor fetal growth**
Maternal care for known or suspected light-for-dates NOS
Maternal care for known or suspected small-for-dates NOS
- ● ♀ +7th **O36.591 Maternal care for other known or suspected poor fetal growth, first trimester**
- ● ♀ +7th **O36.592 Maternal care for other known or suspected poor fetal growth, second trimester**
- ● ♀ +7th **O36.593 Maternal care for other known or suspected poor fetal growth, third trimester**
- ● ♀ +7th **O36.599 Maternal care for other known or suspected poor fetal growth, unspecified trimester**

+ **O36.6 Maternal care for excessive fetal growth**
Maternal care for known or suspected large-for-dates
- ● ♀ X+7th **O36.60 Maternal care for excessive fetal growth, unspecified trimester**
- ● ♀ X+7th **O36.61 Maternal care for excessive fetal growth, first trimester**
- ● ♀ X+7th **O36.62 Maternal care for excessive fetal growth, second trimester**
- ● ♀ X+7th **O36.63 Maternal care for excessive fetal growth, third trimester**

+ **O36.7 Maternal care for viable fetus in abdominal pregnancy**
- ● ♀ X+7th **O36.70 Maternal care for viable fetus in abdominal pregnancy, unspecified trimester**
- ● ♀ X+7th **O36.71 Maternal care for viable fetus in abdominal pregnancy, first trimester**
- ● ♀ X+7th **O36.72 Maternal care for viable fetus in abdominal pregnancy, second trimester**
- ● ♀ X+7th **O36.73 Maternal care for viable fetus in abdominal pregnancy, third trimester**

+ **O36.8 Maternal care for other specified fetal problems**
● ♀ X+7th **O36.80 Pregnancy with inconclusive fetal viability**
Encounter to determine fetal viability of pregnancy

+ **O36.81 Decreased fetal movements**
- ● ♀ +7th **O36.812 Decreased fetal movements, second trimester**
- ● ♀ +7th **O36.813 Decreased fetal movements, third trimester**
- ● ♀ +7th **O36.819 Decreased fetal movements, unspecified trimester**

+ **O36.82 Fetal anemia and thrombocytopenia**
- ● ♀ +7th **O36.821 Fetal anemia and thrombocytopenia, first trimester**
- ● ♀ +7th **O36.822 Fetal anemia and thrombocytopenia, second trimester**
- ● ♀ +7th **O36.823 Fetal anemia and thrombocytopenia, third trimester**
- ● ♀ +7th **O36.829 Fetal anemia and thrombocytopenia, unspecified trimester**

+ **O36.89 Maternal care for other specified fetal problems**
- ● ♀ +7th **O36.891 Maternal care for other specified fetal problems, first trimester**
- ● ♀ +7th **O36.892 Maternal care for other specified fetal problems, second trimester**
- ● ♀ +7th **O36.893 Maternal care for other specified fetal problems, third trimester**
- ● ♀ +7th **O36.899 Maternal care for other specified fetal problems, unspecified trimester**

+ **O36.9 Maternal care for fetal problem, unspecified**
- ● ♀ X+7th **O36.90 Maternal care for fetal problem, unspecified, unspecified trimester**
- ● ♀ X+7th **O36.91 Maternal care for fetal problem, unspecified, first trimester**
- ● ♀ X+7th **O36.92 Maternal care for fetal problem, unspecified, second trimester**
- ● ♀ X+7th **O36.93 Maternal care for fetal problem, unspecified, third trimester**

O40 Polyhydramnios

Includes: hydramnios
Excludes1: *encounter for suspected maternal and fetal conditions ruled out (Z03.7-)*

One of the following 7th characters is to be assigned to each code under category O40. 7th character 0 is for single gestations and multiple gestations where the fetus is unspecified. 7th characters 1 through 9 are for cases of multiple gestations to identify the fetus for which the code applies. The appropriate code from category O30, Multiple gestation, must also be assigned when assigning a code from category O40 that h a 7th character of 1 through 9.
0 - not applicable or unspecified
1 - fetus 1
2 - fetus 2
3 - fetus 3
4 - fetus 4
5 - fetus 5
9 - other fetus

- ● ♀ X+7th **O40.1 Polyhydramnios, first trimester**
- ● ♀ X+7th **O40.2 Polyhydramnios, second trimester**
- ● ♀ X+7th **O40.3 Polyhydramnios, third trimester**
- ● ♀ X+7th **O40.9 Polyhydramnios, unspecified trimester**

O41 Other disorders of amniotic fluid and membranes

Excludes1: *encounter for suspected maternal and fetal conditions ruled out (Z03.7-)*

One of the following 7th characters is to be assigned to each code under category O41. 7th character 0 is for single gestations and multiple gestations where the fetus is unspecified. 7th characters 1 through 9 are for cases of multiple gestations to identify the fetus for which the code applies. The appropriate code from category O30, Multiple gestation, must also be assigned when assigning a code from category O41 that h a 7th character of 1 through 9.
0 - not applicable or unspecified
1 - fetus 1
2 - fetus 2
3 - fetus 3
4 - fetus 4
5 - fetus 5
9 - other fetus

+ **O41.0 Oligohydramnios**
Oligohydramnios without rupture of membranes
- ● ♀ X+7th **O41.00 Oligohydramnios, unspecified trimester**
- ● ♀ CC X+7th **O41.01 Oligohydramnios, first trimester**
  CC Exclusion for all 7th characters see Appendix A PDX collection 0982
- ● ♀ CC X+7th **O41.02 Oligohydramnios, second trimester**
  CC Exclusion for all 7th characters see Appendix A PDX collection 0982
- ● ♀ CC X+7th **O41.03 Oligohydramnios, third trimester**
  CC Exclusion for all 7th characters see Appendix A PDX collection 0982

+ **O41.1 Infection of amniotic sac and membranes**
+ **O41.10 Infection of amniotic sac and membranes, unspecified**
● ♀ MCC +7th **O41.101 Infection of amniotic sac and membranes, unspecified, first trimester**
MCC Exclusion for all 7th characters see Appendix A PDX collection 0983

• ♀ MCC +7th **O41.102 Infection of amniotic sac and membranes, unspecified, second trimester**
MCC Exclusion for all 7th characters see Appendix A PDX collection 0983

• ♀ MCC +7th **O41.103 Infection of amniotic sac and membranes, unspecified, third trimester**
MCC Exclusion for all 7th characters see Appendix A PDX collection 0983

• ♀ +7th **O41.109 Infection of amniotic sac and membranes, unspecified, unspecified trimester**

\+ **O41.12 Chorioamnionitis**

• ♀ MCC +7th **O41.121 Chorioamnionitis, first trimester**
MCC Exclusion for all 7th characters see Appendix A PDX collection 0983

• ♀ MCC +7th **O41.122 Chorioamnionitis, second trimester**
MCC Exclusion for all 7th characters see Appendix A PDX collection 0983

• ♀ MCC +7th **O41.123 Chorioamnionitis, third trimester**
MCC Exclusion for all 7th characters see Appendix A PDX collection 0983

• ♀ +7th **O41.129 Chorioamnionitis, unspecified trimester**

\+ **O41.14 Placentitis**

• ♀ MCC +7th **O41.141 Placentitis, first trimester**
MCC Exclusion for all 7th characters see Appendix A PDX collection 0983

• ♀ MCC +7th **O41.142 Placentitis, second trimester**
MCC Exclusion for all 7th characters see Appendix A PDX collection 0983

• ♀ MCC +7th **O41.143 Placentitis, third trimester**
MCC Exclusion for all 7th characters see Appendix A PDX collection 0983

• ♀ +7th **O41.149 Placentitis, unspecified trimester**

\+ **O41.8 Other specified disorders of amniotic fluid and membranes**

\+ **O41.8X Other specified disorders of amniotic fluid and membranes**

• ♀ +7th **O41.8X1 Other specified disorders of amniotic fluid and membranes, first trimester**

• ♀ +7th **O41.8X2 Other specified disorders of amniotic fluid and membranes, second trimester**

• ♀ +7th **O41.8X3 Other specified disorders of amniotic fluid and membranes, third trimester**

• ♀ +7th **O41.8X9 Other specified disorders of amniotic fluid and membranes, unspecified trimester**

\+ **O41.9 Disorder of amniotic fluid and membranes, unspecified**

• ♀ X+7th **O41.90 Disorder of amniotic fluid and membranes, unspecified, unspecified trimester**

• ♀ X+7th **O41.91 Disorder of amniotic fluid and membranes, unspecified, first trimester**

• ♀ X+7th **O41.92 Disorder of amniotic fluid and membranes, unspecified, second trimester**

• ♀ X+7th **O41.93 Disorder of amniotic fluid and membranes, unspecified, third trimester**

O42 Premature rupture of membranes

\+ **O42.0 Premature rupture of membranes, onset of labor within 24 hours of rupture**

• ♀ **O42.00 Premature rupture of membranes, onset of labor within 24 hours of rupture, unspecified weeks of gestation**

\+ **O42.01 Preterm premature rupture of membranes, onset of labor within 24 hours of rupture**
Premature rupture of membranes before 37 completed weeks of gestation

• ♀ **O42.011 Preterm premature rupture of membranes, onset of labor within 24 hours of rupture, first trimester**

• ♀ **O42.012 Preterm premature rupture of membranes, onset of labor within 24 hours of rupture, second trimester**

• ♀ **O42.013 Preterm premature rupture of membranes, onset of labor within 24 hours of rupture, third trimester**

• ♀ **O42.019 Preterm premature rupture of membranes, onset of labor within 24 hours of rupture, unspecified trimester**

• ♀ **O42.02 Full-term premature rupture of membranes, onset of labor within 24 hours of rupture**
Premature rupture of membranes after 37 completed weeks of gestation

\+ **O42.1 Premature rupture of membranes, onset of labor more than 24 hours following rupture**

• ♀ **O42.10 Premature rupture of membranes, onset of labor more than 24 hours following rupture, unspecified weeks of gestation**

\+ **O42.11 Preterm premature rupture of membranes, onset of labor more than 24 hours following rupture**
Premature rupture of membranes before 37 completed weeks of gestation

• ♀ **O42.111 Preterm premature rupture of membranes, onset of labor more than 24 hours following rupture, first trimester**

• ♀ **O42.112 Preterm premature rupture of membranes, onset of labor more than 24 hours following rupture, second trimester**

• ♀ **O42.113 Preterm premature rupture of membranes, onset of labor more than 24 hours following rupture, third trimester**

• ♀ **O42.119 Preterm premature rupture of membranes, onset of labor more than 24 hours following rupture, unspecified trimester**

• ♀ **O42.12 Full-term premature rupture of membranes, onset of labor more than 24 hours following rupture**
Premature rupture of membranes after 37 completed weeks of gestation

\+ **O42.9 Premature rupture of membranes, unspecified as to length of time between rupture and onset of labor**

• ♀ **O42.90 Premature rupture of membranes, unspecified as to length of time between rupture and onset of labor, unspecified weeks of gestation**

\+ **O42.91 Preterm premature rupture of membranes, unspecified as to length of time between rupture and onset of labor**
Premature rupture of membranes before 37 completed weeks of gestation

• ♀ **O42.911 Preterm premature rupture of membranes, unspecified as to length of time between rupture and onset of labor, first trimester**

• ♀ **O42.912 Preterm premature rupture of membranes, unspecified as to length of time between rupture and onset of labor, second trimester**

• ♀ **O42.913 Preterm premature rupture of membranes, unspecified as to length of time between rupture and onset of labor, third trimester**

• ♀ **O42.919 Preterm premature rupture of membranes, unspecified as to length of time between rupture and onset of labor, unspecified trimester**

• ♀ **O42.92 Full-term premature rupture of membranes, unspecified as to length of time between rupture and onset of labor**
Premature rupture of membranes after 37 completed weeks of gestation

O43 Placental disorders

Excludes2: *maternal care for poor fetal growth due to placental insufficiency (O36.5-)*
placenta previa (O44.-)
placental polyp (O90.89)
placentitis (O41.14-)
premature separation of placenta [abruptio placentae] (O45.-)

\+ **O43.0 Placental transfusion syndromes**

\+ **O43.01 Fetomaternal placental transfusion syndrome**
Maternofetal placental transfusion syndrome

• ♀ **O43.011 Fetomaternal placental transfusion syndrome, first trimester**

• ♀ **O43.012 Fetomaternal placental transfusion syndrome, second trimester**

• ♀ **O43.013 Fetomaternal placental transfusion syndrome, third trimester**

• ♀ **O43.019 Fetomaternal placental transfusion syndrome, unspecified trimester**

\+ **O43.02 Fetus-to-fetus placental transfusion syndrome**

• ♀ **O43.021 Fetus-to-fetus placental transfusion syndrome, first trimester**

• ♀ **O43.022 Fetus-to-fetus placental transfusion syndrome, second trimester**

• ♀ **O43.023 Fetus-to-fetus placental transfusion syndrome, third trimester**

• ♀ **O43.029 Fetus-to-fetus placental transfusion syndrome, unspecified trimester**

+ **O43.1 Malformation of placenta**
+ **O43.10 Malformation of placenta, unspecified**
  Abnormal placenta NOS
- ♀ **O43.101 Malformation of placenta, unspecified, first trimester**
- ♀ **O43.102 Malformation of placenta, unspecified, second trimester**
- ♀ **O43.103 Malformation of placenta, unspecified, third trimester**
- ♀ **O43.109 Malformation of placenta, unspecified, unspecified trimester**

+ **O43.11 Circumvallate placenta**
- ♀ **O43.111 Circumvallate placenta, first trimester**
- ♀ **O43.112 Circumvallate placenta, second trimester**
- ♀ **O43.113 Circumvallate placenta, third trimester**
- ♀ **O43.119 Circumvallate placenta, unspecified trimester**

+ **O43.12 Velamentous insertion of umbilical cord**
- ♀ **O43.121 Velamentous insertion of umbilical cord, first trimester**
- ♀ **O43.122 Velamentous insertion of umbilical cord, second trimester**
- ♀ **O43.123 Velamentous insertion of umbilical cord, third trimester**
- ♀ **O43.129 Velamentous insertion of umbilical cord, unspecified trimester**

+ **O43.19 Other malformation of placenta**
- ♀ **O43.191 Other malformation of placenta, first trimester**
- ♀ **O43.192 Other malformation of placenta, second trimester**
- ♀ **O43.193 Other malformation of placenta, third trimester**
- ♀ **O43.199 Other malformation of placenta, unspecified trimester**

+ **O43.2 Morbidly adherent placenta**
  Code also associated third stage postpartum hemorrhage, if applicable (O72.0)
  Excludes1: *retained placenta (O73.-)*
+ **O43.21 Placenta accreta**
- ♀ **O43.211 Placenta accreta, first trimester**
- ♀ **O43.212 Placenta accreta, second trimester**
- ♀ **O43.213 Placenta accreta, third trimester**
- ♀ **O43.219 accreta, unspecified trimester**

+ **O43.22 Placenta increta**
- ♀ **O43.221 Placenta increta, first trimester**
- ♀ **O43.222 Placenta increta, second trimester**
- ♀ **O43.223 Placenta increta, third trimester**
- ♀ **O43.229 Placenta increta, unspecified trimester**

+ **O43.23 Placenta percreta**
- ♀ **O43.231 Placenta percreta, first trimester**
- ♀ **O43.232 Placenta percreta, second trimester**
- ♀ **O43.233 Placenta percreta, third trimester**
- ♀ **O43.239 Placenta percreta, unspecified trimester**

+ **O43.8 Other placental disorders**
+ **O43.81 Placental infarction**
- ♀ **O43.811 Placental infarction, first trimester**
- ♀ **O43.812 Placental infarction, second trimester**
- ♀ **O43.813 Placental infarction, third trimester**
- ♀ **O43.819 Placental infarction, unspecified trimester**

+ **O43.89 Other placental disorders**
  Placental dysfunction
- ♀ **O43.891 Other placental disorders, first trimester**
- ♀ **O43.892 Other placental disorders, second trimester**
- ♀ **O43.893 Other placental disorders, third trimester**
- ♀ **O43.899 Other placental disorders, unspecified trimester**

+ **O43.9 Unspecified placental disorder**
- ♀ **O43.90 Unspecified placental disorder, unspecified trimester**
- ♀ **O43.91 Unspecified placental disorder, first trimester**
- ♀ **O43.92 Unspecified placental disorder, second trimester**
- ♀ **O43.93 Unspecified placental disorder, third trimester**

O44 Placenta previa

+ **O44.0 Placenta previa specified as without hemorrhage**
  Low implantation of placenta specified as without hemorrhage
- ♀ **O44.00 Placenta previa specified as without hemorrhage, unspecified trimester**
- ♀ CC **O44.01 Placenta previa specified as without hemorrhage, first trimester**
  CC Exclusion see Appendix A PDX collection 0966
- ♀ CC **O44.02 Placenta previa specified as without hemorrhage, second trimester**
  CC Exclusion see Appendix A PDX collection 0966
- ♀ CC **O44.03 Placenta previa specified as without hemorrhage, t trimester**
  CC Exclusion see Appendix A PDX collection 0966

+ **O44.1 Placenta previa with hemorrhage**
  Low implantation of placenta, NOS or with hemorrhage
  Marginal placenta previa, NOS or with hemorrhage
  Partial placenta previa, NOS or with hemorrhage
  Total placenta previa, NOS or with hemorrhage
  Excludes1: *labor and delivery complicated by hemorrhage f vasa previa (O69.4)*
- ♀ **O44.10 Placenta previa with hemorrhage, unspecified trimester**
- ♀ MCC **O44.11 Placenta previa with hemorrhage, first trimester**
  MCC Exclusion see Appendix A PDX collection 0966
- ♀ MCC **O44.12 Placenta previa with hemorrhage, second trimester**
  MCC Exclusion see Appendix A PDX collection 0966
- ♀ MCC **O44.13 Placenta previa with hemorrhage, third trimester**
  MCC Exclusion see Appendix A PDX collection 0966

O45 Premature separation of placenta [abruptio placentae]

+ **O45.0 Premature separation of placenta with coagulation defect**
+ **O45.00 Premature separation of placenta with coagulation defect, unspecified**
- ♀ MCC **O45.001 Premature separation of placenta with coagulation defect, unspecified, first trimester**
  MCC Exclusion see Appendix A PDX collecti 0985
- ♀ MCC **O45.002 Premature separation of placenta with coagulation defect, unspecified, second trimester**
  MCC Exclusion see Appendix A PDX collecti 0985
- ♀ MCC **O45.003 Premature separation of placenta with coagulation defect, unspecified, third trimester**
  MCC Exclusion see Appendix A PDX collecti 0985
- ♀ **O45.009 Premature separation of placenta with coagulation defect, unspecified, unspecifi trimester**

+ **O45.01 Premature separation of placenta with afibrinogenemia**
  Premature separation of placenta with hypofibrinogenemia
- ♀ MCC **O45.011 Premature separation of placenta with afibrinogenemia, first trimester**
  MCC Exclusion see Appendix A PDX collecti 0985
- ♀ MCC **O45.012 Premature separation of placenta with afibrinogenemia, second trimester**
  MCC Exclusion see Appendix A PDX collecti 0985
- ♀ MCC **O45.013 Premature separation of placenta with afibrinogenemia, third trimester**
  MCC Exclusion see Appendix A PDX collecti 0985
- ♀ **O45.019 Premature separation of placenta with afibrinogenemia, unspecified trimester**

+ **O45.02 Premature separation of placenta with disseminated intravascular coagulation**
- ♀ MCC **O45.021 Premature separation of placenta with disseminated intravascular coagulation, trimester**
  MCC Exclusion see Appendix A PDX collecti 0985
- ♀ MCC **O45.022 Premature separation of placenta with disseminated intravascular coagulation, second trimester**
  MCC Exclusion see Appendix A PDX collecti 0985
- ♀ MCC **O45.023 Premature separation of placenta with disseminated intravascular coagulation, third trimester**
  MCC Exclusion see Appendix A PDX collecti 0985
- ♀ **O45.029 Premature separation of placenta with disseminated intravascular coagulation, unspecified trimester**

O45.09 Premature separation of placenta with other coagulation defect

• ♀ MCC **O45.091 Premature separation of placenta with other coagulation defect, first trimester**
MCC Exclusion see Appendix A PDX collection 0985

• ♀ MCC **O45.092 Premature separation of placenta with other coagulation defect, second trimester**
MCC Exclusion see Appendix A PDX collection 0985

• ♀ MCC **O45.093 Premature separation of placenta with other coagulation defect, third trimester**
MCC Exclusion see Appendix A PDX collection 0985

• ♀ **O45.099 Premature separation of placenta with other coagulation defect, unspecified trimester**

+ **O45.8 Other premature separation of placenta**

+ **O45.8X Other premature separation of placenta**

• ♀ MCC **O45.8X1 Other premature separation of placenta, first trimester**
MCC Exclusion see Appendix A PDX collection 0986

• ♀ MCC **O45.8X2 Other premature separation of placenta, second trimester**
MCC Exclusion see Appendix A PDX collection 0986

• ♀ MCC **O45.8X3 Other premature separation of placenta, third trimester**
MCC Exclusion see Appendix A PDX collection 0986

• ♀ **O45.8X9 Other premature separation of placenta, unspecified trimester**

+ **O45.9 Premature separation of placenta, unspecified**
Abruptio placentae NOS

• ♀ **O45.90 Premature separation of placenta, unspecified, unspecified trimester**

• ♀ MCC **O45.91 Premature separation of placenta, unspecified, first trimester**
MCC Exclusion see Appendix A PDX collection 0986

• ♀ MCC **O45.92 Premature separation of placenta, unspecified, second trimester**
MCC Exclusion see Appendix A PDX collection 0986

• ♀ MCC **O45.93 Premature separation of placenta, unspecified, third trimester**
MCC Exclusion see Appendix A PDX collection 0986

O46 Antepartum hemorrhage, not elsewhere classified

Excludes1: *hemorrhage in early pregnancy (O20.-)*
intrapartum hemorrhage NEC (O67.-)
placenta previa (O44.-)
premature separation of placenta [abruptio placentae] (O45.-)

+ **O46.0 Antepartum hemorrhage with coagulation defect**

+ **O46.00 Antepartum hemorrhage with coagulation defect, unspecified**

• ♀ MCC **O46.001 Antepartum hemorrhage with coagulation defect, unspecified, first trimester**
MCC Exclusion see Appendix A PDX collection 0985

• ♀ MCC **O46.002 Antepartum hemorrhage with coagulation defect, unspecified, second trimester**
MCC Exclusion see Appendix A PDX collection 0985

• ♀ MCC **O46.003 Antepartum hemorrhage with coagulation defect, unspecified, third trimester**
MCC Exclusion see Appendix A PDX collection 0985

• ♀ **O46.009 Antepartum hemorrhage with coagulation defect, unspecified, unspecified trimester**

+ **O46.01 Antepartum hemorrhage with afibrinogenemia**
Antepartum hemorrhage with hypofibrinogenemia

• ♀ MCC **O46.011 Antepartum hemorrhage with afibrinogenemia, first trimester**
MCC Exclusion see Appendix A PDX collection 0985

• ♀ MCC **O46.012 Antepartum hemorrhage with afibrinogenemia, second trimester**
MCC Exclusion see Appendix A PDX collection 0985

• ♀ MCC **O46.013 Antepartum hemorrhage with afibrinogenemia, third trimester**
MCC Exclusion see Appendix A PDX collection 0985

• ♀ **O46.019 Antepartum hemorrhage with afibrinogenemia, unspecified trimester**

+ **O46.02 Antepartum hemorrhage with disseminated intravascular coagulation**

• ♀ MCC **O46.021 Antepartum hemorrhage with disseminated intravascular coagulation, first trimester**
MCC Exclusion see Appendix A PDX collection 0985

• ♀ MCC **O46.022 Antepartum hemorrhage with disseminated intravascular coagulation, second trimester**
MCC Exclusion see Appendix A PDX collection 0985

• ♀ MCC **O46.023 Antepartum hemorrhage with disseminated intravascular coagulation, third trimester**
MCC Exclusion see Appendix A PDX collection 0985

• ♀ **O46.029 Antepartum hemorrhage with disseminated intravascular coagulation, unspecified trimester**

+ **O46.09 Antepartum hemorrhage with other coagulation defect**

• ♀ MCC **O46.091 Antepartum hemorrhage with other coagulation defect, first trimester**
MCC Exclusion see Appendix A PDX collection 0985

• ♀ MCC **O46.092 Antepartum hemorrhage with other coagulation defect, second trimester**
MCC Exclusion see Appendix A PDX collection 0985

• ♀ MCC **O46.093 Antepartum hemorrhage with other coagulation defect, third trimester**
MCC Exclusion see Appendix A PDX collection 0985

• ♀ **O46.099 Antepartum hemorrhage with other coagulation defect, unspecified trimester**

+ **O46.8 Other antepartum hemorrhage**

+ **O46.8X Other antepartum hemorrhage**

• ♀ **O46.8X1 Other antepartum hemorrhage, first trimester**

• ♀ **O46.8X2 Other antepartum hemorrhage, second trimester**

• ♀ **O46.8X3 Other antepartum hemorrhage, third trimester**

• ♀ **O46.8X9 Other antepartum hemorrhage, unspecified trimester**

+ **O46.9 Antepartum hemorrhage, unspecified**

• ♀ **O46.90 Antepartum hemorrhage, unspecified, unspecified trimester**

• ♀ **O46.91 Antepartum hemorrhage, unspecified, first trimester**

• ♀ **O46.92 Antepartum hemorrhage, unspecified, second trimester**

• ♀ **O46.93 Antepartum hemorrhage, unspecified, third trimester**

O47 False labor

Includes: Braxton Hicks contractions
threatened labor

Excludes1: *preterm labor (O60.-)*

+ **O47.0 False labor before 37 completed weeks of gestation**

• ♀ **O47.00 False labor before 37 completed weeks of gestation, unspecified trimester**

• ♀ CC **O47.02 False labor before 37 completed weeks of gestation, second trimester**
CC Exclusion see Appendix A PDX collection 0987

• ♀ CC **O47.03 False labor before 37 completed weeks of gestation, third trimester**
CC Exclusion see Appendix A PDX collection 0987

• ♀ CC **O47.1 False labor at or after 37 completed weeks of gestation**
CC Exclusion see Appendix A PDX collection 0987

• ♀ **O47.9 False labor, unspecified**

O48 Late pregnancy

• ♀ **O48.0 Post-term pregnancy**
Pregnancy over 40 completed weeks to 42 completed weeks gestation

• ♀ **O48.1 Prolonged pregnancy**
Pregnancy which has advanced beyond 42 completed weeks gestation

Complications of labor and delivery (O60-O77)

O60 Preterm labor

Includes: onset (spontaneous) of labor before 37 completed weeks of gestation

Excludes1: *false labor (O47.0-)*
threatened labor NOS (O47.0-)

\+ **O60.0 Preterm labor without delivery**

• ♀ **O60.00 Preterm labor without delivery, unspecified trimester**

• ♀ MCC **O60.02 Preterm labor without delivery, second trimester**
MCC Exclusion see Appendix A PDX collection 0987

• ♀ MCC **O60.03 Preterm labor without delivery, third trimester**
MCC Exclusion see Appendix A PDX collection 0987

\+ **O60.1 Preterm labor with preterm delivery**

One of the following 7th characters is to be assigned to each code under subcategory O60.1. 7th character 0 is for single gestations and multiple gestations where the fetus is unspecified. 7th characters 1 through 9 are for cases of multiple gestations to identify the fetus for which the code applies. The appropriate code from category O30, Multiple gestation, must also be assigned when assigning a code from subcategory O60.1 that has a 7th character of 1 through 9.

- 0 - not applicable or unspecified
- 1 - fetus 1
- 2 - fetus 2
- 3 - fetus 3
- 4 - fetus 4
- 5 - fetus 5
- 9 - other fetus

• ♀ CC X+7th **O60.10 Preterm labor with preterm delivery, unspecified trimester**
Preterm labor with delivery NOS
CC Exclusion for all 7th characters see Appendix A PDX collection 0987

• ♀ MCC X+7th **O60.12 Preterm labor second trimester with preterm delivery second trimester**
MCC Exclusion for all 7th characters see Appendix A PDX collection 0987

• ♀ MCC X+7th **O60.13 Preterm labor second trimester with preterm delivery third trimester**
MCC Exclusion for all 7th characters see Appendix A PDX collection 0987

• ♀ MCC X+7th **O60.14 Preterm labor third trimester with preterm delivery third trimester**
MCC Exclusion for all 7th characters see Appendix A PDX collection 0987

\+ **O60.2 Term delivery with preterm labor**

One of the following 7th characters is to be assigned to each code under subcategory O60.2. 7th character 0 is for single gestations and multiple gestations where the fetus is unspecified. 7th characters 1 through 9 are for cases of multiple gestations to identify the fetus for which the code applies. The appropriate code from category O30, Multiple gestation, must also be assigned when assigning a code from subcategory O60.2 that has a 7th character of 1 through 9.

- 0 - not applicable or unspecified
- 1 - fetus 1
- 2 - fetus 2
- 3 - fetus 3
- 4 - fetus 4
- 5 - fetus 5
- 9 - other fetus

• ♀ CC X+7th **O60.20 Term delivery with preterm labor, unspecified trimester**
CC Exclusion for all 7th characters see Appendix A PDX collection 0987

• ♀ MCC X+7th **O60.22 Term delivery with preterm labor, second trimester**
MCC Exclusion for all 7th characters see Appendix A PDX collection 0987

• ♀ MCC X+7th **O60.23 Term delivery with preterm labor, third trimester**
MCC Exclusion for all 7th characters see Appendix A PDX collection 0987

O61 Failed induction of labor

• ♀ **O61.0 Failed medical induction of labor**
Failed induction (of labor) by oxytocin
Failed induction (of labor) by prostaglandins

• ♀ **O61.1 Failed instrumental induction of labor**
Failed mechanical induction (of labor)
Failed surgical induction (of labor)

• ♀ **O61.8 Other failed induction of labor**

• ♀ **O61.9 Failed induction of labor, unspecified**

O62 Abnormalities of forces of labor

• ♀ **O62.0 Primary inadequate contractions**
Failure of cervical dilatation
Primary hypotonic uterine dysfunction
Uterine inertia during latent phase of labor

• ♀ **O62.1 Secondary uterine inertia**
Arrested active phase of labor
Secondary hypotonic uterine dysfunction

• ♀ **O62.2 Other uterine inertia**
Atony of uterus without hemorrhage
Atony of uterus NOS
Desultory labor
Hypotonic uterine dysfunction NOS
Irregular labor
Poor contractions
Slow slope active phase of labor
Uterine inertia NOS
Excludes1: *atony of uterus with hemorrhage (postpartum) (O72.1)*
postpartum atony of uterus without hemorrhage (O75.89)

• ♀ **O62.3 Precipitate labor**

• ♀ **O62.4 Hypertonic, incoordinate, and prolonged uterine contractions**
Cervical spasm
Contraction ring dystocia
Dyscoordinate labor
Hour-glass contraction of uterus
Hypertonic uterine dysfunction
Incoordinate uterine action
Tetanic contractions
Uterine dystocia NOS
Uterine spasm
Excludes1: *dystocia (fetal) (maternal) NOS (O66.9)*

• ♀ **O62.8 Other abnormalities of forces of labor**

• ♀ **O62.9 Abnormality of forces of labor, unspecified**

O63 Long labor

• ♀ **O63.0 Prolonged first stage (of labor)**

• ♀ **O63.1 Prolonged second stage (of labor)**

• ♀ **O63.2 Delayed delivery of second twin, triplet, etc.**

• ♀ CC **O63.9 Long labor, unspecified**
Prolonged labor NOS
CC Exclusion see Appendix A PDX collection 0988

O64 Obstructed labor due to malposition and malpresentation of fetus

One of the following 7th characters is to be assigned to each code under category O64. 7th character 0 is for single gestations and multiple gestations where the fetus is unspecified. 7th characters 1 through 9 are for cases of multiple gestations to identify the fetus for which the code applies. The appropriate code from category O30, Multiple gestation, mu[st] also be assigned when assigning a code from category O64 that has a 7th character of 1 through 9.

- 0 - not applicable or unspecified
- 1 - fetus 1
- 2 - fetus 2
- 3 - fetus 3
- 4 - fetus 4
- 5 - fetus 5
- 9 - other fetus

• ♀ X+7th **O64.0 Obstructed labor due to incomplete rotation of fetal head**
Deep transverse arrest
Obstructed labor due to persistent occipitoiliac (position)
Obstructed labor due to persistent occipitoposterior (position)
Obstructed labor due to persistent occipitosacral (position)
Obstructed labor due to persistent occipitotransverse (position)

• ♀ X+7th **O64.1 Obstructed labor due to breech presentation**
Obstructed labor due to buttocks presentation
Obstructed labor due to complete breech presentation
Obstructed labor due to frank breech presentation

• ♀ X+7th **O64.2 Obstructed labor due to face presentation**
Obstructed labor due to chin presentation

• ♀ X+7th **O64.3 Obstructed labor due to brow presentation**

• ♀ X+7th **O64.4 Obstructed labor due to shoulder presentation**
Prolapsed arm
Excludes1: *impacted shoulders (O66.0)*
shoulder dystocia (O66.0)

♀ X+7th **O64.5 Obstructed labor due to compound presentation**
♀ X+7th **O64.8 Obstructed labor due to other malposition and malpresentation**
Obstructed labor due to footling presentation
Obstructed labor due to incomplete breech presentation
♀ X+7th **O64.9 Obstructed labor due to malposition and malpresentation, unspecified**

O65 Obstructed labor due to maternal pelvic abnormality

• ♀ **O65.0 Obstructed labor due to deformed pelvis**
• ♀ **O65.1 Obstructed labor due to generally contracted pelvis**
• ♀ **O65.2 Obstructed labor due to pelvic inlet contraction**
• ♀ **O65.3 Obstructed labor due to pelvic outlet and mid-cavity contraction**
• ♀ **O65.4 Obstructed labor due to fetopelvic disproportion, unspecified**
Excludes1: *dystocia due to abnormality of fetus (O66.2-O66.3)*
• ♀ **O65.5 Obstructed labor due to abnormality of maternal pelvic organs**
Obstructed labor due to conditions listed in O34.-
Use additional code to identify abnormality of pelvic organs O34.-
• ♀ **O65.8 Obstructed labor due to other maternal pelvic abnormalities**
• ♀ **O65.9 Obstructed labor due to maternal pelvic abnormality, unspecified**

O66 Other obstructed labor

• ♀ **O66.0 Obstructed labor due to shoulder dystocia**
Impacted shoulders
• ♀ **O66.1 Obstructed labor due to locked twins**
• ♀ **O66.2 Obstructed labor due to unusually large fetus**
• ♀ **O66.3 Obstructed labor due to other abnormalities of fetus**
Dystocia due to fetal ascites
Dystocia due to fetal hydrops
Dystocia due to fetal meningomyelocele
Dystocia due to fetal sacral teratoma
Dystocia due to fetal tumor
Dystocia due to hydrocephalic fetus
Use additional code to identify cause of obstruction
+ **O66.4 Failed trial of labor**
• ♀ **O66.40 Failed trial of labor, unspecified**
• ♀ **O66.41 Failed attempted vaginal birth after previous cesarean delivery**
Code first rupture of uterus, if applicable (O71.0-, O71.1)
• ♀ **O66.5 Attempted application of vacuum extractor and forceps**
Attempted application of vacuum or forceps, with subsequent delivery by forceps or cesarean delivery
• ♀ **O66.6 Obstructed labor due to other multiple fetuses**
• ♀ **O66.8 Other specified obstructed labor**
Use additional code to identify cause of obstruction
• ♀ **O66.9 Obstructed labor, unspecified**
Dystocia NOS
Fetal dystocia NOS
Maternal dystocia NOS

O67 Labor and delivery complicated by intrapartum hemorrhage, not elsewhere classified

Excludes1: *antepartum hemorrhage NEC (O46.-)*
placenta previa (O44.-)
premature separation of placenta [abruptio placentae] (O45.-)
Excludes2: *postpartum hemorrhage (O72.-)*
♀ MCC **O67.0 Intrapartum hemorrhage with coagulation defect**
Intrapartum hemorrhage (excessive) associated with afibrinogenemia
Intrapartum hemorrhage (excessive) associated with disseminated intravascular coagulation
Intrapartum hemorrhage (excessive) associated with hyperfibrinolysis
Intrapartum hemorrhage (excessive) associated with hypofibrinogenemia
MCC Exclusion see Appendix A PDX collection 0985
• ♀ **O67.8 Other intrapartum hemorrhage**
Excessive intrapartum hemorrhage
• ♀ **O67.9 Intrapartum hemorrhage, unspecified**

• ♀ CC **O68 Labor and delivery complicated by abnormality of fetal acid-base balance**
Fetal acidemia complicating labor and delivery
Fetal acidosis complicating labor and delivery
Fetal alkalosis complicating labor and delivery
Fetal metabolic acidemia complicating labor and delivery
Excludes1: *fetal stress NOS (O77.9)*
labor and delivery complicated by electrocardiographic evidence of fetal stress (O77.8)
labor and delivery complicated by ultrasonic evidence of fetal stress (O77.8)
Excludes2: *abnormality in fetal heart rate or rhythm (O76)*
labor and delivery complicated by meconium in amniotic fluid (O77.0)
CC Exclusion see Appendix A PDX collection 0989
Valid 3-character code, no further characters required

O69 Labor and delivery complicated by umbilical cord complications

One of the following 7th characters is to be assigned to each code under category O69. 7th character 0 is for single gestations and multiple gestations where the fetus is unspecified. 7th characters 1 through 9 are for cases of multiple gestations to identify the fetus for which the code applies. The appropriate code from category O30, Multiple gestation, must also be assigned when assigning a code from category O69 that has a 7th character of 1 through 9.
0 - not applicable or unspecified
1 - fetus 1
2 - fetus 2
3 - fetus 3
4 - fetus 4
5 - fetus 5
9 - other fetus

• ♀ X+7th **O69.0 Labor and delivery complicated by prolapse of cord**
• ♀ X+7th **O69.1 Labor and delivery complicated by cord around neck, with compression**
Excludes1: *labor and delivery complicated by cord around neck, without compression (O69.81)*
• ♀ X+7th **O69.2 Labor and delivery complicated by other cord entanglement, with compression**
Labor and delivery complicated by compression of cord NOS
Labor and delivery complicated by entanglement of cords of twins in monoamniotic sac
Labor and delivery complicated by knot in cord
Excludes1: *labor and delivery complicated by other cordentanglement,withoutcompression(O69.82)*
• ♀ X+7th **O69.3 Labor and delivery complicated by short cord**
• ♀ X+7th **O69.4 Labor and delivery complicated by vasa previa**
Labor and delivery complicated by hemorrhage from vasa previa
• ♀ X+7th **O69.5 Labor and delivery complicated by vascular lesion of cord**
Labor and delivery complicated by cord bruising
Labor and delivery complicated by cord hematoma
Labor and delivery complicated by thrombosis of umbilical vessels
X+7th **O69.8 Labor and delivery complicated by other cord complications**
• ♀ X+7th **O69.81 Labor and delivery complicated by cord around neck, without compression**
• ♀ X+7th **O69.82 Labor and delivery complicated by other cord entanglement, without compression**
• ♀ X+7th **O69.89 Labor and delivery complicated by other cord complications**
• ♀ X+7th **O69.9 Labor and delivery complicated by cord complication, unspecified**

O70 Perineal laceration during delivery

Includes: episiotomy extended by laceration
Excludes1: *obstetric high vaginal laceration alone (O71.4)*
• ♀ **O70.0 First degree perineal laceration during delivery**
Perineal laceration, rupture or tear involving fourchette during delivery
Perineal laceration, rupture or tear involving labia during delivery
Perineal laceration, rupture or tear involving skin during delivery
Perineal laceration, rupture or tear involving vagina during delivery
Perineal laceration, rupture or tear involving vulva during delivery
Slight perineal laceration, rupture or tear during delivery

• ♀ **O70.1 Second degree perineal laceration during delivery**
Perineal laceration, rupture or tear during delivery as in O70.0, also involving pelvic floor
Perineal laceration, rupture or tear during delivery as in O70.0, also involving perineal muscles
Perineal laceration, rupture or tear during delivery as in O70.0, also involving vaginal muscles
Excludes1: *perineal laceration involving anal sphincter (O70.2)*

• ♀ CC **O70.2 Third degree perineal laceration during delivery**
Perineal laceration, rupture or tear during delivery as in O70.1, also involving anal sphincter
Perineal laceration, rupture or tear during delivery as in O70.1, also involving rectovaginal septum
Perineal laceration, rupture or tear during delivery as in O70.1, also involving sphincter NOS
Excludes1: *anal sphincter tear during delivery without third degree perineal laceration (O70.4)*
perineal laceration involving anal or rectal mucosa (O70.3)
CC Exclusion see Appendix A PDX collection 0990

• ♀ CC **O70.3 Fourth degree perineal laceration during delivery**
Perineal laceration, rupture or tear during delivery as in O70.2, also involving anal mucosa
Perineal laceration, rupture or tear during delivery as in O70.2, also involving rectal mucosa
CC Exclusion see Appendix A PDX collection 0991

• ♀ CC **O70.4 Anal sphincter tear complicating delivery, not associated with third degree laceration**
Excludes1: *anal sphincter tear with third degree perineal laceration (O70.2)*
CC Exclusion see Appendix A PDX collection 0992

• ♀ **O70.9 Perineal laceration during delivery, unspecified**

O71 Other obstetric trauma

Includes: obstetric damage from instruments

\+ **O71.0 Rupture of uterus (spontaneous) before onset of labor**
Excludes1: *disruption of (current) cesarean delivery wound (O90.0)*
laceration of uterus, NEC (O71.81)

• ♀ **O71.00 Rupture of uterus before onset of labor, unspecified trimester**

• ♀ MCC **O71.02 Rupture of uterus before onset of labor, second trimester**
MCC Exclusion see Appendix A PDX collection 0993

• ♀ MCC **O71.03 Rupture of uterus before onset of labor, third trimester**
MCC Exclusion see Appendix A PDX collection 0993

• ♀ MCC **O71.1 Rupture of uterus during labor**
Rupture of uterus not stated as occurring before onset of labor
Excludes1: *disruption of cesarean delivery wound (O90.0)*
laceration of uterus, NEC (O71.81)
MCC Exclusion see Appendix A PDX collection 0993

• ♀ CC **O71.2 Postpartum inversion of uterus**
CC Exclusion see Appendix A PDX collection 0994

• ♀ CC **O71.3 Obstetric laceration of cervix**
Annular detachment of cervix
CC Exclusion see Appendix A PDX collection 0995

• ♀ CC **O71.4 Obstetric high vaginal laceration alone**
Laceration of vaginal wall without perineal laceration
Excludes1: *obstetric high vaginal laceration with perineal laceration (O70.-)*
CC Exclusion see Appendix A PDX collection 0996

• ♀ CC **O71.5 Other obstetric injury to pelvic organs**
Obstetric injury to bladder
Obstetric injury to urethra
Excludes2: *obstetric periurethral trauma (O71.82)*
CC Exclusion see Appendix A PDX collection 0993

• ♀ CC **O71.6 Obstetric damage to pelvic joints and ligaments**
Obstetric avulsion of inner symphyseal cartilage
Obstetric damage to coccyx
CC Exclusion see Appendix A PDX collection 0997
Obstetric traumatic separation of symphysis (pubis)

• ♀ CC **O71.7 Obstetric hematoma of pelvis**
Obstetric hematoma of perineum
Obstetric hematoma of vagina
Obstetric hematoma of vulva
CC Exclusion see Appendix A PDX collection 0998

\+ **O71.8 Other specified obstetric trauma**

• ♀ **O71.81 Laceration of uterus, not elsewhere classified**

• ♀ **O71.82 Other specified trauma to perineum and vulva**
Obstetric periurethral trauma

• ♀ **O71.89 Other specified obstetric trauma**

• ♀ **O71.9 Obstetric trauma, unspecified**

O72 Postpartum hemorrhage

Includes: hemorrhage after delivery of fetus or infant

• ♀ CC **O72.0 Third-stage hemorrhage**
Hemorrhage associated with retained, trapped or adherent placenta
Retained placenta NOS
Code also type of adherent placenta (O43.2-)
CC Exclusion see Appendix A PDX collection 0999

• ♀ CC **O72.1 Other immediate postpartum hemorrhage**
Hemorrhage following delivery of placenta
Postpartum hemorrhage (atonic) NOS
Uterine atony with hemorrhage
Excludes1: *uterine atony NOS (O62.2)*
uterine atony without hemorrhage (O62.2)
postpartum atony of uterus without hemorrhag (O75.89)
CC Exclusion see Appendix A PDX collection 1000

• ♀ CC **O72.2 Delayed and secondary postpartum hemorrhage**
Hemorrhage associated with retained portions of placenta or membranes after the first 24 hours following delivery of placenta
Retained products of conception NOS, following delivery
CC Exclusion see Appendix A PDX collection 1001

• ♀ **O72.3 Postpartum coagulation defects**
Postpartum afibrinogenemia
Postpartum fibrinolysis

O73 Retained placenta and membranes, without hemorrhage

Excludes1: *placenta accreta (O43.21-)*
placenta increta (O43.22-)
placenta percreta (O43.23-)

• ♀ **O73.0 Retained placenta without hemorrhage**
Adherent placenta, without hemorrhage
Trapped placenta without hemorrhage

• ♀ **O73.1 Retained portions of placenta and membranes, without hemorrhage**
Retained products of conception following delivery, without hemorrhage

O74 Complications of anesthesia during labor and delivery

Includes: maternal complications arising from the administration of a general, regional or local anesthetic, analgesic or other sedation during labor and delivery
Use additional code, if applicable, to identify specific complication

• ♀ **O74.0 Aspiration pneumonitis due to anesthesia during labor and delivery**
Inhalation of stomach contents or secretions NOS due to anesthesia during labor and delivery
Mendelson's syndrome due to anesthesia during labor and delivery

• ♀ **O74.1 Other pulmonary complications of anesthesia during labor a delivery**

• ♀ **O74.2 Cardiac complications of anesthesia during labor and deliver**

• ♀ **O74.3 Central nervous system complications of anesthesia during la and delivery**

• ♀ **O74.4 Toxic reaction to local anesthesia during labor and delivery**

• ♀ **O74.5 Spinal and epidural anesthesia-induced headache during lab and delivery**

• ♀ **O74.6 Other complications of spinal and epidural anesthesia during labor and delivery**

• ♀ **O74.7 Failed or difficult intubation for anesthesia during labor and delivery**

• ♀ **O74.8 Other complications of anesthesia during labor and delivery**

• ♀ **O74.9 Complication of anesthesia during labor and delivery, unspecified**

O75 Other complications of labor and delivery, not elsewhere classified

Excludes2: *puerperal (postpartum) infection (O86.-)*
puerperal (postpartum) sepsis (O85)

• ♀ **O75.0 Maternal distress during labor and delivery**

• ♀ MCC **O75.1 Shock during or following labor and delivery**
Obstetric shock following labor and delivery
MCC Exclusion see Appendix A PDX collection 1002

• ♀ CC **O75.2 Pyrexia during labor, not elsewhere classified**
CC Exclusion see Appendix A PDX collection 1003

• ♀ MCC **O75.3 Other infection during labor**
Sepsis during labor
Use additional code (B95-B97), to identify infectious agent
MCC Exclusion see Appendix A PDX collection 1004
Review coding guideline C.15.j

• ♀ **O75.4 Other complications of obstetric surgery and procedures**
Cardiac arrest following obstetric surgery or procedures
Cardiac failure following obstetric surgery or procedures
Cerebral anoxia following obstetric surgery or procedures
Pulmonary edema following obstetric surgery or procedures
Use additional code to identify specific complication
Excludes2: *complications of anesthesia during labor and delivery (O74.-)*
disruption of obstetrical (surgical) wound (O90.0-O90.1)
hematoma of obstetrical (surgical) wound (O90.2)
infection of obstetrical (surgical) wound (O86.0)

• ♀ **O75.5 Delayed delivery after artificial rupture of membranes**

\+ **O75.8 Other specified complications of labor and delivery**

• ♀ **O75.81 Maternal exhaustion complicating labor and delivery**

• ♀ **O75.82 Onset (spontaneous) of labor after 37 completed weeks of gestation but before 39 completed weeks gestation, with delivery by (planned) cesarean section**
Delivery by (planned) cesarean section occurring after 37 completed weeks of gestation but before 39 completed weeks gestation due to (spontaneous) onset of labor
Code first to specify reason for planned cesarean section such as:
cephalopelvic disproportion (normally formed fetus) (O33.9)
previous cesarean delivery (O34.21)

• ♀ **O75.89 Other specified complications of labor and delivery**

• ♀ **O75.9 Complication of labor and delivery, unspecified**

O76 Abnormality in fetal heart rate and rhythm complicating labor and delivery
Depressed fetal heart rate tones complicating labor and delivery
Fetal bradycardia complicating labor and delivery
Fetal heart rate decelerations complicating labor and delivery
Fetal heart rate irregularity complicating labor and delivery
Fetal heart rate abnormal variability complicating labor and delivery
Fetal tachycardia complicating labor and delivery
Non-reassuring fetal heart rate or rhythm complicating labor and delivery
Excludes1: *fetal stress NOS (O77.9)*
labor and delivery complicated by electrocardiographic evidence of fetal stress (O77.8)
labor and delivery complicated by ultrasonic evidence of fetal stress (O77.8)
Excludes2: *fetal metabolic acidemia (O68)*
other fetal stress (O77.0-O77.1)
Valid 3-character code, no further characters required

O77 Other fetal stress complicating labor and delivery

• ♀ **O77.0 Labor and delivery complicated by meconium in amniotic fluid**
AHA CC: 4Q, 2013, 118

• ♀ **O77.1 Fetal stress in labor or delivery due to drug administration**

• ♀ **O77.8 Labor and delivery complicated by other evidence of fetal stress**
Labor and delivery complicated by electrocardiographic evidence of fetal stress
Labor and delivery complicated by ultrasonic evidence of fetal stress
Excludes1: *abnormality of fetal acid-base balance (O68)*
abnormality in fetal heart rate or rhythm (O76)
fetal metabolic acidemia (O68)

• ♀ **O77.9 Labor and delivery complicated by fetal stress, unspecified**
Excludes1: *abnormality of fetal acid-base balance (O68)*
abnormality in fetal heart rate or rhythm (O76)
fetal metabolic acidemia (O68)

ncounter for delivery (O80-O82)

♀ **O80 Encounter for full-term uncomplicated delivery**
Delivery requiring minimal or no assistance, with or without episiotomy, without fetal manipulation [e.g., rotation version] or instrumentation [forceps] of a spontaneous, cephalic, vaginal, full-term, single, live-born infant. This code is for use as a single diagnosis code and is not to be used with any other code from chapter 15.
Use additional code to indicate outcome of delivery (Z37.0)
AHA CC: 2Q, 2014, 9
Review coding guideline C.15.n
Valid 3-character code, no further characters required

♀ **O82 Encounter for cesarean delivery without indication**
Use additional code to indicate outcome of delivery (Z37.0)
Valid 3-character code, no further characters required

Complications predominantly related to the puerperium (O85-O92)

Excludes2: *mental and behavioral disorders associated with the puerperium (F53)*
obstetrical tetanus (A34)
puerperal osteomalacia (M83.0)

MCC • ♀ **O85 Puerperal sepsis**
Postpartum sepsis
Puerperal peritonitis
Puerperal pyemia
Use additional code (B95-B97), to identify infectious agent
Use additional code (R65.2-) to identify severe sepsis, if applicable
Excludes1: *fever of unknown origin following delivery (O86.4)*
genital tract infection following delivery (O86.1-)
obstetric pyemic and septic embolism (O88.3-)
puerperal septic thrombophlebitis (O86.81)
urinary tract infection following delivery (O86.2-)
Excludes2: *sepsis during labor (O75.3)*
Review coding guideline C.15.k
MCC Exclusion see Appendix A PDX collection 1005
Valid 3-character code, no further characters required

O86 Other puerperal infections
Use additional code (B95-B97), to identify infectious agent
Excludes2: *infection during labor (O75.3)*
obstetrical tetanus (A34)

• ♀ **O86.0 Infection of obstetric surgical wound**
Infected cesarean delivery wound following delivery
Infected perineal repair following delivery
Review coding guideline C.1.d.5

\+ **O86.1 Other infection of genital tract following delivery**

• ♀ CC **O86.11 Cervicitis following delivery**
CC Exclusion see Appendix A PDX collection 0968

• ♀ CC **O86.12 Endometritis following delivery**
CC Exclusion see Appendix A PDX collection 1005

• ♀ CC **O86.13 Vaginitis following delivery**
CC Exclusion see Appendix A PDX collection 0968

• ♀ CC **O86.19 Other infection of genital tract following delivery**
CC Exclusion see Appendix A PDX collection 0968

\+ **O86.2 Urinary tract infection following delivery**

• ♀ CC **O86.20 Urinary tract infection following delivery, unspecified**
Puerperal urinary tract infection NOS
CC Exclusion see Appendix A PDX collection 0968

• ♀ CC **O86.21 Infection of kidney following delivery**
CC Exclusion see Appendix A PDX collection 0968

• ♀ CC **O86.22 Infection of bladder following delivery**
Infection of urethra following delivery
CC Exclusion see Appendix A PDX collection 0968

• ♀ CC **O86.29 Other urinary tract infection following delivery**
CC Exclusion see Appendix A PDX collection 0968

• ♀ CC **O86.4 Pyrexia of unknown origin following delivery**
Puerperal infection NOS following delivery
Puerperal pyrexia NOS following delivery
Excludes2: *pyrexia during labor (O75.2)*
CC Exclusion see Appendix A PDX collection 1006

\+ **O86.8 Other specified puerperal infections**

• ♀ MCC **O86.81 Puerperal septic thrombophlebitis**
MCC Exclusion see Appendix A PDX collection 1005

• ♀ MCC **O86.89 Other specified puerperal infections**
MCC Exclusion see Appendix A PDX collection 1005

O87 Venous complications and hemorrhoids in the puerperium
Includes: venous complications in labor, delivery and the puerperium
Excludes2: *obstetric embolism (O88.-)*
puerperal septic thrombophlebitis (O86.81)
venous complications in pregnancy (O22.-)

• ♀ CC **O87.0 Superficial thrombophlebitis in the puerperium**
Puerperal phlebitis NOS
Puerperal thrombosis NOS
CC Exclusion see Appendix A PDX collection 0967

• ♀ MCC **O87.1 Deep phlebothrombosis in the puerperium**
Deep vein thrombosis, postpartum
Pelvic thrombophlebitis, postpartum
Use additional code to identify the deep vein thrombosis (I82.4-, I82.5-, I82.62-, I82.72-)
Use additional code, if applicable, for associated long-term (current) use of anticoagulants (Z79.01)
MCC Exclusion see Appendix A PDX collection 0967

• ♀ CC **O87.2 Hemorrhoids in the puerperium**
CC Exclusion see Appendix A PDX collection 0967

• ♀ CC **O87.3 Cerebral venous thrombosis in the puerperium**
Cerebrovenous sinus thrombosis in the puerperium
CC Exclusion see Appendix A PDX collection 0967

• ♀ **O87.4 Varicose veins of lower extremity in the puerperium**

• ♀ CC **O87.8 Other venous complications in the puerperium**
Genital varices in the puerperium
CC Exclusion see Appendix A PDX collection 0967

• ♀ **O87.9 Venous complication in the puerperium, unspecified**
Puerperal phlebopathy NOS

O88 Obstetric embolism

Excludes1: *embolism complicating abortion NOS (O03.2)*
embolism complicating ectopic or molar pregnancy (O08.2)
embolism complicating failed attempted abortion (O07.2)
embolism complicating induced abortion (O04.7)
embolism complicating spontaneous abortion (O03.2, O03.7)

\+ **O88.0 Obstetric air embolism**

\+ **O88.01 Obstetric air embolism in pregnancy**

• ♀ MCC **O88.011 Air embolism in pregnancy, first trimester**
MCC Exclusion see Appendix A PDX collection 1007

• ♀ MCC **O88.012 Air embolism in pregnancy, second trimester**
MCC Exclusion see Appendix A PDX collection 1007

• ♀ MCC **O88.013 Air embolism in pregnancy, third trimester**
MCC Exclusion see Appendix A PDX collection 1007

• ♀ **O88.019 Air embolism in pregnancy, unspecified trimester**

• ♀ MCC **O88.02 Air embolism in childbirth**
MCC Exclusion see Appendix A PDX collection 1007

• ♀ MCC **O88.03 Air embolism in the puerperium**
MCC Exclusion see Appendix A PDX collection 1007

\+ **O88.1 Amniotic fluid embolism**
Anaphylactoid syndrome in pregnancy

\+ **O88.11 Amniotic fluid embolism in pregnancy**

• ♀ MCC **O88.111 Amniotic fluid embolism in pregnancy, first trimester**
MCC Exclusion see Appendix A PDX collection 1007

• ♀ MCC **O88.112 Amniotic fluid embolism in pregnancy, second trimester**
MCC Exclusion see Appendix A PDX collection 1007

• ♀ MCC **O88.113 Amniotic fluid embolism in pregnancy, third trimester**
MCC Exclusion see Appendix A PDX collection 1007

• ♀ **O88.119 Amniotic fluid embolism in pregnancy, unspecified trimester**

• ♀ MCC **O88.12 Amniotic fluid embolism in childbirth**
MCC Exclusion see Appendix A PDX collection 1007

• ♀ MCC **O88.13 Amniotic fluid embolism in the puerperium**
MCC Exclusion see Appendix A PDX collection 1007

\+ **O88.2 Obstetric thromboembolism**

\+ **O88.21 Thromboembolism in pregnancy**
Obstetric (pulmonary) embolism NOS

• ♀ MCC **O88.211 Thromboembolism in pregnancy, first trimester**
MCC Exclusion see Appendix A PDX collection 1007

• ♀ MCC **O88.212 Thromboembolism in pregnancy, second trimester**
MCC Exclusion see Appendix A PDX collection 1007

• ♀ MCC **O88.213 Thromboembolism in pregnancy, third trimester**
MCC Exclusion see Appendix A PDX collection 1007

• ♀ **O88.219 Thromboembolism in pregnancy, unspecified trimester**

• ♀ MCC **O88.22 Thromboembolism in childbirth**
MCC Exclusion see Appendix A PDX collection 1007

• ♀ MCC **O88.23 Thromboembolism in the puerperium**
Puerperal (pulmonary) embolism NOS
MCC Exclusion see Appendix A PDX collection 1007

\+ **O88.3 Obstetric pyemic and septic embolism**

\+ **O88.31 Pyemic and septic embolism in pregnancy**

• ♀ MCC **O88.311 Pyemic and septic embolism in pregnancy, first trimester**
MCC Exclusion see Appendix A PDX collection 1007

• ♀ MCC **O88.312 Pyemic and septic embolism in pregnancy, second trimester**
MCC Exclusion see Appendix A PDX collection 1007

• ♀ MCC **O88.313 Pyemic and septic embolism in pregnancy, third trimester**
MCC Exclusion see Appendix A PDX collection 1007

• ♀ **O88.319 Pyemic and septic embolism in pregnancy, unspecified trimester**

• ♀ MCC **O88.32 Pyemic and septic embolism in childbirth**
MCC Exclusion see Appendix A PDX collection 1007

• ♀ MCC **O88.33 Pyemic and septic embolism in the puerperium**
MCC Exclusion see Appendix A PDX collection 1007

\+ **O88.8 Other obstetric embolism**
Obstetric fat embolism

\+ **O88.81 Other embolism in pregnancy**

• ♀ MCC **O88.811 Other embolism in pregnancy, first trimester**
MCC Exclusion see Appendix A PDX collection 1007

• ♀ MCC **O88.812 Other embolism in pregnancy, second trimester**
MCC Exclusion see Appendix A PDX collection 1007

• ♀ MCC **O88.813 Other embolism in pregnancy, third trimester**
MCC Exclusion see Appendix A PDX collection 1007

• ♀ CC **O88.819 Other embolism in pregnancy, unspecified trimester**
CC Exclusion see Appendix A PDX collection 1007

• ♀ MCC **O88.82 Other embolism in childbirth**
MCC Exclusion see Appendix A PDX collection 1007

• ♀ MCC **O88.83 Other embolism in the puerperium**
MCC Exclusion see Appendix A PDX collection 1007

O89 Complications of anesthesia during the puerperium

Includes: maternal complications arising from the administration of a general, regional or local anesthetic, analgesic or other sedation during the puerperium

Use additional code, if applicable, to identify specific complication

\+ **O89.0 Pulmonary complications of anesthesia during the puerperium**

• ♀ **O89.01 Aspiration pneumonitis due to anesthesia during the puerperium**
Inhalation of stomach contents or secretions NOS due to anesthesia during the puerperium
Mendelson's syndrome due to anesthesia during the puerperium

• ♀ **O89.09 Other pulmonary complications of anesthesia during the puerperium**

• ♀ **O89.1 Cardiac complications of anesthesia during the puerperium**

• ♀ **O89.2 Central nervous system complications of anesthesia during the puerperium**

• ♀ **O89.3 Toxic reaction to local anesthesia during the puerperium**

• ♀ **O89.4 Spinal and epidural anesthesia-induced headache during the puerperium**

• ♀ **O89.5 Other complications of spinal and epidural anesthesia during the puerperium**

• ♀ **O89.6 Failed or difficult intubation for anesthesia during the puerperium**

• ♀ **O89.8 Other complications of anesthesia during the puerperium**

• ♀ **O89.9 Complication of anesthesia during the puerperium, unspecified**

O90 Complications of the puerperium, not elsewhere classified

• ♀ **O90.0 Disruption of cesarean delivery wound**
Dehiscence of cesarean delivery wound
Excludes1: *rupture of uterus (spontaneous) before onset of labor (O71.0-)*
rupture of uterus during labor (O71.1)

• ♀ **O90.1 Disruption of perineal obstetric wound**
Disruption of wound of episiotomy
Disruption of wound of perineal laceration
Secondary perineal tear

• ♀ **O90.2 Hematoma of obstetric wound**

• ♀ MCC **O90.3 Peripartum cardiomyopathy**
Conditions in I42.- arising during pregnancy and the puerperium
Excludes1: *pre-existing heart disease complicating pregnancy and the puerperium (O99.4-)*
MCC Exclusion see Appendix A PDX collection 1008
Review coding guideline C.15.o.5

♀ MCC **O90.4 Postpartum acute kidney failure**
Hepatorenal syndrome following labor and delivery
MCC Exclusion see Appendix A PDX collection 1009

• ♀ **O90.5 Postpartum thyroiditis**

• ♀ **O90.6 Postpartum mood disturbance**
Postpartum blues
Postpartum dysphoria
Postpartum sadness
Excludes1: *postpartum depression (F53)*
puerperal psychosis (F53)

\+ **O90.8 Other complications of the puerperium, not elsewhere classified**

• ♀ **O90.81 Anemia of the puerperium**
Postpartum anemia NOS
Excludes1: *pre-existing anemia complicating the puerperium (O99.03)*

• ♀ **O90.89 Other complications of the puerperium, not elsewhere classified**
Placental polyp

• ♀ **O90.9 Complication of the puerperium, unspecified**

O91 Infections of breast associated with pregnancy, the puerperium and lactation
Use additional code to identify infection

\+ **O91.0 Infection of nipple associated with pregnancy, the puerperium and lactation**

\+ **O91.01 Infection of nipple associated with pregnancy**
Gestational abscess of nipple

• ♀ **O91.011 Infection of nipple associated with pregnancy, first trimester**

• ♀ **O91.012 Infection of nipple associated with pregnancy, second trimester**

• ♀ **O91.013 Infection of nipple associated with pregnancy, third trimester**

• ♀ **O91.019 Infection of nipple associated with pregnancy, unspecified trimester**

• ♀ **O91.02 Infection of nipple associated with the puerperium**
Puerperal abscess of nipple

• ♀ **O91.03 Infection of nipple associated with lactation**
Abscess of nipple associated with lactation

\+ **O91.1 Abscess of breast associated with pregnancy, the puerperium and lactation**

\+ **O91.11 Abscess of breast associated with pregnancy**
Gestational mammary abscess
Gestational purulent mastitis
Gestational subareolar abscess

• ♀ **O91.111 Abscess of breast associated with pregnancy, first trimester**

• ♀ **O91.112 Abscess of breast associated with pregnancy, second trimester**

• ♀ **O91.113 Abscess of breast associated with pregnancy, third trimester**

• ♀ **O91.119 Abscess of breast associated with pregnancy, unspecified trimester**

O91.12 Abscess of breast associated with the puerperium
Puerperal mammary abscess
Puerperal purulent mastitis
Puerperal subareolar abscess

• ♀ **O91.13 Abscess of breast associated with lactation**
Mammary abscess associated with lactation
Purulent mastitis associated with lactation
Subareolar abscess associated with lactation

\+ **O91.2 Nonpurulent mastitis associated with pregnancy, the puerperium and lactation**

\+ **O91.21 Nonpurulent mastitis associated with pregnancy**
Gestational interstitial mastitis
Gestational lymphangitis of breast
Gestational mastitis NOS
Gestational parenchymatous mastitis

• ♀ **O91.211 Nonpurulent mastitis associated with pregnancy, first trimester**

• ♀ **O91.212 Nonpurulent mastitis associated with pregnancy, second trimester**

• ♀ **O91.213 Nonpurulent mastitis associated with pregnancy, third trimester**

• ♀ **O91.219 Nonpurulent mastitis associated with pregnancy, unspecified trimester**

• ♀ **O91.22 Nonpurulent mastitis associated with the puerperium**
Puerperal interstitial mastitis
Puerperal lymphangitis of breast
Puerperal mastitis NOS
Puerperal parenchymatous mastitis

• ♀ **O91.23 Nonpurulent mastitis associated with lactation**
Interstitial mastitis associated with lactation
Lymphangitis of breast associated with lactation
Mastitis NOS associated with lactation
Parenchymatous mastitis associated with lactation

O92 Other disorders of breast and disorders of lactation associated with pregnancy and the puerperium

\+ **O92.0 Retracted nipple associated with pregnancy, the puerperium, and lactation**

\+ **O92.01 Retracted nipple associated with pregnancy**

• ♀ **O92.011 Retracted nipple associated with pregnancy, first trimester**

• ♀ **O92.012 Retracted nipple associated with pregnancy, second trimester**

• ♀ **O92.013 Retracted nipple associated with pregnancy, third trimester**

• ♀ **O92.019 Retracted nipple associated with pregnancy, unspecified trimester**

• ♀ **O92.02 Retracted nipple associated with the puerperium**

• ♀ **O92.03 Retracted nipple associated with lactation**

\+ **O92.1 Cracked nipple associated with pregnancy, the puerperium, and lactation**
Fissure of nipple, gestational or puerperal

\+ **O92.11 Cracked nipple associated with pregnancy**

• ♀ **O92.111 Cracked nipple associated with pregnancy, first trimester**

• ♀ **O92.112 Cracked nipple associated with pregnancy, second trimester**

• ♀ **O92.113 Cracked nipple associated with pregnancy, third trimester**

• ♀ **O92.119 Cracked nipple associated with pregnancy, unspecified trimester**

• ♀ **O92.12 Cracked nipple associated with the puerperium**

• ♀ **O92.13 Cracked nipple associated with lactation**

\+ **O92.2 Other and unspecified disorders of breast associated with pregnancy and the puerperium**

• ♀ **O92.20 Unspecified disorder of breast associated with pregnancy and the puerperium**

• ♀ **O92.29 Other disorders of breast associated with pregnancy and the puerperium**

• ♀ **O92.3 Agalactia**
Primary agalactia
Excludes1: *Elective agalactia (O92.5)*
Secondary agalactia (O92.5)
Therapeutic agalactia (O92.5)

• ♀ **O92.4 Hypogalactia**

• ♀ **O92.5 Suppressed lactation**
Elective agalactia
Secondary agalactia
Therapeutic agalactia
Excludes1: *primary agalactia (O92.3)*

• ♀ **O92.6 Galactorrhea**

\+ **O92.7 Other and unspecified disorders of lactation**

• ♀ **O92.70 Unspecified disorders of lactation**

• ♀ **O92.79 Other disorders of lactation**
Puerperal galactocele

Other obstetric conditions, not elsewhere classified (O94-O9A)

• ♀ **O94 Sequelae of complication of pregnancy, childbirth, and the puerperium**

NOTE This category is to be used to indicate conditions in O00-O77.-, O85-O94 and O98-O9A.- as the cause of late effects. The sequelae include conditions specified as such, or as late effects, which may occur at any time after the puerperium

Code first condition resulting from (sequela) of complication of pregnancy, childbirth, and the puerperium
Review coding guideline C.15.p

O98 Maternal infectious and parasitic diseases classifiable elsewhere but complicating pregnancy, childbirth and the puerperium

Includes: the listed conditions when complicating the pregnant state, when aggravated by the pregnancy, or as a reason for obstetric care

Use additional code (Chapter 1), to identify specific infectious or parasitic disease

Excludes2: *herpes gestationis (O26.4-)*
infectious carrier state (O99.82-, O99.83-)
obstetrical tetanus (A34)
puerperal infection (O86.-)
puerperal sepsis (O85)
when the reason for maternal care is that the disease is known or suspected to have affected the fetus (O35-O36)

\+ **O98.0 Tuberculosis complicating pregnancy, childbirth and the puerperium**
Conditions in A15-A19

\+ **O98.01 Tuberculosis complicating pregnancy**

• ♀ CC **O98.011 Tuberculosis complicating pregnancy, first trimester**
CC Exclusion see Appendix A PDX collection 1011

• ♀ CC **O98.012 Tuberculosis complicating pregnancy, second trimester**
CC Exclusion see Appendix A PDX collection 1011

• ♀ CC **O98.013 Tuberculosis complicating pregnancy, third trimester**
CC Exclusion see Appendix A PDX collection 1011

• ♀ **O98.019 Tuberculosis complicating pregnancy, unspecified trimester**

• ♀ CC **O98.02 Tuberculosis complicating childbirth**
CC Exclusion see Appendix A PDX collection 1011

• ♀ CC **O98.03 Tuberculosis complicating the puerperium**
CC Exclusion see Appendix A PDX collection 1011

\+ **O98.1 Syphilis complicating pregnancy, childbirth and the puerperium**
Conditions in A50-A53

\+ **O98.11 Syphilis complicating pregnancy**

• ♀ CC **O98.111 Syphilis complicating pregnancy, first trimester**
CC Exclusion see Appendix A PDX collection 1012

• ♀ CC **O98.112 Syphilis complicating pregnancy, second trimester**
CC Exclusion see Appendix A PDX collection 1012

• ♀ CC **O98.113 Syphilis complicating pregnancy, third trimester**
CC Exclusion see Appendix A PDX collection 1012

• ♀ **O98.119 Syphilis complicating pregnancy, unspecified trimester**

• ♀ CC **O98.12 Syphilis complicating childbirth**
CC Exclusion see Appendix A PDX collection 1012

• ♀ CC **O98.13 Syphilis complicating the puerperium**
CC Exclusion see Appendix A PDX collection 1012

\+ **O98.2 Gonorrhea complicating pregnancy, childbirth and the puerperium**
Conditions in A54.-

\+ **O98.21 Gonorrhea complicating pregnancy**

• ♀ CC **O98.211 Gonorrhea complicating pregnancy, first trimester**
CC Exclusion see Appendix A PDX collection 1012

• ♀ CC **O98.212 Gonorrhea complicating pregnancy, second trimester**
CC Exclusion see Appendix A PDX collection 1012

• ♀ CC **O98.213 Gonorrhea complicating pregnancy, third trimester**
CC Exclusion see Appendix A PDX collection 1012

• ♀ **O98.219 Gonorrhea complicating pregnancy, unspecified trimester**

• ♀ CC **O98.22 Gonorrhea complicating childbirth**
CC Exclusion see Appendix A PDX collection 1012

• ♀ CC **O98.23 Gonorrhea complicating the puerperium**
CC Exclusion see Appendix A PDX collection 1012

\+ **O98.3 Other infections with a predominantly sexual mode of transmission complicating pregnancy, childbirth and the puerperium**
Conditions in A55-A64

\+ **O98.31 Other infections with a predominantly sexual mode transmission complicating pregnancy**

• ♀ CC **O98.311 Other infections with a predominantly sexual mode of transmission complicating pregnancy, first trimester**
CC Exclusion see Appendix A PDX collection 1012

• ♀ CC **O98.312 Other infections with a predominantly sexual mode of transmission complicating pregnancy, second trimester**
CC Exclusion see Appendix A PDX collection 1012

• ♀ CC **O98.313 Other infections with a predominantly sexual mode of transmission complicating pregnancy, third trimester**
CC Exclusion see Appendix A PDX collection 1012

• ♀ **O98.319 Other infections with a predominantly sexual mode of transmission complicating pregnancy, unspecified trimester**

• ♀ CC **O98.32 Other infections with a predominantly sexual mode transmission complicating childbirth**
CC Exclusion see Appendix A PDX collection 1012

• ♀ CC **O98.33 Other infections with a predominantly sexual mode transmission complicating the puerperium**
CC Exclusion see Appendix A PDX collection 1012

\+ **O98.4 Viral hepatitis complicating pregnancy, childbirth and the puerperium**
Conditions in B15-B19

\+ **O98.41 Viral hepatitis complicating pregnancy**

• ♀ CC **O98.411 Viral hepatitis complicating pregnancy, fir trimester**
CC Exclusion see Appendix A PDX collection 1013

• ♀ CC **O98.412 Viral hepatitis complicating pregnancy, second trimester**
CC Exclusion see Appendix A PDX collection 1013

• ♀ CC **O98.413 Viral hepatitis complicating pregnancy, thi trimester**
CC Exclusion see Appendix A PDX collection 1013

• ♀ **O98.419 Viral hepatitis complicating pregnancy, unspecified trimester**

• ♀ CC **O98.42 Viral hepatitis complicating childbirth**
CC Exclusion see Appendix A PDX collection 1013

• ♀ CC **O98.43 Viral hepatitis complicating the puerperium**
CC Exclusion see Appendix A PDX collection 1013

\+ **O98.5 Other viral diseases complicating pregnancy, childbirth and th puerperium**
Conditions in A80-B09, B25-B34, R87.81-, R87.82-
Excludes1: *human immunodeficiency virus [HIV] disease complicating pregnancy, childbirth and the puerperium (O98.7-)*

\+ **O98.51 Other viral diseases complicating pregnancy**

• ♀ CC **O98.511 Other viral diseases complicating pregnan first trimester**
CC Exclusion see Appendix A PDX collection 1013

• ♀ CC **O98.512 Other viral diseases complicating pregnan second trimester**
CC Exclusion see Appendix A PDX collection 1013

• ♀ CC **O98.513 Other viral diseases complicating pregnan third trimester**
CC Exclusion see Appendix A PDX collection 1013

• ♀ **O98.519 Other viral diseases complicating pregnan unspecified trimester**

• ♀ CC **O98.52 Other viral diseases complicating childbirth**
CC Exclusion see Appendix A PDX collection 1013

• ♀ CC **O98.53 Other viral diseases complicating the puerperium**
CC Exclusion see Appendix A PDX collection 1013

+ **O98.6 Protozoal diseases complicating pregnancy, childbirth and the puerperium**
Conditions in B50-B64
+ **O98.61 Protozoal diseases complicating pregnancy**
• ♀ CC **O98.611 Protozoal diseases complicating pregnancy, first trimester**
CC Exclusion see Appendix A PDX collection 1014
• ♀ CC **O98.612 Protozoal diseases complicating pregnancy, second trimester**
CC Exclusion see Appendix A PDX collection 1014
• ♀ CC **O98.613 Protozoal diseases complicating pregnancy, third trimester**
CC Exclusion see Appendix A PDX collection 1014
• ♀ **O98.619 Protozoal diseases complicating pregnancy, unspecified trimester**
• ♀ CC **O98.62 Protozoal diseases complicating childbirth**
CC Exclusion see Appendix A PDX collection 1015
• ♀ CC **O98.63 Protozoal diseases complicating the puerperium**
CC Exclusion see Appendix A PDX collection 1015
+ **O98.7 Human immunodeficiency virus [HIV] disease complicating pregnancy, childbirth and the puerperium**
Use additional code to identify the type of HIV disease:
Acquired immune deficiency syndrome (AIDS) (B20)
Asymptomatic HIV status (Z21)
HIV positive NOS (Z21)
Symptomatic HIV disease (B20)
Review coding guideline C.1.a.2.g
Review coding guideline C.15.f
+ **O98.71 Human immunodeficiency virus [HIV] disease complicating pregnancy**
• ♀ CC **O98.711 Human immunodeficiency virus [HIV] disease complicating pregnancy, first trimester**
CC Exclusion see Appendix A PDX collection 1013
• ♀ CC **O98.712 Human immunodeficiency virus [HIV] disease complicating pregnancy, second trimester**
CC Exclusion see Appendix A PDX collection 1013
• ♀ CC **O98.713 Human immunodeficiency virus [HIV] disease complicating pregnancy, third trimester**
CC Exclusion see Appendix A PDX collection 1013
• ♀ **O98.719 Human immunodeficiency virus [HIV] disease complicating pregnancy, unspecified trimester**
• ♀ CC **O98.72 Human immunodeficiency virus [HIV] disease complicating childbirth**
CC Exclusion see Appendix A PDX collection 1013
• ♀ CC **O98.73 Human immunodeficiency virus [HIV] disease complicating the puerperium**
CC Exclusion see Appendix A PDX collection 1013
+ **O98.8 Other maternal infectious and parasitic diseases complicating pregnancy, childbirth and the puerperium**
+ **O98.81 Other maternal infectious and parasitic diseases complicating pregnancy**
• ♀ CC **O98.811 Other maternal infectious and parasitic diseases complicating pregnancy, first trimester**
CC Exclusion see Appendix A PDX collection 1013
• ♀ CC **O98.812 Other maternal infectious and parasitic diseases complicating pregnancy, second trimester**
CC Exclusion see Appendix A PDX collection 1013
• ♀ CC **O98.813 Other maternal infectious and parasitic diseases complicating pregnancy, third trimester**
CC Exclusion see Appendix A PDX collection 1013
• ♀ **O98.819 Other maternal infectious and parasitic diseases complicating pregnancy, unspecified trimester**
• ♀ CC **O98.82 Other maternal infectious and parasitic diseases complicating childbirth**
CC Exclusion see Appendix A PDX collection 1013
• ♀ CC **O98.83 Other maternal infectious and parasitic diseases complicating the puerperium**
CC Exclusion see Appendix A PDX collection 1013
+ **O98.9 Unspecified maternal infectious and parasitic disease complicating pregnancy, childbirth and the puerperium**
+ **O98.91 Unspecified maternal infectious and parasitic disease complicating pregnancy**
• ♀ CC **O98.911 Unspecified maternal infectious and parasitic disease complicating pregnancy, first trimester**
CC Exclusion see Appendix A PDX collection 1013
• ♀ CC **O98.912 Unspecified maternal infectious and parasitic disease complicating pregnancy, second trimester**
CC Exclusion see Appendix A PDX collection 1013
• ♀ CC **O98.913 Unspecified maternal infectious and parasitic disease complicating pregnancy, third trimester**
CC Exclusion see Appendix A PDX collection 1013
• ♀ **O98.919 Unspecified maternal infectious and parasitic disease complicating pregnancy, unspecified trimester**
• ♀ CC **O98.92 Unspecified maternal infectious and parasitic disease complicating childbirth**
CC Exclusion see Appendix A PDX collection 1013
• ♀ CC **O98.93 Unspecified maternal infectious and parasitic disease complicating the puerperium**
CC Exclusion see Appendix A PDX collection 1013

O99 Other maternal diseases classifiable elsewhere but complicating pregnancy, childbirth and the puerperium
Includes: conditions which complicate the pregnant state, are aggravated by the pregnancy or are a main reason for obstetric care
Use additional code to identify specific condition
Excludes2: *when the reason for maternal care is that the condition is known or suspected to have affected the fetus (O35-O36)*
+ **O99.0 Anemia complicating pregnancy, childbirth and the puerperium**
Conditions in D50-D64
Excludes1: *anemia arising in the puerperium (O90.81)*
postpartum anemia NOS (O90.81)
+ **O99.01 Anemia complicating pregnancy**
• ♀ **O99.011 Anemia complicating pregnancy, first trimester**
• ♀ **O99.012 Anemia complicating pregnancy, second trimester**
• ♀ **O99.013 Anemia complicating pregnancy, third trimester**
• ♀ **O99.019 Anemia complicating pregnancy, unspecified trimester**
• ♀ **O99.02 Anemia complicating childbirth**
• ♀ **O99.03 Anemia complicating the puerperium**
Excludes1: *postpartum anemia not pre-existing prior to delivery (O90.81)*
+ **O99.1 Other diseases of the blood and blood-forming organs and certain disorders involving the immune mechanism complicating pregnancy, childbirth and the puerperium**
Conditions in D65-D89
Excludes2: *hemorrhage with coagulation defects (O45.-, O46.0-, O67.0, O72.3)*
+ **O99.11 Other diseases of the blood and blood-forming organs and certain disorders involving the immune mechanism complicating pregnancy**
• ♀ CC **O99.111 Other diseases of the blood and blood-forming organs and certain disorders involving the immune mechanism complicating pregnancy, first trimester**
CC Exclusion see Appendix A PDX collection 1016
• ♀ CC **O99.112 Other diseases of the blood and blood-forming organs and certain disorders involving the immune mechanism complicating pregnancy, second trimester**
CC Exclusion see Appendix A PDX collection 1016
• ♀ CC **O99.113 Other diseases of the blood and blood-forming organs and certain disorders involving the immune mechanism complicating pregnancy, third trimester**
CC Exclusion see Appendix A PDX collection 1016

- • ♀ CC **O99.119 Other diseases of the blood and blood-forming organs and certain disorders involving the immune mechanism complicating pregnancy, unspecified trimester**
  CC Exclusion see Appendix A PDX collection 1017
- • ♀ CC **O99.12 Other diseases of the blood and blood-forming organs and certain disorders involving the immune mechanism complicating childbirth**
  CC Exclusion see Appendix A PDX collection 1016
- • ♀ CC **O99.13 Other diseases of the blood and blood-forming organs and certain disorders involving the immune mechanism complicating the puerperium**
  CC Exclusion see Appendix A PDX collection 1016

+ **O99.2 Endocrine, nutritional and metabolic diseases complicating pregnancy, childbirth and the puerperium**
  Conditions in E00-E88
  Excludes2: *diabetes mellitus (O24.-)*
  malnutrition (O25.-)
  postpartum thyroiditis (O90.5)

+ **O99.21 Obesity complicating pregnancy, childbirth, and the puerperium**
  Use additional code to identify the type of obesity (E66.-)
- • ♀ **O99.210 Obesity complicating pregnancy, unspecified trimester**
- • ♀ **O99.211 Obesity complicating pregnancy, first trimester**
- • ♀ **O99.212 Obesity complicating pregnancy, second trimester**
- • ♀ **O99.213 Obesity complicating pregnancy, third trimester**
- • ♀ **O99.214 Obesity complicating childbirth**
- • ♀ **O99.215 Obesity complicating the puerperium**

+ **O99.28 Other endocrine, nutritional and metabolic diseases complicating pregnancy, childbirth and the puerperium**
- • ♀ **O99.280 Endocrine, nutritional and metabolic diseases complicating pregnancy, unspecified trimester**
- • ♀ **O99.281 Endocrine, nutritional and metabolic diseases complicating pregnancy, first trimester**
- • ♀ **O99.282 Endocrine, nutritional and metabolic diseases complicating pregnancy, second trimester**
- • ♀ **O99.283 Endocrine, nutritional and metabolic diseases complicating pregnancy, third trimester**
- • ♀ **O99.284 Endocrine, nutritional and metabolic diseases complicating childbirth**
- • ♀ **O99.285 Endocrine, nutritional and metabolic diseases complicating the puerperium**

+ **O99.3 Mental disorders and diseases of the nervous system complicating pregnancy, childbirth and the puerperium**

+ **O99.31 Alcohol use complicating pregnancy, childbirth, and the puerperium**
  Use additional code(s) from F10 to identify manifestations of the alcohol use
  Review coding guideline C.15.l.1
- • ♀ **O99.310 Alcohol use complicating pregnancy, unspecified trimester**
- • ♀ **O99.311 Alcohol use complicating pregnancy, first trimester**
- • ♀ **O99.312 Alcohol use complicating pregnancy, second trimester**
- • ♀ **O99.313 Alcohol use complicating pregnancy, third trimester**
- • ♀ **O99.314 Alcohol use complicating childbirth**
- • ♀ **O99.315 Alcohol use complicating the puerperium**

+ **O99.32 Drug use complicating pregnancy, childbirth, and the puerperium**
  Use additional code(s) from F11-F16 and F18-F19 to identify manifestations of the drug use
- • ♀ **O99.320 Drug use complicating pregnancy, unspecified trimester**
- • ♀ CC **O99.321 Drug use complicating pregnancy, first trimester**
  CC Exclusion see Appendix A PDX collection 1018
- • ♀ CC **O99.322 Drug use complicating pregnancy, second trimester**
  CC Exclusion see Appendix A PDX collection 1018
- • ♀ CC **O99.323 Drug use complicating pregnancy, third trimester**
  CC Exclusion see Appendix A PDX collection 1018
- • ♀ CC **O99.324 Drug use complicating childbirth**
  CC Exclusion see Appendix A PDX collection 1018
- • ♀ CC **O99.325 Drug use complicating the puerperium**
  CC Exclusion see Appendix A PDX collection 1018

+ **O99.33 Smoking (tobacco) complicating pregnancy, childbirth, and the puerperium**
  Use additional code from F17 to identify type of toba
  Review coding guideline C.15.l.2
- • ♀ **O99.330 Smoking (tobacco) complicating pregnan unspecified trimester**
- • ♀ **O99.331 Smoking (tobacco) complicating pregnan first trimester**
- • ♀ **O99.332 Smoking (tobacco) complicating pregnan second trimester**
- • ♀ **O99.333 Smoking (tobacco) complicating pregnan third trimester**
- • ♀ **O99.334 Smoking (tobacco) complicating childbir**
- • ♀ **O99.335 Smoking (tobacco) complicating the puerperium**

+ **O99.34 Other mental disorders complicating pregnancy, childbirth, and the puerperium**
  Conditions in F01-F09 and F20-F99
  Excludes2: *postpartum mood disturbance (O90.6)*
  postnatal psychosis (F53)
  puerperal psychosis (F53)
- • ♀ **O99.340 Other mental disorders complicating pregnancy, unspecified trimester**
- • ♀ **O99.341 Other mental disorders complicating pregnancy, first trimester**
- • ♀ **O99.342 Other mental disorders complicating pregnancy, second trimester**
- • ♀ **O99.343 Other mental disorders complicating pregnancy, third trimester**
- • ♀ **O99.344 Other mental disorders complicating childbirth**
- • ♀ **O99.345 Other mental disorders complicating the puerperium**

+ **O99.35 Diseases of the nervous system complicating pregnancy, childbirth, and the puerperium**
  Conditions in G00-G99
  Excludes2: *pregnancy related peripheral neuritis (O26.8-)*
- • ♀ **O99.350 Diseases of the nervous system complicati pregnancy, unspecified trimester**
- • ♀ **O99.351 Diseases of the nervous system complicati pregnancy, first trimester**
- • ♀ **O99.352 Diseases of the nervous system complicati pregnancy, second trimester**
- • ♀ **O99.353 Diseases of the nervous system complicati pregnancy, third trimester**
- • ♀ CC **O99.354 Diseases of the nervous system complicati childbirth**
  CC Exclusion see Appendix A PDX collection 1016
- • ♀ CC **O99.355 Diseases of the nervous system complicati the puerperium**
  CC Exclusion see Appendix A PDX collection 1016

+ **O99.4 Diseases of the circulatory system complicating pregnancy, childbirth and the puerperium**
  Conditions in I00-I99
  Excludes1: *peripartum cardiomyopathy (O90.3)*
  Excludes2: *hypertensive disorders (O10-O16)*
  obstetric embolism (O88.-)
  venous complications and cerebrovenous sinus thrombosis in labor, childbirth and the puerperium (O87.-)
  venous complications and cerebrovenous sinus thrombosis in pregnancy (O22.-)

+ **O99.41 Diseases of the circulatory system complicating pregnancy**
- ● ♀ CC **O99.411 Diseases of the circulatory system complicating pregnancy, first trimester**
  CC Exclusion see Appendix A PDX collection 1019
- ● ♀ CC **O99.412 Diseases of the circulatory system complicating pregnancy, second trimester**
  CC Exclusion see Appendix A PDX collection 1019
- ● ♀ CC **O99.413 Diseases of the circulatory system complicating pregnancy, third trimester**
  CC Exclusion see Appendix A PDX collection 1019
- ● ♀ **O99.419 Diseases of the circulatory system complicating pregnancy, unspecified trimester**

● ♀ MCC **O99.42 Diseases of the circulatory system complicating childbirth**
MCC Exclusion see Appendix A PDX collection 1008

● ♀ CC **O99.43 Diseases of the circulatory system complicating the puerperium**
CC Exclusion see Appendix A PDX collection 1019

+ **O99.5 Diseases of the respiratory system complicating pregnancy, childbirth and the puerperium**
  Conditions in J00-J99

+ **O99.51 Diseases of the respiratory system complicating pregnancy**
- ● ♀ **O99.511 Diseases of the respiratory system complicating pregnancy, first trimester**
- ● ♀ **O99.512 Diseases of the respiratory system complicating pregnancy, second trimester**
- ● ♀ **O99.513 Diseases of the respiratory system complicating pregnancy, third trimester**
- ● ♀ **O99.519 Diseases of the respiratory system complicating pregnancy, unspecified trimester**

● ♀ **O99.52 Diseases of the respiratory system complicating childbirth**

● ♀ **O99.53 Diseases of the respiratory system complicating the puerperium**

+ **O99.6 Diseases of the digestive system complicating pregnancy, childbirth and the puerperium**
  Conditions in K00-K93
  Excludes2: *liver and biliary tract disorders in pregnancy, childbirth and the puerperium (O26.6-)*

+ **O99.61 Diseases of the digestive system complicating pregnancy**
- ● ♀ **O99.611 Diseases of the digestive system complicating pregnancy, first trimester**
- ● ♀ **O99.612 Diseases of the digestive system complicating pregnancy, second trimester**
- ● ♀ **O99.613 Diseases of the digestive system complicating pregnancy, third trimester**
- ● ♀ **O99.619 Diseases of the digestive system complicating pregnancy, unspecified trimester**

● ♀ **O99.62 Diseases of the digestive system complicating childbirth**

● ♀ **O99.63 Diseases of the digestive system complicating the puerperium**

+ **O99.7 Diseases of the skin and subcutaneous tissue complicating pregnancy, childbirth and the puerperium**
  Conditions in L00-L99
  Excludes2: *herpes gestationis (O26.4)*
  pruritic urticarial papules and plaques of pregnancy (PUPPP) (O26.86)

+ **O99.71 Diseases of the skin and subcutaneous tissue complicating pregnancy**
- ● ♀ **O99.711 Diseases of the skin and subcutaneous tissue complicating pregnancy, first trimester**
- ● ♀ **O99.712 Diseases of the skin and subcutaneous tissue complicating pregnancy, second trimester**
- ● ♀ **O99.713 Diseases of the skin and subcutaneous tissue complicating pregnancy, third trimester**
- ● ♀ **O99.719 Diseases of the skin and subcutaneous tissue complicating pregnancy, unspecified trimester**

● ♀ **O99.72 Diseases of the skin and subcutaneous tissue complicating childbirth**

● ♀ **O99.73 Diseases of the skin and subcutaneous tissue complicating the puerperium**

+ **O99.8 Other specified diseases and conditions complicating pregnancy, childbirth and the puerperium**
  Conditions in D00-D48, H00-H95, M00-N99, and Q00-Q99
  Use additional code to identify condition
  Excludes2: *genitourinary infections in pregnancy (O23.-)*
  infection of genitourinary tract following delivery (O86.1-O86.3)
  malignant neoplasm complicating pregnancy, childbirth and the puerperium (O9A.1-)
  maternal care for known or suspected abnormality of maternal pelvic organs (O34.-)
  postpartum acute kidney failure (O90.4)
  traumatic injuries in pregnancy (O9A.2-)

+ **O99.81 Abnormal glucose complicating pregnancy, childbirth and the puerperium**
  Excludes1: *gestational diabetes (O24.4-)*
  Review coding guideline C.15.i
- ● ♀ **O99.810 Abnormal glucose complicating pregnancy**
- ● ♀ **O99.814 Abnormal glucose complicating childbirth**
- ● ♀ **O99.815 Abnormal glucose complicating the puerperium**

+ **O99.82 Streptococcus B carrier state complicating pregnancy, childbirth and the puerperium**
- ● ♀ **O99.820 Streptococcus B carrier state complicating pregnancy**
- ● ♀ **O99.824 Streptococcus B carrier state complicating childbirth**
- ● ♀ **O99.825 Streptococcus B carrier state complicating the puerperium**

+ **O99.83 Other infection carrier state complicating pregnancy, childbirth and the puerperium**
  Use additional code to identify the carrier state (Z22.-)
- ● ♀ CC **O99.830 Other infection carrier state complicating pregnancy**
  CC Exclusion see Appendix A PDX collection 1013
- ● ♀ CC **O99.834 Other infection carrier state complicating childbirth**
  CC Exclusion see Appendix A PDX collection 1013
- ● ♀ CC **O99.835 Other infection carrier state complicating the puerperium**
  CC Exclusion see Appendix A PDX collection 1013

+ **O99.84 Bariatric surgery status complicating pregnancy, childbirth and the puerperium**
  Gastric banding status complicating pregnancy, childbirth and the puerperium
  Gastric bypass status for obesity complicating pregnancy, childbirth and the puerperium
  Obesity surgery status complicating pregnancy, childbirth and the puerperium
- ● ♀ **O99.840 Bariatric surgery status complicating pregnancy, unspecified trimester**
- ● ♀ **O99.841 Bariatric surgery status complicating pregnancy, first trimester**
- ● ♀ **O99.842 Bariatric surgery status complicating pregnancy, second trimester**
- ● ♀ **O99.843 Bariatric surgery status complicating pregnancy, third trimester**
- ● ♀ **O99.844 Bariatric surgery status complicating childbirth**
- ● ♀ **O99.845 Bariatric surgery status complicating the puerperium**

● ♀ **O99.89 Other specified diseases and conditions complicating pregnancy, childbirth and the puerperium**

O9A Maternal malignant neoplasms, traumatic injuries and abuse classifiable elsewhere but complicating pregnancy, childbirth and the puerperium

+ **O9A.1 Malignant neoplasm complicating pregnancy, childbirth and the puerperium**
  Conditions in C00-C96
  Use additional code to identify neoplasm
  Excludes2: *maternal care for benign tumor of corpus uteri (O34.1-)*
  maternal care for benign tumor of cervix (O34.4-)
  Review coding guideline C.2.l.3

+ **O9A.11 Malignant neoplasm complicating pregnancy**
- ● ♀ **O9A.111 Malignant neoplasm complicating pregnancy, first trimester**
- ● ♀ **O9A.112 Malignant neoplasm complicating pregnancy, second trimester**

- ● ♀ **O9A.113 Malignant neoplasm complicating pregnancy, third trimester**
- ● ♀ **O9A.119 Malignant neoplasm complicating pregnancy, unspecified trimester**
- ● ♀ **O9A.12 Malignant neoplasm complicating childbirth**
- ● ♀ **O9A.13 Malignant neoplasm complicating the puerperium**

\+ **O9A.2 Injury, poisoning and certain other consequences of external causes complicating pregnancy, childbirth and the puerperium**

Conditions in S00-T88, except T74 and T76

Use additional code(s) to identify the injury or poisoning

Excludes2: *physical, sexual and psychological abuse complicating pregnancy, childbirth and the puerperium (O9A.3-, O9A.4-, O9A.5-)*

Review coding guideline C.15.m

\+ **O9A.21 Injury, poisoning and certain other consequences of external causes complicating pregnancy**
- ● ♀ **O9A.211 Injury, poisoning and certain other consequences of external causes complicating pregnancy, first trimester**
- ● ♀ **O9A.212 Injury, poisoning and certain other consequences of external causes complicating pregnancy, second trimester**
- ● ♀ **O9A.213 Injury, poisoning and certain other consequences of external causes complicating pregnancy, third trimester**
- ● ♀ **O9A.219 Injury, poisoning and certain other consequences of external causes complicating pregnancy, unspecified trimester**
- ● ♀ **O9A.22 Injury, poisoning and certain other consequences of external causes complicating childbirth**
- ● ♀ **O9A.23 Injury, poisoning and certain other consequences of external causes complicating the puerperium**

\+ **O9A.3 Physical abuse complicating pregnancy, childbirth and the puerperium**

Conditions in T74.11 or T76.11

Use additional code (if applicable):

to identify any associated current injury due to physical abuse

to identify the perpetrator of abuse (Y07.-)

Excludes2: *sexual abuse complicating pregnancy, childbirth and the puerperium (O9A.4)*

Review coding guideline C.15.r

\+ **O9A.31 Physical abuse complicating pregnancy**
- ● ♀ **O9A.311 Physical abuse complicating pregnancy, first trimester**
- ● ♀ **O9A.312 Physical abuse complicating pregnancy, second trimester**
- ● ♀ **O9A.313 Physical abuse complicating pregnancy, third trimester**
- ● ♀ **O9A.319 Physical abuse complicating pregnancy, unspecified trimester**
- ● ♀ **O9A.32 Physical abuse complicating childbirth**
- ● ♀ **O9A.33 Physical abuse complicating the puerperium**

\+ **O9A.4 Sexual abuse complicating pregnancy, childbirth and the puerperium**

Conditions in T74.21 or T76.21

Use additional code (if applicable):

to identify any associated current injury due to sexual abuse

to identify the perpetrator of abuse (Y07.-)

Review coding guideline C.15.r

\+ **O9A.41 Sexual abuse complicating pregnancy**
- ● ♀ **O9A.411 Sexual abuse complicating pregnancy, first trimester**
- ● ♀ **O9A.412 Sexual abuse complicating pregnancy, second trimester**
- ● ♀ **O9A.413 Sexual abuse complicating pregnancy, third trimester**
- ● ♀ **O9A.419 Sexual abuse complicating pregnancy, unspecified trimester**
- ● ♀ **O9A.42 Sexual abuse complicating childbirth**
- ● ♀ **O9A.43 Sexual abuse complicating the puerperium**

\+ **O9A.5 Psychological abuse complicating pregnancy, childbirth and the puerperium**

Conditions in T74.31 or T76.31

Use additional code to identify the perpetrator of abuse (Y07.-)

Review coding guideline C.15.r

\+ **O9A.51 Psychological abuse complicating pregnancy**
- ● ♀ **O9A.511 Psychological abuse complicating pregnancy, first trimester**
- ● ♀ **O9A.512 Psychological abuse complicating pregnancy, second trimester**
- ● ♀ **O9A.513 Psychological abuse complicating pregnancy, third trimester**
- ● ♀ **O9A.519 Psychological abuse complicating pregnancy, unspecified trimester**
- ● ♀ **O9A.52 Psychological abuse complicating childbirth**
- ● ♀ **O9A.53 Psychological abuse complicating the puerperium**

hapter 16: Certain Conditions Originating in the erinatal Period (P00-P96)

OTE Codes from this chapter are for use on newborn records only, never on maternal records

cludes: conditions that have their origin in the fetal or perinatal period (before birth through the first 28 days after birth) even if morbidity occurs later

cludes2: *congenital malformations, deformations and chromosomal abnormalities (Q00-Q99)*
endocrine, nutritional and metabolic diseases (E00-E88)
injury, poisoning and certain other consequences of external causes (S00-T88)
neoplasms (C00-D49)
tetanus neonatorum (A33)

is chapter contains the following category blocks:

- P00-P04 Newborn affected by maternal factors and by complications of pregnancy, labor, and delivery
- P05-P08 Disorders of newborn related to length of gestation and fetal growth
- P09 Abnormal findings on neonatal screening
- P10-P15 Birth trauma
- P19-P29 Respiratory and cardiovascular disorders specific to the perinatal period
- P35-P39 Infections specific to the perinatal period
- P50-P61 Hemorrhagic and hematological disorders of newborn
- P70-P74 Transitory endocrine and metabolic disorders specific to newborn
- P76-P78 Digestive system disorders of newborn
- P80-P83 Conditions involving the integument and temperature regulation of newborn
- P84 Other problems with newborn
- P90-P96 Other disorders originating in the perinatal period

Chapter-Specific Coding Guidelines

addition to general coding guidelines, there are guidelines for specific diagnoses d/or conditions in the classification. Unless otherwise indicated, these guidelines ply to all health care settings. Please refer to Section II for guidelines on the ection of principal diagnosis.

. Chapter 16: Certain Conditions Originating in the Perinatal Period (P00-P96)

For coding and reporting purposes the perinatal period is defined as before birth through the 28th day following birth. The following guidelines are provided for reporting purposes

a. General Perinatal Rules

1) Use of Chapter 16 Codes

Codes in this chapter are <u>never</u> for use on the maternal record. Codes from Chapter 15, the obstetric chapter, are never permitted on the newborn record. Chapter 16 codes may be used throughout the life of the patient if the condition is still present.

2) Principal Diagnosis for Birth Record

When coding the birth episode in a newborn record, assign a code from category Z38, Liveborn infants according to place of birth and type of delivery, as the principal diagnosis. A code from category Z38 is assigned only once, to a newborn at the time of birth. If a newborn is transferred to another institution, a code from category Z38 should not be used at the receiving hospital.

A code from category Z38 is used only on the newborn record, not on the mother's record.

3) Use of Codes from other Chapters with Codes from Chapter 16

Codes from other chapters may be used with codes from chapter 16 if the codes from the other chapters provide more specific detail. Codes for signs and symptoms may be assigned when a definitive diagnosis has not been established. If the reason for the encounter is a perinatal condition, the code from chapter 16 should be sequenced first.

4) Use of Chapter 16 Codes after the Perinatal Period

Should a condition originate in the perinatal period, and continue throughout the life of the patient, the perinatal code should continue to be used regardless of the patient's age.

5) Birth process or community acquired conditions

If a newborn has a condition that may be either due to the birth process or community acquired and the documentation does not indicate which it is, the default is due to the birth process and the code from Chapter 16 should be used. If the condition is community-acquired, a code from Chapter 16 should not be assigned.

6) Code all clinically significant conditions

All clinically significant conditions noted on routine newborn examination should be coded. A condition is clinically significant if it requires:

- clinical evaluation; or
- therapeutic treatment; or
- diagnostic procedures; or
- extended length of hospital stay; or
- increased nursing care and/or monitoring; or
- has implications for future health care needs

Note: The perinatal guidelines listed above are the same as the general coding guidelines for "additional diagnoses", except for the final point regarding implications for future health care needs. Codes should be assigned for conditions that have been specified by the provider as having implications for future health care needs.

b. Observation and Evaluation of Newborns for Suspected Conditions not Found

Reserved for future expansion

c. Coding Additional Perinatal Diagnoses

1) Assigning codes for conditions that require treatment

Assign codes for conditions that require treatment or further investigation, prolong the length of stay, or require resource utilization.

2) Codes for conditions specified as having implications for future health care needs

Assign codes for conditions that have been specified by the provider as having implications for future health care needs.

Note: This guideline should not be used for adult patients.

d. Prematurity and Fetal Growth Retardation

Providers utilize different criteria in determining prematurity. A code for prematurity should not be assigned unless it is documented. Assignment of codes in categories P05, Disorders of newborn related to slow fetal growth and fetal malnutrition, and P07, Disorders of newborn related to short gestation and low birth weight, not elsewhere classified, should be based on the recorded birth weight and estimated gestational age. Codes from category P05 should not be assigned with codes from category P07.

When both birth weight and gestational age are available, two codes from category P07 should be assigned, with the code for birth weight sequenced before the code for gestational age.

e. Low birth weight and immaturity status

Codes from category P07, Disorders of newborn related to short gestation and low birth weight, not elsewhere classified, are for use for a child or adult who was premature or had a low birth weight as a newborn and this is affecting the patient's current health status.

See Section I.C.21. Factors influencing health status and contact with health services, Status.

f. Bacterial Sepsis of Newborn

Category P36, Bacterial sepsis of newborn, includes congenital sepsis. If a perinate is documented as having sepsis without documentation of congenital or community acquired, the default is congenital and a code from category P36 should be assigned. If the P36 code includes the causal organism, an additional code from category B95, Streptococcus, Staphylococcus, and Enterococcus as the cause of diseases classified elsewhere, or B96, Other bacterial agents as the cause of diseases classified elsewhere, should not be assigned. If the P36 code does not include the causal organism, assign an additional code from category B96. If applicable, use additional codes to identify severe sepsis (R65.2-) and any associated acute organ dysfunction.

g. Stillbirth

Code P95, Stillbirth, is only for use in institutions that maintain separate records for stillbirths. No other code should be used with P95. Code P95 should not be used on the mother's record.

Newborn affected by maternal factors and by complications of pregnancy, labor, and delivery (P00-P04)

NOTE These codes are for use when the listed maternal conditions are specified as the cause of confirmed morbidity or potential morbidity which have their origin in the perinatal period (before birth through the first 28 days after birth). Codes from these categories are also for use for newborns who are suspected of having an abnormal condition resulting from exposure from the mother or the birth process, but without signs or symptoms, and, which after examination and observation, is found not to exist. These codes may be used even if treatment is begun for a suspected condition that is ruled out.

P00 Newborn (suspected to be) affected by maternal conditions that may be unrelated to present pregnancy

Code first any current condition in newborn

Excludes2: *newborn (suspected to be) affected by maternal complications of pregnancy (P01.-)*
newborn affected by maternal endocrine and metabolic disorders (P70-P74)
newborn affected by noxious substances transmitted via placenta or breast milk (P04.-)

- **P00.0 Newborn (suspected to be) affected by maternal hypertensive disorders**
  Newborn (suspected to be) affected by maternal conditions classifiable to O10-O11, O13-O16
- **P00.1 Newborn (suspected to be) affected by maternal renal and urinary tract diseases**
  Newborn (suspected to be) affected by maternal conditions classifiable to N00-N39
- **P00.2 Newborn (suspected to be) affected by maternal infectious and parasitic diseases**
  Newborn (suspected to be) affected by maternal infectious disease classifiable to A00-B99, J09 and J10
  Excludes1: *infections specific to the perinatal period (P35-P39)*
  maternal genital tract or other localized infections (P00.8)
- **P00.3 Newborn (suspected to be) affected by other maternal circulatory and respiratory diseases**
  Newborn (suspected to be) affected by maternal conditions classifiable to I00-I99, J00-J99, Q20-Q34 and not included in P00.0, P00.2
- **P00.4 Newborn (suspected to be) affected by maternal nutritional disorders**
  Newborn (suspected to be) affected by maternal disorders classifiable to E40-E64
  Maternal malnutrition NOS
- **P00.5 Newborn (suspected to be) affected by maternal injury**
  Newborn (suspected to be) affected by maternal conditions classifiable to O9A.2-
- **P00.6 Newborn (suspected to be) affected by surgical procedure on mother**
  Newborn (suspected to be) affected by amniocentesis
  Excludes1: *Cesarean delivery for present delivery (P03.4)*
  damage to placenta from amniocentesis, Cesarean delivery or surgical induction (P02.1)
  previous surgery to uterus or pelvic organs (P03.89)
  Excludes2: *newborn affected by complication of (fetal) intrauterine procedure (P96.5)*
- **P00.7 Newborn (suspected to be) affected by other medical procedures on mother, not elsewhere classified**
  Newborn (suspected to be) affected by radiation to mother
  Excludes1: *damage to placenta from amniocentesis, cesarean delivery or surgical induction (P02.1)*
  newborn affected by other complications of labor and delivery (P03.-)

+ **P00.8 Newborn (suspected to be) affected by other maternal conditions**
  - **P00.81 Newborn (suspected to be) affected by periodontal disease in mother**
  - **P00.89 Newborn (suspected to be) affected by other maternal conditions**
    Newborn (suspected to be) affected by conditions classifiable to T80-T88
    Newborn (suspected to be) affected by maternal genital tract or other localized infections
    Newborn (suspected to be) affected by maternal systemic lupus erythematosus
- **P00.9 Newborn (suspected to be) affected by unspecified maternal condition**

P01 Newborn (suspected to be) affected by maternal complications of pregnancy

Code first any current condition in newborn

- **P01.0 Newborn (suspected to be) affected by incompetent cervix**
- **P01.1 Newborn (suspected to be) affected by premature rupture of membranes**
- **P01.2 Newborn (suspected to be) affected by oligohydramnios**
  Excludes1: *oligohydramnios due to premature rupture of membranes (P01.1)*
- **P01.3 Newborn (suspected to be) affected by polyhydramnios**
  Newborn (suspected to be) affected by hydramnios
- **P01.4 Newborn (suspected to be) affected by ectopic pregnancy**
  Newborn (suspected to be) affected by abdominal pregnancy
- **P01.5 Newborn (suspected to be) affected by multiple pregnancy**
  Newborn (suspected to be) affected by triplet (pregnancy)
  Newborn (suspected to be) affected by twin (pregnancy)
- **P01.6 Newborn (suspected to be) affected by maternal death**
- **P01.7 Newborn (suspected to be) affected by malpresentation before labor**
  Newborn (suspected to be) affected by breech presentation before labor
  Newborn (suspected to be) affected by external version before labor
  Newborn (suspected to be) affected by face presentation before labor
  Newborn (suspected to be) affected by transverse lie before labor
  Newborn (suspected to be) affected by unstable lie before labor
- **P01.8 Newborn (suspected to be) affected by other maternal complications of pregnancy**
- **P01.9 Newborn (suspected to be) affected by maternal complication of pregnancy, unspecified**

P02 Newborn (suspected to be) affected by complications of placenta, cord and membranes

Code first any current condition in newborn

- **P02.0 Newborn (suspected to be) affected by placenta previa**
- **P02.1 Newborn (suspected to be) affected by other forms of placental separation and hemorrhage**
  Newborn (suspected to be) affected by abruptio placenta
  Newborn (suspected to be) affected by accidental hemorrhage
  Newborn (suspected to be) affected by antepartum hemorrhage
  Newborn (suspected to be) affected by damage to placenta from amniocentesis, cesarean delivery or surgical induction
  Newborn (suspected to be) affected by maternal blood loss
  Newborn (suspected to be) affected by premature separation of placenta

+ **P02.2 Newborn (suspected to be) affected by other and unspecified morphological and functional abnormalities of placenta**
  - **P02.20 Newborn (suspected to be) affected by unspecified morphological and functional abnormalities of placenta**
  - **P02.29 Newborn (suspected to be) affected by other morphological and functional abnormalities of placenta**
    Newborn (suspected to be) affected by placental dysfunction
    Newborn (suspected to be) affected by placental infarction
    Newborn (suspected to be) affected by placental insufficiency
- **P02.3 Newborn (suspected to be) affected by placental transfusion syndromes**
  Newborn (suspected to be) affected by placental and cord abnormalities resulting in twin-to-twin or other transplacental transfusion
- **P02.4 Newborn (suspected to be) affected by prolapsed cord**
- **P02.5 Newborn (suspected to be) affected by other compression of umbilical cord**
  Newborn (suspected to be) affected by umbilical cord (tightly) around neck
  Newborn (suspected to be) affected by entanglement of umbilical cord
  Newborn (suspected to be) affected by knot in umbilical cord

+ **P02.6 Newborn (suspected to be) affected by other and unspecified conditions of umbilical cord**
- **P02.60 Newborn (suspected to be) affected by unspecified conditions of umbilical cord**
- **P02.69 Newborn (suspected to be) affected by other conditions of umbilical cord**
  Newborn (suspected to be) affected by short umbilical cord
  Newborn (suspected to be) affected by vasa previa
  Excludes1: *newborn affected by single umbilical artery (Q27.0)*
- **P02.7 Newborn (suspected to be) affected by chorioamnionitis**
  Newborn (suspected to be) affected by amnionitis
  Newborn (suspected to be) affected by membranitis
  Newborn (suspected to be) affected by placentitis
- **P02.8 Newborn (suspected to be) affected by other abnormalities of membranes**
- **P02.9 Newborn (suspected to be) affected by abnormality of membranes, unspecified**

P03 Newborn (suspected to be) affected by other complications of labor and delivery

Code first any current condition in newborn
- **P03.0 Newborn (suspected to be) affected by breech delivery and extraction**
- **P03.1 Newborn (suspected to be) affected by other malpresentation, malposition and disproportion during labor and delivery**
  Newborn (suspected to be) affected by contracted pelvis
  Newborn (suspected to be) affected by conditions classifiable to O64-O66
  Newborn (suspected to be) affected by persistent occipitoposterior
  Newborn (suspected to be) affected by transverse lie
- **P03.2 Newborn (suspected to be) affected by forceps delivery**
- **P03.3 Newborn (suspected to be) affected by delivery by vacuum extractor [ventouse]**
- **P03.4 Newborn (suspected to be) affected by Cesarean delivery**
- **P03.5 Newborn (suspected to be) affected by precipitate delivery**
  Newborn (suspected to be) affected by rapid second stage
- **P03.6 Newborn (suspected to be) affected by abnormal uterine contractions**
  Newborn (suspected to be) affected by conditions classifiable to O62.-, except O62.3
  Newborn (suspected to be) affected by hypertonic labor
  Newborn (suspected to be) affected by uterine inertia

+ **P03.8 Newborn (suspected to be) affected by other specified complications of labor and delivery**

+ **P03.81 Newborn (suspected to be) affected by abnormality in fetal (intrauterine) heart rate or rhythm**
  Excludes1: *neonatal cardiac dysrhythmia (P29.1-)*
- **P03.810 Newborn (suspected to be) affected by abnormality in fetal (intrauterine) heart rate or rhythm before the onset of labor**
- **P03.811 Newborn (suspected to be) affected by abnormality in fetal (intrauterine) heart rate or rhythm during labor**
- **P03.819 Newborn (suspected to be) affected by abnormality in fetal (intrauterine) heart rate or rhythm, unspecified as to time of onset**
- **P03.82 Meconium passage during delivery**
  Excludes1: *meconium aspiration (P24.00, P24.01)*
  meconium staining (P96.83)
- **P03.89 Newborn (suspected to be) affected by other specified complications of labor and delivery**
  Newborn (suspected to be) affected by abnormality of maternal soft tissues
  Newborn (suspected to be) affected by conditions classifiable to O60-O75 and by procedures used in labor and delivery not included in P02.- and P03.0-P03.6
  Newborn (suspected to be) affected by induction of labor
- **P03.9 Newborn (suspected to be) affected by complication of labor and delivery, unspecified**

P04 Newborn (suspected to be) affected by noxious substances transmitted via placenta or breast milk

Includes: nonteratogenic effects of substances transmitted via placenta
Excludes2: *congenital malformations (Q00-Q99)*
neonatal jaundice from excessive hemolysis due to drugs or toxins transmitted from mother (P58.4)
newborn in contact with and (suspected) exposures hazardous to health not transmitted via placenta or breast milk (Z77.-)

- **P04.0 Newborn (suspected to be) affected by maternal anesthesia and analgesia in pregnancy, labor and delivery**
  Newborn (suspected to be) affected by reactions and intoxications from maternal opiates and tranquilizers administered during labor and delivery
- **P04.1 Newborn (suspected to be) affected by other maternal medication**
  Newborn (suspected to be) affected by cancer chemotherapy
  Newborn (suspected to be) affected by cytotoxic drugs
  Excludes1: *dysmorphism due to warfarin (Q86.2)*
  fetal hydantoin syndrome (Q86.1)
  maternal use of drugs of addiction (P04.4-)
- **P04.2 Newborn (suspected to be) affected by maternal use of tobacco**
  Newborn (suspected to be) affected by exposure in utero to tobacco smoke
  Excludes2: *newborn exposure to environmental tobacco smoke (P96.81)*
- **P04.3 Newborn (suspected to be) affected by maternal use of alcohol**
  Excludes1: *fetal alcohol syndrome (Q86.0)*

+ **P04.4 Newborn (suspected to be) affected by maternal use of drugs of addiction**
- **P04.41 Newborn (suspected to be) affected by maternal use of cocaine**
  'Crack baby'
- **P04.49 Newborn (suspected to be) affected by maternal use of other drugs of addiction**
  Excludes2: *newborn (suspected to be) affected by maternal anesthesia and analgesia (P04.0)*
  withdrawal symptoms from maternal use of drugs of addiction (P96.1)
- **P04.5 Newborn (suspected to be) affected by maternal use of nutritional chemical substances**
- **P04.6 Newborn (suspected to be) affected by maternal exposure to environmental chemical substances**
- **P04.8 Newborn (suspected to be) affected by other maternal noxious substances**
- **P04.9 Newborn (suspected to be) affected by maternal noxious substance, unspecified**

Disorders of newborn related to length of gestation and fetal growth (P05-P08)

P05 Disorders of newborn related to slow fetal growth and fetal malnutrition

Review coding guideline C.16.d

+ **P05.0 Newborn light for gestational age**
  Newborn light-for-dates
- **P05.00 Newborn light for gestational age, unspecified weight**
- **P05.01 Newborn light for gestational age, less than 500 grams**
- **P05.02 Newborn light for gestational age, 500-749 grams**
- **P05.03 Newborn light for gestational age, 750-999 grams**
- **P05.04 Newborn light for gestational age, 1000-1249 grams**
- **P05.05 Newborn light for gestational age, 1250-1499 grams**
- **P05.06 Newborn light for gestational age, 1500-1749 grams**
- **P05.07 Newborn light for gestational age, 1750-1999 grams**
- **P05.08 Newborn light for gestational age, 2000-2499 grams**

+ **P05.1 Newborn small for gestational age**
  Newborn small-and-light-for-dates
  Newborn small-for-dates
- **P05.10 Newborn small for gestational age, unspecified weight**
- **P05.11 Newborn small for gestational age, less than 500 grams**
- **P05.12 Newborn small for gestational age, 500-749 grams**
- **P05.13 Newborn small for gestational age, 750-999 grams**
- **P05.14 Newborn small for gestational age, 1000-1249 grams**
- **P05.15 Newborn small for gestational age, 1250-1499 grams**
- **P05.16 Newborn small for gestational age, 1500-1749 grams**

• **P05.17 Newborn small for gestational age, 1750-1999 grams**

• **P05.18 Newborn small for gestational age, 2000-2499 grams**

• **P05.2 Newborn affected by fetal (intrauterine) malnutrition not light or small for gestational age**
Infant, not light or small for gestational age, showing signs of fetal malnutrition, such as dry, peeling skin and loss of subcutaneous tissue
Excludes1: *newborn affected by fetal malnutrition with light for gestational age (P05.0-)*
newborn affected by fetal malnutrition with small for gestational age (P05.1-)

• **P05.9 Newborn affected by slow intrauterine growth, unspecified**
Newborn affected by fetal growth retardation NOS

P07 Disorders of newborn related to short gestation and low birth weight, not elsewhere classified

NOTE When both birth weight and gestational age of the newborn are available, both should be coded with birth weight sequenced before gestational age

Includes: the listed conditions, without further specification, as the cause of morbidity or additional care, in newborn

Excludes1: *low birth weight due to slow fetal growth and fetal malnutrition (P05.-)*

Review coding guidelines C.16.d and C.16.e

+ **P07.0 Extremely low birth weight newborn**
Newborn birth weight 999 g. or less

• **P07.00 Extremely low birth weight newborn, unspecified weight**

• **P07.01 Extremely low birth weight newborn, less than 500 grams**

• **P07.02 Extremely low birth weight newborn, 500-749 grams**

• **P07.03 Extremely low birth weight newborn, 750-999 grams**

+ **P07.1 Other low birth weight newborn**
Newborn birth weight 1000-2499 g.

• **P07.10 Other low birth weight newborn, unspecified weight**

• **P07.14 Other low birth weight newborn, 1000-1249 grams**

• **P07.15 Other low birth weight newborn, 1250-1499 grams**

• **P07.16 Other low birth weight newborn, 1500-1749 grams**

• **P07.17 Other low birth weight newborn, 1750-1999 grams**

• **P07.18 Other low birth weight newborn, 2000-2499 grams**

+ **P07.2 Extreme immaturity of newborn**
Less than 28 completed weeks (less than 196 completed days) of gestation.

• **P07.20 Extreme immaturity of newborn, unspecified weeks of gestation**
Gestational age less than 28 completed weeks NOS

• **P07.21 Extreme immaturity of newborn, gestational age less than 23 completed weeks**
Extreme immaturity of newborn, gestational age less than 23 weeks, 0 days

• **P07.22 Extreme immaturity of newborn, gestational age 23 completed weeks**
Extreme immaturity of newborn, gestational age 23 weeks, 0 days through 23 weeks, 6 days

• **P07.23 Extreme immaturity of newborn, gestational age 24 completed weeks**
Extreme immaturity of newborn, gestational age 24 weeks, 0 days through 24 weeks, 6 days

• **P07.24 Extreme immaturity of newborn, gestational age 25 completed weeks**
Extreme immaturity of newborn, gestational age 25 weeks, 0 days through 25 weeks, 6 days

• **P07.25 Extreme immaturity of newborn, gestational age 26 completed weeks**
Extreme immaturity of newborn, gestational age 26 weeks, 0 days through 26 weeks, 6 days

• **P07.26 Extreme immaturity of newborn, gestational age 27 completed weeks**
Extreme immaturity of newborn, gestational age 27 weeks, 0 days through 27 weeks, 6 days

+ **P07.3 Preterm [premature] newborn [other]**
28 completed weeks or more but less than 37 completed weeks (196 completed days but less than 259 completed days) of gestation.
Prematurity NOS

• **P07.30 Preterm newborn, unspecified weeks of gestation**

• **P07.31 Preterm newborn, gestational age 28 completed weeks**
Preterm newborn, gestational age 28 weeks, 0 days through 28 weeks, 6 days

• **P07.32 Preterm newborn, gestational age 29 completed weeks**
Preterm newborn, gestational age 29 weeks, 0 days through 29 weeks, 6 days

• **P07.33 Preterm newborn, gestational age 30 completed weeks**
Preterm newborn, gestational age 30 weeks, 0 days through 30 weeks, 6 days

• **P07.34 Preterm newborn, gestational age 31 completed weeks**
Preterm newborn, gestational age 31 weeks, 0 days through 31 weeks, 6 days

• **P07.35 Preterm newborn, gestational age 32 completed weeks**
Preterm newborn, gestational age 32 weeks, 0 days through 32 weeks, 6 days

• **P07.36 Preterm newborn, gestational age 33 completed weeks**
Preterm newborn, gestational age 33 weeks, 0 days through 33 weeks, 6 days

• **P07.37 Preterm newborn, gestational age 34 completed weeks**
Preterm newborn, gestational age 34 weeks, 0 days through 34 weeks, 6 days

• **P07.38 Preterm newborn, gestational age 35 completed weeks**
Preterm newborn, gestational age 35 weeks, 0 days through 35 weeks, 6 days

• **P07.39 Preterm newborn, gestational age 36 completed weeks**
Preterm newborn, gestational age 36 weeks, 0 days through 36 weeks, 6 days

P08 Disorders of newborn related to long gestation and high birth weight

NOTE When both birth weight and gestational age of the newborn are available, priority of assignment should be given to birth weight

Includes: the listed conditions, without further specification, as causes of morbidity or additional care, in newborn

• **P08.0 Exceptionally large newborn baby**
Usually implies a birth weight of 4500 g. or more
Excludes1: *syndrome of infant of diabetic mother (P70.1)*
syndrome of infant of mother with gestational diabetes (P70.0)

• **P08.1 Other heavy for gestational age newborn**
Other newborn heavy- or large-for-dates regardless of period of gestation
Usually implies a birth weight of 4000 g. to 4499 g.
Excludes1: *newborn with a birth weight of 4500 or more (P08.0)*
syndrome of infant of diabetic mother (P70.1)
syndrome of infant of mother with gestational diabetes (P70.0).

+ **P08.2 Late newborn, not heavy for gestational age**

• **P08.21 Post-term newborn**
Newborn with gestation period over 40 completed weeks to 42 completed weeks
AHA CC: 1Q, 2014, 14

• **P08.22 Prolonged gestation of newborn**
Newborn with gestation period over 42 completed weeks (294 days or more), not heavy- or large-for-dates.
Postmaturity NOS
AHA CC: 1Q, 2014, 14

Abnormal findings on neonatal screening (P09)

• **P09 Abnormal findings on neonatal screening**
Use additional code to identify signs, symptoms and conditions associated with the screening
Excludes2: *nonspecific serologic evidence of human immunodeficiency virus [HIV] (R75)*
Valid 3-character code, no further characters required

Birth trauma (P10-P15)

P10 Intracranial laceration and hemorrhage due to birth injury
Excludes1: *intracranial hemorrhage of newborn NOS (P52.9)*
intracranial hemorrhage of newborn due to anoxia or hypoxia (P52.-)
nontraumatic intracranial hemorrhage of newborn (P52.-)

• **MCC P10.0 Subdural hemorrhage due to birth injury**
Subdural hematoma (localized) due to birth injury
Excludes1: *subdural hemorrhage accompanying tentorial tear (P10.4)*
MCC Exclusion see Appendix A PDX collection 1020

• **MCC P10.1 Cerebral hemorrhage due to birth injury**
MCC Exclusion see Appendix A PDX collection 1020

• **CC P10.2 Intraventricular hemorrhage due to birth injury**
CC Exclusion see Appendix A PDX collection 1021

• MCC **P10.3 Subarachnoid hemorrhage due to birth injury**
MCC Exclusion see Appendix A PDX collection 1022
• MCC **P10.4 Tentorial tear due to birth injury**
MCC Exclusion see Appendix A PDX collection 1020
• MCC **P10.8 Other intracranial lacerations and hemorrhages due to birth injury**
MCC Exclusion see Appendix A PDX collection 1020
• MCC **P10.9 Unspecified intracranial laceration and hemorrhage due to birth injury**
MCC Exclusion see Appendix A PDX collection 1020

P11 Other birth injuries to central nervous system

• MCC **P11.0 Cerebral edema due to birth injury**
MCC Exclusion see Appendix A PDX collection 1020
• **P11.1 Other specified brain damage due to birth injury**
• MCC **P11.2 Unspecified brain damage due to birth injury**
MCC Exclusion see Appendix A PDX collection 1020
• **P11.3 Birth injury to facial nerve**
Facial palsy due to birth injury
• **P11.4 Birth injury to other cranial nerves**
• **P11.5 Birth injury to spine and spinal cord**
Fracture of spine due to birth injury
• MCC **P11.9 Birth injury to central nervous system, unspecified**
MCC Exclusion see Appendix A PDX collection 1020

P12 Birth injury to scalp

• **P12.0 Cephalhematoma due to birth injury**
• **P12.1 Chignon (from vacuum extraction) due to birth injury**
• CC **P12.2 Epicranial subaponeurotic hemorrhage due to birth injury**
Subgaleal hemorrhage
CC Exclusion see Appendix A PDX collection 1023
• **P12.3 Bruising of scalp due to birth injury**
• **P12.4 Injury of scalp of newborn due to monitoring equipment**
Sampling incision of scalp of newborn
Scalp clip (electrode) injury of newborn
+ **P12.8 Other birth injuries to scalp**
• **P12.81 Caput succedaneum**
• **P12.89 Other birth injuries to scalp**
• **P12.9 Birth injury to scalp, unspecified**

P13 Birth injury to skeleton

Excludes2: *birth injury to spine (P11.5)*
• **P13.0 Fracture of skull due to birth injury**
• **P13.1 Other birth injuries to skull**
Excludes1: *cephalhematoma (P12.0)*
• **P13.2 Birth injury to femur**
• **P13.3 Birth injury to other long bones**
• **P13.4 Fracture of clavicle due to birth injury**
• **P13.8 Birth injuries to other parts of skeleton**
• **P13.9 Birth injury to skeleton, unspecified**

P14 Birth injury to peripheral nervous system

• **P14.0 Erb's paralysis due to birth injury**
• **P14.1 Klumpke's paralysis due to birth injury**
• **P14.2 Phrenic nerve paralysis due to birth injury**
• **P14.3 Other brachial plexus birth injuries**
• **P14.8 Birth injuries to other parts of peripheral nervous system**
• **P14.9 Birth injury to peripheral nervous system, unspecified**

P15 Other birth injuries

• **P15.0 Birth injury to liver**
Rupture of liver due to birth injury
• **P15.1 Birth injury to spleen**
Rupture of spleen due to birth injury
• **P15.2 Sternomastoid injury due to birth injury**
• **P15.3 Birth injury to eye**
Subconjunctival hemorrhage due to birth injury
Traumatic glaucoma due to birth injury
• **P15.4 Birth injury to face**
Facial congestion due to birth injury
• **P15.5 Birth injury to external genitalia**
• **P15.6 Subcutaneous fat necrosis due to birth injury**
• **P15.8 Other specified birth injuries**
• **P15.9 Birth injury, unspecified**

Respiratory and cardiovascular disorders specific to the perinatal period (P19-P29)

P19 Metabolic acidemia in newborn

Includes: metabolic acidemia in newborn
• **P19.0 Metabolic acidemia in newborn first noted before onset of labor**
• **P19.1 Metabolic acidemia in newborn first noted during labor**
• **P19.2 Metabolic acidemia noted at birth**
• **P19.9 Metabolic acidemia, unspecified**

P22 Respiratory distress of newborn

Excludes1: *respiratory arrest of newborn (P28.81)*
respiratory failure of newborn NOS (P28.5)
• MCC **P22.0 Respiratory distress syndrome of newborn**
Cardiorespiratory distress syndrome of newborn
Hyaline membrane disease
Idiopathic respiratory distress syndrome [IRDS or RDS] of newborn
Pulmonary hypoperfusion syndrome
Respiratory distress syndrome, type I
MCC Exclusion see Appendix A PDX collection 0748
• **P22.1 Transient tachypnea of newborn**
Idiopathic tachypnea of newborn
Respiratory distress syndrome, type II
Wet lung syndrome
• **P22.8 Other respiratory distress of newborn**
• **P22.9 Respiratory distress of newborn, unspecified**

P23 Congenital pneumonia

Includes: infective pneumonia acquired in utero or during birth
Excludes1: *neonatal pneumonia resulting from aspiration (P24.-)*
• MCC **P23.0 Congenital pneumonia due to viral agent**
Use additional code (B97) to identify organism
Excludes1: *congenital rubella pneumonitis (P35.0)*
MCC Exclusion see Appendix A PDX collection 0748
• MCC **P23.1 Congenital pneumonia due to Chlamydia**
MCC Exclusion see Appendix A PDX collection 0748
• MCC **P23.2 Congenital pneumonia due to staphylococcus**
MCC Exclusion see Appendix A PDX collection 0748
• MCC **P23.3 Congenital pneumonia due to streptococcus, group B**
MCC Exclusion see Appendix A PDX collection 0748
• MCC **P23.4 Congenital pneumonia due to Escherichia coli**
MCC Exclusion see Appendix A PDX collection 0748
• MCC **P23.5 Congenital pneumonia due to Pseudomonas**
• MCC **P23.6 Congenital pneumonia due to other bacterial agents**
Congenital pneumonia due to Hemophilus influenzae
Congenital pneumonia due to Klebsiella pneumoniae
Congenital pneumonia due to Mycoplasma
Congenital pneumonia due to Streptococcus, except group B
Use additional code (B95-B96) to identify organism
MCC Exclusion see Appendix A PDX collection 0748
• MCC **P23.8 Congenital pneumonia due to other organisms**
MCC Exclusion see Appendix A PDX collection 0748
• MCC **P23.9 Congenital pneumonia, unspecified**
MCC Exclusion see Appendix A PDX collection 0748

P24 Neonatal aspiration

Includes: aspiration in utero and during delivery
+ **P24.0 Meconium aspiration**
Excludes1: *meconium passage (without aspiration) during delivery (P03.82)*
meconium staining (P96.83)
• **P24.00 Meconium aspiration without respiratory symptoms**
Meconium aspiration NOS
• MCC **P24.01 Meconium aspiration with respiratory symptoms**
Meconium aspiration pneumonia
Meconium aspiration pneumonitis
Meconium aspiration syndrome NOS
Use additional code to identify any secondary pulmonary hypertension, if applicable (I27.2)
MCC Exclusion see Appendix A PDX collection 0748
+ **P24.1 Neonatal aspiration of (clear) amniotic fluid and mucus**
Neonatal aspiration of liquor (amnii)
• **P24.10 Neonatal aspiration of (clear) amniotic fluid and mucus without respiratory symptoms**
Neonatal aspiration of amniotic fluid and mucus NOS
• MCC **P24.11 Neonatal aspiration of (clear) amniotic fluid and mucus with respiratory symptoms**
Neonatal aspiration of amniotic fluid and mucus with pneumonia
Neonatal aspiration of amniotic fluid and mucus with pneumonitis
Use additional code to identify any secondary pulmonary hypertension, if applicable (I27.2)
MCC Exclusion see Appendix A PDX collection 0748
+ **P24.2 Neonatal aspiration of blood**
• **P24.20 Neonatal aspiration of blood without respiratory symptoms**
Neonatal aspiration of blood NOS

• MCC **P24.21 Neonatal aspiration of blood with respiratory symptoms**
Neonatal aspiration of blood with pneumonia
Neonatal aspiration of blood with pneumonitis
Use additional code to identify any secondary pulmonary hypertension, if applicable (I27.2)
MCC Exclusion see Appendix A PDX collection 0748

\+ **P24.3 Neonatal aspiration of milk and regurgitated food**
Neonatal aspiration of stomach contents

• **P24.30 Neonatal aspiration of milk and regurgitated food without respiratory symptoms**
Neonatal aspiration of milk and regurgitated food NOS

• MCC **P24.31 Neonatal aspiration of milk and regurgitated food with respiratory symptoms**
Neonatal aspiration of milk and regurgitated food with pneumonia
Neonatal aspiration of milk and regurgitated food with pneumonitis
Use additional code to identify any secondary pulmonary hypertension, if applicable (I27.2)
MCC Exclusion see Appendix A PDX collection 0748

\+ **P24.8 Other neonatal aspiration**

• **P24.80 Other neonatal aspiration without respiratory symptoms**
Neonatal aspiration NEC

• MCC **P24.81 Other neonatal aspiration with respiratory symptoms**
Neonatal aspiration pneumonia NEC
Neonatal aspiration with pneumonitis NEC
Neonatal aspiration with pneumonia NOS
Neonatal aspiration with pneumonitis NOS
Use additional code to identify any secondary pulmonary hypertension, if applicable (I27.2)
MCC Exclusion see Appendix A PDX collection 0748

• **P24.9 Neonatal aspiration, unspecified**

P25 Interstitial emphysema and related conditions originating in the perinatal period

• MCC **P25.0 Interstitial emphysema originating in the perinatal period**
MCC Exclusion see Appendix A PDX collection 0748

• MCC **P25.1 Pneumothorax originating in the perinatal period**
MCC Exclusion see Appendix A PDX collection 0748

• MCC **P25.2 Pneumomediastinum originating in the perinatal period**
MCC Exclusion see Appendix A PDX collection 0748

• MCC **P25.3 Pneumopericardium originating in the perinatal period**
MCC Exclusion see Appendix A PDX collection 0748

• MCC **P25.8 Other conditions related to interstitial emphysema originating in the perinatal period**
MCC Exclusion see Appendix A PDX collection 0748

P26 Pulmonary hemorrhage originating in the perinatal period

Excludes1: *acute idiopathic hemorrhage in infants over 28 days old (R04.81)*

• MCC **P26.0 Tracheobronchial hemorrhage originating in the perinatal period**
MCC Exclusion see Appendix A PDX collection 0748

• MCC **P26.1 Massive pulmonary hemorrhage originating in the perinatal period**
MCC Exclusion see Appendix A PDX collection 0748

• MCC **P26.8 Other pulmonary hemorrhages originating in the perinatal period**
MCC Exclusion see Appendix A PDX collection 0748

• MCC **P26.9 Unspecified pulmonary hemorrhage originating in the perinatal period**
MCC Exclusion see Appendix A PDX collection 0748

P27 Chronic respiratory disease originating in the perinatal period

Excludes1: *respiratory distress of newborn (P22.0-P22.9)*

MCC **P27.0 Wilson-Mikity syndrome**
Pulmonary dysmaturity
MCC Exclusion see Appendix A PDX collection 0748

MCC **P27.1 Bronchopulmonary dysplasia originating in the perinatal period**
MCC Exclusion see Appendix A PDX collection 0748

MCC **P27.8 Other chronic respiratory diseases originating in the perinatal period**
Congenital pulmonary fibrosis
Ventilator lung in newborn
MCC Exclusion see Appendix A PDX collection 0748

MCC **P27.9 Unspecified chronic respiratory disease originating in the perinatal period**
MCC Exclusion see Appendix A PDX collection 0748

P28 Other respiratory conditions originating in the perinatal period

Excludes1: *congenital malformations of the respiratory system (Q30-Q34)*

• CC **P28.0 Primary atelectasis of newborn**
Primary failure to expand terminal respiratory units
Pulmonary hypoplasia associated with short gestation
Pulmonary immaturity NOS
CC Exclusion see Appendix A PDX collection 0748

\+ **P28.1 Other and unspecified atelectasis of newborn**

• CC **P28.10 Unspecified atelectasis of newborn**
Atelectasis of newborn NOS
CC Exclusion see Appendix A PDX collection 0748

• CC **P28.11 Resorption atelectasis without respiratory distress syndrome**
Excludes1: *resorption atelectasis with respiratory distress syndrome (P22.0)*
CC Exclusion see Appendix A PDX collection 0748

• CC **P28.19 Other atelectasis of newborn**
Partial atelectasis of newborn
Secondary atelectasis of newborn
CC Exclusion see Appendix A PDX collection 0748

• CC **P28.2 Cyanotic attacks of newborn**
Excludes1: *apnea of newborn (P28.3-P28.4)*
CC Exclusion see Appendix A PDX collection 1024

• CC **P28.3 Primary sleep apnea of newborn**
Central sleep apnea of newborn
Obstructive sleep apnea of newborn
Sleep apnea of newborn NOS
CC Exclusion see Appendix A PDX collection 1025

• CC **P28.4 Other apnea of newborn**
Apnea of prematurity
Obstructive apnea of newborn
Excludes1: *obstructive sleep apnea of newborn (P28.3)*
CC Exclusion see Appendix A PDX collection 1026

• MCC **P28.5 Respiratory failure of newborn**
Excludes1: *respiratory arrest of newborn (P28.81)*
respiratory distress of newborn (P22.0-)
MCC Exclusion see Appendix A PDX collection 0748

\+ **P28.8 Other specified respiratory conditions of newborn**

• MCC **P28.81 Respiratory arrest of newborn**
MCC Exclusion see Appendix A PDX collection 1027

• **P28.89 Other specified respiratory conditions of newborn**
Congenital laryngeal stridor
Sniffles in newborn
Snuffles in newborn
Excludes1: *early congenital syphilitic rhinitis (A50.05)*

• **P28.9 Respiratory condition of newborn, unspecified**
Respiratory depression in newborn

P29 Cardiovascular disorders originating in the perinatal period

Excludes1: *congenital malformations of the circulatory system (Q20-Q28)*

• **P29.0 Neonatal cardiac failure**

\+ **P29.1 Neonatal cardiac dysrhythmia**

• **P29.11 Neonatal tachycardia**

• **P29.12 Neonatal bradycardia**

• **P29.2 Neonatal hypertension**

• MCC **P29.3 Persistent fetal circulation**
Delayed closure of ductus arteriosus
(Persistent) pulmonary hypertension of newborn
MCC Exclusion see Appendix A PDX collection 1028

• **P29.4 Transient myocardial ischemia in newborn**

\+ **P29.8 Other cardiovascular disorders originating in the perinatal period**

• MCC **P29.81 Cardiac arrest of newborn**
MCC Exclusion see Appendix A PDX collection 1029

• **P29.89 Other cardiovascular disorders originating in the perinatal period**

• **P29.9 Cardiovascular disorder originating in the perinatal period, unspecified**

Infections specific to the perinatal period (P35-P39)

Infections acquired in utero, during birth via the umbilicus, or during the first 28 days after birth

Excludes2: *asymptomatic human immunodeficiency virus [HIV] infection status (Z21)*
congenital gonococcal infection (A54.-)
congenital pneumonia (P23.-)
congenital syphilis (A50.-)
human immunodeficiency virus [HIV] disease (B20)
infant botulism (A48.51)
infectious diseases not specific to the perinatal period (A00-B99, J09, J10.-)
intestinal infectious disease (A00-A09)
laboratory evidence of human immunodeficiency virus [HIV] (R75)
tetanus neonatorum (A33)

P35 Congenital viral diseases

Includes: infections acquired in utero or during birth

- CC **P35.0 Congenital rubella syndrome**
  Congenital rubella pneumonitis
  CC Exclusion see Appendix A PDX collection 1030
- MCC **P35.1 Congenital cytomegalovirus infection**
  MCC Exclusion see Appendix A PDX collection 1030
- MCC **P35.2 Congenital herpesviral [herpes simplex] infection**
  MCC Exclusion see Appendix A PDX collection 0562
- MCC **P35.3 Congenital viral hepatitis**
  MCC Exclusion see Appendix A PDX collection 0562
- MCC **P35.8 Other congenital viral diseases**
  Congenital varicella [chickenpox]
  MCC Exclusion see Appendix A PDX collection 0562
- MCC **P35.9 Congenital viral disease, unspecified**
  MCC Exclusion see Appendix A PDX collection 0562

P36 Bacterial sepsis of newborn

Includes: congenital sepsis
Use additional code(s), if applicable, to identify severe sepsis (R65.2-) and associated acute organ dysfunction(s)
Review coding guideline C.1.d and C.16.f

- MCC **P36.0 Sepsis of newborn due to streptococcus, group B**
  MCC Exclusion see Appendix A PDX collection 1031
- + **P36.1 Sepsis of newborn due to other and unspecified streptococci**
  - MCC **P36.10 Sepsis of newborn due to unspecified streptococci**
    MCC Exclusion see Appendix A PDX collection 1031
  - MCC **P36.19 Sepsis of newborn due to other streptococci**
    MCC Exclusion see Appendix A PDX collection 1031
- MCC **P36.2 Sepsis of newborn due to Staphylococcus aureus**
  MCC Exclusion see Appendix A PDX collection 1031
- + **P36.3 Sepsis of newborn due to other and unspecified staphylococci**
  - MCC **P36.30 Sepsis of newborn due to unspecified staphylococci**
    MCC Exclusion see Appendix A PDX collection 1031
  - MCC **P36.39 Sepsis of newborn due to other staphylococci**
    MCC Exclusion see Appendix A PDX collection 1031
- MCC **P36.4 Sepsis of newborn due to Escherichia coli**
  MCC Exclusion see Appendix A PDX collection 1031
- MCC **P36.5 Sepsis of newborn due to anaerobes**
  MCC Exclusion see Appendix A PDX collection 1031
- MCC **P36.8 Other bacterial sepsis of newborn**
  Use additional code from category B96 to identify organism
  MCC Exclusion see Appendix A PDX collection 1031
- MCC **P36.9 Bacterial sepsis of newborn, unspecified**
  MCC Exclusion see Appendix A PDX collection 1031

P37 Other congenital infectious and parasitic diseases

Excludes2: *congenital syphilis (A50.-)*
infectious neonatal diarrhea (A00-A09)
necrotizing enterocolitis in newborn (P77.-)
noninfectious neonatal diarrhea (P78.3)
ophthalmia neonatorum due to gonococcus (A54.31)
tetanus neonatorum (A33)

- MCC **P37.0 Congenital tuberculosis**
  MCC Exclusion see Appendix A PDX collection 0562
- MCC **P37.1 Congenital toxoplasmosis**
  Hydrocephalus due to congenital toxoplasmosis
  MCC Exclusion see Appendix A PDX collection 0562
- MCC **P37.2 Neonatal (disseminated) listeriosis**
  MCC Exclusion see Appendix A PDX collection 0562
- MCC **P37.3 Congenital falciparum malaria**
  MCC Exclusion see Appendix A PDX collection 0562
- MCC **P37.4 Other congenital malaria**
  MCC Exclusion see Appendix A PDX collection 0562
- **P37.5 Neonatal candidiasis**
- MCC **P37.8 Other specified congenital infectious and parasitic diseases**
  MCC Exclusion see Appendix A PDX collection 0562
- MCC **P37.9 Congenital infectious or parasitic disease, unspecified**
  MCC Exclusion see Appendix A PDX collection 0562

P38 Omphalitis of newborn

Excludes1: *omphalitis not of newborn (L08.82)*
tetanus omphalitis (A33)
umbilical hemorrhage of newborn (P51.-)

- CC **P38.1 Omphalitis with mild hemorrhage**
  CC Exclusion see Appendix A PDX collection 1032
- CC **P38.9 Omphalitis without hemorrhage**
  Omphalitis of newborn NOS
  CC Exclusion see Appendix A PDX collection 1032

P39 Other infections specific to the perinatal period

Use additional code to identify organism or specific infection

- CC **P39.0 Neonatal infective mastitis**
  Excludes1: *breast engorgement of newborn (P83.4)*
  noninfective mastitis of newborn (P83.4)
  CC Exclusion see Appendix A PDX collection 1032
- **P39.1 Neonatal conjunctivitis and dacryocystitis**
  Neonatal chlamydial conjunctivitis
  Ophthalmia neonatorum NOS
  Excludes1: *gonococcal conjunctivitis (A54.31)*
- CC **P39.2 Intra-amniotic infection affecting newborn, not elsewhere classified**
  CC Exclusion see Appendix A PDX collection 1034
- CC **P39.3 Neonatal urinary tract infection**
  CC Exclusion see Appendix A PDX collection 1033
- CC **P39.4 Neonatal skin infection**
  Neonatal pyoderma
  Excludes1: *pemphigus neonatorum (L00)*
  staphylococcal scalded skin syndrome (L00)
  CC Exclusion see Appendix A PDX collection 1033
- CC **P39.8 Other specified infections specific to the perinatal period**
  CC Exclusion see Appendix A PDX collection 1033
- CC **P39.9 Infection specific to the perinatal period, unspecified**
  CC Exclusion see Appendix A PDX collection 1033

Hemorrhagic and hematological disorders of newborn (P50-P61)

Excludes1: *congenital stenosis and stricture of bile ducts (Q44.3)*
Crigler-Najjar syndrome (E80.5)
Dubin-Johnson syndrome (E80.6)
Gilbert syndrome (E80.4)
hereditary hemolytic anemias (D55-D58)

P50 Newborn affected by intrauterine (fetal) blood loss

Excludes1: *congenital anemia from intrauterine (fetal) blood loss (P61.3)*

- **P50.0 Newborn affected by intrauterine (fetal) blood loss from vasa previa**
- **P50.1 Newborn affected by intrauterine (fetal) blood loss from ruptured cord**
- **P50.2 Newborn affected by intrauterine (fetal) blood loss from placenta**
- **P50.3 Newborn affected by hemorrhage into co-twin**
- **P50.4 Newborn affected by hemorrhage into maternal circulation**
- **P50.5 Newborn affected by intrauterine (fetal) blood loss from cut end of co-twin's cord**
- **P50.8 Newborn affected by other intrauterine (fetal) blood loss**
- **P50.9 Newborn affected by intrauterine (fetal) blood loss, unspecified**
  Newborn affected by fetal hemorrhage NOS

P51 Umbilical hemorrhage of newborn

Excludes1: *omphalitis with mild hemorrhage (P38.1)*
umbilical hemorrhage from cut end of co-twins cord (P50.5)

- **P51.0 Massive umbilical hemorrhage of newborn**
- **P51.8 Other umbilical hemorrhages of newborn**
  Slipped umbilical ligature NOS
- **P51.9 Umbilical hemorrhage of newborn, unspecified**

P52 Intracranial nontraumatic hemorrhage of newborn

Includes: intracranial hemorrhage due to anoxia or hypoxia
Excludes1: *intracranial hemorrhage due to birth injury (P10.-)*
intracranial hemorrhage due to other injury (S06.-)

- CC **P52.0 Intraventricular (nontraumatic) hemorrhage, grade 1, of newborn**
  Subependymal hemorrhage (without intraventricular extension)
  Bleeding into germinal matrix
  CC Exclusion see Appendix A PDX collection 1021

• CC **P52.1 Intraventricular (nontraumatic) hemorrhage, grade 2, of newborn**
Subependymal hemorrhage with intraventricular extension
Bleeding into ventricle
CC Exclusion see Appendix A PDX collection 1021

+ **P52.2 Intraventricular (nontraumatic) hemorrhage, grade 3 and grade 4, of newborn**

• MCC **P52.21 Intraventricular (nontraumatic) hemorrhage, grade 3, of newborn**
Subependymal hemorrhage with intraventricular extension with enlargement of ventricle
MCC Exclusion see Appendix A PDX collection 1021

• MCC **P52.22 Intraventricular (nontraumatic) hemorrhage, grade 4, of newborn**
Bleeding into cerebral cortex
Subependymal hemorrhage with intracerebral extension
MCC Exclusion see Appendix A PDX collection 1021

• CC **P52.3 Unspecified intraventricular (nontraumatic) hemorrhage of newborn**
CC Exclusion see Appendix A PDX collection 1021

• MCC **P52.4 Intracerebral (nontraumatic) hemorrhage of newborn**
MCC Exclusion see Appendix A PDX collection 1020

• MCC **P52.5 Subarachnoid (nontraumatic) hemorrhage of newborn**
MCC Exclusion see Appendix A PDX collection 1022

• MCC **P52.6 Cerebellar (nontraumatic) and posterior fossa hemorrhage of newborn**
MCC Exclusion see Appendix A PDX collection 1020

• MCC **P52.8 Other intracranial (nontraumatic) hemorrhages of newborn**
MCC Exclusion see Appendix A PDX collection 1020

• MCC **P52.9 Intracranial (nontraumatic) hemorrhage of newborn, unspecified**
MCC Exclusion see Appendix A PDX collection 1020

• CC **P53 Hemorrhagic disease of newborn**
Vitamin K deficiency of newborn
CC Exclusion see Appendix A PDX collection 1035
Valid 3-character code, no further characters required

P54 Other neonatal hemorrhages

Excludes1: *newborn affected by (intrauterine) blood loss (P50.-)*
pulmonary hemorrhage originating in the perinatal period (P26.-)

• **P54.0 Neonatal hematemesis**
Excludes1: *neonatal hematemesis due to swallowed maternal blood (P78.2)*

• MCC **P54.1 Neonatal melena**
Excludes1: *neonatal melena due to swallowed maternal blood (P78.2)*
MCC Exclusion see Appendix A PDX collection 1036

• MCC **P54.2 Neonatal rectal hemorrhage**
MCC Exclusion see Appendix A PDX collection 1036

• MCC **P54.3 Other neonatal gastrointestinal hemorrhage**
MCC Exclusion see Appendix A PDX collection 1036

• CC **P54.4 Neonatal adrenal hemorrhage**
CC Exclusion see Appendix A PDX collection 1036

• **P54.5 Neonatal cutaneous hemorrhage**
Neonatal bruising
Neonatal ecchymoses
Neonatal petechiae
Neonatal superficial hematomata
Excludes2: *bruising of scalp due to birth injury (P12.3)*
cephalhematoma due to birth injury (P12.0)

• ♀ **P54.6 Neonatal vaginal hemorrhage**
Neonatal pseudomenses

• **P54.8 Other specified neonatal hemorrhages**

• **P54.9 Neonatal hemorrhage, unspecified**

P55 Hemolytic disease of newborn

• **P55.0 Rh isoimmunization of newborn**
• **P55.1 ABO isoimmunization of newborn**
• **P55.8 Other hemolytic diseases of newborn**
• **P55.9 Hemolytic disease of newborn, unspecified**

P56 Hydrops fetalis due to hemolytic disease

Excludes1: *hydrops fetalis NOS (P83.2)*

• MCC **P56.0 Hydrops fetalis due to isoimmunization**
MCC Exclusion see Appendix A PDX collection 1037

+ **P56.9 Hydrops fetalis due to other and unspecified hemolytic disease**

• MCC **P56.90 Hydrops fetalis due to unspecified hemolytic disease**
MCC Exclusion see Appendix A PDX collection 1037

• MCC **P56.99 Hydrops fetalis due to other hemolytic disease**
MCC Exclusion see Appendix A PDX collection 1037

P57 Kernicterus

• MCC **P57.0 Kernicterus due to isoimmunization**
MCC Exclusion see Appendix A PDX collection 1037

• MCC **P57.8 Other specified kernicterus**
Excludes1: *Crigler-Najjar syndrome (E80.5)*
MCC Exclusion see Appendix A PDX collection 1038

• MCC **P57.9 Kernicterus, unspecified**
MCC Exclusion see Appendix A PDX collection 1038

P58 Neonatal jaundice due to other excessive hemolysis

Excludes1: *jaundice due to isoimmunization (P55-P57)*

• **P58.0 Neonatal jaundice due to bruising**
• **P58.1 Neonatal jaundice due to bleeding**
• **P58.2 Neonatal jaundice due to infection**
• **P58.3 Neonatal jaundice due to polycythemia**

+ **P58.4 Neonatal jaundice due to drugs or toxins transmitted from mother or given to newborn**
Code first poisoning due to drug or toxin, if applicable (T36-T65 with fifth or sixth character 1-4 or 6)

Use additional code for adverse effect, if applicable, to identify drug (T36-T50 with fifth or sixth character 5)

• **P58.41 Neonatal jaundice due to drugs or toxins transmitted from mother**

• **P58.42 Neonatal jaundice due to drugs or toxins given to newborn**

• **P58.5 Neonatal jaundice due to swallowed maternal blood**
• **P58.8 Neonatal jaundice due to other specified excessive hemolysis**
• **P58.9 Neonatal jaundice due to excessive hemolysis, unspecified**

P59 Neonatal jaundice from other and unspecified causes

Excludes1: *jaundice due to inborn errors of metabolism (E70-E88)*
kernicterus (P57.-)

• **P59.0 Neonatal jaundice associated with preterm delivery**
Hyperbilirubinemia of prematurity
Jaundice due to delayed conjugation associated with preterm delivery

• MCC **P59.1 Inspissated bile syndrome**
MCC Exclusion see Appendix A PDX collection 1038

+ **P59.2 Neonatal jaundice from other and unspecified hepatocellular damage**
Excludes1: *congenital viral hepatitis (P35.3)*

• MCC **P59.20 Neonatal jaundice from unspecified hepatocellular damage**
MCC Exclusion see Appendix A PDX collection 1038

• MCC **P59.29 Neonatal jaundice from other hepatocellular damage**
Neonatal giant cell hepatitis
Neonatal (idiopathic) hepatitis
MCC Exclusion see Appendix A PDX collection 1038

• **P59.3 Neonatal jaundice from breast milk inhibitor**
• **P59.8 Neonatal jaundice from other specified causes**
• **P59.9 Neonatal jaundice, unspecified**
Neonatal physiological jaundice (intense)(prolonged) NOS

MCC • **P60 Disseminated intravascular coagulation of newborn**
Defibrination syndrome of newborn
MCC Exclusion see Appendix A PDX collection 1035
Valid 3-character code, no further characters required

P61 Other perinatal hematological disorders

Excludes1: *transient hypogammaglobulinemia of infancy (D80.7)*

• MCC **P61.0 Transient neonatal thrombocytopenia**
Neonatal thrombocytopenia due to exchange transfusion
Neonatal thrombocytopenia due to idiopathic maternal thrombocytopenia
Neonatal thrombocytopenia due to isoimmunization
MCC Exclusion see Appendix A PDX collection 1035

• **P61.1 Polycythemia neonatorum**

• CC **P61.2 Anemia of prematurity**
CC Exclusion see Appendix A PDX collection 1039

• CC **P61.3 Congenital anemia from fetal blood loss**
CC Exclusion see Appendix A PDX collection 1039

• CC **P61.4 Other congenital anemias, not elsewhere classified**
Congenital anemia NOS
CC Exclusion see Appendix A PDX collection 1039

• MCC **P61.5 Transient neonatal neutropenia**
Excludes1: *congenital neutropenia (nontransient) (D70.0)*
MCC Exclusion see Appendix A PDX collection 1040

• CC **P61.6 Other transient neonatal disorders of coagulation**
CC Exclusion see Appendix A PDX collection 1035

• **P61.8 Other specified perinatal hematological disorders**
• **P61.9 Perinatal hematological disorder, unspecified**

ransitory endocrine and metabolic disorders specific to ewborn (P70-P74)

cludes: transitory endocrine and metabolic disturbances caused by the infant's response to maternal endocrine and metabolic factors, or its adjustment to extrauterine environment

P70 Transitory disorders of carbohydrate metabolism specific to newborn

- **P70.0 Syndrome of infant of mother with gestational diabetes**
  Newborn (with hypoglycemia) affected by maternal gestational diabetes
  Excludes1: *newborn (with hypoglycemia) affected by maternal (pre-existing) diabetes mellitus (P70.1)*
  syndrome of infant of a diabetic mother (P70.1)
- **P70.1 Syndrome of infant of a diabetic mother**
  Newborn (with hypoglycemia) affected by maternal (pre-existing) diabetes mellitus
  Excludes1: *newborn (with hypoglycemia) affected by maternal gestational diabetes (P70.0)*
  syndrome of infant of mother with gestational diabetes (P70.0)
- CC **P70.2 Neonatal diabetes mellitus**
  CC Exclusion see Appendix A PDX collection 1041
- **P70.3 Iatrogenic neonatal hypoglycemia**
- **P70.4 Other neonatal hypoglycemia**
  Transitory neonatal hypoglycemia
- CC **P70.8 Other transitory disorders of carbohydrate metabolism of newborn**
  CC Exclusion see Appendix A PDX collection 1042
- **P70.9 Transitory disorder of carbohydrate metabolism of newborn, unspecified**

P71 Transitory neonatal disorders of calcium and magnesium metabolism

- CC **P71.0 Cow's milk hypocalcemia in newborn**
  CC Exclusion see Appendix A PDX collection 1041
- CC **P71.1 Other neonatal hypocalcemia**
  Excludes1: *neonatal hypoparathyroidism (P71.4)*
  CC Exclusion see Appendix A PDX collection 1041
- CC **P71.2 Neonatal hypomagnesemia**
  CC Exclusion see Appendix A PDX collection 1041
- CC **P71.3 Neonatal tetany without calcium or magnesium deficiency**
  Neonatal tetany NOS
  CC Exclusion see Appendix A PDX collection 1041
- CC **P71.4 Transitory neonatal hypoparathyroidism**
  CC Exclusion see Appendix A PDX collection 1041
- CC **P71.8 Other transitory neonatal disorders of calcium and magnesium metabolism**
  CC Exclusion see Appendix A PDX collection 1041
- CC **P71.9 Transitory neonatal disorder of calcium and magnesium metabolism, unspecified**
  CC Exclusion see Appendix A PDX collection 1041

P72 Other transitory neonatal endocrine disorders

Excludes1: *congenital hypothyroidism with or without goiter (E03.0-E03.1)*
dyshormogenetic goiter (E07.1)
Pendred's syndrome (E07.1)

- CC **P72.0 Neonatal goiter, not elsewhere classified**
  Transitory congenital goiter with normal functioning
  CC Exclusion see Appendix A PDX collection 1042
- CC **P72.1 Transitory neonatal hyperthyroidism**
  Neonatal thyrotoxicosis
  CC Exclusion see Appendix A PDX collection 1041
- CC **P72.2 Other transitory neonatal disorders of thyroid function, not elsewhere classified**
  Transitory neonatal hypothyroidism
  CC Exclusion see Appendix A PDX collection 1042
- CC **P72.8 Other specified transitory neonatal endocrine disorders**
  CC Exclusion see Appendix A PDX collection 1042
- **P72.9 Transitory neonatal endocrine disorder, unspecified**

P74 Other transitory neonatal electrolyte and metabolic disturbances

- MCC **P74.0 Late metabolic acidosis of newborn**
  Excludes1: *(fetal) metabolic acidosis of newborn (P19)*
  MCC Exclusion see Appendix A PDX collection 1041
- **P74.1 Dehydration of newborn**
- **P74.2 Disturbances of sodium balance of newborn**
- **P74.3 Disturbances of potassium balance of newborn**
- **P74.4 Other transitory electrolyte disturbances of newborn**
- CC **P74.5 Transitory tyrosinemia of newborn**
  CC Exclusion see Appendix A PDX collection 1042
- CC **P74.6 Transitory hyperammonemia of newborn**
  CC Exclusion see Appendix A PDX collection 1042
- CC **P74.8 Other transitory metabolic disturbances of newborn**
  Amino-acid metabolic disorders described as transitory
  CC Exclusion see Appendix A PDX collection 1042
- **P74.9 Transitory metabolic disturbance of newborn, unspecified**

Digestive system disorders of newborn (P76-P78)

P76 Other intestinal obstruction of newborn

- **P76.0 Meconium plug syndrome**
  Meconium ileus NOS
  Excludes1: *meconium ileus in cystic fibrosis (E84.11)*
- CC **P76.1 Transitory ileus of newborn**
  Excludes1: *Hirschsprung's disease (Q43.1)*
  CC Exclusion see Appendix A PDX collection 1043
- **P76.2 Intestinal obstruction due to inspissated milk**
- **P76.8 Other specified intestinal obstruction of newborn**
  Excludes1: *intestinal obstruction classifiable to K56.-*
- **P76.9 Intestinal obstruction of newborn, unspecified**

P77 Necrotizing enterocolitis of newborn

- MCC **P77.1 Stage 1 necrotizing enterocolitis in newborn**
  Necrotizing enterocolitis without pneumatosis, without perforation
  MCC Exclusion see Appendix A PDX collection 1044
- MCC **P77.2 Stage 2 necrotizing enterocolitis in newborn**
  Necrotizing enterocolitis with pneumatosis, without perforation
  MCC Exclusion see Appendix A PDX collection 1044
- MCC **P77.3 Stage 3 necrotizing enterocolitis in newborn**
  Necrotizing enterocolitis with perforation
  Necrotizing enterocolitis with pneumatosis and perforation
  MCC Exclusion see Appendix A PDX collection 1044
- MCC **P77.9 Necrotizing enterocolitis in newborn, unspecified**
  Necrotizing enterocolitis in newborn, NOS
  MCC Exclusion see Appendix A PDX collection 1044

P78 Other perinatal digestive system disorders

Excludes1: *cystic fibrosis (E84.0-E84.9)*
neonatal gastrointestinal hemorrhages (P54.0-P54.3)

- MCC **P78.0 Perinatal intestinal perforation**
  Meconium peritonitis
  MCC Exclusion see Appendix A PDX collection 1044
- **P78.1 Other neonatal peritonitis**
  Neonatal peritonitis NOS
- **P78.2 Neonatal hematemesis and melena due to swallowed maternal blood**
- **P78.3 Noninfective neonatal diarrhea**
  Neonatal diarrhea NOS
- + **P78.8 Other specified perinatal digestive system disorders**
  - **P78.81 Congenital cirrhosis (of liver)**
  - **P78.82 Peptic ulcer of newborn**
  - **P78.83 Newborn esophageal reflux**
    Neonatal esophageal reflux
  - **P78.89 Other specified perinatal digestive system disorders**
- **P78.9 Perinatal digestive system disorder, unspecified**

Conditions involving the integument and temperature regulation of newborn (P80-P83)

P80 Hypothermia of newborn

- **P80.0 Cold injury syndrome**
  Severe and usually chronic hypothermia associated with a pink flushed appearance, edema and neurological and biochemical abnormalities.
  Excludes1: *mild hypothermia of newborn (P80.8)*
- **P80.8 Other hypothermia of newborn**
  Mild hypothermia of newborn
- **P80.9 Hypothermia of newborn, unspecified**

P81 Other disturbances of temperature regulation of newborn

- **P81.0 Environmental hyperthermia of newborn**
- **P81.8 Other specified disturbances of temperature regulation of newborn**
- **P81.9 Disturbance of temperature regulation of newborn, unspecified**
  Fever of newborn NOS

P83 Other conditions of integument specific to newborn

Excludes1: *congenital malformations of skin and integument (Q80-Q84)*
hydrops fetalis due to hemolytic disease (P56.-)
neonatal skin infection (P39.4)
staphylococcal scalded skin syndrome (L00)
Excludes2: *cradle cap (L21.0)*
diaper [napkin] dermatitis (L22)

- • CC **P83.0 Sclerema neonatorum**
  CC Exclusion see Appendix A PDX collection 1045
- • **P83.1 Neonatal erythema toxicum**
- • MCC **P83.2 Hydrops fetalis not due to hemolytic disease**
  Hydrops fetalis NOS
  MCC Exclusion see Appendix A PDX collection 1046
- + **P83.3 Other and unspecified edema specific to newborn**
  - • CC **P83.30 Unspecified edema specific to newborn**
    CC Exclusion see Appendix A PDX collection 1047
  - • CC **P83.39 Other edema specific to newborn**
    CC Exclusion see Appendix A PDX collection 1047
- • **P83.4 Breast engorgement of newborn**
  Noninfective mastitis of newborn
- ♂ **P83.5 Congenital hydrocele**
- • **P83.6 Umbilical polyp of newborn**
- • **P83.8 Other specified conditions of integument specific to newborn**
  Bronze baby syndrome
  Neonatal scleroderma
  Urticaria neonatorum
- • **P83.9 Condition of the integument specific to newborn, unspecified**

Other problems with newborn (P84)

- • **P84 Other problems with newborn**
  Acidemia of newborn
  Acidosis of newborn
  Anoxia of newborn NOS
  Asphyxia of newborn NOS
  Hypercapnia of newborn
  Hypoxemia of newborn
  Hypoxia of newborn NOS
  Mixed metabolic and respiratory acidosis of newborn
  Excludes1: *intracranial hemorrhage due to anoxia or hypoxia (P52.-)*
  hypoxic ischemic encephalopathy [HIE] (P91.6-)
  late metabolic acidosis of newborn (P74.0)
  Valid 3-character code, no further characters required

Other disorders originating in the perinatal period (P90-P96)

- • MCC **P90 Convulsions of newborn**
  Excludes1: *benign myoclonic epilepsy in infancy (G40.3-)*
  benign neonatal convulsions (familial) (G40.3-)
  MCC Exclusion see Appendix A PDX collection 1048
  Valid 3-character code, no further characters required

P91 Other disturbances of cerebral status of newborn

- • MCC **P91.0 Neonatal cerebral ischemia**
  MCC Exclusion see Appendix A PDX collection 1049
- • MCC **P91.1 Acquired periventricular cysts of newborn**
  MCC Exclusion see Appendix A PDX collection 1049
- • MCC **P91.2 Neonatal cerebral leukomalacia**
  Periventricular leukomalacia
  MCC Exclusion see Appendix A PDX collection 1022
- • MCC **P91.3 Neonatal cerebral irritability**
  MCC Exclusion see Appendix A PDX collection 1049
- • MCC **P91.4 Neonatal cerebral depression**
  MCC Exclusion see Appendix A PDX collection 1049
- • MCC **P91.5 Neonatal coma**
  MCC Exclusion see Appendix A PDX collection 1049
- + **P91.6 Hypoxic ischemic encephalopathy [HIE]**
  - • CC **P91.60 Hypoxic ischemic encephalopathy [HIE], unspecified**
    CC Exclusion see Appendix A PDX collection 1050
  - • CC **P91.61 Mild hypoxic ischemic encephalopathy [HIE]**
    CC Exclusion see Appendix A PDX collection 1050
  - • **P91.62 Moderate hypoxic ischemic encephalopathy [HIE]**
  - • MCC **P91.63 Severe hypoxic ischemic encephalopathy [HIE]**
    MCC Exclusion see Appendix A PDX collection 1050
- • **P91.8 Other specified disturbances of cerebral status of newborn**
- • **P91.9 Disturbance of cerebral status of newborn, unspecified**

P92 Feeding problems of newborn

Excludes1: *feeding problems in child over 28 days old (R63.3)*

- + **P92.0 Vomiting of newborn**
  Excludes1: *vomiting of child over 28 days old (R11.-)*
  - • MCC **P92.01 Bilious vomiting of newborn**
    Excludes1: *bilious vomiting in child over 28 days old (R11.14)*
    MCC Exclusion see Appendix A PDX collection 1051
  - • **P92.09 Other vomiting of newborn**
    Excludes1: *regurgitation of food in newborn (P92.1)*
- • **P92.1 Regurgitation and rumination of newborn**
- • **P92.2 Slow feeding of newborn**
- • **P92.3 Underfeeding of newborn**
- • **P92.4 Overfeeding of newborn**
- • **P92.5 Neonatal difficulty in feeding at breast**
- • **P92.6 Failure to thrive in newborn**
  Excludes1: *failure to thrive in child over 28 days old (R62.51)*
- • **P92.8 Other feeding problems of newborn**
- • **P92.9 Feeding problem of newborn, unspecified**

P93 Reactions and intoxications due to drugs administered to newborn

Includes: reactions and intoxications due to drugs administered to fetus affecting newborn
Excludes1: *jaundice due to drugs or toxins transmitted from mother or given to newborn (P58.4-)*
reactions and intoxications from maternal opiates, tranquilizers and other medication (P04.0-P04.1, P04.4)
withdrawal symptoms from maternal use of drugs of addiction (P96.1)
withdrawal symptoms from therapeutic use of drugs in newborn (P96.2)

- • CC **P93.0 Grey baby syndrome**
  Grey syndrome from chloramphenicol administration in newbor
  CC Exclusion see Appendix A PDX collection 1052
- • CC **P93.8 Other reactions and intoxications due to drugs administered to newborn**
  Use additional code for adverse effect, if applicable, to identify drug (T36-T50 with fifth or sixth character 5)
  CC Exclusion see Appendix A PDX collection 1052

P94 Disorders of muscle tone of newborn

- • CC **P94.0 Transient neonatal myasthenia gravis**
  Excludes1: *myasthenia gravis (G70.0)*
  CC Exclusion see Appendix A PDX collection 1041
- • **P94.1 Congenital hypertonia**
- • **P94.2 Congenital hypotonia**
  Floppy baby syndrome, unspecified
- • **P94.8 Other disorders of muscle tone of newborn**
- • **P94.9 Disorder of muscle tone of newborn,unspecified**

- • **P95 Stillbirth**
  Deadborn fetus NOS
  Fetal death of unspecified cause
  Stillbirth NOS
  Excludes1: *maternal care for intrauterine death (O36.4)*
  missed abortion (O02.1)
  outcome of delivery, stillbirth (Z37.1, Z37.3, Z37.4, Z37.7)
  Review coding guideline C.16.g
  Valid 3-character code, no further characters required

P96 Other conditions originating in the perinatal period

- • **P96.0 Congenital renal failure**
  Uremia of newborn
- • CC **P96.1 Neonatal withdrawal symptoms from maternal use of drugs of addiction**
  Drug withdrawal syndrome in infant of dependent mother
  Neonatal abstinence syndrome
  Excludes1: *reactions and intoxications from maternal opiates and tranquilizers administered during labor and delivery (P04.0)*
  CC Exclusion see Appendix A PDX collection 1052
- • CC **P96.2 Withdrawal symptoms from therapeutic use of drugs in newborn**
  CC Exclusion see Appendix A PDX collection 1052
- • **P96.3 Wide cranial sutures of newborn**
  Neonatal craniotabes
- • **P96.5 Complication to newborn due to (fetal) intrauterine procedure**
  Excludes2: *newborn (suspected to be) affected by amniocentesis (P00.6)*
- + **P96.8 Other specified conditions originating in the perinatal period**
  - **P96.81 Exposure to (parental) (environmental) tobacco smoke in the perinatal period**
    Excludes2: *newborn affected by in utero exposure to tobacco (P04.2)*
    exposure to environmental tobacco smoke after the perinatal period (Z77.22)
  - • **P96.82 Delayed separation of umbilical cord**
  - • **P96.83 Meconium staining**
    Excludes1: *meconium aspiration (P24.00, P24.01)*
    meconium passage during delivery (P03.82
  - • **P96.89 Other specified conditions originating in the perinatal period**
    Use additional code to specify condition
- • **P96.9 Condition originating in the perinatal period, unspecified**
  Congenital debility NOS

hapter 17: Congenital Malformations, Deformations nd Chromosomal Abnormalities (Q00-Q99)

TE Codes from this chapter are not for use on maternal or fetal records

cludes2: *inborn errors of metabolism (E70-E88)*

is chapter contains the following category blocks:

Q00-Q07 Congenital malformations of the nervous system
Q10-Q18 Congenital malformations of eye, ear, face and neck
Q20-Q28 Congenital malformations of the circulatory system
Q30-Q34 Congenital malformations of the respiratory system
Q35-Q37 Cleft lip and cleft palate
Q38-Q45 Other congenital malformations of the digestive system
Q50-Q56 Congenital malformations of genital organs
Q60-Q64 Congenital malformations of the urinary system
Q65-Q79 Congenital malformations and deformations of the musculoskeletal system
Q80-Q89 Other congenital malformations
Q90-Q99 Chromosomal abnormalities, not elsewhere classified

Chapter-Specific Coding Guidelines

addition to general coding guidelines, there are guidelines for specific diagnoses d/or conditions in the classification. Unless otherwise indicated, these guidelines ply to all health care settings. Please refer to Section II for guidelines on the ection of principal diagnosis.

. Chapter 17: Congenital Malformations, Deformations and Chromosomal Abnormalities (Q00-Q99)

Assign an appropriate code(s) from categories Q00-Q99, Congenital malformations, deformations, and chromosomal abnormalities when a malformation/deformation or chromosomal abnormality is documented. A malformation/deformation/or chromosomal abnormality may be the principal/first-listed diagnosis on a record or a secondary diagnosis.

When a malformation/deformation/or chromosomal abnormality does not have a unique code assignment, assign additional code(s) for any manifestations that may be present.

When the code assignment specifically identifies the malformation/deformation/or chromosomal abnormality, manifestations that are an inherent component of the anomaly should not be coded separately. Additional codes should be assigned for manifestations that are not an inherent component.

Codes from Chapter 17 may be used throughout the life of the patient. If a congenital malformation or deformity has been corrected, a personal history code should be used to identify the history of the malformation or deformity. Although present at birth, malformation/deformation/or chromosomal abnormality may not be identified until later in life. Whenever the condition is diagnosed by the physician, it is appropriate to assign a code from codes Q00-Q99. For the birth admission, the appropriate code from category Z38, Liveborn infants, according to place of birth and type of delivery, should be sequenced as the principal diagnosis, followed by any congenital anomaly codes, Q00-Q99.

ongenital malformations of the nervous system (Q00-Q07)

Q00 Anencephaly and similar malformations

MCC **Q00.0 Anencephaly**
Acephaly
Acrania
Amyelencephaly
Hemianencephaly
Hemicephaly
MCC Exclusion see Appendix A PDX collection 1053

MCC **Q00.1 Craniorachischisis**
MCC Exclusion see Appendix A PDX collection 1053

MCC **Q00.2 Iniencephaly**
MCC Exclusion see Appendix A PDX collection 1053

Q01 Encephalocele

Includes: Arnold-Chiari syndrome, type III
encephalocystocele
encephalomyelocele
hydroencephalocele
hydromeningocele, cranial
meningocele, cerebral
meningoencephalocele

Excludes1: *Meckel-Gruber syndrome (Q61.9)*

CC **Q01.0 Frontal encephalocele**
CC Exclusion see Appendix A PDX collection 1054

CC **Q01.1 Nasofrontal encephalocele**
CC Exclusion see Appendix A PDX collection 1054

CC **Q01.2 Occipital encephalocele**
CC Exclusion see Appendix A PDX collection 1054

CC **Q01.8 Encephalocele of other sites**
CC Exclusion see Appendix A PDX collection 1054

CC **Q01.9 Encephalocele, unspecified**
CC Exclusion see Appendix A PDX collection 1054

Q02 Microcephaly

Includes: hydromicrocephaly
micrencephalon

Excludes1: *Meckel-Gruber syndrome (Q61.9)*

Valid 3-character code, no further characters required

Q03 Congenital hydrocephalus

Includes: hydrocephalus in newborn

Excludes1: *Arnold-Chiari syndrome, type II (Q07.0-)*
acquired hydrocephalus (G91.-)
hydrocephalus due to congenital toxoplasmosis (P37.1)
hydrocephalus with spina bifida (Q05.0-Q05.4)

Q03.0 Malformations of aqueduct of Sylvius
Anomaly of aqueduct of Sylvius
Obstruction of aqueduct of Sylvius, congenital
Stenosis of aqueduct of Sylvius

Q03.1 Atresia of foramina of Magendie and Luschka
Dandy-Walker syndrome

Q03.8 Other congenital hydrocephalus

Q03.9 Congenital hydrocephalus, unspecified

Q04 Other congenital malformations of brain

Excludes1: *cyclopia (Q87.0)*
macrocephaly (Q75.3)

MCC **Q04.0 Congenital malformations of corpus callosum**
Agenesis of corpus callosum
MCC Exclusion see Appendix A PDX collection 1054

MCC **Q04.1 Arhinencephaly**
MCC Exclusion see Appendix A PDX collection 1054

MCC **Q04.2 Holoprosencephaly**
MCC Exclusion see Appendix A PDX collection 1054

MCC **Q04.3 Other reduction deformities of brain**
Absence of part of brain
Agenesis of part of brain
Agyria
Aplasia of part of brain
Hydranencephaly
Hypoplasia of part of brain
Lissencephaly
Microgyria
Pachygyria
Excludes1: *congenital malformations of corpus callosum (Q04.0)*
MCC Exclusion see Appendix A PDX collection 1054

CC **Q04.4 Septo-optic dysplasia of brain**
CC Exclusion see Appendix A PDX collection 1055

CC **Q04.5 Megalencephaly**
CC Exclusion see Appendix A PDX collection 1055

CC **Q04.6 Congenital cerebral cysts**
Porencephaly
Schizencephaly
Excludes1: *acquired porencephalic cyst (G93.0)*
CC Exclusion see Appendix A PDX collection 1055

CC **Q04.8 Other specified congenital malformations of brain**
Arnold-Chiari syndrome, type IV
Macrogyria
CC Exclusion see Appendix A PDX collection 1055

Q04.9 Congenital malformation of brain, unspecified
Congenital anomaly NOS of brain
Congenital deformity NOS of brain
Congenital disease or lesion NOS of brain
Multiple anomalies NOS of brain, congenital

Q05 Spina bifida

Includes: hydromeningocele (spinal)
meningocele (spinal)
meningomyelocele
myelocele
myelomeningocele
rachischisis
spina bifida (aperta)(cystica)
syringomyelocele

Use additional code for any associated paraplegia (paraparesis) (G82.2-)

Excludes1: *Arnold-Chiari syndrome, type II (Q07.0-)*
spina bifida occulta (Q76.0)

CC **Q05.0 Cervical spina bifida with hydrocephalus**
CC Exclusion see Appendix A PDX collection 1056

CC **Q05.1 Thoracic spina bifida with hydrocephalus**
Dorsal spina bifida with hydrocephalus
Thoracolumbar spina bifida with hydrocephalus
CC Exclusion see Appendix A PDX collection 1056

CC **Q05.2 Lumbar spina bifida with hydrocephalus**
CC Exclusion see Appendix A PDX collection 1056
Lumbosacral spina bifida with hydrocephalus
CC Exclusion see Appendix A PDX collection 1056

CC **Q05.3 Sacral spina bifida with hydrocephalus**
CC Exclusion see Appendix A PDX collection 1056

CC **Q05.4 Unspecified spina bifida with hydrocephalus**
CC Exclusion see Appendix A PDX collection 1056

Q05.5 Cervical spina bifida without hydrocephalus

Q05.6 Thoracic spina bifida without hydrocephalus
Dorsal spina bifida NOS
Thoracolumbar spina bifida NOS

Q05.7 Lumbar spina bifida without hydrocephalus
Lumbosacral spina bifida NOS

Q05.8 Sacral spina bifida without hydrocephalus

Q05.9 Spina bifida, unspecified

Q06 Other congenital malformations of spinal cord

Q06.0 Amyelia

Q06.1 Hypoplasia and dysplasia of spinal cord
Atelomyelia
Myelatelia
Myelodysplasia of spinal cord

Q06.2 Diastematomyelia

Q06.3 Other congenital cauda equina malformations

Q06.4 Hydromyelia
Hydrorachis

Q06.8 Other specified congenital malformations of spinal cord

Q06.9 Congenital malformation of spinal cord, unspecified
Congenital anomaly NOS of spinal cord
Congenital deformity NOS of spinal cord
Congenital disease or lesion NOS of spinal cord

Q07 Other congenital malformations of nervous system

Excludes2: *congenital central alveolar hypoventilation syndrome (G47.35)*
familial dysautonomia [Riley-Day] (G90.1)
neurofibromatosis (nonmalignant) (Q85.0-)

\+ **Q07.0 Arnold-Chiari syndrome**
Arnold-Chiari syndrome, type II
Excludes1: *Arnold-Chiari syndrome, type III (Q01.-)*
Arnold-Chiari syndrome, type IV (Q04.8)

Q07.00 Arnold-Chiari syndrome without spina bifida or hydrocephalus

Q07.01 Arnold-Chiari syndrome with spina bifida

CC **Q07.02 Arnold-Chiari syndrome with hydrocephalus**
CC Exclusion see Appendix A PDX collection 1056

CC **Q07.03 Arnold-Chiari syndrome with spina bifida and hydrocephalus**
CC Exclusion see Appendix A PDX collection 1056

Q07.8 Other specified congenital malformations of nervous system
Agenesis of nerve
Displacement of brachial plexus
Jaw-winking syndrome
Marcus Gunn's syndrome

Q07.9 Congenital malformation of nervous system, unspecified
Congenital anomaly NOS of nervous system
Congenital deformity NOS of nervous system
Congenital disease or lesion NOS of nervous system

Congenital malformations of eye, ear, face and neck (Q10-Q18)

Excludes2: *cleft lip and cleft palate (Q35-Q37)*
congenital malformation of cervical spine (Q05.0, Q05.5, Q67.5, Q76.0-Q76.4)
congenital malformation of larynx (Q31.-)
congenital malformation of lip NEC (Q38.0)
congenital malformation of nose (Q30.-)
congenital malformation of parathyroid gland (Q89.2)
congenital malformation of thyroid gland (Q89.2)

Q10 Congenital malformations of eyelid, lacrimal apparatus and orbit

Excludes1: *cryptophthalmos NOS (Q11.2)*
cryptophthalmos syndrome (Q87.0)

Q10.0 Congenital ptosis

Q10.1 Congenital ectropion

Q10.2 Congenital entropion

Q10.3 Other congenital malformations of eyelid
Ablepharon
Blepharophimosis, congenital
Coloboma of eyelid
Congenital absence or agenesis of cilia
Congenital absence or agenesis of eyelid
Congenital accessory eyelid
Congenital accessory eye muscle
Congenital malformation of eyelid NOS

Q10.4 Absence and agenesis of lacrimal apparatus
Congenital absence of punctum lacrimale

Q10.5 Congenital stenosis and stricture of lacrimal duct

Q10.6 Other congenital malformations of lacrimal apparatus
Congenital malformation of lacrimal apparatus NOS

Q10.7 Congenital malformation of orbit

Q11 Anophthalmos, microphthalmos and macrophthalmos

Q11.0 Cystic eyeball

Q11.1 Other anophthalmos
Anophthalmos NOS
Agenesis of eye
Aplasia of eye

Q11.2 Microphthalmos
Cryptophthalmos NOS
Dysplasia of eye
Hypoplasia of eye
Rudimentary eye
Excludes1: *cryptophthalmos syndrome (Q87.0)*

Q11.3 Macrophthalmos
Excludes1: *macrophthalmos in congenital glaucoma (Q15.0)*

Q12 Congenital lens malformations

CC **Q12.0 Congenital cataract**
CC Exclusion see Appendix A PDX collection 1057

CC **Q12.1 Congenital displaced lens**
CC Exclusion see Appendix A PDX collection 1058

CC **Q12.2 Coloboma of lens**
CC Exclusion see Appendix A PDX collection 1057

Q12.3 Congenital aphakia

Q12.4 Spherophakia

Q12.8 Other congenital lens malformations
Microphakia

Q12.9 Congenital lens malformation, unspecified

Q13 Congenital malformations of anterior segment of eye

Q13.0 Coloboma of iris
Coloboma NOS

Q13.1 Absence of iris
Aniridia
Use additional code for associated glaucoma (H42)

Q13.2 Other congenital malformations of iris
Anisocoria, congenital
Atresia of pupil
Congenital malformation of iris NOS
Corectopia

Q13.3 Congenital corneal opacity

Q13.4 Other congenital corneal malformations
Congenital malformation of cornea NOS
Microcornea
Peter's anomaly

Q13.5 Blue sclera

Q13.8 Other congenital malformations of anterior segment of eye

Q13.81 Rieger's anomaly
Use additional code for associated glaucoma (H42)

Q13.89 Other congenital malformations of anterior segment of eye

Q13.9 Congenital malformation of anterior segment of eye, unspecified

Q14 Congenital malformations of posterior segment of eye

Excludes2: *optic nerve hypoplasia (H47.03-)*

Q14.0 Congenital malformation of vitreous humor
Congenital vitreous opacity

Q14.1 Congenital malformation of retina
Congenital retinal aneurysm

Q14.2 Congenital malformation of optic disc
Coloboma of optic disc

Q14.3 Congenital malformation of choroid

Q14.8 Other congenital malformations of posterior segment of eye
Coloboma of the fundus

Q14.9 Congenital malformation of posterior segment of eye, unspecified

Q15 Other congenital malformations of eye

Excludes1: *congenital nystagmus (H55.01)*
ocular albinism (E70.31-)
optic nerve hypoplasia (H47.03-)
retinitis pigmentosa (H35.52)

Q15.0 Congenital glaucoma
Axenfeld's anomaly
Buphthalmos
Glaucoma of childhood
Glaucoma of newborn
Hydrophthalmos
Keratoglobus, congenital, with glaucoma
Macrocornea with glaucoma
Macrophthalmos in congenital glaucoma
Megalocornea with glaucoma

Q15.8 Other specified congenital malformations of eye

Q15.9 Congenital malformation of eye, unspecified
Congenital anomaly of eye
Congenital deformity of eye

Q16 Congenital malformations of ear causing impairment of hearing

Excludes1: *congenital deafness (H90.-)*

Q16.0 Congenital absence of (ear) auricle

Q16.1 Congenital absence, atresia and stricture of auditory canal (external)
Congenital atresia or stricture of osseous meatus

Q16.2 Absence of eustachian tube

Q16.3 Congenital malformation of ear ossicles
Congenital fusion of ear ossicles

Q16.4 Other congenital malformations of middle ear
Congenital malformation of middle ear NOS

Q16.5 Congenital malformation of inner ear
Congenital anomaly of membranous labyrinth
Congenital anomaly of organ of Corti

Q16.9 Congenital malformation of ear causing impairment of hearing, unspecified
Congenital absence of ear NOS

Q17 Other congenital malformations of ear

Excludes1: *congenital malformations of ear with impairment of hearing (Q16.0-Q16.9)*
preauricular sinus (Q18.1)

Q17.0 Accessory auricle
Accessory tragus
Polyotia
Preauricular appendage or tag
Supernumerary ear
Supernumerary lobule

Q17.1 Macrotia

Q17.2 Microtia

Q17.3 Other misshapen ear
Pointed ear

Q17.4 Misplaced ear
Low-set ears
Excludes1: *cervical auricle (Q18.2)*

Q17.5 Prominent ear
Bat ear

Q17.8 Other specified congenital malformations of ear
Congenital absence of lobe of ear

Q17.9 Congenital malformation of ear, unspecified
Congenital anomaly of ear NOS

Q18 Other congenital malformations of face and neck

Excludes1: *cleft lip and cleft palate (Q35-Q37)*
conditions classified to Q67.0-Q67.4
congenital malformations of skull and face bones (Q75.-)
cyclopia (Q87.0)
dentofacial anomalies [including malocclusion] (M26.-)
malformation syndromes affecting facial appearance (Q87.0)
persistent thyroglossal duct (Q89.2)

Q18.0 Sinus, fistula and cyst of branchial cleft
Branchial vestige

Q18.1 Preauricular sinus and cyst
Fistula of auricle, congenital
Cervicoaural fistula

Q18.2 Other branchial cleft malformations
Branchial cleft malformation NOS
Cervical auricle
Otocephaly

Q18.3 Webbing of neck
Pterygium colli

Q18.4 Macrostomia

Q18.5 Microstomia

Q18.6 Macrocheilia
Hypertrophy of lip, congenital

Q18.7 Microcheilia

Q18.8 Other specified congenital malformations of face and neck
Medial cyst of face and neck
Medial fistula of face and neck
Medial sinus of face and neck

Q18.9 Congenital malformation of face and neck, unspecified
Congenital anomaly NOS of face and neck

Congenital malformations of the circulatory system (Q20-Q28)

Q20 Congenital malformations of cardiac chambers and connections

Excludes1: *dextrocardia with situs inversus (Q89.3)*
mirror-image atrial arrangement with situs inversus (Q89.3)

MCC **Q20.0 Common arterial trunk**
Persistent truncus arteriosus
Excludes1: *aortic septal defect (Q21.4)*
MCC Exclusion see Appendix A PDX collection 1057

MCC **Q20.1 Double outlet right ventricle**
Taussig-Bing syndrome
MCC Exclusion see Appendix A PDX collection 1057

MCC **Q20.2 Double outlet left ventricle**
MCC Exclusion see Appendix A PDX collection 1057

MCC **Q20.3 Discordant ventriculoarterial connection**
Dextrotransposition of aorta
Transposition of great vessels (complete)
MCC Exclusion see Appendix A PDX collection 1057

MCC **Q20.4 Double inlet ventricle**
Common ventricle
Cor triloculare biatriatum
Single ventricle
MCC Exclusion see Appendix A PDX collection 1057

CC **Q20.5 Discordant atrioventricular connection**
Corrected transposition
Levotransposition
Ventricular inversion
CC Exclusion see Appendix A PDX collection 1057

Q20.6 Isomerism of atrial appendages
Isomerism of atrial appendages with asplenia or polysplenia

Q20.8 Other congenital malformations of cardiac chambers and connections
Cor binoculare

Q20.9 Congenital malformation of cardiac chambers and connections, unspecified

Q21 Congenital malformations of cardiac septa

Excludes1: *acquired cardiac septal defect (I51.0)*

Q21.0 Ventricular septal defect
Roger's disease

Q21.1 Atrial septal defect
Coronary sinus defect
Patent or persistent foramen ovale
Patent or persistent ostium secundum defect (type II)
Patent or persistent sinus venosus defect

Q21.2 Atrioventricular septal defect
Common atrioventricular canal
Endocardial cushion defect
Ostium primum atrial septal defect (type I)

MCC **Q21.3 Tetralogy of Fallot**
Ventricular septal defect with pulmonary stenosis or atresia, dextroposition of aorta and hypertrophy of right ventricle.
MCC Exclusion see Appendix A PDX collection 1057

Q21.4 Aortopulmonary septal defect
Aortic septal defect
Aortopulmonary window

Q21.8 Other congenital malformations of cardiac septa
Eisenmenger's defect
Pentalogy of Fallot
Excludes1: *Eisenmenger's complex (I27.8)*
Eisenmenger's syndrome (I27.8)

Q21.9 Congenital malformation of cardiac septum, unspecified
Septal (heart) defect NOS

Q22 Congenital malformations of pulmonary and tricuspid valves

MCC **Q22.0 Pulmonary valve atresia**
MCC Exclusion see Appendix A PDX collection 1059

CC **Q22.1 Congenital pulmonary valve stenosis**
CC Exclusion see Appendix A PDX collection 1060

CC **Q22.2 Congenital pulmonary valve insufficiency**
Congenital pulmonary valve regurgitation
CC Exclusion see Appendix A PDX collection 1060

CC **Q22.3 Other congenital malformations of pulmonary valve**
Congenital malformation of pulmonary valve NOS
Supernumerary cusps of pulmonary valve
CC Exclusion see Appendix A PDX collection 1060

MCC **Q22.4 Congenital tricuspid stenosis**
Congenital tricuspid atresia
MCC Exclusion see Appendix A PDX collection 1061

MCC **Q22.5 Ebstein's anomaly**
MCC Exclusion see Appendix A PDX collection 1061

MCC **Q22.6 Hypoplastic right heart syndrome**
MCC Exclusion see Appendix A PDX collection 1061

MCC **Q22.8 Other congenital malformations of tricuspid valve**
MCC Exclusion see Appendix A PDX collection 1061

MCC **Q22.9 Congenital malformation of tricuspid valve, unspecified**
MCC Exclusion see Appendix A PDX collection 1061

Q23 Congenital malformations of aortic and mitral valves

CC **Q23.0 Congenital stenosis of aortic valve**
Congenital aortic atresia
Congenital aortic stenosis NOS
Excludes1: *congenital stenosis of aortic valve in hypoplastic left heart syndrome (Q23.4)*
congenital subaortic stenosis (Q24.4)
supravalvular aortic stenosis (congenital) (Q25.3)
CC Exclusion see Appendix A PDX collection 1061

CC **Q23.1 Congenital insufficiency of aortic valve**
Bicuspid aortic valve
Congenital aortic insufficiency
CC Exclusion see Appendix A PDX collection 1061

CC **Q23.2 Congenital mitral stenosis**
Congenital mitral atresia
CC Exclusion see Appendix A PDX collection 1061

CC **Q23.3 Congenital mitral insufficiency**
CC Exclusion see Appendix A PDX collection 1061

MCC **Q23.4 Hypoplastic left heart syndrome**
MCC Exclusion see Appendix A PDX collection 1063

CC **Q23.8 Other congenital malformations of aortic and mitral valves**

CC **Q23.9 Congenital malformation of aortic and mitral valves, unspecified**

Q24 Other congenital malformations of heart

Excludes1: *endocardial fibroelastosis (I42.4)*

CC **Q24.0 Dextrocardia**
Excludes1: *dextrocardia with situs inversus (Q89.3)*
isomerism of atrial appendages (with asplenia or polysplenia) (Q20.6)
mirror-image atrial arrangement with situs inversus (Q89.3)
CC Exclusion see Appendix A PDX collection 1062

CC **Q24.1 Levocardia**
CC Exclusion see Appendix A PDX collection 1062

MCC **Q24.2 Cor triatriatum**
MCC Exclusion see Appendix A PDX collection 1063

CC **Q24.3 Pulmonary infundibular stenosis**
Subvalvular pulmonic stenosis
CC Exclusion see Appendix A PDX collection 1063

MCC **Q24.4 Congenital subaortic stenosis**
MCC Exclusion see Appendix A PDX collection 1063

CC **Q24.5 Malformation of coronary vessels**
Congenital coronary (artery) aneurysm
CC Exclusion see Appendix A PDX collection 1064

MCC **Q24.6 Congenital heart block**
MCC Exclusion see Appendix A PDX collection 1065

Q24.8 Other specified congenital malformations of heart
Congenital diverticulum of left ventricle
Congenital malformation of myocardium
Congenital malformation of pericardium
Malposition of heart
Uhl's disease

Q24.9 Congenital malformation of heart, unspecified
Congenital anomaly of heart
Congenital disease of heart

Q25 Congenital malformations of great arteries

CC **Q25.0 Patent ductus arteriosus**
Patent ductus Botallo
Persistent ductus arteriosus
CC Exclusion see Appendix A PDX collection 1066

CC **Q25.1 Coarctation of aorta**
Coarctation of aorta (preductal) (postductal)
CC Exclusion see Appendix A PDX collection 1067

CC **Q25.2 Atresia of aorta**
CC Exclusion see Appendix A PDX collection 1068

CC **Q25.3 Supravalvular aortic stenosis**
Excludes1: *congenital aortic stenosis NOS (Q23.0)*
congenital stenosis of aortic valve (Q23.0)
CC Exclusion see Appendix A PDX collection 1068

CC **Q25.4 Other congenital malformations of aorta**
Absence of aorta
Aneurysm of sinus of Valsalva (ruptured)
Aplasia of aorta
Congenital aneurysm of aorta
Congenital malformations of aorta
Congenital dilatation of aorta
Double aortic arch [vascular ring of aorta]
Hypoplasia of aorta
Persistent convolutions of aortic arch
Persistent right aortic arch
Excludes1: *hypoplasia of aorta in hypoplastic left heart syndrome (Q23.4)*
CC Exclusion see Appendix A PDX collection 1069

MCC **Q25.5 Atresia of pulmonary artery**
MCC Exclusion see Appendix A PDX collection 1070

MCC **Q25.6 Stenosis of pulmonary artery**
Supravalvular pulmonary stenosis
MCC Exclusion see Appendix A PDX collection 1070

\+ **Q25.7 Other congenital malformations of pulmonary artery**

MCC **Q25.71 Coarctation of pulmonary artery**
MCC Exclusion see Appendix A PDX collection 1070

MCC **Q25.72 Congenital pulmonary arteriovenous malformation**
Congenital pulmonary arteriovenous aneurysm
MCC Exclusion see Appendix A PDX collection 1070

MCC **Q25.79 Other congenital malformations of pulmonary artery**
Aberrant pulmonary artery
Agenesis of pulmonary artery
Congenital aneurysm of pulmonary artery
Congenital anomaly of pulmonary artery
Hypoplasia of pulmonary artery
MCC Exclusion see Appendix A PDX collection 1070

Q25.8 Other congenital malformations of other great arteries
CC Exclusion see Appendix A PDX collection 1069

CC **Q25.9 Congenital malformation of great arteries, unspecified**
CC Exclusion see Appendix A PDX collection 1069

Q26 Congenital malformations of great veins

CC **Q26.0 Congenital stenosis of vena cava**
Congenital stenosis of vena cava (inferior)(superior)
CC Exclusion see Appendix A PDX collection 1071

CC **Q26.1 Persistent left superior vena cava**
CC Exclusion see Appendix A PDX collection 1071

CC **Q26.2 Total anomalous pulmonary venous connection**
Total anomalous pulmonary venous return [TAPVR], subdiaphragmatic
Total anomalous pulmonary venous return [TAPVR], supradiaphragmatic
CC Exclusion see Appendix A PDX collection 1072

CC **Q26.3 Partial anomalous pulmonary venous connection**
Partial anomalous pulmonary venous return
CC Exclusion see Appendix A PDX collection 1073

CC **Q26.4 Anomalous pulmonary venous connection, unspecified**
CC Exclusion see Appendix A PDX collection 1073

Q26.5 Anomalous portal venous connection

Q26.6 Portal vein-hepatic artery fistula

CC **Q26.8 Other congenital malformations of great veins**
Absence of vena cava (inferior) (superior)
Azygos continuation of inferior vena cava
Persistent left posterior cardinal vein
Scimitar syndrome
CC Exclusion see Appendix A PDX collection 1071

CC **Q26.9 Congenital malformation of great vein, unspecified**
Congenital anomaly of vena cava (inferior) (superior) NOS
CC Exclusion see Appendix A PDX collection 1074

Q27 Other congenital malformations of peripheral vascular system

Excludes2: *anomalies of cerebral and precerebral vessels (Q28.0-Q28.3)*
anomalies of coronary vessels (Q24.5)
anomalies of pulmonary artery (Q25.5-Q25.7)
congenital retinal aneurysm (Q14.1)
hemangioma and lymphangioma (D18.-)

Q27.0 Congenital absence and hypoplasia of umbilical artery
Single umbilical artery

Q27.1 Congenital renal artery stenosis

Q27.2 Other congenital malformations of renal artery
Congenital malformation of renal artery NOS
Multiple renal arteries

+ **Q27.3 Arteriovenous malformation (peripheral)**
Arteriovenous aneurysm
Excludes1: *acquired arteriovenous aneurysm (I77.0)*
Excludes2: *arteriovenous malformation of cerebral vessels (Q28.2)*
arteriovenous malformation of precerebral vessels (Q28.0)

CC **Q27.30 Arteriovenous malformation, site unspecified**
CC Exclusion see Appendix A PDX collection 1075

Q27.31 Arteriovenous malformation of vessel of upper limb

Q27.32 Arteriovenous malformation of vessel of lower limb

Q27.33 Arteriovenous malformation of digestive system vessel

Q27.34 Arteriovenous malformation of renal vessel

Q27.39 Arteriovenous malformation, other site

CC **Q27.4 Congenital phlebectasia**
CC Exclusion see Appendix A PDX collection 1075

Q27.8 Other specified congenital malformations of peripheral vascular system
Absence of peripheral vascular system
Atresia of peripheral vascular system
Congenital aneurysm (peripheral)
Congenital stricture, artery
Congenital varix
Excludes1: *arteriovenous malformation (Q27.3-)*

Q27.9 Congenital malformation of peripheral vascular system, unspecified
Anomaly of artery or vein NOS

Q28 Other congenital malformations of circulatory system

Excludes1: *congenital aneurysm NOS (Q27.8)*
congenital coronary aneurysm (Q24.5)
ruptured cerebral arteriovenous malformation (I60.8)
ruptured malformation of precerebral vessels (I72.0)
Excludes2: *congenital peripheral aneurysm (Q27.8)*
congenital pulmonary aneurysm (Q25.79)
congenital retinal aneurysm (Q14.1)

CC **Q28.0 Arteriovenous malformation of precerebral vessels**
Congenital arteriovenous precerebral aneurysm (nonruptured)
CC Exclusion see Appendix A PDX collection 1075

CC **Q28.1 Other malformations of precerebral vessels**
Congenital malformation of precerebral vessels NOS
Congenital precerebral aneurysm (nonruptured)
CC Exclusion see Appendix A PDX collection 1075

MCC **Q28.2 Arteriovenous malformation of cerebral vessels**
Arteriovenous malformation of brain NOS
Congenital arteriovenous cerebral aneurysm (nonruptured)
MCC Exclusion see Appendix A PDX collection 1076

MCC **Q28.3 Other malformations of cerebral vessels**
Congenital cerebral aneurysm (nonruptured)
Congenital malformation of cerebral vessels NOS
Developmental venous anomaly
MCC Exclusion see Appendix A PDX collection 1076

CC **Q28.8 Other specified congenital malformations of circulatory system**
Congenital aneurysm, specified site NEC
Spinal vessel anomaly
CC Exclusion see Appendix A PDX collection 1075

CC **Q28.9 Congenital malformation of circulatory system, unspecified**
CC Exclusion see Appendix A PDX collection 1077

Congenital malformations of the respiratory system (Q30-Q34)

Q30 Congenital malformations of nose

Excludes1: *congenital deviation of nasal septum (Q67.4)*

Q30.0 Choanal atresia
Atresia of nares (anterior) (posterior)
Congenital stenosis of nares (anterior) (posterior)

Q30.1 Agenesis and underdevelopment of nose
Congenital absent of nose

Q30.2 Fissured, notched and cleft nose

Q30.3 Congenital perforated nasal septum

Q30.8 Other congenital malformations of nose
Accessory nose
Congenital anomaly of nasal sinus wall

Q30.9 Congenital malformation of nose, unspecified

Q31 Congenital malformations of larynx

Excludes1: *congenital laryngeal stridor NOS (P28.89)*

Q31.0 Web of larynx
Glottic web of larynx
Subglottic web of larynx
Web of larynx NOS

CC **Q31.1 Congenital subglottic stenosis**
CC Exclusion see Appendix A PDX collection 1078

CC **Q31.2 Laryngeal hypoplasia**
CC Exclusion see Appendix A PDX collection 1078

CC **Q31.3 Laryngocele**
CC Exclusion see Appendix A PDX collection 1078

CC **Q31.5 Congenital laryngomalacia**
CC Exclusion see Appendix A PDX collection 1078

CC **Q31.8 Other congenital malformations of larynx**
Absence of larynx
Agenesis of larynx
Atresia of larynx
Congenital cleft thyroid cartilage
Congenital fissure of epiglottis
Congenital stenosis of larynx NEC
Posterior cleft of cricoid cartilage
CC Exclusion see Appendix A PDX collection 1078

CC **Q31.9 Congenital malformation of larynx, unspecified**
CC Exclusion see Appendix A PDX collection 1078

Q32 Congenital malformations of trachea and bronchus

Excludes1: *congenital bronchiectasis (Q33.4)*

CC **Q32.0 Congenital tracheomalacia**
CC Exclusion see Appendix A PDX collection 1078

CC **Q32.1 Other congenital malformations of trachea**
Atresia of trachea
Congenital anomaly of tracheal cartilage
Congenital dilatation of trachea
Congenital malformation of trachea
Congenital stenosis of trachea
Congenital tracheocele
CC Exclusion see Appendix A PDX collection 1078

CC **Q32.2 Congenital bronchomalacia**
CC Exclusion see Appendix A PDX collection 1078

CC **Q32.3 Congenital stenosis of bronchus**
CC Exclusion see Appendix A PDX collection 1078

CC **Q32.4 Other congenital malformations of bronchus**
Absence of bronchus
Agenesis of bronchus
Atresia of bronchus
Congenital diverticulum of bronchus
Congenital malformation of bronchus NOS
CC Exclusion see Appendix A PDX collection 1078

Q33 Congenital malformations of lung

CC **Q33.0 Congenital cystic lung**
Congenital cystic lung disease
Congenital honeycomb lung
Congenital polycystic lung disease
Excludes1: *cystic fibrosis (E84.0)*
cystic lung disease, acquired or unspecified (J98.4)
CC Exclusion see Appendix A PDX collection 1079

Q33.1 Accessory lobe of lung
Azygos lobe (fissured), lung

MCC **Q33.2 Sequestration of lung**
MCC Exclusion see Appendix A PDX collection 1079

MCC **Q33.3 Agenesis of lung**
Congenital absence of lung (lobe)
MCC Exclusion see Appendix A PDX collection 1079

CC **Q33.4 Congenital bronchiectasis**
CC Exclusion see Appendix A PDX collection 1080

Q33.5 Ectopic tissue in lung

MCC **Q33.6 Congenital hypoplasia and dysplasia of lung**
Excludes1: *pulmonary hypoplasia associated with short gestation (P28.0)*
MCC Exclusion see Appendix A PDX collection 1079

Q33.8 Other congenital malformations of lung

Q33.9 Congenital malformation of lung, unspecified

Q34 Other congenital malformations of respiratory system

Excludes2: *congenital central alveolar hypoventilation syndrome (G47.35)*

Q34.0 Anomaly of pleura

Q34.1 Congenital cyst of mediastinum
Q34.8 Other specified congenital malformations of respiratory system
Atresia of nasopharynx
Q34.9 Congenital malformation of respiratory system, unspecified
Congenital absence of respiratory system
Congenital anomaly of respiratory system NOS

Cleft lip and cleft palate (Q35-Q37)

Use additional code to identify associated malformation of the nose (Q30.2)

Excludes1: *Robin's syndrome (Q87.0)*

Q35 Cleft palate

Includes: fissure of palate
palatoschisis

Excludes1: *cleft palate with cleft lip (Q37.-)*

Q35.1 Cleft hard palate
Q35.3 Cleft soft palate
Q35.5 Cleft hard palate with cleft soft palate
Q35.7 Cleft uvula
Q35.9 Cleft palate, unspecified
Cleft palate NOS

Q36 Cleft lip

Includes: cheiloschisis
congenital fissure of lip
harelip
labium leporinum

Excludes1: *cleft lip with cleft palate (Q37.-)*

Q36.0 Cleft lip, bilateral
Q36.1 Cleft lip, median
Q36.9 Cleft lip, unilateral
Cleft lip NOS

Q37 Cleft palate with cleft lip

Includes: cheilopalatoschisis

Q37.0 Cleft hard palate with bilateral cleft lip
Q37.1 Cleft hard palate with unilateral cleft lip
Cleft hard palate with cleft lip NOS
Q37.2 Cleft soft palate with bilateral cleft lip
Q37.3 Cleft soft palate with unilateral cleft lip
Cleft soft palate with cleft lip NOS
Q37.4 Cleft hard and soft palate with bilateral cleft lip
Q37.5 Cleft hard and soft palate with unilateral cleft lip
Cleft hard and soft palate with cleft lip NOS
Q37.8 Unspecified cleft palate with bilateral cleft lip
Q37.9 Unspecified cleft palate with unilateral cleft lip
Cleft palate with cleft lip NOS

Other congenital malformations of the digestive system (Q38-Q45)

Q38 Other congenital malformations of tongue, mouth and pharynx

Excludes1: *dentofacial anomalies (M26.-)*
macrostomia (Q18.4)
microstomia (Q18.5)

Q38.0 Congenital malformations of lips, not elsewhere classified
Congenital fistula of lip
Congenital malformation of lip NOS
Van der Woude's syndrome
Excludes1: *cleft lip (Q36.-)*
cleft lip with cleft palate (Q37.-)
macrocheilia (Q18.6)
microcheilia (Q18.7)
Q38.1 Ankyloglossia
Tongue tie
Q38.2 Macroglossia
Congenital hypertrophy of tongue
Q38.3 Other congenital malformations of tongue
Aglossia
Bifid tongue
Congenital adhesion of tongue
Congenital fissure of tongue
Congenital malformation of tongue NOS
Double tongue
Hypoglossia
Hypoplasia of tongue
Microglossia
Q38.4 Congenital malformations of salivary glands and ducts
Atresia of salivary glands and ducts
Congenital absence of salivary glands and ducts
Congenital accessory salivary glands and ducts
Congenital fistula of salivary gland
Q38.5 Congenital malformations of palate, not elsewhere classified
Congenital absence of uvula
Congenital malformation of palate NOS
Congenital high arched palate
Excludes1: *cleft palate (Q35.-)*
cleft palate with cleft lip (Q37.-)
Q38.6 Other congenital malformations of mouth
Congenital malformation of mouth NOS
Q38.7 Congenital pharyngeal pouch
Congenital diverticulum of pharynx
Excludes1: *pharyngeal pouch syndrome (D82.1)*
Q38.8 Other congenital malformations of pharynx
Congenital malformation of pharynx NOS
Imperforate pharynx

Q39 Congenital malformations of esophagus

MCC **Q39.0 Atresia of esophagus without fistula**
Atresia of esophagus NOS
MCC Exclusion see Appendix A PDX collection 1081
MCC **Q39.1 Atresia of esophagus with tracheo-esophageal fistula**
Atresia of esophagus with broncho-esophageal fistula
MCC Exclusion see Appendix A PDX collection 1081
MCC **Q39.2 Congenital tracheo-esophageal fistula without atresia**
Congenital tracheo-esophageal fistula NOS
MCC Exclusion see Appendix A PDX collection 1081
MCC **Q39.3 Congenital stenosis and stricture of esophagus**
MCC Exclusion see Appendix A PDX collection 1081
MCC **Q39.4 Esophageal web**
MCC Exclusion see Appendix A PDX collection 1081
CC **Q39.5 Congenital dilatation of esophagus**
Congenital cardiospasm
CC Exclusion see Appendix A PDX collection 1082
CC **Q39.6 Congenital diverticulum of esophagus**
Congenital esophageal pouch
CC Exclusion see Appendix A PDX collection 1082
CC **Q39.8 Other congenital malformations of esophagus**
Congenital absence of esophagus
Congenital displacement of esophagus
Congenital duplication of esophagus
CC Exclusion see Appendix A PDX collection 1082
CC **Q39.9 Congenital malformation of esophagus, unspecified**
CC Exclusion see Appendix A PDX collection 1082

Q40 Other congenital malformations of upper alimentary tract

Q40.0 Congenital hypertrophic pyloric stenosis
Congenital or infantile constriction
Congenital or infantile hypertrophy
Congenital or infantile spasm
Congenital or infantile stenosis
Congenital or infantile stricture
Q40.1 Congenital hiatus hernia
Congenital displacement of cardia through esophageal hiatus
Excludes1: *congenital diaphragmatic hernia (Q79.0)*
Q40.2 Other specified congenital malformations of stomach
Congenital displacement of stomach
Congenital diverticulum of stomach
Congenital hourglass stomach
Congenital duplication of stomach
Megalogastria
Microgastria
Q40.3 Congenital malformation of stomach, unspecified
Q40.8 Other specified congenital malformations of upper alimentary tract
Q40.9 Congenital malformation of upper alimentary tract, unspecified
Congenital anomaly of upper alimentary tract
Congenital deformity of upper alimentary tract

Q41 Congenital absence, atresia and stenosis of small intestine

Includes: congenital obstruction, occlusion or stricture of small intestine or intestine NOS

Excludes1: *cystic fibrosis with intestinal manifestation (E84.11)*
meconium ileus NOS (without cystic fibrosis) (P76.0)

CC **Q41.0 Congenital absence, atresia and stenosis of duodenum**
CC Exclusion see Appendix A PDX collection 1083
CC **Q41.1 Congenital absence, atresia and stenosis of jejunum**
Apple peel syndrome
Imperforate jejunum
CC Exclusion see Appendix A PDX collection 1083
CC **Q41.2 Congenital absence, atresia and stenosis of ileum**
CC Exclusion see Appendix A PDX collection 1083
CC **Q41.8 Congenital absence, atresia and stenosis of other specified parts of small intestine**
CC Exclusion see Appendix A PDX collection 1083

CC **Q41.9 Congenital absence, atresia and stenosis of small intestine, part unspecified**
Congenital absence, atresia and stenosis of intestine NOS
CC Exclusion see Appendix A PDX collection 1083

Q42 Congenital absence, atresia and stenosis of large intestine
Includes: congenital obstruction, occlusion and stricture of large intestine

CC **Q42.0 Congenital absence, atresia and stenosis of rectum with fistula**
CC Exclusion see Appendix A PDX collection 1084

CC **Q42.1 Congenital absence, atresia and stenosis of rectum without fistula**
Imperforate rectum
CC Exclusion see Appendix A PDX collection 1084

CC **Q42.2 Congenital absence, atresia and stenosis of anus with fistula**
CC Exclusion see Appendix A PDX collection 1084

CC **Q42.3 Congenital absence, atresia and stenosis of anus without fistula**
Imperforate anus
CC Exclusion see Appendix A PDX collection 1084

CC **Q42.8 Congenital absence, atresia and stenosis of other parts of large intestine**
CC Exclusion see Appendix A PDX collection 1084

CC **Q42.9 Congenital absence, atresia and stenosis of large intestine, part unspecified**
CC Exclusion see Appendix A PDX collection 1084

Q43 Other congenital malformations of intestine

Q43.0 Meckel's diverticulum (displaced) (hypertrophic)
Persistent omphalomesenteric duct
Persistent vitelline duct

CC **Q43.1 Hirschsprung's disease**
Aganglionosis
Congenital (aganglionic) megacolon
CC Exclusion see Appendix A PDX collection 1085

CC **Q43.2 Other congenital functional disorders of colon**
Congenital dilatation of colon
CC Exclusion see Appendix A PDX collection 1085

CC **Q43.3 Congenital malformations of intestinal fixation**
Congenital omental, anomalous adhesions [bands]
Congenital peritoneal adhesions [bands]
Incomplete rotation of cecum and colon
Insufficient rotation of cecum and colon
Jackson's membrane
Malrotation of colon
Rotation failure of cecum and colon
Universal mesentery
CC Exclusion see Appendix A PDX collection 1086

CC **Q43.4 Duplication of intestine**
CC Exclusion see Appendix A PDX collection 1087

CC **Q43.5 Ectopic anus**
CC Exclusion see Appendix A PDX collection 1087

CC **Q43.6 Congenital fistula of rectum and anus**
Excludes1: *congenital fistula of anus with absence, atresia and stenosis (Q42.2)*
congenital fistula of rectum with absence, atresia and stenosis (Q42.0)
congenital rectovaginal fistula (Q52.2)
congenital urethrorectal fistula (Q64.73)
pilonidal fistula or sinus (L05.-)
CC Exclusion see Appendix A PDX collection 1087

CC **Q43.7 Persistent cloaca**
Cloaca NOS
CC Exclusion see Appendix A PDX collection 1087

CC **Q43.8 Other specified congenital malformations of intestine**
Congenital blind loop syndrome
Congenital diverticulitis, colon
Congenital diverticulum, intestine
Dolichocolon
Megaloappendix
Megaloduodenum
Microcolon
Transposition of appendix
Transposition of colon
Transposition of intestine
CC Exclusion see Appendix A PDX collection 1087
AHA CC: 2Q, 2013, 31

CC **Q43.9 Congenital malformation of intestine, unspecified**
CC Exclusion see Appendix A PDX collection 1087

Q44 Congenital malformations of gallbladder, bile ducts and liver

CC **Q44.0 Agenesis, aplasia and hypoplasia of gallbladder**
Congenital absence of gallbladder
CC Exclusion see Appendix A PDX collection 1088

CC **Q44.1 Other congenital malformations of gallbladder**
Congenital malformation of gallbladder NOS
Intrahepatic gallbladder
CC Exclusion see Appendix A PDX collection 1088

MCC **Q44.2 Atresia of bile ducts**
MCC Exclusion see Appendix A PDX collection 1089

MCC **Q44.3 Congenital stenosis and stricture of bile ducts**
MCC Exclusion see Appendix A PDX collection 1089

CC **Q44.4 Choledochal cyst**
CC Exclusion see Appendix A PDX collection 1088

CC **Q44.5 Other congenital malformations of bile ducts**
Accessory hepatic duct
Biliary duct duplication
Congenital malformation of bile duct NOS
Cystic duct duplication
CC Exclusion see Appendix A PDX collection 1088

CC **Q44.6 Cystic disease of liver**
Fibrocystic disease of liver
CC Exclusion see Appendix A PDX collection 1090

CC **Q44.7 Other congenital malformations of liver**
Accessory liver
Alagille's syndrome
Congenital absence of liver
Congenital hepatomegaly
Congenital malformation of liver NOS
CC Exclusion see Appendix A PDX collection 1088

Q45 Other congenital malformations of digestive system
Excludes2: *congenital diaphragmatic hernia (Q79.0)*
congenital hiatus hernia (Q40.1)

CC **Q45.0 Agenesis, aplasia and hypoplasia of pancreas**
Congenital absence of pancreas
CC Exclusion see Appendix A PDX collection 1091

CC **Q45.1 Annular pancreas**
CC Exclusion see Appendix A PDX collection 1091

CC **Q45.2 Congenital pancreatic cyst**
CC Exclusion see Appendix A PDX collection 1091

Q45.3 Other congenital malformations of pancreas and pancreatic duct
Accessory pancreas
Congenital malformation of pancreas or pancreatic duct NOS
Excludes1: *congenital diabetes mellitus (E10.-)*
cystic fibrosis (E84.0-E84.9)
fibrocystic disease of pancreas (E84.-)
neonatal diabetes mellitus (P70.2)
CC Exclusion see Appendix A PDX collection 1091

Q45.8 Other specified congenital malformations of digestive system
Absence (complete) (partial) of alimentary tract NOS
Duplication of digestive system
Malposition, congenital of digestive system

Q45.9 Congenital malformation of digestive system, unspecified
Congenital anomaly of digestive system
Congenital deformity of digestive system

Congenital malformations of genital organs (Q50-Q56)

Excludes1: *androgen insensitivity syndrome (E34.5-)*
syndromes associated with anomalies in the number and form of chromosomes (Q90-Q99)

Q50 Congenital malformations of ovaries, fallopian tubes and broad ligaments

\+ **Q50.0 Congenital absence of ovary**
Excludes1: *Turner's syndrome (Q96.-)*
♀ **Q50.01 Congenital absence of ovary, unilateral**
♀ **Q50.02 Congenital absence of ovary, bilateral**

♀ **Q50.1 Developmental ovarian cyst**

♀ **Q50.2 Congenital torsion of ovary**

\+ **Q50.3 Other congenital malformations of ovary**
♀ **Q50.31 Accessory ovary**
♀ **Q50.32 Ovarian streak**
46, XX with streak gonads
♀ **Q50.39 Other congenital malformation of ovary**
Congenital malformation of ovary NOS

♀ **Q50.4 Embryonic cyst of fallopian tube**
Fimbrial cyst

♀ **Q50.5 Embryonic cyst of broad ligament**
Epoophoron cyst
Parovarian cyst

♀ **Q50.6 Other congenital malformations of fallopian tube and broad ligament**
Absence of fallopian tube and broad ligament
Accessory fallopian tube and broad ligament
Atresia of fallopian tube and broad ligament
Congenital malformation of fallopian tube or broad ligament NOS

Q51 Congenital malformations of uterus and cervix

♀ **Q51.0 Agenesis and aplasia of uterus**
Congenital absence of uterus
\+ **Q51.1 Doubling of uterus with doubling of cervix and vagina**
♀ **Q51.10 Doubling of uterus with doubling of cervix and vagina without obstruction**
Doubling of uterus with doubling of cervix and vagina NOS
♀ **Q51.11 Doubling of uterus with doubling of cervix and vagina with obstruction**
♀ **Q51.2 Other doubling of uterus**
Doubling of uterus NOS
Septate uterus, complete or partial
♀ **Q51.3 Bicornate uterus**
Bicornate uterus, complete or partial
♀ **Q51.4 Unicornate uterus**
Unicornate uterus with or without a separate uterine horn
Uterus with only one functioning horn
♀ **Q51.5 Agenesis and aplasia of cervix**
Congenital absence of cervix
♀ **Q51.6 Embryonic cyst of cervix**
♀ **Q51.7 Congenital fistulae between uterus and digestive and urinary tracts**
\+ **Q51.8 Other congenital malformations of uterus and cervix**
\+ **Q51.81 Other congenital malformations of uterus**
♀ **Q51.810 Arcuate uterus**
Arcuatus uterus
♀ **Q51.811 Hypoplasia of uterus**
♀ **Q51.818 Other congenital malformations of uterus**
Müllerian anomaly of uterus NEC
\+ **Q51.82 Other congenital malformations of cervix**
♀ **Q51.820 Cervical duplication**
♀ **Q51.821 Hypoplasia of cervix**
♀ **Q51.828 Other congenital malformations of cervix**
♀ **Q51.9 Congenital malformation of uterus and cervix, unspecified**

Q52 Other congenital malformations of female genitalia

♀ **Q52.0 Congenital absence of vagina**
Vaginal agenesis, total or partial
\+ **Q52.1 Doubling of vagina**
Excludes1: *doubling of vagina with doubling of uterus and cervix (Q51.1-)*
♀ **Q52.10 Doubling of vagina, unspecified**
Septate vagina NOS
♀ **Q52.11 Transverse vaginal septum**
♀ **Q52.12 Longitudinal vaginal septum**
Longitudinal vaginal septum with or without obstruction
♀ **Q52.2 Congenital rectovaginal fistula**
Excludes1: *cloaca (Q43.7)*
♀ **Q52.3 Imperforate hymen**
♀ **Q52.4 Other congenital malformations of vagina**
Canal of Nuck cyst, congenital
Congenital malformation of vagina NOS
Embryonic vaginal cyst
Gartner's duct cyst
♀ **Q52.5 Fusion of labia**
♀ **Q52.6 Congenital malformation of clitoris**
\+ **Q52.7 Other and unspecified congenital malformations of vulva**
♀ **Q52.70 Unspecified congenital malformations of vulva**
Congenital malformation of vulva NOS
♀ **Q52.71 Congenital absence of vulva**
♀ **Q52.79 Other congenital malformations of vulva**
Congenital cyst of vulva
♀ **Q52.8 Other specified congenital malformations of female genitalia**
♀ **Q52.9 Congenital malformation of female genitalia, unspecified**

Q53 Undescended and ectopic testicle

\+ **Q53.0 Ectopic testis**
♂ **Q53.00 Ectopic testis, unspecified**
♂ **Q53.01 Ectopic testis, unilateral**
♂ **Q53.02 Ectopic testes, bilateral**
\+ **Q53.1 Undescended testicle, unilateral**
♂ **Q53.10 Unspecified undescended testicle, unilateral**
♂ **Q53.11 Abdominal testis, unilateral**
♂ **Q53.12 Ectopic perineal testis, unilateral**
\+ **Q53.2 Undescended testicle, bilateral**
♂ **Q53.20 Undescended testicle, unspecified, bilateral**
♂ **Q53.21 Abdominal testis, bilateral**
♂ **Q53.22 Ectopic perineal testis, bilateral**
♂ **Q53.9 Undescended testicle, unspecified**
Cryptorchism NOS

Q54 Hypospadias

Excludes1: *epispadias (Q64.0)*
♂ **Q54.0 Hypospadias, balanic**
Hypospadias, coronal
Hypospadias, glandular
♂ **Q54.1 Hypospadias, penile**
♂ **Q54.2 Hypospadias, penoscrotal**
♂ **Q54.3 Hypospadias, perineal**
♂ **Q54.4 Congenital chordee**
Chordee without hypospadias
♂ **Q54.8 Other hypospadias**
Hypospadias with intersex state
♂ **Q54.9 Hypospadias, unspecified**

Q55 Other congenital malformations of male genital organs

Excludes1: *congenital hydrocele (P83.5)*
hypospadias (Q54.-)
♂ **Q55.0 Absence and aplasia of testis**
Monorchism
♂ **Q55.1 Hypoplasia of testis and scrotum**
Fusion of testes
\+ **Q55.2 Other and unspecified congenital malformations of testis and scrotum**
♂ **Q55.20 Unspecified congenital malformations of testis and scrotum**
Congenital malformation of testis or scrotum NOS
♂ **Q55.21 Polyorchism**
♂ **Q55.22 Retractile testis**
♂ **Q55.23 Scrotal transposition**
♂ **Q55.29 Other congenital malformations of testis and scrotum**
♂ **Q55.3 Atresia of vas deferens**
Code first any associated cystic fibrosis (E84.-)
♂ **Q55.4 Other congenital malformations of vas deferens, epididymis, seminal vesicles and prostate**
Absence or aplasia of prostate
Absence or aplasia of spermatic cord
Congenital malformation of vas deferens, epididymis, seminal vesicles or prostate NOS
♂ **Q55.5 Congenital absence and aplasia of penis**
\+ **Q55.6 Other congenital malformations of penis**
♂ **Q55.61 Curvature of penis (lateral)**
♂ **Q55.62 Hypoplasia of penis**
Micropenis
♂ **Q55.63 Congenital torsion of penis**
Excludes1: *acquired torsion of penis (N48.82)*
♂ **Q55.64 Hidden penis**
Buried penis
Concealed penis
Excludes1: *acquired buried penis (N48.83)*
♂ **Q55.69 Other congenital malformation of penis**
Congenital malformation of penis NOS
♂ **Q55.7 Congenital vasocutaneous fistula**
♂ **Q55.8 Other specified congenital malformations of male genital organ**
♂ **Q55.9 Congenital malformation of male genital organ, unspecified**
Congenital anomaly of male genital organ
Congenital deformity of male genital organ

Q56 Indeterminate sex and pseudohermaphroditism

Excludes1: *46,XX true hermaphrodite (Q99.1)*
androgen insensitivity syndrome (E34.5-)
chimera 46,XX/46,XY true hermaphrodite (Q99.0)
female pseudohermaphroditism with adrenocortical disorder (E25.-)
pseudohermaphroditism with specified chromosomal anomaly (Q96-Q99)
pure gonadal dysgenesis (Q99.1)
Q56.0 Hermaphroditism, not elsewhere classified
Ovotestis
♂ **Q56.1 Male pseudohermaphroditism, not elsewhere classified**
46, XY with streak gonads
Male pseudohermaphroditism NOS
♀ **Q56.2 Female pseudohermaphroditism, not elsewhere classified**
Female pseudohermaphroditism NOS
Q56.3 Pseudohermaphroditism, unspecified
Q56.4 Indeterminate sex, unspecified
Ambiguous genitalia

ongenital malformations of the urinary system (Q60-Q64)

Q60 Renal agenesis and other reduction defects of kidney

Includes: congenital absence of kidney
congenital atrophy of kidney
infantile atrophy of kidney

CC **Q60.0 Renal agenesis, unilateral**
CC Exclusion see Appendix A PDX collection 1092

CC **Q60.1 Renal agenesis, bilateral**
CC Exclusion see Appendix A PDX collection 1092

CC **Q60.2 Renal agenesis, unspecified**
CC Exclusion see Appendix A PDX collection 1092

CC **Q60.3 Renal hypoplasia, unilateral**
CC Exclusion see Appendix A PDX collection 1092

CC **Q60.4 Renal hypoplasia, bilateral**
CC Exclusion see Appendix A PDX collection 1092

CC **Q60.5 Renal hypoplasia, unspecified**
CC Exclusion see Appendix A PDX collection 1092

CC **Q60.6 Potter's syndrome**
CC Exclusion see Appendix A PDX collection 1092

Q61 Cystic kidney disease

Excludes1: *acquired cyst of kidney (N28.1)*
Potter's syndrome (Q60.6)

+ **Q61.0 Congenital renal cyst**

CC **Q61.00 Congenital renal cyst, unspecified**
Cyst of kidney NOS (congenital)
CC Exclusion see Appendix A PDX collection 1093

CC **Q61.01 Congenital single renal cyst**
CC Exclusion see Appendix A PDX collection 1094

CC **Q61.02 Congenital multiple renal cysts**
CC Exclusion see Appendix A PDX collection 1095

+ **Q61.1 Polycystic kidney, infantile type**
Polycystic kidney, autosomal recessive

CC **Q61.11 Cystic dilatation of collecting ducts**
CC Exclusion see Appendix A PDX collection 1096

CC **Q61.19 Other polycystic kidney, infantile type**
CC Exclusion see Appendix A PDX collection 1096

CC **Q61.2 Polycystic kidney, adult type**
Polycystic kidney, autosomal dominant
CC Exclusion see Appendix A PDX collection 1096

CC **Q61.3 Polycystic kidney, unspecified**
CC Exclusion see Appendix A PDX collection 1096

CC **Q61.4 Renal dysplasia**
Multicystic dysplastic kidney
Multicystic kidney (development)
Multicystic kidney disease
Multicystic renal dysplasia
Excludes1: *polycystic kidney disease (Q61.11-Q61.3)*
CC Exclusion see Appendix A PDX collection 1097

CC **Q61.5 Medullary cystic kidney**
Nephronopthisis
Sponge kidney NOS
CC Exclusion see Appendix A PDX collection 1095

CC **Q61.8 Other cystic kidney diseases**
Fibrocystic kidney
Fibrocystic renal degeneration or disease
CC Exclusion see Appendix A PDX collection 1095

CC **Q61.9 Cystic kidney disease, unspecified**
Meckel-Gruber syndrome
CC Exclusion see Appendix A PDX collection 1093

Q62 Congenital obstructive defects of renal pelvis and congenital malformations of ureter

CC **Q62.0 Congenital hydronephrosis**
CC Exclusion see Appendix A PDX collection 1098

+ **Q62.1 Congenital occlusion of ureter**
Atresia and stenosis of ureter

CC **Q62.10 Congenital occlusion of ureter, unspecified**
CC Exclusion see Appendix A PDX collection 1098

CC **Q62.11 Congenital occlusion of ureteropelvic junction**
CC Exclusion see Appendix A PDX collection 1098

CC **Q62.12 Congenital occlusion of ureterovesical orifice**
CC Exclusion see Appendix A PDX collection 1098

Q62.2 Congenital megaureter
Congenital dilatation of ureter
CC Exclusion see Appendix A PDX collection 1098

+ **Q62.3 Other obstructive defects of renal pelvis and ureter**

CC **Q62.31 Congenital ureterocele, orthotopic**
CC Exclusion see Appendix A PDX collection 1098

CC **Q62.32 Cecoureterocele**
Ectopic ureterocele
CC Exclusion see Appendix A PDX collection 1098

CC **Q62.39 Other obstructive defects of renal pelvis and ureter**
Ureteropelvic junction obstruction NOS
CC Exclusion see Appendix A PDX collection 1098

Q62.4 Agenesis of ureter
Congenital absence ureter

Q62.5 Duplication of ureter
Accessory ureter
Double ureter

+ **Q62.6 Malposition of ureter**

Q62.60 Malposition of ureter, unspecified

Q62.61 Deviation of ureter

Q62.62 Displacement of ureter

Q62.63 Anomalous implantation of ureter
Ectopia of ureter
Ectopic ureter

Q62.69 Other malposition of ureter

Q62.7 Congenital vesico-uretero-renal reflux

Q62.8 Other congenital malformations of ureter
Anomaly of ureter NOS

Q63 Other congenital malformations of kidney

Excludes1: *congenital nephrotic syndrome (N04.-)*

Q63.0 Accessory kidney

Q63.1 Lobulated, fused and horseshoe kidney

Q63.2 Ectopic kidney
Congenital displaced kidney
Malrotation of kidney

Q63.3 Hyperplastic and giant kidney
Compensatory hypertrophy of kidney

Q63.8 Other specified congenital malformations of kidney
Congenital renal calculi

Q63.9 Congenital malformation of kidney, unspecified

Q64 Other congenital malformations of urinary system

♂ **Q64.0 Epispadias**
Excludes1: *hypospadias (Q54.-)*

+ **Q64.1 Exstrophy of urinary bladder**

CC **Q64.10 Exstrophy of urinary bladder, unspecified**
Ectopia vesicae
CC Exclusion see Appendix A PDX collection 1099

CC **Q64.11 Supravesical fissure of urinary bladder**
CC Exclusion see Appendix A PDX collection 1099

CC **Q64.12 Cloacal extrophy of urinary bladder**
CC Exclusion see Appendix A PDX collection 1099

CC **Q64.19 Other exstrophy of urinary bladder**
Extroversion of bladder
CC Exclusion see Appendix A PDX collection 1099

CC **Q64.2 Congenital posterior urethral valves**
CC Exclusion see Appendix A PDX collection 1100

+ **Q64.3 Other atresia and stenosis of urethra and bladder neck**

CC **Q64.31 Congenital bladder neck obstruction**
Congenital obstruction of vesicourethral orifice
CC Exclusion see Appendix A PDX collection 1100

CC **Q64.32 Congenital stricture of urethra**
CC Exclusion see Appendix A PDX collection 1100

CC **Q64.33 Congenital stricture of urinary meatus**
CC Exclusion see Appendix A PDX collection 1100

CC **Q64.39 Other atresia and stenosis of urethra and bladder neck**
Atresia and stenosis of urethra and bladder neck NOS
CC Exclusion see Appendix A PDX collection 1100

Q64.4 Malformation of urachus
Cyst of urachus
Patent urachus
Prolapse of urachus

Q64.5 Congenital absence of bladder and urethra

Q64.6 Congenital diverticulum of bladder

+ **Q64.7 Other and unspecified congenital malformations of bladder and urethra**
Excludes1: *congenital prolapse of bladder (mucosa) (Q79.4)*

Q64.70 Unspecified congenital malformation of bladder and urethra
Malformation of bladder or urethra NOS

Q64.71 Congenital prolapse of urethra

Q64.72 Congenital prolapse of urinary meatus

Q64.73 Congenital urethrorectal fistula

Q64.74 Double urethra

Q64.75 Double urinary meatus

Q64.79 Other congenital malformations of bladder and urethra

Q64.8 Other specified congenital malformations of urinary system

Q64.9 Congenital malformation of urinary system, unspecified
Congenital anomaly NOS of urinary system
Congenital deformity NOS of urinary system

Congenital malformations and deformations of the musculoskeletal system (Q65-Q79)

Q65 Congenital deformities of hip

Excludes1: *clicking hip (R29.4)*

+ **Q65.0 Congenital dislocation of hip, unilateral**
  - **Q65.00 Congenital dislocation of unspecified hip, unilateral**
  - **Q65.01 Congenital dislocation of right hip, unilateral**
  - **Q65.02 Congenital dislocation of left hip, unilateral**

Q65.1 Congenital dislocation of hip, bilateral

Q65.2 Congenital dislocation of hip, unspecified

+ **Q65.3 Congenital partial dislocation of hip, unilateral**
  - **Q65.30 Congenital partial dislocation of unspecified hip, unilateral**
  - **Q65.31 Congenital partial dislocation of right hip, unilateral**
  - **Q65.32 Congenital partial dislocation of left hip, unilateral**

Q65.4 Congenital partial dislocation of hip, bilateral

Q65.5 Congenital partial dislocation of hip, unspecified

Q65.6 Congenital unstable hip

Congenital dislocatable hip

+ **Q65.8 Other congenital deformities of hip**
  - **Q65.81 Congenital coxa valga**
  - **Q65.82 Congenital coxa vara**
  - **Q65.89 Other specified congenital deformities of hip**
    Anteversion of femoral neck
    Congenital acetabular dysplasia

Q65.9 Congenital deformity of hip, unspecified

Q66 Congenital deformities of feet

Excludes1: *reduction defects of feet (Q72.-)*
valgus deformities (acquired) (M21.0-)
varus deformities (acquired) (M21.1-)

Q66.0 Congenital talipes equinovarus

Q66.1 Congenital talipes calcaneovarus

Q66.2 Congenital metatarsus (primus) varus

Q66.3 Other congenital varus deformities of feet

Hallux varus, congenital

Q66.4 Congenital talipes calcaneovalgus

+ **Q66.5 Congenital pes planus**
  Congenital flat foot
  Congenital rigid flat foot
  Congenital spastic (everted) flat foot
  Excludes1: *pes planus, acquired (M21.4)*
  - **Q66.50 Congenital pes planus, unspecified foot**
  - **Q66.51 Congenital pes planus, right foot**
  - **Q66.52 Congenital pes planus, left foot**

Q66.6 Other congenital valgus deformities of feet

Congenital metatarsus valgus

Q66.7 Congenital pes cavus

+ **Q66.8 Other congenital deformities of feet**
  - **Q66.80 Congenital vertical talus deformity, unspecified foot**
  - **Q66.81 Congenital vertical talus deformity, right foot**
  - **Q66.82 Congenital vertical talus deformity, left foot**
  - **Q66.89 Other specified congenital deformities of feet**
    Congenital asymmetric talipes
    Congenital clubfoot NOS
    Congenital talipes NOS
    Congenital tarsal coalition
    Hammer toe, congenital

Q66.9 Congenital deformity of feet, unspecified

Q67 Congenital musculoskeletal deformities of head, face, spine and chest

Excludes1: *congenital malformation syndromes classified to Q87.-*
Potter's syndrome (Q60.6)

Q67.0 Congenital facial asymmetry

Q67.1 Congenital compression facies

Q67.2 Dolichocephaly

Q67.3 Plagiocephaly

Q67.4 Other congenital deformities of skull, face and jaw

Congenital depressions in skull
Congenital hemifacial atrophy or hypertrophy
Deviation of nasal septum, congenital
Squashed or bent nose, congenital
Excludes1: *dentofacial anomalies [including malocclusion] (M26.-)*
syphilitic saddle nose (A50.5)

CC **Q67.5 Congenital deformity of spine**

Congenital postural scoliosis
Congenital scoliosis NOS
Excludes1: *infantile idiopathic scoliosis (M41.0)*
scoliosis due to congenital bony malformation (Q76.3)
CC Exclusion see Appendix A PDX collection 1101

Q67.6 Pectus excavatum

Congenital funnel chest

Q67.7 Pectus carinatum

Congenital pigeon chest

CC **Q67.8 Other congenital deformities of chest**

Congenital deformity of chest wall NOS
CC Exclusion see Appendix A PDX collection 1102

Q68 Other congenital musculoskeletal deformities

Excludes1: *reduction defects of limb(s) (Q71-Q73)*
Excludes2: *congenital myotonic chondrodystrophy (G71.13)*

Q68.0 Congenital deformity of sternocleidomastoid muscle

Congenital contracture of sternocleidomastoid (muscle)
Congenital (sternomastoid) torticollis
Sternomastoid tumor (congenital)

CC **Q68.1 Congenital deformity of finger(s) and hand**

Congenital clubfinger
Spade-like hand (congenital)
CC Exclusion see Appendix A PDX collection 1102

Q68.2 Congenital deformity of knee

Congenital dislocation of knee
Congenital genu recurvatum

Q68.3 Congenital bowing of femur

Excludes1: *anteversion of femur (neck) (Q65.89)*

Q68.4 Congenital bowing of tibia and fibula

Q68.5 Congenital bowing of long bones of leg, unspecified

Q68.6 Discoid meniscus

Q68.8 Other specified congenital musculoskeletal deformities

Congenital deformity of clavicle
Congenital deformity of elbow
Congenital deformity of forearm
Congenital deformity of scapula
Congenital deformity of wrist
Congenital dislocation of elbow
Congenital dislocation of shoulder
Congenital dislocation of wrist

Q69 Polydactyly

Q69.0 Accessory finger(s)

Q69.1 Accessory thumb(s)

Q69.2 Accessory toe(s)

Accessory hallux

Q69.9 Polydactyly, unspecified

Supernumerary digit(s) NOS

Q70 Syndactyly

+ **Q70.0 Fused fingers**
  Complex syndactyly of fingers with synostosis
  - **Q70.00 Fused fingers, unspecified hand**
  - **Q70.01 Fused fingers, right hand**
  - **Q70.02 Fused fingers, left hand**
  - **Q70.03 Fused fingers, bilateral**
+ **Q70.1 Webbed fingers**
  Simple syndactyly of fingers without synostosis
  - **Q70.10 Webbed fingers, unspecified hand**
  - **Q70.11 Webbed fingers, right hand**
  - **Q70.12 Webbed fingers, left hand**
  - **Q70.13 Webbed fingers, bilateral**
+ **Q70.2 Fused toes**
  Complex syndactyly of toes with synostosis
  - **Q70.20 Fused toes, unspecified foot**
  - **Q70.21 Fused toes, right foot**
  - **Q70.22 Fused toes, left foot**
  - **Q70.23 Fused toes, bilateral**
+ **Q70.3 Webbed toes**
  Simple syndactyly of toes without synostosis
  - **Q70.30 Webbed toes, unspecified foot**
  - **Q70.31 Webbed toes, right foot**
  - **Q70.32 Webbed toes, left foot**
  - **Q70.33 Webbed toes, bilateral**

Q70.4 Polysyndactyly, unspecified

Excludes1: *specified syndactyly of hand and feet - code to specified conditions (Q70.0-Q70.3-)*

Q70.9 Syndactyly, unspecified

Symphalangy NOS

Q71 Reduction defects of upper limb

+ **Q71.0 Congenital complete absence of upper limb**
  - **Q71.00 Congenital complete absence of unspecified upper limb**
  - **Q71.01 Congenital complete absence of right upper limb**
  - **Q71.02 Congenital complete absence of left upper limb**
  - **Q71.03 Congenital complete absence of upper limb, bilateral**

+ **Q71.1 Congenital absence of upper arm and forearm with hand present**
  - **Q71.10 Congenital absence of unspecified upper arm and forearm with hand present**
  - **Q71.11 Congenital absence of right upper arm and forearm with hand present**
  - **Q71.12 Congenital absence of left upper arm and forearm with hand present**
  - **Q71.13 Congenital absence of upper arm and forearm with hand present, bilateral**

+ **Q71.2 Congenital absence of both forearm and hand**
  - **Q71.20 Congenital absence of both forearm and hand, unspecified upper limb**
  - **Q71.21 Congenital absence of both forearm and hand, right upper limb**
  - **Q71.22 Congenital absence of both forearm and hand, left upper limb**
  - **Q71.23 Congenital absence of both forearm and hand, bilateral**

+ **Q71.3 Congenital absence of hand and finger**
  - **Q71.30 Congenital absence of unspecified hand and finger**
  - **Q71.31 Congenital absence of right hand and finger**
  - **Q71.32 Congenital absence of left hand and finger**
  - **Q71.33 Congenital absence of hand and finger, bilateral**

+ **Q71.4 Longitudinal reduction defect of radius**
  Clubhand (congenital)
  Radial clubhand
  - **Q71.40 Longitudinal reduction defect of unspecified radius**
  - **Q71.41 Longitudinal reduction defect of right radius**
  - **Q71.42 Longitudinal reduction defect of left radius**
  - **Q71.43 Longitudinal reduction defect of radius, bilateral**

+ **Q71.5 Longitudinal reduction defect of ulna**
  - **Q71.50 Longitudinal reduction defect of unspecified ulna**
  - **Q71.51 Longitudinal reduction defect of right ulna**
  - **Q71.52 Longitudinal reduction defect of left ulna**
  - **Q71.53 Longitudinal reduction defect of ulna, bilateral**

+ **Q71.6 Lobster-claw hand**
  - **Q71.60 Lobster-claw hand, unspecified hand**
  - **Q71.61 Lobster-claw right hand**
  - **Q71.62 Lobster-claw left hand**
  - **Q71.63 Lobster-claw hand, bilateral**

+ **Q71.8 Other reduction defects of upper limb**
  + **Q71.81 Congenital shortening of upper limb**
    - **Q71.811 Congenital shortening of right upper limb**
    - **Q71.812 Congenital shortening of left upper limb**
    - **Q71.813 Congenital shortening of upper limb, bilateral**
    - **Q71.819 Congenital shortening of unspecified upper limb**
  + **Q71.89 Other reduction defects of upper limb**
    - **Q71.891 Other reduction defects of right upper limb**
    - **Q71.892 Other reduction defects of left upper limb**
    - **Q71.893 Other reduction defects of upper limb, bilateral**
    - **Q71.899 Other reduction defects of unspecified upper limb**

+ **Q71.9 Unspecified reduction defect of upper limb**
  - **Q71.90 Unspecified reduction defect of unspecified upper limb**
  - **Q71.91 Unspecified reduction defect of right upper limb**
  - **Q71.92 Unspecified reduction defect of left upper limb**
  - **Q71.93 Unspecified reduction defect of upper limb, bilateral**

Q72 Reduction defects of lower limb

+ **Q72.0 Congenital complete absence of lower limb**
  - **Q72.00 Congenital complete absence of unspecified lower limb**
  - **Q72.01 Congenital complete absence of right lower limb**
  - **Q72.02 Congenital complete absence of left lower limb**
  - **Q72.03 Congenital complete absence of lower limb, bilateral**

+ **Q72.1 Congenital absence of thigh and lower leg with foot present**
  - **Q72.10 Congenital absence of unspecified thigh and lower leg with foot present**
  - **Q72.11 Congenital absence of right thigh and lower leg with foot present**
  - **Q72.12 Congenital absence of left thigh and lower leg with foot present**
  - **Q72.13 Congenital absence of thigh and lower leg with foot present, bilateral**

+ **Q72.2 Congenital absence of both lower leg and foot**
  - **Q72.20 Congenital absence of both lower leg and foot, unspecified lower limb**
  - **Q72.21 Congenital absence of both lower leg and foot, right lower limb**
  - **Q72.22 Congenital absence of both lower leg and foot, left lower limb**
  - **Q72.23 Congenital absence of both lower leg and foot, bilateral**

+ **Q72.3 Congenital absence of foot and toe(s)**
  - **Q72.30 Congenital absence of unspecified foot and toe(s)**
  - **Q72.31 Congenital absence of right foot and toe(s)**
  - **Q72.32 Congenital absence of left foot and toe(s)**
  - **Q72.33 Congenital absence of foot and toe(s), bilateral**

+ **Q72.4 Longitudinal reduction defect of femur**
  Proximal femoral focal deficiency
  - **Q72.40 Longitudinal reduction defect of unspecified femur**
  - **Q72.41 Longitudinal reduction defect of right femur**
  - **Q72.42 Longitudinal reduction defect of left femur**
  - **Q72.43 Longitudinal reduction defect of femur, bilateral**

+ **Q72.5 Longitudinal reduction defect of tibia**
  - **Q72.50 Longitudinal reduction defect of unspecified tibia**
  - **Q72.51 Longitudinal reduction defect of right tibia**
  - **Q72.52 Longitudinal reduction defect of left tibia**
  - **Q72.53 Longitudinal reduction defect of tibia, bilateral**

+ **Q72.6 Longitudinal reduction defect of fibula**
  - **Q72.60 Longitudinal reduction defect of unspecified fibula**
  - **Q72.61 Longitudinal reduction defect of right fibula**
  - **Q72.62 Longitudinal reduction defect of left fibula**
  - **Q72.63 Longitudinal reduction defect of fibula, bilateral**

+ **Q72.7 Split foot**
  - **Q72.70 Split foot, unspecified lower limb**
  - **Q72.71 Split foot, right lower limb**
  - **Q72.72 Split foot, left lower limb**
  - **Q72.73 Split foot, bilateral**

+ **Q72.8 Other reduction defects of lower limb**
  + **Q72.81 Congenital shortening of lower limb**
    - **Q72.811 Congenital shortening of right lower limb**
    - **Q72.812 Congenital shortening of left lower limb**
    - **Q72.813 Congenital shortening of lower limb, bilateral**
    - **Q72.819 Congenital shortening of unspecified lower limb**
  + **Q72.89 Other reduction defects of lower limb**
    - **Q72.891 Other reduction defects of right lower limb**
    - **Q72.892 Other reduction defects of left lower limb**
    - **Q72.893 Other reduction defects of lower limb, bilateral**
    - **Q72.899 Other reduction defects of unspecified lower limb**

+ **Q72.9 Unspecified reduction defect of lower limb**
  - **Q72.90 Unspecified reduction defect of unspecified lower limb**
  - **Q72.91 Unspecified reduction defect of right lower limb**
  - **Q72.92 Unspecified reduction defect of left lower limb**
  - **Q72.93 Unspecified reduction defect of lower limb, bilateral**

Q73 Reduction defects of unspecified limb

Q73.0 Congenital absence of unspecified limb(s)
Amelia NOS

Q73.1 Phocomelia, unspecified limb(s)
Phocomelia NOS

Q73.8 Other reduction defects of unspecified limb(s)
Longitudinal reduction deformity of unspecified limb(s)
Ectromelia of limb NOS
Hemimelia of limb NOS
Reduction defect of limb NOS

Q74 Other congenital malformations of limb(s)

Excludes1: *polydactyly (Q69.-)*
reduction defect of limb (Q71-Q73)
syndactyly (Q70.-)

Q74.0 Other congenital malformations of upper limb(s), including shoulder girdle
Accessory carpal bones
Cleidocranial dysostosis
Congenital pseudarthrosis of clavicle
Macrodactylia (fingers)
Madelung's deformity
Radioulnar synostosis
Sprengel's deformity
Triphalangeal thumb

Q74.1 Congenital malformation of knee
Congenital absence of patella
Congenital dislocation of patella
Congenital genu valgum
Congenital genu varum
Rudimentary patella
Excludes1: *congenital dislocation of knee (Q68.2)*
congenital genu recurvatum (Q68.2)
nail patella syndrome (Q87.2)

Q74.2 Other congenital malformations of lower limb(s), including pelvic girdle
Congenital fusion of sacroiliac joint
Congenital malformation of ankle joint
Congenital malformation of sacroiliac joint
Excludes1: *anteversion of femur (neck) (Q65.89)*

CC **Q74.3 Arthrogryposis multiplex congenita**
CC Exclusion see Appendix A PDX collection 1102

Q74.8 Other specified congenital malformations of limb(s)

Q74.9 Unspecified congenital malformation of limb(s)
Congenital anomaly of limb(s) NOS

Q75 Other congenital malformations of skull and face bones

Excludes1: *congenital malformation of face NOS (Q18.-)*
congenital malformation syndromes classified to Q87.-
dentofacial anomalies [including malocclusion] (M26.-)
musculoskeletal deformities of head and face (Q67.0-Q67.4)
skull defects associated with congenital anomalies of brain such as:
anencephaly (Q00.0)
encephalocele (Q01.-)
hydrocephalus (Q03.-)
microcephaly (Q02)

Q75.0 Craniosynostosis
Acrocephaly
Imperfect fusion of skull
Oxycephaly
Trigonocephaly

Q75.1 Craniofacial dysostosis
Crouzon's disease

Q75.2 Hypertelorism

Q75.3 Macrocephaly

Q75.4 Mandibulofacial dysostosis
Franceschetti syndrome
Treacher Collins syndrome

Q75.5 Oculomandibular dysostosis

Q75.8 Other specified congenital malformations of skull and face bones
Absence of skull bone, congenital
Congenital deformity of forehead
Platybasia

Q75.9 Congenital malformation of skull and face bones, unspecified
Congenital anomaly of face bones NOS
Congenital anomaly of skull NOS

Q76 Congenital malformations of spine and bony thorax

Excludes1: *congenital musculoskeletal deformities of spine and chest (Q67.5-Q67.8)*

Q76.0 Spina bifida occulta
Excludes1: *meningocele (spinal) (Q05.-)*
spina bifida (aperta) (cystica) (Q05.-)

Q76.1 Klippel-Feil syndrome
Cervical fusion syndrome

Q76.2 Congenital spondylolisthesis
Congenital spondylolysis
Excludes1: *spondylolisthesis (acquired) (M43.1-)*
spondylolysis (acquired) (M43.0-)

CC **Q76.3 Congenital scoliosis due to congenital bony malformation**
Hemivertebra fusion or failure of segmentation with scoliosis
CC Exclusion see Appendix A PDX collection 1101

\+ **Q76.4 Other congenital malformations of spine, not associated with scoliosis**

\+ **Q76.41 Congenital kyphosis**

Q76.411 Congenital kyphosis, occipito-atlanto-axial region

Q76.412 Congenital kyphosis, cervical region

Q76.413 Congenital kyphosis, cervicothoracic region

Q76.414 Congenital kyphosis, thoracic region

Q76.415 Congenital kyphosis, thoracolumbar region

Q76.419 Congenital kyphosis, unspecified region

\+ **Q76.42 Congenital lordosis**

CC **Q76.425 Congenital lordosis, thoracolumbar region**
CC Exclusion see Appendix A PDX collection 1101

CC **Q76.426 Congenital lordosis, lumbar region**
CC Exclusion see Appendix A PDX collection 1101

CC **Q76.427 Congenital lordosis, lumbosacral region**
CC Exclusion see Appendix A PDX collection 1101

CC **Q76.428 Congenital lordosis, sacral and sacrococcygeal region**
CC Exclusion see Appendix A PDX collection 1101

CC **Q76.429 Congenital lordosis, unspecified region**
CC Exclusion see Appendix A PDX collection 1101

Q76.49 Other congenital malformations of spine, not associated with scoliosis
Congenital absence of vertebra NOS
Congenital fusion of spine NOS
Congenital malformation of lumbosacral (joint) (regi[on]) NOS
Congenital malformation of spine NOS
Hemivertebra NOS
Malformation of spine NOS
Platyspondylisis NOS
Supernumerary vertebra NOS

Q76.5 Cervical rib
Supernumerary rib in cervical region

CC **Q76.6 Other congenital malformations of ribs**
Accessory rib
Congenital absence of rib
Congenital fusion of ribs
Congenital malformation of ribs NOS
Excludes1: *short rib syndrome (Q77.2)*
CC Exclusion see Appendix A PDX collection 1103

CC **Q76.7 Congenital malformation of sternum**
Congenital absence of sternum
Sternum bifidum
CC Exclusion see Appendix A PDX collection 1103

CC **Q76.8 Other congenital malformations of bony thorax**
CC Exclusion see Appendix A PDX collection 1103

CC **Q76.9 Congenital malformation of bony thorax, unspecified**
CC Exclusion see Appendix A PDX collection 1103

Q77 Osteochondrodysplasia with defects of growth of tubular bones and spine

Excludes1: *mucopolysaccharidosis (E76.0-E76.3)*
Excludes2: *congenital myotonic chondrodystrophy (G71.13)*

Q77.0 Achondrogenesis
Hypochondrogenesis

Q77.1 Thanatophoric short stature

CC **Q77.2 Short rib syndrome**
Asphyxiating thoracic dysplasia [Jeune]
CC Exclusion see Appendix A PDX collection 1103

Q77.3 Chondrodysplasia punctata
Excludes1: *Rhizomelic chondrodysplasia punctata (E71.43)*

Q77.4 Achondroplasia
Hypochondroplasia
Osteosclerosis congenita

Q77.5 Diastrophic dysplasia

Q77.6 Chondroectodermal dysplasia
Ellis-van Creveld syndrome

Q77.7 Spondyloepiphyseal dysplasia

Q77.8 Other osteochondrodysplasia with defects of growth of tubular bones and spine

Q77.9 Osteochondrodysplasia with defects of growth of tubular bones and spine, unspecified

Q78 Other osteochondrodysplasias

Excludes2: *congenital myotonic chondrodystrophy (G71.13)*

CC **Q78.0 Osteogenesis imperfecta**
Fragilitas ossium
Osteopsathyrosis
CC Exclusion see Appendix A PDX collection 1104

Q78.1 Polyostotic fibrous dysplasia
Albright(-McCune)(-Sternberg) syndrome

CC **Q78.2 Osteopetrosis**
Albers-Schönberg syndrome
Osteosclerosis NOS
CC Exclusion see Appendix A PDX collection 1104

Q78.3 Progressive diaphyseal dysplasia
Camurati-Engelmann syndrome

Q78.4 Enchondromatosis
Maffucci's syndrome
Ollier's disease

Q78.5 Metaphyseal dysplasia
Pyle's syndrome

Q78.6 Multiple congenital exostoses
Diaphyseal aclasis

Q78.8 Other specified osteochondrodysplasias
Osteopoikilosis
Q78.9 Osteochondrodysplasia, unspecified
Chondrodystrophy NOS
Osteodystrophy NOS

Q79 Congenital malformations of musculoskeletal system, not elsewhere classified
Excludes2: *congenital (sternomastoid) torticollis (Q68.0)*
MCC **Q79.0 Congenital diaphragmatic hernia**
Excludes1: *congenital hiatus hernia (Q40.1)*
MCC Exclusion see Appendix A PDX collection 1105
MCC **Q79.1 Other congenital malformations of diaphragm**
Absence of diaphragm
Congenital malformation of diaphragm NOS
Eventration of diaphragm
MCC Exclusion see Appendix A PDX collection 1105
MCC **Q79.2 Exomphalos**
Omphalocele
Excludes1: *umbilical hernia (K42.-)*
MCC Exclusion see Appendix A PDX collection 1106
MCC **Q79.3 Gastroschisis**
MCC Exclusion see Appendix A PDX collection 1106
MCC **Q79.4 Prune belly syndrome**
Congenital prolapse of bladder mucosa
Eagle-Barrett syndrome
MCC Exclusion see Appendix A PDX collection 1106
\+ **Q79.5 Other congenital malformations of abdominal wall**
Excludes1: *umbilical hernia (K42.-)*
MCC **Q79.51 Congenital hernia of bladder**
MCC Exclusion see Appendix A PDX collection 1106
MCC **Q79.59 Other congenital malformations of abdominal wall**
MCC Exclusion see Appendix A PDX collection 1106
CC **Q79.6 Ehlers-Danlos syndrome**
CC Exclusion see Appendix A PDX collection 1107
Q79.8 Other congenital malformations of musculoskeletal system
Absence of muscle
Absence of tendon
Accessory muscle
Amyotrophia congenita
Congenital constricting bands
Congenital shortening of tendon
Poland syndrome
Q79.9 Congenital malformation of musculoskeletal system, unspecified
Congenital anomaly of musculoskeletal system NOS
Congenital deformity of musculoskeletal system NOS

Other congenital malformations (Q80-Q89)

Q80 Congenital ichthyosis
Excludes1: *Refsum's disease (G60.1)*
Q80.0 Ichthyosis vulgaris
Q80.1 X-linked ichthyosis
Q80.2 Lamellar ichthyosis
Collodion baby
Q80.3 Congenital bullous ichthyosiform erythroderma
Q80.4 Harlequin fetus
Q80.8 Other congenital ichthyosis
Q80.9 Congenital ichthyosis, unspecified

Q81 Epidermolysis bullosa
Q81.0 Epidermolysis bullosa simplex
Excludes1: *Cockayne's syndrome (Q87.1)*
Q81.1 Epidermolysis bullosa letalis
Herlitz' syndrome
Q81.2 Epidermolysis bullosa dystrophica
Q81.8 Other epidermolysis bullosa
Q81.9 Epidermolysis bullosa, unspecified

Q82 Other congenital malformations of skin
Excludes1: *acrodermatitis enteropathica (E83.2)*
congenital erythropoietic porphyria (E80.0)
pilonidal cyst or sinus (L05.-)
Sturge-Weber (-Dimitri) syndrome (Q85.8)
Q82.0 Hereditary lymphedema
Q82.1 Xeroderma pigmentosum
Q82.2 Mastocytosis
Urticaria pigmentosa
Excludes1: *malignant mastocytosis (C96.2)*
Q82.3 Incontinentia pigmenti
Q82.4 Ectodermal dysplasia (anhidrotic)
Excludes1: *Ellis-van Creveld syndrome (Q77.6)*
Q82.5 Congenital non-neoplastic nevus
Birthmark NOS
Flammeus Nevus
Portwine Nevus
Sanguineous Nevus
Strawberry Nevus
Vascular Nevus NOS
Verrucous Nevus
Excludes2: *Café au lait spots (L81.3)*
lentigo (L81.4)
nevus NOS (D22.-)
araneus nevus (I78.1)
melanocytic nevus (D22.-)
pigmented nevus (D22.-)
spider nevus (I78.1)
stellar nevus (I78.1)
Q82.8 Other specified congenital malformations of skin
Abnormal palmar creases
Accessory skin tags
Benign familial pemphigus [Hailey-Hailey]
Congenital poikiloderma
Cutis laxa (hyperelastica)
Dermatoglyphic anomalies
Inherited keratosis palmaris et plantaris
Keratosis follicularis [Darier-White]
Excludes1: *Ehlers-Danlos syndrome (Q79.6)*
Q82.9 Congenital malformation of skin, unspecified

Q83 Congenital malformations of breast
Excludes2: *absence of pectoral muscle (Q79.8)*
hypoplasia of breast (N64.82)
micromastia (N64.82)
Q83.0 Congenital absence of breast with absent nipple
Q83.1 Accessory breast
Supernumerary breast
Q83.2 Absent nipple
Q83.3 Accessory nipple
Supernumerary nipple
Q83.8 Other congenital malformations of breast
Q83.9 Congenital malformation of breast, unspecified

Q84 Other congenital malformations of integument
Q84.0 Congenital alopecia
Congenital atrichosis
Q84.1 Congenital morphological disturbances of hair, not elsewhere classified
Beaded hair
Monilethrix
Pili annulati
Excludes1: *Menkes' kinky hair syndrome (E83.0)*
Q84.2 Other congenital malformations of hair
Congenital hypertrichosis
Congenital malformation of hair NOS
Persistent lanugo
Q84.3 Anonychia
Excludes1: *nail patella syndrome (Q87.2)*
Q84.4 Congenital leukonychia
Q84.5 Enlarged and hypertrophic nails
Congenital onychauxis
Pachyonychia
Q84.6 Other congenital malformations of nails
Congenital clubnail
Congenital koilonychia
Congenital malformation of nail NOS
Q84.8 Other specified congenital malformations of integument
Aplasia cutis congenita
Q84.9 Congenital malformation of integument, unspecified
Congenital anomaly of integument NOS
Congenital deformity of integument NOS

Q85 Phakomatoses, not elsewhere classified
Excludes1: *ataxia telangiectasia [Louis-Bar] (G11.3)*
familial dysautonomia [Riley-Day] (G90.1)
\+ **Q85.0 Neurofibromatosis (nonmalignant)**
Q85.00 Neurofibromatosis, unspecified
Q85.01 Neurofibromatosis, type 1
Von Recklinghausen disease
Q85.02 Neurofibromatosis, type 2
Acoustic neurofibromatosis
Q85.03 Schwannomatosis
Q85.09 Other neurofibromatosis

CC **Q85.1 Tuberous sclerosis**
Bourneville's disease
Epiloia
CC Exclusion see Appendix A PDX collection 1108

CC **Q85.8 Other phakomatoses, not elsewhere classified**
Peutz-Jeghers Syndrome
Sturge-Weber(-Dimitri) syndrome
von Hippel-Lindau syndrome
Excludes1: *Meckel-Gruber syndrome (Q61.9)*
CC Exclusion see Appendix A PDX collection 1109

CC **Q85.9 Phakomatosis, unspecified**
Hamartosis NOS
CC Exclusion see Appendix A PDX collection 1109

Q86 Congenital malformation syndromes due to known exogenous causes, not elsewhere classified

Excludes2: *iodine-deficiency-related hypothyroidism (E00-E02)*
nonteratogenic effects of substances transmitted via placenta or breast milk (P04.-)

Q86.0 Fetal alcohol syndrome (dysmorphic)

● **Q86.1 Fetal hydantoin syndrome**
Meadow's syndrome

Q86.2 Dysmorphism due to warfarin

Q86.8 Other congenital malformation syndromes due to known exogenous causes

Q87 Other specified congenital malformation syndromes affecting multiple systems

Use additional code(s) to identify all associated manifestations

Q87.0 Congenital malformation syndromes predominantly affecting facial appearance
Acrocephalopolysyndactyly
Acrocephalosyndactyly [Apert]
Cryptophthalmos syndrome
Cyclopia
Goldenhar syndrome
Moebius syndrome
Oro-facial-digital syndrome
Robin syndrome
Whistling face

CC **Q87.1 Congenital malformation syndromes predominantly associated with short stature**
Aarskog syndrome
Cockayne syndrome
De Lange syndrome
Dubowitz syndrome
Noonan syndrome
Prader-Willi syndrome
Robinow-Silverman-Smith syndrome
Russell-Silver syndrome
Seckel syndrome
Excludes1: *Ellis-van Creveld syndrome (Q77.6)*
Smith-Lemli-Opitz syndrome (E78.72)
CC Exclusion see Appendix A PDX collection 1110

CC **Q87.2 Congenital malformation syndromes predominantly involving limbs**
Holt-Oram syndrome
Klippel-Trenaunay-Weber syndrome
Nail patella syndrome
Rubinstein-Taybi syndrome
Sirenomelia syndrome
Thrombocytopenia with absent radius [TAR] syndrome
VATER syndrome
CC Exclusion see Appendix A PDX collection 0540

CC **Q87.3 Congenital malformation syndromes involving early overgrowth**
Beckwith-Wiedemann syndrome
Sotos syndrome
Weaver syndrome
CC Exclusion see Appendix A PDX collection 0540

\+ **Q87.4 Marfan's syndrome**

CC **Q87.40 Marfan's syndrome, unspecified**
CC Exclusion see Appendix A PDX collection 1110

\+ **Q87.41 Marfan's syndrome with cardiovascular manifestations**

CC **Q87.410 Marfan's syndrome with aortic dilation**
CC Exclusion see Appendix A PDX collection 1110

CC **Q87.418 Marfan's syndrome with other cardiovascular manifestations**
CC Exclusion see Appendix A PDX collection 1110

CC **Q87.42 Marfan's syndrome with ocular manifestations**
CC Exclusion see Appendix A PDX collection 1110

CC **Q87.43 Marfan's syndrome with skeletal manifestation**
CC Exclusion see Appendix A PDX collection 1110

CC **Q87.5 Other congenital malformation syndromes with other skeletal changes**
CC Exclusion see Appendix A PDX collection 0540

\+ **Q87.8 Other specified congenital malformation syndromes, not elsewhere classified**
Excludes1: *Zellweger syndrome (E71.510)*

CC **Q87.81 Alport syndrome**
Use additional code to identify stage of chronic kidney disease (N18.1-N18.6)
CC Exclusion see Appendix A PDX collection 0540

CC **Q87.89 Other specified congenital malformation syndromes, not elsewhere classified**
Laurence-Moon (-Bardet)-Biedl syndrome
CC Exclusion see Appendix A PDX collection 0540

Q89 Other congenital malformations, not elsewhere classified

\+ **Q89.0 Congenital absence and malformations of spleen**
Excludes1: *isomerism of atrial appendages (with asplenia or polysplenia) (Q20.6)*

CC **Q89.01 Asplenia (congenital)**
CC Exclusion see Appendix A PDX collection 1111

CC **Q89.09 Congenital malformations of spleen**
Congenital splenomegaly
CC Exclusion see Appendix A PDX collection 1111

Q89.1 Congenital malformations of adrenal gland
Excludes1: *adrenogenital disorders (E25.-)*
congenital adrenal hyperplasia (E25.0)

Q89.2 Congenital malformations of other endocrine glands
Congenital malformation of parathyroid or thyroid gland
Persistent thyroglossal duct
Thyroglossal cyst
Excludes1: *congenital goiter (E03.0)*
congenital hypothyroidism (E03.1)

CC **Q89.3 Situs inversus**
Dextrocardia with situs inversus
Mirror-image atrial arrangement with situs inversus
Situs inversus or transversus abdominalis
Situs inversus or transversus thoracis
Transposition of abdominal viscera
Transposition of thoracic viscera
Excludes1: *dextrocardia NOS (Q24.0)*
CC Exclusion see Appendix A PDX collection 1112

MCC **Q89.4 Conjoined twins**
Craniopagus
Dicephaly
Pygopagus
Thoracopagus
MCC Exclusion see Appendix A PDX collection 1113

CC **Q89.7 Multiple congenital malformations, not elsewhere classified**
Multiple congenital anomalies NOS
Multiple congenital deformities NOS
Excludes1: *congenital malformation syndromes affecting multiple systems (Q87.-)*
CC Exclusion see Appendix A PDX collection 1112

CC **Q89.8 Other specified congenital malformations**
Use additional code(s) to identify all associated manifestations
CC Exclusion see Appendix A PDX collection 0540

Q89.9 Congenital malformation, unspecified
Congenital anomaly NOS
Congenital deformity NOS

Chromosomal abnormalities, not elsewhere classified (Q90-Q99)

Excludes2: *mitochondrial metabolic disorders (E88.4-)*

Q90 Down syndrome

Use additional code(s) to identify any associated physical conditions and degree of intellectual disabilities (F70-F79)

Q90.0 Trisomy 21, nonmosaicism (meiotic nondisjunction)
Q90.1 Trisomy 21, mosaicism (mitotic nondisjunction)
Q90.2 Trisomy 21, translocation
Q90.9 Down syndrome, unspecified
Trisomy 21 NOS

Q91 Trisomy 18 and Trisomy 13

CC **Q91.0 Trisomy 18, nonmosaicism (meiotic nondisjunction)**
CC Exclusion see Appendix A PDX collection 1114

CC **Q91.1 Trisomy 18, mosaicism (mitotic nondisjunction)**
CC Exclusion see Appendix A PDX collection 1114

CC **Q91.2 Trisomy 18, translocation**
CC Exclusion see Appendix A PDX collection 1114

CC **Q91.3 Trisomy 18, unspecified**
CC Exclusion see Appendix A PDX collection 1114

CC **Q91.4 Trisomy 13, nonmosaicism (meiotic nondisjunction)**
CC Exclusion see Appendix A PDX collection 1114

CC **Q91.5 Trisomy 13, mosaicism (mitotic nondisjunction)**
CC Exclusion see Appendix A PDX collection 1114

CC **Q91.6 Trisomy 13, translocation**
CC Exclusion see Appendix A PDX collection 1114

CC **Q91.7 Trisomy 13, unspecified**
CC Exclusion see Appendix A PDX collection 1114

Q92 Other trisomies and partial trisomies of the autosomes, not elsewhere classified

Includes: unbalanced translocations and insertions
Excludes1: *trisomies of chromosomes 13, 18, 21 (Q90-Q91)*

Q92.0 Whole chromosome trisomy, nonmosaicism (meiotic nondisjunction)

Q92.1 Whole chromosome trisomy, mosaicism (mitotic nondisjunction)

Q92.2 Partial trisomy
Less than whole arm duplicated
Whole arm or more duplicated
Excludes1: *partial trisomy due to unbalanced translocation (Q92.5)*

Q92.5 Duplications with other complex rearrangements
Partial trisomy due to unbalanced translocations
Code also any associated deletions due to unbalanced translocations, inversions and insertions (Q93.7)

\+ **Q92.6 Marker chromosomes**
Trisomies due to dicentrics
Trisomies due to extra rings
Trisomies due to isochromosomes
Individual with marker heterochromatin

Q92.61 Marker chromosomes in normal individual

Q92.62 Marker chromosomes in abnormal individual

Q92.7 Triploidy and polyploidy

Q92.8 Other specified trisomies and partial trisomies of autosomes
Duplications identified by fluorescence in situ hybridization (FISH)
Duplications identified by in situ hybridization (ISH)
Duplications seen only at prometaphase

Q92.9 Trisomy and partial trisomy of autosomes, unspecified

Q93 Monosomies and deletions from the autosomes, not elsewhere classified

Q93.0 Whole chromosome monosomy, nonmosaicism (meiotic nondisjunction)

Q93.1 Whole chromosome monosomy, mosaicism (mitotic nondisjunction)

Q93.2 Chromosome replaced with ring, dicentric or isochromosome

CC **Q93.3 Deletion of short arm of chromosome 4**
Wolff-Hirschorn syndrome
CC Exclusion see Appendix A PDX collection 1115

CC **Q93.4 Deletion of short arm of chromosome 5**
Cri-du-chat syndrome
CC Exclusion see Appendix A PDX collection 1116

CC **Q93.5 Other deletions of part of a chromosome**
Angelman syndrome
CC Exclusion see Appendix A PDX collection 1115

CC **Q93.7 Deletions with other complex rearrangements**
Deletions due to unbalanced translocations, inversions and insertions
Code also any associated duplications due to unbalanced translocations, inversions and insertions (Q92.5)
CC Exclusion see Appendix A PDX collection 1115

\+ **Q93.8 Other deletions from the autosomes**

MCC **Q93.81 Velo-cardio-facial syndrome**
Deletion 22q11.2
MCC Exclusion see Appendix A PDX collection 1117

CC **Q93.88 Other microdeletions**
Miller-Dieker syndrome
Smith-Magenis syndrome
CC Exclusion see Appendix A PDX collection 1118

CC **Q93.89 Other deletions from the autosomes**
Deletions identified by fluorescence in situ hybridization (FISH)
Deletions identified by in situ hybridization (ISH)
Deletions seen only at prometaphase
CC Exclusion see Appendix A PDX collection 1115

CC **Q93.9 Deletion from autosomes, unspecified**
CC Exclusion see Appendix A PDX collection 1115

Q95 Balanced rearrangements and structural markers, not elsewhere classified

Includes: Robertsonian and balanced reciprocal translocations and insertions

Q95.0 Balanced translocation and insertion in normal individual

Q95.1 Chromosome inversion in normal individual

Q95.2 Balanced autosomal rearrangement in abnormal individual

Q95.3 Balanced sex/autosomal rearrangement in abnormal individual

Q95.5 Individual with autosomal fragile site

Q95.8 Other balanced rearrangements and structural markers

Q95.9 Balanced rearrangement and structural marker, unspecified

Q96 Turner's syndrome

Excludes1: *Noonan syndrome (Q87.1)*

♀ **Q96.0 Karyotype 45, X**

♀ **Q96.1 Karyotype 46, X iso (Xq)**
Karyotype 46, isochromosome Xq

♀ **Q96.2 Karyotype 46, X with abnormal sex chromosome, except iso (Xq)**
Karyotype 46, X with abnormal sex chromosome, except isochromosome Xq

♀ **Q96.3 Mosaicism, 45, X/46, XX or XY**

♀ **Q96.4 Mosaicism, 45, X/other cell line(s) with abnormal sex chromosome**

♀ **Q96.8 Other variants of Turner's syndrome**

♀ **Q96.9 Turner's syndrome, unspecified**

Q97 Other sex chromosome abnormalities, female phenotype, not elsewhere classified

Excludes1: *Turner's syndrome (Q96.-)*

♀ **Q97.0 Karyotype 47, XXX**

♀ **Q97.1 Female with more than three X chromosomes**

♀ **Q97.2 Mosaicism, lines with various numbers of X chromosomes**

♀ **Q97.3 Female with 46, XY karyotype**

♀ **Q97.8 Other specified sex chromosome abnormalities, female phenotype**

♀ **Q97.9 Sex chromosome abnormality, female phenotype, unspecified**

Q98 Other sex chromosome abnormalities, male phenotype, not elsewhere classified

♂ **Q98.0 Klinefelter syndrome karyotype 47, XXY**

♂ **Q98.1 Klinefelter syndrome, male with more than two X chromosomes**

♂ **Q98.3 Other male with 46, XX karyotype**

♂ **Q98.4 Klinefelter syndrome, unspecified**

Q98.5 Karyotype 47, XYY

♂ **Q98.6 Male with structurally abnormal sex chromosome**

♂ **Q98.7 Male with sex chromosome mosaicism**

♂ **Q98.8 Other specified sex chromosome abnormalities, male phenotype**

♂ **Q98.9 Sex chromosome abnormality, male phenotype, unspecified**

Q99 Other chromosome abnormalities, not elsewhere classified

Q99.0 Chimera 46, XX/46, XY
Chimera 46, XX/46, XY true hermaphrodite

Q99.1 46, XX true hermaphrodite
46, XX with streak gonads
46, XY with streak gonads
Pure gonadal dysgenesis

Q99.2 Fragile X chromosome
Fragile X syndrome

Q99.8 Other specified chromosome abnormalities

Q99.9 Chromosomal abnormality, unspecified

Chapter 18: Symptoms, Signs and Abnormal Clinical and Laboratory Findings, Not Elsewhere Classified (R00-R99)

NOTE This chapter includes symptoms, signs, abnormal results of clinical or other investigative procedures, and ill-defined conditions regarding which no diagnosis classifiable elsewhere is recorded.

Signs and symptoms that point rather definitely to a given diagnosis have been assigned to a category in other chapters of the classification. In general, categories in this chapter include the less well-defined conditions and symptoms that, without the necessary study of the case to establish a final diagnosis, point perhaps equally to two or more diseases or to two or more systems of the body. Practically all categories in the chapter could be designated 'not otherwise specified', 'unknown etiology' or 'transient'. The Alphabetical Index should be consulted to determine which symptoms and signs are to be allocated here and which to other chapters. The residual subcategories, numbered .8, are generally provided for other relevant symptoms that cannot be allocated elsewhere in the classification.

The conditions and signs or symptoms included in categories R00-R94 consist of:
(a) cases for which no more specific diagnosis can be made even after all the facts bearing on the case have been investigated;
(b) signs or symptoms existing at the time of initial encounter that proved to be transient and whose causes could not be determined;
(c) provisional diagnosis in a patient who failed to return for further investigation or care;
(d) cases referred elsewhere for investigation or treatment before the diagnosis was made;
(e) cases in which a more precise diagnosis was not available for any other reason;
(f) certain symptoms, for which supplementary information is provided, that represent important problems in medical care in their own right.

Excludes2: *abnormal findings on antenatal screening of mother (O28.-)*
certain conditions originating in the perinatal period (P04-P96)
signs and symptoms classified in the body system chapters
signs and symptoms of breast (N63, N64.5)

This chapter contains the following category blocks:

R00-R09 Symptoms and signs involving the circulatory and respiratory systems
R10-R19 Symptoms and signs involving the digestive system and abdomen
R20-R23 Symptoms and signs involving the skin and subcutaneous tissue
R25-R29 Symptoms and signs involving the nervous and musculoskeletal systems
R30-R39 Symptoms and signs involving the genitourinary system
R40-R46 Symptoms and signs involving cognition, perception, emotional state and behavior
R47-R49 Symptoms and signs involving speech and voice
R50-R69 General symptoms and signs
R70-R79 Abnormal findings on examination of blood, without diagnosis
R80-R82 Abnormal findings on examination of urine, without diagnosis
R83-R89 Abnormal findings on examination of other body fluids, substances and tissues, without diagnosis
R90-R94 Abnormal findings on diagnostic imaging and in function studies, without diagnosis
R97 Abnormal tumor markers
R99 Ill-defined and unknown cause of mortality

C. Chapter-Specific Coding Guidelines

In addition to general coding guidelines, there are guidelines for specific diagnoses and/or conditions in the classification. Unless otherwise indicated, these guidelines apply to all health care settings. Please refer to Section II for guidelines on the selection of principal diagnosis.

18. Chapter 18: Symptoms, Signs, and Abnormal Clinical and Laboratory Findings, Not Elsewhere Classified (R00-R99)

Chapter 18 includes symptoms, signs, abnormal results of clinical or other investigative procedures, and ill-defined conditions regarding which no diagnosis classifiable elsewhere is recorded. Signs and symptoms that point to a specific diagnosis have been assigned to a category in other chapters of the classification.

a. Use of symptom codes

Codes that describe symptoms and signs are acceptable for reporting purposes when a related definitive diagnosis has not been established (confirmed) by the provider.

b. Use of a symptom code with a definitive diagnosis code

Codes for signs and symptoms may be reported in addition to a related definitive diagnosis when the sign or symptom is not routinely associated with that diagnosis, such as the various signs and symptoms associated with complex syndromes. The definitive diagnosis code should be sequenced before the symptom code.

Signs or symptoms that are associated routinely with a disease pro should not be assigned as additional codes, unless otherwise instructed by classification.

c. Combination codes that include symptoms

ICD-10-CM contains a number of combination codes that identify both definitive diagnosis and common symptoms of that diagnosis. When using of these combination codes, an additional code should not be assigned for symptom.

d. Repeated falls

Code R29.6, Repeated falls, is for use for encounters when a patient has rece fallen and the reason for the fall is being investigated.

Code Z91.81, History of falling, is for use when a patient has fallen in the and is at risk for future falls. When appropriate, both codes R29.6 and Z91 may be assigned together.

e. Coma scale

The coma scale codes (R40.2-) can be used in conjunction with traumatic b injury codes, acute cerebrovascular disease or sequelae of cerebrovasc disease codes. These codes are primarily for use by trauma registries, but may be used in any setting where this information is collected. The coma sc codes should be sequenced after the diagnosis code(s).

These codes, one from each subcategory, are needed to complete the scale. 7th character indicates when the scale was recorded. The 7th character sho match for all three codes.

At a minimum, report the initial score documented on presentation at y facility. This may be a score from the emergency medicine technician (EM or in the emergency department. If desired, a facility may choose to cap multiple coma scale scores.

Assign code R40.24, Glasgow coma scale, total score, when only the total sc is documented in the medical record and not the individual score(s).

f. Functional quadriplegia

Functional quadriplegia (code R53.2) is the lack of ability to use one's limb to ambulate due to extreme debility. It is not associated with neurologic defici injury, and code R53.2 should not be used for cases of neurologic quadriple It should only be assigned if functional quadriplegia is specifically documen in the medical record.

g. SIRS due to Non-Infectious Process

The systemic inflammatory response syndrome (SIRS) can develop as a resul certain non-infectious disease processes, such as trauma, malignant neopla or pancreatitis. When SIRS is documented with a noninfectious condition, no subsequent infection is documented, the code for the underlying conditi such as an injury, should be assigned, followed by code R65.10, Syster inflammatory response syndrome (SIRS) of non-infectious origin without ac organ dysfunction, or code R65.11, Systemic inflammatory response syndro (SIRS) of non-infectious origin with acute organ dysfunction. If an associa acute organ dysfunction is documented, the appropriate code(s) for the spec type of organ dysfunction(s) should be assigned in addition to code R65.11 acute organ dysfunction is documented, but it cannot be determined if the ac organ dysfunction is associated with SIRS or due to another condition (e directly due to the trauma), the provider should be queried.

h. Death NOS

Code R99, Ill-defined and unknown cause of mortality, is only for use in very limited circumstance when a patient who has already died is brought i an emergency department or other healthcare facility and is pronounced de upon arrival. It does not represent the discharge disposition of death.

Symptoms and signs involving the circulatory and respiratory systems (R00-R09)

R00 Abnormalities of heart beat

Excludes1: *abnormalities originating in the perinatal period (P29.1-)*
specified arrhythmias (I47-I49)

R00.0 Tachycardia, unspecified
Rapid heart beat
Sinoauricular tachycardia NOS
Sinus [sinusal] tachycardia NOS
Excludes1: *neonatal tachycardia (P29.11)*
paroxysmal tachycardia (I47.-)

R00.1 Bradycardia, unspecified
Sinoatrial bradycardia
Sinus bradycardia
Slow heart beat
Vagal bradycardia
Use additional code for adverse effect, if applicable, to identify drug (T36-T50 with fifth or sixth character 5)
Excludes1: *neonatal bradycardia (P29.12)*

R00.2 Palpitations
Awareness of heart beat
R00.8 Other abnormalities of heart beat
R00.9 Unspecified abnormalities of heart beat

R01 Cardiac murmurs and other cardiac sounds
Excludes1: *cardiac murmurs and sounds originating in the perinatal period (P29.8)*
R01.0 Benign and innocent cardiac murmurs
Functional cardiac murmur
R01.1 Cardiac murmur, unspecified
Cardiac bruit NOS
Heart murmur NOS
R01.2 Other cardiac sounds
Cardiac dullness, increased or decreased
Precordial friction

R03 Abnormal blood-pressure reading, without diagnosis
R03.0 Elevated blood-pressure reading, without diagnosis of hypertension
NOTE This category is to be used to record an episode of elevated blood pressure in a patient in whom no formal diagnosis of hypertension has been made, or as an isolated incidental finding.
Review coding guideline C.9.a.7
R03.1 Nonspecific low blood-pressure reading
Excludes1: *hypotension (I95.-)*
maternal hypotension syndrome (O26.5-)
neurogenic orthostatic hypotension (G90.3)

R04 Hemorrhage from respiratory passages
R04.0 Epistaxis
Hemorrhage from nose
Nosebleed
R04.1 Hemorrhage from throat
Excludes2: *hemoptysis (R04.2)*
CC **R04.2 Hemoptysis**
Blood-stained sputum
Cough with hemorrhage
CC Exclusion see Appendix A PDX collection 1119
AHA CC: 4Q, 2013, 118
\+ **R04.8 Hemorrhage from other sites in respiratory passages**
• CC **R04.81 Acute idiopathic pulmonary hemorrhage in infants**
AIPHI
Acute idiopathic hemorrhage in infants over 28 days old
Excludes1: *perinatal pulmonary hemorrhage (P26.-)*
von Willebrand's disease (D68.0)
CC Exclusion see Appendix A PDX collection 1119
CC **R04.89 Hemorrhage from other sites in respiratory passages**
Pulmonary hemorrhage NOS
CC Exclusion see Appendix A PDX collection 1119
CC **R04.9 Hemorrhage from respiratory passages, unspecified**
CC Exclusion see Appendix A PDX collection 1119

R05 Cough
Excludes1: *cough with hemorrhage (R04.2)*
smoker's cough (J41.0)
Valid 3-character code, no further characters required

R06 Abnormalities of breathing
Excludes1: *acute respiratory distress syndrome (J80)*
respiratory arrest (R09.2)
respiratory arrest of newborn (P28.81)
respiratory distress syndrome of newborn (P22.-)
respiratory failure (J96.-)
respiratory failure of newborn (P28.5)
\+ **R06.0 Dyspnea**
Excludes1: *tachypnea NOS (R06.82)*
transient tachypnea of newborn (P22.1)
R06.00 Dyspnea, unspecified
R06.01 Orthopnea
R06.02 Shortness of breath
R06.09 Other forms of dyspnea
R06.1 Stridor
Excludes1: *congenital laryngeal stridor (P28.89)*
laryngismus (stridulus) (J38.5)
R06.2 Wheezing
Excludes1: *Asthma (J45.-)*
CC **R06.3 Periodic breathing**
Cheyne-Stokes breathing
CC Exclusion see Appendix A PDX collection 1120
R06.4 Hyperventilation
Excludes1: *psychogenic hyperventilation (F45.8)*
R06.5 Mouth breathing
Excludes2: *dry mouth NOS (R68.2)*
R06.6 Hiccough
Excludes1: *psychogenic hiccough (F45.8)*
R06.7 Sneezing
\+ **R06.8 Other abnormalities of breathing**
R06.81 Apnea, not elsewhere classified
Apnea NOS
Excludes1: *apnea (of) newborn (P28.4)*
sleep apnea (G47.3-)
sleep apnea of newborn (primary) (P28.3)
R06.82 Tachypnea, not elsewhere classified
Tachypnea NOS
Excludes1: *transitory tachypnea of newborn (P22.1)*
R06.83 Snoring
R06.89 Other abnormalities of breathing
Breath-holding (spells)
Sighing
R06.9 Unspecified abnormalities of breathing

R07 Pain in throat and chest
Excludes1: *epidemic myalgia (B33.0)*
Excludes2: *jaw pain R68.84*
pain in breast (N64.4)
R07.0 Pain in throat
Excludes1: *chronic sore throat (J31.2)*
sore throat (acute) NOS (J02.9)
Excludes2: *dysphagia (R13.1-)*
pain in neck (M54.2)
R07.1 Chest pain on breathing
Painful respiration
R07.2 Precordial pain
\+ **R07.8 Other chest pain**
R07.81 Pleurodynia
Pleurodynia NOS
Excludes1: *epidemic pleurodynia (B33.0)*
R07.82 Intercostal pain
R07.89 Other chest pain
Anterior chest-wall pain NOS
R07.9 Chest pain, unspecified

R09 Other symptoms and signs involving the circulatory and respiratory system
Excludes1: *acute respiratory distress syndrome (J80)*
respiratory arrest of newborn (P28.81)
respiratory distress syndrome of newborn (P22.0)
respiratory failure (J96.-)
respiratory failure of newborn (P28.5)
\+ **R09.0 Asphyxia and hypoxemia**
Excludes1: *asphyxia due to carbon monoxide (T58.-)*
asphyxia due to foreign body in respiratory tract (T17.-)
birth (intrauterine) asphyxia (P84)
hypercapnia (R06.4)
hyperventilation (R06.4)
traumatic asphyxia (T71-)
CC **R09.01 Asphyxia**
CC Exclusion see Appendix A PDX collection 1121
R09.02 Hypoxemia
R09.1 Pleurisy
Excludes1: *pleurisy with effusion (J90)*
MCC **R09.2 Respiratory arrest**
Cardiorespiratory failure
Excludes1: *cardiac arrest (I46.-)*
respiratory arrest of newborn (P28.81)
respiratory distress of newborn (P22.0)
respiratory failure (J96.-)
respiratory failure of newborn (P28.5)
respiratory insufficiency (R06.89)
respiratory insufficiency of newborn (P28.5)
MCC Exclusion see Appendix A PDX collection 1121
R09.3 Abnormal sputum
Abnormal amount of sputum
Abnormal color of sputum
Abnormal odor of sputum
Excessive sputum
Excludes1: *blood-stained sputum (R04.2)*
\+ **R09.8 Other specified symptoms and signs involving the circulatory and respiratory systems**
R09.81 Nasal congestion
R09.82 Postnasal drip

R09.89 Other specified symptoms and signs involving the circulatory and respiratory systems
Bruit (arterial)
Abnormal chest percussion
Feeling of foreign body in throat
Friction sounds in chest
Chest tympany
Choking sensation
Rales
Weak pulse
Excludes2: *foreign body in throat (T17.2-)*
wheezing (R06.2)

Symptoms and signs involving the digestive system and abdomen (R10-R19)

Excludes1: *congenital or infantile pylorospasm (Q40.0)*
gastrointestinal hemorrhage (K92.0-K92.2)
intestinal obstruction (K56.-)
newborn gastrointestinal hemorrhage (P54.0-P54.3)
newborn intestinal obstruction (P76.-)
pylorospasm (K31.3)
signs and symptoms involving the urinary system (R30-R39)
symptoms referable to female genital organs (N94.-)
symptoms referable to male genital organs male (N48-N50)

R10 Abdominal and pelvic pain
Excludes1: *renal colic (N23)*
Excludes2: *dorsalgia (M54.-)*
flatulence and related conditions (R14.-)

R10.0 Acute abdomen
Severe abdominal pain (generalized) (with abdominal rigidity)
Excludes1: *abdominal rigidity NOS (R19.3)*
generalized abdominal pain NOS (R10.84)
localized abdominal pain (R10.1-R10.3-)

\+ **R10.1 Pain localized to upper abdomen**
R10.10 Upper abdominal pain, unspecified
R10.11 Right upper quadrant pain
R10.12 Left upper quadrant pain
R10.13 Epigastric pain
Dyspepsia
Excludes1: *functional dyspepsia (K30)*

R10.2 Pelvic and perineal pain
Excludes1: *vulvodynia (N94.81)*

\+ **R10.3 Pain localized to other parts of lower abdomen**
R10.30 Lower abdominal pain, unspecified
R10.31 Right lower quadrant pain
R10.32 Left lower quadrant pain
R10.33 Periumbilical pain

\+ **R10.8 Other abdominal pain**
\+ **R10.81 Abdominal tenderness**
Abdominal tenderness NOS
R10.811 Right upper quadrant abdominal tenderness
R10.812 Left upper quadrant abdominal tenderness
R10.813 Right lower quadrant abdominal tenderness
R10.814 Left lower quadrant abdominal tenderness
R10.815 Periumbilic abdominal tenderness
R10.816 Epigastric abdominal tenderness
R10.817 Generalized abdominal tenderness
R10.819 Abdominal tenderness, unspecified site

\+ **R10.82 Rebound abdominal tenderness**
R10.821 Right upper quadrant rebound abdominal tenderness
R10.822 Left upper quadrant rebound abdominal tenderness
R10.823 Right lower quadrant rebound abdominal tenderness
R10.824 Left lower quadrant rebound abdominal tenderness
R10.825 Periumbilic rebound abdominal tenderness
R10.826 Epigastric rebound abdominal tenderness
R10.827 Generalized rebound abdominal tenderness
R10.829 Rebound abdominal tenderness, unspecified site

• **R10.83 Colic**
Colic NOS
Infantile colic
Excludes1: *colic in adult and child over 12 months old (R10.84)*

R10.84 Generalized abdominal pain
Excludes1: *generalized abdominal pain associated acute abdomen (R10.0)*

R10.9 Unspecified abdominal pain

R11 Nausea and vomiting
Excludes1: *cyclical vomiting associated with migraine (G43.A-)*
excessive vomiting in pregnancy (O21.-)
hematemesis (K92.0)
neonatal hematemesis (P54.0)
newborn vomiting (P92.0-)
psychogenic vomiting (F50.8)
vomiting associated with bulimia nervosa (F50.2)
vomiting following gastrointestinal surgery (K91.0)

R11.0 Nausea
Nausea NOS
Nausea without vomiting

\+ **R11.1 Vomiting**
R11.10 Vomiting, unspecified
Vomiting NOS
R11.11 Vomiting without nausea
R11.12 Projectile vomiting
R11.13 Vomiting of fecal matter
R11.14 Bilious vomiting
Bilious emesis

R11.2 Nausea with vomiting, unspecified
Persistent nausea with vomiting NOS

R12 Heartburn
Excludes1: *dyspepsia NOS (R10.13)*
functional dyspepsia (K30)
Valid 3-character code, no further characters required

R13 Aphagia and dysphagia
R13.0 Aphagia
Inability to swallow
Excludes1: *psychogenic aphagia (F50.9)*

\+ **R13.1 Dysphagia**
Code first if applicable, dysphagia following cerebrovascular disease (I69. with final characters -91)
Excludes1: *psychogenic dysphagia (F45.8)*
R13.10 Dysphagia, unspecified
Difficulty in swallowing NOS
R13.11 Dysphagia, oral phase
R13.12 Dysphagia, oropharyngeal phase
R13.13 Dysphagia, pharyngeal phase
R13.14 Dysphagia, pharyngoesophageal phase
R13.19 Other dysphagia
Cervical dysphagia
Neurogenic dysphagia

R14 Flatulence and related conditions
Excludes1: *psychogenic aerophagy (F45.8)*
R14.0 Abdominal distension (gaseous)
Bloating
Tympanites (abdominal) (intestinal)
R14.1 Gas pain
R14.2 Eructation
R14.3 Flatulence

R15 Fecal incontinence
Includes: encopresis NOS
Excludes1: *fecal incontinence of nonorganic origin (F98.1)*
R15.0 Incomplete defecation
Excludes1: *constipation (K59.0-)*
fecal impaction (K56.41)
R15.1 Fecal smearing
Fecal soiling
R15.2 Fecal urgency
R15.9 Full incontinence of feces
Fecal incontinence NOS

R16 Hepatomegaly and splenomegaly, not elsewhere classified
R16.0 Hepatomegaly, not elsewhere classified
Hepatomegaly NOS
R16.1 Splenomegaly, not elsewhere classified
Splenomegaly NOS
R16.2 Hepatomegaly with splenomegaly, not elsewhere classified
Hepatosplenomegaly NOS

R17 Unspecified jaundice

Excludes1: *neonatal jaundice (P55, P57-P59)*
CC Exclusion see Appendix A PDX collection 1122
Valid 3-character code, no further characters required

R18 Ascites

Includes: fluid in peritoneal cavity
Excludes1: *ascites in alcoholic cirrhosis (K70.31)*
ascites in alcoholic hepatitis (K70.11)
ascites in toxic liver disease with chronic active hepatitis (K71.51)
CC Exclusion see Appendix A PDX collection 1123

CC **R18.0 Malignant ascites**
Code first malignancy, such as:
malignant neoplasm of ovary (C56.-)
secondary malignant neoplasm of retroperitoneum and peritoneum (C78.6)
CC Exclusion see Appendix A PDX collection 1123

CC **R18.8 Other ascites**
Ascites NOS
Peritoneal effusion (chronic)
CC Exclusion see Appendix A PDX collection 1123

R19 Other symptoms and signs involving the digestive system and abdomen

Excludes1: *acute abdomen (R10.0)*

\+ **R19.0 Intra-abdominal and pelvic swelling, mass and lump**
Excludes1: *abdominal distension (gaseous) (R14.-)*
ascites (R18.-)
R19.00 Intra-abdominal and pelvic swelling, mass and lump, unspecified site
R19.01 Right upper quadrant abdominal swelling, mass and lump
R19.02 Left upper quadrant abdominal swelling, mass and lump
R19.03 Right lower quadrant abdominal swelling, mass and lump
R19.04 Left lower quadrant abdominal swelling, mass and lump
R19.05 Periumbilic swelling, mass or lump
Diffuse or generalized umbilical swelling or mass
R19.06 Epigastric swelling, mass or lump
R19.07 Generalized intra-abdominal and pelvic swelling, mass and lump
Diffuse or generalized intra-abdominal swelling or mass NOS
Diffuse or generalized pelvic swelling or mass NOS
R19.09 Other intra-abdominal and pelvic swelling, mass and lump

\+ **R19.1 Abnormal bowel sounds**
R19.11 Absent bowel sounds
R19.12 Hyperactive bowel sounds
R19.15 Other abnormal bowel sounds
Abnormal bowel sounds NOS

R19.2 Visible peristalsis
Hyperperistalsis

\+ **R19.3 Abdominal rigidity**
Excludes1: *abdominal rigidity with severe abdominal pain (R10.0)*
R19.30 Abdominal rigidity, unspecified site
R19.31 Right upper quadrant abdominal rigidity
R19.32 Left upper quadrant abdominal rigidity
R19.33 Right lower quadrant abdominal rigidity
R19.34 Left lower quadrant abdominal rigidity
R19.35 Periumbilic abdominal rigidity
R19.36 Epigastric abdominal rigidity
R19.37 Generalized abdominal rigidity

R19.4 Change in bowel habit
Excludes1: *constipation (K59.0-)*
functional diarrhea (K59.1)

R19.5 Other fecal abnormalities
Abnormal stool color
Bulky stools
Mucus in stools
Occult blood in feces
Occult blood in stools
Excludes1: *melena (K92.1)*
neonatal melena (P54.1)

R19.6 Halitosis

R19.7 Diarrhea, unspecified
Diarrhea NOS
Excludes1: *functional diarrhea (K59.1)*
neonatal diarrhea (P78.3)
psychogenic diarrhea (F45.8)

R19.8 Other specified symptoms and signs involving the digestive system and abdomen

Symptoms and signs involving the skin and subcutaneous tissue (R20-R23)

Excludes2: *symptoms relating to breast (N64.4-N64.5)*

R20 Disturbances of skin sensation

Excludes1: *dissociative anesthesia and sensory loss (F44.6)*
psychogenic disturbances (F45.8)
R20.0 Anesthesia of skin
R20.1 Hypoesthesia of skin
R20.2 Paresthesia of skin
Formication
Pins and needles
Tingling skin
Excludes1: *acroparesthesia (I73.8)*
R20.3 Hyperesthesia
R20.8 Other disturbances of skin sensation
R20.9 Unspecified disturbances of skin sensation

R21 Rash and other nonspecific skin eruption

Includes: rash NOS
Excludes1: *specified type of rash- code to condition vesicular eruption (R23.8)*
Valid 3-character code, no further characters required

R22 Localized swelling, mass and lump of skin and subcutaneous tissue

Includes: subcutaneous nodules (localized)(superficial)
Excludes1: *abnormal findings on diagnostic imaging (R90-R93)*
edema (R60.-)
enlarged lymph nodes (R59.-)
localized adiposity (E65)
swelling of joint (M25.4-)
R22.0 Localized swelling, mass and lump, head
R22.1 Localized swelling, mass and lump, neck
R22.2 Localized swelling, mass and lump, trunk
Excludes1: *intra-abdominal or pelvic mass and lump (R19.0-)*
intra-abdominal or pelvic swelling (R19.0-)
Excludes2: *breast mass and lump (N63)*

\+ **R22.3 Localized swelling, mass and lump, upper limb**
R22.30 Localized swelling, mass and lump, unspecified upper limb
R22.31 Localized swelling, mass and lump, right upper limb
R22.32 Localized swelling, mass and lump, left upper limb
R22.33 Localized swelling, mass and lump, upper limb, bilateral

\+ **R22.4 Localized swelling, mass and lump, lower limb**
R22.40 Localized swelling, mass and lump, unspecified lower limb
R22.41 Localized swelling, mass and lump, right lower limb
R22.42 Localized swelling, mass and lump, left lower limb
R22.43 Localized swelling, mass and lump, lower limb, bilateral

R22.9 Localized swelling, mass and lump, unspecified

R23 Other skin changes

R23.0 Cyanosis
Excludes1: *acrocyanosis (I73.8)*
cyanotic attacks of newborn (P28.2)
R23.1 Pallor
Clammy skin
R23.2 Flushing
Excessive blushing
Code first, if applicable, menopausal and female climacteric states (N95.1)
R23.3 Spontaneous ecchymoses
Petechiae
Excludes1: *ecchymoses of newborn (P54.5)*
purpura (D69.-)
R23.4 Changes in skin texture
Desquamation of skin
Induration of skin
Scaling of skin
Excludes1: *epidermal thickening NOS (L85.9)*
R23.8 Other skin changes
R23.9 Unspecified skin changes

Symptoms and signs involving the nervous and musculoskeletal systems (R25-R29)

R25 Abnormal involuntary movements

Excludes1: *specific movement disorders (G20-G26)*
stereotyped movement disorders (F98.4)
tic disorders (F95.-)

R25.0 Abnormal head movements
R25.1 Tremor, unspecified
Excludes1: *chorea NOS (G25.5)*
essential tremor (G25.0)
hysterical tremor (F44.4)
intention tremor (G25.2)
R25.2 Cramp and spasm
Excludes2: *carpopedal spasm (R29.0)*
charley-horse (M62.831)
infantile spasms (G40.4-)
muscle spasm of back (M62.830)
muscle spasm of calf (M62.831)
R25.3 Fasciculation
Twitching NOS
R25.8 Other abnormal involuntary movements
R25.9 Unspecified abnormal involuntary movements

R26 Abnormalities of gait and mobility

Excludes1: *ataxia NOS (R27.0)*
hereditary ataxia (G11.-)
locomotor (syphilitic) ataxia (A52.11)
immobility syndrome (paraplegic) (M62.3)

R26.0 Ataxic gait
Staggering gait
R26.1 Paralytic gait
Spastic gait
R26.2 Difficulty in walking, not elsewhere classified
Excludes1: *falling (R29.6)*
unsteadiness on feet (R26.81)
R26.8 Other abnormalities of gait and mobility
R26.81 Unsteadiness on feet
R26.89 Other abnormalities of gait and mobility
R26.9 Unspecified abnormalities of gait and mobility

R27 Other lack of coordination

Excludes1: *ataxic gait (R26.0)*
hereditary ataxia (G11.-)
vertigo NOS (R42)

R27.0 Ataxia, unspecified
Excludes1: *ataxia following cerebrovascular disease (I69. with final characters -93)*
R27.8 Other lack of coordination
R27.9 Unspecified lack of coordination

R29 Other symptoms and signs involving the nervous and musculoskeletal systems

CC **R29.0 Tetany**
Carpopedal spasm
Excludes1: *hysterical tetany (F44.5)*
neonatal tetany (P71.3)
parathyroid tetany (E20.9)
post-thyroidectomy tetany (E89.2)
CC Exclusion see Appendix A PDX collection 1124
CC **R29.1 Meningismus**
CC Exclusion see Appendix A PDX collection 1125
R29.2 Abnormal reflex
Excludes2: *abnormal pupillary reflex (H57.0)*
hyperactive gag reflex (J39.2)
vasovagal reaction or syncope (R55)
R29.3 Abnormal posture
R29.4 Clicking hip
Excludes1: *congenital deformities of hip (Q65.-)*
CC **R29.5 Transient paralysis**
Code first any associated spinal cord injury (S14.0, S14.1-, S24.0, S24.1-, S34.0-, S34.1-)
Excludes1: *transient ischemic attack (G45.9)*
CC Exclusion see Appendix A PDX collection 1126
R29.6 Repeated falls
Falling
Tendency to fall
Excludes2: *at risk for falling (Z91.81)*
history of falling (Z91.81)
Review coding guideline C.18.d

\+ **R29.8 Other symptoms and signs involving the nervous and musculoskeletal systems**
\+ **R29.81 Other symptoms and signs involving the nervous system**
R29.810 Facial weakness
Facial droop
Excludes1: *Bell's palsy (G51.0)*
facial weakness following cerebrovascular disease (I69. with final characters -92)
R29.818 Other symptoms and signs involving the nervous system
\+ **R29.89 Other symptoms and signs involving the musculoskeletal system**
Excludes2: *pain in limb (M79.6-)*
R29.890 Loss of height
Excludes1: *osteoporosis (M80-M81)*
R29.891 Ocular torticollis
Excludes1: *congenital (sternomastoid) torticollis Q68.0*
psychogenic torticollis (F45.8)
spasmodic torticollis (G24.3)
torticollis due to birth injury (P15.8)
torticollis NOS M43.6
R29.898 Other symptoms and signs involving the musculoskeletal system
\+ **R29.9 Unspecified symptoms and signs involving the nervous and musculoskeletal systems**
R29.90 Unspecified symptoms and signs involving the nervous system
R29.91 Unspecified symptoms and signs involving the musculoskeletal system

Symptoms and signs involving the genitourinary system (R30-R39)

R30 Pain associated with micturition

Excludes1: *psychogenic pain associated with micturition (F45.8)*

R30.0 Dysuria
Strangury
R30.1 Vesical tenesmus
R30.9 Painful micturition, unspecified
Painful urination NOS

R31 Hematuria

Excludes1: *hematuria included with underlying conditions, such as:*
acute cystitis with hematuria (N30.01)
recurrent and persistent hematuria in glomerular diseases (N02.-)

R31.0 Gross hematuria
R31.1 Benign essential microscopic hematuria
R31.2 Other microscopic hematuria
R31.9 Hematuria, unspecified

R32 Unspecified urinary incontinence

Enuresis NOS
Excludes1: *functional urinary incontinence (R39.81)*
nonorganic enuresis (F98.0)
stress incontinence and other specified urinary incontinence (N39.3-N39.4-)
urinary incontinence associated with cognitive impairment (R39.81)
Valid 3-character code, no further characters required

R33 Retention of urine

Excludes1: *psychogenic retention of urine (F45.8)*

R33.0 Drug induced retention of urine
Use additional code for adverse effect, if applicable, to identify drug (T36-T50 with fifth or sixth character 5)
R33.8 Other retention of urine
Code first if applicable, any causal condition, such as:
enlarged prostate (N40.1)
R33.9 Retention of urine, unspecified

R34 Anuria and oliguria

Excludes1: *anuria and oliguria complicating abortion or ectopic or molar pregnancy (O00-O07, O08.4)*
anuria and oliguria complicating pregnancy (O26.83-)
anuria and oliguria complicating the puerperium (O90.4)
Valid 3-character code, no further characters required

R35 Polyuria

Code first if applicable, any causal condition, such as:
enlarged prostate (N40.1)

Excludes1: *psychogenic polyuria (F45.8)*

R35.0 Frequency of micturition

R35.1 Nocturia

R35.8 Other polyuria

Polyuria NOS

R36 Urethral discharge

R36.0 Urethral discharge without blood

♂ **R36.1 Hematospermia**

R36.9 Urethral discharge, unspecified

Penile discharge NOS
Urethrorrhea

R37 Sexual dysfunction, unspecified

Valid 3-character code, no further characters required

R39 Other and unspecified symptoms and signs involving the genitourinary system

CC **R39.0 Extravasation of urine**

CC Exclusion see Appendix A PDX collection 1127

+ **R39.1 Other difficulties with micturition**

Code first if applicable, any causal condition, such as:
enlarged prostate (N40.1)

R39.11 Hesitancy of micturition

R39.12 Poor urinary stream

Weak urinary steam

R39.13 Splitting of urinary stream

R39.14 Feeling of incomplete bladder emptying

R39.15 Urgency of urination

Excludes1: *urge incontinence (N39.41, N39.46)*

R39.16 Straining to void

R39.19 Other difficulties with micturition

R39.2 Extrarenal uremia

Prerenal uremia

Excludes1: *uremia NOS (N19)*

+ **R39.8 Other symptoms and signs involving the genitourinary system**

R39.81 Functional urinary incontinence

Urinary incontinence due to cognitive impairment, or severe physical disability or immobility

Excludes1: *stress incontinence and other specified urinary incontinence (N39.3-N39.4-)*
urinary incontinence NOS (R32)

R39.89 Other symptoms and signs involving the genitourinary system

R39.9 Unspecified symptoms and signs involving the genitourinary system

mptoms and signs involving cognition, perception, emotional ate and behavior (R40-R46)

cludes1: *symptoms and signs constituting part of a pattern of mental disorder (F01-F99)*

R40 Somnolence, stupor and coma

Excludes1: *neonatal coma (P91.5)*
somnolence, stupor and coma in diabetes (E08-E13)
somnolence, stupor and coma in hepatic failure (K72.-)
somnolence, stupor and coma in hypoglycemia (nondiabetic) (E15)

R40.0 Somnolence

Drowsiness

Excludes1: *coma (R40.2-)*

R40.1 Stupor

Catatonic stupor
Semicoma

Excludes1: *catatonic schizophrenia (F20.2)*
coma (R40.2-)
depressive stupor (F31-F33)
dissociative stupor (F44.2)
manic stupor (F30.2)

+ **R40.2 Coma**

Code first any associated:
fracture of skull (S02.-)
intracranial injury (S06.-)

NOTE One code from subcategories R40.21-R40.23 is required to complete the coma scale

Review coding guideline C.18.e

AHA CC: 1Q, 2014, 19-20

MCC X+7th **R40.20 Unspecified coma**

Coma NOS
Unconsciousness NOS

MCC Exclusion see Appendix A PDX collection 0515

+ **R40.21 Coma scale, eyes open**

The appropriate 7th character is to be added to each code from subcategory R40.21-:
0 unspecified time
1 in the field [EMT or ambulance]
2 at arrival to emergency department
3 at hospital admission
4 24 hours or more after hospital admission

MCC +7th **R40.211 Coma scale, eyes open, never**

MCC Exclusion for all 7th characters see Appendix A PDX collection 0515

MCC +7th **R40.212 Coma scale, eyes open, to pain**

MCC Exclusion for all 7th characters see Appendix A PDX collection 0515

+7th **R40.213 Coma scale, eyes open, to sound**

+7th **R40.214 Coma scale, eyes open, spontaneous**

+ **R40.22 Coma scale, best verbal response**

The appropriate 7th character is to be added to each code from subcategory R40.22-:
0 unspecified time
1 in the field [EMT or ambulance]
2 at arrival to emergency department
3 at hospital admission
4 24 hours or more after hospital admission

MCC +7th **R40.221 Coma scale, best verbal response, none**

MCC Exclusion for all 7th characters see Appendix A PDX collection 0515

MCC +7th **R40.222 Coma scale, best verbal response, incomprehensible words**

MCC Exclusion for all 7th characters see Appendix A PDX collection 0515

+7th **R40.223 Coma scale, best verbal response, inappropriate words**

+7th **R40.224 Coma scale, best verbal response, confused conversation**

+7th **R40.225 Coma scale, best verbal response, oriented**

+ **R40.23 Coma scale, best motor response**

The appropriate 7th character is to be added to each code from subcategory R40.23-:
0 unspecified time
1 in the field [EMT or ambulance]
2 at arrival to emergency department
3 at hospital admission
4 24 hours or more after hospital admission

MCC +7th **R40.231 Coma scale, best motor response, none**

MCC Exclusion for all 7th characters see Appendix A PDX collection 0515

MCC +7th **R40.232 Coma scale, best motor response, extension**

MCC Exclusion for all 7th characters see Appendix A PDX collection 0515

+7th **R40.233 Coma scale, best motor response, abnormal**

MCC +7th **R40.234 Coma scale, best motor response, flexion withdrawal**

MCC Exclusion for all 7th characters see Appendix A PDX collection 0515

+7th **R40.235 Coma scale, best motor response, localizes pain**

+7th **R40.236 Coma scale, best motor response, obeys commands**

+ **R40.24 Glasgow coma scale, total score**

Use codes R40.21- through R40.23- only when the individual score(s) are documented

R40.241 Glasgow coma scale score 13-15

R40.242 Glasgow coma scale score 9-12

R40.243 Glasgow coma scale score 3-8

R40.244 Other coma, without documented Glasgow coma scale score, or with partial score reported

CC **R40.3 Persistent vegetative state**

CC Exclusion see Appendix A PDX collection 0515

R40.4 Transient alteration of awareness

R41 Other symptoms and signs involving cognitive functions and awareness

Excludes1: *dissociative [conversion] disorders (F44.-)*
mild cognitive impairment, so stated (G31.84)

R41.0 Disorientation, unspecified
Confusion NOS
Delirium NOS
R41.1 Anterograde amnesia
R41.2 Retrograde amnesia
R41.3 Other amnesia
Amnesia NOS
Memory loss NOS
Excludes1: *amnestic disorder due to known physiologic condition (F04)*
amnestic syndrome due to psychoactive substance use (F10-F19 with 5th character .6)
mild memory disturbance due to known physiological condition (F06.8)
transient global amnesia (G45.4)

CC **R41.4 Neurologic neglect syndrome**
Asomatognosia
Hemi-akinesia
Hemi-inattention
Hemispatial neglect
Left-sided neglect
Sensory neglect
Visuospatial neglect
Excludes1: *visuospatial deficit (R41.842)*
CC Exclusion see Appendix A PDX collection 1128

+ **R41.8 Other symptoms and signs involving cognitive functions and awareness**
• **R41.81 Age-related cognitive decline**
Senility NOS
R41.82 Altered mental status, unspecified
Change in mental status NOS
Excludes1: *altered level of consciousness (R40.-)*
altered mental status due to known condition - code to condition delirium NOS (R41.0)
AHA CC: 4Q, 2012, 98
R41.83 Borderline intellectual functioning
IQ level 71 to 84
Excludes1: *intellectual disabilities (F70-F79)*
+ **R41.84 Other specified cognitive deficit**
R41.840 Attention and concentration deficit
Excludes1: *attention-deficit hyperactivity disorders (F90.-)*
R41.841 Cognitive communication deficit
R41.842 Visuospatial deficit
R41.843 Psychomotor deficit
R41.844 Frontal lobe and executive function deficit
R41.89 Other symptoms and signs involving cognitive functions and awareness
Anosognosia
R41.9 Unspecified symptoms and signs involving cognitive functions and awareness

R42 Dizziness and giddiness

Light-headedness
Vertigo NOS
Excludes1: *vertiginous syndromes (H81.-)*
vertigo from infrasound (T75.23)
Valid 3-character code, no further characters required

R43 Disturbances of smell and taste

R43.0 Anosmia
R43.1 Parosmia
R43.2 Parageusia
R43.8 Other disturbances of smell and taste
Mixed disturbance of smell and taste
R43.9 Unspecified disturbances of smell and taste

R44 Other symptoms and signs involving general sensations and perceptions

Excludes1: *alcoholic hallucinations (F1.5)*
hallucinations in drug psychosis (F11-F19 with .5)
hallucinations in mood disorders with psychotic symptoms (F30.2, F31.5, F32.3, F33.3)
hallucinations in schizophrenia, schizotypal and delusional disorders (F20-F29)
Excludes2: *disturbances of skin sensation (R20.-)*

CC **R44.0 Auditory hallucinations**
CC Exclusion see Appendix A PDX collection 1129
R44.1 Visual hallucinations
CC **R44.2 Other hallucinations**
CC Exclusion see Appendix A PDX collection 1129
CC **R44.3 Hallucinations, unspecified**
CC Exclusion see Appendix A PDX collection 1129
R44.8 Other symptoms and signs involving general sensations and perceptions
R44.9 Unspecified symptoms and signs involving general sensations and perceptions

R45 Symptoms and signs involving emotional state

R45.0 Nervousness
Nervous tension
R45.1 Restlessness and agitation
R45.2 Unhappiness
R45.3 Demoralization and apathy
Excludes1: *anhedonia (R45.84)*
R45.4 Irritability and anger
R45.5 Hostility
R45.6 Violent behavior
R45.7 State of emotional shock and stress, unspecified
+ **R45.8 Other symptoms and signs involving emotional state**
R45.81 Low self-esteem
R45.82 Worries
R45.83 Excessive crying of child, adolescent or adult
Excludes1: *excessive crying of infant (baby) R68.11*
R45.84 Anhedonia
+ **R45.85 Homicidal and suicidal ideations**
Excludes1: *suicide attempt (T14.91)*
R45.850 Homicidal ideations
CC **R45.851 Suicidal ideations**
CC Exclusion see Appendix A PDX collection 1130
R45.86 Emotional lability
R45.87 Impulsiveness
R45.89 Other symptoms and signs involving emotional state

R46 Symptoms and signs involving appearance and behavior

Excludes1: *appearance and behavior in schizophrenia, schizotypal and delusional disorders (F20-F29)*
mental and behavioral disorders (F01-F99)

R46.0 Very low level of personal hygiene
R46.1 Bizarre personal appearance
R46.2 Strange and inexplicable behavior
R46.3 Overactivity
R46.4 Slowness and poor responsiveness
Excludes1: *stupor (R40.1)*
R46.5 Suspiciousness and marked evasiveness
R46.6 Undue concern and preoccupation with stressful events
R46.7 Verbosity and circumstantial detail obscuring reason for contact
+ **R46.8 Other symptoms and signs involving appearance and behavior**
R46.81 Obsessive-compulsive behavior
Excludes1: *obsessive-compulsive disorder (F42)*
R46.89 Other symptoms and signs involving appearance and behavior

Symptoms and signs involving speech and voice (R47-R49)

R47 Speech disturbances, not elsewhere classified

Excludes1: *autism (F84.0)*
cluttering (F80.81)
specific developmental disorders of speech and language (F80.-)
stuttering (F80.81)

+ **R47.0 Dysphasia and aphasia**
CC **R47.01 Aphasia**
Excludes1: *aphasia following cerebrovascular disease (I69. with final characters -20)*
progressive isolated aphasia (G31.01)
CC Exclusion see Appendix A PDX collection 1131
R47.02 Dysphasia
Excludes1: *dysphasia following cerebrovascular disease (I69. with final characters -21)*
R47.1 Dysarthria and anarthria
Excludes1: *dysarthria following cerebrovascular disease (I69. with final characters -22)*
+ **R47.8 Other speech disturbances**
Excludes1: *dysarthria following cerebrovascular disease (I69. with final characters -28)*
R47.81 Slurred speech

R47.82 Fluency disorder in conditions classified elsewhere
Stuttering in conditions classified elsewhere
Code first underlying disease or condition, such as:
Parkinson's disease (G20)
Excludes1: *adult onset fluency disorder (F98.5)*
childhood onset fluency disorder (F80.81)
fluency disorder (stuttering) following cerebrovascular disease (I69. with final characters -23)

R47.89 Other speech disturbances

R47.9 Unspecified speech disturbances

R48 Dyslexia and other symbolic dysfunctions, not elsewhere classified

Excludes1: *specific developmental disorders of scholastic skills (F81.-)*

R48.0 Dyslexia and alexia

R48.1 Agnosia
Astereognosia (astereognosis)
Autotopagnosia
Excludes1: *visual object agnosia (R48.3)*

R48.2 Apraxia
Excludes1: *apraxia following cerebrovascular disease (I69. with final characters -90)*

R48.3 Visual agnosia
Prosopagnosia
Simultanagnosia (asimultagnosia)

R48.8 Other symbolic dysfunctions
Acalculia
Agraphia

R48.9 Unspecified symbolic dysfunctions

R49 Voice and resonance disorders

Excludes1: *psychogenic voice and resonance disorders (F44.4)*

R49.0 Dysphonia
Hoarseness

R49.1 Aphonia
Loss of voice

\+ **R49.2 Hypernasality and hyponasality**

R49.21 Hypernasality

R49.22 Hyponasality

R49.8 Other voice and resonance disorders

R49.9 Unspecified voice and resonance disorder
Change in voice NOS
Resonance disorder NOS

eneral symptoms and signs (R50-R69)

R50 Fever of other and unknown origin

Excludes1: *chills without fever (R68.83)*
febrile convulsions (R56.0-)
fever of unknown origin during labor (O75.2)
fever of unknown origin in newborn (P81.9)
hypothermia due to illness (R68.0)
malignant hyperthermia due to anesthesia (T88.3)
puerperal pyrexia NOS (O86.4)

R50.2 Drug induced fever
Use additional code for adverse effect, if applicable, to identify drug (T36-T50 with fifth or sixth character 5)
Excludes1: *postvaccination (postimmunization) fever (R50.83)*

\+ **R50.8 Other specified fever**

R50.81 Fever presenting with conditions classified elsewhere
Code first underlying condition when associated fever is present, such as with:
leukemia (C91-C95)
neutropenia (D70.-)
sickle-cell disease (D57.-)

R50.82 Postprocedural fever
Excludes1: *postprocedural infection (T81.4)*
posttransfusion fever (R50.84)
postvaccination (postimmunization) fever (R50.83)

R50.83 Postvaccination fever
Postimmunization fever

R50.84 Febrile nonhemolytic transfusion reaction
FNHTR
Posttransfusion fever

R50.9 Fever, unspecified
Fever NOS
Fever of unknown origin [FUO]
Fever with chills
Fever with rigors
Hyperpyrexia NOS
Persistent fever
Pyrexia NOS

R51 Headache

Facial pain NOS
Excludes1: *atypical face pain (G50.1)*
migraine and other headache syndromes (G43-G44)
trigeminal neuralgia (G50.0)
Valid 3-character code, no further characters required

R52 Pain, unspecified

Acute pain NOS
Generalized pain NOS
Pain NOS
Excludes1: *acute and chronic pain, not elsewhere classified (G89.-)*
localized pain, unspecified type - code to pain by site, such as:
abdomen pain (R10.-)
back pain (M54.9)
breast pain (N64.4)
chest pain (R07.1-R07.9)
ear pain (H92.0-)
eye pain (H57.1)
headache (R51)
joint pain (M25.5-)
limb pain (M79.6-)
lumbar region pain (M54.5)
pelvic and perineal pain (R10.2)
shoulder pain (M25.51-)
spine pain (M54.-)
throat pain (R07.0)
tongue pain (K14.6)
tooth pain (K08.8)
renal colic (N23)
pain disorders exclusively related to psychological factors (F45.41)
Valid 3-character code, no further characters required

R53 Malaise and fatigue

R53.0 Neoplastic (malignant) related fatigue
Code first associated neoplasm

R53.1 Weakness
Asthenia NOS
Excludes1: *age-related weakness (R54)*
muscle weakness (M62.8-)
senile asthenia (R54)

MCC **R53.2 Functional quadriplegia**
Complete immobility due to severe physical disability or frailty
Excludes1: *frailty NOS (R54)*
hysterical paralysis (F44.4)
immobility syndrome (M62.3)
neurologic quadriplegia (G82.5-)
quadriplegia (G82.50)
MCC Exclusion see Appendix A PDX collection 0595
Review coding guideline C.18.f

\+ **R53.8 Other malaise and fatigue**
Excludes1: *combat exhaustion and fatigue (F43.0)*
congenital debility (P96.9)
exhaustion and fatigue due to depressive episode (F32.-)
exhaustion and fatigue due to excessive exertion (T73.3)
exhaustion and fatigue due to exposure (T73.2)
exhaustion and fatigue due to heat (T67.-)
exhaustion and fatigue due to pregnancy (O26.8-)
exhaustion and fatigue due to recurrent depressive episode (F33)
exhaustion and fatigue due to senile debility (R54)

R53.81 Other malaise
Chronic debility
Debility NOS
General physical deterioration
Malaise NOS
Nervous debility
Excludes1: *age-related physical debility (R54)*

R53.82 Chronic fatigue, unspecified
Chronic fatigue syndrome NOS
Excludes1: *postviral fatigue syndrome (G93.3)*

R53.83 Other fatigue
Fatigue NOS
Lack of energy
Lethargy
Tiredness

• **R54 Age-related physical debility**
Frailty
Old age
Senescence
Senile asthenia
Senile debility
Excludes1: *age-related cognitive decline (R41.81)*
senile psychosis (F03)
senility NOS (R41.81)
Valid 3-character code, no further characters required

R55 Syncope and collapse
Blackout
Fainting
Vasovagal attack
Excludes1: *cardiogenic shock (R57.0)*
carotid sinus syncope (G90.01)
heat syncope (T67.1)
neurocirculatory asthenia (F45.8)
neurogenic orthostatic hypotension (G90.3)
orthostatic hypotension (I95.1)
postprocedural shock (T81.1-)
psychogenic syncope (F48.8)
shock NOS (R57.9)
shock complicating or following abortion or ectopic or molar pregnancy (O00-O07, O08.3)
shock complicating or following labor and delivery (O75.1)
Stokes-Adams attack (I45.9)
unconsciousness NOS (R40.2-)
Valid 3-character code, no further characters required

R56 Convulsions, not elsewhere classified
Excludes1: *dissociative convulsions and seizures (F44.5)*
epileptic convulsions and seizures (G40.-)
newborn convulsions and seizures (P90)
\+ **R56.0 Febrile convulsions**
CC **R56.00 Simple febrile convulsions**
Febrile convulsion NOS
Febrile seizure NOS
CC Exclusion see Appendix A PDX collection 1132
CC **R56.01 Complex febrile convulsions**
Atypical febrile seizure
Complex febrile seizure
Complicated febrile seizure
Excludes1: *status epilepticus (G40.901)*
CC Exclusion see Appendix A PDX collection 1132
CC **R56.1 Post traumatic seizures**
Excludes1: *post traumatic epilepsy (G40.-)*
CC Exclusion see Appendix A PDX collection 0582
R56.9 Unspecified convulsions
Convulsion disorder
Fit NOS
Recurrent convulsions
Seizure(s) (convulsive) NOS

R57 Shock, not elsewhere classified
Excludes1: *anaphylactic shock NOS (T78.2)*
anaphylactic reaction or shock due to adverse food reaction (T78.0-)
anaphylactic shock due to adverse effect of correct drug or medicament properly administered (T88.6)
anaphylactic shock due to serum (T80.5-)
anesthetic shock (T88.3)
electric shock (T75.4)
obstetric shock (O75.1)
postprocedural shock (T81.1-)
psychic shock (F43.0)
septic shock (R65.21)
shock complicating or following ectopic or molar pregnancy (O00-O07, O08.3)
shock due to lightning (T75.01)
traumatic shock (T79.4)
toxic shock syndrome (A48.3)
MCC **R57.0 Cardiogenic shock**
MCC Exclusion see Appendix A PDX collection 1133
MCC **R57.1 Hypovolemic shock**
MCC Exclusion see Appendix A PDX collection 1133
MCC **R57.8 Other shock**
MCC Exclusion see Appendix A PDX collection 1133
CC **R57.9 Shock, unspecified**
Failure of peripheral circulation NOS
CC Exclusion see Appendix A PDX collection 1133

R58 Hemorrhage, not elsewhere classified
Hemorrhage NOS
Excludes1: *hemorrhage included with underlying conditions, such as:*
acute duodenal ulcer with hemorrhage (K26.0)
acute gastritis with bleeding (K29.01)
ulcerative enterocolitis with rectal bleeding (K51.01)
Valid 3-character code, no further characters required

R59 Enlarged lymph nodes
Includes: swollen glands
Excludes1: *lymphadenitis NOS (I88.9)*
acute lymphadenitis (L04.-)
chronic lymphadenitis (I88.1)
mesenteric (acute) (chronic) lymphadenitis (I88.0)
R59.0 Localized enlarged lymph nodes
R59.1 Generalized enlarged lymph nodes
Lymphadenopathy NOS
R59.9 Enlarged lymph nodes, unspecified

R60 Edema, not elsewhere classified
Excludes1: *angioneurotic edema (T78.3)*
ascites (R18.-)
cerebral edema (G93.6)
cerebral edema due to birth injury (P11.0)
edema of larynx (J38.4)
edema of nasopharynx (J39.2)
edema of pharynx (J39.2)
gestational edema (O12.0-)
hereditary edema (Q82.0)
hydrops fetalis NOS (P83.2)
hydrothorax (J94.8)
nutritional edema (E40-E46)
hydrops fetalis NOS (P83.2)
newborn edema (P83.3)
pulmonary edema (J81.-)
R60.0 Localized edema
R60.1 Generalized edema
R60.9 Edema, unspecified
Fluid retention NOS

R61 Generalized hyperhidrosis
Excessive sweating
Night sweats
Secondary hyperhidrosis
Code first if applicable, menopausal and female climacteric states (N95.1
Excludes1: *focal (primary) (secondary) hyperhidrosis (L74.5-)*
Frey's syndrome (L74.52)
localized (primary) (secondary) hyperhidrosis (L74.5-)
Valid 3-character code, no further characters required

R62 Lack of expected normal physiological development in childhood an adults
Excludes1: *delayed puberty (E30.0)*
gonadal dysgenesis (Q99.1)
hypopituitarism (E23.0)
• **R62.0 Delayed milestone in childhood**
Delayed attainment of expected physiological developmental stage
Late talker
Late walker
\+ **R62.5 Other and unspecified lack of expected normal physiological development in childhood**
Excludes1: *HIV disease resulting in failure to thrive (B20)*
physical retardation due to malnutrition (E45)
• **R62.50 Unspecified lack of expected normal physiological development in childhood**
Infantilism NOS
• **R62.51 Failure to thrive (child)**
Failure to gain weight
Excludes1: *failure to thrive in child under 28 days ol (P92.6)*
• **R62.52 Short stature (child)**
Lack of growth
Physical retardation
Short stature NOS
Excludes1: *short stature due to endocrine disorder (E34.3)*
• **R62.59 Other lack of expected normal physiological development in childhood**
• **R62.7 Adult failure to thrive**

R63 Symptoms and signs concerning food and fluid intake
Excludes1: *bulimia NOS (F50.2)*
eating disorders of nonorganic origin (F50.-)
malnutrition (E40-E46)

R63.0 Anorexia
Loss of appetite
Excludes1: *anorexia nervosa (F50.0-)*
loss of appetite of nonorganic origin (F50.8)

R63.1 Polydipsia
Excessive thirst

R63.2 Polyphagia
Excessive eating
Hyperalimentation NOS

R63.3 Feeding difficulties
Feeding problem (elderly) (infant) NOS
Excludes1: *feeding problems of newborn (P92.-)*
infant feeding disorder of nonorganic origin (F98.2-)

R63.4 Abnormal weight loss

R63.5 Abnormal weight gain
Excludes1: *excessive weight gain in pregnancy (O26.0-)*
obesity (E66.-)

R63.6 Underweight
Use additional code to identify body mass index (BMI), if known (Z68.-)
Excludes1: *abnormal weight loss (R63.4)*
anorexia nervosa (F50.0-)
malnutrition (E40-E46)

R63.8 Other symptoms and signs concerning food and fluid intake

C **R64 Cachexia**
Wasting syndrome
Code first underlying condition, if known
Excludes1: *abnormal weight loss (R63.4)*
nutritional marasmus (E41)
CC Exclusion see Appendix A PDX collection 1134
Valid 3-character code, no further characters required

R65 Symptoms and signs specifically associated with systemic inflammation and infection

\+ **R65.1 Systemic inflammatory response syndrome (SIRS) of non-infectious origin**
Code first underlying condition, such as:
heatstroke (T67.0)
injury and trauma (S00-T88)
Excludes1: *sepsis- code to infection*
severe sepsis (R65.2)

CC **R65.10 Systemic inflammatory response syndrome (SIRS) of non-infectious origin without acute organ dysfunction**
Systemic inflammatory response syndrome (SIRS) NOS
CC Exclusion see Appendix A PDX collection 0071
Review coding guideline C.18.g

MCC **R65.11 Systemic inflammatory response syndrome (SIRS) of non-infectious origin with acute organ dysfunction**
Use additional code to identify specific acute organ dysfunction, such as:
acute kidney failure (N17.-)
acute respiratory failure (J96.0-)
critical illness myopathy (G72.81)
critical illness polyneuropathy (G62.81)
disseminated intravascular coagulopathy [DIC] (D65)
encephalopathy (metabolic) (septic) (G93.41)
hepatic failure (K72.0-)
MCC Exclusion see Appendix A PDX collection 0071
Review coding guideline C.18.g

\+ **R65.2 Severe sepsis**
Infection with associated acute organ dysfunction
Sepsis with acute organ dysfunction
Sepsis with multiple organ dysfunction
Systemic inflammatory response syndrome due to infectious process with acute organ dysfunction
Code first underlying infection, such as:
infection following a procedure (T81.4)
infections following infusion, transfusion and therapeutic injection (T80.2-)
puerperal sepsis (O85)
sepsis following complete or unspecified spontaneous abortion (O03.87)
sepsis following ectopic and molar pregnancy (O08.82)
sepsis following incomplete spontaneous abortion (O03.37)
sepsis following (induced) termination of pregnancy (O04.87)
sepsis NOS (A41.9)

Use additional code to identify specific acute organ dysfunction, such as:
acute kidney failure (N17.-)
acute respiratory failure (J96.0-)
critical illness myopathy (G72.81)
critical illness polyneuropathy (G62.81)
disseminated intravascular coagulopathy [DIC] (D65)
encephalopathy (metabolic) (septic) (G93.41)
hepatic failure (K72.0-)
Review coding guideline C.1.d

MCC **R65.20 Severe sepsis without septic shock**
Severe sepsis NOS
MCC Exclusion see Appendix A PDX collection 0071

MCC **R65.21 Severe sepsis with septic shock**
MCC Exclusion see Appendix A PDX collection 1133
Review coding guideline C.1.d.2

R68 Other general symptoms and signs

R68.0 Hypothermia, not associated with low environmental temperature
Excludes1: *hypothermia NOS (accidental) (T68)*
hypothermia due to anesthesia (T88.51)
hypothermia due to low environmental temperature (T68)
newborn hypothermia (P80.-)

\+ **R68.1 Nonspecific symptoms peculiar to infancy**
Excludes1: *colic, infantile (R10.83)*
neonatal cerebral irritability (P91.3)
teething syndrome (K00.7)

• **R68.11 Excessive crying of infant (baby)**
Excludes1: *excessive crying of child, adolescent, or adult (R45.83)*

• **R68.12 Fussy infant (baby)**
Irritable infant

• **R68.13 Apparent life threatening event in infant (ALTE)**
Apparent life threatening event in newborn
Code first confirmed diagnosis, if known

Use additional code(s) for associated signs and symptoms if no confirmed diagnosis established, or if signs and symptoms are not associated routinely with confirmed diagnosis, or provide additional information for cause of ALTE

• **R68.19 Other nonspecific symptoms peculiar to infancy**

R68.2 Dry mouth, unspecified
Excludes1: *dry mouth due to dehydration (E86.0)*
dry mouth due to sicca syndrome [Sjögren] (M35.0-)
salivary gland hyposecretion (K11.7)

R68.3 Clubbing of fingers
Clubbing of nails
Excludes1: *congenital clubfinger (Q68.1)*

\+ **R68.8 Other general symptoms and signs**

R68.81 Early satiety

• **R68.82 Decreased libido**
Decreased sexual desire

R68.83 Chills (without fever)
Chills NOS
Excludes1: *chills with fever (R50.9)*

R68.84 Jaw pain
Mandibular pain
Maxilla pain
Excludes1: *temporomandibular joint arthralgia (M26.62)*

R68.89 Other general symptoms and signs

R69 Illness, unspecified

Unknown and unspecified cases of morbidity
Valid 3-character code, no further characters required

Abnormal findings on examination of blood, without diagnosis (R70-R79)

Excludes1: *abnormalities (of)(on):*
abnormal findings on antenatal screening of mother (O28.-)
coagulation hemorrhagic disorders (D65-D68)
lipids (E78.-)
platelets and thrombocytes (D69.-)
white blood cells classified elsewhere (D70-D72)
diagnostic abnormal findings classified elsewhere - see Alphabetical Index
hemorrhagic and hematological disorders of newborn (P50-P61)

R70 Elevated erythrocyte sedimentation rate and abnormality of plasma viscosity

R70.0 Elevated erythrocyte sedimentation rate
R70.1 Abnormal plasma viscosity

R71 Abnormality of red blood cells

Excludes1: *anemias (D50-D64)*
anemia of premature infant (P61.2)
benign (familial) polycythemia (D75.0)
congenital anemias (P61.2-P61.4)
newborn anemia due to isoimmunization (P55.-)
polycythemia neonatorum (P61.1)
polycythemia NOS (D75.1)
polycythemia vera (D45)
secondary polycythemia (D75.1)

CC **R71.0 Precipitous drop in hematocrit**
Drop (precipitous) in hemoglobin
Drop in hematocrit
CC Exclusion see Appendix A PDX collection 1135

R71.8 Other abnormality of red blood cells
Abnormal red-cell morphology NOS
Abnormal red-cell volume NOS
Anisocytosis
Poikilocytosis

R73 Elevated blood glucose level

Excludes1: *diabetes mellitus (E08-E13)*
diabetes mellitus in pregnancy, childbirth and the puerperium (O24.-)
neonatal disorders (P70.0-P70.2)
postsurgical hypoinsulinemia (E89.1)

\+ **R73.0 Abnormal glucose**
Excludes1: *abnormal glucose in pregnancy (O99.81-)*
diabetes mellitus (E08-E13)
dysmetabolic syndrome X (E88.81)
gestational diabetes (O24.4-)
glycosuria (R81)
hypoglycemia (E16.2)

R73.01 Impaired fasting glucose
Elevated fasting glucose

R73.02 Impaired glucose tolerance (oral)
Elevated glucose tolerance

R73.09 Other abnormal glucose
Abnormal glucose NOS
Abnormal non-fasting glucose tolerance
Latent diabetes
Prediabetes

R73.9 Hyperglycemia, unspecified

R74 Abnormal serum enzyme levels

R74.0 Nonspecific elevation of levels of transaminase and lactic acid dehydrogenase [LDH]

R74.8 Abnormal levels of other serum enzymes
Abnormal level of acid phosphatase
Abnormal level of alkaline phosphatase
Abnormal level of amylase
Abnormal level of lipase [triacylglycerol lipase]

R74.9 Abnormal serum enzyme level, unspecified

R75 Inconclusive laboratory evidence of human immunodeficiency virus [HIV]

Nonconclusive HIV-test finding in infants
Excludes1: *asymptomatic human immunodeficiency virus [HIV] infection status (Z21)*
human immunodeficiency virus [HIV] disease (B20)
Review coding guidelines C.1.a.2.e and C.1.a.2.f
Valid 3-character code, no further characters required

R76 Other abnormal immunological findings in serum

R76.0 Raised antibody titer
Excludes1: *isoimmunization in pregnancy (O36.0-O36.1)*
isoimmunization affecting newborn (P55.-)

\+ **R76.1 Nonspecific reaction to test for tuberculosis**

R76.11 Nonspecific reaction to tuberculin skin test without active tuberculosis
Abnormal result of Mantoux test
PPD positive
Tuberculin (skin test) positive
Tuberculin (skin test) reactor
Excludes1: *nonspecific reaction to cell mediated immunity measurement of gamma interferon antigen response without active tuberculosis (R76.12)*

R76.12 Nonspecific reaction to cell mediated immunity measurement of gamma interferon antigen response without active tuberculosis
Nonspecific reaction to QuantiFERON-TB test (QFT) without active tuberculosis
Excludes1: *nonspecific reaction to tuberculin skin test without active tuberculosis (R76.11)*
positive tuberculin skin test (R76.11)

R76.8 Other specified abnormal immunological findings in serum
Raised level of immunoglobulins NOS

R76.9 Abnormal immunological finding in serum, unspecified

R77 Other abnormalities of plasma proteins

Excludes1: *disorders of plasma-protein metabolism (E88.0)*

R77.0 Abnormality of albumin
R77.1 Abnormality of globulin
Hyperglobulinemia NOS
R77.2 Abnormality of alphafetoprotein
R77.8 Other specified abnormalities of plasma proteins
R77.9 Abnormality of plasma protein, unspecified

R78 Findings of drugs and other substances, not normally found in blood

Use additional code to identify the any retained foreign body, if applicable (Z18.-)
Excludes1: *mental or behavioral disorders due to psychoactive substance use (F10-F19)*

R78.0 Finding of alcohol in blood
external cause code (Y90.-), for detail regarding alcohol level.
R78.1 Finding of opiate drug in blood
R78.2 Finding of cocaine in blood
R78.3 Finding of hallucinogen in blood
R78.4 Finding of other drugs of addictive potential in blood
R78.5 Finding of other psychotropic drug in blood
R78.6 Finding of steroid agent in blood

\+ **R78.7 Finding of abnormal level of heavy metals in blood**

R78.71 Abnormal lead level in blood
Excludes1: *lead poisoning (T56.0-)*

R78.79 Finding of abnormal level of heavy metals in blood

\+ **R78.8 Finding of other specified substances, not normally found in blood**

CC **R78.81 Bacteremia**
Excludes1: *sepsis-code to specified infection (A00-B99)*
CC Exclusion see Appendix A PDX collection 1136

R78.89 Finding of other specified substances, not normally found in blood
Finding of abnormal level of lithium in blood

R78.9 Finding of unspecified substance, not normally found in blood

R79 Other abnormal findings of blood chemistry
Use additional code to identify any retained foreign body, if applicable (Z18.-)
Excludes1: *abnormality of fluid, electrolyte or acid-base balance (E86-E87)*
asymptomatic hyperuricemia (E79.0)
hyperglycemia NOS (R73.9)
hypoglycemia NOS (E16.2)
neonatal hypoglycemia (P70.3-P70.4)
specific findings indicating disorder of amino-acid metabolism (E70-E72)
specific findings indicating disorder of carbohydrate metabolism (E73-E74)
specific findings indicating disorder of lipid metabolism (E75.-)

R79.0 Abnormal level of blood mineral
Abnormal blood level of cobalt
Abnormal blood level of copper
Abnormal blood level of iron
Abnormal blood level of magnesium
Abnormal blood level of mineral NEC
Abnormal blood level of zinc
Excludes1: *abnormal level of lithium (R78.89)*
disorders of mineral metabolism (E83.-)
neonatal hypomagnesemia (P71.2)
nutritional mineral deficiency (E58-E61)

R79.1 Abnormal coagulation profile
Abnormal or prolonged bleeding time
Abnormal or prolonged coagulation time
Abnormal or prolonged partial thromboplastin time [PTT]
Abnormal or prolonged prothrombin time [PT]
Excludes1: *coagulation defects (D68.-)*

\+ **R79.8 Other specified abnormal findings of blood chemistry**
R79.81 Abnormal blood-gas level
R79.82 Elevated C-reactive protein (CRP)
R79.89 Other specified abnormal findings of blood chemistry

R79.9 Abnormal finding of blood chemistry, unspecified

Abnormal findings on examination of urine, without diagnosis (R80-R82)

Excludes1: *abnormal findings on antenatal screening of mother (O28.-)*
diagnostic abnormal findings classified elsewhere - see Alphabetical Index
specific findings indicating disorder of amino-acid metabolism (E70-E72)
specific findings indicating disorder of carbohydrate metabolism (E73-E74)

R80 Proteinuria
Excludes1: *gestational proteinuria (O12.1-)*

R80.0 Isolated proteinuria
Idiopathic proteinuria
Excludes1: *isolated proteinuria with specific morphological lesion (N06.-)*

R80.1 Persistent proteinuria, unspecified
R80.2 Orthostatic proteinuria, unspecified
Postural proteinuria
R80.3 Bence Jones proteinuria
R80.8 Other proteinuria
R80.9 Proteinuria, unspecified
Albuminuria NOS

R81 Glycosuria
Excludes1: *renal glycosuria (E74.8)*
Valid 3-character code, no further characters required

R82 Other and unspecified abnormal findings in urine
Includes: chromoabnormalities in urine
Use additional code to identify any retained foreign body, if applicable (Z18.-)
Excludes2: *hematuria (R31.-)*

CC **R82.0 Chyluria**
Excludes1: *filarial chyluria (B74.-)*
CC Exclusion see Appendix A PDX collection 1137

CC **R82.1 Myoglobinuria**
CC Exclusion see Appendix A PDX collection 1138

R82.2 Biliuria

R82.3 Hemoglobinuria
Excludes1: *hemoglobinuria due to hemolysis from external causes NEC (D59.6)*
hemoglobinuria due to paroxysmal nocturnal [Marchiafava-Micheli] (D59.5)

R82.4 Acetonuria
Ketonuria

R82.5 Elevated urine levels of drugs, medicaments and biological substances
Elevated urine levels of catecholamines
Elevated urine levels of indoleacetic acid
Elevated urine levels of 17-ketosteroids
Elevated urine levels of steroids

R82.6 Abnormal urine levels of substances chiefly nonmedicinal as to source
Abnormal urine level of heavy metals

R82.7 Abnormal findings on microbiological examination of urine
Positive culture findings of urine
Excludes1: *colonization status (Z22.-)*

R82.8 Abnormal findings on cytological and histological examination of urine

\+ **R82.9 Other and unspecified abnormal findings in urine**
R82.90 Unspecified abnormal findings in urine
R82.91 Other chromoabnormalities of urine
Chromoconversion (dipstick)
Idiopathic dipstick converts positive for blood with no cellular forms in sediment
Excludes1: *hemoglobinuria (R82.3)*
myoglobinuria (R82.1)
R82.99 Other abnormal findings in urine
Cells and casts in urine
Crystalluria
Melanuria

Abnormal findings on examination of other body fluids, substances and tissues, without diagnosis (R83-R89)

Excludes1: *abnormal findings on antenatal screening of mother (O28.-)*
diagnostic abnormal findings classified elsewhere - see Alphabetical Index

Excludes2: *abnormal findings on examination of blood, without diagnosis (R70-R79)*
abnormal findings on examination of urine, without diagnosis (R80-R82)
abnormal tumor markers (R97.-)

R83 Abnormal findings in cerebrospinal fluid
R83.0 Abnormal level of enzymes in cerebrospinal fluid
R83.1 Abnormal level of hormones in cerebrospinal fluid
R83.2 Abnormal level of other drugs, medicaments and biological substances in cerebrospinal fluid
R83.3 Abnormal level of substances chiefly nonmedicinal as to source in cerebrospinal fluid
R83.4 Abnormal immunological findings in cerebrospinal fluid
R83.5 Abnormal microbiological findings in cerebrospinal fluid
Positive culture findings in cerebrospinal fluid
Excludes1: *colonization status (Z22.-)*
R83.6 Abnormal cytological findings in cerebrospinal fluid
R83.8 Other abnormal findings in cerebrospinal fluid
Abnormal chromosomal findings in cerebrospinal fluid
R83.9 Unspecified abnormal finding in cerebrospinal fluid

R84 Abnormal findings in specimens from respiratory organs and thorax
Includes: abnormal findings in bronchial washings
abnormal findings in nasal secretions
abnormal findings in pleural fluid
abnormal findings in sputum
abnormal findings in throat scrapings
Excludes1: *blood-stained sputum (R04.2)*

R84.0 Abnormal level of enzymes in specimens from respiratory organs and thorax
R84.1 Abnormal level of hormones in specimens from respiratory organs and thorax
R84.2 Abnormal level of other drugs, medicaments and biological substances in specimens from respiratory organs and thorax
R84.3 Abnormal level of substances chiefly nonmedicinal as to source in specimens from respiratory organs and thorax
R84.4 Abnormal immunological findings in specimens from respiratory organs and thorax

R84.5 Abnormal microbiological findings in specimens from respiratory organs and thorax
Positive culture findings in specimens from respiratory organs and thorax
Excludes1: *colonization status (Z22.-)*

R84.6 Abnormal cytological findings in specimens from respiratory organs and thorax

R84.7 Abnormal histological findings in specimens from respiratory organs and thorax

R84.8 Other abnormal findings in specimens from respiratory organs and thorax
Abnormal chromosomal findings in specimens from respiratory organs and thorax

R84.9 Unspecified abnormal finding in specimens from respiratory organs and thorax

R85 Abnormal findings in specimens from digestive organs and abdominal cavity

Includes: abnormal findings in peritoneal fluid
abnormal findings in saliva
Excludes1: *cloudy peritoneal dialysis effluent (R88.0)*
fecal abnormalities (R19.5)

R85.0 Abnormal level of enzymes in specimens from digestive organs and abdominal cavity

R85.1 Abnormal level of hormones in specimens from digestive organs and abdominal cavity

R85.2 Abnormal level of other drugs, medicaments and biological substances in specimens from digestive organs and abdominal cavity

R85.3 Abnormal level of substances chiefly nonmedicinal as to source in specimens from digestive organs and abdominal cavity

R85.4 Abnormal immunological findings in specimens from digestive organs and abdominal cavity

R85.5 Abnormal microbiological findings in specimens from digestive organs and abdominal cavity
Positive culture findings in specimens from digestive organs and abdominal cavity
Excludes1: *colonization status (Z22.-)*

\+ **R85.6 Abnormal cytological findings in specimens from digestive organs and abdominal cavity**

\+ **R85.61 Abnormal cytologic smear of anus**
Excludes1: *abnormal cytological findings in specimens from other digestive organs and abdominal cavity (R85.69)*
carcinoma in situ of anus (histologically confirmed) (D01.3)
anal intraepithelial neoplasia I [AIN I] (K62.82)
anal intraepithelial neoplasia II [AIN II] (K62.82)
anal intraepithelial neoplasia III [AIN III] (D01.3)
dysplasia (mild) (moderate) of anus (histologically confirmed) (K62.82)
severe dysplasia of anus (histologically confirmed) (D01.3)
Excludes2: *anal high risk human papillomavirus (HPV) DNA test positive (R85.81)*
anal low risk human papillomavirus (HPV) DNA test positive (R85.82)

R85.610 Atypical squamous cells of undetermined significance on cytologic smear of anus (ASC-US)

R85.611 Atypical squamous cells cannot exclude high grade squamous intraepithelial lesion on cytologic smear of anus (ASC-H)

R85.612 Low grade squamous intraepithelial lesion on cytologic smear of anus (LGSIL)

R85.613 High grade squamous intraepithelial lesion on cytologic smear of anus (HGSIL)

R85.614 Cytologic evidence of malignancy on smear of anus

R85.615 Unsatisfactory cytologic smear of anus
Inadequate sample of cytologic smear of anus

R85.616 Satisfactory anal smear but lacking transformation zone

R85.618 Other abnormal cytological findings on specimens from anus

R85.619 Unspecified abnormal cytological findings in specimens from anus
Abnormal anal cytology NOS
Atypical glandular cells of anus NOS

R85.69 Abnormal cytological findings in specimens from other digestive organs and abdominal cavity

R85.7 Abnormal histological findings in specimens from digestive organs and abdominal cavity

\+ **R85.8 Other abnormal findings in specimens from digestive organs and abdominal cavity**

R85.81 Anal high risk human papillomavirus (HPV) DNA test positive
Excludes1: *anogenital warts due to human papillomavirus (HPV) (A63.0)*
condyloma acuminatum (A63.0)

R85.82 Anal low risk human papillomavirus (HPV) DNA test positive
Use additional code for associated human papillomavirus (B97.7)

R85.89 Other abnormal findings in specimens from digestive organs and abdominal cavity
Abnormal chromosomal findings in specimens from digestive organs and abdominal cavity

R85.9 Unspecified abnormal finding in specimens from digestive organs and abdominal cavity

R86 Abnormal findings in specimens from male genital organs

Includes: abnormal findings in prostatic secretions
abnormal findings in semen, seminal fluid
abnormal spermatozoa
Excludes1: *azoospermia (N46.0-)*
oligospermia (N46.1-)

♂ **R86.0 Abnormal level of enzymes in specimens from male genital organs**

♂ **R86.1 Abnormal level of hormones in specimens from male genital organs**

♂ **R86.2 Abnormal level of other drugs, medicaments and biological substances in specimens from male genital organs**

♂ **R86.3 Abnormal level of substances chiefly nonmedicinal as to source in specimens from male genital organs**

♂ **R86.4 Abnormal immunological findings in specimens from male genital organs**

♂ **R86.5 Abnormal microbiological findings in specimens from male genital organs**
Positive culture findings in specimens from male genital organs
Excludes1: *colonization status (Z22.-)*

♂ **R86.6 Abnormal cytological findings in specimens from male genital organs**

♂ **R86.7 Abnormal histological findings in specimens from male genital organs**

♂ **R86.8 Other abnormal findings in specimens from male genital organs**
Abnormal chromosomal findings in specimens from male genital organs

♂ **R86.9 Unspecified abnormal finding in specimens from male genital organs**

R87 Abnormal findings in specimens from female genital organs

Includes: abnormal findings in secretion and smears from cervix uteri
abnormal findings in secretion and smears from vagina
abnormal findings in secretion and smears from vulva

♀ **R87.0 Abnormal level of enzymes in specimens from female genital organs**

♀ **R87.1 Abnormal level of hormones in specimens from female genital organs**

♀ **R87.2 Abnormal level of other drugs, medicaments and biological substances in specimens from female genital organs**

♀ **R87.3 Abnormal level of substances chiefly nonmedicinal as to source in specimens from female genital organs**

♀ **R87.4 Abnormal immunological findings in specimens from female genital organs**

♀ **R87.5 Abnormal microbiological findings in specimens from female genital organs**
Positive culture findings in specimens from female genital organs
Excludes1: *colonization status (Z22.-)*

+ **R87.6 Abnormal cytological findings in specimens from female genital organs**

+ **R87.61 Abnormal cytological findings in specimens from cervix uteri**

Excludes1: *abnormal cytological findings in specimens from other female genital organs (R87.69)*
abnormal cytological findings in specimens from vagina (R87.62-)
carcinoma in situ of cervix uteri (histologically confirmed) (D06.-)
cervical intraepithelial neoplasia I [CIN I] (N87.0)
cervical intraepithelial neoplasia II [CIN II] (N87.1)
cervical intraepithelial neoplasia III [CIN III] (D06.-)
dysplasia (mild) (moderate) of cervix uteri (histologically confirmed) (N87.-)
severe dysplasia of cervix uteri (histologically confirmed) (D06.-)

Excludes2: *cervical high risk human papillomavirus (HPV) DNA test positive (R87.810)*
cervical low risk human papillomavirus (HPV) DNA test positive (R87.820)

♀ **R87.610 Atypical squamous cells of undetermined significance on cytologic smear of cervix (ASC-US)**

♀ **R87.611 Atypical squamous cells cannot exclude high grade squamous intraepithelial lesion on cytologic smear of cervix (ASC-H)**

♀ **R87.612 Low grade squamous intraepithelial lesion on cytologic smear of cervix (LGSIL)**

♀ **R87.613 High grade squamous intraepithelial lesion on cytologic smear of cervix (HGSIL)**

♀ **R87.614 Cytologic evidence of malignancy on smear of cervix**

♀ **R87.615 Unsatisfactory cytologic smear of cervix**
Inadequate sample of cytologic smear of cervix

♀ **R87.616 Satisfactory cervical smear but lacking transformation zone**

♀ **R87.618 Other abnormal cytological findings on specimens from cervix uteri**

♀ **R87.619 Unspecified abnormal cytological findings in specimens from cervix uteri**
Abnormal cervical cytology NOS
Abnormal Papanicolaou smear of cervix NOS
Abnormal thin preparation smear of cervix NOS
Atypical endocervial cells of cervix NOS
Atypical endometrial cells of cervix NOS
Atypical glandular cells of cervix NOS

+ **R87.62 Abnormal cytological findings in specimens from vagina**
Use additional code to identify acquired absence of uterus and cervix, if applicable (Z90.71-)

Excludes1: *abnormal cytological findings in specimens from cervix uteri (R87.61-)*
abnormal cytological findings in specimens from other female genital organs (R87.69)
carcinoma in situ of vagina (histologically confirmed) (D07.2)
vaginal intraepithelial neoplasia I [VAIN I] (N89.0)
vaginal intraepithelial neoplasia II [VAIN II] (N89.1)
vaginal intraepithelial neoplasia III [VAIN III] (D07.2)
dysplasia (mild) (moderate) of vagina (histologically confirmed) (N89.-)
severe dysplasia of vagina (histologically confirmed) (D07.2)

Excludes2: *vaginal high risk human papillomavirus (HPV) DNA test positive (R87.811)*
vaginal low risk human papillomavirus (HPV) DNA test positive (R87.821)

♀ **R87.620 Atypical squamous cells of undetermined significance on cytologic smear of vagina (ASC-US)**

♀ **R87.621 Atypical squamous cells cannot exclude high grade squamous intraepithelial lesion on cytologic smear of vagina (ASC-H)**

♀ **R87.622 Low grade squamous intraepithelial lesion on cytologic smear of vagina (LGSIL)**

♀ **R87.623 High grade squamous intraepithelial lesion on cytologic smear of vagina (HGSIL)**

♀ **R87.624 Cytologic evidence of malignancy on smear of vagina**

♀ **R87.625 Unsatisfactory cytologic smear of vagina**
Inadequate sample of cytologic smear of vagina

♀ **R87.628 Other abnormal cytological findings on specimens from vagina**

♀ **R87.629 Unspecified abnormal cytological findings in specimens from vagina**
Abnormal Papanicolaou smear of vagina NOS
Abnormal thin preparation smear of vagina NOS
Abnormal vaginal cytology NOS
Atypical endocervical cells of vagina NOS
Atypical endometrial cells of vagina NOS
Atypical glandular cells of vagina NOS

♀ **R87.69 Abnormal cytological findings in specimens from other female genital organs**
Abnormal cytological findings in specimens from female genital organs NOS

Excludes1: *dysplasia of vulva (histologically confirmed) (N90.0-N90.3)*

♀ **R87.7 Abnormal histological findings in specimens from female genital organs**

Excludes1: *carcinoma in situ (histologically confirmed) of female genital organs (D06-D07.3)*
cervical intraepithelial neoplasia I [CIN I] (N87.0)
cervical intraepithelial neoplasia II [CIN II] (N87.1)
cervical intraepithelial neoplasia III [CIN III] (D06.-)
dysplasia (mild) (moderate) of cervix uteri (histologically confirmed) (N87.-)
dysplasia (mild) (moderate) of vagina (histologically confirmed) (N89.-)
vaginal intraepithelial neoplasia I [VAIN I] (N89.0)
vaginal intraepithelial neoplasia II [VAIN II] (N89.1)
vaginal intraepithelial neoplasia III [VAIN III] (D07.2)
severe dysplasia of cervix uteri (histologically confirmed) (D06.-)
severe dysplasia of vagina (histologically confirmed) (D07.2)

+ **R87.8 Other abnormal findings in specimens from female genital organs**

+ **R87.81 High risk human papillomavirus (HPV) DNA test positive from female genital organs**

Excludes1: *anogenital warts due to human papillomavirus (HPV) (A63.0)*
condyloma acuminatum (A63.0)

♀ **R87.810 Cervical high risk human papillomavirus (HPV) DNA test positive**

♀ **R87.811 Vaginal high risk human papillomavirus (HPV) DNA test positive**

+ **R87.82 Low risk human papillomavirus (HPV) DNA test positive from female genital organs**
Use additional code for associated human papillomavirus (B97.7)

♀ **R87.820 Cervical low risk human papillomavirus (HPV) DNA test positive**

♀ **R87.821 Vaginal low risk human papillomavirus (HPV) DNA test positive**

♀ **R87.89 Other abnormal findings in specimens from female genital organs**
Abnormal chromosomal findings in specimens from female genital organs

♀ **R87.9 Unspecified abnormal finding in specimens from female genital organs**

R88 Abnormal findings in other body fluids and substances

R88.0 Cloudy (hemodialysis) (peritoneal) dialysis effluent

R88.8 Abnormal findings in other body fluids and substances

R89 Abnormal findings in specimens from other organs, systems and tissues

Includes: abnormal findings in nipple discharge
abnormal findings in synovial fluid
abnormal findings in wound secretions

R89.0 Abnormal level of enzymes in specimens from other organs, systems and tissues

R89.1 Abnormal level of hormones in specimens from other organs, systems and tissues

R89.2 Abnormal level of other drugs, medicaments and biological substances in specimens from other organs, systems and tissues

R89.3 Abnormal level of substances chiefly nonmedicinal as to source in specimens from other organs, systems and tissues

R89.4 Abnormal immunological findings in specimens from other organs, systems and tissues

R89.5 Abnormal microbiological findings in specimens from other organs, systems and tissues
Positive culture findings in specimens from other organs, systems and tissues
Excludes1: *colonization status (Z22.-)*

R89.6 Abnormal cytological findings in specimens from other organs, systems and tissues

R89.7 Abnormal histological findings in specimens from other organs, systems and tissues

R89.8 Other abnormal findings in specimens from other organs, systems and tissues
Abnormal chromosomal findings in specimens from other organs, systems and tissues

R89.9 Unspecified abnormal finding in specimens from other organs, systems and tissues

Abnormal findings on diagnostic imaging and in function studies, without diagnosis (R90-R94)

Includes: nonspecific abnormal findings on diagnostic imaging by computerized axial tomography [CAT scan]
nonspecific abnormal findings on diagnostic imaging by magnetic resonance imaging [MRI][NMR]
nonspecific abnormal findings on diagnostic imaging by positron emission tomography [PET scan]
nonspecific abnormal findings on diagnostic imaging by thermography
nonspecific abnormal findings on diagnostic imaging by ultrasound [echogram]
nonspecific abnormal findings on diagnostic imaging by X-ray examination

Excludes1: *abnormal findings on antenatal screening of mother (O28.-)*
diagnostic abnormal findings classified elsewhere - see Alphabetical Index

R90 Abnormal findings on diagnostic imaging of central nervous system

R90.0 Intracranial space-occupying lesion found on diagnostic imaging of central nervous system

\+ **R90.8 Other abnormal findings on diagnostic imaging of central nervous system**

R90.81 Abnormal echoencephalogram

R90.82 White matter disease, unspecified

R90.89 Other abnormal findings on diagnostic imaging of central nervous system
Other cerebrovascular abnormality found on diagnostic imaging of central nervous system

R91 Abnormal findings on diagnostic imaging of lung

R91.1 Solitary pulmonary nodule
Coin lesion lung
Solitary pulmonary nodule, subsegmental branch of the bronchial tree

R91.8 Other nonspecific abnormal finding of lung field
Lung mass NOS found on diagnostic imaging of lung
Pulmonary infiltrate NOS
Shadow, lung

R92 Abnormal and inconclusive findings on diagnostic imaging of breast

R92.0 Mammographic microcalcification found on diagnostic imaging of breast
Excludes2: *mammographic calcification (calculus) found on diagnostic imaging of breast (R92.1)*

R92.1 Mammographic calcification found on diagnostic imaging of breast
Mammographic calculus found on diagnostic imaging of breast

R92.2 Inconclusive mammogram
Dense breasts NOS
Inconclusive mammogram NEC
Inconclusive mammography due to dense breasts
Inconclusive mammography NEC

R92.8 Other abnormal and inconclusive findings on diagnostic imag of breast

R93 Abnormal findings on diagnostic imaging of other body structures

R93.0 Abnormal findings on diagnostic imaging of skull and head, n elsewhere classified
Excludes1: *intracranial space-occupying lesion found on diagnostic imaging (R90.0)*

R93.1 Abnormal findings on diagnostic imaging of heart and corona circulation
Abnormal echocardiogram NOS
Abnormal heart shadow

R93.2 Abnormal findings on diagnostic imaging of liver and biliary tract
Nonvisualization of gallbladder

R93.3 Abnormal findings on diagnostic imaging of other parts of digestive tract

R93.4 Abnormal findings on diagnostic imaging of urinary organs
Filling defect of bladder found on diagnostic imaging
Filling defect of kidney found on diagnostic imaging
Filling defect of ureter found on diagnostic imaging
Excludes1: *hypertrophy of kidney (N28.81)*

R93.5 Abnormal findings on diagnostic imaging of other abdominal regions, including retroperitoneum

R93.6 Abnormal findings on diagnostic imaging of limbs
Excludes2: *abnormal finding in skin and subcutaneous tissue (R93.8)*

R93.7 Abnormal findings on diagnostic imaging of other parts of musculoskeletal system
Excludes2: *abnormal findings on diagnostic imaging of skull (R93.0)*

R93.8 Abnormal findings on diagnostic imaging of other specified bo structures
Abnormal finding by radioisotope localization of placenta
Abnormal radiological finding in skin and subcutaneous tissue
Mediastinal shift

R93.9 Diagnostic imaging inconclusive due to excess body fat of pati

R94 Abnormal results of function studies

Includes: abnormal results of radionuclide [radioisotope] uptake studi
abnormal results of scintigraphy

\+ **R94.0 Abnormal results of function studies of central nervous syste**

R94.01 Abnormal electroencephalogram [EEG]

R94.02 Abnormal brain scan

R94.09 Abnormal results of other function studies of centra nervous system

\+ **R94.1 Abnormal results of function studies of peripheral nervous system and special senses**

\+ **R94.11 Abnormal results of function studies of eye**

R94.110 Abnormal electro-oculogram [EOG]

R94.111 Abnormal electroretinogram [ERG]
Abnormal retinal function study

R94.112 Abnormal visually evoked potential [VEP]

R94.113 Abnormal oculomotor study

R94.118 Abnormal results of other function studies of eye

\+ **R94.12 Abnormal results of function studies of ear and othe special senses**

R94.120 Abnormal auditory function study

R94.121 Abnormal vestibular function study

R94.128 Abnormal results of other function studies of ear and other special senses

\+ **R94.13 Abnormal results of function studies of peripheral nervous system**

R94.130 Abnormal response to nerve stimulation, unspecified

R94.131 Abnormal electromyogram [EMG]
Excludes1: *electromyogram of eye (R94.1*

R94.138 Abnormal results of other function studies peripheral nervous system

R94.2 Abnormal results of pulmonary function studies
Reduced ventilatory capacity
Reduced vital capacity

+ **R94.3 Abnormal results of cardiovascular function studies**
  - **R94.30 Abnormal result of cardiovascular function study, unspecified**
  - **R94.31 Abnormal electrocardiogram [ECG] [EKG]**
    Excludes1: *long QT syndrome (I45.81)*
  - **R94.39 Abnormal result of other cardiovascular function study**
    Abnormal electrophysiological intracardiac studies
    Abnormal phonocardiogram
    Abnormal vectorcardiogram

R94.4 Abnormal results of kidney function studies
Abnormal renal function test

R94.5 Abnormal results of liver function studies

R94.6 Abnormal results of thyroid function studies

R94.7 Abnormal results of other endocrine function studies
Excludes2: *abnormal glucose (R73.0-)*

R94.8 Abnormal results of function studies of other organs and systems
Abnormal basal metabolic rate [BMR]
Abnormal bladder function test
Abnormal splenic function test

Abnormal tumor markers (R97)

R97 Abnormal tumor markers

Elevated tumor associated antigens [TAA]
Elevated tumor specific antigens [TSA]

R97.0 Elevated carcinoembryonic antigen [CEA]
♀ **R97.1 Elevated cancer antigen 125 [CA 125]**
● ♂ **R97.2 Elevated prostate specific antigen [PSA]**
R97.8 Other abnormal tumor markers

Ill-defined and unknown cause of mortality (R99)

R99 Ill-defined and unknown cause of mortality

Death (unexplained) NOS
Unspecified cause of mortality
Review coding guideline C.18.h
Valid 3-character code, no further characters required

Muscles

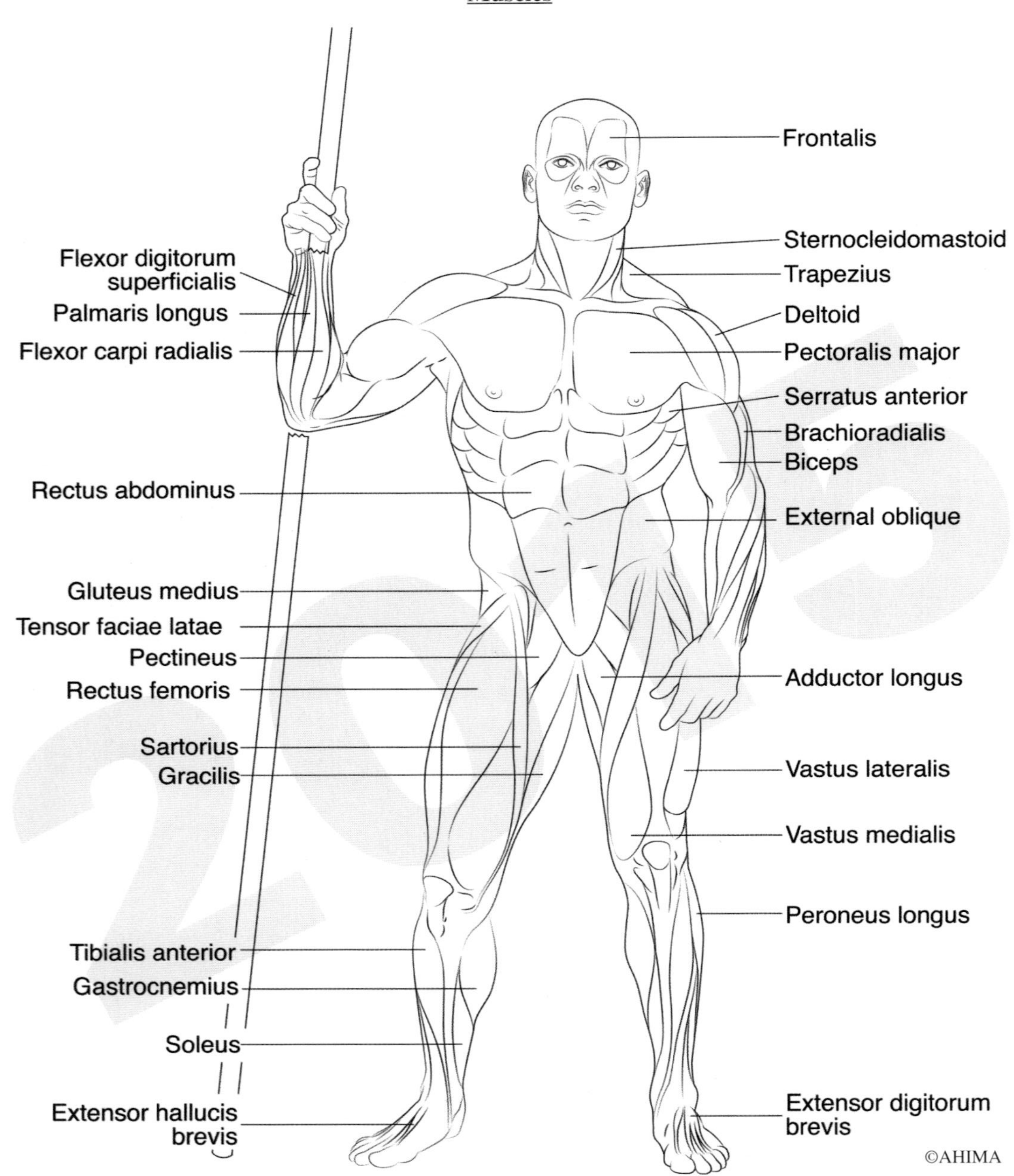
Frontalis
Sternocleidomastoid
Trapezius
Deltoid
Pectoralis major
Serratus anterior
Brachioradialis
Biceps
External oblique
Adductor longus
Vastus lateralis
Vastus medialis
Peroneus longus
Extensor digitorum brevis
Flexor digitorum superficialis
Palmaris longus
Flexor carpi radialis
Rectus abdominus
Gluteus medius
Tensor faciae latae
Pectineus
Rectus femoris
Sartorius
Gracilis
Tibialis anterior
Gastrocnemius
Soleus
Extensor hallucis brevis
©AHIMA

Skeleton - Front and Side Views

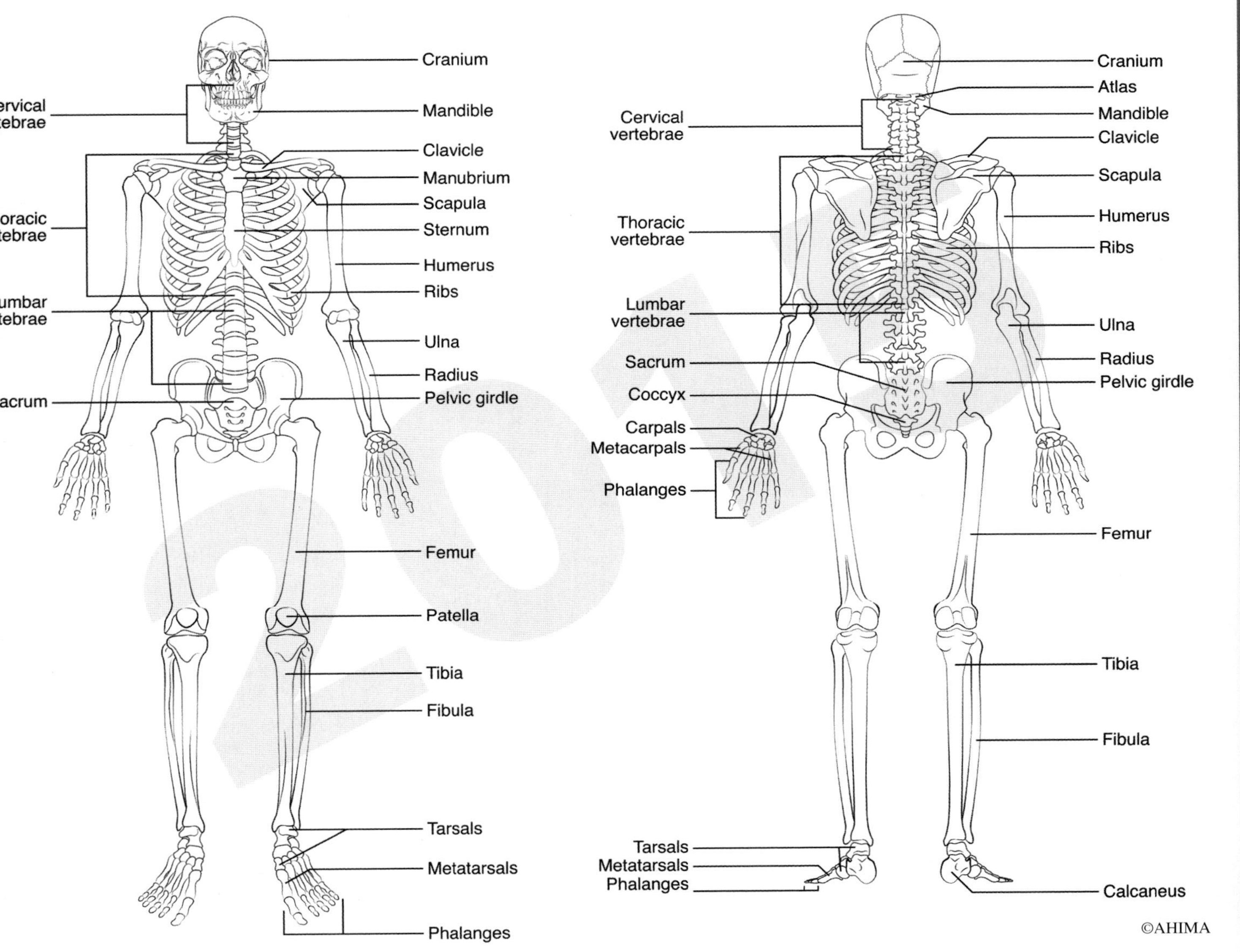

Chapter 19: Injury, Poisoning and Certain Other Consequences of External Causes (S00-T88)

NOTE Use secondary code(s) from Chapter 20, External causes of morbidity, to indicate cause of injury. Codes within the T-section that include the external cause do not require an additional external cause code

Use additional code to identify any retained foreign body, if applicable (Z18.-)

Excludes1: *birth trauma (P10-P15)*
obstetric trauma (O70-O71)

NOTE The chapter uses the S-section for coding different types of injuries related to single body regions and the T-section to cover injuries to unspecified body regions as well as poisoning and certain other consequences of external causes.

This chapter contains the following category blocks:

- S00-S09 Injuries to the head
- S10-S19 Injuries to the neck
- S20-S29 Injuries to the thorax
- S30-S39 Injuries to the abdomen, lower back, lumbar spine, pelvis and external genitals
- S40-S49 Injuries to the shoulder and upper arm
- S50-S59 Injuries to the elbow and forearm
- S60-S69 Injuries to the wrist, hand and fingers
- S70-S79 Injuries to the hip and thigh
- S80-S89 Injuries to the knee and lower leg
- S90-S99 Injuries to the ankle and foot
- T07 Injuries involving multiple body regions
- T14 Injury of unspecified body region
- T15-T19 Effects of foreign body entering through natural orifice
- T20-T32 Burns and corrosions
- T20-T25 Burns and corrosions of external body surface, specified by site
- T26-T28 Burns and corrosions confined to eye and internal organs
- T30-T32 Burns and corrosions of multiple and unspecified body regions
- T33-T34 Frostbite
- T36-T50 Poisoning by, adverse effect of and underdosing of drugs, medicaments and biological substances
- T51-T65 Toxic effects of substances chiefly nonmedicinal as to source
- T66-T78 Other and unspecified effects of external causes
- T79 Certain early complications of trauma
- T80-T88 Complications of surgical and medical care, not elsewhere classified

C. Chapter-Specific Coding Guidelines

In addition to general coding guidelines, there are guidelines for specific diagnoses and/or conditions in the classification. Unless otherwise indicated, these guidelines apply to all health care settings. Please refer to Section II for guidelines on the selection of principal diagnosis.

19. Chapter 19: Injury, Poisoning and Certain Other Consequences of External Causes (S00-T88)

a. Application of 7th Characters in Chapter 19

Most categories in chapter 19 have a 7th character requirement for each applicable code. Most categories in this chapter have three 7th character values (with the exception of fractures): A, initial encounter, D, subsequent encounter and S, sequela. Categories for traumatic fractures have additional 7th character values. **While the patient may be seen by a new or different provider over the course of treatment for an injury, assignment of the 7th character is based on whether the patient is undergoing active treatment and not whether the provider is seeing the patient for the first time.**

For complication codes, active treatment refers to treatment for the condition described by the code, even though it may be related to an earlier precipitating problem. For example, code T84.50XA, Infection and inflammatory reaction due to unspecified internal joint prosthesis, initial encounter, is used when active treatment is provided for the infection, even though the condition relates to the prosthetic device, implant or graft that was placed at a previous encounter.

7th character "A", initial encounter is used while the patient is receiving active treatment for the condition. Examples of active treatment are: surgical treatment, emergency department encounter, and **continuing** treatment by the **same or a different** physician.

7th character "D" subsequent encounter is used for encounters after the patient has received active treatment of the condition and is receiving routine care for the condition during the healing or recovery phase. Examples of subsequent care are: cast change or removal, **an x-ray to check healing status of fracture** removal of external or internal fixation device, medication adjustment, other aftercare and follow up visits following treatment of the injury or condition.

The aftercare Z codes should not be used for aftercare for conditions such as injuries or poisonings, where 7th characters are provided to identify subsequent care. For example, for aftercare of an injury, assign the acute injury code with the 7th character "D" (subsequent encounter).

7th character "S", sequela, is for use for complications or conditions that arise as a direct result of a condition, such as scar formation after a burn. The scars are sequelae of the burn. When using 7th character "S", it is necessary to use both the injury code that precipitated the sequela and the code for the sequela its[elf]. The "S" is added only to the injury code, not the sequela code. The 7th charac[ter] "S" identifies the injury responsible for the sequela. The specific type of sequ[ela] (e.g. scar) is sequenced first, followed by the injury code.

b. Coding of Injuriesv

When coding injuries, assign separate codes for each injury unless a combinati[on] code is provided, in which case the combination code is assigned. Code T[07], Unspecified multiple injuries should not be assigned in the inpatient setti[ng] unless information for a more specific code is not available. Traumatic inj[ury] codes (S00-T14.9) are not to be used for normal, healing surgical wounds or [to] identify complications of surgical wounds.

The code for the most serious injury, as determined by the provider and [the] focus of treatment, is sequenced first.

1) Superficial injuries

Superficial injuries such as abrasions or contusions are not coded wh[en] associated with more severe injuries of the same site.

2) Primary injury with damage to nerves/blood vessels

When a primary injury results in minor damage to peripheral nerves or blo[od] vessels, the primary injury is sequenced first with additional code(s) [for] injuries to nerves and spinal cord (such as category S04), and/or injury [to] blood vessels (such as category S15). When the primary injury is to the blo[od] vessels or nerves, that injury should be sequenced first.

c. Coding of Traumatic Fractures

The principles of multiple coding of injuries should be followed in codi[ng] fractures. Fractures of specified sites are coded individually by site in accordan[ce] with both the provisions within categories S02, S12, S22, S32, S42, S49, S[52], S59, S62, S72, S79, S82, S89, S92 and the level of detail furnished by medi[cal] record content.

A fracture not indicated as open or closed should be coded to closed. A fractu[re] not indicated whether displaced or not displaced should be coded to displace[d].

More specific guidelines are as follows:

1) Initial vs. Subsequent Encounter for Fractures

Traumatic fractures are coded using the appropriate 7th character for init[ial] encounter (A, B, C) while the patient is receiving active treatment for t[he] fracture. Examples of active treatment are: surgical treatment, emergen[cy] department encounter, and evaluation and **continued** (**ongoing**) treatme[nt] by the **same or different** physician. The appropriate 7th character [for] initial encounter should also be assigned for a patient who delayed seeki[ng] treatment for the fracture or nonunion.

Fractures are coded using the appropriate 7th character for subsequent care [for] encounters after the patient has completed active treatment of the fracture a[nd] is receiving routine care for the fracture during the healing or recovery pha[se]. Examples of fracture aftercare are: cast change or removal, **an x-ray to che[ck] healing status of fracture** removal of external or internal fixation devic[e], medication adjustment, and follow-up visits following fracture treatment.

Care for complications of surgical treatment for fracture repairs during t[he] healing or recovery phase should be coded with the appropriate complicati[on] codes.

Care of complications of fractures, such as malunion and nonunion, shou[ld] be reported with the appropriate 7th character for subsequent care wi[th] nonunion (K, M, N,) or subsequent care with malunion (P, Q, R).

<u>Malunion/nonunion: The appropriate 7th character for initial encount[er] should also be assigned for a patient who delayed seeking treatment for t[he] fracture or nonunion.</u>

A code from category M80, not a traumatic fracture code, should be us[ed] for any patient with known osteoporosis who suffers a fracture, even if t[he] patient had a minor fall or trauma, if that fall or trauma would not usual[ly] break a normal, healthy bone.

See Section I.C.13. Osteoporosis.

The aftercare Z codes should not be used for aftercare for traumatic fracture[s]. For aftercare of a traumatic fracture, assign the acute fracture code with t[he] appropriate 7th character.

2) Multiple fractures sequencing

Multiple fractures are sequenced in accordance with the severity of t[he] fracture.

d. Coding of Burns and Corrosions

The ICD-10-CM makes a distinction between burns and corrosions. The bu[rn] codes are for thermal burns, except sunburns, that come from a heat sourc[e], such as a fire or hot appliance. The burn codes are also for burns resulting fro[m] electricity and radiation. Corrosions are burns due to chemicals. The guidelin[es] are the same for burns and corrosions.

Current burns (T20-T25) are classified by depth, extent and by agent ([X] code). Burns are classified by depth as first degree (erythema), second degre[e] (blistering), and third degree (full-thickness involvement). Burns of the eye an[d] internal organs (T26-T28) are classified by site, but not by degree.

1) Sequencing of burn and related condition codes

Sequence first the code that reflects the highest degree of burn when mo[re] than one burn is present.

a. When the reason for the admission or encounter is for treatment of external multiple burns, sequence first the code that reflects the burn of the highest degree.

b. When a patient has both internal and external burns, the circumstances of admission govern the selection of the principal diagnosis or first-listed diagnosis.

c. When a patient is admitted for burn injuries and other related conditions such as smoke inhalation and/or respiratory failure, the circumstances of admission govern the selection of the principal or first-listed diagnosis.

2) Burns of the same local site

Classify burns of the same local site (three-character category level, T20-T28) but of different degrees to the subcategory identifying the highest degree recorded in the diagnosis.

3) Non-healing burns

Non-healing burns are coded as acute burns.

Necrosis of burned skin should be coded as a non-healed burn.

4) Infected Burn

For any documented infected burn site, use an additional code for the infection.

5) Assign separate codes for each burn site

When coding burns, assign separate codes for each burn site. Category T30, Burn and corrosion, body region unspecified is extremely vague and should rarely be used.

6) Burns and Corrosions Classified According to Extent of Body Surface Involved

Assign codes from category T31, Burns classified according to extent of body surface involved, or T32, Corrosions classified according to extent of body surface involved, when the site of the burn is not specified or when there is a need for additional data. It is advisable to use category T31 as additional coding when needed to provide data for evaluating burn mortality, such as that needed by burn units. It is also advisable to use category T31 as an additional code for reporting purposes when there is mention of a third-degree burn involving 20 percent or more of the body surface.

Categories T31 and T32 are based on the classic "rule of nines" in estimating body surface involved: head and neck are assigned nine percent, each arm nine percent, each leg 18 percent, the anterior trunk 18 percent, posterior trunk 18 percent, and genitalia one percent. Providers may change these percentage assignments where necessary to accommodate infants and children who have proportionately larger heads than adults, and patients who have large buttocks, thighs, or abdomen that involve burns.

7) Encounters for treatment of sequela of burns

Encounters for the treatment of the late effects of burns or corrosions (i.e., scars or joint contractures) should be coded with a burn or corrosion code with the 7th character "S" for sequela.

8) Sequelae with a late effect code and current burn

When appropriate, both a code for a current burn or corrosion with 7th character "A" or "D" and a burn or corrosion code with 7th character "S" may be assigned on the same record (when both a current burn and sequelae of an old burn exist). Burns and corrosions do not heal at the same rate and a current healing wound may still exist with sequela of a healed burn or corrosion. ***See Section I.B.10 Sequela (Late Effects)***

9) Use of an external cause code with burns and corrosions

An external cause code should be used with burns and corrosions to identify the source and intent of the burn, as well as the place where it occurred.

e. Adverse Effects, Poisoning, Underdosing and Toxic Effects

Codes in categories T36-T65 are combination codes that include the substance that was taken as well as the intent. No additional external cause code is required for poisonings, toxic effects, adverse effects and underdosing codes.

1) Do not code directly from the Table of Drugs

Do not code directly from the Table of Drugs and Chemicals. Always refer back to the Tabular List.

2) Use as many codes as necessary to describe

Use as many codes as necessary to describe completely all drugs, medicinal or biological substances.

3) If the same code would describe the causative agent

If the same code would describe the causative agent for more than one adverse reaction, poisoning, toxic effect or underdosing, assign the code only once.

4) If two or more drugs, medicinal or biological substances

If two or more drugs, medicinal or biological substances are reported, code each individually unless a combination code is listed in the Table of Drugs and Chemicals.

5) The occurrence of drug toxicity is classified in ICD-10-CM as follows:

(a) Adverse Effect

When coding an adverse effect of a drug that has been correctly prescribed and properly administered, assign the appropriate code for the nature of the adverse effect followed by the appropriate code for the adverse effect of the drug (T36-T50). The code for the drug should have a 5th or 6th character "5" (for example T36.0X5-) Examples of the nature of an adverse effect are tachycardia, delirium, gastrointestinal hemorrhaging, vomiting, hypokalemia, hepatitis, renal failure, or respiratory failure.

(b) Poisoning

When coding a poisoning or reaction to the improper use of a medication (e.g., overdose, wrong substance given or taken in error, wrong route of administration), first assign the appropriate code from categories T36-T50. The poisoning codes have an associated intent as their 5th or 6th character (accidental, intentional self-harm, assault and undetermined. Use additional code(s) for all manifestations of poisonings.

If there is also a diagnosis of abuse or dependence of the substance, the abuse or dependence is assigned as an additional code.

Examples of poisoning include:

(i) Error was made in drug prescription

Errors made in drug prescription or in the administration of the drug by provider, nurse, patient, or other person.

(ii) Overdose of a drug intentionally taken

If an overdose of a drug was intentionally taken or administered and resulted in drug toxicity, it would be coded as a poisoning.

(iii) Nonprescribed drug taken with correctly prescribed and properly administered drug

If a nonprescribed drug or medicinal agent was taken in combination with a correctly prescribed and properly administered drug, any drug toxicity or other reaction resulting from the interaction of the two drugs would be classified as a poisoning.

(iv) Interaction of drug(s) and alcohol

When a reaction results from the interaction of a drug(s) and alcohol, this would be classified as poisoning.

See Section I.C.4. if poisoning is the result of insulin pump malfunctions.

(c) Underdosing

Underdosing refers to taking less of a medication than is prescribed by a provider or a manufacturer's instruction. For underdosing, assign the code from categories T36-T50 (fifth or sixth character "6").

Codes for underdosing should never be assigned as principal or first-listed codes. If a patient has a relapse or exacerbation of the medical condition for which the drug is prescribed because of the reduction in dose, then the medical condition itself should be coded.

Noncompliance (Z91.12-, Z91.13-) or complication of care (Y63.6-Y63.9) codes are to be used with an underdosing code to indicate intent, if known.

(d) Toxic Effects

When a harmful substance is ingested or comes in contact with a person, this is classified as a toxic effect. The toxic effect codes are in categories T51-T65.

Toxic effect codes have an associated intent: accidental, intentional self-harm, assault and undetermined.

f. Adult and child abuse, neglect and other maltreatment

Sequence first the appropriate code from categories T74.- (Adult and child abuse, neglect and other maltreatment, confirmed) or T76.- (Adult and child abuse, neglect and other maltreatment, suspected) for abuse, neglect and other maltreatment, followed by any accompanying mental health or injury code(s).

If the documentation in the medical record states abuse or neglect it is coded as confirmed (T74.-). It is coded as suspected if it is documented as suspected (T76.-).

For cases of confirmed abuse or neglect an external cause code from the assault section (X92-Y08) should be added to identify the cause of any physical injuries. A perpetrator code (Y07) should be added when the perpetrator of the abuse is known. For suspected cases of abuse or neglect, do not report external cause or perpetrator code.

If a suspected case of abuse, neglect or mistreatment is ruled out during an encounter code Z04.71, Encounter for examination and observation following alleged physical adult abuse, ruled out, or code Z04.72, Encounter for examination and observation following alleged child physical abuse, ruled out, should be used, not a code from T76.

If a suspected case of alleged rape or sexual abuse is ruled out during an encounter code Z04.41, Encounter for examination and observation following alleged physical adult abuse, ruled out, or code Z04.42, Encounter for examination and observation following alleged rape or sexual abuse, ruled out, should be used, not a code from T76.

See Section I.C.15. Abuse in a pregnant patient.

g. Complications of care

1) General guidelines for complications of care

(a) Documentation of complications of care

See Section I.B.16. for information on documentation of complications of care.

2) Pain due to medical devices

Pain associated with devices, implants or grafts left in a surgical site (for example painful hip prosthesis) is assigned to the appropriate code(s) found in Chapter 19, Injury, poisoning, and certain other consequences of external causes. Specific codes for pain due to medical devices are found in the T code section of the ICD-10-CM. Use additional code(s) from category G89 to identify acute or chronic pain due to presence of the device, implant or graft (G89.18 or G89.28).

3) Transplant complications

(a) Transplant complications other than kidney

Codes under category T86, Complications of transplanted organs and tissues, are for use for both complications and rejection of transplanted organs. A transplant complication code is only assigned if the complication affects the function of the transplanted organ. Two codes are required to fully describe a transplant complication: the appropriate code from category T86 and a secondary code that identifies the complication.

Pre-existing conditions or conditions that develop after the transplant are not coded as complications unless they affect the function of the transplanted organs.

See I.C.21. for transplant organ removal status.

See I.C.2. for malignant neoplasm associated with transplanted organ.

(b) Kidney transplant complications

Patients who have undergone kidney transplant may still have some form of chronic kidney disease (CKD) because the kidney transplant may not fully restore kidney function. Code T86.1- should be assigned for documented complications of a kidney transplant, such as transplant failure or rejection or other transplant complication. Code T86.1- should not be assigned for post kidney transplant patients who have chronic kidney (CKD) unless a transplant complication such as transplant failure or rejection is documented. If the documentation is unclear as to whether the patient has a complication of the transplant, query the provider.

Conditions that affect the function of the transplanted kidney, other than CKD, should be assigned a code from subcategory T86.1, Complications of transplanted organ, Kidney, and a secondary code that identifies the complication.

For patients with CKD following a kidney transplant, but who do not have a complication such as failure or rejection, *see section I.C.14. Chronic kidney disease and kidney transplant status.*

4) Complication codes that include the external cause

As with certain other T codes, some of the complications of care codes have the external cause included in the code. The code includes the nature of the complication as well as the type of procedure that caused the complication. No external cause code indicating the type of procedure is necessary for these codes.

5) Complications of care codes within the body system chapters

Intraoperative and postprocedural complication codes are found within the body system chapters with codes specific to the organs and structures of that body system. These codes should be sequenced first, followed by a code(s) for the specific complication, if applicable.

Injuries to the head (S00-S09)

Includes: *injuries of ear*
injuries of eye
injuries of face [any part]
injuries of gum
injuries of jaw
injuries of oral cavity
injuries of palate
injuries of periocular area
injuries of scalp
injuries of temporomandibular joint area
injuries of tongue
injuries of tooth

Code also for any associated infection

Excludes2: *burns and corrosions (T20-T32)*
effects of foreign body in ear (T16)
effects of foreign body in larynx (T17.3)
effects of foreign body in mouth NOS (T18.0)
effects of foreign body in nose (T17.0-T17.1)
effects of foreign body in pharynx (T17.2)
effects of foreign body on external eye (T15.-)
frostbite (T33-T34)
insect bite or sting, venomous (T63.4)

S00 Superficial injury of head

Excludes1: *diffuse cerebral contusion (S06.2-)*
focal cerebral contusion (S06.3-)
injury of eye and orbit (S05.-)
open wound of head (S01.-)

The appropriate 7th character is to be added to each code from category S00
A initial encounter
D subsequent encounter
S sequela

\+ **S00.0 Superficial injury of scalp**
X+7th **S00.00 Unspecified superficial injury of scalp**
X+7th **S00.01 Abrasion of scalp**
X+7th **S00.02 Blister (nonthermal) of scalp**
X+7th **S00.03 Contusion of scalp**
Bruise of scalp
Hematoma of scalp
X+7th **S00.04 External constriction of part of scalp**
X+7th **S00.05 Superficial foreign body of scalp**
Splinter in the scalp
X+7th **S00.06 Insect bite (nonvenomous) of scalp**
X+7th **S00.07 Other superficial bite of scalp**
Excludes1: *open bite of scalp (S01.05)*

\+ **S00.1 Contusion of eyelid and periocular area**
Black eye
Excludes2: *contusion of eyeball and orbital tissues (S05.1)*
X+7th **S00.10 Contusion of unspecified eyelid and periocular area**
X+7th **S00.11 Contusion of right eyelid and periocular area**
X+7th **S00.12 Contusion of left eyelid and periocular area**

\+ **S00.2 Other and unspecified superficial injuries of eyelid and periocular area**
Excludes2: *superficial injury of conjunctiva and cornea (S05.0-*
\+ **S00.20 Unspecified superficial injury of eyelid and periocular area**
+7th **S00.201 Unspecified superficial injury of right eyelid and periocular area**
+7th **S00.202 Unspecified superficial injury of left eyelid and periocular area**
+7th **S00.209 Unspecified superficial injury of unspecified eyelid and periocular area**
\+ **S00.21 Abrasion of eyelid and periocular area**
+7th **S00.211 Abrasion of right eyelid and periocular area**
+7th **S00.212 Abrasion of left eyelid and periocular area**
+7th **S00.219 Abrasion of unspecified eyelid and periocular area**
\+ **S00.22 Blister (nonthermal) of eyelid and periocular area**
+7th **S00.221 Blister (nonthermal) of right eyelid and periocular area**
+7th **S00.222 Blister (nonthermal) of left eyelid and periocular area**
+7th **S00.229 Blister (nonthermal) of unspecified eyelid and periocular area**
\+ **S00.24 External constriction of eyelid and periocular area**
+7th **S00.241 External constriction of right eyelid and periocular area**
+7th **S00.242 External constriction of left eyelid and periocular area**
+7th **S00.249 External constriction of unspecified eyelid and periocular area**
\+ **S00.25 Superficial foreign body of eyelid and periocular area**
Splinter of eyelid and periocular area
Excludes2: *retained foreign body in eyelid (H02.81-)*
+7th **S00.251 Superficial foreign body of right eyelid and periocular area**
+7th **S00.252 Superficial foreign body of left eyelid and periocular area**
+7th **S00.259 Superficial foreign body of unspecified eyelid and periocular area**
\+ **S00.26 Insect bite (nonvenomous) of eyelid and periocular area**
+7th **S00.261 Insect bite (nonvenomous) of right eyelid and periocular area**
+7th **S00.262 Insect bite (nonvenomous) of left eyelid and periocular area**
+7th **S00.269 Insect bite (nonvenomous) of unspecified eyelid and periocular area**

+ **S00.27 Other superficial bite of eyelid and periocular area**
 Excludes1: *open bite of eyelid and periocular area (S01.15)*
 +7th **S00.271 Other superficial bite of right eyelid and periocular area**
 +7th **S00.272 Other superficial bite of left eyelid and periocular area**
 +7th **S00.279 Other superficial bite of unspecified eyelid and periocular area**

+ **S00.3 Superficial injury of nose**
 X+7th **S00.30 Unspecified superficial injury of nose**
 X+7th **S00.31 Abrasion of nose**
 X+7th **S00.32 Blister (nonthermal) of nose**
 X+7th **S00.33 Contusion of nose**
 Bruise of nose
 Hematoma of nose
 X+7th **S00.34 External constriction of nose**
 X+7th **S00.35 Superficial foreign body of nose**
 Splinter in the nose
 X+7th **S00.36 Insect bite (nonvenomous) of nose**
 X+7th **S00.37 Other superficial bite of nose**
 Excludes1: *open bite of nose (S01.25)*

+ **S00.4 Superficial injury of ear**
 + **S00.40 Unspecified superficial injury of ear**
 +7th **S00.401 Unspecified superficial injury of right ear**
 +7th **S00.402 Unspecified superficial injury of left ear**
 +7th **S00.409 Unspecified superficial injury of unspecified ear**
 + **S00.41 Abrasion of ear**
 +7th **S00.411 Abrasion of right ear**
 +7th **S00.412 Abrasion of left ear**
 +7th **S00.419 Abrasion of unspecified ear**
 + **S00.42 Blister (nonthermal) of ear**
 +7th **S00.421 Blister (nonthermal) of right ear**
 +7th **S00.422 Blister (nonthermal) of left ear**
 +7th **S00.429 Blister (nonthermal) of unspecified ear**
 + **S00.43 Contusion of ear**
 Bruise of ear
 Hematoma of ear
 +7th **S00.431 Contusion of right ear**
 +7th **S00.432 Contusion of left ear**
 +7th **S00.439 Contusion of unspecified ear**
 + **S00.44 External constriction of ear**
 +7th **S00.441 External constriction of right ear**
 +7th **S00.442 External constriction of left ear**
 +7th **S00.449 External constriction of unspecified ear**
 + **S00.45 Superficial foreign body of ear**
 Splinter in the ear
 +7th **S00.451 Superficial foreign body of right ear**
 +7th **S00.452 Superficial foreign body of left ear**
 +7th **S00.459 Superficial foreign body of unspecified ear**
 + **S00.46 Insect bite (nonvenomous) of ear**
 +7th **S00.461 Insect bite (nonvenomous) of right ear**
 +7th **S00.462 Insect bite (nonvenomous) of left ear**
 +7th **S00.469 Insect bite (nonvenomous) of unspecified ear**
 + **S00.47 Other superficial bite of ear**
 Excludes1: *open bite of ear (S01.35)*
 +7th **S00.471 Other superficial bite of right ear**
 +7th **S00.472 Other superficial bite of left ear**
 +7th **S00.479 Other superficial bite of unspecified ear**

+ **S00.5 Superficial injury of lip and oral cavity**
 + **S00.50 Unspecified superficial injury of lip and oral cavity**
 +7th **S00.501 Unspecified superficial injury of lip**
 +7th **S00.502 Unspecified superficial injury of oral cavity**
 + **S00.51 Abrasion of lip and oral cavity**
 +7th **S00.511 Abrasion of lip**
 +7th **S00.512 Abrasion of oral cavity**
 + **S00.52 Blister (nonthermal) of lip and oral cavity**
 +7th **S00.521 Blister (nonthermal) of lip**
 +7th **S00.522 Blister (nonthermal) of oral cavity**
 + **S00.53 Contusion of lip and oral cavity**
 +7th **S00.531 Contusion of lip**
 Bruise of lip
 Hematoma of oral cavity
 +7th **S00.532 Contusion of oral cavity**
 Bruise of lip
 Hematoma of oral cavity
 + **S00.54 External constriction of lip and oral cavity**
 +7th **S00.541 External constriction of lip**
 +7th **S00.542 External constriction of oral cavity**
 + **S00.55 Superficial foreign body of lip and oral cavity**
 +7th **S00.551 Superficial foreign body of lip**
 Splinter of lip and oral cavity
 +7th **S00.552 Superficial foreign body of oral cavity**
 Splinter of lip and oral cavity
 + **S00.56 Insect bite (nonvenomous) of lip and oral cavity**
 +7th **S00.561 Insect bite (nonvenomous) of lip**
 +7th **S00.562 Insect bite (nonvenomous) of oral cavity**
 + **S00.57 Other superficial bite of lip and oral cavity**
 +7th **S00.571 Other superficial bite of lip**
 Excludes1: *open bite of lip (S01.551)*
 +7th **S00.572 Other superficial bite of oral cavity**
 Excludes1: *open bite of oral cavity (S01.552)*

+ **S00.8 Superficial injury of other parts of head**
 X+7th **S00.80 Unspecified superficial injury of other part of head**
 X+7th **S00.81 Abrasion of other part of head**
 X+7th **S00.82 Blister (nonthermal) of other part of head**
 X+7th **S00.83 Contusion of other part of head**
 Bruise of other part of head
 Hematoma of other part of head
 X+7th **S00.84 External constriction of other part of head**
 X+7th **S00.85 Superficial foreign body of other part of head**
 Splinter in other part of head
 X+7th **S00.86 Insect bite (nonvenomous) of other part of head**
 X+7th **S00.87 Other superficial bite of other part of head**
 Excludes1: *open bite of other part of head (S01.85)*

+ **S00.9 Superficial injury of unspecified part of head**
 X+7th **S00.90 Unspecified superficial injury of unspecified part of head**
 X+7th **S00.91 Abrasion of unspecified part of head**
 X+7th **S00.92 Blister (nonthermal) of unspecified part of head**
 X+7th **S00.93 Contusion of unspecified part of head**
 Bruise of head
 Hematoma of head
 X+7th **S00.94 External constriction of unspecified part of head**
 X+7th **S00.95 Superficial foreign body of unspecified part of head**
 Splinter of head
 X+7th **S00.96 Insect bite (nonvenomous) of unspecified part of head**
 X+7th **S00.97 Other superficial bite of unspecified part of head**
 Excludes1: *open bite of head (S01.95)*

S01 Open wound of head

Code also any associated:
injury of cranial nerve (S04.-)
injury of muscle and tendon of head (S09.1-)
intracranial injury (S06.-)
wound infection

Excludes1: *open skull fracture (S02.- with 7th character B)*
Excludes2: *injury of eye and orbit (S05.-)*
traumatic amputation of part of head (S08.-)

The appropriate 7th character is to be added to each code from category S01
A initial encounter
D subsequent encounter
S sequela

+ **S01.0 Open wound of scalp**
 Excludes1: *avulsion of scalp (S08.0)*
 X+7th **S01.00 Unspecified open wound of scalp**
 X+7th **S01.01 Laceration without foreign body of scalp**
 X+7th **S01.02 Laceration with foreign body of scalp**
 X+7th **S01.03 Puncture wound without foreign body of scalp**
 X+7th **S01.04 Puncture wound with foreign body of scalp**
 X+7th **S01.05 Open bite of scalp**
 Bite of scalp NOS
 Excludes1: *superficial bite of scalp (S00.06, S00.07-)*

+ **S01.1 Open wound of eyelid and periocular area**
 Open wound of eyelid and periocular area with or without involvement of lacrimal passages
 + **S01.10 Unspecified open wound of eyelid and periocular area**
 CC +7th **S01.101 Unspecified open wound of right eyelid and periocular area**
 CC Exclusion 7th character A see Appendix A
 PDX collection 1139
 CC +7th **S01.102 Unspecified open wound of left eyelid and periocular area**
 CC Exclusion 7th character A see Appendix A
 PDX collection 1139
 CC +7th **S01.109 Unspecified open wound of unspecified eyelid and periocular area**
 CC Exclusion 7th character A see Appendix A
 PDX collection 1139

+ **S01.11 Laceration without foreign body of eyelid and periocular area**

+7th **S01.111 Laceration without foreign body of right eyelid and periocular area**

+7th **S01.112 Laceration without foreign body of left eyelid and periocular area**

+7th **S01.119 Laceration without foreign body of unspecified eyelid and periocular area**

+ **S01.12 Laceration with foreign body of eyelid and periocular area**

+7th **S01.121 Laceration with foreign body of right eyelid and periocular area**

+7th **S01.122 Laceration with foreign body of left eyelid and periocular area**

+7th **S01.129 Laceration with foreign body of unspecified eyelid and periocular area**

+ **S01.13 Puncture wound without foreign body of eyelid and periocular area**

+7th **S01.131 Puncture wound without foreign body of right eyelid and periocular area**

+7th **S01.132 Puncture wound without foreign body of left eyelid and periocular area**

+7th **S01.139 Puncture wound without foreign body of unspecified eyelid and periocular area**

+ **S01.14 Puncture wound with foreign body of eyelid and periocular area**

+7th **S01.141 Puncture wound with foreign body of right eyelid and periocular area**

+7th **S01.142 Puncture wound with foreign body of left eyelid and periocular area**

+7th **S01.149 Puncture wound with foreign body of unspecified eyelid and periocular area**

+ **S01.15 Open bite of eyelid and periocular area**

Bite of eyelid and periocular area NOS

Excludes1: *superficial bite of eyelid and periocular area (S00.26, S00.27)*

+7th **S01.151 Open bite of right eyelid and periocular area**

+7th **S01.152 Open bite of left eyelid and periocular area**

+7th **S01.159 Open bite of unspecified eyelid and periocular area**

+ **S01.2 Open wound of nose**

X+7th **S01.20 Unspecified open wound of nose**

X+7th **S01.21 Laceration without foreign body of nose**

X+7th **S01.22 Laceration with foreign body of nose**

X+7th **S01.23 Puncture wound without foreign body of nose**

X+7th **S01.24 Puncture wound with foreign body of nose**

X+7th **S01.25 Open bite of nose**

Bite of nose NOS

Excludes1: *superficial bite of nose (S00.36, S00.37)*

+ **S01.3 Open wound of ear**

+ **S01.30 Unspecified open wound of ear**

+7th **S01.301 Unspecified open wound of right ear**

+7th **S01.302 Unspecified open wound of left ear**

+7th **S01.309 Unspecified open wound of unspecified ear**

+ **S01.31 Laceration without foreign body of ear**

+7th **S01.311 Laceration without foreign body of right ear**

+7th **S01.312 Laceration without foreign body of left ear**

+7th **S01.319 Laceration without foreign body of unspecified ear**

+ **S01.32 Laceration with foreign body of ear**

+7th **S01.321 Laceration with foreign body of right ear**

+7th **S01.322 Laceration with foreign body of left ear**

+7th **S01.329 Laceration with foreign body of unspecified ear**

+ **S01.33 Puncture wound without foreign body of ear**

+7th **S01.331 Puncture wound without foreign body of right ear**

+7th **S01.332 Puncture wound without foreign body of left ear**

+7th **S01.339 Puncture wound without foreign body of unspecified ear**

+ **S01.34 Puncture wound with foreign body of ear**

+7th **S01.341 Puncture wound with foreign body of right ear**

+7th **S01.342 Puncture wound with foreign body of left ear**

+7th **S01.349 Puncture wound with foreign body of unspecified ear**

+ **S01.35 Open bite of ear**

Bite of ear NOS

Excludes1: *superficial bite of ear (S00.46, S00.47)*

+7th **S01.351 Open bite of right ear**

+7th **S01.352 Open bite of left ear**

+7th **S01.359 Open bite of unspecified ear**

+ **S01.4 Open wound of cheek and temporomandibular area**

+ **S01.40 Unspecified open wound of cheek and temporomandibular area**

+7th **S01.401 Unspecified open wound of right cheek and temporomandibular area**

+7th **S01.402 Unspecified open wound of left cheek and temporomandibular area**

+7th **S01.409 Unspecified open wound of unspecified che and temporomandibular area**

+ **S01.41 Laceration without foreign body of cheek and temporomandibular area**

+7th **S01.411 Laceration without foreign body of right cheek and temporomandibular area**

+7th **S01.412 Laceration without foreign body of left che and temporomandibular area**

+7th **S01.419 Laceration without foreign body of unspecified cheek and temporomandibular area**

+ **S01.42 Laceration with foreign body of cheek and temporomandibular area**

+7th **S01.421 Laceration with foreign body of right cheek and temporomandibular area**

+7th **S01.422 Laceration with foreign body of left cheek and temporomandibular area**

+7th **S01.429 Laceration with foreign body of unspecified cheek and temporomandibular area**

+ **S01.43 Puncture wound without foreign body of cheek and temporomandibular area**

+7th **S01.431 Puncture wound without foreign body of right cheek and temporomandibular area**

+7th **S01.432 Puncture wound without foreign body of le cheek and temporomandibular area**

+7th **S01.439 Puncture wound without foreign body of unspecified cheek and temporomandibular area**

+ **S01.44 Puncture wound with foreign body of cheek and temporomandibular area**

+7th **S01.441 Puncture wound with foreign body of right cheek and temporomandibular area**

+7th **S01.442 Puncture wound with foreign body of left cheek and temporomandibular area**

+7th **S01.449 Puncture wound with foreign body of unspecified cheek and temporomandibular area**

+ **S01.45 Open bite of cheek and temporomandibular area**

Bite of cheek and temporomandibular area NOS

Excludes2: *superficial bite of cheek and temporomandibular area (S00.86, S00.87)*

+7th **S01.451 Open bite of right cheek and temporomandibular area**

+7th **S01.452 Open bite of left cheek and temporomandibular area**

+7th **S01.459 Open bite of unspecified cheek and temporomandibular area**

+ **S01.5 Open wound of lip and oral cavity**

Excludes2: *tooth dislocation (S03.2)*
tooth fracture (S02.5)

+ **S01.50 Unspecified open wound of lip and oral cavity**

+7th **S01.501 Unspecified open wound of lip**

+7th **S01.502 Unspecified open wound of oral cavity**

+ **S01.51 Laceration of lip and oral cavity without foreign body**

+7th **S01.511 Laceration without foreign body of lip**

+7th **S01.512 Laceration without foreign body of oral cavit**

+ **S01.52 Laceration of lip and oral cavity with foreign body**

+7th **S01.521 Laceration with foreign body of lip**

+7th **S01.522 Laceration with foreign body of oral cavity**

+ **S01.53 Puncture wound of lip and oral cavity without foreign body**

+7th **S01.531 Puncture wound without foreign body of lip**

+7th **S01.532 Puncture wound without foreign body of oral cavity**

+ **S01.54 Puncture wound of lip and oral cavity with foreign body**

+7th **S01.541 Puncture wound with foreign body of lip**

+7th **S01.542 Puncture wound with foreign body of oral cavity**

+ **S01.55 Open bite of lip and oral cavity**
+7th **S01.551 Open bite of lip**
Bite of lip NOS
Excludes1: *superficial bite of lip (S00.571)*
+7th **S01.552 Open bite of oral cavity**
Bite of oral cavity NOS
Excludes1: *superficial bite of oral cavity (S00.572)*

+ **S01.8 Open wound of other parts of head**
X+7th **S01.80 Unspecified open wound of other part of head**
X+7th **S01.81 Laceration without foreign body of other part of head**
X+7th **S01.82 Laceration with foreign body of other part of head**
X+7th **S01.83 Puncture wound without foreign body of other part of head**
X+7th **S01.84 Puncture wound with foreign body of other part of head**
X+7th **S01.85 Open bite of other part of head**
Bite of other part of head NOS
Excludes1: *superficial bite of other part of head (S00.85)*

+ **S01.9 Open wound of unspecified part of head**
X+7th **S01.90 Unspecified open wound of unspecified part of head**
X+7th **S01.91 Laceration without foreign body of unspecified part of head**
X+7th **S01.92 Laceration with foreign body of unspecified part of head**
X+7th **S01.93 Puncture wound without foreign body of unspecified part of head**
X+7th **S01.94 Puncture wound with foreign body of unspecified part of head**
X+7th **S01.95 Open bite of unspecified part of head**
Bite of head NOS
Excludes1: *superficial bite of head NOS (S00.97)*

S02 Fracture of skull and facial bones

NOTE A fracture not indicated as open or closed should be coded to closed

Code also any associated intracranial injury (S06.-)

The appropriate 7th character is to be added to each code from category S02
A initial encounter for closed fracture
B initial encounter for open fracture
D subsequent encounter for fracture with routine healing
G subsequent encounter for fracture with delayed healing
K subsequent encounter for fracture with nonunion
S sequela

Review coding guideline C.19.c

X+7th MCC CC **S02.0 Fracture of vault of skull**
Fracture of frontal bone
Fracture of parietal bone
CC Exclusion 7th character A see Appendix A PDX collection 1140
CC Exclusion 7th character K see Appendix A PDX collection 0897
MCC Exclusion 7th character B see Appendix A PDX collection 1140
HAC 7th characters A & B see Appendix B for HAC conditional logic

+ **S02.1 Fracture of base of skull**
Excludes1: *orbit NOS (S02.8)*
Excludes2: *orbital floor (S02.3-)*
CC MCC X+7th **S02.10 Unspecified fracture of base of skull**
CC Exclusion 7th character A see Appendix A PDX collection 1140
CC Exclusion 7th character K see Appendix A PDX collection 0897
MCC Exclusion 7th character B see Appendix A PDX collection 1140
HAC 7th characters A & B see Appendix B for HAC conditional logic

+ **S02.11 Fracture of occiput**
CC MCC +7th **S02.110 Type I occipital condyle fracture**
CC Exclusion 7th character A see Appendix A PDX collection 1140
CC Exclusion 7th character K see Appendix A PDX collection 0897
MCC Exclusion 7th character B see Appendix A PDX collection 1140
HAC 7th characters A & B see Appendix B for HAC conditional logic
CC MCC +7th **S02.111 Type II occipital condyle fracture**
CC Exclusion 7th character A see Appendix A PDX collection 1140
CC Exclusion 7th character K see Appendix A PDX collection 0897
MCC Exclusion 7th character B see Appendix A PDX collection 1140
HAC 7th characters A & B see Appendix B for HAC conditional logic
CC MCC +7th **S02.112 Type III occipital condyle fracture**
CC Exclusion 7th character A see Appendix A PDX collection 1140
CC Exclusion 7th character K see Appendix A PDX collection 0897
MCC Exclusion 7th character B see Appendix A PDX collection 1140
HAC 7th characters A & B see Appendix B for HAC conditional logic
CC MCC +7th **S02.113 Unspecified occipital condyle fracture**
CC Exclusion 7th character A see Appendix A PDX collection 1140
CC Exclusion 7th character K see Appendix A PDX collection 0897
MCC Exclusion 7th character B see Appendix A PDX collection 1140
HAC 7th characters A & B see Appendix B for HAC conditional logic
CC MCC +7th **S02.118 Other fracture of occiput**
CC Exclusion 7th character A see Appendix A PDX collection 1140
CC Exclusion 7th character K see Appendix A PDX collection 0897
MCC Exclusion 7th character B see Appendix A PDX collection 1140
HAC 7th characters A & B see Appendix B for HAC conditional logic
CC MCC +7th **S02.119 Unspecified fracture of occiput**
CC Exclusion 7th character A see Appendix A PDX collection 1140
CC Exclusion 7th character K see Appendix A PDX collection 0897
MCC Exclusion 7th character B see Appendix A PDX collection 1140
HAC 7th characters A & B see Appendix B for HAC conditional logic

CC MCC X+7th **S02.19 Other fracture of base of skull**
Fracture of anterior fossa of base of skull
Fracture of ethmoid sinus
Fracture of frontal sinus
Fracture of middle fossa of base of skull
Fracture of orbital roof
Fracture of posterior fossa of base of skull
Fracture of sphenoid
Fracture of temporal bone
CC Exclusion 7th character A see Appendix A PDX collection 1140
CC Exclusion 7th character K see Appendix A PDX collection 0897
MCC Exclusion 7th character B see Appendix A PDX collection 1140
HAC 7th characters A & B see Appendix B for HAC conditional logic

CC X+7th **S02.2 Fracture of nasal bones**
CC Exclusion 7th character B see Appendix A PDX collection 1141
CC Exclusion 7th character K see Appendix A PDX collection 0897
HAC 7th character B see Appendix B for HAC conditional logic

CC X+7th **S02.3 Fracture of orbital floor**
Excludes1: *orbit NOS (S02.8)*
Excludes2: *orbital roof (S02.1-)*
CC Exclusion 7th characters A & B see Appendix A PDX collection 1142
CC Exclusion 7th character K see Appendix A PDX collection 0897
HAC 7th characters A & B see Appendix B for HAC conditional logic

+ **S02.4 Fracture of malar, maxillary and zygoma bones**
Fracture of superior maxilla
Fracture of upper jaw (bone)
Fracture of zygomatic process of temporal bone
+ **S02.40 Fracture of malar, maxillary and zygoma bones, unspecified**
CC +7th **S02.400 Malar fracture unspecified**
CC Exclusion 7th characters A & B see Appendix A PDX collection 1143
CC Exclusion 7th character K see Appendix A PDX collection 0897
HAC 7th characters A & B see Appendix B for HAC conditional logic
CC +7th **S02.401 Maxillary fracture, unspecified**
CC Exclusion 7th characters A & B see Appendix A PDX collection 1143
CC Exclusion 7th character K see Appendix A PDX collection 0897
HAC 7th characters A & B see Appendix B for HAC conditional logic

Head and Facial Bones - Side View

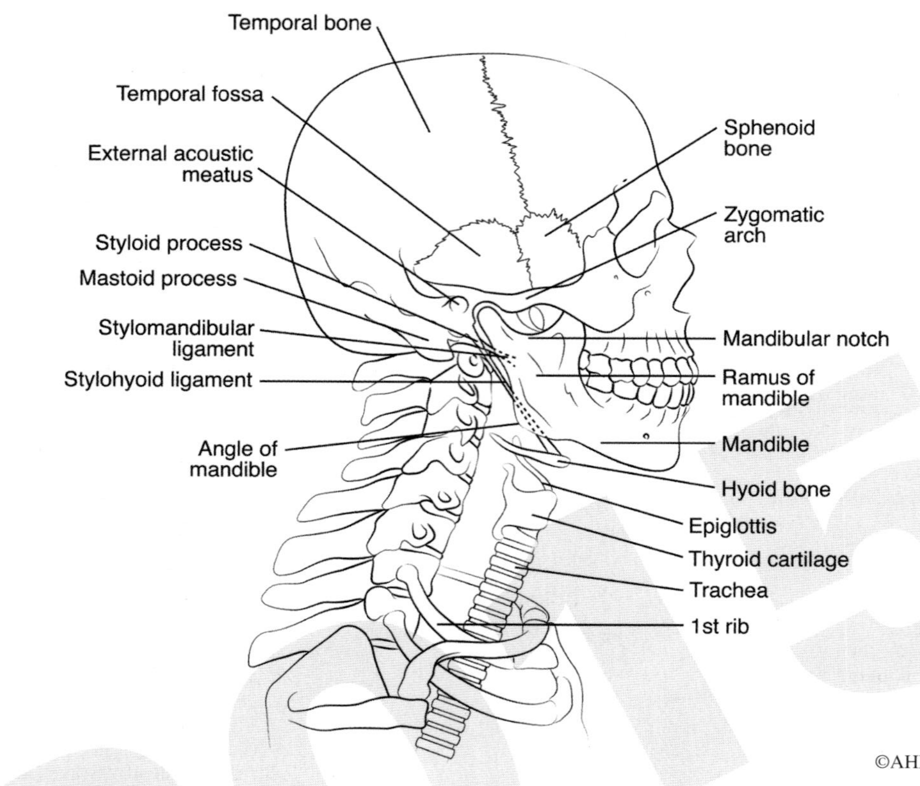
Temporal bone
Temporal fossa
External acoustic meatus
Styloid process
Mastoid process
Stylomandibular ligament
Stylohyoid ligament
Angle of mandible
Sphenoid bone
Zygomatic arch
Mandibular notch
Ramus of mandible
Mandible
Hyoid bone
Epiglottis
Thyroid cartilage
Trachea
1st rib
©AHIMA

Head and Facial Bones - Side View

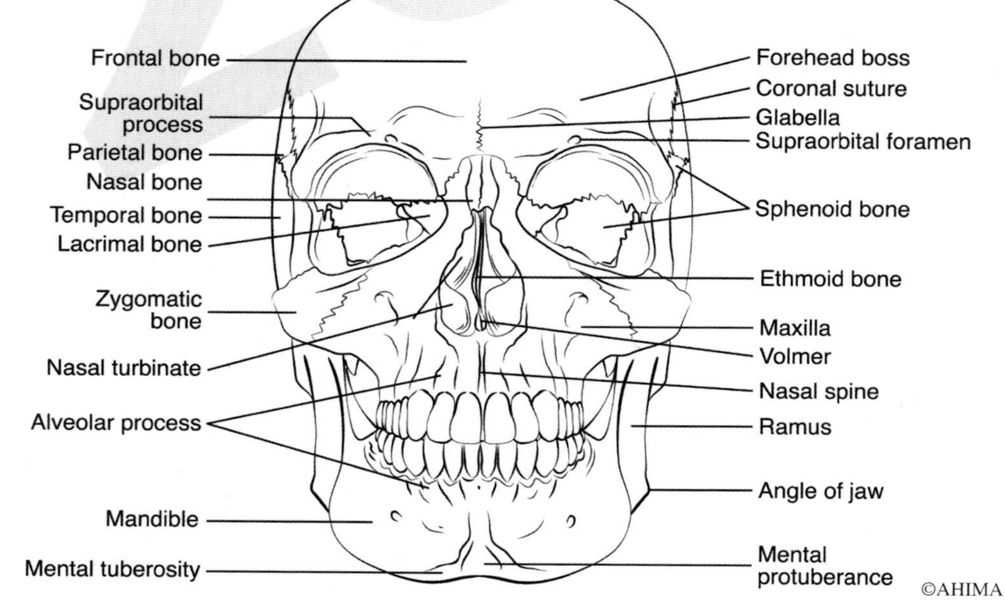
Frontal bone
Supraorbital process
Parietal bone
Nasal bone
Temporal bone
Lacrimal bone
Zygomatic bone
Nasal turbinate
Alveolar process
Mandible
Mental tuberosity
Forehead boss
Coronal suture
Glabella
Supraorbital foramen
Sphenoid bone
Ethmoid bone
Maxilla
Volmer
Nasal spine
Ramus
Angle of jaw
Mental protuberance
©AHIMA

CC +7th **S02.402 Zygomatic fracture, unspecified**
CC Exclusion 7th characters A & B see Appendix A PDX collection 1143
CC Exclusion 7th character K see Appendix A PDX collection 0897
HAC 7th characters A & B see Appendix B for HAC conditional logic

+ **S02.41 LeFort fracture**

CC +7th **S02.411 LeFort I fracture**
CC Exclusion 7th characters A & B see Appendix A PDX collection 1143
CC Exclusion 7th character K see Appendix A PDX collection 0897
HAC 7th characters A & B see Appendix B for HAC conditional logic

CC +7th **S02.412 LeFort II fracture**
CC Exclusion 7th characters A & B see Appendix A PDX collection 1143
CC Exclusion 7th character K see Appendix A PDX collection 0897
HAC 7th characters A & B see Appendix B for HAC conditional logic

CC +7th **S02.413 LeFort III fracture**
CC Exclusion 7th characters A & B see Appendix A PDX collection 1143
CC Exclusion 7th character K see Appendix A PDX collection 0897
HAC 7th characters A & B see Appendix B for HAC conditional logic

CC X+7th **S02.42 Fracture of alveolus of maxilla**
CC Exclusion 7th characters A & B see Appendix A PDX collection 1142
CC Exclusion 7th character K see Appendix A PDX collection 0897
HAC 7th characters A & B see Appendix B for HAC conditional logic

CC X+7th **S02.5 Fracture of tooth (traumatic)**
Broken tooth
Excludes1: *cracked tooth (nontraumatic) (K03.81)*
CC Exclusion 7th character K see Appendix A PDX collection 0897

+ **S02.6 Fracture of mandible**
Fracture of lower jaw (bone)

+ **S02.60 Fracture of mandible, unspecified**

CC **S02.600 Fracture of unspecified part of body of mandible**
CC Exclusion 7th characters A & B see Appendix A PDX collection 1143
CC Exclusion 7th character K see Appendix A PDX collection 0897
HAC 7th characters A & B see Appendix B for HAC conditional logic

CC **S02.609 Fracture of mandible, unspecified**
CC Exclusion 7th characters A & B see Appendix A PDX collection 1143
CC Exclusion 7th character K see Appendix A PDX collection 0897
HAC 7th characters A & B see Appendix B for HAC conditional logic

CC X+7th **S02.61 Fracture of condylar process of mandible**
CC Exclusion 7th characters A & B see Appendix A PDX collection 1143
CC Exclusion 7th character K see Appendix A PDX collection 0897
HAC 7th characters A & B see Appendix B for HAC conditional logic

CC X+7th **S02.62 Fracture of subcondylar process of mandible**
CC Exclusion 7th characters A & B see Appendix A PDX collection 1143
CC Exclusion 7th character K see Appendix A PDX collection 0897
HAC 7th characters A & B see Appendix B for HAC conditional logic

CC X+7th **S02.63 Fracture of coronoid process of mandible**
CC Exclusion 7th characters A & B see Appendix A PDX collection 1143
CC Exclusion 7th character K see Appendix A PDX collection 0897
HAC 7th characters A & B see Appendix B for HAC conditional logic

CC X+7th **S02.64 Fracture of ramus of mandible**
CC Exclusion 7th characters A & B see Appendix A PDX collection 1143
CC Exclusion 7th character K see Appendix A PDX collection 0897
HAC 7th characters A & B see Appendix B for HAC conditional logic

CC X+7th **S02.65 Fracture of angle of mandible**
CC Exclusion 7th characters A & B see Appendix A PDX collection 1143
CC Exclusion 7th character K see Appendix A PDX collection 0897
HAC 7th characters A & B see Appendix B for HAC conditional logic

CC X+7th **S02.66 Fracture of symphysis of mandible**
CC Exclusion 7th characters A & B see Appendix A PDX collection 1143
CC Exclusion 7th character K see Appendix A PDX collection 0897
HAC 7th characters A & B see Appendix B for HAC conditional logic

CC X+7th **S02.67 Fracture of alveolus of mandible**
CC Exclusion 7th characters A & B see Appendix A PDX collection 1143
CC Exclusion 7th character K see Appendix A PDX collection 0897
HAC 7th characters A & B see Appendix B for HAC conditional logic

CC X+7th **S02.69 Fracture of mandible of other specified site**
CC Exclusion 7th characters A & B see Appendix A PDX collection 1143
CC Exclusion 7th character K see Appendix A PDX collection 0897
HAC 7th characters A & B see Appendix B for HAC conditional logic

CC X+7th **S02.8 Fractures of other specified skull and facial bones**
Fracture of orbit NOS
Fracture of palate
Excludes1: *fracture of orbital floor (S02.3-)*
fracture of orbital roof (S02.1-)
CC Exclusion 7th characters A & B see Appendix A PDX collection 1142
CC Exclusion 7th character K see Appendix A PDX collection 0897
HAC 7th characters A & B see Appendix B for HAC conditional logic

+ **S02.9 Fracture of unspecified skull and facial bones**

CC MCC X+7th **S02.91 Unspecified fracture of skull**
CC Exclusion 7th character A see Appendix A PDX collection 1140
CC Exclusion 7th character K see Appendix A PDX collection 0897
MCC Exclusion 7th character B see Appendix A PDX collection 1140
HAC 7th characters A & B see Appendix B for HAC conditional logic

CC X+7th **S02.92 Unspecified fracture of facial bones**
CC Exclusion 7th characters A & B see Appendix A PDX collection 1142
CC Exclusion 7th character K see Appendix A PDX collection 0897
HAC 7th characters A & B see Appendix B for HAC conditional logic

S03 Dislocation and sprain of joints and ligaments of head

Includes: avulsion of joint (capsule) or ligament of head
laceration of cartilage, joint (capsule) or ligament of head
sprain of cartilage, joint (capsule) or ligament of head
traumatic hemarthrosis of joint or ligament of head
traumatic rupture of joint or ligament of head
traumatic subluxation of joint or ligament of head
traumatic tear of joint or ligament of head

Code also any associated open wound
Excludes2: *Strain of muscle or tendon of head (S09.1)*

The appropriate 7th character is to be added to each code from category S03
A initial encounter
D subsequent encounter
S sequela

X+7th **S03.0 Dislocation of jaw**
Dislocation of jaw (cartilage) (meniscus)
Dislocation of mandible
Dislocation of temporomandibular (joint)

X+7th **S03.1 Dislocation of septal cartilage of nose**
X+7th **S03.2 Dislocation of tooth**
X+7th **S03.4 Sprain of jaw**
Sprain of temporomandibular (joint) (ligament)
X+7th **S03.8 Sprain of joints and ligaments of other parts of head**
X+7th **S03.9 Sprain of joints and ligaments of unspecified parts of head**

S04 Injury of cranial nerve

The selection of side should be based on the side of the body being affected

Code first any associated intracranial injury (S06.-)

Code also any associated:
open wound of head (S01.-)
skull fracture (S02.-)

The appropriate 7th character is to be added to each code from category S04
A initial encounter
D subsequent encounter
S sequela

+ **S04.0 Injury of optic nerve and pathways**
Use additional code to identify any visual field defect or blindness (H53.4-, H54)

+ **S04.01 Injury of optic nerve**
Injury of 2nd cranial nerve

CC +7th **S04.011 Injury of optic nerve, right eye**
CC Exclusion 7th character A see Appendix A PDX collection 1144

CC +7th **S04.012 Injury of optic nerve, left eye**
CC Exclusion 7th character A see Appendix A PDX collection 1144

CC +7th **S04.019 Injury of optic nerve, unspecified eye**
Injury of optic nerve NOS
CC Exclusion 7th character A see Appendix A PDX collection 1144

CC X+7th **S04.02 Injury of optic chiasm**
CC Exclusion 7th character A see Appendix A PDX collection 1144

+ **S04.03 Injury of optic tract and pathways**
Injury of optic radiation

CC +7th **S04.031 Injury of optic tract and pathways, right eye**
CC Exclusion 7th character A see Appendix A PDX collection 1144

CC +7th **S04.032 Injury of optic tract and pathways, left eye**
CC Exclusion 7th character A see Appendix A PDX collection 1144

CC +7th **S04.039 Injury of optic tract and pathways, unspecified eye**
Injury of optic tract and pathways NOS
CC Exclusion 7th character A see Appendix A PDX collection 1144

+ **S04.04 Injury of visual cortex**

CC +7th **S04.041 Injury of visual cortex, right eye**
CC Exclusion 7th character A see Appendix A PDX collection 1144

CC +7th **S04.042 Injury of visual cortex, left eye**
CC Exclusion 7th character A see Appendix A PDX collection 1144

CC +7th **S04.049 Injury of visual cortex, unspecified eye**
Injury of visual cortex NOS
CC Exclusion 7th character A see Appendix A PDX collection 1144

+ **S04.1 Injury of oculomotor nerve**
Injury of 3rd cranial nerve

CC X+7th **S04.10 Injury of oculomotor nerve, unspecified side**
CC Exclusion 7th character A see Appendix A PDX collection 1145

CC X+7th **S04.11 Injury of oculomotor nerve, right side**
CC Exclusion 7th character A see Appendix A PDX collection 1145

CC X+7th **S04.12 Injury of oculomotor nerve, left side**
CC Exclusion 7th character A see Appendix A PDX collection 1145

+ **S04.2 Injury of trochlear nerve**
Injury of 4th cranial nerve

CC X+7th **S04.20 Injury of trochlear nerve, unspecified side**
CC Exclusion 7th character A see Appendix A PDX collection 1146

CC X+7th **S04.21 Injury of trochlear nerve, right side**
CC Exclusion 7th character A see Appendix A PDX collection 1146

CC X+7th **S04.22 Injury of trochlear nerve, left side**
CC Exclusion 7th character A see Appendix A PDX collection 1146

+ **S04.3 Injury of trigeminal nerve**
Injury of 5th cranial nerve

CC X+7th **S04.30 Injury of trigeminal nerve, unspecified side**
CC Exclusion 7th character A see Appendix A PDX collection 1147

CC X+7th **S04.31 Injury of trigeminal nerve, right side**
CC Exclusion 7th character A see Appendix A PDX collection 1147

CC X+7th **S04.32 Injury of trigeminal nerve, left side**
CC Exclusion 7th character A see Appendix A PDX collection 1147

+ **S04.4 Injury of abducent nerve**
Injury of 6th cranial nerve

CC X+7th **S04.40 Injury of abducent nerve, unspecified side**
CC Exclusion 7th character A see Appendix A PDX collection 1148

CC X+7th **S04.41 Injury of abducent nerve, right side**
CC Exclusion 7th character A see Appendix A PDX collection 1148

CC X+7th **S04.42 Injury of abducent nerve, left side**
CC Exclusion 7th character A see Appendix A PDX collection 1148

+ **S04.5 Injury of facial nerve**
Injury of 7th cranial nerve

CC X+7th **S04.50 Injury of facial nerve, unspecified side**
CC Exclusion 7th character A see Appendix A PDX collection 1149

CC X+7th **S04.51 Injury of facial nerve, right side**
CC Exclusion 7th character A see Appendix A PDX collection 1149

CC X+7th **S04.52 Injury of facial nerve, left side**
CC Exclusion 7th character A see Appendix A PDX collection 1149

+ **S04.6 Injury of acoustic nerve**
Injury of auditory nerve
Injury of 8th cranial nerve

CC X+7th **S04.60 Injury of acoustic nerve, unspecified side**
CC Exclusion 7th character A see Appendix A PDX collection 1150

CC X+7th **S04.61 Injury of acoustic nerve, right side**
CC Exclusion 7th character A see Appendix A PDX collection 1150

CC X+7th **S04.62 Injury of acoustic nerve, left side**
CC Exclusion 7th character A see Appendix A PDX collection 1150

+ **S04.7 Injury of accessory nerve**
Injury of 11th cranial nerve

CC X+7th **S04.70 Injury of accessory nerve, unspecified side**
CC Exclusion 7th character A see Appendix A PDX collection 1151

CC X+7th **S04.71 Injury of accessory nerve, right side**
CC Exclusion 7th character A see Appendix A PDX collection 1151

CC X+7th **S04.72 Injury of accessory nerve, left side**
CC Exclusion 7th character A see Appendix A PDX collection 1151

+ **S04.8 Injury of other cranial nerves**

+ **S04.81 Injury of olfactory [1st] nerve**

CC +7th **S04.811 Injury of olfactory [1st] nerve, right side**
CC Exclusion 7th character A see Appendix A PDX collection 1152

CC +7th **S04.812 Injury of olfactory [1st] nerve, left side**
CC Exclusion 7th character A see Appendix A PDX collection 1152

CC +7th **S04.819 Injury of olfactory [1st] nerve, unspecified side**
CC Exclusion 7th character A see Appendix A PDX collection 1152

+ **S04.89 Injury of other cranial nerves**
Injury of vagus [10th] nerve

CC +7th **S04.891 Injury of other cranial nerves, right side**
CC Exclusion 7th character A see Appendix A PDX collection 1152

CC +7th **S04.892 Injury of other cranial nerves, left side**
CC Exclusion 7th character A see Appendix A PDX collection 1152

CC +7th **S04.899 Injury of other cranial nerves, unspecified si[de]**
CC Exclusion 7th character A see Appendix A PDX collection 1152

CC X+7th **S04.9 Injury of unspecified cranial nerve**
CC Exclusion 7th character A see Appendix A PDX collection 1152

S05 Injury of eye and orbit

Includes: open wound of eye and orbit
Excludes2: *2nd cranial [optic] nerve injury (S04.0-)*
3rd cranial [oculomotor] nerve injury (S04.1-)
open wound of eyelid and periocular area (S01.1-)
orbital bone fracture (S02.1-, S02.3-, S02.8-)
superficial injury of eyelid (S00.1-S00.2)

The appropriate 7th character is to be added to each code from category S05
A initial encounter
D subsequent encounter
S sequela

\+ **S05.0 Injury of conjunctiva and corneal abrasion without foreign body**
Excludes1: *foreign body in conjunctival sac (T15.1)*
foreign body in cornea (T15.0)
X+7th **S05.00 Injury of conjunctiva and corneal abrasion without foreign body, unspecified eye**
X+7th **S05.01 Injury of conjunctiva and corneal abrasion without foreign body, right eye**
X+7th **S05.02 Injury of conjunctiva and corneal abrasion without foreign body, left eye**

\+ **S05.1 Contusion of eyeball and orbital tissues**
Traumatic hyphema
Excludes2: *black eye NOS (S00.1)*
contusion of eyelid and periocular area (S00.1)
X+7th **S05.10 Contusion of eyeball and orbital tissues, unspecified eye**
X+7th **S05.11 Contusion of eyeball and orbital tissues, right eye**
X+7th **S05.12 Contusion of eyeball and orbital tissues, left eye**

\+ **S05.2 Ocular laceration and rupture with prolapse or loss of intraocular tissue**
CC X+7th **S05.20 Ocular laceration and rupture with prolapse or loss of intraocular tissue, unspecified eye**
CC Exclusion 7th character A see Appendix A PDX collection 1139
CC X+7th **S05.21 Ocular laceration and rupture with prolapse or loss of intraocular tissue, right eye**
CC Exclusion 7th character A see Appendix A PDX collection 1139
CC X+7th **S05.22 Ocular laceration and rupture with prolapse or loss of intraocular tissue, left eye**
CC Exclusion 7th character A see Appendix A PDX collection 1139

\+ **S05.3 Ocular laceration without prolapse or loss of intraocular tissue**
Laceration of eye NOS
CC X+7th **S05.30 Ocular laceration without prolapse or loss of intraocular tissue, unspecified eye**
CC Exclusion 7th character A see Appendix A PDX collection 1139
CC X+7th **S05.31 Ocular laceration without prolapse or loss of intraocular tissue, right eye**
CC Exclusion 7th character A see Appendix A PDX collection 1139
CC X+7th **S05.32 Ocular laceration without prolapse or loss of intraocular tissue, left eye**
CC Exclusion 7th character A see Appendix A PDX collection 1139

\+ **S05.4 Penetrating wound of orbit with or without foreign body**
Excludes2: *retained (old) foreign body following penetrating wound in orbit (H05.5-)*
CC X+7th **S05.40 Penetrating wound of orbit with or without foreign body, unspecified eye**
CC Exclusion 7th character A see Appendix A PDX collection 1139
CC X+7th **S05.41 Penetrating wound of orbit with or without foreign body, right eye**
CC Exclusion 7th character A see Appendix A PDX collection 1139
CC X+7th **S05.42 Penetrating wound of orbit with or without foreign body, left eye**
CC Exclusion 7th character A see Appendix A PDX collection 1139

\+ **S05.5 Penetrating wound with foreign body of eyeball**
Excludes2: *retained (old) intraocular foreign body (H44.6-, H44.7)*
CC X+7th **S05.50 Penetrating wound with foreign body of unspecified eyeball**
CC Exclusion 7th character A see Appendix A PDX collection 1153
CC X+7th **S05.51 Penetrating wound with foreign body of right eyeball**
CC Exclusion 7th character A see Appendix A PDX collection 1153
CC X+7th **S05.52 Penetrating wound with foreign body of left eyeball**
CC Exclusion 7th character A see Appendix A PDX collection 1153

\+ **S05.6 Penetrating wound without foreign body of eyeball**
Ocular penetration NOS
X+7th **S05.60 Penetrating wound without foreign body of unspecified eyeball**
X+7th **S05.61 Penetrating wound without foreign body of right eyeball**
X+7th **S05.62 Penetrating wound without foreign body of left eyeball**

\+ **S05.7 Avulsion of eye**
Traumatic enucleation
CC X+7th **S05.70 Avulsion of unspecified eye**
CC Exclusion 7th character A see Appendix A PDX collection 1139
CC X+7th **S05.71 Avulsion of right eye**
CC Exclusion 7th character A see Appendix A PDX collection 1139
CC X+7th **S05.72 Avulsion of left eye**
CC Exclusion 7th character A see Appendix A PDX collection 1139

CC + **S05.8 Other injuries of eye and orbit**
Lacrimal duct injury
CC Exclusion 7th character A see Appendix A PDX collection 1139
\+ **S05.8X Other injuries of eye and orbit**
+7th **S05.8X1 Other injuries of right eye and orbit**
+7th **S05.8X2 Other injuries of left eye and orbit**
+7th **S05.8X9 Other injuries of unspecified eye and orbit**

\+ **S05.9 Unspecified injury of eye and orbit**
Injury of eye NOS
X+7th **S05.90 Unspecified injury of unspecified eye and orbit**
CC X+7th **S05.91 Unspecified injury of right eye and orbit**
CC Exclusion 7th character A see Appendix A PDX collection 1139
CC X+7th **S05.92 Unspecified injury of left eye and orbit**
CC Exclusion 7th character A see Appendix A PDX collection 1139

S06 Intracranial injury

Includes: traumatic brain injury
Code also any associated:
open wound of head (S01.-)
skull fracture (S02.-)
Excludes1: *head injury NOS (S09.90)*

The appropriate 7th character is to be added to each code from category S06
A initial encounter
D subsequent encounter
S sequela

CC + **S06.0 Concussion**
Commotio cerebri
Excludes1: *concussion with other intracranial injuries classified in category S06- code to specified intracranial injury*
CC Exclusion 7th character A see Appendix A PDX collection 1154
\+ **S06.0X Concussion**
+7th **S06.0X0 Concussion without loss of consciousness**
HAC 7th character A see Appendix B for HAC conditional logic
+7th **S06.0X1 Concussion with loss of consciousness of 30 minutes or less**
HAC 7th character A see Appendix B for HAC conditional logic
+7th **S06.0X2 Concussion with loss of consciousness of 31 minutes to 59 minutes**
HAC 7th character A see Appendix B for HAC conditional logic
+7th **S06.0X3 Concussion with loss of consciousness of 1 hour to 5 hours 59 minutes**
HAC 7th character A see Appendix B for HAC conditional logic
+7th **S06.0X4 Concussion with loss of consciousness of 6 hours to 24 hours**
HAC 7th character A see Appendix B for HAC conditional logic
+7th **S06.0X5 Concussion with loss of consciousness greater than 24 hours with return to pre-existing conscious level**
HAC 7th character A see Appendix B for HAC conditional logic

MCC +7th **S06.0X6 Concussion with loss of consciousness greater than 24 hours without return to pre-existing conscious level with patient surviving**
MCC Exclusion 7th character A see Appendix A PDX collection 1154
HAC 7th character A see Appendix B for HAC conditional logic

+7th **S06.0X7 Concussion with loss of consciousness of any duration with death due to brain injury prior to regaining consciousness**
HAC 7th character A see Appendix B for HAC conditional logic

+7th **S06.0X8 Concussion with loss of consciousness of any duration with death due to other cause prior to regaining consciousness**
HAC 7th character A see Appendix B for HAC conditional logic

+7th **S06.0X9 Concussion with loss of consciousness of unspecified duration**
Concussion NOS
HAC 7th character A see Appendix B for HAC conditional logic

\+ **S06.1 Traumatic cerebral edema**
Diffuse traumatic cerebral edema
Focal traumatic cerebral edema

\+ **S06.1X Traumatic cerebral edema**

MCC +7th **S06.1X0 Traumatic cerebral edema without loss of consciousness**
MCC Exclusion 7th character A see Appendix A PDX collection 0612
HAC 7th character A see Appendix B for HAC conditional logic

MCC +7th **S06.1X1 Traumatic cerebral edema with loss of consciousness of 30 minutes or less**
MCC Exclusion 7th character A see Appendix A PDX collection 1155
HAC 7th character A see Appendix B for HAC conditional logic

MCC +7th **S06.1X2 Traumatic cerebral edema with loss of consciousness of 31 minutes to 59 minutes**
MCC Exclusion 7th character A see Appendix A PDX collection 1155
HAC 7th character A see Appendix B for HAC conditional logic

MCC +7th **S06.1X3 Traumatic cerebral edema with loss of consciousness of 1 hour to 5 hours 59 minutes**
MCC Exclusion 7th character A see Appendix A PDX collection 1155
HAC 7th character A see Appendix B for HAC conditional logic

MCC +7th **S06.1X4 Traumatic cerebral edema with loss of consciousness of 6 hours to 24 hours**
MCC Exclusion 7th character A see Appendix A PDX collection 1155
HAC 7th character A see Appendix B for HAC conditional logic

MCC +7th **S06.1X5 Traumatic cerebral edema with loss of consciousness greater than 24 hours with return to pre-existing conscious level**
MCC Exclusion 7th character A see Appendix A PDX collection 1155
HAC 7th character A see Appendix B for HAC conditional logic

MCC +7th **S06.1X6 Traumatic cerebral edema with loss of consciousness greater than 24 hours without return to pre-existing conscious level with patient surviving**
MCC Exclusion 7th character A see Appendix A PDX collection 1154
HAC 7th character A see Appendix B for HAC conditional logic

MCC +7th **S06.1X7 Traumatic cerebral edema with loss of consciousness of any duration with death due to brain injury prior to regaining consciousness**
MCC Exclusion 7th character A see Appendix A PDX collection 1154
HAC 7th character A see Appendix B for HAC conditional logic

MCC +7th **S06.1X8 Traumatic cerebral edema with loss of consciousness of any duration with death due to other cause prior to regaining consciousness**
MCC Exclusion 7th character A see Appendix A PDX collection 1154
HAC 7th character A see Appendix B for HAC conditional logic

MCC +7th **S06.1X9 Traumatic cerebral edema with loss of consciousness of unspecified duration**
Traumatic cerebral edema NOS
MCC Exclusion 7th character A see Appendix A PDX collection 1155
HAC 7th character A see Appendix B for HAC conditional logic

CC + **S06.2 Diffuse traumatic brain injury**
Diffuse axonal brain injury
Excludes1: *traumatic diffuse cerebral edema (S06.1X-)*
CC Exclusion 7th character A see Appendix A PDX collection 1154

\+ **S06.2X Diffuse traumatic brain injury**

+7th **S06.2X0 Diffuse traumatic brain injury without loss of consciousness**
HAC 7th character A see Appendix B for HAC conditional logic

+7th **S06.2X1 Diffuse traumatic brain injury with loss of consciousness of 30 minutes or less**
HAC 7th character A see Appendix B for HAC conditional logic

+7th **S06.2X2 Diffuse traumatic brain injury with loss of consciousness of 31 minutes to 59 minutes**
HAC 7th character A see Appendix B for HAC conditional logic

+7th **S06.2X3 Diffuse traumatic brain injury with loss of consciousness of 1 hour to 5 hours 59 minutes**
HAC 7th character A see Appendix B for HAC conditional logic

+7th **S06.2X4 Diffuse traumatic brain injury with loss of consciousness of 6 hours to 24 hours**
HAC 7th character A see Appendix B for HAC conditional logic

+7th **S06.2X5 Diffuse traumatic brain injury with loss of consciousness greater than 24 hours with return to pre-existing conscious levels**
HAC 7th character A see Appendix B for HAC conditional logic

MCC +7th **S06.2X6 Diffuse traumatic brain injury with loss of consciousness greater than 24 hours without return to pre-existing conscious level with patient surviving**
MCC Exclusion 7th character A see Appendix A PDX collection 1154
HAC 7th character A see Appendix B for HAC conditional logic

MCC +7th **S06.2X7 Diffuse traumatic brain injury with loss of consciousness of any duration with death due to brain injury prior to regaining consciousness**
MCC Exclusion 7th character A see Appendix A PDX collection 1154
HAC 7th character A see Appendix B for HAC conditional logic

MCC +7th **S06.2X8 Diffuse traumatic brain injury with loss of consciousness of any duration with death due to other cause prior to regaining consciousness**
MCC Exclusion 7th character A see Appendix A PDX collection 1154
HAC 7th character A see Appendix B for HAC conditional logic

+7th **S06.2X9 Diffuse traumatic brain injury with loss of consciousness of unspecified duration**
Diffuse traumatic brain injury NOS
HAC 7th character A see Appendix B for HAC conditional logic

\+ **S06.3 Focal traumatic brain injury**
Excludes1: *any condition classifiable to S06.4-S06.6*
focal cerebral edema (S06.1)

\+ **S06.30 Unspecified focal traumatic brain injury**

+7th **S06.300 Unspecified focal traumatic brain injury without loss of consciousness**

CC +7th **S06.301 Unspecified focal traumatic brain injury with loss of consciousness of 30 minutes or less**
CC Exclusion 7th character A see Appendix A PDX collection 1154
HAC 7th character A see Appendix B for HAC conditional logic

CC +7th **S06.302 Unspecified focal traumatic brain injury with loss of consciousness of 31 minutes to 59 minutes**
CC Exclusion 7th character A see Appendix A PDX collection 1154
HAC 7th character A see Appendix B for HAC conditional logic

CC +7th **S06.303 Unspecified focal traumatic brain injury with loss of consciousness of 1 hour to 5 hours 59 minutes**
CC Exclusion 7th character A see Appendix A
PDX collection 1154
HAC 7th character A see Appendix B for HAC conditional logic

CC +7th **S06.304 Unspecified focal traumatic brain injury with loss of consciousness of 6 hours to 24 hours**
CC Exclusion 7th character A see Appendix A
PDX collection 1154
HAC 7th character A see Appendix B for HAC conditional logic

CC +7th **S06.305 Unspecified focal traumatic brain injury with loss of consciousness greater than 24 hours with return to pre-existing conscious level**
CC Exclusion 7th character A see Appendix A
PDX collection 1154
HAC 7th character A see Appendix B for HAC conditional logic

MCC +7th **S06.306 Unspecified focal traumatic brain injury with loss of consciousness greater than 24 hours without return to pre-existing conscious level with patient surviving**
MCC Exclusion 7th character A see Appendix A
PDX collection 1154
HAC 7th character A see Appendix B for HAC conditional logic

MCC +7th **S06.307 Unspecified focal traumatic brain injury with loss of consciousness of any duration with death due to brain injury prior to regaining consciousness**
MCC Exclusion 7th character A see Appendix A
PDX collection 1154
HAC 7th character A see Appendix B for HAC conditional logic

MCC +7th **S06.308 Unspecified focal traumatic brain injury with loss of consciousness of any duration with death due to other cause prior to regaining consciousness**
MCC Exclusion 7th character A see Appendix A
PDX collection 1154
HAC 7th character A see Appendix B for HAC conditional logic

CC +7th **S06.309 Unspecified focal traumatic brain injury with loss of consciousness of unspecified duration**
Unspecified focal traumatic brain injury NOS
CC Exclusion 7th character A see Appendix A
PDX collection 1154
HAC 7th character A see Appendix B for HAC conditional logic

+ S06.31 Contusion and laceration of right cerebrum

MCC +7th **S06.310 Contusion and laceration of right cerebrum without loss of consciousness**
MCC Exclusion 7th character A see Appendix A
PDX collection 1154
HAC 7th character A see Appendix B for HAC conditional logic

MCC +7th **S06.311 Contusion and laceration of right cerebrum with loss of consciousness of 30 minutes or less**
MCC Exclusion 7th character A see Appendix A
PDX collection 1154
HAC 7th character A see Appendix B for HAC conditional logic

MCC +7th **S06.312 Contusion and laceration of right cerebrum with loss of consciousness of 31 minutes to 59 minutes**
MCC Exclusion 7th character A see Appendix A
PDX collection 1154
HAC 7th character A see Appendix B for HAC conditional logic

MCC +7th **S06.313 Contusion and laceration of right cerebrum with loss of consciousness of 1 hour to 5 hours 59 minutes**
MCC Exclusion 7th character A see Appendix A
PDX collection 1154
HAC 7th character A see Appendix B for HAC conditional logic

MCC +7th **S06.314 Contusion and laceration of right cerebrum with loss of consciousness of 6 hours to 24 hours**
MCC Exclusion 7th character A see Appendix A
PDX collection 1154
HAC 7th character A see Appendix B for HAC conditional logic

MCC +7th **S06.315 Contusion and laceration of right cerebrum with loss of consciousness greater than 24 hours with return to pre-existing conscious level**
MCC Exclusion 7th character A see Appendix A
PDX collection 1154
HAC 7th character A see Appendix B for HAC conditional logic

MCC +7th **S06.316 Contusion and laceration of right cerebrum with loss of consciousness greater than 24 hours without return to pre-existing conscious level with patient surviving**
MCC Exclusion 7th character A see Appendix A
PDX collection 1154
HAC 7th character A see Appendix B for HAC conditional logic

MCC +7th **S06.317 Contusion and laceration of right cerebrum with loss of consciousness of any duration with death due to brain injury prior to regaining consciousness**
MCC Exclusion 7th character A see Appendix A
PDX collection 1154
HAC 7th character A see Appendix B for HAC conditional logic

MCC +7th **S06.318 Contusion and laceration of right cerebrum with loss of consciousness of any duration with death due to other cause prior to regaining consciousness**
MCC Exclusion 7th character A see Appendix A
PDX collection 1154
HAC 7th character A see Appendix B for HAC conditional logic

MCC +7th **S06.319 Contusion and laceration of right cerebrum with loss of consciousness of unspecified duration**
Contusion and laceration of right cerebrum NOS
MCC Exclusion 7th character A see Appendix A
PDX collection 1154
HAC 7th character A see Appendix B for HAC conditional logic

+ S06.32 Contusion and laceration of left cerebrum

MCC +7th **S06.320 Contusion and laceration of left cerebrum without loss of consciousness**
MCC Exclusion 7th character A see Appendix A
PDX collection 1154
HAC 7th character A see Appendix B for HAC conditional logic

MCC +7th **S06.321 Contusion and laceration of left cerebrum with loss of consciousness of 30 minutes or less**
MCC Exclusion 7th character A see Appendix A
PDX collection 1154
HAC 7th character A see Appendix B for HAC conditional logic

MCC +7th **S06.322 Contusion and laceration of left cerebrum with loss of consciousness of 31 minutes to 59 minutes**
MCC Exclusion 7th character A see Appendix A
PDX collection 1154
HAC 7th character A see Appendix B for HAC conditional logic

MCC +7th **S06.323 Contusion and laceration of left cerebrum with loss of consciousness of 1 hour to 5 hours 59 minutes**
MCC Exclusion 7th character A see Appendix A
PDX collection 1154
HAC 7th character A see Appendix B for HAC conditional logic

MCC +7th **S06.324 Contusion and laceration of left cerebrum with loss of consciousness of 6 hours to 24 hours**
MCC Exclusion 7th character A see Appendix A
PDX collection 1154
HAC 7th character A see Appendix B for HAC conditional logic

MCC +7th **S06.325 Contusion and laceration of left cerebrum with loss of consciousness greater than 24 hours with return to pre-existing conscious level**
MCC Exclusion 7th character A see Appendix A
PDX collection 1154
HAC 7th character A see Appendix B for HAC conditional logic

MCC +7th **S06.326 Contusion and laceration of left cerebrum with loss of consciousness greater than 24 hours without return to pre-existing conscious level with patient surviving**
MCC Exclusion 7th character A see Appendix A
PDX collection 1154
HAC 7th character A see Appendix B for HAC conditional logic

MCC +7th **S06.327 Contusion and laceration of left cerebrum with loss of consciousness of any duration with death due to brain injury prior to regaining consciousness**
MCC Exclusion 7th character A see Appendix A
PDX collection 1154
HAC 7th character A see Appendix B for HAC conditional logic

MCC +7th **S06.328 Contusion and laceration of left cerebrum with loss of consciousness of any duration with death due to other cause prior to regaining consciousness**
MCC Exclusion 7th character A see Appendix A
PDX collection 1154
HAC 7th character A see Appendix B for HAC conditional logic

MCC +7th **S06.329 Contusion and laceration of left cerebrum with loss of consciousness of unspecified duration**
Contusion and laceration of left cerebrum NOS
MCC Exclusion 7th character A see Appendix A
PDX collection 1154
HAC 7th character A see Appendix B for HAC conditional logic

\+ **S06.33 Contusion and laceration of cerebrum, unspecified**

MCC +7th **S06.330 Contusion and laceration of cerebrum, unspecified, without loss of consciousness**
MCC Exclusion 7th character A see Appendix A
PDX collection 1154
HAC 7th character A see Appendix B for HAC conditional logic

MCC +7th **S06.331 Contusion and laceration of cerebrum, unspecified, with loss of consciousness of 30 minutes or less**
MCC Exclusion 7th character A see Appendix A
PDX collection 1154
HAC 7th character A see Appendix B for HAC conditional logic

MCC +7th **S06.332 Contusion and laceration of cerebrum, unspecified, with loss of consciousness of 31 minutes to 59 minutes**
MCC Exclusion 7th character A see Appendix A
PDX collection 1154
HAC 7th character A see Appendix B for HAC conditional logic

MCC +7th **S06.333 Contusion and laceration of cerebrum, unspecified, with loss of consciousness of 1 hour to 5 hours 59 minutes**
MCC Exclusion 7th character A see Appendix A
PDX collection 1154
HAC 7th character A see Appendix B for HAC conditional logic

MCC +7th **S06.334 Contusion and laceration of cerebrum, unspecified, with loss of consciousness of 6 hours to 24 hours**
MCC Exclusion 7th character A see Appendix A
PDX collection 1154
HAC 7th character A see Appendix B for HAC conditional logic

MCC +7th **S06.335 Contusion and laceration of cerebrum, unspecified, with loss of consciousness greater than 24 hours with return to pre-existing conscious level**
MCC Exclusion 7th character A see Appendix A
PDX collection 1154
HAC 7th character A see Appendix B for HAC conditional logic

MCC +7th **S06.336 Contusion and laceration of cerebrum, unspecified, with loss of consciousness greater than 24 hours without return to pre-existing conscious level with patient surviving**
MCC Exclusion 7th character A see Appendix A
PDX collection 1154
HAC 7th character A see Appendix B for HAC conditional logic

MCC +7th **S06.337 Contusion and laceration of cerebrum, unspecified, with loss of consciousness of any duration with death due to brain injury prior to regaining consciousness**
MCC Exclusion 7th character A see Appendix A
PDX collection 1154
HAC 7th character A see Appendix B for HAC conditional logic

MCC +7th **S06.338 Contusion and laceration of cerebrum, unspecified, with loss of consciousness of any duration with death due to other cause prior to regaining consciousness**
MCC Exclusion 7th character A see Appendix A
PDX collection 1154
HAC 7th character A see Appendix B for HAC conditional logic

MCC +7th **S06.339 Contusion and laceration of cerebrum, unspecified, with loss of consciousness of unspecified duration**
Contusion and laceration of cerebrum NOS
MCC Exclusion 7th character A see Appendix A
PDX collection 1154
HAC 7th character A see Appendix B for HAC conditional logic

\+ **S06.34 Traumatic hemorrhage of right cerebrum**
Traumatic intracerebral hemorrhage and hematoma of right cerebrum

MCC +7th **S06.340 Traumatic hemorrhage of right cerebrum without loss of consciousness**
MCC Exclusion 7th character A see Appendix A
PDX collection 1154
HAC 7th character A see Appendix B for HAC conditional logic

MCC +7th **S06.341 Traumatic hemorrhage of right cerebrum with loss of consciousness of 30 minutes or less**
MCC Exclusion 7th character A see Appendix A
PDX collection 1154
HAC 7th character A see Appendix B for HAC conditional logic

MCC +7th **S06.342 Traumatic hemorrhage of right cerebrum with loss of consciousness of 31 minutes to 59 minutes**
MCC Exclusion 7th character A see Appendix A
PDX collection 1154
HAC 7th character A see Appendix B for HAC conditional logic

MCC +7th **S06.343 Traumatic hemorrhage of right cerebrum with loss of consciousness of 1 hours to 5 hours 59 minutes**
MCC Exclusion 7th character A see Appendix A
PDX collection 1154
HAC 7th character A see Appendix B for HAC conditional logic

MCC +7th **S06.344 Traumatic hemorrhage of right cerebrum with loss of consciousness of 6 hours to 24 hours**
MCC Exclusion 7th character A see Appendix A
PDX collection 1154
HAC 7th character A see Appendix B for HAC conditional logic

MCC +7th **S06.345 Traumatic hemorrhage of right cerebrum with loss of consciousness greater than 24 hours with return to pre-existing conscious level**
MCC Exclusion 7th character A see Appendix A
PDX collection 1154
HAC 7th character A see Appendix B for HAC conditional logic

MCC +7th **S06.346 Traumatic hemorrhage of right cerebrum with loss of consciousness greater than 24 hours without return to pre-existing conscious level with patient surviving**
MCC Exclusion 7th character A see Appendix A
PDX collection 1154
HAC 7th character A see Appendix B for HAC conditional logic

MCC +7th **S06.347 Traumatic hemorrhage of right cerebrum with loss of consciousness of any duration with death due to brain injury prior to regaining consciousness**
MCC Exclusion 7th character A see Appendix A
PDX collection 1154
HAC 7th character A see Appendix B for HAC conditional logic

MCC +7th **S06.348 Traumatic hemorrhage of right cerebrum with loss of consciousness of any duration with death due to other cause prior to regaining consciousness**
MCC Exclusion 7th character A see Appendix A
PDX collection 1154
HAC 7th character A see Appendix B for HAC conditional logic

MCC +7th **S06.349 Traumatic hemorrhage of right cerebrum with loss of consciousness of unspecified duration**
Traumatic hemorrhage of right cerebrum NOS
MCC Exclusion 7th character A see Appendix A
PDX collection 1154
HAC 7th character A see Appendix B for HAC conditional logic

+ **S06.35 Traumatic hemorrhage of left cerebrum**
Traumatic intracerebral hemorrhage and hematoma of left cerebrum

MCC +7th **S06.350 Traumatic hemorrhage of left cerebrum without loss of consciousness**
MCC Exclusion 7th character A see Appendix A
PDX collection 1154
HAC 7th character A see Appendix B for HAC conditional logic

MCC +7th **S06.351 Traumatic hemorrhage of left cerebrum with loss of consciousness of 30 minutes or less**
MCC Exclusion 7th character A see Appendix A
PDX collection 1154
HAC 7th character A see Appendix B for HAC conditional logic

MCC +7th **S06.352 Traumatic hemorrhage of left cerebrum with loss of consciousness of 31 minutes to 59 minutes**
MCC Exclusion 7th character A see Appendix A
PDX collection 1154
HAC 7th character A see Appendix B for HAC conditional logic

MCC +7th **S06.353 Traumatic hemorrhage of left cerebrum with loss of consciousness of 1 hours to 5 hours 59 minutes**
MCC Exclusion 7th character A see Appendix A
PDX collection 1154
HAC 7th character A see Appendix B for HAC conditional logic

MCC +7th **S06.354 Traumatic hemorrhage of left cerebrum with loss of consciousness of 6 hours to 24 hours**
MCC Exclusion 7th character A see Appendix A
PDX collection 1154
HAC 7th character A see Appendix B for HAC conditional logic

MCC +7th **S06.355 Traumatic hemorrhage of left cerebrum with loss of consciousness greater than 24 hours with return to pre-existing conscious level**
MCC Exclusion 7th character A see Appendix A
PDX collection 1154
HAC 7th character A see Appendix B for HAC conditional logic

MCC +7th **S06.356 Traumatic hemorrhage of left cerebrum with loss of consciousness greater than 24 hours without return to pre-existing conscious level with patient surviving**
MCC Exclusion 7th character A see Appendix A
PDX collection 1154
HAC 7th character A see Appendix B for HAC conditional logic

MCC +7th **S06.357 Traumatic hemorrhage of left cerebrum with loss of consciousness of≈any duration with death due to brain injury prior to regaining consciousness**
MCC Exclusion 7th character A see Appendix A
PDX collection 1154
HAC 7th character A see Appendix B for HAC conditional logic

MCC +7th **S06.358 Traumatic hemorrhage of left cerebrum with loss of consciousness of any duration with death due to other cause prior to regaining consciousness**
MCC Exclusion 7th character A see Appendix A
PDX collection 1154
HAC 7th character A see Appendix B for HAC conditional logic

MCC +7th **S06.359 Traumatic hemorrhage of left cerebrum with loss of consciousness of unspecified duration**
Traumatic hemorrhage of left cerebrum NOS
MCC Exclusion 7th character A see Appendix A
PDX collection 1154
HAC 7th character A see Appendix B for HAC conditional logic

+ **S06.36 Traumatic hemorrhage of cerebrum, unspecified**
Traumatic intracerebral hemorrhage and hematoma, unspecified

MCC +7th **S06.360 Traumatic hemorrhage of cerebrum, unspecified, without loss of consciousness**
MCC Exclusion 7th character A see Appendix A
PDX collection 1154
HAC 7th character A see Appendix B for HAC conditional logic

MCC +7th **S06.361 Traumatic hemorrhage of cerebrum, unspecified, with loss of consciousness of 30 minutes or less**
MCC Exclusion 7th character A see Appendix A
PDX collection 1154
HAC 7th character A see Appendix B for HAC conditional logic

MCC +7th **S06.362 Traumatic hemorrhage of cerebrum, unspecified, with loss of consciousness of 31 minutes to 59 minutes**
MCC Exclusion 7th character A see Appendix A
PDX collection 1154
HAC 7th character A see Appendix B for HAC conditional logic

MCC +7th **S06.363 Traumatic hemorrhage of cerebrum, unspecified, with loss of consciousness of 1 hours to 5 hours 59 minutes**
MCC Exclusion 7th character A see Appendix A
PDX collection 1154
HAC 7th character A see Appendix B for HAC conditional logic

MCC +7th **S06.364 Traumatic hemorrhage of cerebrum, unspecified, with loss of consciousness of 6 hours to 24 hours**
MCC Exclusion 7th character A see Appendix A
PDX collection 1154
HAC 7th character A see Appendix B for HAC conditional logic

MCC +7th **S06.365 Traumatic hemorrhage of cerebrum, unspecified, with loss of consciousness greater than 24 hours with return to pre-existing conscious level**
MCC Exclusion 7th character A see Appendix A
PDX collection 1154
HAC 7th character A see Appendix B for HAC conditional logic

MCC +7th **S06.366 Traumatic hemorrhage of cerebrum, unspecified, with loss of consciousness greater than 24 hours without return to pre-existing conscious level with patient surviving**
MCC Exclusion 7th character A see Appendix A
PDX collection 1154
HAC 7th character A see Appendix B for HAC conditional logic

MCC +7th **S06.367 Traumatic hemorrhage of cerebrum, unspecified, with loss of consciousness of any duration with death due to brain injury prior to regaining consciousness**
MCC Exclusion 7th character A see Appendix A
PDX collection 1154
HAC 7th character A see Appendix B for HAC conditional logic

MCC +7th **S06.368 Traumatic hemorrhage of cerebrum, unspecified, with loss of consciousness of any duration with death due to other cause prior to regaining consciousness**
MCC Exclusion 7th character A see Appendix A
PDX collection 1154
HAC 7th character A see Appendix B for HAC conditional logic

MCC +7th **S06.369 Traumatic hemorrhage of cerebrum, unspecified, with loss of consciousness of unspecified duration**
Traumatic hemorrhage of cerebrum NOS
MCC Exclusion 7th character A see Appendix A
PDX collection 1154
HAC 7th character A see Appendix B for HAC conditional logic

+ **S06.37 Contusion, laceration, and hemorrhage of cerebellum**

MCC +7th **S06.370 Contusion, laceration, and hemorrhage of cerebellum without loss of consciousness**
No MCC Exclusions
HAC 7th character A see Appendix B for HAC conditional logic

CC +7th **S06.371 Contusion, laceration, and hemorrhage of cerebellum with loss of consciousness of 30 minutes or less**
CC Exclusion 7th character A see Appendix A
PDX collection 1154
HAC 7th character A see Appendix B for HAC conditional logic

CC +7th **S06.372 Contusion, laceration, and hemorrhage of cerebellum with loss of consciousness of 31 minutes to 59 minutes**
CC Exclusion 7th character A see Appendix A
PDX collection 1154
HAC 7th character A see Appendix B for HAC conditional logic

CC +7th **S06.373 Contusion, laceration, and hemorrhage of cerebellum with loss of consciousness of 1 hour to 5 hours 59 minutes**
CC Exclusion 7th character A see Appendix A
PDX collection 1154
HAC 7th character A see Appendix B for HAC conditional logic

CC +7th **S06.374 Contusion, laceration, and hemorrhage of cerebellum with loss of consciousness of 6 hours to 24 hours**
CC Exclusion 7th character A see Appendix A
PDX collection 1154
HAC 7th character A see Appendix B for HAC conditional logic

CC +7th **S06.375 Contusion, laceration, and hemorrhage of cerebellum with loss of consciousness greater than 24 hours with return to pre-existing conscious level**
CC Exclusion 7th character A see Appendix A
PDX collection 1154
HAC 7th character A see Appendix B for HAC conditional logic

MCC +7th **S06.376 Contusion, laceration, and hemorrhage of cerebellum with loss of consciousness greater than 24 hours without return to pre-existing conscious level with patient surviving**
MCC Exclusion 7th character A see Appendix A
PDX collection 1154
HAC 7th character A see Appendix B for HAC conditional logic

MCC +7th **S06.377 Contusion, laceration, and hemorrhage of cerebellum with loss of consciousness of any duration with death due to brain injury prior to regaining consciousness**
MCC Exclusion 7th character A see Appendix A
PDX collection 1154
HAC 7th character A see Appendix B for HAC conditional logic

MCC +7th **S06.378 Contusion, laceration, and hemorrhage of cerebellum with loss of consciousness of any duration with death due to other cause prior to regaining consciousness**
MCC Exclusion 7th character A see Appendix A
PDX collection 1154
HAC 7th character A see Appendix B for HAC conditional logic

CC +7th **S06.379 Contusion, laceration, and hemorrhage of cerebellum with loss of consciousness of unspecified duration**
Contusion, laceration, and hemorrhage of cerebellum NOS
CC Exclusion 7th character A see Appendix A
PDX collection 1154
HAC 7th character A see Appendix B for HAC conditional logic

+ **S06.38 Contusion, laceration, and hemorrhage of brainstem**

MCC +7th **S06.380 Contusion, laceration, and hemorrhage of brainstem without loss of consciousness**
No MCC Exclusions
HAC 7th character A see Appendix B for HAC conditional logic

CC +7th **S06.381 Contusion, laceration, and hemorrhage of brainstem with loss of consciousness of 30 minutes or less**
CC Exclusion 7th character A see Appendix A
PDX collection 1154
HAC 7th character A see Appendix B for HAC conditional logic

CC +7th **S06.382 Contusion, laceration, and hemorrhage of brainstem with loss of consciousness of 31 minutes to 59 minutes**
CC Exclusion 7th character A see Appendix A
PDX collection 1154
HAC 7th character A see Appendix B for HAC conditional logic

CC +7th **S06.383 Contusion, laceration, and hemorrhage of brainstem with loss of consciousness of 1 hour to 5 hours 59 minutes**
CC Exclusion 7th character A see Appendix A
PDX collection 1154
HAC 7th character A see Appendix B for HAC conditional logic

CC +7th **S06.384 Contusion, laceration, and hemorrhage of brainstem with loss of consciousness of 6 hours to 24 hours**
CC Exclusion 7th character A see Appendix A
PDX collection 1154
HAC 7th character A see Appendix B for HAC conditional logic

CC +7th **S06.385 Contusion, laceration, and hemorrhage of brainstem with loss of consciousness greater than 24 hours with return to pre-existing conscious level**
CC Exclusion 7th character A see Appendix A
PDX collection 1154
HAC 7th character A see Appendix B for HAC conditional logic

MCC +7th **S06.386 Contusion, laceration, and hemorrhage of brainstem with loss of consciousness greater than 24 hours without return to pre-existing conscious level with patient surviving**
MCC Exclusion 7th character A see Appendix A
PDX collection 1154
HAC 7th character A see Appendix B for HAC conditional logic

MCC +7th **S06.387 Contusion, laceration, and hemorrhage of brainstem with loss of consciousness of any duration with death due to brain injury prior to regaining consciousness**
MCC Exclusion 7th character A see Appendix A
PDX collection 1154
HAC 7th character A see Appendix B for HAC conditional logic

MCC +7th **S06.388 Contusion, laceration, and hemorrhage of brainstem with loss of consciousness of any duration with death due to other cause prior to regaining consciousness**
MCC Exclusion 7th character A see Appendix A
PDX collection 1154
HAC 7th character A see Appendix B for HAC conditional logic

CC +7th **S06.389 Contusion, laceration, and hemorrhage of brainstem with loss of consciousness of unspecified duration**
Contusion, laceration, and hemorrhage of brainstem NOS
CC Exclusion 7th character A see Appendix A
PDX collection 1154
HAC 7th character A see Appendix B for HAC conditional logic

+ **S06.4 Epidural hemorrhage**
Extradural hemorrhage NOS
Extradural hemorrhage (traumatic)

+ **S06.4X Epidural hemorrhage**

MCC +7th **S06.4X0 Epidural hemorrhage without loss of consciousness**
MCC Exclusion 7th character A see Appendix A
PDX collection 1154
HAC 7th character A see Appendix B for HAC conditional logic

MCC +7th **S06.4X1 Epidural hemorrhage with loss of consciousness of 30 minutes or less**
MCC Exclusion 7th character A see Appendix A
PDX collection 1154
HAC 7th character A see Appendix B for HAC conditional logic

MCC +7th **S06.4X2 Epidural hemorrhage with loss of consciousness of 31 minutes to 59 minutes**
MCC Exclusion 7th character A see Appendix A
PDX collection 1154
HAC 7th character A see Appendix B for HAC conditional logic

MCC +7th **S06.4X3 Epidural hemorrhage with loss of consciousness of 1 hour to 5 hours 59 minutes**
MCC Exclusion 7th character A see Appendix A
PDX collection 1154
HAC 7th character A see Appendix B for HAC conditional logic

MCC +7th **S06.4X4 Epidural hemorrhage with loss of consciousness of 6 hours to 24 hours**
MCC Exclusion 7th character A see Appendix A
PDX collection 1154
HAC 7th character A see Appendix B for HAC conditional logic

MCC +7th **S06.4X5 Epidural hemorrhage with loss of consciousness greater than 24 hours with return to pre-existing conscious level**
MCC Exclusion 7th character A see Appendix A
PDX collection 1154
HAC 7th character A see Appendix B for HAC conditional logic

MCC +7th **S06.4X6 Epidural hemorrhage with loss of consciousness greater than 24 hours without return to pre-existing conscious level with patient surviving**
MCC Exclusion 7th character A see Appendix A
PDX collection 1154
HAC 7th character A see Appendix B for HAC conditional logic

MCC +7th **S06.4X7 Epidural hemorrhage with loss of consciousness of any duration with death due to brain injury prior to regaining consciousness**
MCC Exclusion 7th character A see Appendix A
PDX collection 1154
HAC 7th character A see Appendix B for HAC conditional logic

MCC +7th **S06.4X8 Epidural hemorrhage with loss of consciousness of any duration with death due to other causes prior to regaining consciousness**
MCC Exclusion 7th character A see Appendix A
PDX collection 1154
HAC 7th character A see Appendix B for HAC conditional logic

MCC +7th **S06.4X9 Epidural hemorrhage with loss of consciousness of unspecified duration**
Epidural hemorrhage NOS
MCC Exclusion 7th character A see Appendix A
PDX collection 1154
HAC 7th character A see Appendix B for HAC conditional logic

\+ **S06.5 Traumatic subdural hemorrhage**

\+ **S06.5X Traumatic subdural hemorrhage**

MCC +7th **S06.5X0 Traumatic subdural hemorrhage without loss of consciousness**
MCC Exclusion 7th character A see Appendix A
PDX collection 1154
HAC 7th character A see Appendix B for HAC conditional logic

MCC +7th **S06.5X1 Traumatic subdural hemorrhage with loss of consciousness of 30 minutes or less**
MCC Exclusion 7th character A see Appendix A
PDX collection 1154
HAC 7th character A see Appendix B for HAC conditional logic

MCC +7th **S06.5X2 Traumatic subdural hemorrhage with loss of consciousness of 31 minutes to 59 minutes**
MCC Exclusion 7th character A see Appendix A
PDX collection 1154
HAC 7th character A see Appendix B for HAC conditional logic

MCC +7th **S06.5X3 Traumatic subdural hemorrhage with loss of consciousness of 1 hour to 5 hours 59 minutes**
MCC Exclusion 7th character A see Appendix A
PDX collection 1154
HAC 7th character A see Appendix B for HAC conditional logic

MCC +7th **S06.5X4 Traumatic subdural hemorrhage with loss of consciousness of 6 hours to 24 hours**
MCC Exclusion 7th character A see Appendix A
PDX collection 1154
HAC 7th character A see Appendix B for HAC conditional logic

MCC +7th **S06.5X5 Traumatic subdural hemorrhage with loss of consciousness greater than 24 hours with return to pre-existing conscious level**
MCC Exclusion 7th character A see Appendix A
PDX collection 1154
HAC 7th character A see Appendix B for HAC conditional logic

MCC +7th **S06.5X6 Traumatic subdural hemorrhage with loss of consciousness greater than 24 hours without return to pre-existing conscious level with patient surviving**
MCC Exclusion 7th character A see Appendix A
PDX collection 1154
HAC 7th character A see Appendix B for HAC conditional logic

MCC +7th **S06.5X7 Traumatic subdural hemorrhage with loss of consciousness of any duration with death due to brain injury before regaining consciousness**
MCC Exclusion 7th character A see Appendix A
PDX collection 1154
HAC 7th character A see Appendix B for HAC conditional logic

MCC +7th **S06.5X8 Traumatic subdural hemorrhage with loss of consciousness of any duration with death due to other cause before regaining consciousness**
MCC Exclusion 7th character A see Appendix A
PDX collection 1154
HAC 7th character A see Appendix B for HAC conditional logic

MCC +7th **S06.5X9 Traumatic subdural hemorrhage with loss of consciousness of unspecified duration**
Traumatic subdural hemorrhage NOS
MCC Exclusion 7th character A see Appendix A
PDX collection 1154
HAC 7th character A see Appendix B for HAC conditional logic

\+ **S06.6 Traumatic subarachnoid hemorrhage**

\+ **S06.6X Traumatic subarachnoid hemorrhage**

MCC +7th **S06.6X0 Traumatic subarachnoid hemorrhage without loss of consciousness**
MCC Exclusion 7th character A see Appendix A
PDX collection 1154
HAC 7th character A see Appendix B for HAC conditional logic

MCC +7th **S06.6X1 Traumatic subarachnoid hemorrhage with loss of consciousness of 30 minutes or less**
MCC Exclusion 7th character A see Appendix A
PDX collection 1154
HAC 7th character A see Appendix B for HAC conditional logic

MCC +7th **S06.6X2 Traumatic subarachnoid hemorrhage with loss of consciousness of 31 minutes to 59 minutes**
MCC Exclusion 7th character A see Appendix A
PDX collection 1154
HAC 7th character A see Appendix B for HAC conditional logic

MCC +7th **S06.6X3 Traumatic subarachnoid hemorrhage with loss of consciousness of 1 hour to 5 hours 59 minutes**
MCC Exclusion 7th character A see Appendix A
PDX collection 1154
HAC 7th character A see Appendix B for HAC conditional logic

MCC +7th **S06.6X4 Traumatic subarachnoid hemorrhage with loss of consciousness of 6 hours to 24 hours**
MCC Exclusion 7th character A see Appendix A
PDX collection 1154
HAC 7th character A see Appendix B for HAC conditional logic

MCC +7th **S06.6X5 Traumatic subarachnoid hemorrhage with loss of consciousness greater than 24 hours with return to pre-existing conscious level**
MCC Exclusion 7th character A see Appendix A
PDX collection 1154
HAC 7th character A see Appendix B for HAC conditional logic

MCC +7th **S06.6X6 Traumatic subarachnoid hemorrhage with loss of consciousness greater than 24 hours without return to pre-existing conscious level with patient surviving**
MCC Exclusion 7th character A see Appendix A
PDX collection 1154
HAC 7th character A see Appendix B for HAC conditional logic

MCC +7th **S06.6X7 Traumatic subarachnoid hemorrhage with loss of consciousness of any duration with death due to brain injury prior to regaining consciousness**
MCC Exclusion 7th character A see Appendix A
PDX collection 1154
HAC 7th character A see Appendix B for HAC conditional logic

MCC +7th **S06.6X8 Traumatic subarachnoid hemorrhage with loss of consciousness of any duration with death due to other cause prior to regaining consciousness**
MCC Exclusion 7th character A see Appendix A
PDX collection 1154
HAC 7th character A see Appendix B for HAC conditional logic

MCC +7th **S06.6X9 Traumatic subarachnoid hemorrhage with loss of consciousness of unspecified duration**
Traumatic subarachnoid hemorrhage NOS
MCC Exclusion 7th character A see Appendix A
PDX collection 1154
HAC 7th character A see Appendix B for HAC conditional logic

+ **S06.8 Other specified intracranial injuries**

+ **S06.81 Injury of right internal carotid artery, intracranial portion, not elsewhere classified**

+7th **S06.810 Injury of right internal carotid artery, intracranial portion, not elsewhere classified without loss of consciousness**

CC +7th **S06.811 Injury of right internal carotid artery, intracranial portion, not elsewhere classified with loss of consciousness of 30 minutes or less**
CC Exclusion 7th character A see Appendix A
PDX collection 1154
HAC 7th character A see Appendix B for HAC conditional logic

CC +7th **S06.812 Injury of right internal carotid artery, intracranial portion, not elsewhere classified with loss of consciousness of 31 minutes to 59 minutes**
CC Exclusion 7th character A see Appendix A
PDX collection 1154
HAC 7th character A see Appendix B for HAC conditional logic

CC +7th **S06.813 Injury of right internal carotid artery, intracranial portion, not elsewhere classified with loss of consciousness of 1 hour to 5 hours 59 minutes**
CC Exclusion 7th character A see Appendix A
PDX collection 1154
HAC 7th character A see Appendix B for HAC conditional logic

CC +7th **S06.814 Injury of right internal carotid artery, intracranial portion, not elsewhere classified with loss of consciousness of 6 hours to 24 hours**
CC Exclusion 7th character A see Appendix A
PDX collection 1154
HAC 7th character A see Appendix B for HAC conditional logic

CC +7th **S06.815 Injury of right internal carotid artery, intracranial portion, not elsewhere classified with loss of consciousness greater than 24 hours with return to pre-existing conscious level**
CC Exclusion 7th character A see Appendix A
PDX collection 1154
HAC 7th character A see Appendix B for HAC conditional logic

MCC +7th **S06.816 Injury of right internal carotid artery, intracranial portion, not elsewhere classified with loss of consciousness greater than 24 hours without return to pre-existing conscious level with patient surviving**
MCC Exclusion 7th character A see Appendix A
PDX collection 1154
HAC 7th character A see Appendix B for HAC conditional logic

MCC +7th **S06.817 Injury of right internal carotid artery, intracranial portion, not elsewhere classified with loss of consciousness of any duration with death due to brain injury prior to regaining consciousness**
MCC Exclusion 7th character A see Appendix A
PDX collection 1154
HAC 7th character A see Appendix B for HAC conditional logic

MCC +7th **S06.818 Injury of right internal carotid artery, intracranial portion, not elsewhere classified with loss of consciousness of any duration with death due to other cause prior to regaining consciousness**
MCC Exclusion 7th character A see Appendix A
PDX collection 1154
HAC 7th character A see Appendix B for HAC conditional logic

CC +7th **S06.819 Injury of right internal carotid artery, intracranial portion, not elsewhere classified with loss of consciousness of unspecified duration**
Injury of right internal carotid artery, intracranial portion, not elsewhere classified NOS
CC Exclusion 7th character A see Appendix A
PDX collection 1154
HAC 7th character A see Appendix B for HAC conditional logic

+ **S06.82 Injury of left internal carotid artery, intracranial portion, not elsewhere classified**

+7th **S06.820 Injury of left internal carotid artery, intracranial portion, not elsewhere classified without loss of consciousness**

CC +7th **S06.821 Injury of left internal carotid artery, intracranial portion, not elsewhere classified with loss of consciousness of 30 minutes or less**
CC Exclusion 7th character A see Appendix A
PDX collection 1154
HAC 7th character A see Appendix B for HAC conditional logic

CC +7th **S06.822 Injury of left internal carotid artery, intracranial portion, not elsewhere classified with loss of consciousness of 31 minutes to 59 minutes**
CC Exclusion 7th character A see Appendix A
PDX collection 1154
HAC 7th character A see Appendix B for HAC conditional logic

CC +7th **S06.823 Injury of left internal carotid artery, intracranial portion, not elsewhere classified with loss of consciousness of 1 hour to 5 hours 59 minutes**
CC Exclusion 7th character A see Appendix A
PDX collection 1154
HAC 7th character A see Appendix B for HAC conditional logic

CC +7th **S06.824 Injury of left internal carotid artery, intracranial portion, not elsewhere classified with loss of consciousness of 6 hours to 24 hours**
CC Exclusion 7th character A see Appendix A
PDX collection 1154
HAC 7th character A see Appendix B for HAC conditional logic

CC +7th **S06.825 Injury of left internal carotid artery, intracranial portion, not elsewhere classified with loss of consciousness greater than 24 hours with return to pre-existing conscious level**
CC Exclusion 7th character A see Appendix A
PDX collection 1154
HAC 7th character A see Appendix B for HAC conditional logic

MCC +7th **S06.826 Injury of left internal carotid artery, intracranial portion, not elsewhere classified with loss of consciousness greater than 24 hours without return to pre-existing conscious level with patient surviving**
MCC Exclusion 7th character A see Appendix A
PDX collection 1154
HAC 7th character A see Appendix B for HAC conditional logic

MCC +7th **S06.827** **Injury of left internal carotid artery, intracranial portion, not elsewhere classified with loss of consciousness of any duration with death due to brain injury prior to regaining consciousness**
MCC Exclusion 7th character A see Appendix A PDX collection 1154
HAC 7th character A see Appendix B for HAC conditional logic

MCC +7th **S06.828** **Injury of left internal carotid artery, intracranial portion, not elsewhere classified with loss of consciousness of any duration with death due to other cause prior to regaining consciousness**
MCC Exclusion 7th character A see Appendix A PDX collection 1154
HAC 7th character A see Appendix B for HAC conditional logic

CC +7th **S06.829** **Injury of left internal carotid artery, intracranial portion, not elsewhere classified with loss of consciousness of unspecified duration**
Injury of left internal carotid artery, intracranial portion, not elsewhere classified NOS
CC Exclusion 7th character A see Appendix A PDX collection 1154
HAC 7th character A see Appendix B for HAC conditional logic

\+ **S06.89** **Other specified intracranial injury**

+7th **S06.890** **Other specified intracranial injury without loss of consciousness**

CC +7th **S06.891** **Other specified intracranial injury with loss of consciousness of 30 minutes or less**
CC Exclusion 7th character A see Appendix A PDX collection 1154
HAC 7th character A see Appendix B for HAC conditional logic

CC +7th **S06.892** **Other specified intracranial injury with loss of consciousness of 31 minutes to 59 minutes**
CC Exclusion 7th character A see Appendix A PDX collection 1154
HAC 7th character A see Appendix B for HAC conditional logic

CC +7th **S06.893** **Other specified intracranial injury with loss of consciousness of 1 hour to 5 hours 59 minutes**
CC Exclusion 7th character A see Appendix A PDX collection 1154
HAC 7th character A see Appendix B for HAC conditional logic

CC +7th **S06.894** **Other specified intracranial injury with loss of consciousness of 6 hours to 24 hours**
CC Exclusion 7th character A see Appendix A PDX collection 1154
HAC 7th character A see Appendix B for HAC conditional logic

CC +7th **S06.895** **Other specified intracranial injury with loss of consciousness greater than 24 hours with return to pre-existing conscious level**
CC Exclusion 7th character A see Appendix A PDX collection 1154
HAC 7th character A see Appendix B for HAC conditional logic

MCC +7th **S06.896** **Other specified intracranial injury with loss of consciousness greater than 24 hours without return to pre-existing conscious level with patient surviving**
MCC Exclusion 7th character A see Appendix A PDX collection 1154
HAC 7th character A see Appendix B for HAC conditional logic

MCC +7th **S06.897** **Other specified intracranial injury with loss of consciousness of any duration with death due to brain injury prior to regaining consciousness**
MCC Exclusion 7th character A see Appendix A PDX collection 1154
HAC 7th character A see Appendix B for HAC conditional logic

MCC +7th **S06.898** **Other specified intracranial injury with loss of consciousness of any duration with death due to other cause prior to regaining consciousness**
MCC Exclusion 7th character A see Appendix A PDX collection 1154
HAC 7th character A see Appendix B for HAC conditional logic

CC +7th **S06.899** **Other specified intracranial injury with loss of consciousness of unspecified duration**
CC Exclusion 7th character A see Appendix A PDX collection 1154
HAC 7th character A see Appendix B for HAC conditional logic

CC + **S06.9** **Unspecified intracranial injury**
Brain injury NOS
Head injury NOS with loss of consciousness
Excludes1: *head injury NOS (S09.90)*
CC Exclusion 7th character A see Appendix A PDX collection 1154

\+ **S06.9X** **Unspecified intracranial injury**

+7th **S06.9X0** **Unspecified intracranial injury without loss of consciousness**
HAC 7th character A see Appendix B for HAC conditional logic

+7th **S06.9X1** **Unspecified intracranial injury with loss of consciousness of 30 minutes or less**
HAC 7th character A see Appendix B for HAC conditional logic

+7th **S06.9X2** **Unspecified intracranial injury with loss of consciousness of 31 minutes to 59 minutes**
HAC 7th character A see Appendix B for HAC conditional logic

+7th **S06.9X3** **Unspecified intracranial injury with loss of consciousness of 1 hour to 5 hours 59 minutes**
HAC 7th character A see Appendix B for HAC conditional logic

+7th **S06.9X4** **Unspecified intracranial injury with loss of consciousness of 6 hours to 24 hours**
HAC 7th character A see Appendix B for HAC conditional logic

+7th **S06.9X5** **Unspecified intracranial injury with loss of consciousness greater than 24 hours with return to pre-existing conscious level**
HAC 7th character A see Appendix B for HAC conditional logic

MCC +7th **S06.9X6** **Unspecified intracranial injury with loss of consciousness greater than 24 hours without return to pre-existing conscious level with patient surviving**
MCC Exclusion 7th character A see Appendix A PDX collection 1154
HAC 7th character A see Appendix B for HAC conditional logic

MCC +7th **S06.9X7** **Unspecified intracranial injury with loss of consciousness of any duration with death due to brain injury prior to regaining consciousness**
MCC Exclusion 7th character A see Appendix A PDX collection 1154
HAC 7th character A see Appendix B for HAC conditional logic

MCC +7th **S06.9X8** **Unspecified intracranial injury with loss of consciousness of any duration with death due to other cause prior to regaining consciousness**
MCC Exclusion 7th character A see Appendix A PDX collection 1154
HAC 7th character A see Appendix B for HAC conditional logic

+7th **S06.9X9** **Unspecified intracranial injury with loss of consciousness of unspecified duration**
HAC 7th character A see Appendix B for HAC conditional logic

S07 **Crushing injury of head**
Use additional code for all associated injuries, such as:
intracranial injuries (S06.-)
skull fractures (S02.-)

The appropriate 7th character is to be added to each code from category S07
A initial encounter
D subsequent encounter
S sequela

CC X+7th **S07.0** **Crushing injury of face**
CC Exclusion 7th character A see Appendix A PDX collection 1156
HAC 7th character A see Appendix B for HAC conditional logic

CC X+7th **S07.1** **Crushing injury of skull**
CC Exclusion 7th character A see Appendix A PDX collection 1156
HAC 7th character A see Appendix B for HAC conditional logic

CC X+7th **S07.8** **Crushing injury of other parts of head**
CC Exclusion 7th character A see Appendix A PDX collection 1156
HAC 7th character A see Appendix B for HAC conditional logic

CC X+7th **S07.9** **Crushing injury of head, part unspecified**
CC Exclusion 7th character A see Appendix A PDX collection 1156
HAC 7th character A see Appendix B for HAC conditional logic

S08 Avulsion and traumatic amputation of part of head

An amputation not identified as partial or complete should be coded to complete

The appropriate 7th character is to be added to each code from category S08
A initial encounter
D subsequent encounter
S sequela

X+7th **S08.0 Avulsion of scalp**
+ **S08.1 Traumatic amputation of ear**
+ **S08.11 Complete traumatic amputation of ear**
+7th **S08.111 Complete traumatic amputation of right ear**
+7th **S08.112 Complete traumatic amputation of left ear**
+7th **S08.119 Complete traumatic amputation of unspecified ear**
+ **S08.12 Partial traumatic amputation of ear**
+7th **S08.121 Partial traumatic amputation of right ear**
+7th **S08.122 Partial traumatic amputation of left ear**
+7th **S08.129 Partial traumatic amputation of unspecified ear**
+ **S08.8 Traumatic amputation of other parts of head**
+ **S08.81 Traumatic amputation of nose**
+7th **S08.811 Complete traumatic amputation of nose**
+7th **S08.812 Partial traumatic amputation of nose**
X+7th **S08.89 Traumatic amputation of other parts of head**

S09 Other and unspecified injuries of head

The appropriate 7th character is to be added to each code from category S09
A initial encounter
D subsequent encounter
S sequela

CC X+7th **S09.0 Injury of blood vessels of head, not elsewhere classified**
Excludes1: *injury of cerebral blood vessels (S06.-)*
injury of precerebral blood vessels (S15.-)
CC Exclusion 7th character A see Appendix A PDX collection 1157
+ **S09.1 Injury of muscle and tendon of head**
Code also any associated open wound (S01.-)
Excludes2: *sprain to joints and ligament of head (S03.9)*
X+7th **S09.10 Unspecified injury of muscle and tendon of head**
Injury of muscle and tendon of head NOS
X+7th **S09.11 Strain of muscle and tendon of head**
X+7th **S09.12 Laceration of muscle and tendon of head**
X+7th **S09.19 Other specified injury of muscle and tendon of head**
+ **S09.2 Traumatic rupture of ear drum**
Excludes1: *traumatic rupture of ear drum due to blast injury (S09.31-)*
CC X+7th **S09.20 Traumatic rupture of unspecified ear drum**
CC Exclusion 7th character A see Appendix A PDX collection 1158
CC X+7th **S09.21 Traumatic rupture of right ear drum**
CC Exclusion 7th character A see Appendix A PDX collection 1158
CC X+7th **S09.22 Traumatic rupture of left ear drum**
CC Exclusion 7th character A see Appendix A PDX collection 1158
+ **S09.3 Other specified and unspecified injury of middle and inner ear**
Excludes1: *injury to ear NOS (S09.91-)*
Excludes2: *injury to external ear (S00.4-, S01.3-, S08.1-)*
+ **S09.30 Unspecified injury of middle and inner ear**
CC +7th **S09.301 Unspecified injury of right middle and inner ear**
CC Exclusion 7th character A see Appendix A PDX collection 1158
CC +7th **S09.302 Unspecified injury of left middle and inner ear**
CC Exclusion 7th character A see Appendix A PDX collection 1158
CC +7th **S09.309 Unspecified injury of unspecified middle and inner ear**
CC Exclusion 7th character A see Appendix A PDX collection 1158
+ **S09.31 Primary blast injury of ear**
Blast injury of ear NOS
CC +7th **S09.311 Primary blast injury of right ear**
CC Exclusion 7th character A see Appendix A PDX collection 1158
CC +7th **S09.312 Primary blast injury of left ear**
CC Exclusion 7th character A see Appendix A PDX collection 1158
CC +7th **S09.313 Primary blast injury of ear, bilateral**
CC Exclusion 7th character A see Appendix A PDX collection 1158
CC +7th **S09.319 Primary blast injury of unspecified ear**
CC Exclusion 7th character A see Appendix A PDX collection 1158
+ **S09.39 Other specified injury of middle and inner ear**
Secondary blast injury to ear
CC +7th **S09.391 Other specified injury of right middle and inner ear**
CC Exclusion 7th character A see Appendix A PDX collection 1158
CC +7th **S09.392 Other specified injury of left middle and inner ear**
CC Exclusion 7th character A see Appendix A PDX collection 1158
CC +7th **S09.399 Other specified injury of unspecified middle and inner ear**
CC Exclusion 7th character A see Appendix A PDX collection 1158
X+7th **S09.8 Other specified injuries of head**
+ **S09.9 Unspecified injury of face and head**
X+7th **S09.90 Unspecified injury of head**
Head injury NOS
Excludes1: *brain injury NOS (S06.9-)*
head injury NOS with loss of consciousness (S06.9-)
intracranial injury NOS (S06.9-)
X+7th **S09.91 Unspecified injury of ear**
Injury of ear NOS
X+7th **S09.92 Unspecified injury of nose**
Injury of nose NOS
X+7th **S09.93 Unspecified injury of face**
Injury of face NOS

Injuries to the neck (S10-S19)

Includes: injuries of nape
injuries of supraclavicular region
injuries of throat

Excludes2: *burns and corrosions (T20-T32)*
effects of foreign body in esophagus (T18.1)
effects of foreign body in larynx (T17.3)
effects of foreign body in pharynx (T17.2)
effects of foreign body in trachea (T17.4)
frostbite (T33-T34)
insect bite or sting, venomous (T63.4)

S10 Superficial injury of neck

The appropriate 7th character is to be added to each code from category S10
A initial encounter
D subsequent encounter
S sequela

X+7th **S10.0 Contusion of throat**
Contusion of cervical esophagus
Contusion of larynx
Contusion of pharynx
Contusion of trachea
+ **S10.1 Other and unspecified superficial injuries of throat**
X+7th **S10.10 Unspecified superficial injuries of throat**
X+7th **S10.11 Abrasion of throat**
X+7th **S10.12 Blister (nonthermal) of throat**
X+7th **S10.14 External constriction of part of throat**
X+7th **S10.15 Superficial foreign body of throat**
Splinter in the throat
X+7th **S10.16 Insect bite (nonvenomous) of throat**
X+7th **S10.17 Other superficial bite of throat**
Excludes1: *open bite of throat (S11.85)*
+ **S10.8 Superficial injury of other specified parts of neck**
X+7th **S10.80 Unspecified superficial injury of other specified part of neck**
X+7th **S10.81 Abrasion of other specified part of neck**
X+7th **S10.82 Blister (nonthermal) of other specified part of neck**
X+7th **S10.83 Contusion of other specified part of neck**
X+7th **S10.84 External constriction of other specified part of neck**
X+7th **S10.85 Superficial foreign body of other specified part of neck**
Splinter in other specified part of neck
X+7th **S10.86 Insect bite of other specified part of neck**
X+7th **S10.87 Other superficial bite of other specified part of neck**
Excludes1: *open bite of other specified parts of neck (S11.85)*

+ **S10.9 Superficial injury of unspecified part of neck**
X+7th **S10.90 Unspecified superficial injury of unspecified part of neck**
X+7th **S10.91 Abrasion of unspecified part of neck**
X+7th **S10.92 Blister (nonthermal) of unspecified part of neck**
X+7th **S10.93 Contusion of unspecified part of neck**
X+7th **S10.94 External constriction of unspecified part of neck**
X+7th **S10.95 Superficial foreign body of unspecified part of neck**
X+7th **S10.96 Insect bite of unspecified part of neck**
X+7th **S10.97 Other superficial bite of unspecified part of neck**

S11 Open wound of neck

Code also any associated:
spinal cord injury (S14.0, S14.1-)
wound infection

Excludes2: *open fracture of vertebra (S12.- with 7th character B)*

The appropriate 7th character is to be added to each code from category S11
A initial encounter
D subsequent encounter
S sequela

+ **S11.0 Open wound of larynx and trachea**
+ **S11.01 Open wound of larynx**
Excludes2: *open wound of vocal cord (S11.03)*
MCC +7th **S11.011 Laceration without foreign body of larynx**
MCC Exclusion 7th character A see Appendix A PDX collection 1159
MCC +7th **S11.012 Laceration with foreign body of larynx**
MCC Exclusion 7th character A see Appendix A PDX collection 1159
MCC +7th **S11.013 Puncture wound without foreign body of larynx**
MCC Exclusion 7th character A see Appendix A PDX collection 1159
MCC +7th **S11.014 Puncture wound with foreign body of larynx**
MCC Exclusion 7th character A see Appendix A PDX collection 1159
MCC +7th **S11.015 Open bite of larynx**
Bite of larynx NOS
MCC Exclusion 7th character A see Appendix A PDX collection 1159
MCC +7th **S11.019 Unspecified open wound of larynx**
MCC Exclusion 7th character A see Appendix A PDX collection 1159
+ **S11.02 Open wound of trachea**
Open wound of cervical trachea
Open wound of trachea NOS
Excludes2: *open wound of thoracic trachea (S27.5-)*
MCC +7th **S11.021 Laceration without foreign body of trachea**
MCC Exclusion 7th character A see Appendix A PDX collection 1159
MCC +7th **S11.022 Laceration with foreign body of trachea**
MCC Exclusion 7th character A see Appendix A PDX collection 1159
MCC +7th **S11.023 Puncture wound without foreign body of trachea**
MCC Exclusion 7th character A see Appendix A PDX collection 1159
MCC +7th **S11.024 Puncture wound with foreign body of trachea**
MCC Exclusion 7th character A see Appendix A PDX collection 1159
MCC +7th **S11.025 Open bite of trachea**
Bite of trachea NOS
MCC Exclusion 7th character A see Appendix A PDX collection 1159
MCC +7th **S11.029 Unspecified open wound of trachea**
MCC Exclusion 7th character A see Appendix A PDX collection 1159
+ **S11.03 Open wound of vocal cord**
MCC +7th **S11.031 Laceration without foreign body of vocal cord**
MCC Exclusion 7th character A see Appendix A PDX collection 1159
MCC +7th **S11.032 Laceration with foreign body of vocal cord**
MCC Exclusion 7th character A see Appendix A PDX collection 1159
MCC +7th **S11.033 Puncture wound without foreign body of vocal cord**
MCC Exclusion 7th character A see Appendix A PDX collection 1159
MCC +7th **S11.034 Puncture wound with foreign body of vocal cord**
MCC Exclusion 7th character A see Appendix A PDX collection 1159
MCC +7th **S11.035 Open bite of vocal cord**
Bite of vocal cord NOS
MCC Exclusion 7th character A see Appendix A PDX collection 1159
MCC +7th **S11.039 Unspecified open wound of vocal cord**
MCC Exclusion 7th character A see Appendix A PDX collection 1159

+ **S11.1 Open wound of thyroid gland**
CC X+7th **S11.10 Unspecified open wound of thyroid gland**
CC Exclusion 7th character A see Appendix A PDX collection 1160
CC X+7th **S11.11 Laceration without foreign body of thyroid gland**
CC Exclusion 7th character A see Appendix A PDX collection 1160
CC X+7th **S11.12 Laceration with foreign body of thyroid gland**
CC Exclusion 7th character A see Appendix A PDX collection 1161
CC X+7th **S11.13 Puncture wound without foreign body of thyroid gland**
CC Exclusion 7th character A see Appendix A PDX collection 1160
CC X+7th **S11.14 Puncture wound with foreign body of thyroid gland**
CC Exclusion 7th character A see Appendix A PDX collection 1161
CC X+7th **S11.15 Open bite of thyroid gland**
Bite of thyroid gland NOS
CC Exclusion 7th character A see Appendix A PDX collection 1160

+ **S11.2 Open wound of pharynx and cervical esophagus**
Excludes1: *open wound of esophagus NOS (S27.8-)*
CC X+7th **S11.20 Unspecified open wound of pharynx and cervical esophagus**
CC Exclusion 7th character A see Appendix A PDX collection 1162
CC X+7th **S11.21 Laceration without foreign body of pharynx and cervical esophagus**
CC Exclusion 7th character A see Appendix A PDX collection 1162
CC X+7th **S11.22 Laceration with foreign body of pharynx and cervical esophagus**
CC Exclusion 7th character A see Appendix A PDX collection 1163
CC X+7th **S11.23 Puncture wound without foreign body of pharynx and cervical esophagus**
CC Exclusion 7th character A see Appendix A PDX collection 1162
CC X+7th **S11.24 Puncture wound with foreign body of pharynx and cervical esophagus**
CC Exclusion 7th character A see Appendix A PDX collection 1163
CC X+7th **S11.25 Open bite of pharynx and cervical esophagus**
Bite of pharynx and cervical esophagus NOS
CC Exclusion 7th character A see Appendix A PDX collection 1162

+ **S11.8 Open wound of other specified parts of neck**
X+7th **S11.80 Unspecified open wound of other specified part of neck**
X+7th **S11.81 Laceration without foreign body of other specified part of neck**
X+7th **S11.82 Laceration with foreign body of other specified part of neck**
X+7th **S11.83 Puncture wound without foreign body of other specified part of neck**
X+7th **S11.84 Puncture wound with foreign body of other specified part of neck**
X+7th **S11.85 Open bite of other specified part of neck**
Bite of other specified part of neck NOS
Excludes1: *superficial bite of other specified part of neck (S10.87)*
S11.89 Other open wound of other specified part of neck

+ **S11.9 Open wound of unspecified part of neck**
X+7th **S11.90 Unspecified open wound of unspecified part of neck**
X+7th **S11.91 Laceration without foreign body of unspecified part of neck**
X+7th **S11.92 Laceration with foreign body of unspecified part of neck**
X+7th **S11.93 Puncture wound without foreign body of unspecified part of neck**
X+7th **S11.94 Puncture wound with foreign body of unspecified part of neck**
X+7th **S11.95 Open bite of unspecified part of neck**
Bite of neck NOS
Excludes1: *superficial bite of neck (S10.97)*

S12 Fracture of cervical vertebra and other parts of neck

NOTE A fracture not indicated as displaced or nondisplaced should be coded to displaced

A fracture not indicated as open or closed should be coded to closed

Includes: fracture of cervical neural arch
fracture of cervical spine
fracture of cervical spinous process
fracture of cervical transverse process
fracture of cervical vertebral arch
fracture of neck

Code first any associated cervical spinal cord injury (S14.0, S14.1-)

The appropriate 7th character is to be added to all codes from subcategories S12.0-S12.6
- A initial encounter for closed fracture
- B initial encounter for open fracture
- D subsequent encounter for fracture with routine healing
- G subsequent encounter for fracture with delayed healing
- K subsequent encounter for fracture with nonunion
- S sequela

Review coding guideline C.19.c

+ **S12.0 Fracture of first cervical vertebra**
Atlas

+ **S12.00 Unspecified fracture of first cervical vertebra**

CC MCC +7th **S12.000 Unspecified displaced fracture of first cervical vertebra**
CC Exclusion 7th character A see Appendix A PDX collection 1164
CC Exclusion 7th character K see Appendix A PDX collection 0897
MCC Exclusion 7th character B see Appendix A PDX collection 1164
HAC 7th characters A & B see Appendix B for HAC conditional logic

CC MCC +7th **S12.001 Unspecified nondisplaced fracture of first cervical vertebra**
CC Exclusion 7th character A see Appendix A PDX collection 1164
CC Exclusion 7th character K see Appendix A PDX collection 0897
MCC Exclusion 7th character B see Appendix A PDX collection 1164
HAC 7th characters A & B see Appendix B for HAC conditional logic

CC MCC X+7th **S12.01 Stable burst fracture of first cervical vertebra**
CC Exclusion 7th character A see Appendix A PDX collection 1164
CC Exclusion 7th character K see Appendix A PDX collection 0897
MCC Exclusion 7th character B see Appendix A PDX collection 1164
HAC 7th characters A & B see Appendix B for HAC conditional logic

CC MCC X+7th **S12.02 Unstable burst fracture of first cervical vertebra**
CC Exclusion 7th character A see Appendix A PDX collection 1164
CC Exclusion 7th character K see Appendix A PDX collection 0897
MCC Exclusion 7th character B see Appendix A PDX collection 1164
HAC 7th characters A & B see Appendix B for HAC conditional logic

+ **S12.03 Posterior arch fracture of first cervical vertebra**

CC MCC +7th **S12.030 Displaced posterior arch fracture of first cervical vertebra**
CC Exclusion 7th character A see Appendix A PDX collection 1164
CC Exclusion 7th character K see Appendix A PDX collection 0897
MCC Exclusion 7th character B see Appendix A PDX collection 1164
HAC 7th characters A & B see Appendix B for HAC conditional logic

Vertebrae

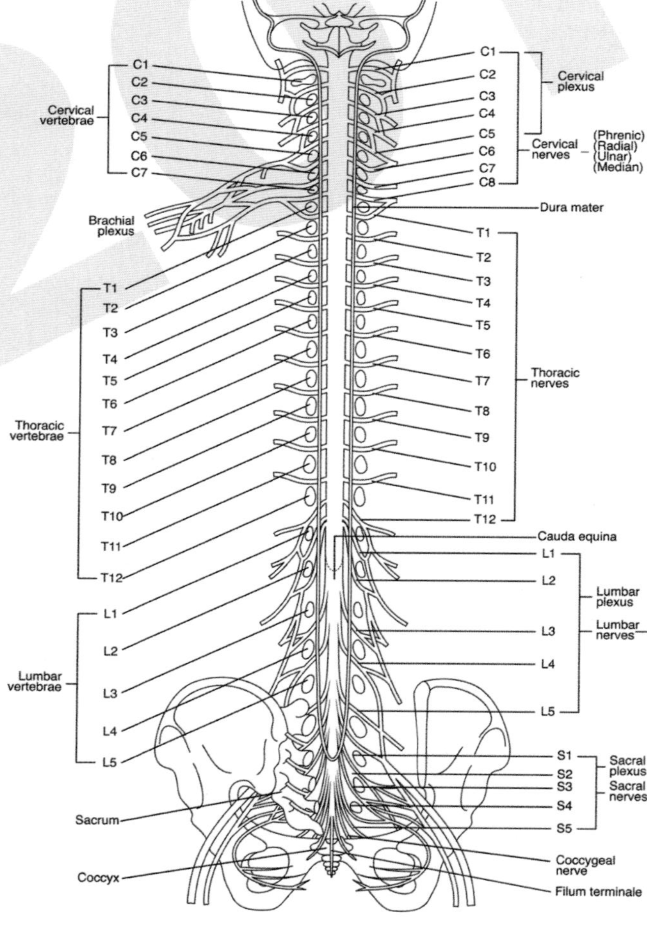

©AHIMA

CC MCC +7th **S12.031 Nondisplaced posterior arch fracture of first cervical vertebra**
CC Exclusion 7th character A see Appendix A
PDX collection 1164
CC Exclusion 7th character K see Appendix A
PDX collection 0897
MCC Exclusion 7th character B see Appendix A
PDX collection 1164
HAC 7th characters A & B see Appendix B for HAC conditional logic

+ S12.04 Lateral mass fracture of first cervical vertebra

CC MCC +7th **S12.040 Displaced lateral mass fracture of first cervical vertebra**
CC Exclusion 7th character A see Appendix A
PDX collection 1164
CC Exclusion 7th character K see Appendix A
PDX collection 0897
MCC Exclusion 7th character B see Appendix A
PDX collection 1164
HAC 7th characters A & B see Appendix B for HAC conditional logic

CC MCC +7th **S12.041 Nondisplaced lateral mass fracture of first cervical vertebra**
CC Exclusion 7th character A see Appendix A
PDX collection 1164
CC Exclusion 7th character K see Appendix A
PDX collection 0897
MCC Exclusion 7th character B see Appendix A
PDX collection 1164
HAC 7th characters A & B see Appendix B for HAC conditional logic

+ S12.09 Other fracture of first cervical vertebra

CC MCC +7th **S12.090 Other displaced fracture of first cervical vertebra**
CC Exclusion 7th character A see Appendix A
PDX collection 1164
CC Exclusion 7th character K see Appendix A
PDX collection 0897
MCC Exclusion 7th character B see Appendix A
PDX collection 1164
HAC 7th characters A & B see Appendix B for HAC conditional logic

CC MCC +7th **S12.091 Other nondisplaced fracture of first cervical vertebra**
CC Exclusion 7th character A see Appendix A
PDX collection 1164
CC Exclusion 7th character K see Appendix A
PDX collection 0897
MCC Exclusion 7th character B see Appendix A
PDX collection 1164
HAC 7th characters A & B see Appendix B for HAC conditional logic

+ S12.1 Fracture of second cervical vertebra
Axis

+ S12.10 Unspecified fracture of second cervical vertebra

CC MCC +7th **S12.100 Unspecified displaced fracture of second cervical vertebra**
CC Exclusion 7th character A see Appendix A
PDX collection 1164
CC Exclusion 7th character K see Appendix A
PDX collection 0897
MCC Exclusion 7th character B see Appendix A
PDX collection 1164
HAC 7th characters A & B see Appendix B for HAC conditional logic

CC MCC +7th **S12.101 Unspecified nondisplaced fracture of second cervical vertebra**
CC Exclusion 7th character A see Appendix A
PDX collection 1164
CC Exclusion 7th character K see Appendix A
PDX collection 0897
MCC Exclusion 7th character B see Appendix A
PDX collection 1164
HAC 7th characters A & B see Appendix B for HAC conditional logic

+ S12.11 Type II dens fracture

CC MCC +7th **S12.110 Anterior displaced Type II dens fracture**
CC Exclusion 7th character A see Appendix A
PDX collection 1164
CC Exclusion 7th character K see Appendix A
PDX collection 0897
MCC Exclusion 7th character B see Appendix A
PDX collection 1164
HAC 7th characters A & B see Appendix B for HAC conditional logic

CC MCC +7th **S12.111 Posterior displaced Type II dens fracture**
CC Exclusion 7th character A see Appendix A
PDX collection 1164
CC Exclusion 7th character K see Appendix A
PDX collection 0897
MCC Exclusion 7th character B see Appendix A
PDX collection 1164
HAC 7th characters A & B see Appendix B for HAC conditional logic

CC MCC +7th **S12.112 Nondisplaced Type II dens fracture**
CC Exclusion 7th character A see Appendix A
PDX collection 1164
CC Exclusion 7th character K see Appendix A
PDX collection 0897
MCC Exclusion 7th character B see Appendix A
PDX collection 1164
HAC 7th characters A & B see Appendix B for HAC conditional logic

+ S12.12 Other dens fracture

CC MCC +7th **S12.120 Other displaced dens fracture**
CC Exclusion 7th character A see Appendix A
PDX collection 1164
CC Exclusion 7th character K see Appendix A
PDX collection 0897
MCC Exclusion 7th character B see Appendix A
PDX collection 1164
HAC 7th characters A & B see Appendix B for HAC conditional logic

CC MCC +7th **S12.121 Other nondisplaced dens fracture**
CC Exclusion 7th character A see Appendix A
PDX collection 1164
CC Exclusion 7th character K see Appendix A
PDX collection 0897
MCC Exclusion 7th character B see Appendix A
PDX collection 1164
HAC 7th characters A & B see Appendix B for HAC conditional logic

+ S12.13 Unspecified traumatic spondylolisthesis of second cervical vertebra

CC MCC +7th **S12.130 Unspecified traumatic displaced spondylolisthesis of second cervical vertebra**
CC Exclusion 7th character A see Appendix A
PDX collection 1164
CC Exclusion 7th character K see Appendix A
PDX collection 0897
MCC Exclusion 7th character B see Appendix A
PDX collection 1164
HAC 7th characters A & B see Appendix B for HAC conditional logic

CC MCC +7th **S12.131 Unspecified traumatic nondisplaced spondylolisthesis of second cervical vertebra**
CC Exclusion 7th character A see Appendix A
PDX collection 1164
CC Exclusion 7th character K see Appendix A
PDX collection 0897
MCC Exclusion 7th character B see Appendix A
PDX collection 1164
HAC 7th characters A & B see Appendix B for HAC conditional logic

CC MCC X+7th **S12.14 Type III traumatic spondylolisthesis of second cervical vertebra**
CC Exclusion 7th character A see Appendix A PDX collection 1164
CC Exclusion 7th character K see Appendix A PDX collection 0897
MCC Exclusion 7th character B see Appendix A PDX collection 1164
HAC 7th characters A & B see Appendix B for HAC conditional logic

+ S12.15 Other traumatic spondylolisthesis of second cervical vertebra

CC MCC +7th **S12.150 Other traumatic displaced spondylolisthesis of second cervical vertebra**
CC Exclusion 7th character A see Appendix A
PDX collection 1164
CC Exclusion 7th character K see Appendix A
PDX collection 0897
MCC Exclusion 7th character B see Appendix A
PDX collection 1164
HAC 7th characters A & B see Appendix B for HAC conditional logic

CC MCC +7th **S12.151 Other traumatic nondisplaced spondylolisthesis of second cervical vertebra**
CC Exclusion 7th character A see Appendix A
PDX collection 1164
CC Exclusion 7th character K see Appendix A
PDX collection 0897
MCC Exclusion 7th character B see Appendix A
PDX collection 1164
HAC 7th characters A & B see Appendix B for HAC conditional logic

+ S12.19 Other fracture of second cervical vertebra

CC MCC +7th **S12.190 Other displaced fracture of second cervical vertebra**
CC Exclusion 7th character A see Appendix A
PDX collection 1164
CC Exclusion 7th character K see Appendix A
PDX collection 0897
MCC Exclusion 7th character B see Appendix A
PDX collection 1164
HAC 7th characters A & B see Appendix B for HAC conditional logic

CC MCC +7th **S12.191 Other nondisplaced fracture of second cervical vertebra**
CC Exclusion 7th character A see Appendix A
PDX collection 1164
CC Exclusion 7th character K see Appendix A
PDX collection 0897
MCC Exclusion 7th character B see Appendix A
PDX collection 1164
HAC 7th characters A & B see Appendix B for HAC conditional logic

+ S12.2 Fracture of third cervical vertebra

+ S12.20 Unspecified fracture of third cervical vertebra

CC MCC +7th **S12.200 Unspecified displaced fracture of third cervical vertebra**
CC Exclusion 7th character A see Appendix A
PDX collection 1164
CC Exclusion 7th character K see Appendix A
PDX collection 0897
MCC Exclusion 7th character B see Appendix A
PDX collection 1164
HAC 7th characters A & B see Appendix B for HAC conditional logic

CC MCC +7th **S12.201 Unspecified nondisplaced fracture of third cervical vertebra**
CC Exclusion 7th character A see Appendix A
PDX collection 1164
CC Exclusion 7th character K see Appendix A
PDX collection 0897
MCC Exclusion 7th character B see Appendix A
PDX collection 1164
HAC 7th characters A & B see Appendix B for HAC conditional logic

+ S12.23 Unspecified traumatic spondylolisthesis of third cervical vertebra

CC MCC +7th **S12.230 Unspecified traumatic displaced spondylolisthesis of third cervical vertebra**
CC Exclusion 7th character A see Appendix A
PDX collection 1164
CC Exclusion 7th character K see Appendix A
PDX collection 0897
MCC Exclusion 7th character B see Appendix A
PDX collection 1164
HAC 7th characters A & B see Appendix B for HAC conditional logic

CC MCC +7th **S12.231 Unspecified traumatic nondisplaced spondylolisthesis of third cervical vertebra**
CC Exclusion 7th character A see Appendix A
PDX collection 1164
CC Exclusion 7th character K see Appendix A
PDX collection 0897
MCC Exclusion 7th character B see Appendix A
PDX collection 1164
HAC 7th characters A & B see Appendix B for HAC conditional logic

CC MCC X+7th **S12.24 Type III traumatic spondylolisthesis of third cervical vertebra**
CC Exclusion 7th character A see Appendix A PDX collection 1164
CC Exclusion 7th character K see Appendix A PDX collection 0897
MCC Exclusion 7th character B see Appendix A PDX collection 1164
HAC 7th characters A & B see Appendix B for HAC conditional logic

+ S12.25 Other traumatic spondylolisthesis of third cervical vertebra

CC MCC +7th **S12.250 Other traumatic displaced spondylolisthesis of third cervical vertebra**
CC Exclusion 7th character A see Appendix A
PDX collection 1164
CC Exclusion 7th character K see Appendix A
PDX collection 0897
MCC Exclusion 7th character B see Appendix A
PDX collection 1164
HAC 7th characters A & B see Appendix B for HAC conditional logic

CC MCC +7th **S12.251 Other traumatic nondisplaced spondylolisthesis of third cervical vertebra**
CC Exclusion 7th character A see Appendix A
PDX collection 1164
CC Exclusion 7th character K see Appendix A
PDX collection 0897
MCC Exclusion 7th character B see Appendix A
PDX collection 1164
HAC 7th characters A & B see Appendix B for HAC conditional logic

+ S12.29 Other fracture of third cervical vertebra

CC MCC +7th **S12.290 Other displaced fracture of third cervical vertebra**
CC Exclusion 7th character A see Appendix A
PDX collection 1164
CC Exclusion 7th character K see Appendix A
PDX collection 0897
MCC Exclusion 7th character B see Appendix A
PDX collection 1164
HAC 7th characters A & B see Appendix B for HAC conditional logic

CC MCC +7th **S12.291 Other nondisplaced fracture of third cervical vertebra**
CC Exclusion 7th character A see Appendix A
PDX collection 1164
CC Exclusion 7th character K see Appendix A
PDX collection 0897
MCC Exclusion 7th character B see Appendix A
PDX collection 1164
HAC 7th characters A & B see Appendix B for HAC conditional logic

+ S12.3 Fracture of fourth cervical vertebra

+ S12.30 Unspecified fracture of fourth cervical vertebra

CC MCC +7th **S12.300 Unspecified displaced fracture of fourth cervical vertebra**
CC Exclusion 7th character A see Appendix A
PDX collection 1164
CC Exclusion 7th character K see Appendix A
PDX collection 0897
MCC Exclusion 7th character B see Appendix A
PDX collection 1164
HAC 7th characters A & B see Appendix B for HAC conditional logic

CC MCC +7th **S12.301 Unspecified nondisplaced fracture of fourth cervical vertebra**
CC Exclusion 7th character A see Appendix A
PDX collection 1164
CC Exclusion 7th character K see Appendix A
PDX collection 0897
MCC Exclusion 7th character B see Appendix A
PDX collection 1164
HAC 7th characters A & B see Appendix B for HAC conditional logic

+ S12.33 Unspecified traumatic spondylolisthesis of fourth cervical vertebra

CC MCC +7th **S12.330 Unspecified traumatic displaced spondylolisthesis of fourth cervical vertebra**
CC Exclusion 7th character A see Appendix A
PDX collection 1164
CC Exclusion 7th character K see Appendix A
PDX collection 0897
MCC Exclusion 7th character B see Appendix A
PDX collection 1164
HAC 7th characters A & B see Appendix B for HAC conditional logic

CC MCC +7th **S12.331 Unspecified traumatic nondisplaced spondylolisthesis of fourth cervical vertebra**
CC Exclusion 7th character A see Appendix A
PDX collection 1164
CC Exclusion 7th character K see Appendix A
PDX collection 0897
MCC Exclusion 7th character B see Appendix A
PDX collection 1164
HAC 7th characters A & B see Appendix B for HAC conditional logic

CC MCC X+7th **S12.34 Type III traumatic spondylolisthesis of fourth cervical vertebra**
CC Exclusion 7th character A see Appendix A PDX collection 1164
CC Exclusion 7th character K see Appendix A PDX collection 0897
MCC Exclusion 7th character B see Appendix A PDX collection 1164
HAC 7th characters A & B see Appendix B for HAC conditional logic

+ **S12.35 Other traumatic spondylolisthesis of fourth cervical vertebra**

CC MCC +7th **S12.350 Other traumatic displaced spondylolisthesis of fourth cervical vertebra**
CC Exclusion 7th character A see Appendix A PDX collection 1164
CC Exclusion 7th character K see Appendix A PDX collection 0897
MCC Exclusion 7th character B see Appendix A PDX collection 1164
HAC 7th characters A & B see Appendix B for HAC conditional logic

CC MCC +7th **S12.351 Other traumatic nondisplaced spondylolisthesis of fourth cervical vertebra**
CC Exclusion 7th character A see Appendix A PDX collection 1164
CC Exclusion 7th character K see Appendix A PDX collection 0897
MCC Exclusion 7th character B see Appendix A PDX collection 1164
HAC 7th characters A & B see Appendix B for HAC conditional logic

+ **S12.39 Other fracture of fourth cervical vertebra**

CC MCC +7th **S12.390 Other displaced fracture of fourth cervical vertebra**
CC Exclusion 7th character A see Appendix A PDX collection 1164
CC Exclusion 7th character K see Appendix A PDX collection 0897
MCC Exclusion 7th character B see Appendix A PDX collection 1164
HAC 7th characters A & B see Appendix B for HAC conditional logic

CC MCC +7th **S12.391 Other nondisplaced fracture of fourth cervical vertebra**
CC Exclusion 7th character A see Appendix A PDX collection 1164
CC Exclusion 7th character K see Appendix A PDX collection 0897
MCC Exclusion 7th character B see Appendix A PDX collection 1164
HAC 7th characters A & B see Appendix B for HAC conditional logic

+ **S12.4 Fracture of fifth cervical vertebra**

+ **S12.40 Unspecified fracture of fifth cervical vertebra**

CC MCC +7th **S12.400 Unspecified displaced fracture of fifth cervical vertebra**
CC Exclusion 7th character A see Appendix A PDX collection 1164
CC Exclusion 7th character K see Appendix A PDX collection 0897
MCC Exclusion 7th character B see Appendix A PDX collection 1164
HAC 7th characters A & B see Appendix B for HAC conditional logic

CC MCC +7th **S12.401 Unspecified nondisplaced fracture of fifth cervical vertebra**
CC Exclusion 7th character A see Appendix A PDX collection 1164
CC Exclusion 7th character K see Appendix A PDX collection 0897
MCC Exclusion 7th character B see Appendix A PDX collection 1164
HAC 7th characters A & B see Appendix B for HAC conditional logic

+ **S12.43 Unspecified traumatic spondylolisthesis of fifth cervical vertebra**

CC MCC +7th **S12.430 Unspecified traumatic displaced spondylolisthesis of fifth cervical vertebra**
CC Exclusion 7th character A see Appendix A PDX collection 1164
CC Exclusion 7th character K see Appendix A PDX collection 0897
MCC Exclusion 7th character B see Appendix A PDX collection 1164
HAC 7th characters A & B see Appendix B for HAC conditional logic

CC MCC +7th **S12.431 Unspecified traumatic nondisplaced spondylolisthesis of fifth cervical vertebra**
CC Exclusion 7th character A see Appendix A PDX collection 1164
CC Exclusion 7th character K see Appendix A PDX collection 0897
MCC Exclusion 7th character B see Appendix A PDX collection 1164
HAC 7th characters A & B see Appendix B for HAC conditional logic

CC MCC X+7th **S12.44 Type III traumatic spondylolisthesis of fifth cervical vertebra**
CC Exclusion 7th character A see Appendix A PDX collection 1164
CC Exclusion 7th character K see Appendix A PDX collection 0897
MCC Exclusion 7th character B see Appendix A PDX collection 1164
HAC 7th characters A & B see Appendix B for HAC conditional logic

+ **S12.45 Other traumatic spondylolisthesis of fifth cervical vertebra**

CC MCC +7th **S12.450 Other traumatic displaced spondylolisthesis of fifth cervical vertebra**
CC Exclusion 7th character A see Appendix A PDX collection 1164
CC Exclusion 7th character K see Appendix A PDX collection 0897
MCC Exclusion 7th character B see Appendix A PDX collection 1164
HAC 7th characters A & B see Appendix B for HAC conditional logic

CC MCC +7th **S12.451 Other traumatic nondisplaced spondylolisthesis of fifth cervical vertebra**
CC Exclusion 7th character A see Appendix A PDX collection 1164
CC Exclusion 7th character K see Appendix A PDX collection 0897
MCC Exclusion 7th character B see Appendix A PDX collection 1164
HAC 7th characters A & B see Appendix B for HAC conditional logic

+ **S12.49 Other fracture of fifth cervical vertebra**

CC MCC +7th **S12.490 Other displaced fracture of fifth cervical vertebra**
CC Exclusion 7th character A see Appendix A PDX collection 1164
CC Exclusion 7th character K see Appendix A PDX collection 0897
MCC Exclusion 7th character B see Appendix A PDX collection 1164
HAC 7th characters A & B see Appendix B for HAC conditional logic

CC MCC +7th **S12.491 Other nondisplaced fracture of fifth cervical vertebra**
CC Exclusion 7th character A see Appendix A PDX collection 1164
CC Exclusion 7th character K see Appendix A PDX collection 0897
MCC Exclusion 7th character B see Appendix A PDX collection 1164
HAC 7th characters A & B see Appendix B for HAC conditional logic

+ **S12.5 Fracture of sixth cervical vertebra**

+ **S12.50 Unspecified fracture of sixth cervical vertebra**

CC MCC +7th **S12.500 Unspecified displaced fracture of sixth cervical vertebra**
CC Exclusion 7th character A see Appendix A PDX collection 1164
CC Exclusion 7th character K see Appendix A PDX collection 0897
MCC Exclusion 7th character B see Appendix A PDX collection 1164
HAC 7th characters A & B see Appendix B for HAC conditional logic

CC MCC +7th **S12.501 Unspecified nondisplaced fracture of sixth cervical vertebra**
CC Exclusion 7th character A see Appendix A PDX collection 1164
CC Exclusion 7th character K see Appendix A PDX collection 0897
MCC Exclusion 7th character B see Appendix A PDX collection 1164
HAC 7th characters A & B see Appendix B for HAC conditional logic

+ S12.53 Unspecified traumatic spondylolisthesis of sixth cervical vertebra

CC MCC +7th **S12.530 Unspecified traumatic displaced spondylolisthesis of sixth cervical vertebra**
CC Exclusion 7th character A see Appendix A PDX collection 1164
CC Exclusion 7th character K see Appendix A PDX collection 0897
MCC Exclusion 7th character B see Appendix A PDX collection 1164
HAC 7th characters A & B see Appendix B for HAC conditional logic

CC MCC +7th **S12.531 Unspecified traumatic nondisplaced spondylolisthesis of sixth cervical vertebra**
CC Exclusion 7th character A see Appendix A PDX collection 1164
CC Exclusion 7th character K see Appendix A PDX collection 0897
MCC Exclusion 7th character B see Appendix A PDX collection 1164
HAC 7th characters A & B see Appendix B for HAC conditional logic

CC MCC X+7th **S12.54 Type III traumatic spondylolisthesis of sixth cervical vertebra**
CC Exclusion 7th character A see Appendix A PDX collection 1164
CC Exclusion 7th character K see Appendix A PDX collection 0897
MCC Exclusion 7th character B see Appendix A PDX collection 1164
HAC 7th characters A & B see Appendix B for HAC conditional logic

+ S12.55 Other traumatic spondylolisthesis of sixth cervical vertebra

CC MCC +7th **S12.550 Other traumatic displaced spondylolisthesis of sixth cervical vertebra**
CC Exclusion 7th character A see Appendix A PDX collection 1164
CC Exclusion 7th character K see Appendix A PDX collection 0897
MCC Exclusion 7th character B see Appendix A PDX collection 1164
HAC 7th characters A & B see Appendix B for HAC conditional logic

CC MCC +7th **S12.551 Other traumatic nondisplaced spondylolisthesis of sixth cervical vertebra**
CC Exclusion 7th character A see Appendix A PDX collection 1164
CC Exclusion 7th character K see Appendix A PDX collection 0897
MCC Exclusion 7th character B see Appendix A PDX collection 1164
HAC 7th characters A & B see Appendix B for HAC conditional logic

+ S12.59 Other fracture of sixth cervical vertebra

CC MCC +7th **S12.590 Other displaced fracture of sixth cervical vertebra**
CC Exclusion 7th character A see Appendix A PDX collection 1164
CC Exclusion 7th character K see Appendix A PDX collection 0897
MCC Exclusion 7th character B see Appendix A PDX collection 1164
HAC 7th characters A & B see Appendix B for HAC conditional logic

CC MCC +7th **S12.591 Other nondisplaced fracture of sixth cervical vertebra**
CC Exclusion 7th character A see Appendix A PDX collection 1164
CC Exclusion 7th character K see Appendix A PDX collection 0897
MCC Exclusion 7th character B see Appendix A PDX collection 1164
HAC 7th characters A & B see Appendix B for HAC conditional logic

+ S12.6 Fracture of seventh cervical vertebra

+ S12.60 Unspecified fracture of seventh cervical vertebra

CC MCC +7th **S12.600 Unspecified displaced fracture of seventh cervical vertebra**
CC Exclusion 7th character A see Appendix A PDX collection 1164
CC Exclusion 7th character K see Appendix A PDX collection 0897
MCC Exclusion 7th character B see Appendix A PDX collection 1164
HAC 7th characters A & B see Appendix B for HAC conditional logic

CC MCC +7th **S12.601 Unspecified nondisplaced fracture of seventh cervical vertebra**
CC Exclusion 7th character A see Appendix A PDX collection 1164
CC Exclusion 7th character K see Appendix A PDX collection 0897
MCC Exclusion 7th character B see Appendix A PDX collection 1164
HAC 7th characters A & B see Appendix B for HAC conditional logic

+ S12.63 Unspecified traumatic spondylolisthesis of seventh cervical vertebra

CC MCC +7th **S12.630 Unspecified traumatic displaced spondylolisthesis of seventh cervical vertebra**
CC Exclusion 7th character A see Appendix A PDX collection 1164
CC Exclusion 7th character K see Appendix A PDX collection 0897
MCC Exclusion 7th character B see Appendix A PDX collection 1164
HAC 7th characters A & B see Appendix B for HAC conditional logic

CC MCC +7th **S12.631 Unspecified traumatic nondisplaced spondylolisthesis of seventh cervical vertebra**
CC Exclusion 7th character A see Appendix A PDX collection 1164
CC Exclusion 7th character K see Appendix A PDX collection 0897
MCC Exclusion 7th character B see Appendix A PDX collection 1164
HAC 7th characters A & B see Appendix B for HAC conditional logic

CC MCC X+7th **S12.64 Type III traumatic spondylolisthesis of seventh cervical vertebra**
CC Exclusion 7th character A see Appendix A PDX collection 1164
CC Exclusion 7th character K see Appendix A PDX collection 0897
MCC Exclusion 7th character B see Appendix A PDX collection 1164
HAC 7th characters A & B see Appendix B for HAC conditional logic

+ S12.65 Other traumatic spondylolisthesis of seventh cervical vertebra

CC MCC +7th **S12.650 Other traumatic displaced spondylolisthesis of seventh cervical vertebra**
CC Exclusion 7th character A see Appendix A PDX collection 1164
CC Exclusion 7th character A see Appendix A PDX collection 1164
MCC Exclusion 7th character B see Appendix A PDX collection 1164
HAC 7th characters A & B see Appendix B for HAC conditional logic

CC MCC +7th **S12.651 Other traumatic nondisplaced spondylolisthesis of seventh cervical vertebra**
CC Exclusion 7th character A see Appendix A PDX collection 1164
CC Exclusion 7th character K see Appendix A PDX collection 0897
MCC Exclusion 7th character B see Appendix A PDX collection 1164
HAC 7th characters A & B see Appendix B for HAC conditional logic

+ S12.69 Other fracture of seventh cervical vertebra

CC MCC +7th **S12.690 Other displaced fracture of seventh cervical vertebra**
CC Exclusion 7th character A see Appendix A PDX collection 1164
CC Exclusion 7th character K see Appendix A PDX collection 0897
MCC Exclusion 7th character B see Appendix A PDX collection 1164
HAC 7th characters A & B see Appendix B for HAC conditional logic

CC MCC +7th **S12.691 Other nondisplaced fracture of seventh cervical vertebra**
CC Exclusion 7th character A see Appendix A PDX collection 1164
CC Exclusion 7th character K see Appendix A PDX collection 0897
MCC Exclusion 7th character B see Appendix A PDX collection 1164
HAC 7th characters A & B see Appendix B for HAC conditional logic

C X+7th **S12.8 Fracture of other parts of neck**

The appropriate 7th character is to be added to code S12.8
A initial encounter
D subsequent encounter
S sequela

Hyoid bone
Larynx
Thyroid cartilage
Trachea
MCC Exclusion 7th character A see Appendix A PDX collection 1165
HAC 7th character A see Appendix B for HAC conditional logic

C X+7th **S12.9 Fracture of neck, unspecified**

The appropriate 7th character is to be added to code S12.9
A initial encounter
D subsequent encounter
S sequela

Fracture of neck NOS
Fracture of cervical spine NOS
Fracture of cervical vertebra NOS
CC Exclusion 7th character A see Appendix A PDX collection 1164
HAC 7th character A see Appendix B for HAC conditional logic

S13 Dislocation and sprain of joints and ligaments at neck level

Includes: avulsion of joint or ligament at neck level
laceration of cartilage, joint or ligament at neck level
sprain of cartilage, joint or ligament at neck level
traumatic hemarthrosis of joint or ligament at neck level
traumatic rupture of joint or ligament at neck level
traumatic subluxation of joint or ligament at neck level
traumatic tear of joint or ligament at neck level

Code also any associated open wound

Excludes2: *strain of muscle or tendon at neck level (S16.1)*

The appropriate 7th character is to be added to each code from category S13
A initial encounter
D subsequent encounter
S sequela

CC X+7th **S13.0 Traumatic rupture of cervical intervertebral disc**
Excludes1: *rupture or displacement (nontraumatic) of cervical intervertebral disc NOS (M50.-)*
CC Exclusion 7th character A see Appendix A PDX collection 0913
HAC 7th character A see Appendix B for HAC conditional logic

+ **S13.1 Subluxation and dislocation of cervical vertebrae**
Code also any associated:
open wound of neck (S11.-)
spinal cord injury (S14.1-)
Excludes2: *fracture of cervical vertebrae (S12.0-S12.3-)*

+ **S13.10 Subluxation and dislocation of unspecified cervical vertebrae**

CC +7th **S13.100 Subluxation of unspecified cervical vertebrae**
CC Exclusion 7th character A see Appendix A PDX collection 0913
HAC 7th character A see Appendix B for HAC conditional logic

CC +7th **S13.101 Dislocation of unspecified cervical vertebrae**
CC Exclusion 7th character A see Appendix A PDX collection 0913
HAC 7th character A see Appendix B for HAC conditional logic

+ **S13.11 Subluxation and dislocation of C0/C1 cervical vertebrae**
Subluxation and dislocation of atlantooccipital joint
Subluxation and dislocation of atloidooccipital joint
Subluxation and dislocation of occipitoatloid joint

CC +7th **S13.110 Subluxation of C0/C1 cervical vertebrae**
CC Exclusion 7th character A see Appendix A PDX collection 0913
HAC 7th character A see Appendix B for HAC conditional logic

CC +7th **S13.111 Dislocation of C0/C1 cervical vertebrae**
CC Exclusion 7th character A see Appendix A PDX collection 0913
HAC 7th character A see Appendix B for HAC conditional logic

+ **S13.12 Subluxation and dislocation of C1/C2 cervical vertebrae**
Subluxation and dislocation of atlantoaxial joint

CC +7th **S13.120 Subluxation of C1/C2 cervical vertebrae**
CC Exclusion 7th character A see Appendix A PDX collection 0913
HAC 7th character A see Appendix B for HAC conditional logic

CC +7th **S13.121 Dislocation of C1/C2 cervical vertebrae**
CC Exclusion 7th character A see Appendix A PDX collection 0913
HAC 7th character A see Appendix B for HAC conditional logic

+ **S13.13 Subluxation and dislocation of C2/C3 cervical vertebrae**

CC +7th **S13.130 Subluxation of C2/C3 cervical vertebrae**
CC Exclusion 7th character A see Appendix A PDX collection 0913
HAC 7th character A see Appendix B for HAC conditional logic

CC +7th **S13.131 Dislocation of C2/C3 cervical vertebrae**
CC Exclusion 7th character A see Appendix A PDX collection 0913
HAC 7th character A see Appendix B for HAC conditional logic

+ **S13.14 Subluxation and dislocation of C3/C4 cervical vertebrae**

CC +7th **S13.140 Subluxation of C3/C4 cervical vertebrae**
CC Exclusion 7th character A see Appendix A PDX collection 0913
HAC 7th character A see Appendix B for HAC conditional logic

CC +7th **S13.141 Dislocation of C3/C4 cervical vertebrae**
CC Exclusion 7th character A see Appendix A PDX collection 0913
HAC 7th character A see Appendix B for HAC conditional logic

+ **S13.15 Subluxation and dislocation of C4/C5 cervical vertebrae**

CC +7th **S13.150 Subluxation of C4/C5 cervical vertebrae**
CC Exclusion 7th character A see Appendix A PDX collection 0913
HAC 7th character A see Appendix B for HAC conditional logic

CC +7th **S13.151 Dislocation of C4/C5 cervical vertebrae**
CC Exclusion 7th character A see Appendix A PDX collection 0913
HAC 7th character A see Appendix B for HAC conditional logic

+ **S13.16 Subluxation and dislocation of C5/C6 cervical vertebrae**

CC +7th **S13.160 Subluxation of C5/C6 cervical vertebrae**
CC Exclusion 7th character A see Appendix A PDX collection 0913
HAC 7th character A see Appendix B for HAC conditional logic

CC +7th **S13.161 Dislocation of C5/C6 cervical vertebrae**
CC Exclusion 7th character A see Appendix A PDX collection 0913
HAC 7th character A see Appendix B for HAC conditional logic

+ **S13.17 Subluxation and dislocation of C6/C7 cervical vertebrae**

CC +7th **S13.170 Subluxation of C6/C7 cervical vertebrae**
CC Exclusion 7th character A see Appendix A PDX collection 0913
HAC 7th character A see Appendix B for HAC conditional logic

CC +7th **S13.171 Dislocation of C6/C7 cervical vertebrae**
CC Exclusion 7th character A see Appendix A PDX collection 0913
HAC 7th character A see Appendix B for HAC conditional logic

+ **S13.18 Subluxation and dislocation of C7/T1 cervical vertebrae**

CC +7th **S13.180 Subluxation of C7/T1 cervical vertebrae**
CC Exclusion 7th character A see Appendix A PDX collection 0913
HAC 7th character A see Appendix B for HAC conditional logic

CC +7th **S13.181 Dislocation of C7/T1 cervical vertebrae**
CC Exclusion 7th character A see Appendix A PDX collection 0913
HAC 7th character A see Appendix B for HAC conditional logic

+ S13.2 Dislocation of other and unspecified parts of neck

CC X+7th S13.20 Dislocation of unspecified parts of neck

CC Exclusion 7th character A see Appendix A PDX collection 0913

HAC 7th character A see Appendix B for HAC conditional logic

CC X+7th S13.29 Dislocation of other parts of neck

CC Exclusion 7th character A see Appendix A PDX collection 0913

HAC 7th character A see Appendix B for HAC conditional logic

X+7th S13.4 Sprain of ligaments of cervical spine

Sprain of anterior longitudinal (ligament), cervical
Sprain of atlanto-axial (joints)
Sprain of atlanto-occipital (joints)
Whiplash injury of cervical spine

X+7th S13.5 Sprain of thyroid region

Sprain of cricoarytenoid (joint) (ligament)
Sprain of cricothyroid (joint) (ligament)
Sprain of thyroid cartilage

X+7th S13.8 Sprain of joints and ligaments of other parts of neck

X+7th S13.9 Sprain of joints and ligaments of unspecified parts of neck

S14 Injury of nerves and spinal cord at neck level

NOTE Code to highest level of cervical cord injury
Code also any associated:
fracture of cervical vertebra (S12.0--S12.6.-)
open wound of neck (S11.-)
transient paralysis (R29.5)

The appropriate 7th character is to be added to each code from category S14
A initial encounter
D subsequent encounter
S sequela

MCC X+7th S14.0 Concussion and edema of cervical spinal cord

MCC Exclusion 7th character A see Appendix A PDX collection 1166

+ S14.1 Other and unspecified injuries of cervical spinal cord

+ S14.10 Unspecified injury of cervical spinal cord

MCC +7th S14.101 Unspecified injury at C1 level of cervical spinal cord

MCC Exclusion 7th character A see Appendix A PDX collection 1166

HAC 7th character A see Appendix B for HAC conditional logic

MCC +7th S14.102 Unspecified injury at C2 level of cervical spinal cord

MCC Exclusion 7th character A see Appendix A PDX collection 1166

HAC 7th character A see Appendix B for HAC conditional logic

MCC +7th S14.103 Unspecified injury at C3 level of cervical spinal cord

MCC Exclusion 7th character A see Appendix A PDX collection 1166

HAC 7th character A see Appendix B for HAC conditional logic

MCC +7th S14.104 Unspecified injury at C4 level of cervical spinal cord

MCC Exclusion 7th character A see Appendix A PDX collection 1166

HAC 7th character A see Appendix B for HAC conditional logic

MCC +7th S14.105 Unspecified injury at C5 level of cervical spinal cord

MCC Exclusion 7th character A see Appendix A PDX collection 1166

HAC 7th character A see Appendix B for HAC conditional logic

MCC +7th S14.106 Unspecified injury at C6 level of cervical spinal cord

MCC Exclusion 7th character A see Appendix A PDX collection 1166

HAC 7th character A see Appendix B for HAC conditional logic

MCC +7th S14.107 Unspecified injury at C7 level of cervical spinal cord

MCC Exclusion 7th character A see Appendix A PDX collection 1166

HAC 7th character A see Appendix B for HAC conditional logic

MCC +7th S14.108 Unspecified injury at C8 level of cervical spinal cord

MCC Exclusion 7th character A see Appendix A PDX collection 1166

+7th S14.109 Unspecified injury at unspecified level of cervical spinal cord

Injury of cervical spinal cord NOS

HAC 7th character A see Appendix B for HAC conditional logic

+ S14.11 Complete lesion of cervical spinal cord

MCC +7th S14.111 Complete lesion at C1 level of cervical spin cord

MCC Exclusion 7th character A see Appendix A PDX collection 1166

HAC 7th character A see Appendix B for HAC conditional logic

MCC +7th S14.112 Complete lesion at C2 level of cervical spina cord

MCC Exclusion 7th character A see Appendix A PDX collection 1166

HAC 7th character A see Appendix B for HAC conditional logic

MCC +7th S14.113 Complete lesion at C3 level of cervical spina cord

MCC Exclusion 7th character A see Appendix A PDX collection 1166

HAC 7th character A see Appendix B for HAC conditional logic

MCC +7th S14.114 Complete lesion at C4 level of cervical spina cord

MCC Exclusion 7th character A see Appendix A PDX collection 1166

HAC 7th character A see Appendix B for HAC conditional logic

MCC +7th S14.115 Complete lesion at C5 level of cervical spina cord

MCC Exclusion 7th character A see Appendix A PDX collection 1166

HAC 7th character A see Appendix B for HAC conditional logic

MCC +7th S14.116 Complete lesion at C6 level of cervical spina cord

MCC Exclusion 7th character A see Appendix A PDX collection 1166

HAC 7th character A see Appendix B for HAC conditional logic

MCC +7th S14.117 Complete lesion at C7 level of cervical spina cord

MCC Exclusion 7th character A see Appendix A PDX collection 1166

HAC 7th character A see Appendix B for HAC conditional logic

MCC +7th S14.118 Complete lesion at C8 level of cervical spinal cord

MCC Exclusion 7th character A see Appendix A PDX collection 1166

+7th S14.119 Complete lesion at unspecified level of cervical spinal cord

+ S14.12 Central cord syndrome of cervical spinal cord

MCC +7th S14.121 Central cord syndrome at C1 level of cervical spinal cord

MCC Exclusion 7th character A see Appendix A PDX collection 1166

HAC 7th character A see Appendix B for HAC conditional logic

MCC +7th S14.122 Central cord syndrome at C2 level of cervical spinal cord

MCC Exclusion 7th character A see Appendix A PDX collection 1166

HAC 7th character A see Appendix B for HAC conditional logic

MCC +7th S14.123 Central cord syndrome at C3 level of cervical spinal cord

MCC Exclusion 7th character A see Appendix A PDX collection 1166

HAC 7th character A see Appendix B for HAC conditional logic

MCC +7th S14.124 Central cord syndrome at C4 level of cervical spinal cord

MCC Exclusion 7th character A see Appendix A PDX collection 1166

HAC 7th character A see Appendix B for HAC conditional logic

MCC +7th S14.125 Central cord syndrome at C5 level of cervical spinal cord

MCC Exclusion 7th character A see Appendix A PDX collection 1166

HAC 7th character A see Appendix B for HAC conditional logic

MCC +7th **S14.126 Central cord syndrome at C6 level of cervical spinal cord**
MCC Exclusion 7th character A see Appendix A
PDX collection 1166
HAC 7th character A see Appendix B for HAC conditional logic

MCC +7th **S14.127 Central cord syndrome at C7 level of cervical spinal cord**
MCC Exclusion 7th character A see Appendix A
PDX collection 1166
HAC 7th character A see Appendix B for HAC conditional logic

MCC +7th **S14.128 Central cord syndrome at C8 level of cervical spinal cord**
MCC Exclusion 7th character A see Appendix A
PDX collection 1166

+7th **S14.129 Central cord syndrome at unspecified level of cervical spinal cord**

+ **S14.13 Anterior cord syndrome of cervical spinal cord**

MCC +7th **S14.131 Anterior cord syndrome at C1 level of cervical spinal cord**
MCC Exclusion 7th character A see Appendix A
PDX collection 1166
HAC 7th character A see Appendix B for HAC conditional logic

MCC +7th **S14.132 Anterior cord syndrome at C2 level of cervical spinal cord**
MCC Exclusion 7th character A see Appendix A
PDX collection 1166
HAC 7th character A see Appendix B for HAC conditional logic

MCC +7th **S14.133 Anterior cord syndrome at C3 level of cervical spinal cord**
MCC Exclusion 7th character A see Appendix A
PDX collection 1166
HAC 7th character A see Appendix B for HAC conditional logic

MCC +7th **S14.134 Anterior cord syndrome at C4 level of cervical spinal cord**
MCC Exclusion 7th character A see Appendix A
PDX collection 1166
HAC 7th character A see Appendix B for HAC conditional logic

MCC +7th **S14.135 Anterior cord syndrome at C5 level of cervical spinal cord**
MCC Exclusion 7th character A see Appendix A
PDX collection 1166
HAC 7th character A see Appendix B for HAC conditional logic

MCC +7th **S14.136 Anterior cord syndrome at C6 level of cervical spinal cord**
MCC Exclusion 7th character A see Appendix A
PDX collection 1166
HAC 7th character A see Appendix B for HAC conditional logic

MCC +7th **S14.137 Anterior cord syndrome at C7 level of cervical spinal cord**
MCC Exclusion 7th character A see Appendix A
PDX collection 1166
HAC 7th character A see Appendix B for HAC conditional logic

MCC +7th **S14.138 Anterior cord syndrome at C8 level of cervical spinal cord**
MCC Exclusion 7th character A see Appendix A
PDX collection 1166

+7th **S14.139 Anterior cord syndrome at unspecified level of cervical spinal cord**

+ **S14.14 Brown-Séquard syndrome of cervical spinal cord**

MCC +7th **S14.141 Brown-Séquard syndrome at C1 level of cervical spinal cord**
MCC Exclusion 7th character A see Appendix A
PDX collection 1166

MCC +7th **S14.142 Brown-Séquard syndrome at C2 level of cervical spinal cord**
MCC Exclusion 7th character A see Appendix A
PDX collection 1166

MCC +7th **S14.143 Brown-Séquard syndrome at C3 level of cervical spinal cord**
MCC Exclusion 7th character A see Appendix A
PDX collection 1166

MCC +7th **S14.144 Brown-Séquard syndrome at C4 level of cervical spinal cord**
MCC Exclusion 7th character A see Appendix A
PDX collection 1166

MCC +7th **S14.145 Brown-Séquard syndrome at C5 level of cervical spinal cord**
MCC Exclusion 7th character A see Appendix A
PDX collection 1166

MCC +7th **S14.146 Brown-Séquard syndrome at C6 level of cervical spinal cord**
MCC Exclusion 7th character A see Appendix A
PDX collection 1166

MCC +7th **S14.147 Brown-Séquard syndrome at C7 level of cervical spinal cord**
MCC Exclusion 7th character A see Appendix A
PDX collection 1166

MCC +7th **S14.148 Brown-Séquard syndrome at C8 level of cervical spinal cord**
MCC Exclusion 7th character A see Appendix A
PDX collection 1166

+7th **S14.149 Brown-Séquard syndrome at unspecified level of cervical spinal cord**

+ **S14.15 Other incomplete lesions of cervical spinal cord**
Incomplete lesion of cervical spinal cord NOS
Posterior cord syndrome of cervical spinal cord

MCC +7th **S14.151 Other incomplete lesion at C1 level of cervical spinal cord**
MCC Exclusion 7th character A see Appendix A
PDX collection 1166
HAC 7th character A see Appendix B for HAC conditional logic

MCC +7th **S14.152 Other incomplete lesion at C2 level of cervical spinal cord**
MCC Exclusion 7th character A see Appendix A
PDX collection 1166
HAC 7th character A see Appendix B for HAC conditional logic

MCC +7th **S14.153 Other incomplete lesion at C3 level of cervical spinal cord**
MCC Exclusion 7th character A see Appendix A
PDX collection 1166
HAC 7th character A see Appendix B for HAC conditional logic

MCC +7th **S14.154 Other incomplete lesion at C4 level of cervical spinal cord**
MCC Exclusion 7th character A see Appendix A
PDX collection 1166
HAC 7th character A see Appendix B for HAC conditional logic

MCC +7th **S14.155 Other incomplete lesion at C5 level of cervical spinal cord**
MCC Exclusion 7th character A see Appendix A
PDX collection 1166
HAC 7th character A see Appendix B for HAC conditional logic

MCC +7th **S14.156 Other incomplete lesion at C6 level of cervical spinal cord**
MCC Exclusion 7th character A see Appendix A
PDX collection 1166
HAC 7th character A see Appendix B for HAC conditional logic

MCC +7th **S14.157 Other incomplete lesion at C7 level of cervical spinal cord**
MCC Exclusion 7th character A see Appendix A
PDX collection 1166
HAC 7th character A see Appendix B for HAC conditional logic

MCC +7th **S14.158 Other incomplete lesion at C8 level of cervical spinal cord**
MCC Exclusion 7th character A see Appendix A
PDX collection 1166

+7th **S14.159 Other incomplete lesion at unspecified level of cervical spinal cord**

X+7th **S14.2 Injury of nerve root of cervical spine**
X+7th **S14.3 Injury of brachial plexus**
X+7th **S14.4 Injury of peripheral nerves of neck**
X+7th **S14.5 Injury of cervical sympathetic nerves**
X+7th **S14.8 Injury of other specified nerves of neck**
X+7th **S14.9 Injury of unspecified nerves of neck**

S15 Injury of blood vessels at neck level
Code also any associated open wound (S11.-)

The appropriate 7th character is to be added to each code from category S15
A initial encounter
D subsequent encounter
S sequela

+ **S15.0 Injury of carotid artery of neck**
Injury of carotid artery (common) (external) (internal, extracranial portion)
Injury of carotid artery NOS
Excludes1: *injury of internal carotid artery, intracranial portion (S06.8)*

+ **S15.00 Unspecified injury of carotid artery**
CC +7th **S15.001 Unspecified injury of right carotid artery**
CC Exclusion 7th character A see Appendix A
PDX collection 1167
CC +7th **S15.002 Unspecified injury of left carotid artery**
CC Exclusion 7th character A see Appendix A
PDX collection 1167
CC +7th **S15.009 Unspecified injury of unspecified carotid artery**
CC Exclusion 7th character A see Appendix A
PDX collection 1167
+ **S15.01 Minor laceration of carotid artery**
Incomplete transection of carotid artery
Laceration of carotid artery NOS
Superficial laceration of carotid artery
CC +7th **S15.011 Minor laceration of right carotid artery**
CC Exclusion 7th character A see Appendix A
PDX collection 1167
CC +7th **S15.012 Minor laceration of left carotid artery**
CC Exclusion 7th character A see Appendix A
PDX collection 1167
CC +7th **S15.019 Minor laceration of unspecified carotid artery**
CC Exclusion 7th character A see Appendix A
PDX collection 1167
+ **S15.02 Major laceration of carotid artery**
Complete transection of carotid artery
Traumatic rupture of carotid artery
CC +7th **S15.021 Major laceration of right carotid artery**
CC Exclusion 7th character A see Appendix A
PDX collection 1167
CC +7th **S15.022 Major laceration of left carotid artery**
CC Exclusion 7th character A see Appendix A
PDX collection 1167
CC +7th **S15.029 Major laceration of unspecified carotid artery**
CC Exclusion 7th character A see Appendix A
PDX collection 1167
+ **S15.09 Other specified injury of carotid artery**
CC +7th **S15.091 Other specified injury of right carotid artery**
CC Exclusion 7th character A see Appendix A
PDX collection 1167
CC +7th **S15.092 Other specified injury of left carotid artery**
CC Exclusion 7th character A see Appendix A
PDX collection 1167
CC +7th **S15.099 Other specified injury of unspecified carotid artery**
CC Exclusion 7th character A see Appendix A
PDX collection 1167
+ **S15.1 Injury of vertebral artery**
+ **S15.10 Unspecified injury of vertebral artery**
CC +7th **S15.101 Unspecified injury of right vertebral artery**
CC Exclusion 7th character A see Appendix A
PDX collection 1157
CC +7th **S15.102 Unspecified injury of left vertebral artery**
CC Exclusion 7th character A see Appendix A
PDX collection 1157
CC +7th **S15.109 Unspecified injury of unspecified vertebral artery**
CC Exclusion 7th character A see Appendix A
PDX collection 1157
+ **S15.11 Minor laceration of vertebral artery**
Incomplete transection of vertebral artery
Laceration of vertebral artery NOS
Superficial laceration of vertebral artery
CC +7th **S15.111 Minor laceration of right vertebral artery**
CC Exclusion 7th character A see Appendix A
PDX collection 1157
CC +7th **S15.112 Minor laceration of left vertebral artery**
CC Exclusion 7th character A see Appendix A
PDX collection 1157
CC +7th **S15.119 Minor laceration of unspecified vertebral artery**
CC Exclusion 7th character A see Appendix A
PDX collection 1157
+ **S15.12 Major laceration of vertebral artery**
Complete transection of vertebral artery
Traumatic rupture of vertebral artery
CC +7th **S15.121 Major laceration of right vertebral artery**
CC Exclusion 7th character A see Appendix A
PDX collection 1157
CC +7th **S15.122 Major laceration of left vertebral artery**
CC Exclusion 7th character A see Appendix A
PDX collection 1157
CC +7th **S15.129 Major laceration of unspecified vertebral artery**
CC Exclusion 7th character A see Appendix A
PDX collection 1157
+ **S15.19 Other specified injury of vertebral artery**
CC +7th **S15.191 Other specified injury of right vertebral artery**
CC Exclusion 7th character A see Appendix A
PDX collection 1157
CC +7th **S15.192 Other specified injury of left vertebral arte**
CC Exclusion 7th character A see Appendix A
PDX collection 1157
CC +7th **S15.199 Other specified injury of unspecified vertebral artery**
CC Exclusion 7th character A see Appendix A
PDX collection 1157
+ **S15.2 Injury of external jugular vein**
+ **S15.20 Unspecified injury of external jugular vein**
CC +7th **S15.201 Unspecified injury of right external jugular vein**
CC Exclusion 7th character A see Appendix A
PDX collection 1157
CC +7th **S15.202 Unspecified injury of left external jugular vein**
CC Exclusion 7th character A see Appendix A
PDX collection 1157
CC +7th **S15.209 Unspecified injury of unspecified external jugular vein**
CC Exclusion 7th character A see Appendix A
PDX collection 1157
+ **S15.21 Minor laceration of external jugular vein**
Incomplete transection of external jugular vein
Laceration of external jugular vein NOS
Superficial laceration of external jugular vein
CC +7th **S15.211 Minor laceration of right external jugular vein**
CC Exclusion 7th character A see Appendix A
PDX collection 1157
CC +7th **S15.212 Minor laceration of left external jugular vei**
CC Exclusion 7th character A see Appendix A
PDX collection 1157
CC +7th **S15.219 Minor laceration of unspecified external jugular vein**
CC Exclusion 7th character A see Appendix A
PDX collection 1157
+ **S15.22 Major laceration of external jugular vein**
Complete transection of external jugular vein
Traumatic rupture of external jugular vein
CC +7th **S15.221 Major laceration of right external jugular vein**
CC Exclusion 7th character A see Appendix A
PDX collection 1157
CC +7th **S15.222 Major laceration of left external jugular vein**
CC Exclusion 7th character A see Appendix A
PDX collection 1157
CC +7th **S15.229 Major laceration of unspecified external jugular vein**
CC Exclusion 7th character A see Appendix A
PDX collection 1157
+ **S15.29 Other specified injury of external jugular vein**
CC +7th **S15.291 Other specified injury of right external jugular vein**
CC Exclusion 7th character A see Appendix A
PDX collection 1157
CC +7th **S15.292 Other specified injury of left external jugular vein**
CC Exclusion 7th character A see Appendix A
PDX collection 1157
CC +7th **S15.299 Other specified injury of unspecified external jugular vein**
CC Exclusion 7th character A see Appendix A
PDX collection 1157
+ **S15.3 Injury of internal jugular vein**
+ **S15.30 Unspecified injury of internal jugular vein**
CC +7th **S15.301 Unspecified injury of right internal jugular vein**
CC Exclusion 7th character A see Appendix A
PDX collection 1157
CC +7th **S15.302 Unspecified injury of left internal jugular vein**
CC Exclusion 7th character A see Appendix A
PDX collection 1157

CC +7th **S15.309 Unspecified injury of unspecified internal jugular vein**
CC Exclusion 7th character A see Appendix A PDX collection 1157

\+ **S15.31 Minor laceration of internal jugular vein**
Incomplete transection of internal jugular vein
Laceration of internal jugular vein NOS
Superficial laceration of internal jugular vein

CC +7th **S15.311 Minor laceration of right internal jugular vein**
CC Exclusion 7th character A see Appendix A PDX collection 1157

CC +7th **S15.312 Minor laceration of left internal jugular vein**
CC Exclusion 7th character A see Appendix A PDX collection 1157

CC +7th **S15.319 Minor laceration of unspecified internal jugular vein**
CC Exclusion 7th character A see Appendix A PDX collection 1157

\+ **S15.32 Major laceration of internal jugular vein**
Complete transection of internal jugular vein
Traumatic rupture of internal jugular vein

CC +7th **S15.321 Major laceration of right internal jugular vein**
CC Exclusion 7th character A see Appendix A PDX collection 1157

CC +7th **S15.322 Major laceration of left internal jugular vein**
CC Exclusion 7th character A see Appendix A PDX collection 1157

CC +7th **S15.329 Major laceration of unspecified internal jugular vein**
CC Exclusion 7th character A see Appendix A PDX collection 1157

\+ **S15.39 Other specified injury of internal jugular vein**

CC +7th **S15.391 Other specified injury of right internal jugular vein**
CC Exclusion 7th character A see Appendix A PDX collection 1157

CC +7th **S15.392 Other specified injury of left internal jugular vein**
CC Exclusion 7th character A see Appendix A PDX collection 1157

CC +7th **S15.399 Other specified injury of unspecified internal jugular vein**
CC Exclusion 7th character A see Appendix A PDX collection 1157

CC X+7th **S15.8 Injury of other specified blood vessels at neck level**
CC Exclusion 7th character A see Appendix A PDX collection 1157

CC X+7th **S15.9 Injury of unspecified blood vessel at neck level**
CC Exclusion 7th character A see Appendix A PDX collection 1157

S16 Injury of muscle, fascia and tendon at neck level
Code also any associated open wound (S11.-)
Excludes2: *sprain of joint or ligament at neck level (S13.9)*

The appropriate 7th character is to be added to each code from category S16
A initial encounter
D subsequent encounter
S sequela

X+7th **S16.1 Strain of muscle, fascia and tendon at neck level**
X+7th **S16.2 Laceration of muscle, fascia and tendon at neck level**
X+7th **S16.8 Other specified injury of muscle, fascia and tendon at neck level**
X+7th **S16.9 Unspecified injury of muscle, fascia and tendon at neck level**

S17 Crushing injury of neck
Use additional code for all associated injuries, such as:
injury of blood vessels (S15.-)
open wound of neck (S11.-)
spinal cord injury (S14.0, S14.1-)
vertebral fracture (S12.0--S12.3-)

The appropriate 7th character is to be added to each code from category S17
A initial encounter
D subsequent encounter
S sequela

CC X+7th **S17.0 Crushing injury of larynx and trachea**
CC Exclusion 7th character A see Appendix A PDX collection 1156
HAC 7th character A see Appendix B for HAC conditional logic

CC X+7th **S17.8 Crushing injury of other specified parts of neck**
CC Exclusion 7th character A see Appendix A PDX collection 1156
HAC 7th character A see Appendix B for HAC conditional logic

CC X+7th **S17.9 Crushing injury of neck, part unspecified**
CC Exclusion 7th character A see Appendix A PDX collection 1156
HAC 7th character A see Appendix B for HAC conditional logic

S19 Other specified and unspecified injuries of neck

The appropriate 7th character is to be added to each code from category S19
A initial encounter
D subsequent encounter
S sequela

\+ **S19.8 Other specified injuries of neck**
X+7th **S19.80 Other specified injuries of unspecified part of neck**
X+7th **S19.81 Other specified injuries of larynx**
X+7th **S19.82 Other specified injuries of cervical trachea**
Excludes2: *other specified injury of thoracic trachea (S27.5-)*
X+7th **S19.83 Other specified injuries of vocal cord**
X+7th **S19.84 Other specified injuries of thyroid gland**
X+7th **S19.85 Other specified injuries of pharynx and cervical esophagus**
X+7th **S19.89 Other specified injuries of other specified part of neck**

X+7th **S19.9 Unspecified injury of neck**

Injuries to the thorax (S20-S29)

Includes: injuries of breast
injuries of chest (wall)
injuries of interscapular area

Excludes2: *burns and corrosions (T20-T32)*
effects of foreign body in bronchus (T17.5)
effects of foreign body in esophagus (T18.1)
effects of foreign body in lung (T17.8)
effects of foreign body in trachea (T17.4)
frostbite (T33-T34)
injuries of axilla
injuries of clavicle
injuries of scapular region
injuries of shoulder
insect bite or sting, venomous (T63.4)

S20 Superficial injury of thorax

The appropriate 7th character is to be added to each code from category S20
A initial encounter
D subsequent encounter
S sequela

\+ **S20.0 Contusion of breast**
X+7th **S20.00 Contusion of breast, unspecified breast**
X+7th **S20.01 Contusion of right breast**
X+7th **S20.02 Contusion of left breast**

\+ **S20.1 Other and unspecified superficial injuries of breast**

\+ **S20.10 Unspecified superficial injuries of breast**
+7th **S20.101 Unspecified superficial injuries of breast, right breast**
+7th **S20.102 Unspecified superficial injuries of breast, left breast**
+7th **S20.109 Unspecified superficial injuries of breast, unspecified breast**

\+ **S20.11 Abrasion of breast**
+7th **S20.111 Abrasion of breast, right breast**
+7th **S20.112 Abrasion of breast, left breast**
+7th **S20.119 Abrasion of breast, unspecified breast**

\+ **S20.12 Blister (nonthermal) of breast**
+7th **S20.121 Blister (nonthermal) of breast, right breast**
+7th **S20.122 Blister (nonthermal) of breast, left breast**
+7th **S20.129 Blister (nonthermal) of breast, unspecified breast**

\+ **S20.14 External constriction of part of breast**
+7th **S20.141 External constriction of part of breast, right breast**
+7th **S20.142 External constriction of part of breast, left breast**
+7th **S20.149 External constriction of part of breast, unspecified breast**

\+ **S20.15 Superficial foreign body of breast**
Splinter in the breast
+7th **S20.151 Superficial foreign body of breast, right breast**
+7th **S20.152 Superficial foreign body of breast, left breast**
+7th **S20.159 Superficial foreign body of breast, unspecified breast**

\+ **S20.16 Insect bite (nonvenomous) of breast**
+7th **S20.161 Insect bite (nonvenomous) of breast, right breast**

+7th **S20.162 Insect bite (nonvenomous) of breast, left breast**
+7th **S20.169 Insect bite (nonvenomous) of breast, unspecified breast**
\+ **S20.17 Other superficial bite of breast**
Excludes1: *open bite of breast (S21.05-)*
+7th **S20.171 Other superficial bite of breast, right breast**
+7th **S20.172 Other superficial bite of breast, left breast**
+7th **S20.179 Other superficial bite of breast, unspecified breast**

\+ **S20.2 Contusion of thorax**
X+7th **S20.20 Contusion of thorax, unspecified**
\+ **S20.21 Contusion of front wall of thorax**
+7th **S20.211 Contusion of right front wall of thorax**
+7th **S20.212 Contusion of left front wall of thorax**
+7th **S20.219 Contusion of unspecified front wall of thorax**
\+ **S20.22 Contusion of back wall of thorax**
+7th **S20.221 Contusion of right back wall of thorax**
+7th **S20.222 Contusion of left back wall of thorax**
+7th **S20.229 Contusion of unspecified back wall of thorax**

\+ **S20.3 Other and unspecified superficial injuries of front wall of thorax**
\+ **S20.30 Unspecified superficial injuries of front wall of thorax**
+7th **S20.301 Unspecified superficial injuries of right front wall of thorax**
+7th **S20.302 Unspecified superficial injuries of left front wall of thorax**
+7th **S20.309 Unspecified superficial injuries of unspecified front wall of thorax**
\+ **S20.31 Abrasion of front wall of thorax**
+7th **S20.311 Abrasion of right front wall of thorax**
+7th **S20.312 Abrasion of left front wall of thorax**
+7th **S20.319 Abrasion of unspecified front wall of thorax**
\+ **S20.32 Blister (nonthermal) of front wall of thorax**
+7th **S20.321 Blister (nonthermal) of right front wall of thorax**
+7th **S20.322 Blister (nonthermal) of left front wall of thorax**
+7th **S20.329 Blister (nonthermal) of unspecified front wall of thorax**
\+ **S20.34 External constriction of front wall of thorax**
+7th **S20.341 External constriction of right front wall of thorax**
+7th **S20.342 External constriction of left front wall of thorax**
+7th **S20.349 External constriction of unspecified front wall of thorax**
\+ **S20.35 Superficial foreign body of front wall of thorax**
Splinter in front wall of thorax
+7th **S20.351 Superficial foreign body of right front wall of thorax**
+7th **S20.352 Superficial foreign body of left front wall of thorax**
+7th **S20.359 Superficial foreign body of unspecified front wall of thorax**
\+ **S20.36 Insect bite (nonvenomous) of front wall of thorax**
+7th **S20.361 Insect bite (nonvenomous) of right front wall of thorax**
+7th **S20.362 Insect bite (nonvenomous) of left front wall of thorax**
+7th **S20.369 Insect bite (nonvenomous) of unspecified front wall of thorax**
\+ **S20.37 Other superficial bite of front wall of thorax**
Excludes1: *open bite of front wall of thorax (S21.14)*
+7th **S20.371 Other superficial bite of right front wall of thorax**
+7th **S20.372 Other superficial bite of left front wall of thorax**
+7th **S20.379 Other superficial bite of unspecified front wall of thorax**

\+ **S20.4 Other and unspecified superficial injuries of back wall of thorax**
\+ **S20.40 Unspecified superficial injuries of back wall of thorax**
+7th **S20.401 Unspecified superficial injuries of right back wall of thorax**
+7th **S20.402 Unspecified superficial injuries of left back wall of thorax**
+7th **S20.409 Unspecified superficial injuries of unspecified back wall of thorax**
\+ **S20.41 Abrasion of back wall of thorax**
+7th **S20.411 Abrasion of right back wall of thorax**
+7th **S20.412 Abrasion of left back wall of thorax**
+7th **S20.419 Abrasion of unspecified back wall of thorax**
\+ **S20.42 Blister (nonthermal) of back wall of thorax**
+7th **S20.421 Blister (nonthermal) of right back wall of thorax**
+7th **S20.422 Blister (nonthermal) of left back wall of thorax**
+7th **S20.429 Blister (nonthermal) of unspecified back w of thorax**
\+ **S20.44 External constriction of back wall of thorax**
+7th **S20.441 External constriction of right back wall of thorax**
+7th **S20.442 External constriction of left back wall of thorax**
+7th **S20.449 External constriction of unspecified back wall of thorax**
\+ **S20.45 Superficial foreign body of back wall of thorax**
Splinter of back wall of thorax
+7th **S20.451 Superficial foreign body of right back wall thorax**
+7th **S20.452 Superficial foreign body of left back wall of thorax**
+7th **S20.459 Superficial foreign body of unspecified bacl wall of thorax**
\+ **S20.46 Insect bite (nonvenomous) of back wall of thorax**
+7th **S20.461 Insect bite (nonvenomous) of right back wa of thorax**
+7th **S20.462 Insect bite (nonvenomous) of left back wall of thorax**
+7th **S20.469 Insect bite (nonvenomous) of unspecified back wall of thorax**
\+ **S20.47 Other superficial bite of back wall of thorax**
Excludes1: *open bite of back wall of thorax (S21.24)*
+7th **S20.471 Other superficial bite of right back wall of thorax**
+7th **S20.472 Other superficial bite of left back wall of thorax**
+7th **S20.479 Other superficial bite of unspecified back wall of thorax**

\+ **S20.9 Superficial injury of unspecified parts of thorax**
Excludes1: *contusion of thorax NOS (S20.20)*
X+7th **S20.90 Unspecified superficial injury of unspecified parts of thorax**
Superficial injury of thoracic wall NOS
X+7th **S20.91 Abrasion of unspecified parts of thorax**
X+7th **S20.92 Blister (nonthermal) of unspecified parts of thorax**
X+7th **S20.94 External constriction of unspecified parts of thorax**
X+7th **S20.95 Superficial foreign body of unspecified parts of thorax**
Splinter in thorax NOS
X+7th **S20.96 Insect bite (nonvenomous) of unspecified parts of thorax**
X+7th **S20.97 Other superficial bite of unspecified parts of thorax**
Excludes1: *open bite of thorax NOS (S21.95)*

S21 Open wound of thorax

Code also any associated injury, such as:
injury of heart (S26.-)
injury of intrathoracic organs (S27.-)
rib fracture (S22.3-, S22.4-)
spinal cord injury (S24.0-, S24.1-)
traumatic hemothorax (S27.1)
traumatic hemopneumothorax (S27.3)
traumatic pneumothorax (S27.0)
wound infection
Excludes1: *traumatic amputation (partial) of thorax (S28.1)*

The appropriate 7th character is to be added to each code from category S21
A initial encounter
D subsequent encounter
S sequela

\+ **S21.0 Open wound of breast**
\+ **S21.00 Unspecified open wound of breast**
+7th **S21.001 Unspecified open wound of right breast**
+7th **S21.002 Unspecified open wound of left breast**
+7th **S21.009 Unspecified open wound of unspecified breast**
\+ **S21.01 Laceration without foreign body of breast**
+7th **S21.011 Laceration without foreign body of right breast**
+7th **S21.012 Laceration without foreign body of left breast**
+7th **S21.019 Laceration without foreign body of unspecified breast**

+ **S21.02 Laceration with foreign body of breast**
  - +7th **S21.021 Laceration with foreign body of right breast**
  - +7th **S21.022 Laceration with foreign body of left breast**
  - +7th **S21.029 Laceration with foreign body of unspecified breast**

+ **S21.03 Puncture wound without foreign body of breast**
  - +7th **S21.031 Puncture wound without foreign body of right breast**
  - +7th **S21.032 Puncture wound without foreign body of left breast**
  - +7th **S21.039 Puncture wound without foreign body of unspecified breast**

+ **S21.04 Puncture wound with foreign body of breast**
  - +7th **S21.041 Puncture wound with foreign body of right breast**
  - +7th **S21.042 Puncture wound with foreign body of left breast**
  - +7th **S21.049 Puncture wound with foreign body of unspecified breast**

+ **S21.05 Open bite of breast**
  Bite of breast NOS
  Excludes1: *superficial bite of breast (S20.17)*
  - **S21.051 Open bite of right breast**
  - **S21.052 Open bite of left breast**
  - **S21.059 Open bite of unspecified breast**

+ **S21.1 Open wound of front wall of thorax without penetration into thoracic cavity**
  Open wound of chest without penetration into thoracic cavity

+ **S21.10 Unspecified open wound of front wall of thorax without penetration into thoracic cavity**
  - CC +7th **S21.101 Unspecified open wound of right front wall of thorax without penetration into thoracic cavity**
    CC Exclusion 7th character A see Appendix A
    PDX collection 1168
  - CC +7th **S21.102 Unspecified open wound of left front wall of thorax without penetration into thoracic cavity**
    CC Exclusion 7th character A see Appendix A
    PDX collection 1168
  - CC +7th **S21.109 Unspecified open wound of unspecified front wall of thorax without penetration into thoracic cavity**
    CC Exclusion 7th character A see Appendix A
    PDX collection 1168

+ **S21.11 Laceration without foreign body of front wall of thorax without penetration into thoracic cavity**
  - CC +7th **S21.111 Laceration without foreign body of right front wall of thorax without penetration into thoracic cavity**
    CC Exclusion 7th character A see Appendix A
    PDX collection 1168
  - CC +7th **S21.112 Laceration without foreign body of left front wall of thorax without penetration into thoracic cavity**
    CC Exclusion 7th character A see Appendix A
    PDX collection 1168
  - CC +7th **S21.119 Laceration without foreign body of unspecified front wall of thorax without penetration into thoracic cavity**
    CC Exclusion 7th character A see Appendix A
    PDX collection 1168

+ **S21.12 Laceration with foreign body of front wall of thorax without penetration into thoracic cavity**
  - CC +7th **S21.121 Laceration with foreign body of right front wall of thorax without penetration into thoracic cavity**
    CC Exclusion 7th character A see Appendix A
    PDX collection 1168
  - CC +7th **S21.122 Laceration with foreign body of left front wall of thorax without penetration into thoracic cavity**
    CC Exclusion 7th character A see Appendix A
    PDX collection 1168
  - CC +7th **S21.129 Laceration with foreign body of unspecified front wall of thorax without penetration into thoracic cavity**
    CC Exclusion 7th character A see Appendix A
    PDX collection 1168

+ **S21.13 Puncture wound without foreign body of front wall of thorax without penetration into thoracic cavity**
  - CC +7th **S21.131 Puncture wound without foreign body of right front wall of thorax without penetration into thoracic cavity**
    CC Exclusion 7th character A see Appendix A
    PDX collection 1168
  - CC +7th **S21.132 Puncture wound without foreign body of left front wall of thorax without penetration into thoracic cavity**
    CC Exclusion 7th character A see Appendix A
    PDX collection 1168
  - CC +7th **S21.139 Puncture wound without foreign body of unspecified front wall of thorax without penetration into thoracic cavity**
    CC Exclusion 7th character A see Appendix A
    PDX collection 1168

+ **S21.14 Puncture wound with foreign body of front wall of thorax without penetration into thoracic cavity**
  - CC +7th **S21.141 Puncture wound with foreign body of right front wall of thorax without penetration into thoracic cavity**
    CC Exclusion 7th character A see Appendix A
    PDX collection 1168
  - CC +7th **S21.142 Puncture wound with foreign body of left front wall of thorax without penetration into thoracic cavity**
    CC Exclusion 7th character A see Appendix A
    PDX collection 1168
  - CC +7th **S21.149 Puncture wound with foreign body of unspecified front wall of thorax without penetration into thoracic cavity**
    CC Exclusion 7th character A see Appendix A
    PDX collection 1168

+ **S21.15 Open bite of front wall of thorax without penetration into thoracic cavity**
  Bite of front wall of thorax NOS
  Excludes1: *superficial bite of front wall of thorax (S20.37)*
  - CC +7th **S21.151 Open bite of right front wall of thorax without penetration into thoracic cavity**
    CC Exclusion 7th character A see Appendix A
    PDX collection 1168
  - CC +7th **S21.152 Open bite of left front wall of thorax without penetration into thoracic cavity**
    CC Exclusion 7th character A see Appendix A
    PDX collection 1168
  - CC +7th **S21.159 Open bite of unspecified front wall of thorax without penetration into thoracic cavity**
    CC Exclusion 7th character A see Appendix A
    PDX collection 1168

+ **S21.2 Open wound of back wall of thorax without penetration into thoracic cavity**

+ **S21.20 Unspecified open wound of back wall of thorax without penetration into thoracic cavity**
  - +7th **S21.201 Unspecified open wound of right back wall of thorax without penetration into thoracic cavity**
  - +7th **S21.202 Unspecified open wound of left back wall of thorax without penetration into thoracic cavity**
  - +7th **S21.209 Unspecified open wound of unspecified back wall of thorax without penetration into thoracic cavity**

+ **S21.21 Laceration without foreign body of back wall of thorax without penetration into thoracic cavity**
  - +7th **S21.211 Laceration without foreign body of right back wall of thorax without penetration into thoracic cavity**
  - +7th **S21.212 Laceration without foreign body of left back wall of thorax without penetration into thoracic cavity**
  - +7th **S21.219 Laceration without foreign body of unspecified back wall of thorax without penetration into thoracic cavity**

+ S21.22 Laceration with foreign body of back wall of thorax without penetration into thoracic cavity

+7th **S21.221 Laceration with foreign body of right back wall of thorax without penetration into thoracic cavity**

+7th **S21.222 Laceration with foreign body of left back wall of thorax without penetration into thoracic cavity**

+7th **S21.229 Laceration with foreign body of unspecified back wall of thorax without penetration into thoracic cavity**

+ S21.23 Puncture wound without foreign body of back wall of thorax without penetration into thoracic cavity

+7th **S21.231 Puncture wound without foreign body of right back wall of thorax without penetration into thoracic cavity**

+7th **S21.232 Puncture wound without foreign body of left back wall of thorax without penetration into thoracic cavity**

+7th **S21.239 Puncture wound without foreign body of unspecified back wall of thorax without penetration into thoracic cavity**

+ S21.24 Puncture wound with foreign body of back wall of thorax without penetration into thoracic cavity

+7th **S21.241 Puncture wound with foreign body of right back wall of thorax without penetration into thoracic cavity**

+7th **S21.242 Puncture wound with foreign body of left back wall of thorax without penetration into thoracic cavity**

+7th **S21.249 Puncture wound with foreign body of unspecified back wall of thorax without penetration into thoracic cavity**

+ S21.25 Open bite of back wall of thorax without penetration into thoracic cavity

Bite of back wall of thorax NOS

Excludes1: *superficial bite of back wall of thorax (S20.47)*

+7th **S21.251 Open bite of right back wall of thorax without penetration into thoracic cavity**

+7th **S21.252 Open bite of left back wall of thorax without penetration into thoracic cavity**

+7th **S21.259 Open bite of unspecified back wall of thorax without penetration into thoracic cavity**

+ S21.3 Open wound of front wall of thorax with penetration into thoracic cavity

Open wound of chest with penetration into thoracic cavity

+ S21.30 Unspecified open wound of front wall of thorax with penetration into thoracic cavity

MCC +7th **S21.301 Unspecified open wound of right front wall of thorax with penetration into thoracic cavity**

MCC Exclusion 7th character A see Appendix A PDX collection 1169

MCC +7th **S21.302 Unspecified open wound of left front wall of thorax with penetration into thoracic cavity**

MCC Exclusion 7th character A see Appendix A PDX collection 1169

MCC +7th **S21.309 Unspecified open wound of unspecified front wall of thorax with penetration into thoracic cavity**

MCC Exclusion 7th character A see Appendix A PDX collection 1170

+ S21.31 Laceration without foreign body of front wall of thorax with penetration into thoracic cavity

MCC +7th **S21.311 Laceration without foreign body of right front wall of thorax with penetration into thoracic cavity**

MCC Exclusion 7th character A see Appendix A PDX collection 1169

MCC +7th **S21.312 Laceration without foreign body of left front wall of thorax with penetration into thoracic cavity**

MCC Exclusion 7th character A see Appendix A PDX collection 1169

MCC +7th **S21.319 Laceration without foreign body of unspecified front wall of thorax with penetration into thoracic cavity**

MCC Exclusion 7th character A see Appendix A PDX collection 1169

+ S21.32 Laceration with foreign body of front wall of thorax with penetration into thoracic cavity

MCC +7th **S21.321 Laceration with foreign body of right front wall of thorax with penetration into thoracic cavity**

MCC Exclusion 7th character A see Appendix A PDX collection 1169

MCC +7th **S21.322 Laceration with foreign body of left front wall of thorax with penetration into thoracic cavity**

MCC Exclusion 7th character A see Appendix A PDX collection 1169

MCC +7th **S21.329 Laceration with foreign body of unspecified front wall of thorax with penetration into thoracic cavity**

MCC Exclusion 7th character A see Appendix A PDX collection 1169

+ S21.33 Puncture wound without foreign body of front wall of thorax with penetration into thoracic cavity

MCC +7th **S21.331 Puncture wound without foreign body of right front wall of thorax with penetration into thoracic cavity**

MCC Exclusion 7th character A see Appendix A PDX collection 1169

MCC +7th **S21.332 Puncture wound without foreign body of left front wall of thorax with penetration into thoracic cavity**

MCC Exclusion 7th character A see Appendix A PDX collection 1169

MCC +7th **S21.339 Puncture wound without foreign body of unspecified front wall of thorax with penetration into thoracic cavity**

MCC Exclusion 7th character A see Appendix A PDX collection 1169

+ S21.34 Puncture wound with foreign body of front wall of thorax with penetration into thoracic cavity

MCC +7th **S21.341 Puncture wound with foreign body of right front wall of thorax with penetration into thoracic cavity**

MCC Exclusion 7th character A see Appendix A PDX collection 1169

MCC +7th **S21.342 Puncture wound with foreign body of left front wall of thorax with penetration into thoracic cavity**

MCC Exclusion 7th character A see Appendix A PDX collection 1169

MCC +7th **S21.349 Puncture wound with foreign body of unspecified front wall of thorax with penetration into thoracic cavity**

MCC Exclusion 7th character A see Appendix A PDX collection 1169

+ S21.35 Open bite of front wall of thorax with penetration into thoracic cavity

Excludes1: *superficial bite of front wall of thorax (S20.37)*

MCC +7th **S21.351 Open bite of right front wall of thorax with penetration into thoracic cavity**

MCC Exclusion 7th character A see Appendix A PDX collection 1169

MCC +7th **S21.352 Open bite of left front wall of thorax with penetration into thoracic cavity**

MCC Exclusion 7th character A see Appendix A PDX collection 1169

MCC +7th **S21.359 Open bite of unspecified front wall of thorax with penetration into thoracic cavity**

MCC Exclusion 7th character A see Appendix A PDX collection 1169

+ S21.4 Open wound of back wall of thorax with penetration into thoracic cavity

+ S21.40 Unspecified open wound of back wall of thorax with penetration into thoracic cavity

MCC +7th **S21.401 Unspecified open wound of right back wall of thorax with penetration into thoracic cavity**

MCC Exclusion 7th character A see Appendix A PDX collection 1169

MCC +7th **S21.402 Unspecified open wound of left back wall of thorax with penetration into thoracic cavity**

MCC Exclusion 7th character A see Appendix A PDX collection 1169

MCC +7th **S21.409 Unspecified open wound of unspecified back wall of thorax with penetration into thoracic cavity**
MCC Exclusion 7th character A see Appendix A PDX collection 1169

\+ **S21.41 Laceration without foreign body of back wall of thorax with penetration into thoracic cavity**

MCC +7th **S21.411 Laceration without foreign body of right back wall of thorax with penetration into thoracic cavity**
MCC Exclusion 7th character A see Appendix A PDX collection 1169

MCC +7th **S21.412 Laceration without foreign body of left back wall of thorax with penetration into thoracic cavity**
MCC Exclusion 7th character A see Appendix A PDX collection 1169

MCC +7th **S21.419 Laceration without foreign body of unspecified back wall of thorax with penetration into thoracic cavity**
MCC Exclusion 7th character A see Appendix A PDX collection 1169

\+ **S21.42 Laceration with foreign body of back wall of thorax with penetration into thoracic cavity**

MCC +7th **S21.421 Laceration with foreign body of right back wall of thorax with penetration into thoracic cavity**
MCC Exclusion 7th character A see Appendix A PDX collection 1169

MCC +7th **S21.422 Laceration with foreign body of left back wall of thorax with penetration into thoracic cavity**
MCC Exclusion 7th character A see Appendix A PDX collection 1169

MCC +7th **S21.429 Laceration with foreign body of unspecified back wall of thorax with penetration into thoracic cavity**
MCC Exclusion 7th character A see Appendix A PDX collection 1169

\+ **S21.43 Puncture wound without foreign body of back wall of thorax with penetration into thoracic cavity**

MCC +7th **S21.431 Puncture wound without foreign body of right back wall of thorax with penetration into thoracic cavity**
MCC Exclusion 7th character A see Appendix A PDX collection 1169

MCC +7th **S21.432 Puncture wound without foreign body of left back wall of thorax with penetration into thoracic cavity**
MCC Exclusion 7th character A see Appendix A PDX collection 1169

MCC +7th **S21.439 Puncture wound without foreign body of unspecified back wall of thorax with penetration into thoracic cavity**
MCC Exclusion 7th character A see Appendix A PDX collection 1169

\+ **S21.44 Puncture wound with foreign body of back wall of thorax with penetration into thoracic cavity**

MCC +7th **S21.441 Puncture wound with foreign body of right back wall of thorax with penetration into thoracic cavity**
MCC Exclusion 7th character A see Appendix A PDX collection 1169

MCC +7th **S21.442 Puncture wound with foreign body of left back wall of thorax with penetration into thoracic cavity**
MCC Exclusion 7th character A see Appendix A PDX collection 1169

MCC +7th **S21.449 Puncture wound with foreign body of unspecified back wall of thorax with penetration into thoracic cavity**
MCC Exclusion 7th character A see Appendix A PDX collection 1169

\+ **S21.45 Open bite of back wall of thorax with penetration into thoracic cavity**
Bite of back wall of thorax NOS
Excludes1: *superficial bite of back wall of thorax (S20.47)*

MCC +7th **S21.451 Open bite of right back wall of thorax with penetration into thoracic cavity**
MCC Exclusion 7th character A see Appendix A PDX collection 1169

MCC +7th **S21.452 Open bite of left back wall of thorax with penetration into thoracic cavity**
MCC Exclusion 7th character A see Appendix A PDX collection 1169

MCC +7th **S21.459 Open bite of unspecified back wall of thorax with penetration into thoracic cavity**
MCC Exclusion 7th character A see Appendix A PDX collection 1169

\+ **S21.9 Open wound of unspecified part of thorax**
Open wound of thoracic wall NOS

CC X+7th **S21.90 Unspecified open wound of unspecified part of thorax**
CC Exclusion 7th character A see Appendix A PDX collection 1168

CC X+7th **S21.91 Laceration without foreign body of unspecified part of thorax**
CC Exclusion 7th character A see Appendix A PDX collection 1168

CC X+7th **S21.92 Laceration with foreign body of unspecified part of thorax**
CC Exclusion 7th character A see Appendix A PDX collection 1168

CC X+7th **S21.93 Puncture wound without foreign body of unspecified part of thorax**
CC Exclusion 7th character A see Appendix A PDX collection 1168

CC X+7th **S21.94 Puncture wound with foreign body of unspecified part of thorax**
CC Exclusion 7th character A see Appendix A PDX collection 1168

CC X+7th **S21.95 Open bite of unspecified part of thorax**
Excludes1: *superficial bite of thorax (S20.97)*
CC Exclusion 7th character A see Appendix A PDX collection 1168

See page 916 for Vertebrae Illustration.

S22 Fracture of rib(s), sternum and thoracic spine

NOTE A fracture not indicated as displaced or nondisplaced should be coded to displaced
A fracture not indicated as open or closed should be coded to closed

Includes: fracture of thoracic neural arch
fracture of thoracic spinous process
fracture of thoracic transverse process
fracture of thoracic vertebra
fracture of thoracic vertebral arch

Code first any associated:
injury of intrathoracic organ (S27.-)
spinal cord injury (S24.0-, S24.1-)

Excludes1: *transection of thorax (S28.1)*
Excludes2: *fracture of clavicle (S42.0-)*
fracture of scapula (S42.1-)

The appropriate 7th character is to be added to each code from category S22
A initial encounter for closed fracture
B initial encounter for open fracture
D subsequent encounter for fracture with routine healing
G subsequent encounter for fracture with delayed healing
K subsequent encounter for fracture with nonunion
S sequela

Review coding guideline C.19.c

\+ **S22.0 Fracture of thoracic vertebra**

\+ **S22.00 Fracture of unspecified thoracic vertebra**

CC MCC +7th **S22.000 Wedge compression fracture of unspecified thoracic vertebra**
CC Exclusion 7th character A see Appendix A PDX collection 1171
CC Exclusion 7th character K see Appendix A PDX collection 0897
MCC Exclusion 7th character B see Appendix A PDX collection 1171
HAC 7th characters A & B see Appendix B for HAC conditional logic

CC MCC +7th **S22.001 Stable burst fracture of unspecified thoracic vertebra**
CC Exclusion 7th character A see Appendix A PDX collection 1171
CC Exclusion 7th character K see Appendix A PDX collection 0897
MCC Exclusion 7th character B see Appendix A PDX collection 1171
HAC 7th characters A & B see Appendix B for HAC conditional logic

CC MCC +7th **S22.002 Unstable burst fracture of unspecified thoracic vertebra**
CC Exclusion 7th character A see Appendix A
PDX collection 1171
CC Exclusion 7th character K see Appendix A
PDX collection 0897
MCC Exclusion 7th character B see Appendix A
PDX collection 1171
HAC 7th characters A & B see Appendix B for HAC conditional logic

CC MCC +7th **S22.008 Other fracture of unspecified thoracic vertebra**
CC Exclusion 7th character A see Appendix A
PDX collection 1171
CC Exclusion 7th character K see Appendix A
PDX collection 0897
MCC Exclusion 7th character B see Appendix A
PDX collection 1171
HAC 7th characters A & B see Appendix B for HAC conditional logic

CC MCC +7th **S22.009 Unspecified fracture of unspecified thoracic vertebra**
CC Exclusion 7th character A see Appendix A
PDX collection 1171
CC Exclusion 7th character K see Appendix A
PDX collection 0897
MCC Exclusion 7th character B see Appendix A
PDX collection 1171
HAC 7th characters A & B see Appendix B for HAC conditional logic

\+ **S22.01 Fracture of first thoracic vertebra**

CC MCC +7th **S22.010 Wedge compression fracture of first thoracic vertebra**
CC Exclusion 7th character A see Appendix A
PDX collection 1171
CC Exclusion 7th character K see Appendix A
PDX collection 0897
MCC Exclusion 7th character B see Appendix A
PDX collection 1171
HAC 7th characters A & B see Appendix B for HAC conditional logic

CC MCC +7th **S22.011 Stable burst fracture of first thoracic vertebra**
CC Exclusion 7th character A see Appendix A
PDX collection 1171
CC Exclusion 7th character K see Appendix A
PDX collection 0897
MCC Exclusion 7th character B see Appendix A
PDX collection 1171
HAC 7th characters A & B see Appendix B for HAC conditional logic

CC MCC +7th **S22.012 Unstable burst fracture of first thoracic vertebra**
CC Exclusion 7th character A see Appendix A
PDX collection 1171
CC Exclusion 7th character K see Appendix A
PDX collection 0897
MCC Exclusion 7th character B see Appendix A
PDX collection 1171
HAC 7th characters A & B see Appendix B for HAC conditional logic

CC MCC +7th **S22.018 Other fracture of first thoracic vertebra**
CC Exclusion 7th character A see Appendix A
PDX collection 1171
CC Exclusion 7th character K see Appendix A
PDX collection 0897
MCC Exclusion 7th character B see Appendix A
PDX collection 1171
HAC 7th characters A & B see Appendix B for HAC conditional logic

CC MCC +7th **S22.019 Unspecified fracture of first thoracic vertebra**
CC Exclusion 7th character A see Appendix A
PDX collection 1171
CC Exclusion 7th character K see Appendix A
PDX collection 0897
MCC Exclusion 7th character B see Appendix A
PDX collection 1171
HAC 7th characters A & B see Appendix B for HAC conditional logic

\+ **S22.02 Fracture of second thoracic vertebra**

CC MCC +7th **S22.020 Wedge compression fracture of second thoracic vertebra**
CC Exclusion 7th character A see Appendix A
PDX collection 1171
CC Exclusion 7th character K see Appendix A
PDX collection 0897
MCC Exclusion 7th character B see Appendix A
PDX collection 1171
HAC 7th characters A & B see Appendix B for HAC conditional logic

CC MCC +7th **S22.021 Stable burst fracture of second thoracic vertebra**
CC Exclusion 7th character A see Appendix A
PDX collection 1171
CC Exclusion 7th character K see Appendix A
PDX collection 0897
MCC Exclusion 7th character B see Appendix A
PDX collection 1171
HAC 7th characters A & B see Appendix B for HAC conditional logic

CC MCC +7th **S22.022 Unstable burst fracture of second thoracic vertebra**
CC Exclusion 7th character A see Appendix A
PDX collection 1171
CC Exclusion 7th character K see Appendix A
PDX collection 0897
MCC Exclusion 7th character B see Appendix A
PDX collection 1171
HAC 7th characters A & B see Appendix B for HAC conditional logic

CC MCC +7th **S22.028 Other fracture of second thoracic vertebra**
CC Exclusion 7th character A see Appendix A
PDX collection 1171
CC Exclusion 7th character K see Appendix A
PDX collection 0897
MCC Exclusion 7th character B see Appendix A
PDX collection 1171
HAC 7th characters A & B see Appendix B for HAC conditional logic

CC MCC +7th **S22.029 Unspecified fracture of second thoracic vertebra**
CC Exclusion 7th character A see Appendix A
PDX collection 1171
CC Exclusion 7th character K see Appendix A
PDX collection 0897
MCC Exclusion 7th character B see Appendix A
PDX collection 1171
HAC 7th characters A & B see Appendix B for HAC conditional logic

\+ **S22.03 Fracture of third thoracic vertebra**

CC MCC +7th **S22.030 Wedge compression fracture of third thoracic vertebra**
CC Exclusion 7th character A see Appendix A
PDX collection 1171
CC Exclusion 7th character K see Appendix A
PDX collection 0897
MCC Exclusion 7th character B see Appendix A
PDX collection 1171
HAC 7th characters A & B see Appendix B for HAC conditional logic

CC MCC +7th **S22.031 Stable burst fracture of third thoracic vertebra**
CC Exclusion 7th character A see Appendix A
PDX collection 1171
CC Exclusion 7th character K see Appendix A
PDX collection 0897
MCC Exclusion 7th character B see Appendix A
PDX collection 1171
HAC 7th characters A & B see Appendix B for HAC conditional logic

CC MCC +7th **S22.032 Unstable burst fracture of third thoracic vertebra**
CC Exclusion 7th character A see Appendix A
PDX collection 1171
CC Exclusion 7th character K see Appendix A
PDX collection 0897
MCC Exclusion 7th character B see Appendix A
PDX collection 1171
HAC 7th characters A & B see Appendix B for HAC conditional logic

CC MCC +7th **S22.038 Other fracture of third thoracic vertebra**
CC Exclusion 7th character A see Appendix A
PDX collection 1171
CC Exclusion 7th character K see Appendix A
PDX collection 0897
MCC Exclusion 7th character B see Appendix A
PDX collection 1171
HAC 7th characters A & B see Appendix B for HAC conditional logic

CC MCC +7th **S22.039 Unspecified fracture of third thoracic vertebra**
CC Exclusion 7th character A see Appendix A
PDX collection 1171
CC Exclusion 7th character K see Appendix A
PDX collection 0897
MCC Exclusion 7th character B see Appendix A
PDX collection 1171
HAC 7th characters A & B see Appendix B for HAC conditional logic

+ S22.04 Fracture of fourth thoracic vertebra

CC MCC +7th S22.040 Wedge compression fracture of fourth thoracic vertebra

CC Exclusion 7th character A see Appendix A

PDX collection 1171

CC Exclusion 7th character K see Appendix A

PDX collection 0897

MCC Exclusion 7th character B see Appendix A

PDX collection 1171

HAC 7th characters A & B see Appendix B for HAC conditional logic

CC MCC +7th S22.041 Stable burst fracture of fourth thoracic vertebra

CC Exclusion 7th character A see Appendix A

PDX collection 1171

CC Exclusion 7th character K see Appendix A

PDX collection 0897

MCC Exclusion 7th character B see Appendix A

PDX collection 1171

HAC 7th characters A & B see Appendix B for HAC conditional logic

CC MCC +7th S22.042 Unstable burst fracture of fourth thoracic vertebra

CC Exclusion 7th character A see Appendix A

PDX collection 1171

CC Exclusion 7th character K see Appendix A

PDX collection 0897

MCC Exclusion 7th character B see Appendix A

PDX collection 1171

HAC 7th characters A & B see Appendix B for HAC conditional logic

CC MCC +7th S22.048 Other fracture of fourth thoracic vertebra

CC Exclusion 7th character A see Appendix A

PDX collection 1171

CC Exclusion 7th character K see Appendix A

PDX collection 0897

MCC Exclusion 7th character B see Appendix A

PDX collection 1171

HAC 7th characters A & B see Appendix B for HAC conditional logic

CC MCC +7th S22.049 Unspecified fracture of fourth thoracic vertebra

CC Exclusion 7th character A see Appendix A

PDX collection 1171

CC Exclusion 7th character K see Appendix A

PDX collection 0897

MCC Exclusion 7th character B see Appendix A

PDX collection 1171

HAC 7th characters A & B see Appendix B for HAC conditional logic

+ S22.05 Fracture of T5-T6 vertebra

CC MCC +7th S22.050 Wedge compression fracture of T5-T6 vertebra

CC Exclusion 7th character A see Appendix A

PDX collection 1171

CC Exclusion 7th character K see Appendix A

PDX collection 0897

MCC Exclusion 7th character B see Appendix A

PDX collection 1171

HAC 7th characters A & B see Appendix B for HAC conditional logic

CC MCC +7th S22.051 Stable burst fracture of T5-T6 vertebra

CC Exclusion 7th character A see Appendix A

PDX collection 1171

CC Exclusion 7th character K see Appendix A

PDX collection 0897

MCC Exclusion 7th character B see Appendix A

PDX collection 1171

HAC 7th characters A & B see Appendix B for HAC conditional logic

CC MCC +7th S22.052 Unstable burst fracture of T5-T6 vertebra

CC Exclusion 7th character A see Appendix A

PDX collection 1171

CC Exclusion 7th character K see Appendix A

PDX collection 0897

MCC Exclusion 7th character B see Appendix A

PDX collection 1171

HAC 7th characters A & B see Appendix B for HAC conditional logic

CC MCC +7th S22.058 Other fracture of T5-T6 vertebra

CC Exclusion 7th character A see Appendix A

PDX collection 1171

CC Exclusion 7th character K see Appendix A

PDX collection 0897

MCC Exclusion 7th character B see Appendix A

PDX collection 1171

HAC 7th characters A & B see Appendix B for HAC conditional logic

CC MCC +7th S22.059 Unspecified fracture of T5-T6 vertebra

CC Exclusion 7th character A see Appendix A

PDX collection 1171

CC Exclusion 7th character K see Appendix A

PDX collection 0897

MCC Exclusion 7th character B see Appendix A

PDX collection 1171

HAC 7th characters A & B see Appendix B for HAC conditional logic

+ S22.06 Fracture of T7-T8 vertebra

CC MCC +7th S22.060 Wedge compression fracture of T7-T8 vertebra

CC Exclusion 7th character A see Appendix A

PDX collection 1171

CC Exclusion 7th character K see Appendix A

PDX collection 0897

MCC Exclusion 7th character B see Appendix A

PDX collection 1171

HAC 7th characters A & B see Appendix B for HAC conditional logic

CC MCC +7th S22.061 Stable burst fracture of T7-T8 vertebra

CC Exclusion 7th character A see Appendix A

PDX collection 1171

CC Exclusion 7th character K see Appendix A

PDX collection 0897

MCC Exclusion 7th character B see Appendix A

PDX collection 1171

HAC 7th characters A & B see Appendix B for HAC conditional logic

CC MCC +7th S22.062 Unstable burst fracture of T7-T8 vertebra

CC Exclusion 7th character A see Appendix A

PDX collection 1171

CC Exclusion 7th character K see Appendix A

PDX collection 0897

MCC Exclusion 7th character B see Appendix A

PDX collection 1171

HAC 7th characters A & B see Appendix B for HAC conditional logic

CC MCC +7th S22.068 Other fracture of T7-T8 thoracic vertebra

CC Exclusion 7th character A see Appendix A

PDX collection 1171

CC Exclusion 7th character K see Appendix A

PDX collection 0897

MCC Exclusion 7th character B see Appendix A

PDX collection 1171

HAC 7th characters A & B see Appendix B for HAC conditional logic

CC MCC +7th S22.069 Unspecified fracture of T7-T8 vertebra

CC Exclusion 7th character A see Appendix A

PDX collection 1171

CC Exclusion 7th character K see Appendix A

PDX collection 0897

MCC Exclusion 7th character B see Appendix A

PDX collection 1171

HAC 7th characters A & B see Appendix B for HAC conditional logic

+ S22.07 Fracture of T9-T10 vertebra

CC MCC +7th S22.070 Wedge compression fracture of T9-T10 vertebra

CC Exclusion 7th character A see Appendix A

PDX collection 1171

CC Exclusion 7th character K see Appendix A

PDX collection 0897

MCC Exclusion 7th character B see Appendix A

PDX collection 1171

HAC 7th characters A & B see Appendix B for HAC conditional logic

CC MCC +7th S22.071 Stable burst fracture of T9-T10 vertebra

CC Exclusion 7th character A see Appendix A

PDX collection 1171

CC Exclusion 7th character K see Appendix A

PDX collection 0897

MCC Exclusion 7th character B see Appendix A

PDX collection 1171

HAC 7th characters A & B see Appendix B for HAC conditional logic

CC MCC +7th S22.072 Unstable burst fracture of T9-T10 vertebra

CC Exclusion 7th character A see Appendix A

PDX collection 1171

CC Exclusion 7th character K see Appendix A

PDX collection 0897

MCC Exclusion 7th character B see Appendix A

PDX collection 1171

HAC 7th characters A & B see Appendix B for HAC conditional logic

CC MCC +7th **S22.078 Other fracture of T9-T10 vertebra**
- CC Exclusion 7th character A see Appendix A PDX collection 1171
- CC Exclusion 7th character K see Appendix A PDX collection 0897
- MCC Exclusion 7th character B see Appendix A PDX collection 1171
- HAC 7th characters A & B see Appendix B for HAC conditional logic

CC MCC +7th **S22.079 Unspecified fracture of T9-T10 vertebra**
- CC Exclusion 7th character A see Appendix A PDX collection 1171
- CC Exclusion 7th character K see Appendix A PDX collection 0897
- MCC Exclusion 7th character B see Appendix A PDX collection 1171
- HAC 7th characters A & B see Appendix B for HAC conditional logic

+ **S22.08 Fracture of T11-T12 vertebra**

CC MCC +7th **S22.080 Wedge compression fracture of T11-T12 vertebra**
- CC Exclusion 7th character A see Appendix A PDX collection 1171
- CC Exclusion 7th character K see Appendix A PDX collection 0897
- MCC Exclusion 7th character B see Appendix A PDX collection 1171
- HAC 7th characters A & B see Appendix B for HAC conditional logic

CC MCC +7th **S22.081 Stable burst fracture of T11-T12 vertebra**
- CC Exclusion 7th character A see Appendix A PDX collection 1171
- CC Exclusion 7th character K see Appendix A PDX collection 0897
- MCC Exclusion 7th character B see Appendix A PDX collection 1171
- HAC 7th characters A & B see Appendix B for HAC conditional logic

CC MCC +7th **S22.082 Unstable burst fracture of T11-T12 vertebra**
- CC Exclusion 7th character A see Appendix A PDX collection 1171
- CC Exclusion 7th character K see Appendix A PDX collection 0897
- MCC Exclusion 7th character B see Appendix A PDX collection 1171
- HAC 7th characters A & B see Appendix B for HAC conditional logic

CC MCC +7th **S22.088 Other fracture of T11-T12 vertebra**
- CC Exclusion 7th character A see Appendix A PDX collection 1171
- CC Exclusion 7th character K see Appendix A PDX collection 0897
- MCC Exclusion 7th character B see Appendix A PDX collection 1171
- HAC 7th characters A & B see Appendix B for HAC conditional logic

CC MCC +7th **S22.089 Unspecified fracture of T11-T12 vertebra**
- CC Exclusion 7th character A see Appendix A PDX collection 1171
- CC Exclusion 7th character K see Appendix A PDX collection 0897
- MCC Exclusion 7th character B see Appendix A PDX collection 1171
- HAC 7th characters A & B see Appendix B for HAC conditional logic

+ **S22.2 Fracture of sternum**

CC MCC X+7th **S22.20 Unspecified fracture of sternum**
- CC Exclusion 7th character A see Appendix A PDX collection 1172
- CC Exclusion 7th character K see Appendix A PDX collection 0897
- MCC Exclusion 7th character B see Appendix A PDX collection 1172
- HAC 7th characters A & B see Appendix B for HAC conditional logic

CC MCC X+7th **S22.21 Fracture of manubrium**
- CC Exclusion 7th character A see Appendix A PDX collection 1172
- CC Exclusion 7th character K see Appendix A PDX collection 0897
- MCC Exclusion 7th character B see Appendix A PDX collection 1172
- HAC 7th characters A & B see Appendix B for HAC conditional logic

CC MCC X+7th **S22.22 Fracture of body of sternum**
- CC Exclusion 7th character A see Appendix A PDX collection 1172
- CC Exclusion 7th character K see Appendix A PDX collection 0897
- MCC Exclusion 7th character B see Appendix A PDX collection 1172
- HAC 7th characters A & B see Appendix B for HAC conditional logic

CC MCC X+7th **S22.23 Sternal manubrial dissociation**
- CC Exclusion 7th character A see Appendix A PDX collection 1172
- CC Exclusion 7th character K see Appendix A PDX collection 0897
- MCC Exclusion 7th character B see Appendix A PDX collection 1172
- HAC 7th characters A & B see Appendix B for HAC conditional logic

CC MCC X+7th **S22.24 Fracture of xiphoid process**
- CC Exclusion 7th character A see Appendix A PDX collection 1172
- CC Exclusion 7th character K see Appendix A PDX collection 0897
- MCC Exclusion 7th character B see Appendix A PDX collection 1172
- HAC 7th characters A & B see Appendix B for HAC conditional logic

+ **S22.3 Fracture of one rib**

CC MCC X+7th **S22.31 Fracture of one rib, right side**
- CC Exclusion 7th character A see Appendix A PDX collection 1173
- CC Exclusion 7th character K see Appendix A PDX collection 0897
- MCC Exclusion 7th character B see Appendix A PDX collection 1174
- HAC 7th characters A & B see Appendix B for HAC conditional logic

CC MCC X+7th **S22.32 Fracture of one rib, left side**
- CC Exclusion 7th character A see Appendix A PDX collection 1173
- CC Exclusion 7th character K see Appendix A PDX collection 0897
- MCC Exclusion 7th character B see Appendix A PDX collection 1174
- HAC 7th characters A & B see Appendix B for HAC conditional logic

CC MCC X+7th **S22.39 Fracture of one rib, unspecified side**
- CC Exclusion 7th character A see Appendix A PDX collection 1173
- CC Exclusion 7th character K see Appendix A PDX collection 0897
- MCC Exclusion 7th character B see Appendix A PDX collection 1174
- HAC 7th characters A & B see Appendix B for HAC conditional logic

+ **S22.4 Multiple fractures of ribs**

Fractures of two or more ribs

Excludes1: *flail chest (S22.5-)*

CC MCC X+7th **S22.41 Multiple fractures of ribs, right side**
- CC Exclusion 7th character A see Appendix A PDX collection 1174
- CC Exclusion 7th character K see Appendix A PDX collection 0897
- MCC Exclusion 7th character B see Appendix A PDX collection 1174
- HAC 7th characters A & B see Appendix B for HAC conditional logic

CC MCC X+7th **S22.42 Multiple fractures of ribs, left side**
- CC Exclusion 7th character A see Appendix A PDX collection 1174
- CC Exclusion 7th character K see Appendix A PDX collection 0897
- MCC Exclusion 7th character B see Appendix A PDX collection 1174
- HAC 7th characters A & B see Appendix B for HAC conditional logic

CC MCC X+7th **S22.43 Multiple fractures of ribs, bilateral**
- CC Exclusion 7th character A see Appendix A PDX collection 1174
- CC Exclusion 7th character K see Appendix A PDX collection 0897
- MCC Exclusion 7th character B see Appendix A PDX collection 1174
- HAC 7th characters A & B see Appendix B for HAC conditional logic

C MCC X+7th **S22.49 Multiple fractures of ribs, unspecified side**
CC Exclusion 7th character A see Appendix A PDX collection 1174
CC Exclusion 7th character K see Appendix A PDX collection 0897
No MCC Exclusions
HAC 7th characters A & B see Appendix B for HAC conditional logic

X+7th CC **S22.5 Flail chest**
CC Exclusion 7th character K see Appendix A PDX collection 0897
MCC Exclusion 7th characters A & B see Appendix A PDX collection 1175
HAC 7th characters A & B see Appendix B for HAC conditional logic

X+7th CC **S22.9 Fracture of bony thorax, part unspecified**
CC Exclusion 7th character A see Appendix A PDX collection 1176
CC Exclusion 7th character K see Appendix A PDX collection 0897
MCC Exclusion 7th character B see Appendix A PDX collection 1176
HAC 7th characters A & B see Appendix B for HAC conditional logic

S23 Dislocation and sprain of joints and ligaments of thorax

Includes: avulsion of joint or ligament of thorax
laceration of cartilage, joint or ligament of thorax
sprain of cartilage, joint or ligament of thorax
traumatic hemarthrosis of joint or ligament of thorax
traumatic rupture of joint or ligament of thorax
traumatic subluxation of joint or ligament of thorax
traumatic tear of joint or ligament of thorax

Code also any associated open wound

Excludes2: *dislocation, sprain of sternoclavicular joint (S43.2, S43.6)*
strain of muscle or tendon of thorax (S29.01-)

The appropriate 7th character is to be added to each code from category S23
A initial encounter
D subsequent encounter
S sequela

X+7th **S23.0 Traumatic rupture of thoracic intervertebral disc**
Excludes1: *rupture or displacement (nontraumatic) of thoracic intervertebral disc NOS (M51.- with fifth character 4)*

+ **S23.1 Subluxation and dislocation of thoracic vertebra**
Code also any associated
open wound of thorax (S21.-)
spinal cord injury (S24.0-, S24.1-)
Excludes2: *fracture of thoracic vertebrae (S22.0-)*

+ **S23.10 Subluxation and dislocation of unspecified thoracic vertebra**
+7th **S23.100 Subluxation of unspecified thoracic vertebra**
+7th **S23.101 Dislocation of unspecified thoracic vertebra**

+ **S23.11 Subluxation and dislocation of T1/T2 thoracic vertebra**
+7th **S23.110 Subluxation of T1/T2 thoracic vertebra**
+7th **S23.111 Dislocation of T1/T2 thoracic vertebra**

+ **S23.12 Subluxation and dislocation of T2/T3-T3/T4 thoracic vertebra**
+7th **S23.120 Subluxation of T2/T3 thoracic vertebra**
+7th **S23.121 Dislocation of T2/T3 thoracic vertebra**
+7th **S23.122 Subluxation of T3/T4 thoracic vertebra**
+7th **S23.123 Dislocation of T3/T4 thoracic vertebra**

+ **S23.13 Subluxation and dislocation of T4/T5-T5/T6 thoracic vertebra**
+7th **S23.130 Subluxation of T4/T5 thoracic vertebra**
+7th **S23.131 Dislocation of T4/T5 thoracic vertebra**
+7th **S23.132 Subluxation of T5/T6 thoracic vertebra**
+7th **S23.133 Dislocation of T5/T6 thoracic vertebra**

+ **S23.14 Subluxation and dislocation of T6/T7-T7/T8 thoracic vertebra**
+7th **S23.140 Subluxation of T6/T7 thoracic vertebra**
+7th **S23.141 Dislocation of T6/T7 thoracic vertebra**
+7th **S23.142 Subluxation of T7/T8 thoracic vertebra**
+7th **S23.143 Dislocation of T7/T8 thoracic vertebra**

+ **S23.15 Subluxation and dislocation of T8/T9-T9/T10 thoracic vertebra**
+7th **S23.150 Subluxation of T8/T9 thoracic vertebra**
+7th **S23.151 Dislocation of T8/T9 thoracic vertebra**
+7th **S23.152 Subluxation of T9/T10 thoracic vertebra**
+7th **S23.153 Dislocation of T9/T10 thoracic vertebra**

+ **S23.16 Subluxation and dislocation of T10/T11-T11/T12 thoracic vertebra**
+7th **S23.160 Subluxation of T10/T11 thoracic vertebra**
+7th **S23.161 Dislocation of T10/T11 thoracic vertebra**
+7th **S23.162 Subluxation of T11/T12 thoracic vertebra**
+7th **S23.163 Dislocation of T11/T12 thoracic vertebra**

+ **S23.17 Subluxation and dislocation of T12/L1 thoracic vertebra**
+7th **S23.170 Subluxation of T12/L1 thoracic vertebra**
+7th **S23.171 Dislocation of T12/L1 thoracic vertebra**

+ **S23.2 Dislocation of other and unspecified parts of thorax**
X+7th **S23.20 Dislocation of unspecified part of thorax**
X+7th **S23.29 Dislocation of other parts of thorax**

X+7th **S23.3 Sprain of ligaments of thoracic spine**

+ **S23.4 Sprain of ribs and sternum**
X+7th **S23.41 Sprain of ribs**
+ **S23.42 Sprain of sternum**
+7th **S23.420 Sprain of sternoclavicular (joint) (ligament)**
+7th **S23.421 Sprain of chondrosternal joint**
+7th **S23.428 Other sprain of sternum**
+7th **S23.429 Unspecified sprain of sternum**

X+7th **S23.8 Sprain of other specified parts of thorax**
X+7th **S23.9 Sprain of unspecified parts of thorax**

S24 Injury of nerves and spinal cord at thorax level

NOTE Code to highest level of thoracic spinal cord injury
Injuries to the spinal cord (S24.0 and S24.1) refer to the cord level and not bone level injury, and can affect nerve roots at and below the level given.

Code also any associated:
fracture of thoracic vertebra (S22.0-)
open wound of thorax (S21.-)
transient paralysis (R29.5)

Excludes2: *injury of brachial plexus (S14.3)*

The appropriate 7th character is to be added to each code from category S24
A initial encounter
D subsequent encounter
S sequela

MCC X+7th **S24.0 Concussion and edema of thoracic spinal cord**
MCC Exclusion 7th character A see Appendix A PDX collection 1177

+ **S24.1 Other and unspecified injuries of thoracic spinal cord**
+ **S24.10 Unspecified injury of thoracic spinal cord**

MCC +7th **S24.101 Unspecified injury at T1 level of thoracic spinal cord**
MCC Exclusion 7th character A see Appendix A PDX collection 1177
HAC 7th character A see Appendix B for HAC conditional logic

MCC +7th **S24.102 Unspecified injury at T2-T6 level of thoracic spinal cord**
MCC Exclusion 7th character A see Appendix A PDX collection 1177
HAC 7th character A see Appendix B for HAC conditional logic

MCC +7th **S24.103 Unspecified injury at T7-T10 level of thoracic spinal cord**
MCC Exclusion 7th character A see Appendix A PDX collection 1177
HAC 7th character A see Appendix B for HAC conditional logic

MCC +7th **S24.104 Unspecified injury at T11-T12 level of thoracic spinal cord**
MCC Exclusion 7th character A see Appendix A PDX collection 1177
HAC 7th character A see Appendix B for HAC conditional logic

+7th **S24.109 Unspecified injury at unspecified level of thoracic spinal cord**
Injury of thoracic spinal cord NOS
HAC 7th character A see Appendix B for HAC conditional logic

+ **S24.11 Complete lesion of thoracic spinal cord**

MCC +7th **S24.111 Complete lesion at T1 level of thoracic spinal cord**
MCC Exclusion 7th character A see Appendix A PDX collection 1177
HAC 7th character A see Appendix B for HAC conditional logic

MCC +7th **S24.112 Complete lesion at T2-T6 level of thoracic spinal cord**
MCC Exclusion 7th character A see Appendix A PDX collection 1177
HAC 7th character A see Appendix B for HAC conditional logic

MCC +7th **S24.113 Complete lesion at T7-T10 level of thoracic spinal cord**
MCC Exclusion 7th character A see Appendix A PDX collection 1177
HAC 7th character A see Appendix B for HAC conditional logic

MCC +7th **S24.114 Complete lesion at T11-T12 level of thoracic spinal cord**
MCC Exclusion 7th character A see Appendix A PDX collection 1177
HAC 7th character A see Appendix B for HAC conditional logic

+7th **S24.119 Complete lesion at unspecified level of thoracic spinal cord**

+ **S24.13 Anterior cord syndrome of thoracic spinal cord**

MCC +7th **S24.131 Anterior cord syndrome at T1 level of thoracic spinal cord**
MCC Exclusion 7th character A see Appendix A PDX collection 1177
HAC 7th character A see Appendix B for HAC conditional logic

MCC +7th **S24.132 Anterior cord syndrome at T2-T6 level of thoracic spinal cord**
MCC Exclusion 7th character A see Appendix A PDX collection 1177
HAC 7th character A see Appendix B for HAC conditional logic

MCC +7th **S24.133 Anterior cord syndrome at T7-T10 level of thoracic spinal cord**
MCC Exclusion 7th character A see Appendix A PDX collection 1177
HAC 7th character A see Appendix B for HAC conditional logic

MCC +7th **S24.134 Anterior cord syndrome at T11-T12 level of thoracic spinal cord**
MCC Exclusion 7th character A see Appendix A PDX collection 1177
HAC 7th character A see Appendix B for HAC conditional logic

+7th **S24.139 Anterior cord syndrome at unspecified level of thoracic spinal cord**

+ **S24.14 Brown-Séquard syndrome of thoracic spinal cord**

MCC +7th **S24.141 Brown-Séquard syndrome at T1 level of thoracic spinal cord**
MCC Exclusion 7th character A see Appendix A PDX collection 1177

MCC +7th **S24.142 Brown-Séquard syndrome at T2-T6 level of thoracic spinal cord**
MCC Exclusion 7th character A see Appendix A PDX collection 1177

MCC +7th **S24.143 Brown-Séquard syndrome at T7-T10 level of thoracic spinal cord**
MCC Exclusion 7th character A see Appendix A PDX collection 1177

MCC +7th **S24.144 Brown-Séquard syndrome at T11-T12 level of thoracic spinal cord**
MCC Exclusion 7th character A see Appendix A PDX collection 1177

+7th **S24.149 Brown-Séquard syndrome at unspecified level of thoracic spinal cord**

+ **S24.15 Other incomplete lesions of thoracic spinal cord**
Incomplete lesion of thoracic spinal cord NOS
Posterior cord syndrome of thoracic spinal cord

MCC +7th **S24.151 Other incomplete lesion at T1 level of thoracic spinal cord**
MCC Exclusion 7th character A see Appendix A PDX collection 1177
HAC 7th character A see Appendix B for HAC conditional logic

MCC +7th **S24.152 Other incomplete lesion at T2-T6 level of thoracic spinal cord**
MCC Exclusion 7th character A see Appendix A PDX collection 1177
HAC 7th character A see Appendix B for HAC conditional logic

MCC +7th **S24.153 Other incomplete lesion at T7-T10 level of thoracic spinal cord**
MCC Exclusion 7th character A see Appendix A PDX collection 1177
HAC 7th character A see Appendix B for HAC conditional logic

MCC +7th **S24.154 Other incomplete lesion at T11-T12 level of thoracic spinal cord**
MCC Exclusion 7th character A see Appendix A PDX collection 1177
HAC 7th character A see Appendix B for HAC conditional logic

+7th **S24.159 Other incomplete lesion at unspecified level of thoracic spinal cord**

X+7th **S24.2 Injury of nerve root of thoracic spine**

X+7th **S24.3 Injury of peripheral nerves of thorax**

X+7th **S24.4 Injury of thoracic sympathetic nervous system**
Injury of cardiac plexus
Injury of esophageal plexus
Injury of pulmonary plexus
Injury of stellate ganglion
Injury of thoracic sympathetic ganglion

X+7th **S24.8 Injury of other specified nerves of thorax**

X+7th **S24.9 Injury of unspecified nerve of thorax**

S25 Injury of blood vessels of thorax

Code also any associated open wound (S21.-)

The appropriate 7th character is to be added to each code from category S25
A initial encounter
D subsequent encounter
S sequela

+ **S25.0 Injury of thoracic aorta**
Injury of aorta NOS

MCC X+7th **S25.00 Unspecified injury of thoracic aorta**
MCC Exclusion 7th character A see Appendix A PDX collection 1178

MCC X+7th **S25.01 Minor laceration of thoracic aorta**
Incomplete transection of thoracic aorta
Laceration of thoracic aorta NOS
Superficial laceration of thoracic aorta
MCC Exclusion 7th character A see Appendix A PDX collection 1178

MCC X+7th **S25.02 Major laceration of thoracic aorta**
Complete transection of thoracic aorta
Traumatic rupture of thoracic aorta
MCC Exclusion 7th character A see Appendix A PDX collection 1178

MCC X+7th **S25.09 Other specified injury of thoracic aorta**
MCC Exclusion 7th character A see Appendix A PDX collection 1178

+ **S25.1 Injury of innominate or subclavian artery**

+ **S25.10 Unspecified injury of innominate or subclavian artery**

MCC +7th **S25.101 Unspecified injury of right innominate or subclavian artery**
MCC Exclusion 7th character A see Appendix A PDX collection 1179

MCC +7th **S25.102 Unspecified injury of left innominate or subclavian artery**
MCC Exclusion 7th character A see Appendix A PDX collection 1179

MCC +7th **S25.109 Unspecified injury of unspecified innominate or subclavian artery**
MCC Exclusion 7th character A see Appendix A PDX collection 1179

+ **S25.11 Minor laceration of innominate or subclavian artery**
Incomplete transection of innominate or subclavian artery
Laceration of innominate or subclavian artery NOS
Superficial laceration of innominate or subclavian artery

MCC +7th **S25.111 Minor laceration of right innominate or subclavian artery**
MCC Exclusion 7th character A see Appendix A PDX collection 1179

MCC +7th **S25.112 Minor laceration of left innominate or subclavian artery**
MCC Exclusion 7th character A see Appendix A PDX collection 1179

MCC +7th **S25.119 Minor laceration of unspecified innominate or subclavian artery**
MCC Exclusion 7th character A see Appendix A PDX collection 1179

+ **S25.12 Major laceration of innominate or subclavian artery**
Complete transection of innominate or subclavian artery
Traumatic rupture of innominate or subclavian artery

MCC +7th **S25.121 Major laceration of right innominate or subclavian artery**
MCC Exclusion 7th character A see Appendix A PDX collection 1179

MCC +7th **S25.122 Major laceration of left innominate or subclavian artery**
MCC Exclusion 7th character A see Appendix A PDX collection 1179

MCC +7th **S25.129 Major laceration of unspecified innominate or subclavian artery**
MCC Exclusion 7th character A see Appendix A PDX collection 1179

+ **S25.19 Other specified injury of innominate or subclavian artery**

MCC +7th **S25.191 Other specified injury of right innominate or subclavian artery**
MCC Exclusion 7th character A see Appendix A PDX collection 1179

MCC +7th **S25.192 Other specified injury of left innominate or subclavian artery**
MCC Exclusion 7th character A see Appendix A PDX collection 1179

MCC +7th **S25.199 Other specified injury of unspecified innominate or subclavian artery**
MCC Exclusion 7th character A see Appendix A PDX collection 1179

+ **S25.2 Injury of superior vena cava**
Injury of vena cava NOS

MCC X+7th **S25.20 Unspecified injury of superior vena cava**
MCC Exclusion 7th character A see Appendix A PDX collection 1180

MCC X+7th **S25.21 Minor laceration of superior vena cava**
Incomplete transection of superior vena cava
Laceration of superior vena cava NOS
Superficial laceration of superior vena cava
MCC Exclusion 7th character A see Appendix A PDX collection 1180

MCC X+7th **S25.22 Major laceration of superior vena cava**
Complete transection of superior vena cava
Traumatic rupture of superior vena cava
MCC Exclusion 7th character A see Appendix A PDX collection 1180

MCC X+7th **S25.29 Other specified injury of superior vena cava**
MCC Exclusion 7th character A see Appendix A PDX collection 1180

+ **S25.3 Injury of innominate or subclavian vein**

+ **S25.30 Unspecified injury of innominate or subclavian vein**

MCC +7th **S25.301 Unspecified injury of right innominate or subclavian vein**
MCC Exclusion 7th character A see Appendix A PDX collection 1181

MCC +7th **S25.302 Unspecified injury of left innominate or subclavian vein**
MCC Exclusion 7th character A see Appendix A PDX collection 1181

CC

MCC +7th **S25.309 Unspecified injury of unspecified innominate or subclavian vein**
MCC Exclusion 7th character A see Appendix A PDX collection 1181

CC

+ **S25.31 Minor laceration of innominate or subclavian vein**
Incomplete transection of innominate or subclavian vein
Laceration of innominate or subclavian vein NOS
Superficial laceration of innominate or subclavian vein

MCC +7th **S25.311 Minor laceration of right innominate or subclavian vein**
MCC Exclusion 7th character A see Appendix A PDX collection 1181

MCC +7th **S25.312 Minor laceration of left innominate or subclavian vein**
MCC Exclusion 7th character A see Appendix A PDX collection 1181

MCC +7th **S25.319 Minor laceration of unspecified innominate or subclavian vein**
MCC Exclusion 7th character A see Appendix A PDX collection 1181

+ **S25.32 Major laceration of innominate or subclavian vein**
Complete transection of innominate or subclavian vein
Traumatic rupture of innominate or subclavian vein

MCC +7th **S25.321 Major laceration of right innominate or subclavian vein**
MCC Exclusion 7th character A see Appendix A PDX collection 1181

MCC +7th **S25.322 Major laceration of left innominate or subclavian vein**
MCC Exclusion 7th character A see Appendix A PDX collection 1181

MCC +7th **S25.329 Major laceration of unspecified innominate or subclavian vein**
MCC Exclusion 7th character A see Appendix A PDX collection 1181

+ **S25.39 Other specified injury of innominate or subclavian vein**

MCC +7th **S25.391 Other specified injury of right innominate or subclavian vein**
MCC Exclusion 7th character A see Appendix A PDX collection 1181

MCC +7th **S25.392 Other specified injury of left innominate or subclavian vein**
MCC Exclusion 7th character A see Appendix A PDX collection 1181

MCC +7th **S25.399 Other specified injury of unspecified innominate or subclavian vein**
MCC Exclusion 7th character A see Appendix A PDX collection 1181

+ **S25.4 Injury of pulmonary blood vessels**

+ **S25.40 Unspecified injury of pulmonary blood vessels**

MCC +7th **S25.401 Unspecified injury of right pulmonary blood vessels**
MCC Exclusion 7th character A see Appendix A PDX collection 1182

MCC +7th **S25.402 Unspecified injury of left pulmonary blood vessels**
MCC Exclusion 7th character A see Appendix A PDX collection 1182

MCC +7th **S25.409 Unspecified injury of unspecified pulmonary blood vessels**
MCC Exclusion 7th character A see Appendix A PDX collection 1182

+ **S25.41 Minor laceration of pulmonary blood vessels**
Incomplete transection of pulmonary blood vessels
Laceration of pulmonary blood vessels NOS
Superficial laceration of pulmonary blood vessels

MCC +7th **S25.411 Minor laceration of right pulmonary blood vessels**
MCC Exclusion 7th character A see Appendix A PDX collection 1182

MCC +7th **S25.412 Minor laceration of left pulmonary blood vessels**
MCC Exclusion 7th character A see Appendix A PDX collection 1182

MCC +7th **S25.419 Minor laceration of unspecified pulmonary blood vessels**
MCC Exclusion 7th character A see Appendix A PDX collection 1182

+ **S25.42 Major laceration of pulmonary blood vessels**
Complete transection of pulmonary blood vessels
Traumatic rupture of pulmonary blood vessels

MCC +7th **S25.421 Major laceration of right pulmonary blood vessels**
MCC Exclusion 7th character A see Appendix A PDX collection 1183

MCC +7th **S25.422 Major laceration of left pulmonary blood vessels**
MCC Exclusion 7th character A see Appendix A PDX collection 1182

MCC +7th **S25.429 Major laceration of unspecified pulmonary blood vessels**
MCC Exclusion 7th character A see Appendix A PDX collection 1182

+ **S25.49 Other specified injury of pulmonary blood vessels**

MCC +7th **S25.491 Other specified injury of right pulmonary blood vessels**
MCC Exclusion 7th character A see Appendix A PDX collection 1182

MCC +7th **S25.492 Other specified injury of left pulmonary blood vessels**
MCC Exclusion 7th character A see Appendix A PDX collection 1182

MCC +7th **S25.499 Other specified injury of unspecified pulmonary blood vessels**
MCC Exclusion 7th character A see Appendix A PDX collection 1182

+ **S25.5 Injury of intercostal blood vessels**

+ **S25.50 Unspecified injury of intercostal blood vessels**

CC +7th **S25.501 Unspecified injury of intercostal blood vessels, right side**
CC Exclusion 7th character A see Appendix A PDX collection 1184

CC +7th **S25.502 Unspecified injury of intercostal blood vessels, left side**
CC Exclusion 7th character A see Appendix A PDX collection 1184

CC +7th **S25.509 Unspecified injury of intercostal blood vessels, unspecified side**
CC Exclusion 7th character A see Appendix A PDX collection 1184

+ **S25.51 Laceration of intercostal blood vessels**
CC +7th **S25.511 Laceration of intercostal blood vessels, right side**
CC Exclusion 7th character A see Appendix A PDX collection 1184
CC +7th **S25.512 Laceration of intercostal blood vessels, left side**
CC Exclusion 7th character A see Appendix A PDX collection 1184
CC +7th **S25.519 Laceration of intercostal blood vessels, unspecified side**
CC Exclusion 7th character A see Appendix A PDX collection 1184

+ **S25.59 Other specified injury of intercostal blood vessels**
CC +7th **S25.591 Other specified injury of intercostal blood vessels, right side**
CC Exclusion 7th character A see Appendix A PDX collection 1184
CC +7th **S25.592 Other specified injury of intercostal blood vessels, left side**
CC Exclusion 7th character A see Appendix A PDX collection 1184
CC +7th **S25.599 Other specified injury of intercostal blood vessels, unspecified side**
CC Exclusion 7th character A see Appendix A PDX collection 1184

+ **S25.8 Injury of other blood vessels of thorax**
Injury of azygos vein
Injury of mammary artery or vein

+ **S25.80 Unspecified injury of other blood vessels of thorax**
CC +7th **S25.801 Unspecified injury of other blood vessels of thorax, right side**
CC Exclusion 7th character A see Appendix A PDX collection 1185
CC +7th **S25.802 Unspecified injury of other blood vessels of thorax, left side**
CC Exclusion 7th character A see Appendix A PDX collection 1185
CC +7th **S25.809 Unspecified injury of other blood vessels of thorax, unspecified side**
CC Exclusion 7th character A see Appendix A PDX collection 1185

+ **S25.81 Laceration of other blood vessels of thorax**
CC +7th **S25.811 Laceration of other blood vessels of thorax, right side**
CC Exclusion 7th character A see Appendix A PDX collection 1185
CC +7th **S25.812 Laceration of other blood vessels of thorax, left side**
CC Exclusion 7th character A see Appendix A PDX collection 1185
CC +7th **S25.819 Laceration of other blood vessels of thorax, unspecified side**
CC Exclusion 7th character A see Appendix A PDX collection 1185

+ **S25.89 Other specified injury of other blood vessels of thorax**
CC +7th **S25.891 Other specified injury of other blood vessels of thorax, right side**
CC Exclusion 7th character A see Appendix A PDX collection 1185
CC +7th **S25.892 Other specified injury of other blood vessels of thorax, left side**
CC Exclusion 7th character A see Appendix A PDX collection 1185
CC +7th **S25.899 Other specified injury of other blood vessels of thorax, unspecified side**
CC Exclusion 7th character A see Appendix A PDX collection 1185

+ **S25.9 Injury of unspecified blood vessel of thorax**
CC X+7th **S25.90 Unspecified injury of unspecified blood vessel of thorax**
CC Exclusion 7th character A see Appendix A PDX collection 1185
CC X+7th **S25.91 Laceration of unspecified blood vessel of thorax**
CC Exclusion 7th character A see Appendix A PDX collection 1185
CC X+7th **S25.99 Other specified injury of unspecified blood vessel of thorax**
CC Exclusion 7th character A see Appendix A PDX collection 1185

S26 Injury of heart

Code also any associated:
open wound of thorax (S21.-)
traumatic hemopneumothorax (S27.2)
traumatic hemothorax (S27.1)
traumatic pneumothorax (S27.0)

The appropriate 7th character is to be added to each code from category S26
A initial encounter
D subsequent encounter
S sequela

+ **S26.0 Injury of heart with hemopericardium**
CC X+7th **S26.00 Unspecified injury of heart with hemopericardium**
CC Exclusion 7th character A see Appendix A PDX collection 1186
CC X+7th **S26.01 Contusion of heart with hemopericardium**
CC Exclusion 7th character A see Appendix A PDX collection 1187

+ **S26.02 Laceration of heart with hemopericardium**
MCC +7th **S26.020 Mild laceration of heart with hemopericardium**
Laceration of heart without penetration of heart chamber
MCC Exclusion 7th character A see Appendix PDX collection 1187
MCC +7th **S26.021 Moderate laceration of heart with hemopericardium**
Laceration of heart with penetration of hear chamber
MCC Exclusion 7th character A see Appendix PDX collection 1187
MCC +7th **S26.022 Major laceration of heart with hemopericardium**
Laceration of heart with penetration of multiple heart chambers
MCC Exclusion 7th character A see Appendix PDX collection 1187
CC X+7th **S26.09 Other injury of heart with hemopericardium**
CC Exclusion 7th character A see Appendix A PDX collection 1186

+ **S26.1 Injury of heart without hemopericardium**
CC X+7th **S26.10 Unspecified injury of heart without hemopericardiu**
CC Exclusion 7th character A see Appendix A PDX collection 1186
CC X+7th **S26.11 Contusion of heart without hemopericardium**
CC Exclusion 7th character A see Appendix A PDX collection 1187
MCC X+7th **S26.12 Laceration of heart without hemopericardium**
MCC Exclusion 7th character A see Appendix A PDX collection 1187
CC X+7th **S26.19 Other injury of heart without hemopericardium**
CC Exclusion 7th character A see Appendix A PDX collection 1186

+ **S26.9 Injury of heart, unspecified with or without hemopericardium**
CC X+7th **S26.90 Unspecified injury of heart, unspecified with or without hemopericardium**
CC Exclusion 7th character A see Appendix A PDX collection 1186
CC X+7th **S26.91 Contusion of heart, unspecified with or without hemopericardium**
CC Exclusion 7th character A see Appendix A PDX collection 1187
MCC X+7th **S26.92 Laceration of heart, unspecified with or without hemopericardium**
Laceration of heart NOS
MCC Exclusion 7th character A see Appendix A PDX collection 1187
CC X+7th **S26.99 Other injury of heart, unspecified with or without hemopericardium**
CC Exclusion 7th character A see Appendix A PDX collection 1186

S27 Injury of other and unspecified intrathoracic organs

Code also associated open wound of thorax (S21.-)
Excludes2: *injury of cervical esophagus (S10-S19)*
injury of trachea (cervical) (S10-S19)

The appropriate 7th character is to be added to each code from category S27
A initial encounter
D subsequent encounter
S sequela

X+7th **S27.0 Traumatic pneumothorax**
Excludes1: spontaneous pneumothorax (J93.-)
CC Exclusion 7th character A see Appendix A PDX collection 1188

X+7th **S27.1 Traumatic hemothorax**
MCC Exclusion 7th character A see Appendix A PDX collection 1188

X+7th **S27.2 Traumatic hemopneumothorax**
MCC Exclusion 7th character A see Appendix A PDX collection 1188

S27.3 Other and unspecified injuries of lung

+ **S27.30 Unspecified injury of lung**

CC +7th **S27.301 Unspecified injury of lung, unilateral**
CC Exclusion 7th character A see Appendix A PDX collection 1189

CC +7th **S27.302 Unspecified injury of lung, bilateral**
CC Exclusion 7th character A see Appendix A PDX collection 1189

CC +7th **S27.309 Unspecified injury of lung, unspecified**
CC Exclusion 7th character A see Appendix A PDX collection 1189

+ **S27.31 Primary blast injury of lung**
Blast injury of lung NOS

CC +7th **S27.311 Primary blast injury of lung, unilateral**
CC Exclusion 7th character A see Appendix A PDX collection 1189

CC +7th **S27.312 Primary blast injury of lung, bilateral**
CC Exclusion 7th character A see Appendix A PDX collection 1189

CC +7th **S27.319 Primary blast injury of lung, unspecified**
CC Exclusion 7th character A see Appendix A PDX collection 1189

+ **S27.32 Contusion of lung**

CC +7th **S27.321 Contusion of lung, unilateral**
CC Exclusion 7th character A see Appendix A PDX collection 1189

CC +7th **S27.322 Contusion of lung, bilateral**
CC Exclusion 7th character A see Appendix A PDX collection 1189

CC +7th **S27.329 Contusion of lung, unspecified**
CC Exclusion 7th character A see Appendix A PDX collection 1189

+ **S27.33 Laceration of lung**

MCC +7th **S27.331 Laceration of lung, unilateral**
MCC Exclusion 7th character A see Appendix A PDX collection 1190

MCC +7th **S27.332 Laceration of lung, bilateral**
MCC Exclusion 7th character A see Appendix A PDX collection 1190

MCC +7th **S27.339 Laceration of lung, unspecified**
MCC Exclusion 7th character A see Appendix A PDX collection 1190

+ **S27.39 Other injuries of lung**
Secondary blast injury of lung

CC +7th **S27.391 Other injuries of lung, unilateral**
CC Exclusion 7th character A see Appendix A PDX collection 1189

CC +7th **S27.392 Other injuries of lung, bilateral**
CC Exclusion 7th character A see Appendix A PDX collection 1189

CC +7th **S27.399 Other injuries of lung, unspecified**
CC Exclusion 7th character A see Appendix A PDX collection 1189

S27.4 Injury of bronchus

+ **S27.40 Unspecified injury of bronchus**

MCC +7th **S27.401 Unspecified injury of bronchus, unilateral**
MCC Exclusion 7th character A see Appendix A PDX collection 1191

MCC +7th **S27.402 Unspecified injury of bronchus, bilateral**
MCC Exclusion 7th character A see Appendix A PDX collection 1191

MCC +7th **S27.409 Unspecified injury of bronchus, unspecified**
MCC Exclusion 7th character A see Appendix A PDX collection 1191

+ **S27.41 Primary blast injury of bronchus**
Blast injury of bronchus NOS

MCC +7th **S27.411 Primary blast injury of bronchus, unilateral**
MCC Exclusion 7th character A see Appendix A PDX collection 1191

MCC +7th **S27.412 Primary blast injury of bronchus, bilateral**
MCC Exclusion 7th character A see Appendix A PDX collection 1191

MCC +7th **S27.419 Primary blast injury of bronchus, unspecified**
MCC Exclusion 7th character A see Appendix A PDX collection 1191

+ **S27.42 Contusion of bronchus**

MCC +7th **S27.421 Contusion of bronchus, unilateral**
MCC Exclusion 7th character A see Appendix A PDX collection 1191

MCC +7th **S27.422 Contusion of bronchus, bilateral**
MCC Exclusion 7th character A see Appendix A PDX collection 1191

MCC +7th **S27.429 Contusion of bronchus, unspecified**
MCC Exclusion 7th character A see Appendix A PDX collection 1191

+ **S27.43 Laceration of bronchus**

MCC +7th **S27.431 Laceration of bronchus, unilateral**
MCC Exclusion 7th character A see Appendix A PDX collection 1191

MCC +7th **S27.432 Laceration of bronchus, bilateral**
MCC Exclusion 7th character A see Appendix A PDX collection 1191

MCC +7th **S27.439 Laceration of bronchus, unspecified**
MCC Exclusion 7th character A see Appendix A PDX collection 1191

+ **S27.49 Other injury of bronchus**
Secondary blast injury of bronchus

MCC +7th **S27.491 Other injury of bronchus, unilateral**
MCC Exclusion 7th character A see Appendix A PDX collection 1191

MCC +7th **S27.492 Other injury of bronchus, bilateral**
MCC Exclusion 7th character A see Appendix A PDX collection 1191

MCC +7th **S27.499 Other injury of bronchus, unspecified**
MCC Exclusion 7th character A see Appendix A PDX collection 1191

+ **S27.5 Injury of thoracic trachea**

CC X+7th **S27.50 Unspecified injury of thoracic trachea**
CC Exclusion 7th character A see Appendix A PDX collection 1169

CC X+7th **S27.51 Primary blast injury of thoracic trachea**
Blast injury of thoracic trachea NOS
CC Exclusion 7th character A see Appendix A PDX collection 1169

CC X+7th **S27.52 Contusion of thoracic trachea**
CC Exclusion 7th character A see Appendix A PDX collection 1169

CC X+7th **S27.53 Laceration of thoracic trachea**
CC Exclusion 7th character A see Appendix A PDX collection 1169

CC X+7th **S27.59 Other injury of thoracic trachea**
Secondary blast injury of thoracic trachea
CC Exclusion 7th character A see Appendix A PDX collection 1169

+ **S27.6 Injury of pleura**

CC X+7th **S27.60 Unspecified injury of pleura**
CC Exclusion 7th character A see Appendix A PDX collection 1169

CC X+7th **S27.63 Laceration of pleura**
CC Exclusion 7th character A see Appendix A PDX collection 1169

CC X+7th **S27.69 Other injury of pleura**
CC Exclusion 7th character A see Appendix A PDX collection 1169

+ **S27.8 Injury of other specified intrathoracic organs**

+ **S27.80 Injury of diaphragm**

CC +7th **S27.802 Contusion of diaphragm**
CC Exclusion 7th character A see Appendix A PDX collection 1192

CC +7th **S27.803 Laceration of diaphragm**
CC Exclusion 7th character A see Appendix A PDX collection 1192

CC +7th **S27.808 Other injury of diaphragm**
CC Exclusion 7th character A see Appendix A PDX collection 1192

CC +7th **S27.809 Unspecified injury of diaphragm**
CC Exclusion 7th character A see Appendix A PDX collection 1192

+ **S27.81 Injury of esophagus (thoracic part)**

MCC +7th **S27.812 Contusion of esophagus (thoracic part)**
MCC Exclusion 7th character A see Appendix A PDX collection 1193

MCC +7th **S27.813 Laceration of esophagus (thoracic part)**
MCC Exclusion 7th character A see Appendix A PDX collection 1193

MCC +7th **S27.818 Other injury of esophagus (thoracic part)**
MCC Exclusion 7th character A see Appendix A PDX collection 1193

MCC +7th **S27.819 Unspecified injury of esophagus (thoracic part)**
MCC Exclusion 7th character A see Appendix A PDX collection 1193

+ **S27.89 Injury of other specified intrathoracic organs**
Injury of lymphatic thoracic duct
Injury of thymus gland
CC +7th **S27.892 Contusion of other specified intrathoracic organs**
CC Exclusion 7th character A see Appendix A PDX collection 1169
CC +7th **S27.893 Laceration of other specified intrathoracic organs**
CC Exclusion 7th character A see Appendix A PDX collection 1169
CC +7th **S27.898 Other injury of other specified intrathoracic organs**
CC Exclusion 7th character A see Appendix A PDX collection 1169
CC +7th **S27.899 Unspecified injury of other specified intrathoracic organs**
CC Exclusion 7th character A see Appendix A PDX collection 1169
CC X+7th **S27.9 Injury of unspecified intrathoracic organ**
CC Exclusion 7th character A see Appendix A PDX collection 1194

S28 Crushing injury of thorax, and traumatic amputation of part of thorax

The appropriate 7th character is to be added to each code from category S28
A initial encounter
D subsequent encounter
S sequela

X+7th **S28.0 Crushed chest**
Use additional code for all associated injuries
Excludes1: *flail chest (S22.5)*
CC X+7th **S28.1 Traumatic amputation (partial) of part of thorax, except breast**
CC Exclusion 7th character A see Appendix A PDX collection 1168
+ **S28.2 Traumatic amputation of breast**
+ **S28.21 Complete traumatic amputation of breast**
Traumatic amputation of breast NOS
+7th **S28.211 Complete traumatic amputation of right breast**
+7th **S28.212 Complete traumatic amputation of left breast**
+7th **S28.219 Complete traumatic amputation of unspecified breast**
+ **S28.22 Partial traumatic amputation of breast**
+7th **S28.221 Partial traumatic amputation of right breast**
+7th **S28.222 Partial traumatic amputation of left breast**
+7th **S28.229 Partial traumatic amputation of unspecified breast**

S29 Other and unspecified injuries of thorax
Code also any associated open wound (S21.-)

The appropriate 7th character is to be added to each code from category S29
A initial encounter
D subsequent encounter
S sequela

+ **S29.0 Injury of muscle and tendon at thorax level**
+ **S29.00 Unspecified injury of muscle and tendon of thorax**
+7th **S29.001 Unspecified injury of muscle and tendon of front wall of thorax**
+7th **S29.002 Unspecified injury of muscle and tendon of back wall of thorax**
+7th **S29.009 Unspecified injury of muscle and tendon of unspecified wall of thorax**
+ **S29.01 Strain of muscle and tendon of thorax**
+7th **S29.011 Strain of muscle and tendon of front wall of thorax**
+7th **S29.012 Strain of muscle and tendon of back wall of thorax**
+7th **S29.019 Strain of muscle and tendon of unspecified wall of thorax**
+ **S29.02 Laceration of muscle and tendon of thorax**
CC +7th **S29.021 Laceration of muscle and tendon of front wall of thorax**
CC Exclusion 7th character A see Appendix A PDX collection 1168
+7th **S29.022 Laceration of muscle and tendon of back wall of thorax**
CC +7th **S29.029 Laceration of muscle and tendon of unspecified wall of thorax**
CC Exclusion 7th character A see Appendix A PDX collection 1168
+ **S29.09 Other injury of muscle and tendon of thorax**
+7th **S29.091 Other injury of muscle and tendon of front wall of thorax**
+7th **S29.092 Other injury of muscle and tendon of back wall of thorax**
+7th **S29.099 Other injury of muscle and tendon of unspecified wall of thorax**
X+7th **S29.8 Other specified injuries of thorax**
X+7th **S29.9 Unspecified injury of thorax**

Injuries to the abdomen, lower back, lumbar spine, pelvis and external genitals (S30-S39)

Includes: injuries to the abdominal wall
injuries to the anus
injuries to the buttock
injuries to the external genitalia
injuries to the flank
injuries to the groin

Excludes2: *burns and corrosions (T20-T32)*
effects of foreign body in anus and rectum (T18.5)
effects of foreign body in genitourinary tract (T19.-)
effects of foreign body in stomach, small intestine and colon (T18.2-T18.4)
frostbite (T33-T34)
insect bite or sting, venomous (T63.4)

S30 Superficial injury of abdomen, lower back, pelvis and external genitals
Excludes2: *superficial injury of hip (S70.-)*

The appropriate 7th character is to be added to each code from category S30
A initial encounter
D subsequent encounter
S sequela

X+7th **S30.0 Contusion of lower back and pelvis**
Contusion of buttock
X+7th **S30.1 Contusion of abdominal wall**
Contusion of flank
Contusion of groin
+ **S30.2 Contusion of external genital organs**
+ **S30.20 Contusion of unspecified external genital organ**
♂ +7th **S30.201 Contusion of unspecified external genital organ, male**
♀ +7th **S30.202 Contusion of unspecified external genital organ, female**
♂ X+7th **S30.21 Contusion of penis**
♂ X+7th **S30.22 Contusion of scrotum and testes**
♀ X+7th **S30.23 Contusion of vagina and vulva**
X+7th **S30.3 Contusion of anus**
X+7th **S30.8 Other superficial injuries of abdomen, lower back, pelvis and external genitals**
+ **S30.81 Abrasion of abdomen, lower back, pelvis and external genitals**
+7th **S30.810 Abrasion of lower back and pelvis**
+7th **S30.811 Abrasion of abdominal wall**
♂ +7th **S30.812 Abrasion of penis**
♂ +7th **S30.813 Abrasion of scrotum and testes**
♀ +7th **S30.814 Abrasion of vagina and vulva**
♂ +7th **S30.815 Abrasion of unspecified external genital organs, male**
♀ +7th **S30.816 Abrasion of unspecified external genital organs, female**
+7th **S30.817 Abrasion of anus**
+ **S30.82 Blister (nonthermal) of abdomen, lower back, pelvis and external genitals**
+7th **S30.820 Blister (nonthermal) of lower back and pelvis**
+7th **S30.821 Blister (nonthermal) of abdominal wall**
♂ +7th **S30.822 Blister (nonthermal) of penis**
♂ +7th **S30.823 Blister (nonthermal) of scrotum and testes**
♀ +7th **S30.824 Blister (nonthermal) of vagina and vulva**
♂ +7th **S30.825 Blister (nonthermal) of unspecified external genital organs, male**
♀ +7th **S30.826 Blister (nonthermal) of unspecified external genital organs, female**
+7th **S30.827 Blister (nonthermal) of anus**
+ **S30.84 External constriction of abdomen, lower back, pelvis and external genitals**
+7th **S30.840 External constriction of lower back and pelvis**
+7th **S30.841 External constriction of abdominal wall**

♂ +7th **S30.842** **External constriction of penis**
Hair tourniquet syndrome of penis
Use additional cause code to identify the constricting item (W49.0-)
♂ +7th **S30.843** **External constriction of scrotum and testes**
♀ +7th **S30.844** **External constriction of vagina and vulva**
♂ +7th **S30.845** **External constriction of unspecified external genital organs, male**
♀ +7th **S30.846** **External constriction of unspecified external genital organs, female**

+ **S30.85** **Superficial foreign body of abdomen, lower back, pelvis and external genitals**
Splinter in the abdomen, lower back, pelvis and external genitals
+7th **S30.850** **Superficial foreign body of lower back and pelvis**
+7th **S30.851** **Superficial foreign body of abdominal wall**
♂ +7th **S30.852** **Superficial foreign body of penis**
♂ +7th **S30.853** **Superficial foreign body of scrotum and testes**
♀ +7th **S30.854** **Superficial foreign body of vagina and vulva**
♂ +7th **S30.855** **Superficial foreign body of unspecified external genital organs, male**
♀ +7th **S30.856** **Superficial foreign body of unspecified external genital organs, female**
+7th **S30.857** **Superficial foreign body of anus**

+ **S30.86** **Insect bite (nonvenomous) of abdomen, lower back, pelvis and external genitals**
+7th **S30.860** **Insect bite (nonvenomous) of lower back and pelvis**
+7th **S30.861** **Insect bite (nonvenomous) of abdominal wall**
♂ +7th **S30.862** **Insect bite (nonvenomous) of penis**
♂ +7th **S30.863** **Insect bite (nonvenomous) of scrotum and testes**
♀ +7th **S30.864** **Insect bite (nonvenomous) of vagina and vulva**
♂ +7th **S30.865** **Insect bite (nonvenomous) of unspecified external genital organs, male**
♀ +7th **S30.866** **Insect bite (nonvenomous) of unspecified external genital organs, female**
+7th **S30.867** **Insect bite (nonvenomous) of anus**

+ **S30.87** **Other superficial bite of abdomen, lower back, pelvis and external genitals**
Excludes1: *open bite of abdomen, lower back, pelvis and external genitals (S31.05, S31.15, S31.25, S31.35, S31.45, S31.55)*
+7th **S30.870** **Other superficial bite of lower back and pelvis**
+7th **S30.871** **Other superficial bite of abdominal wall**
♂ +7th **S30.872** **Other superficial bite of penis**
♂ +7th **S30.873** **Other superficial bite of scrotum and testes**
♀ +7th **S30.874** **Other superficial bite of vagina and vulva**
♂ +7th **S30.875** **Other superficial bite of unspecified external genital organs, male**
♀ +7th **S30.876** **Other superficial bite of unspecified external genital organs, female**
+7th **S30.877** **Other superficial bite of anus**

+ **S30.9** **Unspecified superficial injury of abdomen, lower back, pelvis and external genitals**
X+7th **S30.91** **Unspecified superficial injury of lower back and pelvis**
X+7th **S30.92** **Unspecified superficial injury of abdominal wall**
♂ X+7th **S30.93** **Unspecified superficial injury of penis**
♂ X+7th **S30.94** **Unspecified superficial injury of scrotum and testes**
♀ X+7th **S30.95** **Unspecified superficial injury of vagina and vulva**
♂ X+7th **S30.96** **Unspecified superficial injury of unspecified external genital organs, male**
♀ X+7th **S30.97** **Unspecified superficial injury of unspecified external genital organs, female**
X+7th **S30.98** **Unspecified superficial injury of anus**

S31 Open wound of abdomen, lower back, pelvis and external genitals

Code also any associated:
spinal cord injury (S24.0, S24.1-, S34.0-, S34.1-)
wound infection

Excludes1: *traumatic amputation of part of abdomen, lower back and pelvis (S38.2-, S38.3)*
Excludes2: *open wound of hip (S71.00-S71.02)*
open fracture of pelvis (S32.1--S32.9 with 7th character B)

The appropriate 7th character is to be added to each code from category S31
A initial encounter
D subsequent encounter
S sequela

+ **S31.0** **Open wound of lower back and pelvis**
+ **S31.00** **Unspecified open wound of lower back and pelvis**
+7th **S31.000** **Unspecified open wound of lower back and pelvis without penetration into retroperitoneum**
Unspecified open wound of lower back and pelvis NOS
MCC +7th **S31.001** **Unspecified open wound of lower back and pelvis with penetration into retroperitoneum**
MCC Exclusion 7th character A see Appendix A PDX collection 1195

+ **S31.01** **Laceration without foreign body of lower back and pelvis**
+7th **S31.010** **Laceration without foreign body of lower back and pelvis without penetration into retroperitoneum**
Laceration without foreign body of lower back and pelvis NOS
MCC +7th **S31.011** **Laceration without foreign body of lower back and pelvis with penetration into retroperitoneum**
MCC Exclusion 7th character A see Appendix A PDX collection 1195

+ **S31.02** **Laceration with foreign body of lower back and pelvis**
+7th **S31.020** **Laceration with foreign body of lower back and pelvis without penetration into retroperitoneum**
Laceration with foreign body of lower back and pelvis NOS
MCC +7th **S31.021** **Laceration with foreign body of lower back and pelvis with penetration into retroperitoneum**
MCC Exclusion 7th character A see Appendix A PDX collection 1195

+ **S31.03** **Puncture wound without foreign body of lower back and pelvis**
+7th **S31.030** **Puncture wound without foreign body of lower back and pelvis without penetration into retroperitoneum**
Puncture wound without foreign body of lower back and pelvis NOS
MCC +7th **S31.031** **Puncture wound without foreign body of lower back and pelvis with penetration into retroperitoneum**
MCC Exclusion 7th character A see Appendix A PDX collection 1195

+ **S31.04** **Puncture wound with foreign body of lower back and pelvis**
+7th **S31.040** **Puncture wound with foreign body of lower back and pelvis without penetration into retroperitoneum**
Puncture wound with foreign body of lower back and pelvis NOS
MCC +7th **S31.041** **Puncture wound with foreign body of lower back and pelvis with penetration into retroperitoneum**
MCC Exclusion 7th character A see Appendix A PDX collection 1195

+ **S31.05** **Open bite of lower back and pelvis**
Bite of lower back and pelvis NOS
Excludes1: *superficial bite of lower back and pelvis (S30.860, S30.870)*
+7th **S31.050** **Open bite of lower back and pelvis without penetration into retroperitoneum**
Open bite of lower back and pelvis NOS
MCC +7th **S31.051** **Open bite of lower back and pelvis with penetration into retroperitoneum**
MCC Exclusion 7th character A see Appendix A PDX collection 1195

+ **S31.1 Open wound of abdominal wall without penetration into peritoneal cavity**
Open wound of abdominal wall NOS
Excludes2: *open wound of abdominal wall with penetration into peritoneal cavity (S31.6-)*

+ **S31.10 Unspecified open wound of abdominal wall without penetration into peritoneal cavity**
+7th **S31.100 Unspecified open wound of abdominal wall, right upper quadrant without penetration into peritoneal cavity**
+7th **S31.101 Unspecified open wound of abdominal wall, left upper quadrant without penetration into peritoneal cavity**
+7th **S31.102 Unspecified open wound of abdominal wall, epigastric region without penetration into peritoneal cavity**
+7th **S31.103 Unspecified open wound of abdominal wall, right lower quadrant without penetration into peritoneal cavity**
+7th **S31.104 Unspecified open wound of abdominal wall, left lower quadrant without penetration into peritoneal cavity**
+7th **S31.105 Unspecified open wound of abdominal wall, periumbilic region without penetration into peritoneal cavity**
+7th **S31.109 Unspecified open wound of abdominal wall, unspecified quadrant without penetration into peritoneal cavity**
Unspecified open wound of abdominal wall NOS

+ **S31.11 Laceration without foreign body of abdominal wall without penetration into peritoneal cavity**
+7th **S31.110 Laceration without foreign body of abdominal wall, right upper quadrant without penetration into peritoneal cavity**
+7th **S31.111 Laceration without foreign body of abdominal wall, left upper quadrant without penetration into peritoneal cavity**
+7th **S31.112 Laceration without foreign body of abdominal wall, epigastric region without penetration into peritoneal cavity**
+7th **S31.113 Laceration without foreign body of abdominal wall, right lower quadrant without penetration into peritoneal cavity**
+7th **S31.114 Laceration without foreign body of abdominal wall, left lower quadrant without penetration into peritoneal cavity**
+7th **S31.115 Laceration without foreign body of abdominal wall, periumbilic region without penetration into peritoneal cavity**
+7th **S31.119 Laceration without foreign body of abdominal wall, unspecified quadrant without penetration into peritoneal cavity**

+ **S31.12 Laceration with foreign body of abdominal wall without penetration into peritoneal cavity**
+7th **S31.120 Laceration of abdominal wall with foreign body, right upper quadrant without penetration into peritoneal cavity**
+7th **S31.121 Laceration of abdominal wall with foreign body, left upper quadrant without penetration into peritoneal cavity**
+7th **S31.122 Laceration of abdominal wall with foreign body, epigastric region without penetration into peritoneal cavity**
+7th **S31.123 Laceration of abdominal wall with foreign body, right lower quadrant without penetration into peritoneal cavity**
+7th **S31.124 Laceration of abdominal wall with foreign body, left lower quadrant without penetration into peritoneal cavity**
+7th **S31.125 Laceration of abdominal wall with foreign body, periumbilic region without penetration into peritoneal cavity**
+7th **S31.129 Laceration of abdominal wall with foreign body, unspecified quadrant without penetration into peritoneal cavity**

+ **S31.13 Puncture wound of abdominal wall without foreign body without penetration into peritoneal cavity**
+7th **S31.130 Puncture wound of abdominal wall without foreign body, right upper quadrant without penetration into peritoneal cavity**
+7th **S31.131 Puncture wound of abdominal wall witho foreign body, left upper quadrant withou penetration into peritoneal cavity**
+7th **S31.132 Puncture wound of abdominal wall witho foreign body, epigastric region without penetration into peritoneal cavity**
+7th **S31.133 Puncture wound of abdominal wall witho foreign body, right lower quadrant witho penetration into peritoneal cavity**
+7th **S31.134 Puncture wound of abdominal wall witho foreign body, left lower quadrant without penetration into peritoneal cavity**
+7th **S31.135 Puncture wound of abdominal wall witho foreign body, periumbilic region without penetration into peritoneal cavity**
+7th **S31.139 Puncture wound of abdominal wall witho foreign body, unspecified quadrant witho penetration into peritoneal cavity**

+ **S31.14 Puncture wound of abdominal wall with foreign bo without penetration into peritoneal cavity**
+7th **S31.140 Puncture wound of abdominal wall with foreign body, right upper quadrant witho penetration into peritoneal cavity**
+7th **S31.141 Puncture wound of abdominal wall with foreign body, left upper quadrant withou penetration into peritoneal cavity**
+7th **S31.142 Puncture wound of abdominal wall with foreign body, epigastric region without penetration into peritoneal cavity**
+7th **S31.143 Puncture wound of abdominal wall with foreign body, right lower quadrant witho penetration into peritoneal cavity**
+7th **S31.144 Puncture wound of abdominal wall with foreign body, left lower quadrant without penetration into peritoneal cavity**
+7th **S31.145 Puncture wound of abdominal wall with foreign body, periumbilic region without penetration into peritoneal cavity**
+7th **S31.149 Puncture wound of abdominal wall with foreign body, unspecified quadrant witho penetration into peritoneal cavity**

+ **S31.15 Open bite of abdominal wall without penetration in peritoneal cavity**
Bite of abdominal wall NOS
Excludes1: *superficial bite of abdominal wall (S30.8*
+7th **S31.150 Open bite of abdominal wall, right upper quadrant without penetration into perito cavity**
+7th **S31.151 Open bite of abdominal wall, left upper quadrant without penetration into perito cavity**
+7th **S31.152 Open bite of abdominal wall, epigastric reg without penetration into peritoneal cavity**
+7th **S31.153 Open bite of abdominal wall, right lower quadrant without penetration into perito cavity**
+7th **S31.154 Open bite of abdominal wall, left lower quadrant without penetration into periton cavity**
+7th **S31.155 Open bite of abdominal wall, periumbilic region without penetration into peritoneal cavity**
+7th **S31.159 Open bite of abdominal wall, unspecified quadrant without penetration into periton cavity**

+ **S31.2 Open wound of penis**
♂ X+7th **S31.20 Unspecified open wound of penis**
♂ X+7th **S31.21 Laceration without foreign body of penis**
♂ X+7th **S31.22 Laceration with foreign body of penis**
♂ X+7th **S31.23 Puncture wound without foreign body of penis**
♂ X+7th **S31.24 Puncture wound with foreign body of penis**
♂ X+7th **S31.25 Open bite of penis**
Bite of penis NOS
Excludes1: *superficial bite of penis (S30.862, S30.87*

+ **S31.3 Open wound of scrotum and testes**
♂ X+7th **S31.30 Unspecified open wound of scrotum and testes**
♂ X+7th **S31.31 Laceration without foreign body of scrotum and test**
♂ X+7th **S31.32 Laceration with foreign body of scrotum and testes**
♂ X+7th **S31.33 Puncture wound without foreign body of scrotum ar testes**
♂ X+7th **S31.34 Puncture wound with foreign body of scrotum and testes**

♂ X+7th **S31.35 Open bite of scrotum and testes**
Bite of scrotum and testes NOS
Excludes1: *superficial bite of scrotum and testes (S30.863, S30.873)*

\+ **S31.4 Open wound of vagina and vulva**
Excludes1: *injury to vagina and vulva during delivery (O70.-, O71.4)*

♀ X+7th **S31.40 Unspecified open wound of vagina and vulva**
♀ X+7th **S31.41 Laceration without foreign body of vagina and vulva**
♀ X+7th **S31.42 Laceration with foreign body of vagina and vulva**
♀ X+7th **S31.43 Puncture wound without foreign body of vagina and vulva**
♀ X+7th **S31.44 Puncture wound with foreign body of vagina and vulva**
♀ X+7th **S31.45 Open bite of vagina and vulva**
Bite of vagina and vulva NOS
Excludes1: *superficial bite of vagina and vulva (S30.864, S30.874)*

\+ **S31.5 Open wound of unspecified external genital organs**
Excludes1: *traumatic amputation of external genital organs (S38.21, S38.22)*

\+ **S31.50 Unspecified open wound of unspecified external genital organs**
♂ +7th **S31.501 Unspecified open wound of unspecified external genital organs, male**
♀ +7th **S31.502 Unspecified open wound of unspecified external genital organs, female**

\+ **S31.51 Laceration without foreign body of unspecified external genital organs**
♂ +7th **S31.511 Laceration without foreign body of unspecified external genital organs, male**
♀ +7th **S31.512 Laceration without foreign body of unspecified external genital organs, female**

\+ **S31.52 Laceration with foreign body of unspecified external genital organs**
♂ +7th **S31.521 Laceration with foreign body of unspecified external genital organs, male**
♀ +7th **S31.522 Laceration with foreign body of unspecified external genital organs, female**

\+ **S31.53 Puncture wound without foreign body of unspecified external genital organs**
♂ +7th **S31.531 Puncture wound without foreign body of unspecified external genital organs, male**
♀ +7th **S31.532 Puncture wound without foreign body of unspecified external genital organs, female**

\+ **S31.54 Puncture wound with foreign body of unspecified external genital organs**
♂ +7th **S31.541 Puncture wound with foreign body of unspecified external genital organs, male**
♀ +7th **S31.542 Puncture wound with foreign body of unspecified external genital organs, female**

\+ **S31.55 Open bite of unspecified external genital organs**
Bite of unspecified external genital organs NOS
Excludes1: *superficial bite of unspecified external genital organs (S30.865, S30.866, S30.875, S30.876)*
♂ +7th **S31.551 Open bite of unspecified external genital organs, male**
♀ +7th **S31.552 Open bite of unspecified external genital organs, female**

\+ **S31.6 Open wound of abdominal wall with penetration into peritoneal cavity**

\+ **S31.60 Unspecified open wound of abdominal wall with penetration into peritoneal cavity**

MCC +7th **S31.600 Unspecified open wound of abdominal wall, right upper quadrant with penetration into peritoneal cavity**
MCC Exclusion 7th character A see Appendix A
PDX collection 1195

MCC +7th **S31.601 Unspecified open wound of abdominal wall, left upper quadrant with penetration into peritoneal cavity**
MCC Exclusion 7th character A see Appendix A
PDX collection 1195

MCC +7th **S31.602 Unspecified open wound of abdominal wall, epigastric region with penetration into peritoneal cavity**
MCC Exclusion 7th character A see Appendix A
PDX collection 1195

MCC +7th **S31.603 Unspecified open wound of abdominal wall, right lower quadrant with penetration into peritoneal cavity**
MCC Exclusion 7th character A see Appendix A
PDX collection 1195

MCC +7th **S31.604 Unspecified open wound of abdominal wall, left lower quadrant with penetration into peritoneal cavity**
MCC Exclusion 7th character A see Appendix A
PDX collection 1195

MCC +7th **S31.605 Unspecified open wound of abdominal wall, periumbilic region with penetration into peritoneal cavity**
MCC Exclusion 7th character A see Appendix A
PDX collection 1195

MCC +7th **S31.609 Unspecified open wound of abdominal wall, unspecified quadrant with penetration into peritoneal cavity**
MCC Exclusion 7th character A see Appendix A
PDX collection 1195

\+ **S31.61 Laceration without foreign body of abdominal wall with penetration into peritoneal cavity**

MCC +7th **S31.610 Laceration without foreign body of abdominal wall, right upper quadrant with penetration into peritoneal cavity**
MCC Exclusion 7th character A see Appendix A
PDX collection 1195

MCC +7th **S31.611 Laceration without foreign body of abdominal wall, left upper quadrant with penetration into peritoneal cavity**
MCC Exclusion 7th character A see Appendix A
PDX collection 1195

MCC +7th **S31.612 Laceration without foreign body of abdominal wall, epigastric region with penetration into peritoneal cavity**
MCC Exclusion 7th character A see Appendix A
PDX collection 1195

MCC +7th **S31.613 Laceration without foreign body of abdominal wall, right lower quadrant with penetration into peritoneal cavity**
MCC Exclusion 7th character A see Appendix A
PDX collection 1195

MCC +7th **S31.614 Laceration without foreign body of abdominal wall, left lower quadrant with penetration into peritoneal cavity**
MCC Exclusion 7th character A see Appendix A
PDX collection 1195

MCC +7th **S31.615 Laceration without foreign body of abdominal wall, periumbilic region with penetration into peritoneal cavity**
MCC Exclusion 7th character A see Appendix A
PDX collection 1195

MCC +7th **S31.619 Laceration without foreign body of abdominal wall, unspecified quadrant with penetration into peritoneal cavity**
MCC Exclusion 7th character A see Appendix A
PDX collection 1195

\+ **S31.62 Laceration with foreign body of abdominal wall with penetration into peritoneal cavity**

MCC +7th **S31.620 Laceration with foreign body of abdominal wall, right upper quadrant with penetration into peritoneal cavity**
MCC Exclusion 7th character A see Appendix A
PDX collection 1195

MCC +7th **S31.621 Laceration with foreign body of abdominal wall, left upper quadrant with penetration into peritoneal cavity**
MCC Exclusion 7th character A see Appendix A
PDX collection 1195

MCC +7th **S31.622 Laceration with foreign body of abdominal wall, epigastric region with penetration into peritoneal cavity**
MCC Exclusion 7th character A see Appendix A
PDX collection 1195

MCC +7th **S31.623 Laceration with foreign body of abdominal wall, right lower quadrant with penetration into peritoneal cavity**
MCC Exclusion 7th character A see Appendix A
PDX collection 1195

MCC +7th **S31.624 Laceration with foreign body of abdominal wall, left lower quadrant with penetration into peritoneal cavity**
MCC Exclusion 7th character A see Appendix A
PDX collection 1195

MCC +7th **S31.625 Laceration with foreign body of abdominal wall, periumbilic region with penetration into peritoneal cavity**
MCC Exclusion 7th character A see Appendix A
PDX collection 1195

MCC +7th **S31.629** **Laceration with foreign body of abdominal wall, unspecified quadrant with penetration into peritoneal cavity**
MCC Exclusion 7th character A see Appendix A
PDX collection 1195

\+ **S31.63** **Puncture wound without foreign body of abdominal wall with penetration into peritoneal cavity**

MCC +7th **S31.630** **Puncture wound without foreign body of abdominal wall, right upper quadrant with penetration into peritoneal cavity**
MCC Exclusion 7th character A see Appendix A
PDX collection 1195

MCC +7th **S31.631** **Puncture wound without foreign body of abdominal wall, left upper quadrant with penetration into peritoneal cavity**
MCC Exclusion 7th character A see Appendix A
PDX collection 1195

MCC +7th **S31.632** **Puncture wound without foreign body of abdominal wall, epigastric region with penetration into peritoneal cavity**
MCC Exclusion 7th character A see Appendix A
PDX collection 1195

MCC +7th **S31.633** **Puncture wound without foreign body of abdominal wall, right lower quadrant with penetration into peritoneal cavity**
MCC Exclusion 7th character A see Appendix A
PDX collection 1195

MCC +7th **S31.634** **Puncture wound without foreign body of abdominal wall, left lower quadrant with penetration into peritoneal cavity**
MCC Exclusion 7th character A see Appendix A
PDX collection 1195

MCC +7th **S31.635** **Puncture wound without foreign body of abdominal wall, periumbilic region with penetration into peritoneal cavity**
MCC Exclusion 7th character A see Appendix A
PDX collection 1195

MCC +7th **S31.639** **Puncture wound without foreign body of abdominal wall, unspecified quadrant with penetration into peritoneal cavity**
MCC Exclusion 7th character A see Appendix A
PDX collection 1195

\+ **S31.64** **Puncture wound with foreign body of abdominal wall with penetration into peritoneal cavity**

MCC +7th **S31.640** **Puncture wound with foreign body of abdominal wall, right upper quadrant with penetration into peritoneal cavity**
MCC Exclusion 7th character A see Appendix A
PDX collection 1195

MCC +7th **S31.641** **Puncture wound with foreign body of abdominal wall, left upper quadrant with penetration into peritoneal cavity**
MCC Exclusion 7th character A see Appendix A
PDX collection 1195

MCC +7th **S31.642** **Puncture wound with foreign body of abdominal wall, epigastric region with penetration into peritoneal cavity**
MCC Exclusion 7th character A see Appendix A
PDX collection 1195

MCC +7th **S31.643** **Puncture wound with foreign body of abdominal wall, right lower quadrant with penetration into peritoneal cavity**
MCC Exclusion 7th character A see Appendix A
PDX collection 1195

MCC +7th **S31.644** **Puncture wound with foreign body of abdominal wall, left lower quadrant with penetration into peritoneal cavity**
MCC Exclusion 7th character A see Appendix A
PDX collection 1195

MCC +7th **S31.645** **Puncture wound with foreign body of abdominal wall, periumbilic region with penetration into peritoneal cavity**
MCC Exclusion 7th character A see Appendix A
PDX collection 1195

MCC +7th **S31.649** **Puncture wound with foreign body of abdominal wall, unspecified quadrant with penetration into peritoneal cavity**
MCC Exclusion 7th character A see Appendix A
PDX collection 1195

\+ **S31.65** **Open bite of abdominal wall with penetration into peritoneal cavity**
Excludes1: *superficial bite of abdominal wall (S30.861, S30.871)*

MCC +7th **S31.650** **Open bite of abdominal wall, right upper quadrant with penetration into peritoneal cavity**
MCC Exclusion 7th character A see Appendix A
PDX collection 1195

MCC +7th **S31.651** **Open bite of abdominal wall, left upper quadrant with penetration into peritoneal cavity**
MCC Exclusion 7th character A see Appendix A
PDX collection 1195

MCC +7th **S31.652** **Open bite of abdominal wall, epigastric region with penetration into peritoneal cavity**
MCC Exclusion 7th character A see Appendix A
PDX collection 1195

MCC +7th **S31.653** **Open bite of abdominal wall, right lower quadrant with penetration into peritoneal cavity**
MCC Exclusion 7th character A see Appendix A
PDX collection 1195

MCC +7th **S31.654** **Open bite of abdominal wall, left lower quadrant with penetration into peritoneal cavity**
MCC Exclusion 7th character A see Appendix A
PDX collection 1195

MCC +7th **S31.655** **Open bite of abdominal wall, periumbilic region with penetration into peritoneal cavity**
MCC Exclusion 7th character A see Appendix A
PDX collection 1195

MCC +7th **S31.659** **Open bite of abdominal wall, unspecified quadrant with penetration into peritoneal cavity**
MCC Exclusion 7th character A see Appendix A
PDX collection 1195

\+ **S31.8** **Open wound of other parts of abdomen, lower back and pelvis**

\+ **S31.80** **Open wound of unspecified buttock**

+7th **S31.801** **Laceration without foreign body of unspecified buttock**

+7th **S31.802** **Laceration with foreign body of unspecified buttock**

+7th **S31.803** **Puncture wound without foreign body of unspecified buttock**

+7th **S31.804** **Puncture wound with foreign body of unspecified buttock**

+7th **S31.805** **Open bite of unspecified buttock**
Bite of buttock NOS
Excludes1: *superficial bite of buttock (S30.870)*

S31.809 **Unspecified open wound of unspecified buttock**

\+ **S31.81** **Open wound of right buttock**

+7th **S31.811** **Laceration without foreign body of right buttock**

+7th **S31.812** **Laceration with foreign body of right buttock**

+7th **S31.813** **Puncture wound without foreign body of right buttock**

+7th **S31.814** **Puncture wound with foreign body of right buttock**

+7th **S31.815** **Open bite of right buttock**
Bite of right buttock NOS
Excludes1: *superficial bite of buttock (S30.870)*

S31.819 **Unspecified open wound of right buttock**

\+ **S31.82** **Open wound of left buttock**

+7th **S31.821** **Laceration without foreign body of left buttock**

+7th **S31.822** **Laceration with foreign body of left buttock**

+7th **S31.823** **Puncture wound without foreign body of left buttock**

+7th **S31.824** **Puncture wound with foreign body of left buttock**

+7th **S31.825** **Open bite of left buttock**
Bite of left buttock NOS
Excludes1: *superficial bite of buttock (S30.870)*

S31.829 **Unspecified open wound of left buttock**

\+ **S31.83** **Open wound of anus**

+7th **S31.831** **Laceration without foreign body of anus**

+7th **S31.832** **Laceration with foreign body of anus**

+7th **S31.833** **Puncture wound without foreign body of anus**

+7th **S31.834 Puncture wound with foreign body of anus**

+7th **S31.835 Open bite of anus**
Bite of anus NOS
Excludes1: *superficial bite of anus (S30.877)*

+7th **S31.839 Unspecified open wound of anus**

See page 916 for Vertebrae Illustration.

S32 Fracture of lumbar spine and pelvis

NOTE A fracture not indicated as displaced or nondisplaced should be coded to displaced
A fracture not indicated as opened or closed should be coded to closed

Includes: fracture of lumbosacral neural arch
fracture of lumbosacral spinous process
fracture of lumbosacral transverse process
fracture of lumbosacral vertebra
fracture of lumbosacral vertebral arch

Code first any associated spinal cord and spinal nerve injury (S34.-)
Excludes1: *transection of abdomen (S38.3)*
Excludes2: *fracture of hip NOS (S72.0-)*

The appropriate 7th character is to be added to each code from category S32
A initial encounter for closed fracture
B initial encounter for open fracture
D subsequent encounter for fracture with routine healing
G subsequent encounter for fracture with delayed healing
K subsequent encounter for fracture with nonunion
S sequela

Review coding guideline C.19.c

+ **S32.0 Fracture of lumbar vertebra**
Fracture of lumbar spine NOS

+ **S32.00 Fracture of unspecified lumbar vertebra**

CC MCC +7th **S32.000 Wedge compression fracture of unspecified lumbar vertebra**
CC Exclusion 7th character A see Appendix A
PDX collection 1196
CC Exclusion 7th character K see Appendix A
PDX collection 0897
MCC Exclusion 7th character B see Appendix A
PDX collection 1196
HAC 7th characters A & B see Appendix B for HAC conditional logic

CC MCC +7th **S32.001 Stable burst fracture of unspecified lumbar vertebra**
CC Exclusion 7th character A see Appendix A
PDX collection 1196
CC Exclusion 7th character K see Appendix A
PDX collection 0897
MCC Exclusion 7th character B see Appendix A
PDX collection 1196
HAC 7th characters A & B see Appendix B for HAC conditional logic

CC MCC +7th **S32.002 Unstable burst fracture of unspecified lumbar vertebra**
CC Exclusion 7th character A see Appendix A
PDX collection 1196
CC Exclusion 7th character K see Appendix A
PDX collection 0897
MCC Exclusion 7th character B see Appendix A
PDX collection 1196
HAC 7th characters A & B see Appendix B for HAC conditional logic

CC MCC +7th **S32.008 Other fracture of unspecified lumbar vertebra**
CC Exclusion 7th character A see Appendix A
PDX collection 1196
CC Exclusion 7th character K see Appendix A
PDX collection 0897
MCC Exclusion 7th character B see Appendix A
PDX collection 1196
HAC 7th characters A & B see Appendix B for HAC conditional logic

CC MCC +7th **S32.009 Unspecified fracture of unspecified lumbar vertebra**
CC Exclusion 7th character A see Appendix A
PDX collection 1196
CC Exclusion 7th character K see Appendix A
PDX collection 0897
MCC Exclusion 7th character B see Appendix A
PDX collection 1196
HAC 7th characters A & B see Appendix B for HAC conditional logic

+ **S32.01 Fracture of first lumbar vertebra**

CC MCC +7th **S32.010 Wedge compression fracture of first lumbar vertebra**
CC Exclusion 7th character A see Appendix A
PDX collection 1196
CC Exclusion 7th character K see Appendix A
PDX collection 0897
MCC Exclusion 7th character B see Appendix A
PDX collection 1196
HAC 7th characters A & B see Appendix B for HAC conditional logic

CC MCC +7th **S32.011 Stable burst fracture of first lumbar vertebra**
CC Exclusion 7th character A see Appendix A
PDX collection 1196
CC Exclusion 7th character K see Appendix A
PDX collection 0897
MCC Exclusion 7th character B see Appendix A
PDX collection 1196
HAC 7th characters A & B see Appendix B for HAC conditional logic

CC MCC +7th **S32.012 Unstable burst fracture of first lumbar vertebra**
CC Exclusion 7th character A see Appendix A
PDX collection 1196
CC Exclusion 7th character K see Appendix A
PDX collection 0897
MCC Exclusion 7th character B see Appendix A
PDX collection 1196
HAC 7th characters A & B see Appendix B for HAC conditional logic

CC MCC +7th **S32.018 Other fracture of first lumbar vertebra**
CC Exclusion 7th character A see Appendix A
PDX collection 1196
CC Exclusion 7th character K see Appendix A
PDX collection 0897
MCC Exclusion 7th character B see Appendix A
PDX collection 1196
HAC 7th characters A & B see Appendix B for HAC conditional logic

CC MCC +7th **S32.019 Unspecified fracture of first lumbar vertebra**
CC Exclusion 7th character A see Appendix A
PDX collection 1196
CC Exclusion 7th character K see Appendix A
PDX collection 0897
MCC Exclusion 7th character B see Appendix A
PDX collection 1196
HAC 7th characters A & B see Appendix B for HAC conditional logic

+ **S32.02 Fracture of second lumbar vertebra**

CC MCC +7th **S32.020 Wedge compression fracture of second lumbar vertebra**
CC Exclusion 7th character A see Appendix A
PDX collection 1196
CC Exclusion 7th character K see Appendix A
PDX collection 0897
MCC Exclusion 7th character B see Appendix A
PDX collection 1196
HAC 7th characters A & B see Appendix B for HAC conditional logic

CC MCC +7th **S32.021 Stable burst fracture of second lumbar vertebra**
CC Exclusion 7th character A see Appendix A
PDX collection 1196
CC Exclusion 7th character K see Appendix A
PDX collection 0897
MCC Exclusion 7th character B see Appendix A
PDX collection 1196
HAC 7th characters A & B see Appendix B for HAC conditional logic

CC MCC +7th **S32.022 Unstable burst fracture of second lumbar vertebra**
CC Exclusion 7th character A see Appendix A
PDX collection 1196
CC Exclusion 7th character K see Appendix A
PDX collection 0897
MCC Exclusion 7th character B see Appendix A
PDX collection 1196
HAC 7th characters A & B see Appendix B for HAC conditional logic

CC MCC +7th **S32.028 Other fracture of second lumbar vertebra**
CC Exclusion 7th character A see Appendix A
PDX collection 1196
CC Exclusion 7th character K see Appendix A
PDX collection 0897
MCC Exclusion 7th character B see Appendix A
PDX collection 1196
HAC 7th characters A & B see Appendix B for HAC conditional logic

CC MCC +7th **S32.029 Unspecified fracture of second lumbar vertebra**
- **CC Exclusion 7th character A see Appendix A PDX collection 1196**
- **CC Exclusion 7th character K see Appendix A PDX collection 0897**
- **MCC Exclusion 7th character B see Appendix A PDX collection 1196**
- HAC 7th characters A & B see Appendix B for HAC conditional logic

\+ **S32.03 Fracture of third lumbar vertebra**

CC MCC +7th **S32.030 Wedge compression fracture of third lumbar vertebra**
- **CC Exclusion 7th character A see Appendix A PDX collection 1196**
- **CC Exclusion 7th character K see Appendix A PDX collection 0897**
- **MCC Exclusion 7th character B see Appendix A PDX collection 1196**
- HAC 7th characters A & B see Appendix B for HAC conditional logic

CC MCC +7th **S32.031 Stable burst fracture of third lumbar vertebra**
- **CC Exclusion 7th character A see Appendix A PDX collection 1196**
- **CC Exclusion 7th character K see Appendix A PDX collection 0897**
- **MCC Exclusion 7th character B see Appendix A PDX collection 1196**
- HAC 7th characters A & B see Appendix B for HAC conditional logic

CC MCC +7th **S32.032 Unstable burst fracture of third lumbar vertebra**
- **CC Exclusion 7th character A see Appendix A PDX collection 1196**
- **CC Exclusion 7th character K see Appendix A PDX collection 0897**
- **MCC Exclusion 7th character B see Appendix A PDX collection 1196**
- HAC 7th characters A & B see Appendix B for HAC conditional logic

CC MCC +7th **S32.038 Other fracture of third lumbar vertebra**
- **CC Exclusion 7th character A see Appendix A PDX collection 1196**
- **CC Exclusion 7th character K see Appendix A PDX collection 0897**
- **MCC Exclusion 7th character B see Appendix A PDX collection 1196**
- HAC 7th characters A & B see Appendix B for HAC conditional logic

CC MCC +7th **S32.039 Unspecified fracture of third lumbar vertebra**
- **CC Exclusion 7th character A see Appendix A PDX collection 1196**
- **CC Exclusion 7th character K see Appendix A PDX collection 0897**
- **MCC Exclusion 7th character B see Appendix A PDX collection 1196**
- HAC 7th characters A & B see Appendix B for HAC conditional logic

\+ **S32.04 Fracture of fourth lumbar vertebra**

CC MCC +7th **S32.040 Wedge compression fracture of fourth lumbar vertebra**
- **CC Exclusion 7th character A see Appendix A PDX collection 1196**
- **CC Exclusion 7th character K see Appendix A PDX collection 0897**
- **MCC Exclusion 7th character B see Appendix A PDX collection 1196**
- HAC 7th characters A & B see Appendix B for HAC conditional logic

CC MCC +7th **S32.041 Stable burst fracture of fourth lumbar vertebra**
- **CC Exclusion 7th character A see Appendix A PDX collection 1196**
- **CC Exclusion 7th character K see Appendix A PDX collection 0897**
- **MCC Exclusion 7th character B see Appendix A PDX collection 1196**
- HAC 7th characters A & B see Appendix B for HAC conditional logic

CC MCC +7th **S32.042 Unstable burst fracture of fourth lumbar vertebra**
- **CC Exclusion 7th character A see Appendix A PDX collection 1196**
- **CC Exclusion 7th character K see Appendix A PDX collection 0897**
- **MCC Exclusion 7th character B see Appendix A PDX collection 1196**
- HAC 7th characters A & B see Appendix B for HAC conditional logic

CC MCC +7th **S32.048 Other fracture of fourth lumbar vertebra**
- **CC Exclusion 7th character A see Appendix A PDX collection 1196**
- **CC Exclusion 7th character K see Appendix A PDX collection 0897**
- **MCC Exclusion 7th character B see Appendix PDX collection 1196**
- HAC 7th characters A & B see Appendix B for HAC conditional logic

CC MCC +7th **S32.049 Unspecified fracture of fourth lumbar vertebra**
- **CC Exclusion 7th character A see Appendix A PDX collection 1196**
- **CC Exclusion 7th character K see Appendix A PDX collection 0897**
- **MCC Exclusion 7th character B see Appendix PDX collection 1196**
- HAC 7th characters A & B see Appendix B for HAC conditional logic

\+ **S32.05 Fracture of fifth lumbar vertebra**

CC MCC +7th **S32.050 Wedge compression fracture of fifth lumbar vertebra**
- **CC Exclusion 7th character A see Appendix A PDX collection 1196**
- **CC Exclusion 7th character K see Appendix A PDX collection 0897**
- **MCC Exclusion 7th character B see Appendix PDX collection 1196**
- HAC 7th characters A & B see Appendix B for HAC conditional logic

CC MCC +7th **S32.051 Stable burst fracture of fifth lumbar vertebra**
- **CC Exclusion 7th character A see Appendix A PDX collection 1196**
- **CC Exclusion 7th character K see Appendix A PDX collection 0897**
- **MCC Exclusion 7th character B see Appendix A PDX collection 1196**
- HAC 7th characters A & B see Appendix B for HAC conditional logic

CC MCC +7th **S32.052 Unstable burst fracture of fifth lumbar vertebra**
- **CC Exclusion 7th character A see Appendix A PDX collection 1196**
- **CC Exclusion 7th character K see Appendix A PDX collection 0897**
- **MCC Exclusion 7th character B see Appendix A PDX collection 1196**
- HAC 7th characters A & B see Appendix B for HAC conditional logic

CC MCC +7th **S32.058 Other fracture of fifth lumbar vertebra**
- **CC Exclusion 7th character A see Appendix A PDX collection 1196**
- **CC Exclusion 7th character K see Appendix A PDX collection 0897**
- **MCC Exclusion 7th character B see Appendix A PDX collection 1196**
- HAC 7th characters A & B see Appendix B for HAC conditional logic

CC MCC +7th **S32.059 Unspecified fracture of fifth lumbar vertebra**
- **CC Exclusion 7th character A see Appendix A PDX collection 1196**
- **CC Exclusion 7th character K see Appendix A PDX collection 0897**
- **MCC Exclusion 7th character B see Appendix A PDX collection 1196**
- HAC 7th characters A & B see Appendix B for HAC conditional logic

\+ **S32.1 Fracture of sacrum**

NOTE For vertical fractures, code to most medial fracture extension
Use two codes if both a vertical and transverse fracture are present

Code also any associated fracture of pelvic ring (S32.8-)

CC MCC X+7th **S32.10 Unspecified fracture of sacrum**
- **CC Exclusion 7th character A see Appendix A PDX collection 1197**
- **CC Exclusion 7th character K see Appendix A PDX collection 0897**
- **MCC Exclusion 7th character B see Appendix A PDX collection 1197**
- HAC 7th characters A & B see Appendix B for HAC conditional logic

\+ **S32.11 Zone I fracture of sacrum**
Vertical sacral ala fracture of sacrum

CC MCC +7th **S32.110 Nondisplaced Zone I fracture of sacrum**
CC Exclusion 7th character A see Appendix A PDX collection 1197
CC Exclusion 7th character K see Appendix A PDX collection 0897
MCC Exclusion 7th character B see Appendix A PDX collection 1197
HAC 7th characters A & B see Appendix B for HAC conditional logic

CC MCC +7th **S32.111 Minimally displaced Zone I fracture of sacrum**
CC Exclusion 7th character A see Appendix A PDX collection 1197
CC Exclusion 7th character K see Appendix A PDX collection 0897
MCC Exclusion 7th character B see Appendix A PDX collection 1197
HAC 7th characters A & B see Appendix B for HAC conditional logic

CC MCC +7th **S32.112 Severely displaced Zone I fracture of sacrum**
CC Exclusion 7th character A see Appendix A PDX collection 1197
CC Exclusion 7th character K see Appendix A PDX collection 0897
MCC Exclusion 7th character B see Appendix A PDX collection 1197
HAC 7th characters A & B see Appendix B for HAC conditional logic

CC MCC +7th **S32.119 Unspecified Zone I fracture of sacrum**
CC Exclusion 7th character A see Appendix A PDX collection 1197
CC Exclusion 7th character K see Appendix A PDX collection 0897
MCC Exclusion 7th character B see Appendix A PDX collection 1197
HAC 7th characters A & B see Appendix B for HAC conditional logic

\+ **S32.12 Zone II fracture of sacrum**
Vertical foraminal region fracture of sacrum

CC MCC +7th **S32.120 Nondisplaced Zone II fracture of sacrum**
CC Exclusion 7th character A see Appendix A PDX collection 1197
CC Exclusion 7th character K see Appendix A PDX collection 0897
MCC Exclusion 7th character B see Appendix A PDX collection 1197
HAC 7th characters A & B see Appendix B for HAC conditional logic

CC MCC +7th **S32.121 Minimally displaced Zone II fracture of sacrum**
CC Exclusion 7th character A see Appendix A PDX collection 1197
CC Exclusion 7th character K see Appendix A PDX collection 0897
MCC Exclusion 7th character B see Appendix A PDX collection 1197
HAC 7th characters A & B see Appendix B for HAC conditional logic

CC MCC +7th **S32.122 Severely displaced Zone II fracture of sacrum**
CC Exclusion 7th character A see Appendix A PDX collection 1197
CC Exclusion 7th character K see Appendix A PDX collection 0897
MCC Exclusion 7th character B see Appendix A PDX collection 1197
HAC 7th characters A & B see Appendix B for HAC conditional logic

CC MCC +7th **S32.129 Unspecified Zone II fracture of sacrum**
CC Exclusion 7th character A see Appendix A PDX collection 1197
CC Exclusion 7th character K see Appendix A PDX collection 0897
MCC Exclusion 7th character B see Appendix A PDX collection 1197
HAC 7th characters A & B see Appendix B for HAC conditional logic

\+ **S32.13 Zone III fracture of sacrum**
Vertical fracture into spinal canal region of sacrum

CC MCC +7th **S32.130 Nondisplaced Zone III fracture of sacrum**
CC Exclusion 7th character A see Appendix A PDX collection 1197
CC Exclusion 7th character K see Appendix A PDX collection 0897
MCC Exclusion 7th character B see Appendix A PDX collection 1197
HAC 7th characters A & B see Appendix B for HAC conditional logic

CC MCC +7th **S32.131 Minimally displaced Zone III fracture of sacrum**
CC Exclusion 7th character A see Appendix A PDX collection 1197
CC Exclusion 7th character K see Appendix A PDX collection 0897
MCC Exclusion 7th character B see Appendix A PDX collection 1197
HAC 7th characters A & B see Appendix B for HAC conditional logic

CC MCC +7th **S32.132 Severely displaced Zone III fracture of sacrum**
CC Exclusion 7th character A see Appendix A PDX collection 1197
CC Exclusion 7th character K see Appendix A PDX collection 0897
MCC Exclusion 7th character B see Appendix A PDX collection 1197
HAC 7th characters A & B see Appendix B for HAC conditional logic

CC MCC +7th **S32.139 Unspecified Zone III fracture of sacrum**
CC Exclusion 7th character A see Appendix A PDX collection 1197
CC Exclusion 7th character K see Appendix A PDX collection 0897
MCC Exclusion 7th character B see Appendix A PDX collection 1197
HAC 7th characters A & B see Appendix B for HAC conditional logic

CC MCC X+7th **S32.14 Type 1 fracture of sacrum**
Transverse flexion fracture of sacrum without displacement
CC Exclusion 7th character A see Appendix A PDX collection 1197
CC Exclusion 7th character K see Appendix A PDX collection 0897
MCC Exclusion 7th character B see Appendix A PDX collection 1197
HAC 7th characters A & B see Appendix B for HAC conditional logic

CC MCC X+7th **S32.15 Type 2 fracture of sacrum**
Transverse flexion fracture of sacrum with posterior displacement
CC Exclusion 7th character A see Appendix A PDX collection 1197
CC Exclusion 7th character K see Appendix A PDX collection 0897
MCC Exclusion 7th character B see Appendix A PDX collection 1197
HAC 7th characters A & B see Appendix B for HAC conditional logic

CC MCC X+7th **S32.16 Type 3 fracture of sacrum**
Transverse extension fracture of sacrum with anterior displacement
CC Exclusion 7th character A see Appendix A PDX collection 1197
CC Exclusion 7th character K see Appendix A PDX collection 0897
MCC Exclusion 7th character B see Appendix A PDX collection 1197
HAC 7th characters A & B see Appendix B for HAC conditional logic

CC MCC X+7th **S32.17 Type 4 fracture of sacrum**
Transverse segmental comminution of upper sacrum
CC Exclusion 7th character A see Appendix A PDX collection 1197
CC Exclusion 7th character K see Appendix A PDX collection 0897
MCC Exclusion 7th character B see Appendix A PDX collection 1197
HAC 7th characters A & B see Appendix B for HAC conditional logic

CC MCC X+7th **S32.19 Other fracture of sacrum**
CC Exclusion 7th character A see Appendix A PDX collection 1197
CC Exclusion 7th character K see Appendix A PDX collection 0897
MCC Exclusion 7th character B see Appendix A PDX collection 1197
HAC 7th characters A & B see Appendix B for HAC conditional logic

X+7th CC MCC **S32.2 Fracture of coccyx**
CC Exclusion 7th character A see Appendix A PDX collection 1197
CC Exclusion 7th character K see Appendix A PDX collection 0897
MCC Exclusion 7th character B see Appendix A PDX collection 1197
HAC 7th characters A & B see Appendix B for HAC conditional logic

+ S32.3 Fracture of ilium
Excludes1: fracture of ilium with associated disruption of pelvic ring (S32.8-)

+ S32.30 Unspecified fracture of ilium

CC MCC +7th **S32.301 Unspecified fracture of right ilium**
CC Exclusion 7th character A see Appendix A
PDX collection 1176
CC Exclusion 7th character K see Appendix A
PDX collection 0897
MCC Exclusion 7th character B see Appendix A
PDX collection 1198
HAC 7th characters A & B see Appendix B for HAC conditional logic

CC MCC +7th **S32.302 Unspecified fracture of left ilium**
CC Exclusion 7th character A see Appendix A
PDX collection 1176
CC Exclusion 7th character K see Appendix A
PDX collection 0897
MCC Exclusion 7th character B see Appendix A
PDX collection 1198
HAC 7th characters A & B see Appendix B for HAC conditional logic

CC MCC +7th **S32.309 Unspecified fracture of unspecified ilium**
CC Exclusion 7th character A see Appendix A
PDX collection 1176
CC Exclusion 7th character K see Appendix A
PDX collection 0897
MCC Exclusion 7th character B see Appendix A
PDX collection 1198
HAC 7th characters A & B see Appendix B for HAC conditional logic

+ S32.31 Avulsion fracture of ilium

CC MCC +7th **S32.311 Displaced avulsion fracture of right ilium**
CC Exclusion 7th character A see Appendix A
PDX collection 1176
CC Exclusion 7th character K see Appendix A
PDX collection 0897
MCC Exclusion 7th character B see Appendix A
PDX collection 1198
HAC 7th characters A & B see Appendix B for HAC conditional logic

CC MCC +7th **S32.312 Displaced avulsion fracture of left ilium**
CC Exclusion 7th character A see Appendix A
PDX collection 1176
CC Exclusion 7th character K see Appendix A
PDX collection 0897
MCC Exclusion 7th character B see Appendix A
PDX collection 1198
HAC 7th characters A & B see Appendix B for HAC conditional logic

CC MCC +7th **S32.313 Displaced avulsion fracture of unspecified ilium**
CC Exclusion 7th character A see Appendix A
PDX collection 1176
CC Exclusion 7th character K see Appendix A
PDX collection 0897
MCC Exclusion 7th character B see Appendix A
PDX collection 1198
HAC 7th characters A & B see Appendix B for HAC conditional logic

CC MCC +7th **S32.314 Nondisplaced avulsion fracture of right ilium**
CC Exclusion 7th character A see Appendix A
PDX collection 1176
CC Exclusion 7th character K see Appendix A
PDX collection 0897
MCC Exclusion 7th character B see Appendix A
PDX collection 1198
HAC 7th characters A & B see Appendix B for HAC conditional logic

CC MCC +7th **S32.315 Nondisplaced avulsion fracture of left ilium**
CC Exclusion 7th character A see Appendix A
PDX collection 1176
CC Exclusion 7th character K see Appendix A
PDX collection 0897
MCC Exclusion 7th character B see Appendix A
PDX collection 1198
HAC 7th characters A & B see Appendix B for HAC conditional logic

CC MCC +7th **S32.316 Nondisplaced avulsion fracture of unspecified ilium**
CC Exclusion 7th character A see Appendix A
PDX collection 1176
CC Exclusion 7th character K see Appendix A
PDX collection 0897
MCC Exclusion 7th character B see Appendix A
PDX collection 1198
HAC 7th characters A & B see Appendix B for HAC conditional logic

+ S32.39 Other fracture of ilium

CC MCC +7th **S32.391 Other fracture of right ilium**
CC Exclusion 7th character A see Appendix A
PDX collection 1176
CC Exclusion 7th character K see Appendix A
PDX collection 0897
MCC Exclusion 7th character B see Appendix A
PDX collection 1198
HAC 7th characters A & B see Appendix B for HAC conditional logic

CC MCC +7th **S32.392 Other fracture of left ilium**
CC Exclusion 7th character A see Appendix A
PDX collection 1176
CC Exclusion 7th character K see Appendix A
PDX collection 0897
MCC Exclusion 7th character B see Appendix A
PDX collection 1198
HAC 7th characters A & B see Appendix B for HAC conditional logic

CC MCC +7th **S32.399 Other fracture of unspecified ilium**
CC Exclusion 7th character A see Appendix A
PDX collection 1176
CC Exclusion 7th character K see Appendix A
PDX collection 0897
MCC Exclusion 7th character B see Appendix A
PDX collection 1198
HAC 7th characters A & B see Appendix B for HAC conditional logic

+ S32.4 Fracture of acetabulum
Code also any associated fracture of pelvic ring (S32.8-)

+ S32.40 Unspecified fracture of acetabulum

CC MCC +7th **S32.401 Unspecified fracture of right acetabulum**
CC Exclusion 7th character K see Appendix A
PDX collection 0897
MCC Exclusion 7th character A see Appendix A
PDX collection 1199
MCC Exclusion 7th character B see Appendix A
PDX collection 1200
HAC 7th characters A & B see Appendix B for HAC conditional logic

CC MCC +7th **S32.402 Unspecified fracture of left acetabulum**
CC Exclusion 7th character K see Appendix A
PDX collection 0897
MCC Exclusion 7th character A see Appendix A
PDX collection 1199
MCC Exclusion 7th character B see Appendix A
PDX collection 1200
HAC 7th characters A & B see Appendix B for HAC conditional logic

CC MCC +7th **S32.409 Unspecified fracture of unspecified acetabulum**
CC Exclusion 7th character K see Appendix A
PDX collection 0897
MCC Exclusion 7th character A see Appendix A
PDX collection 1199
MCC Exclusion 7th character B see Appendix A
PDX collection 1200
HAC 7th characters A & B see Appendix B for HAC conditional logic

S32.41 Fracture of anterior wall of acetabulum

CC MCC +7th **S32.411 Displaced fracture of anterior wall of right acetabulum**
CC Exclusion 7th character K see Appendix A
PDX collection 0897
MCC Exclusion 7th character A see Appendix A
PDX collection 1199
MCC Exclusion 7th character B see Appendix A
PDX collection 1200
HAC 7th characters A & B see Appendix B for HAC conditional logic

CC MCC +7th **S32.412 Displaced fracture of anterior wall of left acetabulum**
CC Exclusion 7th character K see Appendix A
PDX collection 0897
MCC Exclusion 7th character A see Appendix A
PDX collection 1199
MCC Exclusion 7th character B see Appendix A
PDX collection 1200
HAC 7th characters A & B see Appendix B for HAC conditional logic

CC MCC +7th **S32.413 Displaced fracture of anterior wall of unspecified acetabulum**
CC Exclusion 7th character K see Appendix A
PDX collection 0897
MCC Exclusion 7th character A see Appendix A
PDX collection 1199
MCC Exclusion 7th character B see Appendix A
PDX collection 1200
HAC 7th characters A & B see Appendix B for HAC conditional logic

CC MCC +7th **S32.414 Nondisplaced fracture of anterior wall of right acetabulum**
CC Exclusion 7th character K see Appendix A
PDX collection 0897
MCC Exclusion 7th character A see Appendix A
PDX collection 1199
MCC Exclusion 7th character B see Appendix A
PDX collection 1200
HAC 7th characters A & B see Appendix B for HAC conditional logic

CC MCC +7th **S32.415 Nondisplaced fracture of anterior wall of left acetabulum**
CC Exclusion 7th character K see Appendix A
PDX collection 0897
MCC Exclusion 7th character A see Appendix A
PDX collection 1199
MCC Exclusion 7th character B see Appendix A
PDX collection 1200
HAC 7th characters A & B see Appendix B for HAC conditional logic

CC MCC +7th **S32.416 Nondisplaced fracture of anterior wall of unspecified acetabulum**
CC Exclusion 7th character K see Appendix A
PDX collection 0897
MCC Exclusion 7th character A see Appendix A
PDX collection 1199
MCC Exclusion 7th character B see Appendix A
PDX collection 1200
HAC 7th characters A & B see Appendix B for HAC conditional logic

\+ **S32.42 Fracture of posterior wall of acetabulum**

CC MCC +7th **S32.421 Displaced fracture of posterior wall of right acetabulum**
CC Exclusion 7th character K see Appendix A
PDX collection 0897
MCC Exclusion 7th character A see Appendix A
PDX collection 1199
MCC Exclusion 7th character B see Appendix A
PDX collection 1200
HAC 7th characters A & B see Appendix B for HAC conditional logic

CC MCC +7th **S32.422 Displaced fracture of posterior wall of left acetabulum**
CC Exclusion 7th character K see Appendix A
PDX collection 0897
MCC Exclusion 7th character A see Appendix A
PDX collection 1199
MCC Exclusion 7th character B see Appendix A
PDX collection 1200
HAC 7th characters A & B see Appendix B for HAC conditional logic

CC MCC +7th **S32.423 Displaced fracture of posterior wall of unspecified acetabulum**
CC Exclusion 7th character K see Appendix A
PDX collection 0897
MCC Exclusion 7th character A see Appendix A
PDX collection 1199
MCC Exclusion 7th character B see Appendix A
PDX collection 1200
HAC 7th characters A & B see Appendix B for HAC conditional logic

CC MCC +7th **S32.424 Nondisplaced fracture of posterior wall of right acetabulum**
CC Exclusion 7th character K see Appendix A
PDX collection 0897
MCC Exclusion 7th character A see Appendix A
PDX collection 1199
MCC Exclusion 7th character B see Appendix A
PDX collection 1200
HAC 7th characters A & B see Appendix B for HAC conditional logic

CC MCC +7th **S32.425 Nondisplaced fracture of posterior wall of left acetabulum**
CC Exclusion 7th character K see Appendix A
PDX collection 0897
MCC Exclusion 7th character A see Appendix A
PDX collection 1199
MCC Exclusion 7th character B see Appendix A
PDX collection 1200
HAC 7th characters A & B see Appendix B for HAC conditional logic

CC MCC +7th **S32.426 Nondisplaced fracture of posterior wall of unspecified acetabulum**
CC Exclusion 7th character K see Appendix A
PDX collection 0897
MCC Exclusion 7th character A see Appendix A
PDX collection 1199
MCC Exclusion 7th character B see Appendix A
PDX collection 1200
HAC 7th characters A & B see Appendix B for HAC conditional logic

\+ **S32.43 Fracture of anterior column [iliopubic] of acetabulum**

CC MCC +7th **S32.431 Displaced fracture of anterior column [iliopubic] of right acetabulum**
CC Exclusion 7th character K see Appendix A
PDX collection 0897
MCC Exclusion 7th character A see Appendix A
PDX collection 1199
MCC Exclusion 7th character B see Appendix A
PDX collection 1200
HAC 7th characters A & B see Appendix B for HAC conditional logic

CC MCC +7th **S32.432 Displaced fracture of anterior column [iliopubic] of left acetabulum**
CC Exclusion 7th character K see Appendix A
PDX collection 0897
MCC Exclusion 7th character A see Appendix A
PDX collection 1199
MCC Exclusion 7th character B see Appendix A
PDX collection 1200
HAC 7th characters A & B see Appendix B for HAC conditional logic

CC MCC +7th **S32.433 Displaced fracture of anterior column [iliopubic] of unspecified acetabulum**
CC Exclusion 7th character K see Appendix A
PDX collection 0897
MCC Exclusion 7th character A see Appendix A
PDX collection 1199
MCC Exclusion 7th character B see Appendix A
PDX collection 1200
HAC 7th characters A & B see Appendix B for HAC conditional logic

CC MCC +7th **S32.434 Nondisplaced fracture of anterior column [iliopubic] of right acetabulum**
CC Exclusion 7th character K see Appendix A
PDX collection 0897
MCC Exclusion 7th character A see Appendix A
PDX collection 1199
MCC Exclusion 7th character B see Appendix A
PDX collection 1200
HAC 7th characters A & B see Appendix B for HAC conditional logic

CC MCC +7th **S32.435 Nondisplaced fracture of anterior column [iliopubic] of left acetabulum**
CC Exclusion 7th character K see Appendix A
PDX collection 0897
MCC Exclusion 7th character A see Appendix A
PDX collection 1199
MCC Exclusion 7th character B see Appendix A
PDX collection 1200
HAC 7th characters A & B see Appendix B for HAC conditional logic

CC MCC +7th **S32.436 Nondisplaced fracture of anterior column [iliopubic] of unspecified acetabulum**
CC Exclusion 7th character K see Appendix A
PDX collection 0897
MCC Exclusion 7th character A see Appendix A
PDX collection 1199
MCC Exclusion 7th character B see Appendix A
PDX collection 1200
HAC 7th characters A & B see Appendix B for HAC conditional logic

\+ **S32.44 Fracture of posterior column [ilioischial] of acetabulum**

CC MCC +7th **S32.441 Displaced fracture of posterior column [ilioischial] of right acetabulum**
CC Exclusion 7th character K see Appendix A
PDX collection 0897
MCC Exclusion 7th character A see Appendix A
PDX collection 1199
MCC Exclusion 7th character B see Appendix A
PDX collection 1200
HAC 7th characters A & B see Appendix B for HAC conditional logic

CC MCC +7th **S32.442 Displaced fracture of posterior column [ilioischial] of left acetabulum**
CC Exclusion 7th character K see Appendix A
PDX collection 0897
MCC Exclusion 7th character A see Appendix A
PDX collection 1199
MCC Exclusion 7th character B see Appendix A
PDX collection 1200
HAC 7th characters A & B see Appendix B for HAC conditional logic

CC MCC +7th **S32.443 Displaced fracture of posterior column [ilioischial] of unspecified acetabulum**
- CC Exclusion 7th character K see Appendix A PDX collection 0897
- MCC Exclusion 7th character A see Appendix A PDX collection 1199
- MCC Exclusion 7th character B see Appendix A PDX collection 1200
- HAC 7th characters A & B see Appendix B for HAC conditional logic

CC MCC +7th **S32.444 Nondisplaced fracture of posterior column [ilioischial] of right acetabulum**
- CC Exclusion 7th character K see Appendix A PDX collection 0897
- MCC Exclusion 7th character A see Appendix A PDX collection 1199
- MCC Exclusion 7th character B see Appendix A PDX collection 1200
- HAC 7th characters A & B see Appendix B for HAC conditional logic

CC MCC +7th **S32.445 Nondisplaced fracture of posterior column [ilioischial] of left acetabulum**
- CC Exclusion 7th character K see Appendix A PDX collection 0897
- MCC Exclusion 7th character A see Appendix A PDX collection 1199
- MCC Exclusion 7th character B see Appendix A PDX collection 1200
- HAC 7th characters A & B see Appendix B for HAC conditional logic

CC MCC +7th **S32.446 Nondisplaced fracture of posterior column [ilioischial] of unspecified acetabulum**
- CC Exclusion 7th character K see Appendix A PDX collection 0897
- MCC Exclusion 7th character A see Appendix A PDX collection 1199
- MCC Exclusion 7th character B see Appendix A PDX collection 1200
- HAC 7th characters A & B see Appendix B for HAC conditional logic

+ S32.45 Transverse fracture of acetabulum

CC MCC +7th **S32.451 Displaced transverse fracture of right acetabulum**
- CC Exclusion 7th character K see Appendix A PDX collection 0897
- MCC Exclusion 7th character A see Appendix A PDX collection 1199
- MCC Exclusion 7th character B see Appendix A PDX collection 1200
- HAC 7th characters A & B see Appendix B for HAC conditional logic

CC MCC +7th **S32.452 Displaced transverse fracture of left acetabulum**
- CC Exclusion 7th character K see Appendix A PDX collection 0897
- MCC Exclusion 7th character A see Appendix A PDX collection 1199
- MCC Exclusion 7th character B see Appendix A PDX collection 1200
- HAC 7th characters A & B see Appendix B for HAC conditional logic

CC MCC +7th **S32.453 Displaced transverse fracture of unspecified acetabulum**
- CC Exclusion 7th character K see Appendix A PDX collection 0897
- MCC Exclusion 7th character A see Appendix A PDX collection 1199
- MCC Exclusion 7th character B see Appendix A PDX collection 1200
- HAC 7th characters A & B see Appendix B for HAC conditional logic

CC MCC +7th **S32.454 Nondisplaced transverse fracture of right acetabulum**
- CC Exclusion 7th character K see Appendix A PDX collection 0897
- MCC Exclusion 7th character A see Appendix A PDX collection 1199
- MCC Exclusion 7th character B see Appendix A PDX collection 1200
- HAC 7th characters A & B see Appendix B for HAC conditional logic

CC MCC +7th **S32.455 Nondisplaced transverse fracture of left acetabulum**
- CC Exclusion 7th character K see Appendix A PDX collection 0897
- MCC Exclusion 7th character A see Appendix A PDX collection 1199
- MCC Exclusion 7th character B see Appendix A PDX collection 1200
- HAC 7th characters A & B see Appendix B for HAC conditional logic

CC MCC +7th **S32.456 Nondisplaced transverse fracture of unspecified acetabulum**
- CC Exclusion 7th character K see Appendix A PDX collection 0897
- MCC Exclusion 7th character A see Appendix A PDX collection 1199
- MCC Exclusion 7th character B see Appendix A PDX collection 1200
- HAC 7th characters A & B see Appendix B for HAC conditional logic

+ S32.46 Associated transverse-posterior fracture of acetabulum

CC MCC +7th **S32.461 Displaced associated transverse-posterior fracture of right acetabulum**
- CC Exclusion 7th character K see Appendix A PDX collection 0897
- MCC Exclusion 7th character A see Appendix A PDX collection 1199
- MCC Exclusion 7th character B see Appendix A PDX collection 1200
- HAC 7th characters A & B see Appendix B for HAC conditional logic

CC MCC +7th **S32.462 Displaced associated transverse-posterior fracture of left acetabulum**
- CC Exclusion 7th character K see Appendix A PDX collection 0897
- MCC Exclusion 7th character A see Appendix A PDX collection 1199
- MCC Exclusion 7th character B see Appendix A PDX collection 1200
- HAC 7th characters A & B see Appendix B for HAC conditional logic

CC MCC +7th **S32.463 Displaced associated transverse-posterior fracture of unspecified acetabulum**
- CC Exclusion 7th character K see Appendix A PDX collection 0897
- MCC Exclusion 7th character A see Appendix A PDX collection 1199
- MCC Exclusion 7th character B see Appendix A PDX collection 1200
- HAC 7th characters A & B see Appendix B for HAC conditional logic

CC MCC +7th **S32.464 Nondisplaced associated transverse-posterior fracture of right acetabulum**
- CC Exclusion 7th character K see Appendix A PDX collection 0897
- MCC Exclusion 7th character A see Appendix A PDX collection 1199
- MCC Exclusion 7th character B see Appendix A PDX collection 1200
- HAC 7th characters A & B see Appendix B for HAC conditional logic

CC MCC +7th **S32.465 Nondisplaced associated transverse-posterior fracture of left acetabulum**
- CC Exclusion 7th character K see Appendix A PDX collection 0897
- MCC Exclusion 7th character A see Appendix A PDX collection 1199
- MCC Exclusion 7th character B see Appendix A PDX collection 1200
- HAC 7th characters A & B see Appendix B for HAC conditional logic

CC MCC +7th **S32.466 Nondisplaced associated transverse-posterior fracture of unspecified acetabulum**
- CC Exclusion 7th character K see Appendix A PDX collection 0897
- MCC Exclusion 7th character A see Appendix A PDX collection 1199
- MCC Exclusion 7th character B see Appendix A PDX collection 1200
- HAC 7th characters A & B see Appendix B for HAC conditional logic

+ S32.47 Fracture of medial wall of acetabulum

CC MCC +7th **S32.471 Displaced fracture of medial wall of right acetabulum**
CC Exclusion 7th character K see Appendix A
PDX collection 0897
MCC Exclusion 7th character A see Appendix A
PDX collection 1199
MCC Exclusion 7th character B see Appendix A
PDX collection 1200
HAC 7th characters A & B see Appendix B for HAC conditional logic

CC MCC +7th **S32.472 Displaced fracture of medial wall of left acetabulum**
CC Exclusion 7th character K see Appendix A
PDX collection 0897
MCC Exclusion 7th character A see Appendix A
PDX collection 1199
MCC Exclusion 7th character B see Appendix A
PDX collection 1200
HAC 7th characters A & B see Appendix B for HAC conditional logic

CC MCC +7th **S32.473 Displaced fracture of medial wall of unspecified acetabulum**
CC Exclusion 7th character K see Appendix A
PDX collection 0897
MCC Exclusion 7th character A see Appendix A
PDX collection 1199
MCC Exclusion 7th character B see Appendix A
PDX collection 1200
HAC 7th characters A & B see Appendix B for HAC conditional logic

CC MCC +7th **S32.474 Nondisplaced fracture of medial wall of right acetabulum**
CC Exclusion 7th character K see Appendix A
PDX collection 0897
MCC Exclusion 7th character A see Appendix A
PDX collection 1199
MCC Exclusion 7th character B see Appendix A
PDX collection 1200
HAC 7th characters A & B see Appendix B for HAC conditional logic

CC MCC +7th **S32.475 Nondisplaced fracture of medial wall of left acetabulum**
CC Exclusion 7th character K see Appendix A
PDX collection 0897
MCC Exclusion 7th character A see Appendix A
PDX collection 1199
MCC Exclusion 7th character B see Appendix A
PDX collection 1200
HAC 7th characters A & B see Appendix B for HAC conditional logic

CC MCC +7th **S32.476 Nondisplaced fracture of medial wall of unspecified acetabulum**
CC Exclusion 7th character K see Appendix A
PDX collection 0897
MCC Exclusion 7th character A see Appendix A
PDX collection 1199
MCC Exclusion 7th character B see Appendix A
PDX collection 1200
HAC 7th characters A & B see Appendix B for HAC conditional logic

+ S32.48 Dome fracture of acetabulum

CC MCC +7th **S32.481 Displaced dome fracture of right acetabulum**
CC Exclusion 7th character K see Appendix A
PDX collection 0897
MCC Exclusion 7th character A see Appendix A
PDX collection 1199
MCC Exclusion 7th character B see Appendix A
PDX collection 1200
HAC 7th characters A & B see Appendix B for HAC conditional logic

CC MCC +7th **S32.482 Displaced dome fracture of left acetabulum**
CC Exclusion 7th character K see Appendix A
PDX collection 0897
MCC Exclusion 7th character A see Appendix A
PDX collection 1199
MCC Exclusion 7th character B see Appendix A
PDX collection 1200
HAC 7th characters A & B see Appendix B for HAC conditional logic

CC MCC +7th **S32.483 Displaced dome fracture of unspecified acetabulum**
CC Exclusion 7th character K see Appendix A
PDX collection 0897
MCC Exclusion 7th character A see Appendix A
PDX collection 1199
MCC Exclusion 7th character B see Appendix A
PDX collection 1200
HAC 7th characters A & B see Appendix B for HAC conditional logic

CC MCC +7th **S32.484 Nondisplaced dome fracture of right acetabulum**
CC Exclusion 7th character K see Appendix A
PDX collection 0897
MCC Exclusion 7th character A see Appendix A
PDX collection 1199
MCC Exclusion 7th character B see Appendix A
PDX collection 1200
HAC 7th characters A & B see Appendix B for HAC conditional logic

CC MCC +7th **S32.485 Nondisplaced dome fracture of left acetabulum**
CC Exclusion 7th character K see Appendix A
PDX collection 0897
MCC Exclusion 7th character A see Appendix A
PDX collection 1199
MCC Exclusion 7th character B see Appendix A
PDX collection 1200
HAC 7th characters A & B see Appendix B for HAC conditional logic

CC MCC +7th **S32.486 Nondisplaced dome fracture of unspecified acetabulum**
CC Exclusion 7th character K see Appendix A
PDX collection 0897
MCC Exclusion 7th character A see Appendix A
PDX collection 1199
MCC Exclusion 7th character B see Appendix A
PDX collection 1200
HAC 7th characters A & B see Appendix B for HAC conditional logic

+ S32.49 Other specified fracture of acetabulum

CC MCC +7th **S32.491 Other specified fracture of right acetabulum**
CC Exclusion 7th character K see Appendix A
PDX collection 0897
MCC Exclusion 7th character A see Appendix A
PDX collection 1199
MCC Exclusion 7th character B see Appendix A
PDX collection 1200
HAC 7th characters A & B see Appendix B for HAC conditional logic

CC MCC +7th **S32.492 Other specified fracture of left acetabulum**
CC Exclusion 7th character K see Appendix A
PDX collection 0897
MCC Exclusion 7th character A see Appendix A
PDX collection 1199
MCC Exclusion 7th character B see Appendix A
PDX collection 1200
HAC 7th characters A & B see Appendix B for HAC conditional logic

CC MCC +7th **S32.499 Other specified fracture of unspecified acetabulum**
CC Exclusion 7th character K see Appendix A
PDX collection 0897
MCC Exclusion 7th character A see Appendix A
PDX collection 1199
MCC Exclusion 7th character B see Appendix A
PDX collection 1200
HAC 7th characters A & B see Appendix B for HAC conditional logic

+ S32.5 Fracture of pubis

Excludes1: *fracture of pubis with associated disruption of pelvic ring (S32.8-)*

+ S32.50 Unspecified fracture of pubis

CC MCC +7th **S32.501 Unspecified fracture of right pubis**
CC Exclusion 7th character A see Appendix A
PDX collection 1201
CC Exclusion 7th character K see Appendix A
PDX collection 0897
MCC Exclusion 7th character B see Appendix A
PDX collection 1201
HAC 7th characters A & B see Appendix B for HAC conditional logic

CC MCC +7th **S32.502 Unspecified fracture of left pubis**
CC Exclusion 7th character A see Appendix A
PDX collection 1201
CC Exclusion 7th character K see Appendix A
PDX collection 0897
MCC Exclusion 7th character B see Appendix A
PDX collection 1201
HAC 7th characters A & B see Appendix B for HAC conditional logic

CC MCC +7th **S32.509 Unspecified fracture of unspecified pubis**
CC Exclusion 7th character A see Appendix A
PDX collection 1201
CC Exclusion 7th character K see Appendix A
PDX collection 0897
MCC Exclusion 7th character B see Appendix A
PDX collection 1201
HAC 7th characters A & B see Appendix B for HAC conditional logic

+ **S32.51 Fracture of superior rim of pubis**

CC MCC +7th **S32.511 Fracture of superior rim of right pubis**
CC Exclusion 7th character A see Appendix A
PDX collection 1201
CC Exclusion 7th character K see Appendix A
PDX collection 0897
MCC Exclusion 7th character B see Appendix A
PDX collection 1201
HAC 7th characters A & B see Appendix B for HAC conditional logic

CC MCC +7th **S32.512 Fracture of superior rim of left pubis**
CC Exclusion 7th character A see Appendix A
PDX collection 1201
CC Exclusion 7th character K see Appendix A
PDX collection 0897
MCC Exclusion 7th character B see Appendix A
PDX collection 1201
HAC 7th characters A & B see Appendix B for HAC conditional logic

CC MCC +7th **S32.519 Fracture of superior rim of unspecified pubis**
CC Exclusion 7th character A see Appendix A
PDX collection 1201
CC Exclusion 7th character K see Appendix A
PDX collection 0897
MCC Exclusion 7th character B see Appendix A
PDX collection 1201
HAC 7th characters A & B see Appendix B for HAC conditional logic

+ **S32.59 Other specified fracture of pubis**

CC MCC +7th **S32.591 Other specified fracture of right pubis**
CC Exclusion 7th character A see Appendix A
PDX collection 1201
CC Exclusion 7th character K see Appendix A
PDX collection 0897
MCC Exclusion 7th character B see Appendix A
PDX collection 1201
HAC 7th characters A & B see Appendix B for HAC conditional logic

CC MCC +7th **S32.592 Other specified fracture of left pubis**
CC Exclusion 7th character A see Appendix A
PDX collection 1201
CC Exclusion 7th character K see Appendix A
PDX collection 0897
MCC Exclusion 7th character B see Appendix A
PDX collection 1201
HAC 7th characters A & B see Appendix B for HAC conditional logic

CC MCC +7th **S32.599 Other specified fracture of unspecified pubis**
CC Exclusion 7th character A see Appendix A
PDX collection 1201
CC Exclusion 7th character K see Appendix A
PDX collection 0897
MCC Exclusion 7th character B see Appendix A
PDX collection 1201
HAC 7th characters A & B see Appendix B for HAC conditional logic

+ **S32.6 Fracture of ischium**
Excludes1: *fracture of ischium with associated disruption of pelvic ring (S32.8-)*

+ **S32.60 Unspecified fracture of ischium**

CC MCC +7th **S32.601 Unspecified fracture of right ischium**
CC Exclusion 7th character A see Appendix A
PDX collection 1202
CC Exclusion 7th character K see Appendix A
PDX collection 0897
MCC Exclusion 7th character B see Appendix A
PDX collection 1203
HAC 7th characters A & B see Appendix B for HAC conditional logic

CC MCC +7th **S32.602 Unspecified fracture of left ischium**
CC Exclusion 7th character A see Appendix A
PDX collection 1202
CC Exclusion 7th character K see Appendix A
PDX collection 0897
MCC Exclusion 7th character B see Appendix A
PDX collection 1203
HAC 7th characters A & B see Appendix B for HAC conditional logic

CC MCC +7th **S32.609 Unspecified fracture of unspecified ischium**
CC Exclusion 7th character A see Appendix A
PDX collection 1202
CC Exclusion 7th character K see Appendix A
PDX collection 0897
MCC Exclusion 7th character B see Appendix A
PDX collection 1203
HAC 7th characters A & B see Appendix B for HAC conditional logic

+ **S32.61 Avulsion fracture of ischium**

CC MCC +7th **S32.611 Displaced avulsion fracture of right ischium**
CC Exclusion 7th character A see Appendix A
PDX collection 1202
CC Exclusion 7th character K see Appendix A
PDX collection 0897
MCC Exclusion 7th character B see Appendix A
PDX collection 1203
HAC 7th characters A & B see Appendix B for HAC conditional logic

CC MCC +7th **S32.612 Displaced avulsion fracture of left ischium**
CC Exclusion 7th character A see Appendix A
PDX collection 1202
CC Exclusion 7th character K see Appendix A
PDX collection 0897
MCC Exclusion 7th character B see Appendix A
PDX collection 1203
HAC 7th characters A & B see Appendix B for HAC conditional logic

CC MCC +7th **S32.613 Displaced avulsion fracture of unspecified ischium**
CC Exclusion 7th character A see Appendix A
PDX collection 1202
CC Exclusion 7th character K see Appendix A
PDX collection 0897
MCC Exclusion 7th character B see Appendix A
PDX collection 1203
HAC 7th characters A & B see Appendix B for HAC conditional logic

CC MCC +7th **S32.614 Nondisplaced avulsion fracture of right ischium**
CC Exclusion 7th character A see Appendix A
PDX collection 1202
CC Exclusion 7th character K see Appendix A
PDX collection 0897
MCC Exclusion 7th character B see Appendix A
PDX collection 1203
HAC 7th characters A & B see Appendix B for HAC conditional logic

CC MCC +7th **S32.615 Nondisplaced avulsion fracture of left ischium**
CC Exclusion 7th character A see Appendix A
PDX collection 1202
CC Exclusion 7th character K see Appendix A
PDX collection 0897
MCC Exclusion 7th character B see Appendix A
PDX collection 1203
HAC 7th characters A & B see Appendix B for HAC conditional logic

CC MCC +7th **S32.616 Nondisplaced avulsion fracture of unspecified ischium**
CC Exclusion 7th character A see Appendix A
PDX collection 1202
CC Exclusion 7th character K see Appendix A
PDX collection 0897
MCC Exclusion 7th character B see Appendix A
PDX collection 1203
HAC 7th characters A & B see Appendix B for HAC conditional logic

+ **S32.69 Other specified fracture of ischium**

CC MCC +7th **S32.691 Other specified fracture of right ischium**
CC Exclusion 7th character A see Appendix A
PDX collection 1202
CC Exclusion 7th character K see Appendix A
PDX collection 0897
MCC Exclusion 7th character B see Appendix A
PDX collection 1203
HAC 7th characters A & B see Appendix B for HAC conditional logic

CC MCC +7th **S32.692 Other specified fracture of left ischium**
CC Exclusion 7th character A see Appendix A
PDX collection 1202
CC Exclusion 7th character K see Appendix A
PDX collection 0897
MCC Exclusion 7th character B see Appendix A
PDX collection 1203
HAC 7th characters A & B see Appendix B for HAC conditional logic

CC MCC +7th **S32.699 Other specified fracture of unspecified ischium**
CC Exclusion 7th character A see Appendix A
PDX collection 1202
CC Exclusion 7th character K see Appendix A
PDX collection 0897
MCC Exclusion 7th character B see Appendix A
PDX collection 1203
HAC 7th characters A & B see Appendix B for HAC conditional logic

\+ **S32.8 Fracture of other parts of pelvis**
Code also any associated:
fracture of acetabulum (S32.4-)
sacral fracture (S32.1-)

\+ **S32.81 Multiple fractures of pelvis with disruption of pelvic ring**
Multiple pelvic fractures with disruption of pelvic circle

CC MCC +7th **S32.810 Multiple fractures of pelvis with stable disruption of pelvic ring**
CC Exclusion 7th character A see Appendix A PDX collection 1204
CC Exclusion 7th character K see Appendix A PDX collection 0897
MCC Exclusion 7th character B see Appendix A PDX collection 1204
HAC 7th characters A & B see Appendix B for HAC conditional logic

CC MCC +7th **S32.811 Multiple fractures of pelvis with unstable disruption of pelvic ring**
CC Exclusion 7th character A see Appendix A PDX collection 1204
CC Exclusion 7th character K see Appendix A PDX collection 0897
MCC Exclusion 7th character B see Appendix A PDX collection 1204
HAC 7th characters A & B see Appendix B for HAC conditional logic

C MCC X+7th **S32.82 Multiple fractures of pelvis without disruption of pelvic ring**
Multiple pelvic fractures without disruption of pelvic circle
CC Exclusion 7th character A see Appendix A PDX collection 1205
CC Exclusion 7th character K see Appendix A PDX collection 0897
MCC Exclusion 7th character B see Appendix A PDX collection 1205
HAC 7th characters A & B see Appendix B for HAC conditional logic

MCC X+7th **S32.89 Fracture of other parts of pelvis**
CC Exclusion 7th character A see Appendix A PDX collection 1206
CC Exclusion 7th character K see Appendix A PDX collection 0897
MCC Exclusion 7th character B see Appendix A PDX collection 1206
HAC 7th characters A & B see Appendix B for HAC conditional logic

+7th **S32.9 Fracture of unspecified parts of lumbosacral spine and pelvis**
Fracture of lumbosacral spine NOS
Fracture of pelvis NOS
CC Exclusion 7th character A see Appendix A PDX collection 1204
CC Exclusion 7th character K see Appendix A PDX collection 0897
MCC Exclusion 7th character B see Appendix A PDX collection 1204
HAC 7th characters A & B see Appendix B for HAC conditional logic

33 Dislocation and sprain of joints and ligaments of lumbar spine and pelvis

Includes: avulsion of joint or ligament of lumbar spine and pelvis
laceration of cartilage, joint or ligament of lumbar spine and pelvis
sprain of cartilage, joint or ligament of lumbar spine and pelvis
traumatic hemarthrosis of joint or ligament of lumbar spine and pelvis
traumatic rupture of joint or ligament of lumbar spine and pelvis
traumatic subluxation of joint or ligament of lumbar spine and pelvis
traumatic tear of joint or ligament of lumbar spine and pelvis

Code also any associated open wound

Excludes1: *nontraumatic rupture or displacement of lumbar intervertebral disc NOS (M51.-)*
obstetric damage to pelvic joints and ligaments (O71.6)

Excludes2: *dislocation and sprain of joints and ligaments of hip (S73.-)*
strain of muscle of lower back and pelvis (S39.01-)

The appropriate 7th character is to be added to each code from category S33
A initial encounter
D subsequent encounter
S sequela

-7th **S33.0 Traumatic rupture of lumbar intervertebral disc**
Excludes1: *rupture or displacement (nontraumatic) of lumbar intervertebral disc NOS (M51.- with fifth character 6)*

\+ **S33.1 Subluxation and dislocation of lumbar vertebra**
Code also any associated:
open wound of abdomen, lower back and pelvis (S31)
spinal cord injury (S24.0, S24.1-, S34.0-, S34.1-)
Excludes2: *fracture of lumbar vertebrae (S32.0-)*

\+ **S33.10 Subluxation and dislocation of unspecified lumbar vertebra**
+7th **S33.100 Subluxation of unspecified lumbar vertebra**
+7th **S33.101 Dislocation of unspecified lumbar vertebra**

\+ **S33.11 Subluxation and dislocation of L1/L2 lumbar vertebra**
+7th **S33.110 Subluxation of L1/L2 lumbar vertebra**
+7th **S33.111 Dislocation of L1/L2 lumbar vertebra**

\+ **S33.12 Subluxation and dislocation of L2/L3 lumbar vertebra**
+7th **S33.120 Subluxation of L2/L3 lumbar vertebra**
+7th **S33.121 Dislocation of L2/L3 lumbar vertebra**

\+ **S33.13 Subluxation and dislocation of L3/L4 lumbar vertebra**
+7th **S33.130 Subluxation of L3/L4 lumbar vertebra**
+7th **S33.131 Dislocation of L3/L4 lumbar vertebra**

\+ **S33.14 Subluxation and dislocation of L4/L5 lumbar vertebra**
+7th **S33.140 Subluxation of L4/L5 lumbar vertebra**
+7th **S33.141 Dislocation of L4/L5 lumbar vertebra**

X+7th **S33.2 Dislocation of sacroiliac and sacrococcygeal joint**

\+ **S33.3 Dislocation of other and unspecified parts of lumbar spine and pelvis**
X+7th **S33.30 Dislocation of unspecified parts of lumbar spine and pelvis**
X+7th **S33.39 Dislocation of other parts of lumbar spine and pelvis**

X+7th **S33.4 Traumatic rupture of symphysis pubis**
X+7th **S33.5 Sprain of ligaments of lumbar spine**
X+7th **S33.6 Sprain of sacroiliac joint**
X+7th **S33.8 Sprain of other parts of lumbar spine and pelvis**
X+7th **S33.9 Sprain of unspecified parts of lumbar spine and pelvis**

S34 Injury of lumbar and sacral spinal cord and nerves at abdomen, lower back and pelvis level

NOTE Code to highest level of lumbar cord injury
Injuries to the spinal cord (S34.0 and S34.1) refer to the cord level and not bone level injury, and can affect nerve roots at and below the level given.

Code also any associated:
fracture of vertebra (S22.0-, S32.0-)
open wound of abdomen, lower back and pelvis (S31.-)
transient paralysis (R29.5)

The appropriate 7th character is to be added to each code from category S34
A initial encounter
D subsequent encounter
S sequela

\+ **S34.0 Concussion and edema of lumbar and sacral spinal cord**

MCC X+7th **S34.01 Concussion and edema of lumbar spinal cord**
MCC Exclusion 7th character A see Appendix A PDX collection 1207

MCC X+7th **S34.02 Concussion and edema of sacral spinal cord**
Concussion and edema of conus medullaris
MCC Exclusion 7th character A see Appendix A PDX collection 1208

\+ **S34.1 Other and unspecified injury of lumbar and sacral spinal cord**
\+ **S34.10 Unspecified injury to lumbar spinal cord**

MCC +7th **S34.101 Unspecified injury to L1 level of lumbar spinal cord**
MCC Exclusion 7th character A see Appendix A PDX collection 1207
HAC 7th character A see Appendix B for HAC conditional logic

MCC +7th **S34.102 Unspecified injury to L2 level of lumbar spinal cord**
MCC Exclusion 7th character A see Appendix A PDX collection 1207
HAC 7th character A see Appendix B for HAC conditional logic

MCC +7th **S34.103 Unspecified injury to L3 level of lumbar spinal cord**
MCC Exclusion 7th character A see Appendix A PDX collection 1207
HAC 7th character A see Appendix B for HAC conditional logic

MCC +7th **S34.104 Unspecified injury to L4 level of lumbar spinal cord**
MCC Exclusion 7th character A see Appendix A PDX collection 1207
HAC 7th character A see Appendix B for HAC conditional logic

MCC +7th **S34.105 Unspecified injury to L5 level of lumbar spinal cord**
MCC Exclusion 7th character A see Appendix A PDX collection 1207
HAC 7th character A see Appendix B for HAC conditional logic

MCC +7th **S34.109 Unspecified injury to unspecified level of lumbar spinal cord**
MCC Exclusion 7th character A see Appendix A PDX collection 1207
HAC 7th character A see Appendix B for HAC conditional logic

\+ **S34.11 Complete lesion of lumbar spinal cord**

MCC +7th **S34.111 Complete lesion of L1 level of lumbar spinal cord**
MCC Exclusion 7th character A see Appendix A PDX collection 1207
HAC 7th character A see Appendix B for HAC conditional logic

MCC +7th **S34.112 Complete lesion of L2 level of lumbar spinal cord**
MCC Exclusion 7th character A see Appendix A PDX collection 1207
HAC 7th character A see Appendix B for HAC conditional logic

MCC +7th **S34.113 Complete lesion of L3 level of lumbar spinal cord**
MCC Exclusion 7th character A see Appendix A PDX collection 1207
HAC 7th character A see Appendix B for HAC conditional logic

MCC +7th **S34.114 Complete lesion of L4 level of lumbar spinal cord**
MCC Exclusion 7th character A see Appendix A PDX collection 1207
HAC 7th character A see Appendix B for HAC conditional logic

MCC +7th **S34.115 Complete lesion of L5 level of lumbar spinal cord**
MCC Exclusion 7th character A see Appendix A PDX collection 1207
HAC 7th character A see Appendix B for HAC conditional logic

MCC +7th **S34.119 Complete lesion of unspecified level of lumbar spinal cord**
MCC Exclusion 7th character A see Appendix A PDX collection 1207
HAC 7th character A see Appendix B for HAC conditional logic

\+ **S34.12 Incomplete lesion of lumbar spinal cord**

MCC +7th **S34.121 Incomplete lesion of L1 level of lumbar spinal cord**
MCC Exclusion 7th character A see Appendix A PDX collection 1207
HAC 7th character A see Appendix B for HAC conditional logic

MCC +7th **S34.122 Incomplete lesion of L2 level of lumbar spinal cord**
MCC Exclusion 7th character A see Appendix A PDX collection 1207
HAC 7th character A see Appendix B for HAC conditional logic

MCC +7th **S34.123 Incomplete lesion of L3 level of lumbar spinal cord**
MCC Exclusion 7th character A see Appendix A PDX collection 1207
HAC 7th character A see Appendix B for HAC conditional logic

MCC +7th **S34.124 Incomplete lesion of L4 level of lumbar spinal cord**
MCC Exclusion 7th character A see Appendix A PDX collection 1207
HAC 7th character A see Appendix B for HAC conditional logic

MCC +7th **S34.125 Incomplete lesion of L5 level of lumbar spinal cord**
MCC Exclusion 7th character A see Appendi PDX collection 1207
HAC 7th character A see Appendix B for HAC conditional logic

MCC +7th **S34.129 Incomplete lesion of unspecified level of lumbar spinal cord**
MCC Exclusion 7th character A see Appendi PDX collection 1207
HAC 7th character A see Appendix B for HAC conditional logic

\+ **S34.13 Other and unspecified injury to sacral spinal cord**
Other injury to conus medullaris

MCC +7th **S34.131 Complete lesion of sacral spinal cord**
Complete lesion of conus medullaris
MCC Exclusion 7th character A see Appendix PDX collection 1208
HAC 7th character A see Appendix B for HAC conditional logic

MCC +7th **S34.132 Incomplete lesion of sacral spinal cord**
Incomplete lesion of conus medullaris
MCC Exclusion 7th character A see Appendix PDX collection 1208
HAC 7th character A see Appendix B for HAC conditional logic

MCC +7th **S34.139 Unspecified injury to sacral spinal cord**
Unspecified injury of conus medullaris
MCC Exclusion 7th character A see Appendix PDX collection 1208
HAC 7th character A see Appendix B for HAC conditional logic

\+ **S34.2 Injury of nerve root of lumbar and sacral spine**

X+7th **S34.21 Injury of nerve root of lumbar spine**

X+7th **S34.22 Injury of nerve root of sacral spine**

MCC X+7th **S34.3 Injury of cauda equina**
MCC Exclusion 7th character A see Appendix A PDX collection 12
HAC 7th character A see Appendix B for HAC conditional logic

X+7th **S34.4 Injury of lumbosacral plexus**

X+7th **S34.5 Injury of lumbar, sacral and pelvic sympathetic nerves**
Injury of celiac ganglion or plexus
Injury of hypogastric plexus
Injury of mesenteric plexus (inferior) (superior)
Injury of splanchnic nerve

X+7th **S34.6 Injury of peripheral nerve(s) at abdomen, lower back and pe level**

X+7th **S34.8 Injury of other nerves at abdomen, lower back and pelvis lev**

X+7th **S34.9 Injury of unspecified nerves at abdomen, lower back and pel level**

S35 Injury of blood vessels at abdomen, lower back and pelvis level

Code also any associated open wound (S31.-)

The appropriate 7th character is to be added to each code from category S35
A initial encounter
D subsequent encounter
S sequela

\+ **S35.0 Injury of abdominal aorta**
Excludes1: *injury of aorta NOS (S25.0)*

MCC X+7th **S35.00 Unspecified injury of abdominal aorta**
MCC Exclusion 7th character A see Appendix A PDX collection 1209

MCC X+7th **S35.01 Minor laceration of abdominal aorta**
Incomplete transection of abdominal aorta
Laceration of abdominal aorta NOS
Superficial laceration of abdominal aorta
MCC Exclusion 7th character A see Appendix A PDX collection 1209

MCC X+7th **S35.02 Major laceration of abdominal aorta**
Complete transection of abdominal aorta
Traumatic rupture of abdominal aorta
MCC Exclusion 7th character A see Appendix A PDX collection 1209

MCC X+7th **S35.09 Other injury of abdominal aorta**
MCC Exclusion 7th character A see Appendix A PDX collection 1209

\+ **S35.1 Injury of inferior vena cava**
Injury of hepatic vein
Excludes1: *injury of vena cava NOS (S25.2)*

MCC X+7th **S35.10 Unspecified injury of inferior vena cava**
MCC Exclusion 7th character A see Appendix A PDX collection 1210

MCC X+7th **S35.11 Minor laceration of inferior vena cava**
Incomplete transection of inferior vena cava
Laceration of inferior vena cava NOS
Superficial laceration of inferior vena cava
MCC Exclusion 7th character A see Appendix A PDX collection 1210

MCC X+7th **S35.12 Major laceration of inferior vena cava**
Complete transection of inferior vena cava
Traumatic rupture of inferior vena cava
MCC Exclusion 7th character A see Appendix A PDX collection 1210

MCC X+7th **S35.19 Other injury of inferior vena cava**
MCC Exclusion 7th character A see Appendix A PDX collection 1210

+ **S35.2 Injury of celiac or mesenteric artery and branches**

+ **S35.21 Injury of celiac artery**

MCC +7th **S35.211 Minor laceration of celiac artery**
Incomplete transection of celiac artery
Laceration of celiac artery NOS
Superficial laceration of celiac artery
MCC Exclusion 7th character A see Appendix A PDX collection 1211

MCC +7th **S35.212 Major laceration of celiac artery**
Complete transection of celiac artery
Traumatic rupture of celiac artery
MCC Exclusion 7th character A see Appendix A PDX collection 1211

MCC +7th **S35.218 Other injury of celiac artery**
MCC Exclusion 7th character A see Appendix A PDX collection 1211

MCC +7th **S35.219 Unspecified injury of celiac artery**
MCC Exclusion 7th character A see Appendix A PDX collection 1211

+ **S35.22 Injury of superior mesenteric artery**

MCC +7th **S35.221 Minor laceration of superior mesenteric artery**
Incomplete transection of superior mesenteric artery
Laceration of superior mesenteric artery NOS
Superficial laceration of superior mesenteric artery
MCC Exclusion 7th character A see Appendix A PDX collection 1212

MCC +7th **S35.222 Major laceration of superior mesenteric artery**
Complete transection of superior mesenteric artery
Traumatic rupture of superior mesenteric artery
MCC Exclusion 7th character A see Appendix A PDX collection 1212

MCC +7th **S35.228 Other injury of superior mesenteric artery**
MCC Exclusion 7th character A see Appendix A PDX collection 1212

MCC +7th **S35.229 Unspecified injury of superior mesenteric artery**
MCC Exclusion 7th character A see Appendix A PDX collection 1212

+ **S35.23 Injury of inferior mesenteric artery**

MCC +7th **S35.231 Minor laceration of inferior mesenteric artery**
Incomplete transection of inferior mesenteric artery
Laceration of inferior mesenteric artery NOS
Superficial laceration of inferior mesenteric artery
MCC Exclusion 7th character A see Appendix A PDX collection 1213

MCC +7th **S35.232 Major laceration of inferior mesenteric artery**
Complete transection of inferior mesenteric artery
Traumatic rupture of inferior mesenteric artery
MCC Exclusion 7th character A see Appendix A PDX collection 1213

MCC +7th **S35.238 Other injury of inferior mesenteric artery**
MCC Exclusion 7th character A see Appendix A PDX collection 1213

MCC +7th **S35.239 Unspecified injury of inferior mesenteric artery**
MCC Exclusion 7th character A see Appendix A PDX collection 1213

+ **S35.29 Injury of branches of celiac and mesenteric artery**
Injury of gastric artery
Injury of gastroduodenal artery
Injury of hepatic artery
Injury of splenic artery

MCC +7th **S35.291 Minor laceration of branches of celiac and mesenteric artery**
Incomplete transection of branches of celiac and mesenteric artery
Laceration of branches of celiac and mesenteric artery NOS
Superficial laceration of branches of celiac and mesenteric artery
MCC Exclusion 7th character A see Appendix A PDX collection 1214

MCC +7th **S35.292 Major laceration of branches of celiac and mesenteric artery**
Complete transection of branches of celiac and mesenteric artery
Traumatic rupture of branches of celiac and mesenteric artery
MCC Exclusion 7th character A see Appendix A PDX collection 1215

MCC +7th **S35.298 Other injury of branches of celiac and mesenteric artery**
MCC Exclusion 7th character A see Appendix A PDX collection 1215

MCC +7th **S35.299 Unspecified injury of branches of celiac and mesenteric artery**
MCC Exclusion 7th character A see Appendix A PDX collection 1216

+ **S35.3 Injury of portal or splenic vein and branches**

+ **S35.31 Injury of portal vein**

MCC +7th **S35.311 Laceration of portal vein**
MCC Exclusion 7th character A see Appendix A PDX collection 1217

MCC +7th **S35.318 Other specified injury of portal vein**
MCC Exclusion 7th character A see Appendix A PDX collection 1217

MCC +7th **S35.319 Unspecified injury of portal vein**
MCC Exclusion 7th character A see Appendix A PDX collection 1217

+ **S35.32 Injury of splenic vein**

MCC +7th **S35.321 Laceration of splenic vein**
MCC Exclusion 7th character A see Appendix A PDX collection 1218

MCC +7th **S35.328 Other specified injury of splenic vein**
MCC Exclusion 7th character A see Appendix A PDX collection 1218

MCC +7th **S35.329 Unspecified injury of splenic vein**
MCC Exclusion 7th character A see Appendix A PDX collection 1218

+ **S35.33 Injury of superior mesenteric vein**

MCC +7th **S35.331 Laceration of superior mesenteric vein**
MCC Exclusion 7th character A see Appendix A PDX collection 1219

MCC +7th **S35.338 Other specified injury of superior mesenteric vein**
MCC Exclusion 7th character A see Appendix A PDX collection 1219

MCC +7th **S35.339 Unspecified injury of superior mesenteric vein**
MCC Exclusion 7th character A see Appendix A PDX collection 1219

+ **S35.34 Injury of inferior mesenteric vein**

MCC +7th **S35.341 Laceration of inferior mesenteric vein**
MCC Exclusion 7th character A see Appendix A PDX collection 1220

MCC +7th **S35.348 Other specified injury of inferior mesenteric vein**
MCC Exclusion 7th character A see Appendix A PDX collection 1220

MCC +7th **S35.349 Unspecified injury of inferior mesenteric vein**
MCC Exclusion 7th character A see Appendix A PDX collection 1220

+ **S35.4 Injury of renal blood vessels**

+ **S35.40 Unspecified injury of renal blood vessel**

MCC +7th **S35.401 Unspecified injury of right renal artery**
MCC Exclusion 7th character A see Appendix A PDX collection 1221

MCC +7th **S35.402 Unspecified injury of left renal artery**
MCC Exclusion 7th character A see Appendix A PDX collection 1221

MCC +7th **S35.403 Unspecified injury of unspecified renal artery**
MCC Exclusion 7th character A see Appendix A PDX collection 1221

MCC +7th **S35.404 Unspecified injury of right renal vein**
MCC Exclusion 7th character A see Appendix A PDX collection 1222

MCC +7th **S35.405 Unspecified injury of left renal vein**
MCC Exclusion 7th character A see Appendix A PDX collection 1222

MCC +7th **S35.406 Unspecified injury of unspecified renal vein**
MCC Exclusion 7th character A see Appendix A PDX collection 1222

\+ **S35.41 Laceration of renal blood vessel**

MCC +7th **S35.411 Laceration of right renal artery**
MCC Exclusion 7th character A see Appendix A PDX collection 1221

MCC +7th **S35.412 Laceration of left renal artery**
MCC Exclusion 7th character A see Appendix A PDX collection 1221

MCC +7th **S35.413 Laceration of unspecified renal artery**
MCC Exclusion 7th character A see Appendix A PDX collection 1221

MCC +7th **S35.414 Laceration of right renal vein**
MCC Exclusion 7th character A see Appendix A PDX collection 1222

MCC +7th **S35.415 Laceration of left renal vein**
MCC Exclusion 7th character A see Appendix A PDX collection 1222

MCC +7th **S35.416 Laceration of unspecified renal vein**
MCC Exclusion 7th character A see Appendix A PDX collection 1222

\+ **S35.49 Other specified injury of renal blood vessel**

MCC +7th **S35.491 Other specified injury of right renal artery**
MCC Exclusion 7th character A see Appendix A PDX collection 1221

MCC +7th **S35.492 Other specified injury of left renal artery**
MCC Exclusion 7th character A see Appendix A PDX collection 1221

MCC +7th **S35.493 Other specified injury of unspecified renal artery**
MCC Exclusion 7th character A see Appendix A PDX collection 1221

MCC +7th **S35.494 Other specified injury of right renal vein**
MCC Exclusion 7th character A see Appendix A PDX collection 1222

MCC +7th **S35.495 Other specified injury of left renal vein**
MCC Exclusion 7th character A see Appendix A PDX collection 1222

MCC +7th **S35.496 Other specified injury of unspecified renal vein**
MCC Exclusion 7th character A see Appendix A PDX collection 1222

\+ **S35.5 Injury of iliac blood vessels**

MCC X+7th **S35.50 Injury of unspecified iliac blood vessel(s)**
MCC Exclusion 7th character A see Appendix A PDX collection 1223

\+ **S35.51 Injury of iliac artery or vein**
Injury of hypogastric artery or vein

MCC +7th **S35.511 Injury of right iliac artery**
MCC Exclusion 7th character A see Appendix A PDX collection 1224

MCC +7th **S35.512 Injury of left iliac artery**
MCC Exclusion 7th character A see Appendix A PDX collection 1224

MCC +7th **S35.513 Injury of unspecified iliac artery**
MCC Exclusion 7th character A see Appendix A PDX collection 1224

MCC +7th **S35.514 Injury of right iliac vein**
MCC Exclusion 7th character A see Appendix A PDX collection 1225

MCC +7th **S35.515 Injury of left iliac vein**
MCC Exclusion 7th character A see Appendix A PDX collection 1225

MCC +7th **S35.516 Injury of unspecified iliac vein**
MCC Exclusion 7th character A see Appendix A PDX collection 1225

\+ **S35.53 Injury of uterine artery or vein**

♀ CC +7th **S35.531 Injury of right uterine artery**
CC Exclusion 7th character A see Appendix A PDX collection 1226

♀ CC +7th **S35.532 Injury of left uterine artery**
CC Exclusion 7th character A see Appendix A PDX collection 1226

♀ CC +7th **S35.533 Injury of unspecified uterine artery**
CC Exclusion 7th character A see Appendix A PDX collection 1226

♀ CC +7th **S35.534 Injury of right uterine vein**
CC Exclusion 7th character A see Appendix A PDX collection 1227

♀ CC +7th **S35.535 Injury of left uterine vein**
CC Exclusion 7th character A see Appendix A PDX collection 1227

♀ CC +7th **S35.536 Injury of unspecified uterine vein**
CC Exclusion 7th character A see Appendix A PDX collection 1227

MCC X+7th **S35.59 Injury of other iliac blood vessels**
MCC Exclusion 7th character A see Appendix A PDX collection 1223

CC + **S35.8 Injury of other blood vessels at abdomen, lower back and pelvis level**
Injury of ovarian artery or vein
CC Exclusion 7th character A see Appendix A PDX collection 1228

\+ **S35.8X Injury of other blood vessels at abdomen, lower back and pelvis level**

+7th **S35.8X1 Laceration of other blood vessels at abdomen, lower back and pelvis level**

+7th **S35.8X8 Other specified injury of other blood vessels at abdomen, lower back and pelvis level**

+7th **S35.8X9 Unspecified injury of other blood vessels at abdomen, lower back and pelvis level**

\+ **S35.9 Injury of unspecified blood vessel at abdomen, lower back and pelvis level**

CC X+7th **S35.90 Unspecified injury of unspecified blood vessel at abdomen, lower back and pelvis level**
CC Exclusion 7th character A see Appendix A PDX collection 1229

CC X+7th **S35.91 Laceration of unspecified blood vessel at abdomen, lower back and pelvis level**
CC Exclusion 7th character A see Appendix A PDX collection 1229

CC X+7th **S35.99 Other specified injury of unspecified blood vessel at abdomen, lower back and pelvis level**
CC Exclusion 7th character A see Appendix A PDX collection 1229

S36 Injury of intra-abdominal organs

Code also any associated open wound (S31.-)

The appropriate 7th character is to be added to each code from category S36
A initial encounter
D subsequent encounter
S sequela

\+ **S36.0 Injury of spleen**

CC X+7th **S36.00 Unspecified injury of spleen**
CC Exclusion 7th character A see Appendix A PDX collection 1230

\+ **S36.02 Contusion of spleen**

CC +7th **S36.020 Minor contusion of spleen**
Contusion of spleen less than 2 cm
CC Exclusion 7th character A see Appendix A PDX collection 1230

CC +7th **S36.021 Major contusion of spleen**
Contusion of spleen greater than 2 cm
CC Exclusion 7th character A see Appendix A PDX collection 1230

CC +7th **S36.029 Unspecified contusion of spleen**
CC Exclusion 7th character A see Appendix A PDX collection 1230

\+ **S36.03 Laceration of spleen**

CC +7th **S36.030 Superficial (capsular) laceration of spleen**
Laceration of spleen less than 1 cm
Minor laceration of spleen
CC Exclusion 7th character A see Appendix A PDX collection 1230

MCC +7th **S36.031 Moderate laceration of spleen**
Laceration of spleen 1 to 3 cm
MCC Exclusion 7th character A see Appendix A PDX collection 1230

MCC +7th **S36.032 Major laceration of spleen**
Avulsion of spleen
Laceration of spleen greater than 3 cm
Massive laceration of spleen
Multiple moderate lacerations of spleen
Stellate laceration of spleen
MCC Exclusion 7th character A see Appendix A PDX collection 1230

CC +7th **S36.039 Unspecified laceration of spleen**
CC Exclusion 7th character A see Appendix A PDX collection 1230

CC X+7th **S36.09 Other injury of spleen**
CC Exclusion 7th character A see Appendix A PDX collection 1230

+ **S36.1 Injury of liver and gallbladder and bile duct**

+ **S36.11 Injury of liver**

CC +7th **S36.112 Contusion of liver**
CC Exclusion 7th character A see Appendix A PDX collection 1231

CC +7th **S36.113 Laceration of liver, unspecified degree**
CC Exclusion 7th character A see Appendix A PDX collection 1231

CC +7th **S36.114 Minor laceration of liver**
Laceration involving capsule only, or, without significant involvement of hepatic parenchyma [i.e., less than 1 cmdeep]
CC Exclusion 7th character A see Appendix A PDX collection 1231

MCC +7th **S36.115 Moderate laceration of liver**
Laceration involving parenchyma but without major disruption of parenchyma [i.e., less than 10 cm long and less than 3 cm deep]
MCC Exclusion 7th character A see Appendix A PDX collection 1231

MCC +7th **S36.116 Major laceration of liver**
Laceration with significant disruption of hepatic parenchyma [i.e., greater than 10 cm long and 3 cm deep]
Multiple moderate lacerations, with or without hematoma
Stellate laceration of liver
MCC Exclusion 7th character A see Appendix A PDX collection 1231

CC +7th **S36.118 Other injury of liver**
CC Exclusion 7th character A see Appendix A PDX collection 1231

CC +7th **S36.119 Unspecified injury of liver**
CC Exclusion 7th character A see Appendix A PDX collection 1231

+ **S36.12 Injury of gallbladder**

CC +7th **S36.122 Contusion of gallbladder**
CC Exclusion 7th character A see Appendix A PDX collection 1232

CC +7th **S36.123 Laceration of gallbladder**
CC Exclusion 7th character A see Appendix A PDX collection 1232

CC +7th **S36.128 Other injury of gallbladder**
CC Exclusion 7th character A see Appendix A PDX collection 1232

CC +7th **S36.129 Unspecified injury of gallbladder**
CC Exclusion 7th character A see Appendix A PDX collection 1232

CC X+7th **S36.13 Injury of bile duct**
CC Exclusion 7th character A see Appendix A PDX collection 1232

+ **S36.2 Injury of pancreas**

+ **S36.20 Unspecified injury of pancreas**

CC +7th **S36.200 Unspecified injury of head of pancreas**
CC Exclusion 7th character A see Appendix A PDX collection 1233

CC +7th **S36.201 Unspecified injury of body of pancreas**
CC Exclusion 7th character A see Appendix A PDX collection 1233

CC +7th **S36.202 Unspecified injury of tail of pancreas**
CC Exclusion 7th character A see Appendix A PDX collection 1233

CC +7th **S36.209 Unspecified injury of unspecified part of pancreas**
CC Exclusion 7th character A see Appendix A PDX collection 1233

+ **S36.22 Contusion of pancreas**

CC **S36.220 Contusion of head of pancreas**
CC Exclusion 7th character A see Appendix A PDX collection 1233

CC **S36.221 Contusion of body of pancreas**
CC Exclusion 7th character A see Appendix A PDX collection 1233

CC **S36.222 Contusion of tail of pancreas**
CC Exclusion 7th character A see Appendix A PDX collection 1233

CC **S36.229 Contusion of unspecified part of pancreas**
CC Exclusion 7th character A see Appendix A PDX collection 1233

+ **S36.23 Laceration of pancreas, unspecified degree**

CC +7th **S36.230 Laceration of head of pancreas, unspecified degree**
CC Exclusion 7th character A see Appendix A PDX collection 1233

CC +7th **S36.231 Laceration of body of pancreas, unspecified degree**
CC Exclusion 7th character A see Appendix A PDX collection 1233

CC +7th **S36.232 Laceration of tail of pancreas, unspecified degree**
CC Exclusion 7th character A see Appendix A PDX collection 1233

CC +7th **S36.239 Laceration of unspecified part of pancreas, unspecified degree**
CC Exclusion 7th character A see Appendix A PDX collection 1233

+ **S36.24 Minor laceration of pancreas**

CC +7th **S36.240 Minor laceration of head of pancreas**
CC Exclusion 7th character A see Appendix A PDX collection 1233

CC +7th **S36.241 Minor laceration of body of pancreas**
CC Exclusion 7th character A see Appendix A PDX collection 1233

CC +7th **S36.242 Minor laceration of tail of pancreas**
CC Exclusion 7th character A see Appendix A PDX collection 1233

CC +7th **S36.249 Minor laceration of unspecified part of pancreas**
CC Exclusion 7th character A see Appendix A PDX collection 1233

+ **S36.25 Moderate laceration of pancreas**

CC +7th **S36.250 Moderate laceration of head of pancreas**
CC Exclusion 7th character A see Appendix A PDX collection 1233

CC +7th **S36.251 Moderate laceration of body of pancreas**
CC Exclusion 7th character A see Appendix A PDX collection 1233

CC +7th **S36.252 Moderate laceration of tail of pancreas**
CC Exclusion 7th character A see Appendix A PDX collection 1233

CC +7th **S36.259 Moderate laceration of unspecified part of pancreas**
CC Exclusion 7th character A see Appendix A PDX collection 1233

+ **S36.26 Major laceration of pancreas**

CC +7th **S36.260 Major laceration of head of pancreas**
CC Exclusion 7th character A see Appendix A PDX collection 1233

CC +7th **S36.261 Major laceration of body of pancreas**
CC Exclusion 7th character A see Appendix A PDX collection 1233

CC +7th **S36.262 Major laceration of tail of pancreas**
CC Exclusion 7th character A see Appendix A PDX collection 1233

CC +7th **S36.269 Major laceration of unspecified part of pancreas**
CC Exclusion 7th character A see Appendix A PDX collection 1233

+ **S36.29 Other injury of pancreas**

CC +7th **S36.290 Other injury of head of pancreas**
CC Exclusion 7th character A see Appendix A PDX collection 1233

CC +7th **S36.291 Other injury of body of pancreas**
CC Exclusion 7th character A see Appendix A PDX collection 1233

CC +7th **S36.292 Other injury of tail of pancreas**
CC Exclusion 7th character A see Appendix A PDX collection 1233

CC +7th **S36.299 Other injury of unspecified part of pancreas**
CC Exclusion 7th character A see Appendix A PDX collection 1233

+ **S36.3 Injury of stomach**

CC X+7th **S36.30 Unspecified injury of stomach**
CC Exclusion 7th character A see Appendix A PDX collection 1234

CC X+7th **S36.32 Contusion of stomach**
CC Exclusion 7th character A see Appendix A PDX collection 1234

CC X+7th **S36.33 Laceration of stomach**
CC Exclusion 7th character A see Appendix A PDX collection 1234

CC X+7th **S36.39 Other injury of stomach**
CC Exclusion 7th character A see Appendix A PDX collection 1234

+ **S36.4 Injury of small intestine**

+ **S36.40 Unspecified injury of small intestine**

CC +7th **S36.400 Unspecified injury of duodenum**
CC Exclusion 7th character A see Appendix A PDX collection 1235

CC +7th **S36.408 Unspecified injury of other part of small intestine**
CC Exclusion 7th character A see Appendix A
PDX collection 1235

CC +7th **S36.409 Unspecified injury of unspecified part of small intestine**
CC Exclusion 7th character A see Appendix A
PDX collection 1235

\+ **S36.41 Primary blast injury of small intestine**
Blast injury of small intestine NOS

CC +7th **S36.410 Primary blast injury of duodenum**
CC Exclusion 7th character A see Appendix A
PDX collection 1235

CC +7th **S36.418 Primary blast injury of other part of small intestine**
CC Exclusion 7th character A see Appendix A
PDX collection 1235

CC +7th **S36.419 Primary blast injury of unspecified part of small intestine**
CC Exclusion 7th character A see Appendix A
PDX collection 1235

\+ **S36.42 Contusion of small intestine**

CC +7th **S36.420 Contusion of duodenum**
CC Exclusion 7th character A see Appendix A
PDX collection 1235

CC +7th **S36.428 Contusion of other part of small intestine**
CC Exclusion 7th character A see Appendix A
PDX collection 1235

CC +7th **S36.429 Contusion of unspecified part of small intestine**
CC Exclusion 7th character A see Appendix A
PDX collection 1235

\+ **S36.43 Laceration of small intestine**

CC +7th **S36.430 Laceration of duodenum**
CC Exclusion 7th character A see Appendix A
PDX collection 1235

CC +7th **S36.438 Laceration of other part of small intestine**
CC Exclusion 7th character A see Appendix A
PDX collection 1235

CC +7th **S36.439 Laceration of unspecified part of small intestine**
CC Exclusion 7th character A see Appendix A
PDX collection 1235

\+ **S36.49 Other injury of small intestine**

CC +7th **S36.490 Other injury of duodenum**
CC Exclusion 7th character A see Appendix A
PDX collection 1235

CC +7th **S36.498 Other injury of other part of small intestine**
CC Exclusion 7th character A see Appendix A
PDX collection 1235

CC +7th **S36.499 Other injury of unspecified part of small intestine**
CC Exclusion 7th character A see Appendix A
PDX collection 1235

S36.5 Injury of colon
Excludes2: *injury of rectum (S36.6-)*

\+ **S36.50 Unspecified injury of colon**

CC +7th **S36.500 Unspecified injury of ascending [right] colon**
CC Exclusion 7th character A see Appendix A
PDX collection 1236

CC +7th **S36.501 Unspecified injury of transverse colon**
CC Exclusion 7th character A see Appendix A
PDX collection 1236

CC +7th **S36.502 Unspecified injury of descending [left] colon**
CC Exclusion 7th character A see Appendix A
PDX collection 1236

CC +7th **S36.503 Unspecified injury of sigmoid colon**
CC Exclusion 7th character A see Appendix A
PDX collection 1236

CC +7th **S36.508 Unspecified injury of other part of colon**
CC Exclusion 7th character A see Appendix A
PDX collection 1236

CC +7th **S36.509 Unspecified injury of unspecified part of colon**
CC Exclusion 7th character A see Appendix A
PDX collection 1236

\+ **S36.51 Primary blast injury of colon**
Blast injury of colon NOS

CC +7th **S36.510 Primary blast injury of ascending [right] colon**
CC Exclusion 7th character A see Appendix A
PDX collection 1236

CC +7th **S36.511 Primary blast injury of transverse colon**
CC Exclusion 7th character A see Appendix A
PDX collection 1236

CC +7th **S36.512 Primary blast injury of descending [left] colon**
CC Exclusion 7th character A see Appendix A
PDX collection 1236

CC +7th **S36.513 Primary blast injury of sigmoid colon**
CC Exclusion 7th character A see Appendix A
PDX collection 1236

CC +7th **S36.518 Primary blast injury of other part of colon**
CC Exclusion 7th character A see Appendix A
PDX collection 1236

CC +7th **S36.519 Primary blast injury of unspecified part of colon**
CC Exclusion 7th character A see Appendix A
PDX collection 1236

\+ **S36.52 Contusion of colon**

CC +7th **S36.520 Contusion of ascending [right] colon**
CC Exclusion 7th character A see Appendix A
PDX collection 1236

CC +7th **S36.521 Contusion of transverse colon**
CC Exclusion 7th character A see Appendix A
PDX collection 1236

CC +7th **S36.522 Contusion of descending [left] colon**
CC Exclusion 7th character A see Appendix A
PDX collection 1236

CC +7th **S36.523 Contusion of sigmoid colon**
CC Exclusion 7th character A see Appendix A
PDX collection 1236

CC +7th **S36.528 Contusion of other part of colon**
CC Exclusion 7th character A see Appendix A
PDX collection 1236

CC +7th **S36.529 Contusion of unspecified part of colon**
CC Exclusion 7th character A see Appendix A
PDX collection 1236

\+ **S36.53 Laceration of colon**

CC +7th **S36.530 Laceration of ascending [right] colon**
CC Exclusion 7th character A see Appendix A
PDX collection 1236

CC +7th **S36.531 Laceration of transverse colon**
CC Exclusion 7th character A see Appendix A
PDX collection 1236

CC +7th **S36.532 Laceration of descending [left] colon**
CC Exclusion 7th character A see Appendix A
PDX collection 1236

CC +7th **S36.533 Laceration of sigmoid colon**
CC Exclusion 7th character A see Appendix A
PDX collection 1236

CC +7th **S36.538 Laceration of other part of colon**
CC Exclusion 7th character A see Appendix A
PDX collection 1236

CC +7th **S36.539 Laceration of unspecified part of colon**
CC Exclusion 7th character A see Appendix A
PDX collection 1236

\+ **S36.59 Other injury of colon**
Secondary blast injury of colon

CC +7th **S36.590 Other injury of ascending [right] colon**
CC Exclusion 7th character A see Appendix A
PDX collection 1236

CC +7th **S36.591 Other injury of transverse colon**
CC Exclusion 7th character A see Appendix A
PDX collection 1236

CC +7th **S36.592 Other injury of descending [left] colon**
CC Exclusion 7th character A see Appendix A
PDX collection 1236

CC +7th **S36.593 Other injury of sigmoid colon**
CC Exclusion 7th character A see Appendix A
PDX collection 1236

CC +7th **S36.598 Other injury of other part of colon**
CC Exclusion 7th character A see Appendix A
PDX collection 1236

CC +7th **S36.599 Other injury of unspecified part of colon**
CC Exclusion 7th character A see Appendix A
PDX collection 1236

\+ **S36.6 Injury of rectum**

CC X+7th **S36.60 Unspecified injury of rectum**
CC Exclusion 7th character A see Appendix A PDX collection 1236

CC X+7th **S36.61 Primary blast injury of rectum**
Blast injury of rectum NOS
CC Exclusion 7th character A see Appendix A PDX collection 1236

CC X+7th **S36.62 Contusion of rectum**
CC Exclusion 7th character A see Appendix A PDX collection 1236

CC X+7th **S36.63 Laceration of rectum**
CC Exclusion 7th character A see Appendix A PDX collection 1236

CC X+7th **S36.69 Other injury of rectum**
Secondary blast injury of rectum
CC Exclusion 7th character A see Appendix A PDX collection 1236

+ **S36.8 Injury of other intra-abdominal organs**

CC X+7th **S36.81 Injury of peritoneum**
CC Exclusion 7th character A see Appendix A PDX collection 1195

+ **S36.89 Injury of other intra-abdominal organs**
Injury of retroperitoneum

CC +7th **S36.892 Contusion of other intra-abdominal organs**
CC Exclusion 7th character A see Appendix A PDX collection 1195

CC +7th **S36.893 Laceration of other intra-abdominal organs**
CC Exclusion 7th character A see Appendix A PDX collection 1195

CC +7th **S36.898 Other injury of other intra-abdominal organs**
CC Exclusion 7th character A see Appendix A PDX collection 1195

CC +7th **S36.899 Unspecified injury of other intra-abdominal organs**
CC Exclusion 7th character A see Appendix A PDX collection 1195

+ **S36.9 Injury of unspecified intra-abdominal organ**

CC X+7th **S36.90 Unspecified injury of unspecified intra-abdominal organ**
CC Exclusion 7th character A see Appendix A PDX collection 1195

CC X+7th **S36.92 Contusion of unspecified intra-abdominal organ**
CC Exclusion 7th character A see Appendix A PDX collection 1195

CC X+7th **S36.93 Laceration of unspecified intra-abdominal organ**
CC Exclusion 7th character A see Appendix A PDX collection 1195

CC X+7th **S36.99 Other injury of unspecified intra-abdominal organ**
CC Exclusion 7th character A see Appendix A PDX collection 1195

S37 Injury of urinary and pelvic organs

Code also any associated open wound (S31.-)
Excludes1: *obstetric trauma to pelvic organs (O71.-)*
Excludes2: *injury of peritoneum (S36.81)*
injury of retroperitoneum (S36.89-)

The appropriate 7th character is to be added to each code from category S37
A initial encounter
D subsequent encounter
S sequela

+ **S37.0 Injury of kidney**
Excludes2: *acute kidney injury (nontraumatic) (N17.9)*

+ **S37.00 Unspecified injury of kidney**

CC +7th **S37.001 Unspecified injury of right kidney**
CC Exclusion 7th character A see Appendix A PDX collection 1237

CC +7th **S37.002 Unspecified injury of left kidney**
CC Exclusion 7th character A see Appendix A PDX collection 1237

CC +7th **S37.009 Unspecified injury of unspecified kidney**
CC Exclusion 7th character A see Appendix A PDX collection 1237

+ **S37.01 Minor contusion of kidney**
Contusion of kidney less than 2 cm
Contusion of kidney NOS

CC +7th **S37.011 Minor contusion of right kidney**
CC Exclusion 7th character A see Appendix A PDX collection 1237

CC +7th **S37.012 Minor contusion of left kidney**
CC Exclusion 7th character A see Appendix A PDX collection 1237

CC +7th **S37.019 Minor contusion of unspecified kidney**
CC Exclusion 7th character A see Appendix A PDX collection 1237

+ **S37.02 Major contusion of kidney**
Contusion of kidney greater than 2 cm

CC +7th **S37.021 Major contusion of right kidney**
CC Exclusion 7th character A see Appendix A PDX collection 1237

CC +7th **S37.022 Major contusion of left kidney**
CC Exclusion 7th character A see Appendix A PDX collection 1237

CC +7th **S37.029 Major contusion of unspecified kidney**
CC Exclusion 7th character A see Appendix A PDX collection 1237

+ **S37.03 Laceration of kidney, unspecified degree**

CC +7th **S37.031 Laceration of right kidney, unspecified degree**
CC Exclusion 7th character A see Appendix A PDX collection 1237

CC +7th **S37.032 Laceration of left kidney, unspecified degree**
CC Exclusion 7th character A see Appendix A PDX collection 1237

CC +7th **S37.039 Laceration of unspecified kidney, unspecified degree**
CC Exclusion 7th character A see Appendix A PDX collection 1237

+ **S37.04 Minor laceration of kidney**
Laceration of kidney less than 1 cm

CC +7th **S37.041 Minor laceration of right kidney**
CC Exclusion 7th character A see Appendix A PDX collection 1237

CC +7th **S37.042 Minor laceration of left kidney**
CC Exclusion 7th character A see Appendix A PDX collection 1237

CC +7th **S37.049 Minor laceration of unspecified kidney**
CC Exclusion 7th character A see Appendix A PDX collection 1237

+ **S37.05 Moderate laceration of kidney**
Laceration of kidney 1 to 3 cm

CC +7th **S37.051 Moderate laceration of right kidney**
CC Exclusion 7th character A see Appendix A PDX collection 1237

CC +7th **S37.052 Moderate laceration of left kidney**
CC Exclusion 7th character A see Appendix A PDX collection 1237

CC +7th **S37.059 Moderate laceration of unspecified kidney**
CC Exclusion 7th character A see Appendix A PDX collection 1237

+ **S37.06 Major laceration of kidney**
Avulsion of kidney
Laceration of kidney greater than 3 cm
Massive laceration of kidney
Multiple moderate lacerations of kidney
Stellate laceration of kidney

MCC +7th **S37.061 Major laceration of right kidney**
MCC Exclusion 7th character A see Appendix A PDX collection 1237

MCC +7th **S37.062 Major laceration of left kidney**
MCC Exclusion 7th character A see Appendix A PDX collection 1237

MCC +7th **S37.069 Major laceration of unspecified kidney**
MCC Exclusion 7th character A see Appendix A PDX collection 1237

+ **S37.09 Other injury of kidney**

MCC +7th **S37.091 Other injury of right kidney**
MCC Exclusion 7th character A see Appendix A PDX collection 1237

MCC +7th **S37.092 Other injury of left kidney**
MCC Exclusion 7th character A see Appendix A PDX collection 1237

MCC +7th **S37.099 Other injury of unspecified kidney**
MCC Exclusion 7th character A see Appendix A PDX collection 1237

+ **S37.1 Injury of ureter**

CC X+7th **S37.10 Unspecified injury of ureter**
CC Exclusion 7th character A see Appendix A PDX collection 1238

CC X+7th **S37.12 Contusion of ureter**
CC Exclusion 7th character A see Appendix A PDX collection 1238

CC X+7th **S37.13 Laceration of ureter**
CC Exclusion 7th character A see Appendix A PDX collection 1238

CC X+7th **S37.19 Other injury of ureter**
CC Exclusion 7th character A see Appendix A PDX collection 1238

+ **S37.2 Injury of bladder**

CC X+7th **S37.20 Unspecified injury of bladder**
CC Exclusion 7th character A see Appendix A PDX collection 1239

CC X+7th **S37.22 Contusion of bladder**
CC Exclusion 7th character A see Appendix A PDX collection 1239

CC X+7th **S37.23 Laceration of bladder**
CC Exclusion 7th character A see Appendix A PDX collection 1239

CC X+7th **S37.29 Other injury of bladder**
CC Exclusion 7th character A see Appendix A PDX collection 1239

\+ **S37.3 Injury of urethra**
CC X+7th **S37.30 Unspecified injury of urethra**
CC Exclusion 7th character A see Appendix A PDX collection 1239
CC X+7th **S37.32 Contusion of urethra**
CC Exclusion 7th character A see Appendix A PDX collection 1239
CC X+7th **S37.33 Laceration of urethra**
CC Exclusion 7th character A see Appendix A PDX collection 1239
CC X+7th **S37.39 Other injury of urethra**
CC Exclusion 7th character A see Appendix A PDX collection 1239
\+ **S37.4 Injury of ovary**
\+ **S37.40 Unspecified injury of ovary**
♀ +7th **S37.401 Unspecified injury of ovary, unilateral**
♀ +7th **S37.402 Unspecified injury of ovary, bilateral**
♀ +7th **S37.409 Unspecified injury of ovary, unspecified**
\+ **S37.42 Contusion of ovary**
♀ +7th **S37.421 Contusion of ovary, unilateral**
♀ +7th **S37.422 Contusion of ovary, bilateral**
♀ +7th **S37.429 Contusion of ovary, unspecified**
\+ **S37.43 Laceration of ovary**
♀ +7th **S37.431 Laceration of ovary, unilateral**
♀ +7th **S37.432 Laceration of ovary, bilateral**
♀ +7th **S37.439 Laceration of ovary, unspecified**
\+ **S37.49 Other injury of ovary**
♀ +7th **S37.491 Other injury of ovary, unilateral**
♀ +7th **S37.492 Other injury of ovary, bilateral**
♀ +7th **S37.499 Other injury of ovary, unspecified**
\+ **S37.5 Injury of fallopian tube**
\+ **S37.50 Unspecified injury of fallopian tube**
♀ +7th **S37.501 Unspecified injury of fallopian tube, unilateral**
♀ +7th **S37.502 Unspecified injury of fallopian tube, bilateral**
♀ +7th **S37.509 Unspecified injury of fallopian tube, unspecified**
\+ **S37.51 Primary blast injury of fallopian tube**
Blast injury of fallopian tube NOS
♀ +7th **S37.511 Primary blast injury of fallopian tube, unilateral**
♀ +7th **S37.512 Primary blast injury of fallopian tube, bilateral**
♀ +7th **S37.519 Primary blast injury of fallopian tube, unspecified**
\+ **S37.52 Contusion of fallopian tube**
♀ +7th **S37.521 Contusion of fallopian tube, unilateral**
♀ +7th **S37.522 Contusion of fallopian tube, bilateral**
♀ +7th **S37.529 Contusion of fallopian tube, unspecified**
\+ **S37.53 Laceration of fallopian tube**
♀ +7th **S37.531 Laceration of fallopian tube, unilateral**
♀ +7th **S37.532 Laceration of fallopian tube, bilateral**
♀ +7th **S37.539 Laceration of fallopian tube, unspecified**
\+ **S37.59 Other injury of fallopian tube**
Secondary blast injury of fallopian tube
♀ +7th **S37.591 Other injury of fallopian tube, unilateral**
♀ +7th **S37.592 Other injury of fallopian tube, bilateral**
♀ +7th **S37.599 Other injury of fallopian tube, unspecified**
\+ **S37.6 Injury of uterus**
Excludes1: *injury to gravid uterus (O9A.2-)*
injury to uterus during delivery (O71.-)
♀ CC X+7th **S37.60 Unspecified injury of uterus**
CC Exclusion 7th character A see Appendix A PDX collection 1240
♀ CC X+7th **S37.62 Contusion of uterus**
CC Exclusion 7th character A see Appendix A PDX collection 1240
♀ CC X+7th **S37.63 Laceration of uterus**
CC Exclusion 7th character A see Appendix A PDX collection 1240
♀ CC X+7th **S37.69 Other injury of uterus**
CC Exclusion 7th character A see Appendix A PDX collection 1240
\+ **S37.8 Injury of other urinary and pelvic organs**
\+ **S37.81 Injury of adrenal gland**
CC +7th **S37.812 Contusion of adrenal gland**
CC Exclusion 7th character A see Appendix A PDX collection 1241
CC +7th **S37.813 Laceration of adrenal gland**
CC Exclusion 7th character A see Appendix A PDX collection 1241
CC +7th **S37.818 Other injury of adrenal gland**
CC Exclusion 7th character A see Appendix A PDX collection 1241
CC +7th **S37.819 Unspecified injury of adrenal gland**
CC Exclusion 7th character A see Appendix A PDX collection 1241
\+ **S37.82 Injury of prostate**
♂ +7th **S37.822 Contusion of prostate**
♂ +7th **S37.823 Laceration of prostate**
♂ +7th **S37.828 Other injury of prostate**
♂ +7th **S37.829 Unspecified injury of prostate**
\+ **S37.89 Injury of other urinary and pelvic organ**
CC +7th **S37.892 Contusion of other urinary and pelvic org**
CC Exclusion 7th character A see Appendix A PDX collection 1242
CC +7th **S37.893 Laceration of other urinary and pelvic or**
CC Exclusion 7th character A see Appendix A PDX collection 1242
CC +7th **S37.898 Other injury of other urinary and pelvic organ**
CC Exclusion 7th character A see Appendix A PDX collection 1242
CC +7th **S37.899 Unspecified injury of other urinary and pelvic organ**
CC Exclusion 7th character A see Appendix A PDX collection 1242
\+ **S37.9 Injury of unspecified urinary and pelvic organ**
CC X+7th **S37.90 Unspecified injury of unspecified urinary and pelvic organ**
CC Exclusion 7th character A see Appendix A PDX collection 1242
CC X+7th **S37.92 Contusion of unspecified urinary and pelvic organ**
CC Exclusion 7th character A see Appendix A PDX collection 1242
CC X+7th **S37.93 Laceration of unspecified urinary and pelvic organ**
CC Exclusion 7th character A see Appendix A PDX collection 1242
CC X+7th **S37.99 Other injury of unspecified urinary and pelvic orga**
CC Exclusion 7th character A see Appendix A PDX collection 1242

S38 Crushing injury and traumatic amputation of abdomen, lower back pelvis and external genitals

An amputation not identified as partial or complete should be coded to complete

The appropriate 7th character is to be added to each code from category S38
A initial encounter
D subsequent encounter
S sequela

\+ **S38.0 Crushing injury of external genital organs**
Use additional code for any associated injuries
\+ **S38.00 Crushing injury of unspecified external genital orga**
♂ +7th **S38.001 Crushing injury of unspecified external genital organs, male**
♀ +7th **S38.002 Crushing injury of unspecified external genital organs, female**
♂ X+7th **S38.01 Crushing injury of penis**
♂ X+7th **S38.02 Crushing injury of scrotum and testis**
♀ X+7th **S38.03 Crushing injury of vulva**
X+7th **S38.1 Crushing injury of abdomen, lower back, and pelvis**
Use additional code for all associated injuries, such as:
fracture of thoracic or lumbar spine and pelvis (S22.0-, S32.-
injury to intra-abdominal organs (S36.-)
injury to urinary and pelvic organs (S37.-)
open wound of abdominal wall (S31.-)
spinal cord injury (S34.0, S34.1-)
Excludes2: *crushing injury of external genital organs (S38.0-)*
\+ **S38.2 Traumatic amputation of external genital organs**
\+ **S38.21 Traumatic amputation of female external genital organs**
Traumatic amputation of clitoris
Traumatic amputation of labium (majus) (minus)
Traumatic amputation of vulva
♀ +7th **S38.211 Complete traumatic amputation of female external genital organs**
♀ +7th **S38.212 Partial traumatic amputation of female external genital organs**
\+ **S38.22 Traumatic amputation of penis**
♂ +7th **S38.221 Complete traumatic amputation of penis**
♂ +7th **S38.222 Partial traumatic amputation of penis**

+ **S38.23 Traumatic amputation of scrotum and testis**
  - ♂ +7th **S38.231 Complete traumatic amputation of scrotum and testis**
  - ♂ +7th **S38.232 Partial traumatic amputation of scrotum and testis**

X+7th **S38.3 Transection (partial) of abdomen**

S39 Other and unspecified injuries of abdomen, lower back, pelvis and external genitals

Code also any associated open wound (S31.-)

Excludes2: *sprain of joints and ligaments of lumbar spine and pelvis (S33.-)*

The appropriate 7th character is to be added to each code from category S39
A initial encounter
D subsequent encounter
S sequela

+ **S39.0 Injury of muscle, fascia and tendon of abdomen, lower back and pelvis**
  + **S39.00 Unspecified injury of muscle, fascia and tendon of abdomen, lower back and pelvis**
    - +7th **S39.001 Unspecified injury of muscle, fascia and tendon of abdomen**
    - +7th **S39.002 Unspecified injury of muscle, fascia and tendon of lower back**
    - +7th **S39.003 Unspecified injury of muscle, fascia and tendon of pelvis**
  + **S39.01 Strain of muscle, fascia and tendon of abdomen, lower back and pelvis**
    - +7th **S39.011 Strain of muscle, fascia and tendon of abdomen**
    - +7th **S39.012 Strain of muscle, fascia and tendon of lower back**
    - +7th **S39.013 Strain of muscle, fascia and tendon of pelvis**
  + **S39.02 Laceration of muscle, fascia and tendon of abdomen, lower back and pelvis**
    - +7th **S39.021 Laceration of muscle, fascia and tendon of abdomen**
    - +7th **S39.022 Laceration of muscle, fascia and tendon of lower back**
    - +7th **S39.023 Laceration of muscle, fascia and tendon of pelvis**
  + **S39.09 Other injury of muscle, fascia and tendon of abdomen, lower back and pelvis**
    - +7th **S39.091 Other injury of muscle, fascia and tendon of abdomen**
    - +7th **S39.092 Other injury of muscle, fascia and tendon of lower back**
    - +7th **S39.093 Other injury of muscle, fascia and tendon of pelvis**

+ **S39.8 Other specified injuries of abdomen, lower back, pelvis and external genitals**
  - X+7th **S39.81 Other specified injuries of abdomen**
  - X+7th **S39.82 Other specified injuries of lower back**
  - X+7th **S39.83 Other specified injuries of pelvis**
  + **S39.84 Other specified injuries of external genitals**
    - ♂ X+7th **S39.840 Fracture of corpus cavernosum penis**
    - X+7th **S39.848 Other specified injuries of external genitals**

+ **S39.9 Unspecified injury of abdomen, lower back, pelvis and external genitals**
  - X+7th **S39.91 Unspecified injury of abdomen**
  - X+7th **S39.92 Unspecified injury of lower back**
  - X+7th **S39.93 Unspecified injury of pelvis**
  - X+7th **S39.94 Unspecified injury of external genitals**

juries to the shoulder and upper arm (S40-S49)

cludes: injuries of axilla
injuries of scapular region

cludes2: *and corrosions (T20-T32)*
frostbite (T33-T34)
injuries of elbow (S50-S59)
insect bite or sting, venomous (T63.4)

S40 Superficial injury of shoulder and upper arm

The appropriate 7th character is to be added to each code from category S40
A initial encounter
D subsequent encounter
S sequela

+ **S40.0 Contusion of shoulder and upper arm**
  + **S40.01 Contusion of shoulder**
    - +7th **S40.011 Contusion of right shoulder**
    - +7th **S40.012 Contusion of left shoulder**
    - +7th **S40.019 Contusion of unspecified shoulder**
  + **S40.02 Contusion of upper arm**
    - +7th **S40.021 Contusion of right upper arm**
    - +7th **S40.022 Contusion of left upper arm**
    - +7th **S40.029 Contusion of unspecified upper arm**

+ **S40.2 Other superficial injuries of shoulder**
  + **S40.21 Abrasion of shoulder**
    - +7th **S40.211 Abrasion of right shoulder**
    - +7th **S40.212 Abrasion of left shoulder**
    - +7th **S40.219 Abrasion of unspecified shoulder**
  + **S40.22 Blister (nonthermal) of shoulder**
    - +7th **S40.221 Blister (nonthermal) of right shoulder**
    - +7th **S40.222 Blister (nonthermal) of left shoulder**
    - +7th **S40.229 Blister (nonthermal) of unspecified shoulder**
  + **S40.24 External constriction of shoulder**
    - +7th **S40.241 External constriction of right shoulder**
    - +7th **S40.242 External constriction of left shoulder**
    - +7th **S40.249 External constriction of unspecified shoulder**
  + **S40.25 Superficial foreign body of shoulder**
    Splinter in the shoulder
    - +7th **S40.251 Superficial foreign body of right shoulder**
    - +7th **S40.252 Superficial foreign body of left shoulder**
    - +7th **S40.259 Superficial foreign body of unspecified shoulder**
  + **S40.26 Insect bite (nonvenomous) of shoulder**
    - +7th **S40.261 Insect bite (nonvenomous) of right shoulder**
    - +7th **S40.262 Insect bite (nonvenomous) of left shoulder**
    - +7th **S40.269 Insect bite (nonvenomous) of unspecified shoulder**
  + **S40.27 Other superficial bite of shoulder**
    Excludes1: *open bite of shoulder (S41.05)*
    - +7th **S40.271 Other superficial bite of right shoulder**
    - +7th **S40.272 Other superficial bite of left shoulder**
    - +7th **S40.279 Other superficial bite of unspecified shoulder**

+ **S40.8 Other superficial injuries of upper arm**
  + **S40.81 Abrasion of upper arm**
    - +7th **S40.811 Abrasion of right upper arm**
    - +7th **S40.812 Abrasion of left upper arm**
    - +7th **S40.819 Abrasion of unspecified upper arm**
  + **S40.82 Blister (nonthermal) of upper arm**
    - +7th **S40.821 Blister (nonthermal) of right upper arm**
    - +7th **S40.822 Blister (nonthermal) of left upper arm**
    - +7th **S40.829 Blister (nonthermal) of unspecified upper arm**
  + **S40.84 External constriction of upper arm**
    - +7th **S40.841 External constriction of right upper arm**
    - +7th **S40.842 External constriction of left upper arm**
    - +7th **S40.849 External constriction of unspecified upper arm**
  + **S40.85 Superficial foreign body of upper arm**
    Splinter in the upper arm
    - +7th **S40.851 Superficial foreign body of right upper arm**
    - +7th **S40.852 Superficial foreign body of left upper arm**
    - +7th **S40.859 Superficial foreign body of unspecified upper arm**
  + **S40.86 Insect bite (nonvenomous) of upper arm**
    - +7th **S40.861 Insect bite (nonvenomous) of right upper arm**
    - +7th **S40.862 Insect bite (nonvenomous) of left upper arm**
    - +7th **S40.869 Insect bite (nonvenomous) of unspecified upper arm**
  + **S40.87 Other superficial bite of upper arm**
    Excludes1: *open bite of upper arm (S41.14)*
    Excludes2: *other superficial bite of shoulder (S40.27-)*
    - +7th **S40.871 Other superficial bite of right upper arm**
    - +7th **S40.872 Other superficial bite of left upper arm**
    - +7th **S40.879 Other superficial bite of unspecified upper arm**

+ **S40.9 Unspecified superficial injury of shoulder and upper arm**
  + **S40.91 Unspecified superficial injury of shoulder**
    - +7th **S40.911 Unspecified superficial injury of right shoulder**
    - +7th **S40.912 Unspecified superficial injury of left shoulder**
    - +7th **S40.919 Unspecified superficial injury of unspecified shoulder**

Shoulder

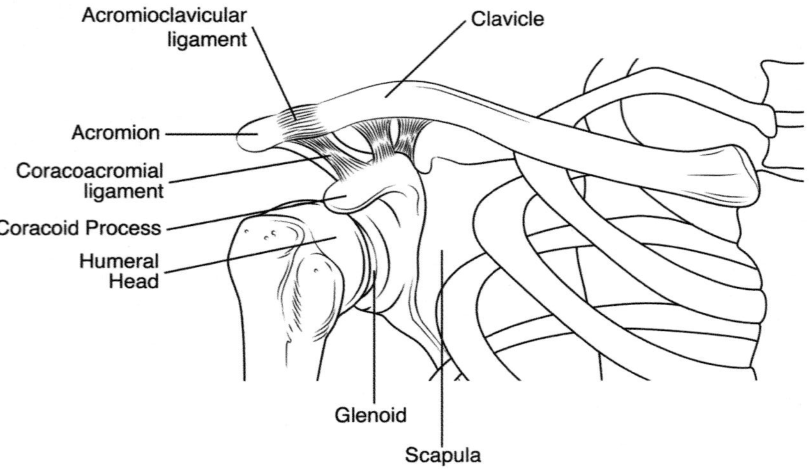
Acromioclavicular ligament
Clavicle
Acromion
Coracoacromial ligament
Coracoid Process
Humeral Head
Glenoid
Scapula

©AHIMA

Shoulder Tendons

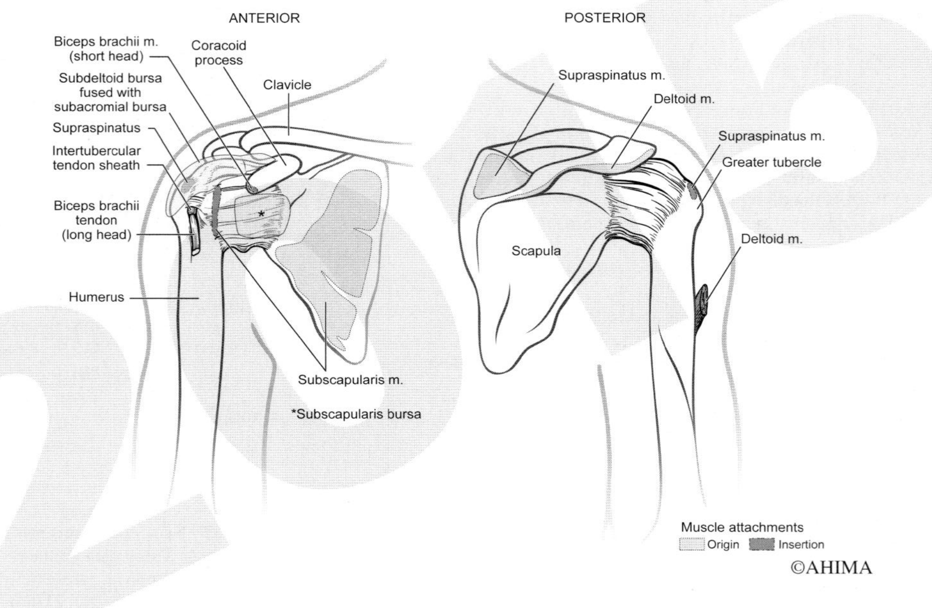
ANTERIOR
POSTERIOR
Biceps brachii m. (short head)
Coracoid process
Clavicle
Subdeltoid bursa fused with subacromial bursa
Supraspinatus
Intertubercular tendon sheath
Biceps brachii tendon (long head)
Humerus
Subscapularis m.
*Subscapularis bursa
Supraspinatus m.
Deltoid m.
Supraspinatus m.
Greater tubercle
Scapula
Deltoid m.
Muscle attachments
Origin
Insertion

©AHIMA

Shoulder Ligaments

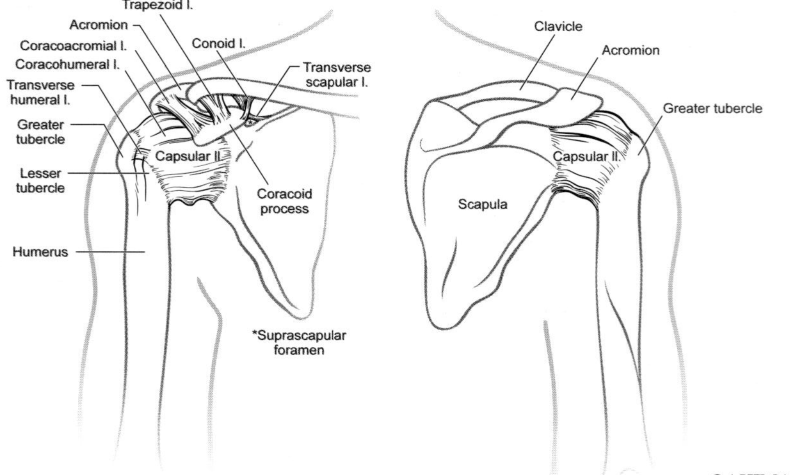
ANTERIOR
POSTERIOR
Trapezoid l.
Acromion
Conoid l.
Coracoacromial l.
Coracohumeral l.
Transverse scapular l.
Transverse humeral l.
Greater tubercle
Capsular ll.
Lesser tubercle
Coracoid process
Humerus
*Suprascapular foramen
Clavicle
Acromion
Greater tubercle
Capsular ll.
Scapula

©AHIMA

+ S40.92 Unspecified superficial injury of upper arm
- **+7th S40.921 Unspecified superficial injury of right upper arm**
- **+7th S40.922 Unspecified superficial injury of left upper arm**
- **+7th S40.929 Unspecified superficial injury of unspecified upper arm**

S41 Open wound of shoulder and upper arm

Code also any associated wound infection

Excludes1: *traumatic amputation of shoulder and upper arm (S48.-)*

Excludes2: *open fracture of shoulder and upper arm (S42.- with 7th character B or C)*

The appropriate 7th character is to be added to each code from category S41
- A initial encounter
- D subsequent encounter
- S sequela

+ S41.0 Open wound of shoulder
- **+ S41.00 Unspecified open wound of shoulder**
  - **+7th S41.001 Unspecified open wound of right shoulder**
  - **+7th S41.002 Unspecified open wound of left shoulder**
  - **+7th S41.009 Unspecified open wound of unspecified shoulder**
- **+ S41.01 Laceration without foreign body of shoulder**
  - **+7th S41.011 Laceration without foreign body of right shoulder**
  - **+7th S41.012 Laceration without foreign body of left shoulder**
  - **+7th S41.019 Laceration without foreign body of unspecified shoulder**
- **+ S41.02 Laceration with foreign body of shoulder**
  - **+7th S41.021 Laceration with foreign body of right shoulder**
  - **+7th S41.022 Laceration with foreign body of left shoulder**
  - **+7th S41.029 Laceration with foreign body of unspecified shoulder**
- **+ S41.03 Puncture wound without foreign body of shoulder**
  - **+7th S41.031 Puncture wound without foreign body of right shoulder**
  - **+7th S41.032 Puncture wound without foreign body of left shoulder**
  - **+7th S41.039 Puncture wound without foreign body of unspecified shoulder**
- **+ S41.04 Puncture wound with foreign body of shoulder**
  - **+7th S41.041 Puncture wound with foreign body of right shoulder**
  - **+7th S41.042 Puncture wound with foreign body of left shoulder**
  - **+7th S41.049 Puncture wound with foreign body of unspecified shoulder**
- **+ S41.05 Open bite of shoulder**

  Bite of shoulder NOS

  Excludes1: *superficial bite of shoulder (S40.27)*
  - **+7th S41.051 Open bite of right shoulder**
  - **+7th S41.052 Open bite of left shoulder**
  - **+7th S41.059 Open bite of unspecified shoulder**

+ S41.1 Open wound of upper arm
- **+ S41.10 Unspecified open wound of upper arm**
  - **+7th S41.101 Unspecified open wound of right upper arm**
  - **+7th S41.102 Unspecified open wound of left upper arm**
  - **+7th S41.109 Unspecified open wound of unspecified upper arm**
- **+ S41.11 Laceration without foreign body of upper arm**
  - **S41.111 Laceration without foreign body of right upper arm**
  - **S41.112 Laceration without foreign body of left upper arm**
  - **S41.119 Laceration without foreign body of unspecified upper arm**
- **+ S41.12 Laceration with foreign body of upper arm**
  - **+7th S41.121 Laceration with foreign body of right upper arm**
  - **+7th S41.122 Laceration with foreign body of left upper arm**
  - **+7th S41.129 Laceration with foreign body of unspecified upper arm**
- **+ S41.13 Puncture wound without foreign body of upper arm**
  - **+7th S41.131 Puncture wound without foreign body of right upper arm**
  - **+7th S41.132 Puncture wound without foreign body of left upper arm**
  - **+7th S41.139 Puncture wound without foreign body of unspecified upper arm**
- **+ S41.14 Puncture wound with foreign body of upper arm**
  - **+7th S41.141 Puncture wound with foreign body of right upper arm**
  - **+7th S41.142 Puncture wound with foreign body of left upper arm**
  - **+7th S41.149 Puncture wound with foreign body of unspecified upper arm**
- **+ S41.15 Open bite of upper arm**

  Bite of upper arm NOS

  Excludes1: *superficial bite of upper arm (S40.87)*
  - **+7th S41.151 Open bite of right upper arm**
  - **+7th S41.152 Open bite of left upper arm**
  - **+7th S41.159 Open bite of unspecified upper arm**

S42 Fracture of shoulder and upper arm

NOTE A fracture not indicated as displaced or nondisplaced should be coded to displaced

A fracture not indicated as open or closed should be coded to closed unless otherwise indicated.

Excludes1: *traumatic amputation of shoulder and upper arm (S48.-)*

The appropriate 7th character is to be added to all codes from category S42
- A initial encounter for closed fracture
- B initial encounter for open fracture
- D subsequent encounter for fracture with routine healing
- G subsequent encounter for fracture with delayed healing
- K subsequent encounter for fracture with nonunion
- P subsequent encounter for fracture with malunion
- S sequela

Review coding guideline C.19.c

+ S42.0 Fracture of clavicle
- **+ S42.00 Fracture of unspecified part of clavicle**
  - **CC +7th S42.001 Fracture of unspecified part of right clavicle**
    - **CC Exclusion 7th character B see Appendix A PDX collection 1243**
    - **CC Exclusion 7th characters K & P see Appendix A PDX collection 0897**
    - HAC 7th character B see Appendix B for HAC conditional logic
  - **CC +7th S42.002 Fracture of unspecified part of left clavicle**
    - **CC Exclusion 7th character B see Appendix A PDX collection 1243**
    - **CC Exclusion 7th characters K & P see Appendix A PDX collection 0897**
    - HAC 7th character B see Appendix B for HAC conditional logic
  - **CC +7th S42.009 Fracture of unspecified part of unspecified clavicle**
    - **CC Exclusion 7th character B see Appendix A PDX collection 1243**
    - **CC Exclusion 7th characters K & P see Appendix A PDX collection 0897**
    - HAC 7th character B see Appendix B for HAC conditional logic
- **+ S42.01 Fracture of sternal end of clavicle**
  - **CC +7th S42.011 Anterior displaced fracture of sternal end of right clavicle**
    - **CC Exclusion 7th character B see Appendix A PDX collection 1243**
    - **CC Exclusion 7th characters K & P see Appendix A PDX collection 0897**
    - HAC 7th character B see Appendix B for HAC conditional logic
  - **CC +7th S42.012 Anterior displaced fracture of sternal end of left clavicle**
    - **CC Exclusion 7th character B see Appendix A PDX collection 1243**
    - **CC Exclusion 7th characters K & P see Appendix A PDX collection 0897**
    - HAC 7th character B see Appendix B for HAC conditional logic

CC +7th **S42.013 Anterior displaced fracture of sternal end of unspecified clavicle**
Displaced fracture of sternal end of clavicle NOS
CC Exclusion 7th character B see Appendix A PDX collection 1243
CC Exclusion 7th characters K & P see Appendix A PDX collection 0897
HAC 7th character B see Appendix B for HAC conditional logic

CC +7th **S42.014 Posterior displaced fracture of sternal end of right clavicle**
CC Exclusion 7th character B see Appendix A PDX collection 1243
CC Exclusion 7th characters K & P see Appendix A PDX collection 0897
HAC 7th character B see Appendix B for HAC conditional logic

CC +7th **S42.015 Posterior displaced fracture of sternal end of left clavicle**
CC Exclusion 7th character B see Appendix A PDX collection 1243
CC Exclusion 7th characters K & P see Appendix A PDX collection 0897
HAC 7th character B see Appendix B for HAC conditional logic

CC +7th **S42.016 Posterior displaced fracture of sternal end of unspecified clavicle**
CC Exclusion 7th character B see Appendix A PDX collection 1243
CC Exclusion 7th characters K & P see Appendix A PDX collection 0897
HAC 7th character B see Appendix B for HAC conditional logic

CC +7th **S42.017 Nondisplaced fracture of sternal end of right clavicle**
CC Exclusion 7th character B see Appendix A PDX collection 1243
CC Exclusion 7th characters K & P see Appendix A PDX collection 0897
HAC 7th character B see Appendix B for HAC conditional logic

CC +7th **S42.018 Nondisplaced fracture of sternal end of left clavicle**
CC Exclusion 7th character B see Appendix A PDX collection 1243
CC Exclusion 7th characters K & P see Appendix A PDX collection 0897
HAC 7th character B see Appendix B for HAC conditional logic

CC +7th **S42.019 Nondisplaced fracture of sternal end of unspecified clavicle**
CC Exclusion 7th character B see Appendix A PDX collection 1243
CC Exclusion 7th characters K & P see Appendix A PDX collection 0897
HAC 7th character B see Appendix B for HAC conditional logic

+ S42.02 Fracture of shaft of clavicle

CC +7th **S42.021 Displaced fracture of shaft of right clavicle**
CC Exclusion 7th character B see Appendix A PDX collection 1243
CC Exclusion 7th characters K & P see Appendix A PDX collection 0897
HAC 7th character B see Appendix B for HAC conditional logic

CC +7th **S42.022 Displaced fracture of shaft of left clavicle**
CC Exclusion 7th character B see Appendix A PDX collection 1243
CC Exclusion 7th characters K & P see Appendix A PDX collection 0897
HAC 7th character B see Appendix B for HAC conditional logic

CC +7th **S42.023 Displaced fracture of shaft of unspecified clavicle**
CC Exclusion 7th character B see Appendix A PDX collection 1243
CC Exclusion 7th characters K & P see Appendix A PDX collection 0897
HAC 7th character B see Appendix B for HAC conditional logic

CC +7th **S42.024 Nondisplaced fracture of shaft of right clavicle**
CC Exclusion 7th character B see Appendix A PDX collection 1243
CC Exclusion 7th characters K & P see Appendix A PDX collection 0897
HAC 7th character B see Appendix B for HAC conditional logic

CC +7th **S42.025 Nondisplaced fracture of shaft of left clav**
CC Exclusion 7th character B see Appendix A PDX collection 1243
CC Exclusion 7th characters K & P see Appendix A PDX collection 0897
HAC 7th character B see Appendix B for HAC conditional logic

CC +7th **S42.026 Nondisplaced fracture of shaft of unspeci clavicle**
CC Exclusion 7th character B see Appendix A PDX collection 1243
CC Exclusion 7th characters K & P see Appendix A PDX collection 0897
HAC 7th character B see Appendix B for HAC conditional logic

+ S42.03 Fracture of lateral end of clavicle
Fracture of acromial end of clavicle

CC +7th **S42.031 Displaced fracture of lateral end of right clavicle**
CC Exclusion 7th character B see Appendix A PDX collection 1243
CC Exclusion 7th characters K & P see Appendix A PDX collection 0897
HAC 7th character B see Appendix B for HAC conditional logic

CC +7th **S42.032 Displaced fracture of lateral end of left clavicle**
CC Exclusion 7th character B see Appendix A PDX collection 1243
CC Exclusion 7th characters K & P see Appendix A PDX collection 0897
HAC 7th character B see Appendix B for HAC conditional logic

CC +7th **S42.033 Displaced fracture of lateral end of unspecified clavicle**
CC Exclusion 7th character B see Appendix A PDX collection 1243
CC Exclusion 7th characters K & P see Appendix A PDX collection 0897
HAC 7th character B see Appendix B for HAC conditional logic

CC +7th **S42.034 Nondisplaced fracture of lateral end of rig clavicle**
CC Exclusion 7th character B see Appendix A PDX collection 1243
CC Exclusion 7th characters K & P see Appendix A PDX collection 0897
HAC 7th character B see Appendix B for HAC conditional logic

CC +7th **S42.035 Nondisplaced fracture of lateral end of lef clavicle**
CC Exclusion 7th character B see Appendix A PDX collection 1243
CC Exclusion 7th characters K & P see Appendix A PDX collection 0897
HAC 7th character B see Appendix B for HAC conditional logic

CC +7th **S42.036 Nondisplaced fracture of lateral end of unspecified clavicle**
CC Exclusion 7th character B see Appendix A PDX collection 1243
CC Exclusion 7th characters K & P see Appendix A PDX collection 0897
HAC 7th character B see Appendix B for HAC conditional logic

+ S42.1 Fracture of scapula

+ S42.10 Fracture of unspecified part of scapula

CC +7th **S42.101 Fracture of unspecified part of scapula, rig shoulder**
CC Exclusion 7th character B see Appendix A PDX collection 1244
CC Exclusion 7th characters K & P see Appendix A PDX collection 0897
HAC 7th character B see Appendix B for HAC conditional logic

CC +7th **S42.102 Fracture of unspecified part of scapula, lef shoulder**
CC Exclusion 7th character B see Appendix A PDX collection 1244
CC Exclusion 7th characters K & P see Appendix A PDX collection 0897
HAC 7th character B see Appendix B for HAC conditional logic

CC +7th **S42.109 Fracture of unspecified part of scapula, unspecified shoulder**
CC Exclusion 7th character B see Appendix A PDX collection 1244
CC Exclusion 7th characters K & P see Appendix A PDX collection 0897
HAC 7th character B see Appendix B for HAC conditional logic

+ **S42.11 Fracture of body of scapula**

CC +7th **S42.111 Displaced fracture of body of scapula, right shoulder**
CC Exclusion 7th character B see Appendix A PDX collection 1244
CC Exclusion 7th characters K & P see Appendix A PDX collection 0897
HAC 7th character B see Appendix B for HAC conditional logic

CC +7th **S42.112 Displaced fracture of body of scapula, left shoulder**
CC Exclusion 7th character B see Appendix A PDX collection 1244
CC Exclusion 7th characters K & P see Appendix A PDX collection 0897
HAC 7th character B see Appendix B for HAC conditional logic

CC +7th **S42.113 Displaced fracture of body of scapula, unspecified shoulder**
CC Exclusion 7th character B see Appendix A PDX collection 1244
CC Exclusion 7th characters K & P see Appendix A PDX collection 0897
HAC 7th character B see Appendix B for HAC conditional logic

CC +7th **S42.114 Nondisplaced fracture of body of scapula, right shoulder**
CC Exclusion 7th character B see Appendix A PDX collection 1244
CC Exclusion 7th characters K & P see Appendix A PDX collection 0897
HAC 7th character B see Appendix B for HAC conditional logic

CC +7th **S42.115 Nondisplaced fracture of body of scapula, left shoulder**
CC Exclusion 7th character B see Appendix A PDX collection 1244
CC Exclusion 7th characters K & P see Appendix A PDX collection 0897
HAC 7th character B see Appendix B for HAC conditional logic

CC +7th **S42.116 Nondisplaced fracture of body of scapula, unspecified shoulder**
CC Exclusion 7th character B see Appendix A PDX collection 1244
CC Exclusion 7th characters K & P see Appendix A PDX collection 0897
HAC 7th character B see Appendix B for HAC conditional logic

+ **S42.12 Fracture of acromial process**

CC +7th **S42.121 Displaced fracture of acromial process, right shoulder**
CC Exclusion 7th character B see Appendix A PDX collection 1244
CC Exclusion 7th characters K & P see Appendix A PDX collection 0897
HAC 7th character B see Appendix B for HAC conditional logic

CC +7th **S42.122 Displaced fracture of acromial process, left shoulder**
CC Exclusion 7th character B see Appendix A PDX collection 1244
CC Exclusion 7th characters K & P see Appendix A PDX collection 0897
HAC 7th character B see Appendix B for HAC conditional logic

CC +7th **S42.123 Displaced fracture of acromial process, unspecified shoulder**
CC Exclusion 7th character B see Appendix A PDX collection 1244
CC Exclusion 7th characters K & P see Appendix A PDX collection 0897
HAC 7th character B see Appendix B for HAC conditional logic

CC +7th **S42.124 Nondisplaced fracture of acromial process, right shoulder**
CC Exclusion 7th character B see Appendix A PDX collection 1244
CC Exclusion 7th characters K & P see Appendix A PDX collection 0897
HAC 7th character B see Appendix B for HAC conditional logic

CC +7th **S42.125 Nondisplaced fracture of acromial process, left shoulder**
CC Exclusion 7th character B see Appendix A PDX collection 1244
CC Exclusion 7th characters K & P see Appendix A PDX collection 0897
HAC 7th character B see Appendix B for HAC conditional logic

CC +7th **S42.126 Nondisplaced fracture of acromial process, unspecified shoulder**
CC Exclusion 7th character B see Appendix A PDX collection 1244
CC Exclusion 7th characters K & P see Appendix A PDX collection 0897
HAC 7th character B see Appendix B for HAC conditional logic

+ **S42.13 Fracture of coracoid process**

CC +7th **S42.131 Displaced fracture of coracoid process, right shoulder**
CC Exclusion 7th character B see Appendix A PDX collection 1244
CC Exclusion 7th characters K & P see Appendix A PDX collection 0897
HAC 7th character B see Appendix B for HAC conditional logic

CC +7th **S42.132 Displaced fracture of coracoid process, left shoulder**
CC Exclusion 7th character B see Appendix A PDX collection 1244
CC Exclusion 7th characters K & P see Appendix A PDX collection 0897
HAC 7th character B see Appendix B for HAC conditional logic

CC +7th **S42.133 Displaced fracture of coracoid process, unspecified shoulder**
CC Exclusion 7th character B see Appendix A PDX collection 1244
CC Exclusion 7th characters K & P see Appendix A PDX collection 0897
HAC 7th character B see Appendix B for HAC conditional logic

CC +7th **S42.134 Nondisplaced fracture of coracoid process, right shoulder**
CC Exclusion 7th character B see Appendix A PDX collection 1244
CC Exclusion 7th characters K & P see Appendix A PDX collection 0897
HAC 7th character B see Appendix B for HAC conditional logic

CC +7th **S42.135 Nondisplaced fracture of coracoid process, left shoulder**
CC Exclusion 7th character B see Appendix A PDX collection 1244
CC Exclusion 7th characters K & P see Appendix A PDX collection 0897
HAC 7th character B see Appendix B for HAC conditional logic

CC +7th **S42.136 Nondisplaced fracture of coracoid process, unspecified shoulder**
CC Exclusion 7th character B see Appendix A PDX collection 1244
CC Exclusion 7th characters K & P see Appendix A PDX collection 0897
HAC 7th character B see Appendix B for HAC conditional logic

+ **S42.14 Fracture of glenoid cavity of scapula**

CC +7th **S42.141 Displaced fracture of glenoid cavity of scapula, right shoulder**
CC Exclusion 7th character B see Appendix A PDX collection 1244
CC Exclusion 7th characters K & P see Appendix A PDX collection 0897
HAC 7th character B see Appendix B for HAC conditional logic

CC +7th **S42.142 Displaced fracture of glenoid cavity of scapula, left shoulder**
CC Exclusion 7th character B see Appendix A PDX collection 1244
CC Exclusion 7th characters K & P see Appendix A PDX collection 0897
HAC 7th character B see Appendix B for HAC conditional logic

CC +7th **S42.143 Displaced fracture of glenoid cavity of scapula, unspecified shoulder**
CC Exclusion 7th character B see Appendix A PDX collection 1244
CC Exclusion 7th characters K & P see Appendix A PDX collection 0897
HAC 7th character B see Appendix B for HAC conditional logic

CC +7th **S42.144 Nondisplaced fracture of glenoid cavity of scapula, right shoulder**
CC Exclusion 7th character B see Appendix A PDX collection 1244
CC Exclusion 7th characters K & P see Appendix A PDX collection 0897
HAC 7th character B see Appendix B for HAC conditional logic

CC +7th **S42.145 Nondisplaced fracture of glenoid cavity of scapula, left shoulder**
CC Exclusion 7th character B see Appendix A PDX collection 1244
CC Exclusion 7th characters K & P see Appendix A PDX collection 0897
HAC 7th character B see Appendix B for HAC conditional logic

CC +7th **S42.146 Nondisplaced fracture of glenoid cavity of scapula, unspecified shoulder**
CC Exclusion 7th character B see Appendix A PDX collection 1244
CC Exclusion 7th characters K & P see Appendix A PDX collection 0897
HAC 7th character B see Appendix B for HAC conditional logic

\+ **S42.15 Fracture of neck of scapula**

CC +7th **S42.151 Displaced fracture of neck of scapula, right shoulder**
CC Exclusion 7th character B see Appendix A PDX collection 1244
CC Exclusion 7th characters K & P see Appendix A PDX collection 0897
HAC 7th character B see Appendix B for HAC conditional logic

CC +7th **S42.152 Displaced fracture of neck of scapula, left shoulder**
CC Exclusion 7th character B see Appendix A PDX collection 1244
CC Exclusion 7th characters K & P see Appendix A PDX collection 0897
HAC 7th character B see Appendix B for HAC conditional logic

CC +7th **S42.153 Displaced fracture of neck of scapula, unspecified shoulder**
CC Exclusion 7th character B see Appendix A PDX collection 1244
CC Exclusion 7th characters K & P see Appendix A PDX collection 0897
HAC 7th character B see Appendix B for HAC conditional logic

CC +7th **S42.154 Nondisplaced fracture of neck of scapula, right shoulder**
CC Exclusion 7th character B see Appendix A PDX collection 1244
CC Exclusion 7th characters K & P see Appendix A PDX collection 0897
HAC 7th character B see Appendix B for HAC conditional logic

CC +7th **S42.155 Nondisplaced fracture of neck of scapula, left shoulder**
CC Exclusion 7th character B see Appendix A PDX collection 1244
CC Exclusion 7th characters K & P see Appendix A PDX collection 0897
HAC 7th character B see Appendix B for HAC conditional logic

CC +7th **S42.156 Nondisplaced fracture of neck of scapula, unspecified shoulder**
CC Exclusion 7th character B see Appendix A PDX collection 1244
CC Exclusion 7th characters K & P see Appendix A PDX collection 0897
HAC 7th character B see Appendix B for HAC conditional logic

\+ **S42.19 Fracture of other part of scapula**

CC +7th **S42.191 Fracture of other part of scapula, right shoulder**
CC Exclusion 7th character B see Appendix A PDX collection 1244
CC Exclusion 7th characters K & P see Appendix A PDX collection 0897
HAC 7th character B see Appendix B for HAC conditional logic

CC +7th **S42.192 Fracture of other part of scapula, left shoulder**
CC Exclusion 7th character B see Appendix A PDX collection 1244
CC Exclusion 7th characters K & P see Appendix A PDX collection 0897
HAC 7th character B see Appendix B for HAC conditional logic

CC +7th **S42.199 Fracture of other part of scapula, unspecified shoulder**
CC Exclusion 7th character B see Appendix A PDX collection 1244
CC Exclusion 7th characters K & P see Appendix A PDX collection 0897
HAC 7th character B see Appendix B for HAC conditional logic

\+ **S42.2 Fracture of upper end of humerus**
Fracture of proximal end of humerus
Excludes2: *fracture of shaft of humerus (S42.3-)*
physeal fracture of upper end of humerus (S49.0-)

\+ **S42.20 Unspecified fracture of upper end of humerus**

CC MCC +7th **S42.201 Unspecified fracture of upper end of right humerus**
CC Exclusion 7th character A see Appendix A PDX collection 1245
CC Exclusion 7th characters K & P see Appendix A PDX collection 0897
MCC Exclusion 7th character B see Appendix A PDX collection 1246
HAC 7th characters A & B see Appendix B for HAC conditional logic

CC MCC +7th **S42.202 Unspecified fracture of upper end of left humerus**
CC Exclusion 7th character A see Appendix A PDX collection 1247
CC Exclusion 7th characters K & P see Appendix A PDX collection 0897
MCC Exclusion 7th character B see Appendix A PDX collection 1246
HAC 7th characters A & B see Appendix B for HAC conditional logic

CC MCC +7th **S42.209 Unspecified fracture of upper end of unspecified humerus**
CC Exclusion 7th character A see Appendix A PDX collection 1248
CC Exclusion 7th characters K & P see Appendix A PDX collection 0897
MCC Exclusion 7th character B see Appendix A PDX collection 1246
HAC 7th characters A & B see Appendix B for HAC conditional logic

\+ **S42.21 Unspecified fracture of surgical neck of humerus**
Fracture of neck of humerus NOS

CC MCC +7th **S42.211 Unspecified displaced fracture of surgical neck of right humerus**
CC Exclusion 7th character A see Appendix A PDX collection 1245
CC Exclusion 7th characters K & P see Appendix A PDX collection 0897
MCC Exclusion 7th character B see Appendix A PDX collection 1246
HAC 7th characters A & B see Appendix B for HAC conditional logic

CC MCC +7th **S42.212 Unspecified displaced fracture of surgical neck of left humerus**
CC Exclusion 7th character A see Appendix A PDX collection 1247
CC Exclusion 7th characters K & P see Appendix A PDX collection 0897
MCC Exclusion 7th character B see Appendix A PDX collection 1246

CC MCC +7th **S42.213 Unspecified displaced fracture of surgical neck of unspecified humerus**
CC Exclusion 7th character A see Appendix A PDX collection 1248
CC Exclusion 7th characters K & P see Appendix A PDX collection 0897
MCC Exclusion 7th character B see Appendix A PDX collection 1246
HAC 7th characters A & B see Appendix B for HAC conditional logic

CC MCC +7th **S42.214 Unspecified nondisplaced fracture of surgical neck of right humerus**
CC Exclusion 7th character A see Appendix A PDX collection 1245
CC Exclusion 7th characters K & P see Appendix A PDX collection 0897
MCC Exclusion 7th character B see Appendix A PDX collection 1246
HAC 7th characters A & B see Appendix B for HAC conditional logic

CC MCC +7th **S42.215 Unspecified nondisplaced fracture of surgical neck of left humerus**
CC Exclusion 7th character A see Appendix A PDX collection 1247
CC Exclusion 7th characters K & P see Appendix A PDX collection 0897
MCC Exclusion 7th character B see Appendix A PDX collection 1246
HAC 7th characters A & B see Appendix B for HAC conditional logic

CC MCC +7th **S42.216 Unspecified nondisplaced fracture of surgical neck of unspecified humerus**
CC Exclusion 7th character A see Appendix A PDX collection 1248
CC Exclusion 7th characters K & P see Appendix A PDX collection 0897
MCC Exclusion 7th character B see Appendix A PDX collection 1246
HAC 7th characters A & B see Appendix B for HAC conditional logic

+ **S42.22 2-part fracture of surgical neck of humerus**

CC MCC +7th **S42.221 2-part displaced fracture of surgical neck of right humerus**
CC Exclusion 7th character A see Appendix A PDX collection 1245
CC Exclusion 7th characters K & P see Appendix A PDX collection 0897
MCC Exclusion 7th character B see Appendix A PDX collection 1246
HAC 7th characters A & B see Appendix B for HAC conditional logic

CC MCC +7th **S42.222 2-part displaced fracture of surgical neck of left humerus**
CC Exclusion 7th character A see Appendix A PDX collection 1247
CC Exclusion 7th characters K & P see Appendix A PDX collection 0897
MCC Exclusion 7th character B see Appendix A PDX collection 1246
HAC 7th characters A & B see Appendix B for HAC conditional logic

CC MCC +7th **S42.223 2-part displaced fracture of surgical neck of unspecified humerus**
CC Exclusion 7th character A see Appendix A PDX collection 1248
CC Exclusion 7th characters K & P see Appendix A PDX collection 0897
MCC Exclusion 7th character B see Appendix A PDX collection 1246
HAC 7th characters A & B see Appendix B for HAC conditional logic

CC MCC +7th **S42.224 2-part nondisplaced fracture of surgical neck of right humerus**
CC Exclusion 7th character A see Appendix A PDX collection 1245
CC Exclusion 7th characters K & P see Appendix A PDX collection 0897
MCC Exclusion 7th character B see Appendix A PDX collection 1246
HAC 7th characters A & B see Appendix B for HAC conditional logic

CC MCC +7th **S42.225 2-part nondisplaced fracture of surgical neck of left humerus**
CC Exclusion 7th character A see Appendix A PDX collection 1247
CC Exclusion 7th characters K & P see Appendix A PDX collection 0897
MCC Exclusion 7th character B see Appendix A PDX collection 1246
HAC 7th characters A & B see Appendix B for HAC conditional logic

CC MCC +7th **S42.226 2-part nondisplaced fracture of surgical neck of unspecified humerus**
CC Exclusion 7th character A see Appendix A PDX collection 1248
CC Exclusion 7th characters K & P see Appendix A PDX collection 0897
MCC Exclusion 7th character B see Appendix A PDX collection 1246
HAC 7th characters A & B see Appendix B for HAC conditional logic

+ **S42.23 3-part fracture of surgical neck of humerus**

CC MCC +7th **S42.231 3-part fracture of surgical neck of right humerus**
CC Exclusion 7th character A see Appendix A PDX collection 1245
CC Exclusion 7th characters K & P see Appendix A PDX collection 0897
MCC Exclusion 7th character B see Appendix A PDX collection 1246
HAC 7th characters A & B see Appendix B for HAC conditional logic

CC MCC +7th **S42.232 3-part fracture of surgical neck of left humerus**
CC Exclusion 7th character A see Appendix A PDX collection 1247
CC Exclusion 7th characters K & P see Appendix A PDX collection 0897
MCC Exclusion 7th character B see Appendix A PDX collection 1246
HAC 7th characters A & B see Appendix B for HAC conditional logic

CC MCC +7th **S42.239 3-part fracture of surgical neck of unspecified humerus**
CC Exclusion 7th character A see Appendix A PDX collection 1248
CC Exclusion 7th characters K & P see Appendix A PDX collection 0897
MCC Exclusion 7th character B see Appendix A PDX collection 1246
HAC 7th characters A & B see Appendix B for HAC conditional logic

+ **S42.24 4-part fracture of surgical neck of humerus**

CC MCC +7th **S42.241 4-part fracture of surgical neck of right humerus**
CC Exclusion 7th character A see Appendix A PDX collection 1245
CC Exclusion 7th characters K & P see Appendix A PDX collection 0897
MCC Exclusion 7th character B see Appendix A PDX collection 1246
HAC 7th characters A & B see Appendix B for HAC conditional logic

CC MCC +7th **S42.242 4-part fracture of surgical neck of left humerus**
CC Exclusion 7th character A see Appendix A PDX collection 1247
CC Exclusion 7th characters K & P see Appendix A PDX collection 0897
MCC Exclusion 7th character B see Appendix A PDX collection 1246
HAC 7th characters A & B see Appendix B for HAC conditional logic

CC MCC +7th **S42.249 4-part fracture of surgical neck of unspecified humerus**
CC Exclusion 7th character A see Appendix A PDX collection 1248
CC Exclusion 7th characters K & P see Appendix A PDX collection 0897
MCC Exclusion 7th character B see Appendix A PDX collection 1246
HAC 7th characters A & B see Appendix B for HAC conditional logic

+ **S42.25 Fracture of greater tuberosity of humerus**

CC MCC +7th **S42.251 Displaced fracture of greater tuberosity of right humerus**
CC Exclusion 7th character A see Appendix A PDX collection 1245
CC Exclusion 7th characters K & P see Appendix A PDX collection 0897
MCC Exclusion 7th character B see Appendix A PDX collection 1246
HAC 7th characters A & B see Appendix B for HAC conditional logic

CC MCC +7th **S42.252 Displaced fracture of greater tuberosity of left humerus**
CC Exclusion 7th character A see Appendix A PDX collection 1247
CC Exclusion 7th characters K & P see Appendix A PDX collection 0897
MCC Exclusion 7th character B see Appendix A PDX collection 1246
HAC 7th characters A & B see Appendix B for HAC conditional logic

CC MCC +7th **S42.253 Displaced fracture of greater tuberosity of unspecified humerus**
CC Exclusion 7th character A see Appendix A PDX collection 1248
CC Exclusion 7th characters K & P see Appendix A PDX collection 0897
MCC Exclusion 7th character B see Appendix A PDX collection 1246
HAC 7th characters A & B see Appendix B for HAC conditional logic

CC MCC +7th **S42.254 Nondisplaced fracture of greater tuberosity of right humerus**
CC Exclusion 7th character A see Appendix A PDX collection 1245
CC Exclusion 7th characters K & P see Appendix A PDX collection 0897
MCC Exclusion 7th character B see Appendix A PDX collection 1246
HAC 7th characters A & B see Appendix B for HAC conditional logic

CC MCC +7th **S42.255 Nondisplaced fracture of greater tuberosity of left humerus**
CC Exclusion 7th character A see Appendix A PDX collection 1247
CC Exclusion 7th characters K & P see Appendix A PDX collection 0897
MCC Exclusion 7th character B see Appendix A PDX collection 1246
HAC 7th characters A & B see Appendix B for HAC conditional logic

CC MCC +7th **S42.256 Nondisplaced fracture of greater tuberosity of unspecified humerus**
CC Exclusion 7th character A see Appendix A PDX collection 1248
CC Exclusion 7th characters K & P see Appendix A PDX collection 0897
MCC Exclusion 7th character B see Appendix A PDX collection 1246
HAC 7th characters A & B see Appendix B for HAC conditional logic

+ S42.26 Fracture of lesser tuberosity of humerus

CC MCC +7th **S42.261 Displaced fracture of lesser tuberosity of right humerus**
CC Exclusion 7th character A see Appendix A PDX collection 1245
CC Exclusion 7th characters K & P see Appendix A PDX collection 0897
MCC Exclusion 7th character B see Appendix A PDX collection 1246
HAC 7th characters A & B see Appendix B for HAC conditional logic

CC MCC +7th **S42.262 Displaced fracture of lesser tuberosity of left humerus**
CC Exclusion 7th character A see Appendix A PDX collection 1247
CC Exclusion 7th characters K & P see Appendix A PDX collection 0897
MCC Exclusion 7th character B see Appendix A PDX collection 1246
HAC 7th characters A & B see Appendix B for HAC conditional logic

CC MCC +7th **S42.263 Displaced fracture of lesser tuberosity of unspecified humerus**
CC Exclusion 7th character A see Appendix A PDX collection 1248
CC Exclusion 7th characters K & P see Appendix A PDX collection 0897
MCC Exclusion 7th character B see Appendix A PDX collection 1246
HAC 7th characters A & B see Appendix B for HAC conditional logic

CC MCC +7th **S42.264 Nondisplaced fracture of lesser tuberosity of right humerus**
CC Exclusion 7th character A see Appendix A PDX collection 1245
CC Exclusion 7th characters K & P see Appendix A PDX collection 0897
MCC Exclusion 7th character B see Appendix A PDX collection 1246
HAC 7th characters A & B see Appendix B for HAC conditional logic

CC MCC +7th **S42.265 Nondisplaced fracture of lesser tuberosity left humerus**
CC Exclusion 7th character A see Appendix A PDX collection 1247
CC Exclusion 7th characters K & P see Appendix A PDX collection 0897
MCC Exclusion 7th character B see Appendix PDX collection 1246
HAC 7th characters A & B see Appendix B for HAC conditional logic

CC MCC +7th **S42.266 Nondisplaced fracture of lesser tuberosity unspecified humerus**
CC Exclusion 7th character A see Appendix A PDX collection 1248
CC Exclusion 7th characters K & P see Appendix A PDX collection 0897
MCC Exclusion 7th character B see Appendix PDX collection 1246
HAC 7th characters A & B see Appendix B for HAC conditional logic

+ S42.27 Torus fracture of upper end of humerus

The appropriate 7th character is to be added to all codes in subcategory S42.27
- A initial encounter for closed fracture
- D subsequent encounter for fracture with routine healing
- G subsequent encounter for fracture with delayed healing
- K subsequent encounter for fracture with nonunion
- P subsequent encounter for fracture with malunion
- S sequela

CC +7th **S42.271 Torus fracture of upper end of right humerus**
CC Exclusion 7th character A see Appendix A PDX collection 1245
CC Exclusion 7th characters K & P see Appendix A PDX collection 0897
HAC 7th character A see Appendix B for HAC conditional logic

CC +7th **S42.272 Torus fracture of upper end of left humerus**
CC Exclusion 7th character A see Appendix A PDX collection 1247
CC Exclusion 7th characters K & P see Appendix A PDX collection 0897
HAC 7th character A see Appendix B for HAC conditional logic

CC +7th **S42.279 Torus fracture of upper end of unspecified humerus**
CC Exclusion 7th character A see Appendix A PDX collection 1248
CC Exclusion 7th characters K & P see Appendix A PDX collection 0897
HAC 7th character A see Appendix B for HAC conditional logic

+ S42.29 Other fracture of upper end of humerus
Fracture of anatomical neck of humerus
Fracture of articular head of humerus

CC MCC +7th **S42.291 Other displaced fracture of upper end of right humerus**
CC Exclusion 7th character A see Appendix A PDX collection 1245
CC Exclusion 7th characters K & P see Appendix A PDX collection 0897
MCC Exclusion 7th character B see Appendix A PDX collection 1246
HAC 7th characters A & B see Appendix B for HAC conditional logic

CC MCC +7th **S42.292 Other displaced fracture of upper end of le humerus**
CC Exclusion 7th character A see Appendix A PDX collection 1247
CC Exclusion 7th characters K & P see Appendix A PDX collection 0897
MCC Exclusion 7th character B see Appendix A PDX collection 1246
HAC 7th characters A & B see Appendix B for HAC conditional logic

CC MCC +7th **S42.293 Other displaced fracture of upper end of unspecified humerus**
CC Exclusion 7th character A see Appendix A PDX collection 1248
CC Exclusion 7th characters K & P see Appendix A PDX collection 0897
MCC Exclusion 7th character B see Appendix A PDX collection 1246
HAC 7th characters A & B see Appendix B for HAC conditional logic

CC MCC +7th **S42.294 Other nondisplaced fracture of upper end of right humerus**
CC Exclusion 7th character A see Appendix A PDX collection 1245
CC Exclusion 7th characters K & P see Appendix A PDX collection 0897
MCC Exclusion 7th character B see Appendix A PDX collection 1246
HAC 7th characters A & B see Appendix B for HAC conditional logic

CC MCC +7th **S42.295 Other nondisplaced fracture of upper end of left humerus**
CC Exclusion 7th character A see Appendix A PDX collection 1247
CC Exclusion 7th characters K & P see Appendix A PDX collection 0897
MCC Exclusion 7th character B see Appendix A PDX collection 1246
HAC 7th characters A & B see Appendix B for HAC conditional logic

CC MCC +7th **S42.296 Other nondisplaced fracture of upper end of unspecified humerus**
CC Exclusion 7th character A see Appendix A PDX collection 1248
CC Exclusion 7th characters K & P see Appendix A PDX collection 0897
MCC Exclusion 7th character B see Appendix A PDX collection 1246
HAC 7th characters A & B see Appendix B for HAC conditional logic

\+ **S42.3 Fracture of shaft of humerus**
Fracture of humerus NOS
Fracture of upper arm NOS
Excludes2: *physeal fractures of upper end of humerus (S49.0-)*
physeal fractures of lower end of humerus (S49.1-)

\+ **S42.30 Unspecified fracture of shaft of humerus**

CC MCC +7th **S42.301 Unspecified fracture of shaft of humerus, right arm**
CC Exclusion 7th character A see Appendix A PDX collection 1245
CC Exclusion 7th characters K & P see Appendix A PDX collection 0897
MCC Exclusion 7th character B see Appendix A PDX collection 1246
HAC 7th characters A & B see Appendix B for HAC conditional logic

CC MCC +7th **S42.302 Unspecified fracture of shaft of humerus, left arm**
CC Exclusion 7th character A see Appendix A PDX collection 1247
CC Exclusion 7th characters K & P see Appendix A PDX collection 0897
MCC Exclusion 7th character B see Appendix A PDX collection 1246
HAC 7th characters A & B see Appendix B for HAC conditional logic

CC MCC +7th **S42.309 Unspecified fracture of shaft of humerus, unspecified arm**
CC Exclusion 7th character A see Appendix A PDX collection 1248
CC Exclusion 7th characters K & P see Appendix A PDX collection 0897
MCC Exclusion 7th character B see Appendix A PDX collection 1246
HAC 7th characters A & B see Appendix B for HAC conditional logic

\+ **S42.31 Greenstick fracture of shaft of humerus**
The appropriate 7th character is to be added to all codes in subcategory S42.31
A initial encounter for closed fracture
D subsequent encounter for fracture with routine healing
G subsequent encounter for fracture with delayed healing
K subsequent encounter for fracture with nonunion
P subsequent encounter for fracture with malunion
S sequela

CC +7th **S42.311 Greenstick fracture of shaft of humerus, right arm**
CC Exclusion 7th character A see AppendixA PDX collection 1249
CC Exclusion 7th characters K & P see Appendix A PDX collection 0897
HAC 7th character A see Appendix B for HAC conditional logic

CC +7th **S42.312 Greenstick fracture of shaft of humerus, left arm**
CC Exclusion 7th character A see Appendix A PDX collection 1250
CC Exclusion 7th characters K & P see Appendix A PDX collection 0897
HAC 7th character A see Appendix B for HAC conditional logic

CC +7th **S42.319 Greenstick fracture of shaft of humerus, unspecified arm**
CC Exclusion 7th character A see Appendix A PDX collection 1251
CC Exclusion 7th characters K & P see Appendix A PDX collection 0897
HAC 7th character A see Appendix B for HAC conditional logic

\+ **S42.32 Transverse fracture of shaft of humerus**

CC MCC +7th **S42.321 Displaced transverse fracture of shaft of humerus, right arm**
CC Exclusion 7th character A see Appendix A PDX collection 1249
CC Exclusion 7th characters K & P see Appendix A PDX collection 0897
MCC Exclusion 7th character B see Appendix A PDX collection 1246
HAC 7th characters A & B see Appendix B for HAC conditional logic

CC MCC +7th **S42.322 Displaced transverse fracture of shaft of humerus, left arm**
CC Exclusion 7th character A see Appendix A PDX collection 1250
CC Exclusion 7th characters K & P see Appendix A PDX collection 0897
MCC Exclusion 7th character B see Appendix A PDX collection 1246
HAC 7th characters A & B see Appendix B for HAC conditional logic

CC MCC +7th **S42.323 Displaced transverse fracture of shaft of humerus, unspecified arm**
CC Exclusion 7th character A see Appendix A PDX collection 1251
CC Exclusion 7th characters K & P see Appendix A PDX collection 0897
MCC Exclusion 7th character B see Appendix A PDX collection 1246
HAC 7th characters A & B see Appendix B for HAC conditional logic

CC MCC +7th **S42.324 Nondisplaced transverse fracture of shaft of humerus, right arm**
CC Exclusion 7th character A see Appendix A PDX collection 1249
CC Exclusion 7th characters K & P see Appendix A PDX collection 0897
MCC Exclusion 7th character B see Appendix A PDX collection 1246
HAC 7th characters A & B see Appendix B for HAC conditional logic

CC MCC +7th **S42.325 Nondisplaced transverse fracture of shaft of humerus, left arm**
CC Exclusion 7th character A see Appendix A PDX collection 1250
CC Exclusion 7th characters K & P see Appendix A PDX collection 0897
MCC Exclusion 7th character B see Appendix A PDX collection 1246
HAC 7th characters A & B see Appendix B for HAC conditional logic

CC MCC +7th **S42.326 Nondisplaced transverse fracture of shaft of humerus, unspecified arm**
CC Exclusion 7th character A see Appendix A PDX collection 1251
CC Exclusion 7th characters K & P see Appendix A PDX collection 0897
MCC Exclusion 7th character B see Appendix A PDX collection 1246
HAC 7th characters A & B see Appendix B for HAC conditional logic

+ S42.33 Oblique fracture of shaft of humerus

CC MCC +7th **S42.331 Displaced oblique fracture of shaft of humerus, right arm**
- CC Exclusion 7th character A see Appendix A PDX collection 1249
- CC Exclusion 7th characters K & P see Appendix A PDX collection 0897
- MCC Exclusion 7th character B see Appendix A PDX collection 1246
- HAC 7th characters A & B see Appendix B for HAC conditional logic

CC MCC +7th **S42.332 Displaced oblique fracture of shaft of humerus, left arm**
- CC Exclusion 7th character A see Appendix A PDX collection 1250
- CC Exclusion 7th characters K & P see Appendix A PDX collection 0897
- MCC Exclusion 7th character B see Appendix A PDX collection 1246
- HAC 7th characters A & B see Appendix B for HAC conditional logic

CC MCC +7th **S42.333 Displaced oblique fracture of shaft of humerus, unspecified arm**
- CC Exclusion 7th character A see Appendix A PDX collection 1251
- CC Exclusion 7th characters K & P see Appendix A PDX collection 0897
- MCC Exclusion 7th character B see Appendix A PDX collection 1246
- HAC 7th characters A & B see Appendix B for HAC conditional logic

CC MCC +7th **S42.334 Nondisplaced oblique fracture of shaft of humerus, right arm**
- CC Exclusion 7th character A see Appendix A PDX collection 1249
- CC Exclusion 7th characters K & P see Appendix A PDX collection 0897
- MCC Exclusion 7th character B see Appendix A PDX collection 1246
- HAC 7th characters A & B see Appendix B for HAC conditional logic

CC MCC +7th **S42.335 Nondisplaced oblique fracture of shaft of humerus, left arm**
- CC Exclusion 7th character A see Appendix A PDX collection 1250
- CC Exclusion 7th characters K & P see Appendix A PDX collection 0897
- MCC Exclusion 7th character B see Appendix A PDX collection 1246
- HAC 7th characters A & B see Appendix B for HAC conditional logic

CC MCC +7th **S42.336 Nondisplaced oblique fracture of shaft of humerus, unspecified arm**
- CC Exclusion 7th character A see Appendix A PDX collection 1251
- CC Exclusion 7th characters K & P see Appendix A PDX collection 0897
- MCC Exclusion 7th character B see Appendix A PDX collection 1246
- HAC 7th characters A & B see Appendix B for HAC conditional logic

+ S42.34 Spiral fracture of shaft of humerus

CC MCC +7th **S42.341 Displaced spiral fracture of shaft of humerus, right arm**
- CC Exclusion 7th character A see Appendix A PDX collection 1249
- CC Exclusion 7th characters K & P see Appendix A PDX collection 0897
- MCC Exclusion 7th character B see Appendix A PDX collection 1246
- HAC 7th characters A & B see Appendix B for HAC conditional logic

CC MCC +7th **S42.342 Displaced spiral fracture of shaft of humerus, left arm**
- CC Exclusion 7th character A see Appendix A PDX collection 1250
- CC Exclusion 7th characters K & P see Appendix A PDX collection 0897
- MCC Exclusion 7th character B see Appendix A PDX collection 1246
- HAC 7th characters A & B see Appendix B for HAC conditional logic

CC MCC +7th **S42.343 Displaced spiral fracture of shaft of humerus, unspecified arm**
- CC Exclusion 7th character A see Appendix A PDX collection 1251
- CC Exclusion 7th characters K & P see Appendix A PDX collection 0897
- MCC Exclusion 7th character B see Appendix PDX collection 1246
- HAC 7th characters A & B see Appendix B for HAC conditional logic

CC MCC +7th **S42.344 Nondisplaced spiral fracture of shaft of humerus, right arm**
- CC Exclusion 7th character A see Appendix A PDX collection 1249
- CC Exclusion 7th characters K & P see Appendix A PDX collection 0897
- MCC Exclusion 7th character B see Appendix PDX collection 1246
- HAC 7th characters A & B see Appendix B for HAC conditional logic

CC MCC +7th **S42.345 Nondisplaced spiral fracture of shaft of humerus, left arm**
- CC Exclusion 7th character A see Appendix A PDX collection 1250
- CC Exclusion 7th characters K & P see Appendix A PDX collection 0897
- MCC Exclusion 7th character B see Appendix PDX collection 1246
- HAC 7th characters A & B see Appendix B for HAC conditional logic

CC MCC +7th **S42.346 Nondisplaced spiral fracture of shaft of humerus, unspecified arm**
- CC Exclusion 7th character A see Appendix A PDX collection 1251
- CC Exclusion 7th characters K & P see Appendix A PDX collection 0897
- MCC Exclusion 7th character B see Appendix PDX collection 1246
- HAC 7th characters A & B see Appendix B for HAC conditional logic

+ S42.35 Comminuted fracture of shaft of humerus

CC MCC +7th **S42.351 Displaced comminuted fracture of shaft of humerus, right arm**
- CC Exclusion 7th character A see Appendix A PDX collection 1249
- CC Exclusion 7th characters K & P see Appendix A PDX collection 0897
- MCC Exclusion 7th character B see Appendix PDX collection 1246
- HAC 7th characters A & B see Appendix B for HAC conditional logic

CC MCC +7th **S42.352 Displaced comminuted fracture of shaft of humerus, left arm**
- CC Exclusion 7th character A see Appendix A PDX collection 1250
- CC Exclusion 7th characters K & P see Appendix A PDX collection 0897
- MCC Exclusion 7th character B see Appendix PDX collection 1246
- HAC 7th characters A & B see Appendix B for HAC conditional logic

CC MCC +7th **S42.353 Displaced comminuted fracture of shaft of humerus, unspecified arm**
- CC Exclusion 7th character A see Appendix A PDX collection 1251
- CC Exclusion 7th characters K & P see Appendix A PDX collection 0897
- MCC Exclusion 7th character B see Appendix PDX collection 1246
- HAC 7th characters A & B see Appendix B for HAC conditional logic

CC MCC +7th **S42.354 Nondisplaced comminuted fracture of shaft of humerus, right arm**
- CC Exclusion 7th character A see Appendix A PDX collection 1249
- CC Exclusion 7th characters K & P see Appendix A PDX collection 0897
- MCC Exclusion 7th character B see Appendix PDX collection 1246
- HAC 7th characters A & B see Appendix B for HAC conditional logic

CC MCC +7th **S42.355 Nondisplaced comminuted fracture of shaft of humerus, left arm**
- CC Exclusion 7th character A see Appendix A PDX collection 1250
- CC Exclusion 7th characters K & P see Appendix A PDX collection 0897
- MCC Exclusion 7th character B see Appendix PDX collection 1246
- HAC 7th characters A & B see Appendix B for HAC conditional logic

CC MCC +7th **S42.356 Nondisplaced comminuted fracture of shaft of humerus, unspecified arm**
CC Exclusion 7th character A see Appendix A PDX collection 1251
CC Exclusion 7th characters K & P see Appendix A PDX collection 0897
MCC Exclusion 7th character B see Appendix A PDX collection 1246
HAC 7th characters A & B see Appendix B for HAC conditional logic

+ **S42.36 Segmental fracture of shaft of humerus**

CC MCC +7th **S42.361 Displaced segmental fracture of shaft of humerus, right arm**
CC Exclusion 7th character A see Appendix A PDX collection 1249
CC Exclusion 7th characters K & P see Appendix A PDX collection 0897
MCC Exclusion 7th character B see Appendix A PDX collection 1246
HAC 7th characters A & B see Appendix B for HAC conditional logic

CC MCC +7th **S42.362 Displaced segmental fracture of shaft of humerus, left arm**
CC Exclusion 7th character A see Appendix A PDX collection 1250
CC Exclusion 7th characters K & P see Appendix A PDX collection 0897
MCC Exclusion 7th character B see Appendix A PDX collection 1246
HAC 7th characters A & B see Appendix B for HAC conditional logic

CC MCC +7th **S42.363 Displaced segmental fracture of shaft of humerus, unspecified arm**
CC Exclusion 7th character A see Appendix A PDX collection 1251
CC Exclusion 7th characters K & P see Appendix A PDX collection 0897
MCC Exclusion 7th character B see Appendix A PDX collection 1246
HAC 7th characters A & B see Appendix B for HAC conditional logic

CC MCC +7th **S42.364 Nondisplaced segmental fracture of shaft of humerus, right arm**
CC Exclusion 7th character A see Appendix A PDX collection 1249
CC Exclusion 7th characters K & P see Appendix A PDX collection 0897
MCC Exclusion 7th character B see Appendix A PDX collection 1246
HAC 7th characters A & B see Appendix B for HAC conditional logic

CC MCC +7th **S42.365 Nondisplaced segmental fracture of shaft of humerus, left arm**
CC Exclusion 7th character A see Appendix A PDX collection 1250
CC Exclusion 7th characters K & P see Appendix A PDX collection 0897
MCC Exclusion 7th character B see Appendix A PDX collection 1246
HAC 7th characters A & B see Appendix B for HAC conditional logic

CC MCC +7th **S42.366 Nondisplaced segmental fracture of shaft of humerus, unspecified arm**
CC Exclusion 7th character A see Appendix A PDX collection 1251
CC Exclusion 7th characters K & P see Appendix A PDX collection 0897
MCC Exclusion 7th character B see Appendix A PDX collection 1246
HAC 7th characters A & B see Appendix B for HAC conditional logic

+ **S42.39 Other fracture of shaft of humerus**

CC MCC +7th **S42.391 Other fracture of shaft of right humerus**
CC Exclusion 7th character A see Appendix A PDX collection 1249
CC Exclusion 7th characters K & P see Appendix A PDX collection 0897
MCC Exclusion 7th character B see Appendix A PDX collection 1246
HAC 7th characters A & B see Appendix B for HAC conditional logic

CC MCC +7th **S42.392 Other fracture of shaft of left humerus**
CC Exclusion 7th character A see Appendix A PDX collection 1250
CC Exclusion 7th characters K & P see Appendix A PDX collection 0897
MCC Exclusion 7th character B see Appendix A PDX collection 1246
HAC 7th characters A & B see Appendix B for HAC conditional logic

CC MCC +7th **S42.399 Other fracture of shaft of unspecified humerus**
CC Exclusion 7th character A see Appendix A PDX collection 1251
CC Exclusion 7th characters K & P see Appendix A PDX collection 0897
MCC Exclusion 7th character B see Appendix A PDX collection 1246
HAC 7th characters A & B see Appendix B for HAC conditional logic

+ **S42.4 Fracture of lower end of humerus**
Fracture of distal end of humerus
Excludes2: *fracture of shaft of humerus (S42.3-)*
physeal fracture of lower end of humerus (S49.1-)

+ **S42.40 Unspecified fracture of lower end of humerus**
Fracture of elbow NOS

CC MCC +7th **S42.401 Unspecified fracture of lower end of right humerus**
CC Exclusion 7th character A see Appendix A PDX collection 1245
CC Exclusion 7th characters K & P see Appendix A PDX collection 0897
MCC Exclusion 7th character B see Appendix A PDX collection 1246
HAC 7th characters A & B see Appendix B for HAC conditional logic

CC MCC +7th **S42.402 Unspecified fracture of lower end of left humerus**
CC Exclusion 7th character A see Appendix A PDX collection 1247
CC Exclusion 7th characters K & P see Appendix A PDX collection 0897
MCC Exclusion 7th character B see Appendix A PDX collection 1246
HAC 7th characters A & B see Appendix B for HAC conditional logic

CC MCC +7th **S42.409 Unspecified fracture of lower end of unspecified humerus**
CC Exclusion 7th character A see Appendix A PDX collection 1248
CC Exclusion 7th characters K & P see Appendix A PDX collection 0897
MCC Exclusion 7th character B see Appendix A PDX collection 1246
HAC 7th characters A & B see Appendix B for HAC conditional logic

+ **S42.41 Simple supracondylar fracture without intercondylar fracture of humerus**

CC MCC +7th **S42.411 Displaced simple supracondylar fracture without intercondylar fracture of right humerus**
CC Exclusion 7th character A see Appendix A PDX collection 1245
CC Exclusion 7th characters K & P see Appendix A PDX collection 0897
MCC Exclusion 7th character B see Appendix A PDX collection 1246
HAC 7th characters A & B see Appendix B for HAC conditional logic

CC MCC +7th **S42.412 Displaced simple supracondylar fracture without intercondylar fracture of left humerus**
CC Exclusion 7th character A see Appendix A PDX collection 1247
CC Exclusion 7th characters K & P see Appendix A PDX collection 0897
MCC Exclusion 7th character B see Appendix A PDX collection 1246
HAC 7th characters A & B see Appendix B for HAC conditional logic

CC MCC +7th **S42.413 Displaced simple supracondylar fracture without intercondylar fracture of unspecified humerus**
CC Exclusion 7th character A see Appendix A PDX collection 1248
CC Exclusion 7th characters K & P see Appendix A PDX collection 0897
MCC Exclusion 7th character B see Appendix A PDX collection 1246
HAC 7th characters A & B see Appendix B for HAC conditional logic

CC MCC +7th **S42.414 Nondisplaced simple supracondylar fracture without intercondylar fracture of right humerus**
- CC Exclusion 7th character A see Appendix A PDX collection 1245
- CC Exclusion 7th characters K & P see Appendix A PDX collection 0897
- MCC Exclusion 7th character B see Appendix A PDX collection 1246
- HAC 7th characters A & B see Appendix B for HAC conditional logic

CC MCC +7th **S42.415 Nondisplaced simple supracondylar fracture without intercondylar fracture of left humerus**
- CC Exclusion 7th character A see Appendix A PDX collection 1247
- CC Exclusion 7th characters K & P see Appendix A PDX collection 0897
- MCC Exclusion 7th character B see Appendix A PDX collection 1246
- HAC 7th characters A & B see Appendix B for HAC conditional logic

CC MCC +7th **S42.416 Nondisplaced simple supracondylar fracture without intercondylar fracture of unspecified humerus**
- CC Exclusion 7th character A see Appendix A PDX collection 1248
- CC Exclusion 7th characters K & P see Appendix A PDX collection 0897
- MCC Exclusion 7th character B see Appendix A PDX collection 1246
- HAC 7th characters A & B see Appendix B for HAC conditional logic

+ **S42.42 Comminuted supracondylar fracture without intercondylar fracture of humerus**

CC MCC +7th **S42.421 Displaced comminuted supracondylar fracture without intercondylar fracture of right humerus**
- CC Exclusion 7th character A see Appendix A PDX collection 1245
- CC Exclusion 7th characters K & P see Appendix A PDX collection 0897
- MCC Exclusion 7th character B see Appendix A PDX collection 1246
- HAC 7th characters A & B see Appendix B for HAC conditional logic

CC MCC +7th **S42.422 Displaced comminuted supracondylar fracture without intercondylar fracture of left humerus**
- CC Exclusion 7th character A see Appendix A PDX collection 1247
- CC Exclusion 7th characters K & P see Appendix A PDX collection 0897
- MCC Exclusion 7th character B see Appendix A PDX collection 1246
- HAC 7th characters A & B see Appendix B for HAC conditional logic

CC MCC +7th **S42.423 Displaced comminuted supracondylar fracture without intercondylar fracture of unspecified humerus**
- CC Exclusion 7th character A see Appendix A PDX collection 1248
- CC Exclusion 7th characters K & P see Appendix A PDX collection 0897
- MCC Exclusion 7th character B see Appendix A PDX collection 1246
- HAC 7th characters A & B see Appendix B for HAC conditional logic

CC MCC +7th **S42.424 Nondisplaced comminuted supracondylar fracture without intercondylar fracture of right humerus**
- CC Exclusion 7th character A see Appendix A PDX collection 1245
- CC Exclusion 7th characters K & P see Appendix A PDX collection 0897
- MCC Exclusion 7th character B see Appendix A PDX collection 1246
- HAC 7th characters A & B see Appendix B for HAC conditional logic

CC MCC +7th **S42.425 Nondisplaced comminuted supracondylar fracture without intercondylar fracture of left humerus**
- CC Exclusion 7th character A see Appendix A PDX collection 1247
- CC Exclusion 7th characters K & P see Appendix A PDX collection 0897
- MCC Exclusion 7th character B see Appendix A PDX collection 1246
- HAC 7th characters A & B see Appendix B for HAC conditional logic

CC MCC +7th **S42.426 Nondisplaced comminuted supracondylar fracture without intercondylar fracture of unspecified humerus**
- CC Exclusion 7th character A see Appendix A PDX collection 1248
- CC Exclusion 7th characters K & P see Appendix A PDX collection 0897
- MCC Exclusion 7th character B see Appendix A PDX collection 1246
- HAC 7th characters A & B see Appendix B for HAC conditional logic

+ **S42.43 Fracture (avulsion) of lateral epicondyle of humerus**

CC MCC +7th **S42.431 Displaced fracture (avulsion) of lateral epicondyle of right humerus**
- CC Exclusion 7th character A see Appendix A PDX collection 1245
- CC Exclusion 7th characters K & P see Appendix A PDX collection 0897
- MCC Exclusion 7th character B see Appendix A PDX collection 1246
- HAC 7th characters A & B see Appendix B for HAC conditional logic

CC MCC +7th **S42.432 Displaced fracture (avulsion) of lateral epicondyle of left humerus**
- CC Exclusion 7th character A see Appendix A PDX collection 1247
- CC Exclusion 7th characters K & P see Appendix A PDX collection 0897
- MCC Exclusion 7th character B see Appendix A PDX collection 1246
- HAC 7th characters A & B see Appendix B for HAC conditional logic

CC MCC +7th **S42.433 Displaced fracture (avulsion) of lateral epicondyle of unspecified humerus**
- CC Exclusion 7th character A see Appendix A PDX collection 1248
- CC Exclusion 7th characters K & P see Appendix A PDX collection 0897
- MCC Exclusion 7th character B see Appendix A PDX collection 1246
- HAC 7th characters A & B see Appendix B for HAC conditional logic

CC MCC +7th **S42.434 Nondisplaced fracture (avulsion) of lateral epicondyle of right humerus**
- CC Exclusion 7th character A see Appendix A PDX collection 1245
- CC Exclusion 7th characters K & P see Appendix A PDX collection 0897
- MCC Exclusion 7th character B see Appendix A PDX collection 1246
- HAC 7th characters A & B see Appendix B for HAC conditional logic

CC MCC +7th **S42.435 Nondisplaced fracture (avulsion) of lateral epicondyle of left humerus**
- CC Exclusion 7th character A see Appendix A PDX collection 1247
- CC Exclusion 7th characters K & P see Appendix A PDX collection 0897
- MCC Exclusion 7th character B see Appendix A PDX collection 1246
- HAC 7th characters A & B see Appendix B for HAC conditional logic

CC MCC +7th **S42.436 Nondisplaced fracture (avulsion) of lateral epicondyle of unspecified humerus**
- CC Exclusion 7th character A see Appendix A PDX collection 1248
- CC Exclusion 7th characters K & P see Appendix A PDX collection 0897
- MCC Exclusion 7th character B see Appendix A PDX collection 1246
- HAC 7th characters A & B see Appendix B for HAC conditional logic

+ **S42.44 Fracture (avulsion) of medial epicondyle of humerus**

CC MCC +7th **S42.441 Displaced fracture (avulsion) of medial epicondyle of right humerus**
- CC Exclusion 7th character A see Appendix A PDX collection 1245
- CC Exclusion 7th characters K & P see Appendix A PDX collection 0897
- MCC Exclusion 7th character B see Appendix A PDX collection 1246
- HAC 7th characters A & B see Appendix B for HAC conditional logic

CC MCC +7th **S42.442 Displaced fracture (avulsion) of medial epicondyle of left humerus**
CC Exclusion 7th character A see Appendix A PDX collection 1247
CC Exclusion 7th characters K & P see Appendix A PDX collection 0897
MCC Exclusion 7th character B see Appendix A PDX collection 1246
HAC 7th characters A & B see Appendix B for HAC conditional logic

CC MCC +7th **S42.443 Displaced fracture (avulsion) of medial epicondyle of unspecified humerus**
CC Exclusion 7th character A see Appendix A PDX collection 1248
CC Exclusion 7th characters K & P see Appendix A PDX collection 0897
MCC Exclusion 7th character B see Appendix A PDX collection 1246
HAC 7th characters A & B see Appendix B for HAC conditional logic

CC MCC +7th **S42.444 Nondisplaced fracture (avulsion) of medial epicondyle of right humerus**
CC Exclusion 7th character A see Appendix A PDX collection 1245
CC Exclusion 7th characters K & P see Appendix A PDX collection 0897
MCC Exclusion 7th character B see Appendix A PDX collection 1246
HAC 7th characters A & B see Appendix B for HAC conditional logic

CC MCC +7th **S42.445 Nondisplaced fracture (avulsion) of medial epicondyle of left humerus**
CC Exclusion 7th character A see Appendix A PDX collection 1247
CC Exclusion 7th characters K & P see Appendix A PDX collection 0897
MCC Exclusion 7th character B see Appendix A PDX collection 1246
HAC 7th characters A & B see Appendix B for HAC conditional logic

CC MCC +7th **S42.446 Nondisplaced fracture (avulsion) of medial epicondyle of unspecified humerus**
CC Exclusion 7th character A see Appendix A PDX collection 1248
CC Exclusion 7th characters K & P see Appendix A PDX collection 0897
MCC Exclusion 7th character B see Appendix A PDX collection 1246
HAC 7th characters A & B see Appendix B for HAC conditional logic

CC MCC +7th **S42.447 Incarcerated fracture (avulsion) of medial epicondyle of right humerus**
CC Exclusion 7th character A see Appendix A PDX collection 1245
CC Exclusion 7th characters K & P see Appendix A PDX collection 0897
MCC Exclusion 7th character B see Appendix A PDX collection 1246
HAC 7th characters A & B see Appendix B for HAC conditional logic

CC MCC +7th **S42.448 Incarcerated fracture (avulsion) of medial epicondyle of left humerus**
CC Exclusion 7th character A see Appendix A PDX collection 1247
CC Exclusion 7th characters K & P see Appendix A PDX collection 0897
MCC Exclusion 7th character B see Appendix A PDX collection 1246
HAC 7th characters A & B see Appendix B for HAC conditional logic

CC MCC +7th **S42.449 Incarcerated fracture (avulsion) of medial epicondyle of unspecified humerus**
CC Exclusion 7th character A see Appendix A PDX collection 1248
CC Exclusion 7th characters K & P see Appendix A PDX collection 0897
MCC Exclusion 7th character B see Appendix A PDX collection 1246
HAC 7th characters A & B see Appendix B for HAC conditional logic

+ **S42.45 Fracture of lateral condyle of humerus**
Fracture of capitellum of humerus

CC MCC +7th **S42.451 Displaced fracture of lateral condyle of right humerus**
CC Exclusion 7th character A see Appendix A PDX collection 1245
CC Exclusion 7th characters K & P see Appendix A PDX collection 0897
MCC Exclusion 7th character B see Appendix A PDX collection 1246
HAC 7th characters A & B see Appendix B for HAC conditional logic

CC MCC +7th **S42.452 Displaced fracture of lateral condyle of left humerus**
CC Exclusion 7th character A see Appendix A PDX collection 1247
CC Exclusion 7th characters K & P see Appendix A PDX collection 0897
MCC Exclusion 7th character B see Appendix A PDX collection 1246
HAC 7th characters A & B see Appendix B for HAC conditional logic

CC MCC +7th **S42.453 Displaced fracture of lateral condyle of unspecified humerus**
CC Exclusion 7th character A see Appendix A PDX collection 1248
CC Exclusion 7th characters K & P see Appendix A PDX collection 0897
MCC Exclusion 7th character B see Appendix A PDX collection 1246
HAC 7th characters A & B see Appendix B for HAC conditional logic

CC MCC +7th **S42.454 Nondisplaced fracture of lateral condyle of right humerus**
CC Exclusion 7th character A see Appendix A PDX collection 1245
CC Exclusion 7th characters K & P see Appendix A PDX collection 0897
MCC Exclusion 7th character B see Appendix A PDX collection 1246
HAC 7th characters A & B see Appendix B for HAC conditional logic

CC MCC +7th **S42.455 Nondisplaced fracture of lateral condyle of left humerus**
CC Exclusion 7th character A see Appendix A PDX collection 1247
CC Exclusion 7th characters K & P see Appendix A PDX collection 0897
MCC Exclusion 7th character B see Appendix A PDX collection 1246
HAC 7th characters A & B see Appendix B for HAC conditional logic

CC MCC +7th **S42.456 Nondisplaced fracture of lateral condyle of unspecified humerus**
CC Exclusion 7th character A see Appendix A PDX collection 1248
CC Exclusion 7th characters K & P see Appendix A PDX collection 0897
MCC Exclusion 7th character B see Appendix A PDX collection 1246
HAC 7th characters A & B see Appendix B for HAC conditional logic

+ **S42.46 Fracture of medial condyle of humerus**
Trochlea fracture of humerus

CC MCC +7th **S42.461 Displaced fracture of medial condyle of right humerus**
CC Exclusion 7th character A see Appendix A PDX collection 1245
CC Exclusion 7th characters K & P see Appendix A PDX collection 0897
MCC Exclusion 7th character B see Appendix A PDX collection 1246
HAC 7th characters A & B see Appendix B for HAC conditional logic

CC MCC +7th **S42.462 Displaced fracture of medial condyle of left humerus**
CC Exclusion 7th character A see Appendix A PDX collection 1247
CC Exclusion 7th characters K & P see Appendix A PDX collection 0897
MCC Exclusion 7th character B see Appendix A PDX collection 1246
HAC 7th characters A & B see Appendix B for HAC conditional logic

CC MCC +7th **S42.463 Displaced fracture of medial condyle of unspecified humerus**
CC Exclusion 7th character A see Appendix A PDX collection 1248
CC Exclusion 7th characters K & P see Appendix A PDX collection 0897
MCC Exclusion 7th character B see Appendix A PDX collection 1246
HAC 7th characters A & B see Appendix B for HAC conditional logic

CC MCC +7th **S42.464 Nondisplaced fracture of medial condyle of right humerus**
CC Exclusion 7th character A see Appendix A PDX collection 1245
CC Exclusion 7th characters K & P see Appendix A PDX collection 0897
MCC Exclusion 7th character B see Appendix A PDX collection 1246
HAC 7th characters A & B see Appendix B for HAC conditional logic

CC MCC +7th **S42.465 Nondisplaced fracture of medial condyle of left humerus**
CC Exclusion 7th character A see Appendix A PDX collection 1247
CC Exclusion 7th characters K & P see Appendix A PDX collection 0897
MCC Exclusion 7th character B see Appendix A PDX collection 1246
HAC 7th characters A & B see Appendix B for HAC conditional logic

CC MCC +7th **S42.466 Nondisplaced fracture of medial condyle of unspecified humerus**
CC Exclusion 7th character A see Appendix A PDX collection 1248
CC Exclusion 7th characters K & P see Appendix A PDX collection 0897
MCC Exclusion 7th character B see Appendix A PDX collection 1246
HAC 7th characters A & B see Appendix B for HAC conditional logic

\+ **S42.47 Transcondylar fracture of humerus**

CC MCC +7th **S42.471 Displaced transcondylar fracture of right humerus**
CC Exclusion 7th character A see Appendix A PDX collection 1245
CC Exclusion 7th characters K & P see Appendix A PDX collection 0897
MCC Exclusion 7th character B see Appendix A PDX collection 1246
HAC 7th characters A & B see Appendix B for HAC conditional logic

CC MCC +7th **S42.472 Displaced transcondylar fracture of left humerus**
CC Exclusion 7th character A see Appendix A PDX collection 1247
CC Exclusion 7th characters K & P see Appendix A PDX collection 0897
MCC Exclusion 7th character B see Appendix A PDX collection 1246
HAC 7th characters A & B see Appendix B for HAC conditional logic

CC MCC +7th **S42.473 Displaced transcondylar fracture of unspecified humerus**
CC Exclusion 7th character A see Appendix A PDX collection 1248
CC Exclusion 7th characters K & P see Appendix A PDX collection 0897
MCC Exclusion 7th character B see Appendix A PDX collection 1246
HAC 7th characters A & B see Appendix B for HAC conditional logic

CC MCC +7th **S42.474 Nondisplaced transcondylar fracture of right humerus**
CC Exclusion 7th character A see Appendix A PDX collection 1245
CC Exclusion 7th characters K & P see Appendix A PDX collection 0897
MCC Exclusion 7th character B see Appendix A PDX collection 1246
HAC 7th characters A & B see Appendix B for HAC conditional logic

CC MCC +7th **S42.475 Nondisplaced transcondylar fracture of left humerus**
CC Exclusion 7th character A see Appendix A PDX collection 1247
CC Exclusion 7th characters K & P see Appendix A PDX collection 0897
MCC Exclusion 7th character B see Appendix A PDX collection 1246
HAC 7th characters A & B see Appendix B for HAC conditional logic

CC MCC +7th **S42.476 Nondisplaced transcondylar fracture of unspecified humerus**
CC Exclusion 7th character A see Appendix A PDX collection 1248
CC Exclusion 7th characters K & P see Appendix A PDX collection 0897
MCC Exclusion 7th character B see Appendix A PDX collection 1246
HAC 7th characters A & B see Appendix B for HAC conditional logic

\+ **S42.48 Torus fracture of lower end of humerus**

The appropriate 7th character is to be added to all codes in subcategory S42.48
A initial encounter for closed fracture
D subsequent encounter for fracture with routine healing
G subsequent encounter for fracture with delayed healing
K subsequent encounter for fracture with nonunion
P subsequent encounter for fracture with malunion
S sequela

CC +7th **S42.481 Torus fracture of lower end of right humerus**
CC Exclusion 7th character A see Appendix A PDX collection 1245
CC Exclusion 7th characters K & P see Appendix A PDX collection 0897
HAC 7th character A see Appendix B for HAC conditional logic

CC +7th **S42.482 Torus fracture of lower end of left humerus**
CC Exclusion 7th character A see Appendix A PDX collection 1247
CC Exclusion 7th characters K & P see Appendix A PDX collection 0897
HAC 7th character A see Appendix B for HAC conditional logic

CC +7th **S42.489 Torus fracture of lower end of unspecified humerus**
CC Exclusion 7th character A see Appendix A PDX collection 1248
CC Exclusion 7th characters K & P see Appendix A PDX collection 0897
HAC 7th character A see Appendix B for HAC conditional logic

\+ **S42.49 Other fracture of lower end of humerus**

CC MCC +7th **S42.491 Other displaced fracture of lower end of right humerus**
CC Exclusion 7th character A see Appendix A PDX collection 1245
CC Exclusion 7th characters K & P see Appendix A PDX collection 0897
MCC Exclusion 7th character B see Appendix A PDX collection 1246
HAC 7th characters A & B see Appendix B for HAC conditional logic

CC MCC +7th **S42.492 Other displaced fracture of lower end of left humerus**
CC Exclusion 7th character A see Appendix A PDX collection 1247
CC Exclusion 7th characters K & P see Appendix A PDX collection 0897
MCC Exclusion 7th character B see Appendix A PDX collection 1246
HAC 7th characters A & B see Appendix B for HAC conditional logic

CC MCC +7th **S42.493 Other displaced fracture of lower end of unspecified humerus**
CC Exclusion 7th character A see Appendix A PDX collection 1248
CC Exclusion 7th characters K & P see Appendix A PDX collection 0897
MCC Exclusion 7th character B see Appendix A PDX collection 1246
HAC 7th characters A & B see Appendix B for HAC conditional logic

CC MCC +7th **S42.494 Other nondisplaced fracture of lower end of right humerus**
CC Exclusion 7th character A see Appendix A PDX collection 1245
CC Exclusion 7th characters K & P see Appendix A PDX collection 0897
MCC Exclusion 7th character B see Appendix A PDX collection 1246
HAC 7th characters A & B see Appendix B for HAC conditional logic

CC MCC +7th **S42.495 Other nondisplaced fracture of lower end of left humerus**
CC Exclusion 7th character A see Appendix A PDX collection 1247
CC Exclusion 7th characters K & P see Appendix A PDX collection 0897
MCC Exclusion 7th character B see Appendix A PDX collection 1246
HAC 7th characters A & B see Appendix B for HAC conditional logic

CC MCC +7th **S42.496 Other nondisplaced fracture of lower end of unspecified humerus**
CC Exclusion 7th character A see Appendix A PDX collection 1248
CC Exclusion 7th characters K & P see Appendix A PDX collection 0897
MCC Exclusion 7th character B see Appendix A PDX collection 1246
HAC 7th characters A & B see Appendix B for HAC conditional logic

\+ **S42.9 Fracture of shoulder girdle, part unspecified**
Fracture of shoulder NOS

CC MCC X+7th **S42.90 Fracture of unspecified shoulder girdle, part unspecified**
CC Exclusion 7th character A see Appendix A PDX collection 1248
CC Exclusion 7th characters K & P see Appendix A PDX collection 0897
MCC Exclusion 7th character B see Appendix A PDX collection 1246
HAC 7th characters A & B see Appendix B for HAC conditional logic

CC MCC X+7th **S42.91 Fracture of right shoulder girdle, part unspecified**
CC Exclusion 7th character A see Appendix A PDX collection 1248
CC Exclusion 7th characters K & P see Appendix A PDX collection 0897
MCC Exclusion 7th character B see Appendix A PDX collection 1246
HAC 7th characters A & B see Appendix B for HAC conditional logic

CC MCC X+7th **S42.92 Fracture of left shoulder girdle, part unspecified**
CC Exclusion 7th character A see Appendix A PDX collection 1248
CC Exclusion 7th characters K & P see Appendix A PDX collection 0897
MCC Exclusion 7th character B see Appendix A PDX collection 1246
HAC 7th characters A & B see Appendix B for HAC conditional logic

S43 Dislocation and sprain of joints and ligaments of shoulder girdle

Includes: avulsion of joint or ligament of shoulder girdle
laceration of cartilage, joint or ligament of shoulder girdle
sprain of cartilage, joint or ligament of shoulder girdle
traumatic hemarthrosis of joint or ligament of shoulder girdle
traumatic rupture of joint or ligament of shoulder girdle
traumatic subluxation of joint or ligament of shoulder girdle
traumatic tear of joint or ligament of shoulder girdle

Code also any associated open wound

Excludes2: *strain of muscle, fascia and tendon of shoulder and upper arm (S46.-)*

The appropriate 7th character is to be added to each code from category S43
A initial encounter
D subsequent encounter
S sequela

\+ **S43.0 Subluxation and dislocation of shoulder joint**
Dislocation of glenohumeral joint
Subluxation of glenohumeral joint

\+ **S43.00 Unspecified subluxation and dislocation of shoulder joint**
Dislocation of humerus NOS
Subluxation of humerus NOS

+7th **S43.001 Unspecified subluxation of right shoulder joint**
+7th **S43.002 Unspecified subluxation of left shoulder joint**
+7th **S43.003 Unspecified subluxation of unspecified shoulder joint**
+7th **S43.004 Unspecified dislocation of right shoulder joint**
+7th **S43.005 Unspecified dislocation of left shoulder joint**
+7th **S43.006 Unspecified dislocation of unspecified shoulder joint**

\+ **S43.01 Anterior subluxation and dislocation of humerus**
+7th **S43.011 Anterior subluxation of right humerus**
+7th **S43.012 Anterior subluxation of left humerus**
+7th **S43.013 Anterior subluxation of unspecified humerus**
+7th **S43.014 Anterior dislocation of right humerus**
+7th **S43.015 Anterior dislocation of left humerus**
+7th **S43.016 Anterior dislocation of unspecified humerus**

\+ **S43.02 Posterior subluxation and dislocation of humerus**
+7th **S43.021 Posterior subluxation of right humerus**
+7th **S43.022 Posterior subluxation of left humerus**
+7th **S43.023 Posterior subluxation of unspecified humerus**
+7th **S43.024 Posterior dislocation of right humerus**
+7th **S43.025 Posterior dislocation of left humerus**
+7th **S43.026 Posterior dislocation of unspecified humerus**

\+ **S43.03 Inferior subluxation and dislocation of humerus**
+7th **S43.031 Inferior subluxation of right humerus**
+7th **S43.032 Inferior subluxation of left humerus**
+7th **S43.033 Inferior subluxation of unspecified humerus**
+7th **S43.034 Inferior dislocation of right humerus**
+7th **S43.035 Inferior dislocation of left humerus**
+7th **S43.036 Inferior dislocation of unspecified humerus**

\+ **S43.08 Other subluxation and dislocation of shoulder joint**
+7th **S43.081 Other subluxation of right shoulder joint**
+7th **S43.082 Other subluxation of left shoulder joint**
+7th **S43.083 Other subluxation of unspecified shoulder joint**
+7th **S43.084 Other dislocation of right shoulder joint**
+7th **S43.085 Other dislocation of left shoulder joint**
+7th **S43.086 Other dislocation of unspecified shoulder joint**

\+ **S43.1 Subluxation and dislocation of acromioclavicular joint**

\+ **S43.10 Unspecified dislocation of acromioclavicular joint**
+7th **S43.101 Unspecified dislocation of right acromioclavicular joint**
+7th **S43.102 Unspecified dislocation of left acromioclavicular joint**
+7th **S43.109 Unspecified dislocation of unspecified acromioclavicular joint**

\+ **S43.11 Subluxation of acromioclavicular joint**
+7th **S43.111 Subluxation of right acromioclavicular joint**
+7th **S43.112 Subluxation of left acromioclavicular joint**
+7th **S43.119 Subluxation of unspecified acromioclavicular joint**

\+ **S43.12 Dislocation of acromioclavicular joint, 100%-200% displacement**
+7th **S43.121 Dislocation of right acromioclavicular joint, 100%-200% displacement**
+7th **S43.122 Dislocation of left acromioclavicular joint, 100%-200% displacement**
+7th **S43.129 Dislocation of unspecified acromioclavicular joint, 100%-200% displacement**

\+ **S43.13 Dislocation of acromioclavicular joint, greater than 200% displacement**
+7th **S43.131 Dislocation of right acromioclavicular joint, greater than 200% displacement**
+7th **S43.132 Dislocation of left acromioclavicular joint, greater than 200% displacement**
+7th **S43.139 Dislocation of unspecified acromioclavicular joint, greater than 200% displacement**

\+ **S43.14 Inferior dislocation of acromioclavicular joint**
+7th **S43.141 Inferior dislocation of right acromioclavicular joint**
+7th **S43.142 Inferior dislocation of left acromioclavicular joint**
+7th **S43.149 Inferior dislocation of unspecified acromioclavicular joint**

\+ **S43.15 Posterior dislocation of acromioclavicular joint**
+7th **S43.151 Posterior dislocation of right acromioclavicular joint**
+7th **S43.152 Posterior dislocation of left acromioclavicular joint**
+7th **S43.159 Posterior dislocation of unspecified acromioclavicular joint**

+ **S43.2 Subluxation and dislocation of sternoclavicular joint**

+ **S43.20 Unspecified subluxation and dislocation of sternoclavicular joint**

CC +7th **S43.201 Unspecified subluxation of right sternoclavicular joint**
CC Exclusion 7th character A see Appendix A
PDX collection 1252
HAC 7th character A see Appendix B for HAC conditional logic

CC +7th **S43.202 Unspecified subluxation of left sternoclavicular joint**
CC Exclusion 7th character A see Appendix A
PDX collection 1253
HAC 7th character A see Appendix B for HAC conditional logic

CC +7th **S43.203 Unspecified subluxation of unspecified sternoclavicular joint**
CC Exclusion 7th character A see Appendix A
PDX collection 0914
HAC 7th character A see Appendix B for HAC conditional logic

CC +7th **S43.204 Unspecified dislocation of right sternoclavicular joint**
CC Exclusion 7th character A see Appendix A
PDX collection 1252
HAC 7th character A see Appendix B for HAC conditional logic

CC +7th **S43.205 Unspecified dislocation of left sternoclavicular joint**
CC Exclusion 7th character A see Appendix A
PDX collection 1253
HAC 7th character A see Appendix B for HAC conditional logic

CC +7th **S43.206 Unspecified dislocation of unspecified sternoclavicular joint**
CC Exclusion 7th character A see Appendix A
PDX collection 0914
HAC 7th character A see Appendix B for HAC conditional logic

+ **S43.21 Anterior subluxation and dislocation of sternoclavicular joint**

CC +7th **S43.211 Anterior subluxation of right sternoclavicular joint**
CC Exclusion 7th character A see Appendix A
PDX collection 1252
HAC 7th character A see Appendix B for HAC conditional logic

CC +7th **S43.212 Anterior subluxation of left sternoclavicular joint**
CC Exclusion 7th character A see Appendix A
PDX collection 1253
HAC 7th character A see Appendix B for HAC conditional logic

CC +7th **S43.213 Anterior subluxation of unspecified sternoclavicular joint**
CC Exclusion 7th character A see Appendix A
PDX collection 0914
HAC 7th character A see Appendix B for HAC conditional logic

CC +7th **S43.214 Anterior dislocation of right sternoclavicular joint**
CC Exclusion 7th character A see Appendix A
PDX collection 1252
HAC 7th character A see Appendix B for HAC conditional logic

CC +7th **S43.215 Anterior dislocation of left sternoclavicular joint**
CC Exclusion 7th character A see Appendix A
PDX collection 1253
HAC 7th character A see Appendix B for HAC conditional logic

CC +7th **S43.216 Anterior dislocation of unspecified sternoclavicular joint**
CC Exclusion 7th character A see Appendix A
PDX collection 0914
HAC 7th character A see Appendix B for HAC conditional logic

+ **S43.22 Posterior subluxation and dislocation of sternoclavicular joint**

CC +7th **S43.221 Posterior subluxation of right sternoclavicular joint**
CC Exclusion 7th character A see Appendix A
PDX collection 1252
HAC 7th character A see Appendix B for HAC conditional logic

CC +7th **S43.222 Posterior subluxation of left sternoclavicular joint**
CC Exclusion 7th character A see Appendix A
PDX collection 1253
HAC 7th character A see Appendix B for HAC conditional logic

CC +7th **S43.223 Posterior subluxation of unspecified sternoclavicular joint**
CC Exclusion 7th character A see Appendix A
PDX collection 0914
HAC 7th character A see Appendix B for HAC conditional logic

CC +7th **S43.224 Posterior dislocation of right sternoclavicular joint**
CC Exclusion 7th character A see Appendix A
PDX collection 1252
HAC 7th character A see Appendix B for HAC conditional logic

CC +7th **S43.225 Posterior dislocation of left sternoclavicular joint**
CC Exclusion 7th character A see Appendix A
PDX collection 1253
HAC 7th character A see Appendix B for HAC conditional logic

CC +7th **S43.226 Posterior dislocation of unspecified sternoclavicular joint**
CC Exclusion 7th character A see Appendix A
PDX collection 0914

+ **S43.3 Subluxation and dislocation of other and unspecified parts of shoulder girdle**

+ **S43.30 Subluxation and dislocation of unspecified parts of shoulder girdle**
Dislocation of shoulder girdle NOS
Subluxation of shoulder girdle NOS

+7th **S43.301 Subluxation of unspecified parts of right shoulder girdle**
+7th **S43.302 Subluxation of unspecified parts of left shoulder girdle**
+7th **S43.303 Subluxation of unspecified parts of unspecified shoulder girdle**
+7th **S43.304 Dislocation of unspecified parts of right shoulder girdle**
+7th **S43.305 Dislocation of unspecified parts of left shoulder girdle**
+7th **S43.306 Dislocation of unspecified parts of unspecified shoulder girdle**

+ **S43.31 Subluxation and dislocation of scapula**
+7th **S43.311 Subluxation of right scapula**
+7th **S43.312 Subluxation of left scapula**
+7th **S43.313 Subluxation of unspecified scapula**
+7th **S43.314 Dislocation of right scapula**
+7th **S43.315 Dislocation of left scapula**
+7th **S43.316 Dislocation of unspecified scapula**

+ **S43.39 Subluxation and dislocation of other parts of shoulder girdle**
+7th **S43.391 Subluxation of other parts of right shoulder girdle**
+7th **S43.392 Subluxation of other parts of left shoulder girdle**
+7th **S43.393 Subluxation of other parts of unspecified shoulder girdle**
+7th **S43.394 Dislocation of other parts of right shoulder girdle**
+7th **S43.395 Dislocation of other parts of left shoulder girdle**
+7th **S43.396 Dislocation of other parts of unspecified shoulder girdle**

+ **S43.4 Sprain of shoulder joint**

+ **S43.40 Unspecified sprain of shoulder joint**
+7th **S43.401 Unspecified sprain of right shoulder joint**
+7th **S43.402 Unspecified sprain of left shoulder joint**
+7th **S43.409 Unspecified sprain of unspecified shoulder joint**

+ **S43.41 Sprain of coracohumeral (ligament)**
+7th **S43.411 Sprain of right coracohumeral (ligament)**
+7th **S43.412 Sprain of left coracohumeral (ligament)**
+7th **S43.419 Sprain of unspecified coracohumeral (ligament)**

+ **S43.42 Sprain of rotator cuff capsule**
Excludes1: *rotator cuff syndrome (complete) (incomplete), not specified as traumatic (M75.1-)*
Excludes2: *injury of tendon of rotator cuff (S46.0-)*
+7th **S43.421 Sprain of right rotator cuff capsule**

+7th **S43.422 Sprain of left rotator cuff capsule**
+7th **S43.429 Sprain of unspecified rotator cuff capsule**
+ **S43.43 Superior glenoid labrum lesion**
SLAP lesion
+7th **S43.431 Superior glenoid labrum lesion of right shoulder**
+7th **S43.432 Superior glenoid labrum lesion of left shoulder**
+7th **S43.439 Superior glenoid labrum lesion of unspecified shoulder**
+ **S43.49 Other sprain of shoulder joint**
S43.491 Other sprain of right shoulder joint
S43.492 Other sprain of left shoulder joint
S43.499 Other sprain of unspecified shoulder joint
+ **S43.5 Sprain of acromioclavicular joint**
Sprain of acromioclavicular ligament
X+7th **S43.50 Sprain of unspecified acromioclavicular joint**
X+7th **S43.51 Sprain of right acromioclavicular joint**
X+7th **S43.52 Sprain of left acromioclavicular joint**
+ **S43.6 Sprain of sternoclavicular joint**
X+7th **S43.60 Sprain of unspecified sternoclavicular joint**
X+7th **S43.61 Sprain of right sternoclavicular joint**
X+7th **S43.62 Sprain of left sternoclavicular joint**
+ **S43.8 Sprain of other specified parts of shoulder girdle**
X+7th **S43.80 Sprain of other specified parts of unspecified shoulder girdle**
X+7th **S43.81 Sprain of other specified parts of right shoulder girdle**
X+7th **S43.82 Sprain of other specified parts of left shoulder girdle**
+ **S43.9 Sprain of unspecified parts of shoulder girdle**
X+7th **S43.90 Sprain of unspecified parts of unspecified shoulder girdle**
Sprain of shoulder girdle NOS
X+7th **S43.91 Sprain of unspecified parts of right shoulder girdle**
X+7th **S43.92 Sprain of unspecified parts of left shoulder girdle**

S44 Injury of nerves at shoulder and upper arm level

Code also any associated open wound (S41.-)
Excludes2: *injury of brachial plexus (S14.3-)*

The appropriate 7th character is to be added to each code from category S44
A initial encounter
D subsequent encounter
S sequela

+ **S44.0 Injury of ulnar nerve at upper arm level**
Excludes1: *ulnar nerve NOS (S54.0)*
X+7th **S44.00 Injury of ulnar nerve at upper arm level, unspecified arm**
X+7th **S44.01 Injury of ulnar nerve at upper arm level, right arm**
X+7th **S44.02 Injury of ulnar nerve at upper arm level, left arm**
+ **S44.1 Injury of median nerve at upper arm level**
Excludes1: *median nerve NOS (S54.1)*
X+7th **S44.10 Injury of median nerve at upper arm level, unspecified arm**
X+7th **S44.11 Injury of median nerve at upper arm level, right arm**
X+7th **S44.12 Injury of median nerve at upper arm level, left arm**
+ **S44.2 Injury of radial nerve at upper arm level**
Excludes1: *radial nerve NOS (S54.2)*
X+7th **S44.20 Injury of radial nerve at upper arm level, unspecified arm**
X+7th **S44.21 Injury of radial nerve at upper arm level, right arm**
X+7th **S44.22 Injury of radial nerve at upper arm level, left arm**
+ **S44.3 Injury of axillary nerve**
X+7th **S44.30 Injury of axillary nerve, unspecified arm**
X+7th **S44.31 Injury of axillary nerve, right arm**
X+7th **S44.32 Injury of axillary nerve, left arm**
+ **S44.4 Injury of musculocutaneous nerve**
X+7th **S44.40 Injury of musculocutaneous nerve, unspecified arm**
X+7th **S44.41 Injury of musculocutaneous nerve, right arm**
X+7th **S44.42 Injury of musculocutaneous nerve, left arm**
+ **S44.5 Injury of cutaneous sensory nerve at shoulder and upper arm level**
X+7th **S44.50 Injury of cutaneous sensory nerve at shoulder and upper arm level, unspecified arm**
X+7th **S44.51 Injury of cutaneous sensory nerve at shoulder and upper arm level, right arm**
X+7th **S44.52 Injury of cutaneous sensory nerve at shoulder and upper arm level, left arm**
+ **S44.8 Injury of other nerves at shoulder and upper arm level**
+ **S44.8X Injury of other nerves at shoulder and upper arm level**
+7th **S44.8X1 Injury of other nerves at shoulder and upper arm level, right arm**
+7th **S44.8X2 Injury of other nerves at shoulder and upper arm level, left arm**
+7th **S44.8X9 Injury of other nerves at shoulder and upper arm level, unspecified arm**
+ **S44.9 Injury of unspecified nerve at shoulder and upper arm level**
X+7th **S44.90 Injury of unspecified nerve at shoulder and upper arm level, unspecified arm**
X+7th **S44.91 Injury of unspecified nerve at shoulder and upper arm level, right arm**
X+7th **S44.92 Injury of unspecified nerve at shoulder and upper arm level, left arm**

S45 Injury of blood vessels at shoulder and upper arm level

Code also any associated open wound (S41.-)
Excludes2: *injury of subclavian artery (S25.1)*
injury of subclavian vein (S25.3)

The appropriate 7th character is to be added to each code from category S45
A initial encounter
D subsequent encounter
S sequela

+ **S45.0 Injury of axillary artery**
+ **S45.00 Unspecified injury of axillary artery**
MCC +7th **S45.001 Unspecified injury of axillary artery, right side**
MCC Exclusion 7th character A see Appendix A
PDX collection 1254
MCC +7th **S45.002 Unspecified injury of axillary artery, left side**
MCC Exclusion 7th character A see Appendix A
PDX collection 1255
MCC +7th **S45.009 Unspecified injury of axillary artery, unspecified side**
MCC Exclusion 7th character A see Appendix A
PDX collection 1256
+ **S45.01 Laceration of axillary artery**
MCC +7th **S45.011 Laceration of axillary artery, right side**
MCC Exclusion 7th character A see Appendix A
PDX collection 1254
MCC +7th **S45.012 Laceration of axillary artery, left side**
MCC Exclusion 7th character A see Appendix A
PDX collection 1255
MCC +7th **S45.019 Laceration of axillary artery, unspecified side**
MCC Exclusion 7th character A see Appendix A
PDX collection 1256
+ **S45.09 Other specified injury of axillary artery**
MCC +7th **S45.091 Other specified injury of axillary artery, right side**
MCC Exclusion 7th character A see Appendix A
PDX collection 1254
MCC +7th **S45.092 Other specified injury of axillary artery, left side**
MCC Exclusion 7th character A see Appendix A
PDX collection 1255
MCC +7th **S45.099 Other specified injury of axillary artery, unspecified side**
MCC Exclusion 7th character A see Appendix A
PDX collection 1256
+ **S45.1 Injury of brachial artery**
+ **S45.10 Unspecified injury of brachial artery**
CC +7th **S45.101 Unspecified injury of brachial artery, right side**
CC Exclusion 7th character A see Appendix A
PDX collection 1257
CC +7th **S45.102 Unspecified injury of brachial artery, left side**
CC Exclusion 7th character A see Appendix A
PDX collection 1258
CC +7th **S45.109 Unspecified injury of brachial artery, unspecified side**
CC Exclusion 7th character A see Appendix A
PDX collection 1259
+ **S45.11 Laceration of brachial artery**
CC +7th **S45.111 Laceration of brachial artery, right side**
CC Exclusion 7th character A see Appendix A
PDX collection 1257

CC +7th **S45.112** Laceration of brachial artery, left side
CC Exclusion 7th character A see Appendix A
PDX collection 1258

CC +7th **S45.119** Laceration of brachial artery, unspecified side
CC Exclusion 7th character A see Appendix A
PDX collection 1259

+ **S45.19** Other specified injury of brachial artery

CC +7th **S45.191** Other specified injury of brachial artery, right side
CC Exclusion 7th character A see Appendix A
PDX collection 1257

CC +7th **S45.192** Other specified injury of brachial artery, left side
CC Exclusion 7th character A see Appendix A
PDX collection 1258

CC +7th **S45.199** Other specified injury of brachial artery, unspecified side
CC Exclusion 7th character A see Appendix A
PDX collection 1259

+ **S45.2** Injury of axillary or brachial vein

+ **S45.20** Unspecified injury of axillary or brachial vein

CC +7th **S45.201** Unspecified injury of axillary or brachial vein, right side
CC Exclusion 7th character A see Appendix A
PDX collection 1257

CC +7th **S45.202** Unspecified injury of axillary or brachial vein, left side
CC Exclusion 7th character A see Appendix A
PDX collection 1258

CC +7th **S45.209** Unspecified injury of axillary or brachial vein, unspecified side
CC Exclusion 7th character A see Appendix A
PDX collection 1259

+ **S45.21** Laceration of axillary or brachial vein

CC +7th **S45.211** Laceration of axillary or brachial vein, right side
CC Exclusion 7th character A see Appendix A
PDX collection 1257

CC +7th **S45.212** Laceration of axillary or brachial vein, left side
CC Exclusion 7th character A see Appendix A
PDX collection 1258

CC +7th **S45.219** Laceration of axillary or brachial vein, unspecified side
CC Exclusion 7th character A see Appendix A
PDX collection 1259

+ **S45.29** Other specified injury of axillary or brachial vein

CC +7th **S45.291** Other specified injury of axillary or brachial vein, right side
CC Exclusion 7th character A see Appendix A
PDX collection 1257

CC +7th **S45.292** Other specified injury of axillary or brachial vein, left side
CC Exclusion 7th character A see Appendix A
PDX collection 1258

CC +7th **S45.299** Other specified injury of axillary or brachial vein, unspecified side
CC Exclusion 7th character A see Appendix A
PDX collection 1259

+ **S45.3** Injury of superficial vein at shoulder and upper arm level

+ **S45.30** Unspecified injury of superficial vein at shoulder and upper arm level

CC +7th **S45.301** Unspecified injury of superficial vein at shoulder and upper arm level, right arm
CC Exclusion 7th character A see Appendix A
PDX collection 1260

CC +7th **S45.302** Unspecified injury of superficial vein at shoulder and upper arm level, left arm
CC Exclusion 7th character A see Appendix A
PDX collection 1261

CC +7th **S45.309** Unspecified injury of superficial vein at shoulder and upper arm level, unspecified arm
CC Exclusion 7th character A see Appendix A
PDX collection 1262

+ **S45.31** Laceration of superficial vein at shoulder and upper arm level

CC +7th **S45.311** Laceration of superficial vein at shoulder and upper arm level, right arm
CC Exclusion 7th character A see Appendix A
PDX collection 1260

CC +7th **S45.312** Laceration of superficial vein at shoulder and upper arm level, left arm
CC Exclusion 7th character A see Appendix A
PDX collection 1261

CC +7th **S45.319** Laceration of superficial vein at shoulder and upper arm level, unspecified arm
CC Exclusion 7th character A see Appendix A
PDX collection 1262

+ **S45.39** Other specified injury of superficial vein at shoulder and upper arm level

CC +7th **S45.391** Other specified injury of superficial vein at shoulder and upper arm level, right arm
CC Exclusion 7th character A see Appendix A
PDX collection 1260

CC +7th **S45.392** Other specified injury of superficial vein at shoulder and upper arm level, left arm
CC Exclusion 7th character A see Appendix A
PDX collection 1261

CC +7th **S45.399** Other specified injury of superficial vein at shoulder and upper arm level, unspecified arm
CC Exclusion 7th character A see Appendix A
PDX collection 1262

+ **S45.8** Injury of other specified blood vessels at shoulder and upper arm level

+ **S45.80** Unspecified injury of other specified blood vessels at shoulder and upper arm level

CC +7th **S45.801** Unspecified injury of other specified blood vessels at shoulder and upper arm level, right arm
CC Exclusion 7th character A see Appendix A
PDX collection 1260

CC +7th **S45.802** Unspecified injury of other specified blood vessels at shoulder and upper arm level, left arm
CC Exclusion 7th character A see Appendix A
PDX collection 1261

CC +7th **S45.809** Unspecified injury of other specified blood vessels at shoulder and upper arm level, unspecified arm
CC Exclusion 7th character A see Appendix A
PDX collection 1262

+ **S45.81** Laceration of other specified blood vessels at shoulder and upper arm level

CC +7th **S45.811** Laceration of other specified blood vessels at shoulder and upper arm level, right arm
CC Exclusion 7th character A see Appendix A
PDX collection 1260

CC +7th **S45.812** Laceration of other specified blood vessels at shoulder and upper arm level, left arm
CC Exclusion 7th character A see Appendix A
PDX collection 1261

CC +7th **S45.819** Laceration of other specified blood vessels at shoulder and upper arm level, unspecified arm
CC Exclusion 7th character A see Appendix A
PDX collection 1262

+ **S45.89** Other specified injury of other specified blood vessels at shoulder and upper arm level

CC +7th **S45.891** Other specified injury of other specified blood vessels at shoulder and upper arm level, right arm
CC Exclusion 7th character A see Appendix A
PDX collection 1260

CC +7th **S45.892** Other specified injury of other specified blood vessels at shoulder and upper arm level, left arm
CC Exclusion 7th character A see Appendix A
PDX collection 1261

CC +7th **S45.899** Other specified injury of other specified blood vessels at shoulder and upper arm level, unspecified arm
CC Exclusion 7th character A see Appendix A
PDX collection 1262

+ **S45.9** Injury of unspecified blood vessel at shoulder and upper arm level

+ **S45.90** Unspecified injury of unspecified blood vessel at shoulder and upper arm level

CC +7th **S45.901** Unspecified injury of unspecified blood vessel at shoulder and upper arm level, right arm
CC Exclusion 7th character A see Appendix A
PDX collection 1260

CC +7th **S45.902** Unspecified injury of unspecified blood vessel at shoulder and upper arm level, left arm
CC Exclusion 7th character A see Appendix A
PDX collection 1261

CC +7th **S45.909 Unspecified injury of unspecified blood vessel at shoulder and upper arm level, unspecified arm**
CC Exclusion 7th character A see Appendix A
PDX collection 1262

\+ **S45.91 Laceration of unspecified blood vessel at shoulder and upper arm level**

CC +7th **S45.911 Laceration of unspecified blood vessel at shoulder and upper arm level, right arm**
CC Exclusion 7th character A see Appendix A
PDX collection 1260

CC +7th **S45.912 Laceration of unspecified blood vessel at shoulder and upper arm level, left arm**
CC Exclusion 7th character A see Appendix A
PDX collection 1261

CC +7th **S45.919 Laceration of unspecified blood vessel at shoulder and upper arm level, unspecified arm**
CC Exclusion 7th character A see Appendix A
PDX collection 1262

\+ **S45.99 Other specified injury of unspecified blood vessel at shoulder and upper arm level**

CC +7th **S45.991 Other specified injury of unspecified blood vessel at shoulder and upper arm level, right arm**
CC Exclusion 7th character A see Appendix A
PDX collection 1260

CC +7th **S45.992 Other specified injury of unspecified blood vessel at shoulder and upper arm level, left arm**
CC Exclusion 7th character A see Appendix A
PDX collection 1261

CC +7th **S45.999 Other specified injury of unspecified blood vessel at shoulder and upper arm level, unspecified arm**
CC Exclusion 7th character A see Appendix A
PDX collection 1262

S46 Injury of muscle, fascia and tendon at shoulder and upper arm level

Code also any associated open wound (S41.-)

Excludes2: *injury of muscle, fascia and tendon at elbow (S56.-)*
sprain of joints and ligaments of shoulder girdle (S43.9)

The appropriate 7th character is to be added to each code from category S46
A initial encounter
D subsequent encounter
S sequela

\+ **S46.0 Injury of muscle(s) and tendon(s) of the rotator cuff of shoulder**

\+ **S46.00 Unspecified injury of muscle(s) and tendon(s) of the rotator cuff of shoulder**

+7th **S46.001 Unspecified injury of muscle(s) and tendon(s) of the rotator cuff of right shoulder**

+7th **S46.002 Unspecified injury of muscle(s) and tendon(s) of the rotator cuff of left shoulder**

+7th **S46.009 Unspecified injury of muscle(s) and tendon(s) of the rotator cuff of unspecified shoulder**

\+ **S46.01 Strain of muscle(s) and tendon(s) of the rotator cuff of shoulder**

+7th **S46.011 Strain of muscle(s) and tendon(s) of the rotator cuff of right shoulder**

+7th **S46.012 Strain of muscle(s) and tendon(s) of the rotator cuff of left shoulder**

+7th **S46.019 Strain of muscle(s) and tendon(s) of the rotator cuff of unspecified shoulder**

\+ **S46.02 Laceration of muscle(s) and tendon(s) of the rotator cuff of shoulder**

CC +7th **S46.021 Laceration of muscle(s) and tendon(s) of the rotator cuff of right shoulder**
CC Exclusion 7th character A see Appendix A
PDX collection 1263

CC +7th **S46.022 Laceration of muscle(s) and tendon(s) of the rotator cuff of left shoulder**
CC Exclusion 7th character A see Appendix A
PDX collection 1264

CC +7th **S46.029 Laceration of muscle(s) and tendon(s) of the rotator cuff of unspecified shoulder**
CC Exclusion 7th character A see Appendix A
PDX collection 1265

\+ **S46.09 Other injury of muscle(s) and tendon(s) of the rotator cuff of shoulder**

+7th **S46.091 Other injury of muscle(s) and tendon(s) of the rotator cuff of right shoulder**

+7th **S46.092 Other injury of muscle(s) and tendon(s) of the rotator cuff of left shoulder**

+7th **S46.099 Other injury of muscle(s) and tendon(s) of the rotator cuff of unspecified shoulder**

\+ **S46.1 Injury of muscle, fascia and tendon of long head of biceps**

\+ **S46.10 Unspecified injury of muscle, fascia and tendon of long head of biceps**

+7th **S46.101 Unspecified injury of muscle, fascia and tendon of long head of biceps, right arm**

+7th **S46.102 Unspecified injury of muscle, fascia and tendon of long head of biceps, left arm**

+7th **S46.109 Unspecified injury of muscle, fascia and tendon of long head of biceps, unspecified arm**

\+ **S46.11 Strain of muscle, fascia and tendon of long head of biceps**

+7th **S46.111 Strain of muscle, fascia and tendon of long head of biceps, right arm**

+7th **S46.112 Strain of muscle, fascia and tendon of long head of biceps, left arm**

+7th **S46.119 Strain of muscle, fascia and tendon of long head of biceps, unspecified arm**

\+ **S46.12 Laceration of muscle, fascia and tendon of long head of biceps**

CC +7th **S46.121 Laceration of muscle, fascia and tendon of long head of biceps, right arm**
CC Exclusion 7th character A see Appendix A
PDX collection 1263

CC +7th **S46.122 Laceration of muscle, fascia and tendon of long head of biceps, left arm**
CC Exclusion 7th character A see Appendix A
PDX collection 1264

CC +7th **S46.129 Laceration of muscle, fascia and tendon of long head of biceps, unspecified arm**
CC Exclusion 7th character A see Appendix A
PDX collection 1265

\+ **S46.19 Other injury of muscle, fascia and tendon of long head of biceps**

+7th **S46.191 Other injury of muscle, fascia and tendon of long head of biceps, right arm**

+7th **S46.192 Other injury of muscle, fascia and tendon of long head of biceps, left arm**

+7th **S46.199 Other injury of muscle, fascia and tendon of long head of biceps, unspecified arm**

\+ **S46.2 Injury of muscle, fascia and tendon of other parts of biceps**

\+ **S46.20 Unspecified injury of muscle, fascia and tendon of other parts of biceps**

+7th **S46.201 Unspecified injury of muscle, fascia and tendon of other parts of biceps, right arm**

+7th **S46.202 Unspecified injury of muscle, fascia and tendon of other parts of biceps, left arm**

+7th **S46.209 Unspecified injury of muscle, fascia and tendon of other parts of biceps, unspecified arm**

\+ **S46.21 Strain of muscle, fascia and tendon of other parts of biceps**

+7th **S46.211 Strain of muscle, fascia and tendon of other parts of biceps, right arm**

+7th **S46.212 Strain of muscle, fascia and tendon of other parts of biceps, left arm**

+7th **S46.219 Strain of muscle, fascia and tendon of other parts of biceps, unspecified arm**

\+ **S46.22 Laceration of muscle, fascia and tendon of other parts of biceps**

CC +7th **S46.221 Laceration of muscle, fascia and tendon of other parts of biceps, right arm**
CC Exclusion 7th character A see Appendix A
PDX collection 1263

CC +7th **S46.222 Laceration of muscle, fascia and tendon of other parts of biceps, left arm**
CC Exclusion 7th character A see Appendix A
PDX collection 1264

CC +7th **S46.229 Laceration of muscle, fascia and tendon of other parts of biceps, unspecified arm**
CC Exclusion 7th character A see Appendix A
PDX collection 1265

+ S46.29 Other injury of muscle, fascia and tendon of other parts of biceps

+7th **S46.291 Other injury of muscle, fascia and tendon of other parts of biceps, right arm**

+7th **S46.292 Other injury of muscle, fascia and tendon of other parts of biceps, left arm**

+7th **S46.299 Other injury of muscle, fascia and tendon of other parts of biceps, unspecified arm**

+ S46.3 Injury of muscle, fascia and tendon of triceps

+ S46.30 Unspecified injury of muscle, fascia and tendon of triceps

+7th **S46.301 Unspecified injury of muscle, fascia and tendon of triceps, right arm**

+7th **S46.302 Unspecified injury of muscle, fascia and tendon of triceps, left arm**

+7th **S46.309 Unspecified injury of muscle, fascia and tendon of triceps, unspecified arm**

+ S46.31 Strain of muscle, fascia and tendon of triceps

+7th **S46.311 Strain of muscle, fascia and tendon of triceps, right arm**

+7th **S46.312 Strain of muscle, fascia and tendon of triceps, left arm**

+7th **S46.319 Strain of muscle, fascia and tendon of triceps, unspecified arm**

+ S46.32 Laceration of muscle, fascia and tendon of triceps

CC +7th **S46.321 Laceration of muscle, fascia and tendon of triceps, right arm**
CC Exclusion 7th character A see Appendix A PDX collection 1263

CC +7th **S46.322 Laceration of muscle, fascia and tendon of triceps, left arm**
CC Exclusion 7th character A see Appendix A PDX collection 1264

CC +7th **S46.329 Laceration of muscle, fascia and tendon of triceps, unspecified arm**
CC Exclusion 7th character A see Appendix A PDX collection 1265

+ S46.39 Other injury of muscle, fascia and tendon of triceps

+7th **S46.391 Other injury of muscle, fascia and tendon of triceps, right arm**

+7th **S46.392 Other injury of muscle, fascia and tendon of triceps, left arm**

+7th **S46.399 Other injury of muscle, fascia and tendon of triceps, unspecified arm**

+ S46.8 Injury of other muscles, fascia and tendons at shoulder and upper arm level

+ S46.80 Unspecified injury of other muscles, fascia and tendons at shoulder and upper arm level

+7th **S46.801 Unspecified injury of other muscles, fascia and tendons at shoulder and upper arm level, right arm**

+7th **S46.802 Unspecified injury of other muscles, fascia and tendons at shoulder and upper arm level, left arm**

+7th **S46.809 Unspecified injury of other muscles, fascia and tendons at shoulder and upper arm level, unspecified arm**

+ S46.81 Strain of other muscles, fascia and tendons at shoulder and upper arm level

+7th **S46.811 Strain of other muscles, fascia and tendons at shoulder and upper arm level, right arm**

+7th **S46.812 Strain of other muscles, fascia and tendons at shoulder and upper arm level, left arm**

+7th **S46.819 Strain of other muscles, fascia and tendons at shoulder and upper arm level, unspecified arm**

+ S46.82 Laceration of other muscles, fascia and tendons at shoulder and upper arm level

CC +7th **S46.821 Laceration of other muscles, fascia and tendons at shoulder and upper arm level, right arm**
CC Exclusion 7th character A see Appendix A PDX collection 1263

CC +7th **S46.822 Laceration of other muscles, fascia and tendons at shoulder and upper arm level, left arm**
CC Exclusion 7th character A see Appendix A PDX collection 1264

CC +7th **S46.829 Laceration of other muscles, fascia and tendons at shoulder and upper arm level, unspecified arm**
CC Exclusion 7th character A see Appendix A PDX collection 1265

+ S46.89 Other injury of other muscles, fascia and tendons at shoulder and upper arm level

+7th **S46.891 Other injury of other muscles, fascia and tendons at shoulder and upper arm level, right arm**

+7th **S46.892 Other injury of other muscles, fascia and tendons at shoulder and upper arm level, left arm**

+7th **S46.899 Other injury of other muscles, fascia and tendons at shoulder and upper arm level, unspecified arm**

+ S46.9 Injury of unspecified muscle, fascia and tendon at shoulder a upper arm level

+ S46.90 Unspecified injury of unspecified muscle, fascia and tendon at shoulder and upper arm level

+7th **S46.901 Unspecified injury of unspecified muscle, fascia and tendon at shoulder and upper arm level, right arm**

+7th **S46.902 Unspecified injury of unspecified muscle, fascia and tendon at shoulder and upper arm level, left arm**

+7th **S46.909 Unspecified injury of unspecified muscle, fascia and tendon at shoulder and upper arm level, unspecified arm**

+ S46.91 Strain of unspecified muscle, fascia and tendon at shoulder and upper arm level

+7th **S46.911 Strain of unspecified muscle, fascia and tendon at shoulder and upper arm level, right arm**

+7th **S46.912 Strain of unspecified muscle, fascia and tendon at shoulder and upper arm level, l arm**

+7th **S46.919 Strain of unspecified muscle, fascia and tendon at shoulder and upper arm level, unspecified arm**

+ S46.92 Laceration of unspecified muscle, fascia and tendon shoulder and upper arm level

CC +7th **S46.921 Laceration of unspecified muscle, fascia a tendon at shoulder and upper arm level, right arm**
CC Exclusion 7th character A see Appendix A PDX collection 1263

CC +7th **S46.922 Laceration of unspecified muscle, fascia a tendon at shoulder and upper arm level, l arm**
CC Exclusion 7th character A see Appendix A PDX collection 1264

CC +7th **S46.929 Laceration of unspecified muscle, fascia a tendon at shoulder and upper arm level, unspecified arm**
CC Exclusion 7th character A see Appendix A PDX collection 1265

+ S46.99 Other injury of unspecified muscle, fascia and tend at shoulder and upper arm level

+7th **S46.991 Other injury of unspecified muscle, fascia and tendon at shoulder and upper arm le right arm**

+7th **S46.992 Other injury of unspecified muscle, fascia and tendon at shoulder and upper arm le left arm**

+7th **S46.999 Other injury of unspecified muscle, fascia and tendon at shoulder and upper arm le unspecified arm**

S47 Crushing injury of shoulder and upper arm

Use additional code for all associated injuries

Excludes2: *crushing injury of elbow (S57.0-)*

The appropriate 7th character is to be added to each code from category S47
A initial encounter
D subsequent encounter
S sequela

X+7th **S47.1 Crushing injury of right shoulder and upper arm**

X+7th **S47.2 Crushing injury of left shoulder and upper arm**

X+7th **S47.9 Crushing injury of shoulder and upper arm, unspecified arm**

S48 Traumatic amputation of shoulder and upper arm

An amputation not identified as partial or complete should be coded to complete

Excludes1: *traumatic amputation at elbow level (S58.0)*

The appropriate 7th character is to be added to each code from category S48
A initial encounter
D subsequent encounter
S sequela

+ **S48.0 Traumatic amputation at shoulder joint**
+ **S48.01 Complete traumatic amputation at shoulder joint**

CC +7th **S48.011 Complete traumatic amputation at right shoulder joint**
CC Exclusion 7th character A see Appendix A PDX collection 1266

CC +7th **S48.012 Complete traumatic amputation at left shoulder joint**
CC Exclusion 7th character A see Appendix A PDX collection 1267

CC +7th **S48.019 Complete traumatic amputation at unspecified shoulder joint**
CC Exclusion 7th character A see Appendix A PDX collection 1268

+ **S48.02 Partial traumatic amputation at shoulder joint**

CC **S48.021 Partial traumatic amputation at right shoulder joint**
CC Exclusion 7th character A see Appendix A PDX collection 1266

CC **S48.022 Partial traumatic amputation at left shoulder joint**
CC Exclusion 7th character A see Appendix A PDX collection 1267

CC **S48.029 Partial traumatic amputation at unspecified shoulder joint**
CC Exclusion 7th character A see Appendix A PDX collection 1268

+ **S48.1 Traumatic amputation at level between shoulder and elbow**
+ **S48.11 Complete traumatic amputation at level between shoulder and elbow**

CC +7th **S48.111 Complete traumatic amputation at level between right shoulder and elbow**
CC Exclusion 7th character A see Appendix A PDX collection 1266

CC +7th **S48.112 Complete traumatic amputation at level between left shoulder and elbow**
CC Exclusion 7th character A see Appendix A PDX collection 1267

CC +7th **S48.119 Complete traumatic amputation at level between unspecified shoulder and elbow**
CC Exclusion 7th character A see Appendix A PDX collection 1268

+ **S48.12 Partial traumatic amputation at level between shoulder and elbow**

CC +7th **S48.121 Partial traumatic amputation at level between right shoulder and elbow**
CC Exclusion 7th character A see Appendix A PDX collection 1266

CC +7th **S48.122 Partial traumatic amputation at level between left shoulder and elbow**
CC Exclusion 7th character A see Appendix A PDX collection 1267

CC +7th **S48.129 Partial traumatic amputation at level between unspecified shoulder and elbow**
CC Exclusion 7th character A see Appendix A PDX collection 1268

+ **S48.9 Traumatic amputation of shoulder and upper arm, level unspecified**
+ **S48.91 Complete traumatic amputation of shoulder and upper arm, level unspecified**

CC +7th **S48.911 Complete traumatic amputation of right shoulder and upper arm, level unspecified**
CC Exclusion 7th character A see Appendix A PDX collection 1266

CC +7th **S48.912 Complete traumatic amputation of left shoulder and upper arm, level unspecified**
CC Exclusion 7th character A see Appendix A PDX collection 1267

CC +7th **S48.919 Complete traumatic amputation of unspecified shoulder and upper arm, level unspecified**
CC Exclusion 7th character A see Appendix A PDX collection 1268

+ **S48.92 Partial traumatic amputation of shoulder and upper arm, level unspecified**

CC +7th **S48.921 Partial traumatic amputation of right shoulder and upper arm, level unspecified**
CC Exclusion 7th character A see Appendix A PDX collection 1266

CC +7th **S48.922 Partial traumatic amputation of left shoulder and upper arm, level unspecified**
CC Exclusion 7th character A see Appendix A PDX collection 1267

CC +7th **S48.929 Partial traumatic amputation of unspecified shoulder and upper arm, level unspecified**
CC Exclusion 7th character A see Appendix A PDX collection 1268

S49 Other and unspecified injuries of shoulder and upper arm

The appropriate 7th character is to be added to each code from subcategories S49.0 and S49.1
A initial encounter for closed fracture
D subsequent encounter for fracture with routine healing
G subsequent encounter for fracture with delayed healing
K subsequent encounter for fracture with nonunion
P subsequent encounter for fracture with malunion
S sequela

Review coding guideline C.19.c

+ **S49.0 Physeal fracture of upper end of humerus**
+ **S49.00 Unspecified physeal fracture of upper end of humerus**

CC +7th **S49.001 Unspecified physeal fracture of upper end of humerus, right arm**
CC Exclusion 7th character A see Appendix A PDX collection 1245
CC Exclusion 7th characters K & P see Appendix A PDX collection 0897
HAC 7th character A see Appendix B for HAC conditional logic

CC +7th **S49.002 Unspecified physeal fracture of upper end of humerus, left arm**
CC Exclusion 7th character A see Appendix A PDX collection 1247
CC Exclusion 7th characters K & P see Appendix A PDX collection 0897
HAC 7th character A see Appendix B for HAC conditional logic

CC +7th **S49.009 Unspecified physeal fracture of upper end of humerus, unspecified arm**
CC Exclusion 7th character A see Appendix A PDX collection 1248
CC Exclusion 7th characters K & P see Appendix A PDX collection 0897
HAC 7th character A see Appendix B for HAC conditional logic

+ **S49.01 Salter-Harris Type I physeal fracture of upper end of humerus**

CC +7th **S49.011 Salter-Harris Type I physeal fracture of upper end of humerus, right arm**
CC Exclusion 7th character A see Appendix A PDX collection 1245
CC Exclusion 7th characters K & P see Appendix A PDX collection 0897
HAC 7th character A see Appendix B for HAC conditional logic

CC +7th **S49.012 Salter-Harris Type I physeal fracture of upper end of humerus, left arm**
CC Exclusion 7th character A see Appendix A PDX collection 1247
CC Exclusion 7th characters K & P see Appendix A PDX collection 0897
HAC 7th character A see Appendix B for HAC conditional logic

CC +7th **S49.019 Salter-Harris Type I physeal fracture of upper end of humerus, unspecified arm**
CC Exclusion 7th character A see Appendix A PDX collection 1248
CC Exclusion 7th characters K & P see Appendix A PDX collection 0897
HAC 7th character A see Appendix B for HAC conditional logic

+ **S49.02 Salter-Harris Type II physeal fracture of upper end of humerus**

CC +7th **S49.021 Salter-Harris Type II physeal fracture of upper end of humerus, right arm**
CC Exclusion 7th character A see Appendix A PDX collection 1245
CC Exclusion 7th characters K & P see Appendix A PDX collection 0897
HAC 7th character A see Appendix B for HAC conditional logic

CC +7th **S49.022** **Salter-Harris Type II physeal fracture of upper end of humerus, left arm**
CC Exclusion 7th character A see Appendix A PDX collection 1247
CC Exclusion 7th characters K & P see Appendix A PDX collection 0897
HAC 7th character A see Appendix B for HAC conditional logic

CC +7th **S49.029** **Salter-Harris Type II physeal fracture of upper end of humerus, unspecified arm**
CC Exclusion 7th character A see Appendix A PDX collection 1248
CC Exclusion 7th characters K & P see Appendix A PDX collection 0897
HAC 7th character A see Appendix B for HAC conditional logic

\+ **S49.03** **Salter-Harris Type III physeal fracture of upper end of humerus**

CC +7th **S49.031** **Salter Harris Type III physeal fracture of upper end of humerus, right arm**
CC Exclusion 7th character A see Appendix A PDX collection 1245
CC Exclusion 7th characters K & P see Appendix A PDX collection 0897
HAC 7th character A see Appendix B for HAC conditional logic

CC +7th **S49.032** **Salter Harris Type III physeal fracture of upper end of humerus, left arm**
CC Exclusion 7th character A see Appendix A PDX collection 1247
CC Exclusion 7th characters K & P see Appendix A PDX collection 0897
HAC 7th character A see Appendix B for HAC conditional logic

CC +7th **S49.039** **Salter Harris Type III physeal fracture of upper end of humerus, unspecified arm**
CC Exclusion 7th character A see Appendix A PDX collection 1248
CC Exclusion 7th characters K & P see Appendix A PDX collection 0897
HAC 7th character A see Appendix B for HAC conditional logic

\+ **S49.04** **Salter-Harris Type IV physeal fracture of upper end of humerus**

CC +7th **S49.041** **Salter-Harris Type IV physeal fracture of upper end of humerus, right arm**
CC Exclusion 7th character A see Appendix A PDX collection 1245
CC Exclusion 7th characters K & P see Appendix A PDX collection 0897
HAC 7th character A see Appendix B for HAC conditional logic

CC +7th **S49.042** **Salter-Harris Type IV physeal fracture of upper end of humerus, left arm**
CC Exclusion 7th character A see Appendix A PDX collection 1247
CC Exclusion 7th characters K & P see Appendix A PDX collection 0897
HAC 7th character A see Appendix B for HAC conditional logic

CC +7th **S49.049** **Salter-Harris Type IV physeal fracture of upper end of humerus, unspecified arm**
CC Exclusion 7th character A see Appendix A PDX collection 1248
CC Exclusion 7th characters K & P see Appendix A PDX collection 0897
HAC 7th character A see Appendix B for HAC conditional logic

\+ **S49.09** **Other physeal fracture of upper end of humerus**

CC +7th **S49.091** **Other physeal fracture of upper end of humerus, right arm**
CC Exclusion 7th character A see Appendix A PDX collection 1245
CC Exclusion 7th characters K & P see Appendix A PDX collection 0897
HAC 7th character A see Appendix B for HAC conditional logic

CC +7th **S49.092** **Other physeal fracture of upper end of humerus, left arm**
CC Exclusion 7th character A see Appendix A PDX collection 1247
CC Exclusion 7th characters K & P see Appendix A PDX collection 0897
HAC 7th character A see Appendix B for HAC conditional logic

CC +7th **S49.099** **Other physeal fracture of upper end of humerus, unspecified arm**
CC Exclusion 7th character A see Appendix A PDX collection 1248
CC Exclusion 7th characters K & P see Appendix A PDX collection 0897
HAC 7th character A see Appendix B for HAC conditional logic

\+ **S49.1** **Physeal fracture of lower end of humerus**

\+ **S49.10** **Unspecified physeal fracture of lower end of humeru**

CC +7th **S49.101** **Unspecified physeal fracture of lower end o humerus, right arm**
CC Exclusion 7th character A see Appendix A PDX collection 1245
CC Exclusion 7th characters K & P see Appendix A PDX collection 0897
HAC 7th character A see Appendix B for HAC conditional logic

CC +7th **S49.102** **Unspecified physeal fracture of lower end o humerus, left arm**
CC Exclusion 7th character A see Appendix A PDX collection 1247
CC Exclusion 7th characters K & P see Appendix A PDX collection 0897
HAC 7th character A see Appendix B for HAC conditional logic

CC +7th **S49.109** **Unspecified physeal fracture of lower end o humerus, unspecified arm**
CC Exclusion 7th character A see Appendix A PDX collection 1248
CC Exclusion 7th characters K & P see Appendix A PDX collection 0897
HAC 7th character A see Appendix B for HAC conditional logic

\+ **S49.11** **Salter-Harris Type I physeal fracture of lower end of humerus**

CC +7th **S49.111** **Salter-Harris Type I physeal fracture of lower end of humerus, right arm**
CC Exclusion 7th character A see Appendix A PDX collection 1245
CC Exclusion 7th characters K & P see Appendix A PDX collection 0897
HAC 7th character A see Appendix B for HAC conditional logic

CC +7th **S49.112** **Salter-Harris Type I physeal fracture of lower end of humerus, left arm**
CC Exclusion 7th character A see Appendix A PDX collection 1247
CC Exclusion 7th characters K & P see Appendix A PDX collection 0897
HAC 7th character A see Appendix B for HAC conditional logic

CC +7th **S49.119** **Salter-Harris Type I physeal fracture of lower end of humerus, unspecified arm**
CC Exclusion 7th character A see Appendix A PDX collection 1248
CC Exclusion 7th characters K & P see Appendix A PDX collection 0897
HAC 7th character A see Appendix B for HAC conditional logic

\+ **S49.12** **Salter-Harris Type II physeal fracture of lower end o humerus**

CC +7th **S49.121** **Salter-Harris Type II physeal fracture of lower end of humerus, right arm**
CC Exclusion 7th character A see Appendix A PDX collection 1245
CC Exclusion 7th characters K & P see Appendix A PDX collection 0897
HAC 7th character A see Appendix B for HAC conditional logic

CC +7th **S49.122** **Salter-Harris Type II physeal fracture of lower end of humerus, left arm**
CC Exclusion 7th character A see Appendix A PDX collection 1247
CC Exclusion 7th characters K & P see Appendix A PDX collection 0897
HAC 7th character A see Appendix B for HAC conditional logic

CC +7th **S49.129** **Salter-Harris Type II physeal fracture of lower end of humerus, unspecified arm**
CC Exclusion 7th character A see Appendix A PDX collection 1248
CC Exclusion 7th characters K & P see Appendix A PDX collection 0897
HAC 7th character A see Appendix B for HAC conditional logic

+ **S49.13 Salter Harris Type III physeal fracture of lower end of humerus**

CC +7th **S49.131 Salter Harris Type III physeal fracture of lower end of humerus, right arm**
CC Exclusion 7th character A see Appendix A PDX collection 1245
CC Exclusion 7th characters K & P see Appendix A PDX collection 0897
HAC 7th character A see Appendix B for HAC conditional logic

CC +7th **S49.132 Salter Harris Type III physeal fracture of lower end of humerus, left arm**
CC Exclusion 7th character A see Appendix A PDX collection 1247
CC Exclusion 7th characters K & P see Appendix A PDX collection 0897
HAC 7th character A see Appendix B for HAC conditional logic

CC +7th **S49.139 Salter Harris Type III physeal fracture of lower end of humerus, unspecified arm**
CC Exclusion 7th character A see Appendix A PDX collection 1248
CC Exclusion 7th characters K & P see Appendix A PDX collection 0897
HAC 7th character A see Appendix B for HAC conditional logic

+ **S49.14 Salter-Harris Type IV physeal fracture of lower end of humerus**

CC +7th **S49.141 Salter-Harris Type IV physeal fracture of lower end of humerus, right arm**
CC Exclusion 7th character A see Appendix A PDX collection 1245
CC Exclusion 7th characters K & P see Appendix A PDX collection 0897
HAC 7th character A see Appendix B for HAC conditional logic

CC +7th **S49.142 Salter-Harris Type IV physeal fracture of lower end of humerus, left arm**
CC Exclusion 7th character A see Appendix A PDX collection 1247
CC Exclusion 7th characters K & P see Appendix A PDX collection 0897
HAC 7th character A see Appendix B for HAC conditional logic

CC +7th **S49.149 Salter-Harris Type IV physeal fracture of lower end of humerus, unspecified arm**
CC Exclusion 7th character A see Appendix A PDX collection 1248
CC Exclusion 7th characters K & P see Appendix A PDX collection 0897
HAC 7th character A see Appendix B for HAC conditional logic

+ **S49.19 Other physeal fracture of lower end of humerus**

CC +7th **S49.191 Other physeal fracture of lower end of humerus, right arm**
CC Exclusion 7th character A see Appendix A PDX collection 1245
CC Exclusion 7th characters K & P see Appendix A PDX collection 0897
HAC 7th character A see Appendix B for HAC conditional logic

CC +7th **S49.192 Other physeal fracture of lower end of humerus, left arm**
CC Exclusion 7th character A see Appendix A PDX collection 1247
CC Exclusion 7th characters K & P see Appendix A PDX collection 0897
HAC 7th character A see Appendix B for HAC conditional logic

CC +7th **S49.199 Other physeal fracture of lower end of humerus, unspecified arm**
CC Exclusion 7th character A see Appendix A PDX collection 1248
CC Exclusion 7th characters K & P see Appendix A PDX collection 0897
HAC 7th character A see Appendix B for HAC conditional logic

+ **S49.8 Other specified injuries of shoulder and upper arm**

The appropriate 7th character is to be added to each code in subcategory S49.8
A initial encounter
D subsequent encounter
S sequela

X+7th **S49.80 Other specified injuries of shoulder and upper arm, unspecified arm**
X+7th **S49.81 Other specified injuries of right shoulder and upper arm**
X+7th **S49.82 Other specified injuries of left shoulder and upper arm**

+ **S49.9 Unspecified injury of shoulder and upper arm**

The appropriate 7th character is to be added to each code in subcategory S49.9
A initial encounter
D subsequent encounter
S sequela

X+7th **S49.90 Unspecified injury of shoulder and upper arm, unspecified arm**
X+7th **S49.91 Unspecified injury of right shoulder and upper arm**
X+7th **S49.92 Unspecified injury of left shoulder and upper arm**

Injuries to the elbow and forearm (S50-S59)

Excludes2: *burns and corrosions (T20-T32)*
frostbite (T33-T34)
injuries of wrist and hand (S60-S69)
insect bite or sting, venomous (T63.4)

S50 Superficial injury of elbow and forearm

Excludes2: *superficial injury of wrist and hand (S60.-)*

The appropriate 7th character is to be added to each code from category S50
A initial encounter
D subsequent encounter
S sequela

+ **S50.0 Contusion of elbow**
X+7th **S50.00 Contusion of unspecified elbow**
X+7th **S50.01 Contusion of right elbow**
X+7th **S50.02 Contusion of left elbow**

+ **S50.1 Contusion of forearm**
X+7th **S50.10 Contusion of unspecified forearm**
X+7th **S50.11 Contusion of right forearm**
X+7th **S50.12 Contusion of left forearm**

+ **S50.3 Other superficial injuries of elbow**

+ **S50.31 Abrasion of elbow**
+7th **S50.311 Abrasion of right elbow**
+7th **S50.312 Abrasion of left elbow**
+7th **S50.319 Abrasion of unspecified elbow**

+ **S50.32 Blister (nonthermal) of elbow**
+7th **S50.321 Blister (nonthermal) of right elbow**
+7th **S50.322 Blister (nonthermal) of left elbow**
+7th **S50.329 Blister (nonthermal) of unspecified elbow**

+ **S50.34 External constriction of elbow**
+7th **S50.341 External constriction of right elbow**
+7th **S50.342 External constriction of left elbow**
+7th **S50.349 External constriction of unspecified elbow**

+ **S50.35 Superficial foreign body of elbow**
Splinter in the elbow
+7th **S50.351 Superficial foreign body of right elbow**
+7th **S50.352 Superficial foreign body of left elbow**
+7th **S50.359 Superficial foreign body of unspecified elbow**

+ **S50.36 Insect bite (nonvenomous) of elbow**
+7th **S50.361 Insect bite (nonvenomous) of right elbow**
+7th **S50.362 Insect bite (nonvenomous) of left elbow**
+7th **S50.369 Insect bite (nonvenomous) of unspecified elbow**

+ **S50.37 Other superficial bite of elbow**
Excludes1: *open bite of elbow (S51.04)*
+7th **S50.371 Other superficial bite of right elbow**
+7th **S50.372 Other superficial bite of left elbow**
+7th **S50.379 Other superficial bite of unspecified elbow**

+ **S50.8 Other superficial injuries of forearm**

+ **S50.81 Abrasion of forearm**
+7th **S50.811 Abrasion of right forearm**
+7th **S50.812 Abrasion of left forearm**
+7th **S50.819 Abrasion of unspecified forearm**

+ **S50.82 Blister (nonthermal) of forearm**
+7th **S50.821 Blister (nonthermal) of right forearm**
+7th **S50.822 Blister (nonthermal) of left forearm**
+7th **S50.829 Blister (nonthermal) of unspecified forearm**

+ **S50.84 External constriction of forearm**
+7th **S50.841 External constriction of right forearm**
+7th **S50.842 External constriction of left forearm**
+7th **S50.849 External constriction of unspecified forearm**

+ **S50.85 Superficial foreign body of forearm**
Splinter in the forearm
+7th **S50.851 Superficial foreign body of right forearm**
+7th **S50.852 Superficial foreign body of left forearm**
+7th **S50.859 Superficial foreign body of unspecified forearm**

Elbow

+ **S50.86 Insect bite (nonvenomous) of forearm**
  - +7th **S50.861 Insect bite (nonvenomous) of right forearm**
  - +7th **S50.862 Insect bite (nonvenomous) of left forearm**
  - +7th **S50.869 Insect bite (nonvenomous) of unspecified forearm**

+ **S50.87 Other superficial bite of forearm**
  Excludes1: *open bite of forearm (S51.84)*
  - +7th **S50.871 Other superficial bite of right forearm**
  - +7th **S50.872 Other superficial bite of left forearm**
  - +7th **S50.879 Other superficial bite of unspecified forearm**

+ **S50.9 Unspecified superficial injury of elbow and forearm**

+ **S50.90 Unspecified superficial injury of elbow**
  - +7th **S50.901 Unspecified superficial injury of right elbow**
  - +7th **S50.902 Unspecified superficial injury of left elbow**
  - +7th **S50.909 Unspecified superficial injury of unspecified elbow**

+ **S50.91 Unspecified superficial injury of forearm**
  - **S50.911 Unspecified superficial injury of right forearm**
  - **S50.912 Unspecified superficial injury of left forearm**
  - **S50.919 Unspecified superficial injury of unspecified forearm**

S51 Open wound of elbow and forearm

Code also any associated wound infection
Excludes1: *open fracture of elbow and forearm (S52.- with open fracture 7th character)*
traumatic amputation of elbow and forearm (S58.-)
Excludes2: *open wound of wrist and hand (S61.-)*

The appropriate 7th character is to be added to each code from category S51
A initial encounter
D subsequent encounter
S sequela

+ **S51.0 Open wound of elbow**

+ **S51.00 Unspecified open wound of elbow**
  - +7th **S51.001 Unspecified open wound of right elbow**
    AHA CC: 4Q, 2012, 108
  - +7th **S51.002 Unspecified open wound of left elbow**
  - +7th **S51.009 Unspecified open wound of unspecified elbow**
    Open wound of elbow NOS

+ **S51.01 Laceration without foreign body of elbow**
  - +7th **S51.011 Laceration without foreign body of right elbow**
  - +7th **S51.012 Laceration without foreign body of left elbow**
  - +7th **S51.019 Laceration without foreign body of unspecified elbow**

+ **S51.02 Laceration with foreign body of elbow**
  - +7th **S51.021 Laceration with foreign body of right elbow**
  - +7th **S51.022 Laceration with foreign body of left elbow**
  - +7th **S51.029 Laceration with foreign body of unspecified elbow**

+ **S51.03 Puncture wound without foreign body of elbow**
  - +7th **S51.031 Puncture wound without foreign body of right elbow**
  - +7th **S51.032 Puncture wound without foreign body of left elbow**
  - +7th **S51.039 Puncture wound without foreign body of unspecified elbow**

+ **S51.04 Puncture wound with foreign body of elbow**
  - +7th **S51.041 Puncture wound with foreign body of right elbow**
  - +7th **S51.042 Puncture wound with foreign body of left elbow**
  - +7th **S51.049 Puncture wound with foreign body of unspecified elbow**

+ **S51.05 Open bite of elbow**
  Bite of elbow NOS
  Excludes1: *superficial bite of elbow (S50.36, S50.37)*
  - +7th **S51.051 Open bite, right elbow**
  - +7th **S51.052 Open bite, left elbow**
  - +7th **S51.059 Open bite, unspecified elbow**

+ **S51.8 Open wound of forearm**
  Excludes2: *open wound of elbow (S51.0-)*

+ **S51.80 Unspecified open wound of forearm**
  - +7th **S51.801 Unspecified open wound of right forearm**
  - +7th **S51.802 Unspecified open wound of left forearm**
  - +7th **S51.809 Unspecified open wound of unspecified forearm**
    Open wound of forearm NOS

+ **S51.81 Laceration without foreign body of forearm**
  - +7th **S51.811 Laceration without foreign body of right forearm**
  - +7th **S51.812 Laceration without foreign body of left forearm**
  - +7th **S51.819 Laceration without foreign body of unspecified forearm**

+ **S51.82 Laceration with foreign body of forearm**
  - +7th **S51.821 Laceration with foreign body of right forearm**

+7th **S51.822 Laceration with foreign body of left forearm**
+7th **S51.829 Laceration with foreign body of unspecified forearm**
+ **S51.83 Puncture wound without foreign body of forearm**
+7th **S51.831 Puncture wound without foreign body of right forearm**
+7th **S51.832 Puncture wound without foreign body of left forearm**
+7th **S51.839 Puncture wound without foreign body of unspecified forearm**
+ **S51.84 Puncture wound with foreign body of forearm**
+7th **S51.841 Puncture wound with foreign body of right forearm**
+7th **S51.842 Puncture wound with foreign body of left forearm**
+7th **S51.849 Puncture wound with foreign body of unspecified forearm**
+ **S51.85 Open bite of forearm**
Bite of forearm NOS
Excludes1: *superficial bite of forearm (S50.86, S50.87)*
+7th **S51.851 Open bite of right forearm**
+7th **S51.852 Open bite of left forearm**
+7th **S51.859 Open bite of unspecified forearm**

S52 Fracture of forearm

NOTE A fracture not indicated as displaced or nondisplaced should be coded to displaced
A fracture not indicated as open or closed should be coded to closed
The open fracture designations are based on the Gustilo open fracture classification

Excludes1: *traumatic amputation of forearm (S58.-)*
Excludes2: *fracture at wrist and hand level (S62.-)*

The appropriate 7th character is to be added to all codes from category S52
- A initial encounter for closed fracture
- B initial encounter for open fracture type I or II initial encounter for open fracture NOS
- C initial encounter for open fracture type IIIA, IIIB, or IIIC
- D subsequent encounter for closed fracture with routine healing
- E subsequent encounter for open fracture type I or II with routine healing
- F subsequent encounter for open fracture type IIIA, IIIB, or IIIC with routine healing
- G subsequent encounter for closed fracture with delayed healing
- H subsequent encounter for open fracture type I or II with delayed healing
- J subsequent encounter for open fracture type IIIA, IIIB, or IIIC with delayed healing
- K subsequent encounter for closed fracture with nonunion
- M subsequent encounter for open fracture type I or II with nonunion
- N subsequent encounter for open fracture type IIIA, IIIB, or IIIC with nonunion
- P subsequent encounter for closed fracture with malunion
- Q subsequent encounter for open fracture type I or II with malunion
- R subsequent encounter for open fracture type IIIA, IIIB, or IIIC with malunion
- S sequela

Review coding guideline C.19.c

+ **S52.0 Fracture of upper end of ulna**
Fracture of proximal end of ulna
Excludes2: *fracture of elbow NOS (S42.40-)*
fractures of shaft of ulna (S52.2-)

+ **S52.00 Unspecified fracture of upper end of ulna**

CC MCC +7th **S52.001 Unspecified fracture of upper end of right ulna**
CC Exclusion 7th characters K - R see Appendix A PDX collection 0897
MCC Exclusion 7th characters B & C see Appendix A PDX collection 1269
HAC 7th characters B & C see Appendix B for HAC conditional logic

CC MCC +7th **S52.002 Unspecified fracture of upper end of left ulna**
CC Exclusion 7th characters K - R see Appendix A PDX collection 0897
MCC Exclusion 7th characters B & C see Appendix A PDX collection 1269
HAC 7th characters B & C see Appendix B for HAC conditional logic

CC MCC +7th **S52.009 Unspecified fracture of upper end of unspecified ulna**
CC Exclusion 7th characters K - R see Appendix A PDX collection 0897
MCC Exclusion 7th characters B & C see Appendix A PDX collection 1269
HAC 7th characters B & C see Appendix B for HAC conditional logic

+ **S52.01 Torus fracture of upper end of ulna**

The appropriate 7th character is to be added to all codes in subcategory S52.01
- A initial encounter for closed fracture
- D subsequent encounter for fracture with routine healing
- G subsequent encounter for fracture with delayed healing
- K subsequent encounter for fracture with nonunion
- P - subsequent encounter for fracture with malunion
- S - sequela

CC +7th **S52.011 Torus fracture of upper end of right ulna**
CC Exclusion 7th character A see Appendix A PDX collection 1270
CC Exclusion 7th characters K & P see Appendix A PDX collection 0897
HAC 7th character A see Appendix B for HAC conditional logic

CC +7th **S52.012 Torus fracture of upper end of left ulna**
CC Exclusion 7th character A see Appendix A PDX collection 1271
CC Exclusion 7th characters K & P see Appendix A PDX collection 0897
HAC 7th character A see Appendix B for HAC conditional logic

CC +7th **S52.019 Torus fracture of upper end of unspecified ulna**
CC Exclusion 7th character A see Appendix A PDX collection 1272
CC Exclusion 7th characters K & P see Appendix A PDX collection 0897
HAC 7th character A see Appendix B for HAC conditional logic

+ **S52.02 Fracture of olecranon process without intraarticular extension of ulna**

CC MCC +7th **S52.021 Displaced fracture of olecranon process without intraarticular extension of right ulna**
CC Exclusion 7th characters K - R see Appendix A PDX collection 0897
MCC Exclusion 7th characters B & C see Appendix A PDX collection 1273
HAC 7th characters B & C see Appendix B for HAC conditional logic

CC MCC +7th **S52.022 Displaced fracture of olecranon process without intraarticular extension of left ulna**
CC Exclusion 7th characters K - R see Appendix A PDX collection 0897
MCC Exclusion 7th characters B & C see Appendix A PDX collection 1273
HAC 7th characters B & C see Appendix B for HAC conditional logic

CC MCC +7th **S52.023 Displaced fracture of olecranon process without intraarticular extension of unspecified ulna**
CC Exclusion 7th characters K - R see Appendix A PDX collection 0897
MCC Exclusion 7th characters B & C see Appendix A PDX collection 1273
HAC 7th characters B & C see Appendix B for HAC conditional logic

CC MCC +7th **S52.024 Nondisplaced fracture of olecranon process without intraarticular extension of right ulna**
CC Exclusion 7th characters K - R see Appendix A PDX collection 0897
MCC Exclusion 7th characters B & C see Appendix A PDX collection 1273
HAC 7th characters B & C see Appendix B for HAC conditional logic

CC MCC +7th **S52.025 Nondisplaced fracture of olecranon process without intraarticular extension of left ulna**
CC Exclusion 7th characters K - R see Appendix A PDX collection 0897
MCC Exclusion 7th characters B & C see Appendix A PDX collection 1273
HAC 7th characters B & C see Appendix B for HAC conditional logic

CC MCC +7th S52.026 Nondisplaced fracture of olecranon process without intraarticular extension of unspecified ulna
CC Exclusion 7th characters K - R see Appendix A PDX collection 0897
MCC Exclusion 7th characters B & C see Appendix A PDX collection 1273
HAC 7th characters B & C see Appendix B for HAC conditional logic

+ S52.03 Fracture of olecranon process with intraarticular extension of ulna

CC MCC +7th S52.031 Displaced fracture of olecranon process with intraarticular extension of right ulna
CC Exclusion 7th characters K - R see Appendix A PDX collection 0897
MCC Exclusion 7th characters B & C see Appendix A PDX collection 1273
HAC 7th characters B & C see Appendix B for HAC conditional logic

CC MCC +7th S52.032 Displaced fracture of olecranon process with intraarticular extension of left ulna
CC Exclusion 7th characters K - R see Appendix A PDX collection 0897
MCC Exclusion 7th characters B & C see Appendix A PDX collection 1273
HAC 7th characters B & C see Appendix B for HAC conditional logic

CC MCC +7th S52.033 Displaced fracture of olecranon process with intraarticular extension of unspecified ulna
CC Exclusion 7th characters K - R see Appendix A PDX collection 0897
MCC Exclusion 7th characters B & C see Appendix A PDX collection 1273
HAC 7th characters B & C see Appendix B for HAC conditional logic

CC MCC +7th S52.034 Nondisplaced fracture of olecranon process with intraarticular extension of right ulna
CC Exclusion 7th characters K - R see Appendix A PDX collection 0897
MCC Exclusion 7th characters B & C see Appendix A PDX collection 1273
HAC 7th characters B & C see Appendix B for HAC conditional logic

CC MCC +7th S52.035 Nondisplaced fracture of olecranon process with intraarticular extension of left ulna
CC Exclusion 7th characters K - R see Appendix A PDX collection 0897
MCC Exclusion 7th characters B & C see Appendix A PDX collection 1273
HAC 7th characters B & C see Appendix B for HAC conditional logic

CC MCC +7th S52.036 Nondisplaced fracture of olecranon process with intraarticular extension of unspecified ulna
CC Exclusion 7th characters K - R see Appendix A PDX collection 0897
MCC Exclusion 7th characters B & C see Appendix A PDX collection 1273
HAC 7th characters B & C see Appendix B for HAC conditional logic

+ S52.04 Fracture of coronoid process of ulna

CC MCC +7th S52.041 Displaced fracture of coronoid process of right ulna
CC Exclusion 7th characters K - R see Appendix A PDX collection 0897
MCC Exclusion 7th characters B & C see Appendix A PDX collection 1269
HAC 7th characters B & C see Appendix B for HAC conditional logic

CC MCC +7th S52.042 Displaced fracture of coronoid process of left ulna
CC Exclusion 7th characters K - R see Appendix A PDX collection 0897
MCC Exclusion 7th characters B & C see Appendix A PDX collection 1269
HAC 7th characters B & C see Appendix B for HAC conditional logic

CC MCC +7th S52.043 Displaced fracture of coronoid process of unspecified ulna
CC Exclusion 7th characters K - R see Appendix A PDX collection 0897
MCC Exclusion 7th characters B & C see Appendix A PDX collection 1269
HAC 7th characters B & C see Appendix B for HAC conditional logic

CC MCC +7th S52.044 Nondisplaced fracture of coronoid process o right ulna
CC Exclusion 7th characters K - R see Appendix A PDX collection 0897
MCC Exclusion 7th characters B & C see Appendix A PDX collection 1269
HAC 7th characters B & C see Appendix B for HAC conditional logic

CC MCC +7th S52.045 Nondisplaced fracture of coronoid process o left ulna
CC Exclusion 7th characters K - R see Appendix A PDX collection 0897
MCC Exclusion 7th characters B & C see Appendix A PDX collection 1269
HAC 7th characters B & C see Appendix B for HAC conditional logic

CC MCC +7th S52.046 Nondisplaced fracture of coronoid process o unspecified ulna
CC Exclusion 7th characters K - R see Appendix A PDX collection 0897
MCC Exclusion 7th characters B & C see Appendix A PDX collection 1269
HAC 7th characters B & C see Appendix B for HAC conditional logic

+ S52.09 Other fracture of upper end of ulna

CC MCC +7th S52.091 Other fracture of upper end of right ulna
CC Exclusion 7th characters K - R see Appendix A PDX collection 0897
MCC Exclusion 7th characters B & C see Appendix A PDX collection 1269
HAC 7th characters B & C see Appendix B for HAC conditional logic

CC MCC +7th S52.092 Other fracture of upper end of left ulna
CC Exclusion 7th characters K - R see Appendix A PDX collection 0897
MCC Exclusion 7th characters B & C see Appendix A PDX collection 1269
HAC 7th characters B & C see Appendix B for HAC conditional logic

CC MCC +7th S52.099 Other fracture of upper end of unspecified ulna
CC Exclusion 7th characters K - R see Appendix A PDX collection 0897
MCC Exclusion 7th characters B & C see Appendix A PDX collection 1269
HAC 7th characters B & C see Appendix B for HAC conditional logic

+ S52.1 Fracture of upper end of radius
Fracture of proximal end of radius
Excludes2: *physeal fractures of upper end of radius (S59.2-)*
fracture of shaft of radius (S52.3-)

+ S52.10 Unspecified fracture of upper end of radius

CC MCC +7th S52.101 Unspecified fracture of upper end of right radius
CC Exclusion 7th characters K - R see Appendix A PDX collection 0897
MCC Exclusion 7th characters B & C see Appendix A PDX collection 1269
HAC 7th characters B & C see Appendix B for HAC conditional logic

CC MCC +7th S52.102 Unspecified fracture of upper end of left radius
CC Exclusion 7th characters K - R see Appendix A PDX collection 0897
MCC Exclusion 7th characters B & C see Appendix A PDX collection 1269
HAC 7th characters B & C see Appendix B for HAC conditional logic

CC MCC +7th S52.109 Unspecified fracture of upper end of unspecified radius
CC Exclusion 7th characters K - R see Appendix A PDX collection 0897
MCC Exclusion 7th characters B & C see Appendix A PDX collection 1269
HAC 7th characters B & C see Appendix B for HAC conditional logic

+ S52.11 Torus fracture of upper end of radius

The appropriate 7th character is to be added to all codes in subcategory S52.11
A initial encounter for closed fracture
D subsequent encounter for fracture with routine healing
G subsequent encounter for fracture with delayed healing
K subsequent encounter for fracture with nonunion
P subsequent encounter for fracture with malunion
S sequela

CC +7th **S52.111 Torus fracture of upper end of right radius**
CC Exclusion 7th character A see Appendix A PDX collection 1270
CC Exclusion 7th characters K & P see Appendix A PDX collection 0897
HAC 7th character A see Appendix B for HAC conditional logic

CC +7th **S52.112 Torus fracture of upper end of left radius**
CC Exclusion 7th character A see Appendix A PDX collection 1271
CC Exclusion 7th characters K & P see Appendix A PDX collection 0897
HAC 7th character A see Appendix B for HAC conditional logic

CC +7th **S52.119 Torus fracture of upper end of unspecified radius**
CC Exclusion 7th character A see Appendix A PDX collection 1272
CC Exclusion 7th characters K & P see Appendix A PDX collection 0897
HAC 7th character A see Appendix B for HAC conditional logic

+ S52.12 Fracture of head of radius

CC MCC +7th **S52.121 Displaced fracture of head of right radius**
CC Exclusion 7th characters K - R see Appendix A PDX collection 0897
MCC Exclusion 7th characters B & C see Appendix A PDX collection 1269
HAC 7th characters B & C see Appendix B for HAC conditional logic

CC MCC +7th **S52.122 Displaced fracture of head of left radius**
CC Exclusion 7th characters K - R see Appendix A PDX collection 0897
MCC Exclusion 7th characters B & C see Appendix A PDX collection 1269
HAC 7th characters B & C see Appendix B for HAC conditional logic

CC MCC +7th **S52.123 Displaced fracture of head of unspecified radius**
CC Exclusion 7th characters K - R see Appendix A PDX collection 0897
MCC Exclusion 7th characters B & C see Appendix A PDX collection 1269
HAC 7th characters B & C see Appendix B for HAC conditional logic

CC MCC +7th **S52.124 Nondisplaced fracture of head of right radius**
CC Exclusion 7th characters K - R see Appendix A PDX collection 0897
MCC Exclusion 7th characters B & C see Appendix A PDX collection 1269
HAC 7th characters B & C see Appendix B for HAC conditional logic

CC MCC +7th **S52.125 Nondisplaced fracture of head of left radius**
CC Exclusion 7th characters K - R see Appendix A PDX collection 0897
MCC Exclusion 7th characters B & C see Appendix A PDX collection 1269
HAC 7th characters B & C see Appendix B for HAC conditional logic

CC MCC +7th **S52.126 Nondisplaced fracture of head of unspecified radius**
CC Exclusion 7th characters K - R see Appendix A PDX collection 0897
MCC Exclusion 7th characters B & C see Appendix A PDX collection 1269
HAC 7th characters B & C see Appendix B for HAC conditional logic

+ S52.13 Fracture of neck of radius

CC MCC +7th **S52.131 Displaced fracture of neck of right radius**
CC Exclusion 7th characters K - R see Appendix A PDX collection 0897
MCC Exclusion 7th characters B & C see Appendix A PDX collection 1269
HAC 7th characters B & C see Appendix B for HAC conditional logic

CC MCC +7th **S52.132 Displaced fracture of neck of left radius**
CC Exclusion 7th characters K - R see Appendix A PDX collection 0897
MCC Exclusion 7th characters B & C see Appendix A PDX collection 1269
HAC 7th characters B & C see Appendix B for HAC conditional logic

CC MCC +7th **S52.133 Displaced fracture of neck of unspecified radius**
CC Exclusion 7th characters K - R see Appendix A PDX collection 0897
MCC Exclusion 7th characters B & C see Appendix A PDX collection 1269
HAC 7th characters B & C see Appendix B for HAC conditional logic

CC MCC +7th **S52.134 Nondisplaced fracture of neck of right radius**
CC Exclusion 7th characters K - R see Appendix A PDX collection 0897
MCC Exclusion 7th characters B & C see Appendix A PDX collection 1269
HAC 7th characters B & C see Appendix B for HAC conditional logic

CC MCC +7th **S52.135 Nondisplaced fracture of neck of left radius**
CC Exclusion 7th characters K - R see Appendix A PDX collection 0897
MCC Exclusion 7th characters B & C see Appendix A PDX collection 1269
HAC 7th characters B & C see Appendix B for HAC conditional logic

CC MCC +7th **S52.136 Nondisplaced fracture of neck of unspecified radius**
CC Exclusion 7th characters K - R see Appendix A PDX collection 0897
MCC Exclusion 7th characters B & C see Appendix A PDX collection 1269
HAC 7th characters B & C see Appendix B for HAC conditional logic

+ S52.18 Other fracture of upper end of radius

CC MCC +7th **S52.181 Other fracture of upper end of right radius**
CC Exclusion 7th characters K - R see Appendix A PDX collection 0897
MCC Exclusion 7th characters B & C see Appendix A PDX collection 1269
HAC 7th characters B & C see Appendix B for HAC conditional logic

CC MCC +7th **S52.182 Other fracture of upper end of left radius**
CC Exclusion 7th characters K - R see Appendix A PDX collection 0897
MCC Exclusion 7th characters B & C see Appendix A PDX collection 1269
HAC 7th characters B & C see Appendix B for HAC conditional logic

CC MCC +7th **S52.189 Other fracture of upper end of unspecified radius**
CC Exclusion 7th characters K - R see Appendix A PDX collection 0897
MCC Exclusion 7th characters B & C see Appendix A PDX collection 1269
HAC 7th characters B & C see Appendix B for HAC conditional logic

+ S52.2 Fracture of shaft of ulna

+ S52.20 Unspecified fracture of shaft of ulna
Fracture of ulna NOS

CC MCC +7th **S52.201 Unspecified fracture of shaft of right ulna**
CC Exclusion 7th character A see Appendix A PDX collection 1270
CC Exclusion 7th characters K - R see Appendix A PDX collection 0897
MCC Exclusion 7th characters B & C see Appendix A PDX collection 1269
HAC 7th characters A - C see Appendix B for HAC conditional logic

CC MCC +7th **S52.202 Unspecified fracture of shaft of left ulna**
CC Exclusion 7th character A see Appendix A PDX collection 1271
CC Exclusion 7th characters K - R see Appendix A PDX collection 0897
MCC Exclusion 7th characters B & C see Appendix A PDX collection 1269
HAC 7th characters A - C see Appendix B for HAC conditional logic

CC MCC +7th **S52.209 Unspecified fracture of shaft of unspecified ulna**
- **CC Exclusion 7th character A see Appendix A PDX collection 1272**
- **CC Exclusion 7th characters K - R see Appendix A PDX collection 0897**
- **MCC Exclusion 7th characters B & C see Appendix A PDX collection 1269**
- HAC 7th characters A - C see Appendix B for HAC conditional logic

\+ **S52.21 Greenstick fracture of shaft of ulna**

The appropriate 7th character is to be added to all codes in subcategory S52.21
A initial encounter for closed fracture
D subsequent encounter for fracture with routine healing
G subsequent encounter for fracture with delayed healing
K subsequent encounter for fracture with nonunion
P subsequent encounter for fracture with malunion
S sequela

CC +7th **S52.211 Greenstick fracture of shaft of right ulna**
- **CC Exclusion 7th character A see Appendix A PDX collection 1270**
- **CC Exclusion 7th characters K - R see Appendix A PDX collection 0897**
- HAC 7th character A see Appendix B for HAC conditional logic

CC +7th **S52.212 Greenstick fracture of shaft of left ulna**
- **CC Exclusion 7th character A see Appendix A PDX collection 1271**
- **CC Exclusion 7th characters K - R see Appendix A PDX collection 0897**
- HAC 7th character A see Appendix B for HAC conditional logic

CC +7th **S52.219 Greenstick fracture of shaft of unspecified ulna**
- **CC Exclusion 7th character A see Appendix A PDX collection 1272**
- **CC Exclusion 7th characters K - R see Appendix A PDX collection 0897**
- HAC 7th character A see Appendix B for HAC conditional logic

\+ **S52.22 Transverse fracture of shaft of ulna**

CC MCC +7th **S52.221 Displaced transverse fracture of shaft of right ulna**
- **CC Exclusion 7th character A see Appendix A PDX collection 1270**
- **CC Exclusion 7th characters K - R see Appendix A PDX collection 0897**
- **MCC Exclusion 7th characters B & C see Appendix A PDX collection 1269**
- HAC 7th characters A - C see Appendix B for HAC conditional logic

CC MCC +7th **S52.222 Displaced transverse fracture of shaft of left ulna**
- **CC Exclusion 7th character A see Appendix A PDX collection 1271**
- **CC Exclusion 7th characters K - R see Appendix A PDX collection 0897**
- **MCC Exclusion 7th characters B & C see Appendix A PDX collection 1269**
- HAC 7th characters A - C see Appendix B for HAC conditional logic

CC MCC +7th **S52.223 Displaced transverse fracture of shaft of unspecified ulna**
- **CC Exclusion 7th character A see Appendix A PDX collection 1272**
- **CC Exclusion 7th characters K - R see Appendix A PDX collection 0897**
- **MCC Exclusion 7th characters B & C see Appendix A PDX collection 1269**
- HAC 7th characters A - C see Appendix B for HAC conditional logic

CC MCC +7th **S52.224 Nondisplaced transverse fracture of shaft of right ulna**
- **CC Exclusion 7th character A see Appendix A PDX collection 1270**
- **CC Exclusion 7th characters K - R see Appendix A PDX collection 0897**
- **MCC Exclusion 7th characters B & C see Appendix A PDX collection 1269**
- HAC 7th characters A - C see Appendix B for HAC conditional logic

CC MCC +7th **S52.225 Nondisplaced transverse fracture of shaft of left ulna**
- **CC Exclusion 7th character A see Appendix A PDX collection 1271**
- **CC Exclusion 7th characters K - R see Appendix A PDX collection 0897**
- **MCC Exclusion 7th characters B & C see Appendix A PDX collection 1269**
- HAC 7th characters A - C see Appendix B for HAC conditional logic

CC MCC +7th **S52.226 Nondisplaced transverse fracture of shaft of unspecified ulna**
- **CC Exclusion 7th character A see Appendix A PDX collection 1272**
- **CC Exclusion 7th characters K - R see Appendix A PDX collection 0897**
- **MCC Exclusion 7th characters B & C see Appendix A PDX collection 1269**
- HAC 7th characters A - C see Appendix B for HAC conditional logic

\+ **S52.23 Oblique fracture of shaft of ulna**

CC MCC +7th **S52.231 Displaced oblique fracture of shaft of right ulna**
- **CC Exclusion 7th character A see Appendix A PDX collection 1270**
- **CC Exclusion 7th characters K - R see Appendix A PDX collection 0897**
- **MCC Exclusion 7th characters B & C see Appendix A PDX collection 1269**
- HAC 7th characters A - C see Appendix B for HAC conditional logic

CC MCC +7th **S52.232 Displaced oblique fracture of shaft of left ulna**
- **CC Exclusion 7th character A see Appendix A PDX collection 1271**
- **CC Exclusion 7th characters K - R see Appendix A PDX collection 0897**
- **MCC Exclusion 7th characters B & C see Appendix A PDX collection 1269**
- HAC 7th characters A - C see Appendix B for HAC conditional logic

CC MCC +7th **S52.233 Displaced oblique fracture of shaft of unspecified ulna**
- **CC Exclusion 7th character A see Appendix A PDX collection 1272**
- **CC Exclusion 7th characters K - R see Appendix A PDX collection 0897**
- **MCC Exclusion 7th characters B & C see Appendix A PDX collection 1269**
- HAC 7th characters A - C see Appendix B for HAC conditional logic

CC MCC +7th **S52.234 Nondisplaced oblique fracture of shaft of right ulna**
- **CC Exclusion 7th character A see Appendix A PDX collection 1270**
- **CC Exclusion 7th characters K - R see Appendix A PDX collection 0897**
- **MCC Exclusion 7th characters B & C see Appendix A PDX collection 1269**
- HAC 7th characters A - C see Appendix B for HAC conditional logic

CC MCC +7th **S52.235 Nondisplaced oblique fracture of shaft of left ulna**
- **CC Exclusion 7th character A see Appendix A PDX collection 1271**
- **CC Exclusion 7th characters K - R see Appendix A PDX collection 0897**
- **MCC Exclusion 7th characters B & C see Appendix A PDX collection 1269**
- HAC 7th characters A - C see Appendix B for HAC conditional logic

CC MCC +7th **S52.236 Nondisplaced oblique fracture of shaft of unspecified ulna**
- **CC Exclusion 7th character A see Appendix A PDX collection 1272**
- **CC Exclusion 7th characters K - R see Appendix A PDX collection 0897**
- **MCC Exclusion 7th characters B & C see Appendix A PDX collection 1269**
- HAC 7th characters A - C see Appendix B for HAC conditional logic

\+ **S52.24 Spiral fracture of shaft of ulna**

CC MCC +7th **S52.241 Displaced spiral fracture of shaft of ulna, right arm**
- CC Exclusion 7th character A see Appendix A PDX collection 1270
- CC Exclusion 7th characters K - R see Appendix A PDX collection 0897
- MCC Exclusion 7th characters B & C see Appendix A PDX collection 1269
- HAC 7th characters A - C see Appendix B for HAC conditional logic

CC MCC +7th **S52.242 Displaced spiral fracture of shaft of ulna, left arm**
- CC Exclusion 7th character A see Appendix A PDX collection 1271
- CC Exclusion 7th characters K - R see Appendix A PDX collection 0897
- MCC Exclusion 7th characters B & C see Appendix A PDX collection 1269
- HAC 7th characters A - C see Appendix B for HAC conditional logic

CC MCC +7th **S52.243 Displaced spiral fracture of shaft of ulna, unspecified arm**
- CC Exclusion 7th character A see Appendix A PDX collection 1272
- CC Exclusion 7th characters K - R see Appendix A PDX collection 0897
- MCC Exclusion 7th characters B & C see Appendix A PDX collection 1269
- HAC 7th characters A - C see Appendix B for HAC conditional logic

CC MCC +7th **S52.244 Nondisplaced spiral fracture of shaft of ulna, right arm**
- CC Exclusion 7th character A see Appendix A PDX collection 1270
- CC Exclusion 7th characters K - R see Appendix A PDX collection 0897
- MCC Exclusion 7th characters B & C see Appendix A PDX collection 1269
- HAC 7th characters A - C see Appendix B for HAC conditional logic

CC MCC +7th **S52.245 Nondisplaced spiral fracture of shaft of ulna, left arm**
- CC Exclusion 7th character A see Appendix A PDX collection 1271
- CC Exclusion 7th characters K - R see Appendix A PDX collection 0897
- MCC Exclusion 7th characters B & C see Appendix A PDX collection 1269
- HAC 7th characters A - C see Appendix B for HAC conditional logic

CC MCC +7th **S52.246 Nondisplaced spiral fracture of shaft of ulna, unspecified arm**
- CC Exclusion 7th character A see Appendix A PDX collection 1272
- CC Exclusion 7th characters K - R see Appendix A PDX collection 0897
- MCC Exclusion 7th characters B & C see Appendix A PDX collection 1269
- HAC 7th characters A - C see Appendix B for HAC conditional logic

\+ **S52.25 Comminuted fracture of shaft of ulna**

CC MCC +7th **S52.251 Displaced comminuted fracture of shaft of ulna, right arm**
- CC Exclusion 7th character A see Appendix A PDX collection 1270
- CC Exclusion 7th characters K - R see Appendix A PDX collection 0897
- MCC Exclusion 7th characters B & C see Appendix A PDX collection 1269
- HAC 7th characters A - C see Appendix B for HAC conditional logic

CC MCC +7th **S52.252 Displaced comminuted fracture of shaft of ulna, left arm**
- CC Exclusion 7th character A see Appendix A PDX collection 1271
- CC Exclusion 7th characters K - R see Appendix A PDX collection 0897
- MCC Exclusion 7th characters B & C see Appendix A PDX collection 1269
- HAC 7th characters A - C see Appendix B for HAC conditional logic

CC MCC +7th **S52.253 Displaced comminuted fracture of shaft of ulna, unspecified arm**
- CC Exclusion 7th character A see Appendix A PDX collection 1272
- CC Exclusion 7th characters K - R see Appendix A PDX collection 0897
- MCC Exclusion 7th characters B & C see Appendix A PDX collection 1269
- HAC 7th characters A - C see Appendix B for HAC conditional logic

CC MCC +7th **S52.254 Nondisplaced comminuted fracture of shaft of ulna, right arm**
- CC Exclusion 7th character A see Appendix A PDX collection 1270
- CC Exclusion 7th characters K - R see Appendix A PDX collection 0897
- MCC Exclusion 7th characters B & C see Appendix A PDX collection 1269
- HAC 7th characters A - C see Appendix B for HAC conditional logic

CC MCC +7th **S52.255 Nondisplaced comminuted fracture of shaft of ulna, left arm**
- CC Exclusion 7th character A see Appendix A PDX collection 1271
- CC Exclusion 7th characters K - R see Appendix A PDX collection 0897
- MCC Exclusion 7th characters B & C see Appendix A PDX collection 1269
- HAC 7th characters A - C see Appendix B for HAC conditional logic

CC MCC +7th **S52.256 Nondisplaced comminuted fracture of shaft of ulna, unspecified arm**
- CC Exclusion 7th character A see Appendix A PDX collection 1272
- CC Exclusion 7th characters K - R see Appendix A PDX collection 0897
- MCC Exclusion 7th characters B & C see Appendix A PDX collection 1269
- HAC 7th characters A - C see Appendix B for HAC conditional logic

\+ **S52.26 Segmental fracture of shaft of ulna**

CC MCC +7th **S52.261 Displaced segmental fracture of shaft of ulna, right arm**
- CC Exclusion 7th character A see Appendix A PDX collection 1270
- CC Exclusion 7th characters K - R see Appendix A PDX collection 0897
- MCC Exclusion 7th characters B & C see Appendix A PDX collection 1269
- HAC 7th characters A - C see Appendix B for HAC conditional logic

CC MCC +7th **S52.262 Displaced segmental fracture of shaft of ulna, left arm**
- CC Exclusion 7th character A see Appendix A PDX collection 1271
- CC Exclusion 7th characters K - R see Appendix A PDX collection 0897
- MCC Exclusion 7th characters B & C see Appendix A PDX collection 1269
- HAC 7th characters A - C see Appendix B for HAC conditional logic

CC MCC +7th **S52.263 Displaced segmental fracture of shaft of ulna, unspecified arm**
- CC Exclusion 7th character A see Appendix A PDX collection 1272
- CC Exclusion 7th characters K - R see Appendix A PDX collection 0897
- MCC Exclusion 7th characters B & C see Appendix A PDX collection 1269
- HAC 7th characters A - C see Appendix B for HAC conditional logic

CC MCC +7th **S52.264 Nondisplaced segmental fracture of shaft of ulna, right arm**
- CC Exclusion 7th character A see Appendix A PDX collection 1270
- CC Exclusion 7th characters K - R see Appendix A PDX collection 0897
- MCC Exclusion 7th characters B & C see Appendix A PDX collection 1269
- HAC 7th characters A - C see Appendix B for HAC conditional logic

CC MCC +7th **S52.265 Nondisplaced segmental fracture of shaft of ulna, left arm**
CC Exclusion 7th character A see Appendix A PDX collection 1271
CC Exclusion 7th characters K - R see Appendix A PDX collection 0897
MCC Exclusion 7th characters B & C see Appendix A PDX collection 1269
HAC 7th characters A - C see Appendix B for HAC conditional logic

CC MCC +7th **S52.266 Nondisplaced segmental fracture of shaft of ulna, unspecified arm**
CC Exclusion 7th character A see Appendix A PDX collection 1272
CC Exclusion 7th characters K - R see Appendix A PDX collection 0897
MCC Exclusion 7th characters B & C see Appendix A PDX collection 1269
HAC 7th characters A - C see Appendix B for HAC conditional logic

+ **S52.27 Monteggia's fracture of ulna**
Fracture of upper shaft of ulna with dislocation of radial head

CC MCC +7th **S52.271 Monteggia's fracture of right ulna**
CC Exclusion 7th characters K - R see Appendix A PDX collection 0897
MCC Exclusion 7th characters B & C see Appendix A PDX collection 1269
HAC 7th characters B & C see Appendix B for HAC conditional logic

CC MCC +7th **S52.272 Monteggia's fracture of left ulna**
CC Exclusion 7th characters K - R see Appendix A PDX collection 0897
MCC Exclusion 7th characters B & C see Appendix A PDX collection 1269
HAC 7th characters B & C see Appendix B for HAC conditional logic

CC MCC +7th **S52.279 Monteggia's fracture of unspecified ulna**
CC Exclusion 7th characters K - R see Appendix A PDX collection 0897
MCC Exclusion 7th characters B & C see Appendix A PDX collection 1269
HAC 7th characters B & C see Appendix B for HAC conditional logic

+ **S52.28 Bent bone of ulna**

CC MCC +7th **S52.281 Bent bone of right ulna**
CC Exclusion 7th character A see Appendix A PDX collection 1270
CC Exclusion 7th characters K - R see Appendix A PDX collection 0897
MCC Exclusion 7th characters B & C see Appendix A PDX collection 1269
HAC 7th characters A - C see Appendix B for HAC conditional logic

CC MCC +7th **S52.282 Bent bone of left ulna**
CC Exclusion 7th character A see Appendix A PDX collection 1271
CC Exclusion 7th characters K - R see Appendix A PDX collection 0897
MCC Exclusion 7th characters B & C see Appendix A PDX collection 1269
HAC 7th characters A - C see Appendix B for HAC conditional logic

CC MCC +7th **S52.283 Bent bone of unspecified ulna**
CC Exclusion 7th character A see Appendix A PDX collection 1272
CC Exclusion 7th characters K - R see Appendix A PDX collection 0897
MCC Exclusion 7th characters B & C see Appendix A PDX collection 1269
HAC 7th characters A - C see Appendix B for HAC conditional logic

+ **S52.29 Other fracture of shaft of ulna**

CC MCC +7th **S52.291 Other fracture of shaft of right ulna**
CC Exclusion 7th character A see Appendix A PDX collection 1270
CC Exclusion 7th characters K - R see Appendix A PDX collection 0897
MCC Exclusion 7th characters B & C see Appendix A PDX collection 1269
HAC 7th characters A - C see Appendix B for HAC conditional logic

CC MCC +7th **S52.292 Other fracture of shaft of left ulna**
CC Exclusion 7th character A see Appendix A PDX collection 1271
CC Exclusion 7th characters K - R see Appendix A PDX collection 0897
MCC Exclusion 7th characters B & C see Appendix A PDX collection 1269
HAC 7th characters A - C see Appendix B for HAC conditional logic

CC MCC +7th **S52.299 Other fracture of shaft of unspecified ulna**
CC Exclusion 7th character A see Appendix A PDX collection 1272
CC Exclusion 7th characters K - R see Appendix A PDX collection 0897
MCC Exclusion 7th characters B & C see Appendix A PDX collection 1269
HAC 7th characters A - C see Appendix B for HAC conditional logic

+ **S52.3 Fracture of shaft of radius**

+ **S52.30 Unspecified fracture of shaft of radius**

CC MCC +7th **S52.301 Unspecified fracture of shaft of right radius**
CC Exclusion 7th character A see Appendix A PDX collection 1270
CC Exclusion 7th characters K - R see Appendix A PDX collection 0897
MCC Exclusion 7th characters B & C see Appendix A PDX collection 1269
HAC 7th characters A - C see Appendix B for HAC conditional logic

CC MCC +7th **S52.302 Unspecified fracture of shaft of left radius**
CC Exclusion 7th character A see Appendix A PDX collection 1271
CC Exclusion 7th characters K - R see Appendix A PDX collection 0897
MCC Exclusion 7th characters B & C see Appendix A PDX collection 1269
HAC 7th characters A - C see Appendix B for HAC conditional logic

CC MCC +7th **S52.309 Unspecified fracture of shaft of unspecified radius**
CC Exclusion 7th character A see Appendix A PDX collection 1272
CC Exclusion 7th characters K - R see Appendix A PDX collection 0897
MCC Exclusion 7th characters B & C see Appendix A PDX collection 1269
HAC 7th characters A - C see Appendix B for HAC conditional logic

+ **S52.31 Greenstick fracture of shaft of radius**

The appropriate 7th character is to be added to all codes in subcategory S52.31
A initial encounter for closed fracture
D subsequent encounter for fracture with routine healing
G subsequent encounter for fracture with delayed healing
K subsequent encounter for fracture with nonunion
P subsequent encounter for fracture with malunion
S sequela

CC +7th **S52.311 Greenstick fracture of shaft of radius, right arm**
CC Exclusion 7th character A see Appendix A PDX collection 1270
CC Exclusion 7th characters K - R see Appendix A PDX collection 0897
HAC 7th character A see Appendix B for HAC conditional logic

CC +7th **S52.312 Greenstick fracture of shaft of radius, left arm**
CC Exclusion 7th character A see Appendix A PDX collection 1271
CC Exclusion 7th characters K - R see Appendix A PDX collection 0897
HAC 7th character A see Appendix B for HAC conditional logic

CC +7th **S52.319 Greenstick fracture of shaft of radius, unspecified arm**
CC Exclusion 7th character A see Appendix A PDX collection 1272
CC Exclusion 7th characters K - R see Appendix A PDX collection 0897
HAC 7th character A see Appendix B for HAC conditional logic

+ **S52.32 Transverse fracture of shaft of radius**

CC MCC +7th **S52.321 Displaced transverse fracture of shaft of right radius**
CC Exclusion 7th character A see Appendix A PDX collection 1270
CC Exclusion 7th characters K - R see Appendix A PDX collection 0897
MCC Exclusion 7th characters B & C see Appendix A PDX collection 1269
HAC 7th characters A - C see Appendix B for HAC conditional logic

CC MCC +7th **S52.322 Displaced transverse fracture of shaft of left radius**
CC Exclusion 7th character A see Appendix A PDX collection 1271
CC Exclusion 7th characters K - R see Appendix A PDX collection 0897
MCC Exclusion 7th characters B & C see Appendix A PDX collection 1269
HAC 7th characters A - C see Appendix B for HAC conditional logic

CC MCC +7th **S52.323 Displaced transverse fracture of shaft of unspecified radius**
CC Exclusion 7th character A see Appendix A PDX collection 1272
CC Exclusion 7th characters K - R see Appendix A PDX collection 0897
MCC Exclusion 7th characters B & C see Appendix A PDX collection 1269
HAC 7th characters A - C see Appendix B for HAC conditional logic

CC MCC +7th **S52.324 Nondisplaced transverse fracture of shaft of right radius**
CC Exclusion 7th character A see Appendix A PDX collection 1270
CC Exclusion 7th characters K - R see Appendix A PDX collection 0897
MCC Exclusion 7th characters B & C see Appendix A PDX collection 1269
HAC 7th characters A - C see Appendix B for HAC conditional logic

CC MCC +7th **S52.325 Nondisplaced transverse fracture of shaft of left radius**
CC Exclusion 7th character A see Appendix A PDX collection 1271
CC Exclusion 7th characters K - R see Appendix A PDX collection 0897
MCC Exclusion 7th characters B & C see Appendix A PDX collection 1269
HAC 7th characters A - C see Appendix B for HAC conditional logic

CC MCC +7th **S52.326 Nondisplaced transverse fracture of shaft of unspecified radius**
CC Exclusion 7th character A see Appendix A PDX collection 1272
CC Exclusion 7th characters K - R see Appendix A PDX collection 0897
MCC Exclusion 7th characters B & C see Appendix A PDX collection 1269
HAC 7th characters A - C see Appendix B for HAC conditional logic

\+ **S52.33 Oblique fracture of shaft of radius**

CC MCC +7th **S52.331 Displaced oblique fracture of shaft of right radius**
CC Exclusion 7th character A see Appendix A PDX collection 1270
CC Exclusion 7th characters K - R see Appendix A PDX collection 0897
MCC Exclusion 7th characters B & C see Appendix A PDX collection 1269
HAC 7th characters A - C see Appendix B for HAC conditional logic

CC MCC +7th **S52.332 Displaced oblique fracture of shaft of left radius**
CC Exclusion 7th character A see Appendix A PDX collection 1271
CC Exclusion 7th characters K - R see Appendix A PDX collection 0897
MCC Exclusion 7th characters B & C see Appendix A PDX collection 1269
HAC 7th characters A - C see Appendix B for HAC conditional logic

CC MCC +7th **S52.333 Displaced oblique fracture of shaft of unspecified radius**
CC Exclusion 7th character A see Appendix A PDX collection 1272
CC Exclusion 7th characters K - R see Appendix A PDX collection 0897
MCC Exclusion 7th characters B & C see Appendix A PDX collection 1269
HAC 7th characters A - C see Appendix B for HAC conditional logic

CC MCC +7th **S52.334 Nondisplaced oblique fracture of shaft of right radius**
CC Exclusion 7th character A see Appendix A PDX collection 1270
CC Exclusion 7th characters K - R see Appendix A PDX collection 0897
MCC Exclusion 7th characters B & C see Appendix A PDX collection 1269
HAC 7th characters A - C see Appendix B for HAC conditional logic

CC MCC +7th **S52.335 Nondisplaced oblique fracture of shaft of left radius**
CC Exclusion 7th character A see Appendix A PDX collection 1271
CC Exclusion 7th characters K - R see Appendix A PDX collection 0897
MCC Exclusion 7th characters B & C see Appendix A PDX collection 1269
HAC 7th characters A - C see Appendix B for HAC conditional logic

CC MCC +7th **S52.336 Nondisplaced oblique fracture of shaft of unspecified radius**
CC Exclusion 7th character A see Appendix A PDX collection 1272
CC Exclusion 7th characters K - R see Appendix A PDX collection 0897
MCC Exclusion 7th characters B & C see Appendix A PDX collection 1269
HAC 7th characters A - C see Appendix B for HAC conditional logic

\+ **S52.34 Spiral fracture of shaft of radius**

CC MCC +7th **S52.341 Displaced spiral fracture of shaft of radius, right arm**
CC Exclusion 7th character A see Appendix A PDX collection 1270
CC Exclusion 7th characters K - R see Appendix A PDX collection 0897
MCC Exclusion 7th characters B & C see Appendix A PDX collection 1269
HAC 7th characters A - C see Appendix B for HAC conditional logic

CC MCC +7th **S52.342 Displaced spiral fracture of shaft of radius, left arm**
CC Exclusion 7th character A see Appendix A PDX collection 1271
CC Exclusion 7th characters K - R see Appendix A PDX collection 0897
MCC Exclusion 7th characters B & C see Appendix A PDX collection 1269
HAC 7th characters A - C see Appendix B for HAC conditional logic

CC MCC +7th **S52.343 Displaced spiral fracture of shaft of radius, unspecified arm**
CC Exclusion 7th character A see Appendix A PDX collection 1272
CC Exclusion 7th characters K - R see Appendix A PDX collection 0897
MCC Exclusion 7th characters B & C see Appendix A PDX collection 1269
HAC 7th characters A - C see Appendix B for HAC conditional logic

CC MCC +7th **S52.344 Nondisplaced spiral fracture of shaft of radius, right arm**
CC Exclusion 7th character A see Appendix A PDX collection 1270
CC Exclusion 7th characters K - R see Appendix A PDX collection 0897
MCC Exclusion 7th characters B & C see Appendix A PDX collection 1269
HAC 7th characters A - C see Appendix B for HAC conditional logic

CC MCC +7th **S52.345 Nondisplaced spiral fracture of shaft of radius, left arm**
CC Exclusion 7th character A see Appendix A PDX collection 1271
CC Exclusion 7th characters K - R see Appendix A PDX collection 0897
MCC Exclusion 7th characters B & C see Appendix A PDX collection 1269
HAC 7th characters A - C see Appendix B for HAC conditional logic

CC MCC +7th **S52.346 Nondisplaced spiral fracture of shaft of radius, unspecified arm**
CC Exclusion 7th character A see Appendix A PDX collection 1272
CC Exclusion 7th characters K - R see Appendix A PDX collection 0897
MCC Exclusion 7th characters B & C see Appendix A PDX collection 1269
HAC 7th characters A - C see Appendix B for HAC conditional logic

\+ **S52.35 Comminuted fracture of shaft of radius**

CC MCC +7th **S52.351 Displaced comminuted fracture of shaft of radius, right arm**
CC Exclusion 7th character A see Appendix A PDX collection 1270
CC Exclusion 7th characters K - R see Appendix A PDX collection 0897
MCC Exclusion 7th characters B & C see Appendix A PDX collection 1269
HAC 7th characters A - C see Appendix B for HAC conditional logic

CC MCC +7th **S52.352 Displaced comminuted fracture of shaft of radius, left arm**
CC Exclusion 7th character A see Appendix A PDX collection 1271
CC Exclusion 7th characters K - R see Appendix A PDX collection 0897
MCC Exclusion 7th characters B & C see Appendix A PDX collection 1269
HAC 7th characters A - C see Appendix B for HAC conditional logic

CC MCC +7th **S52.353 Displaced comminuted fracture of shaft of radius, unspecified arm**
CC Exclusion 7th character A see Appendix A PDX collection 1272
CC Exclusion 7th characters K - R see Appendix A PDX collection 0897
MCC Exclusion 7th characters B & C see Appendix A PDX collection 1269
HAC 7th characters A - C see Appendix B for HAC conditional logic

CC MCC +7th **S52.354 Nondisplaced comminuted fracture of shaft of radius, right arm**
CC Exclusion 7th character A see Appendix A PDX collection 1270
CC Exclusion 7th characters K - R see Appendix A PDX collection 0897
MCC Exclusion 7th characters B & C see Appendix A PDX collection 1269
HAC 7th characters A - C see Appendix B for HAC conditional logic

CC MCC +7th **S52.355 Nondisplaced comminuted fracture of shaft of radius, left arm**
CC Exclusion 7th character A see Appendix A PDX collection 1271
CC Exclusion 7th characters K - R see Appendix A PDX collection 0897
MCC Exclusion 7th characters B & C see Appendix A PDX collection 1269
HAC 7th characters A - C see Appendix B for HAC conditional logic

CC MCC +7th **S52.356 Nondisplaced comminuted fracture of shaft of radius, unspecified arm**
CC Exclusion 7th character A see Appendix A PDX collection 1272
CC Exclusion 7th characters K - R see Appendix A PDX collection 0897
MCC Exclusion 7th characters B & C see Appendix A PDX collection 1269
HAC 7th characters A - C see Appendix B for HAC conditional logic

\+ **S52.36 Segmental fracture of shaft of radius**

CC MCC +7th **S52.361 Displaced segmental fracture of shaft of radius, right arm**
CC Exclusion 7th character A see Appendix A PDX collection 1270
CC Exclusion 7th characters K - R see Appendix A PDX collection 0897
MCC Exclusion 7th characters B & C see Appendix A PDX collection 1269
HAC 7th characters A - C see Appendix B for HAC conditional logic

CC MCC +7th **S52.362 Displaced segmental fracture of shaft of radius, left arm**
CC Exclusion 7th character A see Appendix A PDX collection 1271
CC Exclusion 7th characters K - R see Appendix A PDX collection 0897
MCC Exclusion 7th characters B & C see Appendix A PDX collection 1269
HAC 7th characters A - C see Appendix B for HAC conditional logic

CC MCC +7th **S52.363 Displaced segmental fracture of shaft of radius, unspecified arm**
CC Exclusion 7th character A see Appendix A PDX collection 1272
CC Exclusion 7th characters K - R see Appendix A PDX collection 0897
MCC Exclusion 7th characters B & C see Appendix A PDX collection 1269
HAC 7th characters A - C see Appendix B for HAC conditional logic

CC MCC +7th **S52.364 Nondisplaced segmental fracture of shaft of radius, right arm**
CC Exclusion 7th character A see Appendix A PDX collection 1270
CC Exclusion 7th characters K - R see Appendix A PDX collection 0897
MCC Exclusion 7th characters B & C see Appendix A PDX collection 1269
HAC 7th characters A - C see Appendix B for HAC conditional logic

CC MCC +7th **S52.365 Nondisplaced segmental fracture of shaft of radius, left arm**
CC Exclusion 7th character A see Appendix A PDX collection 1271
CC Exclusion 7th characters K - R see Appendix A PDX collection 0897
MCC Exclusion 7th characters B & C see Appendix A PDX collection 1269
HAC 7th characters A - C see Appendix B for HAC conditional logic

CC MCC +7th **S52.366 Nondisplaced segmental fracture of shaft of radius, unspecified arm**
CC Exclusion 7th character A see Appendix A PDX collection 1272
CC Exclusion 7th characters K - R see Appendix A PDX collection 0897
MCC Exclusion 7th characters B & C see Appendix A PDX collection 1269
HAC 7th characters A - C see Appendix B for HAC conditional logic

\+ **S52.37 Galeazzi's fracture**
Fracture of lower shaft of radius with radioulnar joint dislocation

CC MCC +7th **S52.371 Galeazzi's fracture of right radius**
CC Exclusion 7th character A see Appendix A PDX collection 1270
CC Exclusion 7th characters K - R see Appendix A PDX collection 0897
MCC Exclusion 7th characters B & C see Appendix A PDX collection 1269
HAC 7th characters A - C see Appendix B for HAC conditional logic

CC MCC +7th **S52.372 Galeazzi's fracture of left radius**
CC Exclusion 7th character A see Appendix A PDX collection 1271
CC Exclusion 7th characters K - R see Appendix A PDX collection 0897
MCC Exclusion 7th characters B & C see Appendix A PDX collection 1269
HAC 7th characters A - C see Appendix B for HAC conditional logic

CC MCC +7th **S52.379 Galeazzi's fracture of unspecified radius**
CC Exclusion 7th character A see Appendix A PDX collection 1272
CC Exclusion 7th characters K - R see Appendix A PDX collection 0897
MCC Exclusion 7th characters B & C see Appendix A PDX collection 1269
HAC 7th characters A - C see Appendix B for HAC conditional logic

+ **S52.38 Bent bone of radius**

CC MCC +7th **S52.381 Bent bone of right radius**
CC Exclusion 7th character A see Appendix A PDX collection 1270
CC Exclusion 7th characters K - R see Appendix A PDX collection 0897
MCC Exclusion 7th characters B & C see Appendix A PDX collection 1269
HAC 7th characters A - C see Appendix B for HAC conditional logic

CC MCC +7th **S52.382 Bent bone of left radius**
CC Exclusion 7th character A see Appendix A PDX collection 1271
CC Exclusion 7th characters K - R see Appendix A PDX collection 0897
MCC Exclusion 7th characters B & C see Appendix A PDX collection 1269
HAC 7th characters A - C see Appendix B for HAC conditional logic

CC MCC +7th **S52.389 Bent bone of unspecified radius**
CC Exclusion 7th character A see Appendix A PDX collection 1272
CC Exclusion 7th characters K - R see Appendix A PDX collection 0897
MCC Exclusion 7th characters B & C see Appendix A PDX collection 1269
HAC 7th characters A - C see Appendix B for HAC conditional logic

+ **S52.39 Other fracture of shaft of radius**

CC MCC +7th **S52.391 Other fracture of shaft of radius, right arm**
CC Exclusion 7th character A see Appendix A PDX collection 1270
CC Exclusion 7th characters K - R see Appendix A PDX collection 0897
MCC Exclusion 7th characters B & C see Appendix A PDX collection 1269
HAC 7th characters A - C see Appendix B for HAC conditional logic

CC MCC +7th **S52.392 Other fracture of shaft of radius, left arm**
CC Exclusion 7th character A see Appendix A PDX collection 1271
CC Exclusion 7th characters K - R see Appendix A PDX collection 0897
MCC Exclusion 7th characters B & C see Appendix A PDX collection 1269
HAC 7th characters A - C see Appendix B for HAC conditional logic

CC MCC +7th **S52.399 Other fracture of shaft of radius, unspecified arm**
CC Exclusion 7th character A see Appendix A PDX collection 1272
CC Exclusion 7th characters K - R see Appendix A PDX collection 0897
MCC Exclusion 7th characters B & C see Appendix A PDX collection 1269
HAC 7th characters A - C see Appendix B for HAC conditional logic

+ **S52.5 Fracture of lower end of radius**
Fracture of distal end of radius
Excludes2: *physeal fractures of lower end of radius (S59.2-)*

+ **S52.50 Unspecified fracture of the lower end of radius**

CC MCC +7th **S52.501 Unspecified fracture of the lower end of right radius**
CC Exclusion 7th character A see Appendix A PDX collection 1270
CC Exclusion 7th characters K - R see Appendix A PDX collection 0897
MCC Exclusion 7th characters B & C see Appendix A PDX collection 1269
HAC 7th characters A - C see Appendix B for HAC conditional logic

CC MCC +7th **S52.502 Unspecified fracture of the lower end of left radius**
CC Exclusion 7th character A see Appendix A PDX collection 1271
CC Exclusion 7th characters K - R see Appendix A PDX collection 0897
MCC Exclusion 7th characters B & C see Appendix A PDX collection 1269
HAC 7th characters A - C see Appendix B for HAC conditional logic

CC MCC +7th **S52.509 Unspecified fracture of the lower end of unspecified radius**
CC Exclusion 7th character A see Appendix A PDX collection 1272
CC Exclusion 7th characters K - R see Appendix A PDX collection 0897
MCC Exclusion 7th characters B & C see Appendix A PDX collection 1269
HAC 7th characters A - C see Appendix B for HAC conditional logic

+ **S52.51 Fracture of radial styloid process**

CC MCC +7th **S52.511 Displaced fracture of right radial styloid process**
CC Exclusion 7th character A see Appendix A PDX collection 1270
CC Exclusion 7th characters K - R see Appendix A PDX collection 0897
MCC Exclusion 7th characters B & C see Appendix A PDX collection 1269
HAC 7th characters A - C see Appendix B for HAC conditional logic

CC MCC +7th **S52.512 Displaced fracture of left radial styloid process**
CC Exclusion 7th character A see Appendix A PDX collection 1271
CC Exclusion 7th characters K - R see Appendix A PDX collection 0897
MCC Exclusion 7th characters B & C see Appendix A PDX collection 1269
HAC 7th characters A - C see Appendix B for HAC conditional logic

CC MCC +7th **S52.513 Displaced fracture of unspecified radial styloid process**
CC Exclusion 7th character A see Appendix A PDX collection 1272
CC Exclusion 7th characters K - R see Appendix A PDX collection 0897
MCC Exclusion 7th characters B & C see Appendix A PDX collection 1269
HAC 7th characters A - C see Appendix B for HAC conditional logic

CC MCC +7th **S52.514 Nondisplaced fracture of right radial styloid process**
CC Exclusion 7th character A see Appendix A PDX collection 1270
CC Exclusion 7th characters K - R see Appendix A PDX collection 0897
MCC Exclusion 7th characters B & C see Appendix A PDX collection 1269
HAC 7th characters A - C see Appendix B for HAC conditional logic

CC MCC +7th **S52.515 Nondisplaced fracture of left radial styloid process**
CC Exclusion 7th character A see Appendix A PDX collection 1271
CC Exclusion 7th characters K - R see Appendix A PDX collection 0897
MCC Exclusion 7th characters B & C see Appendix A PDX collection 1269
HAC 7th characters A - C see Appendix B for HAC conditional logic

CC MCC +7th **S52.516 Nondisplaced fracture of unspecified radial styloid process**
CC Exclusion 7th character A see Appendix A PDX collection 1272
CC Exclusion 7th characters K - R see Appendix A PDX collection 0897
MCC Exclusion 7th characters B & C see Appendix A PDX collection 1269
HAC 7th characters A - C see Appendix B for HAC conditional logic

+ **S52.52 Torus fracture of lower end of radius**

The appropriate 7th character is to be added to all codes in subcategory S52.52
A initial encounter for closed fracture
D subsequent encounter for fracture with routine healing
G subsequent encounter for fracture with delayed healing
K subsequent encounter for fracture with nonunion
P subsequent encounter for fracture with malunion
S sequela

CC +7th **S52.521 Torus fracture of lower end of right radius**
CC Exclusion 7th character A see Appendix A PDX collection 1270
CC Exclusion 7th characters K - R see Appendix A PDX collection 0897
HAC 7th character A see Appendix B for HAC conditional logic

CC $+7^{th}$ **S52.522 Torus fracture of lower end of left radius**
CC Exclusion 7th character A see Appendix A PDX collection 1271
CC Exclusion 7th characters K - R see Appendix A PDX collection 0897
HAC 7th character A see Appendix B for HAC conditional logic

CC $+7^{th}$ **S52.529 Torus fracture of lower end of unspecified radius**
CC Exclusion 7th character A see Appendix A PDX collection 1272
CC Exclusion 7th characters K - R see Appendix A PDX collection 0897
HAC 7th character A see Appendix B for HAC conditional logic

\+ **S52.53 Colles' fracture**

CC MCC $+7^{th}$ **S52.531 Colles' fracture of right radius**
CC Exclusion 7th character A see Appendix A PDX collection 1270
CC Exclusion 7th characters K - R see Appendix A PDX collection 0897
MCC Exclusion 7th characters B & C see Appendix A PDX collection 1269
HAC 7th characters A - C see Appendix B for HAC conditional logic

CC MCC $+7^{th}$ **S52.532 Colles' fracture of left radius**
CC Exclusion 7th character A see Appendix A PDX collection 1271
CC Exclusion 7th characters K - R see Appendix A PDX collection 0897
MCC Exclusion 7th characters B & C see Appendix A PDX collection 1269
HAC 7th characters A - C see Appendix B for HAC conditional logic

CC MCC $+7^{th}$ **S52.539 Colles' fracture of unspecified radius**
CC Exclusion 7th character A see Appendix A PDX collection 1272
CC Exclusion 7th characters K - R see Appendix A PDX collection 0897
MCC Exclusion 7th characters B & C see Appendix A PDX collection 1269
HAC 7th characters A - C see Appendix B for HAC conditional logic

\+ **S52.54 Smith's fracture**

CC MCC $+7^{th}$ **S52.541 Smith's fracture of right radius**
CC Exclusion 7th character A see Appendix A PDX collection 1270
CC Exclusion 7th characters K - R see Appendix A PDX collection 0897
MCC Exclusion 7th characters B & C see Appendix A PDX collection 1269
HAC 7th characters A - C see Appendix B for HAC conditional logic

CC MCC $+7^{th}$ **S52.542 Smith's fracture of left radius**
CC Exclusion 7th character A see Appendix A PDX collection 1271
CC Exclusion 7th characters K - R see Appendix A PDX collection 0897
MCC Exclusion 7th characters B & C see Appendix A PDX collection 1269
HAC 7th characters A - C see Appendix B for HAC conditional logic

CC MCC $+7^{th}$ **S52.549 Smith's fracture of unspecified radius**
CC Exclusion 7th character A see Appendix A PDX collection 1272
CC Exclusion 7th characters K - R see Appendix A PDX collection 0897
MCC Exclusion 7th characters B & C see Appendix A PDX collection 1269
HAC 7th characters A - C see Appendix B for HAC conditional logic

\+ **S52.55 Other extraarticular fracture of lower end of radius**

CC MCC $+7^{th}$ **S52.551 Other extraarticular fracture of lower end of right radius**
CC Exclusion 7th character A see Appendix A PDX collection 1270
CC Exclusion 7th characters K - R see Appendix A PDX collection 0897
MCC Exclusion 7th characters B & C see Appendix A PDX collection 1269
HAC 7th characters A - C see Appendix B for HAC conditional logic

CC MCC $+7^{th}$ **S52.552 Other extraarticular fracture of lower end left radius**
CC Exclusion 7th character A see Appendix A PDX collection 1271
CC Exclusion 7th characters K - R see Appendix A PDX collection 0897
MCC Exclusion 7th characters B & C see Appendix A PDX collection 1269
HAC 7th characters A - C see Appendix B for H conditional logic

CC MCC $+7^{th}$ **S52.559 Other extraarticular fracture of lower end unspecified radius**
CC Exclusion 7th character A see Appendix A PDX collection 1272
CC Exclusion 7th characters K - R see Appendix A PDX collection 0897
MCC Exclusion 7th characters B & C see Appendix A PDX collection 1269
HAC 7th characters A - C see Appendix B for H conditional logic

\+ **S52.56 Barton's fracture**

CC MCC $+7^{th}$ **S52.561 Barton's fracture of right radius**
CC Exclusion 7th character A see Appendix A PDX collection 1270
CC Exclusion 7th characters K - R see Appendix A PDX collection 0897
MCC Exclusion 7th characters B & C see Appendix A PDX collection 1269
HAC 7th characters A - C see Appendix B for H conditional logic

CC MCC $+7^{th}$ **S52.562 Barton's fracture of left radius**
CC Exclusion 7th character A see Appendix A PDX collection 1271
CC Exclusion 7th characters K - R see Appendix A PDX collection 0897
MCC Exclusion 7th characters B & C see Appendix A PDX collection 1269
HAC 7th characters A - C see Appendix B for H conditional logic

CC MCC $+7^{th}$ **S52.569 Barton's fracture of unspecified radius**
CC Exclusion 7th character A see Appendix A PDX collection 1272
CC Exclusion 7th characters K - R see Appendix A PDX collection 0897
MCC Exclusion 7th characters B & C see Appendix A PDX collection 1269
HAC 7th characters A - C see Appendix B for HA conditional logic

\+ **S52.57 Other intraarticular fracture of lower end of radius**

CC MCC $+7^{th}$ **S52.571 Other intraarticular fracture of lower end right radius**
CC Exclusion 7th character A see Appendix A PDX collection 1270
CC Exclusion 7th characters K - R see Appendix A PDX collection 0897
MCC Exclusion 7th characters B & C see Appendix A PDX collection 1269
HAC 7th characters A - C see Appendix B for HA conditional logic

CC MCC $+7^{th}$ **S52.572 Other intraarticular fracture of lower end left radius**
CC Exclusion 7th character A see Appendix A PDX collection 1271
CC Exclusion 7th characters K - R see Appendix A PDX collection 0897
MCC Exclusion 7th characters B & C see Appendix A PDX collection 1269
HAC 7th characters A - C see Appendix B for HA conditional logic

CC MCC $+7^{th}$ **S52.579 Other intraarticular fracture of lower end unspecified radius**
CC Exclusion 7th character A see Appendix A PDX collection 1272
CC Exclusion 7th characters K - R see Appendix A PDX collection 0897
MCC Exclusion 7th characters B & C see Appendix A PDX collection 1269
HAC 7th characters A - C see Appendix B for HA conditional logic

\+ **S52.59 Other fractures of lower end of radius**

CC MCC $+7^{th}$ **S52.591 Other fractures of lower end of right radius**
CC Exclusion 7th character A see Appendix A PDX collection 1270
CC Exclusion 7th characters K - R see Appendix A PDX collection 0897
MCC Exclusion 7th characters B & C see Appendix A PDX collection 1269
HAC 7th characters A - C see Appendix B for HAC conditional logic

CC MCC +7th **S52.592 Other fractures of lower end of left radius**
CC Exclusion 7th character A see Appendix A PDX collection 1271
CC Exclusion 7th characters K - R see Appendix A PDX collection 0897
MCC Exclusion 7th characters B & C see Appendix A PDX collection 1269
HAC 7th characters A - C see Appendix B for HAC conditional logic

CC MCC +7th **S52.599 Other fractures of lower end of unspecified radius**
CC Exclusion 7th character A see Appendix A PDX collection 1272
CC Exclusion 7th characters K - R see Appendix A PDX collection 0897
MCC Exclusion 7th characters B & C see Appendix A PDX collection 1269
HAC 7th characters A - C see Appendix B for HAC conditional logic

+ **S52.6 Fracture of lower end of ulna**

+ **S52.60 Unspecified fracture of lower end of ulna**

CC MCC +7th **S52.601 Unspecified fracture of lower end of right ulna**
CC Exclusion 7th character A see Appendix A PDX collection 1270
CC Exclusion 7th characters K - R see Appendix A PDX collection 0897
MCC Exclusion 7th characters B & C see Appendix A PDX collection 1269
HAC 7th characters A - C see Appendix B for HAC conditional logic

CC MCC +7th **S52.602 Unspecified fracture of lower end of left ulna**
CC Exclusion 7th character A see Appendix A PDX collection 1271
CC Exclusion 7th characters K - R see Appendix A PDX collection 0897
MCC Exclusion 7th characters B & C see Appendix A PDX collection 1269
HAC 7th characters A - C see Appendix B for HAC conditional logic

CC MCC +7th **S52.609 Unspecified fracture of lower end of unspecified ulna**
CC Exclusion 7th character A see Appendix A PDX collection 1272
CC Exclusion 7th characters K - R see Appendix A PDX collection 0897
MCC Exclusion 7th characters B & C see Appendix A PDX collection 1269
HAC 7th characters A - C see Appendix B for HAC conditional logic

+ **S52.61 Fracture of ulna styloid process**

CC MCC +7th **S52.611 Displaced fracture of right ulna styloid process**
CC Exclusion 7th character A see Appendix A PDX collection 1270
CC Exclusion 7th characters K - R see Appendix A PDX collection 0897
MCC Exclusion 7th characters B & C see Appendix A PDX collection 1269
HAC 7th characters A - C see Appendix B for HAC conditional logic

CC MCC +7th **S52.612 Displaced fracture of left ulna styloid process**
CC Exclusion 7th character A see Appendix A PDX collection 1271
CC Exclusion 7th characters K - R see Appendix A PDX collection 0897
MCC Exclusion 7th characters B & C see Appendix A PDX collection 1269
HAC 7th characters A - C see Appendix B for HAC conditional logic

CC MCC +7th **S52.613 Displaced fracture of unspecified ulna styloid process**
CC Exclusion 7th character A see Appendix A PDX collection 1272
CC Exclusion 7th characters K - R see Appendix A PDX collection 0897
MCC Exclusion 7th characters B & C see Appendix A PDX collection 1269
HAC 7th characters A - C see Appendix B for HAC conditional logic

CC MCC +7th **S52.614 Nondisplaced fracture of right ulna styloid process**
CC Exclusion 7th character A see Appendix A PDX collection 1270
CC Exclusion 7th characters K - R see Appendix A PDX collection 0897
MCC Exclusion 7th characters B & C see Appendix A PDX collection 1269
HAC 7th characters A - C see Appendix B for HAC conditional logic

CC MCC +7th **S52.615 Nondisplaced fracture of left ulna styloid process**
CC Exclusion 7th character A see Appendix A PDX collection 1271
CC Exclusion 7th characters K - R see Appendix A PDX collection 0897
MCC Exclusion 7th characters B & C see Appendix A PDX collection 1269
HAC 7th characters A - C see Appendix B for HAC conditional logic

CC MCC +7th **S52.616 Nondisplaced fracture of unspecified ulna styloid process**
CC Exclusion 7th character A see Appendix A PDX collection 1272
CC Exclusion 7th characters K - R see Appendix A PDX collection 0897
MCC Exclusion 7th characters B & C see Appendix A PDX collection 1269
HAC 7th characters A - C see Appendix B for HAC conditional logic

+ **S52.62 Torus fracture of lower end of ulna**

The appropriate 7th character is to be added to all codes in subcategory S52.62
A initial encounter for closed fracture
D subsequent encounter for fracture with routine healing
G subsequent encounter for fracture with delayed healing
K subsequent encounter for fracture with nonunion
P subsequent encounter for fracture with malunion
S sequela

CC +7th **S52.621 Torus fracture of lower end of right ulna**
CC Exclusion 7th character A see Appendix A PDX collection 1270
CC Exclusion 7th characters K - R see Appendix A PDX collection 0897
HAC 7th character A see Appendix B for HAC conditional logic

CC +7th **S52.622 Torus fracture of lower end of left ulna**
CC Exclusion 7th character A see Appendix A PDX collection 1271
CC Exclusion 7th characters K - R see Appendix A PDX collection 0897
HAC 7th character A see Appendix B for HAC conditional logic

CC +7th **S52.629 Torus fracture of lower end of unspecified ulna**
CC Exclusion 7th character A see Appendix A PDX collection 1272
CC Exclusion 7th characters K - R see Appendix A PDX collection 0897
HAC 7th character A see Appendix B for HAC conditional logic

+ **S52.69 Other fracture of lower end of ulna**

CC MCC +7th **S52.691 Other fracture of lower end of right ulna**
CC Exclusion 7th character A see Appendix A PDX collection 1270
CC Exclusion 7th characters K - R see Appendix A PDX collection 0897
MCC Exclusion 7th characters B & C see Appendix A PDX collection 1269
HAC 7th characters A - C see Appendix B for HAC conditional logic

CC MCC +7th **S52.692 Other fracture of lower end of left ulna**
CC Exclusion 7th character A see Appendix A PDX collection 1271
CC Exclusion 7th characters K - R see Appendix A PDX collection 0897
MCC Exclusion 7th characters B & C see Appendix A PDX collection 1269
HAC 7th characters A - C see Appendix B for HAC conditional logic

CC MCC +7th **S52.699 Other fracture of lower end of unspecified ulna**
CC Exclusion 7th character A see Appendix A PDX collection 1272
CC Exclusion 7th characters K - R see Appendix A PDX collection 0897
MCC Exclusion 7th characters B & C see Appendix A PDX collection 1269
HAC 7th characters A - C see Appendix B for HAC conditional logic

\+ **S52.9 Unspecified fracture of forearm**

CC MCC X+7th **S52.90 Unspecified fracture of unspecified forearm**
CC Exclusion 7th character A see Appendix A PDX collection 1272
CC Exclusion 7th characters K - R see Appendix A PDX collection 0897
MCC Exclusion 7th characters B & C see Appendix A PDX collection 1269
HAC 7th characters A - C see Appendix B for HAC conditional logic

CC MCC X+7th **S52.91 Unspecified fracture of right forearm**
CC Exclusion 7th character A see Appendix A PDX collection 1272
CC Exclusion 7th characters K - R see Appendix A PDX collection 0897
MCC Exclusion 7th characters B & C see Appendix A PDX collection 1269
HAC 7th characters A - C see Appendix B for HAC conditional logic

CC MCC X+7th **S52.92 Unspecified fracture of left forearm**
CC Exclusion 7th character A see Appendix A PDX collection 1272
CC Exclusion 7th characters K - R see Appendix A PDX collection 0897
MCC Exclusion 7th characters B & C see Appendix A PDX collection 1269
HAC 7th characters A - C see Appendix B for HAC conditional logic

S53 Dislocation and sprain of joints and ligaments of elbow

Includes: avulsion of joint or ligament of elbow
laceration of cartilage, joint or ligament of elbow
sprain of cartilage, joint or ligament of elbow
traumatic hemarthrosis of joint or ligament of elbow
traumatic rupture of joint or ligament of elbow
traumatic subluxation of joint or ligament of elbow
traumatic tear of joint or ligament of elbow

Code also any associated open wound

Excludes2: *strain of muscle, fascia and tendon at forearm level (S56.-)*

The appropriate 7th character is to be added to each code from category S53
A initial encounter
D subsequent encounter
S sequela

\+ **S53.0 Subluxation and dislocation of radial head**
Dislocation of radiohumeral joint
Subluxation of radiohumeral joint
Excludes1: *Monteggia's fracture-dislocation (S52.27-)*

\+ **S53.00 Unspecified subluxation and dislocation of radial head**
+7th **S53.001 Unspecified subluxation of right radial head**
+7th **S53.002 Unspecified subluxation of left radial head**
+7th **S53.003 Unspecified subluxation of unspecified radial head**
+7th **S53.004 Unspecified dislocation of right radial head**
+7th **S53.005 Unspecified dislocation of left radial head**
+7th **S53.006 Unspecified dislocation of unspecified radial head**

\+ **S53.01 Anterior subluxation and dislocation of radial head**
Anteriomedial subluxation and dislocation of radial head
+7th **S53.011 Anterior subluxation of right radial head**
+7th **S53.012 Anterior subluxation of left radial head**
+7th **S53.013 Anterior subluxation of unspecified radial head**
+7th **S53.014 Anterior dislocation of right radial head**
+7th **S53.015 Anterior dislocation of left radial head**
+7th **S53.016 Anterior dislocation of unspecified radial head**

\+ **S53.02 Posterior subluxation and dislocation of radial head**
Posteriolateral subluxation and dislocation of radial head
+7th **S53.021 Posterior subluxation of right radial head**
+7th **S53.022 Posterior subluxation of left radial head**
+7th **S53.023 Posterior subluxation of unspecified radial head**
+7th **S53.024 Posterior dislocation of right radial head**
+7th **S53.025 Posterior dislocation of left radial head**
+7th **S53.026 Posterior dislocation of unspecified radial head**

\+ **S53.03 Nursemaid's elbow**
+7th **S53.031 Nursemaid's elbow, right elbow**
+7th **S53.032 Nursemaid's elbow, left elbow**
+7th **S53.033 Nursemaid's elbow, unspecified elbow**

\+ **S53.09 Other subluxation and dislocation of radial head**
+7th **S53.091 Other subluxation of right radial head**
+7th **S53.092 Other subluxation of left radial head**
+7th **S53.093 Other subluxation of unspecified radial head**
+7th **S53.094 Other dislocation of right radial head**
+7th **S53.095 Other dislocation of left radial head**
+7th **S53.096 Other dislocation of unspecified radial head**

\+ **S53.1 Subluxation and dislocation of ulnohumeral joint**
Subluxation and dislocation of elbow NOS
Excludes1: *dislocation of radial head alone (S53.0-)*

\+ **S53.10 Unspecified subluxation and dislocation of ulnohumeral joint**
+7th **S53.101 Unspecified subluxation of right ulnohumeral joint**
+7th **S53.102 Unspecified subluxation of left ulnohumeral joint**
+7th **S53.103 Unspecified subluxation of unspecified ulnohumeral joint**
+7th **S53.104 Unspecified dislocation of right ulnohumeral joint**
+7th **S53.105 Unspecified dislocation of left ulnohumeral joint**
+7th **S53.106 Unspecified dislocation of unspecified ulnohumeral joint**

\+ **S53.11 Anterior subluxation and dislocation of ulnohumeral joint**
+7th **S53.111 Anterior subluxation of right ulnohumeral joint**
+7th **S53.112 Anterior subluxation of left ulnohumeral joint**
+7th **S53.113 Anterior subluxation of unspecified ulnohumeral joint**
+7th **S53.114 Anterior dislocation of right ulnohumeral joint**
AHA CC: 4Q, 2012, 108
+7th **S53.115 Anterior dislocation of left ulnohumeral joint**
+7th **S53.116 Anterior dislocation of unspecified ulnohumeral joint**

\+ **S53.12 Posterior subluxation and dislocation of ulnohumeral joint**
+7th **S53.121 Posterior subluxation of right ulnohumeral joint**
+7th **S53.122 Posterior subluxation of left ulnohumeral joint**
+7th **S53.123 Posterior subluxation of unspecified ulnohumeral joint**
+7th **S53.124 Posterior dislocation of right ulnohumeral joint**
+7th **S53.125 Posterior dislocation of left ulnohumeral joint**
+7th **S53.126 Posterior dislocation of unspecified ulnohumeral joint**

\+ **S53.13 Medial subluxation and dislocation of ulnohumeral joint**
+7th **S53.131 Medial subluxation of right ulnohumeral joint**
+7th **S53.132 Medial subluxation of left ulnohumeral joint**
+7th **S53.133 Medial subluxation of unspecified ulnohumeral joint**
+7th **S53.134 Medial dislocation of right ulnohumeral joint**
+7th **S53.135 Medial dislocation of left ulnohumeral joint**
+7th **S53.136 Medial dislocation of unspecified ulnohumeral joint**

\+ **S53.14 Lateral subluxation and dislocation of ulnohumeral joint**
+7th **S53.141 Lateral subluxation of right ulnohumeral joint**
+7th **S53.142 Lateral subluxation of left ulnohumeral joint**
+7th **S53.143 Lateral subluxation of unspecified ulnohumeral joint**
+7th **S53.144 Lateral dislocation of right ulnohumeral joint**

+7th **S53.145 Lateral dislocation of left ulnohumeral joint**
+7th **S53.146 Lateral dislocation of unspecified ulnohumeral joint**
+ **S53.19 Other subluxation and dislocation of ulnohumeral joint**
+7th **S53.191 Other subluxation of right ulnohumeral joint**
+7th **S53.192 Other subluxation of left ulnohumeral joint**
+7th **S53.193 Other subluxation of unspecified ulnohumeral joint**
+7th **S53.194 Other dislocation of right ulnohumeral joint**
+7th **S53.195 Other dislocation of left ulnohumeral joint**
+7th **S53.196 Other dislocation of unspecified ulnohumeral joint**
+ **S53.2 Traumatic rupture of radial collateral ligament**
Excludes1: *sprain of radial collateral ligament NOS (S53.43-)*
X+7th **S53.20 Traumatic rupture of unspecified radial collateral ligament**
X+7th **S53.21 Traumatic rupture of right radial collateral ligament**
X+7th **S53.22 Traumatic rupture of left radial collateral ligament**
+ **S53.3 Traumatic rupture of ulnar collateral ligament**
Excludes1: *sprain of ulnar collateral ligament (S53.44-)*
X+7th **S53.30 Traumatic rupture of unspecified ulnar collateral ligament**
X+7th **S53.31 Traumatic rupture of right ulnar collateral ligament**
X+7th **S53.32 Traumatic rupture of left ulnar collateral ligament**
+ **S53.4 Sprain of elbow**
Excludes2: *traumatic rupture of radial collateral ligament (S53.2-)*
traumatic rupture of ulnar collateral ligament (S53.3-)
+ **S53.40 Unspecified sprain of elbow**
+7th **S53.401 Unspecified sprain of right elbow**
+7th **S53.402 Unspecified sprain of left elbow**
+7th **S53.409 Unspecified sprain of unspecified elbow**
Sprain of elbow NOS
+ **S53.41 Radiohumeral (joint) sprain**
+7th **S53.411 Radiohumeral (joint) sprain of right elbow**
+7th **S53.412 Radiohumeral (joint) sprain of left elbow**
+7th **S53.419 Radiohumeral (joint) sprain of unspecified elbow**
+ **S53.42 Ulnohumeral (joint) sprain**
+7th **S53.421 Ulnohumeral (joint) sprain of right elbow**
+7th **S53.422 Ulnohumeral (joint) sprain of left elbow**
+7th **S53.429 Ulnohumeral (joint) sprain of unspecified elbow**
+ **S53.43 Radial collateral ligament sprain**
+7th **S53.431 Radial collateral ligament sprain of right elbow**
+7th **S53.432 Radial collateral ligament sprain of left elbow**
+7th **S53.439 Radial collateral ligament sprain of unspecified elbow**
+ **S53.44 Ulnar collateral ligament sprain**
+7th **S53.441 Ulnar collateral ligament sprain of right elbow**
+7th **S53.442 Ulnar collateral ligament sprain of left elbow**
+7th **S53.449 Ulnar collateral ligament sprain of unspecified elbow**
+ **S53.49 Other sprain of elbow**
+7th **S53.491 Other sprain of right elbow**
+7th **S53.492 Other sprain of left elbow**
+7th **S53.499 Other sprain of unspecified elbow**

S54 Injury of nerves at forearm level
Code also any associated open wound (S51.-)
Excludes2: *injury of nerves at wrist and hand level (S64.-)*

The appropriate 7th character is to be added to each code from category S54
A initial encounter
D subsequent encounter
S sequela

+ **S54.0 Injury of ulnar nerve at forearm level**
Injury of ulnar nerve NOS
X+7th **S54.00 Injury of ulnar nerve at forearm level, unspecified arm**
X+7th **S54.01 Injury of ulnar nerve at forearm level, right arm**
X+7th **S54.02 Injury of ulnar nerve at forearm level, left arm**
+ **S54.1 Injury of median nerve at forearm level**
Injury of median nerve NOS
X+7th **S54.10 Injury of median nerve at forearm level, unspecified arm**
X+7th **S54.11 Injury of median nerve at forearm level, right arm**
X+7th **S54.12 Injury of median nerve at forearm level, left arm**
+ **S54.2 Injury of radial nerve at forearm level**
Injury of radial nerve NOS
X+7th **S54.20 Injury of radial nerve at forearm level, unspecified arm**
X+7th **S54.21 Injury of radial nerve at forearm level, right arm**
X+7th **S54.22 Injury of radial nerve at forearm level, left arm**
+ **S54.3 Injury of cutaneous sensory nerve at forearm level**
X+7th **S54.30 Injury of cutaneous sensory nerve at forearm level, unspecified arm**
X+7th **S54.31 Injury of cutaneous sensory nerve at forearm level, right arm**
X+7th **S54.32 Injury of cutaneous sensory nerve at forearm level, left arm**
+ **S54.8 Injury of other nerves at forearm level**
+ **S54.8X Unspecified injury of other nerves at forearm level**
+7th **S54.8X1 Unspecified injury of other nerves at forearm level, right arm**
+7th **S54.8X2 Unspecified injury of other nerves at forearm level, left arm**
+7th **S54.8X9 Unspecified injury of other nerves at forearm level, unspecified arm**
+ **S54.9 Injury of unspecified nerve at forearm level**
X+7th **S54.90 Injury of unspecified nerve at forearm level, unspecified arm**
X+7th **S54.91 Injury of unspecified nerve at forearm level, right arm**
X+7th **S54.92 Injury of unspecified nerve at forearm level, left arm**

S55 Injury of blood vessels at forearm level
Code also any associated open wound (S51.-)
Excludes2: *injury of blood vessels at wrist and hand level (S65.-)*
injury of brachial vessels (S45.1-S45.2)

The appropriate 7th character is to be added to each code from category S55
A initial encounter
D subsequent encounter
S sequela

+ **S55.0 Injury of ulnar artery at forearm level**
+ **S55.00 Unspecified injury of ulnar artery at forearm level**
CC +7th **S55.001 Unspecified injury of ulnar artery at forearm level, right arm**
CC Exclusion 7th character A see Appendix A
PDX collection 1274
CC +7th **S55.002 Unspecified injury of ulnar artery at forearm level, left arm**
CC Exclusion 7th character A see Appendix A
PDX collection 1275
CC +7th **S55.009 Unspecified injury of ulnar artery at forearm level, unspecified arm**
CC Exclusion 7th character A see Appendix A
PDX collection 1276
+ **S55.01 Laceration of ulnar artery at forearm level**
CC +7th **S55.011 Laceration of ulnar artery at forearm level, right arm**
CC Exclusion 7th character A see Appendix A
PDX collection 1274
CC +7th **S55.012 Laceration of ulnar artery at forearm level, left arm**
CC Exclusion 7th character A see Appendix A
PDX collection 1275
CC +7th **S55.019 Laceration of ulnar artery at forearm level, unspecified arm**
CC Exclusion 7th character A see Appendix A
PDX collection 1276
+ **S55.09 Other specified injury of ulnar artery at forearm level**
CC +7th **S55.091 Other specified injury of ulnar artery at forearm level, right arm**
CC Exclusion 7th character A see Appendix A
PDX collection 1274
CC +7th **S55.092 Other specified injury of ulnar artery at forearm level, left arm**
CC Exclusion 7th character A see Appendix A
PDX collection 1275
CC +7th **S55.099 Other specified injury of ulnar artery at forearm level, unspecified arm**
CC Exclusion 7th character A see Appendix A
PDX collection 1276
+ **S55.1 Injury of radial artery at forearm level**
+ **S55.10 Unspecified injury of radial artery at forearm level**
CC +7th **S55.101 Unspecified injury of radial artery at forearm level, right arm**
CC Exclusion 7th character A see Appendix A
PDX collection 1277

CC +7th **S55.102** **Unspecified injury of radial artery at forearm level, left arm**
CC Exclusion 7th character A see Appendix A
PDX collection 1278

CC +7th **S55.109** **Unspecified injury of radial artery at forearm level, unspecified arm**
CC Exclusion 7th character A see Appendix A
PDX collection 1279

\+ **S55.11** **Laceration of radial artery at forearm level**

CC +7th **S55.111** **Laceration of radial artery at forearm level, right arm**
CC Exclusion 7th character A see Appendix A
PDX collection 1277

CC +7th **S55.112** **Laceration of radial artery at forearm level, left arm**
CC Exclusion 7th character A see Appendix A
PDX collection 1278

CC +7th **S55.119** **Laceration of radial artery at forearm level, unspecified arm**
CC Exclusion 7th character A see Appendix A
PDX collection 1279

\+ **S55.19** **Other specified injury of radial artery at forearm level**

CC +7th **S55.191** **Other specified injury of radial artery at forearm level, right arm**
CC Exclusion 7th character A see Appendix A
PDX collection 1277

CC +7th **S55.192** **Other specified injury of radial artery at forearm level, left arm**
CC Exclusion 7th character A see Appendix A
PDX collection 1278

CC +7th **S55.199** **Other specified injury of radial artery at forearm level, unspecified arm**
CC Exclusion 7th character A see Appendix A
PDX collection 1279

\+ **S55.2** **Injury of vein at forearm level**

\+ **S55.20** **Unspecified injury of vein at forearm level**

CC +7th **S55.201** **Unspecified injury of vein at forearm level, right arm**
CC Exclusion 7th character A see Appendix A
PDX collection 1260

CC +7th **S55.202** **Unspecified injury of vein at forearm level, left arm**
CC Exclusion 7th character A see Appendix A
PDX collection 1261

CC +7th **S55.209** **Unspecified injury of vein at forearm level, unspecified arm**
CC Exclusion 7th character A see Appendix A
PDX collection 1262

\+ **S55.21** **Laceration of vein at forearm level**

CC +7th **S55.211** **Laceration of vein at forearm level, right arm**
CC Exclusion 7th character A see Appendix A
PDX collection 1260

CC +7th **S55.212** **Laceration of vein at forearm level, left arm**
CC Exclusion 7th character A see Appendix A
PDX collection 1261

CC +7th **S55.219** **Laceration of vein at forearm level, unspecified arm**
CC Exclusion 7th character A see Appendix A
PDX collection 1262

\+ **S55.29** **Other specified injury of vein at forearm level**

CC +7th **S55.291** **Other specified injury of vein at forearm level, right arm**
CC Exclusion 7th character A see Appendix A
PDX collection 1260

CC +7th **S55.292** **Other specified injury of vein at forearm level, left arm**
CC Exclusion 7th character A see Appendix A
PDX collection 1261

CC +7th **S55.299** **Other specified injury of vein at forearm level, unspecified arm**
CC Exclusion 7th character A see Appendix A
PDX collection 1262

\+ **S55.8** **Injury of other blood vessels at forearm level**

\+ **S55.80** **Unspecified injury of other blood vessels at forearm level**

CC +7th **S55.801** **Unspecified injury of other blood vessels at forearm level, right arm**
CC Exclusion 7th character A see Appendix A
PDX collection 1260

CC +7th **S55.802** **Unspecified injury of other blood vessels at forearm level, left arm**
CC Exclusion 7th character A see Appendix A
PDX collection 1261

CC +7th **S55.809** **Unspecified injury of other blood vessels at forearm level, unspecified arm**
CC Exclusion 7th character A see Appendix A
PDX collection 1262

\+ **S55.81** **Laceration of other blood vessels at forearm level**

CC +7th **S55.811** **Laceration of other blood vessels at forearm level, right arm**
CC Exclusion 7th character A see Appendix A
PDX collection 1260

CC +7th **S55.812** **Laceration of other blood vessels at forearm level, left arm**
CC Exclusion 7th character A see Appendix A
PDX collection 1261

CC +7th **S55.819** **Laceration of other blood vessels at forearm level, unspecified arm**
CC Exclusion 7th character A see Appendix A
PDX collection 1262

\+ **S55.89** **Other specified injury of other blood vessels at forearm level**

CC +7th **S55.891** **Other specified injury of other blood vessels at forearm level, right arm**
CC Exclusion 7th character A see Appendix A
PDX collection 1260

CC +7th **S55.892** **Other specified injury of other blood vessels at forearm level, left arm**
CC Exclusion 7th character A see Appendix A
PDX collection 1261

CC +7th **S55.899** **Other specified injury of other blood vessels at forearm level, unspecified arm**
CC Exclusion 7th character A see Appendix A
PDX collection 1262

\+ **S55.9** **Injury of unspecified blood vessel at forearm level**

\+ **S55.90** **Unspecified injury of unspecified blood vessel at forearm level**

CC +7th **S55.901** **Unspecified injury of unspecified blood vessel at forearm level, right arm**
CC Exclusion 7th character A see Appendix A
PDX collection 1260

CC +7th **S55.902** **Unspecified injury of unspecified blood vessel at forearm level, left arm**
CC Exclusion 7th character A see Appendix A
PDX collection 1261

CC +7th **S55.909** **Unspecified injury of unspecified blood vessel at forearm level, unspecified arm**
CC Exclusion 7th character A see Appendix A
PDX collection 1262

\+ **S55.91** **Laceration of unspecified blood vessel at forearm level**

CC +7th **S55.911** **Laceration of unspecified blood vessel at forearm level, right arm**
CC Exclusion 7th character A see Appendix A
PDX collection 1260

CC +7th **S55.912** **Laceration of unspecified blood vessel at forearm level, left arm**
CC Exclusion 7th character A see Appendix A
PDX collection 1261

CC +7th **S55.919** **Laceration of unspecified blood vessel at forearm level, unspecified arm**
CC Exclusion 7th character A see Appendix A
PDX collection 1262

\+ **S55.99** **Other specified injury of unspecified blood vessel at forearm level**

CC +7th **S55.991** **Other specified injury of unspecified blood vessel at forearm level, right arm**
CC Exclusion 7th character A see Appendix A
PDX collection 1260

CC +7th **S55.992** **Other specified injury of unspecified blood vessel at forearm level, left arm**
CC Exclusion 7th character A see Appendix A
PDX collection 1261

CC +7th **S55.999** **Other specified injury of unspecified blood vessel at forearm level, unspecified arm**
CC Exclusion 7th character A see Appendix A
PDX collection 1262

S56 Injury of muscle, fascia and tendon at forearm level

Code also any associated open wound (S51.-)

Excludes2: *injury of muscle, fascia and tendon at or below wrist (S66.-)*
sprain of joints and ligaments of elbow (S53.4-)

The appropriate 7th character is to be added to each code from category S56
A initial encounter
D subsequent encounter
S sequela

+ **S56.0 Injury of flexor muscle, fascia and tendon of thumb at forearm level**
  + **S56.00 Unspecified injury of flexor muscle, fascia and tendon of thumb at forearm level**
    - +7th **S56.001 Unspecified injury of flexor muscle, fascia and tendon of right thumb at forearm level**
    - +7th **S56.002 Unspecified injury of flexor muscle, fascia and tendon of left thumb at forearm level**
    - +7th **S56.009 Unspecified injury of flexor muscle, fascia and tendon of unspecified thumb at forearm level**
  + **S56.01 Strain of flexor muscle, fascia and tendon of thumb at forearm level**
    - +7th **S56.011 Strain of flexor muscle, fascia and tendon of right thumb at forearm level**
    - +7th **S56.012 Strain of flexor muscle, fascia and tendon of left thumb at forearm level**
    - +7th **S56.019 Strain of flexor muscle, fascia and tendon of unspecified thumb at forearm level**
  + **S56.02 Laceration of flexor muscle, fascia and tendon of thumb at forearm level**
    - CC +7th **S56.021 Laceration of flexor muscle, fascia and tendon of right thumb at forearm level**
      CC Exclusion 7th character A see Appendix A
      PDX collection 1280
    - CC +7th **S56.022 Laceration of flexor muscle, fascia and tendon of left thumb at forearm level**
      CC Exclusion 7th character A see Appendix A
      PDX collection 1281
    - CC +7th **S56.029 Laceration of flexor muscle, fascia and tendon of unspecified thumb at forearm level**
      CC Exclusion 7th character A see Appendix A
      PDX collection 1282
  + **S56.09 Other injury of flexor muscle, fascia and tendon of thumb at forearm level**
    - +7th **S56.091 Other injury of flexor muscle, fascia and tendon of right thumb at forearm level**
    - +7th **S56.092 Other injury of flexor muscle, fascia and tendon of left thumb at forearm level**
    - +7th **S56.099 Other injury of flexor muscle, fascia and tendon of unspecified thumb at forearm level**

+ **S56.1 Injury of flexor muscle, fascia and tendon of other and unspecified finger at forearm level**
  + **S56.10 Unspecified injury of flexor muscle, fascia and tendon of other and unspecified finger at forearm level**
    - +7th **S56.101 Unspecified injury of flexor muscle, fascia and tendon of right index finger at forearm level**
    - +7th **S56.102 Unspecified injury of flexor muscle, fascia and tendon of left index finger at forearm level**
    - +7th **S56.103 Unspecified injury of flexor muscle, fascia and tendon of right middle finger at forearm level**
    - +7th **S56.104 Unspecified injury of flexor muscle, fascia and tendon of left middle finger at forearm level**
    - +7th **S56.105 Unspecified injury of flexor muscle, fascia and tendon of right ring finger at forearm level**
    - +7th **S56.106 Unspecified injury of flexor muscle, fascia and tendon of left ring finger at forearm level**
    - +7th **S56.107 Unspecified injury of flexor muscle, fascia and tendon of right little finger at forearm level**
    - +7th **S56.108 Unspecified injury of flexor muscle, fascia and tendon of left little finger at forearm level**
    - +7th **S56.109 Unspecified injury of flexor muscle, fascia and tendon of unspecified finger at forearm level**
  + **S56.11 Strain of flexor muscle, fascia and tendon of other and unspecified finger at forearm level**
    - +7th **S56.111 Strain of flexor muscle, fascia and tendon of right index finger at forearm level**
    - +7th **S56.112 Strain of flexor muscle, fascia and tendon of left index finger at forearm level**
    - +7th **S56.113 Strain of flexor muscle, fascia and tendon of right middle finger at forearm level**
    - +7th **S56.114 Strain of flexor muscle, fascia and tendon of left middle finger at forearm level**
    - +7th **S56.115 Strain of flexor muscle, fascia and tendon of right ring finger at forearm level**
    - +7th **S56.116 Strain of flexor muscle, fascia and tendon of left ring finger at forearm level**
    - +7th **S56.117 Strain of flexor muscle, fascia and tendon of right little finger at forearm level**
    - +7th **S56.118 Strain of flexor muscle, fascia and tendon of left little finger at forearm level**
    - +7th **S56.119 Strain of flexor muscle, fascia and tendon of finger of unspecified finger at forearm level**
  + **S56.12 Laceration of flexor muscle, fascia and tendon of other and unspecified finger at forearm level**
    - CC +7th **S56.121 Laceration of flexor muscle, fascia and tendon of right index finger at forearm level**
      CC Exclusion 7th character A see Appendix A
      PDX collection 1280
    - CC +7th **S56.122 Laceration of flexor muscle, fascia and tendon of left index finger at forearm level**
      CC Exclusion 7th character A see Appendix A
      PDX collection 1281
    - CC +7th **S56.123 Laceration of flexor muscle, fascia and tendon of right middle finger at forearm level**
      CC Exclusion 7th character A see Appendix A
      PDX collection 1280
    - CC +7th **S56.124 Laceration of flexor muscle, fascia and tendon of left middle finger at forearm level**
      CC Exclusion 7th character A see Appendix A
      PDX collection 1281
    - CC +7th **S56.125 Laceration of flexor muscle, fascia and tendon of right ring finger at forearm level**
      CC Exclusion 7th character A see Appendix A
      PDX collection 1280
    - CC +7th **S56.126 Laceration of flexor muscle, fascia and tendon of left ring finger at forearm level**
      CC Exclusion 7th character A see Appendix A
      PDX collection 1281
    - CC +7th **S56.127 Laceration of flexor muscle, fascia and tendon of right little finger at forearm level**
      CC Exclusion 7th character A see Appendix A
      PDX collection 1280
    - CC +7th **S56.128 Laceration of flexor muscle, fascia and tendon of left little finger at forearm level**
      CC Exclusion 7th character A see Appendix A
      PDX collection 1281
    - CC +7th **S56.129 Laceration of flexor muscle, fascia and tendon of unspecified finger at forearm level**
      CC Exclusion 7th character A see Appendix A
      PDX collection 1282
  + **S56.19 Other injury of flexor muscle, fascia and tendon of other and unspecified finger at forearm level**
    - +7th **S56.191 Other injury of flexor muscle, fascia and tendon of right index finger at forearm level**
    - +7th **S56.192 Other injury of flexor muscle, fascia and tendon of left index finger at forearm level**
    - +7th **S56.193 Other injury of flexor muscle, fascia and tendon of right middle finger at forearm level**
    - +7th **S56.194 Other injury of flexor muscle, fascia and tendon of left middle finger at forearm level**
    - +7th **S56.195 Other injury of flexor muscle, fascia and tendon of right ring finger at forearm level**
    - +7th **S56.196 Other injury of flexor muscle, fascia and tendon of left ring finger at forearm level**
    - +7th **S56.197 Other injury of flexor muscle, fascia and tendon of right little finger at forearm level**
    - +7th **S56.198 Other injury of flexor muscle, fascia and tendon of left little finger at forearm level**
    - +7th **S56.199 Other injury of flexor muscle, fascia and tendon of unspecified finger at forearm level**

+ S56.2 Injury of other flexor muscle, fascia and tendon at forearm level
+ S56.20 Unspecified injury of other flexor muscle, fascia and tendon at forearm level
+7th S56.201 Unspecified injury of other flexor muscle, fascia and tendon at forearm level, right arm
+7th S56.202 Unspecified injury of other flexor muscle, fascia and tendon at forearm level, left arm
+7th S56.209 Unspecified injury of other flexor muscle, fascia and tendon at forearm level, unspecified arm
+ S56.21 Strain of other flexor muscle, fascia and tendon at forearm level
+7th S56.211 Strain of other flexor muscle, fascia and tendon at forearm level, right arm
+7th S56.212 Strain of other flexor muscle, fascia and tendon at forearm level, left arm
+7th S56.219 Strain of other flexor muscle, fascia and tendon at forearm level, unspecified arm
+ S56.22 Laceration of other flexor muscle, fascia and tendon at forearm level
CC +7th S56.221 Laceration of other flexor muscle, fascia and tendon at forearm level, right arm
CC Exclusion 7th character A see Appendix A PDX collection 1280
CC +7th S56.222 Laceration of other flexor muscle, fascia and tendon at forearm level, left arm
CC Exclusion 7th character A see Appendix A PDX collection 1281
CC +7th S56.229 Laceration of other flexor muscle, fascia and tendon at forearm level, unspecified arm
CC Exclusion 7th character A see Appendix A PDX collection 1282
+ S56.29 Other injury of other flexor muscle, fascia and tendon at forearm level
+7th S56.291 Other injury of other flexor muscle, fascia and tendon at forearm level, right arm
+7th S56.292 Other injury of other flexor muscle, fascia and tendon at forearm level, left arm
+7th S56.299 Other injury of other flexor muscle, fascia and tendon at forearm level, unspecified arm
+ S56.3 Injury of extensor or abductor muscles, fascia and tendons of thumb at forearm level
+ S56.30 Unspecified injury of extensor or abductor muscles, fascia and tendons of thumb at forearm level
+7th S56.301 Unspecified injury of extensor or abductor muscles, fascia and tendons of right thumb at forearm level
+7th S56.302 Unspecified injury of extensor or abductor muscles, fascia and tendons of left thumb at forearm level
+7th S56.309 Unspecified injury of extensor or abductor muscles, fascia and tendons of unspecified thumb at forearm level
+ S56.31 Strain of extensor or abductor muscles, fascia and tendons of thumb at forearm level
+7th S56.311 Strain of extensor or abductor muscles, fascia and tendons of right thumb at forearm level
+7th S56.312 Strain of extensor or abductor muscles, fascia and tendons of left thumb at forearm level
+7th S56.319 Strain of extensor or abductor muscles, fascia and tendons of unspecified thumb at forearm level
+ S56.32 Laceration of extensor or abductor muscles, fascia and tendons of thumb at forearm level
CC +7th S56.321 Laceration of extensor or abductor muscles, fascia and tendons of right thumb at forearm level
CC Exclusion 7th character A see Appendix A PDX collection 1280
CC +7th S56.322 Laceration of extensor or abductor muscles, fascia and tendons of left thumb at forearm level
CC Exclusion 7th character A see Appendix A PDX collection 1281
CC +7th S56.329 Laceration of extensor or abductor muscles, fascia and tendons of unspecified thumb at forearm level
CC Exclusion 7th character A see Appendix A PDX collection 1282
+ S56.39 Other injury of extensor or abductor muscles, fascia and tendons of thumb at forearm level
+7th S56.391 Other injury of extensor or abductor muscles, fascia and tendons of right thumb at forearm level
+7th S56.392 Other injury of extensor or abductor muscles, fascia and tendons of left thumb at forearm level
+7th S56.399 Other injury of extensor or abductor muscles, fascia and tendons of unspecified thumb at forearm level
+ S56.4 Injury of extensor muscle, fascia and tendon of other and unspecified finger at forearm level
+ S56.40 Unspecified injury of extensor muscle, fascia and tendon of other and unspecified finger at forearm level
+7th S56.401 Unspecified injury of extensor muscle, fascia and tendon of right index finger at forearm level
+7th S56.402 Unspecified injury of extensor muscle, fascia and tendon of left index finger at forearm level
+7th S56.403 Unspecified injury of extensor muscle, fascia and tendon of right middle finger at forearm level
+7th S56.404 Unspecified injury of extensor muscle, fascia and tendon of left middle finger at forearm level
+7th S56.405 Unspecified injury of extensor muscle, fascia and tendon of right ring finger at forearm level
+7th S56.406 Unspecified injury of extensor muscle, fascia and tendon of left ring finger at forearm level
+7th S56.407 Unspecified injury of extensor muscle, fascia and tendon of right little finger at forearm level
+7th S56.408 Unspecified injury of extensor muscle, fascia and tendon of left little finger at forearm level
+7th S56.409 Unspecified injury of extensor muscle, fascia and tendon of unspecified finger at forearm level
+ S56.41 Strain of extensor muscle, fascia and tendon of other and unspecified finger at forearm level
+7th S56.411 Strain of extensor muscle, fascia and tendon of right index finger at forearm level
+7th S56.412 Strain of extensor muscle, fascia and tendon of left index finger at forearm level
+7th S56.413 Strain of extensor muscle, fascia and tendon of right middle finger at forearm level
+7th S56.414 Strain of extensor muscle, fascia and tendon of left middle finger at forearm level
+7th S56.415 Strain of extensor muscle, fascia and tendon of right ring finger at forearm level
+7th S56.416 Strain of extensor muscle, fascia and tendon of left ring finger at forearm level
+7th S56.417 Strain of extensor muscle, fascia and tendon of right little finger at forearm level
+7th S56.418 Strain of extensor muscle, fascia and tendon of left little finger at forearm level
+7th S56.419 Strain of extensor muscle, fascia and tendon of finger, unspecified finger at forearm level
+ S56.42 Laceration of extensor muscle, fascia and tendon of other and unspecified finger at forearm level
CC +7th S56.421 Laceration of extensor muscle, fascia and tendon of right index finger at forearm level
CC Exclusion 7th character A see Appendix A PDX collection 1280
CC +7th S56.422 Laceration of extensor muscle, fascia and tendon of left index finger at forearm level
CC Exclusion 7th character A see Appendix A PDX collection 1281
CC +7th S56.423 Laceration of extensor muscle, fascia and tendon of right middle finger at forearm level
CC Exclusion 7th character A see Appendix A PDX collection 1280
CC +7th S56.424 Laceration of extensor muscle, fascia and tendon of left middle finger at forearm level
CC Exclusion 7th character A see Appendix A PDX collection 1281

CC +7th **S56.425** Laceration of extensor muscle, fascia and tendon of right ring finger at forearm level
CC Exclusion 7th character A see Appendix A
PDX collection 1280

CC +7th **S56.426** Laceration of extensor muscle, fascia and tendon of left ring finger at forearm level
CC Exclusion 7th character A see Appendix A
PDX collection 1281

CC +7th **S56.427** Laceration of extensor muscle, fascia and tendon of right little finger at forearm level
CC Exclusion 7th character A see Appendix A
PDX collection 1280

CC +7th **S56.428** Laceration of extensor muscle, fascia and tendon of left little finger at forearm level
CC Exclusion 7th character A see Appendix A
PDX collection 1281

CC +7th **S56.429** Laceration of extensor muscle, fascia and tendon of unspecified finger at forearm level
CC Exclusion 7th character A see Appendix A
PDX collection 1282

\+ **S56.49** Other injury of extensor muscle, fascia and tendon of other and unspecified finger at forearm level

+7th **S56.491** Other injury of extensor muscle, fascia and tendon of right index finger at forearm level

+7th **S56.492** Other injury of extensor muscle, fascia and tendon of left index finger at forearm level

+7th **S56.493** Other injury of extensor muscle, fascia and tendon of right middle finger at forearm level

+7th **S56.494** Other injury of extensor muscle, fascia and tendon of left middle finger at forearm level

+7th **S56.495** Other injury of extensor muscle, fascia and tendon of right ring finger at forearm level

+7th **S56.496** Other injury of extensor muscle, fascia and tendon of left ring finger at forearm level

+7th **S56.497** Other injury of extensor muscle, fascia and tendon of right little finger at forearm level

+7th **S56.498** Other injury of extensor muscle, fascia and tendon of left little finger at forearm level

+7th **S56.499** Other injury of extensor muscle, fascia and tendon of unspecified finger at forearm level

\+ **S56.5** Injury of other extensor muscle, fascia and tendon at forearm level

\+ **S56.50** Unspecified injury of other extensor muscle, fascia and tendon at forearm level

+7th **S56.501** Unspecified injury of other extensor muscle, fascia and tendon at forearm level, right arm

+7th **S56.502** Unspecified injury of other extensor muscle, fascia and tendon at forearm level, left arm

+7th **S56.509** Unspecified injury of other extensor muscle, fascia and tendon at forearm level, unspecified arm

\+ **S56.51** Strain of other extensor muscle, fascia and tendon at forearm level

+7th **S56.511** Strain of other extensor muscle, fascia and tendon at forearm level, right arm

+7th **S56.512** Strain of other extensor muscle, fascia≈and tendon at forearm level, left arm

+7th **S56.519** Strain of other extensor muscle, fascia and tendon at forearm level, unspecified arm

\+ **S56.52** Laceration of other extensor muscle, fascia and tendon at forearm level

CC +7th **S56.521** Laceration of other extensor muscle, fascia and tendon at forearm level, right arm
CC Exclusion 7th character A see Appendix A
PDX collection 1280

CC +7th **S56.522** Laceration of other extensor muscle, fascia and tendon at forearm level, left arm
CC Exclusion 7th character A see Appendix A
PDX collection 1281

CC +7th **S56.529** Laceration of other extensor muscle, fascia and tendon at forearm level, unspecified arm
CC Exclusion 7th character A see Appendix A
PDX collection 1282

\+ **S56.59** Other injury of other extensor muscle, fascia and tendon at forearm level

+7th **S56.591** Other injury of other extensor muscle, fascia and tendon at forearm level, right arm

+7th **S56.592** Other injury of other extensor muscle, fascia and tendon at forearm level, left arm

+7th **S56.599** Other injury of other extensor muscle, fascia and tendon at forearm level, unspecified arm

\+ **S56.8** Injury of other muscles, fascia and tendons at forearm level

\+ **S56.80** Unspecified injury of other muscles, fascia and tendons at forearm level

+7th **S56.801** Unspecified injury of other muscles, fascia and tendons at forearm level, right arm

+7th **S56.802** Unspecified injury of other muscles, fascia and tendons at forearm level, left arm

+7th **S56.809** Unspecified injury of other muscles, fascia and tendons at forearm level, unspecified arm

\+ **S56.81** Strain of other muscles, fascia and tendons at forearm level

+7th **S56.811** Strain of other muscles, fascia and tendons at forearm level, right arm

+7th **S56.812** Strain of other muscles, fascia and tendons at forearm level, left arm

+7th **S56.819** Strain of other muscles, fascia and tendons at forearm level, unspecified arm

\+ **S56.82** Laceration of other muscles, fascia and tendons at forearm level

CC +7th **S56.821** Laceration of other muscles, fascia and tendons at forearm level, right arm
CC Exclusion 7th character A see Appendix A
PDX collection 1280

CC +7th **S56.822** Laceration of other muscles, fascia and tendons at forearm level, left arm
CC Exclusion 7th character A see Appendix A
PDX collection 1281

CC +7th **S56.829** Laceration of other muscles, fascia and tendons at forearm level, unspecified arm
CC Exclusion 7th character A see Appendix A
PDX collection 1282

\+ **S56.89** Other injury of other muscles, fascia and tendons at forearm level

+7th **S56.891** Other injury of other muscles, fascia and tendons at forearm level, right arm

+7th **S56.892** Other injury of other muscles, fascia and tendons at forearm level, left arm

+7th **S56.899** Other injury of other muscles, fascia and tendons at forearm level, unspecified arm

\+ **S56.9** Injury of unspecified muscles, fascia and tendons at forearm level

\+ **S56.90** Unspecified injury of unspecified muscles, fascia and tendons at forearm level

+7th **S56.901** Unspecified injury of unspecified muscles, fascia and tendons at forearm level, right arm

+7th **S56.902** Unspecified injury of unspecified muscles, fascia and tendons at forearm level, left arm

+7th **S56.909** Unspecified injury of unspecified muscles, fascia and tendons at forearm level, unspecified arm

\+ **S56.91** Strain of unspecified muscles, fascia and tendons at forearm level

+7th **S56.911** Strain of unspecified muscles, fascia and tendons at forearm level, right arm

+7th **S56.912** Strain of unspecified muscles, fascia and tendons at forearm level, left arm

+7th **S56.919** Strain of unspecified muscles, fascia and tendons at forearm level, unspecified arm

\+ **S56.92** Laceration of unspecified muscles, fascia and tendons at forearm level

CC +7th **S56.921** Laceration of unspecified muscles, fascia and tendons at forearm level, right arm
CC Exclusion 7th character A see Appendix A
PDX collection 1280

CC +7th **S56.922** Laceration of unspecified muscles, fascia and tendons at forearm level, left arm
CC Exclusion 7th character A see Appendix A
PDX collection 1281

CC +7th **S56.929** Laceration of unspecified muscles, fascia and tendons at forearm level, unspecified arm
CC Exclusion 7th character A see Appendix A
PDX collection 1282

\+ **S56.99** Other injury of unspecified muscles, fascia and tendons at forearm level

+7th **S56.991** Other injury of unspecified muscles, fascia and tendons at forearm level, right arm

+7th **S56.992** Other injury of unspecified muscles, fascia and tendons at forearm level, left arm

+7th **S56.999** Other injury of unspecified muscles, fascia and tendons at forearm level, unspecified arm

S57 Crushing injury of elbow and forearm

Use additional code(s) for all associated injuries

Excludes2: *crushing injury of wrist and hand (S67.-)*

The appropriate 7th character is to be added to each code from category S57
A initial encounter
D subsequent encounter
S sequela

+ S57.0 Crushing injury of elbow
- **X+7th S57.00 Crushing injury of unspecified elbow**
- **X+7th S57.01 Crushing injury of right elbow**
- **X+7th S57.02 Crushing injury of left elbow**

+ S57.8 Crushing injury of forearm
- **X+7th S57.80 Crushing injury of unspecified forearm**
- **X+7th S57.81 Crushing injury of right forearm**
- **X+7th S57.82 Crushing injury of left forearm**

S58 Traumatic amputation of elbow and forearm

An amputation not identified as partial or complete should be coded to complete

Excludes1: *traumatic amputation of wrist and hand (S68.-)*

The appropriate 7th character is to be added to each code from category S58
A initial encounter
D subsequent encounter
S sequela

+ S58.0 Traumatic amputation at elbow level

+ S58.01 Complete traumatic amputation at elbow level

CC +7th S58.011 Complete traumatic amputation at elbow level, right arm
CC Exclusion 7th character A see Appendix A PDX collection 1266

CC +7th S58.012 Complete traumatic amputation at elbow level, left arm
CC Exclusion 7th character A see Appendix A PDX collection 1267

CC +7th S58.019 Complete traumatic amputation at elbow level, unspecified arm
CC Exclusion 7th character A see Appendix A PDX collection 1268

+ S58.02 Partial traumatic amputation at elbow level

CC +7th S58.021 Partial traumatic amputation at elbow level, right arm
CC Exclusion 7th character A see Appendix A PDX collection 1266

CC +7th S58.022 Partial traumatic amputation at elbow level, left arm
CC Exclusion 7th character A see Appendix A PDX collection 1267

CC +7th S58.029 Partial traumatic amputation at elbow level, unspecified arm
CC Exclusion 7th character A see Appendix A PDX collection 1268

+ S58.1 Traumatic amputation at level between elbow and wrist

+ S58.11 Complete traumatic amputation at level between elbow and wrist

CC +7th S58.111 Complete traumatic amputation at level between elbow and wrist, right arm
CC Exclusion 7th character A see Appendix A PDX collection 1266

CC +7th S58.112 Complete traumatic amputation at level between elbow and wrist, left arm
CC Exclusion 7th character A see Appendix A PDX collection 1267

CC +7th S58.119 Complete traumatic amputation at level between elbow and wrist, unspecified arm
CC Exclusion 7th character A see Appendix A PDX collection 1268

+ S58.12 Partial traumatic amputation at level between elbow and wrist

CC +7th S58.121 Partial traumatic amputation at level between elbow and wrist, right arm
CC Exclusion 7th character A see Appendix A PDX collection 1266

CC +7th S58.122 Partial traumatic amputation at level between elbow and wrist, left arm
CC Exclusion 7th character A see Appendix A PDX collection 1267

CC +7th S58.129 Partial traumatic amputation at level between elbow and wrist, unspecified arm
CC Exclusion 7th character A see Appendix A PDX collection 1268

+ S58.9 Traumatic amputation of forearm, level unspecified

Excludes1: *traumatic amputation of wrist (S68.-)*

+ S58.91 Complete traumatic amputation of forearm, level unspecified

CC +7th S58.911 Complete traumatic amputation of right forearm, level unspecified
CC Exclusion 7th character A see Appendix A PDX collection 1266

CC +7th S58.912 Complete traumatic amputation of left forearm, level unspecified
CC Exclusion 7th character A see Appendix A PDX collection 1267

CC +7th S58.919 Complete traumatic amputation of unspecified forearm, level unspecified
CC Exclusion 7th character A see Appendix A PDX collection 1268

+ S58.92 Partial traumatic amputation of forearm, level unspecified

CC +7th S58.921 Partial traumatic amputation of right forearm, level unspecified
CC Exclusion 7th character A see Appendix A PDX collection 1266

CC +7th S58.922 Partial traumatic amputation of left forearm, level unspecified
CC Exclusion 7th character A see Appendix A PDX collection 1267

CC +7th S58.929 Partial traumatic amputation of unspecified forearm, level unspecified
CC Exclusion 7th character A see Appendix A PDX collection 1268

S59 Other and unspecified injuries of elbow and forearm

Excludes2: *other and unspecified injuries of wrist and hand (S69.-)*

The appropriate 7th character is to be added to each code from subcategories S59.0, S59.1, and S59.2
A initial encounter for closed fracture
D subsequent encounter for fracture with routine healing
G subsequent encounter for fracture with delayed healing
K subsequent encounter for fracture with nonunion
P subsequent encounter for fracture with malunion
S sequela

Review coding guideline C.19.c

+ S59.0 Physeal fracture of lower end of ulna

+ S59.00 Unspecified physeal fracture of lower end of ulna

CC +7th S59.001 Unspecified physeal fracture of lower end of ulna, right arm
CC Exclusion 7th character A see Appendix A PDX collection 1270
CC Exclusion 7th characters K & P see Appendix A PDX collection 0897
HAC 7th character A see Appendix B for HAC conditional logic

CC +7th S59.002 Unspecified physeal fracture of lower end of ulna, left arm
CC Exclusion 7th character A see Appendix A PDX collection 1271
CC Exclusion 7th characters K & P see Appendix A PDX collection 0897
HAC 7th character A see Appendix B for HAC conditional logic

CC +7th S59.009 Unspecified physeal fracture of lower end of ulna, unspecified arm
CC Exclusion 7th character A see Appendix A PDX collection 1272
CC Exclusion 7th characters K & P see Appendix A PDX collection 0897
HAC 7th character A see Appendix B for HAC conditional logic

+ S59.01 Salter-Harris Type I physeal fracture of lower end of ulna

CC +7th S59.011 Salter-Harris Type I physeal fracture of lower end of ulna, right arm
CC Exclusion 7th character A see Appendix A PDX collection 1270
CC Exclusion 7th characters K & P see Appendix A PDX collection 0897
HAC 7th character A see Appendix B for HAC conditional logic

CC +7th S59.012 Salter-Harris Type I physeal fracture of lower end of ulna, left arm
CC Exclusion 7th character A see Appendix A PDX collection 1271
CC Exclusion 7th characters K & P see Appendix A PDX collection 0897
HAC 7th character A see Appendix B for HAC conditional logic

CC +7th **S59.019 Salter-Harris Type I physeal fracture of lower end of ulna, unspecified arm**
CC Exclusion 7th character A see Appendix A PDX collection 1272
CC Exclusion 7th characters K & P see Appendix A PDX collection 0897
HAC 7th character A see Appendix B for HAC conditional logic

+ **S59.02 Salter-Harris Type II physeal fracture of lower end of ulna**

CC +7th **S59.021 Salter-Harris Type II physeal fracture of lower end of ulna, right arm**
CC Exclusion 7th character A see Appendix A PDX collection 1270
CC Exclusion 7th characters K & P see Appendix A PDX collection 0897
HAC 7th character A see Appendix B for HAC conditional logic

CC +7th **S59.022 Salter-Harris Type II physeal fracture of lower end of ulna, left arm**
CC Exclusion 7th character A see Appendix A PDX collection 1271
CC Exclusion 7th characters K & P see Appendix A PDX collection 0897
HAC 7th character A see Appendix B for HAC conditional logic

CC +7th **S59.029 Salter-Harris Type II physeal fracture of lower end of ulna, unspecified arm**
CC Exclusion 7th character A see Appendix A PDX collection 1272
CC Exclusion 7th characters K & P see Appendix A PDX collection 0897
HAC 7th character A see Appendix B for HAC conditional logic

+ **S59.03 Salter-Harris Type III physeal fracture of lower end of ulna**

CC +7th **S59.031 Salter-Harris Type III physeal fracture of lower end of ulna, right arm**
CC Exclusion 7th character A see Appendix A PDX collection 1270
CC Exclusion 7th characters K & P see Appendix A PDX collection 0897
HAC 7th character A see Appendix B for HAC conditional logic

CC +7th **S59.032 Salter-Harris Type III physeal fracture of lower end of ulna, left arm**
CC Exclusion 7th character A see Appendix A PDX collection 1271
CC Exclusion 7th characters K & P see Appendix A PDX collection 0897
HAC 7th character A see Appendix B for HAC conditional logic

CC +7th **S59.039 Salter-Harris Type III physeal fracture of lower end of ulna, unspecified arm**
CC Exclusion 7th character A see Appendix A PDX collection 1272
CC Exclusion 7th characters K & P see Appendix A PDX collection 0897
HAC 7th character A see Appendix B for HAC conditional logic

+ **S59.04 Salter-Harris Type IV physeal fracture of lower end of ulna**

CC +7th **S59.041 Salter-Harris Type IV physeal fracture of lower end of ulna, right arm**
CC Exclusion 7th character A see Appendix A PDX collection 1270
CC Exclusion 7th characters K & P see Appendix A PDX collection 0897
HAC 7th character A see Appendix B for HAC conditional logic

CC +7th **S59.042 Salter-Harris Type IV physeal fracture of lower end of ulna, left arm**
CC Exclusion 7th character A see Appendix A PDX collection 1271
CC Exclusion 7th characters K & P see Appendix A PDX collection 0897
HAC 7th character A see Appendix B for HAC conditional logic

CC +7th **S59.049 Salter-Harris Type IV physeal fracture of lower end of ulna, unspecified arm**
CC Exclusion 7th character A see Appendix A PDX collection 1272
CC Exclusion 7th characters K & P see Appendix A PDX collection 0897
HAC 7th character A see Appendix B for HAC conditional logic

+ **S59.09 Other physeal fracture of lower end of ulna**

CC +7th **S59.091 Other physeal fracture of lower end of ulna, right arm**
CC Exclusion 7th character A see Appendix A PDX collection 1270
CC Exclusion 7th characters K & P see Appendix A PDX collection 0897
HAC 7th character A see Appendix B for HAC conditional logic

CC +7th **S59.092 Other physeal fracture of lower end of ulna, left arm**
CC Exclusion 7th character A see Appendix A PDX collection 1271
CC Exclusion 7th characters K & P see Appendix A PDX collection 0897
HAC 7th character A see Appendix B for HAC conditional logic

CC +7th **S59.099 Other physeal fracture of lower end of ulna, unspecified arm**
CC Exclusion 7th character A see Appendix A PDX collection 1272
CC Exclusion 7th characters K & P see Appendix A PDX collection 0897
HAC 7th character A see Appendix B for HAC conditional logic

+ **S59.1 Physeal fracture of upper end of radius**

+ **S59.10 Unspecified physeal fracture of upper end of radius**

CC +7th **S59.101 Unspecified physeal fracture of upper end of radius, right arm**
CC Exclusion 7th characters K & P see Appendix A PDX collection 0897

CC +7th **S59.102 Unspecified physeal fracture of upper end of radius, left arm**
CC Exclusion 7th characters K & P see Appendix A PDX collection 0897

CC +7th **S59.109 Unspecified physeal fracture of upper end of radius, unspecified arm**
CC Exclusion 7th characters K & P see Appendix A PDX collection 0897

+ **S59.11 Salter-Harris Type I physeal fracture of upper end of radius**

CC +7th **S59.111 Salter-Harris Type I physeal fracture of upper end of radius, right arm**
CC Exclusion 7th characters K & P see Appendix A PDX collection 0897

CC +7th **S59.112 Salter-Harris Type I physeal fracture of upper end of radius, left arm**
CC Exclusion 7th characters K & P see Appendix A PDX collection 0897

CC +7th **S59.119 Salter-Harris Type I physeal fracture of upper end of radius, unspecified arm**
CC Exclusion 7th characters K & P see Appendix A PDX collection 0897

+ **S59.12 Salter-Harris Type II physeal fracture of upper end of radius**

CC +7th **S59.121 Salter-Harris Type II physeal fracture of upper end of radius, right arm**
CC Exclusion 7th characters K & P see Appendix A PDX collection 0897

CC +7th **S59.122 Salter-Harris Type II physeal fracture of upper end of radius, left arm**
CC Exclusion 7th characters K & P see Appendix A PDX collection 0897

CC +7th **S59.129 Salter-Harris Type II physeal fracture of upper end of radius, unspecified arm**
CC Exclusion 7th characters K & P see Appendix A PDX collection 0897

+ **S59.13 Salter-Harris Type III physeal fracture of upper end of radius**

CC +7th **S59.131 Salter-Harris Type III physeal fracture of upper end of radius, right arm**
CC Exclusion 7th characters K & P see Appendix A PDX collection 0897

CC +7th **S59.132 Salter-Harris Type III physeal fracture of upper end of radius, left arm**
CC Exclusion 7th characters K & P see Appendix A PDX collection 0897

CC +7th **S59.139 Salter-Harris Type III physeal fracture of upper end of radius, unspecified arm**
CC Exclusion 7th characters K & P see Appendix A PDX collection 0897

+ **S59.14 Salter-Harris Type IV physeal fracture of upper end of radius**

CC +7th **S59.141 Salter-Harris Type IV physeal fracture of upper end of radius, right arm**
CC Exclusion 7th characters K & P see Appendix A PDX collection 0897

CC +7th **S59.142 Salter-Harris Type IV physeal fracture of upper end of radius, left arm**
CC Exclusion 7th characters K & P see Appendix A PDX collection 0897

CC +7th **S59.149 Salter-Harris Type IV physeal fracture of upper end of radius, unspecified arm**
CC Exclusion 7th characters K & P see Appendix A PDX collection 0897

+ **S59.19 Other physeal fracture of upper end of radius**

CC +7th **S59.191 Other physeal fracture of upper end of radius, right arm**
CC Exclusion 7th characters K & P see Appendix A PDX collection 0897

CC +7th **S59.192 Other physeal fracture of upper end of radius, left arm**
CC Exclusion 7th characters K & P see Appendix A PDX collection 0897

CC +7th **S59.199 Other physeal fracture of upper end of radius, unspecified arm**
CC Exclusion 7th characters K & P see Appendix A PDX collection 0897

+ **S59.2 Physeal fracture of lower end of radius**

+ **S59.20 Unspecified physeal fracture of lower end of radius**

CC +7th **S59.201 Unspecified physeal fracture of lower end of radius, right arm**
CC Exclusion 7th character A see Appendix A PDX collection 1270
CC Exclusion 7th characters K & P see Appendix A PDX collection 0897
HAC 7th character A see Appendix B for HAC conditional logic

CC +7th **S59.202 Unspecified physeal fracture of lower end of radius, left arm**
CC Exclusion 7th character A see Appendix A PDX collection 1271
CC Exclusion 7th characters K & P see Appendix A PDX collection 0897
HAC 7th character A see Appendix B for HAC conditional logic

CC +7th **S59.209 Unspecified physeal fracture of lower end of radius, unspecified arm**
CC Exclusion 7th character A see Appendix A PDX collection 1272
CC Exclusion 7th characters K & P see Appendix A PDX collection 0897
HAC 7th character A see Appendix B for HAC conditional logic

+ **S59.21 Salter-Harris Type I physeal fracture of lower end of radius**

CC +7th **S59.211 Salter-Harris Type I physeal fracture of lower end of radius, right arm**
CC Exclusion 7th character A see Appendix A PDX collection 1270
CC Exclusion 7th characters K & P see Appendix A PDX collection 0897
HAC 7th character A see Appendix B for HAC conditional logic

CC +7th **S59.212 Salter-Harris Type I physeal fracture of lower end of radius, left arm**
CC Exclusion 7th character A see Appendix A PDX collection 1271
CC Exclusion 7th characters K & P see Appendix A PDX collection 0897
HAC 7th character A see Appendix B for HAC conditional logic

CC +7th **S59.219 Salter-Harris Type I physeal fracture of lower end of radius, unspecified arm**
CC Exclusion 7th character A see Appendix A PDX collection 1272
CC Exclusion 7th characters K & P see Appendix A PDX collection 0897
HAC 7th character A see Appendix B for HAC conditional logic

+ **S59.22 Salter-Harris Type II physeal fracture of lower end radius**

CC +7th **S59.221 Salter-Harris Type II physeal fracture of lower end of radius, right arm**
CC Exclusion 7th character A see Appendix A PDX collection 1270
CC Exclusion 7th characters K & P see Appendix A PDX collection 0897
HAC 7th character A see Appendix B for HAC conditional logic

CC +7th **S59.222 Salter-Harris Type II physeal fracture of lower end of radius, left arm**
CC Exclusion 7th character A see Appendix A PDX collection 1271
CC Exclusion 7th characters K & P see Appendix A PDX collection 0897
HAC 7th character A see Appendix B for HAC conditional logic

CC +7th **S59.229 Salter-Harris Type II physeal fracture of lower end of radius, unspecified arm**
CC Exclusion 7th character A see Appendix A PDX collection 1272
CC Exclusion 7th characters K & P see Appendix A PDX collection 0897
HAC 7th character A see Appendix B for HAC conditional logic

+ **S59.23 Salter-Harris Type III physeal fracture of lower end radius**

CC +7th **S59.231 Salter-Harris Type III physeal fracture of lower end of radius, right arm**
CC Exclusion 7th character A see Appendix A PDX collection 1270
CC Exclusion 7th characters K & P see Appendix A PDX collection 0897
HAC 7th character A see Appendix B for HAC conditional logic

CC +7th **S59.232 Salter-Harris Type III physeal fracture of lower end of radius, left arm**
CC Exclusion 7th character A see Appendix A PDX collection 1271
CC Exclusion 7th characters K & P see Appendix A PDX collection 0897
HAC 7th character A see Appendix B for HAC conditional logic

CC +7th **S59.239 Salter-Harris Type III physeal fracture of lower end of radius, unspecified arm**
CC Exclusion 7th character A see Appendix A PDX collection 1272
CC Exclusion 7th characters K & P see Appendix A PDX collection 0897
HAC 7th character A see Appendix B for HAC conditional logic

+ **S59.24 Salter-Harris Type IV physeal fracture of lower end of radius**

CC +7th **S59.241 Salter-Harris Type IV physeal fracture of lower end of radius, right arm**
CC Exclusion 7th character A see Appendix A PDX collection 1270
CC Exclusion 7th characters K & P see Appendix A PDX collection 0897
HAC 7th character A see Appendix B for HAC conditional logic

CC +7th **S59.242 Salter-Harris Type IV physeal fracture of lower end of radius, left arm**
CC Exclusion 7th character A see Appendix A PDX collection 1271
CC Exclusion 7th characters K & P see Appendix A PDX collection 0897
HAC 7th character A see Appendix B for HAC conditional logic

CC +7th **S59.249 Salter-Harris Type IV physeal fracture of lower end of radius, unspecified arm**
CC Exclusion 7th character A see Appendix A PDX collection 1272
CC Exclusion 7th characters K & P see Appendix A PDX collection 0897
HAC 7th character A see Appendix B for HAC conditional logic

+ **S59.29 Other physeal fracture of lower end of radius**

CC +7th **S59.291 Other physeal fracture of lower end of radius, right arm**
CC Exclusion 7th character A see Appendix A PDX collection 1270
CC Exclusion 7th characters K & P see Appendix A PDX collection 0897
HAC 7th character A see Appendix B for HAC conditional logic

CC +7th **S59.292 Other physeal fracture of lower end of radius, left arm**
CC Exclusion 7th character A see Appendix A PDX collection 1271
CC Exclusion 7th characters K & P see Appendix A PDX collection 0897
HAC 7th character A see Appendix B for HAC conditional logic

CC +7th **S59.299 Other physeal fracture of lower end of radius, unspecified arm**
CC Exclusion 7th character A see Appendix A PDX collection 1272
CC Exclusion 7th characters K & P see Appendix A PDX collection 0897
HAC 7th character A see Appendix B for HAC conditional logic

\+ **S59.8 Other specified injuries of elbow and forearm**

The appropriate 7th character is to be added to each code in subcategory S59.8
A initial encounter
D subsequent encounter
S sequela

\+ **S59.80 Other specified injuries of elbow**
+7th **S59.801 Other specified injuries of right elbow**
+7th **S59.802 Other specified injuries of left elbow**
+7th **S59.809 Other specified injuries of unspecified elbow**

\+ **S59.81 Other specified injuries of forearm**
+7th **S59.811 Other specified injuries right forearm**
+7th **S59.812 Other specified injuries left forearm**
+7th **S59.819 Other specified injuries unspecified forearm**

\+ **S59.9 Unspecified injury of elbow and forearm**

The appropriate 7th character is to be added to each code in subcategory S59.9
A initial encounter
D subsequent encounter
S sequela

\+ **S59.90 Unspecified injury of elbow**
+7th **S59.901 Unspecified injury of right elbow**
+7th **S59.902 Unspecified injury of left elbow**
+7th **S59.909 Unspecified injury of unspecified elbow**

\+ **S59.91 Unspecified injury of forearm**
+7th **S59.911 Unspecified injury of right forearm**
+7th **S59.912 Unspecified injury of left forearm**
+7th **S59.919 Unspecified injury of unspecified forearm**

njuries to the wrist, hand and fingers (S60-S69)

xcludes2: *burns and corrosions (T20-T32)*
frostbite (T33-T34)
insect bite or sting, venomous (T63.4)

S60 Superficial injury of wrist, hand and fingers

The appropriate 7th character is to be added to each code from category S60
A initial encounter
D subsequent encounter
S sequela

\+ **S60.0 Contusion of finger without damage to nail**
Excludes1: *contusion involving nail (matrix) (S60.1)*
X+7th **S60.00 Contusion of unspecified finger without damage to nail**
Contusion of finger(s) NOS

\+ **S60.01 Contusion of thumb without damage to nail**
+7th **S60.011 Contusion of right thumb without damage to nail**
+7th **S60.012 Contusion of left thumb without damage to nail**
+7th **S60.019 Contusion of unspecified thumb without damage to nail**

\+ **S60.02 Contusion of index finger without damage to nail**
+7th **S60.021 Contusion of right index finger without damage to nail**
+7th **S60.022 Contusion of left index finger without damage to nail**
+7th **S60.029 Contusion of unspecified index finger without damage to nail**

\+ **S60.03 Contusion of middle finger without damage to nail**
+7th **S60.031 Contusion of right middle finger without damage to nail**
+7th **S60.032 Contusion of left middle finger without damage to nail**
+7th **S60.039 Contusion of unspecified middle finger without damage to nail**

\+ **S60.04 Contusion of ring finger without damage to nail**
+7th **S60.041 Contusion of right ring finger without damage to nail**
+7th **S60.042 Contusion of left ring finger without damage to nail**
+7th **S60.049 Contusion of unspecified ring finger without damage to nail**

\+ **S60.05 Contusion of little finger without damage to nail**
+7th **S60.051 Contusion of right little finger without damage to nail**
+7th **S60.052 Contusion of left little finger without damage to nail**
+7th **S60.059 Contusion of unspecified little finger without damage to nail**

\+ **S60.1 Contusion of finger with damage to nail**
X+7th **S60.10 Contusion of unspecified finger with damage to nail**

\+ **S60.11 Contusion of thumb with damage to nail**
+7th **S60.111 Contusion of right thumb with damage to nail**
+7th **S60.112 Contusion of left thumb with damage to nail**
+7th **S60.119 Contusion of unspecified thumb with damage to nail**

\+ **S60.12 Contusion of index finger with damage to nail**
+7th **S60.121 Contusion of right index finger with damage to nail**
+7th **S60.122 Contusion of left index finger with damage to nail**
+7th **S60.129 Contusion of unspecified index finger with damage to nail**

\+ **S60.13 Contusion of middle finger with damage to nail**
+7th **S60.131 Contusion of right middle finger with damage to nail**
+7th **S60.132 Contusion of left middle finger with damage to nail**
+7th **S60.139 Contusion of unspecified middle finger with damage to nail**

\+ **S60.14 Contusion of ring finger with damage to nail**
+7th **S60.141 Contusion of right ring finger with damage to nail**
+7th **S60.142 Contusion of left ring finger with damage to nail**
+7th **S60.149 Contusion of unspecified ring finger with damage to nail**

\+ **S60.15 Contusion of little finger with damage to nail**
+7th **S60.151 Contusion of right little finger with damage to nail**
+7th **S60.152 Contusion of left little finger with damage to nail**
+7th **S60.159 Contusion of unspecified little finger with damage to nail**

\+ **S60.2 Contusion of wrist and hand**
Excludes2: *contusion of fingers (S60.0-, S60.1-)*

\+ **S60.21 Contusion of wrist**
+7th **S60.211 Contusion of right wrist**
+7th **S60.212 Contusion of left wrist**
+7th **S60.219 Contusion of unspecified wrist**

\+ **S60.22 Contusion of hand**
+7th **S60.221 Contusion of right hand**
+7th **S60.222 Contusion of left hand**
+7th **S60.229 Contusion of unspecified hand**

\+ **S60.3 Other superficial injuries of thumb**

\+ **S60.31 Abrasion of thumb**
+7th **S60.311 Abrasion of right thumb**
+7th **S60.312 Abrasion of left thumb**
+7th **S60.319 Abrasion of unspecified thumb**

\+ **S60.32 Blister (nonthermal) of thumb**
+7th **S60.321 Blister (nonthermal) of right thumb**
+7th **S60.322 Blister (nonthermal) of left thumb**
+7th **S60.329 Blister (nonthermal) of unspecified thumb**

\+ **S60.34 External constriction of thumb**
Hair tourniquet syndrome of thumb
Use additional cause code to identify the constricting item (W49.0-)
+7th **S60.341 External constriction of right thumb**
+7th **S60.342 External constriction of left thumb**
+7th **S60.349 External constriction of unspecified thumb**

\+ **S60.35 Superficial foreign body of thumb**
Splinter in the thumb
+7th **S60.351 Superficial foreign body of right thumb**
+7th **S60.352 Superficial foreign body of left thumb**
+7th **S60.359 Superficial foreign body of unspecified thumb**

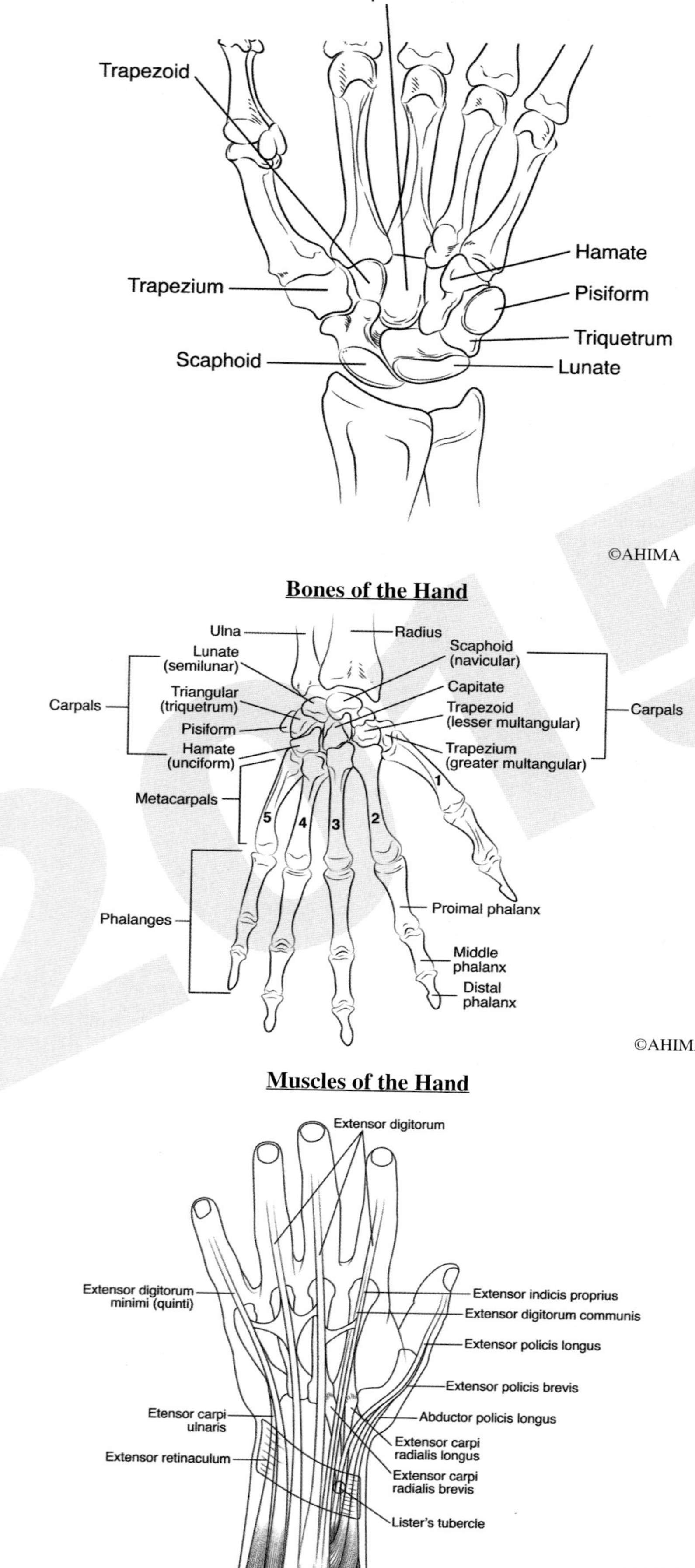
Wrist
Capitate
Trapezoid
Hamate
Trapezium
Pisiform
Triquetrum
Scaphoid
Lunate
©AHIMA
Bones of the Hand
Ulna
Radius
Lunate (semilunar)
Scaphoid (navicular)
Carpals
Capitate
Triangular (triquetrum)
Trapezoid (lesser multangular)
Carpals
Pisiform
Hamate (unciform)
Trapezium (greater multangular)
1
Metacarpals
5
4
3
2
Phalanges
Proimal phalanx
Middle phalanx
Distal phalanx
©AHIMA
Muscles of the Hand
Extensor digitorum
Extensor digitorum minimi (quinti)
Extensor indicis proprius
Extensor digitorum communis
Extensor policis longus
Extensor policis brevis
Etensor carpi ulnaris
Abductor policis longus
Extensor carpi radialis longus
Extensor retinaculum
Extensor carpi radialis brevis
Lister's tubercle
©AHIMA

+ **S60.36 Insect bite (nonvenomous) of thumb**
  - +7th **S60.361 Insect bite (nonvenomous) of right thumb**
  - +7th **S60.362 Insect bite (nonvenomous) of left thumb**
  - +7th **S60.369 Insect bite (nonvenomous) of unspecified thumb**

+ **S60.37 Other superficial bite of thumb**
  Excludes1: *open bite of thumb (S61.05-, S61.15-)*
  - +7th **S60.371 Other superficial bite of right thumb**
  - +7th **S60.372 Other superficial bite of left thumb**
  - +7th **S60.379 Other superficial bite of unspecified thumb**

+ **S60.39 Other superficial injuries of thumb**
  - +7th **S60.391 Other superficial injuries of right thumb**
  - +7th **S60.392 Other superficial injuries of left thumb**
  - +7th **S60.399 Other superficial injuries of unspecified thumb**

+ **S60.4 Other superficial injuries of other fingers**

+ **S60.41 Abrasion of fingers**
  - **S60.410 Abrasion of right index finger**
  - +7th **S60.411 Abrasion of left index finger**
  - +7th **S60.412 Abrasion of right middle finger**
  - +7th **S60.413 Abrasion of left middle finger**
  - +7th **S60.414 Abrasion of right ring finger**
  - +7th **S60.415 Abrasion of left ring finger**
  - +7th **S60.416 Abrasion of right little finger**
  - +7th **S60.417 Abrasion of left little finger**
  - +7th **S60.418 Abrasion of other finger**
    Abrasion of specified finger with unspecified laterality
  - +7th **S60.419 Abrasion of unspecified finger**

+ **S60.42 Blister (nonthermal) of fingers**
  - **S60.420 Blister (nonthermal) of right index finger**
  - +7th **S60.421 Blister (nonthermal) of left index finger**
  - +7th **S60.422 Blister (nonthermal) of right middle finger**
  - +7th **S60.423 Blister (nonthermal) of left middle finger**
  - +7th **S60.424 Blister (nonthermal) of right ring finger**
  - +7th **S60.425 Blister (nonthermal) of left ring finger**
  - +7th **S60.426 Blister (nonthermal) of right little finger**
  - +7th **S60.427 Blister (nonthermal) of left little finger**
  - +7th **S60.428 Blister (nonthermal) of other finger**
    Blister (nonthermal) of specified finger with unspecified laterality
  - +7th **S60.429 Blister (nonthermal) of unspecified finger**

+ **S60.44 External constriction of fingers**
  Hair tourniquet syndrome of finger
  Use additional cause code to identify the constricting item (W49.0-)
  - **S60.440 External constriction of right index finger**
  - +7th **S60.441 External constriction of left index finger**
  - +7th **S60.442 External constriction of right middle finger**
  - +7th **S60.443 External constriction of left middle finger**
  - +7th **S60.444 External constriction of right ring finger**
  - +7th **S60.445 External constriction of left ring finger**
  - +7th **S60.446 External constriction of right little finger**
  - +7th **S60.447 External constriction of left little finger**
  - +7th **S60.448 External constriction of other finger**
    External constriction of specified finger with unspecified laterality
  - +7th **S60.449 External constriction of unspecified finger**

+ **S60.45 Superficial foreign body of fingers**
  Splinter in the finger(s)
  - **S60.450 Superficial foreign body of right index finger**
  - +7th **S60.451 Superficial foreign body of left index finger**
  - +7th **S60.452 Superficial foreign body of right middle finger**
  - +7th **S60.453 Superficial foreign body of left middle finger**
  - +7th **S60.454 Superficial foreign body of right ring finger**
  - +7th **S60.455 Superficial foreign body of left ring finger**
  - +7th **S60.456 Superficial foreign body of right little finger**
  - +7th **S60.457 Superficial foreign body of left little finger**
  - +7th **S60.458 Superficial foreign body of other finger**
    Superficial foreign body of specified finger with unspecified laterality
  - +7th **S60.459 Superficial foreign body of unspecified finger**

+ **S60.46 Insect bite (nonvenomous) of fingers**
  - **S60.460 Insect bite (nonvenomous) of right index finger**
  - +7th **S60.461 Insect bite (nonvenomous) of left index finger**
  - +7th **S60.462 Insect bite (nonvenomous) of right middle finger**
  - +7th **S60.463 Insect bite (nonvenomous) of left middle finger**
  - +7th **S60.464 Insect bite (nonvenomous) of right ring finger**
  - +7th **S60.465 Insect bite (nonvenomous) of left ring finger**
  - +7th **S60.466 Insect bite (nonvenomous) of right little finger**
  - +7th **S60.467 Insect bite (nonvenomous) of left little finger**
  - +7th **S60.468 Insect bite (nonvenomous) of other finger**
    Insect bite (nonvenomous) of specified finger with unspecified laterality
  - +7th **S60.469 Insect bite (nonvenomous) of unspecified finger**

+ **S60.47 Other superficial bite of fingers**
  Excludes1: *open bite of fingers (S61.25-, S61.35-)*
  - **S60.470 Other superficial bite of right index finger**
  - +7th **S60.471 Other superficial bite of left index finger**
  - +7th **S60.472 Other superficial bite of right middle finger**
  - +7th **S60.473 Other superficial bite of left middle finger**
  - +7th **S60.474 Other superficial bite of right ring finger**
  - +7th **S60.475 Other superficial bite of left ring finger**
  - +7th **S60.476 Other superficial bite of right little finger**
  - +7th **S60.477 Other superficial bite of left little finger**
  - +7th **S60.478 Other superficial bite of other finger**
    Other superficial bite of specified finger with unspecified laterality
  - +7th **S60.479 Other superficial bite of unspecified finger**

+ **S60.5 Other superficial injuries of hand**
  Excludes2: *superficial injuries of fingers (S60.3-, S60.4-)*

+ **S60.51 Abrasion of hand**
  - +7th **S60.511 Abrasion of right hand**
  - +7th **S60.512 Abrasion of left hand**
  - +7th **S60.519 Abrasion of unspecified hand**

+ **S60.52 Blister (nonthermal) of hand**
  - +7th **S60.521 Blister (nonthermal) of right hand**
  - +7th **S60.522 Blister (nonthermal) of left hand**
  - +7th **S60.529 Blister (nonthermal) of unspecified hand**

+ **S60.54 External constriction of hand**
  - +7th **S60.541 External constriction of right hand**
  - +7th **S60.542 External constriction of left hand**
  - +7th **S60.549 External constriction of unspecified hand**

+ **S60.55 Superficial foreign body of hand**
  Splinter in the hand
  - +7th **S60.551 Superficial foreign body of right hand**
  - +7th **S60.552 Superficial foreign body of left hand**
  - +7th **S60.559 Superficial foreign body of unspecified hand**

+ **S60.56 Insect bite (nonvenomous) of hand**
  - +7th **S60.561 Insect bite (nonvenomous) of right hand**
  - +7th **S60.562 Insect bite (nonvenomous) of left hand**
  - +7th **S60.569 Insect bite (nonvenomous) of unspecified hand**

+ **S60.57 Other superficial bite of hand**
  Excludes1: *open bite of hand (S61.45-)*
  - +7th **S60.571 Other superficial bite of hand of right hand**
  - +7th **S60.572 Other superficial bite of hand of left hand**
  - +7th **S60.579 Other superficial bite of hand of unspecified hand**

+ **S60.8 Other superficial injuries of wrist**

+ **S60.81 Abrasion of wrist**
  - +7th **S60.811 Abrasion of right wrist**
  - +7th **S60.812 Abrasion of left wrist**
  - +7th **S60.819 Abrasion of unspecified wrist**

+ **S60.82 Blister (nonthermal) of wrist**
  - +7th **S60.821 Blister (nonthermal) of right wrist**
  - +7th **S60.822 Blister (nonthermal) of left wrist**
  - +7th **S60.829 Blister (nonthermal) of unspecified wrist**

+ **S60.84 External constriction of wrist**
  - +7th **S60.841 External constriction of right wrist**
  - +7th **S60.842 External constriction of left wrist**
  - +7th **S60.849 External constriction of unspecified wrist**

+ **S60.85 Superficial foreign body of wrist**
  Splinter in the wrist
  - +7th **S60.851 Superficial foreign body of right wrist**
  - +7th **S60.852 Superficial foreign body of left wrist**
  - +7th **S60.859 Superficial foreign body of unspecified wrist**

+ **S60.86 Insect bite (nonvenomous) of wrist**
  - +7th **S60.861 Insect bite (nonvenomous) of right wrist**
  - +7th **S60.862 Insect bite (nonvenomous) of left wrist**
  - +7th **S60.869 Insect bite (nonvenomous) of unspecified wrist**

+ **S60.87 Other superficial bite of wrist**
Excludes1: *open bite of wrist (S61.55)*
+7th **S60.871 Other superficial bite of right wrist**
+7th **S60.872 Other superficial bite of left wrist**
+7th **S60.879 Other superficial bite of unspecified wrist**
+ **S60.9 Unspecified superficial injury of wrist, hand and fingers**
+ **S60.91 Unspecified superficial injury of wrist**
+7th **S60.911 Unspecified superficial injury of right wrist**
+7th **S60.912 Unspecified superficial injury of left wrist**
+7th **S60.919 Unspecified superficial injury of unspecified wrist**
+ **S60.92 Unspecified superficial injury of hand**
+7th **S60.921 Unspecified superficial injury of right hand**
+7th **S60.922 Unspecified superficial injury of left hand**
+7th **S60.929 Unspecified superficial injury of unspecified hand**
+ **S60.93 Unspecified superficial injury of thumb**
+7th **S60.931 Unspecified superficial injury of right thumb**
+7th **S60.932 Unspecified superficial injury of left thumb**
+7th **S60.939 Unspecified superficial injury of unspecified thumb**
+ **S60.94 Unspecified superficial injury of other fingers**
S60.940 Unspecified superficial injury of right index finger
+7th **S60.941 Unspecified superficial injury of left index finger**
+7th **S60.942 Unspecified superficial injury of right middle finger**
+7th **S60.943 Unspecified superficial injury of left middle finger**
+7th **S60.944 Unspecified superficial injury of right ring finger**
+7th **S60.945 Unspecified superficial injury of left ring finger**
+7th **S60.946 Unspecified superficial injury of right little finger**
+7th **S60.947 Unspecified superficial injury of left little finger**
+7th **S60.948 Unspecified superficial injury of other finger**
Unspecified superficial injury of specified finger with unspecified laterality
+7th **S60.949 Unspecified superficial injury of unspecified finger**

S61 Open wound of wrist, hand and fingers
Code also any associated wound infection
Excludes1: *open fracture of wrist, hand and finger (S62.- with 7th character B)*
traumatic amputation of wrist and hand (S68.-)

The appropriate 7th character is to be added to each code from category S61
A initial encounter
D subsequent encounter
S sequela

+ **S61.0 Open wound of thumb without damage to nail**
Excludes1: *open wound of thumb with damage to nail (S61.1-)*
+ **S61.00 Unspecified open wound of thumb without damage to nail**
+7th **S61.001 Unspecified open wound of right thumb without damage to nail**
+7th **S61.002 Unspecified open wound of left thumb without damage to nail**
+7th **S61.009 Unspecified open wound of unspecified thumb without damage to nail**
+ **S61.01 Laceration without foreign body of thumb without damage to nail**
+7th **S61.011 Laceration without foreign body of right thumb without damage to nail**
+7th **S61.012 Laceration without foreign body of left thumb without damage to nail**
+7th **S61.019 Laceration without foreign body of unspecified thumb without damage to nail**
+ **S61.02 Laceration with foreign body of thumb without damage to nail**
+7th **S61.021 Laceration with foreign body of right thumb without damage to nail**
+7th **S61.022 Laceration with foreign body of left thumb without damage to nail**
+7th **S61.029 Laceration with foreign body of unspecified thumb without damage to nail**
+ **S61.03 Puncture wound without foreign body of thumb without damage to nail**
+7th **S61.031 Puncture wound without foreign body of right thumb without damage to nail**
+7th **S61.032 Puncture wound without foreign body of le[ft] thumb without damage to nail**
+7th **S61.039 Puncture wound without foreign body of unspecified thumb without damage to nail**
+ **S61.04 Puncture wound with foreign body of thumb withou[t] damage to nail**
+7th **S61.041 Puncture wound with foreign body of right thumb without damage to nail**
+7th **S61.042 Puncture wound with foreign body of left thumb without damage to nail**
+7th **S61.049 Puncture wound with foreign body of unspecified thumb without damage to nail**
+ **S61.05 Open bite of thumb without damage to nail**
Bite of thumb NOS
Excludes1: *superficial bite of thumb (S60.36-, S60.37-)*
+7th **S61.051 Open bite of right thumb without damage t[o] nail**
+7th **S61.052 Open bite of left thumb without damage to nail**
+7th **S61.059 Open bite of unspecified thumb without damage to nail**
+ **S61.1 Open wound of thumb with damage to nail**
+ **S61.10 Unspecified open wound of thumb with damage to na[il]**
+7th **S61.101 Unspecified open wound of right thumb wit[h] damage to nail**
+7th **S61.102 Unspecified open wound of left thumb with damage to nail**
+7th **S61.109 Unspecified open wound of unspecified thumb with damage to nail**
+ **S61.11 Laceration without foreign body of thumb with damage to nail**
+7th **S61.111 Laceration without foreign body of right thumb with damage to nail**
+7th **S61.112 Laceration without foreign body of left thumb with damage to nail**
+7th **S61.119 Laceration without foreign body of unspecified thumb with damage to nail**
+ **S61.12 Laceration with foreign body of thumb with damage to nail**
+7th **S61.121 Laceration with foreign body of right thumb with damage to nail**
+7th **S61.122 Laceration with foreign body of left thumb with damage to nail**
+7th **S61.129 Laceration with foreign body of unspecified thumb with damage to nail**
+ **S61.13 Puncture wound without foreign body of thumb with damage to nail**
+7th **S61.131 Puncture wound without foreign body of right thumb with damage to nail**
+7th **S61.132 Puncture wound without foreign body of left thumb with damage to nail**
+7th **S61.139 Puncture wound without foreign body of unspecified thumb with damage to nail**
+ **S61.14 Puncture wound with foreign body of thumb with damage to nail**
+7th **S61.141 Puncture wound with foreign body of right thumb with damage to nail**
+7th **S61.142 Puncture wound with foreign body of left thumb with damage to nail**
+7th **S61.149 Puncture wound with foreign body of unspecified thumb with damage to nail**
+ **S61.15 Open bite of thumb with damage to nail**
Bite of thumb with damage to nail NOS
Excludes1: *superficial bite of thumb (S60.36-, S60.37-)*
+7th **S61.151 Open bite of right thumb with damage to nail**
+7th **S61.152 Open bite of left thumb with damage to nail**
+7th **S61.159 Open bite of unspecified thumb with damage to nail**

+ **S61.2 Open wound of other finger without damage to nail**
Excludes1: *open wound of finger involving nail (matrix) (S61.3-)*
Excludes2: *open wound of thumb without damage to nail (S61.0-)*

+ **S61.20 Unspecified open wound of other finger without damage to nail**
S61.200 Unspecified open wound of right index finger without damage to nail
+7th **S61.201 Unspecified open wound of left index finger without damage to nail**
+7th **S61.202 Unspecified open wound of right middle finger without damage to nail**
+7th **S61.203 Unspecified open wound of left middle finger without damage to nail**
+7th **S61.204 Unspecified open wound of right ring finger without damage to nail**
+7th **S61.205 Unspecified open wound of left ring finger without damage to nail**
+7th **S61.206 Unspecified open wound of right little finger without damage to nail**
+7th **S61.207 Unspecified open wound of left little finger without damage to nail**
+7th **S61.208 Unspecified open wound of other finger without damage to nail**
Unspecified open wound of specified finger with unspecified laterality without damage to nail
+7th **S61.209 Unspecified open wound of unspecified finger without damage to nail**

+ **S61.21 Laceration without foreign body of finger without damage to nail**
S61.210 Laceration without foreign body of right index finger without damage to nail
+7th **S61.211 Laceration without foreign body of left index finger without damage to nail**
+7th **S61.212 Laceration without foreign body of right middle finger without damage to nail**
+7th **S61.213 Laceration without foreign body of left middle finger without damage to nail**
+7th **S61.214 Laceration without foreign body of right ring finger without damage to nail**
+7th **S61.215 Laceration without foreign body of left ring finger without damage to nail**
+7th **S61.216 Laceration without foreign body of right little finger without damage to nail**
+7th **S61.217 Laceration without foreign body of left little finger without damage to nail**
+7th **S61.218 Laceration without foreign body of other finger without damage to nail**
Laceration without foreign body of specified finger with unspecified laterality without damage to nail
+7th **S61.219 Laceration without foreign body of unspecified finger without damage to nail**

+ **S61.22 Laceration with foreign body of finger without damage to nail**
S61.220 Laceration with foreign body of right index finger without damage to nail
+7th **S61.221 Laceration with foreign body of left index finger without damage to nail**
+7th **S61.222 Laceration with foreign body of right middle finger without damage to nail**
+7th **S61.223 Laceration with foreign body of left middle finger without damage to nail**
+7th **S61.224 Laceration with foreign body of right ring finger without damage to nail**
+7th **S61.225 Laceration with foreign body of left ring finger without damage to nail**
+7th **S61.226 Laceration with foreign body of right little finger without damage to nail**
+7th **S61.227 Laceration with foreign body of left little finger without damage to nail**
+7th **S61.228 Laceration with foreign body of other finger without damage to nail**
Laceration with foreign body of specified finger with unspecified laterality without damage to nail
+7th **S61.229 Laceration with foreign body of unspecified finger without damage to nail**

+ **S61.23 Puncture wound without foreign body of finger without damage to nail**
S61.230 Puncture wound without foreign body of right index finger without damage to nail
+7th **S61.231 Puncture wound without foreign body of left index finger without damage to nail**
+7th **S61.232 Puncture wound without foreign body of right middle finger without damage to nail**
+7th **S61.233 Puncture wound without foreign body of left middle finger without damage to nail**
+7th **S61.234 Puncture wound without foreign body of right ring finger without damage to nail**
+7th **S61.235 Puncture wound without foreign body of left ring finger without damage to nail**
+7th **S61.236 Puncture wound without foreign body of right little finger without damage to nail**
+7th **S61.237 Puncture wound without foreign body of left little finger without damage to nail**
+7th **S61.238 Puncture wound without foreign body of other finger without damage to nail**
Puncture wound without foreign body of specified finger with unspecified laterality without damage to nail
+7th **S61.239 Puncture wound without foreign body of unspecified finger without damage to nail**

+ **S61.24 Puncture wound with foreign body of finger without damage to nail**
S61.240 Puncture wound with foreign body of right index finger without damage to nail
+7th **S61.241 Puncture wound with foreign body of left index finger without damage to nail**
+7th **S61.242 Puncture wound with foreign body of right middle finger without damage to nail**
+7th **S61.243 Puncture wound with foreign body of left middle finger without damage to nail**
+7th **S61.244 Puncture wound with foreign body of right ring finger without damage to nail**
+7th **S61.245 Puncture wound with foreign body of left ring finger without damage to nail**
+7th **S61.246 Puncture wound with foreign body of right little finger without damage to nail**
+7th **S61.247 Puncture wound with foreign body of left little finger without damage to nail**
+7th **S61.248 Puncture wound with foreign body of other finger without damage to nail**
Puncture wound with foreign body of specified finger with unspecified laterality without damage to nail
+7th **S61.249 Puncture wound with foreign body of unspecified finger without damage to nail**

+ **S61.25 Open bite of finger without damage to nail**
Bite of finger without damage to nail NOS
Excludes1: *superficial bite of finger (S60.46-, S60.47-)*
S61.250 Open bite of right index finger without damage to nail
+7th **S61.251 Open bite of left index finger without damage to nail**
+7th **S61.252 Open bite of right middle finger without damage to nail**
+7th **S61.253 Open bite of left middle finger without damage to nail**
+7th **S61.254 Open bite of right ring finger without damage to nail**
+7th **S61.255 Open bite of left ring finger without damage to nail**
+7th **S61.256 Open bite of right little finger without damage to nail**
+7th **S61.257 Open bite of left little finger without damage to nail**
+7th **S61.258 Open bite of other finger without damage to nail**
Open bite of specified finger with unspecified laterality without damage to nail
+7th **S61.259 Open bite of unspecified finger without damage to nail**

+ **S61.3 Open wound of other finger with damage to nail**
+ **S61.30 Unspecified open wound of finger with damage to nail**
S61.300 Unspecified open wound of right index finger with damage to nail
+7th **S61.301 Unspecified open wound of left index finger with damage to nail**

+7th S61.302 **Unspecified open wound of right middle finger with damage to nail**
+7th S61.303 **Unspecified open wound of left middle finger with damage to nail**
+7th S61.304 **Unspecified open wound of right ring finger with damage to nail**
+7th S61.305 **Unspecified open wound of left ring finger with damage to nail**
+7th S61.306 **Unspecified open wound of right little finger with damage to nail**
+7th S61.307 **Unspecified open wound of left little finger with damage to nail**
+7th S61.308 **Unspecified open wound of other finger with damage to nail**
Unspecified open wound of specified finger with unspecified laterality with damage to nail
+7th S61.309 **Unspecified open wound of unspecified finger with damage to nail**

+ **S61.31 Laceration without foreign body of finger with damage to nail**
S61.310 **Laceration without foreign body of right index finger with damage to nail**
+7th S61.311 **Laceration without foreign body of left index finger with damage to nail**
+7th S61.312 **Laceration without foreign body of right middle finger with damage to nail**
+7th S61.313 **Laceration without foreign body of left middle finger with damage to nail**
+7th S61.314 **Laceration without foreign body of right ring finger with damage to nail**
+7th S61.315 **Laceration without foreign body of left ring finger with damage to nail**
+7th S61.316 **Laceration without foreign body of right little finger with damage to nail**
+7th S61.317 **Laceration without foreign body of left little finger with damage to nail**
+7th S61.318 **Laceration without foreign body of other finger with damage to nail**
Laceration without foreign body of specified finger with unspecified laterality with damage to nail
+7th S61.319 **Laceration without foreign body of unspecified finger with damage to nail**

+ **S61.32 Laceration with foreign body of finger with damage to nail**
S61.320 **Laceration with foreign body of right index finger with damage to nail**
+7th S61.321 **Laceration with foreign body of left index finger with damage to nail**
+7th S61.322 **Laceration with foreign body of right middle finger with damage to nail**
+7th S61.323 **Laceration with foreign body of left middle finger with damage to nail**
+7th S61.324 **Laceration with foreign body of right ring finger with damage to nail**
+7th S61.325 **Laceration with foreign body of left ring finger with damage to nail**
+7th S61.326 **Laceration with foreign body of right little finger with damage to nail**
+7th S61.327 **Laceration with foreign body of left little finger with damage to nail**
+7th S61.328 **Laceration with foreign body of other finger with damage to nail**
Laceration with foreign body of specified finger with unspecified laterality with damage to nail
+7th S61.329 **Laceration with foreign body of unspecified finger with damage to nail**

+ **S61.33 Puncture wound without foreign body of finger with damage to nail**
S61.330 **Puncture wound without foreign body of right index finger with damage to nail**
+7th S61.331 **Puncture wound without foreign body of left index finger with damage to nail**
+7th S61.332 **Puncture wound without foreign body of right middle finger with damage to nail**
+7th S61.333 **Puncture wound without foreign body of left middle finger with damage to nail**
+7th S61.334 **Puncture wound without foreign body of right ring finger with damage to nail**
+7th S61.335 **Puncture wound without foreign body of left ring finger with damage to nail**
+7th S61.336 **Puncture wound without foreign body of right little finger with damage to nail**
+7th S61.337 **Puncture wound without foreign body of left little finger with damage to nail**
+7th S61.338 **Puncture wound without foreign body of other finger with damage to nail**
Puncture wound without foreign body of specified finger with unspecified laterality with damage to nail
+7th S61.339 **Puncture wound without foreign body of unspecified finger with damage to nail**

+ **S61.34 Puncture wound with foreign body of finger with damage to nail**
S61.340 **Puncture wound with foreign body of right index finger with damage to nail**
+7th S61.341 **Puncture wound with foreign body of left index finger with damage to nail**
+7th S61.342 **Puncture wound with foreign body of right middle finger with damage to nail**
+7th S61.343 **Puncture wound with foreign body of left middle finger with damage to nail**
+7th S61.344 **Puncture wound with foreign body of right ring finger with damage to nail**
+7th S61.345 **Puncture wound with foreign body of left ring finger with damage to nail**
+7th S61.346 **Puncture wound with foreign body of right little finger with damage to nail**
+7th S61.347 **Puncture wound with foreign body of left little finger with damage to nail**
+7th S61.348 **Puncture wound with foreign body of other finger with damage to nail**
Puncture wound with foreign body of specified finger with unspecified laterality with damage to nail
+7th S61.349 **Puncture wound with foreign body of unspecified finger with damage to nail**

+ **S61.35 Open bite of finger with damage to nail**
Bite of finger with damage to nail NOS
Excludes1: *superficial bite of finger (S60.46-, S60.47-)*
S61.350 **Open bite of right index finger with damage to nail**
+7th S61.351 **Open bite of left index finger with damage to nail**
+7th S61.352 **Open bite of right middle finger with damage to nail**
+7th S61.353 **Open bite of left middle finger with damage to nail**
+7th S61.354 **Open bite of right ring finger with damage to nail**
+7th S61.355 **Open bite of left ring finger with damage to nail**
+7th S61.356 **Open bite of right little finger with damage to nail**
+7th S61.357 **Open bite of left little finger with damage to nail**
+7th S61.358 **Open bite of other finger with damage to nail**
Open bite of specified finger with unspecified laterality with damage to nail
+7th S61.359 **Open bite of unspecified finger with damage to nail**

+ **S61.4 Open wound of hand**
+ **S61.40 Unspecified open wound of hand**
+7th S61.401 **Unspecified open wound of right hand**
+7th S61.402 **Unspecified open wound of left hand**
+7th S61.409 **Unspecified open wound of unspecified hand**
+ **S61.41 Laceration without foreign body of hand**
+7th S61.411 **Laceration without foreign body of right hand**
+7th S61.412 **Laceration without foreign body of left hand**
+7th S61.419 **Laceration without foreign body of unspecified hand**
+ **S61.42 Laceration with foreign body of hand**
+7th S61.421 **Laceration with foreign body of right hand**
+7th S61.422 **Laceration with foreign body of left hand**
+7th S61.429 **Laceration with foreign body of unspecified hand**
+ **S61.43 Puncture wound without foreign body of hand**
+7th S61.431 **Puncture wound without foreign body of right hand**

+7th **S61.432 Puncture wound without foreign body of left hand**
+7th **S61.439 Puncture wound without foreign body of unspecified hand**
+ **S61.44 Puncture wound with foreign body of hand**
+7th **S61.441 Puncture wound with foreign body of right hand**
+7th **S61.442 Puncture wound with foreign body of left hand**
+7th **S61.449 Puncture wound with foreign body of unspecified hand**
+ **S61.45 Open bite of hand**
Bite of hand NOS
Excludes1: *superficial bite of hand (S60.56-, S60.57-)*
+7th **S61.451 Open bite of right hand**
+7th **S61.452 Open bite of left hand**
+7th **S61.459 Open bite of unspecified hand**
+ **S61.5 Open wound of wrist**
+ **S61.50 Unspecified open wound of wrist**
+7th **S61.501 Unspecified open wound of right wrist**
+7th **S61.502 Unspecified open wound of left wrist**
+7th **S61.509 Unspecified open wound of unspecified wrist**
+ **S61.51 Laceration without foreign body of wrist**
+7th **S61.511 Laceration without foreign body of right wrist**
+7th **S61.512 Laceration without foreign body of left wrist**
+7th **S61.519 Laceration without foreign body of unspecified wrist**
+ **S61.52 Laceration with foreign body of wrist**
+7th **S61.521 Laceration with foreign body of right wrist**
+7th **S61.522 Laceration with foreign body of left wrist**
+7th **S61.529 Laceration with foreign body of unspecified wrist**
+ **S61.53 Puncture wound without foreign body of wrist**
+7th **S61.531 Puncture wound without foreign body of right wrist**
+7th **S61.532 Puncture wound without foreign body of left wrist**
+7th **S61.539 Puncture wound without foreign body of unspecified wrist**
+ **S61.54 Puncture wound with foreign body of wrist**
+7th **S61.541 Puncture wound with foreign body of right wrist**
+7th **S61.542 Puncture wound with foreign body of left wrist**
+7th **S61.549 Puncture wound with foreign body of unspecified wrist**
+ **S61.55 Open bite of wrist**
Bite of wrist NOS
Excludes1: *superficial bite of wrist (S60.86-, S60.87-)*
+7th **S61.551 Open bite of right wrist**
+7th **S61.552 Open bite of left wrist**
+7th **S61.559 Open bite of unspecified wrist**

S62 Fracture at wrist and hand level

NOTE A fracture not indicated as displaced or nondisplaced should be coded to displaced
A fracture not indicated as open or closed should be coded to closed

Excludes1: *traumatic amputation of wrist and hand (S68.-)*
Excludes2: *fracture of distal parts of ulna and radius (S52.-)*

The appropriate 7th character is to be added to each code from category S62
A initial encounter for closed fracture
B initial encounter for open fracture
D subsequent encounter for fracture with routine healing
G subsequent encounter for fracture with delayed healing
K subsequent encounter for fracture with nonunion
P subsequent encounter for fracture with malunion
S sequela

Review coding guideline C.19.c

+ **S62.0 Fracture of navicular [scaphoid] bone of wrist**
+ **S62.00 Unspecified fracture of navicular [scaphoid] bone of wrist**
CC +7th **S62.001 Unspecified fracture of navicular [scaphoid] bone of right wrist**
CC Exclusion 7th character B see Appendix A PDX collection 1283
CC Exclusion 7th characters K & P see Appendix A PDX collection 0897
HAC 7th character B see Appendix B for HAC conditional logic
CC +7th **S62.002 Unspecified fracture of navicular [scaphoid] bone of left wrist**
CC Exclusion 7th character B see Appendix A PDX collection 1283
CC Exclusion 7th characters K & P see Appendix A PDX collection 0897
AHA CC: 4Q, 2012, 106
HAC 7th character B see Appendix B for HAC conditional logic
CC +7th **S62.009 Unspecified fracture of navicular [scaphoid] bone of unspecified wrist**
CC Exclusion 7th character B see Appendix A PDX collection 1283
CC Exclusion 7th characters K & P see Appendix A PDX collection 0897
HAC 7th character B see Appendix B for HAC conditional logic
+ **S62.01 Fracture of distal pole of navicular [scaphoid] bone of wrist**
Fracture of volar tuberosity of navicular [scaphoid] bone of wrist
CC +7th **S62.011 Displaced fracture of distal pole of navicular [scaphoid] bone of right wrist**
CC Exclusion 7th character B see Appendix A PDX collection 1283
CC Exclusion 7th characters K & P see Appendix A PDX collection 0897
HAC 7th character B see Appendix B for HAC conditional logic
CC +7th **S62.012 Displaced fracture of distal pole of navicular [scaphoid] bone of left wrist**
CC Exclusion 7th character B see Appendix A PDX collection 1283
CC Exclusion 7th characters K & P see Appendix A PDX collection 0897
HAC 7th character B see Appendix B for HAC conditional logic
CC +7th **S62.013 Displaced fracture of distal pole of navicular [scaphoid] bone of unspecified wrist**
CC Exclusion 7th character B see Appendix A PDX collection 1283
CC Exclusion 7th characters K & P see Appendix A PDX collection 0897
HAC 7th character B see Appendix B for HAC conditional logic
CC +7th **S62.014 Nondisplaced fracture of distal pole of navicular [scaphoid] bone of right wrist**
CC Exclusion 7th character B see Appendix A PDX collection 1283
CC Exclusion 7th characters K & P see Appendix A PDX collection 0897
HAC 7th character B see Appendix B for HAC conditional logic
CC +7th **S62.015 Nondisplaced fracture of distal pole of navicular [scaphoid] bone of left wrist**
CC Exclusion 7th character B see Appendix A PDX collection 1283
CC Exclusion 7th characters K & P see Appendix A PDX collection 0897
HAC 7th character B see Appendix B for HAC conditional logic
CC +7th **S62.016 Nondisplaced fracture of distal pole of navicular [scaphoid] bone of unspecified wrist**
CC Exclusion 7th character B see Appendix A PDX collection 1283
CC Exclusion 7th characters K & P see Appendix A PDX collection 0897
HAC 7th character B see Appendix B for HAC conditional logic
+ **S62.02 Fracture of middle third of navicular [scaphoid] bone of wrist**
CC +7th **S62.021 Displaced fracture of middle third of navicular [scaphoid] bone of right wrist**
CC Exclusion 7th character B see Appendix A PDX collection 1283
CC Exclusion 7th characters K & P see Appendix A PDX collection 0897
HAC 7th character B see Appendix B for HAC conditional logic
CC +7th **S62.022 Displaced fracture of middle third of navicular [scaphoid] bone of left wrist**
CC Exclusion 7th character B see Appendix A PDX collection 1283
CC Exclusion 7th characters K & P see Appendix A PDX collection 0897
HAC 7th character B see Appendix B for HAC conditional logic

CC +7th **S62.023 Displaced fracture of middle third of navicular [scaphoid] bone of unspecified wrist**
- **CC Exclusion 7th character B see Appendix A PDX collection 1283**
- **CC Exclusion 7th characters K & P see Appendix A PDX collection 0897**
- HAC 7th character B see Appendix B for HAC conditional logic

CC +7th **S62.024 Nondisplaced fracture of middle third of navicular [scaphoid] bone of right wrist**
- **CC Exclusion 7th character B see Appendix A PDX collection 1283**
- **CC Exclusion 7th characters K & P see Appendix A PDX collection 0897**
- HAC 7th character B see Appendix B for HAC conditional logic

CC +7th **S62.025 Nondisplaced fracture of middle third of navicular [scaphoid] bone of left wrist**
- **CC Exclusion 7th character B see Appendix A PDX collection 1283**
- **CC Exclusion 7th characters K & P see Appendix A PDX collection 0897**
- HAC 7th character B see Appendix B for HAC conditional logic

CC +7th **S62.026 Nondisplaced fracture of middle third of navicular [scaphoid] bone of unspecified wrist**
- **CC Exclusion 7th character B see Appendix A PDX collection 1283**
- **CC Exclusion 7th characters K & P see Appendix A PDX collection 0897**
- HAC 7th character B see Appendix B for HAC conditional logic

+ **S62.03 Fracture of proximal third of navicular [scaphoid] bone of wrist**

CC +7th **S62.031 Displaced fracture of proximal third of navicular [scaphoid] bone of right wrist**
- **CC Exclusion 7th character B see Appendix A PDX collection 1283**
- **CC Exclusion 7th characters K & P see Appendix A PDX collection 0897**
- HAC 7th character B see Appendix B for HAC conditional logic

CC +7th **S62.032 Displaced fracture of proximal third of navicular [scaphoid] bone of left wrist**
- **CC Exclusion 7th character B see Appendix A PDX collection 1283**
- **CC Exclusion 7th characters K & P see Appendix A PDX collection 0897**
- HAC 7th character B see Appendix B for HAC conditional logic

CC +7th **S62.033 Displaced fracture of proximal third of navicular [scaphoid] bone of unspecified wrist**
- **CC Exclusion 7th character B see Appendix A PDX collection 1283**
- **CC Exclusion 7th characters K & P see Appendix A PDX collection 0897**
- HAC 7th character B see Appendix B for HAC conditional logic

CC +7th **S62.034 Nondisplaced fracture of proximal third of navicular [scaphoid] bone of right wrist**
- **CC Exclusion 7th character B see Appendix A PDX collection 1283**
- **CC Exclusion 7th characters K & P see Appendix A PDX collection 0897**
- HAC 7th character B see Appendix B for HAC conditional logic

CC +7th **S62.035 Nondisplaced fracture of proximal third of navicular [scaphoid] bone of left wrist**
- **CC Exclusion 7th character B see Appendix A PDX collection 1283**
- **CC Exclusion 7th characters K & P see Appendix A PDX collection 0897**
- HAC 7th character B see Appendix B for HAC conditional logic

CC +7th **S62.036 Nondisplaced fracture of proximal third of navicular [scaphoid] bone of unspecified wrist**
- **CC Exclusion 7th character B see Appendix A PDX collection 1283**
- **CC Exclusion 7th characters K & P see Appendix A PDX collection 0897**
- HAC 7th character B see Appendix B for HAC conditional logic

+ **S62.1 Fracture of other and unspecified carpal bone(s)**

Excludes2: *fracture of scaphoid of wrist (S62.0-)*

+ **S62.10 Fracture of unspecified carpal bone**

Fracture of wrist NOS

CC +7th **S62.101 Fracture of unspecified carpal bone, right wrist**
- **CC Exclusion 7th character B see Appendix A PDX collection 1283**
- **CC Exclusion 7th characters K & P see Appendix A PDX collection 0897**
- HAC 7th character B see Appendix B for HAC conditional logic

CC +7th **S62.102 Fracture of unspecified carpal bone, left wrist**
- **CC Exclusion 7th character B see Appendix A PDX collection 1283**
- **CC Exclusion 7th characters K & P see Appendix A PDX collection 0897**
- *AHA CC: 4Q, 2012, 95-96*
- HAC 7th character B see Appendix B for HAC conditional logic

CC +7th **S62.109 Fracture of unspecified carpal bone, unspecified wrist**
- **CC Exclusion 7th character B see Appendix A PDX collection 1283**
- **CC Exclusion 7th characters K & P see Appendix A PDX collection 0897**
- HAC 7th character B see Appendix B for HAC conditional logic

+ **S62.11 Fracture of triquetrum [cuneiform] bone of wrist**

CC +7th **S62.111 Displaced fracture of triquetrum [cuneiform] bone, right wrist**
- **CC Exclusion 7th character B see Appendix A PDX collection 1283**
- **CC Exclusion 7th characters K & P see Appendix A PDX collection 0897**
- HAC 7th character B see Appendix B for HAC conditional logic

CC +7th **S62.112 Displaced fracture of triquetrum [cuneiform] bone, left wrist**
- **CC Exclusion 7th character B see Appendix A PDX collection 1283**
- **CC Exclusion 7th characters K & P see Appendix A PDX collection 0897**
- HAC 7th character B see Appendix B for HAC conditional logic

CC +7th **S62.113 Displaced fracture of triquetrum [cuneiform] bone, unspecified wrist**
- **CC Exclusion 7th character B see Appendix A PDX collection 1283**
- **CC Exclusion 7th characters K & P see Appendix A PDX collection 0897**
- HAC 7th character B see Appendix B for HAC conditional logic

CC +7th **S62.114 Nondisplaced fracture of triquetrum [cuneiform] bone, right wrist**
- **CC Exclusion 7th character B see Appendix A PDX collection 1283**
- **CC Exclusion 7th characters K & P see Appendix A PDX collection 0897**
- HAC 7th character B see Appendix B for HAC conditional logic

CC +7th **S62.115 Nondisplaced fracture of triquetrum [cuneiform] bone, left wrist**
- **CC Exclusion 7th character B see Appendix A PDX collection 1283**
- **CC Exclusion 7th characters K & P see Appendix A PDX collection 0897**
- HAC 7th character B see Appendix B for HAC conditional logic

CC +7th **S62.116 Nondisplaced fracture of triquetrum [cuneiform] bone, unspecified wrist**
- **CC Exclusion 7th character B see Appendix A PDX collection 1283**
- **CC Exclusion 7th characters K & P see Appendix A PDX collection 0897**
- HAC 7th character B see Appendix B for HAC conditional logic

+ **S62.12 Fracture of lunate [semilunar]**

CC +7th **S62.121 Displaced fracture of lunate [semilunar], right wrist**
- **CC Exclusion 7th character B see Appendix A PDX collection 1283**
- **CC Exclusion 7th characters K & P see Appendix A PDX collection 0897**
- HAC 7th character B see Appendix B for HAC conditional logic

CC +7th **S62.122 Displaced fracture of lunate [semilunar], left wrist**
CC Exclusion 7th character B see Appendix A PDX collection 1283
CC Exclusion 7th characters K & P see Appendix A PDX collection 0897
HAC 7th character B see Appendix B for HAC conditional logic

CC +7th **S62.123 Displaced fracture of lunate [semilunar], unspecified wrist**
CC Exclusion 7th character B see Appendix A PDX collection 1283
CC Exclusion 7th characters K & P see Appendix A PDX collection 0897
HAC 7th character B see Appendix B for HAC conditional logic

CC +7th **S62.124 Nondisplaced fracture of lunate [semilunar], right wrist**
CC Exclusion 7th character B see Appendix A PDX collection 1283
CC Exclusion 7th characters K & P see Appendix A PDX collection 0897
HAC 7th character B see Appendix B for HAC conditional logic

CC +7th **S62.125 Nondisplaced fracture of lunate [semilunar], left wrist**
CC Exclusion 7th character B see Appendix A PDX collection 1283
CC Exclusion 7th characters K & P see Appendix A PDX collection 0897
HAC 7th character B see Appendix B for HAC conditional logic

CC +7th **S62.126 Nondisplaced fracture of lunate [semilunar], unspecified wrist**
CC Exclusion 7th character B see Appendix A PDX collection 1283
CC Exclusion 7th characters K & P see Appendix A PDX collection 0897
HAC 7th character B see Appendix B for HAC conditional logic

\+ **S62.13 Fracture of capitate [os magnum] bone**

CC +7th **S62.131 Displaced fracture of capitate [os magnum] bone, right wrist**
CC Exclusion 7th character B see Appendix A PDX collection 1283
CC Exclusion 7th characters K & P see Appendix A PDX collection 0897
HAC 7th character B see Appendix B for HAC conditional logic

CC +7th **S62.132 Displaced fracture of capitate [os magnum] bone, left wrist**
CC Exclusion 7th character B see Appendix A PDX collection 1283
CC Exclusion 7th characters K & P see Appendix A PDX collection 0897
HAC 7th character B see Appendix B for HAC conditional logic

CC +7th **S62.133 Displaced fracture of capitate [os magnum] bone, unspecified wrist**
CC Exclusion 7th character B see Appendix A PDX collection 1283
CC Exclusion 7th characters K & P see Appendix A PDX collection 0897
HAC 7th character B see Appendix B for HAC conditional logic

CC +7th **S62.134 Nondisplaced fracture of capitate [os magnum] bone, right wrist**
CC Exclusion 7th character B see Appendix A PDX collection 1283
CC Exclusion 7th characters K & P see Appendix A PDX collection 0897
HAC 7th character B see Appendix B for HAC conditional logic

CC +7th **S62.135 Nondisplaced fracture of capitate [os magnum] bone, left wrist**
CC Exclusion 7th character B see Appendix A PDX collection 1283
CC Exclusion 7th characters K & P see Appendix A PDX collection 0897
HAC 7th character B see Appendix B for HAC conditional logic

CC +7th **S62.136 Nondisplaced fracture of capitate [os magnum] bone, unspecified wrist**
CC Exclusion 7th character B see Appendix A PDX collection 1283
CC Exclusion 7th characters K & P see Appendix A PDX collection 0897
HAC 7th character B see Appendix B for HAC conditional logic

\+ **S62.14 Fracture of body of hamate [unciform] bone**
Fracture of hamate [unciform] bone NOS

CC +7th **S62.141 Displaced fracture of body of hamate [unciform] bone, right wrist**
CC Exclusion 7th character B see Appendix A PDX collection 1283
CC Exclusion 7th characters K & P see Appendix A PDX collection 0897
HAC 7th character B see Appendix B for HAC conditional logic

CC +7th **S62.142 Displaced fracture of body of hamate [unciform] bone, left wrist**
CC Exclusion 7th character B see Appendix A PDX collection 1283
CC Exclusion 7th characters K & P see Appendix A PDX collection 0897
HAC 7th character B see Appendix B for HAC conditional logic

CC +7th **S62.143 Displaced fracture of body of hamate [unciform] bone, unspecified wrist**
CC Exclusion 7th character B see Appendix A PDX collection 1283
CC Exclusion 7th characters K & P see Appendix A PDX collection 0897
HAC 7th character B see Appendix B for HAC conditional logic

CC +7th **S62.144 Nondisplaced fracture of body of hamate [unciform] bone, right wrist**
CC Exclusion 7th character B see Appendix A PDX collection 1283
CC Exclusion 7th characters K & P see Appendix A PDX collection 0897
HAC 7th character B see Appendix B for HAC conditional logic

CC +7th **S62.145 Nondisplaced fracture of body of hamate [unciform] bone, left wrist**
CC Exclusion 7th character B see Appendix A PDX collection 1283
CC Exclusion 7th characters K & P see Appendix A PDX collection 0897
HAC 7th character B see Appendix B for HAC conditional logic

CC +7th **S62.146 Nondisplaced fracture of body of hamate [unciform] bone, unspecified wrist**
CC Exclusion 7th character B see Appendix A PDX collection 1283
CC Exclusion 7th characters K & P see Appendix A PDX collection 0897
HAC 7th character B see Appendix B for HAC conditional logic

\+ **S62.15 Fracture of hook process of hamate [unciform] bone**
Fracture of unciform process of hamate [unciform] bone

CC +7th **S62.151 Displaced fracture of hook process of hamate [unciform] bone, right wrist**
CC Exclusion 7th character B see Appendix A PDX collection 1283
CC Exclusion 7th characters K & P see Appendix A PDX collection 0897
HAC 7th character B see Appendix B for HAC conditional logic

CC +7th **S62.152 Displaced fracture of hook process of hamate [unciform] bone, left wrist**
CC Exclusion 7th character B see Appendix A PDX collection 1283
CC Exclusion 7th characters K & P see Appendix A PDX collection 0897
HAC 7th character B see Appendix B for HAC conditional logic

CC +7th **S62.153 Displaced fracture of hook process of hamate [unciform] bone, unspecified wrist**
CC Exclusion 7th character B see Appendix A PDX collection 1283
CC Exclusion 7th characters K & P see Appendix A PDX collection 0897
HAC 7th character B see Appendix B for HAC conditional logic

CC +7th **S62.154 Nondisplaced fracture of hook process of hamate [unciform] bone, right wrist**
CC Exclusion 7th character B see Appendix A PDX collection 1283
CC Exclusion 7th characters K & P see Appendix A PDX collection 0897
HAC 7th character B see Appendix B for HAC conditional logic

CC +7th **S62.155 Nondisplaced fracture of hook process of hamate [unciform] bone, left wrist**
CC Exclusion 7th character B see Appendix A PDX collection 1283
CC Exclusion 7th characters K & P see Appendix A PDX collection 0897
HAC 7th character B see Appendix B for HAC conditional logic

CC +7th **S62.156 Nondisplaced fracture of hook process of hamate [unciform] bone, unspecified wrist**
CC Exclusion 7th character B see Appendix A PDX collection 1283
CC Exclusion 7th characters K & P see Appendix A PDX collection 0897
HAC 7th character B see Appendix B for HAC conditional logic

\+ **S62.16 Fracture of pisiform**

CC +7th **S62.161 Displaced fracture of pisiform, right wrist**
CC Exclusion 7th character B see Appendix A PDX collection 1283
CC Exclusion 7th characters K & P see Appendix A PDX collection 0897
HAC 7th character B see Appendix B for HAC conditional logic

CC +7th **S62.162 Displaced fracture of pisiform, left wrist**
CC Exclusion 7th character B see Appendix A PDX collection 1283
CC Exclusion 7th characters K & P see Appendix A PDX collection 0897
HAC 7th character B see Appendix B for HAC conditional logic

CC +7th **S62.163 Displaced fracture of pisiform, unspecified wrist**
CC Exclusion 7th character B see Appendix A PDX collection 1283
CC Exclusion 7th characters K & P see Appendix A PDX collection 0897
HAC 7th character B see Appendix B for HAC conditional logic

CC +7th **S62.164 Nondisplaced fracture of pisiform, right wrist**
CC Exclusion 7th character B see Appendix A PDX collection 1283
CC Exclusion 7th characters K & P see Appendix A PDX collection 0897
HAC 7th character B see Appendix B for HAC conditional logic

CC +7th **S62.165 Nondisplaced fracture of pisiform, left wrist**
CC Exclusion 7th character B see Appendix A PDX collection 1283
CC Exclusion 7th characters K & P see Appendix A PDX collection 0897
HAC 7th character B see Appendix B for HAC conditional logic

CC +7th **S62.166 Nondisplaced fracture of pisiform, unspecified wrist**
CC Exclusion 7th character B see Appendix A PDX collection 1283
CC Exclusion 7th characters K & P see Appendix A PDX collection 0897
HAC 7th character B see Appendix B for HAC conditional logic

\+ **S62.17 Fracture of trapezium [larger multangular]**

CC +7th **S62.171 Displaced fracture of trapezium [larger multangular], right wrist**
CC Exclusion 7th character B see Appendix A PDX collection 1283
CC Exclusion 7th characters K & P see Appendix A PDX collection 0897
HAC 7th character B see Appendix B for HAC conditional logic

CC +7th **S62.172 Displaced fracture of trapezium [larger multangular], left wrist**
CC Exclusion 7th character B see Appendix A PDX collection 1283
CC Exclusion 7th characters K & P see Appendix A PDX collection 0897
HAC 7th character B see Appendix B for HAC conditional logic

CC +7th **S62.173 Displaced fracture of trapezium [larger multangular], unspecified wrist**
CC Exclusion 7th character B see Appendix A PDX collection 1283
CC Exclusion 7th characters K & P see Appendix A PDX collection 0897
HAC 7th character B see Appendix B for HAC conditional logic

CC +7th **S62.174 Nondisplaced fracture of trapezium [larger multangular], right wrist**
CC Exclusion 7th character B see Appendix A PDX collection 1283
CC Exclusion 7th characters K & P see Appendix A PDX collection 0897
HAC 7th character B see Appendix B for HAC conditional logic

CC +7th **S62.175 Nondisplaced fracture of trapezium [larger multangular], left wrist**
CC Exclusion 7th character B see Appendix A PDX collection 1283
CC Exclusion 7th characters K & P see Appendix A PDX collection 0897
HAC 7th character B see Appendix B for HAC conditional logic

CC +7th **S62.176 Nondisplaced fracture of trapezium [larger multangular], unspecified wrist**
CC Exclusion 7th character B see Appendix A PDX collection 1283
CC Exclusion 7th characters K & P see Appendix A PDX collection 0897
HAC 7th character B see Appendix B for HAC conditional logic

\+ **S62.18 Fracture of trapezoid [smaller multangular]**

CC +7th **S62.181 Displaced fracture of trapezoid [smaller multangular], right wrist**
CC Exclusion 7th character B see Appendix A PDX collection 1283
CC Exclusion 7th characters K & P see Appendix A PDX collection 0897
HAC 7th character B see Appendix B for HAC conditional logic

CC +7th **S62.182 Displaced fracture of trapezoid [smaller multangular], left wrist**
CC Exclusion 7th character B see Appendix A PDX collection 1283
CC Exclusion 7th characters K & P see Appendix A PDX collection 0897
HAC 7th character B see Appendix B for HAC conditional logic

CC +7th **S62.183 Displaced fracture of trapezoid [smaller multangular], unspecified wrist**
CC Exclusion 7th character B see Appendix A PDX collection 1283
CC Exclusion 7th characters K & P see Appendix A PDX collection 0897
HAC 7th character B see Appendix B for HAC conditional logic

CC +7th **S62.184 Nondisplaced fracture of trapezoid [smaller multangular], right wrist**
CC Exclusion 7th character B see Appendix A PDX collection 1283
CC Exclusion 7th characters K & P see Appendix A PDX collection 0897
HAC 7th character B see Appendix B for HAC conditional logic

CC +7th **S62.185 Nondisplaced fracture of trapezoid [smaller multangular], left wrist**
CC Exclusion 7th character B see Appendix A PDX collection 1283
CC Exclusion 7th characters K & P see Appendix A PDX collection 0897
HAC 7th character B see Appendix B for HAC conditional logic

CC +7th **S62.186 Nondisplaced fracture of trapezoid [smaller multangular], unspecified wrist**
CC Exclusion 7th character B see Appendix A PDX collection 1283
CC Exclusion 7th characters K & P see Appendix A PDX collection 0897
HAC 7th character B see Appendix B for HAC conditional logic

\+ **S62.2 Fracture of first metacarpal bone**

\+ **S62.20 Unspecified fracture of first metacarpal bone**

CC +7th **S62.201 Unspecified fracture of first metacarpal bone, right hand**
CC Exclusion 7th character B see Appendix A PDX collection 1284
CC Exclusion 7th characters K & P see Appendix A PDX collection 0897
HAC 7th character B see Appendix B for HAC conditional logic

CC +7th **S62.202 Unspecified fracture of first metacarpal bone, left hand**
CC Exclusion 7th character B see Appendix A PDX collection 1284
CC Exclusion 7th characters K & P see Appendix A PDX collection 0897
HAC 7th character B see Appendix B for HAC conditional logic

CC +7th **S62.209 Unspecified fracture of first metacarpal bone, unspecified hand**
CC Exclusion 7th character B see Appendix A PDX collection 1284
CC Exclusion 7th characters K & P see Appendix A PDX collection 0897
HAC 7th character B see Appendix B for HAC conditional logic

+ **S62.21 Bennett's fracture**

CC +7th **S62.211 Bennett's fracture, right hand**
CC Exclusion 7th character B see Appendix A PDX collection 1284
CC Exclusion 7th characters K & P see Appendix A PDX collection 0897
HAC 7th character B see Appendix B for HAC conditional logic

CC +7th **S62.212 Bennett's fracture, left hand**
CC Exclusion 7th character B see Appendix A PDX collection 1284
CC Exclusion 7th characters K & P see Appendix A PDX collection 0897
HAC 7th character B see Appendix B for HAC conditional logic

CC +7th **S62.213 Bennett's fracture, unspecified hand**
CC Exclusion 7th character B see Appendix A PDX collection 1284
CC Exclusion 7th characters K & P see Appendix A PDX collection 0897
HAC 7th character B see Appendix B for HAC conditional logic

+ **S62.22 Rolando's fracture**

CC +7th **S62.221 Displaced Rolando's fracture, right hand**
CC Exclusion 7th character B see Appendix A PDX collection 1284
CC Exclusion 7th characters K & P see Appendix A PDX collection 0897
HAC 7th character B see Appendix B for HAC conditional logic

CC +7th **S62.222 Displaced Rolando's fracture, left hand**
CC Exclusion 7th character B see Appendix A PDX collection 1284
CC Exclusion 7th characters K & P see Appendix A PDX collection 0897
HAC 7th character B see Appendix B for HAC conditional logic

CC +7th **S62.223 Displaced Rolando's fracture, unspecified hand**
CC Exclusion 7th character B see Appendix A PDX collection 1284
CC Exclusion 7th characters K & P see Appendix A PDX collection 0897
HAC 7th character B see Appendix B for HAC conditional logic

CC +7th **S62.224 Nondisplaced Rolando's fracture, right hand**
CC Exclusion 7th character B see Appendix A PDX collection 1284
CC Exclusion 7th characters K & P see Appendix A PDX collection 0897
HAC 7th character B see Appendix B for HAC conditional logic

CC +7th **S62.225 Nondisplaced Rolando's fracture, left hand**
CC Exclusion 7th character B see Appendix A PDX collection 1284
CC Exclusion 7th characters K & P see Appendix A PDX collection 0897
HAC 7th character B see Appendix B for HAC conditional logic

CC +7th **S62.226 Nondisplaced Rolando's fracture, unspecified hand**
CC Exclusion 7th character B see Appendix A PDX collection 1284
CC Exclusion 7th characters K & P see Appendix A PDX collection 0897
HAC 7th character B see Appendix B for HAC conditional logic

+ **S62.23 Other fracture of base of first metacarpal bone**

CC +7th **S62.231 Other displaced fracture of base of first metacarpal bone, right hand**
CC Exclusion 7th character B see Appendix A PDX collection 1284
CC Exclusion 7th characters K & P see Appendix A PDX collection 0897
HAC 7th character B see Appendix B for HAC conditional logic

CC +7th **S62.232 Other displaced fracture of base of first metacarpal bone, left hand**
CC Exclusion 7th character B see Appendix A PDX collection 1284
CC Exclusion 7th characters K & P see Appendix A PDX collection 0897
HAC 7th character B see Appendix B for HAC conditional logic

CC +7th **S62.233 Other displaced fracture of base of first metacarpal bone, unspecified hand**
CC Exclusion 7th character B see Appendix A PDX collection 1284
CC Exclusion 7th characters K & P see Appendix A PDX collection 0897
HAC 7th character B see Appendix B for HAC conditional logic

CC +7th **S62.234 Other nondisplaced fracture of base of first metacarpal bone, right hand**
CC Exclusion 7th character B see Appendix A PDX collection 1284
CC Exclusion 7th characters K & P see Appendix A PDX collection 0897
HAC 7th character B see Appendix B for HAC conditional logic

CC +7th **S62.235 Other nondisplaced fracture of base of first metacarpal bone, left hand**
CC Exclusion 7th character B see Appendix A PDX collection 1284
CC Exclusion 7th characters K & P see Appendix A PDX collection 0897
HAC 7th character B see Appendix B for HAC conditional logic

CC +7th **S62.236 Other nondisplaced fracture of base of first metacarpal bone, unspecified hand**
CC Exclusion 7th character B see Appendix A PDX collection 1284
CC Exclusion 7th characters K & P see Appendix A PDX collection 0897
HAC 7th character B see Appendix B for HAC conditional logic

+ **S62.24 Fracture of shaft of first metacarpal bone**

CC +7th **S62.241 Displaced fracture of shaft of first metacarpal bone, right hand**
CC Exclusion 7th character B see Appendix A PDX collection 1284
CC Exclusion 7th characters K & P see Appendix A PDX collection 0897
HAC 7th character B see Appendix B for HAC conditional logic

CC +7th **S62.242 Displaced fracture of shaft of first metacarpal bone, left hand**
CC Exclusion 7th character B see Appendix A PDX collection 1284
CC Exclusion 7th characters K & P see Appendix A PDX collection 0897
HAC 7th character B see Appendix B for HAC conditional logic

CC +7th **S62.243 Displaced fracture of shaft of first metacarpal bone, unspecified hand**
CC Exclusion 7th character B see Appendix A PDX collection 1284
CC Exclusion 7th characters K & P see Appendix A PDX collection 0897
HAC 7th character B see Appendix B for HAC conditional logic

CC +7th **S62.244 Nondisplaced fracture of shaft of first metacarpal bone, right hand**
CC Exclusion 7th character B see Appendix A PDX collection 1284
CC Exclusion 7th characters K & P see Appendix A PDX collection 0897
HAC 7th character B see Appendix B for HAC conditional logic

CC +7th **S62.245 Nondisplaced fracture of shaft of first metacarpal bone, left hand**
CC Exclusion 7th character B see Appendix A PDX collection 1284
CC Exclusion 7th characters K & P see Appendix A PDX collection 0897
HAC 7th character B see Appendix B for HAC conditional logic

CC +7th **S62.246 Nondisplaced fracture of shaft of first metacarpal bone, unspecified hand**
CC Exclusion 7th character B see Appendix A PDX collection 1284
CC Exclusion 7th characters K & P see Appendix A PDX collection 0897
HAC 7th character B see Appendix B for HAC conditional logic

+ **S62.25 Fracture of neck of first metacarpal bone**

CC +7th **S62.251 Displaced fracture of neck of first metacarpal bone, right hand**
CC Exclusion 7th character B see Appendix A PDX collection 1284
CC Exclusion 7th characters K & P see Appendix A PDX collection 0897
HAC 7th character B see Appendix B for HAC conditional logic

CC +7th **S62.252 Displaced fracture of neck of first metacarpal bone, left hand**
CC Exclusion 7th character B see Appendix A PDX collection 1284
CC Exclusion 7th characters K & P see Appendix A PDX collection 0897
HAC 7th character B see Appendix B for HAC conditional logic

CC +7th **S62.253 Displaced fracture of neck of first metacarpal bone, unspecified hand**
CC Exclusion 7th character B see Appendix A PDX collection 1284
CC Exclusion 7th characters K & P see Appendix A PDX collection 0897
HAC 7th character B see Appendix B for HAC conditional logic

CC +7th **S62.254 Nondisplaced fracture of neck of first metacarpal bone, right hand**
CC Exclusion 7th character B see Appendix A PDX collection 1284
CC Exclusion 7th characters K & P see Appendix A PDX collection 0897
HAC 7th character B see Appendix B for HAC conditional logic

CC +7th **S62.255 Nondisplaced fracture of neck of first metacarpal bone, left hand**
CC Exclusion 7th character B see Appendix A PDX collection 1284
CC Exclusion 7th characters K & P see Appendix A PDX collection 0897
HAC 7th character B see Appendix B for HAC conditional logic

CC +7th **S62.256 Nondisplaced fracture of neck of first metacarpal bone, unspecified hand**
CC Exclusion 7th character B see Appendix A PDX collection 1284
CC Exclusion 7th characters K & P see Appendix A PDX collection 0897
HAC 7th character B see Appendix B for HAC conditional logic

+ **S62.29 Other fracture of first metacarpal bone**

CC +7th **S62.291 Other fracture of first metacarpal bone, right hand**
CC Exclusion 7th character B see Appendix A PDX collection 1284
CC Exclusion 7th characters K & P see Appendix A PDX collection 0897
HAC 7th character B see Appendix B for HAC conditional logic

CC +7th **S62.292 Other fracture of first metacarpal bone, left hand**
CC Exclusion 7th character B see Appendix A PDX collection 1284
CC Exclusion 7th characters K & P see Appendix A PDX collection 0897
HAC 7th character B see Appendix B for HAC conditional logic

CC +7th **S62.299 Other fracture of first metacarpal bone, unspecified hand**
CC Exclusion 7th character B see Appendix A PDX collection 1284
CC Exclusion 7th characters K & P see Appendix A PDX collection 0897
HAC 7th character B see Appendix B for HAC conditional logic

+ **S62.3 Fracture of other and unspecified metacarpal bone**
Excludes2: *fracture of first metacarpal bone (S62.2-)*

+ **S62.30 Unspecified fracture of other metacarpal bone**

CC +7th **S62.300 Unspecified fracture of second metacarpal bone, right hand**
CC Exclusion 7th character B see Appendix A PDX collection 1284
CC Exclusion 7th characters K & P see Appendix A PDX collection 0897
HAC 7th character B see Appendix B for HAC conditional logic

CC +7th **S62.301 Unspecified fracture of second metacarpal bone, left hand**
CC Exclusion 7th character B see Appendix A PDX collection 1284
CC Exclusion 7th characters K & P see Appendix A PDX collection 0897
HAC 7th character B see Appendix B for HAC conditional logic

CC +7th **S62.302 Unspecified fracture of third metacarpal bone, right hand**
CC Exclusion 7th character B see Appendix A PDX collection 1284
CC Exclusion 7th characters K & P see Appendix A PDX collection 0897
HAC 7th character B see Appendix B for HAC conditional logic

CC +7th **S62.303 Unspecified fracture of third metacarpal bone, left hand**
CC Exclusion 7th character B see Appendix A PDX collection 1284
CC Exclusion 7th characters K & P see Appendix A PDX collection 0897
HAC 7th character B see Appendix B for HAC conditional logic

CC +7th **S62.304 Unspecified fracture of fourth metacarpal bone, right hand**
CC Exclusion 7th character B see Appendix A PDX collection 1284
CC Exclusion 7th characters K & P see Appendix A PDX collection 0897
HAC 7th character B see Appendix B for HAC conditional logic

CC +7th **S62.305 Unspecified fracture of fourth metacarpal bone, left hand**
CC Exclusion 7th character B see Appendix A PDX collection 1284
CC Exclusion 7th characters K & P see Appendix A PDX collection 0897
HAC 7th character B see Appendix B for HAC conditional logic

CC +7th **S62.306 Unspecified fracture of fifth metacarpal bone, right hand**
CC Exclusion 7th character B see Appendix A PDX collection 1284
CC Exclusion 7th characters K & P see Appendix A PDX collection 0897
HAC 7th character B see Appendix B for HAC conditional logic

CC +7th **S62.307 Unspecified fracture of fifth metacarpal bone, left hand**
CC Exclusion 7th character B see Appendix A PDX collection 1284
CC Exclusion 7th characters K & P see Appendix A PDX collection 0897
HAC 7th character B see Appendix B for HAC conditional logic

CC +7th **S62.308 Unspecified fracture of other metacarpal bone**
Unspecified fracture of specified metacarpal bone with unspecified laterality
CC Exclusion 7th character B see Appendix A PDX collection 1284
CC Exclusion 7th characters K & P see Appendix A PDX collection 0897
HAC 7th character B see Appendix B for HAC conditional logic

CC +7th **S62.309 Unspecified fracture of unspecified metacarpal bone**
CC Exclusion 7th character B see Appendix A PDX collection 1284
CC Exclusion 7th characters K & P see Appendix A PDX collection 0897
HAC 7th character B see Appendix B for HAC conditional logic

+ S62.31 Displaced fracture of base of other metacarpal bone

CC +7th **S62.310 Displaced fracture of base of second metacarpal bone, right hand**
CC Exclusion 7th character B see Appendix A PDX collection 1284
CC Exclusion 7th characters K & P see Appendix A PDX collection 0897
HAC 7th character B see Appendix B for HAC conditional logic

CC +7th **S62.311 Displaced fracture of base of second metacarpal bone. left hand**
CC Exclusion 7th character B see Appendix A PDX collection 1284
CC Exclusion 7th characters K & P see Appendix A PDX collection 0897
HAC 7th character B see Appendix B for HAC conditional logic

CC +7th **S62.312 Displaced fracture of base of third metacarpal bone, right hand**
CC Exclusion 7th character B see Appendix A PDX collection 1284
CC Exclusion 7th characters K & P see Appendix A PDX collection 0897
HAC 7th character B see Appendix B for HAC conditional logic

CC +7th **S62.313 Displaced fracture of base of third metacarpal bone, left hand**
CC Exclusion 7th character B see Appendix A PDX collection 1284
CC Exclusion 7th characters K & P see Appendix A PDX collection 0897
HAC 7th character B see Appendix B for HAC conditional logic

CC +7th **S62.314 Displaced fracture of base of fourth metacarpal bone, right hand**
CC Exclusion 7th character B see Appendix A PDX collection 1284
CC Exclusion 7th characters K & P see Appendix A PDX collection 0897
HAC 7th character B see Appendix B for HAC conditional logic

CC +7th **S62.315 Displaced fracture of base of fourth metacarpal bone, left hand**
CC Exclusion 7th character B see Appendix A PDX collection 1284
CC Exclusion 7th characters K & P see Appendix A PDX collection 0897
HAC 7th character B see Appendix B for HAC conditional logic

CC +7th **S62.316 Displaced fracture of base of fifth metacarpal bone, right hand**
CC Exclusion 7th character B see Appendix A PDX collection 1284
CC Exclusion 7th characters K & P see Appendix A PDX collection 0897
HAC 7th character B see Appendix B for HAC conditional logic

CC +7th **S62.317 Displaced fracture of base of fifth metacarpal bone. left hand**
CC Exclusion 7th character B see Appendix A PDX collection 1284
CC Exclusion 7th characters K & P see Appendix A PDX collection 0897
HAC 7th character B see Appendix B for HAC conditional logic

CC +7th **S62.318 Displaced fracture of base of other metacarpal bone**
Displaced fracture of base of specified metacarpal bone with unspecified laterality
CC Exclusion 7th character B see Appendix A PDX collection 1284
CC Exclusion 7th characters K & P see Appendix A PDX collection 0897
HAC 7th character B see Appendix B for HAC conditional logic

CC +7th **S62.319 Displaced fracture of base of unspecified metacarpal bone**
CC Exclusion 7th character B see Appendix A PDX collection 1284
CC Exclusion 7th characters K & P see Appendix A PDX collection 0897
HAC 7th character B see Appendix B for HAC conditional logic

+ S62.32 Displaced fracture of shaft of other metacarpal bone

CC +7th **S62.320 Displaced fracture of shaft of second metacarpal bone, right hand**
CC Exclusion 7th character B see Appendix A PDX collection 1284
CC Exclusion 7th characters K & P see Appendix A PDX collection 0897
HAC 7th character B see Appendix B for HAC conditional logic

CC +7th **S62.321 Displaced fracture of shaft of second metacarpal bone, left hand**
CC Exclusion 7th character B see Appendix A PDX collection 1284
CC Exclusion 7th characters K & P see Appendix A PDX collection 0897
HAC 7th character B see Appendix B for HAC conditional logic

CC +7th **S62.322 Displaced fracture of shaft of third metacarpal bone, right hand**
CC Exclusion 7th character B see Appendix A PDX collection 1284
CC Exclusion 7th characters K & P see Appendix A PDX collection 0897
HAC 7th character B see Appendix B for HAC conditional logic

CC +7th **S62.323 Displaced fracture of shaft of third metacarpal bone, left hand**
CC Exclusion 7th character B see Appendix A PDX collection 1284
CC Exclusion 7th characters K & P see Appendix A PDX collection 0897
HAC 7th character B see Appendix B for HAC conditional logic

CC +7th **S62.324 Displaced fracture of shaft of fourth metacarpal bone, right hand**
CC Exclusion 7th character B see Appendix A PDX collection 1284
CC Exclusion 7th characters K & P see Appendix A PDX collection 0897
HAC 7th character B see Appendix B for HAC conditional logic

CC +7th **S62.325 Displaced fracture of shaft of fourth metacarpal bone, left hand**
CC Exclusion 7th character B see Appendix A PDX collection 1284
CC Exclusion 7th characters K & P see Appendix A PDX collection 0897
HAC 7th character B see Appendix B for HAC conditional logic

CC +7th **S62.326 Displaced fracture of shaft of fifth metacarpal bone, right hand**
CC Exclusion 7th character B see Appendix A PDX collection 1284
CC Exclusion 7th characters K & P see Appendix A PDX collection 0897
HAC 7th character B see Appendix B for HAC conditional logic

CC +7th **S62.327 Displaced fracture of shaft of fifth metacarpal bone, left hand**
CC Exclusion 7th character B see Appendix A PDX collection 1284
CC Exclusion 7th characters K & P see Appendix A PDX collection 0897
HAC 7th character B see Appendix B for HAC conditional logic

CC +7th **S62.328 Displaced fracture of shaft of other metacarpal bone**
Displaced fracture of shaft of specified metacarpal bone with unspecified laterality
CC Exclusion 7th character B see Appendix A PDX collection 1284
CC Exclusion 7th characters K & P see Appendix A PDX collection 0897
HAC 7th character B see Appendix B for HAC conditional logic

CC +7th **S62.329 Displaced fracture of shaft of unspecified metacarpal bone**
CC Exclusion 7th character B see Appendix A PDX collection 1284
CC Exclusion 7th characters K & P see Appendix A PDX collection 0897
HAC 7th character B see Appendix B for HAC conditional logic

+ S62.33 Displaced fracture of neck of other metacarpal bone

CC +7th **S62.330 Displaced fracture of neck of second metacarpal bone, right hand**
- **CC Exclusion 7th character B see Appendix A PDX collection 1284**
- **CC Exclusion 7th characters K & P see Appendix A PDX collection 0897**
- HAC 7th character B see Appendix B for HAC conditional logic

CC +7th **S62.331 Displaced fracture of neck of second metacarpal bone, left hand**
- **CC Exclusion 7th character B see Appendix A PDX collection 1284**
- **CC Exclusion 7th characters K & P see Appendix A PDX collection 0897**
- HAC 7th character B see Appendix B for HAC conditional logic

CC +7th **S62.332 Displaced fracture of neck of third metacarpal bone, right hand**
- **CC Exclusion 7th character B see Appendix A PDX collection 1284**
- **CC Exclusion 7th characters K & P see Appendix A PDX collection 0897**
- HAC 7th character B see Appendix B for HAC conditional logic

CC +7th **S62.333 Displaced fracture of neck of third metacarpal bone, left hand**
- **CC Exclusion 7th character B see Appendix A PDX collection 1284**
- **CC Exclusion 7th characters K & P see Appendix A PDX collection 0897**
- HAC 7th character B see Appendix B for HAC conditional logic

CC +7th **S62.334 Displaced fracture of neck of fourth metacarpal bone, right hand**
- **CC Exclusion 7th character B see Appendix A PDX collection 1284**
- **CC Exclusion 7th characters K & P see Appendix A PDX collection 0897**
- HAC 7th character B see Appendix B for HAC conditional logic

CC +7th **S62.335 Displaced fracture of neck of fourth metacarpal bone, left hand**
- **CC Exclusion 7th character B see Appendix A PDX collection 1284**
- **CC Exclusion 7th characters K & P see Appendix A PDX collection 0897**
- HAC 7th character B see Appendix B for HAC conditional logic

CC +7th **S62.336 Displaced fracture of neck of fifth metacarpal bone, right hand**
- **CC Exclusion 7th character B see Appendix A PDX collection 1284**
- **CC Exclusion 7th characters K & P see Appendix A PDX collection 0897**
- HAC 7th character B see Appendix B for HAC conditional logic

CC +7th **S62.337 Displaced fracture of neck of fifth metacarpal bone, left hand**
- **CC Exclusion 7th character B see Appendix A PDX collection 1284**
- **CC Exclusion 7th characters K & P see Appendix A PDX collection 0897**
- HAC 7th character B see Appendix B for HAC conditional logic

CC +7th **S62.338 Displaced fracture of neck of other metacarpal bone**
- Displaced fracture of neck of specified metacarpal bone with unspecified laterality
- **CC Exclusion 7th character B see Appendix A PDX collection 1284**
- **CC Exclusion 7th characters K & P see Appendix A PDX collection 0897**
- HAC 7th character B see Appendix B for HAC conditional logic

CC +7th **S62.339 Displaced fracture of neck of unspecified metacarpal bone**
- **CC Exclusion 7th character B see Appendix A PDX collection 1284**
- **CC Exclusion 7th characters K & P see Appendix A PDX collection 0897**
- HAC 7th character B see Appendix B for HAC conditional logic

+ S62.34 Nondisplaced fracture of base of other metacarpal bone

CC +7th **S62.340 Nondisplaced fracture of base of second metacarpal bone, right hand**
- **CC Exclusion 7th character B see Appendix A PDX collection 1284**
- **CC Exclusion 7th characters K & P see Appendix A PDX collection 0897**
- HAC 7th character B see Appendix B for HAC conditional logic

CC +7th **S62.341 Nondisplaced fracture of base of second metacarpal bone. left hand**
- **CC Exclusion 7th character B see Appendix A PDX collection 1284**
- **CC Exclusion 7th characters K & P see Appendix A PDX collection 0897**
- HAC 7th character B see Appendix B for HAC conditional logic

CC +7th **S62.342 Nondisplaced fracture of base of third metacarpal bone, right hand**
- **CC Exclusion 7th character B see Appendix A PDX collection 1284**
- **CC Exclusion 7th characters K & P see Appendix A PDX collection 0897**
- HAC 7th character B see Appendix B for HAC conditional logic

CC +7th **S62.343 Nondisplaced fracture of base of third metacarpal bone, left hand**
- **CC Exclusion 7th character B see Appendix A PDX collection 1284**
- **CC Exclusion 7th characters K & P see Appendix A PDX collection 0897**
- HAC 7th character B see Appendix B for HAC conditional logic

CC +7th **S62.344 Nondisplaced fracture of base of fourth metacarpal bone, right hand**
- **CC Exclusion 7th character B see Appendix A PDX collection 1284**
- **CC Exclusion 7th characters K & P see Appendix A PDX collection 0897**
- HAC 7th character B see Appendix B for HAC conditional logic

CC +7th **S62.345 Nondisplaced fracture of base of fourth metacarpal bone, left hand**
- **CC Exclusion 7th character B see Appendix A PDX collection 1284**
- **CC Exclusion 7th characters K & P see Appendix A PDX collection 0897**
- HAC 7th character B see Appendix B for HAC conditional logic

CC +7th **S62.346 Nondisplaced fracture of base of fifth metacarpal bone, right hand**
- **CC Exclusion 7th character B see Appendix A PDX collection 1284**
- **CC Exclusion 7th characters K & P see Appendix A PDX collection 0897**
- HAC 7th character B see Appendix B for HAC conditional logic

CC +7th **S62.347 Nondisplaced fracture of base of fifth metacarpal bone. left hand**
- **CC Exclusion 7th character B see Appendix A PDX collection 1284**
- **CC Exclusion 7th characters K & P see Appendix A PDX collection 0897**
- HAC 7th character B see Appendix B for HAC conditional logic

CC +7th **S62.348 Nondisplaced fracture of base of other metacarpal bone**
- Nondisplaced fracture of base of specified metacarpal bone with unspecified lateral
- **CC Exclusion 7th character B see Appendix A PDX collection 1284**
- **CC Exclusion 7th characters K & P see Appendix A PDX collection 0897**
- HAC 7th character B see Appendix B for HAC conditional logic

CC +7th **S62.349 Nondisplaced fracture of base of unspecifi metacarpal bone**
- **CC Exclusion 7th character B see Appendix A PDX collection 1284**
- **CC Exclusion 7th characters K & P see Appendix A PDX collection 0897**
- HAC 7th character B see Appendix B for HAC conditional logic

+ S62.35 Nondisplaced fracture of shaft of other metacarpal bone

CC +7th **S62.350 Nondisplaced fracture of shaft of second metacarpal bone, right hand**
CC Exclusion 7th character B see Appendix A PDX collection 1284
CC Exclusion 7th characters K & P see Appendix A PDX collection 0897
HAC 7th character B see Appendix B for HAC conditional logic

CC +7th **S62.351 Nondisplaced fracture of shaft of second metacarpal bone, left hand**
CC Exclusion 7th character B see Appendix A PDX collection 1284
CC Exclusion 7th characters K & P see Appendix A PDX collection 0897
HAC 7th character B see Appendix B for HAC conditional logic

CC +7th **S62.352 Nondisplaced fracture of shaft of third metacarpal bone, right hand**
CC Exclusion 7th character B see Appendix A PDX collection 1284
CC Exclusion 7th characters K & P see Appendix A PDX collection 0897
HAC 7th character B see Appendix B for HAC conditional logic

CC +7th **S62.353 Nondisplaced fracture of shaft of third metacarpal bone, left hand**
CC Exclusion 7th character B see Appendix A PDX collection 1284
CC Exclusion 7th characters K & P see Appendix A PDX collection 0897
HAC 7th character B see Appendix B for HAC conditional logic

CC +7th **S62.354 Nondisplaced fracture of shaft of fourth metacarpal bone, right hand**
CC Exclusion 7th character B see Appendix A PDX collection 1284
CC Exclusion 7th characters K & P see Appendix A PDX collection 0897
HAC 7th character B see Appendix B for HAC conditional logic

CC +7th **S62.355 Nondisplaced fracture of shaft of fourth metacarpal bone, left hand**
CC Exclusion 7th character B see Appendix A PDX collection 1284
CC Exclusion 7th characters K & P see Appendix A PDX collection 0897
HAC 7th character B see Appendix B for HAC conditional logic

CC +7th **S62.356 Nondisplaced fracture of shaft of fifth metacarpal bone, right hand**
CC Exclusion 7th character B see Appendix A PDX collection 1284
CC Exclusion 7th characters K & P see Appendix A PDX collection 0897
HAC 7th character B see Appendix B for HAC conditional logic

CC +7th **S62.357 Nondisplaced fracture of shaft of fifth metacarpal bone, left hand**
CC Exclusion 7th character B see Appendix A PDX collection 1284
CC Exclusion 7th characters K & P see Appendix A PDX collection 0897
HAC 7th character B see Appendix B for HAC conditional logic

CC +7th **S62.358 Nondisplaced fracture of shaft of other metacarpal bone**
Nondisplaced fracture of shaft of specified metacarpal bone with unspecified laterality
CC Exclusion 7th character B see Appendix A PDX collection 1284
CC Exclusion 7th characters K & P see Appendix A PDX collection 0897
HAC 7th character B see Appendix B for HAC conditional logic

CC +7th **S62.359 Nondisplaced fracture of shaft of unspecified metacarpal bone**
CC Exclusion 7th character B see Appendix A PDX collection 1284
CC Exclusion 7th characters K & P see Appendix A PDX collection 0897
HAC 7th character B see Appendix B for HAC conditional logic

+ S62.36 Nondisplaced fracture of neck of other metacarpal bone

CC +7th **S62.360 Nondisplaced fracture of neck of second metacarpal bone, right hand**
CC Exclusion 7th character B see Appendix A PDX collection 1284
CC Exclusion 7th characters K & P see Appendix A PDX collection 0897
HAC 7th character B see Appendix B for HAC conditional logic

CC +7th **S62.361 Nondisplaced fracture of neck of second metacarpal bone, left hand**
CC Exclusion 7th character B see Appendix A PDX collection 1284
CC Exclusion 7th characters K & P see Appendix A PDX collection 0897
HAC 7th character B see Appendix B for HAC conditional logic

CC +7th **S62.362 Nondisplaced fracture of neck of third metacarpal bone, right hand**
CC Exclusion 7th character B see Appendix A PDX collection 1284
CC Exclusion 7th characters K & P see Appendix A PDX collection 0897
HAC 7th character B see Appendix B for HAC conditional logic

CC +7th **S62.363 Nondisplaced fracture of neck of third metacarpal bone, left hand**
CC Exclusion 7th character B see Appendix A PDX collection 1284
CC Exclusion 7th characters K & P see Appendix A PDX collection 0897
HAC 7th character B see Appendix B for HAC conditional logic

CC +7th **S62.364 Nondisplaced fracture of neck of fourth metacarpal bone, right hand**
CC Exclusion 7th character B see Appendix A PDX collection 1284
CC Exclusion 7th characters K & P see Appendix A PDX collection 0897
HAC 7th character B see Appendix B for HAC conditional logic

CC +7th **S62.365 Nondisplaced fracture of neck of fourth metacarpal bone, left hand**
CC Exclusion 7th character B see Appendix A PDX collection 1284
CC Exclusion 7th characters K & P see Appendix A PDX collection 0897
HAC 7th character B see Appendix B for HAC conditional logic

CC +7th **S62.366 Nondisplaced fracture of neck of fifth metacarpal bone, right hand**
CC Exclusion 7th character B see Appendix A PDX collection 1284
CC Exclusion 7th characters K & P see Appendix A PDX collection 0897
HAC 7th character B see Appendix B for HAC conditional logic

CC +7th **S62.367 Nondisplaced fracture of neck of fifth metacarpal bone, left hand**
CC Exclusion 7th character B see Appendix A PDX collection 1284
CC Exclusion 7th characters K & P see Appendix A PDX collection 0897
HAC 7th character B see Appendix B for HAC conditional logic

CC +7th **S62.368 Nondisplaced fracture of neck of other metacarpal bone**
Nondisplaced fracture of neck of specified metacarpal bone with unspecified laterality
CC Exclusion 7th character B see Appendix A PDX collection 1284
CC Exclusion 7th characters K & P see Appendix A PDX collection 0897
HAC 7th character B see Appendix B for HAC conditional logic

CC +7th **S62.369 Nondisplaced fracture of neck of unspecified metacarpal bone**
CC Exclusion 7th character B see Appendix A PDX collection 1284
CC Exclusion 7th characters K & P see Appendix A PDX collection 0897
HAC 7th character B see Appendix B for HAC conditional logic

+ S62.39 Other fracture of other metacarpal bone

CC +7th **S62.390 Other fracture of second metacarpal bone, right hand**
CC Exclusion 7th character B see Appendix A PDX collection 1284
CC Exclusion 7th characters K & P see Appendix A PDX collection 0897
HAC 7th character B see Appendix B for HAC conditional logic

CC +7th **S62.391 Other fracture of second metacarpal bone, left hand**
CC Exclusion 7th character B see Appendix A PDX collection 1284
CC Exclusion 7th characters K & P see Appendix A PDX collection 0897
HAC 7th character B see Appendix B for HAC conditional logic

CC +7th **S62.392 Other fracture of third metacarpal bone, right hand**
CC Exclusion 7th character B see Appendix A PDX collection 1284
CC Exclusion 7th characters K & P see Appendix A PDX collection 0897
HAC 7th character B see Appendix B for HAC conditional logic

CC +7th **S62.393 Other fracture of third metacarpal bone, left hand**
CC Exclusion 7th character B see Appendix A PDX collection 1284
CC Exclusion 7th characters K & P see Appendix A PDX collection 0897
HAC 7th character B see Appendix B for HAC conditional logic

CC +7th **S62.394 Other fracture of fourth metacarpal bone, right hand**
CC Exclusion 7th character B see Appendix A PDX collection 1284
CC Exclusion 7th characters K & P see Appendix A PDX collection 0897
HAC 7th character B see Appendix B for HAC conditional logic

CC +7th **S62.395 Other fracture of fourth metacarpal bone, left hand**
CC Exclusion 7th character B see Appendix A PDX collection 1284
CC Exclusion 7th characters K & P see Appendix A PDX collection 0897
HAC 7th character B see Appendix B for HAC conditional logic

CC +7th **S62.396 Other fracture of fifth metacarpal bone, right hand**
CC Exclusion 7th character B see Appendix A PDX collection 1284
CC Exclusion 7th characters K & P see Appendix A PDX collection 0897
HAC 7th character B see Appendix B for HAC conditional logic

CC +7th **S62.397 Other fracture of fifth metacarpal bone, left hand**
CC Exclusion 7th character B see Appendix A PDX collection 1284
CC Exclusion 7th characters K & P see Appendix A PDX collection 0897
HAC 7th character B see Appendix B for HAC conditional logic

CC +7th **S62.398 Other fracture of other metacarpal bone**
Other fracture of specified metacarpal bone with unspecified laterality
CC Exclusion 7th character B see Appendix A PDX collection 1284
CC Exclusion 7th characters K & P see Appendix A PDX collection 0897
HAC 7th character B see Appendix B for HAC conditional logic

CC +7th **S62.399 Other fracture of unspecified metacarpal bone**
CC Exclusion 7th character B see Appendix A PDX collection 1284
CC Exclusion 7th characters K & P see Appendix A PDX collection 0897
HAC 7th character B see Appendix B for HAC conditional logic

+ S62.5 Fracture of thumb

+ S62.50 Fracture of unspecified phalanx of thumb

CC +7th **S62.501 Fracture of unspecified phalanx of right thumb**
CC Exclusion 7th character B see Appendix A PDX collection 1285
CC Exclusion 7th characters K & P see Appendix A PDX collection 0897
HAC 7th character B see Appendix B for HAC conditional logic

CC +7th **S62.502 Fracture of unspecified phalanx of left thumb**
CC Exclusion 7th character B see Appendix A PDX collection 1285
CC Exclusion 7th characters K & P see Appendix A PDX collection 0897
HAC 7th character B see Appendix B for HAC conditional logic

CC +7th **S62.509 Fracture of unspecified phalanx of unspecified thumb**
CC Exclusion 7th character B see Appendix A PDX collection 1285
CC Exclusion 7th characters K & P see Appendix A PDX collection 0897
HAC 7th character B see Appendix B for HAC conditional logic

+ S62.51 Fracture of proximal phalanx of thumb

CC +7th **S62.511 Displaced fracture of proximal phalanx o right thumb**
CC Exclusion 7th character B see Appendix A PDX collection 1285
CC Exclusion 7th characters K & P see Appendix A PDX collection 0897
HAC 7th character B see Appendix B for HAC conditional logic

CC +7th **S62.512 Displaced fracture of proximal phalanx o left thumb**
CC Exclusion 7th character B see Appendix A PDX collection 1285
CC Exclusion 7th characters K & P see Appendix A PDX collection 0897
HAC 7th character B see Appendix B for HAC conditional logic

CC +7th **S62.513 Displaced fracture of proximal phalanx o unspecified thumb**
CC Exclusion 7th character B see Appendix A PDX collection 1285
CC Exclusion 7th characters K & P see Appendix A PDX collection 0897
HAC 7th character B see Appendix B for HAC conditional logic

CC +7th **S62.514 Nondisplaced fracture of proximal phala of right thumb**
CC Exclusion 7th character B see Appendix A PDX collection 1285
CC Exclusion 7th characters K & P see Appendix A PDX collection 0897
HAC 7th character B see Appendix B for HAC conditional logic

CC +7th **S62.515 Nondisplaced fracture of proximal phala of left thumb**
CC Exclusion 7th character B see Appendix A PDX collection 1285
CC Exclusion 7th characters K & P see Appendix A PDX collection 0897
HAC 7th character B see Appendix B for HAC conditional logic

CC +7th **S62.516 Nondisplaced fracture of proximal phala of unspecified thumb**
CC Exclusion 7th character B see Appendix A PDX collection 1285
CC Exclusion 7th characters K & P see Appendix A PDX collection 0897
HAC 7th character B see Appendix B for HAC conditional logic

+ S62.52 Fracture of distal phalanx of thumb

CC +7th **S62.521 Displaced fracture of distal phalanx of ri thumb**
CC Exclusion 7th character B see Appendix A PDX collection 1285
CC Exclusion 7th characters K & P see Appendix A PDX collection 0897
HAC 7th character B see Appendix B for HAC conditional logic

CC +7th **S62.522 Displaced fracture of distal phalanx of left thumb**
CC Exclusion 7th character B see Appendix A PDX collection 1285
CC Exclusion 7th characters K & P see Appendix A PDX collection 0897
HAC 7th character B see Appendix B for HAC conditional logic

CC +7th **S62.523 Displaced fracture of distal phalanx of unspecified thumb**
CC Exclusion 7th character B see Appendix A PDX collection 1285
CC Exclusion 7th characters K & P see Appendix A PDX collection 0897
HAC 7th character B see Appendix B for HAC conditional logic

CC +7th **S62.524 Nondisplaced fracture of distal phalanx of right thumb**
CC Exclusion 7th character B see Appendix A PDX collection 1285
CC Exclusion 7th characters K & P see Appendix A PDX collection 0897
HAC 7th character B see Appendix B for HAC conditional logic

CC +7th **S62.525 Nondisplaced fracture of distal phalanx of left thumb**
CC Exclusion 7th character B see Appendix A PDX collection 1285
CC Exclusion 7th characters K & P see Appendix A PDX collection 0897
HAC 7th character B see Appendix B for HAC conditional logic

CC +7th **S62.526 Nondisplaced fracture of distal phalanx of unspecified thumb**
CC Exclusion 7th character B see Appendix A PDX collection 1285
CC Exclusion 7th characters K & P see Appendix A PDX collection 0897
HAC 7th character B see Appendix B for HAC conditional logic

\+ **S62.6 Fracture of other and unspecified finger(s)**
Excludes2: *fracture of thumb (S62.5-)*

\+ **S62.60 Fracture of unspecified phalanx of finger**

CC +7th **S62.600 Fracture of unspecified phalanx of right index finger**
CC Exclusion 7th character B see Appendix A PDX collection 1285
CC Exclusion 7th characters K & P see Appendix A PDX collection 0897
HAC 7th character B see Appendix B for HAC conditional logic

CC +7th **S62.601 Fracture of unspecified phalanx of left index finger**
CC Exclusion 7th character B see Appendix A PDX collection 1285
CC Exclusion 7th characters K & P see Appendix A PDX collection 0897
HAC 7th character B see Appendix B for HAC conditional logic

CC +7th **S62.602 Fracture of unspecified phalanx of right middle finger**
CC Exclusion 7th character B see Appendix A PDX collection 1285
CC Exclusion 7th characters K & P see Appendix A PDX collection 0897
HAC 7th character B see Appendix B for HAC conditional logic

CC +7th **S62.603 Fracture of unspecified phalanx of left middle finger**
CC Exclusion 7th character B see Appendix A PDX collection 1285
CC Exclusion 7th characters K & P see Appendix A PDX collection 0897
HAC 7th character B see Appendix B for HAC conditional logic

CC +7th **S62.604 Fracture of unspecified phalanx of right ring finger**
CC Exclusion 7th character B see Appendix A PDX collection 1285
CC Exclusion 7th characters K & P see Appendix A PDX collection 0897
HAC 7th character B see Appendix B for HAC conditional logic

CC +7th **S62.605 Fracture of unspecified phalanx of left ring finger**
CC Exclusion 7th character B see Appendix A PDX collection 1285
CC Exclusion 7th characters K & P see Appendix A PDX collection 0897
HAC 7th character B see Appendix B for HAC conditional logic

CC +7th **S62.606 Fracture of unspecified phalanx of right little finger**
CC Exclusion 7th character B see Appendix A PDX collection 1285
CC Exclusion 7th characters K & P see Appendix A PDX collection 0897
HAC 7th character B see Appendix B for HAC conditional logic

CC +7th **S62.607 Fracture of unspecified phalanx of left little finger**
CC Exclusion 7th character B see Appendix A PDX collection 1285
CC Exclusion 7th characters K & P see Appendix A PDX collection 0897
HAC 7th character B see Appendix B for HAC conditional logic

CC +7th **S62.608 Fracture of unspecified phalanx of other finger**
Fracture of unspecified phalanx of specified finger with unspecified laterality
CC Exclusion 7th character B see Appendix A PDX collection 1285
CC Exclusion 7th characters K & P see Appendix A PDX collection 0897
HAC 7th character B see Appendix B for HAC conditional logic

CC +7th **S62.609 Fracture of unspecified phalanx of unspecified finger**
CC Exclusion 7th character B see Appendix A PDX collection 1285
CC Exclusion 7th characters K & P see Appendix A PDX collection 0897
HAC 7th character B see Appendix B for HAC conditional logic

\+ **S62.61 Displaced fracture of proximal phalanx of finger**

CC +7th **S62.610 Displaced fracture of proximal phalanx of right index finger**
CC Exclusion 7th character B see Appendix A PDX collection 1285
CC Exclusion 7th characters K & P see Appendix A PDX collection 0897
HAC 7th character B see Appendix B for HAC conditional logic

CC +7th **S62.611 Displaced fracture of proximal phalanx of left index finger**
CC Exclusion 7th character B see Appendix A PDX collection 1285
CC Exclusion 7th characters K & P see Appendix A PDX collection 0897
HAC 7th character B see Appendix B for HAC conditional logic

CC +7th **S62.612 Displaced fracture of proximal phalanx of right middle finger**
CC Exclusion 7th character B see Appendix A PDX collection 1285
CC Exclusion 7th characters K & P see Appendix A PDX collection 0897
HAC 7th character B see Appendix B for HAC conditional logic

CC +7th **S62.613 Displaced fracture of proximal phalanx of left middle finger**
CC Exclusion 7th character B see Appendix A PDX collection 1285
CC Exclusion 7th characters K & P see Appendix A PDX collection 0897
HAC 7th character B see Appendix B for HAC conditional logic

CC +7th **S62.614 Displaced fracture of proximal phalanx of right ring finger**
CC Exclusion 7th character B see Appendix A PDX collection 1285
CC Exclusion 7th characters K & P see Appendix A PDX collection 0897
HAC 7th character B see Appendix B for HAC conditional logic

CC +7th **S62.615** **Displaced fracture of proximal phalanx of left ring finger**
CC Exclusion 7th character B see Appendix A PDX collection 1285
CC Exclusion 7th characters K & P see Appendix A PDX collection 0897
HAC 7th character B see Appendix B for HAC conditional logic

CC +7th **S62.616** **Displaced fracture of proximal phalanx of right little finger**
CC Exclusion 7th character B see Appendix A PDX collection 1285
CC Exclusion 7th characters K & P see Appendix A PDX collection 0897
HAC 7th character B see Appendix B for HAC conditional logic

CC +7th **S62.617** **Displaced fracture of proximal phalanx of left little finger**
CC Exclusion 7th character B see Appendix A PDX collection 1285
CC Exclusion 7th characters K & P see Appendix A PDX collection 0897
HAC 7th character B see Appendix B for HAC conditional logic

CC +7th **S62.618** **Displaced fracture of proximal phalanx of other finger**
Displaced fracture of proximal phalanx of specified finger with unspecified laterality
CC Exclusion 7th character B see Appendix A PDX collection 1285
CC Exclusion 7th characters K & P see Appendix A PDX collection 0897
HAC 7th character B see Appendix B for HAC conditional logic

CC +7th **S62.619** **Displaced fracture of proximal phalanx of unspecified finger**
CC Exclusion 7th character B see Appendix A PDX collection 1285
CC Exclusion 7th characters K & P see Appendix A PDX collection 0897
HAC 7th character B see Appendix B for HAC conditional logic

\+ **S62.62** **Displaced fracture of medial phalanx of finger**

CC +7th **S62.620** **Displaced fracture of medial phalanx of right index finger**
CC Exclusion 7th character B see Appendix A PDX collection 1285
CC Exclusion 7th characters K & P see Appendix A PDX collection 0897
HAC 7th character B see Appendix B for HAC conditional logic

CC +7th **S62.621** **Displaced fracture of medial phalanx of left index finger**
CC Exclusion 7th character B see Appendix A PDX collection 1285
CC Exclusion 7th characters K & P see Appendix A PDX collection 0897
HAC 7th character B see Appendix B for HAC conditional logic

CC +7th **S62.622** **Displaced fracture of medial phalanx of right middle finger**
CC Exclusion 7th character B see Appendix A PDX collection 1285
CC Exclusion 7th characters K & P see Appendix A PDX collection 0897
HAC 7th character B see Appendix B for HAC conditional logic

CC +7th **S62.623** **Displaced fracture of medial phalanx of left middle finger**
CC Exclusion 7th character B see Appendix A PDX collection 1285
CC Exclusion 7th characters K & P see Appendix A PDX collection 0897
HAC 7th character B see Appendix B for HAC conditional logic

CC +7th **S62.624** **Displaced fracture of medial phalanx of right ring finger**
CC Exclusion 7th character B see Appendix A PDX collection 1285
CC Exclusion 7th characters K & P see Appendix A PDX collection 0897
HAC 7th character B see Appendix B for HAC conditional logic

CC +7th **S62.625** **Displaced fracture of medial phalanx of ring finger**
CC Exclusion 7th character B see Appendix A PDX collection 1285
CC Exclusion 7th characters K & P see Appendix A PDX collection 0897
HAC 7th character B see Appendix B for HAC conditional logic

CC +7th **S62.626** **Displaced fracture of medial phalanx of right little finger**
CC Exclusion 7th character B see Appendix A PDX collection 1285
CC Exclusion 7th characters K & P see Appendix A PDX collection 0897
HAC 7th character B see Appendix B for HAC conditional logic

CC +7th **S62.627** **Displaced fracture of medial phalanx of little finger**
CC Exclusion 7th character B see Appendix A PDX collection 1285
CC Exclusion 7th characters K & P see Appendix A PDX collection 0897
HAC 7th character B see Appendix B for HAC conditional logic

CC +7th **S62.628** **Displaced fracture of medial phalanx of other finger**
Displaced fracture of medial phalanx of specified finger with unspecified laterality
CC Exclusion 7th character B see Appendix A PDX collection 1285
CC Exclusion 7th characters K & P see Appendix A PDX collection 0897
HAC 7th character B see Appendix B for HAC conditional logic

CC +7th **S62.629** **Displaced fracture of medial phalanx of unspecified finger**
CC Exclusion 7th character B see Appendix A PDX collection 1285
CC Exclusion 7th characters K & P see Appendix A PDX collection 0897
HAC 7th character B see Appendix B for HAC conditional logic

\+ **S62.63** **Displaced fracture of distal phalanx of finger**

CC +7th **S62.630** **Displaced fracture of distal phalanx of ri index finger**
CC Exclusion 7th character B see Appendix A PDX collection 1285
CC Exclusion 7th characters K & P see Appendix A PDX collection 0897
HAC 7th character B see Appendix B for HAC conditional logic

CC +7th **S62.631** **Displaced fracture of distal phalanx of le index finger**
CC Exclusion 7th character B see Appendix A PDX collection 1285
CC Exclusion 7th characters K & P see Appendix A PDX collection 0897
HAC 7th character B see Appendix B for HAC conditional logic

CC +7th **S62.632** **Displaced fracture of distal phalanx of ri middle finger**
CC Exclusion 7th character B see Appendix A PDX collection 1285
CC Exclusion 7th characters K & P see Appendix A PDX collection 0897
HAC 7th character B see Appendix B for HAC conditional logic

CC +7th **S62.633** **Displaced fracture of distal phalanx of le middle finger**
CC Exclusion 7th character B see Appendix A PDX collection 1285
CC Exclusion 7th characters K & P see Appendix A PDX collection 0897
HAC 7th character B see Appendix B for HAC conditional logic

CC +7th **S62.634** **Displaced fracture of distal phalanx of ri ring finger**
CC Exclusion 7th character B see Appendix A PDX collection 1285
CC Exclusion 7th characters K & P see Appendix A PDX collection 0897
HAC 7th character B see Appendix B for HAC conditional logic

CC +7th **S62.635 Displaced fracture of distal phalanx of left ring finger**
CC Exclusion 7th character B see Appendix A PDX collection 1285
CC Exclusion 7th characters K & P see Appendix A PDX collection 0897
HAC 7th character B see Appendix B for HAC conditional logic

CC +7th **S62.636 Displaced fracture of distal phalanx of right little finger**
CC Exclusion 7th character B see Appendix A PDX collection 1285
CC Exclusion 7th characters K & P see Appendix A PDX collection 0897
HAC 7th character B see Appendix B for HAC conditional logic

CC +7th **S62.637 Displaced fracture of distal phalanx of left little finger**
CC Exclusion 7th character B see Appendix A PDX collection 1285
CC Exclusion 7th characters K & P see Appendix A PDX collection 0897
HAC 7th character B see Appendix B for HAC conditional logic

CC +7th **S62.638 Displaced fracture of distal phalanx of other finger**
Displaced fracture of distal phalanx of specified finger with unspecified laterality
CC Exclusion 7th character B see Appendix A PDX collection 1285
CC Exclusion 7th characters K & P see Appendix A PDX collection 0897
HAC 7th character B see Appendix B for HAC conditional logic

CC +7th **S62.639 Displaced fracture of distal phalanx of unspecified finger**
CC Exclusion 7th character B see Appendix A PDX collection 1285
CC Exclusion 7th characters K & P see Appendix A PDX collection 0897
HAC 7th character B see Appendix B for HAC conditional logic

\+ **S62.64 Nondisplaced fracture of proximal phalanx of finger**

CC +7th **S62.640 Nondisplaced fracture of proximal phalanx of right index finger**
CC Exclusion 7th character B see Appendix A PDX collection 1285
CC Exclusion 7th characters K & P see Appendix A PDX collection 0897
HAC 7th character B see Appendix B for HAC conditional logic

CC +7th **S62.641 Nondisplaced fracture of proximal phalanx of left index finger**
CC Exclusion 7th character B see Appendix A PDX collection 1285
CC Exclusion 7th characters K & P see Appendix A PDX collection 0897
HAC 7th character B see Appendix B for HAC conditional logic

CC +7th **S62.642 Nondisplaced fracture of proximal phalanx of right middle finger**
CC Exclusion 7th character B see Appendix A PDX collection 1285
CC Exclusion 7th characters K & P see Appendix A PDX collection 0897
HAC 7th character B see Appendix B for HAC conditional logic

CC +7th **S62.643 Nondisplaced fracture of proximal phalanx of left middle finger**
CC Exclusion 7th character B see Appendix A PDX collection 1285
CC Exclusion 7th characters K & P see Appendix A PDX collection 0897
HAC 7th character B see Appendix B for HAC conditional logic

CC +7th **S62.644 Nondisplaced fracture of proximal phalanx of right ring finger**
CC Exclusion 7th character B see Appendix A PDX collection 1285
CC Exclusion 7th characters K & P see Appendix A PDX collection 0897
HAC 7th character B see Appendix B for HAC conditional logic

CC +7th **S62.645 Nondisplaced fracture of proximal phalanx of left ring finger**
CC Exclusion 7th character B see Appendix A PDX collection 1285
CC Exclusion 7th characters K & P see Appendix A PDX collection 0897
HAC 7th character B see Appendix B for HAC conditional logic

CC +7th **S62.646 Nondisplaced fracture of proximal phalanx of right little finger**
CC Exclusion 7th character B see Appendix A PDX collection 1285
CC Exclusion 7th characters K & P see Appendix A PDX collection 0897
HAC 7th character B see Appendix B for HAC conditional logic

CC +7th **S62.647 Nondisplaced fracture of proximal phalanx of left little finger**
CC Exclusion 7th character B see Appendix A PDX collection 1285
CC Exclusion 7th characters K & P see Appendix A PDX collection 0897
HAC 7th character B see Appendix B for HAC conditional logic

CC +7th **S62.648 Nondisplaced fracture of proximal phalanx of other finger**
Nondisplaced fracture of proximal phalanx of specified finger with unspecified laterality
CC Exclusion 7th character B see Appendix A PDX collection 1285
CC Exclusion 7th characters K & P see Appendix A PDX collection 0897
HAC 7th character B see Appendix B for HAC conditional logic

CC +7th **S62.649 Nondisplaced fracture of proximal phalanx of unspecified finger**
CC Exclusion 7th character B see Appendix A PDX collection 1285
CC Exclusion 7th characters K & P see Appendix A PDX collection 0897
HAC 7th character B see Appendix B for HAC conditional logic

\+ **S62.65 Nondisplaced fracture of medial phalanx of finger**

CC +7th **S62.650 Nondisplaced fracture of medial phalanx of right index finger**
CC Exclusion 7th character B see Appendix A PDX collection 1285
CC Exclusion 7th characters K & P see Appendix A PDX collection 0897
HAC 7th character B see Appendix B for HAC conditional logic

CC +7th **S62.651 Nondisplaced fracture of medial phalanx of left index finger**
CC Exclusion 7th character B see Appendix A PDX collection 1285
CC Exclusion 7th characters K & P see Appendix A PDX collection 0897
HAC 7th character B see Appendix B for HAC conditional logic

CC +7th **S62.652 Nondisplaced fracture of medial phalanx of right middle finger**
CC Exclusion 7th character B see Appendix A PDX collection 1285
CC Exclusion 7th characters K & P see Appendix A PDX collection 0897
HAC 7th character B see Appendix B for HAC conditional logic

CC +7th **S62.653 Nondisplaced fracture of medial phalanx of left middle finger**
CC Exclusion 7th character B see Appendix A PDX collection 1285
CC Exclusion 7th characters K & P see Appendix A PDX collection 0897
HAC 7th character B see Appendix B for HAC conditional logic

CC +7th **S62.654 Nondisplaced fracture of medial phalanx of right ring finger**
CC Exclusion 7th character B see Appendix A PDX collection 1285
CC Exclusion 7th characters K & P see Appendix A PDX collection 0897
HAC 7th character B see Appendix B for HAC conditional logic

CC +7th **S62.655 Nondisplaced fracture of medial phalanx of left ring finger**
CC Exclusion 7th character B see Appendix A PDX collection 1285
CC Exclusion 7th characters K & P see Appendix A PDX collection 0897
HAC 7th character B see Appendix B for HAC conditional logic

CC +7th **S62.656 Nondisplaced fracture of medial phalanx of right little finger**
CC Exclusion 7th character B see Appendix A PDX collection 1285
CC Exclusion 7th characters K & P see Appendix A PDX collection 0897
HAC 7th character B see Appendix B for HAC conditional logic

CC +7th **S62.657 Nondisplaced fracture of medial phalanx of left little finger**
CC Exclusion 7th character B see Appendix A PDX collection 1285
CC Exclusion 7th characters K & P see Appendix A PDX collection 0897
HAC 7th character B see Appendix B for HAC conditional logic

CC +7th **S62.658 Nondisplaced fracture of medial phalanx of other finger**
Nondisplaced fracture of medial phalanx of specified finger with unspecified laterality
CC Exclusion 7th character B see Appendix A PDX collection 1285
CC Exclusion 7th characters K & P see Appendix A PDX collection 0897
HAC 7th character B see Appendix B for HAC conditional logic

CC +7th **S62.659 Nondisplaced fracture of medial phalanx of unspecified finger**
CC Exclusion 7th character B see Appendix A PDX collection 1285
CC Exclusion 7th characters K & P see Appendix A PDX collection 0897
HAC 7th character B see Appendix B for HAC conditional logic

\+ **S62.66 Nondisplaced fracture of distal phalanx of finger**

CC +7th **S62.660 Nondisplaced fracture of distal phalanx of right index finger**
CC Exclusion 7th character B see Appendix A PDX collection 1285
CC Exclusion 7th characters K & P see Appendix A PDX collection 0897
HAC 7th character B see Appendix B for HAC conditional logic

CC +7th **S62.661 Nondisplaced fracture of distal phalanx of left index finger**
CC Exclusion 7th character B see Appendix A PDX collection 1285
CC Exclusion 7th characters K & P see Appendix A PDX collection 0897
HAC 7th character B see Appendix B for HAC conditional logic

CC +7th **S62.662 Nondisplaced fracture of distal phalanx of right middle finger**
CC Exclusion 7th character B see Appendix A PDX collection 1285
CC Exclusion 7th characters K & P see Appendix A PDX collection 0897
HAC 7th character B see Appendix B for HAC conditional logic

CC +7th **S62.663 Nondisplaced fracture of distal phalanx of left middle finger**
CC Exclusion 7th character B see Appendix A PDX collection 1285
CC Exclusion 7th characters K & P see Appendix A PDX collection 0897
HAC 7th character B see Appendix B for HAC conditional logic

CC +7th **S62.664 Nondisplaced fracture of distal phalanx of right ring finger**
CC Exclusion 7th character B see Appendix A PDX collection 1285
CC Exclusion 7th characters K & P see Appendix A PDX collection 0897
HAC 7th character B see Appendix B for HAC conditional logic

CC +7th **S62.665 Nondisplaced fracture of distal phalanx of left ring finger**
CC Exclusion 7th character B see Appendix A PDX collection 1285
CC Exclusion 7th characters K & P see Appendix A PDX collection 0897
HAC 7th character B see Appendix B for HAC conditional logic

CC +7th **S62.666 Nondisplaced fracture of distal phalanx of right little finger**
CC Exclusion 7th character B see Appendix A PDX collection 1285
CC Exclusion 7th characters K & P see Appendix A PDX collection 0897
HAC 7th character B see Appendix B for HAC conditional logic

CC +7th **S62.667 Nondisplaced fracture of distal phalanx of left little finger**
CC Exclusion 7th character B see Appendix A PDX collection 1285
CC Exclusion 7th characters K & P see Appendix A PDX collection 0897
HAC 7th character B see Appendix B for HAC conditional logic

CC +7th **S62.668 Nondisplaced fracture of distal phalanx of other finger**
Nondisplaced fracture of distal phalanx of specified finger with unspecified laterali
CC Exclusion 7th character B see Appendix A PDX collection 1285
CC Exclusion 7th characters K & P see Appendix A PDX collection 0897
HAC 7th character B see Appendix B for HAC conditional logic

CC +7th **S62.669 Nondisplaced fracture of distal phalanx o unspecified finger**
CC Exclusion 7th character B see Appendix A PDX collection 1285
CC Exclusion 7th characters K & P see Appendix A PDX collection 0897
HAC 7th character B see Appendix B for HAC conditional logic

\+ **S62.9 Unspecified fracture of wrist and hand**

CC X+7th **S62.90 Unspecified fracture of unspecified wrist and hand**
CC Exclusion 7th character B see Appendix A PDX collection 1286
CC Exclusion 7th characters K & P see Appendix A PDX collection 0897
HAC 7th character B see Appendix B for HAC conditional logic

CC X+7th **S62.91 Unspecified fracture of right wrist and hand**
CC Exclusion 7th character B see Appendix A PDX collection 1287
CC Exclusion 7th characters K & P see Appendix A PDX collection 0897
HAC 7th character B see Appendix B for HAC conditional logic

CC X+7th **S62.92 Unspecified fracture of left wrist and hand**
CC Exclusion 7th character B see Appendix A PDX collection 1287
CC Exclusion 7th characters K & P see Appendix A PDX collection 0897
HAC 7th character B see Appendix B for HAC conditional logic

S63 Dislocation and sprain of joints and ligaments at wrist and hand lev

Includes: avulsion of joint or ligament at wrist and hand level
laceration of cartilage, joint or ligament at wrist and hand le
sprain of cartilage, joint or ligament at wrist and hand level
traumatic hemarthrosis of joint or ligament at wrist and han level
traumatic rupture of joint or ligament at wrist and hand leve
traumatic subluxation of joint or ligament at wrist and hand le
traumatic tear of joint or ligament at wrist and hand level

Code also any associated open wound

Excludes2: *strain of muscle, fascia and tendon of wrist and hand (S66.-*

The appropriate 7th character is to be added to each code from category S63
A initial encounter
D subsequent encounter
S sequela

\+ **S63.0 Subluxation and dislocation of wrist and hand joints**

\+ **S63.00 Unspecified subluxation and dislocation of wrist and hand**
Dislocation of carpal bone NOS
Dislocation of distal end of radius NOS
Subluxation of carpal bone NOS

Subluxation of distal end of radius NOS

+7th **S63.001** **Unspecified subluxation of right wrist and hand**
+7th **S63.002** **Unspecified subluxation of left wrist and hand**
+7th **S63.003** **Unspecified subluxation of unspecified wrist and hand**
+7th **S63.004** **Unspecified dislocation of right wrist and hand**
+7th **S63.005** **Unspecified dislocation of left wrist and hand**
+7th **S63.006** **Unspecified dislocation of unspecified wrist and hand**

+ **S63.01** **Subluxation and dislocation of distal radioulnar joint**
+7th **S63.011** **Subluxation of distal radioulnar joint of right wrist**
+7th **S63.012** **Subluxation of distal radioulnar joint of left wrist**
+7th **S63.013** **Subluxation of distal radioulnar joint of unspecified wrist**
+7th **S63.014** **Dislocation of distal radioulnar joint of right wrist**
+7th **S63.015** **Dislocation of distal radioulnar joint of left wrist**
+7th **S63.016** **Dislocation of distal radioulnar joint of unspecified wrist**

+ **S63.02** **Subluxation and dislocation of radiocarpal joint**
+7th **S63.021** **Subluxation of radiocarpal joint of right wrist**
+7th **S63.022** **Subluxation of radiocarpal joint of left wrist**
+7th **S63.023** **Subluxation of radiocarpal joint of unspecified wrist**
+7th **S63.024** **Dislocation of radiocarpal joint of right wrist**
+7th **S63.025** **Dislocation of radiocarpal joint of left wrist**
+7th **S63.026** **Dislocation of radiocarpal joint of unspecified wrist**

+ **S63.03** **Subluxation and dislocation of midcarpal joint**
+7th **S63.031** **Subluxation of midcarpal joint of right wrist**
+7th **S63.032** **Subluxation of midcarpal joint of left wrist**
+7th **S63.033** **Subluxation of midcarpal joint of unspecified wrist**
+7th **S63.034** **Dislocation of midcarpal joint of right wrist**
+7th **S63.035** **Dislocation of midcarpal joint of left wrist**
+7th **S63.036** **Dislocation of midcarpal joint of unspecified wrist**

+ **S63.04** **Subluxation and dislocation of carpometacarpal joint of thumb**

Excludes2: *interphalangeal subluxation and dislocation of thumb (S63.1-)*

+7th **S63.041** **Subluxation of carpometacarpal joint of right thumb**
+7th **S63.042** **Subluxation of carpometacarpal joint of left thumb**
+7th **S63.043** **Subluxation of carpometacarpal joint of unspecified thumb**
+7th **S63.044** **Dislocation of carpometacarpal joint of right thumb**
+7th **S63.045** **Dislocation of carpometacarpal joint of left thumb**
+7th **S63.046** **Dislocation of carpometacarpal joint of unspecified thumb**

+ **S63.05** **Subluxation and dislocation of other carpometacarpal joint**

Excludes2: *subluxation and dislocation of carpometacarpaljointofthumb(S63.04-)*

+7th **S63.051** **Subluxation of other carpometacarpal joint of right hand**
+7th **S63.052** **Subluxation of other carpometacarpal joint of left hand**
+7th **S63.053** **Subluxation of other carpometacarpal joint of unspecified hand**
+7th **S63.054** **Dislocation of other carpometacarpal joint of right hand**
+7th **S63.055** **Dislocation of other carpometacarpal joint of left hand**
+7th **S63.056** **Dislocation of other carpometacarpal joint of unspecified hand**

+ **S63.06** **Subluxation and dislocation of metacarpal (bone), proximal end**
+7th **S63.061** **Subluxation of metacarpal (bone), proximal end of right hand**
+7th **S63.062** **Subluxation of metacarpal (bone), proximal end of left hand**
+7th **S63.063** **Subluxation of metacarpal (bone), proximal end of unspecified hand**
+7th **S63.064** **Dislocation of metacarpal (bone), proximal end of right hand**
+7th **S63.065** **Dislocation of metacarpal (bone), proximal end of left hand**
+7th **S63.066** **Dislocation of metacarpal (bone), proximal end of unspecified hand**

+ **S63.07** **Subluxation and dislocation of distal end of ulna**
+7th **S63.071** **Subluxation of distal end of right ulna**
+7th **S63.072** **Subluxation of distal end of left ulna**
+7th **S63.073** **Subluxation of distal end of unspecified ulna**
+7th **S63.074** **Dislocation of distal end of right ulna**
+7th **S63.075** **Dislocation of distal end of left ulna**
+7th **S63.076** **Dislocation of distal end of unspecified ulna**

+ **S63.09** **Other subluxation and dislocation of wrist and hand**
+7th **S63.091** **Other subluxation of right wrist and hand**
+7th **S63.092** **Other subluxation of left wrist and hand**
+7th **S63.093** **Other subluxation of unspecified wrist and hand**
+7th **S63.094** **Other dislocation of right wrist and hand**
+7th **S63.095** **Other dislocation of left wrist and hand**
+7th **S63.096** **Other dislocation of unspecified wrist and hand**

+ **S63.1** **Subluxation and dislocation of thumb**

+ **S63.10** **Unspecified subluxation and dislocation of thumb**
+7th **S63.101** **Unspecified subluxation of right thumb**
+7th **S63.102** **Unspecified subluxation of left thumb**
+7th **S63.103** **Unspecified subluxation of unspecified thumb**
+7th **S63.104** **Unspecified dislocation of right thumb**
+7th **S63.105** **Unspecified dislocation of left thumb**
+7th **S63.106** **Unspecified dislocation of unspecified thumb**

+ **S63.11** **Subluxation and dislocation of metacarpophalangeal joint of thumb**
+7th **S63.111** **Subluxation of metacarpophalangeal joint of right thumb**
+7th **S63.112** **Subluxation of metacarpophalangeal joint of left thumb**
+7th **S63.113** **Subluxation of metacarpophalangeal joint of unspecified thumb**
+7th **S63.114** **Dislocation of metacarpophalangeal joint of right thumb**
+7th **S63.115** **Dislocation of metacarpophalangeal joint of left thumb**
+7th **S63.116** **Dislocation of metacarpophalangeal joint of unspecified thumb**

+ **S63.12** **Subluxation and dislocation of unspecified interphalangeal joint of thumb**
+7th **S63.121** **Subluxation of unspecified interphalangeal joint of right thumb**
+7th **S63.122** **Subluxation of unspecified interphalangeal joint of left thumb**
+7th **S63.123** **Subluxation of unspecified interphalangeal joint of unspecified thumb**
+7th **S63.124** **Dislocation of unspecified interphalangeal joint of right thumb**
+7th **S63.125** **Dislocation of unspecified interphalangeal joint of left thumb**
+7th **S63.126** **Dislocation of unspecified interphalangeal joint of unspecified thumb**

+ **S63.13** **Subluxation and dislocation of proximal interphalangeal joint of thumb**
+7th **S63.131** **Subluxation of proximal interphalangeal joint of right thumb**
+7th **S63.132** **Subluxation of proximal interphalangeal joint of left thumb**
+7th **S63.133** **Subluxation of proximal interphalangeal joint of unspecified thumb**
+7th **S63.134** **Dislocation of proximal interphalangeal joint of right thumb**
+7th **S63.135** **Dislocation of proximal interphalangeal joint of left thumb**
+7th **S63.136** **Dislocation of proximal interphalangeal joint of unspecified thumb**

+ **S63.14** **Subluxation and dislocation of distal interphalangeal joint of thumb**
+7th **S63.141** **Subluxation of distal interphalangeal joint of right thumb**
+7th **S63.142** **Subluxation of distal interphalangeal joint of left thumb**
+7th **S63.143** **Subluxation of distal interphalangeal joint of unspecified thumb**
+7th **S63.144** **Dislocation of distal interphalangeal joint of right thumb**

+7th **S63.145** **Dislocation of distal interphalangeal joint of left thumb**

+7th **S63.146** **Dislocation of distal interphalangeal joint of unspecified thumb**

\+ **S63.2** **Subluxation and dislocation of other finger(s)**

Excludes2: *subluxation and dislocation of thumb (S63.1-)*

\+ **S63.20** **Unspecified subluxation of other finger**

+7th **S63.200** **Unspecified subluxation of right index finger**

+7th **S63.201** **Unspecified subluxation of left index finger**

+7th **S63.202** **Unspecified subluxation of right middle finger**

+7th **S63.203** **Unspecified subluxation of left middle finger**

+7th **S63.204** **Unspecified subluxation of right ring finger**

+7th **S63.205** **Unspecified subluxation of left ring finger**

+7th **S63.206** **Unspecified subluxation of right little finger**

+7th **S63.207** **Unspecified subluxation of left little finger**

+7th **S63.208** **Unspecified subluxation of other finger**

Unspecified subluxation of specified finger with unspecified laterality

+7th **S63.209** **Unspecified subluxation of unspecified finger**

\+ **S63.21** **Subluxation of metacarpophalangeal joint of finger**

+7th **S63.210** **Subluxation of metacarpophalangeal joint of right index finger**

+7th **S63.211** **Subluxation of metacarpophalangeal joint of left index finger**

+7th **S63.212** **Subluxation of metacarpophalangeal joint of right middle finger**

+7th **S63.213** **Subluxation of metacarpophalangeal joint of left middle finger**

+7th **S63.214** **Subluxation of metacarpophalangeal joint of right ring finger**

+7th **S63.215** **Subluxation of metacarpophalangeal joint of left ring finger**

+7th **S63.216** **Subluxation of metacarpophalangeal joint of right little finger**

+7th **S63.217** **Subluxation of metacarpophalangeal joint of left little finger**

+7th **S63.218** **Subluxation of metacarpophalangeal joint of other finger**

Subluxation of metacarpophalangeal joint of specified finger with unspecified laterality

+7th **S63.219** **Subluxation of metacarpophalangeal joint of unspecified finger**

\+ **S63.22** **Subluxation of unspecified interphalangeal joint of finger**

+7th **S63.220** **Subluxation of unspecified interphalangeal joint of right index finger**

+7th **S63.221** **Subluxation of unspecified interphalangeal joint of left index finger**

+7th **S63.222** **Subluxation of unspecified interphalangeal joint of right middle finger**

+7th **S63.223** **Subluxation of unspecified interphalangeal joint of left middle finger**

+7th **S63.224** **Subluxation of unspecified interphalangeal joint of right ring finger**

+7th **S63.225** **Subluxation of unspecified interphalangeal joint of left ring finger**

+7th **S63.226** **Subluxation of unspecified interphalangeal joint of right little finger**

+7th **S63.227** **Subluxation of unspecified interphalangeal joint of left little finger**

+7th **S63.228** **Subluxation of unspecified interphalangeal joint of other finger**

Subluxation of unspecified interphalangeal joint of specified finger with unspecified laterality

+7th **S63.229** **Subluxation of unspecified interphalangeal joint of unspecified finger**

\+ **S63.23** **Subluxation of proximal interphalangeal joint of finger**

+7th **S63.230** **Subluxation of proximal interphalangeal joint of right index finger**

+7th **S63.231** **Subluxation of proximal interphalangeal joint of left index finger**

+7th **S63.232** **Subluxation of proximal interphalangeal joint of right middle finger**

+7th **S63.233** **Subluxation of proximal interphalangeal joint of left middle finger**

+7th **S63.234** **Subluxation of proximal interphalangeal joint of right ring finger**

+7th **S63.235** **Subluxation of proximal interphalangeal joint of left ring finger**

+7th **S63.236** **Subluxation of proximal interphalangeal joint of right little finger**

+7th **S63.237** **Subluxation of proximal interphalangeal joint of left little finger**

+7th **S63.238** **Subluxation of proximal interphalangeal joint of other finger**

Subluxation of proximal interphalangeal joint of specified finger with unspecified laterality

+7th **S63.239** **Subluxation of proximal interphalangeal joint of unspecified finger**

\+ **S63.24** **Subluxation of distal interphalangeal joint of finger**

+7th **S63.240** **Subluxation of distal interphalangeal join right index finger**

+7th **S63.241** **Subluxation of distal interphalangeal join left index finger**

+7th **S63.242** **Subluxation of distal interphalangeal join right middle finger**

+7th **S63.243** **Subluxation of distal interphalangeal join left middle finger**

+7th **S63.244** **Subluxation of distal interphalangeal join right ring finger**

+7th **S63.245** **Subluxation of distal interphalangeal join left ring finger**

+7th **S63.246** **Subluxation of distal interphalangeal join right little finger**

+7th **S63.247** **Subluxation of distal interphalangeal join left little finger**

+7th **S63.248** **Subluxation of distal interphalangeal join other finger**

Subluxation of distal interphalangeal joint specified finger with unspecified lateralit

+7th **S63.249** **Subluxation of distal interphalangeal join unspecified finger**

\+ **S63.25** **Unspecified dislocation of other finger**

+7th **S63.250** **Unspecified dislocation of right index fing**

+7th **S63.251** **Unspecified dislocation of left index finger**

+7th **S63.252** **Unspecified dislocation of right middle fin**

+7th **S63.253** **Unspecified dislocation of left middle fing**

+7th **S63.254** **Unspecified dislocation of right ring finge**

+7th **S63.255** **Unspecified dislocation of left ring finger**

+7th **S63.256** **Unspecified dislocation of right little finge**

+7th **S63.257** **Unspecified dislocation of left little finger**

+7th **S63.258** **Unspecified dislocation of other finger**

Unspecified dislocation of specified finger with unspecified laterality

+7th **S63.259** **Unspecified dislocation of unspecified fing**

Unspecified dislocation of specified finger with unspecified laterality

\+ **S63.26** **Dislocation of metacarpophalangeal joint of finger**

+7th **S63.260** **Dislocation of metacarpophalangeal joint right index finger**

+7th **S63.261** **Dislocation of metacarpophalangeal joint left index finger**

+7th **S63.262** **Dislocation of metacarpophalangeal joint right middle finger**

+7th **S63.263** **Dislocation of metacarpophalangeal joint left middle finger**

+7th **S63.264** **Dislocation of metacarpophalangeal joint right ring finger**

+7th **S63.265** **Dislocation of metacarpophalangeal joint left ring finger**

+7th **S63.266** **Dislocation of metacarpophalangeal joint right little finger**

+7th **S63.267** **Dislocation of metacarpophalangeal joint left little finger**

+7th **S63.268** **Dislocation of metacarpophalangeal joint other finger**

Dislocation of metacarpophalangeal joint o specified finger with unspecified lateralit

+7th **S63.269** **Dislocation of metacarpophalangeal joint unspecified finger**

\+ **S63.27** **Dislocation of unspecified interphalangeal joint of finger**

+7th **S63.270** **Dislocation of unspecified interphalangeal joint of right index finger**

+7th **S63.271** **Dislocation of unspecified interphalangeal joint of left index finger**

+7th **S63.272** **Dislocation of unspecified interphalangeal joint of right middle finger**

+7th **S63.273** **Dislocation of unspecified interphalangeal joint of left middle finger**

+7th **S63.274 Dislocation of unspecified interphalangeal joint of right ring finger**
+7th **S63.275 Dislocation of unspecified interphalangeal joint of left ring finger**
+7th **S63.276 Dislocation of unspecified interphalangeal joint of right little finger**
+7th **S63.277 Dislocation of unspecified interphalangeal joint of left little finger**
+7th **S63.278 Dislocation of unspecified interphalangeal joint of other finger**
Dislocation of unspecified interphalangeal joint of specified finger with unspecified laterality
+7th **S63.279 Dislocation of unspecified interphalangeal joint of unspecified finger**
Dislocation of unspecified interphalangeal joint of specified finger without specified laterality

+ **S63.28 Dislocation of proximal interphalangeal joint of finger**
+7th **S63.280 Dislocation of proximal interphalangeal joint of right index finger**
+7th **S63.281 Dislocation of proximal interphalangeal joint of left index finger**
+7th **S63.282 Dislocation of proximal interphalangeal joint of right middle finger**
+7th **S63.283 Dislocation of proximal interphalangeal joint of left middle finger**
+7th **S63.284 Dislocation of proximal interphalangeal joint of right ring finger**
+7th **S63.285 Dislocation of proximal interphalangeal joint of left ring finger**
+7th **S63.286 Dislocation of proximal interphalangeal joint of right little finger**
+7th **S63.287 Dislocation of proximal interphalangeal joint of left little finger**
+7th **S63.288 Dislocation of proximal interphalangeal joint of other finger**
Dislocation of proximal interphalangeal joint of specified finger with unspecified laterality
+7th **S63.289 Dislocation of proximal interphalangeal joint of unspecified finger**

+ **S63.29 Dislocation of distal interphalangeal joint of finger**
+7th **S63.290 Dislocation of distal interphalangeal joint of right index finger**
+7th **S63.291 Dislocation of distal interphalangeal joint of left index finger**
+7th **S63.292 Dislocation of distal interphalangeal joint of right middle finger**
+7th **S63.293 Dislocation of distal interphalangeal joint of left middle finger**
+7th **S63.294 Dislocation of distal interphalangeal joint of right ring finger**
+7th **S63.295 Dislocation of distal interphalangeal joint of left ring finger**
+7th **S63.296 Dislocation of distal interphalangeal joint of right little finger**
+7th **S63.297 Dislocation of distal interphalangeal joint of left little finger**
+7th **S63.298 Dislocation of distal interphalangeal joint of other finger**
Dislocation of distal interphalangeal joint of specified finger with unspecified laterality
+7th **S63.299 Dislocation of distal interphalangeal joint of unspecified finger**

+ **S63.3 Traumatic rupture of ligament of wrist**
+ **S63.30 Traumatic rupture of unspecified ligament of wrist**
+7th **S63.301 Traumatic rupture of unspecified ligament of right wrist**
+7th **S63.302 Traumatic rupture of unspecified ligament of left wrist**
+7th **S63.309 Traumatic rupture of unspecified ligament of unspecified wrist**

+ **S63.31 Traumatic rupture of collateral ligament of wrist**
+7th **S63.311 Traumatic rupture of collateral ligament of right wrist**
+7th **S63.312 Traumatic rupture of collateral ligament of left wrist**
+7th **S63.319 Traumatic rupture of collateral ligament of unspecified wrist**

+ **S63.32 Traumatic rupture of radiocarpal ligament**
+7th **S63.321 Traumatic rupture of right radiocarpal ligament**
+7th **S63.322 Traumatic rupture of left radiocarpal ligament**
+7th **S63.329 Traumatic rupture of unspecified radiocarpal ligament**

+ **S63.33 Traumatic rupture of ulnocarpal (palmar) ligament**
+7th **S63.331 Traumatic rupture of right ulnocarpal (palmar) ligament**
+7th **S63.332 Traumatic rupture of left ulnocarpal (palmar) ligament**
+7th **S63.339 Traumatic rupture of unspecified ulnocarpal (palmar) ligament**

+ **S63.39 Traumatic rupture of other ligament of wrist**
+7th **S63.391 Traumatic rupture of other ligament of right wrist**
+7th **S63.392 Traumatic rupture of other ligament of left wrist**
+7th **S63.399 Traumatic rupture of other ligament of unspecified wrist**

+ **S63.4 Traumatic rupture of ligament of finger at metacarpophalangeal and interphalangeal joint(s)**
+ **S63.40 Traumatic rupture of unspecified ligament of finger at metacarpophalangeal and interphalangeal joint**
+7th **S63.400 Traumatic rupture of unspecified ligament of right index finger at metacarpophalangeal and interphalangeal joint**
+7th **S63.401 Traumatic rupture of unspecified ligament of left index finger at metacarpophalangeal and interphalangeal joint**
+7th **S63.402 Traumatic rupture of unspecified ligament of right middle finger at metacarpophalangeal and interphalangeal joint**
+7th **S63.403 Traumatic rupture of unspecified ligament of left middle finger at metacarpophalangeal and interphalangeal joint**
+7th **S63.404 Traumatic rupture of unspecified ligament of right ring finger at metacarpophalangeal and interphalangeal joint**
+7th **S63.405 Traumatic rupture of unspecified ligament of left ring finger at metacarpophalangeal and interphalangeal joint**
+7th **S63.406 Traumatic rupture of unspecified ligament of right little finger at metacarpophalangeal and interphalangeal joint**
+7th **S63.407 Traumatic rupture of unspecified ligament of left little finger at metacarpophalangeal and interphalangeal joint**
+7th **S63.408 Traumatic rupture of unspecified ligament of other finger at metacarpophalangeal and interphalangeal joint**
Traumatic rupture of unspecified ligament of specified finger with unspecified laterality at metacarpophalangeal and interphalangeal joint
+7th **S63.409 Traumatic rupture of unspecified ligament of unspecified finger at metacarpophalangeal and interphalangeal joint**

+ **S63.41 Traumatic rupture of collateral ligament of finger at metacarpophalangeal and interphalangeal joint**
+7th **S63.410 Traumatic rupture of collateral ligament of right index finger at metacarpophalangeal and interphalangeal joint**
+7th **S63.411 Traumatic rupture of collateral ligament of left index finger at metacarpophalangeal and interphalangeal joint**
+7th **S63.412 Traumatic rupture of collateral ligament of right middle finger at metacarpophalangeal and interphalangeal joint**
+7th **S63.413 Traumatic rupture of collateral ligament of left middle finger at metacarpophalangeal and interphalangeal joint**
+7th **S63.414 Traumatic rupture of collateral ligament of right ring finger at metacarpophalangeal and interphalangeal joint**
+7th **S63.415 Traumatic rupture of collateral ligament of left ring finger at metacarpophalangeal and interphalangeal joint**
+7th **S63.416 Traumatic rupture of collateral ligament of right little finger at metacarpophalangeal and interphalangeal joint**
+7th **S63.417 Traumatic rupture of collateral ligament of left little finger at metacarpophalangeal and interphalangeal joint**

+7th **S63.418 Traumatic rupture of collateral ligament of other finger at metacarpophalangeal and interphalangeal joint**
Traumatic rupture of collateral ligament of specified finger with unspecified laterality at metacarpophalangeal and interphalangeal joint

+7th **S63.419 Traumatic rupture of collateral ligament of unspecified finger at metacarpophalangeal and interphalangeal joint**

\+ **S63.42 Traumatic rupture of palmar ligament of finger at metacarpophalangeal and interphalangeal joint**

+7th **S63.420 Traumatic rupture of palmarligament of right index finger at metacarpophalangeal and interphalangeal joint**

+7th **S63.421 Traumatic rupture of palmar ligament of left index finger at metacarpophalangeal and interphalangeal joint**

+7th **S63.422 Traumatic rupture of palmar ligament of right middle finger at metacarpophalangeal and interphalangeal joint**

+7th **S63.423 Traumatic rupture of palmar ligament of left middle finger at metacarpophalangeal and interphalangeal joint**

+7th **S63.424 Traumatic rupture of palmar ligament of right ring finger at metacarpophalangeal and interphalangeal joint**

+7th **S63.425 Traumatic rupture of palmar ligament of left ring finger at metacarpophalangeal and interphalangeal joint**

+7th **S63.426 Traumatic rupture of palmar ligament of right little finger at metacarpophalangeal and interphalangeal joint**

+7th **S63.427 Traumatic rupture of palmar ligament of left little finger at metacarpophalangeal and interphalangeal joint**

+7th **S63.428 Traumatic rupture of palmar ligament of other finger at metacarpophalangeal and interphalangeal joint**
Traumatic rupture of palmar ligament of specified finger with unspecified laterality at metacarpophalangeal and interphalangeal joint

+7th **S63.429 Traumatic rupture of palmar ligament of unspecified finger at metacarpophalangeal and interphalangeal joint**

\+ **S63.43 Traumatic rupture of volar plate of finger at metacarpophalangeal and interphalangeal joint**

+7th **S63.430 Traumatic rupture of volar plate of right index finger at metacarpophalangeal and interphalangeal joint**

+7th **S63.431 Traumatic rupture of volar plate of left index finger at metacarpophalangeal and interphalangeal joint**

+7th **S63.432 Traumatic rupture of volar plate of right middle finger at metacarpophalangeal and interphalangeal joint**

+7th **S63.433 Traumatic rupture of volar plate of left middle finger at metacarpophalangeal and interphalangeal joint**

+7th **S63.434 Traumatic rupture of volar plate of right ring finger at metacarpophalangeal and interphalangeal joint**

+7th **S63.435 Traumatic rupture of volar plate of left ring finger at metacarpophalangeal and interphalangeal joint**

+7th **S63.436 Traumatic rupture of volar plate of right little finger at metacarpophalangeal and interphalangeal joint**

+7th **S63.437 Traumatic rupture of volar plate of left little finger at metacarpophalangeal and interphalangeal joint**

+7th **S63.438 Traumatic rupture of volar plate of other finger at metacarpophalangeal and interphalangeal joint**
Traumatic rupture of volar plate of specified finger with unspecified laterality at metacarpophalangeal and interphalangeal joint

+7th **S63.439 Traumatic rupture of volar plate of unspecified finger at metacarpophalangeal and interphalangeal joint**

\+ **S63.49 Traumatic rupture of other ligament of finger at metacarpophalangeal and interphalangeal joint**

+7th **S63.490 Traumatic rupture of other ligament of r index finger at metacarpophalangeal and interphalangeal joint**

+7th **S63.491 Traumatic rupture of other ligament of l index finger at metacarpophalangeal and interphalangeal joint**

+7th **S63.492 Traumatic rupture of other ligament of r middle finger at metacarpophalangeal an interphalangeal joint**

+7th **S63.493 Traumatic rupture of other ligament of l middle finger at metacarpophalangeal an interphalangeal joint**

+7th **S63.494 Traumatic rupture of other ligament of r ring finger at metacarpophalangeal and interphalangeal joint**

+7th **S63.495 Traumatic rupture of other ligament of l ring finger at metacarpophalangeal and interphalangeal joint**

+7th **S63.496 Traumatic rupture of other ligament of r little finger at metacarpophalangeal and interphalangeal joint**

+7th **S63.497 Traumatic rupture of other ligament of l little finger at metacarpophalangeal and interphalangeal joint**

+7th **S63.498 Traumatic rupture of other ligament of other finger at metacarpophalangeal and interphalangeal joint**
Traumatic rupture of ligament of specified finger with unspecified laterality at metacarpophalangeal and interphalange joint

+7th **S63.499 Traumatic rupture of other ligament of unspecified finger at metacarpophalange and interphalangeal joint**

\+ **S63.5 Other and unspecified sprain of wrist**

\+ **S63.50 Unspecified sprain of wrist**

+7th **S63.501 Unspecified sprain of right wrist**

+7th **S63.502 Unspecified sprain of left wrist**

+7th **S63.509 Unspecified sprain of unspecified wrist**

\+ **S63.51 Sprain of carpal (joint)**

+7th **S63.511 Sprain of carpal joint of right wrist**

+7th **S63.512 Sprain of carpal joint of left wrist**

+7th **S63.519 Sprain of carpal joint of unspecified wris**

\+ **S63.52 Sprain of radiocarpal joint**
Excludes1: *traumatic rupture of radiocarpal ligame (S63.32-)*

+7th **S63.521 Sprain of radiocarpal joint of right wrist**

+7th **S63.522 Sprain of radiocarpal joint of left wrist**

+7th **S63.529 Sprain of radiocarpal joint of unspecified wrist**

\+ **S63.59 Other specified sprain of wrist**

+7th **S63.591 Other specified sprain of right wrist**

+7th **S63.592 Other specified sprain of left wrist**

+7th **S63.599 Other specified sprain of unspecified wri**

\+ **S63.6 Other and unspecified sprain of finger(s)**
Excludes1: *traumatic rupture of ligament of finger at metacarpophalangealandinterphalangealjoint((S63.4-)*

\+ **S63.60 Unspecified sprain of thumb**

+7th **S63.601 Unspecified sprain of right thumb**

+7th **S63.602 Unspecified sprain of left thumb**

+7th **S63.609 Unspecified sprain of unspecified thumb**

\+ **S63.61 Unspecified sprain of other and unspecified finger(**

+7th **S63.610 Unspecified sprain of right index finger**

+7th **S63.611 Unspecified sprain of left index finger**

+7th **S63.612 Unspecified sprain of right middle finger**

+7th **S63.613 Unspecified sprain of left middle finger**

+7th **S63.614 Unspecified sprain of right ring finger**

+7th **S63.615 Unspecified sprain of left ring finger**

+7th **S63.616 Unspecified sprain of right little finger**

+7th **S63.617 Unspecified sprain of left little finger**

+7th **S63.618 Unspecified sprain of other finger**
Unspecified sprain of specified finger with unspecified laterality

+7th **S63.619 Unspecified sprain of unspecified finger**

\+ **S63.62 Sprain of interphalangeal joint of thumb**

+7th **S63.621 Sprain of interphalangeal joint of right thumb**

+7th **S63.622 Sprain of interphalangeal joint of left thu**

+7th **S63.629 Sprain of interphalangeal joint of unspecified thumb**
+ **S63.63 Sprain of interphalangeal joint of other and unspecified finger(s)**
+7th **S63.630 Sprain of interphalangeal joint of right index finger**
+7th **S63.631 Sprain of interphalangeal joint of left index finger**
+7th **S63.632 Sprain of interphalangeal joint of right middle finger**
+7th **S63.633 Sprain of interphalangeal joint of left middle finger**
+7th **S63.634 Sprain of interphalangeal joint of right ring finger**
+7th **S63.635 Sprain of interphalangeal joint of left ring finger**
+7th **S63.636 Sprain of interphalangeal joint of right little finger**
+7th **S63.637 Sprain of interphalangeal joint of left little finger**
+7th **S63.638 Sprain of interphalangeal joint of other finger**
+7th **S63.639 Sprain of interphalangeal joint of unspecified finger**
+ **S63.64 Sprain of metacarpophalangeal joint of thumb**
+7th **S63.641 Sprain of metacarpophalangeal joint of right thumb**
+7th **S63.642 Sprain of metacarpophalangeal joint of left thumb**
+7th **S63.649 Sprain of metacarpophalangeal joint of unspecified thumb**
+ **S63.65 Sprain of metacarpophalangeal joint of other and unspecified finger(s)**
+7th **S63.650 Sprain of metacarpophalangeal joint of right index finger**
+7th **S63.651 Sprain of metacarpophalangeal joint of left index finger**
+7th **S63.652 Sprain of metacarpophalangeal joint of right middle finger**
+7th **S63.653 Sprain of metacarpophalangeal joint of left middle finger**
+7th **S63.654 Sprain of metacarpophalangeal joint of right ring finger**
+7th **S63.655 Sprain of metacarpophalangeal joint of left ring finger**
+7th **S63.656 Sprain of metacarpophalangeal joint of right little finger**
+7th **S63.657 Sprain of metacarpophalangeal joint of left little finger**
+7th **S63.658 Sprain of metacarpophalangeal joint of other finger**
Sprain of metacarpophalangeal joint of specified finger with unspecified laterality
+7th **S63.659 Sprain of metacarpophalangeal joint of unspecified finger**
+ **S63.68 Other sprain of thumb**
+7th **S63.681 Other sprain of right thumb**
+7th **S63.682 Other sprain of left thumb**
+7th **S63.689 Other sprain of unspecified thumb**
+ **S63.69 Other sprain of other and unspecified finger(s)**
+7th **S63.690 Other sprain of right index finger**
+7th **S63.691 Other sprain of left index finger**
+7th **S63.692 Other sprain of right middle finger**
+7th **S63.693 Other sprain of left middle finger**
+7th **S63.694 Other sprain of right ring finger**
+7th **S63.695 Other sprain of left ring finger**
+7th **S63.696 Other sprain of right little finger**
+7th **S63.697 Other sprain of left little finger**
+7th **S63.698 Other sprain of other finger**
Other sprain of specified finger with unspecified laterality
+7th **S63.699 Other sprain of unspecified finger**
+ **S63.8 Sprain of other part of wrist and hand**
+ **S63.8X Sprain of other part of wrist and hand**
+7th **S63.8X1 Sprain of other part of right wrist and hand**
+7th **S63.8X2 Sprain of other part of left wrist and hand**
+7th **S63.8X9 Sprain of other part of unspecified wrist and hand**
+ **S63.9 Sprain of unspecified part of wrist and hand**
X+7th **S63.90 Sprain of unspecified part of unspecified wrist and hand**
X+7th **S63.91 Sprain of unspecified part of right wrist and hand**
X+7th **S63.92 Sprain of unspecified part of left wrist and hand**

S64 Injury of nerves at wrist and hand level

Code also any associated open wound (S61.-)

The appropriate 7th character is to be added to each code from category S64
A initial encounter
D subsequent encounter
S sequela

+ **S64.0 Injury of ulnar nerve at wrist and hand level**
X+7th **S64.00 Injury of ulnar nerve at wrist and hand level of unspecified arm**
X+7th **S64.01 Injury of ulnar nerve at wrist and hand level of right arm**
X+7th **S64.02 Injury of ulnar nerve at wrist and hand level of left arm**
+ **S64.1 Injury of median nerve at wrist and hand level**
X+7th **S64.10 Injury of median nerve at wrist and hand level of unspecified arm**
X+7th **S64.11 Injury of median nerve at wrist and hand level of right arm**
X+7th **S64.12 Injury of median nerve at wrist and hand level of left arm**
+ **S64.2 Injury of radial nerve at wrist and hand level**
X+7th **S64.20 Injury of radial nerve at wrist and hand level of unspecified arm**
X+7th **S64.21 Injury of radial nerve at wrist and hand level of right arm**
X+7th **S64.22 Injury of radial nerve at wrist and hand level of left arm**
+ **S64.3 Injury of digital nerve of thumb**
X+7th **S64.30 Injury of digital nerve of unspecified thumb**
X+7th **S64.31 Injury of digital nerve of right thumb**
X+7th **S64.32 Injury of digital nerve of left thumb**
+ **S64.4 Injury of digital nerve of other and unspecified finger**
X+7th **S64.40 Injury of digital nerve of unspecified finger**
+ **S64.49 Injury of digital nerve of other finger**
+7th **S64.490 Injury of digital nerve of right index finger**
+7th **S64.491 Injury of digital nerve of left index finger**
+7th **S64.492 Injury of digital nerve of right middle finger**
+7th **S64.493 Injury of digital nerve of left middle finger**
+7th **S64.494 Injury of digital nerve of right ring finger**
+7th **S64.495 Injury of digital nerve of left ring finger**
+7th **S64.496 Injury of digital nerve of right little finger**
+7th **S64.497 Injury of digital nerve of left little finger**
+7th **S64.498 Injury of digital nerve of other finger**
Injury of digital nerve of specified finger with unspecified laterality
+ **S64.8 Injury of other nerves at wrist and hand level**
+ **S64.8X Injury of other nerves at wrist and hand level**
+7th **S64.8X1 Injury of other nerves at wrist and hand level of right arm**
+7th **S64.8X2 Injury of other nerves at wrist and hand level of left arm**
+7th **S64.8X9 Injury of other nerves at wrist and hand level of unspecified arm**
+ **S64.9 Injury of unspecified nerve at wrist and hand level**
X+7th **S64.90 Injury of unspecified nerve at wrist and hand level of unspecified arm**
X+7th **S64.91 Injury of unspecified nerve at wrist and hand level of right arm**
X+7th **S64.92 Injury of unspecified nerve at wrist and hand level of left arm**

S65 Injury of blood vessels at wrist and hand level

Code also any associated open wound (S61.-)

The appropriate 7th character is to be added to each code from category S65
A initial encounter
D subsequent encounter
S sequela

+ **S65.0 Injury of ulnar artery at wrist and hand level**
+ **S65.00 Unspecified injury of ulnar artery at wrist and hand level**
CC +7th **S65.001 Unspecified injury of ulnar artery at wrist and hand level of right arm**
CC Exclusion 7th character A see Appendix A PDX collection 1274
CC +7th **S65.002 Unspecified injury of ulnar artery at wrist and hand level of left arm**
CC Exclusion 7th character A see Appendix A PDX collection 1275

CC +7th **S65.009** **Unspecified injury of ulnar artery at wrist and hand level of unspecified arm**
CC Exclusion 7th character A see Appendix A
PDX collection 1276

+ **S65.01** **Laceration of ulnar artery at wrist and hand level**

CC +7th **S65.011** **Laceration of ulnar artery at wrist and hand level of right arm**
CC Exclusion 7th character A see Appendix A
PDX collection 1274

CC +7th **S65.012** **Laceration of ulnar artery at wrist and hand level of left arm**
CC Exclusion 7th character A see Appendix A
PDX collection 1275

CC +7th **S65.019** **Laceration of ulnar artery at wrist and hand level of unspecified arm**
CC Exclusion 7th character A see Appendix A
PDX collection 1276

+ **S65.09** **Other specified injury of ulnar artery at wrist and hand level**

CC +7th **S65.091** **Other specified injury of ulnar artery at wrist and hand level of right arm**
CC Exclusion 7th character A see Appendix A
PDX collection 1274

CC +7th **S65.092** **Other specified injury of ulnar artery at wrist and hand level of left arm**
CC Exclusion 7th character A see Appendix A
PDX collection 1275

CC +7th **S65.099** **Other specified injury of ulnar artery at wrist and hand level of unspecified arm**
CC Exclusion 7th character A see Appendix A
PDX collection 1276

+ **S65.1** **Injury of radial artery at wrist and hand level**

+ **S65.10** **Unspecified injury of radial artery at wrist and hand level**

CC +7th **S65.101** **Unspecified injury of radial artery at wrist and hand level of right arm**
CC Exclusion 7th character A see Appendix A
PDX collection 1277

CC +7th **S65.102** **Unspecified injury of radial artery at wrist and hand level of left arm**
CC Exclusion 7th character A see Appendix A
PDX collection 1278

CC +7th **S65.109** **Unspecified injury of radial artery at wrist and hand level of unspecified arm**
CC Exclusion 7th character A see Appendix A
PDX collection 1279

+ **S65.11** **Laceration of radial artery at wrist and hand level**

CC +7th **S65.111** **Laceration of radial artery at wrist and hand level of right arm**
CC Exclusion 7th character A see Appendix A
PDX collection 1277

CC +7th **S65.112** **Laceration of radial artery at wrist and hand level of left arm**
CC Exclusion 7th character A see Appendix A
PDX collection 1278

CC +7th **S65.119** **Laceration of radial artery at wrist and hand level of unspecified arm**
CC Exclusion 7th character A see Appendix A
PDX collection 1279

+ **S65.19** **Other specified injury of radial artery at wrist and hand level**

CC +7th **S65.191** **Other specified injury of radial artery at wrist and hand level of right arm**
CC Exclusion 7th character A see Appendix A
PDX collection 1277

CC +7th **S65.192** **Other specified injury of radial artery at wrist and hand level of left arm**
CC Exclusion 7th character A see Appendix A
PDX collection 1278

CC +7th **S65.199** **Other specified injury of radial artery at wrist and hand level of unspecified arm**
CC Exclusion 7th character A see Appendix A
PDX collection 1279

+ **S65.2** **Injury of superficial palmar arch**

+ **S65.20** **Unspecified injury of superficial palmar arch**

CC +7th **S65.201** **Unspecified injury of superficial palmar arch of right hand**
CC Exclusion 7th character A see Appendix A
PDX collection 1288

CC +7th **S65.202** **Unspecified injury of superficial palmar arch of left hand**
CC Exclusion 7th character A see Appendix A
PDX collection 1289

CC +7th **S65.209** **Unspecified injury of superficial palmar a[rch] of unspecified hand**
CC Exclusion 7th character A see Appendix A
PDX collection 1290

+ **S65.21** **Laceration of superficial palmar arch**

CC +7th **S65.211** **Laceration of superficial palmar arch of right hand**
CC Exclusion 7th character A see Appendix A
PDX collection 1288

CC +7th **S65.212** **Laceration of superficial palmar arch of le[ft] hand**
CC Exclusion 7th character A see Appendix A
PDX collection 1289

CC +7th **S65.219** **Laceration of superficial palmar arch of unspecified hand**
CC Exclusion 7th character A see Appendix A
PDX collection 1290

+ **S65.29** **Other specified injury of superficial palmar arch**

CC +7th **S65.291** **Other specified injury of superficial palma[r] arch of right hand**
CC Exclusion 7th character A see Appendix A
PDX collection 1288

CC +7th **S65.292** **Other specified injury of superficial palma[r] arch of left hand**
CC Exclusion 7th character A see Appendix A
PDX collection 1289

CC +7th **S65.299** **Other specified injury of superficial palma[r] arch of unspecified hand**
CC Exclusion 7th character A see Appendix A
PDX collection 1290

+ **S65.3** **Injury of deep palmar arch**

+ **S65.30** **Unspecified injury of deep palmar arch**

CC +7th **S65.301** **Unspecified injury of deep palmar arch of right hand**
CC Exclusion 7th character A see Appendix A
PDX collection 1288

CC +7th **S65.302** **Unspecified injury of deep palmar arch of left hand**
CC Exclusion 7th character A see Appendix A
PDX collection 1289

CC +7th **S65.309** **Unspecified injury of deep palmar arch of unspecified hand**
CC Exclusion 7th character A see Appendix A
PDX collection 1290

+ **S65.31** **Laceration of deep palmar arch**

CC +7th **S65.311** **Laceration of deep palmar arch of right hand**
CC Exclusion 7th character A see Appendix A
PDX collection 1288

CC +7th **S65.312** **Laceration of deep palmar arch of left han[d]**
CC Exclusion 7th character A see Appendix A
PDX collection 1289

CC +7th **S65.319** **Laceration of deep palmar arch of unspecified hand**
CC Exclusion 7th character A see Appendix A
PDX collection 1290

+ **S65.39** **Other specified injury of deep palmar arch**

CC +7th **S65.391** **Other specified injury of deep palmar arch of right hand**
CC Exclusion 7th character A see Appendix A
PDX collection 1288

CC +7th **S65.392** **Other specified injury of deep palmar arch of left hand**
CC Exclusion 7th character A see Appendix A
PDX collection 1289

CC +7th **S65.399** **Other specified injury of deep palmar arch of unspecified hand**
CC Exclusion 7th character A see Appendix A
PDX collection 1290

+ **S65.4** **Injury of blood vessel of thumb**

+ **S65.40** **Unspecified injury of blood vessel of thumb**

CC +7th **S65.401** **Unspecified injury of blood vessel of right thumb**
CC Exclusion 7th character A see Appendix A
PDX collection 1291

CC +7th **S65.402** **Unspecified injury of blood vessel of left thumb**
CC Exclusion 7th character A see Appendix A
PDX collection 1292

CC +7th **S65.409** **Unspecified injury of blood vessel of unspecified thumb**
CC Exclusion 7th character A see Appendix A
PDX collection 1293

+ S65.41 Laceration of blood vessel of thumb

CC +7th **S65.411 Laceration of blood vessel of right thumb**
CC Exclusion 7th character A see Appendix A
PDX collection 1291

CC +7th **S65.412 Laceration of blood vessel of left thumb**
CC Exclusion 7th character A see Appendix A
PDX collection 1292

CC +7th **S65.419 Laceration of blood vessel of unspecified thumb**
CC Exclusion 7th character A see Appendix A
PDX collection 1293

+ S65.49 Other specified injury of blood vessel of thumb

CC +7th **S65.491 Other specified injury of blood vessel of right thumb**
CC Exclusion 7th character A see Appendix A
PDX collection 1291

CC +7th **S65.492 Other specified injury of blood vessel of left thumb**
CC Exclusion 7th character A see Appendix A
PDX collection 1292

CC +7th **S65.499 Other specified injury of blood vessel of unspecified thumb**
CC Exclusion 7th character A see Appendix A
PDX collection 1293

+ S65.5 Injury of blood vessel of other and unspecified finger

+ S65.50 Unspecified injury of blood vessel of other and unspecified finger

CC +7th **S65.500 Unspecified injury of blood vessel of right index finger**
CC Exclusion 7th character A see Appendix A
PDX collection 1291

CC +7th **S65.501 Unspecified injury of blood vessel of left index finger**
CC Exclusion 7th character A see Appendix A
PDX collection 1292

CC +7th **S65.502 Unspecified injury of blood vessel of right middle finger**
CC Exclusion 7th character A see Appendix A
PDX collection 1291

CC +7th **S65.503 Unspecified injury of blood vessel of left middle finger**
CC Exclusion 7th character A see Appendix A
PDX collection 1292

CC +7th **S65.504 Unspecified injury of blood vessel of right ring finger**
CC Exclusion 7th character A see Appendix A
PDX collection 1291

CC +7th **S65.505 Unspecified injury of blood vessel of left ring finger**
CC Exclusion 7th character A see Appendix A
PDX collection 1292

CC +7th **S65.506 Unspecified injury of blood vessel of right little finger**
CC Exclusion 7th character A see Appendix A
PDX collection 1291

CC +7th **S65.507 Unspecified injury of blood vessel of left little finger**
CC Exclusion 7th character A see Appendix A
PDX collection 1292

CC +7th **S65.508 Unspecified injury of blood vessel of other finger**
Unspecified injury of blood vessel of specified finger with unspecified laterality
CC Exclusion 7th character A see Appendix A
PDX collection 1293

CC +7th **S65.509 Unspecified injury of blood vessel of unspecified finger**
CC Exclusion 7th character A see Appendix A
PDX collection 1293

+ S65.51 Laceration of blood vessel of other and unspecified finger

CC +7th **S65.510 Laceration of blood vessel of right index finger**
CC Exclusion 7th character A see Appendix A
PDX collection 1291

CC +7th **S65.511 Laceration of blood vessel of left index finger**
CC Exclusion 7th character A see Appendix A
PDX collection 1292

CC +7th **S65.512 Laceration of blood vessel of right middle finger**
CC Exclusion 7th character A see Appendix A
PDX collection 1291

CC +7th **S65.513 Laceration of blood vessel of left middle finger**
CC Exclusion 7th character A see Appendix A
PDX collection 1292

CC +7th **S65.514 Laceration of blood vessel of right ring finger**
CC Exclusion 7th character A see Appendix A
PDX collection 1291

CC +7th **S65.515 Laceration of blood vessel of left ring finger**
CC Exclusion 7th character A see Appendix A
PDX collection 1292

CC +7th **S65.516 Laceration of blood vessel of right little finger**
CC Exclusion 7th character A see Appendix A
PDX collection 1291

CC +7th **S65.517 Laceration of blood vessel of left little finger**
CC Exclusion 7th character A see Appendix A
PDX collection 1292

CC +7th **S65.518 Laceration of blood vessel of other finger**
Laceration of blood vessel of specified finger with unspecified laterality
CC Exclusion 7th character A see Appendix A
PDX collection 1293

CC +7th **S65.519 Laceration of blood vessel of unspecified finger**
CC Exclusion 7th character A see Appendix A
PDX collection 1293

+ S65.59 Other specified injury of blood vessel of other and unspecified finger

CC +7th **S65.590 Other specified injury of blood vessel of right index finger**
CC Exclusion 7th character A see Appendix A
PDX collection 1291

CC +7th **S65.591 Other specified injury of blood vessel of left index finger**
CC Exclusion 7th character A see Appendix A
PDX collection 1292

CC +7th **S65.592 Other specified injury of blood vessel of right middle finger**
CC Exclusion 7th character A see Appendix A
PDX collection 1291

CC +7th **S65.593 Other specified injury of blood vessel of left middle finger**
CC Exclusion 7th character A see Appendix A
PDX collection 1292

CC +7th **S65.594 Other specified injury of blood vessel of right ring finger**
CC Exclusion 7th character A see Appendix A
PDX collection 1291

CC +7th **S65.595 Other specified injury of blood vessel of left ring finger**
CC Exclusion 7th character A see Appendix A
PDX collection 1292

CC +7th **S65.596 Other specified injury of blood vessel of right little finger**
CC Exclusion 7th character A see Appendix A
PDX collection 1291

CC +7th **S65.597 Other specified injury of blood vessel of left little finger**
CC Exclusion 7th character A see Appendix A
PDX collection 1292

CC +7th **S65.598 Other specified injury of blood vessel of other finger**
Other specified injury of blood vessel of specified finger with unspecified laterality
CC Exclusion 7th character A see Appendix A
PDX collection 1293

CC +7th **S65.599 Other specified injury of blood vessel of unspecified finger**
CC Exclusion 7th character A see Appendix A
PDX collection 1293

+ S65.8 Injury of other blood vessels at wrist and hand level

+ S65.80 Unspecified injury of other blood vessels at wrist and hand level

CC +7th **S65.801 Unspecified injury of other blood vessels at wrist and hand level of right arm**
CC Exclusion 7th character A see Appendix A
PDX collection 1260

CC +7th **S65.802 Unspecified injury of other blood vessels at wrist and hand level of left arm**
CC Exclusion 7th character A see Appendix A
PDX collection 1261

CC +7th **S65.809 Unspecified injury of other blood vessels at wrist and hand level of unspecified arm**
CC Exclusion 7th character A see Appendix A
PDX collection 1262

+ **S65.81 Laceration of other blood vessels at wrist and hand level**
  - CC +7th **S65.811 Laceration of other blood vessels at wrist and hand level of right arm**
    CC Exclusion 7th character A see Appendix A PDX collection 1260
  - CC +7th **S65.812 Laceration of other blood vessels at wrist and hand level of left arm**
    CC Exclusion 7th character A see Appendix A PDX collection 1261
  - CC +7th **S65.819 Laceration of other blood vessels at wrist and hand level of unspecified arm**
    CC Exclusion 7th character A see Appendix A PDX collection 1262

+ **S65.89 Other specified injury of other blood vessels at wrist and hand level**
  - CC +7th **S65.891 Other specified injury of other blood vessels at wrist and hand level of right arm**
    CC Exclusion 7th character A see Appendix A PDX collection 1260
  - CC +7th **S65.892 Other specified injury of other blood vessels at wrist and hand level of left arm**
    CC Exclusion 7th character A see Appendix A PDX collection 1261
  - CC +7th **S65.899 Other specified injury of other blood vessels at wrist and hand level of unspecified arm**
    CC Exclusion 7th character A see Appendix A PDX collection 1262

+ **S65.9 Injury of unspecified blood vessel at wrist and hand level**

+ **S65.90 Unspecified injury of unspecified blood vessel at wrist and hand level**
  - CC +7th **S65.901 Unspecified injury of unspecified blood vessel at wrist and hand level of right arm**
    CC Exclusion 7th character A see Appendix A PDX collection 1260
  - CC +7th **S65.902 Unspecified injury of unspecified blood vessel at wrist and hand level of left arm**
    CC Exclusion 7th character A see Appendix A PDX collection 1261
  - CC +7th **S65.909 Unspecified injury of unspecified blood vessel at wrist and hand level of unspecified arm**
    CC Exclusion 7th character A see Appendix A PDX collection 1262

+ **S65.91 Laceration of unspecified blood vessel at wrist and hand level**
  - CC +7th **S65.911 Laceration of unspecified blood vessel at wrist and hand level of right arm**
    CC Exclusion 7th character A see Appendix A PDX collection 1260
  - CC +7th **S65.912 Laceration of unspecified blood vessel at wrist and hand level of left arm**
    CC Exclusion 7th character A see Appendix A PDX collection 1261
  - CC +7th **S65.919 Laceration of unspecified blood vessel at wrist and hand level of unspecified arm**
    CC Exclusion 7th character A see Appendix A PDX collection 1262

+ **S65.99 Other specified injury of unspecified blood vessel at wrist and hand level**
  - CC +7th **S65.991 Other specified injury of unspecified blood vessel at wrist and hand of right arm**
    CC Exclusion 7th character A see Appendix A PDX collection 1260
  - CC +7th **S65.992 Other specified injury of unspecified blood vessel at wrist and hand of left arm**
    CC Exclusion 7th character A see Appendix A PDX collection 1261
  - CC +7th **S65.999 Other specified injury of unspecified blood vessel at wrist and hand of unspecified arm**
    CC Exclusion 7th character A see Appendix A PDX collection 1262

S66 Injury of muscle, fascia and tendon at wrist and hand level

Code also any associated open wound (S61.-)

Excludes2: *sprain of joints and ligaments of wrist and hand (S63.-)*

The appropriate 7th character is to be added to each code from category S66
A initial encounter
D subsequent encounter
S sequela

+ **S66.0 Injury of long flexor muscle, fascia and tendon of thumb at wrist and hand level**

+ **S66.00 Unspecified injury of long flexor muscle, fascia and tendon of thumb at wrist and hand level**
  - +7th **S66.001 Unspecified injury of long flexor muscle, fascia and tendon of right thumb at wrist and hand level**
  - +7th **S66.002 Unspecified injury of long flexor muscle, fascia and tendon of left thumb at wrist and hand level**
  - +7th **S66.009 Unspecified injury of long flexor muscle, fascia and tendon of unspecified thumb at wrist and hand level**

+ **S66.01 Strain of long flexor muscle, fascia and tendon of thumb at wrist and hand level**
  - +7th **S66.011 Strain of long flexor muscle, fascia and tendon of right thumb at wrist and hand level**
  - +7th **S66.012 Strain of long flexor muscle, fascia and tendon of left thumb at wrist and hand level**
  - +7th **S66.019 Strain of long flexor muscle, fascia and tendon of unspecified thumb at wrist and hand level**

+ **S66.02 Laceration of long flexor muscle, fascia and tendon of thumb at wrist and hand level**
  - CC +7th **S66.021 Laceration of long flexor muscle, fascia and tendon of right thumb at wrist and hand level**
    CC Exclusion 7th character A see Appendix A PDX collection 1294
  - CC +7th **S66.022 Laceration of long flexor muscle, fascia and tendon of left thumb at wrist and hand level**
    CC Exclusion 7th character A see Appendix A PDX collection 1295
  - CC +7th **S66.029 Laceration of long flexor muscle, fascia and tendon of unspecified thumb at wrist and hand level**
    CC Exclusion 7th character A see Appendix A PDX collection 1296

+ **S66.09 Other specified injury of long flexor muscle, fascia and tendon of thumb at wrist and hand level**
  - +7th **S66.091 Other specified injury of long flexor muscle, fascia and tendon of right thumb at wrist and hand level**
  - +7th **S66.092 Other specified injury of long flexor muscle, fascia and tendon of left thumb at wrist and hand level**
  - +7th **S66.099 Other specified injury of long flexor muscle, fascia and tendon of unspecified thumb at wrist and hand level**

+ **S66.1 Injury of flexor muscle, fascia and tendon of other and unspecified finger at wrist and hand level**

  Excludes2: *Injury of long flexor muscle, fascia and tendon of thumb at wrist and hand level (S66.0-)*

+ **S66.10 Unspecified injury of flexor muscle, fascia and tendon of other and unspecified finger at wrist and hand level**
  - +7th **S66.100 Unspecified injury of flexor muscle, fascia and tendon of right index finger at wrist and hand level**
  - +7th **S66.101 Unspecified injury of flexor muscle, fascia and tendon of left index finger at wrist and hand level**
  - +7th **S66.102 Unspecified injury of flexor muscle, fascia and tendon of right middle finger at wrist and hand level**
  - +7th **S66.103 Unspecified injury of flexor muscle, fascia and tendon of left middle finger at wrist and hand level**
  - +7th **S66.104 Unspecified injury of flexor muscle, fascia and tendon of right ring finger at wrist and hand level**

+7th **S66.105** **Unspecified injury of flexor muscle, fascia and tendon of left ring finger at wrist and hand level**

+7th **S66.106** **Unspecified injury of flexor muscle, fascia and tendon of right little finger at wrist and hand level**

+7th **S66.107** **Unspecified injury of flexor muscle, fascia and tendon of left little finger at wrist and hand level**

+7th **S66.108** **Unspecified injury of flexor muscle, fascia and tendon of other finger at wrist and hand level**
Unspecified injury of flexor muscle, fascia and tendon of specified finger with unspecified laterality at wrist and hand level

+7th **S66.109** **Unspecified injury of flexor muscle, fascia and tendon of unspecified finger at wrist and hand level**

\+ **S66.11** **Strain of flexor muscle, fascia and tendon of other and unspecified finger at wrist and hand level**

+7th **S66.110** **Strain of flexor muscle, fascia and tendon of right index finger at wrist and hand level**

+7th **S66.111** **Strain of flexor muscle, fascia and tendon of left index finger at wrist and hand level**

+7th **S66.112** **Strain of flexor muscle, fascia and tendon of right middle finger at wrist and hand level**

+7th **S66.113** **Strain of flexor muscle, fascia and tendon of left middle finger at wrist and hand level**

+7th **S66.114** **Strain of flexor muscle, fascia and tendon of right ring finger at wrist and hand level**

+7th **S66.115** **Strain of flexor muscle, fascia and tendon of left ring finger at wrist and hand level**

+7th **S66.116** **Strain of flexor muscle, fascia and tendon of right little finger at wrist and hand level**

+7th **S66.117** **Strain of flexor muscle, fascia and tendon of left little finger at wrist and hand level**

+7th **S66.118** **Strain of flexor muscle, fascia and tendon of other finger at wrist and hand level**
Strain of flexor muscle, fascia and tendon of specified finger with unspecified laterality at wrist and hand level

+7th **S66.119** **Strain of flexor muscle, fascia and tendon of unspecified finger at wrist and hand level**

\+ **S66.12** **Laceration of flexor muscle, fascia and tendon of other and unspecified finger at wrist and hand level**

CC +7th **S66.120** **Laceration of flexor muscle, fascia and tendon of right index finger at wrist and hand level**
CC Exclusion 7th character A see Appendix A
PDX collection 1294

CC +7th **S66.121** **Laceration of flexor muscle, fascia and tendon of left index finger at wrist and hand level**
CC Exclusion 7th character A see Appendix A
PDX collection 1295

CC +7th **S66.122** **Laceration of flexor muscle, fascia and tendon of right middle finger at wrist and hand level**
CC Exclusion 7th character A see Appendix A
PDX collection 1294

CC +7th **S66.123** **Laceration of flexor muscle, fascia and tendon of left middle finger at wrist and hand level**
CC Exclusion 7th character A see Appendix A
PDX collection 1295

CC +7th **S66.124** **Laceration of flexor muscle, fascia and tendon of right ring finger at wrist and hand level**
CC Exclusion 7th character A see Appendix A
PDX collection 1294

CC +7th **S66.125** **Laceration of flexor muscle, fascia and tendon of left ring finger at wrist and hand level**
CC Exclusion 7th character A see Appendix A
PDX collection 1295

CC +7th **S66.126** **Laceration of flexor muscle, fascia and tendon of right little finger at wrist and hand level**
CC Exclusion 7th character A see Appendix A
PDX collection 1294

CC +7th **S66.127** **Laceration of flexor muscle, fascia and tendon of left little finger at wrist and hand level**
CC Exclusion 7th character A see Appendix A
PDX collection 1295

CC +7th **S66.128** **Laceration of flexor muscle, fascia and tendon of other finger at wrist and hand level**
Laceration of flexor muscle, fascia and tendon of specified finger with unspecified laterality at wrist and hand level
CC Exclusion 7th character A see Appendix A
PDX collection 1296

CC +7th **S66.129** **Laceration of flexor muscle, fascia and tendon of unspecified finger at wrist and hand level**
CC Exclusion 7th character A see Appendix A
PDX collection 1296

\+ **S66.19** **Other injury of flexor muscle, fascia and tendon of other and unspecified finger at wrist and hand level**

+7th **S66.190** **Other injury of flexor muscle, fascia and tendon of right index finger at wrist and hand level**

+7th **S66.191** **Other injury of flexor muscle, fascia and tendon of left index finger at wrist and hand level**

+7th **S66.192** **Other injury of flexor muscle, fascia and tendon of right middle finger at wrist and hand level**

+7th **S66.193** **Other injury of flexor muscle, fascia and tendon of left middle finger at wrist and hand level**

+7th **S66.194** **Other injury of flexor muscle, fascia and tendon of right ring finger at wrist and hand level**

+7th **S66.195** **Other injury of flexor muscle, fascia and tendon of left ring finger at wrist and hand level**

+7th **S66.196** **Other injury of flexor muscle, fascia and tendon of right little finger at wrist and hand level**

+7th **S66.197** **Other injury of flexor muscle, fascia and tendon of left little finger at wrist and hand level**

+7th **S66.198** **Other injury of flexor muscle, fascia and tendon of other finger at wrist and hand level**
Other injury of flexor muscle, fascia and tendon of specified finger with unspecified laterality at wrist and hand level

+7th **S66.199** **Other injury of flexor muscle, fascia and tendon of unspecified finger at wrist and hand level**

\+ **S66.2** **Injury of extensor muscle, fascia and tendon of thumb at wrist and hand level**

\+ **S66.20** **Unspecified injury of extensor muscle, fascia and tendon of thumb at wrist and hand level**

+7th **S66.201** **Unspecified injury of extensor muscle, fascia and tendon of right thumb at wrist and hand level**

+7th **S66.202** **Unspecified injury of extensor muscle, fascia and tendon of left thumb at wrist and hand level**

+7th **S66.209** **Unspecified injury of extensor muscle, fascia and tendon of unspecified thumb at wrist and hand level**

\+ **S66.21** **Strain of extensor muscle, fascia and tendon of thumb at wrist and hand level**

+7th **S66.211** **Strain of extensor muscle, fascia and tendon of right thumb at wrist and hand level**

+7th **S66.212** **Strain of extensor muscle, fascia and tendon of left thumb at wrist and hand level**

+7th **S66.219** **Strain of extensor muscle, fascia and tendon of unspecified thumb at wrist and hand level**

\+ **S66.22** **Laceration of extensor muscle, fascia and tendon of thumb at wrist and hand level**

CC +7th **S66.221** **Laceration of extensor muscle, fascia and tendon of right thumb at wrist and hand level**
CC Exclusion 7th character A see Appendix A
PDX collection 1294

CC +7th **S66.222** **Laceration of extensor muscle, fascia and tendon of left thumb at wrist and hand level**
CC Exclusion 7th character A see Appendix A
PDX collection 1295

CC +7th **S66.229 Laceration of extensor muscle, fascia and tendon of unspecified thumb at wrist and hand level**
CC Exclusion 7th character A see Appendix A PDX collection 1296

\+ **S66.29 Other specified injury of extensor muscle, fascia and tendon of thumb at wrist and hand level**

+7th **S66.291 Other specified injury of extensor muscle, fascia and tendon of right thumb at wrist and hand level**

+7th **S66.292 Other specified injury of extensor muscle, fascia and tendon of left thumb at wrist and hand level**

+7th **S66.299 Other specified injury of extensor muscle, fascia and tendon of unspecified thumb at wrist and hand level**

\+ **S66.3 Injury of extensor muscle, fascia and tendon of other and unspecified finger at wrist and hand level**
Excludes2: *Injury of extensor muscle, fascia and tendon of thumb at wrist and hand level (S66.2-)*

\+ **S66.30 Unspecified injury of extensor muscle, fascia and tendon of other and unspecified finger at wrist and hand level**

+7th **S66.300 Unspecified injury of extensor muscle, fascia and tendon of right index finger at wrist and hand level**

+7th **S66.301 Unspecified injury of extensor muscle, fascia and tendon of left index finger at wrist and hand level**

+7th **S66.302 Unspecified injury of extensor muscle, fascia and tendon of right middle finger at wrist and hand level**

+7th **S66.303 Unspecified injury of extensor muscle, fascia and tendon of left middle finger at wrist and hand level**

+7th **S66.304 Unspecified injury of extensor muscle, fascia and tendon of right ring finger at wrist and hand level**

+7th **S66.305 Unspecified injury of extensor muscle, fascia and tendon of left ring finger at wrist and hand level**

+7th **S66.306 Unspecified injury of extensor muscle, fascia and tendon of right little finger at wrist and hand level**

+7th **S66.307 Unspecified injury of extensor muscle, fascia and tendon of left little finger at wrist and hand level**

+7th **S66.308 Unspecified injury of extensor muscle, fascia and tendon of other finger at wrist and hand level**
Unspecified injury of extensor muscle, fascia and tendon of specified finger with unspecified laterality at wrist and hand level

+7th **S66.309 Unspecified injury of extensor muscle, fascia and tendon of unspecified finger at wrist and hand level**

\+ **S66.31 Strain of extensor muscle, fascia and tendon of other and unspecified finger at wrist and hand level**

+7th **S66.310 Strain of extensor muscle, fascia and tendon of right index finger at wrist and hand level**

+7th **S66.311 Strain of extensor muscle, fascia and tendon of left index finger at wrist and hand level**

+7th **S66.312 Strain of extensor muscle, fascia and tendon of right middle finger at wrist and hand level**

+7th **S66.313 Strain of extensor muscle, fascia and tendon of left middle finger at wrist and hand level**

+7th **S66.314 Strain of extensor muscle, fascia and tendon of right ring finger at wrist and hand level**

+7th **S66.315 Strain of extensor muscle, fascia and tendon of left ring finger at wrist and hand level**

+7th **S66.316 Strain of extensor muscle, fascia and tendon of right little finger at wrist and hand level**

+7th **S66.317 Strain of extensor muscle, fascia and tendon of left little finger at wrist and hand level**

+7th **S66.318 Strain of extensor muscle, fascia and tendon of other finger at wrist and hand level**
Strain of extensor muscle, fascia and tendon of specified finger with unspecified laterality at wrist and hand level

+7th **S66.319 Strain of extensor muscle, fascia and tendon of unspecified finger at wrist and hand level**

\+ **S66.32 Laceration of extensor muscle, fascia and tendon of other and unspecified finger at wrist and hand level**

CC +7th **S66.320 Laceration of extensor muscle, fascia and tendon of right index finger at wrist and hand level**
CC Exclusion 7th character A see Appendix A PDX collection 1294

CC +7th **S66.321 Laceration of extensor muscle, fascia and tendon of left index finger at wrist and hand level**
CC Exclusion 7th character A see Appendix A PDX collection 1295

CC +7th **S66.322 Laceration of extensor muscle, fascia and tendon of right middle finger at wrist and hand level**
CC Exclusion 7th character A see Appendix A PDX collection 1294

CC +7th **S66.323 Laceration of extensor muscle, fascia and tendon of left middle finger at wrist and hand level**
CC Exclusion 7th character A see Appendix A PDX collection 1295

CC +7th **S66.324 Laceration of extensor muscle, fascia and tendon of right ring finger at wrist and hand level**
CC Exclusion 7th character A see Appendix A PDX collection 1294

CC +7th **S66.325 Laceration of extensor muscle, fascia and tendon of left ring finger at wrist and hand level**
CC Exclusion 7th character A see Appendix A PDX collection 1295

CC +7th **S66.326 Laceration of extensor muscle, fascia and tendon of right little finger at wrist and hand level**
CC Exclusion 7th character A see Appendix A PDX collection 1294

CC +7th **S66.327 Laceration of extensor muscle, fascia and tendon of left little finger at wrist and hand level**
CC Exclusion 7th character A see Appendix A PDX collection 1295

CC +7th **S66.328 Laceration of extensor muscle, fascia and tendon of other finger at wrist and hand level**
Laceration of extensor muscle, fascia and tendon of specified finger with unspecified laterality at wrist and hand level
CC Exclusion 7th character A see Appendix A PDX collection 1296

CC +7th **S66.329 Laceration of extensor muscle, fascia and tendon of unspecified finger at wrist and hand level**
CC Exclusion 7th character A see Appendix A PDX collection 1296

\+ **S66.39 Other injury of extensor muscle, fascia and tendon of other and unspecified finger at wrist and hand level**

+7th **S66.390 Other injury of extensor muscle, fascia and tendon of right index finger at wrist and hand level**

+7th **S66.391 Other injury of extensor muscle, fascia and tendon of left index finger at wrist and hand level**

+7th **S66.392 Other injury of extensor muscle, fascia and tendon of right middle finger at wrist and hand level**

+7th **S66.393 Other injury of extensor muscle, fascia and tendon of left middle finger at wrist and hand level**

+7th **S66.394 Other injury of extensor muscle, fascia and tendon of right ring finger at wrist and hand level**

+7th **S66.395 Other injury of extensor muscle, fascia and tendon of left ring finger at wrist and hand level**

+7th **S66.396 Other injury of extensor muscle, fascia and tendon of right little finger at wrist and hand level**

+7th **S66.397 Other injury of extensor muscle, fascia and tendon of left little finger at wrist and hand level**

+7th **S66.398 Other injury of extensor muscle, fascia and tendon of other finger at wrist and hand level**
Other injury of extensor muscle, fascia and tendon of specified finger with unspecified laterality at wrist and hand level

+7th **S66.399 Other injury of extensor muscle, fascia and tendon of unspecified finger at wrist and hand level**

\+ **S66.4 Injury of intrinsic muscle, fascia and tendon of thumb at wrist and hand level**

\+ **S66.40 Unspecified injury of intrinsic muscle, fascia and tendon of thumb at wrist and hand level**

+7th **S66.401 Unspecified injury of intrinsic muscle, fascia and tendon of right thumb at wrist and hand level**

+7th **S66.402 Unspecified injury of intrinsic muscle, fascia and tendon of left thumb at wrist and hand level**

+7th **S66.409 Unspecified injury of intrinsic muscle, fascia and tendon of unspecified thumb at wrist and hand level**

\+ **S66.41 Strain of intrinsic muscle, fascia and tendon of thumb at wrist and hand level**

+7th **S66.411 Strain of intrinsic muscle, fascia and tendon of right thumb at wrist and hand level**

+7th **S66.412 Strain of intrinsic muscle, fascia and tendon of left thumb at wrist and hand level**

+7th **S66.419 Strain of intrinsic muscle, fascia and tendon of unspecified thumb at wrist and hand level**

\+ **S66.42 Laceration of intrinsic muscle, fascia and tendon of thumb at wrist and hand level**

CC +7th **S66.421 Laceration of intrinsic muscle, fascia and tendon of right thumb at wrist and hand level**
CC Exclusion 7th character A see Appendix A
PDX collection 1294

CC +7th **S66.422 Laceration of intrinsic muscle, fascia and tendon of left thumb at wrist and hand level**
CC Exclusion 7th character A see Appendix A
PDX collection 1295

CC +7th **S66.429 Laceration of intrinsic muscle, fascia and tendon of unspecified thumb at wrist and hand level**
CC Exclusion 7th character A see Appendix A
PDX collection 1296

\+ **S66.49 Other specified injury of intrinsic muscle, fascia and tendon of thumb at wrist and hand level**

+7th **S66.491 Other specified injury of intrinsic muscle, fascia and tendon of right thumb at wrist and hand level**

+7th **S66.492 Other specified injury of intrinsic muscle, fascia and tendon of left thumb at wrist and hand level**

+7th **S66.499 Other specified injury of intrinsic muscle, fascia and tendon of unspecified thumb at wrist and hand level**

\+ **S66.5 Injury of intrinsic muscle, fascia and tendon of other and unspecified finger at wrist and hand level**
Excludes2: *injury of intrinsic muscle, fascia and tendon of thumb at wrist and hand level (S66.4-)*

\+ **S66.50 Unspecified injury of intrinsic muscle, fascia and tendon of other and unspecified finger at wrist and hand level**

+7th **S66.500 Unspecified injury of intrinsic muscle, fascia and tendon of right index finger at wrist and hand level**

+7th **S66.501 Unspecified injury of intrinsic muscle, fascia and tendon of left index finger at wrist and hand level**

+7th **S66.502 Unspecified injury of intrinsic muscle, fascia and tendon of right middle finger at wrist and hand level**

+7th **S66.503 Unspecified injury of intrinsic muscle, fascia and tendon of left middle finger at wrist and hand level**

+7th **S66.504 Unspecified injury of intrinsic muscle, fascia and tendon of right ring finger at wrist and hand level**

+7th **S66.505 Unspecified injury of intrinsic muscle, fascia and tendon of left ring finger at wrist and hand level**

+7th **S66.506 Unspecified injury of intrinsic muscle, fascia and tendon of right little finger at wrist and hand level**

+7th **S66.507 Unspecified injury of intrinsic muscle, fascia and tendon of left little finger at wrist and hand level**

+7th **S66.508 Unspecified injury of intrinsic muscle, fascia and tendon of other finger at wrist and hand level**
Unspecified injury of intrinsic muscle, fascia and tendon of specified finger with unspecified laterality at wrist and hand level

+7th **S66.509 Unspecified injury of intrinsic muscle, fascia and tendon of unspecified finger at wrist and hand level**

\+ **S66.51 Strain of intrinsic muscle, fascia and tendon of other and unspecified finger at wrist and hand level**

+7th **S66.510 Strain of intrinsic muscle, fascia and tendon of right index finger at wrist and hand level**

+7th **S66.511 Strain of intrinsic muscle, fascia and tendon of left index finger at wrist and hand level**

+7th **S66.512 Strain of intrinsic muscle, fascia and tendon of right middle finger at wrist and hand level**

+7th **S66.513 Strain of intrinsic muscle, fascia and tendon of left middle finger at wrist and hand level**

+7th **S66.514 Strain of intrinsic muscle, fascia and tendon of right ring finger at wrist and hand level**

+7th **S66.515 Strain of intrinsic muscle, fascia and tendon of left ring finger at wrist and hand level**

+7th **S66.516 Strain of intrinsic muscle, fascia and tendon of right little finger at wrist and hand level**

+7th **S66.517 Strain of intrinsic muscle, fascia and tendon of left little finger at wrist and hand level**

+7th **S66.518 Strain of intrinsic muscle, fascia and tendon of other finger at wrist and hand level**
Strain of intrinsic muscle, fascia and tendon of specified finger with unspecified laterality at wrist and hand level

+7th **S66.519 Strain of intrinsic muscle, fascia and tendon of unspecified finger at wrist and hand level**

\+ **S66.52 Laceration of intrinsic muscle, fascia and tendon of other and unspecified finger at wrist and hand level**

CC +7th **S66.520 Laceration of intrinsic muscle, fascia and tendon of right index finger at wrist and hand level**
CC Exclusion 7th character A see Appendix A
PDX collection 1294

CC +7th **S66.521 Laceration of intrinsic muscle, fascia and tendon of left index finger at wrist and hand level**
CC Exclusion 7th character A see Appendix A
PDX collection 1295

CC +7th **S66.522 Laceration of intrinsic muscle, fascia and tendon of right middle finger at wrist and hand level**
CC Exclusion 7th character A see Appendix A
PDX collection 1294

CC +7th **S66.523 Laceration of intrinsic muscle, fascia and tendon of left middle finger at wrist and hand level**
CC Exclusion 7th character A see Appendix A
PDX collection 1295

CC +7th **S66.524 Laceration of intrinsic muscle, fascia and tendon of right ring finger at wrist and hand level**
CC Exclusion 7th character A see Appendix A
PDX collection 1294

CC +7th **S66.525 Laceration of intrinsic muscle, fascia and tendon of left ring finger at wrist and hand level**
CC Exclusion 7th character A see Appendix A
PDX collection 1295

CC +7th **S66.526 Laceration of intrinsic muscle, fascia and tendon of right little finger at wrist and hand level**
CC Exclusion 7th character A see Appendix A
PDX collection 1294

CC +7th **S66.527 Laceration of intrinsic muscle, fascia and tendon of left little finger at wrist and hand level**
CC Exclusion 7th character A see Appendix A
PDX collection 1295

CC +7th **S66.528 Laceration of intrinsic muscle, fascia and tendon of other finger at wrist and hand level**
Laceration of intrinsic muscle, fascia and tendon of specified finger with unspecified laterality at wrist and hand level
CC Exclusion 7th character A see Appendix A PDX collection 1296

CC +7th **S66.529 Laceration of intrinsic muscle, fascia and tendon of unspecified finger at wrist and hand level**
CC Exclusion 7th character A see Appendix A PDX collection 1296

\+ **S66.59 Other injury of intrinsic muscle, fascia and tendon of other and unspecified finger at wrist and hand level**

+7th **S66.590 Other injury of intrinsic muscle, fascia and tendon of right index finger at wrist and hand level**

+7th **S66.591 Other injury of intrinsic muscle, fascia and tendon of left index finger at wrist and hand level**

+7th **S66.592 Other injury of intrinsic muscle, fascia and tendon of right middle finger at wrist and hand level**

+7th **S66.593 Other injury of intrinsic muscle, fascia and tendon of left middle finger at wrist and hand level**

+7th **S66.594 Other injury of intrinsic muscle, fascia and tendon of right ring finger at wrist and hand level**

+7th **S66.595 Other injury of intrinsic muscle, fascia and tendon of left ring finger at wrist and hand level**

+7th **S66.596 Other injury of intrinsic muscle, fascia and tendon of right little finger at wrist and hand level**

+7th **S66.597 Other injury of intrinsic muscle, fascia and tendon of left little finger at wrist and hand level**

+7th **S66.598 Other injury of intrinsic muscle, fascia and tendon of other finger at wrist and hand level**
Other injury of intrinsic muscle, fascia and tendon of specified finger with unspecified laterality at wrist and hand level

+7th **S66.599 Other injury of intrinsic muscle, fascia and tendon of unspecified finger at wrist and hand level**

\+ **S66.8 Injury of other specified muscles, fascia and tendons at wrist and hand level**

\+ **S66.80 Unspecified injury of other specified muscles, fascia and tendons at wrist and hand level**

+7th **S66.801 Unspecified injury of other specified muscles, fascia and tendons at wrist and hand level, right hand**

+7th **S66.802 Unspecified injury of other specified muscles, fascia and tendons at wrist and hand level, left hand**

+7th **S66.809 Unspecified injury of other specified muscles, fascia and tendons at wrist and hand level, unspecified hand**

\+ **S66.81 Strain of other specified muscles, fascia and tendons at wrist and hand level**

+7th **S66.811 Strain of other specified muscles, fascia and tendons at wrist and hand level, right hand**

+7th **S66.812 Strain of other specified muscles, fascia and tendons at wrist and hand level, left hand**

+7th **S66.819 Strain of other specified muscles, fascia and tendons at wrist and hand level, unspecified hand**

\+ **S66.82 Laceration of other specified muscles, fascia and tendons at wrist and hand level**

CC +7th **S66.821 Laceration of other specified muscles, fascia and tendons at wrist and hand level, right hand**
CC Exclusion 7th character A see Appendix A PDX collection 1294

CC +7th **S66.822 Laceration of other specified muscles, fascia and tendons at wrist and hand level, left hand**
CC Exclusion 7th character A see Appendix A PDX collection 1295

CC +7th **S66.829 Laceration of other specified muscles, fascia and tendons at wrist and hand level, unspecified hand**
CC Exclusion 7th character A see Appendix A PDX collection 1296

\+ **S66.89 Other injury of other specified muscles, fascia and tendons at wrist and hand level**

+7th **S66.891 Other injury of other specified muscles, fascia and tendons at wrist and hand level, right hand**

+7th **S66.892 Other injury of other specified muscles, fascia and tendons at wrist and hand level, left hand**

+7th **S66.899 Other injury of other specified muscles, fascia and tendons at wrist and hand level, unspecified hand**

\+ **S66.9 Injury of unspecified muscle, fascia and tendon at wrist and hand level**

\+ **S66.90 Unspecified injury of unspecified muscle, fascia and tendon at wrist and hand level**

+7th **S66.901 Unspecified injury of unspecified muscle, fascia and tendon at wrist and hand level, right hand**

+7th **S66.902 Unspecified injury of unspecified muscle, fascia and tendon at wrist and hand level, left hand**

+7th **S66.909 Unspecified injury of unspecified muscle, fascia and tendon at wrist and hand level, unspecified hand**

\+ **S66.91 Strain of unspecified muscle, fascia and tendon at wrist and hand level**

+7th **S66.911 Strain of unspecified muscle, fascia and tendon at wrist and hand level, right hand**

+7th **S66.912 Strain of unspecified muscle, fascia and tendon at wrist and hand level, left hand**

+7th **S66.919 Strain of unspecified muscle, fascia and tendon at wrist and hand level, unspecified hand**

\+ **S66.92 Laceration of unspecified muscle, fascia and tendon at wrist and hand level**

CC +7th **S66.921 Laceration of unspecified muscle, fascia and tendon at wrist and hand level, right hand**
CC Exclusion 7th character A see Appendix A PDX collection 1294

CC +7th **S66.922 Laceration of unspecified muscle, fascia and tendon at wrist and hand level, left hand**
CC Exclusion 7th character A see Appendix A PDX collection 1295

CC +7th **S66.929 Laceration of unspecified muscle, fascia and tendon at wrist and hand level, unspecified hand**
CC Exclusion 7th character A see Appendix A PDX collection 1296

\+ **S66.99 Other injury of unspecified muscle, fascia and tendon at wrist and hand level**

+7th **S66.991 Other injury of unspecified muscle, fascia and tendon at wrist and hand level, right hand**

+7th **S66.992 Other injury of unspecified muscle, fascia and tendon at wrist and hand level, left hand**

+7th **S66.999 Other injury of unspecified muscle, fascia and tendon at wrist and hand level, unspecified hand**

S67 **Crushing injury of wrist, hand and fingers**

Use additional code for all associated injuries, such as:
fracture of wrist and hand (S62.-)
open wound of wrist and hand (S61.-)

The appropriate 7th character is to be added to each code from category S67
A initial encounter
D subsequent encounter
S sequela

\+ **S67.0 Crushing injury of thumb**

X+7th **S67.00 Crushing injury of unspecified thumb**

X+7th **S67.01 Crushing injury of right thumb**

X+7th **S67.02 Crushing injury of left thumb**

\+ **S67.1 Crushing injury of other and unspecified finger(s)**
Excludes2: *crushing injury of thumb (S67.0-)*

X+7th **S67.10 Crushing injury of unspecified finger(s)**

\+ **S67.19 Crushing injury of other finger(s)**

+7th **S67.190 Crushing injury of right index finger**

+7th **S67.191 Crushing injury of left index finger**

+7th **S67.192 Crushing injury of right middle finger**
+7th **S67.193 Crushing injury of left middle finger**
+7th **S67.194 Crushing injury of right ring finger**
+7th **S67.195 Crushing injury of left ring finger**
+7th **S67.196 Crushing injury of right little finger**
+7th **S67.197 Crushing injury of left little finger**
+7th **S67.198 Crushing injury of other finger**
Crushing injury of specified finger with unspecified laterality

+ **S67.2 Crushing injury of hand**
Excludes2: *crushing injury of fingers (S67.1-)*
crushing injury of thumb (S67.0-)
X+7th **S67.20 Crushing injury of unspecified hand**
X+7th **S67.21 Crushing injury of right hand**
X+7th **S67.22 Crushing injury of left hand**

+ **S67.3 Crushing injury of wrist**
X+7th **S67.30 Crushing injury of unspecified wrist**
X+7th **S67.31 Crushing injury of right wrist**
X+7th **S67.32 Crushing injury of left wrist**

+ **S67.4 Crushing injury of wrist and hand**
Excludes1: *crushing injury of hand alone (S67.2-)*
crushing injury of wrist alone (S67.3-)
Excludes2: *crushing injury of fingers (S67.1-)*
crushing injury of thumb (S67.0-)
X+7th **S67.40 Crushing injury of unspecified wrist and hand**
X+7th **S67.41 Crushing injury of right wrist and hand**
X+7th **S67.42 Crushing injury of left wrist and hand**

+ **S67.9 Crushing injury of unspecified part(s) of wrist, hand and fingers**
X+7th **S67.90 Crushing injury of unspecified part(s) of unspecified wrist, hand and fingers**
X+7th **S67.91 Crushing injury of unspecified part(s) of right wrist, hand and fingers**
X+7th **S67.92 Crushing injury of unspecified part(s) of left wrist, hand and fingers**

S68 Traumatic amputation of wrist, hand and fingers

An amputation not identified as partial or complete should be coded to complete

The appropriate 7th character is to be added to each code from category S68
A initial encounter
D subsequent encounter
S sequela

+ **S68.0 Traumatic metacarpophalangeal amputation of thumb**
Traumatic amputation of thumb NOS
+ **S68.01 Complete traumatic metacarpophalangeal amputation of thumb**
+7th **S68.011 Complete traumatic metacarpophalangeal amputation of right thumb**
+7th **S68.012 Complete traumatic metacarpophalangeal amputation of left thumb**
+7th **S68.019 Complete traumatic metacarpophalangeal amputation of unspecified thumb**
+ **S68.02 Partial traumatic metacarpophalangeal amputation of thumb**
+7th **S68.021 Partial traumatic metacarpophalangeal amputation of right thumb**
+7th **S68.022 Partial traumatic metacarpophalangeal amputation of left thumb**
+7th **S68.029 Partial traumatic metacarpophalangeal amputation of unspecified thumb**

+ **S68.1 Traumatic metacarpophalangeal amputation of other and unspecified finger**
Traumatic amputation of finger NOS
Excludes2: *traumatic metacarpophalangeal amputation of thumb (S68.0-)*
+ **S68.11 Complete traumatic metacarpophalangeal amputation of other and unspecified finger**
+7th **S68.110 Complete traumatic metacarpophalangeal amputation of right index finger**
+7th **S68.111 Complete traumatic metacarpophalangeal amputation of left index finger**
+7th **S68.112 Complete traumatic metacarpophalangeal amputation of right middle finger**
+7th **S68.113 Complete traumatic metacarpophalangeal amputation of left middle finger**
+7th **S68.114 Complete traumatic metacarpophalangeal amputation of right ring finger**
+7th **S68.115 Complete traumatic metacarpophalangeal amputation of left ring finger**
+7th **S68.116 Complete traumatic metacarpophalangeal amputation of right little finger**
+7th **S68.117 Complete traumatic metacarpophalangeal amputation of left little finger**
+7th **S68.118 Complete traumatic metacarpophalangeal amputation of other finger**
Complete traumatic metacarpophalangeal amputation of specified finger with unspecified laterality
+7th **S68.119 Complete traumatic metacarpophalangeal amputation of unspecified finger**
+ **S68.12 Partial traumatic metacarpophalangeal amputation of other and unspecified finger**
+7th **S68.120 Partial traumatic metacarpophalangeal amputation of right index finger**
+7th **S68.121 Partial traumatic metacarpophalangeal amputation of left index finger**
+7th **S68.122 Partial traumatic metacarpophalangeal amputation of right middle finger**
+7th **S68.123 Partial traumatic metacarpophalangeal amputation of left middle finger**
+7th **S68.124 Partial traumatic metacarpophalangeal amputation of right ring finger**
+7th **S68.125 Partial traumatic metacarpophalangeal amputation of left ring finger**
+7th **S68.126 Partial traumatic metacarpophalangeal amputation of right little finger**
+7th **S68.127 Partial traumatic metacarpophalangeal amputation of left little finger**
+7th **S68.128 Partial traumatic metacarpophalangeal amputation of other finger**
Partial traumatic metacarpophalangeal amputation of specified finger with unspecified laterality
+7th **S68.129 Partial traumatic metacarpophalangeal amputation of unspecified finger**

+ **S68.4 Traumatic amputation of hand at wrist level**
Traumatic amputation of hand NOS
Traumatic amputation of wrist
+ **S68.41 Complete traumatic amputation of hand at wrist level**
CC +7th **S68.411 Complete traumatic amputation of right hand at wrist level**
CC Exclusion 7th character A see Appendix A PDX collection 1266
CC +7th **S68.412 Complete traumatic amputation of left hand at wrist level**
CC Exclusion 7th character A see Appendix A PDX collection 1267
CC +7th **S68.419 Complete traumatic amputation of unspecified hand at wrist level**
CC Exclusion 7th character A see Appendix A PDX collection 1268
+ **S68.42 Partial traumatic amputation of hand at wrist level**
CC +7th **S68.421 Partial traumatic amputation of right hand at wrist level**
CC Exclusion 7th character A see Appendix A PDX collection 1266
CC +7th **S68.422 Partial traumatic amputation of left hand at wrist level**
CC Exclusion 7th character A see Appendix A PDX collection 1267
CC +7th **S68.429 Partial traumatic amputation of unspecified hand at wrist level**
CC Exclusion 7th character A see Appendix A PDX collection 1268

+ **S68.5 Traumatic transphalangeal amputation of thumb**
Traumatic interphalangeal joint amputation of thumb
+ **S68.51 Complete traumatic transphalangeal amputation of thumb**
+7th **S68.511 Complete traumatic transphalangeal amputation of right thumb**
+7th **S68.512 Complete traumatic transphalangeal amputation of left thumb**
+7th **S68.519 Complete traumatic transphalangeal amputation of unspecified thumb**
+ **S68.52 Partial traumatic transphalangeal amputation of thumb**
+7th **S68.521 Partial traumatic transphalangeal amputation of right thumb**

+7th **S68.522** **Partial traumatic transphalangeal amputation of left thumb**
+7th **S68.529** **Partial traumatic transphalangeal amputation of unspecified thumb**

+ **S68.6** **Traumatic transphalangeal amputation of other and unspecified finger**

+ **S68.61** **Complete traumatic transphalangeal amputation of other and unspecified finger(s)**

+7th **S68.610** **Complete traumatic transphalangeal amputation of right index finger**
+7th **S68.611** **Complete traumatic transphalangeal amputation of left index finger**
+7th **S68.612** **Complete traumatic transphalangeal amputation of right middle finger**
+7th **S68.613** **Complete traumatic transphalangeal amputation of left middle finger**
+7th **S68.614** **Complete traumatic transphalangeal amputation of right ring finger**
+7th **S68.615** **Complete traumatic transphalangeal amputation of left ring finger**
+7th **S68.616** **Complete traumatic transphalangeal amputation of right little finger**
+7th **S68.617** **Complete traumatic transphalangeal amputation of left little finger**
+7th **S68.618** **Complete traumatic transphalangeal amputation of other finger**
Complete traumatic transphalangeal amputation of specified finger with unspecified laterality
+7th **S68.619** **Complete traumatic transphalangeal amputation of unspecified finger**

+ **S68.62** **Partial traumatic transphalangeal amputation of other and unspecified finger**

+7th **S68.620** **Partial traumatic transphalangeal amputation of right index finger**
+7th **S68.621** **Partial traumatic transphalangeal amputation of left index finger**
+7th **S68.622** **Partial traumatic transphalangeal amputation of right middle finger**
+7th **S68.623** **Partial traumatic transphalangeal amputation of left middle finger**
+7th **S68.624** **Partial traumatic transphalangeal amputation of right ring finger**
+7th **S68.625** **Partial traumatic transphalangeal amputation of left ring finger**
+7th **S68.626** **Partial traumatic transphalangeal amputation of right little finger**
+7th **S68.627** **Partial traumatic transphalangeal amputation of left little finger**
+7th **S68.628** **Partial traumatic transphalangeal amputation of other finger**
Partial traumatic transphalangeal amputation of specified finger with unspecified laterality
+7th **S68.629** **Partial traumatic transphalangeal amputation of unspecified finger**

+ **S68.7** **Traumatic transmetacarpal amputation of hand**

+ **S68.71** **Complete traumatic transmetacarpal amputation of hand**

CC +7th **S68.711** **Complete traumatic transmetacarpal amputation of right hand**
CC Exclusion 7th character A see Appendix A PDX collection 1266
CC +7th **S68.712** **Complete traumatic transmetacarpal amputation of left hand**
CC Exclusion 7th character A see Appendix A PDX collection 1267
CC +7th **S68.719** **Complete traumatic transmetacarpal amputation of unspecified hand**
CC Exclusion 7th character A see Appendix A PDX collection 1268

+ **S68.72** **Partial traumatic transmetacarpal amputation of hand**

CC +7th **S68.721** **Partial traumatic transmetacarpal amputation of right hand**
CC Exclusion 7th character A see Appendix A PDX collection 1266
CC +7th **S68.722** **Partial traumatic transmetacarpal amputation of left hand**
CC Exclusion 7th character A see Appendix A PDX collection 1267
CC +7th **S68.729** **Partial traumatic transmetacarpal amputation of unspecified hand**
CC Exclusion 7th character A see Appendix A PDX collection 1268

S69 **Other and unspecified injuries of wrist, hand and finger(s)**

The appropriate 7th character is to be added to each code from category S69
A initial encounter
D subsequent encounter
S sequela

+ **S69.8** **Other specified injuries of wrist, hand and finger(s)**
X+7th **S69.80** **Other specified injuries of unspecified wrist, hand an finger(s)**
X+7th **S69.81** **Other specified injuries of right wrist, hand and finger(s)**
X+7th **S69.82** **Other specified injuries of left wrist, hand and finger(s)**

+ **S69.9** **Unspecified injury of wrist, hand and finger(s)**
X+7th **S69.90** **Unspecified injury of unspecified wrist, hand and finger(s)**
X+7th **S69.91** **Unspecified injury of right wrist, hand and finger(s)**
X+7th **S69.92** **Unspecified injury of left wrist, hand and finger(s)**

Injuries to the hip and thigh (S70-S79)

Excludes2: *burns and corrosions (T20-T32)*
frostbite (T33-T34)
snake bite (T63.0-)
venomous insect bite or sting (T63.4-)

S70 **Superficial injury of hip and thigh**

The appropriate 7th character is to be added to each code from category S70
A initial encounter
D subsequent encounter
S sequela

+ **S70.0** **Contusion of hip**
X+7th **S70.00** **Contusion of unspecified hip**
X+7th **S70.01** **Contusion of right hip**
X+7th **S70.02** **Contusion of left hip**

+ **S70.1** **Contusion of thigh**
X+7th **S70.10** **Contusion of unspecified thigh**
X+7th **S70.11** **Contusion of right thigh**
X+7th **S70.12** **Contusion of left thigh**

+ **S70.2** **Other superficial injuries of hip**

+ **S70.21** **Abrasion of hip**
+7th **S70.211** **Abrasion, right hip**
+7th **S70.212** **Abrasion, left hip**
+7th **S70.219** **Abrasion, unspecified hip**

+ **S70.22** **Blister (nonthermal) of hip**
+7th **S70.221** **Blister (nonthermal), right hip**
+7th **S70.222** **Blister (nonthermal), left hip**
+7th **S70.229** **Blister (nonthermal), unspecified hip**

+ **S70.24** **External constriction of hip**
+7th **S70.241** **External constriction, right hip**
+7th **S70.242** **External constriction, left hip**
+7th **S70.249** **External constriction, unspecified hip**

+ **S70.25** **Superficial foreign body of hip**
Splinter in the hip
+7th **S70.251** **Superficial foreign body, right hip**
+7th **S70.252** **Superficial foreign body, left hip**
+7th **S70.259** **Superficial foreign body, unspecified hip**

+ **S70.26** **Insect bite (nonvenomous) of hip**
+7th **S70.261** **Insect bite (nonvenomous), right hip**
+7th **S70.262** **Insect bite (nonvenomous), left hip**
+7th **S70.269** **Insect bite (nonvenomous), unspecified hip**

+ **S70.27** **Other superficial bite of hip**
Excludes1: *open bite of hip (S71.05-)*
+7th **S70.271** **Other superficial bite of hip, right hip**
+7th **S70.272** **Other superficial bite of hip, left hip**
+7th **S70.279** **Other superficial bite of hip, unspecified hip**

+ **S70.3** **Other superficial injuries of thigh**

+ **S70.31** **Abrasion of thigh**
+7th **S70.311** **Abrasion, right thigh**
+7th **S70.312** **Abrasion, left thigh**
+7th **S70.319** **Abrasion, unspecified thigh**

+ **S70.32** **Blister (nonthermal) of thigh**
+7th **S70.321** **Blister (nonthermal), right thigh**
+7th **S70.322** **Blister (nonthermal), left thigh**
+7th **S70.329** **Blister (nonthermal), unspecified thigh**

+ **S70.34** **External constriction of thigh**
+7th **S70.341** **External constriction, right thigh**
+7th **S70.342** **External constriction, left thigh**
+7th **S70.349** **External constriction, unspecified thigh**

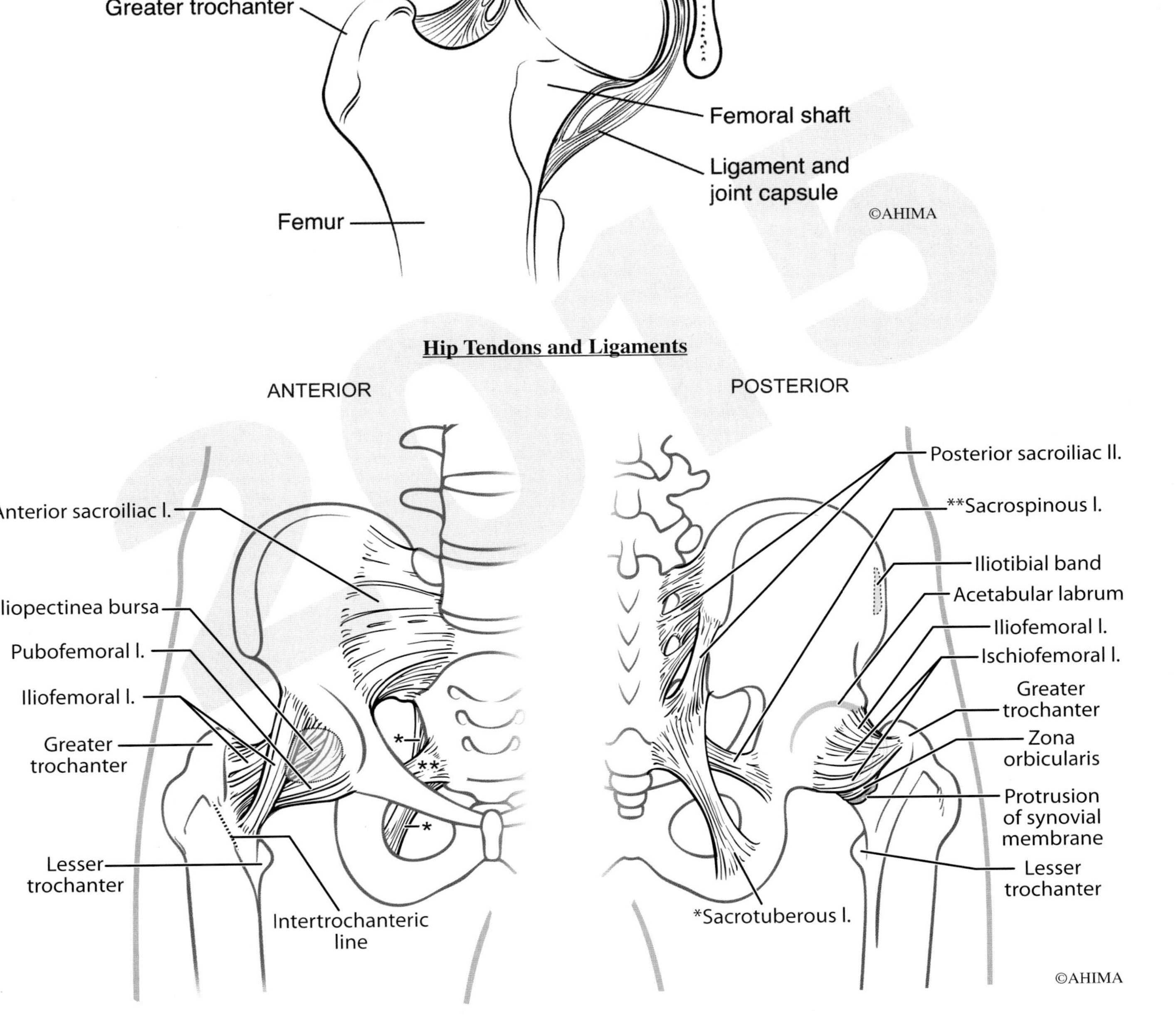
Hip Joint
Synovial fluid
Articular cartilage
Femoral head
Ligament and joint capsule
Acetabulum
Greater trochanter
Femoral shaft
Ligament and joint capsule
Femur
©AHIMA
Hip Tendons and Ligaments
ANTERIOR
POSTERIOR
Anterior sacroiliac l.
Iliopectinea bursa
Pubofemoral l.
Iliofemoral l.
Greater trochanter
Lesser trochanter
Intertrochanteric line
Posterior sacroiliac ll.
**Sacrospinous l.
Iliotibial band
Acetabular labrum
Iliofemoral l.
Ischiofemoral l.
Greater trochanter
Zona orbicularis
Protrusion of synovial membrane
Lesser trochanter
*Sacrotuberous l.
©AHIMA

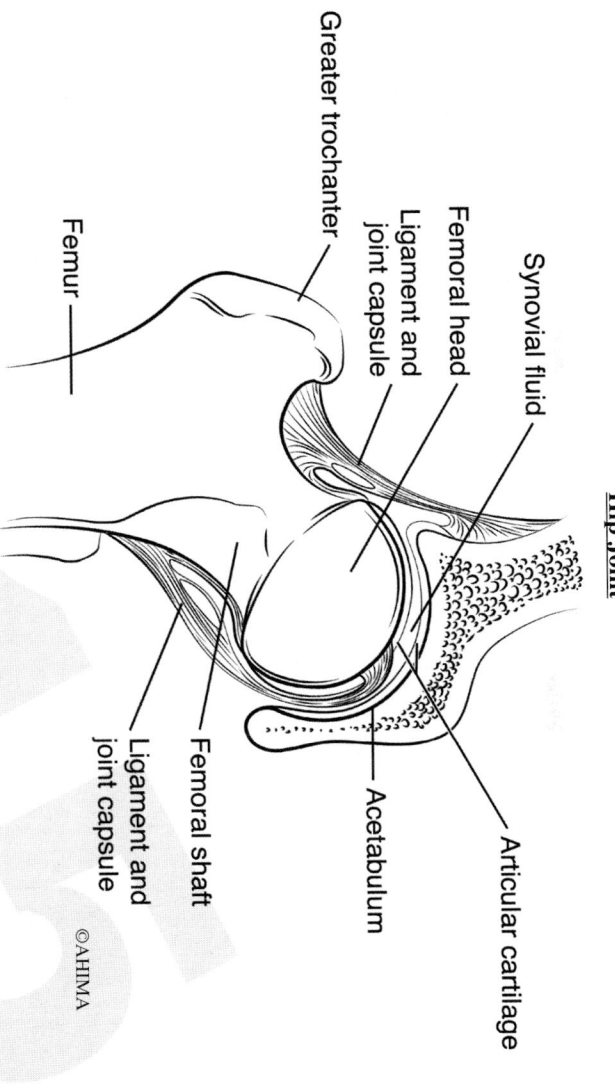

+ **S70.35 Superficial foreign body of thigh**
  Splinter in the thigh
  +7th **S70.351 Superficial foreign body, right thigh**
  +7th **S70.352 Superficial foreign body, left thigh**
  +7th **S70.359 Superficial foreign body, unspecified thigh**
+ **S70.36 Insect bite (nonvenomous) of thigh**
  +7th **S70.361 Insect bite (nonvenomous), right thigh**
  +7th **S70.362 Insect bite (nonvenomous), left thigh**
  +7th **S70.369 Insect bite (nonvenomous), unspecified thigh**
+ **S70.37 Other superficial bite of thigh**
  Excludes1: *open bite of thigh (S71.15)*
  +7th **S70.371 Other superficial bite of right thigh**
  +7th **S70.372 Other superficial bite of left thigh**
  +7th **S70.379 Other superficial bite of unspecified thigh**
+ **S70.9 Unspecified superficial injury of hip and thigh**
+ **S70.91 Unspecified superficial injury of hip**
  +7th **S70.911 Unspecified superficial injury of right hip**
  +7th **S70.912 Unspecified superficial injury of left hip**
  +7th **S70.919 Unspecified superficial injury of unspecified hip**
+ **S70.92 Unspecified superficial injury of thigh**
  +7th **S70.921 Unspecified superficial injury of right thigh**
  +7th **S70.922 Unspecified superficial injury of left thigh**
  +7th **S70.929 Unspecified superficial injury of unspecified thigh**

S71 Open wound of hip and thigh

Code also any associated wound infection
Excludes1: *open fracture of hip and thigh (S72.-)*
traumatic amputation of hip and thigh (S78.-)
Excludes2: *bite of venomous animal (T63.-)*
open wound of ankle, foot and toes (S91.-)
open wound of knee and lower leg (S81.-)

The appropriate 7th character is to be added to each code from category S71
A initial encounter
D subsequent encounter
S sequela

+ **S71.0 Open wound of hip**
+ **S71.00 Unspecified open wound of hip**
  +7th **S71.001 Unspecified open wound, right hip**
  +7th **S71.002 Unspecified open wound, left hip**
  +7th **S71.009 Unspecified open wound, unspecified hip**
+ **S71.01 Laceration without foreign body of hip**
  +7th **S71.011 Laceration without foreign body, right hip**
  +7th **S71.012 Laceration without foreign body, left hip**
  +7th **S71.019 Laceration without foreign body, unspecified hip**
+ **S71.02 Laceration with foreign body of hip**
  +7th **S71.021 Laceration with foreign body, right hip**
  +7th **S71.022 Laceration with foreign body, left hip**
  +7th **S71.029 Laceration with foreign body, unspecified hip**
+ **S71.03 Puncture wound without foreign body of hip**
  +7th **S71.031 Puncture wound without foreign body, right hip**
  +7th **S71.032 Puncture wound without foreign body, left hip**
  +7th **S71.039 Puncture wound without foreign body, unspecified hip**
+ **S71.04 Puncture wound with foreign body of hip**
  +7th **S71.041 Puncture wound with foreign body, right hip**
  +7th **S71.042 Puncture wound with foreign body, left hip**
  +7th **S71.049 Puncture wound with foreign body, unspecified hip**
+ **S71.05 Open bite of hip**
  Bite of hip NOS
  Excludes1: *superficial bite of hip (S70.26, S70.27)*
  +7th **S71.051 Open bite, right hip**
  +7th **S71.052 Open bite, left hip**
  +7th **S71.059 Open bite, unspecified hip**
+ **S71.1 Open wound of thigh**
+ **S71.10 Unspecified open wound of thigh**
  +7th **S71.101 Unspecified open wound, right thigh**
  +7th **S71.102 Unspecified open wound, left thigh**
  +7th **S71.109 Unspecified open wound, unspecified thigh**
+ **S71.11 Laceration without foreign body of thigh**
  +7th **S71.111 Laceration without foreign body, right thigh**
  +7th **S71.112 Laceration without foreign body, left thigh**
  +7th **S71.119 Laceration without foreign body, unspecified thigh**
+ **S71.12 Laceration with foreign body of thigh**
  +7th **S71.121 Laceration with foreign body, right thigh**
  +7th **S71.122 Laceration with foreign body, left thigh**
  +7th **S71.129 Laceration with foreign body, unspecified thigh**
+ **S71.13 Puncture wound without foreign body of thigh**
  +7th **S71.131 Puncture wound without foreign body, right thigh**
  +7th **S71.132 Puncture wound without foreign body, left thigh**
  +7th **S71.139 Puncture wound without foreign body, unspecified thigh**
+ **S71.14 Puncture wound with foreign body of thigh**
  +7th **S71.141 Puncture wound with foreign body, right thigh**
  +7th **S71.142 Puncture wound with foreign body, left thigh**
  +7th **S71.149 Puncture wound with foreign body, unspecified thigh**
+ **S71.15 Open bite of thigh**
  Bite of thigh NOS
  Excludes1: *superficial bite of thigh (S70.37-)*
  +7th **S71.151 Open bite, right thigh**
  +7th **S71.152 Open bite, left thigh**
  +7th **S71.159 Open bite, unspecified thigh**

S72 Fracture of femur

NOTE A fracture not indicated as displaced or nondisplaced should be coded to displaced
A fracture not indicated as open or closed should be coded to closed
The open fracture designations are based on the Gustilo open fracture classification

Excludes1: *traumatic amputation of hip and thigh (S78.-)*
Excludes2: *fracture of lower leg and ankle (S82.-)*
fracture of foot (S92.-)
periprosthetic fracture of prosthetic implant of hip (T84.040, T84.041)

The appropriate 7th character is to be added to all codes from category S72
A initial encounter for closed fracture
B initial encounter for open fracture type I or II
initial encounter for open fracture NOS
C initial encounter for open fracture type IIIA, IIIB, or IIIC
D subsequent encounter for closed fracture with routine healing
E subsequent encounter for open fracture type I or II with routine healing
F subsequent encounter for open fracture type IIIA, IIIB, or IIIC with routine healing
G subsequent encounter for closed fracture with delayed healing
H subsequent encounter for open fracture type I or II with delayed healing
J subsequent encounter for open fracture type IIIA, IIIB, or IIIC with delayed healing
K subsequent encounter for closed fracture with nonunion
M subsequent encounter for open fracture type I or II with nonunion
N subsequent encounter for open fracture type IIIA, IIIB, or IIIC with nonunion
P subsequent encounter for closed fracture with malunion
Q subsequent encounter for open fracture type I or II with malunion
R subsequent encounter for open fracture type IIIA, IIIB, or IIIC with malunion
S sequela

Review coding guideline C.19.c

+ **S72.0 Fracture of head and neck of femur**
  Excludes2: *physeal fracture of upper end of femur (S79.0-)*
+ **S72.00 Fracture of unspecified part of neck of femur**
  Fracture of hip NOS
  Fracture of neck of femur NOS
  CC MCC +7th **S72.001 Fracture of unspecified part of neck of right femur**
  CC Exclusion 7th characters K - R see Appendix A PDX collection 0897
  MCC Exclusion 7th character A see Appendix A PDX collection 1297
  MCC Exclusion 7th characters B & C see Appendix A PDX collection 1298
  HAC 7th characters A - C see Appendix B for HAC conditional logic

CC MCC +7th **S72.002 Fracture of unspecified part of neck of left femur**
CC Exclusion 7th characters K - R see Appendix A PDX collection 0897
MCC Exclusion 7th character A see Appendix A PDX collection 1299
MCC Exclusion 7th characters B & C see Appendix A PDX collection 1298
HAC 7th characters A - C see Appendix B for HAC conditional logic

CC MCC +7th **S72.009 Fracture of unspecified part of neck of unspecified femur**
CC Exclusion 7th characters K - R see Appendix A PDX collection 0897
MCC Exclusion 7th characters A - C see Appendix A PDX collection 1298
HAC 7th characters A - C see Appendix B for HAC conditional logic

+ **S72.01 Unspecified intracapsular fracture of femur**
Subcapital fracture of femur

CC MCC +7th **S72.011 Unspecified intracapsular fracture of right femur**
CC Exclusion 7th characters K - R see Appendix A PDX collection 0897
MCC Exclusion 7th character A see Appendix A PDX collection 1297
MCC Exclusion 7th characters B & C see Appendix A PDX collection 1298
HAC 7th characters A - C see Appendix B for HAC conditional logic

CC MCC +7th **S72.012 Unspecified intracapsular fracture of left femur**
CC Exclusion 7th characters K - R see Appendix A PDX collection 0897
MCC Exclusion 7th character A see Appendix A PDX collection 1299
MCC Exclusion 7th characters B & C see Appendix A PDX collection 1298
HAC 7th characters A - C see Appendix B for HAC conditional logic

CC MCC +7th **S72.019 Unspecified intracapsular fracture of unspecified femur**
CC Exclusion 7th characters K - R see Appendix A PDX collection 0897
MCC Exclusion 7th characters A - C see Appendix A PDX collection 1298
HAC 7th characters A - C see Appendix B for HAC conditional logic

+ **S72.02 Fracture of epiphysis (separation) (upper) of femur**
Transepiphyseal fracture of femur
Excludes1: *capital femoral epiphyseal fracture (pediatric) of femur (S79.01-)*
Salter-Harris Type I physeal fracture of upper end of femur (S79.01-)

CC MCC +7th **S72.021 Displaced fracture of epiphysis (separation) (upper) of right femur**
CC Exclusion 7th characters K - R see Appendix A PDX collection 0897
MCC Exclusion 7th character A see Appendix A PDX collection 1297
MCC Exclusion 7th characters B & C see Appendix A PDX collection 1298
HAC 7th characters A - C see Appendix B for HAC conditional logic

CC MCC +7th **S72.022 Displaced fracture of epiphysis (separation) (upper) of left femur**
CC Exclusion 7th characters K - R see Appendix A PDX collection 0897
MCC Exclusion 7th character A see Appendix A PDX collection 1299
MCC Exclusion 7th characters B & C see Appendix A PDX collection 1298
HAC 7th characters A - C see Appendix B for HAC conditional logic

CC MCC +7th **S72.023 Displaced fracture of epiphysis (separation) (upper) of unspecified femur**
CC Exclusion 7th characters K - R see Appendix A PDX collection 0897
MCC Exclusion 7th characters A - C see Appendix A PDX collection 1298
HAC 7th characters A - C see Appendix B for HAC conditional logic

CC MCC +7th **S72.024 Nondisplaced fracture of epiphysis (separation) (upper) of right femur**
CC Exclusion 7th characters K - R see Appendix A PDX collection 0897
MCC Exclusion 7th character A see Appendix A PDX collection 1297
MCC Exclusion 7th characters B & C see Appendix A PDX collection 1298
HAC 7th characters A - C see Appendix B for HAC conditional logic

CC MCC +7th **S72.025 Nondisplaced fracture of epiphysis (separation) (upper) of left femur**
CC Exclusion 7th characters K - R see Appendix A PDX collection 0897
MCC Exclusion 7th character A see Appendix A PDX collection 1299
MCC Exclusion 7th characters B & C see Appendix A PDX collection 1298
HAC 7th characters A - C see Appendix B for HAC conditional logic

CC MCC +7th **S72.026 Nondisplaced fracture of epiphysis (separation) (upper) of unspecified femur**
CC Exclusion 7th characters K - R see Appendix A PDX collection 0897
MCC Exclusion 7th characters A - C see Appendix A PDX collection 1298
HAC 7th characters A - C see Appendix B for HAC conditional logic

+ **S72.03 Midcervical fracture of femur**
Transcervical fracture of femur NOS

CC MCC +7th **S72.031 Displaced midcervical fracture of right femur**
CC Exclusion 7th characters K - R see Appendix A PDX collection 0897
MCC Exclusion 7th character A see Appendix A PDX collection 1297
MCC Exclusion 7th characters B & C see Appendix A PDX collection 1298
HAC 7th characters A - C see Appendix B for HAC conditional logic

CC MCC +7th **S72.032 Displaced midcervical fracture of left femur**
CC Exclusion 7th characters K - R see Appendix A PDX collection 0897
MCC Exclusion 7th character A see Appendix A PDX collection 1299
MCC Exclusion 7th characters B & C see Appendix A PDX collection 1298
HAC 7th characters A - C see Appendix B for HAC conditional logic

CC MCC +7th **S72.033 Displaced midcervical fracture of unspecified femur**
CC Exclusion 7th characters K - R see Appendix A PDX collection 0897
MCC Exclusion 7th characters A - C see Appendix A PDX collection 1298
HAC 7th characters A - C see Appendix B for HAC conditional logic

CC MCC +7th **S72.034 Nondisplaced midcervical fracture of right femur**
CC Exclusion 7th characters K - R see Appendix A PDX collection 0897
MCC Exclusion 7th character A see Appendix A PDX collection 1297
MCC Exclusion 7th characters B & C see Appendix A PDX collection 1298
HAC 7th characters A - C see Appendix B for HAC conditional logic

CC MCC +7th **S72.035 Nondisplaced midcervical fracture of left femur**
CC Exclusion 7th characters K - R see Appendix A PDX collection 0897
MCC Exclusion 7th character A see Appendix A PDX collection 1299
MCC Exclusion 7th characters B & C see Appendix A PDX collection 1298
HAC 7th characters A - C see Appendix B for HAC conditional logic

CC MCC +7th **S72.036 Nondisplaced midcervical fracture of unspecified femur**
CC Exclusion 7th characters K - R see Appendix A PDX collection 0897
MCC Exclusion 7th characters A - C see Appendix A PDX collection 1298
HAC 7th characters A - C see Appendix B for HAC conditional logic

+ **S72.04 Fracture of base of neck of femur**
Cervicotrochanteric fracture of femur

CC MCC +7th **S72.041 Displaced fracture of base of neck of right femur**
CC Exclusion 7th characters K - R see Appendix A PDX collection 0897
MCC Exclusion 7th character A see Appendix A PDX collection 1297
MCC Exclusion 7th characters B & C see Appendix A PDX collection 1298
HAC 7th characters A - C see Appendix B for HAC conditional logic

CC MCC +7th **S72.042 Displaced fracture of base of neck of left femur**
CC Exclusion 7th characters K - R see Appendix A PDX collection 0897
MCC Exclusion 7th character A see Appendix A PDX collection 1299
MCC Exclusion 7th characters B & C see Appendix A PDX collection 1298
HAC 7th characters A - C see Appendix B for HAC conditional logic

CC MCC +7th **S72.043 Displaced fracture of base of neck of unspecified femur**
CC Exclusion 7th characters K - R see Appendix A PDX collection 0897
MCC Exclusion 7th characters A - C see Appendix A PDX collection 1298
HAC 7th characters A - C see Appendix B for HAC conditional logic

CC MCC +7th **S72.044 Nondisplaced fracture of base of neck of right femur**
CC Exclusion 7th characters K - R see Appendix A PDX collection 0897
MCC Exclusion 7th character A see Appendix A PDX collection 1297
MCC Exclusion 7th characters B & C see Appendix A PDX collection 1298
HAC 7th characters A - C see Appendix B for HAC conditional logic

CC MCC +7th **S72.045 Nondisplaced fracture of base of neck of left femur**
CC Exclusion 7th characters K - R see Appendix A PDX collection 0897
MCC Exclusion 7th character A see Appendix A PDX collection 1299
MCC Exclusion 7th characters B & C see Appendix A PDX collection 1298
HAC 7th characters A - C see Appendix B for HAC conditional logic

CC MCC +7th **S72.046 Nondisplaced fracture of base of neck of unspecified femur**
CC Exclusion 7th characters K - R see Appendix A PDX collection 0897
MCC Exclusion 7th characters A - C see Appendix A PDX collection 1298
HAC 7th characters A - C see Appendix B for HAC conditional logic

+ **S72.05 Unspecified fracture of head of femur**
Fracture of head of femur NOS

CC MCC +7th **S72.051 Unspecified fracture of head of right femur**
CC Exclusion 7th characters K - R see Appendix A PDX collection 0897
MCC Exclusion 7th character A see Appendix A PDX collection 1297
MCC Exclusion 7th characters B & C see Appendix A PDX collection 1298
HAC 7th characters A - C see Appendix B for HAC conditional logic

CC MCC +7th **S72.052 Unspecified fracture of head of left femur**
CC Exclusion 7th characters K - R see Appendix A PDX collection 0897
MCC Exclusion 7th character A see Appendix A PDX collection 1299
MCC Exclusion 7th characters B & C see Appendix A PDX collection 1298
HAC 7th characters A - C see Appendix B for HAC conditional logic

CC MCC +7th **S72.059 Unspecified fracture of head of unspecified femur**
CC Exclusion 7th characters K - R see Appendix A PDX collection 0897
MCC Exclusion 7th characters A - C see Appendix A PDX collection 1298
HAC 7th characters A - C see Appendix B for HAC conditional logic

+ **S72.06 Articular fracture of head of femur**

CC MCC +7th **S72.061 Displaced articular fracture of head of right femur**
CC Exclusion 7th characters K - R see Appendix A PDX collection 0897
MCC Exclusion 7th character A see Appendix A PDX collection 1297
MCC Exclusion 7th characters B & C see Appendix A PDX collection 1298
HAC 7th characters A - C see Appendix B for HAC conditional logic

CC MCC +7th **S72.062 Displaced articular fracture of head of left femur**
CC Exclusion 7th characters K - R see Appendix A PDX collection 0897
MCC Exclusion 7th character A see Appendix A PDX collection 1299
MCC Exclusion 7th characters B & C see Appendix A PDX collection 1298
HAC 7th characters A - C see Appendix B for HAC conditional logic

CC MCC +7th **S72.063 Displaced articular fracture of head of unspecified femur**
CC Exclusion 7th characters K - R see Appendix A PDX collection 0897
MCC Exclusion 7th characters A - C see Appendix A PDX collection 1298
HAC 7th characters A - C see Appendix B for HAC conditional logic

CC MCC +7th **S72.064 Nondisplaced articular fracture of head of right femur**
CC Exclusion 7th characters K - R see Appendix A PDX collection 0897
MCC Exclusion 7th character A see Appendix A PDX collection 1297
MCC Exclusion 7th characters B & C see Appendix A PDX collection 1298
HAC 7th characters A - C see Appendix B for HAC conditional logic

CC MCC +7th **S72.065 Nondisplaced articular fracture of head of left femur**
CC Exclusion 7th characters K - R see Appendix A PDX collection 0897
MCC Exclusion 7th character A see Appendix A PDX collection 1299
MCC Exclusion 7th characters B & C see Appendix A PDX collection 1298
HAC 7th characters A - C see Appendix B for HAC conditional logic

CC MCC +7th **S72.066 Nondisplaced articular fracture of head of unspecified femur**
CC Exclusion 7th characters K - R see Appendix A PDX collection 0897
MCC Exclusion 7th characters A - C see Appendix A PDX collection 1298
HAC 7th characters A - C see Appendix B for HAC conditional logic

+ **S72.09 Other fracture of head and neck of femur**

CC MCC +7th **S72.091 Other fracture of head and neck of right femur**
CC Exclusion 7th characters K - R see Appendix A PDX collection 0897
MCC Exclusion 7th character A see Appendix A PDX collection 1297
MCC Exclusion 7th characters B & C see Appendix A PDX collection 1298
HAC 7th characters A - C see Appendix B for HAC conditional logic

CC MCC +7th **S72.092 Other fracture of head and neck of left femur**
CC Exclusion 7th characters K - R see Appendix A PDX collection 0897
MCC Exclusion 7th character A see Appendix A PDX collection 1299
MCC Exclusion 7th characters B & C see Appendix A PDX collection 1298
HAC 7th characters A - C see Appendix B for HAC conditional logic

CC MCC +7th **S72.099 Other fracture of head and neck of unspecified femur**
CC Exclusion 7th characters K - R see Appendix A PDX collection 0897
MCC Exclusion 7th characters A - C see Appendix A PDX collection 1298
HAC 7th characters A - C see Appendix B for HAC conditional logic

+ S72.1 Pertrochanteric fracture

+ S72.10 Unspecified trochanteric fracture of femur
Fracture of trochanter NOS

CC MCC **S72.101 Unspecified trochanteric fracture of right femur**
CC Exclusion 7th characters K - R see Appendix A PDX collection 0897
MCC Exclusion 7th character A see Appendix A PDX collection 1297
MCC Exclusion 7th characters B & C see Appendix A PDX collection 1298
HAC 7th characters A - C see Appendix B for HAC conditional logic

CC MCC **S72.102 Unspecified trochanteric fracture of left femur**
CC Exclusion 7th characters K - R see Appendix A PDX collection 0897
MCC Exclusion 7th character A see Appendix A PDX collection 1299
MCC Exclusion 7th characters B & C see Appendix A PDX collection 1298
HAC 7th characters A - C see Appendix B for HAC conditional logic

CC MCC **S72.109 Unspecified trochanteric fracture of unspecified femur**
CC Exclusion 7th characters K - R see Appendix A PDX collection 0897
MCC Exclusion 7th characters A - C see Appendix A PDX collection 1298
HAC 7th characters A - C see Appendix B for HAC conditional logic

+ S72.11 Fracture of greater trochanter of femur

CC MCC +7th **S72.111 Displaced fracture of greater trochanter of right femur**
CC Exclusion 7th characters K - R see Appendix A PDX collection 0897
MCC Exclusion 7th character A see Appendix A PDX collection 1297
MCC Exclusion 7th characters B & C see Appendix A PDX collection 1298
HAC 7th characters A - C see Appendix B for HAC conditional logic

CC MCC +7th **S72.112 Displaced fracture of greater trochanter of left femur**
CC Exclusion 7th characters K - R see Appendix A PDX collection 0897
MCC Exclusion 7th character A see Appendix A PDX collection 1299
MCC Exclusion 7th characters B & C see Appendix A PDX collection 1298
HAC 7th characters A - C see Appendix B for HAC conditional logic

CC MCC +7th **S72.113 Displaced fracture of greater trochanter of unspecified femur**
CC Exclusion 7th characters K - R see Appendix A PDX collection 0897
MCC Exclusion 7th characters A - C see Appendix A PDX collection 1298
HAC 7th characters A - C see Appendix B for HAC conditional logic

CC MCC +7th **S72.114 Nondisplaced fracture of greater trochanter of right femur**
CC Exclusion 7th characters K - R see Appendix A PDX collection 0897
MCC Exclusion 7th character A see Appendix A PDX collection 1297
MCC Exclusion 7th characters B & C see Appendix A PDX collection 1298
HAC 7th characters A - C see Appendix B for HAC conditional logic

CC MCC +7th **S72.115 Nondisplaced fracture of greater trochanter of left femur**
CC Exclusion 7th characters K - R see Appendix A PDX collection 0897
MCC Exclusion 7th character A see Appendix A PDX collection 1299
MCC Exclusion 7th characters B & C see Appendix A PDX collection 1298
HAC 7th characters A - C see Appendix B for HAC conditional logic

CC MCC +7th **S72.116 Nondisplaced fracture of greater trochanter of unspecified femur**
CC Exclusion 7th characters K - R see Appendix A PDX collection 0897
MCC Exclusion 7th characters A - C see Appendix A PDX collection 1298
HAC 7th characters A - C see Appendix B for HAC conditional logic

+ S72.12 Fracture of lesser trochanter of femur

CC MCC +7th **S72.121 Displaced fracture of lesser trochanter of right femur**
CC Exclusion 7th characters K - R see Appendix A PDX collection 0897
MCC Exclusion 7th character A see Appendix A PDX collection 1297
MCC Exclusion 7th characters B & C see Appendix A PDX collection 1298
HAC 7th characters A - C see Appendix B for HAC conditional logic

CC MCC +7th **S72.122 Displaced fracture of lesser trochanter of left femur**
CC Exclusion 7th characters K - R see Appendix A PDX collection 0897
MCC Exclusion 7th character A see Appendix A PDX collection 1299
MCC Exclusion 7th characters B & C see Appendix A PDX collection 1298
HAC 7th characters A - C see Appendix B for HAC conditional logic

CC MCC +7th **S72.123 Displaced fracture of lesser trochanter of unspecified femur**
CC Exclusion 7th characters K - R see Appendix A PDX collection 0897
MCC Exclusion 7th characters A - C see Appendix A PDX collection 1298
HAC 7th characters A - C see Appendix B for HAC conditional logic

CC MCC +7th **S72.124 Nondisplaced fracture of lesser trochanter of right femur**
CC Exclusion 7th characters K - R see Appendix A PDX collection 0897
MCC Exclusion 7th character A see Appendix A PDX collection 1297
MCC Exclusion 7th characters B & C see Appendix A PDX collection 1298
HAC 7th characters A - C see Appendix B for HAC conditional logic

CC MCC +7th **S72.125 Nondisplaced fracture of lesser trochanter of left femur**
CC Exclusion 7th characters K - R see Appendix A PDX collection 0897
MCC Exclusion 7th character A see Appendix A PDX collection 1299
MCC Exclusion 7th characters B & C see Appendix A PDX collection 1298
HAC 7th characters A - C see Appendix B for HAC conditional logic

CC MCC +7th **S72.126 Nondisplaced fracture of lesser trochanter of unspecified femur**
CC Exclusion 7th characters K - R see Appendix A PDX collection 0897
MCC Exclusion 7th characters A - C see Appendix A PDX collection 1298
HAC 7th characters A - C see Appendix B for HAC conditional logic

+ S72.13 Apophyseal fracture of femur
Excludes1: *chronic (nontraumatic) slipped upper femoral epiphysis (M93.0-)*

CC MCC +7th **S72.131 Displaced apophyseal fracture of right femur**
CC Exclusion 7th characters K - R see Appendix A PDX collection 0897
MCC Exclusion 7th character A see Appendix A PDX collection 1297
MCC Exclusion 7th characters B & C see Appendix A PDX collection 1298
HAC 7th characters A - C see Appendix B for HAC conditional logic

CC MCC +7th **S72.132 Displaced apophyseal fracture of left femur**
CC Exclusion 7th characters K - R see Appendix A PDX collection 0897
MCC Exclusion 7th character A see Appendix A PDX collection 1299
MCC Exclusion 7th characters B & C see Appendix A PDX collection 1298
HAC 7th characters A - C see Appendix B for HAC conditional logic

CC MCC +7th **S72.133 Displaced apophyseal fracture of unspecified femur**
CC Exclusion 7th characters K - R see Appendix A PDX collection 0897
MCC Exclusion 7th characters A - C see Appendix A PDX collection 1298
HAC 7th characters A - C see Appendix B for HAC conditional logic

CC MCC +7th **S72.134 Nondisplaced apophyseal fracture of right femur**
CC Exclusion 7th characters K - R see Appendix A PDX collection 0897
MCC Exclusion 7th character A see Appendix A PDX collection 1297
MCC Exclusion 7th characters B & C see Appendix A PDX collection 1298
HAC 7th characters A - C see Appendix B for HAC conditional logic

CC MCC +7th **S72.135 Nondisplaced apophyseal fracture of left femur**
CC Exclusion 7th characters K - R see Appendix A PDX collection 0897
MCC Exclusion 7th character A see Appendix A PDX collection 1299
MCC Exclusion 7th characters B & C see Appendix A PDX collection 1298
HAC 7th characters A - C see Appendix B for HAC conditional logic

CC MCC +7th **S72.136 Nondisplaced apophyseal fracture of unspecified femur**
CC Exclusion 7th characters K - R see Appendix A PDX collection 0897
MCC Exclusion 7th characters A - C see Appendix A PDX collection 1298
HAC 7th characters A - C see Appendix B for HAC conditional logic

+ **S72.14 Intertrochanteric fracture of femur**

CC MCC +7th **S72.141 Displaced intertrochanteric fracture of right femur**
CC Exclusion 7th characters K - R see Appendix A PDX collection 0897
MCC Exclusion 7th character A see Appendix A PDX collection 1297
MCC Exclusion 7th characters B & C see Appendix A PDX collection 1298
AHA CC: 4Q, 2013, 128-129
HAC 7th characters A - C see Appendix B for HAC conditional logic

CC MCC +7th **S72.142 Displaced intertrochanteric fracture of left femur**
CC Exclusion 7th characters K - R see Appendix A PDX collection 0897
MCC Exclusion 7th character A see Appendix A PDX collection 1299
MCC Exclusion 7th characters B & C see Appendix A PDX collection 1298
HAC 7th characters A - C see Appendix B for HAC conditional logic

CC MCC +7th **S72.143 Displaced intertrochanteric fracture of unspecified femur**
CC Exclusion 7th characters K - R see Appendix A PDX collection 0897
MCC Exclusion 7th characters A - C see Appendix A PDX collection 1298
HAC 7th characters A - C see Appendix B for HAC conditional logic

CC MCC +7th **S72.144 Nondisplaced intertrochanteric fracture of right femur**
CC Exclusion 7th characters K - R see Appendix A PDX collection 0897
MCC Exclusion 7th character A see Appendix A PDX collection 1297
MCC Exclusion 7th characters B & C see Appendix A PDX collection 1298
HAC 7th characters A - C see Appendix B for HAC conditional logic

CC MCC +7th **S72.145 Nondisplaced intertrochanteric fracture of left femur**
CC Exclusion 7th characters K - R see Appendix A PDX collection 0897
MCC Exclusion 7th character A see Appendix A PDX collection 1299
MCC Exclusion 7th characters B & C see Appendix A PDX collection 1298
HAC 7th characters A - C see Appendix B for HAC conditional logic

CC MCC +7th **S72.146 Nondisplaced intertrochanteric fracture of unspecified femur**
CC Exclusion 7th characters K - R see Appendix A PDX collection 0897
MCC Exclusion 7th characters A - C see Appendix A PDX collection 1298
HAC 7th characters A - C see Appendix B for HAC conditional logic

+ **S72.2 Subtrochanteric fracture of femur**

CC MCC X+7th **S72.21 Displaced subtrochanteric fracture of right femur**
CC Exclusion 7th characters K - R see Appendix A PDX collection 0897
MCC Exclusion 7th characters A - C see Appendix A PDX collection 1298
HAC 7th characters A - C see Appendix B for HAC conditional logic

CC MCC X+7th **S72.22 Displaced subtrochanteric fracture of left femur**
CC Exclusion 7th characters K - R see Appendix A PDX collection 0897
MCC Exclusion 7th characters A - C see Appendix A PDX collection 1298
HAC 7th characters A - C see Appendix B for HAC conditional logic

CC MCC X+7th **S72.23 Displaced subtrochanteric fracture of unspecified femur**
CC Exclusion 7th characters K - R see Appendix A PDX collection 0897
MCC Exclusion 7th characters A - C see Appendix A PDX collection 1298
HAC 7th characters A - C see Appendix B for HAC conditional logic

CC MCC X+7th **S72.24 Nondisplaced subtrochanteric fracture of right femur**
CC Exclusion 7th characters K - R see Appendix A PDX collection 0897
MCC Exclusion 7th characters A - C see Appendix A PDX collection 1298
HAC 7th characters A - C see Appendix B for HAC conditional logic

CC MCC X+7th **S72.25 Nondisplaced subtrochanteric fracture of left femur**
CC Exclusion 7th characters K - R see Appendix A PDX collection 0897
MCC Exclusion 7th characters A - C see Appendix A PDX collection 1298
HAC 7th characters A - C see Appendix B for HAC conditional logic

CC MCC X+7th **S72.26 Nondisplaced subtrochanteric fracture of unspecified femur**
CC Exclusion 7th characters K - R see Appendix A PDX collection 0897
MCC Exclusion 7th characters A - C see Appendix A PDX collection 1298
HAC 7th characters A - C see Appendix B for HAC conditional logic

+ **S72.3 Fracture of shaft of femur**

+ **S72.30 Unspecified fracture of shaft of femur**

CC MCC +7th **S72.301 Unspecified fracture of shaft of right femur**
CC Exclusion 7th characters K - R see Appendix A PDX collection 0897
MCC Exclusion 7th character A see Appendix A PDX collection 1297
MCC Exclusion 7th characters B & C see Appendix A PDX collection 1298
HAC 7th characters A - C see Appendix B for HAC conditional logic

CC MCC +7th **S72.302 Unspecified fracture of shaft of left femur**
CC Exclusion 7th characters K - R see Appendix A PDX collection 0897
MCC Exclusion 7th character A see Appendix A PDX collection 1299
MCC Exclusion 7th characters B & C see Appendix A PDX collection 1298
HAC 7th characters A - C see Appendix B for HAC conditional logic

CC MCC +7th **S72.309 Unspecified fracture of shaft of unspecified femur**
CC Exclusion 7th characters K - R see Appendix A PDX collection 0897
MCC Exclusion 7th characters A - C see Appendix A PDX collection 1298
HAC 7th characters A - C see Appendix B for HAC conditional logic

+ **S72.32 Transverse fracture of shaft of femur**

CC MCC +7th **S72.321 Displaced transverse fracture of shaft of right femur**
CC Exclusion 7th characters K - R see Appendix A PDX collection 0897
MCC Exclusion 7th character A see Appendix A PDX collection 1297
MCC Exclusion 7th characters B & C see Appendix A PDX collection 1298
HAC 7th characters A - C see Appendix B for HAC conditional logic

CC MCC +7th **S72.322 Displaced transverse fracture of shaft of left femur**
CC Exclusion 7th characters K - R see Appendix A PDX collection 0897
MCC Exclusion 7th character A see Appendix A PDX collection 1299
MCC Exclusion 7th characters B & C see Appendix A PDX collection 1298
HAC 7th characters A - C see Appendix B for HAC conditional logic

CC MCC +7th **S72.323 Displaced transverse fracture of shaft of unspecified femur**
CC Exclusion 7th characters K - R see Appendix A PDX collection 0897
MCC Exclusion 7th characters A - C see Appendix A PDX collection 1298
HAC 7th characters A - C see Appendix B for HAC conditional logic

CC MCC +7th **S72.324 Nondisplaced transverse fracture of shaft of right femur**
CC Exclusion 7th characters K - R see Appendix A PDX collection 0897
MCC Exclusion 7th character A see Appendix A PDX collection 1297
MCC Exclusion 7th characters B & C see Appendix A PDX collection 1298
HAC 7th characters A - C see Appendix B for HAC conditional logic

CC MCC +7th **S72.325 Nondisplaced transverse fracture of shaft of left femur**
CC Exclusion 7th characters K - R see Appendix A PDX collection 0897
MCC Exclusion 7th character A see Appendix A PDX collection 1299
MCC Exclusion 7th characters B & C see Appendix A PDX collection 1298
HAC 7th characters A - C see Appendix B for HAC conditional logic

CC MCC +7th **S72.326 Nondisplaced transverse fracture of shaft of unspecified femur**
CC Exclusion 7th characters K - R see Appendix A PDX collection 0897
MCC Exclusion 7th characters A - C see Appendix A PDX collection 1298
HAC 7th characters A - C see Appendix B for HAC conditional logic

\+ **S72.33 Oblique fracture of shaft of femur**

CC MCC +7th **S72.331 Displaced oblique fracture of shaft of right femur**
CC Exclusion 7th characters K - R see Appendix A PDX collection 0897
MCC Exclusion 7th character A see Appendix A PDX collection 1297
MCC Exclusion 7th characters B & C see Appendix A PDX collection 1298
HAC 7th characters A - C see Appendix B for HAC conditional logic

CC MCC +7th **S72.332 Displaced oblique fracture of shaft of left femur**
CC Exclusion 7th characters K - R see Appendix A PDX collection 0897
MCC Exclusion 7th character A see Appendix A PDX collection 1299
MCC Exclusion 7th characters B & C see Appendix A PDX collection 1298
HAC 7th characters A - C see Appendix B for HAC conditional logic

CC MCC +7th **S72.333 Displaced oblique fracture of shaft of unspecified femur**
CC Exclusion 7th characters K - R see Appendix A PDX collection 0897
MCC Exclusion 7th characters A - C see Appendix A PDX collection 1298
HAC 7th characters A - C see Appendix B for HAC conditional logic

CC MCC +7th **S72.334 Nondisplaced oblique fracture of shaft of right femur**
CC Exclusion 7th characters K - R see Appendix A PDX collection 0897
MCC Exclusion 7th character A see Appendix A PDX collection 1297
MCC Exclusion 7th characters B & C see Appendix A PDX collection 1298
HAC 7th characters A - C see Appendix B for HAC conditional logic

CC MCC +7th **S72.335 Nondisplaced oblique fracture of shaft of left femur**
CC Exclusion 7th characters K - R see Appendix A PDX collection 0897
MCC Exclusion 7th character A see Appendix A PDX collection 1299
MCC Exclusion 7th characters B & C see Appendix A PDX collection 1298
HAC 7th characters A - C see Appendix B for HAC conditional logic

CC MCC +7th **S72.336 Nondisplaced oblique fracture of shaft of unspecified femur**
CC Exclusion 7th characters K - R see Appendix A PDX collection 0897
MCC Exclusion 7th characters A - C see Appendix A PDX collection 1298
HAC 7th characters A - C see Appendix B for HAC conditional logic

\+ **S72.34 Spiral fracture of shaft of femur**

CC MCC +7th **S72.341 Displaced spiral fracture of shaft of right femur**
CC Exclusion 7th characters K - R see Appendix A PDX collection 0897
MCC Exclusion 7th character A see Appendix A PDX collection 1297
MCC Exclusion 7th characters B & C see Appendix A PDX collection 1298
HAC 7th characters A - C see Appendix B for HAC conditional logic

CC MCC +7th **S72.342 Displaced spiral fracture of shaft of left femur**
CC Exclusion 7th characters K - R see Appendix A PDX collection 0897
MCC Exclusion 7th character A see Appendix A PDX collection 1299
MCC Exclusion 7th characters B & C see Appendix A PDX collection 1298
HAC 7th characters A - C see Appendix B for HAC conditional logic

CC MCC +7th **S72.343 Displaced spiral fracture of shaft of unspecified femur**
CC Exclusion 7th characters K - R see Appendix A PDX collection 0897
MCC Exclusion 7th characters A - C see Appendix A PDX collection 1298
HAC 7th characters A - C see Appendix B for HAC conditional logic

CC MCC +7th **S72.344 Nondisplaced spiral fracture of shaft of right femur**
CC Exclusion 7th characters K - R see Appendix A PDX collection 0897
MCC Exclusion 7th character A see Appendix A PDX collection 1297
MCC Exclusion 7th characters B & C see Appendix A PDX collection 1298
HAC 7th characters A - C see Appendix B for HAC conditional logic

CC MCC +7th **S72.345 Nondisplaced spiral fracture of shaft of left femur**
CC Exclusion 7th characters K - R see Appendix A PDX collection 0897
MCC Exclusion 7th character A see Appendix A PDX collection 1299
MCC Exclusion 7th characters B & C see Appendix A PDX collection 1298
HAC 7th characters A - C see Appendix B for HAC conditional logic

CC MCC +7th **S72.346 Nondisplaced spiral fracture of shaft of unspecified femur**
CC Exclusion 7th characters K - R see Appendix A PDX collection 0897
MCC Exclusion 7th characters A - C see Appendix A PDX collection 1298
HAC 7th characters A - C see Appendix B for HAC conditional logic

\+ **S72.35 Comminuted fracture of shaft of femur**

CC MCC +7th **S72.351 Displaced comminuted fracture of shaft of right femur**
CC Exclusion 7th characters K - R see Appendix A PDX collection 0897
MCC Exclusion 7th character A see Appendix A PDX collection 1297
MCC Exclusion 7th characters B & C see Appendix A PDX collection 1298
HAC 7th characters A - C see Appendix B for HAC conditional logic

CC MCC +7th **S72.352 Displaced comminuted fracture of shaft of left femur**
CC Exclusion 7th characters K - R see Appendix A PDX collection 0897
MCC Exclusion 7th character A see Appendix A PDX collection 1299
MCC Exclusion 7th characters B & C see Appendix A PDX collection 1298
HAC 7th characters A - C see Appendix B for HAC conditional logic

CC MCC +7th **S72.353 Displaced comminuted fracture of shaft of unspecified femur**
CC Exclusion 7th characters K - R see Appendix A PDX collection 0897
MCC Exclusion 7th characters A - C see Appendix A PDX collection 1298
HAC 7th characters A - C see Appendix B for HAC conditional logic

CC MCC +7th **S72.354 Nondisplaced comminuted fracture of shaft of right femur**
CC Exclusion 7th characters K - R see Appendix A PDX collection 0897
MCC Exclusion 7th character A see Appendix A PDX collection 1297
MCC Exclusion 7th characters B & C see Appendix A PDX collection 1298
HAC 7th characters A - C see Appendix B for HAC conditional logic

CC MCC +7th **S72.355 Nondisplaced comminuted fracture of shaft of left femur**
CC Exclusion 7th characters K - R see Appendix A PDX collection 0897
MCC Exclusion 7th character A see Appendix A PDX collection 1299
MCC Exclusion 7th characters B & C see Appendix A PDX collection 1298
HAC 7th characters A - C see Appendix B for HAC conditional logic

CC MCC +7th **S72.356 Nondisplaced comminuted fracture of shaft of unspecified femur**
CC Exclusion 7th characters K - R see Appendix A PDX collection 0897
MCC Exclusion 7th characters A - C see Appendix A PDX collection 1298
HAC 7th characters A - C see Appendix B for HAC conditional logic

+ **S72.36 Segmental fracture of shaft of femur**

CC MCC +7th **S72.361 Displaced segmental fracture of shaft of right femur**
CC Exclusion 7th characters K - R see Appendix A PDX collection 0897
MCC Exclusion 7th character A see Appendix A PDX collection 1297
MCC Exclusion 7th characters B & C see Appendix A PDX collection 1298
HAC 7th characters A - C see Appendix B for HAC conditional logic

CC MCC +7th **S72.362 Displaced segmental fracture of shaft of left femur**
CC Exclusion 7th characters K - R see Appendix A PDX collection 0897
MCC Exclusion 7th character A see Appendix A PDX collection 1299
MCC Exclusion 7th characters B & C see Appendix A PDX collection 1298
HAC 7th characters A - C see Appendix B for HAC conditional logic

CC MCC +7th **S72.363 Displaced segmental fracture of shaft of unspecified femur**
CC Exclusion 7th characters K - R see Appendix A PDX collection 0897
MCC Exclusion 7th characters A - C see Appendix A PDX collection 1298
HAC 7th characters A - C see Appendix B for HAC conditional logic

CC MCC +7th **S72.364 Nondisplaced segmental fracture of shaft of right femur**
CC Exclusion 7th characters K - R see Appendix A PDX collection 0897
MCC Exclusion 7th character A see Appendix A PDX collection 1297
MCC Exclusion 7th characters B & C see Appendix A PDX collection 1298
HAC 7th characters A - C see Appendix B for HAC conditional logic

CC MCC +7th **S72.365 Nondisplaced segmental fracture of shaft of left femur**
CC Exclusion 7th characters K - R see Appendix A PDX collection 0897
MCC Exclusion 7th character A see Appendix A PDX collection 1299
MCC Exclusion 7th characters B & C see Appendix A PDX collection 1298
HAC 7th characters A - C see Appendix B for HAC conditional logic

CC MCC +7th **S72.366 Nondisplaced segmental fracture of shaft of unspecified femur**
CC Exclusion 7th characters K - R see Appendix A PDX collection 0897
MCC Exclusion 7th characters A - C see Appendix A PDX collection 1298
HAC 7th characters A - C see Appendix B for HAC conditional logic

+ **S72.39 Other fracture of shaft of femur**

CC MCC +7th **S72.391 Other fracture of shaft of right femur**
CC Exclusion 7th characters K - R see Appendix A PDX collection 0897
MCC Exclusion 7th character A see Appendix A PDX collection 1297
MCC Exclusion 7th characters B & C see Appendix A PDX collection 1298
HAC 7th characters A - C see Appendix B for HAC conditional logic

CC MCC +7th **S72.392 Other fracture of shaft of left femur**
CC Exclusion 7th characters K - R see Appendix A PDX collection 0897
MCC Exclusion 7th character A see Appendix A PDX collection 1299
MCC Exclusion 7th characters B & C see Appendix A PDX collection 1298
HAC 7th characters A - C see Appendix B for HAC conditional logic

CC MCC +7th **S72.399 Other fracture of shaft of unspecified femur**
CC Exclusion 7th characters K - R see Appendix A PDX collection 0897
MCC Exclusion 7th characters A - C see Appendix A PDX collection 1298
HAC 7th characters A - C see Appendix B for HAC conditional logic

+ **S72.4 Fracture of lower end of femur**
Fracture of distal end of femur
Excludes2: *fracture of shaft of femur (S72.3-)*
physeal fracture of lower end of femur (S79.1-)

+ **S72.40 Unspecified fracture of lower end of femur**

CC MCC +7th **S72.401 Unspecified fracture of lower end of right femur**
CC Exclusion 7th character A see Appendix A PDX collection 1300
CC Exclusion 7th characters K - R see Appendix A PDX collection 0897
MCC Exclusion 7th characters B & C see Appendix A PDX collection 1301
HAC 7th characters A - C see Appendix B for HAC conditional logic

CC MCC +7th **S72.402 Unspecified fracture of lower end of left femur**
CC Exclusion 7th character A see Appendix A PDX collection 1302
CC Exclusion 7th characters K - R see Appendix A PDX collection 0897
MCC Exclusion 7th characters B & C see Appendix A PDX collection 1301
HAC 7th characters A - C see Appendix B for HAC conditional logic

CC MCC +7th **S72.409 Unspecified fracture of lower end of unspecified femur**
CC Exclusion 7th character A see Appendix A PDX collection 1301
CC Exclusion 7th characters K - R see Appendix A PDX collection 0897
MCC Exclusion 7th characters B & C see Appendix A PDX collection 1301
HAC 7th characters A - C see Appendix B for HAC conditional logic

+ **S72.41 Unspecified condyle fracture of lower end of femur**
Condyle fracture of femur NOS

CC MCC +7th **S72.411 Displaced unspecified condyle fracture of lower end of right femur**
CC Exclusion 7th character A see Appendix A PDX collection 1300
CC Exclusion 7th characters K - R see Appendix A PDX collection 0897
MCC Exclusion 7th characters B & C see Appendix A PDX collection 1301
HAC 7th characters A - C see Appendix B for HAC conditional logic

CC MCC +7th **S72.412 Displaced unspecified condyle fracture of lower end of left femur**
CC Exclusion 7th character A see Appendix A PDX collection 1302
CC Exclusion 7th characters K - R see Appendix A PDX collection 0897
MCC Exclusion 7th characters B & C see Appendix A PDX collection 1301
HAC 7th characters A - C see Appendix B for HAC conditional logic

CC MCC +7th **S72.413 Displaced unspecified condyle fracture of lower end of unspecified femur**
CC Exclusion 7th character A see Appendix A PDX collection 1301
CC Exclusion 7th characters K - R see Appendix A PDX collection 0897
MCC Exclusion 7th characters B & C see Appendix A PDX collection 1301
HAC 7th characters A - C see Appendix B for HAC conditional logic

CC MCC +7th **S72.414 Nondisplaced unspecified condyle fracture of lower end of right femur**
CC Exclusion 7th character A see Appendix A PDX collection 1300
CC Exclusion 7th characters K - R see Appendix A PDX collection 0897
MCC Exclusion 7th characters B & C see Appendix A PDX collection 1301
HAC 7th characters A - C see Appendix B for HAC conditional logic

CC MCC +7th **S72.415 Nondisplaced unspecified condyle fracture of lower end of left femur**
CC Exclusion 7th character A see Appendix A PDX collection 1302
CC Exclusion 7th characters K - R see Appendix A PDX collection 0897
MCC Exclusion 7th characters B & C see Appendix A PDX collection 1301
HAC 7th characters A - C see Appendix B for HAC conditional logic

CC MCC +7th **S72.416 Nondisplaced unspecified condyle fracture of lower end of unspecified femur**
CC Exclusion 7th character A see Appendix A PDX collection 1301
CC Exclusion 7th characters K - R see Appendix A PDX collection 0897
MCC Exclusion 7th characters B & C see Appendix A PDX collection 1301
HAC 7th characters A - C see Appendix B for HAC conditional logic

+ **S72.42 Fracture of lateral condyle of femur**

CC MCC +7th **S72.421 Displaced fracture of lateral condyle of right femur**
CC Exclusion 7th character A see Appendix A PDX collection 1300
CC Exclusion 7th characters K - R see Appendix A PDX collection 0897
MCC Exclusion 7th characters B & C see Appendix A PDX collection 1301
HAC 7th characters A - C see Appendix B for HAC conditional logic

CC MCC +7th **S72.422 Displaced fracture of lateral condyle of left femur**
CC Exclusion 7th character A see Appendix A PDX collection 1302
CC Exclusion 7th characters K - R see Appendix A PDX collection 0897
MCC Exclusion 7th characters B & C see Appendix A PDX collection 1301
HAC 7th characters A - C see Appendix B for HAC conditional logic

CC MCC +7th **S72.423 Displaced fracture of lateral condyle of unspecified femur**
CC Exclusion 7th character A see Appendix A PDX collection 1301
CC Exclusion 7th characters K - R see Appendix A PDX collection 0897
MCC Exclusion 7th characters B & C see Appendix A PDX collection 1301
HAC 7th characters A - C see Appendix B for HAC conditional logic

CC MCC +7th **S72.424 Nondisplaced fracture of lateral condyle of right femur**
CC Exclusion 7th character A see Appendix A PDX collection 1300
CC Exclusion 7th characters K - R see Appendix A PDX collection 0897
MCC Exclusion 7th characters B & C see Appendix A PDX collection 1301
HAC 7th characters A - C see Appendix B for HAC conditional logic

CC MCC +7th **S72.425 Nondisplaced fracture of lateral condyle of left femur**
CC Exclusion 7th character A see Appendix A PDX collection 1302
CC Exclusion 7th characters K - R see Appendix A PDX collection 0897
MCC Exclusion 7th characters B & C see Appendix A PDX collection 1301
HAC 7th characters A - C see Appendix B for HAC conditional logic

CC MCC +7th **S72.426 Nondisplaced fracture of lateral condyle of unspecified femur**
CC Exclusion 7th character A see Appendix A PDX collection 1301
CC Exclusion 7th characters K - R see Appendix A PDX collection 0897
MCC Exclusion 7th characters B & C see Appendix A PDX collection 1301
HAC 7th characters A - C see Appendix B for HAC conditional logic

+ **S72.43 Fracture of medial condyle of femur**

CC MCC +7th **S72.431 Displaced fracture of medial condyle of right femur**
CC Exclusion 7th character A see Appendix A PDX collection 1300
CC Exclusion 7th characters K - R see Appendix A PDX collection 0897
MCC Exclusion 7th characters B & C see Appendix A PDX collection 1301
HAC 7th characters A - C see Appendix B for HAC conditional logic

CC MCC +7th **S72.432 Displaced fracture of medial condyle of left femur**
CC Exclusion 7th character A see Appendix A PDX collection 1302
CC Exclusion 7th characters K - R see Appendix A PDX collection 0897
MCC Exclusion 7th characters B & C see Appendix A PDX collection 1301
HAC 7th characters A - C see Appendix B for HAC conditional logic

CC MCC +7th **S72.433 Displaced fracture of medial condyle of unspecified femur**
CC Exclusion 7th character A see Appendix A PDX collection 1301
CC Exclusion 7th characters K - R see Appendix A PDX collection 0897
MCC Exclusion 7th characters B & C see Appendix A PDX collection 1301
HAC 7th characters A - C see Appendix B for HAC conditional logic

CC MCC +7th **S72.434 Nondisplaced fracture of medial condyle of right femur**
CC Exclusion 7th character A see Appendix A PDX collection 1300
CC Exclusion 7th characters K - R see Appendix A PDX collection 0897
MCC Exclusion 7th characters B & C see Appendix A PDX collection 1301
HAC 7th characters A - C see Appendix B for HAC conditional logic

CC MCC +7th **S72.435 Nondisplaced fracture of medial condyle of left femur**
CC Exclusion 7th character A see Appendix A PDX collection 1302
CC Exclusion 7th characters K - R see Appendix A PDX collection 0897
MCC Exclusion 7th characters B & C see Appendix A PDX collection 1301
HAC 7th characters A - C see Appendix B for HAC conditional logic

CC MCC +7th **S72.436 Nondisplaced fracture of medial condyle of unspecified femur**
CC Exclusion 7th character A see Appendix A PDX collection 1301
CC Exclusion 7th characters K - R see Appendix A PDX collection 0897
MCC Exclusion 7th characters B & C see Appendix A PDX collection 1301
HAC 7th characters A - C see Appendix B for HAC conditional logic

+ **S72.44 Fracture of lower epiphysis (separation) of femur**
Excludes1: *Salter-Harris Type I physeal fracture of lower end of femur (S79.11-)*

CC MCC +7th **S72.441 Displaced fracture of lower epiphysis (separation) of right femur**
CC Exclusion 7th character A see Appendix A PDX collection 1300
CC Exclusion 7th characters K - R see Appendix A PDX collection 0897
MCC Exclusion 7th characters B & C see Appendix A PDX collection 1301
HAC 7th characters A - C see Appendix B for HAC conditional logic

CC MCC +7th **S72.442 Displaced fracture of lower epiphysis (separation) of left femur**
CC Exclusion 7th character A see Appendix A PDX collection 1302
CC Exclusion 7th characters K - R see Appendix A PDX collection 0897
MCC Exclusion 7th characters B & C see Appendix A PDX collection 1301
HAC 7th characters A - C see Appendix B for HAC conditional logic

CC MCC +7th **S72.443 Displaced fracture of lower epiphysis (separation) of unspecified femur**
CC Exclusion 7th character A see Appendix A PDX collection 1301
CC Exclusion 7th characters K - R see Appendix A PDX collection 0897
MCC Exclusion 7th characters B & C see Appendix A PDX collection 1301
HAC 7th characters A - C see Appendix B for HAC conditional logic

CC MCC +7th **S72.444 Nondisplaced fracture of lower epiphysis (separation) of right femur**
CC Exclusion 7th character A see Appendix A PDX collection 1300
CC Exclusion 7th characters K - R see Appendix A PDX collection 0897
MCC Exclusion 7th characters B & C see Appendix A PDX collection 1301
HAC 7th characters A - C see Appendix B for HAC conditional logic

CC MCC +7th **S72.445 Nondisplaced fracture of lower epiphysis (separation) of left femur**
CC Exclusion 7th character A see Appendix A PDX collection 1302
CC Exclusion 7th characters K - R see Appendix A PDX collection 0897
MCC Exclusion 7th characters B & C see Appendix A PDX collection 1301
HAC 7th characters A - C see Appendix B for HAC conditional logic

CC MCC +7th **S72.446 Nondisplaced fracture of lower epiphysis (separation) of unspecified femur**
CC Exclusion 7th character A see Appendix A PDX collection 1303
CC Exclusion 7th characters K - R see Appendix A PDX collection 0897
MCC Exclusion 7th characters B & C see Appendix A PDX collection 1301
HAC 7th characters A - C see Appendix B for HAC conditional logic

+ **S72.45 Supracondylar fracture without intracondylar extension of lower end of femur**
Supracondylar fracture of lower end of femur NOS
Excludes1: *supracondylar fracture with intracondylar extension of lower end of femur (S72.46-)*

CC MCC +7th **S72.451 Displaced supracondylar fracture without intracondylar extension of lower end of right femur**
CC Exclusion 7th character A see Appendix A PDX collection 1300
CC Exclusion 7th characters K - R see Appendix A PDX collection 0897
MCC Exclusion 7th characters B & C see Appendix A PDX collection 1301
HAC 7th characters A - C see Appendix B for HAC conditional logic

CC MCC +7th **S72.452 Displaced supracondylar fracture without intracondylar extension of lower end of left femur**
CC Exclusion 7th character A see Appendix A PDX collection 1302
CC Exclusion 7th characters K - R see Appendix A PDX collection 0897
MCC Exclusion 7th characters B & C see Appendix A PDX collection 1301
HAC 7th characters A - C see Appendix B for HAC conditional logic

CC MCC +7th **S72.453 Displaced supracondylar fracture without intracondylar extension of lower end of unspecified femur**
CC Exclusion 7th character A see Appendix A PDX collection 1301
CC Exclusion 7th characters K - R see Appendix A PDX collection 0897
MCC Exclusion 7th characters B & C see Appendix A PDX collection 1301
HAC 7th characters A - C see Appendix B for HAC conditional logic

CC MCC +7th **S72.454 Nondisplaced supracondylar fracture without intracondylar extension of lower end of right femur**
CC Exclusion 7th character A see Appendix A PDX collection 1300
CC Exclusion 7th characters K - R see Appendix A PDX collection 0897
MCC Exclusion 7th characters B & C see Appendix A PDX collection 1301
HAC 7th characters A - C see Appendix B for HAC conditional logic

CC MCC +7th **S72.455 Nondisplaced supracondylar fracture without intracondylar extension of lower end of left femur**
CC Exclusion 7th character A see Appendix A PDX collection 1302
CC Exclusion 7th characters K - R see Appendix A PDX collection 0897
MCC Exclusion 7th characters B & C see Appendix A PDX collection 1301
HAC 7th characters A - C see Appendix B for HAC conditional logic

CC MCC +7th **S72.456 Nondisplaced supracondylar fracture without intracondylar extension of lower end of unspecified femur**
CC Exclusion 7th character A see Appendix A PDX collection 1301
CC Exclusion 7th characters K - R see Appendix A PDX collection 0897
MCC Exclusion 7th characters B & C see Appendix A PDX collection 1301
HAC 7th characters A - C see Appendix B for HAC conditional logic

+ **S72.46 Supracondylar fracture with intracondylar extension of lower end of femur**
Excludes1: *supracondylar fracture without intracondylar extension of lower end of femur (S72.45-)*

CC MCC +7th **S72.461 Displaced supracondylar fracture with intracondylar extension of lower end of right femur**
CC Exclusion 7th character A see Appendix A PDX collection 1300
CC Exclusion 7th characters K - R see Appendix A PDX collection 0897
MCC Exclusion 7th characters B & C see Appendix A PDX collection 1301
HAC 7th characters A - C see Appendix B for HAC conditional logic

CC MCC +7th **S72.462 Displaced supracondylar fracture with intracondylar extension of lower end of left femur**
CC Exclusion 7th character A see Appendix A PDX collection 1302
CC Exclusion 7th characters K - R see Appendix A PDX collection 0897
MCC Exclusion 7th characters B & C see Appendix A PDX collection 1301
HAC 7th characters A - C see Appendix B for HAC conditional logic

CC MCC +7th **S72.463 Displaced supracondylar fracture with intracondylar extension of lower end of unspecified femur**
CC Exclusion 7th character A see Appendix A PDX collection 1301
CC Exclusion 7th characters K - R see Appendix A PDX collection 0897
MCC Exclusion 7th characters B & C see Appendix A PDX collection 1301
HAC 7th characters A - C see Appendix B for HAC conditional logic

CC MCC +7th **S72.464 Nondisplaced supracondylar fracture with intracondylar extension of lower end of right femur**
CC Exclusion 7th character A see Appendix A PDX collection 1300
CC Exclusion 7th characters K - R see Appendix A PDX collection 0897
MCC Exclusion 7th characters B & C see Appendix A PDX collection 1301
HAC 7th characters A - C see Appendix B for HAC conditional logic

CC MCC +7th **S72.465 Nondisplaced supracondylar fracture with intracondylar extension of lower end of left femur**
CC Exclusion 7th character A see Appendix A PDX collection 1302
CC Exclusion 7th characters K - R see Appendix A PDX collection 0897
MCC Exclusion 7th characters B & C see Appendix A PDX collection 1301
HAC 7th characters A - C see Appendix B for HAC conditional logic

CC MCC +7th **S72.466 Nondisplaced supracondylar fracture with intracondylar extension of lower end of unspecified femur**
CC Exclusion 7th character A see Appendix A PDX collection 1301
CC Exclusion 7th characters K - R see Appendix A PDX collection 0897
MCC Exclusion 7th characters B & C see Appendix A PDX collection 1301
HAC 7th characters A - C see Appendix B for HAC conditional logic

\+ **S72.47 Torus fracture of lower end of femur**

The appropriate 7th character is to be added to all codes in subcategory S72.47
A - initial encounter for closed fracture
D - subsequent encounter for fracture with routine healing
G - subsequent encounter for fracture with delayed healing
K - subsequent encounter for fracture with nonunion
P - subsequent encounter for fracture with malunion
S - sequela

CC +7th **S72.471 Torus fracture of lower end of right femur**
CC Exclusion 7th character A see Appendix A PDX collection 1300
CC Exclusion 7th characters K - R see Appendix A PDX collection 0897
HAC 7th character A see Appendix B for HAC conditional logic

CC +7th **S72.472 Torus fracture of lower end of left femur**
CC Exclusion 7th character A see Appendix A PDX collection 1302
CC Exclusion 7th characters K - R see Appendix A PDX collection 0897
HAC 7th character A see Appendix B for HAC conditional logic

CC +7th **S72.479 Torus fracture of lower end of unspecified femur**
CC Exclusion 7th character A see Appendix A PDX collection 1301
CC Exclusion 7th characters K - R see Appendix A PDX collection 0897
HAC 7th character A see Appendix B for HAC conditional logic

\+ **S72.49 Other fracture of lower end of femur**

CC MCC +7th **S72.491 Other fracture of lower end of right femur**
CC Exclusion 7th character A see Appendix A PDX collection 1300
CC Exclusion 7th characters K - R see Appendix A PDX collection 0897
MCC Exclusion 7th characters B & C see Appendix A PDX collection 1303
HAC 7th characters A - C see Appendix B for HAC conditional logic

CC MCC +7th **S72.492 Other fracture of lower end of left femur**
CC Exclusion 7th character A see Appendix A PDX collection 1302
CC Exclusion 7th characters K - R see Appendix A PDX collection 0897
MCC Exclusion 7th characters B & C see Appendix A PDX collection 1303
HAC 7th characters A - C see Appendix B for HAC conditional logic

CC MCC +7th **S72.499 Other fracture of lower end of unspecified femur**
CC Exclusion 7th character A see Appendix A PDX collection 1301
CC Exclusion 7th characters K - R see Appendix A PDX collection 0897
MCC Exclusion 7th characters B & C see Appendix A PDX collection 1303
HAC 7th characters A - C see Appendix B for HAC conditional logic

CC MCC + **S72.8 Other fracture of femur**
CC Exclusion 7th characters K - R see Appendix A PDX collection 0897
MCC Exclusion 7th characters A - C see Appendix A PDX collection 1298
HAC 7th characters A - C see Appendix B for HAC conditional logic

\+ **S72.8X Other fracture of femur**
+7th **S72.8X1 Other fracture of right femur**
+7th **S72.8X2 Other fracture of left femur**
+7th **S72.8X9 Other fracture of unspecified femur**

\+ **S72.9 Unspecified fracture of femur**
Fracture of thigh NOS
Fracture of upper leg NOS
Excludes1: *fracture of hip NOS (S72.00-, S72.01-)*

CC MCC X+7th **S72.90 Unspecified fracture of unspecified femur**
CC Exclusion 7th characters K - R see Appendix A PDX collection 0897
MCC Exclusion 7th characters A - C see Appendix A PDX collection 1298
AHA CC: 4Q, 2012, 93-94
HAC 7th characters A - C see Appendix B for HAC conditional logic

CC MCC X+7th **S72.91 Unspecified fracture of right femur**
CC Exclusion 7th characters K - R see Appendix A PDX collection 0897
MCC Exclusion 7th characters A - C see Appendix A PDX collection 1298
HAC 7th characters A - C see Appendix B for HAC conditional logic

CC MCC X+7th **S72.92 Unspecified fracture of left femur**
CC Exclusion 7th characters K - R see Appendix A PDX collection 0897
MCC Exclusion 7th characters A - C see Appendix A PDX collection 1298
HAC 7th characters A - C see Appendix B for HAC conditional logic

S73 Dislocation and sprain of joint and ligaments of hip

Includes: avulsion of joint or ligament of hip
lacervw ation of cartilage, joint or ligament of hip
sprain of cartilage, joint or ligament of hip
traumatic hemarthrosis of joint or ligament of hip
traumatic rupture of joint or ligament of hip
traumatic subluxation of joint or ligament of hip
traumatic tear of joint or ligament of hip

Code also any associated open wound
Excludes2: *strain of muscle, fascia and tendon of hip and thigh (S76.-)*

The appropriate 7th character is to be added to each code from category S73
A initial encounter
D subsequent encounter
S sequela

+ S73.0 Subluxation and dislocation of hip
Excludes2: *dislocation and subluxation of hip prosthesis (T84.020, T84.021)*

+ S73.00 Unspecified subluxation and dislocation of hip
Dislocation of hip NOS
Subluxation of hip NOS

CC +7th **S73.001 Unspecified subluxation of right hip**
CC Exclusion 7th character A see Appendix A
PDX collection 1304
HAC 7th character A see Appendix B for HAC conditional logic

CC +7th **S73.002 Unspecified subluxation of left hip**
CC Exclusion 7th character A see Appendix A
PDX collection 1305
HAC 7th character A see Appendix B for HAC conditional logic

CC +7th **S73.003 Unspecified subluxation of unspecified hip**
CC Exclusion 7th character A see Appendix A
PDX collection 1306
HAC 7th character A see Appendix B for HAC conditional logic

CC +7th **S73.004 Unspecified dislocation of right hip**
CC Exclusion 7th character A see Appendix A
PDX collection 1304
HAC 7th character A see Appendix B for HAC conditional logic

CC +7th **S73.005 Unspecified dislocation of left hip**
CC Exclusion 7th character A see Appendix A
PDX collection 1305
HAC 7th character A see Appendix B for HAC conditional logic

CC +7th **S73.006 Unspecified dislocation of unspecified hip**
CC Exclusion 7th character A see Appendix A
PDX collection 1306
HAC 7th character A see Appendix B for HAC conditional logic

+ S73.01 Posterior subluxation and dislocation of hip

CC +7th **S73.011 Posterior subluxation of right hip**
CC Exclusion 7th character A see Appendix A
PDX collection 1307
HAC 7th character A see Appendix B for HAC conditional logic

CC +7th **S73.012 Posterior subluxation of left hip**
CC Exclusion 7th character A see Appendix A
PDX collection 1308
HAC 7th character A see Appendix B for HAC conditional logic

CC +7th **S73.013 Posterior subluxation of unspecified hip**
CC Exclusion 7th character A see Appendix A
PDX collection 1309
HAC 7th character A see Appendix B for HAC conditional logic

CC +7th **S73.014 Posterior dislocation of right hip**
CC Exclusion 7th character A see Appendix A
PDX collection 1307
HAC 7th character A see Appendix B for HAC conditional logic

CC +7th **S73.015 Posterior dislocation of left hip**
CC Exclusion 7th character A see Appendix A
PDX collection 1308
HAC 7th character A see Appendix B for HAC conditional logic

CC +7th **S73.016 Posterior dislocation of unspecified hip**
CC Exclusion 7th character A see Appendix A
PDX collection 1309
HAC 7th character A see Appendix B for HAC conditional logic

+ S73.02 Obturator subluxation and dislocation of hip

CC +7th **S73.021 Obturator subluxation of right hip**
CC Exclusion 7th character A see Appendix A
PDX collection 1310
HAC 7th character A see Appendix B for HAC conditional logic

CC +7th **S73.022 Obturator subluxation of left hip**
CC Exclusion 7th character A see Appendix A
PDX collection 1311
HAC 7th character A see Appendix B for HAC conditional logic

CC +7th **S73.023 Obturator subluxation of unspecified hip**
CC Exclusion 7th character A see Appendix A
PDX collection 1312
HAC 7th character A see Appendix B for HAC conditional logic

CC +7th **S73.024 Obturator dislocation of right hip**
CC Exclusion 7th character A see Appendix A
PDX collection 1310
HAC 7th character A see Appendix B for HAC conditional logic

CC +7th **S73.025 Obturator dislocation of left hip**
CC Exclusion 7th character A see Appendix A
PDX collection 1311
HAC 7th character A see Appendix B for HAC conditional logic

CC +7th **S73.026 Obturator dislocation of unspecified hip**
CC Exclusion 7th character A see Appendix A
PDX collection 1312
HAC 7th character A see Appendix B for HAC conditional logic

+ S73.03 Other anterior dislocation of hip

CC +7th **S73.031 Other anterior subluxation of right hip**
CC Exclusion 7th character A see Appendix A
PDX collection 1313
HAC 7th character A see Appendix B for HAC conditional logic

CC +7th **S73.032 Other anterior subluxation of left hip**
CC Exclusion 7th character A see Appendix A
PDX collection 1314
HAC 7th character A see Appendix B for HAC conditional logic

CC +7th **S73.033 Other anterior subluxation of unspecified hip**
CC Exclusion 7th character A see Appendix A
PDX collection 1315
HAC 7th character A see Appendix B for HAC conditional logic

CC +7th **S73.034 Other anterior dislocation of right hip**
CC Exclusion 7th character A see Appendix A
PDX collection 1313
HAC 7th character A see Appendix B for HAC conditional logic

CC +7th **S73.035 Other anterior dislocation of left hip**
CC Exclusion 7th character A see Appendix A
PDX collection 1314
HAC 7th character A see Appendix B for HAC conditional logic

CC +7th **S73.036 Other anterior dislocation of unspecified hip**
CC Exclusion 7th character A see Appendix A
PDX collection 1315
HAC 7th character A see Appendix B for HAC conditional logic

+ S73.04 Central dislocation of hip

CC +7th **S73.041 Central subluxation of right hip**
CC Exclusion 7th character A see Appendix A
PDX collection 1304
HAC 7th character A see Appendix B for HAC conditional logic

CC +7th **S73.042 Central subluxation of left hip**
CC Exclusion 7th character A see Appendix A
PDX collection 1305
HAC 7th character A see Appendix B for HAC conditional logic

CC +7th **S73.043 Central subluxation of unspecified hip**
CC Exclusion 7th character A see Appendix A
PDX collection 1306
HAC 7th character A see Appendix B for HAC conditional logic

CC +7th **S73.044 Central dislocation of right hip**
CC Exclusion 7th character A see Appendix A
PDX collection 1304
HAC 7th character A see Appendix B for HAC conditional logic

CC +7th **S73.045 Central dislocation of left hip**
CC Exclusion 7th character A see Appendix A
PDX collection 1305
HAC 7th character A see Appendix B for HAC conditional logic

CC +7th **S73.046 Central dislocation of unspecified hip**
CC Exclusion 7th character A see Appendix A
PDX collection 1306
HAC 7th character A see Appendix B for HAC conditional logic

+ S73.1 Sprain of hip

+ S73.10 Unspecified sprain of hip
+7th **S73.101 Unspecified sprain of right hip**
+7th **S73.102 Unspecified sprain of left hip**
+7th **S73.109 Unspecified sprain of unspecified hip**

+ S73.11 Iliofemoral ligament sprain of hip
+7th **S73.111 Iliofemoral ligament sprain of right hip**
+7th **S73.112 Iliofemoral ligament sprain of left hip**
+7th **S73.119 Iliofemoral ligament sprain of unspecified hip**

+ S73.12 Ischiocapsular (ligament) sprain of hip
+7th **S73.121 Ischiocapsular ligament sprain of right hip**
+7th **S73.122 Ischiocapsular ligament sprain of left hip**
+7th **S73.129 Ischiocapsular ligament sprain of unspecified hip**

+ **S73.19 Other sprain of hip**
  - +7th **S73.191 Other sprain of right hip**
  - +7th **S73.192 Other sprain of left hip**
  - +7th **S73.199 Other sprain of unspecified hip**

S74 Injury of nerves at hip and thigh level

Code also any associated open wound (S71.-)

Excludes2: *injury of nerves at ankle and foot level (S94.-)*
injury of nerves at lower leg level (S84.-)

The appropriate 7th character is to be added to each code from category S74
A initial encounter
D subsequent encounter
S sequela

+ **S74.0 Injury of sciatic nerve at hip and thigh level**
  - X+7th **S74.00 Injury of sciatic nerve at hip and thigh level, unspecified leg**
  - X+7th **S74.01 Injury of sciatic nerve at hip and thigh level, right leg**
  - X+7th **S74.02 Injury of sciatic nerve at hip and thigh level, left leg**

+ **S74.1 Injury of femoral nerve at hip and thigh level**
  - X+7th **S74.10 Injury of femoral nerve at hip and thigh level, unspecified leg**
  - X+7th **S74.11 Injury of femoral nerve at hip and thigh level, right leg**
  - X+7th **S74.12 Injury of femoral nerve at hip and thigh level, left leg**

+ **S74.2 Injury of cutaneous sensory nerve at hip and thigh level**
  - X+7th **S74.20 Injury of cutaneous sensory nerve at hip and thigh level, unspecified leg**
  - X+7th **S74.21 Injury of cutaneous sensory nerve at hip and high level, right leg**
  - X+7th **S74.22 Injury of cutaneous sensory nerve at hip and thigh level, left leg**

+ **S74.8 Injury of other nerves at hip and thigh level**
  + **S74.8X Injury of other nerves at hip and thigh level**
    - +7th **S74.8X1 Injury of other nerves at hip and thigh level, right leg**
    - +7th **S74.8X2 Injury of other nerves at hip and thigh level, left leg**
    - +7th **S74.8X9 Injury of other nerves at hip and thigh level, unspecified leg**

+ **S74.9 Injury of unspecified nerve at hip and thigh level**
  - X+7th **S74.90 Injury of unspecified nerve at hip and thigh level, unspecified leg**
  - X+7th **S74.91 Injury of unspecified nerve at hip and thigh level, right leg**
  - X+7th **S74.92 Injury of unspecified nerve at hip and thigh level, left leg**

S75 Injury of blood vessels at hip and thigh level

Code also any associated open wound (S71.-)

Excludes2: *injury of blood vessels at lower leg level (S85.-)*
injury of popliteal artery (S85.0)

The appropriate 7th character is to be added to each code from category S75
A initial encounter
D subsequent encounter
S sequela

+ **S75.0 Injury of femoral artery**
  + **S75.00 Unspecified injury of femoral artery**
    - MCC +7th **S75.001 Unspecified injury of femoral artery, right leg**
      MCC Exclusion 7th character A see Appendix A
      PDX collection 1316
    - MCC +7th **S75.002 Unspecified injury of femoral artery, left leg**
      MCC Exclusion 7th character A see Appendix A
      PDX collection 1317
    - MCC +7th **S75.009 Unspecified injury of femoral artery, unspecified leg**
      MCC Exclusion 7th character A see Appendix A
      PDX collection 1318
  + **S75.01 Minor laceration of femoral artery**
    Incomplete transection of femoral artery
    Laceration of femoral artery NOS
    Superficial laceration of femoral artery
    - MCC +7th **S75.011 Minor laceration of femoral artery, right leg**
      MCC Exclusion 7th character A see Appendix A
      PDX collection 1316
    - MCC +7th **S75.012 Minor laceration of femoral artery, left leg**
      MCC Exclusion 7th character A see Appendix A
      PDX collection 1317
    - MCC +7th **S75.019 Minor laceration of femoral artery, unspecified leg**
      MCC Exclusion 7th character A see Appendix A
      PDX collection 1318
  + **S75.02 Major laceration of femoral artery**
    Complete transection of femoral artery
    Traumatic rupture of femoral artery
    - MCC +7th **S75.021 Major laceration of femoral artery, right leg**
      MCC Exclusion 7th character A see Appendix A
      PDX collection 1316
    - MCC +7th **S75.022 Major laceration of femoral artery, left leg**
      MCC Exclusion 7th character A see Appendix A
      PDX collection 1317
    - MCC +7th **S75.029 Major laceration of femoral artery, unspecified leg**
      MCC Exclusion 7th character A see Appendix A
      PDX collection 1318
  + **S75.09 Other specified injury of femoral artery**
    - MCC +7th **S75.091 Other specified injury of femoral artery, right leg**
      MCC Exclusion 7th character A see Appendix A
      PDX collection 1316
    - MCC +7th **S75.092 Other specified injury of femoral artery, left leg**
      MCC Exclusion 7th character A see Appendix A
      PDX collection 1317
    - MCC +7th **S75.099 Other specified injury of femoral artery, unspecified leg**
      MCC Exclusion 7th character A see Appendix A
      PDX collection 1318

+ **S75.1 Injury of femoral vein at hip and thigh level**
  + **S75.10 Unspecified injury of femoral vein at hip and thigh level**
    - MCC +7th **S75.101 Unspecified injury of femoral vein at hip and thigh level, right leg**
      MCC Exclusion 7th character A see Appendix A
      PDX collection 1319
    - MCC +7th **S75.102 Unspecified injury of femoral vein at hip and thigh level, left leg**
      MCC Exclusion 7th character A see Appendix A
      PDX collection 1320
    - MCC +7th **S75.109 Unspecified injury of femoral vein at hip and thigh level, unspecified leg**
      MCC Exclusion 7th character A see Appendix A
      PDX collection 1321
  + **S75.11 Minor laceration of femoral vein at hip and thigh level**
    Incomplete transection of femoral vein at hip and thigh level
    Laceration of femoral vein at hip and thigh level NOS
    Superficial laceration of femoral vein at hip and thigh level
    - MCC +7th **S75.111 Minor laceration of femoral vein at hip and thigh level, right leg**
      MCC Exclusion 7th character A see Appendix A
      PDX collection 1319
    - MCC +7th **S75.112 Minor laceration of femoral vein at hip and thigh level, left leg**
      MCC Exclusion 7th character A see Appendix A
      PDX collection 1320
    - MCC +7th **S75.119 Minor laceration of femoral vein at hip and thigh level, unspecified leg**
      MCC Exclusion 7th character A see Appendix A
      PDX collection 1321
  + **S75.12 Major laceration of femoral vein at hip and thigh level**
    Complete transection of femoral vein at hip and thigh level
    Traumatic rupture of femoral vein at hip and thigh level
    - MCC +7th **S75.121 Major laceration of femoral vein at hip and thigh level, right leg**
      MCC Exclusion 7th character A see Appendix A
      PDX collection 1319
    - MCC +7th **S75.122 Major laceration of femoral vein at hip and thigh level, left leg**
      MCC Exclusion 7th character A see Appendix A
      PDX collection 1320
    - MCC +7th **S75.129 Major laceration of femoral vein at hip and thigh level, unspecified leg**
      MCC Exclusion 7th character A see Appendix A
      PDX collection 1321
  + **S75.19 Other specified injury of femoral vein at hip and thigh level**
    - MCC +7th **S75.191 Other specified injury of femoral vein at hip and thigh level, right leg**
      MCC Exclusion 7th character A see Appendix A
      PDX collection 1319

MCC +7th **S75.192** **Other specified injury of femoral vein at hip and thigh level, left leg**
MCC Exclusion 7th character A see Appendix A
PDX collection 1320

MCC +7th **S75.199** **Other specified injury of femoral vein at hip and thigh level, unspecified leg**
MCC Exclusion 7th character A see Appendix A
PDX collection 1321

\+ **S75.2** **Injury of greater saphenous vein at hip and thigh level**
Excludes1: *greater saphenous vein NOS (S85.3)*

\+ **S75.20** **Unspecified injury of greater saphenous vein at hip and thigh level**

CC +7th **S75.201** **Unspecified injury of greater saphenous vein at hip and thigh level, right leg**
CC Exclusion 7th character A see Appendix A
PDX collection 1322

CC +7th **S75.202** **Unspecified injury of greater saphenous vein at hip and thigh level, left leg**
CC Exclusion 7th character A see Appendix A
PDX collection 1323

CC +7th **S75.209** **Unspecified injury of greater saphenous vein at hip and thigh level, unspecified leg**
CC Exclusion 7th character A see Appendix A
PDX collection 1324

\+ **S75.21** **Minor laceration of greater saphenous vein at hip and thigh level**
Incomplete transection of greater saphenous vein at hip and thigh level
Laceration of greater saphenous vein at hip and thigh level NOS
Superficial laceration of greater saphenous vein at hip and thigh level

CC +7th **S75.211** **Minor laceration of greater saphenous vein at hip and thigh level, right leg**
CC Exclusion 7th character A see Appendix A
PDX collection 1322

CC +7th **S75.212** **Minor laceration of greater saphenous vein at hip and thigh level, left leg**
CC Exclusion 7th character A see Appendix A
PDX collection 1323

CC +7th **S75.219** **Minor laceration of greater saphenous vein at hip and thigh level, unspecified leg**
CC Exclusion 7th character A see Appendix A
PDX collection 1324

\+ **S75.22** **Major laceration of greater saphenous vein at hip and thigh level**
Complete transection of greater saphenous vein at hip and thigh level
Traumatic rupture of greater saphenous vein at hip and thigh level

CC +7th **S75.221** **Major laceration of greater saphenous vein at hip and thigh level, right leg**
CC Exclusion 7th character A see Appendix A
PDX collection 1322

CC +7th **S75.222** **Major laceration of greater saphenous vein at hip and thigh level, left leg**
CC Exclusion 7th character A see Appendix A
PDX collection 1323

CC +7th **S75.229** **Major laceration of greater saphenous vein at hip and thigh level, unspecified leg**
CC Exclusion 7th character A see Appendix A
PDX collection 1324

\+ **S75.29** **Other specified injury of greater saphenous vein at hip and thigh level**

CC +7th **S75.291** **Other specified injury of greater saphenous vein at hip and thigh level, right leg**
CC Exclusion 7th character A see Appendix A
PDX collection 1322

CC +7th **S75.292** **Other specified injury of greater saphenous vein at hip and thigh level, left leg**
CC Exclusion 7th character A see Appendix A
PDX collection 1323

CC +7th **S75.299** **Other specified injury of greater saphenous vein at hip and thigh level, unspecified leg**
CC Exclusion 7th character A see Appendix A
PDX collection 1324

\+ **S75.8** **Injury of other blood vessels at hip and thigh level**

\+ **S75.80** **Unspecified injury of other blood vessels at hip and thigh level**

CC +7th **S75.801** **Unspecified injury of other blood vessels at hip and thigh level, right leg**
CC Exclusion 7th character A see Appendix A
PDX collection 1325

CC +7th **S75.802** **Unspecified injury of other blood vessels a hip and thigh level, left leg**
CC Exclusion 7th character A see Appendix A
PDX collection 1326

CC +7th **S75.809** **Unspecified injury of other blood vessels a hip and thigh level, unspecified leg**
CC Exclusion 7th character A see Appendix A
PDX collection 1327

\+ **S75.81** **Laceration of other blood vessels at hip and thigh le**

CC +7th **S75.811** **Laceration of other blood vessels at hip an thigh level, right leg**
CC Exclusion 7th character A see Appendix A
PDX collection 1325

CC +7th **S75.812** **Laceration of other blood vessels at hip an thigh level, left leg**
CC Exclusion 7th character A see Appendix A
PDX collection 1326

CC +7th **S75.819** **Laceration of other blood vessels at hip an thigh level, unspecified leg**
CC Exclusion 7th character A see Appendix A
PDX collection 1327

\+ **S75.89** **Other specified injury of other blood vessels at hip a thigh level**

CC +7th **S75.891** **Other specified injury of other blood vesse at hip and thigh level, right leg**
CC Exclusion 7th character A see Appendix A
PDX collection 1325

CC +7th **S75.892** **Other specified injury of other blood vesse at hip and thigh level, left leg**
CC Exclusion 7th character A see Appendix A
PDX collection 1326

CC +7th **S75.899** **Other specified injury of other blood vesse at hip and thigh level, unspecified leg**
CC Exclusion 7th character A see Appendix A
PDX collection 1327

\+ **S75.9** **Injury of unspecified blood vessel at hip and thigh level**

\+ **S75.90** **Unspecified injury of unspecified blood vessel at hip and thigh level**

CC +7th **S75.901** **Unspecified injury of unspecified blood vessel at hip and thigh level, right leg**
CC Exclusion 7th character A see Appendix A
PDX collection 1325

CC +7th **S75.902** **Unspecified injury of unspecified blood vessel at hip and thigh level, left leg**
CC Exclusion 7th character A see Appendix A
PDX collection 1326

CC +7th **S75.909** **Unspecified injury of unspecified blood vessel at hip and thigh level, unspecified leg**
CC Exclusion 7th character A see Appendix A
PDX collection 1327

\+ **S75.91** **Laceration of unspecified blood vessel at hip and thig level**

CC +7th **S75.911** **Laceration of unspecified blood vessel at hi and thigh level, right leg**
CC Exclusion 7th character A see Appendix A
PDX collection 1325

CC +7th **S75.912** **Laceration of unspecified blood vessel at hi and thigh level, left leg**
CC Exclusion 7th character A see Appendix A
PDX collection 1326

CC +7th **S75.919** **Laceration of unspecified blood vessel at hi and thigh level, unspecified leg**
CC Exclusion 7th character A see Appendix A
PDX collection 1327

\+ **S75.99** **Other specified injury of unspecified blood vessel at hip and thigh level**

CC +7th **S75.991** **Other specified injury of unspecified blood vessel at hip and thigh level, right leg**
CC Exclusion 7th character A see Appendix A
PDX collection 1325

CC +7th **S75.992** **Other specified injury of unspecified blood vessel at hip and thigh level, left leg**
CC Exclusion 7th character A see Appendix A
PDX collection 1326

CC +7th **S75.999** **Other specified injury of unspecified blood vessel at hip and thigh level, unspecified leg**
CC Exclusion 7th character A see Appendix A
PDX collection 1327

S76 Injury of muscle, fascia and tendon at hip and thigh level

Code also any associated open wound (S71.-)

Excludes2: *injury of muscle, fascia and tendon at lower leg level (S86)*
sprain of joint and ligament of hip (S73.1)

The appropriate 7th character is to be added to each code from category S76
A initial encounter
D subsequent encounter
S sequela

+ **S76.0 Injury of muscle, fascia and tendon of hip**
  + **S76.00 Unspecified injury of muscle, fascia and tendon of hip**
    +7th **S76.001 Unspecified injury of muscle, fascia and tendon of right hip**
    +7th **S76.002 Unspecified injury of muscle, fascia and tendon of left hip**
    +7th **S76.009 Unspecified injury of muscle, fascia and tendon of unspecified hip**
  + **S76.01 Strain of muscle, fascia and tendon of hip**
    +7th **S76.011 Strain of muscle, fascia and tendon of right hip**
    +7th **S76.012 Strain of muscle, fascia and tendon of left hip**
    +7th **S76.019 Strain of muscle, fascia and tendon of unspecified hip**
  + **S76.02 Laceration of muscle, fascia and tendon of hip**
    CC +7th **S76.021 Laceration of muscle, fascia and tendon of right hip**
    CC Exclusion 7th character A see Appendix A
    PDX collection 1328
    CC +7th **S76.022 Laceration of muscle, fascia and tendon of left hip**
    CC Exclusion 7th character A see Appendix A
    PDX collection 1329
    CC +7th **S76.029 Laceration of muscle, fascia and tendon of unspecified hip**
    CC Exclusion 7th character A see Appendix A
    PDX collection 1330
  + **S76.09 Other specified injury of muscle, fascia and tendon of hip**
    +7th **S76.091 Other specified injury of muscle, fascia and tendon of right hip**
    +7th **S76.092 Other specified injury of muscle, fascia and tendon of left hip**
    +7th **S76.099 Other specified injury of muscle, fascia and tendon of unspecified hip**

+ **S76.1 Injury of quadriceps muscle, fascia and tendon**
  Injury of patellar ligament (tendon)
  + **S76.10 Unspecified injury of quadriceps muscle, fascia and tendon**
    +7th **S76.101 Unspecified injury of right quadriceps muscle, fascia and tendon**
    +7th **S76.102 Unspecified injury of left quadriceps muscle, fascia and tendon**
    +7th **S76.109 Unspecified injury of unspecified quadriceps muscle, fascia and tendon**
  + **S76.11 Strain of quadriceps muscle, fascia and tendon**
    +7th **S76.111 Strain of right quadriceps muscle, fascia and tendon**
    +7th **S76.112 Strain of left quadriceps muscle, fascia and tendon**
    +7th **S76.119 Strain of unspecified quadriceps muscle, fascia and tendon**
  + **S76.12 Laceration of quadriceps muscle, fascia and tendon**
    CC +7th **S76.121 Laceration of right quadriceps muscle, fascia and tendon**
    CC Exclusion 7th character A see Appendix A
    PDX collection 1328
    CC +7th **S76.122 Laceration of left quadriceps muscle, fascia and tendon**
    CC Exclusion 7th character A see Appendix A
    PDX collection 1329
    CC +7th **S76.129 Laceration of unspecified quadriceps muscle, fascia and tendon**
    CC Exclusion 7th character A see Appendix A
    PDX collection 1330
  + **S76.19 Other specified injury of quadriceps muscle, fascia and tendon**
    +7th **S76.191 Other specified injury of right quadriceps muscle, fascia and tendon**
    +7th **S76.192 Other specified injury of left quadriceps muscle, fascia and tendon**
    +7th **S76.199 Other specified injury of unspecified quadriceps muscle, fascia and tendon**

+ **S76.2 Injury of adductor muscle, fascia and tendon of thigh**
  + **S76.20 Unspecified injury of adductor muscle, fascia and tendon of thigh**
    +7th **S76.201 Unspecified injury of adductor muscle, fascia and tendon of right thigh**
    +7th **S76.202 Unspecified injury of adductor muscle, fascia and tendon of left thigh**
    +7th **S76.209 Unspecified injury of adductor muscle, fascia and tendon of unspecified thigh**
  + **S76.21 Strain of adductor muscle, fascia and tendon of thigh**
    +7th **S76.211 Strain of adductor muscle, fascia and tendon of right thigh**
    +7th **S76.212 Strain of adductor muscle, fascia and tendon of left thigh**
    +7th **S76.219 Strain of adductor muscle, fascia and tendon of unspecified thigh**
  + **S76.22 Laceration of adductor muscle, fascia and tendon of thigh**
    CC +7th **S76.221 Laceration of adductor muscle, fascia and tendon of right thigh**
    CC Exclusion 7th character A see Appendix A
    PDX collection 1328
    CC +7th **S76.222 Laceration of adductor muscle, fascia and tendon of left thigh**
    CC Exclusion 7th character A see Appendix A
    PDX collection 1329
    CC +7th **S76.229 Laceration of adductor muscle, fascia and tendon of unspecified thigh**
    CC Exclusion 7th character A see Appendix A
    PDX collection 1330
  + **S76.29 Other injury of adductor muscle, fascia and tendon of thigh**
    +7th **S76.291 Other injury of adductor muscle, fascia and tendon of right thigh**
    +7th **S76.292 Other injury of adductor muscle, fascia and tendon of left thigh**
    +7th **S76.299 Other injury of adductor muscle, fascia and tendon of unspecified thigh**

+ **S76.3 Injury of muscle, fascia and tendon of the posterior muscle group at thigh level**
  + **S76.30 Unspecified injury of muscle, fascia and tendon of the posterior muscle group at thigh level**
    +7th **S76.301 Unspecified injury of muscle, fascia and tendon of the posterior muscle group at thigh level, right thigh**
    +7th **S76.302 Unspecified injury of muscle, fascia and tendon of the posterior muscle group at thigh level, left thigh**
    +7th **S76.309 Unspecified injury of muscle, fascia and tendon of the posterior muscle group at thigh level, unspecified thigh**
  + **S76.31 Strain of muscle, fascia and tendon of the posterior muscle group at thigh level**
    +7th **S76.311 Strain of muscle, fascia and tendon of the posterior muscle group at thigh level, right thigh**
    +7th **S76.312 Strain of muscle, fascia and tendon of the posterior muscle group at thigh level, left thigh**
    +7th **S76.319 Strain of muscle, fascia and tendon of the posterior muscle group at thigh level, unspecified thigh**
  + **S76.32 Laceration of muscle, fascia and tendon of the posterior muscle group at thigh level**
    CC +7th **S76.321 Laceration of muscle, fascia and tendon of the posterior muscle group at thigh level, right thigh**
    CC Exclusion 7th character A see Appendix A
    PDX collection 1328
    CC +7th **S76.322 Laceration of muscle, fascia and tendon of the posterior muscle group at thigh level, left thigh**
    CC Exclusion 7th character A see Appendix A
    PDX collection 1329
    CC +7th **S76.329 Laceration of muscle, fascia and tendon of the posterior muscle group at thigh level, unspecified thigh**
    CC Exclusion 7th character A see Appendix A
    PDX collection 1330

+ **S76.39 Other specified injury of muscle, fascia and tendon of the posterior muscle group at thigh level**
  - +7th **S76.391 Other specified injury of muscle, fascia and tendon of the posterior muscle group at thigh level, right thigh**
  - +7th **S76.392 Other specified injury of muscle, fascia and tendon of the posterior muscle group at thigh level, left thigh**
  - +7th **S76.399 Other specified injury of muscle, fascia and tendon of the posterior muscle group at thigh level, unspecified thigh**

+ **S76.8 Injury of other specified muscles, fascia and tendons at thigh level**
  - + **S76.80 Unspecified injury of other specified muscles, fascia and tendons at thigh level**
    - +7th **S76.801 Unspecified injury of other specified muscles, fascia and tendons at thigh level, right thigh**
    - +7th **S76.802 Unspecified injury of other specified muscles, fascia and tendons at thigh level, left thigh**
    - +7th **S76.809 Unspecified injury of other specified muscles, fascia and tendons at thigh level, unspecified thigh**
  - + **S76.81 Strain of other specified muscles, fascia and tendons at thigh level**
    - +7th **S76.811 Strain of other specified muscles, fascia and tendons at thigh level, right thigh**
    - +7th **S76.812 Strain of other specified muscles, fascia and tendons at thigh level, left thigh**
    - +7th **S76.819 Strain of other specified muscles, fascia and tendons at thigh level, unspecified thigh**
  - + **S76.82 Laceration of other specified muscles, fascia and tendons at thigh level**
    - CC +7th **S76.821 Laceration of other specified muscles, fascia and tendons at thigh level, right thigh**
      CC Exclusion 7th character A see Appendix A PDX collection 1328
    - CC +7th **S76.822 Laceration of other specified muscles, fascia and tendons at thigh level, left thigh**
      CC Exclusion 7th character A see Appendix A PDX collection 1329
    - CC +7th **S76.829 Laceration of other specified muscles, fascia and tendons at thigh level, unspecified thigh**
      CC Exclusion 7th character A see Appendix A PDX collection 1330
  - + **S76.89 Other injury of other specified muscles, fascia and tendons at thigh level**
    - +7th **S76.891 Other injury of other specified muscles, fascia and tendons at thigh level, right thigh**
    - +7th **S76.892 Other injury of other specified muscles, fascia and tendons at thigh level, left thigh**
    - +7th **S76.899 Other injury of other specified muscles, fascia and tendons at thigh level, unspecified thigh**

+ **S76.9 Injury of unspecified muscles, fascia and tendons at thigh level**
  - + **S76.90 Unspecified injury of unspecified muscles, fascia and tendons at thigh level**
    - +7th **S76.901 Unspecified injury of unspecified muscles, fascia and tendons at thigh level, right thigh**
    - +7th **S76.902 Unspecified injury of unspecified muscles, fascia and tendons at thigh level, left thigh**
    - +7th **S76.909 Unspecified injury of unspecified muscles, fascia and tendons at thigh level, unspecified thigh**
  - + **S76.91 Strain of unspecified muscles, fascia and tendons at thigh level**
    - +7th **S76.911 Strain of unspecified muscles, fascia and tendons at thigh level, right thigh**
    - +7th **S76.912 Strain of unspecified muscles, fascia and tendons at thigh level, left thigh**
    - +7th **S76.919 Strain of unspecified muscles, fascia and tendons at thigh level, unspecified thigh**
  - + **S76.92 Laceration of unspecified muscles, fascia and tendons at thigh level**
    - CC +7th **S76.921 Laceration of unspecified muscles, fascia and tendons at thigh level, right thigh**
      CC Exclusion 7th character A see Appendix A PDX collection 1328
    - CC +7th **S76.922 Laceration of unspecified muscles, fascia and tendons at thigh level, left thigh**
      CC Exclusion 7th character A see Appendix A PDX collection 1329
    - CC +7th **S76.929 Laceration of unspecified muscles, fascia and tendons at thigh level, unspecified thigh**
      CC Exclusion 7th character A see Appendix A PDX collection 1330
  - + **S76.99 Other specified injury of unspecified muscles, fascia and tendons at thigh level**
    - +7th **S76.991 Other specified injury of unspecified muscles, fascia and tendons at thigh level, right thigh**
    - +7th **S76.992 Other specified injury of unspecified muscles, fascia and tendons at thigh level, left thigh**
    - +7th **S76.999 Other specified injury of unspecified muscles, fascia and tendons at thigh level, unspecified thigh**

S77 Crushing injury of hip and thigh

Use additional code(s) for all associated injuries

Excludes2: *crushing injury of ankle and foot (S97.-)*
crushing injury of lower leg (S87.-)

The appropriate 7th character is to be added to each code from category S77
A initial encounter
D subsequent encounter
S sequela

+ **S77.0 Crushing injury of hip**
  - CC X+7th **S77.00 Crushing injury of unspecified hip**
    CC Exclusion 7th character A see Appendix A PDX collection 1331
    HAC 7th character A see Appendix B for HAC conditional logic
  - CC X+7th **S77.01 Crushing injury of right hip**
    CC Exclusion 7th character A see Appendix A PDX collection 1331
    HAC 7th character A see Appendix B for HAC conditional logic
  - CC X+7th **S77.02 Crushing injury of left hip**
    CC Exclusion 7th character A see Appendix A PDX collection 1331
    HAC 7th character A see Appendix B for HAC conditional logic

+ **S77.1 Crushing injury of thigh**
  - CC X+7th **S77.10 Crushing injury of unspecified thigh**
    CC Exclusion 7th character A see Appendix A PDX collection 1331
    HAC 7th character A see Appendix B for HAC conditional logic
  - CC X+7th **S77.11 Crushing injury of right thigh**
    CC Exclusion 7th character A see Appendix A PDX collection 1331
    HAC 7th character A see Appendix B for HAC conditional logic
  - CC X+7th **S77.12 Crushing injury of left thigh**
    CC Exclusion 7th character A see Appendix A PDX collection 1331
    HAC 7th character A see Appendix B for HAC conditional logic

+ **S77.2 Crushing injury of hip with thigh**
  - X+7th **S77.20 Crushing injury of unspecified hip with thigh**
  - X+7th **S77.21 Crushing injury of right hip with thigh**
  - X+7th **S77.22 Crushing injury of left hip with thigh**

S78 Traumatic amputation of hip and thigh

An amputation not identified as partial or complete should be coded to complete

Excludes1: *traumatic amputation of knee (S88.0-)*

The appropriate 7th character is to be added to each code from category S78
A initial encounter
D subsequent encounter
S sequela

+ **S78.0 Traumatic amputation at hip joint**
  - + **S78.01 Complete traumatic amputation at hip joint**
    - CC +7th **S78.011 Complete traumatic amputation at right hip joint**
      CC Exclusion 7th character A see Appendix A PDX collection 1333
    - CC +7th **S78.012 Complete traumatic amputation at left hip joint**
      CC Exclusion 7th character A see Appendix A PDX collection 1334
    - CC +7th **S78.019 Complete traumatic amputation at unspecified hip joint**
      CC Exclusion 7th character A see Appendix A PDX collection 1335

+ **S78.02 Partial traumatic amputation at hip joint**
  - CC +7th **S78.021 Partial traumatic amputation at right hip joint**
    - CC Exclusion 7th character A see Appendix A PDX collection 1333
  - CC +7th **S78.022 Partial traumatic amputation at left hip joint**
    - CC Exclusion 7th character A see Appendix A PDX collection 1334
  - CC +7th **S78.029 Partial traumatic amputation at unspecified hip joint**
    - CC Exclusion 7th character A see Appendix A PDX collection 1335

+ **S78.1 Traumatic amputation at level between hip and knee**
  Excludes1: *traumatic amputation of knee (S88.0-)*
  + **S78.11 Complete traumatic amputation at level between hip and knee**
    - CC +7th **S78.111 Complete traumatic amputation at level between right hip and knee**
      - CC Exclusion 7th character A see Appendix A PDX collection 1333
    - CC +7th **S78.112 Complete traumatic amputation at level between left hip and knee**
      - CC Exclusion 7th character A see Appendix A PDX collection 1334
    - CC +7th **S78.119 Complete traumatic amputation at level between unspecified hip and knee**
      - CC Exclusion 7th character A see Appendix A PDX collection 1335
  + **S78.12 Partial traumatic amputation at level between hip and knee**
    - CC +7th **S78.121 Partial traumatic amputation at level between right hip and knee**
      - CC Exclusion 7th character A see Appendix A PDX collection 1333
    - CC +7th **S78.122 Partial traumatic amputation at level between left hip and knee**
      - CC Exclusion 7th character A see Appendix A PDX collection 1334
    - CC +7th **S78.129 Partial traumatic amputation at level between unspecified hip and knee**
      - CC Exclusion 7th character A see Appendix A PDX collection 1335

+ **S78.9 Traumatic amputation of hip and thigh, level unspecified**
  + **S78.91 Complete traumatic amputation of hip and thigh, level unspecified**
    - CC +7th **S78.911 Complete traumatic amputation of right hip and thigh, level unspecified**
      - CC Exclusion 7th character A see Appendix A PDX collection 1333
    - CC +7th **S78.912 Complete traumatic amputation of left hip and thigh, level unspecified**
      - CC Exclusion 7th character A see Appendix A PDX collection 1334
    - CC +7th **S78.919 Complete traumatic amputation of unspecified hip and thigh, level unspecified**
      - CC Exclusion 7th character A see Appendix A PDX collection 1335
  + **S78.92 Partial traumatic amputation of hip and thigh, level unspecified**
    - CC +7th **S78.921 Partial traumatic amputation of right hip and thigh, level unspecified**
      - CC Exclusion 7th character A see Appendix A PDX collection 1333
    - CC +7th **S78.922 Partial traumatic amputation of left hip and thigh, level unspecified**
      - CC Exclusion 7th character A see Appendix A PDX collection 1334
    - CC +7th **S78.929 Partial traumatic amputation of unspecified hip and thigh, level unspecified**
      - CC Exclusion 7th character A see Appendix A PDX collection 1335

S79 Other and unspecified injuries of hip and thigh

NOTE A fracture not indicated as open or closed should be coded to closed

The appropriate 7th character is to be added to each code from subcategories S79.0 and S79.1
A initial encounter for closed fracture
D subsequent encounter for fracture with routine healing
G subsequent encounter for fracture with delayed healing
K subsequent encounter for fracture with nonunion
P subsequent encounter for fracture with malunion
S sequela

Review coding guideline C.19.c

+ **S79.0 Physeal fracture of upper end of femur**
  Excludes1: *apophyseal fracture of upper end of femur (S72.13-)*
  nontraumatic slipped upper femoral epiphysis (M93.0-)
  + **S79.00 Unspecified physeal fracture of upper end of femur**
    - CC MCC +7th **S79.001 Unspecified physeal fracture of upper end of right femur**
      - **CC Exclusion 7th characters K & P see Appendix A PDX collection 0897**
      - **MCC Exclusion 7th character A see Appendix A PDX collection 1297**
      - HAC 7th character A see Appendix B for HAC conditional logic
    - CC MCC +7th **S79.002 Unspecified physeal fracture of upper end of left femur**
      - **CC Exclusion 7th characters K & P see Appendix A PDX collection 0897**
      - **MCC Exclusion 7th character A see Appendix A PDX collection 1299**
      - HAC 7th character A see Appendix B for HAC conditional logic
    - CC MCC +7th **S79.009 Unspecified physeal fracture of upper end of unspecified femur**
      - **CC Exclusion 7th characters K & P see Appendix A PDX collection 0897**
      - **MCC Exclusion 7th character A see Appendix A PDX collection 1298**
      - HAC 7th character A see Appendix B for HAC conditional logic
  + **S79.01 Salter-Harris Type I physeal fracture of upper end of femur**
    Acute on chronic slipped capital femoral epiphysis (traumatic)
    Acute slipped capital femoral epiphysis (traumatic)
    Capital femoral epiphyseal fracture
    Excludes1: *chronic slipped upper femoral epiphysis (nontraumatic) (M93.02-)*
    - CC MCC +7th **S79.011 Salter-Harris Type I physeal fracture of upper end of right femur**
      - **CC Exclusion 7th characters K & P see Appendix A PDX collection 0897**
      - **MCC Exclusion 7th character A see Appendix A PDX collection 1297**
      - HAC 7th character A see Appendix B for HAC conditional logic
    - CC MCC +7th **S79.012 Salter-Harris Type I physeal fracture of upper end of left femur**
      - **CC Exclusion 7th characters K & P see Appendix A PDX collection 0897**
      - **MCC Exclusion 7th character A see Appendix A PDX collection 1299**
      - HAC 7th character A see Appendix B for HAC conditional logic
    - CC MCC +7th **S79.019 Salter-Harris Type I physeal fracture of upper end of unspecified femur**
      - **CC Exclusion 7th characters K & P see Appendix A PDX collection 0897**
      - **MCC Exclusion 7th character A see Appendix A PDX collection 1298**
      - HAC 7th character A see Appendix B for HAC conditional logic
  + **S79.09 Other physeal fracture of upper end of femur**
    - CC MCC +7th **S79.091 Other physeal fracture of upper end of right femur**
      - **CC Exclusion 7th characters K & P see Appendix A PDX collection 0897**
      - **MCC Exclusion 7th character A see Appendix A PDX collection 1297**
      - HAC 7th character A see Appendix B for HAC conditional logic

CC MCC +7th **S79.092 Other physeal fracture of upper end of left femur**
CC Exclusion 7th characters K & P see Appendix A PDX collection 0897
MCC Exclusion 7th character A see Appendix A PDX collection 1299
HAC 7th character A see Appendix B for HAC conditional logic

CC MCC +7th **S79.099 Other physeal fracture of upper end of unspecified femur**
CC Exclusion 7th characters K & P see Appendix A PDX collection 0897
MCC Exclusion 7th character A see Appendix A PDX collection 1298
HAC 7th character A see Appendix B for HAC conditional logic

\+ **S79.1 Physeal fracture of lower end of femur**

\+ **S79.10 Unspecified physeal fracture of lower end of femur**

CC +7th **S79.101 Unspecified physeal fracture of lower end of right femur**
CC Exclusion 7th character A see Appendix A PDX collection 1300
CC Exclusion 7th characters K & P see Appendix A PDX collection 0897
HAC 7th character A see Appendix B for HAC conditional logic

CC +7th **S79.102 Unspecified physeal fracture of lower end of left femur**
CC Exclusion 7th character A see Appendix A PDX collection 1302
CC Exclusion 7th characters K & P see Appendix A PDX collection 0897
HAC 7th character A see Appendix B for HAC conditional logic

CC +7th **S79.109 Unspecified physeal fracture of lower end of unspecified femur**
CC Exclusion 7th character A see Appendix A PDX collection 1301
CC Exclusion 7th characters K & P see Appendix A PDX collection 0897
HAC 7th character A see Appendix B for HAC conditional logic

\+ **S79.11 Salter-Harris Type I physeal fracture of lower end of femur**

CC +7th **S79.111 Salter-Harris Type I physeal fracture of lower end of right femur**
CC Exclusion 7th character A see Appendix A PDX collection 1300
CC Exclusion 7th characters K & P see Appendix A PDX collection 0897
HAC 7th character A see Appendix B for HAC conditional logic

CC +7th **S79.112 Salter-Harris Type I physeal fracture of lower end of left femur**
CC Exclusion 7th character A see Appendix A PDX collection 1302
CC Exclusion 7th characters K & P see Appendix A PDX collection 0897
HAC 7th character A see Appendix B for HAC conditional logic

CC +7th **S79.119 Salter-Harris Type I physeal fracture of lower end of unspecified femur**
CC Exclusion 7th character A see Appendix A PDX collection 1301
CC Exclusion 7th characters K & P see Appendix A PDX collection 0897
HAC 7th character A see Appendix B for HAC conditional logic

\+ **S79.12 Salter-Harris Type II physeal fracture of lower end of femur**

CC +7th **S79.121 Salter-Harris Type II physeal fracture of lower end of right femur**
CC Exclusion 7th character A see Appendix A PDX collection 1300
CC Exclusion 7th characters K & P see Appendix A PDX collection 0897
HAC 7th character A see Appendix B for HAC conditional logic

CC +7th **S79.122 Salter-Harris Type II physeal fracture of lower end of left femur**
CC Exclusion 7th character A see Appendix A PDX collection 1302
CC Exclusion 7th characters K & P see Appendix A PDX collection 0897
HAC 7th character A see Appendix B for HAC conditional logic

CC +7th **S79.129 Salter-Harris Type II physeal fracture of lower end of unspecified femur**
CC Exclusion 7th character A see Appendix A PDX collection 1301
CC Exclusion 7th characters K & P see Appendix A PDX collection 0897
HAC 7th character A see Appendix B for HAC conditional logic

\+ **S79.13 Salter-Harris Type III physeal fracture of lower end femur**

CC +7th **S79.131 Salter-Harris Type III physeal fracture of lower end of right femur**
CC Exclusion 7th character A see Appendix A PDX collection 1300
CC Exclusion 7th characters K & P see Appendix A PDX collection 0897
HAC 7th character A see Appendix B for HAC conditional logic

CC +7th **S79.132 Salter-Harris Type III physeal fracture of lower end of left femur**
CC Exclusion 7th character A see Appendix A PDX collection 1302
CC Exclusion 7th characters K & P see Appendix A PDX collection 0897
HAC 7th character A see Appendix B for HAC conditional logic

CC +7th **S79.139 Salter-Harris Type III physeal fracture of lower end of unspecified femur**
CC Exclusion 7th character A see Appendix A PDX collection 1301
CC Exclusion 7th characters K & P see Appendix A PDX collection 0897
HAC 7th character A see Appendix B for HAC conditional logic

\+ **S79.14 Salter-Harris Type IV physeal fracture of lower end femur**

CC +7th **S79.141 Salter-Harris Type IV physeal fracture of lower end of right femur**
CC Exclusion 7th character A see Appendix A PDX collection 1300
CC Exclusion 7th characters K & P see Appendix A PDX collection 0897
HAC 7th character A see Appendix B for HAC conditional logic

CC +7th **S79.142 Salter-Harris Type IV physeal fracture of lower end of left femur**
CC Exclusion 7th character A see Appendix A PDX collection 1302
CC Exclusion 7th characters K & P see Appendix A PDX collection 0897
HAC 7th character A see Appendix B for HAC conditional logic

CC +7th **S79.149 Salter-Harris Type IV physeal fracture of lower end of unspecified femur**
CC Exclusion 7th character A see Appendix A PDX collection 1301
CC Exclusion 7th characters K & P see Appendix A PDX collection 0897
HAC 7th character A see Appendix B for HAC conditional logic

\+ **S79.19 Other physeal fracture of lower end of femur**

CC +7th **S79.191 Other physeal fracture of lower end of right femur**
CC Exclusion 7th character A see Appendix A PDX collection 1300
CC Exclusion 7th characters K & P see Appendix A PDX collection 0897
HAC 7th character A see Appendix B for HAC conditional logic

CC +7th **S79.192 Other physeal fracture of lower end of left femur**
CC Exclusion 7th character A see Appendix A PDX collection 1302
CC Exclusion 7th characters K & P see Appendix A PDX collection 0897
HAC 7th character A see Appendix B for HAC conditional logic

CC +7th **S79.199 Other physeal fracture of lower end of unspecified femur**
CC Exclusion 7th character A see Appendix A PDX collection 1301
CC Exclusion 7th characters K & P see Appendix A PDX collection 0897
HAC 7th character A see Appendix B for HAC conditional logic

+ **S79.8 Other specified injuries of hip and thigh**

The appropriate 7th character is to be added to each code in subcategory S79.8
A initial encounter
D subsequent encounter
S sequela

+ **S79.81 Other specified injuries of hip**
  - +7th **S79.811 Other specified injuries of right hip**
  - +7th **S79.812 Other specified injuries of left hip**
  - +7th **S79.819 Other specified injuries of unspecified hip**

+ **S79.82 Other specified injuries of thigh**
  - +7th **S79.821 Other specified injuries of right thigh**
  - +7th **S79.822 Other specified injuries of left thigh**
  - +7th **S79.829 Other specified injuries of unspecified thigh**

+ **S79.9 Unspecified injury of hip and thigh**

The appropriate 7th character is to be added to each code in subcategory S79.9
A - initial encounter
D - subsequent encounter
S - sequela

+ **S79.91 Unspecified injury of hip**
  - +7th **S79.911 Unspecified injury of right hip**
  - +7th **S79.912 Unspecified injury of left hip**
  - +7th **S79.919 Unspecified injury of unspecified hip**

+ **S79.92 Unspecified injury of thigh**
  - +7th **S79.921 Unspecified injury of right thigh**
  - +7th **S79.922 Unspecified injury of left thigh**
  - +7th **S79.929 Unspecified injury of unspecified thigh**

Knee Tendons and Ligaments

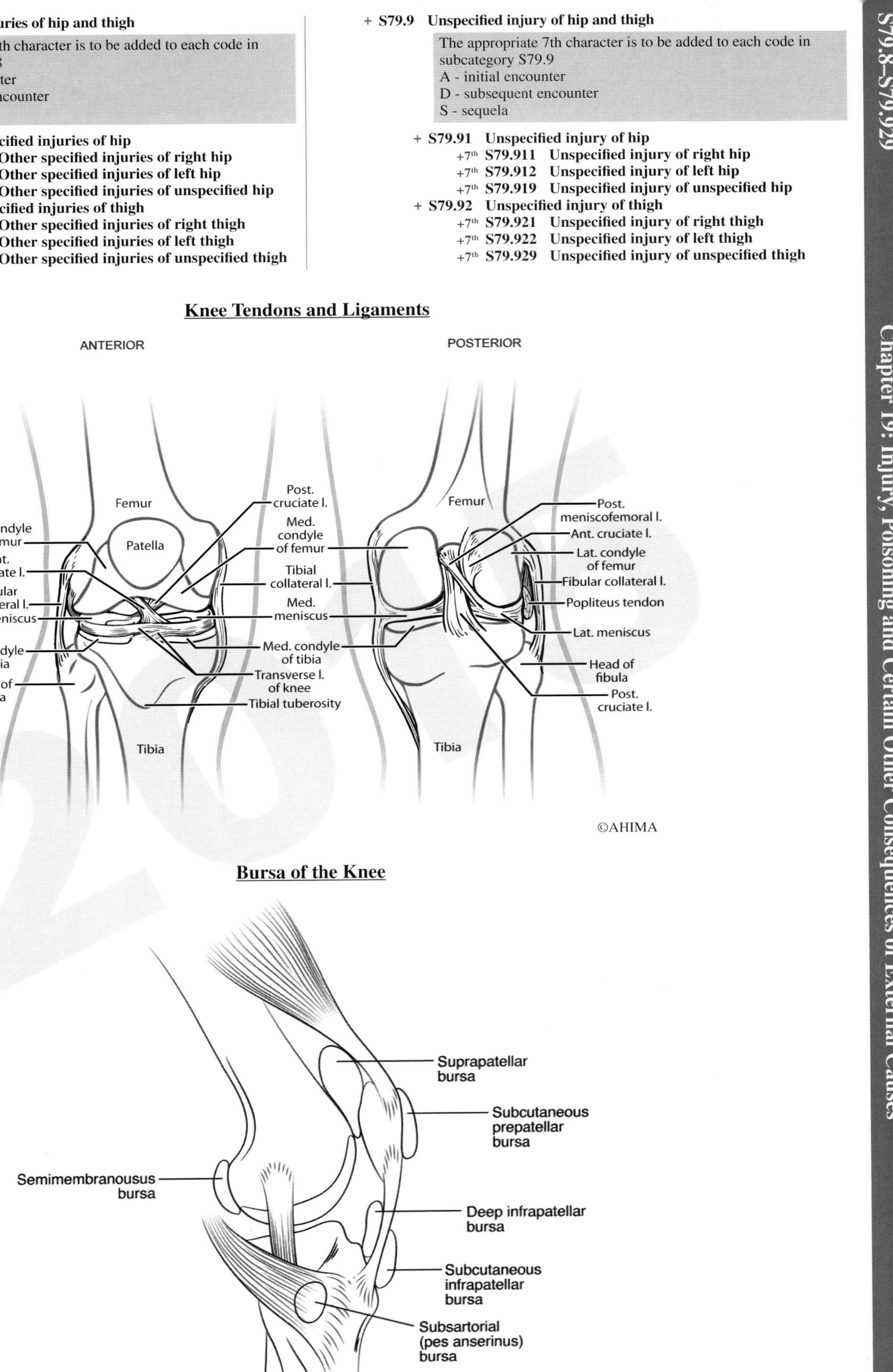

Bursa of the Knee

Injuries to the knee and lower leg (S80-S89)

Excludes2: *burns and corrosions (T20-T32)*
frostbite (T33-T34)
injuries of ankle and foot, except fracture of ankle and malleolus (S90-S99)
insect bite or sting, venomous (T63.4)

S80 Superficial injury of knee and lower leg

Excludes2: *superficial injury of ankle and foot (S90.-)*

The appropriate 7th character is to be added to each code from category S80
A initial encounter
D subsequent encounter
S sequela

+ **S80.0 Contusion of knee**
  - X+7th **S80.00 Contusion of unspecified knee**
  - X+7th **S80.01 Contusion of right knee**
  - X+7th **S80.02 Contusion of left knee**

+ **S80.1 Contusion of lower leg**
  - X+7th **S80.10 Contusion of unspecified lower leg**
  - X+7th **S80.11 Contusion of right lower leg**
  - X+7th **S80.12 Contusion of left lower leg**

+ **S80.2 Other superficial injuries of knee**
  - + **S80.21 Abrasion of knee**
    - +7th **S80.211 Abrasion, right knee**
    - +7th **S80.212 Abrasion, left knee**
    - +7th **S80.219 Abrasion, unspecified knee**
  - + **S80.22 Blister (nonthermal) of knee**
    - +7th **S80.221 Blister (nonthermal), right knee**
    - +7th **S80.222 Blister (nonthermal), left knee**
    - +7th **S80.229 Blister (nonthermal), unspecified knee**
  - + **S80.24 External constriction of knee**
    - +7th **S80.241 External constriction, right knee**
    - +7th **S80.242 External constriction, left knee**
    - +7th **S80.249 External constriction, unspecified knee**
  - + **S80.25 Superficial foreign body of knee**
    Splinter in the knee
    - +7th **S80.251 Superficial foreign body, right knee**
    - +7th **S80.252 Superficial foreign body, left knee**
    - +7th **S80.259 Superficial foreign body, unspecified knee**
  - + **S80.26 Insect bite (nonvenomous) of knee**
    - +7th **S80.261 Insect bite (nonvenomous), right knee**
    - +7th **S80.262 Insect bite (nonvenomous), left knee**
    - +7th **S80.269 Insect bite (nonvenomous), unspecified knee**
  - + **S80.27 Other superficial bite of knee**
    Excludes1: *open bite of knee (S81.05-)*
    - +7th **S80.271 Other superficial bite of right knee**
    - +7th **S80.272 Other superficial bite of left knee**
    - +7th **S80.279 Other superficial bite of unspecified knee**

+ **S80.8 Other superficial injuries of lower leg**
  - + **S80.81 Abrasion of lower leg**
    - +7th **S80.811 Abrasion, right lower leg**
    - +7th **S80.812 Abrasion, left lower leg**
    - +7th **S80.819 Abrasion, unspecified lower leg**
  - + **S80.82 Blister (nonthermal) of lower leg**
    - +7th **S80.821 Blister (nonthermal), right lower leg**
    - +7th **S80.822 Blister (nonthermal), left lower leg**
    - +7th **S80.829 Blister (nonthermal), unspecified lower leg**
  - + **S80.84 External constriction of lower leg**
    - +7th **S80.841 External constriction, right lower leg**
    - +7th **S80.842 External constriction, left lower leg**
    - +7th **S80.849 External constriction, unspecified lower leg**
  - + **S80.85 Superficial foreign body of lower leg**
    Splinter in the lower leg
    - +7th **S80.851 Superficial foreign body, right lower leg**
    - +7th **S80.852 Superficial foreign body, left lower leg**
    - +7th **S80.859 Superficial foreign body, unspecified lower leg**
  - + **S80.86 Insect bite (nonvenomous) of lower leg**
    - +7th **S80.861 Insect bite (nonvenomous), right lower leg**
    - +7th **S80.862 Insect bite (nonvenomous), left lower leg**
    - +7th **S80.869 Insect bite (nonvenomous), unspecified lower leg**
  - + **S80.87 Other superficial bite of lower leg**
    Excludes1: *open bite of lower leg (S81.85-)*
    - +7th **S80.871 Other superficial bite, right lower leg**
    - +7th **S80.872 Other superficial bite, left lower leg**
    - +7th **S80.879 Other superficial bite, unspecified lower leg**

+ **S80.9 Unspecified superficial injury of knee and lower leg**
  - + **S80.91 Unspecified superficial injury of knee**
    - +7th **S80.911 Unspecified superficial injury of right kne**
    - +7th **S80.912 Unspecified superficial injury of left knee**
    - +7th **S80.919 Unspecified superficial injury of unspecifi knee**
  - + **S80.92 Unspecified superficial injury of lower leg**
    - +7th **S80.921 Unspecified superficial injury of right low leg**
    - +7th **S80.922 Unspecified superficial injury of left lower**
    - +7th **S80.929 Unspecified superficial injury of unspecifie lower leg**

S81 Open wound of knee and lower leg

Code also any associated wound infection
Excludes1: *open fracture of knee and lower leg (S82.-)*
traumatic amputation of lower leg (S88.-)
Excludes2: *open wound of ankle and foot (S91.-)*

The appropriate 7th character is to be added to each code from category S81
A initial encounter
D subsequent encounter
S sequela

+ **S81.0 Open wound of knee**
  - + **S81.00 Unspecified open wound of knee**
    - +7th **S81.001 Unspecified open wound, right knee**
    - +7th **S81.002 Unspecified open wound, left knee**
    - +7th **S81.009 Unspecified open wound, unspecified knee**
  - + **S81.01 Laceration without foreign body of knee**
    - +7th **S81.011 Laceration without foreign body, right kne**
    - +7th **S81.012 Laceration without foreign body, left knee**
    - +7th **S81.019 Laceration without foreign body, unspecifie knee**
  - + **S81.02 Laceration with foreign body of knee**
    - +7th **S81.021 Laceration with foreign body, right knee**
    - +7th **S81.022 Laceration with foreign body, left knee**
    - +7th **S81.029 Laceration with foreign body, unspecified knee**
  - + **S81.03 Puncture wound without foreign body of knee**
    - +7th **S81.031 Puncture wound without foreign body, righ knee**
    - +7th **S81.032 Puncture wound without foreign body, left knee**
    - +7th **S81.039 Puncture wound without foreign body, unspecified knee**
  - + **S81.04 Puncture wound with foreign body of knee**
    - +7th **S81.041 Puncture wound with foreign body, right knee**
    - +7th **S81.042 Puncture wound with foreign body, left kne**
    - +7th **S81.049 Puncture wound with foreign body, unspecified knee**
  - + **S81.05 Open bite of knee**
    Bite of knee NOS
    Excludes1: *superficial bite of knee (S80.27-)*
    - +7th **S81.051 Open bite, right knee**
    - +7th **S81.052 Open bite, left knee**
    - +7th **S81.059 Open bite, unspecified knee**

+ **S81.8 Open wound of lower leg**
  - + **S81.80 Unspecified open wound of lower leg**
    - +7th **S81.801 Unspecified open wound, right lower leg**
    - +7th **S81.802 Unspecified open wound, left lower leg**
    - +7th **S81.809 Unspecified open wound, unspecified lower leg**
  - + **S81.81 Laceration without foreign body of lower leg**
    - +7th **S81.811 Laceration without foreign body, right lower leg**
    - +7th **S81.812 Laceration without foreign body, left lower leg**
    - +7th **S81.819 Laceration without foreign body, unspecified lower leg**
  - + **S81.82 Laceration with foreign body of lower leg**
    - +7th **S81.821 Laceration with foreign body, right lower leg**
    - +7th **S81.822 Laceration with foreign body, left lower leg**
    - +7th **S81.829 Laceration with foreign body, unspecified lower leg**
  - + **S81.83 Puncture wound without foreign body of lower leg**
    - +7th **S81.831 Puncture wound without foreign body, right lower leg**
    - +7th **S81.832 Puncture wound without foreign body, left lower leg**
    - +7th **S81.839 Puncture wound without foreign body, unspecified lower leg**

\+ **S81.84 Puncture wound with foreign body of lower leg**

+7th **S81.841 Puncture wound with foreign body, right lower leg**

+7th **S81.842 Puncture wound with foreign body, left lower leg**

+7th **S81.849 Puncture wound with foreign body, unspecified lower leg**

\+ **S81.85 Open bite of lower leg**

Bite of lower leg NOS

Excludes1: *superficial bite of lower leg (S80.86-, S80.87-)*

+7th **S81.851 Open bite, right lower leg**

+7th **S81.852 Open bite, left lower leg**

+7th **S81.859 Open bite, unspecified lower leg**

S82 Fracture of lower leg, including ankle

NOTE A fracture not indicated as displaced or nondisplaced should be coded to displaced

A fracture not indicated as open or closed should be coded to closed

The open fracture designations are based on the Gustilo open fracture classification

Includes: fracture of malleolus

Excludes1: *traumatic amputation of lower leg (S88.-)*

Excludes2: *fracture of foot, except ankle (S92.-)*

periprosthetic fracture of prosthetic implant of knee (T84.042, T84.043)

The appropriate 7th character is to be added to all codes from category S82

A initial encounter for closed fracture

B initial encounter for open fracture type I or II
initial encounter for open fracture NOS

C initial encounter for open fracture type IIIA, IIIB, or IIIC

D subsequent encounter for closed fracture with routine healing

E subsequent encounter for open fracture type I or II with routine healing

F subsequent encounter for open fracture type IIIA, IIIB, or IIIC with routine healing

G subsequent encounter for closed fracture with delayed healing

H subsequent encounter for open fracture type I or II with delayed healing

J subsequent encounter for open fracture type IIIA, IIIB, or IIIC with delayed healing

K subsequent encounter for closed fracture with nonunion

M subsequent encounter for open fracture type I or II with nonunion

N subsequent encounter for open fracture type IIIA, IIIB, or IIIC with nonunion

P subsequent encounter for closed fracture with malunion

Q subsequent encounter for open fracture type I or II with malunion

R subsequent encounter for open fracture type IIIA, IIIB, or IIIC with malunion

S sequela

Review coding guideline C.19.c

\+ **S82.0 Fracture of patella**

Knee cap

\+ **S82.00 Unspecified fracture of patella**

CC +7th **S82.001 Unspecified fracture of right patella**

CC Exclusion 7th character A see Appendix A PDX collection 1336

CC Exclusion 7th characters B & C see Appendix A PDX collection 1337

CC Exclusion 7th characters K - R see Appendix A PDX collection 0897

HAC 7th characters A - C see Appendix B for HAC conditional logic

CC +7th **S82.002 Unspecified fracture of left patella**

CC Exclusion 7th character A see Appendix A PDX collection 1338

CC Exclusion 7th characters B & C see Appendix A PDX collection 1337

CC Exclusion 7th characters K - R see Appendix A PDX collection 0897

HAC 7th characters A - C see Appendix B for HAC conditional logic

CC +7th **S82.009 Unspecified fracture of unspecified patella**

CC Exclusion 7th character A see Appendix A PDX collection 1339

CC Exclusion 7th characters B & C see Appendix A PDX collection 1337

CC Exclusion 7th characters K - R see Appendix A PDX collection 0897

HAC 7th characters A - C see Appendix B for HAC conditional logic

\+ **S82.01 Osteochondral fracture of patella**

CC +7th **S82.011 Displaced osteochondral fracture of right patella**

CC Exclusion 7th character A see Appendix A PDX collection 1336

CC Exclusion 7th characters B & C see Appendix A PDX collection 1337

CC Exclusion 7th characters K - R see Appendix A PDX collection 0897

HAC 7th characters A - C see Appendix B for HAC conditional logic

CC +7th **S82.012 Displaced osteochondral fracture of left patella**

CC Exclusion 7th character A see Appendix A PDX collection 1338

CC Exclusion 7th characters B & C see Appendix A PDX collection 1337

CC Exclusion 7th characters K - R see Appendix A PDX collection 0897

HAC 7th characters A - C see Appendix B for HAC conditional logic

CC +7th **S82.013 Displaced osteochondral fracture of unspecified patella**

CC Exclusion 7th character A see Appendix A PDX collection 1339

CC Exclusion 7th characters B & C see Appendix A PDX collection 1337

CC Exclusion 7th characters K - R see Appendix A PDX collection 0897

HAC 7th characters A - C see Appendix B for HAC conditional logic

CC +7th **S82.014 Nondisplaced osteochondral fracture of right patella**

CC Exclusion 7th character A see Appendix A PDX collection 1336

CC Exclusion 7th characters B & C see Appendix A PDX collection 1337

CC Exclusion 7th characters K - R see Appendix A PDX collection 0897

HAC 7th characters A - C see Appendix B for HAC conditional logic

CC +7th **S82.015 Nondisplaced osteochondral fracture of left patella**

CC Exclusion 7th character A see Appendix A PDX collection 1338

CC Exclusion 7th characters B & C see Appendix A PDX collection 1337

CC Exclusion 7th characters K - R see Appendix A PDX collection 0897

HAC 7th characters A - C see Appendix B for HAC conditional logic

CC +7th **S82.016 Nondisplaced osteochondral fracture of unspecified patella**

CC Exclusion 7th character A see Appendix A PDX collection 1339

CC Exclusion 7th characters B & C see Appendix A PDX collection 1337

CC Exclusion 7th characters K - R see Appendix A PDX collection 0897

HAC 7th characters A - C see Appendix B for HAC conditional logic

\+ **S82.02 Longitudinal fracture of patella**

CC +7th **S82.021 Displaced longitudinal fracture of right patella**

CC Exclusion 7th character A see Appendix A PDX collection 1336

CC Exclusion 7th characters B & C see Appendix A PDX collection 1337

CC Exclusion 7th characters K - R see Appendix A PDX collection 0897

HAC 7th characters A - C see Appendix B for HAC conditional logic

CC +7th **S82.022 Displaced longitudinal fracture of left patella**

CC Exclusion 7th character A see Appendix A PDX collection 1338

CC Exclusion 7th characters B & C see Appendix A PDX collection 1337

CC Exclusion 7th characters K - R see Appendix A PDX collection 0897

HAC 7th characters A - C see Appendix B for HAC conditional logic

CC +7th **S82.023 Displaced longitudinal fracture of unspecified patella**
CC Exclusion 7th character A see Appendix A PDX collection 1339
CC Exclusion 7th characters B & C see Appendix A PDX collection 1337
CC Exclusion 7th characters K - R see Appendix A PDX collection 0897
HAC 7th characters A - C see Appendix B for HAC conditional logic

CC +7th **S82.024 Nondisplaced longitudinal fracture of right patella**
CC Exclusion 7th character A see Appendix A PDX collection 1336
CC Exclusion 7th characters B & C see Appendix A PDX collection 1337
CC Exclusion 7th characters K - R see Appendix A PDX collection 0897
HAC 7th characters A - C see Appendix B for HAC conditional logic

CC +7th **S82.025 Nondisplaced longitudinal fracture of left patella**
CC Exclusion 7th character A see Appendix A PDX collection 1338
CC Exclusion 7th characters B & C see Appendix A PDX collection 1337
CC Exclusion 7th characters K - R see Appendix A PDX collection 0897
HAC 7th characters A - C see Appendix B for HAC conditional logic

CC +7th **S82.026 Nondisplaced longitudinal fracture of unspecified patella**
CC Exclusion 7th character A see Appendix A PDX collection 1339
CC Exclusion 7th characters B & C see Appendix A PDX collection 1337
CC Exclusion 7th characters K - R see Appendix A PDX collection 0897
HAC 7th characters A - C see Appendix B for HAC conditional logic

+ **S82.03 Transverse fracture of patella**

CC +7th **S82.031 Displaced transverse fracture of right patella**
CC Exclusion 7th character A see Appendix A PDX collection 1336
CC Exclusion 7th characters B & C see Appendix A PDX collection 1337
CC Exclusion 7th characters K - R see Appendix A PDX collection 0897
HAC 7th characters A - C see Appendix B for HAC conditional logic

CC +7th **S82.032 Displaced transverse fracture of left patella**
CC Exclusion 7th character A see Appendix A PDX collection 1338
CC Exclusion 7th characters B & C see Appendix A PDX collection 1337
CC Exclusion 7th characters K - R see Appendix A PDX collection 0897
HAC 7th characters A - C see Appendix B for HAC conditional logic

CC +7th **S82.033 Displaced transverse fracture of unspecified patella**
CC Exclusion 7th character A see Appendix A PDX collection 1339
CC Exclusion 7th characters B & C see Appendix A PDX collection 1337
CC Exclusion 7th characters K - R see Appendix A PDX collection 0897
HAC 7th characters A - C see Appendix B for HAC conditional logic

CC +7th **S82.034 Nondisplaced transverse fracture of right patella**
CC Exclusion 7th character A see Appendix A PDX collection 1336
CC Exclusion 7th characters B & C see Appendix A PDX collection 1337
CC Exclusion 7th characters K - R see Appendix A PDX collection 0897
HAC 7th characters A - C see Appendix B for HAC conditional logic

CC +7th **S82.035 Nondisplaced transverse fracture of left patella**
CC Exclusion 7th character A see Appendix A PDX collection 1338
CC Exclusion 7th characters B & C see Appendix A PDX collection 1337
CC Exclusion 7th characters K - R see Appendix A PDX collection 0897
HAC 7th characters A - C see Appendix B for HAC conditional logic

CC +7th **S82.036 Nondisplaced transverse fracture of unspecified patella**
CC Exclusion 7th character A see Appendix A PDX collection 1339
CC Exclusion 7th characters B & C see Appendix A PDX collection 1337
CC Exclusion 7th characters K - R see Appendix A PDX collection 0897
HAC 7th characters A - C see Appendix B for HAC conditional logic

+ **S82.04 Comminuted fracture of patella**

CC +7th **S82.041 Displaced comminuted fracture of right patella**
CC Exclusion 7th character A see Appendix A PDX collection 1336
CC Exclusion 7th characters B & C see Appendix A PDX collection 1337
CC Exclusion 7th characters K - R see Appendix A PDX collection 0897
HAC 7th characters A - C see Appendix B for HAC conditional logic

CC +7th **S82.042 Displaced comminuted fracture of left patella**
CC Exclusion 7th character A see Appendix A PDX collection 1338
CC Exclusion 7th characters B & C see Appendix A PDX collection 1337
CC Exclusion 7th characters K - R see Appendix A PDX collection 0897
HAC 7th characters A - C see Appendix B for HAC conditional logic

CC +7th **S82.043 Displaced comminuted fracture of unspecified patella**
CC Exclusion 7th character A see Appendix A PDX collection 1339
CC Exclusion 7th characters B & C see Appendix A PDX collection 1337
CC Exclusion 7th characters K - R see Appendix A PDX collection 0897
HAC 7th characters A - C see Appendix B for HAC conditional logic

CC +7th **S82.044 Nondisplaced comminuted fracture of right patella**
CC Exclusion 7th character A see Appendix A PDX collection 1336
CC Exclusion 7th characters B & C see Appendix A PDX collection 1337
CC Exclusion 7th characters K - R see Appendix A PDX collection 0897
HAC 7th characters A - C see Appendix B for HAC conditional logic

CC +7th **S82.045 Nondisplaced comminuted fracture of left patella**
CC Exclusion 7th character A see Appendix A PDX collection 1338
CC Exclusion 7th characters B & C see Appendix A PDX collection 1337
CC Exclusion 7th characters K - R see Appendix A PDX collection 0897
HAC 7th characters A - C see Appendix B for HAC conditional logic

CC +7th **S82.046 Nondisplaced comminuted fracture of unspecified patella**
CC Exclusion 7th character A see Appendix A PDX collection 1339
CC Exclusion 7th characters B & C see Appendix A PDX collection 1337
CC Exclusion 7th characters K - R see Appendix A PDX collection 0897
HAC 7th characters A - C see Appendix B for HAC conditional logic

+ **S82.09 Other fracture of patella**

CC +7th **S82.091 Other fracture of right patella**
CC Exclusion 7th character A see Appendix A PDX collection 1336
CC Exclusion 7th characters B & C see Appendix A PDX collection 1337
CC Exclusion 7th characters K - R see Appendix A PDX collection 0897
HAC 7th characters A - C see Appendix B for HAC conditional logic

CC +7th **S82.092 Other fracture of left patella**
CC Exclusion 7th character A see Appendix A PDX collection 1338
CC Exclusion 7th characters B & C see Appendix A PDX collection 1337
CC Exclusion 7th characters K - R see Appendix A PDX collection 0897
HAC 7th characters A - C see Appendix B for HAC conditional logic

CC +7th **S82.099 Other fracture of unspecified patella**
CC Exclusion 7th character A see Appendix A PDX collection 1339
CC Exclusion 7th characters B & C see Appendix A PDX collection 1337
CC Exclusion 7th characters K - R see Appendix A PDX collection 0897
HAC 7th characters A - C see Appendix B for HAC conditional logic

+ **S82.1 Fracture of upper end of tibia**
Fracture of proximal end of tibia
Excludes2: *fracture of shaft of tibia (S82.2-)*
physeal fracture of upper end of tibia (S89.0-)

+ **S82.10 Unspecified fracture of upper end of tibia**

CC MCC +7th **S82.101 Unspecified fracture of upper end of right tibia**
CC Exclusion 7th character A see Appendix A PDX collection 1340
CC Exclusion 7th characters K - R see Appendix A PDX collection 0897
MCC Exclusion 7th characters B & C see Appendix A PDX collection 1341
HAC 7th characters A - C see Appendix B for HAC conditional logic

CC MCC +7th **S82.102 Unspecified fracture of upper end of left tibia**
CC Exclusion 7th character A see Appendix A PDX collection 1342
CC Exclusion 7th characters K - R see Appendix A PDX collection 0897
MCC Exclusion 7th characters B & C see Appendix A PDX collection 1341
HAC 7th characters A - C see Appendix B for HAC conditional logic

CC MCC +7th **S82.109 Unspecified fracture of upper end of unspecified tibia**
CC Exclusion 7th character A see Appendix A PDX collection 1341
CC Exclusion 7th characters K - R see Appendix A PDX collection 0897
MCC Exclusion 7th characters B & C see Appendix A PDX collection 1341
HAC 7th characters A - C see Appendix B for HAC conditional logic

+ **S82.11 Fracture of tibial spine**

CC MCC +7th **S82.111 Displaced fracture of right tibial spine**
CC Exclusion 7th character A see Appendix A PDX collection 1340
CC Exclusion 7th characters K - R see Appendix A PDX collection 0897
MCC Exclusion 7th characters B & C see Appendix A PDX collection 1341
HAC 7th characters A - C see Appendix B for HAC conditional logic

CC MCC +7th **S82.112 Displaced fracture of left tibial spine**
CC Exclusion 7th character A see Appendix A PDX collection 1342
CC Exclusion 7th characters K - R see Appendix A PDX collection 0897
MCC Exclusion 7th characters B & C see Appendix A PDX collection 1341
HAC 7th characters A - C see Appendix B for HAC conditional logic

CC MCC +7th **S82.113 Displaced fracture of unspecified tibial spine**
CC Exclusion 7th character A see Appendix A PDX collection 1341
CC Exclusion 7th characters K - R see Appendix A PDX collection 0897
MCC Exclusion 7th characters B & C see Appendix A PDX collection 1341
HAC 7th characters A - C see Appendix B for HAC conditional logic

CC MCC +7th **S82.114 Nondisplaced fracture of right tibial spine**
CC Exclusion 7th character A see Appendix A PDX collection 1340
CC Exclusion 7th characters K - R see Appendix A PDX collection 0897
MCC Exclusion 7th characters B & C see Appendix A PDX collection 1341
HAC 7th characters A - C see Appendix B for HAC conditional logic

CC MCC +7th **S82.115 Nondisplaced fracture of left tibial spine**
CC Exclusion 7th character A see Appendix A PDX collection 1342
CC Exclusion 7th characters K - R see Appendix A PDX collection 0897
MCC Exclusion 7th characters B & C see Appendix A PDX collection 1341
HAC 7th characters A - C see Appendix B for HAC conditional logic

CC MCC +7th **S82.116 Nondisplaced fracture of unspecified tibial spine**
CC Exclusion 7th character A see Appendix A PDX collection 1341
CC Exclusion 7th characters K - R see Appendix A PDX collection 0897
MCC Exclusion 7th characters B & C see Appendix A PDX collection 1341
HAC 7th characters A - C see Appendix B for HAC conditional logic

+ **S82.12 Fracture of lateral condyle of tibia**

CC MCC +7th **S82.121 Displaced fracture of lateral condyle of right tibia**
CC Exclusion 7th character A see Appendix A PDX collection 1340
CC Exclusion 7th characters K - R see Appendix A PDX collection 0897
MCC Exclusion 7th characters B & C see Appendix A PDX collection 1341
HAC 7th characters A - C see Appendix B for HAC conditional logic

CC MCC +7th **S82.122 Displaced fracture of lateral condyle of left tibia**
CC Exclusion 7th character A see Appendix A PDX collection 1342
CC Exclusion 7th characters K - R see Appendix A PDX collection 0897
MCC Exclusion 7th characters B & C see Appendix A PDX collection 1341
HAC 7th characters A - C see Appendix B for HAC conditional logic

CC MCC +7th **S82.123 Displaced fracture of lateral condyle of unspecified tibia**
CC Exclusion 7th character A see Appendix A PDX collection 1341
CC Exclusion 7th characters K - R see Appendix A PDX collection 0897
MCC Exclusion 7th characters B & C see Appendix A PDX collection 1341
HAC 7th characters A - C see Appendix B for HAC conditional logic

CC MCC +7th **S82.124 Nondisplaced fracture of lateral condyle of right tibia**
CC Exclusion 7th character A see Appendix A PDX collection 1340
CC Exclusion 7th characters K - R see Appendix A PDX collection 0897
MCC Exclusion 7th characters B & C see Appendix A PDX collection 1341
HAC 7th characters A - C see Appendix B for HAC conditional logic

CC MCC +7th S82.125 **Nondisplaced fracture of lateral condyle of left tibia**
CC Exclusion 7th character A see Appendix A PDX collection 1342
CC Exclusion 7th characters K - R see Appendix A PDX collection 0897
MCC Exclusion 7th characters B & C see Appendix A PDX collection 1341
HAC 7th characters A - C see Appendix B for HAC conditional logic

CC MCC +7th **S82.126 Nondisplaced fracture of lateral condyle of unspecified tibia**
CC Exclusion 7th character A see Appendix A PDX collection 1341
CC Exclusion 7th characters K - R see Appendix A PDX collection 0897
MCC Exclusion 7th characters B & C see Appendix A PDX collection 1341
HAC 7th characters A - C see Appendix B for HAC conditional logic

\+ **S82.13 Fracture of medial condyle of tibia**

CC MCC +7th **S82.131 Displaced fracture of medial condyle of right tibia**
CC Exclusion 7th character A see Appendix A PDX collection 1340
CC Exclusion 7th characters K - R see Appendix A PDX collection 0897
MCC Exclusion 7th characters B & C see Appendix A PDX collection 1341
HAC 7th characters A - C see Appendix B for HAC conditional logic

CC MCC +7th **S82.132 Displaced fracture of medial condyle of left tibia**
CC Exclusion 7th character A see Appendix A PDX collection 1342
CC Exclusion 7th characters K - R see Appendix A PDX collection 0897
MCC Exclusion 7th characters B & C see Appendix A PDX collection 1341
HAC 7th characters A - C see Appendix B for HAC conditional logic

CC MCC +7th **S82.133 Displaced fracture of medial condyle of unspecified tibia**
CC Exclusion 7th character A see Appendix A PDX collection 1341
CC Exclusion 7th characters K - R see Appendix A PDX collection 0897
MCC Exclusion 7th characters B & C see Appendix A PDX collection 1341
HAC 7th characters A - C see Appendix B for HAC conditional logic

CC MCC +7th **S82.134 Nondisplaced fracture of medial condyle of right tibia**
CC Exclusion 7th character A see Appendix A PDX collection 1340
CC Exclusion 7th characters K - R see Appendix A PDX collection 0897
MCC Exclusion 7th characters B & C see Appendix A PDX collection 1341
HAC 7th characters A - C see Appendix B for HAC conditional logic

CC MCC +7th **S82.135 Nondisplaced fracture of medial condyle of left tibia**
CC Exclusion 7th character A see Appendix A PDX collection 1342
CC Exclusion 7th characters K - R see Appendix A PDX collection 0897
MCC Exclusion 7th characters B & C see Appendix A PDX collection 1341
HAC 7th characters A - C see Appendix B for HAC conditional logic

CC MCC +7th **S82.136 Nondisplaced fracture of medial condyle of unspecified tibia**
CC Exclusion 7th character A see Appendix A PDX collection 1341
CC Exclusion 7th characters K - R see Appendix A PDX collection 0897
MCC Exclusion 7th characters B & C see Appendix A PDX collection 1341
HAC 7th characters A - C see Appendix B for HAC conditional logic

\+ **S82.14 Bicondylar fracture of tibia**
Fracture of tibial plateau NOS

CC MCC +7th **S82.141 Displaced bicondylar fracture of right tibi**
CC Exclusion 7th character A see Appendix A PDX collection 1340
CC Exclusion 7th characters K - R see Appendix A PDX collection 0897
MCC Exclusion 7th characters B & C see Appendix A PDX collection 1341
HAC 7th characters A - C see Appendix B for H conditional logic

CC MCC +7th **S82.142 Displaced bicondylar fracture of left tibia**
CC Exclusion 7th character A see Appendix A PDX collection 1342
CC Exclusion 7th characters K - R see Appendix A PDX collection 0897
MCC Exclusion 7th characters B & C see Appendix A PDX collection 1341
HAC 7th characters A - C see Appendix B for H conditional logic

CC MCC +7th **S82.143 Displaced bicondylar fracture of unspecifi tibia**
CC Exclusion 7th character A see Appendix A PDX collection 1341
CC Exclusion 7th characters K - R see Appendix A PDX collection 0897
MCC Exclusion 7th characters B & C see Appendix A PDX collection 1341
HAC 7th characters A - C see Appendix B for H conditional logic

CC MCC +7th **S82.144 Nondisplaced bicondylar fracture of right tibia**
CC Exclusion 7th character A see Appendix A PDX collection 1340
CC Exclusion 7th characters K - R see Appendix A PDX collection 0897
MCC Exclusion 7th characters B & C see Appendix A PDX collection 1341
HAC 7th characters A - C see Appendix B for HA conditional logic

CC MCC +7th **S82.145 Nondisplaced bicondylar fracture of left tibia**
CC Exclusion 7th character A see Appendix A PDX collection 1342
CC Exclusion 7th characters K - R see Appendix A PDX collection 0897
MCC Exclusion 7th characters B & C see Appendix A PDX collection 1341
HAC 7th characters A - C see Appendix B for HA conditional logic

CC MCC +7th **S82.146 Nondisplaced bicondylar fracture of unspecified tibia**
CC Exclusion 7th character A see Appendix A PDX collection 1341
CC Exclusion 7th characters K - R see Appendix A PDX collection 0897
MCC Exclusion 7th characters B & C see Appendix A PDX collection 1341
HAC 7th characters A - C see Appendix B for HA conditional logic

\+ **S82.15 Fracture of tibial tuberosity**

CC MCC +7th **S82.151 Displaced fracture of right tibial tuberosity**
CC Exclusion 7th character A see Appendix A PDX collection 1340
CC Exclusion 7th characters K - R see Appendix A PDX collection 0897
MCC Exclusion 7th characters B & C see Appendix A PDX collection 1341
HAC 7th characters A - C see Appendix B for HAC conditional logic

CC MCC +7th **S82.152 Displaced fracture of left tibial tuberosity**
CC Exclusion 7th character A see Appendix A PDX collection 1342
CC Exclusion 7th characters K - R see Appendix A PDX collection 0897
MCC Exclusion 7th characters B & C see Appendix A PDX collection 1341
HAC 7th characters A - C see Appendix B for HAC conditional logic

CC MCC +7th **S82.153 Displaced fracture of unspecified tibial tuberosity**
CC Exclusion 7th character A see Appendix A PDX collection 1341
CC Exclusion 7th characters K - R see Appendix A PDX collection 0897
MCC Exclusion 7th characters B & C see Appendix A PDX collection 1341
HAC 7th characters A - C see Appendix B for HAC conditional logic

CC MCC +7th **S82.154 Nondisplaced fracture of right tibial tuberosity**
CC Exclusion 7th character A see Appendix A PDX collection 1340
CC Exclusion 7th characters K - R see Appendix A PDX collection 0897
MCC Exclusion 7th characters B & C see Appendix A PDX collection 1341
HAC 7th characters A - C see Appendix B for HAC conditional logic

CC MCC +7th **S82.155 Nondisplaced fracture of left tibial tuberosity**
CC Exclusion 7th character A see Appendix A PDX collection 1342
CC Exclusion 7th characters K - R see Appendix A PDX collection 0897
MCC Exclusion 7th characters B & C see Appendix A PDX collection 1341
HAC 7th characters A - C see Appendix B for HAC conditional logic

CC MCC +7th **S82.156 Nondisplaced fracture of unspecified tibial tuberosity**
CC Exclusion 7th character A see Appendix A PDX collection 1341
CC Exclusion 7th characters K - R see Appendix A PDX collection 0897
MCC Exclusion 7th characters B & C see Appendix A PDX collection 1341
HAC 7th characters A - C see Appendix B for HAC conditional logic

\+ **S82.16 Torus fracture of upper end of tibia**

The appropriate 7th character is to be added to all codes in subcategory S82.16
A initial encounter for closed fracture
D subsequent encounter for fracture with routine healing
G subsequent encounter for fracture with delayed healing
K subsequent encounter for fracture with nonunion
P subsequent encounter for fracture with malunion
S sequela

CC +7th **S82.161 Torus fracture of upper end of right tibia**
CC Exclusion 7th character A see Appendix A PDX collection 1343
CC Exclusion 7th characters K & P see Appendix A PDX collection 0897
HAC 7th character A see Appendix B for HAC conditional logic

CC +7th **S82.162 Torus fracture of upper end of left tibia**
CC Exclusion 7th character A see Appendix A PDX collection 1344
CC Exclusion 7th characters K & P see Appendix A PDX collection 0897
HAC 7th character A see Appendix B for HAC conditional logic

CC +7th **S82.169 Torus fracture of upper end of unspecified tibia**
CC Exclusion 7th character A see Appendix A PDX collection 1345
CC Exclusion 7th characters K & P see Appendix A PDX collection 0897
HAC 7th character A see Appendix B for HAC conditional logic

\+ **S82.19 Other fracture of upper end of tibia**

CC MCC +7th **S82.191 Other fracture of upper end of right tibia**
CC Exclusion 7th character A see Appendix A PDX collection 1340
CC Exclusion 7th characters K - R see Appendix A PDX collection 0897
MCC Exclusion 7th characters B & C see Appendix A PDX collection 1341
HAC 7th characters A - C see Appendix B for HAC conditional logic

CC MCC +7th **S82.192 Other fracture of upper end of left tibia**
CC Exclusion 7th character A see Appendix A PDX collection 1342
CC Exclusion 7th characters K - R see Appendix A PDX collection 0897
MCC Exclusion 7th characters B & C see Appendix A PDX collection 1341
HAC 7th characters A - C see Appendix B for HAC conditional logic

CC MCC +7th **S82.199 Other fracture of upper end of unspecified tibia**
CC Exclusion 7th character A see Appendix A PDX collection 1341
CC Exclusion 7th characters K - R see Appendix A PDX collection 0897
MCC Exclusion 7th characters B & C see Appendix A PDX collection 1341
HAC 7th characters A - C see Appendix B for HAC conditional logic

\+ **S82.2 Fracture of shaft of tibia**

\+ **S82.20 Unspecified fracture of shaft of tibia**
Fracture of tibia NOS

CC MCC +7th **S82.201 Unspecified fracture of shaft of right tibia**
CC Exclusion 7th character A see Appendix A PDX collection 1346
CC Exclusion 7th characters K - R see Appendix A PDX collection 0897
MCC Exclusion 7th characters B & C see Appendix A PDX collection 1341
HAC 7th characters A - C see Appendix B for HAC conditional logic

CC MCC +7th **S82.202 Unspecified fracture of shaft of left tibia**
CC Exclusion 7th character A see Appendix A PDX collection 1342
CC Exclusion 7th characters K - R see Appendix A PDX collection 0897
MCC Exclusion 7th characters B & C see Appendix A PDX collection 1341
HAC 7th characters A - C see Appendix B for HAC conditional logic

CC MCC +7th **S82.209 Unspecified fracture of shaft of unspecified tibia**
CC Exclusion 7th character A see Appendix A PDX collection 1341
CC Exclusion 7th characters K - R see Appendix A PDX collection 0897
MCC Exclusion 7th characters B & C see Appendix A PDX collection 1341
HAC 7th characters A - C see Appendix B for HAC conditional logic

\+ **S82.22 Transverse fracture of shaft of tibia**

CC MCC +7th **S82.221 Displaced transverse fracture of shaft of right tibia**
CC Exclusion 7th character A see Appendix A PDX collection 1340
CC Exclusion 7th characters K - R see Appendix A PDX collection 0897
MCC Exclusion 7th characters B & C see Appendix A PDX collection 1341
HAC 7th characters A - C see Appendix B for HAC conditional logic

CC MCC +7th **S82.222 Displaced transverse fracture of shaft of left tibia**
CC Exclusion 7th character A see Appendix A PDX collection 1342
CC Exclusion 7th characters K - R see Appendix A PDX collection 0897
MCC Exclusion 7th characters B & C see Appendix A PDX collection 1341
HAC 7th characters A - C see Appendix B for HAC conditional logic

CC MCC +7th **S82.223 Displaced transverse fracture of shaft of unspecified tibia**
CC Exclusion 7th character A see Appendix A PDX collection 1341
CC Exclusion 7th characters K - R see Appendix A PDX collection 0897
MCC Exclusion 7th characters B & C see Appendix A PDX collection 1341
HAC 7th characters A - C see Appendix B for HAC conditional logic

CC MCC +7th **S82.224 Nondisplaced transverse fracture of shaft of right tibia**
CC Exclusion 7th character A see Appendix A PDX collection 1340
CC Exclusion 7th characters K - R see Appendix A PDX collection 0897
MCC Exclusion 7th characters B & C see Appendix A PDX collection 1341
HAC 7th characters A - C see Appendix B for HAC conditional logic

CC MCC +7th **S82.225 Nondisplaced transverse fracture of shaft of left tibia**
- **CC Exclusion 7th character A see Appendix A PDX collection 1342**
- **CC Exclusion 7th characters K - R see Appendix A PDX collection 0897**
- **MCC Exclusion 7th characters B & C see Appendix A PDX collection 1341**
- HAC 7th characters A - C see Appendix B for HAC conditional logic

CC MCC +7th **S82.226 Nondisplaced transverse fracture of shaft of unspecified tibia**
- **CC Exclusion 7th character A see Appendix A PDX collection 1341**
- **CC Exclusion 7th characters K - R see Appendix A PDX collection 0897**
- **MCC Exclusion 7th characters B & C see Appendix A PDX collection 1341**
- HAC 7th characters A - C see Appendix B for HAC conditional logic

\+ **S82.23 Oblique fracture of shaft of tibia**

CC MCC +7th **S82.231 Displaced oblique fracture of shaft of right tibia**
- **CC Exclusion 7th character A see Appendix A PDX collection 1340**
- **CC Exclusion 7th characters K - R see Appendix A PDX collection 0897**
- **MCC Exclusion 7th characters B & C see Appendix A PDX collection 1341**
- HAC 7th characters A - C see Appendix B for HAC conditional logic

CC MCC +7th **S82.232 Displaced oblique fracture of shaft of left tibia**
- **CC Exclusion 7th character A see Appendix A PDX collection 1342**
- **CC Exclusion 7th characters K - R see Appendix A PDX collection 0897**
- **MCC Exclusion 7th characters B & C see Appendix A PDX collection 1341**
- HAC 7th characters A - C see Appendix B for HAC conditional logic

CC MCC +7th **S82.233 Displaced oblique fracture of shaft of unspecified tibia**
- **CC Exclusion 7th character A see Appendix A PDX collection 1341**
- **CC Exclusion 7th characters K - R see Appendix A PDX collection 0897**
- **MCC Exclusion 7th characters B & C see Appendix A PDX collection 1341**
- HAC 7th characters A - C see Appendix B for HAC conditional logic

CC MCC +7th **S82.234 Nondisplaced oblique fracture of shaft of right tibia**
- **CC Exclusion 7th character A see Appendix A PDX collection 1340**
- **CC Exclusion 7th characters K - R see Appendix A PDX collection 0897**
- **MCC Exclusion 7th characters B & C see Appendix A PDX collection 1341**
- HAC 7th characters A - C see Appendix B for HAC conditional logic

CC MCC +7th **S82.235 Nondisplaced oblique fracture of shaft of left tibia**
- **CC Exclusion 7th character A see Appendix A PDX collection 1342**
- **CC Exclusion 7th characters K - R see Appendix A PDX collection 0897**
- **MCC Exclusion 7th characters B & C see Appendix A PDX collection 1341**
- HAC 7th characters A - C see Appendix B for HAC conditional logic

CC MCC +7th **S82.236 Nondisplaced oblique fracture of shaft of unspecified tibia**
- **CC Exclusion 7th character A see Appendix A PDX collection 1341**
- **CC Exclusion 7th characters K - R see Appendix A PDX collection 0897**
- **MCC Exclusion 7th characters B & C see Appendix A PDX collection 1341**
- HAC 7th characters A - C see Appendix B for HAC conditional logic

\+ **S82.24 Spiral fracture of shaft of tibia**
Toddler fracture

CC MCC +7th **S82.241 Displaced spiral fracture of shaft of right tibia**
- **CC Exclusion 7th character A see Appendix A PDX collection 1340**
- **CC Exclusion 7th characters K - R see Appendix A PDX collection 0897**
- **MCC Exclusion 7th characters B & C see Appendix A PDX collection 1341**
- HAC 7th characters A - C see Appendix B for HA conditional logic

CC MCC +7th **S82.242 Displaced spiral fracture of shaft of left tibi**
- **CC Exclusion 7th character A see Appendix A PDX collection 1342**
- **CC Exclusion 7th characters K - R see Appendix A PDX collection 0897**
- **MCC Exclusion 7th characters B & C see Appendix A PDX collection 1341**
- HAC 7th characters A - C see Appendix B for HA conditional logic

CC MCC +7th **S82.243 Displaced spiral fracture of shaft of unspecified tibia**
- **CC Exclusion 7th character A see Appendix A PDX collection 1341**
- **CC Exclusion 7th characters K - R see Appendix A PDX collection 0897**
- **MCC Exclusion 7th characters B & C see Appendix A PDX collection 1341**
- HAC 7th characters A - C see Appendix B for HA conditional logic

CC MCC +7th **S82.244 Nondisplaced spiral fracture of shaft of righ tibia**
- **CC Exclusion 7th character A see Appendix A PDX collection 1340**
- **CC Exclusion 7th characters K - R see Appendix A PDX collection 0897**
- **MCC Exclusion 7th characters B & C see Appendix A PDX collection 1341**
- HAC 7th characters A - C see Appendix B for HA conditional logic

CC MCC +7th **S82.245 Nondisplaced spiral fracture of shaft of left tibia**
- **CC Exclusion 7th character A see Appendix A PDX collection 1342**
- **CC Exclusion 7th characters K - R see Appendix A PDX collection 0897**
- **MCC Exclusion 7th characters B & C see Appendix A PDX collection 1341**
- HAC 7th characters A - C see Appendix B for HAC conditional logic

CC MCC +7th **S82.246 Nondisplaced spiral fracture of shaft of unspecified tibia**
- **CC Exclusion 7th character A see Appendix A PDX collection 1341**
- **CC Exclusion 7th characters K - R see Appendix A PDX collection 0897**
- **MCC Exclusion 7th characters B & C see Appendix A PDX collection 1341**
- HAC 7th characters A - C see Appendix B for HAC conditional logic

\+ **S82.25 Comminuted fracture of shaft of tibia**

CC MCC +7th **S82.251 Displaced comminuted fracture of shaft of right tibia**
- **CC Exclusion 7th character A see Appendix A PDX collection 1340**
- **CC Exclusion 7th characters K - R see Appendix A PDX collection 0897**
- **MCC Exclusion 7th characters B & C see Appendix A PDX collection 1341**
- HAC 7th characters A - C see Appendix B for HAC conditional logic

CC MCC +7th **S82.252 Displaced comminuted fracture of shaft of left tibia**
- **CC Exclusion 7th character A see Appendix A PDX collection 1342**
- **CC Exclusion 7th characters K - R see Appendix A PDX collection 0897**
- **MCC Exclusion 7th characters B & C see Appendix A PDX collection 1341**
- HAC 7th characters A - C see Appendix B for HAC conditional logic

CC MCC +7th **S82.253 Displaced comminuted fracture of shaft of unspecified tibia**
CC Exclusion 7th character A see Appendix A PDX collection 1341
CC Exclusion 7th characters K - R see Appendix A PDX collection 0897
MCC Exclusion 7th characters B & C see Appendix A PDX collection 1341
HAC 7th characters A - C see Appendix B for HAC conditional logic

CC MCC +7th **S82.254 Nondisplaced comminuted fracture of shaft of right tibia**
CC Exclusion 7th character A see Appendix A PDX collection 1340
CC Exclusion 7th characters K - R see Appendix A PDX collection 0897
MCC Exclusion 7th characters B & C see Appendix A PDX collection 1341
HAC 7th characters A - C see Appendix B for HAC conditional logic

CC MCC +7th **S82.255 Nondisplaced comminuted fracture of shaft of left tibia**
CC Exclusion 7th character A see Appendix A PDX collection 1342
CC Exclusion 7th characters K - R see Appendix A PDX collection 0897
MCC Exclusion 7th characters B & C see Appendix A PDX collection 1341
HAC 7th characters A - C see Appendix B for HAC conditional logic

CC MCC +7th **S82.256 Nondisplaced comminuted fracture of shaft of unspecified tibia**
CC Exclusion 7th character A see Appendix A PDX collection 1341
CC Exclusion 7th characters K - R see Appendix A PDX collection 0897
MCC Exclusion 7th characters B & C see Appendix A PDX collection 1341
HAC 7th characters A - C see Appendix B for HAC conditional logic

+ **S82.26 Segmental fracture of shaft of tibia**

CC MCC +7th **S82.261 Displaced segmental fracture of shaft of right tibia**
CC Exclusion 7th character A see Appendix A PDX collection 1340
CC Exclusion 7th characters K - R see Appendix A PDX collection 0897
MCC Exclusion 7th characters B & C see Appendix A PDX collection 1341
HAC 7th characters A - C see Appendix B for HAC conditional logic

CC MCC +7th **S82.262 Displaced segmental fracture of shaft of left tibia**
CC Exclusion 7th character A see Appendix A PDX collection 1342
CC Exclusion 7th characters K - R see Appendix A PDX collection 0897
MCC Exclusion 7th characters B & C see Appendix A PDX collection 1341
HAC 7th characters A - C see Appendix B for HAC conditional logic

CC MCC +7th **S82.263 Displaced segmental fracture of shaft of unspecified tibia**
CC Exclusion 7th character A see Appendix A PDX collection 1341
CC Exclusion 7th characters K - R see Appendix A PDX collection 0897
MCC Exclusion 7th characters B & C see Appendix A PDX collection 1341
HAC 7th characters A - C see Appendix B for HAC conditional logic

CC MCC +7th **S82.264 Nondisplaced segmental fracture of shaft of right tibia**
CC Exclusion 7th character A see Appendix A PDX collection 1340
CC Exclusion 7th characters K - R see Appendix A PDX collection 0897
MCC Exclusion 7th characters B & C see Appendix A PDX collection 1341
HAC 7th characters A - C see Appendix B for HAC conditional logic

CC MCC +7th **S82.265 Nondisplaced segmental fracture of shaft of left tibia**
CC Exclusion 7th character A see Appendix A PDX collection 1342
CC Exclusion 7th characters K - R see Appendix A PDX collection 0897
MCC Exclusion 7th characters B & C see Appendix A PDX collection 1341
HAC 7th characters A - C see Appendix B for HAC conditional logic

CC MCC +7th **S82.266 Nondisplaced segmental fracture of shaft of unspecified tibia**
CC Exclusion 7th character A see Appendix A PDX collection 1341
CC Exclusion 7th characters K - R see Appendix A PDX collection 0897
MCC Exclusion 7th characters B & C see Appendix A PDX collection 1341
HAC 7th characters A - C see Appendix B for HAC conditional logic

+ **S82.29 Other fracture of shaft of tibia**

CC MCC +7th **S82.291 Other fracture of shaft of right tibia**
CC Exclusion 7th character A see Appendix A PDX collection 1340
CC Exclusion 7th characters K - R see Appendix A PDX collection 0897
MCC Exclusion 7th characters B & C see Appendix A PDX collection 1341
HAC 7th characters A - C see Appendix B for HAC conditional logic

CC MCC +7th **S82.292 Other fracture of shaft of left tibia**
CC Exclusion 7th character A see Appendix A PDX collection 1342
CC Exclusion 7th characters K - R see Appendix A PDX collection 0897
MCC Exclusion 7th characters B & C see Appendix A PDX collection 1341
HAC 7th characters A - C see Appendix B for HAC conditional logic

CC MCC +7th **S82.299 Other fracture of shaft of unspecified tibia**
CC Exclusion 7th character A see Appendix A PDX collection 1341
CC Exclusion 7th characters K - R see Appendix A PDX collection 0897
MCC Exclusion 7th characters B & C see Appendix A PDX collection 1341
HAC 7th characters A - C see Appendix B for HAC conditional logic

+ **S82.3 Fracture of lower end of tibia**
Excludes1: *bimalleolar fracture of lower leg (S82.84-)*
fracture of medial malleolus alone (S82.5-)
Maisonneuve's fracture (S82.86-)
pilon fracture of distal tibia (S82.87-)
trimalleolar fractures of lower leg (S82.85-)

+ **S82.30 Unspecified fracture of lower end of tibia**

CC +7th **S82.301 Unspecified fracture of lower end of right tibia**
CC Exclusion 7th characters B & C see Appendix A PDX collection 1347
CC Exclusion 7th characters K - R see Appendix A PDX collection 0897
HAC 7th characters B & C see Appendix B for HAC conditional logic

CC +7th **S82.302 Unspecified fracture of lower end of left tibia**
CC Exclusion 7th characters B & C see Appendix A PDX collection 1347
CC Exclusion 7th characters K - R see Appendix A PDX collection 0897
HAC 7th characters B & C see Appendix B for HAC conditional logic

CC +7th **S82.309 Unspecified fracture of lower end of unspecified tibia**
CC Exclusion 7th characters B & C see Appendix A PDX collection 1347
CC Exclusion 7th characters K - R see Appendix A PDX collection 0897
HAC 7th characters B & C see Appendix B for HAC conditional logic

\+ **S82.31 Torus fracture of lower end of tibia**

The appropriate 7th character is to be added to all codes in subcategory S82.31
A initial encounter for closed fracture
D subsequent encounter for fracture with routine healing
G subsequent encounter for fracture with delayed healing
K subsequent encounter for fracture with nonunion
P subsequent encounter for fracture with malunion
S sequela

CC +7th **S82.311 Torus fracture of lower end of right tibia**
CC Exclusion 7th character A see Appendix A PDX collection 1343
CC Exclusion 7th characters K & P see Appendix A PDX collection 0897
HAC 7th character A see Appendix B for HAC conditional logic

CC +7th **S82.312 Torus fracture of lower end of left tibia**
CC Exclusion 7th character A see Appendix A PDX collection 1344
CC Exclusion 7th characters K & P see Appendix A PDX collection 0897
HAC 7th character A see Appendix B for HAC conditional logic

CC +7th **S82.319 Torus fracture of lower end of unspecified tibia**
CC Exclusion 7th character A see Appendix A PDX collection 1345
CC Exclusion 7th characters K & P see Appendix A PDX collection 0897
HAC 7th character A see Appendix B for HAC conditional logic

\+ **S82.39 Other fracture of lower end of tibia**

CC +7th **S82.391 Other fracture of lower end of right tibia**
CC Exclusion 7th characters B & C see Appendix A PDX collection 1347
CC Exclusion 7th characters K - R see Appendix A PDX collection 0897
HAC 7th characters B & C see Appendix B for HAC conditional logic

CC +7th **S82.392 Other fracture of lower end of left tibia**
CC Exclusion 7th characters B & C see Appendix A PDX collection 1347
CC Exclusion 7th characters K - R see Appendix A PDX collection 0897
HAC 7th characters B & C see Appendix B for HAC conditional logic

CC +7th **S82.399 Other fracture of lower end of unspecified tibia**
CC Exclusion 7th characters B & C see Appendix A PDX collection 1347
CC Exclusion 7th characters K - R see Appendix A PDX collection 0897
HAC 7th characters B & C see Appendix B for HAC conditional logic

\+ **S82.4 Fracture of shaft of fibula**
Excludes2: *fracture of lateral malleolus alone (S82.6-)*

\+ **S82.40 Unspecified fracture of shaft of fibula**

+7th **S82.401 Unspecified fracture of shaft of right fibula**
CC Exclusion 7th characters K - R see Appendix A PDX collection 0897
MCC Exclusion 7th characters B & C see Appendix A PDX collection 1341
HAC 7th characters B & C see Appendix B for HAC conditional logic

CC MCC +7th **S82.402 Unspecified fracture of shaft of left fibula**
CC Exclusion 7th characters K - R see Appendix A PDX collection 0897
MCC Exclusion 7th characters B & C see Appendix A PDX collection 1341
HAC 7th characters B & C see Appendix B for HAC conditional logic

CC MCC +7th **S82.409 Unspecified fracture of shaft of unspecified fibula**
CC Exclusion 7th characters K - R see Appendix A PDX collection 0897
MCC Exclusion 7th characters B & C see Appendix A PDX collection 1341
HAC 7th characters B & C see Appendix B for HAC conditional logic

\+ **S82.42 Transverse fracture of shaft of fibula**

CC MCC +7th **S82.421 Displaced transverse fracture of shaft of right fibula**
CC Exclusion 7th characters K - R see Appendix A PDX collection 0897
MCC Exclusion 7th characters B & C see Appendix A PDX collection 1341
HAC 7th characters B & C see Appendix B for HAC conditional logic

CC MCC +7th **S82.422 Displaced transverse fracture of shaft of left fibula**
CC Exclusion 7th characters K - R see Appendix A PDX collection 0897
MCC Exclusion 7th characters B & C see Appendix A PDX collection 1341
HAC 7th characters B & C see Appendix B for HAC conditional logic

CC MCC +7th **S82.423 Displaced transverse fracture of shaft of unspecified fibula**
CC Exclusion 7th characters K - R see Appendix A PDX collection 0897
MCC Exclusion 7th characters B & C see Appendix A PDX collection 1341
HAC 7th characters B & C see Appendix B for HAC conditional logic

CC MCC +7th **S82.424 Nondisplaced transverse fracture of shaft of right fibula**
CC Exclusion 7th characters K - R see Appendix A PDX collection 0897
MCC Exclusion 7th characters B & C see Appendix A PDX collection 1341
HAC 7th characters B & C see Appendix B for HAC conditional logic

CC MCC +7th **S82.425 Nondisplaced transverse fracture of shaft of left fibula**
CC Exclusion 7th characters K - R see Appendix A PDX collection 0897
MCC Exclusion 7th characters B & C see Appendix A PDX collection 1341
HAC 7th characters B & C see Appendix B for HAC conditional logic

CC MCC +7th **S82.426 Nondisplaced transverse fracture of shaft of unspecified fibula**
CC Exclusion 7th characters K - R see Appendix A PDX collection 0897
MCC Exclusion 7th characters B & C see Appendix A PDX collection 1341
HAC 7th characters B & C see Appendix B for HAC conditional logic

\+ **S82.43 Oblique fracture of shaft of fibula**

CC MCC +7th **S82.431 Displaced oblique fracture of shaft of right fibula**
CC Exclusion 7th characters K - R see Appendix A PDX collection 0897
MCC Exclusion 7th characters B & C see Appendix A PDX collection 1341
HAC 7th characters B & C see Appendix B for HAC conditional logic

CC MCC +7th **S82.432 Displaced oblique fracture of shaft of left fibula**
CC Exclusion 7th characters K - R see Appendix A PDX collection 0897
MCC Exclusion 7th characters B & C see Appendix A PDX collection 1341
HAC 7th characters B & C see Appendix B for HAC conditional logic

CC MCC +7th **S82.433 Displaced oblique fracture of shaft of unspecified fibula**
CC Exclusion 7th characters K - R see Appendix A PDX collection 0897
MCC Exclusion 7th characters B & C see Appendix A PDX collection 1341
HAC 7th characters B & C see Appendix B for HAC conditional logic

CC MCC +7th **S82.434 Nondisplaced oblique fracture of shaft of right fibula**
CC Exclusion 7th characters K - R see Appendix A PDX collection 0897
MCC Exclusion 7th characters B & C see Appendix A PDX collection 1341
HAC 7th characters B & C see Appendix B for HAC conditional logic

CC MCC +7th **S82.435 Nondisplaced oblique fracture of shaft of left fibula**
CC Exclusion 7th characters K - R see Appendix A PDX collection 0897
MCC Exclusion 7th characters B & C see Appendix A PDX collection 1341
HAC 7th characters B & C see Appendix B for HAC conditional logic

CC MCC +7th **S82.436 Nondisplaced oblique fracture of shaft of unspecified fibula**
CC Exclusion 7th characters K - R see Appendix A PDX collection 0897
MCC Exclusion 7th characters B & C see Appendix A PDX collection 1341
HAC 7th characters B & C see Appendix B for HAC conditional logic

\+ **S82.44 Spiral fracture of shaft of fibula**

CC MCC +7th **S82.441 Displaced spiral fracture of shaft of right fibula**
CC Exclusion 7th characters K - R see Appendix A PDX collection 0897
MCC Exclusion 7th characters B & C see Appendix A PDX collection 1341
HAC 7th characters B & C see Appendix B for HAC conditional logic

CC MCC +7th **S82.442 Displaced spiral fracture of shaft of left fibula**
CC Exclusion 7th characters K - R see Appendix A PDX collection 0897
MCC Exclusion 7th characters B & C see Appendix A PDX collection 1341
HAC 7th characters B & C see Appendix B for HAC conditional logic

CC MCC +7th **S82.443 Displaced spiral fracture of shaft of unspecified fibula**
CC Exclusion 7th characters K - R see Appendix A PDX collection 0897
MCC Exclusion 7th characters B & C see Appendix A PDX collection 1341
HAC 7th characters B & C see Appendix B for HAC conditional logic

CC MCC +7th **S82.444 Nondisplaced spiral fracture of shaft of right fibula**
CC Exclusion 7th characters K - R see Appendix A PDX collection 0897
MCC Exclusion 7th characters B & C see Appendix A PDX collection 1341
HAC 7th characters B & C see Appendix B for HAC conditional logic

CC MCC +7th **S82.445 Nondisplaced spiral fracture of shaft of left fibula**
CC Exclusion 7th characters K - R see Appendix A PDX collection 0897
MCC Exclusion 7th characters B & C see Appendix A PDX collection 1341
HAC 7th characters B & C see Appendix B for HAC conditional logic

CC MCC +7th **S82.446 Nondisplaced spiral fracture of shaft of unspecified fibula**
CC Exclusion 7th characters K - R see Appendix A PDX collection 0897
MCC Exclusion 7th characters B & C see Appendix A PDX collection 1341
HAC 7th characters B & C see Appendix B for HAC conditional logic

\+ **S82.45 Comminuted fracture of shaft of fibula**

CC MCC +7th **S82.451 Displaced comminuted fracture of shaft of right fibula**
CC Exclusion 7th characters K - R see Appendix A PDX collection 0897
MCC Exclusion 7th characters B & C see Appendix A PDX collection 1341
HAC 7th characters B & C see Appendix B for HAC conditional logic

CC MCC +7th **S82.452 Displaced comminuted fracture of shaft of left fibula**
CC Exclusion 7th characters K - R see Appendix A PDX collection 0897
MCC Exclusion 7th characters B & C see Appendix A PDX collection 1341
HAC 7th characters B & C see Appendix B for HAC conditional logic

CC MCC +7th **S82.453 Displaced comminuted fracture of shaft of unspecified fibula**
CC Exclusion 7th characters K - R see Appendix A PDX collection 0897
MCC Exclusion 7th characters B & C see Appendix A PDX collection 1341
HAC 7th characters B & C see Appendix B for HAC conditional logic

CC MCC +7th **S82.454 Nondisplaced comminuted fracture of shaft of right fibula**
CC Exclusion 7th characters K - R see Appendix A PDX collection 0897
MCC Exclusion 7th characters B & C see Appendix A PDX collection 1341
HAC 7th characters B & C see Appendix B for HAC conditional logic

CC MCC +7th **S82.455 Nondisplaced comminuted fracture of shaft of left fibula**
CC Exclusion 7th characters K - R see Appendix A PDX collection 0897
MCC Exclusion 7th characters B & C see Appendix A PDX collection 1341
HAC 7th characters B & C see Appendix B for HAC conditional logic

CC MCC +7th **S82.456 Nondisplaced comminuted fracture of shaft of unspecified fibula**
CC Exclusion 7th characters K - R see Appendix A PDX collection 0897
MCC Exclusion 7th characters B & C see Appendix A PDX collection 1341
HAC 7th characters B & C see Appendix B for HAC conditional logic

\+ **S82.46 Segmental fracture of shaft of fibula**

CC MCC +7th **S82.461 Displaced segmental fracture of shaft of right fibula**
CC Exclusion 7th characters K - R see Appendix A PDX collection 0897
MCC Exclusion 7th characters B & C see Appendix A PDX collection 1341
HAC 7th characters B & C see Appendix B for HAC conditional logic

CC MCC +7th **S82.462 Displaced segmental fracture of shaft of left fibula**
CC Exclusion 7th characters K - R see Appendix A PDX collection 0897
MCC Exclusion 7th characters B & C see Appendix A PDX collection 1341
HAC 7th characters B & C see Appendix B for HAC conditional logic

CC MCC +7th **S82.463 Displaced segmental fracture of shaft of unspecified fibula**
CC Exclusion 7th characters K - R see Appendix A PDX collection 0897
MCC Exclusion 7th characters B & C see Appendix A PDX collection 1341
HAC 7th characters B & C see Appendix B for HAC conditional logic

CC MCC +7th **S82.464 Nondisplaced segmental fracture of shaft of right fibula**
CC Exclusion 7th characters K - R see Appendix A PDX collection 0897
MCC Exclusion 7th characters B & C see Appendix A PDX collection 1341
HAC 7th characters B & C see Appendix B for HAC conditional logic

CC MCC +7th **S82.465 Nondisplaced segmental fracture of shaft of left fibula**
CC Exclusion 7th characters K - R see Appendix A PDX collection 0897
MCC Exclusion 7th characters B & C see Appendix A PDX collection 1341
HAC 7th characters B & C see Appendix B for HAC conditional logic

CC MCC +7th **S82.466 Nondisplaced segmental fracture of shaft of unspecified fibula**
CC Exclusion 7th characters K - R see Appendix A PDX collection 0897
MCC Exclusion 7th characters B & C see Appendix A PDX collection 1341
HAC 7th characters B & C see Appendix B for HAC conditional logic

+ **S82.49 Other fracture of shaft of fibula**

CC MCC +7th **S82.491 Other fracture of shaft of right fibula**
CC Exclusion 7th characters K - R see Appendix A PDX collection 0897
MCC Exclusion 7th characters B & C see Appendix A PDX collection 1341
HAC 7th characters B & C see Appendix B for HAC conditional logic

CC MCC +7th **S82.492 Other fracture of shaft of left fibula**
CC Exclusion 7th characters K - R see Appendix A PDX collection 0897
MCC Exclusion 7th characters B & C see Appendix A PDX collection 1341
HAC 7th characters B & C see Appendix B for HAC conditional logic

CC MCC +7th **S82.499 Other fracture of shaft of unspecified fibula**
CC Exclusion 7th characters K - R see Appendix A PDX collection 0897
MCC Exclusion 7th characters B & C see Appendix A PDX collection 1341
HAC 7th characters B & C see Appendix B for HAC conditional logic

+ **S82.5 Fracture of medial malleolus**
Excludes1: *pilon fracture of distal tibia (S82.87-)*
Salter-Harris type III of lower end of tibia (S89.13-)
Salter-Harris type IV of lower end of tibia (S89.14-)

CC X+7th **S82.51 Displaced fracture of medial malleolus of right tibia**
CC Exclusion 7th characters B & C see Appendix A PDX collection 1347
CC Exclusion 7th characters K - R see Appendix A PDX collection 0897
HAC 7th characters B & C see Appendix B for HAC conditional logic

CC X+7th **S82.52 Displaced fracture of medial malleolus of left tibia**
CC Exclusion 7th characters B & C see Appendix A PDX collection 1347
CC Exclusion 7th characters K - R see Appendix A PDX collection 0897
HAC 7th characters B & C see Appendix B for HAC conditional logic

CC X+7th **S82.53 Displaced fracture of medial malleolus of unspecified tibia**
CC Exclusion 7th characters B & C see Appendix A PDX collection 1347
CC Exclusion 7th characters K - R see Appendix A PDX collection 0897
HAC 7th characters B & C see Appendix B for HAC conditional logic

CC X+7th **S82.54 Nondisplaced fracture of medial malleolus of right tibia**
CC Exclusion 7th characters B & C see Appendix A PDX collection 1347
CC Exclusion 7th characters K - R see Appendix A PDX collection 0897
HAC 7th characters B & C see Appendix B for HAC conditional logic

CC X+7th **S82.55 Nondisplaced fracture of medial malleolus of left tibia**
CC Exclusion 7th characters B & C see Appendix A PDX collection 1347
CC Exclusion 7th characters K - R see Appendix A PDX collection 0897
HAC 7th characters B & C see Appendix B for HAC conditional logic

CC X+7th **S82.56 Nondisplaced fracture of medial malleolus of unspecified tibia**
CC Exclusion 7th characters B & C see Appendix A PDX collection 1347
CC Exclusion 7th characters K - R see Appendix A PDX collection 0897
HAC 7th characters B & C see Appendix B for HAC conditional logic

+ **S82.6 Fracture of lateral malleolus**
Excludes1: *pilon fracture of distal tibia (S82.87-)*

CC X+7th **S82.61 Displaced fracture of lateral malleolus of right fibula**
CC Exclusion 7th characters B & C see Appendix A PDX collection 1347
CC Exclusion 7th characters K - R see Appendix A PDX collection 0897
HAC 7th characters B & C see Appendix B for HAC conditional logic

CC X+7th **S82.62 Displaced fracture of lateral malleolus of left fibula**
CC Exclusion 7th characters B & C see Appendix A PDX collection 1347
CC Exclusion 7th characters K - R see Appendix A PDX collection 0897
HAC 7th characters B & C see Appendix B for HAC conditional logic

CC X+7th **S82.63 Displaced fracture of lateral malleolus of unspecified fibula**
CC Exclusion 7th characters B & C see Appendix A PDX collection 1347
CC Exclusion 7th characters K - R see Appendix A PDX collection 0897
HAC 7th characters B & C see Appendix B for HAC conditional logic

CC X+7th **S82.64 Nondisplaced fracture of lateral malleolus of right fibula**
CC Exclusion 7th characters B & C see Appendix A PDX collection 1347
CC Exclusion 7th characters K - R see Appendix A PDX collection 0897
HAC 7th characters B & C see Appendix B for HAC conditional logic

CC X+7th **S82.65 Nondisplaced fracture of lateral malleolus of left fibu**
CC Exclusion 7th characters B & C see Appendix A PDX collection 1347
CC Exclusion 7th characters K - R see Appendix A PDX collection 0897
HAC 7th characters B & C see Appendix B for HAC conditional logic

CC X+7th **S82.66 Nondisplaced fracture of lateral malleolus of unspecified fibula**
CC Exclusion 7th characters B & C see Appendix A PDX collection 1347
CC Exclusion 7th characters K - R see Appendix A PDX collection 0897
HAC 7th characters B & C see Appendix B for HAC conditional logic

+ **S82.8 Other fractures of lower leg**

+ **S82.81 Torus fracture of upper end of fibula**

The appropriate 7th character is to be added to all codes in subcategory S82.82
A initial encounter for closed fracture
D subsequent encounter for fracture with routine healing
G subsequent encounter for fracture with delayed healing
K subsequent encounter for fracture with nonunion
P subsequent encounter for fracture with malunion
S sequela

CC +7th **S82.811 Torus fracture of upper end of right fibula**
CC Exclusion 7th characters K & P see Appendix A PDX collection 0897

CC +7th **S82.812 Torus fracture of upper end of left fibula**
CC Exclusion 7th characters K & P see Appendix A PDX collection 0897

CC +7th **S82.819 Torus fracture of upper end of unspecified fibula**
CC Exclusion 7th characters K & P see Appendix A PDX collection 0897

+ **S82.82 Torus fracture of lower end of fibula**

The appropriate 7th character is to be added to all codes in subcategory S82.82
A initial encounter for closed fracture
D subsequent encounter for fracture with routine healing
G subsequent encounter for fracture with delayed healing
K subsequent encounter for fracture with nonunion
P subsequent encounter for fracture with malunion
S sequela

CC +7th **S82.821 Torus fracture of lower end of right fibula**
CC Exclusion 7th characters K & P see Appendix A PDX collection 0897

CC +7th **S82.822 Torus fracture of lower end of left fibula**
CC Exclusion 7th characters K & P see Appendix A PDX collection 0897

CC +7th **S82.829 Torus fracture of lower end of unspecified fibula**
CC Exclusion 7th characters K & P see Appendix A PDX collection 0897

+ **S82.83 Other fracture of upper and lower end of fibula**

CC MCC +7th **S82.831 Other fracture of upper and lower end of right fibula**
CC Exclusion 7th characters K - R see Appendix A PDX collection 0897
MCC Exclusion 7th characters B & C see Appendix A PDX collection 1341
HAC 7th characters B & C see Appendix B for HAC conditional logic

CC MCC +7th **S82.832 Other fracture of upper and lower end of left fibula**
CC Exclusion 7th characters K - R see Appendix A PDX collection 0897
MCC Exclusion 7th characters B & C see Appendix A PDX collection 1341
HAC 7th characters B & C see Appendix B for HAC conditional logic

CC MCC +7th **S82.839 Other fracture of upper and lower end of unspecified fibula**
CC Exclusion 7th characters K - R see Appendix A PDX collection 0897
MCC Exclusion 7th characters B & C see Appendix A PDX collection 1341
HAC 7th characters B & C see Appendix B for HAC conditional logic

+ **S82.84 Bimalleolar fracture of lower leg**

CC +7th **S82.841 Displaced bimalleolar fracture of right lower leg**
CC Exclusion 7th characters B & C see Appendix A PDX collection 1347
CC Exclusion 7th characters K - R see Appendix A PDX collection 0897
HAC 7th characters B & C see Appendix B for HAC conditional logic

CC +7th **S82.842 Displaced bimalleolar fracture of left lower leg**
CC Exclusion 7th characters B & C see Appendix A PDX collection 1347
CC Exclusion 7th characters K - R see Appendix A PDX collection 0897
HAC 7th characters B & C see Appendix B for HAC conditional logic

CC +7th **S82.843 Displaced bimalleolar fracture of unspecified lower leg**
CC Exclusion 7th characters B & C see Appendix A PDX collection 1347
CC Exclusion 7th characters K - R see Appendix A PDX collection 0897
HAC 7th characters B & C see Appendix B for HAC conditional logic

CC +7th **S82.844 Nondisplaced bimalleolar fracture of right lower leg**
CC Exclusion 7th characters B & C see Appendix A PDX collection 1347
CC Exclusion 7th characters K - R see Appendix A PDX collection 0897
HAC 7th characters B & C see Appendix B for HAC conditional logic

CC +7th **S82.845 Nondisplaced bimalleolar fracture of left lower leg**
CC Exclusion 7th characters B & C see Appendix A PDX collection 1347
CC Exclusion 7th characters K - R see Appendix A PDX collection 0897
HAC 7th characters B & C see Appendix B for HAC conditional logic

CC +7th **S82.846 Nondisplaced bimalleolar fracture of unspecified lower leg**
CC Exclusion 7th characters B & C see Appendix A PDX collection 1347
CC Exclusion 7th characters K - R see Appendix A PDX collection 0897
HAC 7th characters B & C see Appendix B for HAC conditional logic

+ **S82.85 Trimalleolar fracture of lower leg**

CC +7th **S82.851 Displaced trimalleolar fracture of right lower leg**
CC Exclusion 7th characters B & C see Appendix A PDX collection 1347
CC Exclusion 7th characters K - R see Appendix A PDX collection 0897
HAC 7th characters B & C see Appendix B for HAC conditional logic

CC +7th **S82.852 Displaced trimalleolar fracture of left lower leg**
CC Exclusion 7th characters B & C see Appendix A PDX collection 1347
CC Exclusion 7th characters K - R see Appendix A PDX collection 0897
HAC 7th characters B & C see Appendix B for HAC conditional logic

CC +7th **S82.853 Displaced trimalleolar fracture of unspecified lower leg**
CC Exclusion 7th characters B & C see Appendix A PDX collection 1347
CC Exclusion 7th characters K - R see Appendix A PDX collection 0897
HAC 7th characters B & C see Appendix B for HAC conditional logic

CC +7th **S82.854 Nondisplaced trimalleolar fracture of right lower leg**
CC Exclusion 7th characters B & C see Appendix A PDX collection 1347
CC Exclusion 7th characters K - R see Appendix A PDX collection 0897
HAC 7th characters B & C see Appendix B for HAC conditional logic

CC +7th **S82.855 Nondisplaced trimalleolar fracture of left lower leg**
CC Exclusion 7th characters B & C see Appendix A PDX collection 1347
CC Exclusion 7th characters K - R see Appendix A PDX collection 0897
HAC 7th characters B & C see Appendix B for HAC conditional logic

CC +7th **S82.856 Nondisplaced trimalleolar fracture of unspecified lower leg**
CC Exclusion 7th characters B & C see Appendix A PDX collection 1347
CC Exclusion 7th characters K - R see Appendix A PDX collection 0897
HAC 7th characters B & C see Appendix B for HAC conditional logic

+ **S82.86 Maisonneuve's fracture**

CC MCC +7th **S82.861 Displaced Maisonneuve's fracture of right leg**
CC Exclusion 7th characters K - R see Appendix A PDX collection 0897
MCC Exclusion 7th characters B & C see Appendix A PDX collection 1341
HAC 7th characters B & C see Appendix B for HAC conditional logic

CC MCC +7th **S82.862 Displaced Maisonneuve's fracture of left leg**
CC Exclusion 7th characters K - R see Appendix A PDX collection 0897
MCC Exclusion 7th characters B & C see Appendix A PDX collection 1341
HAC 7th characters B & C see Appendix B for HAC conditional logic

CC MCC +7th **S82.863 Displaced Maisonneuve's fracture of unspecified leg**
CC Exclusion 7th characters K - R see Appendix A PDX collection 0897
MCC Exclusion 7th characters B & C see Appendix A PDX collection 1341
HAC 7th characters B & C see Appendix B for HAC conditional logic

CC MCC +7th **S82.864 Nondisplaced Maisonneuve's fracture of right leg**
CC Exclusion 7th characters K - R see Appendix A PDX collection 0897
MCC Exclusion 7th characters B & C see Appendix A PDX collection 1341
HAC 7th characters B & C see Appendix B for HAC conditional logic

CC MCC +7th **S82.865 Nondisplaced Maisonneuve's fracture of left leg**
CC Exclusion 7th characters K - R see Appendix A PDX collection 0897
MCC Exclusion 7th characters B & C see Appendix A PDX collection 1341
HAC 7th characters B & C see Appendix B for HAC conditional logic

CC MCC +7th **S82.866 Nondisplaced Maisonneuve's fracture of unspecified leg**
CC Exclusion 7th characters K - R see Appendix A PDX collection 0897
MCC Exclusion 7th characters B & C see Appendix A PDX collection 1341
HAC 7th characters B & C see Appendix B for HAC conditional logic

+ **S82.87 Pilon fracture of tibia**

CC +7th **S82.871 Displaced pilon fracture of right tibia**
CC Exclusion 7th characters B & C see Appendix A PDX collection 1347
CC Exclusion 7th characters K - R see Appendix A PDX collection 0897
HAC 7th characters B & C see Appendix B for HAC conditional logic

CC +7th **S82.872 Displaced pilon fracture of left tibia**
CC Exclusion 7th characters B & C see Appendix A PDX collection 1347
CC Exclusion 7th characters K - R see Appendix A PDX collection 0897
HAC 7th characters B & C see Appendix B for HAC conditional logic

CC +7th **S82.873 Displaced pilon fracture of unspecified tibia**
CC Exclusion 7th characters B & C see Appendix A PDX collection 1347
CC Exclusion 7th characters K - R see Appendix A PDX collection 0897
HAC 7th characters B & C see Appendix B for HAC conditional logic

CC +7th **S82.874 Nondisplaced pilon fracture of right tibia**
CC Exclusion 7th characters B & C see Appendix A PDX collection 1347
CC Exclusion 7th characters K - R see Appendix A PDX collection 0897
HAC 7th characters B & C see Appendix B for HAC conditional logic

CC +7th **S82.875 Nondisplaced pilon fracture of left tibia**
CC Exclusion 7th characters B & C see Appendix A PDX collection 1347
CC Exclusion 7th characters K - R see Appendix A PDX collection 0897
HAC 7th characters B & C see Appendix B for HAC conditional logic

CC +7th **S82.876 Nondisplaced pilon fracture of unspecified tibia**
CC Exclusion 7th characters B & C see Appendix A PDX collection 1347
CC Exclusion 7th characters K - R see Appendix A PDX collection 0897
HAC 7th characters B & C see Appendix B for HAC conditional logic

+ **S82.89 Other fractures of lower leg**
Fracture of ankle NOS

CC +7th **S82.891 Other fracture of right lower leg**
CC Exclusion 7th characters B & C see Appendix A PDX collection 1347
CC Exclusion 7th characters K - R see Appendix A PDX collection 0897
HAC 7th characters B & C see Appendix B for HAC conditional logic

CC +7th **S82.892 Other fracture of left lower leg**
CC Exclusion 7th characters B & C see Appendix A PDX collection 1347
CC Exclusion 7th characters K - R see Appendix A PDX collection 0897
HAC 7th characters B & C see Appendix B for HAC conditional logic

CC +7th **S82.899 Other fracture of unspecified lower leg**
CC Exclusion 7th characters B & C see Appendix A PDX collection 1347
CC Exclusion 7th characters K - R see Appendix A PDX collection 0897
HAC 7th characters B & C see Appendix B for HAC conditional logic

+ **S82.9 Unspecified fracture of lower leg**

CC X+7th **S82.90 Unspecified fracture of unspecified lower leg**
CC Exclusion 7th characters B & C see Appendix A PDX collection 1348
CC Exclusion 7th characters K - R see Appendix A PDX collection 0897
HAC 7th characters B & C see Appendix B for HAC conditional logic

CC X+7th **S82.91 Unspecified fracture of right lower leg**
CC Exclusion 7th characters B & C see Appendix A PDX collection 1348
CC Exclusion 7th characters K - R see Appendix A PDX collection 0897
HAC 7th characters B & C see Appendix B for HAC conditional logic

CC X+7th **S82.92 Unspecified fracture of left lower leg**
CC Exclusion 7th characters B & C see Appendix A PDX collection 1348
CC Exclusion 7th characters K - R see Appendix A PDX collection 0897
HAC 7th characters B & C see Appendix B for HAC conditional logic

S83 Dislocation and sprain of joints and ligaments of knee

Includes: avulsion of joint or ligament of knee
laceration of cartilage, joint or ligament of knee
sprain of cartilage, joint or ligament of knee
traumatic hemarthrosis of joint or ligament of knee
traumatic rupture of joint or ligament of knee
traumatic subluxation of joint or ligament of knee
traumatic tear of joint or ligament of knee

Code also any associated open wound

Excludes1: *derangement of patella (M22.0-M22.3)*
injury of patellar ligament (tendon) (S76.1-)
internal derangement of knee (M23.-)
old dislocation of knee (M24.36)
pathological dislocation of knee (M24.36)
recurrent dislocation of knee (M22.0)

Excludes2: *strain of muscle, fascia and tendon of lower leg (S86.-)*

The appropriate 7th character is to be added to each code from category S83
A initial encounter
D subsequent encounter
S sequela

+ **S83.0 Subluxation and dislocation of patella**
+ **S83.00 Unspecified subluxation and dislocation of patella**
+7th **S83.001 Unspecified subluxation of right patella**
+7th **S83.002 Unspecified subluxation of left patella**
+7th **S83.003 Unspecified subluxation of unspecified patella**
+7th **S83.004 Unspecified dislocation of right patella**
+7th **S83.005 Unspecified dislocation of left patella**
+7th **S83.006 Unspecified dislocation of unspecified patella**
+ **S83.01 Lateral subluxation and dislocation of patella**
+7th **S83.011 Lateral subluxation of right patella**
+7th **S83.012 Lateral subluxation of left patella**
+7th **S83.013 Lateral subluxation of unspecified patella**
+7th **S83.014 Lateral dislocation of right patella**
+7th **S83.015 Lateral dislocation of left patella**
+7th **S83.016 Lateral dislocation of unspecified patella**
+ **S83.09 Other subluxation and dislocation of patella**
+7th **S83.091 Other subluxation of right patella**
+7th **S83.092 Other subluxation of left patella**
+7th **S83.093 Other subluxation of unspecified patella**
+7th **S83.094 Other dislocation of right patella**
+7th **S83.095 Other dislocation of left patella**
+7th **S83.096 Other dislocation of unspecified patella**

+ **S83.1 Subluxation and dislocation of knee**
Excludes2: *instability of knee prosthesis (T84.022, T84.023)*
+ **S83.10 Unspecified subluxation and dislocation of knee**
+7th **S83.101 Unspecified subluxation of right knee**
+7th **S83.102 Unspecified subluxation of left knee**
+7th **S83.103 Unspecified subluxation of unspecified knee**
+7th **S83.104 Unspecified dislocation of right knee**
+7th **S83.105 Unspecified dislocation of left knee**
+7th **S83.106 Unspecified dislocation of unspecified knee**
+ **S83.11 Anterior subluxation and dislocation of proximal end of tibia**
Posterior subluxation and dislocation of distal end of femur
+7th **S83.111 Anterior subluxation of proximal end of tibia, right knee**
+7th **S83.112 Anterior subluxation of proximal end of tibia, left knee**
+7th **S83.113 Anterior subluxation of proximal end of tibia, unspecified knee**
+7th **S83.114 Anterior dislocation of proximal end of tibia, right knee**
+7th **S83.115 Anterior dislocation of proximal end of tibia, left knee**
+7th **S83.116 Anterior dislocation of proximal end of tibia, unspecified knee**
+ **S83.12 Posterior subluxation and dislocation of proximal end of tibia**
Anterior dislocation of distal end of femur
+7th **S83.121 Posterior subluxation of proximal end of tibia, right knee**

+7th **S83.122** **Posterior subluxation of proximal end of tibia, left knee**
+7th **S83.123** **Posterior subluxation of proximal end of tibia, unspecified knee**
+7th **S83.124** **Posterior dislocation of proximal end of tibia, right knee**
+7th **S83.125** **Posterior dislocation of proximal end of tibia, left knee**
+7th **S83.126** **Posterior dislocation of proximal end of tibia, unspecified knee**

\+ **S83.13** **Medial subluxation and dislocation of proximal end of tibia**
+7th **S83.131** **Medial subluxation of proximal end of tibia, right knee**
+7th **S83.132** **Medial subluxation of proximal end of tibia, left knee**
+7th **S83.133** **Medial subluxation of proximal end of tibia, unspecified knee**
+7th **S83.134** **Medial dislocation of proximal end of tibia, right knee**
+7th **S83.135** **Medial dislocation of proximal end of tibia, left knee**
+7th **S83.136** **Medial dislocation of proximal end of tibia, unspecified knee**

\+ **S83.14** **Lateral subluxation and dislocation of proximal end of tibia**
+7th **S83.141** **Lateral subluxation of proximal end of tibia, right knee**
+7th **S83.142** **Lateral subluxation of proximal end of tibia, left knee**
+7th **S83.143** **Lateral subluxation of proximal end of tibia, unspecified knee**
+7th **S83.144** **Lateral dislocation of proximal end of tibia, right knee**
+7th **S83.145** **Lateral dislocation of proximal end of tibia, left knee**
+7th **S83.146** **Lateral dislocation of proximal end of tibia, unspecified knee**

\+ **S83.19** **Other subluxation and dislocation of knee**
+7th **S83.191** **Other subluxation of right knee**
+7th **S83.192** **Other subluxation of left knee**
+7th **S83.193** **Other subluxation of unspecified knee**
+7th **S83.194** **Other dislocation of right knee**
+7th **S83.195** **Other dislocation of left knee**
+7th **S83.196** **Other dislocation of unspecified knee**

\+ **S83.2** **Tear of meniscus, current injury**
Excludes1: *old bucket-handle tear (M23.2)*

\+ **S83.20** **Tear of unspecified meniscus, current injury**
Tear of meniscus of knee NOS
+7th **S83.200** **Bucket-handle tear of unspecified meniscus, current injury, right knee**
+7th **S83.201** **Bucket-handle tear of unspecified meniscus, current injury, left knee**
+7th **S83.202** **Bucket-handle tear of unspecified meniscus, current injury, unspecified knee**
+7th **S83.203** **Other tear of unspecified meniscus, current injury, right knee**
+7th **S83.204** **Other tear of unspecified meniscus, current injury, left knee**
+7th **S83.205** **Other tear of unspecified meniscus, current injury, unspecified knee**
+7th **S83.206** **Unspecified tear of unspecified meniscus, current injury, right knee**
+7th **S83.207** **Unspecified tear of unspecified meniscus, current injury, left knee**
+7th **S83.209** **Unspecified tear of unspecified meniscus, current injury, unspecified knee**

\+ **S83.21** **Bucket-handle tear of medial meniscus, current injury**
+7th **S83.211** **Bucket-handle tear of medial meniscus, current injury, right knee**
+7th **S83.212** **Bucket-handle tear of medial meniscus, current injury, left knee**
+7th **S83.219** **Bucket-handle tear of medial meniscus, current injury, unspecified knee**

\+ **S83.22** **Peripheral tear of medial meniscus, current injury**
+7th **S83.221** **Peripheral tear of medial meniscus, current injury, right knee**
+7th **S83.222** **Peripheral tear of medial meniscus, current injury, left knee**
+7th **S83.229** **Peripheral tear of medial meniscus, current injury, unspecified knee**

\+ **S83.23** **Complex tear of medial meniscus, current injury**
+7th **S83.231** **Complex tear of medial meniscus, current injury, right knee**
+7th **S83.232** **Complex tear of medial meniscus, current injury, left knee**
+7th **S83.239** **Complex tear of medial meniscus, current injury, unspecified knee**

\+ **S83.24** **Other tear of medial meniscus, current injury**
+7th **S83.241** **Other tear of medial meniscus, current injury, right knee**
+7th **S83.242** **Other tear of medial meniscus, current injury, left knee**
+7th **S83.249** **Other tear of medial meniscus, current injury, unspecified knee**

\+ **S83.25** **Bucket-handle tear of lateral meniscus, current injury**
+7th **S83.251** **Bucket-handle tear of lateral meniscus, current injury, right knee**
+7th **S83.252** **Bucket-handle tear of lateral meniscus, current injury, left knee**
+7th **S83.259** **Bucket-handle tear of lateral meniscus, current injury, unspecified knee**

\+ **S83.26** **Peripheral tear of lateral meniscus, current injury**
+7th **S83.261** **Peripheral tear of lateral meniscus, current injury, right knee**
+7th **S83.262** **Peripheral tear of lateral meniscus, current injury, left knee**
+7th **S83.269** **Peripheral tear of lateral meniscus, current injury, unspecified knee**

\+ **S83.27** **Complex tear of lateral meniscus, current injury**
+7th **S83.271** **Complex tear of lateral meniscus, current injury, right knee**
+7th **S83.272** **Complex tear of lateral meniscus, current injury, left knee**
+7th **S83.279** **Complex tear of lateral meniscus, current injury, unspecified knee**

\+ **S83.28** **Other tear of lateral meniscus, current injury**
+7th **S83.281** **Other tear of lateral meniscus, current injury, right knee**
+7th **S83.282** **Other tear of lateral meniscus, current injury, left knee**
+7th **S83.289** **Other tear of lateral meniscus, current injury, unspecified knee**

\+ **S83.3** **Tear of articular cartilage of knee, current**
X+7th **S83.30** **Tear of articular cartilage of unspecified knee, current**
X+7th **S83.31** **Tear of articular cartilage of right knee, current**
X+7th **S83.32** **Tear of articular cartilage of left knee, current**

\+ **S83.4** **Sprain of collateral ligament of knee**

\+ **S83.40** **Sprain of unspecified collateral ligament of knee**
+7th **S83.401** **Sprain of unspecified collateral ligament of right knee**
+7th **S83.402** **Sprain of unspecified collateral ligament of left knee**
+7th **S83.409** **Sprain of unspecified collateral ligament of unspecified knee**

\+ **S83.41** **Sprain of medial collateral ligament of knee**
Sprain of tibial collateral ligament
+7th **S83.411** **Sprain of medial collateral ligament of right knee**
+7th **S83.412** **Sprain of medial collateral ligament of left knee**
+7th **S83.419** **Sprain of medial collateral ligament of unspecified knee**

\+ **S83.42** **Sprain of lateral collateral ligament of knee**
Sprain of fibular collateral ligament
+7th **S83.421** **Sprain of lateral collateral ligament of right knee**
+7th **S83.422** **Sprain of lateral collateral ligament of left knee**
+7th **S83.429** **Sprain of lateral collateral ligament of unspecified knee**

\+ **S83.5** **Sprain of cruciate ligament of knee**

\+ **S83.50** **Sprain of unspecified cruciate ligament of knee**
+7th **S83.501** **Sprain of unspecified cruciate ligament of right knee**
+7th **S83.502** **Sprain of unspecified cruciate ligament of left knee**
+7th **S83.509** **Sprain of unspecified cruciate ligament of unspecified knee**

+ **S83.51 Sprain of anterior cruciate ligament of knee**
  - +7th **S83.511 Sprain of anterior cruciate ligament of right knee**
  - +7th **S83.512 Sprain of anterior cruciate ligament of left knee**
  - +7th **S83.519 Sprain of anterior cruciate ligament of unspecified knee**

+ **S83.52 Sprain of posterior cruciate ligament of knee**
  - +7th **S83.521 Sprain of posterior cruciate ligament of right knee**
  - +7th **S83.522 Sprain of posterior cruciate ligament of left knee**
  - +7th **S83.529 Sprain of posterior cruciate ligament of unspecified knee**

+ **S83.6 Sprain of the superior tibiofibular joint and ligament**
  - X+7th **S83.60 Sprain of the superior tibiofibular joint and ligament, unspecified knee**
  - X+7th **S83.61 Sprain of the superior tibiofibular joint and ligament, right knee**
  - X+7th **S83.62 Sprain of the superior tibiofibular joint and ligament, left knee**

+ **S83.8 Sprain of other specified parts of knee**
  + **S83.8X Sprain of other specified parts of knee**
    - +7th **S83.8X1 Sprain of other specified parts of right knee**
    - +7th **S83.8X2 Sprain of other specified parts of left knee**
    - +7th **S83.8X9 Sprain of other specified parts of unspecified knee**

+ **S83.9 Sprain of unspecified site of knee**
  - X+7th **S83.90 Sprain of unspecified site of unspecified knee**
  - X+7th **S83.91 Sprain of unspecified site of right knee**
  - X+7th **S83.92 Sprain of unspecified site of left knee**

S84 Injury of nerves at lower leg level

Code also any associated open wound (S81.-)

Excludes2: *injury of nerves at ankle and foot level (S94.-)*

The appropriate 7th character is to be added to each code from category S84
- A initial encounter
- D subsequent encounter
- S sequela

+ **S84.0 Injury of tibial nerve at lower leg level**
  - X+7th **S84.00 Injury of tibial nerve at lower leg level, unspecified leg**
  - X+7th **S84.01 Injury of tibial nerve at lower leg level, right leg**
  - X+7th **S84.02 Injury of tibial nerve at lower leg level, left leg**

+ **S84.1 Injury of peroneal nerve at lower leg level**
  - X+7th **S84.10 Injury of peroneal nerve at lower leg level, unspecified leg**
  - X+7th **S84.11 Injury of peroneal nerve at lower leg level, right leg**
  - X+7th **S84.12 Injury of peroneal nerve at lower leg level, left leg**

+ **S84.2 Injury of cutaneous sensory nerve at lower leg level**
  - X+7th **S84.20 Injury of cutaneous sensory nerve at lower leg level, unspecified leg**
  - X+7th **S84.21 Injury of cutaneous sensory nerve at lower leg level, right leg**
  - X+7th **S84.22 Injury of cutaneous sensory nerve at lower leg level, left leg**

+ **S84.8 Injury of other nerves at lower leg level**
  + **S84.80 Injury of other nerves at lower leg level**
    - +7th **S84.801 Injury of other nerves at lower leg level, right leg**
    - +7th **S84.802 Injury of other nerves at lower leg level, left leg**
    - +7th **S84.809 Injury of other nerves at lower leg level, unspecified leg**

+ **S84.9 Injury of unspecified nerve at lower leg level**
  - X+7th **S84.90 Injury of unspecified nerve at lower leg level, unspecified leg**
  - X+7th **S84.91 Injury of unspecified nerve at lower leg level, right leg**
  - X+7th **S84.92 Injury of unspecified nerve at lower leg level, left leg**

S85 Injury of blood vessels at lower leg level

Code also any associated open wound (S81.-)

Excludes2: *injury of blood vessels at ankle and foot level (S95.-)*

The appropriate 7th character is to be added to each code from category S85
- A initial encounter
- D subsequent encounter
- S sequela

+ **S85.0 Injury of popliteal artery**
  + **S85.00 Unspecified injury of popliteal artery**
    - MCC +7th **S85.001 Unspecified injury of popliteal artery, right leg**
      MCC Exclusion 7th character A see Appendix A PDX collection 1349
    - MCC +7th **S85.002 Unspecified injury of popliteal artery, left leg**
      MCC Exclusion 7th character A see Appendix A PDX collection 1350
    - MCC +7th **S85.009 Unspecified injury of popliteal artery, unspecified leg**
      MCC Exclusion 7th character A see Appendix A PDX collection 1351
  + **S85.01 Laceration of popliteal artery**
    - MCC +7th **S85.011 Laceration of popliteal artery, right leg**
      MCC Exclusion 7th character A see Appendix A PDX collection 1349
    - MCC +7th **S85.012 Laceration of popliteal artery, left leg**
      MCC Exclusion 7th character A see Appendix A PDX collection 1350
    - MCC +7th **S85.019 Laceration of popliteal artery, unspecified leg**
      MCC Exclusion 7th character A see Appendix A PDX collection 1351
  + **S85.09 Other specified injury of popliteal artery**
    - MCC +7th **S85.091 Other specified injury of popliteal artery, right leg**
      MCC Exclusion 7th character A see Appendix A PDX collection 1349
    - MCC +7th **S85.092 Other specified injury of popliteal artery, left leg**
      MCC Exclusion 7th character A see Appendix A PDX collection 1350
    - MCC +7th **S85.099 Other specified injury of popliteal artery, unspecified leg**
      MCC Exclusion 7th character A see Appendix A PDX collection 1351

+ **S85.1 Injury of tibial artery**
  + **S85.10 Unspecified injury of unspecified tibial artery**
    Injury of tibial artery NOS
    - CC +7th **S85.101 Unspecified injury of unspecified tibial artery, right leg**
      CC Exclusion 7th character A see Appendix A PDX collection 1352
    - CC +7th **S85.102 Unspecified injury of unspecified tibial artery, left leg**
      CC Exclusion 7th character A see Appendix A PDX collection 1353
    - CC +7th **S85.109 Unspecified injury of unspecified tibial artery, unspecified leg**
      CC Exclusion 7th character A see Appendix A PDX collection 1354
  + **S85.11 Laceration of unspecified tibial artery**
    - CC +7th **S85.111 Laceration of unspecified tibial artery, right leg**
      CC Exclusion 7th character A see Appendix A PDX collection 1352
    - CC +7th **S85.112 Laceration of unspecified tibial artery, left leg**
      CC Exclusion 7th character A see Appendix A PDX collection 1353
    - CC +7th **S85.119 Laceration of unspecified tibial artery, unspecified leg**
      CC Exclusion 7th character A see Appendix A PDX collection 1354
  + **S85.12 Other specified injury of unspecified tibial artery**
    - CC +7th **S85.121 Other specified injury of unspecified tibial artery, right leg**
      CC Exclusion 7th character A see Appendix A PDX collection 1352
    - CC +7th **S85.122 Other specified injury of unspecified tibial artery, left leg**
      CC Exclusion 7th character A see Appendix A PDX collection 1353

CC +7th **S85.129 Other specified injury of unspecified tibial artery, unspecified leg**
CC Exclusion 7th character A see Appendix A
PDX collection 1354

+ **S85.13 Unspecified injury of anterior tibial artery**
CC +7th **S85.131 Unspecified injury of anterior tibial artery, right leg**
CC Exclusion 7th character A see Appendix A
PDX collection 1355
CC +7th **S85.132 Unspecified injury of anterior tibial artery, left leg**
CC Exclusion 7th character A see Appendix A
PDX collection 1356
CC +7th **S85.139 Unspecified injury of anterior tibial artery, unspecified leg**
CC Exclusion 7th character A see Appendix A
PDX collection 1357

+ **S85.14 Laceration of anterior tibial artery**
CC +7th **S85.141 Laceration of anterior tibial artery, right leg**
CC Exclusion 7th character A see Appendix A
PDX collection 1355
CC +7th **S85.142 Laceration of anterior tibial artery, left leg**
CC Exclusion 7th character A see Appendix A
PDX collection 1356
CC +7th **S85.149 Laceration of anterior tibial artery, unspecified leg**
CC Exclusion 7th character A see Appendix A
PDX collection 1357

+ **S85.15 Other specified injury of anterior tibial artery**
CC +7th **S85.151 Other specified injury of anterior tibial artery, right leg**
CC Exclusion 7th character A see Appendix A
PDX collection 1355
CC +7th **S85.152 Other specified injury of anterior tibial artery, left leg**
CC Exclusion 7th character A see Appendix A
PDX collection 1356
CC +7th **S85.159 Other specified injury of anterior tibial artery, unspecified leg**
CC Exclusion 7th character A see Appendix A
PDX collection 1357

+ **S85.16 Unspecified injury of posterior tibial artery**
CC +7th **S85.161 Unspecified injury of posterior tibial artery, right leg**
CC Exclusion 7th character A see Appendix A
PDX collection 1358
CC +7th **S85.162 Unspecified injury of posterior tibial artery, left leg**
CC Exclusion 7th character A see Appendix A
PDX collection 1359
CC +7th **S85.169 Unspecified injury of posterior tibial artery, unspecified leg**
CC Exclusion 7th character A see Appendix A
PDX collection 1360

+ **S85.17 Laceration of posterior tibial artery**
CC +7th **S85.171 Laceration of posterior tibial artery, right leg**
CC Exclusion 7th character A see Appendix A
PDX collection 1358
CC +7th **S85.172 Laceration of posterior tibial artery, left leg**
CC Exclusion 7th character A see Appendix A
PDX collection 1359
CC +7th **S85.179 Laceration of posterior tibial artery, unspecified leg**
CC Exclusion 7th character A see Appendix A
PDX collection 1360

+ **S85.18 Other specified injury of posterior tibial artery**
CC +7th **S85.181 Other specified injury of posterior tibial artery, right leg**
CC Exclusion 7th character A see Appendix A
PDX collection 1358
CC +7th **S85.182 Other specified injury of posterior tibial artery, left leg**
CC Exclusion 7th character A see Appendix A
PDX collection 1359
CC +7th **S85.189 Other specified injury of posterior tibial artery, unspecified leg**
CC Exclusion 7th character A see Appendix A
PDX collection 1360

+ **S85.2 Injury of peroneal artery**
+ **S85.20 Unspecified injury of peroneal artery**
CC +7th **S85.201 Unspecified injury of peroneal artery, right leg**
CC Exclusion 7th character A see Appendix A
PDX collection 1325
CC +7th **S85.202 Unspecified injury of peroneal artery, left leg**
CC Exclusion 7th character A see Appendix A
PDX collection 1326
CC +7th **S85.209 Unspecified injury of peroneal artery, unspecified leg**
CC Exclusion 7th character A see Appendix A
PDX collection 1327

+ **S85.21 Laceration of peroneal artery**
CC +7th **S85.211 Laceration of peroneal artery, right leg**
CC Exclusion 7th character A see Appendix A
PDX collection 1325
CC +7th **S85.212 Laceration of peroneal artery, left leg**
CC Exclusion 7th character A see Appendix A
PDX collection 1326
CC +7th **S85.219 Laceration of peroneal artery, unspecified leg**
CC Exclusion 7th character A see Appendix A
PDX collection 1327

+ **S85.29 Other specified injury of peroneal artery**
CC +7th **S85.291 Other specified injury of peroneal artery, right leg**
CC Exclusion 7th character A see Appendix A
PDX collection 1325
CC +7th **S85.292 Other specified injury of peroneal artery, left leg**
CC Exclusion 7th character A see Appendix A
PDX collection 1326
CC +7th **S85.299 Other specified injury of peroneal artery, unspecified leg**
CC Exclusion 7th character A see Appendix A
PDX collection 1327

+ **S85.3 Injury of greater saphenous vein at lower leg level**
Injury of greater saphenous vein NOS
Injury of saphenous vein NOS
+ **S85.30 Unspecified injury of greater saphenous vein at lower leg level**
CC +7th **S85.301 Unspecified injury of greater saphenous vein at lower leg level, right leg**
CC Exclusion 7th character A see Appendix A
PDX collection 1322
CC +7th **S85.302 Unspecified injury of greater saphenous vein at lower leg level, left leg**
CC Exclusion 7th character A see Appendix A
PDX collection 1323
CC +7th **S85.309 Unspecified injury of greater saphenous vein at lower leg level, unspecified leg**
CC Exclusion 7th character A see Appendix A
PDX collection 1324

+ **S85.31 Laceration of greater saphenous vein at lower leg level**
CC +7th **S85.311 Laceration of greater saphenous vein at lower leg level, right leg**
CC Exclusion 7th character A see Appendix A
PDX collection 1322
CC +7th **S85.312 Laceration of greater saphenous vein at lower leg level, left leg**
CC Exclusion 7th character A see Appendix A
PDX collection 1323
CC +7th **S85.319 Laceration of greater saphenous vein at lower leg level, unspecified leg**
CC Exclusion 7th character A see Appendix A
PDX collection 1324

+ **S85.39 Other specified injury of greater saphenous vein at lower leg level**
CC +7th **S85.391 Other specified injury of greater saphenous vein at lower leg level, right leg**
CC Exclusion 7th character A see Appendix A
PDX collection 1322
CC +7th **S85.392 Other specified injury of greater saphenous vein at lower leg level, left leg**
CC Exclusion 7th character A see Appendix A
PDX collection 1323
CC +7th **S85.399 Other specified injury of greater saphenous vein at lower leg level, unspecified leg**
CC Exclusion 7th character A see Appendix A
PDX collection 1324

+ **S85.4 Injury of lesser saphenous vein at lower leg level**
+ **S85.40 Unspecified injury of lesser saphenous vein at lower leg level**
CC +7th **S85.401 Unspecified injury of lesser saphenous vein at lower leg level, right leg**
CC Exclusion 7th character A see Appendix A
PDX collection 1322
CC +7th **S85.402 Unspecified injury of lesser saphenous vein at lower leg level, left leg**
CC Exclusion 7th character A see Appendix A
PDX collection 1323

CC +7th **S85.409 Unspecified injury of lesser saphenous vein at lower leg level, unspecified leg**
CC Exclusion 7th character A see Appendix A
PDX collection 1324

+ **S85.41 Laceration of lesser saphenous vein at lower leg level**

CC +7th **S85.411 Laceration of lesser saphenous vein at lower leg level, right leg**
CC Exclusion 7th character A see Appendix A
PDX collection 1322

CC +7th **S85.412 Laceration of lesser saphenous vein at lower leg level, left leg**
CC Exclusion 7th character A see Appendix A
PDX collection 1323

CC +7th **S85.419 Laceration of lesser saphenous vein at lower leg level, unspecified leg**
CC Exclusion 7th character A see Appendix A
PDX collection 1324

+ **S85.49 Other specified injury of lesser saphenous vein at lower leg level**

CC +7th **S85.491 Other specified injury of lesser saphenous vein at lower leg level, right leg**
CC Exclusion 7th character A see Appendix A
PDX collection 1322

CC +7th **S85.492 Other specified injury of lesser saphenous vein at lower leg level, left leg**
CC Exclusion 7th character A see Appendix A
PDX collection 1323

CC +7th **S85.499 Other specified injury of lesser saphenous vein at lower leg level, unspecified leg**
CC Exclusion 7th character A see Appendix A
PDX collection 1324

+ **S85.5 Injury of popliteal vein**

+ **S85.50 Unspecified injury of popliteal vein**

MCC +7th **S85.501 Unspecified injury of popliteal vein, right leg**
MCC Exclusion 7th character A see Appendix A
PDX collection 1361

MCC +7th **S85.502 Unspecified injury of popliteal vein, left leg**
MCC Exclusion 7th character A see Appendix A
PDX collection 1362

MCC +7th **S85.509 Unspecified injury of popliteal vein, unspecified leg**
MCC Exclusion 7th character A see Appendix A
PDX collection 1363

+ **S85.51 Laceration of popliteal vein**

MCC +7th **S85.511 Laceration of popliteal vein, right leg**
MCC Exclusion 7th character A see Appendix A
PDX collection 1361

MCC +7th **S85.512 Laceration of popliteal vein, left leg**
MCC Exclusion 7th character A see Appendix A
PDX collection 1362

MCC +7th **S85.519 Laceration of popliteal vein, unspecified leg**
MCC Exclusion 7th character A see Appendix A
PDX collection 1363

+ **S85.59 Other specified injury of popliteal vein**

MCC +7th **S85.591 Other specified injury of popliteal vein, right leg**
MCC Exclusion 7th character A see Appendix A
PDX collection 1361

MCC +7th **S85.592 Other specified injury of popliteal vein, left leg**
MCC Exclusion 7th character A see Appendix A
PDX collection 1362

MCC +7th **S85.599 Other specified injury of popliteal vein, unspecified leg**
MCC Exclusion 7th character A see Appendix A
PDX collection 1363

+ **S85.8 Injury of other blood vessels at lower leg level**

+ **S85.80 Unspecified injury of other blood vessels at lower leg level**

CC +7th **S85.801 Unspecified injury of other blood vessels at lower leg level, right leg**
CC Exclusion 7th character A see Appendix A
PDX collection 1325

CC +7th **S85.802 Unspecified injury of other blood vessels at lower leg level, left leg**
CC Exclusion 7th character A see Appendix A
PDX collection 1326

CC +7th **S85.809 Unspecified injury of other blood vessels at lower leg level, unspecified leg**
CC Exclusion 7th character A see Appendix A
PDX collection 1327

+ **S85.81 Laceration of other blood vessels at lower leg level**

CC +7th **S85.811 Laceration of other blood vessels at lower leg level, right leg**
CC Exclusion 7th character A see Appendix A
PDX collection 1325

CC +7th **S85.812 Laceration of other blood vessels at lower level, left leg**
CC Exclusion 7th character A see Appendix A
PDX collection 1326

CC +7th **S85.819 Laceration of other blood vessels at lower level, unspecified leg**
CC Exclusion 7th character A see Appendix A
PDX collection 1327

+ **S85.89 Other specified injury of other blood vessels at lower leg level**

CC +7th **S85.891 Other specified injury of other blood vessel at lower leg level, right leg**
CC Exclusion 7th character A see Appendix A
PDX collection 1325

CC +7th **S85.892 Other specified injury of other blood vessel at lower leg level, left leg**
CC Exclusion 7th character A see Appendix A
PDX collection 1326

CC +7th **S85.899 Other specified injury of other blood vessel at lower leg level, unspecified leg**
CC Exclusion 7th character A see Appendix A
PDX collection 1327

+ **S85.9 Injury of unspecified blood vessel at lower leg level**

+ **S85.90 Unspecified injury of unspecified blood vessel at lowe leg level**

CC +7th **S85.901 Unspecified injury of unspecified blood vessel at lower leg level, right leg**
CC Exclusion 7th character A see Appendix A
PDX collection 1325

CC +7th **S85.902 Unspecified injury of unspecified blood vessel at lower leg level, left leg**
CC Exclusion 7th character A see Appendix A
PDX collection 1326

CC +7th **S85.909 Unspecified injury of unspecified blood vessel at lower leg level, unspecified leg**
CC Exclusion 7th character A see Appendix A
PDX collection 1327

+ **S85.91 Laceration of unspecified blood vessel at lower leg level**

CC +7th **S85.911 Laceration of unspecified blood vessel at lower leg level, right leg**
CC Exclusion 7th character A see Appendix A
PDX collection 1325

CC +7th **S85.912 Laceration of unspecified blood vessel at lower leg level, left leg**
CC Exclusion 7th character A see Appendix A
PDX collection 1326

CC +7th **S85.919 Laceration of unspecified blood vessel at lower leg level, unspecified leg**
CC Exclusion 7th character A see Appendix A
PDX collection 1327

+ **S85.99 Other specified injury of unspecified blood vessel at lower leg level**

CC +7th **S85.991 Other specified injury of unspecified blood vessel at lower leg level, right leg**
CC Exclusion 7th character A see Appendix A
PDX collection 1325

CC +7th **S85.992 Other specified injury of unspecified blood vessel at lower leg level, left leg**
CC Exclusion 7th character A see Appendix A
PDX collection 1326

CC +7th **S85.999 Other specified injury of unspecified blood vessel at lower leg level, unspecified leg**
CC Exclusion 7th character A see Appendix A
PDX collection 1327

S86 Injury of muscle, fascia and tendon at lower leg level

Code also any associated open wound (S81.-)

Excludes2: *injury of muscle, fascia and tendon at ankle (S96.-)*
injury of patellar ligament (tendon) (S76.1-)
sprain of joints and ligaments of knee (S83.-)

The appropriate 7th character is to be added to each code from category S86
A initial encounter
D subsequent encounter
S sequela

+ **S86.0 Injury of Achilles tendon**

+ **S86.00 Unspecified injury of Achilles tendon**

+7th **S86.001 Unspecified injury of right Achilles tendon**
+7th **S86.002 Unspecified injury of left Achilles tendon**
+7th **S86.009 Unspecified injury of unspecified Achilles tendon**

+ **S86.01 Strain of Achilles tendon**

+7th **S86.011 Strain of right Achilles tendon**

+7th S86.012 Strain of left Achilles tendon
+7th S86.019 Strain of unspecified Achilles tendon
+ S86.02 Laceration of Achilles tendon
CC +7th S86.021 Laceration of right Achilles tendon
CC Exclusion 7th character A see Appendix A
PDX collection 1364
CC +7th S86.022 Laceration of left Achilles tendon
CC Exclusion 7th character A see Appendix A
PDX collection 1365
CC +7th S86.029 Laceration of unspecified Achilles tendon
CC Exclusion 7th character A see Appendix A
PDX collection 1366
+ S86.09 Other specified injury of Achilles tendon
+7th S86.091 Other specified injury of right Achilles tendon
+7th S86.092 Other specified injury of left Achilles tendon
+7th S86.099 Other specified injury of unspecified Achilles tendon
+ S86.1 Injury of other muscle(s) and tendon(s) of posterior muscle group at lower leg level
+ S86.10 Unspecified injury of other muscle(s) and tendon(s) of posterior muscle group at lower leg level
+7th S86.101 Unspecified injury of other muscle(s) and tendon(s) of posterior muscle group at lower leg level, right leg
+7th S86.102 Unspecified injury of other muscle(s) and tendon(s) of posterior muscle group at lower leg level, left leg
+7th S86.109 Unspecified injury of other muscle(s) and tendon(s) of posterior muscle group at lower leg level, unspecified leg
+ S86.11 Strain of other muscle(s) and tendon(s) of posterior muscle group at lower leg level
+7th S86.111 Strain of other muscle(s) and tendon(s) of posterior muscle group at lower leg level, right leg
+7th S86.112 Strain of other muscle(s) and tendon(s) of posterior muscle group at lower leg level, left leg
+7th S86.119 Strain of other muscle(s) and tendon(s) of posterior muscle group at lower leg level, unspecified leg
+ S86.12 Laceration of other muscle(s) and tendon(s) of posterior muscle group at lower leg level
CC +7th S86.121 Laceration of other muscle(s) and tendon(s) of posterior muscle group at lower leg level, right leg
CC Exclusion 7th character A see Appendix A
PDX collection 1364
CC +7th S86.122 Laceration of other muscle(s) and tendon(s) of posterior muscle group at lower leg level, left leg
CC Exclusion 7th character A see Appendix A
PDX collection 1365
CC +7th S86.129 Laceration of other muscle(s) and tendon(s) of posterior muscle group at lower leg level, unspecified leg
CC Exclusion 7th character A see Appendix A
PDX collection 1366
+ S86.19 Other injury of other muscle(s) and tendon(s) of posterior muscle group at lower leg level
+7th S86.191 Other injury of other muscle(s) and tendon(s) of posterior muscle group at lower leg level, right leg
+7th S86.192 Other injury of other muscle(s) and tendon(s) of posterior muscle group at lower leg level, left leg
+7th S86.199 Other injury of other muscle(s) and tendon(s) of posterior muscle group at lower leg level, unspecified leg
+ S86.2 Injury of muscle(s) and tendon(s) of anterior muscle group at lower leg level
+ S86.20 Unspecified injury of muscle(s) and tendon(s) of anterior muscle group at lower leg level
+7th S86.201 Unspecified injury of muscle(s) and tendon(s) of anterior muscle group at lower leg level, right leg
+7th S86.202 Unspecified injury of muscle(s) and tendon(s) of anterior muscle group at lower leg level, left leg
+7th S86.209 Unspecified injury of muscle(s) and tendon(s) of anterior muscle group at lower leg level, unspecified leg
+ S86.21 Strain of muscle(s) and tendon(s) of anterior muscle group at lower leg level
+7th S86.211 Strain of muscle(s) and tendon(s) of anterior muscle group at lower leg level, right leg
+7th S86.212 Strain of muscle(s) and tendon(s) of anterior muscle group at lower leg level, left leg
+7th S86.219 Strain of muscle(s) and tendon(s) of anterior muscle group at lower leg level, unspecified leg
+ S86.22 Laceration of muscle(s) and tendon(s) of anterior muscle group at lower leg level
CC +7th S86.221 Laceration of muscle(s) and tendon(s) of anterior muscle group at lower leg level, right leg
CC Exclusion 7th character A see Appendix A
PDX collection 1364
CC +7th S86.222 Laceration of muscle(s) and tendon(s) of anterior muscle group at lower leg level, left leg
CC Exclusion 7th character A see Appendix A
PDX collection 1365
CC +7th S86.229 Laceration of muscle(s) and tendon(s) of anterior muscle group at lower leg level, unspecified leg
CC Exclusion 7th character A see Appendix A
PDX collection 1366
+ S86.29 Other injury of muscle(s) and tendon(s) of anterior muscle group at lower leg level
+7th S86.291 Other injury of muscle(s) and tendon(s) of anterior muscle group at lower leg level, right leg
+7th S86.292 Other injury of muscle(s) and tendon(s) of anterior muscle group at lower leg level, left leg
+7th S86.299 Other injury of muscle(s) and tendon(s) of anterior muscle group at lower leg level, unspecified leg
+ S86.3 Injury of muscle(s) and tendon(s) of peroneal muscle group at lower leg level
+ S86.30 Unspecified injury of muscle(s) and tendon(s) of peroneal muscle group at lower leg level
+7th S86.301 Unspecified injury of muscle(s) and tendon(s) of peroneal muscle group at lower leg level, right leg
+7th S86.302 Unspecified injury of muscle(s) and tendon(s) of peroneal muscle group at lower leg level, left leg
+7th S86.309 Unspecified injury of muscle(s) and tendon(s) of peroneal muscle group at lower leg level, unspecified leg
+ S86.31 Strain of muscle(s) and tendon(s) of peroneal muscle group at lower leg level
+7th S86.311 Strain of muscle(s) and tendon(s) of peroneal muscle group at lower leg level, right leg
+7th S86.312 Strain of muscle(s) and tendon(s) of peroneal muscle group at lower leg level, left leg
+7th S86.319 Strain of muscle(s) and tendon(s) of peroneal muscle group at lower leg level, unspecified leg
+ S86.32 Laceration of muscle(s) and tendon(s) of peroneal muscle group at lower leg level
CC +7th S86.321 Laceration of muscle(s) and tendon(s) of peroneal muscle group at lower leg level, right leg
CC Exclusion 7th character A see Appendix A
PDX collection 1364
CC +7th S86.322 Laceration of muscle(s) and tendon(s) of peroneal muscle group at lower leg level, left leg
CC Exclusion 7th character A see Appendix A
PDX collection 1365
CC +7th S86.329 Laceration of muscle(s) and tendon(s) of peroneal muscle group at lower leg level, unspecified leg
CC Exclusion 7th character A see Appendix A
PDX collection 1366
+ S86.39 Other injury of muscle(s) and tendon(s) of peroneal muscle group at lower leg level
+7th S86.391 Other injury of muscle(s) and tendon(s) of peroneal muscle group at lower leg level, right leg

+7th S86.392 **Other injury of muscle(s) and tendon(s) of peroneal muscle group at lower leg level, left leg**
+7th S86.399 **Other injury of muscle(s) and tendon(s) of peroneal muscle group at lower leg level, unspecified leg**

\+ **S86.8 Injury of other muscles and tendons at lower leg level**
\+ **S86.80 Unspecified injury of other muscles and tendons at lower leg level**
\+ **S86.801 Unspecified injury of other muscle(s) and tendon(s) at lower leg level, right leg**
\+ **S86.802 Unspecified injury of other muscle(s) and tendon(s) at lower leg level, left leg**
\+ **S86.809 Unspecified injury of other muscle(s) and tendon(s) at lower leg level, unspecified leg**
\+ **S86.81 Strain of other muscles and tendons at lower leg level**
+7th **S86.811 Strain of other muscle(s) and tendon(s) at lower leg level, right leg**
+7th **S86.812 Strain of other muscle(s) and tendon(s) at lower leg level, left leg**
+7th **S86.819 Strain of other muscle(s) and tendon(s) at lower leg level, unspecified leg**
\+ **S86.82 Laceration of other muscles and tendons at lower leg level**
CC +7th **S86.821 Laceration of other muscle(s) and tendon(s) at lower leg level, right leg**
CC Exclusion 7th character A see Appendix A PDX collection 1364
CC +7th **S86.822 Laceration of other muscle(s) and tendon(s) at lower leg level, left leg**
CC Exclusion 7th character A see Appendix A PDX collection 1365
CC +7th **S86.829 Laceration of other muscle(s) and tendon(s) at lower leg level, unspecified leg**
CC Exclusion 7th character A see Appendix A PDX collection 1366
\+ **S86.89 Other injury of other muscles and tendons at lower leg level**
+7th **S86.891 Other injury of other muscle(s) and tendon(s) at lower leg level, right leg**
+7th **S86.892 Other injury of other muscle(s) and tendon(s) at lower leg level, left leg**
+7th **S86.899 Other injury of other muscle(s) and tendon(s) at lower leg level, unspecified leg**

\+ **S86.9 Injury of unspecified muscle and tendon at lower leg level**
\+ **S86.90 Unspecified injury of unspecified muscle and tendon at lower leg level**
+7th **S86.901 Unspecified injury of unspecified muscle(s) and tendon(s) at lower leg level, right leg**
+7th **S86.902 Unspecified injury of unspecified muscle(s) and tendon(s) at lower leg level, left leg**
+7th **S86.909 Unspecified injury of unspecified muscle(s) and tendon(s) at lower leg level, unspecified leg**
\+ **S86.91 Strain of unspecified muscle and tendon at lower leg level**
+7th **S86.911 Strain of unspecified muscle(s) and tendon(s) at lower leg level, right leg**
+7th **S86.912 Strain of unspecified muscle(s) and tendon(s) at lower leg level, left leg**
+7th **S86.919 Strain of unspecified muscle(s) and tendon(s) at lower leg level, unspecified leg**
\+ **S86.92 Laceration of unspecified muscle and tendon at lower leg level**
CC +7th **S86.921 Laceration of unspecified muscle(s) and tendon(s) at lower leg level, right leg**
CC Exclusion 7th character A see Appendix A PDX collection 1364
CC +7th **S86.922 Laceration of unspecified muscle(s) and tendon(s) at lower leg level, left leg**
CC Exclusion 7th character A see Appendix A PDX collection 1365
CC +7th **S86.929 Laceration of unspecified muscle(s) and tendon(s) at lower leg level, unspecified leg**
CC Exclusion 7th character A see Appendix A PDX collection 1366
\+ **S86.99 Other injury of unspecified muscle and tendon at lower leg level**
+7th **S86.991 Other injury of unspecified muscle(s) and tendon(s) at lower leg level, right leg**
+7th **S86.992 Other injury of unspecified muscle(s) and tendon(s) at lower leg level, left leg**
+7th **S86.999 Other injury of unspecified muscle(s) and tendon(s) at lower leg level, unspecified leg**

S87 Crushing injury of lower leg

Use additional code(s) for all associated injuries

Excludes2: *crushing injury of ankle and foot (S97.-)*

The appropriate 7th character is to be added to each code from category S87
A initial encounter
D subsequent encounter
S sequela

\+ **S87.0 Crushing injury of knee**
X+7th **S87.00 Crushing injury of unspecified knee**
X+7th **S87.01 Crushing injury of right knee**
X+7th **S87.02 Crushing injury of left knee**
\+ **S87.8 Crushing injury of lower leg**
X+7th **S87.80 Crushing injury of unspecified lower leg**
X+7th **S87.81 Crushing injury of right lower leg**
X+7th **S87.82 Crushing injury of left lower leg**

S88 Traumatic amputation of lower leg

NOTE An amputation not identified as partial or complete should be coded to complete

Excludes1: *traumatic amputation of ankle and foot (S98.-)*

The appropriate 7th character is to be added to each code from category S88
A initial encounter
D subsequent encounter
S sequela

\+ **S88.0 Traumatic amputation at knee level**
\+ **S88.01 Complete traumatic amputation at knee level**
CC +7th **S88.011 Complete traumatic amputation at knee level, right lower leg**
CC Exclusion 7th character A see Appendix A PDX collection 1333
CC +7th **S88.012 Complete traumatic amputation at knee level, left lower leg**
CC Exclusion 7th character A see Appendix A PDX collection 1334
CC +7th **S88.019 Complete traumatic amputation at knee level, unspecified lower leg**
CC Exclusion 7th character A see Appendix A PDX collection 1335
\+ **S88.02 Partial traumatic amputation at knee level**
CC +7th **S88.021 Partial traumatic amputation at knee level, right lower leg**
CC Exclusion 7th character A see Appendix A PDX collection 1333
CC +7th **S88.022 Partial traumatic amputation at knee level, left lower leg**
CC Exclusion 7th character A see Appendix A PDX collection 1334
CC +7th **S88.029 Partial traumatic amputation at knee level, unspecified lower leg**
CC Exclusion 7th character A see Appendix A PDX collection 1335

\+ **S88.1 Traumatic amputation at level between knee and ankle**
\+ **S88.11 Complete traumatic amputation at level between knee and ankle**
CC +7th **S88.111 Complete traumatic amputation at level between knee and ankle, right lower leg**
CC Exclusion 7th character A see Appendix A PDX collection 1333
CC +7th **S88.112 Complete traumatic amputation at level between knee and ankle, left lower leg**
CC Exclusion 7th character A see Appendix A PDX collection 1334
CC +7th **S88.119 Complete traumatic amputation at level between knee and ankle, unspecified lower leg**
CC Exclusion 7th character A see Appendix A PDX collection 1335
\+ **S88.12 Partial traumatic amputation at level between knee and ankle**
CC +7th **S88.121 Partial traumatic amputation at level between knee and ankle, right lower leg**
CC Exclusion 7th character A see Appendix A PDX collection 1333
CC +7th **S88.122 Partial traumatic amputation at level between knee and ankle, left lower leg**
CC Exclusion 7th character A see Appendix A PDX collection 1334

CC +7th **S88.129 Partial traumatic amputation at level between knee and ankle, unspecified lower leg**
CC Exclusion 7th character A see Appendix A PDX collection 1335

+ **S88.9 Traumatic amputation of lower leg, level unspecified**

+ **S88.91 Complete traumatic amputation of lower leg, level unspecified**

CC +7th **S88.911 Complete traumatic amputation of right lower leg, level unspecified**
CC Exclusion 7th character A see Appendix A PDX collection 1333

CC +7th **S88.912 Complete traumatic amputation of left lower leg, level unspecified**
CC Exclusion 7th character A see Appendix A PDX collection 1334

CC +7th **S88.919 Complete traumatic amputation of unspecified lower leg, level unspecified**
CC Exclusion 7th character A see Appendix A PDX collection 1335

+ **S88.92 Partial traumatic amputation of lower leg, level unspecified**

CC +7th **S88.921 Partial traumatic amputation of right lower leg, level unspecified**
CC Exclusion 7th character A see Appendix A PDX collection 1333

CC +7th **S88.922 Partial traumatic amputation of left lower leg, level unspecified**
CC Exclusion 7th character A see Appendix A PDX collection 1334

CC +7th **S88.929 Partial traumatic amputation of unspecified lower leg, level unspecified**
CC Exclusion 7th character A see Appendix A PDX collection 1335

S89 Other and unspecified injuries of lower leg

NOTE A fracture not indicated as open or closed should be coded to closed

Excludes2: *other and unspecified injuries of ankle and foot (S99.-)*

The appropriate 7th character is to be added to each code from subcategories S89.0, S89.1, S89.2, and S89.3
A initial encounter for closed fracture
D subsequent encounter for fracture with routine healing
G subsequent encounter for fracture with delayed healing
K subsequent encounter for fracture with nonunion
P subsequent encounter for fracture with malunion
S sequela

Review coding guideline C.19.c

+ **S89.0 Physeal fracture of upper end of tibia**

+ **S89.00 Unspecified physeal fracture of upper end of tibia**

CC +7th **S89.001 Unspecified physeal fracture of upper end of right tibia**
CC Exclusion 7th character A see Appendix A PDX collection 1340
CC Exclusion 7th characters K & P see Appendix A PDX collection 0897
HAC 7th character A see Appendix B for HAC conditional logic

CC +7th **S89.002 Unspecified physeal fracture of upper end of left tibia**
CC Exclusion 7th character A see Appendix A PDX collection 1342
CC Exclusion 7th characters K & P see Appendix A PDX collection 0897
HAC 7th character A see Appendix B for HAC conditional logic

CC +7th **S89.009 Unspecified physeal fracture of upper end of unspecified tibia**
CC Exclusion 7th character A see Appendix A PDX collection 1341
CC Exclusion 7th characters K & P see Appendix A PDX collection 0897
HAC 7th character A see Appendix B for HAC conditional logic

+ **S89.01 Salter-Harris Type I physeal fracture of upper end of tibia**

CC +7th **S89.011 Salter-Harris Type I physeal fracture of upper end of right tibia**
CC Exclusion 7th character A see Appendix A PDX collection 1340
CC Exclusion 7th characters K & P see Appendix A PDX collection 0897
HAC 7th character A see Appendix B for HAC conditional logic

CC +7th **S89.012 Salter-Harris Type I physeal fracture of upper end of left tibia**
CC Exclusion 7th character A see Appendix A PDX collection 1342
CC Exclusion 7th characters K & P see Appendix A PDX collection 0897
HAC 7th character A see Appendix B for HAC conditional logic

CC +7th **S89.019 Salter-Harris Type I physeal fracture of upper end of unspecified tibia**
CC Exclusion 7th character A see Appendix A PDX collection 1341
CC Exclusion 7th characters K & P see Appendix A PDX collection 0897
HAC 7th character A see Appendix B for HAC conditional logic

+ **S89.02 Salter-Harris Type II physeal fracture of upper end of tibia**

CC +7th **S89.021 Salter-Harris Type II physeal fracture of upper end of right tibia**
CC Exclusion 7th character A see Appendix A PDX collection 1340
CC Exclusion 7th characters K & P see Appendix A PDX collection 0897
HAC 7th character A see Appendix B for HAC conditional logic

CC +7th **S89.022 Salter-Harris Type II physeal fracture of upper end of left tibia**
CC Exclusion 7th character A see Appendix A PDX collection 1342
CC Exclusion 7th characters K & P see Appendix A PDX collection 0897
HAC 7th character A see Appendix B for HAC conditional logic

CC +7th **S89.029 Salter-Harris Type II physeal fracture of upper end of unspecified tibia**
CC Exclusion 7th character A see Appendix A PDX collection 1341
CC Exclusion 7th characters K & P see Appendix A PDX collection 0897
HAC 7th character A see Appendix B for HAC conditional logic

+ **S89.03 Salter-Harris Type III physeal fracture of upper end of tibia**

CC +7th **S89.031 Salter-Harris Type III physeal fracture of upper end of right tibia**
CC Exclusion 7th character A see Appendix A PDX collection 1340
CC Exclusion 7th characters K & P see Appendix A PDX collection 0897
HAC 7th character A see Appendix B for HAC conditional logic

CC +7th **S89.032 Salter-Harris Type III physeal fracture of upper end of left tibia**
CC Exclusion 7th character A see Appendix A PDX collection 1342
CC Exclusion 7th characters K & P see Appendix A PDX collection 0897
HAC 7th character A see Appendix B for HAC conditional logic

CC +7th **S89.039 Salter-Harris Type III physeal fracture of upper end of unspecified tibia**
CC Exclusion 7th character A see Appendix A PDX collection 1341
CC Exclusion 7th characters K & P see Appendix A PDX collection 0897
HAC 7th character A see Appendix B for HAC conditional logic

+ **S89.04 Salter-Harris Type IV physeal fracture of upper end of tibia**

CC +7th **S89.041 Salter-Harris Type IV physeal fracture of upper end of right tibia**
CC Exclusion 7th character A see Appendix A PDX collection 1340
CC Exclusion 7th characters K & P see Appendix A PDX collection 0897
HAC 7th character A see Appendix B for HAC conditional logic

CC +7th **S89.042 Salter-Harris Type IV physeal fracture of upper end of left tibia**
CC Exclusion 7th character A see Appendix A PDX collection 1342
CC Exclusion 7th characters K & P see Appendix A PDX collection 0897
HAC 7th character A see Appendix B for HAC conditional logic

CC +7th **S89.049** **Salter-Harris Type IV physeal fracture of upper end of unspecified tibia**
CC Exclusion 7th character A see Appendix A PDX collection 1341
CC Exclusion 7th characters K & P see Appendix A PDX collection 0897
HAC 7th character A see Appendix B for HAC conditional logic

\+ **S89.09** **Other physeal fracture of upper end of tibia**

CC +7th **S89.091** **Other physeal fracture of upper end of right tibia**
CC Exclusion 7th character A see Appendix A PDX collection 1340
CC Exclusion 7th characters K & P see Appendix A PDX collection 0897
HAC 7th character A see Appendix B for HAC conditional logic

CC +7th **S89.092** **Other physeal fracture of upper end of left tibia**
CC Exclusion 7th character A see Appendix A PDX collection 1342
CC Exclusion 7th characters K & P see Appendix A PDX collection 0897
HAC 7th character A see Appendix B for HAC conditional logic

CC +7th **S89.099** **Other physeal fracture of upper end of unspecified tibia**
CC Exclusion 7th character A see Appendix A PDX collection 1341
CC Exclusion 7th characters K & P see Appendix A PDX collection 0897
HAC 7th character A see Appendix B for HAC conditional logic

\+ **S89.1** **Physeal fracture of lower end of tibia**

\+ **S89.10** **Unspecified physeal fracture of lower end of tibia**

CC +7th **S89.101** **Unspecified physeal fracture of lower end of right tibia**
CC Exclusion 7th characters K & P see Appendix A PDX collection 0897

CC +7th **S89.102** **Unspecified physeal fracture of lower end of left tibia**
CC Exclusion 7th characters K & P see Appendix A PDX collection 0897

CC +7th **S89.109** **Unspecified physeal fracture of lower end of unspecified tibia**
CC Exclusion 7th characters K & P see Appendix A PDX collection 0897

\+ **S89.11** **Salter-Harris Type I physeal fracture of lower end of tibia**

CC +7th **S89.111** **Salter-Harris Type I physeal fracture of lower end of right tibia**
CC Exclusion 7th characters K & P see Appendix A PDX collection 0897

CC +7th **S89.112** **Salter-Harris Type I physeal fracture of lower end of left tibia**
CC Exclusion 7th characters K & P see Appendix A PDX collection 0897

CC +7th **S89.119** **Salter-Harris Type I physeal fracture of lower end of unspecified tibia**
CC Exclusion 7th characters K & P see Appendix A PDX collection 0897

\+ **S89.12** **Salter-Harris Type II physeal fracture of lower end of tibia**

CC +7th **S89.121** **Salter-Harris Type II physeal fracture of lower end of right tibia**
CC Exclusion 7th characters K & P see Appendix A PDX collection 0897

CC +7th **S89.122** **Salter-Harris Type II physeal fracture of lower end of left tibia**
CC Exclusion 7th characters K & P see Appendix A PDX collection 0897

CC +7th **S89.129** **Salter-Harris Type II physeal fracture of lower end of unspecified tibia**
CC Exclusion 7th characters K & P see Appendix A PDX collection 0897

\+ **S89.13** **Salter-Harris Type III physeal fracture of lower end of tibia**
Excludes1: *fracture of medial malleolus (adult) (S82.5-)*

CC +7th **S89.131** **Salter-Harris Type III physeal fracture of lower end of right tibia**
CC Exclusion 7th characters K & P see Appendix A PDX collection 0897

CC +7th **S89.132** **Salter-Harris Type III physeal fracture of lower end of left tibia**
CC Exclusion 7th characters K & P see Appendix A PDX collection 0897

CC +7th **S89.139** **Salter-Harris Type III physeal fracture of lower end of unspecified tibia**
CC Exclusion 7th characters K & P see Appendix A PDX collection 0897

\+ **S89.14** **Salter-Harris Type IV physeal fracture of lower end tibia**
Excludes1: *fracture of medial malleolus (adult) (S82.*

CC +7th **S89.141** **Salter-Harris Type IV physeal fracture of lower end of right tibia**
CC Exclusion 7th characters K & P see Appendix A PDX collection 0897

CC +7th **S89.142** **Salter-Harris Type IV physeal fracture of lower end of left tibia**
CC Exclusion 7th characters K & P see Appendix A PDX collection 0897

CC +7th **S89.149** **Salter-Harris Type IV physeal fracture of lower end of unspecified tibia**
CC Exclusion 7th characters K & P see Appendix A PDX collection 0897

\+ **S89.19** **Other physeal fracture of lower end of tibia**

CC +7th **S89.191** **Other physeal fracture of lower end of righ tibia**
CC Exclusion 7th characters K & P see Appendix A PDX collection 0897

CC +7th **S89.192** **Other physeal fracture of lower end of left tibia**
CC Exclusion 7th characters K & P see Appendix A PDX collection 0897

CC +7th **S89.199** **Other physeal fracture of lower end of unspecified tibia**
CC Exclusion 7th characters K & P see Appendix A PDX collection 0897

\+ **S89.2** **Physeal fracture of upper end of fibula**

\+ **S89.20** **Unspecified physeal fracture of upper end of fibula**

CC +7th **S89.201** **Unspecified physeal fracture of upper end c right fibula**
CC Exclusion 7th characters K & P see Appendix A PDX collection 0897

CC +7th **S89.202** **Unspecified physeal fracture of upper end o left fibula**
CC Exclusion 7th characters K & P see Appendix A PDX collection 0897

CC +7th **S89.209** **Unspecified physeal fracture of upper end o unspecified fibula**
CC Exclusion 7th characters K & P see Appendix A PDX collection 0897

\+ **S89.21** **Salter-Harris Type I physeal fracture of upper end of fibula**

CC +7th **S89.211** **Salter-Harris Type I physeal fracture of upper end of right fibula**
CC Exclusion 7th characters K & P see Appendix A PDX collection 0897

CC +7th **S89.212** **Salter-Harris Type I physeal fracture of upper end of left fibula**
CC Exclusion 7th characters K & P see Appendix A PDX collection 0897

CC +7th **S89.219** **Salter-Harris Type I physeal fracture of upper end of unspecified fibula**
CC Exclusion 7th characters K & P see Appendix A PDX collection 0897

\+ **S89.22** **Salter-Harris Type II physeal fracture of upper end of fibula**

CC +7th **S89.221** **Salter-Harris Type II physeal fracture of upper end of right fibula**
CC Exclusion 7th characters K & P see Appendix A PDX collection 0897

CC +7th **S89.222** **Salter-Harris Type II physeal fracture of upper end of left fibula**
CC Exclusion 7th characters K & P see Appendix A PDX collection 0897

CC +7th **S89.229** **Salter-Harris Type II physeal fracture of upper end of unspecified fibula**
CC Exclusion 7th characters K & P see Appendix A PDX collection 0897

\+ **S89.29** **Other physeal fracture of upper end of fibula**

CC +7th **S89.291** **Other physeal fracture of upper end of right fibula**
CC Exclusion 7th characters K & P see Appendix A PDX collection 0897

CC +7th **S89.292** **Other physeal fracture of upper end of left fibula**
CC Exclusion 7th characters K & P see Appendix A PDX collection 0897

CC +7th **S89.299** **Other physeal fracture of upper end of unspecified fibula**
CC Exclusion 7th characters K & P see Appendix A PDX collection 0897

\+ **S89.3** **Physeal fracture of lower end of fibula**

\+ **S89.30** **Unspecified physeal fracture of lower end of fibula**

CC +7th **S89.301** **Unspecified physeal fracture of lower end of right fibula**
CC Exclusion 7th characters K & P see Appendix A PDX collection 0897

CC +7th **S89.302** **Unspecified physeal fracture of lower end of left fibula**
CC Exclusion 7th characters K & P see Appendix A PDX collection 0897

CC +7th **S89.309** **Unspecified physeal fracture of lower end of unspecified fibula**
CC Exclusion 7th characters K & P see Appendix A PDX collection 0897

\+ **S89.31** **Salter-Harris Type I physeal fracture of lower end of fibula**

CC +7th **S89.311** **Salter-Harris Type I physeal fracture of lower end of right fibula**
CC Exclusion 7th characters K & P see Appendix A PDX collection 0897

CC +7th **S89.312** **Salter-Harris Type I physeal fracture of lower end of left fibula**
CC Exclusion 7th characters K & P see Appendix A PDX collection 0897

CC +7th **S89.319** **Salter-Harris Type I physeal fracture of lower end of unspecified fibula**
CC Exclusion 7th characters K & P see Appendix A PDX collection 0897

\+ **S89.32** **Salter-Harris Type II physeal fracture of lower end of fibula**

CC +7th **S89.321** **Salter-Harris Type II physeal fracture of lower end of right fibula**
CC Exclusion 7th characters K & P see Appendix A PDX collection 0897

CC +7th **S89.322** **Salter-Harris Type II physeal fracture of lower end of left fibula**
CC Exclusion 7th characters K & P see Appendix A PDX collection 0897

CC +7th **S89.329** **Salter-Harris Type II physeal fracture of lower end of unspecified fibula**
CC Exclusion 7th characters K & P see Appendix A PDX collection 0897

\+ **S89.39** **Other physeal fracture of lower end of fibula**

CC +7th **S89.391** **Other physeal fracture of lower end of right fibula**
CC Exclusion 7th characters K & P see Appendix A PDX collection 0897

CC +7th **S89.392** **Other physeal fracture of lower end of left fibula**
CC Exclusion 7th characters K & P see Appendix A PDX collection 0897

CC +7th **S89.399** **Other physeal fracture of lower end of unspecified fibula**
CC Exclusion 7th characters K & P see Appendix A PDX collection 0897

\+ **S89.8** **Other specified injuries of lower leg**

The appropriate 7th character is to be added to each code in subcategory S89.8
A initial encounter
D subsequent encounter
S sequela

X+7th **S89.80** **Other specified injuries of unspecified lower leg**
X+7th **S89.81** **Other specified injuries of right lower leg**
X+7th **S89.82** **Other specified injuries of left lower leg**

\+ **S89.9** **Unspecified injury of lower leg**

The appropriate 7th character is to be added to each code in subcategory S89.9
A initial encounter
D subsequent encounter
S sequela

X+7th **S89.90** **Unspecified injury of unspecified lower leg**
X+7th **S89.91** **Unspecified injury of right lower leg**
X+7th **S89.92** **Unspecified injury of left lower leg**

Injuries to the ankle and foot (S90-S99)

Excludes2: *burns and corrosions (T20-T32)*
fracture of ankle and malleolus (S82.-)
frostbite (T33-T34)
insect bite or sting, venomous (T63.4)

S90 **Superficial injury of ankle, foot and toes**

The appropriate 7th character is to be added to each code from category S90
A initial encounter
D subsequent encounter
S sequela

\+ **S90.0** **Contusion of ankle**
X+7th **S90.00** **Contusion of unspecified ankle**
X+7th **S90.01** **Contusion of right ankle**
X+7th **S90.02** **Contusion of left ankle**

\+ **S90.1** **Contusion of toe without damage to nail**

\+ **S90.11** **Contusion of great toe without damage to nail**
+7th **S90.111** **Contusion of right great toe without damage to nail**
+7th **S90.112** **Contusion of left great toe without damage to nail**
+7th **S90.119** **Contusion of unspecified great toe without damage to nail**

\+ **S90.12** **Contusion of lesser toe without damage to nail**
+7th **S90.121** **Contusion of right lesser toe(s) without damage to nail**
+7th **S90.122** **Contusion of left lesser toe(s) without damage to nail**
+7th **S90.129** **Contusion of unspecified lesser toe(s) without damage to nail**
Contusion of toe NOS

\+ **S90.2** **Contusion of toe with damage to nail**

\+ **S90.21** **Contusion of great toe with damage to nail**
+7th **S90.211** **Contusion of right great toe with damage to nail**
+7th **S90.212** **Contusion of left great toe with damage to nail**
+7th **S90.219** **Contusion of unspecified great toe with damage to nail**

\+ **S90.22** **Contusion of lesser toe with damage to nail**
+7th **S90.221** **Contusion of right lesser toe(s) with damage to nail**
+7th **S90.222** **Contusion of left lesser toe(s) with damage to nail**
+7th **S90.229** **Contusion of unspecified lesser toe(s) with damage to nail**

\+ **S90.3** **Contusion of foot**
Excludes2: *contusion of toes (S90.1-, S90.2-)*
X+7th **S90.30** **Contusion of unspecified foot**
Contusion of foot NOS
X+7th **S90.31** **Contusion of right foot**
X+7th **S90.32** **Contusion of left foot**

\+ **S90.4** **Other superficial injuries of toe**

\+ **S90.41** **Abrasion of toe**
+7th **S90.411** **Abrasion, right great toe**
+7th **S90.412** **Abrasion, left great toe**
+7th **S90.413** **Abrasion, unspecified great toe**
+7th **S90.414** **Abrasion, right lesser toe(s)**
+7th **S90.415** **Abrasion, left lesser toe(s)**
+7th **S90.416** **Abrasion, unspecified lesser toe(s)**

\+ **S90.42** **Blister (nonthermal) of toe**
+7th **S90.421** **Blister (nonthermal), right great toe**
+7th **S90.422** **Blister (nonthermal), left great toe**
+7th **S90.423** **Blister (nonthermal), unspecified great toe**
+7th **S90.424** **Blister (nonthermal), right lesser toe(s)**
+7th **S90.425** **Blister (nonthermal), left lesser toe(s)**
+7th **S90.426** **Blister (nonthermal), unspecified lesser toe(s)**

\+ **S90.44** **External constriction of toe**
Hair tourniquet syndrome of toe
+7th **S90.441** **External constriction, right great toe**
+7th **S90.442** **External constriction, left great toe**
+7th **S90.443** **External constriction, unspecified great toe**
+7th **S90.444** **External constriction, right lesser toe(s)**
+7th **S90.445** **External constriction, left lesser toe(s)**
+7th **S90.446** **External constriction, unspecified lesser toe(s)**

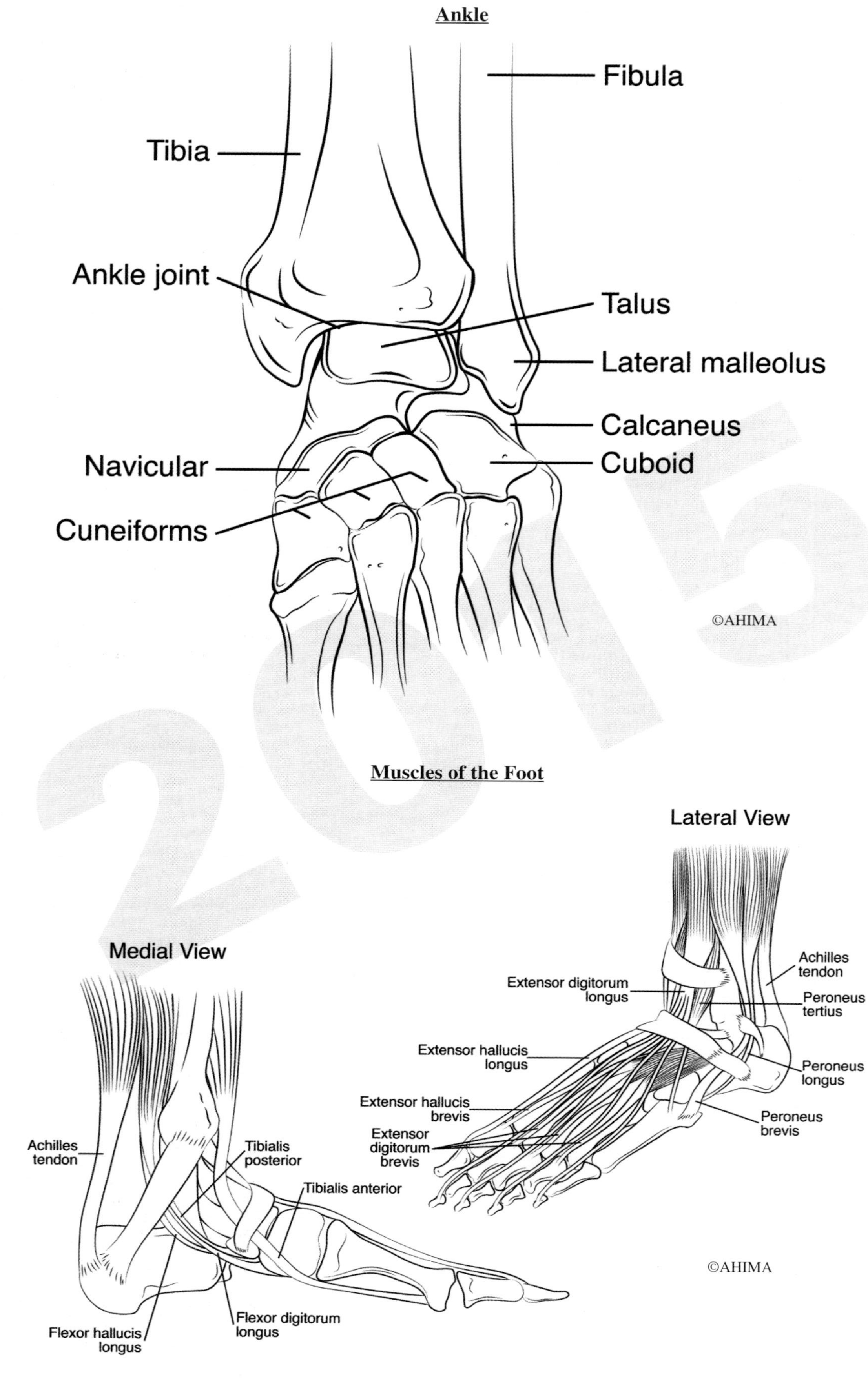
Ankle
Fibula
Tibia
Ankle joint
Talus
Lateral malleolus
Calcaneus
Navicular
Cuboid
Cuneiforms
©AHIMA
Muscles of the Foot
Lateral View
Medial View
Achilles tendon
Extensor digitorum longus
Peroneus tertius
Extensor hallucis longus
Peroneus longus
Extensor hallucis brevis
Peroneus brevis
Extensor digitorum brevis
Achilles tendon
Tibialis posterior
Tibialis anterior
Flexor digitorum longus
Flexor hallucis longus
©AHIMA

+ **S90.45 Superficial foreign body of toe**
  Splinter in the toe
  - +7th **S90.451 Superficial foreign body, right great toe**
  - +7th **S90.452 Superficial foreign body, left great toe**
  - +7th **S90.453 Superficial foreign body, unspecified great toe**
  - +7th **S90.454 Superficial foreign body, right lesser toe(s)**
  - +7th **S90.455 Superficial foreign body, left lesser toe(s)**
  - +7th **S90.456 Superficial foreign body, unspecified lesser toe(s)**

+ **S90.46 Insect bite (nonvenomous) of toe**
  - +7th **S90.461 Insect bite (nonvenomous), right great toe**
  - +7th **S90.462 Insect bite (nonvenomous), left great toe**
  - +7th **S90.463 Insect bite (nonvenomous), unspecified great toe**
  - +7th **S90.464 Insect bite (nonvenomous), right lesser toe(s)**
  - +7th **S90.465 Insect bite (nonvenomous), left lesser toe(s)**
  - +7th **S90.466 Insect bite (nonvenomous), unspecified lesser toe(s)**

+ **S90.47 Other superficial bite of toe**
  Excludes1: *open bite of toe (S91.15-, S91.25-)*
  - +7th **S90.471 Other superficial bite of right great toe**
  - +7th **S90.472 Other superficial bite of left great toe**
  - +7th **S90.473 Other superficial bite of unspecified great toe**
  - +7th **S90.474 Other superficial bite of right lesser toe(s)**
  - +7th **S90.475 Other superficial bite of left lesser toe(s)**
  - +7th **S90.476 Other superficial bite of unspecified lesser toe(s)**

+ **S90.5 Other superficial injuries of ankle**

+ **S90.51 Abrasion of ankle**
  - +7th **S90.511 Abrasion, right ankle**
  - +7th **S90.512 Abrasion, left ankle**
  - +7th **S90.519 Abrasion, unspecified ankle**

+ **S90.52 Blister (nonthermal) of ankle**
  - +7th **S90.521 Blister (nonthermal), right ankle**
  - +7th **S90.522 Blister (nonthermal), left ankle**
  - +7th **S90.529 Blister (nonthermal), unspecified ankle**

+ **S90.54 External constriction of ankle**
  - +7th **S90.541 External constriction, right ankle**
  - +7th **S90.542 External constriction, left ankle**
  - +7th **S90.549 External constriction, unspecified ankle**

+ **S90.55 Superficial foreign body of ankle**
  Splinter in the ankle
  - +7th **S90.551 Superficial foreign body, right ankle**
  - +7th **S90.552 Superficial foreign body, left ankle**
  - +7th **S90.559 Superficial foreign body, unspecified ankle**

+ **S90.56 Insect bite (nonvenomous) of ankle**
  - +7th **S90.561 Insect bite (nonvenomous), right ankle**
  - +7th **S90.562 Insect bite (nonvenomous), left ankle**
  - +7th **S90.569 Insect bite (nonvenomous), unspecified ankle**

+ **S90.57 Other superficial bite of ankle**
  Excludes1: *open bite of ankle (S91.05-)*
  - +7th **S90.571 Other superficial bite of ankle, right ankle**
  - +7th **S90.572 Other superficial bite of ankle, left ankle**
  - +7th **S90.579 Other superficial bite of ankle, unspecified ankle**

+ **S90.8 Other superficial injuries of foot**

+ **S90.81 Abrasion of foot**
  - +7th **S90.811 Abrasion, right foot**
  - +7th **S90.812 Abrasion, left foot**
  - +7th **S90.819 Abrasion, unspecified foot**

+ **S90.82 Blister (nonthermal) of foot**
  - +7th **S90.821 Blister (nonthermal), right foot**
  - +7th **S90.822 Blister (nonthermal), left foot**
  - +7th **S90.829 Blister (nonthermal), unspecified foot**

+ **S90.84 External constriction of foot**
  - +7th **S90.841 External constriction, right foot**
  - +7th **S90.842 External constriction, left foot**
  - +7th **S90.849 External constriction, unspecified foot**

+ **S90.85 Superficial foreign body of foot**
  Splinter in the foot
  - +7th **S90.851 Superficial foreign body, right foot**
  - +7th **S90.852 Superficial foreign body, left foot**
  - +7th **S90.859 Superficial foreign body, unspecified foot**

+ **S90.86 Insect bite (nonvenomous) of foot**
  - +7th **S90.861 Insect bite (nonvenomous), right foot**
  - +7th **S90.862 Insect bite (nonvenomous), left foot**
  - +7th **S90.869 Insect bite (nonvenomous), unspecified foot**

+ **S90.87 Other superficial bite of foot**
  Excludes1: *open bite of foot (S91.35-)*
  - +7th **S90.871 Other superficial bite of right foot**
  - +7th **S90.872 Other superficial bite of left foot**
  - +7th **S90.879 Other superficial bite of unspecified foot**

+ **S90.9 Unspecified superficial injury of ankle, foot and toe**

+ **S90.91 Unspecified superficial injury of ankle**
  - +7th **S90.911 Unspecified superficial injury of right ankle**
  - +7th **S90.912 Unspecified superficial injury of left ankle**
  - +7th **S90.919 Unspecified superficial injury of unspecified ankle**

+ **S90.92 Unspecified superficial injury of foot**
  - +7th **S90.921 Unspecified superficial injury of right foot**
  - +7th **S90.922 Unspecified superficial injury of left foot**
  - +7th **S90.929 Unspecified superficial injury of unspecified foot**

+ **S90.93 Unspecified superficial injury of toes**
  - +7th **S90.931 Unspecified superficial injury of right great toe**
  - +7th **S90.932 Unspecified superficial injury of left great toe**
  - +7th **S90.933 Unspecified superficial injury of unspecified great toe**
  - +7th **S90.934 Unspecified superficial injury of right lesser toe(s)**
  - +7th **S90.935 Unspecified superficial injury of left lesser toe(s)**
  - +7th **S90.936 Unspecified superficial injury of unspecified lesser toe(s)**

S91 Open wound of ankle, foot and toes

Code also any associated wound infection
Excludes1: *open fracture of ankle, foot and toes (S92.-with 7th character B)*
traumatic amputation of ankle and foot (S98.-)

The appropriate 7th character is to be added to each code from category S91
A initial encounter
D subsequent encounter
S sequela

+ **S91.0 Open wound of ankle**

+ **S91.00 Unspecified open wound of ankle**
  - +7th **S91.001 Unspecified open wound, right ankle**
  - +7th **S91.002 Unspecified open wound, left ankle**
  - +7th **S91.009 Unspecified open wound, unspecified ankle**

+ **S91.01 Laceration without foreign body of ankle**
  - +7th **S91.011 Laceration without foreign body, right ankle**
  - +7th **S91.012 Laceration without foreign body, left ankle**
  - +7th **S91.019 Laceration without foreign body, unspecified ankle**

+ **S91.02 Laceration with foreign body of ankle**
  - +7th **S91.021 Laceration with foreign body, right ankle**
  - +7th **S91.022 Laceration with foreign body, left ankle**
  - +7th **S91.029 Laceration with foreign body, unspecified ankle**

+ **S91.03 Puncture wound without foreign body of ankle**
  - +7th **S91.031 Puncture wound without foreign body, right ankle**
  - +7th **S91.032 Puncture wound without foreign body, left ankle**
  - +7th **S91.039 Puncture wound without foreign body, unspecified ankle**

+ **S91.04 Puncture wound with foreign body of ankle**
  - +7th **S91.041 Puncture wound with foreign body, right ankle**
  - +7th **S91.042 Puncture wound with foreign body, left ankle**
  - +7th **S91.049 Puncture wound with foreign body, unspecified ankle**

+ **S91.05 Open bite of ankle**
  Excludes1: *superficial bite of ankle (S90.56-, S90.57-)*
  - +7th **S91.051 Open bite, right ankle**
  - +7th **S91.052 Open bite, left ankle**
  - +7th **S91.059 Open bite, unspecified ankle**

+ **S91.1 Open wound of toe without damage to nail**

+ **S91.10 Unspecified open wound of toe without damage to nail**
  - +7th **S91.101 Unspecified open wound of right great toe without damage to nail**
  - +7th **S91.102 Unspecified open wound of left great toe without damage to nail**
  - +7th **S91.103 Unspecified open wound of unspecified great toe without damage to nail**
  - +7th **S91.104 Unspecified open wound of right lesser toe(s) without damage to nail**
  - +7th **S91.105 Unspecified open wound of left lesser toe(s) without damage to nail**

+7th S91.106 Unspecified open wound of unspecified lesser toe(s) without damage to nail
+7th S91.109 Unspecified open wound of unspecified toe(s) without damage to nail
+ S91.11 Laceration without foreign body of toe without damage to nail
+7th S91.111 Laceration without foreign body of right great toe without damage to nail
+7th S91.112 Laceration without foreign body of left great toe without damage to nail
+7th S91.113 Laceration without foreign body of unspecified great toe without damage to nail
+7th S91.114 Laceration without foreign body of right lesser toe(s) without damage to nail
+7th S91.115 Laceration without foreign body of left lesser toe(s) without damage to nail
+7th S91.116 Laceration without foreign body of unspecified lesser toe(s) without damage to nail
+7th S91.119 Laceration without foreign body of unspecified toe without damage to nail
+ S91.12 Laceration with foreign body of toe without damage to nail
+7th S91.121 Laceration with foreign body of right great toe without damage to nail
+7th S91.122 Laceration with foreign body of left great toe without damage to nail
+7th S91.123 Laceration with foreign body of unspecified great toe without damage to nail
+7th S91.124 Laceration with foreign body of right lesser toe(s) without damage to nail
+7th S91.125 Laceration with foreign body of left lesser toe(s) without damage to nail
+7th S91.126 Laceration with foreign body of unspecified lesser toe(s) without damage to nail
+7th S91.129 Laceration with foreign body of unspecified toe(s) without damage to nail
+ S91.13 Puncture wound without foreign body of toe without damage to nail
+7th S91.131 Puncture wound without foreign body of right great toe without damage to nail
+7th S91.132 Puncture wound without foreign body of left great toe without damage to nail
+7th S91.133 Puncture wound without foreign body of unspecified great toe without damage to nail
+7th S91.134 Puncture wound without foreign body of right lesser toe(s) without damage to nail
+7th S91.135 Puncture wound without foreign body of left lesser toe(s) without damage to nail
+7th S91.136 Puncture wound without foreign body of unspecified lesser toe(s) without damage to nail
+7th S91.139 Puncture wound without foreign body of unspecified toe(s) without damage to nail
+ S91.14 Puncture wound with foreign body of toe without damage to nail
+7th S91.141 Puncture wound with foreign body of right great toe without damage to nail
+7th S91.142 Puncture wound with foreign body of left great toe without damage to nail
+7th S91.143 Puncture wound with foreign body of unspecified great toe without damage to nail
+7th S91.144 Puncture wound with foreign body of right lesser toe(s) without damage to nail
+7th S91.145 Puncture wound with foreign body of left lesser toe(s) without damage to nail
+7th S91.146 Puncture wound with foreign body of unspecified lesser toe(s) without damage to nail
+7th S91.149 Puncture wound with foreign body of unspecified toe(s) without damage to nail
+ S91.15 Open bite of toe without damage to nail
Bite of toe NOS
Excludes1: *superficial bite of toe (S90.46-, S90.47-)*
+7th S91.151 Open bite of right great toe without damage to nail
+7th S91.152 Open bite of left great toe without damage to nail
+7th S91.153 Open bite of unspecified great toe without damage to nail
+7th S91.154 Open bite of right lesser toe(s) without damage to nail
+7th S91.155 Open bite of left lesser toe(s) without damage to nail
+7th S91.156 Open bite of unspecified lesser toe(s) without damage to nail
+7th S91.159 Open bite of unspecified toe(s) without damage to nail
+ S91.2 Open wound of toe with damage to nail
+ S91.20 Unspecified open wound of toe with damage to nail
+7th S91.201 Unspecified open wound of right great toe with damage to nail
+7th S91.202 Unspecified open wound of left great toe with damage to nail
+7th S91.203 Unspecified open wound of unspecified great toe with damage to nail
+7th S91.204 Unspecified open wound of right lesser toe(s) with damage to nail
+7th S91.205 Unspecified open wound of left lesser toe(s) with damage to nail
+7th S91.206 Unspecified open wound of unspecified lesser toe(s) with damage to nail
+7th S91.209 Unspecified open wound of unspecified toe(s) with damage to nail
+ S91.21 Laceration without foreign body of toe with damage to nail
+7th S91.211 Laceration without foreign body of right great toe with damage to nail
+7th S91.212 Laceration without foreign body of left great toe with damage to nail
+7th S91.213 Laceration without foreign body of unspecified great toe with damage to nail
+7th S91.214 Laceration without foreign body of right lesser toe(s) with damage to nail
+7th S91.215 Laceration without foreign body of left lesser toe(s) with damage to nail
+7th S91.216 Laceration without foreign body of unspecified lesser toe(s) with damage to nail
+7th S91.219 Laceration without foreign body of unspecified toe(s) with damage to nail
+ S91.22 Laceration with foreign body of toe with damage to nail
+7th S91.221 Laceration with foreign body of right great toe with damage to nail
+7th S91.222 Laceration with foreign body of left great toe with damage to nail
+7th S91.223 Laceration with foreign body of unspecified great toe with damage to nail
+7th S91.224 Laceration with foreign body of right lesser toe(s) with damage to nail
+7th S91.225 Laceration with foreign body of left lesser toe(s) with damage to nail
+7th S91.226 Laceration with foreign body of unspecified lesser toe(s) with damage to nail
+7th S91.229 Laceration with foreign body of unspecified toe(s) with damage to nail
+ S91.23 Puncture wound without foreign body of toe with damage to nail
+7th S91.231 Puncture wound without foreign body of right great toe with damage to nail
+7th S91.232 Puncture wound without foreign body of left great toe with damage to nail
+7th S91.233 Puncture wound without foreign body of unspecified great toe with damage to nail
+7th S91.234 Puncture wound without foreign body of right lesser toe(s) with damage to nail
+7th S91.235 Puncture wound without foreign body of left lesser toe(s) with damage to nail
+7th S91.236 Puncture wound without foreign body of unspecified lesser toe(s) with damage to nail
+7th S91.239 Puncture wound without foreign body of unspecified toe(s) with damage to nail
+ S91.24 Puncture wound with foreign body of toe with damage to nail
+7th S91.241 Puncture wound with foreign body of right great toe with damage to nail
+7th S91.242 Puncture wound with foreign body of left great toe with damage to nail
+7th S91.243 Puncture wound with foreign body of unspecified great toe with damage to nail
+7th S91.244 Puncture wound with foreign body of right lesser toe(s) with damage to nail
+7th S91.245 Puncture wound with foreign body of left lesser toe(s) with damage to nail

+7th **S91.246 Puncture wound with foreign body of unspecified lesser toe(s) with damage to nail**
+7th **S91.249 Puncture wound with foreign body of unspecified toe(s) with damage to nail**

\+ **S91.25 Open bite of toe with damage to nail**
Bite of toe with damage to nail NOS
Excludes1: *superficial bite of toe (S90.46-, S90.47-)*

+7th **S91.251 Open bite of right great toe with damage to nail**
+7th **S91.252 Open bite of left great toe with damage to nail**
+7th **S91.253 Open bite of unspecified great toe with damage to nail**
+7th **S91.254 Open bite of right lesser toe(s) with damage to nail**
+7th **S91.255 Open bite of left lesser toe(s) with damage to nail**
+7th **S91.256 Open bite of unspecified lesser toe(s) with damage to nail**
+7th **S91.259 Open bite of unspecified toe(s) with damage to nail**

\+ **S91.3 Open wound of foot**

\+ **S91.30 Unspecified open wound of foot**
+7th **S91.301 Unspecified open wound, right foot**
+7th **S91.302 Unspecified open wound, left foot**
+7th **S91.309 Unspecified open wound, unspecified foot**

\+ **S91.31 Laceration without foreign body of foot**
+7th **S91.311 Laceration without foreign body, right foot**
+7th **S91.312 Laceration without foreign body, left foot**
+7th **S91.319 Laceration without foreign body, unspecified foot**

\+ **S91.32 Laceration with foreign body of foot**
+7th **S91.321 Laceration with foreign body, right foot**
+7th **S91.322 Laceration with foreign body, left foot**
+7th **S91.329 Laceration with foreign body, unspecified foot**

\+ **S91.33 Puncture wound without foreign body of foot**
+7th **S91.331 Puncture wound without foreign body, right foot**
+7th **S91.332 Puncture wound without foreign body, left foot**
+7th **S91.339 Puncture wound without foreign body, unspecified foot**

\+ **S91.34 Puncture wound with foreign body of foot**
+7th **S91.341 Puncture wound with foreign body, right foot**
+7th **S91.342 Puncture wound with foreign body, left foot**
+7th **S91.349 Puncture wound with foreign body, unspecified foot**

\+ **S91.35 Open bite of foot**
Excludes1: *superficial bite of foot (S90.86-, S90.87-)*
+7th **S91.351 Open bite, right foot**
+7th **S91.352 Open bite, left foot**
+7th **S91.359 Open bite, unspecified foot**

S92 Fracture of foot and toe, except ankle

NOTE A fracture not indicated as displaced or nondisplaced should be coded to displaced
A fracture not indicated as open or closed should be coded to closed

Excludes1: *traumatic amputation of ankle and foot (S98.-)*
Excludes2: *fracture of ankle (S82.-)*
fracture of malleolus (S82.-)

The appropriate 7th character is to be added to each code from category S92
A initial encounter for closed fracture
B initial encounter for open fracture
D subsequent encounter for fracture with routine healing
G subsequent encounter for fracture with delayed healing
K subsequent encounter for fracture with nonunion
P subsequent encounter for fracture with malunion
S sequela

Review coding guideline C.19.c

\+ **S92.0 Fracture of calcaneus**
Heel bone
Os calcis

\+ **S92.00 Unspecified fracture of calcaneus**

CC +7th **S92.001 Unspecified fracture of right calcaneus**
CC Exclusion 7th character B see Appendix A PDX collection 1367
CC Exclusion 7th characters K & P see Appendix A PDX collection 0897
HAC 7th character B see Appendix B for HAC conditional logic

CC +7th **S92.002 Unspecified fracture of left calcaneus**
CC Exclusion 7th character B see Appendix A PDX collection 1367
CC Exclusion 7th characters K & P see Appendix A PDX collection 0897
HAC 7th character B see Appendix B for HAC conditional logic

CC +7th **S92.009 Unspecified fracture of unspecified calcaneus**
CC Exclusion 7th character B see Appendix A PDX collection 1367
CC Exclusion 7th characters K & P see Appendix A PDX collection 0897
HAC 7th character B see Appendix B for HAC conditional logic

\+ **S92.01 Fracture of body of calcaneus**

CC +7th **S92.011 Displaced fracture of body of right calcaneus**
CC Exclusion 7th character B see Appendix A PDX collection 1367
CC Exclusion 7th characters K & P see Appendix A PDX collection 0897
HAC 7th character B see Appendix B for HAC conditional logic

CC +7th **S92.012 Displaced fracture of body of left calcaneus**
CC Exclusion 7th character B see Appendix A PDX collection 1367
CC Exclusion 7th characters K & P see Appendix A PDX collection 0897
HAC 7th character B see Appendix B for HAC conditional logic

CC +7th **S92.013 Displaced fracture of body of unspecified calcaneus**
CC Exclusion 7th character B see Appendix A PDX collection 1367
CC Exclusion 7th characters K & P see Appendix A PDX collection 0897
HAC 7th character B see Appendix B for HAC conditional logic

CC +7th **S92.014 Nondisplaced fracture of body of right calcaneus**
CC Exclusion 7th character B see Appendix A PDX collection 1367
CC Exclusion 7th characters K & P see Appendix A PDX collection 0897
HAC 7th character B see Appendix B for HAC conditional logic

CC +7th **S92.015 Nondisplaced fracture of body of left calcaneus**
CC Exclusion 7th character B see Appendix A PDX collection 1367
CC Exclusion 7th characters K & P see Appendix A PDX collection 0897
HAC 7th character B see Appendix B for HAC conditional logic

CC +7th **S92.016 Nondisplaced fracture of body of unspecified calcaneus**
CC Exclusion 7th character B see Appendix A PDX collection 1367
CC Exclusion 7th characters K & P see Appendix A PDX collection 0897
HAC 7th character B see Appendix B for HAC conditional logic

\+ **S92.02 Fracture of anterior process of calcaneus**

CC +7th **S92.021 Displaced fracture of anterior process of right calcaneus**
CC Exclusion 7th character B see Appendix A PDX collection 1367
CC Exclusion 7th characters K & P see Appendix A PDX collection 0897
HAC 7th character B see Appendix B for HAC conditional logic

CC +7th **S92.022 Displaced fracture of anterior process of left calcaneus**
CC Exclusion 7th character B see Appendix A PDX collection 1367
CC Exclusion 7th characters K & P see Appendix A PDX collection 0897
HAC 7th character B see Appendix B for HAC conditional logic

CC +7th **S92.023 Displaced fracture of anterior process of unspecified calcaneus**
CC Exclusion 7th character B see Appendix A PDX collection 1367
CC Exclusion 7th characters K & P see Appendix A PDX collection 0897
HAC 7th character B see Appendix B for HAC conditional logic

CC +7th **S92.024 Nondisplaced fracture of anterior process of right calcaneus**
- **CC Exclusion 7th character B see Appendix A PDX collection 1367**
- **CC Exclusion 7th characters K & P see Appendix A PDX collection 0897**
- HAC 7th character B see Appendix B for HAC conditional logic

CC +7th **S92.025 Nondisplaced fracture of anterior process of left calcaneus**
- **CC Exclusion 7th character B see Appendix A PDX collection 1367**
- **CC Exclusion 7th characters K & P see Appendix A PDX collection 0897**
- HAC 7th character B see Appendix B for HAC conditional logic

CC +7th **S92.026 Nondisplaced fracture of anterior process of unspecified calcaneus**
- **CC Exclusion 7th character B see Appendix A PDX collection 1367**
- **CC Exclusion 7th characters K & P see Appendix A PDX collection 0897**
- HAC 7th character B see Appendix B for HAC conditional logic

\+ **S92.03 Avulsion fracture of tuberosity of calcaneus**

CC +7th **S92.031 Displaced avulsion fracture of tuberosity of right calcaneus**
- **CC Exclusion 7th character B see Appendix A PDX collection 1367**
- **CC Exclusion 7th characters K & P see Appendix A PDX collection 0897**
- HAC 7th character B see Appendix B for HAC conditional logic

CC +7th **S92.032 Displaced avulsion fracture of tuberosity of left calcaneus**
- **CC Exclusion 7th character B see Appendix A PDX collection 1367**
- **CC Exclusion 7th characters K & P see Appendix A PDX collection 0897**
- HAC 7th character B see Appendix B for HAC conditional logic

CC +7th **S92.033 Displaced avulsion fracture of tuberosity of unspecified calcaneus**
- **CC Exclusion 7th character B see Appendix A PDX collection 1367**
- **CC Exclusion 7th characters K & P see Appendix A PDX collection 0897**
- HAC 7th character B see Appendix B for HAC conditional logic

CC +7th **S92.034 Nondisplaced avulsion fracture of tuberosity of right calcaneus**
- **CC Exclusion 7th character B see Appendix A PDX collection 1367**
- **CC Exclusion 7th characters K & P see Appendix A PDX collection 0897**
- HAC 7th character B see Appendix B for HAC conditional logic

CC +7th **S92.035 Nondisplaced avulsion fracture of tuberosity of left calcaneus**
- **CC Exclusion 7th character B see Appendix A PDX collection 1367**
- **CC Exclusion 7th characters K & P see Appendix A PDX collection 0897**
- HAC 7th character B see Appendix B for HAC conditional logic

CC +7th **S92.036 Nondisplaced avulsion fracture of tuberosity of unspecified calcaneus**
- **CC Exclusion 7th character B see Appendix A PDX collection 1367**
- **CC Exclusion 7th characters K & P see Appendix A PDX collection 0897**
- HAC 7th character B see Appendix B for HAC conditional logic

\+ **S92.04 Other fracture of tuberosity of calcaneus**

CC +7th **S92.041 Displaced other fracture of tuberosity of right calcaneus**
- **CC Exclusion 7th character B see Appendix A PDX collection 1367**
- **CC Exclusion 7th characters K & P see Appendix A PDX collection 0897**
- HAC 7th character B see Appendix B for HAC conditional logic

CC +7th **S92.042 Displaced other fracture of tuberosity of le calcaneus**
- **CC Exclusion 7th character B see Appendix A PDX collection 1367**
- **CC Exclusion 7th characters K & P see Appendix A PDX collection 0897**
- HAC 7th character B see Appendix B for HAC conditional logic

CC +7th **S92.043 Displaced other fracture of tuberosity of unspecified calcaneus**
- **CC Exclusion 7th character B see Appendix A PDX collection 1367**
- **CC Exclusion 7th characters K & P see Appendix A PDX collection 0897**
- HAC 7th character B see Appendix B for HAC conditional logic

CC +7th **S92.044 Nondisplaced other fracture of tuberosity o right calcaneus**
- **CC Exclusion 7th character B see Appendix A PDX collection 1367**
- **CC Exclusion 7th characters K & P see Appendix A PDX collection 0897**
- HAC 7th character B see Appendix B for HAC conditional logic

CC +7th **S92.045 Nondisplaced other fracture of tuberosity o left calcaneus**
- **CC Exclusion 7th character B see Appendix A PDX collection 1367**
- **CC Exclusion 7th characters K & P see Appendix A PDX collection 0897**
- HAC 7th character B see Appendix B for HAC conditional logic

CC +7th **S92.046 Nondisplaced other fracture of tuberosity o unspecified calcaneus**
- **CC Exclusion 7th character B see Appendix A PDX collection 1367**
- **CC Exclusion 7th characters K & P see Appendix A PDX collection 0897**
- HAC 7th character B see Appendix B for HAC conditional logic

\+ **S92.05 Other extraarticular fracture of calcaneus**

CC +7th **S92.051 Displaced other extraarticular fracture of right calcaneus**
- **CC Exclusion 7th character B see Appendix A PDX collection 1367**
- **CC Exclusion 7th characters K & P see Appendix A PDX collection 0897**
- HAC 7th character B see Appendix B for HAC conditional logic

CC +7th **S92.052 Displaced other extraarticular fracture of left calcaneus**
- **CC Exclusion 7th character B see Appendix A PDX collection 1367**
- **CC Exclusion 7th characters K & P see Appendix A PDX collection 0897**
- HAC 7th character B see Appendix B for HAC conditional logic

CC +7th **S92.053 Displaced other extraarticular fracture of unspecified calcaneus**
- **CC Exclusion 7th character B see Appendix A PDX collection 1367**
- **CC Exclusion 7th characters K & P see Appendix A PDX collection 0897**
- HAC 7th character B see Appendix B for HAC conditional logic

CC +7th **S92.054 Nondisplaced other extraarticular fracture of right calcaneus**
- **CC Exclusion 7th character B see Appendix A PDX collection 1367**
- **CC Exclusion 7th characters K & P see Appendix A PDX collection 0897**
- HAC 7th character B see Appendix B for HAC conditional logic

CC +7th **S92.055 Nondisplaced other extraarticular fracture of left calcaneus**
- **CC Exclusion 7th character B see Appendix A PDX collection 1367**
- **CC Exclusion 7th characters K & P see Appendix A PDX collection 0897**
- HAC 7th character B see Appendix B for HAC conditional logic

CC +7th **S92.056 Nondisplaced other extraarticular fracture of unspecified calcaneus**
CC Exclusion 7th character B see Appendix A PDX collection 1367
CC Exclusion 7th characters K & P see Appendix A PDX collection 0897
HAC 7th character B see Appendix B for HAC conditional logic

\+ **S92.06 Intraarticular fracture of calcaneus**

CC +7th **S92.061 Displaced intraarticular fracture of right calcaneus**
CC Exclusion 7th character B see Appendix A PDX collection 1367
CC Exclusion 7th characters K & P see Appendix A PDX collection 0897
HAC 7th character B see Appendix B for HAC conditional logic

CC +7th **S92.062 Displaced intraarticular fracture of left calcaneus**
CC Exclusion 7th character B see Appendix A PDX collection 1367
CC Exclusion 7th characters K & P see Appendix A PDX collection 0897
HAC 7th character B see Appendix B for HAC conditional logic

CC +7th **S92.063 Displaced intraarticular fracture of unspecified calcaneus**
CC Exclusion 7th character B see Appendix A PDX collection 1367
CC Exclusion 7th characters K & P see Appendix A PDX collection 0897
HAC 7th character B see Appendix B for HAC conditional logic

CC +7th **S92.064 Nondisplaced intraarticular fracture of right calcaneus**
CC Exclusion 7th character B see Appendix A PDX collection 1367
CC Exclusion 7th characters K & P see Appendix A PDX collection 0897
HAC 7th character B see Appendix B for HAC conditional logic

CC +7th **S92.065 Nondisplaced intraarticular fracture of left calcaneus**
CC Exclusion 7th character B see Appendix A PDX collection 1367
CC Exclusion 7th characters K & P see Appendix A PDX collection 0897
HAC 7th character B see Appendix B for HAC conditional logic

CC +7th **S92.066 Nondisplaced intraarticular fracture of unspecified calcaneus**
CC Exclusion 7th character B see Appendix A PDX collection 1367
CC Exclusion 7th characters K & P see Appendix A PDX collection 0897
HAC 7th character B see Appendix B for HAC conditional logic

\+ **S92.1 Fracture of talus**
Astragalus

\+ **S92.10 Unspecified fracture of talus**

CC +7th **S92.101 Unspecified fracture of right talus**
CC Exclusion 7th character B see Appendix A PDX collection 1368
CC Exclusion 7th characters K & P see Appendix A PDX collection 0897
HAC 7th character B see Appendix B for HAC conditional logic

CC +7th **S92.102 Unspecified fracture of left talus**
CC Exclusion 7th character B see Appendix A PDX collection 1368
CC Exclusion 7th characters K & P see Appendix A PDX collection 0897
HAC 7th character B see Appendix B for HAC conditional logic

CC +7th **S92.109 Unspecified fracture of unspecified talus**
CC Exclusion 7th character B see Appendix A PDX collection 1368
CC Exclusion 7th characters K & P see Appendix A PDX collection 0897
HAC 7th character B see Appendix B for HAC conditional logic

\+ **S92.11 Fracture of neck of talus**

CC +7th **S92.111 Displaced fracture of neck of right talus**
CC Exclusion 7th character B see Appendix A PDX collection 1368
CC Exclusion 7th characters K & P see Appendix A PDX collection 0897
HAC 7th character B see Appendix B for HAC conditional logic

CC +7th **S92.112 Displaced fracture of neck of left talus**
CC Exclusion 7th character B see Appendix A PDX collection 1368
CC Exclusion 7th characters K & P see Appendix A PDX collection 0897

CC +7th **S92.113 Displaced fracture of neck of unspecified talus**
CC Exclusion 7th character B see Appendix A PDX collection 1368
CC Exclusion 7th characters K & P see Appendix A PDX collection 0897
HAC 7th character B see Appendix B for HAC conditional logic

CC +7th **S92.114 Nondisplaced fracture of neck of right talus**
CC Exclusion 7th character B see Appendix A PDX collection 1368
CC Exclusion 7th characters K & P see Appendix A PDX collection 0897
HAC 7th character B see Appendix B for HAC conditional logic

CC +7th **S92.115 Nondisplaced fracture of neck of left talus**
CC Exclusion 7th character B see Appendix A PDX collection 1368
CC Exclusion 7th characters K & P see Appendix A PDX collection 0897
HAC 7th character B see Appendix B for HAC conditional logic

CC +7th **S92.116 Nondisplaced fracture of neck of unspecified talus**
CC Exclusion 7th character B see Appendix A PDX collection 1368
CC Exclusion 7th characters K & P see Appendix A PDX collection 0897
HAC 7th character B see Appendix B for HAC conditional logic

\+ **S92.12 Fracture of body of talus**

CC +7th **S92.121 Displaced fracture of body of right talus**
CC Exclusion 7th character B see Appendix A PDX collection 1368
CC Exclusion 7th characters K & P see Appendix A PDX collection 0897
HAC 7th character B see Appendix B for HAC conditional logic

CC +7th **S92.122 Displaced fracture of body of left talus**
CC Exclusion 7th character B see Appendix A PDX collection 1368
CC Exclusion 7th characters K & P see Appendix A PDX collection 0897
HAC 7th character B see Appendix B for HAC conditional logic

CC +7th **S92.123 Displaced fracture of body of unspecified talus**
CC Exclusion 7th character B see Appendix A PDX collection 1368
CC Exclusion 7th characters K & P see Appendix A PDX collection 0897
HAC 7th character B see Appendix B for HAC conditional logic

CC +7th **S92.124 Nondisplaced fracture of body of right talus**
CC Exclusion 7th character B see Appendix A PDX collection 1368
CC Exclusion 7th characters K & P see Appendix A PDX collection 0897
HAC 7th character B see Appendix B for HAC conditional logic

CC +7th **S92.125 Nondisplaced fracture of body of left talus**
CC Exclusion 7th character B see Appendix A PDX collection 1368
CC Exclusion 7th characters K & P see Appendix A PDX collection 0897
HAC 7th character B see Appendix B for HAC conditional logic

CC +7th **S92.126 Nondisplaced fracture of body of unspecified talus**
CC Exclusion 7th character B see Appendix A PDX collection 1368
CC Exclusion 7th characters K & P see Appendix A PDX collection 0897
HAC 7th character B see Appendix B for HAC conditional logic

\+ **S92.13 Fracture of posterior process of talus**

CC +7th **S92.131 Displaced fracture of posterior process of right talus**
CC Exclusion 7th character B see Appendix A PDX collection 1368
CC Exclusion 7th characters K & P see Appendix A PDX collection 0897
HAC 7th character B see Appendix B for HAC conditional logic

CC +7th **S92.132 Displaced fracture of posterior process of left talus**
CC Exclusion 7th character B see Appendix A PDX collection 1368
CC Exclusion 7th characters K & P see Appendix A PDX collection 0897
HAC 7th character B see Appendix B for HAC conditional logic

CC +7th **S92.133 Displaced fracture of posterior process of unspecified talus**
CC Exclusion 7th character B see Appendix A PDX collection 1368
CC Exclusion 7th characters K & P see Appendix A PDX collection 0897
HAC 7th character B see Appendix B for HAC conditional logic

CC +7th **S92.134 Nondisplaced fracture of posterior process of right talus**
CC Exclusion 7th character B see Appendix A PDX collection 1368
CC Exclusion 7th characters K & P see Appendix A PDX collection 0897
HAC 7th character B see Appendix B for HAC conditional logic

CC +7th **S92.135 Nondisplaced fracture of posterior process of left talus**
CC Exclusion 7th character B see Appendix A PDX collection 1368
CC Exclusion 7th characters K & P see Appendix A PDX collection 0897
HAC 7th character B see Appendix B for HAC conditional logic

CC +7th **S92.136 Nondisplaced fracture of posterior process of unspecified talus**
CC Exclusion 7th character B see Appendix A PDX collection 1368
CC Exclusion 7th characters K & P see Appendix A PDX collection 0897
HAC 7th character B see Appendix B for HAC conditional logic

\+ **S92.14 Dome fracture of talus**
Excludes1: *osteochondritis dissecans (M93.2)*

CC +7th **S92.141 Displaced dome fracture of right talus**
CC Exclusion 7th character B see Appendix A PDX collection 1368
CC Exclusion 7th characters K & P see Appendix A PDX collection 0897
HAC 7th character B see Appendix B for HAC conditional logic

CC +7th **S92.142 Displaced dome fracture of left talus**
CC Exclusion 7th character B see Appendix A PDX collection 1368
CC Exclusion 7th characters K & P see Appendix A PDX collection 0897
HAC 7th character B see Appendix B for HAC conditional logic

CC +7th **S92.143 Displaced dome fracture of unspecified talus**
CC Exclusion 7th character B see Appendix A PDX collection 1368
CC Exclusion 7th characters K & P see Appendix A PDX collection 0897
HAC 7th character B see Appendix B for HAC conditional logic

CC +7th **S92.144 Nondisplaced dome fracture of right talus**
CC Exclusion 7th character B see Appendix A PDX collection 1368
CC Exclusion 7th characters K & P see Appendix A PDX collection 0897
HAC 7th character B see Appendix B for HAC conditional logic

CC +7th **S92.145 Nondisplaced dome fracture of left talus**
CC Exclusion 7th character B see Appendix A PDX collection 1368
CC Exclusion 7th characters K & P see Appendix A PDX collection 0897
HAC 7th character B see Appendix B for HAC conditional logic

CC +7th **S92.146 Nondisplaced dome fracture of unspecified talus**
CC Exclusion 7th character B see Appendix A PDX collection 1368
CC Exclusion 7th characters K & P see Appendix A PDX collection 0897
HAC 7th character B see Appendix B for HAC conditional logic

\+ **S92.15 Avulsion fracture (chip fracture) of talus**

CC +7th **S92.151 Displaced avulsion fracture (chip fracture) of right talus**
CC Exclusion 7th character B see Appendix A PDX collection 1368
CC Exclusion 7th characters K & P see Appendix A PDX collection 0897
HAC 7th character B see Appendix B for HAC conditional logic

CC +7th **S92.152 Displaced avulsion fracture (chip fracture) of left talus**
CC Exclusion 7th character B see Appendix A PDX collection 1368
CC Exclusion 7th characters K & P see Appendix A PDX collection 0897
HAC 7th character B see Appendix B for HAC conditional logic

CC +7th **S92.153 Displaced avulsion fracture (chip fracture) of unspecified talus**
CC Exclusion 7th character B see Appendix A PDX collection 1368
CC Exclusion 7th characters K & P see Appendix A PDX collection 0897
HAC 7th character B see Appendix B for HAC conditional logic

CC +7th **S92.154 Nondisplaced avulsion fracture (chip fracture) of right talus**
CC Exclusion 7th character B see Appendix A PDX collection 1368
CC Exclusion 7th characters K & P see Appendix A PDX collection 0897
HAC 7th character B see Appendix B for HAC conditional logic

CC +7th **S92.155 Nondisplaced avulsion fracture (chip fracture) of left talus**
CC Exclusion 7th character B see Appendix A PDX collection 1368
CC Exclusion 7th characters K & P see Appendix A PDX collection 0897
HAC 7th character B see Appendix B for HAC conditional logic

CC +7th **S92.156 Nondisplaced avulsion fracture (chip fracture) of unspecified talus**
CC Exclusion 7th character B see Appendix A PDX collection 1368
CC Exclusion 7th characters K & P see Appendix A PDX collection 0897
HAC 7th character B see Appendix B for HAC conditional logic

\+ **S92.19 Other fracture of talus**

CC +7th **S92.191 Other fracture of right talus**
CC Exclusion 7th character B see Appendix A PDX collection 1368
CC Exclusion 7th characters K & P see Appendix A PDX collection 0897
HAC 7th character B see Appendix B for HAC conditional logic

CC +7th **S92.192 Other fracture of left talus**
CC Exclusion 7th character B see Appendix A PDX collection 1368
CC Exclusion 7th characters K & P see Appendix A PDX collection 0897
HAC 7th character B see Appendix B for HAC conditional logic

CC +7th **S92.199 Other fracture of unspecified talus**
CC Exclusion 7th character B see Appendix A PDX collection 1368
CC Exclusion 7th characters K & P see Appendix A PDX collection 0897
HAC 7th character B see Appendix B for HAC conditional logic

+ **S92.2 Fracture of other and unspecified tarsal bone(s)**

+ **S92.20 Fracture of unspecified tarsal bone(s)**

CC +7th **S92.201 Fracture of unspecified tarsal bone(s) of right foot**
CC Exclusion 7th character B see Appendix A PDX collection 1369
CC Exclusion 7th characters K & P see Appendix A PDX collection 0897
HAC 7th character B see Appendix B for HAC conditional logic

CC +7th **S92.202 Fracture of unspecified tarsal bone(s) of left foot**
CC Exclusion 7th character B see Appendix A PDX collection 1369
CC Exclusion 7th characters K & P see Appendix A PDX collection 0897
HAC 7th character B see Appendix B for HAC conditional logic

CC +7th **S92.209 Fracture of unspecified tarsal bone(s) of unspecified foot**
CC Exclusion 7th character B see Appendix A PDX collection 1369
CC Exclusion 7th characters K & P see Appendix A PDX collection 0897
HAC 7th character B see Appendix B for HAC conditional logic

+ **S92.21 Fracture of cuboid bone**

CC +7th **S92.211 Displaced fracture of cuboid bone of right foot**
CC Exclusion 7th character B see Appendix A PDX collection 1368
CC Exclusion 7th characters K & P see Appendix A PDX collection 0897
HAC 7th character B see Appendix B for HAC conditional logic

CC +7th **S92.212 Displaced fracture of cuboid bone of left foot**
CC Exclusion 7th character B see Appendix A PDX collection 1368
CC Exclusion 7th characters K & P see Appendix A PDX collection 0897
HAC 7th character B see Appendix B for HAC conditional logic

CC +7th **S92.213 Displaced fracture of cuboid bone of unspecified foot**
CC Exclusion 7th character B see Appendix A PDX collection 1368
CC Exclusion 7th characters K & P see Appendix A PDX collection 0897
HAC 7th character B see Appendix B for HAC conditional logic

CC +7th **S92.214 Nondisplaced fracture of cuboid bone of right foot**
CC Exclusion 7th character B see Appendix A PDX collection 1368
CC Exclusion 7th characters K & P see Appendix A PDX collection 0897
HAC 7th character B see Appendix B for HAC conditional logic

CC +7th **S92.215 Nondisplaced fracture of cuboid bone of left foot**
CC Exclusion 7th character B see Appendix A PDX collection 1368
CC Exclusion 7th characters K & P see Appendix A PDX collection 0897
HAC 7th character B see Appendix B for HAC conditional logic

CC +7th **S92.216 Nondisplaced fracture of cuboid bone of unspecified foot**
CC Exclusion 7th character B see Appendix A PDX collection 1368
CC Exclusion 7th characters K & P see Appendix A PDX collection 0897
HAC 7th character B see Appendix B for HAC conditional logic

+ **S92.22 Fracture of lateral cuneiform**

CC +7th **S92.221 Displaced fracture of lateral cuneiform of right foot**
CC Exclusion 7th character B see Appendix A PDX collection 1368
CC Exclusion 7th characters K & P see Appendix A PDX collection 0897
HAC 7th character B see Appendix B for HAC conditional logic

CC +7th **S92.222 Displaced fracture of lateral cuneiform of left foot**
CC Exclusion 7th character B see Appendix A PDX collection 1368
CC Exclusion 7th characters K & P see Appendix A PDX collection 0897
HAC 7th character B see Appendix B for HAC conditional logic

CC +7th **S92.223 Displaced fracture of lateral cuneiform of unspecified foot**
CC Exclusion 7th character B see Appendix A PDX collection 1368
CC Exclusion 7th characters K & P see Appendix A PDX collection 0897
HAC 7th character B see Appendix B for HAC conditional logic

CC +7th **S92.224 Nondisplaced fracture of lateral cuneiform of right foot**
CC Exclusion 7th character B see Appendix A PDX collection 1368
CC Exclusion 7th characters K & P see Appendix A PDX collection 0897
HAC 7th character B see Appendix B for HAC conditional logic

CC +7th **S92.225 Nondisplaced fracture of lateral cuneiform of left foot**
CC Exclusion 7th character B see Appendix A PDX collection 1368
CC Exclusion 7th characters K & P see Appendix A PDX collection 0897
HAC 7th character B see Appendix B for HAC conditional logic

CC +7th **S92.226 Nondisplaced fracture of lateral cuneiform of unspecified foot**
CC Exclusion 7th character B see Appendix A PDX collection 1368
CC Exclusion 7th characters K & P see Appendix A PDX collection 0897
HAC 7th character B see Appendix B for HAC conditional logic

+ **S92.23 Fracture of intermediate cuneiform**

CC +7th **S92.231 Displaced fracture of intermediate cuneiform of right foot**
CC Exclusion 7th character B see Appendix A PDX collection 1368
CC Exclusion 7th characters K & P see Appendix A PDX collection 0897
HAC 7th character B see Appendix B for HAC conditional logic

CC +7th **S92.232 Displaced fracture of intermediate cuneiform of left foot**
CC Exclusion 7th character B see Appendix A PDX collection 1368
CC Exclusion 7th characters K & P see Appendix A PDX collection 0897
HAC 7th character B see Appendix B for HAC conditional logic

CC +7th **S92.233 Displaced fracture of intermediate cuneiform of unspecified foot**
CC Exclusion 7th character B see Appendix A PDX collection 1368
CC Exclusion 7th characters K & P see Appendix A PDX collection 0897
HAC 7th character B see Appendix B for HAC conditional logic

CC +7th **S92.234 Nondisplaced fracture of intermediate cuneiform of right foot**
CC Exclusion 7th character B see Appendix A PDX collection 1368
CC Exclusion 7th characters K & P see Appendix A PDX collection 0897
HAC 7th character B see Appendix B for HAC conditional logic

CC +7th **S92.235 Nondisplaced fracture of intermediate cuneiform of left foot**
CC Exclusion 7th character B see Appendix A PDX collection 1368
CC Exclusion 7th characters K & P see Appendix A PDX collection 0897
HAC 7th character B see Appendix B for HAC conditional logic

CC +7th **S92.236 Nondisplaced fracture of intermediate cuneiform of unspecified foot**
CC Exclusion 7th character B see Appendix A PDX collection 1368
CC Exclusion 7th characters K & P see Appendix A PDX collection 0897
HAC 7th character B see Appendix B for HAC conditional logic

\+ **S92.24 Fracture of medial cuneiform**

CC +7th **S92.241 Displaced fracture of medial cuneiform of right foot**
CC Exclusion 7th character B see Appendix A PDX collection 1368
CC Exclusion 7th characters K & P see Appendix A PDX collection 0897
HAC 7th character B see Appendix B for HAC conditional logic

CC +7th **S92.242 Displaced fracture of medial cuneiform of left foot**
CC Exclusion 7th character B see Appendix A PDX collection 1368
CC Exclusion 7th characters K & P see Appendix A PDX collection 0897
HAC 7th character B see Appendix B for HAC conditional logic

CC +7th **S92.243 Displaced fracture of medial cuneiform of unspecified foot**
CC Exclusion 7th character B see Appendix A PDX collection 1368
CC Exclusion 7th characters K & P see Appendix A PDX collection 0897
HAC 7th character B see Appendix B for HAC conditional logic

CC +7th **S92.244 Nondisplaced fracture of medial cuneiform of right foot**
CC Exclusion 7th character B see Appendix A PDX collection 1368
CC Exclusion 7th characters K & P see Appendix A PDX collection 0897
HAC 7th character B see Appendix B for HAC conditional logic

CC +7th **S92.245 Nondisplaced fracture of medial cuneiform of left foot**
CC Exclusion 7th character B see Appendix A PDX collection 1368
CC Exclusion 7th characters K & P see Appendix A PDX collection 0897
HAC 7th character B see Appendix B for HAC conditional logic

CC +7th **S92.246 Nondisplaced fracture of medial cuneiform of unspecified foot**
CC Exclusion 7th character B see Appendix A PDX collection 1368
CC Exclusion 7th characters K & P see Appendix A PDX collection 0897
HAC 7th character B see Appendix B for HAC conditional logic

\+ **S92.25 Fracture of navicular [scaphoid] of foot**

CC +7th **S92.251 Displaced fracture of navicular [scaphoid] of right foot**
CC Exclusion 7th character B see Appendix A PDX collection 1368
CC Exclusion 7th characters K & P see Appendix A PDX collection 0897
HAC 7th character B see Appendix B for HAC conditional logic

CC +7th **S92.252 Displaced fracture of navicular [scaphoid] of left foot**
CC Exclusion 7th character B see Appendix A PDX collection 1368
CC Exclusion 7th characters K & P see Appendix A PDX collection 0897
HAC 7th character B see Appendix B for HAC conditional logic

CC +7th **S92.253 Displaced fracture of navicular [scaphoid] of unspecified foot**
CC Exclusion 7th character B see Appendix A PDX collection 1368
CC Exclusion 7th characters K & P see Appendix A PDX collection 0897
HAC 7th character B see Appendix B for HAC conditional logic

CC +7th **S92.254 Nondisplaced fracture of navicular [scaphoid] of right foot**
CC Exclusion 7th character B see Appendix A PDX collection 1368
CC Exclusion 7th characters K & P see Appendix A PDX collection 0897
HAC 7th character B see Appendix B for HAC conditional logic

CC +7th **S92.255 Nondisplaced fracture of navicular [scaphoid] of left foot**
CC Exclusion 7th character B see Appendix A PDX collection 1368
CC Exclusion 7th characters K & P see Appendix A PDX collection 0897
HAC 7th character B see Appendix B for HAC conditional logic

CC +7th **S92.256 Nondisplaced fracture of navicular [scaphoid] of unspecified foot**
CC Exclusion 7th character B see Appendix A PDX collection 1368
CC Exclusion 7th characters K & P see Appendix A PDX collection 0897
HAC 7th character B see Appendix B for HAC conditional logic

\+ **S92.3 Fracture of metatarsal bone(s)**

\+ **S92.30 Fracture of unspecified metatarsal bone(s)**

CC +7th **S92.301 Fracture of unspecified metatarsal bone(s), right foot**
CC Exclusion 7th character B see Appendix A PDX collection 1368
CC Exclusion 7th characters K & P see Appendix A PDX collection 0897
HAC 7th character B see Appendix B for HAC conditional logic

CC +7th **S92.302 Fracture of unspecified metatarsal bone(s), left foot**
CC Exclusion 7th character B see Appendix A PDX collection 1368
CC Exclusion 7th characters K & P see Appendix A PDX collection 0897
HAC 7th character B see Appendix B for HAC conditional logic

CC +7th **S92.309 Fracture of unspecified metatarsal bone(s), unspecified foot**
CC Exclusion 7th character B see Appendix A PDX collection 1368
CC Exclusion 7th characters K & P see Appendix A PDX collection 0897

\+ **S92.31 Fracture of first metatarsal bone**

CC +7th **S92.311 Displaced fracture of first metatarsal bone, right foot**
CC Exclusion 7th character B see Appendix A PDX collection 1368
CC Exclusion 7th characters K & P see Appendix A PDX collection 0897
HAC 7th character B see Appendix B for HAC conditional logic

CC +7th **S92.312 Displaced fracture of first metatarsal bone, left foot**
CC Exclusion 7th character B see Appendix A PDX collection 1368
CC Exclusion 7th characters K & P see Appendix A PDX collection 0897
HAC 7th character B see Appendix B for HAC conditional logic

CC +7th **S92.313 Displaced fracture of first metatarsal bone, unspecified foot**
CC Exclusion 7th character B see Appendix A PDX collection 1368
CC Exclusion 7th characters K & P see Appendix A PDX collection 0897
HAC 7th character B see Appendix B for HAC conditional logic

CC +7th **S92.314 Nondisplaced fracture of first metatarsal bone, right foot**
CC Exclusion 7th character B see Appendix A PDX collection 1368
CC Exclusion 7th characters K & P see Appendix A PDX collection 0897
HAC 7th character B see Appendix B for HAC conditional logic

CC +7th **S92.315 Nondisplaced fracture of first metatarsal bone, left foot**
CC Exclusion 7th character B see Appendix A PDX collection 1368
CC Exclusion 7th characters K & P see Appendix A PDX collection 0897
HAC 7th character B see Appendix B for HAC conditional logic

CC +7th **S92.316 Nondisplaced fracture of first metatarsal bone, unspecified foot**
CC Exclusion 7th character B see Appendix A PDX collection 1368
CC Exclusion 7th characters K & P see Appendix A PDX collection 0897
HAC 7th character B see Appendix B for HAC conditional logic

\+ **S92.32 Fracture of second metatarsal bone**

CC +7th **S92.321 Displaced fracture of second metatarsal bone, right foot**
CC Exclusion 7th character B see Appendix A PDX collection 1368
CC Exclusion 7th characters K & P see Appendix A PDX collection 0897
HAC 7th character B see Appendix B for HAC conditional logic

CC +7th **S92.322 Displaced fracture of second metatarsal bone, left foot**
CC Exclusion 7th character B see Appendix A PDX collection 1368
CC Exclusion 7th characters K & P see Appendix A PDX collection 0897
HAC 7th character B see Appendix B for HAC conditional logic

CC +7th **S92.323 Displaced fracture of second metatarsal bone, unspecified foot**
CC Exclusion 7th character B see Appendix A PDX collection 1368
CC Exclusion 7th characters K & P see Appendix A PDX collection 0897
HAC 7th character B see Appendix B for HAC conditional logic

CC +7th **S92.324 Nondisplaced fracture of second metatarsal bone, right foot**
CC Exclusion 7th character B see Appendix A PDX collection 1368
CC Exclusion 7th characters K & P see Appendix A PDX collection 0897
HAC 7th character B see Appendix B for HAC conditional logic

CC +7th **S92.325 Nondisplaced fracture of second metatarsal bone, left foot**
CC Exclusion 7th character B see Appendix A PDX collection 1368
CC Exclusion 7th characters K & P see Appendix A PDX collection 0897
HAC 7th character B see Appendix B for HAC conditional logic

CC +7th **S92.326 Nondisplaced fracture of second metatarsal bone, unspecified foot**
CC Exclusion 7th character B see Appendix A PDX collection 1368
CC Exclusion 7th characters K & P see Appendix A PDX collection 0897
HAC 7th character B see Appendix B for HAC conditional logic

\+ **S92.33 Fracture of third metatarsal bone**

CC +7th **S92.331 Displaced fracture of third metatarsal bone, right foot**
CC Exclusion 7th character B see Appendix A PDX collection 1368
CC Exclusion 7th characters K & P see Appendix A PDX collection 0897
HAC 7th character B see Appendix B for HAC conditional logic

CC +7th **S92.332 Displaced fracture of third metatarsal bone, left foot**
CC Exclusion 7th character B see Appendix A PDX collection 1368
CC Exclusion 7th characters K & P see Appendix A PDX collection 0897
HAC 7th character B see Appendix B for HAC conditional logic

CC +7th **S92.333 Displaced fracture of third metatarsal bone, unspecified foot**
CC Exclusion 7th character B see Appendix A PDX collection 1368
CC Exclusion 7th characters K & P see Appendix A PDX collection 0897
HAC 7th character B see Appendix B for HAC conditional logic

CC +7th **S92.334 Nondisplaced fracture of third metatarsal bone, right foot**
CC Exclusion 7th character B see Appendix A PDX collection 1368
CC Exclusion 7th characters K & P see Appendix A PDX collection 0897
HAC 7th character B see Appendix B for HAC conditional logic

CC +7th **S92.335 Nondisplaced fracture of third metatarsal bone, left foot**
CC Exclusion 7th character B see Appendix A PDX collection 1368
CC Exclusion 7th characters K & P see Appendix A PDX collection 0897
HAC 7th character B see Appendix B for HAC conditional logic

CC +7th **S92.336 Nondisplaced fracture of third metatarsal bone, unspecified foot**
CC Exclusion 7th character B see Appendix A PDX collection 1368
CC Exclusion 7th characters K & P see Appendix A PDX collection 0897
HAC 7th character B see Appendix B for HAC conditional logic

\+ **S92.34 Fracture of fourth metatarsal bone**

CC +7th **S92.341 Displaced fracture of fourth metatarsal bone, right foot**
CC Exclusion 7th character B see Appendix A PDX collection 1368
CC Exclusion 7th characters K & P see Appendix A PDX collection 0897
HAC 7th character B see Appendix B for HAC conditional logic

CC +7th **S92.342 Displaced fracture of fourth metatarsal bone, left foot**
CC Exclusion 7th character B see Appendix A PDX collection 1368
CC Exclusion 7th characters K & P see Appendix A PDX collection 0897
HAC 7th character B see Appendix B for HAC conditional logic

CC +7th **S92.343 Displaced fracture of fourth metatarsal bone, unspecified foot**
CC Exclusion 7th character B see Appendix A PDX collection 1368
CC Exclusion 7th characters K & P see Appendix A PDX collection 0897
HAC 7th character B see Appendix B for HAC conditional logic

CC +7th **S92.344 Nondisplaced fracture of fourth metatarsal bone, right foot**
CC Exclusion 7th character B see Appendix A PDX collection 1368
CC Exclusion 7th characters K & P see Appendix A PDX collection 0897
HAC 7th character B see Appendix B for HAC conditional logic

CC +7th **S92.345 Nondisplaced fracture of fourth metatarsal bone, left foot**
CC Exclusion 7th character B see Appendix A PDX collection 1368
CC Exclusion 7th characters K & P see Appendix A PDX collection 0897
HAC 7th character B see Appendix B for HAC conditional logic

CC +7th **S92.346 Nondisplaced fracture of fourth metatarsal bone, unspecified foot**
CC Exclusion 7th character B see Appendix A PDX collection 1368
CC Exclusion 7th characters K & P see Appendix A PDX collection 0897
HAC 7th character B see Appendix B for HAC conditional logic

+ **S92.35 Fracture of fifth metatarsal bone**

CC +7th **S92.351 Displaced fracture of fifth metatarsal bone, right foot**
CC Exclusion 7th character B see Appendix A PDX collection 1368
CC Exclusion 7th characters K & P see Appendix A PDX collection 0897
HAC 7th character B see Appendix B for HAC conditional logic

CC +7th **S92.352 Displaced fracture of fifth metatarsal bone, left foot**
CC Exclusion 7th character B see Appendix A PDX collection 1368
CC Exclusion 7th characters K & P see Appendix A PDX collection 0897
HAC 7th character B see Appendix B for HAC conditional logic

CC +7th **S92.353 Displaced fracture of fifth metatarsal bone, unspecified foot**
CC Exclusion 7th character B see Appendix A PDX collection 1368
CC Exclusion 7th characters K & P see Appendix A PDX collection 0897
HAC 7th character B see Appendix B for HAC conditional logic

CC +7th **S92.354 Nondisplaced fracture of fifth metatarsal bone, right foot**
CC Exclusion 7th character B see Appendix A PDX collection 1368
CC Exclusion 7th characters K & P see Appendix A PDX collection 0897
HAC 7th character B see Appendix B for HAC conditional logic

CC +7th **S92.355 Nondisplaced fracture of fifth metatarsal bone, left foot**
CC Exclusion 7th character B see Appendix A PDX collection 1368
CC Exclusion 7th characters K & P see Appendix A PDX collection 0897
HAC 7th character B see Appendix B for HAC conditional logic

CC +7th **S92.356 Nondisplaced fracture of fifth metatarsal bone, unspecified foot**
CC Exclusion 7th character B see Appendix A PDX collection 1368
CC Exclusion 7th characters K & P see Appendix A PDX collection 0897
HAC 7th character B see Appendix B for HAC conditional logic

+ **S92.4 Fracture of great toe**

+ **S92.40 Unspecified fracture of great toe**

CC +7th **S92.401 Displaced unspecified fracture of right great toe**
CC Exclusion 7th characters K & P see Appendix A PDX collection 0897

CC +7th **S92.402 Displaced unspecified fracture of left great toe**
CC Exclusion 7th characters K & P see Appendix A PDX collection 0897

CC +7th **S92.403 Displaced unspecified fracture of unspecified great toe**
CC Exclusion 7th characters K & P see Appendix A PDX collection 0897

CC +7th **S92.404 Nondisplaced unspecified fracture of right great toe**
CC Exclusion 7th characters K & P see Appendix A PDX collection 0897

CC +7th **S92.405 Nondisplaced unspecified fracture of left great toe**
CC Exclusion 7th characters K & P see Appendix A PDX collection 0897

CC +7th **S92.406 Nondisplaced unspecified fracture of unspecified great toe**
CC Exclusion 7th characters K & P see Appendix A PDX collection 0897

+ **S92.41 Fracture of proximal phalanx of great toe**

CC +7th **S92.411 Displaced fracture of proximal phalanx of right great toe**
CC Exclusion 7th characters K & P see Appendix A PDX collection 0897

CC +7th **S92.412 Displaced fracture of proximal phalanx of left great toe**
CC Exclusion 7th characters K & P see Appendix A PDX collection 0897

CC +7th **S92.413 Displaced fracture of proximal phalanx of unspecified great toe**
CC Exclusion 7th characters K & P see Appendix A PDX collection 0897

CC +7th **S92.414 Nondisplaced fracture of proximal phalanx of right great toe**
CC Exclusion 7th characters K & P see Appendix A PDX collection 0897

CC +7th **S92.415 Nondisplaced fracture of proximal phalanx of left great toe**
CC Exclusion 7th characters K & P see Appendix A PDX collection 0897

CC +7th **S92.416 Nondisplaced fracture of proximal phalanx of unspecified great toe**
CC Exclusion 7th characters K & P see Appendix A PDX collection 0897

+ **S92.42 Fracture of distal phalanx of great toe**

CC +7th **S92.421 Displaced fracture of distal phalanx of right great toe**
CC Exclusion 7th characters K & P see Appendix A PDX collection 0897

CC +7th **S92.422 Displaced fracture of distal phalanx of left great toe**
CC Exclusion 7th characters K & P see Appendix A PDX collection 0897

CC +7th **S92.423 Displaced fracture of distal phalanx of unspecified great toe**
CC Exclusion 7th characters K & P see Appendix A PDX collection 0897

CC +7th **S92.424 Nondisplaced fracture of distal phalanx of right great toe**
CC Exclusion 7th characters K & P see Appendix A PDX collection 0897

CC +7th **S92.425 Nondisplaced fracture of distal phalanx of left great toe**
CC Exclusion 7th characters K & P see Appendix A PDX collection 0897

CC +7th **S92.426 Nondisplaced fracture of distal phalanx of unspecified great toe**
CC Exclusion 7th characters K & P see Appendix A PDX collection 0897

+ **S92.49 Other fracture of great toe**

CC +7th **S92.491 Other fracture of right great toe**
CC Exclusion 7th characters K & P see Appendix A PDX collection 0897

CC +7th **S92.492 Other fracture of left great toe**
CC Exclusion 7th characters K & P see Appendix A PDX collection 0897

CC +7th **S92.499 Other fracture of unspecified great toe**
CC Exclusion 7th characters K & P see Appendix A PDX collection 0897

+ **S92.5 Fracture of lesser toe(s)**

+ **S92.50 Unspecified fracture of lesser toe(s)**

CC +7th **S92.501 Displaced unspecified fracture of right lesser toe(s)**
CC Exclusion 7th characters K & P see Appendix A PDX collection 0897

CC +7th **S92.502 Displaced unspecified fracture of left lesser toe(s)**
CC Exclusion 7th characters K & P see Appendix A PDX collection 0897

CC +7th **S92.503 Displaced unspecified fracture of unspecified lesser toe(s)**
CC Exclusion 7th characters K & P see Appendix A PDX collection 0897

CC +7th **S92.504 Nondisplaced unspecified fracture of right lesser toe(s)**
CC Exclusion 7th characters K & P see Appendix A PDX collection 0897

CC +7th **S92.505 Nondisplaced unspecified fracture of left lesser toe(s)**
CC Exclusion 7th characters K & P see Appendix A PDX collection 0897

CC +7th **S92.506 Nondisplaced unspecified fracture of unspecified lesser toe(s)**
CC Exclusion 7th characters K & P see Appendix A PDX collection 0897

+ **S92.51 Fracture of proximal phalanx of lesser toe(s)**

CC +7th **S92.511 Displaced fracture of proximal phalanx of right lesser toe(s)**
CC Exclusion 7th characters K & P see Appendix A PDX collection 0897

CC +7th **S92.512 Displaced fracture of proximal phalanx of left lesser toe(s)**
CC Exclusion 7th characters K & P see Appendix A PDX collection 0897

CC +7th **S92.513 Displaced fracture of proximal phalanx of unspecified lesser toe(s)**
CC Exclusion 7th characters K & P see Appendix A PDX collection 0897

CC +7th **S92.514 Nondisplaced fracture of proximal phalanx of right lesser toe(s)**
CC Exclusion 7th characters K & P see Appendix A PDX collection 0897

CC +7th **S92.515 Nondisplaced fracture of proximal phalanx of left lesser toe(s)**
CC Exclusion 7th characters K & P see Appendix A PDX collection 0897

CC +7th **S92.516 Nondisplaced fracture of proximal phalanx of unspecified lesser toe(s)**
CC Exclusion 7th characters K & P see Appendix A PDX collection 0897

\+ **S92.52 Fracture of medial phalanx of lesser toe(s)**

CC +7th **S92.521 Displaced fracture of medial phalanx of right lesser toe(s)**
CC Exclusion 7th characters K & P see Appendix A PDX collection 0897

CC +7th **S92.522 Displaced fracture of medial phalanx of left lesser toe(s)**
CC Exclusion 7th characters K & P see Appendix A PDX collection 0897

CC +7th **S92.523 Displaced fracture of medial phalanx of unspecified lesser toe(s)**
CC Exclusion 7th characters K & P see Appendix A PDX collection 0897

CC +7th **S92.524 Nondisplaced fracture of medial phalanx of right lesser toe(s)**
CC Exclusion 7th characters K & P see Appendix A PDX collection 0897

CC +7th **S92.525 Nondisplaced fracture of medial phalanx of left lesser toe(s)**
CC Exclusion 7th characters K & P see Appendix A PDX collection 0897

CC +7th **S92.526 Nondisplaced fracture of medial phalanx of unspecified lesser toe(s)**
CC Exclusion 7th characters K & P see Appendix A PDX collection 0897

\+ **S92.53 Fracture of distal phalanx of lesser toe(s)**

CC +7th **S92.531 Displaced fracture of distal phalanx of right lesser toe(s)**
CC Exclusion 7th characters K & P see Appendix A PDX collection 0897

CC +7th **S92.532 Displaced fracture of distal phalanx of left lesser toe(s)**
CC Exclusion 7th characters K & P see Appendix A PDX collection 0897

CC +7th **S92.533 Displaced fracture of distal phalanx of unspecified lesser toe(s)**
CC Exclusion 7th characters K & P see Appendix A PDX collection 0897

CC +7th **S92.534 Nondisplaced fracture of distal phalanx of right lesser toe(s)**
CC Exclusion 7th characters K & P see Appendix A PDX collection 0897

CC +7th **S92.535 Nondisplaced fracture of distal phalanx of left lesser toe(s)**
CC Exclusion 7th characters K & P see Appendix A PDX collection 0897

CC +7th **S92.536 Nondisplaced fracture of distal phalanx of unspecified lesser toe(s)**
CC Exclusion 7th characters K & P see Appendix A PDX collection 0897

\+ **S92.59 Other fracture of lesser toe(s)**

CC +7th **S92.591 Other fracture of right lesser toe(s)**
CC Exclusion 7th characters K & P see Appendix A PDX collection 0897

CC +7th **S92.592 Other fracture of left lesser toe(s)**
CC Exclusion 7th characters K & P see Appendix A PDX collection 0897

CC +7th **S92.599 Other fracture of unspecified lesser toe(s)**
CC Exclusion 7th characters K & P see Appendix A PDX collection 0897

\+ **S92.9 Unspecified fracture of foot and toe**

\+ **S92.90 Unspecified fracture of foot**

CC +7th **S92.901 Unspecified fracture of right foot**
CC Exclusion 7th character B see Appendix A PDX collection 1369
CC Exclusion 7th characters K & P see Appendix A PDX collection 0897
HAC 7th character B see Appendix B for HAC conditional logic

CC +7th **S92.902 Unspecified fracture of left foot**
CC Exclusion 7th character B see Appendix A PDX collection 1369
CC Exclusion 7th characters K & P see Appendix A PDX collection 0897
HAC 7th character B see Appendix B for HAC conditional logic

CC +7th **S92.909 Unspecified fracture of unspecified foot**
CC Exclusion 7th character B see Appendix A PDX collection 1369
CC Exclusion 7th characters K & P see Appendix A PDX collection 0897
HAC 7th character B see Appendix B for HAC conditional logic

\+ **S92.91 Unspecified fracture of toe**

CC +7th **S92.911 Unspecified fracture of right toe(s)**
CC Exclusion 7th characters K & P see Appendix A PDX collection 0897

CC +7th **S92.912 Unspecified fracture of left toe(s)**
CC Exclusion 7th characters K & P see Appendix A PDX collection 0897

CC +7th **S92.919 Unspecified fracture of unspecified toe(s)**
CC Exclusion 7th characters K & P see Appendix A PDX collection 0897

S93 Dislocation and sprain of joints and ligaments at ankle, foot and toe level

Includes: avulsion of joint or ligament of ankle, foot and toe
laceration of cartilage, joint or ligament of ankle, foot and toe
sprain of cartilage, joint or ligament of ankle, foot and toe
traumatic hemarthrosis of joint or ligament of ankle, foot and toe
traumatic rupture of joint or ligament of ankle, foot and toe
traumatic subluxation of joint or ligament of ankle, foot and toe
traumatic tear of joint or ligament of ankle, foot and toe

Code also any associated open wound

Excludes2: *strain of muscle and tendon of ankle and foot (S96.-)*

The appropriate 7th character is to be added to each code from category S93
A initial encounter
D subsequent encounter
S sequela

\+ **S93.0 Subluxation and dislocation of ankle joint**
Subluxation and dislocation of astragalus
Subluxation and dislocation of fibula, lower end
Subluxation and dislocation of talus
Subluxation and dislocation of tibia, lower end

X+7th **S93.01 Subluxation of right ankle joint**
X+7th **S93.02 Subluxation of left ankle joint**
X+7th **S93.03 Subluxation of unspecified ankle joint**
X+7th **S93.04 Dislocation of right ankle joint**
X+7th **S93.05 Dislocation of left ankle joint**
X+7th **S93.06 Dislocation of unspecified ankle joint**

\+ **S93.1 Subluxation and dislocation of toe**

\+ **S93.10 Unspecified subluxation and dislocation of toe**
Dislocation of toe NOS
Subluxation of toe NOS

+7th **S93.101 Unspecified subluxation of right toe(s)**
+7th **S93.102 Unspecified subluxation of left toe(s)**
+7th **S93.103 Unspecified subluxation of unspecified toe(s)**
+7th **S93.104 Unspecified dislocation of right toe(s)**
+7th **S93.105 Unspecified dislocation of left toe(s)**
+7th **S93.106 Unspecified dislocation of unspecified toe(s)**

\+ **S93.11 Dislocation of interphalangeal joint**

+7th **S93.111 Dislocation of interphalangeal joint of right great toe**
+7th **S93.112 Dislocation of interphalangeal joint of left great toe**
+7th **S93.113 Dislocation of interphalangeal joint of unspecified great toe**
+7th **S93.114 Dislocation of interphalangeal joint of right lesser toe(s)**
+7th **S93.115 Dislocation of interphalangeal joint of left lesser toe(s)**
+7th **S93.116 Dislocation of interphalangeal joint of unspecified lesser toe(s)**
+7th **S93.119 Dislocation of interphalangeal joint of unspecified toe(s)**

\+ **S93.12 Dislocation of metatarsophalangeal joint**

+7th **S93.121 Dislocation of metatarsophalangeal joint of right great toe**

+7th **S93.122** **Dislocation of metatarsophalangeal joint of left great toe**
+7th **S93.123** **Dislocation of metatarsophalangeal joint of unspecified great toe**
+7th **S93.124** **Dislocation of metatarsophalangeal joint of right lesser toe(s)**
+7th **S93.125** **Dislocation of metatarsophalangeal joint of left lesser toe(s)**
+7th **S93.126** **Dislocation of metatarsophalangeal joint of unspecified lesser toe(s)**
+7th **S93.129** **Dislocation of metatarsophalangeal joint of unspecified toe(s)**

\+ **S93.13** **Subluxation of interphalangeal joint**
+7th **S93.131** **Subluxation of interphalangeal joint of right great toe**
+7th **S93.132** **Subluxation of interphalangeal joint of left great toe**
+7th **S93.133** **Subluxation of interphalangeal joint of unspecified great toe**
+7th **S93.134** **Subluxation of interphalangeal joint of right lesser toe(s)**
+7th **S93.135** **Subluxation of interphalangeal joint of left lesser toe(s)**
+7th **S93.136** **Subluxation of interphalangeal joint of unspecified lesser toe(s)**
+7th **S93.139** **Subluxation of interphalangeal joint of unspecified toe(s)**

\+ **S93.14** **Subluxation of metatarsophalangeal joint**
+7th **S93.141** **Subluxation of metatarsophalangeal joint of right great toe**
+7th **S93.142** **Subluxation of metatarsophalangeal joint of left great toe**
+7th **S93.143** **Subluxation of metatarsophalangeal joint of unspecified great toe**
+7th **S93.144** **Subluxation of metatarsophalangeal joint of right lesser toe(s)**
+7th **S93.145** **Subluxation of metatarsophalangeal joint of left lesser toe(s)**
+7th **S93.146** **Subluxation of metatarsophalangeal joint of unspecified lesser toe(s)**
+7th **S93.149** **Subluxation of metatarsophalangeal joint of unspecified toe(s)**

\+ **S93.3** **Subluxation and dislocation of foot**
Excludes2: *dislocation of toe (S93.1-)*

\+ **S93.30** **Unspecified subluxation and dislocation of foot**
Dislocation of foot NOS
Subluxation of foot NOS
+7th **S93.301** **Unspecified subluxation of right foot**
+7th **S93.302** **Unspecified subluxation of left foot**
+7th **S93.303** **Unspecified subluxation of unspecified foot**
+7th **S93.304** **Unspecified dislocation of right foot**
+7th **S93.305** **Unspecified dislocation of left foot**
+7th **S93.306** **Unspecified dislocation of unspecified foot**

\+ **S93.31** **Subluxation and dislocation of tarsal joint**
+7th **S93.311** **Subluxation of tarsal joint of right foot**
+7th **S93.312** **Subluxation of tarsal joint of left foot**
+7th **S93.313** **Subluxation of tarsal joint of unspecified foot**
+7th **S93.314** **Dislocation of tarsal joint of right foot**
+7th **S93.315** **Dislocation of tarsal joint of left foot**
+7th **S93.316** **Dislocation of tarsal joint of unspecified foot**

\+ **S93.32** **Subluxation and dislocation of tarsometatarsal joint**
+7th **S93.321** **Subluxation of tarsometatarsal joint of right foot**
+7th **S93.322** **Subluxation of tarsometatarsal joint of left foot**
+7th **S93.323** **Subluxation of tarsometatarsal joint of unspecified foot**
+7th **S93.324** **Dislocation of tarsometatarsal joint of right foot**
+7th **S93.325** **Dislocation of tarsometatarsal joint of left foot**
+7th **S93.326** **Dislocation of tarsometatarsal joint of unspecified foot**

\+ **S93.33** **Other subluxation and dislocation of foot**
+7th **S93.331** **Other subluxation of right foot**
+7th **S93.332** **Other subluxation of left foot**
+7th **S93.333** **Other subluxation of unspecified foot**
+7th **S93.334** **Other dislocation of right foot**
+7th **S93.335** **Other dislocation of left foot**
+7th **S93.336** **Other dislocation of unspecified foot**

\+ **S93.4** **Sprain of ankle**
Excludes2: *injury of Achilles tendon (S86.0-)*

\+ **S93.40** **Sprain of unspecified ligament of ankle**
Sprain of ankle NOS
Sprained ankle NOS
+7th **S93.401** **Sprain of unspecified ligament of right ank**
+7th **S93.402** **Sprain of unspecified ligament of left ankle**
+7th **S93.409** **Sprain of unspecified ligament of unspecifie ankle**

\+ **S93.41** **Sprain of calcaneofibular ligament**
+7th **S93.411** **Sprain of calcaneofibular ligament of right ankle**
+7th **S93.412** **Sprain of calcaneofibular ligament of left ankle**
+7th **S93.419** **Sprain of calcaneofibular ligament of unspecified ankle**

\+ **S93.42** **Sprain of deltoid ligament**
+7th **S93.421** **Sprain of deltoid ligament of right ankle**
+7th **S93.422** **Sprain of deltoid ligament of left ankle**
+7th **S93.429** **Sprain of deltoid ligament of unspecified ankle**

\+ **S93.43** **Sprain of tibiofibular ligament**
+7th **S93.431** **Sprain of tibiofibular ligament of right ank**
+7th **S93.432** **Sprain of tibiofibular ligament of left ankle**
+7th **S93.439** **Sprain of tibiofibular ligament of unspecifie ankle**

\+ **S93.49** **Sprain of other ligament of ankle**
Sprain of internal collateral ligament
Sprain of talofibular ligament
+7th **S93.491** **Sprain of other ligament of right ankle**
+7th **S93.492** **Sprain of other ligament of left ankle**
+7th **S93.499** **Sprain of other ligament of unspecified ank**

\+ **S93.5** **Sprain of toe**

\+ **S93.50** **Unspecified sprain of toe**
+7th **S93.501** **Unspecified sprain of right great toe**
+7th **S93.502** **Unspecified sprain of left great toe**
+7th **S93.503** **Unspecified sprain of unspecified great toe**
+7th **S93.504** **Unspecified sprain of right lesser toe(s)**
+7th **S93.505** **Unspecified sprain of left lesser toe(s)**
+7th **S93.506** **Unspecified sprain of unspecified lesser toe(s)**
+7th **S93.509** **Unspecified sprain of unspecified toe(s)**

\+ **S93.51** **Sprain of interphalangeal joint of toe**
+7th **S93.511** **Sprain of interphalangeal joint of right great toe**
+7th **S93.512** **Sprain of interphalangeal joint of left great to**
+7th **S93.513** **Sprain of interphalangeal joint of unspecified great toe**
+7th **S93.514** **Sprain of interphalangeal joint of right lesser toe(s)**
+7th **S93.515** **Sprain of interphalangeal joint of left lesser toe(s)**
+7th **S93.516** **Sprain of interphalangeal joint of unspecified lesser toe(s)**
+7th **S93.519** **Sprain of interphalangeal joint of unspecified toe(s)**

\+ **S93.52** **Sprain of metatarsophalangeal joint of toe**
+7th **S93.521** **Sprain of metatarsophalangeal joint of right great toe**
+7th **S93.522** **Sprain of metatarsophalangeal joint of left great toe**
+7th **S93.523** **Sprain of metatarsophalangeal joint of unspecified great toe**
+7th **S93.524** **Sprain of metatarsophalangeal joint of right lesser toe(s)**
+7th **S93.525** **Sprain of metatarsophalangeal joint of left lesser toe(s)**
+7th **S93.526** **Sprain of metatarsophalangeal joint of unspecified lesser toe(s)**
+7th **S93.529** **Sprain of metatarsophalangeal joint of unspecified toe(s)**

\+ **S93.6** **Sprain of foot**
Excludes2: *sprain of metatarsophalangeal joint of toe (S93.52-)*
sprain of toe (S93.5-)

\+ **S93.60** **Unspecified sprain of foot**
+7th **S93.601** **Unspecified sprain of right foot**
+7th **S93.602** **Unspecified sprain of left foot**
+7th **S93.609** **Unspecified sprain of unspecified foot**

\+ **S93.61** **Sprain of tarsal ligament of foot**
+7th **S93.611** **Sprain of tarsal ligament of right foot**
+7th **S93.612** **Sprain of tarsal ligament of left foot**
+7th **S93.619** **Sprain of tarsal ligament of unspecified foot**

+ **S93.62 Sprain of tarsometatarsal ligament of foot**
  - +7th **S93.621 Sprain of tarsometatarsal ligament of right foot**
  - +7th **S93.622 Sprain of tarsometatarsal ligament of left foot**
  - +7th **S93.629 Sprain of tarsometatarsal ligament of unspecified foot**

+ **S93.69 Other sprain of foot**
  - +7th **S93.691 Other sprain of right foot**
  - +7th **S93.692 Other sprain of left foot**
  - +7th **S93.699 Other sprain of unspecified foot**

S94 Injury of nerves at ankle and foot level

Code also any associated open wound (S91.-)

The appropriate 7th character is to be added to each code from category S94
A initial encounter
D subsequent encounter
S sequela

+ **S94.0 Injury of lateral plantar nerve**
  - X+7th **S94.00 Injury of lateral plantar nerve, unspecified leg**
  - X+7th **S94.01 Injury of lateral plantar nerve, right leg**
  - X+7th **S94.02 Injury of lateral plantar nerve, left leg**

+ **S94.1 Injury of medial plantar nerve**
  - X+7th **S94.10 Injury of medial plantar nerve, unspecified leg**
  - X+7th **S94.11 Injury of medial plantar nerve, right leg**
  - X+7th **S94.12 Injury of medial plantar nerve, left leg**

+ **S94.2 Injury of deep peroneal nerve at ankle and foot level**
  Injury of terminal, lateral branch of deep peroneal nerve
  - X+7th **S94.20 Injury of deep peroneal nerve at ankle and foot level, unspecified leg**
  - X+7th **S94.21 Injury of deep peroneal nerve at ankle and foot level, right leg**
  - X+7th **S94.22 Injury of deep peroneal nerve at ankle and foot level, left leg**

+ **S94.3 Injury of cutaneous sensory nerve at ankle and foot level**
  - X+7th **S94.30 Injury of cutaneous sensory nerve at ankle and foot level, unspecified leg**
  - X+7th **S94.31 Injury of cutaneous sensory nerve at ankle and foot level, right leg**
  - X+7th **S94.32 Injury of cutaneous sensory nerve at ankle and foot level, left leg**

+ **S94.8 Injury of other nerves at ankle and foot level**
  + **S94.8X Injury of other nerves at ankle and foot level**
    - +7th **S94.8X1 Injury of other nerves at ankle and foot level, right leg**
    - +7th **S94.8X2 Injury of other nerves at ankle and foot level, left leg**
    - +7th **S94.8X9 Injury of other nerves at ankle and foot level, unspecified leg**

+ **S94.9 Injury of unspecified nerve at ankle and foot level**
  - X+7th **S94.90 Injury of unspecified nerve at ankle and foot level, unspecified leg**
  - X+7th **S94.91 Injury of unspecified nerve at ankle and foot level, right leg**
  - X+7th **S94.92 Injury of unspecified nerve at ankle and foot level, left leg**

S95 Injury of blood vessels at ankle and foot level

Code also any associated open wound (S91.-)
Excludes2: *injury of posterior tibial artery and vein (S85.1-, S85.8-)*

The appropriate 7th character is to be added to each code from category S95
A initial encounter
D subsequent encounter
S sequela

+ **S95.0 Injury of dorsal artery of foot**
  + **S95.00 Unspecified injury of dorsal artery of foot**
    - CC +7th **S95.001 Unspecified injury of dorsal artery of right foot**
      CC Exclusion 7th character A see Appendix A
      PDX collection 1325
    - CC +7th **S95.002 Unspecified injury of dorsal artery of left foot**
      CC Exclusion 7th character A see Appendix A
      PDX collection 1326
    - CC +7th **S95.009 Unspecified injury of dorsal artery of unspecified foot**
      CC Exclusion 7th character A see Appendix A
      PDX collection 1327
  + **S95.01 Laceration of dorsal artery of foot**
    - CC +7th **S95.011 Laceration of dorsal artery of right foot**
      CC Exclusion 7th character A see Appendix A
      PDX collection 1325
    - CC +7th **S95.012 Laceration of dorsal artery of left foot**
      CC Exclusion 7th character A see Appendix A
      PDX collection 1326
    - CC +7th **S95.019 Laceration of dorsal artery of unspecified foot**
      CC Exclusion 7th character A see Appendix A
      PDX collection 1327
  + **S95.09 Other specified injury of dorsal artery of foot**
    - CC +7th **S95.091 Other specified injury of dorsal artery of right foot**
      CC Exclusion 7th character A see Appendix A
      PDX collection 1325
    - CC +7th **S95.092 Other specified injury of dorsal artery of left foot**
      CC Exclusion 7th character A see Appendix A
      PDX collection 1326
    - CC +7th **S95.099 Other specified injury of dorsal artery of unspecified foot**
      CC Exclusion 7th character A see Appendix A
      PDX collection 1327

+ **S95.1 Injury of plantar artery of foot**
  + **S95.10 Unspecified injury of plantar artery of foot**
    - CC +7th **S95.101 Unspecified injury of plantar artery of right foot**
      CC Exclusion 7th character A see Appendix A
      PDX collection 1370
    - CC +7th **S95.102 Unspecified injury of plantar artery of left foot**
      CC Exclusion 7th character A see Appendix A
      PDX collection 1371
    - CC +7th **S95.109 Unspecified injury of plantar artery of unspecified foot**
      CC Exclusion 7th character A see Appendix A
      PDX collection 1372
  + **S95.11 Laceration of plantar artery of foot**
    - CC +7th **S95.111 Laceration of plantar artery of right foot**
      CC Exclusion 7th character A see Appendix A
      PDX collection 1370
    - CC +7th **S95.112 Laceration of plantar artery of left foot**
      CC Exclusion 7th character A see Appendix A
      PDX collection 1371
    - CC +7th **S95.119 Laceration of plantar artery of unspecified foot**
      CC Exclusion 7th character A see Appendix A
      PDX collection 1372
  + **S95.19 Other specified injury of plantar artery of foot**
    - CC +7th **S95.191 Other specified injury of plantar artery of right foot**
      CC Exclusion 7th character A see Appendix A
      PDX collection 1370
    - CC +7th **S95.192 Other specified injury of plantar artery of left foot**
      CC Exclusion 7th character A see Appendix A
      PDX collection 1371
    - CC +7th **S95.199 Other specified injury of plantar artery of unspecified foot**
      CC Exclusion 7th character A see Appendix A
      PDX collection 1372

+ **S95.2 Injury of dorsal vein of foot**
  + **S95.20 Unspecified injury of dorsal vein of foot**
    - CC +7th **S95.201 Unspecified injury of dorsal vein of right foot**
      CC Exclusion 7th character A see Appendix A
      PDX collection 1325
    - CC +7th **S95.202 Unspecified injury of dorsal vein of left foot**
      CC Exclusion 7th character A see Appendix A
      PDX collection 1326
    - CC +7th **S95.209 Unspecified injury of dorsal vein of unspecified foot**
      CC Exclusion 7th character A see Appendix A
      PDX collection 1327
  + **S95.21 Laceration of dorsal vein of foot**
    - CC +7th **S95.211 Laceration of dorsal vein of right foot**
      CC Exclusion 7th character A see Appendix A
      PDX collection 1325
    - CC +7th **S95.212 Laceration of dorsal vein of left foot**
      CC Exclusion 7th character A see Appendix A
      PDX collection 1326
    - CC +7th **S95.219 Laceration of dorsal vein of unspecified foot**
      CC Exclusion 7th character A see Appendix A
      PDX collection 1327

+ **S95.29 Other specified injury of dorsal vein of foot**
CC +7th **S95.291 Other specified injury of dorsal vein of right foot**
CC Exclusion 7th character A see Appendix A
PDX collection 1325
CC +7th **S95.292 Other specified injury of dorsal vein of left foot**
CC Exclusion 7th character A see Appendix A
PDX collection 1326
CC +7th **S95.299 Other specified injury of dorsal vein of unspecified foot**
CC Exclusion 7th character A see Appendix A
PDX collection 1327

S95.8 Injury of other blood vessels at ankle and foot level
+ **S95.80 Unspecified injury of other blood vessels at ankle and foot level**
CC +7th **S95.801 Unspecified injury of other blood vessels at ankle and foot level, right leg**
CC Exclusion 7th character A see Appendix A
PDX collection 1325
CC +7th **S95.802 Unspecified injury of other blood vessels at ankle and foot level, left leg**
CC Exclusion 7th character A see Appendix A
PDX collection 1326
CC +7th **S95.809 Unspecified injury of other blood vessels at ankle and foot level, unspecified leg**
CC Exclusion 7th character A see Appendix A
PDX collection 1327
+ **S95.81 Laceration of other blood vessels at ankle and foot level**
CC +7th **S95.811 Laceration of other blood vessels at ankle and foot level, right leg**
CC Exclusion 7th character A see Appendix A
PDX collection 1325
CC +7th **S95.812 Laceration of other blood vessels at ankle and foot level, left leg**
CC Exclusion 7th character A see Appendix A
PDX collection 1326
CC +7th **S95.819 Laceration of other blood vessels at ankle and foot level, unspecified leg**
CC Exclusion 7th character A see Appendix A
PDX collection 1327
+ **S95.89 Other specified injury of other blood vessels at ankle and foot level**
CC +7th **S95.891 Other specified injury of other blood vessels at ankle and foot level, right leg**
CC Exclusion 7th character A see Appendix A
PDX collection 1325
CC +7th **S95.892 Other specified injury of other blood vessels at ankle and foot level, left leg**
CC Exclusion 7th character A see Appendix A
PDX collection 1326
CC +7th **S95.899 Other specified injury of other blood vessels at ankle and foot level, unspecified leg**
CC Exclusion 7th character A see Appendix A
PDX collection 1327

+ **S95.9 Injury of unspecified blood vessel at ankle and foot level**
+ **S95.90 Unspecified injury of unspecified blood vessel at ankle and foot level**
CC +7th **S95.901 Unspecified injury of unspecified blood vessel at ankle and foot level, right leg**
CC Exclusion 7th character A see Appendix A
PDX collection 1325
CC +7th **S95.902 Unspecified injury of unspecified blood vessel at ankle and foot level, left leg**
CC Exclusion 7th character A see Appendix A
PDX collection 1326
CC +7th **S95.909 Unspecified injury of unspecified blood vessel at ankle and foot level, unspecified leg**
CC Exclusion 7th character A see Appendix A
PDX collection 1327
+ **S95.91 Laceration of unspecified blood vessel at ankle and foot level**
CC +7th **S95.911 Laceration of unspecified blood vessel at ankle and foot level, right leg**
CC Exclusion 7th character A see Appendix A
PDX collection 1325
CC +7th **S95.912 Laceration of unspecified blood vessel at ankle and foot level, left leg**
CC Exclusion 7th character A see Appendix A
PDX collection 1326
CC +7th **S95.919 Laceration of unspecified blood vessel at ankle and foot level, unspecified leg**
CC Exclusion 7th character A see Appendix A
PDX collection 1327
+ **S95.99 Other specified injury of unspecified blood vessel at ankle and foot level**
CC +7th **S95.991 Other specified injury of unspecified blood vessel at ankle and foot level, right leg**
CC Exclusion 7th character A see Appendix A
PDX collection 1325
CC +7th **S95.992 Other specified injury of unspecified blood vessel at ankle and foot level, left leg**
CC Exclusion 7th character A see Appendix A
PDX collection 1326
CC +7th **S95.999 Other specified injury of unspecified blood vessel at ankle and foot level, unspecified leg**
CC Exclusion 7th character A see Appendix A
PDX collection 1327

S96 Injury of muscle and tendon at ankle and foot level

Code also any associated open wound (S91.-)
Excludes2: *injury of Achilles tendon (S86.0-)*
sprain of joints and ligaments of ankle and foot (S93.-)

The appropriate 7th character is to be added to each code from category S96
A initial encounter
D subsequent encounter
S sequela

+ **S96.0 Injury of muscle and tendon of long flexor muscle of toe at ankle and foot level**
+ **S96.00 Unspecified injury of muscle and tendon of long flexor muscle of toe at ankle and foot level**
+7th **S96.001 Unspecified injury of muscle and tendon of long flexor muscle of toe at ankle and foot level, right foot**
+7th **S96.002 Unspecified injury of muscle and tendon of long flexor muscle of toe at ankle and foot level, left foot**
+7th **S96.009 Unspecified injury of muscle and tendon of long flexor muscle of toe at ankle and foot level, unspecified foot**
+ **S96.01 Strain of muscle and tendon of long flexor muscle of toe at ankle and foot level**
+7th **S96.011 Strain of muscle and tendon of long flexor muscle of toe at ankle and foot level, right foot**
+7th **S96.012 Strain of muscle and tendon of long flexor muscle of toe at ankle and foot level, left foot**
+7th **S96.019 Strain of muscle and tendon of long flexor muscle of toe at ankle and foot level, unspecified foot**
+ **S96.02 Laceration of muscle and tendon of long flexor muscle of toe at ankle and foot level**
CC +7th **S96.021 Laceration of muscle and tendon of long flexor muscle of toe at ankle and foot level, right foot**
CC Exclusion 7th character A see Appendix A
PDX collection 1364
CC +7th **S96.022 Laceration of muscle and tendon of long flexor muscle of toe at ankle and foot level, left foot**
CC Exclusion 7th character A see Appendix A
PDX collection 1365
CC +7th **S96.029 Laceration of muscle and tendon of long flexor muscle of toe at ankle and foot level, unspecified foot**
CC Exclusion 7th character A see Appendix A
PDX collection 1366
+ **S96.09 Other injury of muscle and tendon of long flexor muscle of toe at ankle and foot level**
+7th **S96.091 Other injury of muscle and tendon of long flexor muscle of toe at ankle and foot level, right foot**
+7th **S96.092 Other injury of muscle and tendon of long flexor muscle of toe at ankle and foot level, left foot**
+7th **S96.099 Other injury of muscle and tendon of long flexor muscle of toe at ankle and foot level, unspecified foot**

+ **S96.1 Injury of muscle and tendon of long extensor muscle of toe at ankle and foot level**
+ **S96.10 Unspecified injury of muscle and tendon of long extensor muscle of toe at ankle and foot level**
+7th **S96.101 Unspecified injury of muscle and tendon of long extensor muscle of toe at ankle and foot level, right foot**

+7th **S96.102** **Unspecified injury of muscle and tendon of long extensor muscle of toe at ankle and foot level, left foot**

+7th **S96.109** **Unspecified injury of muscle and tendon of long extensor muscle of toe at ankle and foot level, unspecified foot**

+ **S96.11** **Strain of muscle and tendon of long extensor muscle of toe at ankle and foot level**

+7th **S96.111** **Strain of muscle and tendon of long extensor muscle of toe at ankle and foot level, right foot**

+7th **S96.112** **Strain of muscle and tendon of long extensor muscle of toe at ankle and foot level, left foot**

+7th **S96.119** **Strain of muscle and tendon of long extensor muscle of toe at ankle and foot level, unspecified foot**

+ **S96.12** **Laceration of muscle and tendon of long extensor muscle of toe at ankle and foot level**

CC +7th **S96.121** **Laceration of muscle and tendon of long extensor muscle of toe at ankle and foot level, right foot**
CC Exclusion 7th character A see Appendix A
PDX collection 1364

CC +7th **S96.122** **Laceration of muscle and tendon of long extensor muscle of toe at ankle and foot level, left foot**
CC Exclusion 7th character A see Appendix A
PDX collection 1365

CC +7th **S96.129** **Laceration of muscle and tendon of long extensor muscle of toe at ankle and foot level, unspecified foot**
CC Exclusion 7th character A see Appendix A
PDX collection 1366

+ **S96.19** **Other specified injury of muscle and tendon of long extensor muscle of toe at ankle and foot level**

+7th **S96.191** **Other specified injury of muscle and tendon of long extensor muscle of toe at ankle and foot level, right foot**

+7th **S96.192** **Other specified injury of muscle and tendon of long extensor muscle of toe at ankle and foot level, left foot**

+7th **S96.199** **Other specified injury of muscle and tendon of long extensor muscle of toe at ankle and foot level, unspecified foot**

+ **S96.2** **Injury of intrinsic muscle and tendon at ankle and foot level**

+ **S96.20** **Unspecified injury of intrinsic muscle and tendon at ankle and foot level**

+7th **S96.201** **Unspecified injury of intrinsic muscle and tendon at ankle and foot level, right foot**

+7th **S96.202** **Unspecified injury of intrinsic muscle and tendon at ankle and foot level, left foot**

+7th **S96.209** **Unspecified injury of intrinsic muscle and tendon at ankle and foot level, unspecified foot**

+ **S96.21** **Strain of intrinsic muscle and tendon at ankle and foot level**

+7th **S96.211** **Strain of intrinsic muscle and tendon at ankle and foot level, right foot**

+7th **S96.212** **Strain of intrinsic muscle and tendon at ankle and foot level, left foot**

+7th **S96.219** **Strain of intrinsic muscle and tendon at ankle and foot level, unspecified foot**

+ **S96.22** **Laceration of intrinsic muscle and tendon at ankle and foot level**

CC +7th **S96.221** **Laceration of intrinsic muscle and tendon at ankle and foot level, right foot**
CC Exclusion 7th character A see Appendix A
PDX collection 1364

CC +7th **S96.222** **Laceration of intrinsic muscle and tendon at ankle and foot level, left foot**
CC Exclusion 7th character A see Appendix A
PDX collection 1365

CC +7th **S96.229** **Laceration of intrinsic muscle and tendon at ankle and foot level, unspecified foot**
CC Exclusion 7th character A see Appendix A
PDX collection 1366

+ **S96.29** **Other specified injury of intrinsic muscle and tendon at ankle and foot level**

+7th **S96.291** **Other specified injury of intrinsic muscle and tendon at ankle and foot level, right foot**

+7th **S96.292** **Other specified injury of intrinsic muscle and tendon at ankle and foot level, left foot**

+7th **S96.299** **Other specified injury of intrinsic muscle and tendon at ankle and foot level, unspecified foot**

+ **S96.8** **Injury of other specified muscles and tendons at ankle and foot level**

+ **S96.80** **Unspecified injury of other specified muscles and tendons at ankle and foot level**

+7th **S96.801** **Unspecified injury of other specified muscles and tendons at ankle and foot level, right foot**

+7th **S96.802** **Unspecified injury of other specified muscles and tendons at ankle and foot level, left foot**

+7th **S96.809** **Unspecified injury of other specified muscles and tendons at ankle and foot level, unspecified foot**

+ **S96.81** **Strain of other specified muscles and tendons at ankle and foot level**

+7th **S96.811** **Strain of other specified muscles and tendons at ankle and foot level, right foot**

+7th **S96.812** **Strain of other specified muscles and tendons at ankle and foot level, left foot**

+7th **S96.819** **Strain of other specified muscles and tendons at ankle and foot level, unspecified foot**

+ **S96.82** **Laceration of other specified muscles and tendons at ankle and foot level**

CC +7th **S96.821** **Laceration of other specified muscles and tendons at ankle and foot level, right foot**
CC Exclusion 7th character A see Appendix A
PDX collection 1364

CC +7th **S96.822** **Laceration of other specified muscles and tendons at ankle and foot level, left foot**
CC Exclusion 7th character A see Appendix A
PDX collection 1365

CC +7th **S96.829** **Laceration of other specified muscles and tendons at ankle and foot level, unspecified foot**
CC Exclusion 7th character A see Appendix A
PDX collection 1366

+ **S96.89** **Other specified injury of other specified muscles and tendons at ankle and foot level**

+7th **S96.891** **Other specified injury of other specified muscles and tendons at ankle and foot level, right foot**

+7th **S96.892** **Other specified injury of other specified muscles and tendons at ankle and foot level, left foot**

+7th **S96.899** **Other specified injury of other specified muscles and tendons at ankle and foot level, unspecified foot**

+ **S96.9** **Injury of unspecified muscle and tendon at ankle and foot level**

+ **S96.90** **Unspecified injury of unspecified muscle and tendon at ankle and foot level**

+7th **S96.901** **Unspecified injury of unspecified muscle and tendon at ankle and foot level, right foot**

+7th **S96.902** **Unspecified injury of unspecified muscle and tendon at ankle and foot level, left foot**

+7th **S96.909** **Unspecified injury of unspecified muscle and tendon at ankle and foot level, unspecified foot**

+ **S96.91** **Strain of unspecified muscle and tendon at ankle and foot level**

+7th **S96.911** **Strain of unspecified muscle and tendon at ankle and foot level, right foot**

+7th **S96.912** **Strain of unspecified muscle and tendon at ankle and foot level, left foot**

+7th **S96.919** **Strain of unspecified muscle and tendon at ankle and foot level, unspecified foot**

+ **S96.92** **Laceration of unspecified muscle and tendon at ankle and foot level**

CC +7th **S96.921** **Laceration of unspecified muscle and tendon at ankle and foot level, right foot**
CC Exclusion 7th character A see Appendix A
PDX collection 1364

CC +7th **S96.922** **Laceration of unspecified muscle and tendon at ankle and foot level, left foot**
CC Exclusion 7th character A see Appendix A
PDX collection 1365

CC +7th **S96.929** **Laceration of unspecified muscle and tendon at ankle and foot level, unspecified foot**
CC Exclusion 7th character A see Appendix A
PDX collection 1366

\+ **S96.99 Other specified injury of unspecified muscle and tendon at ankle and foot level**
+7th **S96.991 Other specified injury of unspecified muscle and tendon at ankle and foot level, right foot**
+7th **S96.992 Other specified injury of unspecified muscle and tendon at ankle and foot level, left foot**
+7th **S96.999 Other specified injury of unspecified muscle and tendon at ankle and foot level, unspecified foot**

S97 Crushing injury of ankle and foot
Use additional code(s) for all associated injuries

The appropriate 7th character is to be added to each code from category S97
A initial encounter
D subsequent encounter
S sequela

\+ **S97.0 Crushing injury of ankle**
X+7th **S97.00 Crushing injury of unspecified ankle**
X+7th **S97.01 Crushing injury of right ankle**
X+7th **S97.02 Crushing injury of left ankle**
\+ **S97.1 Crushing injury of toe**
\+ **S97.10 Crushing injury of unspecified toe(s)**
+7th **S97.101 Crushing injury of unspecified right toe(s)**
+7th **S97.102 Crushing injury of unspecified left toe(s)**
+7th **S97.109 Crushing injury of unspecified toe(s)**
Crushing injury of toe NOS
\+ **S97.11 Crushing injury of great toe**
+7th **S97.111 Crushing injury of right great toe**
+7th **S97.112 Crushing injury of left great toe**
+7th **S97.119 Crushing injury of unspecified great toe**
\+ **S97.12 Crushing injury of lesser toe(s)**
+7th **S97.121 Crushing injury of right lesser toe(s)**
+7th **S97.122 Crushing injury of left lesser toe(s)**
+7th **S97.129 Crushing injury of unspecified lesser toe(s)**
\+ **S97.8 Crushing injury of foot**
X+7th **S97.80 Crushing injury of unspecified foot**
Crushing injury of foot NOS
X+7th **S97.81 Crushing injury of right foot**
X+7th **S97.82 Crushing injury of left foot**

S98 Traumatic amputation of ankle and foot
An amputation not identified as partial or complete should be coded to complete

The appropriate 7th character is to be added to each code from category S98
A initial encounter
D subsequent encounter
S sequela

\+ **S98.0 Traumatic amputation of foot at ankle level**
\+ **S98.01 Complete traumatic amputation of foot at ankle level**
CC +7th **S98.011 Complete traumatic amputation of right foot at ankle level**
CC Exclusion 7th character A see Appendix A PDX collection 1333
CC +7th **S98.012 Complete traumatic amputation of left foot at ankle level**
CC Exclusion 7th character A see Appendix A PDX collection 1334
CC +7th **S98.019 Complete traumatic amputation of unspecified foot at ankle level**
CC Exclusion 7th character A see Appendix A PDX collection 1335
\+ **S98.02 Partial traumatic amputation of foot at ankle level**
CC +7th **S98.021 Partial traumatic amputation of right foot at ankle level**
CC Exclusion 7th character A see Appendix A PDX collection 1333
CC +7th **S98.022 Partial traumatic amputation of left foot at ankle level**
CC Exclusion 7th character A see Appendix A PDX collection 1334
CC +7th **S98.029 Partial traumatic amputation of unspecified foot at ankle level**
CC Exclusion 7th character A see Appendix A PDX collection 1335
\+ **S98.1 Traumatic amputation of one toe**
\+ **S98.11 Complete traumatic amputation of great toe**
+7th **S98.111 Complete traumatic amputation of right great toe**
+7th **S98.112 Complete traumatic amputation of left great toe**
+7th **S98.119 Complete traumatic amputation of unspecified great toe**
\+ **S98.12 Partial traumatic amputation of great toe**
+7th **S98.121 Partial traumatic amputation of right grea toe**
+7th **S98.122 Partial traumatic amputation of left great toe**
+7th **S98.129 Partial traumatic amputation of unspecifie great toe**
\+ **S98.13 Complete traumatic amputation of one lesser toe**
Traumatic amputation of toe NOS
+7th **S98.131 Complete traumatic amputation of one rig lesser toe**
+7th **S98.132 Complete traumatic amputation of one left lesser toe**
+7th **S98.139 Complete traumatic amputation of one unspecified lesser toe**
\+ **S98.14 Partial traumatic amputation of one lesser toe**
+7th **S98.141 Partial traumatic amputation of one right lesser toe**
+7th **S98.142 Partial traumatic amputation of one left lesser toe**
+7th **S98.149 Partial traumatic amputation of one unspecified lesser toe**
\+ **S98.2 Traumatic amputation of two or more lesser toes**
\+ **S98.21 Complete traumatic amputation of two or more lesse toes**
+7th **S98.211 Complete traumatic amputation of two or more right lesser toes**
+7th **S98.212 Complete traumatic amputation of two or more left lesser toes**
+7th **S98.219 Complete traumatic amputation of two or more unspecified lesser toes**
\+ **S98.22 Partial traumatic amputation of two or more lesser toes**
+7th **S98.221 Partial traumatic amputation of two or mo right lesser toes**
+7th **S98.222 Partial traumatic amputation of two or mo left lesser toes**
+7th **S98.229 Partial traumatic amputation of two or mo unspecified lesser toes**
\+ **S98.3 Traumatic amputation of midfoot**
\+ **S98.31 Complete traumatic amputation of midfoot**
CC +7th **S98.311 Complete traumatic amputation of right midfoot**
CC Exclusion 7th character A see Appendix A PDX collection 1333
CC +7th **S98.312 Complete traumatic amputation of left midfoot**
CC Exclusion 7th character A see Appendix A PDX collection 1334
CC +7th **S98.319 Complete traumatic amputation of unspecified midfoot**
CC Exclusion 7th character A see Appendix A PDX collection 1335
\+ **S98.32 Partial traumatic amputation of midfoot**
CC +7th **S98.321 Partial traumatic amputation of right midfoot**
CC Exclusion 7th character A see Appendix A PDX collection 1333
CC +7th **S98.322 Partial traumatic amputation of left midfoo**
CC Exclusion 7th character A see Appendix A PDX collection 1334
CC +7th **S98.329 Partial traumatic amputation of unspecified midfoot**
CC Exclusion 7th character A see Appendix A PDX collection 1335
\+ **S98.9 Traumatic amputation of foot, level unspecified**
\+ **S98.91 Complete traumatic amputation of foot, level unspecified**
CC +7th **S98.911 Complete traumatic amputation of right foot, level unspecified**
CC Exclusion 7th character A see Appendix A PDX collection 1333
CC +7th **S98.912 Complete traumatic amputation of left foot, level unspecified**
CC Exclusion 7th character A see Appendix A PDX collection 1334
CC +7th **S98.919 Complete traumatic amputation of unspecified foot, level unspecified**
CC Exclusion 7th character A see Appendix A PDX collection 1335

\+ **S98.92 Partial traumatic amputation of foot, level unspecified**

CC +7th **S98.921 Partial traumatic amputation of right foot, level unspecified**

CC Exclusion 7th character A see Appendix A

PDX collection 1333

CC +7th **S98.922 Partial traumatic amputation of left foot, level unspecified**

CC Exclusion 7th character A see Appendix A

PDX collection 1334

CC +7th **S98.929 Partial traumatic amputation of unspecified foot, level unspecified**

CC Exclusion 7th character A see Appendix A

PDX collection 1335

S99 Other and unspecified injuries of ankle and foot

The appropriate 7th character is to be added to each code from category S99
A initial encounter
D subsequent encounter
S sequela

\+ **S99.8 Other specified injuries of ankle and foot**

\+ **S99.81 Other specified injuries of ankle**

+7th **S99.811 Other specified injuries of right ankle**

+7th **S99.812 Other specified injuries of left ankle**

+7th **S99.819 Other specified injuries of unspecified ankle**

\+ **S99.82 Other specified injuries of foot**

+7th **S99.821 Other specified injuries of right foot**

+7th **S99.822 Other specified injuries of left foot**

+7th **S99.829 Other specified injuries of unspecified foot**

\+ **S99.9 Unspecified injury of ankle and foot**

\+ **S99.91 Unspecified injury of ankle**

+7th **S99.911 Unspecified injury of right ankle**

+7th **S99.912 Unspecified injury of left ankle**

+7th **S99.919 Unspecified injury of unspecified ankle**

\+ **S99.92 Unspecified injury of foot**

+7th **S99.921 Unspecified injury of right foot**

+7th **S99.922 Unspecified injury of left foot**

+7th **S99.929 Unspecified injury of unspecified foot**

INJURY, POISONING AND CERTAIN OTHER CONSEQUENCES OF EXTERNAL CAUSES (T07-T88)

juries involving multiple body regions (T07)

cludes1: *burns and corrosions (T20-T32)*
frostbite (T33-T34)
insect bite or sting, venomous (T63.4)
sunburn (L55.-)

T07 Unspecified multiple injuries

Excludes1: *injury NOS (T14)*

Review coding guideline C.19.b

Valid 3-character code, no further characters required

jury of unspecified body region (T14)

T14 Injury of unspecified body region

Excludes1: *multiple unspecified injuries (T07)*

T14.8 Other injury of unspecified body region

Abrasion NOS
Contusion NOS
Crush injury NOS
Fracture NOS
Skin injury NOS
Vascular injury NOS

\+ **T14.9 Unspecified injury**

T14.90 Injury, unspecified

Injury NOS

T14.91 Suicide attempt

Attempted suicide NOS

Effects of foreign body entering through natural orifice (T15-T19)

Excludes2: *foreign body accidentally left in operation wound (T81.5-)*
foreign body in penetrating wound - See open wound by body region
residual foreign body in soft tissue (M79.5)
splinter, without open wound - See superficial injury by body region

T15 Foreign body on external eye

Excludes2: *foreign body in penetrating wound of orbit and eye ball (S05.4-, S05.5-)*
open wound of eyelid and periocular area (S01.1-)
retained foreign body in eyelid (H02.8-)
retained (old) foreign body in penetrating wound of orbit and eye ball (H05.5-, H44.6-, H44.7-)
superficial foreign body of eyelid and periocular area (S00.25-)

The appropriate 7th character is to be added to each code from category T15
A initial encounter
D subsequent encounter
S sequela

\+ **T15.0 Foreign body in cornea**

X+7th **T15.00 Foreign body in cornea, unspecified eye**

X+7th **T15.01 Foreign body in cornea, right eye**

X+7th **T15.02 Foreign body in cornea, left eye**

\+ **T15.1 Foreign body in conjunctival sac**

X+7th **T15.10 Foreign body in conjunctival sac, unspecified eye**

X+7th **T15.11 Foreign body in conjunctival sac, right eye**

X+7th **T15.12 Foreign body in conjunctival sac, left eye**

\+ **T15.8 Foreign body in other and multiple parts of external eye**

Foreign body in lacrimal punctum

X+7th **T15.80 Foreign body in other and multiple parts of external eye, unspecified eye**

X+7th **T15.81 Foreign body in other and multiple parts of external eye, right eye**

X+7th **T15.82 Foreign body in other and multiple parts of external eye, left eye**

\+ **T15.9 Foreign body on external eye, part unspecified**

X+7th **T15.90 Foreign body on external eye, part unspecified, unspecified eye**

X+7th **T15.91 Foreign body on external eye, part unspecified, right eye**

X+7th **T15.92 Foreign body on external eye, part unspecified, left eye**

T16 Foreign body in ear

Includes: foreign body in auditory canal

The appropriate 7th character is to be added to each code from category T16
A initial encounter
D subsequent encounter
S sequela

X+7th **T16.1 Foreign body in right ear**

X+7th **T16.2 Foreign body in left ear**

X+7th **T16.9 Foreign body in ear, unspecified ear**

T17 Foreign body in respiratory tract

The appropriate 7th character is to be added to each code from category T17
A initial encounter
D subsequent encounter
S sequela

X+7th **T17.0 Foreign body in nasal sinus**

X+7th **T17.1 Foreign body in nostril**

Foreign body in nose NOS

\+ **T17.2 Foreign body in pharynx**

Foreign body in nasopharynx
Foreign body in throat NOS

\+ **T17.20 Unspecified foreign body in pharynx**

+7th **T17.200 Unspecified foreign body in pharynx causing asphyxiation**

+7th **T17.208 Unspecified foreign body in pharynx causing other injury**

\+ **T17.21 Gastric contents in pharynx**

Aspiration of gastric contents into pharynx
Vomitus in pharynx

+7th **T17.210 Gastric contents in pharynx causing asphyxiation**

+7th **T17.218 Gastric contents in pharynx causing other injury**

+ **T17.22 Food in pharynx**
  Bones in pharynx
  Seeds in pharynx
  +7th **T17.220 Food in pharynx causing asphyxiation**
  +7th **T17.228 Food in pharynx causing other injury**

+ **T17.29 Other foreign object in pharynx**
  +7th **T17.290 Other foreign object in pharynx causing asphyxiation**
  +7th **T17.298 Other foreign object in pharynx causing other injury**

+ **T17.3 Foreign body in larynx**

+ **T17.30 Unspecified foreign body in larynx**
  +7th **T17.300 Unspecified foreign body in larynx causing asphyxiation**
  +7th **T17.308 Unspecified foreign body in larynx causing other injury**

+ **T17.31 Gastric contents in larynx**
  Aspiration of gastric contents into larynx
  Vomitus in larynx
  +7th **T17.310 Gastric contents in larynx causing asphyxiation**
  +7th **T17.318 Gastric contents in larynx causing other injury**

+ **T17.32 Food in larynx**
  Bones in larynx
  Seeds in larynx
  +7th **T17.320 Food in larynx causing asphyxiation**
  +7th **T17.328 Food in larynx causing other injury**

+ **T17.39 Other foreign object in larynx**
  +7th **T17.390 Other foreign object in larynx causing asphyxiation**
  +7th **T17.398 Other foreign object in larynx causing other injury**

+ **T17.4 Foreign body in trachea**

+ **T17.40 Unspecified foreign body in trachea**
  CC +7th **T17.400 Unspecified foreign body in trachea causing asphyxiation**
  CC Exclusion 7th character A see Appendix A
  PDX collection 1373
  CC +7th **T17.408 Unspecified foreign body in trachea causing other injury**
  CC Exclusion 7th character A see Appendix A
  PDX collection 1373

+ **T17.41 Gastric contents in trachea**
  Aspiration of gastric contents into trachea
  Vomitus in trachea
  CC +7th **T17.410 Gastric contents in trachea causing asphyxiation**
  CC Exclusion 7th character A see Appendix A
  PDX collection 1373
  CC +7th **T17.418 Gastric contents in trachea causing other injury**
  CC Exclusion 7th character A see Appendix A
  PDX collection 1373

+ **T17.42 Food in trachea**
  Bones in trachea
  Seeds in trachea
  CC +7th **T17.420 Food in trachea causing asphyxiation**
  CC Exclusion 7th character A see Appendix A
  PDX collection 1373
  CC +7th **T17.428 Food in trachea causing other injury**
  CC Exclusion 7th character A see Appendix A
  PDX collection 1373

+ **T17.49 Other foreign object in trachea**
  CC +7th **T17.490 Other foreign object in trachea causing asphyxiation**
  CC Exclusion 7th character A see Appendix A
  PDX collection 1373
  CC +7th **T17.498 Other foreign object in trachea causing other injury**
  CC Exclusion 7th character A see Appendix A
  PDX collection 1373

+ **T17.5 Foreign body in bronchus**

+ **T17.50 Unspecified foreign body in bronchus**
  CC +7th **T17.500 Unspecified foreign body in bronchus causing asphyxiation**
  CC Exclusion 7th character A see Appendix A
  PDX collection 1374
  CC +7th **T17.508 Unspecified foreign body in bronchus causing other injury**
  CC Exclusion 7th character A see Appendix A
  PDX collection 1374

+ **T17.51 Gastric contents in bronchus**
  Aspiration of gastric contents into bronchus
  Vomitus in bronchus
  CC +7th **T17.510 Gastric contents in bronchus causing asphyxiation**
  CC Exclusion 7th character A see Appendix A
  PDX collection 1374
  CC +7th **T17.518 Gastric contents in bronchus causing othe injury**
  CC Exclusion 7th character A see Appendix A
  PDX collection 1374

+ **T17.52 Food in bronchus**
  Bones in bronchus
  Seeds in bronchus
  CC +7th **T17.520 Food in bronchus causing asphyxiation**
  CC Exclusion 7th character A see Appendix A
  PDX collection 1374
  CC +7th **T17.528 Food in bronchus causing other injury**
  CC Exclusion 7th character A see Appendix A
  PDX collection 1374

+ **T17.59 Other foreign object in bronchus**
  CC +7th **T17.590 Other foreign object in bronchus causing asphyxiation**
  CC Exclusion 7th character A see Appendix A
  PDX collection 1374
  CC +7th **T17.598 Other foreign object in bronchus causing other injury**
  CC Exclusion 7th character A see Appendix A
  PDX collection 1374

+ **T17.8 Foreign body in other parts of respiratory tract**
  Foreign body in bronchioles
  Foreign body in lung

+ **T17.80 Unspecified foreign body in other parts of respirator tract**
  CC +7th **T17.800 Unspecified foreign body in other parts of respiratory tract causing asphyxiation**
  CC Exclusion 7th character A see Appendix A
  PDX collection 1374
  CC +7th **T17.808 Unspecified foreign body in other parts of respiratory tract causing other injury**
  CC Exclusion 7th character A see Appendix A
  PDX collection 1374

+ **T17.81 Gastric contents in other parts of respiratory tract**
  Aspiration of gastric contents into other parts of respiratory tract
  Vomitus in other parts of respiratory tract
  CC +7th **T17.810 Gastric contents in other parts of respirato tract causing asphyxiation**
  CC Exclusion 7th character A see Appendix A
  PDX collection 1374
  CC +7th **T17.818 Gastric contents in other parts of respirato tract causing other injury**
  CC Exclusion 7th character A see Appendix A
  PDX collection 1374

+ **T17.82 Food in other parts of respiratory tract**
  Bones in other parts of respiratory tract
  Seeds in other parts of respiratory tract
  CC +7th **T17.820 Food in other parts of respiratory tract causing asphyxiation**
  CC Exclusion 7th character A see Appendix A
  PDX collection 1374
  CC +7th **T17.828 Food in other parts of respiratory tract causing other injury**
  CC Exclusion 7th character A see Appendix A
  PDX collection 1374

+ **T17.89 Other foreign object in other parts of respiratory tra**
  CC +7th **T17.890 Other foreign object in other parts of respiratory tract causing asphyxiation**
  CC Exclusion 7th character A see Appendix A
  PDX collection 1374
  CC +7th **T17.898 Other foreign object in other parts of respiratory tract causing other injury**
  CC Exclusion 7th character A see Appendix A
  PDX collection 1374

T17.9 Foreign body in respiratory tract, part unspecified

+ **T17.90 Unspecified foreign body in respiratory tract, part unspecified**
  +7th **T17.900 Unspecified foreign body in respiratory tract, part unspecified causing asphyxiation**
  +7th **T17.908 Unspecified foreign body in respiratory tract, part unspecified causing other injury**

\+ **T17.91 Gastric contents in respiratory tract, part unspecified**
Aspiration of gastric contents into respiratory tract, part unspecified
Vomitus in trachea respiratory tract, part unspecified
+7th **T17.910 Gastric contents in respiratory tract, part unspecified causing asphyxiation**
+7th **T17.918 Gastric contents in respiratory tract, part unspecified causing other injury**

\+ **T17.92 Food in respiratory tract, part unspecified**
Bones in respiratory tract, part unspecified
Seeds in respiratory tract, part unspecified
+7th **T17.920 Food in respiratory tract, part unspecified causing asphyxiation**
+7th **T17.928 Food in respiratory tract, part unspecified causing other injury**

\+ **T17.99 Other foreign object in respiratory tract, part unspecified**
+7th **T17.990 Other foreign object in respiratory tract, part unspecified in causing asphyxiation**
+7th **T17.998 Other foreign object in respiratory tract, part unspecified causing other injury**

T18 Foreign body in alimentary tract

Excludes2: *foreign body in pharynx (T17.2-)*

The appropriate 7th character is to be added to each code from category T18
A initial encounter
D subsequent encounter
S sequela

X+7th **T18.0 Foreign body in mouth**
\+ **T18.1 Foreign body in esophagus**
Excludes2: *foreign body in respiratory tract (T17.-)*
\+ **T18.10 Unspecified foreign body in esophagus**
+7th **T18.100 Unspecified foreign body in esophagus causing compression of trachea**
Unspecified foreign body in esophagus causing obstruction of respiration
+7th **T18.108 Unspecified foreign body in esophagus causing other injury**
\+ **T18.11 Gastric contents in esophagus**
Vomitus in esophagus
+7th **T18.110 Gastric contents in esophagus causing compression of trachea**
Gastric contents in esophagus causing obstruction of respiration
+7th **T18.118 Gastric contents in esophagus causing other injury**
\+ **T18.12 Food in esophagus**
Bones in esophagus
Seeds in esophagus
+7th **T18.120 Food in esophagus causing compression of trachea**
Food in esophagus causing obstruction of respiration
+7th **T18.128 Food in esophagus causing other injury**
\+ **T18.19 Other foreign object in esophagus**
+7th **T18.190 Other foreign object in esophagus causing compression of trachea**
Other foreign body in esophagus causing obstruction of respiration
+7th **T18.198 Other foreign object in esophagus causing other injury**

X+7th **T18.2 Foreign body in stomach**
X+7th **T18.3 Foreign body in small intestine**
X+7th **T18.4 Foreign body in colon**
X+7th **T18.5 Foreign body in anus and rectum**
Foreign body in rectosigmoid (junction)
X+7th **T18.8 Foreign body in other parts of alimentary tract**
X+7th **T18.9 Foreign body of alimentary tract, part unspecified**
Foreign body in digestive system NOS
Swallowed foreign body NOS

T19 Foreign body in genitourinary tract

Excludes2: *complications due to implanted mesh (T83.7-)*
mechanical complications of contraceptive device (intrauterine) (vaginal) (T83.3-)
presence of contraceptive device (intrauterine) (vaginal) (Z97.5)

The appropriate 7th character is to be added to each code from category T19
A initial encounter
D subsequent encounter
S sequela

X+7th **T19.0 Foreign body in urethra**
X+7th **T19.1 Foreign body in bladder**
X+7th **T19.2 Foreign body in vulva and vagina**
X+7th **T19.3 Foreign body in uterus**
♂ X+7th **T19.4 Foreign body in penis**
X+7th **T19.8 Foreign body in other parts of genitourinary tract**
X+7th **T19.9 Foreign body in genitourinary tract, part unspecified**

BURNS AND CORROSIONS (T20-T32)

Includes: burns (thermal) from electrical heating appliances
burns (thermal) from electricity
burns (thermal) from flame
burns (thermal) from friction
burns (thermal) from hot air and hot gases
burns (thermal) from hot objects
burns (thermal) from lightning
burns (thermal) from radiation
chemical burn [corrosion] (external) (internal)
scalds

Excludes2: *erythema [dermatitis] ab igne (L59.0)*
radiation-related disorders of the skin and subcutaneous tissue (L55-L59)
sunburn (L55.-)

Burns and corrosions of external body surface, specified by site (T20-T25)

Includes: burns and corrosions of first degree [erythema]
burns and corrosions of second degree [blisters][epidermal loss]
burns and corrosions of third degree [deep necrosis of underlying tissue] [full- thickness skin loss]

Use additional code from category T31 or T32 to identify extent of body surface involved

Review coding guideline C.19.d

T20 Burn and corrosion of head, face, and neck

Excludes2: *burn and corrosion of ear drum (T28.41, T28.91)*
burn and corrosion of eye and adnexa (T26.-)
burn and corrosion of mouth and pharynx (T28.0)

The appropriate 7th character is to be added to each code from category T20
A initial encounter
D subsequent encounter
S sequela

\+ **T20.0 Burn of unspecified degree of head, face, and neck**
Use additional external cause code to identify the source, place and intent of the burn (X00-X19, X75-X77, X96-X98, Y92)
X+7th **T20.00 Burn of unspecified degree of head, face, and neck, unspecified site**
\+ **T20.01 Burn of unspecified degree of ear [any part, except ear drum]**
Excludes2: *burn of ear drum (T28.41-)*
+7th **T20.011 Burn of unspecified degree of right ear [any part, except ear drum]**
+7th **T20.012 Burn of unspecified degree of left ear [any part, except ear drum]**
+7th **T20.019 Burn of unspecified degree of unspecified ear [any part, except ear drum]**
X+7th **T20.02 Burn of unspecified degree of lip(s)**
X+7th **T20.03 Burn of unspecified degree of chin**
X+7th **T20.04 Burn of unspecified degree of nose (septum)**
X+7th **T20.05 Burn of unspecified degree of scalp [any part]**
X+7th **T20.06 Burn of unspecified degree of forehead and cheek**
X+7th **T20.07 Burn of unspecified degree of neck**
X+7th **T20.09 Burn of unspecified degree of multiple sites of head, face, and neck**

+ **T20.1 Burn of first degree of head, face, and neck**
Use additional external cause code to identify the source, place and intent of the burn (X00-X19, X75-X77, X96-X98, Y92)
X+7th **T20.10 Burn of first degree of head, face, and neck, unspecified site**
+ **T20.11 Burn of first degree of ear [any part, except ear drum]**
Excludes2: *burn of ear drum (T28.41-)*
+7th **T20.111 Burn of first degree of right ear [any part, except ear drum]**
+7th **T20.112 Burn of first degree of left ear [any part, except ear drum]**
+7th **T20.119 Burn of first degree of unspecified ear [any part, except ear drum]**
X+7th **T20.12 Burn of first degree of lip(s)**
X+7th **T20.13 Burn of first degree of chin**
X+7th **T20.14 Burn of first degree of nose (septum)**
X+7th **T20.15 Burn of first degree of scalp [any part]**
X+7th **T20.16 Burn of first degree of forehead and cheek**
X+7th **T20.17 Burn of first degree of neck**
X+7th **T20.19 Burn of first degree of multiple sites of head, face, and neck**

+ **T20.2 Burn of second degree of head, face, and neck**
Use additional external cause code to identify the source, place and intent of the burn (X00-X19, X75-X77, X96-X98, Y92)
X+7th **T20.20 Burn of second degree of head, face, and neck, unspecified site**
+ **T20.21 Burn of second degree of ear [any part, except ear drum]**
Excludes2: *burn of ear drum (T28.41-)*
+7th **T20.211 Burn of second degree of right ear [any part, except ear drum]**
+7th **T20.212 Burn of second degree of left ear [any part, except ear drum]**
+7th **T20.219 Burn of second degree of unspecified ear [any part, except ear drum]**
X+7th **T20.22 Burn of second degree of lip(s)**
X+7th **T20.23 Burn of second degree of chin**
X+7th **T20.24 Burn of second degree of nose (septum)**
X+7th **T20.25 Burn of second degree of scalp [any part]**
X+7th **T20.26 Burn of second degree of forehead and cheek**
X+7th **T20.27 Burn of second degree of neck**
X+7th **T20.29 Burn of second degree of multiple sites of head, face, and neck**

+ **T20.3 Burn of third degree of head, face, and neck**
Use additional external cause code to identify the source, place and intent of the burn (X00-X19, X75-X77, X96-X98, Y92)
CC X+7th **T20.30 Burn of third degree of head, face, and neck, unspecified site**
CC Exclusion 7th character A see Appendix A PDX collection 1375
HAC 7th character A see Appendix B for HAC conditional logic
+ **T20.31 Burn of third degree of ear [any part, except ear drum]**
Excludes2: *burn of ear drum (T28.41-)*
CC +7th **T20.311 Burn of third degree of right ear [any part, except ear drum]**
CC Exclusion 7th character A see Appendix A PDX collection 1376
HAC 7th character A see Appendix B for HAC conditional logic
CC +7th **T20.312 Burn of third degree of left ear [any part, except ear drum]**
CC Exclusion 7th character A see Appendix A PDX collection 1376
HAC 7th character A see Appendix B for HAC conditional logic
CC +7th **T20.319 Burn of third degree of unspecified ear [any part, except ear drum]**
CC Exclusion 7th character A see Appendix A PDX collection 1376
HAC 7th character A see Appendix B for HAC conditional logic
CC X+7th **T20.32 Burn of third degree of lip(s)**
CC Exclusion 7th character A see Appendix A PDX collection 1377
HAC 7th character A see Appendix B for HAC conditional logic
CC X+7th **T20.33 Burn of third degree of chin**
CC Exclusion 7th character A see Appendix A PDX collection 1378
HAC 7th character A see Appendix B for HAC conditional logic
CC X+7th **T20.34 Burn of third degree of nose (septum)**
CC Exclusion 7th character A see Appendix A PDX collection 1379
HAC 7th character A see Appendix B for HAC conditional logic
CC X+7th **T20.35 Burn of third degree of scalp [any part]**
CC Exclusion 7th character A see Appendix A PDX collection 1380
HAC 7th character A see Appendix B for HAC conditional logic
CC X+7th **T20.36 Burn of third degree of forehead and cheek**
CC Exclusion 7th character A see Appendix A PDX collection 1381
HAC 7th character A see Appendix B for HAC conditional lo
CC X+7th **T20.37 Burn of third degree of neck**
CC Exclusion 7th character A see Appendix A PDX collection 1382
HAC 7th character A see Appendix B for HAC conditional lo
CC X+7th **T20.39 Burn of third degree of multiple sites of head, face, and neck**
CC Exclusion 7th character A see Appendix A PDX collection 1383
HAC 7th character A see Appendix B for HAC conditional log

+ **T20.4 Corrosion of unspecified degree of head, face, and neck**
Code first (T51-T65) to identify chemical and intent external cause code to identify place (Y92)
X+7th **T20.40 Corrosion of unspecified degree of head, face, and neck, unspecified site**
+ **T20.41 Corrosion of unspecified degree of ear [any part, except ear drum]**
Excludes2: *corrosion of ear drum (T28.91-)*
+7th **T20.411 Corrosion of unspecified degree of right ea[r] [any part, except ear drum]**
+7th **T20.412 Corrosion of unspecified degree of left ear [any part, except ear drum]**
+7th **T20.419 Corrosion of unspecified degree of unspecified ear [any part, except ear drum]**
X+7th **T20.42 Corrosion of unspecified degree of lip(s)**
X+7th **T20.43 Corrosion of unspecified degree of chin**
X+7th **T20.44 Corrosion of unspecified degree of nose (septum)**
X+7th **T20.45 Corrosion of unspecified degree of scalp [any part]**
X+7th **T20.46 Corrosion of unspecified degree of forehead and chee[k]**
X+7th **T20.47 Corrosion of unspecified degree of neck**
X+7th **T20.49 Corrosion of unspecified degree of multiple sites of head, face, and neck**

+ **T20.5 Corrosion of first degree of head, face, and neck**
Code first (T51-T65) to identify chemical and intent

Use additional external cause code to identify place (Y92)
X+7th **T20.50 Corrosion of first degree of head, face, and neck, unspecified site**
+ **T20.51 Corrosion of first degree of ear [any part, except ear drum]**
Excludes2: *corrosion of ear drum (T28.91-)*
+7th **T20.511 Corrosion of first degree of right ear [any part, except ear drum]**
+7th **T20.512 Corrosion of first degree of left ear [any part, except ear drum]**
+7th **T20.519 Corrosion of first degree of unspecified ear [any part, except ear drum]**
X+7th **T20.52 Corrosion of first degree of lip(s)**
X+7th **T20.53 Corrosion of first degree of chin**
X+7th **T20.54 Corrosion of first degree of nose (septum)**
X+7th **T20.55 Corrosion of first degree of scalp [any part]**
X+7th **T20.56 Corrosion of first degree of forehead and cheek**
X+7th **T20.57 Corrosion of first degree of neck**
X+7th **T20.59 Corrosion of first degree of multiple sites of head, fac[e] and neck**

+ **T20.6 Corrosion of second degree of head, face, and neck**
Code first (T51-T65) to identify chemical and intent

Use additional external cause code to identify place (Y92)
X+7th **T20.60 Corrosion of second degree of head, face, and neck, unspecified site**
+ **T20.61 Corrosion of second degree of ear [any part, except ear drum]**
Excludes2: *corrosion of ear drum (T28.91-)*
+7th **T20.611 Corrosion of second degree of right ear [any part, except ear drum]**
+7th **T20.612 Corrosion of second degree of left ear [any part, except ear drum]**
+7th **T20.619 Corrosion of second degree of unspecified ear [any part, except ear drum]**

X+7th **T20.62 Corrosion of second degree of lip(s)**
X+7th **T20.63 Corrosion of second degree of chin**
X+7th **T20.64 Corrosion of second degree of nose (septum)**
X+7th **T20.65 Corrosion of second degree of scalp [any part]**
X+7th **T20.66 Corrosion of second degree of forehead and cheek**
X+7th **T20.67 Corrosion of second degree of neck**
X+7th **T20.69 Corrosion of second degree of multiple sites of head, face, and neck**

\+ **T20.7 Corrosion of third degree of head, face, and neck**
Code first (T51-T65) to identify chemical and intent
Use additional external cause code to identify place (Y92)

CC X+7th **T20.70 Corrosion of third degree of head, face, and neck, unspecified site**
CC Exclusion 7th character A see Appendix A PDX collection 1375
HAC 7th character A see Appendix B for HAC conditional logic

\+ **T20.71 Corrosion of third degree of ear [any part, except ear drum]**
Excludes2: *corrosion of ear drum (T28.91-)*

CC +7th **T20.711 Corrosion of third degree of right ear [any part, except ear drum]**
CC Exclusion 7th character A see Appendix A PDX collection 1376
HAC 7th character A see Appendix B for HAC conditional logic

CC +7th **T20.712 Corrosion of third degree of left ear [any part, except ear drum]**
CC Exclusion 7th character A see Appendix A PDX collection 1376
HAC 7th character A see Appendix B for HAC conditional logic

CC +7th **T20.719 Corrosion of third degree of unspecified ear [any part, except ear drum]**
CC Exclusion 7th character A see Appendix A PDX collection 1376
HAC 7th character A see Appendix B for HAC conditional logic

CC X+7th **T20.72 Corrosion of third degree of lip(s)**
CC Exclusion 7th character A see Appendix A PDX collection 1377
HAC 7th character A see Appendix B for HAC conditional logic

CC X+7th **T20.73 Corrosion of third degree of chin**
CC Exclusion 7th character A see Appendix A PDX collection 1378
HAC 7th character A see Appendix B for HAC conditional logic

CC X+7th **T20.74 Corrosion of third degree of nose (septum)**
CC Exclusion 7th character A see Appendix A PDX collection 1379
HAC 7th character A see Appendix B for HAC conditional logic

CC X+7th **T20.75 Corrosion of third degree of scalp [any part]**
CC Exclusion 7th character A see Appendix A PDX collection 1380
HAC 7th character A see Appendix B for HAC conditional logic

CC X+7th **T20.76 Corrosion of third degree of forehead and cheek**
CC Exclusion 7th character A see Appendix A PDX collection 1381
HAC 7th character A see Appendix B for HAC conditional logic

CC X+7th **T20.77 Corrosion of third degree of neck**
CC Exclusion 7th character A see Appendix A PDX collection 1382
HAC 7th character A see Appendix B for HAC conditional logic

CC X+7th **T20.79 Corrosion of third degree of multiple sites of head, face, and neck**
CC Exclusion 7th character A see Appendix A PDX collection 1383
HAC 7th character A see Appendix B for HAC conditional logic

T21 Burn and corrosion of trunk
Includes: burns and corrosion of hip region
Excludes2: *burns and corrosion of axilla (T22.- with fifth character 4)*
burns and corrosion of scapular region (T22.- with fifth character 6)
burns and corrosion of shoulder (T22.- with fifth character 5)

The appropriate 7th character is to be added to each code from category T21
A initial encounter
D subsequent encounter
S sequela

\+ **T21.0 Burn of unspecified degree of trunk**
Use external cause code to identify the source, place and intent of the burn (X00-X19, X75-X77, X96-X98, Y92)

X+7th **T21.00 Burn of unspecified degree of trunk, unspecified site**
X+7th **T21.01 Burn of unspecified degree of chest wall**
Burn of of unspecified degree of breast
X+7th **T21.02 Burn of unspecified degree of abdominal wall**
Burn of unspecified degree of flank
Burn of unspecified degree of groin
X+7th **T21.03 Burn of unspecified degree of upper back**
Burn of unspecified degree of interscapular region
X+7th **T21.04 Burn of unspecified degree of lower back**
X+7th **T21.05 Burn of unspecified degree of buttock**
Burn of unspecified degree of anus
♂ X+7th **T21.06 Burn of unspecified degree of male genital region**
Burn of unspecified degree of penis
Burn of unspecified degree of scrotum
Burn of unspecified degree of testis
♀ X+7th **T21.07 Burn of unspecified degree of female genital region**
Burn of unspecified degree of labium (majus) (minus)
Burn of unspecified degree of perineum
Burn of unspecified degree of vulva
Excludes2: *burn of vagina (T28.3)*
X+7th **T21.09 Burn of unspecified degree of other site of trunk**

\+ **T21.1 Burn of first degree of trunk**
Use external cause code to identify the source, place and intent of the burn (X00-X19, X75-X77, X96-X98, Y92)

X+7th **T21.10 Burn of first degree of trunk, unspecified site**
X+7th **T21.11 Burn of first degree of chest wall**
Burn of first degree of breast
X+7th **T21.12 Burn of first degree of abdominal wall**
Burn of first degree of flank
Burn of first degree of groin
X+7th **T21.13 Burn of first degree of upper back**
Burn of first degree of interscapular region
X+7th **T21.14 Burn of first degree of lower back**
X+7th **T21.15 Burn of first degree of buttock**
Burn of first degree of anus
♂ X+7th **T21.16 Burn of first degree of male genital region**
Burn of first degree of penis
Burn of first degree of scrotum
Burn of first degree of testis
♀ X+7th **T21.17 Burn of first degree of female genital region**
Burn of first degree of labium (majus) (minus)
Burn of first degree of perineum
Burn of first degree of vulva
Excludes2: *burn of vagina (T28.3)*
X+7th **T21.19 Burn of first degree of other site of trunk**

\+ **T21.2 Burn of second degree of trunk**
Use external cause code to identify the source, place and intent of the burn (X00-X19, X75-X77, X96-X98, Y92)

X+7th **T21.20 Burn of second degree of trunk, unspecified site**
X+7th **T21.21 Burn of second degree of chest wall**
Burn of second degree of breast
X+7th **T21.22 Burn of second degree of abdominal wall**
Burn of second degree of flank
Burn of second degree of groin
X+7th **T21.23 Burn of second degree of upper back**
Burn of second degree of interscapular region
X+7th **T21.24 Burn of second degree of lower back**
X+7th **T21.25 Burn of second degree of buttock**
Burn of second degree of anus
♂ X+7th **T21.26 Burn of second degree of male genital region**
Burn of second degree of penis
Burn of second degree of scrotum
Burn of second degree of testis

♀ X+7th **T21.27 Burn of second degree of female genital region**
Burn of second degree of labium (majus) (minus)
Burn of second degree of perineum
Burn of second degree of vulva
Excludes2: *burn of vagina (T28.3)*

X+7th **T21.29 Burn of second degree of other site of trunk**

\+ **T21.3 Burn of third degree of trunk**
Use additional external cause code to identify the source, place and intent of the burn (X00-X19, X75-X77, X96-X98, Y92)

CC X+7th **T21.30 Burn of third degree of trunk, unspecified site**
CC Exclusion 7th character A see Appendix A PDX collection 1384
HAC 7th character A see Appendix B for HAC conditional logic

CC X+7th **T21.31 Burn of third degree of chest wall**
Burn of third degree of breast
CC Exclusion 7th character A see Appendix A PDX collection 1385
HAC 7th character A see Appendix B for HAC conditional logic

CC X+7th **T21.32 Burn of third degree of abdominal wall**
Burn of third degree of flank
Burn of third degree of groin
CC Exclusion 7th character A see Appendix A PDX collection 1386
HAC 7th character A see Appendix B for HAC conditional logic

CC X+7th **T21.33 Burn of third degree of upper back**
Burn of third degree of interscapular region
CC Exclusion 7th character A see Appendix A PDX collection 1387
HAC 7th character A see Appendix B for HAC conditional logic

CC X+7th **T21.34 Burn of third degree of lower back**
CC Exclusion 7th character A see Appendix A PDX collection 1387
HAC 7th character A see Appendix B for HAC conditional logic

CC X+7th **T21.35 Burn of third degree of buttock**
Burn of third degree of anus
CC Exclusion 7th character A see Appendix A PDX collection 1387
HAC 7th character A see Appendix B for HAC conditional logic

CC X+7th **T21.36 Burn of third degree of male genital region**
Burn of third degree of penis
Burn of third degree of scrotum
Burn of third degree of testis
CC Exclusion 7th character A see Appendix A PDX collection 1388
HAC 7th character A see Appendix B for HAC conditional logic

CC X+7th **T21.37 Burn of third degree of female genital region**
Burn of third degree of labium (majus) (minus)
Burn of third degree of perineum
Burn of third degree of vulva
Excludes2: *burn of vagina (T28.3)*
CC Exclusion 7th character A see Appendix A PDX collection 1388
HAC 7th character A see Appendix B for HAC conditional logic

CC X+7th **T21.39 Burn of third degree of other site of trunk**
CC Exclusion 7th character A see Appendix A PDX collection 1384
HAC 7th character A see Appendix B for HAC conditional logic

\+ **T21.4 Corrosion of unspecified degree of trunk**
Code first (T51-T65) to identify chemical and intent
Use additional external cause code to identify place (Y92)

X+7th **T21.40 Corrosion of unspecified degree of trunk, unspecified site**

X+7th **T21.41 Corrosion of unspecified degree of chest wall**
Corrosion of unspecified degree of breast

X+7th **T21.42 Corrosion of unspecified degree of abdominal wall**
Corrosion of unspecified degree of flank
Corrosion of unspecified degree of groin

X+7th **T21.43 Corrosion of unspecified degree of upper back**
Corrosion of unspecified degree of interscapular region

X+7th **T21.44 Corrosion of unspecified degree of lower back**

X+7th **T21.45 Corrosion of unspecified degree of buttock**
Corrosion of unspecified degree of anus

♂ X+7th **T21.46 Corrosion of unspecified degree of male genital region**
Corrosion of unspecified degree of penis
Corrosion of unspecified degree of scrotum
Corrosion of unspecified degree of testis

♀ X+7th **T21.47 Corrosion of unspecified degree of female genital region**
Corrosion of unspecified degree of labium (majus) (min
Corrosion of unspecified degree of perineum
Corrosion of unspecified degree of vulva
Excludes2: *corrosion of vagina (T28.8)*

X+7th **T21.49 Corrosion of unspecified degree of other site of trun**

\+ **T21.5 Corrosion of first degree of trunk**
Code first (T51-T65) to identify chemical and intent

Use additional external cause code to identify place (Y92)

X+7th **T21.50 Corrosion of first degree of trunk, unspecified site**

X+7th **T21.51 Corrosion of first degree of chest wall**
Corrosion of first degree of breast

X+7th **T21.52 Corrosion of first degree of abdominal wall**
Corrosion of first degree of flank
Corrosion of first degree of groin

X+7th **T21.53 Corrosion of first degree of upper back**
Corrosion of first degree of interscapular region

X+7th **T21.54 Corrosion of first degree of lower back**

X+7th **T21.55 Corrosion of first degree of buttock**
Corrosion of first degree of anus

♂ X+7th **T21.56 Corrosion of first degree of male genital region**
Corrosion of first degree of penis
Corrosion of first degree of scrotum
Corrosion of first degree of testis

♀ X+7th **T21.57 Corrosion of first degree of female genital region**
Corrosion of first degree of labium (majus) (minus)
Corrosion of first degree of perineum
Corrosion of first degree of vulva
Excludes2: *corrosion of vagina (T28.8)*

X+7th **T21.59 Corrosion of first degree of other site of trunk**

\+ **T21.6 Corrosion of second degree of trunk**
Code first (T51-T65) to identify chemical and intent

Use additional external cause code to identify place (Y92)

X+7th **T21.60 Corrosion of second degree of trunk, unspecified site**

X+7th **T21.61 Corrosion of second degree of chest wall**
Corrosion of second degree of breast

X+7th **T21.62 Corrosion of second degree of abdominal wall**
Corrosion of second degree of flank
Corrosion of second degree of groin

X+7th **T21.63 Corrosion of second degree of upper back**
Corrosion of second degree of interscapular region

X+7th **T21.64 Corrosion of second degree of lower back**

X+7th **T21.65 Corrosion of second degree of buttock**
Corrosion of second degree of anus

♂ X+7th **T21.66 Corrosion of second degree of male genital region**
Corrosion of second degree of penis
Corrosion of second degree of scrotum
Corrosion of second degree of testis

♀ X+7th **T21.67 Corrosion of second degree of female genital region**
Corrosion of second degree of labium (majus) (minus)
Corrosion of second degree of perineum
Corrosion of second degree of vulva
Excludes2: *corrosion of vagina (T28.8)*

X+7th **T21.69 Corrosion of second degree of other site of trunk**

\+ **T21.7 Corrosion of third degree of trunk**
Code first (T51-T65) to identify chemical and intent

Use additional external cause code to identify place (Y92)

CC X+7th **T21.70 Corrosion of third degree of trunk, unspecified site**
CC Exclusion 7th character A see Appendix A PDX collection 1384
HAC 7th character A see Appendix B for HAC conditional log

CC X+7th **T21.71 Corrosion of third degree of chest wall**
Corrosion of third degree of breast
CC Exclusion 7th character A see Appendix A PDX collection 1385
HAC 7th character A see Appendix B for HAC conditional logic

CC X+7th **T21.72 Corrosion of third degree of abdominal wall**
Corrosion of third degree of flank
Corrosion of third degree of groin
CC Exclusion 7th character A see Appendix A PDX collection 1386
HAC 7th character A see Appendix B for HAC conditional logic

CC X+7th **T21.73 Corrosion of third degree of upper back**
Corrosion of third degree of interscapular region
CC Exclusion 7th character A see Appendix A PDX collection 1387
HAC 7th character A see Appendix B for HAC conditional logic

CC X+7th **T21.74 Corrosion of third degree of lower back**
CC Exclusion 7th character A see Appendix A PDX collection 1387
HAC 7th character A see Appendix B for HAC conditional logic

CC X+7th **T21.75 Corrosion of third degree of buttock**
Corrosion of third degree of anus
CC Exclusion 7th character A see Appendix A PDX collection 1387
HAC 7th character A see Appendix B for HAC conditional logic

CC X+7th **T21.76 Corrosion of third degree of male genital region**
Corrosion of third degree of penis
Corrosion of third degree of scrotum
Corrosion of third degree of testis
CC Exclusion 7th character A see Appendix A PDX collection 1388
HAC 7th character A see Appendix B for HAC conditional logic

CC X+7th **T21.77 Corrosion of third degree of female genital region**
Corrosion of third degree of labium (majus) (minus)
Corrosion of third degree of perineum
Corrosion of third degree of vulva
Excludes2: *corrosion of vagina (T28.8)*
CC Exclusion 7th character A see Appendix A PDX collection 1388
HAC 7th character A see Appendix B for HAC conditional logic

CC X+7th **T21.79 Corrosion of third degree of other site of trunk**
CC Exclusion 7th character A see Appendix A PDX collection 1384
HAC 7th character A see Appendix B for HAC conditional logic

T22 Burn and corrosion of shoulder and upper limb, except wrist and hand

Excludes2: *burn and corrosion of interscapular region (T21.-)*
burn and corrosion of wrist and hand (T23.-)

The appropriate 7th character is to be added to each code from category T22
A initial encounter
D subsequent encounter
S sequela

\+ **T22.0 Burn of unspecified degree of shoulder and upper limb, except wrist and hand**
Use additional external cause code to identify the source, place and intent of the burn (X00-X19, X75-X77, X96-X98, Y92)
X+7th **T22.00 Burn of unspecified degree of shoulder and upper limb, except wrist and hand, unspecified site**
\+ **T22.01 Burn of unspecified degree of forearm**
+7th **T22.011 Burn of unspecified degree of right forearm**
+7th **T22.012 Burn of unspecified degree of left forearm**
+7th **T22.019 Burn of unspecified degree of unspecified forearm**
\+ **T22.02 Burn of unspecified degree of elbow**
+7th **T22.021 Burn of unspecified degree of right elbow**
+7th **T22.022 Burn of unspecified degree of left elbow**
+7th **T22.029 Burn of unspecified degree of unspecified elbow**
\+ **T22.03 Burn of unspecified degree of upper arm**
+7th **T22.031 Burn of unspecified degree of right upper arm**
+7th **T22.032 Burn of unspecified degree of left upper arm**
+7th **T22.039 Burn of unspecified degree of unspecified upper arm**
\+ **T22.04 Burn of unspecified degree of axilla**
+7th **T22.041 Burn of unspecified degree of right axilla**
+7th **T22.042 Burn of unspecified degree of left axilla**
+7th **T22.049 Burn of unspecified degree of unspecified axilla**
\+ **T22.05 Burn of unspecified degree of shoulder**
+7th **T22.051 Burn of unspecified degree of right shoulder**
+7th **T22.052 Burn of unspecified degree of left shoulder**
+7th **T22.059 Burn of unspecified degree of unspecified shoulder**
\+ **T22.06 Burn of unspecified degree of scapular region**
+7th **T22.061 Burn of unspecified degree of right scapular region**
+7th **T22.062 Burn of unspecified degree of left scapular region**
+7th **T22.069 Burn of unspecified degree of unspecified scapular region**
\+ **T22.09 Burn of unspecified degree of multiple sites of shoulder and upper limb, except wrist and hand**
+7th **T22.091 Burn of unspecified degree of multiple sites of right shoulder and upper limb, except wrist and hand**
+7th **T22.092 Burn of unspecified degree of multiple sites of left shoulder and upper limb, except wrist and hand**
+7th **T22.099 Burn of unspecified degree of multiple sites of unspecified shoulder and upper limb, except wrist and hand**

\+ **T22.1 Burn of first degree of shoulder and upper limb, except wrist and hand**
Use additional external cause code to identify the source, place and intent of the burn (X00-X19, X75-X77, X96-X98, Y92)
X+7th **T22.10 Burn of first degree of shoulder and upper limb, except wrist and hand, unspecified site**
\+ **T22.11 Burn of first degree of forearm**
+7th **T22.111 Burn of first degree of right forearm**
+7th **T22.112 Burn of first degree of left forearm**
+7th **T22.119 Burn of first degree of unspecified forearm**
\+ **T22.12 Burn of first degree of elbow**
+7th **T22.121 Burn of first degree of right elbow**
+7th **T22.122 Burn of first degree of left elbow**
+7th **T22.129 Burn of first degree of unspecified elbow**
\+ **T22.13 Burn of first degree of upper arm**
+7th **T22.131 Burn of first degree of right upper arm**
+7th **T22.132 Burn of first degree of left upper arm**
+7th **T22.139 Burn of first degree of unspecified upper arm**
\+ **T22.14 Burn of first degree of axilla**
+7th **T22.141 Burn of first degree of right axilla**
+7th **T22.142 Burn of first degree of left axilla**
+7th **T22.149 Burn of first degree of unspecified axilla**
\+ **T22.15 Burn of first degree of shoulder**
+7th **T22.151 Burn of first degree of right shoulder**
+7th **T22.152 Burn of first degree of left shoulder**
+7th **T22.159 Burn of first degree of unspecified shoulder**
\+ **T22.16 Burn of first degree of scapular region**
+7th **T22.161 Burn of first degree of right scapular region**
+7th **T22.162 Burn of first degree of left scapular region**
+7th **T22.169 Burn of first degree of unspecified scapular region**
\+ **T22.19 Burn of first degree of multiple sites of shoulder and upper limb, except wrist and hand**
+7th **T22.191 Burn of first degree of multiple sites of right shoulder and upper limb, except wrist and hand**
+7th **T22.192 Burn of first degree of multiple sites of left shoulder and upper limb, except wrist and hand**
+7th **T22.199 Burn of first degree of multiple sites of unspecified shoulder and upper limb, except wrist and hand**

\+ **T22.2 Burn of second degree of shoulder and upper limb, except wrist and hand**
Use additional external cause code to identify the source, place and intent of the burn (X00-X19, X75-X77, X96-X98, Y92)
X+7th **T22.20 Burn of second degree of shoulder and upper limb, except wrist and hand, unspecified site**
\+ **T22.21 Burn of second degree of forearm**
+7th **T22.211 Burn of second degree of right forearm**
+7th **T22.212 Burn of second degree of left forearm**
+7th **T22.219 Burn of second degree of unspecified forearm**
\+ **T22.22 Burn of second degree of elbow**
+7th **T22.221 Burn of second degree of right elbow**
+7th **T22.222 Burn of second degree of left elbow**
+7th **T22.229 Burn of second degree of unspecified elbow**
\+ **T22.23 Burn of second degree of upper arm**
+7th **T22.231 Burn of second degree of right upper arm**
+7th **T22.232 Burn of second degree of left upper arm**
+7th **T22.239 Burn of second degree of unspecified upper arm**
\+ **T22.24 Burn of second degree of axilla**
+7th **T22.241 Burn of second degree of right axilla**
+7th **T22.242 Burn of second degree of left axilla**
+7th **T22.249 Burn of second degree of unspecified axilla**
\+ **T22.25 Burn of second degree of shoulder**
+7th **T22.251 Burn of second degree of right shoulder**
+7th **T22.252 Burn of second degree of left shoulder**

+7th **T22.259 Burn of second degree of unspecified shoulder**

\+ **T22.26 Burn of second degree of scapular region**

+7th **T22.261 Burn of second degree of right scapular region**

+7th **T22.262 Burn of second degree of left scapular region**

+7th **T22.269 Burn of second degree of unspecified scapular region**

\+ **T22.29 Burn of second degree of multiple sites of shoulder and upper limb, except wrist and hand**

+7th **T22.291 Burn of second degree of multiple sites of right shoulder and upper limb, except wrist and hand**

+7th **T22.292 Burn of second degree of multiple sites of left shoulder and upper limb, except wrist and hand**

+7th **T22.299 Burn of second degree of multiple sites of unspecified shoulder and upper limb, except wrist and hand**

\+ **T22.3 Burn of third degree of shoulder and upper limb, except wrist and hand**

Use additional external cause code to identify the source, place and intent of the burn (X00-X19, X75-X77, X96-X98, Y92)

CC X+7th **T22.30 Burn of third degree of shoulder and upper limb, except wrist and hand, unspecified site**
CC Exclusion 7th character A see Appendix A PDX collection 1389
HAC 7th character A see Appendix B for HAC conditional logic

\+ **T22.31 Burn of third degree of forearm**

CC +7th **T22.311 Burn of third degree of right forearm**
CC Exclusion 7th character A see Appendix A PDX collection 1390
HAC 7th character A see Appendix B for HAC conditional logic

CC +7th **T22.312 Burn of third degree of left forearm**
CC Exclusion 7th character A see Appendix A PDX collection 1390
HAC 7th character A see Appendix B for HAC conditional logic

CC +7th **T22.319 Burn of third degree of unspecified forearm**
CC Exclusion 7th character A see Appendix A PDX collection 1390
HAC 7th character A see Appendix B for HAC conditional logic

\+ **T22.32 Burn of third degree of elbow**

CC +7th **T22.321 Burn of third degree of right elbow**
CC Exclusion 7th character A see Appendix A PDX collection 1391
HAC 7th character A see Appendix B for HAC conditional logic

CC +7th **T22.322 Burn of third degree of left elbow**
CC Exclusion 7th character A see Appendix A PDX collection 1391
HAC 7th character A see Appendix B for HAC conditional logic

CC +7th **T22.329 Burn of third degree of unspecified elbow**
CC Exclusion 7th character A see Appendix A PDX collection 1391
HAC 7th character A see Appendix B for HAC conditional logic

\+ **T22.33 Burn of third degree of upper arm**

CC +7th **T22.331 Burn of third degree of right upper arm**
CC Exclusion 7th character A see Appendix A PDX collection 1392
HAC 7th character A see Appendix B for HAC conditional logic

CC +7th **T22.332 Burn of third degree of left upper arm**
CC Exclusion 7th character A see Appendix A PDX collection 1392
HAC 7th character A see Appendix B for HAC conditional logic

CC +7th **T22.339 Burn of third degree of unspecified upper arm**
CC Exclusion 7th character A see Appendix A PDX collection 1392
HAC 7th character A see Appendix B for HAC conditional logic

\+ **T22.34 Burn of third degree of axilla**

CC +7th **T22.341 Burn of third degree of right axilla**
CC Exclusion 7th character A see Appendix A PDX collection 1393
HAC 7th character A see Appendix B for HAC conditional logic

CC +7th **T22.342 Burn of third degree of left axilla**
CC Exclusion 7th character A see Appendix A PDX collection 1393
HAC 7th character A see Appendix B for HAC conditional logic

CC +7th **T22.349 Burn of third degree of unspecified axilla**
CC Exclusion 7th character A see Appendix A PDX collection 1393
HAC 7th character A see Appendix B for HAC conditional logic

\+ **T22.35 Burn of third degree of shoulder**

CC +7th **T22.351 Burn of third degree of right shoulder**
CC Exclusion 7th character A see Appendix A PDX collection 1394
HAC 7th character A see Appendix B for HAC conditional logic

CC +7th **T22.352 Burn of third degree of left shoulder**
CC Exclusion 7th character A see Appendix A PDX collection 1394
HAC 7th character A see Appendix B for HAC conditional logic

CC +7th **T22.359 Burn of third degree of unspecified should**
CC Exclusion 7th character A see Appendix A PDX collection 1394
HAC 7th character A see Appendix B for HAC conditional logic

\+ **T22.36 Burn of third degree of scapular region**

CC +7th **T22.361 Burn of third degree of right scapular regi**
CC Exclusion 7th character A see Appendix A PDX collection 1395
HAC 7th character A see Appendix B for HAC conditional logic

CC +7th **T22.362 Burn of third degree of left scapular region**
CC Exclusion 7th character A see Appendix A PDX collection 1395
HAC 7th character A see Appendix B for HAC conditional logic

CC +7th **T22.369 Burn of third degree of unspecified scapula region**
CC Exclusion 7th character A see Appendix A PDX collection 1395
HAC 7th character A see Appendix B for HAC conditional logic

\+ **T22.39 Burn of third degree of multiple sites of shoulder and upper limb, except wrist and hand**

CC +7th **T22.391 Burn of third degree of multiple sites of rig shoulder and upper limb, except wrist and hand**
CC Exclusion 7th character A see Appendix A PDX collection 1389
HAC 7th character A see Appendix B for HAC conditional logic

CC +7th **T22.392 Burn of third degree of multiple sites of left shoulder and upper limb, except wrist and hand**
CC Exclusion 7th character A see Appendix A PDX collection 1389
HAC 7th character A see Appendix B for HAC conditional logic

CC +7th **T22.399 Burn of third degree of multiple sites of unspecified shoulder and upper limb, excep wrist and hand**
CC Exclusion 7th character A see Appendix A PDX collection 1389
HAC 7th character A see Appendix B for HAC conditional logic

\+ **T22.4 Corrosion of unspecified degree of shoulder and upper limb, except wrist and hand**

Code first (T51-T65) to identify chemical and intent

Use additional external cause code to identify place (Y92)

X+7th **T22.40 Corrosion of unspecified degree of shoulder and uppe limb, except wrist and hand, unspecified site**

\+ **T22.41 Corrosion of unspecified degree of forearm**

+7th **T22.411 Corrosion of unspecified degree of right forearm**

+7th **T22.412 Corrosion of unspecified degree of left forearm**

+7th **T22.419 Corrosion of unspecified degree of unspecified forearm**

\+ **T22.42 Corrosion of unspecified degree of elbow**

+7th **T22.421 Corrosion of unspecified degree of right elbow**

+7th **T22.422 Corrosion of unspecified degree of left elbow**

+7th **T22.429 Corrosion of unspecified degree of unspecified elbow**

+ **T22.43 Corrosion of unspecified degree of upper arm**
  - +7th **T22.431 Corrosion of unspecified degree of right upper arm**
  - +7th **T22.432 Corrosion of unspecified degree of left upper arm**
  - +7th **T22.439 Corrosion of unspecified degree of unspecified upper arm**

+ **T22.44 Corrosion of unspecified degree of axilla**
  - +7th **T22.441 Corrosion of unspecified degree of right axilla**
  - +7th **T22.442 Corrosion of unspecified degree of left axilla**
  - +7th **T22.449 Corrosion of unspecified degree of unspecified axilla**

+ **T22.45 Corrosion of unspecified degree of shoulder**
  - +7th **T22.451 Corrosion of unspecified degree of right shoulder**
  - +7th **T22.452 Corrosion of unspecified degree of left shoulder**
  - +7th **T22.459 Corrosion of unspecified degree of unspecified shoulder**

+ **T22.46 Corrosion of unspecified degree of scapular region**
  - +7th **T22.461 Corrosion of unspecified degree of right scapular region**
  - +7th **T22.462 Corrosion of unspecified degree of left scapular region**
  - +7th **T22.469 Corrosion of unspecified degree of unspecified scapular region**

+ **T22.49 Corrosion of unspecified degree of multiple sites of shoulder and upper limb, except wrist and hand**
  - +7th **T22.491 Corrosion of unspecified degree of multiple sites of right shoulder and upper limb, except wrist and hand**
  - +7th **T22.492 Corrosion of unspecified degree of multiple sites of left shoulder and upper limb, except wrist and hand**
  - +7th **T22.499 Corrosion of unspecified degree of multiple sites of unspecified shoulder and upper limb, except wrist and hand**

+ **T22.5 Corrosion of first degree of shoulder and upper limb, except wrist and hand**

Code first (T51-T65) to identify chemical and intent

Use additional external cause code to identify place (Y92)

X+7th **T22.50 Corrosion of first degree of shoulder and upper limb, except wrist and hand unspecified site**

+ **T22.51 Corrosion of first degree of forearm**
  - +7th **T22.511 Corrosion of first degree of right forearm**
  - +7th **T22.512 Corrosion of first degree of left forearm**
  - +7th **T22.519 Corrosion of first degree of unspecified forearm**

+ **T22.52 Corrosion of first degree of elbow**
  - +7th **T22.521 Corrosion of first degree of right elbow**
  - +7th **T22.522 Corrosion of first degree of left elbow**
  - +7th **T22.529 Corrosion of first degree of unspecified elbow**

+ **T22.53 Corrosion of first degree of upper arm**
  - +7th **T22.531 Corrosion of first degree of right upper arm**
  - +7th **T22.532 Corrosion of first degree of left upper arm**
  - +7th **T22.539 Corrosion of first degree of unspecified upper arm**

+ **T22.54 Corrosion of first degree of axilla**
  - +7th **T22.541 Corrosion of first degree of right axilla**
  - +7th **T22.542 Corrosion of first degree of left axilla**
  - +7th **T22.549 Corrosion of first degree of unspecified axilla**

+ **T22.55 Corrosion of first degree of shoulder**
  - +7th **T22.551 Corrosion of first degree of right shoulder**
  - +7th **T22.552 Corrosion of first degree of left shoulder**
  - +7th **T22.559 Corrosion of first degree of unspecified shoulder**

+ **T22.56 Corrosion of first degree of scapular region**
  - +7th **T22.561 Corrosion of first degree of right scapular region**
  - +7th **T22.562 Corrosion of first degree of left scapular region**
  - +7th **T22.569 Corrosion of first degree of unspecified scapular region**

+ **T22.59 Corrosion of first degree of multiple sites of shoulder and upper limb, except wrist and hand**
  - +7th **T22.591 Corrosion of first degree of multiple sites of right shoulder and upper limb, except wrist and hand**
  - +7th **T22.592 Corrosion of first degree of multiple sites of left shoulder and upper limb, except wrist and hand**
  - +7th **T22.599 Corrosion of first degree of multiple sites of unspecified shoulder and upper limb, except wrist and hand**

+ **T22.6 Corrosion of second degree of shoulder and upper limb, except wrist and hand**

Code first (T51-T65) to identify chemical and intent

Use additional external cause code to identify place (Y92)

X+7th **T22.60 Corrosion of second degree of shoulder and upper limb, except wrist and hand, unspecified site**

+ **T22.61 Corrosion of second degree of forearm**
  - +7th **T22.611 Corrosion of second degree of right forearm**
  - +7th **T22.612 Corrosion of second degree of left forearm**
  - +7th **T22.619 Corrosion of second degree of unspecified forearm**

+ **T22.62 Corrosion of second degree of elbow**
  - +7th **T22.621 Corrosion of second degree of right elbow**
  - +7th **T22.622 Corrosion of second degree of left elbow**
  - +7th **T22.629 Corrosion of second degree of unspecified elbow**

+ **T22.63 Corrosion of second degree of upper arm**
  - +7th **T22.631 Corrosion of second degree of right upper arm**
  - +7th **T22.632 Corrosion of second degree of left upper arm**
  - +7th **T22.639 Corrosion of second degree of unspecified upper arm**

+ **T22.64 Corrosion of second degree of axilla**
  - +7th **T22.641 Corrosion of second degree of right axilla**
  - +7th **T22.642 Corrosion of second degree of left axilla**
  - +7th **T22.649 Corrosion of second degree of unspecified axilla**

+ **T22.65 Corrosion of second degree of shoulder**
  - +7th **T22.651 Corrosion of second degree of right shoulder**
  - +7th **T22.652 Corrosion of second degree of left shoulder**
  - +7th **T22.659 Corrosion of second degree of unspecified shoulder**

+ **T22.66 Corrosion of second degree of scapular region**
  - +7th **T22.661 Corrosion of second degree of right scapular region**
  - +7th **T22.662 Corrosion of second degree of left scapular region**
  - +7th **T22.669 Corrosion of second degree of unspecified scapular region**

+ **T22.69 Corrosion of second degree of multiple sites of shoulder and upper limb, except wrist and hand**
  - +7th **T22.691 Corrosion of second degree of multiple sites of right shoulder and upper limb, except wrist and hand**
  - +7th **T22.692 Corrosion of second degree of multiple sites of left shoulder and upper limb, except wrist and hand**
  - +7th **T22.699 Corrosion of second degree of multiple sites of unspecified shoulder and upper limb, except wrist and hand**

+ **T22.7 Corrosion of third degree of shoulder and upper limb, except wrist and hand**

Code first (T51-T65) to identify chemical and intent external cause code to identify place (Y92)

CC X+7th **T22.70 Corrosion of third degree of shoulder and upper limb, except wrist and hand, unspecified site**

CC Exclusion 7th character A see Appendix A PDX collection 1389

HAC 7th character A see Appendix B for HAC conditional logic

+ **T22.71 Corrosion of third degree of forearm**
  - CC +7th **T22.711 Corrosion of third degree of right forearm**
    CC Exclusion 7th character A see Appendix A PDX collection 1390
    HAC 7th character A see Appendix B for HAC conditional logic
  - CC +7th **T22.712 Corrosion of third degree of left forearm**
    CC Exclusion 7th character A see Appendix A PDX collection 1390
    HAC 7th character A see Appendix B for HAC conditional logic
  - CC +7th **T22.719 Corrosion of third degree of unspecified forearm**
    CC Exclusion 7th character A see Appendix A PDX collection 1390
    HAC 7th character A see Appendix B for HAC conditional logic

+ **T22.72 Corrosion of third degree of elbow**
- CC +7th **T22.721 Corrosion of third degree of right elbow**
  - **CC Exclusion 7th character A see Appendix A PDX collection 1391**
  - HAC 7th character A see Appendix B for HAC conditional logic
- CC +7th **T22.722 Corrosion of third degree of left elbow**
  - **CC Exclusion 7th character A see Appendix A PDX collection 1391**
  - HAC 7th character A see Appendix B for HAC conditional logic
- CC +7th **T22.729 Corrosion of third degree of unspecified elbow**
  - **CC Exclusion 7th character A see Appendix A PDX collection 1391**
  - HAC 7th character A see Appendix B for HAC conditional logic

+ **T22.73 Corrosion of third degree of upper arm**
- CC +7th **T22.731 Corrosion of third degree of right upper arm**
  - **CC Exclusion 7th character A see Appendix A PDX collection 1392**
  - HAC 7th character A see Appendix B for HAC conditional logic
- CC +7th **T22.732 Corrosion of third degree of left upper arm**
  - **CC Exclusion 7th character A see Appendix A PDX collection 1392**
  - HAC 7th character A see Appendix B for HAC conditional logic
- CC +7th **T22.739 Corrosion of third degree of unspecified upper arm**
  - **CC Exclusion 7th character A see Appendix A PDX collection 1392**
  - HAC 7th character A see Appendix B for HAC conditional logic

+ **T22.74 Corrosion of third degree of axilla**
- CC +7th **T22.741 Corrosion of third degree of right axilla**
  - **CC Exclusion 7th character A see Appendix A PDX collection 1393**
  - HAC 7th character A see Appendix B for HAC conditional logic
- CC +7th **T22.742 Corrosion of third degree of left axilla**
  - **CC Exclusion 7th character A see Appendix A PDX collection 1393**
  - HAC 7th character A see Appendix B for HAC conditional logic
- CC +7th **T22.749 Corrosion of third degree of unspecified axilla**
  - **CC Exclusion 7th character A see Appendix A PDX collection 1393**
  - HAC 7th character A see Appendix B for HAC conditional logic

+ **T22.75 Corrosion of third degree of shoulder**
- CC +7th **T22.751 Corrosion of third degree of right shoulder**
  - **CC Exclusion 7th character A see Appendix A PDX collection 1394**
  - HAC 7th character A see Appendix B for HAC conditional logic
- CC +7th **T22.752 Corrosion of third degree of left shoulder**
  - **CC Exclusion 7th character A see Appendix A PDX collection 1394**
  - HAC 7th character A see Appendix B for HAC conditional logic
- CC +7th **T22.759 Corrosion of third degree of unspecified shoulder**
  - **CC Exclusion 7th character A see Appendix A PDX collection 1394**
  - HAC 7th character A see Appendix B for HAC conditional logic

+ **T22.76 Corrosion of third degree of scapular region**
- CC +7th **T22.761 Corrosion of third degree of right scapular region**
  - **CC Exclusion 7th character A see Appendix A PDX collection 1395**
  - HAC 7th character A see Appendix B for HAC conditional logic
- CC +7th **T22.762 Corrosion of third degree of left scapular region**
  - **CC Exclusion 7th character A see Appendix A PDX collection 1395**
  - HAC 7th character A see Appendix B for HAC conditional logic
- CC +7th **T22.769 Corrosion of third degree of unspecified scapular region**
  - **CC Exclusion 7th character A see Appendix A PDX collection 1395**
  - HAC 7th character A see Appendix B for HAC conditional logic

+ **T22.79 Corrosion of third degree of multiple sites of shoulder and upper limb, except wrist and hand**
- CC +7th **T22.791 Corrosion of third degree of multiple sites of right shoulder and upper limb, except wrist and hand**
  - **CC Exclusion 7th character A see Appendix A PDX collection 1389**
  - HAC 7th character A see Appendix B for HAC conditional logic
- CC +7th **T22.792 Corrosion of third degree of multiple sites of left shoulder and upper limb, except wrist and hand**
  - **CC Exclusion 7th character A see Appendix A PDX collection 1389**
  - HAC 7th character A see Appendix B for HAC conditional logic
- CC +7th **T22.799 Corrosion of third degree of multiple sites of unspecified shoulder and upper limb, except wrist and hand**
  - **CC Exclusion 7th character A see Appendix A PDX collection 1389**
  - HAC 7th character A see Appendix B for HAC conditional logic

T23 Burn and corrosion of wrist and hand

The appropriate 7th character is to be added to each code from category T23
- A initial encounter
- D subsequent encounter
- S sequela

+ **T23.0 Burn of unspecified degree of wrist and hand**
  Use additional external cause code to identify the source, place and intent of the burn (X00-X19, X75-X77, X96-X98, Y92)
  + **T23.00 Burn of unspecified degree of hand, unspecified site**
    - +7th **T23.001 Burn of unspecified degree of right hand, unspecified site**
    - +7th **T23.002 Burn of unspecified degree of left hand, unspecified site**
    - +7th **T23.009 Burn of unspecified degree of unspecified hand, unspecified site**
  + **T23.01 Burn of unspecified degree of thumb (nail)**
    - +7th **T23.011 Burn of unspecified degree of right thumb (nail)**
    - +7th **T23.012 Burn of unspecified degree of left thumb (nail)**
    - +7th **T23.019 Burn of unspecified degree of unspecified thumb (nail)**
  + **T23.02 Burn of unspecified degree of single finger (nail) except thumb**
    - +7th **T23.021 Burn of unspecified degree of single right finger (nail) except thumb**
    - +7th **T23.022 Burn of unspecified degree of single left finger (nail) except thumb**
    - +7th **T23.029 Burn of unspecified degree of unspecified single finger (nail) except thumb**
  + **T23.03 Burn of unspecified degree of multiple fingers (nail), not including thumb**
    - +7th **T23.031 Burn of unspecified degree of multiple right fingers (nail), not including thumb**
    - +7th **T23.032 Burn of unspecified degree of multiple left fingers (nail), not including thumb**
    - +7th **T23.039 Burn of unspecified degree of unspecified multiple fingers (nail), not including thumb**
  + **T23.04 Burn of unspecified degree of multiple fingers (nail), including thumb**
    - +7th **T23.041 Burn of unspecified degree of multiple right fingers (nail), including thumb**
    - +7th **T23.042 Burn of unspecified degree of multiple left fingers (nail), including thumb**
    - +7th **T23.049 Burn of unspecified degree of unspecified multiple fingers (nail), including thumb**
  + **T23.05 Burn of unspecified degree of palm**
    - +7th **T23.051 Burn of unspecified degree of right palm**
    - +7th **T23.052 Burn of unspecified degree of left palm**
    - +7th **T23.059 Burn of unspecified degree of unspecified palm**

+ **T23.06 Burn of unspecified degree of back of hand**
  - +7th **T23.061 Burn of unspecified degree of back of right hand**
  - +7th **T23.062 Burn of unspecified degree of back of left hand**
  - +7th **T23.069 Burn of unspecified degree of back of unspecified hand**

+ **T23.07 Burn of unspecified degree of wrist**
  - +7th **T23.071 Burn of unspecified degree of right wrist**
  - +7th **T23.072 Burn of unspecified degree of left wrist**
  - +7th **T23.079 Burn of unspecified degree of unspecified wrist**

+ **T23.09 Burn of unspecified degree of multiple sites of wrist and hand**
  - +7th **T23.091 Burn of unspecified degree of multiple sites of right wrist and hand**
  - +7th **T23.092 Burn of unspecified degree of multiple sites of left wrist and hand**
  - +7th **T23.099 Burn of unspecified degree of multiple sites of unspecified wrist and hand**

+ **T23.1 Burn of first degree of wrist and hand**

  Use additional external cause code to identify the source, place and intent of the burn (X00-X19, X75-X77, X96-X98, Y92)

+ **T23.10 Burn of first degree of hand, unspecified site**
  - +7th **T23.101 Burn of first degree of right hand, unspecified site**
  - +7th **T23.102 Burn of first degree of left hand, unspecified site**
  - +7th **T23.109 Burn of first degree of unspecified hand, unspecified site**

+ **T23.11 Burn of first degree of thumb (nail)**
  - +7th **T23.111 Burn of first degree of right thumb (nail)**
  - +7th **T23.112 Burn of first degree of left thumb (nail)**
  - +7th **T23.119 Burn of first degree of unspecified thumb (nail)**

+ **T23.12 Burn of first degree of single finger (nail) except thumb**
  - +7th **T23.121 Burn of first degree of single right finger (nail) except thumb**
  - +7th **T23.122 Burn of first degree of single left finger (nail) except thumb**
  - +7th **T23.129 Burn of first degree of unspecified single finger (nail) except thumb**

+ **T23.13 Burn of first degree of multiple fingers (nail), not including thumb**
  - +7th **T23.131 Burn of first degree of multiple right fingers (nail), not including thumb**
  - +7th **T23.132 Burn of first degree of multiple left fingers (nail), not including thumb**
  - +7th **T23.139 Burn of first degree of unspecified multiple fingers (nail), not including thumb**

+ **T23.14 Burn of first degree of multiple fingers (nail), including thumb**
  - +7th **T23.141 Burn of first degree of multiple right fingers (nail), including thumb**
  - +7th **T23.142 Burn of first degree of multiple left fingers (nail), including thumb**
  - +7th **T23.149 Burn of first degree of unspecified multiple fingers (nail), including thumb**

+ **T23.15 Burn of first degree of palm**
  - +7th **T23.151 Burn of first degree of right palm**
  - +7th **T23.152 Burn of first degree of left palm**
  - +7th **T23.159 Burn of first degree of unspecified palm**

+ **T23.16 Burn of first degree of back of hand**
  - +7th **T23.161 Burn of first degree of back of right hand**
  - +7th **T23.162 Burn of first degree of back of left hand**
  - +7th **T23.169 Burn of first degree of back of unspecified hand**

+ **T23.17 Burn of first degree of wrist**
  - +7th **T23.171 Burn of first degree of right wrist**
  - +7th **T23.172 Burn of first degree of left wrist**
  - +7th **T23.179 Burn of first degree of unspecified wrist**

+ **T23.19 Burn of first degree of multiple sites of wrist and hand**
  - +7th **T23.191 Burn of first degree of multiple sites of right wrist and hand**
  - +7th **T23.192 Burn of first degree of multiple sites of left wrist and hand**
  - +7th **T23.199 Burn of first degree of multiple sites of unspecified wrist and hand**

+ **T23.2 Burn of second degree of wrist and hand**

  Use additional external cause code to identify the source, place and intent of the burn (X00-X19, X75-X77, X96-X98, Y92)

+ **T23.20 Burn of second degree of hand, unspecified site**
  - +7th **T23.201 Burn of second degree of right hand, unspecified site**
  - +7th **T23.202 Burn of second degree of left hand, unspecified site**
  - +7th **T23.209 Burn of second degree of unspecified hand, unspecified site**

+ **T23.21 Burn of second degree of thumb (nail)**
  - +7th **T23.211 Burn of second degree of right thumb (nail)**
  - +7th **T23.212 Burn of second degree of left thumb (nail)**
  - +7th **T23.219 Burn of second degree of unspecified thumb (nail)**

+ **T23.22 Burn of second degree of single finger (nail) except thumb**
  - +7th **T23.221 Burn of second degree of single right finger (nail) except thumb**
  - +7th **T23.222 Burn of second degree of single left finger (nail) except thumb**
  - +7th **T23.229 Burn of second degree of unspecified single finger (nail) except thumb**

+ **T23.23 Burn of second degree of multiple fingers (nail), not including thumb**
  - +7th **T23.231 Burn of second degree of multiple right fingers (nail), not including thumb**
  - +7th **T23.232 Burn of second degree of multiple left fingers (nail), not including thumb**
  - +7th **T23.239 Burn of second degree of unspecified multiple fingers (nail), not including thumb**

+ **T23.24 Burn of second degree of multiple fingers (nail), including thumb**
  - +7th **T23.241 Burn of second degree of multiple right fingers (nail), including thumb**
  - +7th **T23.242 Burn of second degree of multiple left fingers (nail), including thumb**
  - +7th **T23.249 Burn of second degree of unspecified multiple fingers (nail), including thumb**

+ **T23.25 Burn of second degree of palm**
  - +7th **T23.251 Burn of second degree of right palm**
  - +7th **T23.252 Burn of second degree of left palm**
  - +7th **T23.259 Burn of second degree of unspecified palm**

+ **T23.26 Burn of second degree of back of hand**
  - +7th **T23.261 Burn of second degree of back of right hand**
  - +7th **T23.262 Burn of second degree of back of left hand**
  - +7th **T23.269 Burn of second degree of back of unspecified hand**

+ **T23.27 Burn of second degree of wrist**
  - +7th **T23.271 Burn of second degree of right wrist**
  - +7th **T23.272 Burn of second degree of left wrist**
  - +7th **T23.279 Burn of second degree of unspecified wrist**

+ **T23.29 Burn of second degree of multiple sites of wrist and hand**
  - +7th **T23.291 Burn of second degree of multiple sites of right wrist and hand**
  - +7th **T23.292 Burn of second degree of multiple sites of left wrist and hand**
  - +7th **T23.299 Burn of second degree of multiple sites of unspecified wrist and hand**

+ **T23.3 Burn of third degree of wrist and hand**

  Use additional external cause code to identify the source, place and intent of the burn (X00-X19, X75-X77, X96-X98, Y92)

+ **T23.30 Burn of third degree of hand, unspecified site**
  - CC +7th **T23.301 Burn of third degree of right hand, unspecified site**

    CC Exclusion 7th character A see Appendix A PDX collection 1396

    HAC 7th character A see Appendix B for HAC conditional logic
  - CC +7th **T23.302 Burn of third degree of left hand, unspecified site**

    CC Exclusion 7th character A see Appendix A PDX collection 1396

    HAC 7th character A see Appendix B for HAC conditional logic
  - CC +7th **T23.309 Burn of third degree of unspecified hand, unspecified site**

    CC Exclusion 7th character A see Appendix A PDX collection 1396

    HAC 7th character A see Appendix B for HAC conditional logic

+ **T23.31 Burn of third degree of thumb (nail)**

CC +7th **T23.311 Burn of third degree of right thumb (nail)**
CC Exclusion 7th character A see Appendix A
PDX collection 1397
HAC 7th character A see Appendix B for HAC conditional logic

CC +7th **T23.312 Burn of third degree of left thumb (nail)**
CC Exclusion 7th character A see Appendix A
PDX collection 1397
HAC 7th character A see Appendix B for HAC conditional logic

CC +7th **T23.319 Burn of third degree of unspecified thumb (nail)**
CC Exclusion 7th character A see Appendix A
PDX collection 1397
HAC 7th character A see Appendix B for HAC conditional logic

+ **T23.32 Burn of third degree of single finger (nail) except thumb**

CC +7th **T23.321 Burn of third degree of single right finger (nail) except thumb**
CC Exclusion 7th character A see Appendix A
PDX collection 1398
HAC 7th character A see Appendix B for HAC conditional logic

CC +7th **T23.322 Burn of third degree of single left finger (nail) except thumb**
CC Exclusion 7th character A see Appendix A
PDX collection 1398
HAC 7th character A see Appendix B for HAC conditional logic

CC +7th **T23.329 Burn of third degree of unspecified single finger (nail) except thumb**
CC Exclusion 7th character A see Appendix A
PDX collection 1398
HAC 7th character A see Appendix B for HAC conditional logic

+ **T23.33 Burn of third degree of multiple fingers (nail), not including thumb**

CC +7th **T23.331 Burn of third degree of multiple right fingers (nail), not including thumb**
CC Exclusion 7th character A see Appendix A
PDX collection 1399
HAC 7th character A see Appendix B for HAC conditional logic

CC +7th **T23.332 Burn of third degree of multiple left fingers (nail), not including thumb**
CC Exclusion 7th character A see Appendix A
PDX collection 1399
HAC 7th character A see Appendix B for HAC conditional logic

CC +7th **T23.339 Burn of third degree of unspecified multiple fingers (nail), not including thumb**
CC Exclusion 7th character A see Appendix A
PDX collection 1399

+ **T23.34 Burn of third degree of multiple fingers (nail), including thumb**

CC +7th **T23.341 Burn of third degree of multiple right fingers (nail), including thumb**
CC Exclusion 7th character A see Appendix A
PDX collection 1400
HAC 7th character A see Appendix B for HAC conditional logic

CC +7th **T23.342 Burn of third degree of multiple left fingers (nail), including thumb**
CC Exclusion 7th character A see Appendix A
PDX collection 1400
HAC 7th character A see Appendix B for HAC conditional logic

CC +7th **T23.349 Burn of third degree of unspecified multiple fingers (nail), including thumb**
CC Exclusion 7th character A see Appendix A
PDX collection 1400
HAC 7th character A see Appendix B for HAC conditional logic

+ **T23.35 Burn of third degree of palm**

CC +7th **T23.351 Burn of third degree of right palm**
CC Exclusion 7th character A see Appendix A
PDX collection 1401
HAC 7th character A see Appendix B for HAC conditional logic

CC +7th **T23.352 Burn of third degree of left palm**
CC Exclusion 7th character A see Appendix A
PDX collection 1401
HAC 7th character A see Appendix B for HAC conditional logic

CC +7th **T23.359 Burn of third degree of unspecified palm**
CC Exclusion 7th character A see Appendix A
PDX collection 1401
HAC 7th character A see Appendix B for HAC conditional logic

+ **T23.36 Burn of third degree of back of hand**

CC +7th **T23.361 Burn of third degree of back of right hand**
CC Exclusion 7th character A see Appendix A
PDX collection 1402
HAC 7th character A see Appendix B for HAC conditional logic

CC +7th **T23.362 Burn of third degree of back of left hand**
CC Exclusion 7th character A see Appendix A
PDX collection 1402
HAC 7th character A see Appendix B for HAC conditional logic

CC +7th **T23.369 Burn of third degree of back of unspecified hand**
CC Exclusion 7th character A see Appendix A
PDX collection 1402
HAC 7th character A see Appendix B for HAC conditional logic

+ **T23.37 Burn of third degree of wrist**

CC +7th **T23.371 Burn of third degree of right wrist**
CC Exclusion 7th character A see Appendix A
PDX collection 1403
HAC 7th character A see Appendix B for HAC conditional logic

CC +7th **T23.372 Burn of third degree of left wrist**
CC Exclusion 7th character A see Appendix A
PDX collection 1403
HAC 7th character A see Appendix B for HAC conditional logic

CC +7th **T23.379 Burn of third degree of unspecified wrist**
CC Exclusion 7th character A see Appendix A
PDX collection 1403
HAC 7th character A see Appendix B for HAC conditional logic

+ **T23.39 Burn of third degree of multiple sites of wrist and hand**

CC +7th **T23.391 Burn of third degree of multiple sites of rig wrist and hand**
CC Exclusion 7th character A see Appendix A
PDX collection 1396
HAC 7th character A see Appendix B for HAC conditional logic

CC +7th **T23.392 Burn of third degree of multiple sites of left wrist and hand**
CC Exclusion 7th character A see Appendix A
PDX collection 1396
HAC 7th character A see Appendix B for HAC conditional logic

CC +7th **T23.399 Burn of third degree of multiple sites of unspecified wrist and hand**
CC Exclusion 7th character A see Appendix A
PDX collection 1396
HAC 7th character A see Appendix B for HAC conditional logic

+ **T23.4 Corrosion of unspecified degree of wrist and hand**
Code first (T51-T65) to identify chemical and intent

Use additional external cause code to identify place (Y92)

+ **T23.40 Corrosion of unspecified degree of hand, unspecified si**

+7th **T23.401 Corrosion of unspecified degree of right hand, unspecified site**

+7th **T23.402 Corrosion of unspecified degree of left hand unspecified site**

+7th **T23.409 Corrosion of unspecified degree of unspecified hand, unspecified site**

+ **T23.41 Corrosion of unspecified degree of thumb (nail)**

+7th **T23.411 Corrosion of unspecified degree of right thumb (nail)**

+7th **T23.412 Corrosion of unspecified degree of left thumb (nail)**

+7th **T23.419 Corrosion of unspecified degree of unspecified thumb (nail)**

+ **T23.42 Corrosion of unspecified degree of single finger (nail) except thumb**

+7th **T23.421 Corrosion of unspecified degree of single right finger (nail) except thumb**

+7th **T23.422** **Corrosion of unspecified degree of single left finger (nail) except thumb**
+7th **T23.429** **Corrosion of unspecified degree of unspecified single finger (nail) except thumb**
+ **T23.43** **Corrosion of unspecified degree of multiple fingers (nail), not including thumb**
+7th **T23.431** **Corrosion of unspecified degree of multiple right fingers (nail), not including thumb**
+7th **T23.432** **Corrosion of unspecified degree of multiple left fingers (nail), not including thumb**
+7th **T23.439** **Corrosion of unspecified degree of unspecified multiple fingers (nail), not including thumb**
+ **T23.44** **Corrosion of unspecified degree of multiple fingers (nail), including thumb**
+7th **T23.441** **Corrosion of unspecified degree of multiple right fingers (nail), including thumb**
+7th **T23.442** **Corrosion of unspecified degree of multiple left fingers (nail), including thumb**
+7th **T23.449** **Corrosion of unspecified degree of unspecified multiple fingers (nail), including thumb**
+ **T23.45** **Corrosion of unspecified degree of palm**
+7th **T23.451** **Corrosion of unspecified degree of right palm**
+7th **T23.452** **Corrosion of unspecified degree of left palm**
+7th **T23.459** **Corrosion of unspecified degree of unspecified palm**
+ **T23.46** **Corrosion of unspecified degree of back of hand**
+7th **T23.461** **Corrosion of unspecified degree of back of right hand**
+7th **T23.462** **Corrosion of unspecified degree of back of left hand**
+7th **T23.469** **Corrosion of unspecified degree of back of unspecified hand**
+ **T23.47** **Corrosion of unspecified degree of wrist**
+7th **T23.471** **Corrosion of unspecified degree of right wrist**
+7th **T23.472** **Corrosion of unspecified degree of left wrist**
+7th **T23.479** **Corrosion of unspecified degree of unspecified wrist**
+ **T23.49** **Corrosion of unspecified degree of multiple sites of wrist and hand**
+7th **T23.491** **Corrosion of unspecified degree of multiple sites of right wrist and hand**
+7th **T23.492** **Corrosion of unspecified degree of multiple sites of left wrist and hand**
+7th **T23.499** **Corrosion of unspecified degree of multiple sites of unspecified wrist and hand**

+ **T23.5** **Corrosion of first degree of wrist and hand**
Code first (T51-T65) to identify chemical and intent

Use additional external cause code to identify place (Y92)

+ **T23.50** **Corrosion of first degree of hand, unspecified site**
+7th **T23.501** **Corrosion of first degree of right hand, unspecified site**
+7th **T23.502** **Corrosion of first degree of left hand, unspecified site**
+7th **T23.509** **Corrosion of first degree of unspecified hand, unspecified site**
+ **T23.51** **Corrosion of first degree of thumb (nail)**
+7th **T23.511** **Corrosion of first degree of right thumb (nail)**
+7th **T23.512** **Corrosion of first degree of left thumb (nail)**
+7th **T23.519** **Corrosion of first degree of unspecified thumb (nail)**
+ **T23.52** **Corrosion of first degree of single finger (nail) except thumb**
+7th **T23.521** **Corrosion of first degree of single right finger (nail) except thumb**
+7th **T23.522** **Corrosion of first degree of single left finger (nail) except thumb**
+7th **T23.529** **Corrosion of first degree of unspecified single finger (nail) except thumb**
+ **T23.53** **Corrosion of first degree of multiple fingers (nail), not including thumb**
+7th **T23.531** **Corrosion of first degree of multiple right fingers (nail), not including thumb**
+7th **T23.532** **Corrosion of first degree of multiple left fingers (nail), not including thumb**
+7th **T23.539** **Corrosion of first degree of unspecified multiple fingers (nail), not including thumb**
+ **T23.54** **Corrosion of first degree of multiple fingers (nail), including thumb**
+7th **T23.541** **Corrosion of first degree of multiple right fingers (nail), including thumb**
+7th **T23.542** **Corrosion of first degree of multiple left fingers (nail), including thumb**
+7th **T23.549** **Corrosion of first degree of unspecified multiple fingers (nail), including thumb**
+ **T23.55** **Corrosion of first degree of palm**
+7th **T23.551** **Corrosion of first degree of right palm**
+7th **T23.552** **Corrosion of first degree of left palm**
+7th **T23.559** **Corrosion of first degree of unspecified palm**
+ **T23.56** **Corrosion of first degree of back of hand**
+7th **T23.561** **Corrosion of first degree of back of right hand**
+7th **T23.562** **Corrosion of first degree of back of left hand**
+7th **T23.569** **Corrosion of first degree of back of unspecified hand**
+ **T23.57** **Corrosion of first degree of wrist**
+7th **T23.571** **Corrosion of first degree of right wrist**
+7th **T23.572** **Corrosion of first degree of left wrist**
+7th **T23.579** **Corrosion of first degree of unspecified wrist**
+ **T23.59** **Corrosion of first degree of multiple sites of wrist and hand**
+7th **T23.591** **Corrosion of first degree of multiple sites of right wrist and hand**
+7th **T23.592** **Corrosion of first degree of multiple sites of left wrist and hand**
+7th **T23.599** **Corrosion of first degree of multiple sites of unspecified wrist and hand**

+ **T23.6** **Corrosion of second degree of wrist and hand**
Code first (T51-T65) to identify chemical and intent

Use additionalexternal cause code to identify place (Y92)

+ **T23.60** **Corrosion of second degree of hand, unspecified site**
+7th **T23.601** **Corrosion of second degree of right hand, unspecified site**
+7th **T23.602** **Corrosion of second degree of left hand, unspecified site**
+7th **T23.609** **Corrosion of second degree of unspecified hand, unspecified site**
+ **T23.61** **Corrosion of second degree of thumb (nail)**
+7th **T23.611** **Corrosion of second degree of right thumb (nail)**
+7th **T23.612** **Corrosion of second degree of left thumb (nail)**
+7th **T23.619** **Corrosion of second degree of unspecified thumb (nail)**
+ **T23.62** **Corrosion of second degree of single finger (nail) except thumb**
+7th **T23.621** **Corrosion of second degree of single right finger (nail) except thumb**
+7th **T23.622** **Corrosion of second degree of single left finger (nail) except thumb**
+7th **T23.629** **Corrosion of second degree of unspecified single finger (nail) except thumb**
+ **T23.63** **Corrosion of second degree of multiple fingers (nail), not including thumb**
+7th **T23.631** **Corrosion of second degree of multiple right fingers (nail), not including thumb**
+7th **T23.632** **Corrosion of second degree of multiple left fingers (nail), not including thumb**
+7th **T23.639** **Corrosion of second degree of unspecified multiple fingers (nail), not including thumb**
+ **T23.64** **Corrosion of second degree of multiple fingers (nail), including thumb**
+7th **T23.641** **Corrosion of second degree of multiple right fingers (nail), including thumb**
+7th **T23.642** **Corrosion of second degree of multiple left fingers (nail), including thumb**
+7th **T23.649** **Corrosion of second degree of unspecified multiple fingers (nail), including thumb**
+ **T23.65** **Corrosion of second degree of palm**
+7th **T23.651** **Corrosion of second degree of right palm**
+7th **T23.652** **Corrosion of second degree of left palm**
+7th **T23.659** **Corrosion of second degree of unspecified palm**
+ **T23.66** **Corrosion of second degree of back of hand**
+7th **T23.661** **Corrosion of second degree back of right hand**
+7th **T23.662** **Corrosion of second degree back of left hand**
+7th **T23.669** **Corrosion of second degree back of unspecified hand**

+ **T23.67 Corrosion of second degree of wrist**
  - +7th **T23.671 Corrosion of second degree of right wrist**
  - +7th **T23.672 Corrosion of second degree of left wrist**
  - +7th **T23.679 Corrosion of second degree of unspecified wrist**

+ **T23.69 Corrosion of second degree of multiple sites of wrist and hand**
  - +7th **T23.691 Corrosion of second degree of multiple sites of right wrist and hand**
  - +7th **T23.692 Corrosion of second degree of multiple sites of left wrist and hand**
  - +7th **T23.699 Corrosion of second degree of multiple sites of unspecified wrist and hand**

+ **T23.7 Corrosion of third degree of wrist and hand**

Code first (T51-T65) to identify chemical and intent

Use additional external cause code to identify place (Y92)

+ **T23.70 Corrosion of third degree of hand, unspecified site**
  - CC +7th **T23.701 Corrosion of third degree of right hand, unspecified site**
    - **CC Exclusion 7th character A see Appendix A PDX collection 1396**
    - HAC 7th character A see Appendix B for HAC conditional logic
  - CC +7th **T23.702 Corrosion of third degree of left hand, unspecified site**
    - **CC Exclusion 7th character A see Appendix A PDX collection 1396**
    - HAC 7th character A see Appendix B for HAC conditional logic
  - CC +7th **T23.709 Corrosion of third degree of unspecified hand, unspecified site**
    - **CC Exclusion 7th character A see Appendix A PDX collection 1396**
    - HAC 7th character A see Appendix B for HAC conditional logic

+ **T23.71 Corrosion of third degree of thumb (nail)**
  - CC +7th **T23.711 Corrosion of third degree of right thumb (nail)**
    - **CC Exclusion 7th character A see Appendix A PDX collection 1397**
    - HAC 7th character A see Appendix B for HAC conditional logic
  - CC +7th **T23.712 Corrosion of third degree of left thumb (nail)**
    - **CC Exclusion 7th character A see Appendix A PDX collection 1397**
    - HAC 7th character A see Appendix B for HAC conditional logic
  - CC +7th **T23.719 Corrosion of third degree of unspecified thumb (nail)**
    - **CC Exclusion 7th character A see Appendix A PDX collection 1397**
    - HAC 7th character A see Appendix B for HAC conditional logic

+ **T23.72 Corrosion of third degree of single finger (nail) except thumb**
  - CC +7th **T23.721 Corrosion of third degree of single right finger (nail) except thumb**
    - **CC Exclusion 7th character A see Appendix A PDX collection 1398**
    - HAC 7th character A see Appendix B for HAC conditional logic
  - CC +7th **T23.722 Corrosion of third degree of single left finger (nail) except thumb**
    - **CC Exclusion 7th character A see Appendix A PDX collection 1398**
    - HAC 7th character A see Appendix B for HAC conditional logic
  - CC +7th **T23.729 Corrosion of third degree of unspecified single finger (nail) except thumb**
    - **CC Exclusion 7th character A see Appendix A PDX collection 1398**
    - HAC 7th character A see Appendix B for HAC conditional logic

+ **T23.73 Corrosion of third degree of multiple fingers (nail), not including thumb**
  - CC +7th **T23.731 Corrosion of third degree of multiple right fingers (nail), not including thumb**
    - **CC Exclusion 7th character A see Appendix A PDX collection 1399**
    - HAC 7th character A see Appendix B for HAC conditional logic
  - CC +7th **T23.732 Corrosion of third degree of multiple left fingers (nail), not including thumb**
    - **CC Exclusion 7th character A see Appendix A PDX collection 1399**
    - HAC 7th character A see Appendix B for HAC conditional logic
  - CC +7th **T23.739 Corrosion of third degree of unspecified multiple fingers (nail), not including thumb**
    - **CC Exclusion 7th character A see Appendix A PDX collection 1399**
    - HAC 7th character A see Appendix B for HAC conditional logic

+ **T23.74 Corrosion of third degree of multiple fingers (nail), including thumb**
  - CC +7th **T23.741 Corrosion of third degree of multiple right fingers (nail), including thumb**
    - **CC Exclusion 7th character A see Appendix A PDX collection 1400**
    - HAC 7th character A see Appendix B for HAC conditional logic
  - CC +7th **T23.742 Corrosion of third degree of multiple left fingers (nail), including thumb**
    - **CC Exclusion 7th character A see Appendix A PDX collection 1400**
    - HAC 7th character A see Appendix B for HAC conditional logic
  - CC +7th **T23.749 Corrosion of third degree of unspecified multiple fingers (nail), including thumb**
    - **CC Exclusion 7th character A see Appendix A PDX collection 1400**
    - HAC 7th character A see Appendix B for HAC conditional logic

+ **T23.75 Corrosion of third degree of palm**
  - CC +7th **T23.751 Corrosion of third degree of right palm**
    - **CC Exclusion 7th character A see Appendix A PDX collection 1401**
    - HAC 7th character A see Appendix B for HAC conditional logic
  - CC +7th **T23.752 Corrosion of third degree of left palm**
    - **CC Exclusion 7th character A see Appendix A PDX collection 1401**
    - HAC 7th character A see Appendix B for HAC conditional logic
  - CC +7th **T23.759 Corrosion of third degree of unspecified palm**
    - **CC Exclusion 7th character A see Appendix A PDX collection 1401**
    - HAC 7th character A see Appendix B for HAC conditional logic

+ **T23.76 Corrosion of third degree of back of hand**
  - CC +7th **T23.761 Corrosion of third degree of back of right hand**
    - **CC Exclusion 7th character A see Appendix A PDX collection 1402**
    - HAC 7th character A see Appendix B for HAC conditional logic
  - CC +7th **T23.762 Corrosion of third degree of back of left hand**
    - **CC Exclusion 7th character A see Appendix A PDX collection 1402**
    - HAC 7th character A see Appendix B for HAC conditional logic
  - CC +7th **T23.769 Corrosion of third degree back of unspecified hand**
    - **CC Exclusion 7th character A see Appendix A PDX collection 1402**
    - HAC 7th character A see Appendix B for HAC conditional logic

+ **T23.77 Corrosion of third degree of wrist**
  - CC +7th **T23.771 Corrosion of third degree of right wrist**
    - **CC Exclusion 7th character A see Appendix A PDX collection 1403**
    - HAC 7th character A see Appendix B for HAC conditional logic
  - CC +7th **T23.772 Corrosion of third degree of left wrist**
    - **CC Exclusion 7th character A see Appendix A PDX collection 1403**
    - HAC 7th character A see Appendix B for HAC conditional logic
  - CC +7th **T23.779 Corrosion of third degree of unspecified wrist**
    - **CC Exclusion 7th character A see Appendix A PDX collection 1403**
    - HAC 7th character A see Appendix B for HAC conditional logic

+ **T23.79 Corrosion of third degree of multiple sites of wrist and hand**

CC +7th **T23.791 Corrosion of third degree of multiple sites of right wrist and hand**
CC Exclusion 7th character A see Appendix A
PDX collection 1396
HAC 7th character A see Appendix B for HAC conditional logic

CC +7th **T23.792 Corrosion of third degree of multiple sites of left wrist and hand**
CC Exclusion 7th character A see Appendix A
PDX collection 1396
HAC 7th character A see Appendix B for HAC conditional logic

CC +7th **T23.799 Corrosion of third degree of multiple sites of unspecified wrist and hand**
CC Exclusion 7th character A see Appendix A
PDX collection 1396
HAC 7th character A see Appendix B for HAC conditional logic

T24 Burn and corrosion of lower limb, except ankle and foot

Excludes2: *burn and corrosion of ankle and foot (T25.-)*
burn and corrosion of hip region (T21.-)

The appropriate 7th character is to be added to each code from category T24
A initial encounter
D subsequent encounter
S sequela

+ **T24.0 Burn of unspecified degree of lower limb, except ankle and foot**
Use additional external cause code to identify the source, place and intent of the burn (X00-X19, X75-X77, X96-X98, Y92)

+ **T24.00 Burn of unspecified degree of unspecified site of lower limb, except ankle and foot**
+7th **T24.001 Burn of unspecified degree of unspecified site of right lower limb, except ankle and foot**
+7th **T24.002 Burn of unspecified degree of unspecified site of left lower limb, except ankle and foot**
+7th **T24.009 Burn of unspecified degree of unspecified site of unspecified lower limb, except ankle and foot**

+ **T24.01 Burn of unspecified degree of thigh**
+7th **T24.011 Burn of unspecified degree of right thigh**
+7th **T24.012 Burn of unspecified degree of left thigh**
+7th **T24.019 Burn of unspecified degree of unspecified thigh**

+ **T24.02 Burn of unspecified degree of knee**
+7th **T24.021 Burn of unspecified degree of right knee**
+7th **T24.022 Burn of unspecified degree of left knee**
+7th **T24.029 Burn of unspecified degree of unspecified knee**

+ **T24.03 Burn of unspecified degree of lower leg**
+7th **T24.031 Burn of unspecified degree of right lower leg**
+7th **T24.032 Burn of unspecified degree of left lower leg**
+7th **T24.039 Burn of unspecified degree of unspecified lower leg**

+ **T24.09 Burn of unspecified degree of multiple sites of lower limb, except ankle and foot**
+7th **T24.091 Burn of unspecified degree of multiple sites of right lower limb, except ankle and foot**
+7th **T24.092 Burn of unspecified degree of multiple sites of left lower limb, except ankle and foot**
+7th **T24.099 Burn of unspecified degree of multiple sites of unspecified lower limb, except ankle and foot**

+ **T24.1 Burn of first degree of lower limb, except ankle and foot**
Use additional external cause code to identify the source, place and intent of the burn (X00-X19, X75-X77, X96-X98, Y92)

+ **T24.10 Burn of first degree of unspecified site of lower limb, except ankle and foot**
+7th **T24.101 Burn of first degree of unspecified site of right lower limb, except ankle and foot**
+7th **T24.102 Burn of first degree of unspecified site of left lower limb, except ankle and foot**
+7th **T24.109 Burn of first degree of unspecified site of unspecified lower limb, except ankle and foot**

+ **T24.11 Burn of first degree of thigh**
+7th **T24.111 Burn of first degree of right thigh**
+7th **T24.112 Burn of first degree of left thigh**
+7th **T24.119 Burn of first degree of unspecified thigh**

+ **T24.12 Burn of first degree of knee**
+7th **T24.121 Burn of first degree of right knee**
+7th **T24.122 Burn of first degree of left knee**
+7th **T24.129 Burn of first degree of unspecified knee**

+ **T24.13 Burn of first degree of lower leg**
+7th **T24.131 Burn of first degree of right lower leg**
+7th **T24.132 Burn of first degree of left lower leg**
+7th **T24.139 Burn of first degree of unspecified lower leg**

+ **T24.19 Burn of first degree of multiple sites of lower limb, except ankle and foot**
+7th **T24.191 Burn of first degree of multiple sites of right lower limb, except ankle and foot**
+7th **T24.192 Burn of first degree of multiple sites of left lower limb, except ankle and foot**
+7th **T24.199 Burn of first degree of multiple sites of unspecified lower limb, except ankle and foot**

+ **T24.2 Burn of second degree of lower limb, except ankle and foot**
Use additional external cause code to identify the source, place and intent of the burn (X00-X19, X75-X77, X96-X98, Y92)

+ **T24.20 Burn of second degree of unspecified site of lower limb, except ankle and foot**
+7th **T24.201 Burn of second degree of unspecified site of right lower limb, except ankle and foot**
+7th **T24.202 Burn of second degree of unspecified site of left lower limb, except ankle and foot**
+7th **T24.209 Burn of second degree of unspecified site of unspecified lower limb, except ankle and foot**

+ **T24.21 Burn of second degree of thigh**
+7th **T24.211 Burn of second degree of right thigh**
+7th **T24.212 Burn of second degree of left thigh**
+7th **T24.219 Burn of second degree of unspecified thigh**

+ **T24.22 Burn of second degree of knee**
+7th **T24.221 Burn of second degree of right knee**
+7th **T24.222 Burn of second degree of left knee**
+7th **T24.229 Burn of second degree of unspecified knee**

+ **T24.23 Burn of second degree of lower leg**
+7th **T24.231 Burn of second degree of right lower leg**
+7th **T24.232 Burn of second degree of left lower leg**
+7th **T24.239 Burn of second degree of unspecified lower leg**

+ **T24.29 Burn of second degree of multiple sites of lower limb, except ankle and foot**
+7th **T24.291 Burn of second degree of multiple sites of right lower limb, except ankle and foot**
+7th **T24.292 Burn of second degree of multiple sites of left lower limb, except ankle and foot**
+7th **T24.299 Burn of second degree of multiple sites of unspecified lower limb, except ankle and foot**

+ **T24.3 Burn of third degree of lower limb, except ankle and foot**
Use additional external cause code to identify the source, place and intent of the burn (X00-X19, X75-X77, X96-X98, Y92)

+ **T24.30 Burn of third degree of unspecified site of lower limb, except ankle and foot**

CC +7th **T24.301 Burn of third degree of unspecified site of right lower limb, except ankle and foot**
CC Exclusion 7th character A see Appendix A
PDX collection 1404
HAC 7th character A see Appendix B for HAC conditional logic

CC +7th **T24.302 Burn of third degree of unspecified site of left lower limb, except ankle and foot**
CC Exclusion 7th character A see Appendix A
PDX collection 1404
HAC 7th character A see Appendix B for HAC conditional logic

CC +7th **T24.309 Burn of third degree of unspecified site of unspecified lower limb, except ankle and foot**
CC Exclusion 7th character A see Appendix A
PDX collection 1404
HAC 7th character A see Appendix B for HAC conditional logic

+ **T24.31 Burn of third degree of thigh**

CC +7th **T24.311 Burn of third degree of right thigh**
CC Exclusion 7th character A see Appendix A
PDX collection 1405
HAC 7th character A see Appendix B for HAC conditional logic

CC +7th **T24.312 Burn of third degree of left thigh**
CC Exclusion 7th character A see Appendix A
PDX collection 1405
HAC 7th character A see Appendix B for HAC conditional logic

CC +7th **T24.319 Burn of third degree of unspecified thigh**
CC Exclusion 7th character A see Appendix A
PDX collection 1405
HAC 7th character A see Appendix B for HAC conditional logic

+ **T24.32 Burn of third degree of knee**

CC +7th **T24.321 Burn of third degree of right knee**
CC Exclusion 7th character A see Appendix A
PDX collection 1406
HAC 7th character A see Appendix B for HAC conditional logic

CC +7th **T24.322 Burn of third degree of left knee**
CC Exclusion 7th character A see Appendix A
PDX collection 1406
HAC 7th character A see Appendix B for HAC conditional logic

CC +7th **T24.329 Burn of third degree of unspecified knee**
CC Exclusion 7th character A see Appendix A
PDX collection 1406
HAC 7th character A see Appendix B for HAC conditional logic

+ **T24.33 Burn of third degree of lower leg**

CC +7th **T24.331 Burn of third degree of right lower leg**
CC Exclusion 7th character A see Appendix A
PDX collection 1407
HAC 7th character A see Appendix B for HAC conditional logic

CC +7th **T24.332 Burn of third degree of left lower leg**
CC Exclusion 7th character A see Appendix A
PDX collection 1407
HAC 7th character A see Appendix B for HAC conditional logic

CC +7th **T24.339 Burn of third degree of unspecified lower leg**
CC Exclusion 7th character A see Appendix A
PDX collection 1407
HAC 7th character A see Appendix B for HAC conditional logic

+ **T24.39 Burn of third degree of multiple sites of lower limb, except ankle and foot**

CC +7th **T24.391 Burn of third degree of multiple sites of right lower limb, except ankle and foot**
CC Exclusion 7th character A see Appendix A
PDX collection 1404
HAC 7th character A see Appendix B for HAC conditional logic

CC +7th **T24.392 Burn of third degree of multiple sites of left lower limb, except ankle and foot**
CC Exclusion 7th character A see Appendix A
PDX collection 1404
HAC 7th character A see Appendix B for HAC conditional logic

CC +7th **T24.399 Burn of third degree of multiple sites of unspecified lower limb, except ankle and foot**
CC Exclusion 7th character A see Appendix A
PDX collection 1404
HAC 7th character A see Appendix B for HAC conditional logic

+ **T24.4 Corrosion of unspecified degree of lower limb, except ankle and foot**
Code first (T51-T65) to identify chemical and intent

Use additional external cause code to identify place (Y92)

+ **T24.40 Corrosion of unspecified degree of unspecified site of lower limb, except ankle and foot**
+7th **T24.401 Corrosion of unspecified degree of unspecified site of right lower limb, except ankle and foot**
+7th **T24.402 Corrosion of unspecified degree of unspecified site of left lower limb, except ankle and foot**
+7th **T24.409 Corrosion of unspecified degree of unspecified site of unspecified lower limb, except ankle and foot**

+ **T24.41 Corrosion of unspecified degree of thigh**
+7th **T24.411 Corrosion of unspecified degree of right thigh**
+7th **T24.412 Corrosion of unspecified degree of left thigh**
+7th **T24.419 Corrosion of unspecified degree of unspecified thigh**

+ **T24.42 Corrosion of unspecified degree of knee**
+7th **T24.421 Corrosion of unspecified degree of right knee**
+7th **T24.422 Corrosion of unspecified degree of left knee**
+7th **T24.429 Corrosion of unspecified degree of unspecified knee**

+ **T24.43 Corrosion of unspecified degree of lower leg**
+7th **T24.431 Corrosion of unspecified degree of right lower leg**
+7th **T24.432 Corrosion of unspecified degree of left lower leg**
+7th **T24.439 Corrosion of unspecified degree of unspecified lower leg**

+ **T24.49 Corrosion of unspecified degree of multiple sites of lower limb, except ankle and foot**
+7th **T24.491 Corrosion of unspecified degree of multiple sites of right lower limb, except ankle and foot**
+7th **T24.492 Corrosion of unspecified degree of multiple sites of left lower limb, except ankle and foot**
+7th **T24.499 Corrosion of unspecified degree of multiple sites of unspecified lower limb, except ankle and foot**

+ **T24.5 Corrosion of first degree of lower limb, except ankle and foot**
Code first (T51-T65) to identify chemical and intent

Use additional external cause code to identify place (Y92)

+ **T24.50 Corrosion of first degree of unspecified site of lower limb, except ankle and foot**
+7th **T24.501 Corrosion of first degree of unspecified site of right lower limb, except ankle and foot**
+7th **T24.502 Corrosion of first degree of unspecified site of left lower limb, except ankle and foot**
+7th **T24.509 Corrosion of first degree of unspecified site of unspecified lower limb, except ankle and foot**

+ **T24.51 Corrosion of first degree of thigh**
+7th **T24.511 Corrosion of first degree of right thigh**
+7th **T24.512 Corrosion of first degree of left thigh**
+7th **T24.519 Corrosion of first degree of unspecified thigh**

+ **T24.52 Corrosion of first degree of knee**
+7th **T24.521 Corrosion of first degree of right knee**
+7th **T24.522 Corrosion of first degree of left knee**
+7th **T24.529 Corrosion of first degree of unspecified knee**

+ **T24.53 Corrosion of first degree of lower leg**
+7th **T24.531 Corrosion of first degree of right lower leg**
+7th **T24.532 Corrosion of first degree of left lower leg**
+7th **T24.539 Corrosion of first degree of unspecified lower leg**

+ **T24.59 Corrosion of first degree of multiple sites of lower limb, except ankle and foot**
+7th **T24.591 Corrosion of first degree of multiple sites of right lower limb, except ankle and foot**
+7th **T24.592 Corrosion of first degree of multiple sites of left lower limb, except ankle and foot**
+7th **T24.599 Corrosion of first degree of multiple sites of unspecified lower limb, except ankle and foot**

+ **T24.6 Corrosion of second degree of lower limb, except ankle and foot**
Code first (T51-T65) to identify chemical and intent

Use additional external cause code to identify place (Y92)

+ **T24.60 Corrosion of second degree of unspecified site of lower limb, except ankle and foot**
+7th **T24.601 Corrosion of second degree of unspecified site of right lower limb, except ankle and foot**
+7th **T24.602 Corrosion of second degree of unspecified site of left lower limb, except ankle and foot**
+7th **T24.609 Corrosion of second degree of unspecified site of unspecified lower limb, except ankle and foot**

+ **T24.61 Corrosion of second degree of thigh**
+7th **T24.611 Corrosion of second degree of right thigh**
+7th **T24.612 Corrosion of second degree of left thigh**
+7th **T24.619 Corrosion of second degree of unspecified thigh**

+ **T24.62 Corrosion of second degree of knee**
+7th **T24.621 Corrosion of second degree of right knee**
+7th **T24.622 Corrosion of second degree of left knee**
+7th **T24.629 Corrosion of second degree of unspecified knee**

+ **T24.63 Corrosion of second degree of lower leg**
+7th **T24.631 Corrosion of second degree of right lower leg**
+7th **T24.632 Corrosion of second degree of left lower leg**
+7th **T24.639 Corrosion of second degree of unspecified lower leg**

+ **T24.69 Corrosion of second degree of multiple sites of lower limb, except ankle and foot**
+7th **T24.691 Corrosion of second degree of multiple sites of right lower limb, except ankle and foot**

+7th **T24.692** **Corrosion of second degree of multiple sites of left lower limb, except ankle and foot**

+7th **T24.699** **Corrosion of second degree of multiple sites of unspecified lower limb, except ankle and foot**

\+ **T24.7** **Corrosion of third degree of lower limb, except ankle and foot**
Code first (T51-T65) to identify chemical and intent

Use additional external cause code to identify place (Y92)

\+ **T24.70** **Corrosion of third degree of unspecified site of lower limb, except ankle and foot**

CC +7th **T24.701** **Corrosion of third degree of unspecified site of right lower limb, except ankle and foot**
CC Exclusion 7th character A see Appendix A
PDX collection 1404
HAC 7th character A see Appendix B for HAC conditional logic

CC +7th **T24.702** **Corrosion of third degree of unspecified site of left lower limb, except ankle and foot**
CC Exclusion 7th character A see Appendix A
PDX collection 1404
HAC 7th character A see Appendix B for HAC conditional logic

CC +7th **T24.709** **Corrosion of third degree of unspecified site of unspecified lower limb, except ankle and foot**
CC Exclusion 7th character A see Appendix A
PDX collection 1404
HAC 7th character A see Appendix B for HAC conditional logic

\+ **T24.71** **Corrosion of third degree of thigh**

CC +7th **T24.711** **Corrosion of third degree of right thigh**
CC Exclusion 7th character A see Appendix A
PDX collection 1405
HAC 7th character A see Appendix B for HAC conditional logic

CC +7th **T24.712** **Corrosion of third degree of left thigh**
CC Exclusion 7th character A see Appendix A
PDX collection 1405
HAC 7th character A see Appendix B for HAC conditional logic

CC +7th **T24.719** **Corrosion of third degree of unspecified thigh**
CC Exclusion 7th character A see Appendix A
PDX collection 1405
HAC 7th character A see Appendix B for HAC conditional logic

\+ **T24.72** **Corrosion of third degree of knee**

CC +7th **T24.721** **Corrosion of third degree of right knee**
CC Exclusion 7th character A see Appendix A
PDX collection 1406
HAC 7th character A see Appendix B for HAC conditional logic

CC +7th **T24.722** **Corrosion of third degree of left knee**
CC Exclusion 7th character A see Appendix A
PDX collection 1406
HAC 7th character A see Appendix B for HAC conditional logic

CC +7th **T24.729** **Corrosion of third degree of unspecified knee**
CC Exclusion 7th character A see Appendix A
PDX collection 1406
HAC 7th character A see Appendix B for HAC conditional logic

\+ **T24.73** **Corrosion of third degree of lower leg**

CC +7th **T24.731** **Corrosion of third degree of right lower leg**
CC Exclusion 7th character A see Appendix A
PDX collection 1407
HAC 7th character A see Appendix B for HAC conditional logic

CC +7th **T24.732** **Corrosion of third degree of left lower leg**
CC Exclusion 7th character A see Appendix A
PDX collection 1407
HAC 7th character A see Appendix B for HAC conditional logic

CC +7th **T24.739** **Corrosion of third degree of unspecified lower leg**
CC Exclusion 7th character A see Appendix A
PDX collection 1407
HAC 7th character A see Appendix B for HAC conditional logic

\+ **T24.79** **Corrosion of third degree of multiple sites of lower limb, except ankle and foot**

CC +7th **T24.791** **Corrosion of third degree of multiple sites of right lower limb, except ankle and foot**
CC Exclusion 7th character A see Appendix A
PDX collection 1404
HAC 7th character A see Appendix B for HAC conditional logic

CC +7th **T24.792** **Corrosion of third degree of multiple sites of left lower limb, except ankle and foot**
CC Exclusion 7th character A see Appendix A
PDX collection 1404
HAC 7th character A see Appendix B for HAC conditional logic

CC +7th **T24.799** **Corrosion of third degree of multiple sites of unspecified lower limb, except ankle and foot**
CC Exclusion 7th character A see Appendix A
PDX collection 1404
HAC 7th character A see Appendix B for HAC conditional logic

T25 Burn and corrosion of ankle and foot

The appropriate 7th character is to be added to each code from category T25
A initial encounter
D subsequent encounter
S sequela

\+ **T25.0** **Burn of unspecified degree of ankle and foot**
Use additional external cause code to identify the source, place and intent of the burn (X00-X19, X75-X77, X96-X98, Y92)

\+ **T25.01** **Burn of unspecified degree of ankle**

+7th **T25.011** **Burn of unspecified degree of right ankle**

+7th **T25.012** **Burn of unspecified degree of left ankle**

+7th **T25.019** **Burn of unspecified degree of unspecified ankle**

\+ **T25.02** **Burn of unspecified degree of foot**
Excludes2: *burn of unspecified degree of toe(s) (nail) (T25.03-)*

+7th **T25.021** **Burn of unspecified degree of right foot**

+7th **T25.022** **Burn of unspecified degree of left foot**

+7th **T25.029** **Burn of unspecified degree of unspecified foot**

\+ **T25.03** **Burn of unspecified degree of toe(s) (nail)**

+7th **T25.031** **Burn of unspecified degree of right toe(s) (nail)**

+7th **T25.032** **Burn of unspecified degree of left toe(s) (nail)**

+7th **T25.039** **Burn of unspecified degree of unspecified toe(s) (nail)**

\+ **T25.09** **Burn of unspecified degree of multiple sites of ankle and foot**

+7th **T25.091** **Burn of unspecified degree of multiple sites of right ankle and foot**

+7th **T25.092** **Burn of unspecified degree of multiple sites of left ankle and foot**

+7th **T25.099** **Burn of unspecified degree of multiple sites of unspecified ankle and foot**

\+ **T25.1** **Burn of first degree of ankle and foot**
Use additional external cause code to identify the source, place and intent of the burn (X00-X19, X75-X77, X96-X98, Y92)

\+ **T25.11** **Burn of first degree of ankle**

+7th **T25.111** **Burn of first degree of right ankle**

+7th **T25.112** **Burn of first degree of left ankle**

+7th **T25.119** **Burn of first degree of unspecified ankle**

\+ **T25.12** **Burn of first degree of foot**
Excludes2: *burn of first degree of toe(s) (nail) (T25.13-)*

+7th **T25.121** **Burn of first degree of right foot**

+7th **T25.122** **Burn of first degree of left foot**

+7th **T25.129** **Burn of first degree of unspecified foot**

\+ **T25.13** **Burn of first degree of toe(s) (nail)**

+7th **T25.131** **Burn of first degree of right toe(s) (nail)**

+7th **T25.132** **Burn of first degree of left toe(s) (nail)**

+7th **T25.139** **Burn of first degree of unspecified toe(s) (nail)**

\+ **T25.19** **Burn of first degree of multiple sites of ankle and foot**

+7th **T25.191** **Burn of first degree of multiple sites of right ankle and foot**

+7th **T25.192** **Burn of first degree of multiple sites of left ankle and foot**

+7th **T25.199** **Burn of first degree of multiple sites of unspecified ankle and foot**

+ **T25.2 Burn of second degree of ankle and foot**
Use additional external cause code to identify the source, place and intent of the burn (X00-X19, X75-X77, X96-X98, Y92)
+ **T25.21 Burn of second degree of ankle**
+7th **T25.211 Burn of second degree of right ankle**
+7th **T25.212 Burn of second degree of left ankle**
+7th **T25.219 Burn of second degree of unspecified ankle**
+ **T25.22 Burn of second degree of foot**
Excludes2: *burn of second degree of toe(s) (nail) (T25.23-)*
+7th **T25.221 Burn of second degree of right foot**
+7th **T25.222 Burn of second degree of left foot**
+7th **T25.229 Burn of second degree of unspecified foot**
+ **T25.23 Burn of second degree of toe(s) (nail)**
+7th **T25.231 Burn of second degree of right toe(s) (nail)**
+7th **T25.232 Burn of second degree of left toe(s) (nail)**
+7th **T25.239 Burn of second degree of unspecified toe(s) (nail)**
+ **T25.29 Burn of second degree of multiple sites of ankle and foot**
+7th **T25.291 Burn of second degree of multiple sites of right ankle and foot**
+7th **T25.292 Burn of second degree of multiple sites of left ankle and foot**
+7th **T25.299 Burn of second degree of multiple sites of unspecified ankle and foot**
+ **T25.3 Burn of third degree of ankle and foot**
Use external cause code to identify the source, place and intent of the burn (X00-X19, X75-X77, X96-X98, Y92)
+ **T25.31 Burn of third degree of ankle**
CC +7th **T25.311 Burn of third degree of right ankle**
CC Exclusion 7th character A see Appendix A PDX collection 1408
HAC 7th character A see Appendix B for HAC conditional logic
CC +7th **T25.312 Burn of third degree of left ankle**
CC Exclusion 7th character A see Appendix A PDX collection 1408
HAC 7th character A see Appendix B for HAC conditional logic
CC +7th **T25.319 Burn of third degree of unspecified ankle**
CC Exclusion 7th character A see Appendix A PDX collection 1408
HAC 7th character A see Appendix B for HAC conditional logic
+ **T25.32 Burn of third degree of foot**
Excludes2: *burn of third degree of toe(s) (nail) (T25.33-)*
CC +7th **T25.321 Burn of third degree of right foot**
CC Exclusion 7th character A see Appendix A PDX collection 1409
HAC 7th character A see Appendix B for HAC conditional logic
CC +7th **T25.322 Burn of third degree of left foot**
CC Exclusion 7th character A see Appendix A PDX collection 1409
HAC 7th character A see Appendix B for HAC conditional logic
CC +7th **T25.329 Burn of third degree of unspecified foot**
CC Exclusion 7th character A see Appendix A PDX collection 1409
HAC 7th character A see Appendix B for HAC conditional logic
+ **T25.33 Burn of third degree of toe(s) (nail)**
CC +7th **T25.331 Burn of third degree of right toe(s) (nail)**
CC Exclusion 7th character A see Appendix A PDX collection 1410
HAC 7th character A see Appendix B for HAC conditional logic
CC +7th **T25.332 Burn of third degree of left toe(s) (nail)**
CC Exclusion 7th character A see Appendix A PDX collection 1410
HAC 7th character A see Appendix B for HAC conditional logic
CC +7th **T25.339 Burn of third degree of unspecified toe(s) (nail)**
CC Exclusion 7th character A see Appendix A PDX collection 1410
HAC 7th character A see Appendix B for HAC conditional logic
+ **T25.39 Burn of third degree of multiple sites of ankle and foot**
CC +7th **T25.391 Burn of third degree of multiple sites of right ankle and foot**
CC Exclusion 7th character A see Appendix A PDX collection 1404
HAC 7th character A see Appendix B for HAC conditional logic
CC +7th **T25.392 Burn of third degree of multiple sites of left ankle and foot**
CC Exclusion 7th character A see Appendix A PDX collection 1404
HAC 7th character A see Appendix B for HAC conditional logic
CC +7th **T25.399 Burn of third degree of multiple sites of unspecified ankle and foot**
CC Exclusion 7th character A see Appendix A PDX collection 1404
HAC 7th character A see Appendix B for HAC conditional logic
+ **T25.4 Corrosion of unspecified degree of ankle and foot**
Code first (T51-T65) to identify chemical and intent

Use additional external cause code to identify place (Y92)
+ **T25.41 Corrosion of unspecified degree of ankle**
+7th **T25.411 Corrosion of unspecified degree of right ankle**
+7th **T25.412 Corrosion of unspecified degree of left ankle**
+7th **T25.419 Corrosion of unspecified degree of unspecified ankle**
+ **T25.42 Corrosion of unspecified degree of foot**
Excludes2: *corrosion of unspecified degree of toe(s) (nail) (T25.43-)*
+7th **T25.421 Corrosion of unspecified degree of right foot**
+7th **T25.422 Corrosion of unspecified degree of left foot**
+7th **T25.429 Corrosion of unspecified degree of unspecified foot**
+ **T25.43 Corrosion of unspecified degree of toe(s) (nail)**
+7th **T25.431 Corrosion of unspecified degree of right toe(s) (nail)**
+7th **T25.432 Corrosion of unspecified degree of left toe(s) (nail)**
+7th **T25.439 Corrosion of unspecified degree of unspecified toe(s) (nail)**
+ **T25.49 Corrosion of unspecified degree of multiple sites of ankle and foot**
+7th **T25.491 Corrosion of unspecified degree of multiple sites of right ankle and foot**
+7th **T25.492 Corrosion of unspecified degree of multiple sites of left ankle and foot**
+7th **T25.499 Corrosion of unspecified degree of multiple sites of unspecified ankle and foot**
+ **T25.5 Corrosion of first degree of ankle and foot**
Code first (T51-T65) to identify chemical and intent

Use additional external cause code to identify place (Y92)
+ **T25.51 Corrosion of first degree of ankle**
+7th **T25.511 Corrosion of first degree of right ankle**
+7th **T25.512 Corrosion of first degree of left ankle**
+7th **T25.519 Corrosion of first degree of unspecified ankle**
+ **T25.52 Corrosion of first degree of foot**
Excludes2: *corrosion of first degree of toe(s) (nail) (T25.53-)*
+7th **T25.521 Corrosion of first degree of right foot**
+7th **T25.522 Corrosion of first degree of left foot**
+7th **T25.529 Corrosion of first degree of unspecified foot**
+ **T25.53 Corrosion of first degree of toe(s) (nail)**
+7th **T25.531 Corrosion of first degree of right toe(s) (nail)**
+7th **T25.532 Corrosion of first degree of left toe(s) (nail)**
+7th **T25.539 Corrosion of first degree of unspecified toe(s) (nail)**
+ **T25.59 Corrosion of first degree of multiple sites of ankle and foot**
+7th **T25.591 Corrosion of first degree of multiple sites of right ankle and foot**
+7th **T25.592 Corrosion of first degree of multiple sites of left ankle and foot**
+7th **T25.599 Corrosion of first degree of multiple sites of unspecified ankle and foot**
+ **T25.6 Corrosion of second degree of ankle and foot**
Code first (T51-T65) to identify chemical and intent

Use additional external cause code to identify place (Y92)
+ **T25.61 Corrosion of second degree of ankle**
+7th **T25.611 Corrosion of second degree of right ankle**

+7th **T25.612 Corrosion of second degree of left ankle**
+7th **T25.619 Corrosion of second degree of unspecified ankle**

\+ **T25.62 Corrosion of second degree of foot**
Excludes2: *corrosion of second degree of toe(s) (nail) (T25.63-)*

+7th **T25.621 Corrosion of second degree of right foot**
+7th **T25.622 Corrosion of second degree of left foot**
+7th **T25.629 Corrosion of second degree of unspecified foot**

\+ **T25.63 Corrosion of second degree of toe(s) (nail)**

+7th **T25.631 Corrosion of second degree of right toe(s) (nail)**
+7th **T25.632 Corrosion of second degree of left toe(s) (nail)**
+7th **T25.639 Corrosion of second degree of unspecified toe(s) (nail)**

\+ **T25.69 Corrosion of second degree of multiple sites of ankle and foot**

+7th **T25.691 Corrosion of second degree of right ankle and foot**
+7th **T25.692 Corrosion of second degree of left ankle and foot**
+7th **T25.699 Corrosion of second degree of unspecified ankle and foot**

\+ **T25.7 Corrosion of third degree of ankle and foot**
Code first (T51-T65) to identify chemical and intent

Use additional external cause code to identify place (Y92)

\+ **T25.71 Corrosion of third degree of ankle**

CC +7th **T25.711 Corrosion of third degree of right ankle**
CC Exclusion 7th character A see Appendix A
PDX collection 1408
HAC 7th character A see Appendix B for HAC conditional logic

CC +7th **T25.712 Corrosion of third degree of left ankle**
CC Exclusion 7th character A see Appendix A
PDX collection 1408
HAC 7th character A see Appendix B for HAC conditional logic

CC +7th **T25.719 Corrosion of third degree of unspecified ankle**
CC Exclusion 7th character A see Appendix A
PDX collection 1408
HAC 7th character A see Appendix B for HAC conditional logic

\+ **T25.72 Corrosion of third degree of foot**
Excludes2: *corrosion of third degree of toe(s) (nail) (T25.73-)*

CC +7th **T25.721 Corrosion of third degree of right foot**
CC Exclusion 7th character A see Appendix A
PDX collection 1409
HAC 7th character A see Appendix B for HAC conditional logic

CC +7th **T25.722 Corrosion of third degree of left foot**
CC Exclusion 7th character A see Appendix A
PDX collection 1409
HAC 7th character A see Appendix B for HAC conditional logic

CC +7th **T25.729 Corrosion of third degree of unspecified foot**
CC Exclusion 7th character A see Appendix A
PDX collection 1409
HAC 7th character A see Appendix B for HAC conditional logic

\+ **T25.73 Corrosion of third degree of toe(s) (nail)**

CC +7th **T25.731 Corrosion of third degree of right toe(s) (nail)**
CC Exclusion 7th character A see Appendix A
PDX collection 1410
HAC 7th character A see Appendix B for HAC conditional logic

CC +7th **T25.732 Corrosion of third degree of left toe(s) (nail)**
CC Exclusion 7th character A see Appendix A
PDX collection 1410
HAC 7th character A see Appendix B for HAC conditional logic

CC +7th **T25.739 Corrosion of third degree of unspecified toe(s) (nail)**
CC Exclusion 7th character A see Appendix A
PDX collection 1410
HAC 7th character A see Appendix B for HAC conditional logic

\+ **T25.79 Corrosion of third degree of multiple sites of ankle and foot**

CC +7th **T25.791 Corrosion of third degree of multiple sites of right ankle and foot**
CC Exclusion 7th character A see Appendix A
PDX collection 1404
HAC 7th character A see Appendix B for HAC conditional logic

CC +7th **T25.792 Corrosion of third degree of multiple sites of left ankle and foot**
CC Exclusion 7th character A see Appendix A
PDX collection 1404
HAC 7th character A see Appendix B for HAC conditional logic

CC +7th **T25.799 Corrosion of third degree of multiple sites of unspecified ankle and foot**
CC Exclusion 7th character A see Appendix A
PDX collection 1404
HAC 7th character A see Appendix B for HAC conditional logic

Burns and corrosions confined to eye and internal organs (T26-T28)

Review coding guideline C.19.d

T26 Burn and corrosion confined to eye and adnexa

The appropriate 7th character is to be added to each code from category T26
A initial encounter
D subsequent encounter
S sequela

\+ **T26.0 Burn of eyelid and periocular area**
Use additional external cause code to identify the source, place and intent of the burn (X00-X19, X75-X77, X96-X98, Y92)

X+7th **T26.00 Burn of unspecified eyelid and periocular area**
X+7th **T26.01 Burn of right eyelid and periocular area**
X+7th **T26.02 Burn of left eyelid and periocular area**

\+ **T26.1 Burn of cornea and conjunctival sac**
Use additional external cause code to identify the source, place and intent of the burn (X00-X19, X75-X77, X96-X98, Y92)

X+7th **T26.10 Burn of cornea and conjunctival sac, unspecified eye**
X+7th **T26.11 Burn of cornea and conjunctival sac, right eye**
X+7th **T26.12 Burn of cornea and conjunctival sac, left eye**

\+ **T26.2 Burn with resulting rupture and destruction of eyeball**
Use additional external cause code to identify the source, place and intent of the burn (X00-X19, X75-X77, X96-X98, Y92)

CC X+7th **T26.20 Burn with resulting rupture and destruction of unspecified eyeball**
No CC Exclusions
HAC 7th character A see Appendix B for HAC conditional logic

CC X+7th **T26.21 Burn with resulting rupture and destruction of right eyeball**
No CC Exclusions
HAC 7th character A see Appendix B for HAC conditional logic

CC X+7th **T26.22 Burn with resulting rupture and destruction of left eyeball**
No CC Exclusions
HAC 7th character A see Appendix B for HAC conditional logic

\+ **T26.3 Burns of other specified parts of eye and adnexa**
Use additional external cause code to identify the source, place and intent of the burn (X00-X19, X75-X77, X96-X98, Y92)

X+7th **T26.30 Burns of other specified parts of unspecified eye and adnexa**
X+7th **T26.31 Burns of other specified parts of right eye and adnexa**
X+7th **T26.32 Burns of other specified parts of left eye and adnexa**

\+ **T26.4 Burn of eye and adnexa, part unspecified**
Use additional external cause code to identify the source, place and intent of the burn (X00-X19, X75-X77, X96-X98, Y92)

X+7th **T26.40 Burn of unspecified eye and adnexa, part unspecified**
X+7th **T26.41 Burn of right eye and adnexa, part unspecified**
X+7th **T26.42 Burn of left eye and adnexa, part unspecified**

\+ **T26.5 Corrosion of eyelid and periocular area**
Code first (T51-T65) to identify chemical and intent

Use additional external cause code to identify place (Y92)

X+7th **T26.50 Corrosion of unspecified eyelid and periocular area**
X+7th **T26.51 Corrosion of right eyelid and periocular area**
X+7th **T26.52 Corrosion of left eyelid and periocular area**

+ **T26.6 Corrosion of cornea and conjunctival sac**
Code first (T51-T65) to identify chemical and intent

Use additional external cause code to identify place (Y92)

X+7th **T26.60 Corrosion of cornea and conjunctival sac, unspecified eye**
X+7th **T26.61 Corrosion of cornea and conjunctival sac, right eye**
X+7th **T26.62 Corrosion of cornea and conjunctival sac, left eye**

+ **T26.7 Corrosion with resulting rupture and destruction of eyeball**
Code first (T51-T65) to identify chemical and intent

Use additional external cause code to identify place (Y92)

CC X+7th **T26.70 Corrosion with resulting rupture and destruction of unspecified eyeball**
No CC Exclusions
HAC 7th character A see Appendix B for HAC conditional logic

CC X+7th **T26.71 Corrosion with resulting rupture and destruction of right eyeball**
No CC Exclusions
HAC 7th character A see Appendix B for HAC conditional logic

CC X+7th **T26.72 Corrosion with resulting rupture and destruction of left eyeball**
No CC Exclusions
HAC 7th character A see Appendix B for HAC conditional logic

+ **T26.8 Corrosions of other specified parts of eye and adnexa**
Code first (T51-T65) to identify chemical and intent

Use add itional external cause code to identify place (Y92)

X+7th **T26.80 Corrosions of other specified parts of unspecified eye and adnexa**
X+7th **T26.81 Corrosions of other specified parts of right eye and adnexa**
X+7th **T26.82 Corrosions of other specified parts of left eye and adnexa**

+ **T26.9 Corrosion of eye and adnexa, part unspecified**
Code first (T51-T65) to identify chemical and intent

Use additional external cause code to identify place (Y92)

X+7th **T26.90 Corrosion of unspecified eye and adnexa, part unspecified**
X+7th **T26.91 Corrosion of right eye and adnexa, part unspecified**
X+7th **T26.92 Corrosion of left eye and adnexa, part unspecified**

T27 Burn and corrosion of respiratory tract

Use additional external cause code to identify the source and intent of the burn (X00-X19, X75-X77, X96-X98)

Use external cause code to identify place (Y92)

The appropriate 7th character is to be added to each code from category T27
A initial encounter
D subsequent encounter
S sequela

CC X+7th **T27.0 Burn of larynx and trachea**
CC Exclusion 7th character A see Appendix A PDX collection 1411
HAC 7th character A see Appendix B for HAC conditional logic

CC X+7th **T27.1 Burn involving larynx and trachea with lung**
CC Exclusion 7th character A see Appendix A PDX collection 1411
HAC 7th character A see Appendix B for HAC conditional logic

CC X+7th **T27.2 Burn of other parts of respiratory tract**
Burn of thoracic cavity
CC Exclusion 7th character A see Appendix A PDX collection 1411
HAC 7th character A see Appendix B for HAC conditional logic

CC X+7th **T27.3 Burn of respiratory tract, part unspecified**
Code first (T51-T65) to identify chemical and intent for codes T27.4-T27.7
CC Exclusion 7th character A see Appendix A PDX collection 1411
HAC 7th character A see Appendix B for HAC conditional logic

CC X+7th **T27.4 Corrosion of larynx and trachea**
CC Exclusion 7th character A see Appendix A PDX collection 1411
HAC 7th character A see Appendix B for HAC conditional logic

CC X+7th **T27.5 Corrosion involving larynx and trachea with lung**
CC Exclusion 7th character A see Appendix A PDX collection 1411
HAC 7th character A see Appendix B for HAC conditional logic

CC X+7th **T27.6 Corrosion of other parts of respiratory tract**
CC Exclusion 7th character A see Appendix A PDX collection 1411
HAC 7th character A see Appendix B for HAC conditional logic

CC X+7th **T27.7 Corrosion of respiratory tract, part unspecified**
CC Exclusion 7th character A see Appendix A PDX collection 1411
HAC 7th character A see Appendix B for HAC conditional logic

T28 Burn and corrosion of other internal organs

Use additional external cause code to identify the source and intent of th burn (X00-X19, X75-X77, X96-X98)

Use external cause code to identify place (Y92)

The appropriate 7th character is to be added to each code from category T28
A initial encounter
D subsequent encounter
S sequela

X+7th **T28.0 Burn of mouth and pharynx**
CC X+7th **T28.1 Burn of esophagus**
CC Exclusion 7th character A see Appendix A PDX collection 1412
HAC 7th character A see Appendix B for HAC conditional logic

CC X+7th **T28.2 Burn of other parts of alimentary tract**
CC Exclusion 7th character A see Appendix A PDX collection 1413
HAC 7th character A see Appendix B for HAC conditional logic

X+7th **T28.3 Burn of internal genitourinary organs**
+ **T28.4 Burns of other and unspecified internal organs**
X+7th **T28.40 Burn of unspecified internal organ**
+ **T28.41 Burn of ear drum**
+7th **T28.411 Burn of right ear drum**
+7th **T28.412 Burn of left ear drum**
+7th **T28.419 Burn of unspecified ear drum**
X+7th **T28.49 Burn of other internal organ**
Code first (T51-T65) to identify chemical and intent for T28.5-T28.9-

X+7th **T28.5 Corrosion of mouth and pharynx**
CC X+7th **T28.6 Corrosion of esophagus**
CC Exclusion 7th character A see Appendix A PDX collection 1412
HAC 7th character A see Appendix B for HAC conditional logic

CC X+7th **T28.7 Corrosion of other parts of alimentary tract**
CC Exclusion 7th character A see Appendix A PDX collection 1413
HAC 7th character A see Appendix B for HAC conditional logic

X+7th **T28.8 Corrosion of internal genitourinary organs**
+ **T28.9 Corrosions of other and unspecified internal organs**
X+7th **T28.90 Corrosions of unspecified internal organs**
+ **T28.91 Corrosions of ear drum**
+7th **T28.911 Corrosions of right ear drum**
+7th **T28.912 Corrosions of left ear drum**
+7th **T28.919 Corrosions of unspecified ear drum**
X+7th **T28.99 Corrosions of other internal organs**

Burns and corrosions of multiple and unspecified body regions (T30-T32)

T30 Burn and corrosion, body region unspecified

Review coding guideline C.19.d.5

T30.0 Burn of unspecified body region, unspecified degree
This code is not for inpatient use. Code to specified site and degree of burns
Burn NOS
Multiple burns NOS

T30.4 Corrosion of unspecified body region, unspecified degree
This code is not for inpatient use. Code to specified site and degree of corrosion
Corrosion NOS
Multiple corrosion NOS

T31 Burns classified according to extent of body surface involved

NOTE This category is to be used as the primary code only when the site of the burn is unspecified. It should be used as a supplementary code with categories T20-T25 when the site is specified.

Review coding guideline C.19.d.6

T31.0 Burns involving less than 10% of body surface
+ **T31.1 Burns involving 10-19% of body surface**
CC **T31.10 Burns involving 10-19% of body surface with 0% to 9% third degree burns**
Burns involving 10-19% of body surface NOS
CC Exclusion see Appendix A PDX collection 1414
HAC see Appendix B for HAC conditional logic

CC **T31.11 Burns involving 10-19% of body surface with 10-19% third degree burns**
CC Exclusion see Appendix A PDX collection 1414
HAC see Appendix B for HAC conditional logic

+ **T31.2 Burns involving 20-29% of body surface**
CC **T31.20 Burns involving 20-29% of body surface with 0% to 9% third degree burns**
Burns involving 20-29% of body surface NOS
CC Exclusion see Appendix A PDX collection 1414
HAC see Appendix B for HAC conditional logic

MCC **T31.21 Burns involving 20-29% of body surface with 10-19% third degree burns**
MCC Exclusion see Appendix A PDX collection 1414
HAC see Appendix B for HAC conditional logic

MCC **T31.22 Burns involving 20-29% of body surface with 20-29% third degree burns**
MCC Exclusion see Appendix A PDX collection 1414
HAC see Appendix B for HAC conditional logic

\+ **T31.3 Burns involving 30-39% of body surface**

CC **T31.30 Burns involving 30-39% of body surface with 0% to 9% third degree burns**
Burns involving 30-39% of body surface NOS
CC Exclusion see Appendix A PDX collection 1414
HAC see Appendix B for HAC conditional logic

MCC **T31.31 Burns involving 30-39% of body surface with 10-19% third degree burns**
MCC Exclusion see Appendix A PDX collection 1414
HAC see Appendix B for HAC conditional logic

MCC **T31.32 Burns involving 30-39% of body surface with 20-29% third degree burns**
MCC Exclusion see Appendix A PDX collection 1414
HAC see Appendix B for HAC conditional logic

MCC **T31.33 Burns involving 30-39% of body surface with 30-39% third degree burns**
MCC Exclusion see Appendix A PDX collection 1414
HAC see Appendix B for HAC conditional logic

\+ **T31.4 Burns involving 40-49% of body surface**

CC **T31.40 Burns involving 40-49% of body surface with 0% to 9% third degree burns**
Burns involving 40-49% of body surface NOS
CC Exclusion see Appendix A PDX collection 1414
HAC see Appendix B for HAC conditional logic

MCC **T31.41 Burns involving 40-49% of body surface with 10-19% third degree burns**
MCC Exclusion see Appendix A PDX collection 1414
HAC see Appendix B for HAC conditional logic

MCC **T31.42 Burns involving 40-49% of body surface with 20-29% third degree burns**
MCC Exclusion see Appendix A PDX collection 1414
HAC see Appendix B for HAC conditional logic

MCC **T31.43 Burns involving 40-49% of body surface with 30-39% third degree burns**
MCC Exclusion see Appendix A PDX collection 1414
HAC see Appendix B for HAC conditional logic

MCC **T31.44 Burns involving 40-49% of body surface with 40-49% third degree burns**
MCC Exclusion see Appendix A PDX collection 1414
HAC see Appendix B for HAC conditional logic

\+ **T31.5 Burns involving 50-59% of body surface**

CC **T31.50 Burns involving 50-59% of body surface with 0% to 9% third degree burns**
Burns involving 50-59% of body surface NOS
CC Exclusion see Appendix A PDX collection 1414
HAC see Appendix B for HAC conditional logic

MCC **T31.51 Burns involving 50-59% of body surface with 10-19% third degree burns**
MCC Exclusion see Appendix A PDX collection 1414
HAC see Appendix B for HAC conditional logic

MCC **T31.52 Burns involving 50-59% of body surface with 20-29% third degree burns**
MCC Exclusion see Appendix A PDX collection 1414
HAC see Appendix B for HAC conditional logic

MCC **T31.53 Burns involving 50-59% of body surface with 30-39% third degree burns**
MCC Exclusion see Appendix A PDX collection 1414
HAC see Appendix B for HAC conditional logic

MCC **T31.54 Burns involving 50-59% of body surface with 40-49% third degree burns**
MCC Exclusion see Appendix A PDX collection 1414
HAC see Appendix B for HAC conditional logic

MCC **T31.55 Burns involving 50-59% of body surface with 50-59% third degree burns**
MCC Exclusion see Appendix A PDX collection 1414
HAC see Appendix B for HAC conditional logic

\+ **T31.6 Burns involving 60-69% of body surface**

CC **T31.60 Burns involving 60-69% of body surface with 0% to 9% third degree burns**
Burns involving 60-69% of body surface NOS
CC Exclusion see Appendix A PDX collection 1414
HAC see Appendix B for HAC conditional logic

MCC **T31.61 Burns involving 60-69% of body surface with 10-19% third degree burns**
MCC Exclusion see Appendix A PDX collection 1414
HAC see Appendix B for HAC conditional logic

MCC **T31.62 Burns involving 60-69% of body surface with 20-29% third degree burns**
MCC Exclusion see Appendix A PDX collection 1414
HAC see Appendix B for HAC conditional logic

MCC **T31.63 Burns involving 60-69% of body surface with 30-39% third degree burns**
MCC Exclusion see Appendix A PDX collection 1414
HAC see Appendix B for HAC conditional logic

MCC **T31.64 Burns involving 60-69% of body surface with 40-49% third degree burns**
MCC Exclusion see Appendix A PDX collection 1414
HAC see Appendix B for HAC conditional logic

MCC **T31.65 Burns involving 60-69% of body surface with 50-59% third degree burns**
MCC Exclusion see Appendix A PDX collection 1414
HAC see Appendix B for HAC conditional logic

MCC **T31.66 Burns involving 60-69% of body surface with 60-69% third degree burns**
MCC Exclusion see Appendix A PDX collection 1414
HAC see Appendix B for HAC conditional logic

\+ **T31.7 Burns involving 70-79% of body surface**

CC **T31.70 Burns involving 70-79% of body surface with 0% to 9% third degree burns**
Burns involving 70-79% of body surface NOS
CC Exclusion see Appendix A PDX collection 1414
HAC see Appendix B for HAC conditional logic

MCC **T31.71 Burns involving 70-79% of body surface with 10-19% third degree burns**
MCC Exclusion see Appendix A PDX collection 1414
HAC see Appendix B for HAC conditional logic

MCC **T31.72 Burns involving 70-79% of body surface with 20-29% third degree burns**
MCC Exclusion see Appendix A PDX collection 1414
HAC see Appendix B for HAC conditional logic

MCC **T31.73 Burns involving 70-79% of body surface with 30-39% third degree burns**
MCC Exclusion see Appendix A PDX collection 1414
HAC see Appendix B for HAC conditional logic

MCC **T31.74 Burns involving 70-79% of body surface with 40-49% third degree burns**
MCC Exclusion see Appendix A PDX collection 1414
HAC see Appendix B for HAC conditional logic

MCC **T31.75 Burns involving 70-79% of body surface with 50-59% third degree burns**
MCC Exclusion see Appendix A PDX collection 1414
HAC see Appendix B for HAC conditional logic

MCC **T31.76 Burns involving 70-79% of body surface with 60-69% third degree burns**
MCC Exclusion see Appendix A PDX collection 1414
HAC see Appendix B for HAC conditional logic

MCC **T31.77 Burns involving 70-79% of body surface with 70-79% third degree burns**
MCC Exclusion see Appendix A PDX collection 1414
HAC see Appendix B for HAC conditional logic

\+ **T31.8 Burns involving 80-89% of body surface**

CC **T31.80 Burns involving 80-89% of body surface with 0% to 9% third degree burns**
Burns involving 80-89% of body surface NOS
CC Exclusion see Appendix A PDX collection 1414
HAC see Appendix B for HAC conditional logic

MCC **T31.81 Burns involving 80-89% of body surface with 10-19% third degree burns**
MCC Exclusion see Appendix A PDX collection 1414
HAC see Appendix B for HAC conditional logic

MCC **T31.82 Burns involving 80-89% of body surface with 20-29% third degree burns**
MCC Exclusion see Appendix A PDX collection 1414
HAC see Appendix B for HAC conditional logic

MCC **T31.83 Burns involving 80-89% of body surface with 30-39% third degree burns**
MCC Exclusion see Appendix A PDX collection 1414
HAC see Appendix B for HAC conditional logic

MCC **T31.84 Burns involving 80-89% of body surface with 40-49% third degree burns**
MCC Exclusion see Appendix A PDX collection 1414
HAC see Appendix B for HAC conditional logic

MCC **T31.85** **Burns involving 80-89% of body surface with 50-59% third degree burns**
MCC **Exclusion see Appendix A PDX collection 1414**
HAC see Appendix B for HAC conditional logic

MCC **T31.86** **Burns involving 80-89% of body surface with 60-69% third degree burns**
MCC **Exclusion see Appendix A PDX collection 1414**
HAC see Appendix B for HAC conditional logic

MCC **T31.87** **Burns involving 80-89% of body surface with 70-79% third degree burns**
MCC **Exclusion see Appendix A PDX collection 1414**
HAC see Appendix B for HAC conditional logic

MCC **T31.88** **Burns involving 80-89% of body surface with 80-89% third degree burns**
MCC **Exclusion see Appendix A PDX collection 1414**
HAC see Appendix B for HAC conditional logic

+ **T31.9** **Burns involving 90% or more of body surface**

CC **T31.90** **Burns involving 90% or more of body surface with 0% to 9% third degree burns**
Burns involving 90% or more of body surface NOS
CC **Exclusion see Appendix A PDX collection 1414**
HAC see Appendix B for HAC conditional logic

MCC **T31.91** **Burns involving 90% or more of body surface with 10-19% third degree burns**
MCC **Exclusion see Appendix A PDX collection 1414**
HAC see Appendix B for HAC conditional logic

MCC **T31.92** **Burns involving 90% or more of body surface with 20-29% third degree burns**
MCC **Exclusion see Appendix A PDX collection 1414**
HAC see Appendix B for HAC conditional logic

MCC **T31.93** **Burns involving 90% or more of body surface with 30-39% third degree burns**
MCC **Exclusion see Appendix A PDX collection 1414**
HAC see Appendix B for HAC conditional logic

MCC **T31.94** **Burns involving 90% or more of body surface with 40-49% third degree burns**
MCC **Exclusion see Appendix A PDX collection 1414**
HAC see Appendix B for HAC conditional logic

MCC **T31.95** **Burns involving 90% or more of body surface with 50-59% third degree burns**
MCC **Exclusion see Appendix A PDX collection 1414**
HAC see Appendix B for HAC conditional logic

MCC **T31.96** **Burns involving 90% or more of body surface with 60-69% third degree burns**
MCC **Exclusion see Appendix A PDX collection 1414**
HAC see Appendix B for HAC conditional logic

MCC **T31.97** **Burns involving 90% or more of body surface with 70-79% third degree burns**
MCC **Exclusion see Appendix A PDX collection 1414**
HAC see Appendix B for HAC conditional logic

MCC **T31.98** **Burns involving 90% or more of body surface with 80-89% third degree burns**
MCC **Exclusion see Appendix A PDX collection 1414**
HAC see Appendix B for HAC conditional logic

MCC **T31.99** **Burns involving 90% or more of body surface with 90% or more third degree burns**
MCC **Exclusion see Appendix A PDX collection 1414**
HAC see Appendix B for HAC conditional logic

T32 **Corrosions classified according to extent of body surface involved**

NOTE This category is to be used as the primary code only when the site of the corrosion is unspecified. It may be used as a supplementary code with categories T20-T25 when the site is specified.

Review coding guideline C.19.d.6

T32.0 **Corrosions involving less than 10% of body surface**

+ **T32.1** **Corrosions involving 10-19% of body surface**

CC **T32.10** **Corrosions involving 10-19% of body surface with 0% to 9% third degree corrosion**
Corrosions involving 10-19% of body surface NOS
CC **Exclusion see Appendix A PDX collection 1414**
HAC see Appendix B for HAC conditional logic

CC **T32.11** **Corrosions involving 10-19% of body surface with 10-19% third degree corrosion**
CC **Exclusion see Appendix A PDX collection 1414**
HAC see Appendix B for HAC conditional logic

+ **T32.2** **Corrosions involving 20-29% of body surface**

CC **T32.20** **Corrosions involving 20-29% of body surface with 0% to 9% third degree corrosion**
CC **Exclusion see Appendix A PDX collection 1414**
HAC see Appendix B for HAC conditional logic

MCC **T32.21** **Corrosions involving 20-29% of body surface with 10-19% third degree corrosion**
MCC **Exclusion see Appendix A PDX collection 1414**
HAC see Appendix B for HAC conditional logic

MCC **T32.22** **Corrosions involving 20-29% of body surface with 20-29% third degree corrosion**
MCC **Exclusion see Appendix A PDX collection 1414**
HAC see Appendix B for HAC conditional logic

+ **T32.3** **Corrosions involving 30-39% of body surface**

CC **T32.30** **Corrosions involving 30-39% of body surface with 0% to 9% third degree corrosion**
CC **Exclusion see Appendix A PDX collection 1414**
HAC see Appendix B for HAC conditional logic

MCC **T32.31** **Corrosions involving 30-39% of body surface with 10-19% third degree corrosion**
MCC **Exclusion see Appendix A PDX collection 1414**
HAC see Appendix B for HAC conditional logic

MCC **T32.32** **Corrosions involving 30-39% of body surface with 20-29% third degree corrosion**
MCC **Exclusion see Appendix A PDX collection 1414**
HAC see Appendix B for HAC conditional logic

MCC **T32.33** **Corrosions involving 30-39% of body surface with 30-39% third degree corrosion**
MCC **Exclusion see Appendix A PDX collection 1414**
HAC see Appendix B for HAC conditional logic

+ **T32.4** **Corrosions involving 40-49% of body surface**

CC **T32.40** **Corrosions involving 40-49% of body surface with 0% to 9% third degree corrosion**
CC **Exclusion see Appendix A PDX collection 1414**
HAC see Appendix B for HAC conditional logic

MCC **T32.41** **Corrosions involving 40-49% of body surface with 10-19% third degree corrosion**
MCC **Exclusion see Appendix A PDX collection 1414**
HAC see Appendix B for HAC conditional logic

MCC **T32.42** **Corrosions involving 40-49% of body surface with 20-29% third degree corrosion**
MCC **Exclusion see Appendix A PDX collection 1414**
HAC see Appendix B for HAC conditional logic

MCC **T32.43** **Corrosions involving 40-49% of body surface with 30-39% third degree corrosion**
MCC **Exclusion see Appendix A PDX collection 1414**
HAC see Appendix B for HAC conditional logic

MCC **T32.44** **Corrosions involving 40-49% of body surface with 40-49% third degree corrosion**
MCC **Exclusion see Appendix A PDX collection 1414**
HAC see Appendix B for HAC conditional logic

+ **T32.5** **Corrosions involving 50-59% of body surface**

CC **T32.50** **Corrosions involving 50-59% of body surface with 0% to 9% third degree corrosion**
CC **Exclusion see Appendix A PDX collection 1414**
HAC see Appendix B for HAC conditional logic

MCC **T32.51** **Corrosions involving 50-59% of body surface with 10-19% third degree corrosion**
MCC **Exclusion see Appendix A PDX collection 1414**
HAC see Appendix B for HAC conditional logic

MCC **T32.52** **Corrosions involving 50-59% of body surface with 20-29% third degree corrosion**
MCC **Exclusion see Appendix A PDX collection 1414**
HAC see Appendix B for HAC conditional logic

MCC **T32.53** **Corrosions involving 50-59% of body surface with 30-39% third degree corrosion**
MCC **Exclusion see Appendix A PDX collection 1414**
HAC see Appendix B for HAC conditional logic

MCC **T32.54** **Corrosions involving 50-59% of body surface with 40-49% third degree corrosion**
MCC **Exclusion see Appendix A PDX collection 1414**
HAC see Appendix B for HAC conditional logic

MCC **T32.55** **Corrosions involving 50-59% of body surface with 50-59% third degree corrosion**
MCC **Exclusion see Appendix A PDX collection 1414**
HAC see Appendix B for HAC conditional logic

+ **T32.6** **Corrosions involving 60-69% of body surface**

CC **T32.60** **Corrosions involving 60-69% of body surface with 0% to 9% third degree corrosion**
CC **Exclusion see Appendix A PDX collection 1414**
HAC see Appendix B for HAC conditional logic

MCC **T32.61** **Corrosions involving 60-69% of body surface with 10-19% third degree corrosion**
MCC **Exclusion see Appendix A PDX collection 1414**
HAC see Appendix B for HAC conditional logic

MCC **T32.62 Corrosions involving 60-69% of body surface with 20-29% third degree corrosion**
MCC Exclusion see Appendix A PDX collection 1414
HAC see Appendix B for HAC conditional logic

MCC **T32.63 Corrosions involving 60-69% of body surface with 30-39% third degree corrosion**
MCC Exclusion see Appendix A PDX collection 1414
HAC see Appendix B for HAC conditional logic

MCC **T32.64 Corrosions involving 60-69% of body surface with 40-49% third degree corrosion**
MCC Exclusion see Appendix A PDX collection 1414
HAC see Appendix B for HAC conditional logic

MCC **T32.65 Corrosions involving 60-69% of body surface with 50-59% third degree corrosion**
MCC Exclusion see Appendix A PDX collection 1414
HAC see Appendix B for HAC conditional logic

MCC **T32.66 Corrosions involving 60-69% of body surface with 60-69% third degree corrosion**
MCC Exclusion see Appendix A PDX collection 1414
HAC see Appendix B for HAC conditional logic

\+ **T32.7 Corrosions involving 70-79% of body surface**

CC **T32.70 Corrosions involving 70-79% of body surface with 0% to 9% third degree corrosion**
CC Exclusion see Appendix A PDX collection 1414
HAC see Appendix B for HAC conditional logic

MCC **T32.71 Corrosions involving 70-79% of body surface with 10-19% third degree corrosion**
MCC Exclusion see Appendix A PDX collection 1414
HAC see Appendix B for HAC conditional logic

MCC **T32.72 Corrosions involving 70-79% of body surface with 20-29% third degree corrosion**
MCC Exclusion see Appendix A PDX collection 1414
HAC see Appendix B for HAC conditional logic

MCC **T32.73 Corrosions involving 70-79% of body surface with 30-39% third degree corrosion**
MCC Exclusion see Appendix A PDX collection 1414
HAC see Appendix B for HAC conditional logic

MCC **T32.74 Corrosions involving 70-79% of body surface with 40-49% third degree corrosion**
MCC Exclusion see Appendix A PDX collection 1414
HAC see Appendix B for HAC conditional logic

MCC **T32.75 Corrosions involving 70-79% of body surface with 50-59% third degree corrosion**
MCC Exclusion see Appendix A PDX collection 1414
HAC see Appendix B for HAC conditional logic

MCC **T32.76 Corrosions involving 70-79% of body surface with 60-69% third degree corrosion**
MCC Exclusion see Appendix A PDX collection 1414
HAC see Appendix B for HAC conditional logic

MCC **T32.77 Corrosions involving 70-79% of body surface with 70-79% third degree corrosion**
MCC Exclusion see Appendix A PDX collection 1414
HAC see Appendix B for HAC conditional logic

\+ **T32.8 Corrosions involving 80-89% of body surface**

CC **T32.80 Corrosions involving 80-89% of body surface with 0% to 9% third degree corrosion**
CC Exclusion see Appendix A PDX collection 1414
HAC see Appendix B for HAC conditional logic

MCC **T32.81 Corrosions involving 80-89% of body surface with 10-19% third degree corrosion**
MCC Exclusion see Appendix A PDX collection 1414
HAC see Appendix B for HAC conditional logic

MCC **T32.82 Corrosions involving 80-89% of body surface with 20-29% third degree corrosion**
MCC Exclusion see Appendix A PDX collection 1414
HAC see Appendix B for HAC conditional logic

MCC **T32.83 Corrosions involving 80-89% of body surface with 30-39% third degree corrosion**
MCC Exclusion see Appendix A PDX collection 1414
HAC see Appendix B for HAC conditional logic

MCC **T32.84 Corrosions involving 80-89% of body surface with 40-49% third degree corrosion**
MCC Exclusion see Appendix A PDX collection 1414
HAC see Appendix B for HAC conditional logic

MCC **T32.85 Corrosions involving 80-89% of body surface with 50-59% third degree corrosion**
MCC Exclusion see Appendix A PDX collection 1414
HAC see Appendix B for HAC conditional logic

MCC **T32.86 Corrosions involving 80-89% of body surface with 60-69% third degree corrosion**
MCC Exclusion see Appendix A PDX collection 1414
HAC see Appendix B for HAC conditional logic

MCC **T32.87 Corrosions involving 80-89% of body surface with 70-79% third degree corrosion**
MCC Exclusion see Appendix A PDX collection 1414
HAC see Appendix B for HAC conditional logic

MCC **T32.88 Corrosions involving 80-89% of body surface with 80-89% third degree corrosion**
MCC Exclusion see Appendix A PDX collection 1414
HAC see Appendix B for HAC conditional logic

\+ **T32.9 Corrosions involving 90% or more of body surface**

CC **T32.90 Corrosions involving 90% or more of body surface with 0% to 9% third degree corrosion**
CC Exclusion see Appendix A PDX collection 1414
HAC see Appendix B for HAC conditional logic

MCC **T32.91 Corrosions involving 90% or more of body surface with 10-19% third degree corrosion**
MCC Exclusion see Appendix A PDX collection 1414
HAC see Appendix B for HAC conditional logic

MCC **T32.92 Corrosions involving 90% or more of body surface with 20-29% third degree corrosion**
MCC Exclusion see Appendix A PDX collection 1414
HAC see Appendix B for HAC conditional logic

MCC **T32.93 Corrosions involving 90% or more of body surface with 30-39% third degree corrosion**
MCC Exclusion see Appendix A PDX collection 1414
HAC see Appendix B for HAC conditional logic

MCC **T32.94 Corrosions involving 90% or more of body surface with 40-49% third degree corrosion**
MCC Exclusion see Appendix A PDX collection 1414
HAC see Appendix B for HAC conditional logic

MCC **T32.95 Corrosions involving 90% or more of body surface with 50-59% third degree corrosion**
MCC Exclusion see Appendix A PDX collection 1414
HAC see Appendix B for HAC conditional logic

MCC **T32.96 Corrosions involving 90% or more of body surface with 60-69% third degree corrosion**
MCC Exclusion see Appendix A PDX collection 1414
HAC see Appendix B for HAC conditional logic

MCC **T32.97 Corrosions involving 90% or more of body surface with 70-79% third degree corrosion**
MCC Exclusion see Appendix A PDX collection 1414
HAC see Appendix B for HAC conditional logic

MCC **T32.98 Corrosions involving 90% or more of body surface with 80-89% third degree corrosion**
MCC Exclusion see Appendix A PDX collection 1414
HAC see Appendix B for HAC conditional logic

MCC **T32.99 Corrosions involving 90% or more of body surface with 90% or more third degree corrosion**
MCC Exclusion see Appendix A PDX collection 1414
HAC see Appendix B for HAC conditional logic

Frostbite (T33-T34)

Excludes2: *hypothermia and other effects of reduced temperature (T68, T69.-)*

T33 Superficial frostbite

Includes: frostbite with partial thickness skin loss

The appropriate 7th character is to be added to each code from category T33
A initial encounter
D subsequent encounter
S sequela

\+ **T33.0 Superficial frostbite of head**

\+ **T33.01 Superficial frostbite of ear**

CC +7th **T33.011 Superficial frostbite of right ear**
CC Exclusion 7th character A see Appendix A PDX collection 1415
HAC 7th character A see Appendix B for HAC conditional logic

CC +7th **T33.012 Superficial frostbite of left ear**
CC Exclusion 7th character A see Appendix A PDX collection 1415
HAC 7th character A see Appendix B for HAC conditional logic

CC +7th **T33.019 Superficial frostbite of unspecified ear**
CC Exclusion 7th character A see Appendix A PDX collection 1415
HAC 7th character A see Appendix B for HAC conditional logic

CC x+7th **T33.02 Superficial frostbite of nose**
CC Exclusion 7th character A see Appendix A PDX collection 1415
HAC 7th character A see Appendix B for HAC conditional logic

CC x+7th **T33.09 Superficial frostbite of other part of head**
CC Exclusion 7th character A see Appendix A PDX collection 1415
HAC 7th character A see Appendix B for HAC conditional logic

CC x+7th **T33.1 Superficial frostbite of neck**
CC Exclusion 7th character A see Appendix A PDX collection 1415
HAC 7th character A see Appendix B for HAC conditional logic

CC x+7th **T33.2 Superficial frostbite of thorax**
CC Exclusion 7th character A see Appendix A PDX collection 1416
HAC 7th character A see Appendix B for HAC conditional logic

CC x+7th **T33.3 Superficial frostbite of abdominal wall, lower back and pelvis**
CC Exclusion 7th character A see Appendix A PDX collection 1416
HAC 7th character A see Appendix B for HAC conditional logic

\+ **T33.4 Superficial frostbite of arm**
Excludes2: *superficial frostbite of wrist and hand (T33.5-)*

CC x+7th **T33.40 Superficial frostbite of unspecified arm**
CC Exclusion 7th character A see Appendix A PDX collection 1416
HAC 7th character A see Appendix B for HAC conditional logic

CC x+7th **T33.41 Superficial frostbite of right arm**
CC Exclusion 7th character A see Appendix A PDX collection 1416
HAC 7th character A see Appendix B for HAC conditional logic

CC x+7th **T33.42 Superficial frostbite of left arm**
CC Exclusion 7th character A see Appendix A PDX collection 1416
HAC 7th character A see Appendix B for HAC conditional logic

\+ **T33.5 Superficial frostbite of wrist, hand, and fingers**

\+ **T33.51 Superficial frostbite of wrist**

CC +7th **T33.511 Superficial frostbite of right wrist**
CC Exclusion 7th character A see Appendix A PDX collection 1417
HAC 7th character A see Appendix B for HAC conditional logic

CC +7th **T33.512 Superficial frostbite of left wrist**
CC Exclusion 7th character A see Appendix A PDX collection 1417
HAC 7th character A see Appendix B for HAC conditional logic

CC +7th **T33.519 Superficial frostbite of unspecified wrist**
CC Exclusion 7th character A see Appendix A PDX collection 1417
HAC 7th character A see Appendix B for HAC conditional logic

\+ **T33.52 Superficial frostbite of hand**
Excludes2: *superficial frostbite of fingers (T33.53-)*

CC +7th **T33.521 Superficial frostbite of right hand**
CC Exclusion 7th character A see Appendix A PDX collection 1417
HAC 7th character A see Appendix B for HAC conditional logic

CC +7th **T33.522 Superficial frostbite of left hand**
CC Exclusion 7th character A see Appendix A PDX collection 1417
HAC 7th character A see Appendix B for HAC conditional logic

CC +7th **T33.529 Superficial frostbite of unspecified hand**
CC Exclusion 7th character A see Appendix A PDX collection 1417
HAC 7th character A see Appendix B for HAC conditional logic

\+ **T33.53 Superficial frostbite of finger(s)**

CC +7th **T33.531 Superficial frostbite of right finger(s)**
CC Exclusion 7th character A see Appendix A PDX collection 1417
HAC 7th character A see Appendix B for HAC conditional logic

CC +7th **T33.532 Superficial frostbite of left finger(s)**
CC Exclusion 7th character A see Appendix A PDX collection 1417
HAC 7th character A see Appendix B for HAC conditional logic

CC +7th **T33.539 Superficial frostbite of unspecified finger(s)**
CC Exclusion 7th character A see Appendix A PDX collection 1417
HAC 7th character A see Appendix B for HAC conditional logic

\+ **T33.6 Superficial frostbite of hip and thigh**

CC x+7th **T33.60 Superficial frostbite of unspecified hip and thigh**
CC Exclusion 7th character A see Appendix A PDX collection 1416
HAC 7th character A see Appendix B for HAC conditional logic

CC x+7th **T33.61 Superficial frostbite of right hip and thigh**
CC Exclusion 7th character A see Appendix A PDX collection 1416
HAC 7th character A see Appendix B for HAC conditional logic

CC x+7th **T33.62 Superficial frostbite of left hip and thigh**
CC Exclusion 7th character A see Appendix A PDX collection 1416
HAC 7th character A see Appendix B for HAC conditional logic

\+ **T33.7 Superficial frostbite of knee and lower leg**
Excludes2: *superficial frostbite of ankle and foot (T33.8-)*

CC x+7th **T33.70 Superficial frostbite of unspecified knee and lower leg**
CC Exclusion 7th character A see Appendix A PDX collection 1416
HAC 7th character A see Appendix B for HAC conditional logic

CC x+7th **T33.71 Superficial frostbite of right knee and lower leg**
CC Exclusion 7th character A see Appendix A PDX collection 1416
HAC 7th character A see Appendix B for HAC conditional logic

CC x+7th **T33.72 Superficial frostbite of left knee and lower leg**
CC Exclusion 7th character A see Appendix A PDX collection 1416
HAC 7th character A see Appendix B for HAC conditional logic

\+ **T33.8 Superficial frostbite of ankle, foot, and toe(s)**

\+ **T33.81 Superficial frostbite of ankle**

CC +7th **T33.811 Superficial frostbite of right ankle**
CC Exclusion 7th character A see Appendix A PDX collection 1418
HAC 7th character A see Appendix B for HAC conditional logic

CC +7th **T33.812 Superficial frostbite of left ankle**
CC Exclusion 7th character A see Appendix A PDX collection 1418
HAC 7th character A see Appendix B for HAC conditional logic

CC +7th **T33.819 Superficial frostbite of unspecified ankle**
CC Exclusion 7th character A see Appendix A PDX collection 1418
HAC 7th character A see Appendix B for HAC conditional logic

\+ **T33.82 Superficial frostbite of foot**

CC +7th **T33.821 Superficial frostbite of right foot**
CC Exclusion 7th character A see Appendix A PDX collection 1418
HAC 7th character A see Appendix B for HAC conditional logic

CC +7th **T33.822 Superficial frostbite of left foot**
CC Exclusion 7th character A see Appendix A PDX collection 1418
HAC 7th character A see Appendix B for HAC conditional logic

CC +7th **T33.829 Superficial frostbite of unspecified foot**
CC Exclusion 7th character A see Appendix A PDX collection 1418
HAC 7th character A see Appendix B for HAC conditional logic

\+ **T33.83 Superficial frostbite of toe(s)**

CC +7th **T33.831 Superficial frostbite of right toe(s)**
CC Exclusion 7th character A see Appendix A PDX collection 1418
HAC 7th character A see Appendix B for HAC conditional logic

CC +7th **T33.832 Superficial frostbite of left toe(s)**
CC Exclusion 7th character A see Appendix A PDX collection 1418
HAC 7th character A see Appendix B for HAC conditional logic

CC +7th **T33.839 Superficial frostbite of unspecified toe(s)**
CC Exclusion 7th character A see Appendix A PDX collection 1418
HAC 7th character A see Appendix B for HAC conditional logic

+ **T33.9 Superficial frostbite of other and unspecified sites**

CC x+7th **T33.90 Superficial frostbite of unspecified sites**
Superficial frostbite NOS
CC Exclusion 7th character A see Appendix A PDX collection 1416
HAC 7th character A see Appendix B for HAC conditional logic

CC x+7th **T33.99 Superficial frostbite of other sites**
Superficial frostbite of leg NOS
Superficial frostbite of trunk NOS
CC Exclusion 7th character A see Appendix A PDX collection 1416
HAC 7th character A see Appendix B for HAC conditional logic

T34 Frostbite with tissue necrosis

The appropriate 7th character is to be added to each code from category T34
A initial encounter
D subsequent encounter
S sequela

+ **T34.0 Frostbite with tissue necrosis of head**

+ **T34.01 Frostbite with tissue necrosis of ear**

CC +7th **T34.011 Frostbite with tissue necrosis of right ear**
CC Exclusion 7th character A see Appendix A PDX collection 1415
HAC 7th character A see Appendix B for HAC conditional logic

CC +7th **T34.012 Frostbite with tissue necrosis of left ear**
CC Exclusion 7th character A see Appendix A PDX collection 1415
HAC 7th character A see Appendix B for HAC conditional logic

CC +7th **T34.019 Frostbite with tissue necrosis of unspecified ear**
CC Exclusion 7th character A see Appendix A PDX collection 1415
HAC 7th character A see Appendix B for HAC conditional logic

CC x+7th **T34.02 Frostbite with tissue necrosis of nose**
CC Exclusion 7th character A see Appendix A PDX collection 1415
HAC 7th character A see Appendix B for HAC conditional logic

CC x+7th **T34.09 Frostbite with tissue necrosis of other part of head**
CC Exclusion 7th character A see Appendix A PDX collection 1415
HAC 7th character A see Appendix B for HAC conditional logic

CC x+7th **T34.1 Frostbite with tissue necrosis of neck**
CC Exclusion 7th character A see Appendix A PDX collection 1415
HAC 7th character A see Appendix B for HAC conditional logic

CC x+7th **T34.2 Frostbite with tissue necrosis of thorax**
CC Exclusion 7th character A see Appendix A PDX collection 1416
HAC 7th character A see Appendix B for HAC conditional logic

CC x+7th **T34.3 Frostbite with tissue necrosis of abdominal wall, lower back and pelvis**
CC Exclusion 7th character A see Appendix A PDX collection 1416
HAC 7th character A see Appendix B for HAC conditional logic

+ **T34.4 Frostbite with tissue necrosis of arm**
Excludes2: *frostbite with tissue necrosis of wrist and hand (T34.5-)*

CC x+7th **T34.40 Frostbite with tissue necrosis of unspecified arm**
CC Exclusion 7th character A see Appendix A PDX collection 1416
HAC 7th character A see Appendix B for HAC conditional logic

CC x+7th **T34.41 Frostbite with tissue necrosis of right arm**
CC Exclusion 7th character A see Appendix A PDX collection 1416
HAC 7th character A see Appendix B for HAC conditional logic

CC x+7th **T34.42 Frostbite with tissue necrosis of left arm**
CC Exclusion 7th character A see Appendix A PDX collection 1416
HAC 7th character A see Appendix B for HAC conditional logic

+ **T34.5 Frostbite with tissue necrosis of wrist, hand, and finger(s)**

+ **T34.51 Frostbite with tissue necrosis of wrist**

CC +7th **T34.511 Frostbite with tissue necrosis of right wrist**
CC Exclusion 7th character A see Appendix A PDX collection 1417
HAC 7th character A see Appendix B for HAC conditional logic

CC +7th **T34.512 Frostbite with tissue necrosis of left wrist**
CC Exclusion 7th character A see Appendix A PDX collection 1417
HAC 7th character A see Appendix B for HAC conditional logic

CC +7th **T34.519 Frostbite with tissue necrosis of unspecified wrist**
CC Exclusion 7th character A see Appendix A PDX collection 1417
HAC 7th character A see Appendix B for HAC conditional logic

+ **T34.52 Frostbite with tissue necrosis of hand**
Excludes2: *frostbite with tissue necrosis of finger(s) (T34.53-)*

CC +7th **T34.521 Frostbite with tissue necrosis of right hand**
CC Exclusion 7th character A see Appendix A PDX collection 1417
HAC 7th character A see Appendix B for HAC conditional logic

CC +7th **T34.522 Frostbite with tissue necrosis of left hand**
CC Exclusion 7th character A see Appendix A PDX collection 1417
HAC 7th character A see Appendix B for HAC conditional logic

CC +7th **T34.529 Frostbite with tissue necrosis of unspecified hand**
CC Exclusion 7th character A see Appendix A PDX collection 1417
HAC 7th character A see Appendix B for HAC conditional logic

+ **T34.53 Frostbite with tissue necrosis of finger(s)**

CC +7th **T34.531 Frostbite with tissue necrosis of right finger(s)**
CC Exclusion 7th character A see Appendix A PDX collection 1417
HAC 7th character A see Appendix B for HAC conditional logic

CC +7th **T34.532 Frostbite with tissue necrosis of left finger(s)**
CC Exclusion 7th character A see Appendix A PDX collection 1417
HAC 7th character A see Appendix B for HAC conditional logic

CC +7th **T34.539 Frostbite with tissue necrosis of unspecified finger(s)**
CC Exclusion 7th character A see Appendix A PDX collection 1417
HAC 7th character A see Appendix B for HAC conditional logic

+ **T34.6 Frostbite with tissue necrosis of hip and thigh**

CC x+7th **T34.60 Frostbite with tissue necrosis of unspecified hip and thigh**
CC Exclusion 7th character A see Appendix A PDX collection 1416
HAC 7th character A see Appendix B for HAC conditional logic

CC x+7th **T34.61 Frostbite with tissue necrosis of right hip and thigh**
CC Exclusion 7th character A see Appendix A PDX collection 1416
HAC 7th character A see Appendix B for HAC conditional logic

CC x+7th **T34.62 Frostbite with tissue necrosis of left hip and thigh**
CC Exclusion 7th character A see Appendix A PDX collection 1416
HAC 7th character A see Appendix B for HAC conditional logic

+ **T34.7 Frostbite with tissue necrosis of knee and lower leg**
Excludes2: *frostbite with tissue necrosis of ankle and foot (T34.8-)*

CC x+7th **T34.70 Frostbite with tissue necrosis of unspecified knee and lower leg**
CC Exclusion 7th character A see Appendix A PDX collection 1416
HAC 7th character A see Appendix B for HAC conditional logic

CC x+7th **T34.71 Frostbite with tissue necrosis of right knee and lower leg**
CC Exclusion 7th character A see Appendix A PDX collection 1416
HAC 7th character A see Appendix B for HAC conditional logic

CC x+7th **T34.72 Frostbite with tissue necrosis of left knee and lower leg**
CC Exclusion 7th character A see Appendix A PDX collection 1416
HAC 7th character A see Appendix B for HAC conditional logic

+ **T34.8 Frostbite with tissue necrosis of ankle, foot, and toe(s)**
+ **T34.81 Frostbite with tissue necrosis of ankle**
CC +7th **T34.811 Frostbite with tissue necrosis of right ankle**
CC Exclusion 7th character A see Appendix A PDX collection 1418
HAC 7th character A see Appendix B for HAC conditional logic
CC +7th **T34.812 Frostbite with tissue necrosis of left ankle**
CC Exclusion 7th character A see Appendix A PDX collection 1418
HAC 7th character A see Appendix B for HAC conditional logic
CC +7th **T34.819 Frostbite with tissue necrosis of unspecified ankle**
CC Exclusion 7th character A see Appendix A PDX collection 1418
HAC 7th character A see Appendix B for HAC conditional logic
+ **T34.82 Frostbite with tissue necrosis of foot**
CC +7th **T34.821 Frostbite with tissue necrosis of right foot**
CC Exclusion 7th character A see Appendix A PDX collection 1418
HAC 7th character A see Appendix B for HAC conditional logic
CC +7th **T34.822 Frostbite with tissue necrosis of left foot**
CC Exclusion 7th character A see Appendix A PDX collection 1418
HAC 7th character A see Appendix B for HAC conditional logic
CC +7th **T34.829 Frostbite with tissue necrosis of unspecified foot**
CC Exclusion 7th character A see Appendix A PDX collection 1418
HAC 7th character A see Appendix B for HAC conditional logic
+ **T34.83 Frostbite with tissue necrosis of toe(s)**
CC +7th **T34.831 Frostbite with tissue necrosis of right toe(s)**
CC Exclusion 7th character A see Appendix A PDX collection 1418
HAC 7th character A see Appendix B for HAC conditional logic
CC +7th **T34.832 Frostbite with tissue necrosis of left toe(s)**
CC Exclusion 7th character A see Appendix A PDX collection 1418
HAC 7th character A see Appendix B for HAC conditional logic
CC +7th **T34.839 Frostbite with tissue necrosis of unspecified toe(s)**
CC Exclusion 7th character A see Appendix A PDX collection 1418
HAC 7th character A see Appendix B for HAC conditional logic

+ **T34.9 Frostbite with tissue necrosis of other and unspecified sites**
CC x+7th **T34.90 Frostbite with tissue necrosis of unspecified sites**
Frostbite with tissue necrosis NOS
CC Exclusion 7th character A see Appendix A PDX collection 1416
HAC 7th character A see Appendix B for HAC conditional logic
CC x+7th **T34.99 Frostbite with tissue necrosis of other sites**
Frostbite with tissue necrosis of leg NOS
Frostbite with tissue necrosis of trunk NOS
CC Exclusion 7th character A see Appendix A PDX collection 1416
HAC 7th character A see Appendix B for HAC conditional logic

Poisoning by, adverse effects of and underdosing of drugs, medicaments and biological substances (T36-T50)

Includes: adverse effect of correct substance properly administered
poisoning by overdose of substance
poisoning by wrong substance given or taken in error
underdosing by (inadvertently) (deliberately) taking less substance than prescribed or instructed

Code first: for adverse effects, the nature of the adverse effect, such as:
adverse effect NOS (T88.7)
aspirin gastritis (K29.-)
blood disorders (D56-D76)
contact dermatitis (L23-L25)
dermatitis due to substances taken internally (L27.-)
nephropathy (N14.0-N14.2)

NOTE The drug giving rise to the adverse effect should be identified by use of codes from categories T36-T50 with fifth or sixth character 5.

Use additional: code(s) to specify:
manifestations of poisoning
underdosing or failure in dosage during medical and surgical care (Y63.6, Y63.8-Y63.9)
underdosing of medication regimen (Z91.12-, Z91.13-)

Excludes1: *toxic reaction to local anesthesia in pregnancy (O29.3-)*

Excludes2: *abuse and dependence of psychoactive substances (F10-F19)*
abuse of non-dependence-producing substances (F55.-)
drug reaction and poisoning affecting newborn (P00-P96)
pathological drug intoxication (inebriation) (F10-F19)

Review coding guideline C.19.e

T36 Poisoning by, adverse effect of and underdosing of systemic antibiotics
Excludes1: *antineoplastic antibiotics (T45.1-)*
locally applied antibiotic NEC (T49.0)
topically used antibiotic for ear, nose and throat (T49.6)
topically used antibiotic for eye (T49.5)

The appropriate 7th character is to be added to each code from category T36
A initial encounter
D subsequent encounter
S sequela

+ **T36.0 Poisoning by, adverse effect of and underdosing of penicillins**
+ **T36.0X Poisoning by, adverse effect of and underdosing of penicillins**
+7th **T36.0X1 Poisoning by penicillins, accidental (unintentional)**
Poisoning by penicillins NOS
+7th **T36.0X2 Poisoning by penicillins, intentional self-harm**
+7th **T36.0X3 Poisoning by penicillins, assault**
+7th **T36.0X4 Poisoning by penicillins, undetermined**
+7th **T36.0X5 Adverse effect of penicillins**
+7th **T36.0X6 Underdosing of penicillins**
+ **T36.1 Poisoning by, adverse effect of and underdosing of cephalosporins and other beta-lactam antibiotics**
+ **T36.1X Poisoning by, adverse effect of and underdosing of cephalosporins and other beta-lactam antibiotics**
+7th **T36.1X1 Poisoning by cephalosporins and other beta-lactam antibiotics, accidental (unintentional)**
Poisoning by cephalosporins and other beta-lactam antibiotics NOS
+7th **T36.1X2 Poisoning by cephalosporins and other beta-lactam antibiotics, intentional self-harm**
+7th **T36.1X3 Poisoning by cephalosporins and other beta-lactam antibiotics, assault**
+7th **T36.1X4 Poisoning by cephalosporins and other beta-lactam antibiotics, undetermined**
+7th **T36.1X5 Adverse effect of cephalosporins and other beta-lactam antibiotics**
+7th **T36.1X6 Underdosing of cephalosporins and other beta-lactam antibiotics**
+ **T36.2 Poisoning by, adverse effect of and underdosing of chloramphenicol group**
+ **T36.2X Poisoning by, adverse effect of and underdosing of chloramphenicol group**
+7th **T36.2X1 Poisoning by chloramphenicol group, accidental (unintentional)**
Poisoning by chloramphenicol group NOS
+7th **T36.2X2 Poisoning by chloramphenicol group, intentional self-harm**

+7th **T36.2X3 Poisoning by chloramphenicol group, assault**
+7th **T36.2X4 Poisoning by chloramphenicol group, undetermined**
+7th **T36.2X5 Adverse effect of chloramphenicol group**
+7th **T36.2X6 Underdosing of chloramphenicol group**

+ **T36.3 Poisoning by, adverse effect of and underdosing of macrolides**
+ **T36.3X Poisoning by, adverse effect of and underdosing of macrolides**
+7th **T36.3X1 Poisoning by macrolides, accidental (unintentional)**
Poisoning by macrolides NOS
+7th **T36.3X2 Poisoning by macrolides, intentional self-harm**
+7th **T36.3X3 Poisoning by macrolides, assault**
+7th **T36.3X4 Poisoning by macrolides, undetermined**
+7th **T36.3X5 Adverse effect of macrolides**
+7th **T36.3X6 Underdosing of macrolides**

+ **T36.4 Poisoning by, adverse effect of and underdosing of tetracyclines**
+ **T36.4X Poisoning by, adverse effect of and underdosing of tetracyclines**
+7th **T36.4X1 Poisoning by tetracyclines, accidental (unintentional)**
Poisoning by tetracyclines NOS
+7th **T36.4X2 Poisoning by tetracyclines, intentional self-harm**
+7th **T36.4X3 Poisoning by tetracyclines, assault**
+7th **T36.4X4 Poisoning by tetracyclines, undetermined**
+7th **T36.4X5 Adverse effect of tetracyclines**
+7th **T36.4X6 Underdosing of tetracyclines**

+ **T36.5 Poisoning by, adverse effect of and underdosing of aminoglycosides**
Poisoning by, adverse effect of and underdosing of streptomycin
+ **T36.5X Poisoning by, adverse effect of and underdosing of aminoglycosides**
+7th **T36.5X1 Poisoning by aminoglycosides, accidental (unintentional)**
Poisoning by aminoglycosides NOS
+7th **T36.5X2 Poisoning by aminoglycosides, intentional self-harm**
+7th **T36.5X3 Poisoning by aminoglycosides, assault**
+7th **T36.5X4 Poisoning by aminoglycosides, undetermined**
+7th **T36.5X5 Adverse effect of aminoglycosides**
+7th **T36.5X6 Underdosing of aminoglycosides**

+ **T36.6 Poisoning by, adverse effect of and underdosing of rifampicins**
+ **T36.6X Poisoning by, adverse effect of and underdosing of rifampicins**
+7th **T36.6X1 Poisoning by rifampicins, accidental (unintentional)**
Poisoning by rifampicins NOS
+7th **T36.6X2 Poisoning by rifampicins, intentional self-harm**
+7th **T36.6X3 Poisoning by rifampicins, assault**
+7th **T36.6X4 Poisoning by rifampicins, undetermined**
+7th **T36.6X5 Adverse effect of rifampicins**
+7th **T36.6X6 Underdosing of rifampicins**

+ **T36.7 Poisoning by, adverse effect of and underdosing of antifungal antibiotics, systemically used**
+ **T36.7X Poisoning by, adverse effect of and underdosing of antifungal antibiotics, systemically used**
+7th **T36.7X1 Poisoning by antifungal antibiotics, systemically used, accidental (unintentional)**
Poisoning by antifungal antibiotics, systemically used NOS
+7th **T36.7X2 Poisoning by antifungal antibiotics, systemically used, intentional self-harm**
+7th **T36.7X3 Poisoning by antifungal antibiotics, systemically used, assault**
+7th **T36.7X4 Poisoning by antifungal antibiotics, systemically used, undetermined**
+7th **T36.7X5 Adverse effect of antifungal antibiotics, systemically used**
+7th **T36.7X6 Underdosing of antifungal antibiotics, systemically used**

+ **T36.8 Poisoning by, adverse effect of and underdosing of other systemic antibiotics**
+ **T36.8X Poisoning by, adverse effect of and underdosing of other systemic antibiotics**
+7th **T36.8X1 Poisoning by other systemic antibiotics, accidental (unintentional)**
Poisoning by other systemic antibiotics NOS
+7th **T36.8X2 Poisoning by other systemic antibiotics, intentional self-harm**
+7th **T36.8X3 Poisoning by other systemic antibiotics, assault**
+7th **T36.8X4 Poisoning by other systemic antibiotics, undetermined**
+7th **T36.8X5 Adverse effect of other systemic antibiotics**
+7th **T36.8X6 Underdosing of other systemic antibiotics**

+ **T36.9 Poisoning by, adverse effect of and underdosing of unspecified systemic antibiotic**
x+7th **T36.91 Poisoning by unspecified systemic antibiotic, accidental (unintentional)**
Poisoning by systemic antibiotic NOS
x+7th **T36.92 Poisoning by unspecified systemic antibiotic, intentional self-harm**
x+7th **T36.93 Poisoning by unspecified systemic antibiotic, assault**
x+7th **T36.94 Poisoning by unspecified systemic antibiotic, undetermined**
x+7th **T36.95 Adverse effect of unspecified systemic antibiotic**
x+7th **T36.96 Underdosing of unspecified systemic antibiotic**

T37 Poisoning by, adverse effect of and underdosing of other systemic anti-infectives and antiparasitics

Excludes1: *anti-infectives topically used for ear, nose and throat (T49.6-)*
anti-infectives topically used for eye (T49.5-)
locally applied anti-infectives NEC (T49.0-)

The appropriate 7th character is to be added to each code from category T37
A initial encounter
D subsequent encounter
S sequela

+ **T37.0 Poisoning by, adverse effect of and underdosing of sulfonamides**
+ **T37.0X Poisoning by, adverse effect of and underdosing of sulfonamides**
+7th **T37.0X1 Poisoning by sulfonamides, accidental (unintentional)**
Poisoning by sulfonamides NOS
+7th **T37.0X2 Poisoning by sulfonamides, intentional self-harm**
+7th **T37.0X3 Poisoning by sulfonamides, assault**
+7th **T37.0X4 Poisoning by sulfonamides, undetermined**
+7th **T37.0X5 Adverse effect of sulfonamides**
+7th **T37.0X6 Underdosing of sulfonamides**

+ **T37.1 Poisoning by, adverse effect of and underdosing of antimycobacterial drugs**
Excludes1: *rifampicins (T36.6-)*
streptomycin (T36.5-)
+ **T37.1X Poisoning by, adverse effect of and underdosing of antimycobacterial drugs**
+7th **T37.1X1 Poisoning by antimycobacterial drugs, accidental (unintentional)**
Poisoning by antimycobacterial drugs NOS
+7th **T37.1X2 Poisoning by antimycobacterial drugs, intentional self-harm**
+7th **T37.1X3 Poisoning by antimycobacterial drugs, assault**
+7th **T37.1X4 Poisoning by antimycobacterial drugs, undetermined**
+7th **T37.1X5 Adverse effect of antimycobacterial drugs**
+7th **T37.1X6 Underdosing of antimycobacterial drugs**

+ **T37.2 Poisoning by, adverse effect of and underdosing of antimalarials and drugs acting on other blood protozoa**
Excludes1: *hydroxyquinoline derivatives (T37.8-)*
+ **T37.2X Poisoning by, adverse effect of and underdosing of antimalarials and drugs acting on other blood protozoa**
+7th **T37.2X1 Poisoning by antimalarials and drugs acting on other blood protozoa, accidental (unintentional)**
Poisoning by antimalarials and drugs acting on other blood protozoa NOS

+7th **T37.2X2 Poisoning by antimalarials and drugs acting on other blood protozoa, intentional self-harm**
+7th **T37.2X3 Poisoning by antimalarials and drugs acting on other blood protozoa, assault**
+7th **T37.2X4 Poisoning by antimalarials and drugs acting on other blood protozoa, undetermined**
+7th **T37.2X5 Adverse effect of antimalarials and drugs acting on other blood protozoa**
+7th **T37.2X6 Underdosing of antimalarials and drugs acting on other blood protozoa**

+ **T37.3 Poisoning by, adverse effect of and underdosing of other antiprotozoal drugs**
+ **T37.3X Poisoning by, adverse effect of and underdosing of other antiprotozoal drugs**
+7th **T37.3X1 Poisoning by other antiprotozoal drugs, accidental (unintentional)**
Poisoning by other antiprotozoal drugs NOS
+7th **T37.3X2 Poisoning by other antiprotozoal drugs, intentional self-harm**
+7th **T37.3X3 Poisoning by other antiprotozoal drugs, assault**
+7th **T37.3X4 Poisoning by other antiprotozoal drugs, undetermined**
+7th **T37.3X5 Adverse effect of other antiprotozoal drugs**
+7th **T37.3X6 Underdosing of other antiprotozoal drugs**

+ **T37.4 Poisoning by, adverse effect of and underdosing of anthelminthics**
+ **T37.4X Poisoning by, adverse effect of and underdosing of anthelminthics**
+7th **T37.4X1 Poisoning by anthelminthics, accidental (unintentional)**
Poisoning by anthelminthics NOS
+7th **T37.4X2 Poisoning by anthelminthics, intentional self-harm**
+7th **T37.4X3 Poisoning by anthelminthics, assault**
+7th **T37.4X4 Poisoning by anthelminthics, undetermined**
+7th **T37.4X5 Adverse effect of anthelminthics**
+7th **T37.4X6 Underdosing of anthelminthics**

+ **T37.5 Poisoning by, adverse effect of and underdosing of antiviral drugs**
Excludes1: *amantadine (T42.8-)*
cytarabine (T45.1-)
+ **T37.5X Poisoning by, adverse effect of and underdosing of antiviral drugs**
+7th **T37.5X1 Poisoning by antiviral drugs, accidental (unintentional)**
Poisoning by antiviral drugs NOS
+7th **T37.5X2 Poisoning by antiviral drugs, intentional self-harm**
+7th **T37.5X3 Poisoning by antiviral drugs, assault**
+7th **T37.5X4 Poisoning by antiviral drugs, undetermined**
+7th **T37.5X5 Adverse effect of antiviral drugs**
+7th **T37.5X6 Underdosing of antiviral drugs**

+ **T37.8 Poisoning by, adverse effect of and underdosing of other specified systemic anti-infectives and antiparasitics**
Poisoning by, adverse effect of and underdosing of hydroxyquinoline derivatives
Excludes1: *antimalarial drugs (T37.2-)*
+ **T37.8X Poisoning by, adverse effect of and underdosing of other specified systemic anti-infectives and antiparasitics**
+7th **T37.8X1 Poisoning by other specified systemic anti-infectives and antiparasitics, accidental (unintentional)**
Poisoning by other specified systemic anti-infectives and antiparasitics NOS
+7th **T37.8X2 Poisoning by other specified systemic anti-infectives and antiparasitics, intentional self-harm**
+7th **T37.8X3 Poisoning by other specified systemic anti-infectives and antiparasitics, assault**
+7th **T37.8X4 Poisoning by other specified systemic anti-infectives and antiparasitics, undetermined**
+7th **T37.8X5 Adverse effect of other specified systemic anti-infectives and antiparasitics**
+7th **T37.8X6 Underdosing of other specified systemic anti-infectives and antiparasitics**

+ **T37.9 Poisoning by, adverse effect of and underdosing of unspecified systemic anti-infective and antiparasitics**
X+7th **T37.91 Poisoning by unspecified systemic anti-infective and antiparasitics, accidental (unintentional)**
Poisoning by, adverse effect of and underdosing of systemic anti-infective and antiparasitics NOS
X+7th **T37.92 Poisoning by unspecified systemic anti-infective and antiparasitics, intentional self-harm**
X+7th **T37.93 Poisoning by unspecified systemic anti-infective and antiparasitics, assault**
X+7th **T37.94 Poisoning by unspecified systemic anti-infective and antiparasitics, undetermined**
X+7th **T37.95 Adverse effect of unspecified systemic anti-infective and antiparasitic**
X+7th **T37.96 Underdosing of unspecified systemic anti-infectives and antiparasitics**

T38 Poisoning by, adverse effect of and underdosing of hormones and their synthetic substitutes and antagonists, not elsewhere classified

Excludes1: *mineralocorticoids and their antagonists (T50.0-)*
oxytocic hormones (T48.0-)
parathyroid hormones and derivatives (T50.9-)

The appropriate 7th character is to be added to each code from category T38
A initial encounter
D subsequent encounter
S sequela

+ **T38.0 Poisoning by, adverse effect of and underdosing of glucocorticoids and synthetic analogues**
Excludes1: *glucocorticoids, topically used (T49.-)*
+ **T38.0X Poisoning by, adverse effect of and underdosing of glucocorticoids and synthetic analogues**
+7th **T38.0X1 Poisoning by glucocorticoids and synthetic analogues, accidental (unintentional)**
Poisoning by glucocorticoids and synthetic analogues NOS
+7th **T38.0X2 Poisoning by glucocorticoids and synthetic analogues, intentional self-harm**
+7th **T38.0X3 Poisoning by glucocorticoids and synthetic analogues, assault**
+7th **T38.0X4 Poisoning by glucocorticoids and synthetic analogues, undetermined**
+7th **T38.0X5 Adverse effect of glucocorticoids and synthetic analogues**
+7th **T38.0X6 Underdosing of glucocorticoids and synthetic analogues**

+ **T38.1 Poisoning by, adverse effect of and underdosing of thyroid hormones and substitutes**
+ **T38.1X Poisoning by, adverse effect of and underdosing of thyroid hormones and substitutes**
+7th **T38.1X1 Poisoning by thyroid hormones and substitutes, accidental (unintentional)**
Poisoning by thyroid hormones and substitutes NOS
+7th **T38.1X2 Poisoning by thyroid hormones and substitutes, intentional self-harm**
+7th **T38.1X3 Poisoning by thyroid hormones and substitutes, assault**
+7th **T38.1X4 Poisoning by thyroid hormones and substitutes, undetermined**
+7th **T38.1X5 Adverse effect of thyroid hormones and substitutes**
+7th **T38.1X6 Underdosing of thyroid hormones and substitutes**

+ **T38.2 Poisoning by, adverse effect of and underdosing of antithyroid drugs**
+ **T38.2X Poisoning by, adverse effect of and underdosing of antithyroid drugs**
+7th **T38.2X1 Poisoning by antithyroid drugs, accidental (unintentional)**
Poisoning by antithyroid drugs NOS
+7th **T38.2X2 Poisoning by antithyroid drugs, intentional self-harm**
+7th **T38.2X3 Poisoning by antithyroid drugs, assault**
+7th **T38.2X4 Poisoning by antithyroid drugs, undetermined**
+7th **T38.2X5 Adverse effect of antithyroid drugs**
+7th **T38.2X6 Underdosing of antithyroid drugs**

+ **T38.3 Poisoning by, adverse effect of and underdosing of insulin and oral hypoglycemic [antidiabetic] drugs**
  + **T38.3X Poisoning by, adverse effect of and underdosing of insulin and oral hypoglycemic [antidiabetic] drugs**
    - +7th **T38.3X1 Poisoning by insulin and oral hypoglycemic [antidiabetic] drugs, accidental (unintentional)**
      Poisoning by insulin and oral hypoglycemic [antidiabetic] drugs NOS
      Review coding guideline C.4.a.5.b
    - +7th **T38.3X2 Poisoning by insulin and oral hypoglycemic [antidiabetic] drugs, intentional self-harm**
    - +7th **T38.3X3 Poisoning by insulin and oral hypoglycemic [antidiabetic] drugs, assault**
    - +7th **T38.3X4 Poisoning by insulin and oral hypoglycemic [antidiabetic] drugs, undetermined**
    - +7th **T38.3X5 Adverse effect of insulin and oral hypoglycemic [antidiabetic] drugs**
    - +7th **T38.3X6 Underdosing of insulin and oral hypoglycemic [antidiabetic] drugs**
      Review coding guideline C.4.a.5.a

+ **T38.4 Poisoning by, adverse effect of and underdosing of oral contraceptives**
  Poisoning by, adverse effect of and underdosing of multiple- and single-ingredient oral contraceptive preparations
  + **T38.4X Poisoning by, adverse effect of and underdosing of oral contraceptives**
    - +7th **T38.4X1 Poisoning by oral contraceptives, accidental (unintentional)**
      Poisoning by oral contraceptives NOS
    - +7th **T38.4X2 Poisoning by oral contraceptives, intentional self-harm**
    - +7th **T38.4X3 Poisoning by oral contraceptives, assault**
    - +7th **T38.4X4 Poisoning by oral contraceptives, undetermined**
    - +7th **T38.4X5 Adverse effect of oral contraceptives**
    - +7th **T38.4X6 Underdosing of oral contraceptives**

+ **T38.5 Poisoning by, adverse effect of and underdosing of other estrogens and progestogens**
  Poisoning by, adverse effect of and underdosing of estrogens and progestogens mixtures and substitutes
  + **T38.5X Poisoning by, adverse effect of and underdosing of other estrogens and progestogens**
    - +7th **T38.5X1 Poisoning by other estrogens and progestogens, accidental (unintentional)**
      Poisoning by other estrogens and progestogens NOS
    - +7th **T38.5X2 Poisoning by other estrogens and progestogens, intentional self-harm**
    - +7th **T38.5X3 Poisoning by other estrogens and progestogens, assault**
    - +7th **T38.5X4 Poisoning by other estrogens and progestogens, undetermined**
    - +7th **T38.5X5 Adverse effect of other estrogens and progestogens**
    - +7th **T38.5X6 Underdosing of other estrogens and progestogens**

+ **T38.6 Poisoning by, adverse effect of and underdosing of antigonadotrophins, antiestrogens, antiandrogens, not elsewhere classified**
  Poisoning by, adverse effect of and underdosing of tamoxifen
  + **T38.6X Poisoning by, adverse effect of and underdosing of antigonadotrophins, antiestrogens, antiandrogens, not elsewhere classified**
    - +7th **T38.6X1 Poisoning by antigonadotrophins, antiestrogens, antiandrogens, not elsewhere classified, accidental (unintentional)**
      Poisoning by antigonadotrophins, antiestrogens, antiandrogens, not elsewhere classified NOS
    - +7th **T38.6X2 Poisoning by antigonadotrophins, antiestrogens, antiandrogens, not elsewhere classified, intentional self-harm**
    - +7th **T38.6X3 Poisoning by antigonadotrophins, antiestrogens, antiandrogens, not elsewhere classified, assault**
    - +7th **T38.6X4 Poisoning by antigonadotrophins, antiestrogens, antiandrogens, not elsewhere classified, undetermined**
    - +7th **T38.6X5 Adverse effect of antigonadotrophins, antiestrogens, antiandrogens, not elsewhere classified**
    - +7th **T38.6X6 Underdosing of antigonadotrophins, antiestrogens, antiandrogens, not elsewhere classified**

+ **T38.7 Poisoning by, adverse effect of and underdosing of androgens and anabolic congeners**
  + **T38.7X Poisoning by, adverse effect of and underdosing of androgens and anabolic congeners**
    - +7th **T38.7X1 Poisoning by androgens and anabolic congeners, accidental (unintentional)**
      Poisoning by androgens and anabolic congeners NOS
    - +7th **T38.7X2 Poisoning by androgens and anabolic congeners, intentional self-harm**
    - +7th **T38.7X3 Poisoning by androgens and anabolic congeners, assault**
    - +7th **T38.7X4 Poisoning by androgens and anabolic congeners, undetermined**
    - +7th **T38.7X5 Adverse effect of androgens and anabolic congeners**
    - +7th **T38.7X6 Underdosing of androgens and anabolic congeners**

+ **T38.8 Poisoning by, adverse effect of and underdosing of other and unspecified hormones and synthetic substitutes**
  + **T38.80 Poisoning by, adverse effect of and underdosing of unspecified hormones and synthetic substitutes**
    - +7th **T38.801 Poisoning by unspecified hormones and synthetic substitutes, accidental (unintentional)**
      Poisoning by unspecified hormones and synthetic substitutes NOS
    - +7th **T38.802 Poisoning by unspecified hormones and synthetic substitutes, intentional self-harm**
    - +7th **T38.803 Poisoning by unspecified hormones and synthetic substitutes, assault**
    - +7th **T38.804 Poisoning by unspecified hormones and synthetic substitutes, undetermined**
    - +7th **T38.805 Adverse effect of unspecified hormones and synthetic substitutes**
    - +7th **T38.806 Underdosing of unspecified hormones and synthetic substitutes**
  + **T38.81 Poisoning by, adverse effect of and underdosing of anterior pituitary [adenohypophyseal] hormones**
    - +7th **T38.811 Poisoning by anterior pituitary [adenohypophyseal] hormones, accidental (unintentional)**
      Poisoning by anterior pituitary [adenohypophyseal] hormones NOS
    - +7th **T38.812 Poisoning by anterior pituitary [adenohypophyseal] hormones, intentional self-harm**
    - +7th **T38.813 Poisoning by anterior pituitary [adenohypophyseal] hormones, assault**
    - +7th **T38.814 Poisoning by anterior pituitary [adenohypophyseal] hormones, undetermined**
    - +7th **T38.815 Adverse effect of anterior pituitary [adenohypophyseal] hormones**
    - +7th **T38.816 Underdosing of anterior pituitary [adenohypophyseal] hormones**
  + **T38.89 Poisoning by, adverse effect of and underdosing of other hormones and synthetic substitutes**
    - +7th **T38.891 Poisoning by other hormones and synthetic substitutes, accidental (unintentional)**
      Poisoning by other hormones and synthetic substitutes NOS
    - +7th **T38.892 Poisoning by other hormones and synthetic substitutes, intentional self-harm**
    - +7th **T38.893 Poisoning by other hormones and synthetic substitutes, assault**
    - +7th **T38.894 Poisoning by other hormones and synthetic substitutes, undetermined**
    - +7th **T38.895 Adverse effect of other hormones and synthetic substitutes**
    - +7th **T38.896 Underdosing of other hormones and synthetic substitutes**

+ **T38.9 Poisoning by, adverse effect of and underdosing of other and unspecified hormone antagonists**

+ **T38.90 Poisoning by, adverse effect of and underdosing of unspecified hormone antagonists**

+7th **T38.901 Poisoning by unspecified hormone antagonists, accidental (unintentional)**

Poisoning by unspecified hormone antagonists NOS

+7th **T38.902 Poisoning by unspecified hormone antagonists, intentional self-harm**

+7th **T38.903 Poisoning by unspecified hormone antagonists, assault**

+7th **T38.904 Poisoning by unspecified hormone antagonists, undetermined**

+7th **T38.905 Adverse effect of unspecified hormone antagonists**

+7th **T38.906 Underdosing of unspecified hormone antagonists**

+ **T38.99 Poisoning by, adverse effect of and underdosing of other hormone antagonists**

+7th **T38.991 Poisoning by other hormone antagonists, accidental (unintentional)**

Poisoning by other hormone antagonists NOS

+7th **T38.992 Poisoning by other hormone antagonists, intentional self-harm**

+7th **T38.993 Poisoning by other hormone antagonists, assault**

+7th **T38.994 Poisoning by other hormone antagonists, undetermined**

+7th **T38.995 Adverse effect of other hormone antagonists**

+7th **T38.996 Underdosing of other hormone antagonists**

T39 Poisoning by, adverse effect of and underdosing of nonopioid analgesics, antipyretics and antirheumatics

The appropriate 7th character is to be added to each code from category T39
A initial encounter
D subsequent encounter
S sequela

+ **T39.0 Poisoning by, adverse effect of and underdosing of salicylates**

+ **T39.01 Poisoning by, adverse effect of and underdosing of aspirin**

Poisoning by, adverse effect of and underdosing of acetylsalicylic acid

+7th **T39.011 Poisoning by aspirin, accidental (unintentional)**

+7th **T39.012 Poisoning by aspirin, intentional self-harm**

+7th **T39.013 Poisoning by aspirin, assault**

+7th **T39.014 Poisoning by aspirin, undetermined**

+7th **T39.015 Adverse effect of aspirin**

+7th **T39.016 Underdosing of aspirin**

+ **T39.09 Poisoning by, adverse effect of and underdosing of other salicylates**

+7th **T39.091 Poisoning by salicylates, accidental (unintentional)**

Poisoning by salicylates NOS

+7th **T39.092 Poisoning by salicylates, intentional self-harm**

+7th **T39.093 Poisoning by salicylates, assault**

+7th **T39.094 Poisoning by salicylates, undetermined**

+7th **T39.095 Adverse effect of salicylates**

+7th **T39.096 Underdosing of salicylates**

+ **T39.1 Poisoning by, adverse effect of and underdosing of 4-Aminophenol derivatives**

+ **T39.1X Poisoning by, adverse effect of and underdosing of 4-Aminophenol derivatives**

+7th **T39.1X1 Poisoning by 4-Aminophenol derivatives, accidental (unintentional)**

Poisoning by 4-Aminophenol derivatives NOS

+7th **T39.1X2 Poisoning by 4-Aminophenol derivatives, intentional self-harm**

+7th **T39.1X3 Poisoning by 4-Aminophenol derivatives, assault**

+7th **T39.1X4 Poisoning by 4-Aminophenol derivatives, undetermined**

+7th **T39.1X5 Adverse effect of 4-Aminophenol derivatives**

+7th **T39.1X6 Underdosing of 4-Aminophenol derivatives**

+ **T39.2 Poisoning by, adverse effect of and underdosing of pyrazolone derivatives**

+ **T39.2X Poisoning by, adverse effect of and underdosing of pyrazolone derivatives**

+7th **T39.2X1 Poisoning by pyrazolone derivatives, accidental (unintentional)**

Poisoning by pyrazolone derivatives NOS

+7th **T39.2X2 Poisoning by pyrazolone derivatives, intentional self-harm**

+7th **T39.2X3 Poisoning by pyrazolone derivatives, assault**

+7th **T39.2X4 Poisoning by pyrazolone derivatives, undetermined**

+7th **T39.2X5 Adverse effect of pyrazolone derivatives**

+7th **T39.2X6 Underdosing of pyrazolone derivatives**

+ **T39.3 Poisoning by, adverse effect of and underdosing of other nonsteroidal anti-inflammatory drugs [NSAID]**

+ **T39.31 Poisoning by, adverse effect of and underdosing of propionic acid derivatives**

Poisoning by, adverse effect of and underdosing of fenoprofen

Poisoning by, adverse effect of and underdosing of flurbiprofen

Poisoning by, adverse effect of and underdosing of ibuprofen

Poisoning by, adverse effect of and underdosing of ketoprofen

Poisoning by, adverse effect of and underdosing of naproxen

Poisoning by, adverse effect of and underdosing of oxaprozin

+7th **T39.311 Poisoning by propionic acid derivatives, accidental (unintentional)**

+7th **T39.312 Poisoning by propionic acid derivatives, intentional self-harm**

+7th **T39.313 Poisoning by propionic acid derivatives, assault**

+7th **T39.314 Poisoning by propionic acid derivatives, undetermined**

+7th **T39.315 Adverse effect of propionic acid derivatives**

+7th **T39.316 Underdosing of propionic acid derivatives**

+ **T39.39 Poisoning by, adverse effect of and underdosing of other nonsteroidal anti-inflammatory drugs [NSAID]**

+7th **T39.391 Poisoning by other nonsteroidal anti-inflammatory drugs [NSAID], accidental (unintentional)**

Poisoning by other nonsteroidal anti-inflammatory drugs NOS

+7th **T39.392 Poisoning by other nonsteroidal anti-inflammatory drugs [NSAID], intentional self-harm**

+7th **T39.393 Poisoning by other nonsteroidal anti-inflammatory drugs [NSAID], assault**

+7th **T39.394 Poisoning by other nonsteroidal anti-inflammatory drugs [NSAID], undetermined**

+7th **T39.395 Adverse effect of other nonsteroidal anti-inflammatory drugs [NSAID]**

+7th **T39.396 Underdosing of other nonsteroidal anti-inflammatory drugs [NSAID]**

+ **T39.4 Poisoning by, adverse effect of and underdosing of antirheumatics, not elsewhere classified**

Excludes1: *poisoning by, adverse effect of and underdosing of glucocorticoids (T38.0-)*
poisoning by, adverse effect of and underdosing of salicylates (T39.0-)

+ **T39.4X Poisoning by, adverse effect of and underdosing of antirheumatics, not elsewhere classified**

+7th **T39.4X1 Poisoning by antirheumatics, not elsewhere classified, accidental (unintentional)**

Poisoning by antirheumatics, not elsewhere classified NOS

+7th **T39.4X2 Poisoning by antirheumatics, not elsewhere classified, intentional self-harm**

+7th **T39.4X3 Poisoning by antirheumatics, not elsewhere classified, assault**

+7th **T39.4X4 Poisoning by antirheumatics, not elsewhere classified, undetermined**

+7th **T39.4X5 Adverse effect of antirheumatics, not elsewhere classified**

+7th **T39.4X6 Underdosing of antirheumatics, not elsewhere classified**

+ **T39.8 Poisoning by, adverse effect of and underdosing of other nonopioid analgesics and antipyretics, not elsewhere classified**
  + **T39.8X Poisoning by, adverse effect of and underdosing of other nonopioid analgesics and antipyretics, not elsewhere classified**
    +7th **T39.8X1 Poisoning by other nonopioid analgesics and antipyretics, not elsewhere classified, accidental (unintentional)**
      Poisoning by other nonopioid analgesics and antipyretics, not elsewhere classified NOS
    +7th **T39.8X2 Poisoning by other nonopioid analgesics and antipyretics, not elsewhere classified, intentional self-harm**
    +7th **T39.8X3 Poisoning by other nonopioid analgesics and antipyretics, not elsewhere classified, assault**
    +7th **T39.8X4 Poisoning by other nonopioid analgesics and antipyretics, not elsewhere classified, undetermined**
    +7th **T39.8X5 Adverse effect of other nonopioid analgesics and antipyretics, not elsewhere classified**
    +7th **T39.8X6 Underdosing of other nonopioid analgesics and antipyretics, not elsewhere classified**

+ **T39.9 Poisoning by, adverse effect of and underdosing of unspecified nonopioid analgesic, antipyretic and antirheumatic**
  x+7th **T39.91 Poisoning by unspecified nonopioid analgesic, antipyretic and antirheumatic, accidental (unintentional)**
    Poisoning by nonopioid analgesic, antipyretic and antirheumatic NOS
  x+7th **T39.92 Poisoning by unspecified nonopioid analgesic, antipyretic and antirheumatic, intentional self-harm**
  x+7th **T39.93 Poisoning by unspecified nonopioid analgesic, antipyretic and antirheumatic, assault**
  x+7th **T39.94 Poisoning by unspecified nonopioid analgesic, antipyretic and antirheumatic, undetermined**
  x+7th **T39.95 Adverse effect of unspecified nonopioid analgesic, antipyretic and antirheumatic**
  x+7th **T39.96 Underdosing of unspecified nonopioid analgesic, antipyretic and antirheumatic**

T40 Poisoning by, adverse effect of and underdosing of narcotics and psychodysleptics [hallucinogens]

Excludes2: *drug dependence and related mental and behavioral disorders due to psychoactive substance use (F10.-F19.-)*

The appropriate 7th character is to be added to each code from category T40
A initial encounter
D subsequent encounter
S sequela

+ **T40.0 Poisoning by, adverse effect of and underdosing of opium**
  + **T40.0X Poisoning by, adverse effect of and underdosing of opium**
    +7th **T40.0X1 Poisoning by opium, accidental (unintentional)**
      Poisoning by opium NOS
    +7th **T40.0X2 Poisoning by opium, intentional self-harm**
    +7th **T40.0X3 Poisoning by opium, assault**
    +7th **T40.0X4 Poisoning by opium, undetermined**
    +7th **T40.0X5 Adverse effect of opium**
    +7th **T40.0X6 Underdosing of opium**

+ **T40.1 Poisoning by and adverse effect of heroin**
  + **T40.1X Poisoning by and adverse effect of heroin**
    +7th **T40.1X1 Poisoning by heroin, accidental (unintentional)**
      Poisoning by heroin NOS
    +7th **T40.1X2 Poisoning by heroin, intentional self-harm**
    +7th **T40.1X3 Poisoning by heroin, assault**
    +7th **T40.1X4 Poisoning by heroin, undetermined**

+ **T40.2 Poisoning by, adverse effect of and underdosing of other opioids**
  + **T40.2X Poisoning by, adverse effect of and underdosing of other opioids**
    +7th **T40.2X1 Poisoning by other opioids, accidental (unintentional)**
      Poisoning by other opioids NOS
    +7th **T40.2X2 Poisoning by other opioids, intentional self-harm**
    +7th **T40.2X3 Poisoning by other opioids, assault**
    +7th **T40.2X4 Poisoning by other opioids, undetermined**
    +7th **T40.2X5 Adverse effect of other opioids**
    +7th **T40.2X6 Underdosing of other opioids**

+ **T40.3 Poisoning by, adverse effect of and underdosing of methadone**
  + **T40.3X Poisoning by, adverse effect of and underdosing of methadone**
    +7th **T40.3X1 Poisoning by methadone, accidental (unintentional)**
      Poisoning by methadone NOS
    +7th **T40.3X2 Poisoning by methadone, intentional self-harm**
    +7th **T40.3X3 Poisoning by methadone, assault**
    +7th **T40.3X4 Poisoning by methadone, undetermined**
    +7th **T40.3X5 Adverse effect of methadone**
    +7th **T40.3X6 Underdosing of methadone**

+ **T40.4 Poisoning by, adverse effect of and underdosing of other synthetic narcotics**
  + **T40.4X Poisoning by, adverse effect of and underdosing of other synthetic narcotics**
    +7th **T40.4X1 Poisoning by other synthetic narcotics, accidental (unintentional)**
      Poisoning by other synthetic narcotics NOS
    +7th **T40.4X2 Poisoning by other synthetic narcotics, intentional self-harm**
    +7th **T40.4X3 Poisoning by other synthetic narcotics, assault**
    +7th **T40.4X4 Poisoning by other synthetic narcotics, undetermined**
    +7th **T40.4X5 Adverse effect of other synthetic narcotics**
    +7th **T40.4X6 Underdosing of other synthetic narcotics**

+ **T40.5 Poisoning by, adverse effect of and underdosing of cocaine**
  + **T40.5X Poisoning by, adverse effect of and underdosing of cocaine**
    +7th **T40.5X1 Poisoning by cocaine, accidental (unintentional)**
      Poisoning by cocaine NOS
    +7th **T40.5X2 Poisoning by cocaine, intentional self-harm**
    +7th **T40.5X3 Poisoning by cocaine, assault**
    +7th **T40.5X4 Poisoning by cocaine, undetermined**
    +7th **T40.5X5 Adverse effect of cocaine**
    +7th **T40.5X6 Underdosing of cocaine**

+ **T40.6 Poisoning by, adverse effect of and underdosing of other and unspecified narcotics**
  + **T40.60 Poisoning by, adverse effect of and underdosing of unspecified narcotics**
    +7th **T40.601 Poisoning by unspecified narcotics, accidental (unintentional)**
      Poisoning by narcotics NOS
    +7th **T40.602 Poisoning by unspecified narcotics, intentional self-harm**
    +7th **T40.603 Poisoning by unspecified narcotics, assault**
    +7th **T40.604 Poisoning by unspecified narcotics, undetermined**
    +7th **T40.605 Adverse effect of unspecified narcotics**
    +7th **T40.606 Underdosing of unspecified narcotics**
  + **T40.69 Poisoning by, adverse effect of and underdosing of other narcotics**
    +7th **T40.691 Poisoning by other narcotics, accidental (unintentional)**
      Poisoning by other narcotics NOS
    +7th **T40.692 Poisoning by other narcotics, intentional self-harm**
    +7th **T40.693 Poisoning by other narcotics, assault**
    +7th **T40.694 Poisoning by other narcotics, undetermined**
    +7th **T40.695 Adverse effect of other narcotics**
    +7th **T40.696 Underdosing of other narcotics**

+ **T40.7 Poisoning by, adverse effect of and underdosing of cannabis (derivatives)**
  + **T40.7X Poisoning by, adverse effect of and underdosing of cannabis (derivatives)**
    +7th **T40.7X1 Poisoning by cannabis (derivatives), accidental (unintentional)**
      Poisoning by cannabis NOS
    +7th **T40.7X2 Poisoning by cannabis (derivatives), intentional self-harm**
    +7th **T40.7X3 Poisoning by cannabis (derivatives), assault**
    +7th **T40.7X4 Poisoning by cannabis (derivatives), undetermined**
    +7th **T40.7X5 Adverse effect of cannabis (derivatives)**
    +7th **T40.7X6 Underdosing of cannabis (derivatives)**

+ **T40.8 Poisoning by and adverse effect of lysergide [LSD]**
+ **T40.8X Poisoning by and adverse effect of lysergide [LSD]**
+7th **T40.8X1 Poisoning by lysergide [LSD], accidental (unintentional)**
Poisoning by lysergide [LSD]NOS
+7th **T40.8X2 Poisoning by lysergide [LSD], intentional self-harm**
+7th **T40.8X3 Poisoning by lysergide [LSD], assault**
+7th **T40.8X4 Poisoning by lysergide [LSD], undetermined**
+ **T40.9 Poisoning by, adverse effect of and underdosing of other and unspecified psychodysleptics [hallucinogens]**
+ **T40.90 Poisoning by, adverse effect of and underdosing of unspecified psychodysleptics [hallucinogens]**
+7th **T40.901 Poisoning by unspecified psychodysleptics [hallucinogens], accidental (unintentional)**
+7th **T40.902 Poisoning by unspecified psychodysleptics [hallucinogens], intentional self-harm**
+7th **T40.903 Poisoning by unspecified psychodysleptics [hallucinogens], assault**
+7th **T40.904 Poisoning by unspecified psychodysleptics [hallucinogens], undetermined**
+7th **T40.905 Adverse effect of unspecified psychodysleptics [hallucinogens]**
+7th **T40.906 Underdosing of unspecified psychodysleptics**
+ **T40.99 Poisoning by, adverse effect of and underdosing of other psychodysleptics [hallucinogens]**
+7th **T40.991 Poisoning by other psychodysleptics [hallucinogens], accidental (unintentional)**
Poisoning by other psychodysleptics [hallucinogens] NOS
+7th **T40.992 Poisoning by other psychodysleptics [hallucinogens], intentional self-harm**
+7th **T40.993 Poisoning by other psychodysleptics [hallucinogens], assault**
+7th **T40.994 Poisoning by other psychodysleptics [hallucinogens], undetermined**
+7th **T40.995 Adverse effect of other psychodysleptics [hallucinogens]**
+7th **T40.996 Underdosing of other psychodysleptics**

T41 Poisoning by, adverse effect of and underdosing of anesthetics and therapeutic gases

Excludes1: *benzodiazepines (T42.4-)*
cocaine (T40.5-)
complications of anesthesia during pregnancy (O29.-)
complications of anesthesia during labor and delivery (O74.-)
complications of anesthesia during the puerperium (O89.-)
opioids (T40.0-T40.2-)

The appropriate 7th character is to be added to each code from category T41
A initial encounter
D subsequent encounter
S sequela

+ **T41.0 Poisoning by, adverse effect of and underdosing of inhaled anesthetics**
Excludes1: *oxygen (T41.5-)*
+ **T41.0X Poisoning by, adverse effect of and underdosing of inhaled anesthetics**
+7th **T41.0X1 Poisoning by inhaled anesthetics, accidental (unintentional)**
Poisoning by inhaled anesthetics NOS
+7th **T41.0X2 Poisoning by inhaled anesthetics, intentional self-harm**
+7th **T41.0X3 Poisoning by inhaled anesthetics, assault**
+7th **T41.0X4 Poisoning by inhaled anesthetics, undetermined**
+7th **T41.0X5 Adverse effect of inhaled anesthetics**
+7th **T41.0X6 Underdosing of inhaled anesthetics**
+ **T41.1 Poisoning by, adverse effect of and underdosing of intravenous anesthetics**
Poisoning by, adverse effect of and underdosing of thiobarbiturates
+ **T41.1X Poisoning by, adverse effect of and underdosing of intravenous anesthetics**
+7th **T41.1X1 Poisoning by intravenous anesthetics, accidental (unintentional)**
Poisoning by intravenous anesthetics NOS
+7th **T41.1X2 Poisoning by intravenous anesthetics, intentional self-harm**
+7th **T41.1X3 Poisoning by intravenous anesthetics, assa**
+7th **T41.1X4 Poisoning by intravenous anesthetics, undetermined**
+7th **T41.1X5 Adverse effect of intravenous anesthetics**
+7th **T41.1X6 Underdosing of intravenous anesthetics**
+ **T41.2 Poisoning by, adverse effect of and underdosing of other and unspecified general anesthetics**
+ **T41.20 Poisoning by, adverse effect of and underdosing of unspecified general anesthetics**
+7th **T41.201 Poisoning by unspecified general anestheti accidental (unintentional)**
Poisoning by general anesthetics NOS
+7th **T41.202 Poisoning by unspecified general anestheti intentional self-harm**
+7th **T41.203 Poisoning by unspecified general anestheti assault**
+7th **T41.204 Poisoning by unspecified general anestheti undetermined**
+7th **T41.205 Adverse effect of unspecified general anesthetics**
+7th **T41.206 Underdosing of unspecified general anesthetics**
+ **T41.29 Poisoning by, adverse effect of and underdosing of other general anesthetics**
+7th **T41.291 Poisoning by other general anesthetics, accidental (unintentional)**
Poisoning by other general anesthetics NOS
+7th **T41.292 Poisoning by other general anesthetics, intentional self-harm**
+7th **T41.293 Poisoning by other general anesthetics, assault**
+7th **T41.294 Poisoning by other general anesthetics, undetermined**
+7th **T41.295 Adverse effect of other general anesthetics**
+7th **T41.296 Underdosing of other general anesthetics**
+ **T41.3 Poisoning by, adverse effect of and underdosing of local anesthetics**
Cocaine (topical)
Excludes2: *poisoning by cocaine used as a central nervous system stimulant (T40.5X1-T40.5X4)*
+ **T41.3X Poisoning by, adverse effect of and underdosing of local anesthetics**
+7th **T41.3X1 Poisoning by local anesthetics, accidental (unintentional)**
Poisoning by local anesthetics NOS
+7th **T41.3X2 Poisoning by local anesthetics, intentional self-harm**
+7th **T41.3X3 Poisoning by local anesthetics, assault**
+7th **T41.3X4 Poisoning by local anesthetics, undetermine**
+7th **T41.3X5 Adverse effect of local anesthetics**
+7th **T41.3X6 Underdosing of local anesthetics**
+ **T41.4 Poisoning by, adverse effect of and underdosing of unspecified anesthetic**
X+7th **T41.41 Poisoning by unspecified anesthetic, accidental (unintentional)**
Poisoning by anesthetic NOS
X+7th **T41.42 Poisoning by unspecified anesthetic, intentional self-harm**
X+7th **T41.43 Poisoning by unspecified anesthetic, assault**
X+7th **T41.44 Poisoning by unspecified anesthetic, undetermined**
X+7th **T41.45 Adverse effect of unspecified anesthetic**
X+7th **T41.46 Underdosing of unspecified anesthetics**
+ **T41.5 Poisoning by, adverse effect of and underdosing of therapeutic gases**
+ **T41.5X Poisoning by, adverse effect of and underdosing of therapeutic gases**
+7th **T41.5X1 Poisoning by therapeutic gases, accidental (unintentional)**
Poisoning by therapeutic gases NOS
+7th **T41.5X2 Poisoning by therapeutic gases, intentional self-harm**
+7th **T41.5X3 Poisoning by therapeutic gases, assault**
+7th **T41.5X4 Poisoning by therapeutic gases, undetermined**
+7th **T41.5X5 Adverse effect of therapeutic gases**
+7th **T41.5X6 Underdosing of therapeutic gases**

T42 Poisoning by, adverse effect of and underdosing of antiepileptic, sedative- hypnotic and antiparkinsonism drugs

Excludes2: *drug dependence and related mental and behavioral disorders due to psychoactive substance use (F10.--F19.-)*

The appropriate 7th character is to be added to each code from category T42
A initial encounter
D subsequent encounter
S sequela

+ **T42.0 Poisoning by, adverse effect of and underdosing of hydantoin derivatives**
+ **T42.0X Poisoning by, adverse effect of and underdosing of hydantoin derivatives**
+7th **T42.0X1 Poisoning by hydantoin derivatives, accidental (unintentional)**
Poisoning by hydantoin derivatives NOS
+7th **T42.0X2 Poisoning by hydantoin derivatives, intentional self-harm**
+7th **T42.0X3 Poisoning by hydantoin derivatives, assault**
+7th **T42.0X4 Poisoning by hydantoin derivatives, undetermined**
+7th **T42.0X5 Adverse effect of hydantoin derivatives**
+7th **T42.0X6 Underdosing of hydantoin derivatives**

+ **T42.1 Poisoning by, adverse effect of and underdosing of iminostilbenes**
Poisoning by, adverse effect of and underdosing of carbamazepine
+ **T42.1X Poisoning by, adverse effect of and underdosing of iminostilbenes**
+7th **T42.1X1 Poisoning by iminostilbenes, accidental (unintentional)**
Poisoning by iminostilbenes NOS
+7th **T42.1X2 Poisoning by iminostilbenes, intentional self-harm**
+7th **T42.1X3 Poisoning by iminostilbenes, assault**
+7th **T42.1X4 Poisoning by iminostilbenes, undetermined**
+7th **T42.1X5 Adverse effect of iminostilbenes**
+7th **T42.1X6 Underdosing of iminostilbenes**

+ **T42.2 Poisoning by, adverse effect of and underdosing of succinimides and oxazolidinediones**
+ **T42.2X Poisoning by, adverse effect of and underdosing of succinimides and oxazolidinediones**
+7th **T42.2X1 Poisoning by succinimides and oxazolidinediones, accidental (unintentional)**
Poisoning by succinimides and oxazolidinediones NOS
+7th **T42.2X2 Poisoning by succinimides and oxazolidinediones, intentional self-harm**
+7th **T42.2X3 Poisoning by succinimides and oxazolidinediones, assault**
+7th **T42.2X4 Poisoning by succinimides and oxazolidinediones, undetermined**
+7th **T42.2X5 Adverse effect of succinimides and oxazolidinediones**
+7th **T42.2X6 Underdosing of succinimides and oxazolidinediones**

+ **T42.3 Poisoning by, adverse effect of and underdosing of barbiturates**
Excludes1: *poisoning by, adverse effect of and underdosing of thiobarbiturates (T41.1-)*
+ **T42.3X Poisoning by, adverse effect of and underdosing of barbiturates**
+7th **T42.3X1 Poisoning by barbiturates, accidental (unintentional)**
Poisoning by barbiturates NOS
+7th **T42.3X2 Poisoning by barbiturates, intentional self-harm**
+7th **T42.3X3 Poisoning by barbiturates, assault**
+7th **T42.3X4 Poisoning by barbiturates, undetermined**
+7th **T42.3X5 Adverse effect of barbiturates**
+7th **T42.3X6 Underdosing of barbiturates**

+ **T42.4 Poisoning by, adverse effect of and underdosing of benzodiazepines**
+ **T42.4X Poisoning by, adverse effect of and underdosing of benzodiazepines**
+7th **T42.4X1 Poisoning by benzodiazepines, accidental (unintentional)**
Poisoning by benzodiazepines NOS
+7th **T42.4X2 Poisoning by benzodiazepines, intentional self-harm**
+7th **T42.4X3 Poisoning by benzodiazepines, assault**
+7th **T42.4X4 Poisoning by benzodiazepines, undetermined**
+7th **T42.4X5 Adverse effect of benzodiazepines**
+7th **T42.4X6 Underdosing of benzodiazepines**

+ **T42.5 Poisoning by, adverse effect of and underdosing of mixed antiepileptics**
+ **T42.5X Poisoning by, adverse effect of and underdosing of antiepileptics**
+7th **T42.5X1 Poisoning by mixed antiepileptics, accidental (unintentional)**
Poisoning by mixed antiepileptics NOS
+7th **T42.5X2 Poisoning by mixed antiepileptics, intentional self-harm**
+7th **T42.5X3 Poisoning by mixed antiepileptics, assault**
+7th **T42.5X4 Poisoning by mixed antiepileptics, undetermined**
+7th **T42.5X5 Adverse effect of mixed antiepileptics**
+7th **T42.5X6 Underdosing of mixed antiepileptics**

+ **T42.6 Poisoning by, adverse effect of and underdosing of other antiepileptic and sedative-hypnotic drugs**
Poisoning by, adverse effect of and underdosing of methaqualone
Poisoning by, adverse effect of and underdosing of valproic acid
Excludes1: *poisoning by, adverse effect of and underdosing of carbamazepine (T42.1-)*
+ **T42.6X Poisoning by, adverse effect of and underdosing of other antiepileptic and sedative-hypnotic drugs**
+7th **T42.6X1 Poisoning by other antiepileptic and sedative-hypnotic drugs, accidental (unintentional)**
Poisoning by other antiepileptic and sedative-hypnotic drugs NOS
+7th **T42.6X2 Poisoning by other antiepileptic and sedative-hypnotic drugs, intentional self-harm**
+7th **T42.6X3 Poisoning by other antiepileptic and sedative-hypnotic drugs, assault**
+7th **T42.6X4 Poisoning by other antiepileptic and sedative-hypnotic drugs, undetermined**
+7th **T42.6X5 Adverse effect of other antiepileptic and sedative-hypnotic drugs**
+7th **T42.6X6 Underdosing of other antiepileptic and sedative-hypnotic drugs**

+ **T42.7 Poisoning by, adverse effect of and underdosing of unspecified antiepileptic and sedative-hypnotic drugs**
X+7th **T42.71 Poisoning by unspecified antiepileptic and sedative-hypnotic drugs, accidental (unintentional)**
Poisoning by antiepileptic and sedative-hypnotic drugs NOS
X+7th **T42.72 Poisoning by unspecified antiepileptic and sedative-hypnotic drugs, intentional self-harm**
X+7th **T42.73 Poisoning by unspecified antiepileptic and sedative-hypnotic drugs, assault**
X+7th **T42.74 Poisoning by unspecified antiepileptic and sedative-hypnotic drugs, undetermined**
X+7th **T42.75 Adverse effect of unspecified antiepileptic and sedative-hypnotic drugs**
X+7th **T42.76 Underdosing of unspecified antiepileptic and sedative-hypnotic drugs**

+ **T42.8 Poisoning by, adverse effect of and underdosing of antiparkinsonism drugs and other central muscle-tone depressants**
Poisoning by, adverse effect of and underdosing of amantadine
+ **T42.8X Poisoning by, adverse effect of and underdosing of antiparkinsonism drugs and other central muscle-tone depressants**
+7th **T42.8X1 Poisoning by antiparkinsonism drugs and other central muscle-tone depressants, accidental (unintentional)**
Poisoning by antiparkinsonism drugs and other central muscle-tone depressants NOS
+7th **T42.8X2 Poisoning by antiparkinsonism drugs and other central muscle-tone depressants, intentional self-harm**
+7th **T42.8X3 Poisoning by antiparkinsonism drugs and other central muscle-tone depressants, assault**
+7th **T42.8X4 Poisoning by antiparkinsonism drugs and other central muscle-tone depressants, undetermined**
+7th **T42.8X5 Adverse effect of antiparkinsonism drugs and other central muscle-tone depressants**
+7th **T42.8X6 Underdosing of antiparkinsonism drugs and other central muscle-tone depressants**

T43 Poisoning by, adverse effect of and underdosing of psychotropic drugs, not elsewhere classified

Excludes1: *appetite depressants (T50.5-)*
barbiturates (T42.3-)
benzodiazepines (T42.4-)
methaqualone (T42.6-)
psychodysleptics [hallucinogens] (T40.7-T40.9-)

Excludes2: *drug dependence and related mental and behavioral disorders due to psychoactive substance use (F10.- -F19.-)*

The appropriate 7th character is to be added to each code from category T43
A initial encounter
D subsequent encounter
S sequela

+ **T43.0 Poisoning by, adverse effect of and underdosing of tricyclic and tetracyclic antidepressants**
+ **T43.01 Poisoning by, adverse effect of and underdosing of tricyclic antidepressants**
+7th **T43.011 Poisoning by tricyclic antidepressants, accidental (unintentional)**
Poisoning by tricyclic antidepressants NOS
+7th **T43.012 Poisoning by tricyclic antidepressants, intentional self-harm**
+7th **T43.013 Poisoning by tricyclic antidepressants, assault**
+7th **T43.014 Poisoning by tricyclic antidepressants, undetermined**
+7th **T43.015 Adverse effect of tricyclic antidepressants**
+7th **T43.016 Underdosing of tricyclic antidepressants**
+ **T43.02 Poisoning by, adverse effect of and underdosing of tetracyclic antidepressants**
+7th **T43.021 Poisoning by tetracyclic antidepressants, accidental (unintentional)**
Poisoning by tetracyclic antidepressants NOS
+7th **T43.022 Poisoning by tetracyclic antidepressants, intentional self-harm**
+7th **T43.023 Poisoning by tetracyclic antidepressants, assault**
+7th **T43.024 Poisoning by tetracyclic antidepressants, undetermined**
+7th **T43.025 Adverse effect of tetracyclic antidepressants**
+7th **T43.026 Underdosing of tetracyclic antidepressants**
+ **T43.1 Poisoning by, adverse effect of and underdosing of monoamine-oxidase-inhibitor antidepressants**
+ **T43.1X Poisoning by, adverse effect of and underdosing of monoamine-oxidase-inhibitor antidepressants**
+7th **T43.1X1 Poisoning by monoamine-oxidase-inhibitor antidepressants, accidental (unintentional)**
Poisoning by monoamine-oxidase-inhibitor antidepressants NOS
+7th **T43.1X2 Poisoning by monoamine-oxidase-inhibitor antidepressants, intentional self-harm**
+7th **T43.1X3 Poisoning by monoamine-oxidase-inhibitor antidepressants, assault**
+7th **T43.1X4 Poisoning by monoamine-oxidase-inhibitor antidepressants, undetermined**
+7th **T43.1X5 Adverse effect of monoamine-oxidase-inhibitor antidepressants**
+7th **T43.1X6 Underdosing of monoamine-oxidase-inhibitor antidepressants**
+ **T43.2 Poisoning by, adverse effect of and underdosing of other and unspecified antidepressants**
+ **T43.20 Poisoning by, adverse effect of and underdosing of unspecified antidepressants**
+7th **T43.201 Poisoning by unspecified antidepressants, accidental (unintentional)**
Poisoning by antidepressants NOS
+7th **T43.202 Poisoning by unspecified antidepressants, intentional self-harm**
+7th **T43.203 Poisoning by unspecified antidepressants, assault**
+7th **T43.204 Poisoning by unspecified antidepressants, undetermined**
+7th **T43.205 Adverse effect of unspecified antidepressants**
+7th **T43.206 Underdosing of unspecified antidepressants**
+ **T43.21 Poisoning by, adverse effect of and underdosing of selective serotonin and norepinephrine reuptake inhibitors**
Poisoning by, adverse effect of and underdosing of SSNRI antidepressants
+7th **T43.211 Poisoning by selective serotonin and norepinephrine reuptake inhibitors, accidental (unintentional)**
+7th **T43.212 Poisoning by selective serotonin and norepinephrine reuptake inhibitors, intentional self-harm**
+7th **T43.213 Poisoning by selective serotonin and norepinephrine reuptake inhibitors, assaul**
+7th **T43.214 Poisoning by selective serotonin and norepinephrine reuptake inhibitors, undetermined**
+7th **T43.215 Adverse effect of selective serotonin and norepinephrine reuptake inhibitors**
+7th **T43.216 Underdosing of selective serotonin and norepinephrine reuptake inhibitors**
+ **T43.22 Poisoning by, adverse effect of and underdosing of selective serotonin reuptake inhibitors**
Poisoning by, adverse effect of and underdosing of SS antidepressants
+7th **T43.221 Poisoning by selective serotonin reuptake inhibitors, accidental (unintentional)**
+7th **T43.222 Poisoning by selective serotonin reuptake inhibitors, intentional self-harm**
+7th **T43.223 Poisoning by selective serotonin reuptake inhibitors, assault**
+7th **T43.224 Poisoning by selective serotonin reuptake inhibitors, undetermined**
+7th **T43.225 Adverse effect of selective serotonin reupta inhibitors**
+7th **T43.226 Underdosing of selective serotonin reuptak inhibitors**
+ **T43.29 Poisoning by, adverse effect of and underdosing of other antidepressants**
+7th **T43.291 Poisoning by other antidepressants, accidental (unintentional)**
Poisoning by other antidepressants NOS
+7th **T43.292 Poisoning by other antidepressants, intentional self-harm**
+7th **T43.293 Poisoning by other antidepressants, assault**
+7th **T43.294 Poisoning by other antidepressants, undetermined**
+7th **T43.295 Adverse effect of other antidepressants**
+7th **T43.296 Underdosing of other antidepressants**
+ **T43.3 Poisoning by, adverse effect of and underdosing of phenothiazin antipsychotics and neuroleptics**
+ **T43.3X Poisoning by, adverse effect of and underdosing of phenothiazine antipsychotics and neuroleptics**
+7th **T43.3X1 Poisoning by phenothiazine antipsychotics and neuroleptics, accidental (unintentional)**
Poisoning by phenothiazine antipsychotics and neuroleptics NOS
+7th **T43.3X2 Poisoning by phenothiazine antipsychotics and neuroleptics, intentional self-harm**
+7th **T43.3X3 Poisoning by phenothiazine antipsychotics and neuroleptics, assault**
+7th **T43.3X4 Poisoning by phenothiazine antipsychotics and neuroleptics, undetermined**
+7th **T43.3X5 Adverse effect of phenothiazine antipsychotics and neuroleptics**
+7th **T43.3X6 Underdosing of phenothiazine antipsychotic and neuroleptics**
+ **T43.4 Poisoning by, adverse effect of and underdosing of butyrophenone and thiothixene neuroleptics**
+ **T43.4X Poisoning by, adverse effect of and underdosing of butyrophenone and thiothixene neuroleptics**
+7th **T43.4X1 Poisoning by butyrophenone and thiothixene neuroleptics, accidental (unintentional)**
Poisoning by butyrophenone and thiothixene neuroleptics NOS
+7th **T43.4X2 Poisoning by butyrophenone and thiothixene neuroleptics, intentional self-harm**
+7th **T43.4X3 Poisoning by butyrophenone and thiothixene neuroleptics, assault**
+7th **T43.4X4 Poisoning by butyrophenone and thiothixene neuroleptics, undetermined**

+7th **T43.4X5** **Adverse effect of butyrophenone and thiothixene neuroleptics**
+7th **T43.4X6** **Underdosing of butyrophenone and thiothixene neuroleptics**

+ **T43.5** **Poisoning by, adverse effect of and underdosing of other and unspecified antipsychotics and neuroleptics**
Excludes1: *poisoning by, adverse effect of and underdosing of rauwolfia (T46.5-)*

+ **T43.50** **Poisoning by, adverse effect of and underdosing of unspecified antipsychotics and neuroleptics**
+7th **T43.501** **Poisoning by unspecified antipsychotics and neuroleptics, accidental (unintentional)**
Poisoning by antipsychotics and neuroleptics NOS
+7th **T43.502** **Poisoning by unspecified antipsychotics and neuroleptics, intentional self-harm**
+7th **T43.503** **Poisoning by unspecified antipsychotics and neuroleptics, assault**
+7th **T43.504** **Poisoning by unspecified antipsychotics and neuroleptics, undetermined**
+7th **T43.505** **Adverse effect of unspecified antipsychotics and neuroleptics**
+7th **T43.506** **Underdosing of unspecified antipsychotics and neuroleptics**

+ **T43.59** **Poisoning by, adverse effect of and underdosing of other antipsychotics and neuroleptics**
+7th **T43.591** **Poisoning by other antipsychotics and neuroleptics, accidental (unintentional)**
Poisoning by other antipsychotics and neuroleptics NOS
+7th **T43.592** **Poisoning by other antipsychotics and neuroleptics, intentional self-harm**
+7th **T43.593** **Poisoning by other antipsychotics and neuroleptics, assault**
+7th **T43.594** **Poisoning by other antipsychotics and neuroleptics, undetermined**
+7th **T43.595** **Adverse effect of other antipsychotics and neuroleptics**
+7th **T43.596** **Underdosing of other antipsychotics and neuroleptics**

+ **T43.6** **Poisoning by, adverse effect of and underdosing of psychostimulants**
Excludes1: *poisoning by, adverse effect of and underdosing of cocaine (T40.5-)*

+ **T43.60** **Poisoning by, adverse effect of and underdosing of unspecified psychostimulant**
+7th **T43.601** **Poisoning by unspecified psychostimulants, accidental (unintentional)**
Poisoning by psychostimulants NOS
+7th **T43.602** **Poisoning by unspecified psychostimulants, intentional self-harm**
+7th **T43.603** **Poisoning by unspecified psychostimulants, assault**
+7th **T43.604** **Poisoning by unspecified psychostimulants, undetermined**
+7th **T43.605** **Adverse effect of unspecified psychostimulants**
+7th **T43.606** **Underdosing of unspecified psychostimulants**

+ **T43.61** **Poisoning by, adverse effect of and underdosing of caffeine**
+7th **T43.611** **Poisoning by caffeine, accidental (unintentional)**
Poisoning by caffeine NOS
+7th **T43.612** **Poisoning by caffeine, intentional self-harm**
+7th **T43.613** **Poisoning by caffeine, assault**
+7th **T43.614** **Poisoning by caffeine, undetermined**
+7th **T43.615** **Adverse effect of caffeine**
+7th **T43.616** **Underdosing of caffeine**

+ **T43.62** **Poisoning by, adverse effect of and underdosing of amphetamines**
Poisoning by, adverse effect of and underdosing of methamphetamines
+7th **T43.621** **Poisoning by amphetamines, accidental (unintentional)**
Poisoning by amphetamines NOS
+7th **T43.622** **Poisoning by amphetamines, intentional self-harm**
+7th **T43.623** **Poisoning by amphetamines, assault**
+7th **T43.624** **Poisoning by amphetamines, undetermined**
+7th **T43.625** **Adverse effect of amphetamines**
+7th **T43.626** **Underdosing of amphetamines**

+ **T43.63** **Poisoning by, adverse effect of and underdosing of methylphenidate**
+7th **T43.631** **Poisoning by methylphenidate, accidental (unintentional)**
Poisoning by methylphenidate NOS
+7th **T43.632** **Poisoning by methylphenidate, intentional self-harm**
+7th **T43.633** **Poisoning by methylphenidate, assault**
+7th **T43.634** **Poisoning by methylphenidate, undetermined**
+7th **T43.635** **Adverse effect of methylphenidate**
+7th **T43.636** **Underdosing of methylphenidate**

+ **T43.69** **Poisoning by, adverse effect of and underdosing of other psychostimulants**
+7th **T43.691** **Poisoning by other psychostimulants, accidental (unintentional)**
Poisoning by other psychostimulants NOS
+7th **T43.692** **Poisoning by other psychostimulants, intentional self-harm**
+7th **T43.693** **Poisoning by other psychostimulants, assault**
+7th **T43.694** **Poisoning by other psychostimulants, undetermined**
+7th **T43.695** **Adverse effect of other psychostimulants**
+7th **T43.696** **Underdosing of other psychostimulants**

+ **T43.8** **Poisoning by, adverse effect of and underdosing of other psychotropic drugs**
+ **T43.8X** **Poisoning by, adverse effect of and underdosing of other psychotropic drugs**
+7th **T43.8X1** **Poisoning by other psychotropic drugs, accidental (unintentional)**
Poisoning by other psychotropic drugs NOS
+7th **T43.8X2** **Poisoning by other psychotropic drugs, intentional self-harm**
+7th **T43.8X3** **Poisoning by other psychotropic drugs, assault**
+7th **T43.8X4** **Poisoning by other psychotropic drugs, undetermined**
+7th **T43.8X5** **Adverse effect of other psychotropic drugs**
+7th **T43.8X6** **Underdosing of other psychotropic drugs**

+ **T43.9** **Poisoning by, adverse effect of and underdosing of unspecified psychotropic drug**
x+7th **T43.91** **Poisoning by unspecified psychotropic drug, accidental (unintentional)**
Poisoning by psychotropic drug NOS
x+7th **T43.92** **Poisoning by unspecified psychotropic drug, intentional self-harm**
x+7th **T43.93** **Poisoning by unspecified psychotropic drug, assault**
x+7th **T43.94** **Poisoning by unspecified psychotropic drug, undetermined**
x+7th **T43.95** **Adverse effect of unspecified psychotropic drug**
x+7th **T43.96** **Underdosing of unspecified psychotropic drug**

T44 **Poisoning by, adverse effect of and underdosing of drugs primarily affecting the autonomic nervous system**

The appropriate 7th character is to be added to each code from category T44
A initial encounter
D subsequent encounter
S sequela

+ **T44.0** **Poisoning by, adverse effect of and underdosing of anticholinesterase agents**
+ **T44.0X** **Poisoning by, adverse effect of and underdosing of anticholinesterase agents**
+7th **T44.0X1** **Poisoning by anticholinesterase agents, accidental (unintentional)**
Poisoning by anticholinesterase agents NOS
+7th **T44.0X2** **Poisoning by anticholinesterase agents, intentional self-harm**
+7th **T44.0X3** **Poisoning by anticholinesterase agents, assault**
+7th **T44.0X4** **Poisoning by anticholinesterase agents, undetermined**
+7th **T44.0X5** **Adverse effect of anticholinesterase agents**
+7th **T44.0X6** **Underdosing of anticholinesterase agents**

+ **T44.1** **Poisoning by, adverse effect of and underdosing of other parasympathomimetics [cholinergics]**
+ **T44.1X** **Poisoning by, adverse effect of and underdosing of other parasympathomimetics [cholinergics]**
+7th **T44.1X1** **Poisoning by other parasympathomimetics [cholinergics], accidental (unintentional)**
Poisoning by other parasympathomimetics [cholinergics] NOS

+7th **T44.1X2 Poisoning by other parasympathomimetics [cholinergics], intentional self-harm**

+7th **T44.1X3 Poisoning by other parasympathomimetics [cholinergics], assault**

+7th **T44.1X4 Poisoning by other parasympathomimetics [cholinergics], undetermined**

+7th **T44.1X5 Adverse effect of other parasympathomimetics [cholinergics]**

+7th **T44.1X6 Underdosing of other parasympathomimetics**

\+ **T44.2 Poisoning by, adverse effect of and underdosing of ganglionic blocking drugs**

\+ **T44.2X Poisoning by, adverse effect of and underdosing of ganglionic blocking drugs**

+7th **T44.2X1 Poisoning by ganglionic blocking drugs, accidental (unintentional)**

Poisoning by ganglionic blocking drugs NOS

+7th **T44.2X2 Poisoning by ganglionic blocking drugs, intentional self-harm**

+7th **T44.2X3 Poisoning by ganglionic blocking drugs, assault**

+7th **T44.2X4 Poisoning by ganglionic blocking drugs, undetermined**

+7th **T44.2X5 Adverse effect of ganglionic blocking drugs**

+7th **T44.2X6 Underdosing of ganglionic blocking drugs**

\+ **T44.3 Poisoning by, adverse effect of and underdosing of other parasympatholytics [anticholinergics and antimuscarinics] and spasmolytics**

Poisoning by, adverse effect of and underdosing of papaverine

\+ **T44.3X Poisoning by, adverse effect of and underdosing of other parasympatholytics [anticholinergics and antimuscarinics] and spasmolytics**

+7th **T44.3X1 Poisoning by other parasympatholytics [anticholinergics and antimuscarinics] and spasmolytics, accidental (unintentional)**

Poisoning by other parasympatholytics [anticholinergics and antimuscarinics] and spasmolytics NOS

+7th **T44.3X2 Poisoning by other parasympatholytics [anticholinergics and antimuscarinics] and spasmolytics, intentional self-harm**

+7th **T44.3X3 Poisoning by other parasympatholytics [anticholinergics and antimuscarinics] and spasmolytics, assault**

+7th **T44.3X4 Poisoning by other parasympatholytics [anticholinergics and antimuscarinics] and spasmolytics, undetermined**

+7th **T44.3X5 Adverse effect of other parasympatholytics [anticholinergics and antimuscarinics] and spasmolytics**

+7th **T44.3X6 Underdosing of other parasympatholytics [anticholinergics and antimuscarinics] and spasmolytics**

\+ **T44.4 Poisoning by, adverse effect of and underdosing of predominantly alpha-adrenoreceptor agonists**

Poisoning by, adverse effect of and underdosing of metaraminol

\+ **T44.4X Poisoning by, adverse effect of and underdosing of predominantly alpha-adrenoreceptor agonists**

+7th **T44.4X1 Poisoning by predominantly alpha-adrenoreceptor agonists, accidental (unintentional)**

Poisoning by predominantly alpha-adrenoreceptor agonists NOS

+7th **T44.4X2 Poisoning by predominantly alpha-adrenoreceptor agonists, intentional self-harm**

+7th **T44.4X3 Poisoning by predominantly alpha-adrenoreceptor agonists, assault**

+7th **T44.4X4 Poisoning by predominantly alpha-adrenoreceptor agonists, undetermined**

+7th **T44.4X5 Adverse effect of predominantly alpha-adrenoreceptor agonists**

+7th **T44.4X6 Underdosing of predominantly alpha-adrenoreceptor agonists**

\+ **T44.5 Poisoning by, adverse effect of and underdosing of predominantly beta-adrenoreceptor agonists**

Excludes1: *poisoning by, adverse effect of and underdosing of beta-adrenoreceptor agonists used in asthma therapy (T48.6-)*

\+ **T44.5X Poisoning by, adverse effect of and underdosing of predominantly beta-adrenoreceptor agonists**

+7th **T44.5X1 Poisoning by predominantly beta-adrenoreceptor agonists, accidental (unintentional)**

Poisoning by predominantly beta-adrenoreceptor agonists NOS

+7th **T44.5X2 Poisoning by predominantly beta-adrenoreceptor agonists, intentional self-harm**

+7th **T44.5X3 Poisoning by predominantly beta-adrenoreceptor agonists, assault**

+7th **T44.5X4 Poisoning by predominantly beta-adrenoreceptor agonists, undetermined**

+7th **T44.5X5 Adverse effect of predominantly beta-adrenoreceptor agonists**

+7th **T44.5X6 Underdosing of predominantly beta-adrenoreceptor agonists**

\+ **T44.6 Poisoning by, adverse effect of and underdosing of alpha-adrenoreceptor antagonists**

Excludes1: *poisoning by, adverse effect of and underdosing of ergot alkaloids (T48.0)*

\+ **T44.6X Poisoning by, adverse effect of and underdosing of alpha-adrenoreceptor antagonists**

+7th **T44.6X1 Poisoning by alpha-adrenoreceptor antagonists, accidental (unintentional)**

Poisoning by alpha-adrenoreceptor antagonists NOS

+7th **T44.6X2 Poisoning by alpha-adrenoreceptor antagonists, intentional self-harm**

+7th **T44.6X3 Poisoning by alpha-adrenoreceptor antagonists, assault**

+7th **T44.6X4 Poisoning by alpha-adrenoreceptor antagonists, undetermined**

+7th **T44.6X5 Adverse effect of alpha-adrenoreceptor antagonists**

+7th **T44.6X6 Underdosing of alpha-adrenoreceptor antagonists**

\+ **T44.7 Poisoning by, adverse effect of and underdosing of beta-adrenoreceptor antagonists**

\+ **T44.7X Poisoning by, adverse effect of and underdosing of beta-adrenoreceptor antagonists**

+7th **T44.7X1 Poisoning by beta-adrenoreceptor antagonists, accidental (unintentional)**

Poisoning by beta-adrenoreceptor antagonists NOS

+7th **T44.7X2 Poisoning by beta-adrenoreceptor antagonists, intentional self-harm**

+7th **T44.7X3 Poisoning by beta-adrenoreceptor antagonists, assault**

+7th **T44.7X4 Poisoning by beta-adrenoreceptor antagonists, undetermined**

+7th **T44.7X5 Adverse effect of beta-adrenoreceptor antagonists**

+7th **T44.7X6 Underdosing of beta-adrenoreceptor antagonists**

\+ **T44.8 Poisoning by, adverse effect of and underdosing of centrally-acting and adrenergic-neuron- blocking agents**

Excludes1: *poisoning by, adverse effect of and underdosing of clonidine (T46.5)*

poisoning by, adverse effect of and underdosing of guanethidine (T46.5)

\+ **T44.8X Poisoning by, adverse effect of and underdosing of centrally-acting and adrenergic- neuron-blocking agents**

+7th **T44.8X1 Poisoning by centrally-acting and adrenergic-neuron-blocking agents, accidental (unintentional)**

Poisoning by centrally-acting and adrenergic-neuron-blocking agents NOS

+7th **T44.8X2 Poisoning by centrally-acting and adrenergic-neuron-blocking agents, intentional self-harm**

+7th **T44.8X3 Poisoning by centrally-acting and adrenergic-neuron-blocking agents, assault**

+7th **T44.8X4 Poisoning by centrally-acting and adrenergic-neuron-blocking agents, undetermined**

+7th **T44.8X5 Adverse effect of centrally-acting and adrenergic-neuron-blocking agents**

+7th **T44.8X6 Underdosing of centrally-acting and adrenergic-neuron-blocking agents**

\+ **T44.9 Poisoning by, adverse effect of and underdosing of other and unspecified drugs primarily affecting the autonomic nervous system**
Poisoning by, adverse effect of and underdosing of drug stimulating both alpha and beta-adrenoreceptors

\+ **T44.90 Poisoning by, adverse effect of and underdosing of unspecified drugs primarily affecting the autonomic nervous system**

+7th **T44.901 Poisoning by unspecified drugs primarily affecting the autonomic nervous system, accidental (unintentional)**
Poisoning by unspecified drugs primarily affecting the autonomic nervous system NOS

+7th **T44.902 Poisoning by unspecified drugs primarily affecting the autonomic nervous system, intentional self-harm**

+7th **T44.903 Poisoning by unspecified drugs primarily affecting the autonomic nervous system, assault**

+7th **T44.904 Poisoning by unspecified drugs primarily affecting the autonomic nervous system, undetermined**

+7th **T44.905 Adverse effect of unspecified drugs primarily affecting the autonomic nervous system**

+7th **T44.906 Underdosing of unspecified drugs primarily affecting the autonomic nervous system**

\+ **T44.99 Poisoning by, adverse effect of and underdosing of other drugs primarily affecting the autonomic nervous system**

+7th **T44.991 Poisoning by other drug primarily affecting the autonomic nervous system, accidental (unintentional)**
Poisoning by other drugs primarily affecting the autonomic nervous system NOS

+7th **T44.992 Poisoning by other drug primarily affecting the autonomic nervous system, intentional self-harm**

+7th **T44.993 Poisoning by other drug primarily affecting the autonomic nervous system, assault**

+7th **T44.994 Poisoning by other drug primarily affecting the autonomic nervous system, undetermined**

+7th **T44.995 Adverse effect of other drug primarily affecting the autonomic nervous system**

+7th **T44.996 Underdosing of other drug primarily affecting the autonomic nervous system**

T45 Poisoning by, adverse effect of and underdosing of primarily systemic and hematological agents, not elsewhere classified

The appropriate 7th character is to be added to each code from category T45
A initial encounter
D subsequent encounter
S sequela

\+ **T45.0 Poisoning by, adverse effect of and underdosing of antiallergic and antiemetic drugs**
Excludes1: *poisoning by, adverse effect of and underdosing of phenothiazine-based neuroleptics (T43.3)*

\+ **T45.0X Poisoning by, adverse effect of and underdosing of antiallergic and antiemetic drugs**

+7th **T45.0X1 Poisoning by antiallergic and antiemetic drugs, accidental (unintentional)**
Poisoning by antiallergic and antiemetic drugs NOS

+7th **T45.0X2 Poisoning by antiallergic and antiemetic drugs, intentional self-harm**

+7th **T45.0X3 Poisoning by antiallergic and antiemetic drugs, assault**

+7th **T45.0X4 Poisoning by antiallergic and antiemetic drugs, undetermined**

+7th **T45.0X5 Adverse effect of antiallergic and antiemetic drugs**

+7th **T45.0X6 Underdosing of antiallergic and antiemetic drugs**

\+ **T45.1 Poisoning by, adverse effect of and underdosing of antineoplastic and immunosuppressive drugs**
Excludes1: *poisoning by, adverse effect of and underdosing of tamoxifen (T38.6)*

\+ **T45.1X Poisoning by, adverse effect of and underdosing of antineoplastic and immunosuppressive drugs**

+7th **T45.1X1 Poisoning by antineoplastic and immunosuppressive drugs, accidental (unintentional)**
Poisoning by antineoplastic and immunosuppressive drugs NOS

+7th **T45.1X2 Poisoning by antineoplastic and immunosuppressive drugs, intentional self-harm**

+7th **T45.1X3 Poisoning by antineoplastic and immunosuppressive drugs, assault**

+7th **T45.1X4 Poisoning by antineoplastic and immunosuppressive drugs, undetermined**

+7th **T45.1X5 Adverse effect of antineoplastic and immunosuppressive drugs**
Review coding guideline C.2.c.2

+7th **T45.1X6 Underdosing of antineoplastic and immunosuppressive drugs**

\+ **T45.2 Poisoning by, adverse effect of and underdosing of vitamins**
Excludes2: *poisoning by, adverse effect of and underdosing of nicotinic acid (derivatives) (T46.7)*
poisoning by, adverse effect of and underdosing of iron (T45.4)
poisoning by, adverse effect of and underdosing of vitamin K (T45.7)

\+ **T45.2X Poisoning by, adverse effect of and underdosing of vitamins**

+7th **T45.2X1 Poisoning by vitamins, accidental (unintentional)**
Poisoning by vitamins NOS

+7th **T45.2X2 Poisoning by vitamins, intentional self-harm**

+7th **T45.2X3 Poisoning by vitamins, assault**

+7th **T45.2X4 Poisoning by vitamins, undetermined**

+7th **T45.2X5 Adverse effect of vitamins**

+7th **T45.2X6 Underdosing of vitamins**
Excludes1: *vitamin deficiencies (E50-E56)*

\+ **T45.3 Poisoning by, adverse effect of and underdosing of enzymes**

\+ **T45.3X Poisoning by, adverse effect of and underdosing of enzymes**

+7th **T45.3X1 Poisoning by enzymes, accidental (unintentional)**
Poisoning by enzymes NOS

+7th **T45.3X2 Poisoning by enzymes, intentional self-harm**

+7th **T45.3X3 Poisoning by enzymes, assault**

+7th **T45.3X4 Poisoning by enzymes, undetermined**

+7th **T45.3X5 Adverse effect of enzymes**

+7th **T45.3X6 Underdosing of enzymes**

\+ **T45.4 Poisoning by, adverse effect of and underdosing of iron and its compounds**

\+ **T45.4X Poisoning by, adverse effect of and underdosing of iron and its compounds**

+7th **T45.4X1 Poisoning by iron and its compounds, accidental (unintentional)**
Poisoning by iron and its compounds NOS

+7th **T45.4X2 Poisoning by iron and its compounds, intentional self-harm**

+7th **T45.4X3 Poisoning by iron and its compounds, assault**

+7th **T45.4X4 Poisoning by iron and its compounds, undetermined**

+7th **T45.4X5 Adverse effect of iron and its compounds**

+7th **T45.4X6 Underdosing of iron and its compounds**
Excludes1: *iron deficiency (E61.1)*

\+ **T45.5 Poisoning by, adverse effect of and underdosing of anticoagulants and antithrombotic drugs**

\+ **T45.51 Poisoning by, adverse effect of and underdosing of anticoagulants**

+7th **T45.511 Poisoning by anticoagulants, accidental (unintentional)**
Poisoning by anticoagulants NOS

+7th **T45.512 Poisoning by anticoagulants, intentional self-harm**

+7th **T45.513 Poisoning by anticoagulants, assault**

+7th **T45.514 Poisoning by anticoagulants, undetermined**

+7th **T45.515 Adverse effect of anticoagulants**
AHA CC: 2Q, 2013, 34-35

+7th **T45.516 Underdosing of anticoagulants**

+ **T45.52 Poisoning by, adverse effect of and underdosing of antithrombotic drugs**
Poisoning by, adverse effect of and underdosing of antiplatelet drugs
Excludes2: *poisoning by, adverse effect of and underdosing of aspirin (T39.01-)*
poisoning by, adverse effect of and underdosing of acetylsalicylic acid (T39.01-)

+7th **T45.521 Poisoning by antithrombotic drugs, accidental (unintentional)**
Poisoning by antithrombotic drug NOS

+7th **T45.522 Poisoning by antithrombotic drugs, intentional self-harm**

+7th **T45.523 Poisoning by antithrombotic drugs, assault**

+7th **T45.524 Poisoning by antithrombotic drugs, undetermined**

+7th **T45.525 Adverse effect of antithrombotic drugs**

+7th **T45.526 Underdosing of antithrombotic drugs**

+ **T45.6 Poisoning by, adverse effect of and underdosing of fibrinolysis-affecting drugs**

+ **T45.60 Poisoning by, adverse effect of and underdosing of unspecified fibrinolysis-affecting drugs**

+7th **T45.601 Poisoning by unspecified fibrinolysis-affecting drugs, accidental (unintentional)**
Poisoning by fibrinolysis-affecting drug NOS

+7th **T45.602 Poisoning by unspecified fibrinolysis-affecting drugs, intentional self-harm**

+7th **T45.603 Poisoning by unspecified fibrinolysis-affecting drugs, assault**

+7th **T45.604 Poisoning by unspecified fibrinolysis-affecting drugs, undetermined**

+7th **T45.605 Adverse effect of unspecified fibrinolysis-affecting drugs**

+7th **T45.606 Underdosing of unspecified fibrinolysis-affecting drugs**

+ **T45.61 Poisoning by, adverse effect of and underdosing of thrombolytic drugs**

+7th **T45.611 Poisoning by thrombolytic drug, accidental (unintentional)**
Poisoning by thrombolytic drug NOS

+7th **T45.612 Poisoning by thrombolytic drug, intentional self-harm**

+7th **T45.613 Poisoning by thrombolytic drug, assault**

+7th **T45.614 Poisoning by thrombolytic drug, undetermined**

+7th **T45.615 Adverse effect of thrombolytic drugs**

+7th **T45.616 Underdosing of thrombolytic drugs**

+ **T45.62 Poisoning by, adverse effect of and underdosing of hemostatic drugs**

+7th **T45.621 Poisoning by hemostatic drug, accidental (unintentional)**
Poisoning by hemostatic drug NOS

+7th **T45.622 Poisoning by hemostatic drug, intentional self-harm**

+7th **T45.623 Poisoning by hemostatic drug, assault**

+7th **T45.624 Poisoning by hemostatic drug, undetermined**

+7th **T45.625 Adverse effect of hemostatic drug**

+7th **T45.626 Underdosing of hemostatic drugs**

+ **T45.69 Poisoning by, adverse effect of and underdosing of other fibrinolysis-affecting drugs**

+7th **T45.691 Poisoning by other fibrinolysis-affecting drugs, accidental (unintentional)**
Poisoning by other fibrinolysis-affecting drug NOS

+7th **T45.692 Poisoning by other fibrinolysis-affecting drugs, intentional self-harm**

+7th **T45.693 Poisoning by other fibrinolysis-affecting drugs, assault**

+7th **T45.694 Poisoning by other fibrinolysis-affecting drugs, undetermined**

+7th **T45.695 Adverse effect of other fibrinolysis-affecting drugs**

+7th **T45.696 Underdosing of other fibrinolysis-affecting drugs**

+ **T45.7 Poisoning by, adverse effect of and underdosing of anticoagulant antagonists, vitamin K and other coagulants**

+ **T45.7X Poisoning by, adverse effect of and underdosing of anticoagulant antagonists, vitamin K and other coagulants**

+7th **T45.7X1 Poisoning by anticoagulant antagonists, vitamin K and other coagulants, accidenta (unintentional)**
Poisoning by anticoagulant antagonists, vitamin K and other coagulants NOS

+7th **T45.7X2 Poisoning by anticoagulant antagonists, vitamin K and other coagulants, intentiona self-harm**

+7th **T45.7X3 Poisoning by anticoagulant antagonists, vitamin K and other coagulants, assault**

+7th **T45.7X4 Poisoning by anticoagulant antagonists, vitamin K and other coagulants, undetermined**

+7th **T45.7X5 Adverse effect of anticoagulant antagonist vitamin K and other coagulants**

+7th **T45.7X6 Underdosing of anticoagulant antagonist, vitamin K and other coagulants**
Excludes1: *vitamin K deficiency (E56.1)*

+ **T45.8 Poisoning by, adverse effect of and underdosing of other primarily systemic and hematological agents**
Poisoning by, adverse effect of and underdosing of liver preparations and other antianemic agents
Poisoning by, adverse effect of and underdosing of natural bloo and blood products
Poisoning by, adverse effect of and underdosing of plasma substit
Excludes2: *poisoning by, adverse effect of and underdosing of immunoglobulin (T50.Z1)*
poisoning by, adverse effect of and underdosing of iron (T45.4)
transfusion reactions (T80.-)

+ **T45.8X Poisoning by, adverse effect of and underdosing of other primarily systemic and hematological agents**

+7th **T45.8X1 Poisoning by other primarily systemic and hematological agents, accidental (unintentional)**
Poisoning by other primarily systemic and hematological agents NOS

+7th **T45.8X2 Poisoning by other primarily systemic and hematological agents, intentional self-harm**

+7th **T45.8X3 Poisoning by other primarily systemic and hematological agents, assault**

+7th **T45.8X4 Poisoning by other primarily systemic and hematological agents, undetermined**

+7th **T45.8X5 Adverse effect of other primarily systemic and hematological agents**

+7th **T45.8X6 Underdosing of other primarily systemic an hematological agents**

+ **T45.9 Poisoning by, adverse effect of and underdosing of unspecified primarily systemic and hematological agent**

X+7th **T45.91 Poisoning by unspecified primarily systemic and hematological agent, accidental (unintentional)**
Poisoning by primarily systemic and hematological agent NOS

X+7th **T45.92 Poisoning by unspecified primarily systemic and hematological agent, intentional self-harm**

X+7th **T45.93 Poisoning by unspecified primarily systemic and hematological agent, assault**

X+7th **T45.94 Poisoning by unspecified primarily systemic and hematological agent, undetermined**

X+7th **T45.95 Adverse effect of unspecified primarily systemic and hematological agent**

X+7th **T45.96 Underdosing of unspecified primarily systemic and hematological agent**

T46 Poisoning by, adverse effect of and underdosing of agents primarily affecting the cardiovascular system

Excludes1: *poisoning by, adverse effect of and underdosing of metaraminol (T44.4)*

The appropriate 7th character is to be added to each code from category T46
A initial encounter
D subsequent encounter
S sequela

+ **T46.0 Poisoning by, adverse effect of and underdosing of cardiac-stimulant glycosides and drugs of similar action**

+ **T46.0X Poisoning by, adverse effect of and underdosing of cardiac-stimulant glycosides and drugs of similar action**

+7th **T46.0X1 Poisoning by cardiac-stimulant glycosides and drugs of similar action, accidental (unintentional)**
Poisoning by cardiac-stimulant glycosides and drugs of similar action NOS

+7th **T46.0X2 Poisoning by cardiac-stimulant glycosides and drugs of similar action, intentional self-harm**
+7th **T46.0X3 Poisoning by cardiac-stimulant glycosides and drugs of similar action, assault**
+7th **T46.0X4 Poisoning by cardiac-stimulant glycosides and drugs of similar action, undetermined**
+7th **T46.0X5 Adverse effect of cardiac-stimulant glycosides and drugs of similar action**
+7th **T46.0X6 Underdosing of cardiac-stimulant glycosides and drugs of similar action**

+ **T46.1 Poisoning by, adverse effect of and underdosing of calcium-channel blockers**
+ **T46.1X Poisoning by, adverse effect of and underdosing of calcium-channel blockers**
+7th **T46.1X1 Poisoning by calcium-channel blockers, accidental (unintentional)**
Poisoning by calcium-channel blockers NOS
+7th **T46.1X2 Poisoning by calcium-channel blockers, intentional self-harm**
+7th **T46.1X3 Poisoning by calcium-channel blockers, assault**
+7th **T46.1X4 Poisoning by calcium-channel blockers, undetermined**
+7th **T46.1X5 Adverse effect of calcium-channel blockers**
+7th **T46.1X6 Underdosing of calcium-channel blockers**

+ **T46.2 Poisoning by, adverse effect of and underdosing of other antidysrhythmic drugs, not elsewhere classified**
Excludes1: *poisoning by, adverse effect of and underdosing of beta-adrenoreceptor antagonists (T44.7-)*
+ **T46.2X Poisoning by, adverse effect of and underdosing of other antidysrhythmic drugs**
+7th **T46.2X1 Poisoning by other antidysrhythmic drugs, accidental (unintentional)**
Poisoning by other antidysrhythmic drugs NOS
+7th **T46.2X2 Poisoning by other antidysrhythmic drugs, intentional self-harm**
+7th **T46.2X3 Poisoning by other antidysrhythmic drugs, assault**
+7th **T46.2X4 Poisoning by other antidysrhythmic drugs, undetermined**
+7th **T46.2X5 Adverse effect of other antidysrhythmic drugs**
+7th **T46.2X6 Underdosing of other antidysrhythmic drugs**

+ **T46.3 Poisoning by, adverse effect of and underdosing of coronary vasodilators**
Poisoning by, adverse effect of and underdosing of dipyridamole
Excludes1: *poisoning by, adverse effect of and underdosing of calcium-channel blockers (T46.1)*
+ **T46.3X Poisoning by, adverse effect of and underdosing of coronary vasodilators**
+7th **T46.3X1 Poisoning by coronary vasodilators, accidental (unintentional)**
Poisoning by coronary vasodilators NOS
+7th **T46.3X2 Poisoning by coronary vasodilators, intentional self-harm**
+7th **T46.3X3 Poisoning by coronary vasodilators, assault**
+7th **T46.3X4 Poisoning by coronary vasodilators, undetermined**
+7th **T46.3X5 Adverse effect of coronary vasodilators**
+7th **T46.3X6 Underdosing of coronary vasodilators**

+ **T46.4 Poisoning by, adverse effect of and underdosing of angiotensin-converting-enzyme inhibitors**
+ **T46.4X Poisoning by, adverse effect of and underdosing of angiotensin-converting-enzyme inhibitors**
+7th **T46.4X1 Poisoning by angiotensin-converting-enzyme inhibitors, accidental (unintentional)**
Poisoning by angiotensin-converting-enzyme inhibitors NOS
+7th **T46.4X2 Poisoning by angiotensin-converting-enzyme inhibitors, intentional self-harm**
+7th **T46.4X3 Poisoning by angiotensin-converting-enzyme inhibitors, assault**
+7th **T46.4X4 Poisoning by angiotensin-converting-enzyme inhibitors, undetermined**
+7th **T46.4X5 Adverse effect of angiotensin-converting-enzyme inhibitors**
+7th **T46.4X6 Underdosing of angiotensin-converting-enzyme inhibitors**

+ **T46.5 Poisoning by, adverse effect of and underdosing of other antihypertensive drugs**
Excludes2: *poisoning by, adverse effect of and underdosing of beta-adrenoreceptor antagonists (T44.7)*
poisoning by, adverse effect of and underdosing of calcium-channel blockers (T46.1)
poisoning by, adverse effect of and underdosing of diuretics (T50.0-T50.2)
+ **T46.5X Poisoning by, adverse effect of and underdosing of other antihypertensive drugs**
+7th **T46.5X1 Poisoning by other antihypertensive drugs, accidental (unintentional)**
Poisoning by other antihypertensive drugs NOS
+7th **T46.5X2 Poisoning by other antihypertensive drugs, intentional self-harm**
+7th **T46.5X3 Poisoning by other antihypertensive drugs, assault**
+7th **T46.5X4 Poisoning by other antihypertensive drugs, undetermined**
+7th **T46.5X5 Adverse effect of other antihypertensive drugs**
+7th **T46.5X6 Underdosing of other antihypertensive drugs**

+ **T46.6 Poisoning by, adverse effect of and underdosing of antihyperlipidemic and antiarteriosclerotic drugs**
+ **T46.6X Poisoning by, adverse effect of and underdosing of antihyperlipidemic and antiarteriosclerotic drugs**
+7th **T46.6X1 Poisoning by antihyperlipidemic and antiarteriosclerotic drugs, accidental (unintentional)**
Poisoning by antihyperlipidemic and antiarteriosclerotic drugs NOS
+7th **T46.6X2 Poisoning by antihyperlipidemic and antiarteriosclerotic drugs, intentional self-harm**
+7th **T46.6X3 Poisoning by antihyperlipidemic and antiarteriosclerotic drugs, assault**
+7th **T46.6X4 Poisoning by antihyperlipidemic and antiarteriosclerotic drugs, undetermined**
+7th **T46.6X5 Adverse effect of antihyperlipidemic and antiarteriosclerotic drugs**
+7th **T46.6X6 Underdosing of antihyperlipidemic and antiarteriosclerotic drugs**

+ **T46.7 Poisoning by, adverse effect of and underdosing of peripheral vasodilators**
Poisoning by, adverse effect of and underdosing of nicotinic acid (derivatives)
Excludes1: *poisoning by, adverse effect of and underdosing of papaverine (T44.3)*
+ **T46.7X Poisoning by, adverse effect of and underdosing of peripheral vasodilators**
+7th **T46.7X1 Poisoning by peripheral vasodilators, accidental (unintentional)**
Poisoning by peripheral vasodilators NOS
+7th **T46.7X2 Poisoning by peripheral vasodilators, intentional self-harm**
+7th **T46.7X3 Poisoning by peripheral vasodilators, assault**
+7th **T46.7X4 Poisoning by peripheral vasodilators, undetermined**
+7th **T46.7X5 Adverse effect of peripheral vasodilators**
+7th **T46.7X6 Underdosing of peripheral vasodilators**

+ **T46.8 Poisoning by, adverse effect of and underdosing of antivaricose drugs, including sclerosing agents**
+ **T46.8X Poisoning by, adverse effect of and underdosing of antivaricose drugs, including sclerosing agents**
+7th **T46.8X1 Poisoning by antivaricose drugs, including sclerosing agents, accidental (unintentional)**
Poisoning by antivaricose drugs, including sclerosing agents NOS
+7th **T46.8X2 Poisoning by antivaricose drugs, including sclerosing agents, intentional self-harm**
+7th **T46.8X3 Poisoning by antivaricose drugs, including sclerosing agents, assault**
+7th **T46.8X4 Poisoning by antivaricose drugs, including sclerosing agents, undetermined**
+7th **T46.8X5 Adverse effect of antivaricose drugs, including sclerosing agents**
+7th **T46.8X6 Underdosing of antivaricose drugs, including sclerosing agents**

+ **T46.9 Poisoning by, adverse effect of and underdosing of other and unspecified agents primarily affecting the cardiovascular system**

+ **T46.90 Poisoning by, adverse effect of and underdosing of unspecified agents primarily affecting the cardiovascular system**

+7th **T46.901 Poisoning by unspecified agents primarily affecting the cardiovascular system, accidental (unintentional)**

+7th **T46.902 Poisoning by unspecified agents primarily affecting the cardiovascular system, intentional self-harm**

+7th **T46.903 Poisoning by unspecified agents primarily affecting the cardiovascular system, assault**

+7th **T46.904 Poisoning by unspecified agents primarily affecting the cardiovascular system, undetermined**

+7th **T46.905 Adverse effect of unspecified agents primarily affecting the cardiovascular system**

+7th **T46.906 Underdosing of unspecified agents primarily affecting the cardiovascular system**

+ **T46.99 Poisoning by, adverse effect of and underdosing of other agents primarily affecting the cardiovascular system**

+7th **T46.991 Poisoning by other agents primarily affecting the cardiovascular system, accidental (unintentional)**

+7th **T46.992 Poisoning by other agents primarily affecting the cardiovascular system, intentional self-harm**

+7th **T46.993 Poisoning by other agents primarily affecting the cardiovascular system, assault**

+7th **T46.994 Poisoning by other agents primarily affecting the cardiovascular system, undetermined**

+7th **T46.995 Adverse effect of other agents primarily affecting the cardiovascular system**

+7th **T46.996 Underdosing of other agents primarily affecting the cardiovascular system**

T47 Poisoning by, adverse effect of and underdosing of agents primarily affecting the gastrointestinal system

The appropriate 7th character is to be added to each code from category T47
A initial encounter
D subsequent encounter
S sequela

+ **T47.0 Poisoning by, adverse effect of and underdosing of histamine H2-receptor blockers**

+ **T47.0X Poisoning by, adverse effect of and underdosing of histamine H2-receptor blockers**

+7th **T47.0X1 Poisoning by histamine H2-receptor blockers, accidental (unintentional)**
Poisoning by histamine H2-receptor blockers NOS

+7th **T47.0X2 Poisoning by histamine H2-receptor blockers, intentional self-harm**

+7th **T47.0X3 Poisoning by histamine H2-receptor blockers, assault**

+7th **T47.0X4 Poisoning by histamine H2-receptor blockers, undetermined**

+7th **T47.0X5 Adverse effect of histamine H2-receptor blockers**

+7th **T47.0X6 Underdosing of histamine H2-receptor blockers**

+ **T47.1 Poisoning by, adverse effect of and underdosing of other antacids and anti-gastric-secretion drugs**

+ **T47.1X Poisoning by, adverse effect of and underdosing of other antacids and anti-gastric-secretion drugs**

+7th **T47.1X1 Poisoning by other antacids and anti-gastric-secretion drugs, accidental (unintentional)**
Poisoning by other antacids and anti-gastric-secretion drugs NOS

+7th **T47.1X2 Poisoning by other antacids and anti-gastric-secretion drugs, intentional self-harm**

+7th **T47.1X3 Poisoning by other antacids and anti-gastric-secretion drugs, assault**

+7th **T47.1X4 Poisoning by other antacids and anti-gastric-secretion drugs, undetermined**

+7th **T47.1X5 Adverse effect of other antacids and anti-gastric-secretion drugs**

+7th **T47.1X6 Underdosing of other antacids and anti-gastric-secretion drugs**

+ **T47.2 Poisoning by, adverse effect of and underdosing of stimulant laxatives**

+ **T47.2X Poisoning by, adverse effect of and underdosing of stimulant laxatives**

+7th **T47.2X1 Poisoning by stimulant laxatives, accidental (unintentional)**
Poisoning by stimulant laxatives NOS

+7th **T47.2X2 Poisoning by stimulant laxatives, intentional self-harm**

+7th **T47.2X3 Poisoning by stimulant laxatives, assault**

+7th **T47.2X4 Poisoning by stimulant laxatives, undetermined**

+7th **T47.2X5 Adverse effect of stimulant laxatives**

+7th **T47.2X6 Underdosing of stimulant laxatives**

+ **T47.3 Poisoning by, adverse effect of and underdosing of saline and osmotic laxatives**

+ **T47.3X Poisoning by and adverse effect of saline and osmotic laxatives**

+7th **T47.3X1 Poisoning by saline and osmotic laxatives, accidental (unintentional)**
Poisoning by saline and osmotic laxatives NOS

+7th **T47.3X2 Poisoning by saline and osmotic laxatives, intentional self-harm**

+7th **T47.3X3 Poisoning by saline and osmotic laxatives, assault**

+7th **T47.3X4 Poisoning by saline and osmotic laxatives, undetermined**

+7th **T47.3X5 Adverse effect of saline and osmotic laxatives**

+7th **T47.3X6 Underdosing of saline and osmotic laxatives**

+ **T47.4 Poisoning by, adverse effect of and underdosing of other laxatives**

+ **T47.4X Poisoning by, adverse effect of and underdosing of other laxatives**

+7th **T47.4X1 Poisoning by other laxatives, accidental (unintentional)**
Poisoning by other laxatives NOS

+7th **T47.4X2 Poisoning by other laxatives, intentional self-harm**

+7th **T47.4X3 Poisoning by other laxatives, assault**

+7th **T47.4X4 Poisoning by other laxatives, undetermined**

+7th **T47.4X5 Adverse effect of other l axatives**

+7th **T47.4X6 Underdosing of other laxatives**

+ **T47.5 Poisoning by, adverse effect of and underdosing of digestants**

+ **T47.5X Poisoning by, adverse effect of and underdosing of digestants**

+7th **T47.5X1 Poisoning by digestants, accidental (unintentional)**
Poisoning by digestants NOS

+7th **T47.5X2 Poisoning by digestants, intentional self-harm**

+7th **T47.5X3 Poisoning by digestants, assault**

+7th **T47.5X4 Poisoning by digestants, undetermined**

+7th **T47.5X5 Adverse effect of digestants**

+7th **T47.5X6 Underdosing of digestants**

+ **T47.6 Poisoning by, adverse effect of and underdosing of antidiarrheal drugs**

Excludes2: *poisoning by, adverse effect of and underdosing of systemic antibiotics and other anti-infectives (T36-T37)*

+ **T47.6X Poisoning by, adverse effect of and underdosing of antidiarrheal drugs**

+7th **T47.6X1 Poisoning by antidiarrheal drugs, accidental (unintentional)**
Poisoning by antidiarrheal drugs NOS

+7th **T47.6X2 Poisoning by antidiarrheal drugs, intentional self-harm**

+7th **T47.6X3 Poisoning by antidiarrheal drugs, assault**

+7th **T47.6X4 Poisoning by antidiarrheal drugs, undetermined**

+7th **T47.6X5 Adverse effect of antidiarrheal drugs**

+7th **T47.6X6 Underdosing of antidiarrheal drugs**

+ **T47.7 Poisoning by, adverse effect of and underdosing of emetics**
  + **T47.7X Poisoning by, adverse effect of and underdosing of emetics**
    - +7th **T47.7X1 Poisoning by emetics, accidental (unintentional)**
      Poisoning by emetics NOS
    - +7th **T47.7X2 Poisoning by emetics, intentional self-harm**
    - +7th **T47.7X3 Poisoning by emetics, assault**
    - +7th **T47.7X4 Poisoning by emetics, undetermined**
    - +7th **T47.7X5 Adverse effect of emetics**
    - +7th **T47.7X6 Underdosing of emetics**

+ **T47.8 Poisoning by, adverse effect of and underdosing of other agents primarily affecting gastrointestinal system**
  + **T47.8X Poisoning by, adverse effect of and underdosing of other agents primarily affecting gastrointestinal system**
    - +7th **T47.8X1 Poisoning by other agents primarily affecting gastrointestinal system, accidental (unintentional)**
      Poisoning by other agents primarily affecting gastrointestinal system NOS
    - +7th **T47.8X2 Poisoning by other agents primarily affecting gastrointestinal system, intentional self-harm**
    - +7th **T47.8X3 Poisoning by other agents primarily affecting gastrointestinal system, assault**
    - +7th **T47.8X4 Poisoning by other agents primarily affecting gastrointestinal system, undetermined**
    - +7th **T47.8X5 Adverse effect of other agents primarily affecting gastrointestinal system**
    - +7th **T47.8X6 Underdosing of other agents primarily affecting gastrointestinal system**

+ **T47.9 Poisoning by, adverse effect of and underdosing of unspecified agents primarily affecting the gastrointestinal system**
  - X+7th **T47.91 Poisoning by unspecified agents primarily affecting the gastrointestinal system, accidental (unintentional)**
    Poisoning by agents primarily affecting the gastrointestinal system NOS
  - X+7th **T47.92 Poisoning by unspecified agents primarily affecting the gastrointestinal system, intentional self-harm**
  - X+7th **T47.93 Poisoning by unspecified agents primarily affecting the gastrointestinal system, assault**
  - X+7th **T47.94 Poisoning by unspecified agents primarily affecting the gastrointestinal system, undetermined**
  - X+7th **T47.95 Adverse effect of unspecified agents primarily affecting the gastrointestinal system**
  - X+7th **T47.96 Underdosing of unspecified agents primarily affecting the gastrointestinal system**

T48 Poisoning by, adverse effect of and underdosing of agents primarily acting on smooth and skeletal muscles and the respiratory system

The appropriate 7th character is to be added to each code from category T48
A initial encounter
D subsequent encounter
S sequela

+ **T48.0 Poisoning by, adverse effect of and underdosing of oxytocic drugs**
  Excludes1: *poisoning by, adverse effect of and underdosing of estrogens, progestogens and antagonists (T38.4-T38.6)*
  + **T48.0X Poisoning by, adverse effect of and underdosing of oxytocic drugs**
    - +7th **T48.0X1 Poisoning by oxytocic drugs, accidental (unintentional)**
      Poisoning by oxytocic drugs NOS
    - +7th **T48.0X2 Poisoning by oxytocic drugs, intentional self-harm**
    - +7th **T48.0X3 Poisoning by oxytocic drugs, assault**
    - +7th **T48.0X4 Poisoning by oxytocic drugs, undetermined**
    - +7th **T48.0X5 Adverse effect of oxytocic drugs**
    - +7th **T48.0X6 Underdosing of oxytocic drugs**

+ **T48.1 Poisoning by, adverse effect of and underdosing of skeletal muscle relaxants [neuromuscular blocking agents]**
  + **T48.1X Poisoning by, adverse effect of and underdosing of skeletal muscle relaxants [neuromuscular blocking agents]**
    - +7th **T48.1X1 Poisoning by skeletal muscle relaxants [neuromuscular blocking agents], accidental (unintentional)**
      Poisoning by skeletal muscle relaxants [neuromuscular blocking agents] NOS
    - +7th **T48.1X2 Poisoning by skeletal muscle relaxants [neuromuscular blocking agents], intentional self-harm**
    - +7th **T48.1X3 Poisoning by skeletal muscle relaxants [neuromuscular blocking agents], assault**
    - +7th **T48.1X4 Poisoning by skeletal muscle relaxants [neuromuscular blocking agents], undetermined**
    - +7th **T48.1X5 Adverse effect of skeletal muscle relaxants [neuromuscular blocking agents]**
    - +7th **T48.1X6 Underdosing of skeletal muscle relaxants [neuromuscular blocking agents]**

+ **T48.2 Poisoning by, adverse effect of and underdosing of other and unspecified drugs acting on muscles**
  + **T48.20 Poisoning by, adverse effect of and underdosing of unspecified drugs acting on muscles**
    - +7th **T48.201 Poisoning by unspecified drugs acting on muscles, accidental (unintentional)**
      Poisoning by unspecified drugs acting on muscles NOS
    - +7th **T48.202 Poisoning by unspecified drugs acting on muscles, intentional self-harm**
    - +7th **T48.203 Poisoning by unspecified drugs acting on muscles, assault**
    - +7th **T48.204 Poisoning by unspecified drugs acting on muscles, undetermined**
    - +7th **T48.205 Adverse effect of unspecified drugs acting on muscles**
    - +7th **T48.206 Underdosing of unspecified drugs acting on muscles**
  + **T48.29 Poisoning by, adverse effect of and underdosing of other drugs acting on muscles**
    - +7th **T48.291 Poisoning by other drugs acting on muscles, accidental (unintentional)**
      Poisoning by other drugs acting on muscles NOS
    - +7th **T48.292 Poisoning by other drugs acting on muscles, intentional self-harm**
    - +7th **T48.293 Poisoning by other drugs acting on muscles, assault**
    - +7th **T48.294 Poisoning by other drugs acting on muscles, undetermined**
    - +7th **T48.295 Adverse effect of other drugs acting on muscles**
    - +7th **T48.296 Underdosing of other drugs acting on muscles**

+ **T48.3 Poisoning by, adverse effect of and underdosing of antitussives**
  + **T48.3X Poisoning by, adverse effect of and underdosing of antitussives**
    - +7th **T48.3X1 Poisoning by antitussives, accidental (unintentional)**
      Poisoning by antitussives NOS
    - +7th **T48.3X2 Poisoning by antitussives, intentional self-harm**
    - +7th **T48.3X3 Poisoning by antitussives, assault**
    - +7th **T48.3X4 Poisoning by antitussives, undetermined**
    - +7th **T48.3X5 Adverse effect of antitussives**
    - +7th **T48.3X6 Underdosing of antitussives**

+ **T48.4 Poisoning by, adverse effect of and underdosing of expectorants**
  + **T48.4X Poisoning by, adverse effect of and underdosing of expectorants**
    - +7th **T48.4X1 Poisoning by expectorants, accidental (unintentional)**
      Poisoning by expectorants NOS
    - +7th **T48.4X2 Poisoning by expectorants, intentional self-harm**
    - +7th **T48.4X3 Poisoning by expectorants, assault**
    - +7th **T48.4X4 Poisoning by expectorants, undetermined**
    - +7th **T48.4X5 Adverse effect of expectorants**
    - +7th **T48.4X6 Underdosing of expectorants**

+ **T48.5 Poisoning by, adverse effect of and underdosing of other anti-common-cold drugs**
Poisoning by, adverse effect of and underdosing of decongestants
Excludes2: *poisoning by, adverse effect of and underdosing of antipyretics, NEC (T39.9-)*
poisoning by, adverse effect of and underdosing of non-steroidal antiinflammatory drugs (T39.3-)
poisoning by, adverse effect of and underdosing of salicylates (T39.0-)

+ **T48.5X Poisoning by, adverse effect of and underdosing of other anti-common-cold drugs**
+7th **T48.5X1 Poisoning by other anti-common-cold drugs, accidental (unintentional)**
Poisoning by other anti-common-cold drugs NOS
+7th **T48.5X2 Poisoning by other anti-common-cold drugs, intentional self-harm**
+7th **T48.5X3 Poisoning by other anti-common-cold drugs, assault**
+7th **T48.5X4 Poisoning by other anti-common-cold drugs, undetermined**
+7th **T48.5X5 Adverse effect of other anti-common-cold drugs**
+7th **T48.5X6 Underdosing of other anti-common-cold drugs**

+ **T48.6 Poisoning by, adverse effect of and underdosing of antiasthmatics, not elsewhere classified**
Poisoning by, adverse effect of and underdosing of beta-adrenoreceptor agonists used in asthma therapy
Excludes1: *poisoning by, adverse effect of and underdosing of beta-adrenoreceptor agonists not used in asthma therapy (T44.5)*
poisoning by, adverse effect of and underdosing of anterior pituitary [adenohypophyseal] hormones (T38.8)

+ **T48.6X Poisoning by, adverse effect of and underdosing of antiasthmatics**
+7th **T48.6X1 Poisoning by antiasthmatics, accidental (unintentional)**
Poisoning by antiasthmatics NOS
+7th **T48.6X2 Poisoning by antiasthmatics, intentional self-harm**
+7th **T48.6X3 Poisoning by antiasthmatics, assault**
+7th **T48.6X4 Poisoning by antiasthmatics, undetermined**
+7th **T48.6X5 Adverse effect of antiasthmatics**
+7th **T48.6X6 Underdosing of antiasthmatics**

+ **T48.9 Poisoning by, adverse effect of and underdosing of other and unspecified agents primarily acting on the respiratory system**
+ **T48.90 Poisoning by, adverse effect of and underdosing of unspecified agents primarily acting on the respiratory system**
+7th **T48.901 Poisoning by unspecified agents primarily acting on the respiratory system, accidental (unintentional)**
+7th **T48.902 Poisoning by unspecified agents primarily acting on the respiratory system, intentional self-harm**
+7th **T48.903 Poisoning by unspecified agents primarily acting on the respiratory system, assault**
+7th **T48.904 Poisoning by unspecified agents primarily acting on the respiratory system, undetermined**
+7th **T48.905 Adverse effect of unspecified agents primarily acting on the respiratory system**
+7th **T48.906 Underdosing of unspecified agents primarily acting on the respiratory system**
+ **T48.99 Poisoning by, adverse effect of and underdosing of other agents primarily acting on the respiratory system**
+7th **T48.991 Poisoning by other agents primarily acting on the respiratory system, accidental (unintentional)**
+7th **T48.992 Poisoning by other agents primarily acting on the respiratory system, intentional self-harm**
+7th **T48.993 Poisoning by other agents primarily acting on the respiratory system, assault**
+7th **T48.994 Poisoning by other agents primarily acting on the respiratory system, undetermined**
+7th **T48.995 Adverse effect of other agents primarily acting on the respiratory system**
+7th **T48.996 Underdosing of other agents primarily acting on the respiratory system**

T49 Poisoning by, adverse effect of and underdosing of topical agents primarily affecting skin and mucous membrane and by ophthalmological, otorhinorlaryngological and dental drugs
Includes: poisoning by, adverse effect of and underdosing of glucocorticoids, topically used

The appropriate 7th character is to be added to each code from category T49
A initial encounter
D subsequent encounter
S sequela

+ **T49.0 Poisoning by, adverse effect of and underdosing of local antifungal, anti-infective and anti-inflammatory drugs**
+ **T49.0X Poisoning by, adverse effect of and underdosing of local antifungal, anti-infective and anti-inflammatory drugs**
+7th **T49.0X1 Poisoning by local antifungal, anti-infective and anti-inflammatory drugs, accidental (unintentional)**
Poisoning by local antifungal, anti-infective and anti-inflammatory drugs NOS
+7th **T49.0X2 Poisoning by local antifungal, anti-infective and anti-inflammatory drugs, intentional self-harm**
+7th **T49.0X3 Poisoning by local antifungal, anti-infective and anti-inflammatory drugs, assault**
+7th **T49.0X4 Poisoning by local antifungal, anti-infective and anti-inflammatory drugs, undetermined**
+7th **T49.0X5 Adverse effect of local antifungal, anti-infective and anti-inflammatory drugs**
+7th **T49.0X6 Underdosing of local antifungal, anti-infective and anti-inflammatory drugs**

+ **T49.1 Poisoning by, adverse effect of and underdosing of antipruritics**
+ **T49.1X Poisoning by, adverse effect of and underdosing of antipruritics**
+7th **T49.1X1 Poisoning by antipruritics, accidental (unintentional)**
Poisoning by antipruritics NOS
+7th **T49.1X2 Poisoning by antipruritics, intentional self-harm**
+7th **T49.1X3 Poisoning by antipruritics, assault**
+7th **T49.1X4 Poisoning by antipruritics, undetermined**
+7th **T49.1X5 Adverse effect of antipruritics**
+7th **T49.1X6 Underdosing of antipruritics**

+ **T49.2 Poisoning by, adverse effect of and underdosing of local astringents and local detergents**
+ **T49.2X Poisoning by, adverse effect of and underdosing of local astringents and local detergents**
+7th **T49.2X1 Poisoning by local astringents and local detergents, accidental (unintentional)**
Poisoning by local astringents and local detergents NOS
+7th **T49.2X2 Poisoning by local astringents and local detergents, intentional self-harm**
+7th **T49.2X3 Poisoning by local astringents and local detergents, assault**
+7th **T49.2X4 Poisoning by local astringents and local detergents, undetermined**
+7th **T49.2X5 Adverse effect of local astringents and local detergents**
+7th **T49.2X6 Underdosing of local astringents and local detergents**

+ **T49.3 Poisoning by, adverse effect of and underdosing of emollients, demulcents and protectants**
+ **T49.3X Poisoning by, adverse effect of and underdosing of emollients, demulcents and protectants**
+7th **T49.3X1 Poisoning by emollients, demulcents and protectants, accidental (unintentional)**
Poisoning by emollients, demulcents and protectants NOS
+7th **T49.3X2 Poisoning by emollients, demulcents and protectants, intentional self-harm**
+7th **T49.3X3 Poisoning by emollients, demulcents and protectants, assault**
+7th **T49.3X4 Poisoning by emollients, demulcents and protectants, undetermined**
+7th **T49.3X5 Adverse effect of emollients, demulcents and protectants**
+7th **T49.3X6 Underdosing of emollients, demulcents and protectants**

+ **T49.4 Poisoning by, adverse effect of and underdosing of keratolytics, keratoplastics, and other hair treatment drugs and preparations**

+ **T49.4X Poisoning by, adverse effect of and underdosing of keratolytics, keratoplastics, and other hair treatment drugs and preparations**

+7th **T49.4X1 Poisoning by keratolytics, keratoplastics, and other hair treatment drugs and preparations, accidental (unintentional)**
Poisoning by keratolytics, keratoplastics, and other hair treatment drugs and preparations NOS

+7th **T49.4X2 Poisoning by keratolytics, keratoplastics, and other hair treatment drugs and preparations, intentional self-harm**

+7th **T49.4X3 Poisoning by keratolytics, keratoplastics, and other hair treatment drugs and preparations, assault**

+7th **T49.4X4 Poisoning by keratolytics, keratoplastics, and other hair treatment drugs and preparations, undetermined**

+7th **T49.4X5 Adverse effect of keratolytics, keratoplastics, and other hair treatment drugs and preparations**

+7th **T49.4X6 Underdosing of keratolytics, keratoplastics, and other hair treatment drugs and preparations**

+ **T49.5 Poisoning by, adverse effect of and underdosing of ophthalmological drugs and preparations**

+ **T49.5X Poisoning by, adverse effect of and underdosing of ophthalmological drugs and preparations**

+7th **T49.5X1 Poisoning by ophthalmological drugs and preparations, accidental (unintentional)**
Poisoning by ophthalmological drugs and preparations NOS

+7th **T49.5X2 Poisoning by ophthalmological drugs and preparations, intentional self-harm**

+7th **T49.5X3 Poisoning by ophthalmological drugs and preparations, assault**

+7th **T49.5X4 Poisoning by ophthalmological drugs and preparations, undetermined**

+7th **T49.5X5 Adverse effect of ophthalmological drugs and preparations**

+7th **T49.5X6 Underdosing of ophthalmological drugs and preparations**

+ **T49.6 Poisoning by, adverse effect of and underdosing of otorhinolaryngological drugs and preparations**

+ **T49.6X Poisoning by, adverse effect of and underdosing of otorhinolaryngological drugs and preparations**

+7th **T49.6X1 Poisoning by otorhinolaryngological drugs and preparations, accidental (unintentional)**
Poisoning by otorhinolaryngological drugs and preparations NOS

+7th **T49.6X2 Poisoning by otorhinolaryngological drugs and preparations, intentional self-harm**

+7th **T49.6X3 Poisoning by otorhinolaryngological drugs and preparations, assault**

+7th **T49.6X4 Poisoning by otorhinolaryngological drugs and preparations, undetermined**

+7th **T49.6X5 Adverse effect of otorhinolaryngological drugs and preparations**

+7th **T49.6X6 Underdosing of otorhinolaryngological drugs and preparations**

+ **T49.7 Poisoning by, adverse effect of and underdosing of dental drugs, topically applied**

+ **T49.7X Poisoning by, adverse effect of and underdosing of dental drugs, topically applied**

+7th **T49.7X1 Poisoning by dental drugs, topically applied, accidental (unintentional)**
Poisoning by dental drugs, topically applied NOS

+7th **T49.7X2 Poisoning by dental drugs, topically applied, intentional self-harm**

+7th **T49.7X3 Poisoning by dental drugs, topically applied, assault**

+7th **T49.7X4 Poisoning by dental drugs, topically applied, undetermined**

+7th **T49.7X5 Adverse effect of dental drugs, topically applied**

+7th **T49.7X6 Underdosing of dental drugs, topically applied**

+ **T49.8 Poisoning by, adverse effect of and underdosing of other topical agents**
Poisoning by, adverse effect of and underdosing of spermicides

+ **T49.8X Poisoning by, adverse effect of and underdosing of other topical agents**

+7th **T49.8X1 Poisoning by other topical agents, accidental (unintentional)**
Poisoning by other topical agents NOS

+7th **T49.8X2 Poisoning by other topical agents, intentional self-harm**

+7th **T49.8X3 Poisoning by other topical agents, assault**

+7th **T49.8X4 Poisoning by other topical agents, undetermined**

+7th **T49.8X5 Adverse effect of other topical agents**

+7th **T49.8X6 Underdosing of other topical agents**

+ **T49.9 Poisoning by, adverse effect of and underdosing of unspecified topical agent**

X+7th **T49.91 Poisoning by unspecified topical agent, accidental (unintentional)**

X+7th **T49.92 Poisoning by unspecified topical agent, intentional self-harm**

X+7th **T49.93 Poisoning by unspecified topical agent, assault**

X+7th **T49.94 Poisoning by unspecified topical agent, undetermined**

X+7th **T49.95 Adverse effect of unspecified topical agent**

X+7th **T49.96 Underdosing of unspecified topical agent**

T50 Poisoning by, adverse effect of and underdosing of diuretics and other and unspecified drugs, medicaments and biological substances

The appropriate 7th character is to be added to each code from category T50
A initial encounter
D subsequent encounter
S sequela

+ **T50.0 Poisoning by, adverse effect of and underdosing of mineralocorticoids and their antagonists**

+ **T50.0X Poisoning by, adverse effect of and underdosing of mineralocorticoids and their antagonists**

+7th **T50.0X1 Poisoning by mineralocorticoids and their antagonists, accidental (unintentional)**
Poisoning by mineralocorticoids and their antagonists NOS

+7th **T50.0X2 Poisoning by mineralocorticoids and their antagonists, intentional self-harm**

+7th **T50.0X3 Poisoning by mineralocorticoids and their antagonists, assault**

+7th **T50.0X4 Poisoning by mineralocorticoids and their antagonists, undetermined**

+7th **T50.0X5 Adverse effect of mineralocorticoids and their antagonists**

+7th **T50.0X6 Underdosing of mineralocorticoids and their antagonists**

+ **T50.1 Poisoning by, adverse effect of and underdosing of loop [high-ceiling] diuretics**

+ **T50.1X Poisoning by, adverse effect of and underdosing of loop [high-ceiling] diuretics**

+7th **T50.1X1 Poisoning by loop [high-ceiling] diuretics, accidental (unintentional)**
Poisoning by loop [high-ceiling] diuretics NOS

+7th **T50.1X2 Poisoning by loop [high-ceiling] diuretics, intentional self-harm**

+7th **T50.1X3 Poisoning by loop [high-ceiling] diuretics, assault**

+7th **T50.1X4 Poisoning by loop [high-ceiling] diuretics, undetermined**

+7th **T50.1X5 Adverse effect of loop [high-ceiling] diuretics**

+7th **T50.1X6 Underdosing of loop [high-ceiling] diuretics**

+ **T50.2 Poisoning by, adverse effect of and underdosing of carbonic-anhydrase inhibitors, benzothiadiazides and other diuretics**
Poisoning by, adverse effect of and underdosing of acetazolamide

+ **T50.2X Poisoning by, adverse effect of and underdosing of carbonic-anhydrase inhibitors, benzothiadiazides and other diuretics**

+7th **T50.2X1 Poisoning by carbonic-anhydrase inhibitors, benzothiadiazides and other diuretics, accidental (unintentional)**
Poisoning by carbonic-anhydrase inhibitors, benzothiadiazides and other diuretics NOS

+7th **T50.2X2 Poisoning by carbonic-anhydrase inhibitors, benzothiadiazides and other diuretics, intentional self-harm**

+7th T50.2X3 Poisoning by carbonic-anhydrase inhibitors, benzothiadiazides and other diuretics, assault

+7th T50.2X4 Poisoning by carbonic-anhydrase inhibitors, benzothiadiazides and other diuretics, undetermined

+7th T50.2X5 Adverse effect of carbonic-anhydrase inhibitors, benzothiadiazides and other diuretics

+7th T50.2X6 Underdosing of carbonic-anhydrase inhibitors, benzothiadiazides and other diuretics

+ T50.3 Poisoning by, adverse effect of and underdosing of electrolytic, caloric and water-balance agents

Poisoning by, adverse effect of and underdosing of oral rehydration salts

+ T50.3X Poisoning by, adverse effect of and underdosing of electrolytic, caloric and water-balance agents

+7th T50.3X1 Poisoning by electrolytic, caloric and water-balance agents, accidental (unintentional)

Poisoning by electrolytic, caloric and water-balance agents NOS

+7th T50.3X2 Poisoning by electrolytic, caloric and water-balance agents, intentional self-harm

+7th T50.3X3 Poisoning by electrolytic, caloric and water-balance agents, assault

+7th T50.3X4 Poisoning by electrolytic, caloric and water-balance agents, undetermined

+7th T50.3X5 Adverse effect of electrolytic, caloric and water-balance agents

+7th T50.3X6 Underdosing of electrolytic, caloric and water-balance agents

+ T50.4 Poisoning by, adverse effect of and underdosing of drugs affecting uric acid metabolism

+ T50.4X Poisoning by, adverse effect of and underdosing of drugs affecting uric acid metabolism

+7th T50.4X1 Poisoning by drugs affecting uric acid metabolism, accidental (unintentional)

Poisoning by drugs affecting uric acid metabolism NOS

+7th T50.4X2 Poisoning by drugs affecting uric acid metabolism, intentional self-harm

+7th T50.4X3 Poisoning by drugs affecting uric acid metabolism, assault

+7th T50.4X4 Poisoning by drugs affecting uric acid metabolism, undetermined

+7th T50.4X5 Adverse effect of drugs affecting uric acid metabolism

+7th T50.4X6 Underdosing of drugs affecting uric acid metabolism

+ T50.5 Poisoning by, adverse effect of and underdosing of appetite depressants

+ T50.5X Poisoning by, adverse effect of and underdosing of appetite depressants

+7th T50.5X1 Poisoning by appetite depressants, accidental (unintentional)

Poisoning by appetite depressants NOS

+7th T50.5X2 Poisoning by appetite depressants, intentional self-harm

+7th T50.5X3 Poisoning by appetite depressants, assault

+7th T50.5X4 Poisoning by appetite depressants, undetermined

+7th T50.5X5 Adverse effect of appetite depressants

+7th T50.5X6 Underdosing of appetite depressants

+ T50.6 Poisoning by, adverse effect of and underdosing of antidotes and chelating agents

Poisoning by, adverse effect of and underdosing of alcohol deterrents

+ T50.6X Poisoning by, adverse effect of and underdosing of antidotes and chelating agents

+7th T50.6X1 Poisoning by antidotes and chelatingagents, accidental (unintentional)

Poisoning by antidotes and chelating agents NOS

+7th T50.6X2 Poisoning by antidotes and chelating agents, intentional self-harm

+7th T50.6X3 Poisoning by antidotes and chelating agents, assault

+7th T50.6X4 Poisoning by antidotes and chelating agents, undetermined

+7th T50.6X5 Adverse effect of antidotes and chelating agents

+7th T50.6X6 Underdosing of antidotes and chelating agents

+ T50.7 Poisoning by, adverse effect of and underdosing of analeptics and opioid receptor antagonists

+ T50.7X Poisoning by, adverse effect of and underdosing of analeptics and opioid receptor antagonists

+7th T50.7X1 Poisoning by analeptics and opioid receptor antagonists, accidental (unintentional)

Poisoning by analeptics and opioid receptor antagonists NOS

+7th T50.7X2 Poisoning by analeptics and opioid receptor antagonists, intentional self-harm

+7th T50.7X3 Poisoning by analeptics and opioid receptor antagonists, assault

+7th T50.7X4 Poisoning by analeptics and opioid receptor antagonists, undetermined

+7th T50.7X5 Adverse effect of analeptics and opioid receptor antagonists

+7th T50.7X6 Underdosing of analeptics and opioid receptor antagonists

+ T50.8 Poisoning by, adverse effect of and underdosing of diagnostic agents

+ T50.8X Poisoning by, adverse effect of and underdosing of diagnostic agents

+7th T50.8X1 Poisoning by diagnostic agents, accidental (unintentional)

Poisoning by diagnostic agents NOS

+7th T50.8X2 Poisoning by diagnostic agents, intentional self-harm

+7th T50.8X3 Poisoning by diagnostic agents, assault

+7th T50.8X4 Poisoning by diagnostic agents, undetermined

+7th T50.8X5 Adverse effect of diagnostic agents

+7th T50.8X6 Underdosing of diagnostic agents

+ T50.A Poisoning by, adverse effect of and underdosing of bacterial vaccines

+ T50.A1 Poisoning by, adverse effect of and underdosing of pertussis vaccine, including combinations with a pertussis component

+7th T50.A11 Poisoning by pertussis vaccine, including combinations with a pertussis component, accidental (unintentional)

+7th T50.A12 Poisoning by pertussis vaccine, including combinations with a pertussis component, intentional self-harm

+7th T50.A13 Poisoning by pertussis vaccine, including combinations with a pertussis component, assault

+7th T50.A14 Poisoning by pertussis vaccine, including combinations with a pertussis component, undetermined

+7th T50.A15 Adverse effect of pertussis vaccine, including combinations with a pertussis component

+7th T50.A16 Underdosing of pertussis vaccine, including combinations with a pertussis component

+ T50.A2 Poisoning by, adverse effect of and underdosing of mixed bacterial vaccines without a pertussis component

+7th T50.A21 Poisoning by mixed bacterial vaccines without a pertussis component, accidental (unintentional)

+7th T50.A22 Poisoning by mixed bacterial vaccines without a pertussis component, intentional self-harm

+7th T50.A23 Poisoning by mixed bacterial vaccines without a pertussis component, assault

+7th T50.A24 Poisoning by mixed bacterial vaccines without a pertussis component, undetermined

+7th T50.A25 Adverse effect of mixed bacterial vaccines without a pertussis component

+7th T50.A26 Underdosing of mixed bacterial vaccines without a pertussis component

+ T50.A9 Poisoning by, adverse effect of and underdosing of other bacterial vaccines

+7th T50.A91 Poisoning by other bacterial vaccines, accidental (unintentional)

+7th T50.A92 Poisoning by other bacterial vaccines, intentional self-harm

+7th **T50.A93** **Poisoning by other bacterial vaccines, assault**
+7th **T50.A94** **Poisoning by other bacterial vaccines, undetermined**
+7th **T50.A95** **Adverse effect of other bacterial vaccines**
+7th **T50.A96** **Underdosing of other bacterial vaccines**

+ **T50.B** **Poisoning by, adverse effect of and underdosing of viral vaccines**
+ **T50.B1** **Poisoning by, adverse effect of and underdosing of smallpox vaccines**
+7th **T50.B11** **Poisoning by smallpox vaccines, accidental (unintentional)**
+7th **T50.B12** **Poisoning by smallpox vaccines, intentional self-harm**
+7th **T50.B13** **Poisoning by smallpox vaccines, assault**
+7th **T50.B14** **Poisoning by smallpox vaccines, undetermined**
+7th **T50.B15** **Adverse effect of smallpox vaccines**
+7th **T50.B16** **Underdosing of smallpox vaccines**
+ **T50.B9** **Poisoning by, adverse effect of and underdosing of other viral vaccines**
+7th **T50.B91** **Poisoning by other viral vaccines, accidental (unintentional)**
+7th **T50.B92** **Poisoning by other viral vaccines, intentional self-harm**
+7th **T50.B93** **Poisoning by other viral vaccines, assault**
+7th **T50.B94** **Poisoning by other viral vaccines, undetermined**
+7th **T50.B95** **Adverse effect of other viral vaccines**
+7th **T50.B96** **Underdosing of other viral vaccines**

+ **T50.Z** **Poisoning by, adverse effect of and underdosing of other vaccines and biological substances**
+ **T50.Z1** **Poisoning by, adverse effect of and underdosing of immunoglobulin**
+7th **T50.Z11** **Poisoning by immunoglobulin, accidental (unintentional)**
+7th **T50.Z12** **Poisoning by immunoglobulin, intentional self-harm**
+7th **T50.Z13** **Poisoning by immunoglobulin, assault**
+7th **T50.Z14** **Poisoning by immunoglobulin, undetermined**
+7th **T50.Z15** **Adverse effect of immunoglobulin**
+7th **T50.Z16** **Underdosing of immunoglobulin**
+ **T50.Z9** **Poisoning by, adverse effect of and underdosing of other vaccines and biological substances**
+7th **T50.Z91** **Poisoning by other vaccines and biological substances, accidental (unintentional)**
+7th **T50.Z92** **Poisoning by other vaccines and biological substances, intentional self-harm**
+7th **T50.Z93** **Poisoning by other vaccines and biological substances, assault**
+7th **T50.Z94** **Poisoning by other vaccines and biological substances, undetermined**
+7th **T50.Z95** **Adverse effect of other vaccines and biological substances**
+7th **T50.Z96** **Underdosing of other vaccines and biological substances**

+ **T50.9** **Poisoning by, adverse effect of and underdosing of other and unspecified drugs, medicaments and biological substances**
+ **T50.90** **Poisoning by, adverse effect of and underdosing of unspecified drugs, medicaments and biological substances**
+7th **T50.901** **Poisoning by unspecified drugs, medicaments and biological substances, accidental (unintentional)**
+7th **T50.902** **Poisoning by unspecified drugs, medicaments and biological substances, intentional self-harm**
+7th **T50.903** **Poisoning by unspecified drugs, medicaments and biological substances, assault**
+7th **T50.904** **Poisoning by unspecified drugs, medicaments and biological substances, undetermined**
+7th **T50.905** **Adverse effect of unspecified drugs, medicaments and biological substances**
+7th **T50.906** **Underdosing of unspecified drugs, medicaments and biological substances**
+ **T50.99** **Poisoning by, adverse effect of and underdosing of other drugs, medicaments and biological substances**
+7th **T50.991** **Poisoning by other drugs, medicaments and biological substances, accidental (unintentional)**
+7th **T50.992** **Poisoning by other drugs, medicaments and biological substances, intentional self-harm**
+7th **T50.993** **Poisoning by other drugs, medicaments and biological substances, assault**
+7th **T50.994** **Poisoning by other drugs, medicaments and biological substances, undetermined**
+7th **T50.995** **Adverse effect of other drugs, medicaments and biological substances**
+7th **T50.996** **Underdosing of other drugs, medicaments and biological substances**

Toxic effects of substances chiefly nonmedicinal as to source (T51-T65)

NOTE When no intent is indicated code to accidental. Undetermined intent is only for use when there is specific documentation in the record that the intent of the toxic effect cannot be determined.

Use additional code(s):
for all associated manifestations of toxic effect, such as: respiratory conditions due to external agents (J60-J70)
personal history of foreign body fully removed (Z87.821)
to identify any retained foreign body, if applicable (Z18.-)

Excludes1: *contact with and (suspected) exposure to toxic substances (Z77.-)*

Review coding guideline C.19.e

T51 **Toxic effect of alcohol**

The appropriate 7th character is to be added to each code from category T51
A initial encounter
D subsequent encounter
S sequela

+ **T51.0** **Toxic effect of ethanol**
Toxic effect of ethyl alcohol
Excludes2: acute alcohol intoxication or 'hangover' effects (F10.129, F10.229, F10.929) drunkenness (F10.129, F10.229, F10.929) pathological alcohol intoxication (F10.129, F10.229, F10.929)
+ **T51.0X** **Toxic effect of ethanol**
+7th **T51.0X1** **Toxic effect of ethanol, accidental (unintentional)**
Toxic effect of ethanol NOS
+7th **T51.0X2** **Toxic effect of ethanol, intentional self-harm**
+7th **T51.0X3** **Toxic effect of ethanol, assault**
+7th **T51.0X4** **Toxic effect of ethanol, undetermined**

+ **T51.1** **Toxic effect of methanol**
Toxic effect of methyl alcohol
+ **T51.1X** **Toxic effect of methanol**
+7th **T51.1X1** **Toxic effect of methanol, accidental (unintentional)**
Toxic effect of methanol NOS
+7th **T51.1X2** **Toxic effect of methanol, intentional self-harm**
+7th **T51.1X3** **Toxic effect of methanol, assault**
+7th **T51.1X4** **Toxic effect of methanol, undetermined**

+ **T51.2** **Toxic effect of 2-Propanol**
Toxic effect of isopropyl alcohol
+ **T51.2X** **Toxic effect of 2-Propanol**
+7th **T51.2X1** **Toxic effect of 2-Propanol, accidental (unintentional)**
Toxic effect of 2-Propanol NOS
+7th **T51.2X2** **Toxic effect of 2-Propanol, intentional self-harm**
+7th **T51.2X3** **Toxic effect of 2-Propanol, assault**
+7th **T51.2X4** **Toxic effect of 2-Propanol, undetermined**

+ **T51.3** **Toxic effect of fusel oil**
Toxic effect of amyl alcohol
Toxic effect of butyl [1-butanol] alcohol
Toxic effect of propyl [1-propanol] alcohol
+ **T51.3X** **Toxic effect of fusel oil**
+7th **T51.3X1** **Toxic effect of fusel oil, accidental (unintentional)**
Toxic effect of fusel oil NOS
+7th **T51.3X2** **Toxic effect of fusel oil, intentional self-harm**
+7th **T51.3X3** **Toxic effect of fusel oil, assault**
+7th **T51.3X4** **Toxic effect of fusel oil, undetermined**

+ **T51.8** **Toxic effect of other alcohols**
+ **T51.8X** **Toxic effect of other alcohols**
+7th **T51.8X1** **Toxic effect of other alcohols, accidental (unintentional)**
Toxic effect of other alcohols NOS

+7th **T51.8X2 Toxic effect of other alcohols, intentional self-harm**
+7th **T51.8X3 Toxic effect of other alcohols, assault**
+7th **T51.8X4 Toxic effect of other alcohols, undetermined**
+ T51.9 Toxic effect of unspecified alcohol
X+7th **T51.91 Toxic effect of unspecified alcohol, accidental (unintentional)**
X+7th **T51.92 Toxic effect of unspecified alcohol, intentional self-harm**
X+7th **T51.93 Toxic effect of unspecified alcohol, assault**
X+7th **T51.94 Toxic effect of unspecified alcohol, undetermined**

T52 Toxic effect of organic solvents

Excludes1: *halogen derivatives of aliphatic and aromatic hydrocarbons (T53.-)*

The appropriate 7th character is to be added to each code from category T52
A initial encounter
D subsequent encounter
S sequela

+ T52.0 Toxic effects of petroleum products
Toxic effects of gasoline [petrol]
Toxic effects of kerosene [paraffin oil]
Toxic effects of paraffin wax
Toxic effects of ether petroleum
Toxic effects of naphtha petroleum
Toxic effects of spirit petroleum
+ T52.0X Toxic effects of petroleum products
+7th **T52.0X1 Toxic effect of petroleum products, accidental (unintentional)**
Toxic effects of petroleum products NOS
+7th **T52.0X2 Toxic effect of petroleum products, intentional self-harm**
+7th **T52.0X3 Toxic effect of petroleum products, assault**
+7th **T52.0X4 Toxic effect of petroleum products, undetermined**

+ T52.1 Toxic effects of benzene
Excludes1: *homologues of benzene (T52.2)*
nitroderivatives and aminoderivatives of benzene and its homologues (T65.3)
+ T52.1X Toxic effects of benzene
+7th **T52.1X1 Toxic effect of benzene, accidental (unintentional)**
Toxic effects of benzene NOS
+7th **T52.1X2 Toxic effect of benzene, intentional self-harm**
+7th **T52.1X3 Toxic effect of benzene, assault**
+7th **T52.1X4 Toxic effect of benzene, undetermined**

+ T52.2 Toxic effects of homologues of benzene
Toxic effects of toluene [methylbenzene]
Toxic effects of xylene [dimethylbenzene]
+ T52.2X Toxic effects of homologues of benzene
+7th **T52.2X1 Toxic effect of homologues of benzene, accidental (unintentional)**
Toxic effects of homologues of benzene NOS
+7th **T52.2X2 Toxic effect of homologues of benzene, intentional self-harm**
+7th **T52.2X3 Toxic effect of homologues of benzene, assault**
+7th **T52.2X4 Toxic effect of homologues of benzene, undetermined**

+ T52.3 Toxic effects of glycols
+ T52.3X Toxic effects of glycols
+7th **T52.3X1 Toxic effect of glycols, accidental (unintentional)**
Toxic effects of glycols NOS
+7th **T52.3X2 Toxic effect of glycols, intentional self-harm**
+7th **T52.3X3 Toxic effect of glycols, assault**
+7th **T52.3X4 Toxic effect of glycols, undetermined**

+ T52.4 Toxic effects of ketones
+ T52.4X Toxic effects of ketones
+7th **T52.4X1 Toxic effect of ketones, accidental (unintentional)**
Toxic effects of ketones NOS
+7th **T52.4X2 Toxic effect of ketones, intentional self-harm**
+7th **T52.4X3 Toxic effect of ketones, assault**
+7th **T52.4X4 Toxic effect of ketones, undetermined**

+ T52.8 Toxic effects of other organic solvents
+ T52.8X Toxic effects of other organic solvents
+7th **T52.8X1 Toxic effect of other organic solvents, accidental (unintentional)**
Toxic effects of other organic solvents NOS
+7th **T52.8X2 Toxic effect of other organic solvents, intentional self-harm**
+7th **T52.8X3 Toxic effect of other organic solvents, assa**
+7th **T52.8X4 Toxic effect of other organic solvents, undetermined**

+ T52.9 Toxic effects of unspecified organic solvent
X+7th **T52.91 Toxic effect of unspecified organic solvent, accidenta (unintentional)**
X+7th **T52.92 Toxic effect of unspecified organic solvent, intention self-harm**
X+7th **T52.93 Toxic effect of unspecified organic solvent, assault**
X+7th **T52.94 Toxic effect of unspecified organic solvent, undetermined**

T53 Toxic effect of halogen derivatives of aliphatic and aromatic hydrocarbons

The appropriate 7th character is to be added to each code from category T53
A initial encounter
D subsequent encounter
S sequela

+ T53.0 Toxic effects of carbon tetrachloride
Toxic effects of tetrachloromethane
+ T53.0X Toxic effects of carbon tetrachloride
+7th **T53.0X1 Toxic effect of carbon tetrachloride, accidental (unintentional)**
Toxic effects of carbon tetrachloride NOS
+7th **T53.0X2 Toxic effect of carbon tetrachloride, intentional self-harm**
+7th **T53.0X3 Toxic effect of carbon tetrachloride, assaul**
+7th **T53.0X4 Toxic effect of carbon tetrachloride, undetermined**

+ T53.1 Toxic effects of chloroform
Toxic effects of trichloromethane
+ T53.1X Toxic effects of chloroform
+7th **T53.1X1 Toxic effect of chloroform, accidental (unintentional)**
Toxic effects of chloroform NOS
+7th **T53.1X2 Toxic effect of chloroform, intentional self-harm**
+7th **T53.1X3 Toxic effect of chloroform, assault**
+7th **T53.1X4 Toxic effect of chloroform, undetermined**

+ T53.2 Toxic effects of trichloroethylene
Toxic effects of trichloroethene
+ T53.2X Toxic effects of trichloroethylene
+7th **T53.2X1 Toxic effect of trichloroethylene, accidental (unintentional)**
Toxic effects of trichloroethylene NOS
+7th **T53.2X2 Toxic effect of trichloroethylene, intentiona self-harm**
+7th **T53.2X3 Toxic effect of trichloroethylene, assault**
+7th **T53.2X4 Toxic effect of trichloroethylene, undetermined**

+ T53.3 Toxic effects of tetrachloroethylene
Toxic effects of perchloroethylene
Toxic effect of tetrachloroethene
+ T53.3X Toxic effects of tetrachloroethylene
+7th **T53.3X1 Toxic effect of tetrachloroethylene, accidental (unintentional)**
Toxic effects of tetrachloroethylene NOS
+7th **T53.3X2 Toxic effect of tetrachloroethylene, intentional self-harm**
+7th **T53.3X3 Toxic effect of tetrachloroethylene, assault**
+7th **T53.3X4 Toxic effect of tetrachloroethylene, undetermined**

+ T53.4 Toxic effects of dichloromethane
Toxic effects of methylene chloride
+ T53.4X Toxic effects of dichloromethane
+7th **T53.4X1 Toxic effect of dichloromethane, accidental (unintentional)**
Toxic effects of dichloromethane NOS
+7th **T53.4X2 Toxic effect of dichloromethane, intentional self-harm**
+7th **T53.4X3 Toxic effect of dichloromethane, assault**
+7th **T53.4X4 Toxic effect of dichloromethane, undetermined**

+ T53.5 Toxic effects of chlorofluorocarbons
+ T53.5X Toxic effects of chlorofluorocarbons
+7th **T53.5X1 Toxic effect of chlorofluorocarbons, accidental (unintentional)**
Toxic effects of chlorofluorocarbons NOS

+7th **T53.5X2 Toxic effect of chlorofluorocarbons, intentional self-harm**
+7th **T53.5X3 Toxic effect of chlorofluorocarbons, assault**
+7th **T53.5X4 Toxic effect of chlorofluorocarbons, undetermined**

\+ **T53.6 Toxic effects of other halogen derivatives of aliphatic hydrocarbons**
\+ **T53.6X Toxic effects of other halogen derivatives of aliphatic hydrocarbons**
+7th **T53.6X1 Toxic effect of other halogen derivatives of aliphatic hydrocarbons, accidental (unintentional)**
Toxic effects of other halogen derivatives of aliphatic hydrocarbons NOS
+7th **T53.6X2 Toxic effect of other halogen derivatives of aliphatic hydrocarbons, intentional self-harm**
+7th **T53.6X3 Toxic effect of other halogen derivatives of aliphatic hydrocarbons, assault**
+7th **T53.6X4 Toxic effect of other halogen derivatives of aliphatic hydrocarbons, undetermined**

\+ **T53.7 Toxic effects of other halogen derivatives of aromatic hydrocarbons**
\+ **T53.7X Toxic effects of other halogen derivatives of aromatic hydrocarbons**
+7th **T53.7X1 Toxic effect of other halogen derivatives of aromatic hydrocarbons, accidental (unintentional)**
Toxic effects of other halogen derivatives of aromatic hydrocarbons NOS
+7th **T53.7X2 Toxic effect of other halogen derivatives of aromatic hydrocarbons, intentional self-harm**
+7th **T53.7X3 Toxic effect of other halogen derivatives of aromatic hydrocarbons, assault**
+7th **T53.7X4 Toxic effect of other halogen derivatives of aromatic hydrocarbons, undetermined**

\+ **T53.9 Toxic effects of unspecified halogen derivatives of aliphatic and aromatic hydrocarbons**
X+7th **T53.91 Toxic effect of unspecified halogen derivatives of aliphatic and aromatic hydrocarbons, accidental (unintentional)**
X+7th **T53.92 Toxic effect of unspecified halogen derivatives of aliphatic and aromatic hydrocarbons, intentional self-harm**
X+7th **T53.93 Toxic effect of unspecified halogen derivatives of aliphatic and aromatic hydrocarbons, assault**
X+7th **T53.94 Toxic effect of unspecified halogen derivatives of aliphatic and aromatic hydrocarbons, undetermined**

T54 Toxic effect of corrosive substances

The appropriate 7th character is to be added to each code from category T54
A initial encounter
D subsequent encounter
S sequela

\+ **T54.0 Toxic effects of phenol and phenol homologues**
\+ **T54.0X Toxic effects of phenol and phenol homologues**
+7th **T54.0X1 Toxic effect of phenol and phenol homologues, accidental (unintentional)**
Toxic effects of phenol and phenol homologues NOS
+7th **T54.0X2 Toxic effect of phenol and phenol homologues, intentional self-harm**
+7th **T54.0X3 Toxic effect of phenol and phenol homologues, assault**
+7th **T54.0X4 Toxic effect of phenol and phenol homologues, undetermined**

\+ **T54.1 Toxic effects of other corrosive organic compounds**
\+ **T54.1X Toxic effects of other corrosive organic compounds**
+7th **T54.1X1 Toxic effect of other corrosive organic compounds, accidental (unintentional)**
Toxic effects of other corrosive organic compounds NOS
+7th **T54.1X2 Toxic effect of other corrosive organic compounds, intentional self-harm**
+7th **T54.1X3 Toxic effect of other corrosive organic compounds, assault**
+7th **T54.1X4 Toxic effect of other corrosive organic compounds, undetermined**

\+ **T54.2 Toxic effects of corrosive acids and acid-like substances**
Toxic effects of hydrochloric acid
Toxic effects of sulfuric acid
\+ **T54.2X Toxic effects of corrosive acids and acid-like substances**
+7th **T54.2X1 Toxic effect of corrosive acids and acid-like substances, accidental (unintentional)**
Toxic effects of corrosive acids and acid-like substances NOS
+7th **T54.2X2 Toxic effect of corrosive acids and acid-like substances, intentional self-harm**
+7th **T54.2X3 Toxic effect of corrosive acids and acid-like substances, assault**
+7th **T54.2X4 Toxic effect of corrosive acids and acid-like substances, undetermined**

\+ **T54.3 Toxic effects of corrosive alkalis and alkali-like substances**
Toxic effects of potassium hydroxide
Toxic effects of sodium hydroxide
\+ **T54.3X Toxic effects of corrosive alkalis and alkali-like substances**
+7th **T54.3X1 Toxic effect of corrosive alkalis and alkali-like substances, accidental (unintentional)**
Toxic effects of corrosive alkalis and alkali-like substances NOS
+7th **T54.3X2 Toxic effect of corrosive alkalis and alkali-like substances, intentional self-harm**
+7th **T54.3X3 Toxic effect of corrosive alkalis and alkali-like substances, assault**
+7th **T54.3X4 Toxic effect of corrosive alkalis and alkali-like substances, undetermined**

\+ **T54.9 Toxic effects of unspecified corrosive substance**
X+7th **T54.91 Toxic effect of unspecified corrosive substance, accidental (unintentional)**
X+7th **T54.92 Toxic effect of unspecified corrosive substance, intentional self-harm**
X+7th **T54.93 Toxic effect of unspecified corrosive substance, assault**
X+7th **T54.94 Toxic effect of unspecified corrosive substance, undetermined**

T55 Toxic effect of soaps and detergents

The appropriate 7th character is to be added to each code from category T55
A initial encounter
D subsequent encounter
S sequela

\+ **T55.0 Toxic effect of soaps**
\+ **T55.0X Toxic effect of soaps**
+7th **T55.0X1 Toxic effect of soaps, accidental (unintentional)**
Toxic effect of soaps NOS
+7th **T55.0X2 Toxic effect of soaps, intentional self-harm**
+7th **T55.0X3 Toxic effect of soaps, assault**
+7th **T55.0X4 Toxic effect of soaps, undetermined**

\+ **T55.1 Toxic effect of detergents**
\+ **T55.1X Toxic effect of detergents**
+7th **T55.1X1 Toxic effect of detergents, accidental (unintentional)**
Toxic effect of detergents NOS
+7th **T55.1X2 Toxic effect of detergents, intentional self-harm**
+7th **T55.1X3 Toxic effect of detergents, assault**
+7th **T55.1X4 Toxic effect of detergents, undetermined**

T56 Toxic effect of metals

Includes: toxic effects of fumes and vapors of metals
toxic effects of metals from all sources, except medicinal substances

Use additional code to identify any retained metal foreign body, if applicable (Z18.0-, T18.1-)

Excludes1: *arsenic and its compounds (T57.0)*
manganese and its compounds (T57.2)

The appropriate 7th character is to be added to each code from category T56
A initial encounter
D subsequent encounter
S sequela

\+ **T56.0 Toxic effects of lead and its compounds**
\+ **T56.0X Toxic effects of lead and its compounds**
+7th **T56.0X1 Toxic effect of lead and its compounds, accidental (unintentional)**
Toxic effects of lead and its compounds NOS

+7th **T56.0X2 Toxic effect of lead and its compounds, intentional self-harm**
+7th **T56.0X3 Toxic effect of lead and its compounds, assault**
+7th **T56.0X4 Toxic effect of lead and its compounds, undetermined**

+ T56.1 Toxic effects of mercury and its compounds
+ T56.1X Toxic effects of mercury and its compounds
+7th **T56.1X1 Toxic effect of mercury and its compounds, accidental (unintentional)**
Toxic effects of mercury and its compounds NOS
+7th **T56.1X2 Toxic effect of mercury and its compounds, intentional self-harm**
+7th **T56.1X3 Toxic effect of mercury and its compounds, assault**
+7th **T56.1X4 Toxic effect of mercury and its compounds, undetermined**

+ T56.2 Toxic effects of chromium and its compounds
+ T56.2X Toxic effects of chromium and its compounds
+7th **T56.2X1 Toxic effect of chromium and its compounds, accidental (unintentional)**
Toxic effects of chromium and its compounds NOS
+7th **T56.2X2 Toxic effect of chromium and its compounds, intentional self-harm**
+7th **T56.2X3 Toxic effect of chromium and its compounds, assault**
+7th **T56.2X4 Toxic effect of chromium and its compounds, undetermined**

+ T56.3 Toxic effects of cadmium and its compounds
+ T56.3X Toxic effects of cadmium and its compounds
+7th **T56.3X1 Toxic effect of cadmium and its compounds, accidental (unintentional)**
Toxic effects of cadmium and its compounds NOS
+7th **T56.3X2 Toxic effect of cadmium and its compounds, intentional self-harm**
+7th **T56.3X3 Toxic effect of cadmium and its compounds, assault**
+7th **T56.3X4 Toxic effect of cadmium and its compounds, undetermined**

+ T56.4 Toxic effects of copper and its compounds
+ T56.4X Toxic effects of copper and its compounds
+7th **T56.4X1 Toxic effect of copper and its compounds, accidental (unintentional)**
Toxic effects of copper and its compounds NOS
+7th **T56.4X2 Toxic effect of copper and its compounds, intentional self-harm**
+7th **T56.4X3 Toxic effect of copper and its compounds, assault**
+7th **T56.4X4 Toxic effect of copper and its compounds, undetermined**

+ T56.5 Toxic effects of zinc and its compounds
+ T56.5X Toxic effects of zinc and its compounds
+7th **T56.5X1 Toxic effect of zinc and its compounds, accidental (unintentional)**
Toxic effects of zinc and its compounds NOS
+7th **T56.5X2 Toxic effect of zinc and its compounds, intentional self-harm**
+7th **T56.5X3 Toxic effect of zinc and its compounds, assault**
+7th **T56.5X4 Toxic effect of zinc and its compounds, undetermined**

+ T56.6 Toxic effects of tin and its compounds
+ T56.6X Toxic effects of tin and its compounds
+7th **T56.6X1 Toxic effect of tin and its compounds, accidental (unintentional)**
Toxic effects of tin and its compounds NOS
+7th **T56.6X2 Toxic effect of tin and its compounds, intentional self-harm**
+7th **T56.6X3 Toxic effect of tin and its compounds, assault**
+7th **T56.6X4 Toxic effect of tin and its compounds, undetermined**

+ T56.7 Toxic effects of beryllium and its compounds
+ T56.7X Toxic effects of beryllium and its compounds
+7th **T56.7X1 Toxic effect of beryllium and its compounds, accidental (unintentional)**
Toxic effects of beryllium and its compounds NOS
+7th **T56.7X2 Toxic effect of beryllium and its compounds, intentional self-harm**
+7th **T56.7X3 Toxic effect of beryllium and its compounds, assault**
+7th **T56.7X4 Toxic effect of beryllium and its compounds undetermined**

+ T56.8 Toxic effects of other metals
+ T56.81 Toxic effect of thallium
+7th **T56.811 Toxic effect of thallium, accidental (unintentional)**
Toxic effect of thallium NOS
+7th **T56.812 Toxic effect of thallium, intentional self-harm**
+7th **T56.813 Toxic effect of thallium, assault**
+7th **T56.814 Toxic effect of thallium, undetermined**
+ T56.89 Toxic effects of other metals
+7th **T56.891 Toxic effect of other metals, accidental (unintentional)**
Toxic effects of other metals NOS
+7th **T56.892 Toxic effect of other metals, intentional self-harm**
+7th **T56.893 Toxic effect of other metals, assault**
+7th **T56.894 Toxic effect of other metals, undetermined**

+ T56.9 Toxic effects of unspecified metal
X+7th **T56.91 Toxic effect of unspecified metal, accidental (unintentional)**
X+7th **T56.92 Toxic effect of unspecified metal, intentional self-harm**
X+7th **T56.93 Toxic effect of unspecified metal, assault**
X+7th **T56.94 Toxic effect of unspecified metal, undetermined**

T57 Toxic effect of other inorganic substances

The appropriate 7th character is to be added to each code from category T57
A initial encounter
D subsequent encounter
S sequela

+ T57.0 Toxic effect of arsenic and its compounds
+ T57.0X Toxic effect of arsenic and its compounds
+7th **T57.0X1 Toxic effect of arsenic and its compounds, accidental (unintentional)**
Toxic effect of arsenic and its compounds NOS
+7th **T57.0X2 Toxic effect of arsenic and its compounds, intentional self-harm**
+7th **T57.0X3 Toxic effect of arsenic and its compounds, assault**
+7th **T57.0X4 Toxic effect of arsenic and its compounds, undetermined**

+ T57.1 Toxic effect of phosphorus and its compounds
Excludes1: *organophosphate insecticides (T60.0)*
+ T57.1X Toxic effect of phosphorus and its compounds
+7th **T57.1X1 Toxic effect of phosphorus and its compounds, accidental (unintentional)**
Toxic effect of phosphorus and its compounds NOS
+7th **T57.1X2 Toxic effect of phosphorus and its compounds, intentional self-harm**
+7th **T57.1X3 Toxic effect of phosphorus and its compounds, assault**
+7th **T57.1X4 Toxic effect of phosphorus and its compounds, undetermined**

+ T57.2 Toxic effect of manganese and its compounds
+ T57.2X Toxic effect of manganese and its compounds
+7th **T57.2X1 Toxic effect of manganese and its compounds, accidental (unintentional)**
Toxic effect of manganese and its compounds NOS
+7th **T57.2X2 Toxic effect of manganese and its compounds, intentional self-harm**
+7th **T57.2X3 Toxic effect of manganese and its compounds, assault**
+7th **T57.2X4 Toxic effect of manganese and its compounds, undetermined**

+ T57.3 Toxic effect of hydrogen cyanide
+ T57.3X Toxic effect of hydrogen cyanide
+7th **T57.3X1 Toxic effect of hydrogen cyanide, accidental (unintentional)**
Toxic effect of hydrogen cyanide NOS
+7th **T57.3X2 Toxic effect of hydrogen cyanide, intentional self-harm**
+7th **T57.3X3 Toxic effect of hydrogen cyanide, assault**

+7th **T57.3X4 Toxic effect of hydrogen cyanide, undetermined**

+ **T57.8 Toxic effect of other specified inorganic substances**

+ **T57.8X Toxic effect of other specified inorganic substances**

+7th **T57.8X1 Toxic effect of other specified inorganic substances, accidental (unintentional)**
Toxic effect of other specified inorganic substances NOS

+7th **T57.8X2 Toxic effect of other specified inorganic substances, intentional self-harm**

+7th **T57.8X3 Toxic effect of other specified inorganic substances, assault**

+7th **T57.8X4 Toxic effect of other specified inorganic substances, undetermined**

+ **T57.9 Toxic effect of unspecified inorganic substance**

X+7th **T57.91 Toxic effect of unspecified inorganic substance, accidental (unintentional)**

X+7th **T57.92 Toxic effect of unspecified inorganic substance, intentional self-harm**

X+7th **T57.93 Toxic effect of unspecified inorganic substance, assault**

X+7th **T57.94 Toxic effect of unspecified inorganic substance, undetermined**

T58 Toxic effect of carbon monoxide

Includes: asphyxiation from carbon monoxide
toxic effect of carbon monoxide from all sources

The appropriate 7th character is to be added to each code from category T58
A initial encounter
D subsequent encounter
S sequela

+ **T58.0 Toxic effect of carbon monoxide from motor vehicle exhaust**
Toxic effect of exhaust gas from gas engine
Toxic effect of exhaust gas from motor pump

X+7th **T58.01 Toxic effect of carbon monoxide from motor vehicle exhaust, accidental (unintentional)**

X+7th **T58.02 Toxic effect of carbon monoxide from motor vehicle exhaust, intentional self-harm**

X+7th **T58.03 Toxic effect of carbon monoxide from motor vehicle exhaust, assault**

X+7th **T58.04 Toxic effect of carbon monoxide from motor vehicle exhaust, undetermined**

+ **T58.1 Toxic effect of carbon monoxide from utility gas**
Toxic effect of acetylene
Toxic effect of gas NOS used for lighting, heating, cooking
Toxic effect of water gas

X+7th **T58.11 Toxic effect of carbon monoxide from utility gas, accidental (unintentional)**

X+7th **T58.12 Toxic effect of carbon monoxide from utility gas, intentional self-harm**

X+7th **T58.13 Toxic effect of carbon monoxide from utility gas, assault**

X+7th **T58.14 Toxic effect of carbon monoxide from utility gas, undetermined**

+ **T58.2 Toxic effect of carbon monoxide from incomplete combustion of other domestic fuels**
Toxic effect of carbon monoxide from incomplete combustion of coal, coke, kerosene, wood

+ **T58.2X Toxic effect of carbon monoxide from incomplete combustion of other domestic fuels**

+7th **T58.2X1 Toxic effect of carbon monoxide from incomplete combustion of other domestic fuels, accidental (unintentional)**

+7th **T58.2X2 Toxic effect of carbon monoxide from incomplete combustion of other domestic fuels, intentional self-harm**

+7th **T58.2X3 Toxic effect of carbon monoxide from incomplete combustion of other domestic fuels, assault**

+7th **T58.2X4 Toxic effect of carbon monoxide from incomplete combustion of other domestic fuels, undetermined**

+ **T58.8 Toxic effect of carbon monoxide from other source**
Toxic effect of carbon monoxide from blast furnace gas
Toxic effect of carbon monoxide from fuels in industrial use
Toxic effect of carbon monoxide from kiln vapor

+ **T58.8X Toxic effect of carbon monoxide from other source**

+7th **T58.8X1 Toxic effect of carbon monoxide from other source, accidental (unintentional)**

+7th **T58.8X2 Toxic effect of carbon monoxide from other source, intentional self-harm**

+7th **T58.8X3 Toxic effect of carbon monoxide from other source, assault**

+7th **T58.8X4 Toxic effect of carbon monoxide from other source, undetermined**

+ **T58.9 Toxic effect of carbon monoxide from unspecified source**

X+7th **T58.91 Toxic effect of carbon monoxide from unspecified source, accidental (unintentional)**

X+7th **T58.92 Toxic effect of carbon monoxide from unspecified source, intentional self-harm**

X+7th **T58.93 Toxic effect of carbon monoxide from unspecified source, assault**

X+7th **T58.94 Toxic effect of carbon monoxide from unspecified source, undetermined**

T59 Toxic effect of other gases, fumes and vapors

Includes: aerosol propellants
Excludes1: *chlorofluorocarbons (T53.5)*

The appropriate 7th character is to be added to each code from category T59
A initial encounter
D subsequent encounter
S sequela

+ **T59.0 Toxic effect of nitrogen oxides**

+ **T59.0X Toxic effect of nitrogen oxides**

+7th **T59.0X1 Toxic effect of nitrogen oxides, accidental (unintentional)**
Toxic effect of nitrogen oxides NOS

+7th **T59.0X2 Toxic effect of nitrogen oxides, intentional self-harm**

+7th **T59.0X3 Toxic effect of nitrogen oxides, assault**

+7th **T59.0X4 Toxic effect of nitrogen oxides, undetermined**

+ **T59.1 Toxic effect of sulfur dioxide**

+ **T59.1X Toxic effect of sulfur dioxide**

+7th **T59.1X1 Toxic effect of sulfur dioxide, accidental (unintentional)**
Toxic effect of sulfur dioxide NOS

+7th **T59.1X2 Toxic effect of sulfur dioxide, intentional self-harm**

+7th **T59.1X3 Toxic effect of sulfur dioxide, assault**

+7th **T59.1X4 Toxic effect of sulfur dioxide, undetermined**

+ **T59.2 Toxic effect of formaldehyde**

+ **T59.2X Toxic effect of formaldehyde**

+7th **T59.2X1 Toxic effect of formaldehyde, accidental (unintentional)**
Toxic effect of formaldehyde NOS

+7th **T59.2X2 Toxic effect of formaldehyde, intentional self-harm**

+7th **T59.2X3 Toxic effect of formaldehyde, assault**

+7th **T59.2X4 Toxic effect of formaldehyde, undetermined**

+ **T59.3 Toxic effect of lacrimogenic gas**
Toxic effect of tear gas

+ **T59.3X Toxic effect of lacrimogenic gas**

+7th **T59.3X1 Toxic effect of lacrimogenic gas, accidental (unintentional)**
Toxic effect of lacrimogenic gas NOS

+7th **T59.3X2 Toxic effect of lacrimogenic gas, intentional self-harm**

+7th **T59.3X3 Toxic effect of lacrimogenic gas, assault**

+7th **T59.3X4 Toxic effect of lacrimogenic gas, undetermined**

+ **T59.4 Toxic effect of chlorine gas**

+ **T59.4X Toxic effect of chlorine gas**

+7th **T59.4X1 Toxic effect of chlorine gas, accidental (unintentional)**
Toxic effect of chlorine gas NOS

+7th **T59.4X2 Toxic effect of chlorine gas, intentional self-harm**

+7th **T59.4X3 Toxic effect of chlorine gas, assault**

+7th **T59.4X4 Toxic effect of chlorine gas, undetermined**

+ **T59.5 Toxic effect of fluorine gas and hydrogen fluoride**

+ **T59.5X Toxic effect of fluorine gas and hydrogen fluoride**

+7th **T59.5X1 Toxic effect of fluorine gas and hydrogen fluoride, accidental (unintentional)**
Toxic effect of fluorine gas and hydrogen fluoride NOS

+7th **T59.5X2 Toxic effect of fluorine gas and hydrogen fluoride, intentional self-harm**

+7th **T59.5X3 Toxic effect of fluorine gas and hydrogen fluoride, assault**

+7th **T59.5X4 Toxic effect of fluorine gas and hydrogen fluoride, undetermined**

+ **T59.6 Toxic effect of hydrogen sulfide**
+ **T59.6X Toxic effect of hydrogen sulfide**
+7th **T59.6X1 Toxic effect of hydrogen sulfide, accidental (unintentional)**
Toxic effect of hydrogen sulfide NOS
+7th **T59.6X2 Toxic effect of hydrogen sulfide, intentional self-harm**
+7th **T59.6X3 Toxic effect of hydrogen sulfide, assault**
+7th **T59.6X4 Toxic effect of hydrogen sulfide, undetermined**
+ **T59.7 Toxic effect of carbon dioxide**
+ **T59.7X Toxic effect of carbon dioxide**
+7th **T59.7X1 Toxic effect of carbon dioxide, accidental (unintentional)**
Toxic effect of carbon dioxide NOS
+7th **T59.7X2 Toxic effect of carbon dioxide, intentional self-harm**
+7th **T59.7X3 Toxic effect of carbon dioxide, assault**
+7th **T59.7X4 Toxic effect of carbon dioxide, undetermined**
+ **T59.8 Toxic effect of other specified gases, fumes and vapors**
+ **T59.81 Toxic effect of smoke**
Smoke inhalation
Excludes2: *toxic effect of cigarette (tobacco) smoke (T65.22-)*
+7th **T59.811 Toxic effect of smoke, accidental (unintentional)**
Toxic effect of smoke NOS
+7th **T59.812 Toxic effect of smoke, intentional self-harm**
+7th **T59.813 Toxic effect of smoke, assault**
+7th **T59.814 Toxic effect of smoke, undetermined**
+ **T59.89 Toxic effect of other specified gases, fumes and vapors**
+7th **T59.891 Toxic effect of other specified gases, fumes and vapors, accidental (unintentional)**
+7th **T59.892 Toxic effect of other specified gases, fumes and vapors, intentional self-harm**
+7th **T59.893 Toxic effect of other specified gases, fumes and vapors, assault**
+7th **T59.894 Toxic effect of other specified gases, fumes and vapors, undetermined**
+ **T59.9 Toxic effect of unspecified gases, fumes and vapors**
X+7th **T59.91 Toxic effect of unspecified gases, fumes and vapors, accidental (unintentional)**
X+7th **T59.92 Toxic effect of unspecified gases, fumes and vapors, intentional self-harm**
X+7th **T59.93 Toxic effect of unspecified gases, fumes and vapors, assault**
X+7th **T59.94 Toxic effect of unspecified gases, fumes and vapors, undetermined**

T60 Toxic effect of pesticides

Includes: toxic effect of wood preservatives

The appropriate 7th character is to be added to each code from category T60
A initial encounter
D subsequent encounter
S sequela

+ **T60.0 Toxic effect of organophosphate and carbamate insecticides**
+ **T60.0X Toxic effect of organophosphate and carbamate insecticides**
+7th **T60.0X1 Toxic effect of organophosphate and carbamate insecticides, accidental (unintentional)**
Toxic effect of organophosphate and carbamate insecticides NOS
+7th **T60.0X2 Toxic effect of organophosphate and carbamate insecticides, intentional self-harm**
+7th **T60.0X3 Toxic effect of organophosphate and carbamate insecticides, assault**
+7th **T60.0X4 Toxic effect of organophosphate and carbamate insecticides, undetermined**
+ **T60.1 Toxic effect of halogenated insecticides**
Excludes1: *chlorinated hydrocarbon (T53.-)*
+ **T60.1X Toxic effect of halogenated insecticides**
+7th **T60.1X1 Toxic effect of halogenated insecticides, accidental (unintentional)**
Toxic effect of halogenated insecticides NOS
+7th **T60.1X2 Toxic effect of halogenated insecticides, intentional self-harm**
+7th **T60.1X3 Toxic effect of halogenated insecticides, assault**
+7th **T60.1X4 Toxic effect of halogenated insecticides, undetermined**
+ **T60.2 Toxic effect of other insecticides**
+ **T60.2X Toxic effect of other insecticides**
+7th **T60.2X1 Toxic effect of other insecticides, accidental (unintentional)**
Toxic effect of other insecticides NOS
+7th **T60.2X2 Toxic effect of other insecticides, intentional self-harm**
+7th **T60.2X3 Toxic effect of other insecticides, assault**
+7th **T60.2X4 Toxic effect of other insecticides, undetermined**
+ **T60.3 Toxic effect of herbicides and fungicides**
+ **T60.3X Toxic effect of herbicides and fungicides**
+7th **T60.3X1 Toxic effect of herbicides and fungicides, accidental (unintentional)**
Toxic effect of herbicides and fungicides NOS
+7th **T60.3X2 Toxic effect of herbicides and fungicides, intentional self-harm**
+7th **T60.3X3 Toxic effect of herbicides and fungicides, assault**
+7th **T60.3X4 Toxic effect of herbicides and fungicides, undetermined**
+ **T60.4 Toxic effect of rodenticides**
Excludes1: *strychnine and its salts (T65.1)*
thallium (T56.81-)
+ **T60.4X Toxic effect of rodenticides**
+7th **T60.4X1 Toxic effect of rodenticides, accidental (unintentional)**
Toxic effect of rodenticides NOS
+7th **T60.4X2 Toxic effect of rodenticides, intentional self-harm**
+7th **T60.4X3 Toxic effect of rodenticides, assault**
+7th **T60.4X4 Toxic effect of rodenticides, undetermined**
+ **T60.8 Toxic effect of other pesticides**
+ **T60.8X Toxic effect of other pesticides**
+7th **T60.8X1 Toxic effect of other pesticides, accidental (unintentional)**
Toxic effect of other pesticides NOS
+7th **T60.8X2 Toxic effect of other pesticides, intentional self-harm**
+7th **T60.8X3 Toxic effect of other pesticides, assault**
+7th **T60.8X4 Toxic effect of other pesticides, undetermined**
+ **T60.9 Toxic effect of unspecified pesticide**
X+7th **T60.91 Toxic effect of unspecified pesticide, accidental (unintentional)**
X+7th **T60.92 Toxic effect of unspecified pesticide, intentional self-harm**
X+7th **T60.93 Toxic effect of unspecified pesticide, assault**
X+7th **T60.94 Toxic effect of unspecified pesticide, undetermined**

T61 Toxic effect of noxious substances eaten as seafood

Excludes1: *allergic reaction to food, such as:*
anaphylactic reaction or shock due to adverse food reaction (T78.0-)
dermatitis (L23.6, L25.4, L27.2)
bacterial foodborne intoxications (A05.-)
gastroenteritis (noninfective) (K52.2)
toxic effect of aflatoxin and other mycotoxins (T64)
toxic effect of cyanides (T65.0-)
toxic effect of harmful algae bloom (T65.82-)
toxic effect of hydrogen cyanide (T57.3-)
toxic effect of mercury (T56.1-)
toxic effect of red tide (T65.82-)

The appropriate 7th character is to be added to each code from category T61
A initial encounter
D subsequent encounter
S sequela

+ **T61.0 Ciguatera fish poisoning**
X+7th **T61.01 Ciguatera fish poisoning, accidental (unintentional)**
X+7th **T61.02 Ciguatera fish poisoning, intentional self-harm**
X+7th **T61.03 Ciguatera fish poisoning, assault**
X+7th **T61.04 Ciguatera fish poisoning, undetermined**
+ **T61.1 Scombroid fish poisoning**
Histamine-like syndrome
X+7th **T61.11 Scombroid fish poisoning, accidental (unintentional)**
X+7th **T61.12 Scombroid fish poisoning, intentional self-harm**
X+7th **T61.13 Scombroid fish poisoning, assault**
X+7th **T61.14 Scombroid fish poisoning, undetermined**

+ **T61.7 Other fish and shellfish poisoning**
  + **T61.77 Other fish poisoning**
    - +7th **T61.771 Other fish poisoning, accidental (unintentional)**
    - +7th **T61.772 Other fish poisoning, intentional self-harm**
    - +7th **T61.773 Other fish poisoning, assault**
    - +7th **T61.774 Other fish poisoning, undetermined**
  + **T61.78 Other shellfish poisoning**
    - +7th **T61.781 Other shellfish poisoning, accidental (unintentional)**
    - +7th **T61.782 Other shellfish poisoning, intentional self-harm**
    - +7th **T61.783 Other shellfish poisoning, assault**
    - +7th **T61.784 Other shellfish poisoning, undetermined**

+ **T61.8 Toxic effect of other seafood**
  + **T61.8X Toxic effect of other seafood**
    - +7th **T61.8X1 Toxic effect of other seafood, accidental (unintentional)**
    - +7th **T61.8X2 Toxic effect of other seafood, intentional self-harm**
    - +7th **T61.8X3 Toxic effect of other seafood, assault**
    - +7th **T61.8X4 Toxic effect of other seafood, undetermined**

+ **T61.9 Toxic effect of unspecified seafood**
  - X+7th **T61.91 Toxic effect of unspecified seafood, accidental (unintentional)**
  - X+7th **T61.92 Toxic effect of unspecified seafood, intentional self-harm**
  - X+7th **T61.93 Toxic effect of unspecified seafood, assault**
  - X+7th **T61.94 Toxic effect of unspecified seafood, undetermined**

T62 Toxic effect of other noxious substances eaten as food

Excludes1: *allergic reaction to food, such as:*
anaphylactic shock (reaction) due to adverse food reaction (T78.0-)
dermatitis (L23.6, L25.4, L27.2)
gastroenteritis (noninfective) (K52.2)
bacterial food borne intoxications (A05.-)
toxic effect of aflatoxin and other mycotoxins (T64)
toxic effect of cyanides (T65.0-)
toxic effect of hydrogen cyanide (T57.3-)
toxic effect of mercury (T56.1-)

The appropriate 7th character is to be added to each code from category T62
A initial encounter
D subsequent encounter
S sequela

+ **T62.0 Toxic effect of ingested mushrooms**
  + **T62.0X Toxic effect of ingested mushrooms**
    - +7th **T62.0X1 Toxic effect of ingested mushrooms, accidental (unintentional)**
      Toxic effect of ingested mushrooms NOS
    - +7th **T62.0X2 Toxic effect of ingested mushrooms, intentional self-harm**
    - +7th **T62.0X3 Toxic effect of ingested mushrooms, assault**
    - +7th **T62.0X4 Toxic effect of ingested mushrooms, undetermined**

+ **T62.1 Toxic effect of ingested berries**
  + **T62.1X Toxic effect of ingested berries**
    - +7th **T62.1X1 Toxic effect of ingested berries, accidental (unintentional)**
      Toxic effect of ingested berries NOS
    - +7th **T62.1X2 Toxic effect of ingested berries, intentional self-harm**
    - +7th **T62.1X3 Toxic effect of ingested berries, assault**
    - +7th **T62.1X4 Toxic effect of ingested berries, undetermined**

+ **T62.2 Toxic effect of other ingested (parts of) plant(s)**
  + **T62.2X Toxic effect of other ingested (parts of) plant(s)**
    - +7th **T62.2X1 Toxic effect of other ingested (parts of) plant(s), accidental (unintentional)**
      Toxic effect of other ingested (parts of) plant(s) NOS
    - +7th **T62.2X2 Toxic effect of other ingested (parts of) plant(s), intentional self-harm**
    - +7th **T62.2X3 Toxic effect of other ingested (parts of) plant(s), assault**
    - +7th **T62.2X4 Toxic effect of other ingested (parts of) plant(s), undetermined**

+ **T62.8 Toxic effect of other specified noxious substances eaten as food**
  + **T62.8X Toxic effect of other specified noxious substances eaten as food**
    - +7th **T62.8X1 Toxic effect of other specified noxious substances eaten as food, accidental (unintentional)**
      Toxic effect of other specified noxious substances eaten as food NOS
    - +7th **T62.8X2 Toxic effect of other specified noxious substances eaten as food, intentional self-harm**
    - +7th **T62.8X3 Toxic effect of other specified noxious substances eaten as food, assault**
    - +7th **T62.8X4 Toxic effect of other specified noxious substances eaten as food, undetermined**

+ **T62.9 Toxic effect of unspecified noxious substance eaten as food**
  - X+7th **T62.91 Toxic effect of unspecified noxious substance eaten as food, accidental (unintentional)**
    Toxic effect of unspecified noxious substance eaten as food NOS
  - X+7th **T62.92 Toxic effect of unspecified noxious substance eaten as food, intentional self-harm**
  - X+7th **T62.93 Toxic effect of unspecified noxious substance eaten as food, assault**
  - X+7th **T62.94 Toxic effect of unspecified noxious substance eaten as food, undetermined**

T63 Toxic effect of contact with venomous animals and plants

Includes: bite or touch of venomous animal
pricked or stuck by thorn or leaf

Excludes2: *ingestion of toxic animal or plant (T61.-, T62.-)*

The appropriate 7th character is to be added to each code from category T63
A initial encounter
D subsequent encounter
S sequela

+ **T63.0 Toxic effect of snake venom**
  + **T63.00 Toxic effect of unspecified snake venom**
    - +7th **T63.001 Toxic effect of unspecified snake venom, accidental (unintentional)**
      Toxic effect of unspecified snake venom NOS
    - +7th **T63.002 Toxic effect of unspecified snake venom, intentional self-harm**
    - +7th **T63.003 Toxic effect of unspecified snake venom, assault**
    - +7th **T63.004 Toxic effect of unspecified snake venom, undetermined**
  + **T63.01 Toxic effect of rattlesnake venom**
    - +7th **T63.011 Toxic effect of rattlesnake venom, accidental (unintentional)**
      Toxic effect of rattlesnake venom NOS
    - +7th **T63.012 Toxic effect of rattlesnake venom, intentional self-harm**
    - +7th **T63.013 Toxic effect of rattlesnake venom, assault**
    - +7th **T63.014 Toxic effect of rattlesnake venom, undetermined**
  + **T63.02 Toxic effect of coral snake venom**
    - +7th **T63.021 Toxic effect of coral snake venom, accidental (unintentional)**
      Toxic effect of coral snake venom NOS
    - +7th **T63.022 Toxic effect of coral snake venom, intentional self-harm**
    - +7th **T63.023 Toxic effect of coral snake venom, assault**
    - +7th **T63.024 Toxic effect of coral snake venom, undetermined**
  + **T63.03 Toxic effect of taipan venom**
    - +7th **T63.031 Toxic effect of taipan venom, accidental (unintentional)**
      Toxic effect of taipan venom NOS
    - +7th **T63.032 Toxic effect of taipan venom, intentional self-harm**
    - +7th **T63.033 Toxic effect of taipan venom, assault**
    - +7th **T63.034 Toxic effect of taipan venom, undetermined**
  + **T63.04 Toxic effect of cobra venom**
    - +7th **T63.041 Toxic effect of cobra venom, accidental (unintentional)**
      Toxic effect of cobra venom NOS
    - +7th **T63.042 Toxic effect of cobra venom, intentional self-harm**
    - +7th **T63.043 Toxic effect of cobra venom, assault**
    - +7th **T63.044 Toxic effect of cobra venom, undetermined**

+ **T63.06 Toxic effect of venom of other North and South American snake**
  - +7th **T63.061 Toxic effect of venom of other North and South American snake, accidental (unintentional)**
    Toxic effect of venom of other North and South American snake NOS
  - +7th **T63.062 Toxic effect of venom of other North and South American snake, intentional self-harm**
  - +7th **T63.063 Toxic effect of venom of other North and South American snake, assault**
  - +7th **T63.064 Toxic effect of venom of other North and South American snake, undetermined**

+ **T63.07 Toxic effect of venom of other Australian snake**
  - +7th **T63.071 Toxic effect of venom of other Australian snake, accidental (unintentional)**
    Toxic effect of venom of other Australian snake NOS
  - +7th **T63.072 Toxic effect of venom of other Australian snake, intentional self-harm**
  - +7th **T63.073 Toxic effect of venom of other Australian snake, assault**
  - +7th **T63.074 Toxic effect of venom of other Australian snake, undetermined**

+ **T63.08 Toxic effect of venom of other African and Asian snake**
  - +7th **T63.081 Toxic effect of venom of other African and Asian snake, accidental (unintentional)**
    Toxic effect of venom of other African and Asian snake NOS
  - +7th **T63.082 Toxic effect of venom of other African and Asian snake, intentional self-harm**
  - +7th **T63.083 Toxic effect of venom of other African and Asian snake, assault**
  - +7th **T63.084 Toxic effect of venom of other African and Asian snake, undetermined**

+ **T63.09 Toxic effect of venom of other snake**
  - +7th **T63.091 Toxic effect of venom of other snake, accidental (unintentional)**
    Toxic effect of venom of other snake NOS
  - +7th **T63.092 Toxic effect of venom of other snake, intentional self-harm**
  - +7th **T63.093 Toxic effect of venom of other snake, assault**
  - +7th **T63.094 Toxic effect of venom of other snake, undetermined**

+ **T63.1 Toxic effect of venom of other reptiles**

+ **T63.11 Toxic effect of venom of gila monster**
  - +7th **T63.111 Toxic effect of venom of gila monster, accidental (unintentional)**
    Toxic effect of venom of gila monster NOS
  - +7th **T63.112 Toxic effect of venom of gila monster, intentional self-harm**
  - +7th **T63.113 Toxic effect of venom of gila monster, assault**
  - +7th **T63.114 Toxic effect of venom of gila monster, undetermined**

+ **T63.12 Toxic effect of venom of other venomous lizard**
  - +7th **T63.121 Toxic effect of venom of other venomous lizard, accidental (unintentional)**
    Toxic effect of venom of other venomous lizard NOS
  - +7th **T63.122 Toxic effect of venom of other venomous lizard, intentional self-harm**
  - +7th **T63.123 Toxic effect of venom of other venomous lizard, assault**
  - +7th **T63.124 Toxic effect of venom of other venomous lizard, undetermined**

+ **T63.19 Toxic effect of venom of other reptiles**
  - +7th **T63.191 Toxic effect of venom of other reptiles, accidental (unintentional)**
    Toxic effect of venom of other reptiles NOS
  - +7th **T63.192 Toxic effect of venom of other reptiles, intentional self-harm**
  - +7th **T63.193 Toxic effect of venom of other reptiles, assault**
  - +7th **T63.194 Toxic effect of venom of other reptiles, undetermined**

+ **T63.2 Toxic effect of venom of scorpion**

+ **T63.2X Toxic effect of venom of scorpion**
  - +7th **T63.2X1 Toxic effect of venom of scorpion, accidental (unintentional)**
    Toxic effect of venom of scorpion NOS
  - +7th **T63.2X2 Toxic effect of venom of scorpion, intentional self-harm**
  - +7th **T63.2X3 Toxic effect of venom of scorpion, assault**
  - +7th **T63.2X4 Toxic effect of venom of scorpion, undetermined**

+ **T63.3 Toxic effect of venom of spider**

+ **T63.30 Toxic effect of unspecified spider venom**
  - +7th **T63.301 Toxic effect of unspecified spider venom, accidental (unintentional)**
  - +7th **T63.302 Toxic effect of unspecified spider venom, intentional self-harm**
  - +7th **T63.303 Toxic effect of unspecified spider venom, assault**
  - +7th **T63.304 Toxic effect of unspecified spider venom, undetermined**

+ **T63.31 Toxic effect of venom of black widow spider**
  - +7th **T63.311 Toxic effect of venom of black widow spider, accidental (unintentional)**
  - +7th **T63.312 Toxic effect of venom of black widow spider, intentional self-harm**
  - +7th **T63.313 Toxic effect of venom of black widow spider, assault**
  - +7th **T63.314 Toxic effect of venom of black widow spider, undetermined**

+ **T63.32 Toxic effect of venom of tarantula**
  - +7th **T63.321 Toxic effect of venom of tarantula, accidental (unintentional)**
  - +7th **T63.322 Toxic effect of venom of tarantula, intentional self-harm**
  - +7th **T63.323 Toxic effect of venom of tarantula, assault**
  - +7th **T63.324 Toxic effect of venom of tarantula, undetermined**

+ **T63.33 Toxic effect of venom of brown recluse spider**
  - +7th **T63.331 Toxic effect of venom of brown recluse spider, accidental (unintentional)**
  - +7th **T63.332 Toxic effect of venom of brown recluse spider, intentional self-harm**
  - +7th **T63.333 Toxic effect of venom of brown recluse spider, assault**
  - +7th **T63.334 Toxic effect of venom of brown recluse spider, undetermined**

+ **T63.39 Toxic effect of venom of other spider**
  - +7th **T63.391 Toxic effect of venom of other spider, accidental (unintentional)**
  - +7th **T63.392 Toxic effect of venom of other spider, intentional self-harm**
  - +7th **T63.393 Toxic effect of venom of other spider, assault**
  - +7th **T63.394 Toxic effect of venom of other spider, undetermined**

+ **T63.4 Toxic effect of venom of other arthropods**

+ **T63.41 Toxic effect of venom of centipedes and venomous millipedes**
  - +7th **T63.411 Toxic effect of venom of centipedes and venomous millipedes, accidental (unintentional)**
  - +7th **T63.412 Toxic effect of venom of centipedes and venomous millipedes, intentional self-harm**
  - +7th **T63.413 Toxic effect of venom of centipedes and venomous millipedes, assault**
  - +7th **T63.414 Toxic effect of venom of centipedes and venomous millipedes, undetermined**

+ **T63.42 Toxic effect of venom of ants**
  - +7th **T63.421 Toxic effect of venom of ants, accidental (unintentional)**
  - +7th **T63.422 Toxic effect of venom of ants, intentional self-harm**
  - +7th **T63.423 Toxic effect of venom of ants, assault**
  - +7th **T63.424 Toxic effect of venom of ants, undetermined**

+ **T63.43 Toxic effect of venom of caterpillars**
  - +7th **T63.431 Toxic effect of venom of caterpillars, accidental (unintentional)**
  - +7th **T63.432 Toxic effect of venom of caterpillars, intentional self-harm**
  - +7th **T63.433 Toxic effect of venom of caterpillars, assault**
  - +7th **T63.434 Toxic effect of venom of caterpillars, undetermined**

+ **T63.44 Toxic effect of venom of bees**
  - +7th **T63.441 Toxic effect of venom of bees, accidental (unintentional)**
  - +7th **T63.442 Toxic effect of venom of bees, intentional self-harm**
  - +7th **T63.443 Toxic effect of venom of bees, assault**
  - +7th **T63.444 Toxic effect of venom of bees, undetermined**

+ **T63.45** **Toxic effect of venom of hornets**
- +7th **T63.451** **Toxic effect of venom of hornets, accidental (unintentional)**
- +7th **T63.452** **Toxic effect of venom of hornets, intentional self-harm**
- +7th **T63.453** **Toxic effect of venom of hornets, assault**
- +7th **T63.454** **Toxic effect of venom of hornets, undetermined**

+ **T63.46** **Toxic effect of venom of wasps**
  Toxic effect of yellow jacket
- +7th **T63.461** **Toxic effect of venom of wasps, accidental (unintentional)**
- +7th **T63.462** **Toxic effect of venom of wasps, intentional self-harm**
- +7th **T63.463** **Toxic effect of venom of wasps, assault**
- +7th **T63.464** **Toxic effect of venom of wasps, undetermined**

+ **T63.48** **Toxic effect of venom of other arthropod**
- +7th **T63.481** **Toxic effect of venom of other arthropod, accidental (unintentional)**
- +7th **T63.482** **Toxic effect of venom of other arthropod, intentional self-harm**
- +7th **T63.483** **Toxic effect of venom of other arthropod, assault**
- +7th **T63.484** **Toxic effect of venom of other arthropod, undetermined**

+ **T63.5** **Toxic effect of contact with venomous fish**
  Excludes2: *poisoning by ingestion of fish (T61.-)*

+ **T63.51** **Toxic effect of contact with stingray**
- +7th **T63.511** **Toxic effect of contact with stingray, accidental (unintentional)**
- +7th **T63.512** **Toxic effect of contact with stingray, intentional self-harm**
- +7th **T63.513** **Toxic effect of contact with stingray, assault**
- +7th **T63.514** **Toxic effect of contact with stingray, undetermined**

+ **T63.59** **Toxic effect of contact with other venomous fish**
- +7th **T63.591** **Toxic effect of contact with other venomous fish, accidental (unintentional)**
- +7th **T63.592** **Toxic effect of contact with other venomous fish, intentional self-harm**
- +7th **T63.593** **Toxic effect of contact with other venomous fish, assault**
- +7th **T63.594** **Toxic effect of contact with other venomous fish, undetermined**

+ **T63.6** **Toxic effect of contact with other venomous marine animals**
  Excludes1: *sea-snake venom (T63.09)*
  Excludes2: *poisoning by ingestion of shellfish (T61.78-)*

+ **T63.61** **Toxic effect of contact with Portugese Man-o-war**
  Toxic effect of contact with bluebottle
- +7th **T63.611** **Toxic effect of contact with Portugese Man-o-war, accidental (unintentional)**
- +7th **T63.612** **Toxic effect of contact with Portugese Man-o-war, intentional self-harm**
- +7th **T63.613** **Toxic effect of contact with Portugese Man-o-war, assault**
- +7th **T63.614** **Toxic effect of contact with Portugese Man-o-war, undetermined**

+ **T63.62** **Toxic effect of contact with other jellyfish**
- +7th **T63.621** **Toxic effect of contact with other jellyfish, accidental (unintentional)**
- +7th **T63.622** **Toxic effect of contact with other jellyfish, intentional self-harm**
- +7th **T63.623** **Toxic effect of contact with other jellyfish, assault**
- +7th **T63.624** **Toxic effect of contact with other jellyfish, undetermined**

+ **T63.63** **Toxic effect of contact with sea anemone**
- +7th **T63.631** **Toxic effect of contact with sea anemone, accidental (unintentional)**
- +7th **T63.632** **Toxic effect of contact with sea anemone, intentional self-harm**
- +7th **T63.633** **Toxic effect of contact with sea anemone, assault**
- +7th **T63.634** **Toxic effect of contact with sea anemone, undetermined**

+ **T63.69** **Toxic effect of contact with other venomous marine animals**
- +7th **T63.691** **Toxic effect of contact with other venomous marine animals, accidental (unintentional)**
- +7th **T63.692** **Toxic effect of contact with other venomous marine animals, intentional self-harm**
- +7th **T63.693** **Toxic effect of contact with other venomous marine animals, assault**
- +7th **T63.694** **Toxic effect of contact with other venomous marine animals, undetermined**

+ **T63.7** **Toxic effect of contact with venomous plant**

+ **T63.71** **Toxic effect of contact with venomous marine plant**
- +7th **T63.711** **Toxic effect of contact with venomous marine plant, accidental (unintentional)**
- +7th **T63.712** **Toxic effect of contact with venomous marine plant, intentional self-harm**
- +7th **T63.713** **Toxic effect of contact with venomous marine plant, assault**
- +7th **T63.714** **Toxic effect of contact with venomous marine plant, undetermined**

+ **T63.79** **Toxic effect of contact with other venomous plant**
- +7th **T63.791** **Toxic effect of contact with other venomous plant, accidental (unintentional)**
- +7th **T63.792** **Toxic effect of contact with other venomous plant, intentional self-harm**
- +7th **T63.793** **Toxic effect of contact with other venomous plant, assault**
- +7th **T63.794** **Toxic effect of contact with other venomous plant, undetermined**

+ **T63.8** **Toxic effect of contact with other venomous animals**

+ **T63.81** **Toxic effect of contact with venomous frog**
  Excludes1: *contact with nonvenomous frog (W62.0)*
- +7th **T63.811** **Toxic effect of contact with venomous frog, accidental (unintentional)**
- +7th **T63.812** **Toxic effect of contact with venomous frog, intentional self-harm**
- +7th **T63.813** **Toxic effect of contact with venomous frog, assault**
- +7th **T63.814** **Toxic effect of contact with venomous frog, undetermined**

+ **T63.82** **Toxic effect of contact with venomous toad**
  Excludes1: *contact with nonvenomous toad (W62.1)*
- +7th **T63.821** **Toxic effect of contact with venomous toad, accidental (unintentional)**
- +7th **T63.822** **Toxic effect of contact with venomous toad, intentional self-harm**
- +7th **T63.823** **Toxic effect of contact with venomous toad, assault**
- +7th **T63.824** **Toxic effect of contact with venomous toad, undetermined**

+ **T63.83** **Toxic effect of contact with other venomous amphibian**
  Excludes1: *contact with nonvenomous amphibian (W62.9)*
- +7th **T63.831** **Toxic effect of contact with other venomous amphibian, accidental (unintentional)**
- +7th **T63.832** **Toxic effect of contact with other venomous amphibian, intentional self-harm**
- +7th **T63.833** **Toxic effect of contact with other venomous amphibian, assault**
- +7th **T63.834** **Toxic effect of contact with other venomous amphibian, undetermined**

+ **T63.89** **Toxic effect of contact with other venomous animals**
- +7th **T63.891** **Toxic effect of contact with other venomous animals, accidental (unintentional)**
- +7th **T63.892** **Toxic effect of contact with other venomous animals, intentional self-harm**
- +7th **T63.893** **Toxic effect of contact with other venomous animals, assault**
- +7th **T63.894** **Toxic effect of contact with other venomous animals, undetermined**

+ **T63.9** **Toxic effect of contact with unspecified venomous animal**
- X+7th **T63.91** **Toxic effect of contact with unspecified venomous animal, accidental (unintentional)**
- X+7th **T63.92** **Toxic effect of contact with unspecified venomous animal, intentional self-harm**
- X+7th **T63.93** **Toxic effect of contact with unspecified venomous animal, assault**
- X+7th **T63.94** **Toxic effect of contact with unspecified venomous animal, undetermined**

T64 Toxic effect of aflatoxin and other mycotoxin food contaminants

The appropriate 7th character is to be added to each code from category T64
A initial encounter
D subsequent encounter
S sequela

+ **T64.0 Toxic effect of aflatoxin**
X+7th **T64.01 Toxic effect of aflatoxin, accidental (unintentional)**
X+7th **T64.02 Toxic effect of aflatoxin, intentional self-harm**
X+7th **T64.03 Toxic effect of aflatoxin, assault**
X+7th **T64.04 Toxic effect of aflatoxin, undetermined**
+ **T64.8 Toxic effect of other mycotoxin food contaminants**
X+7th **T64.81 Toxic effect of other mycotoxin food contaminants, accidental (unintentional)**
X+7th **T64.82 Toxic effect of other mycotoxin food contaminants, intentional self-harm**
X+7th **T64.83 Toxic effect of other mycotoxin food contaminants, assault**
X+7th **T64.84 Toxic effect of other mycotoxin food contaminants, undetermined**

T65 Toxic effect of other and unspecified substances

The appropriate 7th character is to be added to each code from category T65
A initial encounter
D subsequent encounter
S sequela

+ **T65.0 Toxic effect of cyanides**
Excludes1: *hydrogen cyanide (T57.3-)*
+ **T65.0X Toxic effect of cyanides**
+7th **T65.0X1 Toxic effect of cyanides, accidental (unintentional)**
Toxic effect of cyanides NOS
+7th **T65.0X2 Toxic effect of cyanides, intentional self-harm**
+7th **T65.0X3 Toxic effect of cyanides, assault**
+7th **T65.0X4 Toxic effect of cyanides, undetermined**
+ **T65.1 Toxic effect of strychnine and its salts**
+ **T65.1X Toxic effect of strychnine and its salts**
+7th **T65.1X1 Toxic effect of strychnine and its salts, accidental (unintentional)**
Toxic effect of strychnine and its salts NOS
+7th **T65.1X2 Toxic effect of strychnine and its salts, intentional self-harm**
+7th **T65.1X3 Toxic effect of strychnine and its salts, assault**
+7th **T65.1X4 Toxic effect of strychnine and its salts, undetermined**
+ **T65.2 Toxic effect of tobacco and nicotine**
Excludes2: *nicotine dependence (F17.-)*
+ **T65.21 Toxic effect of chewing tobacco**
+7th **T65.211 Toxic effect of chewing tobacco, accidental (unintentional)**
Toxic effect of chewing tobacco NOS
+7th **T65.212 Toxic effect of chewing tobacco, intentional self-harm**
+7th **T65.213 Toxic effect of chewing tobacco, assault**
+7th **T65.214 Toxic effect of chewing tobacco, undetermined**
+ **T65.22 Toxic effect of tobacco cigarettes**
Toxic effect of tobacco smoke
Use additional code for exposure to second hand tobacco smoke (Z57.31, Z77.22)
+7th **T65.221 Toxic effect of tobacco cigarettes, accidental (unintentional)**
Toxic effect of tobacco cigarettes NOS
+7th **T65.222 Toxic effect of tobacco cigarettes, intentional self-harm**
+7th **T65.223 Toxic effect of tobacco cigarettes, assault**
+7th **T65.224 Toxic effect of tobacco cigarettes, undetermined**
+ **T65.29 Toxic effect of other tobacco and nicotine**
+7th **T65.291 Toxic effect of other tobacco and nicotine, accidental (unintentional)**
Toxic effect of other tobacco and nicotine NOS
+7th **T65.292 Toxic effect of other tobacco and nicotine, intentional self-harm**
+7th **T65.293 Toxic effect of other tobacco and nicotine, assault**
+7th **T65.294 Toxic effect of other tobacco and nicotine, undetermined**

+ **T65.3 Toxic effect of nitroderivatives and aminoderivatives of benzene and its homologues**
Toxic effect of anilin [benzenamine]
Toxic effect of nitrobenzene
Toxic effect of trinitrotoluene
+ **T65.3X Toxic effect of nitroderivatives and aminoderivatives of benzene and its homologues**
+7th **T65.3X1 Toxic effect of nitroderivatives and aminoderivatives of benzene and its homologues, accidental (unintentional)**
Toxic effect of nitroderivatives and aminoderivatives of benzene and its homologues NOS
+7th **T65.3X2 Toxic effect of nitroderivatives and aminoderivatives of benzene and its homologues, intentional self-harm**
+7th **T65.3X3 Toxic effect of nitroderivatives and aminoderivatives of benzene and its homologues, assault**
+7th **T65.3X4 Toxic effect of nitroderivatives and aminoderivatives of benzene and its homologues, undetermined**
+ **T65.4 Toxic effect of carbon disulfide**
+ **T65.4X Toxic effect of carbon disulfide**
+7th **T65.4X1 Toxic effect of carbon disulfide, accidental (unintentional)**
Toxic effect of carbon disulfide NOS
+7th **T65.4X2 Toxic effect of carbon disulfide, intentional self-harm**
+7th **T65.4X3 Toxic effect of carbon disulfide, assault**
+7th **T65.4X4 Toxic effect of carbon disulfide, undetermined**
+ **T65.5 Toxic effect of nitroglycerin and other nitric acids and esters**
Toxic effect of 1,2,3-Propanetriol trinitrate
+ **T65.5X Toxic effect of nitroglycerin and other nitric acids and esters**
+7th **T65.5X1 Toxic effect of nitroglycerin and other nitric acids and esters, accidental (unintentional)**
Toxic effect of nitroglycerin and other nitric acids and esters NOS
+7th **T65.5X2 Toxic effect of nitroglycerin and other nitric acids and esters, intentional self-harm**
+7th **T65.5X3 Toxic effect of nitroglycerin and other nitric acids and esters, assault**
+7th **T65.5X4 Toxic effect of nitroglycerin and other nitric acids and esters, undetermined**
+ **T65.6 Toxic effect of paints and dyes, not elsewhere classified**
+ **T65.6X Toxic effect of paints and dyes, not elsewhere classified**
+7th **T65.6X1 Toxic effect of paints and dyes, not elsewhere classified, accidental (unintentional)**
Toxic effect of paints and dyes NOS
+7th **T65.6X2 Toxic effect of paints and dyes, not elsewhere classified, intentional self-harm**
+7th **T65.6X3 Toxic effect of paints and dyes, not elsewhere classified, assault**
+7th **T65.6X4 Toxic effect of paints and dyes, not elsewhere classified, undetermined**
+ **T65.8 Toxic effect of other specified substances**
+ **T65.81 Toxic effect of latex**
+7th **T65.811 Toxic effect of latex, accidental (unintentional)**
Toxic effect of latex NOS
+7th **T65.812 Toxic effect of latex, intentional self-harm**
+7th **T65.813 Toxic effect of latex, assault**
+7th **T65.814 Toxic effect of latex, undetermined**
+ **T65.82 Toxic effect of harmful algae and algae toxins**
Toxic effect of (harmful) algae bloom NOS
Toxic effect of blue-green algae bloom
Toxic effect of brown tide
Toxic effect of cyanobacteria bloom
Toxic effect of Florida red tide
Toxic effect of pfiesteria piscicida
Toxic effect of red tide
+7th **T65.821 Toxic effect of harmful algae and algae toxins, accidental (unintentional)**
Toxic effect of harmful algae and algae toxins NOS
+7th **T65.822 Toxic effect of harmful algae and algae toxins, intentional self-harm**
+7th **T65.823 Toxic effect of harmful algae and algae toxins, assault**
+7th **T65.824 Toxic effect of harmful algae and algae toxins, undetermined**

+ **T65.83 Toxic effect of fiberglass**
+7th **T65.831 Toxic effect of fiberglass, accidental (unintentional)**
Toxic effect of fiberglass NOS
+7th **T65.832 Toxic effect of fiberglass, intentional self-harm**
+7th **T65.833 Toxic effect of fiberglass, assault**
+7th **T65.834 Toxic effect of fiberglass, undetermined**
+ **T65.89 Toxic effect of other specified substances**
+7th **T65.891 Toxic effect of other specified substances, accidental (unintentional)**
Toxic effect of other specified substances NOS
+7th **T65.892 Toxic effect of other specified substances, intentional self-harm**
+7th **T65.893 Toxic effect of other specified substances, assault**
+7th **T65.894 Toxic effect of other specified substances, undetermined**
+ **T65.9 Toxic effect of unspecified substance**
X+7th **T65.91 Toxic effect of unspecified substance, accidental (unintentional)**
Poisoning NOS
X+7th **T65.92 Toxic effect of unspecified substance, intentional self-harm**
X+7th **T65.93 Toxic effect of unspecified substance, assault**
X+7th **T65.94 Toxic effect of unspecified substance, undetermined**

Other and unspecified effects of external causes (T66-T78)

7th **T66 Radiation sickness, unspecified**

Excludes1: *specified adverse effects of radiation, such as:*
burns (T20-T31)
leukemia (C91-C95)
radiation gastroenteritis and colitis (K52.0)
radiation pneumonitis (J70.0)
radiation related disorders of the skin and subcutaneous tissue (L55-L59)
sunburn (L55.-)

The appropriate 7th character is to be added to code T66
A initial encounter
D subsequent encounter
S sequela

T67 Effects of heat and light

Excludes1: *erythema [dermatitis] ab igne (L59.0)*
malignant hyperpyrexia due to anesthesia (T88.3)
radiation-related disorders of the skin and subcutaneous tissue (L55-L59)
Excludes2: *burns (T20-T31)*
sunburn (L55.-)
sweat disorder due to heat (L74-L75)

The appropriate 7th character is to be added to each code from category T67
A initial encounter
D subsequent encounter
S sequela

CC X+7th **T67.0 Heatstroke and sunstroke**
Heat apoplexy
Heat pyrexia
Siriasis
Thermoplegia
Use additional code(s) to identify any associated complications of heatstroke, such as:
coma and stupor (R40.-)
systemic inflammatory response syndrome (R65.1-)
CC Exclusion 7th character A see Appendix A PDX collection 1419
HAC 7th character A see Appendix B for HAC conditional logic
X+7th **T67.1 Heat syncope**
Heat collapse
X+7th **T67.2 Heat cramp**
X+7th **T67.3 Heat exhaustion, anhydrotic**
Heat prostration due to water depletion
Excludes1: *heat exhaustion due to salt depletion (T67.4)*
X+7th **T67.4 Heat exhaustion due to salt depletion**
Heat prostration due to salt (and water) depletion
X+7th **T67.5 Heat exhaustion, unspecified**
Heat prostration NOS
X+7th **T67.6 Heat fatigue, transient**
X+7th **T67.7 Heat edema**
X+7th **T67.8 Other effects of heat and light**
X+7th **T67.9 Effect of heat and light, unspecified**

X+7th **T68 Hypothermia**
Accidental hypothermia
Hypothermia NOS
Use additional code to identify source of exposure:
Exposure to excessive cold of man-made origin (W93)
Exposure to excessive cold of natural origin (X31)
Excludes1: *hypothermia following anesthesia (T88.51)*
hypothermia not associated with low environmental temperature (R68.0)
hypothermia of newborn (P80.-)
Excludes2: *frostbite (T33-T34)*

The appropriate 7th character is to be added to code T68
A initial encounter
D subsequent encounter
S sequela

T69 Other effects of reduced temperature

Use additional code to identify source of exposure:
Exposure to excessive cold of man-made origin (W93)
Exposure to excessive cold of natural origin (X31)
Excludes2: *frostbite (T33-T34)*

The appropriate 7th character is to be added to each code from category T69
A initial encounter
D subsequent encounter
S sequela

+ **T69.0 Immersion hand and foot**
+ **T69.01 Immersion hand**
+7th **T69.011 Immersion hand, right hand**
+7th **T69.012 Immersion hand, left hand**
+7th **T69.019 Immersion hand, unspecified hand**
+ **T69.02 Immersion foot**
Trench foot
CC +7th **T69.021 Immersion foot, right foot**
CC Exclusion 7th character A see Appendix A PDX collection 1420
HAC 7th character A see Appendix B for HAC conditional logic
CC +7th **T69.022 Immersion foot, left foot**
CC Exclusion 7th character A see Appendix A PDX collection 1420
HAC 7th character A see Appendix B for HAC conditional logic
CC +7th **T69.029 Immersion foot, unspecified foot**
CC Exclusion 7th character A see Appendix A PDX collection 1420
HAC 7th character A see Appendix B for HAC conditional logic
X+7th **T69.1 Chilblains**
X+7th **T69.8 Other specified effects of reduced temperature**
X+7th **T69.9 Effect of reduced temperature, unspecified**

T70 Effects of air pressure and water pressure

The appropriate 7th character is to be added to each code from category T70
A initial encounter
D subsequent encounter
S sequela

X+7th **T70.0 Otitic barotrauma**
Aero-otitis media
Effects of change in ambient atmospheric pressure or water pressure on ears
X+7th **T70.1 Sinus barotrauma**
Aerosinusitis
Effects of change in ambient atmospheric pressure on sinuses
+ **T70.2 Other and unspecified effects of high altitude**
Excludes2: *polycythemia due to high altitude (D75.1)*
X+7th **T70.20 Unspecified effects of high altitude**
X+7th **T70.29 Other effects of high altitude**
Alpine sickness
Anoxia due to high altitude
Barotrauma NOS
Hypobaropathy
Mountain sickness
CC X+7th **T70.3 Caisson disease [decompression sickness]**
Compressed-air disease
Diver's palsy or paralysis
CC Exclusion 7th character A see Appendix A PDX collection 1421
HAC 7th character A see Appendix B for HAC conditional logic

X+7th **T70.4 Effects of high-pressure fluids**
Hydraulic jet injection (industrial)
Pneumatic jet injection (industrial)
Traumatic jet injection (industrial)

X+7th **T70.8 Other effects of air pressure and water pressure**

X+7th **T70.9 Effect of air pressure and water pressure, unspecified**

T71 Asphyxiation
Mechanical suffocation
Traumatic suffocation
Excludes1: *acute respiratory distress (syndrome) (J80)*
anoxia due to high altitude (T70.2)
asphyxia NOS (R09.01)
asphyxia from carbon monoxide (T58.-)
asphyxia from inhalation of food or foreign body (T17.-)
asphyxia from other gases, fumes and vapors (T59.-)
respiratory distress (syndrome) in newborn (P22.-)

The appropriate 7th character is to be added to each code from category T71
A initial encounter
D subsequent encounter
S sequela

\+ **T71.1 Asphyxiation due to mechanical threat to breathing**
Suffocation due to mechanical threat to breathing

\+ **T71.11 Asphyxiation due to smothering under pillow**

CC +7th **T71.111 Asphyxiation due to smothering under pillow, accidental**
Asphyxiation due to smothering under pillow NOS
CC Exclusion 7th character A see Appendix A PDX collection 1422
HAC 7th character A see Appendix B for HAC conditional logic

CC +7th **T71.112 Asphyxiation due to smothering under pillow, intentional self-harm**
CC Exclusion 7th character A see Appendix A PDX collection 1422
HAC 7th character A see Appendix B for HAC conditional logic

CC +7th **T71.113 Asphyxiation due to smothering under pillow, assault**
CC Exclusion 7th character A see Appendix A PDX collection 1422
HAC 7th character A see Appendix B for HAC conditional logic

CC +7th **T71.114 Asphyxiation due to smothering under pillow, undetermined**
CC Exclusion 7th character A see Appendix A PDX collection 1422
HAC 7th character A see Appendix B for HAC conditional logic

\+ **T71.12 Asphyxiation due to plastic bag**

CC +7th **T71.121 Asphyxiation due to plastic bag, accidental**
Asphyxiation due to plastic bag NOS
CC Exclusion 7th character A see Appendix A PDX collection 1422
HAC 7th character A see Appendix B for HAC conditional logic

CC +7th **T71.122 Asphyxiation due to plastic bag, intentional self-harm**
CC Exclusion 7th character A see Appendix A PDX collection 1422
HAC 7th character A see Appendix B for HAC conditional logic

CC +7th **T71.123 Asphyxiation due to plastic bag, assault**
CC Exclusion 7th character A see Appendix A PDX collection 1422
HAC 7th character A see Appendix B for HAC conditional logic

CC +7th **T71.124 Asphyxiation due to plastic bag, undetermined**
CC Exclusion 7th character A see Appendix A PDX collection 1422
HAC 7th character A see Appendix B for HAC conditional logic

\+ **T71.13 Asphyxiation due to being trapped in bed linens**

CC +7th **T71.131 Asphyxiation due to being trapped in bed linens, accidental**
Asphyxiation due to being trapped in bed linens NOS
CC Exclusion 7th character A see Appendix A PDX collection 1422
HAC 7th character A see Appendix B for HAC conditional logic

CC +7th **T71.132 Asphyxiation due to being trapped in bed linens, intentional self-harm**
CC Exclusion 7th character A see Appendix A PDX collection 1422
HAC 7th character A see Appendix B for HAC conditional logic

CC +7th **T71.133 Asphyxiation due to being trapped in bed linens, assault**
CC Exclusion 7th character A see Appendix A PDX collection 1422
HAC 7th character A see Appendix B for HAC conditional logic

CC +7th **T71.134 Asphyxiation due to being trapped in bed linens, undetermined**
CC Exclusion 7th character A see Appendix A PDX collection 1422
HAC 7th character A see Appendix B for HAC conditional logic

\+ **T71.14 Asphyxiation due to smothering under another person's body (in bed)**

CC +7th **T71.141 Asphyxiation due to smothering under another person's body (in bed), accidental**
Asphyxiation due to smothering under anoth[er] person's body (in bed) NOS
CC Exclusion 7th character A see Appendix A PDX collection 1422
HAC 7th character A see Appendix B for HAC conditional logic

CC +7th **T71.143 Asphyxiation due to smothering under another person's body (in bed), assault**
CC Exclusion 7th character A see Appendix A PDX collection 1422
HAC 7th character A see Appendix B for HAC conditional logic

CC +7th **T71.144 Asphyxiation due to smothering under another person's body (in bed), undetermined**
CC Exclusion 7th character A see Appendix A PDX collection 1422
HAC 7th character A see Appendix B for HAC conditional logic

\+ **T71.15 Asphyxiation due to smothering in furniture**

CC +7th **T71.151 Asphyxiation due to smothering in furniture, accidental**
Asphyxiation due to smothering in furniture NOS
CC Exclusion 7th character A see Appendix A PDX collection 1422
HAC 7th character A see Appendix B for HAC conditional logic

CC +7th **T71.152 Asphyxiation due to smothering in furniture, intentional self-harm**
CC Exclusion 7th character A see Appendix A PDX collection 1422
HAC 7th character A see Appendix B for HAC conditional logic

CC +7th **T71.153 Asphyxiation due to smothering in furniture, assault**
CC Exclusion 7th character A see Appendix A PDX collection 1422
HAC 7th character A see Appendix B for HAC conditional logic

CC +7th **T71.154 Asphyxiation due to smothering in furniture, undetermined**
CC Exclusion 7th character A see Appendix A PDX collection 1422
HAC 7th character A see Appendix B for HAC conditional logic

+ **T71.16 Asphyxiation due to hanging**
Hanging by window shade cord
Use additional code for any associated injuries, such as:
crushing injury of neck (S17.-)
fracture of cervical vertebrae (S12.0-S12.2-)
open wound of neck (S11.-)

CC +7th **T71.161 Asphyxiation due to hanging, accidental**
Asphyxiation due to hanging NOS
Hanging NOS
CC Exclusion 7th character A see Appendix A PDX collection 1422
HAC 7th character A see Appendix B for HAC conditional logic

CC +7th **T71.162 Asphyxiation due to hanging, intentional self-harm**
CC Exclusion 7th character A see Appendix A PDX collection 1422
HAC 7th character A see Appendix B for HAC conditional logic

CC +7th **T71.163 Asphyxiation due to hanging, assault**
CC Exclusion 7th character A see Appendix A PDX collection 1422
HAC 7th character A see Appendix B for HAC conditional logic

CC +7th **T71.164 Asphyxiation due to hanging, undetermined**
CC Exclusion 7th character A see Appendix A PDX collection 1422
HAC 7th character A see Appendix B for HAC conditional logic

+ **T71.19 Asphyxiation due to mechanical threat to breathing due to other causes**

CC +7th **T71.191 Asphyxiation due to mechanical threat to breathing due to other causes, accidental**
Asphyxiation due to other causes NOS
CC Exclusion 7th character A see Appendix A PDX collection 1422
HAC 7th character A see Appendix B for HAC conditional logic

CC +7th **T71.192 Asphyxiation due to mechanical threat to breathing due to other causes, intentional self-harm**
CC Exclusion 7th character A see Appendix A PDX collection 1422
HAC 7th character A see Appendix B for HAC conditional logic

CC +7th **T71.193 Asphyxiation due to mechanical threat to breathing due to other causes, assault**
CC Exclusion 7th character A see Appendix A PDX collection 1422
HAC 7th character A see Appendix B for HAC conditional logic

CC +7th **T71.194 Asphyxiation due to mechanical threat to breathing due to other causes, undetermined**
CC Exclusion 7th character A see Appendix A PDX collection 1422
HAC 7th character A see Appendix B for HAC conditional logic

+ **T71.2 Asphyxiation due to systemic oxygen deficiency due to low oxygen content in ambient air**
Suffocation due to systemic oxygen deficiency due to low oxygen content in ambient air

CC X+7th **T71.20 Asphyxiation due to systemic oxygen deficiency due to low oxygen content in ambient air due to unspecified cause**
CC Exclusion 7th character A see Appendix A PDX collection 1422
HAC 7th character A see Appendix B for HAC conditional logic

CC X+7th **T71.21 Asphyxiation due to cave-in or falling earth**
Use additional code for any associated cataclysm (X34-X38)
CC Exclusion 7th character A see Appendix A PDX collection 1422
HAC 7th character A see Appendix B for HAC conditional logic

+ **T71.22 Asphyxiation due to being trapped in a car trunk**

CC +7th **T71.221 Asphyxiation due to being trapped in a car trunk, accidental**
CC Exclusion 7th character A see Appendix A PDX collection 1422

CC +7th **T71.222 Asphyxiation due to being trapped in a car trunk, intentional self-harm**
CC Exclusion 7th character A see Appendix A PDX collection 1422

CC +7th **T71.223 Asphyxiation due to being trapped in a car trunk, assault**
CC Exclusion 7th character A see Appendix A PDX collection 1422

CC +7th **T71.224 Asphyxiation due to being trapped in a car trunk, undetermined**
CC Exclusion 7th character A see Appendix A PDX collection 1422

+ **T71.23 Asphyxiation due to being trapped in a (discarded) refrigerator**

CC +7th **T71.231 Asphyxiation due to being trapped in a (discarded) refrigerator, accidental**
CC Exclusion 7th character A see Appendix A PDX collection 1422

CC +7th **T71.232 Asphyxiation due to being trapped in a (discarded) refrigerator, intentional self-harm**
CC Exclusion 7th character A see Appendix A PDX collection 1422

CC +7th **T71.233 Asphyxiation due to being trapped in a (discarded) refrigerator, assault**
CC Exclusion 7th character A see Appendix A PDX collection 1422

CC +7th **T71.234 Asphyxiation due to being trapped in a (discarded) refrigerator, undetermined**
CC Exclusion 7th character A see Appendix A PDX collection 1422

CC X+7th **T71.29 Asphyxiation due to being trapped in other low oxygen environment**
CC Exclusion 7th character A see Appendix A PDX collection 1422
HAC 7th character A see Appendix B for HAC conditional logic

CC X+7th **T71.9 Asphyxiation due to unspecified cause**
Suffocation (by strangulation) due to unspecified cause
Suffocation NOS
Systemic oxygen deficiency due to low oxygen content in ambient air due to unspecified cause
Systemic oxygen deficiency due to mechanical threat to breathing due to unspecified cause
Traumatic asphyxia NOS
CC Exclusion 7th character A see Appendix A PDX collection 1422
HAC 7th character A see Appendix B for HAC conditional logic

T73 Effects of other deprivation

The appropriate 7th character is to be added to each code from category T73
A initial encounter
D subsequent encounter
S sequela

T73.0 Starvation
Deprivation of food

X+7th **T73.1 Deprivation of water**
X+7th **T73.2 Exhaustion due to exposure**
X+7th **T73.3 Exhaustion due to excessive exertion**
Exhaustion due to overexertion
X+7th **T73.8 Other effects of deprivation**
X+7th **T73.9 Effect of deprivation, unspecified**

T74 Adult and child abuse, neglect and other maltreatment, confirmed
Use additional code, if applicable, to identify any associated current injury external cause code to identify perpetrator, if known (Y07.-)
Excludes1: *abuse and maltreatment in pregnancy (O9A.3-, O9A.4-, O9A.5-)*
adult and child maltreatment, suspected (T76.-)

The appropriate 7th character is to be added to each code from category T74
A initial encounter
D subsequent encounter
S sequela

Review coding guideline C.19.f

+ **T74.0 Neglect or abandonment, confirmed**

• CC X+7th **T74.01 Adult neglect or abandonment, confirmed**
CC Exclusion 7th character A see Appendix A PDX collection 1423

• CC X+7th **T74.02 Child neglect or abandonment, confirmed**
CC Exclusion 7th character A see Appendix A PDX collection 1423

+ **T74.1 Physical abuse, confirmed**
Excludes2: *sexual abuse (T74.2-)*

• CC X+7th **T74.11 Adult physical abuse, confirmed**
CC Exclusion 7th character A see Appendix A PDX collection 1423

• CC X+7th **T74.12 Child physical abuse, confirmed**
Excludes2: *shaken infant syndrome (T74.4)*
CC Exclusion 7th character A see Appendix A PDX collection 1423

\+ **T74.2 Sexual abuse, confirmed**
Rape, confirmed
Sexual assault, confirmed

• CC X+7th **T74.21 Adult sexual abuse, confirmed**
CC Exclusion 7th character A see Appendix A PDX collection 1423

• CC X+7th **T74.22 Child sexual abuse, confirmed**
CC Exclusion 7th character A see Appendix A PDX collection 1423

\+ **T74.3 Psychological abuse, confirmed**
CC Exclusion 7th character A see Appendix A PDX collection 1423

• X+7th **T74.31 Adult psychological abuse, confirmed**
CC Exclusion 7th character A see Appendix A PDX collection 1423

• CC X+7th **T74.32 Child psychological abuse, confirmed**
CC Exclusion 7th character A see Appendix A PDX collection 1423

• CC X+7th **T74.4 Shaken infant syndrome**
CC Exclusion 7th character A see Appendix A PDX collection 1423

\+ **T74.9 Unspecified maltreatment, confirmed**

• CC X+7th **T74.91 Unspecified adult maltreatment, confirmed**
CC Exclusion 7th character A see Appendix A PDX collection 1424

• CC X+7th **T74.92 Unspecified child maltreatment, confirmed**
CC Exclusion 7th character A see Appendix A PDX collection 1423

T75 Other and unspecified effects of other external causes

Excludes1: *adverse effects NEC (T78.-)*
Excludes2: *burns (electric) (T20-T31)*

The appropriate 7th character is to be added to each code from category T75
A initial encounter
D subsequent encounter
S sequela

\+ **T75.0 Effects of lightning**
Struck by lightning

X+7th **T75.00 Unspecified effects of lightning**
Struck by lightning NOS

X+7th **T75.01 Shock due to being struck by lightning**

X+7th **T75.09 Other effects of lightning**
Use additional code for other effects of lightning

CC X+7th **T75.1 Unspecified effects of drowning and nonfatal submersion**
Immersion
Excludes1: *specified effects of drowning- code to effects*
CC Exclusion 7th character A see Appendix A PDX collection 1425
HAC 7th character A see Appendix B for HAC conditional logic

\+ **T75.2 Effects of vibration**

X+7th **T75.20 Unspecified effects of vibration**

X+7th **T75.21 Pneumatic hammer syndrome**

X+7th **T75.22 Traumatic vasospastic syndrome**

X+7th **T75.23 Vertigo from infrasound**
Excludes1: *vertigo NOS (R42)*

X+7th **T75.29 Other effects of vibration**

X+7th **T75.3 Motion sickness**
Airsickness
Seasickness
Travel sickness
Use additional external cause code to identify vehicle or type of motion (Y92.81-, Y93.5-)

X+7th **T75.4 Electrocution**
Shock from electric current
Shock from electroshock gun (taser)

\+ **T75.8 Other specified effects of external causes**

X+7th **T75.81 Effects of abnormal gravitation [G] forces**

X+7th **T75.82 Effects of weightlessness**

X+7th **T75.89 Other specified effects of external causes**

T76 Adult and child abuse, neglect and other maltreatment, suspected

Use additional code, if applicable, to identify any associated current injur
Excludes1: adult and child maltreatment, confirmed (T74.-)
suspected abuse and maltreatment in pregnancy (O9A.3-, O9A.4-, O9A.5-)
suspected adult physical abuse, ruled out (Z04.71)
suspected adult sexual abuse, ruled out (Z04.41)
suspected child physical abuse, ruled out (Z04.72)
suspected child sexual abuse, ruled out (Z04.42)

The appropriate 7th character is to be added to each code from category T7
A initial encounter
D subsequent encounter
S sequela

Review coding guideline C.19.f

\+ **T76.0 Neglect or abandonment, suspected**

• CC X+7th **T76.01 Adult neglect or abandonment, suspected**
CC Exclusion 7th character A see Appendix A PDX collection 1423

• CC X+7th **T76.02 Child neglect or abandonment, suspected**
CC Exclusion 7th character A see Appendix A PDX collection 1423

\+ **T76.1 Physical abuse, suspected**

• CC X+7th **T76.11 Adult physical abuse, suspected**
CC Exclusion 7th character A see Appendix A PDX collection 1423

• CC X+7th **T76.12 Child physical abuse, suspected**
CC Exclusion 7th character A see Appendix A PDX collection 1423

\+ **T76.2 Sexual abuse, suspected**
Rape, suspected
Sexual abuse, suspected
Excludes1: *alleged abuse, ruled out (Z04.7)*

• CC X+7th **T76.21 Adult sexual abuse, suspected**
CC Exclusion 7th character A see Appendix A PDX collection 1423

• CC X+7th **T76.22 Child sexual abuse, suspected**
CC Exclusion 7th character A see Appendix A PDX collection 1423

\+ **T76.3 Psychological abuse, suspected**

• X+7th **T76.31 Adult psychological abuse, suspected**

• CC X+7th **T76.32 Child psychological abuse, suspected**
CC Exclusion 7th character A see Appendix A PDX collection 1423

\+ **T76.9 Unspecified maltreatment, suspected**

• CC X+7th **T76.91 Unspecified adult maltreatment, suspected**
CC Exclusion 7th character A see Appendix A PDX collection 1424

• CC X+7th **T76.92 Unspecified child maltreatment, suspected**
CC Exclusion 7th character A see Appendix A PDX collection 1423

T78 Adverse effects, not elsewhere classified

Excludes2: *complications of surgical and medical care NEC (T80-T88)*

The appropriate 7th character is to be added to each code from category T78
A initial encounter
D subsequent encounter
S sequela

\+ **T78.0 Anaphylactic reaction due to food**
Anaphylactic reaction due to adverse food reaction
Anaphylactic shock or reaction due to nonpoisonous foods
Anaphylactoid reaction due to food

CC X+7th **T78.00 Anaphylactic reaction due to unspecified food**
CC Exclusion 7th character A see Appendix A PDX collection 1426

CC X+7th **T78.01 Anaphylactic reaction due to peanuts**
CC Exclusion 7th character A see Appendix A PDX collection 1426

CC X+7th **T78.02 Anaphylactic reaction due to shellfish (crustaceans)**
CC Exclusion 7th character A see Appendix A PDX collection 1426

CC X+7th **T78.03 Anaphylactic reaction due to other fish**
CC Exclusion 7th character A see Appendix A PDX collection 1426

CC X+7th **T78.04 Anaphylactic reaction due to fruits and vegetables**
CC Exclusion 7th character A see Appendix A PDX collection 1426

CC X+7th **T78.05 Anaphylactic reaction due to tree nuts and seeds**
Excludes1: *anaphylactic reaction due to peanuts (T78.01)*
CC Exclusion 7th character A see Appendix A PDX collection 1426

CC X+7th **T78.06 Anaphylactic reaction due to food additives**
CC Exclusion 7th character A see Appendix A PDX collection 1426

CC X+7th **T78.07 Anaphylactic reaction due to milk and dairy products**
CC Exclusion 7th character A see Appendix A PDX collection 1426

CC X+7th **T78.08 Anaphylactic reaction due to eggs**
CC Exclusion 7th character A see Appendix A PDX collection 1426

CC X+7th **T78.09 Anaphylactic reaction due to other food products**
CC Exclusion 7th character A see Appendix A PDX collection 1426

X+7th **T78.1 Other adverse food reactions, not elsewhere classified**
Use additional code to identify the type of reaction
Excludes1: *anaphylactic reaction or shock due to adverse food reaction (T78.0-)*
anaphylactic reaction due to food (T78.0-)
bacterial food borne intoxications (A05.-)
Excludes2: *allergic and dietetic gastroenteritis and colitis (K52.2)*
allergic rhinitis due to food (J30.5)
dermatitis due to food in contact with skin (L23.6, L24.6, L25.4)
dermatitis due to ingested food (L27.2)

CC X+7th **T78.2 Anaphylactic shock, unspecified**
Allergic shock
Anaphylactic reaction
Anaphylaxis
Excludes1: *anaphylactic reaction or shock due to adverse effect of correct medicinal substance properly administered (T88.6)*
anaphylactic reaction or shock due to adverse food reaction (T78.0-)
anaphylactic reaction or shock due to serum (T80.5-)
CC Exclusion 7th character A see Appendix A PDX collection 1426

X+7th **T78.3 Angioneurotic edema**
Allergic angioedema
Giant urticaria
Quincke's edema
Excludes1: *serum urticaria (T80.6-)*
urticaria (L50.-)

\+ **T78.4 Other and unspecified allergy**
Excludes1: *specified types of allergic reaction such as:*
allergic diarrhea (K52.2)
allergic gastroenteritis and colitis (K52.2)
dermatitis (L23-L25, L27.-)
hay fever (J30.1)

X+7th **T78.40 Allergy, unspecified**
Allergic reaction NOS
Hypersensitivity NOS

X+7th **T78.41 Arthus phenomenon**
Arthus reaction

X+7th **T78.49 Other allergy**

X+7th **T78.8 Other adverse effects, not elsewhere classified**

Certain early complications of trauma (T79)

T79 Certain early complications of trauma, not elsewhere classified
Excludes2: *acute respiratory distress syndrome (J80)*
complications occurring during or following medical procedures (T80-T88)
complications of surgical and medical care NEC (T80-T88)
newborn respiratory distress syndrome (P22.0)

The appropriate 7th character is to be added to each code from category T79
A initial encounter
D subsequent encounter
S sequela

CC X+7th **T79.0 Air embolism (traumatic)**
Excludes1: *air embolism complicating abortion or ectopic or molar pregnancy (O00-O07, O08.2)*
air embolism complicating pregnancy, childbirth and the puerperium (O88.0)
air embolism following infusion, transfusion, and therapeutic injection (T80.0)
air embolism following procedure NEC (T81.7-)
MCC Exclusion 7th character A see Appendix A PDX collection 1427

CC X+7th **T79.1 Fat embolism (traumatic)**
Excludes1: *fat embolism complicating:*
abortion or ectopic or molar pregnancy (O00-O07, O08.2)
pregnancy, childbirth and the puerperium (O88.8)
MCC Exclusion 7th character A see Appendix A PDX collection 1428

CC X+7th **T79.2 Traumatic secondary and recurrent hemorrhage and seroma**
CC Exclusion 7th character A see Appendix A PDX collection 1429

MCC X+7th **T79.4 Traumatic shock**
Shock (immediate) (delayed) following injury
Excludes1: *anaphylactic shock due to adverse food reaction (T78.0-)*
anaphylactic shock due to correct medicinal substance properly administered (T88.6)
anaphylactic shock due to serum (T80.5-)
anaphylactic shock NOS (T78.2)
anesthetic shock (T88.2)
electric shock (T75.4)
nontraumatic shock NEC (R57.-)
obstetric shock (O75.1)
postprocedural shock (T81.1-)
septic shock (R65.21)
shock complicating abortion or ectopic or molar pregnancy (O00-O07, O08.3)
shock due to lightning (T75.01)
shock NOS (R57.9)
MCC Exclusion 7th character A see Appendix A PDX collection 1430

MCC X+7th **T79.5 Traumatic anuria**
Crush syndrome
Renal failure following crushing
MCC Exclusion 7th character A see Appendix A PDX collection 1431

X+7th **T79.6 Traumatic ischemia of muscle**
Traumatic rhabdomyolysis
Volkmann's ischemic contracture
Excludes2: *anterior tibial syndrome (M76.8)*
compartment syndrome (traumatic) (T79.A-)
nontraumatic ischemia of muscle (M62.2-)

CC X+7th **T79.7 Traumatic subcutaneous emphysema**
Excludes1: *emphysema NOS (J43)*
emphysema (subcutaneous) resulting from a procedure (T81.82)
CC Exclusion 7th character A see Appendix A PDX collection 1432

\+ **T79.A Traumatic compartment syndrome**
Excludes1: *fibromyalgia (M79.7)*
nontraumatic compartment syndrome (M79.A-)
traumatic ischemic infarction of muscle (T79.6)

CC X+7th **T79.A0 Compartment syndrome, unspecified**
Compartment syndrome NOS
CC Exclusion 7th character A see Appendix A PDX collection 0896

\+ **T79.A1 Traumatic compartment syndrome of upper extremity**
Traumatic compartment syndrome of shoulder, arm, forearm, wrist, hand, and fingers

CC +7th **T79.A11 Traumatic compartment syndrome of right upper extremity**
CC Exclusion 7th character A see Appendix A PDX collection 1433

CC +7th **T79.A12 Traumatic compartment syndrome of left upper extremity**
CC Exclusion 7th character A see Appendix A PDX collection 1433

CC +7th **T79.A19 Traumatic compartment syndrome of unspecified upper extremity**
CC Exclusion 7th character A see Appendix A PDX collection 1433

\+ **T79.A2 Traumatic compartment syndrome of lower extremity**
Traumatic compartment syndrome of hip, buttock, thigh, leg, foot, and toes

CC +7th **T79.A21 Traumatic compartment syndrome of right lower extremity**
CC Exclusion 7th character A see Appendix A PDX collection 1433

CC +7th **T79.A22 Traumatic compartment syndrome of left lower extremity**
CC Exclusion 7th character A see Appendix A PDX collection 1433

CC +7th **T79.A29 Traumatic compartment syndrome of unspecified lower extremity**
CC Exclusion 7th character A see Appendix A PDX collection 1433

CC X+7th **T79.A3 Traumatic compartment syndrome of abdomen**
CC Exclusion 7th character A see Appendix A PDX collection 1434

CC X+7th **T79.A9 Traumatic compartment syndrome of other sites**
CC Exclusion 7th character A see Appendix A PDX collection 0896

X+7th **T79.8 Other early complications of trauma**

X+7th **T79.9 Unspecified early complication of trauma**

Complications of surgical and medical care, not elsewhere classified (T80-T88)

Use additional code for adverse effect, if applicable, to identify drug (T36-T50 with fifth or sixth character 5)

Use additional code(s) to identify the specified condition resulting from the complication

Use additional code to identify devices involved and details of circumstances (Y62-Y82)

Excludes2: *any encounters with medical care for postprocedural conditions in which no complications are present, such as:*
artificial opening status (Z93.-)
closure of external stoma (Z43.-)
fitting and adjustment of external prosthetic device (Z44.-)
burns and corrosions from local applications and irradiation (T20-T32)
complications of surgical procedures during pregnancy, childbirth and the puerperium (O00-O9A)
mechanical complication of respirator [ventilator] (J95.850)
poisoning and toxic effects of drugs and chemicals (T36-T65 with fifth or sixth character 1-4 or 6)
postprocedural fever (R50.82)
specified complications classified elsewhere, such as:
cerebrospinal fluid leak from spinal puncture (G97.0)
colostomy malfunction (K94.0-)
disorders of fluid and electrolyte imbalance (E86-E87)
functional disturbances following cardiac surgery (I97.0-I97.1)
intraoperative and postprocedural complications of specified body systems (D78.-, E36.-, E89.-, G97.3-, G97.4, H59.3-, H59.-, H95.2-, H95.3, I97.4-, I97.5, J95.6-, J95.7, K91.6-, L76.-, M96.-, N99.-)
ostomy complications (J95.0-, K94.-, N99.5-)
postgastric surgery syndromes (K91.1)
postlaminectomy syndrome NEC (M96.1)
postmastectomy lymphedema syndrome (I97.2)
postsurgical blind-loop syndrome (K91.2)
ventilator associated pneumonia (J95.851)

T80 Complications following infusion, transfusion and therapeutic injection

Includes: complications following perfusion
Excludes2: *bone marrow transplant rejection (T86.01)*
febrile nonhemolytic transfusion reaction (R50.84)
fluid overload due to transfusion (E87.71)
posttransfusion purpura (D69.51)
transfusion associated circulatory overload (TACO) (E87.71)
transfusion (red blood cell) associated hemochromatosis (E83.111)
transfusion related acute lung injury (TRALI) (J95.84)

The appropriate 7th character is to be added to each code from category T80
A initial encounter
D subsequent encounter
S sequela

MCC X+7th **T80.0 Air embolism following infusion, transfusion and therapeutic injection**
MCC Exclusion 7th character A see Appendix A PDX collection 1435
HAC 7th character A see Appendix B for HAC conditional logic

CC X+7th **T80.1 Vascular complications following infusion, transfusion and therapeutic injection**
Use additional code to identify the vascular complication
Excludes2: *extravasation of vesicant agent (T80.81-)*
infiltration of vesicant agent (T80.81-)
vascular complications specified as due to prosthetic devices, implants and grafts (T82.8-, T83.8, T84.8-, T85.8)
postprocedural vascular complications (T81.7-)
CC Exclusion 7th character A see Appendix A PDX collection 1436

\+ **T80.2 Infections following infusion, transfusion and therapeutic injection**
Use additional code to identify the specific infection, such as: sepsis (A41.9)
Use additional code (R65.2-) to identify severe sepsis, if applicable
Excludes2: *infections specified as due to prosthetic devices, implants and grafts (T82.6-T82.7, T83.5-T83.6, T84.5-T84.7, T85.7)*
postprocedural infections (T81.4)
Review coding guideline C.1.d.5

\+ **T80.21 Infection due to central venous catheter**

CC +7th **T80.211 Bloodstream infection due to central venous catheter**
Catheter-related bloodstream infection (CRBSI) NOS
Central line-associated bloodstream infection (CLABSI)
Bloodstream infection due to Hickman catheter
Bloodstream infection due to peripherally inserted central catheter (PICC)
Bloodstream infection due to portacath (port-a-cath)
Bloodstream infection due to triple lumen catheter
Bloodstream infection due to umbilical venous catheter
CC Exclusion 7th character A see Appendix A PDX collection 0948
HAC 7th character A see Appendix B for HAC conditional logic

CC +7th **T80.212 Local infection due to central venous catheter**
Exit or insertion site infection
Local infection due to Hickman catheter
Local infection due to peripherally inserted central catheter (PICC)
Local infection due to portacath (port-a-cath)
Local infection due to triple lumen catheter
Local infection due to umbilical venous catheter
Port or reservoir infection
Tunnel infection
CC Exclusion 7th character A see Appendix A PDX collection 0948
HAC 7th character A see Appendix B for HAC conditional logic

CC +7th **T80.218 Other infection due to central venous catheter**
Other central line-associated infection
Other infection due to Hickman catheter
Other infection due to peripherally inserted central catheter (PICC)
Other infection due to portacath (port-a-cath)
Other infection due to triple lumen catheter
Other infection due to umbilical venous catheter
CC Exclusion 7th character A see Appendix A PDX collection 0948
HAC 7th character A see Appendix B for HAC conditional logic

CC +7th **T80.219 Unspecified infection due to central venous catheter**
Central line-associated infection NOS
Unspecified infection due to Hickman catheter
Unspecified infection due to peripherally inserted central catheter (PICC)
Unspecified infection due to portacath (port-a-cath)
Unspecified infection due to triple lumen catheter
Unspecified infection due to umbilical venous catheter
CC Exclusion 7th character A see Appendix A PDX collection 0948
HAC 7th character A see Appendix B for HAC conditional logic

CC X+7th **T80.22 Acute infection following transfusion, infusion, or injection of blood and blood products**
CC Exclusion 7th character A see Appendix A PDX collection 0948

CC X+7th **T80.29 Infection following other infusion, transfusion and therapeutic injection**
CC Exclusion 7th character A see Appendix A PDX collection 0948

\+ **T80.3 ABO incompatibility reaction due to transfusion of blood or blood products**
Excludes1: *minor blood group antigens reactions (Duffy) (E) (K(ell)) (Kidd) (Lewis) (M) (N) (P) (S) (T80.A)*

CC X+7th **T80.30 ABO incompatibility reaction due to transfusion of blood or blood products, unspecified**
ABO incompatibility blood transfusion NOS
Reaction to ABO incompatibility from transfusion NOS
CC Exclusion 7th character A see Appendix A PDX collection 1437
HAC 7th character A see Appendix B for HAC conditional logic

\+ **T80.31 ABO incompatibility with hemolytic transfusion reaction**

CC +7th **T80.310 ABO incompatibility with acute hemolytic transfusion reaction**
ABO incompatibility with hemolytic transfusion reaction less than 24 hours after transfusion
Acute hemolytic transfusion reaction (AHTR) due to ABO incompatibility
CC Exclusion 7th character A see Appendix A PDX collection 1437
HAC 7th character A see Appendix B for HAC conditional logic

CC +7th **T80.311 ABO incompatibility with delayed hemolytic transfusion reaction**
ABO incompatibility with hemolytic transfusion reaction 24 hours or more after transfusion
Delayed hemolytic transfusion reaction (DHTR) due to ABO incompatibility
CC Exclusion 7th character A see Appendix A PDX collection 1437
HAC 7th character A see Appendix B for HAC conditional logic

CC +7th **T80.319 ABO incompatibility with hemolytic transfusion reaction, unspecified**
ABO incompatibility with hemolytic transfusion reaction at unspecified time after transfusion
Hemolytic transfusion reaction (HTR) due to ABO incompatibility NOS
CC Exclusion 7th character A see Appendix A PDX collection 1437
HAC 7th character A see Appendix B for HAC conditional logic

CC X+7th **T80.39 Other ABO incompatibility reaction due to transfusion of blood or blood products**
Delayed serologic transfusion reaction (DSTR) from ABO incompatibility
Other ABO incompatible blood transfusion
Other reaction to ABO incompatible blood transfusion
CC Exclusion 7th character A see Appendix A PDX collection 1437
HAC 7th character A see Appendix B for HAC conditional logic

\+ **T80.4 Rh incompatibility reaction due to transfusion of blood or blood products**
Reaction due to incompatibility of Rh antigens (C) (c) (D) (E) (e)

CC X+7th **T80.40 Rh incompatibility reaction due to transfusion of blood or blood products, unspecified**
Reaction due to Rh factor in transfusion NOS
Rh incompatible blood transfusion NOS
CC Exclusion 7th character A see Appendix A PDX collection 1437

\+ **T80.41 Rh incompatibility with hemolytic transfusion reaction**

CC +7th **T80.410 Rh incompatibility with acute hemolytic transfusion reaction**
Acute hemolytic transfusion reaction (AHTR) due to Rh incompatibility
Rh incompatibility with hemolytic transfusion reaction less than 24 hours after transfusion
CC Exclusion 7th character A see Appendix A PDX collection 1437

CC +7th **T80.411 Rh incompatibility with delayed hemolytic transfusion reaction**
Delayed hemolytic transfusion reaction (DHTR) due to Rh incompatibility
Rh incompatibility with hemolytic transfusion reaction 24 hours or more after transfusion
CC Exclusion 7th character A see Appendix A PDX collection 1437

CC +7th **T80.419 Rh incompatibility with hemolytic transfusion reaction, unspecified**
Rh incompatibility with hemolytic transfusion reaction at unspecified time after transfusion
Hemolytic transfusion reaction (HTR) due to Rh incompatibility NOS
CC Exclusion 7th character A see Appendix A PDX collection 1437

CC X+7th **T80.49 Other Rh incompatibility reaction due to transfusion of blood or blood products**
Delayed serologic transfusion reaction (DSTR) from Rh incompatibility
Other reaction to Rh incompatible blood transfusion
CC Exclusion 7th character A see Appendix A PDX collection 1438

\+ **T80.A Non-ABO incompatibility reaction due to transfusion of blood or blood products**
Reaction due to incompatibility of minor antigens (Duffy) (Kell) (Kidd) (Lewis) (M) (N) (P) (S)

CC X+7th **T80.A0 Non-ABO incompatibility reaction due to transfusion of blood or blood products, unspecified**
Non-ABO antigen incompatibility reaction from transfusion NOS
CC Exclusion 7th character A see Appendix A PDX collection 1438

\+ **T80.A1 Non-ABO incompatibility with hemolytic transfusion reaction**

CC +7th **T80.A10 Non-ABO incompatibility with acute hemolytic transfusion reaction**
Acute hemolytic transfusion reaction (AHTR) due to non-ABO incompatibility
Non-ABO incompatibility with hemolytic transfusion reaction less than 24 hours after transfusion
CC Exclusion 7th character A see Appendix A PDX collection 1438

CC +7th **T80.A11 Non-ABO incompatibility with delayed hemolytic transfusion reaction**
Delayed hemolytic transfusion reaction (DHTR) due to non-ABO incompatibility
Non-ABO incompatibility with hemolytic transfusion reaction 24 or more hours after transfusion
CC Exclusion 7th character A see Appendix A PDX collection 1438

CC +7th **T80.A19 Non-ABO incompatibility with hemolytic transfusion reaction, unspecified**
Hemolytic transfusion reaction (HTR) due to non-ABO incompatibility NOS
Non-ABO incompatibility with hemolytic transfusion reaction at unspecified time after transfusion
CC Exclusion 7th character A see Appendix A PDX collection 1438

CC X+7th **T80.A9 Other non-ABO incompatibility reaction due to transfusion of blood or blood products**
Delayed serologic transfusion reaction (DSTR) from non-ABO incompatibility
Other reaction to non-ABO incompatible blood transfusion
CC Exclusion 7th character A see Appendix A PDX collection 1437

\+ **T80.5 Anaphylactic reaction due to serum**
Allergic shock due to serum
Anaphylactic shock due to serum
Anaphylactoid reaction due to serum
Anaphylaxis due to serum
Excludes1: *ABO incompatibility reaction due to transfusion of blood or blood products (T80.3-)*
allergic reaction or shock NOS (T78.2)
anaphylactic reaction or shock NOS (T78.2)
anaphylactic reaction or shock due to adverse effect of correct medicinal substance properly administered (T88.6)
other serum reaction (T80.6-)

CC X+7th **T80.51 Anaphylactic reaction due to administration of blood and blood products**
CC Exclusion 7th character A see Appendix A PDX collection 1439

CC X+7th **T80.52 Anaphylactic reaction due to vaccination**
CC Exclusion 7th character A see Appendix A PDX collection 1439

CC X+7th **T80.59 Anaphylactic reaction due to other serum**
CC Exclusion 7th character A see Appendix A PDX collection 1439

\+ **T80.6 Other serum reactions**
Intoxication by serum
Protein sickness
Serum rash
Serum sickness
Serum urticaria
Excludes2: *serum hepatitis (B16.-)*

CC X+7th **T80.61 Other serum reaction due to administration of blood and blood products**
CC Exclusion 7th character A see Appendix A PDX collection 1439

CC X+7th **T80.62 Other serum reaction due to vaccination**
CC Exclusion 7th character A see Appendix A PDX collection 1439

CC X+7th **T80.69 Other serum reaction due to other serum**
CC Exclusion 7th character A see Appendix A PDX collection 1440

\+ **T80.8 Other complications following infusion, transfusion and therapeutic injection**

\+ **T80.81 Extravasation of vesicant agent**
Infiltration of vesicant agent

CC +7th **T80.810 Extravasation of vesicant antineoplastic chemotherapy**
Infiltration of vesicant antineoplastic chemotherapy
CC Exclusion 7th character A see Appendix A PDX collection 1436

CC +7th **T80.818 Extravasation of other vesicant agent**
Infiltration of other vesicant agent
CC Exclusion 7th character A see Appendix A PDX collection 1436

X+7th **T80.89 Other complications following infusion, transfusion and therapeutic injection**
Delayed serologic transfusion reaction (DSTR), unspecified incompatibility
Use additional code to identify graft-versus-host reaction, if applicable, (D89.81-)

\+ **T80.9 Unspecified complication following infusion, transfusion and therapeutic injection**

X+7th **T80.90 Unspecified complication following infusion and therapeutic injection**

\+ **T80.91 Hemolytic transfusion reaction, unspecified incompatibility**
Excludes1: *ABO incompatibility with hemolytic transfusion reaction (T80.31-)*
Non-ABO incompatibility with hemolytic transfusion reaction (T80.A1-)
Rh incompatibility with hemolytic transfusion reaction (T80.41-)

CC +7th **T80.910 Acute hemolytic transfusion reaction, unspecified incompatibility**
CC Exclusion 7th character A see Appendix A PDX collection 1437

CC +7th **T80.911 Delayed hemolytic transfusion reaction, unspecified incompatibility**
CC Exclusion 7th character A see Appendix A PDX collection 1437

CC +7th **T80.919 Hemolytic transfusion reaction, unspecified incompatibility, unspecified as acute or delayed**
Hemolytic transfusion reaction NOS
CC Exclusion 7th character A see Appendix A PDX collection 1437

X+7th **T80.92 Unspecified transfusion reaction**
Transfusion reaction NOS

T81 Complications of procedures, not elsewhere classified
Use additional code for adverse effect, if applicable, to identify drug (T36-T50 with fifth or sixth character 5)
Excludes2: *complications following immunization (T88.0-T88.1)*
complications following infusion, transfusion and therapeutic injection (T80.-)
complications of transplanted organs and tissue (T86.-)
specified complications classified elsewhere, such as:
complication of prosthetic devices, implants and grafts (T82-T85)
dermatitis due to drugs and medicaments (L23.3, L24.4, L25.1, L27.0-L27.1)
endosseous dental implant failure (M27.6-)
floppy iris syndrome (IFIS) (intraoperative) H21.81
intraoperative and postprocedural complications of specific body system (D78.-, E36.-, E89.-, G97.3-, G97.4, H59.3-, H59.-, H95.2-, H95.3, I97.4-, I97.5, J95, K91.-, L76.-, M96.-, N99.-)
ostomy complications (J95.0-, K94.-, N99.5-)
plateau iris syndrome (post-iridectomy) (postprocedural) H21.82
poisoning and toxic effects of drugs and chemicals (T36-T65 with fifth or sixth character 1-4 or 6)

The appropriate 7th character is to be added to each code from category T81
A initial encounter
D subsequent encounter
S sequela

\+ **T81.1 Postprocedural shock**
Shock during or resulting from a procedure, not elsewhere classified
Excludes1: *anaphylactic shock NOS (T78.2)*
anaphylactic shock due to correct substance properly administered (T88.6)
anaphylactic shock due to serum (T80.5-)
anesthetic shock (T88.2)
electric shock (T75.4)
obstetric shock (O75.1)
septic shock (R65.21)
shock following abortion or ectopic or molar pregnancy (O00-O07, O08.3)
traumatic shock (T79.4)

CC X+7th **T81.10 Postprocedural shock unspecified**
Collapse NOS during or resulting from a procedure, not elsewhere classified
Postprocedural failure of peripheral circulation
Postprocedural shock NOS
CC Exclusion 7th character A see Appendix A PDX collection 1441

MCC X+7th **T81.11 Postprocedural cardiogenic shock**
MCC Exclusion 7th character A see Appendix A PDX collection 1441

MCC X+7th **T81.12 Postprocedural septic shock**
Postprocedural endotoxic shock during or resulting from a procedure, not elsewhere classified
Postprocedural gram-negative shock during or resulting from a procedure, not elsewhere classified
Code first underlying infection
Use additional code, to identify any associated acute organ dysfunction, if applicable
MCC Exclusion 7th character A see Appendix A PDX collection 1441
Review coding guideline C.1.d.2

MCC X+7th **T81.19 Other postprocedural shock**
Postprocedural hypovolemic shock
MCC Exclusion 7th character A see Appendix A PDX collection 1441

+ T81.3 Disruption of wound, not elsewhere classified
Disruption of any suture materials or other closure methods
Excludes1: *breakdown (mechanical) of permanent sutures (T85.612)*
displacement of permanent sutures (T85.622)
disruption of cesarean delivery wound (O90.0)
disruption of perineal obstetric wound (O90.1)
mechanical complication of permanent sutures NEC (T85.692)
AHA CC: 1Q, 2014, 23

CC X+7th **T81.30 Disruption of wound, unspecified**
Disruption of wound NOS
CC Exclusion 7th character A see Appendix A PDX collection 1442

CC X+7th **T81.31 Disruption of external operation (surgical) wound, not elsewhere classified**
Dehiscence of operation wound NOS
Disruption of operation wound NOS
Disruption or dehiscence of closure of cornea
Disruption or dehiscence of closure of mucosa
Disruption or dehiscence of closure of skin and subcutaneous tissue
Full-thickness skin disruption or dehiscence
Superficial disruption or dehiscence of operation wound
Excludes1: *dehiscence of amputation stump (T87.81)*
CC Exclusion 7th character A see Appendix A PDX collection 1442

CC X+7th **T81.32 Disruption of internal operation (surgical) wound, not elsewhere classified**
Deep disruption or dehiscence of operation wound NOS
Disruption or dehiscence of closure of internal organ or other internal tissue
Disruption or dehiscence of closure of muscle or muscle flap
Disruption or dehiscence of closure of ribs or rib cage
Disruption or dehiscence of closure of skull or craniotomy
Disruption or dehiscence of closure of sternum or sternotomy
Disruption or dehiscence of closure of tendon or ligament
Disruption or dehiscence of closure of superficial or muscular fascia
CC Exclusion 7th character A see Appendix A PDX collection 1442

CC X+7th **T81.33 Disruption of traumatic injury wound repair**
Disruption or dehiscence of closure of traumatic laceration (external) (internal)
CC Exclusion 7th character A see Appendix A PDX collection 1442

C X+7th **T81.4 Infection following a procedure**
Intra-abdominal abscess following a procedure
Postprocedural infection, not elsewhere classified
Sepsis following a procedure
Stitch abscess following a procedure
Subphrenic abscess following a procedure
Wound abscess following a procedure
Use additional code to identify infection
Use additional code (R65.2-) to identify severe sepsis, if applicable
Excludes1: *obstetric surgical wound infection (O86.0)*
postprocedural fever NOS (R50.82)
postprocedural retroperitoneal abscess (K68.11)
Excludes2: *bleb associated endophthalmitis (H59.4-)*
infection due to infusion, transfusion and therapeutic injection (T80.2-)
infection due to prosthetic devices, implants and grafts (T82.6-T82.7, T83.5-T83.6, T84.5-T84.7, T85.7)
CC Exclusion 7th character A see Appendix A PDX collection 0805
HAC 7th character A see Appendix B for HAC conditional logic
AHA CC: 1Q, 2014, 23
Review coding guideline C.1.d.5

+ T81.5 Complications of foreign body accidentally left in body following procedure

+ T81.50 Unspecified complication of foreign body accidentally left in body following procedure

CC +7th **T81.500 Unspecified complication of foreign body accidentally left in body following surgical operation**
CC Exclusion 7th character A see Appendix A PDX collection 1443
HAC 7th character A see Appendix B for HAC conditional logic

CC +7th **T81.501 Unspecified complication of foreign body accidentally left in body following infusion or transfusion**
CC Exclusion 7th character A see Appendix A PDX collection 1443
HAC 7th character A see Appendix B for HAC conditional logic

CC +7th **T81.502 Unspecified complication of foreign body accidentally left in body following kidney dialysis**
CC Exclusion 7th character A see Appendix A PDX collection 1443
HAC 7th character A see Appendix B for HAC conditional logic

CC +7th **T81.503 Unspecified complication of foreign body accidentally left in body following injection or immunization**
CC Exclusion 7th character A see Appendix A PDX collection 1443
HAC 7th character A see Appendix B for HAC conditional logic

CC +7th **T81.504 Unspecified complication of foreign body accidentally left in body following endoscopic examination**
CC Exclusion 7th character A see Appendix A PDX collection 1443
HAC 7th character A see Appendix B for HAC conditional logic

CC +7th **T81.505 Unspecified complication of foreign body accidentally left in body following heart catheterization**
CC Exclusion 7th character A see Appendix A PDX collection 1443
HAC 7th character A see Appendix B for HAC conditional logic

CC +7th **T81.506 Unspecified complication of foreign body accidentally left in body following aspiration, puncture or other catheterization**
CC Exclusion 7th character A see Appendix A PDX collection 1443
HAC 7th character A see Appendix B for HAC conditional logic

CC +7th **T81.507 Unspecified complication of foreign body accidentally left in body following removal of catheter or packing**
CC Exclusion 7th character A see Appendix A PDX collection 1443
HAC 7th character A see Appendix B for HAC conditional logic

CC +7th **T81.508 Unspecified complication of foreign body accidentally left in body following other procedure**
CC Exclusion 7th character A see Appendix A PDX collection 1443
HAC 7th character A see Appendix B for HAC conditional logic

CC +7th **T81.509 Unspecified complication of foreign body accidentally left in body following unspecified procedure**
CC Exclusion 7th character A see Appendix A PDX collection 1443
HAC 7th character A see Appendix B for HAC conditional logic

+ T81.51 Adhesions due to foreign body accidentally left in body following procedure

CC +7th **T81.510 Adhesions due to foreign body accidentally left in body following surgical operation**
CC Exclusion 7th character A see Appendix A PDX collection 1443
HAC 7th character A see Appendix B for HAC conditional logic

CC +7th **T81.511 Adhesions due to foreign body accidentally left in body following infusion or transfusion**
CC Exclusion 7th character A see Appendix A PDX collection 1443
HAC 7th character A see Appendix B for HAC conditional logic

CC +7th **T81.512 Adhesions due to foreign body accidentally left in body following kidney dialysis**
CC Exclusion 7th character A see Appendix A PDX collection 1443
HAC 7th character A see Appendix B for HAC conditional logic

CC +7th **T81.513 Adhesions due to foreign body accidentally left in body following injection or immunization**
CC Exclusion 7th character A see Appendix A PDX collection 1443
HAC 7th character A see Appendix B for HAC conditional logic

CC +7th **T81.514 Adhesions due to foreign body accidentally left in body following endoscopic examination**
CC Exclusion 7th character A see Appendix A PDX collection 1443
HAC 7th character A see Appendix B for HAC conditional logic

CC +7th **T81.515 Adhesions due to foreign body accidentally left in body following heart catheterization**
CC Exclusion 7th character A see Appendix A PDX collection 1443
HAC 7th character A see Appendix B for HAC conditional logic

CC +7th **T81.516 Adhesions due to foreign body accidentally left in body following aspiration, puncture or other catheterization**
CC Exclusion 7th character A see Appendix A PDX collection 1443
HAC 7th character A see Appendix B for HAC conditional logic

CC +7th **T81.517 Adhesions due to foreign body accidentally left in body following removal of catheter or packing**
CC Exclusion 7th character A see Appendix A PDX collection 1443
HAC 7th character A see Appendix B for HAC conditional logic

CC +7th **T81.518 Adhesions due to foreign body accidentally left in body following other procedure**
CC Exclusion 7th character A see Appendix A PDX collection 1443
HAC 7th character A see Appendix B for HAC conditional logic

CC +7th **T81.519 Adhesions due to foreign body accidentally left in body following unspecified procedure**
CC Exclusion 7th character A see Appendix A PDX collection 1443
HAC 7th character A see Appendix B for HAC conditional logic

+ T81.52 Obstruction due to foreign body accidentally left in body following procedure

CC +7th **T81.520 Obstruction due to foreign body accidentally left in body following surgical operation**
CC Exclusion 7th character A see Appendix A PDX collection 1443
HAC 7th character A see Appendix B for HAC conditional logic

CC +7th **T81.521 Obstruction due to foreign body accidentally left in body following infusion or transfusion**
CC Exclusion 7th character A see Appendix A PDX collection 1443
HAC 7th character A see Appendix B for HAC conditional logic

CC +7th **T81.522 Obstruction due to foreign body accidentally left in body following kidney dialysis**
CC Exclusion 7th character A see Appendix A PDX collection 1443
HAC 7th character A see Appendix B for HAC conditional logic

CC +7th **T81.523 Obstruction due to foreign body accidentally left in body following injection or immunization**
CC Exclusion 7th character A see Appendix A PDX collection 1443
HAC 7th character A see Appendix B for HAC conditional logic

CC +7th **T81.524 Obstruction due to foreign body accidentally left in body following endoscopic examination**
CC Exclusion 7th character A see Appendix A PDX collection 1443
HAC 7th character A see Appendix B for HAC conditional logic

CC +7th **T81.525 Obstruction due to foreign body accidentally left in body following heart catheterization**
CC Exclusion 7th character A see Appendix A PDX collection 1443
HAC 7th character A see Appendix B for HAC conditional logic

CC +7th **T81.526 Obstruction due to foreign body accidental left in body following aspiration, puncture other catheterization**
CC Exclusion 7th character A see Appendix A PDX collection 1443
HAC 7th character A see Appendix B for HAC conditional logic

CC +7th **T81.527 Obstruction due to foreign body accidental left in body following removal of catheter o packing**
CC Exclusion 7th character A see Appendix A PDX collection 1443
HAC 7th character A see Appendix B for HAC conditional logic

CC +7th **T81.528 Obstruction due to foreign body accidental left in body following other procedure**
CC Exclusion 7th character A see Appendix A PDX collection 1443
HAC 7th character A see Appendix B for HAC conditional logic

CC +7th **T81.529 Obstruction due to foreign body accidental left in body following unspecified procedure**
CC Exclusion 7th character A see Appendix A PDX collection 1443
HAC 7th character A see Appendix B for HAC conditional logic

+ T81.53 Perforation due to foreign body accidentally left in body following procedure

CC +7th **T81.530 Perforation due to foreign body accidentally left in body following surgical operation**
CC Exclusion 7th character A see Appendix A PDX collection 1443
HAC 7th character A see Appendix B for HAC conditional logic

CC +7th **T81.531 Perforation due to foreign body accidentally left in body following infusion or transfusio**
CC Exclusion 7th character A see Appendix A PDX collection 1443
HAC 7th character A see Appendix B for HAC conditional logic

+7th **T81.532 Perforation due to foreign body accidentally left in body following kidney dialysis**
CC Exclusion 7th character A see Appendix A PDX collection 1443
HAC 7th character A see Appendix B for HAC conditional logic

CC +7th **T81.533 Perforation due to foreign body accidentally left in body following injection or immunization**
CC Exclusion 7th character A see Appendix A PDX collection 1443
HAC 7th character A see Appendix B for HAC conditional logic

CC +7th **T81.534 Perforation due to foreign body accidentally left in body following endoscopic examination**
CC Exclusion 7th character A see Appendix A PDX collection 1443
HAC 7th character A see Appendix B for HAC conditional logic

CC +7th **T81.535 Perforation due to foreign body accidentally left in body following heart catheterization**
CC Exclusion 7th character A see Appendix A PDX collection 1443
HAC 7th character A see Appendix B for HAC conditional logic

CC +7th **T81.536 Perforation due to foreign body accidentally left in body following aspiration, puncture o other catheterization**
CC Exclusion 7th character A see Appendix A PDX collection 1443
HAC 7th character A see Appendix B for HAC conditional logic

CC +7th **T81.537 Perforation due to foreign body accidentally left in body following removal of catheter or packing**
CC Exclusion 7th character A see Appendix A PDX collection 1443
HAC 7th character A see Appendix B for HAC conditional logic

CC +7th **T81.538 Perforation due to foreign body accidentally left in body following other procedure**
CC Exclusion 7th character A see Appendix A
PDX collection 1443
HAC 7th character A see Appendix B for HAC conditional logic

CC +7th **T81.539 Perforation due to foreign body accidentally left in body following unspecified procedure**
CC Exclusion 7th character A see Appendix A
PDX collection 1443
HAC 7th character A see Appendix B for HAC conditional logic

\+ **T81.59 Other complications of foreign body accidentally left in body following procedure**
Excludes2: *obstruction or perforation due to prosthetic devices and implants intentionally left in body (T82.0-T82.5, T83.0-T83.4, T83.7, T84.0-T84.4, T85.0-T85.6)*

CC +7th **T81.590 Other complications of foreign body accidentally left in body following surgical operation**
CC Exclusion 7th character A see Appendix A
PDX collection 1443
HAC 7th character A see Appendix B for HAC conditional logic

CC +7th **T81.591 Other complications of foreign body accidentally left in body following infusion or transfusion**
CC Exclusion 7th character A see Appendix A
PDX collection 1443
HAC 7th character A see Appendix B for HAC conditional logic

CC +7th **T81.592 Other complications of foreign body accidentally left in body following kidney dialysis**
CC Exclusion 7th character A see Appendix A
PDX collection 1443
HAC 7th character A see Appendix B for HAC conditional logic

CC +7th **T81.593 Other complications of foreign body accidentally left in body following injection or immunization**
CC Exclusion 7th character A see Appendix A
PDX collection 1443
HAC 7th character A see Appendix B for HAC conditional logic

CC +7th **T81.594 Other complications of foreign body accidentally left in body following endoscopic examination**
CC Exclusion 7th character A see Appendix A
PDX collection 1443
HAC 7th character A see Appendix B for HAC conditional logic

CC +7th **T81.595 Other complications of foreign body accidentally left in body following heart catheterization**
CC Exclusion 7th character A see Appendix A
PDX collection 1443
HAC 7th character A see Appendix B for HAC conditional logic

CC +7th **T81.596 Other complications of foreign body accidentally left in body following aspiration, puncture or other catheterization**
CC Exclusion 7th character A see Appendix A
PDX collection 1443
HAC 7th character A see Appendix B for HAC conditional logic

CC +7th **T81.597 Other complications of foreign body accidentally left in body following removal of catheter or packing**
CC Exclusion 7th character A see Appendix A
PDX collection 1443
HAC 7th character A see Appendix B for HAC conditional logic

CC +7th **T81.598 Other complications of foreign body accidentally left in body following other procedure**
CC Exclusion 7th character A see Appendix A
PDX collection 1443
HAC 7th character A see Appendix B for HAC conditional logic

CC +7th **T81.599 Other complications of foreign body accidentally left in body following unspecified procedure**
CC Exclusion 7th character A see Appendix A
PDX collection 1443
HAC 7th character A see Appendix B for HAC conditional logic

\+ **T81.6 Acute reaction to foreign substance accidentally left during a procedure**
Excludes2: *complications of foreign body accidentally left in body cavity or operation wound following procedure (T81.5-)*

CC X+7th **T81.60 Unspecified acute reaction to foreign substance accidentally left during a procedure**
CC Exclusion 7th character A see Appendix A PDX collection 1444
HAC 7th character A see Appendix B for HAC conditional logic

CC X+7th **T81.61 Aseptic peritonitis due to foreign substance accidentally left during a procedure**
Chemical peritonitis
CC Exclusion 7th character A see Appendix A PDX collection 1444
HAC 7th character A see Appendix B for HAC conditional logic

CC X+7th **T81.69 Other acute reaction to foreign substance accidentally left during a procedure**
CC Exclusion 7th character A see Appendix A PDX collection 1444
HAC 7th character A see Appendix B for HAC conditional logic

\+ **T81.7 Vascular complications following a procedure, not elsewhere classified**
Air embolism following procedure NEC
Phlebitis or thrombophlebitis resulting from a procedure
Excludes1: *embolism complicating abortion or ectopic or molar pregnancy (O00-O07, O08.2)*
embolism complicating pregnancy, childbirth and the puerperium (O88.-)
traumatic embolism (T79.0)
Excludes2: *embolism due to prosthetic devices, implants and grafts (T82.8-, T83.8, T84.8-, T85.8)*
embolism following infusion, transfusion and therapeutic injection (T80.0)

\+ **T81.71 Complication of artery following a procedure, not elsewhere classified**

CC +7th **T81.710 Complication of mesenteric artery following a procedure, not elsewhere classified**
CC Exclusion 7th character A see Appendix A
PDX collection 1445

CC +7th **T81.711 Complication of renal artery following a procedure, not elsewhere classified**
CC Exclusion 7th character A see Appendix A
PDX collection 1445

CC +7th **T81.718 Complication of other artery following a procedure, not elsewhere classified**
CC Exclusion 7th character A see Appendix A
PDX collection 1446

CC +7th **T81.719 Complication of unspecified artery following a procedure, not elsewhere classified**
CC Exclusion 7th character A see Appendix A
PDX collection 1446

CC X+7th **T81.72 Complication of vein following a procedure, not elsewhere classified**
CC Exclusion 7th character A see Appendix A PDX collection 1446

\+ **T81.8 Other complications of procedures, not elsewhere classified**
Excludes2: *hypothermia following anesthesia (T88.51)*
malignant hyperpyrexia due to anesthesia (T88.3)

X+7th **T81.81 Complication of inhalation therapy**

X+7th **T81.82 Emphysema (subcutaneous) resulting from a procedure**

CC X+7th **T81.83 Persistent postprocedural fistula**
CC Exclusion 7th character A see Appendix A PDX collection 1447

X+7th **T81.89 Other complications of procedures, not elsewhere classified**
Use additional code to specify complication, such as:
postprocedural delirium (F05)
AHA CC: 1Q, 2014, 23

X+7th **T81.9 Unspecified complication of procedure**

T82 Complications of cardiac and vascular prosthetic devices, implants and grafts

Excludes2: *failure and rejection of transplanted organs and tissue (T86.-)*

The appropriate 7th character is to be added to each code from category T82
A initial encounter
D subsequent encounter
S sequela

+ **T82.0 Mechanical complication of heart valve prosthesis**
Mechanical complication of artificial heart valve
Excludes1: *mechanical complication of biological heart valve graft (T82.22-)*

CC X+7th **T82.01 Breakdown (mechanical) of heart valve prosthesis**
CC Exclusion 7th character A see Appendix A PDX collection 1448

CC X+7th **T82.02 Displacement of heart valve prosthesis**
Malposition of heart valve prosthesis
CC Exclusion 7th character A see Appendix A PDX collection 1448

CC X+7th **T82.03 Leakage of heart valve prosthesis**
CC Exclusion 7th character A see Appendix A PDX collection 1448

CC X+7th **T82.09 Other mechanical complication of heart valve prosthesis**
Obstruction (mechanical) of heart valve prosthesis
Perforation of heart valve prosthesis
Protrusion of heart valve prosthesis
CC Exclusion 7th character A see Appendix A PDX collection 1448

+ **T82.1 Mechanical complication of cardiac electronic device**

+ **T82.11 Breakdown (mechanical) of cardiac electronic device**

CC +7th **T82.110 Breakdown (mechanical) of cardiac electrode**
CC Exclusion 7th character A see Appendix A PDX collection 1449

CC +7th **T82.111 Breakdown (mechanical) of cardiac pulse generator (battery)**
CC Exclusion 7th character A see Appendix A PDX collection 1449

CC +7th **T82.118 Breakdown (mechanical) of other cardiac electronic device**
CC Exclusion 7th character A see Appendix A PDX collection 1449

CC +7th **T82.119 Breakdown (mechanical) of unspecified cardiac electronic device**
CC Exclusion 7th character A see Appendix A PDX collection 1449

+ **T82.12 Displacement of cardiac electronic device**
Malposition of cardiac electronic device

CC +7th **T82.120 Displacement of cardiac electrode**
CC Exclusion 7th character A see Appendix A PDX collection 1449

CC +7th **T82.121 Displacement of cardiac pulse generator (battery)**
CC Exclusion 7th character A see Appendix A PDX collection 1449

CC +7th **T82.128 Displacement of other cardiac electronic device**
CC Exclusion 7th character A see Appendix A PDX collection 1449

CC +7th **T82.129 Displacement of unspecified cardiac electronic device**
CC Exclusion 7th character A see Appendix A PDX collection 1449

+ **T82.19 Other mechanical complication of cardiac electronic device**
Leakage of cardiac electronic device
Obstruction of cardiac electronic device
Perforation of cardiac electronic device
Protrusion of cardiac electronic device

CC +7th **T82.190 Other mechanical complication of cardiac electrode**
CC Exclusion 7th character A see Appendix A PDX collection 1449

CC +7th **T82.191 Other mechanical complication of cardiac pulse generator (battery)**
CC Exclusion 7th character A see Appendix A PDX collection 1449

CC +7th **T82.198 Other mechanical complication of other cardiac electronic device**
CC Exclusion 7th character A see Appendix A PDX collection 1449

CC +7th **T82.199 Other mechanical complication of unspecified cardiac device**
CC Exclusion 7th character A see Appendix A PDX collection 1449

+ **T82.2 Mechanical complication of coronary artery bypass graft and biological heart valve graft**
Excludes1: *mechanical complication of artificial heart valve prosthesis (T82.0-)*

+ **T82.21 Mechanical complication of coronary artery bypass graft**

CC +7th **T82.211 Breakdown (mechanical) of coronary artery bypass graft**
CC Exclusion 7th character A see Appendix A PDX collection 1450

CC +7th **T82.212 Displacement of coronary artery bypass graft**
Malposition of coronary artery bypass graft
CC Exclusion 7th character A see Appendix A PDX collection 1450

CC +7th **T82.213 Leakage of coronary artery bypass graft**
CC Exclusion 7th character A see Appendix A PDX collection 1450

CC +7th **T82.218 Other mechanical complication of coronary artery bypass graft**
Obstruction, mechanical of coronary artery bypass graft
Perforation of coronary artery bypass graft
Protrusion of coronary artery bypass graft
CC Exclusion 7th character A see Appendix A PDX collection 1450

+ **T82.22 Mechanical complication of biological heart valve graft**

CC +7th **T82.221 Breakdown (mechanical) of biological heart valve graft**
CC Exclusion 7th character A see Appendix A PDX collection 1451

CC +7th **T82.222 Displacement of biological heart valve graft**
Malposition of biological heart valve graft
CC Exclusion 7th character A see Appendix A PDX collection 1451

CC +7th **T82.223 Leakage of biological heart valve graft**
CC Exclusion 7th character A see Appendix A PDX collection 1451

CC +7th **T82.228 Other mechanical complication of biological heart valve graft**
Obstruction of biological heart valve graft
Perforation of biological heart valve graft
Protrusion of biological heart valve graft
CC Exclusion 7th character A see Appendix A PDX collection 1451

+ **T82.3 Mechanical complication of other vascular grafts**

+ **T82.31 Breakdown (mechanical) of other vascular grafts**

CC +7th **T82.310 Breakdown (mechanical) of aortic (bifurcation) graft (replacement)**
CC Exclusion 7th character A see Appendix A PDX collection 1452

CC +7th **T82.311 Breakdown (mechanical) of carotid arterial graft (bypass)**
CC Exclusion 7th character A see Appendix A PDX collection 1452

CC +7th **T82.312 Breakdown (mechanical) of femoral arterial graft (bypass)**
CC Exclusion 7th character A see Appendix A PDX collection 1452

CC +7th **T82.318 Breakdown (mechanical) of other vascular grafts**
CC Exclusion 7th character A see Appendix A PDX collection 1452

CC +7th **T82.319 Breakdown (mechanical) of unspecified vascular grafts**
CC Exclusion 7th character A see Appendix A PDX collection 1452

+ **T82.32 Displacement of other vascular grafts**
Malposition of other vascular grafts

CC +7th **T82.320 Displacement of aortic (bifurcation) graft (replacement)**
CC Exclusion 7th character A see Appendix A PDX collection 1452

CC +7th **T82.321 Displacement of carotid arterial graft (bypass)**
CC Exclusion 7th character A see Appendix A PDX collection 1452

CC +7th **T82.322 Displacement of femoral arterial graft (bypass)**
CC Exclusion 7th character A see Appendix A
PDX collection 1452

CC +7th **T82.328 Displacement of other vascular grafts**
CC Exclusion 7th character A see Appendix A
PDX collection 1452

CC +7th **T82.329 Displacement of unspecified vascular grafts**
CC Exclusion 7th character A see Appendix A
PDX collection 1452

+ **T82.33 Leakage of other vascular grafts**

CC +7th **T82.330 Leakage of aortic (bifurcation) graft (replacement)**
CC Exclusion 7th character A see Appendix A
PDX collection 1452

CC +7th **T82.331 Leakage of carotid arterial graft (bypass)**
CC Exclusion 7th character A see Appendix A
PDX collection 1452

CC +7th **T82.332 Leakage of femoral arterial graft (bypass)**
CC Exclusion 7th character A see Appendix A
PDX collection 1452

CC +7th **T82.338 Leakage of other vascular grafts**
CC Exclusion 7th character A see Appendix A
PDX collection 1452

CC +7th **T82.339 Leakage of unspecified vascular graft**
CC Exclusion 7th character A see Appendix A
PDX collection 1452

+ **T82.39 Other mechanical complication of other vascular grafts**
Obstruction (mechanical) of other vascular grafts
Perforation of other vascular grafts
Protrusion of other vascular grafts

CC +7th **T82.390 Other mechanical complication of aortic (bifurcation) graft (replacement)**
CC Exclusion 7th character A see Appendix A
PDX collection 1452

CC +7th **T82.391 Other mechanical complication of carotid arterial graft (bypass)**
CC Exclusion 7th character A see Appendix A
PDX collection 1452

CC +7th **T82.392 Other mechanical complication of femoral arterial graft (bypass)**
CC Exclusion 7th character A see Appendix A
PDX collection 1452

CC +7th **T82.398 Other mechanical complication of other vascular grafts**
CC Exclusion 7th character A see Appendix A
PDX collection 1452

CC +7th **T82.399 Other mechanical complication of unspecified vascular grafts**
CC Exclusion 7th character A see Appendix A
PDX collection 1452

+ **T82.4 Mechanical complication of vascular dialysis catheter**
Mechanical complication of hemodialysis catheter
Excludes1: *mechanical complication of intraperitoneal dialysis catheter (T85.62)*

CC X+7th **T82.41 Breakdown (mechanical) of vascular dialysis catheter**
CC Exclusion 7th character A see Appendix A PDX collection 1452

CC X+7th **T82.42 Displacement of vascular dialysis catheter**
Malposition of vascular dialysis catheter
CC Exclusion 7th character A see Appendix A PDX collection 1452

CC X+7th **T82.43 Leakage of vascular dialysis catheter**
CC Exclusion 7th character A see Appendix A PDX collection 1452

CC X+7th **T82.49 Other complication of vascular dialysis catheter**
Obstruction (mechanical) of vascular dialysis catheter
Perforation of vascular dialysis catheter
Protrusion of vascular dialysis catheter
CC Exclusion 7th character A see Appendix A PDX collection 1452

+ **T82.5 Mechanical complication of other cardiac and vascular devices and implants**
Excludes2: *mechanical complication of epidural and subdural infusion catheter (T85.61)*

+ **T82.51 Breakdown (mechanical) of other cardiac and vascular devices and implants**

CC +7th **T82.510 Breakdown (mechanical) of surgically created arteriovenous fistula**
CC Exclusion 7th character A see Appendix A
PDX collection 1452

CC +7th **T82.511 Breakdown (mechanical) of surgically created arteriovenous shunt**
CC Exclusion 7th character A see Appendix A
PDX collection 1452

CC +7th **T82.512 Breakdown (mechanical) of artificial heart**
CC Exclusion 7th character A see Appendix A
PDX collection 1452

CC +7th **T82.513 Breakdown (mechanical) of balloon (counterpulsation) device**
CC Exclusion 7th character A see Appendix A
PDX collection 1451

CC +7th **T82.514 Breakdown (mechanical) of infusion catheter**
CC Exclusion 7th character A see Appendix A
PDX collection 1452

CC +7th **T82.515 Breakdown (mechanical) of umbrella device**
CC Exclusion 7th character A see Appendix A
PDX collection 1452

CC +7th **T82.518 Breakdown (mechanical) of other cardiac and vascular devices and implants**
CC Exclusion 7th character A see Appendix A
PDX collection 1452

CC +7th **T82.519 Breakdown (mechanical) of unspecified cardiac and vascular devices and implants**
CC Exclusion 7th character A see Appendix A
PDX collection 1453

+ **T82.52 Displacement of other cardiac and vascular devices and implants**
Malposition of other cardiac and vascular devices and implants

CC +7th **T82.520 Displacement of surgically created arteriovenous fistula**
CC Exclusion 7th character A see Appendix A
PDX collection 1452

CC +7th **T82.521 Displacement of surgically created arteriovenous shunt**
CC Exclusion 7th character A see Appendix A
PDX collection 1452

CC +7th **T82.522 Displacement of artificial heart**
CC Exclusion 7th character A see Appendix A
PDX collection 1451

CC +7th **T82.523 Displacement of balloon (counterpulsation) device**
CC Exclusion 7th character A see Appendix A
PDX collection 1452

CC +7th **T82.524 Displacement of infusion catheter**
CC Exclusion 7th character A see Appendix A
PDX collection 1452

CC +7th **T82.525 Displacement of umbrella device**
CC Exclusion 7th character A see Appendix A
PDX collection 1452

CC +7th **T82.528 Displacement of other cardiac and vascular devices and implants**
CC Exclusion 7th character A see Appendix A
PDX collection 1452

CC +7th **T82.529 Displacement of unspecified cardiac and vascular devices and implants**
CC Exclusion 7th character A see Appendix A
PDX collection 1452

+ **T82.53 Leakage of other cardiac and vascular devices and implants**

CC +7th **T82.530 Leakage of surgically created arteriovenous fistula**
CC Exclusion 7th character A see Appendix A
PDX collection 1452

CC +7th **T82.531 Leakage of surgically created arteriovenous shunt**
CC Exclusion 7th character A see Appendix A
PDX collection 1452

CC +7th **T82.532 Leakage of artificial heart**
CC Exclusion 7th character A see Appendix A
PDX collection 1451

CC +7th **T82.533 Leakage of balloon (counterpulsation) device**
CC Exclusion 7th character A see Appendix A
PDX collection 1452

CC +7th **T82.534 Leakage of infusion catheter**
CC Exclusion 7th character A see Appendix A
PDX collection 1452

CC +7th **T82.535 Leakage of umbrella device**
CC Exclusion 7th character A see Appendix A
PDX collection 1452

CC +7th **T82.538 Leakage of other cardiac and vascular devices and implants**
CC Exclusion 7th character A see Appendix A
PDX collection 1452

CC +7th **T82.539 Leakage of unspecified cardiac and vascular devices and implants**
CC Exclusion 7th character A see Appendix A PDX collection 1453

\+ **T82.59 Other mechanical complication of other cardiac and vascular devices and implants**
Obstruction (mechanical) of other cardiac and vascular devices and implants
Perforation of other cardiac and vascular devices and implants
Protrusion of other cardiac and vascular devices and implants

CC +7th **T82.590 Other mechanical complication of surgically created arteriovenous fistula**
CC Exclusion 7th character A see Appendix A PDX collection 1452

CC +7th **T82.591 Other mechanical complication of surgically created arteriovenous shunt**
CC Exclusion 7th character A see Appendix A PDX collection 1452

CC +7th **T82.592 Other mechanical complication of artificial heart**
CC Exclusion 7th character A see Appendix A PDX collection 1451

CC +7th **T82.593 Other mechanical complication of balloon (counterpulsation) device**
CC Exclusion 7th character A see Appendix A PDX collection 1452

CC +7th **T82.594 Other mechanical complication of infusion catheter**
CC Exclusion 7th character A see Appendix A PDX collection 1451

CC +7th **T82.595 Other mechanical complication of umbrella device**
CC Exclusion 7th character A see Appendix A PDX collection 1452

CC +7th **T82.598 Other mechanical complication of other cardiac and vascular devices and implants**
CC Exclusion 7th character A see Appendix A PDX collection 1451

CC +7th **T82.599 Other mechanical complication of unspecified cardiac and vascular devices and implants**
CC Exclusion 7th character A see Appendix A PDX collection 1453

CC X+7th **T82.6 Infection and inflammatory reaction due to cardiac valve prosthesis**
Use additional code to identify infection
CC Exclusion 7th character A see Appendix A PDX collection 1454
HAC 7th character A see Appendix B for HAC conditional logic

CC X+7th **T82.7 Infection and inflammatory reaction due to other cardiac and vascular devices, implants and grafts**
Use additional code to identify infection
CC Exclusion 7th character A see Appendix A PDX collection 1454
HAC 7th character A see Appendix B for HAC conditional logic

T82.8 Other specified complications of cardiac and vascular prosthetic devices, implants and grafts

T82.81 Embolism of cardiac and vascular prosthetic devices, implants and grafts

CC +7th **T82.817 Embolism of cardiac prosthetic devices, implants and grafts**
CC Exclusion 7th character A see Appendix A PDX collection 1455

CC +7th **T82.818 Embolism of vascular prosthetic devices, implants and grafts**
CC Exclusion 7th character A see Appendix A PDX collection 1454

T82.82 Fibrosis of cardiac and vascular prosthetic devices, implants and grafts

CC +7th **T82.827 Fibrosis of cardiac prosthetic devices, implants and grafts**
CC Exclusion 7th character A see Appendix A PDX collection 1455

CC +7th **T82.828 Fibrosis of vascular prosthetic devices, implants and grafts**
CC Exclusion 7th character A see Appendix A PDX collection 1454

\+ **T82.83 Hemorrhage of cardiac and vascular prosthetic devices, implants and grafts**

CC +7th **T82.837 Hemorrhage of cardiac prosthetic devices, implants and grafts**
CC Exclusion 7th character A see Appendix A PDX collection 1455

CC +7th **T82.838 Hemorrhage of vascular prosthetic devices, implants and grafts**
CC Exclusion 7th character A see Appendix A PDX collection 1454

\+ **T82.84 Pain from cardiac and vascular prosthetic devices, implants and grafts**

CC +7th **T82.847 Pain from cardiac prosthetic devices, implants and grafts**
CC Exclusion 7th character A see Appendix A PDX collection 1455

CC +7th **T82.848 Pain from vascular prosthetic devices, implants and grafts**
CC Exclusion 7th character A see Appendix A PDX collection 1454

\+ **T82.85 Stenosis of cardiac and vascular prosthetic devices, implants and grafts**

CC +7th **T82.857 Stenosis of cardiac prosthetic devices, implants and grafts**
CC Exclusion 7th character A see Appendix A PDX collection 1455

CC +7th **T82.858 Stenosis of vascular prosthetic devices, implants and grafts**
CC Exclusion 7th character A see Appendix A PDX collection 1454

\+ **T82.86 Thrombosis of cardiac and vascular prosthetic devices, implants and grafts**

CC +7th **T82.867 Thrombosis of cardiac prosthetic devices, implants and grafts**
CC Exclusion 7th character A see Appendix A PDX collection 1455

CC +7th **T82.868 Thrombosis of vascular prosthetic devices, implants and grafts**
CC Exclusion 7th character A see Appendix A PDX collection 1454

\+ **T82.89 Other specified complication of cardiac and vascular prosthetic devices, implants and grafts**

CC +7th **T82.897 Other specified complication of cardiac prosthetic devices, implants and grafts**
CC Exclusion 7th character A see Appendix A PDX collection 1455

CC +7th **T82.898 Other specified complication of vascular prosthetic devices, implants and grafts**
CC Exclusion 7th character A see Appendix A PDX collection 1454

CC X+7th **T82.9 Unspecified complication of cardiac and vascular prosthetic device, implant and graft**
CC Exclusion 7th character A see Appendix A PDX collection 1455

T83 Complications of genitourinary prosthetic devices, implants and grafts

Excludes2: *failure and rejection of transplanted organs and tissue (T86.*

The appropriate 7th character is to be added to each code from category T83
A initial encounter
D subsequent encounter
S sequela

\+ **T83.0 Mechanical complication of urinary (indwelling) catheter**
Excludes2: *complications of stoma of urinary tract (N99.5-)*

\+ **T83.01 Breakdown (mechanical) of urinary (indwelling) catheter**

CC +7th **T83.010 Breakdown (mechanical) of cystostomy catheter**
CC Exclusion 7th character A see Appendix A PDX collection 1456

+7th **T83.018 Breakdown (mechanical) of other indwelling urethral catheter**

\+ **T83.02 Displacement of urinary (indwelling) catheter**
Malposition of urinary (indwelling) catheter

CC +7th **T83.020 Displacement of cystostomy catheter**
CC Exclusion 7th character A see Appendix A PDX collection 1456

+7th **T83.028 Displacement of other indwelling urethral catheter**

\+ **T83.03 Leakage of urinary (indwelling) catheter**

CC +7th **T83.030 Leakage of cystostomy catheter**
CC Exclusion 7th character A see Appendix A PDX collection 1456

+7th **T83.038 Leakage of other indwelling urethral catheter**

\+ **T83.09 Other mechanical complication of urinary (indwelling) catheter**
Obstruction (mechanical) of urinary (indwelling) catheter
Perforation of urinary (indwelling) catheter
Protrusion of urinary (indwelling) catheter

CC +7th **T83.090 Other mechanical complication of cystostomy catheter**
CC Exclusion 7th character A see Appendix A PDX collection 1456

+7th **T83.098 Other mechanical complication of other indwelling urethral catheter**

+ **T83.1 Mechanical complication of other urinary devices and implants**

+ **T83.11 Breakdown (mechanical) of other urinary devices and implants**

CC +7th **T83.110 Breakdown (mechanical) of urinary electronic stimulator device**
CC Exclusion 7th character A see Appendix A PDX collection 1456

CC +7th **T83.111 Breakdown (mechanical) of urinary sphincter implant**
CC Exclusion 7th character A see Appendix A PDX collection 1456

CC +7th **T83.112 Breakdown (mechanical) of urinary stent**
CC Exclusion 7th character A see Appendix A PDX collection 1456

CC +7th **T83.118 Breakdown (mechanical) of other urinary devices and implants**
CC Exclusion 7th character A see Appendix A PDX collection 1456

+ **T83.12 Displacement of other urinary devices and implants**
Malposition of other urinary devices and implants

CC +7th **T83.120 Displacement of urinary electronic stimulator device**
CC Exclusion 7th character A see Appendix A PDX collection 1456

CC +7th **T83.121 Displacement of urinary sphincter implant**
CC Exclusion 7th character A see Appendix A PDX collection 1456

CC +7th **T83.122 Displacement of urinary stent**
CC Exclusion 7th character A see Appendix A PDX collection 1456

CC +7th **T83.128 Displacement of other urinary devices and implants**
CC Exclusion 7th character A see Appendix A PDX collection 1456

+ **T83.19 Other mechanical complication of other urinary devices and implants**
Leakage of other urinary devices and implants
Obstruction (mechanical) of other urinary devices and implants
Perforation of other urinary devices and implants
Protrusion of other urinary devices and implants

CC +7th **T83.190 Other mechanical complication of urinary electronic stimulator device**
CC Exclusion 7th character A see Appendix A PDX collection 1456

CC +7th **T83.191 Other mechanical complication of urinary sphincter implant**
CC Exclusion 7th character A see Appendix A PDX collection 1456

CC +7th **T83.192 Other mechanical complication of urinary stent**
CC Exclusion 7th character A see Appendix A PDX collection 1456

CC +7th **T83.198 Other mechanical complication of other urinary devices and implants**
CC Exclusion 7th character A see Appendix A PDX collection 1456

+ **T83.2 Mechanical complication of graft of urinary organ**

CC X+7th **T83.21 Breakdown (mechanical) of graft of urinary organ**
CC Exclusion 7th character A see Appendix A PDX collection 1456

CC X+7th **T83.22 Displacement of graft of urinary organ**
Malposition of graft of urinary organ
CC Exclusion 7th character A see Appendix A PDX collection 1456

CC X+7th **T83.23 Leakage of graft of urinary organ**
CC Exclusion 7th character A see Appendix A PDX collection 1456

CC X+7th **T83.29 Other mechanical complication of graft of urinary organ**
Obstruction (mechanical) of graft of urinary organ
Perforation of graft of urinary organ
Protrusion of graft of urinary organ
CC Exclusion 7th character A see Appendix A PDX collection 1456

+ **T83.3 Mechanical complication of intrauterine contraceptive device**

♀ X+7th **T83.31 Breakdown (mechanical) of intrauterine contraceptive device**

♀ X+7th **T83.32 Displacement of intrauterine contraceptive device**
Malposition of intrauterine contraceptive device

♀ X+7th **T83.39 Other mechanical complication of intrauterine contraceptive device**
Leakage of intrauterine contraceptive device
Obstruction (mechanical) of intrauterine contraceptive device
Perforation of intrauterine contraceptive device
Protrusion of intrauterine contraceptive device

+ **T83.4 Mechanical complication of other prosthetic devices, implants and grafts of genital tract**

+ **T83.41 Breakdown (mechanical) of other prosthetic devices, implants and grafts of genital tract**

♂ CC +7th **T83.410 Breakdown (mechanical) of penile (implanted) prosthesis**
CC Exclusion 7th character A see Appendix A PDX collection 1456

CC +7th **T83.418 Breakdown (mechanical) of other prosthetic devices, implants and grafts of genital tract**
CC Exclusion 7th character A see Appendix A PDX collection 1456

+ **T83.42 Displacement of other prosthetic devices, implants and grafts of genital tract**
Malposition of other prosthetic devices, implants and grafts of genital tract

♂ CC +7th **T83.420 Displacement of penile (implanted) prosthesis**
CC Exclusion 7th character A see Appendix A PDX collection 1456

CC +7th **T83.428 Displacement of other prosthetic devices, implants and grafts of genital tract**
CC Exclusion 7th character A see Appendix A PDX collection 1456

+ **T83.49 Other mechanical complication of other prosthetic devices, implants and grafts of genital tract**
Leakage of other prosthetic devices, implants and grafts of genital tract
Obstruction, mechanical of other prosthetic devices, implants and grafts of genital tract
Perforation of other prosthetic devices, implants and grafts of genital tract
Protrusion of other prosthetic devices, implants and grafts of genital tract

♂ CC +7th **T83.490 Other mechanical complication of penile (implanted) prosthesis**
CC Exclusion 7th character A see Appendix A PDX collection 1456

CC +7th **T83.498 Other mechanical complication of other prosthetic devices, implants and grafts of genital tract**
CC Exclusion 7th character A see Appendix A PDX collection 1456

+ **T83.5 Infection and inflammatory reaction due to prosthetic device, implant and graft in urinary system**
Use additional code to identify infection

CC X+7th **T83.51 Infection and inflammatory reaction due to indwelling urinary catheter**
Excludes2: *complications of stoma of urinary tract (N99.5-)*
CC Exclusion 7th character A see Appendix A PDX collection 1457
HAC 7th character A see Appendix B for HAC conditional logic

CC X+7th **T83.59 Infection and inflammatory reaction due to prosthetic device, implant and graft in urinary system**
CC Exclusion 7th character A see Appendix A PDX collection 1458

CC X+7th **T83.6 Infection and inflammatory reaction due to prosthetic device, implant and graft in genital tract**
Use additional code to identify infection
CC Exclusion 7th character A see Appendix A PDX collection 1458

+ **T83.7 Complications due to implanted mesh and other prosthetic materials**

+ **T83.71 Erosion of implanted mesh and other prosthetic materials to surrounding organ or tissue**

♀ +7th **T83.711 Erosion of implanted vaginal mesh and other prosthetic materials to surrounding organ or tissue**
Erosion of implanted vaginal mesh and other prosthetic materials into pelvic floor muscles

CC +7th **T83.718 Erosion of other implanted mesh and other prosthetic materials to surrounding organ or tissue**
CC Exclusion 7th character A see Appendix A PDX collection 1456

+ **T83.72 Exposure of implanted mesh and other prosthetic materials into surrounding organ or tissue**

♀ +7th **T83.721 Exposure of implanted vaginal mesh and other prosthetic materials into vagina**
Exposure of implanted vaginal mesh and other prosthetic materials through vaginal wall

CC +7th **T83.728 Exposure of other implanted mesh and other prosthetic materials to surrounding organ or tissue**
CC Exclusion 7th character A see Appendix A PDX collection 1456

+ **T83.8 Other specified complications of genitourinary prosthetic devices, implants and grafts**

CC X+7th **T83.81 Embolism of genitourinary prosthetic devices, implants and grafts**
CC Exclusion 7th character A see Appendix A PDX collection 1458

CC X+7th **T83.82 Fibrosis of genitourinary prosthetic devices, implants and grafts**
CC Exclusion 7th character A see Appendix A PDX collection 1458

CC X+7th **T83.83 Hemorrhage of genitourinary prosthetic devices, implants and grafts**
CC Exclusion 7th character A see Appendix A PDX collection 1458

CC X+7th **T83.84 Pain from genitourinary prosthetic devices, implants and grafts**
CC Exclusion 7th character A see Appendix A PDX collection 1458

CC X+7th **T83.85 Stenosis of genitourinary prosthetic devices, implants and grafts**
CC Exclusion 7th character A see Appendix A PDX collection 1458

CC X+7th **T83.86 Thrombosis of genitourinary prosthetic devices, implants and grafts**
CC Exclusion 7th character A see Appendix A PDX collection 1458

CC X+7th **T83.89 Other specified complication of genitourinary prosthetic devices, implants and grafts**
CC Exclusion 7th character A see Appendix A PDX collection 1458

CC X+7th **T83.9 Unspecified complication of genitourinary prosthetic device, implant and graft**
CC Exclusion 7th character A see Appendix A PDX collection 1458

T84 Complications of internal orthopedic prosthetic devices, implants and grafts

Excludes2: *failure and rejection of transplanted organs and tissues (T86.-)*
fracture of bone following insertion of orthopedic implant, joint prosthesis or bone plate (M96.6)

The appropriate 7th character is to be added to each code from category T84
A initial encounter
D subsequent encounter
S sequela

+ **T84.0 Mechanical complication of internal joint prosthesis**

+ **T84.01 Broken internal joint prosthesis**
Breakage (fracture) of prosthetic joint
Broken prosthetic joint implant
Excludes1: *periprosthetic joint implant fracture (T84.04)*

CC +7th **T84.010 Broken internal right hip prosthesis**
CC Exclusion 7th character A see Appendix A PDX collection 0911

CC +7th **T84.011 Broken internal left hip prosthesis**
CC Exclusion 7th character A see Appendix A PDX collection 0911

CC +7th **T84.012 Broken internal right knee prosthesis**
CC Exclusion 7th character A see Appendix A PDX collection 0911

CC +7th **T84.013 Broken internal left knee prosthesis**
CC Exclusion 7th character A see Appendix A PDX collection 0911

CC +7th **T84.018 Broken internal joint prosthesis, other site**
Use additional code to identify the joint (Z96.6-)
CC Exclusion 7th character A see Appendix A PDX collection 0911

CC +7th **T84.019 Broken internal joint prosthesis, unspecified site**
CC Exclusion 7th character A see Appendix A PDX collection 0911

+ **T84.02 Dislocation of internal joint prosthesis**
Instability of internal joint prosthesis
Subluxation of internal joint prosthesis

CC +7th **T84.020 Dislocation of internal right hip prosthesis**
CC Exclusion 7th character A see Appendix A PDX collection 0911

CC +7th **T84.021 Dislocation of internal left hip prosthesis**
CC Exclusion 7th character A see Appendix A PDX collection 0911

CC +7th **T84.022 Instability of internal right knee prosthesis**
CC Exclusion 7th character A see Appendix A PDX collection 0911

CC +7th **T84.023 Instability of internal left knee prosthesis**
CC Exclusion 7th character A see Appendix A PDX collection 0911

CC +7th **T84.028 Dislocation of other internal joint prosthesis**
Use additional code to identify the joint (Z96.6
CC Exclusion 7th character A see Appendix A PDX collection 0911

CC +7th **T84.029 Dislocation of unspecified internal joint prosthesis**
CC Exclusion 7th character A see Appendix A PDX collection 0911

+ **T84.03 Mechanical loosening of internal prosthetic joint**
Aseptic loosening of prosthetic joint

CC +7th **T84.030 Mechanical loosening of internal right hip prosthetic joint**
CC Exclusion 7th character A see Appendix A PDX collection 0911

CC +7th **T84.031 Mechanical loosening of internal left hip prosthetic joint**
CC Exclusion 7th character A see Appendix A PDX collection 0911

CC +7th **T84.032 Mechanical loosening of internal right knee prosthetic joint**
CC Exclusion 7th character A see Appendix A PDX collection 0911

CC +7th **T84.033 Mechanical loosening of internal left knee prosthetic joint**
CC Exclusion 7th character A see Appendix A PDX collection 0911

CC +7th **T84.038 Mechanical loosening of other internal prosthetic joint**
Use additional code to identify the joint (Z96.6
CC Exclusion 7th character A see Appendix A PDX collection 0911

CC +7th **T84.039 Mechanical loosening of unspecified internal prosthetic joint**
CC Exclusion 7th character A see Appendix A PDX collection 0911

+ **T84.04 Periprosthetic fracture around internal prosthetic joint**
Excludes2: *breakage (fracture) of prosthetic joint (T84.01)*

CC +7th **T84.040 Periprosthetic fracture around internal prosthetic right hip joint**
CC Exclusion 7th character A see Appendix A PDX collection 0911

CC +7th **T84.041 Periprosthetic fracture around internal prosthetic left hip joint**
CC Exclusion 7th character A see Appendix A PDX collection 0911

CC +7th **T84.042 Periprosthetic fracture around internal prosthetic right knee joint**
CC Exclusion 7th character A see Appendix A PDX collection 0911

CC +7th **T84.043 Periprosthetic fracture around internal prosthetic left knee joint**
CC Exclusion 7th character A see Appendix A PDX collection 0911

CC +7th **T84.048 Periprosthetic fracture around other internal prosthetic joint**
Use additional code to identify the joint (Z96.6
CC Exclusion 7th character A see Appendix A PDX collection 0911

CC +7th **T84.049 Periprosthetic fracture around unspecified internal prosthetic joint**
CC Exclusion 7th character A see Appendix A PDX collection 0911

+ **T84.05 Periprosthetic osteolysis of internal prosthetic joint**
Use additional code to identify major osseous defect, if applicable (M89.7-)
CC Exclusion 7th character A see Appendix A
PDX collection 0911

CC +7th **T84.050 Periprosthetic osteolysis of internal prosthetic right hip joint**
CC Exclusion 7th character A see Appendix A
PDX collection 0911

CC +7th **T84.051 Periprosthetic osteolysis of internal prosthetic left hip joint**
CC Exclusion 7th character A see Appendix A
PDX collection 0911

CC +7th **T84.052 Periprosthetic osteolysis of internal prosthetic right knee joint**
CC Exclusion 7th character A see Appendix A
PDX collection 0911

CC +7th **T84.053 Periprosthetic osteolysis of internal prosthetic left knee joint**
CC Exclusion 7th character A see Appendix A
PDX collection 0911

CC +7th **T84.058 Periprosthetic osteolysis of other internal prosthetic joint**
Use additional code to identify the joint (Z96.6-)
CC Exclusion 7th character A see Appendix A
PDX collection 0911

CC +7th **T84.059 Periprosthetic osteolysis of unspecified internal prosthetic joint**
CC Exclusion 7th character A see Appendix A
PDX collection 0911

+ **T84.06 Wear of articular bearing surface of internal prosthetic joint**

CC +7th **T84.060 Wear of articular bearing surface of internal prosthetic right hip joint**
CC Exclusion 7th character A see Appendix A
PDX collection 0911

CC +7th **T84.061 Wear of articular bearing surface of internal prosthetic left hip joint**
CC Exclusion 7th character A see Appendix A
PDX collection 0911

CC +7th **T84.062 Wear of articular bearing surface of internal prosthetic right knee joint**
CC Exclusion 7th character A see Appendix A
PDX collection 0911

CC +7th **T84.063 Wear of articular bearing surface of internal prosthetic left knee joint**
CC Exclusion 7th character A see Appendix A
PDX collection 0911

CC +7th **T84.068 Wear of articular bearing surface of other internal prosthetic joint**
Use additional code to identify the joint (Z96.6-)
CC Exclusion 7th character A see Appendix A
PDX collection 0911

CC +7th **T84.069 Wear of articular bearing surface of unspecified internal prosthetic joint**
CC Exclusion 7th character A see Appendix A
PDX collection 0911

+ **T84.09 Other mechanical complication of internal joint prosthesis**
Prosthetic joint implant failure NOS

CC +7th **T84.090 Other mechanical complication of internal right hip prosthesis**
CC Exclusion 7th character A see Appendix A
PDX collection 0911

CC +7th **T84.091 Other mechanical complication of internal left hip prosthesis**
CC Exclusion 7th character A see Appendix A
PDX collection 0911

CC +7th **T84.092 Other mechanical complication of internal right knee prosthesis**
CC Exclusion 7th character A see Appendix A
PDX collection 0911

CC +7th **T84.093 Other mechanical complication of internal left knee prosthesis**
CC Exclusion 7th character A see Appendix A
PDX collection 0911

CC +7th **T84.098 Other mechanical complication of other internal joint prosthesis**
Use additional code to identify the joint (Z96.6-)
CC Exclusion 7th character A see Appendix A
PDX collection 0911

CC +7th **T84.099 Other mechanical complication of unspecified internal joint prosthesis**
CC Exclusion 7th character A see Appendix A
PDX collection 0911

+ **T84.1 Mechanical complication of internal fixation device of bones of limb**
Excludes2: *mechanical complication of internal fixation device of bones of feet (T84.2-)*
mechanical complication of internal fixation device of bones of fingers (T84.2-)
mechanical complication of internal fixation device of bones of hands (T84.2-)
mechanical complication of internal fixation device of bones of toes (T84.2-)

+ **T84.11 Breakdown (mechanical) of internal fixation device of bones of limb**

CC +7th **T84.110 Breakdown (mechanical) of internal fixation device of right humerus**
CC Exclusion 7th character A see Appendix A
PDX collection 0911

CC +7th **T84.111 Breakdown (mechanical) of internal fixation device of left humerus**
CC Exclusion 7th character A see Appendix A
PDX collection 0911

CC +7th **T84.112 Breakdown (mechanical) of internal fixation device of bone of right forearm**
CC Exclusion 7th character A see Appendix A
PDX collection 0911

CC +7th **T84.113 Breakdown (mechanical) of internal fixation device of bone of left forearm**
CC Exclusion 7th character A see Appendix A
PDX collection 0911

CC +7th **T84.114 Breakdown (mechanical) of internal fixation device of right femur**
CC Exclusion 7th character A see Appendix A
PDX collection 0911

CC +7th **T84.115 Breakdown (mechanical) of internal fixation device of left femur**
CC Exclusion 7th character A see Appendix A
PDX collection 0911

CC +7th **T84.116 Breakdown (mechanical) of internal fixation device of bone of right lower leg**
CC Exclusion 7th character A see Appendix A
PDX collection 0911

CC +7th **T84.117 Breakdown (mechanical) of internal fixation device of bone of left lower leg**
CC Exclusion 7th character A see Appendix A
PDX collection 0911

CC +7th **T84.119 Breakdown (mechanical) of internal fixation device of unspecified bone of limb**
CC Exclusion 7th character A see Appendix A
PDX collection 0911

+ **T84.12 Displacement of internal fixation device of bones of limb**
Malposition of internal fixation device of bones of limb

CC +7th **T84.120 Displacement of internal fixation device of right humerus**
CC Exclusion 7th character A see Appendix A
PDX collection 0911

CC +7th **T84.121 Displacement of internal fixation device of left humerus**
CC Exclusion 7th character A see Appendix A
PDX collection 0911

CC +7th **T84.122 Displacement of internal fixation device of bone of right forearm**
CC Exclusion 7th character A see Appendix A
PDX collection 0911

CC +7th **T84.123 Displacement of internal fixation device of bone of left forearm**
CC Exclusion 7th character A see Appendix A
PDX collection 0911

CC +7th **T84.124 Displacement of internal fixation device of right femur**
CC Exclusion 7th character A see Appendix A
PDX collection 0911

CC +7th **T84.125 Displacement of internal fixation device of left femur**
CC Exclusion 7th character A see Appendix A
PDX collection 0911

CC +7th **T84.126 Displacement of internal fixation device of bone of right lower leg**
CC Exclusion 7th character A see Appendix A
PDX collection 0911

CC +7th **T84.127 Displacement of internal fixation device of bone of left lower leg**
CC Exclusion 7th character A see Appendix A
PDX collection 0911

CC +7th **T84.129 Displacement of internal fixation device of unspecified bone of limb**
CC Exclusion 7th character A see Appendix A
PDX collection 0911

\+ **T84.19 Other mechanical complication of internal fixation device of bones of limb**
Obstruction (mechanical) of internal fixation device of bones of limb
Perforation of internal fixation device of bones of limb
Protrusion of internal fixation device of bones of limb

CC +7th **T84.190 Other mechanical complication of internal fixation device of right humerus**
CC Exclusion 7th character A see Appendix A
PDX collection 0911

CC +7th **T84.191 Other mechanical complication of internal fixation device of left humerus**
CC Exclusion 7th character A see Appendix A
PDX collection 0911

CC +7th **T84.192 Other mechanical complication of internal fixation device of bone of right forearm**
CC Exclusion 7th character A see Appendix A
PDX collection 0911

CC +7th **T84.193 Other mechanical complication of internal fixation device of bone of left forearm**
CC Exclusion 7th character A see Appendix A
PDX collection 0911

CC +7th **T84.194 Other mechanical complication of internal fixation device of right femur**
CC Exclusion 7th character A see Appendix A
PDX collection 0911

CC +7th **T84.195 Other mechanical complication of internal fixation device of left femur**
CC Exclusion 7th character A see Appendix A
PDX collection 0911

CC +7th **T84.196 Other mechanical complication of internal fixation device of bone of right lower leg**
CC Exclusion 7th character A see Appendix A
PDX collection 0911

CC +7th **T84.197 Other mechanical complication of internal fixation device of bone of left lower leg**
CC Exclusion 7th character A see Appendix A
PDX collection 0911

CC +7th **T84.199 Other mechanical complication of internal fixation device of unspecified bone of limb**
CC Exclusion 7th character A see Appendix A
PDX collection 0911

\+ **T84.2 Mechanical complication of internal fixation device of other bones**

\+ **T84.21 Breakdown (mechanical) of internal fixation device of other bones**

CC +7th **T84.210 Breakdown (mechanical) of internal fixation device of bones of hand and fingers**
CC Exclusion 7th character A see Appendix A
PDX collection 0911

CC +7th **T84.213 Breakdown (mechanical) of internal fixation device of bones of foot and toes**
CC Exclusion 7th character A see Appendix A
PDX collection 0911

CC +7th **T84.216 Breakdown (mechanical) of internal fixation device of vertebrae**
CC Exclusion 7th character A see Appendix A
PDX collection 0911

CC +7th **T84.218 Breakdown (mechanical) of internal fixation device of other bones**
CC Exclusion 7th character A see Appendix A
PDX collection 0911

\+ **T84.22 Displacement of internal fixation device of other bones**
Malposition of internal fixation device of other bones

CC +7th **T84.220 Displacement of internal fixation device of bones of hand and fingers**
CC Exclusion 7th character A see Appendix A
PDX collection 0911

CC +7th **T84.223 Displacement of internal fixation device of bones of foot and toes**
CC Exclusion 7th character A see Appendix A
PDX collection 0911

CC +7th **T84.226 Displacement of internal fixation device of vertebrae**
CC Exclusion 7th character A see Appendix A
PDX collection 0911

CC +7th **T84.228 Displacement of internal fixation device of other bones**
CC Exclusion 7th character A see Appendix A
PDX collection 0911

\+ **T84.29 Other mechanical complication of internal fixation device of other bones**
Obstruction (mechanical) of internal fixation device of other bones
Perforation of internal fixation device of other bones
Protrusion of internal fixation device of other bones

CC +7th **T84.290 Other mechanical complication of internal fixation device of bones of hand and fingers**
CC Exclusion 7th character A see Appendix A
PDX collection 0911

CC +7th **T84.293 Other mechanical complication of internal fixation device of bones of foot and toes**
CC Exclusion 7th character A see Appendix A
PDX collection 0911

CC +7th **T84.296 Other mechanical complication of internal fixation device of vertebrae**
CC Exclusion 7th character A see Appendix A
PDX collection 0911

CC +7th **T84.298 Other mechanical complication of internal fixation device of other bones**
CC Exclusion 7th character A see Appendix A
PDX collection 0911

\+ **T84.3 Mechanical complication of other bone devices, implants and grafts**
Excludes2: *other complications of bone graft (T86.83-)*

\+ **T84.31 Breakdown (mechanical) of other bone devices, implants and grafts**

CC +7th **T84.310 Breakdown (mechanical) of electronic bone stimulator**
CC Exclusion 7th character A see Appendix A
PDX collection 0911

CC +7th **T84.318 Breakdown (mechanical) of other bone devices, implants and grafts**
CC Exclusion 7th character A see Appendix A
PDX collection 0911

\+ **T84.32 Displacement of other bone devices, implants and grafts**
Malposition of other bone devices, implants and grafts

CC +7th **T84.320 Displacement of electronic bone stimulator**
CC Exclusion 7th character A see Appendix A
PDX collection 0911

CC +7th **T84.328 Displacement of other bone devices, implant and grafts**
CC Exclusion 7th character A see Appendix A
PDX collection 0911

\+ **T84.39 Other mechanical complication of other bone devices, implants and grafts**
Obstruction (mechanical) of other bone devices, implants and grafts
Perforation of other bone devices, implants and grafts
Protrusion of other bone devices, implants and grafts

CC +7th **T84.390 Other mechanical complication of electronic bone stimulator**
CC Exclusion 7th character A see Appendix A
PDX collection 0911

CC +7th **T84.398 Other mechanical complication of other bone devices, implants and grafts**
CC Exclusion 7th character A see Appendix A
PDX collection 0911

\+ **T84.4 Mechanical complication of other internal orthopedic devices, implants and grafts**

\+ **T84.41 Breakdown (mechanical) of other internal orthopedic devices, implants and grafts**

CC +7th **T84.410 Breakdown (mechanical) of muscle and tendon graft**
CC Exclusion 7th character A see Appendix A
PDX collection 0911

CC +7th **T84.418 Breakdown (mechanical) of other internal orthopedic devices, implants and grafts**
CC Exclusion 7th character A see Appendix A
PDX collection 0911

\+ **T84.42 Displacement of other internal orthopedic devices, implants and grafts**
Malposition of other internal orthopedic devices, implants and grafts

CC +7th **T84.420 Displacement of muscle and tendon graft**
CC Exclusion 7th character A see Appendix A
PDX collection 0911

CC +7th **T84.428 Displacement of other internal orthopedic devices, implants and grafts**
CC Exclusion 7th character A see Appendix A PDX collection 0911

+ **T84.49 Other mechanical complication of other internal orthopedic devices, implants and grafts**
Mechanical complication of other internal orthopedic devices, implants and grafts NOS
Obstruction (mechanical) of other internal orthopedic devices, implants and grafts
Perforation of other internal orthopedic devices, implants and grafts
Protrusion of other internal orthopedic devices, implants and grafts

CC +7th **T84.490 Other mechanical complication of muscle and tendon graft**
CC Exclusion 7th character A see Appendix A PDX collection 0911

CC +7th **T84.498 Other mechanical complication of other internal orthopedic devices, implants and grafts**
CC Exclusion 7th character A see Appendix A PDX collection 0911

+ **T84.5 Infection and inflammatory reaction due to internal joint prosthesis**
Use additional code to identify infection

CC X+7th **T84.50 Infection and inflammatory reaction due to unspecified internal joint prosthesis**
CC Exclusion 7th character A see Appendix A PDX collection 1459

CC X+7th **T84.51 Infection and inflammatory reaction due to internal right hip prosthesis**
CC Exclusion 7th character A see Appendix A PDX collection 1459

CC X+7th **T84.52 Infection and inflammatory reaction due to internal left hip prosthesis**
CC Exclusion 7th character A see Appendix A PDX collection 1459

CC X+7th **T84.53 Infection and inflammatory reaction due to internal right knee prosthesis**
CC Exclusion 7th character A see Appendix A PDX collection 1459

CC X+7th **T84.54 Infection and inflammatory reaction due to internal left knee prosthesis**
CC Exclusion 7th character A see Appendix A PDX collection 1459

CC X+7th **T84.59 Infection and inflammatory reaction due to other internal joint prosthesis**
CC Exclusion 7th character A see Appendix A PDX collection 1459

+ **T84.6 Infection and inflammatory reaction due to internal fixation device**
Use additional code to identify infection

CC X+7th **T84.60 Infection and inflammatory reaction due to internal fixation device of unspecified site**
CC Exclusion 7th character A see Appendix A PDX collection 1459
HAC 7th character A see Appendix B for HAC conditional logic

+ **T84.61 Infection and inflammatory reaction due to internal fixation device of arm**

CC +7th **T84.610 Infection and inflammatory reaction due to internal fixation device of right humerus**
CC Exclusion 7th character A see Appendix A PDX collection 1459
HAC 7th character A see Appendix B for HAC conditional logic

CC +7th **T84.611 Infection and inflammatory reaction due to internal fixation device of left humerus**
CC Exclusion 7th character A see Appendix A PDX collection 1459
HAC 7th character A see Appendix B for HAC conditional logic

CC +7th **T84.612 Infection and inflammatory reaction due to internal fixation device of right radius**
CC Exclusion 7th character A see Appendix A PDX collection 1459
HAC 7th character A see Appendix B for HAC conditional logic

CC +7th **T84.613 Infection and inflammatory reaction due to internal fixation device of left radius**
CC Exclusion 7th character A see Appendix A PDX collection 1459
HAC 7th character A see Appendix B for HAC conditional logic

CC +7th **T84.614 Infection and inflammatory reaction due to internal fixation device of right ulna**
CC Exclusion 7th character A see Appendix A PDX collection 1459
HAC 7th character A see Appendix B for HAC conditional logic

CC +7th **T84.615 Infection and inflammatory reaction due to internal fixation device of left ulna**
CC Exclusion 7th character A see Appendix A PDX collection 1459
HAC 7th character A see Appendix B for HAC conditional logic

CC +7th **T84.619 Infection and inflammatory reaction due to internal fixation device of unspecified bone of arm**
CC Exclusion 7th character A see Appendix A PDX collection 1459
HAC 7th character A see Appendix B for HAC conditional logic

+ **T84.62 Infection and inflammatory reaction due to internal fixation device of leg**

CC +7th **T84.620 Infection and inflammatory reaction due to internal fixation device of right femur**
CC Exclusion 7th character A see Appendix A PDX collection 1459

CC +7th **T84.621 Infection and inflammatory reaction due to internal fixation device of left femur**
CC Exclusion 7th character A see Appendix A PDX collection 1459

CC +7th **T84.622 Infection and inflammatory reaction due to internal fixation device of right tibia**
CC Exclusion 7th character A see Appendix A PDX collection 1459

CC +7th **T84.623 Infection and inflammatory reaction due to internal fixation device of left tibia**
CC Exclusion 7th character A see Appendix A PDX collection 1459

CC +7th **T84.624 Infection and inflammatory reaction due to internal fixation device of right fibula**
CC Exclusion 7th character A see Appendix A PDX collection 1459

CC +7th **T84.625 Infection and inflammatory reaction due to internal fixation device of left fibula**
CC Exclusion 7th character A see Appendix A PDX collection 1459

CC +7th **T84.629 Infection and inflammatory reaction due to internal fixation device of unspecified bone of leg**
CC Exclusion 7th character A see Appendix A PDX collection 1459

CC X+7th **T84.63 Infection and inflammatory reaction due to internal fixation device of spine**
CC Exclusion 7th character A see Appendix A PDX collection 1459
HAC 7th character A see Appendix B for HAC conditional logic

CC X+7th **T84.69 Infection and inflammatory reaction due to internal fixation device of other site**
CC Exclusion 7th character A see Appendix A PDX collection 1459
HAC 7th character A see Appendix B for HAC conditional logic

CC X+7th **T84.7 Infection and inflammatory reaction due to other internal orthopedic prosthetic devices, implants and grafts**
Use additional code to identify infection
CC Exclusion 7th character A see Appendix A PDX collection 1459
HAC 7th character A see Appendix B for HAC conditional logic

+ **T84.8 Other specified complications of internal orthopedic prosthetic devices, implants and grafts**

CC X+7th **T84.81 Embolism due to internal orthopedic prosthetic devices, implants and grafts**
CC Exclusion 7th character A see Appendix A PDX collection 1459

CC X+7th **T84.82 Fibrosis due to internal orthopedic prosthetic devices, implants and grafts**
CC Exclusion 7th character A see Appendix A PDX collection 1459

CC X+7th **T84.83 Hemorrhage due to internal orthopedic prosthetic devices, implants and grafts**
CC Exclusion 7th character A see Appendix A PDX collection 1459

CC X+7th **T84.84 Pain due to internal orthopedic prosthetic devices, implants and grafts**
CC Exclusion 7th character A see Appendix A PDX collection 1459

CC X+7th **T84.85 Stenosis due to internal orthopedic prosthetic devices, implants and grafts**
CC Exclusion 7th character A see Appendix A PDX collection 1459

CC X+7th **T84.86 Thrombosis due to internal orthopedic prosthetic devices, implants and grafts**
CC Exclusion 7th character A see Appendix A PDX collection 1459

CC X+7th **T84.89 Other specified complication of internal orthopedic prosthetic devices, implants and grafts**
CC Exclusion 7th character A see Appendix A PDX collection 1459

CC X+7th **T84.9 Unspecified complication of internal orthopedic prosthetic device, implant and graft**
CC Exclusion 7th character A see Appendix A PDX collection 1459

T85 Complications of other internal prosthetic devices, implants and grafts
Excludes2: *failure and rejection of transplanted organs and tissue (T86.-)*

The appropriate 7th character is to be added to each code from category T85
A initial encounter
D subsequent encounter
S sequela

\+ **T85.0 Mechanical complication of ventricular intracranial (communicating) shunt**

CC X+7th **T85.01 Breakdown (mechanical) of ventricular intracranial (communicating) shunt**
CC Exclusion 7th character A see Appendix A PDX collection 1460

CC X+7th **T85.02 Displacement of ventricular intracranial (communicating) shunt**
Malposition of ventricular intracranial (communicating) shunt
CC Exclusion 7th character A see Appendix A PDX collection 1460

CC X+7th **T85.03 Leakage of ventricular intracranial (communicating) shunt**
CC Exclusion 7th character A see Appendix A PDX collection 1460

CC X+7th **T85.09 Other mechanical complication of ventricular intracranial (communicating) shunt**
Obstruction (mechanical) of ventricular intracranial (communicating) shunt
Perforation of ventricular intracranial (communicating) shunt
Protrusion of ventricular intracranial (communicating) shunt
CC Exclusion 7th character A see Appendix A PDX collection 1460

\+ **T85.1 Mechanical complication of implanted electronic stimulator of nervous system**

\+ **T85.11 Breakdown (mechanical) of implanted electronic stimulator of nervous system**

CC +7th **T85.110 Breakdown (mechanical) of implanted electronic neurostimulator (electrode) of brain**
CC Exclusion 7th character A see Appendix A PDX collection 1460

CC +7th **T85.111 Breakdown (mechanical) of implanted electronic neurostimulator (electrode) of peripheral nerve**
CC Exclusion 7th character A see Appendix A PDX collection 1460

CC +7th **T85.112 Breakdown (mechanical) of implanted electronic neurostimulator (electrode) of spinal cord**
CC Exclusion 7th character A see Appendix A PDX collection 1460

CC +7th **T85.118 Breakdown (mechanical) of other implanted electronic stimulator of nervous system**
CC Exclusion 7th character A see Appendix A PDX collection 1460

\+ **T85.12 Displacement of implanted electronic stimulator of nervous system**
Malposition of implanted electronic stimulator of nervous system

CC +7th **T85.120 Displacement of implanted electronic neurostimulator (electrode) of brain**
CC Exclusion 7th character A see Appendix A PDX collection 1460

CC +7th **T85.121 Displacement of implanted electronic neurostimulator (electrode) of peripheral nerve**
CC Exclusion 7th character A see Appendix A PDX collection 1460

CC +7th **T85.122 Displacement of implanted electronic neurostimulator (electrode) of spinal cord**
CC Exclusion 7th character A see Appendix A PDX collection 1460

CC +7th **T85.128 Displacement of other implanted electronic stimulator of nervous system**
CC Exclusion 7th character A see Appendix A PDX collection 1460

\+ **T85.19 Other mechanical complication of implanted electronic stimulator of nervous system**
Leakage of implanted electronic stimulator of nervous system
Obstruction (mechanical) of implanted electronic stimulator of nervous system
Perforation of implanted electronic stimulator of nervous system
Protrusion of implanted electronic stimulator of nervous system

CC +7th **T85.190 Other mechanical complication of implanted electronic neurostimulator (electrode) of brain**
CC Exclusion 7th character A see Appendix A PDX collection 1460

CC +7th **T85.191 Other mechanical complication of implanted electronic neurostimulator (electrode) of peripheral nerve**
CC Exclusion 7th character A see Appendix A PDX collection 1460

CC +7th **T85.192 Other mechanical complication of implanted electronic neurostimulator (electrode) of spinal cord**
CC Exclusion 7th character A see Appendix A PDX collection 1460

CC +7th **T85.199 Other mechanical complication of other implanted electronic stimulator of nervous system**
CC Exclusion 7th character A see Appendix A PDX collection 1460

\+ **T85.2 Mechanical complication of intraocular lens**

CC X+7th **T85.21 Breakdown (mechanical) of intraocular lens**
CC Exclusion 7th character A see Appendix A PDX collection 1461

CC X+7th **T85.22 Displacement of intraocular lens**
Malposition of intraocular lens
CC Exclusion 7th character A see Appendix A PDX collection 1461

CC X+7th **T85.29 Other mechanical complication of intraocular lens**
Obstruction (mechanical) of intraocular lens
Perforation of intraocular lens
Protrusion of intraocular lens
CC Exclusion 7th character A see Appendix A PDX collection 1461

\+ **T85.3 Mechanical complication of other ocular prosthetic devices, implants and grafts**
Excludes2: *other complications of corneal graft (T86.84-)*

\+ **T85.31 Breakdown (mechanical) of other ocular prosthetic devices, implants and grafts**

CC +7th **T85.310 Breakdown (mechanical) of prosthetic orbit of right eye**
CC Exclusion 7th character A see Appendix A PDX collection 1462

CC +7th **T85.311 Breakdown (mechanical) of prosthetic orbit of left eye**
CC Exclusion 7th character A see Appendix A PDX collection 1462

+7th **T85.318 Breakdown (mechanical) of other ocular prosthetic devices, implants and grafts**

\+ **T85.32 Displacement of other ocular prosthetic devices, implants and grafts**
Malposition of other ocular prosthetic devices, implants and grafts

CC +7th **T85.320 Displacement of prosthetic orbit of right eye**
CC Exclusion 7th character A see Appendix A PDX collection 1462

CC +7th **T85.321 Displacement of prosthetic orbit of left eye**
CC Exclusion 7th character A see Appendix A PDX collection 1462

+7th **T85.328 Displacement of other ocular prosthetic devices, implants and grafts**

+ **T85.39 Other mechanical complication of other ocular prosthetic devices, implants and grafts**
Obstruction (mechanical) of other ocular prosthetic devices, implants and grafts
Perforation of other ocular prosthetic devices, implants and grafts
Protrusion of other ocular prosthetic devices, implants and grafts

CC +7th **T85.390 Other mechanical complication of prosthetic orbit of right eye**
CC Exclusion 7th character A see Appendix A PDX collection 1462

CC +7th **T85.391 Other mechanical complication of prosthetic orbit of left eye**
CC Exclusion 7th character A see Appendix A PDX collection 1462

+7th **T85.398 Other mechanical complication of other ocular prosthetic devices, implants and grafts**

+ **T85.4 Mechanical complication of breast prosthesis and implant**

CC X+7th **T85.41 Breakdown (mechanical) of breast prosthesis and implant**
CC Exclusion 7th character A see Appendix A PDX collection 1463

CC X+7th **T85.42 Displacement of breast prosthesis and implant**
Malposition of breast prosthesis and implant
CC Exclusion 7th character A see Appendix A PDX collection 1463

CC X+7th **T85.43 Leakage of breast prosthesis and implant**
CC Exclusion 7th character A see Appendix A PDX collection 1463

CC X+7th **T85.44 Capsular contracture of breast implant**
CC Exclusion 7th character A see Appendix A PDX collection 1463

CC X+7th **T85.49 Other mechanical complication of breast prosthesis and implant**
Obstruction (mechanical) of breast prosthesis and implant
Perforation of breast prosthesis and implant
Protrusion of breast prosthesis and implant
CC Exclusion 7th character A see Appendix A PDX collection 1463

+ **T85.5 Mechanical complication of gastrointestinal prosthetic devices, implants and grafts**

+ **T85.51 Breakdown (mechanical) of gastrointestinal prosthetic devices, implants and grafts**

CC +7th **T85.510 Breakdown (mechanical) of bile duct prosthesis**
CC Exclusion 7th character A see Appendix A PDX collection 1464

CC +7th **T85.511 Breakdown (mechanical) of esophageal anti-reflux device**
CC Exclusion 7th character A see Appendix A PDX collection 1464

CC +7th **T85.518 Breakdown (mechanical) of other gastrointestinal prosthetic devices, implants and grafts**
CC Exclusion 7th character A see Appendix A PDX collection 1464

+ **T85.52 Displacement of gastrointestinal prosthetic devices, implants and grafts**
Malposition of gastrointestinal prosthetic devices, implants and grafts

CC +7th **T85.520 Displacement of bile duct prosthesis**
CC Exclusion 7th character A see Appendix A PDX collection 1464

CC +7th **T85.521 Displacement of esophageal anti-reflux device**
CC Exclusion 7th character A see Appendix A PDX collection 1464

CC +7th **T85.528 Displacement of other gastrointestinal prosthetic devices, implants and grafts**
CC Exclusion 7th character A see Appendix A PDX collection 1464

+ **T85.59 Other mechanical complication of gastrointestinal prosthetic devices, implants and**
Obstruction, mechanical of gastrointestinal prosthetic devices, implants and grafts
Perforation of gastrointestinal prosthetic devices, implants and grafts
Protrusion of gastrointestinal prosthetic devices, implants and grafts

CC +7th **T85.590 Other mechanical complication of bile duct prosthesis**
CC Exclusion 7th character A see Appendix A PDX collection 1464

CC +7th **T85.591 Other mechanical complication of esophageal anti-reflux device**
CC Exclusion 7th character A see Appendix A PDX collection 1464

CC +7th **T85.598 Other mechanical complication of other gastrointestinal prosthetic devices, implants and grafts**
CC Exclusion 7th character A see Appendix A PDX collection 1464

+ **T85.6 Mechanical complication of other specified internal and external prosthetic devices, implants and grafts**
Review coding guidelines C.4.a.5.a and C.4.a.5.b

+ **T85.61 Breakdown (mechanical) of other specified internal prosthetic devices, implants and grafts**

CC +7th **T85.610 Breakdown (mechanical) of epidural and subdural infusion catheter**
CC Exclusion 7th character A see Appendix A PDX collection 1465

CC +7th **T85.611 Breakdown (mechanical) of intraperitoneal dialysis catheter**
Excludes1: *mechanical complication of vascular dialysis catheter (T82.4-)*
CC Exclusion 7th character A see Appendix A PDX collection 1466

CC +7th **T85.612 Breakdown (mechanical) of permanent sutures**
Excludes1: *mechanical complication of permanent (wire) suture used in bone repair (T84.1-T84.2)*
CC Exclusion 7th character A see Appendix A PDX collection 1467

CC +7th **T85.613 Breakdown (mechanical) of artificial skin graft and decellularized allodermis**
Failure of artificial skin graft and decellularized allodermis
Non-adherence of artificial skin graft and decellularized allodermis
Poor incorporation of artificial skin graft and decellularized allodermis
Shearing of artificial skin graft and decellularized allodermis
CC Exclusion 7th character A see Appendix A PDX collection 1468

CC +7th **T85.614 Breakdown (mechanical) of insulin pump**
CC Exclusion 7th character A see Appendix A PDX collection 1469

CC +7th **T85.618 Breakdown (mechanical) of other specified internal prosthetic devices, implants and grafts**
CC Exclusion 7th character A see Appendix A PDX collection 1467

+ **T85.62 Displacement of other specified internal prosthetic devices, implants and grafts**
Malposition of other specified internal prosthetic devices, implants and grafts

CC +7th **T85.620 Displacement of epidural and subdural infusion catheter**
CC Exclusion 7th character A see Appendix A PDX collection 1465

CC +7th **T85.621 Displacement of intraperitoneal dialysis catheter**
Excludes1: *mechanical complication of vascular dialysis catheter (T82.4-)*
CC Exclusion 7th character A see Appendix A PDX collection 1466

CC +7th **T85.622 Displacement of permanent sutures**
Excludes1: *mechanical complication of permanent (wire) suture used in bone repair (T84.1-T84.2)*
CC Exclusion 7th character A see Appendix A PDX collection 1467

CC +7th **T85.623 Displacement of artificial skin graft and decellularized allodermis**
Dislodgement of artificial skin graft and decellularized allodermis
Displacement of artificial skin graft and decellularized allodermis
CC Exclusion 7th character A see Appendix A PDX collection 1468

CC +7th **T85.624 Displacement of insulin pump**
CC Exclusion 7th character A see Appendix A PDX collection 1469

CC +7th **T85.628 Displacement of other specified internal prosthetic devices, implants and grafts**
CC Exclusion 7th character A see Appendix A PDX collection 1467

+ **T85.63 Leakage of other specified internal prosthetic devices, implants and grafts**

CC +7th **T85.630 Leakage of epidural and subdural infusion catheter**
CC Exclusion 7th character A see Appendix A PDX collection 1465

CC +7th **T85.631 Leakage of intraperitoneal dialysis catheter**
Excludes1: *mechanical complication of vascular dialysis catheter (T82.4)*
CC Exclusion 7th character A see Appendix A PDX collection 1466

CC +7th **T85.633 Leakage of insulin pump**
CC Exclusion 7th character A see Appendix A PDX collection 1469

CC +7th **T85.638 Leakage of other specified internal prosthetic devices, implants and grafts**
CC Exclusion 7th character A see Appendix A PDX collection 1467

+ **T85.69 Other mechanical complication of other specified internal prosthetic devices, implants and grafts**
Obstruction, mechanical of other specified internal prosthetic devices, implants and grafts
Perforation of other specified internal prosthetic devices, implants and grafts
Protrusion of other specified internal prosthetic devices, implants and grafts

CC +7th **T85.690 Other mechanical complication of epidural and subdural infusion catheter**
CC Exclusion 7th character A see Appendix A PDX collection 1465

CC +7th **T85.691 Other mechanical complication of intraperitoneal dialysis catheter**
Excludes1: *mechanical complication of vascular dialysis catheter (T82.4)*
CC Exclusion 7th character A see Appendix A PDX collection 1466

CC +7th **T85.692 Other mechanical complication of permanent sutures**
Excludes1: *mechanical complication of permanent (wire) suture used in bone repair (T84.1-T84.2)*
CC Exclusion 7th character A see Appendix A PDX collection 1467

CC +7th **T85.693 Other mechanical complication of artificial skin graft and decellularized allodermis**
CC Exclusion 7th character A see Appendix A PDX collection 1468

CC +7th **T85.694 Other mechanical complication of insulin pump**
CC Exclusion 7th character A see Appendix A PDX collection 1469

CC +7th **T85.698 Other mechanical complication of other specified internal prosthetic devices, implants and grafts**
Mechanical complication of nonabsorbable surgical material NOS
CC Exclusion 7th character A see Appendix A PDX collection 1467

+ **T85.7 Infection and inflammatory reaction due to other internal prosthetic devices, implants and grafts**
Use additional code to identify infection

CC X+7th **T85.71 Infection and inflammatory reaction due to peritoneal dialysis catheter**
CC Exclusion 7th character A see Appendix A PDX collection 1467

CC X+7th **T85.72 Infection and inflammatory reaction due to insulin pump**
CC Exclusion 7th character A see Appendix A PDX collection 1470

CC X+7th **T85.79 Infection and inflammatory reaction due to other internal prosthetic devices, implants and grafts**
CC Exclusion 7th character A see Appendix A PDX collection 1470

+ **T85.8 Other specified complications of internal prosthetic devices, implants and grafts, not elsewhere classified**

CC X+7th **T85.81 Embolism due to internal prosthetic devices, implants and grafts, not elsewhere classified**
CC Exclusion 7th character A see Appendix A PDX collection 1470

CC X+7th **T85.82 Fibrosis due to internal prosthetic devices, implants and grafts, not elsewhere classified**
CC Exclusion 7th character A see Appendix A PDX collection 1470

CC X+7th **T85.83 Hemorrhage due to internal prosthetic devices, implants and grafts, not elsewhere classified**
CC Exclusion 7th character A see Appendix A PDX collection 1470

CC X+7th **T85.84 Pain due to internal prosthetic devices, implants and grafts, not elsewhere classified**
CC Exclusion 7th character A see Appendix A PDX collection 1470

CC X+7th **T85.85 Stenosis due to internal prosthetic devices, implants and grafts, not elsewhere classified**
CC Exclusion 7th character A see Appendix A PDX collection 1470

CC X+7th **T85.86 Thrombosis due to internal prosthetic devices, implants and grafts, not elsewhere classified**
CC Exclusion 7th character A see Appendix A PDX collection 1470

CC X+7th **T85.89 Other specified complication of internal prosthetic devices, implants and grafts, not elsewhere classified**
CC Exclusion 7th character A see Appendix A PDX collection 1470

X+7th **T85.9 Unspecified complication of internal prosthetic device, implant and graft**
Complication of internal prosthetic device, implant and graft NOS

T86 Complications of transplanted organs and tissue
Use additional code to identify other transplant complications, such as:
graft-versus-host disease (D89.81-)
malignancy associated with organ transplant (C80.2)
post-transplant lymphoproliferative disorders (PTLD) (D47.Z1)
Review coding guideline C.2.r
Review coding guideline C.19.g.3

+ **T86.0 Complications of bone marrow transplant**

CC **T86.00 Unspecified complication of bone marrow transplant**
CC Exclusion see Appendix A PDX collection 0514

CC **T86.01 Bone marrow transplant rejection**
CC Exclusion see Appendix A PDX collection 0514

CC **T86.02 Bone marrow transplant failure**
CC Exclusion see Appendix A PDX collection 0514

CC **T86.03 Bone marrow transplant infection**
CC Exclusion see Appendix A PDX collection 0514

CC **T86.09 Other complications of bone marrow transplant**
CC Exclusion see Appendix A PDX collection 0514

+ **T86.1 Complications of kidney transplant**
Review coding guideline C.19.g.3.b

CC **T86.10 Unspecified complication of kidney transplant**
CC Exclusion see Appendix A PDX collection 1471

CC **T86.11 Kidney transplant rejection**
CC Exclusion see Appendix A PDX collection 1471

CC **T86.12 Kidney transplant failure**
CC Exclusion see Appendix A PDX collection 1471
AHA CC: 1Q, 2014, 24

CC **T86.13 Kidney transplant infection**
Use additional code to specify infection
CC Exclusion see Appendix A PDX collection 1471

CC **T86.19 Other complication of kidney transplant**
CC Exclusion see Appendix A PDX collection 1471

+ **T86.2 Complications of heart transplant**
Excludes1: *complication of:*
artificial heart device (T82.5)
heart-lung transplant (T86.3)

CC **T86.20 Unspecified complication of heart transplant**
CC Exclusion see Appendix A PDX collection 1472

CC **T86.21 Heart transplant rejection**
CC Exclusion see Appendix A PDX collection 1472

CC **T86.22 Heart transplant failure**
CC Exclusion see Appendix A PDX collection 1472

CC **T86.23 Heart transplant infection**
Use additional code to specify infection
CC Exclusion see Appendix A PDX collection 1472

\+ **T86.29 Other complications of heart transplant**
CC **T86.290 Cardiac allograft vasculopathy**
Excludes1: *atherosclerosis of coronary arteries (I25.75-, I25.76-, I25.81-)*
CC Exclusion see Appendix A PDX collection 1472
CC **T86.298 Other complications of heart transplant**
CC Exclusion see Appendix A PDX collection 1472

\+ **T86.3 Complications of heart-lung transplant**
CC **T86.30 Unspecified complication of heart-lung transplant**
CC Exclusion see Appendix A PDX collection 1472
CC **T86.31 Heart-lung transplant rejection**
CC Exclusion see Appendix A PDX collection 1472
CC **T86.32 Heart-lung transplant failure**
CC Exclusion see Appendix A PDX collection 1472
CC **T86.33 Heart-lung transplant infection**
Use additional code to specify infection
CC Exclusion see Appendix A PDX collection 1472
CC **T86.39 Other complications of heart-lung transplant**
CC Exclusion see Appendix A PDX collection 1472

\+ **T86.4 Complications of liver transplant**
CC **T86.40 Unspecified complication of liver transplant**
CC Exclusion see Appendix A PDX collection 1473
CC **T86.41 Liver transplant rejection**
CC Exclusion see Appendix A PDX collection 1473
CC **T86.42 Liver transplant failure**
CC Exclusion see Appendix A PDX collection 1473
CC **T86.43 Liver transplant infection**
Use additional code to identify infection, such as:
Cytomegalovirus (CMV) infection (B25.-)
CC Exclusion see Appendix A PDX collection 1473
CC **T86.49 Other complications of liver transplant**
CC Exclusion see Appendix A PDX collection 1473

CC **T86.5 Complications of stem cell transplant**
Complications from stem cells from peripheral blood
Complications from stem cells from umbilical cord
CC Exclusion see Appendix A PDX collection 1474

\+ **T86.8 Complications of other transplanted organs and tissues**
\+ **T86.81 Complications of lung transplant**
Excludes1: *complication of heart-lung transplant (T86.3-)*
CC **T86.810 Lung transplant rejection**
CC Exclusion see Appendix A PDX collection 1475
CC **T86.811 Lung transplant failure**
CC Exclusion see Appendix A PDX collection 1475
CC **T86.812 Lung transplant infection**
Use additional code to specify infection
CC Exclusion see Appendix A PDX collection 1475
CC **T86.818 Other complications of lung transplant**
CC Exclusion see Appendix A PDX collection 1475
CC **T86.819 Unspecified complication of lung transplant**
CC Exclusion see Appendix A PDX collection 1475
\+ **T86.82 Complications of skin graft (allograft) (autograft)**
Excludes2: *complication of artificial skin graft (T85.693)*
CC **T86.820 Skin graft (allograft) rejection**
CC Exclusion see Appendix A PDX collection 1476
CC **T86.821 Skin graft (allograft) (autograft) failure**
CC Exclusion see Appendix A PDX collection 1476
CC **T86.822 Skin graft (allograft) (autograft) infection**
Use additional code to specify infection
CC Exclusion see Appendix A PDX collection 1476
CC **T86.828 Other complications of skin graft (allograft) (autograft)**
CC Exclusion see Appendix A PDX collection 1476
CC **T86.829 Unspecified complication of skin graft (allograft) (autograft)**
CC Exclusion see Appendix A PDX collection 1476
\+ **T86.83 Complications of bone graft**
Excludes2: *mechanical complications of bone graft (T84.3-)*
CC **T86.830 Bone graft rejection**
CC Exclusion see Appendix A PDX collection 1477
CC **T86.831 Bone graft failure**
CC Exclusion see Appendix A PDX collection 1477
CC **T86.832 Bone graft infection**
Use additional code to specify infection
CC Exclusion see Appendix A PDX collection 1477
CC **T86.838 Other complications of bone graft**
CC Exclusion see Appendix A PDX collection 1477
CC **T86.839 Unspecified complication of bone graft**
CC Exclusion see Appendix A PDX collection 1477
\+ **T86.84 Complications of corneal transplant**
Excludes2: *mechanical complications of corneal graft (T85.3-)*
CC **T86.840 Corneal transplant rejection**
CC Exclusion see Appendix A PDX collection 1478
CC **T86.841 Corneal transplant failure**
CC Exclusion see Appendix A PDX collection 1478
CC **T86.842 Corneal transplant infection**
Use additional code to specify infection
CC Exclusion see Appendix A PDX collection 1479
CC **T86.848 Other complications of corneal transplant**
CC Exclusion see Appendix A PDX collection 1479
CC **T86.849 Unspecified complication of corneal transplant**
CC Exclusion see Appendix A PDX collection 1479
\+ **T86.85 Complication of intestine transplant**
CC **T86.850 Intestine transplant rejection**
CC Exclusion see Appendix A PDX collection 0495
CC **T86.851 Intestine transplant failure**
CC Exclusion see Appendix A PDX collection 0495
CC **T86.852 Intestine transplant infection**
Use additional code to specify infection
CC Exclusion see Appendix A PDX collection 0495
CC **T86.858 Other complications of intestine transplant**
CC Exclusion see Appendix A PDX collection 0495
CC **T86.859 Unspecified complication of intestine transplant**
CC Exclusion see Appendix A PDX collection 0495
\+ **T86.89 Complications of other transplanted tissue**
Transplant failure or rejection of pancreas
CC **T86.890 Other transplanted tissue rejection**
CC Exclusion see Appendix A PDX collection 1480
CC **T86.891 Other transplanted tissue failure**
CC Exclusion see Appendix A PDX collection 1480
CC **T86.892 Other transplanted tissue infection**
Use additional code to specify infection
CC Exclusion see Appendix A PDX collection 1480
CC **T86.898 Other complications of other transplanted tissue**
CC Exclusion see Appendix A PDX collection 1480
CC **T86.899 Unspecified complication of other transplanted tissue**
CC Exclusion see Appendix A PDX collection 1480

\+ **T86.9 Complication of unspecified transplanted organ and tissue**
CC **T86.90 Unspecified complication of unspecified transplanted organ and tissue**
CC Exclusion see Appendix A PDX collection 0495
CC **T86.91 Unspecified transplanted organ and tissue rejection**
CC Exclusion see Appendix A PDX collection 0495
CC **T86.92 Unspecified transplanted organ and tissue failure**
CC Exclusion see Appendix A PDX collection 0495
CC **T86.93 Unspecified transplanted organ and tissue infection**
Use additional code to specify infection
CC Exclusion see Appendix A PDX collection 0495
CC **T86.99 Other complications of unspecified transplanted organ and tissue**
CC Exclusion see Appendix A PDX collection 0495

T87 Complications peculiar to reattachment and amputation

\+ **T87.0 Complications of reattached (part of) upper extremity**
\+ **T87.0X Complications of reattached (part of) upper extremity**
CC **T87.0X1 Complications of reattached (part of) right upper extremity**
CC Exclusion see Appendix A PDX collection 1481
CC **T87.0X2 Complications of reattached (part of) left upper extremity**
CC Exclusion see Appendix A PDX collection 1481
CC **T87.0X9 Complications of reattached (part of) unspecified upper extremity**
CC Exclusion see Appendix A PDX collection 1481

+ **T87.1 Complications of reattached (part of) lower extremity**
+ **T87.1X Complications of reattached (part of) lower extremity**
CC **T87.1X1 Complications of reattached (part of) right lower extremity**
CC Exclusion see Appendix A PDX collection 1482
CC **T87.1X2 Complications of reattached (part of) left lower extremity**
CC Exclusion see Appendix A PDX collection 1482
CC **T87.1X9 Complications of reattached (part of) unspecified lower extremity**
CC Exclusion see Appendix A PDX collection 1482
CC **T87.2 Complications of other reattached body part**
CC Exclusion see Appendix A PDX collection 1483
+ **T87.3 Neuroma of amputation stump**
T87.30 Neuroma of amputation stump, unspecified extremity
T87.31 Neuroma of amputation stump, right upper extremity
T87.32 Neuroma of amputation stump, left upper extremity
T87.33 Neuroma of amputation stump, right lower extremity
T87.34 Neuroma of amputation stump, left lower extremity
+ **T87.4 Infection of amputation stump**
CC **T87.40 Infection of amputation stump, unspecified extremity**
CC Exclusion see Appendix A PDX collection 1484
CC **T87.41 Infection of amputation stump, right upper extremity**
CC Exclusion see Appendix A PDX collection 1484
CC **T87.42 Infection of amputation stump, left upper extremity**
CC Exclusion see Appendix A PDX collection 1484
CC **T87.43 Infection of amputation stump, right lower extremity**
CC Exclusion see Appendix A PDX collection 1484
CC **T87.44 Infection of amputation stump, left lower extremity**
CC Exclusion see Appendix A PDX collection 1484
+ **T87.5 Necrosis of amputation stump**
T87.50 Necrosis of amputation stump, unspecified extremity
T87.51 Necrosis of amputation stump, right upper extremity
T87.52 Necrosis of amputation stump, left upper extremity
T87.53 Necrosis of amputation stump, right lower extremity
T87.54 Necrosis of amputation stump, left lower extremity
+ **T87.8 Other complications of amputation stump**
T87.81 Dehiscence of amputation stump
T87.89 Other complications of amputation stump
Amputation stump contracture
Amputation stump contracture of next proximal joint
Amputation stump flexion
Amputation stump edema
Amputation stump hematoma
Excludes2: *phantom limb syndrome (G54.6-G54.7)*
T87.9 Unspecified complications of amputation stump

T88 Other complications of surgical and medical care, not elsewhere classified

Excludes2: *complication following infusion, transfusion and therapeutic injection (T80.-)*
complication following procedure NEC (T81.-)
complications of anesthesia in labor and delivery (O74.-)
complications of anesthesia in pregnancy (O29.-)
complications of anesthesia in puerperium (O89.-)
complications of devices, implants and grafts (T82-T85)
complications of obstetric surgery and procedure (O75.4)
dermatitis due to drugs and medicaments (L23.3, L24.4, L25.1, L27.0-L27.1)
poisoning and toxic effects of drugs and chemicals (T36-T65 with fifth or sixth character 1-4 or 6)
specified complications classified elsewhere

The appropriate 7th character is to be added to each code from category T88
A initial encounter
D subsequent encounter
S sequela

CC X+7th **T88.0 Infection following immunization**
Sepsis following immunization
CC Exclusion 7th character A see Appendix A PDX collection 0948
Review coding guideline C.1.d.5

CC X+7th **T88.1 Other complications following immunization, not elsewhere classified**
Generalized vaccinia
Rash following immunization
Excludes1: *vaccinia not from vaccine (B08.011)*
Excludes2: *anaphylactic shock due to serum (T80.5-)*
other serum reactions (T80.6-)
postimmunization arthropathy (M02.2)
postimmunization encephalitis (G04.02)
postimmunization fever (R50.83)
CC Exclusion 7th character A see Appendix A PDX collection 1485
CC X+7th **T88.2 Shock due to anesthesia**
Use additional code for adverse effect, if applicable, to identify drug (T41.- with fifth or sixth character 5)
Excludes1: *complications of anesthesia (in):*
labor and delivery (O74.-)
pregnancy (O29.-)
puerperium (O89.-)
postprocedural shock NOS (T81.1-)
CC Exclusion 7th character A see Appendix A PDX collection 1441
CC X+7th **T88.3 Malignant hyperthermia due to anesthesia**
Use additional code for adverse effect, if applicable, to identify drug (T41.- with fifth or sixth character 5)
CC Exclusion 7th character A see Appendix A PDX collection 1486
X+7th **T88.4 Failed or difficult intubation**
+ **T88.5 Other complications of anesthesia**
Use additional code for adverse effect, if applicable, to identify drug (T41.- with fifth or sixth character 5)
X+7th **T88.51 Hypothermia following anesthesia**
X+7th **T88.52 Failed moderate sedation during procedure**
Failed conscious sedation during procedure
Excludes2: *personal history of failed moderate sedatio (Z92.83)*
X+7th **T88.59 Other complications of anesthesia**
CC X+7th **T88.6 Anaphylactic reaction due to adverse effect of correct drug or medicament properly administered**
Anaphylactic shock due to adverse effect of correct drug or medicament properly administered
Anaphylactoid reaction NOS
Use additional code for adverse effect, if applicable, to identify drug (T36-T50 with fifth or sixth character 5)
Excludes1: *anaphylactic reaction due to serum (T80.5-)*
anaphylactic shock or reaction due to adverse food reaction (T78.0-)
CC Exclusion 7th character A see Appendix A PDX collection 1426
X+7th **T88.7 Unspecified adverse effect of drug or medicament**
Drug hypersensitivity NOS
Drug reaction NOS
Use additional code for adverse effect, if applicable, to identify drug (T36-T50 with fifth or sixth character 5)
Excludes1: *specified adverse effects of drugs and medicaments (A00-R94 and T80-T88.6, T88.8)*
X+7th **T88.8 Other specified complications of surgical and medical care, not elsewhere classified**
Use additional code to identify the complication
X+7th **T88.9 Complication of surgical and medical care, unspecified**

Chapter 20: External Causes of Morbidity (V00-Y99)

NOTE This chapter permits the classification of environmental events and circumstances as the cause of injury, and other adverse effects. Where a code from this section is applicable, it is intended that it shall be used secondary to a code from another chapter of the Classification indicating the nature of the condition. Most often, the condition will be classifiable to Chapter 19, Injury, poisoning and certain other consequences of external causes (S00-T88). Other conditions that may be stated to be due to external causes are classified in Chapters 1 to 18. For these conditions, codes from Chapter 20 should be used to provide additional information as to the cause of the condition.

This chapter contains the following category blocks:

V00-X58	Accidents
V00-V99	Transport accidents
V00-V09	Pedestrian injured in transport accident
V10-V19	Pedal cycle rider injured in transport accident
V20-V29	Motorcycle rider injured in transport accident
V30-V39	Occupant of three-wheeled motor vehicle injured in transport accident
V40-V49	Car occupant injured in transport accident
V50-V59	Occupant of pick-up truck or van injured in transport accident
V60-V69	Occupant of heavy transport vehicle injured in transport accident
V70-V79	Bus occupant injured in transport accident
V80-V89	Other land transport accidents
V90-V94	Water transport accidents
V95-V97	Air and space transport accidents
V98-V99	Other and unspecified transport accidents
W00-X58	Other external causes of accidental injury
W00-W19	Slipping, tripping, stumbling and falls
W20-W49	Exposure to inanimate mechanical forces
W50-W64	Exposure to animate mechanical forces
W65-W74	Accidental non-transport drowning and submersion
W85-W99	Exposure to electric current, radiation and extreme ambient air temperature and pressure
X00-X08	Exposure to smoke, fire and flames
X10-X19	Contact with heat and hot substances
X30-X39	Exposure to forces of nature
X52-X58	Accidental exposure to other specified factors
X71-X83	Intentional self-harm
X92-Y08	Assault
Y21-Y33	Event of undetermined intent
Y35-Y38	Legal intervention, operations of war, military operations, and terrorism
Y62-Y84	Complications of medical and surgical care
Y62-Y69	Misadventures to patients during surgical and medical care
Y70-Y82	Medical devices associated with adverse incidents in diagnostic and therapeutic use
Y83-Y84	Surgical and other medical procedures as the cause of abnormal reaction of the patient, or of later complication, without mention of misadventure at the time of the procedure
Y90-Y99	Supplementary factors related to causes of morbidity classified elsewhere

C. Chapter-Specific Coding Guidelines

In addition to general coding guidelines, there are guidelines for specific diagnoses and/or conditions in the classification. Unless otherwise indicated, these guidelines apply to all health care settings. Please refer to Section II for guidelines on the selection of principal diagnosis.

20. Chapter 20: External Causes of Morbidity (V00-Y99)

The external causes of morbidity codes should never be sequenced as the first-listed or principal diagnosis.

External cause codes are intended to provide data for injury research and evaluation of injury prevention strategies. These codes capture how the injury or health condition happened (cause), the intent (unintentional or accidental; or intentional, such as suicide or assault), the place where the event occurred the activity of the patient at the time of the event, and the person's status (e.g., civilian, military).

There is no national requirement for mandatory ICD-10-CM external cause code reporting. Unless a provider is subject to a state-based external cause code reporting mandate or these codes are required by a particular payer, reporting of ICD-10-CM codes in Chapter 20, External Causes of Morbidity, is not required. In the absence of a mandatory reporting requirement, providers are encouraged to voluntarily report external cause codes, as they provide valuable data for injury research and evaluation of injury prevention strategies.

a. General External Cause Coding Guidelines

1) Used with any code in the range of A00.0-T88.9, Z00-Z99

An external cause code may be used with any code in the range of A00.0-T88.9, Z00-Z99, classification that is a health condition due to an external cause. Though they are most applicable to injuries, they are also valid for use with such things as infections or diseases due to an external source, and other health conditions, such as a heart attack that occurs during strenuous physical activity.

2) External cause code used for length of treatment

Assign the external cause code, with the appropriate 7th character (initial encounter, subsequent encounter or sequela) for each encounter for which the injury or condition is being treated. **Most categories in chapter 20 have a 7th character requirement for each applicable code. Most categories in this chapter have three 7th character values: A, initial encounter, D, subsequent encounter and S, sequela. While the patient may be seen by a new or different provider over the course of treatment for an injury or condition, assignment of the 7th character for external cause should match the 7th character of the code assigned for the associated injury or condition for the encounter.**

3) Use the full range of external cause codes

Use the full range of external cause codes to completely describe the cause, the intent, the place of occurrence, and if applicable, the activity of the patient at the time of the event, and the patient's status, for all injuries, and other health conditions due to an external cause.

4) Assign as many external cause codes as necessary

Assign as many external cause codes as necessary to fully explain each cause. If only one external code can be recorded, assign the code most related to the principal diagnosis.

5) The selection of the appropriate external cause code

The selection of the appropriate external cause code is guided by the Alphabetic Index of External Causes and by Inclusion and Exclusion notes in the Tabular List.

6) External cause code can never be a principal diagnosis

An external cause code can never be a principal (first-listed) diagnosis.

7) Combination external cause codes

Certain of the external cause codes are combination codes that identify sequential events that result in an injury, such as a fall which results in striking against an object. The injury may be due to either event or both. The combination external cause code used should correspond to the sequence of events regardless of which caused the most serious injury.

8) No external cause code needed in certain circumstances

No external cause code from Chapter 20 is needed if the external cause and intent are included in a code from another chapter (e.g. T36.0X1- Poisoning by penicillins, accidental (unintentional)).

b. Place of Occurrence Guideline

Codes from category Y92, Place of occurrence of the external cause, are secondary codes for use after other external cause codes to identify the location of the patient at the time of injury or other condition.

Generally, a place of occurrent code is **assigned** only once, at the initial encounter. **However, in the rare instance that a new injury occurs during hospitalization, an additional place of occurrence code may be assigned.**

A place of occurrence code is used only once, at the initial encounter for treatment. No 7th characters are used for Y92. Only one code from Y92 should be recorded on a medical record.

Do not use place of occurrence code Y92.9 if the place is not stated or is not applicable.

c. Activity Code

Assign a code from category Y93, Activity code, to describe the activity of the patient at the time the injury or other health condition occurred.

An activity code is used only once, at the initial encounter for treatment. Only one code from Y93 should be recorded on a medical record.

The activity codes are not applicable to poisonings, adverse effects, misadventures or sequela.

Do not assign Y93.9, Unspecified activity, if the activity is not stated.

A code from category Y93 is appropriate for use with external cause and intent codes if identifying the activity provides additional information about the event.

d. Place of Occurrence, Activity, and Status Codes Used with other External Cause Code

When applicable, place of occurrence, activity, and external cause status codes are sequenced after the main external cause code(s). Regardless of the number of external cause codes assigned, there should be only one place of occurrence code, one activity code, and one external cause status code assigned to an encounter.

e. If the Reporting Format Limits the Number of External Cause Codes

If the reporting format limits the number of external cause codes that can be used in reporting clinical data, report the code for the cause/intent most related to the principal diagnosis. If the format permits capture of additional external cause codes, the cause/intent, including medical misadventures, of the additional events should be reported rather than the codes for place, activity, or external status.

f. Multiple External Cause Coding Guidelines

More than one external cause code is required to fully describe the external cause of an illness or injury. The assignment of external cause codes should be sequenced in the following priority:

If two or more events cause separate injuries, an external cause code should be assigned for each cause. The first-listed external cause code will be selected in the following order:

External codes for child and adult abuse take priority over all other external cause codes.

See Section I.C.19., Child and Adult abuse guidelines.

External cause codes for terrorism events take priority over all other external cause codes except child and adult abuse.

External cause codes for cataclysmic events take priority over all other external cause codes except child and adult abuse and terrorism.

External cause codes for transport accidents take priority over all other external cause codes except cataclysmic events, child and adult abuse and terrorism.

Activity and external cause status codes are assigned following all causal (intent) external cause codes.

The first-listed external cause code should correspond to the cause of the most serious diagnosis due to an assault, accident, or self-harm, following the order of hierarchy listed above.

g. Child and Adult Abuse Guideline

Adult and child abuse, neglect and maltreatment are classified as assault. Any of the assault codes may be used to indicate the external cause of any injury resulting from the confirmed abuse.

For confirmed cases of abuse, neglect and maltreatment, when the perpetrator is known, a code from Y07, Perpetrator of maltreatment and neglect, should accompany any other assault codes.

See Section I.C.19. Adult and child abuse, neglect and other maltreatment

h. Unknown or Undetermined Intent Guideline

If the intent (accident, self-harm, assault) of the cause of an injury or other condition is unknown or unspecified, code the intent as accidental intent. All transport accident categories assume accidental intent.

1) Use of undetermined intent

External cause codes for events of undetermined intent are only for use if the documentation in the record specifies that the intent cannot be determined.

i. Sequelae (Late Effects) of External Cause Guidelines

1) Sequelae external cause codes

Sequela are reported using the external cause code with the 7th character "S" for sequela. These codes should be used with any report of a late effect or sequela resulting from a previous injury.

See Section I.B.10 Sequela (Late Effects)

2) Sequela external cause code with a related current injury

A sequela external cause code should never be used with a related current nature of injury code.

3) Use of sequela external cause codes for subsequent visits

Use a late effect external cause code for subsequent visits when a late effect of the initial injury is being treated. Do not use a late effect external cause code for subsequent visits for follow- up care (e.g., to assess healing, to receive rehabilitative therapy) of the injury when no late effect of the injury has been documented.

j. Terrorism Guidelines

1) Cause of injury identified by the Federal Government (FBI) as terrorism

When the cause of an injury is identified by the Federal Government (FBI) as terrorism, the first-listed external cause code should be a code from category Y38, Terrorism. The definition of terrorism employed by the FBI is found at the inclusion note at the beginning of category Y38. Use additional code for place of occurrence (Y92.-). More than one Y38 code may be assigned if the injury is the result of more than one mechanism of terrorism.

2) Cause of an injury is suspected to be the result of terrorism

When the cause of an injury is suspected to be the result of terrorism a code from category Y38 should not be assigned. Suspected cases should be classified as assault.

3) Code Y38.9, Terrorism, secondary effects

Assign code Y38.9, Terrorism, secondary effects, for conditions occurring subsequent to the terrorist event. This code should not be assigned for conditions that are due to the initial terrorist act.

It is acceptable to assign code Y38.9 with another code from Y38 if there is an injury due to the initial terrorist event and an injury that is a subsequent result of the terrorist event.

k. External cause status

A code from category Y99, External cause status, should be assigned whenever any other external cause code is assigned for an encounter, including an Activity code, except for the events noted below. Assign a code from category Y99, External cause status, to indicate the work status of the person at the time the event occurred. The status code indicates whether the event occurred during military activity, whether a non-military person was at work, whether an individual including a student or volunteer was involved in a non-work activity at the time of the causal event.

A code from Y99, External cause status, should be assigned, when applicable, with other external cause codes, such as transport accidents and falls. The external cause status codes are not applicable to poisonings, adverse effects, misadventures or late effects. Do not assign a code from category Y99 if no other external cause codes (cause, activity) are applicable for the encounter.

An external cause status code is used only once, at the initial encounter for treatment. Only one code from Y99 should be recorded on a medical record.

Do not assign code Y99.9, Unspecified external cause status, if the status is not stated.

Accidents (V00-X58)

Transport accidents (V00-V99)

Use additional code to identify:
Airbag injury (W22.1)
Type of street or road (Y92.4-)
Use of cellular telephone and other electronic equipment at the time of the transport accident (Y93.C-)

Excludes1: *agricultural vehicles in stationary use or maintenance (W31.-)*
assault by crashing of motor vehicle (Y03.-)
automobile or motor cycle in stationary use or maintenance- code to type of accident
crashing of motor vehicle, undetermined intent (Y32)
intentional self-harm by crashing of motor vehicle (X82)

Excludes2: *transport accidents due to cataclysm (X34-X38)*

NOTE This section is structured in 12 groups. Those relating to land transport accidents (V01-V89) reflect the victim's mode of transport and are subdivided to identify the victim's 'counterpart' or the type of event. The vehicle of which the injured person is an occupant is identified in the first two characters since it is seen as the most important factor to identify for prevention purposes. A transport accident is one in which the vehicle involved must be moving or running or in use for transport purposes at the time of the accident.

Pedestrian injured in transport accident (V00-V09)

Includes: person changing tire on transport vehicle
person examining engine of vehicle broken down in (on side of) road

Excludes1: *fall due to non-transport collision with other person (W03)*
pedestrian on foot falling (slipping) on ice and snow (W00.-)
struck or bumped by another person (W51)

V00 Pedestrian conveyance accident

Use additional place of occurrence and activity external cause codes, if known (Y92.-, Y93.-)

Excludes1: *collision with another person without fall (W51)*
fall due to person on foot colliding with another person on foot (W03)
fall from non-moving wheelchair, nonmotorized scooter and motorized mobility scooter without collision (W05.-)
pedestrian (conveyance) collision with other land transport vehicle (V01-V09)
pedestrian on foot falling (slipping) on ice and snow (W00.-)

The appropriate 7th character is to be added to each code from category V00
A initial encounter
D subsequent encounter
S sequela

\+ **V00.0 Pedestrian on foot injured in collision with pedestrian conveyance**

X+7th **V00.01 Pedestrian on foot injured in collision with roller-skater**

X+7th **V00.02 Pedestrian on foot injured in collision with skateboarder**

X+7th **V00.09 Pedestrian on foot injured in collision with other pedestrian conveyance**

\+ **V00.1 Rolling-type pedestrian conveyance accident**

Excludes1: *accident with babystroller (V00.82-)*
accident with wheelchair (powered) (V00.81-)
accident with motorized mobility scooter (V00.83-)

+ **V00.11 In-line roller-skate accident**
- +7th **V00.111 Fall from in-line roller-skates**
- +7th **V00.112 In-line roller-skater colliding with stationary object**
- +7th **V00.118 Other in-line roller-skate accident**
  Excludes1: *roller-skater collision with other land transport vehicle (V01-V09with5thcharacter1)*

+ **V00.12 Non-in- line roller-skate accident**
- +7th **V00.121 Fall from non-in-line roller-skates**
- +7th **V00.122 Non-in-line roller-skater colliding with stationary object**
- +7th **V00.128 Other non-in-line roller-skating accident**
  Excludes1: *roller-skater collision with other land transport vehicle (V01-V09with5thcharacter1)*

+ **V00.13 Skateboard accident**
- +7th **V00.131 Fall from skateboard**
- +7th **V00.132 Skateboarder colliding with stationary object**
- +7th **V00.138 Other skateboard accident**
  Excludes1: *skateboarder collision with other land transport vehicle (V01-V09with5thcharacter2)*

+ **V00.14 Scooter (nonmotorized) accident**
  Excludes1: *motorscooter accident (V20-V29)*
- +7th **V00.141 Fall from scooter (nonmotorized)**
- +7th **V00.142 Scooter (nonmotorized) colliding with stationary object**
- +7th **V00.148 Other scooter (nonmotorized) accident**
  Excludes1: *scooter (nonmotorized) collision with other land transport vehicle (V01-V09 with fifth character 9)*

+ **V00.15 Heelies accident**
  Rolling shoe
  Wheeled shoe
  Wheelies accident
- +7th **V00.151 Fall from heelies**
- +7th **V00.152 Heelies colliding with stationary object**
- +7th **V00.158 Other heelies accident**

+ **V00.18 Accident on other rolling-type pedestrian conveyance**
- +7th **V00.181 Fall from other rolling-type pedestrian conveyance**
- +7th **V00.182 Pedestrian on other rolling-type pedestrian conveyance colliding with stationary object**
- +7th **V00.188 Other accident on other rolling-type pedestrian conveyance**

+ **V00.2 Gliding-type pedestrian conveyance accident**

+ **V00.21 Ice-skates accident**
- +7th **V00.211 Fall from ice-skates**
- +7th **V00.212 Ice-skater colliding with stationary object**
- +7th **V00.218 Other ice-skates accident**
  Excludes1: *ice-skater collision with other land transport vehicle (V01-V09 with 5th digit 9)*

+ **V00.22 Sled accident**
- +7th **V00.221 Fall from sled**
- +7th **V00.222 Sledder colliding with stationary object**
- +7th **V00.228 Other sled accident**
  Excludes1: *sled collision with other land transport vehicle (V01-V09 with 5th digit 9)*

+ **V00.28 Other gliding-type pedestrian conveyance accident**
- +7th **V00.281 Fall from other gliding-type pedestrian conveyance**
- +7th **V00.282 Pedestrian on other gliding-type pedestrian conveyance colliding with stationary object**
- +7th **V00.288 Other accident on other gliding-type pedestrian conveyance**
  Excludes1: *gliding-type pedestrian conveyance collision with other land transport vehicle (V01-V09 with 5th digit 9)*

+ **V00.3 Flat-bottomed pedestrian conveyance accident**

+ **V00.31 Snowboard accident**
- +7th **V00.311 Fall from snowboard**
- +7th **V00.312 Snowboarder colliding with stationary object**
- +7th **V00.318 Other snowboard accident**
  Excludes1: *snowboarder collision with other land transport vehicle (V01-V09 with 5th digit 9)*

+ **V00.32 Snow-ski accident**
- +7th **V00.321 Fall from snow-skis**
- +7th **V00.322 Snow-skier colliding with stationary object**
- +7th **V00.328 Other snow-ski accident**
  Excludes1: *snow-skier collision with other land transport vehicle (V01-V09 with 5th digit 9)*

+ **V00.38 Other flat-bottomed pedestrian conveyance accident**
- +7th **V00.381 Fall from other flat-bottomed pedestrian conveyance**
- +7th **V00.382 Pedestrian on other flat-bottomed pedestrian conveyance colliding with stationary object**
- +7th **V00.388 Other accident on other flat-bottomed pedestrian conveyance**

+ **V00.8 Accident on other pedestrian conveyance**

+ **V00.81 Accident with wheelchair (powered)**
- +7th **V00.811 Fall from moving wheelchair (powered)**
  Excludes1: *fall from non-moving wheelchair (W05.0)*
- +7th **V00.812 Wheelchair (powered) colliding with stationary object**
- +7th **V00.818 Other accident with wheelchair (powered)**

+ **V00.82 Accident with babystroller**
- +7th **V00.821 Fall from babystroller**
- +7th **V00.822 Babystroller colliding with stationary object**
- +7th **V00.828 Other accident with babystroller**

+ **V00.83 Accident with motorized mobility scooter**
- +7th **V00.831 Fall from motorized mobility scooter**
  Excludes1: *fall from non-moving motorized mobility scooter (W05.2)*
- +7th **V00.832 Motorized mobility scooter colliding with stationary object**
- +7th **V00.838 Other accident with motorized mobility scooter**

+ **V00.89 Accident on other pedestrian conveyance**
- +7th **V00.891 Fall from other pedestrian conveyance**
- +7th **V00.892 Pedestrian on other pedestrian conveyance colliding with stationary object**
- +7th **V00.898 Other accident on other pedestrian conveyance**
  Excludes1: *other pedestrian (conveyance) collision with other land transport vehicle (V01-V09 with 5th digit 9)*

V01 Pedestrian injured in collision with pedal cycle

The appropriate 7th character is to be added to each code from category V01
A initial encounter
D subsequent encounter
S sequela

+ **V01.0 Pedestrian injured in collision with pedal cycle in nontraffic accident**
- X+7th **V01.00 Pedestrian on foot injured in collision with pedal cycle in nontraffic accident**
  Pedestrian NOS injured in collision with pedal cycle in nontraffic accident
- X+7th **V01.01 Pedestrian on roller-skates injured in collision with pedal cycle in nontraffic accident**
- X+7th **V01.02 Pedestrian on skateboard injured in collision with pedal cycle in nontraffic accident**
- X+7th **V01.09 Pedestrian with other conveyance injured in collision with pedal cycle in nontraffic accident**
  Pedestrian with babystroller injured in collision with pedal cycle in nontraffic accident
  Pedestrian on ice-skates injured in collision with pedal cycle in nontraffic accident
  Pedestrian on nonmotorized scooter injured in collision with pedal cycle in nontraffic accident
  Pedestrian on sled injured in collision with pedal cycle in nontraffic accident
  Pedestrian on snowboard injured in collision with pedal cycle in nontraffic accident
  Pedestrian on snow-skis injured in collision with pedal cycle in nontraffic accident
  Pedestrian in wheelchair (powered) injured in collision with pedal cycle in nontraffic accident
  Pedestrian in motorized mobility scooter injured in collision with pedal cycle in nontraffic accident

+ V01.1 Pedestrian injured in collision with pedal cycle in traffic accident

X+7th **V01.10 Pedestrian on foot injured in collision with pedal cycle in traffic accident**
Pedestrian NOS injured in collision with pedal cycle in traffic accident

X+7th **V01.11 Pedestrian on roller-skates injured in collision with pedal cycle in traffic accident**

X+7th **V01.12 Pedestrian on skateboard injured in collision with pedal cycle in traffic accident**

X+7th **V01.19 Pedestrian with other conveyance injured in collision with pedal cycle in traffic accident**
Pedestrian with babystroller injured in collision with pedal cycle in traffic accident
Pedestrian on ice-skates injured in collision with pedal cycle in traffic accident
Pedestrian on nonmotorized scooter injured in collision with pedal cycle in traffic accident
Pedestrian on sled injured in collision with pedal cycle in traffic accident
Pedestrian on snowboard injured in collision with pedal cycle in traffic accident
Pedestrian on snow-skis injured in collision with pedal cycle in traffic accident
Pedestrian in wheelchair (powered) injured in collision with pedal cycle in traffic accident
Pedestrian in motorized mobility scooter injured in collision with pedal cycle in traffic accident

+ V01.9 Pedestrian injured in collision with pedal cycle, unspecified whether traffic or nontraffic accident

X+7th **V01.90 Pedestrian on foot injured in collision with pedal cycle, unspecified whether traffic or nontraffic accident**
Pedestrian NOS injured in collision with pedal cycle, unspecified whether traffic or nontraffic accident

X+7th **V01.91 Pedestrian on roller-skates injured in collision with pedal cycle, unspecified whether traffic or nontraffic accident**

X+7th **V01.92 Pedestrian on skateboard injured in collision with pedal cycle, unspecified whether traffic or nontraffic accident**

X+7th **V01.99 Pedestrian with other conveyance injured in collision with pedal cycle, unspecified whether traffic or nontraffic accident**
Pedestrian with babystroller injured in collision with pedal cycle, unspecified whether traffic or nontraffic accident
Pedestrian on ice-skates injured in collision with pedal cycle unspecified, whether traffic or nontraffic accident
Pedestrian on nonmotorized scooter injured in collision with pedal cycle, unspecified whether traffic or nontraffic accident
Pedestrian on sled injured in collision with pedal cycle unspecified, whether traffic or nontraffic accident
Pedestrian on snowboard injured in collision with pedal cycle, unspecified whether traffic or nontraffic accident
Pedestrian on snow-skis injured in collision with pedal cycle, unspecified whether traffic or nontraffic accident
Pedestrian in wheelchair (powered) injured in collision with pedal cycle, unspecified whether traffic or nontraffic accident
Pedestrian in motorized mobility scooter injured in collision with pedal cycle, unspecified whether traffic or nontraffic accident

V02 Pedestrian injured in collision with two- or three-wheeled motor vehicle

The appropriate 7th character is to be added to each code from category V02
A initial encounter
D subsequent encounter
S sequela

+ V02.0 Pedestrian injured in collision with two- or three-wheeled motor vehicle in nontraffic accident

X+7th **V02.00 Pedestrian on foot injured in collision with two- or three-wheeled motor vehicle in nontraffic accident**
Pedestrian NOS injured in collision with two- or three-wheeled motor vehicle in nontraffic accident

X+7th **V02.01 Pedestrian on roller-skates injured in collision with two- or three-wheeled motor vehicle in nontraffic accident**

X+7th **V02.02 Pedestrian on skateboard injured in collision with two- or three-wheeled motor vehicle in nontraffic accident**

X+7th **V02.09 Pedestrian with other conveyance injured in collision with two- or three-wheeled motor vehicle in nontraffic accident**
Pedestrian with babystroller injured in collision with two- or three-wheeled motor vehicle in nontraffic accident
Pedestrian on ice-skates injured in collision with two- or three-wheeled motor vehicle in nontraffic accident
Pedestrian on nonmotorized scooter injured in collision with two- or three-wheeled motor vehicle in nontraffic accident
Pedestrian on sled injured in collision with two- or three-wheeled motor vehicle in nontraffic accident
Pedestrian on snowboard injured in collision with two- or three-wheeled motor vehicle in nontraffic accident
Pedestrian on snow-skis injured in collision with two- or three-wheeled motor vehicle in nontraffic accident
Pedestrian in wheelchair (powered) injured in collision with two- or three-wheeled motor vehicle in nontraffic accident
Pedestrian in motorized mobility scooter injured in collision with two- or three-wheeled motor vehicle in nontraffic accident

+ V02.1 Pedestrian injured in collision with two- or three-wheeled motor vehicle in traffic accident

X+7th **V02.10 Pedestrian on foot injured in collision with two- or three-wheeled motor vehicle in traffic accident**
Pedestrian NOS injured in collision with two- or three-wheeled motor vehicle in traffic accident

X+7th **V02.11 Pedestrian on roller-skates injured in collision with two- or three-wheeled motor vehicle in traffic accident**

X+7th **V02.12 Pedestrian on skateboard injured in collision with two- or three-wheeled motor vehicle in traffic accident**

V02.19 Pedestrian with other conveyance injured in collision with two- or three-wheeled motor vehicle in traffic accident
Pedestrian with babystroller injured in collision with two- or three-wheeled motor vehicle in traffic accident
Pedestrian on ice-skates injured in collision with two- or three-wheeled motor vehicle in traffic accident
Pedestrian on nonmotorized scooter injured in collision with two- or three-wheeled motor vehicle in traffic accident
Pedestrian on sled injured in collision with two- or three-wheeled motor vehicle in traffic accident
Pedestrian on snowboard injured in collision with two- or three-wheeled motor vehicle in traffic accident
Pedestrian on snow-skis injured in collision with two- or three-wheeled motor vehicle in traffic accident
Pedestrian in wheelchair (powered) injured in collision with two- or three-wheeled motor vehicle in traffic accident
Pedestrian in motorized mobility scooter injured in collision with two- or three-wheeled motor vehicle in traffic accident

+ V02.9 Pedestrian injured in collision with two- or three-wheeled motor vehicle, unspecified whether traffic or nontraffic accident

X+7th **V02.90 Pedestrian on foot injured in collision with two- or three-wheeled motor vehicle, unspecified whether traffic or nontraffic accident**
Pedestrian NOS injured in collision with two- or three-wheeled motor vehicle, unspecified whether traffic or nontraffic accident

X+7th **V02.91 Pedestrian on roller-skates injured in collision with two- or three-wheeled motor vehicle, unspecified whether traffic or nontraffic accident**

X+7th **V02.92 Pedestrian on skateboard injured in collision with two- or three-wheeled motor vehicle, unspecified whether traffic or nontraffic accident**

X+7th **V02.99 Pedestrian with other conveyance injured in collision with two- or three-wheeled motor vehicle, unspecified whether traffic or nontraffic accident**
Pedestrian with babystroller injured in collision with two- or three-wheeled motor vehicle, unspecified whether traffic or nontraffic accident
Pedestrian on ice-skates injured in collision with two- or three-wheeled motor vehicle, unspecified whether traffic or nontraffic accident
Pedestrian on nonmotorized scooter injured in collision with two- or three-wheeled motor vehicle, unspecified whether traffic or nontraffic accident
Pedestrian on sled injured in collision with two- or three-wheeled motor vehicle, unspecified whether traffic or nontraffic accident
Pedestrian on snowboard injured in collision with two- or three-wheeled motor vehicle, unspecified whether traffic or nontraffic accident
Pedestrian on snow-skis injured in collision with two- or three-wheeled motor vehicle, unspecified whether traffic or nontraffic accident
Pedestrian in wheelchair (powered) injured in collision with two- or three-wheeled motor vehicle, unspecified whether traffic or nontraffic accident
Pedestrian in motorized mobility scooter injured in collision with two- or three-wheeled motor vehicle, unspecified whether traffic or nontraffic accident

V03 Pedestrian injured in collision with car, pick-up truck or van

The appropriate 7th character is to be added to each code from category V03
A initial encounter
D subsequent encounter
S sequela

+ **V03.0 Pedestrian injured in collision with car, pick-up truck or van in nontraffic accident**

X+7th **V03.00 Pedestrian on foot injured in collision with car, pick-up truck or van in nontraffic accident**
Pedestrian NOS injured in collision with car, pick-up truck or van in nontraffic accident

X+7th **V03.01 Pedestrian on roller-skates injured in collision with car, pick-up truck or van in nontraffic accident**

X+7th **V03.02 Pedestrian on skateboard injured in collision with car, pick-up truck or van in nontraffic accident**

X+7th **V03.09 Pedestrian with other conveyance injured in collision with car, pick-up truck or van in nontraffic accident**
Pedestrian with babystroller injured in collision with car, pick-up truck or van in nontraffic accident
Pedestrian on ice-skates injured in collision with car, pick-up truck or van in nontraffic accident
Pedestrian on nonmotorized scooter injured in collision with car, pick-up truck or van in nontraffic accident
Pedestrian on sled injured in collision with car, pick-up truck or van in nontraffic accident
Pedestrian on snowboard injured in collision with car, pick-up truck or van in nontraffic accident
Pedestrian on snow-skis injured in collision with car, pick-up truck or van in nontraffic accident
Pedestrian in wheelchair (powered) injured in collision with car, pick-up truck or van in nontraffic accident
Pedestrian in motorized mobility scooter injured in collision with car, pick-up truck or van in nontraffic accident

+ **V03.1 Pedestrian injured in collision with car, pick-up truck or van in traffic accident**

X+7th **V03.10 Pedestrian on foot injured in collision with car, pick-up truck or van in traffic accident**
Pedestrian NOS injured in collision with car, pick-up truck or van in traffic accident

X+7th **V03.11 Pedestrian on roller-skates injured in collision with car, pick-up truck or van in traffic accident**

X+7th **V03.12 Pedestrian on skateboard injured in collision with car, pick-up truck or van in traffic accident**

X+7th **V03.19 Pedestrian with other conveyance injured in collision with car, pick-up truck or van in traffic accident**
Pedestrian with babystroller injured in collision with car, pick-up truck or van in traffic accident
Pedestrian on ice-skates injured in collision with car, pick-up truck or van in traffic accident
Pedestrian on nonmotorized scooter injured in collision with car, pick-up truck or van in traffic accident
Pedestrian on sled injured in collision with car, pick-up truck or van in traffic accident
Pedestrian on snowboard injured in collision with car, pick-up truck or van in traffic accident
Pedestrian on snow-skis injured in collision with car, pick-up truck or van in traffic accident
Pedestrian in wheelchair (powered) injured in collision with car, pick-up truck or van in traffic accident
Pedestrian in motorized mobility scooter injured in collision with car, pick-up truck or van in traffic accident

+ **V03.9 Pedestrian injured in collision with car, pick-up truck or van, unspecified whether traffic or nontraffic accident**

X+7th **V03.90 Pedestrian on foot injured in collision with car, pick-up truck or van, unspecified whether traffic or nontraffic accident**
Pedestrian NOS injured in collision with car, pick-up truck or van, unspecified whether traffic or nontraffic accident

X+7th **V03.91 Pedestrian on roller-skates injured in collision with car, pick-up truck or van, unspecified whether traffic or nontraffic accident**

X+7th **V03.92 Pedestrian on skateboard injured in collision with car, pick-up truck or van, unspecified whether traffic or nontraffic accident**

X+7th **V03.99 Pedestrian with other conveyance injured in collision with car, pick-up truck or van, unspecified whether traffic or nontraffic accident**
Pedestrian with babystroller injured in collision with car, pick-up truck or van, unspecified whether traffic or nontraffic accident
Pedestrian on ice-skates injured in collision with car, pick-up truck or van, unspecified whether traffic or nontraffic accident
Pedestrian on nonmotorized scooter injured in collision with car, pick-up truck or van, unspecified whether traffic or nontraffic accident
Pedestrian on sled injured in collision with car, pick-up truck or van in nontraffic accident
Pedestrian on snowboard injured in collision with car, pick-up truck or van, unspecified whether traffic or nontraffic accident
Pedestrian on snow-skis injured in collision with car, pick-up truck or van, unspecified whether traffic or nontraffic accident
Pedestrian in wheelchair (powered) injured in collision with car, pick-up truck or van, unspecified whether traffic or nontraffic accident
Pedestrian in motorized mobility scooter injured in collision with car, pick-up truck or van, unspecified whether traffic or nontraffic accident

V04 Pedestrian injured in collision with heavy transport vehicle or bus

Excludes1: *pedestrian injured in collision with military vehicle (V09.01, V09.21)*

The appropriate 7th character is to be added to each code from category V04
A initial encounter
D subsequent encounter
S sequela

+ **V04.0 Pedestrian injured in collision with heavy transport vehicle or bus in nontraffic accident**

X+7th **V04.00 Pedestrian on foot injured in collision with heavy transport vehicle or bus in nontraffic accident**
Pedestrian NOS injured in collision with heavy transport vehicle or bus in nontraffic accident

X+7th **V04.01 Pedestrian on roller-skates injured in collision with heavy transport vehicle or bus in nontraffic accident**

X+7th **V04.02 Pedestrian on skateboard injured in collision with heavy transport vehicle or bus in nontraffic accident**

X+7th **V04.09 Pedestrian with other conveyance injured in collision with heavy transport vehicle or bus in nontraffic accident**
Pedestrian with babystroller injured in collision with heavy transport vehicle or bus in nontraffic accident
Pedestrian on ice-skates injured in collision with heavy transport vehicle or bus in nontraffic accident
Pedestrian on nonmotorized scooter injured in collision with heavy transport vehicle or bus in nontraffic accident
Pedestrian on sled injured in collision with heavy transport vehicle or bus in nontraffic accident
Pedestrian on snowboard injured in collision with heavy transport vehicle or bus in nontraffic accident
Pedestrian on snow-skis injured in collision with heavy transport vehicle or bus in nontraffic accident
Pedestrian in wheelchair (powered) injured in collision with heavy transport vehicle or bus in nontraffic accident
Pedestrian in motorized mobility scooter injured in collision with heavy transport vehicle or bus in nontraffic accident

\+ **V04.1 Pedestrian injured in collision with heavy transport vehicle or bus in traffic accident**

X+7th **V04.10 Pedestrian on foot injured in collision with heavy transport vehicle or bus in traffic accident**
Pedestrian NOS injured in collision with heavy transport vehicle or bus in traffic accident

X+7th **V04.11 Pedestrian on roller-skates injured in collision with heavy transport vehicle or bus in traffic accident**

X+7th **V04.12 Pedestrian on skateboard injured in collision with heavy transport vehicle or bus in traffic accident**

X+7th **V04.19 Pedestrian with other conveyance injured in collision with heavy transport vehicle or bus in traffic accident**
Pedestrian with babystroller injured in collision with heavy transport vehicle or bus in traffic accident
Pedestrian on ice-skates injured in collision with heavy transport vehicle or bus in traffic accident
Pedestrian on nonmotorized scooter injured in collision with heavy transport vehicle or bus in traffic accident
Pedestrian on sled injured in collision with heavy transport vehicle or bus in traffic accident
Pedestrian on snowboard injured in collision with heavy transport vehicle or bus in traffic accident
Pedestrian on snow-skis injured in collision with heavy transport vehicle or bus in traffic accident
Pedestrian in wheelchair (powered) injured in collision with heavy transport vehicle or bus in traffic accident
Pedestrian in motorized mobility scooter injured in collision with heavy transport vehicle or bus in traffic accident

\+ **V04.9 Pedestrian injured in collision with heavy transport vehicle or bus, unspecified whether traffic or nontraffic accident**

X+7th **V04.90 Pedestrian on foot injured in collision with heavy transport vehicle or bus, unspecified whether traffic or nontraffic accident**
Pedestrian NOS injured in collision with heavy transport vehicle or bus, unspecified whether traffic or nontraffic accident

X+7th **V04.91 Pedestrian on roller-skates injured in collision with heavy transport vehicle or bus, unspecified whether traffic or nontraffic accident**

X+7th **V04.92 Pedestrian on skateboard injured in collision with heavy transport vehicle or bus, unspecified whether traffic or nontraffic accident**

X+7th **V04.99 Pedestrian with other conveyance injured in collision with heavy transport vehicle or bus, unspecified whether traffic or nontraffic accident**
Pedestrian with babystroller injured in collision with heavy transport vehicle or bus, unspecified whether traffic or nontraffic accident
Pedestrian on ice-skates injured in collision with heavy transport vehicle or bus, unspecified whether traffic or nontraffic accident
Pedestrian on nonmotorized scooter injured in collision with heavy transport vehicle or bus, unspecified whether traffic or nontraffic accident
Pedestrian on sled injured in collision with heavy transport vehicle or bus, unspecified whether traffic or nontraffic accident
Pedestrian on snowboard injured in collision with heavy transport vehicle or bus, unspecified whether traffic or nontraffic accident
Pedestrian on snow-skis injured in collision with heavy transport vehicle or bus, unspecified whether traffic or nontraffic accident
Pedestrian in wheelchair (powered) injured in collision with heavy transport vehicle or bus, unspecified whether traffic or nontraffic accident
Pedestrian in motorized mobility scooter injured in collision with heavy transport vehicle or bus, unspecified whether traffic or nontraffic accident

V05 Pedestrian injured in collision with railway train or railway vehicle

The appropriate 7th character is to be added to each code from category V05
A initial encounter
D subsequent encounter
S sequela

\+ **V05.0 Pedestrian injured in collision with railway train or railway vehicle in nontraffic accident**

X+7th **V05.00 Pedestrian on foot injured in collision with railway train or railway vehicle in nontraffic accident**
Pedestrian NOS injured in collision with railway train or railway vehicle in nontraffic accident

X+7th **V05.01 Pedestrian on roller-skates injured in collision with railway train or railway vehicle in nontraffic accident**

X+7th **V05.02 Pedestrian on skateboard injured in collision with railway train or railway vehicle in nontraffic accident**

X+7th **V05.09 Pedestrian with other conveyance injured in collision with railway train or railway vehicle in nontraffic accident**
Pedestrian with babystroller injured in collision with railway train or railway vehicle in nontraffic accident
Pedestrian on ice-skates injured in collision with railway train or railway vehicle in nontraffic accident
Pedestrian on nonmotorized scooter injured in collision with railway train or railway vehicle in nontraffic accident
Pedestrian on sled injured in collision with railway train or railway vehicle in nontraffic accident
Pedestrian on snowboard injured in collision with railway train or railway vehicle in nontraffic accident
Pedestrian on snow-skis injured in collision with railway train or railway vehicle in nontraffic accident
Pedestrian in wheelchair (powered) injured in collision with railway train or railway vehicle in nontraffic accident
Pedestrian in motorized mobility scooter injured in collision with railway train or railway vehicle in nontraffic accident

\+ **V05.1 Pedestrian injured in collision with railway train or railway vehicle in traffic accident**

X+7th **V05.10 Pedestrian on foot injured in collision with railway train or railway vehicle in traffic accident**
Pedestrian NOS injured in collision with railway train or railway vehicle in traffic accident

X+7th **V05.11 Pedestrian on roller-skates injured in collision with railway train or railway vehicle in traffic accident**

X+7th **V05.12 Pedestrian on skateboard injured in collision with railway train or railway vehicle in traffic accident**

X+7th **V05.19 Pedestrian with other conveyance injured in collision with railway train or railway vehicle in traffic accident**
Pedestrian with babystroller injured in collision with railway train or railway vehicle in traffic accident
Pedestrian on ice-skates injured in collision with railway train or railway vehicle in traffic accident
Pedestrian on nonmotorized scooter injured in collision with railway train or railway vehicle in traffic accident
Pedestrian on sled injured in collision with railway train or railway vehicle in traffic accident
Pedestrian on snowboard injured in collision with railway train or railway vehicle in traffic accident
Pedestrian on snow-skis injured in collision with railway train or railway vehicle in traffic accident
Pedestrian in wheelchair (powered) injured in collision with railway train or railway vehicle in traffic accident
Pedestrian in motorized mobility scooter injured in collision with railway train or railway vehicle in traffic accident

\+ **V05.9 Pedestrian injured in collision with railway train or railway vehicle, unspecified whether traffic or nontraffic accident**

X+7th **V05.90 Pedestrian on foot injured in collision with railway train or railway vehicle, unspecified whether traffic or nontraffic accident**
Pedestrian NOS injured in collision with railway train or railway vehicle, unspecified whether traffic or nontraffic accident

X+7th **V05.91 Pedestrian on roller-skates injured in collision with railway train or railway vehicle, unspecified whether traffic or nontraffic accident**

X+7th **V05.92 Pedestrian on skateboard injured in collision with railway train or railway vehicle, unspecified whether traffic or nontraffic accident**

X+7th **V05.99 Pedestrian with other conveyance injured in collision with railway train or railway vehicle, unspecified whether traffic or nontraffic accident**
Pedestrian with babystroller injured in collision with railway train or railway vehicle, unspecified whether traffic or nontraffic
Pedestrian on ice-skates injured in collision with railway train or railway vehicle, unspecified whether traffic or nontraffic
Pedestrian on nonmotorized scooter injured in collision with railway train or railway vehicle, unspecified whether traffic or nontraffic
Pedestrian on sled injured in collision with railway train or railway vehicle, unspecified whether traffic or nontraffic
Pedestrian on snowboard injured in collision with railway train or railway vehicle, unspecified whether traffic or nontraffic
Pedestrian on snow-skis injured in collision with railway train or railway vehicle, unspecified whether traffic or nontraffic
Pedestrian in wheelchair (powered) injured in collision with railway train or railway vehicle, unspecified whether traffic or nontraffic
Pedestrian in motorized mobility scooter injured in collision with railway train or railway vehicle, unspecified whether traffic or nontraffic

V06 Pedestrian injured in collision with other nonmotor vehicle

Includes: collision with animal-drawn vehicle, animal being ridden, nonpowered streetcar

Excludes1: *pedestrian injured in collision with pedestrian conveyance (V00.0-)*

The appropriate 7th character is to be added to each code from category V06
A initial encounter
D subsequent encounter
S sequela

\+ **V06.0 Pedestrian injured in collision with other nonmotor vehicle in nontraffic accident**

X+7th **V06.00 Pedestrian on foot injured in collision with other nonmotor vehicle in nontraffic accident**
Pedestrian NOS injured in collision with other nonmotor vehicle in nontraffic accident

X+7th **V06.01 Pedestrian on roller-skates injured in collision with other nonmotor vehicle in nontraffic accident**

X+7th **V06.02 Pedestrian on skateboard injured in collision with other nonmotor vehicle in nontraffic accident**

X+7th **V06.09 Pedestrian with other conveyance injured in collision with other nonmotor vehicle in nontraffic accident**
Pedestrian with babystroller injured in collision with other nonmotor vehicle in nontraffic accident
Pedestrian on ice-skates injured in collision with other nonmotor vehicle in nontraffic accident
Pedestrian on nonmotorized scooter injured in collision with other nonmotor vehicle in nontraffic accident
Pedestrian on sled injured in collision with other nonmotor vehicle in nontraffic accident
Pedestrian on snowboard injured in collision with other nonmotor vehicle in nontraffic accident
Pedestrian on snow-skis injured in collision with other nonmotor vehicle in nontraffic accident
Pedestrian in wheelchair (powered) injured in collision with other nonmotor vehicle in nontraffic accident
Pedestrian in motorized mobility scooter injured in collision with other nonmotor vehicle in nontraffic accident

\+ **V06.1 Pedestrian injured in collision with other nonmotor vehicle in traffic accident**

X+7th **V06.10 Pedestrian on foot injured in collision with other nonmotor vehicle in traffic accident**
Pedestrian NOS injured in collision with other nonmotor vehicle in traffic accident

X+7th **V06.11 Pedestrian on roller-skates injured in collision with other nonmotor vehicle in traffic accident**

X+7th **V06.12 Pedestrian on skateboard injured in collision with other nonmotor vehicle in traffic accident**

X+7th **V06.19 Pedestrian with other conveyance injured in collision with other nonmotor vehicle in traffic accident**
Pedestrian with babystroller injured in collision with other nonmotor vehicle in nontraffic accident
Pedestrian on ice-skates injured in collision with other nonmotor vehicle in traffic accident
Pedestrian on nonmotorized scooter injured in collision with other nonmotor vehicle in traffic accident
Pedestrian on sled injured in collision with other nonmotor vehicle in traffic accident
Pedestrian on snowboard injured in collision with other nonmotor vehicle in traffic accident
Pedestrian on snow-skis injured in collision with other nonmotor vehicle in traffic accident
Pedestrian in wheelchair (powered) injured in collision with other nonmotor vehicle in traffic accident
Pedestrian in motorized mobility scooter injured in collision with other nonmotor vehicle in traffic accident

\+ **V06.9 Pedestrian injured in collision with other nonmotor vehicle, unspecified whether traffic or nontraffic accident**

X+7th **V06.90 Pedestrian on foot injured in collision with other nonmotor vehicle, unspecified whether traffic or nontraffic accident**
Pedestrian NOS injured in collision with other nonmotor vehicle, unspecified whether traffic or nontraffic accident

X+7th **V06.91 Pedestrian on roller-skates injured in collision with other nonmotor vehicle, unspecified whether traffic or nontraffic accident**

X+7th **V06.92 Pedestrian on skateboard injured in collision with other nonmotor vehicle, unspecified whether traffic or nontraffic accident**

X+7th **V06.99 Pedestrian with other conveyance injured in collision with other nonmotor vehicle, unspecified whether traffic or nontraffic accident**
Pedestrian with babystroller injured in collision with other nonmotor vehicle, unspecified whether traffic or nontraffic accident
Pedestrian on ice-skates injured in collision with other nonmotor vehicle, unspecified whether traffic or nontraffic accident
Pedestrian on nonmotorized scooter injured in collision with other nonmotor vehicle, unspecified whether traffic or nontraffic accident
Pedestrian on sled injured in collision with other nonmotor vehicle, unspecified whether traffic or nontraffic accident
Pedestrian on snowboard injured in collision with other nonmotor vehicle, unspecified whether traffic or nontraffic accident
Pedestrian on snow-skis injured in collision with other nonmotor vehicle, unspecified whether traffic or nontraffic accident
Pedestrian in wheelchair (powered) injured in collision with other nonmotor vehicle, unspecified whether traffic or nontraffic accident
Pedestrian in motorized mobility scooter injured in collision with other nonmotor vehicle, unspecified whether traffic or nontraffic accident

V09 Pedestrian injured in other and unspecified transport accidents

The appropriate 7th character is to be added to each code from category V09
A initial encounter
D subsequent encounter
S sequela

\+ **V09.0 Pedestrian injured in nontraffic accident involving other and unspecified motor vehicles**
X+7th **V09.00 Pedestrian injured in nontraffic accident involving unspecified motor vehicles**
X+7th **V09.01 Pedestrian injured in nontraffic accident involving military vehicle**
X+7th **V09.09 Pedestrian injured in nontraffic accident involving other motor vehicles**
Pedestrian injured in nontraffic accident by special vehicle
X+7th **V09.1 Pedestrian injured in unspecified nontraffic accident**
\+ **V09.2 Pedestrian injured in traffic accident involving other and unspecified motor vehicles**
X+7th **V09.20 Pedestrian injured in traffic accident involving unspecified motor vehicles**
X+7th **V09.21 Pedestrian injured in traffic accident involving military vehicle**
X+7th **V09.29 Pedestrian injured in traffic accident involving other motor vehicles**
X+7th **V09.3 Pedestrian injured in unspecified traffic accident**
X+7th **V09.9 Pedestrian injured in unspecified transport accident**

Pedal cycle rider injured in transport accident (V10-V19)

Includes: any non-motorized vehicle, excluding an animal-drawn vehicle, or a sidecar or trailer attached to the pedal cycle

Excludes2: *rupture of pedal cycle tire (W37.0)*

V10 Pedal cycle rider injured in collision with pedestrian or animal

Excludes1: *pedal cycle rider collision with animal-drawn vehicle or animal being ridden (V16.-)*

The appropriate 7th character is to be added to each code from category V10
A initial encounter
D subsequent encounter
S sequela

X+7th **V10.0 Pedal cycle driver injured in collision with pedestrian or animal in nontraffic accident**
X+7th **V10.1 Pedal cycle passenger injured in collision with pedestrian or animal in nontraffic accident**
X+7th **V10.2 Unspecified pedal cyclist injured in collision with pedestrian or animal in nontraffic accident**
X+7th **V10.3 Person boarding or alighting a pedal cycle injured in collision with pedestrian or animal**
X+7th **V10.4 Pedal cycle driver injured in collision with pedestrian or animal in traffic accident**
X+7th **V10.5 Pedal cycle passenger injured in collision with pedestrian or animal in traffic accident**
X+7th **V10.9 Unspecified pedal cyclist injured in collision with pedestrian or animal in traffic accident**

V11 Pedal cycle rider injured in collision with other pedal cycle

The appropriate 7th character is to be added to each code from category V11
A initial encounter
D subsequent encounter
S sequela

X+7th **V11.0 Pedal cycle driver injured in collision with other pedal cycle in nontraffic accident**
X+7th **V11.1 Pedal cycle passenger injured in collision with other pedal cycle in nontraffic accident**
X+7th **V11.2 Unspecified pedal cyclist injured in collision with other pedal cycle in nontraffic accident**
X+7th **V11.3 Person boarding or alighting a pedal cycle injured in collision with other pedal cycle**
X+7th **V11.4 Pedal cycle driver injured in collision with other pedal cycle in traffic accident**
X+7th **V11.5 Pedal cycle passenger injured in collision with other pedal cycle in traffic accident**
X+7th **V11.9 Unspecified pedal cyclist injured in collision with other pedal cycle in traffic accident**

V12 Pedal cycle rider injured in collision with two- or three-wheeled motor vehicle

The appropriate 7th character is to be added to each code from category V12
A initial encounter
D subsequent encounter
S sequela

X+7th **V12.0 Pedal cycle driver injured in collision with two- or three-wheeled motor vehicle in nontraffic accident**
X+7th **V12.1 Pedal cycle passenger injured in collision with two- or three-wheeled motor vehicle in nontraffic accident**
X+7th **V12.2 Unspecified pedal cyclist injured in collision with two- or three-wheeled motor vehicle in nontraffic accident**
X+7th **V12.3 Person boarding or alighting a pedal cycle injured in collision with two- or three-wheeled motor vehicle**
X+7th **V12.4 Pedal cycle driver injured in collision with two- or three-wheeled motor vehicle in traffic accident**
X+7th **V12.5 Pedal cycle passenger injured in collision with two- or three-wheeled motor vehicle in traffic accident**
X+7th **V12.9 Unspecified pedal cyclist injured in collision with two- or three-wheeled motor vehicle in traffic accident**

V13 Pedal cycle rider injured in collision with car, pick-up truck or van

The appropriate 7th character is to be added to each code from category V13
A initial encounter
D subsequent encounter
S sequela

X+7th **V13.0 Pedal cycle driver injured in collision with car, pick-up truck or van in nontraffic accident**
X+7th **V13.1 Pedal cycle passenger injured in collision with car, pick-up truck or van in nontraffic accident**
X+7th **V13.2 Unspecified pedal cyclist injured in collision with car, pick-up truck or van in nontraffic accident**
X+7th **V13.3 Person boarding or alighting a pedal cycle injured in collision with car, pick-up truck or van**
X+7th **V13.4 Pedal cycle driver injured in collision with car, pick-up truck or van in traffic accident**
X+7th **V13.5 Pedal cycle passenger injured in collision with car, pick-up truck or van in traffic accident**
X+7th **V13.9 Unspecified pedal cyclist injured in collision with car, pick-up truck or van in traffic accident**

V14 Pedal cycle rider injured in collision with heavy transport vehicle or bus

Excludes1: *pedal cycle rider injured in collision with military vehicle (V19.81)*

The appropriate 7th character is to be added to each code from category V14
A initial encounter
D subsequent encounter
S sequela

X+7th **V14.0 Pedal cycle driver injured in collision with heavy transport vehicle or bus in nontraffic accident**
X+7th **V14.1 Pedal cycle passenger injured in collision with heavy transport vehicle or bus in nontraffic accident**

X+7th **V14.2** **Unspecified pedal cyclist injured in collision with heavy transport vehicle or bus in nontraffic accident**

X+7th **V14.3** **Person boarding or alighting a pedal cycle injured in collision with heavy transport vehicle or bus**

X+7th **V14.4** **Pedal cycle driver injured in collision with heavy transport vehicle or bus in traffic accident**

X+7th **V14.5** **Pedal cycle passenger injured in collision with heavy transport vehicle or bus in traffic accident**

X+7th **V14.9** **Unspecified pedal cyclist injured in collision with heavy transport vehicle or bus in traffic accident**

V15 Pedal cycle rider injured in collision with railway train or railway vehicle

The appropriate 7th character is to be added to each code from category V15
A initial encounter
D subsequent encounter
S sequela

X+7th **V15.0** **Pedal cycle driver injured in collision with railway train or railway vehicle in nontraffic accident**

X+7th **V15.1** **Pedal cycle passenger injured in collision with railway train or railway vehicle in nontraffic accident**

X+7th **V15.2** **Unspecified pedal cyclist injured in collision with railway train or railway vehicle in nontraffic accident**

X+7th **V15.3** **Person boarding or alighting a pedal cycle injured in collision with railway train or railway vehicle**

X+7th **V15.4** **Pedal cycle driver injured in collision with railway train or railway vehicle in traffic accident**

X+7th **V15.5** **Pedal cycle passenger injured in collision with railway train or railway vehicle in traffic accident**

X+7th **V15.9** **Unspecified pedal cyclist injured in collision with railway train or railway vehicle in traffic accident**

V16 Pedal cycle rider injured in collision with other nonmotor vehicle

Includes: collision with animal-drawn vehicle, animal being ridden, streetcar

The appropriate 7th character is to be added to each code from category V16
A initial encounter
D subsequent encounter
S sequela

X+7th **V16.0** **Pedal cycle driver injured in collision with other nonmotor vehicle in nontraffic accident**

X+7th **V16.1** **Pedal cycle passenger injured in collision with other nonmotor vehicle in nontraffic accident**

X+7th **V16.2** **Unspecified pedal cyclist injured in collision with other nonmotor vehicle in nontraffic accident**

X+7th **V16.3** **Person boarding or alighting a pedal cycle injured in collision with other nonmotor vehicle in nontraffic accident**

X+7th **V16.4** **Pedal cycle driver injured in collision with other nonmotor vehicle in traffic accident**

X+7th **V16.5** **Pedal cycle passenger injured in collision with other nonmotor vehicle in traffic accident**

X+7th **V16.9** **Unspecified pedal cyclist injured in collision with other nonmotor vehicle in traffic accident**

V17 Pedal cycle rider injured in collision with fixed or stationary object

The appropriate 7th character is to be added to each code from category V17
A initial encounter
D subsequent encounter
S sequela

X+7th **V17.0** **Pedal cycle driver injured in collision with fixed or stationary object in nontraffic accident**

X+7th **V17.1** **Pedal cycle passenger injured in collision with fixed or stationary object in nontraffic accident**

X+7th **V17.2** **Unspecified pedal cyclist injured in collision with fixed or stationary object in nontraffic accident**

X+7th **V17.3** **Person boarding or alighting a pedal cycle injured in collision with fixed or stationary object**

X+7th **V17.4** **Pedal cycle driver injured in collision with fixed or stationary object in traffic accident**

X+7th **V17.5** **Pedal cycle passenger injured in collision with fixed or stationary object in traffic accident**

X+7th **V17.9** **Unspecified pedal cyclist injured in collision with fixed or stationary object in traffic accident**

V18 Pedal cycle rider injured in noncollision transport accident

Includes: fall or thrown from pedal cycle (without antecedent collision)
overturning pedal cycle NOS
overturning pedal cycle without collision

The appropriate 7th character is to be added to each code from category V18
A initial encounter
D subsequent encounter
S sequela

X+7th **V18.0** **Pedal cycle driver injured in noncollision transport accident in nontraffic accident**

X+7th **V18.1** **Pedal cycle passenger injured in noncollision transport accident in nontraffic accident**

X+7th **V18.2** **Unspecified pedal cyclist injured in noncollision transport accident in nontraffic accident**

X+7th **V18.3** **Person boarding or alighting a pedal cycle injured in noncollision transport accident**

X+7th **V18.4** **Pedal cycle driver injured in noncollision transport accident in traffic accident**

X+7th **V18.5** **Pedal cycle passenger injured in noncollision transport accident in traffic accident**

X+7th **V18.9** **Unspecified pedal cyclist injured in noncollision transport accident in traffic accident**

V19 Pedal cycle rider injured in other and unspecified transport accidents

The appropriate 7th character is to be added to each code from category V19
A initial encounter
D subsequent encounter
S sequela

+ **V19.0** **Pedal cycle driver injured in collision with other and unspecified motor vehicles in nontraffic accident**
  - X+7th **V19.00** **Pedal cycle driver injured in collision with unspecified motor vehicles in nontraffic accident**
  - X+7th **V19.09** **Pedal cycle driver injured in collision with other motor vehicles in nontraffic accident**

+ **V19.1** **Pedal cycle passenger injured in collision with other and unspecified motor vehicles in nontraffic accident**
  - X+7th **V19.10** **Pedal cycle passenger injured in collision with unspecified motor vehicles in nontraffic accident**
  - X+7th **V19.19** **Pedal cycle passenger injured in collision with other motor vehicles in nontraffic accident**

+ **V19.2** **Unspecified pedal cyclist injured in collision with other and unspecified motor vehicles in nontraffic accident**
  - X+7th **V19.20** **Unspecified pedal cyclist injured in collision with unspecified motor vehicles in nontraffic accident**
    Pedal cycle collision NOS, nontraffic
  - X+7th **V19.29** **Unspecified pedal cyclist injured in collision with other motor vehicles in nontraffic accident**

X+7th **V19.3** **Pedal cyclist (driver) (passenger) injured in unspecified nontraffic accident**
Pedal cycle accident NOS, nontraffic
Pedal cyclist injured in nontraffic accident NOS

+ **V19.4** **Pedal cycle driver injured in collision with other and unspecified motor vehicles in traffic accident**
  - X+7th **V19.40** **Pedal cycle driver injured in collision with unspecified motor vehicles in traffic accident**
  - X+7th **V19.49** **Pedal cycle driver injured in collision with other motor vehicles in traffic accident**

+ **V19.5** **Pedal cycle passenger injured in collision with other and unspecified motor vehicles in traffic accident**
  - X+7th **V19.50** **Pedal cycle passenger injured in collision with unspecified motor vehicles in traffic accident**
  - X+7th **V19.59** **Pedal cycle passenger injured in collision with other motor vehicles in traffic accident**

+ **V19.6** **Unspecified pedal cyclist injured in collision with other and unspecified motor vehicles in traffic accident**
  - X+7th **V19.60** **Unspecified pedal cyclist injured in collision with unspecified motor vehicles in traffic accident**
    Pedal cycle collision NOS (traffic)
  - X+7th **V19.69** **Unspecified pedal cyclist injured in collision with other motor vehicles in traffic accident**

+ **V19.8** **Pedal cyclist (driver) (passenger) injured in other specified transport accidents**
  - X+7th **V19.81** **Pedal cyclist (driver) (passenger) injured in transport accident with military vehicle**
  - X+7th **V19.88** **Pedal cyclist (driver) (passenger) injured in other specified transport accidents**

X+7th **V19.9** **Pedal cyclist (driver) (passenger) injured in unspecified traffic accident**
Pedal cycle accident NOS

Motorcycle rider injured in transport accident (V20-V29)

Includes: moped
motorcycle with sidecar
motorized bicycle
motor scooter

Excludes1: *three-wheeled motor vehicle (V30-V39)*

V20 Motorcycle rider injured in collision with pedestrian or animal

Excludes1: *motorcycle rider collision with animal-drawn vehicle or animal being ridden (V26.-)*

The appropriate 7th character is to be added to each code from category V20
A initial encounter
D subsequent encounter
S sequela

X+7th **V20.0 Motorcycle driver injured in collision with pedestrian or animal in nontraffic accident**
X+7th **V20.1 Motorcycle passenger injured in collision with pedestrian or animal in nontraffic accident**
X+7th **V20.2 Unspecified motorcycle rider injured in collision with pedestrian or animal in nontraffic accident**
X+7th **V20.3 Person boarding or alighting a motorcycle injured in collision with pedestrian or animal**
X+7th **V20.4 Motorcycle driver injured in collision with pedestrian or animal in traffic accident**
X+7th **V20.5 Motorcycle passenger injured in collision with pedestrian or animal in traffic accident**
X+7th **V20.9 Unspecified motorcycle rider injured in collision with pedestrian or animal in traffic accident**

V21 Motorcycle rider injured in collision with pedal cycle

The appropriate 7th character is to be added to each code from category V21
A initial encounter
D subsequent encounter
S sequela

X+7th **V21.0 Motorcycle driver injured in collision with pedal cycle in nontraffic accident**
X+7th **V21.1 Motorcycle passenger injured in collision with pedal cycle in nontraffic accident**
X+7th **V21.2 Unspecified motorcycle rider injured in collision with pedal cycle in nontraffic accident**
X+7th **V21.3 Person boarding or alighting a motorcycle injured in collision with pedal cycle**
X+7th **V21.4 Motorcycle driver injured in collision with pedal cycle in traffic accident**
X+7th **V21.5 Motorcycle passenger injured in collision with pedal cycle in traffic accident**
X+7th **V21.9 Unspecified motorcycle rider injured in collision with pedal cycle in traffic accident**

V22 Motorcycle rider injured in collision with two- or three-wheeled motor vehicle

The appropriate 7th character is to be added to each code from category V22
A initial encounter
D subsequent encounter
S sequela

X+7th **V22.0 Motorcycle driver injured in collision with two- or three-wheeled motor vehicle in nontraffic accident**
X+7th **V22.1 Motorcycle passenger injured in collision with two- or three-wheeled motor vehicle in nontraffic accident**
X+7th **V22.2 Unspecified motorcycle rider injured in collision with two- or three-wheeled motor vehicle in nontraffic accident**
X+7th **V22.3 Person boarding or alighting a motorcycle injured in collision with two- or three-wheeled motor vehicle**
X+7th **V22.4 Motorcycle driver injured in collision with two- or three-wheeled motor vehicle in traffic accident**
X+7th **V22.5 Motorcycle passenger injured in collision with two- or three-wheeled motor vehicle in traffic accident**
X+7th **V22.9 Unspecified motorcycle rider injured in collision with two- or three-wheeled motor vehicle in traffic accident**

V23 Motorcycle rider injured in collision with car, pick-up truck or van

The appropriate 7th character is to be added to each code from category V23
A initial encounter
D subsequent encounter
S sequela

X+7th **V23.0 Motorcycle driver injured in collision with car, pick-up truck or van in nontraffic accident**
X+7th **V23.1 Motorcycle passenger injured in collision with car, pick-up truck or van in nontraffic accident**
X+7th **V23.2 Unspecified motorcycle rider injured in collision with car, pick-up truck or van in nontraffic accident**
X+7th **V23.3 Person boarding or alighting a motorcycle injured in collision with car, pick-up truck or van**
X+7th **V23.4 Motorcycle driver injured in collision with car, pick-up truck or van in traffic accident**
X+7th **V23.5 Motorcycle passenger injured in collision with car, pick-up truck or van in traffic accident**
X+7th **V23.9 Unspecified motorcycle rider injured in collision with car, pick-up truck or van in traffic accident**

V24 Motorcycle rider injured in collision with heavy transport vehicle or bus

Excludes1: *motorcycle rider injured in collision with military vehicle (V29.81)*

The appropriate 7th character is to be added to each code from category V24
A initial encounter
D subsequent encounter
S sequela

X+7th **V24.0 Motorcycle driver injured in collision with heavy transport vehicle or bus in nontraffic accident**
X+7th **V24.1 Motorcycle passenger injured in collision with heavy transport vehicle or bus in nontraffic accident**
X+7th **V24.2 Unspecified motorcycle rider injured in collision with heavy transport vehicle or bus in nontraffic accident**
X+7th **V24.3 Person boarding or alighting a motorcycle injured in collision with heavy transport vehicle or bus**
X+7th **V24.4 Motorcycle driver injured in collision with heavy transport vehicle or bus in traffic accident**
X+7th **V24.5 Motorcycle passenger injured in collision with heavy transport vehicle or bus in traffic accident**
X+7th **V24.9 Unspecified motorcycle rider injured in collision with heavy transport vehicle or bus in traffic accident**

V25 Motorcycle rider injured in collision with railway train or railway vehicle

The appropriate 7th character is to be added to each code from category V25
A initial encounter
D subsequent encounter
S sequela

X+7th **V25.0 Motorcycle driver injured in collision with railway train or railway vehicle in nontraffic accident**
X+7th **V25.1 Motorcycle passenger injured in collision with railway train or railway vehicle in nontraffic accident**
X+7th **V25.2 Unspecified motorcycle rider injured in collision with railway train or railway vehicle in nontraffic accident**
X+7th **V25.3 Person boarding or alighting a motorcycle injured in collision with railway train or railway vehicle**
X+7th **V25.4 Motorcycle driver injured in collision with railway train or railway vehicle in traffic accident**
X+7th **V25.5 Motorcycle passenger injured in collision with railway train or railway vehicle in traffic accident**
X+7th **V25.9 Unspecified motorcycle rider injured in collision with railway train or railway vehicle in traffic accident**

V26 Motorcycle rider injured in collision with other nonmotor vehicle

Includes: collision with animal-drawn vehicle, animal being ridden, streetcar

The appropriate 7th character is to be added to each code from category V26
A initial encounter
D subsequent encounter
S sequela

X+7th **V26.0 Motorcycle driver injured in collision with other nonmotor vehicle in nontraffic accident**
X+7th **V26.1 Motorcycle passenger injured in collision with other nonmotor vehicle in nontraffic accident**
X+7th **V26.2 Unspecified motorcycle rider injured in collision with other nonmotor vehicle in nontraffic accident**
X+7th **V26.3 Person boarding or alighting a motorcycle injured in collision with other nonmotor vehicle**
X+7th **V26.4 Motorcycle driver injured in collision with other nonmotor vehicle in traffic accident**
X+7th **V26.5 Motorcycle passenger injured in collision with other nonmotor vehicle in traffic accident**
X+7th **V26.9 Unspecified motorcycle rider injured in collision with other nonmotor vehicle in traffic accident**

V27 Motorcycle rider injured in collision with fixed or stationary object

The appropriate 7th character is to be added to each code from category V27
A initial encounter
D subsequent encounter
S sequela

X+7th **V27.0 Motorcycle driver injured in collision with fixed or stationary object in nontraffic accident**

X+7th **V27.1 Motorcycle passenger injured in collision with fixed or stationary object in nontraffic accident**

X+7th **V27.2 Unspecified motorcycle rider injured in collision with fixed or stationary object in nontraffic accident**

X+7th **V27.3 Person boarding or alighting a motorcycle injured in collision with fixed or stationary object**

X+7th **V27.4 Motorcycle driver injured in collision with fixed or stationary object in traffic accident**

X+7th **V27.5 Motorcycle passenger injured in collision with fixed or stationary object in traffic accident**

X+7th **V27.9 Unspecified motorcycle rider injured in collision with fixed or stationary object in traffic accident**

V28 Motorcycle rider injured in noncollision transport accident

Includes: fall or thrown from motorcycle (without antecedent collision)
overturning motorcycle NOS
overturning motorcycle without collision

The appropriate 7th character is to be added to each code from category V28
A initial encounter
D subsequent encounter
S sequela

X+7th **V28.0 Motorcycle driver injured in noncollision transport accident in nontraffic accident**

X+7th **V28.1 Motorcycle passenger injured in noncollision transport accident in nontraffic accident**

X+7th **V28.2 Unspecified motorcycle rider injured in noncollision transport accident in nontraffic accident**

X+7th **V28.3 Person boarding or alighting a motorcycle injured in noncollision transport accident**

X+7th **V28.4 Motorcycle driver injured in noncollision transport accident in traffic accident**

X+7th **V28.5 Motorcycle passenger injured in noncollision transport accident in traffic accident**

X+7th **V28.9 Unspecified motorcycle rider injured in noncollision transport accident in traffic accident**

V29 Motorcycle rider injured in other and unspecified transport accidents

The appropriate 7th character is to be added to each code from category V29
A initial encounter
D subsequent encounter
S sequela

\+ **V29.0 Motorcycle driver injured in collision with other and unspecified motor vehicles in nontraffic accident**

X+7th **V29.00 Motorcycle driver injured in collision with unspecified motor vehicles in nontraffic accident**

X+7th **V29.09 Motorcycle driver injured in collision with other motor vehicles in nontraffic accident**

\+ **V29.1 Motorcycle passenger injured in collision with other and unspecified motor vehicles in nontraffic accident**

X+7th **V29.10 Motorcycle passenger injured in collision with unspecified motor vehicles in nontraffic accident**

X+7th **V29.19 Motorcycle passenger injured in collision with other motor vehicles in nontraffic accident**

\+ **V29.2 Unspecified motorcycle rider injured in collision with other and unspecified motor vehicles in nontraffic accident**

X+7th **V29.20 Unspecified motorcycle rider injured in collision with unspecified motor vehicles in nontraffic accident**
Motorcycle collision NOS, nontraffic

X+7th **V29.29 Unspecified motorcycle rider injured in collision with other motor vehicles in nontraffic accident**

X+7th **V29.3 Motorcycle rider (driver) (passenger) injured in unspecified nontraffic accident**
Motorcycle accident NOS, nontraffic
Motorcycle rider injured in nontraffic accident NOS

\+ **V29.4 Motorcycle driver injured in collision with other and unspecified motor vehicles in traffic accident**

X+7th **V29.40 Motorcycle driver injured in collision with unspecified motor vehicles in traffic accident**

X+7th **V29.49 Motorcycle driver injured in collision with other motor vehicles in traffic accident**

\+ **V29.5 Motorcycle passenger injured in collision with other and unspecified motor vehicles in traffic accident**

X+7th **V29.50 Motorcycle passenger injured in collision with unspecified motor vehicles in traffic accident**

X+7th **V29.59 Motorcycle passenger injured in collision with other motor vehicles in traffic accident**

\+ **V29.6 Unspecified motorcycle rider injured in collision with other and unspecified motor vehicles in traffic accident**

X+7th **V29.60 Unspecified motorcycle rider injured in collision with unspecified motor vehicles in traffic accident**
Motorcycle collision NOS (traffic)

X+7th **V29.69 Unspecified motorcycle rider injured in collision with other motor vehicles in traffic accident**

\+ **V29.8 Motorcycle rider (driver) (passenger) injured in other specified transport accidents**

X+7th **V29.81 Motorcycle rider (driver) (passenger) injured in transport accident with military vehicle**

X+7th **V29.88 Motorcycle rider (driver) (passenger) injured in other specified transport accidents**

X+7th **V29.9 Motorcycle rider (driver) (passenger) injured in unspecified traffic accident**
Motorcycle accident NOS

Occupant of three-wheeled motor vehicle injured in transport accident (V30-V39)

Includes: motorized tricycle
motorized rickshaw
three-wheeled motor car

Excludes1: *all-terrain vehicles (V86.-)*
motorcycle with sidecar (V20-V29)
vehicle designed primarily for off-road use (V86.-)

V30 Occupant of three-wheeled motor vehicle injured in collision with pedestrian or animal

Excludes1: *three-wheeled motor vehicle collision with animal-drawn vehicle or animal being ridden (V36.-)*

The appropriate 7th character is to be added to each code from category V30
A initial encounter
D subsequent encounter
S sequela

X+7th **V30.0 Driver of three-wheeled motor vehicle injured in collision with pedestrian or animal in nontraffic accident**

X+7th **V30.1 Passenger in three-wheeled motor vehicle injured in collision with pedestrian or animal in nontraffic accident**

X+7th **V30.2 Person on outside of three-wheeled motor vehicle injured in collision with pedestrian or animal in nontraffic accident**

X+7th **V30.3 Unspecified occupant of three-wheeled motor vehicle injured in collision with pedestrian or animal in nontraffic accident**

X+7th **V30.4 Person boarding or alighting a three-wheeled motor vehicle injured in collision with pedestrian or animal**

X+7th **V30.5 Driver of three-wheeled motor vehicle injured in collision with pedestrian or animal in traffic accident**

X+7th **V30.6 Passenger in three-wheeled motor vehicle injured in collision with pedestrian or animal in traffic accident**

X+7th **V30.7 Person on outside of three-wheeled motor vehicle injured in collision with pedestrian or animal in traffic accident**

X+7th **V30.9 Unspecified occupant of three-wheeled motor vehicle injured in collision with pedestrian or animal in traffic accident**

V31 Occupant of three-wheeled motor vehicle injured in collision with pedal cycle

The appropriate 7th character is to be added to each code from category V31
A initial encounter
D subsequent encounter
S sequela

X+7th **V31.0 Driver of three-wheeled motor vehicle injured in collision with pedal cycle in nontraffic accident**

X+7th **V31.1 Passenger in three-wheeled motor vehicle injured in collision with pedal cycle in nontraffic accident**

X+7th **V31.2 Person on outside of three-wheeled motor vehicle injured in collision with pedal cycle in nontraffic accident**

X+7th **V31.3 Unspecified occupant of three-wheeled motor vehicle injured in collision with pedal cycle in nontraffic accident**

X+7th **V31.4 Person boarding or alighting a three-wheeled motor vehicle injured in collision with pedal cycle**

X+7th **V31.5 Driver of three-wheeled motor vehicle injured in collision with pedal cycle in traffic accident**

X+7th **V31.6** **Passenger in three-wheeled motor vehicle injured in collision with pedal cycle in traffic accident**

X+7th **V31.7** **Person on outside of three-wheeled motor vehicle injured in collision with pedal cycle in traffic accident**

X+7th **V31.9** **Unspecified occupant of three-wheeled motor vehicle injured in collision with pedal cycle in traffic accident**

V32 Occupant of three-wheeled motor vehicle injured in collision with two- or three-wheeled motor vehicle

The appropriate 7th character is to be added to each code from category V32
A initial encounter
D subsequent encounter
S sequela

X+7th **V32.0** **Driver of three-wheeled motor vehicle injured in collision with two- or three-wheeled motor vehicle in nontraffic accident**

X+7th **V32.1** **Passenger in three-wheeled motor vehicle injured in collision with two- or three-wheeled motor vehicle in nontraffic accident**

X+7th **V32.2** **Person on outside of three-wheeled motor vehicle injured in collision with two- or three-wheeled motor vehicle in nontraffic accident**

X+7th **V32.3** **Unspecified occupant of three-wheeled motor vehicle injured in collision with two- or three-wheeled motor vehicle in nontraffic accident**

X+7th **V32.4** **Person boarding or alighting a three-wheeled motor vehicle injured in collision with two- or three-wheeled motor vehicle**

X+7th **V32.5** **Driver of three-wheeled motor vehicle injured in collision with two- or three-wheeled motor vehicle in traffic accident**

X+7th **V32.6** **Passenger in three-wheeled motor vehicle injured in collision with two- or three-wheeled motor vehicle in traffic accident**

X+7th **V32.7** **Person on outside of three-wheeled motor vehicle injured in collision with two- or three-wheeled motor vehicle in traffic accident**

X+7th **V32.9** **Unspecified occupant of three-wheeled motor vehicle injured in collision with two- or three-wheeled motor vehicle in traffic accident**

V33 Occupant of three-wheeled motor vehicle injured in collision with car, pick-up truck or van

The appropriate 7th character is to be added to each code from category V33
A initial encounter
D subsequent encounter
S sequela

X+7th **V33.0** **Driver of three-wheeled motor vehicle injured in collision with car, pick-up truck or van in nontraffic accident**

X+7th **V33.1** **Passenger in three-wheeled motor vehicle injured in collision with car, pick-up truck or van in nontraffic accident**

X+7th **V33.2** **Person on outside of three-wheeled motor vehicle injured in collision with car, pick-up truck or van in nontraffic accident**

X+7th **V33.3** **Unspecified occupant of three-wheeled motor vehicle injured in collision with car, pick-up truck or van in nontraffic accident**

X+7th **V33.4** **Person boarding or alighting a three-wheeled motor vehicle injured in collision with car, pick-up truck or van**

X+7th **V33.5** **Driver of three-wheeled motor vehicle injured in collision with car, pick-up truck or van in traffic accident**

X+7th **V33.6** **Passenger in three-wheeled motor vehicle injured in collision with car, pick-up truck or van in traffic accident**

X+7th **V33.7** **Person on outside of three-wheeled motor vehicle injured in collision with car, pick-up truck or van in traffic accident**

X+7th **V33.9** **Unspecified occupant of three-wheeled motor vehicle injured in collision with car, pick-up truck or van in traffic accident**

V34 Occupant of three-wheeled motor vehicle injured in collision with heavy transport vehicle or bus

Excludes1: *occupant of three-wheeled motor vehicle injured in collision with military vehicle (V39.81)*

The appropriate 7th character is to be added to each code from category V34
A initial encounter
D subsequent encounter
S sequela

X+7th **V34.0** **Driver of three-wheeled motor vehicle injured in collision with heavy transport vehicle or bus in nontraffic accident**

X+7th **V34.1** **Passenger in three-wheeled motor vehicle injured in collision with heavy transport vehicle or bus in nontraffic accident**

X+7th **V34.2** **Person on outside of three-wheeled motor vehicle injured in collision with heavy transport vehicle or bus in nontraffic accident**

X+7th **V34.3** **Unspecified occupant of three-wheeled motor vehicle injured in collision with heavy transport vehicle or bus in nontraffic accident**

X+7th **V34.4** **Person boarding or alighting a three-wheeled motor vehicle injured in collision with heavy transport vehicle or bus**

X+7th **V34.5** **Driver of three-wheeled motor vehicle injured in collision with heavy transport vehicle or bus in traffic accident**

X+7th **V34.6** **Passenger in three-wheeled motor vehicle injured in collision with heavy transport vehicle or bus in traffic accident**

X+7th **V34.7** **Person on outside of three-wheeled motor vehicle injured in collision with heavy transport vehicle or bus in traffic accident**

X+7th **V34.9** **Unspecified occupant of three-wheeled motor vehicle injured in collision with heavy transport vehicle or bus in traffic accident**

V35 Occupant of three-wheeled motor vehicle injured in collision with railway train or railway vehicle

The appropriate 7th character is to be added to each code from category V35
A initial encounter
D subsequent encounter
S sequela

X+7th **V35.0** **Driver of three-wheeled motor vehicle injured in collision with railway train or railway vehicle in nontraffic accident**

X+7th **V35.1** **Passenger in three-wheeled motor vehicle injured in collision with railway train or railway vehicle in nontraffic accident**

X+7th **V35.2** **Person on outside of three-wheeled motor vehicle injured in collision with railway train or railway vehicle in nontraffic accident**

X+7th **V35.3** **Unspecified occupant of three-wheeled motor vehicle injured in collision with railway train or railway vehicle in nontraffic accident**

X+7th **V35.4** **Person boarding or alighting a three-wheeled motor vehicle injured in collision with railway train or railway vehicle**

X+7th **V35.5** **Driver of three-wheeled motor vehicle injured in collision with railway train or railway vehicle in traffic accident**

X+7th **V35.6** **Passenger in three-wheeled motor vehicle injured in collision with railway train or railway vehicle in traffic accident**

X+7th **V35.7** **Person on outside of three-wheeled motor vehicle injured in collision with railway train or railway vehicle in traffic accident**

X+7th **V35.9** **Unspecified occupant of three-wheeled motor vehicle injured in collision with railway train or railway vehicle in traffic accident**

V36 Occupant of three-wheeled motor vehicle injured in collision with other nonmotor vehicle

Includes: collision with animal-drawn vehicle, animal being ridden, streetcar

The appropriate 7th character is to be added to each code from category V36
A initial encounter
D subsequent encounter
S sequela

X+7th **V36.0** **Driver of three-wheeled motor vehicle injured in collision with other nonmotor vehicle in nontraffic accident**

X+7th **V36.1** **Passenger in three-wheeled motor vehicle injured in collision with other nonmotor vehicle in nontraffic accident**

X+7th **V36.2** **Person on outside of three-wheeled motor vehicle injured in collision with other nonmotor vehicle in nontraffic accident**

X+7th **V36.3** **Unspecified occupant of three-wheeled motor vehicle injured in collision with other nonmotor vehicle in nontraffic accident**

X+7th **V36.4** **Person boarding or alighting a three-wheeled motor vehicle injured in collision with other nonmotor vehicle**

X+7th **V36.5** **Driver of three-wheeled motor vehicle injured in collision with other nonmotor vehicle in traffic accident**

X+7th **V36.6** **Passenger in three-wheeled motor vehicle injured in collision with other nonmotor vehicle in traffic accident**

X+7th **V36.7** **Person on outside of three-wheeled motor vehicle injured in collision with other nonmotor vehicle in traffic accident**

X+7th **V36.9** **Unspecified occupant of three-wheeled motor vehicle injured in collision with other nonmotor vehicle in traffic accident**

V37 Occupant of three-wheeled motor vehicle injured in collision with fixed or stationary object

The appropriate 7th character is to be added to each code from category V37
A initial encounter
D subsequent encounter
S sequela

X+7th **V37.0** **Driver of three-wheeled motor vehicle injured in collision with fixed or stationary object in nontraffic accident**

X+7th **V37.1** **Passenger in three-wheeled motor vehicle injured in collision with fixed or stationary object in nontraffic accident**

X+7th **V37.2** **Person on outside of three-wheeled motor vehicle injured in collision with fixed or stationary object in nontraffic accident**

X+7th **V37.3** **Unspecified occupant of three-wheeled motor vehicle injured in collision with fixed or stationary object in nontraffic accident**

X+7th **V37.4 Person boarding or alighting a three-wheeled motor vehicle injured in collision with fixed or stationary object**

X+7th **V37.5 Driver of three-wheeled motor vehicle injured in collision with fixed or stationary object in traffic accident**

X+7th **V37.6 Passenger in three-wheeled motor vehicle injured in collision with fixed or stationary object in traffic accident**

X+7th **V37.7 Person on outside of three-wheeled motor vehicle injured in collision with fixed or stationary object in traffic accident**

X+7th **V37.9 Unspecified occupant of three-wheeled motor vehicle injured in collision with fixed or stationary object in traffic accident**

V38 Occupant of three-wheeled motor vehicle injured in noncollision transport accident

Includes: fall or thrown from three-wheeled motor vehicle
overturning of three-wheeled motor vehicle NOS
overturning of three-wheeled motor vehicle without collision

The appropriate 7th character is to be added to each code from category V38
A initial encounter
D subsequent encounter
S sequela

X+7th **V38.0 Driver of three-wheeled motor vehicle injured in noncollision transport accident in nontraffic accident**

X+7th **V38.1 Passenger in three-wheeled motor vehicle injured in noncollision transport accident in nontraffic accident**

X+7th **V38.2 Person on outside of three-wheeled motor vehicle injured in noncollision transport accident in nontraffic accident**

X+7th **V38.3 Unspecified occupant of three-wheeled motor vehicle injured in noncollision transport accident in nontraffic accident**

X+7th **V38.4 Person boarding or alighting a three-wheeled motor vehicle injured in noncollision transport accident**

X+7th **V38.5 Driver of three-wheeled motor vehicle injured in noncollision transport accident in traffic accident**

X+7th **V38.6 Passenger in three-wheeled motor vehicle injured in noncollision transport accident in traffic accident**

X+7th **V38.7 Person on outside of three-wheeled motor vehicle injured in noncollision transport accident in traffic accident**

X+7th **V38.9 Unspecified occupant of three-wheeled motor vehicle injured in noncollision transport accident in traffic accident**

V39 Occupant of three-wheeled motor vehicle injured in other and unspecified transport accidents

The appropriate 7th character is to be added to each code from category V39
A initial encounter
D subsequent encounter
S sequela

\+ **V39.0 Driver of three-wheeled motor vehicle injured in collision with other and unspecified motor vehicles in nontraffic accident**

X+7th **V39.00 Driver of three-wheeled motor vehicle injured in collision with unspecified motor vehicles in nontraffic accident**

X+7th **V39.09 Driver of three-wheeled motor vehicle injured in collision with other motor vehicles in nontraffic accident**

\+ **V39.1 Passenger in three-wheeled motor vehicle injured in collision with other and unspecified motor vehicles in nontraffic accident**

X+7th **V39.10 Passenger in three-wheeled motor vehicle injured in collision with unspecified motor vehicles in nontraffic accident**

X+7th **V39.19 Passenger in three-wheeled motor vehicle injured in collision with other motor vehicles in nontraffic accident**

\+ **V39.2 Unspecified occupant of three-wheeled motor vehicle injured in collision with other and unspecified motor vehicles in nontraffic accident**

X+7th **V39.20 Unspecified occupant of three-wheeled motor vehicle injured in collision with unspecified motor vehicles in nontraffic accident**
Collision NOS involving three-wheeled motor vehicle, nontraffic

X+7th **V39.29 Unspecified occupant of three-wheeled motor vehicle injured in collision with other motor vehicles in nontraffic accident**

X+7th **V39.3 Occupant (driver) (passenger) of three-wheeled motor vehicle injured in unspecified nontraffic accident**
Accident NOS involving three-wheeled motor vehicle, nontraffic
Occupant of three-wheeled motor vehicle injured in nontraffic accident NOS

\+ **V39.4 Driver of three-wheeled motor vehicle injured in collision with other and unspecified motor vehicles in traffic accident**

X+7th **V39.40 Driver of three-wheeled motor vehicle injured in collision with unspecified motor vehicles in traffic accident**

X+7th **V39.49 Driver of three-wheeled motor vehicle injured in collision with other motor vehicles in traffic accident**

\+ **V39.5 Passenger in three-wheeled motor vehicle injured in collision with other and unspecified motor vehicles in traffic accident**

X+7th **V39.50 Passenger in three-wheeled motor vehicle injured in collision with unspecified motor vehicles in traffic accident**

X+7th **V39.59 Passenger in three-wheeled motor vehicle injured in collision with other motor vehicles in traffic accident**

\+ **V39.6 Unspecified occupant of three-wheeled motor vehicle injured in collision with other and unspecified motor vehicles in traffic accident**

X+7th **V39.60 Unspecified occupant of three-wheeled motor vehicle injured in collision with unspecified motor vehicles in traffic accident**
Collision NOS involving three-wheeled motor vehicle (traffic)

X+7th **V39.69 Unspecified occupant of three-wheeled motor vehicle injured in collision with other motor vehicles in traffic accident**

\+ **V39.8 Occupant (driver) (passenger) of three-wheeled motor vehicle injured in other specified transport accidents**

X+7th **V39.81 Occupant (driver) (passenger) of three-wheeled motor vehicle injured in transport accident with military vehicle**

X+7th **V39.89 Occupant (driver) (passenger) of three-wheeled motor vehicle injured in other specified transport accidents**

X+7th **V39.9 Occupant (driver) (passenger) of three-wheeled motor vehicle injured in unspecified traffic accident**
Accident NOS involving three-wheeled motor vehicle

Car occupant injured in transport accident (V40-V49)

Includes: a four-wheeled motor vehicle designed primarily for carrying passengers
automobile (pulling a trailer or camper)

Excludes1: *bus (V50-V59)*
minibus (V50-V59)
minivan (V50-V59)
motorcoach (V70-V79)
pick-up truck (V50-V59)
sport utility vehicle (SUV) (V50-V59)

V40 Car occupant injured in collision with pedestrian or animal

Excludes1: *car collision with animal-drawn vehicle or animal being ridden (V46.-)*

The appropriate 7th character is to be added to each code from category V40
A initial encounter
D subsequent encounter
S sequela

X+7th **V40.0 Car driver injured in collision with pedestrian or animal in nontraffic accident**

X+7th **V40.1 Car passenger injured in collision with pedestrian or animal in nontraffic accident**

X+7th **V40.2 Person on outside of car injured in collision with pedestrian or animal in nontraffic accident**

X+7th **V40.3 Unspecified car occupant injured in collision with pedestrian or animal in nontraffic accident**

X+7th **V40.4 Person boarding or alighting a car injured in collision with pedestrian or animal**

X+7th **V40.5 Car driver injured in collision with pedestrian or animal in traffic accident**

X+7th **V40.6 Car passenger injured in collision with pedestrian or animal in traffic accident**

X+7th **V40.7 Person on outside of car injured in collision with pedestrian or animal in traffic accident**

X+7th **V40.9 Unspecified car occupant injured in collision with pedestrian or animal in traffic accident**

V41 Car occupant injured in collision with pedal cycle

The appropriate 7th character is to be added to each code from category V41
A initial encounter
D subsequent encounter
S sequela

X+7th **V41.0 Car driver injured in collision with pedal cycle in nontraffic accident**

X+7th **V41.1 Car passenger injured in collision with pedal cycle in nontraffic accident**

X+7th **V41.2** **Person on outside of car injured in collision with pedal cycle in nontraffic accident**
X+7th **V41.3** **Unspecified car occupant injured in collision with pedal cycle in nontraffic accident**
X+7th **V41.4** **Person boarding or alighting a car injured in collision with pedal cycle**
X+7th **V41.5** **Car driver injured in collision with pedal cycle in traffic accident**
X+7th **V41.6** **Car passenger injured in collision with pedal cycle in traffic accident**
X+7th **V41.7** **Person on outside of car injured in collision with pedal cycle in traffic accident**
X+7th **V41.9** **Unspecified car occupant injured in collision with pedal cycle in traffic accident**

V42 Car occupant injured in collision with two- or three-wheeled motor vehicle

The appropriate 7th character is to be added to each code from category V42
A initial encounter
D subsequent encounter
S sequela

X+7th **V42.0** **Car driver injured in collision with two- or three-wheeled motor vehicle in nontraffic accident**
X+7th **V42.1** **Car passenger injured in collision with two- or three-wheeled motor vehicle in nontraffic accident**
X+7th **V42.2** **Person on outside of car injured in collision with two- or three-wheeled motor vehicle in nontraffic accident**
X+7th **V42.3** **Unspecified car occupant injured in collision with two- or three-wheeled motor vehicle in nontraffic accident**
X+7th **V42.4** **Person boarding or alighting a car injured in collision with two- or three-wheeled motor vehicle**
X+7th **V42.5** **Car driver injured in collision with two- or three-wheeled motor vehicle in traffic accident**
X+7th **V42.6** **Car passenger injured in collision with two- or three-wheeled motor vehicle in traffic accident**
X+7th **V42.7** **Person on outside of car injured in collision with two- or three-wheeled motor vehicle in traffic accident**
X+7th **V42.9** **Unspecified car occupant injured in collision with two- or three-wheeled motor vehicle in traffic accident**

V43 Car occupant injured in collision with car, pick-up truck or van

The appropriate 7th character is to be added to each code from category V43
A initial encounter
D subsequent encounter
S sequela

\+ **V43.0** **Car driver injured in collision with car, pick-up truck or van in nontraffic accident**
X+7th **V43.01** **Car driver injured in collision with sport utility vehicle in nontraffic accident**
X+7th **V43.02** **Car driver injured in collision with other type car in nontraffic accident**
X+7th **V43.03** **Car driver injured in collision with pick-up truck in nontraffic accident**
X+7th **V43.04** **Car driver injured in collision with van in nontraffic accident**
\+ **V43.1** **Car passenger injured in collision with car, pick-up truck or van in nontraffic accident**
X+7th **V43.11** **Car passenger injured in collision with sport utility vehicle in nontraffic accident**
X+7th **V43.12** **Car passenger injured in collision with other type car in nontraffic accident**
X+7th **V43.13** **Car passenger injured in collision with pick-up in nontraffic accident**
X+7th **V43.14** **Car passenger injured in collision with van in nontraffic accident**
\+ **V43.2** **Person on outside of car injured in collision with car, pick-up truck or van in nontraffic accident**
X+7th **V43.21** **Person on outside of car injured in collision with sport utility vehicle in nontraffic accident**
X+7th **V43.22** **Person on outside of car injured in collision with other type car in nontraffic accident**
X+7th **V43.23** **Person on outside of car injured in collision with pick-up truck in nontraffic accident**
X+7th **V43.24** **Person on outside of car injured in collision with van in nontraffic accident**
\+ **V43.3** **Unspecified car occupant injured in collision with car, pick-up truck or van in nontraffic accident**
X+7th **V43.31** **Unspecified car occupant injured in collision with sport utility vehicle in nontraffic accident**
X+7th **V43.32** **Unspecified car occupant injured in collision with other type car in nontraffic accident**
X+7th **V43.33** **Unspecified car occupant injured in collision with pick-up truck in nontraffic accident**
X+7th **V43.34** **Unspecified car occupant injured in collision with van in nontraffic accident**
\+ **V43.4** **Person boarding or alighting a car injured in collision with car, pick-up truck or van**
X+7th **V43.41** **Person boarding or alighting a car injured in collision with sport utility vehicle**
X+7th **V43.42** **Person boarding or alighting a car injured in collision with other type car**
X+7th **V43.43** **Person boarding or alighting a car injured in collision with pick-up truck**
X+7th **V43.44** **Person boarding or alighting a car injured in collision with van**
\+ **V43.5** **Car driver injured in collision with car, pick-up truck or van in traffic accident**
X+7th **V43.51** **Car driver injured in collision with sport utility vehicle in traffic accident**
X+7th **V43.52** **Car driver injured in collision with other type car in traffic accident**
X+7th **V43.53** **Car driver injured in collision with pick-up truck in traffic accident**
X+7th **V43.54** **Car driver injured in collision with van in traffic accident**
\+ **V43.6** **Car passenger injured in collision with car, pick-up truck or van in traffic accident**
X+7th **V43.61** **Car passenger injured in collision with sport utility vehicle in traffic accident**
X+7th **V43.62** **Car passenger injured in collision with other type car in traffic accident**
X+7th **V43.63** **Car passenger injured in collision with pick-up truck in traffic accident**
X+7th **V43.64** **Car passenger injured in collision with van in traffic accident**
\+ **V43.7** **Person on outside of car injured in collision with car, pick-up truck or van in traffic accident**
X+7th **V43.71** **Person on outside of car injured in collision with sport utility vehicle in traffic accident**
X+7th **V43.72** **Person on outside of car injured in collision with other type car in traffic accident**
X+7th **V43.73** **Person on outside of car injured in collision with pick-up truck in traffic accident**
X+7th **V43.74** **Person on outside of car injured in collision with van in traffic accident**
\+ **V43.9** **Unspecified car occupant injured in collision with car, pick-up truck or van in traffic accident**
X+7th **V43.91** **Unspecified car occupant injured in collision with sport utility vehicle in traffic accident**
X+7th **V43.92** **Unspecified car occupant injured in collision with other type car in traffic accident**
X+7th **V43.93** **Unspecified car occupant injured in collision with pick-up truck in traffic accident**
X+7th **V43.94** **Unspecified car occupant injured in collision with van in traffic accident**

V44 Car occupant injured in collision with heavy transport vehicle or bus

Excludes1: *car occupant injured in collision with military vehicle (V49.81)*

The appropriate 7th character is to be added to each code from category V44
A initial encounter
D subsequent encounter
S sequela

X+7th **V44.0** **Car driver injured in collision with heavy transport vehicle or bus in nontraffic accident**
X+7th **V44.1** **Car passenger injured in collision with heavy transport vehicle or bus in nontraffic accident**
X+7th **V44.2** **Person on outside of car injured in collision with heavy transport vehicle or bus in nontraffic accident**
X+7th **V44.3** **Unspecified car occupant injured in collision with heavy transport vehicle or bus in nontraffic accident**
X+7th **V44.4** **Person boarding or alighting a car injured in collision with heavy transport vehicle or bus**
X+7th **V44.5** **Car driver injured in collision with heavy transport vehicle or bus in traffic accident**
X+7th **V44.6** **Car passenger injured in collision with heavy transport vehicle or bus in traffic accident**
X+7th **V44.7** **Person on outside of car injured in collision with heavy transport vehicle or bus in traffic accident**
X+7th **V44.9** **Unspecified car occupant injured in collision with heavy transport vehicle or bus in traffic accident**

V45 Car occupant injured in collision with railway train or railway vehicle

The appropriate 7th character is to be added to each code from category V45
A initial encounter
D subsequent encounter
S sequela

X+7th **V45.0 Car driver injured in collision with railway train or railway vehicle in nontraffic accident**
X+7th **V45.1 Car passenger injured in collision with railway train or railway vehicle in nontraffic accident**
X+7th **V45.2 Person on outside of car injured in collision with railway train or railway vehicle in nontraffic accident**
X+7th **V45.3 Unspecified car occupant injured in collision with railway train or railway vehicle in nontraffic accident**
X+7th **V45.4 Person boarding or alighting a car injured in collision with railway train or railway vehicle**
X+7th **V45.5 Car driver injured in collision with railway train or railway vehicle in traffic accident**
X+7th **V45.6 Car passenger injured in collision with railway train or railway vehicle in traffic accident**
X+7th **V45.7 Person on outside of car injured in collision with railway train or railway vehicle in traffic accident**
X+7th **V45.9 Unspecified car occupant injured in collision with railway train or railway vehicle in traffic accident**

V46 Car occupant injured in collision with other nonmotor vehicle

Includes: collision with animal-drawn vehicle, animal being ridden, streetcar

The appropriate 7th character is to be added to each code from category V46
A initial encounter
D subsequent encounter
S sequela

X+7th **V46.0 Car driver injured in collision with other nonmotor vehicle in nontraffic accident**
X+7th **V46.1 Car passenger injured in collision with other nonmotor vehicle in nontraffic accident**
X+7th **V46.2 Person on outside of car injured in collision with other nonmotor vehicle in nontraffic accident**
X+7th **V46.3 Unspecified car occupant injured in collision with other nonmotor vehicle in nontraffic accident**
X+7th **V46.4 Person boarding or alighting a car injured in collision with other nonmotor vehicle**
X+7th **V46.5 Car driver injured in collision with other nonmotor vehicle in traffic accident**
X+7th **V46.6 Car passenger injured in collision with other nonmotor vehicle in traffic accident**
X+7th **V46.7 Person on outside of car injured in collision with other nonmotor vehicle in traffic accident**
X+7th **V46.9 Unspecified car occupant injured in collision with other nonmotor vehicle in traffic accident**

V47 Car occupant injured in collision with fixed or stationary object

The appropriate 7th character is to be added to each code from category V47
A initial encounter
D subsequent encounter
S sequela

\+ **V47.0 Car driver injured in collision with fixed or stationary object in nontraffic accident**
X+7th **V47.01 Driver of sport utility vehicle injured in collision with fixed or stationary object in nontraffic accident**
X+7th **V47.02 Driver of other type car injured in collision with fixed or stationary object in nontraffic accident**
\+ **V47.1 Car passenger injured in collision with fixed or stationary object in nontraffic accident**
X+7th **V47.11 Passenger of sport utility vehicle injured in collision with fixed or stationary object in nontraffic accident**
X+7th **V47.12 Passenger of other type car injured in collision with fixed or stationary object in nontraffic accident**
X+7th **V47.2 Person on outside of car injured in collision with fixed or stationary object in nontraffic accident**
\+ **V47.3 Unspecified car occupant injured in collision with fixed or stationary object in nontraffic accident**
X+7th **V47.31 Unspecified occupant of sport utility vehicle injured in collision with fixed or stationary object in nontraffic accident**
X+7th **V47.32 Unspecified occupant of other type car injured in collision with fixed or stationary object in nontraffic accident**
X+7th **V47.4 Person boarding or alighting a car injured in collision with fixed or stationary object**
\+ **V47.5 Car driver injured in collision with fixed or stationary object in traffic accident**
X+7th **V47.51 Driver of sport utility vehicle injured in collision with fixed or stationary object in traffic accident**
X+7th **V47.52 Driver of other type car injured in collision with fixed or stationary object in traffic accident**
\+ **V47.6 Car passenger injured in collision with fixed or stationary object in traffic accident**
X+7th **V47.61 Passenger of sport utility vehicle injured in collision with fixed or stationary object in traffic accident**
X+7th **V47.62 Passenger of other type car injured in collision with fixed or stationary object in traffic accident**
X+7th **V47.7 Person on outside of car injured in collision with fixed or stationary object in traffic accident**
\+ **V47.9 Unspecified car occupant injured in collision with fixed or stationary object in traffic accident**
X+7th **V47.91 Unspecified occupant of sport utility vehicle injured in collision with fixed or stationary object in traffic accident**
X+7th **V47.92 Unspecified occupant of other type car injured in collision with fixed or stationary object in traffic accident**

V48 Car occupant injured in noncollision transport accident

Includes: overturning car NOS
overturning car without collision

The appropriate 7th character is to be added to each code from category V48
A initial encounter
D subsequent encounter
S sequela

X+7th **V48.0 Car driver injured in noncollision transport accident in nontraffic accident**
X+7th **V48.1 Car passenger injured in noncollision transport accident in nontraffic accident**
X+7th **V48.2 Person on outside of car injured in noncollision transport accident in nontraffic accident**
X+7th **V48.3 Unspecified car occupant injured in noncollision transport accident in nontraffic accident**
X+7th **V48.4 Person boarding or alighting a car injured in noncollision transport accident**
X+7th **V48.5 Car driver injured in noncollision transport accident in traffic accident**
X+7th **V48.6 Car passenger injured in noncollision transport accident in traffic accident**
X+7th **V48.7 Person on outside of car injured in noncollision transport accident in traffic accident**
X+7th **V48.9 Unspecified car occupant injured in noncollision transport accident in traffic accident**

V49 Car occupant injured in other and unspecified transport accidents

The appropriate 7th character is to be added to each code from category V49
A initial encounter
D subsequent encounter
S sequela

\+ **V49.0 Driver injured in collision with other and unspecified motor vehicles in nontraffic accident**
X+7th **V49.00 Driver injured in collision with unspecified motor vehicles in nontraffic accident**
X+7th **V49.09 Driver injured in collision with other motor vehicles in nontraffic accident**
\+ **V49.1 Passenger injured in collision with other and unspecified motor vehicles in nontraffic accident**
X+7th **V49.10 Passenger injured in collision with unspecified motor vehicles in nontraffic accident**
X+7th **V49.19 Passenger injured in collision with other motor vehicles in nontraffic accident**
\+ **V49.2 Unspecified car occupant injured in collision with other and unspecified motor vehicles in nontraffic accident**
X+7th **V49.20 Unspecified car occupant injured in collision with unspecified motor vehicles in nontraffic accident**
Car collision NOS, nontraffic
X+7th **V49.29 Unspecified car occupant injured in collision with other motor vehicles in nontraffic accident**
X+7th **V49.3 Car occupant (driver) (passenger) injured in unspecified nontraffic accident**
Car accident NOS, nontraffic
Car occupant injured in nontraffic accident NOS

+ **V49.4 Driver injured in collision with other and unspecified motor vehicles in traffic accident**

X+7th **V49.40 Driver injured in collision with unspecified motor vehicles in traffic accident**

X+7th **V49.49 Driver injured in collision with other motor vehicles in traffic accident**

+ **V49.5 Passenger injured in collision with other and unspecified motor vehicles in traffic accident**

X+7th **V49.50 Passenger injured in collision with unspecified motor vehicles in traffic accident**

X+7th **V49.59 Passenger injured in collision with other motor vehicles in traffic accident**

+ **V49.6 Unspecified car occupant injured in collision with other and unspecified motor vehicles in traffic accident**

X+7th **V49.60 Unspecified car occupant injured in collision with unspecified motor vehicles in traffic accident**
Car collision NOS (traffic)

X+7th **V49.69 Unspecified car occupant injured in collision with other motor vehicles in traffic accident**

+ **V49.8 Car occupant (driver) (passenger) injured in other specified transport accidents**

X+7th **V49.81 Car occupant (driver) (passenger) injured in transport accident with military vehicle**

X+7th **V49.88 Car occupant (driver) (passenger) injured in other specified transport accidents**

X+7th **V49.9 Car occupant (driver) (passenger) injured in unspecified traffic accident**
Car accident NOS

Occupant of pick-up truck or van injured in transport accident (V50-V59)

Includes: a four or six wheel motor vehicle designed primarily for carrying passengers and property but weighing less than the local limit for classification as a heavy goods vehicle
minibus
minivan
sport utility vehicle (SUV)
truck
van

Excludes1: *heavy transport vehicle (V60-V69)*

V50 Occupant of pick-up truck or van injured in collision with pedestrian or animal

Excludes1: *pick-up truck or van collision with animal-drawn vehicle or animal being ridden (V56.-)*

The appropriate 7th character is to be added to each code from category V50
A initial encounter
D subsequent encounter
S sequela

X+7th **V50.0 Driver of pick-up truck or van injured in collision with pedestrian or animal in nontraffic accident**

X+7th **V50.1 Passenger in pick-up truck or van injured in collision with pedestrian or animal in nontraffic accident**

X+7th **V50.2 Person on outside of pick-up truck or van injured in collision with pedestrian or animal in nontraffic accident**

X+7th **V50.3 Unspecified occupant of pick-up truck or van injured in collision with pedestrian or animal in nontraffic accident**

X+7th **V50.4 Person boarding or alighting a pick-up truck or van injured in collision with pedestrian or animal**

X+7th **V50.5 Driver of pick-up truck or van injured in collision with pedestrian or animal in traffic accident**

X+7th **V50.6 Passenger in pick-up truck or van injured in collision with pedestrian or animal in traffic accident**

X+7th **V50.7 Person on outside of pick-up truck or van injured in collision with pedestrian or animal in traffic accident**

X+7th **V50.9 Unspecified occupant of pick-up truck or van injured in collision with pedestrian or animal in traffic accident**

V51 Occupant of pick-up truck or van injured in collision with pedal cycle

The appropriate 7th character is to be added to each code from category V51
A initial encounter
D subsequent encounter
S sequela

X+7th **V51.0 Driver of pick-up truck or van injured in collision with pedal cycle in nontraffic accident**

X+7th **V51.1 Passenger in pick-up truck or van injured in collision with pedal cycle in nontraffic accident**

X+7th **V51.2 Person on outside of pick-up truck or van injured in collision with pedal cycle in nontraffic accident**

X+7th **V51.3 Unspecified occupant of pick-up truck or van injured in collision with pedal cycle in nontraffic accident**

X+7th **V51.4 Person boarding or alighting a pick-up truck or van injured in collision with pedal cycle**

X+7th **V51.5 Driver of pick-up truck or van injured in collision with pedal cycle in traffic accident**

X+7th **V51.6 Passenger in pick-up truck or van injured in collision with pedal cycle in traffic accident**

X+7th **V51.7 Person on outside of pick-up truck or van injured in collision with pedal cycle in traffic accident**

X+7th **V51.9 Unspecified occupant of pick-up truck or van injured in collision with pedal cycle in traffic accident**

V52 Occupant of pick-up truck or van injured in collision with two- or three-wheeled motor vehicle

The appropriate 7th character is to be added to each code from category V52
A initial encounter
D subsequent encounter
S sequela

X+7th **V52.0 Driver of pick-up truck or van injured in collision with two- or three-wheeled motor vehicle in nontraffic accident**

X+7th **V52.1 Passenger in pick-up truck or van injured in collision with two- or three-wheeled motor vehicle in nontraffic accident**

X+7th **V52.2 Person on outside of pick-up truck or van injured in collision with two- or three-wheeled motor vehicle in nontraffic accident**

X+7th **V52.3 Unspecified occupant of pick-up truck or van injured in collision with two- or three-wheeled motor vehicle in nontraffic accident**

X+7th **V52.4 Person boarding or alighting a pick-up truck or van injured in collision with two- or three-wheeled motor vehicle**

X+7th **V52.5 Driver of pick-up truck or van injured in collision with two- or three-wheeled motor vehicle in traffic accident**

X+7th **V52.6 Passenger in pick-up truck or van injured in collision with two- or three-wheeled motor vehicle in traffic accident**

X+7th **V52.7 Person on outside of pick-up truck or van injured in collision with two- or three-wheeled motor vehicle in traffic accident**

X+7th **V52.9 Unspecified occupant of pick-up truck or van injured in collision with two- or three-wheeled motor vehicle in traffic accident**

V53 Occupant of pick-up truck or van injured in collision with car, pick-up truck or van

The appropriate 7th character is to be added to each code from category V53
A initial encounter
D subsequent encounter
S sequela

X+7th **V53.0 Driver of pick-up truck or van injured in collision with car, pick-up truck or van in nontraffic accident**

X+7th **V53.1 Passenger in pick-up truck or van injured in collision with car, pick-up truck or van in nontraffic accident**

X+7th **V53.2 Person on outside of pick-up truck or van injured in collision with car, pick-up truck or van in nontraffic accident**

X+7th **V53.3 Unspecified occupant of pick-up truck or van injured in collision with car, pick-up truck or van in nontraffic accident**

X+7th **V53.4 Person boarding or alighting a pick-up truck or van injured in collision with car, pick-up truck or van**

X+7th **V53.5 Driver of pick-up truck or van injured in collision with car, pick-up truck or van in traffic accident**

X+7th **V53.6 Passenger in pick-up truck or van injured in collision with car, pick-up truck or van in traffic accident**

X+7th **V53.7 Person on outside of pick-up truck or van injured in collision with car, pick-up truck or van in traffic accident**

X+7th **V53.9 Unspecified occupant of pick-up truck or van injured in collision with car, pick-up truck or van in traffic accident**

V54 Occupant of pick-up truck or van injured in collision with heavy transport vehicle or bus

Excludes1: *occupant of pick-up truck or van injured in collision with military vehicle (V59.81)*

The appropriate 7th character is to be added to each code from category V54
A initial encounter
D subsequent encounter
S sequela

X+7th **V54.0 Driver of pick-up truck or van injured in collision with heavy transport vehicle or bus in nontraffic accident**

X+7th **V54.1 Passenger in pick-up truck or van injured in collision with heavy transport vehicle or bus in nontraffic accident**

X+7th **V54.2** **Person on outside of pick-up truck or van injured in collision with heavy transport vehicle or bus in nontraffic accident**

X+7th **V54.3** **Unspecified occupant of pick-up truck or van injured in collision with heavy transport vehicle or bus in nontraffic accident**

X+7th **V54.4** **Person boarding or alighting a pick-up truck or van injured in collision with heavy transport vehicle or bus**

X+7th **V54.5** **Driver of pick-up truck or van injured in collision with heavy transport vehicle or bus in traffic accident**

X+7th **V54.6** **Passenger in pick-up truck or van injured in collision with heavy transport vehicle or bus in traffic accident**

X+7th **V54.7** **Person on outside of pick-up truck or van injured in collision with heavy transport vehicle or bus in traffic accident**

X+7th **V54.9** **Unspecified occupant of pick-up truck or van injured in collision with heavy transport vehicle or bus in traffic accident**

V55 **Occupant of pick-up truck or van injured in collision with railway train or railway vehicle**

The appropriate 7th character is to be added to each code from category V55
A initial encounter
D subsequent encounter
S sequela

X+7th **V55.0** **Driver of pick-up truck or van injured in collision with railway train or railway vehicle in nontraffic accident**

X+7th **V55.1** **Passenger in pick-up truck or van injured in collision with railway train or railway vehicle in nontraffic accident**

X+7th **V55.2** **Person on outside of pick-up truck or van injured in collision with railway train or railway vehicle in nontraffic accident**

X+7th **V55.3** **Unspecified occupant of pick-up truck or van injured in collision with railway train or railway vehicle in nontraffic accident**

X+7th **V55.4** **Person boarding or alighting a pick-up truck or van injured in collision with railway train or railway vehicle**

X+7th **V55.5** **Driver of pick-up truck or van injured in collision with railway train or railway vehicle in traffic accident**

X+7th **V55.6** **Passenger in pick-up truck or van injured in collision with railway train or railway vehicle in traffic accident**

X+7th **V55.7** **Person on outside of pick-up truck or van injured in collision with railway train or railway vehicle in traffic accident**

X+7th **V55.9** **Unspecified occupant of pick-up truck or van injured in collision with railway train or railway vehicle in traffic accident**

V56 **Occupant of pick-up truck or van injured in collision with other nonmotor vehicle**

Includes: collision with animal-drawn vehicle, animal being ridden, streetcar

The appropriate 7th character is to be added to each code from category V56
A initial encounter
D subsequent encounter
S sequela

X+7th **V56.0** **Driver of pick-up truck or van injured in collision with other nonmotor vehicle in nontraffic accident**

X+7th **V56.1** **Passenger in pick-up truck or van injured in collision with other nonmotor vehicle in nontraffic accident**

X+7th **V56.2** **Person on outside of pick-up truck or van injured in collision with other nonmotor vehicle in nontraffic accident**

X+7th **V56.3** **Unspecified occupant of pick-up truck or van injured in collision with other nonmotor vehicle in nontraffic accident**

X+7th **V56.4** **Person boarding or alighting a pick-up truck or van injured in collision with other nonmotor vehicle**

X+7th **V56.5** **Driver of pick-up truck or van injured in collision with other nonmotor vehicle in traffic accident**

X+7th **V56.6** **Passenger in pick-up truck or van injured in collision with other nonmotor vehicle in traffic accident**

X+7th **V56.7** **Person on outside of pick-up truck or van injured in collision with other nonmotor vehicle in traffic accident**

X+7th **V56.9** **Unspecified occupant of pick-up truck or van injured in collision with other nonmotor vehicle in traffic accident**

V57 **Occupant of pick-up truck or van injured in collision with fixed or stationary object**

The appropriate 7th character is to be added to each code from category V57
A initial encounter
D subsequent encounter
S sequela

X+7th **V57.0** **Driver of pick-up truck or van injured in collision with fixed or stationary object in nontraffic accident**

X+7th **V57.1** **Passenger in pick-up truck or van injured in collision with fixed or stationary object in nontraffic accident**

X+7th **V57.2** **Person on outside of pick-up truck or van injured in collision with fixed or stationary object in nontraffic accident**

X+7th **V57.3** **Unspecified occupant of pick-up truck or van injured in collision with fixed or stationary object in nontraffic accident**

X+7th **V57.4** **Person boarding or alighting a pick-up truck or van injured in collision with fixed or stationary object**

X+7th **V57.5** **Driver of pick-up truck or van injured in collision with fixed or stationary object in traffic accident**

X+7th **V57.6** **Passenger in pick-up truck or van injured in collision with fixed or stationary object in traffic accident**

X+7th **V57.7** **Person on outside of pick-up truck or van injured in collision with fixed or stationary object in traffic accident**

X+7th **V57.9** **Unspecified occupant of pick-up truck or van injured in collision with fixed or stationary object in traffic accident**

V58 **Occupant of pick-up truck or van injured in noncollision transport accident**

Includes: overturning pick-up truck or van NOS
overturning pick-up truck or van without collision

The appropriate 7th character is to be added to each code from category V58
A initial encounter
D subsequent encounter
S sequela

X+7th **V58.0** **Driver of pick-up truck or van injured in noncollision transport accident in nontraffic accident**

X+7th **V58.1** **Passenger in pick-up truck or van injured in noncollision transport accident in nontraffic accident**

X+7th **V58.2** **Person on outside of pick-up truck or van injured in noncollision transport accident in nontraffic accident**

X+7th **V58.3** **Unspecified occupant of pick-up truck or van injured in noncollision transport accident in nontraffic accident**

X+7th **V58.4** **Person boarding or alighting a pick-up truck or van injured in noncollision transport accident**

X+7th **V58.5** **Driver of pick-up truck or van injured in noncollision transport accident in traffic accident**

X+7th **V58.6** **Passenger in pick-up truck or van injured in noncollision transport accident in traffic accident**

X+7th **V58.7** **Person on outside of pick-up truck or van injured in noncollision transport accident in traffic accident**

X+7th **V58.9** **Unspecified occupant of pick-up truck or van injured in noncollision transport accident in traffic accident**

V59 **Occupant of pick-up truck or van injured in other and unspecified transport accidents**

The appropriate 7th character is to be added to each code from category V59
A initial encounter
D subsequent encounter
S sequela

\+ **V59.0** **Driver of pick-up truck or van injured in collision with other and unspecified motor vehicles in nontraffic accident**

X+7th **V59.00** **Driver of pick-up truck or van injured in collision with unspecified motor vehicles in nontraffic accident**

X+7th **V59.09** **Driver of pick-up truck or van injured in collision with other motor vehicles in nontraffic accident**

\+ **V59.1** **Passenger in pick-up truck or van injured in collision with other and unspecified motor vehicles in nontraffic accident**

X+7th **V59.10** **Passenger in pick-up truck or van injured in collision with unspecified motor vehicles in nontraffic accident**

X+7th **V59.19** **Passenger in pick-up truck or van injured in collision with other motor vehicles in nontraffic accident**

\+ **V59.2** **Unspecified occupant of pick-up truck or van injured in collision with other and unspecified motor vehicles in nontraffic accident**

X+7th **V59.20** **Unspecified occupant of pick-up truck or van injured in collision with unspecified motor vehicles in nontraffic accident**
Collision NOS involving pick-up truck or van, nontraffic

X+7th **V59.29** **Unspecified occupant of pick-up truck or van injured in collision with other motor vehicles in nontraffic accident**

X+7th **V59.3** **Occupant (driver) (passenger) of pick-up truck or van injured in unspecified nontraffic accident**
Accident NOS involving pick-up truck or van, nontraffic
Occupant of pick-up truck or van injured in nontraffic accident NOS

\+ **V59.4** **Driver of pick-up truck or van injured in collision with other and unspecified motor vehicles in traffic accident**

X+7th **V59.40** **Driver of pick-up truck or van injured in collision with unspecified motor vehicles in traffic accident**

X+7th **V59.49** **Driver of pick-up truck or van injured in collision with other motor vehicles in traffic accident**

+ V59.5 Passenger in pick-up truck or van injured in collision with other and unspecified motor vehicles in traffic accident
- X+7th **V59.50 Passenger in pick-up truck or van injured in collision with unspecified motor vehicles in traffic accident**
- X+7th **V59.59 Passenger in pick-up truck or van injured in collision with other motor vehicles in traffic accident**

+ V59.6 Unspecified occupant of pick-up truck or van injured in collision with other and unspecified motor vehicles in traffic accident
- X+7th **V59.60 Unspecified occupant of pick-up truck or van injured in collision with unspecified motor vehicles in traffic accident**
  Collision NOS involving pick-up truck or van (traffic)
- X+7th **V59.69 Unspecified occupant of pick-up truck or van injured in collision with other motor vehicles in traffic accident**

+ V59.8 Occupant (driver) (passenger) of pick-up truck or van injured in other specified transport accidents
- X+7th **V59.81 Occupant (driver) (passenger) of pick-up truck or van injured in transport accident with military vehicle**
- X+7th **V59.88 Occupant (driver) (passenger) of pick-up truck or van injured in other specified transport accidents**

X+7th **V59.9 Occupant (driver) (passenger) of pick-up truck or van injured in unspecified traffic accident**
Accident NOS involving pick-up truck or van

Occupant of heavy transport vehicle injured in transport accident (V60-V69)

Includes: 18 wheeler
armored car
panel truck

Excludes1: *bus*
motorcoach

V60 Occupant of heavy transport vehicle injured in collision with pedestrian or animal

Excludes1: *heavy transport vehicle collision with animal-drawn vehicle or animal being ridden (V66.-)*

The appropriate 7th character is to be added to each code from category V60
A initial encounter
D subsequent encounter
S sequela

- X+7th **V60.0 Driver of heavy transport vehicle injured in collision with pedestrian or animal in nontraffic accident**
- X+7th **V60.1 Passenger in heavy transport vehicle injured in collision with pedestrian or animal in nontraffic accident**
- X+7th **V60.2 Person on outside of heavy transport vehicle injured in collision with pedestrian or animal in nontraffic accident**
- X+7th **V60.3 Unspecified occupant of heavy transport vehicle injured in collision with pedestrian or animal in nontraffic accident**
- X+7th **V60.4 Person boarding or alighting a heavy transport vehicle injured in collision with pedestrian or animal**
- X+7th **V60.5 Driver of heavy transport vehicle injured in collision with pedestrian or animal in traffic accident**
- X+7th **V60.6 Passenger in heavy transport vehicle injured in collision with pedestrian or animal in traffic accident**
- X+7th **V60.7 Person on outside of heavy transport vehicle injured in collision with pedestrian or animal in traffic accident**
- X+7th **V60.9 Unspecified occupant of heavy transport vehicle injured in collision with pedestrian or animal in traffic accident**

V61 Occupant of heavy transport vehicle injured in collision with pedal cycle

The appropriate 7th character is to be added to each code from category V61
A initial encounter
D subsequent encounter
S sequela

- X+7th **V61.0 Driver of heavy transport vehicle injured in collision with pedal cycle in nontraffic accident**
- X+7th **V61.1 Passenger in heavy transport vehicle injured in collision with pedal cycle in nontraffic accident**
- X+7th **V61.2 Person on outside of heavy transport vehicle injured in collision with pedal cycle in nontraffic accident**
- X+7th **V61.3 Unspecified occupant of heavy transport vehicle injured in collision with pedal cycle in nontraffic accident**
- X+7th **V61.4 Person boarding or alighting a heavy transport vehicle injured in collision with pedal cycle while boarding or alighting**
- X+7th **V61.5 Driver of heavy transport vehicle injured in collision with pedal cycle in traffic accident**
- X+7th **V61.6 Passenger in heavy transport vehicle injured in collision with pedal cycle in traffic accident**
- X+7th **V61.7 Person on outside of heavy transport vehicle injured in collision with pedal cycle in traffic accident**
- X+7th **V61.9 Unspecified occupant of heavy transport vehicle injured in collision with pedal cycle in traffic accident**

V62 Occupant of heavy transport vehicle injured in collision with two- or three-wheeled motor vehicle

The appropriate 7th character is to be added to each code from category V62
A initial encounter
D subsequent encounter
S sequela

- X+7th **V62.0 Driver of heavy transport vehicle injured in collision with two or three-wheeled motor vehicle in nontraffic accident**
- X+7th **V62.1 Passenger in heavy transport vehicle injured in collision with two- or three-wheeled motor vehicle in nontraffic accident**
- X+7th **V62.2 Person on outside of heavy transport vehicle injured in collision with two- or three-wheeled motor vehicle in nontraffic accident**
- X+7th **V62.3 Unspecified occupant of heavy transport vehicle injured in collision with two- or three-wheeled motor vehicle in nontraffic accident**
- X+7th **V62.4 Person boarding or alighting a heavy transport vehicle injured in collision with two- or three-wheeled motor vehicle**
- X+7th **V62.5 Driver of heavy transport vehicle injured in collision with two- or three-wheeled motor vehicle in traffic accident**
- X+7th **V62.6 Passenger in heavy transport vehicle injured in collision with two or three-wheeled motor vehicle in traffic accident**
- X+7th **V62.7 Person on outside of heavy transport vehicle injured in collision with two- or three-wheeled motor vehicle in traffic accident**
- X+7th **V62.9 Unspecified occupant of heavy transport vehicle injured in collision with two- or three-wheeled motor vehicle in traffic accident**

V63 Occupant of heavy transport vehicle injured in collision with car, pick-up truck or van

The appropriate 7th character is to be added to each code from category V63
A initial encounter
D subsequent encounter
S sequela

- X+7th **V63.0 Driver of heavy transport vehicle injured in collision with car, pick-up truck or van in nontraffic accident**
- X+7th **V63.1 Passenger in heavy transport vehicle injured in collision with car, pick-up truck or van in nontraffic accident**
- X+7th **V63.2 Person on outside of heavy transport vehicle injured in collision with car, pick-up truck or van in nontraffic accident**
- X+7th **V63.3 Unspecified occupant of heavy transport vehicle injured in collision with car, pick-up truck or van in nontraffic accident**
- X+7th **V63.4 Person boarding or alighting a heavy transport vehicle injured in collision with car, pick-up truck or van**
- X+7th **V63.5 Driver of heavy transport vehicle injured in collision with car, pick-up truck or van in traffic accident**
- X+7th **V63.6 Passenger in heavy transport vehicle injured in collision with car, pick-up truck or van in traffic accident**
- X+7th **V63.7 Person on outside of heavy transport vehicle injured in collision with car, pick-up truck or van in traffic accident**
- X+7th **V63.9 Unspecified occupant of heavy transport vehicle injured in collision with car, pick-up truck or van in traffic accident**

V64 Occupant of heavy transport vehicle injured in collision with heavy transport vehicle or bus

Excludes1: *occupant of heavy transport vehicle injured in collision with military vehicle (V69.81)*

The appropriate 7th character is to be added to each code from category V64
A initial encounter
D subsequent encounter
S sequela

- X+7th **V64.0 Driver of heavy transport vehicle injured in collision with heavy transport vehicle or bus in nontraffic accident**
- X+7th **V64.1 Passenger in heavy transport vehicle injured in collision with heavy transport vehicle or bus in nontraffic accident**
- X+7th **V64.2 Person on outside of heavy transport vehicle injured in collision with heavy transport vehicle or bus in nontraffic accident**
- X+7th **V64.3 Unspecified occupant of heavy transport vehicle injured in collision with heavy transport vehicle or bus in nontraffic accident**

X+7th **V64.4** **Person boarding or alighting a heavy transport vehicle injured in collision with heavy transport vehicle or bus while boarding or alighting**

X+7th **V64.5** **Driver of heavy transport vehicle injured in collision with heavy transport vehicle or bus in traffic accident**

X+7th **V64.6** **Passenger in heavy transport vehicle injured in collision with heavy transport vehicle or bus in traffic accident**

X+7th **V64.7** **Person on outside of heavy transport vehicle injured in collision with heavy transport vehicle or bus in traffic accident**

X+7th **V64.9** **Unspecified occupant of heavy transport vehicle injured in collision with heavy transport vehicle or bus in traffic accident**

V65 Occupant of heavy transport vehicle injured in collision with railway train or railway vehicle

The appropriate 7th character is to be added to each code from category V65
A initial encounter
D subsequent encounter
S sequela

X+7th **V65.0** **Driver of heavy transport vehicle injured in collision with railway train or railway vehicle in nontraffic accident**

X+7th **V65.1** **Passenger in heavy transport vehicle injured in collision with railway train or railway vehicle in nontraffic accident**

X+7th **V65.2** **Person on outside of heavy transport vehicle injured in collision with railway train or railway vehicle in nontraffic accident**

X+7th **V65.3** **Unspecified occupant of heavy transport vehicle injured in collision with railway train or railway vehicle in nontraffic accident**

X+7th **V65.4** **Person boarding or alighting a heavy transport vehicle injured in collision with railway train or railway vehicle**

X+7th **V65.5** **Driver of heavy transport vehicle injured in collision with railway train or railway vehicle in traffic accident**

X+7th **V65.6** **Passenger in heavy transport vehicle injured in collision with railway train or railway vehicle in traffic accident**

X+7th **V65.7** **Person on outside of heavy transport vehicle injured in collision with railway train or railway vehicle in traffic accident**

X+7th **V65.9** **Unspecified occupant of heavy transport vehicle injured in collision with railway train or railway vehicle in traffic accident**

V66 Occupant of heavy transport vehicle injured in collision with other nonmotor vehicle

Includes: collision with animal-drawn vehicle, animal being ridden, streetcar

The appropriate 7th character is to be added to each code from category V66
A initial encounter
D subsequent encounter
S sequela

X+7th **V66.0** **Driver of heavy transport vehicle injured in collision with other nonmotor vehicle in nontraffic accident**

X+7th **V66.1** **Passenger in heavy transport vehicle injured in collision with other nonmotor vehicle in nontraffic accident**

X+7th **V66.2** **Person on outside of heavy transport vehicle injured in collision with other nonmotor vehicle in nontraffic accident**

X+7th **V66.3** **Unspecified occupant of heavy transport vehicle injured in collision with other nonmotor vehicle in nontraffic accident**

X+7th **V66.4** **Person boarding or alighting a heavy transport vehicle injured in collision with other nonmotor vehicle**

X+7th **V66.5** **Driver of heavy transport vehicle injured in collision with other nonmotor vehicle in traffic accident**

X+7th **V66.6** **Passenger in heavy transport vehicle injured in collision with other nonmotor vehicle in traffic accident**

X+7th **V66.7** **Person on outside of heavy transport vehicle injured in collision with other nonmotor vehicle in traffic accident**

X+7th **V66.9** **Unspecified occupant of heavy transport vehicle injured in collision with other nonmotor vehicle in traffic accident**

V67 Occupant of heavy transport vehicle injured in collision with fixed or stationary object

The appropriate 7th character is to be added to each code from category V67
A initial encounter
D subsequent encounter
S sequela

X+7th **V67.0** **Driver of heavy transport vehicle injured in collision with fixed or stationary object in nontraffic accident**

X+7th **V67.1** **Passenger in heavy transport vehicle injured in collision with fixed or stationary object in nontraffic accident**

X+7th **V67.2** **Person on outside of heavy transport vehicle injured in collision with fixed or stationary object in nontraffic accident**

X+7th **V67.3** **Unspecified occupant of heavy transport vehicle injured in collision with fixed or stationary object in nontraffic accident**

X+7th **V67.4** **Person boarding or alighting a heavy transport vehicle injured in collision with fixed or stationary object**

X+7th **V67.5** **Driver of heavy transport vehicle injured in collision with fixed or stationary object in traffic accident**

X+7th **V67.6** **Passenger in heavy transport vehicle injured in collision with fixed or stationary object in traffic accident**

X+7th **V67.7** **Person on outside of heavy transport vehicle injured in collision with fixed or stationary object in traffic accident**

X+7th **V67.9** **Unspecified occupant of heavy transport vehicle injured in collision with fixed or stationary object in traffic accident**

V68 Occupant of heavy transport vehicle injured in noncollision transport accident

Includes: overturning heavy transport vehicle NOS
overturning heavy transport vehicle without collision

The appropriate 7th character is to be added to each code from category V68
A initial encounter
D subsequent encounter
S sequela

X+7th **V68.0** **Driver of heavy transport vehicle injured in noncollision transport accident in nontraffic accident**

X+7th **V68.1** **Passenger in heavy transport vehicle injured in noncollision transport accident in nontraffic accident**

X+7th **V68.2** **Person on outside of heavy transport vehicle injured in noncollision transport accident in nontraffic accident**

X+7th **V68.3** **Unspecified occupant of heavy transport vehicle injured in noncollision transport accident in nontraffic accident**

X+7th **V68.4** **Person boarding or alighting a heavy transport vehicle injured in noncollision transport accident**

X+7th **V68.5** **Driver of heavy transport vehicle injured in noncollision transport accident in traffic accident**

X+7th **V68.6** **Passenger in heavy transport vehicle injured in noncollision transport accident in traffic accident**

X+7th **V68.7** **Person on outside of heavy transport vehicle injured in noncollision transport accident in traffic accident**

X+7th **V68.9** **Unspecified occupant of heavy transport vehicle injured in noncollision transport accident in traffic accident**

V69 Occupant of heavy transport vehicle injured in other and unspecified transport accidents

The appropriate 7th character is to be added to each code from category V69
A initial encounter
D subsequent encounter
S sequela

+ **V69.0** **Driver of heavy transport vehicle injured in collision with other and unspecified motor vehicles in nontraffic accident**

X+7th **V69.00** **Driver of heavy transport vehicle injured in collision with unspecified motor vehicles in nontraffic accident**

X+7th **V69.09** **Driver of heavy transport vehicle injured in collision with other motor vehicles in nontraffic accident**

+ **V69.1** **Passenger in heavy transport vehicle injured in collision with other and unspecified motor vehicles in nontraffic accident**

X+7th **V69.10** **Passenger in heavy transport vehicle injured in collision with unspecified motor vehicles in nontraffic accident**

X+7th **V69.19** **Passenger in heavy transport vehicle injured in collision with other motor vehicles in nontraffic accident**

+ **V69.2** **Unspecified occupant of heavy transport vehicle injured in collision with other and unspecified motor vehicles in nontraffic accident**

X+7th **V69.20** **Unspecified occupant of heavy transport vehicle injured in collision with unspecified motor vehicles in nontraffic accident**
Collision NOS involving heavy transport vehicle, nontraffic

X+7th **V69.29** **Unspecified occupant of heavy transport vehicle injured in collision with other motor vehicles in nontraffic accident**

X+7th **V69.3** **Occupant (driver) (passenger) of heavy transport vehicle injured in unspecified nontraffic accident**
Accident NOS involving heavy transport vehicle, nontraffic
Occupant of heavy transport vehicle injured in nontraffic accident NOS

+ V69.4 Driver of heavy transport vehicle injured in collision with other and unspecified motor vehicles in traffic accident

X+7th **V69.40 Driver of heavy transport vehicle injured in collision with unspecified motor vehicles in traffic accident**

X+7th **V69.49 Driver of heavy transport vehicle injured in collision with other motor vehicles in traffic accident**

+ V69.5 Passenger in heavy transport vehicle injured in collision with other and unspecified motor vehicles in traffic accident

X+7th **V69.50 Passenger in heavy transport vehicle injured in collision with unspecified motor vehicles in traffic accident**

X+7th **V69.59 Passenger in heavy transport vehicle injured in collision with other motor vehicles in traffic accident**

+ V69.6 Unspecified occupant of heavy transport vehicle injured in collision with other and unspecified motor vehicles in traffic accident

X+7th **V69.60 Unspecified occupant of heavy transport vehicle injured in collision with unspecified motor vehicles in traffic accident**
Collision NOS involving heavy transport vehicle (traffic)

X+7th **V69.69 Unspecified occupant of heavy transport vehicle injured in collision with other motor vehicles in traffic accident**

+ V69.8 Occupant (driver) (passenger) of heavy transport vehicle injured in other specified transport accidents

X+7th **V69.81 Occupant (driver) (passenger) of heavy transport vehicle injured in transport accidents with military vehicle**

X+7th **V69.88 Occupant (driver) (passenger) of heavy transport vehicle injured in other specified transport accidents**

X+7th **V69.9 Occupant (driver) (passenger) of heavy transport vehicle injured in unspecified traffic accident**
Accident NOS involving heavy transport vehicle

Bus occupant injured in transport accident (V70-V79)

Includes: motorcoach

Excludes1: *minibus (V50-V59)*

V70 Bus occupant injured in collision with pedestrian or animal

The appropriate 7th character is to be added to each code from category V70
A initial encounter
D subsequent encounter
S sequela

Excludes1: *bus collision with animal-drawn vehicle or animal being ridden (V76.-)*

X+7th **V70.0 Driver of bus injured in collision with pedestrian or animal in nontraffic accident**

X+7th **V70.1 Passenger on bus injured in collision with pedestrian or animal in nontraffic accident**

X+7th **V70.2 Person on outside of bus injured in collision with pedestrian or animal in nontraffic accident**

X+7th **V70.3 Unspecified occupant of bus injured in collision with pedestrian or animal in nontraffic accident**

X+7th **V70.4 Person boarding or alighting from bus injured in collision with pedestrian or animal**

X+7th **V70.5 Driver of bus injured in collision with pedestrian or animal in traffic accident**

X+7th **V70.6 Passenger on bus injured in collision with pedestrian or animal in traffic accident**

X+7th **V70.7 Person on outside of bus injured in collision with pedestrian or animal in traffic accident**

X+7th **V70.9 Unspecified occupant of bus injured in collision with pedestrian or animal in traffic accident**

V71 Bus occupant injured in collision with pedal cycle

The appropriate 7th character is to be added to each code from category V71
A initial encounter
D subsequent encounter
S sequela

X+7th **V71.0 Driver of bus injured in collision with pedal cycle in nontraffic accident**

X+7th **V71.1 Passenger on bus injured in collision with pedal cycle in nontraffic accident**

X+7th **V71.2 Person on outside of bus injured in collision with pedal cycle in nontraffic accident**

X+7th **V71.3 Unspecified occupant of bus injured in collision with pedal cycle in nontraffic accident**

X+7th **V71.4 Person boarding or alighting from bus injured in collision with pedal cycle**

X+7th **V71.5 Driver of bus injured in collision with pedal cycle in traffic accident**

X+7th **V71.6 Passenger on bus injured in collision with pedal cycle in traffic accident**

X+7th **V71.7 Person on outside of bus injured in collision with pedal cycle in traffic accident**

X+7th **V71.9 Unspecified occupant of bus injured in collision with pedal cycle in traffic accident**

V72 Bus occupant injured in collision with two- or three-wheeled motor vehicle

The appropriate 7th character is to be added to each code from category V72
A initial encounter
D subsequent encounter
S sequela

X+7th **V72.0 Driver of bus injured in collision with two- or three-wheeled motor vehicle in nontraffic accident**

X+7th **V72.1 Passenger on bus injured in collision with two- or three-wheeled motor vehicle in nontraffic accident**

X+7th **V72.2 Person on outside of bus injured in collision with two- or three-wheeled motor vehicle in nontraffic accident**

X+7th **V72.3 Unspecified occupant of bus injured in collision with two- or three-wheeled motor vehicle in nontraffic accident**

X+7th **V72.4 Person boarding or alighting from bus injured in collision with two- or three-wheeled motor vehicle**

X+7th **V72.5 Driver of bus injured in collision with two- or three-wheeled motor vehicle in traffic accident**

X+7th **V72.6 Passenger on bus injured in collision with two- or three-wheeled motor vehicle in traffic accident**

X+7th **V72.7 Person on outside of bus injured in collision with two- or three-wheeled motor vehicle in traffic accident**

X+7th **V72.9 Unspecified occupant of bus injured in collision with two- or three-wheeled motor vehicle in traffic accident**

V73 Bus occupant injured in collision with car, pick-up truck or van

The appropriate 7th character is to be added to each code from category V73
A initial encounter
D subsequent encounter
S sequela

X+7th **V73.0 Driver of bus injured in collision with car, pick-up truck or van in nontraffic accident**

X+7th **V73.1 Passenger on bus injured in collision with car, pick-up truck or van in nontraffic accident**

X+7th **V73.2 Person on outside of bus injured in collision with car, pick-up truck or van in nontraffic accident**

X+7th **V73.3 Unspecified occupant of bus injured in collision with car, pick-up truck or van in nontraffic accident**

X+7th **V73.4 Person boarding or alighting from bus injured in collision with car, pick-up truck or van**

X+7th **V73.5 Driver of bus injured in collision with car, pick-up truck or van in traffic accident**

X+7th **V73.6 Passenger on bus injured in collision with car, pick-up truck or van in traffic accident**

X+7th **V73.7 Person on outside of bus injured in collision with car, pick-up truck or van in traffic accident**

X+7th **V73.9 Unspecified occupant of bus injured in collision with car, pick-up truck or van in traffic accident**

V74 Bus occupant injured in collision with heavy transport vehicle or bus

Excludes1: *bus occupant injured in collision with military vehicle (V79.81)*

The appropriate 7th character is to be added to each code from category V74
A initial encounter
D subsequent encounter
S sequela

X+7th **V74.0 Driver of bus injured in collision with heavy transport vehicle or bus in nontraffic accident**

X+7th **V74.1 Passenger on bus injured in collision with heavy transport vehicle or bus in nontraffic accident**

X+7th **V74.2 Person on outside of bus injured in collision with heavy transport vehicle or bus in nontraffic accident**

X+7th **V74.3 Unspecified occupant of bus injured in collision with heavy transport vehicle or bus in nontraffic accident**

X+7th **V74.4 Person boarding or alighting from bus injured in collision with heavy transport vehicle or bus**

X+7th **V74.5 Driver of bus injured in collision with heavy transport vehicle or bus in traffic accident**

X+7th **V74.6 Passenger on bus injured in collision with heavy transport vehicle or bus in traffic accident**

X+7th **V74.7** **Person on outside of bus injured in collision with heavy transport vehicle or bus in traffic accident**

X+7th **V74.9** **Unspecified occupant of bus injured in collision with heavy transport vehicle or bus in traffic accident**

V75 Bus occupant injured in collision with railway train or railway vehicle

The appropriate 7th character is to be added to each code from category V75
A initial encounter
D subsequent encounter
S sequela

X+7th **V75.0** **Driver of bus injured in collision with railway train or railway vehicle in nontraffic accident**

X+7th **V75.1** **Passenger on bus injured in collision with railway train or railway vehicle in nontraffic accident**

X+7th **V75.2** **Person on outside of bus injured in collision with railway train or railway vehicle in nontraffic accident**

X+7th **V75.3** **Unspecified occupant of bus injured in collision with railway train or railway vehicle in nontraffic accident**

X+7th **V75.4** **Person boarding or alighting from bus injured in collision with railway train or railway vehicle**

X+7th **V75.5** **Driver of bus injured in collision with railway train or railway vehicle in traffic accident**

X+7th **V75.6** **Passenger on bus injured in collision with railway train or railway vehicle in traffic accident**

X+7th **V75.7** **Person on outside of bus injured in collision with railway train or railway vehicle in traffic accident**

X+7th **V75.9** **Unspecified occupant of bus injured in collision with railway train or railway vehicle in traffic accident**

V76 Bus occupant injured in collision with other nonmotor vehicle

Includes: collision with animal-drawn vehicle, animal being ridden, streetcar

The appropriate 7th character is to be added to each code from category V76
A initial encounter
D subsequent encounter
S sequela

X+7th **V76.0** **Driver of bus injured in collision with other nonmotor vehicle in nontraffic accident**

X+7th **V76.1** **Passenger on bus injured in collision with other nonmotor vehicle in nontraffic accident**

X+7th **V76.2** **Person on outside of bus injured in collision with other nonmotor vehicle in nontraffic accident**

X+7th **V76.3** **Unspecified occupant of bus injured in collision with other nonmotor vehicle in nontraffic accident**

X+7th **V76.4** **Person boarding or alighting from bus injured in collision with other nonmotor vehicle**

X+7th **V76.5** **Driver of bus injured in collision with other nonmotor vehicle in traffic accident**

X+7th **V76.6** **Passenger on bus injured in collision with other nonmotor vehicle in traffic accident**

X+7th **V76.7** **Person on outside of bus injured in collision with other nonmotor vehicle in traffic accident**

X+7th **V76.9** **Unspecified occupant of bus injured in collision with other nonmotor vehicle in traffic accident**

V77 Bus occupant injured in collision with fixed or stationary object

The appropriate 7th character is to be added to each code from category V77
A initial encounter
D subsequent encounter
S sequela

X+7th **V77.0** **Driver of bus injured in collision with fixed or stationary object in nontraffic accident**

X+7th **V77.1** **Passenger on bus injured in collision with fixed or stationary object in nontraffic accident**

X+7th **V77.2** **Person on outside of bus injured in collision with fixed or stationary object in nontraffic accident**

X+7th **V77.3** **Unspecified occupant of bus injured in collision with fixed or stationary object in nontraffic accident**

X+7th **V77.4** **Person boarding or alighting from bus injured in collision with fixed or stationary object**

X+7th **V77.5** **Driver of bus injured in collision with fixed or stationary object in traffic accident**

X+7th **V77.6** **Passenger on bus injured in collision with fixed or stationary object in traffic accident**

X+7th **V77.7** **Person on outside of bus injured in collision with fixed or stationary object in traffic accident**

X+7th **V77.9** **Unspecified occupant of bus injured in collision with fixed or stationary object in traffic accident**

V78 Bus occupant injured in noncollision transport accident

Includes: overturning bus NOS
overturning bus without collision

The appropriate 7th character is to be added to each code from category V78
A initial encounter
D subsequent encounter
S sequela

X+7th **V78.0** **Driver of bus injured in noncollision transport accident in nontraffic accident**

X+7th **V78.1** **Passenger on bus injured in noncollision transport accident in nontraffic accident**

X+7th **V78.2** **Person on outside of bus injured in noncollision transport accident in nontraffic accident**

X+7th **V78.3** **Unspecified occupant of bus injured in noncollision transport accident in nontraffic accident**

X+7th **V78.4** **Person boarding or alighting from bus injured in noncollision transport accident**

X+7th **V78.5** **Driver of bus injured in noncollision transport accident in traffic accident**

X+7th **V78.6** **Passenger on bus injured in noncollision transport accident in traffic accident**

X+7th **V78.7** **Person on outside of bus injured in noncollision transport accident in traffic accident**

X+7th **V78.9** **Unspecified occupant of bus injured in noncollision transport accident in traffic accident**

V79 Bus occupant injured in other and unspecified transport accidents

The appropriate 7th character is to be added to each code from category V79
A initial encounter
D subsequent encounter
S sequela

\+ **V79.0** **Driver of bus injured in collision with other and unspecified motor vehicles in nontraffic accident**

X+7th **V79.00** **Driver of bus injured in collision with unspecified motor vehicles in nontraffic accident**

X+7th **V79.09** **Driver of bus injured in collision with other motor vehicles in nontraffic accident**

\+ **V79.1** **Passenger on bus injured in collision with other and unspecified motor vehicles in nontraffic accident**

X+7th **V79.10** **Passenger on bus injured in collision with unspecified motor vehicles in nontraffic accident**

X+7th **V79.19** **Passenger on bus injured in collision with other motor vehicles in nontraffic accident**

\+ **V79.2** **Unspecified bus occupant injured in collision with other and unspecified motor vehicles in nontraffic accident**

X+7th **V79.20** **Unspecified bus occupant injured in collision with unspecified motor vehicles in nontraffic accident**
Bus collision NOS, nontraffic

X+7th **V79.29** **Unspecified bus occupant injured in collision with other motor vehicles in nontraffic accident**

X+7th **V79.3** **Bus occupant (driver) (passenger) injured in unspecified nontraffic accident**
Bus accident NOS, nontraffic
Bus occupant injured in nontraffic accident NOS

\+ **V79.4** **Driver of bus injured in collision with other and unspecified motor vehicles in traffic accident**

X+7th **V79.40** **Driver of bus injured in collision with unspecified motor vehicles in traffic accident**

X+7th **V79.49** **Driver of bus injured in collision with other motor vehicles in traffic accident**

\+ **V79.5** **Passenger on bus injured in collision with other and unspecified motor vehicles in traffic accident**

X+7th **V79.50** **Passenger on bus injured in collision with unspecified motor vehicles in traffic accident**

X+7th **V79.59** **Passenger on bus injured in collision with other motor vehicles in traffic accident**

\+ **V79.6** **Unspecified bus occupant injured in collision with other and unspecified motor vehicles in traffic accident**

X+7th **V79.60** **Unspecified bus occupant injured in collision with unspecified motor vehicles in traffic accident**
Bus collision NOS (traffic)

X+7th **V79.69** **Unspecified bus occupant injured in collision with other motor vehicles in traffic accident**

\+ **V79.8** **Bus occupant (driver) (passenger) injured in other specified transport accidents**

X+7th **V79.81** **Bus occupant (driver) (passenger) injured in transport accidents with military vehicle**

X+7th **V79.88** **Bus occupant (driver) (passenger) injured in other specified transport accidents**

X+7th **V79.9 Bus occupant (driver) (passenger) injured in unspecified traffic accident**
Bus accident NOS

Other land transport accidents (V80-V89)

V80 Animal-rider or occupant of animal-drawn vehicle injured in transport accident

The appropriate 7th character is to be added to each code from category V80
A initial encounter
D subsequent encounter
S sequela

\+ **V80.0 Animal-rider or occupant of animal drawn vehicle injured by fall from or being thrown from animal or animal-drawn vehicle in noncollision accident**
\+ **V80.01 Animal-rider injured by fall from or being thrown from animal in noncollision accident**
+7th **V80.010 Animal-rider injured by fall from or being thrown from horse in noncollision accident**
+7th **V80.018 Animal-rider injured by fall from or being thrown from other animal in noncollision accident**
X+7th **V80.02 Occupant of animal-drawn vehicle injured by fall from or being thrown from animal-drawn vehicle in noncollision accident**
Overturning animal-drawn vehicle NOS
Overturning animal-drawn vehicle without collision
\+ **V80.1 Animal-rider or occupant of animal-drawn vehicle injured in collision with pedestrian or animal**
Excludes1: *animal-rider or animal-drawn vehicle collision with animal-drawn vehicle or animal being ridden (V80.7)*
X+7th **V80.11 Animal-rider injured in collision with pedestrian or animal**
X+7th **V80.12 Occupant of animal-drawn vehicle injured in collision with pedestrian or animal**
\+ **V80.2 Animal-rider or occupant of animal-drawn vehicle injured in collision with pedal cycle**
X+7th **V80.21 Animal-rider injured in collision with pedal cycle**
X+7th **V80.22 Occupant of animal-drawn vehicle injured in collision with pedal cycle**
\+ **V80.3 Animal-rider or occupant of animal-drawn vehicle injured in collision with two- or three-wheeled motor vehicle**
X+7th **V80.31 Animal-rider injured in collision with two- or three-wheeled motor vehicle**
X+7th **V80.32 Occupant of animal-drawn vehicle injured in collision with two- or three-wheeled motor vehicle**
\+ **V80.4 Animal-rider or occupant of animal-drawn vehicle injured in collision with car, pick-up truck, van, heavy transport vehicle or bus**
Excludes1: *animal-rider injured in collision with military vehicle (V80.910)*
occupant of animal-drawn vehicle injured in collision with military vehicle (V80.920)
X+7th **V80.41 Animal-rider injured in collision with car, pick-up truck, van, heavy transport vehicle or bus**
X+7th **V80.42 Occupant of animal-drawn vehicle injured in collision with car, pick-up truck, van, heavy transport vehicle or bus**
\+ **V80.5 Animal-rider or occupant of animal-drawn vehicle injured in collision with other specified motor vehicle**
X+7th **V80.51 Animal-rider injured in collision with other specified motor vehicle**
X+7th **V80.52 Occupant of animal-drawn vehicle injured in collision with other specified motor vehicle**
\+ **V80.6 Animal-rider or occupant of animal-drawn vehicle injured in collision with railway train or railway vehicle**
X+7th **V80.61 Animal-rider injured in collision with railway train or railway vehicle**
X+7th **V80.62 Occupant of animal-drawn vehicle injured in collision with railway train or railway vehicle**
\+ **V80.7 Animal-rider or occupant of animal-drawn vehicle injured in collision with other nonmotor vehicles**
X+7th **V80.71 Animal-rider or occupant of animal-drawn vehicle injured in collision with animal being ridden**
X+7th **V80.710 Animal-rider injured in collision with other animal being ridden**
X+7th **V80.711 Occupant of animal-drawn vehicle injured in collision with animal being ridden**
X+7th **V80.72 Animal-rider or occupant of animal-drawn vehicle injured in collision with other animal-drawn vehicle**
X+7th **V80.720 Animal-rider injured in collision with animal-drawn vehicle**
X+7th **V80.721 Occupant of animal-drawn vehicle injured in collision with other animal-drawn vehicle**
\+ **V80.73 Animal-rider or occupant of animal-drawn vehicle injured in collision with streetcar**
X+7th **V80.730 Animal-rider injured in collision with streetcar**
X+7th **V80.731 Occupant of animal-drawn vehicle injured in collision with streetcar**
X+7th **V80.79 Animal-rider or occupant of animal-drawn vehicle injured in collision with other nonmotor vehicles**
X+7th **V80.790 Animal-rider injured in collision with other nonmotor vehicles**
X+7th **V80.791 Occupant of animal-drawn vehicle injured in collision with other nonmotor vehicles**
\+ **V80.8 Animal-rider or occupant of animal-drawn vehicle injured in collision with fixed or stationary object**
X+7th **V80.81 Animal-rider injured in collision with fixed or stationary object**
X+7th **V80.82 Occupant of animal-drawn vehicle injured in collision with fixed or stationary object**
\+ **V80.9 Animal-rider or occupant of animal-drawn vehicle injured in other and unspecified transport accidents**
\+ **V80.91 Animal-rider injured in other and unspecified transport accidents**
+7th **V80.910 Animal-rider injured in transport accident with military vehicle**
+7th **V80.918 Animal-rider injured in other transport accident**
+7th **V80.919 Animal-rider injured in unspecified transport accident**
Animal rider accident NOS
\+ **V80.92 Occupant of animal-drawn vehicle injured in other and unspecified transport accidents**
+7th **V80.920 Occupant of animal-drawn vehicle injured in transport accident with military vehicle**
+7th **V80.928 Occupant of animal-drawn vehicle injured in other transport accident**
+7th **V80.929 Occupant of animal-drawn vehicle injured in unspecified transport accident**
Animal-drawn vehicle accident NOS

V81 Occupant of railway train or railway vehicle injured in transport accident

Includes: derailment of railway train or railway vehicle
person on outside of train
Excludes1: *streetcar (V82.-)*

The appropriate 7th character is to be added to each code from category V81
A initial encounter
D subsequent encounter
S sequela

X+7th **V81.0 Occupant of railway train or railway vehicle injured in collision with motor vehicle in nontraffic accident**
Excludes1: *Occupant of railway train or railway vehicle injured due to collision with military vehicle (V81.83)*
X+7th **V81.1 Occupant of railway train or railway vehicle injured in collision with motor vehicle in traffic accident**
Excludes1: *Occupant of railway train or railway vehicle injured due to collision with military vehicle (V81.83)*
X+7th **V81.2 Occupant of railway train or railway vehicle injured in collision with or hit by rolling stock**
X+7th **V81.3 Occupant of railway train or railway vehicle injured in collision with other object**
Railway collision NOS
X+7th **V81.4 Person injured while boarding or alighting from railway train or railway vehicle**
X+7th **V81.5 Occupant of railway train or railway vehicle injured by fall in railway train or railway vehicle**
X+7th **V81.6 Occupant of railway train or railway vehicle injured by fall from railway train or railway vehicle**
X+7th **V81.7 Occupant of railway train or railway vehicle injured in derailment without antecedent collision**
\+ **V81.8 Occupant of railway train or railway vehicle injured in other specified railway accidents**
X+7th **V81.81 Occupant of railway train or railway vehicle injured due to explosion or fire on train**

X+7th **V81.82 Occupant of railway train or railway vehicle injured due to object falling onto train**
Occupant of railway train or railway vehicle injured due to falling earth onto train
Occupant of railway train or railway vehicle injured due to falling rocks onto train
Occupant of railway train or railway vehicle injured due to falling snow onto train
Occupant of railway train or railway vehicle injured due to falling trees onto train

X+7th **V81.83 Occupant of railway train or railway vehicle injured due to collision with military vehicle**

X+7th **V81.89 Occupant of railway train or railway vehicle injured due to other specified railway accident**

X+7th **V81.9 Occupant of railway train or railway vehicle injured in unspecified railway accident**
Railway accident NOS

V82 Occupant of powered streetcar injured in transport accident

Includes: interurban electric car
person on outside of streetcar
tram (car)
trolley (car)

Excludes1: *bus (V70-V79)*
motorcoach (V70-V79)
nonpowered streetcar (V76.-)
train (V81.-)

The appropriate 7th character is to be added to each code from category V82
A initial encounter
D subsequent encounter
S sequela

X+7th **V82.0 Occupant of streetcar injured in collision with motor vehicle in nontraffic accident**

X+7th **V82.1 Occupant of streetcar injured in collision with motor vehicle in traffic accident**

X+7th **V82.2 Occupant of streetcar injured in collision with or hit by rolling stock**

X+7th **V82.3 Occupant of streetcar injured in collision with other object**
Excludes1: *collision with animal-drawn vehicle or animal being ridden (V82.8)*

X+7th **V82.4 Person injured while boarding or alighting from streetcar**

X+7th **V82.5 Occupant of streetcar injured by fall in streetcar**
Excludes1: *fall in streetcar:*
while boarding or alighting (V82.4)
with antecedent collision (V82.0-V82.3)

X+7th **V82.6 Occupant of streetcar injured by fall from streetcar**
Excludes1: *fall from streetcar:*
while boarding or alighting (V82.4)
with antecedent collision (V82.0-V82.3)

X+7th **V82.7 Occupant of streetcar injured in derailment without antecedent collision**
Excludes1: *occupant of streetcar injured in derailment with antecedent collision (V82.0-V82.3)*

X+7th **V82.8 Occupant of streetcar injured in other specified transport accidents**
Streetcar collision with military vehicle
Streetcar collision with train or nonmotor vehicles

X+7th **V82.9 Occupant of streetcar injured in unspecified traffic accident**
Streetcar accident NOS

V83 Occupant of special vehicle mainly used on industrial premises injured in transport accident

Includes: battery-powered airport passenger vehicle
battery-powered truck (baggage) (mail)
coal-car in mine
forklift (truck)
logging car
self-propelled industrial truck
station baggage truck (powered)
tram, truck, or tub (powered) in mine or quarry

Excludes1: *special construction vehicles (V85.-)*
special industrial vehicle in stationary use or maintenance (W31.-)

The appropriate 7th character is to be added to each code from category V83
A initial encounter
D subsequent encounter
S sequela

X+7th **V83.0 Driver of special industrial vehicle injured in traffic accident**

X+7th **V83.1 Passenger of special industrial vehicle injured in traffic accident**

X+7th **V83.2 Person on outside of special industrial vehicle injured in traffic accident**

X+7th **V83.3 Unspecified occupant of special industrial vehicle injured in traffic accident**

X+7th **V83.4 Person injured while boarding or alighting from special industrial vehicle**

X+7th **V83.5 Driver of special industrial vehicle injured in nontraffic accident**

X+7th **V83.6 Passenger of special industrial vehicle injured in nontraffic accident**

X+7th **V83.7 Person on outside of special industrial vehicle injured in nontraffic accident**

X+7th **V83.9 Unspecified occupant of special industrial vehicle injured in nontraffic accident**
Special-industrial-vehicle accident NOS

V84 Occupant of special vehicle mainly used in agriculture injured in transport accident

Includes: self-propelled farm machinery
tractor (and trailer)

Excludes1: *animal-powered farm machinery accident (W30.8-)*
contact with combine harvester (W30.0)
special agricultural vehicle in stationary use or maintenance (W30.-)

The appropriate 7th character is to be added to each code from category V84
A initial encounter
D subsequent encounter
S sequela

X+7th **V84.0 Driver of special agricultural vehicle injured in traffic accident**

X+7th **V84.1 Passenger of special agricultural vehicle injured in traffic accident**

X+7th **V84.2 Person on outside of special agricultural vehicle injured in traffic accident**

X+7th **V84.3 Unspecified occupant of special agricultural vehicle injured in traffic accident**

X+7th **V84.4 Person injured while boarding or alighting from special agricultural vehicle**

X+7th **V84.5 Driver of special agricultural vehicle injured in nontraffic accident**

X+7th **V84.6 Passenger of special agricultural vehicle injured in nontraffic accident**

X+7th **V84.7 Person on outside of special agricultural vehicle injured in nontraffic accident**

X+7th **V84.9 Unspecified occupant of special agricultural vehicle injured in nontraffic accident**
Special-agricultural vehicle accident NOS

V85 Occupant of special construction vehicle injured in transport accident

Includes: bulldozer
digger
dump truck
earth-leveller
mechanical shovel
road-roller

Excludes1: *special industrial vehicle (V83.-)*
special construction vehicle in stationary use or maintenance (W31.-)

The appropriate 7th character is to be added to each code from category V85
A initial encounter
D subsequent encounter
S sequela

X+7th **V85.0 Driver of special construction vehicle injured in traffic accident**

X+7th **V85.1 Passenger of special construction vehicle injured in traffic accident**

X+7th **V85.2 Person on outside of special construction vehicle injured in traffic accident**

X+7th **V85.3 Unspecified occupant of special construction vehicle injured in traffic accident**

X+7th **V85.4 Person injured while boarding or alighting from special construction vehicle**

X+7th **V85.5 Driver of special construction vehicle injured in nontraffic accident**

X+7th **V85.6 Passenger of special construction vehicle injured in nontraffic accident**

X+7th **V85.7 Person on outside of special construction vehicle injured in nontraffic accident**

X+7th **V85.9 Unspecified occupant of special construction vehicle injured in nontraffic accident**
Special-construction-vehicle accident NOS

V86 Occupant of special all-terrain or other off-road motor vehicle, injured in transport accident

Excludes1: *special all-terrain vehicle in stationary use or maintenance (W31.-)*
sport-utility vehicle (V50-V59)
three-wheeled motor vehicle designed for on-road use (V30-V39)

The appropriate 7th character is to be added to each code from category V86
A initial encounter
D subsequent encounter
S sequela

\+ **V86.0 Driver of special all-terrain or other off-road motor vehicle injured in traffic accident**
+7th **V86.01 Driver of ambulance or fire engine injured in traffic accident**
+7th **V86.02 Driver of snowmobile injured in traffic accident**
+7th **V86.03 Driver of dune buggy injured in traffic accident**
+7th **V86.04 Driver of military vehicle injured in traffic accident**
+7th **V86.09 Driver of other special all-terrain or other off-road motor vehicle injured in traffic accident**
Driver of dirt bike injured in traffic accident
Driver of go cart injured in traffic accident
Driver of golf cart injured in traffic accident

\+ **V86.1 Passenger of special all-terrain or other off-road motor vehicle injured in traffic accident**
+7th **V86.11 Passenger of ambulance or fire engine injured in traffic accident**
+7th **V86.12 Passenger of snowmobile injured in traffic accident**
+7th **V86.13 Passenger of dune buggy injured in traffic accident**
+7th **V86.14 Passenger of military vehicle injured in traffic accident**
+7th **V86.19 Passenger of other special all-terrain or other off-road motor vehicle injured in traffic accident**
Passenger of dirt bike injured in traffic accident
Passenger of go cart injured in traffic accident
Passenger of golf cart injured in traffic accident

\+ **V86.2 Person on outside of special all-terrain or other off-road motor vehicle injured in traffic accident**
+7th **V86.21 Person on outside of ambulance or fire engine injured in traffic accident**
+7th **V86.22 Person on outside of snowmobile injured in traffic accident**
+7th **V86.23 Person on outside of dune buggy injured in traffic accident**
+7th **V86.24 Person on outside of military vehicle injured in traffic accident**
+7th **V86.29 Person on outside of other special all-terrain or other off-road motor vehicle injured in traffic accident**
Person on outside of dirt bike injured in traffic accident
Person on outside of go cart in traffic accident
Person on outside of golf cart injured in traffic accident

\+ **V86.3 Unspecified occupant of special all-terrain or other off-road motor vehicle injured in traffic accident**
+7th **V86.31 Unspecified occupant of ambulance or fire engine injured in traffic accident**
+7th **V86.32 Unspecified occupant of snowmobile injured in traffic accident**
+7th **V86.33 Unspecified occupant of dune buggy injured in traffic accident**
+7th **V86.34 Unspecified occupant of military vehicle injured in traffic accident**
+7th **V86.39 Unspecified occupant of other special all-terrain or other off-road motor vehicle injured in traffic accident**
Unspecified occupant of dirt bike injured in traffic accident
Unspecified occupant of go cart injured in traffic accident
Unspecified occupant of golf cart injured in traffic accident

\+ **V86.4 Person injured while boarding or alighting from special all-terrain or other off-road motor vehicle**
+7th **V86.41 Person injured while boarding or alighting from ambulance or fire engine**
+7th **V86.42 Person injured while boarding or alighting from snowmobile**
+7th **V86.43 Person injured while boarding or alighting from dune buggy**
+7th **V86.44 Person injured while boarding or alighting from military vehicle**
+7th **V86.49 Person injured while boarding or alighting from othe[r] special all-terrain or other off-road motor vehicle**
Person injured while boarding or alighting from dirt bi[ke]
Person injured while boarding or alighting from go car[t]
Person injured while boarding or alighting from golf ca[rt]

\+ **V86.5 Driver of special all-terrain or other off-road motor vehicle injured in nontraffic accident**
+7th **V86.51 Driver of ambulance or fire engine injured in nontraffic accident**
+7th **V86.52 Driver of snowmobile injured in nontraffic accident**
+7th **V86.53 Driver of dune buggy injured in nontraffic accident**
+7th **V86.54 Driver of military vehicle injured in nontraffic accident**
+7th **V86.59 Driver of other special all-terrain or other off-road motor vehicle injured in nontraffic accident**
Driver of dirt bike injured in nontraffic accident
Driver of go cart injured in nontraffic accident
Driver of golf cart injured in nontraffic accident

\+ **V86.6 Passenger of special all-terrain or other off-road motor vehicle injured in nontraffic accident**
+7th **V86.61 Passenger of ambulance or fire engine injured in nontraffic accident**
+7th **V86.62 Passenger of snowmobile injured in nontraffic accident**
+7th **V86.63 Passenger of dune buggy injured in nontraffic accide[nt]**
+7th **V86.64 Passenger of military vehicle injured in nontraffic accident**
+7th **V86.69 Passenger of other special all-terrain or other off-road motor vehicle injured in nontraffic accident**
Passenger of dirt bike injured in nontraffic accident
Passenger of go cart injured in nontraffic accident
Passenger of golf cart injured in nontraffic accident

\+ **V86.7 Person on outside of special all-terrain or other off-road motor vehicle injured in nontraffic accident**
+7th **V86.71 Person on outside of ambulance or fire engine injured in nontraffic accident**
+7th **V86.72 Person on outside of snowmobile injured in nontraffi[c] accident**
+7th **V86.73 Person on outside of dune buggy injured in nontraffic accident**
+7th **V86.74 Person on outside of military vehicle injured in nontraffic accident**
+7th **V86.79 Person on outside of other special all-terrain or other off-road motor vehicles injured in nontraffic accident**
Person on outside of dirt bike injured in nontraffic accident
Person on outside of go cart injured in nontraffic accident
Person on outside of golf cart injured in nontraffic accident

\+ **V86.9 Unspecified occupant of special all-terrain or other off-road motor vehicle injured in nontraffic accident**
+7th **V86.91 Unspecified occupant of ambulance or fire engine injured in nontraffic accident**
+7th **V86.92 Unspecified occupant of snowmobile injured in nontraffic accident**
+7th **V86.93 Unspecified occupant of dune buggy injured in nontraffic accident**
+7th **V86.94 Unspecified occupant of military vehicle injured in nontraffic accident**
+7th **V86.99 Unspecified occupant of other special all-terrain or other off-road motor vehicle injured in nontraffic accident**
All-terrain motor-vehicle accident NOS
Off-road motor-vehicle accident NOS
Other motor-vehicle accident NOS
Unspecified occupant of dirt bike injured in nontraffic accident
Unspecified occupant of go cart injured in nontraffic accident
Unspecified occupant of golf cart injured in nontraffic accident

V87 Traffic accident of specified type but victim's mode of transport unknown

Excludes1: *collision involving:*
pedal cycle (V10-V19)
pedestrian (V01-V09)

The appropriate 7th character is to be added to each code from category V87
A initial encounter
D subsequent encounter
S sequela

X+7th **V87.0 Person injured in collision between car and two- or three-wheeled powered vehicle (traffic)**
X+7th **V87.1 Person injured in collision between other motor vehicle and two- or three-wheeled motor vehicle (traffic)**
X+7th **V87.2 Person injured in collision between car and pick-up truck or van (traffic)**
X+7th **V87.3 Person injured in collision between car and bus (traffic)**
X+7th **V87.4 Person injured in collision between car and heavy transport vehicle (traffic)**
X+7th **V87.5 Person injured in collision between heavy transport vehicle and bus (traffic)**
X+7th **V87.6 Person injured in collision between railway train or railway vehicle and car (traffic)**
X+7th **V87.7 Person injured in collision between other specified motor vehicles (traffic)**
X+7th **V87.8 Person injured in other specified noncollision transport accidents involving motor vehicle (traffic)**
X+7th **V87.9 Person injured in other specified (collision) (noncollision) transport accidents involving nonmotor vehicle (traffic)**

V88 Nontraffic accident of specified type but victim's mode of transport unknown

Excludes1: *collision involving:*
pedal cycle (V10-V19)
pedestrian (V01-V09)

The appropriate 7th character is to be added to each code from category V88
A initial encounter
D subsequent encounter
S sequela

X+7th **V88.0 Person injured in collision between car and two- or three-wheeled motor vehicle, nontraffic**
X+7th **V88.1 Person injured in collision between other motor vehicle and two- or three-wheeled motor vehicle, nontraffic**
X+7th **V88.2 Person injured in collision between car and pick-up truck or van, nontraffic**
X+7th **V88.3 Person injured in collision between car and bus, nontraffic**
X+7th **V88.4 Person injured in collision between car and heavy transport vehicle, nontraffic**
X+7th **V88.5 Person injured in collision between heavy transport vehicle and bus, nontraffic**
X+7th **V88.6 Person injured in collision between railway train or railway vehicle and car, nontraffic**
X+7th **V88.7 Person injured in collision between other specified motor vehicle, nontraffic**
X+7th **V88.8 Person injured in other specified noncollision transport accidents involving motor vehicle, nontraffic**
X+7th **V88.9 Person injured in other specified (collision)(noncollision) transport accidents involving nonmotor vehicle, nontraffic**

V89 Motor- or nonmotor-vehicle accident, type of vehicle unspecified

The appropriate 7th character is to be added to each code from category V89
A initial encounter
D subsequent encounter
S sequela

X+7th **V89.0 Person injured in unspecified motor-vehicle accident, nontraffic**
Motor-vehicle accident NOS, nontraffic
X+7th **V89.1 Person injured in unspecified nonmotor-vehicle accident, nontraffic**
Nonmotor-vehicle accident NOS (nontraffic)
X+7th **V89.2 Person injured in unspecified motor-vehicle accident, traffic**
Motor-vehicle accident [MVA] NOS
Road (traffic) accident [RTA] NOS
X+7th **V89.3 Person injured in unspecified nonmotor-vehicle accident, traffic**
Nonmotor-vehicle traffic accident NOS
X+7th **V89.9 Person injured in unspecified vehicle accident**
Collision NOS

Water transport accidents (V90-V94)

V90 Drowning and submersion due to accident to watercraft

Excludes1: *civilian water transport accident involving military watercraft (V94.81-)*
fall into water not from watercraft (W16.-)
military watercraft accident in military or war operations (Y36.0-, Y37.0-)
water-transport-related drowning or submersion without accident to watercraft (V92.-)

The appropriate 7th character is to be added to each code from category V90
A initial encounter
D subsequent encounter
S sequela

\+ **V90.0 Drowning and submersion due to watercraft overturning**
X+7th **V90.00 Drowning and submersion due to merchant ship overturning**
X+7th **V90.01 Drowning and submersion due to passenger ship overturning**
Drowning and submersion due to Ferry-boat overturning
Drowning and submersion due to Liner overturning
X+7th **V90.02 Drowning and submersion due to fishing boat overturning**
X+7th **V90.03 Drowning and submersion due to other powered watercraft overturning**
Drowning and submersion due to Hovercraft (on open water) overturning
Drowning and submersion due to Jet ski overturning
X+7th **V90.04 Drowning and submersion due to sailboat overturning**
X+7th **V90.05 Drowning and submersion due to canoe or kayak overturning**
X+7th **V90.06 Drowning and submersion due to (nonpowered) inflatable craft overturning**
X+7th **V90.08 Drowning and submersion due to other unpowered watercraft overturning**
Drowning and submersion due to windsurfer overturning
X+7th **V90.09 Drowning and submersion due to unspecified watercraft overturning**
Drowning and submersion due to boat NOS overturning
Drowning and submersion due to ship NOS overturning
Drowning and submersion due to watercraft NOS overturning

\+ **V90.1 Drowning and submersion due to watercraft sinking**
X+7th **V90.10 Drowning and submersion due to merchant ship sinking**
X+7th **V90.11 Drowning and submersion due to passenger ship sinking**
Drowning and submersion due to Ferry-boat sinking
Drowning and submersion due to Liner sinking
X+7th **V90.12 Drowning and submersion due to fishing boat sinking**
X+7th **V90.13 Drowning and submersion due to other powered watercraft sinking**
Drowning and submersion due to Hovercraft (on open water) sinking
Drowning and submersion due to Jet ski sinking
X+7th **V90.14 Drowning and submersion due to sailboat sinking**
X+7th **V90.15 Drowning and submersion due to canoe or kayak sinking**
X+7th **V90.16 Drowning and submersion due to (nonpowered) inflatable craft sinking**
X+7th **V90.18 Drowning and submersion due to other unpowered watercraft sinking**
X+7th **V90.19 Drowning and submersion due to unspecified watercraft sinking**
Drowning and submersion due to boat NOS sinking
Drowning and submersion due to ship NOS sinking
Drowning and submersion due to watercraft NOS sinking

\+ **V90.2 Drowning and submersion due to falling or jumping from burning watercraft**
X+7th **V90.20 Drowning and submersion due to falling or jumping from burning merchant ship**
X+7th **V90.21 Drowning and submersion due to falling or jumping from burning passenger ship**
Drowning and submersion due to falling or jumping from burning Ferry-boat
Drowning and submersion due to falling or jumping from burning Liner
X+7th **V90.22 Drowning and submersion due to falling or jumping from burning fishing boat**

X+7th **V90.23 Drowning and submersion due to falling or jumping from other burning powered watercraft**
Drowning and submersion due to falling and jumping from burning Hovercraft (on open water)
Drowning and submersion due to falling and jumping from burning Jet ski

X+7th **V90.24 Drowning and submersion due to falling or jumping from burning sailboat**

X+7th **V90.25 Drowning and submersion due to falling or jumping from burning canoe or kayak**

X+7th **V90.26 Drowning and submersion due to falling or jumping from burning (nonpowered) inflatable craft**

X+7th **V90.27 Drowning and submersion due to falling or jumping from burning water-skis**

X+7th **V90.28 Drowning and submersion due to falling or jumping from other burning unpowered watercraft**
Drowning and submersion due to falling and jumping from burning surf-board
Drowning and submersion due to falling and jumping from burning windsurfer

X+7th **V90.29 Drowning and submersion due to falling or jumping from unspecified burning watercraft**
Drowning and submersion due to falling or jumping from burning boat NOS
Drowning and submersion due to falling or jumping from burning ship NOS
Drowning and submersion due to falling or jumping from burning watercraft NOS

+ **V90.3 Drowning and submersion due to falling or jumping from crushed watercraft**

X+7th **V90.30 Drowning and submersion due to falling or jumping from crushed merchant ship**

X+7th **V90.31 Drowning and submersion due to falling or jumping from crushed passenger ship**
Drowning and submersion due to falling and jumping from crushed Ferry boat
Drowning and submersion due to falling and jumping from crushed Liner

X+7th **V90.32 Drowning and submersion due to falling or jumping from crushed fishing boat**

X+7th **V90.33 Drowning and submersion due to falling or jumping from other crushed powered watercraft**
Drowning and submersion due to falling and jumping from crushed Hovercraft
Drowning and submersion due to falling and jumping from crushed Jet ski

X+7th **V90.34 Drowning and submersion due to falling or jumping from crushed sailboat**

X+7th **V90.35 Drowning and submersion due to falling or jumping from crushed canoe or kayak**

X+7th **V90.36 Drowning and submersion due to falling or jumping from crushed (nonpowered) inflatable craft**

X+7th **V90.37 Drowning and submersion due to falling or jumping from crushed water-skis**

X+7th **V90.38 Drowning and submersion due to falling or jumping from other crushed unpowered watercraft**
Drowning and submersion due to falling and jumping from crushed surf-board
Drowning and submersion due to falling and jumping from crushed windsurfer

X+7th **V90.39 Drowning and submersion due to falling or jumping from crushed unspecified watercraft**
Drowning and submersion due to falling and jumping from crushed boat NOS
Drowning and submersion due to falling and jumping from crushed ship NOS
Drowning and submersion due to falling and jumping from crushed watercraft NOS

+ **V90.8 Drowning and submersion due to other accident to watercraft**

X+7th **V90.80 Drowning and submersion due to other accident to merchant ship**

X+7th **V90.81 Drowning and submersion due to other accident to passenger ship**
Drowning and submersion due to other accident to Ferry-boat
Drowning and submersion due to other accident to Liner

X+7th **V90.82 Drowning and submersion due to other accident to fishing boat**

X+7th **V90.83 Drowning and submersion due to other accident to other powered watercraft**
Drowning and submersion due to other accident to Hovercraft (on open water)
Drowning and submersion due to other accident to Jet ski

X+7th **V90.84 Drowning and submersion due to other accident to sailboat**

X+7th **V90.85 Drowning and submersion due to other accident to canoe or kayak**

X+7th **V90.86 Drowning and submersion due to other accident to (nonpowered) inflatable craft**

X+7th **V90.87 Drowning and submersion due to other accident to water-skis**

X+7th **V90.88 Drowning and submersion due to other accident to other unpowered watercraft**
Drowning and submersion due to other accident to surf-board
Drowning and submersion due to other accident to windsurfer

X+7th **V90.89 Drowning and submersion due to other accident to unspecified watercraft**
Drowning and submersion due to other accident to boat NOS
Drowning and submersion due to other accident to ship NOS
Drowning and submersion due to other accident to watercraft NOS

V91 Other injury due to accident to watercraft

Includes: any injury except drowning and submersion as a result of an accident to watercraft

Excludes1: *civilian water transport accident involving military watercraft (V94.81-)*
military watercraft accident in military or war operations (Y36, Y37.-)

Excludes2: *drowning and submersion due to accident to watercraft (V90.-)*

The appropriate 7th character is to be added to each code from category V91
A initial encounter
D subsequent encounter
S sequela

+ **V91.0 Burn due to watercraft on fire**
Excludes1: *burn from localized fire or explosion on board ship without accident to watercraft (V93.-)*

X+7th **V91.00 Burn due to merchant ship on fire**

X+7th **V91.01 Burn due to passenger ship on fire**
Burn due to Ferry-boat on fire
Burn due to Liner on fire

X+7th **V91.02 Burn due to fishing boat on fire**

X+7th **V91.03 Burn due to other powered watercraft on fire**
Burn due to Hovercraft (on open water) on fire
Burn due to Jet ski on fire

X+7th **V91.04 Burn due to sailboat on fire**

X+7th **V91.05 Burn due to canoe or kayak on fire**

X+7th **V91.06 Burn due to (nonpowered) inflatable craft on fire**

X+7th **V91.07 Burn due to water-skis on fire**

X+7th **V91.08 Burn due to other unpowered watercraft on fire**

X+7th **V91.09 Burn due to unspecified watercraft on fire**
Burn due to boat NOS on fire
Burn due to ship NOS on fire
Burn due to watercraft NOS on fire

+ **V91.1 Crushed between watercraft and other watercraft or other object due to collision**
Crushed by lifeboat after abandoning ship in a collision
NOTE select the specified type of watercraft that the victim was on at the time of the collision

X+7th **V91.10 Crushed between merchant ship and other watercraft or other object due to collision**

X+7th **V91.11 Crushed between passenger ship and other watercraft or other object due to collision**
Crushed between Ferry-boat and other watercraft or other object due to collision
Crushed between Liner and other watercraft or other object due to collision

X+7th **V91.12 Crushed between fishing boat and other watercraft or other object due to collision**

X+7th **V91.13 Crushed between other powered watercraft and other watercraft or other object due to collision**
Crushed between Hovercraft (on open water) and other watercraft or other object due to collision
Crushed between Jet ski and other watercraft or other object due to collision

X+7th **V91.14 Crushed between sailboat and other watercraft or other object due to collision**

X+7th **V91.15 Crushed between canoe or kayak and other watercraft or other object due to collision**

X+7th **V91.16 Crushed between (nonpowered) inflatable craft and other watercraft or other object due to collision**

X+7th **V91.18 Crushed between other unpowered watercraft and other watercraft or other object due to collision**
Crushed between surfboard and other watercraft or other object due to collision
Crushed between windsurfer and other watercraft or other object due to collision

X+7th **V91.19 Crushed between unspecified watercraft and other watercraft or other object due to collision**
Crushed between boat NOS and other watercraft or other object due to collision
Crushed between ship NOS and other watercraft or other object due to collision
Crushed between watercraft NOS and other watercraft or other object due to collision

+ **V91.2 Fall due to collision between watercraft and other watercraft or other object**
Fall while remaining on watercraft after collision
NOTE select the specified type of watercraft that the victim was on at the time of the collision
Excludes1: *crushed between watercraft and other watercraft and other object due to collision (V91.1-)*
drowning and submersion due to falling from crushed watercraft (V90.3-)

X+7th **V91.20 Fall due to collision between merchant ship and other watercraft or other object**

X+7th **V91.21 Fall due to collision between passenger ship and other watercraft or other object**
Fall due to collision between Ferry-boat and other watercraft or other object
Fall due to collision between Liner and other watercraft or other object

X+7th **V91.22 Fall due to collision between fishing boat and other watercraft or other object**

X+7th **V91.23 Fall due to collision between other powered watercraft and other watercraft or other object**
Fall due to collision between Hovercraft (on open water) and other watercraft or other object
Fall due to collision between Jet ski and other watercraft or other object

X+7th **V91.24 Fall due to collision between sailboat and other watercraft or other object**

X+7th **V91.25 Fall due to collision between canoe or kayak and other watercraft or other object**

X+7th **V91.26 Fall due to collision between (nonpowered) inflatable craft and other watercraft or other object**

X+7th **V91.29 Fall due to collision between unspecified watercraft and other watercraft or other object**
Fall due to collision between boat NOS and other watercraft or other object
Fall due to collision between ship NOS and other watercraft or other object
Fall due to collision between watercraft NOS and other watercraft or other object

+ **V91.3 Hit or struck by falling object due to accident to watercraft**
Hit or struck by falling object (part of damaged watercraft or other object) after falling or jumping from damaged watercraft
Excludes2: *drowning or submersion due to fall or jumping from damaged watercraft (V90.2-, V90.3-)*

X+7th **V91.30 Hit or struck by falling object due to accident to merchant ship**

X+7th **V91.31 Hit or struck by falling object due to accident to passenger ship**
Hit or struck by falling object due to accident to Ferry-boat
Hit or struck by falling object due to accident to Liner

X+7th **V91.32 Hit or struck by falling object due to accident to fishing boat**

X+7th **V91.33 Hit or struck by falling object due to accident to other powered watercraft**
Hit or struck by falling object due to accident to Hovercraft (on open water)
Hit or struck by falling object due to accident to Jet ski

X+7th **V91.34 Hit or struck by falling object due to accident to sailboat**

X+7th **V91.35 Hit or struck by falling object due to accident to canoe or kayak**

X+7th **V91.36 Hit or struck by falling object due to accident to (nonpowered) inflatable craft**

X+7th **V91.37 Hit or struck by falling object due to accident to water-skis**
Hit by water-skis after jumping off of waterskis

X+7th **V91.38 Hit or struck by falling object due to accident to other unpowered watercraft**
Hit or struck by surf-board after falling off damaged surf-board
Hit or struck by object after falling off damaged windsurfer

X+7th **V91.39 Hit or struck by falling object due to accident to unspecified watercraft**
Hit or struck by falling object due to accident to boat NOS
Hit or struck by falling object due to accident to ship NOS
Hit or struck by falling object due to accident to watercraft NOS

+ **V91.8 Other injury due to other accident to watercraft**

X+7th **V91.80 Other injury due to other accident to merchant ship**

X+7th **V91.81 Other injury due to other accident to passenger ship**
Other injury due to other accident to Ferry-boat
Other injury due to other accident to Liner

X+7th **V91.82 Other injury due to other accident to fishing boat**

X+7th **V91.83 Other injury due to other accident to other powered watercraft**
Other injury due to other accident to Hovercraft (on open water)
Other injury due to other accident to Jet ski

X+7th **V91.84 Other injury due to other accident to sailboat**

X+7th **V91.85 Other injury due to other accident to canoe or kayak**

X+7th **V91.86 Other injury due to other accident to (nonpowered) inflatable craft**

X+7th **V91.87 Other injury due to other accident to water-skis**

X+7th **V91.88 Other injury due to other accident to other unpowered watercraft**
Other injury due to other accident to surf-board
Other injury due to other accident to windsurfer

X+7th **V91.89 Other injury due to other accident to unspecified watercraft**
Other injury due to other accident to boat NOS
Other injury due to other accident to ship NOS
Other injury due to other accident to watercraft NOS

V92 Drowning and submersion due to accident on board watercraft, without accident to watercraft
Excludes1: *civilian water transport accident involving military watercraft (V94.81-)*
drowning or submersion due to accident to watercraft (V90-V91)
drowning or submersion of diver who voluntarily jumps from boat not involved in an accident (W16.711, W16.721)
fall into water without watercraft (W16.-)
military watercraft accident in military or war operations (Y36, Y37)

The appropriate 7th character is to be added to each code from category V92
A initial encounter
D subsequent encounter
S sequela

+ **V92.0 Drowning and submersion due to fall off watercraft**
Drowning and submersion due to fall from gangplank of watercraft
Drowning and submersion due to fall overboard watercraft
Excludes2: *hitting head on object or bottom of body of water due to fall from watercraft (V94.0-)*

X+7th **V92.00 Drowning and submersion due to fall off merchant ship**

X+7th **V92.01 Drowning and submersion due to fall off passenger ship**
Drowning and submersion due to fall off Ferry-boat
Drowning and submersion due to fall off Liner

X+7th **V92.02 Drowning and submersion due to fall off fishing boat**

X+7th **V92.03 Drowning and submersion due to fall off other powered watercraft**
Drowning and submersion due to fall off Hovercraft (on open water)
Drowning and submersion due to fall off Jet ski

X+7th **V92.04 Drowning and submersion due to fall off sailboat**

X+7th **V92.05 Drowning and submersion due to fall off canoe or kayak**

X+7th **V92.06 Drowning and submersion due to fall off (nonpowered) inflatable craft**

X+7th **V92.07 Drowning and submersion due to fall off water-skis**
Excludes1: *drowning and submersion due to falling off burning water-skis (V90.27)*
drowning and submersion due to falling off crushed water-skis (V90.37)
hit by boat while water-skiing NOS (V94.X)

X+7th **V92.08 Drowning and submersion due to fall off other unpowered watercraft**
Drowning and submersion due to fall off surf-board
Drowning and submersion due to fall off windsurfer
Excludes1: *drowning and submersion due to fall off burning unpowered watercraft (V90.28)*
drowning and submersion due to fall off crushed unpowered watercraft (V90.38)
drowning and submersion due to fall off damaged unpowered watercraft (V90.88)
drowning and submersion due to rider of nonpowered watercraft being hit by other watercraft (V94.-)
other injury due to rider of nonpowered watercraft being hit by other watercraft (V94.-)

X+7th **V92.09 Drowning and submersion due to fall off unspecified watercraft**
Drowning and submersion due to fall off boat NOS
Drowning and submersion due to fall off ship
Drowning and submersion due to fall off watercraft NOS

\+ **V92.1 Drowning and submersion due to being thrown overboard by motion of watercraft**
Excludes1: *drowning and submersion due to fall off surf-board (V92.08)*
drowning and submersion due to fall off water-skis (V92.07)
drowning and submersion due to fall off windsurfer (V92.08)

X+7th **V92.10 Drowning and submersion due to being thrown overboard by motion of merchant ship**

X+7th **V92.11 Drowning and submersion due to being thrown overboard by motion of passenger ship**
Drowning and submersion due to being thrown overboard by motion of Ferry-boat
Drowning and submersion due to being thrown overboard by motion of Liner

X+7th **V92.12 Drowning and submersion due to being thrown overboard by motion of fishing boat**

X+7th **V92.13 Drowning and submersion due to being thrown overboard by motion of other powered watercraft**
Drowning and submersion due to being thrown overboard by motion of Hovercraft

X+7th **V92.14 Drowning and submersion due to being thrown overboard by motion of sailboat**

X+7th **V92.15 Drowning and submersion due to being thrown overboard by motion of canoe or kayak**

X+7th **V92.16 Drowning and submersion due to being thrown overboard by motion of (nonpowered) inflatable craft**

X+7th **V92.19 Drowning and submersion due to being thrown overboard by motion of unspecified watercraft**
Drowning and submersion due to being thrown overboard by motion of boat NOS
Drowning and submersion due to being thrown overboard by motion of ship NOS
Drowning and submersion due to being thrown overboard by motion of watercraft NOS

\+ **V92.2 Drowning and submersion due to being washed overboard from watercraft**
Code first any associated cataclysm (X37.0-)

X+7th **V92.20 Drowning and submersion due to being washed overboard from merchant ship**

X+7th **V92.21 Drowning and submersion due to being washed overboard from passenger ship**
Drowning and submersion due to being washed overboard from Ferry-boat
Drowning and submersion due to being washed overboard from Liner

X+7th **V92.22 Drowning and submersion due to being washed overboard from fishing boat**

X+7th **V92.23 Drowning and submersion due to being washed overboard from other powered watercraft**
Drowning and submersion due to being washed overboard from Hovercraft (on open water)
Drowning and submersion due to being washed overboard from Jet ski

X+7th **V92.24 Drowning and submersion due to being washed overboard from sailboat**

X+7th **V92.25 Drowning and submersion due to being washed overboard from canoe or kayak**

X+7th **V92.26 Drowning and submersion due to being washed overboard from (nonpowered) inflatable craft**

X+7th **V92.27 Drowning and submersion due to being washed overboard from water-skis**
Excludes1: *drowning and submersion due to fall off water-skis (V92.07)*

X+7th **V92.28 Drowning and submersion due to being washed overboard from other unpowered watercraft**
Drowning and submersion due to being washed overboard from surf-board
Drowning and submersion due to being washed overboard from windsurfer

X+7th **V92.29 Drowning and submersion due to being washed overboard from unspecified watercraft**
Drowning and submersion due to being washed overboard from boat NOS
Drowning and submersion due to being washed overboard from ship NOS
Drowning and submersion due to being washed overboard from watercraft NOS

V93 Other injury due to accident on board watercraft, without accident t watercraft

Excludes1: *civilian water transport accident involving military watercraft (V94.81-)*
other injury due to accident to watercraft (V91.-)
military watercraft accident in military or war operations (Y36, Y37.-)
Excludes2: *drowning and submersion due to accident on board watercraft, without accident to watercraft (V92.-)*

The appropriate 7th character is to be added to each code from category V93
A initial encounter
D subsequent encounter
S sequela

\+ **V93.0 Burn due to localized fire on board watercraft**
Excludes1: *burn due to watercraft on fire (V91.0-)*

X+7th **V93.00 Burn due to localized fire on board merchant vessel**

X+7th **V93.01 Burn due to localized fire on board passenger vessel**
Burn due to localized fire on board Ferry-boat
Burn due to localized fire on board Liner

X+7th **V93.02 Burn due to localized fire on board fishing boat**

X+7th **V93.03 Burn due to localized fire on board other powered watercraft**
Burn due to localized fire on board Hovercraft
Burn due to localized fire on board Jet ski

X+7th **V93.04 Burn due to localized fire on board sailboat**

X+7th **V93.09 Burn due to localized fire on board unspecified watercraft**
Burn due to localized fire on board boat NOS
Burn due to localized fire on board ship NOS
Burn due to localized fire on board watercraft NOS

\+ **V93.1 Other burn on board watercraft**
Burn due to source other than fire on board watercraft
Excludes1: *burn due to watercraft on fire (V91.0-)*

X+7th **V93.10 Other burn on board merchant vessel**

X+7th **V93.11 Other burn on board passenger vessel**
Other burn on board Ferry-boat
Other burn on board Liner

X+7th **V93.12 Other burn on board fishing boat**

X+7th **V93.13 Other burn on board other powered watercraft**
Other burn on board Hovercraft
Other burn on board Jet ski

X+7th **V93.14 Other burn on board sailboat**

X+7th **V93.19 Other burn on board unspecified watercraft**
Other burn on board boat NOS
Other burn on board ship NOS
Other burn on board watercraft NOS

\+ **V93.2 Heat exposure on board watercraft**
Excludes1: *exposure to man-made heat not aboard watercraft (W92)*
exposure to natural heat while on board watercraft (X30)
exposure to sunlight while on board watercraft (X32)
Excludes2: *burn due to fire on board watercraft (V93.0-)*

X+7th **V93.20 Heat exposure on board merchant ship**

X+7th **V93.21 Heat exposure on board passenger ship**
Heat exposure on board Ferry-boat
Heat exposure on board Liner

X+7th **V93.22 Heat exposure on board fishing boat**

X+7th **V93.23 Heat exposure on board other powered watercraft**
Heat exposure on board hovercraft

X+7th **V93.24 Heat exposure on board sailboat**

X+7th **V93.29 Heat exposure on board unspecified watercraft**
Heat exposure on board boat NOS
Heat exposure on board ship NOS
Heat exposure on board watercraft NOS

\+ **V93.3 Fall on board watercraft**
Excludes1: *fall due to collision of watercraft (V91.2-)*

X+7th **V93.30 Fall on board merchant ship**

X+7th **V93.31 Fall on board passenger ship**
Fall on board Ferry-boat
Fall on board Liner

X+7th **V93.32 Fall on board fishing boat**

X+7th **V93.33 Fall on board other powered watercraft**
Fall on board Hovercraft (on open water)
Fall on board Jet ski

X+7th **V93.34 Fall on board sailboat**

X+7th **V93.35 Fall on board canoe or kayak**

X+7th **V93.36 Fall on board (nonpowered) inflatable craft**

X+7th **V93.38 Fall on board other unpowered watercraft**

X+7th **V93.39 Fall on board unspecified watercraft**
Fall on board boat NOS
Fall on board ship NOS
Fall on board watercraft NOS

\+ **V93.4 Struck by falling object on board watercraft**
Hit by falling object on board watercraft
Excludes1: *struck by falling object due to accident to watercraft (V91.3)*

X+7th **V93.40 Struck by falling object on merchant ship**

X+7th **V93.41 Struck by falling object on passenger ship**
Struck by falling object on Ferry-boat
Struck by falling object on Liner

X+7th **V93.42 Struck by falling object on fishing boat**

X+7th **V93.43 Struck by falling object on other powered watercraft**
Struck by falling object on Hovercraft

X+7th **V93.44 Struck by falling object on sailboat**

X+7th **V93.48 Struck by falling object on other unpowered watercraft**

X+7th **V93.49 Struck by falling object on unspecified watercraft**

\+ **V93.5 Explosion on board watercraft**
Boiler explosion on steamship
Excludes2: *fire on board watercraft (V93.0-)*

X+7th **V93.50 Explosion on board merchant ship**

X+7th **V93.51 Explosion on board passenger ship**
Explosion on board Ferry-boat
Explosion on board Liner

X+7th **V93.52 Explosion on board fishing boat**

X+7th **V93.53 Explosion on board other powered watercraft**
Explosion on board Hovercraft
Explosion on board Jet ski

X+7th **V93.54 Explosion on board sailboat**

X+7th **V93.59 Explosion on board unspecified watercraft**
Explosion on board boat NOS
Explosion on board ship NOS
Explosion on board watercraft NOS

\+ **V93.6 Machinery accident on board watercraft**
Excludes1: *machinery explosion on board watercraft (V93.4-)*
machinery fire on board watercraft (V93.0-)

X+7th **V93.60 Machinery accident on board merchant ship**

X+7th **V93.61 Machinery accident on board passenger ship**
Machinery accident on board Ferry-boat
Machinery accident on board Liner

X+7th **V93.62 Machinery accident on board fishing boat**

X+7th **V93.63 Machinery accident on board other powered watercraft**
Machinery accident on board Hovercraft

X+7th **V93.64 Machinery accident on board sailboat**

X+7th **V93.69 Machinery accident on board unspecified watercraft**
Machinery accident on board boat NOS
Machinery accident on board ship NOS
Machinery accident on board watercraft NOS

\+ **V93.8 Other injury due to other accident on board watercraft**
Accidental poisoning by gases or fumes on watercraft

X+7th **V93.80 Other injury due to other accident on board merchant ship**

X+7th **V93.81 Other injury due to other accident on board passenger ship**
Other injury due to other accident on board Ferry-boat
Other injury due to other accident on board Liner

X+7th **V93.82 Other injury due to other accident on board fishing boat**

X+7th **V93.83 Other injury due to other accident on board other powered watercraft**
Other injury due to other accident on board Hovercraft
Other injury due to other accident on board Jet ski

X+7th **V93.84 Other injury due to other accident on board sailboat**

X+7th **V93.85 Other injury due to other accident on board canoe or kayak**

X+7th **V93.86 Other injury due to other accident on board (nonpowered) inflatable craft**

X+7th **V93.87 Other injury due to other accident on board water-skis**
Hit or struck by object while waterskiing

X+7th **V93.88 Other injury due to other accident on board other unpowered watercraft**
Hit or struck by object while surfing
Hit or struck by object while on board windsurfer

X+7th **V93.89 Other injury due to other accident on board unspecified watercraft**
Other injury due to other accident on board boat NOS
Other injury due to other accident on board ship NOS
Other injury due to other accident on board watercraft NOS

V94 Other and unspecified water transport accidents

Excludes1: *military watercraft accidents in military or war operations (Y36, Y37)*

The appropriate 7th character is to be added to each code from category V94
A initial encounter
D subsequent encounter
S sequela

X+7th **V94.0 Hitting object or bottom of body of water due to fall from watercraft**
Excludes2: *drowning and submersion due to fall from watercraft (V92.0-)*

\+ **V94.1 Bather struck by watercraft**
Swimmer hit by watercraft

X+7th **V94.11 Bather struck by powered watercraft**

X+7th **V94.12 Bather struck by nonpowered watercraft**

\+ **V94.2 Rider of nonpowered watercraft struck by other watercraft**

X+7th **V94.21 Rider of nonpowered watercraft struck by other nonpowered watercraft**
Canoer hit by other nonpowered watercraft
Surfer hit by other nonpowered watercraft
Windsurfer hit by other nonpowered watercraft

X+7th **V94.22 Rider of nonpowered watercraft struck by powered watercraft**
Canoer hit by motorboat
Surfer hit by motorboat
Windsurfer hit by motorboat

\+ **V94.3 Injury to rider of (inflatable) watercraft being pulled behind other watercraft**

X+7th **V94.31 Injury to rider of (inflatable) recreational watercraft being pulled behind other watercraft**
Injury to rider of inner-tube pulled behind motor boat

X+7th **V94.32 Injury to rider of non-recreational watercraft being pulled behind other watercraft**
Injury to occupant of dingy being pulled behind boat or ship
Injury to occupant of life-raft being pulled behind boat or ship

X+7th **V94.4 Injury to barefoot water-skier**
Injury to person being pulled behind boat or ship

\+ **V94.8 Other water transport accident**
\+ **V94.81 Water transport accident involving military watercraft**
+7th **V94.810 Civilian watercraft involved in water transport accident with military watercraft**
Passenger on civilian watercraft injured due to accident with military watercraft
+7th **V94.811 Civilian in water injured by military watercraft**
+7th **V94.818 Other water transport accident involving military watercraft**
X+7th **V94.89 Other water transport accident**
X+7th **V94.9 Unspecified water transport accident**
Water transport accident NOS

Air and space transport accidents (V95-V97)

Excludes1: *military aircraft accidents in military or war operations (Y36, Y37.-)*

V95 Accident to powered aircraft causing injury to occupant

The appropriate 7th character is to be added to each code from category V95
A initial encounter
D subsequent encounter
S sequela

\+ **V95.0 Helicopter accident injuring occupant**
X+7th **V95.00 Unspecified helicopter accident injuring occupant**
X+7th **V95.01 Helicopter crash injuring occupant**
X+7th **V95.02 Forced landing of helicopter injuring occupant**
X+7th **V95.03 Helicopter collision injuring occupant**
Helicopter collision with any object, fixed, movable or moving
X+7th **V95.04 Helicopter fire injuring occupant**
X+7th **V95.05 Helicopter explosion injuring occupant**
X+7th **V95.09 Other helicopter accident injuring occupant**
\+ **V95.1 Ultralight, microlight or powered-glider accident injuring occupant**
X+7th **V95.10 Unspecified ultralight, microlight or powered-glider accident injuring occupant**
X+7th **V95.11 Ultralight, microlight or powered-glider crash injuring occupant**
X+7th **V95.12 Forced landing of ultralight, microlight or powered-glider injuring occupant**
X+7th **V95.13 Ultralight, microlight or powered-glider collision injuring occupant**
Ultralight, microlight or powered-glider collision with any object, fixed, movable or moving
X+7th **V95.14 Ultralight, microlight or powered-glider fire injuring occupant**
X+7th **V95.15 Ultralight, microlight or powered-glider explosion injuring occupant**
X+7th **V95.19 Other ultralight, microlight or powered-glider accident injuring occupant**
\+ **V95.2 Other private fixed-wing aircraft accident injuring occupant**
X+7th **V95.20 Unspecified accident to other private fixed-wing aircraft, injuring occupant**
X+7th **V95.21 Other private fixed-wing aircraft crash injuring occupant**
X+7th **V95.22 Forced landing of other private fixed-wing aircraft injuring occupant**
X+7th **V95.23 Other private fixed-wing aircraft collision injuring occupant**
Other private fixed-wing aircraft collision with any object, fixed, movable or moving
X+7th **V95.24 Other private fixed-wing aircraft fire injuring occupant**
X+7th **V95.25 Other private fixed-wing aircraft explosion injuring occupant**
X+7th **V95.29 Other accident to other private fixed-wing aircraft injuring occupant**
\+ **V95.3 Commercial fixed-wing aircraft accident injuring occupant**
X+7th **V95.30 Unspecified accident to commercial fixed-wing aircraft injuring occupant**
X+7th **V95.31 Commercial fixed-wing aircraft crash injuring occupant**
X+7th **V95.32 Forced landing of commercial fixed-wing aircraft injuring occupant**
X+7th **V95.33 Commercial fixed-wing aircraft collision injuring occupant**
Commercial fixed-wing aircraft collision with any object, fixed, movable or moving
X+7th **V95.34 Commercial fixed-wing aircraft fire injuring occupant**
X+7th **V95.35 Commercial fixed-wing aircraft explosion injuring occupant**
X+7th **V95.39 Other accident to commercial fixed-wing aircraft injuring occupant**
\+ **V95.4 Spacecraft accident injuring occupant**
X+7th **V95.40 Unspecified spacecraft accident injuring occupant**
X+7th **V95.41 Spacecraft crash injuring occupant**
X+7th **V95.42 Forced landing of spacecraft injuring occupant**
X+7th **V95.43 Spacecraft collision injuring occupant**
Spacecraft collision with any object, fixed, moveable or moving
X+7th **V95.44 Spacecraft fire injuring occupant**
X+7th **V95.45 Spacecraft explosion injuring occupant**
X+7th **V95.49 Other spacecraft accident injuring occupant**
X+7th **V95.8 Other powered aircraft accidents injuring occupant**
X+7th **V95.9 Unspecified aircraft accident injuring occupant**
Aircraft accident NOS
Air transport accident NOS

V96 Accident to nonpowered aircraft causing injury to occupant

The appropriate 7th character is to be added to each code from category V96
A initial encounter
D subsequent encounter
S sequela

\+ **V96.0 Balloon accident injuring occupant**
X+7th **V96.00 Unspecified balloon accident injuring occupant**
X+7th **V96.01 Balloon crash injuring occupant**
X+7th **V96.02 Forced landing of balloon injuring occupant**
X+7th **V96.03 Balloon collision injuring occupant**
Balloon collision with any object, fixed, moveable or moving
X+7th **V96.04 Balloon fire injuring occupant**
X+7th **V96.05 Balloon explosion injuring occupant**
X+7th **V96.09 Other balloon accident injuring occupant**
\+ **V96.1 Hang-glider accident injuring occupant**
X+7th **V96.10 Unspecified hang-glider accident injuring occupant**
X+7th **V96.11 Hang-glider crash injuring occupant**
X+7th **V96.12 Forced landing of hang-glider injuring occupant**
X+7th **V96.13 Hang-glider collision injuring occupant**
Hang-glider collision with any object, fixed, moveable or moving
X+7th **V96.14 Hang-glider fire injuring occupant**
X+7th **V96.15 Hang-glider explosion injuring occupant**
X+7th **V96.19 Other hang-glider accident injuring occupant**
\+ **V96.2 Glider (nonpowered) accident injuring occupant**
X+7th **V96.20 Unspecified glider (nonpowered) accident injuring occupant**
X+7th **V96.21 Glider (nonpowered) crash injuring occupant**
X+7th **V96.22 Forced landing of glider (nonpowered) injuring occupant**
X+7th **V96.23 Glider (nonpowered) collision injuring occupant**
Glider (nonpowered) collision with any object, fixed, moveable or moving
X+7th **V96.24 Glider (nonpowered) fire injuring occupant**
V96.25 Glider (nonpowered) explosion injuring occupant
X+7th **V96.29 Other glider (nonpowered) accident injuring occupant**
X+7th **V96.8 Other nonpowered-aircraft accidents injuring occupant**
Kite carrying a person accident injuring occupant
X+7th **V96.9 Unspecified nonpowered-aircraft accident injuring occupant**
Nonpowered-aircraft accident NOS

V97 Other specified air transport accidents

The appropriate 7th character is to be added to each code from category V97
A initial encounter
D subsequent encounter
S sequela

X+7th **V97.0 Occupant of aircraft injured in other specified air transport accidents**
Fall in, on or from aircraft in air transport accident
Excludes1: *accident while boarding or alighting aircraft (V97.1)*
X+7th **V97.1 Person injured while boarding or alighting from aircraft**
\+ **V97.2 Parachutist accident**
X+7th **V97.21 Parachutist entangled in object**
Parachutist landing in tree
X+7th **V97.22 Parachutist injured on landing**
X+7th **V97.29 Other parachutist accident**

+ V97.3 Person on ground injured in air transport accident

X+7th **V97.31 Hit by object falling from aircraft**
Hit by crashing aircraft
Injured by aircraft hitting house
Injured by aircraft hitting car

X+7th **V97.32 Injured by rotating propeller**

X+7th **V97.33 Sucked into jet engine**

X+7th **V97.39 Other injury to person on ground due to air transport accident**

+ V97.8 Other air transport accidents, not elsewhere classified
Excludes1: *aircraft accident NOS (V95.9)*
exposure to changes in air pressure during ascent or descent (W94.-)

+ V97.81 Air transport accident involving military aircraft

+7th **V97.810 Civilian aircraft involved in air transport accident with military aircraft**
Passenger in civilian aircraft injured due to accident with military aircraft

+7th **V97.811 Civilian injured by military aircraft**

+7th **V97.818 Other air transport accident involving military aircraft**

X+7th **V97.89 Other air transport accidents, not elsewhere classified**
Injury from machinery on aircraft

ther and unspecified transport accidents (V98-V99)

cludes1: *vehicle accident, type of vehicle unspecified (V89.-)*

V98 Other specified transport accidents

The appropriate 7th character is to be added to each code from category V98
A initial encounter
D subsequent encounter
S sequela

X+7th **V98.0 Accident to, on or involving cable-car, not on rails**
Caught or dragged by cable-car, not on rails
Fall or jump from cable-car, not on rails
Object thrown from or in cable-car, not on rails

X+7th **V98.1 Accident to, on or involving land-yacht**

X+7th **V98.2 Accident to, on or involving ice yacht**

X+7th **V98.3 Accident to, on or involving ski lift**
Accident to, on or involving ski chair-lift
Accident to, on or involving ski-lift with gondola

X+7th **V98.8 Other specified transport accidents**

th **V99 Unspecified transport accident**

The appropriate 7th character is to be added to code V99
A initial encounter
D subsequent encounter
S sequela

ther external causes of accidental injury (W00-X58)

lipping, tripping, stumbling and falls (W00-W19)

cludes1: *assault involving a fall (Y01-Y02)*
fall from animal (V80.-)
fall (in) (from) machinery (in operation) (W28-W31)
fall (in) (from) transport vehicle (V01-V99)
intentional self-harm involving a fall (X80-X81)

cludes2: *at risk for fall (history of fall) Z91.81*
fall (in) (from) burning building (X00.-)
fall in to fire (X00-X04, X08-X09)

W00 Fall due to ice and snow

Includes: pedestrian on foot falling (slipping) on ice and snow
Excludes1: *fall on (from) ice and snow involving pedestrian conveyance (V00.-)*
fall from stairs and steps not due to ice and snow (W10.-)

The appropriate 7th character is to be added to each code from category W00
A initial encounter
D subsequent encounter
S sequela

X+7th **W00.0 Fall on same level due to ice and snow**

X+7th **W00.1 Fall from stairs and steps due to ice and snow**

X+7th **W00.2 Other fall from one level to another due to ice and snow**

X+7th **W00.9 Unspecified fall due to ice and snow**

W01 Fall on same level from slipping, tripping and stumbling

Includes: fall on moving sidewalk
Excludes1: *fall due to bumping (striking) against object (W18.0-)*
fall in shower or bathtub (W18.2-)
fall on same level NOS (W18.30)
fall on same level from slipping, tripping and stumbling due to ice or snow (W00.0)
fall off or from toilet (W18.1-)
slipping, tripping and stumbling NOS (W18.40)
slipping, tripping and stumbling without falling (W18.4-)

The appropriate 7th character is to be added to each code from category W01
A initial encounter
D subsequent encounter
S sequela

X+7th **W01.0 Fall on same level from slipping, tripping and stumbling without subsequent striking against object**
Falling over animal

+ W01.1 Fall on same level from slipping, tripping and stumbling with subsequent striking against object

X+7th **W01.10 Fall on same level from slipping, tripping and stumbling with subsequent striking against unspecified object**

+ W01.11 Fall on same level from slipping, tripping and stumbling with subsequent striking against sharp object

+7th **W01.110 Fall on same level from slipping, tripping and stumbling with subsequent striking against sharp glass**

+7th **W01.111 Fall on same level from slipping, tripping and stumbling with subsequent striking against power tool or machine**

+7th **W01.118 Fall on same level from slipping, tripping and stumbling with subsequent striking against other sharp object**

+7th **W01.119 Fall on same level from slipping, tripping and stumbling with subsequent striking against unspecified sharp object**

+ W01.19 Fall on same level from slipping, tripping and stumbling with subsequent striking against other object

+7th **W01.190 Fall on same level from slipping, tripping and stumbling with subsequent striking against furniture**

+7th **W01.198 Fall on same level from slipping, tripping and stumbling with subsequent striking against other object**

X+7th **W03 Other fall on same level due to collision with another person**
Fall due to non-transport collision with other person
Excludes1: *collision with another person without fall (W51)*
crushed or pushed by a crowd or human stampede (W52)
fall involving pedestrian conveyance (V00-V09)
fall due to ice or snow (W00)
fall on same level NOS (W18.30)
AHA CC: 4Q, 2012, 108

The appropriate 7th character is to be added to code W03
A initial encounter
D subsequent encounter
S sequela

X+7th **W04 Fall while being carried or supported by other persons**
Accidentally dropped while being carried

The appropriate 7th character is to be added to code W04
A initial encounter
D subsequent encounter
S sequela

W05 Fall from non-movitng wheelchair, nonmotorized scooter and motorized mobility scooter

Excludes1: *fall from moving wheelchair (powered) (V00.811)*
fall from moving motorized mobility scooter (V00.831)
fall from nonmotorized scooter (V00.141)

The appropriate 7th character is to be added to each code from category W05
A initial encounter
D subsequent encounter
S sequela

X+7th **W05.0 Fall from non-moving wheelchair**

X+7th **W05.1 Fall from non-moving nonmotorized scooter**

X+7th **W05.2 Fall from non-moving motorized mobility scooter**

X+7th **W06 Fall from bed**

The appropriate 7th character is to be added to code W06
A initial encounter
D subsequent encounter
S sequela

X+7th **W07 Fall from chair**

The appropriate 7th character is to be added to code W07
A initial encounter
D subsequent encounter
S sequela

X+7th **W08 Fall from other furniture**

The appropriate 7th character is to be added to code W08
A initial encounter
D subsequent encounter
S sequela

W09 Fall on and from playground equipment

Excludes1: *fall involving recreational machinery (W31)*

The appropriate 7th character is to be added to each code from category W09
A initial encounter
D subsequent encounter
S sequela

X+7th **W09.0 Fall on or from playground slide**
X+7th **W09.1 Fall from playground swing**
X+7th **W09.2 Fall on or from jungle gym**
X+7th **W09.8 Fall on or from other playground equipment**

W10 Fall on and from stairs and steps

Excludes1: *Fall from stairs and steps due to ice and snow (W00.1)*

The appropriate 7th character is to be added to each code from category W10
A initial encounter
D subsequent encounter
S sequela

X+7th **W10.0 Fall (on)(from) escalator**
X+7th **W10.1 Fall (on)(from) sidewalk curb**
X+7th **W10.2 Fall (on)(from) incline**
Fall (on) (from) ramp
X+7th **W10.8 Fall (on) (from) other stairs and steps**
X+7th **W10.9 Fall (on) (from) unspecified stairs and steps**

X+7th **W11 Fall on and from ladder**

The appropriate 7th character is to be added to code W11
A initial encounter
D subsequent encounter
S sequela

X+7th **W12 Fall on and from scaffolding**

The appropriate 7th character is to be added to code W12
A initial encounter
D subsequent encounter
S sequela

W13 Fall from, out of or through building or structure

The appropriate 7th character is to be added to each code from category W13
A initial encounter
D subsequent encounter
S sequela

X+7th **W13.0 Fall from, out of or through balcony**
Fall from, out of or through railing
X+7th **W13.1 Fall from, out of or through bridge**
X+7th **W13.2 Fall from, out of or through roof**
X+7th **W13.3 Fall through floor**
X+7th **W13.4 Fall from, out of or through window**
Excludes2: *fall with subsequent striking against sharp glass (W01.110)*
X+7th **W13.8 Fall from, out of or through other building or structure**
Fall from, out of or through viaduct
Fall from, out of or through wall
Fall from, out of or through flag-pole
X+7th **W13.9 Fall from, out of or through building, not otherwise specified**
Excludes1: *collapse of a building or structure (W20.-)*
fall or jump from burning building or structure (X00.-)

X+7th **W14 Fall from tree**

The appropriate 7th character is to be added to code W14
A initial encounter
D subsequent encounter
S sequela

X+7th **W15 Fall from cliff**

The appropriate 7th character is to be added to code W15
A initial encounter
D subsequent encounter
S sequela

W16 Fall, jump or diving into water

Excludes1: *accidental non-watercraft drowning and submersion not involving fall (W65-W74)*
effects of air pressure from diving (W94.-)
fall into water from watercraft (V90-V94)
hitting an object or against bottom when falling from watercraft (V94.0)
Excludes2: *striking or hitting diving board (W21.4)*

The appropriate 7th character is to be added to each code from category W16
A initial encounter
D subsequent encounter
S sequela

\+ **W16.0 Fall into swimming pool**
Fall into swimming pool NOS
Excludes1: *fall into empty swimming pool (W17.3)*
\+ **W16.01 Fall into swimming pool striking water surface**
+7th **W16.011 Fall into swimming pool striking water surface causing drowning and submersion**
Excludes1: *drowning and submersion whi in swimming pool without fal (W67)*
+7th **W16.012 Fall into swimming pool striking water surface causing other injury**
\+ **W16.02 Fall into swimming pool striking bottom**
+7th **W16.021 Fall into swimming pool striking bottom causing drowning and submersion**
Excludes1: *drowning and submersion whil in swimming pool without fal (W67)*
+7th **W16.022 Fall into swimming pool striking bottom causing other injury**
\+ **W16.03 Fall into swimming pool striking wall**
+7th **W16.031 Fall into swimming pool striking wall causing drowning and submersion**
Excludes1: *drowning and submersion whil in swimming pool without fal (W67)*
+7th **W16.032 Fall into swimming pool striking wall causing other injury**

\+ **W16.1 Fall into natural body of water**
Fall into lake
Fall into open sea
Fall into river
Fall into stream
\+ **W16.11 Fall into natural body of water striking water surfac**
+7th **W16.111 Fall into natural body of water striking water surface causing drowning and submersion**
Excludes1: *drowning and submersion whil in natural body of water without fall (W69)*
+7th **W16.112 Fall into natural body of water striking water surface causing other injury**
\+ **W16.12 Fall into natural body of water striking bottom**
+7th **W16.121 Fall into natural body of water striking bottom causing drowning and submersion**
Excludes1: *drowning and submersion while in natural body of water without fall (W69)*
+7th **W16.122 Fall into natural body of water striking bottom causing other injury**
\+ **W16.13 Fall into natural body of water striking side**
+7th **W16.131 Fall into natural body of water striking sid causing drowning and submersion**
Excludes1: *drowning and submersion while in natural body of water without fall (W69)*
+7th **W16.132 Fall into natural body of water striking sid causing other injury**

+ **W16.2 Fall in (into) filled bathtub or bucket of water**
+ **W16.21 Fall in (into) filled bathtub**
Excludes1: *fall into empty bathtub (W18.2)*
+7th **W16.211 Fall in (into) filled bathtub causing drowning and submersion**
Excludes1: drowning and submersion while in filled bathtub without fall (W65)
+7th **W16.212 Fall in (into) filled bathtub causing other injury**
+ **W16.22 Fall in (into) bucket of water**
+7th **W16.221 Fall in (into) bucket of water causing drowning and submersion**
+7th **W16.222 Fall in (into) bucket of water causing other injury**
+ **W16.3 Fall into other water**
Fall into fountain
Fall into reservoir
+ **W16.31 Fall into other water striking water surface**
+7th **W16.311 Fall into other water striking water surface causing drowning and submersion**
Excludes1: drowning and submersion while in other water without fall (W73)
+7th **W16.312 Fall into other water striking water surface causing other injury**
+ **W16.32 Fall into other water striking bottom**
+7th **W16.321 Fall into other water striking bottom causing drowning and submersion**
Excludes1: drowning and submersion while in other water without fall (W73)
+7th **W16.322 Fall into other water striking bottom causing other injury**
+ **W16.33 Fall into other water striking wall**
+7th **W16.331 Fall into other water striking wall causing drowning and submersion**
Excludes1: drowning and submersion while in other water without fall (W73)
+7th **W16.332 Fall into other water striking wall causing other injury**
+ **W16.4 Fall into unspecified water**
X+7th **W16.41 Fall into unspecified water causing drowning and submersion**
X+7th **W16.42 Fall into unspecified water causing other injury**
+ **W16.5 Jumping or diving into swimming pool**
+ **W16.51 Jumping or diving into swimming pool striking water surface**
+7th **W16.511 Jumping or diving into swimming pool striking water surface causing drowning and submersion**
Excludes1: drowning and submersion while in swimming pool without jumping or diving (W67)
+7th **W16.512 Jumping or diving into swimming pool striking water surface causing other injury**
+ **W16.52 Jumping or diving into swimming pool striking bottom**
+7th **W16.521 Jumping or diving into swimming pool striking bottom causing drowning and submersion**
Excludes1: drowning and submersion while in swimming pool without jumping or diving (W67)
+7th **W16.522 Jumping or diving into swimming pool striking bottom causing other injury**
+ **W16.53 Jumping or diving into swimming pool striking wall**
+7th **W16.531 Jumping or diving into swimming pool striking wall causing drowning and submersion**
Excludes1: drowning and submersion while in swimming pool without jumping or diving (W67)
+7th **W16.532 Jumping or diving into swimming pool striking wall causing other injury**
+ **W16.6 Jumping or diving into natural body of water**
Jumping or diving into lake
Jumping or diving into open sea
Jumping or diving into river
Jumping or diving into stream
+ **W16.61 Jumping or diving into natural body of water striking water surface**
+7th **W16.611 Jumping or diving into natural body of water striking water surface causing drowning and submersion**
Excludes1: drowning and submersion while in natural body of water without jumping or diving (W69)
+7th **W16.612 Jumping or diving into natural body of water striking water surface causing other injury**
+ **W16.62 Jumping or diving into natural body of water striking bottom**
+7th **W16.621 Jumping or diving into natural body of water striking bottom causing drowning and submersion**
Excludes1: drowning and submersion while in natural body of water without jumping or diving (W69)
+7th **W16.622 Jumping or diving into natural body of water striking bottom causing other injury**
+ **W16.7 Jumping or diving from boat**
Excludes1: *Fall from boat into water -see watercraft accident (V90-V94)*
+ **W16.71 Jumping or diving from boat striking water surface**
+7th **W16.711 Jumping or diving from boat striking water surface causing drowning and submersion**
+7th **W16.712 Jumping or diving from boat striking water surface causing other injury**
+ **W16.72 Jumping or diving from boat striking bottom**
+7th **W16.721 Jumping or diving from boat striking bottom causing drowning and submersion**
+7th **W16.722 Jumping or diving from boat striking bottom causing other injury**
+ **W16.8 Jumping or diving into other water**
Jumping or diving into fountain
Jumping or diving into reservoir
+ **W16.81 Jumping or diving into other water striking water surface**
+7th **W16.811 Jumping or diving into other water striking water surface causing drowning and submersion**
Excludes1: drowning and submersion while in other water without jumping or diving (W73)
+7th **W16.812 Jumping or diving into other water striking water surface causing other injury**
+ **W16.82 Jumping or diving into other water striking bottom**
+7th **W16.821 Jumping or diving into other water striking bottom causing drowning and submersion**
Excludes1: drowning and submersion while in other water without jumping or diving (W73)
+7th **W16.822 Jumping or diving into other water striking bottom causing other injury**
+ **W16.83 Jumping or diving into other water striking wall**
+7th **W16.831 Jumping or diving into other water striking wall causing drowning and submersion**
Excludes1: drowning and submersion while in other water without jumping or diving (W73)
+7th **W16.832 Jumping or diving into other water striking wall causing other injury**
+ **W16.9 Jumping or diving into unspecified water**
X+7th **W16.91 Jumping or diving into unspecified water causing drowning and submersion**
X+7th **W16.92 Jumping or diving into unspecified water causing other injury**

W17 Other fall from one level to another

The appropriate 7th character is to be added to each code from category W17
A initial encounter
D subsequent encounter
S sequela

X+7th **W17.0 Fall into well**
X+7th **W17.1 Fall into storm drain or manhole**
X+7th **W17.2 Fall into hole**
Fall into pit

X+7th **W17.3 Fall into empty swimming pool**
Excludes1: *fall into filled swimming pool (W16.0-)*
X+7th **W17.4 Fall from dock**
+ **W17.8 Other fall from one level to another**
X+7th **W17.81 Fall down embankment (hill)**
X+7th **W17.82 Fall from (out of) grocery cart**
Fall due to grocery cart tipping over
X+7th **W17.89 Other fall from one level to another**
Fall from cherry picker
Fall from lifting device
Fall from mobile elevated work platform [MEWP]
Fall from sky lift

W18 Other slipping, tripping and stumbling and falls

The appropriate 7th character is to be added to each code from category W18
A initial encounter
D subsequent encounter
S sequela

+ **W18.0 Fall due to bumping against object**
Striking against object with subsequent fall
Excludes1: *fall on same level due to slipping, tripping, or stumbling with subsequent striking against object (W01.1-)*
X+7th **W18.00 Striking against unspecified object with subsequent fall**
X+7th **W18.01 Striking against sports equipment with subsequent fall**
X+7th **W18.02 Striking against glass with subsequent fall**
X+7th **W18.09 Striking against other object with subsequent fall**
+ **W18.1 Fall from or off toilet**
X+7th **W18.11 Fall from or off toilet without subsequent striking against object**
Fall from (off) toilet NOS
X+7th **W18.12 Fall from or off toilet with subsequent striking against object**
X+7th **W18.2 Fall in (into) shower or empty bathtub**
Excludes1: *fall in full bathtub causing drowning or submersion (W16.21-)*
+ **W18.3 Other and unspecified fall on same level**
X+7th **W18.30 Fall on same level, unspecified**
X+7th **W18.31 Fall on same level due to stepping on an object**
Fall on same level due to stepping on an animal
Excludes1: *slipping, tripping and stumbling without fall due to stepping on animal (W18.41)*
X+7th **W18.39 Other fall on same level**
+ **W18.4 Slipping, tripping and stumbling without falling**
Excludes1: *collision with another person without fall (W51)*
X+7th **W18.40 Slipping, tripping and stumbling without falling, unspecified**
X+7th **W18.41 Slipping, tripping and stumbling without falling due to stepping on object**
Slipping, tripping and stumbling without falling due to stepping on animal
Excludes1: *slipping, tripping and stumbling with fall due to stepping on animal (W18.31)*
X+7th **W18.42 Slipping, tripping and stumbling without falling due to stepping into hole or opening**
X+7th **W18.43 Slipping, tripping and stumbling without falling due to stepping from one level to another**
X+7th **W18.49 Other slipping, tripping and stumbling without falling**

X+7th **W19 Unspecified fall**
Accidental fall NOS
AHA CC: 4Q, 2012, 95-96

The appropriate 7th character is to be added to code W19
A initial encounter
D subsequent encounter
S sequela

Exposure to inanimate mechanical forces (W20-W49)

Excludes1: *assault (X92-Y08)*
contact or collision with animals or persons (W50-W64)
exposure to inanimate mechanical forces involving military or war operations (Y36.-, Y37.-)
intentional self-harm (X71-X83)

W20 Struck by thrown, projected or falling object
Code first any associated:
cataclysm (X34-X39)
lightning strike (T75.00)
Excludes1: *falling object in machinery accident (W24, W28-W31)*
falling object in transport accident (V01-V99)
object set in motion by explosion (W35-W40)
object set in motion by firearm (W32-W34)
struck by thrown sports equipment (W21.-)

The appropriate 7th character is to be added to each code from category W20
A initial encounter
D subsequent encounter
S sequela

X+7th **W20.0 Struck by falling object in cave-in**
Excludes2: *asphyxiation due to cave-in (T71.21)*
X+7th **W20.1 Struck by object due to collapse of building**
Excludes1: *struck by object due to collapse of burning building (X00.2, X02.2)*
X+7th **W20.8 Other cause of strike by thrown, projected or falling object**
Excludes1: *struck by thrown sports equipment (W21.-)*

W21 Striking against or struck by sports equipment
Excludes1: *assault with sports equipment (Y08.0-)*
striking against or struck by sports equipment with subsequent fall (W18.01)

The appropriate 7th character is to be added to each code from category W21
A initial encounter
D subsequent encounter
S sequela

+ **W21.0 Struck by hit or thrown ball**
X+7th **W21.00 Struck by hit or thrown ball, unspecified type**
X+7th **W21.01 Struck by football**
X+7th **W21.02 Struck by soccer ball**
X+7th **W21.03 Struck by baseball**
X+7th **W21.04 Struck by golf ball**
X+7th **W21.05 Struck by basketball**
X+7th **W21.06 Struck by volleyball**
X+7th **W21.07 Struck by softball**
X+7th **W21.09 Struck by other hit or thrown ball**
+ **W21.1 Struck by bat, racquet or club**
X+7th **W21.11 Struck by baseball bat**
X+7th **W21.12 Struck by tennis racquet**
X+7th **W21.13 Struck by golf club**
X+7th **W21.19 Struck by other bat, racquet or club**
+ **W21.2 Struck by hockey stick or puck**
+ **W21.21 Struck by hockey stick**
+7th **W21.210 Struck by ice hockey stick**
+7th **W21.211 Struck by field hockey stick**
+ **W21.22 Struck by hockey puck**
X+7th **W21.220 Struck by ice hockey puck**
X+7th **W21.221 Struck by field hockey puck**
+ **W21.3 Struck by sports foot wear**
X+7th **W21.31 Struck by shoe cleats**
Stepped on by shoe cleats
X+7th **W21.32 Struck by skate blades**
Skated over by skate blades
X+7th **W21.39 Struck by other sports foot wear**
X+7th **W21.4 Striking against diving board**
Use additional code for subsequent falling into water, if applicable (W16.-)
+ **W21.8 Striking against or struck by other sports equipment**
X+7th **W21.81 Striking against or struck by football helmet**
X+7th **W21.89 Striking against or struck by other sports equipment**
X+7th **W21.9 Striking against or struck by unspecified sports equipment**

W22 Striking against or struck by other objects
Excludes1: *striking against or struck by object with subsequent fall (W18.09)*

The appropriate 7th character is to be added to each code from category W22
A initial encounter
D subsequent encounter
S sequela

+ **W22.0 Striking against stationary object**
Excludes1: *striking against stationary sports equipment (W21.8)*
X+7th **W22.01 Walked into wall**
X+7th **W22.02 Walked into lamppost**

X+7th **W22.03 Walked into furniture**
+ **W22.04 Striking against wall of swimming pool**
+7th **W22.041 Striking against wall of swimming pool causing drowning and submersion**
Excludes1: *drowning and submersion while swimming without striking against wall (W67)*
+7th **W22.042 Striking against wall of swimming pool causing other injury**
X+7th **W22.09 Striking against other stationary object**
+ **W22.1 Striking against or struck by automobile airbag**
X+7th **W22.10 Striking against or struck by unspecified automobile airbag**
X+7th **W22.11 Striking against or struck by driver side automobile airbag**
X+7th **W22.12 Striking against or struck by front passenger side automobile airbag**
X+7th **W22.19 Striking against or struck by other automobile airbag**
X+7th **W22.8 Striking against or struck by other objects**
Striking against or struck by object NOS
Excludes1: *struck by thrown, projected or falling object (W20.-)*

W23 Caught, crushed, jammed or pinched in or between objects

Excludes1: *injury caused by cutting or piercing instruments (W25-W27)*
injury caused by firearms malfunction (W32.1, W33.1-, W34.1-)
injury caused by lifting and transmission devices (W24.-)
injury caused by machinery (W28-W31)
injury caused by nonpowered hand tools (W27.-)
injury caused by transport vehicle being used as a means of transportation (V01-V99)
injury caused by struck by thrown, projected or falling object (W20.-)

The appropriate 7th character is to be added to each code from category W23
A initial encounter
D subsequent encounter
S sequela

X+7th **W23.0 Caught, crushed, jammed, or pinched between moving objects**
X+7th **W23.1 Caught, crushed, jammed, or pinched between stationary objects**

W24 Contact with lifting and transmission devices, not elsewhere classified

Excludes1: *transport accidents (V01-V99)*

The appropriate 7th character is to be added to each code from category W24
A initial encounter
D subsequent encounter
S sequela

X+7th **W24.0 Contact with lifting devices, not elsewhere classified**
Contact with chain hoist
Contact with drive belt
Contact with pulley (block)
X+7th **W24.1 Contact with transmission devices, not elsewhere classified**
Contact with transmission belt or cable

+7th **W25 Contact with sharp glass**

Code first any associated:
injury due to flying glass from explosion or firearm discharge (W32-W40)
transport accident (V00-V99)
Excludes1: *fall on same level due to slipping, tripping and stumbling with subsequent striking against sharp glass (W01.10)*
striking against sharp glass with subsequent fall (W18.02)

The appropriate 7th character is to be added to code W25
A initial encounter
D subsequent encounter
S sequela

W26 Contact with knife, sword or dagger

The appropriate 7th character is to be added to each code from category W26
A initial encounter
D subsequent encounter
S sequela

X+7th **W26.0 Contact with knife**
Excludes1: *contact with electric knife (W29.1)*
X+7th **W26.1 Contact with sword or dagger**

W27 Contact with nonpowered hand tool

The appropriate 7th character is to be added to each code from category W27
A initial encounter
D subsequent encounter
S sequela

X+7th **W27.0 Contact with workbench tool**
Contact with auger
Contact with axe
Contact with chisel
Contact with handsaw
Contact with screwdriver
X+7th **W27.1 Contact with garden tool**
Contact with hoe
Contact with nonpowered lawn mower
Contact with pitchfork
Contact with rake
X+7th **W27.2 Contact with scissors**
X+7th **W27.3 Contact with needle (sewing)**
Excludes1: *contact with hypodermic needle (W46.-)*
X+7th **W27.4 Contact with kitchen utensil**
Contact with fork
Contact with ice-pick
Contact with can-opener NOS
X+7th **W27.5 Contact with paper-cutter**
X+7th **W27.8 Contact with other nonpowered hand tool**
Contact with nonpowered sewing machine
Contact with shovel

X+7th **W28 Contact with powered lawn mower**

Powered lawn mower (commercial) (residential)
Excludes1: *contact with nonpowered lawn mower (W27.1)*
Excludes2: *exposure to electric current (W86.-)*

The appropriate 7th character is to be added to code W28
A initial encounter
D subsequent encounter
S sequela

W29 Contact with other powered hand tools and household machinery

Excludes1: *contact with commercial machinery (W31.82)*
contact with hot household appliance (X15)
contact with nonpowered hand tool (W27.-)
exposure to electric current (W86)

The appropriate 7th character is to be added to each code from category W29
A initial encounter
D subsequent encounter
S sequela

X+7th **W29.0 Contact with powered kitchen appliance**
Contact with blender
Contact with can-opener
Contact with garbage disposal
Contact with mixer
X+7th **W29.1 Contact with electric knife**
X+7th **W29.2 Contact with other powered household machinery**
Contact with electric fan
Contact with powered dryer (clothes) (powered) (spin)
Contact with washing-machine
Contact with sewing machine
X+7th **W29.3 Contact with powered garden and outdoor hand tools and machinery**
Contact with chainsaw
Contact with edger
Contact with garden cultivator (tiller)
Contact with hedge trimmer
Contact with other powered garden tool
Excludes1: *contact with powered lawn mower (W28)*
X+7th **W29.4 Contact with nail gun**
X+7th **W29.8 Contact with other powered powered hand tools and household machinery**
Contact with do-it-yourself tool NOS

W30 Contact with agricultural machinery

Includes: animal-powered farm machine
Excludes1: *agricultural transport vehicle accident (V01-V99)*
explosion of grain store (W40.8)
exposure to electric current (W86.-)

The appropriate 7th character is to be added to each code from category W30
A initial encounter
D subsequent encounter
S sequela

X+7th **W30.0 Contact with combine harvester**
Contact with reaper
Contact with thresher
X+7th **W30.1 Contact with power take-off devices (PTO)**
X+7th **W30.2 Contact with hay derrick**
X+7th **W30.3 Contact with grain storage elevator**
Excludes1: *explosion of grain store (W40.8)*
\+ **W30.8 Contact with other specified agricultural machinery**
X+7th **W30.81 Contact with agricultural transport vehicle in stationary use**
Contact with agricultural transport vehicle under repair, not on public roadway
Excludes1: *agricultural transport vehicle accident (V01-V99)*
X+7th **W30.89 Contact with other specified agricultural machinery**
X+7th **W30.9 Contact with unspecified agricultural machinery**
Contact with farm machinery NOS

W31 Contact with other and unspecified machinery

Excludes1: *contact with agricultural machinery (W30.-)*
contact with machinery in transport under own power or being towed by a vehicle (V01-V99)
exposure to electric current (W86)

The appropriate 7th character is to be added to each code from category W31
A initial encounter
D subsequent encounter
S sequela

X+7th **W31.0 Contact with mining and earth-drilling machinery**
Contact with bore or drill (land) (seabed)
Contact with shaft hoist
Contact with shaft lift
Contact with undercutter
X+7th **W31.1 Contact with metalworking machines**
Contact with abrasive wheel
Contact with forging machine
Contact with lathe
Contact with mechanical shears
Contact with metal drilling machine
Contact with milling machine
Contact with power press
Contact with rolling-mill
Contact with metal sawing machine
X+7th **W31.2 Contact with powered woodworking and forming machines**
Contact with band saw
Contact with bench saw
Contact with circular saw
Contact with molding machine
Contact with overhead plane
Contact with powered saw
Contact with radial saw
Contact with sander
Excludes1: *nonpowered woodworking tools (W27.0)*
X+7th **W31.3 Contact with prime movers**
Contact with gas turbine
Contact with internal combustion engine
Contact with steam engine
Contact with water driven turbine
\+ **W31.8 Contact with other specified machinery**
X+7th **W31.81 Contact with recreational machinery**
Contact with roller coaster
X+7th **W31.82 Contact with other commercial machinery**
Contact with commercial electric fan
Contact with commercial kitchen appliances
Contact with commercial powered dryer (clothes) (powered) (spin)
Contact with commercial washing-machine
Contact with commercial sewing machine
Excludes1: *contact with household machinery (W29.-)*
contact with powered lawn mower (W28)
X+7th **W31.83 Contact with special construction vehicle in stationary use**
Contact with special construction vehicle under repair, not on public roadway
Excludes1: *special construction vehicle accident (V01-V99)*
X+7th **W31.89 Contact with other specified machinery**
X+7th **W31.9 Contact with unspecified machinery**
Contact with machinery NOS

W32 Accidental handgun discharge and malfunction

Includes: accidental discharge and malfunction of gun for single hand use
accidental discharge and malfunction of pistol
accidental discharge and malfunction of revolver
Handgun discharge and malfunction NOS
Excludes1: *accidental airgun discharge and malfunction (W34.010, W34.110)*
accidental BB gun discharge and malfunction (W34.010, W34.110)
accidental pellet gun discharge and malfunction (W34.010, W34.110)
accidental shotgun discharge and malfunction (W33.01, W33.11)
assault by handgun discharge (X93)
handgun discharge involving legal intervention (Y35.0-)
handgun discharge involving military or war operations (Y36.4-)
intentional self-harm by handgun discharge (X72)
Very pistol discharge and malfunction (W34.09, W34.19)

The appropriate 7th character is to be added to each code from category W32
A initial encounter
D subsequent encounter
S sequela

X+7th **W32.0 Accidental handgun discharge**
X+7th **W32.1 Accidental handgun malfunction**
Injury due to explosion of handgun (parts)
Injury due to malfunction of mechanism or component of handgun
Injury due to recoil of handgun
Powder burn from handgun

W33 Accidental rifle, shotgun and larger firearm discharge and malfunction

Includes: rifle, shotgun and larger firearm discharge and malfunction NOS
Excludes1: *accidental airgun discharge and malfunction (W34.010, W34.110)*
accidental BB gun discharge and malfunction (W34.010, W34.110)
accidental handgun discharge and malfunction (W32.-)
accidental pellet gun discharge and malfunction (W34.010, W34.110)
assault by rifle, shotgun and larger firearm discharge (X94)
firearm discharge involving legal intervention (Y35.0-)
firearm discharge involving military or war operations (Y36.4-)
intentional self-harm by rifle, shotgun and larger firearm discharge (X73)

The appropriate 7th character is to be added to each code from category W33
A initial encounter
D subsequent encounter
S sequela

\+ **W33.0 Accidental rifle, shotgun and larger firearm discharge**
X+7th **W33.00 Accidental discharge of unspecified larger firearm**
Discharge of unspecified larger firearm NOS
X+7th **W33.01 Accidental discharge of shotgun**
Discharge of shotgun NOS
X+7th **W33.02 Accidental discharge of hunting rifle**
Discharge of hunting rifle NOS
X+7th **W33.03 Accidental discharge of machine gun**
Discharge of machine gun NOS
X+7th **W33.09 Accidental discharge of other larger firearm**
Discharge of other larger firearm NOS

+ **W33.1 Accidental rifle, shotgun and larger firearm malfunction**
Injury due to explosion of rifle, shotgun and larger firearm (parts)
Injury due to malfunction of mechanism or component of rifle, shotgun and larger firearm
Injury due to piercing, cutting, crushing or pinching due to (by) slide trigger mechanism, scope or other gun part
Injury due to recoil of rifle, shotgun and larger firearm
Powder burn from rifle, shotgun and larger firearm

X+7th **W33.10 Accidental malfunction of unspecified larger firearm**
Malfunction of unspecified larger firearm NOS

X+7th **W33.11 Accidental malfunction of shotgun**
Malfunction of shotgun NOS

X+7th **W33.12 Accidental malfunction of hunting rifle**
Malfunction of hunting rifle NOS

X+7th **W33.13 Accidental malfunction of machine gun**
Malfunction of machine gun NOS

X+7th **W33.19 Accidental malfunction of other larger firearm**
Malfunction of other larger firearm NOS

W34 Accidental discharge and malfunction from other and unspecified firearms and guns

The appropriate 7th character is to be added to each code from category W34
A initial encounter
D subsequent encounter
S sequela

+ **W34.0 Accidental discharge from other and unspecified firearms and guns**

X+7th **W34.00 Accidental discharge from unspecified firearms or gun**
Discharge from firearm NOS
Gunshot wound NOS
Shot NOS

+ **W34.01 Accidental discharge of gas, air or spring-operated guns**

+7th **W34.010 Accidental discharge of airgun**
Accidental discharge of BB gun
Accidental discharge of pellet gun

+7th **W34.011 Accidental discharge of paintball gun**
Accidental injury due to paintball discharge

+7th **W34.018 Accidental discharge of other gas, air or spring-operated gun**

X+7th **W34.09 Accidental discharge from other specified firearms**
Accidental discharge from Very pistol [flare]

+ **W34.1 Accidental malfunction from other and unspecified firearms and guns**

X+7th **W34.10 Accidental malfunction from unspecified firearms or gun**
Firearm malfunction NOS

+ **W34.11 Accidental malfunction of gas, air or spring-operated guns**

+7th **W34.110 Accidental malfunction of airgun**
Accidental malfunction of BB gun
Accidental malfunction of pellet gun

+7th **W34.111 Accidental malfunction of paintball gun**
Accidental injury due to paintball gun malfunction

+7th **W34.118 Accidental malfunction of other gas, air or spring-operated gun**

X+7th **W34.19 Accidental malfunction from other specified firearms**
Accidental malfunction from Very pistol [flare]

+7th **W35 Explosion and rupture of boiler**

Excludes1: *explosion and rupture of boiler on watercraft (V93.4)*

The appropriate 7th character is to be added to code W35
A initial encounter
D subsequent encounter
S sequela

W36 Explosion and rupture of gas cylinder

The appropriate 7th character is to be added to each code from category W36
A initial encounter
D subsequent encounter
S sequela

X+7th **W36.1 Explosion and rupture of aerosol can**
X+7th **W36.2 Explosion and rupture of air tank**
X+7th **W36.3 Explosion and rupture of pressurized-gas tank**
X+7th **W36.8 Explosion and rupture of other gas cylinder**
X+7th **W36.9 Explosion and rupture of unspecified gas cylinder**

W37 Explosion and rupture of pressurized tire, pipe or hose

The appropriate 7th character is to be added to each code from category W37
A initial encounter
D subsequent encounter
S sequela

X+7th **W37.0 Explosion of bicycle tire**
X+7th **W37.8 Explosion and rupture of other pressurized tire, pipe or hose**

X+7th **W38 Explosion and rupture of other specified pressurized devices**

The appropriate 7th character is to be added to code W38
A initial encounter
D subsequent encounter
S sequela

X+7th **W39 Discharge of firework**

The appropriate 7th character is to be added to code W39
A initial encounter
D subsequent encounter
S sequela

W40 Explosion of other materials

Excludes1: *assault by explosive material (X96)*
explosion involving legal intervention (Y35.1-)
explosion involving military or war operations (Y36.0-, Y36.2-)
intentional self-harm by explosive material (X75)

The appropriate 7th character is to be added to each code from category W40
A initial encounter
D subsequent encounter
S sequela

X+7th **W40.0 Explosion of blasting material**
Explosion of blasting cap
Explosion of detonator
Explosion of dynamite
Explosion of explosive (any) used in blasting operations

X+7th **W40.1 Explosion of explosive gases**
Explosion of acetylene
Explosion of butane
Explosion of coal gas
Explosion in mine NOS
Explosion of explosive gas
Explosion of fire damp
Explosion of gasoline fumes
Explosion of methane
Explosion of propane

X+7th **W40.8 Explosion of other specified explosive materials**
Explosion in dump NOS
Explosion in factory NOS
Explosion in grain store
Explosion in munitions
Excludes1: *explosion involving legal intervention (Y35.1-)*
explosion involving military or war operations (Y36.0-, Y36.2-)

X+7th **W40.9 Explosion of unspecified explosive materials**
Explosion NOS

W42 Exposure to noise

The appropriate 7th character is to be added to each code from category W42
A initial encounter
D subsequent encounter
S sequela

X+7th **W42.0 Exposure to supersonic waves**
X+7th **W42.9 Exposure to other noise**
Exposure to sound waves NOS

W45 Foreign body or object entering through skin

Excludes2: *contact with hand tools (nonpowered) (powered) (W27-W29)*
contact with knife, sword or dagger (W26.-)
contact with sharp glass (W25.-)
struck by objects (W20-W22)

The appropriate 7th character is to be added to each code from category W45
A initial encounter
D subsequent encounter
S sequela

X+7th **W45.0 Nail entering through skin**
X+7th **W45.1 Paper entering through skin**
Paper cut

X+7th **W45.2 Lid of can entering through skin**
X+7th **W45.8 Other foreign body or object entering through skin**
Splinter in skin NOS

W46 Contact with hypodermic needle

The appropriate 7th character is to be added to each code from category W46
A initial encounter
D subsequent encounter
S sequela

X+7th **W46.0 Contact with hypodermic needle**
Hypodermic needle stick NOS
X+7th **W46.1 Contact with contaminated hypodermic needle**

W49 Exposure to other inanimate mechanical forces

Includes: exposure to abnormal gravitational [G] forces
exposure to inanimate mechanical forces NEC
Excludes1: *exposure to inanimate mechanical forces involving military or war operations (Y36.-, Y37.-)*

The appropriate 7th character is to be added to each code from category W49
A initial encounter
D subsequent encounter
S sequela

+ **W49.0 Item causing external constriction**
X+7th **W49.01 Hair causing external constriction**
X+7th **W49.02 String or thread causing external constriction**
X+7th **W49.03 Rubber band causing external constriction**
X+7th **W49.04 Ring or other jewelry causing external constriction**
X+7th **W49.09 Other specified item causing external constriction**
X+7th **W49.9 Exposure to other inanimate mechanical forces**

Exposure to animate mechanical forces (W50-W64)

Excludes1: *Toxic effect of contact with venomous animals and plants (T63.-)*

W50 Accidental hit, strike, kick, twist, bite or scratch by another person

Includes: hit, strike, kick, twist, bite, or scratch by another person NOS
Excludes1: *assault by bodily force (Y04)*
struck by objects (W20-W22)

The appropriate 7th character is to be added to each code from category W50
A initial encounter
D subsequent encounter
S sequela

X+7th **W50.0 Accidental hit or strike by another person**
Hit or strike by another person NOS
X+7th **W50.1 Accidental kick by another person**
Kick by another person NOS
X+7th **W50.2 Accidental twist by another person**
Twist by another person NOS
X+7th **W50.3 Accidental bite by another person**
Human bite
Bite by another person NOS
X+7th **W50.4 Accidental scratch by another person**
Scratch by another person NOS

X+7th **W51 Accidental striking against or bumped into by another person**

Excludes1: *assault by striking against or bumping into by another person (Y04.2)*
fall due to collision with another person (W03)

The appropriate 7th character is to be added to code W51
A initial encounter
D subsequent encounter
S sequela

X+7th **W52 Crushed, pushed or stepped on by crowd or human stampede**

Crushed, pushed or stepped on by crowd or human stampede with or without fall

The appropriate 7th character is to be added to code W52
A initial encounter
D subsequent encounter
S sequela

+ **W53 Contact with rodent**

Includes: contact with saliva, feces or urine of rodent

The appropriate 7th character is to be added to each code from category W53
A initial encounter
D subsequent encounter
S sequela

+ **W53.0 Contact with mouse**
X+7th **W53.01 Bitten by mouse**
X+7th **W53.09 Other contact with mouse**
+ **W53.1 Contact with rat**
X+7th **W53.11 Bitten by rat**
X+7th **W53.19 Other contact with rat**
+ **W53.2 Contact with squirrel**
X+7th **W53.21 Bitten by squirrel**
X+7th **W53.29 Other contact with squirrel**
+ **W53.8 Contact with other rodent**
X+7th **W53.81 Bitten by other rodent**
X+7th **W53.89 Other contact with other rodent**

W54 Contact with dog

Includes: contact with saliva, feces or urine of dog

The appropriate 7th character is to be added to each code from category W54
A initial encounter
D subsequent encounter
S sequela

X+7th **W54.0 Bitten by dog**
X+7th **W54.1 Struck by dog**
Knocked over by dog
X+7th **W54.8 Other contact with dog**

W55 Contact with other mammals

Includes: contact with saliva, feces or urine of mammal
Excludes1: *animal being ridden- see transport accidents*
bitten or struck by dog (W54)
bitten or struck by rodent (W53.-)
contact with marine mammals (W56.-)

The appropriate 7th character is to be added to each code from category W55
A initial encounter
D subsequent encounter
S sequela

+ **W55.0 Contact with cat**
X+7th **W55.01 Bitten by cat**
X+7th **W55.03 Scratched by cat**
X+7th **W55.09 Other contact with cat**
+ **W55.1 Contact with horse**
X+7th **W55.11 Bitten by horse**
X+7th **W55.12 Struck by horse**
X+7th **W55.19 Other contact with horse**
+ **W55.2 Contact with cow**
Contact with bull
X+7th **W55.21 Bitten by cow**
X+7th **W55.22 Struck by cow**
Gored by bull
X+7th **W55.29 Other contact with cow**
+ **W55.3 Contact with other hoof stock**
Contact with goats
Contact with sheep
X+7th **W55.31 Bitten by other hoof stock**
X+7th **W55.32 Struck by other hoof stock**
Gored by goat
Gored by ram
X+7th **W55.39 Other contact with other hoof stock**
+ **W55.4 Contact with pig**
X+7th **W55.41 Bitten by pig**
X+7th **W55.42 Struck by pig**
X+7th **W55.49 Other contact with pig**
+ **W55.5 Contact with raccoon**
X+7th **W55.51 Bitten by raccoon**
X+7th **W55.52 Struck by raccoon**
X+7th **W55.59 Other contact with raccoon**
+ **W55.8 Contact with other mammals**
X+7th **W55.81 Bitten by other mammals**
X+7th **W55.82 Struck by other mammals**
X+7th **W55.89 Other contact with other mammals**

W56 Contact with nonvenomous marine animal

Excludes1: *contact with venomous marine animal (T63.-)*

The appropriate 7th character is to be added to each code from category W56
A initial encounter
D subsequent encounter
S sequela

\+ **W56.0 Contact with dolphin**
X+7th **W56.01 Bitten by dolphin**
X+7th **W56.02 Struck by dolphin**
X+7th **W56.09 Other contact with dolphin**
\+ **W56.1 Contact with sea lion**
X+7th **W56.11 Bitten by sea lion**
X+7th **W56.12 Struck by sea lion**
X+7th **W56.19 Other contact with sea lion**
\+ **W56.2 Contact with orca**
Contact with killer whale
X+7th **W56.21 Bitten by orca**
X+7th **W56.22 Struck by orca**
X+7th **W56.29 Other contact with orca**
\+ **W56.3 Contact with other marine mammals**
X+7th **W56.31 Bitten by other marine mammals**
X+7th **W56.32 Struck by other marine mammals**
X+7th **W56.39 Other contact with other marine mammals**
\+ **W56.4 Contact with shark**
X+7th **W56.41 Bitten by shark**
X+7th **W56.42 Struck by shark**
X+7th **W56.49 Other contact with shark**
\+ **W56.5 Contact with other fish**
X+7th **W56.51 Bitten by other fish**
X+7th **W56.52 Struck by other fish**
X+7th **W56.59 Other contact with other fish**
\+ **W56.8 Contact with other nonvenomous marine animals**
X+7th **W56.81 Bitten by other nonvenomous marine animals**
X+7th **W56.82 Struck by other nonvenomous marine animals**
X+7th **W56.89 Other contact with other nonvenomous marine animals**

+7th **W57 Bitten or stung by nonvenomous insect and other nonvenomous arthropods**

Excludes1: *contact with venomous insects and arthropods (T63.2-, T63.3-, T63.4-)*

The appropriate 7th character is to be added to code W57
A initial encounter
D subsequent encounter
S sequela

W58 Contact with crocodile or alligator

The appropriate 7th character is to be added to each code from category W58
A initial encounter
D subsequent encounter
S sequela

\+ **W58.0 Contact with alligator**
X+7th **W58.01 Bitten by alligator**
X+7th **W58.02 Struck by alligator**
X+7th **W58.03 Crushed by alligator**
X+7th **W58.09 Other contact with alligator**
\+ **W58.1 Contact with crocodile**
X+7th **W58.11 Bitten by crocodile**
X+7th **W58.12 Struck by crocodile**
X+7th **W58.13 Crushed by crocodile**
X+7th **W58.19 Other contact with crocodile**

W59 Contact with other nonvenomous reptiles

Excludes1: *contact with venomous reptile (T63.0-, T63.1-)*

The appropriate 7th character is to be added to each code from category W59
A initial encounter
D subsequent encounter
S sequela

\+ **W59.0 Contact with nonvenomous lizards**
X+7th **W59.01 Bitten by nonvenomous lizards**
X+7th **W59.02 Struck by nonvenomous lizards**
X+7th **W59.09 Other contact with nonvenomous lizards**
Exposure to nonvenomous lizards
\+ **W59.1 Contact with nonvenomous snakes**
X+7th **W59.11 Bitten by nonvenomous snake**
X+7th **W59.12 Struck by nonvenomous snake**
X+7th **W59.13 Crushed by nonvenomous snake**
X+7th **W59.19 Other contact with nonvenomous snake**
\+ **W59.2 Contact with turtles**
Excludes1: *contact with tortoises (W59.8-)*
X+7th **W59.21 Bitten by turtle**
X+7th **W59.22 Struck by turtle**
X+7th **W59.29 Other contact with turtle**
Exposure to turtles
\+ **W59.8 Contact with other nonvenomous reptiles**
X+7th **W59.81 Bitten by other nonvenomous reptiles**
X+7th **W59.82 Struck by other nonvenomous reptiles**
X+7th **W59.83 Crushed by other nonvenomous reptiles**
X+7th **W59.89 Other contact with other nonvenomous reptiles**

X+7th **W60 Contact with nonvenomous plant thorns and spines and sharp leaves**

Excludes1: *Contact with venomous plants (T63.7-)*

The appropriate 7th character is to be added to code W60
A initial encounter
D subsequent encounter
S sequela

W61 Contact with birds (domestic) (wild)

Includes: contact with excreta of birds

The appropriate 7th character is to be added to each code from category W61
A initial encounter
D subsequent encounter
S sequela

\+ **W61.0 Contact with parrot**
X+7th **W61.01 Bitten by parrot**
X+7th **W61.02 Struck by parrot**
X+7th **W61.09 Other contact with parrot**
Exposure to parrots
\+ **W61.1 Contact with macaw**
X+7th **W61.11 Bitten by macaw**
X+7th **W61.12 Struck by macaw**
X+7th **W61.19 Other contact with macaw**
Exposure to macaws
\+ **W61.2 Contact with other psittacines**
X+7th **W61.21 Bitten by other psittacines**
X+7th **W61.22 Struck by other psittacines**
X+7th **W61.29 Other contact with other psittacines**
Exposure to other psittacines
\+ **W61.3 Contact with chicken**
X+7th **W61.32 Struck by chicken**
X+7th **W61.33 Pecked by chicken**
X+7th **W61.39 Other contact with chicken**
Exposure to chickens
\+ **W61.4 Contact with turkey**
X+7th **W61.42 Struck by turkey**
X+7th **W61.43 Pecked by turkey**
X+7th **W61.49 Other contact with turkey**
\+ **W61.5 Contact with goose**
X+7th **W61.51 Bitten by goose**
X+7th **W61.52 Struck by goose**
X+7th **W61.59 Other contact with goose**
\+ **W61.6 Contact with duck**
X+7th **W61.61 Bitten by duck**
X+7th **W61.62 Struck by duck**
X+7th **W61.69 Other contact with duck**
\+ **W61.9 Contact with other birds**
X+7th **W61.91 Bitten by other birds**
X+7th **W61.92 Struck by other birds**
X+7th **W61.99 Other contact with other birds**
Contact with bird NOS

W62 Contact with nonvenomous amphibians

Excludes1: *contact with venomous amphibians (T63.81-R63.83)*

The appropriate 7th character is to be added to each code from category W62
A initial encounter
D subsequent encounter
S sequela

X+7th **W62.0 Contact with nonvenomous frogs**
X+7th **W62.1 Contact with nonvenomous toads**
X+7th **W62.9 Contact with other nonvenomous amphibians**

X+7th **W64 Exposure to other animate mechanical forces**

Includes: exposure to nonvenomous animal NOS
Excludes1: *contact with venomous animal (T63.-)*

The appropriate 7th character is to be added to code W64
A initial encounter
D subsequent encounter
S sequela

Accidental non-transport drowning and submersion (W65-W74)

Excludes1: *accidental drowning and submersion due to fall into water (W16.-)*
accidental drowning and submersion due to water transport accident (V90.-, V92.-)

Excludes2: *accidental drowning and submersion due to cataclysm (X34-X39)*

X+7th **W65 Accidental drowning and submersion while in bath-tub**

Excludes1: *accidental drowning and submersion due to fall in (into) bathtub (W16.211)*

The appropriate 7th character is to be added to code W65
A initial encounter
D subsequent encounter
S sequela

X+7th **W67 Accidental drowning and submersion while in swimming-pool**

Excludes1: *accidental drowning and submersion due to fall into swimming pool (W16.011, W16.021, W16.031)*
accidental drowning and submersion due to striking into wall of swimming pool (W22.041)

The appropriate 7th character is to be added to code W67
A initial encounter
D subsequent encounter
S sequela

X+7th **W69 Accidental drowning and submersion while in natural water**

Accidental drowning and submersion while in lake
Accidental drowning and submersion while in open sea
Accidental drowning and submersion while in river
Accidental drowning and submersion while in stream
Excludes1: *accidental drowning and submersion due to fall into natural body of water (W16.111, W16.121, W16.131)*

The appropriate 7th character is to be added to code W69
A initial encounter
D subsequent encounter
S sequela

X+7th **W73 Other specified cause of accidental non-transport drowning and submersion**

Accidental drowning and submersion while in quenching tank
Accidental drowning and submersion while in reservoir
Excludes1: *accidental drowning and submersion due to fall into other water (W16.311, W16.321, W16.331)*

The appropriate 7th character is to be added to code W73
A initial encounter
D subsequent encounter
S sequela

X+7th **W74 Unspecified cause of accidental drowning and submersion**

Drowning NOS

The appropriate 7th character is to be added to code W74
A initial encounter
D subsequent encounter
S sequela

Exposure to electric current, radiation and extreme ambient air temperature and pressure (W85-W99)

Excludes1: *exposure to:*
failure in dosage of radiation or temperature during surgical and medical care (Y63.2-Y63.5)
lightning (T75.0-)
natural cold (X31)
natural heat (X30)
natural radiation NOS (X39)
radiological procedure and radiotherapy (Y84.2)
sunlight (X32)

X+7th **W85 Exposure to electric transmission lines**

Broken power line

The appropriate 7th character is to be added to code W85
A initial encounter
D subsequent encounter
S sequela

W86 Exposure to other specified electric current

The appropriate 7th character is to be added to each code from category W86
A initial encounter
D subsequent encounter
S sequela

X+7th **W86.0 Exposure to domestic wiring and appliances**
X+7th **W86.1 Exposure to industrial wiring, appliances and electrical machinery**
Exposure to conductors
Exposure to control apparatus
Exposure to electrical equipment and machinery
Exposure to transformers
X+7th **W86.8 Exposure to other electric current**
Exposure to wiring and appliances in or on farm (not farmhouse)
Exposure to wiring and appliances outdoors
Exposure to wiring and appliances in or on public building
Exposure to wiring and appliances in or on residential institutions
Exposure to wiring and appliances in or on schools

W88 Exposure to ionizing radiation

Excludes1: *exposure to sunlight (X32)*

The appropriate 7th character is to be added to each code from category W88
A initial encounter
D subsequent encounter
S sequela

X+7th **W88.0 Exposure to X-rays**
X+7th **W88.1 Exposure to radioactive isotopes**
X+7th **W88.8 Exposure to other ionizing radiation**

W89 Exposure to man-made visible and ultraviolet light

Includes: exposure to welding light (arc)
Excludes2: *exposure to sunlight (X32)*

The appropriate 7th character is to be added to each code from category W89
A initial encounter
D subsequent encounter
S sequela

X+7th **W89.0 Exposure to welding light (arc)**
X+7th **W89.1 Exposure to tanning bed**
X+7th **W89.8 Exposure to other man-made visible and ultraviolet light**
X+7th **W89.9 Exposure to unspecified man-made visible and ultraviolet light**

W90 Exposure to other nonionizing radiation

Excludes1: *exposure to sunlight (X32)*

The appropriate 7th character is to be added to each code from category W90
A initial encounter
D subsequent encounter
S sequela

X+7th **W90.0 Exposure to radiofrequency**
X+7th **W90.1 Exposure to infrared radiation**
X+7th **W90.2 Exposure to laser radiation**
X+7th **W90.8 Exposure to other nonionizing radiation**

X+7th **W92 Exposure to excessive heat of man-made origin**

The appropriate 7th character is to be added to code W92
A initial encounter
D subsequent encounter
S sequela

W93 Exposure to excessive cold of man-made origin

The appropriate 7th character is to be added to each code from category W93
A initial encounter
D subsequent encounter
S sequela

\+ **W93.0 Contact with or inhalation of dry ice**
X+7th **W93.01 Contact with dry ice**
X+7th **W93.02 Inhalation of dry ice**
\+ **W93.1 Contact with or inhalation of liquid air**
X+7th **W93.11 Contact with liquid air**
Contact with liquid hydrogen
Contact with liquid nitrogen
X+7th **W93.12 Inhalation of liquid air**
Inhalation of liquid hydrogen
Inhalation of liquid nitrogen
X+7th **W93.2 Prolonged exposure in deep freeze unit or refrigerator**
X+7th **W93.8 Exposure to other excessive cold of man-made origin**

W94 Exposure to high and low air pressure and changes in air pressure

The appropriate 7th character is to be added to each code from category W94
A initial encounter
D subsequent encounter
S sequela

X+7th **W94.0 Exposure to prolonged high air pressure**
+ **W94.1 Exposure to prolonged low air pressure**
X+7th **W94.11 Exposure to residence or prolonged visit at high altitude**
X+7th **W94.12 Exposure to other prolonged low air pressure**
+ **W94.2 Exposure to rapid changes in air pressure during ascent**
X+7th **W94.21 Exposure to reduction in atmospheric pressure while surfacing from deep-water diving**
X+7th **W94.22 Exposure to reduction in atmospheric pressure while surfacing from underground**
X+7th **W94.23 Exposure to sudden change in air pressure in aircraft during ascent**
X+7th **W94.29 Exposure to other rapid changes in air pressure during ascent**
+ **W94.3 Exposure to rapid changes in air pressure during descent**
X+7th **W94.31 Exposure to sudden change in air pressure in aircraft during descent**
X+7th **W94.32 Exposure to high air pressure from rapid descent in water**
X+7th **W94.39 Exposure to other rapid changes in air pressure during descent**

X+7th **W99 Exposure to other man-made environmental factors**

The appropriate 7th character is to be added to code W99
A initial encounter
D subsequent encounter
S sequela

Exposure to smoke, fire and flames (X00-X08)

Excludes1: *arson (X97)*
Excludes2: *explosions (W35-W40)*
lightning (T75.0-)
transport accident (V01-V99)

X00 Exposure to uncontrolled fire in building or structure

Includes: conflagration in building or structure
Code first any associated cataclysm
Excludes2: *Exposure to ignition or melting of nightwear (X05)*
Exposure to ignition or melting of other clothing and apparel (X06.-)
Exposure to other specified smoke, fire and flames (X08.-)

The appropriate 7th character is to be added to each code from category X00
A initial encounter
D subsequent encounter
S sequela

X+7th **X00.0 Exposure to flames in uncontrolled fire in building or structure**
X+7th **X00.1 Exposure to smoke in uncontrolled fire in building or structure**
X+7th **X00.2 Injury due to collapse of burning building or structure in uncontrolled fire**
Excludes1: *injury due to collapse of building not on fire (W20.1)*
X+7th **X00.3 Fall from burning building or structure in uncontrolled fire**
X+7th **X00.4 Hit by object from burning building or structure in uncontrolled fire**
X+7th **X00.5 Jump from burning building or structure in uncontrolled fire**
X+7th **X00.8 Other exposure to uncontrolled fire in building or structure**

X01 Exposure to uncontrolled fire, not in building or structure

Includes: exposure to forest fire

The appropriate 7th character is to be added to each code from category X01
A initial encounter
D subsequent encounter
S sequela

X+7th **X01.0 Exposure to flames in uncontrolled fire, not in building or structure**
X+7th **X01.1 Exposure to smoke in uncontrolled fire, not in building or structure**
X+7th **X01.3 Fall due to uncontrolled fire, not in building or structure**
X+7th **X01.4 Hit by object due to uncontrolled fire, not in building or structure**
X+7th **X01.8 Other exposure to uncontrolled fire, not in building or structure**

X02 Exposure to controlled fire in building or structure

Includes: exposure to fire in fireplace
exposure to fire in stove

The appropriate 7th character is to be added to each code from category X02
A initial encounter
D subsequent encounter
S sequela

X+7th **X02.0 Exposure to flames in controlled fire in building or structure**
X+7th **X02.1 Exposure to smoke in controlled fire in building or structure**
X+7th **X02.2 Injury due to collapse of burning building or structure in controlled fire**
Excludes1: *injury due to collapse of building not on fire (W20.1)*
X+7th **X02.3 Fall from burning building or structure in controlled fire**
X+7th **X02.4 Hit by object from burning building or structure in controlled fire**
X+7th **X02.5 Jump from burning building or structure in controlled fire**
X+7th **X02.8 Other exposure to controlled fire in building or structure**

X03 Exposure to controlled fire, not in building or structure

Includes: exposure to bon fire
exposure to camp-fire
exposure to trash fire

The appropriate 7th character is to be added to each code from category X03
A initial encounter
D subsequent encounter
S sequela

X+7th **X03.0 Exposure to flames in controlled fire, not in building or structure**
X+7th **X03.1 Exposure to smoke in controlled fire, not in building or structure**
X+7th **X03.3 Fall due to controlled fire, not in building or structure**
X+7th **X03.4 Hit by object due to controlled fire, not in building or structure**
X+7th **X03.8 Other exposure to controlled fire, not in building or structure**

X+7th **X04 Exposure to ignition of highly flammable material**

Exposure to ignition of gasoline
Exposure to ignition of kerosene
Exposure to ignition of petrol
Excludes2: *exposure to ignition or melting of nightwear (X05)*
exposure to ignition or melting of other clothing and apparel (X06)

The appropriate 7th character is to be added to code X04
A initial encounter
D subsequent encounter
S sequela

X+7th **X05 Exposure to ignition or melting of nightwear**

Excludes2: *exposure to uncontrolled fire in building or structure (X00.-)*
exposure to uncontrolled fire, not in building or structure (X01.-)
exposure to controlled fire in building or structure (X02.-)
exposure to controlled fire, not in building or structure (X03.-)
exposure to ignition of highly flammable materials (X04.-)

The appropriate 7th character is to be added to code X05
A initial encounter
D subsequent encounter
S sequela

X06 Exposure to ignition or melting of other clothing and apparel

Excludes2: *exposure to uncontrolled fire in building or structure (X00.-)*
exposure to uncontrolled fire, not in building or structure (X01.-)
exposure to controlled fire in building or structure (X02.-)
exposure to controlled fire, not in building or structure (X03.-)
exposure to ignition of highly flammable materials (X04.-)

The appropriate 7th character is to be added to each code from category X06
A initial encounter
D subsequent encounter
S sequela

X+7th **X06.0 Exposure to ignition of plastic jewelry**
X+7th **X06.1 Exposure to melting of plastic jewelry**
X+7th **X06.2 Exposure to ignition of other clothing and apparel**
X+7th **X06.3 Exposure to melting of other clothing and apparel**

X08 Exposure to other specified smoke, fire and flames

The appropriate 7th character is to be added to each code from category X08
A initial encounter
D subsequent encounter
S sequela

\+ **X08.0 Exposure to bed fire**
Exposure to mattress fire
X+7th **X08.00 Exposure to bed fire due to unspecified burning material**
X+7th **X08.01 Exposure to bed fire due to burning cigarette**
X+7th **X08.09 Exposure to bed fire due to other burning material**
\+ **X08.1 Exposure to sofa fire**
X+7th **X08.10 Exposure to sofa fire due to unspecified burning material**
X+7th **X08.11 Exposure to sofa fire due to burning cigarette**
X+7th **X08.19 Exposure to sofa fire due to other burning material**
\+ **X08.2 Exposure to other furniture fire**
X+7th **X08.20 Exposure to other furniture fire due to unspecified burning material**
X+7th **X08.21 Exposure to other furniture fire due to burning cigarette**
X+7th **X08.29 Exposure to other furniture fire due to other burning material**
X+7th **X08.8 Exposure to other specified smoke, fire and flames**

Contact with heat and hot substances (X10-X19)

Excludes1: *exposure to excessive natural heat (X30)*
exposure to fire and flames (X00-X09)

X10 Contact with hot drinks, food, fats and cooking oils

The appropriate 7th character is to be added to each code from category X10
A initial encounter
D subsequent encounter
S sequela

X+7th **X10.0 Contact with hot drinks**
X+7th **X10.1 Contact with hot food**
X+7th **X10.2 Contact with fats and cooking oils**

X11 Contact with hot tap-water

Includes: contact with boiling tap-water
contact with boiling water NOS
Excludes1: *contact with water heated on stove (X12)*

The appropriate 7th character is to be added to each code from category X11
A initial encounter
D subsequent encounter
S sequela

X+7th **X11.0 Contact with hot water in bath or tub**
Excludes1: *contact with running hot water in bath or tub (X11.1)*
X+7th **X11.1 Contact with running hot water**
Contact with hot water running out of hose
Contact with hot water running out of tap
X+7th **X11.8 Contact with other hot tap-water**
Contact with hot water in bucket
Contact with hot tap-water NOS

X+7th **X12 Contact with other hot fluids**

Contact with water heated on stove
Excludes1: *hot (liquid) metals (X18)*

The appropriate 7th character is to be added to code X12
A initial encounter
D subsequent encounter
S sequela

X13 Contact with steam and other hot vapors

The appropriate 7th character is to be added to each code from category X13
A initial encounter
D subsequent encounter
S sequela

X+7th **X13.0 Inhalation of steam and other hot vapors**
X+7th **X13.1 Other contact with steam and other hot vapors**

X14 Contact with hot air and other hot gases

The appropriate 7th character is to be added to each code from category X14
A initial encounter
D subsequent encounter
S sequela

X+7th **X14.0 Inhalation of hot air and gases**
X+7th **X14.1 Other contact with hot air and other hot gases**

X15 Contact with hot household appliances

Excludes1: *contact with heating appliances (X16)*
contact with powered household appliances (W29.-)
exposure to controlled fire in building or structure due to household appliance (X02.8)
exposure to household appliances electrical current (W86.0

The appropriate 7th character is to be added to each code from category X15
A initial encounter
D subsequent encounter
S sequela

X+7th **X15.0 Contact with hot stove (kitchen)**
X+7th **X15.1 Contact with hot toaster**
X+7th **X15.2 Contact with hotplate**
X+7th **X15.3 Contact with hot saucepan or skillet**
X+7th **X15.8 Contact with other hot household appliances**
Contact with cooker
Contact with kettle
Contact with light bulbs

X+7th **X16 Contact with hot heating appliances, radiators and pipes**

Excludes1: *contact with powered appliances (W29.-)*
exposure to controlled fire in building or structure due to appliance (X02.8)
exposure to industrial appliances electrical current (W86.1)

The appropriate 7th character is to be added to code X16
A initial encounter
D subsequent encounter
S sequela

X+7th **X17 Contact with hot engines, machinery and tools**

Excludes1: *contact with hot heating appliances, radiators and pipes (X16)*
contact with hot household appliances (X15)

The appropriate 7th character is to be added to code X17
A initial encounter
D subsequent encounter
S sequela

X+7th **X18 Contact with other hot metals**

Contact with liquid metal

The appropriate 7th character is to be added to code X18
A initial encounter
D subsequent encounter
S sequela

X+7th **X19 Contact with other heat and hot substances**

Excludes1: *objects that are not normally hot, e.g., an object made hot by a house fire (X00-X09)*

The appropriate 7th character is to be added to code X19
A initial encounter
D subsequent encounter
S sequela

Exposure to forces of nature (X30-X39)

X+7th **X30 Exposure to excessive natural heat**

Exposure to excessive heat as the cause of sunstroke
Exposure to heat NOS
Excludes1: *excessive heat of man-made origin (W92)*
exposure to man-made radiation (W89)
exposure to sunlight (X32)
exposure to tanning bed (W89)

The appropriate 7th character is to be added to code X30
A initial encounter
D subsequent encounter
S sequela

th **X31 Exposure to excessive natural cold**

Excessive cold as the cause of chilblains NOS
Excessive cold as the cause of immersion foot or hand
Exposure to cold NOS
Exposure to weather conditions
Excludes1: *cold of man-made origin (W93.-)*
contact with or inhalation of dry ice (W93.-)
contact with or inhalation of liquefied gas (W93.-)

The appropriate 7th character is to be added to code X31
A initial encounter
D subsequent encounter
S sequela

7th **X32 Exposure to sunlight**

Excludes1: *radiation-related disorders of the skin and subcutaneous tissue (L55-L59)*
man-made radiation (tanning bed) (W89)

The appropriate 7th character is to be added to code X32
A initial encounter
D subsequent encounter
S sequela

7th **X34 Earthquake**

Excludes2: *tidal wave (tsunami) due to earthquake (X37.41)*

The appropriate 7th character is to be added to code X34
A initial encounter
D subsequent encounter
S sequela

7th **X35 Volcanic eruption**

Excludes2: *tidal wave (tsunami) due to volcanic eruption (X37.41)*

The appropriate 7th character is to be added to code X35
A initial encounter
D subsequent encounter
S sequela

7th **X36 Avalanche, landslide and other earth movements**

Includes: victim of mudslide of cataclysmic nature
Excludes1: *earthquake (X34)*
Excludes2: *transport accident involving collision with avalanche or landslide not in motion (V01-V99)*

The appropriate 7th character is to be added to each code from category X36
A initial encounter
D subsequent encounter
S sequela

X36.0 Collapse of dam or man-made structure causing earth movement
X36.1 Avalanche, landslide, or mudslide

X37 Cataclysmic storm

The appropriate 7th character is to be added to each code from category X37
A initial encounter
D subsequent encounter
S sequela

X+7th **X37.0 Hurricane**
Storm surge
Typhoon
X+7th **X37.1 Tornado**
Cyclone
Twister
X+7th **X37.2 Blizzard (snow)(ice)**
X+7th **X37.3 Dust storm**
\+ **X37.4 Tidalwave**
X+7th **X37.41 Tidal wave due to earthquake or volcanic eruption**
Tidal wave NOS
Tsunami
X+7th **X37.42 Tidal wave due to storm**
X+7th **X37.43 Tidal wave due to landslide**
X+7th **X37.8 Other cataclysmic storms**
Cloudburst
Torrential rain
Excludes2: *flood (X38)*
X+7th **X37.9 Unspecified cataclysmic storm**
Storm NOS
Excludes1: *collapse of dam or man-made structure causing earth movement (X39.0)*

X+7th **X38 Flood**

Flood arising from remote storm
Flood of cataclysmic nature arising from melting snow
Flood resulting directly from storm
Excludes1: *collapse of dam or man-made structure causing earth movement (X39.0)*
tidal wave NOS (X37.41)
tidal wave caused by storm (X37.2)

The appropriate 7th character is to be added to code X38
A initial encounter
D subsequent encounter
S sequela

X39 Exposure to other forces of nature

The appropriate 7th character is to be added to each code from category X39
A initial encounter
D subsequent encounter
S sequela

\+ **X39.0 Exposure to natural radiation**
Excludes1: *contact with and (suspected) exposure to radon and other naturally occuring radiation (Z77.122)*
exposure to man-made radiation (W88-W90)
exposure to sunlight (X32)
X+7th **X39.01 Exposure to radon**
X+7th **X39.08 Exposure to other natural radiation**
X+7th **X39.8 Other exposure to forces of nature**

Accidental exposure to other specified factors (X52-X58)

X+7th **X52 Prolonged stay in weightless environment**

Weightlessness in spacecraft (simulator)

The appropriate 7th character is to be added to code X52
A initial encounter
D subsequent encounter
S sequela

X+7th **X58 Exposure to other specified factors**

Accident NOS
Exposure NOS

The appropriate 7th character is to be added to code X58
A initial encounter
D subsequent encounter
S sequela

Intentional self-harm (X71-X83)

Purposely self-inflicted injury
Suicide (attempted)

X71 Intentional self-harm by drowning and submersion

The appropriate 7th character is to be added to each code from category X71
A initial encounter
D subsequent encounter
S sequela

X+7th **X71.0 Intentional self-harm by drowning and submersion while in bathtub**
X+7th **X71.1 Intentional self-harm by drowning and submersion while in swimming pool**
X+7th **X71.2 Intentional self-harm by drowning and submersion after jump into swimming pool**
X+7th **X71.3 Intentional self-harm by drowning and submersion in natural water**
X+7th **X71.8 Other intentional self-harm by drowning and submersion**
X+7th **X71.9 Intentional self-harm by drowning and submersion, unspecified**

X+7th **X72 Intentional self-harm by handgun discharge**

Intentional self-harm by gun for single hand use
Intentional self-harm by pistol
Intentional self-harm by revolver
Excludes1: *Very pistol (X74.8)*

The appropriate 7th character is to be added to code X72
A initial encounter
D subsequent encounter
S sequela

X+7th **X73 Intentional self-harm by rifle, shotgun and larger firearm discharge**

Excludes1: *airgun (X74.01)*

The appropriate 7th character is to be added to each code from category X73
A initial encounter
D subsequent encounter
S sequela

X+7th **X73.0 Intentional self-harm by shotgun discharge**
X+7th **X73.1 Intentional self-harm by hunting rifle discharge**
X+7th **X73.2 Intentional self-harm by machine gun discharge**
X+7th **X73.8 Intentional self-harm by other larger firearm discharge**
X+7th **X73.9 Intentional self-harm by unspecified larger firearm discharge**

X74 Intentional self-harm by other and unspecified firearm and gun discharge

The appropriate 7th character is to be added to each code from category X74
A initial encounter
D subsequent encounter
S sequela

+ **X74.0 Intentional self-harm by gas, air or spring-operated guns**
X+7th **X74.01 Intentional self-harm by airgun**
Intentional self-harm by BB gun discharge
Intentional self-harm by pellet gun discharge
X+7th **X74.02 Intentional self-harm by paintball gun**
X+7th **X74.09 Intentional self-harm by other gas, air or spring-operated gun**
X+7th **X74.8 Intentional self-harm by other firearm discharge**
Intentional self-harm by Very pistol [flare] discharge
X+7th **X74.9 Intentional self-harm by unspecified firearm discharge**

X+7th **X75 Intentional self-harm by explosive material**

The appropriate 7th character is to be added to code X75
A initial encounter
D subsequent encounter
S sequela

X+7th **X76 Intentional self-harm by smoke, fire and flames**

The appropriate 7th character is to be added to code X76
A initial encounter
D subsequent encounter
S sequela

X77 Intentional self-harm by steam, hot vapors and hot objects

The appropriate 7th character is to be added to each code from category X77
A initial encounter
D subsequent encounter
S sequela

X+7th **X77.0 Intentional self-harm by steam or hot vapors**
X+7th **X77.1 Intentional self-harm by hot tap water**
X+7th **X77.2 Intentional self-harm by other hot fluids**
X+7th **X77.3 Intentional self-harm by hot household appliances**
X+7th **X77.8 Intentional self-harm by other hot objects**
X+7th **X77.9 Intentional self-harm by unspecified hot objects**

X78 Intentional self-harm by sharp object

The appropriate 7th character is to be added to each code from category X78
A initial encounter
D subsequent encounter
S sequela

X+7th **X78.0 Intentional self-harm by sharp glass**
X+7th **X78.1 Intentional self-harm by knife**
X+7th **X78.2 Intentional self-harm by sword or dagger**
X+7th **X78.8 Intentional self-harm by other sharp object**
X+7th **X78.9 Intentional self-harm by unspecified sharp object**

X+7th **X79 Intentional self-harm by blunt object**

The appropriate 7th character is to be added to code X79
A initial encounter
D subsequent encounter
S sequela

X+7th **X80 Intentional self-harm by jumping from a high place**

Intentional fall from one level to another

The appropriate 7th character is to be added to code X80
A initial encounter
D subsequent encounter
S sequela

X81 Intentional self-harm by jumping or lying in front of moving object

The appropriate 7th character is to be added to each code from category X81
A initial encounter
D subsequent encounter
S sequela

X+7th **X81.0 Intentional self-harm by jumping or lying in front of motor vehicle**
X+7th **X81.1 Intentional self-harm by jumping or lying in front of (subway) train**
X+7th **X81.8 Intentional self-harm by jumping or lying in front of other moving object**

X82 Intentional self-harm by crashing of motor vehicle

The appropriate 7th character is to be added to each code from category X82
A initial encounter
D subsequent encounter
S sequela

X+7th **X82.0 Intentional collision of motor vehicle with other motor vehicle**
X+7th **X82.1 Intentional collision of motor vehicle with train**
X+7th **X82.2 Intentional collision of motor vehicle with tree**
X+7th **X82.8 Other intentional self-harm by crashing of motor vehicle**

X83 Intentional self-harm by other specified means

Excludes1: *intentional self-harm by poisoning or contact with toxic substance- See Table of Drugs and Chemicals*

The appropriate 7th character is to be added to each code from category X83
A initial encounter
D subsequent encounter
S sequela

X+7th **X83.0 Intentional self-harm by crashing of aircraft**
X+7th **X83.1 Intentional self-harm by electrocution**
X+7th **X83.2 Intentional self-harm by exposure to extremes of cold**
X+7th **X83.8 Intentional self-harm by other specified means**

Assault (X92-Y08)

Includes: homicide
injuries inflicted by another person with intent to injure or kill, by any means

Excludes1: *injuries due to legal intervention (Y35.-)*
injuries due to operations of war (Y36.-)
injuries due to terrorism (Y38.-)

Review coding guideline C.19.f

X92 Assault by drowning and submersion

The appropriate 7th character is to be added to each code from category X92
A initial encounter
D subsequent encounter
S sequela

X+7th **X92.0 Assault by drowning and submersion while in bathtub**
X+7th **X92.1 Assault by drowning and submersion while in swimming pool**
X+7th **X92.2 Assault by drowning and submersion after push into swimming pool**
X+7th **X92.3 Assault by drowning and submersion in natural water**
X+7th **X92.8 Other assault by drowning and submersion**
X+7th **X92.9 Assault by drowning and submersion, unspecified**

X+7th **X93 Assault by handgun discharge**

Assault by discharge of gun for single hand use
Assault by discharge of pistol
Assault by discharge of revolver
Excludes1: *Very pistol (X95.8)*

The appropriate 7th character is to be added to code X93
A initial encounter
D subsequent encounter
S sequela

X94 Assault by rifle, shotgun and larger firearm discharge

Excludes1: *airgun (X95.01)*

The appropriate 7th character is to be added to each code from category X94
A initial encounter
D subsequent encounter
S sequela

X+7th **X94.0 Assault by shotgun**
X+7th **X94.1 Assault by hunting rifle**
X+7th **X94.2 Assault by machine gun**
X+7th **X94.8 Assault by other larger firearm discharge**
X+7th **X94.9 Assault by unspecified larger firearm discharge**

X95 Assault by other and unspecified firearm and gun discharge

The appropriate 7th character is to be added to each code from category X95
A initial encounter
D subsequent encounter
S sequela

\+ **X95.0 Assault by gas, air or spring-operated guns**
X+7th **X95.01 Assault by airgun discharge**
Assault by BB gun discharge
Assault by pellet gun discharge
X+7th **X95.02 Assault by paintball gun discharge**
X+7th **X95.09 Assault by other gas, air or spring-operated gun**
X+7th **X95.8 Assault by other firearm discharge**
Assault by very pistol [flare] discharge
X+7th **X95.9 Assault by unspecified firearm discharge**

X96 Assault by explosive material

Excludes1: *incendiary device (X97)*
terrorism involving explosive material (Y38.2-)

The appropriate 7th character is to be added to each code from category X96
A initial encounter
D subsequent encounter
S sequela

X+7th **X96.0 Assault by antipersonnel bomb**
Excludes1: *antipersonnel bomb use in military or war (Y36.2-)*
X+7th **X96.1 Assault by gasoline bomb**
X+7th **X96.2 Assault by letter bomb**
X+7th **X96.3 Assault by fertilizer bomb**
X+7th **X96.4 Assault by pipe bomb**
X+7th **X96.8 Assault by other specified explosive**
X+7th **X96.9 Assault by unspecified explosive**

X+7th **X97 Assault by smoke, fire and flames**

Assault by arson
Assault by cigarettes
Assault by incendiary device

The appropriate 7th character is to be added to code X97
A initial encounter
D subsequent encounter
S sequela

X98 Assault by steam, hot vapors and hot objects

The appropriate 7th character is to be added to each code from category X98
A initial encounter
D subsequent encounter
S sequela

X+7th **X98.0 Assault by steam or hot vapors**
X+7th **X98.1 Assault by hot tap water**
X+7th **X98.2 Assault by hot fluids**
X+7th **X98.3 Assault by hot household appliances**
X+7th **X98.8 Assault by other hot objects**
X+7th **X98.9 Assault by unspecified hot objects**

X99 Assault by sharp object

Excludes1: *assault by strike by sports equipment (Y08.0-)*

The appropriate 7th character is to be added to each code from category X99
A initial encounter
D subsequent encounter
S sequela

X+7th **X99.0 Assault by sharp glass**
X+7th **X99.1 Assault by knife**
X+7th **X99.2 Assault by sword or dagger**
X+7th **X99.8 Assault by other sharp object**
X+7th **X99.9 Assault by unspecified sharp object**
Assault by stabbing NOS

X+7th **Y00 Assault by blunt object**

Excludes1: *assault by strike by sports equipment (Y08.0-)*

The appropriate 7th character is to be added to code Y00
A initial encounter
D subsequent encounter
S sequela

X+7th **Y01 Assault by pushing from high place**

The appropriate 7th character is to be added to code Y01
A initial encounter
D subsequent encounter
S sequela

Y02 Assault by pushing or placing victim in front of moving object

The appropriate 7th character is to be added to each code from category Y02
A initial encounter
D subsequent encounter
S sequela

X+7th **Y02.0 Assault by pushing or placing victim in front of motor vehicle**
X+7th **Y02.1 Assault by pushing or placing victim in front of (subway) train**
X+7th **Y02.8 Assault by pushing or placing victim in front of other moving object**

Y03 Assault by crashing of motor vehicle

The appropriate 7th character is to be added to each code from category Y03
A initial encounter
D subsequent encounter
S sequela

X+7th **Y03.0 Assault by being hit or run over by motor vehicle**
X+7th **Y03.8 Other assault by crashing of motor vehicle**

Y04 Assault by bodily force

Excludes1: *assault by:*
submersion (X92.-)
use of weapon (X93-X95, X99, Y00)

The appropriate 7th character is to be added to each code from category Y04
A initial encounter
D subsequent encounter
S sequela

X+7th **Y04.0 Assault by unarmed brawl or fight**
X+7th **Y04.1 Assault by human bite**
X+7th **Y04.2 Assault by strike against or bumped into by another person**
X+7th **Y04.8 Assault by other bodily force**
Assault by bodily force NOS

Y07 Perpetrator of assault, maltreatment and neglect

NOTE Codes from this category are for use only in cases of confirmed abuse (T74.-)
Selection of the correct perpetrator code is based on the relationship between the perpetrator and the victim

Includes: perpetrator of abandonment
perpetrator of emotional neglect
perpetrator of mental cruelty
perpetrator of physical abuse
perpetrator of physical neglect
perpetrator of sexual abuse
perpetrator of torture

Review coding guideline C.20.g

\+ **Y07.0 Spouse or partner, perpetrator of maltreatment and neglect**
Spouse or partner, perpetrator of maltreatment and neglect against spouse or partner
Y07.01 Husband, perpetrator of maltreatment and neglect
Y07.02 Wife, perpetrator of maltreatment and neglect
Y07.03 Male partner, perpetrator of maltreatment and neglect
Y07.04 Female partner, perpetrator of maltreatment and neglect

\+ **Y07.1 Parent (adoptive) (biological), perpetrator of maltreatment and neglect**
Y07.11 Biological father, perpetrator of maltreatment and neglect
Y07.12 Biological mother, perpetrator of maltreatment and neglect
Y07.13 Adoptive father, perpetrator of maltreatment and neglect
Y07.14 Adoptive mother, perpetrator of maltreatment and neglect

+ **Y07.4 Other family member, perpetrator of maltreatment and neglect**
+ **Y07.41 Sibling, perpetrator of maltreatment and neglect**
Excludes1: *stepsibling, perpetrator of maltreatment and neglect (Y07.435, Y07.436)*
Y07.410 Brother, perpetrator of maltreatment and neglect
Y07.411 Sister, perpetrator of maltreatment and neglect
+ **Y07.42 Foster parent, perpetrator of maltreatment and neglect**
Y07.420 Foster father, perpetrator of maltreatment and neglect
Y07.421 Foster mother, perpetrator of maltreatment and neglect
+ **Y07.43 Stepparent or stepsibling, perpetrator of maltreatment and neglect**
Y07.430 Stepfather, perpetrator of maltreatment and neglect
Y07.432 Male friend of parent (co-residing in household), perpetrator of maltreatment and neglect
Y07.433 Stepmother, perpetrator of maltreatment and neglect
Y07.434 Female friend of parent (co-residing in household), perpetrator of maltreatment and neglect
Y07.435 Stepbrother, perpetrator or maltreatment and neglect
Y07.436 Stepsister, perpetrator of maltreatment and neglect
+ **Y07.49 Other family member, perpetrator of maltreatment and neglect**
Y07.490 Male cousin, perpetrator of maltreatment and neglect
Y07.491 Female cousin, perpetrator of maltreatment and neglect
Y07.499 Other family member, perpetrator of maltreatment and neglect
+ **Y07.5 Non-family member, perpetrator of maltreatment and neglect**
Y07.50 Unspecified non-family member, perpetrator of maltreatment and neglect
+ **Y07.51 Daycare provider, perpetrator of maltreatment and neglect**
Y07.510 At-home childcare provider, perpetrator of maltreatment and neglect
Y07.511 Daycare center childcare provider, perpetrator of maltreatment and neglect
Y07.512 At-home adultcare provider, perpetrator of maltreatment and neglect
Y07.513 Adultcare center provider, perpetrator of maltreatment and neglect
Y07.519 Unspecified daycare provider, perpetrator of maltreatment and neglect
+ **Y07.52 Healthcare provider, perpetrator of maltreatment and neglect**
Y07.521 Mental health provider, perpetrator of maltreatment and neglect
Y07.528 Other therapist or healthcare provider, perpetrator of maltreatment and neglect
Nurse perpetrator of maltreatment and neglect
Occupational therapist perpetrator of maltreatment and neglect
Physical therapist perpetrator of maltreatment and neglect
Speech therapist perpetrator of maltreatment and neglect
Y07.529 Unspecified healthcare provider, perpetrator of maltreatment and neglect
Y07.53 Teacher or instructor, perpetrator of maltreatment and neglect
Coach, perpetrator of maltreatment and neglect
Y07.59 Other non-family member, perpetrator of maltreatment and neglect
Y07.9 Unspecified perpetrator of maltreatment and neglect

Y08 Assault by other specified means

The appropriate 7th character is to be added to each code from category Y08
A initial encounter
D subsequent encounter
S sequela

+ **Y08.0 Assault by strike by sport equipment**
X+7th **Y08.01 Assault by strike by hockey stick**
X+7th **Y08.02 Assault by strike by baseball bat**
X+7th **Y08.09 Assault by strike by other specified type of sport equipment**
+ **Y08.8 Assault by other specified means**
X+7th **Y08.81 Assault by crashing of aircraft**
X+7th **Y08.89 Assault by other specified means**

Y09 Assault by unspecified means
Assassination (attempted) NOS
Homicide (attempted) NOS
Manslaughter (attempted) NOS
Murder (attempted) NOS
Valid 3-character code, no further characters required

Event of undetermined intent (Y21-Y33)

Undetermined intent is only for use when there is specific documentation in the record that the intent of the injury cannot be determined. If no such documentation is present, code to accidental (unintentional)

Y21 Drowning and submersion, undetermined intent

The appropriate 7th character is to be added to each code from category Y21
A initial encounter
D subsequent encounter
S sequela

X+7th **Y21.0 Drowning and submersion while in bathtub, undetermined intent**
X+7th **Y21.1 Drowning and submersion after fall into bathtub, undetermined intent**
X+7th **Y21.2 Drowning and submersion while in swimming pool, undetermined intent**
X+7th **Y21.3 Drowning and submersion after fall into swimming pool, undetermined intent**
X+7th **Y21.4 Drowning and submersion in natural water, undetermined intent**
X+7th **Y21.8 Other drowning and submersion, undetermined intent**
X+7th **Y21.9 Unspecified drowning and submersion, undetermined intent**

X+7th **Y22 Handgun discharge, undetermined intent**
Discharge of gun for single hand use, undetermined intent
Discharge of pistol, undetermined intent
Discharge of revolver, undetermined intent
Excludes2: *very pistol (Y24.8)*

The appropriate 7th character is to be added to code Y22
A initial encounter
D subsequent encounter
S sequela

Y23 Rifle, shotgun and larger firearm discharge, undetermined intent
Excludes2: *airgun (Y24.0)*

The appropriate 7th character is to be added to each code from category Y23
A initial encounter
D subsequent encounter
S sequela

X+7th **Y23.0 Shotgun discharge, undetermined intent**
X+7th **Y23.1 Hunting rifle discharge, undetermined intent**
X+7th **Y23.2 Military firearm discharge, undetermined intent**
X+7th **Y23.3 Machine gun discharge, undetermined intent**
X+7th **Y23.8 Other larger firearm discharge, undetermined intent**
X+7th **Y23.9 Unspecified larger firearm discharge, undetermined intent**

Y24 Other and unspecified firearm discharge, undetermined intent

The appropriate 7th character is to be added to each code from category Y24
A initial encounter
D subsequent encounter
S sequela

X+7th **Y24.0 Airgun discharge, undetermined intent**
BB gun discharge, undetermined intent
Pellet gun discharge, undetermined intent
X+7th **Y24.8 Other firearm discharge, undetermined intent**
Paintball gun discharge, undetermined intent
Very pistol [flare] discharge, undetermined intent
X+7th **Y24.9 Unspecified firearm discharge, undetermined intent**

+7th **Y25 Contact with explosive material, undetermined intent**

The appropriate 7th character is to be added to code Y25
A initial encounter
D subsequent encounter
S sequela

+7th **Y26 Exposure to smoke, fire and flames, undetermined intent**

The appropriate 7th character is to be added to code Y26
A initial encounter
D subsequent encounter
S sequela

Y27 Contact with steam, hot vapors and hot objects, undetermined intent

The appropriate 7th character is to be added to each code from category Y27
A initial encounter
D subsequent encounter
S sequela

X+7th **Y27.0 Contact with steam and hot vapors, undetermined intent**
X+7th **Y27.1 Contact with hot tap water, undetermined intent**
X+7th **Y27.2 Contact with hot fluids, undetermined intent**
X+7th **Y27.3 Contact with hot household appliance, undetermined intent**
X+7th **Y27.8 Contact with other hot objects, undetermined intent**
X+7th **Y27.9 Contact with unspecified hot objects, undetermined intent**

Y28 Contact with sharp object, undetermined intent

The appropriate 7th character is to be added to each code from category Y28
A initial encounter
D subsequent encounter
S sequela

X+7th **Y28.0 Contact with sharp glass, undetermined intent**
X+7th **Y28.1 Contact with knife, undetermined intent**
X+7th **Y28.2 Contact with sword or dagger, undetermined intent**
X+7th **Y28.8 Contact with other sharp object, undetermined intent**
X+7th **Y28.9 Contact with unspecified sharp object, undetermined intent**

+7th **Y29 Contact with blunt object, undetermined intent**

The appropriate 7th character is to be added to code Y29
A initial encounter
D subsequent encounter
S sequela

+7th **Y30 Falling, jumping or pushed from a high place, undetermined intent**

Victim falling from one level to another, undetermined intent

The appropriate 7th character is to be added to code Y30
A initial encounter
D subsequent encounter
S sequela

+7th **Y31 Falling, lying or running before or into moving object, undetermined intent**

The appropriate 7th character is to be added to code Y31
A initial encounter
D subsequent encounter
S sequela

+7th **Y32 Crashing of motor vehicle, undetermined intent**

The appropriate 7th character is to be added to code Y32
A initial encounter
D subsequent encounter
S sequela

+7th **Y33 Other specified events, undetermined intent**

The appropriate 7th character is to be added to code Y33
A initial encounter
D subsequent encounter
S sequela

Legal intervention, operations of war, military operations, and terrorism (Y35-Y38)

Y35 Legal intervention

Includes: any injury sustained as a result of an encounter with any law enforcement official, serving in any capacity at the time of the encounter, whether on-duty or off-duty. Includes: a injury to law enforcement official, suspect and bystander

The appropriate 7th character is to be added to each code from category Y35
A initial encounter
D subsequent encounter
S sequela

\+ **Y35.0 Legal intervention involving firearm discharge**
\+ **Y35.00 Legal intervention involving unspecified firearm discharge**
Legal intervention involving gunshot wound
Legal intervention involving shot NOS
+7th **Y35.001 Legal intervention involving unspecified firearm discharge, law enforcement official injured**
+7th **Y35.002 Legal intervention involving unspecified firearm discharge, bystander injured**
+7th **Y35.003 Legal intervention involving unspecified firearm discharge, suspect injured**
\+ **Y35.01 Legal intervention involving injury by machine gun**
+7th **Y35.011 Legal intervention involving injury by machine gun, law enforcement official injured**
+7th **Y35.012 Legal intervention involving injury by machine gun, bystander injured**
+7th **Y35.013 Legal intervention involving injury by machine gun, suspect injured**
\+ **Y35.02 Legal intervention involving injury by handgun**
+7th **Y35.021 Legal intervention involving injury by handgun, law enforcement official injured**
+7th **Y35.022 Legal intervention involving injury by handgun, bystander injured**
+7th **Y35.023 Legal intervention involving injury by handgun, suspect injured**
\+ **Y35.03 Legal intervention involving injury by rifle pellet**
+7th **Y35.031 Legal intervention involving injury by rifle pellet, law enforcement official injured**
+7th **Y35.032 Legal intervention involving injury by rifle pellet, bystander injured**
+7th **Y35.033 Legal intervention involving injury by rifle pellet, suspect injured**
\+ **Y35.04 Legal intervention involving injury by rubber bullet**
+7th **Y35.041 Legal intervention involving injury by rubber bullet, law enforcement official injured**
+7th **Y35.042 Legal intervention involving injury by rubber bullet, bystander injured**
+7th **Y35.043 Legal intervention involving injury by rubber bullet, suspect injured**
\+ **Y35.09 Legal intervention involving other firearm discharge**
+7th **Y35.091 Legal intervention involving other firearm discharge, law enforcement official injured**
+7th **Y35.092 Legal intervention involving other firearm discharge, bystander injured**
+7th **Y35.093 Legal intervention involving other firearm discharge, suspect injured**
\+ **Y35.1 Legal intervention involving explosives**
\+ **Y35.10 Legal intervention involving unspecified explosives**
+7th **Y35.101 Legal intervention involving unspecified explosives, law enforcement official injured**
+7th **Y35.102 Legal intervention involving unspecified explosives, bystander injured**
+7th **Y35.103 Legal intervention involving unspecified explosives, suspect injured**
\+ **Y35.11 Legal intervention involving injury by dynamite**
+7th **Y35.111 Legal intervention involving injury by dynamite, law enforcement official injured**
+7th **Y35.112 Legal intervention involving injury by dynamite, bystander injured**
+7th **Y35.113 Legal intervention involving injury by dynamite, suspect injured**
\+ **Y35.12 Legal intervention involving injury by explosive shell**

+7th **Y35.121 Legal intervention involving injury by explosive shell, law enforcement official injured**
+7th **Y35.122 Legal intervention involving injury by explosive shell, bystander injured**
+7th **Y35.123 Legal intervention involving injury by explosive shell, suspect injured**
\+ **Y35.19 Legal intervention involving other explosives**
Legal intervention involving injury by grenade
Legal intervention involving injury by mortar bomb
+7th **Y35.191 Legal intervention involving other explosives, law enforcement official injured**
+7th **Y35.192 Legal intervention involving other explosives, bystander injured**
+7th **Y35.193 Legal intervention involving other explosives, suspect injured**
\+ **Y35.2 Legal intervention involving gas**
Legal intervention involving asphyxiation by gas
Legal intervention involving poisoning by gas
\+ **Y35.20 Legal intervention involving unspecified gas**
+7th **Y35.201 Legal intervention involving unspecified gas, law enforcement official injured**
+7th **Y35.202 Legal intervention involving unspecified gas, bystander injured**
+7th **Y35.203 Legal intervention involving unspecified gas, suspect injured**
\+ **Y35.21 Legal intervention involving injury by tear gas**
+7th **Y35.211 Legal intervention involving injury by tear gas, law enforcement official injured**
+7th **Y35.212 Legal intervention involving injury by tear gas, bystander injured**
+7th **Y35.213 Legal intervention involving injury by tear gas, suspect injured**
\+ **Y35.29 Legal intervention involving other gas**
+7th **Y35.291 Legal intervention involving other gas, law enforcement official injured**
+7th **Y35.292 Legal intervention involving other gas, bystander injured**
+7th **Y35.293 Legal intervention involving other gas, suspect injured**
\+ **Y35.3 Legal intervention involving blunt objects**
Legal intervention involving being hit or struck by blunt object
\+ **Y35.30 Legal intervention involving unspecified blunt objects**
+7th **Y35.301 Legal intervention involving unspecified blunt objects, law enforcement official injured**
+7th **Y35.302 Legal intervention involving unspecified blunt objects, bystander injured**
+7th **Y35.303 Legal intervention involving unspecified blunt objects, suspect injured**
\+ **Y35.31 Legal intervention involving baton**
+7th **Y35.311 Legal intervention involving baton, law enforcement official injured**
+7th **Y35.312 Legal intervention involving baton, bystander injured**
+7th **Y35.313 Legal intervention involving baton, suspect injured**
\+ **Y35.39 Legal intervention involving other blunt objects**
+7th **Y35.391 Legal intervention involving other blunt objects, law enforcement official injured**
+7th **Y35.392 Legal intervention involving other blunt objects, bystander injured**
+7th **Y35.393 Legal intervention involving other blunt objects, suspect injured**
\+ **Y35.4 Legal intervention involving sharp objects**
Legal intervention involving being cut by sharp objects
Legal intervention involving being stabbed by sharp objects
\+ **Y35.40 Legal intervention involving unspecified sharp objects**
+7th **Y35.401 Legal intervention involving unspecified sharp objects, law enforcement official injured**
+7th **Y35.402 Legal intervention involving unspecified sharp objects, bystander injured**
+7th **Y35.403 Legal intervention involving unspecified sharp objects, suspect injured**
\+ **Y35.41 Legal intervention involving bayonet**
+7th **Y35.411 Legal intervention involving bayonet, law enforcement official injured**
+7th **Y35.412 Legal intervention involving bayonet, bystander injured**
+7th **Y35.413 Legal intervention involving bayonet, suspect injured**
\+ **Y35.49 Legal intervention involving other sharp objects**
+7th **Y35.491 Legal intervention involving other sharp objects, law enforcement official injured**
+7th **Y35.492 Legal intervention involving other sharp objects, bystander injured**
+7th **Y35.493 Legal intervention involving other sharp objects, suspect injured**
\+ **Y35.8 Legal intervention involving other specified means**
\+ **Y35.81 Legal intervention involving manhandling**
+7th **Y35.811 Legal intervention involving manhandling, law enforcement official injured**
+7th **Y35.812 Legal intervention involving manhandling, bystander injured**
+7th **Y35.813 Legal intervention involving manhandling, suspect injured**
\+ **Y35.89 Legal intervention involving other specified means**
+7th **Y35.891 Legal intervention involving other specified means, law enforcement official injured**
+7th **Y35.892 Legal intervention involving other specified means, bystanderinjured**
+7th **Y35.893 Legal intervention involving other specified means, suspect injured**
\+ **Y35.9 Legal intervention, means unspecified**
X+7th **Y35.91 Legal intervention, means unspecified, law enforcement official injured**
X+7th **Y35.92 Legal intervention, means unspecified, bystander injured**
X+7th **Y35.93 Legal intervention, means unspecified, suspect injured**

Y36 Operations of war

Includes: injuries to military personnel and civilians caused by war, civil insurrection, and peacekeeping missions

Excludes1: *injury to military personnel occurring during peacetime military operations (Y37.-)*
military vehicles involved in transport accidents with non-military vehicle during peacetime (V09.01, V09.21, V19.81, V29.81, V39.81, V49.81, V59.81, V69.81, V79.81)

The appropriate 7th character is to be added to each code from category Y36
A initial encounter
D subsequent encounter
S sequela

\+ **Y36.0 War operations involving explosion of marine weapons**
\+ **Y36.00 War operations involving explosion of unspecified marine weapon**
War operations involving underwater blast NOS
+7th **Y36.000 War operations involving explosion of unspecified marine weapon, military personnel**
+7th **Y36.001 War operations involving explosion of unspecified marine weapon, civilian**
\+ **Y36.01 War operations involving explosion of depth-charge**
+7th **Y36.010 War operations involving explosion of depth-charge, military personnel**
+7th **Y36.011 War operations involving explosion of depth-charge, civilian**
\+ **Y36.02 War operations involving explosion of marine mine**
War operations involving explosion of marine mine, at sea or in harbor
+7th **Y36.020 War operations involving explosion of marine mine, military personnel**
+7th **Y36.021 War operations involving explosion of marine mine, civilian**
\+ **Y36.03 War operations involving explosion of sea-based artillery shell**
+7th **Y36.030 War operations involving explosion of sea-based artillery shell, military personnel**
+7th **Y36.031 War operations involving explosion of sea-based artillery shell, civilian**
\+ **Y36.04 War operations involving explosion of torpedo**
+7th **Y36.040 War operations involving explosion of torpedo, military personnel**
+7th **Y36.041 War operations involving explosion of torpedo, civilian**

+ **Y36.05 War operations involving accidental detonation of onboard marine weapons**
  - +7th **Y36.050 War operations involving accidental detonation of onboard marine weapons, military personnel**
  - +7th **Y36.051 War operations involving accidental detonation of onboard marine weapons, civilian**

+ **Y36.09 War operations involving explosion of other marine weapons**
  - +7th **Y36.090 War operations involving explosion of other marine weapons, military personnel**
  - +7th **Y36.091 War operations involving explosion of other marine weapons, civilian**

+ **Y36.1 War operations involving destruction of aircraft**

+ **Y36.10 War operations involving unspecified destruction of aircraft**
  - +7th **Y36.100 War operations involving unspecified destruction of aircraft, military personnel**
  - +7th **Y36.101 War operations involving unspecified destruction of aircraft, civilian**

+ **Y36.11 War operations involving destruction of aircraft due to enemy fire or explosives**

  War operations involving destruction of aircraft due to air to air missile
  War operations involving destruction of aircraft due to explosive placed on aircraft
  War operations involving destruction of aircraft due to rocket propelled grenade [RPG]
  War operations involving destruction of aircraft due to small arms fire
  War operations involving destruction of aircraft due to surface to air missile
  - +7th **Y36.110 War operations involving destruction of aircraft due to enemy fire or explosives, military personnel**
  - +7th **Y36.111 War operations involving destruction of aircraft due to enemy fire or explosives, civilian**

+ **Y36.12 War operations involving destruction of aircraft due to collision with other aircraft**
  - +7th **Y36.120 War operations involving destruction of aircraft due to collision with other aircraft, military personnel**
  - +7th **Y36.121 War operations involving destruction of aircraft due to collision with other aircraft, civilian**

+ **Y36.13 War operations involving destruction of aircraft due to onboard fire**
  - +7th **Y36.130 War operations involving destruction of aircraft due to onboard fire, military personnel**
  - +7th **Y36.131 War operations involving destruction of aircraft due to onboard fire, civilian**

+ **Y36.14 War operations involving destruction of aircraft due to accidental detonation of onboard munitions and explosives**
  - +7th **Y36.140 War operations involving destruction of aircraft due to accidental detonation of onboard munitions and explosives, military personnel**
  - +7th **Y36.141 War operations involving destruction of aircraft due to accidental detonation of onboard munitions and explosives, civilian**

+ **Y36.19 War operations involving other destruction of aircraft**
  - +7th **Y36.190 War operations involving other destruction of aircraft, military personnel**
  - +7th **Y36.191 War operations involving other destruction of aircraft, civilian**

+ **Y36.2 War operations involving other explosions and fragments**

  Excludes1: *war operations involving explosion of aircraft (Y36.1-)*
  war operations involving explosion of marine weapons (Y36.0-)
  war operations involving explosion of nuclear weapons (Y36.5-)
  war operations involving explosion occurring after cessation of hostilities (Y36.8-)

+ **Y36.20 War operations involving unspecified explosion and fragments**

  War operations involving air blast NOS
  War operations involving blast NOS
  War operations involving blast fragments NOS
  War operations involving blast wave NOS
  War operations involving blast wind NOS
  War operations involving explosion NOS
  War operations involving explosion of bomb NOS
  - +7th **Y36.200 War operations involving unspecified explosion and fragments, military personnel**
  - +7th **Y36.201 War operations involving unspecified explosion and fragments, civilian**

+ **Y36.21 War operations involving explosion of aerial bomb**
  - +7th **Y36.210 War operations involving explosion of aerial bomb, military personnel**
  - +7th **Y36.211 War operations involving explosion of aerial bomb, civilian**

+ **Y36.22 War operations involving explosion of guided missile**
  - +7th **Y36.220 War operations involving explosion of guided missile, military personnel**
  - +7th **Y36.221 War operations involving explosion of guided missile, civilian**

+ **Y36.23 War operations involving explosion of improvised explosive device [IED]**

  War operations involving explosion of person-borne improvised explosive device [IED]
  War operations involving explosion of vehicle-borne improvised explosive device [IED]
  War operations involving explosion of roadside improvised explosive device [IED]
  - +7th **Y36.230 War operations involving explosion of improvised explosive device [IED], military personnel**
  - +7th **Y36.231 War operations involving explosion of improvised explosive device [IED], civilian**

+ **Y36.24 War operations involving explosion due to accidental detonation and discharge of own munitions or munitions launch device**
  - +7th **Y36.240 War operations involving explosion due to accidental detonation and discharge of own munitions or munitions launch device, military personnel**
  - +7th **Y36.241 War operations involving explosion due to accidental detonation and discharge of own munitions or munitions launch device, civilian**

+ **Y36.25 War operations involving fragments from munitions**
  - +7th **Y36.250 War operations involving fragments from munitions, military personnel**
  - +7th **Y36.251 War operations involving fragments from munitions, civilian**

+ **Y36.26 War operations involving fragments of improvised explosive device [IED]**

  War operations involving fragments of person-borne improvised explosive device [IED]
  War operations involving fragments of vehicle-borne improvised explosive device [IED]
  War operations involving fragments of roadside improvised explosive device [IED]
  - +7th **Y36.260 War operations involving fragments of improvised explosive device [IED], military personnel**
  - +7th **Y36.261 War operations involving fragments of improvised explosive device [IED], civilian**

+ **Y36.27 War operations involving fragments from weapons**
  - +7th **Y36.270 War operations involving fragments from weapons, military personnel**
  - +7th **Y36.271 War operations involving fragments from weapons, civilian**

+ **Y36.29 War operations involving other explosions and fragments**
War operations involving explosion of grenade
War operations involving explosions of land mine
War operations involving shrapnel NOS
+7th **Y36.290 War operations involving other explosions and fragments, military personnel**
+7th **Y36.291 War operations involving other explosions and fragments, civilian**

+ **Y36.3 War operations involving fires, conflagrations and hot substances**
War operations involving smoke, fumes, and heat from fires, conflagrations and hot substances
Excludes1: *war operations involving fires and conflagrations aboard military aircraft (Y36.1-)*
war operations involving fires and conflagrations aboard military watercraft (Y36.0-)
war operations involving fires and conflagrations caused indirectly by conventional weapons (Y36.2-)
war operations involving fires and thermal effects of nuclear weapons (Y36.53-)

+ **Y36.30 War operations involving unspecified fire, conflagration and hot substance**
+7th **Y36.300 War operations involving unspecified fire, conflagration and hot substance, military personnel**
+7th **Y36.301 War operations involving unspecified fire, conflagration and hot substance, civilian**

+ **Y36.31 War operations involving gasoline bomb**
War operations involving incendiary bomb
War operations involving petrol bomb
+7th **Y36.310 War operations involving gasoline bomb, military personnel**
+7th **Y36.311 War operations involving gasoline bomb, civilian**

+ **Y36.32 War operations involving incendiary bullet**
+7th **Y36.320 War operations involving incendiary bullet, military personnel**
+7th **Y36.321 War operations involving incendiary bullet, civilian**

+ **Y36.33 War operations involving flamethrower**
+7th **Y36.330 War operations involving flamethrower, military personnel**
+7th **Y36.331 War operations involving flamethrower, civilian**

+ **Y36.39 War operations involving other fires, conflagrations and hot substances**
+7th **Y36.390 War operations involving other fires, conflagrations and hot substances, military personnel**
+7th **Y36.391 War operations involving other fires, conflagrations and hot substances, civilian**

+ **Y36.4 War operations involving firearm discharge and other forms of conventional warfare**

+ **Y36.41 War operations involving rubber bullets**
+7th **Y36.410 War operations involving rubber bullets, military personnel**
+7th **Y36.411 War operations involving rubber bullets, civilian**

+ **Y36.42 War operations involving firearms pellets**
+7th **Y36.420 War operations involving firearms pellets, military personnel**
+7th **Y36.421 War operations involving firearms pellets, civilian**

+ **Y36.43 War operations involving other firearms discharge**
War operations involving bullets NOS
Excludes1: *war operations involving munitions fragments (Y36.25-)*
war operations involving incendiary bullets (Y36.32-)
+7th **Y36.430 War operations involving other firearms discharge, military personnel**
+7th **Y36.431 War operations involving other firearms discharge, civilian**

+ **Y36.44 War operations involving unarmed hand to hand combat**
Excludes1: *war operations involving combat using blunt or piercing object (Y36.45-)*
war operations involving intentional restriction of air and airway (Y36.46-)
war operations involving unintentional restriction of air and airway (Y36.47-)
+7th **Y36.440 War operations involving unarmed hand to hand combat, military personnel**
+7th **Y36.441 War operations involving unarmed hand to hand combat, civilian**

+ **Y36.45 War operations involving combat using blunt or piercing object**
+7th **Y36.450 War operations involving combat using blunt or piercing object, military personnel**
+7th **Y36.451 War operations involving combat using blunt or piercing object, civilian**

+ **Y36.46 War operations involving intentional restriction of air and airway**
+7th **Y36.460 War operations involving intentional restriction of air and airway, military personnel**
+7th **Y36.461 War operations involving intentional restriction of air and airway, civilian**

+ **Y36.47 War operations involving unintentional restriction of air and airway**
+7th **Y36.470 War operations involving unintentional restriction of air and airway, military personnel**
+7th **Y36.471 War operations involving unintentional restriction of air and airway, civilian**

+ **Y36.49 War operations involving other forms of conventional warfare**
+7th **Y36.490 War operations involving other forms of conventional warfare, military personnel**
+7th **Y36.491 War operations involving other forms of conventional warfare, civilian**

+ **Y36.5 War operations involving nuclear weapons**
War operations involving dirty bomb NOS

+ **Y36.50 War operations involving unspecified effect of nuclear weapon**
+7th **Y36.500 War operations involving unspecified effect of nuclear weapon, military personnel**
+7th **Y36.501 War operations involving unspecified effect of nuclear weapon, civilian**

+ **Y36.51 War operations involving direct blast effect of nuclear weapon**
War operations involving blast pressure of nuclear weapon
+7th **Y36.510 War operations involving direct blast effect of nuclear weapon, military personnel**
+7th **Y36.511 War operations involving direct blast effect of nuclear weapon, civilian**

+ **Y36.52 War operations involving indirect blast effect of nuclear weapon**
War operations involving being thrown by blast of nuclear weapon
War operations involving being struck or crushed by blast debris of nuclear weapon
+7th **Y36.520 War operations involving indirect blast effect of nuclear weapon, military personnel**
+7th **Y36.521 War operations involving indirect blast effect of nuclear weapon, civilian**

+ **Y36.53 War operations involving thermal radiation effect of nuclear weapon**
War operations involving direct heat from nuclear weapon
War operation involving fireball effects from nuclear weapon
+7th **Y36.530 War operations involving thermal radiation effect of nuclear weapon, military personnel**
+7th **Y36.531 War operations involving thermal radiation effect of nuclear weapon, civilian**

+ **Y36.54 War operation involving nuclear radiation effects of nuclear weapon**
War operation involving acute radiation exposure from nuclear weapon
War operation involving exposure to immediate ionizing radiation from nuclear weapon
War operation involving fallout exposure from nuclear weapon
War operation involving secondary effects of nuclear weapons
+7th **Y36.540 War operation involving nuclear radiation effects of nuclear weapon, military personnel**
+7th **Y36.541 War operation involving nuclear radiation effects of nuclear weapon, civilian**
+ **Y36.59 War operation involving other effects of nuclear weapons**
+7th **Y36.590 War operation involving other effects of nuclear weapons, military personnel**
+7th **Y36.591 War operation involving other effects of nuclear weapons, civilian**
+ **Y36.6 War operations involving biological weapons**
+ **Y36.6X War operations involving biological weapons**
+7th **Y36.6X0 War operations involving biological weapons, military personnel**
+7th **Y36.6X1 War operations involving biological weapons, civilian**
+ **Y36.7 War operations involving chemical weapons and other forms of unconventional warfare**
Excludes1: *war operations involving incendiary devices (Y36.3-, Y36.5-)*
+ **Y36.7X War operations involving chemical weapons and other forms of unconventional warfare**
+7th **Y36.7X0 War operations involving chemical weapons and other forms of unconventional warfare, military personnel**
+7th **Y36.7X1 War operations involving chemical weapons and other forms of unconventional warfare, civilian**
+ **Y36.8 War operations occurring after cessation of hostilities**
War operations classifiable to categories Y36.0-Y36.8 but occurring after cessation of hostilities
+ **Y36.81 Explosion of mine placed during war operations but exploding after cessation of hostilities**
+7th **Y36.810 Explosion of mine placed during war operations but exploding after cessation of hostilities, military personnel**
+7th **Y36.811 Explosion of mine placed during war operations but exploding after cessation of hostilities, civilian**
+ **Y36.82 Explosion of bomb placed during war operations but exploding after cessation of hostilities**
+7th **Y36.820 Explosion of bomb placed during war operations but exploding after cessation of hostilities, military personnel**
+7th **Y36.821 Explosion of bomb placed during war operations but exploding after cessation of hostilities, civilian**
+ **Y36.88 Other war operations occurring after cessation of hostilities**
+7th **Y36.880 Other war operations occurring after cessation of hostilities, military personnel**
+7th **Y36.881 Other war operations occurring after cessation of hostilities, civilian**
+ **Y36.89 Unspecified war operations occurring after cessation of hostilities**
+7th **Y36.890 Unspecified war operations occurring after cessation of hostilities, military personnel**
+7th **Y36.891 Unspecified war operations occurring after cessation of hostilities, civilian**
+ **Y36.9 Other and unspecified war operations**
X+7th **Y36.90 War operations, unspecified**
X+7th **Y36.91 War operations involving unspecified weapon of mass destruction [WMD]**
X+7th **Y36.92 War operations involving friendly fire**

Y37 Military operations
Includes: injuries to military personnel and civilians occurring during peacetime on military property and during routine military exercises and operations
Excludes1: *military aircraft involved in aircraft accident with civilian aircraft (V97.81-)*
military vehicles involved in transport accident with civilian vehicle (V09.01, V09.21, V19.81, V29.81, V39.81, V49.81, V59.81, V69.81, V79.81)
military watercraft involved in water transport accident with civilian watercraft (V94.81-)
war operations (Y36.-)

The appropriate 7th character is to be added to each code from category Y37
A initial encounter
D subsequent encounter
S sequela

+ **Y37.0 Military operations involving explosion of marine weapons**
+ **Y37.00 Military operations involving explosion of unspecified marine weapon**
Military operations involving underwater blast NOS
+7th **Y37.000 Military operations involving explosion of unspecified marine weapon, military personnel**
+7th **Y37.001 Military operations involving explosion of unspecified marine weapon, civilian**
+ **Y37.01 Military operations involving explosion of depth-charge**
+7th **Y37.010 Military operations involving explosion of depth-charge, military personnel**
+7th **Y37.011 Military operations involving explosion of depth-charge, civilian**
+ **Y37.02 Military operations involving explosion of marine mine**
Military operations involving explosion of marine mine, at sea or in harbor
+7th **Y37.020 Military operations involving explosion of marine mine, military personnel**
+7th **Y37.021 Military operations involving explosion of marine mine, civilian**
+ **Y37.03 Military operations involving explosion of sea-based artillery shell**
+7th **Y37.030 Military operations involving explosion of sea-based artillery shell, military personnel**
+7th **Y37.031 Military operations involving explosion of sea-based artillery shell, civilian**
+ **Y37.04 Military operations involving explosion of torpedo**
+7th **Y37.040 Military operations involving explosion of torpedo, military personnel**
+7th **Y37.041 Military operations involving explosion of torpedo, civilian**
+ **Y37.05 Military operations involving accidental detonation of onboard marine weapons**
+7th **Y37.050 Military operations involving accidental detonation of onboard marine weapons, military personnel**
+7th **Y37.051 Military operations involving accidental detonation of onboard marine weapons, civilian**
+ **Y37.09 Military operations involving explosion of other marine weapons**
+7th **Y37.090 Military operations involving explosion of other marine weapons, military personnel**
+7th **Y37.091 Military operations involving explosion of other marine weapons, civilian**
+ **Y37.1 Military operations involving destruction of aircraft**
+ **Y37.10 Military operations involving unspecified destruction of aircraft**
+7th **Y37.100 Military operations involving unspecified destruction of aircraft, military personnel**
+7th **Y37.101 Military operations involving unspecified destruction of aircraft, civilian**

+ Y37.11 Military operations involving destruction of aircraft due to enemy fire or explosives
Military operations involving destruction of aircraft due to air to air missile
Military operations involving destruction of aircraft due to explosive placed on aircraft
Military operations involving destruction of aircraft due to rocket propelled grenade [RPG]
Military operations involving destruction of aircraft due to small arms fire
Military operations involving destruction of aircraft due to surface to air missile

+7th **Y37.110 Military operations involving destruction of aircraft due to enemy fire or explosives, military personnel**

+7th **Y37.111 Military operations involving destruction of aircraft due to enemy fire or explosives, civilian**

+ Y37.12 Military operations involving destruction of aircraft due to collision with other aircraft

+7th **Y37.120 Military operations involving destruction of aircraft due to collision with other aircraft, military personnel**

+7th **Y37.121 Military operations involving destruction of aircraft due to collision with other aircraft, civilian**

+ Y37.13 Military operations involving destruction of aircraft due to onboard fire

+7th **Y37.130 Military operations involving destruction of aircraft due to onboard fire, military personnel**

+7th **Y37.131 Military operations involving destruction of aircraft due to onboard fire, civilian**

+ Y37.14 Military operations involving destruction of aircraft due to accidental detonation of onboard munitions and explosives

+7th **Y37.140 Military operations involving destruction of aircraft due to accidental detonation of onboard munitions and explosives, military personnel**

+7th **Y37.141 Military operations involving destruction of aircraft due to accidental detonation of onboard munitions and explosives, civilian**

+ Y37.19 Military operations involving other destruction of aircraft

+7th **Y37.190 Military operations involving other destruction of aircraft, military personnel**

+7th **Y37.191 Military operations involving other destruction of aircraft, civilian**

+ Y37.2 Military operations involving other explosions and fragments
Excludes1: *military operations involving explosion of aircraft (Y37.1-)*
military operations involving explosion of marine weapons (Y37.0-)
military operations involving explosion of nuclear weapons (Y37.5-)

+ Y37.20 Military operations involving unspecified explosion and fragments
Military operations involving air blast NOS
Military operations involving blast NOS
Military operations involving blast fragments NOS
Military operations involving blast wave NOS
Military operations involving blast wind NOS
Military operations involving explosion NOS
Military operations involving explosion of bomb NOS

+7th **Y37.200 Military operations involving unspecified explosion and fragments, military personnel**

+7th **Y37.201 Military operations involving unspecified explosion and fragments, civilian**

+ Y37.21 Military operations involving explosion of aerial bomb

+7th **Y37.210 Military operations involving explosion of aerial bomb, military personnel**

+7th **Y37.211 Military operations involving explosion of aerial bomb, civilian**

+ Y37.22 Military operations involving explosion of guided missile

+7th **Y37.220 Military operations involving explosion of guided missile, military personnel**

+7th **Y37.221 Military operations involving explosion of guided missile, civilian**

+ Y37.23 Military operations involving explosion of improvised explosive device [IED]
Military operations involving explosion of person-borne improvised explosive device [IED]
Military operations involving explosion of vehicle-borne improvised explosive device [IED]
Military operations involving explosion of roadside improvised explosive device [IED]

+7th **Y37.230 Military operations involving explosion of improvised explosive device [IED], military personnel**

+7th **Y37.231 Military operations involving explosion of improvised explosive device [IED], civilian**

+ Y37.24 Military operations involving explosion due to accidental detonation and discharge of own munitions or munitions launch device

+7th **Y37.240 Military operations involving explosion due to accidental detonation and discharge of own munitions or munitions launch device, military personnel**

+7th **Y37.241 Military operations involving explosion due to accidental detonation and discharge of own munitions or munitions launch device, civilian**

+ Y37.25 Military operations involving fragments from munitions

+7th **Y37.250 Military operations involving fragments from munitions, military personnel**

+7th **Y37.251 Military operations involving fragments from munitions, civilian**

+ Y37.26 Military operations involving fragments of improvised explosive device [IED]
Military operations involving fragments of person-borne improvised explosive device [IED]
Military operations involving fragments of vehicle-borne improvised explosive device [IED]
Military operations involving fragments of roadside improvised explosive device [IED]

+7th **Y37.260 Military operations involving fragments of improvised explosive device [IED], military personnel**

+7th **Y37.261 Military operations involving fragments of improvised explosive device [IED], civilian**

+ Y37.27 Military operations involving fragments from weapons

+7th **Y37.270 Military operations involving fragments from weapons, military personnel**

+7th **Y37.271 Military operations involving fragments from weapons, civilian**

+ Y37.29 Military operations involving other explosions and fragments
Military operations involving explosion of grenade
Military operations involving explosions of land mine
Military operations involving shrapnel NOS

+7th **Y37.290 Military operations involving other explosions and fragments, military personnel**

+7th **Y37.291 Military operations involving other explosions and fragments,civilian**

+ Y37.3 Military operations involving fires, conflagrations and hot substances
Military operations involving smoke, fumes, and heat from fires, conflagrations and hot substances
Excludes1: *military operations involving fires and conflagrations aboard military aircraft (Y37.1-)*
military operations involving fires and conflagrations aboard military watercraft (Y37.0-)
military operations involving fires and conflagrations caused indirectly by conventional weapons (Y37.2-)
military operations involving fires and thermal effects of nuclear weapons (Y36.53-)

+ Y37.30 Military operations involving unspecified fire, conflagration and hot substance

+7th **Y37.300 Military operations involving unspecified fire, conflagration and hot substance, military personnel**

+7th **Y37.301 Military operations involving unspecified fire, conflagration and hot substance, civilian**

+ **Y37.31 Military operations involving gasoline bomb**
Military operations involving incendiary bomb
Military operations involving petrol bomb
+7th **Y37.310 Military operations involving gasoline bomb, military personnel**
+7th **Y37.311 Military operations involving gasoline bomb, civilian**
+ **Y37.32 Military operations involving incendiary bullet**
+7th **Y37.320 Military operations involving incendiary bullet, military personnel**
+7th **Y37.321 Military operations involving incendiary bullet, civilian**
+ **Y37.33 Military operations involving flamethrower**
+7th **Y37.330 Military operations involving flamethrower, military personnel**
+7th **Y37.331 Military operations involving flamethrower, civilian**
+ **Y37.39 Military operations involving other fires, conflagrations and hot substances**
+7th **Y37.390 Military operations involving other fires, conflagrations and hot substances, military personnel**
+7th **Y37.391 Military operations involving other fires, conflagrations and hot substances, civilian**
+ **Y37.4 Military operations involving firearm discharge and other forms of conventional warfare**
+ **Y37.41 Military operations involving rubber bullets**
+7th **Y37.410 Military operations involving rubber bullets, military personnel**
+7th **Y37.411 Military operations involving rubber bullets, civilian**
+ **Y37.42 Military operations involving firearms pellets**
+7th **Y37.420 Military operations involving firearms pellets, military personnel**
+7th **Y37.421 Military operations involving firearms pellets, civilian**
+ **Y37.43 Military operations involving other firearms discharge**
Military operations involving bullets NOS
Excludes1: *military operations involving munitions fragments (Y37.25-)*
military operations involving incendiary bullets (Y37.32-)
+7th **Y37.430 Military operations involving other firearms discharge, military personnel**
+7th **Y37.431 Military operations involving other firearms discharge, civilian**
+ **Y37.44 Military operations involving unarmed hand to hand combat**
Excludes1: *military operations involving combat using blunt or piercing object (Y37.45-)*
military operations involving intentional restriction of air and airway (Y37.46-)
military operations involving unintentional restriction of air and airway (Y37.47-)
+7th **Y37.440 Military operations involving unarmed hand to hand combat, military personnel**
+7th **Y37.441 Military operations involving unarmed hand to hand combat, civilian**
+ **Y37.45 Military operations involving combat using blunt or piercing object**
+7th **Y37.450 Military operations involving combat using blunt or piercing object, military personnel**
+7th **Y37.451 Military operations involving combat using blunt or piercing object, civilian**
+ **Y37.46 Military operations involving intentional restriction of air and airway**
+7th **Y37.460 Military operations involving intentional restriction of air and airway, military personnel**
+7th **Y37.461 Military operations involving intentional restriction of air and airway, civilian**
+ **Y37.47 Military operations involving unintentional restriction of air and airway**
+7th **Y37.470 Military operations involving unintentional restriction of air and airway, military personnel**
+7th **Y37.471 Military operations involving unintentional restriction of air and airway, civilian**
+ **Y37.49 Military operations involving other forms of conventional warfare**
+7th **Y37.490 Military operations involving other forms of conventional warfare, military personnel**
+7th **Y37.491 Military operations involving other forms of conventional warfare, civilian**
+ **Y37.5 Military operations involving nuclear weapons**
Military operation involving dirty bomb NOS
+ **Y37.50 Military operations involving unspecified effect of nuclear weapon**
+7th **Y37.500 Military operations involving unspecified effect of nuclear weapon, military personnel**
+7th **Y37.501 Military operations involving unspecified effect of nuclear weapon, civilian**
+ **Y37.51 Military operations involving direct blast effect of nuclear weapon**
Military operations involving blast pressure of nuclear weapon
+7th **Y37.510 Military operations involving direct blast effect of nuclear weapon, military personnel**
+7th **Y37.511 Military operations involving direct blast effect of nuclear weapon, civilian**
+ **Y37.52 Military operations involving indirect blast effect of nuclear weapon**
Military operations involving being thrown by blast of nuclear weapon
Military operations involving being struck or crushed by blast debris of nuclear weapon
+7th **Y37.520 Military operations involving indirect blast effect of nuclear weapon, military personnel**
+7th **Y37.521 Military operations involving indirect blast effect of nuclear weapon, civilian**
+ **Y37.53 Military operations involving thermal radiation effect of nuclear weapon**
Military operations involving direct heat from nuclear weapon
Military operation involving fireball effects from nuclear weapon
+7th **Y37.530 Military operations involving thermal radiation effect of nuclear weapon, military personnel**
+7th **Y37.531 Military operations involving thermal radiation effect of nuclear weapon, civilian**
+ **Y37.54 Military operation involving nuclear radiation effects of nuclear weapon**
Military operation involving acute radiation exposure from nuclear weapon
Military operation involving exposure to immediate ionizing radiation from nuclear weapon
Military operation involving fallout exposure from nuclear weapon
Military operation involving secondary effects of nuclear weapons
+7th **Y37.540 Military operation involving nuclear radiation effects of nuclear weapon, military personnel**
+7th **Y37.541 Military operation involving nuclear radiation effects of nuclear weapon, civilian**
+ **Y37.59 Military operation involving other effects of nuclear weapons**
+7th **Y37.590 Military operation involving other effects of nuclear weapons, military personnel**
+7th **Y37.591 Military operation involving other effects of nuclear weapons, civilian**
+ **Y37.6 Military operations involving biological weapons**
+ **Y37.6X Military operations involving biological weapons**
+7th **Y37.6X0 Military operations involving biological weapons, military personnel**
+7th **Y37.6X1 Military operations involving biological weapons, civilian**
+ **Y37.7 Military operations involving chemical weapons and other forms of unconventional warfare**
Excludes1: *military operations involving incendiary devices (Y36.3-, Y36.5-)*
+ **Y37.7X Military operations involving chemical weapons and other forms of unconventional warfare**
+7th **Y37.7X0 Military operations involving chemical weapons and other forms of unconventional warfare, military personnel**
+7th **Y37.7X1 Military operations involving chemical weapons and other forms of unconventional warfare, civilian**

+ **Y37.9 Other and unspecified military operations**
  - X+7th **Y37.90 Military operations, unspecified**
  - X+7th **Y37.91 Military operations involving unspecified weapon of mass destruction [WMD]**
  - X+7th **Y37.92 Military operations involving friendly fire**

Y38 Terrorism

These codes are for use to identify injuries resulting from the unlawful use of force or violence against persons or property to intimidate or coerce a Government, the civilian population, or any segment thereof, in furtherance of political or social objective

Use additional code for place of occurrence (Y92.-)

The appropriate 7th character is to be added to each code from category Y38
A initial encounter
D subsequent encounter
S sequela

Review coding guideline C.20.j

+ **Y38.0 Terrorism involving explosion of marine weapons**
  Terrorism involving depth-charge
  Terrorism involving marine mine
  Terrorism involving mine NOS, at sea or in harbor
  Terrorism involving sea-based artillery shell
  Terrorism involving torpedo
  Terrorism involving underwater blast
  + **Y38.0X Terrorism involving explosion of marine weapons**
    - +7th **Y38.0X1 Terrorism involving explosion of marine weapons, public safety official injured**
    - +7th **Y38.0X2 Terrorism involving explosion of marine weapons, civilian injured**
    - +7th **Y38.0X3 Terrorism involving explosion of marine weapons, terrorist injured**

+ **Y38.1 Terrorism involving destruction of aircraft**
  Terrorism involving aircraft burned
  Terrorism involving aircraft exploded
  Terrorism involving aircraft being shot down
  Terrorism involving aircraft used as a weapon
  + **Y38.1X Terrorism involving destruction of aircraft**
    - +7th **Y38.1X1 Terrorism involving destruction of aircraft, public safety official injured**
    - +7th **Y38.1X2 Terrorism involving destruction of aircraft, civilian injured**
    - +7th **Y38.1X3 Terrorism involving destruction of aircraft, terrorist injured**

+ **Y38.2 Terrorism involving other explosions and fragments**
  Terrorism involving antipersonnel (fragments) bomb
  Terrorism involving blast NOS
  Terrorism involving explosion NOS
  Terrorism involving explosion of breech block
  Terrorism involving explosion of cannon block
  Terrorism involving explosion (fragments) of artillery shell
  Terrorism involving explosion (fragments) of bomb
  Terrorism involving explosion (fragments) of grenade
  Terrorism involving explosion (fragments) of guided missile
  Terrorism involving explosion (fragments) of land mine
  Terrorism involving explosion of mortar bomb
  Terrorism involving explosion of munitions
  Terrorism involving explosion (fragments) of rocket
  Terrorism involving explosion (fragments) of shell
  Terrorism involving shrapnel
  Terrorism involving mine NOS, on land
  Excludes1: *terrorism involving explosion of nuclear weapon (Y38.5)*
  terrorism involving suicide bomber (Y38.81)
  + **Y38.2X Terrorism involving other explosions and fragments**
    - +7th **Y38.2X1 Terrorism involving other explosions and fragments, public safety official injured**
    - +7th **Y38.2X2 Terrorism involving other explosions and fragments, civilian injured**
    - +7th **Y38.2X3 Terrorism involving other explosions and fragments, terrorist injured**

+ **Y38.3 Terrorism involving fires, conflagration and hot substances**
  Terrorism involving conflagration NOS
  Terrorism involving fire NOS
  Terrorism involving petrol bomb
  Excludes1: *terrorism involving fire or heat of nuclear weapon (Y38.5)*
  + **Y38.3X Terrorism involving fires, conflagration and hot substances**
    - +7th **Y38.3X1 Terrorism involving fires, conflagration and hot substances, public safety official injured**
    - +7th **Y38.3X2 Terrorism involving fires, conflagration and hot substances, civilian injured**
    - +7th **Y38.3X3 Terrorism involving fires, conflagration and hot substances, terrorist injured**

+ **Y38.4 Terrorism involving firearms**
  Terrorism involving carbine bullet
  Terrorism involving machine gun bullet
  Terrorism involving pellets (shotgun)
  Terrorism involving pistol bullet
  Terrorism involving rifle bullet
  Terrorism involving rubber (rifle) bullet
  + **Y38.4X Terrorism involving firearms**
    - +7th **Y38.4X1 Terrorism involving firearms, public safety official injured**
    - +7th **Y38.4X2 Terrorism involving firearms, civilian injured**
    - +7th **Y38.4X3 Terrorism involving firearms, terrorist injured**

+ **Y38.5 Terrorism involving nuclear weapons**
  Terrorism involving blast effects of nuclear weapon
  Terrorism involving exposure to ionizing radiation from nuclear weapon
  Terrorism involving fireball effect of nuclear weapon
  Terrorism involving heat from nuclear weapon
  + **Y38.5X Terrorism involving nuclear weapons**
    - +7th **Y38.5X1 Terrorism involving nuclear weapons, public safety official injured**
    - +7th **Y38.5X2 Terrorism involving nuclear weapons, civilian injured**
    - +7th **Y38.5X3 Terrorism involving nuclear weapons, terrorist injured**

+ **Y38.6 Terrorism involving biological weapons**
  Terrorism involving anthrax
  Terrorism involving cholera
  Terrorism involving smallpox
  + **Y38.6X Terrorism involving biological weapons**
    - +7th **Y38.6X1 Terrorism involving biological weapons, public safety official injured**
    - +7th **Y38.6X2 Terrorism involving biological weapons, civilian injured**
    - +7th **Y38.6X3 Terrorism involving biological weapons, terrorist injured**

+ **Y38.7 Terrorism involving chemical weapons**
  Terrorism involving gases, fumes, chemicals
  Terrorism involving hydrogen cyanide
  Terrorism involving phosgene
  Terrorism involving sarin
  + **Y38.7X Terrorism involving chemical weapons**
    - +7th **Y38.7X1 Terrorism involving chemical weapons, public safety official injured**
    - +7th **Y38.7X2 Terrorism involving chemical weapons, civilian injured**
    - +7th **Y38.7X3 Terrorism involving chemical weapons, terrorist injured**

+ **Y38.8 Terrorism involving other and unspecified means**
  - X+7th **Y38.80 Terrorism involving unspecified means**
    Terrorism NOS
  + **Y38.81 Terrorism involving suicide bomber**
    - +7th **Y38.811 Terrorism involving suicide bomber, public safety official injured**
    - +7th **Y38.812 Terrorism involving suicide bomber, civilian injured**
  + **Y38.89 Terrorism involving other means**
    Terrorism involving drowning and submersion
    Terrorism involving lasers
    Terrorism involving piercing or stabbing instruments
    - +7th **Y38.891 Terrorism involving other means, public safety official injured**
    - +7th **Y38.892 Terrorism involving other means, civilian injured**
    - +7th **Y38.893 Terrorism involving other means, terrorist injured**

+ **Y38.9 Terrorism, secondary effects**
  NOTE This code is for use to identify conditions occurring subsequent to a terrorist attack not those that are due to the initial terrorist attack
  + **Y38.9X Terrorism, secondary effects**
    - +7th **Y38.9X1 Terrorism, secondary effects, public safety official injured**
    - +7th **Y38.9X2 Terrorism, secondary effects, civilian injured**

Complications of medical and surgical care (Y62-Y84)

Includes: complications of medical devices surgical and medical procedures as the cause of abnormal reaction of the patient, or of later complication, without mention of misadventure at the time of the procedure

Misadventures to patients during surgical and medical care (Y62-Y69)

Excludes2: *breakdown or malfunctioning of medical device (during procedure) (after implantation) (ongoing use) (Y70-Y82)*
surgical and medical procedures as the cause of abnormal reaction of the patient, without mention of misadventure at the time of the procedure (Y83-Y84)

Y62 Failure of sterile precautions during surgical and medical care
- **Y62.0 Failure of sterile precautions during surgical operation**
- **Y62.1 Failure of sterile precautions during infusion or transfusion**
- **Y62.2 Failure of sterile precautions during kidney dialysis and other perfusion**
- **Y62.3 Failure of sterile precautions during injection or immunization**
- **Y62.4 Failure of sterile precautions during endoscopic examination**
- **Y62.5 Failure of sterile precautions during heart catheterization**
- **Y62.6 Failure of sterile precautions during aspiration, puncture and other catheterization**
- **Y62.8 Failure of sterile precautions during other surgical and medical care**
- **Y62.9 Failure of sterile precautions during unspecified surgical and medical care**

Y63 Failure in dosage during surgical and medical care

Excludes2: *accidental overdose of drug or wrong drug given in error (T36-T50)*

- **Y63.0 Excessive amount of blood or other fluid given during transfusion or infusion**
- **Y63.1 Incorrect dilution of fluid used during infusion**
- **Y63.2 Overdose of radiation given during therapy**
- **Y63.3 Inadvertent exposure of patient to radiation during medical care**
- **Y63.4 Failure in dosage in electroshock or insulin-shock therapy**
- **Y63.5 Inappropriate temperature in local application and packing**
- **Y63.6 Underdosing and nonadministration of necessary drug, medicament or biological substance**
  Review coding guideline C.19.e.5.c
- **Y63.8 Failure in dosage during other surgical and medical care**
  Review coding guideline C.19.e.5.c
- **Y63.9 Failure in dosage during unspecified surgical and medical care**
  Review coding guideline C.19.e.5.c

Y64 Contaminated medical or biological substances
- **Y64.0 Contaminated medical or biological substance, transfused or infused**
- **Y64.1 Contaminated medical or biological substance, injected or used for immunization**
- **Y64.8 Contaminated medical or biological substance administered by other means**
- **Y64.9 Contaminated medical or biological substance administered by unspecified means**
  Administered contaminated medical or biological substance NOS

Y65 Other misadventures during surgical and medical care
- **Y65.0 Mismatched blood in transfusion**
- **Y65.1 Wrong fluid used in infusion**
- **Y65.2 Failure in suture or ligature during surgical operation**
- **Y65.3 Endotracheal tube wrongly placed during anesthetic procedure**
- **Y65.4 Failure to introduce or to remove other tube or instrument**
- + **Y65.5 Performance of wrong procedure (operation)**
  - **Y65.51 Performance of wrong procedure (operation) on correct patient**
    Wrong device implanted into correct surgical site
    Excludes1: *performance of correct procedure (operation) on wrong side or body part (Y65.53)*
  - **Y65.52 Performance of procedure (operation) on patient not scheduled for surgery**
    Performance of procedure (operation) intended for another patient
    Performance of procedure (operation) on wrong patient
  - **Y65.53 Performance of correct procedure (operation) on wrong side or body part**
    Performance of correct procedure (operation) on wrong side
    Performance of correct procedure (operation) on wrong site
- **Y65.8 Other specified misadventures during surgical and medical care**

Y66 Nonadministration of surgical and medical care

Premature cessation of surgical and medical care
Excludes1: *DNR status (Z66)*
palliative care (Z51.5)
Valid 3-character code, no further characters required

Y69 Unspecified misadventure during surgical and medical care

Valid 3-character code, no further characters required

Medical devices associated with adverse incidents in diagnostic and therapeutic use (Y70-Y82)

Includes: breakdown or malfunction of medical devices (during use) (after implantation) (ongoing use)

Excludes1: *misadventure to patients during surgical and medical care, classifiable to (Y62-Y69)*
later complications following use of medical devices without breakdown or malfunctioning of device (Y83-Y84)

Y70 Anesthesiology devices associated with adverse incidents
- **Y70.0 Diagnostic and monitoring anesthesiology devices associated with adverse incidents**
- **Y70.1 Therapeutic (nonsurgical) and rehabilitative anesthesiology devices associated with adverse incidents**
- **Y70.2 Prosthetic and other implants, materials and accessory anesthesiology devices associated with adverse incidents**
- **Y70.3 Surgical instruments, materials and anesthesiology devices (including sutures) associated with adverse incidents**
- **Y70.8 Miscellaneous anesthesiology devices associated with adverse incidents, not elsewhere classified**

Y71 Cardiovascular devices associated with adverse incidents
- **Y71.0 Diagnostic and monitoring cardiovascular devices associated with adverse incidents**
- **Y71.1 Therapeutic (nonsurgical) and rehabilitative cardiovascular devices associated with adverse incidents**
- **Y71.2 Prosthetic and other implants, materials and accessory cardiovascular devices associated with adverse incidents**
- **Y71.3 Surgical instruments, materials and cardiovascular devices (including sutures) associated with adverse incidents**
- **Y71.8 Miscellaneous cardiovascular devices associated with adverse incidents, not elsewhere classified**

Y72 Otorhinolaryngological devices associated with adverse incidents
- **Y72.0 Diagnostic and monitoring otorhinolaryngological devices associated with adverse incidents**
- **Y72.1 Therapeutic (nonsurgical) and rehabilitative otorhinolaryngological devices associated with adverse incidents**
- **Y72.2 Prosthetic and other implants, materials and accessory otorhinolaryngological devices associated with adverse incidents**
- **Y72.3 Surgical instruments, materials and otorhinolaryngological devices (including sutures) associated with adverse incidents**
- **Y72.8 Miscellaneous otorhinolaryngological devices associated with adverse incidents, not elsewhere classified**

Y73 Gastroenterology and urology devices associated with adverse incidents
- **Y73.0 Diagnostic and monitoring gastroenterology and urology devices associated with adverse incidents**
- **Y73.1 Therapeutic (nonsurgical) and rehabilitative gastroenterology and urology devices associated with adverse incidents**
- **Y73.2 Prosthetic and other implants, materials and accessory gastroenterology and urology devices associated with adverse incidents**
- **Y73.3 Surgical instruments, materials and gastroenterology and urology devices (including sutures) associated with adverse incidents**
- **Y73.8 Miscellaneous gastroenterology and urology devices associated with adverse incidents, not elsewhere classified**

Y74 General hospital and personal-use devices associated with adverse incidents
- **Y74.0 Diagnostic and monitoring general hospital and personal-use devices associated with adverse incidents**
- **Y74.1 Therapeutic (nonsurgical) and rehabilitative general hospital and personal-use devices associated with adverse incidents**
- **Y74.2 Prosthetic and other implants, materials and accessory general hospital and personal-use devices associated with adverse incidents**

Y74.3 Surgical instruments, materials and general hospital and personal-use devices (including sutures) associated with adverse incidents
Y74.8 Miscellaneous general hospital and personal-use devices associated with adverse incidents, not elsewhere classified

Y75 Neurological devices associated with adverse incidents
Y75.0 Diagnostic and monitoring neurological devices associated with adverse incidents
Y75.1 Therapeutic (nonsurgical) and rehabilitative neurological devices associated with adverse incidents
Y75.2 Prosthetic and other implants, materials and neurological devices associated with adverse incidents
Y75.3 Surgical instruments, materials and neurological devices (including sutures) associated with adverse incidents
Y75.8 Miscellaneous neurological devices associated with adverse incidents, not elsewhere classified

Y76 Obstetric and gynecological devices associated with adverse incidents
♀ Y76.0 Diagnostic and monitoring obstetric and gynecological devices associated with adverse incidents
♀ Y76.1 Therapeutic (nonsurgical) and rehabilitative obstetric and gynecological devices associated with adverse incidents
♀ Y76.2 Prosthetic and other implants, materials and accessory obstetric and gynecological devices associated with adverse incidents
♀ Y76.3 Surgical instruments, materials and obstetric and gynecological devices (including sutures) associated with adverse incidents
♀ Y76.8 Miscellaneous obstetric and gynecological devices associated with adverse incidents, not elsewhere classified

Y77 Ophthalmic devices associated with adverse incidents
Y77.0 Diagnostic and monitoring ophthalmic devices associated with adverse incidents
Y77.1 Therapeutic (nonsurgical) and rehabilitative ophthalmic devices associated with adverse incidents
Y77.2 Prosthetic and other implants, materials and accessory ophthalmic devices associated with adverse incidents
Y77.3 Surgical instruments, materials and ophthalmic devices (including sutures) associated with adverse incidents
Y77.8 Miscellaneous ophthalmic devices associated with adverse incidents, not elsewhere classified

Y78 Radiological devices associated with adverse incidents
Y78.0 Diagnostic and monitoring radiological devices associated with adverse incidents
Y78.1 Therapeutic (nonsurgical) and rehabilitative radiological devices associated with adverse incidents
Y78.2 Prosthetic and other implants, materials and accessory radiological devices associated with adverse incidents
Y78.3 Surgical instruments, materials and radiological devices (including sutures) associated with adverse incidents
Y78.8 Miscellaneous radiological devices associated with adverse incidents, not elsewhere classified

Y79 Orthopedic devices associated with adverse incidents
Y79.0 Diagnostic and monitoring orthopedic devices associated with adverse incidents
Y79.1 Therapeutic (nonsurgical) and rehabilitative orthopedic devices associated with adverse incidents
Y79.2 Prosthetic and other implants, materials and accessory orthopedic devices associated with adverse incidents
Y79.3 Surgical instruments, materials and orthopedic devices (including sutures) associated with adverse incidents
Y79.8 Miscellaneous orthopedic devices associated with adverse incidents, not elsewhere classified

Y80 Physical medicine devices associated with adverse incidents
Y80.0 Diagnostic and monitoring physical medicine devices associated with adverse incidents
Y80.1 Therapeutic (nonsurgical) and rehabilitative physical medicine devices associated with adverse incidents
Y80.2 Prosthetic and other implants, materials and accessory physical medicine devices associated with adverse incidents
Y80.3 Surgical instruments, materials and physical medicine devices (including sutures) associated with adverse incidents
Y80.8 Miscellaneous physical medicine devices associated with adverse incidents, not elsewhere classified

Y81 General- and plastic-surgery devices associated with adverse incidents
Y81.0 Diagnostic and monitoring general- and plastic-surgery devices associated with adverse incidents
Y81.1 Therapeutic (nonsurgical) and rehabilitative general- and plastic-surgery devices associated with adverse incidents
Y81.2 Prosthetic and other implants, materials and accessory general- and plastic-surgery devices associated with adverse incidents
Y81.3 Surgical instruments, materials and general- and plastic-surger devices (including sutures) associated with adverse incidents
Y81.8 Miscellaneous general- and plastic-surgery devices associated with adverse incidents, not elsewhere classified

Y82 Other and unspecified medical devices associated with adverse incidents
Y82.8 Other medical devices associated with adverse incidents
Y82.9 Unspecified medical devices associated with adverse incidents

Surgical and other medical procedures as the cause of abnormal reaction of the patient, or of later complication, without mention of misadventure at the time of the procedure (Y83-Y84)

Excludes1: *misadventures to patients during surgical and medical care, classifiable to (Y62-Y69)*

Y83 Surgical operation and other surgical procedures as the cause of abnormal reaction of the patient, or of later complication, without mention of misadventure at the time of the procedure
Y83.0 Surgical operation with transplant of whole organ as the cause of abnormal reaction of the patient, or of later complication, without mention of misadventure at the time of the procedure
Y83.1 Surgical operation with implant of artificial internal device as the cause of abnormal reaction of the patient, or of later complication, without mention of misadventure at the time of the procedure
Y83.2 Surgical operation with anastomosis, bypass or graft as the cause of abnormal reaction of the patient, or of later complication, without mention of misadventure at the time of the procedure
Y83.3 Surgical operation with formation of external stoma as the cause of abnormal reaction of the patient, or of later complication, without mention of misadventure at the time of the procedure
Y83.4 Other reconstructive surgery as the cause of abnormal reaction of the patient, or of later complication, without mention of misadventure at the time of the procedure
Y83.5 Amputation of limb(s) as the cause of abnormal reaction of the patient, or of later complication, without mention of misadventure at the time of the procedure
Y83.6 Removal of other organ (partial) (total) as the cause of abnormal reaction of the patient, or of later complication, without mention of misadventure at the time of the procedure
Y83.8 Other surgical procedures as the cause of abnormal reaction of the patient, or of later complication, without mention of misadventure at the time of the procedure
Y83.9 Surgical procedure, unspecified as the cause of abnormal reaction of the patient, or of later complication, without mention of misadventure at the time of the procedure

Y84 Other medical procedures as the cause of abnormal reaction of the patient, or of later complication, without mention of misadventure at the time of the procedure
Y84.0 Cardiac catheterization as the cause of abnormal reaction of the patient, or of later complication, without mention of misadventure at the time of the procedure
Y84.1 Kidney dialysis as the cause of abnormal reaction of the patient, or of later complication, without mention of misadventure at the time of the procedure
Y84.2 Radiological procedure and radiotherapy as the cause of abnormal reaction of the patient, or of later complication, without mention of misadventure at the time of the procedure
Review coding guideline C.2.c.2
Y84.3 Shock therapy as the cause of abnormal reaction of the patient, or of later complication, without mention of misadventure at the time of the procedure
Y84.4 Aspiration of fluid as the cause of abnormal reaction of the patient, or of later complication, without mention of misadventure at the time of the procedure
Y84.5 Insertion of gastric or duodenal sound as the cause of abnormal reaction of the patient, or of later complication, without mention of misadventure at the time of the procedure
Y84.6 Urinary catheterization as the cause of abnormal reaction of the patient, or of later complication, without mention of misadventure at the time of the procedure
Y84.7 Blood-sampling as the cause of abnormal reaction of the patient, or of later complication, without mention of misadventure at the time of the procedure

Y84.8 **Other medical procedures as the cause of abnormal reaction of the patient, or of later complication, without mention of misadventure at the time of the procedure**

Y84.9 **Medical procedure, unspecified as the cause of abnormal reaction of the patient, or of later complication, without mention of misadventure at the time of the procedure**

Supplementary factors related to causes of morbidity classified elsewhere (Y90-Y99)

NOTE These categories may be used to provide supplementary information concerning causes of morbidity. They are not to be used for single-condition coding.

Y90 **Evidence of alcohol involvement determined by blood alcohol level**

Code first any associated alcohol related disorders (F10)

Y90.0 **Blood alcohol level of less than 20 mg/100 ml**
Y90.1 **Blood alcohol level of 20-39 mg/100 ml**
Y90.2 **Blood alcohol level of 40-59 mg/100 ml**
Y90.3 **Blood alcohol level of 60-79 mg/100 ml**
Y90.4 **Blood alcohol level of 80-99 mg/100 ml**
Y90.5 **Blood alcohol level of 100-119 mg/100 ml**
Y90.6 **Blood alcohol level of 120-199 mg/100 ml**
Y90.7 **Blood alcohol level of 200-239 mg/100 ml**
Y90.8 **Blood alcohol level of 240 mg/100 ml or more**
Y90.9 **Presence of alcohol in blood, level not specified**

Y92 **Place of occurrence of the external cause**

The following category is for use, when relevant, to identify the place of occurrence of the external cause. Use in conjunction with an activity code.

Place of occurrence should be recorded only at the initial encounter for treatment

Review coding guideline C.20.b

+ **Y92.0** **Non-institutional (private) residence as the place of occurrence of the external cause**

Excludes1: *abandoned or derelict house (Y92.89)*
home under construction but not yet occupied (Y92.6-)
institutional place of residence (Y92.1-)

+ **Y92.00** **Unspecified non-institutional (private) residence as the place of occurrence of the external cause**

Y92.000 **Kitchen of unspecified non-institutional (private) residence as the place of occurrence of the external cause**
Y92.001 **Dining room of unspecified non-institutional (private) residence as the place of occurrence of the external cause**
Y92.002 **Bathroom of unspecified non-institutional (private) residence single-family (private) house as the place of occurrence of the external cause**
Y92.003 **Bedroom of unspecified non-institutional (private) residence as the place of occurrence of the external cause**
Y92.007 **Garden or yard of unspecified non-institutional (private) residence as the place of occurrence of the external cause**
Y92.008 **Other place in unspecified non-institutional (private) residence as the place of occurrence of the external cause**
Y92.009 **Unspecified place in unspecified non-institutional (private) residence as the place of occurrence of the external cause**

Home (NOS) as the place of occurrence of the external cause

+ **Y92.01** **Single-family non-institutional (private) house as the place of occurrence of the external cause**

Farmhouse as the place of occurrence of the external cause

Excludes1: *barn (Y92.71)*
chicken coop or hen house (Y92.72)
farm field (Y92.73)
orchard (Y92.74)
single family mobile home or trailer (Y92.02-)
slaughter house (Y92.86)

Y92.010 **Kitchen of single-family (private) house as the place of occurrence of the external cause**
Y92.011 **Dining room of single-family (private) house as the place of occurrence of the external cause**
Y92.012 **Bathroom of single-family (private) house as the place of occurrence of the external cause**
Y92.013 **Bedroom of single-family (private) house as the place of occurrence of the external cause**
Y92.014 **Private driveway to single-family (private) house as the place of occurrence of the external cause**
Y92.015 **Private garage of single-family (private) house as the place of occurrence of the external cause**
Y92.016 **Swimming-pool in single-family (private) house or garden as the place of occurrence of the external cause**
Y92.017 **Garden or yard in single-family (private) house as the place of occurrence of the external cause**
Y92.018 **Other place in single-family (private) house as the place of occurrence of the external cause**
Y92.019 **Unspecified place in single-family (private) house as the place of occurrence of the external cause**

+ **Y92.02** **Mobile home as the place of occurrence of the external cause**

Y92.020 **Kitchen in mobile home as the place of occurrence of the external cause**
Y92.021 **Dining room in mobile home as the place of occurrence of the external cause**
Y92.022 **Bathroom in mobile home as the place of occurrence of the external cause**
Y92.023 **Bedroom in mobile home as the place of occurrence of the external cause**
Y92.024 **Driveway of mobile home as the place of occurrence of the external cause**
Y92.025 **Garage of mobile home as the place of occurrence of the external cause**
Y92.026 **Swimming-pool of mobile home as the place of occurrence of the external cause**
Y92.027 **Garden or yard of mobile home as the place of occurrence of the external cause**
Y92.028 **Other place in mobile home as the place of occurrence of the external cause**
Y92.029 **Unspecified place in mobile home as the place of occurrence of the external cause**

+ **Y92.03** **Apartment as the place of occurrence of the external cause**

Condominium as the place of occurrence of the external cause

Co-op apartment as the place of occurrence of the external cause

Y92.030 **Kitchen in apartment as the place of occurrence of the external cause**
Y92.031 **Bathroom in apartment as the place of occurrence of the external cause**
Y92.032 **Bedroom in apartment as the place of occurrence of the external cause**
Y92.038 **Other place in apartment as the place of occurrence of the external cause**
Y92.039 **Unspecified place in apartment as the place of occurrence of the external cause**

+ **Y92.04** **Boarding-house as the place of occurrence of the external cause**

Y92.040 **Kitchen in boarding-house as the place of occurrence of the external cause**
Y92.041 **Bathroom in boarding-house as the place of occurrence of the external cause**
Y92.042 **Bedroom in boarding-house as the place of occurrence of the external cause**
Y92.043 **Driveway of boarding-house as the place of occurrence of the external cause**
Y92.044 **Garage of boarding-house as the place of occurrence of the external cause**
Y92.045 **Swimming-pool of boarding-house as the place of occurrence of the external cause**
Y92.046 **Garden or yard of boarding-house as the place of occurrence of the external cause**
Y92.048 **Other place in boarding-house as the place of occurrence of the external cause**
Y92.049 **Unspecified place in boarding-house as the place of occurrence of the external cause**

+ Y92.09 Other non-institutional residence as the place of occurrence of the external cause

Y92.090 Kitchen in other non-institutional residence as the place of occurrence of the external cause

Y92.091 Bathroom in other non-institutional residence as the place of occurrence of the external cause

Y92.092 Bedroom in other non-institutional residence as the place of occurrence of the external cause

Y92.093 Driveway of other non-institutional residence as the place of occurrence of the external cause

Y92.094 Garage of other non-institutional residence as the place of occurrence of the external cause

Y92.095 Swimming-pool of other non-institutional residence as the place of occurrence of the external cause

Y92.096 Garden or yard of other non-institutional residence as the place of occurrence of the external cause

Y92.098 Other place in other non-institutional residence as the place of occurrence of the external cause

Y92.099 Unspecified place in other non-institutional residence as the place of occurrence of the external cause

+ Y92.1 Institutional (nonprivate) residence as the place of occurrence of the external cause

Y92.10 Unspecified residential institution as the place of occurrence of the external cause

+ Y92.11 Children's home and orphanage as the place of occurrence of the external cause

Y92.110 Kitchen in children's home and orphanage as the place of occurrence of the external cause

Y92.111 Bathroom in children's home and orphanage as the place of occurrence of the external cause

Y92.112 Bedroom in children's home and orphanage as the place of occurrence of the external cause

Y92.113 Driveway of children's home and orphanage as the place of occurrence of the external cause

Y92.114 Garage of children's home and orphanage as the place of occurrence of the external cause

Y92.115 Swimming-pool of children's home and orphanage as the place of occurrence of the external cause

Y92.116 Garden or yard of children's home and orphanage as the place of occurrence of the external cause

Y92.118 Other place in children's home and orphanage as the place of occurrence of the external cause

Y92.119 Unspecified place in children's home and orphanage as the place of occurrence of the external cause

+ Y92.12 Nursing home as the place of occurrence of the external cause

Home for the sick as the place of occurrence of the external cause

Hospice as the place of occurrence of the external cause

Y92.120 Kitchen in nursing home as the place of occurrence of the external cause

Y92.121 Bathroom in nursing home as the place of occurrence of the external cause

Y92.122 Bedroom in nursing home as the place of occurrence of the external cause

Y92.123 Driveway of nursing home as the place of occurrence of the external cause

Y92.124 Garage of nursing home as the place of occurrence of the external cause

Y92.125 Swimming-pool of nursing home as the place of occurrence of the external cause

Y92.126 Garden or yard of nursing home as the place of occurrence of the external cause

Y92.128 Other place in nursing home as the place of occurrence of the external cause

Y92.129 Unspecified place in nursing home as the place of occurrence of the external cause

+ Y92.13 Military base as the place of occurrence of the external cause

Excludes1: *military training grounds (Y92.83)*

Y92.130 Kitchen on military base as the place of occurrence of the external cause

Y92.131 Mess hall on military base as the place of occurrence of the external cause

Y92.133 Barracks on military base as the place of occurrence of the external cause

Y92.135 Garage on military base as the place of occurrence of the external cause

Y92.136 Swimming-pool on military base as the place of occurrence of the external cause

Y92.137 Garden or yard on military base as the place of occurrence of the external cause

Y92.138 Other place on military base as the place of occurrence of the external cause

Y92.139 Unspecified place military base as the place of occurrence of the external cause

+ Y92.14 Prison as the place of occurrence of the external cause

Y92.140 Kitchen in prison as the place of occurrence of the external cause

Y92.141 Dining room in prison as the place of occurrence of the external cause

Y92.142 Bathroom in prison as the place of occurrence of the external cause

Y92.143 Cell of prison as the place of occurrence of the external cause

Y92.146 Swimming-pool of prison as the place of occurrence of the external cause

Y92.147 Courtyard of prison as the place of occurrence of the external cause

Y92.148 Other place in prison as the place of occurrence of the external cause

Y92.149 Unspecified place in prison as the place of occurrence of the external cause

+ Y92.15 Reform school as the place of occurrence of the external cause

Y92.150 Kitchen in reform school as the place of occurrence of the external cause

Y92.151 Dining room in reform school as the place of occurrence of the external cause

Y92.152 Bathroom in reform school as the place of occurrence of the external cause

Y92.153 Bedroom in reform school as the place of occurrence of the external cause

Y92.154 Driveway of reform school as the place of occurrence of the external cause

Y92.155 Garage of reform school as the place of occurrence of the external cause

Y92.156 Swimming-pool of reform school as the place of occurrence of the external cause

Y92.157 Garden or yard of reform school as the place of occurrence of the external cause

Y92.158 Other place in reform school as the place of occurrence of the external cause

Y92.159 Unspecified place in reform school as the place of occurrence of the external cause

+ Y92.16 School dormitory as the place of occurrence of the external cause

Excludes1: *reform school as the place of occurrence of the external cause (Y92.15-)*
school buildings and grounds as the place of occurrence of the external cause (Y92.2-)
school sports and athletic areas as the place of occurrence of the external cause (Y92.3-)

Y92.160 Kitchen in school dormitory as the place of occurrence of the external cause

Y92.161 Dining room in school dormitory as the place of occurrence of the external cause

Y92.162 Bathroom in school dormitory as the place of occurrence of the external cause

Y92.163 Bedroom in school dormitory as the place of occurrence of the external cause

Y92.168 Other place in school dormitory as the place of occurrence of the external cause

Y92.169 Unspecified place in school dormitory as the place of occurrence of the external cause

+ Y92.19 Other specified residential institution as the place of occurrence of the external cause

Y92.190 Kitchen in other specified residential institution as the place of occurrence of the external cause

Y92.191 Dining room in other specified residential institution as the place of occurrence of the external cause

Y92.192 Bathroom in other specified residential institution as the place of occurrence of the external cause

Y92.193 Bedroom in other specified residential institution as the place of occurrence of the external cause

Y92.194 Driveway of other specified residential institution as the place of occurrence of the external cause

Y92.195 Garage of other specified residential institution as the place of occurrence of the external cause

Y92.196 Pool of other specified residential institution as the place of occurrence of the external cause

Y92.197 Garden or yard of other specified residential institution as the place of occurrence of the external cause

Y92.198 Other place in other specified residential institution as the place of occurrence of the external cause

Y92.199 Unspecified place in other specified residential institution as the place of occurrence of the external cause

+ Y92.2 School, other institution and public administrative area as the place of occurrence of the external cause

Building and adjacent grounds used by the general public or by a particular group of the public

Excludes1: *building under construction as the place of occurrence of the external cause (Y92.6)*
residential institution as the place of occurrence of the external cause (Y92.1)
school dormitory as the place of occurrence of the external cause (Y92.16-)
sports and athletics area of schools as the place of occurrence of the external cause (Y92.3-)

+ Y92.21 School (private) (public) (state) as the place of occurrence of the external cause

Y92.210 Daycare center as the place of occurrence of the external cause

Y92.211 Elementary school as the place of occurrence of the external cause

Kindergarten as the place of occurrence of the external cause

Y92.212 Middle school as the place of occurrence of the external cause

Y92.213 High school as the place of occurrence of the external cause

AHA CC: 4Q, 2012, 108

Y92.214 College as the place of occurrence of the external cause

University as the place of occurrence of the external cause

Y92.215 Trade school as the place of occurrence of the external cause

Y92.218 Other school as the place of occurrence of the external cause

Y92.219 Unspecified school as the place of occurrence of the external cause

+ Y92.22 Religious institution as the place of occurrence of the external cause

Church as the place of occurrence of the external cause
Mosque as the place of occurrence of the external cause
Synagogue as the place of occurrence of the external cause

+ Y92.23 Hospital as the place of occurrence of the external cause

Excludes1: *ambulatory (outpatient) health services establishments (Y92.53-)*
home for the sick as the place of occurrence of the external cause (Y92.12-)
hospice as the place of occurrence of the external cause (Y92.12-)
nursing home as the place of occurrence of the external cause (Y92.12-)

Y92.230 Patient room in hospital as the place of occurrence of the external cause

Y92.231 Patient bathroom in hospital as the place of occurrence of the external cause

Y92.232 Corridor of hospital as the place of occurrence of the external cause

Y92.233 Cafeteria of hospital as the place of occurrence of the external cause

Y92.234 Operating room of hospital as the place of occurrence of the external cause

Y92.238 Other place in hospital as the place of occurrence of the external cause

Y92.239 Unspecified place in hospital as the place of occurrence of the external cause

+ Y92.24 Public administrative building as the place of occurrence of the external cause

Y92.240 Courthouse as the place of occurrence of the external cause

Y92.241 Library as the place of occurrence of the external cause

Y92.242 Post office as the place of occurrence of the external cause

Y92.243 City hall as the place of occurrence of the external cause

Y92.248 Other public administrative building as the place of occurrence of the external cause

+ Y92.25 Cultural building as the place of occurrence of the external cause

Y92.250 Art Gallery as the place of occurrence of the external cause

Y92.251 Museum as the place of occurrence of the external cause

Y92.252 Music hall as the place of occurrence of the external cause

Y92.253 Opera house as the place of occurrence of the external cause

Y92.254 Theater (live) as the place of occurrence of the external cause

Y92.258 Other cultural public building as the place of occurrence of the external cause

Y92.26 Movie house or cinema as the place of occurrence of the external cause

Y92.29 Other specified public building as the place of occurrence of the external cause

Assembly hall as the place of occurrence of the external cause
Clubhouse as the place of occurrence of the external cause

+ Y92.3 Sports and athletics area as the place of occurrence of the external cause

+ Y92.31 Athletic court as the place of occurrence of the external cause

Excludes1: *tennis court in private home or garden (Y92.09)*

Y92.310 Basketball court as the place of occurrence of the external cause

Y92.311 Squash court as the place of occurrence of the external cause

Y92.312 Tennis court as the place of occurrence of the external cause

Y92.318 Other athletic court as the place of occurrence of the external cause

+ Y92.32 Athletic field as the place of occurrence of the external cause

Y92.320 Baseball field as the place of occurrence of the external cause

Y92.321 Football field as the place of occurrence of the external cause

Y92.322 Soccer field as the place of occurrence of the external cause

Y92.328 Other athletic field as the place of occurrence of the external cause
Cricket field as the place of occurrence of the external cause
Hockey field as the place of occurrence of the external cause

+ Y92.33 Skating rink as the place of occurrence of the external cause

Y92.330 Ice skating rink (indoor) (outdoor) as the place of occurrence of the external cause

Y92.331 Roller skating rink as the place of occurrence of the external cause

Y92.34 Swimming pool (public) as the place of occurrence of the external cause
Excludes1: *swimming pool in private home or garden (Y92.016)*

Y92.39 Other specified sports and athletic area as the place of occurrence of the external cause
Golf-course as the place of occurrence of the external cause
Gymnasium as the place of occurrence of the external cause
Riding-school as the place of occurrence of the external cause
Stadium as the place of occurrence of the external cause

+ Y92.4 Street , highway and other paved roadways as the place of occurrence of the external cause
Excludes1: *private driveway of residence (Y92.014, Y92.024, Y92.043, Y92.093, Y92.113, Y92.123, Y92.154, Y92.194)*

+ Y92.41 Street and highway as the place of occurrence of the external cause

Y92.410 Unspecified street and highway as the place of occurrence of the external cause
Road NOS as the place of occurrence of the external cause

Y92.411 Interstate highway as the place of occurrence of the external cause
Freeway as the place of occurrence of the external cause
Motorway as the place of occurrence of the external cause

Y92.412 Parkway as the place of occurrence of the external cause

Y92.413 State road as the place of occurrence of the external cause

Y92.414 Local residential or business street as the place of occurrence of the external cause

Y92.415 Exit ramp or entrance ramp of street or highway as the place of occurrence of the external cause

+ Y92.48 Other paved roadways as the place of occurrence of the external cause

Y92.480 Sidewalk as the place of occurrence of the external cause

Y92.481 Parking lot as the place of occurrence of the external cause

Y92.482 Bike path as the place of occurrence of the external cause

Y92.488 Other paved roadways as the place of occurrence of the external cause

+ Y92.5 Trade and service area as the place of occurrence of the external cause
Excludes1: *garage in private home (Y92.015)*
schools and other public administration buildings (Y92.2-)

+ Y92.51 Private commercial establishments as the place of occurrence of the external cause

Y92.510 Bank as the place of occurrence of the external cause

Y92.511 Restaurant or café as the place of occurrence of the external cause

Y92.512 Supermarket, store or market as the place of occurrence of the external cause

Y92.513 Shop (commercial) as the place of occurrence of the external cause

+ Y92.52 Service areas as the place of occurrence of the external cause

Y92.520 Airport as the place of occurrence of the external cause

Y92.521 Bus station as the place of occurrence of the external cause

Y92.522 Railway station as the place of occurrence of the external cause

Y92.523 Highway rest stop as the place of occurrence of the external cause

Y92.524 Gas station as the place of occurrence of the external cause
Petroleum station as the place of occurrence of the external cause
Service station as the place of occurrence of the external cause

+ Y92.53 Ambulatory health services establishments as the place of occurrence of the external cause

Y92.530 Ambulatory surgery center as the place of occurrence of the external cause
Outpatient surgery center, including that connected with a hospital as the place of occurrence of the external cause
Same day surgery center, including that connected with a hospital as the place of occurrence of the external cause

Y92.531 Health care provider office as the place of occurrence of the external cause
Physician office as the place of occurrence of the external cause

Y92.532 Urgent care center as the place of occurrence of the external cause

Y92.538 Other ambulatory health services establishments as the place of occurrence of the external cause

Y92.59 Other trade areas as the place of occurrence of the external cause
Office building as the place of occurrence of the external cause
Casino as the place of occurrence of the external cause
Garage (commercial) as the place of occurrence of the external cause
Hotel as the place of occurrence of the external cause
Radio or television station as the place of occurrence of the external cause
Shopping mall as the place of occurrence of the external cause
Warehouse as the place of occurrence of the external cause

+ Y92.6 Industrial and construction area as the place of occurrence of the external cause

Y92.61 Building [any] under construction as the place of occurrence of the external cause

Y92.62 Dock or shipyard as the place of occurrence of the external cause
Dockyard as the place of occurrence of the external cause
Dry dock as the place of occurrence of the external cause
Shipyard as the place of occurrence of the external cause

Y92.63 Factory as the place of occurrence of the external cause
Factory building as the place of occurrence of the external cause
Factory premises as the place of occurrence of the external cause
Industrial yard as the place of occurrence of the external cause

Y92.64 Mine or pit as the place of occurrence of the external cause
Mine as the place of occurrence of the external cause

Y92.65 Oil rig as the place of occurrence of the external cause
Pit (coal) (gravel) (sand) as the place of occurrence of the external cause

Y92.69 Other specified industrial and construction area as the place of occurrence of the external cause
Gasworks as the place of occurrence of the external cause
Power-station (coal) (nuclear) (oil) as the place of occurrence of the external cause
Tunnel under construction as the place of occurrence of the external cause
Workshop as the place of occurrence of the external cause

+ Y92.7 Farm as the place of occurrence of the external cause
Ranch as the place of occurrence of the external cause
Excludes1: *farmhouse and home premises of farm (Y92.01-)*
Y92.71 Barn as the place of occurrence of the external cause
Y92.72 Chicken coop as the place of occurrence of the external cause
Hen house as the place of occurrence of the external cause
Y92.73 Farm field as the place of occurrence of the external cause
Y92.74 Orchard as the place of occurrence of the external cause
Y92.79 Other farm location as the place of occurrence of the external cause

+ Y92.8 Other places as the place of occurrence of the external cause
+ Y92.81 Transport vehicle as the place of occurrence of the external cause
Excludes1: *transport accidents (V00-V99)*
Y92.810 Car as the place of occurrence of the external cause
Y92.811 Bus as the place of occurrence of the external cause
Y92.812 Truck as the place of occurrence of the external cause
Y92.813 Airplane as the place of occurrence of the external cause
Y92.814 Boat as the place of occurrence of the external cause
Y92.815 Train as the place of occurrence of the external cause
Y92.816 Subway car as the place of occurrence of the external cause
Y92.818 Other transport vehicle as the place of occurrence of the external cause
+ Y92.82 Wilderness area
Y92.820 Desert as the place of occurrence of the external cause
Y92.821 Forest as the place of occurrence of the external cause
Y92.828 Other wilderness area as the place of occurrence of the external cause
Swamp as the place of occurrence of the external cause
Mountain as the place of occurrence of the external cause
Marsh as the place of occurrence of the external cause
Prairie as the place of occurrence of the external cause
+ Y92.83 Recreation area as the place of occurrence of the external cause
Y92.830 Public park as the place of occurrence of the external cause
Y92.831 Amusement park as the place of occurrence of the external cause
Y92.832 Beach as the place of occurrence of the external cause
Seashore as the place of occurrence of the external cause
Y92.833 Campsite as the place of occurrence of the external cause
Y92.834 Zoological garden (Zoo) as the place of occurrence of the external cause
Y92.838 Other recreation area as the place of occurrence of the external cause
Y92.84 Military training ground as the place of occurrence of the external cause
Y92.85 Railroad track as the place of occurrence of the external cause
Y92.86 Slaughter house as the place of occurrence of the external cause
Y92.89 Other specified places as the place of occurrence of the external cause
Derelict house as the place of occurrence of the external cause

Y92.9 Unspecified place or not applicable

Y93 Activity codes

NOTE Category Y93 is provided for use to indicate the activity of the person seeking healthcare for an injury or health condition, such as a heart attack while shoveling snow, which resulted from, or was contributed to, by the activity. These codes are appropriate for use for both acute injuries, such as those from chapter 19, and conditions that are due to the long-term, cumulative effects of an activity, such as those from chapter 13. They are also appropriate for use with external cause codes for cause and intent if identifying the activity provides additional information on the event. These codes should be used in conjunction with codes for external cause status (Y99) and place of occurrence (Y92).

This section contains the following broad activity categories:
Y93.0 Activities involving walking and running
Y93.1 Activities involving water and water craft
Y93.2 Activities involving ice and snow
Y93.3 Activities involving climbing, rappelling, and jumping off
Y93.4 Activities involving dancing and other rhythmic movement
Y93.5 Activities involving other sports and athletics played individually
Y93.6 Activities involving other sports and athletics played as a team or group
Y93.7 Activities involving other specified sports and athletics
Y93.A Activities involving other cardiorespiratory exercise
Y93.B Activities involving other muscle strengthening exercises
Y93.C Activities involving computer technology and electronic devices
Y93.D Activities involving arts and handcrafts
Y93.E Activities involving personal hygiene and interior property and clothing maintenance
Y93.F Activities involving caregiving
Y93.G Activities involving food preparation, cooking and grilling
Y93.H Activities involving exterior property and land maintenance, building and construction
Y93.I Activities involving roller coasters and other types of external motion
Y93.J Activities involving playing musical instrument
Y93.K Activities involving animal care
Y93.8 Activities, other specified
Y93.9 Activity, unspecified

Review coding guideline C.20.c

+ Y93.0 Activities involving walking and running
Excludes1: *activity, walking an animal (Y93.K1)*
activity, walking or running on a treadmill (Y93.A1)
Y93.01 Activity, walking, marching and hiking
Activity, walking, marching and hiking on level or elevated terrain
Excludes1: *activity, mountain climbing (Y93.31)*
Y93.02 Activity, running

+ Y93.1 Activities involving water and water craft
Excludes1: *activities involving ice (Y93.2-)*
Y93.11 Activity, swimming
Y93.12 Activity, springboard and platform diving
Y93.13 Activity, water polo
Y93.14 Activity, water aerobics and water exercise
Y93.15 Activity, underwater diving and snorkeling
Activity, SCUBA diving
Y93.16 Activity, rowing, canoeing, kayaking, rafting and tubing
Activity, canoeing, kayaking, rafting and tubing in calm and turbulent water
Y93.17 Activity, water skiing and wake boarding
Y93.18 Activity, surfing, windsurfing and boogie boarding
Activity, water sliding
Y93.19 Activity, other involving water and watercraft
Activity involving water NOS
Activity, parasailing
Activity, water survival training and testing

+ Y93.2 Activities involving ice and snow
Excludes1: *activity, shoveling ice and snow (Y93.H1)*
Y93.21 Activity, ice skating
Activity, figure skating (singles) (pairs)
Activity, ice dancing
Excludes1: *activity, ice hockey (Y93.22)*
Y93.22 Activity, ice hockey
Y93.23 Activity, snow (alpine) (downhill) skiing, snow boarding, sledding, tobogganing and snow tubing
Excludes1: *activity, cross country skiing (Y93.24)*
Y93.24 Activity, cross country skiing
Activity, nordic skiing
Y93.29 Activity, other involving ice and snow
Activity involving ice and snow NOS

+ **Y93.3 Activities involving climbing, rappelling and jumping off**
  Excludes1: *activity, hiking on level or elevated terrain (Y93.01)*
  activity, jumping rope (Y93.56)
  activity, trampoline jumping (Y93.44)
  Y93.31 Activity, mountain climbing, rock climbing and wall climbing
  Y93.32 Activity, rappelling
  Y93.33 Activity, BASE jumping
  Activity, Building, Antenna, Span, Earth jumping
  Y93.34 Activity, bungee jumping
  Y93.35 Activity, hang gliding
  Y93.39 Activity, other involving climbing, rappelling and jumping off

+ **Y93.4 Activities involving dancing and other rhythmic movement**
  Excludes1: *activity, martial arts (Y93.75)*
  Y93.41 Activity, dancing
  AHA CC: 4Q, 2012, 108
  Y93.42 Activity, yoga
  Y93.43 Activity, gymnastics
  Activity, rhythmic gymnastics
  Excludes1: *activity, trampolining (Y93.44)*
  Y93.44 Activity, trampolining
  Y93.45 Activity, cheerleading
  Y93.49 Activity, other involving dancing and other rhythmic movements

+ **Y93.5 Activities involving other sports and athletics played individually**
  Excludes1: *activity, dancing (Y93.41)*
  activity, gymnastic (Y93.43)
  activity, trampolining (Y93.44)
  activity, yoga (Y93.42)
  Y93.51 Activity, roller skating (inline) and skateboarding
  Y93.52 Activity, horseback riding
  Y93.53 Activity, golf
  Y93.54 Activity, bowling
  Y93.55 Activity, bike riding
  Y93.56 Activity, jumping rope
  Y93.57 Activity, non-running track and field events
  Excludes1: *activity, running (any form) (Y93.02)*
  Y93.59 Activity, other involving other sports and athletics played individually
  Excludes1: *activities involving climbing, rappelling, and jumping (Y93.3-)*
  activities involving ice and snow (Y93.2-)
  activities involving walking and running (Y93.0-)
  activities involving water and watercraft (Y93.1-)

+ **Y93.6 Activities involving other sports and athletics played as a team or group**
  Excludes1: *activity, ice hockey (Y93.22)*
  activity, water polo (Y93.13)
  Y93.61 Activity, american tackle football
  Activity, football NOS
  Y93.62 Activity, american flag or touch football
  Y93.63 Activity, rugby
  Y93.64 Activity, baseball
  Activity, softball
  Y93.65 Activity, lacrosse and field hockey
  Y93.66 Activity, soccer
  Y93.67 Activity, basketball
  Y93.68 Activity, volleyball (beach) (court)
  • **Y93.6A Activity, physical games generally associated with school recess, summer camp and children**
  Activity, capture the flag
  Activity, dodge ball
  Activity, four square
  Activity, kickball
  Y93.69 Activity, other involving other sports and athletics played as a team or group
  Activity, cricket

+ **Y93.7 Activities involving other specified sports and athletics**
  Y93.71 Activity, boxing
  Y93.72 Activity, wrestling
  Y93.73 Activity, racquet and hand sports
  Activity, handball
  Activity, racquetball
  Activity, squash
  Activity, tennis
  Y93.74 Activity, frisbee
  Activity, ultimate frisbee
  Y93.75 Activity, martial arts
  Activity, combatives
  Y93.79 Activity, other specified sports and athletics
  Excludes1: *sports and athletics activities specified in categories Y93.0-Y93.6*

+ **Y93.A Activities involving other cardiorespiratory exercise**
  Activities involving physical training
  Y93.A1 Activity, exercise machines primarily for cardiorespiratory conditioning
  Activity, elliptical and stepper machines
  Activity, stationary bike
  Activity, treadmill
  Y93.A2 Activity, calisthenics
  Activity, jumping jacks
  Activity, warm up and cool down
  Y93.A3 Activity, aerobic and step exercise
  Y93.A4 Activity, circuit training
  Y93.A5 Activity, obstacle course
  Activity, challenge course
  Activity, confidence course
  Y93.A6 Activity, grass drills
  Activity, guerilla drills
  Y93.A9 Activity, other involving cardiorespiratory exercise
  Excludes1: *activities involving cardiorespiratory exercise specified in categories Y93.0-Y93.7*

+ **Y93.B Activities involving other muscle strengthening exercises**
  Y93.B1 Activity, exercise machines primarily for muscle strengthening
  Y93.B2 Activity, push-ups, pull-ups, sit-ups
  Y93.B3 Activity, free weights
  Activity, barbells
  Activity, dumbbells
  Y93.B4 Activity, pilates
  Y93.B9 Activity, other involving muscle strengthening exercises
  Excludes1: *activities involving muscle strengthening specified in categories Y93.0-Y93.A*

+ **Y93.C Activities involving computer technology and electronic devices**
  Excludes1: *activity, electronic musical keyboard or instruments (Y93.J-)*
  Y93.C1 Activity, computer keyboarding
  Activity, electronic game playing using keyboard or other stationary device
  Y93.C2 Activity, hand held interactive electronic device
  Activity, cellular telephone and communication device
  Activity, electronic game playing using interactive device
  Excludes1: *activity, electronic game playing using keyboardorotherstationarydevice(Y93.C1)*
  Y93.C9 Activity, other involving computer technology and electronic devices

+ **Y93.D Activities involving arts and handcrafts**
  Excludes1: *activities involving playing musical instrument (Y93.J-)*
  Y93.D1 Activity, knitting and crocheting
  Y93.D2 Activity, sewing
  Y93.D3 Activity, furniture building and finishing
  Activity, furniture repair
  Y93.D9 Activity, other involving arts and handcrafts

+ **Y93.E Activities involving personal hygiene and interior property and clothing maintenance**
  Excludes1: *activities involving cooking and grilling (Y93.G-)*
  activities involving exterior property and land maintenance, building and construction (Y93.H-)
  activities involving caregiving (Y93.F-)
  activity, dishwashing (Y93.G1)
  activity, food preparation (Y93.G1)
  activity, gardening (Y93.H2)
  Y93.E1 Activity, personal bathing and showering
  Y93.E2 Activity, laundry
  Y93.E3 Activity, vacuuming
  Y93.E4 Activity, ironing
  Y93.E5 Activity, floor mopping and cleaning
  Y93.E6 Activity, residential relocation
  Activity, packing up and unpacking involved in moving to a new residence
  Y93.E8 Activity, other personal hygiene
  Y93.E9 Activity, other interior property and clothing maintenance

+ **Y93.F Activities involving caregiving**
  Activity involving the provider of caregiving
  Y93.F1 Activity, caregiving, bathing
  Y93.F2 Activity, caregiving, lifting
  Y93.F9 Activity, other caregiving

+ **Y93.G Activities involving food preparation, cooking and grilling**
  Y93.G1 Activity, food preparation and clean up
  Activity, dishwashing
  Y93.G2 Activity, grilling and smoking food
  Y93.G3 Activity, cooking and baking
  Activity, use of stove, oven and microwave oven
  Y93.G9 Activity, other involving cooking and grilling

+ **Y93.H Activities involving exterior property and land maintenance, building and construction**
  Y93.H1 Activity, digging, shoveling and raking
  Activity, dirt digging
  Activity, raking leaves
  Activity, snow shoveling
  Y93.H2 Activity, gardening and landscaping
  Activity, pruning, trimming shrubs, weeding
  Y93.H3 Activity, building and construction
  Y93.H9 Activity, other involving exterior property and land maintenance, building and construction

+ **Y93.I Activities involving roller coasters and other types of external motion**
  Y93.I1 Activity, roller coaster riding
  Y93.I9 Activity, other involving external motion

+ **Y93.J Activities involving playing musical instrument**
  Activity involving playing electric musical instrument
  Y93.J1 Activity, piano playing
  Activity, musical keyboard (electronic) playing
  Y93.J2 Activity, drum and other percussion instrument playing
  Y93.J3 Activity, string instrument playing
  Y93.J4 Activity, winds and brass instrument playing

+ **Y93.K Activities involving animal care**
  Excludes1: *activity, horseback riding (Y93.52)*
  Y93.K1 Activity, walking an animal
  Y93.K2 Activity, milking an animal
  Y93.K3 Activity, grooming and shearing an animal
  Y93.K9 Activity, other involving animal care

+ **Y93.8 Activities, other specified**
  Y93.81 Activity, refereeing a sports activity
  Y93.82 Activity, spectator at an event
  Y93.83 Activity, rough housing and horseplay
  Y93.84 Activity, sleeping
  Y93.89 Activity, other specified

Y93.9 Activity, unspecified

Y95 Nosocomial condition

Valid 3-character code, no further characters required
AHA CC: 4Q, 2013, 119

Y99 External cause status

NOTE A single code from category Y99 should be used in conjunction with the external cause code(s) assigned to a record to indicate the status of the person at the time the event occurred.

Review coding guideline C.20.k

Y99.0 Civilian activity done for income or pay
  Civilian activity done for financial or other compensation
  Excludes1: *military activity (Y99.1)*
  volunteer activity (Y99.2)

Y99.1 Military activity
  Excludes1: *activity of off duty military personnel (Y99.8)*

Y99.2 Volunteer activity
  Excludes1: *activity of child or other family member assisting in compensated work of other family member (Y99.8)*

Y99.8 Other external cause status
  Activity NEC
  Activity of child or other family member assisting in compensated work of other family member
  Hobby not done for income
  Leisure activity
  Off-duty activity of military personnel
  Recreation or sport not for income or while a student
  Student activity
  Excludes1: *civilian activity done for income or compensation (Y99.0)*
  military activity (Y99.1)
  AHA CC: 4Q, 2012, 108

Y99.9 Unspecified external cause status

Chapter 21: Factors Influencing Health Status and Contact with Health Services (Z00-Z99)

NOTE Z codes represent reasons for encounters. A corresponding procedure code must accompany a Z code if a procedure is performed. Categories Z00-Z99 are provided for occasions when circumstances other than a disease, injury or external cause classifiable to categories A00-Y89 are recorded as 'diagnoses' or 'problems'. This can arise in two main ways:
(a) When a person who may or may not be sick encounters the health services for some specific purpose, such as to receive limited care or service for a current condition, to donate an organ or tissue, to receive prophylactic vaccination (immunization), or to discuss a problem which is in itself not a disease or injury.
(b) When some circumstance or problem is present which influences the person's health status but is not in itself a current illness or injury.

This chapter contains the following category blocks:

Z00-Z13 Persons encountering health services for examinations
Z14-Z15 Genetic carrier and genetic susceptibility to disease
Z16 Resistance to antimicrobial drugs
Z17 Estrogen receptor status
Z18 Retained foreign body fragments
Z20-Z28 Persons with potential health hazards related to communicable diseases
Z30-Z39 Persons encountering health services in circumstances related to reproduction
Z40-Z53 Encounters for other specific health care
Z55-Z65 Persons with potential health hazards related to socioeconomic and psychosocial circumstances
Z66 Do not resuscitate status
Z67 Blood type
Z68 Body mass index (BMI)
Z69-Z76 Persons encountering health services in other circumstances
Z77-Z99 Persons with potential health hazards related to family and personal history and certain conditions influencing health status

C. Chapter-Specific Coding Guidelines

In addition to general coding guidelines, there are guidelines for specific diagnoses and/or conditions in the classification. Unless otherwise indicated, these guidelines apply to all health care settings. Please refer to Section II for guidelines on the selection of principal diagnosis.

21. Chapter 21: Factors Influencing Health Status and Contact with Health Services (Z00-Z99)

NOTE The chapter specific guidelines provide additional information about the use of Z codes for specified encounters.

a. Use of Z codes in any healthcare setting

Z codes are for use in any healthcare setting. Z codes may be used as either a first-listed (principal diagnosis code in the inpatient setting) or secondary code, depending on the circumstances of the encounter. Certain Z codes may only be used as first-listed or principal diagnosis.

b. Z Codes indicate a reason for an encounter

Z codes are not procedure codes. A corresponding procedure code must accompany a Z code to describe any procedure performed.

c. Categories of Z Codes

1) Contact/Exposure

Category Z20 indicates contact with, and suspected exposure to, communicable diseases. These codes are for patients who do not show any sign or symptom of a disease but are suspected to have been exposed to it by close personal contact with an infected individual or are in an area where a disease is epidemic.

Category Z77, **Other contact with and (suspected) exposures hazardous to health,** indicates contact with and suspected exposures hazardous to health.

Contact/exposure codes may be used as a first-listed code to explain an encounter for testing, or, more commonly, as a secondary code to identify a potential risk.

2) Inoculations and vaccinations

Code Z23 is for encounters for inoculations and vaccinations. It indicates that a patient is being seen to receive a prophylactic inoculation against a disease. Procedure codes are required to identify the actual administration of the injection and the type(s) of immunizations given. Code Z23 may be used as a secondary code if the inoculation is given as a routine part of preventive health care, such as a well-baby visit.

3) Status

Status codes indicate that a patient is either a carrier of a disease or has the sequelae or residual of a past disease or condition. This includes such things as the presence of prosthetic or mechanical devices resulting from past treatment.

A status code is informative, because the status may affect the course of treatment and its outcome. A status code is distinct from a history code. The history code indicates that the patient no longer has the condition.

A status code should not be used with a diagnosis code from one of the body system chapters, if the diagnosis code includes the information provided by the status code. For example, code Z94.1, Heart transplant status, should not be used with a code from subcategory T86.2, Complications of heart transplant. The status code does not provide additional information. The complication code indicates that the patient is a heart transplant patient.

For encounters for weaning from a mechanical ventilator, assign a code from subcategory J96.1, Chronic respiratory failure, followed by code Z99.11, Dependence on respirator [ventilator] status.

The status Z codes/categories are:

Z14 Genetic carrier
Genetic carrier status indicates that a person carries a gene, associated with a particular disease, which may be passed to offspring who may develop that disease. The person does not have the disease and is not at risk of developing the disease.

Z15 Genetic susceptibility to disease
Genetic susceptibility indicates that a person has a gene that increases the risk of that person developing the disease.

Codes from category Z15 should not be used as principal or first-listed codes. If the patient has the condition to which he/she is susceptible, and that condition is the reason for the encounter, the code for the current condition should be sequenced first. If the patient is being seen for follow-up after completed treatment for this condition, and the condition no longer exists, a follow-up code should be sequenced first, followed by the appropriate personal history and genetic susceptibility codes. If the purpose of the encounter is genetic counseling associated with procreative management, code Z31.5, Encounter for genetic counseling, should be assigned as the first-listed code, followed by a code from category Z15. Additional codes should be assigned for any applicable family or personal history.

Z16 Resistance to antimicrobial drugs
This code indicates that a patient has a condition that is resistant to antimicrobial drug treatment. Sequence the infection code first.

Z17 Estrogen receptor status

Z18 Retained foreign body fragments

Z21 Asymptomatic HIV infection status
This code indicates that a patient has tested positive for HIV but has manifested no signs or symptoms of the disease.

Z22 Carrier of infectious disease
Carrier status indicates that a person harbors the specific organisms of a disease without manifest symptoms and is capable of transmitting the infection.

Z28.3 Underimmunization status

Z33.1 Pregnant state, incidental
This code is a secondary code only for use when the pregnancy is in no way complicating the reason for visit. Otherwise, a code from the obstetric chapter is required.

Z66 Do not resuscitate
This code may be used when it is documented by the provider that a patient is on do not resuscitate status at any time during the stay.

Z67 Blood type

Z68 Body mass index (BMI)

Z74.01 Bed confinement status

Z76.82 Awaiting organ transplant status

Z78 Other specified health status
Code Z78.1, Physical restraint status, may be used when it is documented by the provider that a patient has been put in restraints during the current encounter. Please note that this code should not be reported when it is documented by the provider that a patient is temporarily restrained during a procedure.

Z79 Long-term (current) drug therapy
Codes from this category indicate a patient's continuous use of a prescribed drug (including such things as aspirin therapy) for the long-term treatment of a condition or for prophylactic use. It is not for use for patients who have addictions to drugs. This subcategory is not for use of medications for detoxification or maintenance programs to prevent withdrawal symptoms in patients with drug dependence (e.g., methadone maintenance for opiate dependence). Assign the appropriate code for the drug dependence instead.

Assign a code from Z79 if the patient is receiving a medication for an extended period as a prophylactic measure (such as for the prevention of deep vein thrombosis) or as treatment of a chronic condition (such as arthritis) or a disease requiring a lengthy course of treatment (such as cancer). Do not assign a code from category Z79 for medication being administered for a brief period of time to treat an acute illness or injury (such as a course of antibiotics to treat acute bronchitis).

Z88 Allergy status to drugs, medicaments and biological substances
Except: Z88.9, Allergy status to unspecified drugs, medicaments and biological substances status
Z89 Acquired absence of limb
Z90 Acquired absence of organs, not elsewhere classified
Z91.0- Allergy status, other than to drugs and biological substances
Z92.82 Status post administration of tPA (rtPA) in a different facility within the last 24 hours prior to admission to a current facility

Assign code Z92.82, Status post administration of tPA (rtPA) in a different facility within the last 24 hours prior to admission to current facility, as a secondary diagnosis when a patient is received by transfer into a facility and documentation indicates they were administered tissue plasminogen activator (tPA) within the last 24 hours prior to admission to the current facility.

This guideline applies even if the patient is still receiving the tPA at the time they are received into the current facility.

The appropriate code for the condition for which the tPA was administered (such as cerebrovascular disease or myocardial infarction) should be assigned first.

Code Z92.82 is only applicable to the receiving facility record and not to the transferring facility record.

Z93 Artificial opening status
Z94 Transplanted organ and tissue status
Z95 Presence of cardiac and vascular implants and grafts Z96 Presence of other functional implants
Z97 Presence of other devices
Z98 Other postprocedural states
Assign code Z98.85, Transplanted organ removal status, to indicate that a transplanted organ has been previously removed. This code should not be assigned for the encounter in which the transplanted organ is removed. The complication necessitating removal of the transplant organ should be assigned for that encounter.
See section I.C19. for information on the coding of organ transplant complications.
Z99 Dependence on enabling machines and devices, not elsewhere classified

NOTE Categories Z89-Z90 and Z93-Z99 are for use only if there are no complications or malfunctions of the organ or tissue replaced, the amputation site or the equipment on which the patient is dependent.

4) History (of)

There are two types of history Z codes, personal and family. Personal history codes explain a patient's past medical condition that no longer exists and is not receiving any treatment, but that has the potential for recurrence, and therefore may require continued monitoring.

Family history codes are for use when a patient has a family member(s) who has had a particular disease that causes the patient to be at higher risk of also contracting the disease.

Personal history codes may be used in conjunction with follow- up codes and family history codes may be used in conjunction with screening codes to explain the need for a test or procedure. History codes are also acceptable on any medical record regardless of the reason for visit. A history of an illness, even if no longer present, is important information that may alter the type of treatment ordered.

The history Z code categories are:
Z80 Family history of primary malignant neoplasm
Z81 Family history of mental and behavioral disorders
Z82 Family history of certain disabilities and chronic diseases (leading to disablement)
Z83 Family history of other specific disorders
Z84 Family history of other conditions
Z85 Personal history of malignant neoplasm
Z86 Personal history of certain other diseases
Z87 Personal history of other diseases and conditions
Z91.4- Personal history of psychological trauma, not elsewhere classified
Z91.5 Personal history of self-harm
Z91.8- Other specified personal risk factors, not elsewhere classified
Exception:
Z91.83, Wandering in diseases classified elsewhere
Z92 Personal history of medical treatment
Except: Z92.0, Personal history of contraception Except: Z92.82, Status post administration of tPA (rtPA) in a different facility within the last 24 hours prior to admission to a current facility

5) Screening

Screening is the testing for disease or disease precursors in seemingly well individuals so that early detection and treatment can be provided for those who test positive for the disease (e.g., screening mammogram).

The testing of a person to rule out or confirm a suspected diagnosis because the patient has some sign or symptom is a diagnostic examination, not a screening. In these cases, the sign or symptom is used to explain the reason for the test.

A screening code may be a first-listed code if the reason for the visit is specifically the screening exam. It may also be used as an additional code if the screening is done during an office visit for other health problems. A screening code is not necessary if the screening is inherent to a routine examination, such as a pap smear done during a routine pelvic examination.

Should a condition be discovered during the screening then the code for the condition may be assigned as an additional diagnosis.

The Z code indicates that a screening exam is planned. A procedure code is required to confirm that the screening was performed.

The screening Z codes/categories:
Z11 Encounter for screening for infectious and parasitic diseases
Z12 Encounter for screening for malignant neoplasms
Z13 Encounter for screening for other diseases and disorders
Except: Z13.9, Encounter for screening, unspecified
Z36 Encounter for antenatal screening for mother

6) Observation

There are two observation Z code categories. They are for use in very limited circumstances when a person is being observed for a suspected condition that is ruled out. The observation codes are not for use if an injury or illness or any signs or symptoms related to the suspected condition are present. In such cases the diagnosis/symptom code is used with the corresponding external cause code.

The observation codes are to be used as principal diagnosis only. Additional codes may be used in addition to the observation code but only if they are unrelated to the suspected condition being observed.

Codes from subcategory Z03.7, Encounter for suspected maternal and fetal conditions ruled out, may either be used as a first-listed or as an additional code assignment depending on the case. They are for use in very limited circumstances on a maternal record when an encounter is for a suspected maternal or fetal condition that is ruled out during that encounter (for example, a maternal or fetal condition may be suspected due to an abnormal test result). These codes should not be used when the condition is confirmed. In those cases, the confirmed condition should be coded. In addition, these codes are not for use if an illness or any signs or symptoms related to the suspected condition or problem are present. In such cases the diagnosis/symptom code is used.

Additional codes may be used in addition to the code from subcategory Z03.7, but only if they are unrelated to the suspected condition being evaluated.

Codes from subcategory Z03.7 may not be used for encounters for antenatal screening of mother. *See Section I.C.21. Screening.*

For encounters for suspected fetal condition that are inconclusive following testing and evaluation, assign the appropriate code from category O35, O36, O40 or O41. The observation Z code categories:
Z03 Encounter for medical observation for suspected diseases and conditions ruled out
Z04 Encounter for examination and observation for other reasons
Except: Z04.9, Encounter for examination and observation for unspecified reason

7) Aftercare

Aftercare visit codes cover situations when the initial treatment of a disease has been performed and the patient requires continued care during the healing or recovery phase, or for the long-term consequences of the disease. The aftercare Z code should not be used if treatment is directed at a current, acute disease. The diagnosis code is to be used in these cases. Exceptions to this rule are codes Z51.0, Encounter for antineoplastic radiation therapy, and codes from subcategory Z51.1, Encounter for antineoplastic chemotherapy and immunotherapy. These codes are to be first-listed, followed by the diagnosis code when a patient's encounter is solely to receive radiation therapy, chemotherapy, or immunotherapy for the treatment of a neoplasm. If the reason for the encounter is more than one type of antineoplastic therapy, code Z51.0 and a code from subcategory Z51.1 may be assigned together, in which case one of these codes would be reported as a secondary diagnosis.

The aftercare Z codes should also not be used for aftercare for injuries. For aftercare of an injury, assign the acute injury code with the appropriate 7th character (for subsequent encounter).

The aftercare codes are generally first-listed to explain the specific reason for the encounter. An aftercare code may be used as an additional code when some type of aftercare is provided in addition to the reason for admission and no diagnosis code is applicable. An example of this would be the closure of a colostomy during an encounter for treatment of another condition.

Aftercare codes should be used in conjunction with other aftercare codes or diagnosis codes to provide better detail on the specifics of an aftercare encounter visit, unless otherwise directed by the classification. Should a patient receive multiple types of antineoplastic therapy during the same encounter, code Z51.0, Encounter for antineoplastic radiation therapy, and codes from subcategory Z51.1, Encounter for antineoplastic chemotherapy and immunotherapy, may be used together on a record. The sequencing of multiple aftercare codes depends on the circumstances of the encounter.

Certain aftercare Z code categories need a secondary diagnosis code to describe the resolving condition or sequelae. For others, the condition is included in the code title.

Additional Z code aftercare category terms include fitting and adjustment, and attention to artificial openings.

Status Z codes may be used with aftercare Z codes to indicate the nature of the aftercare. For example code Z95.1, Presence of aortocoronary bypass graft, may be used with code Z48.812, Encounter for surgical aftercare following surgery on the circulatory system, to indicate the surgery for which the aftercare is being performed. A status code should not be used when the aftercare code indicates the type of status, such as using Z43.0, Encounter for attention to tracheostomy, with Z93.0, Tracheostomy status.

The aftercare Z category/codes:

Z42	Encounter for plastic and reconstructive surgery following medical procedure or healed injury
Z43	Encounter for attention to artificial openings
Z44	Encounter for fitting and adjustment of external prosthetic device
Z45	Encounter for adjustment and management of implanted device
Z46	Encounter for fitting and adjustment of other devices
Z47	Orthopedic aftercare
Z48	Encounter for other postprocedural aftercare
Z49	Encounter for care involving renal dialysis
Z51	Encounter for other aftercare

8) Follow-up

The follow-up codes are used to explain continuing surveillance following completed treatment of a disease, condition, or injury. They imply that the condition has been fully treated and no longer exists. They should not be confused with aftercare codes, or injury codes with a 7th character for subsequent encounter, that explain ongoing care of a healing condition or its sequelae. Follow-up codes may be used in conjunction with history codes to provide the full picture of the healed condition and its treatment. The follow-up code is sequenced first, followed by the history code.

A follow-up code may be used to explain multiple visits. Should a condition be found to have recurred on the follow-up visit, then the diagnosis code for the condition should be assigned in place of the follow-up code.

The follow-up Z code categories:

Z08	Encounter for follow-up examination after completed treatment for malignant neoplasm
Z09	Encounter for follow-up examination after completed treatment for conditions other than malignant neoplasm
Z39	Encounter for maternal postpartum care and examination

9) Donor

Codes in category Z52, Donors of organs and tissues, are used for living individuals who are donating blood or other body tissue. These codes are only for individuals donating for others, not for self-donations. They are not used to identify cadaveric donations.

10) Counseling

Counseling Z codes are used when a patient or family member receives assistance in the aftermath of an illness or injury, or when support is required in coping with family or social problems. They are not used in conjunction with a diagnosis code when the counseling component of care is considered integral to standard treatment.

The counseling Z codes/categories:

Z30.0-	Encounter for general counseling and advice on contraception
Z31.5	Encounter for genetic counseling
Z31.6-	Encounter for general counseling and advice on procreation
Z32.2	Encounter for childbirth instruction
Z32.3	Encounter for childcare instruction
Z69	Encounter for mental health services for victim and perpetrator of abuse
Z70	Counseling related to sexual attitude, behavior and orientation
Z71	Persons encountering health services for other counseling and medical advice, not elsewhere classified
Z76.81	Expectant mother prebirth pediatrician visit

11) Encounters for Obstetrical and Reproductive Services

See Section I.C.15. Pregnancy, Childbirth, and the Puerperium, for further instruction on the use of these codes.

Z codes for pregnancy are for use in those circumstances when none of the problems or complications included in the codes from the Obstetrics chapter exist (a routine prenatal visit or postpartum care). Codes in category Z34, Encounter for supervision of normal pregnancy, are always first-listed and are not to be used with any other code from the OB chapter.

Codes in category Z3A, Weeks of gestation, may be assigned to provide additional information about the pregnancy. The date of the admission should be used to determine weeks of gestation for inpatient admissions that encompass more than one gestational week.

The outcome of delivery, category Z37, should be included on all maternal delivery records. It is always a secondary code. Codes in category Z37 should not be used on the newborn record.

Z codes for family planning (contraceptive) or procreative management and counseling should be included on an obstetric record either during the pregnancy or the postpartum stage, if applicable.

Z codes/categories for obstetrical and reproductive services:

Z30	Encounter for contraceptive management
Z31	Encounter for procreative management
Z32.2	Encounter for childbirth instruction
Z32.3	Encounter for childcare instruction
Z33	Pregnant state
Z34	Encounter for supervision of normal pregnancy
Z36	Encounter for antenatal screening of mother
Z3A	Weeks of gestation
Z37	Outcome of delivery
Z39	Encounter for maternal postpartum care and examination
Z76.81	Expectant mother prebirth pediatrician visit

12) Newborns and Infants

See Section I.C.16. Newborn (Perinatal) Guidelines, for further instruction on the use of these codes.

Newborn Z codes/categories:

Z76.1	Encounter for health supervision and care of foundling
Z00.1-	Encounter for routine child health examination
Z38	Liveborn infants according to place of birth and type of delivery

13) Routine and administrative examinations

The Z codes allow for the description of encounters for routine examinations, such as, a general check-up, or, examinations for administrative purposes, such as, a pre-employment physical. The codes are not to be used if the examination is for diagnosis of a suspected condition or for treatment purposes. In such cases the diagnosis code is used. During a routine exam, should a diagnosis or condition be discovered, it should be coded as an additional code. Pre-existing and chronic conditions and history codes may also be included as additional codes as long as the examination is for administrative purposes and not focused on any particular condition.

Some of the codes for routine health examinations distinguish between "with" and "without" abnormal findings. Code assignment depends on the information that is known at the time the encounter is being coded. For example, if no abnormal findings were found during the examination, but the encounter is being coded before test results are back, it is acceptable to assign the code for "without abnormal findings." When assigning a code for "with abnormal findings," additional code(s) should be assigned to identify the specific abnormal finding(s).

Pre-operative examination and pre-procedural laboratory examination Z codes are for use only in those situations when a patient is being cleared for a procedure or surgery and no treatment is given.

The Z codes/categories for routine and administrative examinations:

Z00	Encounter for general examination without complaint, suspected or reported diagnosis
Z01	Encounter for other special examination without complaint, suspected or reported diagnosis
Z02	Encounter for administrative examination Except: Z02.9, Encounter for administrative examinations, unspecified
Z32.0-	Encounter for pregnancy test

14) Miscellaneous Z codes

The miscellaneous Z codes capture a number of other health care encounters that do not fall into one of the other categories. Certain of these codes identify the reason for the encounter; others are for use as additional codes that provide useful information on circumstances that may affect a patient's care and treatment.

Prophylactic Organ Removal

For encounters specifically for prophylactic removal of an organ (such as prophylactic removal of breasts due to a genetic susceptibility to cancer or a family history of cancer), the principal or first-listed code should be a code from category Z40, Encounter for prophylactic surgery, followed by the appropriate codes to identify the associated risk factor (such as genetic susceptibility or family history).

If the patient has a malignancy of one site and is having prophylactic removal at another site to prevent either a new primary malignancy or metastatic disease, a code for the malignancy should also be assigned in addition to a code from subcategory Z40.0, Encounter for prophylactic surgery for risk factors related to malignant neoplasms. A Z40.0 code should not be assigned if the patient is having organ removal for treatment of a malignancy, such as the removal of the testes for the treatment of prostate cancer.

Miscellaneous Z codes/categories:

Z28 Immunization not carried out
Except: Z28.3, Underimmunization status
Z40 Encounter for prophylactic surgery
Z41 Encounter for procedures for purposes other than remedying health state
Except: Z41.9, Encounter for procedure for purposes other than remedying health state, unspecified
Z53 Persons encountering health services for specific procedures and treatment, not carried out
Z55 Problems related to education and literacy
Z56 Problems related to employment and unemployment
Z57 Occupational exposure to risk factors
Z58 Problems related to physical environment
Z59 Problems related to housing and economic circumstances
Z60 Problems related to social environment
Z62 Problems related to upbringing
Z63 Other problems related to primary support group, including family circumstances
Z64 Problems related to certain psychosocial circumstances
Z65 Problems related to other psychosocial circumstances
Z72 Problems related to lifestyle
Z73 Problems related to life management difficulty
Z74 Problems related to care provider dependency
Except: Z74.01, Bed confinement status
Z75 Problems related to medical facilities and other health care
Z76.0 Encounter for issue of repeat prescription
Z76.3 Healthy person accompanying sick person
Z76.4 Other boarder to healthcare facility
Z76.5 Malingerer [conscious simulation]
Z91.1- Patient's noncompliance with medical treatment and regimen
Z91.83 Wandering in diseases classified elsewhere
Z91.89 Other specified personal risk factors, not elsewhere classified

15) Nonspecific Z codes

Certain Z codes are so non-specific, or potentially redundant with other codes in the classification, that there can be little justification for their use in the inpatient setting. Their use in the outpatient setting should be limited to those instances when there is no further documentation to permit more precise coding. Otherwise, any sign or symptom or any other reason for visit that is captured in another code should be used.

Nonspecific Z codes/categories:

Z02.9 Encounter for administrative examinations, unspecified
Z04.9 Encounter for examination and observation for unspecified reason
Z13.9 Encounter for screening, unspecified
Z41.9 Encounter for procedure for purposes other than remedying health state, unspecified
Z52.9 Donor of unspecified organ or tissue
Z86.59 Personal history of other mental and behavioral disorders
Z88.9 Allergy status to unspecified drugs, medicaments and biological substances status
Z92.0 Personal history of contraception

16) Z Codes That May Only be Principal/First-Listed Diagnosis

The following Z codes/categories may only be reported as the principal/first-listed diagnosis, except when there are multiple encounters on the same day and the medical records for the encounters are combined:

Z00 Encounter for general examination without complaint, suspected or reported diagnosis
Except: Z00.6
Z01 Encounter for other special examination without complaint, suspected or reported diagnosis
Z02 Encounter for administrative examination
Z03 Encounter for medical observation for suspected diseases and conditions ruled out
Z04 Encounter for examination and observation for other reasons
Z33.2 Encounter for elective termination of pregnancy
Z31.81 Encounter for male factor infertility in female patient
Z31.82 Encounter for Rh incompatibility status
Z31.83 Encounter for assisted reproductive fertility procedure cycle
Z31.84 Encounter for fertility preservation procedure
Z34 Encounter for supervision of normal pregnancy
Z39 Encounter for maternal postpartum care and examination
Z38 Liveborn infants according to place of birth and type of delivery
Z42 Encounter for plastic and reconstructive surgery following medical procedure or healed injury

Z51.0 Encounter for antineoplastic radiation therapy
Z51.1- Encounter for antineoplastic chemotherapy and immunotherapy
Z52 Donors of organs and tissues
Except: Z52.9, Donor of unspecified organ or tissue
Z76.1 Encounter for health supervision and care of foundling
Z76.2 Encounter for health supervision and care of other healthy infant and child
Z99.12 Encounter for respirator [ventilator] dependence during power failure

Persons encountering health services for examinations (Z00-Z13)

NOTE Nonspecific abnormal findings disclosed at the time of these examinations are classified to categories R70-R94.

Excludes1: *examinations related to pregnancy and reproduction (Z30-Z36, Z39.-)*

Z00 Encounter for general examination without complaint, suspected or reported diagnosis

Excludes1: *encounter for examination for administrative purposes (Z02.-)*
Excludes2: *encounter for pre-procedural examinations (Z01.81-)*
special screening examinations (Z11-Z13)

Review coding guidelines C.21.c.13 and C.21.c.16

+ **Z00.0 Encounter for general adult medical examination**
Encounter for adult periodic examination (annual) (physical) and any associated laboratory and radiologic examinations
Excludes1: *encounter for examination of sign or symptom- code to sign or symptom*
general health check-up of infant or child (Z00.12.-)
• **Z00.00 Encounter for general adult medical examination without abnormal findings**
Encounter for adult health check-up NOS
• **Z00.01 Encounter for general adult medical examination with abnormal findings**
Use additional code to identify abnormal findings

+ **Z00.1 Encounter for newborn, infant and child health examinations**
Review coding guideline C.21.c.12
+ **Z00.11 Newborn health examination**
Health check for child under 29 days old
Use additional code to identify any abnormal findings
Excludes1: *health check for child over 28 days old (Z00.12-)*
• **Z00.110 Health examination for newborn under 8 days old**
Health check for newborn under 8 days old
• **Z00.111 Health examination for newborn 8 to 28 days old**
Health check for newborn 8 to 28 days old
Newborn weight check
+ **Z00.12 Encounter for routine child health examination**
Encounter for development testing of infant or child
Health check (routine) for child over 28 days old
Excludes1: *health check for child under 29 days old (Z00.11-)*
health supervision of foundling or other healthy infant or child (Z76.1-Z76.2)
newborn health examination (Z00.11-)
• **Z00.121 Encounter for routine child health examination with abnormal findings**
Use additional code to identify abnormal findings
• **Z00.129 Encounter for routine child health examination without abnormal findings**
Encounter for routine child health examination NOS

• **Z00.2 Encounter for examination for period of rapid growth in childhood**
• **Z00.3 Encounter for examination for adolescent development state**
Encounter for puberty development state
Z00.5 Encounter for examination of potential donor of organ and tissue
Z00.6 Encounter for examination for normal comparison and control in clinical research program
Examination of participant or control in clinical research program
+ **Z00.7 Encounter for examination for period of delayed growth in childhood**
• **Z00.70 Encounter for examination for period of delayed growth in childhood without abnormal findings**
• **Z00.71 Encounter for examination for period of delayed growth in childhood with abnormal findings**
Use additional code to identify abnormal findings
Z00.8 Encounter for other general examination
Encounter for health examination in population surveys

Z01 Encounter for other special examination without complaint, suspected or reported diagnosis

Includes: routine examination of specific system

NOTE Codes from category Z01 represent the reason for the encounter. A separate procedure code is required to identify any examinations or procedures performed

Excludes1: *encounter for examination for administrative purposes (Z02.-)*
encounter for examination for suspected conditions, proven not to exist (Z03.-)
encounter for laboratory and radiologic examinations as a component of general medical examinations (Z00.0-)
encounter for laboratory, radiologic and imaging examinations for sign(s) and symptom(s) - code to the sign(s) or symptom(s)

Excludes2: *screening examinations (Z11-Z13)*

Review coding guidelines C.21.c.13 and C.21.c.16

+ **Z01.0 Encounter for examination of eyes and vision**
 Excludes1: *examination for driving license (Z02.4)*
 Z01.00 Encounter for examination of eyes and vision without abnormal findings
 Encounter for examination of eyes and vision NOS
 Z01.01 Encounter for examination of eyes and vision with abnormal findings
 Use additional code to identify abnormal findings

+ **Z01.1 Encounter for examination of ears and hearing**
 Z01.10 Encounter for examination of ears and hearing without abnormal findings
 Encounter for examination of ears and hearing NOS
 + **Z01.11 Encounter for examination of ears and hearing with abnormal findings**
 Z01.110 Encounter for hearing examination following failed hearing screening
 Z01.118 Encounter for examination of ears and hearing with other abnormal findings
 Use additional code to identify abnormal findings
 Z01.12 Encounter for hearing conservation and treatment

+ **Z01.2 Encounter for dental examination and cleaning**
 Z01.20 Encounter for dental examination and cleaning without abnormal findings
 Encounter for dental examination and cleaning NOS
 Z01.21 Encounter for dental examination and cleaning with abnormal findings
 Use additional code to identify abnormal findings

+ **Z01.3 Encounter for examination of blood pressure**
 Z01.30 Encounter for examination of blood pressure without abnormal findings
 Encounter for examination of blood pressure NOS
 Z01.31 Encounter for examination of blood pressure with abnormal findings
 Use additional code to identify abnormal findings

+ **Z01.4 Encounter for gynecological examination**
 Excludes2: *pregnancy examination or test (Z32.0-)*
 routine examination for contraceptive maintenance (Z30.4-)
 + **Z01.41 Encounter for routine gynecological examination**
 Encounter for general gynecological examination with or without cervical smear
 Encounter for gynecological examination (general) (routine) NOS
 Encounter for pelvic examination (annual) (periodic)
 Use additional code:
 for screening for human papillomavirus, if applicable, (Z11.51)
 for screening vaginal pap smear, if applicable (Z12.72)
 to identify acquired absence of uterus, if applicable (Z90.71-)
 Excludes1: *gynecologic examination status-post hysterectomy for malignant condition (Z08)*
 screening cervical pap smear not a part of a routine gynecological examination (Z12.4)
 ♀ **Z01.411 Encounter for gynecological examination (general) (routine) with abnormal findings**
 ♀ **Z01.419 Encounter for gynecological examination (general) (routine) without abnormal findings**
 Use additional code to identify abnormal findings
 ♀ **Z01.42 Encounter for cervical smear to confirm findings of recent normal smear following initial abnormal smear**

+ **Z01.8 Encounter for other specified special examinations**
 + **Z01.81 Encounter for preprocedural examinations**
 Encounter for preoperative examinations
 Encounter for radiological and imaging examinations as part of preprocedural examination
 Z01.810 Encounter for preprocedural cardiovascular examination
 Z01.811 Encounter for preprocedural respiratory examination
 Z01.812 Encounter for preprocedural laboratory examination
 Blood and urine tests prior to treatment or procedure
 Z01.818 Encounter for other preprocedural examination
 Encounter for preprocedural examination NOS
 Encounter for examinations prior to antineoplastic chemotherapy
 Z01.82 Encounter for allergy testing
 Excludes1: *encounter for antibody response examination (Z01.84)*
 Z01.83 Encounter for blood typing
 Encounter for Rh typing
 Z01.84 Encounter for antibody response examination
 Encounter for immunity status testing
 Excludes1: *encounter for allergy testing (Z01.82)*
 Z01.89 Encounter for other specified special examinations

Z02 Encounter for administrative examination

Review coding guidelines C.21.c.13 and C.21.c.16

Z02.0 Encounter for examination for admission to educational institution
 Encounter for examination for admission to preschool (education)
 Encounter for examination for re-admission to school following illness or medical treatment
Z02.1 Encounter for pre-employment examination
Z02.2 Encounter for examination for admission to residential institution
 Excludes1: *examination for admission to prison (Z02.89)*
Z02.3 Encounter for examination for recruitment to armed forces
Z02.4 Encounter for examination for driving license
Z02.5 Encounter for examination for participation in sport
 Excludes1: *blood-alcohol and blood-drug test (Z02.83)*
Z02.6 Encounter for examination for insurance purposes
+ **Z02.7 Encounter for issue of medical certificate**
 Excludes1: *encounter for general medical examination (Z00-Z01, Z02.0-Z02.6, Z02.8-Z02.9,)*
 Z02.71 Encounter for disability determination
 Encounter for issue of medical certificate of incapacity
 Encounter for issue of medical certificate of invalidity
 Z02.79 Encounter for issue of other medical certificate
+ **Z02.8 Encounter for other administrative examinations**
 Z02.81 Encounter for paternity testing
 Z02.82 Encounter for adoption services
 Z02.83 Encounter for blood-alcohol and blood-drug test
 Use additional code for findings of alcohol or drugs in blood (R78.-)
 Z02.89 Encounter for other administrative examinations
 Encounter for examination for admission to prison
 Encounter for examination for admission to summer camp
 Encounter for immigration examination
 Encounter for naturalization examination
 Encounter for premarital examination
 Excludes1: *health supervision of foundling or other healthy infant or child (Z76.1-Z76.2)*
Z02.9 Encounter for administrative examinations, unspecified

Z03 Encounter for medical observation for suspected diseases and conditions ruled out

This category is to be used when a person without a diagnosis is suspected of having an abnormal condition, without signs or symptoms, which requires study, but after examination and observation, is ruled out. This category is also for use for administrative and legal observation status.

Excludes1: *contact with and (suspected) exposures hazardous to health (Z77.-)*
newborn observation for suspected condition, ruled out (P00-P04)
person with feared complaint in whom no diagnosis is made (Z71.1)
signs or symptoms under study- code to signs or symptoms

Review coding guidelines C.21.c.6 and C.21.c.16

Z03.6 Encounter for observation for suspected toxic effect from ingested substance ruled out
Encounter for observation for suspected adverse effect from drug
Encounter for observation for suspected poisoning

+ **Z03.7 Encounter for suspected maternal and fetal conditions ruled out**
Encounter for suspected maternal and fetal conditions not found
Excludes1: *known or suspected fetal anomalies affecting management of mother, not ruled out (O26.-, O35.-, O36.-, O40.-, O41.-)*

• ♀ **Z03.71 Encounter for suspected problem with amniotic cavity and membrane ruled out**
Encounter for suspected oligohydramnios ruled out
Encounter for suspected polyhydramnios ruled out

• ♀ **Z03.72 Encounter for suspected placental problem ruled out**

• ♀ **Z03.73 Encounter for suspected fetal anomaly ruled out**

• ♀ **Z03.74 Encounter for suspected problem with fetal growth ruled out**

• ♀ **Z03.75 Encounter for suspected cervical shortening ruled out**

• ♀ **Z03.79 Encounter for other suspected maternal and fetal conditions ruled out**

+ **Z03.8 Encounter for observation for other suspected diseases and conditions ruled out**

Z03.81 Encounter for observation for suspected exposure to biological agents ruled out

Z03.810 Encounter for observation for suspected exposure to anthrax ruled out

Z03.818 Encounter for observation for suspected exposure to other biological agents ruled out

Z03.89 Encounter for observation for other suspected diseases and conditions ruled out

Z04 Encounter for examination and observation for other reasons

Includes: encounter for examination for medicolegal reasons
This category is to be used when a person without a diagnosis is suspected of having an abnormal condition, without signs or symptoms, which requires study, but after examination and observation, is ruled-out. This category is also for use for administrative and legal observation status.
Review coding guidelines C.21.c.6 and C.21.c.16

Z04.1 Encounter for examination and observation following transport accident
Excludes1: *encounter for examination and observation following work accident (Z04.2)*

Z04.2 Encounter for examination and observation following work accident

Z04.3 Encounter for examination and observation following other accident

+ **Z04.4 Encounter for examination and observation following alleged rape**
Encounter for examination and observation of victim following alleged rape
Encounter for examination and observation of victim following alleged sexual abuse

• **Z04.41 Encounter for examination and observation following alleged adult rape**
Suspected adult rape, ruled out
Suspected adult sexual abuse, ruled out
Review coding guideline C.19.f

• **Z04.42 Encounter for examination and observation following alleged child rape**
Suspected child rape, ruled out
Suspected child sexual abuse, ruled out
Review coding guideline C.19.f

Z04.6 Encounter for general psychiatric examination, requested by authority

+ **Z04.7 Encounter for examination and observation following alleged physical abuse**

• **Z04.71 Encounter for examination and observation following alleged adult physical abuse**
Suspected adult physical abuse, ruled out
Excludes1: *confirmed case of adult physical abuse (T74.-)*
encounter for examination and observation following alleged adult sexual abuse (Z04.41)
suspected case of adult physical abuse, not ruled out (T76.-)
Review coding guideline C.19.f

• **Z04.72 Encounter for examination and observation following alleged child physical abuse**
Suspected child physical abuse, ruled out
Excludes1: *confirmed case of child physical abuse (T74.-)*
encounter for examination and observation following alleged child sexual abuse (Z04.42)
suspected case of child physical abuse, not ruled out (T76.-)
Review coding guideline C.19.f

Z04.8 Encounter for examination and observation for other specified reasons
Encounter for examination and observation for request for expert evidence

Z04.9 Encounter for examination and observation for unspecified reason
Encounter for observation NOS

Z08 Encounter for follow-up examination after completed treatment for malignant neoplasm

Medical surveillance following completed treatment
Use additional code to identify any acquired absence of organs (Z90.-)

Use additional code to identify the personal history of malignant neoplasm (Z85.-)
Excludes1: *aftercare following medical care (Z43-Z49, Z51)*
Review coding guideline C.21.c.8
Valid 3-character code, no further characters required

Z09 Encounter for follow-up examination after completed treatment for conditions other than malignant neoplasm

Medical surveillance following completed treatment
Use additional code to identify any applicable history of disease code (Z86.-, Z87.-)
Excludes1: *aftercare following medical care (Z43-Z49, Z51)*
surveillance of contraception (Z30.4-)
surveillance of prosthetic and other medical devices (Z44-Z46)
Review coding guideline C.21.c.8
Valid 3-character code, no further characters required

Z11 Encounter for screening for infectious and parasitic diseases

Screening is the testing for disease or disease precursors in asymptomatic individuals so that early detection and treatment can be provided for those who test positive for the disease.
Excludes1: *encounter for diagnostic examination-code to sign or symptom*
Review coding guideline C.21.c.5

Z11.0 Encounter for screening for intestinal infectious diseases

Z11.1 Encounter for screening for respiratory tuberculosis

Z11.2 Encounter for screening for other bacterial diseases

Z11.3 Encounter for screening for infections with a predominantly sexual mode of transmission
Excludes2: *encounter for screening for human immunodeficiency virus [HIV] (Z11.4)*
encounter for screening for human papillomavirus (Z11.51)

Z11.4 Encounter for screening for human immunodeficiency virus [HIV]
Review coding guideline C.1.a.2.h

+ **Z11.5 Encounter for screening for other viral diseases**
Excludes2: *encounter for screening for viral intestinal disease (Z11.0)*

Z11.51 Encounter for screening for human papillomavirus (HPV)

Z11.59 Encounter for screening for other viral diseases

Z11.6 Encounter for screening for other protozoal diseases and helminthiases
Excludes2: *encounter for screening for protozoal intestinal disease (Z11.0)*

Z11.8 Encounter for screening for other infectious and parasitic diseases
Encounter for screening for chlamydia
Encounter for screening for rickettsial
Encounter for screening for spirochetal
Encounter for screening for mycoses

Z11.9 Encounter for screening for infectious and parasitic diseases, unspecified

Z12 Encounter for screening for malignant neoplasms

Screening is the testing for disease or disease precursors in asymptomatic individuals so that early detection and treatment can be provided for those who test positive for the disease.

Use additional code to identify any family history of malignant neoplasm (Z80.-)

Excludes1: *encounter for diagnostic examination-code to sign or symptom*

Review coding guideline C.21.c.5

Z12.0 Encounter for screening for malignant neoplasm of stomach

\+ **Z12.1 Encounter for screening for malignant neoplasm of intestinal tract**

Z12.10 Encounter for screening for malignant neoplasm of intestinal tract, unspecified

Z12.11 Encounter for screening for malignant neoplasm of colon

Encounter for screening colonoscopy NOS

Z12.12 Encounter for screening for malignant neoplasm of rectum

Z12.13 Encounter for screening for malignant neoplasm of small intestine

Z12.2 Encounter for screening for malignant neoplasm of respiratory organs

\+ **Z12.3 Encounter for screening for malignant neoplasm of breast**

Z12.31 Encounter for screening mammogram for malignant neoplasm of breast

Excludes1: *inconclusive mammogram (R92.2)*

Z12.39 Encounter for other screening for malignant neoplasm of breast

♀ **Z12.4 Encounter for screening for malignant neoplasm of cervix**

Encounter for screening pap smear for malignant neoplasm of cervix

Excludes1: *encounter for screening for human papillomavirus (Z11.51)*

when screening is part of general gynecological examination (Z01.4-)

♂ **Z12.5 Encounter for screening for malignant neoplasm of prostate**

Z12.6 Encounter for screening for malignant neoplasm of bladder

\+ **Z12.7 Encounter for screening for malignant neoplasm of other genitourinary organs**

♂ **Z12.71 Encounter for screening for malignant neoplasm of testis**

♀ **Z12.72 Encounter for screening for malignant neoplasm of vagina**

Vaginal pap smear status-post hysterectomy for non-malignant condition

Use additional code to identify acquired absence of uterus (Z90.71-)

Excludes1: *vaginal pap smear status-post hysterectomy for malignant conditions (Z08)*

♀ **Z12.73 Encounter for screening for malignant neoplasm of ovary**

Z12.79 Encounter for screening for malignant neoplasm of other genitourinary organs

\+ **Z12.8 Encounter for screening for malignant neoplasm of other sites**

Z12.81 Encounter for screening for malignant neoplasm of oral cavity

Z12.82 Encounter for screening for malignant neoplasm of nervous system

Z12.83 Encounter for screening for malignant neoplasm of skin

Z12.89 Encounter for screening for malignant neoplasm of other sites

Z12.9 Encounter for screening for malignant neoplasm, site unspecified

Z13 Encounter for screening for other diseases and disorders

Screening is the testing for disease or disease precursors in asymptomatic individuals so that early detection and treatment can be provided for those who test positive for the disease.

Excludes1: *encounter for diagnostic examination-code to sign or symptom*

Review coding guideline C.21.c.5

Z13.0 Encounter for screening for diseases of the blood and blood-forming organs and certain disorders involving the immune mechanism

Z13.1 Encounter for screening for diabetes mellitus

\+ **Z13.2 Encounter for screening for nutritional, metabolic and other endocrine disorders**

Z13.21 Encounter for screening for nutritional disorder

\+ **Z13.22 Encounter for screening for metabolic disorder**

Z13.220 Encounter for screening for lipoid disorders

Encounter for screening for cholesterol level

Encounter for screening for hypercholesterolemia

Encounter for screening for hyperlipidemia

Z13.228 Encounter for screening for other metabolic disorders

Z13.29 Encounter for screening for other suspected endocrine disorder

Excludes1: *encounter for screening for diabetes mellitus (Z13.1)*

● **Z13.4 Encounter for screening for certain developmental disorders in childhood**

Encounter for screening for developmental handicaps in early childhood

Excludes1: *routine development testing of infant or child (Z00.1-)*

Z13.5 Encounter for screening for eye and ear disorders

Excludes2: *encounter for general hearing examination (Z01.1-)*

encounter for general vision examination (Z01.0-)

Z13.6 Encounter for screening for cardiovascular disorders

\+ **Z13.7 Encounter for screening for genetic and chromosomal anomalies**

Excludes1: *genetic testing for procreative management (Z31.4-)*

Z13.71 Encounter for nonprocreative screening for genetic disease carrier status

Z13.79 Encounter for other screening for genetic and chromosomal anomalies

\+ **Z13.8 Encounter for screening for other specified diseases and disorders**

Excludes2: *screening for malignant neoplasms (Z12.-)*

\+ **Z13.81 Encounter for screening for digestive system disorders**

Z13.810 Encounter for screening for upper gastrointestinal disorder

Z13.811 Encounter for screening for lower gastrointestinal disorder

Excludes1: *encounter for screening for intestinal infectious disease (Z11.0)*

Z13.818 Encounter for screening for other digestive system disorders

\+ **Z13.82 Encounter for screening for musculoskeletal disorder**

Z13.820 Encounter for screening for osteoporosis

Z13.828 Encounter for screening for other musculoskeletal disorder

Z13.83 Encounter for screening for respiratory disorder NEC

Excludes1: *encounter for screening for respiratory tuberculosis (Z11.1)*

Z13.84 Encounter for screening for dental disorders

\+ **Z13.85 Encounter for screening for nervous system disorders**

Z13.850 Encounter for screening for traumatic brain injury

Z13.858 Encounter for screening for other nervous system disorders

Z13.88 Encounter for screening for disorder due to exposure to contaminants

Excludes1: *those exposed to contaminants without suspected disorders (Z57.-, Z77.-)*

Z13.89 Encounter for screening for other disorder

Encounter for screening for genitourinary disorders

Z13.9 Encounter for screening, unspecified

Genetic carrier and genetic susceptibility to disease (Z14-Z15)

Z14 Genetic carrier
Review coding guideline C.21.c.3
+ **Z14.0 Hemophilia A carrier**
  - **Z14.01 Asymptomatic hemophilia A carrier**
  - **Z14.02 Symptomatic hemophilia A carrier**
- **Z14.1 Cystic fibrosis carrier**
- **Z14.8 Genetic carrier of other disease**

Z15 Genetic susceptibility to disease
Includes: confirmed abnormal gene
Use additional code, if applicable, for any associated family history of the disease (Z80-Z84)
Excludes1: *chromosomal anomalies (Q90-Q99)*
Review coding guideline C.21.c.3
+ **Z15.0 Genetic susceptibility to malignant neoplasm**
  Code first , if applicable, any current malignant neoplasm (C00-C75, C81-C96)

  Use additional code, if applicable, for any personal history of malignant neoplasm (Z85.-)
  - **Z15.01 Genetic susceptibility to malignant neoplasm of breast**
  - ♀ **Z15.02 Genetic susceptibility to malignant neoplasm of ovary**
  - ♂ **Z15.03 Genetic susceptibility to malignant neoplasm of prostate**
  - ♀ **Z15.04 Genetic susceptibility to malignant neoplasm of endometrium**
  - **Z15.09 Genetic susceptibility to other malignant neoplasm**
+ **Z15.8 Genetic susceptibility to other disease**
  - **Z15.81 Genetic susceptibility to multiple endocrine neoplasia [MEN]**
    Excludes1: *multiple endocrine neoplasia [MEN] syndromes (E31.2-)*
  - **Z15.89 Genetic susceptibility to other disease**

Resistance to antimicrobial drugs (Z16)

Z16 Resistance to antimicrobial drugs
NOTE The codes in this category are provided for use as additional codes to identify the resistance and non-responsiveness of a condition to antimicrobial drugs.
Code first the infection
Excludes1: *Methicillin resistant Staphylococcus aureus infection (A49.02)*
Methicillin resistant Staphylococcus aureus infection in diseases classified elsewhere (B95.62)
Methicillin resistant Staphylococcus aureus pneumonia (J15.212)
Sepsis due to Methicillin resistant Staphylococcus aureus (A41.02)
Review coding guideline C.1.c
Review coding guideline C.21.c.3
+ **Z16.1 Resistance to beta lactam antibiotics**
  - **Z16.10 Resistance to unspecified beta lactam antibiotics**
  - **Z16.11 Resistance to penicillins**
    Resistance to amoxicillin
    Resistance to ampicillin
    Review coding guidelines C.1.e.1.a and C.1.e.1.b
  - **Z16.12 Extended spectrum beta lactamase (ESBL) resistance**
  - **Z16.19 Resistance to other specified beta lactam antibiotics**
    Resistance to cephalosporins
+ **Z16.2 Resistance to other antibiotics**
  - **Z16.20 Resistance to unspecified antibiotic**
    Resistance to antibiotics NOS
  - **Z16.21 Resistance to vancomycin**
  - **Z16.22 Resistance to vancomycin related antibiotics**
  - **Z16.23 Resistance to quinolones and fluoroquinolones**
  - **Z16.24 Resistance to multiple antibiotics**
  - **Z16.29 Resistance to other single specified antibiotic**
    Resistance to aminoglycosides
    Resistance to macrolides
    Resistance to sulfonamides
    Resistance to tetracyclines
+ **Z16.3 Resistance to other antimicrobial drugs**
  Excludes1: *resistance to antibiotics (Z16.1-, Z16.2-)*
  - **Z16.30 Resistance to unspecified antimicrobial drugs**
    Drug resistance NOS
  - **Z16.31 Resistance to antiparasitic drug(s)**
    Resistance to quinine and related compounds
  - **Z16.32 Resistance to antifungal drug(s)**
  - **Z16.33 Resistance to antiviral drug(s)**
  - + **Z16.34 Resistance to antimycobacterial drug(s)**
    Resistance to tuberculostatics
    - **Z16.341 Resistance to single antimycobacterial drug**
      Resistance to antimycobacterial drug NOS
    - **Z16.342 Resistance to multiple antimycobacterial drugs**
  - **Z16.35 Resistance to multiple antimicrobial drugs**
    Excludes1: *Resistance to multiple antibiotics only (Z16.24)*
  - **Z16.39 Resistance to other specified antimicrobial drug**

Estrogen receptor status (Z17)

Z17 Estrogen receptor status
Code first malignant neoplasm of breast (C50.-)
Review coding guideline C.21.c.3
- **Z17.0 Estrogen receptor positive status [ER+]**
- **Z17.1 Estrogen receptor negative status [ER-]**

Retained foreign body fragments (Z18)

Z18 Retained foreign body fragments
Includes: embedded fragment (status)
embedded splinter (status)
retained foreign body status
Excludes1: *artificial joint prosthesis status (Z96.6-)*
foreign body accidentally left during a procedure (T81.5-)
foreign body entering through orifice (T15-T19)
in situ cardiac device (Z95.-)
organ or tissue replaced by means other than transplant (Z96.-, Z97.-)
organ or tissue replaced by transplant (Z94.-)
personal history of retained foreign body fully removed Z87.821
superficial foreign body (non-embedded splinter) - code to superficial foreign body, by site
Review coding guideline C.21.c.3
+ **Z18.0 Retained radioactive fragments**
  - **Z18.01 Retained depleted uranium fragments**
  - **Z18.09 Other retained radioactive fragments**
    Other retained depleted isotope fragments
    Retained nontherapeutic radioactive fragments
+ **Z18.1 Retained metal fragments**
  Excludes1: *retained radioactive metal fragments (Z18.01-Z18.09)*
  - **Z18.10 Retained metal fragments, unspecified**
    Retained metal fragment NOS
  - **Z18.11 Retained magnetic metal fragments**
  - **Z18.12 Retained nonmagnetic metal fragments**
- **Z18.2 Retained plastic fragments**
  Acrylics fragments
  Diethylhexylphthalates fragments
  Isocyanate fragments
+ **Z18.3 Retained organic fragments**
  - **Z18.31 Retained animal quills or spines**
  - **Z18.32 Retained tooth**
  - **Z18.33 Retained wood fragments**
  - **Z18.39 Other retained organic fragments**
+ **Z18.8 Other specified retained foreign body**
  - **Z18.81 Retained glass fragments**
  - **Z18.83 Retained stone or crystalline fragments**
    Retained concrete or cement fragments
  - **Z18.89 Other specified retained foreign body fragments**
- **Z18.9 Retained foreign body fragments, unspecified material**

Persons with potential health hazards related to communicable diseases (Z20-Z28)

Z20 Contact with and (suspected) exposure to communicable diseases
Excludes1: *carrier of infectious disease (Z22.-)*
diagnosed current infectious or parasitic disease -see Alphabetic Index
Excludes2: *personal history of infectious and parasitic diseases (Z86.1-)*
Review coding guideline C.21.c.1
+ **Z20.0 Contact with and (suspected) exposure to intestinal infectious diseases**
  - **Z20.01 Contact with and (suspected) exposure to intestinal infectious diseases due to Escherichia coli (E. coli)**
  - **Z20.09 Contact with and (suspected) exposure to other intestinal infectious diseases**

Z20.1 **Contact with and (suspected) exposure to tuberculosis**
Z20.2 **Contact with and (suspected) exposure to infections with a predominantly sexual mode of transmission**
Z20.3 **Contact with and (suspected) exposure to rabies**
Z20.4 **Contact with and (suspected) exposure to rubella**
Z20.5 **Contact with and (suspected) exposure to viral hepatitis**
Z20.6 **Contact with and (suspected) exposure to human immunodeficiency virus [HIV]**
Excludes1: *asymptomatic human immunodeficiency virus [HIV] HIV infection status (Z21)*
Z20.7 **Contact with and (suspected) exposure to pediculosis, acariasis and other infestations**
+ **Z20.8** **Contact with and (suspected) exposure to other communicable diseases**
+ **Z20.81** **Contact with and (suspected) exposure to other bacterial communicable diseases**
Z20.810 **Contact with and (suspected) exposure to anthrax**
Z20.811 **Contact with and (suspected) exposure to meningococcus**
Z20.818 **Contact with and (suspected) exposure to other bacterial communicable diseases**
+ **Z20.82** **Contact with and (suspected) exposure to other viral communicable diseases**
Z20.820 **Contact with and (suspected) exposure to varicella**
Z20.828 **Contact with and (suspected) exposure to other viral communicable diseases**
Z20.89 **Contact with and (suspected) exposure to other communicable diseases**
Z20.9 **Contact with and (suspected) exposure to unspecified communicable disease**

Z21 Asymptomatic human immunodeficiency virus [HIV] infection status
HIV positive NOS
Code first Human immunodeficiency virus [HIV] disease complicating pregnancy, childbirth and the puerperium, if applicable (O98.7-)
Excludes1: *acquired immunodeficiency syndrome (B20)*
contact with human immunodeficiency virus [HIV] (Z20.6)
exposure to human immunodeficiency virus [HIV] (Z20.6)
human immunodeficiency virus [HIV] disease (B20)
inconclusive laboratory evidence of human immunodeficiency virus [HIV] (R75)
Review coding guidelines C.1.a.2.d, C.1.a.2.f and C.1.a.2.g
Review coding guideline C.15.f
Review coding guideline C.21.c.3
Valid 3-character code, no further characters required

Z22 Carrier of2 infectious disease
Includes: colonization status
suspected carrier
Review coding guideline C.21.c.3
Z22.0 **Carrier of typhoid**
Z22.1 **Carrier of other intestinal infectious diseases**
Z22.2 **Carrier of diphtheria**
+ **Z22.3** **Carrier of other specified bacterial diseases**
Z22.31 **Carrier of bacterial disease due to meningococci**
+ **Z22.32** **Carrier of bacterial disease due to staphylococci**
Z22.321 **Carrier or suspected carrier of Methicillin susceptible Staphylococcus aureus**
MSSA colonization
Review coding guidelines C.1.e.1.c and C.1.e.1.d
Z22.322 **Carrier or suspected carrier of Methicillin resistant Staphylococcus aureus**
MRSA colonization
Review coding guidelines C.1.e.1.c and C.1.e.1.d
+ **Z22.33** **Carrier of bacterial disease due to streptococci**
Z22.330 **Carrier of Group B streptococcus**
Z22.338 **Carrier of other streptococcus**
Z22.39 **Carrier of other specified bacterial diseases**
Z22.4 **Carrier of infections with a predominantly sexual mode of transmission**
+ **Z22.5** **Carrier of viral hepatitis**
Z22.50 **Carrier of unspecified viral hepatitis**
Z22.51 **Carrier of viral hepatitis B**
Hepatitis B surface antigen [HBsAg] carrier
Z22.52 **Carrier of viral hepatitis C**
Z22.59 **Carrier of other viral hepatitis**
Z22.6 **Carrier of human T-lymphotropic virus type-1 [HTLV-1] infection**
Z22.8 **Carrier of other infectious diseases**
Z22.9 **Carrier of infectious disease, unspecified**

Z23 Encounter for immunization
Code first any routine childhood examination
NOTE procedure codes are required to identify the types of immunizations given
Review coding guideline C.21.c.2
Valid 3-character code, no further characters required

Z28 Immunization not carried out and underimmunization status
Includes: vaccination not carried out
+ **Z28.0** **Immunization not carried out because of contraindication**
Z28.01 **Immunization not carried out because of acute illness of patient**
Z28.02 **Immunization not carried out because of chronic illness or condition of patient**
Z28.03 **Immunization not carried out because of immune compromised state of patient**
Z28.04 **Immunization not carried out because of patient allergy to vaccine or component**
Z28.09 **Immunization not carried out because of other contraindication**
Z28.1 **Immunization not carried out because of patient decision for reasons of belief or group pressure**
Immunization not carried out because of religious belief
+ **Z28.2** **Immunization not carried out because of patient decision for other and unspecified reason**
Z28.20 **Immunization not carried out because of patient decision for unspecified reason**
Z28.21 **Immunization not carried out because of patient refusal**
Z28.29 **Immunization not carried out because of patient decision for other reason**
Z28.3 **Underimmunization status**
Delinquent immunization status
Lapsed immunization schedule status
Review coding guideline C.21.c.3
+ **Z28.8** **Immunization not carried out for other reason**
Z28.81 **Immunization not carried out due to patient having had the disease**
Z28.82 **Immunization not carried out because of caregiver refusal**
Immunization not carried out because of guardian refusal
Immunization not carried out because of parent refusal
Excludes1: *immunization not carried out because of caregiver refusal because of religious belief (Z28.1)*
Z28.89 **Immunization not carried out for other reason**
Z28.9 **Immunization not carried out for unspecified reason**

Persons encountering health services in circumstances related to reproduction (Z30-Z39)

Z30 Encounter for contraceptive management
Review coding guideline C.21.c.11
+ **Z30.0** **Encounter for general counseling and advice on contraception**
Review coding guideline C.21.c.10
+ **Z30.01** **Encounter for initial prescription of contraceptives**
Excludes1: *encounter for surveillance of contraceptives (Z30.4-)*
♀ **Z30.011** **Encounter for initial prescription of contraceptive pills**
♀ **Z30.012** **Encounter for prescription of emergency contraception**
Encounter for postcoital contraception
♀ **Z30.013** **Encounter for initial prescription of injectable contraceptive**
♀ **Z30.014** **Encounter for initial prescription of intrauterine contraceptive device**
Excludes1: *encounter for insertion of intrauterine contraceptive device (Z30.430, Z30.432)*
♀ **Z30.018** **Encounter for initial prescription of other contraceptives**
♀ **Z30.019** **Encounter for initial prescription of contraceptives, unspecified**
Z30.02 **Counseling and instruction in natural family planning to avoid pregnancy**
Z30.09 **Encounter for other general counseling and advice on contraception**
Encounter for family planning advice NOS
Z30.2 **Encounter for sterilization**
+ **Z30.4** **Encounter for surveillance of contraceptives**

Z30.40 **Encounter for surveillance of contraceptives, unspecified**
♀ **Z30.41** **Encounter for surveillance of contraceptive pills**
Encounter for repeat prescription for contraceptive pill
♀ **Z30.42** **Encounter for surveillance of injectable contraceptive**
+ **Z30.43** **Encounter for surveillance of intrauterine contraceptive device**
♀ **Z30.430** **Encounter for insertion of intrauterine contraceptive device**
♀ **Z30.431** **Encounter for routine checking of intrauterine contraceptive device**
♀ **Z30.432** **Encounter for removal of intrauterine contraceptive device**
♀ **Z30.433** **Encounter for removal and reinsertion of intrauterine contraceptive device**
Encounter for replacement of intrauterine contraceptive device
♀ **Z30.49** **Encounter for surveillance of other contraceptives**
Z30.8 **Encounter for other contraceptive management**
Encounter for postvasectomy sperm count
Encounter for routine examination for contraceptive maintenance
Excludes1: *sperm count following sterilization reversal (Z31.42)*
sperm count for fertility testing (Z31.41)
Z30.9 **Encounter for contraceptive management, unspecified**

Z31 **Encounter for procreative management**
Excludes1: *complications associated with artificial fertilization (N98.-)*
female infertility (N97.-)
male infertility (N46.-)
Review coding guideline C.21.c.11
Z31.0 **Encounter for reversal of previous sterilization**
+ **Z31.4** **Encounter for procreative investigation and testing**
Excludes1: *postvasectomy sperm count (Z30.8)*
Z31.41 **Encounter for fertility testing**
Encounter for fallopian tube patency testing
Encounter for sperm count for fertility testing
Z31.42 **Aftercare following sterilization reversal**
Sperm count following sterilization reversal
+ **Z31.43** **Encounter for genetic testing of female for procreative management**
Use additional code for recurrent pregnancy loss, if applicable (N96, O26.2-)
Excludes1: *nonprocreative genetic testing (Z13.7-)*
♀ **Z31.430** **Encounter of female for testing for genetic disease carrier status for procreative management**
♀ **Z31.438** **Encounter for other genetic testing of female for procreative management**
+ **Z31.44** **Encounter for genetic testing of male for procreative management**
Excludes1: *nonprocreative genetic testing (Z13.7-)*
♂ **Z31.440** **Encounter of male for testing for genetic disease carrier status for procreative management**
• ♂ **Z31.441** **Encounter for testing of male partner of patient with recurrent pregnancy loss**
• ♂ **Z31.448** **Encounter for other genetic testing of male for procreative management**
Z31.49 **Encounter for other procreative investigation and testing**
Z31.5 **Encounter for genetic counseling**
Review coding guideline C.21.c.10
+ **Z31.6** **Encounter for general counseling and advice on procreation**
Review coding guideline C.21.c.10
Z31.61 **Procreative counseling and advice using natural family planning**
Z31.62 **Encounter for fertility preservation counseling**
Encounter for fertility preservation counseling prior to cancer therapy
Encounter for fertility preservation counseling prior to surgical removal of gonads
Z31.69 **Encounter for other general counseling and advice on procreation**
+ **Z31.8** **Encounter for other procreative management**
♀ **Z31.81** **Encounter for male factor infertility in female patient**
Review coding guideline C.21.c.16
♀ **Z31.82** **Encounter for Rh incompatibility status**
Review coding guideline C.21.c.16
♀ **Z31.83** **Encounter for assisted reproductive fertility procedure cycle**
Patient undergoing in vitro fertilization cycle
Use additional code to identify the type of infertility
Excludes1: *pre-cycle diagnosis and testing - code to reason for encounter*
Review coding guideline C.21.c.16
Z31.84 **Encounter for fertility preservation procedure**
Encounter for fertility preservation procedure prior to cancer therapy
Encounter for fertility preservation procedure prior to surgical removal of gonads
Review coding guideline C.21.c.16
Z31.89 **Encounter for other procreative management**
Z31.9 **Encounter for procreative management, unspecified**

Z32 **Encounter for pregnancy test and childbirth and childcare instruction**
+ **Z32.0** **Encounter for pregnancy test**
Review coding guideline C.21.c.13
♀ **Z32.00** **Encounter for pregnancy test, result unknown**
Encounter for pregnancy test NOS
• ♀ **Z32.01** **Encounter for pregnancy test, result positive**
♀ **Z32.02** **Encounter for pregnancy test, result negative**
Z32.2 **Encounter for childbirth instruction**
Review coding guidelines C.21.c.10 and C.21.c.11
Z32.3 **Encounter for childcare instruction**
Encounter for prenatal or postpartum childcare instruction
Review coding guidelines C.21.c.10 and C.21.c.11

Z33 **Pregnant state**
Review coding guideline C.21.c.11
• ♀ **Z33.1** **Pregnant state, incidental**
Pregnant state NOS
Excludes1: *complications of pregnancy (O00-O9A)*
Review coding guideline C.15.a.1
Review coding guidelines C.21.c.3
• ♀ **Z33.2** **Encounter for elective termination of pregnancy**
Excludes1: *early fetal death with retention of dead fetus (O02.1)*
late fetal death (O36.4)
spontaneous abortion (O03)
Review coding guidelines C.15.q.1 and C.15.q.2
Review coding guidelines C.21.c.16

Z34 **Encounter for supervision of normal pregnancy**
Excludes1: *any complication of pregnancy (O00-O9A)*
encounter for pregnancy test (Z32.0-)
encounter for supervision of high risk pregnancy (O09.-)
Review coding guideline C.15.b.1
Review coding guidelines C.21.c.11 and C.21.c.16
+ **Z34.0** **Encounter for supervision of normal first pregnancy**
• ♀ **Z34.00** **Encounter for supervision of normal first pregnancy, unspecified trimester**
• ♀ **Z34.01** **Encounter for supervision of normal first pregnancy, first trimester**
• ♀ **Z34.02** **Encounter for supervision of normal first pregnancy, second trimester**
• ♀ **Z34.03** **Encounter for supervision of normal first pregnancy, third trimester**
+ **Z34.8** **Encounter for supervision of other normal pregnancy**
• ♀ **Z34.80** **Encounter for supervision of other normal pregnancy, unspecified trimester**
• ♀ **Z34.81** **Encounter for supervision of other normal pregnancy, first trimester**
• ♀ **Z34.82** **Encounter for supervision of other normal pregnancy, second trimester**
• ♀ **Z34.83** **Encounter for supervision of other normal pregnancy, third trimester**
+ **Z34.9** **Encounter for supervision of normal pregnancy, unspecified**
• ♀ **Z34.90** **Encounter for supervision of normal pregnancy, unspecified, unspecified trimester**
• ♀ **Z34.91** **Encounter for supervision of normal pregnancy, unspecified, first trimester**
• ♀ **Z34.92** **Encounter for supervision of normal pregnancy, unspecified, second trimester**
• ♀ **Z34.93** **Encounter for supervision of normal pregnancy, unspecified, third trimester**

• ♀ **Z36 Encounter for antenatal screening of mother**

Excludes1: *abnormal findings on antenatal screening of mother (O28.-)*
diagnostic examination- code to sign or symptom
encounter for suspected maternal and fetal conditions ruled out (Z03.7-)
suspected fetal condition affecting management of pregnancy - code to condition in Chapter 15

Excludes2: *genetic counseling and testing (Z31.43-, Z31.5)*
routine prenatal care (Z34)

Review coding guidelines C.21.c.5 and C.21.c.11
Valid 3-character code, no further characters required

Z3A Weeks of gestation

NOTE Codes from category Z3A are for use, only on the maternal record, to indicate the weeks of gestation of the pregnancy.

Code first complications of pregnancy, childbirth and the puerperium (O00-O9A)

Review coding guideline C.21.c.11

+ **Z3A.0 Weeks of gestation of pregnancy, unspecified or less than 10 weeks**
  - • ♀ **Z3A.00 Weeks of gestation of pregnancy not specified**
  - • ♀ **Z3A.01 Less than 8 weeks gestation of pregnancy**
  - • ♀ **Z3A.08 8 weeks gestation of pregnancy**
  - • ♀ **Z3A.09 9 weeks gestation of pregnancy**

+ **Z3A.1 Weeks of gestation of pregnancy, weeks 10-19**
  - • ♀ **Z3A.10 10 weeks gestation of pregnancy**
  - • ♀ **Z3A.11 11 weeks gestation of pregnancy**
  - • ♀ **Z3A.12 12 weeks gestation of pregnancy**
  - • ♀ **Z3A.13 13 weeks gestation of pregnancy**
  - • ♀ **Z3A.14 14 weeks gestation of pregnancy**
  - • ♀ **Z3A.15 15 weeks gestation of pregnancy**
  - • ♀ **Z3A.16 16 weeks gestation of pregnancy**
  - • ♀ **Z3A.17 17 weeks gestation of pregnancy**
  - • ♀ **Z3A.18 18 weeks gestation of pregnancy**
  - • ♀ **Z3A.19 19 weeks gestation of pregnancy**

+ **Z3A.2 Weeks of gestation of pregnancy, weeks 20-29**
  - • ♀ **Z3A.20 20 weeks gestation of pregnancy**
  - • ♀ **Z3A.21 21 weeks gestation of pregnancy**
  - • ♀ **Z3A.22 22 weeks gestation of pregnancy**
  - • ♀ **Z3A.23 23 weeks gestation of pregnancy**
  - • ♀ **Z3A.24 24 weeks gestation of pregnancy**
  - • ♀ **Z3A.25 25 weeks gestation of pregnancy**
  - • ♀ **Z3A.26 26 weeks gestation of pregnancy**
  - • ♀ **Z3A.27 27 weeks gestation of pregnancy**
  - • ♀ **Z3A.28 28 weeks gestation of pregnancy**
  - • ♀ **Z3A.29 29 weeks gestation of pregnancy**

+ **Z3A.3 Weeks of gestation of pregnancy, weeks 30-39**
  - • ♀ **Z3A.30 30 weeks gestation of pregnancy**
  - • ♀ **Z3A.31 31 weeks gestation of pregnancy**
  - • ♀ **Z3A.32 32 weeks gestation of pregnancy**
  - • ♀ **Z3A.33 33 weeks gestation of pregnancy**
  - • ♀ **Z3A.34 34 weeks gestation of pregnancy**
  - • ♀ **Z3A.35 35 weeks gestation of pregnancy**
  - • ♀ **Z3A.36 36 weeks gestation of pregnancy**
  - • ♀ **Z3A.37 37 weeks gestation of pregnancy**
  - • ♀ **Z3A.38 38 weeks gestation of pregnancy**
  - • ♀ **Z3A.39 39 weeks gestation of pregnancy**

+ **Z3A.4 Weeks of gestation of pregnancy, weeks 40 or greater**
  - • ♀ **Z3A.40 40 weeks gestation of pregnancy**
    AHA CC: 2Q, 2014, 9
  - • ♀ **Z3A.41 41 weeks gestation of pregnancy**
  - • ♀ **Z3A.42 42 weeks gestation of pregnancy**
  - • ♀ **Z3A.49 Greater than 42 weeks gestation of pregnancy**

Z37 Outcome of delivery

This category is intended for use as an additional code to identify the outcome of delivery on the mother's record. It is not for use on the newborn record.

Excludes1: *stillbirth (P95)*

Review coding guidelines C.15.b.5
Review coding guidelines C.15.n.3 and C.15.q.1
Review coding guidelines C.21.c.11

- • ♀ **Z37.0 Single live birth**
  AHA CC: 2Q, 2014, 9
- • ♀ **Z37.1 Single stillbirth**
- • ♀ **Z37.2 Twins, both liveborn**
- • ♀ **Z37.3 Twins, one liveborn and one stillborn**
- • ♀ **Z37.4 Twins, both stillborn**

+ **Z37.5 Other multiple births, all liveborn**
  - • ♀ **Z37.50 Multiple births, unspecified, all liveborn**
  - • ♀ **Z37.51 Triplets, all liveborn**
  - • ♀ **Z37.52 Quadruplets, all liveborn**
  - • ♀ **Z37.53 Quintuplets, all liveborn**
  - • ♀ **Z37.54 Sextuplets, all liveborn**
  - • ♀ **Z37.59 Other multiple births, all liveborn**

+ **Z37.6 Other multiple births, some liveborn**
  - • ♀ **Z37.60 Multiple births, unspecified, some liveborn**
  - • ♀ **Z37.61 Triplets, some liveborn**
  - • ♀ **Z37.62 Quadruplets, some liveborn**
  - • ♀ **Z37.63 Quintuplets, some liveborn**
  - • ♀ **Z37.64 Sextuplets, some liveborn**
  - • ♀ **Z37.69 Other multiple births, some liveborn**

- • ♀ **Z37.7 Other multiple births, all stillborn**
- • ♀ **Z37.9 Outcome of delivery, unspecified**
  Multiple birth NOS
  Single birth NOS

Z38 Liveborn infants according to place of birth and type of delivery

This category is for use as the principal code on the initial record of a newborn baby. It is to be used for the initial birth record only. It is not to be used on the mother's record.

Review coding guideline C.16.a.2
Review coding guideline C.17
Review coding guidelines C.21.c.12 and C.21.c.16

+ **Z38.0 Single liveborn infant, born in hospital**
  Single liveborn infant, born in birthing center or other health care facility
  - • **Z38.00 Single liveborn infant, delivered vaginally**
  - • **Z38.01 Single liveborn infant, delivered by cesarean**

- • **Z38.1 Single liveborn infant, born outside hospital**
- • **Z38.2 Single liveborn infant, unspecified as to place of birth**
  Single liveborn infant NOS

+ **Z38.3 Twin liveborn infant, born in hospital**
  - • **Z38.30 Twin liveborn infant, delivered vaginally**
  - • **Z38.31 Twin liveborn infant, delivered by cesarean**

- • **Z38.4 Twin liveborn infant, born outside hospital**
- • **Z38.5 Twin liveborn infant, unspecified as to place of birth**

+ **Z38.6 Other multiple liveborn infant, born in hospital**
  - • **Z38.61 Triplet liveborn infant, delivered vaginally**
  - • **Z38.62 Triplet liveborn infant, delivered by cesarean**
  - • **Z38.63 Quadruplet liveborn infant, delivered vaginally**
  - • **Z38.64 Quadruplet liveborn infant, delivered by cesarean**
  - • **Z38.65 Quintuplet liveborn infant, delivered vaginally**
  - • **Z38.66 Quintuplet liveborn infant, delivered by cesarean**
  - • **Z38.68 Other multiple liveborn infant, delivered vaginally**
  - • **Z38.69 Other multiple liveborn infant, delivered by cesarean**

- • **Z38.7 Other multiple liveborn infant, born outside hospital**
- • **Z38.8 Other multiple liveborn infant, unspecified as to place of birth**

Z39 Encounter for maternal postpartum care and examination

Review coding guidelines C.21.c.8, C.21.c.11 and C.21.c.16

- • ♀ **Z39.0 Encounter for care and examination of mother immediately after delivery**
  Care and observation in uncomplicated cases when the delivery occurs outside a healthcare facility
  Excludes1: *care for postpartum complication- see Alphabetic index*
  Review coding guideline C.15.o.4
- • ♀ **Z39.1 Encounter for care and examination of lactating mother**
  Encounter for supervision of lactation
  Excludes1: *disorders of lactation (O92.-)*
- • ♀ **Z39.2 Encounter for routine postpartum follow-up**

Encounters for other specific health care (Z40-Z53)

Categories Z40-Z53 are intended for use to indicate a reason for care. They may be used for patients who have already been treated for a disease or injury, but who are receiving aftercare or prophylactic care, or care to consolidate the treatment, or to deal with a residual state

Excludes2: *follow-up examination for medical surveillance after treatment (Z08-Z09)*

Z40 Encounter for prophylactic surgery

Excludes1: *organ donations (Z52.-)*
therapeutic organ removal-code to condition

Review coding guideline C.21.c.14

+ **Z40.0 Encounter for prophylactic surgery for risk factors related to malignant neoplasms**
  Admission for prophylactic organ removal
  Use additional code to identify risk factor
  - **Z40.00 Encounter for prophylactic removal of unspecified organ**
  - **Z40.01 Encounter for prophylactic removal of breast**
  - ♀ **Z40.02 Encounter for prophylactic removal of ovary**
  - **Z40.09 Encounter for prophylactic removal of other organ**

- **Z40.8 Encounter for other prophylactic surgery**
- **Z40.9 Encounter for prophylactic surgery, unspecified**

Z41 Encounter for procedures for purposes other than remedying health state

Z41.1 Encounter for cosmetic surgery
Encounter for cosmetic breast implant
Encounter for cosmetic procedure
Excludes1: *encounter for plastic and reconstructive surgery following medical procedure or healed injury (Z42.-)*
encounter for post-mastectomy breast implantation (Z42.1)

♂ **Z41.2 Encounter for routine and ritual male circumcision**
Z41.3 Encounter for ear piercing
Z41.8 Encounter for other procedures for purposes other than remedying health state
Z41.9 Encounter for procedure for purposes other than remedying health state, unspecified

Z42 Encounter for plastic and reconstructive surgery following medical procedure or healed injury
Excludes1: *encounter for cosmetic plastic surgery (Z41.1)*
encounter for plastic surgery for treatment of current injury - code to relevent injury
Review coding guidelines C.21.c.7 and C.21.c.16

• **Z42.1 Encounter for breast reconstruction following mastectomy**
Excludes1: *deformity and disproportion of reconstructed breast (N65.1-)*

Z42.8 Encounter for other plastic and reconstructive surgery following medical procedure or healed injury

Z43 Encounter for attention to artificial openings
Includes: closure of artificial openings
passage of sounds or bougies through artificial openings
reforming artificial openings
removal of catheter from artificial openings
toilet or cleansing of artificial openings
Excludes1: *artificial opening status only, without need for care (Z93.-)*
complications of external stoma (J95.0-, K94.-, N99.5-)
Excludes2: *fitting and adjustment of prosthetic and other devices (Z44-Z46)*
Review coding guideline C.21.c.7

Z43.0 Encounter for attention to tracheostomy
CC **Z43.1 Encounter for attention to gastrostomy**
CC Exclusion see Appendix A PDX collection 1487
Z43.2 Encounter for attention to ileostomy
Z43.3 Encounter for attention to colostomy
Z43.4 Encounter for attention to other artificial openings of digestive tract
Z43.5 Encounter for attention to cystostomy
Z43.6 Encounter for attention to other artificial openings of urinary tract
Encounter for attention to nephrostomy
Encounter for attention to ureterostomy
Encounter for attention to urethrostomy
Z43.7 Encounter for attention to artificial vagina
Z43.8 Encounter for attention to other artificial openings
Z43.9 Encounter for attention to unspecified artificial opening

Z44 Encounter for fitting and adjustment of external prosthetic device
Includes: removal or replacement of external prosthetic device
Excludes1: *malfunction or other complications of device - see Alphabetical Index*
presence of prosthetic device (Z97.-)
Review coding guideline C.21.c.7

+ **Z44.0 Encounter for fitting and adjustment of artificial arm**
+ **Z44.00 Encounter for fitting and adjustment of unspecified artificial arm**
Z44.001 Encounter for fitting and adjustment of unspecified right artificial arm
Z44.002 Encounter for fitting and adjustment of unspecified left artificial arm
Z44.009 Encounter for fitting and adjustment of unspecified artificial arm, unspecified arm
+ **Z44.01 Encounter for fitting and adjustment of complete artificial arm**
Z44.011 Encounter for fitting and adjustment of complete right artificial arm
Z44.012 Encounter for fitting and adjustment of complete left artificial arm
Z44.019 Encounter for fitting and adjustment of complete artificial arm, unspecified arm
+ **Z44.02 Encounter for fitting and adjustment of partial artificial arm**
Z44.021 Encounter for fitting and adjustment of partial artificial right arm
Z44.022 Encounter for fitting and adjustment of partial artificial left arm
Z44.029 Encounter for fitting and adjustment of partial artificial arm, unspecified arm
+ **Z44.1 Encounter for fitting and adjustment of artificial leg**
+ **Z44.10 Encounter for fitting and adjustment of unspecified artificial leg**
Z44.101 Encounter for fitting and adjustment of unspecified right artificial leg
Z44.102 Encounter for fitting and adjustment of unspecified left artificial leg
Z44.109 Encounter for fitting and adjustment of unspecified artificial leg, unspecified leg
+ **Z44.11 Encounter for fitting and adjustment of complete artificial leg**
Z44.111 Encounter for fitting and adjustment of complete right artificial leg
Z44.112 Encounter for fitting and adjustment of complete left artificial leg
Z44.119 Encounter for fitting and adjustment of complete artificial leg, unspecified leg
+ **Z44.12 Encounter for fitting and adjustment of partial artificial leg**
Z44.121 Encounter for fitting and adjustment of partial artificial right leg
Z44.122 Encounter for fitting and adjustment of partial artificial left leg
Z44.129 Encounter for fitting and adjustment of partial artificial leg, unspecified leg
+ **Z44.2 Encounter for fitting and adjustment of artificial eye**
Excludes1: *mechanical complication of ocular prosthesis (T85.3)*
Z44.20 Encounter for fitting and adjustment of artificial eye, unspecified
Z44.21 Encounter for fitting and adjustment of artificial right eye
Z44.22 Encounter for fitting and adjustment of artificial left eye
+ **Z44.3 Encounter for fitting and adjustment of external breast prosthesis**
Excludes1: *complications of breast implant (T85.4-)*
encounter for adjustment or removal of breast implant (Z45.81-)
encounter for initial breast implant insertion for cosmetic breast augmentation (Z41.1)
encounter for breast reconstruction following mastectomy (Z42.1)
♀ **Z44.30 Encounter for fitting and adjustment of external breast prosthesis, unspecified breast**
♀ **Z44.31 Encounter for fitting and adjustment of external right breast prosthesis**
♀ **Z44.32 Encounter for fitting and adjustment of external left breast prosthesis**
Z44.8 Encounter for fitting and adjustment of other external prosthetic devices
Z44.9 Encounter for fitting and adjustment of unspecified external prosthetic device

Z45 Encounter for adjustment and management of implanted device
Includes: removal or replacement of implanted device
Excludes1: *malfunction or other complications of device - see Alphabetical Index*
presence of prosthetic and other devices (Z95-Z97)
Excludes2: *encounter for fitting and adjustment of non-implanted device (Z46.-)*
Review coding guideline C.21.c.7

+ **Z45.0 Encounter for adjustment and management of cardiac device**
+ **Z45.01 Encounter for adjustment and management of cardiac pacemaker**
Excludes1: *encounter for adjustment and management of automatic implantable cardiac defibrillator with synchronous cardiac pacemaker (Z45.02)*
Z45.010 Encounter for checking and testing of cardiac pacemaker pulse generator [battery]
Encounter for replacing cardiac pacemaker pulse generator [battery]
Z45.018 Encounter for adjustment and management of other part of cardiac pacemaker

Z45.02 Encounter for adjustment and management of automatic implantable cardiac defibrillator
Encounter for adjustment and management of automatic implantable cardiac defibrillator with synchronous cardiac pacemaker
Z45.09 Encounter for adjustment and management of other cardiac device
Z45.1 Encounter for adjustment and management of infusion pump
Z45.2 Encounter for adjustment and management of vascular access device
Encounter for adjustment and management of vascular catheters
Excludes1: *encounter for adjustment and management of renal dialysis catheter (Z49.01)*
+ **Z45.3 Encounter for adjustment and management of implanted devices of the special senses**
Z45.31 Encounter for adjustment and management of implanted visual substitution device
+ **Z45.32 Encounter for adjustment and management of implanted hearing device**
Excludes1: *Encounter for fitting and adjustment of hearing aide (Z46.1)*
Z45.320 Encounter for adjustment and management of bone conduction device
Z45.321 Encounter for adjustment and management of cochlear device
Z45.328 Encounter for adjustment and management of other implanted hearing device
+ **Z45.4 Encounter for adjustment and management of implanted nervous system device**
Z45.41 Encounter for adjustment and management of cerebrospinal fluid drainage device
Encounter for adjustment and management of cerebral ventricular (communicating) shunt
Z45.42 Encounter for adjustment and management of neuropacemaker (brain) (peripheral nerve) (spinal cord)
Z45.49 Encounter for adjustment and management of other implanted nervous system device
+ **Z45.8 Encounter for adjustment and management of other implanted devices**
+ **Z45.81 Encounter for adjustment or removal of breast implant**
Encounter for elective implant exchange (different material) (different size)
Encounter removal of tissue expander without synchronous insertion of permanent implant
Excludes1: *complications of breast implant (T85.4-)*
encounter for initial breast implant insertion for cosmetic breast augmentation (Z41.1)
encounter for breast reconstruction following mastectomy (Z42.1)
♀ **Z45.811 Encounter for adjustment or removal of right breast implant**
♀ **Z45.812 Encounter for adjustment or removal of left breast implant**
♀ **Z45.819 Encounter for adjustment or removal of unspecified breast implant**
Z45.82 Encounter for adjustment or removal of myringotomy device (stent) (tube)
Z45.89 Encounter for adjustment and management of other implanted devices
Z45.9 Encounter for adjustment and management of unspecified implanted device

Z46 Encounter for fitting and adjustment of other devices
Includes: removal or replacement of other device
Excludes1: *malfunction or other complications of device - see Alphabetical Index*
Excludes2: *encounter for fitting and management of implanted devices (Z45.-)*
issue of repeat prescription only (Z76.0)
presence of prosthetic and other devices (Z95-Z97)
Review coding guideline C.21.c.7
Z46.0 Encounter for fitting and adjustment of spectacles and contact lenses
Z46.1 Encounter for fitting and adjustment of hearing aid
Excludes1: *encounter for adjustment and management of implanted hearing device (Z45.32-)*
Z46.2 Encounter for fitting and adjustment of other devices related to nervous system and special senses
Excludes2: *encounter for adjustment and management of implanted nervous system device (Z45.4-)*
encounter for adjustment and management of implanted visual substitution device (Z45.31)
Z46.3 Encounter for fitting and adjustment of dental prosthetic device
Encounter for fitting and adjustment of dentures
Z46.4 Encounter for fitting and adjustment of orthodontic device
+ **Z46.5 Encounter for fitting and adjustment of other gastrointestinal appliance and device**
Excludes1: *encounter for attention to artificial openings of digestive tract (Z43.1-Z43.4)*
Z46.51 Encounter for fitting and adjustment of gastric lap band
Z46.59 Encounter for fitting and adjustment of other gastrointestinal appliance and device
Z46.6 Encounter for fitting and adjustment of urinary device
Excludes2: *attention to artificial openings of urinary tract (Z43.5, Z43.6)*
+ **Z46.8 Encounter for fitting and adjustment of other specified devices**
Z46.81 Encounter for fitting and adjustment of insulin pump
Encounter for insulin pump titration
Encounter for insulin pump instruction and training
Z46.82 Encounter for fitting and adjustment of non-vascular catheter
Z46.89 Encounter for fitting and adjustment of other specified devices
Encounter for fitting and adjustment of wheelchair
Z46.9 Encounter for fitting and adjustment of unspecified device

Z47 Orthopedic aftercare
Excludes1: *aftercare for healing fracture-code to fracture with 7th character D*
Review coding guideline C.21.c.7
Z47.1 Aftercare following joint replacement surgery
Use additional code to identify the joint (Z96.6-)
Z47.2 Encounter for removal of internal fixation device
Excludes1: *encounter for adjustment of internal fixation device for fracture treatment- code to fracture with appropriate 7th character*
encounter for removal of external fixation device- code to fracture with 7th character D
infection or inflammatory reaction to internal fixation device (T84.6-)
mechanical complication of internal fixation device (T84.1-)
+ **Z47.3 Aftercare following explantation of joint prosthesis**
Aftercare following explantation of joint prosthesis, staged procedure
Encounter for joint prosthesis insertion following prior explantation of joint prosthesis
Z47.31 Aftercare following explantation of shoulder joint prosthesis
Excludes1: *acquired absence of shoulder joint following prior explantation of shoulder joint prosthesis (Z89.23-)*
shoulder joint prosthesis explantation status (Z89.23-)
Z47.32 Aftercare following explantation of hip joint prosthesis
Excludes1: *acquired absence of hip joint following prior explantation of hip joint prosthesis (Z89.62-)*
hip joint prosthesis explantation status (Z89.62-)
Z47.33 Aftercare following explantation of knee joint prosthesis
Excludes1: *acquired absence of knee joint following prior explantation of knee prosthesis (Z89.52-*
knee joint prosthesis explantation status (Z89.52-)
+ **Z47.8 Encounter for other orthopedic aftercare**
Z47.81 Encounter for orthopedic aftercare following surgical amputation
Use additional code to identify the limb amputated (Z89.-)
Z47.82 Encounter for orthopedic aftercare following scoliosis surgery
Z47.89 Encounter for other orthopedic aftercare

Z48 Encounter for other postprocedural aftercare
Excludes1: *encounter for follow-up examination after completed treatment (Z08-Z09)*
Excludes2: *encounter for attention to artificial openings (Z43.-)*
encounter for fitting and adjustment of prosthetic and other devices (Z44-Z46)
Review coding guideline C.21.c.7
+ **Z48.0 Encounter for attention to dressings, sutures and drains**
Excludes1: *encounter for planned postprocedural wound closure (Z48.1)*
Z48.00 Encounter for change or removal of nonsurgical wound dressing
Encounter for change or removal of wound dressing NOS
Z48.01 Encounter for change or removal of surgical wound dressing
Z48.02 Encounter for removal of sutures
Encounter for removal of staples
Z48.03 Encounter for change or removal of drains
Z48.1 Encounter for planned postprocedural wound closure
Excludes1: *encounter for attention to dressings and sutures (Z48.0-)*
+ **Z48.2 Encounter for aftercare following organ transplant**
CC **Z48.21 Encounter for aftercare following heart transplant**
CC Exclusion see Appendix A PDX collection 1488
CC **Z48.22 Encounter for aftercare following kidney transplant**
CC Exclusion see Appendix A PDX collection 1489
CC **Z48.23 Encounter for aftercare following liver transplant**
CC Exclusion see Appendix A PDX collection 1490
CC **Z48.24 Encounter for aftercare following lung transplant**
CC Exclusion see Appendix A PDX collection 1491
+ **Z48.28 Encounter for aftercare following multiple organ transplant**
CC **Z48.280 Encounter for aftercare following heart-lung transplant**
CC Exclusion see Appendix A PDX collection 1488
Z48.288 Encounter for aftercare following multiple organ transplant
+ **Z48.29 Encounter for aftercare following other organ transplant**
CC **Z48.290 Encounter for aftercare following bone marrow transplant**
CC Exclusion see Appendix A PDX collection 1492
Z48.298 Encounter for aftercare following other organ transplant
Z48.3 Aftercare following surgery for neoplasm
Use additional code to identify the neoplasm
+ **Z48.8 Encounter for other specified postprocedural aftercare**
+ **Z48.81 Encounter for surgical aftercare following surgery on specified body systems**
These codes identify the body system requiring aftercare. They are for use in conjunction with other aftercare codes to fully explain the aftercare encounter. The condition treated should also be coded if still present.
Excludes1: *aftercare for injury- code the injury with 7th character D*
aftercare following surgery for neoplasm (Z48.3)
Excludes2: *aftercare following organ transplant (Z48.2-)*
orthopedic aftercare (Z47.-)
Z48.810 Encounter for surgical aftercare following surgery on the sense organs
Z48.811 Encounter for surgical aftercare following surgery on the nervous system
Excludes2: *encounter for surgical aftercare following surgery on the sense organs (Z48.810)*
Z48.812 Encounter for surgical aftercare following surgery on the circulatory system
AHA CC: 4Q, 2012, 96-97
Z48.813 Encounter for surgical aftercare following surgery on the respiratory system
Z48.814 Encounter for surgical aftercare following surgery on the teeth or oral cavity
Z48.815 Encounter for surgical aftercare following surgery on the digestive system
Z48.816 Encounter for surgical aftercare following surgery on the genitourinary system
Excludes1: *encounter for aftercare following sterilization reversal (Z31.42)*
Z48.817 Encounter for surgical aftercare following surgery on the skin and subcutaneous tissue
Z48.89 Encounter for other specified surgical aftercare

Z49 Encounter for5 care involving renal dialysis
Code also associated end stage renal disease (N18.6)
Review coding guideline C.21.c.7
+ **Z49.0 Preparatory care for renal dialysis**
Encounter for dialysis instruction and training
Z49.01 Encounter for fitting and adjustment of extracorporeal dialysis catheter
Removal or replacement of renal dialysis catheter
Toilet or cleansing of renal dialysis catheter
Z49.02 Encounter for fitting and adjustment of peritoneal dialysis catheter
+ **Z49.3 Encounter for adequacy testing for dialysis**
Z49.31 Encounter for adequacy testing for hemodialysis
Z49.32 Encounter for adequacy testing for peritoneal dialysis
Encounter for peritoneal equilibration test

Z51 Encounter for other aftercare
Code also condition requiring care
Excludes1: *follow-up examination after treatment (Z08-Z09)*
Review coding guidelines C.2.a, C.2.e.2 and C.2.e.3
Review coding guideline C.21.c.7
Z51.0 Encounter for antineoplastic radiation therapy
Review coding guidelines C.21.c.7 and C.21.c.16
+ **Z51.1 Encounter for antineoplastic chemotherapy and immunotherapy**
Excludes2: *encounter for chemotherapy and immunotherapy for nonneoplastic condition - code to condition*
Review coding guidelines C.21.c.7 and C21.c.16
Z51.11 Encounter for antineoplastic chemotherapy
Z51.12 Encounter for antineoplastic immunotherapy
Z51.5 Encounter for palliative care
+ **Z51.8 Encounter for other specified aftercare**
Excludes1: *holiday relief care (Z75.5)*
Z51.81 Encounter for therapeutic drug level monitoring
Code also any long-term (current) drug therapy (Z79.-)
Excludes1: *encounter for blood-drug test for administrative or medicolegal reasons (Z02.83)*
Z51.89 Encounter for other specified aftercare
AHA CC: 4Q, 2012, 96-97
Z51.89 is an acceptable PDX when reported with a secondary diagnosis.

Z52 Donors of organs and tissues
Includes: autologous and other living donors
Excludes1: *cadaveric donor - omit code*
examination of potential donor (Z00.5)
Review coding guidelines C.21.c.9 and C.21.c.16
+ **Z52.0 Blood donor**
+ **Z52.00 Unspecified blood donor**
Z52.000 Unspecified donor, whole blood
Z52.001 Unspecified donor, stem cells
Z52.008 Unspecified donor, other blood
+ **Z52.01 Autologous blood donor**
Z52.010 Autologous donor, whole blood
Z52.011 Autologous donor, stem cells
Z52.018 Autologous donor, other blood
+ **Z52.09 Other blood donor**
Volunteer donor
Z52.090 Other blood donor, whole blood
Z52.091 Other blood donor, stem cells
Z52.098 Other blood donor, other blood
+ **Z52.1 Skin donor**
Z52.10 Skin donor, unspecified
Z52.11 Skin donor, autologous
Z52.19 Skin donor, other
+ **Z52.2 Bone donor**
Z52.20 Bone donor, unspecified
Z52.21 Bone donor, autologous
Z52.29 Bone donor, other
Z52.3 Bone marrow donor
Z52.4 Kidney donor
Z52.5 Cornea donor
Z52.6 Liver donor

+ **Z52.8 Donor of other specified organs or tissues**
+ **Z52.81 Egg (Oocyte) donor**
♀ **Z52.810 Egg (Oocyte) donor under age 35, anonymous recipient**
Egg donor under age 35 NOS
♀ **Z52.811 Egg (Oocyte) donor under age 35, designated recipient**
♀ **Z52.812 Egg (Oocyte) donor age 35 and over, anonymous recipient**
Egg donor age 35 and over NOS
♀ **Z52.813 Egg (Oocyte) donor age 35 and over, designated recipient**
♀ **Z52.819 Egg (Oocyte) donor, unspecified**
Z52.89 Donor of other specified organs or tissues
Z52.9 Donor of unspecified organ or tissue
Donor NOS

Z53 Persons encountering health services for specific procedures and treatment, not carried out

+ **Z53.0 Procedure and treatment not carried out because of contraindication**
Z53.01 Procedure and treatment not carried out due to patient smoking
Z53.09 Procedure and treatment not carried out because of other contraindication
Z53.1 Procedure and treatment not carried out because of patient's decision for reasons of belief and group pressure
+ **Z53.2 Procedure and treatment not carried out because of patient's decision for other and unspecified reasons**
Z53.20 Procedure and treatment not carried out because of patient's decision for unspecified reasons
Z53.21 Procedure and treatment not carried out due to patient leaving prior to being seen by health care provider
Z53.29 Procedure and treatment not carried out because of patient's decision for other reasons
Z53.8 Procedure and treatment not carried out for other reasons
Z53.9 Procedure and treatment not carried out, unspecified reason

Persons with potential health hazards related to socioeconomic and psychosocial circumstances (Z55-Z65)

Z55 Problems related to education and literacy

Excludes1: *disorders of psychological development (F80-F89)*
Z55.0 Illiteracy and low-level literacy
Z55.1 Schooling unavailable and unattainable
Z55.2 Failed school examinations
Z55.3 Underachievement in school
Z55.4 Educational maladjustment and discord with teachers and classmates
Z55.8 Other problems related to education and literacy
Problems related to inadequate teaching
Z55.9 Problems related to education and literacy, unspecified
Academic problems NOS

Z56 Problems related to employment and unemployment

Excludes2: *occupational exposure to risk factors (Z57.-)*
problems related to housing and economic circumstances (Z59.-)
Z56.0 Unemployment, unspecified
• **Z56.1 Change of job**
Z56.2 Threat of job loss
Z56.3 Stressful work schedule
Z56.4 Discord with boss and workmates
Z56.5 Uncongenial work environment
Difficult conditions at work
Z56.6 Other physical and mental strain related to work
+ **Z56.8 Other problems related to employment**
Z56.81 Sexual harassment on the job
Z56.82 Military deployment status
Individual (civilian or military) currently deployed in theater or in support of military war, peacekeeping and humanitarian operations
Z56.89 Other problems related to employment
Z56.9 Unspecified problems related to employment
Occupational problems NOS

Z57 Occupational exposure to risk factors

Z57.0 Occupational exposure to noise
Z57.1 Occupational exposure to radiation
Z57.2 Occupational exposure to dust
+ **Z57.3 Occupational exposure to other air contaminants**
Z57.31 Occupational exposure to environmental tobacco smoke
Excludes2: *exposure to environmental tobacco smoke (Z77.22)*
Z57.39 Occupational exposure to other air contaminants
Z57.4 Occupational exposure to toxic agents in agriculture
Occupational exposure to solids, liquids, gases or vapors in agriculture
Z57.5 Occupational exposure to toxic agents in other industries
Occupational exposure to solids, liquids, gases or vapors in other industries
Z57.6 Occupational exposure to extreme temperature
Z57.7 Occupational exposure to vibration
Z57.8 Occupational exposure to other risk factors
Z57.9 Occupational exposure to unspecified risk factor

Z59 Problems related to housing and economic circumstances

Excludes2: *problems related to upbringing (Z62.-)*
Z59.0 Homelessness
Z59.1 Inadequate housing
Lack of heating
Restriction of space
Technical defects in home preventing adequate care
Unsatisfactory surroundings
Excludes1: *problems related to the natural and physical environment (Z77.1-)*
Z59.2 Discord with neighbors, lodgers and landlord
Z59.3 Problems related to living in residential institution
Boarding-school resident
Excludes1: *institutional upbringing (Z62.2)*
Z59.4 Lack of adequate food and safe drinking water
Inadequate drinking water supply
Excludes1: *effects of hunger (T73.0)*
inappropriate diet or eating habits (Z72.4)
malnutrition (E40-E46)
Z59.5 Extreme poverty
Z59.6 Low income
Z59.7 Insufficient social insurance and welfare support
Z59.8 Other problems related to housing and economic circumstances
Foreclosure on loan
Isolated dwelling
Problems with creditors
Z59.9 Problem related to housing and economic circumstances, unspecified

Z60 Problems related to social environment

Z60.0 Problems of adjustment to life-cycle transitions
Empty nest syndrome
Phase of life problem
Problem with adjustment to retirement [pension]
Z60.2 Problems related to living alone
Z60.3 Acculturation difficulty
Problem with migration
Problem with social transplantation
Z60.4 Social exclusion and rejection
Exclusion and rejection on the basis of personal characteristics, such as unusual physical appearance, illness or behavior.
Excludes1: *target of adverse discrimination such as for racial or religious reasons (Z60.5)*
Z60.5 Target of (perceived) adverse discrimination and persecution
Excludes1: *social exclusion and rejection (Z60.4)*
Z60.8 Other problems related to social environment
Z60.9 Problem related to social environment, unspecified

Z62 Problems related to upbringing

Includes: current and past negative life events in childhood
current and past problems of a child related to upbringing
Excludes2: *maltreatment syndrome (T74.-)*
problems related to housing and economic circumstances (Z59.-)
Z62.0 Inadequate parental supervision and control
Z62.1 Parental overprotection
+ **Z62.2 Upbringing away from parents**
Excludes1: *problems with boarding school (Z59.3)*
• **Z62.21 Child in welfare custody**
Child in care of non-parental family member
Child in foster care
Excludes2: *problem for parent due to child in welfare custody (Z63.5)*
Z62.22 Institutional upbringing
Child living in orphanage or group home
Z62.29 Other upbringing away from parents

• **Z62.3 Hostility towards and scapegoating of child**
Z62.6 Inappropriate (excessive) parental pressure
+ **Z62.8 Other specified problems related to upbringing**
+ **Z62.81 Personal history of abuse in childhood**
Z62.810 Personal history of physical and sexual abuse in childhood
Excludes1: *current child physical abuse (T74.12, T76.12)*
current child sexual abuse (T74.22, T76.22)
Z62.811 Personal history of psychological abuse in childhood
Excludes1: *current child psychological abuse (T74.32, T76.32)*
Z62.812 Personal history of neglect in childhood
Excludes1: *current child neglect (T74.02, T76.02)*
Z62.819 Personal history of unspecified abuse in childhood
Excludes1: *current child abuse NOS (T74.92, T76.92)*
+ **Z62.82 Parent-child conflict**
Z62.820 Parent-biological child conflict
Parent-child problem NOS
Z62.821 Parent-adopted child conflict
Z62.822 Parent-foster child conflict
+ **Z62.89 Other specified problems related to upbringing**
Z62.890 Parent-child estrangement NEC
Z62.891 Sibling rivalry
Z62.898 Other specified problems related to upbringing
Z62.9 Problem related to upbringing, unspecified

Z63 Other problems related to primary support group, including family circumstances
Excludes2: *maltreatment syndrome (T74.-, T76)*
parent-child problems (Z62.-)
problems related to negative life events in childhood (Z62.-)
problems related to upbringing (Z62.-)
Z63.0 Problems in relationship with spouse or partner
Excludes1: *counseling for spousal or partner abuse problems (Z69.1)*
counseling related to sexual attitude, behavior, and orientation (Z70.-)
Z63.1 Problems in relationship with in-laws
+ **Z63.3 Absence of family member**
Excludes1: *absence of family member due to disappearance and death (Z63.4)*
absence of family member due to separation and divorce (Z63.5)
Z63.31 Absence of family member due to military deployment
Individual or family affected by other family member being on military deployment
Excludes1: *family disruption due to return of family memberfrommilitarydeployment(Z63.71)*
Z63.32 Other absence of family member
Z63.4 Disappearance and death of family member
Assumed death of family member
Bereavement
AHA CC: 1Q, 2014, 25
Z63.5 Disruption of family by separation and divorce
Marital estrangement
Z63.6 Dependent relative needing care at home
+ **Z63.7 Other stressful life events affecting family and household**
Z63.71 Stress on family due to return of family member from military deployment
Individual or family affected by family member having returned from military deployment (current or past conflict)
Z63.72 Alcoholism and drug addiction in family
Z63.79 Other stressful life events affecting family and household
Anxiety (normal) about sick person in family
Health problems within family
Ill or disturbed family member
Isolated family
Z63.8 Other specified problems related to primary support group
Family discord NOS
Family estrangement NOS
High expressed emotional level within family
Inadequate family support NOS
Inadequate or distorted communication within family
Z63.9 Problem related to primary support group, unspecified
Relationship disorder NOS

Z64 Problems related to certain psychosocial circumstances
• ♀ **Z64.0 Problems related to unwanted pregnancy**
♀ **Z64.1 Problems related to multiparity**
Z64.4 Discord with counselors
Discord with probation officer
Discord with social worker

Z65 Problems related to other psychosocial circumstances
Z65.0 Conviction in civil and criminal proceedings without imprisonment
Z65.1 Imprisonment and other incarceration
Z65.2 Problems related to release from prison
Z65.3 Problems related to other legal circumstances
Arrest
Child custody or support proceedings
Litigation
Prosecution
Z65.4 Victim of crime and terrorism
Victim of torture
• **Z65.5 Exposure to disaster, war and other hostilities**
Excludes1: *target of perceived discrimination or persecution (Z60.5)*
Z65.8 Other specified problems related to psychosocial circumstances
Z65.9 Problem related to unspecified psychosocial circumstances

Do not resuscitate status (Z66)

Z66 Do not resuscitate
DNR status
Review coding guideline C.21.c.3
Valid 3-character code, no further characters required

Blood type (Z67)

Z67 Blood type
Review coding guideline C.21.c.3
+ **Z67.1 Type A blood**
Z67.10 Type A blood, Rh positive
Z67.11 Type A blood, Rh negative
+ **Z67.2 Type B blood**
Z67.20 Type B blood, Rh positive
Z67.21 Type B blood, Rh negative
+ **Z67.3 Type AB blood**
Z67.30 Type AB blood, Rh positive
Z67.31 Type AB blood, Rh negative
+ **Z67.4 Type O blood**
Z67.40 Type O blood, Rh positive
Z67.41 Type O blood, Rh negative
+ **Z67.9 Unspecified blood type**
Z67.90 Unspecified blood type, Rh positive
Z67.91 Unspecified blood type, Rh negative

Body mass index [BMI] (Z68)

Z68 Body mass index [BMI]
Kilograms per meters squared
NOTE BMI adult codes are for use for persons 21 years of age or older
BMI pediatric codes are for use for persons 2-20 years of age.
These percentiles are based on the growth charts published by the Centers for Disease Control and Prevention (CDC)
Review coding guideline C.21.c.3
• CC **Z68.1 Body mass index (BMI) 19 or less, adult**
CC Exclusion see Appendix A PDX collection 1493
+ **Z68.2 Body mass index (BMI) 20-29, adult**
• **Z68.20 Body mass index (BMI) 20.0-20.9, adult**
• **Z68.21 Body mass index (BMI) 21.0-21.9, adult**
• **Z68.22 Body mass index (BMI) 22.0-22.9, adult**
• **Z68.23 Body mass index (BMI) 23.0-23.9, adult**
• **Z68.24 Body mass index (BMI) 24.0-24.9, adult**
• **Z68.25 Body mass index (BMI) 25.0-25.9, adult**
• **Z68.26 Body mass index (BMI) 26.0-26.9, adult**
• **Z68.27 Body mass index (BMI) 27.0-27.9, adult**
• **Z68.28 Body mass index (BMI) 28.0-28.9, adult**
• **Z68.29 Body mass index (BMI) 29.0-29.9, adult**

+ **Z68.3 Body mass index (BMI) 30-39, adult**
- • **Z68.30 Body mass index (BMI) 30.0-30.9, adult**
- • **Z68.31 Body mass index (BMI) 31.0-31.9, adult**
- • **Z68.32 Body mass index (BMI) 32.0-32.9, adult**
- • **Z68.33 Body mass index (BMI) 33.0-33.9, adult**
- • **Z68.34 Body mass index (BMI) 34.0-34.9, adult**
- • **Z68.35 Body mass index (BMI) 35.0-35.9, adult**
- • **Z68.36 Body mass index (BMI) 36.0-36.9, adult**
- • **Z68.37 Body mass index (BMI) 37.0-37.9, adult**
- • **Z68.38 Body mass index (BMI) 38.0-38.9, adult**
- • **Z68.39 Body mass index (BMI) 39.0-39.9, adult**

+ **Z68.4 Body mass index (BMI) 40 or greater, adult**
- • CC **Z68.41 Body mass index (BMI) 40.0-44.9, adult**
  CC Exclusion see Appendix A PDX collection 1494
- • CC **Z68.42 Body mass index (BMI) 45.0-49.9, adult**
  CC Exclusion see Appendix A PDX collection 1494
- • CC **Z68.43 Body mass index (BMI) 50-59.9 , adult**
  CC Exclusion see Appendix A PDX collection 1494
- • CC **Z68.44 Body mass index (BMI) 60.0-69.9, adult**
  CC Exclusion see Appendix A PDX collection 1494
- • CC **Z68.45 Body mass index (BMI) 70 or greater, adult**
  CC Exclusion see Appendix A PDX collection 1494

+ **Z68.5 Body mass index (BMI) pediatric**
- • **Z68.51 Body mass index (BMI) pediatric, less than 5th percentile for age**
- • **Z68.52 Body mass index (BMI) pediatric, 5th percentile to less than 85th percentile for age**
- • **Z68.53 Body mass index (BMI) pediatric, 85th percentile to less than 95th percentile for age**
- • **Z68.54 Body mass index (BMI) pediatric, greater than or equal to 95th percentile for age**

Persons encountering health services in other circumstances (Z69-Z76)

Z69 Encounter for mental health services for victim and perpetrator of abuse

Includes: counseling for victims and perpetrators of abuse
Review coding guideline C.21.c.10

+ **Z69.0 Encounter for mental health services for child abuse problems**
  + **Z69.01 Encounter for mental health services for parental child abuse**
    - • **Z69.010 Encounter for mental health services for victim of parental child abuse**
    - **Z69.011 Encounter for mental health services for perpetrator of parental child abuse**
      Excludes1: *encounter for mental health services for non-parental child abuse (Z69.02-)*
  + **Z69.02 Encounter for mental health services for non-parental child abuse**
    - • **Z69.020 Encounter for mental health services for victim of non-parental child abuse**
    - **Z69.021 Encounter for mental health services for perpetrator of non-parental child abuse**

+ **Z69.1 Encounter for mental health services for spousal or partner abuse problems**
  - **Z69.11 Encounter for mental health services for victim of spousal or partner abuse**
  - **Z69.12 Encounter for mental health services for perpetrator of spousal or partner abuse**

+ **Z69.8 Encounter for mental health services for victim or perpetrator of other abuse**
  - **Z69.81 Encounter for mental health services for victim of other abuse**
    Encounter for rape victim counseling
  - **Z69.82 Encounter for mental health services for perpetrator of other abuse**

Z70 Counseling related to sexual attitude, behavior and orientation

Includes: encounter for mental health services for sexual attitude, behavior and orientation
Excludes2: *contraceptive or procreative counseling (Z30-Z31)*
Review coding guideline C.21.c.10

Z70.0 Counseling related to sexual attitude

Z70.1 Counseling related to patient's sexual behavior and orientation
Patient concerned regarding impotence
Patient concerned regarding non-responsiveness
Patient concerned regarding promiscuity
Patient concerned regarding sexual orientation

Z70.2 Counseling related to sexual behavior and orientation of third party
Advice sought regarding sexual behavior and orientation of child
Advice sought regarding sexual behavior and orientation of partner
Advice sought regarding sexual behavior and orientation of spouse

Z70.3 Counseling related to combined concerns regarding sexual attitude, behavior and orientation

Z70.8 Other sex counseling
Encounter for sex education

Z70.9 Sex counseling, unspecified

Z71 Persons encountering health services for other counseling and medical advice, not elsewhere classified

Excludes2: *contraceptive or procreation counseling (Z30-Z31)*
sex counseling (Z70.-)
Review coding guideline C.21.c.10

Z71.0 Person encountering health services to consult on behalf of another person
Person encountering health services to seek advice or treatment for non-attending third party
Excludes2: *anxiety (normal) about sick person in family (Z63.7)*
expectant (adoptive) parent(s) pre-birth pediatrician visit (Z76.81)

Z71.1 Person with feared health complaint in whom no diagnosis is made
Person encountering health services with feared condition which was not demonstrated
Person encountering health services in which problem was normal state
'Worried well'
Excludes1: *medical observation for suspected diseases and conditions proven not to exist (Z03.-)*

Z71.2 Person consulting for explanation of examination or test findings

Z71.3 Dietary counseling and surveillance
Use additional code for any associated underlying medical condition

Use additional code to identify body mass index (BMI), if known (Z68.-)

+ **Z71.4 Alcohol abuse counseling and surveillance**
  Use additional code for alcohol abuse or dependence (F10.-)
  - **Z71.41 Alcohol abuse counseling and surveillance of alcoholic**
  - **Z71.42 Counseling for family member of alcoholic**
    Counseling for significant other, partner, or friend of alcoholic

+ **Z71.5 Drug abuse counseling and surveillance**
  Use additional code for drug abuse or dependence (F11-F16, F18-F19)
  - **Z71.51 Drug abuse counseling and surveillance of drug abuser**
  - **Z71.52 Counseling for family member of drug abuser**
    Counseling for significant other, partner, or friend of drug abuser

Z71.6 Tobacco abuse counseling
Use additional code for nicotine dependence (F17.-)

Z71.7 Human immunodeficiency virus [HIV] counseling
Review coding guideline C.1.a.2.h

+ **Z71.8 Other specified counseling**
  Excludes2: *counseling for contraception (Z30.0-)*
  counseling for genetics (Z31.5)
  counseling for procreative management (Z31.6-)
  - **Z71.81 Spiritual or religious counseling**
  - **Z71.89 Other specified counseling**

Z71.9 Counseling, unspecified
Encounter for medical advice NOS

Z72 Problems related to lifestyle

Excludes2: *problems related to life-management difficulty (Z73.-)*
problems related to socioeconomic and psychosocial circumstances (Z55-Z65)

Z72.0 Tobacco use
Tobacco use NOS
Excludes1: *history of tobacco dependence (Z87.891)*
nicotine dependence (F17.2-)
tobacco dependence (F17.2-)
tobacco use during pregnancy (O99.33-)
Review coding guideline C.15.l.2

Z72.3 Lack of physical exercise

Z72.4 Inappropriate diet and eating habits
Excludes1: *behavioral eating disorders of infancy or childhood (F98.2-F98.3)*
eating disorders (F50.-)
lack of adequate food (Z59.4)
malnutrition and other nutritional deficiencies (E40-E64)

\+ **Z72.5 High risk sexual behavior**
Promiscuity
Excludes1: *paraphilias (F65)*
Z72.51 High risk heterosexual behavior
Z72.52 High risk homosexual behavior
Z72.53 High risk bisexual behavior

Z72.6 Gambling and betting
Excludes1: *compulsive or pathological gambling (F63.0)*

\+ **Z72.8 Other problems related to lifestyle**
\+ **Z72.81 Antisocial behavior**
Excludes1: *conduct disorders (F91.-)*
• **Z72.810 Child and adolescent antisocial behavior**
Antisocial behavior (child) (adolescent) without manifest psychiatric disorder
Delinquency NOS
Group delinquency
Offenses in the context of gang membership
Stealing in company with others
Truancy from school
• **Z72.811 Adult antisocial behavior**
Adult antisocial behavior without manifest psychiatric disorder
\+ **Z72.82 Problems related to sleep**
Z72.820 Sleep deprivation
Lack of adequate sleep
Excludes1: *insomnia (G47.0-)*
Z72.821 Inadequate sleep hygiene
Bad sleep habits
Irregular sleep habits
Unhealthy sleep wake schedule
Excludes1: *insomnia (F51.0-, G47.0-)*
Z72.89 Other problems related to lifestyle
Self-damaging behavior

Z72.9 Problem related to lifestyle, unspecified

Z73 Problems related to life management difficulty

Excludes2: *problems related to socioeconomic and psychosocial circumstances (Z55-Z65)*

Z73.0 Burn-out
Z73.1 Type A behavior pattern
Z73.2 Lack of relaxation and leisure
Z73.3 Stress, not elsewhere classified
Physical and mental strain NOS
Excludes1: *stress related to employment or unemployment (Z56.-)*
Z73.4 Inadequate social skills, not elsewhere classified
Z73.5 Social role conflict, not elsewhere classified
Z73.6 Limitation of activities due to disability
Excludes1: *care-provider dependency (Z74.-)*

\+ **Z73.8 Other problems related to life management difficulty**
\+ **Z73.81 Behavioral insomnia of childhood**
• **Z73.810 Behavioral insomnia of childhood, sleep-onset association type**
• **Z73.811 Behavioral insomnia of childhood, limit setting type**
• **Z73.812 Behavioral insomnia of childhood, combined type**
• **Z73.819 Behavioral insomnia of childhood, unspecified type**
Z73.82 Dual sensory impairment
Z73.89 Other problems related to life management difficulty

Z73.9 Problem related to life management difficulty, unspecified

Z74 Problems related to care provider dependency

Excludes2: *dependence on enabling machines or devices NEC (Z99.-)*

\+ **Z74.0 Reduced mobility**
Z74.01 Bed confinement status
Bedridden
Review coding guideline C.21.c.3
Z74.09 Other reduced mobility
Chairridden
Reduced mobility NOS
Excludes2: *wheelchair dependence (Z99.3)*

Z74.1 Need for assistance with personal care
Z74.2 Need for assistance at home and no other household member able to render care
Z74.3 Need for continuous supervision
Z74.8 Other problems related to care provider dependency
Z74.9 Problem related to care provider dependency, unspecified

Z75 Problems related to medical facilities and other health care

Z75.0 Medical services not available in home
Excludes1: *no other household member able to render care (Z74.2)*
Z75.1 Person awaiting admission to adequate facility elsewhere
Z75.2 Other waiting period for investigation and treatment
Z75.3 Unavailability and inaccessibility of health-care facilities
Excludes1: *bed unavailable (Z75.1)*
Z75.4 Unavailability and inaccessibility of other helping agencies
Z75.5 Holiday relief care
Z75.8 Other problems related to medical facilities and other health care
Z75.9 Unspecified problem related to medical facilities and other health care

Z76 Persons encountering health services in other circumstances

Z76.0 Encounter for issue of repeat prescription
Encounter for issue of repeat prescription for appliance
Encounter for issue of repeat prescription for medicaments
Encounter for issue of repeat prescription for spectacles
Excludes2: *issue of medical certificate (Z02.7)*
repeat prescription for contraceptive (Z30.4-)

Z76.1 Encounter for health supervision and care of foundling
Review coding guidelines C.21.c.12 and C.21.c.16

• **Z76.2 Encounter for health supervision and care of other healthy infant and child**
Encounter for medical or nursing care or supervision of healthy infant under circumstances such as adverse socioeconomic conditions at home
Encounter for medical or nursing care or supervision of healthy infant under circumstances such as awaiting foster or adoptive placement
Encounter for medical or nursing care or supervision of healthy infant under circumstances such as maternal illness
Encounter for medical or nursing care or supervision of healthy infant under circumstances such as number of children at home preventing or interfering with normal care
Review coding guideline C.21.c.16

Z76.3 Healthy person accompanying sick person
Z76.4 Other boarder to healthcare facility
Excludes1: *homelessness (Z59.0)*
Z76.5 Malingerer [conscious simulation]
Person feigning illness (with obvious motivation)
Excludes1: *factitious disorder (F68.1-)*
peregrinating patient (F68.1-)

\+ **Z76.8 Persons encountering health services in other specified circumstances**
Z76.81 Expectant parent(s) prebirth pediatrician visit
Pre-adoption pediatrician visit for adoptive parent(s)
Review coding guideline C.21.c.10
Z76.82 Awaiting organ transplant status
Patient waiting for organ availability
Review coding guideline C.21.c.3
Z76.89 Persons encountering health services in other specified circumstances
Persons encountering health services NOS
AHA CC: 2Q, 2014, 10

Persons with potential health hazards related to family and personal history and certain conditions influencing health status (Z77-Z99)

Code also any follow-up examination (Z08-Z09)

Z77 Other contact with and (suspected) exposures hazardous to health

Includes: contact with and (suspected) exposures to potential hazards to health

Excludes2: *contact with and (suspected) exposure to communicable diseases (Z20.-)*
exposure to (parental) (environmental) tobacco smoke in the perinatal period (P96.81)
newborn (suspected to be) affected by noxious substances transmitted via placenta or breast milk (P04.-)
occupational exposure to risk factors (Z57.-)
retained foreign body (Z18.-)
retained foreign body fully removed (Z87.821)
toxic effects of substances chiefly nonmedicinal as to source (T51-T65)

Review coding guideline C.21.c.1

+ **Z77.0 Contact with and (suspected) exposure to hazardous, chiefly nonmedicinal, chemicals**

+ **Z77.01 Contact with and (suspected) exposure to hazardous metals**

Z77.010 Contact with and (suspected) exposure to arsenic

Z77.011 Contact with and (suspected) exposure to lead

Z77.012 Contact with and (suspected) exposure to uranium

Excludes1: *retained depleted uranium fragments (Z18.01)*

Z77.018 Contact with and (suspected) exposure to other hazardous metals
Contact with and (suspected) exposure to chromium compounds
Contact with and (suspected) exposure to nickel dust

+ **Z77.02 Contact with and (suspected) exposure to hazardous aromatic compounds**

Z77.020 Contact with and (suspected) exposure to aromatic amines

Z77.021 Contact with and (suspected) exposure to benzene

Z77.028 Contact with and (suspected) exposure to other hazardous aromatic compounds
Aromatic dyes NOS
Polycyclic aromatic hydrocarbons

+ **Z77.09 Contact with and (suspected) exposure to other hazardous, chiefly nonmedicinal, chemicals**

Z77.090 Contact with and (suspected) exposure to asbestos

Z77.098 Contact with and (suspected) exposure to other hazardous, chiefly nonmedicinal, chemicals
Dyes NOS

+ **Z77.1 Contact with and (suspected) exposure to environmental pollution and hazards in the physical environment**

+ **Z77.11 Contact with and (suspected) exposure to environmental pollution**

Z77.110 Contact with and (suspected) exposure to air pollution

Z77.111 Contact with and (suspected) exposure to water pollution

Z77.112 Contact with and (suspected) exposure to soil pollution

Z77.118 Contact with and (suspected) exposure to other environmental pollution

+ **Z77.12 Contact with and (suspected) exposure to hazards in the physical environment**

Z77.120 Contact with and (suspected) exposure to mold (toxic)

Z77.121 Contact with and (suspected) exposure to harmful algae and algae toxins
Contact with and (suspected) exposure to (harmful) algae bloom NOS
Contact with and (suspected) exposure to blue-green algae bloom
Contact with and (suspected) exposure to brown tide
Contact with and (suspected) exposure to cyanobacteria bloom
Contact with and (suspected) exposure to Florida red tide
Contact with and (suspected) exposure to pfiesteria piscicida
Contact with and (suspected) exposure to red tide

Z77.122 Contact with and (suspected) exposure to noise

Z77.123 Contact with and (suspected) exposure to radon and other naturally occuring radiation

Excludes2: *radiation exposure as the cause of a confirmed condition (W88-W90, X39.0-)*
radiation sickness NOS (T66)

Z77.128 Contact with and (suspected) exposure to other hazards in the physical environment

+ **Z77.2 Contact with and (suspected) exposure to other hazardous substances**

Z77.21 Contact with and (suspected) exposure to potentially hazardous body fluids

Z77.22 Contact with and (suspected) exposure to environmental tobacco smoke (acute) (chronic)
Exposure to second hand tobacco smoke (acute) (chronic)
Passive smoking (acute) (chronic)

Excludes1: *nicotine dependence (F17.-)*
tobacco use (Z72.0)

Excludes2: *occupational exposure to environmental tobacco smoke (Z57.31)*

Z77.29 Contact with and (suspected) exposure to other hazardous substances

Z77.9 Other contact with and (suspected) exposures hazardous to health

Z78 Other specified health status

Excludes2: *asymptomatic human immunodeficiency virus [HIV] infection status (Z21)*
postprocedural status (Z93-Z99)
sex reassignment status (Z87.890)

Review coding guideline C.21.c.3

• ♀ **Z78.0 Asymptomatic menopausal state**
Menopausal state NOS
Postmenopausal status NOS

Excludes2: *symptomatic menopausal state (N95.1)*

Z78.1 Physical restraint status

Excludes1: *physical restraint due to a procedure - omit code*

Z78.9 Other specified health status

Z79 Long term (current) drug therapy

Includes: long term (current) drug use for prophylactic purposes
Code also any therapeutic drug level monitoring (Z51.81)

Excludes2: *drug abuse and dependence (F11-F19)*
drug use complicating pregnancy, childbirth, and the puerperium (O99.32-)

Review coding guideline C.21.c.3

+ **Z79.0 Long term (current) use of anticoagulants and antithrombotics/antiplatelets**

Excludes2: *long term (current) use of aspirin (Z79.82)*

Z79.01 Long term (current) use of anticoagulants

Z79.02 Long term (current) use of antithrombotics/antiplatelets

Z79.1 Long term (current) use of non-steroidal anti-inflammatories (NSAID)

Excludes2: *long term (current) use of aspirin (Z79.82)*

Z79.2 Long term (current) use of antibiotics

Z79.3 Long term (current) use of hormonal contraceptives
Long term (current) use of birth control pill or patch

Z79.4 Long term (current) use of insulin
Review coding guideline C.4.a.3
Review coding guidelines C.15.h and C.15.i
+ **Z79.5 Long term (current) use of steroids**
Z79.51 Long term (current) use of inhaled steroids
Z79.52 Long term (current) use of systemic steroids
+ **Z79.8 Other long term (current) drug therapy**
+ **Z79.81 Long term (current) use of agents affecting estrogen receptors and estrogen levels**
Code first if applicable:
malignant neoplasm of breast (C50.-)
malignant neoplasm of prostate (C61)

Use additional code, if applicable, to identify:
estrogen receptor positive status (Z17.0)
family history of breast cancer (Z80.3)
genetic susceptibility to malignant neoplasm (cancer) (Z15.0-)
personal history of breast cancer (Z85.3)
personal history of prostate cancer (Z85.46)
postmenopausal status (Z78.0)
Excludes1: *hormone replacement therapy (postmenopausal) (Z79.890)*
Z79.810 Long term (current) use of selective estrogen receptor modulators (SERMs)
Long term (current) use of raloxifene (Evista)
Long term (current) use of tamoxifen (Nolvadex)
Long term (current) use of toremifene (Fareston)
Z79.811 Long term (current) use of aromatase inhibitors
Long term (current) use of anastrozole (Arimidex)
Long term (current) use of exemestane (Aromasin)
Long term (current) use of letrozole (Femara)
Z79.818 Long term (current) use of other agents affecting estrogen receptors and estrogen levels
Long term (current) use of estrogen receptor downregulators
Long term (current) use of fulvestrant (Faslodex)
Long term (current) use of gonadotropin-releasing hormone (GnRH) agonist
Long term (current) use of goserelin acetate (Zoladex)
Long term (current) use of leuprolide acetate (leuprorelin) (Lupron)
Long term (current) use of megestrol acetate (Megace)
Z79.82 Long term (current) use of aspirin
Z79.83 Long term (current) use of bisphosphonates
+ **Z79.89 Other long term (current) drug therapy**
♀ **Z79.890 Hormone replacement therapy (postmenopausal)**
Z79.891 Long term (current) use of opiate analgesic
Long term (current) use of methadone for pain management
Excludes1: *methodone use NOS (F11.2-)*
use of methodone for treatment of heroin addiction (F11.2-)
Z79.899 Other long term (current) drug therapy

Z80 Family history of primary malignant neoplasm
Review coding guideline C.21.c.4
Z80.0 Family history of malignant neoplasm of digestive organs
Conditions classifiable to C15-C26
Z80.1 Family history of malignant neoplasm of trachea, bronchus and lung
Conditions classifiable to C33-C34
Z80.2 Family history of malignant neoplasm of other respiratory and intrathoracic organs
Conditions classifiable to C30-C32, C37-C39
Z80.3 Family history of malignant neoplasm of breast
Conditions classifiable to C50.-
+ **Z80.4 Family history of malignant neoplasm of genital organs**
Conditions classifiable to C51-C63
♀ **Z80.41 Family history of malignant neoplasm of ovary**
♂ **Z80.42 Family history of malignant neoplasm of prostate**
♂ **Z80.43 Family history of malignant neoplasm of testis**
Z80.49 Family history of malignant neoplasm of other genital organs
+ **Z80.5 Family history of malignant neoplasm of urinary tract**
Conditions classifiable to C64-C68
Z80.51 Family history of malignant neoplasm of kidney
Z80.52 Family history of malignant neoplasm of bladder
Z80.59 Family history of malignant neoplasm of other urinary tract organ
Z80.6 Family history of leukemia
Conditions classifiable to C91-C95
Z80.7 Family history of other malignant neoplasms of lymphoid, hematopoietic and related tissues
Conditions classifiable to C81-C90, C96.-
Z80.8 Family history of malignant neoplasm of other organs or systems
Conditions classifiable to C00-C14, C40-C49, C69-C79
Z80.9 Family history of malignant neoplasm, unspecified
Conditions classifiable to C80.1

Z81 Family history of mental and behavioral disorders
Review coding guideline C.21.c.4
Z81.0 Family history of intellectual disabilities
Conditions classifiable to F70-F79
Z81.1 Family history of alcohol abuse and dependence
Conditions classifiable to F10.-
Z81.2 Family history of tobacco abuse and dependence
Conditions classifiable to F17.-
Z81.3 Family history of other psychoactive substance abuse and dependence
Conditions classifiable to F11-F16, F18-F19
Z81.4 Family history of other substance abuse and dependence
Conditions classifiable to F55
Z81.8 Family history of other mental and behavioral disorders
Conditions classifiable elsewhere in F01-F99

Z82 Family history of certain disabilities and chronic diseases (leading to disablement)
Review coding guideline C.21.c.4
Z82.0 Family history of epilepsy and other diseases of the nervous system
Conditions classifiable to G00-G99
Z82.1 Family history of blindness and visual loss
Conditions classifiable to H54.-
Z82.2 Family history of deafness and hearing loss
Conditions classifiable to H90-H91
Z82.3 Family history of stroke
Conditions classifiable to I60-I64
+ **Z82.4 Family history of ischemic heart disease and other diseases of the circulatory system**
Conditions classifiable to I00-I52, I65-I99
Z82.41 Family history of sudden cardiac death
Z82.49 Family history of ischemic heart disease and other diseases of the circulatory system
Z82.5 Family history of asthma and other chronic lower respiratory diseases
Conditions classifiable to J40-J47
Excludes2: *family history of other diseases of the respiratory system (Z83.6)*
+ **Z82.6 Family history of arthritis and other diseases of the musculoskeletal system and connective tissue**
Conditions classifiable to M00-M99
Z82.61 Family history of arthritis
Z82.62 Family history of osteoporosis
Z82.69 Family history of other diseases of the musculoskeletal system and connective tissue
+ **Z82.7 Family history of congenital malformations, deformations and chromosomal abnormalities**
Conditions classifiable to Q00-Q99
Z82.71 Family history of polycystic kidney
Z82.79 Family history of other congenital malformations, deformations and chromosomal abnormalities
Z82.8 Family history of other disabilities and chronic diseases leading to disablement, not elsewhere classified

Z83 Family history of other specific disorders
Excludes2: *contact with and (suspected) exposure to communicable disease in the family (Z20.-)*
Review coding guideline C.21.c.4
Z83.0 Family history of human immunodeficiency virus [HIV] disease
Conditions classifiable to B20
Z83.1 Family history of other infectious and parasitic diseases
Conditions classifiable to A00-B19, B25-B94, B99

Z83.2 Family history of diseases of the blood and blood-forming organs and certain disorders involving the immune mechanism
Conditions classifiable to D50-D89
Z83.3 Family history of diabetes mellitus
Conditions classifiable to E08-E13
+ Z83.4 Family history of other endocrine, nutritional and metabolic diseases
Conditions classifiable to E00-E07, E15-E88
Z83.41 Family history of multiple endocrine neoplasia [MEN] syndrome
Z83.49 Family history of other endocrine, nutritional and metabolic diseases
+ Z83.5 Family history of eye and ear disorders
+ Z83.51 Family history of eye disorders
Conditions classifiable to H00-H53, H55-H59
Excludes2: *family history of blindness and visual loss (Z82.1)*
Z83.511 Family history of glaucoma
Z83.518 Family history of other specified eye disorder
Z83.52 Family history of ear disorders
Conditions classifiable to H60-H83, H92-H95
Excludes2: *family history of deafness and hearing loss (Z82.2)*
Z83.6 Family history of other diseases of the respiratory system
Conditions classifiable to J00-J39, J60-J99
Excludes2: *family history of asthma and other chronic lower respiratory diseases (Z82.5)*
+ Z83.7 Family history of diseases of the digestive system
Conditions classifiable to K00-K93
Z83.71 Family history of colonic polyps
Excludes1: *family history of malignant neoplasm of digestive organs (Z80.0)*
Z83.79 Family history of other diseases of the digestive system

Z84 Family history of other conditions
Review coding guideline C.21.c.4
Z84.0 Family history of diseases of the skin and subcutaneous tissue
Conditions classifiable to L00-L99
Z84.1 Family history of disorders of kidney and ureter
Conditions classifiable to N00-N29
Z84.2 Family history of other diseases of the genitourinary system
Conditions classifiable to N30-N99
Z84.3 Family history of consanguinity
+ Z84.8 Family history of other specified conditions
Z84.81 Family history of carrier of genetic disease
Z84.89 Family history of other specified conditions

Z85 Personal history of malignant neoplasm
Code first any follow-up examination after treatment of malignant neoplasm (Z08)

Use additional code to identify:
alcohol use and dependence (F10.-)
exposure to environmental tobacco smoke (Z77.22)
history of tobacco use (Z87.891)
occupational exposure to environmental tobacco smoke (Z57.31)
tobacco dependence (F17.-)
tobacco use (Z72.0)
Excludes2: *personal history of benign neoplasm (Z86.01-)*
personal history of carcinoma-in-situ (Z86.00-)
Review coding guidelines C.2.d and C.2.m
Review coding guideline C.21.c.4
+ Z85.0 Personal history of malignant neoplasm of digestive organs
Z85.00 Personal history of malignant neoplasm of unspecified digestive organ
Z85.01 Personal history of malignant neoplasm of esophagus
Conditions classifiable to C15
+ Z85.02 Personal history of malignant neoplasm of stomach
Z85.020 Personal history of malignant carcinoid tumor of stomach
Conditions classifiable to C7A.092
Z85.028 Personal history of other malignant neoplasm of stomach
Conditions classifiable to C16
+ Z85.03 Personal history of malignant neoplasm of large intestine
Z85.030 Personal history of malignant carcinoid tumor of large intestine
Conditions classifiable to C7A.022-C7A.025, C7A.029
Z85.038 Personal history of other malignant neoplasm of large intestine
Conditions classifiable to C18
+ Z85.04 Personal history of malignant neoplasm of rectum, rectosigmoid junction, and anus
Z85.040 Personal history of malignant carcinoid tumor of rectum
Conditions classifiable to C7A.026
Z85.048 Personal history of other malignant neoplasm of rectum, rectosigmoid junction, and anus
Conditions classifiable to C19-C21
Z85.05 Personal history of malignant neoplasm of liver
Conditions classifiable to C22
+ Z85.06 Personal history of malignant neoplasm of small intestine
Z85.060 Personal history of malignant carcinoid tumor of small intestine
Conditions classifiable to C7A.01-
Z85.068 Personal history of other malignant neoplasm of small intestine
Conditions classifiable to C17
Z85.07 Personal history of malignant neoplasm of pancreas
Conditions classifiable to C25
Z85.09 Personal history of malignant neoplasm of other digestive organs
+ Z85.1 Personal history of malignant neoplasm of trachea, bronchus and lung
+ Z85.11 Personal history of malignant neoplasm of bronchus and lung
Z85.110 Personal history of malignant carcinoid tumor of bronchus and lung
Conditions classifiable to C7A.090
Z85.118 Personal history of other malignant neoplasm of bronchus and lung
Conditions classifiable to C34
Z85.12 Personal history of malignant neoplasm of trachea
Conditions classifiable to C33
+ Z85.2 Personal history of malignant neoplasm of other respiratory and intrathoracic organs
Z85.20 Personal history of malignant neoplasm of unspecified respiratory organ
Z85.21 Personal history of malignant neoplasm of larynx
Conditions classifiable to C32
Z85.22 Personal history of malignant neoplasm of nasal cavities, middle ear, and accessory sinuses
Conditions classifiable to C30-C31
+ Z85.23 Personal history of malignant neoplasm of thymus
Z85.230 Personal history of malignant carcinoid tumor of thymus
Conditions classifiable to C7A.091
Z85.238 Personal history of other malignant neoplasm of thymus
Conditions classifiable to C37
Z85.29 Personal history of malignant neoplasm of other respiratory and intrathoracic organs
Z85.3 Personal history of malignant neoplasm of breast
Conditions classifiable to C50.-
+ Z85.4 Personal history of malignant neoplasm of genital organs
Conditions classifiable to C51-C63
♀ **Z85.40 Personal history of malignant neoplasm of unspecified female genital organ**
♀ **Z85.41 Personal history of malignant neoplasm of cervix uteri**
♀ **Z85.42 Personal history of malignant neoplasm of other parts of uterus**
♀ **Z85.43 Personal history of malignant neoplasm of ovary**
♀ **Z85.44 Personal history of malignant neoplasm of other female genital organs**
♂ **Z85.45 Personal history of malignant neoplasm of unspecified male genital organ**
♂ **Z85.46 Personal history of malignant neoplasm of prostate**
♂ **Z85.47 Personal history of malignant neoplasm of testis**
♂ **Z85.48 Personal history of malignant neoplasm of epididymis**
♂ **Z85.49 Personal history of malignant neoplasm of other male genital organs**

+ **Z85.5 Personal history of malignant neoplasm of urinary tract**
Conditions classifiable to C64-C68
Z85.50 Personal history of malignant neoplasm of unspecified urinary tract organ
Z85.51 Personal history of malignant neoplasm of bladder
+ **Z85.52 Personal history of malignant neoplasm of kidney**
Excludes1: *personal history of malignant neoplasm of renal pelvis (Z85.53)*
Z85.520 Personal history of malignant carcinoid tumor of kidney
Conditions classifiable to C7A.093
Z85.528 Personal history of other malignant neoplasm of kidney
Conditions classifiable to C64
Z85.53 Personal history of malignant neoplasm of renal pelvis
Z85.54 Personal history of malignant neoplasm of ureter
Z85.59 Personal history of malignant neoplasm of other urinary tract organ
Z85.6 Personal history of leukemia
Conditions classifiable to C91-C95
Excludes1: *leukemia in remission C91.0-C95.9 with 5th character 1*
Review coding guideline C.2.n
+ **Z85.7 Personal history of other malignant neoplasms of lymphoid, hematopoietic and related tissues**
Z85.71 Personal history of Hodgkin lymphoma
Conditions classifiable to C81
Z85.72 Personal history of non-Hodgkin lymphomas
Conditions classifiable to C82-C85
Z85.79 Personal history of other malignant neoplasms of lymphoid, hematopoietic and related tissues
Conditions classifiable to C88-C90, C96
Excludes1: *multiple myeloma in remission (C90.01)*
plasma cell leukemia in remission (C90.11)
plasmacytoma in remission (C90.21)
Review coding guideline C.2.n
+ **Z85.8 Personal history of malignant neoplasms of other organs and systems**
Conditions classifiable to C00-C14, C40-C49, C69-C79, C7A.098
+ **Z85.81 Personal history of malignant neoplasm of lip, oral cavity, and pharynx**
Z85.810 Personal history of malignant neoplasm of tongue
Z85.818 Personal history of malignant neoplasm of other sites of lip, oral cavity, and pharynx
Z85.819 Personal history of malignant neoplasm of unspecified site of lip, oral cavity, and pharynx
+ **Z85.82 Personal history of malignant neoplasm of skin**
Z85.820 Personal history of malignant melanoma of skin
Conditions classifiable to C43
Z85.821 Personal history of Merkel cell carcinoma
Conditions classifiable to C4A
Z85.828 Personal history of other malignant neoplasm of skin
Conditions classifiable to C44
+ **Z85.83 Personal history of malignant neoplasm of bone and soft tissue**
Z85.830 Personal history of malignant neoplasm of bone
Z85.831 Personal history of malignant neoplasm of soft tissue
Excludes2: *personal history of malignant neoplasm of skin (Z85.82-)*
+ **Z85.84 Personal history of malignant neoplasm of eye and nervous tissue**
Z85.840 Personal history of malignant neoplasm of eye
Z85.841 Personal history of malignant neoplasm of brain
Z85.848 Personal history of malignant neoplasm of other parts of nervous tissue
+ **Z85.85 Personal history of malignant neoplasm of endocrine glands**
Z85.850 Personal history of malignant neoplasm of thyroid
Z85.858 Personal history of malignant neoplasm of other endocrine glands
Z85.89 Personal history of malignant neoplasm of other organs and systems
Z85.9 Personal history of malignant neoplasm, unspecified
Conditions classifiable to C7A.00, C80.1

Z86 Personal history of certain other diseases
Code first any follow-up examination after treatment (Z09)
Review coding guideline C.21.c.4
+ **Z86.0 Personal history of in-situ and benign neoplasms and neoplasms of uncertain behavior**
Excludes2: *personal history of malignant neoplasms (Z85.-)*
+ **Z86.00 Personal history of in-situ neoplasm**
Z86.000 Personal history of in-situ neoplasm of breast
♀ **Z86.001 Personal history of in-situ neoplasm of cervix uteri**
Z86.008 Personal history of in-situ neoplasm of other site
+ **Z86.01 Personal history of benign neoplasm**
Z86.010 Personal history of colonic polyps
Z86.011 Personal history of benign neoplasm of the brain
Z86.012 Personal history of benign carcinoid tumor
Z86.018 Personal history of other benign neoplasm
Z86.03 Personal history of neoplasm of uncertain behavior
+ **Z86.1 Personal history of infectious and parasitic diseases**
Conditions classifiable to A00-B89, B99
Excludes1: *personal history of infectious diseases specific to a body system*
sequelae of infectious and parasitic diseases (B90-B94)
Z86.11 Personal history of tuberculosis
Z86.12 Personal history of poliomyelitis
Z86.13 Personal history of malaria
Z86.14 Personal history of Methicillin resistant Staphylococcus aureus infection
Personal history of MRSA infection
Z86.19 Personal history of other infectious and parasitic diseases
Z86.2 Personal history of diseases of the blood and blood-forming organs and certain disorders involving the immune mechanism
Conditions classifiable to D50-D89
+ **Z86.3 Personal history of endocrine, nutritional and metabolic diseases**
Conditions classifiable to E00-E88
Z86.31 Personal history of diabetic foot ulcer
Excludes2: *current diabetic foot ulcer (E08.621, E09.621, E10.621, E11.621, E13.621)*
♀ **Z86.32 Personal history of gestational diabetes**
Personal history of conditions classifiable to O24.4-
Excludes1: *gestational diabetes mellitus in current pregnancy (O24.4-)*
Z86.39 Personal history of other endocrine, nutritional and metabolic disease
+ **Z86.5 Personal history of mental and behavioral disorders**
Conditions classifiable to F40-F59
• **Z86.51 Personal history of combat and operational stress reaction**
Z86.59 Personal history of other mental and behavioral disorders
+ **Z86.6 Personal history of diseases of the nervous system and sense organs**
Conditions classifiable to G00-G99, H00-H95
Z86.61 Personal history of infections of the central nervous system
Personal history of encephalitis
Personal history of meningitis
Z86.69 Personal history of other diseases of the nervous system and sense organs
+ **Z86.7 Personal history of diseases of the circulatory system**
Conditions classifiable to I00-I99
Excludes2: *old myocardial infarction (I25.2)*
personal history of anaphylactic shock (Z87.892)
postmyocardial infarction syndrome (I24.1)
+ **Z86.71 Personal history of venous thrombosis and embolism**
Z86.711 Personal history of pulmonary embolism
Z86.718 Personal history of other venous thrombosis and embolism
Z86.72 Personal history of thrombophlebitis
Z86.73 Personal history of transient ischemic attack (TIA), and cerebral infarction without residual deficits
Personal history of prolonged reversible ischemic neurological deficit (PRIND)
Personal history of stroke NOS without residual deficits
Excludes1: *personal history of traumatic brain injury (Z87.820)*
sequelae of cerebrovascular disease (I69.-)
Review coding guideline C.9.d.3

Z86.74 Personal history of sudden cardiac arrest
Personal history of sudden cardiac death successfully resuscitated

Z86.79 Personal history of other diseases of the circulatory system

Z87 Personal history of other diseases and conditions
Code first any follow-up examination after treatment (Z09)
Review coding guideline C.21.c.4

+ **Z87.0 Personal history of diseases of the respiratory system**
Conditions classifiable to J00-J99

Z87.01 Personal history of pneumonia (recurrent)

Z87.09 Personal history of other diseases of the respiratory system

+ **Z87.1 Personal history of diseases of the digestive system**
Conditions classifiable to K00-K93

Z87.11 Personal history of peptic ulcer disease

Z87.19 Personal history of other diseases of the digestive system

Z87.2 Personal history of diseases of the skin and subcutaneous tissue
Conditions classifiable to L00-L99
Excludes2: *personal history of diabetic foot ulcer (Z86.31)*

+ **Z87.3 Personal history of diseases of the musculoskeletal system and connective tissue**
Conditions classifiable to M00-M99
Excludes2: *personal history of (healed) traumatic fracture (Z87.81)*

+ **Z87.31 Personal history of (healed) nontraumatic fracture**

Z87.310 Personal history of (healed) osteoporosis fracture
Personal history of (healed) fragility fracture
Personal history of (healed) collapsed vertebra due to osteoporosis
Review coding guideline C.13.d.1

Z87.311 Personal history of (healed) other pathological fracture
Personal history of (healed) collapsed vertebra NOS
Excludes2: *personal history of osteoporosis fracture (Z87.310)*

Z87.312 Personal history of (healed) stress fracture
Personal history of (healed) fatigue fracture

Z87.39 Personal history of other diseases of the musculoskeletal system and connective tissue

+ **Z87.4 Personal history of diseases of genitourinary system**
Conditions classifiable to N00-N99

+ **Z87.41 Personal history of dysplasia of the female genital tract**
Excludes1: *personal history of malignant neoplasm of female genital tract (Z85.40-Z85.44)*

♀ **Z87.410 Personal history of cervical dysplasia**

♀ **Z87.411 Personal history of vaginal dysplasia**

♀ **Z87.412 Personal history of vulvar dysplasia**

♀ **Z87.42 Personal history of other diseases of the female genital tract**

+ **Z87.43 Personal history of diseases of male genital organs**

Z87.430 Personal history of prostatic dysplasia
Excludes1: *personal history of malignant neoplasm of prostate (Z85.46)*

Z87.438 Personal history of other diseases of male genital organs

+ **Z87.44 Personal history of diseases of urinary system**
Excludes1: *personal history of malignant neoplasm of cervix uteri (Z85.41)*

Z87.440 Personal history of urinary (tract) infections

Z87.441 Personal history of nephrotic syndrome

Z87.442 Personal history of urinary calculi
Personal history of kidney stones

Z87.448 Personal history of other diseases of urinary system

+ **Z87.5 Personal history of complications of pregnancy, childbirth and the puerperium**
Conditions classifiable to O00-O9A
Excludes2: *recurrent pregnancy loss (N96)*

♀ **Z87.51 Personal history of pre-term labor**
Excludes1: *current pregnancy with history of pre-term labor (O09.21-)*

♀ **Z87.59 Personal history of other complications of pregnancy, childbirth and the puerperium**
Personal history of trophoblastic disease

+ **Z87.7 Personal history of (corrected) congenital malformations**
Conditions classifiable to Q00-Q89 that have been repaired or corrected
Excludes1: *congenital malformations that have been partially corrected or repair but which still require medical treatment - code to condition*
Excludes2: *other postprocedural states (Z98.-)*
personal history of medical treatment (Z92.-)
presence of cardiac and vascular implants and grafts (Z95.-)
presence of other devices (Z97.-)
presence of other functional implants (Z96.-)
transplanted organ and tissue status (Z94.-)

+ **Z87.71 Personal history of (corrected) congenital malformations of genitourinary system**

♂ **Z87.710 Personal history of (corrected) hypospadias**

Z87.718 Personal history of other specified (corrected) congenital malformations of genitourinary system

+ **Z87.72 Personal history of (corrected) congenital malformations of nervous system and sense organs**

Z87.720 Personal history of (corrected) congenital malformations of eye

Z87.721 Personal history of (corrected) congenital malformations of ear

Z87.728 Personal history of other specified (corrected) congenital malformations of nervous system and sense organs

+ **Z87.73 Personal history of (corrected) congenital malformations of digestive system**

Z87.730 Personal history of (corrected) cleft lip and palate

Z87.738 Personal history of other specified (corrected) congenital malformations of digestive system

Z87.74 Personal history of (corrected) congenital malformations of heart and circulatory system

Z87.75 Personal history of (corrected) congenital malformations of respiratory system

Z87.76 Personal history of (corrected) congenital malformations of integument, limbs and musculoskeletal system

+ **Z87.79 Personal history of other (corrected) congenital malformations**

Z87.790 Personal history of (corrected) congenital malformations of face and neck

Z87.798 Personal history of other (corrected) congenital malformations

+ **Z87.8 Personal history of other specified conditions**
Excludes2: *personal history of self harm (Z91.5)*

Z87.81 Personal history of (healed) traumatic fracture
Excludes2: *personal history of (healed) nontraumatic fracture (Z87.31-)*

+ **Z87.82 Personal history of other (healed) physical injury and trauma**
Conditions classifiable to S00-T88, except traumatic fractures

Z87.820 Personal history of traumatic brain injury
Excludes1: *personal history of transient ischemic attack (TIA), and cerebral infarction without residual deficits (Z86.73)*

Z87.821 Personal history of retained foreign body fully removed

Z87.828 Personal history of other (healed) physical injury and trauma

+ **Z87.89 Personal history of other specified conditions**

Z87.890 Personal history of sex reassignment

Z87.891 Personal history of nicotine dependence
Excludes1: *current nicotine dependence (F17.2-)*

Z87.892 Personal history of anaphylaxis
Code also allergy status such as:
allergy status to drugs, medicaments and biological substances (Z88.-)
allergy status, other than to drugs and biological substances (Z91.0-)

Z87.898 Personal history of other specified conditions
AHA CC: 1Q, 2013, 21

Z88 Allergy status to drugs, medicaments and biological substances

Excludes2: *Allergy status, other than to drugs and biological substances (Z91.0-)*

Review coding guideline C.21.c.3

Z88.0 Allergy status to penicillin

Z88.1 Allergy status to other antibiotic agents status

Z88.2 Allergy status to sulfonamides status

Z88.3 Allergy status to other anti-infective agents status

Z88.4 Allergy status to anesthetic agent status

Z88.5 Allergy status to narcotic agent status

Z88.6 Allergy status to analgesic agent status

Z88.7 Allergy status to serum and vaccine status

Z88.8 Allergy status to other drugs, medicaments and biological substances status

Z88.9 Allergy status to unspecified drugs, medicaments and biological substances status

Z89 Acquired absence of limb

Includes: amputation status
postprocedural loss of limb
post-traumatic loss of limb

Excludes1: *acquired deformities of limbs (M20-M21)*
congenital absence of limbs (Q71-Q73)

Review coding guideline C.21.c.3

+ **Z89.0 Acquired absence of thumb and other finger(s)**

+ **Z89.01 Acquired absence of thumb**

Z89.011 Acquired absence of right thumb

Z89.012 Acquired absence of left thumb

Z89.019 Acquired absence of unspecified thumb

+ **Z89.02 Acquired absence of other finger(s)**

Excludes2: *acquired absence of thumb (Z89.01-)*

Z89.021 Acquired absence of right finger(s)

Z89.022 Acquired absence of left finger(s)

Z89.029 Acquired absence of unspecified finger(s)

+ **Z89.1 Acquired absence of hand and wrist**

+ **Z89.11 Acquired absence of hand**

Z89.111 Acquired absence of right hand

Z89.112 Acquired absence of left hand

Z89.119 Acquired absence of unspecified hand

+ **Z89.12 Acquired absence of wrist**

Disarticulation at wrist

Z89.121 Acquired absence of right wrist

Z89.122 Acquired absence of left wrist

Z89.129 Acquired absence of unspecified wrist

+ **Z89.2 Acquired absence of upper limb above wrist**

+ **Z89.20 Acquired absence of upper limb, unspecified level**

Z89.201 Acquired absence of right upper limb, unspecified level

Z89.202 Acquired absence of left upper limb, unspecified level

Z89.209 Acquired absence of unspecified upper limb, unspecified level

Acquired absence of arm NOS

+ **Z89.21 Acquired absence of upper limb below elbow**

Z89.211 Acquired absence of right upper limb below elbow

Z89.212 Acquired absence of left upper limb below elbow

Z89.219 Acquired absence of unspecified upper limb below elbow

+ **Z89.22 Acquired absence of upper limb above elbow**

Disarticulation at elbow

Z89.221 Acquired absence of right upper limb above elbow

Z89.222 Acquired absence of left upper limb above elbow

Z89.229 Acquired absence of unspecified upper limb above elbow

+ **Z89.23 Acquired absence of shoulder**

Acquired absence of shoulder joint following explantation of shoulder joint prosthesis, with or without presence of antibiotic-impregnated cement spacer

Z89.231 Acquired absence of right shoulder

Z89.232 Acquired absence of left shoulder

Z89.239 Acquired absence of unspecified shoulder

+ **Z89.4 Acquired absence of toe(s), foot, and ankle**

+ **Z89.41 Acquired absence of great toe**

Z89.411 Acquired absence of right great toe

Z89.412 Acquired absence of left great toe

Z89.419 Acquired absence of unspecified great toe

+ **Z89.42 Acquired absence of other toe(s)**

Excludes2: *acquired absence of great toe (Z89.41-)*

Z89.421 Acquired absence of other right toe(s)

Z89.422 Acquired absence of other left toe(s)

Z89.429 Acquired absence of other toe(s), unspecified side

+ **Z89.43 Acquired absence of foot**

Z89.431 Acquired absence of right foot

Z89.432 Acquired absence of left foot

Z89.439 Acquired absence of unspecified foot

+ **Z89.44 Acquired absence of ankle**

Disarticulation of ankle

Z89.441 Acquired absence of right ankle

Z89.442 Acquired absence of left ankle

Z89.449 Acquired absence of unspecified ankle

+ **Z89.5 Acquired absence of leg below knee**

+ **Z89.51 Acquired absence of leg below knee**

Z89.511 Acquired absence of right leg below knee

Z89.512 Acquired absence of left leg below knee

Z89.519 Acquired absence of unspecified leg below knee

+ **Z89.52 Acquired absence of knee**

Acquired absence of knee joint following explantation of knee joint prosthesis, with or without presence of antibiotic-impregnated cement spacer

Z89.521 Acquired absence of right knee

Z89.522 Acquired absence of left knee

Z89.529 Acquired absence of unspecified knee

+ **Z89.6 Acquired absence of leg above knee**

+ **Z89.61 Acquired absence of leg above knee**

Acquired absence of leg NOS
Disarticulation at knee

Z89.611 Acquired absence of right leg above knee

Z89.612 Acquired absence of left leg above knee

Z89.619 Acquired absence of unspecified leg above knee

+ **Z89.62 Acquired absence of hip**

Acquired absence of hip joint following explantation of hip joint prosthesis, with or without presence of antibiotic-impregnated cement spacer
Disarticulation at hip

Z89.621 Acquired absence of right hip joint

Z89.622 Acquired absence of left hip joint

Z89.629 Acquired absence of unspecified hip joint

Z89.9 Acquired absence of limb, unspecified

Z90 Acquired absence of organs, not elsewhere classified

Includes: postprocedural or post-traumatic loss of body part NEC

Excludes1: *congenital absence - see Alphabetical Index*

Excludes2: *postprocedural absence of endocrine glands (E89.-)*

Review coding guideline C.21.c.3

+ **Z90.0 Acquired absence of part of head and neck**

Z90.01 Acquired absence of eye

Z90.02 Acquired absence of larynx

Z90.09 Acquired absence of other part of head and neck

Acquired absence of nose

Excludes2: *teeth (K08.1)*

+ **Z90.1 Acquired absence of breast and nipple**

Z90.10 Acquired absence of unspecified breast and nipple

Z90.11 Acquired absence of right breast and nipple

Z90.12 Acquired absence of left breast and nipple

Z90.13 Acquired absence of bilateral breasts and nipples

Z90.2 Acquired absence of lung [part of]

Z90.3 Acquired absence of stomach [part of]

+ **Z90.4 Acquired absence of other specified parts of digestive tract**

+ **Z90.41 Acquired absence of pancreas**

Use additional code to identify any associated:
insulin use (Z79.4)
diabetes mellitus, postpancreatectomy (E13.-)

Review coding guideline C.4.a.6.b.i

Z90.410 Acquired total absence of pancreas

Acquired absence of pancreas NOS

Z90.411 Acquired partial absence of pancreas

Z90.49 Acquired absence of other specified parts of digestive tract

Z90.5 Acquired absence of kidney

Z90.6 Acquired absence of other parts of urinary tract

Acquired absence of bladder

+ **Z90.7 Acquired absence of genital organ(s)**
Excludes1: personal history of sex reassignment (Z87.890)
Excludes2: female genital mutilation status (N90.81-)
+ **Z90.71 Acquired absence of cervix and uterus**
♀ **Z90.710 Acquired absence of both cervix and uterus**
Acquired absence of uterus NOS
Status post total hysterectomy
♀ **Z90.711 Acquired absence of uterus with remaining cervical stump**
Status post partial hysterectomy with remaining cervical stump
♀ **Z90.712 Acquired absence of cervix with remaining uterus**
+ **Z90.72 Acquired absence of ovaries**
♀ **Z90.721 Acquired absence of ovaries, unilateral**
♀ **Z90.722 Acquired absence of ovaries, bilateral**
Z90.79 Acquired absence of other genital organ(s)
+ **Z90.8 Acquired absence of other organs**
Z90.81 Acquired absence of spleen
Z90.89 Acquired absence of other organs

Z91 Personal risk factors, not elsewhere classified
Excludes2: contact with and (suspected) exposures hazardous to health (Z77.-)
exposure to pollution and other problems related to physical environment (Z77.1-)
personal history of physical injury and trauma (Z87.81, Z87.82-)
occupational exposure to risk factors (Z57.-)
+ **Z91.0 Allergy status, other than to drugs and biological substances**
Excludes2: Allergy status to drugs, medicaments, and biological substances (Z88.-)
Review coding guideline C.21.c.3
+ **Z91.01 Food allergy status**
Excludes2: food additives allergy status (Z91.02)
Z91.010 Allergy to peanuts
Z91.011 Allergy to milk products
Excludes1: lactose intolerance (E73.-)
Z91.012 Allergy to eggs
Z91.013 Allergy to seafood
Allergy to shellfish
Allergy to octopus or squid ink
Z91.018 Allergy to other foods
Allergy to nuts other than peanuts
Z91.02 Food additives allergy status
+ **Z91.03 Insect allergy status**
Z91.030 Bee allergy status
Z91.038 Other insect allergy status
+ **Z91.04 Nonmedicinal substance allergy status**
Z91.040 Latex allergy status
Latex sensitivity status
Z91.041 Radiographic dye allergy status
Allergy status to contrast media used for diagnostic X-ray procedure
Z91.048 Other nonmedicinal substance allergy status
Z91.09 Other allergy status, other than to drugs and biological substances
+ **Z91.1 Patient's noncompliance with medical treatment and regimen**
Z91.11 Patient's noncompliance with dietary regimen
+ **Z91.12 Patient's intentional underdosing of medication regimen**
Code first underdosing of medication (T36-T50) with fifth or sixth character 6
Excludes1: adverse effect of prescribed drug taken as directed- code to adverse effect
poisoning (overdose) -code to poisoning
Review coding guideline C.19.e.5.c
Z91.120 Patient's intentional underdosing of medication regimen due to financial hardship
Z91.128 Patient's intentional underdosing of medication regimen for other reason
+ **Z91.13 Patient's unintentional underdosing of medication regimen**
Code first underdosing of medication (T36-T50) with fifth or sixth character 6
Excludes1: adverse effect of prescribed drug taken as directed- code to adverse effect
poisoning (overdose) -code to poisoning
Review coding guideline C.19.e.5.c
Z91.130 Patient's unintentional underdosing of medication regimen due to age-related debility
Z91.138 Patient's unintentional underdosing of medication regimen for other reason
Z91.14 Patient's other noncompliance with medication regime
Patient's underdosing of medication NOS
Z91.15 Patient's noncompliance with renal dialysis
Z91.19 Patient's noncompliance with other medical treatmen and regimen
+ **Z91.4 Personal history of psychological trauma, not elsewhere classifie**
Review coding guideline C.21.c.4
+ **Z91.41 Personal history of adult abuse**
Excludes2: personal history of abuse in childhood (Z62.81-)
• **Z91.410 Personal history of adult physical and sexua abuse**
Excludes1: current adult physical abuse (T74.11, T76.11)
current adult sexual abuse (T74.21-T76.11)
• **Z91.411 Personal history of adult psychological abus**
• **Z91.412 Personal history of adult neglect**
Excludes1: current adult neglect (T74.01, T76.01)
• **Z91.419 Personal history of unspecified adult abuse**
Z91.49 Other personal history of psychological trauma, not elsewhere classified
Z91.5 Personal history of self-harm
Personal history of parasuicide
Personal history of self-poisoning
Personal history of suicide attempt
Review coding guideline C.21.c.4
+ **Z91.8 Other specified personal risk factors, not elsewhere classified**
Review coding guideline C.21.c.4
Z91.81 History of falling
At risk for falling
Review coding guideline C.18.d
• **Z91.82 Personal history of military deployment**
Individual (civilian or military) with past history of military war, peacekeeping and humanitarian deployment (current or past conflict)
Returned from military deployment
Z91.83 Wandering in diseases classified elsewhere
Code first underlying disorder such as:
Alzheimer's disease (G30.-)
autism or pervasive developmental disorder (F84.-)
intellectual disabilities (F70-F79)
unspecified dementia with behavioral disturbance (F03.9-
Z91.89 Other specified personal risk factors, not elsewhere classified

Z92 Personal history of medical treatment
Excludes2: postprocedural states (Z98.-)
Review coding guideline C.21.c.4
Z92.0 Personal history of contraception
Excludes1: counseling or management of current contraceptive practices (Z30.-)
long term (current) use of contraception (Z79.3)
presence of (intrauterine) contraceptive device (Z97.5
+ **Z92.2 Personal history of drug therapy**
Excludes2: long term (current) drug therapy (Z79.-)
Z92.21 Personal history of antineoplastic chemotherapy
Z92.22 Personal history of monoclonal drug therapy
Z92.23 Personal history of estrogen therapy
+ **Z92.24 Personal history of steroid therapy**
Z92.240 Personal history of inhaled steroid therapy
Z92.241 Personal history of systemic steroid therapy
Personal history of steroid therapy NOS
Z92.25 Personal history of immunosupression therapy
Excludes2: personal history of steroid therapy (Z92.24
Z92.29 Personal history of other drug therapy
Z92.3 Personal history of irradiation
Personal history of exposure to therapeutic radiation
Excludes1: exposure to radiation in the physical environment (Z77.12)
occupational exposure to radiation (Z57.1)
+ **Z92.8 Personal history of other medical treatment**
Z92.81 Personal history of extracorporeal membrane oxygenation (ECMO)
Z92.82 Status post administration of tPA (rtPA) in a different facility within the last 24 hours prior to admission to current facility
Code first condition requiring tPA administration, such as
acute cerebral infarction (I63.-)
acute myocardial infarction (I21.-, I22.-)
AHA CC: 4Q, 2013, 124
Review coding guideline C.21.c.3

Z92.83 **Personal history of failed moderate sedation**
Personal history of failed conscious sedation
Excludes2: *failed moderate sedation during procedure (T88.52)*

Z92.89 **Personal history of other medical treatment**

Z93 Artificial opening status

Excludes1: *artificial openings requiring attention or management (Z43.-)*
complications of external stoma (J95.0-, K94.-, N99.5-)
Review coding guideline C.21.c.3

Z93.0 **Tracheostomy status**
AHA CC: 4Q, 2013, 129
Z93.1 **Gastrostomy status**
Z93.2 **Ileostomy status**
Z93.3 **Colostomy status**
Z93.4 **Other artificial openings of gastrointestinal tract status**
\+ **Z93.5** **Cystostomy status**
Z93.50 **Unspecified cystostomy status**
Z93.51 **Cutaneous-vesicostomy status**
Z93.52 **Appendico-vesicostomy status**
Z93.59 **Other cystostomy status**
Z93.6 **Other artificial openings of urinary tract status**
Nephrostomy status
Ureterostomy status
Urethrostomy status
Z93.8 **Other artificial opening status**
Z93.9 **Artificial opening status, unspecified**

Z94 Transplanted organ and tissue status

Includes: organ or tissue replaced by heterogenous or homogenous transplant
Excludes1: *complications of transplanted organ or tissue - see Alphabetical Index*
Excludes2: *presence of vascular grafts (Z95.-)*
Review coding guideline C.21.c.3

CC **Z94.0** **Kidney transplant status**
CC Exclusion see Appendix A PDX collection 1489
Review coding guideline C.14.a.2
CC **Z94.1** **Heart transplant status**
Excludes1: *artificial heart status (Z95.812)*
heart-valve replacement status (Z95.2-Z95.4)
CC Exclusion see Appendix A PDX collection 1488
CC **Z94.2** **Lung transplant status**
CC Exclusion see Appendix A PDX collection 1491
CC **Z94.3** **Heart and lungs transplant status**
CC Exclusion see Appendix A PDX collection 1488
CC **Z94.4** **Liver transplant status**
CC Exclusion see Appendix A PDX collection 1490
Z94.5 **Skin transplant status**
Autogenous skin transplant status
Z94.6 **Bone transplant status**
Z94.7 **Corneal transplant status**
\+ **Z94.8** **Other transplanted organ and tissue status**
CC **Z94.81** **Bone marrow transplant status**
CC Exclusion see Appendix A PDX collection 1492
CC **Z94.82** **Intestine transplant status**
CC Exclusion see Appendix A PDX collection 1495
CC **Z94.83** **Pancreas transplant status**
CC Exclusion see Appendix A PDX collection 1496
CC **Z94.84** **Stem cells transplant status**
CC Exclusion see Appendix A PDX collection 1497
Z94.89 **Other transplanted organ and tissue status**
Z94.9 **Transplanted organ and tissue status, unspecified**

Z95 Presence of cardiac and vascular implants and grafts

Excludes1: *complications of cardiac and vascular devices, implants and grafts (T82.-)*
Review coding guideline C.21.c.3

Z95.0 **Presence of cardiac pacemaker**
Excludes1: *adjustment or management of cardiac pacemaker (Z45.0)*
presence of automatic (implantable) cardiac defibrillator with synchronous cardiac pacemaker (Z95.810)
Z95.1 **Presence of aortocoronary bypass graft**
Z95.2 **Presence of prosthetic heart valve**
Presence of heart valve NOS
Z95.3 **Presence of xenogenic heart valve**
Z95.4 **Presence of other heart-valve replacement**
Z95.5 **Presence of coronary angioplasty implant and graft**
Excludes1: *coronary angioplasty status without implant and graft (Z98.61)*
\+ **Z95.8** **Presence of other cardiac and vascular implants and grafts**
\+ **Z95.81** **Presence of other cardiac implants and grafts**
Z95.810 **Presence of automatic (implantable) cardiac defibrillator**
Presence of automatic (implantable) cardiac defibrillator with synchronous cardiac pacemaker
CC **Z95.811** **Presence of heart assist device**
CC Exclusion see Appendix A PDX collection 1498
CC **Z95.812** **Presence of fully implantable artificial heart**
CC Exclusion see Appendix A PDX collection 1498
Z95.818 **Presence of other cardiac implants and grafts**
\+ **Z95.82** **Presence of other vascular implants and grafts**
Z95.820 **Peripheral vascular angioplasty status with implants and grafts**
Excludes1: *peripheral vascular angioplasty without implant and graft (Z98.62)*
Z95.828 **Presence of other vascular implants and grafts**
Presence of intravascular prosthesis NEC
Z95.9 **Presence of cardiac and vascular implant and graft, unspecified**

Z96 Presence of other functional implants

Excludes2: *complications of internal prosthetic devices, implants and grafts (T82-T85)*
fitting and adjustment of prosthetic and other devices (Z44-Z46)
Review coding guideline C.21.c.3

Z96.0 **Presence of urogenital implants**
Z96.1 **Presence of intraocular lens**
Presence of pseudophakia
\+ **Z96.2** **Presence of otological and audiological implants**
Z96.20 **Presence of otological and audiological implant, unspecified**
Z96.21 **Cochlear implant status**
Z96.22 **Myringotomy tube(s) status**
Z96.29 **Presence of other otological and audiological implants**
Presence of bone-conduction hearing device
Presence of eustachian tube stent
Stapes replacement
Z96.3 **Presence of artificial larynx**
\+ **Z96.4** **Presence of endocrine implants**
Z96.41 **Presence of insulin pump (external) (internal)**
Z96.49 **Presence of other endocrine implants**
Z96.5 **Presence of tooth-root and mandibular implants**
\+ **Z96.6** **Presence of orthopedic joint implants**
Z96.60 **Presence of unspecified orthopedic joint implant**
\+ **Z96.61** **Presence of artificial shoulder joint**
Z96.611 **Presence of right artificial shoulder joint**
Z96.612 **Presence of left artificial shoulder joint**
Z96.619 **Presence of unspecified artificial shoulder joint**
\+ **Z96.62** **Presence of artificial elbow joint**
Z96.621 **Presence of right artificial elbow joint**
Z96.622 **Presence of left artificial elbow joint**
Z96.629 **Presence of unspecified artificial elbow joint**
\+ **Z96.63** **Presence of artificial wrist joint**
Z96.631 **Presence of right artificial wrist joint**
Z96.632 **Presence of left artificial wrist joint**
Z96.639 **Presence of unspecified artificial wrist joint**
\+ **Z96.64** **Presence of artificial hip joint**
Hip-joint replacement (partial) (total)
Z96.641 **Presence of right artificial hip joint**
Z96.642 **Presence of left artificial hip joint**
Z96.643 **Presence of artificial hip joint, bilateral**
Z96.649 **Presence of unspecified artificial hip joint**
\+ **Z96.65** **Presence of artificial knee joint**
Z96.651 **Presence of right artificial knee joint**
Z96.652 **Presence of left artificial knee joint**
Z96.653 **Presence of artificial knee joint, bilateral**
Z96.659 **Presence of unspecified artificial knee joint**
\+ **Z96.66** **Presence of artificial ankle joint**
Z96.661 **Presence of right artificial ankle joint**
Z96.662 **Presence of left artificial ankle joint**
Z96.669 **Presence of unspecified artificial ankle joint**
\+ **Z96.69** **Presence of other orthopedic joint implants**
Z96.691 **Finger-joint replacement of right hand**
Z96.692 **Finger-joint replacement of left hand**
Z96.693 **Finger-joint replacement, bilateral**
Z96.698 **Presence of other orthopedic joint implants**
Z96.7 **Presence of other bone and tendon implants**
Presence of skull plate

+ **Z96.8 Presence of other specified functional implants**
Z96.81 Presence of artificial skin
Z96.89 Presence of other specified functional implants
Z96.9 Presence of functional implant, unspecified

Z97 Presence of other devices
Excludes1: *complications of internal prosthetic devices, implants and grafts (T82-T85)*
fitting and adjustment of prosthetic and other devices (Z44-Z46)
Excludes2: *presence of cerebrospinal fluid drainage device (Z98.2)*
Review coding guideline C.21.c.3
Z97.0 Presence of artificial eye
+ **Z97.1 Presence of artificial limb (complete) (partial)**
Z97.10 Presence of artificial limb (complete) (partial), unspecified
Z97.11 Presence of artificial right arm (complete) (partial)
Z97.12 Presence of artificial left arm (complete) (partial)
Z97.13 Presence of artificial right leg (complete) (partial)
Z97.14 Presence of artificial left leg (complete) (partial)
Z97.15 Presence of artificial arms, bilateral (complete) (partial)
Z97.16 Presence of artificial legs, bilateral (complete) (partial)
Z97.2 Presence of dental prosthetic device (complete) (partial)
Presence of dentures (complete) (partial)
Z97.3 Presence of spectacles and contact lenses
Z97.4 Presence of external hearing-aid
♀ **Z97.5 Presence of (intrauterine) contraceptive device**
Excludes1: *checking, reinsertion or removal of contraceptive device (Z30.43)*
Z97.8 Presence of other specified devices

Z98 Other postprocedural states
Excludes2: *aftercare (Z43-Z49, Z51)*
follow-up medical care (Z08-Z09)
postprocedural complication - see Alphabetical Index
Review coding guideline C.21.c.3
Z98.0 Intestinal bypass and anastomosis status
Excludes2: *bariatric surgery status (Z98.84)*
gastric bypass status (Z98.84)
obesity surgery status (Z98.84)
Z98.1 Arthrodesis status
Z98.2 Presence of cerebrospinal fluid drainage device
Presence of CSF shunt
Z98.3 Post therapeutic collapse of lung status
Code first underlying disease
+ **Z98.4 Cataract extraction status**
Use additional code to identify intraocular lens implant status (Z96.1)
Excludes1: *aphakia (H27.0)*
Z98.41 Cataract extraction status, right eye
Z98.42 Cataract extraction status, left eye
Z98.49 Cataract extraction status, unspecified eye
+ **Z98.5 Sterilization status**
Excludes1: *female infertility (N97.-)*
male infertility (N46.-)
♀ **Z98.51 Tubal ligation status**
• ♂ **Z98.52 Vasectomy status**
+ **Z98.6 Angioplasty status**
Z98.61 Coronary angioplasty status
Excludes1: *coronary angioplasty status with implant and graft (Z95.5)*
Z98.62 Peripheral vascular angioplasty status
Excludes1: *peripheral vascular angioplasty status with implant and graft (Z95.820)*
+ **Z98.8 Other specified postprocedural states**
+ **Z98.81 Dental procedure status**
Z98.810 Dental sealant status
Z98.811 Dental restoration status
Dental crown status
Dental fillings status
Z98.818 Other dental procedure status
Z98.82 Breast implant status
Excludes1: *breast implant removal status (Z98.86)*
Z98.83 Filtering (vitreous) bleb after glaucoma surgery status
Excludes1: *Inflammation (infection) of postprocedural bleb (H59.4-)*
Z98.84 Bariatric surgery status
Gastric banding status
Gastric bypass status for obesity
Obesity surgery status
Excludes1: *bariatric surgery status complicating pregnancy, childbirth, or the puerperium (O99.84)*
Excludes2: *intestinal bypass and anastomosis status (Z98.0)*
Z98.85 Transplanted organ removal status
Transplanted organ previously removed due to complication, failure, rejection or infection
Excludes1: *encounter for removal of transplanted organ -code to complication of transplanted organ (T86.-)*
Z98.86 Personal history of breast implant removal
+ **Z98.87 Personal history of in utero procedure**
♀ **Z98.870 Personal history of in utero procedure during pregnancy**
Excludes2: *complications from in utero procedure for current pregnancy (O35.7)*
supervision of current pregnancy with history of in utero procedure during previous pregnancy (O09.82-)
Z98.871 Personal history of in utero procedure while a fetus
Z98.89 Other specified postprocedural states
Personal history of surgery, not elsewhere classified

Z99 Dependence on enabling machines and devices, not elsewhere classified
Excludes1: *cardiac pacemaker status (Z95.0)*
Review coding guideline C.21.c.3
Z99.0 Dependence on aspirator
+ **Z99.1 Dependence on respirator**
Dependence on ventilator
CC **Z99.11 Dependence on respirator [ventilator] status**
CC Exclusion see Appendix A PDX collection 0759
CC **Z99.12 Encounter for respirator [ventilator] dependence during power failure**
Excludes1: *mechanical complication of respirator [ventilator] (J95.850)*
CC Exclusion see Appendix A PDX collection 0759
Review coding guideline C.21.c.16
Z99.2 Dependence on renal dialysis
Hemodialysis status
Peritoneal dialysis status
Presence of arteriovenous shunt for dialysis
Renal dialysis status NOS
Excludes1: *encounter for fitting and adjustment of dialysis catheter (Z49.0-)*
noncompliance with renal dialysis (Z91.15)
Z99.3 Dependence on wheelchair
Wheelchair confinement status
Code first cause of dependence, such as:
muscular dystrophy (G71.0)
obesity (E66.-)
+ **Z99.8 Dependence on other enabling machines and devices**
Z99.81 Dependence on supplemental oxygen
Dependence on long-term oxygen
AHA CC: 4Q, 2013, 129
Z99.89 Dependence on other enabling machines and devices
Dependence on machine or device NOS